Praise fo

Secrets of th

"I read it with complete absorption, wholly immersed in its world. It has a palpability and veracity which is quite mesmerising. A tremendous piece of work."
—William Boyd, award-winning author of *The Blue Afternoon* and *Restless*

"Masterful. . . . *Secrets of the Sea* is the delicate account of [two lovers'] coming together and drifting apart. . . . Shakespeare has produced a work of rare beauty."
—*Financial Times*

"Gripping . . . subtle but arresting." —*The Times* (UK)

"If he has not previously earned the right to be considered a world writer, this novel should confirm it. . . . A resonant fiction, affirmative and very human."
—John Linklater, *Sunday Herald*

"A remarkable novel. It is brilliantly successful in portraying the forlorn, claustrophobic, gossipy, defiant little society in which it is set. . . . This latest work shows Shakespeare to be one of our dozen or so best." —*Literary Review*

"Engagement with the sea, . . . its significance in the unplumbed depths of human psyche, is the real, undoubted strength of this novel." —*The Independent*

"Carefully measured storytelling in this enveloping tale of life's small treasures lost and found."
—*The Sunday Times* (UK)

"An impressive, poignant piece of work." —*The Sunday Telegraph*

"An astute portrayal of thoughtful characters. . . . Elegant and enjoyable."
—*The Spectator*

"Nicholas Shakespeare has a magpie's eye for shiny colloquialisms."
—*The Times Literary Supplement*

"It reads absolutely true. . . . A very good novel indeed." —*The Scotsman*

Praise for

The Dancer Upstairs

"Riveting. . . . An intriguing, well-crafted, and powerful novel."
—*Washington Post*

"Astoundingly good. . . . This dramatic, moving story demands you put your life on hold until it is finished."
—*The Guardian*

"A beautifully crafted tale of love, obsession, and terror." —*Baltimore Sun*

"Enviably good, a genuinely fine novel from a writer who possesses real heart and flair."
—Louis de Bernières, *The Sunday Times* (UK)

"A gripping literary thriller. . . . An unusually powerful examination of what animates the souls of those who choose—or are forced—to play upon the stage of history."
—*Publishers Weekly*

"A crackling good yarn—Graham Greene meets Gabriel García Márquez."
—*The Evening Standard*

"Shakespeare explores an explosive situation in Latin America, deftly mingling love and suspense in a powerful, persuasive narrative. . . . Precisely, beautifully detailed, a tale both faithful to its time and utterly timeless."
—*Kirkus Reviews*

"In Nicholas Shakespeare's novel of present-day Peru, where nothing is ever safe and people are almost never what they seem, tracking down a Marxist terrorist can make the labors of Hercules seem easy. . . . In *The Dancer Upstairs*, passion propels the main characters forward."
—*New York Times Book Review*

Praise for *Bruce Chatwin*

"Unimprovable (and unstoppably readable)."
—Pico Iyer, *Time*

"Moving and elegant. . . . A superb portrayal of the restless and randy travel writer brings us as close to his hidden heart as we're likely to get."
—Salon.com

"Shakespeare's engrossing bio does exactly what Chatwin's fans have longed to do: get beneath the alluring but elusive quality of his persona and prose. Grade: A."
—*Entertainment Weekly*

"Immensely readable. . . . Shakespeare portrays a man of colossal energies and intellect in perpetual conflict, whose life was a web of contradiction, controversy, and conundrum. . . . Shakespeare artfully synthesizes what could have been cacophonous voices into an impressively rendered and remarkably coherent portrait."
—*Vogue*

"In Nicholas Shakespeare, Chatwin has found the right biographer. This is a magnificent work of empathy and detection."
—Colin Thubron, *The Sunday Times* (UK)

"Though it runs to five hundred fifty pages, Nicholas Shakespeare's biography feels concise: comprehensively researched, elegantly written, perfectly balanced between the life, the books, and the ideas. It's hard to imagine the Life being better done—or that . . . there is anything now left to say."
—Blake Morrison, *The Independent on Sunday*

"I take my scalp off to Nicholas Shakespeare. Biographies don't come any better than this. . . . A glorious quilt-work of texts, voices, and places, joined together with consummate judgement."
—Justin Wintle, *Financial Times*

"An epic piece of work of immense fascination. In awe-inspiring detail . . . [Shakespeare] does what Chatwin never did and drenches all these worlds in their emotional, human implications."
—Duncan Fallowell, *The Times* (UK)

"This excellent biography is very far removed from Chatwin's own anecdotal concision. However, it is fantastically difficult to fashion a narrative out of the inchoate facts of someone's life. Shakespeare has managed to pull it off."

—Ian Thomson, *The Guardian*

"Vastly enjoyable."

—*The Independent*

"Thoroughly researched and unsparingly revealing. . . . A graphic page-turner."

—*Publishers Weekly*

"Masterful, absorbing . . . simply a brilliant portrait of the artist as a young man."

—*Booklist*

"An ingenious, outsize, myth-meets-facts 'life and works' of the charismatic global citizen and compulsive tale-teller. . . . This spirited tell-all will make newcomers yearn to try his books. An unflinching reconstruction of a singular writer's scorching trajectory through life: Speed makes it concise; fate makes it haunting."

—*Kirkus Reviews*

"Quite simply one of the most beautifully written, painstakingly researched, and cleverly constructed biographies written this decade. Shakespeare has a quite extraordinary empathy for his subject, whom he portrays with humor, warmth, and an eye for telling detail, creating a book almost as original, intelligent, and observant as those by Chatwin himself."

—William Dalrymple, *Literary Review*

Praise for *Snowleg*

"Superb. . . . Beautifully written, rich in character, it displays all the courage for which its hero so desperately wants to be recognized." —*The Economist*

"Superbly evoked. . . . A morality tale which keeps the reader spellbound till the last sentence."

—*Literary Review*

"This novel is one of the finest attempts in English to convey something of two very strange places which no longer appear on the map of Europe . . . Shakespeare has told a very skillful story." —*The Evening Standard*

"Haunting. . . . Compelling. . . . Shakespeare deftly captures both the paranoia and the material and cultural poverty of East Germany." —*Publishers Weekly*

"A brooding, introspective, deftly crafted novel. . . . A moving story that speaks volumes about an era and a political system that is rapidly slipping into the recesses of our memory." —*Washington Post Book World*

"Like Michael Ondaatje in *The English Patient* and Shirley Hazzard in *The Great Fire,* Shakespeare weds a formal, detached prose style to a deeply romantic theme; the result is a powerful, ethereal love story set against the twisted politics of East Germany under Communism. . . . A beautifully written, utterly compelling story of love and politics." —*Booklist* (starred review)

"A volatile cocktail of passion and politics." —*San Francisco Chronicle*

"A richly imagined tale of thwarted romance between characters whose lives have been warped by East German treachery under Communism." —*Kirkus Reviews*

"Elegant, romantic, forceful." —*Library Journal*

"Already my bet for this year's Booker Prize. A superbly achieved and moving novel." —Giles Foden

Praise for *In Tasmania*

"Meticulous, lyrical history of the island. . . . Shakespeare's writing is transcendent—readers will gain a deep understanding not only of Tasmania's history, but of the forces that have shaped its isolated peoples' nature. . . . His skill as a storyteller never wavers." —*Publishers Weekly*

"A beautiful affectionate portrait." —*The Sunday Times* (UK)

Praise for *The Vision of Elena Silves*

"Written with precision, clarity, and rare beauty. . . . Alongside Salman Rushdie and the late Bruce Chatwin, Shakespeare now joins the ranks of the New Exotics school." —*New Statesman*

"A remarkable debut. . . . A story of love and insurrection brilliantly told. . . . One of the best books about the continent written by an outsider." —*The Sunday Times* (UK)

"A novel of action in the best tradition of Conrad and Greene. . . . Love, violence, revolution, and death—a denouement that is unexpected, shocking, and brilliantly conceived. . . . I closed the novel with both satisfaction and regret." —*Literary Review*

Praise for *The High Flyer*

"Wonderful. . . . He tells a story like an angel." —*The Observer*

"Shakespeare's lyricism is all his own, and he raises his lovers to a plateau of passion where Greene never ventured." —*The Sunday Telegraph*

"A deeply satisfying book. I feel quite exceptionally inclined to read it all over again." —Rosemary Stoyle, *Literary Review*

SECRETS OF THE SEA

Also by Nicholas Shakespeare

Fiction

The Vision of Elena Silves
The High Flyer
The Dancer Upstairs
Snowleg

Nonfiction

Bruce Chatwin
In Tasmania

SECRETS OF THE SEA

NICHOLAS SHAKESPEARE

AN ecco BOOK

NEW YORK • LONDON • TORONTO • SYDNEY • NEW DELHI • AUCKLAND

HARPER PERENNIAL

First published in Great Britain in 2007 by Harvill Secker, an imprint of Random House.

P.S.™ is a trademark of HarperCollins Publishers.

FIRST U.S. EDITION

Library of Congress Cataloging-in-Publication Data is available upon request.

ISBN 978-0-06-147470-5

08 09 10 11 12 OFF/RRD 10 9 8 7 6 5 4 3 2 1

To Anne Rood, for introducing me to Dolphin Sands,
and in memory of her husband Trevor (1927–2004)

There is the land-locked valley and the river,
The Western Tiers make distance an emotion,
The gum trees roar in the gale, the poplars shiver
At twilight, the church pines imitate an ocean.

A. D. HOPE

A home is like the sea.

BULGARIAN PROVERB

Your children are not your children. They are the sons and daughters of Life's longing for itself.

KAHLIL GIBRAN, *THE PROPHET*

CONTENTS

PART I

Wellington Point,
February–May 1988

CHAPTER ONE

THE SATURDAY ALEX MET Merridy he had driven to Wellington Point to look for ice-cream sticks in the school rubbish bins.

It was blowing hard when he came out of the playground and he could tell that it was about to rain. Across the narrow lane a movement caught his eye. Two girls helping each other over a high paling fence.

His heart sank.

He knew one of them – Tildy. She was younger than him, nineteen, with a tiny waist and cushiony buttocks and strong, almost manly shoulders. Her hair was dyed blonde, with a severe fringe. From certain angles she looked minx-like. On this afternoon, she wore a familiar tight-fitting green skirt.

It all rushed back – the warm honeysuckle smell of her young-woman's bedroom, the disarray of her bathroom cabinet, his regret. He held tighter to his plastic bag.

She put her bare foot onto the other girl's laced hands, and his attention jolted to the person preparing to lift her up. This one had thick dark hair cut short in a bob. Her lips shone with the same coral gloss as Tildy's, but she looked different.

Before he could slip back the way he had come, Tildy noticed him.

"Hey, Alex . . ." rising up to sit on the fence.

She hauled herself onto the top of it and sat, her legs splayed like a wishbone, and looked down at him. A grin crept over her face, which under her make-up Alex knew to be freckled.

In the light drizzle that had begun to fall, Alex stood where he was, mortified. Feverish, congested, filthy, this is not how he would have chosen to be seen by anyone. He had spent the morning jetting the sheep for fly, and his coat and jeans were spattered with Pyrethrum.

"Hi, Tildy," in a voice hoarse with flu, and watched her squeeze a narrow foot into the shoe.

Because she was a "blow-in", like himself, Tildy was not one of the girls with whom he had played catch-and-kiss in this lane behind the school. She had grown up in the north of Tasmania, before her father bought the Freycinet Court Hotel two years back. She worked in the canteen at the school.

"Where have you *been*, stranger?"

"I've been crook," he said, concentrating on her foot, trying to keep the image of the little balls of pantyhose at bay, but they were there forever, tangled up with the skin-coloured bra, the Kleenex smudged with lipstick.

She gave him another chance: "Were you coming to see me?"

His joints ached. Even his knuckles hurt as he stifled a cough with the back of his hand. "There was something I needed to get from the school," and raised his head.

She nodded at his plastic bag. "Not stealing my tucker, were you?"

"Of course not."

"What's in your bag, Alex?"

"Just sticks."

"Sticks?"

"Yeah, ice-cream sticks."

"What in heaven's name for?"

The other girl walked a pace or two away.

Alex stepped onto the grass where she had stood. "Listen, Tildy," in a low voice, at once ashamed and contrite. "I'm sorry I haven't rung you."

Tildy flexed her foot, studied the drizzle drops accumulating on the toe of her shoe.

Bedridden, with a streaming cold of the sort that he had learned to catch when he was at school in England, Alex had been able to blot out the memory of their evening together, but now it returned in a cloud of heavy pollen.

"I mean it," he said, and coughed again. "I'm really sorry. I couldn't get out of bed for three days, and there were things I had to do on the farm."

She drummed her heel against the side of the fence. "So you *weren't* coming to see me?"

He shook his head unhappily. "Tildy, I'm sorry."

She looked at his pale face and the plastic bag he was hugging to his chest, and looked away.

On a rotary clothes-line over the fence, a damp shirt dipped in the wind. Her friend waited. Whom Tildy now remembered.

"Get your bum over here, Merridy. Meet this great guy," and to him: "Alex, this is Merridy. We grew up together." Then, possibly to boost her appeal: "She's at uni in Melbourne."

Still, the girl did not turn, but crouched as though she were pulling something from the ground. "Perhaps Ray will get the wrong idea," she said over her shoulder. "Maybe you ought to go on your own."

Her voice was almost a sigh, a coming to the surface of someone who was no longer a childhood friend doing something that children did.

It came to Alex where he had seen her. Pushing a wheelchair with a sick-looking man in it, and walking two steps behind had been a gaunt, middle-aged woman, probably her mother. They were making their solemn procession up the main street.

Despite his fever he could still visibly see Mrs Grogan's expression as she backed out of the chemist's with her poodle in her arms, talking to someone, and tripped into the lap of the invalid.

Tildy glanced sharply down. "I told you, I'm not invited. Hey, Alex, give her a leg-up."

The young woman stood and turned.

About white-throated needletail swifts, his father had told him something that Alex had never forgotten: They spend a third of their life in the air before they nest. In the days and weeks ahead, Alex wondered if this did not define his own trajectory, feeding and sleeping on the wing, and alighting on solid earth on the evening he caught sight of Merridy standing against Ray Grogan's fence. For a long while afterwards he would cleave to the idea that his life, halted at the age of eleven by the accident, began humming again in that moment.

Rain making grey the washing. Tildy in her tight skirt manoeuvring her legs to the far side of the high fence. And the sea of sadness within the face that looked at him, and made Alex in that moment feel tall and alone and – in another remembered phrase of his father's – more useless than a second toe.

Her face grew simpler. "Hello, Alex."

Their glances touched, and now she was assessing him through blue eyes wide apart.

The way they stared. It was how wayward people recognised

one another. Whereas on Tildy her lip gloss was part of a riot of colour which harked back to a period of adolescence that Alex would rather forget, this girl's lips had the tinge of the orange lichen on the rock where he went to sit and watch the sea. He turned his eyes from her with huge reluctance, but not for long. He looked up at Tildy, her blonde hair, her gloss, and back to the girl's lips.

Her gaze swam into his and tickled through him and fluttered down.

"Hi, Merridy," he said, and his voice had an unfamiliar note.

She smiled, her expression enigmatic. Already her eyes were pulling away. They did not seek his approval or understanding. She was waiting for someone and it was not him.

"Help her up, Alex," came a tetchy voice from the sky.

The smoke of barbecuing tuna mingled with the aroma of rotting seaweed and the sound of male voices.

"*C'mon.*"

"Right," and cradled his fingers as he had seen Merridy do.

Merridy hesitated. Then slipped off her shoe.

He held his breath, looking away from her knees.

She bent her tanned leg, and rested her rough-textured, rather muddy heel in his knitted palms.

He left them, two girls perched on Ray Grogan's fence. Only when he turned into the main street did it occur to him to wonder why on earth they wanted to be up there.

A minute later Alex climbed into his ute and sat behind the wheel, looking through streaks of rain at the end of the road to the sea and – at the end of the sea – the deep blue line of the horizon. He could still feel the imprint of her heel.

CHAPTER TWO

AT A SMALL, ROUND window – a porthole, really – high above Talbot's store, two eyes observed Alex through a pair of long brass Zeiss binoculars. The brass still had vestiges of camouflage paint on it.

The general store was Wellington Point's largest building as well as the town's main employer, a fortress of brown brick and bluestone that commanded the north end of the street and the jetty. Its proprietor was Albert Talbot, who since his return half a century before from New Guinea, where he had spent nineteen months as a coast-watcher, tracking enemy troop movements day and night from the hills above Blanche Bay, was known to venture downstairs only occasionally, most often for funerals. Otherwise, he sat at the fourth-storey porthole in his eyrie, a tartan blanket across his knees and his mournful eyes presiding over the cricket pitch and golf course, over the waters of the bay beyond, even keeping half an eye on the bowling green.

Mr Talbot was patient for one so spare and strict. From force of habit he made notes of the vessels that arrived at the jetty, of the young men growing up, the girls coming of age. He had no children or wife himself. The few people he regularly spoke to were his manager (who would bring him the gossip and the rumbles); and less frequently his shop-girls, whom he allowed to enjoy the run of the ground floor, but would never invite into his private quarters. Lacking a family, he tended to regard those who shopped at his store as his dependents.

At a desk in what also served as a bedroom, he had a huge skylight above the bed, and watched over by the stars he compiled his weekly *Newsletter*, typing out each word letter by letter – as in the months when he had to send messages over his dry-cell radio set, ten words per minute in Morse code. Talbot's *Newsletter* was distributed free at the tills.

But mainly he looked out at the street – it reminded him of

the old coast road through the plantations – and the townspeople, who in certain respects differed not one jot from the light-skinned Kukakuka headhunters, Pygmy tribes and cannibals amongst whom Mr Talbot had once lived.

There was one road into Wellington Point and one road out. On warm days, it smelled of blueberry muffin and chemist's scent and tractor exhaust. To the west a spine of hills stretched inland, coated in dense Crown forest: an avalanche of bluegums, wattle and sassafras that tumbled down the slopes and drew up at the outlying farms. On the east side lay Oyster Bay and the long rocky arm of the Freycinet Peninsula – a ridge of glittering quartzite that had risen from the ocean bed in the Permian era.

"Just how long ago is that, Alex?" Tildy had asked.

"About two hundred and ninety million years."

Wellington Point was one of the smaller towns on Tasmania's southern east coast and belonged to Australia's oldest rural municipality. That it should have come by a reputation as a retirement village was a source of irritation to those like Mr Talbot who remembered when it was a thriving community the same size as Swansea, across the bay. Now the place was virtually a backwater. In tourist promotions of the island, Wellington Point (pop. 327) was routinely omitted from the map while Swansea was unfailingly labelled "the jewel of the East Coast". In Swansea, they looked upon Wellington Point in the same way as mainland Australia looked on Tasmania. Which is to say, they affected not to notice it.

Like its more successful neighbour over the bay, the township of Wellington Point was a promontory of farmers, pensioners and convalescents drawn here – as was Tildy's mother, now dead – by the absence of winter fog and a high daily average sunshine. Fishermen came for the bream and honeymooners for the view of Oyster Bay, which had once been compared to the Bay of Naples. Among the honeymooners whom Mr Talbot had – years ago now – watched get of their white Ford Zephyr, still hung about with paper streamers, were Alex's parents, Basil and Marjorie Dove.

Basil Dove had had a great-grandfather who fought under

Wellington in the Peninsular Wars. This thread of a connection to the peninsula here may have clinched it for Basil in his decision to strike out with his new bride for the east coast on the morning after their marriage in Hobart. In a hotel lounge in Wellington Point, he would learn from a retired English journalist how veterans of the Napoleonic wars had settled this promontory, which was named by a Captain Greer who had survived the whole campaign in the Peninsula and even fought at Waterloo, and who organised his convicts to axe down the thickets of bluegums and native cherry that grew to the water's edge. Whether it was Basil Dove's grey eyes that he boasted could see "for ivver", like his fellow Cumbrian John Peel, or his romantic spirit, Alex's father was instantly able to picture Greer, surrounded by fallen trees and recalling the battlefield where he had forfeited an ear; the dead bodies of the 88th, his regiment of foot, stretching in all directions. The promontory was now a home to the Greer Golf Club.

The site cleared by Greer and its panorama were spectacularly lovely. The sun rose between the Hazards, sparkling across the bay onto Talbot's on clear days, and, at the south end, onto the Freycinet Court Hotel where Alex's parents had spent their honeymoon: yellowish, mock-Tudor, with narrow windows and a courtyard.

In between, on blocks of identical size, were the primary school where Alex had been schooled until the age of eleven, a charity shop, a newsagent-cum-baker, two bed & breakfasts, the chemist's, the Town Hall, the post office, a real-estate office, a nursing home – where Tildy's mother had died eleven months ago now – a bowls club, a Uniting Church and a Wesleyan chapel.

The chapel of Alex's boyhood was today the Bethel Teahouse, owned by Welsh sisters Rhiannon and Myfanwy from Hay-on-Wye. It was, like Talbot's, one of very few buildings in Wellington Point that did not sit with its back to the bay. There, from a counter at one of the Gothic-shaped windows, Alex could watch the jetty and listen to the log-trucks slapping on their brakes as they approached the school.

CHAPTER THREE

JAZZ SOCIAL
The Louisa Meredith Nursing Home invites you along to a night of entertainment with the well-known Barney Todman and his steel pedal guitar, playing jazz-style music from the Thirties through to the Eighties.

Come along and dance the night away or sing along or just come and listen to the music and have a fun night out with friends.

Where: The Town Hall

When: Saturday 27 February

Tickets: $17 (includes pre-dinner drink and smorgasbord dinner)

Music will start at 7.00 p.m. See you there.

It was another five days before Alex saw Merridy again. On Tuesday afternoon, he sat in the Bethel Teahouse, Darjeeling on counter, and flicked through Talbot's *Newsletter*. It was late summer and Wellington Point was having a dance. He thought of who he might invite to the Jazz Social. The image of Tildy's friend swam into his mind – the flash of a goldfish under a flat still surface – but Alex had no idea where she lived, and he could not very well ask Tildy for her address.

He turned the page.

A warning not to drink the town water. A theft from the bowls club: still no arrest. The local cricket league scores. Sergeant Finter, the lumbering policeman in whose team Alex used to play as a ten-year-old, had scored fifty-four against Swansea. And a poem by Agnes who ran the Op-Shop, a sterilised but nevertheless musty room where Alex had handed over all his parents' clothes.

A white shape went by. He looked up in time to see a van reversing a trailer with quite a nice-looking speedboat towards the jetty. On the side of the van italic letters spelled out *THE LONG HAUL*, and beneath: *Jos. Silkleigh removals.* The van stopped on the ramp and a man in a wetsuit climbed out to unhitch the floating boat, a twenty-foot runabout with a navy-blue hull and trim. He tied her expertly to the jetty. Alex was impressed. It was a cloudless day. The man was going snorkelling. Alex envied him.

He blew on his tea. Beneath Agnes's poem, the next meeting of the Wellington Point reading group: *Mavis Pidd will speak about her recently released autobiography: "A Self-Published Life"*. There was a column on the Summer Flower Show. Mrs Fysshe had taken second prize in the forced rhubarb category. Alex was reading how Harry Ford had won the Betsy Grogan Cup for his assorted chutneys when a face came up to the window.

It was – not immediately, but in lapping ripples – the young woman whom he had helped up onto the fence.

She peered inside. He hoped for a second it was at him, but whoever it was her blue eyes sought she did not see them, and then it became her own reflection that she needed to vet.

He sat very still as she stared at herself, the candid expression of someone who did not know that she was being watched. This afternoon she wore a tortoiseshell comb in her hair, but no lipstick.

Alex was aware of a surge in his chest. Then a voice whisked her round and she was adjusting to an athletic figure who crossed the road at a gallop. Ray Grogan in his brown suit and neat ginger moustache. And – on this particular afternoon – a gold stud in his right ear. Looking at her like a mink about to take a sea trout.

He felt himself rise to his feet as the two of them came inside.

"Hi, Alex," said Ray with a hint of animus, and piloted her to the most distant table.

Alex could not hear their conversation, but he saw that from time to time Merridy shook her head. Ray worked in Tamlyn & Peppiatt on the main street – selling and managing farms far and wide, organising home loans and dealing with holiday rentals – but it was easy to see him on a beach, cutting the throat of a bushranger for the reward while the kookaburras croaked their encouragement. Ray with his glib talk was the only man in town whom Alex categorically disliked.

Then Ray got up and swaggered across the room as if he were

in Parliament and not in a teahouse on the east coast, and through the door that led to the toilet outside.

She was staring at the table.

"Hi," he said.

"Hi." Not looking up.

"Alex Dove. I met you the other day."

"I know," in that voice. "You live at Moulting Lagoon." She lifted her head.

"Anything wrong?" he asked.

"Not really."

"Ray doing a Ray?"

"What's a Ray?"

"If you don't know, you're in the middle of it."

She laughed.

"He's sure got the magic touch," Alex said.

She rocked back in her chair. "Oh, come on. Don't wind me up. He caught me with my guard down. I should have told him to get lost."

"Why don't you?"

"I didn't want to offend him, but there's a certain type of pushy fellow who gets up my nose. I hate feeling passive like that."

"Hi, Mr Dove."

Alex looked around reluctantly.

A boy stood in the centre of the tearoom.

"Rob, if it's your mum you're after, she left ten minutes ago."

The boy went on standing there with a timid expression. "Hey, I just wanted to thank you for the other day. It was tops."

"Glad you had a good time," and explained to Merridy: "Rob came out with his school and watched the sheep being dipped."

"And how to mark them!" raising his leg. Scrawled on his jeans, a faded orange D.

Alex smiled. "You realise what that means, don't you? Now you'll have to work for me. Come again in shearing time and you can write it on a sheep."

When Rob had left, Alex told Merridy how just after Christmas the school's Deputy Head had telephoned him. There had been a falling-out with Jack Fysshe and they were looking for someone to take children in the holidays around a working farm.

Alex had given over a day to Rob's class. He had ridden them each on his tractor. He had lifted them all onto a horse and then shown them how to milk a cow.

She said: "That was kind of you."

"Not really. In England, that's what I was going to be, a teacher," and leaned forward. "What were we talking about?"

"Ray."

"Oh, God . . ." he groaned. "What did he want? What does Ray ever want?" Women somehow did not wish to be attracted to him, but were. By and large, men, of course, found him odious and shallow and vain, but women didn't see that – until it was too late. Merridy, being a little brassier, a little brittler and more consciously tough than most girls in this town, might prove an exception to Ray's motto that a cock could never have too many hens.

"He's invited me to the Jazz Social," Merridy said.

"But you won't go?"

She gazed at Alex and with a slow motion shook her head. But the exasperation might have been aimed at him.

His cheeks boiled. He glanced down at the plastic bag at his feet, containing three bottles retrieved from a bin behind the hotel.

"Would you come out for a meal one night?" he said.

"You mean with you?" Not unkindly, but surprised.

"Right. With me."

She went on sipping at him. It had surprised her less to discover that he had slept with Tildy. At the time when she removed her shoe, she knew nothing about him, but his hands were clearly pleased. "He seems nice," she had said, putting her shoe back on.

"He is. Thoroughly," Tildy had murmured, her interest already shifting to what was happening over the fence. "But it was never going to work out. Even I could see that. I just knew my mother would have really liked him."

Across the table, Alex was smiling. Enjoying her forthright stare.

She thought, looking at him: From the moment I arrived in this place, men have not stopped hitting on me. But Alex's smile inspired confidence. She felt a mysterious sense of relief to see him there. He was tentative and she liked that. And withdrawn. A self-sufficient man but kind, who grazed his cattle and was educated. So Tildy had led her to believe. "He was going on about this ruddy novel. The way he talked about that book, I reckon he'd have preferred to take *it* to bed rather than me!"

Merridy recalled Tildy's indignation and thought of a book she had herself been reading the night before – a reprint on sale in the hotel, written by a Victorian settler to this coast, Louisa Meredith. She had not bought it, but would read a few pages whenever she was not having to help Debbie with the dishes, and it made her tingle with wisdom and unspecified fine feelings. And gentility and uprightness. Everything, in fact, that she had hoped to experience at university.

Yes, I'll come for a meal, under the influence of her book. Is what she meant to say.

"Hey, leave my girl alone!"

She turned her head towards the handsome shouter in his shiny brown tailor's cloth.

"Not your girl, Mr Grogan," she said.

"You don't know what you're missing," replied Ray and glared at Alex. He resumed his place and squeezed her arm with a hand that was large and clean and scrubbed of the blue biro that Alex remembered from the classroom, covered with the correct spellings of English kings and queens and, on one occasion, English trees.

She lowered her head, but did not withdraw her arm.

"Bye, then," said Alex.

"Bye," ordered Ray, clicking his teeth.

Alex looked at them for a moment. He gathered up his bottles and left.

Unable to shake off the sight of Ray Grogan's ginger-freckled fist on Merridy's arm, Alex walked fast from the teahouse and along the footpath that seemed to sway under him like the suspension bridge in the school playground.

The wide shy street was quiet, and behind the hedges and the Norfolk Island pines the owners of the single-storey houses had one eye on the cricket and one on the thin drift of smoke from their barbies. In the early morning the street would stir with log-trucks heading out for Hobart, but at five in the afternoon

Wellington Point contained the promise of the empty road and the faint sewerage smell of seaweed that presaged rain.

Doing his very best to think of anything, anything but the real-estate agent, Alex made his way past the school, along the esplanade, and towards the jetty and the street where he had parked his ute. The tide was out, the sun catching the white tips of the low waves and the mauve dorsal of the peninsula. However down at heart Alex might get to feel on the farm, he would never tire of this view – unlike certain of his schoolmates. He knew one or two who preferred nothing more than to sit slumped with their backs to the bay, their heads in the *Mercury* or peering through wreaths of home-grown marijuana at porn videos bootlegged from Canberra.

A branch creaked above him. The air had been still when he entered the teahouse, but a breeze had blown up. He opened the door of his ute and stopped. The noise of the wind in the pines. Grit in his face. An ice cream wrapper sucked up into the sky. He closed the door and walked on. The thought of the snorkeller drawing him down the concrete boat ramp and onto the jetty.

It was a saw of Miss Pritchard's geography class that the next land mass south was the polar ice cap. As always when Alex walked out on the eighty-yard-long jetty, he was aware of being at the end of the line. With a keener pang than normal, it struck him – surveying the horizon – that he really did live in one of the earth's more remote places. One of the more unvisited, too.

Until the road was finished in 1911, the town was reachable from Hobart only by horse and cart, or by sea: a journey taking up to three days, the steam packet sailing down the Derwent, round the Iron Pot lighthouse, past Betsy Island, Blackjack Reef and across Storm Bay to the canal at Dunalley, coming out north of Eaglehawk Neck, round Hellfire Bluff, through Mercury Passage to Swansea and Wellington Point.

Though this jetty was still here, where the scallop boats had unloaded, the bay had silted up. South-easterly breezes with sand-bearing waves had shallowed what was two fathoms of water at the time of the packet to a mere three feet, so that only shoal-draught boats could tie up alongside. At weekends, out-of-towners launched their tinnies from the ramp, anchoring off Dolphin Sands to catch flat-head, but vessels with a keel avoided Oyster Bay. Talk of a marina every few years invariably petered out in agreement that whoever was going to build it would have to construct an overlapping groin on the other side of the promontory – and have mighty deep pockets. Wellington Point boasted no such entrepreneurs and probably would not have made one coming in from outside welcome. As Alex's father had soon discovered, this was not a Yorkshire village bobbing with life and fishing boats. It was a town on the sea without sea-life, affected by the same elements that affected the farm; and was vulnerable – even on the clearest, calmest day – to southerly busters from Antarctica. Fierce, sudden winds that gusted up without warning, driving the surface of the sea into the bay and giving rise to extreme tides and flooding.

Perhaps this explained Alex's sudden concern for the snorkeller. He had known too many occasions when a mainlander or tourist had misread the weather conditions and set out across a perfectly calm sea, expecting the calmness to last through the weekend.

He reached the end of the jetty – four corroded planks – and looked out, his eyes sweeping the bay for a solitary blue-and-white hull. Past Maria Island, the Hen and Chicks, Schouten . . . but it was no good. All he could see was a young woman sitting at a table. And Ray.

CHAPTER FOUR

SIMPLY TO TOUCH HER reluctant flesh gave Ray a jolt of comfort. He was desperate to seduce Merridy. She had come into his office two weeks ago, on a mild afternoon in early February, wheeling her invalid father.

Ray leaped up, in his enthusiasm to close the door almost slamming it against a foot. He peered around it to see a thin woman, dressed in loose-fitting nylon slacks with an onyx crucifix dangling from her throat.

"You must be Mrs Bowman," and flashed her an indulgent look. "Please, come in."

Still she stood there in her trance. Her face white and lined, with nostrils nipped in and eyes red-rimmed from weeping.

"Mum, this is Mr . . ."

With no effort he shifted his smile to the young woman. "Ray Grogan. But please call me Ray. As in sunshine."

"We've come to inspect one of your retirement units," Merridy continued flatly. "I believe Mr Framley has been in touch."

She wheeled her father up to the desk.

"Ah, yes, yes," Ray addressed the wheelchair. "We've been expecting you, Mr Bowman. Welcome to the heart of Tasmania's relaxed east coast!"

Mr Bowman looked rotten. On this afternoon, he was in pain with a bloodshot eye after he had tried to join his wife and daughter at breakfast and had fallen getting out of bed. His second accident in a week.

Ray asked cheerily: "Can you see me, sir?"

A slow shake of the head.

Ray turned his attention back to Merridy. "I think you'll be pleased with the unit. It's a pioneering scheme. I like to describe the philosophy behind it as 'independence with a sense of well-being'."

He fished in a drawer for a set of keys. "Shall we walk or shall I drive you?"

"Well, where is it? How far?"

"End of the street and across the cricket pitch."

"We'll walk," decided Merridy. "The air might do my father good."

In the eight hundred yards from the office to the retirement unit, Ray sought to engage Merridy in conversation.

Already from Keith Framley, her relative, Ray had learned a fair amount. Merridy's father – the man she propelled up the footpath – had been a mechanical engineer who was electrocuted in Zeehan while installing a lift in the tin mine there. The shock had brought on an aneurysm that slurred his speech. He couldn't complete the simplest sentence – humiliating for someone remembered by Tildy's father as a man who enjoyed nothing more than to recite poetry.

Because of his accident, Mr Bowman's wife, from whom he had been separated, had come back to look after him – as had his daughter, who had taken a year off from her studies at Melbourne University.

"It must be tough for you, leaving your course like that," glancing sideways with keen green eyes.

"I was only in my first year," she said crisply, all her concentration on the asphalt ahead.

"Keith speaks very highly of your Dad."

"My father helped him early on."

"Keith says he remembers your Dad always with a book of poetry in his hand."

"Then he's exaggerating."

"I like poetry myself, I used to read it aloud at school," Ray sailed on. "Did – does your Dad like anyone in particular?"

Merridy twisted her head to look at Ray. "Well, a favourite is Edward Lear."

"Edward Lear?" his eyes boring into hers. He touched his moustache, a soulful expression on his face. "Now that does ring a definite bell."

*

The property to which Ray escorted the Bowmans was called "Otranto", a modern one-storey villa behind Louisa Meredith House. The nursing home had funded the building of three "independent self-care living units", according to Ray's description in the brochure, of which this one was still for sale. Keith, a second cousin of Merridy's father, was on the charity's board. As soon as he learned of her husband's accident he had telephoned Mrs Bowman and encouraged her to bring Leonard immediately to Wellington Point to convalesce, even as he had brought Mrs Framley. The Bowmans could stay at his hotel free of charge while they inspected the unit or until other appropriate accommodation was found. He defied them not to adore Wellington Point. Its recuperative air had performed minor but measurable miracles for his late wife, even if it could not in the end prevent the cancer from spreading to her brain. "It's heaven on a stick! Reminds a lot of people of the Bay of Naples."

"Naples," said Mrs Bowman.

From Zeehan, Merridy called to enquire if there was anything she could do to repay his kindness.

"Nothing!" said Keith, who had never forgotten how helpful her father had been when a bed & breakfast had come up for sale in the Bowmans' street in Ulverstone. "Nothing at all."

But a day later he telephoned to crave a favour. What he wondered was, would Merridy be willing to help out in his newly opened cocktail bar.

Ray drew back the melon-pink curtains and stepped aside for Mrs Bowman to take in the view of Oyster Bay that was only partially obscured by an ochre wall. Beyond the wall was a close-cropped lawn where two people squatted dressed in white.

"It's close to medical facilities. And while you're here you don't pay rates, Hydro, only your own phone bill. Plus, there's a nurse-call system for emergency," and indicated a button on the wall above the pneumatic hospital bed.

Mrs Bowman bent down – crucifix swinging – to her husband. "What do you think, Leonard? Would this suit?"

From the wheelchair came a whining noise incomprehensible to Ray. He paused to plump up a pillow and waited until Mr Bowman fell silent before tapping the door-frame. "The unit is constructed throughout in environmentally friendly materials to minimise energy usage, and there's an irrigated drip system in the landscaped garden. The whole idea is to make you feel very much at home."

"That's nice," said Mrs Bowman, a thin hand mashing the onyx Christ into her throat. She walked over to the window and stood in the alcove, her concentration on the neat lawn and the two white-haired women stooped there. She released her hand from her throat and spread it on the glass.

Ray noted that something in Mrs Bowman had mended. "As you can see, our town has a thriving bowling club. The green is a stone's throw away. And should you wish to join there, my mother is the president! You know, it's funny, but I always find myself telling newcomers to Wellington Point the same thing. Excellence, dignity and respect are the priorities of our little community. And companionship."

"It's perfect, I'm sure," Merridy broke in. "But what happens when we come to sell?"

Ray smiled at her. He could tell who made the decisions in this family! "Should you ever wish to sell," he ploughed on without missing a beat, "the unit reverts back to Louisa Meredith House, and half the profits go to the family." He positioned himself to catch her eye. "I hope that won't be for a long while."

Many years later, when his jaw lifted with pride at the *Mercury*'s description of him as "the David Boon of real estate", Ray would date the recovery in Tasmania's east coast property market to his sale of this retirement unit. Ray took the credit. It was his description of "Otranto", he advised Mr Tamlyn on his return to the office, that had swayed the Bowman family. "You should have seen the lady's expression when I told her about the bowlo."

Since joining the company office seven years before, Ray had discovered that one enjoyable aspect of his work consisted in writing short paragraphs to accompany the half-dozen photographs that Tamlyn & Peppiatt advertised each Friday in the

Mercury's property section. At primary school, his worst subject had been English: it was a standing joke in the class – in which Ray consistently hovered close to the bottom – that Ray Grogan had to cheat to spell his own name. But at his office desk, he developed a knack for describing the most ordinary-looking weatherboard shack in such a way that people would more often than not wish to view it.

It was very simple. Properties were like dogs: they took on the characteristics of their owners. As Ray bade farewell to the Bowman family outside the nursing home, he reflected that Mr Bowman was a ruin that no amount of renovation could restore. His wife, rewired, upgraded and tastefully refurbished, had potential, although her religion might be an obstacle to a quick sale. He perceived her in the same light as he had once viewed the Bethel Teahouse. Not for the faint-hearted, but offering great prospects for enterprising buyers looking to invest in a historical quarter. Renovate. Renovate. Renovate. This dame is just crying out for you to rescue her from her loneliness!

As for the daughter . . . His eyes lingered on Merridy as she wheeled her father around the boundary to the hotel. This gorgeous 1960s prestige home has long been coveted by many, but owned by few. Rarely on the market, an inspection will not disappoint. Do not miss this golden opportunity!

Nothing he could think of, though, quite captured the commanding, grave beauty of the young woman who passed in front of the score-keeper's hut and turned into the hotel courtyard.

Her impregnable and valiant look would have Catherine-wheeled the stumps of most men, but an unhappy woman appealed to Ray's vanity. The fact was that if she were a house, then he had never come up against anything so splendid, so grand, so classical – unless it was Talbot's (which Albert Talbot had made clear that he would never in any circumstance put up for sale, not while there was breath left in his body). No, she was more one of those Crusader castles that he was taught about in his history class. Walls eight metres thick that no amount of cannon-fire could broach, with buckets of boiling tar tipped onto the head of anyone rash enough to scale them.

But where properties were concerned, he had the patience of a snake.

Merridy could feel his eyes like marbles on her neck and shivered. She pushed the wheelchair quicker, her mother following in silent contemplation. Not until they reached the courtyard did her mother say: "What was your honest opinion of that young man?"

"Awful."

"And the place?"

"It will do."

"Couldn't we get a better deal if we rented? If your father . . ."

"Well, we've got to hope he doesn't. Anyway, I think Keith is keen to have his rooms back."

"I will write the cheque tomorrow."

They had arrived at a door with a brass "7" screwed into it. Keith had allocated them a suite in a ground-floor block next to the main building. Merridy opened the door and together the two women lifted Leonard's body out of the wheelchair and onto the bed. Her father's feet had shrunk and his shoes slipped off as they lay him down. A wheezing noise issued from the dry lips, the sound of air bubbling through the fluid on his lungs.

Merridy looked at the bloodshot cye that roved the ceiling, the cracked skin. The lines in his face were inscriptions that had weathered and were now unreadable. "We're making the right decision, Mum," in a quiet voice.

Her gaze remained on her father while her mother rinsed a glass and filled it with tap-water and gulped it down. The walk had tired Mrs Bowman.

Suddenly, she was spitting out.

The noise whipped Merridy around. "Mum! Keith said we're not to drink the tap-water."

Mrs Bowman grimaced, spitting again into the basin. "I forgot," wiping the taste from her lips.

"Over there – I put it over there."

Mrs Bowman drank two glass of water from the bottle and lay down beside her husband. She licked the corners of her mouth. "I found the church, Merridy. There is a late service this evening."

"What time?"

Mrs Bowman checked her watch. "Nine o'clock." Then picked up the photograph that she had propped on the bedside table, a black-and-white photograph of a young boy racing barefoot along a narrow strand.

He would be with her for ever. Her only regret was, every time she turned her eyes to him, that she had not told him how beautiful he had looked in his boots.

"I'll make sure I'm back in time," Merridy said, and sat on her Glory Box – a wooden steamer trunk at the foot of the bed – to take off her shoes. She crossed her arms and stared a moment at the orange lino. Then she stood up, put on a pair of dark tights and the navy-blue skirt and jacket which Keith insisted that she wear, kissed her mother on her forehead and her father on the cheek, and set off across the courtyard, her book under her arm.

There were two places to drink in Wellington Point. The Returned Servicemen's Club on Greer Street and the Freycinet Court Hotel. In a bid to excite more customers, and partly to distract himself in the hollow months after his wife's death, Keith Framley had the previous winter fitted out a cocktail bar at the suggestion of a mate in the hotel trade who overheard at a convention of travel agents in Bali that Tasmania was set to become a destination for the discerning European tourist. His mate had blundered. There *were* no tourists here in 1988, not in Wellington Point. Steady drinkers went to the pub in Swansea for their beer. The odd backpacker misdirected to Framley's cocktail bar at the extremity of the globe almost invariably preferred to join regulars in the public bar on the other side of the hotel.

The only person to disturb Merridy's reading that night, around seven o'clock, was Keith's despondent daughter.

"Hey, Tildy," said Merridy, and closed her book.

"Have you seen Dad?" her face drawn beneath the flawless fringe.

"In Hobart."

"What's he gone to Hobart for?" hunting around in a black handbag until she found her lip gloss.

"The cricket, could it be?"

"Oh, yes, the cricket," in a disappointed voice. She finished touching up her mouth. "Like some?"

"Not really."

"Go on, take it. If you want to get on in this place, you wear lip gloss. That's a fact."

"No, it's an opinion."

"No, no, believe me, it's a fact. Put this on and you'll see. You'll be a hit with it. Hey, what you reading?" She picked it up. "Louisa Meredith. *My Home in Tasmania*." It might have been some unpalatable medicine. "Part of your studies, is it?"

"I borrowed it from the front desk."

"Looks boring," Tildy yawned.

"It's interesting – if you're interested in history."

"I'm not interested in history. What sort of history, anyway?"

"I was learning how they got the feathers off the black swans at Moulting Lagoon."

"Really?" She climbed onto a stool and looked around the bar. "How did they? Someone I know, his family made their money from swan down."

Merridy found the place. She read aloud: "*The general custom was, to take the birds in large quantities in the moulting season, when they are most easily captured and extremely fat; they were then confined in pens*, without any food, *to linger miserably for a time, till ready to die of starvation, because, whilst they are fat, the down can neither be so well stripped off, nor so effectually prepared.*"

The sound of Tildy listening made her look up.

Tildy's lips were trembling. "That's me! That me! Oh, Merridy, I'm no different. I know how those swans feel."

"Why, what's the matter?"

"I have a pain, it's right here," and squeezed under her breast. "Normally if I have a pain there's a good reason. But this pain is different. I can't make it go away. I can't breathe. I can't sleep."

Merridy put the book down. "Maybe it's indigestion."

"I've never felt so bad," said Tildy, and lunged over to a table to seize a paper napkin. She blew her nose and dabbed one eye and then the other.

"Maybe you're in love."

"Oh, Merridy. How can you be so cruel? Now I know how Mr Twelvetrees suffered."

Merridy straightened a brick that was on the counter.

"You haven't forgotten Randal Twelvetrees?" accusingly.

"Oh, no."

"He liked you. My God, he did."

"He was just ill, poor man."

"Obsessed more like," and blew her nose again.

"It was more my mother who affected Randal, Tildy. As I think you know."

"Whatever, whatever. Pointless, I know, to ask about *your* love life. Am I not right?"

Merridy had not taken her eyes from the brick. Baked by a convict and with its frog filled with Redhead matches to strike on the side, it was one of half a dozen that Tildy's father had bought from an antique shop in Battery Point and scattered on tables and counters around the hotel.

She began separating the matches. "My hands are pretty tied at the moment," in a tight voice. "For romance."

"Oh, Merridy, how selfish of me," and Tildy's eyes watered again. "I'm so sorry about your dad."

Merridy lay the back of her hand on Tildy's wrist. "Who is he?"

Tildy's disconsolate face looked up. "Have you a moment? I know you've got a lot on your plate, but I need someone to talk to."

With a nod of her head, Merridy indicated the empty room. "I'm all yours – until ten to nine."

"This is so embarrassing," and went behind the counter. "No, I can do it." She poured herself a double shot of the Captain Morgan – one of the rums that her father had stocked in the bar for discerning customers and which she much preferred to Bundaberg. "You wouldn't keep anything from me, Merridy? I couldn't stand that."

"I wouldn't keep anything from you."

"Well, it's Ray Grogan."

"Ray Grogan?"

"You met him this afternoon. He showed you the unit."

*

Ray, in case Merridy had not already heard, was a man renowned in the district for having bedded most women in Wellington Point – not including Tildy.

His reticence on this score was a source of frustration that Tildy had begun to mistake in herself for passion.

"Why not ignore him?" Merridy suggested.

"I've tried to. Believe me, I've tried to," looking up and down for tonic. "But it's no good," and sniffed.

Around about the time of Merridy's appearance in town, Tildy had decided that the handsome real-estate agent was all she ever wanted. Even though part of her could see clean through him to the other side.

"I was so furious the other night, I up-fronted him: 'You're nothing but a proper slut, Ray. That's all you are.'"

"And his reaction?"

"He told me that I couldn't be more mistaken. But I know Ray." She poured the tonic into her rum and swallowed. "He screws them in his clients' beds or wherever he's showing them around," grimacing. "He's got keys to every house in Wellington Point, I wouldn't be surprised. He even shags them in the score-keeper's hut! Oh, he's a shonk. You should hear his lines. They're the same for every woman."

"Must be good ones," observed Merridy, who had heard enough.

But the bit was between Tildy's teeth. "He was pashing on with Rose-Maree, promising that all he ever wanted was to give her pleasure. And telling Abbygail that she smelled like the Taj Mahal by moonlight. He's nothing but a root-rat. And don't think he minds how old they are! Teresa overheard him at the RSL saying that he knew Mrs Prosser found him attractive because when he put his hand down her pants it was like feeding a horse – and she must be over sixty. Oh, he's disgusting," and shivered.

"But you aren't just disgusted?" toying with the lip gloss that Tildy had left on the counter.

"I don't know. I can't tell you how many times I've said to myself: Right. That's it. Step back, Tildy."

"Have you told him how you feel?"

"No. He has enough tickets on himself." And shivered again. "Such a skite."

"He must have something good hidden away," Merridy said.

"Oh, Merridy, it's not that!" Her voice had risen to a wail at the injustice of it. Beyond the porkies that he told her, beyond his reputation for – in her father's words – "rooting like a leather-punch", Tildy discerned the outline of a different Ray; the Platonic version, as it were. "The truth is, there's a side of Ray which is actually quite sweet and generous."

Merridy was not convinced. "What's in it for you?"

"Well, I'm not alone," her eyes downcast. "And now he's having a birthday party on Saturday. He's invited Rose-Maree and Debbie and Abbygail and Teresa. He's even invited the girls from the Bethel Teahouse. But the bastard hasn't invited me."

She grappled with the upturned rum bottle. Empty.

Merridy plucked the bottle from its holder and dropped it into the bin. Above the counter the clock said 8.55.

"Listen, I've got to go. But if you want my opinion, I think you should have nothing whatever to do with him."

Next morning, first thing, Merridy walked into Tamlyn & Peppiatt and handed over her mother's cheque for the deposit on the unit.

Ray scrutinised Mrs Bowman's signature. He clipped the cheque to the folder on his desk. "What are you doing this Saturday?" light as spray.

"I'm busy," Merridy said.

"Would you like to come to a party?"

"No."

He gave a pleasant laugh. "It would be a chance to meet some locals."

"Why haven't you invited Tildy?"

"Tildy? Do I know a Tildy?"

"Tildy Framley, my cousin."

"Oh, Tildy!" guarded, all of a sudden. "You're right. I haven't."

"Is there a reason?"

He hesitated. "Tildy and I . . . Listen, it's difficult—"

"Invite Tildy to your birthday party and I'll come."

He stared at her, weighing what she had said. "That's blackmail."

"So . . ." At the door, with her back to him, she paused. "Tell me, why don't you like her?" addressing the carpet, its fake Aboriginal design. "She likes you."

"I *do* like her," his voice high-pitched and apologetic. He twisted his moustache. "But . . . But . . ."

She turned, bristling. "But what?"

On that Saturday afternoon, Ray looked up from his tuna steaks – and there she was, head in the wet gum leaves, sitting on his fence right next to Tildy, and gazing down at his family and friends and the barbie that had started to hiss. Despite the damp, the sight of Merridy rekindled furtive hopes.

"Hey, girls, come on down."

"Both of us?"

"Both. Of. You."

After that, he was overly welcoming. He poured a Bloody Mary for Tildy, saying how pleased he was to see her, and took her over to speak with Rhiannon; and a tomato juice for Merridy.

"Here you are." His eyes moved from her lip gloss that emphasised the whiteness of her skin. He had never seen a face so white – like milk to tempt a snake.

She accepted the glass. A pulse of colour darted into her cheeks, then was gone. "I suppose I should say Happy Birthday."

"Couldn't keep away, eh?" swilling the thought of her naked around the bedroom of his mind.

"Lord, I tried," she laughed. "Nothing else to do in this godforsaken village."

He was wearing blue shorts daggered in white slashes, and had a footballer's build, with ginger hairs on his chest, and was tall.

Something puzzled him. "Why the fence? Why not come round the front like everyone else?"

"Fences are for gatecrashers."

"But I invited you."

Her body moved inside her clothes, away from the wet clinging cotton. "Not without her," nodding at her cousin.

"You mean," it began to dawn on him, "you really are here only because of Tildy?"

"What other reason could there be?"

He pretended to study Tildy, who was pretending to talk to the Welsh sisters, although her body faced the wrong way.

"That's not kind," he murmured, hurt, and yet Merridy's annihilating laugh only intensified the appeal of her. He looked at her bust pushing against her damp blue dress. And gave one fiftieth of his concentration to her cousin across the yard and even less to the horizon that he decided to address.

"Merridy, look at the sea, it goes on and on to the South Pole and makes me feel a grain of sand." He adopted a pensive expression and wished that it would stop drizzling. He was talking like a version of himself that he would like to be. It sounded OK. It felt good. He could not understand why she was still laughing. But he was not in her fantastical scheme.

Five days after his party, Ray was removing the details of "Otranto" from his office window when he caught sight of Merridy standing on her own outside the Bethel Teahouse. He seized the moment.

"Hey, Merridy!"

"Oh, Ray. Hi."

"What are you up to?"

"I'm looking for my mother, actually."

"Let me buy you a coffee. There's something I want to ask you."

"What?" standing her ground.

"Do you like jazz?" and pushed open the door.

"It depends. Why?"

"Come on in and I'll tell you."

He could have done, though, without Alex Dove sitting there to witness his humiliation.

"Who was that?" asked Merridy to break the silence after Alex had disappeared out of the Bethel with his clinking bag. She knew, but was curious to know more.

"That," Ray said, "is Piers Dove."

"Piers Dove?" At the same time thinking: But Tildy called him Alex.

"Oh, I can tell you about Piers Dove," too pleased at the sight of her attentive face to be alert to the reason.

"Then tell me."

"He's a Pom," said Ray philosophically. "Although we were at school together."

"He looks all right."

"Yeah, in his sleep," with a murky smile.

"And where does he sleep?"

"Over at Moulting Lagoon."

"With someone?"

"Lives on his own. TV reception's not good. Nor is the bore-water." He grinned, squeezing her arm. "He was crazy even before his parents had an accident," and with his free hand tapped the side of his temple.

She cocked her head. "What accident?" interested where before she had been merely curious.

CHAPTER FIVE

TALBOT'S STORE
We apologise for any inconvenience caused by the refurbishment of the food aisles. From March 3, Bread and Cereals will be relocated to Toiletries.

Deadline for the March 9 Newsletter: *Tuesday, March 1, 5 p.m. All notices and advertisements to Mr Talbot. Donations to offset the cost of production are welcome. Ed.*

The binoculars tracked Alex to the end of the jetty with the same attention as they had observed him reappear in Wellington Point after an absence of twelve years. The scuttlebutt was that young Mr Dove would be gone back to England by the end of the week, once he had sorted out his affairs. Mr Talbot had heard this from his manager, Fred Coggins.

That was four years ago.

Whatever Albert Talbot made of Alex's behaviour, he was unlikely to say. It was his inflexible habit never to make comments about what people did. Only to watch, listen, remember – as in his wartime watches.

"You have one instruction, Sergeant Talbot. And you will reissue it to yourself every morning until the war is over: Make yourself invisible. That way you won't get caught, and you certainly don't want to get caught, son, take it from me. My advice to you, furthermore, would be to keep your head well down vis-à-vis the natives, too. If you're going to live in the bush, you've got to have a very, very clean nose. That means: Don't fraternise, don't take them to your hidey-holes, and – above all – don't borrow any of their women. Natives don't like that, Talbot. But tell you what I do want to see when you get back. I want to see bruises all over your head and body. That's where the wild animals have bumped into you because you'll be invisible."

These had been his orders from Lieutenant Black, a compact watchful type himself who had picked Sergeant Talbot to be the radio-op – "because," he said, "you get on with people." They had met when Albert was taking his St John's Ambulance certificate.

Dropped ashore in Jacquinot Bay, Albert had followed Black's orders to a tee. Safe as in church when sitting up there in the thick scrub, beneath a ceiling of sago palms and a red-and-blue silk parachute in which to catch the creepy-crawlies – or to cut clothes from. Living on swede and yams and dehydrated American rations as he crouched there – with no weapon, with nothing but his brass binoculars – behind a screen of vines and long grass, tracking the least movement of the Japanese. Where they ate, slept, the planes that flew over, the warships that stopped off in Rabaul, plus anything untoward. And twice a day reporting back what he saw on his ATR4 radio, in a code derived from sentences taken from a by-now damp copy of Agatha Christie's *The Secret Adversary*, the words coming back to him in stray and disembodied phrases upon which once upon a time hung the freedom of the Christian world and now no longer made the slightest sense . . . "Repulsive goes the Whole Hog."

Half a century on, Sergeant Talbot's radio was now his *Newsletter.* Together with the general store, it defined his life. Because, wisely or not – and he thought, on balance, not – he had obeyed Lieutenant Black's other stricture: about keeping away from women.

He had had opportunity and provocation galore. In the light of his first-aid training, he was expected to perform minor medical procedures on the natives. Alerted by drums, the women would walk for two days. They came down from the hills and lined up for him. Bent over, each carrying her child in a *bilum,* taking the weight of the string bag in a broad strap around her forehead. They were finely built women, with bold brown eyes that looked straight into his, and black hair that he wanted to touch. He conversed easily with these women – he knew them as *meri* – and spoke to them in proper pidgin taught by the missionaries. They were so immediately welcoming that he did not have to navigate a whole lot of prejudices, because they did not appear to have any. Many had been tortured to extract information about

Australians. He dressed their spear cuts and bullet wounds. He drained their hands which sometimes blew up huge, like inflated rubber gloves. He injected them against fevers and yaws. And yet he had not known intimacy with a single *meri*. (There had been one never-to-be-forgotten occasion when, yes, he had known the desire, but the Japanese had put paid to that.) With the consequence that Sergeant Talbot's detachment had got to be a habit. Educated not to be an encumbrance, he had not been one. But as he grew older he had come bitterly to wonder if, all things considered, he mightn't have preferred to swap his very clean nose for the excitement and mess of an involved heart. The mess that he watched unfold below day by day, and now in Alex Dove.

At the end of the jetty, Alex could see no sign of the snorkeller's boat.

Meanwhile, the wind had toughened, hurling the waves against the pylons and bringing the first pellets of rain. They stung his cheek in the same instant that he heard the whoosh of something rushing past – and a flock of tiny birds flew out of the sun from the direction of Schouten Island.

The end of February and the swifts had come back, their colours radiant as if polished by the breeze on the long journey south. He followed them, one curved wing beating faster than the other, as he had watched them with his father on the top of Barn Hill. Alex had not known his father well, but there were things he had said that Alex could never forget. "Main point in life is to experience life. Some of those swifts may have flown from as far afield as Mongolia to warn us." For they were storm-signal birds, heralds of a humid north-easterly. When you saw them circling high in a thermal and listened to their shrill twittering, it would be only minutes before you heard the first crack of summer thunder.

Immediately, black thoughts flurried in on the backs of the birds. A cramped apartment in a red-brick mansion block in south London. The gloomy, low-ceilinged room and the lift, a vertical coffin that shuddered up past metal grilles through which his eyes fell on tense faces.

He thought: No, I love this place.

Alex felt good. Better than felt. Less than an hour ago, when he had pushed open the door into the teahouse, he was on the point of believing in everything that Ray Grogan said about him. He was a misfit. He would never make a good farmer. He might as well chuck it in and go back to London to teach. But now he was happy. Happy at the sight of the swifts and also at the prospect of a little more rain to put a tinge back on the paddocks. Above all, happy to think of the black-haired young woman in the Bethel. Her smile returned to him over Ray Grogan's arm, a dim light flashing its enigmatic message across the darkening water.

He turned, walked back, crossed Greer Street – a short road with three parked cars and Sergeant Finter eating flat-head – and climbed into his ute and drove home. Twenty minutes on and he still could feel a strange flicker inside him, like the jet of blue flame in the shape of a human figure that in his boyhood Bill Molson, his parents' immediate neighbour, claimed to have observed hovering above the marshes behind Moulting Lagoon; at least, that was the story.

Nor had this feeling diminished when Alex woke. As the day wore on, the prospect of seeing Merridy Bowman pushed every other thought from his head.

Until he met Merridy, Alex had not pictured the kind of woman with whom he wished to share his life, how she might look. Now he discovered her traces everywhere; in the colour of the sand blown up from the beach; in the swallows under the eaves on the back deck; he even heard her voice in the iron windmill. When a helicopter tilted over the house towards Wellington Point he thought maybe she was looking up at it, too.

The next time he saw her in town, bustling out of Tamlyn & Peppiatt surprisingly early on a Thursday morning, she was the averted glance across the road. Walking a purposeful walk that he would have run eight miles to see.

"Hey, Merridy!" He started towards her with the exaggerated carelessness of someone on a vital mission, exhilarated.

She turned. Looking different in profile. Surprised perhaps by his childish trick of opening his arms to attract attention.

"That meal," he said. His breaths came quick. It was absurd how nervous he was. He was seven or eight years older than her, dammit!

"What meal was that?"

He knew what he wanted to say, but it came out wrong. "The other day. I asked you out for a meal."

"Oh, yes," and gave a smile in which there was reticence and relief.

"I was wondering if you would take me up on it . . ." But his words did not fit. They had the looseness of a borrowed garment. He felt them drop about his ankles.

She rescued him. "When would you like?"

"Any time. Are you free Saturday?"

"Where?"

He faced the street for inspiration. "What about . . . what about . . . I know – the hotel?"

She looked at him with a curious expression and seemed on the verge of saying something.

"Or would you prefer somewhere else? Swansea perhaps?"

"No, no, I'll see you at the hotel."

The reason for Merridy's distractedness was the embarrassing night that she had spent with Ray Grogan, the culmination of his energetic campaign to lure her into an empty bedroom in a Tuscanised brick bungalow south of Wellington Point.

He had focused his attentions on her ever since she turned down his invitation to the Jazz Social, sauntering every lunchtime into the cocktail bar on no provocation and ordering a ten-ounce of Boag's that she had little alternative but to pour. And then, because there was never anyone other than himself to serve, engaging her in soft, beseeching talk.

It was perfectly, painfully obvious that Ray's flattery was habitual. It was his vernacular; he was not expressing his passion for her, but making the bed for its possibility, uttering ridiculous compliments in a steady flow until she no longer heard them. She beat him away, and still he came back. He was robust in the face of rejection, and that was somehow attractive.

Failing to interest her in the more recondite aspects of the local property market, Ray resorted to the dependable formulae that he employed for seduction. The lines tripped from his lips with the same ease as the phrases that came to him at his desk and that he taped to the windows of Tamlyn & Peppiatt.

"Confidentially," he said, "how would you like to go out with me?"

She gave him a disagreeable smile. "I don't think so, Mr Grogan. Ginger men always fall for me, but I can't stand them."

"I'll dye my hair for you," he proposed.

She looked at the stud in his ear. Debbie had told her that he had bought it to celebrate the sale of "Otranto": "Green, pink, purple, orange, I won't change my mind."

"Come on, Merridy, at least call me Ray," he pleaded. "I'll show you a wonderful time, really I will," he whispered in a humid, tropical breath, a root-rat with a gold stud. He sensed that this was the wrong tack to take with Merridy, but by force of habit found himself heading there. "Every passionate relationship I've had has begun passionately," he confessed. "But nothing to compare with this, Merridy. Nothing."

"Give me one reason why I should believe a word you say. One good reason."

"No, you're right, perhaps you shouldn't. Yet perhaps you want to. What's more, perhaps you need to."

She laughed. "I've never heard such bullshit." She had met his type in her first year at uni. Ray was an acupuncturist who knew nothing about women, but knew by dull rote the seven spots where to touch them so that in surprisingly more instances than not, and against every instinct, their cheeks dimpled and their skin tingled in a strange way up the insides of their legs.

"You're a clever girl, Merridy. All the same, I'd feel sorry to be your partner."

"Is that so?"

"You know what they say: *If you wish to be loved, love.*"

"'They say' is a big liar." Then: "Have you been reading a manual?"

"You mustn't, Merridy," with a grave face, "judge me by your past experiences."

And so uninsultably on he went. He had the resilience of the punching bag that he was rumoured to keep in his gym. It meant that Merridy could be rude to him and say what she really thought – without that penetrating either.

Until the moment came when she decided that the only way to tackle Ray Grogan was head on.

One Tuesday noon, he struck a match against the convict brick and studied the flame with an earnest expression.

"You're not going to smoke, are you?" she said. "I hate smoking."

"I do appreciate, Merridy, that we don't have much to offer you here."

"What do you mean?" at this new departure.

"Well, you're beautiful, you're intelligent," tuning his voice to a concerned note. "You should be at university, not stuck in Wellington Point."

"I have to be here. My father's dying."

"But one day, maybe sooner than you think, you'll have to think of yourself. And if you look at everyone in Wellington Point, which is a small place, and you take away the gays and the lesbians, of which there are an inappropriately large number, and then you take away the happily married men, of which there are quite a few by the way – that's all they know! – and then you take away the many no-hopers – the drunks, the drugged, the ditsy – then all you're left with is me. And though it hurts me to say this, I'm aware that I'm no catch for the likes of you. So of course, you'll go back to the university. Why wouldn't you?" He blew out the flame and gazed at her with an expression of plausible vulnerability.

It surprised her, what she felt. She expected to feel derision, but she was unexpectedly stirred. He was, after all, physically attractive and touching, and she made a deliberate effort to look at him as though the weight of his stare was a hairy caterpillar crawling over her. "Don't you have any homes to sell?"

"Market's off the boil. Not like me," with a solemn, beery chuckle. He slouched forward. "If you like, I could read you poetry." And tapped his nose.

She could tolerate it no longer. She put down her tray and faced him. "All right, Ray-as-in-sunshine," hand on hip. "Let's go."

The unexpectedness of it caught him by surprise. "Where?"

"Where do you think?" her cheeks dimpling.

A slow smile returned to his face until he was positively beaming. "Listen, there's a house out of town I've got to prepare for inspection. It so happens," and jangled his pocket, "I've got the keys right here. The bedroom has a terrific view of Schouten. A terrific view."

"No," she said so emphatically that he jerked his glass. "I'd like to see *your* house."

"*My* house?" Ray Grogan looked tense, uneasy, not at all prepared for this.

She went up to him where he sat at the bar, laid the back of her hand against his cheek, smelled his dog's breath between the glistening teeth.

"What, the old hunter doesn't want to kill?"

"What about Keith?" he stammered. "Won't he be missing you?"

"Not on my afternoon off," already putting her arms into a coat.

Less than ten minutes later, Merridy stepped into Ray Grogan's lair.

"Do you share this with your parents?" noticing three fibreglass fishing rods behind the door.

"No, I live on my own."

She paused to unbutton her coat in front of a poster of the Taj Mahal. Further along the wall was a poster of the Sphinx, pyramids in the background; and one more, of a glittering gold dome and minarets.

"I always wanted to go to Egypt," taking off his jacket. "Don't know why. It's probably a shit-hole."

Before laying his jacket over the back of a leatherette chair, he slipped a hand into one of its pockets and transferred whatever he found there to his trousers. "Well, what do you think?"

"About what?"

"My place. Here, give me that."

She let him take her coat and sat down on the sofa and looked around. "Oh, nice," she said. "Very nice."

"I bought it off a chemist who had to leave town in a hurry," he said, coming to sit beside her. "I turned the garage into a gym. Maybe you'd like to see?"

"I don't think so."

He edged nearer, stretching a practised arm along the backrest. "You know," he said, "it's wrong what they say about estate agents."

"What do they say?"

"Oh, stupid things," and looked sad and misunderstood. "That we're the least trustworthy profession – after car salesman, mark you, and journalists and policemen."

"I never read those surveys." She leaned forward a little to ease off her shoe.

"Can I tell you something?" stroking her hair and inspecting a lock of it with fierce intent. "You smell like the Taj Mahal looks by moonlight."

"Oh, bull," she laughed and pulled up her jacket.

"Whoa there! What are you doing?"

"Getting ready for your paintbrush," she said merrily. "Isn't that what you want?" And unfastened her bra.

He stared at her breasts, the shadow of the lace curtain falling on them in the pattern of a hot snowflake. She was buxom for someone her height. Even so, he was alarmed by her pace. "Hey," licking his upper lip, "something to drink? When do you have to get back?"

"I don't know. When I've had a wonderful time maybe," and dropped her bra on the carpet and sat back.

He went on staring at her on the leatherette sofa, the bright afternoon light streaming through the front window onto her white arms and breasts, her face without make-up.

"What about some music? I could put on some music. What do you like?"

"Have you any choral hymns?"

He watched for a sign that she was teasing him. But she seemed deadly serious. His mouth parted in a lamentable smile. "I was thinking Leonard Cohen. I'm not actually sure I have any church music."

His arm snaked back along the top of the sofa and he studied her hair again. "You don't want a Campari or something? I've got a bottle somewhere."

"No, I just want you to shove your sash into my gash."

Merridy spoke the words in a clear, pleasant manner. She could have been trying them out for the first time. Or singing a familiar hymn.

An undisguisable fear crept over his face. He spoke in a dry, dazed voice.

"There's something I'd like to understand about you."

But Merridy did not want anyone else's understanding. Least of all Ray Grogan's.

She leaped up and walked fast, across the thick brown carpet, and slipped into the bedroom – the quick, discreet movement of a girl who might have been late for a lecture.

He came in and she was waiting like fate on the bed, shoes already off, eyes looking up at him and her body poised, ready to take notes.

She pointed down at her tights. "All you have to do is take these off and put your hand here."

When, the following morning, Ray did not appear at the usual hour at Tamlyn & Peppiatt, his boss grew worried. Ray was booked to show Mrs Prosser a shack on a three-acre block in Merthyr Drive.

On telephoning his home, Mr Tamlyn discovered that Ray was indisposed.

He asked Teresa: "Was Ray ill yesterday?"

"Not that I saw," she harrumphed.

"He says he's really under the weather. He says he has the flu." Mr Tamlyn cursed and reached for his jacket. "That means I'll have to go. What's Mrs Prosser's number?"

CHAPTER SIX

WELLINGTON POINT BOWLS CLUB
Results for Saturday.
Talbot Shield:

Swansea 79 defeated Wellington Point 63
M. Levings 20 – B. Grogan 17.

Next Saturday will be President's Day/Appreciation Day combined. Old and new members will be made very welcome. Come and join the fun. B. Grogan (Pres. & Sec.).

Shortly before 7 p.m. the following Saturday, Alex drove into Wellington Point to have dinner with Merridy at the Freycinet Court Hotel. It was the night of the Jazz Social and cars were parked bumper to bumper along the main street. He found a space behind Nevin's garage and was locking up his ute when he saw a large woman coming up the alley towards him. Tildy in her war paint. Heading in the direction of the Town Hall.

He remembered that determined, excited walk. Across her bedroom. Both were trying to appease a hunger and fill a stinging blankness. "Why don't you put that down?" she had urged, indicating the novel in his hand. "Harry told me you went to Oxford. Well, I ought to warn you, I don't read much, not unless it's *New Idea.*" He remembered the powdery vanilla smell of the room, like the hay-fever tang of wattle. Quickly, he took in the bottles with their tops off, the stray tampons and hairpins and creams, the magazines that she traded with the shop-girls at Talbot's. He had not had sisters and the exaggerated femininity unsettled him. Had he remained in Wellington Point at the age of eleven, he might have ended up in a thick-scented room like this, with a girl like this. She had dimmed the lights and turned on a tape-recorder and swayed her buttocks, mimicking the words so exactly that it might have been Nina Simone herself who gyrated towards him, her arms reaching out with a hopeful smile, until with a desperate little gasp, she said: "Fuck me, Alex." He had dropped his book to the floor and torn down his pants as if peeling the price off himself so that she would not have to see his cheapness. And remembered how she stood up afterwards, sighed, and went to the bathroom, stretching her lolly-green skirt down over her tights.

She was almost level when she noticed him. "Why . . . Alex," and batted her eyes. "You look like you're dressed for a funeral."

"Tildy . . ." He had changed clothes three times until he found the combination of shirt and trousers that seemed to him just right.

"Are you coming to the Social?"

"No."

"Hope it's not *your* funeral," she said brightly.

"Listen, I want to apologise."

"What for, sweetie?"

"I'm sorry I haven't been in touch."

"Don't worry about it. You were crook. Now I'd love a chat, but I have to meet someone."

He watched her hurry up the street towards the Town Hall, growing small as she climbed the steps, and felt something pop when the door closed behind her. She had come out from under his skin, an ant-sized thorn that no longer hurt or inflamed.

Ticking with anticipation, Alex waited in the empty restaurant. On the corner table where Debbie had placed him was a wine bottle with candle wax all spewed and a laminated menu from which pretty soon he could recite every dish.

He had suggested the Freycinet Court Hotel because there was nowhere else to eat in Wellington Point. But now as he sat there, he realised that there was a sentimental reason, too. His parents' honeymoon. When sorting out their belongings, Alex had come across a 1950s brochure stuck inside an album of wedding photographs. The hotel, ideally situated, in the consideration of the copywriter, boasted gardens and lawns, home cooking, hot and cold water. Plus electric light, wireless and sewerage arrangements, as well as access to a nine-hole golf links. The proprietor had even provided a quote: *No holidaymaker at Wellington Point need fear suffering from ennui.*

The rest Alex had learned from Harry Ford, the retired Fleet Street journalist who was one of his parents' few surviving friends. Towards the end of their honeymoon fortnight, according to Harry, Alex's parents walked along Dolphin Sands and made love in the dunes. On the same day they explored Moulting Lagoon.

Behind a small cemetery they came upon a track. There was a wooden gate with a padlock. Basil Dove knocked the dottle from his pipe and climbed over.

"At the end of the track was this farmhouse for sale. They decided there and then to buy it."

Quite why his father should have divulged these details to Harry – whose great regret was that ill-health had left him unable to advance in newspapers, and who had been in Wellington Point forty years expecting to die – Alex had no idea. Perhaps because he was the only other Englishman in town.

Alex looked again around at the unoccupied tables. The place had altered from his last visit, shortly after his return from England four years ago. Then he had asked the waitress for a mango. He might have asked her for a pre-phylloxeric Lafite from her expression. Two more proprietors and now the hotel was owned by Tildy's father, a blusterer with a grey handlebar moustache who – according to Harry – had been retired from the North Hobart Cricket Club because of his beer gut. Framley's taste was reflected in the green chintz pelmets that stretched over the windows and the chaffinch noise that issued from a concealed alarm when Alex had first come into the dining room, causing Debbie to come scurrying from the kitchen.

"Ah, yes, Mr Dove," smirking. "The discreet table for two." She led him to it. "You're the first," in tones that failed to conceal her curiosity about his guest, Alex Dove being considered quite a catch in her small circle.

Outside, it was still light. Alex listened to the street noises. Fred Coggins, whom he vaguely remembered from school, locking up the Talbot emporium; the skimpy figure of Rose-Maree yelling out to Joe Hollows, a boy who had briefly helped him put up fences; Tom Pidd hooting the horn of his ute as he drove slowly past Abbygail the chemist, a keen golfer who did not disguise her ambition to be elected to the council so that Wellington Point could have a sports complex; the sound of an electric guitar being tuned.

In a corner of the restaurant, the coffee-maker gargled.

Perhaps she had forgotten. At 7.15 he borrowed two coins from Debbie and, not wishing to be overheard, went into the street to the public phone. The mouthpiece stank of vomit, lipstick and fried flat-head. He dialled Louisa Meredith House and was put through to the Bowman unit, but the line was engaged. He waited five minutes before trying again. A couple in evening clothes walked by, laughing at something. He heard the engaged tone and returned to the restaurant.

Twenty minutes later, a voice was saying: "I'm sorry." Two lips shyly kissed his cheek. "The phone rang as I was leaving."

"I didn't mind waiting."

"Liar," and pulled in her chair. "My mother always told me that people count up the faults of those who keep them waiting. Do you lie about other things, too?"

He smiled, relieved to see her sitting there. "Only when I'm hungry," he said.

"That's good." She picked up a menu. "I suppose you've decided."

"I ought to warn you – the choice won't be what you're used to in Melbourne."

"Oh, I don't know."

It warmed him to watch the tanned arm with the unusually fair hairs as she fidgeted with the menu. Her blue dress had something animal about it. Under the thin cotton, her breasts swayed like censers, releasing the incense of her perfume.

"You know what I'd love more than anything?" She looked up. "A plate of oysters."

She saw his expression and immediately reached to touch his hand. "Don't worry," she laughed, but in a kind way. "I've learned never to expect oysters in Great Oyster Bay."

"They're recommending the wallaby."

She gave a quick look around. "I wouldn't," leaning forward. "It's been in the deep freeze six months."

"It says here 'freshly farmed'."

"Keith lies through his teeth and expects the girls to do the same. He tells customers that the ice cream is home-made when in fact it comes out of Peter's tubs which have their labels peeled off. And you mustn't believe that the scones are home-made and oven fresh. They're frozen and microwaved. 'Don't let them hear the ping,'" in Framley's voice.

"You have a spy in the kitchen?"

She studied the menu. "Now if I'm not having oysters, what shall I have?"

But he wanted to know. "How come you're so well informed?"

"Keith Framley is my father's cousin."

"Oh." And realised that he would have known this had he lived in Wellington Point instead of eight miles outside. Or spoken to Tildy. Everyone was related to each other in Tasmania.

"He let us stay in the hotel before we moved into the unit." She was reading the menu. "I also work here in the evenings. Part of the rent."

"So it's not exactly a treat," he said thickly, "bringing you here."

"Of course it is!"

They were interrupted by Debbie coming to take their orders.

"Ready?" arching a brow when she saw who it was. "Sorry, Merridy, didn't see you come in."

"I'll have the chicken satay," Merridy decided.

Unseeing, Alex turned the menu over. "I might have the steak."

"And to drink?" asked Debbie with a starched expression.

"Tea for me."

"You're not drinking?" said Alex.

"What's tea if it's not a drink?"

"And for you, Mr Dove?" said Debbie, making him feel that he had to pay for her disappointment.

"A glass of Coombend red."

When Debbie had left, Merridy put down the menu. She looked him in the eye. "Listen, I'm very happy to be here. And very sorry I'm late. It's a rule of my parents. Never keep anyone waiting. Ever."

Her face responded shinily to the overhead light. He still could not bear to examine it too closely. Her coral mouth. Her blue dress that was devoted to the contour of her breast.

Picking at the candle wax, he asked about her parents.

CHAPTER SEVEN

HOW MUCH MERRIDY TOLD him then became confused with how much he discovered afterwards.

She was twenty years old, born in Ulverstone on Tasmania's north-west coast. Her mother was a Sunday school teacher, the middle child of strict Methodist parents from Adelaide. The Proudlocks had come to where the most neglected souls on earth had called them and because of the wretchedness to be found in Tasmania. They knew that God was exacting. When informed of their daughter's decision to marry Leonard Bowman, a mechanical engineer from Melbourne, Merridy's grandmother gave a sorrowful headshake. "I have asked Him from the bottom of my heart to increase my suffering and He has obliged."

Merridy's father had trained at night school when he was sixteen. He started in workshops, building bus bodies, and then was put in the drawing office. He designed cases for cameras to go down to 10,000 feet, and water tanks and lifts for mine shafts. But there came a hideous moment when none of this engaged him.

As a student in Melbourne, and during the first eight years of his marriage, Leonard had a conviction amounting almost to a religion. He believed that the world was full of patterns and that even human behaviour could be determined by mathematical equations. The motion of the waves on a windy day was determined by an interplay of these equations. They might be immensely complex, but they could be resolved down to a neat truth – and if only the man or woman in the street learned to switch on a certain part of their brain they would not have to stumble along in the dark.

Leonard was two months short of his fortieth birthday when – overnight – he lost his faith. Up to this point, he had lived according to the precept: "Science requires the simple: it won't tolerate the unnecessary." From this time on, the unnecessary gave meaning to his life.

To conquer his grief, he began to write children's stories. He penned and illustrated more than thirty of these over the next decade. But he was keeping a conversation alive that nobody wanted to hear. The editors who returned his manuscripts were unanimous in their admiration of his drawings and also in their judgment that here was a poetry lover who had never progressed beyond doggerel, whose sure limit was Edward Lear. In the saddest period of Merridy's upbringing, he read to her every night from *A Book of Nonsense*, to the eventual consternation of her mother, who one night burst into Merridy's bedroom and screamed at the pair of them that she was fed up with runcible spoons and would live a contented life were she never to hear those detestable verses again.

But not at the beginning. Not at the beginning.

Leticia Proudlock was twenty-one, young, pretty and naïve when she tripped over Leonard on her way to the daffodil show at the Leven Theatre.

The man who restored her to her feet had arrived in Tasmania that week to take up a job in Burnie. The liking was mutual. He admired her purity and her legs. She saw in him a man of sciencc who might give her practical knowledge of a world that so far she had experienced through the rigid filter of the scriptures. She would adore Leonard principally for everything that her parents were not. Plus he was more sophisticated and ten years older. In Melbourne, he had had European friends. He read poetry and loved foreign cuisine, but was not averse to expressing himself in the vernacular of the workshops. Best of all, he was blessed with a rolling laugh that scattered his sense of the ridiculous into the deepest crevices, and specifically the Methodist Hall in Ulverstone where Leticia had passed a hefty proportion of her adolescence.

Four days after their encounter, he arrived at her parents' house bearing gifts of smoked oysters, blue cheese and brown bread that he had had shipped across Bass Strait on the *Abel Tasman*.

On the formica table in the kitchen was a plastic colander. Leonard fitted it on his head.

For the Jumblies came in a Sieve, they did –
Landing at eve near the Zemmery Fidd
Where the Oblong Oysters grow . . .

At 91 Water Street, Leonard's nonsense verse and gifts fell on rocky soil. "Get that vomit cheese out of the fridge!" ordered Leticia's father as soon as Leonard had departed the house. Luke Proudlock was a teetotaller who never failed to refer to the Bible and whose only passion – apart from his God and his briar pipe – was bowls. He refused to eat plum pudding in case it contained brandy, and used words like "yonder" to describe a country that his forefathers had sailed from in 1832 – "as free settlers". He was accustomed to his wife's stodgy cooking, her custard and coddled eggs. He shoved aside a plate of smoked oysters with the words: "It's like eating snot." Served up spaghetti a week later: "I'm not eating this foreign muck."

If Luke Proudlock felt intimidated by Leonard's spaghetti, he was angered by Leonard's atheism. He and his wife abominated this young man from Melbourne for corrupting their untarnished daughter. They had picked out that she would marry Randal Twelvetrees, the son of the local minister, not a Godless mechanical engineer from the mainland who knew *The Hunting of the Snark* by heart, who believed that religion was like alcohol – "It turns ordinary men into heroes, Mr Proudlock, and heroes into ordinary men" – and whose party trick was to read their futures in a Royal Worcester teacup. The marriage was doomed, even if it was the wish of Him who wept for Lazarus.

Their prophecies were not realised until Merridy was five.

"Do you have siblings?" Alex said.

"I had a brother," she said in a small, deliberate voice.

"Had?"

"He disappeared. But I don't want to talk about that."

Alex waited. Once again, he had a sense of the ocean of sadness within her. But she was not going to elucidate. Flatly, she went on: "The shock gave Mum a stroke."

*

Mrs Bowman was bedridden for a year, receiving her husband and daughter in a pale grey nightdress and holding them sobbing to her paralysed chest. Then, once they were safely out of the room, she returned her face to the wall. Another year before she could speak again or move her limbs. As soon as her muscles were restored, she took up bowls to exercise her arms. And spiritualism.

On the third anniversary of her son's disappearance she read an advertisement in the Burnie *Advocate*. "You may have lived on earth before! New places or people you pass may seem oddly familiar to you; have you known them in a previous life?" The notice cautioned that certain secrets of life and mental development could not be divulged indiscriminately. That afternoon, she sent off for a thirty-two-page booklet, *The Mastery of Life*, and a fortnight later was welcomed into the Rosicrucians, hoping through them to be reunited with her missing child, who would now be ten.

For the next four years, she kept in touch with a retired Welsh railway engineer who passed on a series of messages from her son. Then, when Merridy was twelve, Mrs Bowman abandoned Taffy Guest and the Rosicrucians and returned to the faith of her parents. She had come to an excruciating realisation. Her loss was her penalty for disobeying God. Her son had wandered off one Sunday morning when the family ought properly to have been at prayer – not visiting steam engines – and was never seen again. She copied out a passage from the Bible and showed it to Merridy's father: *He was the chosen one for the sacrifice that had to be made and in that fact we may find our guarantee that all is well with him.*

"For goodness' sake," Leonard exploded. "God no more exists than I am a purple giraffe." And quoted David Hume to the effect that the life of a boy, even the life of their precious son, was of no greater importance to the universe than that of an oyster.

"O was an oyster
"Who lived in his shell
"If you let him alone
"He felt perfectly well."

But Mrs Bowman had been shaken by religious fear. Whatever her extravagant feelings for Leonard before their son's abrupt departure from their lives, she now viewed her husband in the clear and unforgiving light of a false shepherd, an idolater, a Satan who had counterfeited the image of Christ. And how was an idolater punished? This she did not show Leonard: *Thou shalt stone him with stones, that he shall die, because he hath sought to thrust thee away from the Lord thy God.*

When her parents argued, Merridy was put in mind of an old pump that had lost its bearings through sucking up so much air and mud.

"Mum used to scold Dad. He was hopelessly entangled in the categories of science. Technological progress had bred pride etc. etc. While Dad kept telling her that she was an idiot for believing in a myth. He hated what he called 'the Methodism in her madness'."

Upon returning to the embrace of her church, Mrs Bowman outdid even her parents in the intensity of her devotion. All the pent-up dicta of her childhood to which she had been pleased to block her ears returned in a furious salvo. Her horror of sexual contact became absolute. Until the evening arrived when Leonard came upon his wife in the hallway, dressed in her peppermint-green coat and zipping up an ancient leather holdall.

"What ho, Lettice?"

"I'm going to stay with Doss."

"When can I expect you back?"

"I'm leaving you, Leonard."

Forced to choose between parents, Merridy elected life with her father, but her mother, who went to lodge with her younger sister in a large, depressing house two streets away, had weekend rights, which invariably commenced with Mrs Bowman escorting Merridy to the Friday-night dance class at the Methodist Hall.

The rest of the weekend was not less grim. In her sister's house on Weybridge Drive, Mrs Bowman bobbed like a decoy duck on the roughened waters of her faith; her features set in an unalterable expression of piety to draw the fire from her Godless husband and wayward daughter.

Her son, on the other hand, was equal unto the angels. But he would be worthy of a part in the Resurrection only if she atoned. So she acknowledged her iniquity. She regretted in her daily prayers that she was a backslider who had gone away from God's ordinances. She had not trained up her child in the way he should have gone. And out of her husband's earshot never tired of reciting to Merridy her favourite verse from Thessalonians: *If we believe that Jesus died and rose again, even so them also which sleep in Jesus will God bring with Him.*

Merridy preferred her father's verses about the Dong with the Luminous Nose. She rejected her mother's petrified morality that nothing could dissipate.

The bitter truth was, once her brother disappeared there was no purpose to life that Merridy could think of. She, too, now inhabited a "yonder" which bore no relation to earth. She was unable to believe in a deity that had removed her favourite person from the face of it. A deity, furthermore, that had turned her mother into a passionless automaton.

Merridy's weekends were an agony for a girl who could recall her mother as a jubilant and loving woman, with a round carefree face. Settled in her new home, Mrs Bowman had the pared-down features of atonement. Once on Saturday, and twice on Sunday, she attended church, the services conducted by the minister whose son she had rejected. Merridy sat in the front row and watched Minister Twelvetrees when he was not looking, his finger pointed upward, his pious face, long and narrow and worn, like the sole of a shoe at the communion rail. What Merridy loved most had been taken from her, and now her mother by God and Minister Twelvetrees.

So she made a promise: she would not allow herself to love again.

Her father, meanwhile, stumbled about his wifeless house, neglecting to eat, refusing to take off his wedding ring. Even though she had deserted him, he treasured the woman he had loved and married, with whom he had fathered two children.

His response to her desertion was to dive back into the hard comforts of science. He threw away his mediocre children's stories, his fanciful drawings, his squeezed-out tubes of Winsor & Newton paint, and concentrated his energies on what he could build in solid three dimensions. God's designs for his servants were never so meticulous as Leonard's plans for the water tower at the paper mill in Burnie, or the mechanised cranes and bulldozers that he once had created for his infant son and now lavished on Merridy, and which she pretended to herself were ponies and dogs. From her father, Merridy adopted her chuckle, her weakness for strong language and her taste for red pasta sauces.

The nearest Leonard came to Christian piety was the respect he taught Merridy for immortal characters like the Dong, the Snark and the Pobble – part of the comforting menagerie of creatures whom she had learned to cherish in the months following her brother's disappearance. And for everything electrical.

Determined to rescue his daughter from her mother's orbit, he encouraged Merridy to apply to a university on the mainland, to move beyond the confines of the Methodist Hall and Edward Lear. "I want you to have the chance of doing something miraculous with your life – even if it's only a tiny miracle."

"What about our sieve?" asked Merridy, half-joking.

"Our sieve?" He had forgotten. "Bloody hell – our sieve!" Colouring, he resumed: "If we're ever going to build it, all the more reason for you to go to university."

She was nineteen when she won a place at Melbourne to study civil engineering. She had completed almost a year when her father was electrocuted.

After attending a morning funeral in Zeehan, he came out of the pump house in level seven at the Renison Bell mine and was convulsed by spasms. A runaway trolley had trapped an exposed wire as it picked up speed and the live part of the wire flailed against the rail that he was following. The resistance of people to electricity varies, and Leonard might not have suffered so badly had he worn his normal shoes. But he was wearing dress shoes and the leather soles had become damp as he tramped up the passage. The 400-volt shock chucked him off the rail and his hand with its wedding ring on clutched at the side of the shaft and touched a metal support. The flashback burned his face and contracted his hand around the metal. His science taught him that he had four chances every second to pull away, but his body was in too violent a spasm at the electricity rushing in, and it was not until his assistant cracked him away with a wooden brush that he fell free. By then, Leonard was unconscious.

He was taken to hospital in Burnie. Two days later the skin hardened on his feet and his right foot started to go black. Burning from the inside out.

The shock that had blackened his foot might have killed another man. Instead, Leonard had what Mrs Bowman liked to describe as a life-after-death experience that lasted six minutes. In a lucid interval he reported to his wife, who out of religious duty had returned to nurse him, that he saw a dark tunnel and light at the end of it and felt calm. He waited until he had Merridy on his own before giving a different version, in which he claimed to have observed a large hill with a one-legged man walking with a goose.

"He wondered if it could be my brother," said Merridy, staring at the dish that Debbie had brought and separating the three sticks of chicken satay.

Her father was a month in intensive care. In September, he returned to Zeehan. He had nowhere else to go – he had sold his property in Ulverstone once Merridy left for university. The mining company agreed that he could occupy the house until the end of the year. But a week after his homecoming Merridy heard a gasping sound.

"No air . . . need oxygen."

She took one look. "Dad, I have to call the ambulance. You realise once I call an ambulance you're out of my hands?"

Two further months in Burnie hospital. Another homecoming. But this time harder to follow the twists of his mind. The aneurysm, apart from slurring his speech, had planted on his face an expression that reminded his daughter of the toeless Pobble.

Leonard's accident was proof positive to Mrs Bowman of the workings of a divine providence. She lost no opportunity to tell him so when Merridy was not looking. He could only respond by thumping the table with his good fist and saying: "O, O, O, O." Once, when Merridy heard her father remonstrating, she raced to see what was up. Accused of upsetting her husband, Mrs Bowman defended herself: "I was only saying how much God loves him," at which he thumped the table again and exclaimed: "O, O, O, O," shaking his head with an agonised frown.

Meanwhile, December approached and with it the end of the lease. When, a week before Christmas, the mining company offered Leonard the house for as long as he wanted, Mrs Bowman declined.

So at the end of January, at Keith Framley's instigation, Merridy packed her father and mother into the family Peugeot and drove south to Wellington Point. Mrs Bowman was indifferent to her surroundings, as she had been in Zeehan and before that in Ulverstone. In her Bible-clouded imagination, Wellington Point was another filthy step on the Scala Santa. The three principal things that she had to ask God's forgiveness for in the year 1988 were her lack of warmth towards her estranged husband, her sensuality towards God, and her want of charity to her daughter.

Merridy had set aside her studies in Melbourne to help her mother look after him. When her father did not die immediately she stayed on against her mother's wishes.

CHAPTER EIGHT

To Merridy, her parents' unhappiness was a scandal that she proposed to avoid. She looked forward to the day when she could resume her degree, have her own room again – like Tildy.

"How long have you known Tildy?" Alex asked.

"I've known her since I was" – flattening her hand, Merridy could have been dowsing a flame – "this high."

They had grown up on the same street in Ulverstone. Tildy's father then ran a bed & breakfast three doors down from Merridy's house. The memory of her cousin was connected with Mandeville Gardens, a wide crescent planted with pear trees, where, on Friday evenings and chaperoned by her mother, Merridy walked to the Methodist Hall for Randal Twelvetrees' dance class. Merridy was the brighter of the two. Books, films, museums – she had seen the Francis Bacon exhibition in Melbourne. Tildy occupied herself, rather, with men.

"She hasn't changed. And now she's fallen for Ray Grogan," Merridy said, her laugh edged with disapproval. Or was it regret?

"Like every girl in Wellington Point," and felt a spark of envy for his old schoolmate.

"You don't like Ray, do you?"

"Oh, Ray's all right." It was just that nothing was interesting to Ray unless he could see it undress. When he contemplated Ray's ornate womanising, Alex wondered if the man was not in fact gay.

"I warned you. One more lie – and I'm leaving."

"No, he's fine," Alex hurried on. "He's done very well with his business. He can sell sand to the seals, can't he? Maybe it's his moustache I don't like. Who does he think he is?"

"Errol Flynn?" she ventured, amused.

"In his mother's dreams."

"Speaking of whom, I met Mrs Grogan last night."

"What, the president of our bowls club?" He thought of the owl-beak nose and asbestos face, soft and grey, and smiled.

"That would be her. She's invited my mother to become a member."

"Everyone suspects her of stealing from the kitty. It wouldn't surprise me." Nothing about the Grogans surprised Alex. "Was it Ray you were speaking to on the phone just now?" looking up.

She lowered her eyes, nodded.

He was unable to stem his thoughts: Merridy appeals to Ray because she's new. Every other girl here he's had, save for Tildy – and that's because they're two peas in a pod.

She said: "You haven't told me why you dislike him?"

"I sat beside him in class when we were kids."

"Is that a crime?"

"He cheated. He wrote the answers to exams on his hands." Afterwards, at school in Cumbria, Alex could never look at the English landscape without seeing interposed Ray's palm. The words written in blue biro in shambolic capitals. Sycamore, beech, elm.

She nodded. "Sounds like Ray. Anything else?" Cheating was not enough?

"Oh, I don't know," and tried to laugh. "Wasn't he bitten on the chin by a tiger-snake who died in agony? I don't think Ray ever lost that ugly look on his face."

"A lot of people find him attractive."

"I don't like the way he treats people, that's all."

"How does he treat them?"

"You'll find out if you let him."

"Maybe it's a local thing. Isn't that how you behaved with Tildy?" Her blue eyes returned a bold stare.

"It's not how I wanted . . . it's not how . . ." he repeated uselessly. At the same time, a need to speak of his lapse with Tildy seized him with the force of a cramp. "No, you're right, it was my fault. I could have said no. I should have said no." But they clinked like kidney stones in a jar, his words.

To the rescue bringing more tea came Debbie, with another glass of red wine for Alex.

Alone again with him, Merridy said: "So Ray cheated. Is that all?"

He did not want to tell. But his expression was crying out.

"Alex . . ."

He jutted his chin, not because he was brave but because other young men did when not wanting to dob.

She had decided. "If you don't tell, I'm going. This minute."

Merridy half-rose from the chair and waited there, suspended. The flesh between her breasts had the unnatural whiteness of the powder that his father laid in trails for ants.

Then to keep her from leaving he was blurting it. A revolting rite of passage devised by Ray for Alex to prove that he was an Aussie who belonged and not a Pommy bastard who had no place here. Even now, sixteen years on, Alex could hear ringing in his ears the voice of Ray Grogan bullying him across the playground, pushing him with all the authority of an eleven-year-old captain of cricket to assault the newest member of class as he set up a pyramid of marbles. And so Alex had strolled up to Jack Cheele – who smiled trustingly at him, "Hi, Piers, wanna go?" who had no idea what was about to occur – and kicked him, hard, in the balls. An action so out of character and committed from a wish to try and include himself in the local hoonery. At least that was his excuse. Ray Grogan had no excuse. He had kneed everyone in the balls all his life. But the astonishment in Cheele's face was something that Alex had carried with him ever since; a pinch of shame in his guts that preyed on his mind at inappropriate moments. "Piers . . ." gasping. Doubled up on the ground. Those anguished, accusing, ineradicable eyes. It was practically Alex's last memory of the school. He never told his parents and they never found out. A week later, they set off in their car for the auction room in Campbell Town.

"And what happened to Cheele?" Merridy was asking, still suspended. Something about the way that he lowered his voice a little, sounding grave, made her believe and forgive him. She saw Alex in that moment as a lion in a poor zoo, prey to teasing boys. Prodded and prodded, until he behaved like a hyena.

"I tried to get in touch when I came back. But like a lot of people at school, he'd left Wellington Point. No one knew where he lived, whether he'd gone interstate, whether he was still in Australia. So I don't know what happened to him, but I composed endless letters in my head."

His answer seemed to satisfy Merridy, who resumed her place.

She poured milk into her tea and stirred. “Tell me, why does Ray call you Piers?”

He looked sharply at her. “You’ve been talking about me to Ray Grogan?”

She blushed.

His turn to come to the rescue. “Because Piers is my first name. But I never use it.”

“Why not? It’s a lovely name.” So English – evoking buckets and spades and music-halls.

He breathed in. “It’s the name I had when I lived here before.”

CHAPTER NINE

ALEX HAD GROWN UP in Wellington Point until he was eleven. Sometimes he looked back, invariably without success, to his boyhood. He had pulped so many memories that whenever he tried to invoke his mother and father, a hopeless distortion overtook him. His parents sprang from their photographs on his bedroom wall, discoloured, in wool clothes saturated with a particular smell, and addressing each other in rotund voices by names that might have come from the movies that they saw at the Prince of Wales on their monthly excursions to Hobart. Marjorie. Basil. Piers.

It was not intentional, his name change. After the accident, he had gone to school in England but arriving at Sedbergh at the start of the Easter term, he was told by his housemaster: "You're not going to be called Piers, old chap. We've got four Pierses."

"My second name is Alexander."

"Alexander is toooo long."

So he became Alex. He even got used to it, wanting nothing more in a way than to live in the present tense. It was only when he came back to Wellington Point that he found himself having to explain to people that for reasons too silly to go into he was now actually Alex – in fact had been Alex longer than he had ever been Piers.

But he could not shake off that frowsy odour of old wool. He still caught a whiff of it when passing Agnes's charity shop. He did not know if the odour was soap or dead skin, or what it was, but whenever he smelled those "pre-loved" clothes he was jolted back to the sight of a wardrobe filled with his father's suits and, next to the bookie's tweeds from Bidencope's, his mother's cropped jackets and angora sheaths. Plus a blueberry Crimplene frock, bought in the Mather summer sale for the occasion of Prince Philip's visit to Hobart.

When, having been away more than a decade, Alex had returned to Tasmania, almost his first action after visiting the farm and observing its neglected state was to remove his parents' clothes from the house and drive the whole lot to Agnes.

Upon leaving her shop he had walked into a man getting out of a new Holden. He was a healthy-looking type, dressed in clerk-grey trousers and a plain white shirt with cufflinks.

"Piers Dove," cunning eyes evaluating him.

"Ray Grogan. I didn't recognise you . . . the moustache."

So they faced each other outside the Op-Shop.

"Fancy meeting you here, Piers," and patted the moustache that gave the impression of a bird hovering over his mouth.

"Living people often meet."

"What brings you back to Wellington Point?" and his green eyes looked searchingly at Alex.

"It's my home, Ray. I was born here," he said stiffly.

"Couldn't make it in the big smoke, eh?"

"Matter of fact, I'm about to go back there."

"How are you earning a crust these days?"

"I'm training to be a teacher."

"What, like Miss Pritchard? You know, that surprises me. You were so raw, Piers, I wouldn't have fed you to my chooks."

"How is Miss Pritchard by the way?"

"She carked it. But they're looking for a teacher. You should apply. You really should."

"Actually, Ray, I'm glad I bumped into you."

"What can I do for you, Piers?"

"I wanted to track down Cheele."

"Cheele? Who the heck's Cheele?" caressing his chin, in the guarded way that he used to do when Miss Pritchard asked him to spell out a word.

"You don't remember Cheele?"

But Ray had spotted something. "What happened to your hand, mate?"

Alex to his chagrin forgot Cheele and looked down at the black sock that he had taken off to bind his torn palm. "I was fixing a windmill," he muttered.

Ray contemplated the makeshift bandage. "Be careful of tetanus. It gives you lockjaw. You won't be able to speak. God, wouldn't that be great?" and the sun glinted gold on a cufflink.

Alex rubbed his hand.

But Ray was on a roll. "Talking of smoke, that place of yours ought to have a match put to it. That's what it wants. It puts me in mind of some of them people in Egypt."

"What, Moulting Lagoon Farm?"

"The house is back to buggery. Not worth a thing."

"You don't know that."

"Oh, yes, I do," and gave a husky chuckle. "I've been looking after it, mate."

"You? But Mr Tamlyn arranged the lease."

"One of my first jobs when I went to work for him was to take care of your place. And know what? I could hardly give it away with a tea bag."

So turning points come in plain clothes. The abysmal state of the crops and fences, the gates that wouldn't swing, the dilapidation of the house – all this, Alex understood, could be blamed on his schoolmate. Ray had had it in his power to walk around the property with the tenant and force him to put things to rights. Instead, he had done nothing with the asset but pocket his 10 per cent. One more thing for which he never would forgive Ray.

And having returned to Wellington Point steeled to get rid of the farm, Alex was all of a sudden determined to keep it.

"That's a pity because I was going to ask Mr Tamlyn to put it on the market."

"Is that so?" Ray leaned back against his car and folded his arms. "I suppose I could do a valuation. Mind you, nobody in their right mind would buy it except maybe a bloody Japanese – who are buying just about everything."

"You please yourself what you do, but if you ever come round there you won't walk away from the place."

"I said I could do a valuation."

"Save your precious time, Ray. I wouldn't wipe my arse with any valuation you did. Just ask Mr Tamlyn to send me back all the keys and papers to do with the lease. I've a damned good mind to give them to a lawyer."

"What? You're going to keep it now, are you?"

"Too right I am. And one more thing."

Ray waited.

"I'm not Piers any more. I'm Alex."

"Can you do that?" said Ray. "I suppose you can. Like a sex-change. But don't think giving a mongrel another name makes him less of a mongrel. You'll always be Piers to me. Always."

"Fuck you, Ray."

At this, Ray laughed. "Not while the dogs are still on the street."

"Hi, Ray."

"Hi, Agnes."

"I must say, it's grand to see Piers again," she smiled, locking up the shop and its new stock.

"I suppose."

They watched her cross the road to Talbot's.

Ray said almost wistfully: "I had a dig in that once," before his curiosity overcame his facetiousness.

But Alex was walking away.

He was passing the chemist's when he heard Ray call out in a different voice. "Hey, Piers? Why keep it?" And when Alex hesitated, he went on. "Hell, Piers . . . Alex . . . whoever you want to be. Why would anyone who's been lucky to get away from here look for a reason to come back? There's nothing to do in Wellington Point 'cept die."

Alex strode on. Into the view he had been about to renounce, and left Ray standing there, his arm frozen in a vague gesture at the bay.

Very possibly Ray was right. Unlike Swansea or Bicheno on the same coast, the town had not grown. Nothing commercial had made it sprawl larger than the backwater it was. Roads of red dirt leading to all sorts of futures, none of them enviable, and crawling with copperheads like Ray who took the colour of the country they lived in.

It had been down one of these roads that a 60-ton semi-articulated Scania log-truck came thundering as Alex's father, already going blind, and his wife beside him, nosed the family's Ford Zephyr out of their drive. Alex could never see a log-truck without imagining that moment: the dragonish smoke streaming from the two vertical exhausts, the air brakes screaming, the old-growth eucalypts tumbling.

The truck had killed his parents outright, picked them off clean like an artillery shell. In the crater that it had left behind, Alex had struggled ever since to find some battered meaning.

His parents had willed everything they owned to him. Instead of their possessions being dispersed, Alex inherited their house, estate, belongings. Right down to a lifetime's subscription to *Bottleship* magazine.

All this he had abandoned until such a time as he felt equal to dealing with it. While in England, he had deliberately put any decision on hold. But by the time of his reappearance in Wellington Point on this hot, dry afternoon, he had made up his mind. He told Agnes that he planned to stay until the weekend, by which time he hoped to have washed his hands of the place.

"So you won't be coming back?" she said.

"No, Agnes. I don't think so."

That was before he bumped into Ray Grogan.

After the conversation outside the Op-Shop, to steady himself, Alex had taken one of his father's rods and driven in his hired car to the mouth of the Swan. The river broadened into an estuarial beach of white sand, dotted with tiny red crabs and patrolled over by pelicans. He walked along it, calculating. It was one thing to change his mind about selling Moulting Lagoon Farm, but what could he do with the property? His parents had lost enough money on the farm, and on a regular basis. Could he, with what little he had inherited, make it work?

Alex tried to bat away the thought. He put up the cane rod and caught a small bream with a prettyfish. He was eleven the last time he had stripped out a line or spent a quiet hour fishing. He could tell it was a bream by the black chevrons on the tail.

He buried the bream head down in the sand after gutting it. The fish flapped for a while on the beach amongst its guts, a headless, tailless, gutless creature trying to fly.

Am I being a pathetic bastard? he asked himself. He looked at the bream and then out across the bay, and there was not a nerve in his body that did not twitch like his line.

By the time he returned to his car an idea had formed. He knew what he was going to do.

*

Until this moment, Alex had assumed that he would continue to live and work in London. On coming down from Oxford with a degree in English he had enrolled at a teacher-training college in Putney. He lived in a rented one-bedroom flat on the sixth floor of a mansion block near Southfields Tube station, and had a girlfriend, Sarah, a teacher on the same course whom he described to his uncle-cum-guardian in Sedbergh as "good for me".

Even so, Moulting Lagoon Farm was always at the back of his mind a refuge; a place where he was in his heart while he was away. He might be living on the other side of the world, but on February nights in London, after two or three months of slanting grey rain, he recalled a jetty on the edge of some sea, and kept alive the notion that he would one day go back there for a visit or maybe longer; maybe even with Sarah.

Since his departure from Tasmania twelve years before, the house and paddocks had been let out to the neighbouring farmer. The call when it came was a letter from Mr Tamlyn, the managing agent, to say that Bill Molson had died and his estate had to sell up. As a result, the trustees wished to terminate the lease on Moulting Lagoon Farm.

The letter was a signal for Alex to face what he had left unresolved. But when he invited Sarah to accompany him to Tasmania, she declined: "I'd be getting in the way." Not until the night before he flew did she enquire with the seriousness of an oldest child what his plans were for the farm, and he went through the motions that he was returning to tidy up various odds and ends. But Sarah sensed the shape of his longing. She knew when he went out the door and stepped into the lift that he did not know what he was going to do.

A large part of her hoped that distance would lend clarity and he would arrive at a decision about their future as well. Nine days later he telephoned from Tasmania and said in a careful voice: "I have something to tell you." But rather than ask her to marry him he announced that he could not see a way of continuing their relationship unless she was prepared to abandon Southfields for the outermost margin of the earth.

"You? A farmer?" Sarah had shouted on the telephone. "I'll tell you one thing what you are. You're completely fucking nuts. All you've ever husbanded is a cold."

From Hobart, he had already called his uncle. "I'm going to do something quite mad."

"I'm so glad," said his uncle, "she sounds the right girl for you."

"No, no, I've decided to keep the farm."

At any rate, he had passed Merridy's peculiar test. She sat down and picked up her cup and looked at him over it.

"Well, whatever happened between you and Tildy, it no longer matters." On Thursday, out of the blue, Ray Grogan had invited Tildy to the Jazz Social at the Town Hall. "She asked me to pass on a message. She says her heart is spoken for."

It sounded like a phrase from one of Tildy's magazines. But what, Alex wanted to know, about Merridy's heart? "Tell me, why was Ray ringing you just now?"

"Oh, just being an idiot," and sat back.

"Did he hope you might change your mind?" Even at the last moment, with Tildy humming to her reflection: Your ship has come in, honey. Your. Ship. Has. Come. In.

"I don't know what Ray thought," Merridy said quickly.

Still, it nagged. "What made you crash his party – if you dislike him so?"

"I didn't crash. I was invited." Her eyes held his and a sly expression came into them. "And maybe I fancy him."

"Do you?"

"He has something."

"Do me a favour," Alex said. "Just explain to me for my peace of mind and my education, what was it between you and Ray? Everywhere I go in this town, I hear about you and that odious fucker."

"Oh, Alex. What is it with you people? He's not odious, he's footling."

"No, he's not footling, he's odious. He has one woman after another." And again saw Ray's face, in the moment when he squeezed Merridy's arm. His expression like that of a farmer in Cumbria who shot badgers in the stomach so that they crawled back to their sett and died there out of reach and without trace.

She tilted her head. Eyes glinting. Not knowing yet whether

she found Alex attractive. But willing to concede that he was intelligent and generous and pleasant to look at, and dependable as the navigation-light beam that she saw from her bedroom, flashing on the tip of Schouten; and that something about him, while being tender beyond belief, was obviously strong enough to wrestle a steer to the ground, and even to punch it on the forehead if need be. And she could talk without strain to him.

"You really want me to tell you why women like Ray? Well, he's one of the few guys in this place who's on the make – and that's sexy. He's hustling, he's ambitious, he works hard, and that isn't very common here. He listens, which is always a bonus. And there's a bit of danger around him."

"Well, I'm sorry . . . I don't see it. I do not see it."

"Then can I ask you to keep this to yourself? I can't have Tildy knowing. At one time, yes, I did have a slight walking-out with Ray, but oh, my, how slight. Tildy wasn't in the picture and anyway she's my best friend. Well, it was appalling. You know what they're like, these men – the engineering faculty was full of them. They're so transparent, but you get used to them. I always knew that if I stopped dead and turned around and said: 'Take your trousers off, let's go to work,' they'd run a mile. Though Ray, I have to say, really got up my nose. I thought: OK, I'll do just that – and I did it. But what you probably don't know is what subsequently happened."

"No, that's not completely convincing."

"Oh, Alex!" shaking her head.

"What?"

She looked at him, then burst out laughing. He had never heard such a laugh. It reverberated through the whole building.

"I was on his bed down to my underpants and he ran away."

Ray would never forget the humiliation in his bedroom.

"I just want to have a cuddle," he told Merridy. "You could lie on top of me. It would be safe. I probably wouldn't even get an erection."

"But I want you to put your hand down my pants," she said hospitably.

Ray sat down heavily on his capacious bed and looked sideways at her. He had thought that he wanted her. But he was not feeling seductive.

He stared down between his legs with a ghostly expression. "I'm . . . not sure I can," he said brokenly.

She went on, musing: "Isn't it funny how we talk about vaginas as the sexual zone rather than the labia?"

It had never happened to him before. "I don't know why you dislike me. I just want to give you pleasure."

She sat in silent thought. "You know what would give me pleasure?"

"What?" His answer was edged with desperation.

"How long have we got?"

"As long as you want. All night – if you want." But his eye did not join in his smile. How fatally he had underestimated Merridy. It would take more cannon-fire than he had bargained for to storm this citadel. A lot more.

"I remember you telling me that you liked to read poetry aloud."

"Yes," in a mossy whisper. And pawed his moustache with his fingers. He might have been checking to see if it was still there.

She sprang from the bed and opened the door and went into the main room. When she came back she was holding her coat. She patted its pockets. "Here we are," and produced a faded blue clothbound book that she handed to him.

He looked at the spine. "*A Book of Nonsense,* by Edward Lear," he mouthed. Already, he smelled the renewed stench of blazing pitch.

"Perhaps you could read to me?" she said.

It was not simply Ray's failure to perform that marked his rupture with Merridy. It was his inability to deal with what, remarkably for him, had not happened.

When, failing to hear from Ray-as-in-sunshine, Merridy paid a special visit to Tamlyn & Peppiatt two days later to assure him that he must not worry, it did not matter, he had addressed her in the tones of a stranger and refused to receive her comfort. His peremptoriness caused Merridy to question whether Ray had been attracted to her in the first place. It was a little blow to her pride and she went away feeling rather stupid, which was the cause of her preoccupied expression when a moment later she ran into Alex. She had got it wrong. She was arrogant. Why should Ray not fancy Tildy, who was, after all, easier and nicer? After that Merridy tried to be happy for her cousin – in fact, *was* happy for her. So that when Ray telephoned – just as she was washing her hands prior to leaving for the hotel – to apologise for behaving like a jerk, and to plead, even at this late hour, for Merridy to change her mind and come as his guest to the Jazz Social, she was grateful for the opportunity to turn him down flat.

Watched impassively by her father, whose bed she sat on to take the call, she informed Ray in an upbeat voice: "Nothing personal, no judgment intended, but it's been a really positive experience. It's taught me a lot to be at the end of a certain sort of behaviour, because it's made me realise it's not what I want right now."

The problem of Ray Grogan dispensed with, Merridy returned to her bedroom. She was late, she was late. That was all she could think as she slipped into her dress, called out goodbye to her parents and dashed from "Otranto", only to stop on the top of the steps – *Put this on and you'll see. You'll be a hit with it.*

Then, re-emerging a few moments later, she had run all the way along the main street to meet Alex Dove for dinner.

"I was also bored," she said, and straightened her back. She glanced around the restaurant at the paper napkins that earlier in the day she had folded into cones. "This isn't a place for anyone under fifty."

"It's not so bad," Alex said.

"I know what Dad would say if he could speak. He'd say it's a one-horse town where even the horse is on its last legs. Everyone's waiting around to die, and when they're not sitting in, waiting for death, or being poisoned by the water, they're waiting for you to fall flat on your face – and then they'll jump right on you. Mum's upset that she let herself be talked into bringing Dad here. She'd like to leave the island altogether. 'What has Tasmania produced except Errol Flynn and he got out as soon as he could,'" in Mrs Bowman's clipped voice.

Merridy's outburst took Alex by surprise. "Oh, come on. It's no different to anywhere else. It's all right once you get to know it."

"Tildy's been here two years. She says unless you have kids no one will talk to you. Then once you have kids, you're no longer part of the in-group. And if you stay on, then people who've left think you're a loser. She says there's no real jobs unless you want to work as a shop-girl in Talbot's or a waitress here." And sat back, breathing in quick breaths. She knew the details like an enemy.

"She says that?" All the same, Merridy's prejudices were ones that he himself had felt.

At Merton, Alex had come upon Henry James's description of Baltimore: "It affected me as a sort of perversely cheerful little city of the dead." There was a period after he reoccupied his childhood home when he looked at Wellington Point through adult eyes accustomed to the Oxford or London metropolis. And found it as depressing as a fairground. A town of flapping gums where no one escaped their neighbour's eye. "Don't do or say anything in this place if you don't want everyone else to know about it next morning," Harry Ford had warned Alex in his first week back, before adding: "Look close and you'll see this coast is full of quartzite. It's why the inhabitants are fractured and double-faced." In Wellington Point, any singularity or achievement – a little beauty or education – was regarded as an excess. In Talbot's, Alex overheard Joe Hollows, the boy who had been helping him fence a paddock, confide to the shop-girl: "He knows fuck all. What was he reading in so-called Oxford – litter-rat-ure? That's going to be all sorts of use down here." In that home of gossip, the Returned Servicemen's Club, local spite had it that Alex consorted with goats. Like any Pom left to himself. As any sensible person tended to leave Poms, which by dint of his parents and his slightly flattened accent Alex was regarded still.

"You can always leave," he told Merridy. He was not yet ready to admit that up until a few days ago he had been considering this option for himself. That when they met in the lane behind the school he was even then debating whether to go back to Southfields.

"Oh, I plan to. As soon as my father . . ." And stared at the backs of her hands that she was washing when Ray telephoned, flecked with the salve that she had rubbed on her father's lips. "He doesn't have long. He's left me an inheritance, not large, but enough to take me away from here." To create her tiny miracle, whatever that was.

"Where will you go?" conscious of a clatter of hooves in his heart.

"Back to Melbourne probably. My mother is pissed off with me for dropping out of uni."

"Do you want to go to Melbourne?"

"Not much. I'd prefer to go to Greece."

"Why Greece?"

"I don't know. I always wanted to go to Greece."

She wanted to find a partner. A Jumbly boy. She had not met anyone, there just had not been the click.

Most convent girls in their first year at uni went – as Tildy enviously had predicted – "besonkers". Engineering students were divided between "the Alfs" – the bogans who were rough as guts – and "the Ralphs", who attended lectures in ties and middle-class tweeds. For the second time in her life, Merridy recognised her power and it was heady. Plucky, slightly thin-skinned, but willing to take on anything, she had had two boyfriends at the same time: a raw and puppyish Ralph, whom she saw during the day, and a more experienced Alf, whom she tormented in the evenings. Unlike the majority of her contemporaries, she had not been to bed with her boyfriends. Part of her knew that they were "practice men". To sleep with either would risk raising the bar of complications and entail a commitment that Merridy was not prepared to make. She might have left Ulverstone and Randal Twelvetrees behind, but she could not forget her adolescent promise to herself. At twenty, she continued to feel her old antagonism to love; a suspicious fear of it that Ray Grogan had absolutely failed to lift, for all his persistence.

Alex Dove was another matter. So far their exchange had been tentative, but the young farmer had begun to spur in her emotions that Merridy suspected of being dangerously close to those she had guarded herself against.

At first, Alex had merely intrigued her. Then Ray told her about what had happened to Alex's parents. The effect was galvanic. She could not help but be attracted to a quality in him to which she responded in spite of herself; his candour and also his loss. She saw this vividly as the evening wore on: how his parents' death was a stone that dragged him down. It was an odd characteristic, unusually intense in both of them, that each would be drawn to a commensurate tragedy in the other.

Prominent in what was appealing about Alex was his instinct to blot out unpleasantness. He lived – it seemed to Merridy – with both feet planted in the present. He did not blame anything on his parents' death. He believed in putting the past behind him; in not looking back. She, on the other hand, only looked back. This was the difference between them. If there is an instinct to chain oneself to the past that leaves even the longest-serving convict howling for mercy, Merridy had it.

Towards the end of the meal a fantasy plucked at her. Somehow to whisk herself into Alex's slipstream and leave her history behind. She did not know what made life worth living, hadn't a clue, but Alex might.

She finished her meal before him. In the darkening room, she watched him chew his steak. "You're a slow eater."

"It's a family curse."

His father had chewed each mouthful sixty-four times, "like Mr Gladstone" – a habit that Alex could not shake. It had resulted in him having his plates endlessly taken away at school and university.

She said: "I still don't understand why you came back from London. I mean, don't you mind being so far away from everywhere? This is the end of the world."

He put down his knife and fork. "If you want to see the end of the world, go up Regent Street on a rainy Sunday afternoon."

"So where is the centre?"

"Wherever each one of us is." He raised his head. "Isn't it?"

"Is that what you believe?"

"Why not?"

"No, I mean, really believe." And suddenly her eyes were less playful than her mouth.

The question having appeared from nowhere hovered like a frightful moth between them.

Immediately, Alex was out of his depth. He had met Merridy two, three times. And yet he felt that somewhat more than the fate of the evening hung on his reply.

He pushed away his plate that had some meat still on it. "If you're talking about God, then no," he said quite fiercely. His heroes might have believed in God. Merridy's mother obviously did. But Alex could not lie, even if it meant losing her.

"I can see from a Darwinian point of view why the Church came into force," he went on, "because we need a body that is not the State to govern our morals. But all those wonderful con tricks about heaven and hell . . ."

Her eyes relaxed. "I think that's all a nonsense, too."

"You do?"

"Yes. I think we're just an accidental growth of moss that's appeared on a rock. To me, it's no coincidence that the vast majority of saints were created before the Middle Ages – when we can't check up on them."

"But you do believe in something?"

She considered his question. "The sea. I could believe in that."

"Any particular aspect of it?" He was smiling again. "It's quite a big place."

Another pause. "I believe that people who go away to sea always come back."

"That sounds poetic." For the first time, he could understand how she might irritate. "But what does it mean?"

"Does one's belief have to mean anything to anyone else? I suppose I have a residual superstition that when we die, we don't die, we're still around somehow. But what about you? You haven't answered my question."

He picked at the candle wax. A piece fell away, the colour of dead flesh. Of something divine, perhaps. And though he did not have an answer, he was terrified to disappoint.

"I believe in bottles."

"You're an alcoholic?" she frowned.

"My father probably was," with humour. "No, not bottles with gin or wine in them. Not anything like that."

"What, then?"

"Ships."

"Ships?" She looked at him.

A chaffinch noise announced Debbie bringing the bill on a willow-pattern saucer. She started to clear the table when Alex reached across and seized all three satay sticks from Merridy's plate and slipped them without explanation into his jacket inside pocket.

The bill settled with a substantial tip, Alex was unwilling to tear himself away. He picked off a last piece of wax. The bottle was now bare of it and the candle shot up straight from the mouth. On the other side of the flame Merridy peered down into her cup.

"What are you looking at?"

She was insolently beautiful to him.

"Tea leaves. You can read the future." Another thing her father had taught her.

"What do they say?" leaning forward, immensely interested. But seeing only warm black wet flakes in the discoloured milk.

Her eyes fluttered towards him through the distorted air. "Not telling."

It was late when Alex walked her home. Past Sergeant Finter sitting in his Ford Falcon on the corner of Radley Street. The policeman looked at her and all but saluted. A woman to make you go crazy, his face said to Alex. Past the Town Hall. Barney Todman playing "Stranger on the Shore" and through tall windows a blur of faces nuzzling into necks and mascaraed eyes half-shut. Up Waterloo Street to Louisa Meredith House and the modest villa with its melon curtains closed and between the gap a bright light on.

He stood beneath the window, the light falling in a stripe across his nose. "Goodnight." Not daring to touch her for fear of bursting.

"Goodnight," said Merridy and for the first time trembled for him. For them both. "Love is a weakness. It peters out, it enfeebles, it has no mandate beyond the appeasement of lust; it is lent and snatched away." So did she remember the words of her mother, who lay on her bed behind the curtain, waiting.

But then her father's words returned:

For day and night he was always there
By the side of the Jumbly Girl so fair . . .

She looked with an intense expression at Alex's forehead where his hairline started. Quickly, she brushed his cheek with the back of her hand. "It's been fun, I must say."

"Will I see you again?" he said.

Merridy smiled at him. "What do you reckon? Small town."

The table radio was still on, playing Bach. Her father lay on his pneumatic bed, eyes closed and a muscle quivering under them. She switched off the motet and waited. When the head on the pillow failed to stir, she dimmed the light that her mother had kept on for the past four nights, ever since her evening with Ray Grogan.

In the Town Hall Barney Todman struck up a faster tune.

Merridy slipped into the room that she shared with her mother. She undressed and got into bed and stretched out, eyes on the ceiling, inhaling the music. The sound of the guitar escorted her back to a drafty barren hall of ugly red brick tacked onto the side of the Methodist church in Ulverstone, and the game that they played on Friday evenings, all the girls and boys; a sort of tribal mating ritual. The ripped copies of the *Advocate* strewn quite prettily about on the floor; the brass-rubbings pinned to the walls; and the surprisingly well-tuned piano on which Randal Twelvetrees, the repressed idiot who might have married her mother and into whose care Mrs Bowman out of some deformed sense of guilt now sought to deliver Merridy, played a jolly tune like "Coming Round the Mountain" that would stop abruptly in mid-note. She recalled the boys in an outer circle, each holding an *Advocate*, and the girls in an inner circle, skipping round in different directions, and – when the music stopped – the rush to grab hold of your partner and open up the newspaper and leap on it, standing very still, waiting for Randal to sweep back the gingerish hair from his eyes and shuffle over to turf off the last pair who had jumped on. She remembered with a cold shiver how he pressed his unblinking face against the bodies that in order to remain upright stood on tiptoe, inspecting for any stray foot that remained off the newspaper, or any part of a foot. The losing pair identified, the surviving couples each tore their newspaper in half and the music started up; and so on, down and down until there were just two couples left, circling each other around a shrinking island of shredded paper, an island no larger than a page, dancing closer and closer together until the piano fell silent. And she remembered what a strong connection you had with the other person if you happened to be one of these last two pairs, which repeatedly she was, so strong was her wish to escape the devouring ginger stare of Randal Twelvetrees. You were not a mob any longer, you were a couple. The girl perspiring under her little armpits and her nervous young breasts pushing against her partner's chest, and yet really enjoying it. The boy, too. It was superb. An ornate and deadly cocktail. "When it gets down to a tram-ticket, you're both of you dry-rooting," laughed Tildy. And then only one couple was left. And she remembered a boy with a massive erection who was too embarrassed to press himself up against her – and so he lost the game. Merridy had felt this thing and wondered what the hell had hit her, but it was nature sorting itself out. She had won him in a way and on those Friday evenings winning was everything. Afterwards, everyone walked home, although Merridy remembered one occasion when she had to plead with the boy to remain behind, until it was time for her mother to collect her, so that she would not be left alone with Randal. Sitting there in the hall beside the boy, not saying anything. Not doing anything either, beyond holding his hand while Randal cleared up bits of newspaper. There was a rural dorkiness about it all that she imagined when she thought of England, but also a thwarted passion.

Merridy remembered this, then looked across at her mother who lay awake, mouthing silent words at the ceiling and the beam that flashed from the lighthouse.

"I've found him."

Her mother's lips went on moving. Where had he got to, her

dearest boy, her firstborn? Was he in trouble? In pain? But he was strong. She wished that he could be here to protect her. Then stopped. "Who?"

"Who did you think?" sighed Merridy and threw back her head on the pillow. The surf boomed. Another spoke of light rotated on the ceiling, raking the night. "The bloody Dong?"

Walking back towards his ute, Alex resembled a bird at the top of its swoop, wings clipped to its side. Chesting the air like a bowsprit.

He drove home. North along the coast road and then down a small trunk road that led, five windy miles later, to his farm. Carrying in his head an image that he wanted never to fade. He hoarded up in his mind the smallest detail of their dinner. Her forthright way of speaking. Her sudden seriousness. Her mannish laugh that made him feel nothing so funny or delightful had ever happened to anyone. He had talked about his past in a way that he was not accustomed to talk with anyone, and said to her all the things that a young man might feel inspired to say who had lost his heart thoroughly. And yet when he pulled into the drive, he had, as inevitably he did on reaching this blind corner, a flashback of a white Ford Zephyr with his parents inside juddering forward.

Five drops of rain splashed onto the windscreen and then others. He shivered, struggling to invoke Merridy, and touched his cheek where she had brushed it with the back of her hand. But his younger self had ambushed him.

CHAPTER TEN

IT WAS FOUR YEARS before. He was twenty-three. He felt raw and nervous as he stood at the edge of the road where out of some superstition he had parked his hired car. Suddenly, he did not want to walk for half a mile up the worn-out drive of pale gravel that had lost its guts; past the windmill and the Oyster Bay pine, to find, as he knew he would, the house as he had left it; he did not want to squeak open the fly-screen into the kitchen; he did not want to stay.

So when he started up the drive, he was more resolved than ever to sell the place.

The house he climbed to was a low brick one with whitewashed walls and a green corrugated-iron roof that sagged at the back. It was single storey and stood next to a farmyard squared off by sheds and barns. On an unmowed lawn in front of it, obscuring the windows, was a large tree. The pine had grown enormous since his childhood, so that its lowermost branches reached out and all but brushed the roof.

He walked through the long grass to the base of the tree and stood before two slabs of Maria Island granite inscribed with the names and dates of his parents. He looked at the simple headstones and thought of his mother and father beneath, their bones blending with the roots.

Something was wrong with the iron windmill. The machinery creaked wildly and gouts of water streamed down from a pipe and into the yard. He delayed going into the house in order to fix the leak. For whatever reason, it was important that he stop the flow of water. But in trying to repair the windmill, he gashed his hand.

The blood oozed out of the cut. He washed his hand under the leaking pipe. Then took off his left boot and sock, and bound the sock around the wound.

He could anticipate Sarah's reaction.

The grassy air was scented with cow dung. He breathed it in and clenched his fingers to dull the throbbing. The water splashed from the pipe.

He leaned against the windmill and took a long look at his childhood home. The house had a flower bed around it over-spilling with bottle-brushes and wild daisies. It lay in a hammock of barley fields and grazing paddocks that rose on either side to hills planted with black wattle and gums; and beyond, into Crown land of thicker bush and old-growth forest. Behind, paddocks sloped down to a windbreak of macrocarpa and through the trees a lagoon glittered. These were the smells and shapes to which he was first exposed. He knew their features better than his own.

He picked his way through the long grass, oppressed by the weight of memories. Their vividness had come to an end when he left Australia for England. Twelve years in that cold, foggy climate had blurred him. Everything that he had succeeded in keeping at bay behind a screen, as it were, of sycamore, beech and elm, threatened now to dart out into the open and overwhelm him.

His thoughts gallivanted off. He had the illusion that he could recall with extraordinary clarity almost every day of his child-hood better than any day at boarding school or university. His memory struggled along a ditch. Was it here that he had sat with his father and watched the eels wriggling across the wet paddocks to the dam? He heard his father ruminating: "You know, no one has ever seen an eel mate." Or over there that the tiger-snake had wrapped itself about his father's leg and only uncoiled after being lured away with the glass of Beefeater that he happened to be holding? Afflicted with the memories, Alex trod across the lawn, ignoring the pain in his hand, ignoring the hives on his legs made by the grass, and opened the fly-screen to the kitchen and went in, to the damp and stringent odours of a house that had not been lived in since he was a boy.

He inhaled. Smells of dripping and Mortein insect spray. Another stink turned out to be a dead possum in the disused rain-water tank, heaving with a fleece of maggots.

Alex dug a hole in the flower bed and buried the rancid corpse with a rusted spade that he discovered in the shearing shed. Then he came back in and sat at the blackwood table and ate the sandwich that he had brought with him.

He looked around. Some things remained in the darkness beyond the lantern glow of memory. Though not the image of his parents playing Scrabble at this table. He heard their shouts as his father got up to refill his glass and upset the letters. His mother saying: "Piers, your legs are younger than mine. Run to my room and get the dictionary." She had been dead set against the idea of a dictionary on ideological grounds. But that was before her husband gave her one for their tenth wedding anniversary. From that moment on, she pored over her dictionary every night, ransacking it for obscure words. Especially words composed of two letters. She never knew what they meant, but was categorical that they did mean something. "Darling," she would say testily, "everyone knows that your luck is determined by the flow of qi" – although, when challenged, it usually transpired that she had confused the Chinese life force with the Egyptian spiritual self or a Vietnamese monetary unit.

Let to Bill Molson, who had lived the other side of Coombend and was interested only in grazing the land, the farmhouse did not show evidence of having been interfered with by any spiritual or human agency. Everything wore an aspect of distress and mismanagement.

There was a black telephone on the table. Alex finished eating his sandwich and picked it up. Dead. But sounds came back to him. The voices of the girls at the manual exchange. The party-line number: three short rings and one long. The occasions when he would listen carefully so as not to answer the neighbours' calls. He gently replaced the receiver.

Piles of mail lay where they had tumbled onto the kitchen floor. Alex started to open the envelopes, but his eyes only followed print that he did not take in. An appeal from Merton College for the renovation of the chapel. A brochure from a hotel in Cumbria addressed to his parents. A postcard from Sarah, sent ten days before he left London – *Hurry home, XXX S* – and bulletins from museums in Denmark and Germany that housed collections of ships in bottles. Plus forty-nine issues of *Bottleship* magazine that someone had stacked on the dresser.

This was the first hour. It caused a glugging in his heart to disentangle the kitchen from his rememberance of it. The sink against which he had groaned as a kid, a boy with the innocence rubbed off, hugging his elbows, watching the water running out clockwise – "In Cumbria," his father maintained, "it drains the other way." The windows that no one had cleaned since that horribly sad day. The Ruber calendar with Waterhouse's *Circe Individuosa* hanging behind the closed door, stuck fast in January 1972. His father liked to keep the grandfather clock half an hour forward, but his mother was the tardy one. She never flipped the page on the calendar until well into the following month. Another three weeks before she hurried into his bedroom on her way to the auction of fine furniture and linen in Campbell Town. "Your cricket whites are on the line, and, Piers, you can offer them breakfast if you like," while his father yelled from the kitchen, "Hista! Marjorie, hista! Unless we leave this *instant* we will miss the auction." About to close the door, his mother had darted back into the room and pulled open the curtains. "We should be back in time for tea," kissing him. "Good luck with the match. Who are you playing? Fingal? Bowl well." In her thick black hair a streak of white and on her breath the scent of something medicinal. Then, louder: "Coming." His last sight of her: from the back, the strong light splintering onto her peacock jacket before he retreated into sleep. The sleep in which he hoped to find the courage to tell Cheele how dreadfully sorry he was.

When he had opened all the mail, Alex stood up and went into the corridor that led to the two bedrooms and his father's workshop. His Blundstone boots were stiff, and the dry boards creaked like ice under his sockless foot. Alert, he avoided looking at the ratty frames of Huon pine that hung along both walls. He knew by heart their homespun wisdom. Occasionally in England, a sentence from within one of these frames had wormed its way into his head and stayed there. And he had gathered together homilies of his own that he might like to put behind glass.

No one reaches the end of their life and wishes they'd spent more time marking papers.

If you want to make the gods laugh, tell them your plans.

When you're skating on thin ice, you might as well dance.

Don't sleep with anyone who has bigger problems than you have.

Holding his breath, he creaked through the rooms. Saliva filled his mouth when he found his parents' clothes hanging in the oak wardrobe. His father's jacket and waistcoat fleece, his mother's blueberry frock. He pushed his face into the tweed suits and dresses, gulping in the odour of mothballs mingled with musty wool, and a shudder ran through him. "Oh, Dad, oh, Mum."

Alex unhooked the clothes from the rail and threw them onto the bed.

He fled into the living room and opened the curtains, sending up puffs of rodent-scented dust. The light slashed into strange, half-remembered furniture and paintings: a sewing machine, a watercolour of the River Tamar by Gladstone Eyre, a Lear lithograph of a cockatoo. Mice had eaten the arm of a red chair, revealing four springs.

He plumped up the cushions, shaking out the dead flies. He had inherited all this, down to the Brussels carpet, but he hardly knew anything about these objects. Except for those in the room at the end.

Alex turned the handle, pushed open the door. His heart pounding.

He stood on the threshold of what resembled an operating theatre. In the centre of the room was a worktop scattered with scalpels, tweezers, twist-drills, long scissors; all from the same surgical suppliers in Melbourne, all left where his father had put them down.

He rubbed his nose vigorously at the familiar smell of varnish and gave a slow look around. Sunlight winked through the window blind on shelves of gin bottles placed horizontally, of light bulbs and injection capsules. Each contained a miniature vessel under full sail.

Upright on the worktop, a bottle with a coin in its mouth.

At the sight of the coin, Alex started forward. His sudden movement disturbed a huntsman spider and a ghost in red braces who sat hunched over the bottle and stared intently at a match that burned at the bottom of it. On hearing Alex enter, the memory looked up and searched for him with fading eyesight: "You need to be original, you need to be different," in a voice curbed by exile. "Not like Johnny-round-the-corner."

It was to this room that Alex now made his way upon returning from his dinner with Merridy. His first act was to sit down at the worktop and retrieve the three satay sticks from his pocket. He reached over to the model of the ship that he had started to piece together and measured the sticks against the hull. Perfect.

Then, about to scrub off the legacy of the dried chicken, he noticed an orange trace on one of them. He pressed it to his lips.

And in the morning sketched a single enormous word on the green vane of the windmill. He read and reread the letters drying in the sun, then put the top back on the marker that he used for identifying sheep and climbed down the ladder.

When Alice came to clean on Monday, she found Alex trying on a new shirt that he had bought a year before and never worn.

"Anything the matter?" she asked, although she had heard some of it already from Debbie.

"No. Why?"

"You look like a washing machine set on spin."

CHAPTER ELEVEN

The WELLINGTON POINT READING GROUP met at the Bethel Teahouse on Tuesday last. The small audience was disappointing. However, the moment was rescued by a wonderful presentation by Mavis Pidd who in response to our suggestion that her talk be abandoned went on with enthusiasm to describe her vibrant and whimsical upbringing in Tomahawk.

Tildy stared across the counter of the cocktail bar and examined the face of her childhood friend with respectful astonishment. "Alex Dove took you to dinner? He's never taken anyone to dinner. You know what I reckon?"

"No."

"It was the lip gloss I lent you!"

"Very probably," laughed Merridy. Whatever had passed between her cousin and Alex, it relieved her to find that she was not upset.

"So. What did you make of him?"

Merridy picked up the brick and wiped the counter under it and put it down. "I liked him."

Tildy's eyes rattled in her head. "Oh, everybody likes Alex Dove. But Ray's right. Say what you want, he's still a Pom. And you know what they say about Poms. Where the heart should be there's a jellyfish."

"He was born in Australia, you goof," said Merridy. But she felt defenceless. Tildy was her employer's daughter. Not for the first time, Merridy resented the position this put her in. To be an object of Keith Framley's charity.

Tildy was not done. She rotated her glass. "Tell him about your brother, did you?"

Merridy frowned. "I did."

"You did?"

"Well, more or less."

"Oh, Merridy," she sighed. Then, matter-of-factly: "I don't think you'll ever get over it."

"Of course I will," flashed Merridy. "You can get over anything. You just have to put your mind to it."

Tildy was not ever going to be able to conceive of getting over Ray Grogan. Not in two hundred and ninety million years.

"Anyway, he'd understand," Merridy went on. Battling to keep the anguish from her voice. "After all, his parents . . . He got over that, didn't he?"

"I suppose so," said Tildy, and stood up. She was on her way to the Returned Servicemen's Club to meet Ray. "I suppose so," retrieving her handbag from the counter. "But you do like him?"

"Like, yes."

Impatient as she was to see Ray, Tildy paused. She had known her cousin long enough to be aware that Merridy's confidence was under siege. Something Tildy had not witnessed before.

"Would you *like* to be in love with him?" with exaggerated patience.

A dry silence. In which Tildy's father could be heard talking in the kitchen to Debbie.

". . . wind's started to blow again. Reckon if it'd stop, we'd fall over."

"We've had winter before we've even had it, Mr Framley . . ."

"Merridy?"

"Of course. Of course," in a whisper.

Tildy looked at the cousin she had danced with as a child and shook her head. "Oh, Merridy, you'd better start living. We're dead an awfully long time. You may not have liked Mr Twelvetrees, but sometimes he was right – 'Unknown makes unloved.'"

Her cousin's words ate into Merridy. She saw the regret in Tildy's eye and it moved her as umpteen young men's entreaties had not succeeded in doing. The following afternoon, she leaned against an ochre wall that suited her colour better than the dark jacket that Keith Framley obliged her to wear behind his bar, and stroked Alex's face again.

"Why do you touch me like that?" he wanted to know.

"Like what?"

He took her hand and showed her.

"It's a family thing. Don't all families do something? Yours must have had its idiosyncrasies. This is one of ours."

He moved forward at her inflection to read the intention in her mouth. Then they were kissing. He felt her breath inside him, warming and expanding, snapping the threads that bound him.

She pulled back. Fighting to catch her breath. And to keep above the surface. "Know what Ray Grogan says about you?"

"What?"

She struggled for distance, but something drew her to him once more. She touched his face with the tips of her fingers, the fair unprotected hairs at the borders of his temples. Like the hairs on a baby's legs.

"Go on," he said. "Tell me." Losing himself in her eyes.

She swallowed and tried to look mean. "He says you're the biggest spurt of piss ever let out of an English prick."

"He said that!"

"Also, you're so tight-arsed that if you rammed a bluegum up your bum it would come out wood chips," and her mouth, with the lipstick overrunning the lips, where she had kissed him, smiled as if he were something that she had in that instant decided to defend to the death.

In a sparsely decorated room less than a hundred yards away, Sister Surrage inspected a plate of melted ice cream. "How are we doing today, Mr Bowman? Not eating, I see." And clucked. "I suppose you know it's home-made?"

Propped up on blue cushions, Leonard Bowman had lost his appetite but not his taste for poetry. His gaze remained fixed to the wall of the bowls club opposite, and the couple kissing there. Unsuspecting on the other side of the wall, his wife scuttled forward two steps and released a black ball onto the grass under the critical eye of her plump partner.

"What's that you're saying?" Sister Surrage hovered with the tray.

He tried to speak, but the words were sewn to his tongue. A

piece of doggerel memorised from the Talbot's *Newsletter,* and adapted.

Who do you see, sister, who do you see?
When you enter this room and stand looking at me:
Are you thinking: a crabby old man, not very wise
Uncertain of habit with faraway eyes
Who dribbles his food and makes no replies?
But inside this old carcass
A young man still dwells
And now and again his battered heart swells
I remember the joys, I remember the pain
And I'm loving and living life over again
So open your eyes, sister, open and see
Not a crabby old man, look closer – see me.

But all Sister Surrage heard was a low steady drone uttered through dry lips.

Moments later, the door handle turned and Merridy came into the room. "All right, nurse. I'll take over."

Once Sister Surrage had left, Merridy dragged over her Glory Box from the foot of the pneumatic bed and sat on it beside her father. She was conscious of the quickness of her breathing. She did not believe what her heart was telling her. The idea was absurd. It was only a kiss. And yet something remained, some strange tingling or taste, a presentiment even, that made her want to see Alex again already.

Another moment before it dawned.

She turned. "Dad, did you just see us?"

Seated in his wheelchair beside her, Mr Bowman had nothing to say. Even so, she heard his thoughts.

Good thing your mother's playing bowls! She wouldn't have understood what I witnessed. Once upon a time, perhaps. But I understand. It sweeps me back to my first sight of Leticia. On her way to a daffodil competition when this impatient young fellow overtakes her. Did I tell you ever about that afternoon? It was raining and we were both trying to get out of the wind. I noticed this girl in front of me, ducking her head and leaning forward at an angle as if she were running from a helicopter, and before I knew it I was tangled up in her legs. We fell head over heels, literally, but I was first on my feet. I pulled her up from the footpath and when I looked into those eyes I couldn't let go of her hand. Simple as that. I was heading out that afternoon to Burnie, but twenty minutes after meeting your mother I called up Mr Bathurst at the pulp mill to say I was crook and that night booked into a B & B – as it happened in the same part of town where she lived, though it took me a few days to track her down. Sometimes you have to act like that, straight away. If I had not cast caution to the wind, I might have missed out on a whole lot of heartbreak and bother, but I would not have had you. My own little miracle. That's what you are to me. You know that, don't you?

Some ice cream had dried on his jersey. Merridy licked the corner of her shirtsleeve and wiped it away. She switched on the table radio that she had bought him after his accident. The Tasmanian Symphony Orchestra playing Sibelius.

"It's all right, Dad. You can go to sleep. Unless you want to watch Mum losing at bowls."

Want your soon-to-be ex-wife's chattels or impedimenta moved to her mother's house? Or your grand piano? Contact THE LONG HAUL. No journey too far or too near. Phone: 62578583

Bang! A black shape tumbled from the gum tree in a blur and clatter of feathers. Bang! Another.

Alex was out with his father's shotgun, shooting crows before they picked out the eyes of the lambs. It gave him no pleasure to kill. Almost his first act on taking on the farm at Moulting Lagoon was to forbid the swan shooters from crossing his land. This had alienated an element in the community, foremost among them Ray Grogan, who had enjoyed unfettered access to the lagoon under Bill Molson's tenancy. Alex also banned 1080 poison, laid by other farmers to prevent marsupials from devouring the young plantations. This meant, though, that he had to cull. Unable to afford a wallaby-proof fence, he depended on his father's Purdey to protect his barley from anything that nibbled.

He left the dead crows for the devils. He picked up the plastic cartridge cases and put them in his pocket and walked home. At this hour, he usually made himself a sandwich, but he had no appetite.

Meanwhile, Alex's hunger for Merridy was a bread that he tore at. He had not expected love. For the first time, he began to find his isolated life depressing. The most trivial excuse took him back into town.

The following afternoon, he was at Nevin's garage filling the ute for the second time in two days, when he caught sight of Tildy's blonde head. She was squeezed into jeans and wore a man's white shirt with the gold cufflinks still in.

"Hi, Tildy," and nodded to her over the sack of Bismarck potatoes and jump-leads and rolls of wire. "How was the Jazz Social?"

"Wonderful," she breathed. She rested her arm on the side of his vehicle before deciding that it would dirty her elbow. "Just wonderful."

"I heard about you and Ray. That's great."

"Thank you," and stretched her arms. "It's the first time I've felt like this. It really is."

"Yes, I know."

She studied him. "OK, who is it?" cunningly.

"Merridy—" and stopped, embarrassed at having spoken – that it was so close to the surface.

Tildy fell silent at the mention of her cousin's name. She folded her arms and waited while Alex hooked the nozzle back on the pump. "Alex . . . a word in your shell-like," very seriously.

"What about?"

She rolled her eyes.

"C'mon. What is it?"

She exhaled. "Don't get involved," biting her lip.

"Who says I'm involved?"

"She's my oldest friend as well as my cousin. But it's not just her. It's the whole situation."

“What whole situation?” And tried to picture it from Tildy’s angle. Merridy’s father refusing to die; her mother a religious nutcase.

“Did she tell you about her brother?”

“She said that he disappeared.”

“Explain what happened, did she?”

“No. Just that he disappeared.”

“Well, I hate to say this, and of my own cousin too, but you’ve got to know something about Merridy.” She whispered, as if to mock her own words: “The fact is, she’s madder than a cut snake.”

“Seems pretty normal to me,” hunting around for the cap.

“Oh, she doesn’t look mad, but she is. Don’t believe me, have a word with Ray.”

“Ray? Are you joking?”

CHAPTER TWELVE

KEITH FRAMLEY ALLOWED MERRIDY one afternoon off a week. At 2.30 p.m. on Tuesday, Alex collected her from the hotel.

It was a cutting cold day. Smells from a recent rain rose from the paddocks and the sky was grey with flotillas of thick cumulus. Early March and Wellington Point was still exposed to sudden showers.

They talked pleasantly about not much at all on the journey. But Alex felt nervous as he rounded Cerney Hill and approached the last bend. It was raining again and he wanted her to like what she was about to see. And Merridy, sensing this, stared out through the windscreen with a concentrated expression, her hands in their gloves of brown wool laced in her lap.

The entrance to Alex's property was on a blind corner concealed between two bluegums.

"I live by myself," he explained unnecessarily.

"Tildy said." But it was Ray who had told about the Scania log-truck. In the Bethel Teahouse, he had described for her the trailer stacked with gigantic eucalypts, careering down this road as though the driver had but a moment to live. She pictured the log-truck swiping the car that emerged from between the trees, and scattering Alex's childhood into fragments.

They jolted over the cattle-grid and up a long drive of white gravel. She watched it dead-end into a tidy lawn in the middle of which was a large and solitary pine. Like a finger pointing upward in the Methodist Hall. Minister Twelvetrees's finger.

Alex parked beside a rotary clothes-line and they climbed out. It was raining heavily now.

She stood on the gravel, looked around, started to walk towards the house.

"No, this way," said Alex.

Ignoring the downpour, he insisted on first showing her the view. A veranda stretched around the back of the house, a deck of cedar planks which the sea salt had blackened. She stood beside him and cast her eyes out over Moulting Lagoon to Oyster Bay. It was, as Alex's father never tired of repeating, a top spot. But not on this day, perhaps.

Rain dripped from the gutters and leaves. A scratching and a whining sounded from inside. Alex opened a door and a young Border collie, jackdaw-coloured, bounded out.

"Hey, Flash!"

Merridy, who was unbuttoning her wet coat, sank to her haunches. "It's all right," shutting her eyes to the dog's tongue.

"I'm still training her."

In the tactile warmth of the kitchen, he twisted the stove on and offered her tea.

"It's Bushells." Not the Glen Valley that his mother insisted on.

"I'd love a cup," shaking the raindrops from her head and throwing off her coat. She wore a green jersey underneath with large yellow daisies knitted into it and the brown gloves that she would not take off.

He brought Merridy her tea, thinking of the tanned arm with the fair hairs.

"You heard about the prang?"

She nodded.

Silence. Just the rain.

"I was standing here," moving to the basin. "I'd just got out of bed and I saw a policeman outside and Miss Pritchard, our teacher. I thought: She's come with the cricket team and do we have enough bacon, and I went out in my pyjamas and I said: 'Hello,' and Miss Pritchard, white as a shirt, came towards me and lifted me up, and I said: 'My parents?'

"'Yes.'

"'Dead?'

"'Yes.'"

The accident had happened out of earshot after Alex had gone back to sleep. Composing an apology to Cheele.

"I must see them," he was moaning, and moaning.

The suddenly orphaned boy.

Merridy sipped her tea. Inside the kitchen, the grey light had solidified with the bacon fat from the stove. She was staring into herself and nodding. That expression again, at once absent and focused. He would have hated it if she had said anything.

"More?"

"I'm doing all right," and looked around. At the Welsh dresser painted green. The cherry pips in a saucer. The view through a rain-streaked window onto the solitary tree.

She moved and a yellow daisy rose. She had noticed the frames.

"My mother collected them," coming up behind.

"What are they?"

"Samplers. Young women made them on the voyage out as proof of a skill."

She stood before the first frame.

Alex went on: "To try and win themselves a husband, I suppose."

"Those were the days! But what kind of man would fall for this one?" Merridy murmured the words, embroidered below deck in coloured wools: *"Emily Highmore, aged 13, December 4, 1840: Early will I seek thee/Now that my journey is just begun/My course but little trod/I'll stay before I further run/And give myself to God."*

Alex smiled. "Someone who's not going to see too much action outside a church?"

She passed to the next. "*Delay of repentance is a cheat upon ourselves.*"

He said: "Mainly they sewed the alphabet. And numbers. My mother liked the ones with verses."

She put down her cup on a cabinet of white-bound *Encyclopaedia Britannicas*. Stitched in a frame above was the line: *Worked by Florrie Winch 1887: There is a mystery in every meeting, and that is God.*

"I like that," tapping the glass.

Excitement was in her now. The samplers drew her further into the leaden reaches of corridor, something in their faded colours arousing her to pause before each, read aloud, move on.

He who says all he knows does not know himself.

Beware the anger of the dove.

Remain a child so that your children will always love you.

At the bottom of the devil's bag, one always finds his bill.

When the moon is full she shines over all.

Beautiful are the heralds, crying, O traveller enter in.

Until she came to his bedroom.

She took in with a quiet glance the wide mahogany bed and the large wardrobe of dark oak with claws for feet.

"That's . . ." She had been about to say "a good piece of furniture", but it did not seem adequate.

"It's my mother's," Alex said. "She brought it with her on the ship from England. I don't know how old it is. She used to boast that it was older than Australia."

The wardrobe was the colour of a blackboard. One of the doors, she could not help noticing, was hinged back against the curtain, reflecting her and Alex, their two shapes.

She moved closer.

Some wind had filled her up and she skimmed over a surface where before she might have sunk. It was a novel sensation not to be repelling someone, a relief.

She closed the door, but it swung back on its hinge. She tested it again, with the same result.

"Doesn't it shut?"

"It was damaged in transit from England. They never got round to fixing it."

She pulled open the other door that was also pierced with a hollow heart and a cross above it, and heard her higher pitched voice: "No key?"

"My mother lost it." Or never had it.

Now both doors gaped. She stared inside at the divided interior: one side for hanging space, the other with five tray shelves.

This velvety darkness. It roused in Merridy a faint remembrance of something, right on the edge of memory. She searched her mind, but whatever it was stayed the other side.

She felt a tightening in her womb and at the same time a pleasant unravelling of herself, a clarity. "Do you want children?"

Merridy had never before said such a thing to a man and did not know how she had managed to utter it. But once the phrase was out of her mouth she followed it.

Beyond the curtain was the whirring of a windmill.

"I'd love children," she said. "Mobs of them." And poked in her head as if already she could hear them crying.

A little while later, she would carry away the soapy smell of his shirts; and the image of him in the tight white underpants, his cock straining.

Now, in the darkness of his folded clothes, she panicked. She wondered if anything she had could be important to Alex, anything at all about herself.

Sensing his gaze on her, she turned, hoping to catch him sneaking a look – at least to have that certainty – but his attention was trapped by the clawed legs of the wardrobe.

"What are they holding?" she wanted to know. "Is it a globe? Or just a ball?"

He might have been in their grip. "Do you always ask so many questions?"

"Don't ask, don't get," she replied in the words of her mother, who had herself mislaid the key to a number of things.

But his eyes daunted her. She looked back inside. Up a shelf. And saw something to make her raise her arms in a way that caught his breath.

"Hey, what have you got there?"

"Oh, those," of the bottles stacked on their sides. "They're my father's. Here, come and have a bopeep."

He piloted her to another room, at the end of the corridor. Opened the door.

"You made these?" staring at the shelves. Ship after ship. Each with its thorn-sized sails and cargo of dreams.

"My father taught me," Alex said, not yet adding that it was a way for him to preserve one of his few unfading impressions of a tall man with crinkled grey eyes who Sunday mornings, early, would drive Alex to the canal in Lauderdale and launch his models in the company of enthusiasts; perhaps his only link, apart from a handful of isolated phrases and a distinct memory of the two of them both sitting under the stars on Barn Hill while his father, smelling richly of Balkan Sobranie, knocked his pipe against the ground and talked about white-throated swifts and eels and the uncommonly clear sky, damn well suited for an astronomer.

Less distinct was an excursion to New Norfolk when Alex was

five or six, to visit the asylum where another fellow Cumbrian had been incarcerated. The composer John Woodcock Graves had written the words to the hunting song that Alex's father was always humming: "*Do you ken John Peel?*"

Otherwise, Basil Dove came to him second-hand through the memories of others, smoking a pipe as he swam in the river and holding a billycan filled with speckled trout. "Your father," Harry Ford said, "could catch fish in a bucket." It was not a memory you could argue with. Over the years Alex had constructed a less bucolic image of his parents. A middle-class English couple who sailed to Australia a decade after the war, married and settled in the outback, and when it ceased to suit them took their consolation in drink. Or so he understood from Harry, who fed him peppery morsels that added up to a depressing picture replicated all over Australia: exile, exacerbated by alcohol and a clinging to outdated habits. Like making ships in bottles. And thought of Harry, with his bomb-shaped head and a touch of malice about him, grinning at Alex over a large glass of South African port: "No shortage of empties!"

Across the room, something was stirring up in Merridy. She stared at a 1,000-watt light bulb that contained a minuscule ship.

Alex lifted the large glass bulb for her to see. "Five-masted clipper. Thirty sails in there. And you have to build them up one by one. I'm never doing that again. It's probably why my father went blind."

"How come it didn't explode?"

"Good luck," and smiled.

"Alex, tell me," impatient. "I know about light bulbs. It ought to have exploded."

He drew closer. "Right. You tap with a screwdriver on the contacts. There's a small sigh as the vacuum escapes," and imitated the sound. "Then you keep chipping till you get down to the filament. Once the filament is removed, you clean the rubbish out."

A vacuum was escaping in her, too. Solemnly, she said: "When I was the size of a deck-fitting, I once designed a boat."

There came back to her an afternoon in Wynyard less than a year after her brother's disappearance. She remembered burningly her mother's blank disinterest, her father's curiosity. "What's that, Merridy?"

"It's what the Jumblies went to sea in. Look, that's him steering."

Animated, her father set about making a model based on Merridy's design. It was a vision they shared. When he retired, he promised to build her a full-scale version. For years she had looked forward to it. His sea-going sieve.

It was not what Alex expected. He was braced for her laugh, not a fantastic floating colander. "This model, how big was it?"

"Oh, no bigger than that," and gestured at a bottle.

"I'd like to see."

"I lost it when my parents separated."

"That's a shame. What did you copy it from, a children's book?"

"It came out of my head. I don't know where it came from, I can't remember much about being six." But she had the original drawing in her Glory Box. A fuel-section measured to scale. The whole thing nearly sixty-five feet in diameter. And her brother at the wheel.

She elaborately averted her glance. "So this is where you work."

"I don't consider it as work," returning the light bulb to its shelf.

She listened to him, his face exposed and fragile in the smell of Super Glue and varnish, his voice the tinkle of something becalmed. Something in a bottle perhaps.

"Seems like work to me!"

He ran his finger over the surface of the table and inspected it. "I really should get Alice to clean this place." The words falling among the crumbs of wood and metal. He did not see that he required another sort of help. Or maybe he did, for his look would not retreat from the raft it had found.

"What's that for?" she asked, puzzled by the round smooth corner of an ice-cream stick pressed against his chin.

"This" – he brandished it like a crucifix – "I use for decks and for stuff that's out of sight, braces and bits and pieces that aren't going to take much weight."

There was the sound of his little stick on a bottle, the tap, tap, tap that she listened to, her heart catching the pulse on the vacant glass until the two sounds beat together.

"What about these?" Protruding out of the same jar she recognised one of the satay sticks that he had snatched so surprisingly from her plate. Still orange with Tildy's lip gloss.

"Satay sticks are good for masts."

It was only natural. People attracted to making boats should be attracted to each other. An unfamiliar creature scampered up and down her ribcage.

On the scarred worktop a green ship lay on its side. She reached out and touched it.

"That's wet. Be careful!"

The sticky varnish was like sap from a black wattle on her wool fingertip, or honey.

Ever so respectful, he scooped the ship from the table and brought it to her.

"The *Otago*. A three-masted barque. Conrad's only command," noticing the fluff she had left on his ship.

"Conrad who?"

"Joseph Conrad. My father loved his novels. Conrad captained the *Otago* for a year and wrote a story about it. She was taken to Hobart and sold for scrap. Otago Bay – it's named after her." He tilted the ship. "See here? Over this side Captain Conrad was leaning when he saw a naked man looking up at him from the sea."

A picture of white legs and arms, desperate, floated into her mind. "Who was he?"

"He had killed a man and jumped overboard. Conrad hid him in his cabin. He risked his ship so that the murderer could swim to the China coast."

She sniffed her finger thoughtfully while Alex explained how he had crafted most of the hull out of Huon pine from the timber yard in Strahan. Two of her masts from Merridy's satay sticks and the main mast from kauri. And the deck out of ice-cream sticks that he had gathered from the bins behind the primary school.

"You saw me—" He started to speak, but she talked over him. She remembered.

"And what on earth are they?" rattling another glass jar.

"Kidney stones." His grandfather, a broom maker in Sedbergh, had collected them, apparently. "They make good cannonballs."

Still the fusillade did not let up. She nodded at what he was cradling. "Where do you get your bottles?" She was thinking of her sieve. She had looked forward to it so idiotically.

"Your hotel, mainly."

"You go through the rubbish there as well?"

He blushed. "That's right."

"I've never seen you." She picked up the rum bottle that he had been tapping. Had she tossed it away herself, into a bin behind the hotel? Something grated and she peered inside. "What's that?"

"A penny." Alex's father had found it in a grave on the edge of his land. The blackened coin had belonged to a family of early settlers who had drowned in Moulting Lagoon, their boat overturning in a sudden gale. "It's old. You couldn't cash it in."

She rattled it. The coin had a face on it, but whether of a man or woman she could not make out. Her lips parted between curiosity to see the face and incredulity as to how it could have got there.

"Just how did you squeeze that in?"

"Ah, that *is* a secret." He spoke in such a serious way that she turned her head. And now she felt his eyes, how they stayed on her, and smiled confusedly.

"But Alex, I want to know. It couldn't possibly fit through this neck."

He stepped closer. Their arms brushing. "Take off your gloves, why don't you?" He wanted to stop her questions. To speak of things that had nothing to do with ships or bottles or coins that today would not pay for a telephone call.

She was staring into the rum bottle.

"Will you come to bed with me?" he said in a flat voice.

She could feel the bone in her denying smile. The horror of the black word forming in her throat. And looked for help at the grating penny.

"You never answered my question." She spoke at random, holding up the bottle and peering through the circular base at Alex. He was so unlike Ray. It was essential not to hurt him. "You *never* answer my questions."

"Which one?"

"Do you want children?" to her magnified brown palms. And thought again how uncanny it was that the uttering of her wish should have created it.

He nodded. Anything she wanted, he wanted too.

But she needed to be sure. "How many?"

"Oh, if they are like you, mobs of them." He took the bottle from her and laid it on the table.

She rubbed at her eye with the scratchy glove.

"Then you'll sleep with me?" His voice was flat, but his eyes shone. She could feel his fingers moving on her shoulders. And with no struggle at all her resolve fled out of her, a wave retreating from the ramparts of a child's sandcastle. She returned the pressure of his body.

Outside, what was going on was the chirring of the windmill.

She looked at him with the eyes of someone who was looking at all the children they would have. She peeled off her gloves and they went back along the corridor and into the bedroom.

Quickly, they undressed. At the touch of her warm skin he felt the blood startle in his hands and chest. His thought was not of the sea, but of the water that serpented along the dry furrow he had dug for his potatoes, the sun on its snake-dark back. It hurt.

She felt the tip of his cock on her chest and pressed herself against him.

In the darker room their bodies were the only light. She caught sight of her raised legs reflected in the patina of the ancient oak wardrobe, his back braced and then flowing into her into her. He could have been swimming for his life.

In shadow his face had grown thinner, his eyes rounder. Sound was the gasp as he replied to her with his whole body, the hiccup of flesh. Smell the varnish from his unfinished deck on her fingertips.

She pulled him to her breast so that he would not see her sadness. She felt no aversion to his neediness, no fear. Part of her had found a berth. Someone to share her obscure hurt. She looked over her arm that held him and envisaged in the colours that she could see through the crack in the curtain – a squalor of reds and blues in a grey sky – the children whom she would make happy with every scrap of love that had been denied her brother and, obviously, Alex.

"She'll be coming round the mountain," sang Mr Twelvetrees in the corner. "Singing Yi Yi Yippy Yippy Yi."

The dog sat under the bed, eating. Through the window, the

sound of the windmill and the clack-clack-clack of the yellow-tailed black cockatoos pecking at damp pine cones.

Sometime later the face on the quilt took the shape of Alex.

"Hello," she smiled and sat up. She had been looking at something on the sheet.

With a finger he traced the scatter of moles on her shoulder as if he was connecting them.

She shivered happily. "Dad used to say that in another life I must have been blasted by grapeshot through a sieve."

"What other life?"

Her silvery voice thinned out. "Don't you believe we were other things before?"

But he had been nailed in too straight; he had grown up in a period of thank-you letters and lace-up shoes and watches that you wound before you slept. At the bottom of his heart he had believed in his parents' love and, he supposed, their God. Until Miss Pritchard came into the kitchen and told him it was best that he stay up at the house, not leave, least not till the policeman returned.

He moved his head. "I don't know. I never really thought about it. Maybe I was something before." He looked down at the feet of his mother's wardrobe and it seemed to Alex that the talons were loosening their grip on whatever it was they had been clinging to.

He caressed her and she turned to him. In her need to be held, his to hold, to love.

They made love again and afterwards dozed. It was six thirty when he woke. Merridy no longer beside him.

His eyes darted around the room. She stood naked in the corner. Inspecting two frames on the wall – photographs of his parents.

Aware of his gaze, she said dutifully: "I can see a likeness. You take more after your mother."

Of greater interest was the hand-coloured lithograph of Baudin's cockatoo. Delicate, accurate, gleeful – it was Alex's favourite of their pictures.

"Edward Lear," she read. "Not the poet, surely?"

"He was a bird artist before he wrote limericks. He was eighteen when he painted that."

“I had no idea he painted birds! Australian birds!” and looked back at the soft undulating feathers, the unblinking eye. Another sign. A sermon could not have said more.

She returned to the bed and leaned over Alex, stroking his temple. “What can I tell you? Is there anything I can tell you?”

“No.” Then: “Yes. I’d like to know how your brother died.”

She gulped. Recovering herself, she rested her head on the dune of his chest and stared across it into the wardrobe.

“You don’t have to tell me,” he said.

“I know,” and went on looking into the wardrobe.

CHAPTER THIRTEEN

FROM ACROSS THE ROOM she could see her mother at the basin, flannelling her brother's forehead. It was his seventh birthday. A Sunday morning at the family's shack near Wynyard on the north-west coast. The sun shining, the wattlebirds singing, the dry fresh scent of the eucalypts.

Nothing had happened, but she knew from a tenseness in her heart that something was about to happen.

"Mummy," he questioned the reflected face, "why is an island not a house?"

"I don't know, darling." Mrs Bowman squeezed out the flannel and rubbed it behind his ears.

In the mirror he caught sight of Merridy, stealing close to watch. With a quick flick of his wrist he dipped his fingers into the basin and splashed her.

"Hey!" closing her eyes and holding up her hands.

"Stop that this minute!" Mrs Bowman rammed a straw boater on his head and tried to fasten the strap under his chin, but gave up.

"Go and wait on the deck. Now, Merridy, your turn."

Her father had organised an outing to see the steam trains at Sheffield.

"We were in high spirits, my brother most of all. He had a new pair of Blundstones that he wanted to wear, a birthday present from Dad. Mum had given him a sailor's hat."

She could see her brother – out on the deck – toying with the strap and wiggling his toes to tell everyone how well his boots fitted.

"Mummy," she asked earnestly, "why is a house not an island?"

He leaned over the deck, staring at something.

"Oh, Merridy!" vigorously scrubbing her daughter's cheek.

What was he staring at?

At last, Merridy was all washed and dressed.

"Go and wait with your brother," and picked up the towel from the floor.

Merridy ran skipping out to join him. She loved her older brother. She looked up to his friends who came to the house, who sat in a row on the top step and flipped his Slinky towards her down the stairs. But not as much as she idolised him, sometimes to the point where she developed a stitch in her side. It did not matter that he believed in the silliest things. Things that existed, as she tried to explain to him, only in the imagination. Like the stalagmites they created out of wet sand that hardened into towers and battlements, where he patrolled with cobweb spear, a sentry visible only to his child's eye. Her brother was always sending his mind into places where she could not follow. At breakfast, when their father asked him: "Have you decided what you want to be, now you're seven?", he had answered with his most serious face that his life's ambition was to be a sailor in one of Edward Lear's drawings. He was a child enchanted by sandcastles and Jumblies.

But he was nowhere to be seen.

"As you yourself know," she said to Alex, "in life anything can happen, anything at all; you can be watching the person you love most in the world and you turn your head for the briefest moment and when you look back they are gone."

She shouted into the shack: "Mum, he's not here."

Mrs Bowman's first thought – he's run off. "Leonard, come quick."

Merridy's father, fiddling with a button on his shirt cuff, went down the steps three at a time. He called out into the bush.

Everyone stood still and listened. A wattlebird answered.

"We went looking through the bush, yelling for him."

The shack was on a sandstone bluff in lava-flow country. Potato fields interspersed with thick woods, along a cliff-face of rich volcanic soil that descended to a pebbled beach. The closest neighbours were a mile away, the closest town a twenty-minute drive in the family Holden. After searching for two hours, Merridy's father drove to Wynyard to get help. Soon a line of seventeen men and women – bushies, fallers, police constables, even some wives and children – fanned out from the deck and pushed their way knee-high through the potato crops and woods.

"We searched all that afternoon, and the next day. We were desperate. For three days, we searched. The only thing we found was his sailor's hat with the strap still loose on it that Mum had promised to mend."

At the sight of the straw hat Mrs Bowman burst into tears. She refused to eat or to sleep. She was aware that her son had not come back. Beyond that, her mind was a blank. She spoke of it as a "real shame" that he should have chosen to keep everyone waiting.

"It was weird at first, and then pretty scary. Everything, from what she was eating to the whole plot-line, was just gone. Daddy had to reiterate everything calmly, three to ten times – no exaggeration."

Eventually, she lost herself in household chores and made it clear that she anticipated her son's return at any moment. He would want his meal, a change of trousers.

"She cooked all his favourite dishes for him, put his best clothes out on his bed."

Then on the fourth day after her brother's disappearance, Merridy was trailing her father along the edge of a cliff about half a mile from the shack, when he halted, paralysed. His lips sucked tight. Like a man who had glugged down a bottle of gin in a minute and was trying to keep it in.

That summer it had rained heavily; the bush became a swamp of chocolate-coloured mud, ponds formed in the paddocks and along the cliff-tops holes appeared where tiger-snakes and devils had burrowed. One hole was bigger than the rest and suggested that an animal of some size had made its lair here. This was the hole before which her father stood.

"Daddy, is it him?" taking a step.

He whirled round. "No! Merridy, no!"

Too late. She had seen for herself the large round hole in the bank, as though something had shrugged its way into the earth – and, on the dead leaves to the side of it, her brother's Blundstone boot.

"Wait here."

Merridy watched him on all fours disappear into the burrow – if that is what it was. She pressed her brother's small boot to her face, recalling the way he had looked down at it, and prayed with every fibre in her body for his safe return. Presently her father reappeared. Shook his head.

She knew what she had to do. She had not kissed her brother goodbye. Thinking that he would always be there, wiggling his toes in his new boots. Or tearing, furious, after Merridy to retrieve a toy tractor that she had snatched. Or growing up to be a sailor in a drawing.

"Let me go," she said. She was small. She might be able to penetrate further.

She crept on, her father's black rubber torch between her teeth. The beam fell on dead leaves and violent green moss and the dart-boards of torn cobwebs. Clay gave way to sand. Smells of fungus and mould to the damp marine scents of the sea. She lowered her head. The passage narrowed until she could crawl no further, ending in a wall of sand. The air was thicker, but when she stopped to catch her breath she could hear a tiny voice calling. It was barely audible and she did not know if it came from inside her head or where it came from. She removed the torch from her mouth and shouted his name. The two syllables rolled along the passage. She listened. Silence. Then a distant sound. The dull roar of the ocean sucking on its rocky teeth and sighing, and somewhere in the middle of this dull seductive roar a small voice persisting.

Merridy never forgot her mother's face when she received the news, the distorted look in her left eye. She seemed to stare at her husband through centuries-old glass.

For the next two days Mrs Bowman sat in a collapsible fisherman's chair and levelled her deranged gaze at the hole in the earth. The round dark entrance became the focal point of her worst fears, her wildest hopes. Her son had gone exploring. He only had to hear her anguished shouts and he would crawl back. It was simply a matter of hours before his sand-streaked face would emerge into the sunlight, and she kept a damp flannel at the ready. But as the hours piled up all sorts of extravagant theories stalked through her head. She feared that her son had been murdered or eaten. The detective from Wynyard had a brother in New Zealand where a feral pig – "as big as the trunk of your car" – attacked lambs and turkeys. Or else he had been plucked from the cliff-top by a bright blue Boss-Woss. Or a giant squid hunting for orange roughy. Or the monster marsupial *Wynyardia bassinia* whose fossil had been discovered in these selfsame cliffs by none other than Professor Theodore Flynn. More recently, the remains of a gigantic mollusc had washed ashore in Stanley, a cephalopod with eight arms each the length of the Bowmans' Holden and two tentacles forty feet long and covered with powerful suckers each larger than a man's palm. The scene tormented her. Her young son on the cliff-top in his golden morning. A kraken rising from the deep. Its dreadful arms encircling him. His unheard shrieks. The monster with its flailing prey sinking with a gargle beneath the waves, leaving behind a few bubbles.

An hour after the little boot was discovered, two policemen equipped with foot straps and waist harnesses, and holding spades and powerful torches, lowered themselves into the hole. A neighbour's Jack Russell was sent down, but picked up no scent. A thorough search revealed no lair of any animal, no trace of any boy; no clothes, no bones. When the search was called off, there was nothing of him to bring home or to bury, save for a straw hat and a scuffed right-footed Blundstone, size two. There was no body.

A month later, the entrance was blasted shut with dynamite and a stone left on the bank engraved with her brother's name.

Every unexplained death has its own peculiar horror. A reporter from the Burnie *Advocate* described the impact of the tragedy on the community: *The sight witnessed in Wynyard when the news became known was pathetic in the extreme. Strong men wept, hands trembled, lips quivered. Voices had an involuntary tremor in them and faces were filled with the deepest expressions of hopelessness.*

The *Advocate* editorialised that the young boy had been murdered and held out hope that the killer would soon be found: *Sooner or later the finger of Providence will point out him who has shed the blood of a fellow creature.* But in the absence of a suspect, or, of course, a body, the newspaper refrained from pointing its own finger.

Her father did all he could to protect Merridy from these speculations. He kept checking to see that she had something to do.

She took to wearing her brother's clothes – his trousers and T-shirt that were too big for her – and to sleeping in his bed. His friends had been her friends. She feared that she would never see them again, because why would they come around with her big brother gone? As far as she was concerned, he had followed the noise of the sea, the sucking seductive roar. But his sudden absence degraded the whole of her life, an acid of loss inside her that she could not expel. When she realised that he might not be coming back, half of her was no more.

It was worse for Mrs Bowman.

Merridy was seven before her mother looked directly at her.

"You don't get over something like that," Merridy said. "The questions are always there. What happened to him? Who took him? A person, an animal? What did they do with him? Where are his bones? Or even – could he have survived? My mother still believes that he's alive somewhere."

"What do you think happened?" asked Alex.

Tears were running from her eyes. She had recoiled from thinking about her brother and had learned never to contrast her life then with her life as it was now; but in the recesses of the memories that she carried from childhood had grown a conviction. An idea gestating in a dark part of her that her brother would one day return, but it was not something she could actually say in words, only feel.

"My father told me the Jumblies had taken him. There was no need to worry. He had gone with them on a great journey."

A fly buzzed into the room and flew out again.

"You haven't told me his name," Alex said.

She had not uttered it for many years. Out of a promise she had so far kept. She was full of ridiculous promises that she made to herself.

She hung her head, prepared, for Alex, to commit the sacrilege.

"Hector."

CHAPTER FOURTEEN

LOUISA MEREDITH NURSING HOME:
Invites community members on Thursday March 17th to 10.30 a.m. morning tea.
Guest speaker: TBA. Topic: "Strokes".
Phone 62578380 if transport is needed.
Everyone welcome. So come along.

On a blustery day in the middle of March, Merridy took Alex to "Otranto" and introduced him to her parents.

To conceal her nervousness, Merridy ran across the room and hugged her mother from behind. Mrs Bowman, in a yellow crocus knit, returned her daughter's greeting with a metronomic pat on the arm while with her right elbow she covered up a letter to her sister in Ulverstone.

In the large hesitant words that she forced herself to write every week, she had revealed her concerns about Merridy. "I won't deny it, Doss. I know that dread is a sign of duty, but sometimes I fear that the crown of all my ills is perched on her head." This was the paragraph that her elbow hid.

"Mum, I want you to meet Alex, who I have told you about," looking at him over the hand-knitted shoulder and winking.

"Alex," repeated the sombre, lined face. The day before she had sat on her reading glasses and today peered out of a crushed frame. "I am grateful to you for making Merridy happy at this time. Our family has been spared its portion of happiness. I expect my daughter has said."

"She has, and I'm sorry."

She gave him a speculative look. "Are you a believer?"

"Mum!"

Alex glanced at Merridy. Her rueful expression.

"Do not ask, do not learn," Mrs Bowman reminded her.

"Well . . . in a manner of speaking. You could say, I suppose . . . that I believe in your daughter."

Mrs Bowman seemed to regroup, decided not to press further. The webbed feet tightened about her eyes as if her dryness was painful to her. She rolled her gaze down his right arm. If she was not likely to see him in the same pew at the Uniting Church, he might at least make a useful partner in the triples.

"I have been explaining you to Merridy's father," and nodded towards the window.

He sat slumped in a wheelchair in the alcove. His skin the shade of a peeled apple going brown, his neck swollen by steroids. He had the posture of someone in pain. A power cut the night before had caused the pneumatic headrest on his bed to snap down.

At Alex's greeting, he gave a slight, wincing nod, his eyes chained redly to the setting sun, where his sieve was – or his wife's God.

Mrs Bowman looked from Alex to Merridy as if she could see through the contours of the doom that awaited them: "I was sharing my opinion that Merridy should go back to university. She has talents that cannot be sharpened in Wellington Point. Nor, perhaps, in Tasmania."

"Not now, Mum."

"Well, that's what I was saying," and to herself: You're going to be ruined like I was. You're going to go against your mother's wishes and be ruined.

Firmly locked at the end of her husband's pneumatic bed was the Huon pine steamer trunk that Mrs Bowman had prepared for Merridy in the hope of a devout future son-in-law – and that she took care to transport with her everywhere against such an eventuality.

The Glory Box was a Proudlock tradition. Into it every birthday, Mrs Bowman would pack an item to supplement Merridy's idiosyncratic dowry: scalloped cotton pillowcases, lace tablecloths, bone-handled fish knives from Sheffield, a Bible and Prayer Book. Merridy called it her "Gory Box". On receipt of its key on her eighteenth birthday, she had added her own stuff. Tucked at the bottom in a plastic bag were her childhood drawing of a sea-going sieve, three scrapbooks, a photograph of her brother and a bright orange feather of a bird of paradise from Papua that had been one of Hector's cherished possessions. Plus a pornographic video that her partner from the dance class in Ulverstone had given her for safekeeping. She never wished to look at it and she never saw him again. But folded away in the linen sheets donated by her Aunt Doss, the presence of *Saucy Sally Sees it Through* took the edge off Merridy's embarrassment, and allowed her to smile in agreement whenever her mother started to voice plans for her.

Mrs Bowman had learned from her mistake in marrying Leonard. It was her unshakeable position that Merridy deserved a churchgoing mainlander with a salary, not a Pom farmer with the most peculiar hobby. Plus, worse – according to her enquiries – an agnostic.

"Of course, you can see that he's educated," Mrs Grogan had remarked accusingly in the course of a conversation in the aisles of Talbot's. "Though goodness knows what he does all day in that house by himself. I mean, anyone can see he's no farmer. I won't even *begin* to tell you what Jack Fysshe says."

The bowls champion was searching for washing powder, but where the soaps used to be an unsmiling member of Albert Talbot's staff had stacked bread. "But getting back to what I was saying. I spoke to Ray and he doesn't once remember seeing him in church."

"No one will ever speak the truth about human nature," sighed Mrs Bowman.

"Ah, here we are!"

CHAPTER FIFTEEN

JUNIOR CRICKET TOURNAMENT
Saturday March 19th. Time: 9.30 a.m.
Players should be able to bowl, bat and be able to score.
Trophy donated by H. Ford.
Dress: cricket attire. Ball and drinks provided.

On Saturday, Alex rode with Merridy over the farm.

It had rained in the night. Puddles everywhere. As if the sky had scraped itself on the ground and left rags of blue and white between the gums. Cattle eating stubble off the barley stood with fresh pats on their sides and mosquitoes bounced in the air.

Near the edge of the Crown forest on the top of Rossall Hill was a copse of four dark macrocarpa that in Alex's judgment boasted the finest view of his property. He dismounted and took Merridy's reins and tied them with his own to a branch.

He dragged over a large fallen bough and they sat on it while Flash rolled on her back between the grazing horses.

Merridy wrapped her arms about her knees and looked down over the clot of farm buildings to the sea. The landscape so different from Ulverstone and Zeehan. Her eyes had never seen anywhere more lovely. It was tremendous.

"See that thicket of gums?" Alex indicated with his riding crop. "A tiger was seen there."

Alex was six when Bill Molson encountered a young female thylacine, not more than ten yards from him.

"He heard a rustle, didn't think much of it, and then this creature emerged. He knew what it was because it had twelve stripes across its back. They stood gawping at each other, and after a few seconds the tiger turned and loped off, leaving only its scent behind."

It was a late February afternoon and Bill never forgot the sour smell: "He said it stank worse than his septic tank."

She peered into the eucalypts. "Do you believe it still exists?"

Alex picked up a pine needle. "It's like believing in anything you can't prove. It's like believing in ghosts. Or God."

"My father is convinced the tiger is extinct," and she imitated the voice that he had lost: "'The last thylacine died in Beaumaris zoo in 1936. Since then there has been no evidence whatsoever to indicate that the species has survived. No scat, no hair, no roadkill—'" And stopped. "I'm sorry. What a tactless thing to say."

"Oddly enough, my father *did* believe in the tiger." But then Basil Dove had believed in an awful lot of things.

CHAPTER SIXTEEN

BASIL DOVE WATCHED HIS olive trench coat – with a sausage roll in its pocket – jerk across the floor and out into the landing. A young cocker spaniel had come into his room in a northern hotel while he was packing. The dog belonged to a firm-bodied young woman in a thick red dress who was going downstairs to the bar. That was how he met his wife.

In Cumbria, his family owned a broom and brush factory. On the death of his father the running of the business was assumed by his eldest brother. Basil decided to emigrate. He was a passionate young man who could romanticise every situation and prosper with it. He had come of age in a rain-drenched valley in a period of blackouts, whale meat, egg powder and petrol coupons. After two years of National Service, he hankered for warmth, space and light.

He was making his way to Tilbury, to sail on the ten-pound scheme to Tasmania, when his coat with the crucial papers scurried from his room. The owner of the liver-and-white cocker was on her way home to Tewkesbury, where her parents dealt in antiques, after breaking off her engagement to an oboist in a Scottish radio orchestra. She was easy-going, but easily deceived and when she discovered that her affections were shared with at least two other female members of the orchestra she had become energetic and philosophical. At the hotel bar, she and Basil fell into conversation. They spoke frankly of their drooping circumstances. Marjorie wanted to make Basil laugh.

Bleakly convinced that she was, at twenty-two, washed up, she had on an impulse – and to the horror of her parents – accepted the oboist's offer of the puppy. She confessed to Basil that although she knew a certain amount about early English oak furniture and nineteenth-century paintings she had never before looked after a dog. Basil fed him the rest of his sausage roll, asked his name, and when informed that he did not have one, and was only three months old, suggested Tethera, in Cumbrian dialect the word for three, and advised her to have his tail docked. "He'll wag it like that and scratch it and then he'll go through brambles and the callus will fall off and he'll be permanently flapping blood, and the sore will never heal." He pointed down with the stem of his pipe: "The skin there is like the skin on your shins," and hoisted his gaze up her leg. "It's that thin."

Marjorie stared wide-eyed. She was persuaded.

Basil had a sympathetic laugh and a fondness for board games. They played Scrabble into the night. Marjorie won.

In the morning they exchanged addresses.

"But why Tasmania?"

He said: "I hear it's a place where you can go away and bury yourself."

Marjorie laughed.

Ten weeks later a letter arrived from Hobart with details of Basil's journey on the *Strathaird* to Aden, Ceylon and Fremantle and then on a Port Line apple boat to Tasmania. He had been one of seventeen passengers on a ship taking out Leyland buses and Morris Oxfords – "There was a great palaver because the leather seats went mouldy in the hold" – and returning to England with fruit. He was full of the sight of a queue of trucks stretching from the wharf into Davey Street, all piled high with apples and pears. He had taken lodgings in Battery Point to plot his next move.

Over the months ahead, Basil's family in Cumbria learned of his intentions to become a fruit-farmer, a boatbuilder, a cattle-breeder. He might even open a bookshop or a coffee house where customers could play Scrabble all day. Or a museum devoted to ships in bottles.

"That's Basil," said his older brother. "Full of brisk, emphatic plans that never materialise."

Only in his plans for Marjorie Fulmar did Basil succeed in realising his wishes. For eight months, the pair wrote weekly letters to one another, until one night the telephone rang in a cluttered hall outside Tewkesbury. A long-distance call from Hobart. By the time Marjorie put down the receiver she was engaged.

"What about Tethera?" her mother asked.

"I'm not leaving him behind. Tethera introduced us."

Fourteen months after their first meeting, Basil Dove waved to his fiancée from the wharf in front of the Henry Jones jam factory. Then Tethera shot down the gangplank and all hell broke loose.

"I see you didn't take my advice," Basil said, returning the cocker to Marjorie, after seeing the long, frantically wagging tail. That was before a terse official whisked the dog away. Another three months before they were able to collect Tethera from the kennels in Quarantine Bay. By then they were Mr and Mrs Dove.

They had married in St David's, and after spending their wedding night at Hadley's Hotel drove out to the east coast. Basil still had no house. He had dithered since his arrival, enthusiastically inspecting properties and then rejecting them. In the end, he had needed Marjorie's approval before he committed himself, as well as the small amount of capital that she brought with her.

Within a month, they had completed the purchase on Moulting Lagoon Farm. He set about building a barn and bought his wife a docile piebald to ride along the beach, and for himself decked out a room where he could indulge in the passion that he had had since boyhood for crafting ships to fit into glass bottles.

The couple envisaged a quality of life that had been denied them in a country ground down by six years of war and years of rationing.

"But they didn't transplant well," Alex said. "My mother never worked – she haunted antique shops. Nor was my father cut-out to be a horny-handed son of toil. Fitting little bits of cedar into bottles was his pastime, that and reading. They soon realised farming wasn't for them and yet they didn't want to return to England. Instead of trying to address the problem they just floated along. Then my father started to go blind."

Basil's last years were dispiriting. His romanticism of himself was quite vast, but fragile at the same time. A self-appointed remittance man, he had deliberately washed up in a place where there was nobody who understood him or how he spoke, save for an ex-journalist in the nearby town. So when his grey eyes that once had seen for ever started to fail him, he took refuge in gin – which he drank with a token dash of tonic – and in his ships. In the bottle, as Harry Ford put it to Alex on more than one occasion, as well as a lot of other things. "Best present your father ever gave you – to die young. Or have I told you that?"

"Several times."

Ten days after the log-truck barrelled into their car, Alex's parents were buried in the lawn beneath the Oyster Bay pine. There was no one to tend the farm. Several months later, the chief stock inspector came on a police launch from Hobart to inspect for disease and parasites. The old white-footed piebald was still in the triangular paddock next to the house, its ribs like the contours of a shipwreck, but pleased to see people; as were the cats. The chickens had been eaten and four cows in Rough Run were so wild they had to be shot. Alex learned these details only on his return.

Alex would have needed to live in Wellington Point a year to soak up the goodwill that his new circumstances created, but within a fortnight his godmother, a midwife who had met his father aboard the *Strathaird,* scooped him off to Sydney. Stranded on the mainland, he spent two terms at a school in Vaucluse. At the start of the following Easter term, his uncle in the north of England paid for Alex to attend a similar establishment in Sedbergh famed for its austerity – "You'll like the motto," he joked. "*Hardness is the nurse of men.*"

He arrived in Sedbergh at night, dressed in his father's National Service trench coat, leather buttons done up against the cold. Only next morning did he see that he had come to a place surrounded by high fells. Where the stone walls ended, grass paths led up to long open ridges from where Alex looked down on a landscape a little like Tasmania: mountainous, close-knit and monarchist, with some farmers still travelling about in horse and cart.

At the time of his arrival, these hills belonged to West Riding, a district of Yorkshire. By the end of the year, to the tremendous indignation of his uncle, they were claimed for the new county of Cumbria. It gave Alex a strange but definite relief to move among a rural population that was itself having to forge an unfamiliar identity and adjust to shifted boundaries.

The school was less austere than its motto suggested. It encouraged pupils to get out and engage with their surroundings. On Sundays after chapel, Alex could take a sandwich lunch and, as long as he did not use a wheeled vehicle, he might go anywhere he liked. Over the next four years, he climbed Winder many times and walked the banks of the Lune, and ran ten-mile cross-country runs. His abiding memory was the smell of sheep shit and the sound of curlews in spring, a sonorous bubbling absolutely lovely cry that echoed all round the fells. He never forgot, either, the friendliness of the people. Caught out in a downpour on Firbank Fell, he was ushered into a low-ceilinged house by a farmer who, noting his drenched blue jersey, introduced Alex to his family as "one of them scholar lads" and a month later invited him to his daughter's wedding. But although outwardly very friendly, Cumbrians shared with Tasmanians a resistance to outsiders. They might welcome him into their homes and dry his clothes before a peat fire, but no matter how passionately he immersed himself in their landscape, no matter how often he bathed the perspiration from his face in the Rawthey or hunted for fossils and dippers and otter trails, to the locals he would always be an off-comer. Someone from off.

Off began fifteen miles from Sedbergh. Tasmania was very off. One or two of the masters had the habit of confusing it with Tanzania.

In Hart House, a forbidding grey stone building on the south side of the cricket pitch, Alex caught his first English flu – deeper, darker and wetter than anything he could remember. On the windowsill in his dormitory, the thermometer recorded minus twenty-one.

It was at Sedbergh, too, that Alex discovered the authors whom he would study again and more at university: Henry James, Joseph Conrad, Samuel Johnson. But he was not convinced of a deeper purpose other than to study and to smile and – after a rain-soaked afternoon on the rugger pitch – to strip off his mud-caked shorts and brown shirt. His time at the school served to intensify a sense he already had of running about a playing field that was parallel to the rest of the world. He might wave at others, and they might see him, but he was never able to reach out and tackle them – however far he stretched, whatever name he was called. This sense, almost of weightlessness, could not wholly be put down to the sudden loss of his parents or to the fact that he arrived at Sedbergh a term late and took longer than others in his year to adapt to the school's idiosyncratic rituals and language; or even to the arbitrary shedding of his first name at the request of a jocular housemaster. It had to do as well with where he was from.

An Australian educated in England, Alex found himself trapped between suppressing emotion and trumpeting it. Prone to fits of impatience, he rarely cried when he hurt himself. He held his breath until he fainted rather than kick out or lose physical control. In scrums and skirmishes, other boys left him alone. Wary of a swallowed-up pain that seemed at odds with the soft-spoken orphan from Down Under.

He went up to Oxford on a scholarship endowed for Tasmanian students. At Merton, when not working hard, he clowned and had girlfriends and gambled and got drunk. But he could never find an intimate circle, the one, two or three friends with whom he might be himself. Somehow it eluded him.

On coming down from Oxford, he was offered an apprenticeship in the broom factory by his uncle. Alex declined. Perhaps hoping to master his reticence, he trained to be a teacher, and was halfway through his course when he abandoned it. He was then twenty-three.

Those he left behind in England were not persuaded that Alex's temperament was suited to live alone behind a stock-fence. The view prevailed that he would soon be back, once he had sorted out certain things. "He's gone to Australia really to learn about England," was how one Merton friend explained his behaviour to Sarah (who wrote Alex an irritated postcard, wondering what to do with his stuff. *Keep it,* he wrote back. *Maybe send me my trench coat*). On others, it had never dawned that Alex could be Australian: "He's living *there*? In Van Diemen's Land? Isn't that where people were packed off who'd done something awful?" But 14,000 miles away, pride and enjoyment in his farm took Alex unawares. In a way that he had not anticipated, it exhilarated him to watch his animals grow fat and healthy above the barley, the blood on the frost at lambing time, and to lay a fresh drive of white gravel that emphasised anyone walking up it.

Even so, his passage into countryman had not been smooth. Unmonitored by Ray Grogan, his tenant Bill Molson had raped the land, flogged it to death. Nor had he made any effort to maintain the buildings. The property was so lamentably run down that a farmer up the road, Jack Fysshe, warned Alex that only a mad rabbit would take it on. "Don't do it, mate, it's not worth the candle," Fysshe said, bumping into Alex outside Talbot's. "But I'm there if you need me. And if you do decide to do it, I had a thing going with your Dad. We used to rent a combine harvester together, three of us." The third was Tom Pidd, who farmed towards Bicheno. "Really, we liked your Dad. A useless farmer, but a nice man. If you want my advice, sell your farm – if you can get any money for it – and go back to Putney, England. But if I can be of any help, ring and I'll be there."

Alex was slightly surprised when, back a month, none of these neighbours had appeared to help him. They just had not turned up.

During his first days home, as he began to think of it, farming was as baffling to him as the pink and green lists at Sedbergh. Twelve years since he had last ridden a tractor or a horse. After five weeks, he decided to call on Fysshe.

The farmer was hardly more encouraging than before. "Now you're back – I couldn't say this when Bill was alive – well, the fact of the matter is he wasn't fair to the land, he took the top right off it. I used to look at your farm and think: When I buy it – which I'm inevitably going to have to do – I shall make an offer for nothing, considering the fortune I'll have to spend on fertiliser."

Eventually, after two or three years, the two of them worked out an arrangement to share a semi-trailer for ewes, but Alex would never scold Jack Fysshe for his generosity.

On Fysshe's advice, Alex spread a load of phosphates on the paddocks and hired a young man out of school to help him repair the fences. On the fifth day, Joe Hollows failed to show up.

"Par for the course," said Fysshe. "Workmen are hard to keep round here."

His own ineffectualness brought Alex closer to his parents. He understood how local traders could have fleeced them with such depressing regularity and cheerfulness. The severest case was a builder he contracted to repair the shearing shed, who ordered an excessive quantity of sandstone, only to abscond with half of it to build himself a house in Marion Bay.

And Alex made plenty of mistakes of his own.

He first thought to plant flax for tanning, but it did not take. Nor did the cash crops that he sowed the following year. A storm blew the oats down. Rust got into the spring barley and the seeds failed to germinate. Misled by climate conditions that were warmer here than in the Central Highlands, he had sowed too late. So in his second year home he started running cattle and sheep.

Alex bought Corriedale and Poleworth as his father had – another mistake, since they were not ideal for wool. Two years on, he was in the process of changing the flock, using merinos from the stud in Triabunna.

Thirty paddocks stretched away down the hill. "I move a mob every two days to a different paddock. That way the grass grows back quickly."

"How many sheep do you have?" asked Merridy.

"Three thousand all up. Plus thirty cows and a bull." The herd of Aberdeen Angus was self-replacing, and caused him the least headache. He sold the calves straight off the cow, keeping five. If there were one or two dry cows, he sold those. He was shortly to get rid of the bull after three years – "Otherwise he'll be going over his daughters."

The ride had loosened Merridy's hair. She unpinned it, threw back her head. "Are you a good farmer?" with the tortoiseshell comb in her mouth. She had met few farmers.

Alex laughed. "Good? No. Tell the truth, I was thinking of chucking it in."

"You mustn't do that," she said involuntarily.

"I don't know, Merridy. Farming's hard. It takes everything out of you."

"Everything? Surely not."

"Well, maybe more than I'm prepared to give. It's a lot of uneducated people, mainly families, trying to live off the land. It's not treated as a business, but it is. And I'm not a businessman. I depend on the goodwill of the bank to survive – utterly."

"I don't care. You can't sell this," nodding at the view.

He was surprised at her vehemence, and pleased. "Perhaps I won't have to," and tossed away the pine needle with which he had dug clean his fingernails. "It could be I've just hit my straps."

Three days after he first encountered Merridy, Alex had secured a contract to sell barley to Cascades brewery. "As of next year, I might even stand to break even."

She pretended to finish mending her hair, but she was admiring his competence. She had guessed that he was hard-working, and that he was strong because he was running this farm all by himself. What she had not appreciated was that he was dying to stay alive. He had no help, and yet help was what he needed.

Alex whistled to Flash, and they rode to where he had knocked down the scrub and burned it; where he had banked and drained the marsh; and where in rough winds the south end still overflowed with salt water.

The hills west of the marsh ran up to Masterman's Tier and paddocks of rich volcanic soil; beyond was all sags and tussocks where the sheep hid themselves. In four years, he had taught himself to be a tolerable counter. When his rams went missing he took a bottle of cold tea and stalked through the kangaroo grass that grew thick as the hair on Flash's back, and down through gullies of red ochre which the Oyster Bay tribe had patted into their faces and hair.

Love made him expansive and articulate. They cantered to the summit of Treasure Hill where in the 1920s a travelling cattle-buyer was discovered dead beside the track. Alex did not know the whole story, but the man was reputed to have been carrying a satchel of gold. To Rough Run, where his first summer back Alex bumped into a seal in the ripened corn. "At full moon, the old fur seals come over from the Isle des Foques to die." He described for her a still winter evening, a grizzled leopard seal and its bellow on being disturbed. And on to Barn Hill, where his father had put up a Cumbrian bank-barn. "He was walking here one clear day, nothing in the sky, when he heard a terrific wind and was struck on the elbow by a hard black object. I've still got the meteorite." Alex paused to unwind a strand of wool caught on a wire. "Lucky it didn't take his arm off."

It was past noon when they galloped back to the homestead. In the field above the house a sheep licked at the umbilical cord of a lamb as it nuzzled to suck its mother's engorged teats.

Merridy swivelled in her stock saddle. "Lambs in March?"

"You can have lambs throughout the year – as long as there's a bit of green feed for the ewes."

Alex watched her fascination rather than the drama enacted on the grass. For him, the lamb's birth was not convincing any more than his parents' car accident had been. But Merridy convinced. As if she had fallen to earth and caused a gale and burned the grass all around.

"Let's have some tucker."

They ate in the kitchen, sandwiches that he had prepared with leftover chicken from his dinner the night before. Half an hour later, he shut the fly-screen behind them, and after checking his dog – gulping at a bone beneath the table – resumed the tour.

The land absorbed Alex's energies, but had he the money he planned to renovate the farm buildings. Beyond a sagging fence stood the convict-built shearers' quarters, put up in the 1870s by an old lag called Fazerlacky who had exchanged his wife for a pair of boots. The shingles on the roof were kept in by wooden staples. Several were adrift and the sky, glimpsed in blue splinters, reminded Alex of yet another thing he had to fix. "The shearers have been complaining that the possums piss in their faces."

To the rear of the building lay the shearing shed. Shears in leather cases and an old turkey-stone, originally the property, it was said, of Wellington Point Sam who could drink a bottle of beer standing on his head and who never sharpened his shears in the open air in case the wind scraped the edge off them.

The lime had drained from the bricks, giving to the exterior a dejected look, but inside it smelled of sweat and dung and wool from the June shearing.

He guided her between stalls carved from thin beams of Oyster Bay pine – and back out again into the open, where meanwhile a warm wind had blown up, a northerly that bowed the macrocarpa on Rossall Hill and skittered through the farmyard. It was answered by the shriek of agonised machinery.

She said, to help: "That sounds crook."

What grated and gnashed was the green-painted windmill.

"It's been crook since I can remember."

According to the angle of the wind, the blades worked intermittently – as now – blurring the field behind into a circle of widening ripples.

He followed her gaze. Propped up against the windmill, a ramshackle ladder led to a narrow viewing platform protected on three sides by a rail, and on the fourth by two strands of wire.

"You can see Oyster Bay from up there," he said.

"Can I look?"

"Here. Let me go first." He took hold of the rungs and the ladder all but toppled from the sky.

Alex's voice climbed ahead of him, explaining the windmill's provenance. His father had bought it on the recommendation of an Anglo-Argentine whom he had met in Hobart, and had it shipped from an *estancia* in Entre Ríos. Two rungs below, Merridy did not catch every word but she gathered that Alex had haggled with its innards since he was a boy.

She hauled herself after him onto the platform and he lifted up a wire for her to crawl under.

The platform had the narrow shape of a ship's bridge and was large enough, just, for the two of them to stand side by side. The motion of the wind made it vibrate. She licked from her mouth a strand of dark hair, and held on to the rail.

Then as abruptly as it had blown up the wind dropped. The blades creaked to a halt and shuddered and with one last grumble fell silent.

She turned her head. Wanting a sudden look at him. Over his shoulder through watery eyes she made out a bright smudge. On the vane in an orange marker, her name.

"Alex. What's that doing there?"

"I wrote it," he said, bashful.

"What does it mean?"

He took her hand. She saw that his nails were clean. "I love you."

She withdrew her hand. "Please don't say that."

"Why, have too many men said it to you?"

She looked down. The platform had shrunk to the size of a newspaper.

"Have you said it?" he wanted to know.

"Yes. I have."

"Lots of times?"

"No. Not very often."

"Last time was when?"

"When I was five."

She twisted away before he could see the consternation on her face. Leaning against the rail, she breathed in. The air smelled as if cleaned in rainwater. It had the stillness of something that had cried itself out.

"I'm sorry."

"It's all right." Then: "It's not you who should be sorry. It has nothing to do with you." Whatever it was.

Subdued, Alex followed her gaze to the scrub that led in one direction to low hills of wattle where Tethera had bitten a snake and been bitten and died, and in the other to shimmery fields over the top of which Oyster Bay unravelled in a turquoise thread.

"Ten miles to civilisation," he murmured.

It was so quiet they could hear a pigeon drooling. Far away, the drilling of a speedboat grated on the sea.

"What?" she was laughing again. "Wellington Point?"

"No, the Hazards," rallying.

"I was going to say. You can't even drink the water."

At her laugh, the prospect of early autumn tinged the distant mountains with a pink glowing promise. "You asked why I stayed," he said. "I'll show you."

They walked along the lagoon towards the beach.

On a slope overlooking the shore was a fenced-off area containing four gravestones with the grass growing over them. He waited for Merridy to read the inscriptions. The names of the family of settlers who had drowned in 1843.

"What happened?"

"They were a couple with two children. They'd been at sea eight months. This was the very last leg. The father took off his shirt to sunbathe when a wind came up and blew it into the lagoon. He dived in to retrieve it and got into difficulties and began to sink. His son stood up to jump in, but the convicts held him back – they thought they'd be charged with his murder. He was watching his father die when the wind capsized the boat. His mother and brother are also buried here, so I presume they saw it all, too. The father's body was never found."

Alex pointed. "My father was tidying up the graves one day when the penny surfaced."

Merridy wanted to linger. She had questions to ask. But Alex was anxious to press on. He grabbed her hand and led the way to a low scalp of lichen-covered rock where, he said, he escaped to sit in the numb days following his parents' car crash, watching the waves in their steady regiments charge in, wanting to be older.

She tensed herself to sit, but he took her arm and guided her away through the emerald boobyalla until they came to a dune weed-choked with startling red flowers.

"There," he said.

They stood on the sand.

The earlier wind had chased a pack of clouds to the horizon so that there appeared no distinction between sky and water.

"What?" he asked.

"I was listening to the sea," and rubbed her sandy heel against his leg.

I am tired of living singly
On this coast so wild and shingly.

He stared back out at the bay. "Almost every day I see something, a cloud, a tree, a bird – and say to myself: Four years ago I wouldn't have looked at that. And I can't help thinking what a chump I was. I was so concerned, I'd forgotten how to look at land or sky or sea. When at last I did open my eyes that was a real moment. I'd just caught a bream, over there" – and waved in the direction of the river mouth – "but instead of the fish I saw hills and space and weather, and it made me want to look at it for a long time."

Alex wondered if he might regret the remark, or if she had ever met a more tedious man, but she touched his face.

He held her hand. "See, you're doing it again."

"Electricity," she explained.

"Electricity?"

Her father had taught her to touch everything with the back of her hand. "Otherwise," and flattened her palm on his wrist, "the hand contracts around the shock." She gripped tight. "And never lets go."

She led him by the hand and they lay down in a clearing in the marram grass. The sun blazed in the absence of wind. She stretched out in the sunlight and felt no shame or shadow as he dusted the sand from her arms and her knees. The two boys she had kissed at uni had touched her with greedy hands and no tenderness. They did not tickle her spine like Alex or stare into her eye as though they wanted to rake the bottom of it, or promise an answer to the dark questions that she would like put to them.

What she felt for the others with whom she had tried to envisage a future had leeched away until all she remembered was something synthetic and mildewed. Her feelings for Alex sprang from her intestines.

The sand squeaked beneath them. The colours poured from him into the sky, the waves hissed out and somewhere in the parrot-feathered dusk a black swan honked its way across the water.

When Alex got to his feet the sun was setting.

In silence they picked their way back to the house. They were halfway across the lawn when she heard the scrape of claws on wire.

"Can you drive me back? My parents will be worrying."

CHAPTER SEVENTEEN

HER FATHER DIED ON Sunday. Merridy sat beside his wheelchair in the alcove, waiting for the next breath. He seemed to come up a long way to search for it. But there was nothing there. His mouth lay open on yellow teeth, his eyes in frozen gaze at the window, as if one of the bulldozers he had made for his son had wound down.

The funeral service was at the Uniting Church. A handful of mourners filled three pews, including a latecomer who was whispered to have been Albert Talbot. Keith Framley, dressed in a suit too tight for him, read the eulogy in which he opined that "death is a turning off of the electric light before dawn", and afterwards there was a wake at the bowls club where Debbie handed out lukewarm sausage rolls and hamburgers that tasted of roo.

TWILIGHT BOWLS – It's already started. Wednesday for 5.00 p.m. and only $3.00 to enter. So come along and have some fun.

Not for another four days did Merridy visit Moulting Lagoon, driving from Wellington Point with her mother in Leonard's 1968 green Peugeot. Mrs Bowman, not trusting their mission to her headstrong daughter, was adamant that she come too. She waited in the car, sitting upright and stiff in the passenger seat and glaring at the tree on the lawn, while Merridy sought out Alex.

Merridy spotted him up a ladder against the shearers' quarters, hammering nails into the shingles. The clouds had speckled over and a pair of wedge-tailed eagles scoured the poppies in a paddock behind.

"Merridy!" He took hold of his pliers and hammer and clambered down the ladder two rungs at a time and ran to her.

But her eye would not fit into his. Tomorrow, her mother was taking Merridy to Ulverstone to visit her aunt.

He looked over her shoulder at the gaunt face peering at them from the parked car, the lank grey hair. "You're back when?"

"In a fortnight."

"That's a very long time."

"No, Alex. To pack up. I'm going back to uni." Obedience to Mrs Bowman's wishes had given her an air of unreality. "I've come to say goodbye."

Numbly, he absorbed the news. "Oh no, that's a disappointment."

"Isn't that the way it is? You meet. You say goodbye. I was always going back to Melbourne. You knew that."

With an injured laugh, he quoted Robert Louis Stevenson. "*I think of Melbourne and I vomit.*"

"Well, it's what my mother wants," said her mouth in the same dutiful voice. "We've put the unit on the market."

He inspected his pliers, opening and closing them. It ought not to have surprised him. She had never concealed her intention to go back to university eventually. She had only stayed on to look after her father, and now she was free. "Isn't there anything that would keep you?"

"Like what?"

He told her. He put his question to her and she felt the pins and needles returning to her heart.

She did not answer. Looked away. A branch dipped on the Oyster Bay pine, releasing a fat black bird.

From the car, a bark: "Merridy!"

She made a strange sound. He thought she was laughing, but stepping closer he saw the tears streaming.

She smiled through them. That enigmatic face. She said with all the conviction that she could muster: "No, Alex. I'm not good for you."

"Rubbish, Merridy, of course you are."

But the promise she had made to herself, it did not permit her to believe in what he offered. She went on in a beseeching voice: "What do you want? I bet it includes a quiet life."

"I suppose so, yes." He was an implicit disciple of the seasons. The security of crops grown and harvested. He would like something durable.

"Then you shouldn't be with me." And remembered Randal Twelvetrees: "You're like your mother. You shouldn't be with anyone – you'll only destroy them."

Or maybe children would stabilise her.

"*Merridy!*"

"Listen, I have to go."

"But I love you," his heart aching for her. He put everything else out of his mind. Her mother calling in a reproachful voice from the car. His leaking roof, his cattle and sheep, his barley and clover, his bottled ships. All his care on the young woman who stood before him and wiped her cheek.

"How can I?" she said, miserable. "I'm not in love with you."

"It'll come, you know, it'll come."

She thought that he was trying to boost her up. She thought that she could easily extract herself as she had done in the past. She did not know what she thought.

"Are you serious, Alex?"

"Yes. I am deadly, deadly serious."

She looked at him and saw the faces of all the men she had repudiated.

Meanwhile, the face that leaned from the car window had never been more contorted. "Merridy! Are. You. Coming?"

His expression sabotaged her. She felt the gummy tentacles of his need. And hers.

"Let me think about it. I'll tell you when I get back."

FOR SALE: 1 pre-loved hospital bed and wheelchair. Enquiries to Sister Surrage at Louisa Meredith.

In her father's cocktail bar that night Tildy could not control her excitement. Someone had seen Ray Grogan in Sargison's jeweller's in Hobart. Buying a ring.

"Is that good news, then?" asked Merridy. Her final evening behind this counter.

"Just so long as it's for me!" and splashed herself another incautious measure of Captain Morgan.

"Silly," putting on a smile. "Who else could it be for?"

"Oh, Merridy, will you be my bridesmaid? I've never told you this, but I know how much I owe you."

"If you didn't ask, I'd never speak to you again."

Tildy drew out a compact from her handbag. Her large eyes looked larger still as – mouth open – she applied her mascara. "By the way, how did Alex take the news?"

On the other side of the counter, Merridy checked the level of the upturned rum bottle.

Tildy glanced up. "Well? You did tell him you're leaving, didn't you? How did he take it?"

Merridy gave a crimped smile. "He asked me to marry him."

"No!" Tildy snapped the compact shut, tucked it back in her bag and brought her stool forward. "Tell me, tell me, tell me. Of course, you've said yes."

"Oh, I don't know." She had never thought she would marry. Even if that was in her mind, she had not thought it through.

"But you like him, you said."

"Like, yes. But I'm not in love with him. You mustn't think that," and put the bottle into the bin. Anyway, twenty was too young.

"It will come, you know, it will come."

"Funny, that's what Alex said," quite pensive.

"Then maybe he listened to me. It's what I told him. It's what I keep telling Ray," and leaned over the counter. "Hey, are you sure that bottle was empty?"

LADIES BIBLE STUDY. If you would like to know about Christianity and/or have fellowship with other ladies then you are invited to the Bethel Teahouse, Monday 6 p.m. Supper (finger food only). New members welcome.

It was strange. Mrs Bowman had had a premonition that Alex was about to propose.

In Ulverstone, she had called on the minister at her old church in Hortle Place, the one to whose son she had been engaged when she met Leonard, and asked him about the advisability of her daughter marrying this Alex Dove boy. Minister Twelvetrees was a wise old man with a long narrow face so worn by the sins it had heard that he had come to resemble a tawny frogmouth. His son Randal had settled down eventually with a girl from Albany and they lived in the bush, more or less content. He studied the photograph that Mrs Bowman showed him, a formal portrait of Alex in Oxford after taking his degree, and replied in a voice that sounded as if it had just sipped communion wine, rich and sweet: "If Mr Dove holds out one hand, you should hold out two."

Merridy was grim-faced for much of the fortnight in Ulverstone. She had felt like a sorcerer's apprentice, handing over to her mother the only photograph that she possessed of Alex. She repeated: "Everyone in Wellington Point speaks well of him, except Ray Grogan, and that's a commendation in itself, God knows."

"Mind your tongue, girl." Mrs Bowman gave a little sniff. "*Woe unto thee when all men shall speak well of thee.*"

In Ulverstone, they stayed with Mrs Bowman's younger sister. Doss had been stricken by polio when an epidemic swept through the state. After she became crippled, having been beautiful, her husband decided to disappear. She lived in a crescent lined with pear trees in what had once been a brothel, subsequently bought by a Mayor of Ulverstone. The house had black-stained wooden banisters; dark varnished doors that caught the dull overhead light – beamed through glass bowls from the 1950s; worn green carpets that reminded Merridy of the Louisa Meredith Nursing Home; and peeling grey wallpaper. It was cold at night. Unable to sleep, she combed her mother's Bible for ammunition. The small print revived her father's grumble: "You can find proof of anything you like in that book. You can prove that Edward Lear wrote *Hamlet.*"

One morning beside her breakfast plate, Mrs Bowman discovered a card with handwriting on it.

"What is this, Merridy?"

"Just read, Mum."

She put on her warped glasses. "*Cast thy cares upon Him for He careth for thee.*"

"Letty, will you have some of this?" interrupted her sister. Her false teeth shining like the two rows of encyclopaedias in her hall.

She had bought them in an extravagant fit after her husband left her and was still paying for them.

"Now, Doss, you know I never eat cream."

Her sister skimmed a wink across the table to Merridy: "*Whatsoever is set before thee, eat, asking no questions, for conscience sake.*"

WELLINGTON POINT RSL & EX-SERVICEMEN'S CLUB
Former intelligence officer (MI5 et alia) reveals "A Life of Intrigue". In the Clubrooms on Friday 25th beginning at 7.30 p.m. Members are urged to attend.
Ask the friendly staff about becoming a member. Tom Pidd (Hon. Sec.).

The fortnight stretched away like fourteen years. Alex waxed the sand-scratched floors of the corridor and kitchen; he finished painting details on the deck and hull of his latest model boat, and to the side of the bridge glued a white life-ring, the size of a Polo mint, with the ship's name, *Otago;* and chores had accumulated in the garden. On the morning that Merridy was due back from Ulverstone, he cleaned out the lime-tinted gunge of a wasps' nest caught in the water tank after February's heavy rain. A few wasps buzzed at the moist green overlap, spiralling on angry wings towards the mouth – which he had blocked off. Clots of soggy drones circulated the surface when he stirred. He netted them out and sprayed with mosquito repellent the pipe that he had taped up, and after a day the mass of them did not return, save for one straggler.

All the time, the thought of Merridy shifted like a heatwave in distorting currents.

He was looking forward to her return so much that he did not hear the car. That evening, a tap on the window as he sat in his workroom. Preoccupied with the ship that he had launched into its rum bottle.

In the kitchen, he turned on the stove.

She did not take off her coat. "What have you been doing?"

"I was working on the *Otago*, mostly."

"Did you finish it?"

He fetched the bottle and laid it on the dresser. Ever prone to expecting the worst, he did not look at her but gabbled.

"This part of the hull is made from the original ship, a piece of timber offcut, would you believe it, from a sawhorse that was still there."

She looked into the glass, a quiet, steady gaze. On deck, a cat sat on the penny and her kittens all in a circle.

"If you want, I could tell you more about ships, as I did the other day . . ." But he was as nervous as she.

"I dare say we'll have time."

"You mean . . ." and his eyes brimmed over with pleasure above a six-inch grin.

There was only one condition. Before giving her consent, Mrs Bowman insisted on viewing the house.

MENOPAUSE INFORMATION SESSIONS. You are not alone. The Pit Stop tent will be erected outside the nursing home between Monday and Friday next week. If you are interested, please drop by to browse or contact Cheryl Surrage on 62578380.

Merridy's mother arrived at Moulting Lagoon Farm dressed in a blouse of hailstone black muslin that had the mysterious effect of making her look a good deal younger than her years. She had come on her own and walked alertly through the rooms, taking everything in. If she had been a man, thought Alex, she would have been a cavalry officer, straight-backed, with a mouth like a tight strap keeping her chin in place. But something in her relaxed to observe the God-fearing gene advertised in the frames along the corridor. Her hostile religious spirit placated by the sight of the samplers, she continued into the living room where Alex had set out tea.

He produced his parents' best china, but Mrs Bowman was not to be bowled over by Spode.

"Mr Dove, I won't beat around the bush. My daughter ought to be at university."

"I quite agree."

"You do not know her yet as I know her, but I am concerned how she will behave if her mind is not occupied."

"Maybe she could do a correspondence course? But do you mind if we get the farm up and running before that? I give you my commitment that then she can not only explore, but achieve."

His promise appeared to mollify Mrs Bowman. She drank her tea and the talk was of her plans, after the marriage ceremony and the sale of "Otranto", to return to Ulverstone where she planned to take up again with her sister.

The single other reference to Merridy was made as she was leaving. Her hand polished the air – she might have been cleaning a candlestick in church.

"My daughter is slovenly, Mr Dove."

"I think she's extremely beautiful."

She gave him a Pentecostal glance. "It's frightening what we think is beautiful."

He opened the door of the Peugeot and she gathered up her black skirt and settled in.

She sat there, gripping the wheel.

"I would be grateful if you could make arrangements to collect Merridy's Glory Box. Naturally, I will meet the costs of the wedding. And, Mr Dove –?" reaching for the door handle. "You should know that her father has left her a small legacy."

In the aisles of Talbot's and at the counters and tables of the Bethel Teahouse they acclaimed the engagement as one of the excitements of the autumn. Agnes wrote a commemorative poem for Talbot's *Newsletter* and the vicar in Swansea was in regular communication with Minister Twelvetrees over arrangements for the wedding service.

They married in the third week of May in the red-roofed Uniting Church at the bottom of Radley Street where, not so long before, a small gathering of nurses and patients had buried her father. Minister Twelvetrees officiated and Mrs Bowman's sister came down from Ulverstone. Alex turned to see Merridy on Keith Framley's arm, and was conscious of everyone craning their necks to catch his own expression: Agnes, Jack Fysshe, Tom Pidd,

Abbygail, Dr Musgrove, Sergeant Finter, Sister Surrage, Mrs Grogan, Debbie, Tildy.

The rain stayed away, as did Ray-as-in-sunshine Grogan. Alex had not wanted to invite him. Merridy was relieved, but it worried her that Ray had still not proposed to her cousin, a prevarication that was the source of comment in the RSL and of a degree of panic in Tildy herself. Invited to be Merridy's bridesmaid, she had caught the bouquet – "as if she was fielding at gully," remarked Sergeant Finter afterwards at the reception in the Freycinet Court Hotel.

It was dark when Alex drove Merridy home. He had to swerve twice to avoid dead animals. Sitting beside him, his wife of three hours looked into the passing trees and remarked that her mother had found it indecent the amount of roadkill that she had had to put up with in Wellington Point. Alex smiled. In his opinion, so much roadkill was proof of a nature in rude health.

Not even at the reception had Mrs Bowman let up, tackling Merridy as she helped to carry the wedding gifts into the back of the ute. "Are you really not going back to uni? How are you going to keep your head alive?"

"I. Will. Manage. Mum."

"Well, I'm going to give you as a wedding present *Engineering World*. Because your father would really want you to finish your degree. This is my way of saying: Please keep using your brain."

At the bottom of the drive Merridy reached over and switched off the headlights. The better to look at the night sky with its gunpowder of stars. At a slow walking pace, the ute crunched up the white gravel that seemed to glow as the vehicle approached the house.

That night the couple made a pact that they would keep for the next sixteen years. The idea was Merridy's. She kept looking at the door ajar on the wardrobe, blackboard-coloured on which to chalk the sum of her wishes. Some memory was hiding there. Like a face she knew but had forgotten from where.

She leaped out of bed and stood before the wardrobe. "We must never shut this door," in her most serious voice. "Ever." She could make out the reflection of her hand, pointing.

"I'm not certain that you *can* shut it."

"Well, from now on we always keep it open."

"Regardless of the consequences?" amused by her earnestness. It reminded him, with some reason, of a parlour game.

"Regardless of the consequences."

Again they made love. Afterwards, she brushed his face with the palm of her hand.

"You're so precious to me," he said huskily.

His heart was so open, his longing so unsettling to her, that she had to close her eyes.

He held her palm against his face. "What do you want to know? Ask me anything."

"Anything?" It would come, hadn't he promised? It would come.

He was stroking the back of her hand. "In the whole wide world and I'll tell you," he said.

She opened her eyes. "How did you get that penny into the bottle?"

"No," and tried to twist away, but she pinned him down.

"You promised!" straddling him.

He studied her face for a long second. "You'll never tell?"

"On my brother's name."

"I'll have to whisper it."

She raised the hair from her ear and lay forward on top of him, her cheek against his face. "Alex, I'm listening," into the pillow.

His fingers running up and down her naked spine – "Oh, yes," she wriggled – Alex breathed into her ear the secret that his father had taught him.

She said nothing.

"Merridy?"

Asleep. With the most tender expression.

PART II

Moulting Lagoon Farm, 1988–2004

CHAPTER ONE

REFURBISHMENT SALE. 5 piece older-style lounge suite $80. Brussels carpet $20. Westinghouse stove and Robin Hood canopy $30. Good condition. Contact: Merridy Dove, PO Box 311.

For a great many months there was nothing wrong with their marriage.

If she thought of herself on occasions like Alex's penny, squeezed by a force beyond her comprehension into an impossibly tight and airless space, Merridy felt safe. She perceived in Alex the outline of an anchor. He had taken away her fear, and though what she felt for him was not love necessarily but comfort, she had trusted him when he had assured her that love – and with it passion – would come.

In the meantime, she threw her energies into renovating the house.

Four years since Alex reoccupied Moulting Lagoon Farm and he had done nothing in the way of decorating. The rooms cried out for her care. The house was cold, even in summer. There were no mirrors and frequently no electric light because of power cuts. In the bad light, it had become natural for Alex to ignore the ramshackle state of things.

First, Merridy unpacked her Gory Box – or most of it. Then two cardboard boxes containing her father's cook books and engineering manuals, plus his first editions of Edward Lear, Lewis Carroll, Charles Kingsley. All these she stacked in the spare bedroom.

Next, she sorted out their wedding presents, and with Alex's help distributed them through the house. She spread Tildy's possum rug before the log fire and moved the Lear cockatoo into the living room, hanging it over the fireplace. She bought new mirrors and Electricare plug-in radiators. She removed her father-in-law's bottles from the sock trays in the wardrobe and rearranged them on shelves in Alex's workshop. By tactful degrees, she tidied up his bachelor's detritus.

"Guess how many cherry pips I threw away today."

"I can't. Ten?"

"Two hundred and forty-seven."

"You counted?"

"It's a habit."

"But your mother warned me how untidy you were."

"My mother specialises in warnings."

"She called you *slovenly*."

"Only around her."

Merridy had the corridor and bedrooms repainted in bright yellows and reds. She stencilled luminous stars on the ceiling of the spare room – for which she ordered a new bed from Hobart – and above the bookshelves that had doubled as his father's drinks cabinet replaced Alex's print of Merton College gardens with her pencil drawing, at the age of six, of a sixty-four-foot steel sieve, for which Alex made the frame.

She installed her father's radio in the kitchen that she refurbished from top to bottom, and set about as one of her goals to learn to cook. In particular, she taught herself how to make pastas that her father might have appreciated. She looked with suspicion at the "Easy Asian" and "Fabulous French" recipes in the *Women's Weekly* that Tildy lent her, and which called for Oxo cubes. Disregarding Alex's indifference to food, she devoted herself to creating the ultimate red sauce, using fresh tomatoes from her garden that she boiled and peeled.

In the garden, too, she stamped her mark. She did not like to think of other hands putting in the seeds and bulbs; she ripped out the wild daisies from the flower bed around the house and planted stylidium and native correa to attract the birds, and deep red peonies that she bought from a nursery near Hobart. As a last touch, she positioned two she-oaks in terracotta pots beside the kitchen entrance.

So in fits and starts did Merridy create an environment – the first that she had known since childhood – where children and friends would be made welcome.

Tildy came often. The cousins spoke regularly on the telephone in the days and weeks after Ray at last, at last proposed. Ray did not visit. Alex never said anything, either to Merridy or Tildy, about how Ray had damagingly neglected the farm, but he kept it in his mind.

In the same way, Merridy never admitted to Alex about the times when she surprised herself thinking about the real-estate agent.

On the first occasion, she was washing her hair in rainwater when there was a power cut. She lit a candle and was shocked to see in the new bathroom mirror just how long her hair had grown. She was trying to cut it herself when the lights flashed on again and she looked down and noticed her hairy legs. It was Ray's moustache that she saw as she shaved them.

And once as she stood planting seeds outside the living-room window in the pearl of winter, the pine trembling, she found herself playing Ray's game and imagining how he might describe Moulting Lagoon Farm in the wholly improbable event of the property coming onto his books. The quiet private location. The classic, balconied home with leadlight windows that could be mistaken for a gamekeeper's cottage in the English countryside. The exceptional views of the sea.

A most welcoming entrance foyer leads to rooms of generous proportions with the character of yesteryear. The master bedroom has high raked ceilings with exposed beams and powder room off. Within easy access, and ideal for the growing family, are two further bedrooms, one at present in use as a workshop . . .

CHAPTER TWO

THE MORE TO LEARN the valley, she walked for an hour, sometimes two, each day, or rode on the pony that Alex had given her. Clutching a discarded hickory rake-shaft for her stick, and with Flash at her side, she strolled out in the early morning or evening, with the breeze at its lowest. She took her bearings from the windmill. Whenever she was down on the beach she could see its blurring blades above the boobyalla line. The green vane that had her name on it.

Merridy spent the best part of a fortnight exploring the property. She sat on Alex's orange, lichen-covered rock and picked the marram grass seeds from her feet, picturing her husband at the age of eleven. She revisited the graveyard on the edge of Moulting Lagoon where Alex's father had found the coin. And several times returned to the copse where Basil Dove's neighbour had encountered the thylacine. The only fragrance she detected was eucalyptus.

She discovered the trembling jetty from which Basil Dove had liked to swim. On the far side of the stream an eddy of air on an otherwise calm day caused a splash. She thought it might be a platypus in the reeds, but it furred the surface, then crossed the water and ruffled the grass on the near bank, coiling it with the force of a small cyclone. Or a spirit passing, she could not help wondering, as she watched the grass twisting up the bank, outside a disused shed and into the field. The grass greener than a mallard's breast and on the hill an ochre shiver of grain.

On her way back to the house, a black horse running wild in a field of yellow grass reminded her of how it was possible to feel.

Away from people, she let her hair grow below her shoulders. She took to wearing the same jumpers and trousers. So relieved to be out of her mother's oppressive clutches, leave aside Keith Framley's uniform, that she stopped seeing herself – to a point where she almost forgot that she was female. It was enough to focus her attention on Alex and her project of turning a dilapidated Federation post office into a late twentieth-century home. A home fit for a young farmer and his family.

When it was breezy, the sounds of the animals reached her in the house. They carried through the fresh-painted rooms with tremendous clarity, like the sounds of something lost. She heard the bellows of the herd, the lowings of the new bull and the clicking of horns. She had never lived close to animals. It took her a while to get used to them.

Three months into her marriage a black swan pecked at Merridy's hand, breaking the skin. She was feeding it corn on the edge of Moulting Lagoon and the swan arched its neck and struck, removing the hard yellow grain pinched from one of Alex's cobs, and leaving a bruise on her palm the size and shape of a postage stamp, a purple one from somewhere foreign.

A month later, she ran into the kitchen with a shower of white excrement on her hair and clothes. A wedge-tailed eagle had shat on her. She had disturbed it in the field below the sheep-race and the droppings on her shirt put Merridy in mind of the bottle in the restaurant where Alex had courted her. She stripped off and threw her shirt in the wash, but the stain did not come out and no amount of soap could remove it. Still, she refused to see it as a sign. Until the day when a cheerful plumber came from Swansea to fix a mixer tap that persisted in clogging with silt.

He was under the sink so long that she asked if he knew a good solution to remove eagle shit from clothes.

"I leave that to me wife, love. She's got a remedy for every stain – and with the kids there's a lot."

Packing his tools back into a bag, he remarked on the tidiness in the kitchen. "Obviously, you don't have kids."

She coughed. The salt air often woke her with a dry throat. "No. I've only been married for four months."

"Wife got up the stick right away. Maybe before!" He closed his bag and looked at her. "Or don't you want children? Some don't."

Merridy was affected by the question. She saw by his expression that he felt sympathy for her, and yet she did not – until that moment – feel sorry for herself. His words upset her and soon afterwards she came off the pill and took notice of her cycles.

Her mother never visited. Mrs Bowman's sense of release following her husband's death did not survive the winter. She used her daughter's marriage as a staircase into a long cathedral of depression. She wrote on the first Sunday of the month, a single-sided letter containing meagre news and the hope that Merridy was enjoying *Engineering World*. On reflection, it had been a mistake to live with her sister; she was looking for a house to rent in Devonport; she had found one. And a PS in which she asked to be remembered to Mrs Grogan and sometimes to Alex. Nothing about grandchildren.

TALBOT'S NEWSLETTER
We have now been able to purchase from the contingency fund a 2nd hand collating machine. This machine should more than halve the time to put the Newsletter together. We hope to be able to increase the number of pages in the near future. Same conditions apply. No advertising detrimental to local employment. All submissions subject to strict size restrictions and editor's discretion. A.T.

In a moment of happy tension she called him Piers.

They sat on the back deck facing the sea, between them a bottle of Coombend Riesling, empty. An autumn evening in April. They had been married almost a year.

He reached for her hand. "Is that what you'd like to call him?"

"Why not?"

"What about Hector?"

He felt the involuntary tug of her arm.

"What if he's a girl?" she said, and left her hand where it was.

He contemplated the Hazards. South, towards Maria Island

and the Antarctic, the dragon-coloured sea went from green to scuffled blue. "Piera sounds nice. Piera Dove."

He was teasing, of course. Or was he? She squeezed his hand, but was intertwined, she felt, with a riddle. Not that she minded, or doubted that he was her answer. "Piers Dove. Piera Dove." She said it lightly. Remembering a book of her father's, of pale Italian frescoes. "I'll settle for either."

He opened her fingers, stared at the mark, like a stigma on her palm. "Does that hurt still?"

"It doesn't hurt at all."

There was a flat croak. They watched the birds passing overhead, their eyes hooked to the rim. They looked as if they had been burned into the sky with a hot blade.

So the sun fell in the menacing pink of Tildy's eyeshadow and the lighthouse glowed earlier and earlier from the tip of Schouten and autumn became winter.

LIONS CLUB OF WELLINGTON POINT have horse manure for sale by the trailer load. For orders and enquiries: phone J. Fysshe 63245668.

Then there were mornings when the wind blew even the clouds away and the sky had the translucence of a membrane. From the kitchen, it stretched so thin that a tap of her hand could break it and the oceans it kept back would tumble her in angry torrents. On these days, walking the nine-mile beach with Flash, she felt that the whole sea was chasing her, flaring with a cold anger to protect its secrets.

Not that she denied herself the vivid pleasure of picking up whatever the sea had dropped. Jellyfish in the shape of Tildy's bras. Mutton-bird feathers pressed into the sand. Necklaces of kelp attached to a single stone that it thrilled her to hurl back at the waves.

In Agnes's Op-Shop, she bought a book on seashells and looked up those that she had collected. They might have been characters from her father's unpublished stories: hairy arks, southern gapers, shining wentletraps, flaming dog cockles, exotic boring venerids. There were also mud-oyster shells from an Aboriginal midden, with round holes punctured into them by borer parasites through which she surveyed the horizon. Reciting to herself preposterously: *He went to sea in a sieve.*

The prettiest oyster shells she brought home to her bedroom and laid out on a blue cloth on her Gory Box. She blocked her ears to the sound of the waves, like pebbles in a drum reminding her: There is no God there is no God there is no God.

DEEP-SEA DIVER GIVES LESSONS. Contact: J. S. Phone 62578583.

She was often alone. Once the kitchen-fitters and decorators had departed, fewer visitors came to the house. Despite her radio, she began to feel out of the eye of the town. It was not an uncomfortable feeling, not to begin with.

When the hay was on, Alex was up at six. Through the bedroom wall, she heard him in the kitchen eating his unvarying breakfast. Three pieces of toast: one Vegemite, one butter, one marmalade. Then the careful closing of the fly-screen and kitchen door and after a few minutes the noise of a machine starting up. She lay in bed, savouring the image of her husband cutting and binding the hay and leaving stooks in the paddocks in the shape of the hourglass with which her grandmother in Ulverstone used to time her husband's eggs. When Alex was cutting hay, it was full on from November to January.

In the early morning, the sun pressed on the southward-facing slopes of Barn Hill. She liked to watch it from the bed, flattening the paddocks and gullies into a long spreading curve. The kangaroo grass that grew in thick clumps along the summit was yellower than custard. Her eyes hunted for the man who had left his shape in the sheets. Who would return for dinner at noon and sometimes not until sunset.

Because, as she quite soon learned to appreciate, Alex was forever occupied. Judging fairs. Buying and selling cattle. Planting and harvesting crops. In January, he dipped the sheep. In February, he drenched for flukey. In March, he sowed for barley. In the first week of April, he prepared his heifers for the autumn calf sale at Pawrenna, to which he brought along Merridy. In May, he sprayed for grubs. She could understand why he declined repeated invitations to become a councillor or a firey or go on a whale-stranding course. He had no time. There was only himself on the farm, and now Merridy – who took it upon herself to look after the horses, cleaning the tackle and boots. And though she suspected that the land had not yet worked itself into her husband's bones, she knew that the management of it consumed him as exhaustively as it consumed every farmer on this coast. He was part of a network of landowners all with the same agent, an unprepossessing fellow with a toupee and false teeth who drove around to see each of his clients every three weeks on what Jack Fysshe drily referred to as the Suicide Run: to stop any of them committing suicide after one of their number a few years back threw himself down a well.

RAY GROGAN is proud to announce the opening of his new office at 7 Waterloo St. "I am always in need of rental properties for short and long lets. I have a long and proven history of providing landlords with good reliable tenants."

What was left poking through the froth once her memory simmered away the first months at Moulting Lagoon Farm was less the deepening dread that she would never conceive, nor the moments when she thought with a pang of Melbourne and her university contemporaries, but the evenings, early on, when they made love on the living-room floor.

Alex lay underneath her, his sandy head on the thick possum rug. He had never seen the colour of firelight on a woman's cheeks. He could not keep it from his smile. How she edified the place.

"What did you do today?" He loved to hear everything. Down to the most basic detail. He welcomed the upset that she brought to his routine. The sight of her tights on the clothes-line. Her finger stirring a red sauce; her inevitable frown when she licked it. Plus, in the days when she was renovating the house, the never-ending trail of plumbers and carpenters who had traipsed through the rooms under her direction, even if Alex took great care to conceal his anxiety when their bills arrived. He drew the money out of his fast-shrinking savings, refusing to let Merridy touch her father's inheritance. It was an article of faith with him. Anyway, the farm remained on track to make a profit. They were in love. It would turn out fine.

"Let's see," rising and falling above him, "I made bread. I finished painting the laundry room. I spoke to Alice about getting some bleach. Oh yes, and started *The Shadow Line* . . ."

She edited out the two letters that she had written to friends in Melbourne, urging them to come and stay (they never did). Or the wistful feeling that she experienced whenever she looked into Alex's study, or opened *Engineering World*, or read one of Alex's books.

In the hard bright sun of those first months the possum rug stood out. She remembered his tongue on her eyelids, between her legs, and was almost persuaded. Love was not sober nor static. It was the supreme example of tenderness in motion. And Alex had taught her.

"You've taken a prune and made it a plum." So she told him.

She kept busy. Thinking of the interaction of their bodies. Thinking of their child. She saw, they saw, a baby plucking daisies off her jersey and staring up at a terracotta ceiling spangled with yellowy green stars that twinkled in the darkness. The Christmas trees they would decorate with cut-outs of shiny paper. The toys they would wrap – water pistols, little red Wellington boots, black felt Tasmanian devils from a shop in Bicheno.

"We are going to have a baby."

Tildy's jaw dropped.

"No, no, I don't mean I'm pregnant. Just that I've gone off the pill."

But it did not come. It was so simple: they could make love, but no child.

Unlike Tildy who now had Zac.

"You will be a godmother, won't you?" looking up from her hospital pillows, barely ten minutes after his birth.

"I'd be hurt if you hadn't asked."

"Here. Hold him, why don't you?"

CHAPTER THREE

One morning, Merridy joined her husband at his dawn breakfast.

"You're up early," cheerfully.

"Alex," clearing her throat. She tightened the cord of her dressing gown and sat down. "I'm going to Launceston for a test."

"A Test? Are England playing?"

"To see if there's something wrong, silly. Dr Musgrove has arranged it."

Alex looked hurt. He was a fierce dog where the body was concerned and certainly not going to submit himself to inspections.

"Well?" he asked ten days later.

She held up the letter from the clinic in Canning Street. "They say nothing's the matter. Not so far as they can tell."

He looked away. "So maybe there isn't." And came and wrapped his arms around her waist, as if she was a mast that he would never let go. "We'll just have to go on rooting like rabbits."

Winter came and Alex exchanged his T-shirt for a dark brown jersey and the trench coat that Sarah had sent back.

He had not thought much about Sarah until in his second year of marriage a letter arrived to say that she was coming out to Australia with a group of teachers, and any chance of their seeing each other? Her schedule was tight. She doubted whether she could make it to Tasmania. Perhaps Alex could hop up to Sydney?

"What, like a kangaroo?" said Merridy, feeling a prickle of jealousy. "Has she looked at the map?"

"She was always hopeless about directions," Alex said.

When he telephoned the number that Sarah had given, she had already left for Australia. They never did meet up.

Meanwhile, there was dribbly-eye in the roos. In June, barely a day went by when he did not press his gun to his shoulder and shoot a wallaby or rabbit. Over on Barn Hill, their neighbour's sheep got into a paddock and spread lice into Alex's flock. He decided to dip the lot, not that it made any difference. All his fleeces had a bit of discolouration that year. Wool prices were the lowest he could remember. He had shorn the ewes in May before lambing, but the market had fallen further by October, when he sheared the wethers. "We need another Cold War, that's what we need," grumbled the classer from Kempton, rubbing a fleece between two blunt oily fingers. The Cold War had been good for wool, the Korean War better still. Peace was an effing disaster.

Once again, children from the local school gathered in the shed to watch. They loved to be there on shearing day – "Getting in the way," grizzled Pat, a stout Aboriginal woman from Flinders, who was very patronising to Merridy, who quite liked her.

The children stood gaping at all the noise and activity: Pat and two other shearers stooped over the sheep; the morose classer feeling the fleeces for strength and texture, eyeing the wool for colour; the wool-roller sorting out the fribs and skin pieces to one side, and the stained wool that he threw into a bin.

"It's all done by feel and eyesight," Alex explained, leading them over to the shearers. He was quite sweet on Pat.

Merridy cooked a big mutton roast for the shed-hands. She would look at them, who had never had to cook in their lives, and see the possum shit in their eyes.

The hurry of the shearers, their pace and physicality – Pat could sweep a sheep from the pen with one arm and on a good day shear 130 fleeces – never failed to impress Merridy, but nothing impressed her more than Alex's natural ability to send children into excitement. In Wellington Point, all round town, there were kids who would walk up to him and say: "Good day, Mr Dove," after spending a morning or afternoon at Moulting Lagoon Farm.

Not only the farm excited the children's curiosity. Once, coming into the shed with a tray of lemonade, Merridy overheard Alex in conversation with two boys and a lanky girl who watched transfixed as he held down a shorn lamb for the taller of the boys to daub with an orange D.

"Oh, Mr Dove, what muscles!" the girl joked admiringly.

"Why don't you have children?" piped up the boy with the marker, and Merridy recognised Rob, who had stood in the Bethel Teahouse.

"Oh, I don't know, I'm doing my best."

"What does doing your best mean?" pressed the girl. "You're obviously not doing it right."

Alex looked up and caught Merridy's eye. "Hi, love," blushing, and released the lamb, which dashed its head against the central pine beam and then shot off, slipping and scratching along the wooden grating. "Here, let me take that."

Wool prices were so low that year that Alex toyed with the idea of going organic and then rejected it. He would persevere. At the end of October, Cascade brewery renewed the contract for his barley.

WELLINGTON POINT MODEL YACHT CLUB.
All those who are interested in forming and joining are invited to attend the inaugural meeting to establish Where and When. 4.30 Tuesday 15th. Greer Street jetty.

Like Mrs Bowman, Ray never came to visit. But Tildy did. Bringing Zac and magazines with recipes.

"I must say, you've done a great job, Merridy," tracing a finger over the new ceramic cooktop. "A great job. But don't you find it dull up here?"

"Not enough moments," borrowing Alex's words. She bent over the pram. "How's his sleep going?"

"I only have to turn over and he wakes." Tildy scanned the novel that Merridy had left open on the dresser. "But who do you speak to? Apart from Alex."

"Oh, the sea, the animals." They had a cat now and some ducks. "Does he need another blanket?"

"No, he's mad for the one you gave him. In fact, Ray's got a mind to cut it in half in case he loses it." The book reminded Tildy. "You know, I went to bed with him."

"Who?" stroking Zac's mottled arm.

"Your husband, sweetie. Who do you think?"

"Oh, Tildy."

"There's me shooting my big mouth off," sighed Tildy, and wondered if she had been on the brink of uttering something profound.

But Merridy was amused. "You forget. You already told me."

"Do you – still?"

"What?" looking up.

Tildy's hair was no longer blonde, after she met a man in flippers who remarked of her dye that the anti-foul he painted on his boat contained less poison. And she was pregnant again. So fat that her arms came out at right angles.

"Like rabbits, you said."

"Oh, yes. Absolutely."

"He wasn't a rabbit before," and Tildy cackled before falling contemplative. "You must have made him one."

Merridy turned back to Zac. Who had the preoccupied smile of a baby filling its nappy.

"I think a new Huggie's in order."

Tildy looked at her cousin without rancour. To think that Merridy anticipated Zac's needs before she did. "There should be one under his pillow."

"Zac just needs a little fuss," said Merridy, changing him.

Tildy sighed. "You're a much finer mother than I am. You connect better. He's just like his father."

Merridy felt her face turning hot. She was tugged away from the pram, like any dog from a smell. "And you, Tildy. What about Ray?"

The Grogans had married two months after them. Tildy had worn black boots under her dress with four-inch heels. "I could only find them high enough in black." The Doves had given as their wedding present a pewter tray.

"Is he what you wanted?" persisted Merridy.

"Oh, and more." Tildy's eyes fell again on the book. "Hey, that reminds me. I need your help. What should I read? I was thinking of joining Agnes's reading group."

"I'll ask Alex."

"Would you? I want to branch out."

"We'll make a list. It'll be fun." It was what they did most evenings, read. They had built up a small library.

Tildy folded her arms. "I must say, I really would go mad up here on my own. But, of course, the way you two carry on you'll soon have family responsibilities."

"I know, I know," and smoothed her stomach. She was not going to tell Tildy, but she would have her baby before long. She had missed her period and already she imagined the shape and growth in her uncorrected body.

She did not tell anyone, not even Alex. She bought a test at the chemist's. It was negative. A week later she bought another test. In the slow days ahead she haunted the bathroom, her excitement intensifying. Her periods were usually very regular. Even so, she was conscious that she lacked Tildy's wholesome peaceful expression.

Draggedy draggedy. Day after dragging day. Like her mother's first steps across the room after her stroke.

One Tuesday, Alex came home late from Launceston to find her standing on the counter, scrubbing the top shelves of the dresser.

"What are you doing, love?"

"Alice never gets up here."

Then the frosty morning, a fortnight after Tildy's visit, when she detected the spotting. Next day her period started. Not a child after all, but a phantom. And felt her womb heavier than ever, a black, empty, bottle-shaped presence inside her.

The next meeting of the poetry group will be on Wednesday August 9th at 2.30 p.m. at Agnes Lettsom's house. The subject is: "Sea" – a word to conjure with!

The end of another August and the boobyalla were covered with little yellow caterpillars of blossom. She collected pine needles to put on the path and lay down the silverweed and old copies of the *Mercury* as mulch, and kept the mulch away from her fruit trees so as not to rot them. She wrapped her apple trees against codlin moth. She sprinkled blood and bone around the roses. She started a herb garden down near the beach – pepperberries, lemon verbena, chives – where she also planted tomatoes, strawberries and rhubarb. Her fingers gloved in dirt, she kneeled on the earth and pressed each seed into the ground. And once or twice lifted her eyes to catch a blue-tongue lizard with a taste for strawberries watching her.

She looked for pleasure in predictability. The daisies – purple and white – that opened during the day and snapped shut in late afternoon. The spinach flopping in large green spades. Her flowers that grew around the house in the colours, it suddenly struck her, of Alex's samplers: in reds, blues and yellows.

Merridy was happiest, though, in the garden that she had created behind the dunes. Nipping the flower stalks in the rhubarb, she thought of the child that they would have. She pictured a boy somewhat like Alex and looked forward to the day when she would be leading him by the hand to inspect her herbs and vegetables. "Your great-grandmother, who was a bit of a battleaxe, used to say to me: 'God gives a herb for every ill.' This is hoarhound for coughs. That's comfrey for bones and bruises. Over there that's broccoli, the everlasting vegetable. High on the list for needing lots of poo." So would she converse with him, and not only about plants. "That's a huntsman spider. They get active before the rain. Take your attention off them and they go away. But they're harmless, unlike a red-back. See under that pot? Never put your fingers in anywhere you can't see." She smiled to contemplate anyone she had known at uni overhearing these private conversations. They would conclude that country life had turned Merridy Bowman Dove quite potty.

And in the evening after they had eaten, she gave herself to Alex in firelight.

"Oh, and I polished your boots," she reminded him one memorable night, opening his hand and pressing his palm against her stomach. Not because he needed to know, or cared even; but it was part of the fabric that wove them. A reason to listen to his plans for the next day.

"That's good," Alex said, looking up at her, serious all of a sudden. "Since I have to go to Hobart."

Her immediate thought – the windmill was playing up again. The complexity of the female body was as mysterious as the guts of Alex's windmill, and as liable to go wrong at any time. His journey, she imagined, was to fetch a spare part. "Can't East Coast Freight deliver?"

"I'm going to take a test."

She stared at him, the meaning of his words reaching her. And was impelled to bend down and squeeze his face so tight that he cried out.

He had made an appointment at the Royal Hobart, combining it with a visit to his bank manager, who for some time had been requesting a meeting, and also to J. R. Stephenson in Campbell Street to buy a new water pump and spear pipe. Plus a feed of oysters for Merridy: "I know – it's insane that you can't get oysters in Oyster Bay."

On his return, Alex laughed at how easy the procedure had been. The soft-lit room, the pile of magazines, the glass jar – and the shutter that opened in the wall and the anonymous white gloves that took away the jar. In a fortnight or so Dr Macbeth would send the results.

And when the envelope came. "Same as yours." A five-inch grin. "Sperm count normal. Motility, too. No reason at all."

"What's motility?"

"I think it's how zippy they are."

Next morning, he was up early for the store-sheep auction at Quoiba. On waking, she rolled over onto his cold side of the bed and hankered for the rocking applause of the springs. It was an enormous relief. To think they might leave it to nature, to the forces that regulated the lambs and the black swans and the wedge-tailed eagles and tiger-snakes. And also not a relief.

CHAPTER FOUR

WELLINGTON POINT PRIMARY SCHOOL is now taking enrolments for children who will be 4 years old on January 1. Enrolment packs are available from the school office.

Two years on and the itinerant workers he employed to shear his sheep had grown balder. The cars roared by with boats on trailers, the names on the sterns sillier and sillier. And still nothing for them to christen Piers or Piera.

The simplest act for some had become very complex. Merridy tried not to indicate to Alex that she was at the most fertile part of the month because she did not want to appear utilitarian, but she found herself seducing him mid-cycle. She shied from looking at his temple, and took her tongue to where she would not have to see his face.

Wild flames they were her lips and hands, but her heart was dark to him. It hovered and seemed not to land. Very occasionally Alex stared down at her neck and the chevron of black hair – and mourned that she did not return his love. Instead, it was her brother's disappearance that ran through her veins like a thick red sauce, and everything always, in the end, came back to it. On these occasions, he was crushed by the idea when he wrapped her in his arms that he was holding nothing more than the locked Glory Box of someone who inwardly fell away to the core of the earth.

Most of the time, though, he believed that they were destined to be together. They transformed loss into trust, disbelief into gratitude. They loved one another.

CHILD CARE CENTRE. Advanced photographer will be taking family portraits at Centre on Friday evening for just $10!

*

Christmas approached. They attended the Cranbrook Fair, a sunny day in a bowl of hills. She watched Alex and Flash in the sheepdog trials and afterwards paid two dollars for a long-bearded man on a turquoise hot rod to give a ride to her godson. "That's from Santa," she told Zac. Afterwards, she bought the boy an Abel Tasman pancake from the side of a van. And bumping into the Welsh sisters, in a tent selling lemon marmalade, accepted their invitation to a girls' night out.

In her garden, cultivating life in terracotta pots, she brushed the back of her hands against the fine hairs of the growing leaves. When a little frog hopped out from underneath a saucer, she helped it off its back. One afternoon, a lamb in the field behind the windmill was stung by a tiger-snake and died within minutes. She watched the snake trickle off through the grass with the gleam of hot tar. Between the bite and the bleat, she thought, I take my pulse, and felt again the heavy vacancy inside her.

Next time she saw a baby copperhead undulating across the drive she took a stone and crashed it down. The snake writhed up bleeding, half its body pinned useless to the gravel in a silvery-red smear. She walked back to the house in erratic steps. Hostile and frightened and also jubilant.

FOR SALE: Toyota diesel 1984. 8 months rego. Cheap reliable car. Lots of history, very clean. Red. $800 Phone: 63456776.

Then there were little things she looked forward to. The long afternoons gazing out to sea. Listening to the radio in the kitchen. The ritual of reading the *Mercury*, especially the crime column and its list of thefts that told her that something was happening in the world. ("Oh, Alex," she would say, her voice rising to a tremolo, "just look at this. Someone's stolen a wheelbarrow in Orford!" He would always chuckle.) The dinner with Rhiannon and Myfanwy, at which Rhiannon served mussels. ("Everything's so phallic," Myfanwy said, squeezing a shell. "It's important to eat girlie food, too.")

There were other dinners, too. With their neighbours, the

Macdonalds, from Queensland, who had bought Bill Molson's property and kept a motorboat in Coles Bay on which, twice a year, the two families sped over to Schouten to picnic on a sheltered beach of smooth pebbles. With a pale, shy potter and his wife who lived across the river in Swanwick. With the rather trying Harry Ford, the friend of Alex's parents, in his bungalow opposite the school. Every so often, Keith Framley treated her and Alex to a large dinner at the RSL. Sometimes Tildy joined them – always when Ray could not.

How it evolved, neither party examined too closely, but it became an unspoken agreement whereby it never entered Tildy's mind to invite the Doves to a meal that might involve Ray; nor did Merridy ever ask Ray to Moulting Lagoon Farm. She sometimes caught sight of him over the grey heads, like blown dandelions, on ANZAC day; or pushing a pram into the golf club; or in line at the chicken counter in Talbot's. But they never spoke. They nodded hello, but they did not speak.

This did not stop Merridy from looking, though. Ray's office was opposite Talbot's and she would guiltily catch herself gazing after him if ever he came into the street, and know that she was lingering too long and try to convince herself that it was an accident. As the years went by he filled out, but even his little paunch suited him. The appeal of a big-boned man.

Once – to her considerable shame – Alex caught her standing red-faced outside the store. Her eyes on a figure down by the jetty who winched a new-looking boat onto a trailer. She had thought that Alex was putting the groceries away in the ute round the back, but he was watching her watching Ray.

"Ray-spotting again?"

She turned round horrified, but he was smiling. He winked at her. "Can't keep your eye off him, can you?"

An uncertain look crept into his face when Alex registered her dismay. It perplexed him. He knew that it was innocent.

Ray accelerated up the ramp as they loaded the last of the shopping bags. Alex braced himself, but the real-estate agent was in no mood to stop. Alex's first impression was of a gold chain around a thick tanned neck. That was before he saw Ray's face. He had a black eye and a cut under his jaw criss-crossed with stitches.

"Did you see that?" after Ray sped off.

"I did."

"I'm surprised someone hasn't clubbed him to death before now."

No one was able to tell Alex who had done it.

Ray Grogan apart, Merridy's life at this period of her marriage was more social than later it became, and certainly more social than she had been accustomed to in Ulverstone or Melbourne. There was an element in town that would never accept her as a resident but part of the geriatric flash-tide who came to Wellington Point, took advantage of the facilities and left; but there was another group, much smaller, who invited her to things: to raise funds for the day care or to meet over a capuccino at the Bethel.

Her ability to get around improved enormously after Alex bought her a second-hand Toyota – until then she had had to rely on his ute. For a time, she helped out Agnes twice a week at the Op-Shop, even if she said no to joining her reading group. She assisted in the Summer Flow Show and in Meals on Wheels when Abbygail fell ill. And though neither she nor Alex went regularly to church, they did religiously attend the ANZAC service at the Uniting Church and afterwards stood on the footpath outside Talbot's to watch the procession of old men in ribboned medals shuffling past like a squad of prisoners.

So the days levelled out. Summer yellowed into autumn and the noise of the wind through the tree on the lawn kept her awake. Sleepless, she conceived further plans for the house, for the garden, for her potager by the sea.

CHAPTER FIVE

RAY GROGAN is proud to announce that he is expanding his services from sales, rentals and property management to professional loans. "Let me help you become a stakeholder in your community!"

One Monday morning a truck arrived from Wellington Point and unloaded oyster shells onto the drive. Merridy had taken the idea from Mrs Macdonald. The shells were soon crunched into fragments, several barrows of which Merridy scattered on the graves of Alex's parents under the Oyster Bay pine, where children played on them, trampling the brittle surface in delighted whoops.

And still the only children to chase each other through the bright painted corridors were the ones who came to visit. The junior class from the primary school – she had let the teacher know that pupils would always be welcome to ride the ponies. The two small Macdonald boys, Don and Mike. And Tildy's children, of course.

"What do ducks eat?" said Zac, the elder, who had been discovered by Tildy at the age of eighteen months with a large spider sticking out of his mouth. The only effect of swallowing the huntsman, so far as Tildy could tell, had been to make Zac fart. Dr Musgrove had said: "Better not make a habit of it."

"Grass, water-beetles," Merridy suggested, although really she had no idea. She was Zac's godmother, but she could never look at his mouth without seeing hairy legs protruding. "Ask Alex, why don't you?"

Alex had an affinity with Zac. He would take the boy on his tractor or into the shearing shed. Zac's greatest pleasure was to race through the stalls, and then stand and shriek at his gargoyle's reflection in the central pillar, a thick beam of Oyster Bay pine that the backs of wriggling sheep had oiled to a dark shine. Leaving Tildy a few moments' peace to push her pram on the lawn.

Once upon hearing Zac's hysterical shrieks, Tildy told her with the tactlessness of an adoring mother: "When something's really bad, you hear silence."

"You're so lucky, Tildy. They're beautiful."

Her tone made Tildy look up sharply. "Well, the more time you spend with them, the more time you want to spend with them. You just want to gobble them up."

"Like peanuts!"

"Exactly!"

Inside the pram the new baby gurgled, woken by her brother's screams. Tildy poked a hand under the hood and adjusted something. "Though where this one's button chin comes from, I don't know." This one was called Montana. She continued to make her noise, like a sleepwalker on the verge of speaking, and then stopped. "It's only in the last two days she's begun sucking her thumb. It's as if she's discovered God."

On another visit, Tildy noticed the sagging fence and said: "Oh, I forgot. Ray told me to tell you that one of his farmers has thirty rolls of chicken wire he doesn't need."

"Alex will be thrilled." Or, would he? She no longer knew with Alex, she had stopped trying to gauge his thoughts from his expression. It pained her to notice how the two of them had settled into a kind of acceptance over the past months. Their words careful and deflective. Kind without being intimate. In the unchanged air of their marriage.

"Then I'll let Ray know, shall I?"

"That would be kind." Merridy looked at her cousin. "How is Ray?"

His photograph appeared every week in the *Mercury*'s property supplement. A beaming mouth and, below it, his telephone number and the words: *Phone now to be spoiled.* He had bought out Tamlyn & Peppiatt the year before and operated under his own name. He specialised in loans over $150,000, under the questionable motto: *Ray's solutions. Why not settle for more?*

"Oh, you know Ray. Busy as a bee. He's even thinking of

standing for the council," but Merridy saw in Tildy the beginning of a disenchantment.

"Come on. What's the matter?" They had trusted each other when they lived in Ulverstone. She was able to tell Tildy not to be such a slut, and Tildy could tick her off for acting like a cock-teasing Vestal Virgin.

Tildy had never spoken ill of Ray, had always been protective of him. But once she started, the floodgates opened. She seemed to relish recounting the worst of their marriage. He was always on his boat when she needed him – "He says he bought it to escape the children's screams, for God's sake. And what am I supposed to do?" When he did come home, he was demanding and took her for granted. "Sometimes I have the feeling he'd like me to peel his grapes for him – and if I don't, he'll trade me in for a spanking new condo."

"Oh, he wouldn't do that," Merridy said. "Not Ray."

"Don't be so sure. He just might. When he's in one of his moods." As he seemed to be in right now.

"What kind of mood?"

"It's like he's had a quarrel with himself and neither side has spoken for a while. He's only truly happy when he's out in the middle of the bay with a rod in his hand."

"It will sort itself out."

"Hah!" said Tildy bitterly. "And Alex?" she added in her new stirred-up mood. It had not escaped her notice. Something unhatched in Merridy's eyes.

"He's good," said Merridy. She took off her wide-brimmed floppy sun hat and wiped her forehead. And looked down into the pram. "Hey, is there a fragrance?"

Zac rubbed his red eyes. "She's done a poo."

"It's all right, I'll go," said Merridy, relieved to have an excuse. She put her sun hat back on and went to fetch a Huggie from the supply that she kept handy in the spare bedroom. At the back of the nappy cupboard was a basket of toys and puzzles from the Op-Shop and a second-hand travel cot in case anyone stayed over. Tildy often dropped her kids off to play. Merridy dug out a Huggie and a Winnie-the-Pooh as an afterthought, and came back outside.

Tildy was content to watch Merridy change Montana's nappy. "Spoon it in one end, mop it up the other. Zac was two before he laid his first firm turds. Weren't you, darling?"

Then Zac came up and grabbed the bear and started pinching his sister's leg.

"If you don't stop doing that," said Tildy seriously, "I'm going to kill you. Slowly. No one will know it's me."

He pinched again.

"Stop it, Zac, you're just tired."

"I'm not tired," he shouted, pressing his knuckles to his tired eyes. Looking in that moment like his father, save that he did not have a moustache or a bangle around his wrist, for by now it was an open secret, how Ray flashed with a new item of gold jewellery every time he sold a sizeable property.

"Well, I am," snapped Tildy. She minded that Zac would not let her hug him. That he answered back. That he used sleep as a weapon in the jealous battle which he raged against his sister. And explained through clenched jaws: "If Ray gets up to give him milk, he won't drink it. So I get up three times every night to give him milk. I've never been so knackered, Merridy. Frankly, it's a stake through the foot." Staring into the pram where the one with Merridy's nappy on had resumed her screaming. "Two stakes, in point of fact."

And suddenly Tildy felt all elephantine and red-faced from the sun, her naturally auburn hair too much in a mess to be tamed by her chemist's comb. "I'm not a stressed person, I don't easily wobble, you know that. But I'll tell you this, Merridy Dove – and it's something you'll discover soon enough – children are crap."

"You don't mean that," Merridy said.

"The crappiest version of yourself. The self you thought you'd left behind but keep on meeting." Tildy stopped herself. "You know, I'd never go on like this with anyone else who didn't have kids. But you're different. You're the only person with no children I could bore like this."

"Oh, I don't mind." And she really didn't. She took an interest in children because she still did expect that she was going to have them. She could afford to be generous with her ear.

In her motherly way, Merridy went to fetch some warm milk for Montana.

"It's her birthday soon, isn't it?" coming back.

"That's right. The twenty-third."

"I'll get her something from Pumpkin Patch."

"You can't keep away from that shop!"

Merridy loved the store in Hobart with its simple fresh colours. She was always buying Tildy's children new outfits. She said: "It even has a maternity section now."

"Nothing I could squeeze into. I always get so huge."

Moments later there was a sudden quiet, as if a mosquito was feeding.

Tildy broke it. "You know Rose-Maree's pregnant?"

And Merridy felt her smile droop. Slacker than the fence and the brim of her shapeless sun hat. "But I thought she never wanted children."

"I don't think she felt comfortable talking to you about it. Oh, God, sorry," noticing Merridy's face. "What an insensitive cow I am."

A girl who worked sometimes at the Op-Shop had told Merridy a few months back of her two abortions. At the time, Merridy did not judge her. Now she found herself hating her. It was one reason why she stopped working for Agnes. She began to nurse a resentment against Indians and Chinese, all those who seemed to multiply like rabbits or took it for granted.

She hated, as well, others' discomfort over her affliction.

"What, you don't have children – oh, I'm sorry," and the person would get embarrassed and she would have to counsel them, as if she were missing an arm or a leg.

"I'm not childless," she taught herself to say. "I'm child-free."

But six months on she passed Rose-Maree's pram unattended outside Talbot's and had the strongest urge to snatch the baby.

This freedom was infrequently discussed with Alex. Maybe it was his English blood to overlook what had not happened. At any rate, he seemed to take it much less to heart than she did. He treated her concerns in the manner of his sheepdog, as things to be herded and corralled. While Merridy fretted, Alex buried himself deeper into his patch of east coast soil, his hopes hinged on rain and an upturn in the wool price. Somehow they never got round to talking about adoption.

But Tildy talked. It irritated Alex, who once glumly observed, "Why does she have to keep two mouths open all the time?"

Now that she had started to discuss Ray, Tildy seemed unable to stop. Each visit or telephone call updated Merridy on Ray's latest mood, their last fight.

"What is it about us that we want nothing so much as to be married, then, no sooner is the ring on our finger than it pops out through our nose? We've been fucked over, Merridy. I never yelled before I had kids. Now listen to me. I've become a screamer." And lifted her head in the direction of the Oyster Bay pine where, in the elliptical shade beneath, two shapes stamped with glee on the oyster shells.

"Zac! Montana!" she brayed. "Here, *now*!"

The children slouched across the lawn towards them. Yes, Montana was her daughter, but sometimes Tildy felt no greater attachment to the girl than if she spouted through a blowhole. As for Zac, he could ignite in her an anger such as she had never imagined a human being capable of. "Ray says it's like having a couple of blue-fin permanently on the line. Right until the last day of your life. If you ask me, they're more aggressive than tuna. They're like tumours. Or mutating viruses," and watched Zac, all thread and chicken bone, try to push the crushed oyster shells down Montana's knickers. But the virus, plainly, was catching. With a fondling look: "He only does that to girls he likes."

In the next breath, Tildy was fierce in wanting Merridy to be a mother. Then she forgot about how her children diminished her, eager for the day when Merridy likewise would be clutched at by a monster with four outstretched arms and two yelling faces tarred with Vegemite. Or six arms and three faces, since, lo and behold, Tildy was pregnant again.

"Why don't you get more tests. What's the problem, Merridy? Why are you so passive? You were never passive before."

"Tildy, we're trying," in a thick voice.

"Well, you'd better go about it in a different way. You could have IVF. I've read about this forty-four-year-old woman in Perth—"

"Listen, this is what we've been dealt. I have a marriage in which I'm happy; you have two lovely children."

"You're not unhappy, then?"

"I'm not unhappy, no, I can honestly say that."

"So it's worked out?"

"Yes," she laughed sadly. "It has worked out."

But for Tildy, who conceived so easily, it was not understandable. "You could always do it on your own, you know. You don't need a man."

"You speak as though it is Alex's fault. It's neither of our faults."

"That is the biggest lorry-load of horse manure I ever heard, girl. You could spread it on your veggie garden for a year."

"Oh, Tildy," and wondered if in fact she did not prefer her cousin in the days when she was single.

Merridy knew that she had not covered all the ground. There were better doctors out there, someone who could tell her what to do, what was wrong. We are in the hinterland here, she thought, with not exactly the latest technology, assigned to a form of ignorance.

She booked another test, in Sydney this time, where Alex, through a medical friend of his godmother, now retired to the Blue Mountains, arranged for Merridy to meet a foetal–maternal specialist in King's Cross. But neither could the doctors on the mainland find anything untoward. Two laparoscopies had revealed her tubes all in place, no past infection, no scarring.

"Sometimes there is no explanation," relaying to Alex what the specialist had said. And yet it upset her to think that there was no obvious physiological reason. A certain sperm and egg had got together and biology had declared this combination was not to be. What did that say for the relationship? Perhaps it was nature's way of saying: Not a good pairing. Perhaps as she had recently read somewhere, their DNA was too alike.

"The doctor did suggest IVF," she said carefully.

Alex gave a groan.

She looked sharply up. "Why not, you do it for cows?"

"You're not a cow."

But the initials had been planted.

In the days ahead, Merridy found out all that she could about IVF. Through Dr Musgrove, she made an appointment with the director of the unit at the Royal Hobart and took Alex to meet him and they both underwent tests. The only sticking point was the fee. She would have to pay, but some of the cost could be reclaimed on Medicare.

Alex asked for a fortnight's grace to raise the amount.

She felt guilty. "Listen, Alex, maybe we can't afford it."

"Don't worry. I can take it out of the farm account."

"There is my father's legacy."

"Absolutely not."

It was another three weeks before he was able to send off the cheque. Within a few days she began her injections. They were self-administered – two in the morning, one at night, and no alcohol, coffee or tea. It all seemed to need precise timing, and Alex had to swallow vitamin pills.

A month later they drove down to St John's in Cascade Road for the egg collection. The anaesthetist led Merridy into the operating theatre. She lay back in the stirrup chair in the most humiliating position she could remember and had her eggs removed – which was excruciatingly painful. As the needle passed through the vaginal walls and into the ovaries, Alex was despatched to provide sperm. Less of a novelty this time. A nurse supplied him with a paper bag and a plastic jar with a label on it that had his wife's name and date of birth. She asked Alex to check to see if the details were correct and showed him where the staff toilet was. He thought, looking around: How am I going to do this? But there were magazines jammed in with the cleaning fluids underneath the sink. Ten minutes later, he popped the sample into the paper bag and wandered along the corridor until he found the nurse.

The pain from the needle was forgotten next morning when the embryologist telephoned to say that of the fifteen eggs collected eight had fertilised. He kept in touch over the next three days, ringing morning and night until the afternoon of the embryo transfer. Alex was allowed with her into the operating theatre. The embryologist brought in a dish containing two embryos and projected them onto a screen. At the sight of the cells splitting and dividing, Merridy looked at Alex and looked away. Then the embryos were put in a large test tube and given to the doctor who injected them into the wall of her womb.

"Take it easy for the next few days," the doctor said afterwards.

"Is that it?" asked Alex.

"Pretty much, that's it. We'll know within a fortnight."

Another two weeks. More injections. Suppositories. Blood-thinners twice a day and a powerful intramuscular in the evening. Another drive to Hobart. Another blood test. And two mornings later, Alex feeding the dog when he heard Merridy dragging her bare feet into the kitchen. Her hands fretted at the table and her eyes had begun to swell.

"I've started my period."

Alex crushed her, sobbing and drivelling, to his chest. "Oh, my darling."

So they tried again. Alex scraped the money together and off they went to Hobart.

Afterwards, she would liken the experience to a roller coaster that she had been on with her father and brother when the Royal Show came to Launceston. She could not get off.

The same result.

"It doesn't matter," through her phlegm and tears, "I never was much good with children. I don't think I ever understood them. Not really." Maybe it was another thing that was not meant to be resolved.

"We'll try again. Of course, we'll try again. You'll think differently in a month."

But after the third occasion Alex could see that she was distressed and something in her eye incinerated. When the nurse telephoned to confirm, very gently, what they already knew – "Sorry, you haven't been lucky this time. It's a negative result" – Merridy could not face going through it all a fourth time. It was too disappointing. They stopped.

CHAPTER SIX

THE MANIFESTATION OF THEIR barrenness dawned more slowly on Alex. It had taken until now for him to understand how deep ran his desire to put something into the future. Imperceptibly but steadily, the thought had developed that he could replace his parents with a son or a daughter. Now, as his father would have put it, he looked forward to neither chick nor child.

Once he had absorbed it, the prospect of not having children attacked him at unexpected moments with the violence of a kidney blow.

He tried to keep it from her, but she noticed. How he hummed to himself as though nothing was amiss. How he walked fast past the spare bedroom. He was a long corridor of doors shut and locked.

And while he bowed to her moods and was tolerant and protective towards her, she was irked by his refusal to communicate. The deeper he burrowed into himself, the more snappish she became.

"Wouldn't you prefer someone else?" she said in one sour moment in the wake of a trivial argument.

"Absolutely not," he spluttered.

"I warned you I wouldn't make you happy."

"But you do!" exasperated.

"You could go off. I'd understand. You must feel free."

"What are you talking about, Merridy?"

"You wanted a child. Lots of children. Mobs of them, as I remember."

"Only because you did."

But she noticed that he had not touched his ships for months.

Instead, it was she who went off.

One cloudless Thursday morning, while Alex was repairing a fence at the bottom of Barn Hill, she slipped out of the house wearing a yellow oilskin, walking down the drive, not once looking back until she reached the bus shelter in Wellington Point.

On the bus to Hobart she listened to a garrulous blonde talk of her bad experience with a guru, a French–Peruvian who called himself Pachamama.

"I met him at a night-class in Battery Point. He'd read a few New Age books and saw this as a way of seducing women, so he started a class in which he told us: 'Your first choice is yourself.' Certain women need to hear that. It gives them permission to be totally selfish. Me, I'm no exception. That's why he was so attractive. 'You should only do things you really want to do. In your heart.' But it's just a bunch of shit. Like his claim he could get it up four times a night. He dressed all in white because white was more – spiritually speaking – enlightening, and never wore sunglasses so that people could always see into the window of his soul. And white tennis shorts, winter through summer. I used to see him sunning his gut – ill-fitting dentures and long greasy hair in a tail. Immigration wouldn't let him in because he's such an old goat. If you bump into him and he asks to live with you, don't. He's only after a permanent visa."

The girl was an ex-hippy from Byron Bay with dead eyes and scars on her wrists.

Merridy had not told Alex, but she had gone to Hobart for a last meeting with a last consultant. In the private clinic in West Hobart, the doctor went straight to the point: "I don't think it's going to work other than by sheer accident. Look, there's not a thing wrong with either of you, but many people have come here and said: 'You're the last port of call; we have a completely clean bill of health, what can we do?' and I say what I'm going to say to you: 'Nothing. It's in God's hands. It's in the lap of the gods.'"

It was a very rum fate being in the lap of the gods. But later that morning, Merridy walked through St David's Park to Salamanca Place. And found herself hunting for a ponytail dressed in white.

The brilliant day drew her down to the sea. She thought: I'll find somewhere to sit for an hour to watch the bay and then I shall buy myself a dress and go home.

The water rocking against the wharves infected her. She picked her way along the dockside, taking in the fishing trawlers and yachts, until she stood outside a chandler's shop. Through the window, a boyish-looking man looked up, and she thought for a fleeting second that it was Alex as she had first seen him, coming out of the school yard with his plastic bag of ice-cream sticks, and her heart began to drum and she felt a surge of anxiety and excitement.

She walked in. Smell of pitch and glints of brass and in a back yard a boat being built.

He was locking up. He had his back to her and was sorting through keys.

"Hi," in her emancipating laugh.

"Good day. How are you doing? How can I be of service?"

"I'm thinking of the sea."

"The sea? What is it exactly you're looking for?"

"I don't know. I was just drawn to the sea."

He looked around, a stranger in a chandler's shop, smiling. "Let's see what we can see."

The young man was due to go out on a trial run, testing an outboard. "I'll show you how it works."

She remembered stepping into the sleek black-hulled boat, putting on the life jacket that he held up, the splutter and take of the engine.

He steered the boat into the Derwent and out of the mouth of the river and into Storm Bay. It had become a blazing hot day. They were halfway to Bruny when he cut the engine. A swell came up and she did not feel terribly good. She stood to take off her life jacket and then her oilskin.

"Are you sure you're all right?"

"Nothing a swim won't cure."

Stripped to her bra and underpants, she went overboard and swam around the boat as he watched. For the first time in her married life she was away from something, anything, that she recognised as her world. She was out in someone else's world.

He helped her back in and the swell toppled them against one another.

She remembered the beat of her pulse and the sweat that oiled his hair and a sense she had that he may have been here before.

They undressed, she in a daze. He had a mole on his foreskin and a small hairless oasis on his scalp. To which she pressed her cheek as he rammed into her.

Afterwards, she said: "We will never see each other again, will we?"

When she came home she found a letter for her tucked under the bottle with the *Otago* in it. In Alex's educated, neat, upright hand. *Without you I am so unhappy, I am.* It was the first letter that he had written to Merridy and she had wondered if he had forgotten how to write, his words saved for sheep and cattle and creatures.

RAY'S SOLUTIONS. Why not settle for more? Phone now to be spoiled. Everything I touch turns to SOLD.

They settled back. Each day another drop of wet sand accumulating beneath her cupped hands into a rising tower from which she gazed out with tightening desperation.

Marriage had been a false passport to tranquillity. She was quite miserable. As was Alex. Neither of them had ever believed that they would find a companion in the storm; when they did find each other, they supposed that a child would be a way out of it, and into a region refreshed by what they had suffered. Instead, it was her father's books that seemed so childish, the little group of six or seven verses which aroused her. In this way, she punished herself.

Silence invaded the house. She was the rustle of the paper, looking for crimes. A tightrope-walker in Zeehan had missed the net. An article on Southend Pier, the longest in the world, reprinted from an English newspaper: *The hunger for piers is strictly nostalgic.* An advertisement that featured a bland-looking man in a suit, staring out: "*Is your memory a sieve?*"

She did her best to forget about the chandler and their moment of frenzy on the bottom of his fast black boat.

While on its shelf on the kitchen dresser, the *Otago* sailed on. A consoling empty bottle with its ship and its obsolete coin.

Through the curved glass of which she saw a murderer swimming in the sea look up at her.

Meanwhile, Alex was out on the farm somewhere. That was his achievement. He was off on his own; unwinding strands of wool from the fence, left there by rubbed necks; or painting slats of red cedar with Madison oil, or at a clearance sale, bargain-hunting for old farm machinery. Or counting sheep in Cumbrian: yan tan tethera methera funf aerter slaerter lowra dowra dick yandick tandick . . .

Like this, he subdued himself further into his land. He had his fields to sow that made it easier to accept his uselessness. He had his barley and his herd of cows. The grazing grass that brushed his legs into hives. The green-painted windmill that had taken on the shape of a mystery whose meaning stayed withheld. But now and again in the shape of a lost animal he caught a glimpse of the mob of children that he had not had, and it slayed him.

About Merridy, he felt a spent resignation. Where had she gone, the forthright girl? He thought of Samuel Johnson on marriage, meaningless to him until now: "The dislike hourly increased by causes too slender for complaint and too numerous for removal." Small acts of will kept him on her side and his love alive. But they were in a new stretch of life and the stubble began to show in their relationship. Their eyes tangled and looked away. Their lips rusted together. Before, they had conversations; now they had arguments. "Dumb stuff, as it usually is," she confided to Tildy. Some comment made the wrong way that boiled up. Some cold exchange, its words worn so thin with repetition as to be transparent.

"Don't put that there," she fluctuated, angry, concerned: under it all, bored. Her husband was a good man. She knew well enough his gentle innocence, but his vision was unpolluted by their sterility; what it was doing to her. She felt her boredom dragging at the corner of her mouth. At the sight of an unwashed plate, she wanted to scream.

Alex, for his part, responded by not touching her, perhaps because he had touched her too much; he scratched his nose and looked at the saucepan heating their minestrone and moved his mug of tea off the neat, clean tablecloth and onto the bare blackwood. And thought of the letters that he kept receiving from the ANZ in Hobart, to advise him that interest rates had risen to 18 per cent, 19 per cent, 20 per cent . . .

Now at night beneath the quilt their bodies lay apart. To Merridy, the hand and mouth that had touched her with such intimacy were nothing but a hard limb and an empty hole smelling of what she had fed him. She piled all her blame on the wardrobe that had filled her with a desire she had never sought and could not satisfy. She had sensations of vertigo, when she wanted nothing so much as to curl up inside and seal the door. But there was also a vital part of her that wanted to remain faithful to the promise which she and Alex had made on their wedding night.

In the meantime, the future lay open and darker than the inside of any Jacobean wardrobe. A future to which neither held the key.

CHAPTER SEVEN

TALBOT'S STORE will be closed on Christmas and Boxing Day. The owner and staff wish all our customers a safe and happy Christmas and New Year. And remember – give the Emergency Services Workers a Christmas present. "Go easy on the Grog" and "Take care with Fires". Cheers everybody. A.T.

The talk that summer was of the drought. It was a time of red poppies and grasshoppers that hiccupped through the barley stalks. In the blaze of sun and salt, conversations flapped and fell, and lips became drier for the heat or worry. A mile up the road a sixteen-year-old girl had twins eight weeks prematurely in a shack that no one had known was there. That summer, it was so hot that it seemed to Merridy everyone was giving birth. Save for the Welsh sisters, who announced what many in the community had all along suspected: they were not sisters.

On an oyster shell in the shade of the pine, the cat paralysed a dragon lizard. Merridy found the lizard going black. She held the shrivelled creature by the tail and was looking around for a place to put it when a hoot sounded from the bottom of the drive and the next moment Tildy's white Honda sped into view.

Merridy had been married six years on the morning in late December when Tildy appeared with Zac, Montana and Savannah for the Doves to babysit during the New Year long weekend. At the very last moment a grateful client of Ray's had presented him with a three-night package at the Freycinet Lodge in Coles Bay. Tildy was looking forward to her first weekend alone with her husband since Zac's birth. All she had to do was find a babysitter.

In the early days, when she assumed that it would happen, Merridy had felt kindly to others and did not mind if Tildy took advantage. Now she experienced a flicker of resentment before agreeing to give up her New Year to childmind her godson and his two sisters.

"We've never had all three to stay at once."

"It's the same as looking after one. And they do adore you."

Merridy came out from the shade of the tree as Zac and Montana spilled from the car and ran to torment the horses. She helped Tildy, who held a sleeping Savannah, to carry the bags into the house.

In the kitchen, it was a lot cooler. Merridy had made little iced muffins, laid out on the table on a plastic sheet, and prepared a jug of lemonade. "You've chosen the hottest day of the year," pouring out five plastic cups. "Any plans?"

"I can't speak for Ray, but I don't intend to leave our room. We're going to go at it," Tildy promised, "like you and Alex. At least, I presume you still . . ." And scrutinised her friend.

"Hey, look at my tail," laughed Merridy, and turned. As much to conceal her face.

Meanwhile, Tildy had spied a wickedness taking place through the window. "Zac!" putting down her cup. "Don't DO that to Montana!" And streaked from the kitchen.

Moments later, she shepherded her children in. Montana wore a top that Merridy had bought her from Pumpkin Patch, now stained brown with banana. She was sobbing: "He said he was going to kill my belly button."

"Zac, wish Merridy a Happy New Year."

"Happy New Year," said Zac sepulchrally.

"Now, I want you all to behave with Merridy," Tildy said, plonking Savannah on the table beside three baskets stuffed with clothes and squidgy toys. "I want no repeat of Christmas."

"Why, what happened at Christmas?"

Tildy rolled her eyeballs. "I decided this year we wouldn't go to church, I'd take them to Louisa Meredith House." Succumbing in a foolish moment to a charitable instinct, Tildy had introduced her children into the nursing home, Zac encased in a scarlet Spider-Man outfit with prominent pectorals, Montana in a fluffy bear suit and Savannah dressed as a fairy. But instead of cheering up the inmates, her son and daughters proceeded to terrorise them. They had punched the emergency button in Doris Prosser's bathroom, switched off the live carol service from King's College, Cambridge, that had mesmerised Sadie Wentworth into a contented rhapsody, and stolen Mr Carr's burgundy fez. No one had seen the hat since.

Tildy inspected the baskets with unseeing eyes. "I reckon you have everything you need. Seeyah all Monday."

Over that weekend, Merridy reached a deeper understanding of why people who had children so often looked distraught; much the same as people desperate to have them.

Barely had Tildy's car disappeared from the drive than Zac vomited. The vomit splashed up from the kitchen floor and a speck of it landed in her mouth.

Montana's nose meanwhile was stubbornly charred with dried snot, infecting Alex with a touch of gastro and a streaming cold that he would not shake off until March.

As for Savannah, she had to be restrained from rushing up to her siblings and plucking at handfuls of hair and then sinking her teeth into their backsides.

"They get on very well," Tildy had said. "They're inseparable, in fact. It's me they have the problem with. Zac *still* won't let me hug him."

Away from their mother, the children did not get on. At lunch Zac pulled away Montana's cup of lemonade. She reacted by tipping it over his head.

"All girls are princesses," Merridy reminded Zac, towelling his carrot-coloured hair. "Boys have to understand that."

"She's not a princess," glowered Zac. "She's a big, fat, hairy triceratops, and I'm going to kill her belly button," and lunging from Merridy's grasp, he slapped Montana on the stomach, hard, with the bread knife.

"Please be nicer to your sister," Merridy implored. The most hopeful words in the English language.

As Montana howled, Zac began tugging at Merridy, speaking with sudden seriousness in a grown-up voice. "Merridy, I think Savannah has a pooey bum."

Savannah had not stopped smelling since her mother deposited her on the kitchen table. But Tildy in her haste to join Ray at Freycinet Lodge had forgotten to leave nappies. By four in the afternoon, Merridy discovered that she had run out of her reserve supply, and so, to distract the children with an expedition, she loaded them into her car, a challenge in itself, and drove to Talbot's where Rose-Maree reacted with a look of feral curiosity to be asked about nappies.

"Row four – where cereals used to be."

Talbot's had sold out of Huggies for girls. The boy's Huggies that Merridy bought would keep slipping down over the weekend.

Merridy had left the three children sitting peacefully in the car, but two of them had managed to undo their seat belts. She found Montana at the wheel and Zac with a gleeful expression switching on and off the headlights and the windscreen wipers going full tilt. With a terrific struggle, she strapped both children back in their seats.

For the rest of the weekend, she supervised the children in the garden, trying to encourage them to paint and fielding questions.

"What's this?" asked Zac.

"A dragon lizard."

"It's not moving."

"No," she agreed. "Bring it over to paint, if you like."

"No thanks," said Zac, who looked as if he might prefer to eat it. He tossed the shrivelled thing behind one of the gravestones. "What about that?"

She gazed at the thin stalk in the earth. "A geranium," she said. And to herself: Still hanging on. Foolishly.

"Looks dead," exultant.

And at breakfast, squinting at the contents of the glass dish: "What's that?"

"Lemon marmalade. Here, have some."

"It's got weeds in it. I don't like weeds."

And at lunch: "I don't like sea-horse tails."

"That's pasta."

"No, it's not. It's sea-horse tails."

"What would you prefer?"

"I'd like Coco Pops."

"But you had them for breakfast."

"No, I didn't."

She glared back at him. Shocked at the distance between this face and the face that she had stroked moments after his birth in the Royal Hobart. You uttered bird-like squawks and when I smelled your breath it was as if it had come up through a dank rock. You opened an eye and it was by far the most ancient thing I'd ever seen. You . . .

But Zac did not appreciate being looked at. It was then that he landed his punch. She was removing his plate when he asked: "Where are your children?"

"I don't have any."

"Why not?"

"Because I don't want them." And sensing herself ill-equipped to be in the presence of a child to whom she had not spoken the truth, she stood up and carried her godson's plate to the sink. But when she turned around Zac's mouth hung open and the hairy legs of his words flailed out of it.

"Does Alex have one?"

"No, he has . . . he has . . ." But what did he have, her husband? Zac's question made her frightened. She had a powerful image of Alex going off with someone as she had gone off with the chandler. She saw her fate with absolute clarity of vision, as described with such relish each week in Tildy's magazines. He would trade her in for a younger model and she would join the great confederacy of unused women.

Her eye stabilised on the Welsh dresser. "He has his ships."

But Zac, staring down into his mug of rainwater, had spotted something floating.

"What's that?" for the first time wanting to know.

She took the mug from him. "A wasp, it looks like."

"I don't like wasps." He pushed back his hair and she caught sight of an ugly scab.

In a new voice full of concern she asked: "Zac, how did you get that?"

*

At night, she calmed them with stories. She did her best to interest Zac in Edward Lear, but he was not having it. Tildy had packed his favourite book. He wanted to be read that.

"Where did your mother find this?"

"The Op-Shop." Like many of Tildy's things.

"Then before I begin, I'm going to ask again. How did you get that scratch?"

"Mummy bit me," looking uncomfortable.

"What do you mean, she bit you?"

"She did. She bit me."

"I don't believe you, Zac."

"It's true," Tildy confirmed later with not a smidgen of shame. "His ear was next to my face. I was so annoyed, I bit it."

Her sleeve was being tugged at. "Get on."

He was asleep before she reached the end. She looked at the smile on the pillow and saw that he did not have his father's mouth but Tildy's and was glad. She read on anyway, reluctant to leave a story unfinished. Even one so derivative.

"*The rider of an old horse who had galloped through the darkness slowed to a canter and then to a trot and reined in above the bay. The man looked down and took brief note of the unusual colours, then spurred his horse and rode off across the sea.*"

On New Year's Eve, Merridy was woken by Zac screaming. The boy stared at her through a veil of sleep and horror and threw an arm across his eyes, moaning. She coaxed him back to sleep in the bed that she had bought in the first months of her marriage, a different child in mind, and thought of Ray and Tildy, in all probability making their fourth baby, and for the first time admitted to herself: Who in their right mind would want *this*? What if it's better the way it is?

Soon it was safe to close the door. On couches in the living room, Tildy's two younger children snored through blocked noses. She opened the window and breathed in. The clear air affronted by the smell of Savannah's nappy.

She crawled back to bed and hugged her husband. The children would be leaving the next day.

“What’s wrong?” he sniffled, half-succumbed to Savannah’s cold.

“It’s all right.”

“What’s all right?”

“We have each other.”

But if she thought it was over, it was not. At breakfast, Tildy telephoned to say that Ray had developed kidney stones. “We have to take him to Hobart. Isn’t it typical? They say this is something that comes the moment you start to relax.” The ambulance was on its way. He would have to be operated on immediately.

Tildy went on: “Listen, I’ve used up all my red chips with Ray’s mother. The truth is, Merridy, no one will take my children. Could you look after them? Please? It’ll only be for a few days. And they do adore you.”

CHAPTER EIGHT

WELLINGTON POINT SUMMER FLOWER SHOW:
Vegetable and fruit: onions over 8oz – H. Ford.
Flower arranging (themed arrangement) – Garden of Eden. Joint First: Rose-Maree Kemp, Merridy Dove.

Thereafter, the subject of their childlessness was added to the list of no-go areas that included Ray Grogan, Merridy's university course, the Doves' car crash, Alex's penny and Hector's disappearance. Something that they did not mention. Like a couple who years before had come to an agreement never to talk about it.

When exactly nine months later, Tildy gave birth to Cherokee, Alex and Merridy consoled themselves in the same unspoken way: They could not afford a child, it would wreck the shape of their lives, it was not meant to be.

Nonetheless, they had had a tough trot, and it might have continued. Alex had his land, and this gave him satisfaction. But what about her? The solidity he found in his farmwork was denied Merridy. It was not enough to redecorate the house, or replant the garden, or potter around in the dunes, or seek the ultimate in red pasta sauces, or once a year cook big mutton roasts for the shearers, or make the daily journey into Wellington Point to collect the *Mercury* and milk, plus a blueberry muffin over which to read the crime column.

But what to do? Her abbreviated time at uni was a broken arrowhead inside her and more excruciating that any kidney stone. She had cancelled her subscription to *Engineering World*, but if ever she glanced at the spines in the spare room – the two shelves of textbooks and, above them, the single row of children's books – a complicated regret assailed her. She felt her father's disappointment that she had not achieved her tiny miracle. Worse, she had not given herself the chance to know even what she would have been good at. And yet too late to go back to college. Besides, to leave Alex on his own was out of the question. So she tried to entertain visions of herself driving the elderly at the wheel of the community bus. As a firey. Or a volunteer for the ambulance service. Or reading stories to children at the day care. But none of these options excited her.

She had become conscious, too, of another no-go area. They were running out of money.

It remained a source of pride with Alex that he had not merely broken even during the first years of their marriage but had steered the farm into modest profit. Then, he could still afford a cleaner once a week: Alice, who brought her blonde, curly-headed daughter to play on the lawn while she ironed his shirts and trousers, or dusted his bottle collection. In the expectation of continued profits, Alex had supported Merridy in her makeover of the house. He had footed the bills for three rounds of IVF treatment and bought her a car and paid her a monthly allowance. But he concealed from his wife that money had since become an issue.

Like other farmers Alex lived on an overdraft, but interest rates had risen so steeply that he was overstretched. He had looked into harvesting different crops – poppies, walnuts, wine, peas – but it would almost certainly take several years before he generated the sort of turnover to satisfy his bank. Meanwhile, income came in twice a year, barley at a different time from cattle and wool sales. And it was not enough.

While Alex had made his share of mistakes, there was no avoiding some costs. He had had to raise the dam by a metre after a bad drought in which the barley failed to come up. A pivot irrigator set him back the equivalent of a year's income. And when his father's ancient tractor expired halfway up Barn Hill, he had little option but to replace it with a John Deere, bought second-hand off Jack Fysshe. That tractor was nearing the end of its life, as often on a block in Nevin's garage as in the paddocks. He could not see any way to affording a new one.

Little by little, Alex had gnawed away at the investments left him by his parents until less than $7,000 remained. A further fall in the price of wool or a hefty garage bill could wipe him out. On top of it all, his bank was making persistent demands that he find ways to reduce his overdraft.

TALBOT'S STORE. Applications are invited for a temporary holiday worker. Some experience in the service industry desirable.

One Thursday towards the end of January, Alice failed to turn up.

"That's unlike her," Merridy said at lunch, and kept turning her eyes to the window.

Until Alex looked from his plate. "I've let her go."

Merridy failed to understand. "Go where?"

In a flat voice, he explained. His father's folks had paid for his education. Now Uncle Matt was dead in Sedbergh, and there was no one in the family whom he could draw on for a loan. "We don't have a brass razoo and the ANZ is saying: 'We own 67 per cent of your farm and we are thinking of making this asset of ours a little bit liquid.'"

"What about Ray? Doesn't he specialise in loans?"

No sooner had she blurted the words than she was chiding herself. Alex would never seek a solution with Ray Grogan, who according to Tildy had made a complete recovery and roared across the bay at the helm of an even faster boat.

In the evening, Merridy came to where Alex sat in the living room.

She reached for his hand. "How's that sunspot?" turning it over and inspecting the back of it. "You should let Dr Musgrove take a look." Then: "Listen, Alex, I've been thinking. Maybe I can kick in."

"You?" moving his stare from the fire. He needed spectacles now, and orange flames licked his lens where she expected to meet his eye. "How?"

She had her father's inheritance, she reminded him. "Take it."

"I can't, Merridy," in a dismal voice.

"Oh, don't be so proud, Alex. I want to help."

"How much is it?"

She told him. And glimpsed behind the reflected firelight the painful modesty of the sum.

"No, Merridy. That's for you. I'll have a word with my agent. He's lent money to Jack before. I'm certain he'll let me borrow off him."

Nonetheless, from this moment she cast about for a way to support her husband.

Alice had been a tolerable cleaner, but her broom rarely troubled anything suspended on a wall. A week after Alex dispensed with Alice's services, Merridy was dusting the mantelpiece in the living room when she observed a cobweb trailing from Lear's cockatoo. The discovery motivated her to take a damp cloth and sponge down each and every picture in the house.

So she washed the samplers in the corridor, the Ackermann of Merton College gardens, the foxed print of Sedbergh chapel, until she progressed to her own pencil drawing in the spare bedroom. She wiped the glass frame – and for the first time in many years found herself rereading her childish handwriting.

Plans of a sieve, series 6. General arrangement. Dimensions: 64ft 3 inches diameter; depth 7ft 6 inches; draft: 6ft.

She was tidying the angle of the frame when the urge overwhelmed her to leave the room, get out of the house.

Merridy walked down to Moulting Lagoon. It was seven weeks after her encounter with the chandler and nothing had happened. Her period had come three weeks later, since when she had tucked him away.

Where the lagoon fed into the river was a picnic spot with a wooden hut and the old jetty from which Alex's father had dived and fished. The lagoon was a part of his property, a part of his life, that Alex was not remotely interested in, and so Merridy had made it hers. She had taken to going there more and more.

Put put put. She was sitting at the end of the jetty when coming up the river was a speedboat with a buoyant-looking face at the wheel. She thought for a heart-stopping moment: What am I going to do?

But it was not the chandler.

She watched the boat approach. There was something odd about the man who threw out the line. He was dressed in a black rubber suit, so he must have been skin-diving.

He stepped onto the deck of yellowed planks, each board scratched and bouncing underfoot, and tied the rope with a dripping hand. Under his wetsuit, it was impossible to gauge how old he was.

Out in the river, something large came to the surface and slurped. For a second, he forgot all about Merridy. "Oh look, oh look," to himself, "a Fizzgiggious Fish."

"*. . . who always walked about upon Stilts because he had no legs.*"

The man turned, surprised, and the smile on his face broadened. "Hey!"

He sat down heavily beside her. He had an accent like Alex's, only more pronounced. A Pom for sure.

"I've always liked the look of this place. Yours, I suppose?"

"My husband's."

"Do you know what, if it were mine, I would do here?" kicking out his rubber legs and contemplating the slightly hairy toes that protruded.

"What would you do?" She was perfectly open, utterly unprepared.

"To my eye, I think it's crying out for oysters."

"I'm just brewing a cup of tea. Would you like one? I've only one cup."

"Don't you worry, madam. I'll take it out of the kettle!"

"Don't be silly."

She lifted the kettle off the Primus stove and poured. They settled down, sipping from the same cup, passing it back and forth.

"What makes you say oysters?" she said.

"Well, it's sheltered, the right size. You've got the ocean and the river. Best of all, it's undisturbed. I've been past here many a time and I've never seen anyone near here."

"Why is your boat called the *Lobster*? Do you fish for them?"

"I used to, in another life, but it keeps me in mind of a French poet, mad as a hatter, who used to walk a lobster on a lead up the Champs-Elysées. Someone asked him what the fuck . . . and he said: 'It doesn't bark and it knows the secrets of the sea.' Rather charming. But what you need right here in this ideal spit is to farm oysters."

"What would one have to do to make an oyster?"

"Not much. A female oyster spawns forty million eggs. The sea does the rest. You need a vessel, low flung, something you can stick things on. As for the tackle, I've got a mucker who's getting out of scallops in Triabunna and would sell his stuff. I was with him two days ago and he said to me: 'How in God's name can I get rid of all this?' He's moving into mussels and throwing out ropes, floats, scallop lanterns, everything you need. I'll ring him tonight, if you like. It's not going to be expensive, and I could collect it in my van and drop it off next time I'm passing."

She looked at him long and hard. This man who had come up out of the sea with a solution. Because in the last seven weeks she had nursed the bubbling hope that an unknown person might have given her a last chance. But it had not happened.

"You could have had his boat, too," he said, handing her back her cup, "except that someone smashed into it. The thing is, you should get it properly made. Design it yourself and it's all yours."

She flew back to the house on eagle's wings. It was so obvious, what he suggested. She had been staring at it ever since her second visit to the farm when she climbed the ladder to the windmill. The view down to Oyster Bay was something that she never tired of, whatever its moods or hers. Why should it *not* contain her future?

That evening Alex came home from drenching the sheep and saw her face. "What?"

"I've decided what to do with Dad's inheritance."

He implored her: "Please don't say you're going to open a B & B?"

She worried that the man in the boat would forget, but a fortnight later there it all was, in a heap inside the shed. Together with a note in a waterproof folded envelope: "Dear Madam, wishing you all the luck in the world. If you would be kind enough to send a cheque to this man . . ." Signed: "Joseph Silkleigh."

She sent off the cheque to Triabunna. She would love to have been able to say thank you. But she never saw Mr Silkleigh again, this strange-looking, slightly scholarly *deus ex aqua* who had seeded in her an idea.

CHAPTER NINE

SHE SPENT A DAY at an oyster farm outside St Helen's, led around by a skinny, introverted man with thinning white hair that the wind blew about, and a patch over his right eye. He had skewered his eyeball when clearing boobyalla on a block near Wellington Point. Les Gatenby knew right enough where she lived. He had started his farm twenty years ago and was happy to lend Merridy all his papers and books – most of which originated in British Columbia, where they had been harvesting Pacific oysters since before the Second World War.

Over the following months, Merridy read everything that she could about oysters. In a way that she never managed to feel when researching into IVF, she had the impression of picking up the degree she had left off. Not since her first term at uni had she experienced such a longing to study, such an elating sense of purpose.

Her confidence returned. Once it grew warm, she moved into Alex's old workshop. He had transferred his office to the post room, a brick building behind the shearing shed. Years had passed since he had occasion to hide himself away among his father's ship collection.

She tidied away the tools onto the shelves, next to the bottles. She took down her father's engineering manuals and spread them on the worktable. And over the following days designed an aluminium catamaran: ten metres long with a big, broad beam and pointed bow, a crane to hold the lanterns, a cabin to keep out the weather, and gutters to make it easier for her to clean the deck.

The naval architect in Launceston to whom she showed her plans was approving. "This one will take on anything."

"That's the idea."

For economy, he would shave out the gutters and cabin. Otherwise, he kept faithfully to her drawings. A month later, his design was ready.

Spending half of her father's inheritance, Merridy commissioned a boat yard in Launceston to build the boat; not Hobart, which was identified in her mind with her last despairing fling.

She named her the *Zemmery Fidd.*

"Where the Oblong Oysters grow," she explained to Alex.

The boat was the main expense. Thanks to Mr Silkleigh she already had tackle. Next to sort out was the lease. The Department of Sea and Fisheries was encouraging. For $2,500 a year, she bought a thirty-year lease from the Crown.

If Alex had misgivings, he suppressed them. It was obvious that his wife's mind was set. Long ago, he had given a promise to her mother. And it took the edge off his worries to support her in a venture about which she felt more and more involved. Merridy's oyster farm would be, as she put it to Tildy, her baby.

The *Zemmery Fidd* was already being built in a shipyard on the Tamar when she arranged the construction of a new shed on the banks of Moulting Lagoon. She looked at seeding her own oysters, but Gatenby warned: "You'll need alarms and water controls and temperature gauges – plus you'll have to work seven days a week." Seedlings were dirt cheap anyway. For an investment of $2,000 she bought 8,000 dozen, two months old, from Shellfish Culture in Bicheno, and spent a weekend rolling them in plastic mesh. Then stapled the ends and floated them temporarily from the jetty in scallop lanterns.

The lanterns were partitioned, with individual trays at different levels, and compactable. They reminded Merridy of her brother's Slinky.

One noon, hauling them up, she heard a shout. "That's a sheila doing that!" Men from the power company, down having their lunch. She waved back, chuffed. Oysters was a blokey industry, like salmon. Not too many sheilas doing handlings.

Everything on the river was done by hand, the labour backbreaking. Initially, she wore baggy men's clothes, but in her second season Merridy found a New Zealand firm to make her a pair of bright green overalls. "I want to feel flattered."

Not that tighter overalls made her feel especially feminine. She felt dirty and ugly and different. And in a way she was different. She changed physically. Around her chest and shoulders she grew bulkier from lifting the ten-kilo lanterns. She found it hard to squeeze into her old clothes.

Regulations forbade Merridy to work on her own, so she employed an assistant, Jason, an absent-minded bass guitarist from Cranbrook who accompanied her on the *Zemmery Fidd.*

The oysters required handling every couple of months. She and Jason hoisted them from the river and sieved them and progressively stored the seedlings in larger meshes until they were ready for the sea. Then they were packed back into the lanterns and loaded onto the boat and relocated to Oyster Bay, where they put on a spurt of growth. At thirty months her first oysters were ready to sell.

Sometimes she imagined Mr Silkleigh coming back up the creek. Merridy would like to have told him about where his suggestion had led. To have shared just a fraction of her exasperation. But he never did reappear. Nor was there anyone she could hire as a consultant – save for Les Gatenby, and he very soon became her competitor. She had to learn by herself.

To begin with, she felt that she was holding the whole project together with nothing stronger than wire. The shed had no electric power. Her first job every morning was to light a fire.

She had no idea how to tie knots. The octopuses were adept at unpicking her ropes, until she met a cray-fisherman in Coles Bay who taught her a slip knot that he called a Grinner. "Just tie this one on everything."

She could not tell the wind direction; it might be blowing on her face and she would not know whether it was a south-easterly or northerly, or what it was.

She knew nothing about tides. That before a sudden change of weather the tide sometimes failed to go out; and sometimes it went out and did not come back in for a couple of days.

"And I never ever seem to have enough gear," she complained to Alex. It was not simply that if she left anything out, a float or a rope, thieves would take it. The oysters grew so fast that she found herself lacking the equipment to put them back in the water.

A lot of the equipment she made herself. She cut out the mesh and folded it into baskets. She unearthed a sewing machine that had belonged to Alex's mother and stitched up the ends of sacks. Life on the jetty improved in the second year when she bought a small generator from the Macdonalds.

There was a dirt track to the shed, but only people who had lost their way ever travelled down it. Because of its location, no one liked to come in to Oblong Oysters. If the outboard engines packed up, she piled them into the flat tray of her Toyota and drove to Gravelly Beach Marine on the Tamar.

Then there were the storms that blasted through and tore up her lines, plunging the lanterns to the bottom. The banks in Hobart and Launceston that told her to go away – "because we don't have any data on your industry". The daunting paperwork that she was required to submit to the Department of Sea and Fisheries.

"Don't you love these abbreviations, especially if you don't read the first paragraph and go skimming. What do you think a tassqap is?"

Alex could not recall it from the Scrabble dictionary. "A native sea slug?"

"A Tasmanian Shellfish Quality Assurance Programme."

Like this, it was nearly two years after Merridy registered her business before she made her first sale. To a wholesaler in Victoria chosen with a pin from an old Melbourne telephone directory.

"No worries, send me two hundred dozen."

Merridy was so particular that it took her all day to pack eight bags. Soon she would be able to pack two hundred dozen oysters in an hour. Not that Anton seemed overly impressed by the stuff she was sending.

They had done business for five months when he telephoned to cancel an order: "We've had to throw out your last shipment."

"Why?"

"It smelled."

"What of?"

"I don't know, a customer didn't like the smell."

"What does that mean?"

"It means we're not paying for it," with an offsider's laugh.

"But, Anton, I've got the POD with your signature. Why wait two weeks to tell me?"

"Sorry, Mrs Dove. If you don't like what I'm saying, feel free to go elsewhere."

"Well, I *don't* like it."

One thousand one hundred dollars down the drain. Another six weeks before she found a new wholesaler, this time through Les Gatenby.

That throughout this period Merridy kept her head above water was chiefly thanks to Alex, who knew about the pitfalls of trespassing into new and unknown territory when you are fired up with passion but have zero expertise. With her husband's support, the goad of her father's memory and the painstaking stewardship of her inheritance, Merridy built up the oyster farm. Until four years after the launch of the *Zemmery Fidd*, Alex discovered a curly-headed young woman in the kitchen ironing his shirts.

He continued down the corridor to his old workroom.

Merridy sat on a swivel chair behind a large new desk, writing. Pinned to a corkboard was a mud-map showing the distribution of her lanterns. Otherwise, the same view through the window onto the edge of the lawn and the Oyster Bay pine. The same fleet of ships on the shelves. And her Gory Box in the corner.

He coughed. "Isn't that Alice's daughter?"

"It is." She signed her name and handed the rectangular piece of paper to Alex.

"What's this?"

"Just read."

He dug his spectacles out of his shirt pocket and put them on. A cheque. Enormous. Made out to P. A. Dove.

"What's this for?"

"A tractor."

TIDY TOWN MEETING. "Keep Australia Beautiful". Snowy Dingle, Tidy Town Judge, Tasmania, will talk about gorse eradication and how to get rid of crack willow in your waterways. Town Hall, Sunday March 7th, 10 a.m. onwards. Information from Tildy Grogan.

*

Merridy suspended her oysters in the sea for their last six months. In the centre of the bay, she laid out seven long lines, made from 600 metres of polypropylene rope. At a man's depth below the surface, she tied the scallop lanterns full of oysters. She floated them with the oysters evenly spaced apart. She had inherited her meticulousness from her father, her stubbornness from her mother.

She had chosen Pacific over natives because of the latter's higher mortality rate. The hole through which she repeatedly had scanned the southern horizon for a fugitive pea-green sail was bored, she learned, by a ferocious little parasite that attached itself to the top of the native shell and killed it, exactly as it had killed off the flat native oysters of England. Pacifics were not susceptible to so many predators. Only if they touched the bottom of the bay.

"If they get to touch bottom, then the whole world comes. It's like a biology lesson," she explained to Alex.

Not just octopus and stingrays and dough-boy scallops galore, but skates and sea urchins and – worst of all – starfish. From now on, scarcely a summer went by without her grizzling to Alex about the starfish. They were like flies, vomiting stomach juices onto the young oyster and breaking down the shell so that the starfish could suck it up.

Protective of her oysters, she regarded Moulting Lagoon as their natural home, but during her fifth season a natural disaster startled Merridy into a realisation that she could not have been more mistaken: the lagoon was holding them back.

A bad rain in the middle of January wiped out 95 per cent of her seedlings. The river grew too hot. Not only that: the rain flooded the river with fresh water and this streamed into Moulting Lagoon. The oysters took a little sip to check if the salt water had returned, and when they discovered that it had not, closed up. Ten days on, and still only fresh water in the lagoon.

Alex could not have been more relieved, but for Merridy the rain that raised the level of his dam and replenished the aquifer beneath Dolphin Sands spelled catastrophe.

In normal conditions, the fresh water sat on top and the seawater ran in underneath. Even during a storm, the salt water would sneak in. This time, no such luck. The lagoon was not emptying. Metres of rain kept coming down, kept flowing from the mountains into the river. More water coming down the mountains than upriver, and no wind to stir it. And the oysters could not wait any longer, they had to feed. But hunger was not their sole concern.

"They think the end of the world's come. They think this is their last chance to reproduce."

Panicked, the oysters opened their shells and drank and tried to spawn. But to drink hot, fresh water was not a good combo.

Exhausted by their premature spawning, the oysters succumbed to bacteria in the hot water. They died at the speed of the bush fire that in the same year raced through Friendly Beaches. Merridy's losses were huge.

She despaired about what to do with the surviving seedlings, only ten weeks old. As a last resort, she telephoned Jason, and they loaded the *Zemmery Fidd*. Merridy had little reason for optimism. She had taken it as Gospel that the species was not evolved enough to survive on pure salt water. That the Pacific oyster did not exist which grew all its life in the ocean. More or less everyone in the industry shared Gatenby's belief: "If you're stupid enough to grow your seedlings in the sea, they'll die in a day." As she dropped the seedlings overboard, she had the notion that she was burying them.

But out in Oyster Bay a miracle happened.

It gave her more intense pleasure even than to buy Alex a tractor. Fifteen months after the flood that all but destroyed her harvest, Merridy brought home a bucket containing two dozen live oysters. The first that she had cultivated from seed in Oyster Bay.

"I guess you could say they're really pretty-looking," passing one to Alex. "A lot more water flow. Not with mud and silt settling on them. I'm getting into feeling glad it happened."

And watching her husband inspect the craggy, purple-white oyster that she had grown in the sea she was overcome by the certainty of her affection for him. They had come out of their tangle and the road stretched ahead; it was not the road they had started on, but she could see where it led and the knowledge no longer made her despondent.

*

Merridy's decision to relocate her lanterns in the bay did more than safeguard the oyster farm: it guaranteed a demand for her produce that was unstoppable. Sure, the rough water rumbled the topmost trays. The oysters in those trays were smaller as a result, their shells more friable. She passed anxious days worrying in case the trade rejected them. On the contrary. The splitters in Melbourne found that they could shuck twice as many of Merridy's thinner-shelled oysters. Around Christmas time, it was her sea-grown oysters that the restaurateurs in St Kilda savoured above their Tasmanian river cousins. Their salty ocean taste and sharpness of flavour and distinct colouring. Most important of all, the customers clamoured for Oblong Oysters – although this would take a while for Merridy to discover.

Dmitri, her new wholesaler in Melbourne, was a Greek of few words, and these reluctantly spoken during their fortnightly telephone conversations. Les Gatenby had recommended him as "a real straight-shooter". They had yet to meet, but Dmitri had made a verbal agreement to take a pallet of 600 dozen a week.

On Monday afternoons, Merridy watched the shipment leave her shed in the East Coast Freight van – always with a tinge of sadness at the sight of the door rolling down on the pallet. The oysters were now out of her care, and she pictured their onward journey with the involved concern of any guardian. Van to Hobart. Into a container. Trucked to Devonport. Across on the *Spirit* and landing at 11.00 a.m. Wednesday in Melbourne fish market where Dmitri's splitters waited.

She had no idea if her competitors bothered much about what happened to their produce once it left their sheds, but Merridy cared. Dmitri's lack of feedback maddened her. "You're a customer, Dmitri, but you're not the final customer. What did you think of that shipment? Was it the right size? What are customers saying?"

"Beautiful oysters – and send me some more next week. Oh, and I like the hessian packaging."

"That's as far as he goes," she raged to Alex. "When I send him crackerjack oysters and he goes, 'Yeah, they're all right, can you send me two extra pallets?' – that's when I know they're fantastic."

One night – he must have been drinking – Dmitri telephoned,

and this time verged on the loquacious. He talked about his health and daughter, and towards the end of his call invited Merridy to Melbourne to discuss a business proposition.

"I don't have time to go to Melbourne, Dmitri. Let's talk about it now."

This was not Dmitri's method. Always in their telephone conversations thereafter he was sure to raise the subject of a meeting – "One to one, no lawyers, just you-me".

His persistence began to irritate. One evening, she declared: "I will never come back to Melbourne – not until you tell me what your customers think of my oysters."

Silence. Then in his grave surly voice: "You ask what the customers say? They say your oysters are so good, you get a stiff neck when you eat them!"

At some point she would have to yield to Dmitri's pleas and fly to Melbourne. For the moment, though, she was happy with their arrangement. Dmitri's guarantee to buy a pallet and a half every week ensured that money flowed in on a regular basis, easing the pressure on Alex. But money was the least of Merridy's pleasures. Every time she emptied out a lantern filled with her Pacific oysters, she felt like a pioneer in the early days of a new industry; and there was the pride she took in her boat.

Because the *Zemmery Fidd* had such a wide beam, she was safe in most weathers. This meant that Merridy was called out to help vessels in distress if the police launch in Bicheno could not reach them in time, or if the sea was too rough for the 18-foot coastguard boat in Swansea. When a high-speed rubber dinghy, on a joyride in Coles Bay, tipped off six people – and there were a few broken bones besides – Sergeant Finter had no sympathy. He chewed out the survivors: "You'd have drowned if it hadn't been for Mrs Dove."

FREYCINET COURT HOTEL. Talbot's Newsletter *would like to extend a warm welcome to Murray Went, the new proprietor. Two licensed bars and restaurant. Open for bookings. "We look forward to seeing you."*

That same summer they lost Flash. The restorative air had given the creature a new lease of life. The lifespan of a Border collie was generally no more than twelve years. Smelly, blind, lame, Flash was almost seventeen when Alex pressed the cold barrel of his Purdey to her trusting neck.

He and Merridy were left desolate. For six weeks, Alex could not bring himself even to begin looking for a replacement. But the farm needed a working dog and he used the occasion of Merridy's birthday to give her a puppy that was part collie, part golden retriever. Rusty had a pedigree from Europe on both sides, said the woman at the Kennel Club – who added what an ass Jennifer was to have left a champion bitch on heat playing behind the clubhouse with Sally's retriever. She pointed out Rusty's extraordinary feet, built to run on sand, and remarked how sensible of Alex to choose this combination of breeds. "I have known this mixture before and they give endless pleasure to children."

She did not have children, but at thirty-six Merridy had never felt so clear-headed, so precise in her thoughts and movements. Whereas before she had melted from life, now she strode towards it. She was confident that her stripe of grief had been removed. Perhaps removed messily as a gland is removed. But removed.

Until one mild early morning when she was steering the *Zemmery Fidd* across the bay, the same uneventful and endless stretch of sea that her marriage had become, the realisation came to her that she was uncomplicatedly content. After so many years of fretfulness and frustration, her anxieties seemed resolved into the sea. At last, it suited her to be on this rim of the world. She no longer scanned the horizon for a phantom sail. She looked down into the sea. At her achievement. There might not be a God, but there was the sound of the waves, now hushed, now loud, galloping on through the day and night for ever.

PART III

Oyster Bay, 12–16 December 2004

CHAPTER ONE

OBSERVATIONS FROM THE FRONT LINE. We have noticed with alarm the growing pilfering by young boys of goods in shops. Maybe names should be named. The editor will give thought to this matter. A.T.

No one forecast the storm. Not on Merridy's radio nor in the *Mercury*. It came out of a day so calm and bright and blue that Ray Grogan had locked his office three hours early to go fishing.

It was such a rare afternoon that as soon as Albert Talbot observed Ray's trailer approaching the ramp, he did what he had not done in a long while. He put down his binoculars, abandoned his customary position at the top-storey porthole and shuffled down the back staircase to watch at close quarters. Ray's gleaming craft was the envy of Talbot's proprietor and put the former coast-watcher in mind of the American patrol-boat that had dropped him ashore in New Britain. Even though it was his basic rule that any time you went down to the coast you struck trouble, there was also a tricky matter that he needed to broach with Ray, about his son Zac. Hired by Talbot's for the holiday season, Merridy's fourteen-year-old godson had been caught in the act of removing a wad of notes from the till.

In the event, Albert did not manage to speak to Ray, but he inched his way along the jetty in time to overhear the following conversation.

Ray stood, hands on the hips of his shorts, beside a white van, waiting for a man in a wetsuit to haul his speedboat out of the water.

"You all done for the day?" Ray called impatiently.

"That's right," said the diver, who had an oxygen cylinder strung from his shoulder and goggles pushed up over his head.

"A bit early in the season to be packing up, isn't it?" and screwed up his eyes to read the make of the boat.

"Well, don't take the blindest piece of notice of me, but there's a gale up ahead, and one you won't want to mess with, you mark my words."

But Ray was more interested in the man's boat. "What is she, actually?"

"A Cobalt runabout with a 260-horsepower Volvo inboard engine. Sometimes known as a Bow Rider because you can sit in front. Really, she's a lake boat, although I do find she's terrific for reefs."

"But there are no reefs around here," objected Ray.

The man stared at him with a strange frankness and replied in a tone of sacramental gravity: "There are reefs, old soul, everywhere."

Ray looked up from the boat to the side of the van. *THE LONG HAUL.* The words reminded him of his marriage. "Where are you from?" puzzled, and tugged at the gold chain around his neck. "You're clearly not from here or you'd still be out there."

The man waved a yellow snorkel at Ray's trailer. "Trust me, you should be keeping yours out, not putting her in."

"Never! You blow-ins don't know your arses from your elbows. If ever there was a perfect afternoon to go and drown a few worms this is it."

"Then all I'm going to say to you, old soul, is slacken your guy ropes."

When Grogan's boat *Follow Me* smashed into the jetty less than two hours later, everyone except Albert was taken by surprise. The old man watched the gusts of wind needling his window, packed with sea-spray and sand to obliterate his view, and mumbled to himself: "I wonder who that clever dick was? How did he know what no one else knew?"

The storm thundered in like a log-truck. It hit the beach late afternoon, the cold wind moaning as it passed through the telegraph wires, clattering off a loose sheet of tin from the shearing shed and popping out the wooden stays.

Its vindictiveness alarmed Merridy. The lagoon had thrown back a clear, pale sky when the van collected the oysters at five. She had left Jason to lock up and driven home to take a shower and afterwards sit in the kitchen, as she liked to do, reading the *Mercury*. She had changed into the soft green jersey that she had bought years before at a trekking shop in Hobart, though it felt small on her, and a pair of new trainers; her long, fine face lined against the no longer transparent afternoon light.

A breeze blew up from the beach, slamming the door, but she was accustomed to strong winds in December. She hardly noticed it filling out Alex's shirts and trousers into bloated equivalents of himself that tossed and twisted against the greying clouds. Nor the new puppy that shivered in its basket.

She turned the pages. The Pope was dying – this time there really was no way back, the doctors were saying; the Navy had intercepted near Broome a second vessel filled with boat people, all claiming to be Afghans; a report on Tasmania's increasing appeal for Japanese property speculators; and a photograph of a two-masted ship under full sail.

Something blundered against the fly-screen. She knew what it would be. Bogan moths with red eyes that liked the rain and banged against the windows and stuck to her when she tried to bat them away. Nor did she bother to look up when another door slammed. A good old southerly buster, that was all.

Soon the Crime Stoppers column absorbed her attention.

Sometime on Saturday, Elle Macpherson underwear was stolen from a garden in Lindisfarne. Her mind tiptoed after the thief to a house in North Hobart, snatching a neckwarmer, ski goggles and a centenary medal. And was emerging from a shed in Moonah tugging a Victa lawnmower when she heard a tremendous clatter.

This time Merridy reacted. She raced outside and saw that the rotary clothes-line was down, the tug of the wind so strong that Alex's airborne trousers and shirts had uprooted the Hills Hoist's concrete base. Her trainers crunched across the gravel to where her husband's clothes lay in the grass. She gathered them up and was running back to the house, arms full and her mouth stuffed with pegs, when she glanced out over the deck. Strung along the south horizon a noose of cloud was drawing in. She looked at Schouten for a telltale flash, but there was none. Only the long low cloud advancing.

Still the wind pounded up the slope to a jingling of tin. It moved at great velocity, filled with grit and dust, quarrelling with all that it touched, frittering her flower beds and unclenching the green fists of the pine tree.

Only when she stepped back inside did Merridy hear the telephone ringing above the gale.

"Mrs Dove?" came the urgent voice. "Pete Finter here."

Groggy from a bout of flu, Alex had not wanted to leave his bed, but the day was so exceptionally mild and sparkling – glisky, they would have called it in Cumbria, one of those bright borrowed days of early autumn – that he had taken advantage of the rain which had fallen in the night to plough a field on the east edge of Moulting Lagoon. For most of the afternoon he had sat warmly wrapped in the cabin of his tractor. The earth felt both squashy and hard, as if cardboard boxes were laid out underneath it and the land was a temporary thing.

Not until he stopped the tractor to swallow down a Paracetamol with a cup of Thermos tea did Alex appreciate how humid it had grown suddenly. How thick and hazy.

Wick wick, wick. A large flock of swifts passed fast overhead. He could hear the wings and the clack clack of their beaks as they fed on a hatch of insects. He was too congested to dwell on the reason for their appearance. He sipped his over-stewed tea, watching them rake the sky against a lens-shaped cloud. Then he screwed the top back on his flask and returned to ploughing the field.

Protected by the pine break, Alex did not feel the force of the wind until he drove his tractor onto the road an hour later. But it was not the wind that made him slam on the brakes.

Less than fifty yards away, right on the edge of David Macdonald's property, a ghost shambled between the gums.

Alex stared into the bush. Heart chugging at the bright white figure that he saw there. The puzzle was the colour. Bill Molson confided to Alex's father that he had seen a blue child hasten along the marshes where the black swans laid their eggs. Possibly he had. Not Alex, though sometimes he looked out for it on those evenings when he walked home beside the lagoon.

He slipped the tractor into neutral and applied the handbrake, mesmerised by the pristine colour. Even as he stepped down, he recalled a matron at his house in Sedbergh who had believed in the Radiant Boy, a luminous apparition that made its appearance with dire results. Now Alex found himself speculating, with all the rational instincts of a forty-three-year-old farmer educated at Oxford, whether the ghost might be one of the family of settlers who had drowned.

A pine cone dropped at his feet. Over the fence, the spirit moved behind a thick trunk of macrocarpa, and Alex saw it for what it was: a Friesian cow with a vertical white mark on its coat that it was easy to mistake for a human being.

He kicked the cone into the bush and climbed back onto his tractor and drove on. But the mark on the cow went with him; it remained silhouetted in his head like the flash when a strong light goes out, and it was still there when he turned into his drive.

Alex watched the house come nearer through the tractor's windscreen. A grey cloud wrapping the ripple-iron roof. The fallen clothes-line. And through the window, Merridy, in oilskins, speaking in heated tones to someone, her hands winnowing the air as always when excited.

In the comfort of his cabin, he considered: What would he tell her, that he had been startled out of his skin by one of their neighbours' cows?

He parked the tractor next to the ute and walked towards the kitchen door, head down, hands pinching the bottom of his Driza-Bone pocket and pushing his smile against the gritty wind. The force of it bent back the pine on the lawn and clacked the blades of the windmill into words that belted out across the distance between Alex and the light in the kitchen, and chided him for his credulity.

*

Through the window Merridy caught sight of Alex struggling up the drive. The pressure of battling against the gale gave him the exaggerated totter of a crippled person.

"Listen, there's Alex. Let me work on him," and slammed down the receiver. She ran across the kitchen and flung open the door.

He raised his head. "You'll never guess—"

Her pressing voice competed with the windmill. "Alex, there's been an accident."

A ship was going down between the Hen and Chicks. The Marine Police in Hobart had picked up the call. They were requesting local volunteers to get into the water without delay. All the professional rescuers were indisposed.

"Finter's asked if we'd take the *Zemmery Fidd.*"

"Where's the police launch?" Alex asked.

"In Hobart for repairs."

"And the Devil cat?"

"Answering another distress call."

"What about Trevor?" Trevor was the fisherman in Coles Bay who had taught Merridy her knot and owned a cray-boat.

"On holiday."

"And David?"

"I just rang him. He's sold his boat." She was unhooking Alex's oilskins from the back door.

"You think we can? What if it's too large a sea?"

"I'm prepared to have a go – if you'll come. How are you feeling?"

"Fine," he said. "Fine."

"Here. I'll go and shut Rusty away. He'll be a wreck with this wind."

Squeezed into his oilskins, Alex followed Merridy outside to the ute. The weather that morning had been unnaturally still and warm when he left the house, the bay the smooth opaque green of a perfume bottle. Now he felt the angry smack of the wind. A sheep rolled over in the next paddock and a kookaburra that had nested in the Oyster Bay pine flew off in a twisted parasol of black and grey feathers.

He climbed in beside Merridy and turned the ignition. He was driving off when he heard a resounding crack.

In the rear-view mirror, the lawn capered and twisted. Then burst apart in a dark clot of roots and earth. The tree had toppled over.

Alex drove fast along the edge of Moulting Lagoon towards the jetty, gravel pinging against the windscreen. The storm was ripening. He had never known such a wind.

"What kind of ship?"

"A brigantine, could it be?"

"A brigantine? In Oyster Bay?"

"She's a replica. It's all over the *Mercury*. She's sailing around the island."

Bored by the idea of yet another project to do with the island's bicentenary, she had glanced at the article only out of respect for her husband and the anachronistic image of a ship that might have sailed straight out of one of his bottles. The *Buffalo* had arrived from Sydney the previous day in George Town, and was modelled on the brigantine that had landed two hundred years ago at the mouth of the Tamar, carrying the first European settlers. *Hoods at sea* ran the headline of the article, which she had not bothered to finish but reminded herself to show to Alex.

He skidded to a halt at the entrance to the oyster shed while Merridy leaped out, unlocked the gate, raced ahead.

In less than five minutes, Alex was reversing the *Zemmery Fidd*, with Merridy on board, down the bank. He aimed the stern at the lagoon and steered the ute, its wheels churning the seaweed and mud, until the aluminium hull clanked loose of its pivot and slid into the choppy water.

Merridy started the engines and nodded at Alex. By the time he had parked the ute at the top of the bank, the *Zemmery Fidd* was rocking at the jetty.

He jumped onto the deck, untied the rope. "OK."

Merridy opened the throttle and the force of the engines threw him against the crane. He held on as the boat sped into the river.

Soon they were out of the river. The *Zemmery Fidd* slammed over the bar-way and twisted into the breakers, the spray falling in heavy sheets.

Merridy punched out towards the tip of Freycinet, keeping close to the shore. The sky had darkened further. The clouds overhead a mass of shadows, now dense, now thinning, and tortured into antedeluvian shapes: hippogriffs, bulls, unicorns.

She yelled: "See anything?"

One arm hugging the crane, Alex looked out. The sea roughened and agitated. The bay rutted with deep waves. The waves not advancing in orderly lines, but frenzied like wild cattle. In the fading light, they came on at a gallop, horns down and backs tossing, sweeping water up the beach in a vivid white foam.

She called to him again. The sea had matted his thinning hair so that the skull shone through. "Well?"

He shook his head. As far as the eye could see waves kicked and reared, churning the horizon.

The boat thumped into a trough, lashing salt water into Alex's face. He ascended higher up the crane. At the crest of the next rise, he picked out Maria Island, the Isle des Foques. Then, to the right of Schouten, before a wave hid it, a tangle of white and black.

"Over there," he bellowed in the direction of the rigging. But the wind grabbed his words. "Merridy, over there."

It took the *Zemmery Fidd* twenty minutes more to reach the *Buffalo*. The brigantine was heeled in to land and lying on her side, the sea breaking over her in all directions.

A yellow shape rolled up and down the quarterdeck. Alex saw with a sick heart that it was a body.

The wind blasted fiercer. He felt his shirt heavy and wet under his oilskin and a cold razor of air slashing his face and hard bullets of rain. The waves frothed and seethed as though flames were burning under them, and the wind swooped the sea up into the sky.

"Look, Alex!" Merridy was pointing.

A dark blue figure clung to the flapping ratlines halfway up the mizzen mast.

Alex shouted.

No response.

Above the stampede, the sky had turned the colour of black lava.

He waved a hand, shouted again. His hoarse throat aching from his flu.

A head turned. A hand detached itself from the mast. And this time waved back.

CHAPTER TWO

It was, everyone agreed – although they were quite surprised, too – an amazing physical achievement. Nobody but a halfwit would have got out of that boat.

Even as Merridy brought the *Zemmery Fidd* alongside, the *Buffalo* began to tilt. The mast that a moment before had pointed up at the sky now stretched at the angle of the horizon, in the direction of Moulting Lagoon Farm. The waves rose in a boiling fountain, snatching and whipping at the man who held on, one leg crossed over the other, one arm over the other, in the stoical attitude, Alex could not help thinking, of a grub clinging under the seed head of a stalk of barley.

"Jump in!" he yelled. "Jump in!" the words funnelling off.

Less than twenty yards away, the mizzen mast juddered. It sank further, towards the grasping sea. Quite soon, it would be pointing down.

A wave licked up and there was a splash.

Already, Alex was stripping off his life jacket, his oilskins. He tugged his shirt over his head and belted his life jacket back on and leaped overboard.

The cold kicked the air out of him. He went up to take a huge breath and was slapped by a wave, inhaling it. He desperately tried to climb to the top of the water, dimly aware at the back of his mind that this was how people drowned, and broke the surface coughing.

Vast waves crashed into the existing swell and lifted him away from the *Zemmery Fidd*, towards the sinking ship.

Ten yards away an arm rose out of the sea. He flopped in its direction.

"You all right?" through his throatful of water, approaching from behind. He knew that a drowning person had nothing to fear. They pushed you down to get themselves up. But the man appeared unconscious. Alex front-crawled towards him and reached an arm under his shoulder. When he lifted the head to clear the airway vomit spewed from the mouth. He started towing the man back, one knee up in case he had to thrust him away. At every second ready for him to revive and thrash around and drag Alex under in his panic.

Alex had indeed nearly drowned, bringing in the man. He was sixteen minutes in the sea with him, before he got him onto the *Zemmery Fidd,* Alex shoving, Merridy tugging, having tied herself to the crane. At last the man rolled under the rail, into the boat.

He was so relieved to let go that Alex was caught unprepared for the wave that knocked him back. The sea filled his mouth and he started to sink. He could make out Merridy's distorted face above him, oscillating, coming and going in particles. He reached up his arm, but already he was subsiding. His fingers were grabbed just as he felt himself disconnecting.

When Alex hung his hands on the rail, he went to jelly, but with a wave helping, he held onto Merridy's wrist and hauled himself as close as possible to the stern.

Merridy pulled Alex into the boat, settling him between the engines, and returned to the body. She had laid him out on the bottom of the *Zemmery Fidd.* She knelt down, a knee on either side, water swilling everywhere, and pressed her head to the cold blue lips and inserted a few puffs of air.

"Is he alive?" between breaths. Feeling the heat of the engines on his skin.

The sea banged into the side, lurching Alex onto her.

She pushed herself up, wiping her mouth. "Have a look while I grab the wheel."

CHAPTER THREE

In Alex's childhood, south-easterlies had cast ashore a giant squid, a sunfish and on one occasion the stringy orange remains of what might have been a coelacanth. But nothing was stranger than the young man whom the Doves rescued from the bay that evening and brought back to the farm. As Merridy later explained to Sergeant Finter: "It would've been madness to try for Wellington Point, the sea running as it was."

They laid him on the bed beneath the stars that she had stencilled all those years before. Small drops of perspiration sprang from his forehead and down his neck, and the breath bubbled awkward under his tongue.

Merridy was put in mind of a horse's nose, tender and pale.

"Where do you think he's from?" unfastening the brass buttons on his jacket of heavy serge. His numbed arms and legs belonged not to any port he might have sailed from, but to some region of his own.

"Could he be a stowaway?" Alex wondered aloud. "One of those Afghans?"

Whoever he was, he looked pretty odd in his uniform, a striped sailor's top under the jacket and navy-blue trousers cut in the style of another century.

But he did not strike Merridy as Afghan. His darkness came off with a flannel, revealing a white man in his late teens. Average height. Short spiky hair dyed blond, and on his left ear a gold earring that made her think of Ray.

Alex looked at his watch. Eleven p.m. They had been away four hours. "I'd better telephone Finter."

"Yes, he ought to be told," squeezing out the flannel into a bowl of hot water.

Merridy had twice radioed Sergeant Finter from the *Zemmery Fidd*. The storm causing so much interference on the VHF that she understood nothing the policeman had said.

At the door, Alex hesitated. "Could we have done more?"

She gave him a brave smile. Remembering his expression as he sank beneath the surface. How she reached down with her whole body to catch his upraised hand. Something told her that if she failed to catch it Alex might not reappear. "No."

Alex left the room and she continued mopping the face. Eyes tight shut and streaks of tar on the scratched cheeks.

His lips opened, sucking in another laboured breath.

With great care, she rubbed at the corner of his mouth where the sand had compacted. His teeth were slanted outwards and chipped, the colour of dirty crabshell, and there was an ugly bump on his forehead.

Another breath. The way he gasped for air, he might have been crawling out from the *Buffalo*'s dark hold.

When she had finished washing his face, she raised him by the shoulders and removed the sailor's top from his limp arms, revealing the surprise of a purple T-shirt printed with a skull and a cigarette dangling from its mouth. She slipped the shirt over his head and shook off his soaked trousers.

His legs. They could have been the flanks of a horse.

And felt the weight of something.

Still he lay there, eyes closed, as Merridy drew it out of his pocket.

A silver rigging knife, well-oiled and sharp. She tested her thumb on it and winced. Then closed the 4-inch steel switchblade and carefully put it on the bedside table.

She covered him with a duvet and went to fetch some disinfectant to dab on that forehead.

The storm blew itself out in the early hours. Rain replaced the wind and then the rain stopped and there was a damp silence. Outside, the windmill stood motionless. The only sound to penetrate the curtain the nervous cough of a foal.

It was still dark when Alex got up.

Merridy smelled his metallic breath before he kissed her cheek, but did not open her eyes. She heard him let Rusty out of the living room. Their footsteps – the scrabbling of a pent-up, excitable animal and her husband's more measured tread – passed along the corridor to the kitchen.

He took down the torch from the Welsh dresser and pushed open the fly-screen and went out. Around the house, pandemonium, as if an angry Zac had thrown a tantrum on the landscape – loose sheets of tin, tree limbs everywhere and dotted here and there in the darkness the white blur of a dead sheep. The most dramatic casualty was the Oyster Bay pine. Its topmost branches had crashed onto the drive a few yards short of the living room. Flashing his torch up and down, Alex saw his parents' gravestones lopsided.

He whistled Rusty away from the exposed earth. Then crossed the lawn and walked through the farm buildings, making an inventory of the damage.

Inside the house, the silence unnerved Merridy. She lay awake, worn out but unable to sleep. Moments later, she heard a throat being cleared and quickly pulled on her clothes and stepped barefoot along the corridor.

The young man sat up as she entered. He glanced over the room, the ceiling. Rubbing his head and turning it in her direction.

She switched on the light.

His mouth hung open, red and vulnerable like a child's shoe. The face of someone who might have become a man too soon. And Merridy half-expected a neigh or a bawl.

"You're awake," looking into his eyes. But there was no bottom to them.

He peered back. With his spiky hair and unseeing eyes, he seemed like something hallucinated.

Then she understood. "Can't you see?"

"My specs," he mumbled. The accent Australian. "I lost them."

She went and fetched Alex's spare glasses.

"Here," she said. "Will these do?" They did. They fitted. They seemed to be made for him.

Glasses on, his eyes prised into her. The sabre of a smile guarding his thin, hesitant face. His eyes particularly white under her husband's lenses.

"Hello," she smiled. "I'm Merridy," and held out a hand. "Merridy Dove."

A long arm rose from the bed. Shaking hands, she could have been gripping a tiller. Then all at once he released his hold and leaned forward, fingers touching her face. Ripped by the splintery wheel or mast, their tips had the feeling of shells.

She heard her young girl's giggle. "No," she hooted, closing her eyes. As if a young boy was splashing water at her.

The kitchen door slammed.

"Alex . . ." fluting. "Could you put on the kettle?" And to him, her hand hiding her flushed throat: "Would you like some tea?"

"I . . . I don't recall."

"Then I would."

At the sound of footsteps coming down the corridor he snatched back his hand and his eyes moved to the door where Alex stood.

With Alex, his mouth was adrift; he had abandoned the certainties of speech.

"What do they call you, mate?" Alex asked, dragging up a chair and sitting down.

Without Merridy in the room, the young man looked worried, alert.

"Kish," he whispered.

When Rusty tried to lick him, he shied back.

"Come on, he's not going to eat you," Alex said gently. "Hey, Rusty, get out."

And when the dog had left: "Where were you heading, Kish?" It was strange to see someone wearing his glasses.

"Hobart Town." Rolling out his gaze from under the overhanging brows and scanning the ceiling for a path out.

Alex gave a surprised snort. "Oh, come on," he said. "Hobart."

"We were told Hobart Town. That's what the captain said."

Alex thought: The bump on his head has caused these convolutions and made him lose his place.

"How long have you been at sea?" he asked.

"We left Port Jackson . . ."

"Port Jackson? Oh, Sydney."

". . . on November the sixteenth, eighteen hundred and four."

Alex looked at him kindly. "It's OK, Kish, you're on dry land now. You can relax."

They were still at it when Merridy came back with the tea.

She poured for him and Alex resumed. "Where were you heading?"

"China. I don't know."

"You mean like those escaped convicts from Sarah Island?" said Alex cleverly.

"Or maybe it was Chile," said Kish.

This game he was playing, it had begun to annoy Alex. The young fellow behaving as though he might have been blown for ever by icy gales in a purgatory of white ridges and penguin crap. His fate to go round and round the pole.

Nonetheless, whoever had instructed him had done their work. The boy had learned his lines so well, they might have become ingrown.

Alex tried to catch him out, but Kish had an answer to everything. Where he did not reply, he deflected Alex's questions with a sawing laugh.

"Speak Dutch, do you?" Alex joked, playing his game.

Kish looked at him over his mug of tea, not speaking. His eyes unreadable. His silence tightening its hold.

Still congested by his flu and now by lack of sleep, Alex leaned forward, trying to anchor and clarify his thoughts.

Was this man having him on? Or did he seriously believe that he was a sailor from the year 1804? If he did, then he was lost in a region where no one could reach him, and certainly no one in Wellington Point. They needed to get him to a doctor.

If Kish was a ghost, his currency was worthless. Worth nothing to anyone. Like an old penny found in a grave. And Alex thought of the cow in the wood and Kish drooling in the pine needles; superfluous and dribbling.

No, he was simple, that's what he was. A simpleton. One of those street kids they took aboard ships to teach teamwork.

But Merridy did not think so. To her, Kish was a lost soul. She wanted to lead him off into a quiet corner and read his face.

"I think he needs to sleep, Alex."

Her husband took another look at the young man he had

saved. He stood up. “I spoke to Finter again. He’s been in touch with the coastguard. It looks like three of the eleven crew are missing.”

The sun had climbed over the Hazards by the time Alex stepped onto Dolphin Sands. He looked towards Maria Island. The sky red as a devil’s ear. But no sign of the *Buffalo*. The only vestige of the night before, the iodine seaweed smell and the havoc on the shoreline.

Down on the severely eroded beach, the dunes had the shapes of cliffs. Scattered all along the sand like small alligators were the blue legs of starfish, ripped from their bodies by the battering surf. And grey sea slugs – dead men’s dicks, as Pam the shearer called them. And the most shiny, perfect shells: yellow, with scribbly-gum motifs, some with the red suckers of the whelk protruding, still alive.

Alex followed two gulls. They picked their way through the seaweed, too bloated to fly until Rusty chased them. Clots of kelp lay drying in rubbery brown wigs or floated in submerged rafts close to shore. At the far end of the beach where it met the Swan River stood a solitary figure by a white van. Someone down early, no doubt to see what they could muster.

He discovered the bodies rolling in a gentle surf. Two young men, both dressed in the same naval uniforms as Kish, and the corpse of an older man, togged up in yellow wet-weather gear and heavy sea-boots with electrical tape on the tops.

Already the sun had reddened the faces, and large flies rose and fell from their lips and eyes.

The tide was coming in, so Alex, with great difficulty, propped them upright, over his shoulder, and one by one carried the bodies to the ute where he covered them with a blue tarp against the flies. He scanned the water for a further hour. The calm procession of waves for some reason reviving a fragment of a poem that his father had liked.

Between the sob and clubbing of gunfire
Someone, it seems, has time for this,

To pluck them from the shallows and bury them in burrows
And tread the sand upon their nakedness . . .

At 7 a.m. Alex drove back to the house. He left the engine running and Rusty panting on the front seat while he went inside to telephone Sergeant Finter.

The *Mercury* was open on the table and the aroma of bacon filled the kitchen. Merridy had prepared a cooked breakfast on the stove. She must have returned to bed.

He was devouring with his fingers a second warm strap of bacon when Finter answered.

"Pete, it's Alex. I have three bodies in the back of my ute."

The policeman was the only copper on this stretch of coast. He had been up all night and his reaction was not what Alex expected. "Hey, you should have left them where you found them and let us deal with that."

"Then you should have warned me about the effing gale," with a streak of irritation. "Anyway, I'd have needed sandbags."

"Fuck you, mate, nobody told me either."

"That storm, Pete, had the ingredients of a hurricane."

"Well, what I'm being told is that it was too compact and fast-moving for anyone to have predicted." Then, calming down: "Listen, Alex, thanks for finding those bodies. I'll let Emergency Services know."

"What about the boy? He needs to see a doctor."

"Can't you bring him in as well?"

"He's the one who shouldn't be moved. Not till someone's seen him."

"Leave him, he'll be right. I'll speak to Dr Musgrove. In the meantime, get those bodies over here."

Alex waited in case Finter had anything further to say, but he did not.

"How are you doing, Pete?" he asked.

Finter's laugh rattled with exhaustion. "It's a fuck-up, Alex. And if it isn't, I reckon I'll keep my eye on it till you get here."

Half an hour later, Alex drove into Wellington Point. He found the policeman's car outside the hotel, parked behind the community ambulance. He drew up alongside and climbed out and rapped on the window.

Sergeant Finter sat slumped behind the wheel. His head at an angle on his large chest. His badged blue shirt covered with sand.

"Hey, Alex," blinking, and shook his head. "Boy, I needed that."

From far away up the street, faces pressed against Talbot's ground-floor window watched Alex and Finter unload the bodies into the hotel.

They carried the dead men across the lobby to the kitchen, their passage over the carpet leaving a widening trail of seawater. They were bringing in the third and heaviest body when a total stranger ran into Alex.

"Hi, Murray," panted Finter. "Hey, have you met Alex Dove?"

"Hi," nodded Alex.

But Murray, a burly man with darting eyes, was in no mood for introductions. "Could you fetch a towel?" he snapped at Debbie who appeared in the lobby at that moment. Then padded after Alex into the kitchen, blenching when he saw the two bodies stretched out on the tiled floor.

"Murray's the new owner," explained Finter, unshouldering the dead man. "He's from near Canberra."

"Congratulations," said Alex.

Tildy's father had died three months previously, since when Ray Grogan had been advertising for a buyer.

In a drained tone, Murray asked Finter: "How long might you want to keep them here?"

"Hard to tell. The captain's got to identify them. Then you've got the coroner, and maybe a pathologist."

"It's not ideal for business, you know."

"No, probably it isn't," agreed Finter.

"How many survived?" asked Alex after Murray had gone to mop up the carpet.

"Seven altogether. With the boy you rescued, eight. They were eleven in total, with these three." Finter studied the bloated, sunburned faces. "Poor bastards. They'd have been better off playing cricket, not going to sea in a fucking brig."

Alex looked down. The skin was starting to peel from a pair of puffed-up lips. "Why did you want them in here?"

"I didn't. Nor did Murray. But Dr Musgrove does. It's the only place with an industrial fridge. The coroner's van isn't due for another few hours and Musgrove's worried about the heat."

"What, you're going to put them in with the wallaby and ice cream?"

Finter laughed. "Who's going to notice? Have you eaten here ever? Anyway, it's up to Musgrove to decide where they go."

"And the survivors?"

"In bed. Where I'd swap this badge to be."

Finter had lodged the captain in a suite in the courtyard; the six remaining crew, who were suffering from hypothermia, in the Louisa Meredith, which was now full. He hunted around for a dishcloth. "Lucky it didn't happen at Easter or I'd be having to unlock the cells," trying to be humorous.

"Have you spoken to the captain?"

"Not yet," wiping the sand from his sleeves. "I was down on Cowrie Beach when he landed in the rowboat. But I need his statement. Ah, that may even be him," at the sound of synthetic birdsong.

Alex followed him into the lobby where Murray was wringing out a towel into a washing-up bowl. "Mind if I listen in?"

Finter stopped. "I don't think so, Alex."

"Come on, Pete."

Finter looked at him and he was no longer a policeman but a boy who used to bowl Alex seamers in the nets behind the school.

"I'd like to hear what happened," Alex persisted.

"That's not the point." Then: "Hell, what am I saying – after what you did last night . . . Actually, I'd be glad of someone with a little nous myself, to help me work out what the fuck happened," and opened the door into the restaurant, setting off a trill of chaffinches. "Jesus fucking Christ, how I abominate that noise."

At a table in the corner, Debbie flustered over the captain, trying to interest him in tea and scones.

He had removed his frock coat and sat tightly wrapped in one of the hotel's green blankets, his body shaking like a rope ladder down which feet continued to trample. His expression shambolic and frayed.

"Thanks," he muttered to Debbie. His mind still at the helm of the *Buffalo*.

"You'll be relieved to know we have another survivor."

At the sound of Sergeant Finter's abrasive voice, he jerked his head. A light flickered in the dazed brown eyes. "Oh, yes?" and looked at Alex as though he might be the one.

"This is Alex Dove. He and his wife rescued one of your crew last night. At considerable risk to themselves."

At Finter's urging, Alex described the young man in his spare bedroom.

"That'll be Kish," and nodded to himself. "So he's alive," subsiding ever so slightly into his blanket. He looked like the left-overs of someone.

"Kish?" said the policeman. "How do you spell it?"

"Oh, that's not his real name," the captain said dully. "It's the name he was given. I don't know what his real name is."

In childish capital letters Sergeant Finter wrote KISH. "Like that?" showing the captain. And the troubled look on the policeman's face brought back a memory of Finter in class, sitting at a desk in front, labouring to spell the name of a medieval English king.

"I suppose so."

"I have to be accurate."

"It was a name that was invented," the captain said, moodily. "If you want to know his real name, ask Mrs Wellard."

"Mrs Wellard?"

"She's the one in charge."

"Wellard." Sergeant Finter slowly wrote out the name and looked at it. "Like it sounds?"

"Fucked if I remember," and screwed up his eyes.

The policeman selected a scone and popped it whole into his mouth. "Why don't I take your statement now?" sitting down. "Debbie, if you would – two more cups."

Debbie looked at Alex and left. Already in the street, through the window that she had obscured, small clumps of dog-walkers discussed the drama of the night and every now and then peered out to sea or pointed.

Alex brought his chair closer.

He pieced together the story from the *Mercury* and from Kish and from the captain's statement.

The three dead men were part of a sixteen-week course run by the Bilgola Mission in Sydney for disadvantaged kids. "A shipload of crims," in Finter's estimation. "People not right in the head who didn't know a boat from a banjo. Frankly, it's a sodding marvel any one of them survived."

The idea was to generate self-esteem and responsibility by sending the boys away for a period of outdoor activity. Some rock-climbed, others chose white-water rafting. This year, seven had seized the chance of joining the *Buffalo* on her circumnavigation of Tasmania. The captain had given Mrs Wellard every confidence that he could handle these "hoodlums", mainly from suburban areas around Sydney who were having trouble at home or with the law. He had led similar excursions in the Caribbean with black kids and Cubans. On such trips, generally speaking, everything went well. There was nowhere to escape to; they had to learn to work together, and while it could take several days to understand that they had to rely on each other, the outcome was nearly always positive.

Because the *Buffalo*'s expedition formed part of Tasmania's bicentenary celebrations, the captain made it his project to be as authentic as possible. He had borrowed the idea from the museum at Port Arthur. His crew were to live on board ship as if the previous two centuries had not been. "It was a lark. To get them interested." He provided each boy with a fresh identity and a biography from the convict era. He had dressed them in authentic uniforms from the period. And had issued his crew, as part of their first-day equipment, with a marine rigger's knife – "so if they fell overboard and got tangled up in ropes, they could cut themselves free. 'Just don't use it on each other,' I urged them."

Sailing down from Sydney, he taught them how to tie knots

and splice and to shake out the reefs; to learn the difference between a dolphin-striker, a fore topgallant studding-sail and a spanker-peak halyard; and to calculate their position by the stars, even though he had on board a Global Positioning System.

"Otherwise, I was just there to point and shout and scream. You wait a couple of days to see who's agile and put them on the wheel. The difficult ones peel potatoes."

"What about Kish?" Alex interrupted. "What did he do?"

On the subject of Kish's duties, the captain was evasive. "He joined us late."

"Why?"

"That you'll have to ask Mrs Wellard. But he didn't have time to settle in."

"Who was Kish?" Alex suddenly wanted to know.

"What?"

"Who was Kish in your game?"

"Alex, I do think this can wait," Sergeant Finter said. More pressing for him to know were details of the shipwreck, what had happened.

Required to relive the events of the past twelve hours, the captain shrank deeper into his green blanket. In a squashed tone he explained how he had sheltered from the south-easterly on the northern side of Maria Island. Then a change in the wind forced him to look for another anchorage. His crew being inexperienced sailors, he had not dared to send them closer on beam than 90 degrees.

"The storm front hit us at 6 p.m.," and recalled the noise, the big sea breathing, the wind shrieking through the rigging. The wind had come in so hard and sudden that the dragging anchor snapped its fluke. "I just didn't want a knock-down. I ordered the others below, all except Reg—"

"Reg?" cut in Finter. He did not need help in spelling that.

"The skipper's mate. I needed him to secure the boom while I kept at the wheel. I was steering through the breakers with water coming up over the bow at me. The wind was meeting the current and it all went to lumping up the waves."

In a small voice, he described how his mate was swept from the mast, onto the deck.

"Reg was crawling along topside when he hit the jackstay. It ran like a dog on a wire and it snarled his legs as a breaking crest hit the boat and he went out straight over the top of the boom, a perfect dive . . ."

The captain managed to bring the ship around, but as he moved to grab hold of Reg, who had plummeted to the deck, the *Buffalo* dropped into a trough and in the next moment struck the unmarked rock. "That rock – it wasn't on the charts, you know."

After an interval, Finter asked: "Do you suppose you could have done anything differently?"

The captain fixed his eyes on the glass bowl of strawberry jam. He wished he had cut away the mast when the *Buffalo* first struck, but the axe was in the hold. Otherwise, no, nothing could have been done. The waves were washing fore and aft the deck. It was as much as grown persons could do to hold on. As for Reg: "I did reach him and keep him on board." But his mate had perished in his arms while the ship broke up about them.

"Why didn't you get the kids to shore at the first signs of the storm?"

"If I could have, I would have," shaking his head. He had been twenty-nine years at sea. He had never experienced such a gale. Nor seen a vessel and people in a more dangerous position.

"And they've been in dangerous positions," noted the policeman.

With the captain's assistance, Finter wrote down the names of the six other survivors. He would take their statements later. "And I'd better speak to this woman at the Bilgola Mission. Mrs . . ." flicking back several pages in his notebook.

"Wellard," said the captain.

There was one further duty to perform. Before leaving the hotel, Alex accompanied the captain and Sergeant Finter into the kitchen to identify the drowned men. The two bodies in their nineteenth-century sailor's breeches looked sad and wet on the floor.

Dead seamen, gone in search of the same landfall . . .

"That's him. That's Reg Hull," the captain said, his features buckling at the sight of his mate propped up against the fridge.

They all stared at the face. The lids had started to swell up and close over bulging bloodshot eyes. Finter said to Alex in a contemplative way: "Know who he reminds me of? Cheele. Remember Cheele?"

"Yes," a little surprised to hear the name.

A yard away, a hand trembled out from under the captain's blanket and touched the sunburned, flyblown forehead. "I held him for ten minutes after he was dead. He'd got more brains than you can imagine."

CHAPTER FOUR

NO SOONER HAD SHE cooked Alex's breakfast than Merridy felt exhausted and went back to bed. On waking several hours later, she telephoned her assistant and left a message on his machine. "Could you grade those lanterns? Oh, and Jayce – I won't be coming out."

It was now after ten. Along the corridor, Kish had lapsed back into sleep, sprawled across the bed, snoring. She watched him breathing. From far away she felt something running towards her, and shivered.

She picked out some of Alex's clothes from the wardrobe and laid them on the chair by Kish's bed, and after a while fitted on her gloves and went into the garden to begin the task of clearing the debris.

When he opened his eyes the first thing he saw were the lemony stars on the ceiling. He put on the spectacles that he had left folded on the bedside table and then the white shirt and the pair of green moleskins, and opened the door into the corridor. He peered into the kitchen. A pan with a cold egg on the stove. Newspaper on the table. He looked at the advertisement on the front page and turned a few pages and closed the newspaper. He opened the fridge and looked inside and sniffed and shut it and went over to the sink. He poured himself a mug of water and drank it and then walked back down the corridor into the living room and sat in a chair with his feet stretched out on the dog-basket. The sun shining onto the cockatoo. He stared at himself in the glass.

An hour later, she came upon him in the kitchen. He stood at the Welsh dresser with his back to her. Alex's shirt stretched across his body.

She waited. Then: "How's your head?"

He said nothing. Touching with awe something high up.

Merridy took off her gloves. "I made some bacon and eggs. I can heat them up."

He remained on tiptoe. "What's this?" and held up the shiny black rock.

"A meteorite. Alex's father found it." And Alex's voice came to her: "One of twenty-four million a day that enters the atmosphere."

He replaced it on the shelf. "Alex – he's your husband?"

"Yes."

Still the corner of the dresser attracted his attention. "And that?"

He squinted into the bottle, at the hull of cracked green paint.

"She's called the *Otago*. My husband made her."

"Where is your husband?"

"He went into town."

But it was the ship that interested him. He took off Alex's glasses, wiped them on his shirt and put them back on again. Polishing the lens had not unclouded his eye.

He placed the bottle on the table and gazed into it. He folded his arms and leaned forward and sat there, gazing.

"Insane," he said approvingly.

She skirted past him and heated the pan and served him his plate.

He picked up two straps of bacon, swallowed them.

"You must be hungry," she said.

"I could eat this all in one gobble."

She watched his mouth open and close. "I'm afraid some of your crew – they weren't so lucky," she said after a while.

"You think I'm lucky?" hurling her an abusive look, but it was a pebble that fell short.

"You could have drowned," she pointed out.

"Yes," and laughed.

She tried another tack. "What about your parents?"

"What about them?"

"Don't you want to telephone them? Tell them you're safe."

"No," he said, chewing. "Not especially."

"Do you have brothers, sisters?"

Again, that sawing laugh. "Not that I know of."

He made her feel that her questions were indecent. As if she had asked a man to show her pictures of his mother naked.

Her tiredness dragged at her all of a sudden. "It's all right, Kish. Don't if you don't want," and opened the door to the corridor.

"Hey, Mrs Dove," slyly.

"What?"

"I like your sneakers."

She looked down. She had bought them in Hobart for her forthcoming trip to Melbourne. "Thank you."

Alex arrived home just before noon. He parked the ute the other side of the fallen pine and climbed over the tree and went inside. Merridy was loading the drier with Kish's sodden clothes.

"Where is he?" Alex asked, anxious.

"I sent him down to the beach. What are we going to do with him? I don't want him here."

He followed her into the kitchen and watched her squeeze out a dishcloth.

"It's all right. Finter's coming with Dr Musgrove to see him."

"When?" Angry as the cloth that attacked the dresser and tabletop and dabbed at the dried bacon fat. Anywhere he might have touched.

"I don't know. This afternoon."

"It doesn't take all day to drive out here, Alex."

"Love, they've got seven others to attend to." But her anger surprised him.

Late in the afternoon Kish returned to the house, bringing from the beach a twisted piece of tidewood. He went to his room and stretched out on the bed. He flicked open his knife and started to whittle the wood and only gave any sign of life when Merridy knocked on his door to tell him that the doctor was here to see him.

Sergeant Finter waited with Alex and Merridy in the living room while Dr Musgrove examined Kish.

"Where will he go?" Merridy wanted to know.

"A woman's coming from the Bilgola Mission," Finter said vaguely. "She'll be here Friday." He was a little overwhelmed. Nothing like this had ever happened in Wellington Point. Nothing remotely like it.

"Not till Friday?"

Alex said: "I'm sure he can stay here. If push comes to shove."

But Finter had registered Merridy's face. "No, no. He'll need to be in touch with his probation officer."

"Where is his probation officer?"

"In Hobart – for a check-up."

"Is he seriously injured?"

"I haven't a clue, but it does means there's no one to look after Kish."

"Shouldn't he be with his mates?" Merridy said.

"The problem is," said Finter thickly, "the hotel's full."

"Full?" Alex did not believe it.

"I had to reserve rooms for the coroner and his clerk. Plus the dive squad." Four divers were driving up to survey and assess the wreck, whether it was a hazard to navigation.

"Surely, they can squeeze in one more person," said Merridy.

"The press have taken every other bed. I should have moved sooner." Finter thought. "Maybe I could try the Malvern."

"Please do," said Merridy, and pointed to the telephone.

Finter dialled the Malvern, but the bed & breakfast, too, had stopped taking bookings. The owner suggested Tasman Cottages. No vacancies there, either.

"He might have to go in the cells after all," Finter said. Wanly, he explained to Merridy: "I was joking to Alex a little while back that if it was Easter I'd have to open up the cells."

Merridy nodded.

At last, a room was found at the Oyster Bay guest house in Swansea. But it would not be free until the morning.

So did Merridy accept the inevitable. "I suppose we *could* look after him for another night."

A knock, and now Dr Musgrove entered. Slightly concerned

about the bump on Kish's forehead – it would need watching. Otherwise, his patient seemed as well as could be expected under the circumstances.

Confused by lack of sleep, Sergeant Finter flipped open his notebook. "My turn."

Kish remained seated at the kitchen table after the visitors had left. He got out his knife and flipped it open and started assaulting the stump of driftwood.

Merridy leaned, arms crossed, against the dresser while Alex explained: "A room has been reserved for you from tomorrow in Swansea."

Kish did not look up, but twisted his head as if reacting to some buzzing or twittering that only he could hear.

"Swansea's just across the bay," Alex said.

Kish scraped a sliver onto the floor. Sullenly, he said: "I'd rather stay here." Which surprised them. "Maybe I could sweep up some leaves."

"Leaves?" said Merridy.

"Why not?" asked Alex.

"You heard what Sergeant Finter said. It's not suitable—"

Kish stabbed his knife into the table.

"Hey, don't do that!" Merridy leaped forward. She seized the knife and snapped shut the blade. "I'm taking this away," and marched out of the kitchen, down the corridor, not knowing where she was going, where to hide the weapon.

Kish looked at her when she came back in, but said nothing. Rusty's head on his lap and his index finger caressing the length of her puppy's muzzle, from the nose to between the eyes, back and forth.

She cupped her hand and swept the shavings into it and dropped them in the bin under the sink. It was clear to her: Kish's good points had died in him some while ago.

"Here, Rusty."

At dinner, he ate with his mouth open. She wanted to smack him. It was a face that was made to look the other way, not like Alex's. The violence of her reaction, what she felt, shocked her. She did not like the way that Rusty had attached himself to Kish.

"What do you think he did?" she asked Alex later in bed.

"No idea. It's like adoption, the same procedure. They don't let you know the sin any more than they tell you the father or mother." And she wondered how he knew.

"That knife will have something to do with it," she said. "I bet you it does."

"He's only had it since he joined the ship," Alex pointed out.

"I wonder if he's quite right in the head?" remembering the way he had batted away something invisible. A gesture – thinking of her mother – that was the prerogative of the insane.

Alex swallowed two Nurofen and switched off his bedside light. "He's probably no different to any of these kids from halfway houses. He goes into pubs and has fights and works things out, and one time he gets caught." He did not tell her about the captain's uncomfortable reaction. Nor about his conversation with Finter as he saw the policeman to his car.

Finter had said: "You'll keep your eye on him, Alex? Strictly speaking, he shouldn't be staying here 'without supervision'. Those were the words. But everything's gone to buggery."

"Then find somewhere else for him to go."

"At any rate, the probation officer has promised to come out to see Kish once the hospital release him, which should be any minute."

"Did you find out what he'd done to be on that boat?"

"He doesn't have a record, if that's what Merridy's doing her melon about."

"Why was he late joining the *Buffalo*?"

"I don't know that, Alex," rubbing his eyes. "He didn't tell me. Nor did I get anything out of the Wellard woman. That was the cxcusc – that they wanted to help him – but I don't know what went on and I don't want to know either. Right now, I just want to catch a few zeds."

That night Merridy lay awake. She felt a heightened alertness since Kish's arrival. He was hard to understand, but he seemed to express something that she could not articulate. Sitting next to him at dinner, she had felt out of breath.

Beside her, also awake, his thoughts inflamed by the Nurofen, Alex indulged himself. The idea was ridiculous, but supposing just for a moment that this man – this Kish – was who he said he was . . . what could Alex tell him that had been learned by men and women over the last two hundred years?

In the room across the corridor, a light was still on. Kish had taken off his borrowed shirt and lay on the bed. He was looking at Merridy's drawing of a sieve and remembering something.

Alex rose later than normal. He ate his three pieces of toast and went outside to start sawing up the tree that blocked the drive. A moment later, he was back.

"Chainsaw's out of fuel, I'll have to go to Swansea hardware," collecting the keys to the ute. "Is he up?"

"No."

"Darling . . ."

She saw his concern and was touched. "I'll be fine. And Alex – I don't see why he can't stay on here. He's spent two nights already. It's only till Friday."

He tossed the keys in the air and caught them. "I'll tell Finter, then."

She watched his ute disappear behind the tree and was wondering what to do about Kish when the telephone rang. Jason, speaking from the boathouse. He had got her message and had graded the oysters. He had also been down on the beach, collecting the remains of oyster trays that the wild weather had broken apart. But he was calling for another reason. A mate had been in touch who worked for Les Gatenby. "He says they've started spawning."

"When?"

"Last week."

Merridy swore. "That's early." She had been hoping that St Helen's would not spawn at least for another fortnight, until after her trip to Melbourne. But if the water temperature and conditions were right anything was possible.

"Do you want a holiday?" without thinking. It would be two

or three months at least before her oysters were back in condition and she could resume selling them to Dmitri. It was a phenomenon that she had mentioned before to Alex: "Once St Helen's goes, it's a rule of thumb that within ten days the jellyfish start turning up in Oyster Bay – and bang, we're gone."

Jason laughed. "Since you ask, I wouldn't mind going up to Flinders." And she remembered a girl at the Taste of Tasmania, a singer in a band from Lady Barron. His utter excitement.

"OK. Take the next fortnight off. You'll love Flinders."

"I didn't know you'd been."

"On my honeymoon, Jayce."

Preoccupied, she returned to her bedroom, where she found Kish.

"Get back from there!"

He stepped away from the wardrobe, Alex's shirt undone on him and pleated from being too big. His eyes alarmed at the fury in her voice.

He touched his earring. "I . . . I was looking for a shower," without conviction.

"Down there," sounding just like her mother.

But instead of reacting to her imperious voice, he walked over to the wardrobe and looked inside.

"Hey, what's wrong with the door?"

"It's always been like that."

She would have told her husband anything, had he asked. Even about the chandler. But he never asked.

"You should get it fixed," Kish said, and poked his fingers through the hollow heart, the cross.

It was uncanny. Dressed in Alex's glasses and clothes, he gave her the distinct impression that he was Alex, only younger. She was looking back through her husband's eyes to a parallel time where what was dead lived.

"Maybe I could fix it."

"Out!"

Still, he lingered. His gaze locked on the wardrobe at which he stared long and hard. Until some inkling of obedience led him in the direction of her pointing hand and into the corridor.

*

She left the door to her study ajar so that she could monitor him taking his shower. Any other day, she might have driven to the oyster shed. But she was not prepared to leave Kish alone in the house. Friday stretched too far away.

It therefore dumbfounded her to see the transformation in the young man who emerged from the spare bathroom. His shirt buttoned and his blond hair brushed back. Lean and narrow-shouldered – with his chipped teeth concealed behind tight-drawn lips – he had the look and smell of a clean, oiled knife.

"Wait here," she relented, and went into her bedroom. She retrieved it from its hiding place and returned to where she had left him standing beside her desk, and gave it back to him.

He opened and closed the blade. He believed in his knife quite fiercely, she could tell. It was his crucifix.

Satisfied, he slipped it into his hip pocket.

She followed him down the corridor to the kitchen.

Restless, he opened the fridge and took out a carton of milk and sniffed it. He put it back and rummaged some more.

"What are these?"

"Oysters." Then: "I grow them."

He looked interested. "You grow scallops too?"

"No."

"Oh," disappointed. He picked one up and studied it. "Get pearls from these?"

"Unfortunately not. Different oyster and warmer water. These are for eating." She shut the fridge door. "Have you eaten them ever?"

"Course I have."

He took out his knife and started to open the one in his hand and all but ripped his thumb.

She showed him how. "Stab it vertically at the end, then work the blade back under the muscle."

He studied the watery grey flesh streaked with black.

"Try it," she urged.

He looked reluctant.

"Go on."

With great caution, he raised it to his lips.

Then spat into the sink.

"Your first one?" amused.

"Course not. But the other was nicer."

"Oh, you won't get nicer than these." Her eyes sparkled. "Our oysters are so good, you get a stiff neck when you eat them."

"Is that all, Mrs Dove?" he said. "Then I'd be pretty right as an oyster farmer. I'd be like walking around with a horn all the time."

She ignored the look that had come into his face, but he was not to be put off. "Aren't oysters supposed to be good for you or something?"

"They have amino acids that you won't find in other foods," in a neutral voice.

For something to do, she opened the cupboard and took out the bread-maker. But even as she prepared ingredients, Merridy was conscious of the watchful eyes behind her husband's spectacles.

Presently, a regular rasping sound made her turn. Kish sat facing her. He was honing his stump of wood and had made a point of creating out of the shavings a neat pile on the table.

"What are you making?"

He twisted his head, and once again Merridy had the idea that he was responding to a noise audible only to him.

"What are you making?" she repeated.

"Nothing," he said, and investigated the thin scrap of driftwood that he had pared down to an entrail.

There was something unplumbable about this young man. At the same time she recognised in his face some sign unknown to Alex, belonging to a sect of which only they were initiates, and it did not make her comfortable. She stepped closer. "Show me."

He held up the fragile length of sassafras for her to see, and snapped it.

Minutes later, Rusty burst into the kitchen, followed by Alex, who scattered onto the table the *Mercury* and a bundle of post. And a black bin liner stuffed with something.

He pushed it towards Kish.

Kish glared over his cup at the bag, suspicious.

"Clothes for you." And to Merridy: "I bumped into Agnes."

Kish showed no desire to inspect this donation from the Op-Shop.

Alex turned to him. "It's probably just as well you're up here. You can't budge in town for journalists and photographers." And when Kish did not say anything: "I spoke to Sergeant Finter. He's put in a request to the Bilgola Mission that you stay here till Mrs Wellard comes on Friday. If we don't hear back by this afternoon, we'll assume it's OK."

Merridy smiled; it seemed the best thing to do. "That's settled then." She held up the pot. "I've just made a brew. Want some?"

"Give me half a cup," Alex said.

"If you don't draw it a bit more, it'll be like possum piss," Kish scowled, and went on stroking Rusty whose head had popped up from under the table.

"Sleep well?" Alex asked benevolently.

"I suppose."

"How are you feeling?"

"All right."

"Want to make yourself useful?"

"How?"

"Come and help me cut up that tree."

"No," Kish said, and picked up a magazine that he had noticed in among the bundle.

"What, it's only leaves you sweep?"

Kish opened the magazine.

Alex exchanged glances with his wife. He accepted the cup from her. "I'll be on the lawn. Come on, Rusty."

Outside, the jaded growl of Alex's chainsaw.

Merridy unfolded the *Mercury*. The front page devoted to the disaster at sea.

Sitting opposite, Kish flicked through the pages of *Bottleship*, the magazine of the European Association of Ships in Bottles.

Why Alex had not cancelled the subscription, Merridy could not fathom. He never looked at it. The only journal he liked to read was the *Wilderness*.

Kish pushed back the magazine as though it might be one of her mother's Methodist tracts.

"Mrs Dove?"

"Yes?"

"Come on, the truth. How do you get it in there?"

"What?" She tore herself from the photographs of the *Buffalo* floating raft-like beneath the water.

"That coin," and swivelled back in his chair, pointing his knife at the bottle on the dresser.

So that was it.

"Oh, that. You'll have to ask Alex."

He observed her with his hard, white inscrutable eyes. "It's against the natural law of things."

"You'll find a lot of things are like that. Especially in Tasmania." As Harry Ford once told her: "We're too far out of reach here to be touched by any God or man-made laws, or even scientific ones." She said to Kish: "In Tasmania, everyone is left to be as idiotic as they please."

"But you know, don't you?"

"I might."

"Then tell me."

"No."

"Why not?"

"Because I promised," she flared.

"Is that all?"

She studied him over the top of the *Mercury*. "First," she said, "you tell me what you did to be on this boat."

He met her stare. "And then you'll tell me?"

"No."

Merridy had the distinct idea that Alex had once explained it to her. Too many years had gone by for her to confess that she had forgotten.

Behind their lenses, Kish's eyes had a tarnished, brash look, and there were dark specks under them like burned spots on a pan. He reminded her of someone, but no longer Alex.

"I could tell you and you'd go white sitting there. You don't want to know, Mrs Dove."

But she did. "What did you do, Kish?"

He gave her an aggressive single-fingered salute and stood. "Catch yez later," and slammed the door.

Shaken, Merridy flicked through the *Mercury*. "*Is your memory a sieve?*" The same bland-looking man in a suit stared out, his black-and-white features unchanged over almost two decades. Next to the advertisement, a study on earthquakes. Men's greatest fear was to be thrown up in the air, women's to be gobbled up by the earth. And all of a sudden a bank of sandy soil stretched out on her inner eye, covered in roots and dried-out leaves, and a hole smelling of must, darker than any wardrobe.

She stood unsteadily and poured herself a glass of water. Again, she was conscious of the silent windmill. It was the constant wind that made her feel silly. You never realised how much it irritated till it stopped. But the noise of the chainsaw had ceased as well. The only sound, the grind and groan of the bread-maker.

On the lawn she saw him talking to Alex.

Her husband had put down the chainsaw and removed his earplugs. He gestured at the fallen pine, the thick trunk that he was cutting into neat slices. Behind them, Rusty had found an interesting smell in the foliage.

Kish sank on his haunches and tentatively reached out a hand to touch the single eyeball of exposed wood. Alex squatted next to him, explaining something, and Kish listened, running his hand up and down over the white surface. He appeared to make a request.

Alex nodded and started up the chainsaw.

"What were you two talking about?" she asked him later.

Alex told her. "There was a lovely, rare treecreeper caught in the branches. I couldn't resist showing it to him. Know what he said? 'That may make your life, Mr Dove, but what I like is a police siren.' Then in the next breath he was asking questions about the tree – why it was called an Oyster Bay pine, whether it grows in groves."

"And does it?" She was so accustomed to the lone pine that she had never bothered to ask.

"Well, you don't often see one independent like this, or so bushy. Normally, they grow up in preference to branching out."

She pondered this. "You cut him a piece, I saw."

"He asked for something to hew." Then, with a boyish conspiratorial smile: "I have an idea that he wants to make a ship."

After dinner, Alex took down the dusty rum bottle covered with dried wasp wings and spiders' droppings that once had contained his horizon.

Childlike, all aggression fled, Kish sat rapt by the fire in the living room as Alex explained how he had crafted the *Otago*. And Merridy, reading the novel that she had put down weeks before, overheard them. Her husband remembering his passion; the young man bombarding him with questions.

"All sailing ships go out of the bottle. See? This is sailing in."

"Why is it sailing in?"

In case Merridy had refused him. But had he ever told her? He looked over at his wife. "Just to be different," he said fondly.

"Did you design it?"

"It was built from a half-mould, so no original plans. I had to draw them and blow them up and cut them to shape."

"What do you make the sails from?"

"Cotton japara, stiffened with water."

"What tools do you use?"

"This pair of tweezers is all I need. You touch them to the neck of the bottle to stop your hand shaking, then put in the sail."

"What's the sea made of?"

"My father used putty. I prefer children's blue plasticine."

"And the deck?"

"Ice-cream sticks. Just like the bowsprit."

"You're kidding!"

"I'm not. Am I, love?"

"No, he isn't," said Merridy from her chair across the room. Years ago she had had the same conversation, asked the same question.

"Ice-cream sticks," repeated Kish, and brought his face closer. "Jeez, man."

And the pleasure in his eyes transported Alex back further than a drizzly day in a playground to a period before he met Merridy.

It's absurd, he thought. A man spends his first forty years trying to escape childhood; his next forty, trying to retrieve it. We grow up, only to want to become children.

"What about the coin, Mr Dove?" The intensity of Kish's question made Merridy look up.

Alex put down the bottle. "That's just something my father found. So much rubbish we use as model builders. You need to be original, you need to be different. Not like Johnny-round-the-corner."

That night she lay curled on her side, legs tucked under, asleep, when she became aware of a pressure on her heel. Alex had it in his palm. In his touch she felt the heat of his desire. He followed the line of her leg up, tracking her, almost like a doctor, following the lineaments, making sure everything was there. When she stirred, he moved his hand to her knee, squeezing it, and there was a safety in that and in the weight of his arm on the outside of her thigh. He rested his chin on her hip and then moved up and pressed her shoulder in the same way, emphasising it. He might have been looking for all the ways to fit himself around her, to find her contours. He cupped her ear and held her forehead with his other palm as if to silence the silence. Barely moving, they slipped together under water. Not wishing to make any sound that Kish would hear. Only when needing to taste his breath she turned and rose above him, thighs, breasts, hair, and caused him at last to shudder, hurting – as though a heel pressed into his heart. While she could have been straddling some bowsprit that he had made for her, rising and falling through the phosphorescent waves. Until she floated.

In the morning, Alex had to leave early to meet his agent in Launceston.

"I ought to ring Finter," he said. "I don't know why the probation officer hasn't been in touch."

"Go. I'll be fine."

"You've got his number. Maybe you could call him?"

"Alex. I'll be fine."

She found Kish lying, legs crossed, on his bed, whittling his piece of pine. He wore a blue-and-white striped shirt from the Op-Shop, an oversized grey cable-knit jersey and a pair of faded brown corduroys the colour of dried figs. Merridy caught the frowsy aroma of dead skin and old wool and too much soap. She had preferred it when he smelled of the sea.

In a voice that she tried to keep vague, she asked: "Why is it called an Oyster Bay pine?"

He laughed. "You don't know?"

She blushed to be caught out. She would know if she had grown up on this coast and not in Ulverstone. He was always catching her out. "Of course, I do."

He went on honing.

"Are you making a ship?" It had upset her when Kish snapped his piece of driftwood. The audacity of his look had made her shudder. She said: "Haven't you had enough of ships?"

He ignored her needling tone. "You have to wait for the wood to tell you what to do with it. That's what Mr Dove says. I'm waiting for it to tell me."

"Well, until it does," she said tartly, "maybe you'd like to help out on a real boat."

A day cooped up in the house and she fretted to be back on the *Zemmery Fidd*.

It was Alex's idea for Kish to join her. Before her husband set off for Launceston she had shared with him her concerns for the fate of her oysters. "I ought to check the lanterns. The storm might have damaged them. But who can I get to help?"

"Why, what's happened to Jason?"

"I've just given him a fortnight off. I can't ring and say I didn't mean it. Anyway, he's gone to Flinders with a girl he's crazy about."

"Take Kish, why not?"

The idea had not crossed her mind. "Kish? Would that be allowed?"

"I don't see anyone rushing to stop you. Until that probation officer turns up, I reckon we can do what we like."

"But won't Kish be terrified?"

"He can always say no. And what else is he going to do until Friday? You could try asking him to repair the Hill's Hoist. But I tell you, he's not going to help me take out that tree unless I'm standing right behind him with a chainsaw in his back."

Against Merridy's every expectation Kish accepted her offer. "OK, Mrs Dove, if you want a hand, I'll give you a hand," and folded away his knife.

Once inside the shed, she fitted him with the orange life jacket that normally Alex wore. For someone who had all but drowned in the bay two days earlier, Kish showed remarkably little apprehension about returning to sea.

"We'll take these lanterns," she pointed. "I'll start the crane, you loop them onto the hook and I'll raise them onto the deck."

The scallop lanterns were stacked adjacent to a large metal perforated tube, through which Kish poked a finger. "What's this for?"

"Do you really want to know?" He was always poking fingers.

"I asked, didn't I?"

The answer shamed her. "That's the rotary grader. It knocks their shells about and stresses them. They think: 'Oh, God, I'm dying, I need to sort myself out.' It makes them concentrate on the inside."

Kish ran his hand over the perforations. He had revealed the same interest in Alex's bottles.

She added: "We call it the wheel of fortune, because it's fortuitous if they survive."

If Merridy feared that her talk would bore him, she was mistaken: his curiosity had only sharpened.

She undid the stitching and plucked an oyster from the lantern. Very well, if he wanted a lesson . . . She indicated the ridges on the shell. "Oysters get handled about ten times in their lives. That's ten shocks. Each touching leaves a stress mark like a tree."

"Why would you want to shock an oyster?"

"Shock is good for them. Gets them working, stops them being lazy, wakes them up. Otherwise, they just grow their shells to be beautiful, but their insides go yukky."

"What does yukky look like?"

"Not much, thin and grey. Here, let me show you."

She opened a couple of oysters until she found one with the telltale watery flesh. She handed it to him. "This one's lazy, needs a bit of a shock."

Kish lifted up the oyster until it was level with his spectacles. "Boo!" he yelled. Then ate it.

Soon the *Zemmery Fidd* was banging out towards the mouth of the Swan. Kish sat in the stern, between the two engines, and looked with a baleful expression at the white breakers curling along the far side of the sandbar.

He nodded at the engines and muttered something.

"What?" Tense, she leaned towards him.

"That's a lot of grunt."

"Seen a Suzuki Ingus on the road?" she shouted. "One of them is one of those."

The boat slammed over the sandbar and twisted into the breakers. Then they were through.

Beyond, the sea stretched calm and windless and it was impossible to conceive that this tranquil plain was where the *Buffalo* had splintered apart. Maria Island sat like a hat on the horizon and a sulphur-crested cockatoo flapped alone through the warm blue sky.

Kish lapsed into silence.

"Better than lying on your back," she shouted, and opened the throttle.

She steered west, parallel with Dolphin Sands towards Wellington Point. The water so clear that she could gaze all the way down to the sandy bed. Ahead, she kept her eye out for the orange buoys that supported her lines.

But something was wrong with the sea.

"Hey!" Kish tapped her shoulder. He had sprung to his feet. An expression of wonder in his face.

She looked around. And suddenly there was no end to the whiteness in which they floated.

Kish leaped forward and gripped the bow-rail, leaning over. "It's like something's burning underwater," excited.

Merridy cut the engine and stared into the white cloud that was the colour and consistency of moonlit fog. Mirages enveloped her. Sea-green faces and sky-blue hands. She tried to pull her eyes away, but an inexpressible longing tugged at her. A vertigo that made her want to jump into the water and dive down, down into the centre of this awful whiteness. Then it dawned. "The oysters are spawning."

"It's like snot," Kish had decided.

In a distant voice, she heard herself say: "It's no different to when coral releases its seeds, or a squid lets go its ink. The same deal. Except white."

Still, it bewildered him. "What is it, actually?"

"Eggs mainly, plus some gonad."

"Gonad?"

"Sperm."

The word carved a raw gap in the air. She burbled on to plug it. "Like everything else, they're born to spawn. Their whole life, they're looking to cast their germ-cells into the water. There may be more living creatures in that cloud than there are human beings on the face of the earth."

Kish peered into the white water and his eyes struggled to penetrate the cloud that could contain so much life. The cocky leer had vanished from his expression. He had a child's thoughtful clear face. A child who listens to everything, sees everything.

"How long do they spawn for?" in a fascinated tone.

"What we're seeing will only last an hour. After this they'll be unsellable for three months. They go without telling you. Don't even leave a note on the fridge."

What Merridy knew of the phenomenon she had learned from Les Gatenby, who had witnessed it once in the shallows off Bruny. But she had never seen it for herself until now. Perhaps the storm was responsible.

She was content to let the boat drift. The only sound the gentle slop against the hull. Even so, she flinched from the whiteness. The sea that was blinding her.

Kish remained at the bow-rail, looking over the side of the

boat, his back to her so that she was unable to make out his expression. Every now and then he expelled a moan, like a child calling out to itself in its sleep. She pretended not to notice, but she could not help what she felt: a strange and intensely painful sensation, not to be compared with anything she had experienced. His stance so like her brother when he looked over the deck that it produced the illusion of Kish being the same person. It seemed to her, at that moment, as if Hector had not died and was standing in front of her, staring over the edge.

"Can you eat them?" he asked.

She retrieved the answer from somewhere. "The French like them, apparently, but no one in Australia will touch them."

He came back and joined her behind the windscreen. "And those eggs" – he might have been waving at all the men, women, children who ever lived – "what happens to them now?"

Hastily, she started the engine. "Let me tell you something interesting about oysters," clinging to the lesson that she had resolved to give him. She knew it by heart.

"In the normal course of events, the egg will spend the next few days trying to get it together with a sperm. Once fertilised, it's called an eye larva. It has one eye and a foot and wanders around for up to three weeks until with its little eye it sees something that it can settle on, like a rock. Then this foot attaches itself to the rock and puts a secretion around the side of it like Super Glue, and for ever after it is attached to that rock. The foot and eye disappear and it changes completely from a free-floating creature to a fixed, sedentary critter. It changes anatomy end to end."

Kish was still listening. As if he had never wanted to know anything so much.

"They trick them in the hatchery," she went on. "They put down ground scallop shell, and the eye larva settles on an individual microscopic piece thinking it's settled on a rock. But out here the process is interrupted. Something stops the larva, so it doesn't get to settling. I don't know what happens. A combination of the wind and grazing. Like everything else in the sea, something's eating something. And in Oyster Bay something's eating an awful lot of larvae – probably zoo plankton that floats on the surface and scoffs them down at a fantastic rate."

She wondered if she had lost him, but he was still there. "Hanging onto your every word," as Tildy used to say of Randal Twelvetrees.

"Something else I'll tell you about oysters. They change sex."

"No!"

"It's true. When I buy them as two-millimetre seedlings they're fifty-fifty male and female. But after eighteen months, there are twenty-three females to each male. The males have converted straight across to female."

"You mean, like Sydney boys at Mardi Gras?"

Merridy burst out laughing. "If you like."

She returned her gaze to the sea, but the cloud had dissolved and the water was almost clear again.

Over to starboard on the western side of the oyster lease Kish had spotted something. "Hey, Mrs Dove, what are those people doing?"

"People?" What was he on about?

Kish flattened his hand against the sun. "Over there – those heads."

Her initial thought: It's a flock of gannets sitting around. Only as the *Zemmery Fidd* motored close did she realise the extent of the carnage. So taken up by the white sea and her lesson to Kish that she had failed to notice the mess of orange floats bunched together on the perimeter line.

"They're not heads," slowly. Rather, evidence that her oyster farm was not unscathed after all. "Stand here, Kish. When I hold up my hand, put this into neutral."

Kish took her place behind the wheel. She picked up a grappling hook and moved to the bow-rail.

Far below, a hideous tangle of rope, buoy and lantern.

It would take a day or two fully to understand what had happened. The storm that had sunk the *Buffalo* had ripped one of Merridy's polypropylene lines from its anchor and swung it south to north, enmeshing all its lanterns around the neighbouring six lines. They criss-crossed in every direction, the web of an aquatic spider.

Merridy hooked what resembled a coffin suspended below the surface and winched it up, the lantern suddenly shrinking as it emerged from the sea.

She made a rapid calculation. "We've got three thousand dozen oysters down there."

"What do you want to do?"

"We'll have to load the lanterns into the boat and transfer them to another line and put them straight back down."

"How long will that take?"

"Three or four full days – of good weather, too."

"Then we'd better not hang around, Mrs Dove. I leave tomorrow, remember?"

They worked until sunset. Tucked behind the windscreen on a plastic-covered clipboard was the mud-map, marking one hundred and thirty-three lanterns on the line. They picked up the easiest, until what they were doing made sense.

Each time she saw a lantern she raised her hand.

"Now reverse. Enough! Got him." And with the grappling hook scooped the line expertly from the water, hitching it over the Kabuki roller.

In this way, they raised and relocated thirty lanterns. They paused once, to refuel from the emergency tank on board.

It was shortly after six o'clock when Merridy cupped a hand into the sea and splashed the sweat from her face. "OK, Kish, let's call it a day."

She replaced the mud-map behind the windscreen and steered the *Zemmery Fidd* towards the river mouth. A hundred lanterns still to untangle. And tomorrow Kish was leaving.

In bed that night, Alex said to her: "Have you noticed a change in him?"

"Not really." Why she did not tell the truth, it was difficult to say.

"You know his course is supposed to last another three months?"

"How does that concern us?"

"I don't think he wants to go back."

She sat bolt upright. "He must. We're not probation officers!"

"He could help finish sorting out your lines. And I could use him on the farm. Anyway, it's not up to us."

Separated from them by the corridor of samplers, Kish lay on his bed with an illustrated book of verse. He had discovered it on the top shelf. He flicked through the pages, looking at the drawings, and when he came to the end he turned out the light and stared at the luminous stars on the ceiling.

CHAPTER FIVE

LATE ON FRIDAY AFTERNOON, a raspberry Hyundai with an Avis sticker on the windscreen advanced hesitantly up the drive and parked at the second attempt. A slender woman with a dumpy face climbed out. She stood and moved her eyes over the ruined lawn, the fallen tree and the figure of Kish on the edge of the grass, spading earth around the base of a clothes-line.

Kish had spent all day with Merridy on the *Zemmery Fidd*. They had been back at the house less than an hour. Before he left Moulting Lagoon Farm for good, he had promised her that he would mend the Hill's Hoist.

Mrs Wellard had flown down from Sydney. In fact, she had been on holiday in Cairns when she heard the news of the shipwreck. She was accompanied by the probation officer who had been on board. He had survived with nothing more serious than a bruised ankle.

Through the kitchen window, Merridy saw them ordering Kish to get ready.

While Kish went to his bedroom, Merridy brought the visitors tea in the living room. The door into the corridor was open and she overheard the man speak in a rough whisper. He was talking about Kish.

"Didn't I warn you? Sheepish as a first-timer."

"I didn't notice."

"I did. I tell you, Mrs Wellard, he's cunning, he's innocent, he's scum. The judge was wrong."

"We don't know if it was him or someone else. Maybe it was the one who drowned?"

"Believe you me, he sent in the razor gangs, cut, cut, cut, no apprentices – though I have to say he did like the sheilas. In Sydney, he was shoving everything."

"Shoving? Say that again, Ricky. I don't recognise the term."

"Local dialect, Mrs Wellard, that's what it is. A wonder he didn't wear his pecker out."

"What do you want me to do, ask him if he screws around? I'm not going to do that, it's a leading question—"

"I hope you don't mind Bushells," Merridy broke in cheerily, nudging open the door with the tray.

She had left the window open; the collar blew up around the man's neck.

"Nothing wrong with Bushells," he said, watching her put the tray down. "Nothing at all."

She pulled Rusty's basket away from the sofa and went to close the window latch. "I'm sorry if it's stuffy. We tend to use this room only in winter. In summer, we keep the dog in here."

The woman sat back as Merridy poured the tea. "A dreadful tragedy," she kept saying. She had plucked at the phrase so often over the past four days that her words sounded loose and twangy. She was called Annette. Her breasts had nudged together like croquet balls under her green wool trouser suit. In Sydney, they had warned that Tasmania would be cold. "But he's as well as could be hoped. Didn't you think so, Ricky?"

"Oh, he seemed fine."

Gangell was the probation officer's name. He was unpleasant and young and had a lean face that emphasised his brown eyes and sharp nose. He looked like a possum.

"We've been expecting you for the last two days, Mr Gangell," Merridy rebuked him.

He shifted uncomfortably, stretching out a leg. "Yes, well, there have been some crossed wires."

It fell to Mrs Wellard to explain. "You see, we were given to understand that a colleague from Child Welfare would be standing in for Ricky."

"I don't know what the trouble was," Merridy said. "I rather think he was waiting for you to contact him. Or maybe it was us. But, yes, it's all been rather chaotic. As you may imagine."

"I hope this hasn't put you out," said Mrs Wellard, "having Kish staying."

"Oh, no. Not at all."

"I was in Hobart for tests," Gangell piped up moodily.

"Nothing serious, I hope."

"Not so far. Not so far."

"How long have you been a probation officer, Mr Gangell?" Merridy asked politely. As anxious to put off the subject of Kish.

"Five years." Before that he had trained as a psychiatric nurse at a remand centre in Brisbane. Screening inmates for suicide risk.

"That must have been hard."

Gangell's palpable relief to be alive made him talkative. "We assessed them, but they got wise to telling us what we wanted to know. 'Oh, I'm cruising, seven out of ten.' Then they killed themselves." Three men had done so, apparently, who had spoken their last words to Gangell. He evinced a horror of being summoned to a coroner's court. "I'd book a ticket to Norway!" In Gangell's hardened opinion the men had been on speed. "Even in the straits they'd find drugs to be on."

"Straits?" said Merridy, and wondered what on earth people in Gangell's charge might be doing in Bass Strait.

"Straitjacket," Gangell explained, accepting a biscuit. He sat back and bit into it, looking above the fireplace at the Lear lithograph. "Is it me or is something wrong with that parrot?"

"I think it's you, Ricky," said Mrs Wellard quickly.

She put down her cup. She could not stop thinking of the dreadful tragedy. "So awful about those boys . . ." Her bony hands were agitated and her face that was the colour of bread mix. Unlike Gangell, she was eager to convey to Merridy just how much the young men had looked forward to their expedition on the *Buffalo*.

"They were terribly excited about the characters they were going to be. You should have seen them rehearsing!"

"It's Reg I feel sorry for," said Gangell. "He used to give me a turn at the wheel. 'Come on, Ricky, why don't you have a go?' He was anxious for everyone to be a part of it. 'Hey, boy, want to take this? Come on, lend a hand here.' If a slack-arse, he'd kick his arse. And there were some slack-arses."

"Really?" said Merridy.

"Oh, yeah. Redfern Aborigines. Rich kids from Bilgola. Some quite savage – knifings and car thefts, all that hoonery." And chewed his biscuit.

"And Kish," Mrs Wellard said at last, picking puppy hair off her green wool knee. "How have you found Kish, Mrs Dove?"

"He was strange to begin with, but he's become friendlier."

"He does find it hard, sometimes, to mix."

"I don't know, he seems to like it here, on the farm."

"Oh, one can never be sure what they like," Gangell said with a grimace. In stretching out his leg he had hit his bad ankle against the dog-basket.

"My husband tells me that Kish is not his real name."

Gangell flashed a significant look at Mrs Wellard. "It's a policy we have."

"I gather he was late in joining the boat."

"That is the case, yes," nodded Gangell, attacking a second biscuit.

"Is it too much to ask what he's done?" This short-sighted knifer.

Gangell looked for a fleeting moment as though nothing would give him greater pleasure than to be able to divulge this to Merridy, but before he could speak Mrs Wellard intervened. A professional tone had returned to her voice. "You will, I am sure, appreciate that we are not at liberty to say."

"Oh," said Merridy, and found herself gazing at the cockatoo. "Then I suppose you're here to take him back?"

Mrs Wellard rocked forward. Her long arms crossed like mallets against her chest. "We are right now in the process of sorting things out. If I may be absolutely truthful with you, Mrs Dove, the whole thing has been rather difficult. You see, the *Buffalo* wasn't expected home for another three months. Most of our regular staff are on leave and it's taking time to organise. None of us could have foreseen such a dreadful . . ."

All at once the painted bird was ruffling its feathers. Merridy turned and looked at Mrs Wellard. "You mean, it might be more convenient if he stayed here?"

On the sofa the thin woman with the fat face blathered on. "That wouldn't be legal. There'd be a lot of administration. You see, when he's not at the Mission he ought to be under supervision."

"*Would* it help if Kish stayed here?"

Mrs Wellard looked at Gangell. "Funnily enough, we were talking about that, weren't we, Ricky?"

"It would not be regular," shaking his head. "For one thing, Mrs Dove, you're not a qualified handler, and Kish, as I ought to make clear, is someone who very much needs careful handling. Anyway, I doubt if he'd want to—"

"Ask him," Merridy interrupted reasonably. "We don't mind looking after him – that is, until you are ready to take him back."

"But what if that's not for several weeks . . . ?" fussed Mrs Wellard.

"I've discussed it with my husband. If Kish does any work for us we'd pay him a wage."

For the first time since Mrs Wellard had sat down a modicum of cheerfulness animated her rotund features.

"What do you think, Ricky? Of course, we would have to get clearance."

Gangell looked at the possum rug and frowned. "I don't know, Annette. This lad, he's not like the rest of them. If I were here to keep tabs on things, it would be different."

"Ricky is taking a sabbatical," Mrs Wellard quickly explained. Which for some reason annoyed Merridy.

"A *sabbatical*?" she said.

"It's actually really rather interesting. I'm going to do a course in biodynamics." And that annoyed her even more. All at once she saw him for what he was. Lackadaisical. There for the trip. Issuing institutionalised warnings to the effect that Kish would never be any better than he was, a savage little bastard.

"Ricky kindly agreed to look after the boys for the first fortnight, until they got their sea legs, so to speak."

Merridy was no longer interested in Gangell or his biodynamics. "If Kish likes it here, why not give him a chance?"

But did he like it?

"Why not, Ricky?" Mrs Wellard echoed. Pleading, almost. "If we get clearance, why not?" And Merridy could see her thinking: If it was a libertine house full of fourteen-year-olds . . . But a nice, childless couple on a farm!

Besides, they wanted to be rid of him, that was obvious. One less statistic.

"Because, in my opinion," Gangell said gruffly, "he needs supervision."

"You could always delay your sabbatical," Merridy suggested brightly.

"Mind you, if he did stay here," said Gangell, beginning, at last, to see certain advantages, "it couldn't be for any longer than the duration of the course."

"I understand," Merridy said. She stood up. "But please, before we go any further, shouldn't we ask Kish?"

She found him, glasses off, lying on his bed. He was wearing his purple T-shirt with its gruesome insignia, and had folded his uniform that Merridy had washed, hung on the line and ironed, into the bin liner. On the floor at the foot of the bed in two neat piles were Alex's clothes that he had borrowed, plus Alex's spectacles on top; and the clothes that Agnes had donated. He was shed of all his possessions save those that he had worn in the sea.

Merridy led him into the living room. She realised that she had no idea what his answer would be.

Mrs Wellard had adopted a formal attitude before the fireplace. "Mrs Dove has kindly invited you to remain at Moulting Lagoon Farm for the moment. Subject to what you would say if this could be arranged."

Kish stood with his mouth open. Uneasy, he turned to Merridy. "You mean you don't want me to go?"

"If you'd like to stay, you may stay – for a little while. You'll have to go eventually, obviously."

"It's only for the time being," Gangell said. "An interim period."

"Sure," he said slowly. "I'll stay."

"Well, that's settled then," said Merridy.

Two hours later Mrs Wellard telephoned from Wellington Point. She had spoken to her superiors. Provided that a probation officer could be in touch once a week, there was no objection to Kish remaining at Moulting Lagoon Farm until 23 March, the date on which the *Buffalo* had been due to drop anchor in Sydney.

PART IV

Moulting Lagoon Farm, 17–20 December 2004

CHAPTER ONE

UNITING CHURCH, WELLINGTON POINT.
Memorial Service next Sunday at 10.00 a.m. All visitors welcome. Captain Vamplugh and his crew again extend their appreciation for the lovely knitted items they have received. With your generous donations of goods and money we raised $940.45. We also have 100 Wellington Point tea-towels for sale with pictures of the village drawn by Myfanwy Davies. Any profits go towards the Bilgola City Mission. Phone to place your order: Rev. Chris Mantle 63526836.

Sister Surrage kept telling him: "You're lucky to be alive." He nodded. He could not forget the force of the waves that had dashed his speedboat against one of the pylons of the jetty, or the fury of the wind that tumbled her up the concrete ramp, to burst apart the hull against Mr Talbot's garage – at which point he had jumped unceremoniously out and run, stumbled and collapsed. All the same, his concussion was not so severe that he could ignore the unprecedented publicity that the storm had attracted in its wake. Despite the constraint of his bandages, he was eager to tap into it.

From his bed in the Louisa Meredith Nursing Home, Ray Grogan, who was now on the council, sent instructions to Tildy to open up the school kitchen and for the playing field to be made available to all camper vans. So many of these vehicles had converged on the promontory that the kids had nicknamed the area behind their playground Winnebago City.

Wellington Point, meanwhile, blinked in the glare of an attention that old-timers could not recall since an aeroplane decapitated two locals in the 1930s. Day-trippers came from Hobart and Launceston. Bushies who never much liked to travel beyond sight of their shacks came from Royal George and Green Ponds and Llandaff, and combed the shore to see if they could spot a few deck boards, as often as not mistaking a fragment of Ray's speedboat for a piece of the *Buffalo*. Eventually, a recovery barge anchored off Schouten and hauled away the wreck.

There were those who pretended to dislike the publicity, but no longer Murray Went, who was forced to bus in extra staff from Swansea after promoting Debbie to manageress; nor anyone else in the hospitality business, for whom the sinking of the *Buffalo* was a bonanza. It was a novel sight for Alex to read the "No vacancy" signs outside the bed & breakfasts, and quite a few houses as well. As for the people thronging the street, Alex had never known such an invasion. The hotel's restaurant and its two bars overspilled with reporters and photographers who had flown in from the mainland and even from abroad, a television crew from the BBC competing with one from Southern Cross to interview eyewitnesses and survivors. Agnes had filled a bin liner of clothes for each and every one of these – whom Merridy could not help remarking that Kish showed no inclination to seek out – so that the captain and his crew resembled members of a visiting cricket team as they sat in the hotel restaurant, dressed in baggy, white, moth-eaten jerseys, some of them from a batch donated by Harry Ford, and struggled to find different answers to the same questions posed over and over again.

In this avid atmosphere, it was inevitable that stories began to circulate of Alex's heroism.

Late one morning, he came up from Moulting Lagoon to find a journalist tapping on the living-room window. The man – mid-forties, brown shoes, pot belly – had paid Rose-Maree the equivalent of a week's salary to drive him out to the farm. She sat in her car, radio blaring, engrossed in *Who Weekly* and a feature about actresses with moles.

"Can I help?"

"Alex Dove?" jerking round. He had a beard and was bald.

"No," said Alex.

"Where could I find Mr Dove?"

"Who are you?"

"Oh, friend of a friend." His brown shoes stepped across the herbaceous border that Merridy had created, squashing a red peony and a white trigger-plant. "Marty Ponting. The *Advocate*." And held out a hand.

"He's out at sea, he won't be back till late."

"I see," and inspected a spiral-bound pad with panicked ferocity. "Actually, it was Mr Cash I wanted to speak to." He frowned at what he had written. "Or Cosh, could it be?"

"They're in the same boat."

Mr Ponting looked at Alex. "Who are you?"

"A friend of Mrs Dove," said Alex for some reason.

"Could you ask either of them to ring this number?" and with his still-unshaken hand opened a wallet that bulged with receipts.

Alex suspected Harry of priming this Ponting. The ex-Fleet Streeter could never forget the heavenly days of his journalistic calling that ill-health had cut short. Alex remembered that Harry, fond as he no doubt was of his mother and father, had orchestrated the newspaper coverage following their death. The morals of an alley cat.

He watched the beard duck back into Rose-Marce's car. Then went inside before she looked up. He ripped up Marty Ponting's card and put the pieces in the compost bin.

CHAPTER TWO

THREE DAYS ON AND the journalists had begun to seep away, leaving their smears behind. And still the Oyster Bay pine disfigured the lawn.

A pile of roots extended over the crater, tangled with stones and clay and Aboriginal shells. The roots had forced things down over the years. Alex picked out animal bones, farm equipment and an old whaling blubber-cutter that had lost its handle. He dreaded to investigate the dark hollow beneath his parents' tombstones. He would attend to their graves once he had dealt with the tree.

Already, he had chainsawed the topmost branches that obstructed the drive; the rest of the trunk balanced in an amputated column on its crushed foliage, a huge evergreen umbrella blown inside out.

Even so, Alex felt a curious reluctance to dispose of the pine on his own. The tree could wait; there were fences to right and roofs to mend and sheep and cattle to find. The thought of Kish out in the bay with Merridy intensified the young man's absence.

Not until Sunday morning late did Merridy and Kish untangle the last lantern. On Monday, it became Alex's turn to claim him.

In the hour before dawn, as he drove his tractor across the darkened fields, Alex startled a bloated devil gorging on a dead cow on the other side of a fallen fence. He discovered the putrefying corpse a yard or two inside the adjacent Crown forest where the animal had blundered in the storm, its hide tined by fangs of barbed wire and a sheet of rusted tin embedded in its neck. He repaired the fence and afterwards dug a trench. Playing with the notion and then dismissing it that this was the very cow he had mistaken for a ghost. He levered the remains into the trench and covered it over with bark and leaves.

The crude burial reminded him of the task that he had postponed, for which he would be glad of Kish's assistance.

Down the corridor he heard a mannish laugh. As he had not heard it in years. He refilled Rusty's bowl with water and sat at the table and finished a piece of cold toast that he had left uneaten, and picking at the marmalade label waited for her to come into the kitchen.

He stood up and kissed her.

"What's that smell?" she said gaily.

He told her about the cow in the wood and the devil that had emerged from its backside, teeth clamped around an intestine.

"Let me wash your clothes," and started to unbutton his shirt.

But he held her hand.

"What's wrong?" noticing his face.

"You're wearing mascara."

"I saw myself in the glass, I look so old."

But the lilt in her voice did not sound right. Her face above her green jersey over-bright and the make-up drawing attention.

"Aren't you going to your shed?" he asked. She was usually out of the house by now, dressed in her work clothes. There were nets and baskets to stitch with baling twine, mud-maps to fill in, outboards to mend. In spawning time, she often told him, you needed to get everything ready for the next run.

"I have to ring Panasonic."

"What the hell for?" releasing her.

She looked at him, surprised at his tone. "I lost a blade."

"What blade?" asked Alex. Her face seemed slimmer under her make-up.

"For the bread-maker. Second time, too! I'm going to have Panasonic send two this time. Oh, and Alex, I almost forgot – the new cleaner's coming today." Alice's daughter having moved with her partner to Longford. "She should have been here at eight."

Alex heard Kish knocking around somewhere in the house and went to talk to him.

By the time he came back in, Merridy had moved to the sink. Both hands held onto his plate that she had dried.

"What's up with Kish?" Alex wanted to know.

"Why? Where is he, anyway?"

"He refuses to leave his room, but right now I could do with his help."

"Just go and tell him you need him," carefully stacking the plate.

"It's that lump of wood I gave him. He can't keep his hands off it."

"A bit obsessive, isn't he?"

The sound of a vehicle brought Alex to the window. "Your cleaner's here."

CHAPTER THREE

HER NAME WAS MADASUN, a Catholic from Devonport. She had advertised in Talbot's *Newsletter*.

She parked at an angle on the far side of the tree and tripped from her car, spilling keys onto the gravel. Her round face obscured by frizzy auburn ringlets that she brushed from wide trusting eyes. She had only recently moved to Wellington Point and had overshot the entrance to the house, ending up 30 kilometres away in Bicheno. She was dressed in blue dungarees and had a large watch on her wrist.

"I was listening about the Pope, poor man."

Merridy showed her where the cleaning things were, and around the house, and introduced her to the figure who stepped into the corridor.

"This is Kish."

"That's a nice name," not put off by the skull on his T-shirt. "Unusual."

"I'll be in here if you want me," said Merridy, and opened the last door.

Barely twenty minutes had passed when the vacuum cleaner was switched off to be replaced by the sound of Madasun's resonant voice. She was conversing with Kish in his bedroom and what they were saying, on that cool, overcast day, reached Merridy in Alex's old workshop. It was clear that Madasun was not going to be efficient in the tradition of Alice or her daughter.

"Where were you heading?"

"Hobart Town."

"No, really?"

"I was, too."

"What were you going to do in Hobart?"

"I dunno, spear a whale or two."

"I thought they'd banned whaling. You're not Japanese, are you?" He laughed.

"I bet you're a Virgo. I always get on with Virgos."

"Who are they?"

"Oh, come on. When were you born?"

He gave a date.

The girl giggled. He was funny, Kish. "I don't think even whales live that long. I'm serious, when were you born? What month?"

He told her again.

"Then that would make you, let's see . . . a Pisces."

Suddenly, he did not want to play her game. He mumbled something.

"Look, if you'd rather not tell, that's OK," she said concerned. "It's not important."

But there was something, clearly, he did want to reveal. He spoke in a halting voice. Too low for Merridy to hear.

"That sounds like head lice," said Madasun. "Maybe you should go to the chemist's."

But it was of a different category, evidently, from nits.

"I know what you mean," Madasun sighed. "I feel like that sometimes. Utterly lost. And with a fiancé, too."

So far as Merridy was able to gather, her fiancé was a fireplace installer from Beaconsfield who had a child by a previous partner. Her parents disapproved, but probably they would marry in October. If not, she had other plans. She would like to write science fiction. She would like to study Aboriginal art. She would like to travel.

Until Merridy got up from her desk.

"Maybe you'd like to get the cobwebs out from behind the fridge," interrupting.

Madasun jumped up from the end of the bed, impervious. "Oh, Mrs Dove, gosh, I was so enjoying listening to Kish that I forgot myself."

Kish lay across the unmade bed. He watched Madasun unplug the vacuum cleaner. Then he folded his knife, picked up his piece of wood and left the room.

Merridy called after him: "Kish, where are you going?"

Over his shoulder: "To help Mr Dove."

*

Merridy returned to her desk and flung herself into the mundane tasks that she had put off for the spawning season. After ordering the blades for the bread-maker, she compiled a list:

– sort out cleaning schedules
– sign and date harvests
– order seedlings

By ten o'clock, she had drawn a fresh mud-map, marking the new positions of the lanterns, and composed letters to the Department of Primary Industries and to Dmitri, apologising for having to postpone her visit to Melbourne. To leave the farm right now was impossible. *I am still dealing with fallout from the storm,* she wrote. *Perhaps I could come next week?*

But it was sand to halt the tide.

In Sydney, he was shoving everything. A wonder he didn't wear his pecker out.

The room she sat in was at the end of the house and the window at an angle to the lawn so that she could only see a tantalising portion of the grass. On another day she might have been too preoccupied to look out. But this morning her eyes kept straying. She watched the lawn as dutifully and carefully as Tildy used to watch Zac. The fallen tree with its massive claw of roots and stones and soil.

Did he notice her figure, her eyes? Some men did and the idea of it made them stupid.

A figure approached the tree. Kish! But it was her husband. He stood talking to someone out of sight.

She watched the familiar face that time had nicked and hollowed. He bore the scars of two carcinoma operations, on his right cheek and right hand where he faced the sun when driving the ute. And all at once had no control over her emotions. Dark thoughts flapped around her.

She forced her eyes to the tree. The simplicity of the fall was dreadful, the massive finger aimed at the sky in the angle of a benediction now pointed, stunted and accusing, at her.

Alex said something and came on towards the house. She heard the fly-screen open and close. The sound of the cistern flushing. Her hands tightened into fists. In that instant she hated him that he could still pull a chain, still shut the fly-screen. He was like the air which she had expelled. And she hated herself even more – for this sudden and unexpected ill-will, this deadness towards her loving, decent husband.

She picked up her pen again. Appalled and shaken that she could be capable of feeling like this. She took a fresh sheet of paper and started writing. *Dear Mum . . .* Drawing in the whole assembly of her mother's church to her sense of shame and guilt. *It has been months since I last wrote.* And rummaged further into herself as if she was the wardrobe in their bedroom, to throw her sinful feelings out and leave only what was pure. But her pen did not know how to go on. What could she tell her mother? She looked outside to find the words – and found Kish.

"A young man washed up on the beach the other day," she murmured aloud. *"En route to harpoon a whale in Hobart Town. I've hexed him with my lantern and he has sky-blue limbs, a shiny silver knife and a ring in his ear, his ear. I surprise myself in the uncomfortable position of wanting to sleep with this man, to taste the sea in his mouth. Do you see my quandary? Please advise, your otherwise faithful daughter, Merridy."*

Her gaze did not move from the enigmatic figure who had appeared from behind the fallen tree. In Alex's jeans and denim hat. He was playing with Rusty.

"Know what you are, Merridy Dove?" she said. "You are a silly, silly cow." But still her eyes fumbled after him.

Partially concealed by foliage, Kish snapped off a branch and threw it across the lawn. Then as Rusty ran to fetch he leaned back against a bough and took something from his hip pocket.

She rolled her chair forward. What was he carving? Whenever she woke, she could hear him through the bedroom wall, working on it. But if she asked what he was making, he told her it was a secret. She had little doubt that it had – obviously – to do with ships. Something about the *Otago* obsessed him. Once, on her way to collect firewood, she had startled him poking his rigger's knife into the bottle, but the blade was too wide. He had leaped back, as when she had found him by the wardrobe.

This time she smiled. "Still trying to get that penny out?"

"Hey, Kish!" It was Alex, reeling him in again. Carrying across the lawn not the chainsaw, but two spades. "Come over here."

They walked to the base of the tree and the pine's roots obscured them.

She looked down and wrote quickly: *It is very sad about the Pope. It doesn't look as though he will survive much longer. I realise he has been a constant all my life.*

After a while her serenity returned.

"Mrs Dove?"

Madasun, knocking on the door. Her three hours up.

Merridy scraped together forty-five dollars from her purse.

"We need some bleach," said Madasun. "If you like, I can get it."

"No, I'll get it."

She had decided to tell Madasun not to come again. But what came out was: "Same time next week?"

After the grateful girl had flustered her relief, Merridy returned to the letter that she was halfway through writing to her mother. *Alex is still counting the damage from the storm. He lost eleven sheep and the roof of the shearers' quarters. I wonder if the winds reached you in Devonport . . .*

By noon Merridy had covered six sides. She folded them into an envelope and went into the kitchen. Kish must have finished whatever he was doing with Alex because his silver knife lay on the Welsh dresser. Engraved into its handle, a name – Marlow – that she had not noticed before. Of the manufacturer, perhaps. Once again she tested its blade. This knife to cut ropes that threatened to entangle him, or her.

"Hey! That's mine."

She had not seen him come in.

He snatched it back. Settled his buttocks in a chair.

"Hungry?" she asked.

"I suppose."

He put his legs up on the table and she felt like a woman in a Western when she snapped at him to get them off.

"I thought of making some pasta," she said.

He yawned.

"Does that mean you don't like pasta?"

"No."

"What do you eat in Sydney?"

"I dunno, meat."

She filled a pot with water and put it on the stove. "Weren't you going to saw up the tree?" staring out of the window. That stagey tree she had never liked for its insistence upon itself. She had supposed that getting rid of it was the priority. So she understood.

"Maybe this afternoon."

"What were you doing just now?"

"Righting some stones."

"Oh," before realising that he meant the granite gravestones.

"Didn't Mr Dove tell you? They were popping out of the ground."

"I know. I could see them from here." She turned back into the room. "Something to drink?"

"I wouldn't say no to some moo-juice."

She opened the fridge and poured him a glass of milk, which he drank down in one gulp.

Her breasts filled out her jersey.

"Hey, don't," he said, over the top of his glass.

"Don't what?"

"Look at me like that."

She took his glass from him, colouring.

Tak, tak, tak. From over by the sink she watched him persecute the wood with his gleaming blade, and compressed her lips. She had worked hard with Kish in the bay, lifting and dropping oysters and altogether too busy for conversation. But after the quiet communion at sea, he had reverted to his former prickliness. All his childish seriousness transferred to Alex.

"What's that you're making? Is it a ship for Alex?" Who had never, she realised, taught her how to put a ship in a bottle. Not even tried to.

He rolled it over in his hand. It could have been a naked man swimming. Or drowning. "It still hasn't told me."

"Then it had better get a move on or there'll be nothing left."

Tak, tak, tak.

"You know, Kish," carefully. "It's not good to tell stories."

"I don't," he frowned.

"I overheard what you said to Madasun. That stuff about you being a long-lost sailor, well, it's not really very funny."

"I wasn't trying to be funny, Mrs Dove." He was giving her a hard time, that was all.

"She's an impressionable girl, Madasun. She might believe you."

"So?"

"It's just that . . . Look, Alex and I, we want to help."

He said nothing. He had pulled into himself.

"How old are you, Kish?"

"Nineteen. How old are you?"

"Thirty-six," she shot back.

"How long have you been married, Mrs Dove?"

She looked at her fingers. There was ink on them. "Almost seventeen years."

"Why don't you have children?"

That fucking question. Again. Always. She hunted around for some soap and picked it up, but it had stuck to the dish.

"Didn't want them." Her answer so harsh that he turned his head.

He studied her face, whiter than the soap dish. "You'd like a child, wouldn't you?"

The energy had retreated from her shoulders and legs into her face. Her eyes shone like a sick person's. She picked up a shaving that he had missed. "What I would like," she said from within her invisible hole, "is for you to throw away your mess into that bin."

At the sound of her distress, he laughed. His sawing laugh that kept away questions.

"Want to know what this is?" He held up his stick of wood, the colour of a dirty collar. "It's a key."

"A key to what?"

"Your wardrobe, I reckon."

On the stove the water bubbled away.

Holding onto the table. "It doesn't need a key."

She'd wanted to wait for Alex but her wish to shut Kish up was stronger. In silence, she prepared his lunch and served it to him.

Two mouthfuls into the meal, Kish poked his fork at something on his plate. "What's this?"

"Anchovies." As her father had taught her.

"I don't think I want antchervees."

"But you've got them, haven't you?"

In which position Alex interrupted them.

"Ah, Kish. Do you have a second?"

"I suppose."

"It's that bloody windmill," to Merridy.

"I thought you'd fixed it."

"Yeah, but it's gone again. I reckon it hasn't worked for days. The storm must have buggered it."

"I've made some seafood pasta." This being Alex's favourite.

"It can keep, love, can't it?"

Merridy looked hard at the bowl. "I suppose."

She waited for him to leave the room. His unshaven chin, his reek of dead cow.

Guided by the snorts of thirsty cattle, their heads scraping empty tin and feed on their damp noses, Alex had only now discovered that the windmill was not pumping water to the troughs.

He hoped that the fault lay with the spear beneath; with Kish's help he pulled up the black plastic tube and staring down saw a little rear-mirror of light and his face taut and stubbly.

It puzzled Alex. "Plenty of water there."

"Can I look?"

Kish kneeled, screwing up his face like a photographer at his reflection. Then he twisted round and nodded at the windmill. "Bet you London to a brick the problem's up there."

"It's always caused grief," Alex acknowledged. Most probably, the storm had been the final straw, the wind pumping the machinery into a frenzy so that a vital part had snapped inside the maze of rods and pistons. This time, Alex was determined to get the thing properly repaired.

As he struggled to his feet, he noticed Kish's eyes still on the ladder. "Want a look?"

They climbed to the viewing platform.

Kish took off the denim sun hat that Alex had lent him and raked a hand through his spiky hair, then put it back on, and shook his head. "Good view, Mr Dove."

The grey sky had gone and the sun was out. From far below, Rusty whined up at them.

"Hi, Rusty!"

His back to the rail, Kish turned and looked the other way.

"Hey, what's that?"

Before Alex could stop him, he bent forward and ran his fingers over the faded orange letters that the wind and salt had all but burned off.

It was hard to believe that this was the same angry and confused young man whose lunch he had interrupted. Unlike Merridy, Alex had not warmed to the arrogance contained in the skull shirt, but as he watched him puzzle out her name that had bled into the rust he was glad that he had insisted on Kish staying.

"Been on a farm before?"

"I have been on one, I think," straightening up. His eyes did not budge from the vane. "But I can't say it was anywhere like this."

Alex checked his watch. Now that he had made his decision, he was impatient to press on, find the right person to fix the windmill. And there was still the pine to clear from the lawn. But he had forgotten how pleasant it was to have company.

He looked at Kish. "Ever sat on a horse?"

For the rest of that afternoon, as he had with Merridy half a lifetime before, Alex rode Kish over the farm.

"Just hang on, he's a tame boy."

Alex led the way, opening and closing gates.

The far side of Barn Hill, a piece of wood came away in his hand. He reined in. Legs the larger for a pair of his own trousers kicked Merridy's horse until it came up beside him.

"Look," showing Kish the decayed fence post. "Mayfly caddis."

Splashing across the rivulet where his father liked to swim, they saw a cormorant take a trout on the wing. Kish watched the bird flash through the air and the wriggling silver fish.

"That's a beaut," a sly respect in his eye. The sun glinted on the lens of the borrowed glasses and on his smooth cheeks. One week on and still no beard.

"Better than a police siren?" asked Alex.

"I reckon."

And Alex, on the horse beside him, felt a shot of paternal pride at how this confused Sydney boy responded to his land, his animals. He indulged in the extravagant idea that he had plucked from the sea a child he had never had. He had stuck a life jacket on him and now he had put him on horseback. And he admitted to himself how much he would have liked as a parent to teach Kish a whole lot more.

Three months, though, would be ample. Because what would Kish turn into if he stayed? He would pick walnuts, work for Nevin at the garage, peddle porn DVDs. Or worse. Look at Zac, loved to death and caught stealing from Talbot's. Or so the rumour had it at the RSL. No, three months would be ample, and sucked on his blade of grass at the prospect.

Over by Moulting Lagoon, Kish watched Alex and Rusty move the herd between paddocks. The cows bellowed, stretching black necks, and swayed reluctantly through the gate.

Alex could hear Kish talking to his horse as he closed the gate. He swung back into his saddle.

"Let's go before it breezes up again."

High up in the clear sky, a flock of tiny birds dipped steeply up and down like a shoal of fish in the air. Alex scratched between his horse's ears and the animal quietened into a lope.

"They're fast," Kish remarked, staring at the birds.

"You'd be fast, too, if you flew a hundred miles an hour."

They rode on at walking pace. The bird's twittering audible above the squeak of leather.

"What are they, actually?" Kish leaned forward in the stock saddle; the jolting had sifted away any last trace of discontent.

"Magic birds. White-throated needletail swifts. They fly everywhere, except the ice cap. And you know the most amazing thing about them? They sleep in the air, they feed in the air – even mate in the air."

"No way!" said Kish.

"It's true. They spend their nights up there on the wing. And only come to earth to perch or nest."

"Where do they nest?"

"Treetops in north Asia. They find a hollow and go down deep into it, or cling to vertical, rough bark. But it has to be vertical."

"What, you mean they don't land on the ground?" in a marvelling tone that reminded Alex of his own reaction as a boy on first hearing this fact.

"Their legs are so tiny, they couldn't stand up. They wouldn't be able to fly off. You could say being on the ground doesn't suit them."

Once again it struck Alex that he had no one to talk to; on his own for most of the time, he lacked opportunities to share his thoughts, his enthusiasms. He had Merridy, but Merridy was not always enough. Especially after she discovered oysters. Not for the first time, it made Alex think that he needed another person about the place.

"What I love about those swifts is that we know so little about them," he said. "There's a lot of people hell-bent on taking the mystery out of life. Bit of a shame, really."

On hearing this, Kish seemed to fall into deep contemplation. He did not speak again for the rest of the ride home.

Growing restless after the two men trotted off, Merridy put on her Driza-Bone and went outside. She had no destination in mind, but once on the lawn she walked across it until she stood before the graves of Alex's parents. The stones upright again, the neat earth patted around and sprinkled with the oyster-shell fragments that always reminded her of chicken claws. Her shoes crunched on the mended soil before the names. Basil. Marjorie.

And without warning thought of Hector.

It was not, in fact, the inscriptions that brought her brother clattering up from under the seashells and pine needles and small woody cones, but the touch of grey feathers.

Merridy hauled herself onto the fallen tree that she had never bothered to climb when it was aimed at the sky, and was rubbing her fingers over the abbreviated trunk, exploring the scarred wood from which Alex had sawed Kish's fragment – when she looked down.

Hemmed in beneath a mattress of browning twigs, the mangled body of a kookaburra.

She had not brooded on her brother since her marriage, nor discussed him with anyone, not even Tildy. Instead, she had created a space where he could not enter. But the longer she had refused to think about him, the more insistent – in a cavity of her mind – the memory of him became. It seemed to Merridy, leaning down to discover the snarl of feathers and crushed bones, that Hector was still there, trapped in the amber. Trapped like this sheltering bird.

So she walked back to the house, as isolated in her thoughts as the two men riding towards her. More isolated even than in the painful months and years when she nursed the infantile idea that her brother might return a stranger from another place and time, but would she recognise him?

Twenty minutes later, she discovered Kish sitting in her chair in the kitchen. He was bent over a white cereal bowl and stabbed at something in it with the tip of his knife.

"I thought I heard the phone. Where's Alex?"

"In his office."

"Enjoy the ride?"

"It was good. Real good."

She looked over his shoulder. A few seconds passed before she absorbed the latest object of his persecution.

"What are you doing, Kish?"

"You don't understand how small we are, Mrs Dove. We want to walk big. Be important. Someone dying, people have this idea it affects the whole world. And yet we're not so much as the smallest scraping off this piece of sand. We're so small, God doesn't even know we're here."

"Don't be silly."

"He doesn't."

"I don't know what He knows and I don't suppose you do either."

"What do you reckon God looks like, Mrs Dove?"

"How would I know? I don't think like that any more."

"You're not listening to me," he said to Merridy who thought that she was. "What do you think He looks like?"

"That's not the point," irritated. "Why? Do you have any good ideas?"

Kish stood up and walked over to the Welsh dresser and took down the *Otago* from the shelf. He held up the ship as though it were a telescope and investigated her through it.

"I'd say He could look like anything. He could look like the face on this coin."

"You don't mean that."

He put down the bottle on the table and stared at the coin. He stared at it and he thought about it. "I do."

"Tea?"

"You know, I'm sick of tea, Mrs Dove." He turned to her. "Ever heard of Rudolf Steiner?"

"No," surprised by this turn in the conversation.

"He must be close to whoever made us. He discovered that when you bury a cow horn with cow manure at a certain time, the manure is fifty times more powerful. It's the same with iron. Gearboxes made for Ford cars in 1977 last for ever. Those made in 1978 go to pieces."

"Honestly, Kish! Where did you hear this?"

"Gangell told me."

She remembered the probation officer with the gammy leg and the face of a possum, how she had disliked him.

At that moment the door opened and Alex strode in, smiling broadly. "It's all on," he said, addressing Kish as much as her. "I've spoken to my agent and he's put me in touch with this bloke in Woolnorth."

She was lost. She had no idea what her husband was talking about. "What bloke?"

He took a bucket from under the sink and filled it with water. "The windmill expert. I caught him in the nick of time. He's about to go to Alice Springs for three months, but he can look at it tomorrow. Only snag is, he refuses to leave Woolnorth. I'll have to take it to him."

"What, dismantle the whole thing? Isn't that excessive?"

"That's what he says. Hey, Kish, fancy a trip to the north-west?"

"You want to do this now?" she said.

"Come on, love, you should see the state of the animals. What choice do we have? Kish and I can drive it up tomorrow."

"But is that allowed – I mean, for Kish to leave here?"

He turned off the tap. "I don't see why not. Not if I'm there to look after him. It's no different to you having him out on the *Zemmery Fidd*. And we'll be back for dinner."

CHAPTER FOUR

IT TOOK UNTIL NINE the next morning to unbolt and collapse the windmill.

With a sense of relief for which she chided herself, Merridy watched Alex and Kish load it onto the ute and leave. "It's not a bad thing that you're going," when Alex asked if she would look after Rusty. There was tack to clean, her trip to organise. "I can spend the rest of the day preparing for Melbourne."

For Dmitri had now insisted on a date. "We want to do promotion. Send photographs, anything you've got to make you look good."

They had been gone four hours when the woman telephoned.

"Mrs Dove?" That mainland voice.

"Mrs Wellard."

"I've rung about Kish. How is he?"

"Kish is fine." Although he had seemed awfully glad to be getting out of the house.

"I spoke to Sean."

"Sean?"

"From Child Welfare."

"Oh, Sean." On Sunday afternoon, Sergeant Finter had arrived with a man who stayed for coffee and had a word with Kish and left.

"He sees no reason why the arrangement can't continue. If you're happy, that is."

"Oh, we're happy," said Merridy.

"Could I speak to Kish?"

"I'm afraid not." Licking her lip. "He's away with my husband."

A pause. "I see. He'll be back when?"

"I'm expecting them for dinner."

"Then I'll ring tonight."

Merridy put down the receiver and returned to the stove.

The onions were almost caramelised. She smashed some garlic

under the flat of a knife and chopped it up and added a pinch of coarse salt and a tin of Italian tomatoes. She pureed the tomatoes and the onions with the potato masher so that Kish would not be able to see them. She was making the kind of sauce she used to make for Tildy's children. Simple, with no evidence of onions. She was an expert in hiding onions.

CHAPTER FIVE

KISH SPOKE HARDLY AT all on the journey to Woolnorth, content to stare out the window. The further north they travelled, the more extreme the impact of the previous week's storm on the landscape. The trees on the east coast were hardened to strong winds from the south-east, had grown to face them. But north beyond Longford, the vegetation faced in the opposite direction, towards Bass Strait. Unaccustomed to fast-bowling gales from the south, the gums and wattles had been spun out of the ground like cricket stumps.

They stopped in Stanley and ate fish and chips on a triangle of grass surrounded by seagulls. Kish soon finished his meal. He watched Alex chewing.

At last, he spoke. "Harry says you can get wonderful pork pies in the north, just like he ate in his youth in England."

"When did you talk to Harry?"

"He came up yesterday to see you."

"Where was I?"

Kish shrugged. "He says Tasmania is a place where you can get things that have vanished from England."

"You shouldn't listen to Harry. What did he want?"

"He didn't say."

Trailed by seagulls, Alex took his paper plate and dropped it into the bin with the remains of the battered trevalla. Across the road, a she-oak had collapsed onto a house.

Alex looked at his watch. "I said we'd be there by two."

The windmill expert lived near Cape Grim, a small cove of black sand. Below, a treacherous sea receded from the cliff in white rags.

"Does it ever get calm?" Alex asked the man, who was called Scantlebury.

"Oh, flat as."

Mr Scantlebury had a well-trimmed beard and a serious face protected by rimless glasses, and was employed at the wind farm.

He was in his workshop when they arrived, a converted hangar next to a whitewashed stone cottage. He walked out to the ute and lifted the tarp and nodded.

"Probably the bearings." He was familiar with the model. He had serviced an identical machine in Gladstone. "The bearings go and no one does anything with them."

Only one thing about Alex's windmill puzzled him.

"You live by a highway or something?"

"No, why?"

He reached out a leathery hand and shifted the vane to reveal the bright, fresh orange letters.

"Reckon someone's been hooning around with a spray can."

It was almost four o'clock when Alex called from Smithton.

He was in a buoyant mood. Mr Scantlebury had inspected the windmill and was confident that he could repair it; furthermore, was prepared to work late to do so. But it would not be ready to collect until the following morning. Rather than waste a journey, Alex planned to stay overnight with Kish in the north. "We should be back by lunch."

"Where will you sleep?"

"Scantlebury's recommending a B & B in Alexandria."

He had not sounded so happy in months.

"So you'll be back by lunch," she said slowly.

"What are you doing?"

"I was making you dinner."

"Then we'll have it tomorrow. We can eat it tomorrow, can't we, love?"

"Oh, I should think so," without force.

"Did you finish all you had to do?"

"Yes, I got everything sorted."

But she felt dowdy. She took the sauce off the stove and the cake out of the oven – it looked cooked through – and went into her bedroom. Nauseated suddenly by the kitchen smells on her clothes, she stripped. *Anything you've got to make you look good.*

As Merridy had not done since a teenager, she found herself appealing to her reflection in the bathroom mirror. She combed back her hair, squirted some three-year-old scent beneath her jawline, polished her nails and put on a bit of make-up. Then rolled on a pair of new stockings and unhooked from the wardrobe the cornflower dress that she had picked out in the Myer winter sale for her trip to Melbourne. And as the clock chimed four on the radio shut Rusty in the living room and climbed into her car to drive to Wellington Point.

She was strapping herself in when she heard the telephone ring in the kitchen. She was on the verge of taking off her seat belt when it crossed her mind that the caller would be Mrs Wellard. So she drove away.

RECENT TRAGIC EVENTS

From Sgt Pete Finter: "The recent tragic events in Oyster Bay have highlighted the necessity of having a suitable local rescue boat in our area, as in Swansea. It's frightening to think that without Alex and Merridy Dove there would have been another death. Merridy's handling of the <u>Zemmery Fidd</u> *(which the young lady designed with her very own hand) was an amazing feat of seawomanship. No less exceptional was Alex Dove's dramatic rescue of a drowning Sydneysider. I know that the whole community takes pride in this brave act. Well done, both of you!"*

In Talbot's, Merridy took a *Newsletter* from the stand next to the till, and then a *Mercury*. On the front page, the same bland-looking man stared out at her with the same unwavering expression: "*Is your memory a sieve?*" Next to him, the photograph of a five-metre boat uncovered in Marion Bay.

Watch out for ghost ships! The wild weather and giant swell which battered Tasmania's coast earlier in the week have already bared the wreck of this long rowing boat in Marion Bay. Anyone who sees a wreck should get in touch with the Parks and Wildlife Service.

Merridy folded the newspaper into her trolley – and turned to Rose-Maree. "Where do I find bleach?"

"Sorry?"

"Bleach, Rose-Maree. Where is the bleach?"

"Oh, it's you, Mrs Dove," said Rose-Maree, thawing. "You look amazing." She pointed out the aisle.

And, searching for bleach, bumped into Tildy.

For a fraction of a second, they failed to recognise each other.

"Merridy!" laughed the oversized figure in a grey coat. The freckles were hard dots in her cheeks and around the thick neck was twisted an orange scarf.

"Tildy!"

"How are you? You look well."

"And you."

"Off somewhere special?"

"Oh, no, not really."

"I like the dress!" rubbing her fingers over the lapel. Her hand was puffy and her face had a peaky look. "Why don't I ever see you?"

"I know, it's ridiculous."

"My God, how long has it been?"

"Your father's funeral, was it?"

Tildy touched Merridy's arm. "But that's three months ago! I reckon we saw each other more when you were in Melbourne."

"There's a lot to catch up on," agreed Merridy and felt a warmth returning. There was so much, suddenly, that she did want to say. "How are the kids?"

"How long have you got?" Tildy groaned.

Now it was her hand on Tildy's arm. "Hey, what are you doing now?"

"You mean right this moment? I've got an X-ray at five, but after that—"

"An X-ray? Is something wrong?"

"No, no. It's the Breast Bus." Ever since Tuesday, a converted coach offering free scans had been parked outside the Louisa Meredith Home. "Ray thought I should go – seeing it doesn't cost a cent. Plus it gets me out of the house."

"Then let's meet afterwards."

"Where would you like? I'd ask you home, except Ray's got Albert Talbot coming round for a chat that's apparently so bloody important we've all had to skedaddle. The girls are having a sleep-over. I'll be free as soon as I've dropped them off."

"What about the hotel?"

Tildy hesitated, as Merridy remembered once hesitating. "I suppose we could."

"Say six o'clock?"

Merridy had parked outside Talbot's. She looked across the street, but no one moved in Ray Grogan's office. With an hour to kill, she put her shopping in the trunk and walked towards the Bethel Teahouse. She longed for a strong coffee.

It was that time of afternoon when the wind had paused and the bay was a plate of blue. Out beyond the jetty a gannet mortared the water for black-backed salmon.

But the tearoom was locked.

Disappointed, Merridy peered through a Gothic window at the sombre interior and recalled the afternoon when she had pressed her face to this very pane probably, and searching inside for her mother spotted Alex.

She did not want to think of her mother, but now that she was reminded she was comforted by the maternal presence. Whatever her warm feelings towards Wellington Point, Merridy had never forgotten her mother's opinion of country people. "There's a jealous streak running through this town, Merridy. There are plenty here who hate success. The slightest cut and they're in there – feeding. Mrs Grogan will tell you no different." (This after Mrs Bowman overheard Rose-Maree caution a woman in Talbot's: "You don't want to have coffee in that place, you might get contaminated.") And now the Bethel Teahouse had chairs stacked high on the tables and a black-and-yellow board outside.

A premonition of this same sign planted outside Oblong Oysters hastened Merridy across the road. She walked up the hill, away from the Tearoom. If she could not have a coffee, she would spend the next hour exploring her town.

It was not so often that Merridy found reason to stray from

the waterfront. Her traditional goat path was the main street. On this still afternoon, striking out up Malvern Road, it struck her forcibly the degree to which Wellington Point had altered.

Early on in their courtship, Alex had walked her around, sketching in the history of the settlement. As if repeating fragments told him by his father.

"That" – the golf course – "is where Captain Greer cut down the trees that reminded him of his dead soldiers at Waterloo."

"No, that's where Tildy lost her virginity."

"What, to a golfer?"

"If you must know – Pete Finter."

"Swansea," pointing seven miles across the bay.

"That's where Ray Grogan really would like to live."

His hand cut the air, encompassing the horizon. "Over there, Maria Island . . . The Hazards . . . Oyster Bay."

"Which those who have never been there bravely liken to the Bay of Naples!"

"Ssshhh."

So had she surrendered herself to his silence. She had been on death-watch ever since driving her father and mother down from Zeehan, and had failed to take in her surroundings. But then she stood beside Alex and made an effort to look at the view through his eyes – and saw that it was indeed spectacularly lovely.

In the intervening years, the weatherboard houses had transformed themselves into spic, modern brick homes: "Wivenhoe" and "Cherwell", and "Bliss House" and "Gay Bowers", with gleaming 4x4s behind their security gates. Some of their owners were unknown to Merridy as were the owners of two or three small businesses that had mushroomed on the fringe of town, employing handfuls of people, filling the school, electing Ray to the council. In the first years of her marriage she had known by name nearly everyone in the community. This afternoon almost the only name that she recognised was the one proliferating on the wasp-striped boards visible up and down the street.

She walked on fast and turned into Worcester Crescent, but neither here could she escape the signs. Wherever she looked the same name rose to challenge her.

Ray Grogan. Why not settle for more? Everything I touch turns to SOLD.

On the dot of six Merridy stepped into the old cocktail bar. She frowned at the room. Seen from the entrance, the place was a chaos of fume and noise. There was a large television screen bracketed to a wall. There was the bray of relaxed males and women squealing, with low lights to bathe the faces. She imagined everyone's breath a different colour, the spewing tangle.

Merridy ordered a tomato juice from a woman with lavender-tinted hair whom she recognised but could not place. Behind the bar, where in her first week working for Tildy's father Merridy had had to pin a postcard of Mount Vesuvius, was a photograph of a log-truck, captioned: *Doze a Greenie*. But it pleased her to see the convict brick on the counter. Still filled with matches.

She paid for her tomato juice and made her way to an empty table under the television.

In the artificial light, a stud on a dog's collar winked. Largely unnoticed on screen, the Pope got on with dying. A spectre in a wheelchair appeared at the Vatican balcony. The twin of a Francis Bacon portrait, a poster of which she had had Blu-Tacked to her wall at uni.

"The world is standing by," a commentator gravely intoned.

"No, we are not, pisspot," snarled a tall, emaciated figure in an old cricket jersey – the only other person watching. And to his dog: "We're not standing by anyone, are we, Paddy?"

He caught Merridy looking at the animal.

"Hi, Harry."

"Do I know you?" in an English accent. He stared at her uncertain. Long years had pushed back his eyes. In the pulsing light they were the colour of the oysters that she once grew in the river. "Ah, Mrs Dove, if I'm not mistaken?" and abruptly grinned.

"That's right. How are you?"

"My days are numbered. I saw my specialist in Hobart," and caught his breath. "It's likely to be soon – and sudden."

"I'm sorry to hear that." Harry Ford had come to Wellington Point in 1957 to die, but . . .

He nodded at the screen. "Pope and I, we're in the same boat," and scowled out of his lined, grey cheeks. "But answer me this, Mrs Dove, if he's going to Heaven, why are they weeping?"

"For themselves, I imagine."

"Hypocrites!" he rasped. "Hypocrites!" and held the dog lead tighter. "And Alex? How's that fine husband of yours?"

"He's good," she said, withdrawing. She had never enjoyed moments spent alone with Harry.

But he was not letting go. "I heard . . . I heard that you have a lodger." And his breathlessness reminded her of the chandler in Hobart and a rocking boat.

"That's right. His name is Kish."

He leaned over her. His teeth were slimy and the pupils in his eyes were black. "You do know that's not his name."

"I do."

"As hot a yo-yo as the world produces. So I'm told. As hot as a pistol."

"Is that right, Harry?" angrily smoothing her dress. And remembered Alex: "If a martian landed on Dolphin Sands, Harry would do his best to interview it for the *Daily Express*."

"And you, my dear, how do you find Mr Kish?"

"He's been a great help to me on my boat."

"So I understand. So I understand." At his feet, eyes bulging at the tightened lead, the dog alone watched the pontiff dying. "But take care. My grandmother used to say: 'Save a thief from the gallows and he will cut your throat.'"

"I don't think Sergeant Finter would have allowed him to stay at Moulting Lagoon Farm if he was worried."

"My dear girl, Pete Finter never solved a crime in his life. You might tell Alex—" But the effort of speaking was too much and his face collapsed in a coughing fit.

"Are you all right, Harry?" Overcoming her distaste, she stood to clap between his shoulder-blades.

But he waved her away. He covered his mouth, and jerking his dog after him beat a retreat through the drinkers in the direction of a door with the outline of a beaming man in a top hat with a cane.

*

Merridy was left looking at the crowd that seemed to expand even as it swallowed up Harry; at the row of men and women at the bar who sat or stood over their stubbies, talking. She recognised barely any of them: the vet, a tapering man with a wife who tore off bottle caps with her teeth; and the lugubrious, bearded face of Sammy the Serb who was said to eat roadkill – Alex had once discovered him plucking a crow. These were all that she knew.

"The insurance salesman came out in me. I rang the Kempton pub and asked: 'Who in Kempton is having a baby?'"

"Harry says the coppers sat on it and the driver kept mum. They're doing sixteen hours a day, those drivers."

"One of the great pontiffs in Vatican history."

"She's so fat now, you could slap her in the dough to make gorilla biscuits."

Merridy stood and listened. She could not quite believe it. This room where she had worked all those years ago, and which she remembered as habitually deserted, was now a thriving bar where the whole of Wellington Point seemed to have convened. Paying no attention to a dying Pope.

Merridy caught the sweet, thick smell of a home-grown joint – not unpleasant – and coughed.

She sat down again. Tildy was late. She sipped the tomato juice and watched out for her cousin. But her image of Tildy was impaired by the suspicious, monitoring faces that stared back at her. Until she was no longer looking for the woman whom she had bumped into earlier in Talbot's, the one with pendulous breasts and chicken's feet scratching at her eyes, but a girl with varnished cedar curls and a Cupid's bow mouth who leans over a garden gate in west Ulverstone and holds out a brown paper bag.

"Hey, want one?"

The bag, Merridy cannot help noticing, is spotted with wet purple bruises. She walks up and reaches in her hand and casts about for a cherry that will not stain her gingham dress.

"Going to the dance tonight?" says the mouth made for love.

"That's right."

"There you are!"

She was waved out of her thoughts by Tildy. Her puffy hand

above the sea of drinkers' heads. Her wool scarf like a shred of orange peel.

"Hi."

"Sorry I'm late."

Thirty-six again, she watched her cousin push her large body through the throng. A face on which the eyes of men no longer clung.

Once upon a time Tildy's father had owned this place, but that counted for nothing now.

Merridy heard a voice say: "You won't hear the telephone ring in that!"

"I couldn't see you," Tildy apologised, bursting free. She put two glasses full of something down on the table. "That'll give a spurt to our juices."

She subsided onto the stool and clinked glasses. "To us."

Merridy reached out, happy to see her again. She did not normally drink alcohol. But she had finished her tomato juice and the hot, smoky room made her thirsty.

"To us," and swallowed. "Mmm. What is it?"

"What you used to serve me. Rum and tonic. Oh, I've wiped myself a couple of times on that, I can tell you – between Captain Morgan's and Bacardi. I don't do it any more. Not since I've been off the slops. But tonight I will make an exception." Tildy crossed two thick legs beneath the India cotton dress. And looked directly at Merridy. "Well?"

"How was the Breast Bus?"

"There's nothing to tell," shrugged Tildy and clutched at her bosoms which moments before a disaffected Canadian nurse had rested on cold glass plates. "She was so bored she might have been arranging fruit. They're bloody freezing still."

"Lump free?"

"Think so – you ought to nip in. Anyway, I have plenty of other things to worry about. Plenty." Tildy poked around in her handbag. "Thank God, you can still smoke in here."

She put a scuffed paperback onto the table and then a packet of cigarettes.

"I didn't know you smoked," Merridy said.

Tildy shrugged. "I just lied on the mammogram questionnaire. Why, do you want one?"

"No."

Tildy tapped one out for herself and went on ferreting in her bag. "At school, I have to stand out in the yard," in a voice distorted by the cigarette between her lips. "But not for much longer."

"What, are you giving that up?"

"Certain aspects of my daily intake are no longer satisfied by catering. I want to do something for myself."

"Like what?"

Very seriously, Tildy said: "You're not to laugh, but I am toying with the idea of going into politics."

"Politics," Merridy repeated, wondering if she had misheard.

"Now don't you sound like that, Merridy Bowman Dove. You are looking at the person who organised our entry for last year's Tidy Town competition. In which, may I remind you, Wellington Point came proximay something or other." She leaned forward. "I'm going to put my name down for the council election in April. Listen, it makes sense. I know everyone. I've fed them all. They can vote for me. At the very least, I'd make a better politician than Ray."

It all seemed odd to Merridy. "Tell me, how's Zac?" falling back on a more reliable subject. In the past, when the two cousins had had nothing to say to each other, they would talk about Tildy's children.

Tildy winced. "Later." But unable to restrain herself, she plucked the unlit cigarette from her mouth. "It was his birthday on Tuesday. Guess how old he is? How old do you think Zac is?"

"He must be—"

"Fifteen!"

"Fifteen . . . And Montana?" Merridy said quickly, to tide her over the fact that she had forgotten Zac's birthday.

"Just started grade eight."

"Alex loves Montana."

"Everyone loves Montana," with that blend of pride and resentment which mothers reserve for daughters who seem to enjoy greater luck with the opposite sex than they can remember having had themselves. "Shit, I was in such a hurry to leave the house I left my lighter behind. I'll get a match."

While she waited for Tildy, Merridy rotated the paperback so she could read the title. *The Shadow Line*, with mild surprise. The girl she knew from Ulverstone was not merely politically illiterate but voraciously unread. Interested only in magazines like *New Idea*. Who whenever she saw someone reading a book felt impelled to distract them.

"I started it on the Breast Bus," Tildy explained, resettling herself. "I remember Alex discussing it." It had stayed with her, his expression as he talked about the book. His concentration fastened on the mystery in his hand that Tildy could not hope to match by undressing. But the passion with which he spoke had made her want to glimpse it for herself, even if it had taken her all this time.

"What do you think of it?" Merridy asked.

"There's a bit of packing. But all writers use packing. Have to make up the numbers. But you just skip and keep on going," and drew on her cigarette.

"I'd no idea you liked Conrad." And yet Merridy had known that there were seams in her.

"Sweetie, you'd know a heap more about me if you bothered to ask. It's all I do now, read." She looked for somewhere to put the dead match before squeezing it under the wrap of her cigarette packet. "Reading gives you four eyes."

"When did this happen?"

"It might have happened a darn sight earlier if you and Alex had got your fingers out. Remember I was thinking of joining Agnes's reading group?"

Now Merridy did. "That's right. And we were going to write you a list. Oh, Tildy, I'm sorry."

"You never gave me a solitary title, either of you," Tildy scolded. "So in the end I was left to make the discovery for myself." She took in a long draught and blew out the smoke through her nostrils, smiling. "I'll tell you and you won't believe it. That New Year when you looked after the children?"

"When you and Ray went to Coles Bay?"

"That's right, for our fuckathon," and her eyes sparkled at the irony. "Well, Ray drank too much and afterwards fell asleep on top of me. Next morning he went out to fish. I was so bored and upset. That's when I found this paperback under the bed. *A Fringe of Leaves.* Well, I didn't have a clue what it was, it could have been a gardening book, but I read the first page, for something to do, I suppose, and flicked through the pages to see if they were the same colour. Anyway, when Ray came back with his flat-head and his kisses I was still reading. At last, I had an idea of what so excited you and Alex. Merridy, I never understood before. It was more exciting than anything Ray could offer. It meant that I had something to occupy myself when he woke up next morning with kidney stones, and we had to rush to Hobart in the ambulance." She coughed. "Smoking, it's worse than snakebite," and took a sip to quell her throat. "Actually, over the years I've meant to ask you for books to borrow."

"Why didn't you?"

"I thought you'd laugh at me. But it's one of the reasons I haven't been out and about so much." She put down her glass and cast her eyes around. "In fact, this is the first time I've been in here since Dad died."

"I don't think I've been here since my wedding reception."

"It's where Ray always comes," Tildy said.

"How is Ray?" Still trying to accommodate the novelty of Tildy the Reader. "I heard he was in the Louisa Meredith."

"Only with a minor concussion. I suppose you know what my fat-head of a husband did? Smashed his *Follow* bloody *Me* all over the boat ramp. Mark you, he learned this morning he'll get 120 per cent of the cost of the frigging thing from the insurance. And did you hear? He'd been bloody *warned* not to go out that afternoon and he told this very kind English gentleman to go and pee all over himself. The pity of it is that he didn't get drowned himself . . ."

"Oh, Tildy, you can't mean that."

"Yes, I do." The weight of her body made the stool squeak.

"I see his name everywhere. *The David Boon of real estate.*"

Tildy nodded. "Listen to him and he's single-handedly responsible for the property boom!"

From the street came the sound of a car horn and the scream of brakes.

"Bloody bogans," someone muttered.

A girl giggled, the enthusiastic giggle of the marijuana smoker.

Tildy cradled her glass with both hands and grew thoughtful. "I meant to say this before. You were right about Ray."

"What makes you say that?" doing her best to remember whatever it was she might have said.

"The way he carries on. He's changed, Merridy," and bit her lip. "Or maybe he is what he always was and only you had the smarts to see it."

"Maybe he's under pressure at work?"

Tildy sipped at her rum. "Only pressure I'm aware of is from other women's cleavages."

"Oh, no."

"Oh, yes," and made a motion with her glass. "Only yesterday I'm having my hair coloured and he comes in and starts carrying on with the hairdresser, who used to work in his office. So there he is, talking to his buxom, hard-headed friend, not knowing it's me sitting across the room with Glad wrap about my head. He's probably been shagging her on the floor of the Bethel or wherever he's meant to be selling."

"Tildy, you don't have proof."

"Don't think she's the only one." Tildy blew out smoke. Cooling the hot dish of her anger. And all at once looked oppressed. "I think one of his tarts has had a baby," in a small voice.

"Good grief!"

"Not anyone we know." Her pink tongue licked an upper lip. "A Japanese girl he met last year," and she gave a mirthless smile. "At a real-estate convention in Melbourne, for pity's sake."

Tildy had received a letter from this woman asking her to release Ray from his marital vows so that they might live together – "'I love him so much, blah, blah, so if you care for him in the slightest, blah, blah, you'll let him be with me, blah, blah, blah'" – and enclosing a photograph of a baby girl looking vaguely like Ray, except with oriental eyes and straight black hair.

"Ray denies it's his, of course. But I don't believe him. Frankly, I've reached a point where I don't care one way or the other. I tell you, when I looked at the photo of that baby I felt the battery acid run through my love channels and I knew that our relationship was busted for ever. But Zac's taken it none too well. He heard us rowing about it and found me all in a heap. I honestly believe that's what made him behave as he did. You heard about Zac, I suppose?"

Merridy nodded. Everyone had heard about her godson. Caught with his fingers in the Talbot's till. "Zac's five-finger discount," Agnes was calling it.

"It was dreadful." Tildy looked around. Then, recognising someone, leaned close. "It wasn't much money, but Ray was furious . . ." Her voice trailed off. Her Cupid's bow snapped. "Mr Talbot's coming around tonight to discuss it. That's why Ray wanted the whole family out of the house. Montana, Savannah, Cherokee, me. All except Zac."

Merridy put an arm around her shoulder. "Oh, Tildy," as two women passed.

"Hi," one of them called out to Tildy.

"Hi," rubbing her nose.

"Who are *they*?" asked Merridy after they had gone by.

"Search me," Tildy said, pulling herself together. "Oh Christ, don't look now. There's Harry Ford."

"I know. I've been talking to him already."

"How is he?"

"Dying, he says."

"He's always dying. He's been given extreme unction so many times the priest in Campbell Town now sends a bill."

It revived Tildy, to laugh at her own joke. She found a tissue in her bag and blew her nose.

"He reminds me a lot of someone," Merridy mused. "But I can't think who."

"Mr Twelvetrees, could it be?"

"Tildy, that's exactly who!"

"Remember his face, how he used to stare?"

"'Miss Framley, I think that's your foot on the floor.'"

"That's him! That's him!"

"'Please remove yourself, Miss Framley. Meanwhile, will all other couples tear their newspapers in half.'"

"Just want to get by you, mate." A man lurched past. She was pushed against Tildy. They were joined again at the shoulder and for a second there was a unity of lines in their faces and conflicting thoughts, and they were friends again. Her hand touched Tildy's skin. They were reconnected.

"She'll be coming round the mountain when she comes," Tildy sang, her face lapped by the television light.

They were both laughing now; rubbing the tears that rolled down their cheeks and causing Harry's dog to bark. They laughed so much, thinking of the Friday dances. Girls again.

"And you were always the one left standing," said Tildy. "You were so attractive. You still are, of course. Everyone wanted you, Master Twelvetrees most of all."

"They did not."

But Tildy was right. Randal Twelvetrees had believed that the two of them were destined. Had got it into his head that her mother's rejection of him years before was God's way of preparing him for his inevitable union with Merridy. There was suddenly projected onto her memory the day that the Minister's son had taken Merridy to a church near Penguin to make a brass rubbing. She saw him kneeling on the floor and the peculiar movement of his Adam's apple as he brushed the lock of red hair from his eyes and declared himself. "You think there isn't a pattern, Merridy. You think we're just a blank sheet to be drawn on. But there *is* a pattern. You only have to rub on it like this. And then it takes shape, what was there all along. Our whole life. Stretching before our eyes. Just waiting to be rubbed over with a piece of black crayon."

"Listen," Tildy said, "I'm getting us another drink. I want to hear your news."

Tildy came back with fresh glasses. She leaned an elbow on the table; she could have been leaning on a garden gate, contemplating cherries. And lifted an eyebrow.

"So tell me, Merridy. About yourself."

They sat awkward, at an angle to each other.

"I don't know there's much to tell," stalling.

"Everyone's talking. That boy you rescued. I hear Alex was so brave."

"He was. He was incredible." And fidgeting on the stool

described for her cousin the night at sea; how Alex threw himself into the waves, and how Kish almost dragged him under as they swam back to the *Zemmery Fidd.*

"They're not talking only about Alex's bravery." Tildy picked her words with care.

"How do you mean?"

Across the table, two eyes shone. "Talk is that you and the boy, you're actually quite close."

"Me and Kish?" She felt the dried tears on her cheek.

"There's me shooting my big mouth off."

The hubbub had receded and the faces of the drinkers bathed in television light and smoke, and the denim-covered legs.

"What are they saying?"

So Tildy repeated what she had heard, about their sordid trampolinings and how Merridy was so sweet on Kish that she hung a white shirt out when it was safe to visit, a purple T-shirt when not.

"But that's absurd," Merridy said, and reached for her glass.

"Oh, I've crossed too many dry creek beds to worry about Wellington Point gossip." Again, an eyebrow raised itself. "Even so, something's wrong, Merridy. I know it is."

"No, it isn't." She finished her drink.

Tildy stood up.

"Hey, where are you off to?" said Merridy.

"I'm getting us another."

"I'm going."

"Stay where you are," Tildy commanded.

"I've had enough," but Merridy sat down.

Tildy went away and presently came back.

Merridy watched her put down two more glasses on the table.

Tildy touched her arm. "Come on, sweetie. Share." This time the cigarette she offered was hand-rolled.

Merridy shook her head. "I don't smoke."

"You don't drink, and you're drinking. C'mon, it'll relax you. Ray used to grow it himself until he became a councillor."

Dully, Merridy accepted the joint. Inhaled.

She looked up at her cousin. Tildy had seen her childhood; to everyone else, even Alex, she covered it up. Miserable, she pushed the words out with the thick, sweet smoke: "I don't know. He reminds me of . . ."

"Of who?" Taking her hand away.

"No, it's stupid. I know it is."

Everyone at that bar, which had shrunk with the crowd of people and the enormous screen and the dimness of the lighting, everyone began to fade.

"Not him?" And Tildy saw that she had hit the mark. "That's crazy, Merridy. Hector is dead," very sharply.

"I know," flinching at the name.

"Well, then." Almost angry now.

"But what if . . . what if he didn't die?"

"Well, he'd be almost forty for a start."

"What if—"

"Oh, tommyrot. He died. I don't know how he died, but he died. Full stop," and sat there in glowing annoyance.

Merridy sucked on the cigarette. She was not strong enough for these memories. "He's dead, of course. It's just that when I'm with Kish . . . this sounds idiotic, but . . ."

"But what?"

"I feel, I don't know . . ." She could not stop them. Tears coloured with mascara and rouge. Tears that followed lines which had not been there when they were young. "I feel like I did when Hector was alive."

"That's a very, very long time ago," Tildy said in a voice that had never sounded so grown-up. And raised her glass.

Merridy was matching Tildy sip for sip. Swallowing more than rum. She was swallowing her fear, her pride, her guilt.

"My turn," said Tildy in a jollier voice and took the joint from her.

Merridy borrowed Tildy's tissue and dabbed at her cheeks. "Have you ever wanted anyone – apart from Ray?"

"Oh, Merridy, aren't you getting any?"

"It's not that," in what had become a trembling whisper. "I know that look, and it's not what you're thinking." Over Tildy's shoulder she could see Harry eyeing them. "Don't you know . . ." but the shame was welling, to suppose that Kish might be any resolution to her hidden anguish.

"Of course I know," Tildy sighed. "But that's in the past now, darling." And tapped the grotty paperback. "This gives me everything I need. Well, almost."

Merridy slumped back. "I don't know why I'm talking about this. It never leads to a good place. Let's forget it."

But Tildy was on a jag. "For God's sake, when *are* we going to talk about it? You know one thing reading has taught me? It's that you may as well talk about it because it's *there*. Everyone has felt dreadful for you over the years, but at a certain point your refusal to talk about Hector has turned to poison. To be honest, until you talk about him no one will ever know you – and can you tell me what is so great about not being known? I bet you don't talk about it with Alex. In fact, I bet you chose Alex because you knew you wouldn't have to talk about it with him." She took a final puff and stubbed it out and picked up her empty glass. "Another?"

At last, Merridy pulled herself to her feet. "I really must go."

"Well, go then."

"You're not staying, are you?"

"I don't know, I might. Just for a little. Like I said, it's been ages. Anyway, Ray's probably not finished his oh-so-important business with Mr Talbot," with an embittered laugh.

"Then I'll say goodbye." She moved unsteadily to kiss Tildy's cheek, but their heads bumped and they were kissing on the lips.

Tildy clung to her. "It was lovely to see you, Merridy. You're still my best friend."

Merridy left her there.

It was dark outside. A harvest moon was slung between the Norfolk pines. The white chips of the whittled clouds that the south-easterly gathered across it provoked a dread in her.

Merridy walked on legs that felt drugged. Gulping the air, she stumbled towards her car when she saw a dog in the middle of the road, hunched over something. And observing the dog, a tall figure silhouetted against the moon.

The English voice spoke half to itself. "Pretends he's deaf when he's eating roadkill. He is deaf anyway, but he's even more deaf then."

"Goodnight, Harry."

"Goodnight, Mrs Dove. Don't forget – my affectionate regards to Alex."

CHAPTER SIX

ALEX WAS SURPRISED THAT there were no other cars at the Alexandria Beach Retreat. All was explained. The guests had fled the convict-built cottages because of the stinking whale.

The owner, a small and talkative nurse from Burnley, had lived twenty-five years on this spit. She was relieved to greet two clients who did not appear to mind the stench.

"I live on a farm," Alex said.

"It got so bad I had to spray the room every half-hour. You had to cover your face. You can still smell it faintly," and sniffed. "There." She stepped back from the reception desk and pointed through French windows to where the adult sperm whale had rolled onto the shore, yards from her hotel. "That whiteness on the rocks was made by the oil. See the sea eagles?" Two grey smudges on the pines at the end of the beach. "I think that's some of the intestines over there. Yes. Bits of intestine are sitting over there."

Cormorants wandered along the sand with pieces of blubber in their beaks.

"It was fifty foot long when Parks and Wildlife did their post-mortem. They think it was the storm that made him lose his way, poor thing."

"Is there a toilet?" asked Kish, face taut.

"Over there." And to Alex: "I'll just get the keys."

She went into another small room. Kish headed straight for the lavatory while Alex looked at the newspaper that she had been reading.

A black-and-white photograph on the front page caught his attention.

He was still arched over the *Advocate* when the woman came back.

"I'm putting you both in the deluxe cottage. It has a spa-bath. I assume you don't mind sharing with your son."

Alex looked up. The colour had drained from his face. "I'm sorry. We are going to have to leave at once. I really am sorry, but this is an emergency. Could I use your phone?"

When Kish returned, he found Alex pacing up and down.

"We're going home."

"What, now? But it's right on dark."

"I have to see Merridy."

"What about?"

"It's about her brother. I can't tell you any more." He did not want to talk at all until he saw her, was with her.

"Then what about your windmill?" a good deal puzzled. "Isn't it going to be ready tomorrow?"

But Alex was already out of the door.

CHAPTER SEVEN

MERRIDY HAD A DANGEROUS drive home. Coming down Cerney Hill, her car hit a wallaby. Startled, she drove on. Around the next corner a possum stared at her, two bright pins of light, then scuttled onto the verge. It seemed that the road would never end.

She was in a tremendous state from more than one source and disturbed by her conversation with Tildy. She was ashamed to have been outed by someone with whom she had always felt safe. What she felt now was exhaustion and darkness – anger even – that she had had a drink and stirred it up in the first place. And overriding it all a feeling of dread, as if it had a force of its own and she was in its grasp.

It had happened long ago, but it was still there in her head. At the mention of Hector, she was overwhelmed by a resurgent grief. As she drove back to Moulting Lagoon Farm, she ached, she physically ached, for her brother.

On the dark, winding coast road she thought of her family's shack near Wynyard. She was standing on the deck, staring into the bush. It was morning, in late summer, and the large gums threw thick shadows. She could hear a wattlebird and the roar of the waves breaking on the stony shore. Her father was in the house, and her mother was saying something to him. She had no reason to think this, but she already knew that she was not going to see Hector again. She knew that the world for which her mother had a moment before been washing her face and grabbing the towel off the floor had altered, and that whatever now happened she was exiled from it.

Her headlights picked out the entrance and swept from the road. She drove through the gate, over the cattle-grid, into the drive. A little drunk, a little floaty, and enormously upset, she switched off the headlights. Her eyes scoured the sky. No stars, nothing but a yawning blankness. Only the white track beckoned, a pale arm that reached down out of that blankness and drew her in.

She followed the gravel drive up. The smell of horse and sheep manure rolled over the paddock. Grasping the wheel and staring at her thumbs, the moonlight on the polished nails, she was conscious of the trees reaching over the drive and animals watching. She shuddered, but she was not cold. Severed from its previous life, her heart had gone to ground. Tugged back into a hole that led to who knew where and was inhabited by God knows what.

Alex drove for five hours, stopping only in Epping Forest for petrol and a cup of bitter coffee and to ring Merridy.

Again, no answer. She had to be down at the oyster shed.

In his distress, he telephoned Tildy. He rehearsed what he would say: "Could you dash to my home? Please go out there and get Merridy before she reads it herself, or is told, or hears it on the radio." He did not want her to hear it on the radio. As he listened to the dialling tone, he thought: What about the *Mercury*? But he was confident that the *Mercury*, being a Hobart newspaper and concerned more with stories from the south, would not yet have reported the discovery.

It was Ray who answered. Rattled when he heard that it was Alex. "No, I have no idea where she is and I'm too busy to go chasing around town . . ."

Alex crunched his paper cup and threw it away. He called over to Kish and they drove on.

Night fell as they came into Campbell Town and turned onto the Lake Leake Highway. The ute's headlights roamed through the bush. In some of the shacks – makeshift cabins set among the she-oaks – Alex could see sofas on the deck and corrugated water tanks. Every now and then a wallaby hopped across the road, stopping to peer at the lights that approached at such speed, and hopped away.

After an extremely long journey, they arrived back at the dark house shortly before ten o'clock. It looked a strange place under the full moon, the windows blacker than overcooked coffee and the light glinting on the ripple-iron roofs. But no sign of Merridy, no sign of her car.

"Well, I'm going to have to see if she's at the shed," he said to Kish. "I'll drop you here."

It crossed his mind to wonder how safe it was to leave Kish alone in the house. He always thought twice about leaving his Purdey around when Kish was at home and had taken to locking the shotgun in his office. But Kish showed little inclination to go inside. He stood on the drive, stretching himself and looking up at the moon.

Alex left him there and drove down the hill, fast, towards Moulting Lagoon.

Her eyes not yet adjusted to the night sky, Merridy parked on the lawn and switched off the engine. The moon had floated into the treetops. It shone with unnatural brightness on the roofs and on the grass, save for a dark patch where the fallen pine soured the land.

She made her way, tripping on the edge of the lawn, towards the house. She could hear the telephone ringing as she opened the kitchen door, and then it stopped.

She undid the top button of her dress, not bothering to turn on the light. The night was hot and the kitchen still smelled of the simple red sauce that she had left on the table and the walnut cake that she had baked for the men's dinner. Relieved to have the house all to herself, she kicked off her shoes and tramped along the corridor. Through her rum eyes the place was alive; the samplers glowed; and the cockatoo looked bigger when she went into the living room where she had shut Rusty. She followed the puppy out of the room and fumbled open the door into her study. The moonlight fell across her Huon pine trunk. With a sigh she sank to her knees and unbolted the lid and plunged her hands inside. Throwing out the cotton sheets and lace curtains that she had never unpacked, now speckled with dead insects, the cassette that she had never watched, until, at the bottom, her fingers encountered the edges of a plastic bag.

She shook the objects onto the floor, and in the lozenge of moonlight picked through them: the orange feather; the photograph of Hector on the beach near Wynyard, taken the day before his seventh birthday and that she had never been able to stick in a book; the scrapbooks of cuttings from local papers; the messages relayed through Taffy; the scuffed Blundstone.

Merridy held the child's boot to her face, in quick breaths inhaling the smell of leather and rubber.

Something moved on the deck with the intimacy of an animal's footfall that had walked there for years. And she heard the dog addressed and the shoe-squeak and the twanging of the closed door.

"Hello," he said, speaking from inside.

Who was it? Not Alex – nor Kish. They were north.

She saw, then, it was Hector.

"Hector?" fluting, and stood. There was the sound of what she had held dropping to the floor. She brought her fingers together in the way people did when they were helping one another over fences.

In that narrow passage lined with admonitions and hopes, he came creaking towards her on the cedar floor.

"Hector . . ." She pronounced it to herself as though licking the bottom of a bowl. For she had never spoken his name, never. Apart from that once. He had survived somewhere in the catacombs.

His shadow blended with the samplers, a long dark blade shucking her.

She had become a little girl again. "Hector," she repeated, licking the last leaves so that she would not have to read a fortune. And felt her hunger and panic rising.

A smile crawled along his face.

"You look nice."

"Hector!" A name to shout through her palms. She could not stop herself. His eyes quivered as if he had heard shots. Never had they seemed so strange and round and listless. His hard, deep mouth like an initial engraved.

He came closer. He smelled of stars. She wanted to tell him how much she had missed him; her brother.

"I was just out looking at the moon," he said and smiled.

She heard her young girl's laugh. The *Advocate* was open on the floor. They were dancing around a newspaper. And over in the corner Mr Twelvetrees was playing the piano.

"You're back." In a voice that she used for another person from another world. And threw a hand over her eyes against any thought of the future. "Thank God, you're back," and ran forward in her drugged state to embrace him. Her shirt was unbuttoned; she was sailing towards him in the *Otago*, the gulls cawing, the spray nicking her face and the wind licking at the ice-cream mast and up between her legs. The whole planet was sailing on a wave across the floor towards him.

"Is something wrong?" he asked.

She plastered herself onto him. Longing enamelled her lips. She had bandaged him away inside herself, but all burst out when she touched him. She kissed his face, squeezed away the years, in the ferment of her passion unbuttoning his shirt, taking off his glasses.

"No, no, nothing's wrong." As sobbing she lost herself in his flesh.

He seemed grateful for her outpouring of affection. For a moment he gave in to her embrace.

But he was so unhappy, or sick. Or burning. His mouth made an ugly shape. "No," he said – like that. When she touched him.

Ungluing, she felt his eyes on her. His trapped look.

She looked at her sky-blue hands on his face. Her fingers like tubes squeezed out. Her capacity to touch had dried like paint.

"No," he simply said. And pushed her.

The illusion that it was Hector passed like a shadow down the corridor. Leaving behind Kish. "Pull yourself together."

"Kish . . . ?" She looked at him, incredulous. "I thought you were someone else." And heard her lunatic words fade away. As he ran from her.

A door slammed.

"Kish."

She flung open the door to his room and stood there, her head dishevelled. Nobody.

"Kish!" She was snivelling now. Suspended between her childhood and Kish.

One by one she flung open the doors along the passage. Until she came to her bedroom. No one there. But something had changed. She looked slowly around. Flicking her eyes back and forth. Before she saw what it was.

The wardrobe door – closed.

She started forward and hammered on it. "Kish . . . let me in." But the door was locked fast, from the inside.

Merridy stooped, peered through the keyhole. Filled with his damned piece of pine. She listened to his breathing. And moaned. "Kish! Let. Me. In."

In the kitchen, the telephone was ringing again.

The gate to Oblong Oysters was locked.

Alex returned along the lower road, stopping now and then to check the troughs. He parked next to the shearing shed and after satisfying himself that the bullocks in the paddock had sufficient feed decided that he was too tired to climb back into the ute. He left the vehicle where it was and walked towards the house through the farmyard.

The route took him past his old workshop. Out of habit he looked up at the window. Still no light on inside the house, but over on the lawn the bright moonlight reflected from the roof of Merridy's Toyota. Thank God, she's back, he thought. But how funny she hasn't turned on the lights. There must be a power cut. He was about to walk on when he heard the sound of someone talking in excited tones. He stepped across the flower bed and pressed his face to the glass. The door to Merridy's study was open.

He could make out Merridy in the corridor. She was standing sideways on, one hand up to her face. Instantly, he had the feeling that had seized him when he first saw her. And remembered her forthright laugh and how gamine she was. He was about to tap the window to get her attention, but something about her posture stayed his hand. Then her knees straightened and she ran towards a figure who stood framed in the kitchen doorway, flinging her arms about his neck and clinging to him.

And the man clinging to her.

The news that Alex had to give her bled away. He stumbled back, tripping over roots, heart thudding. He picked himself up.

A door slammed, then another, excluding him. Not knowing what he was doing, he forced his way through the shrubs and bottle-brushes, obedient to a blind force that dragged him around the house, over the flower bed that encircled it, until he stood outside their bedroom window.

He put his neck forward to the glass as if shaving himself. Merridy was in the room. So, evidently, was the man she had embraced, because she was calling to him in a voice haunting and low – the most entreating sound that Alex had ever heard.

"Kish! Let. Me. In."

Alex had no response, no defence for this situation. He remained where he was, absolutely stationary. A tiny bit surprised that Merridy did not see him as she flew out of the house a moment later.

He was rooted to the spot for as long as it took Merridy to scramble into her car and accelerate away down the drive.

This was too much. He did not want to talk to Kish. He did not know what he wanted. He was going to go away and think to himself what in God's name was he to do with his wife and this young man, who would have to get out of his house at first bloody light.

He blundered off, as on the morning when his parents were killed, letting his body take him in the direction of the sea and the sanctuary of his lichen-spattered rock.

The moon shone white on fields where convicts had been flogged for speaking. Blasted with grief, he roamed the paddock that he had walked through ten minutes before, a different person then. His shadow snaked after him, blending with charred stumps. Startled cattle looked up at him as they might have looked at a spectre. And all the time the thumping in his chest.

He staggered towards his rock.

CHAPTER EIGHT

FROM ITS SHELF HIGH up on the Welsh dresser Kish seized the bottle with the *Otago* in it, and fled the appalling house. Across the drive, the clothes-line reared up. The silhouette of the Hill's Hoist against the moon sharper than any gallows.

He swerved onto the lawn and stood very still, panting. He saw that she had taken her car.

His breathlessness was slow to pass. He could not recall this fear before. Fear, though his legs were fast and his knife was sharp. He felt the wind on his torn fingers. Already he missed his room. The consoling smells of kitchen and puppy and log-fire, not to mention the sensation that came over him whenever his eyes looked into those bottles with their ships, shelf after shelf of them. It was so difficult, believing in an abstract. At Moulting Lagoon Farm he had come as close as he had known to belief. That household had offered him the prospect, if not of a lasting home, then a place he would like to have had as home for a little longer.

Warm memories buzzed in his head. Her car – without any headlights on – braking in a skid on the lawn. The way she had stumbled into the house like a sick animal. The windows he had watched, waiting for her to switch on a light. It had relieved him to be away from the farm all day: he had felt the stirrings of desire, but even if he thought Mrs Dove attractive he was not going to get involved there. When at last he had stood up to follow her inside, it was to see if she needed help. Not to be suffocated by her. Not to be mistaken for someone called Hector. Not to be . . .

So he stood by the tree stump, dazed and offended at the violence that she had disturbed in him. In his chaos, he thought: Ah, fuckit. What am I going to do when Mr Dove gets back? Towards Mr Dove he experienced a mingling of gratitude and respect and even a wish to learn from him. But now he had no idea what to do, where to go. He skirted the upended pine and ran and ran across the grass with the bottle burning his hands, until he could tolerate it no longer. At the bottom of the drive, he flung it into the darkness. But no sooner did he hear the scrape of glass on stone than he sank to his knees and scrambled on all fours searching for the bottle. He was convinced that he had lost or broken it, had given up hope, when in a glint of moon he saw the edge of the penny and the bottle still intact. He grabbed it and lay in the gravel and held it tight against his chest.

CHAPTER NINE

IN THE DEPLETED BAR, Ray lectured a truckie.

"A man is a single person, though he might have a second nature. A woman is twenty-three different people, none of whom can stand to be introduced to each other."

"Fair dinkum," the truckie said, stroking a wide black beard.

"Chap in Melbourne told me that," Ray said. Contentment had made him expansive.

"Mathematician, was he?"

"A businessman, more like." Ray smelled his wine and sipped, rolling it around his mouth before swallowing. "Tell you another thing about sheilas. As soon as they get you, they want to change you. They want to bring out the heavy rollers and the sandpaper and rub off the rough edges."

The truckie finished his glass of Boag's. The crowd had thinned and there was no one left to listen to Ray but him.

At his end of the counter, Ray had had another thought. "Why is it that women ask other women for advice about men? Surely they should ask men, since that's the area they want to know about. It's like asking a colonist about the Aborigines. It really is."

The truckie patted his beard philosophically. But did not dwell on Ray's wisdom. Perturbed still by the strange young man who had flagged him down an hour before. The truckie was coming round a tight corner north of Wellington Point when the man ran out at a crouch. His first thought: A large animal had skittered from the bush. Then in the middle of the road it stood up. Barely human, in the headlights. With the face of a persecuted creature, scary too. Any faster – roadkill. He had slammed on his brakes with every foot he had, skidding across the road and jerking his log-truck to a stop with less than the length of his arm to spare. So had he sat recovering his breath in large gulps, his eyes taking in this creature who nursed to his chest what he saw now was a bottle. A fucking wino! Wearing spectacles and with a ring in his ear and glitter in his hair and on his jeans like he'd been to a party. Except that it wasn't glitter. You could see by the dashboard light when he opened the door and scuttled up into the cabin that it was little flecks of glass. Thousands and thousands of them. The wino had asked for a ride into Wellington Point. Too late to refuse him. He had sat for the next ten minutes, hugging that bottle of his, not speaking, until the truck hissed to a halt outside the hotel. "I'm gonna stop here and have a beer. Wanna beer, mate? Or you can have a gin if you like?" But he shook his head. Cheeks rigid in the street light. Eyes emptier than two cemetery jamjars. Then opened the door and leaped into the night, no word, not even a "Ta-ta, mate".

In ebullient mood, Ray ordered a glass of Merlot for his new friend and another for himself. "You, too, Belinda?"

He had bought a whole carton of it.

"He's celebrating," explained the lavender head.

"Oh," said the truckie, and turned to look at Ray. "Lotto?"

"Not quite."

The truckie nodded. "I was gonna say, because there's nothing in the whole wide world you look less like than a man who's won the lotto."

"But almost," said Ray, straightening a sleeve on which there gleamed a gold cufflink. "Almost."

It was in a different frame of mind that Ray had opened his door to Mr Talbot five hours earlier.

"Ah, Albert, please come in." In a grave voice tinged with surprise. Save at Keith Framley's funeral, he had not seen him so formal. The oversized blue suit brought home to Ray the gravity of his son's offence. As for his eyes! They stared at Ray with a distended look, as if set lengthwise in his face. "Do come in."

Mr Talbot had asked for this private meeting. His manner on the telephone furtive so that Ray immediately divined the reason behind the rendezous. Mr Talbot was going to discuss the problem of Zac, who waited in his bedroom to be summoned, forbidden to leave the house until he had delivered the apology over which father and son had spent time this afternoon rehearsing.

"You'll join me, I hope, in a glass of Craigie Knowe?"

"Don't open it on my account," Mr Talbot said.

"I was going to anyway," smiled Ray, whose terror it was that Mr Talbot would make an official report of Zac's small criminal misdemeanour to Sergeant Finter and so the news would inevitably reach Hobart and the columns of the *Mercury*.

Mr Talbot felt the sofa and sat down. He dragged his morbid gaze around the room, the posters of the pyramids and Sphinx, the shelves double-stacked with books, before his eyes came to rest on the coffee table where there was a tray with six glasses on it. "That's nice," he muttered unenthusiastically, tapping his fat fingers on the pewter surface and rattling the glasses.

"A wedding present."

"Mrs Grogan well?"

"Tildy's out," in a light voice. Ray had furthermore instructed Montana to absent herself. And Savannah. And take Cherokee with her. This was man's business. "She'll be sad to miss you, but she's good," and pulled the cork.

Mr Talbot's eyes commenced a second circuit of the room. "Sorry to hear about your boat," he said.

"Yes, wasn't that sad? But she was fully insured. No damage to your garage, I hope?" At the same time tempted to hope that perhaps, after all, this might be the reason for Mr Talbot's visit.

"Oh, no, I don't think so."

Ray looked agitatedly at the wine label. He would speak first, he decided. "Mr Talbot . . ."

"I'll come to the point." The oversized suit wriggled.

"I'm sure we can reach some accommodation," Ray said.

"That remains to be seen."

"Before you say anything, try this. It's young, but suggestive, I think."

Mr Talbot gulped at the young Cabernet with an indefinable thirst. It was many a year since he had felt this need to drink.

Ray hovered, impatient for his reaction. "Well?"

"It reminds me," Mr Talbot said thickly, "of New Britain."

"I'm sorry?"

"Papua," Mr Talbot said. "Where I was in the war." Waiting for the rum-drop. The alcohol floating out of the bomb-bay in a chaff bag that rolled and rolled and rolled. Sometimes the chute tore and he had to go with a spade and dig the stuff out.

"*Ologeta nau*," he urged the native who stood before him.

Ray said nothing. He wondered if Mr Talbot was having a stroke.

"'All together now'," explained Mr Talbot, and took another gulp. "It's in pidgin."

"It must have been awful," said Ray.

Mr Talbot dipped his eyes to the tray, in which the elongated reflections of glasses seemed to hold some sort of fascination.

"They say you should have won the VC three times over. For what you did. That's what they say at the RSL."

Mr Talbot swallowed more wine. He said: "People think we won the war, but we sat on our arses most of the time. We could have been charged tourist rates. In fact, I wouldn't mind doing it again."

Even so, he did not look happy. Remembering line after line of waiting women, the dried grass sticking out from between their legs like a rooster's tail. The *meri* whom he had treated and sometimes comforted, his forbearance. And a woman and an evening that no quantity of Craigie Knowe could extinguish. Whether it was her sarong of blue-and-red silk, or the baby that she carried in a string bag or her stoicism towards her wound – the Japanese had damn near severed her arm – this young widow had pierced Albert's defences.

He cleared his pleated throat. "I have, as you know, no family."

"Then you are the lucky one," Ray smiled tartly.

But for mournfulness Mr Talbot outdid him. "You are looking, Ray, at the last Talbot. The last one," and slumped back. "It is a responsibility you cannot imagine, to be at the end of the line."

Ray studied the blanched sockets, suspecting them of sheltering a hidden menace. Not finding it, he was uncertain where to settle his anxiety.

"Mr Talbot . . ." he began pacifically, casting about for a line to take. "No one in Wellington Point understands better than I your wish to protect your property. No one."

"No, no, you cannot understand."

She smiled as she put down her *bilum*. In the bag, her baby slept. He remembered the shadow of the fibre mesh on the child's face, the discreet and graceful motion of her arm, the pool of parachute silk on the beaten earth floor.

"As I said, I am prepared to do anything to put this unfortunate business behind us."

"What?" he could just ask.

She stood naked. The skin on her flat stomach palpitating where her heart beat quicker. But not so quick as his heart. She was still smiling. A smile without conditions attached, or secrets.

"No women," his commander's final briefing reminded him.

But did he have the strength to restrain himself? He would never discover.

From outside, from beyond the chieftain's hut, there came – soul-destroyingly – the sound of steady typing.

Nothing would ever seem to him more separating than the vanishing of her smile as she recognised machine-gun fire, or the barbed wire of knotted string behind which a child woke.

He sat motionless. Watching her scrabble to cover her nakedness and gather up the baby with the arm that he had managed to mend, and run for her life. He tried to be more invisible than ever that night.

After an appropriate and respectful silence, Ray said: "Speak frankly. How much would satisfy you?"

"What were we talking about . . . ?" Albert shook his head. "This wine. It's making me forgetful."

"Another glass?"

He let Ray pour. His lips were rather dry.

It was after that night that they killed the members of a Japanese patrol. They watched them walk up the head of the valley and picked them off in the moonlight one by one as they crossed a river – their reflections on the water like a row of glasses on a pewter tray. One man had cried out all night. Albert went down in the morning to treat him and found his body on the riverbank. As he turned round, he became aware of the eyes of a Japanese soldier on him. He was propped against a rock and staring. Albert had raised his hands above his head before he saw that the soldier was dead, shot in the back by his own men. He began to weep then.

His eyes looked at Ray out of their hatched face. "I have decided to sell."

"Sell?" With extreme care, Ray put the bottle down. "What, the store?"

They were sitting side by side on the sofa.

"I want to know what you think it might be worth."

And after Ray had blurted a sum, so relieved that the visit was not about Zac – who would remain forgotten in his room for the rest of the evening, even after his mother arrived home and passed out on the sofa – Albert enquired what advantageous terms Ray might offer in the event that he would agree to act as agent, an agreement reached after a second bottle of Craigie Knowe stood empty on the round pewter tray, but not before Ray had jotted down a few particulars of the building, including its history – and, while he was about it, relieved a by-now tottering Albert of a spare set of keys.

"Give me a couple of days to sink about it."

"Take all the time in the word," said Ray.

"There is just one fibrillation," Mr Talbot slurred as Ray walked him home. "And I'm serious about this." A log-truck coming towards them had jogged his memory. He caught the flash of a drawn pale face and was reminded of another – an oriental woman with a baby, peering anxiously out of her crowded, chauffeur-driven car as she was motored ever so slowly down the main street, ostensibly looking for properties to buy.

"Yes?" – but Ray was not in a listening mood. Thrilled that Zac was off the hook. Thrilled at the prize of Talbot's. So that even as Albert told him very seriously about his one fibrillation, he did not quite grasp the subtext: "Oh, don't worry. That's easily arranged."

All in all, Ray was brimming. He was already thinking along the lines of the development of the bark-mill in Swansea. Perfectly adequate, but a bogan's shack compared to the potential of Mr Talbot's building. There was, in fact, no limit to what he envisaged for the Talbot emporium. His fellow councillors were sure to line up behind him. They were going to be as jealous as bright green cats. He was thinking marina, fish restaurant, bottle-shop, youth hostel, art gallery, a library even! In the morning he would speak to his contact in Melbourne. Pump her up. A once-in-a-lifetime opportunity to invest in the undisputed jewel of east-coast real estate.

"Well, thanks for that, mate," said the truckie. "I have to be in Triabunna." And stood up, leaving his wine untouched and Ray on his own.

CHAPTER TEN

MERRIDY DID NOT KNOW how long she drove around before deciding to head back to the hotel. The bar was deserted, so that now it became possible to forget her visit earlier in the evening; indeed, to believe that no time at all had passed since the first occasion she came into this room, kitted out in Keith Framley's flummery. Step by hesitant step she moved forward in the semi-darkness.

The television was still on. With his back to it, a beefy man sat solitary at the counter.

"Excuse me, but have you seen Tildy Grogan?"

So addressed, the figure rotated. Thickset with a cigar-coloured moustache. His mouth gilded in the television light.

"Why, Merridy!" His eyes seized her, growing wider and brighter.

"Ray . . ."

His scarlet skin was squalid, but it erupted, and she realised, on averting her eyes, that the Pope was being wheeled from the balcony – although not before one last upraised finger that mimicked an obscene gesture. Or a native pine teetering.

Her look said: Jesus bloody wept, but he patted a chair.

Hypnotised, she stood her ground. "I was looking for Tildy." She had driven here with no other plan, only to find her cousin and to ask if she might stay the night.

"Tildy?" and appeared bewildered. "Oh, Tildy."

The lavender-headed woman called over her shoulder: "She was here about an hour ago." And pushed herself through the swing-door.

"There you go, she's not here," Ray said.

For a bad second, all Merridy heard was the grave low buzz of the commentator and tearful American voices. Her foot stepped back. She did not want to stay.

"Hey, don't leave. I've hardly spoken to you. I've hardly seen you."

Last time together in the same room as each other – at the funeral service of Tildy's father, but as per normal they had exchanged not a word. Otherwise, Ray saw her in snatched glimpses when she came out of Talbot's. Or every summer at the Cranbrook Fair, selling oysters. It was amazing, now that he came to think of it, how in seventeen years the two of them never once had occasion to meet on their own; how they had continued to avoid all meaningful contact, beyond: "Hi, Merridy, how ya doing?" "Hi, Ray, not too bad. Yourself?" But he had thought of her, oh yes. From the moment she left him in his bedroom staring down at what, then, was unrevivable.

The stool was hard. He parted his legs. "Like a glass of this? What we're drinking, Belinda and me, is box wine, chateau collapsible."

It had never happened again, his inability to perform.

"I think I won't."

She seemed upset, with a flayed, uneasy look. Her hair springing from her head in tufts. She might have seen a ghost, or been violated. In that dress.

The memory of her, shoes off, sitting on his bed made Ray wince.

"Here, I'll do it," seeing as Belinda had disappeared into the kitchen.

Still, she stood. Her thoughts slamming doors down the corridor of her skull. She was confused, but above all she was loathing his attention. This man who incarnated her own deficiency of character. Who had he been consorting with? That barwoman, she supposed. The hairdresser. A young Japanese businesswoman. And tensed herself to slap him, the complicated loathing like an ecstasy in her. At what he had done to Tildy. At what he might have done to her, had he only been capable. She shuddered. Even in her most unstable moments, she had not gone there.

"Come on," Ray said, in the soothing tone of an acupuncturist.

So that she was left poised between her feeling of repulsion and another feeling, in which all sorts of opportunities for shame rehearsed themselves. Numbly, her rage deserting her, she sat on the patted chair and accepted the glass that he had poured. His kindess was an attrition, but she had no contours, she could blur into anything.

Denting his cheek with a fist, Ray took a longer look at her. He wondered if he would find Merridy so beautiful were he first setting eyes on her. This evening she reminded him, in a way that he had never considered before, of Tildy. But still attractive.

"That's a nice dress," fingering the lapel as his wife had done and picking some fluff off the shoulder.

She rocked back. "I have to go to Melbourne."

"Oh?"

"My wholesaler. He's been pestering me to sign a contract."

He shifted on the hot stool, though it was not lust exactly that rose within him. Rather, the consciousness of a tenderer person who was obscured by this other Ray.

"Well, you've certainly made a name for yourself," giving her a smile. "With your oysters."

"Yes, they do seem popular," she mumbled. But his politeness did not deceive.

"Pity one can't get them locally. Pity you have to go all the way to Melbourne to eat them."

"You only have to call the shed. Jason could deliver. Or I could," reminding herself that he disgusted her.

"You would?" Looking into her eyes that swilled with Captain Morgan and tonic. That stared sightlessly ahead. At the photograph of the log-truck. At the bottles that flickered in the reflected light of an empty balcony in Rome.

In this watery light, a dreadful vista opened up behind her: of untaken roads, unopened doors, unkissed faces. So with a pang she remembered Kish and the absurdity of a passion that she could not now credit, or explain. And most of all the panic that suddenly had seized her in the bedroom. The knowledge that if Kish was home then so too was Alex, and she could not face him in this state.

Ray sat forward. It was important that he told her. It was more vital to him even – in that moment – than the once-in-a-lifetime chance to develop the Talbot emporium. A Mass had started and the music emphasised to him the solemnity of his emotion. He had aimed his passion at her and it had missed its mark, but he had kept Merridy upright in his head, unattainable as an angel.

"You know, Merridy, you always made me feel, somehow . . ." But it was out of reach, what he wanted to say.

"What?" Her tactic of not looking at Ray – as if he would thereby vanish – not working. "What are you saying?" And swivelled her head.

He wore a belt now around his wider waist, and gold cufflinks. Plus gold in a bangle on his wrist and in his ear and in a thin chain around his neck; anywhere visible, it seemed. Apart from the gold, he was older. More sinew about his neck and across his shoulder, and under his chin the adipose fin of a scar. But not so very much changed.

"I'm saying that you always made me feel good."

"Oh, Ray." In her eyes a glint of frost, because of her disdain. But her disgust was not collaborating with her desire.

Ray touched the convict brick on the counter. Matches were still arranged in its hollow for smokers to strike. He laid them out carefully side by side. They might have indicated dead men. Or his conquests.

"It's true," he said, emboldened by the organ music and her gaze. Never had he felt so serious. He wanted her to slice out the tender person encased within him. Whom he glimpsed whenever he tracked the sun as it toppled over Maria Island, or inhaled the wind across the bay; or fished for stripy trumpeter on the continental shelf.

He struck a match. It flared and shrank.

Smiling at the flame in rather a sad way, Ray thought again of how little he had seen of Merridy and of how very much, by contrast, she had consumed his thoughts. She served to remind him that his life was not more wonderful for his success. He would have left Wellington Point years ago if it had not been for Tildy and the children, like five spears through the feet. But also – a little bit – because of Merridy too.

He didn't even bother pretending to himself otherwise. He had dreamed of Merridy so deep on his wedding night, at a self-contained cottage in St Helen's, but all he retrieved from his dream was a sturdy erection that caused him to leap out of bed and race through the house shouting: "Tildy, Tildy," until she relieved him of it against the low bluestone wall of the rented kitchen, pressing her buttocks into his groin until she had rubbed and squeezed it away.

But it was Merridy he was thinking of. Impregnable as Talbot's. Whose image he had continued to summon to any number of creaking beds. Who sat less than a yard away, so close that if he wanted he could reach out and touch her face; who watched the flame eat its way along the matchstick, twisting it, blackening it.

He had such thin wrists, she saw.

Her eyes smarted.

It was Captain Morgan leading her astray. And Tildy's joint. And now the wine. Grape and grain don't mix, her father used to say. She wanted to leave this place and go back to what she knew. The samplers stitched by young girls for future husbands. The cockatoo and the sieve. But Kish was there. Sealed in the wardrobe behind his absurd pine key. What would she have done if he had desired it? If he had permitted? No, she could not go back. Not tonight. Not while she was so indistinct to herself.

He blew out the flame.

So they continued to sit there. Red wine has its own moroseness in a dark room with a television on. There were a number of people she could call on, but when she imagined greeting them at the door she lacked the energy to drag herself away.

While he tossed the dead match behind the counter and waited for her to expose his second nature, the good man she had discovered during a rain-soaked barbecue for his twenty-seventh birthday.

Then Ray, who had lined up his matchsticks like so many years of his life that separated him from that moment, leaned forward.

"You never liked me, Merridy."

"That's not true," studiously not looking at him.

"You saw what you saw and you made up your mind."

She touched her hair. "That's not true."

His lips drank the wine. "What did you want with Tildy, by the way?"

"Oh, nothing that can't wait." It did not seem appropriate, now, to tell Ray that she had hoped to spend the night under his roof.

Bending, he said: "You know, I'm worried about Tildy. I think she's not well. All those books. All she ever does is read."

If Merridy had expected Ray's view of his wife's reading to be contemptuous, his next words surprised her.

"It makes me jealous. It really does. I'd like to be able to understand, too." And thought of his bookish wife on the sofa, her thick legs under her, away in some realm where he could never expect to join her. "Thing is, Merridy, she prefers books to me . . ."

"Oh, come on," and kicked him.

"Aah!" said Ray. "Aaah!"

He rubbed his shin. His face crumpled. And now he longed for her. To win her without cheating. Without the intervention of his outward self, who – he could understand – repelled her.

The muscles softened round her eyes. With pleasurable dread she looked at him. His moustache so close to his mouth, like a mutton-bird gliding low over the water.

His intensity surprised him. He felt an old warmth spreading over him. He felt exalted.

"King Lear, wasn't it – what you read to me? I never forget a name. I tried to get hold of a copy afterwards. But it was different without your voice. It didn't make sense. I mean, why would a king want to give up his throne?"

"That was another Lear, Ray," in spite of herself. "Another species of Lear altogether."

He smiled back and his smile made his eyes small. She could see the gold fillings and the illusion of some bright luminosity.

"Then that explains it!" He was mightily relieved. "I remember there was a fella with a big nose and there was a light attached to it. Come on, how did it go?"

"I thought you knew."

"No, I never knew, I was just boasting," and took another pace unchallenged into the citadel.

His moustache was thicker with straws of grey, but he had not changed. She saw that in some circumstances he might be a comfort.

His mouth opened and all of a sudden the light burst incandescent on his grin and on his neck and wrists and sleeves. He was, in that moment, something holy. She wanted to be sated with that golden light. Her hunger for it had the sharpness of pain.

"And Alex?" he said. With all that that word implied, a weak and infertile Pom.

"In Woolnorth."

"You know," in a voice austere with emotion, "I still can't figure out why you married him."

"No, well, you wouldn't."

At this, the other Ray moved forward to protect Merridy, but the old one elbowed him aside. "All on your own, then?"

She felt her throat tighten.

"Go, Harvey, go, Harvey, go Harvey Norman." On screen the Mass had yielded to a commercial.

"You can turn that down, love," said Ray to the woman behind the bar.

She had come out of the kitchen, giggling and holding a plate at which her fingers pecked. "Hey, didn't I see you earlier?" to Merridy.

"This is Belinda," enlisting her. "I've been trying to persuade her to buy the Tearoom. Belinda, my old friend Merridy."

"Sorry, folks, but I'm going to have to chuck you out. It's eleven o'clock." And, with a finger that she licked, began to snap off the lights one by one.

In the street he was all chivalry. "I'll see you to your car."

No Taj Mahal in this moonlight, she thought. He's afraid I will laugh at him. And under the influence of rum and wine felt a spasm of nostalgia for what might have been.

Mist was coming off the road. There was no sign of anyone. A bilious light in Harry Ford's window suggested the only life.

The houses drifted by. Ray held her arm. He was bigger than Alex. He towered over her, a minaret from a poster she remembered.

She bent forward a little, not in step with herself, and he caught her arm. She straightened her knees.

Then he kissed her. She neither thrust him away nor responded. She thought how his breath was strange and the smell of his skin. But his mouth was warm, not greedy. Her lips relaxed and spread into the kiss.

She was drunk. "You're drunk," she said, wiping and staring.

"No, no, I'm not."

This is not how I saw it, he realised. He continued to hold her, a wobbling minaret of indecision.

But his closeness was contagious. She wanted more of the light that the moon was already discovering in little gold flashes all over him. To have the desperation that was in her taken away.

"Listen, I think you'd better not drive home. You'd better come and stay," he said, as she held onto him.

"Your house is the last place."

So rather than escort Merridy back to his home he applied a pressure on her shoulders in the direction of the Tearoom.

"Then you must sleep it off in here. I have the keys."

"No," she said. "I wouldn't want my mother to see."

"Your mother?" he said, not really asking a question but to keep her steady. It would not do to startle her. "What about Talbot's?" kissing the top of her head. He had Albert's keys in his pocket.

She thought of Rose-Maree and again shook her head.

But Ray had stopped, was gaping upwards. "Look, Merridy," speaking in a careful voice with words like kindling that would leap into flame at the smallest spark. "Look at the moon."

They looked at it together. The moon had sailed free of the Norfolk pines and shone with a penetrating glow on Talbot's. So that it became not a four-storey brick building – erected as a warehouse for wool and skins that were block-and-tackled to the second floor; then closed after the '29 depression and reopened only when Sergeant Talbot returned from the jungles of New Guinea – but a palace that mesmerised, with windows of honey-coloured marble and pillars inlaid with jasper and jade. A memorial to the gods of love whom Ray had invoked ever since he touched Rachael Ehrman on the cheek at the age of fourteen.

Ray had never seen anything like it.

"Merridy . . ."

Holding her hand. Who was thinking:

And at night by the light of the Mulberry moon
They danced to the flute of the Blue Baboon.

"Come with me."

Stroking it.

He looked around for a bench, a wall, somewhere to sit and watch the operation of this moon – its light also falling, he noticed with excitement, on the feldspar of the Freycinet Peninsula and giving to the highest peak the contour of a volcano, perhaps, in the Bay of Naples.

"What about that bus shelter?"

Then Ray squelched on something, disturbing up a smell. In the middle of the road, a dark smear of fur and bone and sleek entrails.

"What's that?" aghast. And stared down at what had been a large animal, but so disfigured that in that light he could not tell if the corpse was that of a dog or feral cat or quoll, or what it was.

All thought of a bench was extinguished, too.

They were opposite a place he recognised.

"I know where you can spend the night!" and walked in confident quick steps across the yard where as a small boy he had rolled marbles, patting his pocket for Tildy's spare key and encountering a condom. "I'll put you in the staffroom. And I'll wake you up tomorrow."

In the schoolroom, standing amid the sloping moonlit desks, the smell of textbooks and furniture wax and cooking oil, Merridy started weeping. Her tears came without warning and surprised herself as much as Ray, who really was about to go.

"Don't leave," she whispered. She needed his shoulder more than anything else.

He touched the top button of her dress.

Her tongue found his teeth and then his tongue. Then her clothes were being pulled inside out and she was following her dress and stockings to the wooden floor.

Ray collapsed on top of her, his hands – that once had all the answers written on them – on her thighs, her breasts. In his groping, a cup of crayons fell. He kneed apart her legs and buried himself between them.

So she ground her face into a hard metallic surface, gusts of pleasure rocking through her, slave to a fatal and lacerating hunger. Shaken by the lust – if that it was – he had outed.

In time, she became aware of Ray pinning her down; and her arms stretched back behind her head, grasping the cold iron legs, black-painted and intricate, of a classroom desk. Images came to her as they used to, sometimes, after prayer. Hector, pulling on a new shoe and looking down at his foot, how it fitted. Upside down, Kish's face staring at her through the window. And Alex, whom she suddenly wanted to run to and kiss, to tell him.

But no prayer.

She moved her leg, which hurt from a splinter when she had opened it wider. Where had Alex sat?

The Blue Baboon stirred in her. Now he was sighing. The gloom of a man who had winged an angel. He had not failed this time, but his lust remained and because of it he was still.

Then he rolled over, leaving his hand awkwardly in hers. He stared at the ceiling, his brown body covered in scrolls of greying hair, and thought of the boy out fishing on his father's boat, the tug on his line as certain as a handshake, and the shiny darkness of the tuna's eye, round and black – he had never seen anything so black, not before or since – a retina that had only ever focused on the deep and now was confronted by Ray. Whose life flapped from him in awe and fear.

She withdrew her hand. The stickiness drying on it. And now she did in fact remember some words of a prayer.

Beside her on the splintery floor, Ray raised his hand that she had been holding and squinted at the freckled back of it, as if to examine answers to questions that he still, after forty-three years on this earth, did not understand the first thing about.

While she, looking at the same ceiling through the interrupted tears that were leaping back to her eyes, mouthed to herself: "*There is a mystery in every meeting, and that is God.*"

"What's that? Did you hear something?" said Ray, his neck alert. Staring at the window.

"No."

It was Ray who got up first. How his ankles were hairy she

saw between the legs of the desk. He could not look at her. Her breasts white as eyeballs. Her glossy cheeks.

She began to pull her clothes towards her. She was awfully cold, though she felt so little for herself that any feeling was a comfort.

"I think that's yours," picking up a cufflink.

She stood on one leg like a stork and put her shoe on. It was untenable, she saw that now, to stay the night here.

Then they were outside and he was throwing something into a bin, muttering: "I'm not sure how safe that was."

The street looked at them. Harry's light had gone out and the world had dwindled to a pitch-dark stain on the road.

She waited for it to absolve her.

High in the sky, a hole – and in the hole a movement.

"What's that?" For she, too, had seen the face. Like the face on a coin.

Behind her, she heard a sound – a muffled explosion almost – in the playground, but she did not turn around.

Ray went on looking at the round fourth-storey window where Albert Talbot stood – the corrected proofs of his *Newsletter* in his hand – swaying slightly. "I'll see you to your car."

CHAPTER ELEVEN

SOMETHING CRUNCHED UNDER HIS Blundstones. Alex found the switch and turned on the light. Cowering under the table, Rusty; and everywhere broken glass.

His eyes moved to the dresser – the *Otago* was missing – to a strange dark redness on the wall.

The clock that had survived this tempest told fifteen minutes after midnight. He had been gone two hours.

"Kish!" he shouted. "Merridy!" and stumbled into the corridor, a channel of shattered glass in which there floated splinters of Huon pine and bits of fluff. He ran into his bedroom and cried out. As for the wardrobe. Both doors wrenched from their hinges and the oak struts gaping open and raw-coloured as if something had exploded with terrific force.

It was easy to follow Kish's path. He had destroyed the house to look like something he knew. He had slashed the sheets and then the samplers. He had next gone into the kitchen and flung the red sauce over the walls and the cappuccino-maker on the floor and the cake down the sink. His ankles trailing coloured strands of ancient wools and letters all jumbled up, he had marched down the corridor to her study and hurled the bottles to the floor. With the exception of the *Otago*, which Tildy would discover next morning in the middle of the school playground, he had trampled to pieces each and every model ship. In his fury, he had then ripped up the photograph of Hector on the beach. He had wrenched open the cassette of *Saucy Sally Sees it Through*. He had taken a bottle of ink and spilled it over the scrapbooks and mud-maps. He had seized Merridy's favourite fountain pen and screwed it into the pages of the novel she was rereading until the nib crossed. In the living room he had snatched the cockatoo from the wall and when Rusty barked at him hurled the lithograph into the fireplace. Only then did he run from the house.

How long Alex sat in the chair by the fire, stroking the puppy that had crawled quivering onto his lap, he had no idea. Kish had gone out of his way to obliterate everything that Alex held most dear, and he waited for his body to make a commensurate response. But – peculiarly – no anger came. Alex's instinct told him that he ought to be crushed by the devastation. Instead, he was overcome by what he could only name as a great inner relief. He was conscious of his chest rising and falling, of the distant boom of the waves, of a devil or a possum screeching on the lawn. He could taste the vanilla scent of some herb or plant – a wattle, perhaps – in the air. He breathed in, feeling not anger but on the contrary a deep and authentic peace, as if a barrier which had not, until that evening, been visible to him had been removed. Under his caressing hand, Rusty snored.

Sometime later, Alex returned to the kitchen and began to clean up. Among the glass shards was a piece of paper all scrunched up. He unfolded it, and was reading the words when the sound of a vehicle brought him to the window.

The car skewed to a halt at a distance from the house. He watched a figure climb out and the small dot growing taller and taller up the drive. Against the white gravel, the cornflower dress looked ashamed.

Merridy stepped into the cast of the bright neon light and tugged open the door and then the fly-screen.

"Alex," she greeted him.

He could see from her eye that something had changed. "Kish has gone."

"Kish?" She went red.

"He's disappeared." And waited for her to explain. He so much wanted to trust her. Maybe there was an explanation.

"What's that?" She did not seem so much interested in Kish. She did not seem to have taken in the destruction. Her eyes anchoring on the scrap of paper that he held in his hand.

"This? Oh, a note I once wrote you." The only message he had ever written her. In a hand that did not know the storm or Kish. For years now, he had stored it under the *Otago*, in the same bottle. Kish must have shaken it out.

"Oh, yes," she said. What was he talking about? She could not remember.

"I forgot that I tucked it inside," he said numbly. All the excitement he had felt on the journey, all the sensations of release, had dissolved into this hollow feeling.

She scratched the side of her leg. There was something hectic in her eye. "You're back early, aren't you? Weren't you staying tonight in Alexandria?"

"I was looking for you. I thought you might be in the shed." He folded the piece of paper and put it away in his hip pocket.

"No, I was in the hotel with Tildy. Oh, my God! What's this? What's happened, Alex?" in an altered voice.

Now he remembered. "Listen, there's something important I have to tell you. Or have you heard?" She looked like someone who had heard something pretty awful.

"My God. What's gone on?" absorbing the mess on the walls, the floor, where contents from her pan had congealed and stuck.

"They've discovered your brother's body."

He took it from his jacket and, after brushing away several bits of glass, laid it flat, a page from the *Advocate.*

"Read this," he said.

And Merridy who thought she heard a cockatoo's cry, read that the high seas during the recent storm had crumbled a cliff west of Wynyard, exposing a cave that contained the bones of a young child.

She was leaning on the table.

"Hector," she said.

"It looks like it. I'm so sorry, love."

They had come together over the newspaper article.

"How do they know?"

There was the picture of a cliff and a cave. They were looking at it.

"They found a shoe. A Blundstone."

Often, when they argued, her face had a twisted look. But never this expression.

Unimaginable: in that cave, there all the time he was.

"I thought maybe he was alive still," she choked.

They were reading the article again.

“No,” said Alex. He wanted to do or say something comforting. But he carried on reading. It had seemed so important that he tell her in person.

A considerable sensation has lately been produced in Wynyard by the discovery of a human skeleton under circumstances which leave no doubt that it is the bones of a child who has been missing for thirty-one years from that neighbourhood. A post-mortem will take place on Tuesday.

For some years it was believed that seven-year-old Hector Bowman was abducted or murdered. An investigation into all circumstances connected with the boy and with his habits of life followed. Dead men tell no tales. It is often remarked that at some time or other every murder that is committed is certain to be brought to light. But it seems that this tragic death did not come about by murder. Rather, it was the result of a young and innocent lad following his nose and getting lost.

On the facing page a lawnmower had been stolen from a shed in North Motton.

She looked outside. The light from the kitchen blotted out the stars.

“I wonder where Kish is,” she murmured absently.

The silence was broken by the telephone ringing.

At last, Alex crossed the room and answered. He listened, nodding. “Yeah, she’s right here,” and handed Merridy the receiver. “It’s your Aunt Doss. She says she’s been trying to get hold of you for the past two days.”

PART V

Melbourne, April 2005; Moulting Lagoon Farm, April–May 2005

CHAPTER ONE

MERRIDY LABOURED UP THE front steps of the grand bluestone house and pressed a bell near a little grate. She stepped back, catching her breath. There were scratch marks on the cinnamon-coloured door.

"Ashfield" lay ninety miles north-east of Melbourne. A white-haired man with some effort dragged a roller up and down the lawn, and beyond the high wrought-iron gate stretched bleak flat open fields with sheep and Friesians and young horses.

The door was opened by an oldish, angular woman. Large sunglasses, loose-fitting jeans, a man's pink shirt. She had on an apron and a little dot of something floury was caught in her nostril.

"Mrs Anselm?"

"Mrs Dove?"

Merridy registered the tentativeness with which each took hold of the other's hand.

"But where's your car?" looking over Merridy's shoulder.

"I told the taxi to come back at five. There's a train at twenty past."

"A taxi! That will cost you . . ."

There was a whimpering sound. A black labrador with a hairless patch on its throat that framed a visible scar squeezed past and investigated Merridy through nervous eyes.

Merridy left her coat in a hallway adjoining the stairs and followed Mrs Anselm and the dog through the living room. Tall-ceilinged with cane furniture and expensive-looking modern paintings. On an upright piano, their likenesses framed in tendrils of silver, were arranged photographs.

"That's him," said Mrs Anselm in a Teutonic accent. She picked up a silver frame and smiled at it. "That's Daniel."

Mrs Anselm was an Austrian who had come to Melbourne after the Second World War. She had worked in a shop, selling children's shoes, and as a freelance reader for a small publisher, and finally as a secretary for a psychologist, in whose clinic she had met her architect husband. He had been building a recital hall in St Kilda. He had invited her to visit the work in progress.

"He asked me to marry him three weeks later. Three weeks."

Merridy saw by the texture of her white skin that Mrs Anselm might have been quite beautiful.

"You must have loved him immediately."

"Oh no, not immediately."

"When did you know?" angling her head the better to study the murdered man's serious, intelligent face.

"I just did – eventually." Mrs Anselm repositioned the photograph.

She had arrived in Melbourne not speaking a word of English, only the words taught by her husband's friends who played such awful tricks on her so that once, when she went to church, she looked at the children in the front row and smiled tenderly at them and said: "Poor little bastards."

Mrs Anselm turned from the piano. "I think it's warm enough to sit outside, don't you?" unknotting her apron.

She led Merridy to a screened-in deck and urged her to choose any of the three chairs to sit in – "They were all designed by my husband" – while she fetched the tea-trolley.

Merridy creaked into a high-backed cane seat and watched the old man rolling the lawn. Shattered after all her activity in Melbourne, she suddenly felt really tired, but the events of the last two days had been intense and they replayed word for word in her mind.

Merridy had spent her first morning at a nursing home in Brighton East, her mother having been admitted soon after the discovery of Hector's remains. Mrs Bowman had been watching *McLeod's Daughters* with her sister when the policewoman called.

"Why don't you sit down, Mrs Bowman."

"Why, what's wrong."

"Please sit down." Then: "It's about your son."

She collapsed when the news sunk in. By the time Aunt Doss

managed to get through to Merridy it was two days later and the *Advocate* had printed the story.

The coroner's inquest was low-key and lasted twenty minutes. Dental records, combined with DNA samples that the doctor was able to take from Mrs Bowman, confirmed that the skeleton in the cliff-face near Wynyard was very likely Hector's. The policewoman had combed the Missing Persons files and discovered a record of what Hector had been wearing. His clothing had lost its colour, but was intact. There were two coins in the pocket of his shorts, minted in England in 1963 and 1957. And there was the discovery, in the same cave, of a left Blundstone boot. Contacted by the forensic anthropologist, a spokesman for the shoe company who examined the boot had no doubt that it was manufactured in the period of Hector's disappearance. From the DNA evidence alone, the chances of the skeleton not being Hector's were less than 1 in 76 million.

Merridy had sat beside her mother's bed in the Sanctuary, holding her hand, not speaking. Mrs Bowman was a husk. Once or twice Merridy began to talk, but her mother squeezed her hand to stop her doing that. Ever since attending the burial ceremony in Ulverstone she had crumpled without warning, like a coat from a hanger, but at the same time a peacefulness filled her to know that Hector's soul was finally at rest and that she had an angel in heaven to plead her case with the Lord. So for three hours they sat in their private grasp. The square of light on the bed growing rhomboid. A young doctor giggling in the corridor. A nurse wiping a Kleenex over Mrs Bowman's Bible on which some cranberry juice had spilled.

Only as Merridy stirred to leave did Mrs Bowman peer into her face: "Aren't you going to tell me?"

Merridy pulled back her hand. "Tell you what?"

Mrs Bowman looked irritated. "I know when you've something on your mind."

"Nothing, nothing."

But the telling was a relief.

Following her fit of candour, Merridy had spent the remainder of the afternoon in Country Road on Lygon Street and then at various boutiques in Chapel Street where she bought herself a yellow dress in a larger size than she was used to wearing, and a pair of expensive suede boots. And a navy-blue, crew-neck jersey for Alex.

Next day, in a busy restaurant not far from the fish market, she arrived early for the long-postponed meeting with her wholesaler. She recognised immediately the figure who advanced between the crowded tables: a huge, swaying, black-bearded Greek with a narrow green tie that did not quite reach his belt of snakeskin.

"Dmitri?"

"Mrs Dove," holding her hand and lingering the better, as he put it, "to put a face to Oblong Oysters".

Dmitri was all politeness over lunch. Merridy let flow over her whatever he was saying. Only towards the end of the meal did he become flirtatious again. "Your ears would go a funny colour if I told you what Les Gatenby said about you."

"Really?"

"They really would. This colour," and pointed at the remains of his crayfish.

"Good. Then Les will have warned you how impossible I am," and smoothed out the contract that Dmitri had been pressing her to sign ever since Christmas.

"As you will see, I have added some conditions."

"Oh, yes?"

"I will make our agreement exclusive only to this state. And, since I'm putting my reputation on the line, I want to see all documents relating to your food standards. And I want to know how you are going to label my oysters."

Dmitri nodded. He ordered a coffee and a grappa. In amongst his beard, his lips were shining. "Is that it?"

"Not quite. You mustn't mix mine with any other product."

Dmitri wiped his mouth with a napkin, first the top lip, then the bottom. "Go on."

"I want you to give me all the names of restaurants and food houses that are going to sell Oblong Oysters – so that I can ring at any stage and see if they're happy with the product and service, and if they're splitting them correctly."

Across the table, Dmitri had folded his arms.

"One more thing," she said.

"Yes?" and lifted his chin.

"You pay electronically fourteen days after receipt. I don't have time any more to go putting cheques into banks."

She signed, after which Dmitri enfolded her in his grappa-permeated arms and asked her to dinner at his favourite place, but she declined.

Upon returning to her hotel she had taken a nap, in the course of which she was visited by an idea so powerful to her that she woke up. She only caught the tail of it, but following a call to the Bilgola Mission, Merridy contacted directory enquiries and eventually was put through to "Ashfield".

This was her idea: if there was one person in the world to whom she must speak, it was this Mrs Anselm.

"How do you like your tea?"

The tea poured, the cake sliced, the two women would converse for a further half-hour before touching on the reason which had brought them together on this windless afternoon on a deck overlooking the Victorian countryside, the paddocks that stretched flatter than an aerodrome towards Broken River.

Anxious to keep her dialogue and mood above the surface, Merridy talked about mothers and shopping and the popularity of oysters, while the roller pressed the lawn into strips of light and dark green. Until the widow, at last, broached the subject.

"They haven't found him?"

"No. He's still at large. He may not have left Tasmania."

"He escaped from your house, you said."

Merridy nodded. She expected that he had gone by the beach. His tracks erased by the new tide. She saw in circling images, like wasps making figures-of-eight above Rusty's bowl: Alex driving away to tell Sergeant Finter; Harry Ford appearing at the door to pant his urgent message – "I have a contact at the *Herald* . . . your Kish is a murder suspect"; the policeman checking through the printout delivered by the telephone company to see who Kish might have contacted. But there was nothing.

*

"Every district is on alert," Sergeant Finter told them. "You guys don't need reminding – this place is second to none at swallowing murderers. If he gets in touch—"

"Oh, he won't," Merridy assured him. "Not with me. I can't speak for Alex." But the commotion in his eyes betrayed just how shaken Alex was. She could not remember when she had seen her husband so angry.

"You let this man stay with us, Pete, knowing what he'd done. How could you?" He looked haggard.

"But, Alex, he'd done nothing. Not officially."

"You believe that?"

"Of course, now it pokes out at everyone like dogs' balls, but not at the time, it didn't."

"You took his statement, for God's sake!"

"Yes, and he had no record – at least to speak of. That's what he kept saying. 'I have no record.' I told him I didn't come down in the last shower, I came down in the shower before – and he was a lying bastard. But what could I do?"

"Did Mrs Wellard tell you he was a murder suspect?"

"Listen, Alex. I understand why you're pissed off. But he wasn't *convicted* of anything. Otherwise, he wouldn't have been on board the *Buffalo*. They don't take people with a record. OK, he had had a number of minor convictions – but that's in Sydney. It's a tougher place. You'd expect him to be a petty criminal in Sydney, for fuck's sake. I'll spell it out again: none of those kids on that ship were involved in cases that had gone to trial."

"Then why was he late in joining the *Buffalo*?"

Sergeant Finter drew a long breath. "He went AWOL from the Bilgola Mission. A week later, an architect is murdered on a farm in Victoria. Kish is picked up as a suspect in Melbourne. There's no evidence. So they let him go. Two days later he's packed off on the *Buffalo* under Gangell's supervision. End of fucking story."

"Is that how the criminal justice system works?"

It was a jibe too much for Sergeant Finter. "Hell, and what do you know about the criminal justice system?" He laughed angrily. "I don't need this."

"Alex, Pete. Please," feeling giddy all of a sudden.

*

There was a creak. In the cane chair opposite, Mrs Anselm sipped her tea and her words seemed hotter. "When I try and go on a ship, I can't pay enough. How come these delinquents get to go – and for free? A nice way to see the country, isn't it? At taxpayers' and victims' expense. Why don't they pay to catch him?"

Merridy was surprised at the level of detail that Mrs Anselm had wanted to go into. She reminded her: "There was no weapon discovered – and you identified someone else."

He had been arrested in St Kilda market knotting balloons into inflated swords for children; his earring and short blond hair matching the description given by Mrs Anselm, who promptly failed to pick him out in the identity parade.

"Pah!" And Mrs Anselm looked helpless and angry out of her sunglasses. "As soon as I left the police station I knew which one it was. I was on the steps and I had to hold my daughter's arm. He was standing right next to the man I had chosen! I went back and told them I had made a mistake, I had accused the wrong person, but they weren't interested. They didn't want to listen."

"You're kidding."

"Exactly." She returned her saucer to the trolley. "Some more?"

"No, thanks."

Mrs Anselm looked with a troubled expression into the milky tea that Merridy had left untouched. "I don't understand. My husband wasn't a bad person. He was only trying to help. You see, I have no experience of such people." She uncrossed her legs and cupped her hands around her knees. "Tell me, Mrs Dove, this boy Kish, what was he like? I hardly saw him – well, a moment only. That's why in the line I didn't recognise him right away. They all looked the same . . ."

A hubbub of memories and longings blasted about Merridy's head. "He was strange. He seemed lost in another world."

"Lost?" sitting back.

"We felt sorry for him." It was not what Merridy intended to say. Nor what the older woman wished to hear.

Mrs Anselm raised her sunglasses. "What do you want with me, Mrs Dove?"

"I thought . . . since I knew your husband's killer, well, it might help . . . for us to talk . . ."

"Talk?" Mrs Anselm looked at her. And Merridy, meeting Mrs Anselm's receded, hurt eyes, was also at a loss. On the train from Melbourne, she had stared at the galahs arranged on the telegraph wires, sheet music for some inaudible melody that was drawing her in, and believed that she understood why she was making this impetuous journey to "Ashfield".

But now she wondered: Can this help either of us?

Less than five feet away, Mrs Anselm readjusted a pair of round dark lenses on the bridge of her nose. She pretended not to see as far as she did. But she had seen. Merridy's halo of anguish.

She picked up the pot.

"Let me tell you, Mrs Dove, what it means to lose the man you love."

"There were two of them. They were standing beside the fence, by that quince tree.

"The only thing he said while lying there: 'Who was it? Was it those boys?'

"They'd come to ask for work. They said they'd do anything – sweep leaves, even. I told them we had nothing for them to do. But Daniel was kinder. He remembered how it was to have no money.

"He said to me: 'Darling, they're still there. Let them sweep leaves.'

"'You speak to them, then.'

"He opened the door. Then the dog started growling – and suddenly I heard a shout and I saw someone lying on the grass – like that, two hands over his head. Daniel. Daphne raced up to him. She kneeled down and kissed her Grandpa and came up with her face and golden hair full of blood.

"The boy had stabbed him. For no reason at all . . . My husband didn't lose his watch, they didn't take his wallet. Like they were just out to kill him, a man they didn't know . . ." Her words were crushed as the grass.

Seconds passed before Mrs Anselm spoke again. "I ran on to the lawn and pulled off his shoes and tried to sit him up, which I should never have done. I screamed at the kids: 'Get back, everything's OK.' Then I held a cloth over him so he'd get a little shade over his head. His arms and legs were drawn up, and his wrist – hanging on a thread. Nine times chopped up. Well, I knew he would never play again. He had trained as a pianist and I prayed, squeezing his shoulder: 'Please, God, for his sake let him die, but for my sake let him live.'

"Of course, to him I said: 'It's OK, darling, everything is OK.'

"Then I ran back to the house and called for an ambulance. The kids were screaming when I came outside. They'd found Ruskin. Your Kish had slashed him, too."

Merridy felt sick. "How do you know it was Kish – not the other one?"

"Because I saw his knife . . ."

Mrs Anselm lifted the pot that she had clasped to her lap, and put it back on its stand. "I thought it would be quicker if we drove Daniel ourselves, so we got him into the car. His head was slit over his left eye. But he died that night. I'm glad they didn't see. He died in agony . . ." and patted away the labrador which had come up with a rubber bone in its mouth. "But *you're* OK now, aren't you, Ruskin?"

The labrador's tail was wagging. Catching sight of his mistress's face, the dog retreated and dropped the bone into Merridy's lap.

"He wants you to throw it." Mrs Anselm's voice sounded as though it was echoing off the plain outside.

Merridy picked up the toy bone that gleamed with slobber, and got to her feet. She studied the quince trees, the striped lawn where out of the blue Kish or whoever had launched his savage attack on a perfectly innocent stranger, and wondered where best to hurl the thing. It was – everything that she had heard – quite overwhelming.

Just at that moment the doorbell rang.

"It'll be the taxi," Merridy said, and put down the bone.

Mrs Anselm saw Merridy out. Not until they stood on the steps did she notice how Merridy's dress fell in uneasy lines across her body.

"Your first?"

"Yes. How can you tell?" quickly doing up her coat.

"You are starting late," and sighed. "I started too young."

"We've been trying for a long time."

"Your husband must be overjoyed."

"He doesn't know."

The driver was opening the door of the taxi.

"You're going to have to tell him soon," searching Merridy's face. She smelled of banana cake and fragility.

"When I get home."

Mrs Anselm relaxed. "There's nothing so wonderful as making a family."

CHAPTER TWO

COUNCIL ELECTIONS. There are a select few who reciprocate, contribute, extend respectability and bestow blessings on our town and its people. Then there are the takers, the ones Councillor Grogan refers to as "stakeholders". Their decisions are arrived at behind closed doors, quietly, secretly, with a select few mucketymucks, the so-called ey-leet and the wanna-bees. They take objection to interference from we "the ordinary people", the "country bumpkins", the so-called "brain-dead" seniors or their supposedly ignorant siblings. I could have sworn we voted Mr Ray Grogan in as our councillor to help us fight for a sports complex. Was that a fantasy? Together let's dismantle our council in April. Ray-as-in-sunshine, ho, ho, ho. Ray-as-in-scorched-earth-policy more likely. (Mr Talbot, could you run this past a lawyer before you print it? Thanks, Abby.)
Abbygail Deverill.

Orange flames blazed in a circle on the lawn. Alex stood the far side of them and kicked a smouldering branch into the pyre of browned foliage. He was burning off the last of the Oyster Bay pine.

Merridy parked beside the ute and even before she had taken off her seat belt Alex was bounding across the grass, followed by Rusty, opening the car door, leaning down. She let him kiss her, but she could feel the whimper in his throat.

"How was Melbourne? I missed you," and kept kissing her face in search of what she was withholding. His kisses had the flavour of woodsmoke and kerosene.

"Hey, let me get my suitcase," extricating herself.

"No, I'll get it."

She waited by the car while he opened the trunk. The air unnaturally still. The twisted sheets of flame. She stood looking up at the pipe-cleaner of smoke rising vertical from the lawn, and followed him inside.

Across the safe distance of the kitchen table, she told Alex about her visit to her mother and her lunch with Dmitri.

"And I bought you a present," she smiled.

Later on, he came into her study wearing the blue jersey.

"Oh, but Alex, that's far too tight!"

"No, it's not," and stubbornly flexed the short arms.

"Really – I can send it back." She stood to help him take off the jersey, before he got it caught on a wire or covered in muck.

"What are you doing?" to deflect her.

Half out of her chair, she looked down at her desk. "I have just put in an order to Shellfish Culture in Bicheno for a hundred thousand seedlings."

"Do you want me to post it?"

It pained her heart, his eagerness to please.

"Only if you're going into town."

"I have to go to Swansea. I need to get a pipe fitting from the hardware."

"Then let me find an envelope."

"Anything else?"

She considered the jersey that hemmed him in. As if she had bought it for someone a good deal younger. "We've nothing for dinner. Maybe you could buy a chicken at Talbot's on the way? And Alex—"

He turned. On either side of him, the walls of the corridor were bare – ever since he had taken the frames to Hobart to be replaced.

She had to sit down. "I know this sounds odd, but I'd love you to get some more Coco Pops."

WELLINGTON POINT GOLF CLUB.
Talbot's Memorial Qualifying Round:
Competition results for Saturday.
Winner: N. Fujita (visitor) 56
Runner-up: R. Grogan 58
Junior: Z. Grogan 65

Due to lack of bookings the Golf Club Annual Dinner has been cancelled.

It was a stunning blue calm afternoon – smell of early autumn, dry pines – and whales splashing in the bay. Their spouting had drawn a small crowd to the railings above the beach.

Alex watched the pod of Southern Rights for a while. Then walked along the esplanade to Talbot's. Taped to the windows, black-and-yellow posters advertised Ray Grogan's forthcoming auction of the general store's contents: *The opportunity to acquire something unique, a part of history.*

At the checkout, Rose-Maree said: "You must be hot in that, Mr Dove."

"My wife gave it to me."

She squinted through knowing eyes at the cereal packet. "Hear you might be starting a family." And her incredulous expression that liked to displease added: After all these years!

"I'd be the last to know," Alex joked with a smile that believed it knew what she was talking about.

He left Talbot's and walked in stiff steps along the main street, past the newsagent, past the Op-Shop, not breathing in so as to avoid the fragrance of old clothes and to suppress the irritation that coiled through his head. You only had to nurse a thought and already Rose-Maree had heard it articulated from Chyna, who worked at the chemist's.

Alex had little doubt that if Merridy had bought a pregnancy test it was for Madasun, their frizzy-haired cleaner – she had probably missed her period yet again. And remembered his wife's exasperation the last time this had happened, after Madasun implored Merridy to visit the chemist's on her behalf.

"My boobies are hurting, Mrs Dove. The nipples are hard and I feel so good. I only had one glass of wine. I thought it was a safe time."

Madasun was in such a state of nerves that while she was peeing she dropped the stick in the loo and Merridy had to go back and buy another test.

"Oh, she annoys me so, that girl. And what's the betting it will turn out negative!"

"Why is she asking *you* to buy it?"

"Her parents are full-on Catholics. She lives in permanent fear that they'll find out she's not a virgin – at thirty-one, heaven help us."

So by the time he climbed the steps into the post office had Alex explained away Rose-Maree's remark.

Immediately she saw him come in, Mrs Grogan leaped out from the queue, tugging the small dark poodle at her feet, her trouser suit giving her the look of a tea cosy. She was dressed in her customary pink and clutched at Alex, one hand imitating the other, but she had not worked out what to say.

Perhaps she was ill; she was not, though. Her mouth ungummed itself. And smiled kindly though she was not by nature a kind person.

"I hear Merridy's having a baby."

In the queue some woman coughed and another copied her.

Meanwhile, Mrs Grogan was smiling so broadly that she might have owned the beach. "My father used to say: 'Barren ground can sometimes be what a seed needs.'"

Hostile eyes recognised Alex for what he was, a cuckolded Pom in a close-fitting jersey. White as a rinsed plate, he said: "It's early days," and added with as much dignity as he was able: "Anything might happen."

Mrs Grogan's face, which speech had animated, was turned wrinkly again. Her hands touched her mulberry frill, like that around her dog's mouth, and then fanned themselves out on Alex's constricted chest.

"If she's pregnant, you must come to tea."

Alex posted Merridy's envelope and walked back along the esplanade, avoiding the crowd, to the ute. The cabin had heated up and he tucked the plastic bag with the cereal and chicken under the seat.

The afternoon sun through the windscreen showed a middle-aged man in spectacles – forty-three years old, broader in the chest than when he met the two cousins by Ray Grogan's fence, and darker, with less hair – who switched on the engine and then switched it off and sat looking out.

Is it mine? It could be mine. Couldn't it? And remembered a doctor saying: "Those who are infertile do sometimes remedy themselves."

The whales had swum close to shore. In an elegant and unhurried gesture, the largest of them raised its tail in the air. Alex expected the tail to slap down, but it remained vertical, a gigantic black hand that set the mood and tempo of the bay, and of all who watched, until it seemed to Alex that he was himself caught up in the whale's own slow, mysterious rhythm that was in defiance of gravity or time.

And felt an ache of uncertainty.

A crawl of fear moved in his chest. Where had his head been? He was not a stupid man. It wasn't as if he had not seen it coming: he knew. He had the evidence and had not confronted her, and now he had to deal with it.

The whale's tail was still poised in the air when he retrieved his sun hat from behind the steering wheel and put it on. He turned the key in the ignition and was about to drive away when – "Alex! Alex!"

Tildy, crossing the road.

He wound down the window. "Hey, congratulations. I hear you're on the town council."

"Did you vote for me?" lowering her head. That had never looked so bubbly.

He smiled. "As far as I remember, it was a secret ballot."

"Anyway, it's you who must be congratulated. Is Merridy with you?" peering into the ute.

"She's at the farm. She got back this morning."

"I haven't hugged you for the pure joy you must be feeling."

Before he could say anything, she thrust her arms through the window and held him in an awkward embrace.

"Tell me more," ever so slowly.

"Oh, come on, stop being British. We're so happy for you, Ray and I. We're thrilled. It's a cousin for me. I'll be Aunty Tildy. Uncle Ray. No, really, it's the best news."

Anyone who has copies of my short stories could they please contact me on: 62568583. Thank you, Agnes Lettsom.

From his porthole, Mr Talbot watched Alex's ute meander out of town towards Swansea. He followed Mrs Grogan following her inescapable poodle from the post office to the bowls club, in time for the five p.m. Twilight Bowls competition. He adjusted his binoculars north to the golf course where Abbygail chatted with Jack Fysshe on the apron of the seventh hole, having done everything she decently could to put a spoke in Tildy's wheel at the recent council election, assuming that Tildy was only standing to further her vile husband's interests. To the lane behind the school where Rose-Maree's son played catch-and-kiss with Cherokee. And back to the main street to survey the faces absorbed in the whales, although not before he spotted Tildy going into Ray Grogan's office.

Mr Talbot put down his binoculars. He felt all tuckered out. At all that he had seen. All that he had reported back and typed out in his steady hand, or simply kept intact in his head. The children whom he had witnessed growing up, courting and marrying. The husbands slinking like possums at dawn from the doors of other men's wives – and sometimes of other husbands! The sausage sizzles, the ANZAC parades, the golf tournaments and cricket matches, the Safe'n'Sound car seats in good condition, the visiting speakers and the funeral services . . .

He closed his eyes. For the first time since he had long, long ago taken up position at this window, Mr Talbot looked forward to quitting his eyrie. Ray Grogan was agitating to show him around a retirement villa on a cliff south of Swansea that sounded congenial to his habits and purposes: it had a view only of the sea. He was tempted to take a look, despite not altogether trusting Ray. He said to himself: Funny how nervous he was that night. He thought I was going to nail him for his horrid little son. And while Ray readily agreed to his sole stipulation, Mr Talbot had kept an eye on the real-estate agent for too many years not to discuss the contract with his lawyer. "This is fine up until – and not a millimetre further than – this devious, untrustworthy person mentions any Nippon corporation. So if he comes to see you . . ." And instructed him to put in a clause to the effect that whoever bought or developed the store could not possibly be Japanese.

Up until that time, there would still be the *Newsletter* to compile, proofs to correct. He opened his eyes and stood at the third go and shuffled over to the table under the skylight.

WELLINGTON POINT RSLA. ANZAC DAY, April 25.
11 a.m. service at the Cenotaph – marchers to assemble at 10.40 a.m. opposite Talbot's Store. Wreaths will be laid out for pick-up at the Uniting Church.

Not until late afternoon did Alex return home. He checked the bonfire for embers and was walking towards the house when he almost trod on a tiny brown object.

Dead on the ground, a beautiful bird.

He picked it up. A young swift. He held it in his palm, but even as he ran his finger over the porcelain-white throat, the minute legs and feet, the wings trembled and a drop of saliva oozed from its black bill.

With the utmost tenderness he placed the bird on its back on the flower bed, and opened the fly-screen and went inside.

Merridy had not left her desk. "I meant to ask you to get olive oil. But there's butter in the freezer. And, Alex, you didn't forget that cereal, did you?" still writing.

He stood behind her. His eyes on her sideways face, the exposed bra strap, the new yellow dress that was too large for her body. Almost seventeen years together and he did not recognise her. She was stranger to him – suddenly – than the young man who had wrecked all the ships in this room.

She felt the force of his glare and twisted in the swivel chair.

"Or did you?" She looked radiant.

He crossed his lead arms. "Are you pregnant?"

She blushed. "Now why would you ask that?"

He looked at her very closely and saw her eyes rocking with new colours. But her gaze did not meet his. Her face eloquent of something that she would rather not reveal, not yet.

"Are you? I was in the post office. Mrs Grogan suggested you were."

"A ridiculous idea." She occupied herself with screwing the top back on her pen. "What a bunch of stickybeaks people are." She did not quite believe it herself.

"Did you buy a pregnancy test?"

With a desperate smile, she said: "Everyone in Wellington Point seems to know what I've done."

"Yes," he said. "They do." But still he waited for her to mention Madasun. When she did not, he said with terrifying gentleness: "I also bumped into Tildy."

"You did? And?"

"I don't want to hear any more until you decide to tell me the truth."

She cooked the chicken for dinner. They were eating in silence when she pushed back her chair and rushed past him, prolonging her smile until she reached the bathroom and then vomited into the basin.

He came into the bedroom a few minutes later, holding a glass of water.

She sat on their bed and stared blankly ahead at the faded wall where the wardrobe had stood. "Perhaps I undercooked it," in a whisper. And watched Alex step in front of her, into the space where Kish had sought to shut himself away.

Alex had sold the wardrobe to an antique shop in Campbell Town. A broken piece of furniture with a promise attached. But Merridy had interpreted it as something mystical and unravelling. The room was bigger without it, both of them smaller.

In silence, she accepted the glass. She did not look at him as she drank.

"Are you?" he repeated, in his gentle voice.

His gentleness had the impact of a cudgel.

"I was going to tell you tonight," her head bowed, clasping the empty glass. The water had wiped the taste of vomit from her mouth.

"Is it mine?"

Her smile fluttered on her lips, then was inert.

"I'm not that stupid. Not a fool," and felt out of breath.

She lifted deadly, sad eyes. Alex's expression was terrible. His face not constructed to express his hurt.

"It's not mine, is it?" blinking against a blow he had yet to receive.

She had trouble getting the word out. "Alex . . ."

The noise of air sucked through a dry throat.

His mouth hung open a little. Around him the silence burned.

"Alex . . ."

But his gaze was crumpling under its load of sadness. As if the moment of illumination would snuff him out.

Now he would ask who was the father. She braced herself to tell him. And stopped. Was there not an outside chance it could be Alex – even after all this time?

But he did not have to ask. He knew. Had seen it with his own eyes.

It was curious. In the four months since Kish's disappearance, Alex's sleep had been largely untroubled, pacified by a not disagreeable sensation that everything was out of his control, and by the parallel conviction that Kish's destruction of his collection of ships had in a sort of way released him. But soon as he woke, before he could reassure himself that all was well: the despair.

Even after Sergeant Finter finished putting his questions to them, Alex did not ask Merridy about the events of that night. The image of her embrace with Kish had not penetrated. It remained suspended, so that a small part of Alex was able to persuade himself he had not seen it. Or rather that what he had seen was of a parcel, somehow, with the ghostly figure suggested by the Friesian cow beneath the macrocarpa, a product of humidity and moonlight, of fever and shadows. A mist-mirage. And so he blotted out that night as he had learned to blot out his parents' death. In the days that followed, he explained it away as something that could not be explained, and did not refer to it again. What else could he do? Kish had gone, vanished off the map. As for Merridy, he could not interpret her face. Her thoughts lay unreadable, like letters on a jolted Scrabble board.

Since the discovery of her brother's remains, Merridy had been careful with Alex and attentive, which made him unhappy. He was reminded of the expression in her eyes at their first encounter, her childlike eyes that found it hard to settle on an adult surface in case they might be scalded. And he, in his turn, avoided looking at her in case he saw what he did not expect. Especially, he did not want to discover how infantile she might still be. Her life so firmly organised in response to her own childhood that she had failed to move beyond her childlike beliefs.

So they settled back into an uneasy truce.

More frequent than moments filled with the image of Merridy and Kish in their shocking embrace were those of immersion in the farm.

The windmill worked. Alex could not decide if he regretted or not that Mr Scantlebury, in the course of stripping it down, had scrubbed Merridy's name from the vane. The main thing was, it drew water to the feeding troughs – and in an uninterrupted flow that his father's cattle had never enjoyed. Alex would look at the spinning blades and see the widening ripples of a trout feeding on mayfly. "Good dog," he would call. As he rounded up sheep below Barn Hill. Driving slowly behind and giving the occasional toot to hurry them up and to make Rusty bark. Trees were in blossom and the mutton-birds were in. Out in the bay the sea was bluer than ever. Once, for no good reason he could think of, a snatch of a football song from Sedbergh came to his lips: *The sunshine is melting the snow on the Calf/And the Rawthey is loud in the dale.* Meaningless now. He went through the motions of living.

While at her desk, or down at the oyster shed, or out in the bay on the *Zemmery Fidd*, Merridy glowed. She did not think of what her body had done on a splintery floor, or that she had betrayed her cousin or husband or herself. It had taken place in a dream, her atrocious outburst of lust or whatever it was, so that the dull fact of its having taken place was all she remembered, and not any history. But her eyes skipped away from the primary school whenever she had to go into Wellington Point.

Above all, she succeeded in driving from her head all thoughts of Hector. It was extraordinary, the degree to which her pregnancy had dissolved her brother's memory. She had discovered that she was pregnant two days after Minister Twelvetrees conducted the burial ceremony in which Hector's friends, all middle-aged and married now, stood with their puzzled children behind Mrs Bowman and Doss and tried to remember the seven-year-old boy and also to imagine him as an adult. From that moment on, it was as if Hector had soared up into the sky to disappear out of her life as emphatically as the young man whom Alex had rescued from the sea.

"Do you know what happened to Kish? Have you seen him? Does anyone know where he is?" she had asked Tildy, to whom she had grown close again.

"Not a thing."

But Alex did not have this consolation. To Alex, Kish was the reason. The awfulness. It was Kish who had made them enemies. Whose child swelled under his wife's yellow dress.

It was therefore a double assault for Alex to look back at the past four months in which he had accommodated and denied what he had seen.

Sudden as a fist jagged into his chest, winding him, and with a lucidity that tore at his heart, he now understood the fury that had slashed his mother's collection of samplers and trampled his father's precious ships into smithereens. The tears trickled down his cheeks.

Merridy could not bear to look. He stood there like something painted on wood. A rattle of breath in a too-small jersey.

She got up from the bed. Her excluding voice saying something. Her mouth running after the words. Trying to sound adequate.

"He will be our child," she said. "We always wanted a child."

He reached to touch her stomach. Their barrenness so often

had caused him pain. Yes, he had wanted a child, a better version of himself. Out of his love for Merridy, he had grown as impatient as she to put something into the future and not to have to look back.

Then stopped in the middle of the bedroom with his hand up, like something farewelled, not able to touch, not able to look. Aware that what Merridy was saying was a snakebite whose venom had yet to reach his heart, but was sluggishly and intently heading that way through his bloodstream, and he knew that he must not encourage it even by the smallest motion.

If only he could concentrate hard enough. He wished he was a boy again so that he could weep without embarrassment or scream his pain at the sea instead of bolting it behind an awkward smile. His hands colliding with a living creature, he stroked the dog.

Slowly, he sank onto the bed. But only for a moment.

He was trembling. He felt the chilled anguish in his soul, a choking. His voice sagging under the weight of what she had done to him, he mumbled stupidly, "I'm going to see if that bird's all right."

He lurched to his feet and manoeuvred past her and she saw, then, the abolished light in his eye.

Her stomach rumbled.

"Alex!" She had never been good at shouting. "Alex, where are you going?" as if they were her last words to him. He walked on. Into the bare corridor. Through the kitchen. Vigorously outside. He was going to the unrevived swift; he had always been at ease with dead things.

When he kneeled to recover the bird, it was gone.

CHAPTER THREE

HE STUMBLED DOWN THE drive. The windmill called after him, and the young dog that he had shut behind the fly-screen, but he pressed on, his feet slipping on the gravel that he scattered, rolled downhill faster by the impetus of the seething in his chest. And did not stop when he reached his boundary fence.

He walked on for two miles, along the Avoca road – gorse hedgerows and a red track bounded by low rolling hills with clumps of dark green eucalypts. Another farm, also empty: the bark of locked-up dogs and horses under blankets.

He heard the sound of a car and hurried on. He pushed his way through the bush. Touching the branches for company; the wire barbs.

The swifts that were spending their night in the sky saw him tracking west beside a river. The gums smoky green, the trunks covered in a tight plumage of ivy. Between the trees, he made out horizons of forest like the coat on Mrs Grogan's poodle. Wads of cloud appeared high up. There was a shower and then the rain stopped.

In a clearing, he passed a white fibro shack. A dog yammered at him and stood still and shivered. More dogs followed, trotting over the ground with their tails up and the dying day in their eyes glinting red from the darkening pools. It rained again, harder this time, and the rain swept across him until he was a figure that had been rubbed out. The lead dog licked a raindrop from its snout and turned back.

At the top of the hill, he heard a thuck thuck thuck and turned to see a figure below, chopping wood. The damp crunch of fire-wood after rain carried the sound of someone axing their own flesh.

An hour later, the shape of the skyline that he had left behind stood black and solid against the grey sky. His boots were soaked through and he felt blisters on his heels. He did not know where he was, didn't care.

Bathed in the light of dead stars he staggered on through the moist undergrowth, a creature in his shambles. Smell of wet rock and Kish's child beneath her freakish yellow dress. Branches snapping and the reek of mould.

In the darkness of the woods, with the fronds scoring his face and his sore feet and a devil growling not far off, he was the Piers of his childhood.

Merridy.

He stopped moving only when fatigue overpowered him. He lay where he had tripped, his cheek resting on a bed of damp leaves. Once, hearing a voice, he looked up. But it was himself gabbling. His words spinning off in a senseless stream, his blubbering orphans, their fading cries inarticulate.

He slid back into sleep.

Waking, he saw that he had slept beneath a pine tree. He blundered through the next day and into the night. He did not stop to differentiate, where he had been, what he had done, and mouthfuls of brackish water and hours on hard ground. Pink tentacles bunched with unripe berries plucked at him. He tore off the berries and crammed them into his mouth. The juice tasted marshy, rancid almost. His scratched hands toned in with the strips of bark and the smell of deserted barns came off his clothes. He remembered the wind blunting the young maize, the sneeze of a gun, a curtain across a room and on the stove a saucepan from which an old woman was about to feed her cat. And all the time the soft pad of wings in his chest.

He imagined his chest sawn open. Merridy had scooped up the swift and freed the terrified bird into his darkness and the scars had healed and this tiny thing flapped and squeaked and tormented its beak on his sides.

Sometimes in the stillness of wind he heard a cockatoo laughing at him, cackling out the word: Kish, Kish, Kish, Kish – Kish.

On the third evening, he climbed a hill and peered into a deserted cottage with a high-pitched shingle roof and small panes, where he slept. The noise of rats in the walls was someone eating crisps in a cinema. In his jealousy, he summoned the unexplained chuckles, her mouth red and contented.

At first light, he stepped from the shack and saw the Midlands

Highway below and the metal roofs of Ross. Out of habit, a bruised hand patted his trousers to check that he still had his wallet. He pulled it out and a piece of damp paper fell to the ground. He read the words written in blurred ink. *Without you I am so unhappy, I am.*

In Ross, he sat in a café with a busload of raucous, fat tourists, the windows fogging up and a westerly coming through.

The tour guide called out: "Do we have any New Zealanders with us? No? Oh, I'm going to have a great day today."

The group hollered dutifully and tucked into their scallop pies, paying no attention to Alex. He looked down at the jersey that Merridy had given him and saw how burrs had stuck to it, how wire had ripped it, how filthy it was. Stenchy with the bitter smell of mud, he waited for his coffee.

Night had fallen when he entered Green Ponds and saw the red lights of the Old Ship Inn. Because of his father, he avoided pubs. Now he dragged himself towards the neon blare.

He pushed open the door and stood blinking in the dowdier light. Then bent his back and crossed the floor to the U-shaped bar.

Sitting over their six-ounce beers, three beards tracked his advance from the far side of the polished counter.

Separate from them at the end of the same counter, a clean-shaven man in a green jacket sat eating a sausage off a paper plate. He, too, studied Alex: his bristly cheeks, his bloodshot eyes, his hair all over the place like slashed wool, the tired swing of his arms as he came up to the bar.

"What can I get you, mate?" asked a pleasant Aboriginal face.

Alex looked at the bottles all hanging upside down, all full. As he remembered them on his father's shelves. And waved at one.

"Shot of that. No, make it a double."

So he drank his father's favourite gin. Smiling back at the uncaring beards. His thoughts with their children's masks on them as if he could disguise his hurt with false cheer.

It was almost the first thing that he had noticed on his return to Tasmania, twelve years after the death of his parents: the sight of so many massive beards. There came into his mind, nudged by the gin, the unkempt face of the man who visited Moulting Lagoon Farm six months after Alex had taken up residence again. Alex had mistaken him for an itinerant Jehovah's Witness: Harry Ford had warned that they were operating in the area.

"Are you Mr Dove?" bunching his hat.

"That depends," Alex said. "Are you seeking contributions?"

"No," said the beard, hopping from one foot to another. In the paddock, the horses lifted their heads and went back to tearing the grass. His eyes kept looking out of their corners at Alex. "I need to know. Are you Piers Dove?"

"That used to be my name, but people generally call me Alex."

The beard braced himself. "I'm George Bird." And when Alex did not react explained that he was the driver of the log-truck that had ended his parents' life and sent them into the next one.

Alex sucked in. Hearing his father in red braces talking about boats; smelling his mother's sherry-scented breath. He came up for air. The only sound his heart, and the grass being torn.

"Do you want to come in?"

"No, I just want to let you know that not a day has passed when I didn't wish it was me in that car."

He swallowed the rest of the gin.

"Go on, Whizz, get your arse moving!"

Over by the pool table, two players in their shirts of wife-beater's tartan cheered the television set. A mouth missing several teeth yelled: "Get on with it, Whizz!"

"One more," thumping his empty glass on the counter. In the trapped warmth of the lounge room. Its brutal cordiality.

He drank. He looked around. The television, with its horse race going on. A counter, scattered with slips and the paraphernalia of betting. And flashing up on screen, the Keno numbers.

At the end of the bar, the man in the green tweed jacket removed something from his eye. He stood up and looked at Alex and went outside.

The cheers had become jeers. Two disappointed faces turned away. A cue was chalked and the thump resumed of ivory against ivory.

"I'm going," Alex said after a while to no one in particular.

The beards at the bar simmered approval.

At the pool table, they were making bets on roadkill. How many dead animals could they notch up on their way home?

"Winner in Swansea! Winner in Swansea!"

Alex walked outside into the car park and pissed between two utes. Out of the ground-floor window another peal of undenticulated laughter.

He was zipping up when he became conscious of someone observing him through the windscreen of a stationary Pajero. The red lights picked out a South Australian number plate.

Alex left the car park and set off along the road, the jeers reverberating through his head, and the shrill announcement of a lucky lottery winner.

Behind, an engine started up. The vehicle turned onto the road and followed Alex at a slow pace until it was alongside. The driver leaned across and the window whirred down.

"How ya doing?"

"Going well, mate."

"Need a lift?"

Alex stopped and looked at the face framed in the open window. He took in a man more or less his own age, fleshy lips and chin, sparse hair, drooping, slightly bulging eyes.

"Why would you do a thing like that?"

"We might be heading in the same direction."

"Where you heading?"

"Orford."

"Which way?"

He considered this. "Lake Leake," after a pause.

Alex stared at the ground. "Could you drop me off near Wellington Point?"

"No trouble."

The man opened the door and Alex climbed in and they drove out of Green Ponds and onto the Midlands Highway.

"I've never been in that pub before," the man said after an interval.

Alex eyed the cloth on the arms that held the steering wheel and was conscious of his torn blue jersey, stiff with dried earth. His eyes moved up the arm to the driver's face. His own face by contrast was covered by an unchecked stubble and he smelled of ditches. “Me neither,” he said.

The man picked his teeth. “I don’t reckon I’ll stop there again. But the ferry into Devonport was two hours late and I was famished. I could have eaten the crotch out of a low-flying duck.”

“Do you live in Orford?” Alex said.

“I live in Adelaide, but my family have a house on Spring Beach.”

He was down here visiting his parents; normally they came to him because they liked to get into better weather.

“What about yours?” he asked Alex.

“I’d like to get into better weather.”

“I mean, what about your folks? Are they still around?”

“No, no, they died a long time ago now.”

“Oh. Sorry.”

Alex looked out at the side of the highway. As if half-expecting to see himself shuffling into the headlights. He had walked beside this road for the best part of the afternoon. “A log-truck.”

The man frowned at the road ahead. “Forgive me for asking, but you’re not Piers Dove, are you?”

Alex looked around. “I might have been.”

“I thought so,” nodding to himself.

“How did you work that out?”

“We were at school together.”

Alex took stock of the driver’s silhouette in the darkness. His double chin, his kind protruding eyes, his sparse hair rumpled like a judge who has removed his wig.

“I remember that accident,” the man went on in a deferential tone. “We were pretty cut up for you. But you’d left town before we had a chance to pay our respects to you and your family.” He paused and cleared his throat awkwardly. “You – that is.”

Still, Alex could not decipher the boy in the double chin. In the adult voice with the mainlander’s vowels.

“Were we in the same class?”

“I sat behind you,” and turned and smiled in a sad way.

Headlights from an oncoming vehicle fell on the man’s cheek and nose.

“Jack Cheele . . . ?”

“That’s right.”

They regarded each other. Thirty-two years disappeared and the lines on the face, and all at once Alex discerned the features of the new boy whom Miss Pritchard was introducing to the class.

"Jack Cheele," he repeated in a voice just as strained.

"You remember my name," chuckling.

A car flashed by.

Alex shook his head. That they should meet in a pub in the middle of nowhere.

"Miss Pritchard told us you'd gone to England. It wasn't till I heard you speak that I knew I was right."

Alex twisted to face him. "Jack, I've thought about you so often."

"Well, here I am."

"No, no, you don't realise," in an urgent voice. "I really have thought about you an awful lot."

"You have?"

"That day in the school yard—"

"When you kicked me in the balls?"

"I'd made up my mind to come and see you, to apologise, and then . . . then it was too late." Everything erased by the accident.

"Well, that's decent of you to tell me."

"I tried to find you."

"We moved to South Australia."

"I bet you haven't forgotten."

Cheele gave another chuckle. "Jesus, no. I haven't. But it didn't do too much damage. Four children later. Anyway, it wasn't your fault."

"What do you mean?"

"Ray Grogan set you up, didn't he?"

"You heard that?"

"He told me so himself. I think what surprised him was that you'd gone along with it." He squinted out at the road. "Hey, don't say this is Campbell Town already."

The headlights picked out Federation houses on either side, an antique shop, and an orange telephone kiosk with a light on. Cheele slowed down. "Sorry, but I've got to just drive. The coppers are brutal here. Last time, I got a ticket for doing seventy."

He put on his indicator and moved into the middle of the road and turned right and did not accelerate again until they had left Campbell Town behind them.

"We should make Wellington Point in an hour," he said. "All right with you?"

"That's fine."

Cheele did not speak for a while. They had passed Lake Leake when he cleared his throat again: "I wouldn't want you to take this in the wrong spirit, but when I saw you tonight in the pub I thought: I recognise that fella. That's Piers Dove. But then I said to myself: You've been driving all day, Jack, you're seeing things. Piers Dove wouldn't be in a place like this any more than you would be – not in the normal course of events. Although, as my wife would say: What is normal these days?" He laughed and when Alex said nothing he looked over at him: "I hope, Piers, you're not offended by what I just said."

Alex wondered if he should let it go. It was a comfort that he had not expected, to be called Piers again.

"No, no, far from it, I'm not offended."

"That's good."

So he sat in silence, content to be Piers for just a small while longer, until he saw the streaks of burned rubber and sat up. "You can drop me here."

"Hey, let me take you to your door," Cheele said. He peered out at the road: the blind corner, the tyre marks still black after four months. "Looks like you've had visitors," he murmured, looking for a turning. "Or else someone's been dodging a kangaroo."

"I mean it," Alex said. "Please drop me here. I'd prefer it."

Cheele parked on the grass. He glanced over again at Alex. "You OK, Piers? You don't look so good. I hope you're not still worrying about that incident. It's history. Forget it."

"Yeah, OK, I will," and opened the door and climbed out.

CHAPTER FOUR

MERRIDY WAS NOT AT home.

Alex drank three glasses of water, one after the other, then opened the fridge and made himself an omelette. Out of habit, he looked around for the dog's bowl. Not seeing it, he called out: "Rusty!" – and when nothing moved realised that she must have taken him with her. Afterwards, he ran a bath and lay in it until the water was cold. It unsettled him to stretch out alone in their bed, but sleep quickly overtook him.

He got up earlier than usual and shaved. He pulled out a clean blue shirt and pair of brown corduroy trousers from the chest of drawers, and dressed. Then he went into the kitchen and made a pot of tea and three pieces of toast, and spread Vegemite and marmalade and butter on them. It was not yet seven when he finished his breakfast and grabbed his hat off the dresser and went out to milk the cows, their udders fit to bursting, and to feed the animals that he had neglected.

For the rest of the morning, he rode over the farm. He was keen to make up the four lost days. The barley was showing signs of sooty mould from a big rain. Along the edge of Moulting Lagoon, the black swans had come in for grain and fouled it up a bit. In the afternoon, he sprayed the barley and moved sheep between paddocks. And as it grew dark fired a gas-gun to scare off the swans.

When the telephone rang in the kitchen that night, he dug out a half-bottle of gin that he kept for guests and poured a tumbler.

Half an hour later the telephone rang again. This time he picked it up.

"Alex?"

He sat back. "Merridy."

"Thank God. I was so worried."

"I'm OK."

"Where were you?" She had driven up and down the Avoca Road, hoping to find him. At one point she had urged Rusty out of the car. "Go look for Alex," in a fraught and rather hysterical tone so that the dog had barked at her.

"I had to clear my head," he said.

"I tried ringing, you've no idea how many times . . . I couldn't think where you might be."

Her husband did not have many close friends. She had telephoned his agent, Agnes, Jack Fysshe, the Macdonalds. She had even – in her despair – contacted Harry Ford. "What's that? No, no, he's not here."

So when Jason enquired – they were drifting in the *Zemmery Fidd* above the oyster lines – "Has Alex run away?" she had no clear answer.

"I'm not sure," replied Merridy, for whom the tangle of ropes, of small knots that fastened the lanterns was suddenly too much. "I haven't seen him since Monday."

Alex took another swallow of gin. "I'm sorry for leaving like that," he said. "I didn't know where I was going myself."

"I'm the one who is sorry. I'm so sorry, Alex. I should have told you before."

"Like I said, I wanted to clear my head."

"I was milking the cows when suddenly I got this idea that you might have been waiting for me to leave. I thought you'd be happier if I wasn't there."

"Probably."

"Alex," she said.

"You've got Rusty?"

"I'll bring him back if you like."

"No, keep him. I bought him for you."

"Alex?"

"Where are you ringing from, anyway?"

"Aunt Doss."

He nodded. "I suppose you'll be there a while?"

"Alex . . ."

"What about Kish? Any news?"

"It's you I love."

"Don't!" and slammed the tumbler on the table, though it was the receiver that he meant to crash down. "I'm sorry, Merridy—" and stood up.

She asked him to hear her out. "Even if you never want to see me again, please listen."

He had spilled gin on the table and it was dripping to the floor. He squeezed the receiver between cheek and shoulder, looking around for a cloth.

"You told me this would happen," her voice was saying, quite hoarse, "and, Alex, it has. Alex, are you there?"

"Yes, I'm here." But he could not see straight. He was thinking: Could it be the gin that's given me this quick fuse? Beefeater had been his father's drink, and he was a novice.

"I've had time to think everything over. I love you, Alex."

"Where do you keep dishcloths?"

"When you first understand something you've not been able to understand for ages – how it all fits together – suddenly everything is obvious . . . What?"

"A dishcloth, where would I get a dishcloth?"

"Third drawer on the left. Alex, did you hear what I just said? You were right. It's happened – as you promised." She sounded elated.

"I've found them. Listen, I'm going to have to go."

When the telephone rang again he did not answer. He mopped up the pool of gin and poured himself another glass and sipped, but did not answer.

He expected her to call again the following night. Before turning in, he picked up the receiver in the kitchen, and then checked the receiver in the living room. Nor did she ring the next night, nor the night after that. He walked up and down. He had forgotten how to live on his own. The house without Merridy, without a dog, without the bottled ships and the wardrobe, with nothing on the walls – no paintings, drawings, samplers – was a place far emptier than the house to which he had returned from England as a young man.

He had his hair cut. He started to read again. He took his rod to the river mouth and fished for flat-head, cooking it with a tin of tomatoes that he found in the larder. But he was lonely for Merridy. He dried his face with her towel and, assaulted by a trace of her perfume, tried in vain to summon her laughter.

FOR SALE: TALBOT'S NEWSLETTER
As a complete operation – including computer, printer, Mita photocopier, Risograph high-speed printer. An ideal occupation for retired or community-concerned persons. Please contact me to discuss what is involved – not much really.
Albert Talbot.

One cold evening, he was cleaning his father's shotgun in the laundry room when he heard a car pull up and then yapping.

"Alex?"

They came into the kitchen at the same time.

"Tildy."

He had been back an hour, after an exhausting day's tractoring, plus a quick walk over the pastures for a hare for his supper, and was pleased to see her. He switched off the radio that had become his only company.

"I won't stay long," she said, and he supposed that she needed his vote for something or was going to put pressure on him to stand for the council.

He turned on the tap. "Merridy's not here," soaping the oil from his hands.

"I know. She called me."

"Tildy," she had said, "I have a favour to ask. Could you scout out the ground and go and see Alex? I do worry about him."

"He's the father of your child. Why don't you go?"

"I have to be here. Please. Just go and hug him for me."

So on this wintry night Tildy had driven out to the farm and now stood in her grey coat beside the blackwood table.

She sent her eyes down the corridor. "Hey, is something different?" She had not been for several months. "I know what it is, you've had a clean-out. That's good. They were a bit too old-fashioned for me, those tapestries."

She picked up a glass on the table, sniffed, put it down.

"Did Merridy tell you? I'm starting a book club. I want you both to be members." She started bandying the titles of books.

"Tildy . . ."

"Oh, it doesn't matter. You aren't going to have the time anyway."

His face had closed a little. He felt quite lonely. Was she trying to smoke something out of him? She sounded unnaturally concerned. How you must miss your wife, her face implied. At this special time. But not to worry, Merridy will be back soon from Ulverstone. In the meantime, don't forget to water the garden.

She looked away, at the Welsh dresser. "Did you hear Mr Talbot is selling the store?" for something to say.

"So I saw in the *Newsletter*."

"Everyone's quite upset. My mother-in-law is talking about the end of an era."

"I don't mind who owns the place so long as they look after it."

"Ray's been given the sale."

Alex nodded.

She said: "Knowing Ray, he'll probably want to subdivide it into mansions or convert it into a Melbourne pensioners' parade."

"Has he got a buyer in mind?" filling the kettle.

"He won't say, but it wouldn't be Ray not to have a developer already lined up."

"She's not Japanese, by any chance?"

Tildy stiffened. "Now why do you think that?"

"I saw him escorting a Japanese woman around Jack Fysshe's property. I thought: Hello, he's trying to sell her farms. That was some months ago."

She crossed her arms. "You don't like my husband, do you? I don't like him much myself."

"No, I don't like Ray a lot. But more than that – and I never quite got over this – he really let this farm go to wrack and ruin when it was his to look after."

"Alex, I never knew that!"

"It's not something I like to talk about. I never told Merridy. I'm just hoping to God that Jack doesn't put his fine acres into Ray's hands, that's all."

He switched the kettle on.

She was thinking about what he had said. "But you've made such a success of it, haven't you? And you have Merridy. And now you're going to have a baby." It might have been Tildy who was having the baby, such a burst of unexpected goodwill did she feel in that moment. Towards him, towards her cousin. All thought of Ray dismissed as she remembered: "Merridy wanted me to hug you for her. I don't mind telling you, Alex, I've often thought of hugging you for myself."

Then, arms outstretched, she was advancing towards him: "Talk to me, Alex, don't go into one of your long silences . . . No, I don't want tea. I want you to talk to me and tell me how happy you are."

And while he had uttered not a word – not one word! – she was moved by his response.

Because what he experienced was an ungovernable wish to put his arms around her and press his cheek against her plump cheek and kiss, out of some tremendous gratitude, the top of her head where she had gathered back her hair to expose a lined, freckled face. Not speaking, just standing in the middle of the kitchen, holding her.

Hair, table, light – all trembled.

Then the fly-screen was squeaking and the door opening with a rush of cold wind and Tildy was leaving.

She wound down the car window and shouted: "I'll tell her you are lovely, Alex. The happiest man in the world, too. Is that what I'll tell her? Get down, Midge, you bastard. You'll scratch the seat."

Merridy ran deep for four days and then on the fifth she called. He was reading beside the fire in the living room when the telephone rang on the little glass-topped table. He picked it up.

"It's me," said her voice. Calm but guarded.

"Yes."

He enquired after Aunt Doss, who had had her hair dyed and looked foxier. He asked Merridy how she was feeling and she replied that she had stopped being sick and added that she was going the following day for an ultrasound scan.

"Tell me how it goes." There was nothing else he could think of to say. He did not really want to hear how it went.

But the following evening he sought her reassurance that the baby was all right. He listened as Merridy told him how Aunt Doss had accompanied her to Dr James. They had sat before a monitor and watched the image of the child.

Dr James had guided Merridy through the body parts: "Nice arch of foot. Spine there is really healthy. Legs look good. That's the ventricle. The cerebellum at the back of the brain is the normal dumb-bell shape. Lips. That black circle there is the stomach." Next to the circle, the heart was beating in flashes. "A very nuclear heart," Dr James said approvingly.

"What did it look like to you?" Alex asked.

The baby – moving within its skirt shape – provoked a stream of disconnected images in Merridy: corn on the cob, frogs' legs, Churchill, a crab, the black-and-white footage of Nagasaki.

"Do you want to know the sex?" she said.

"Not particularly."

"Well, if you change your mind . . ."

"What is it?"

A pause.

"Merridy, tell me."

Another pause. "Boy." She coughed. "A boy." And explained how the midwife had given the game away. "I asked her if you could tell the sex at this stage and she said: 'Oh, yes,' and pointed: 'There's his little penis sticking out.'"

"I thought of him as a boy for some reason," Alex said, unscrewing the cap on the bottle. "What did he look like again?"

"He looked like an old man on his back with a large bald head and his chin tucked in. And, Alex, do you know what his first gesture was? He put his right hand up to his forehead."

Alex could not help but smile. "That's what you do in your sleep."

"Just imagine, Alex. My baby is going to have a very nuclear heart. What do you suppose that means?"

He ran his finger around the lip of the bottle. "I've been thinking," he said.

"Yes?"

He clammed up. But it was not a hostile silence and they both knew it.

So was established a pattern that continued over the days that followed. He only drank gin when they had these telephone calls; the Geneva talks, as he came to think of them. He had bought himself a new bottle and when the telephone rang he poured a tumbler and sat in the living room and sipped. As the gin went down, the warmth rose, but it was not an alcoholic heat. It was something else.

They talked in a way that they had not talked in years, maybe never talked. Merridy started to uncover in him an intimacy, and Alex to renew an old pleasure and sense of possibility. And not really having spoken on the telephone in his life, he now talked himself into closeness. Their nightly conversations were a little shell that both crawled into. Together with Merridy he returned in shy, but increasingly jubilant, steps to their first encounter in the lane behind the school; their honeymoon on Flinders, digging for Killiecrankie diamonds, the film that he had taken her to see in Whitemark, and the low-flying peacock that cracked the windscreen of their hired car. With recovered optimism, they went over and celebrated the work, time, energy that each had invested in the house, the farm, Oblong Oysters. They remembered the rapacity of their bodies.

Distance protected them. He was spared the sight of her belly; it would have been a reality too harsh to see his wife's stomach growing with a baby not his own. On the other hand, when the baby began to kick or had hiccups or Merridy had to go to Dr James for the amniocentesis, he surprised himself with his anxiety.

One evening, getting ready for her call, he was drawing the curtains in the living room when he caught sight of his reflection in the window and teased himself. He had never considered what a dignified cuckold might look like, but now he knew.

Her line was engaged that night. When they spoke the following evening she told him of an emotional conversation with her mother. "I'm trying to make sense of it. She wants to leave the Sanctuary."

"What, and live with Doss?"

"Don't laugh. She plans to move in with an old boyfriend – the man she was engaged to before she met Dad." Randal Twelvetrees had been constrained to get in touch with Mrs Bowman after his father alerted him to the discovery of Hector's remains. The Minister's son explained – in the letter that he wrote from Albany and which was forwarded on by Doss – how he had nursed his wife through a long illness and was now a widower. After speaking with her mother for three hours, Merridy could not tell if she was acting out of a late-flowering need for companionship or out of a long-held guilt, or whether she wanted to repent for Merridy. "All I know is that Randal went to see Mum in the Sanctuary and made this offer. He has a property – she won't tell me where it is, except that it's 'somewhere in Tasmania, somewhere a long way away'. She's already making arrangements to have her stuff moved down there."

It was not long afterwards that Alex reached his decision about Merridy's child. "I'd like to raise him as my own," he told her, and when she started to speak: "I'm not going to ask any questions. I don't want to know. But as far as I'm concerned, this is my child."

Two topics they avoided. The first was the question of her return to Moulting Lagoon Farm. She had left Jason in charge of operations while she stayed with her aunt in Ulverstone. But the oysters were ready to harvest and she had signed a contract.

What Alex did not tell Merridy was that he had taken to going down to the shed. He asked for Jason's discretion: "Let's keep this between ourselves, but I reckon you could do with some assistance."

Wary at first, Jason was grateful to have an extra pair of hands. He taught Alex how to cut out the mesh and repair the lanterns and to tie the special knot that would never let anything go – a knot that Alex knew of old, but he said nothing. While Jason was busy handling and loading the stock, Alex mended buoys. He emptied the lanterns and tipped the oysters into the rotary grader and scrubbed down the keels and deck. And one afternoon, leaning against his ute, paper and pencil in hand, was moved to sketch the *Zemmery Fidd*.

"Why don't you come home?" he said to Merridy one night.

"What?"

He repeated it twice.

"When?"

"What about next week? I've got to go to Launceston for a lamb sale. Come down during that."

"Next week would be good."

"Or is that too soon?"

"No, no, it's not too soon."

"Merridy?"

"Yes."

"I've started preparing," incapable of containing his excitement. In the Talbot's closing-down sale, he had bought a small child's wheelbarrow.

"But, Alex," laughing, then tentative, "you do realise he won't be able to use that for another five years!"

He felt his face grow warm. But he didn't care. It was worth more than he could have anticipated to hear the responsive echo of Merridy's laughter. He treasured it so much that he decided not to tell her about his other surprise, on which he had been working night and day in time for her return.

So Merridy agreed to drive back to Moulting Lagoon Farm the following Tuesday. She felt quite positive. She had passed through the Stations of her Cross. It might not be his child, but Alex would come to love it as his own. Alex loved her and the child in her was the best part of her. And she knew, now, that she loved him. She was certain.

The other topic that was not discussed was Kish.

Merridy, because away from his presence it became easy to forget him. It was almost a convenience to her that Kish had disappeared: she would not have to tell Alex.

Alex, because he needed to forget.

CHAPTER FIVE

HE JUMPED DOWN FROM the cabin and ran off along the main street. Opposite the school was a small wooden bus shelter with a bench. He would catch a couple of hours' sleep, then hitch a ride before the town was up, when the log-trucks started rolling through.

He crawled into the corner and lay on his back, revolving Alex's bottle, turning it slowly in his torn fingers. He brought the glass close to his face, but its contents remained dark to him. Too dark at any rate to divine what it obsessed him to see, though he did not understand why. Frustrated, he tucked the bottle under his head and was falling asleep when he heard a woman's voice.

Instantly alert, he slid from the bench and looked out. Across the road, a man unlocked the door to the school. Standing beside him was Mrs Dove.

A little while later he sat crouched beneath the window. He could hear them on the schoolroom floor. They were not piecing together jigsaws or trying out the alphabet or singing "We are the Vegemites". They were playing doctors and nurses.

Alarmed by the racket, he at one point rose from his hiding place between the rubbish bins and looked down through the glass, down the slope of a desk. The sight snatched his breath. Below him, upside down, Mrs Dove. Her closed eyes running together to form a smile, her breasts whiter than eggs, her mouth a fluttering eye.

And sank noiselessly back.

He had put Alex's bottle on the ground beside him and he stared into it. He rested his elbows on his knees and sat there staring, until Merridy and the man had finished their ruckus and shut the door behind them and left.

The man, lifting the lid to throw something in, did not notice him squeezed up against the bin.

For a few moments more he remained squatting there, his head drowned in his hands and swollen with brackish thoughts. Then holding the bottle by its neck he struck it with one hard blow on the gravel.

There was the tink of imploding glass and the ship sailed onto the playground.

He gripped the broken bottle. The way he brought its jagged jaw to his face, he might have been about to lacerate his forehead to release his pain and to stab at the blowflies or red-eyed moths or whatever it was that kept swishing about in his skull. Then with a conscious effort he let the bottle drop and looked around for the *Otago*.

The hull adhered to a segment of glass on a strip of withered blue plasticine. He flicked open his knife and fell upon the delicate assemblage – varnished pine, triangles of stiffened cotton, ice-cream sticks – and with the tip of the blade gently levered the penny from its deck.

He had never been able, not properly, to make out the face on the coin, but now he held it up to the moon. A severe young woman glared back at him.

Once he had the penny in his hand, his whole being fastened around it. In the front seat of log-trucks he zigzagged his way south to the Huon and spent a fortnight repairing nets for cherry trees on a farm outside Franklin. He made himself useful: dressed in Mr Dove's jeans and shirt, and wearing Alex's spare pair of spectacles, he cleared the paths of duck crap and took the garbage to the tip and watered the horses as he had watched Mrs Dove do. At night, he slept in a room, its walls papered with embossed flax. And for companionship caught flies. Bluebottles that he attracted with duck crap into a plastic bag, which he knotted. In his hand, the bag buzzed like a toy running down and then stilled to a splutter. He would sit on his mattress and hold the bag to his ear while he checked his pocket for the coin that he sometimes produced and stared at through Mr Dove's glasses, and at other times was content to pinch through his trouser leg. As if the sound of the flies was telling him where to go and the penny was courage in his pocket.

In the meantime, while he thought about what he was going to do, he needed to earn a different currency. Money that would enable him to lie low until an opportunity came to leave this freaky island.

In Franklin, he read a notice handwritten in black felt pen and pinned to a board outside a boatbuilder's yard: "MAN WITH VAN NEEDS ANOTHER MAN". The man was a talkative Englishman: fiftyish, small, with a gold propelling pencil clipped to his T-shirt at the throat. He had longish thinning hair and a crease about the eyes. Left some money by his father, he had decided to start a removals business. That was his explanation.

His van was a white U-haul. In the front, there was a potted-plant arrangement-tray filled with geraniums that he watered first thing in the morning. His living accommodation was a bunk-bed in the back, where he slept, more often than not while listening to the radio, surrounded by flippers and goggles and oxygen cylinders. The paraphernalia of a skin-diver.

Next to the bed was an old-fashioned Elsan and a basin where he washed.

"You can sleep in the bottom bunk," he said to Kish, who disliked the van immensely.

Eager to get back outside, Kish stepped onto the tow-bar and jumped down.

But something intrigued him about the polished metal ball. "Do you have a caravan?" he asked.

"A caravan? Honestly!" Insulted. "That's for my boat."

Which, he went onto explain, required a complete overhaul. He had put her into the boat yard in Franklin while he earned the money to pay for this.

For ten weeks, Kish lifted bookshelves and refrigerators and once a piano into the van and drove from one corner of the state to another, unloading, sleeping in the back, listening to the man, who was called Joseph Silkleigh, prattle on about the North African coast, where he had spent time frog-diving; or his father who had blamed his mother for everything, like a bad maid; or the girl he had met on a beach south of Perth who had jilted him, after he had parked his van outside her house once too often. Joseph claimed still to be bruised by the rejection. "She's that rare thing" – he said it wistfully – "a woman with a sense of humour."

Joseph's past was a country that he had fled, he suggested, in tatters. "I was the last man out, old soul." But no experience was ever wasted. All would go into his book. The story of Joseph's life. An astonishing story. That he had begun and abandoned countless times, and always for the same reason: he did not have the right title. "But now I do. Now I do." He turned to Kish with an expression of innocent triumph: "I'm going to call it *The Making of Me*."

Kish frowned and then at his lap. "I don't read much," he said.

"You don't talk much either, Knish, if you don't mind my saying."

"It's Kish."

Joseph nodded as if he did not believe him. "I'm a sod for names. Jewish, are you?"

"No."

"A *knish* is a dumpling with chopped liver."

"I didn't know."

"I'm telling you it is." Then: "Not Canadian, are you?"

"No." He was worse than the blowflies.

"I know, I know. When you are down, even dogs don't come near you. But just how *did* you get down here, old soul, if you don't mind my asking?"

"A sailing ship."

"A sailing ship, eh? Then you're a man after my own heart, Knish. I *love* ships. Spent most of my life on them, wouldn't be surprised. Yawls, yachts, gin palaces, smacks, hermaphrodite-brigantines, you name it." He rubbed his nose. "Only ship I've yet to sail in is a relationship," and gave a sad laugh, but a laugh nonetheless.

They drove through Geeveston.

"What about you, Knish, do you have a girl?"

They were heading south with a van-load of second-hand books.

"Yes."

"A nice girl, is she?"

"She is nice."

"Musical?"

"I don't think so."

"Well, as long as you're happy, old soul," said Joseph. "Are you happy?"

Kish said nothing. He eyed the object that he had dug out of his hip pocket and said nothing.

"What is it with you, Knish? If you're not fiddling with that ruddy knife of yours, you're flipping old coins. Not gold, is it? Here, let me see. I used to be a bit of a numismatist."

He plucked the coin from Kish's hand and framed it against the steering wheel and studied it.

"Victorian Bun Penny. 1841. Cheapest type of copper. I found one of these once. Worthless, like yours. Found it at the bottom of the sea. You might get eleven dollars for it. Ten, more likely." And handed it back. "Now if it was 1843 you'd be in the money. 1843, then you'd be talking, Knish," and chuckled. "Or maybe, if it was you, you wouldn't."

Kish grabbed at it. "You bastard." His eyes blazed with darkness and he jerked out his hand. In which a knife flashed.

For a millisecond there was an offer of violence to Joseph, who with one hand took the knife off him and said in a fantastically calm way: "We're working together, don't fuck about. It means nothing to me whether you kill me. It's quite late on in my life. But while we're here, wake up. I don't give a bugger why you're on the run. Nonetheless, I quite like you. And while I don't mind sharing the back of the van with you, I don't need to share your criminal and emotional baggage."

He slowed down to let two girls in bikinis with dripping hair cross the road. "I say," he murmured, "they rather appeal to my aqueous humour."

He watched the girls pick their way barefoot along the gravel towards a shack and then turned to Kish.

"There you are, there's your knife. And it wouldn't be the worst thing if you took it and found a sheep that we could cut up and cook."

He put the van into gear and drove on, concentrating on the road.

They had been driving in this way for a while when he threw Kish another look. "You all right, old dumpling? You look like the proverbial grave in which something's been spinning."

"I'm OK."

Joseph nodded. "I wonder if—" His sentence broke off, like a pencil pressed too hard. Once more his eyes roved down over Kish's spiky hair, his earring, his spectacles, his oversized white shirt, to the hand that fretted with the coin. "I don't want you to swallow this the wrong way, Knish. But it's struck me on a sudden that we've been sitting here nattering contentedly for the best part of ten weeks, and yet all I know about you is that you're a total orphan who has no idea who his father was or his mother. Absolutely no idea. And that you came to Tasmania under full sail. Oh, and that you have a girl who's not especially musical." Joseph looked back at the road ahead and stared at it in a hurt way. "Now, old soul, I hope you will agree that's not much. I mean, that's not much to show for ten weeks of sharing the same precious space, day in, day out. Not when I've told you all about my life. Know what I'm saying?"

"Why do you have to know anything?" It was almost a hiss.

"Why do I have to know anything?" Joseph repeated slowly. He shook his head. Whatever Kish was, he was not a day at the beach. "Because I'm interested, you oaf. Because it passes the time. Because it's polite. Because I'm a bit of a *uomo universale,* you might say. I mean, what are your interests? I've got my goggles and flippers. Just as you've got your knife and penny. But what do you like doing? That's what I can't work out. What floats your boat, eh?"

Kish leaned back. He slipped the coin into his jeans alongside his knife and glowered. "Don't worry about it."

"Then tell you what. Let's play a game. What do you hate? What sickens you?"

"Fuckwits asking questions."

"Come on. Don't be like that. That's not the point. What are your favourite words? Mine are elbow, biltong, claret."

"What's biltong?" asked Kish.

"Biltong? You don't know what biltong is?"

"No, I don't know what biltong is."

Joseph smiled. "I'll say one thing, old dumpling. You keep your cards pretty close to that chest of yours. Jeepers, I can't tell if you're happy, if you're angry, if you're out of your fucking ugly tree, or what you are."

At any rate, Kish must have thought about what Joseph had said because all of a sudden he flung out his hand over the tray of geraniums and pointed at a green flag that dangled from the driving mirror.

"What's that?"

"Irish. Everyone loves the Irish."

"You don't sound Irish."

"I didn't want to draw attention to a colonial bastard. But, hey, you're getting the point. You don't get anywhere without asking questions. I mean, nowhere."

Then: "What does it mean, The Long Haul?"

"*What does it mean?*" incredulous. "What a question! What. A. Question." But once Joseph had stopped shaking his head, he confessed in a voice more solemn: "Actually, I'm toying with the idea of a name change. And maybe, Knish, you're the one to help. There are myriads of possibilities, as well you may imagine, but after a lot of aggro – a lot of aggro – I've boiled them down to two."

He paused. Now the moment had arrived to reveal his choices, he seemed strangely vulnerable. "Either DELIVERANCE" – he turned to gauge the reaction – "or BUT IT MOVES." And when Kish still looked blank, explained: "*E pur si muove.* Attributed to Galileo after his recantation, although generally conceded to be apocryphal. So which one takes your fancy, eh?"

They were passing a refrigeration plant on the Huon. Kish looked out of the window at two sailing boats and touched his earring and mumbled something. Whatever it was did not reach Joseph.

"Hey, blabbermouth, don't keep it from Silkleigh. Not when your words are such gold."

Kish turned. He said in a hard voice: "I have so much anger that sometimes it can near kill people."

"Is that so, old soul? Is that so?" And picked his nose. He seemed relieved that the subject had moved on. "I used to be angry like that until I realised it was just frustration coming out the wrong way. Ah, here we are. Dover. Now where do you suppose this bookshop is? I'll just park on the dirt and ask that nice old lady."

*

For four months, Kish busted his gut doing manual labour. Punishing, healing, galvanising himself. The whole time flipping the severe young woman into the air and catching her and trying to outstare her. Waiting for her to give him some sort of direction. More direction anyway than BRITANNIA REG FID DEF, whoever that was when she was at home.

A conviction took hold that the letters contained a message that would tell him what to do. He tried patiently to work it out, this loop of meaning, but all he felt was desolation. Like when he was going clean for the first time after using heavily. The effort hardly seemed worth it, it was so hard; and what was to be gained? Such a small plus in the middle of such a big mess.

Once or twice he came close to asking Joseph, but always at the last moment he pulled back. This was something that only he and the woman could settle.

There were moments when he hated her long sharp nose. The ringlets of hair tucked over her ear and gathered into a bun. Sometimes he had the feeling that, like him, the penny was really bad. Most of the time he felt that it was a compass, leading him round in circles, leading him all over the island in his quest for reparation. He still did not know what he ought to do, but he never lost faith that the stern face might one day rouse itself from its coma and fix him in the eye and tell him.

One autumn morning, they were in Gladstone – a tin-mining town in the north-east – to deliver a widow's furniture. He opened the back of the van, waking late after their mutton barbecue, and saw Joseph, legs up on a bench, outside the store in the street where they had parked for the night. He was talking to a bald, red-faced man in wire-framed specs who nervously rolled his gaze over the top of Joseph's knees to Kish.

"Hey, Knish," said Joseph. "This is Mr Beeley."

"Hi."

"I was saying to him I bet this place has a lot of kink."

Mr Beeley gave a frightened laugh.

"I've also been telling him about my book. *The Making of Me.*"

Mr Beeley had three large mosquito bites above his brow and his moustache was frosted with ice cream. "Sounds most intriguing," he said charily, and smiled at Kish. "Talking of books," looking from one to the other, "I had a visitor this morning."

"Really?" said Joseph, suddenly not very interested. He tucked his propelling pencil back into his T-shirt and picked up Mr Beeley's newspaper. "What kind of visitor would that be, pray?" as he scanned the front page headline: *EAST COAST SALE SCUPPERED. Plans to develop Talbot's General Store at Wellington Point mysteriously fell through yesterday when owner 84-year-old Albert Talbot took the property off the market . . .*

"I was just cutting the front lawn when she opened the gate. A nice lady, she'd wanna be on her way to sixty. I thought: Oh dear, oh dear. I said to her, 'Last week, I know I was busy and put you off. But I'm very, very busy today.'"

The sound of rushing air made Joseph raise his eyes. "So who was she?" distracted. He had forgotten to water his geraniums.

"I don't know her name. She lives with Mr Twelvetrees," said Mr Beeley. "But I reckon she's a Jehovah's Witness is what she is."

"How extraordinary," watching the flock of birds move at great speed over the roof of the van.

Kish followed his gaze.

Mr Beeley was not to be distracted.

"Anyhow, she gave me a big thick Bible and said: 'I can help you,' and I said: 'Leave it there.' She said: 'To make sure you know the full gist of what's going on, turn your Bible to Peter, Chapter 1 and you go to Verse 23 here, and that tells you for sure. *Being born again, not of corruptible seed, but of incorruptible, by the word of God, which liveth and abideth for ever.*' Well, I looks at her and I say: 'When you go to the Bible, it's all right up to a point,' and she said: 'What do you mean?' I said: 'Jesus was nailed on the cross and so forth, but if you think it's right to bring Him back, it can't be done.' She said: 'Oh, yes, it can. Where do you think we go when we die?' I said: 'Under the ground.' She said: 'No. God will tell Jesus. He'll instruct him and they'll bring you back to life.' I thought: Oh dear, oh dear. She said: 'If you want to, you can give a donation,' and I said: 'No. You might get a donation next time. But there's a lovely pair of gentlemen over the road. They only arrived last night and I'm sure they'll spare you something. Would you like to see them?'"

"You didn't," murmured Joseph.

"I did, too." Mr Beeley lifted his spectacles and rubbed an eye and giggled. "I'm surprised she hasn't been 'long already."

"When was this?" stirring.

"Round twenty minutes ago."

Joseph's eyes scouted the road both ways. "Time we got going," tossing the newspaper aside and standing up. He consulted his notebook. "Knish and I have a delivery to make," he apologised to Mr Beeley. "Hey, Knish! Let's go and find this Mrs Bowman and give her her furniture."

But Kish was watching the birds. They flew in squabbling circles above the roof of the van and settled on it repeatedly as if the van exerted some sort of pull. He wiped his cheek with his shirt-sleeve and his eyes followed their short glides, one flat curved wing beating faster than the other, and the sound of the wind rushing through their feathers, until they rose from the van and this time circled upwards into the sky in high-pitched screeches.

"Wonder what they are . . ." Joseph said half to himself.

Until the specks were too tiny to see.

Kish dropped the hand that shielded his eyes. He rucked up his trousers. Then he went and closed the back of the U-haul and bolted it. He knew now. He did not know why he wanted to do it, but he wanted to do it. For the solvency of his conscience, he had to go back.

CHAPTER SIX

TALBOT'S NEWSLETTER. EDITORIAL
I think I have an old man and a soldier's right to say that whereas we listen to a great deal of codswallop about the peaceable intentions of our powerful northern neighbours, you can take it from me that the nation that laid waste the New Guinea archipelago, that visited a regime of terrible brutality upon the genuinely peace-loving natives of New Britain – well, I saw it all with my own eyes, so I can say it and to hell with your political correctness – I would just like to put a marker down for the next generation. Don't fall asleep, my friends and fellow citizens. That dragon may rise again. A.T.

On the eve of Merridy's return, Alex walked one last time through the house and checked that there was nothing he might have overlooked. He made a bouquet of her favourite flowers and arranged them in a vase beside the bed: white hammer-headed stylidium gathered from beneath their window, red rugosa from down by the beach, pink tubular correa. He rehung the samplers, back from the framer's and repaired by a seamstress in Sandy Bay, as well as the cockatoo and her pencil drawing. He stocked the fridge with meats from the Wursthaus Kitchen in Hobart. And in the waning light went into the room that he had prepared for the child.

His eyes passed over the cot, the black felt Tasmanian devil on the pillow, the red wheelbarrow, the sieve. The room was cold and he noticed that Madasun had left the window open. Beyond Moulting Lagoon, the sea crashed down with a personal note. He stood listening to the waves before he fastened the latch. Then he turned out the light. The luminous paint had dried on the ceiling that he had retouched that morning, and before he closed the door he waited for the lemony stars to begin competing with the darkness gathering outside.

He waited until last to go into Merridy's study.

For more than a week he had taken to coming in here, shutting himself away once he had finished speaking to her, working without pause, at times until daybreak, hunched over an empty gin bottle. Now his work was finished.

Years had passed since Alex had attempted such a project. And yet something troubled him. He suspected that for all the pains he had taken with this particular ship his wife would be disappointed.

He picked up the bottle from her desk and took it into the living room.

Alex added a log to the fire and sat down under the goose-neck reading light.

He was still inspecting his model of the *Zemmery Fidd* when he heard a noise and saw that the door had opened.

A shadow stretched into the room. As if it had detached itself from one of the frames in the corridor: white shirt, his very own jeans, a rustic satchel and a gold earring.

The room lurched and all sorts of emotional somersaults went through Alex's head when he saw the father of his child. This was the one thing that he had not factored into his resolution to look after Merridy's baby. It never had occurred to him, not once. Kish was a wanderer, a blow-in who had blown out. He had gone and was probably on the mainland. He certainly was not going to come back to Moulting Lagoon Farm.

"Kish?" He rubbed his eyes with his knuckles. "Kish?" and put down the bottle. "Is it you? You've changed."

"Mr Dove, you look a little different, too. How are you, Mr Dove?"

"I'm fine. Where have you been?"

"I've been in the north, in the south, all over the island. I've been with Mr Silkleigh."

"You look all bushed," preparing to get up. "You'd better come and have a cup of tea."

"I don't think so."

"Don't worry, I've had the place cleaned."

"And Mrs Dove, how is Mrs Dove?" unfastening his satchel.

Alex sat back. "Mrs Dove is coming back tomorrow. Mrs Dove is going to have a baby."

"A baby? That's wonderful news."

"Do you think so, Kish? I'm happy to hear you say that. Because I very much hope that you didn't come back to claim this baby. It's taken me a long time, but I've made up my mind to adopt the boy and bring him up as my own."

Kish laughed in disbelief. "You've made a mistake there, Mr Dove. I haven't come back to see your wife."

"Then what are you doing here? What do you want?"

Kish walked across the room and opened his satchel and took something very reverently out of it, wrapped in cotton wool, that he laid on the glass-topped table at Alex's elbow.

"What's this?"

As soon as he let it go, Kish felt a rush of lightness to his head. He sat down opposite Alex and crossed his legs and smiled. "Mr Dove, the only reason I came back is to give you this."

Alex looked from Kish to the cotton wool and picked it up. Inside, a tarnished Queen Victoria, the colour of shoe-leather.

He examined the young monarch's face without taking it in. Then returned his gaze to Kish, who was acting as if he had been a good boy. Pleased that he had done what he had to do and now was waiting to be thanked.

Kish said: "I'm here, too, to tell you that I'm very, very sorry for what I did."

Alex stared at this boy whose life he had saved. Who still wore his – Alex's – clothes, for Christ's sake! Who had done everything to destroy his marriage. Who was suspected of murder.

"You come in as if you own the place," he said slowly, "you sit in my wife's chair . . ."

He should have left him to drown.

And remembered when they brought him in, his pheasant flesh all blue and plucked. His guts expelling an awful, bad breath. He had been so touching in his helplessness.

"I suppose you want a reward for returning my own property?"

"A reward? Mr Dove, I'm not after no reward." His brow crinkled at Alex's misjudgement.

Alex looked again at the copper penny. Competing in his head, treacherous thoughts about Kish – and also a bewildered delight at this tribute or penance. In a very extraordinary way, he was grateful to see Kish. His reappearance rounded the whole thing out.

He put down the coin and it rolled off the edge of the table, onto the possum rug.

Kish stared at it with dismay; Alex impassively, without seeing it.

"I thought you'd be missing it," muttered Kish.

"I don't give a damn about the penny," in a cracked voice. "The penny I care about is in my wife's belly."

Kish frowned.

"That's right," Alex said. "Which you put there."

"Me?" his mouth falling open.

There was a trace even of sadness in Kish's eyes, carried up by the reflected firelight to a dark and private place from which he looked back at Alex. As if he did not know what Alex meant at all.

When Alex noticed his baffled expression, he thought: God help us, will our child be as half-witted?

"Kish, I saw you," and brought his chin forward. "I saw you kiss her," harping on it. "Snogging like rabbits in the house that night we came back."

Kish stiffened at the injustice of the accusation. "Look, Mr Dove . . ."

Alex held the bottle tighter. He thought: It has taken me this long, but I have got over my qualms, and now I know I can live with the idea it's going to be all right.

But he could not help it. He felt his resentment unloading. He looked across at Kish who was, before he set another child in train, in a funny way the child that Alex and Merridy had never had. "And why smash all my ships, for God's sake? My father's ships."

Kish uncrossed his legs and leaned back, emptying a pocket. "I guess I've done a lot of things that I shouldn't have done, Mr Dove, but I'm hoping this makes up for it."

All at once, seeing the wad of dollars, a fierce anger developed in Alex. "I don't want your money, Kish. You'd be better backing your future rather than mine. On the other hand, I would like to know why you rampaged through my house destroying everything."

"I was scared," Kish said, and his eyes jittered. He was agitated now. By Mr Dove's behaviour. By the memory of what had happened in the corridor. He had never been scared like that, not even as the *Buffalo* broke up around him. "Mrs Dove, she upset me. She was like a ghost or something."

"Pah! You were the ghost."

Kish stood up and placed the money on the table. "Look here, Mr Dove, I came to say I'm sorry for what I did. If you won't take this, then I'm not sure what I can do. But I'm off."

"No, you're not." Alex leaped from his chair – and the bottle that was in his lap.

He caught up with Kish at the door. Skinny in the oversized trousers and the firelight dancing on the buttons of his shirt. What was it about such a man that he did not have?

"I save you from the sea. I take you in, dress you, feed you. And you fuck my wife." He shoved him against the wall. He sounded pathetic to himself, so self-pitying.

Kish squirmed out of his grasp. A ruthless look dulled his face and his right arm flexed back. "Don't, Mr Dove."

Be careful, Alex! warned the cockatoo above the fireplace, speaking in Merridy's voice.

As soon as his eyes saw the knife, Alex knew that his next step would determine the rest of his life. He knew this with a clarity that he had not felt since coming face to face with Merridy behind the school.

A log slithered in the grate and untrapped flames glinted on oiled steel. Here, in this room where he remembered two Scrabble players pondering their next word, Alex was on his own. He had outlived both his parents. But over the past few days the prospect of a happiness that they were denied had begun to stretch ahead of him in a precarious but tantalising vista. Blocked suddenly by Kish.

Who started to laugh. His laughter was blended with pity, and the sharp teeth of it prowled closer. "I didn't want to tell you" – his hand sawed back and forth, he could have been carving an ice-cream stick for a brigantine – "I didn't want to tell you, Mr Dove." What he had heard. What he had seen. They were as close to him as . . . as that bird over there, and he looked out of those isolated eyes in which he saw her lying on the classroom floor, the man on top, her legs around his back, two animals.

"I could have had her. I might have done . . ."

Don't listen to him, Alex, the bird entreated. It's you I love. Not Kish, not anyone else. You – Piers Alexander Dove.

Alex must have taken a step forward because he tripped over the bottle, but recovered his balance. He could hear a child's voice and Merridy speaking. She was standing in her garden that she had sculpted from the dunes, and by her side there was a boy. She brushed a leaf against his uptilted face, and Alex saw that the boy looked like him at that age. "Lemon balm," she was explaining. "It gladdens the heart and makes a beautiful tea. Here, give me your hand." She broke off a frond of bracken and cracked it open and rubbed the creamy stem on his wrist – "to protect you against jack-jumper ants". She bent down and nipped a stalk that she had spied in the rhubarb. "Spurge. Now you wash your hands after touching that. There's a white sap under the leaves. Get it in your eye, you end up going blind." And taking him by the wrist led the way deeper into her garden.

A different voice said threateningly: "I warn you, one more step . . ."

Alex hesitated. She had disappeared behind the dune – it was where they had made love – but he could hear her talking, in a voice of such kindness that he was willing to sacrifice his last breath in order to catch what she was saying. "With tomatoes, you give them a big scare. You put them in bad soil and they think they'll have to seed or die, and then you pamper them like anything."

Fingers tightened on the silver handle. "Don't!"

At the sight of the blade, a rage balled up inside Alex to think of everything that he risked losing.

He rammed his knee into Kish's groin.

Kish screamed, dropping the knife.

Alex snatched it up. And kneed him again, putting into his savage kick all the strength that he had saved up since childhood.

A table fell, and a glass and lamp – that stayed on, but spilling light elsewhere.

Smell of gin and burning peppermint gum and firelight flickering on Kish's excruciated face. He was on his knees, burrowing and gasping for breath, his speech blurred like a prayer that he mumbled. "Why did you have to do that? Why?" In a bright red voice, he said: "I brought you your coin back. I thought you'd be pleased."

Alex pressed the blade to his throat and sharply tugged back his head in the position of a wether selected for a mutton roast. If hate had permitted, he would have gouged out those eyes that stared back at him through his own spectacles.

"Listen carefully. Before you went away very suddenly that night, I had made up my mind that I wanted you to be here for a long time, that you could stay here, that you could live with us and we could adopt you, and perhaps give you a home you'd never had before. Don't interrupt – because what I have to say to you is very tough. I want you to go now. And I don't want you ever to come back, because Mrs Dove is returning tomorrow and it would upset her to see you. And now what's happened has happened, it upsets me to see you here. I will repeat this one last time. It did take a while for me to accept, but I have decided to bring this baby up as my own. Have you got that, Kish? My own. Or is there something you wish to say?"

There was. And he was all set to say it, too, once he had got his breath back. He sucked in another quart of air and opened his mouth to speak.

And felt a coppery finger on his lips, shushing him.

He stared back at Alex with a glassy concentrated eye in which all the sea in the bay seemed suddenly to have collected. Because he was not seeing Alex. Vivid images flared inside his head. Birds flying. Oysters spawning. Dunes of sand. A sudden wind was streaming them one into the other, and he had the sensation that he himself was melting into the mix, part of an infinite and dazzling whiteness. The tinnitus buzzing and twittering died away and there was a great silence at his core. A fathering silence in which it dawned on Kish that it was not only the penny that he had to give back to Alex.

Those words that haloed the woman. He thought, then, that he understood. She was whispering it into his head.

So instead of saying, as he had been about to: "Your child is nothing to do with me, there's no way in the world it could have been mine," and revealing what he had witnessed through the schoolroom window, he stifled the denial that had been forming in his throat and stood awkwardly up.

"You know what, Mr Dove, the man who dropped me off here called me Blabbermouth. Actually, he's going to collect me at 10 p.m. He had to do something and he dropped me and we're going on. But before I go, I would like to say this. Whatever you saw, it's not what you think. Nothing happened between me and Mrs Dove. Absolutely nothing. It's you she loves. It's yours, the baby. Whoever else's could it be? It is yours."

CHAPTER SEVEN

IN THE GOLDEN HOUR of dawn, when sails come out of the horizon, Alex launched the *Zemmery Fidd* into the river.

The young oysters that he had fed into the rotary grader were repacked and loaded, ready to be returned to the sea, and though, strictly speaking, another person ought to have been on board to assist, Jason's girlfriend had arrived the previous afternoon and Alex saw no reason to disturb them.

There was a man sitting at the end of the jetty, fishing. He watched Alex start up the engines and bring the boat alongside. He had longish thinning hair and a white T-shirt.

Alex tied up, stepped onto the jetty.

"Wonderful to see so many oysters," said the man, as if he had been waiting for him.

"They're my wife's," recognising an English accent. He looked back at the lanterns on deck, each tray bulging with small shocked oysters, and felt a renewed pride in Merridy's achievement. "She's the oyster-grower."

The man wrote something down in a lined notebook. Beside him, a fish flapped in a bucket.

"Guess how I caught that. Go on. Guess."

The fish was flat and grey, with orange spots.

"I don't know," said Alex. He saw that the jetty was marked around like the fish with circles of orange lichen.

The man pointed his pencil at a large Pacific gull standing on the jetty. The gull was staring into the sun.

"That bird dropped it, so I took it off him. I think it's a flounder. It was too big for him."

Alarmed at the man's propelling pencil, the gull shook open its wings and flew off low over the shore, where a white van was parked.

"Catch you later," said Alex, straightening, and went to drive the tractor up from the water's edge to the shed.

When he came back, the man was stripping in his line, preparing to leave.

"I've left some mussels in the water if you want live bait."

"Thanks, mate," Alex said, casting off the rope. "I'm not fishing today."

CHAPTER EIGHT

In the early afternoon, Merridy's red Toyota scrunched to a halt at the top of the drive.

The door on the driver's side opened and Rusty jumped out and scampered onto the lawn to pee.

Alex watched his wife push herself from the car. He breathed out "Whoa!" at the size of her belly. She looked round, almost comical, and his heart swelled. It pressed with a sharp pain against his ribs, the fullness of his love for her and his tremendous need to protect their child, whatever it took.

She turned and saw him at the kitchen window and gave a small nervous wave. He lifted his hand, as when he had dropped the coin overboard, and then the knife, and observed them spinning towards the ocean floor, the darkness of seaweed and sand and shifting tides, and felt his anger purged. He remembered the lanterns like bodies floating. And how the sea that had delivered him to them, began to roughen, to whiten and toss like something alive.

He opened the fly-screen and ran to embrace her.

ACKNOWLEDGEMENTS

THIS IS A WORK of fiction and none of the characters are drawn from anyone in life. The town of Wellington Point does not exist any more than does Moulting Lagoon Farm or the Bilgola Mission. Nonetheless, I would like to thank the Melrose family, in particular Ian and Cass, for their unflagging goodwill and patience in educating me about oysters; John and Jo Fenn-Smith and Margaret Ann Oldmeadow, for details of farming life on Tasmania's east coast; Murray Bail for his memories of Methodist dances. Jane Devenish-Meares for her forensic expertise; Michael Stutchbury, Adrian Caesar and Rachael Rose for comments on the text. I am grateful to the late Alan Gow for sharing his experiences as a coast-watcher in New Britain. I would like also to thank Niko Hansen, Jenni Burdon, David Scarborough, David Vigar, Dominic Turner, Jon Johnson and, as always, Gillian Johnson; and lastly my editor, Christopher MacLehose, for two decades of friendship, encouragement and support.

The stanza by A. D. Hope is from "Ascent into Hell", written in 1943–44 and published in *The Wandering Islands*, (Edwards and Shaw, 1955), reproduced by arrangement with the licensor, The Estate of AD Hope c/- Curtis Brown (Aust) Pty Ltd.

The lines about black swans are taken from Chapter VI of *My Home in Tasmania*, by Louisa Meredith (reprinted by Sullivan's Cove, Hobart, 1979).

The poem "What do you see, nurse?" is adapted from "A Crabby Old Woman", by an anonymous Scottish woman, that first appeared in the Christmas edition of the *News Magazine of the North Ireland Association for Mental Health*.

The lines of Kenneth Slessor's poem "Beach Burial" are taken from *Kenneth Slessor: poetry, essays, war despatches, journalism, autobiographical material and letters*, edited by D. Haskell (University of Queensland Press: St Lucia, 1991), reproduced courtesy of Paul Slessor.

I would also like to pay tribute to *A Farm at the World's End*, by Thomas Dunbabin (Hobart, 1954) and *The East Coasters*, by Lois Nyman (Launceston, 1990).

About the author

About the book

Read on

Insights, Interviews & More . . .

About the author

Meet Nicholas Shakespeare

Jerry Bauer

NOVELIST AND BIOGRAPHER Nicholas Shakespeare has worked as a journalist and a literary editor. He is the author of five novels, including *The Vision of Elena Silves* (1989), *The High Flyer* (1993), *The Dancer Upstairs* (1995), and *Snowleg* (2004). He has also written a highly acclaimed biography of the writer Bruce Chatwin (1999). He divides his time between England and Tasmania.

Tassie: A Photographic Scrapbook

This is Dolphin Sands, a nine-mile beach that faces Oyster Bay, where Merridy has her oyster lease. You never see anyone on it. It must be one of the cleanest beaches in the world: no tar, no Coca-Cola cans, no plastic bags, no people. Whenever there's a storm, I take my two boys down onto the sand and we look for what the sea has tossed up. It was after a particularly violent storm that my son Max found a piece of porcelain that had come from a shipwreck in 1850. The six drowned bodies of the Large family had rolled ashore here next morning, all except one boy who was missing. The unfound child gave me the idea for the castaway Kish.

Tassie: A Photographic Scrapbook
(continued)

After a storm on Dolphin Sands. "For Europeans, it represents the literal end of the world: if you travel any further you are on your way home again" (Tasmania, *Peter Collenette).*

Tasmania's very remoteness has also protected it, and the absence of "progress," which once made this former British penal colony the butt of so many jokes, has turned into its strongest attraction. Bypassed and undeveloped, this arrestingly beautiful island (which is the size of West Virginia) is enjoying a rediscovery as an Arcadia rather than an Alcatraz.

Much of the island's western half remains a protected wilderness of mountains, impenetrable rainforest and torrential rivers.

A sailor told a newcomer who arrived a century ago: "In half that wilderness no man has put foot since time began." Tasmania has—officially—the cleanest air in the world, all pollution rinsed away by ocean-borne winds that blast in from Patagonia ten thousand miles away. The clarity of the light is what detained me. On clear days you have the illusion that you can see not only to the horizon, but beyond it—back to the days of the first settlers, who came ashore on what was then Van Diemen's Land and promptly mistook it for Paradise. ▶

Tassie: A Photographic Scrapbook

(continued)

Late afternoons, I go down to the river mouth at the end of the beach and fish for bream or flathead. It was here that an old fisherman once collared me and asked my name. "Shakespeare?" He looked at me excited, as if he doubted what he had heard. "Not Shakespeare? You couldn't possibly be related to the family who make the fishing tackle?"

A Conversation with Nicholas Shakespeare

How has the Tasmanian landscape influenced your writing?

Graham Greene puts it well in a letter: "The act of creation's awfully odd & inexplicable like falling in love." I did want in this novel to celebrate the startlingly lovely landscape that I could see from my East Coast window, and that was the prime reason for me uprooting myself four months each year from England. The idea was planted during a visit by my German publisher, who was commissioning authors to write stories about the sea: Was I interested? "Does a fish swim?" I remember replying. Here I was, facing Great Oyster Bay, Maria Island, the Tasman. Hardly a week passed when the waves didn't toss ashore some strange sea creature. Plus, I'm attracted to the idea that each one of us is seventy-two percent salt water. I had no story in mind. The narrative evolved to track the proverb that I chose as the epigraph: "A home is like the sea." Married, with two small boys who were like spears through the feet, I couldn't as in previous novels go traveling to procure material. So I decided to map out the new territory (to me) of domesticity, what Zorba called "the whole catastrophe." When I was single and hadn't been through

"I had no story in mind. The narrative evolved to track the proverb that I chose as the epigraph: 'A home is like the sea.'"

A Conversation with Nicholas Shakespeare ***(continued)***

a hedge or two, I foolishly regarded domestic life as dull. Of course, I understand now that it's dull like Verdi is dull. Actually, it resembles a daily opera—with poisonings, stabbings, bloodcurdling screams and deceits, then a couple of arias and a rapprochement before bed. Every hour of every day I feel I'm living out *Nabucco, Aida, Macbeth, Otello*. . . . I wanted to catch some of this energy while I was still on my feet.

In this novel, there appear to be some resonances to Tasmania being at the end of the world and not just Australia's smallest state. Have you felt this?

Like a lot of blow-ins, I was drawn to Tasmania because of its location on the rim of the world—"beyond the seas." But I swiftly discovered that Tasmania is an invigorating place from which to view the rest of the planet (as Grote Reber, who invented the satellite dish, discovered when he decided on Bothwell as the most advantageous site from which to study the universe). I still can't get out of my head a line that I read in a B&B in Wynyard: "For Europeans, it represents the literal end of the world: if you travel any further you are on your way home again." Except that in my case, as I tried to explain in my previous book, I felt a bewildering sense of homecoming. It's not too much to say that in coming to Tasmania, I found out a lot more about who I was. Probably more than I intended.

By setting the novel in the fictitious Wellington Point, have you tried to explore what it is like for many Tasmanians, living in comparative isolation with relatively poor prospects for work and advancement?

Tasmanians—justifiably—get antsy at outsiders who come on fleeting visits to suck the island's nectar, only to regurgitate the usual Gothic stories. There's another Tasmania that is easy to overlook, but to my mind just as compelling: the day-to-day existence that I've observed among farmers on the East Coast—a hard, unsung, unglamorous relationship to the soil and to the seasons. It echoed the sort of life I led in my adolescence as a cowhand on estancias in Argentina, places so remote that the men I worked with had never set eyes on the sea. This way of living has been celebrated to the hilt in Argentina by writers like Borges and W. H. Hudson, but in Tasmania the material was right there in front of me: fresh, profoundly moving, and more or less untilled in fiction. It took ▸

“It's not too much to say that in coming to Tasmania, I found out a lot more about who I was.”

a while before I realized that this was what I wanted to write about. V. S. Naipaul says it more elegantly in his new book: "It is the better and truer part of the labor of a writer from a new place to work out what his material is, to wring substance from the unwritten-about and unregarded local scene."

Once you start looking, you discover how history in Tasmania lies close to the surface. On Flinders, a woman told me how her father had discovered a pair of old leg-irons when out plowing. But there's another layer of history which appealed to me—resting alongside convict relics and Aboriginal middens—that is composed of flotsam from elsewhere. I have a friend on Dolphin Sands who when in Hobart lives in the house where Darwin spent his twenty-seventh birthday in 1836 and where he lost his pet monkey. Not long ago my friend was digging in his garden to lay a conservatory and came across the skull of a strange animal. He took it to a mate at the university, a professor of zoology, who told him, "That's a monkey skull." It was Darwin's pet monkey. Almost my favorite story concerns a meeting I had at Llandaff, a one-shack town about ten miles from our house. The old man who lived in the shack offered to show me

"Not long ago my friend was digging in his garden to lay a conservatory and came across the skull of a strange animal. . . . It was Darwin's pet monkey."

around the graveyard. We got talking. He said that his parents came over a hundred years ago from London, where the family had owned a hotel, but they had got into difficulties and had had to sell up. "What was the hotel called?" I asked. "Claridge's," he said. "It was named after us." His name was Raymond Charles Claridge. When I told him that Claridge's was still going, was probably the most famous hotel in London, I could see that he didn't believe me. I give these examples to show that every valley in Tasmania contains unexpected and touching narratives. Unlike in my earlier novels, I tried in *Secrets of the Sea* to confine my exploration to a small location, what Faulkner calls the "postage stamp" of one's immediate surroundings. Except, of course, that Wellington Point and its characters are invented. If you try to find the town on a map, it's likely to be submerged in the middle of Great Oyster Bay.

The diaspora from the mainland and elsewhere includes Alex Dove. How are you using him? To what purpose?

Alex is like a number of Tasmanians I've met: born to the land, but of parents from another continent, who came out to make a new life ▸

A Conversation with Nicholas Shakespeare *(continued)*

and somehow it all went belly up. Their sudden death in a collision with a log-truck struck me as a peculiarly Tasmanian fate. Not a month goes by when you don't read of some horrendous accident between a sixty-ton Scandia juggernaut and a meandering tourist car, and then it's all hushed up. So Alex's plight held a poignancy for me, as did the tragedy which scores Merridy, whose brother goes missing in Wynyard when she's five. It's a characteristic of Tasmania that the landscape overwhelms many who settle here, to the point of consuming them. The classic Australian myth is the disappeared body. Patrick White's novel *Voss* is about an explorer who disappears when crossing the outback; *Picnic at Hanging Rock* revolves around the vanishing of Miss McCraw and two of her pupils. More recently there's the example of Nancy Grunwaldt, a twenty-six-year-old German cyclist who went missing near St. Helen's. As a barfly in St. Helen's told me over his stubby: "They'll never find that sheila." In America, the dead body is found shot through and left on the highway; in Canada, frozen in a snowbank; in England, slumped over the billiards table. But in Australia? No body is ever found. And yet without it, as the Antigone

“It's a characteristic of Tasmania that the landscape overwhelms many who settle here, to the point of consuming them.”

story shows, you can't commence your grief. The land remains dead to the mourners. This stripe of melancholy is something I also feel in Tasmania.

Grief seems to play a significant role here. There are the deaths of Alex's parents and Merridy's father and the disappearance of Merridy's brother. In an isolated place, is grief all the more heightened?

As I explained above, when I was seventeen I worked as a cowhand in Argentina near a remote village on the pampas called Hortensia. There was a saying in the village: Small town, big hell. I didn't realize the truth of this until I came to live in the English countryside. As I speak, the village in Wiltshire where I spend half the year is in bloodthirsty uproar because one faction wishes to shoo away some barn owls that are nesting in the church belfry. The same divisions are likely to be found in villages anywhere, wherever *Homo sapiens* gather. But the effect is intense: any argument, death, betrayal, infidelity reverberates through the community in a way that doesn't happen in a city. So a collision with a log-truck or a person going missing touches everyone. ▶

A Conversation with Nicholas Shakespeare *(continued)*

Alex and Merridy fail in their relationship. Why do we not blame either of them?

Both have unhealed—and unexamined—wounds that they hope might be cured by marriage and children. I don't know about you, but I've met countless couples who try and salve their hurts in this way, and it only serves to make the original lesion more infected. My feeling is that Alex and Merridy do eventually earn the love and passion that they sought in each other early on. In that respect, I'm probably influenced by a favorite novel of mine, *Love in the Time of Cholera*. We can have what we want, says García Márquez. But we may have to wait a lifetime to appreciate properly its worth. To be worthy of our desire. I agree with that.

"My feeling is that Alex and Merridy do eventually earn the love and passion that they sought in each other early on."

What is the purpose of Kish? He is a destabilizing influence and the drama shifts to him after his arrival. Why?

I was impressed how Patrick White, in his novel *The Tree of Man*, takes a modest family who are dependent on the land and follows them through the vicissitudes of love, courtship, marriage, children, staleness, infidelity, and back into love. It's a desperately hard trick to pull off, but the challenge excited me: to follow a couple through time, through choppy and becalmed waters, and to make a drama out of the passage. What I needed was a catalyst to shake them up, rather as oysters need to be shocked in order to grow healthily. That's when the idea of Kish formed. He's the grit, as it were, in their oyster, who shocks them back into their skins, into life.

What does Kish represent to Alex and Merridy? The child they never had or something more?

I've got to be careful here. The muscles that one uses to explain what one's done are different to those flexed in the doing. At an obvious level, I'd say that Kish nods back to the convict sailors in whose uniform he's dressed, a phantom spirit in the manner of the Flying Dutchman. But he represents more than a continued preoccupation with the colonial past. He's also emblematic of Merridy's vanished brother, as well as the child that she and Alex never had. He's an impediment to their painfully achieved if sterile equilibrium; at the same time, he holds up the possibility of a deeper happiness. The ending took ages to get right. I spent four months rewriting four pages. In the first version, Kish ▸

“The ending took ages to get right. I spent four months rewriting four pages.”

A Conversation with Nicholas Shakespeare *(continued)*

kills Alex, in the second, Alex kills Kish. Both actions seemed wrong. It was only when Kish insisted on redeeming himself that I felt that I'd got nearer to him. All novels are exercises in failure, so it's still far from successful.

Why did you give the novel such an intense focus on two characters? Was this to highlight the interdependence of Alex and Merridy and the shared pain that links them?

I'm a firm believer that writers are only as good as they dare to be bad. If I look at my worst traits, I'd cite: too many flashbacks, plots that are overly congested, characters that get lost in the decorations—and that's for starters. In *Secrets of the Sea* I conceived the lunatic notion that I could write a story that began *in medias res* and simply continue the action in the here and now. And yet as Glenn McGrath said about landing the ball where he wants it (so that it just hits the top of off-stump): "It's pretty simple stuff, but the complicated thing is to keep it simple." I set off wanting to write an intense love story between two people. I ended up writing about a community.

What role do the secondary characters have here? I'm thinking of Albert.

The main action is observed by two characters: a mysterious English frog-diver, who appears in all my novels. And a former coast-watcher in Papua, who owns the general store and spies on all that goes on. The Englishman is a benign if deliberately infuriating *deus ex aqua*, who dips in and out, nudging the tillers of the central characters; Albert, the store owner, is an invisible and distant observer who merely records what he sees from his top-storey window, without judgment or comment. Ever since my first novel, *The Vision of Elena Silves*, I've been attracted to the idea of a Greek chorus, a witness or set of witnesses who can inject a shot of humor, wisdom, and perspective lacking in the central characters—who are usually too entrapped in the action to see what's happening.

What did you learn about writing in this novel?

I learned all about oysters, and about white-throated swifts, who live most of their lives in the clouds, even mating in the air.

Has being in Tasmania helped you develop your writing?

I do my writing in England, my reading and traveling in Tasmania. To ▸

“Ever since my first novel, *The Vision of Elena Silves*, I've been attracted to the idea of a Greek chorus, a witness or set of witnesses who can inject a shot of humor, wisdom, and perspective lacking in the central characters.”

A Conversation with Nicholas Shakespeare
(continued)

write, you need to read. I find it difficult to read in England: there's a constant static which intrudes, hacking at your attention. Not until I settled into my opossum-infested shed on Dolphin Sands did I find the time to read the authors I should have read. Proust, Patrick White, Faulkner, Thomas Bernhard, Cormac McCarthy, Musil, Vasily Grossman, et cetera. In Tasmania, the only newspapers I look at are *The New Yorker* and the *Mercury*. It's a combination that suits me. I have to say that I'm addicted to the *Mercury*—I especially like poring over the Crimestoppers column, a trait I gave to Merridy.

Alex is damaged because of his parents' death. Does he ever escape?

He escapes in the very moment when he decides to recognize Merridy's child as his own—irrespective of whether it is or not. I was determined to leave open the question of paternity. Alex believes the child to be Kish's and comes to accept this, but the child is more likely to be Ray Grogan's. It could, at a pinch, be Alex's. In a larger sense, it doesn't matter who the father is, just so long as the child is accepted—because our children are not, in an important respect, ours. I think of a line in Kahlil Gibran's *The Prophet*: "Your children are not your children. They are the sons and daughters of Life's longing for itself." Gibran was an alcoholic womanizer who lied about whether he ate lobster, but for some reason that phrase got under my fingernail. And watching my children in action, like two tuna fish wriggling permanently at the end of a rod that I will never be able to put down, I realize how true it is.

Read on

"Going Against My Normal Grain" Nine Years in Tasmania

THE NINE-MILE BEACH where I spend part of each year is as far south as you can travel before striking Antarctica. It is framed, on one side, by the Freycinet Peninsula, a ridge of glittering quartzite that erupted from the ocean bed in the Permian era, 290 million years ago; on the other side, by a largely unspoiled coastline, coated with forests of huge eucalyptus that from a distance resemble poodle fur. The beach itself has to be one of the cleanest in the world: no beer cans, no plastic bags, no tar, no people. The air, too, is the cleanest—officially—that you can breathe on our planet, rinsed by stiff southerlies that blow unimpeded across the ocean from Patagonia, 10,330 miles way. Sometimes these winds reach gusts of 170 kilometers an hour, faster even than Glenn McGrath, tumbling onto the beach creatures that might have sailed right out of the nonsense verses of the Victorian English writer, Edward Lear.

> "The beach itself has to be one of the cleanest in the world: no beer cans, no plastic bags, no tar, no people. The air, too, is the cleanest—officially—that you can breathe on our planet."

In the nine years I have been coming here, the sea has washed up on this coastline innumerable whales, a six-foot sun fish, a sea-leopard, and a giant mollusc with eight arms, each the length of my car, and two tentacles forty feet long and covered with powerful suckers, each larger than a man's palm. Plus various skeletons that no one can put a definition to. Visiting this bay in 1802, the French explorer Nicolas Baudin was conscious that his countrymen back home "will have difficulty in believing that the sea can contain living animals with a form as strange and extraordinary as those we have met." Further along the bay, a farmer's wife, Sarah Mitchell, a century ago found a strange creature which she sent to the Hobart museum. The sea-mouse, the first to be discovered, was named after her: *Sarahi mitchelli.*

A beach, then, where my children can well imagine Jumblies landing in their storm-tossed sieve, creatures whose heads are green and their hands blue. On those eerie nights when the Aurora Australis pulses and flares in a strange moss-colored light, I am put in mind of nothing so much as Lear's lovelorn alter ego, the Dong with the Luminous Nose:

ever keeping his weary eyes on
that pea-green sail on the far horizon.

When my German publisher, Niko Hansen, visited us seven years ago, he was brimming with the sea. During our walks along the beach he outlined with infectious passion his plans for his new publishing house, Marebuch, to be devoted to books about it. He explained his hope to persuade a series of writers each to pen a novella that might be about anything—just ▸

"Going Against My Normal Grain"
(continued)

so long as it featured the sea. Was I interested? "Does a fish swim?" I replied, flattered, and also excited. I didn't have a single seaworthy idea in my head, but here I was, living five months a year by the Tasman Sea. Of course, I was interested. Going against my normal grain—which is to travel in search of material—I decided that for the subject of this novella I would stay put, so to speak. I would write a story that drew only on what I could observe from this beach.

Australia is a vast place that has a tendency to swallow people without trace. It's impossible to spend time here without being aware of how many disappear into its landscape, never to be found again. It's the theme of Patrick White's masterpiece *Voss*, based on the Prussian explorer Ludwig Leichhardt, who in 1848 vanishes into thin air—not even a belt-buckle—while trying to cross the outback. It's the theme of Peter Weir's haunting film *Picnic at Hanging Rock*. It's the drama behind the Falconio case and other tourists who go missing, several on Tasmania's east coast. Every year, somebody somewhere in Australia is spirited away for reasons never satisfactorily explained—as, I learned, was a small boy on the island directly across the bay.

"Going against my normal grain—which is to travel in search of material—I decided that for the subject of this novella I would stay put, so to speak."

Maria Island is almost my favorite

place in Tasmania, a place designated as a sanctuary for its fast-diminishing devil, and before that for the thylacine—one more creature that has disappeared from the face of the earth. On a visit, I discovered this hitherto buried story about a mother who had lived on Maria in the 1920s and who suffered "a dreadful experience," according to a nurse who was later employed to look after her. One Sunday she prepared her four children "to go somewhere very special." She washed her children's faces and dressed them, ordering them onto the deck to wait for her. At last she was ready, but her son, whom she had sent out first, was no longer there. "He had run off somewhere, couldn't be found." Desperate days were spent beating the bush. Nothing. Then this grisly discovery: "the lower part of a boy's leg with his shoe and sock on it." The body was never found. The mother lost her speech, became paralyzed.

The image of the lost boy insinuated itself. What had happened to him? I rehearsed every imaginable fate. Eaten by a pig. Abducted. Plucked from the beach by a bright blue Boss-Woss. Or a giant squid hunting for orange roughy. Or the monster marsupial *Wynyardia bassinia* whose fossil had been discovered on Tasmania's north coast by none ▸

“Then this grisly discovery: 'the lower part of a boy's leg with his shoe and sock on it.'”

"Going Against My Normal Grain"
(continued)

other than Errol Flynn's father, Professor Theodore Flynn. Or—could he still be alive?

His unrecovered body was charged with greater significance when, one morning after a particularly violent storm, I went down onto the beach with my two-year-old son, Max, to pick up seashells. We were walking along, a pair of hooded plovers tripping ahead of us and Max tracking their tiny convict arrowheads in the sand—when he spotted something. Not a shell, but a fragment of blue and white china worn to soapy smoothness.

The piece of china had spilled from a shipwreck. I discovered more. In November 1850, the *Resolution,* a forty-nine-ton smack, forty-five feet long, was chartered by a brewer and his wife to ferry their six small children from Hobart to our local town, Swansea. Before the family could disembark, the boat capsized in a ferocious southeasterly gale and sank. Both parents survived, but all six of their children drowned, their bodies rolling ashore the following day. All except one.

I took Max to the cemetery so that we could read their names. The six names painted on the white-painted tombstone included William, the eight-year-old boy whose body was never recovered. In the local History Room,

I discovered something else: a scrap of paper, with a handwritten paragraph, dated February 2, 1946—a cryptic and infinitely suggestive memory recorded by the discoverer of the sea-mouse, Sarah Mitchell, concerning her brother Edwin: "About 1920 a man came to him with a pack on his back and told him he was the boy that was saved in the sailor's arms, said he was going to see his brother's and sister's graves."

From these two incidents, a boy who disappeared in the 1920s and a long-lost boy who reappeared round about the same time, I began to construct my novella. I conceived of it as a small-scale domestic love story, but it grew and grew, spreading out from the beach, into the bay, to the Tasman Sea beyond, until it was not a novella "that featured the sea," but an ocean-going novel that included Jumblies, Dongs with Luminous Noses, oysters, ships in bottles, castaways, tempests. Until I learned the truth of the proverb: "A home is like the sea."

The foregoing essay, first published in The Melbourne Age, *is reprinted courtesy of Nicholas Shakespeare.*

"In the local History Room, I discovered something else: a scrap of paper, with a handwritten paragraph, dated February 2, 1946—a cryptic and infinitely suggestive memory recorded by the discoverer of the sea-mouse, Sarah Mitchell . . ."

DATE DUE

ENGLISH-RUSSIAN
RUSSIAN-ENGLISH
DICTIONARY

OTHER BOOKS BY KENNETH KATZNER

A Russian Review Text (1962)
The Languages of the World (1975)

ENGLISH-RUSSIAN RUSSIAN-ENGLISH DICTIONARY

KENNETH KATZNER

A Wiley-Interscience Publication

JOHN WILEY & SONS

New York • Chichester • Brisbane • Toronto • Singapore

Composition: Euramerica Translations, Inc.

Library of Congress Cataloging in Publication Data:

Katzner, Kenneth.
English-Russian, Russian-English dictionary.

"A Wiley-Interscience publication."
1. English language—Dictionaries—Russian.

2. Russian language—Dictionaries—English. I. Title.
PG2640. K34 1984 491.73'21 82-24747
ISBN 0-471-86763-2

Printed in the United States of America

10 9 8 7 6 5 4 3 2 1

Preface

An American contribution to the field of Russian-English lexicography is long overdue.

This dictionary constitutes a first in many respects. It is the first full-size English-Russian or Russian-English dictionary to be compiled and published in the United States. It is the first to be based on American, rather than British, English. And it is the first full-size dictionary published anywhere, including the Soviet Union, to contain English-Russian and Russian-English sections in the same volume.

Soviet bilingual dictionaries are generally one-way only, based on British English, and designed primarily for those whose mother tongue is Russian. Many of the English words and phrases they contain (especially in the case of the English-Russian dictionaries) have a quaint nineteenth-century flavor about them, and some of them make one wonder where they could possibly have been found. Furthermore, grammatical information, such as irregular verb endings, is given for English words only, whereas obviously the English speaker needs such information for Russian words.

This dictionary, by contrast, is aimed primarily at the native speaker of English, though Russian speakers will also find much in it that is useful. All explanatory notes are in English, rather than in Russian. All irregularities in Russian verb conjugations and noun declensions appear at the beginning of the entry for the given Russian word. And in the English-Russian section all English words with more than one meaning have each meaning numbered and defined, thus making it clear which meaning is about to be rendered into Russian.

The two halves of the dictionary mirror each other exactly. Any Russian word given as the equivalent of an English word in the first half appears as an entry in the second half, and vice versa.

While the dictionary is based on American English, British usage and spellings have not been ignored. Where the British spelling of a word differs from the American, the British spelling is both cross-referenced to the American spelling and listed as an alternate spelling under the American spelling.

The initial planning of this dictionary was done by the late Albert H. Morehead, with valuable assistance from Waldemar von Zedtwitz and Salvatore Ramondino. I am particularly indebted to Sima Ficks, of George Washington University, who read over the entire manuscript for accuracy of translation and usage. And many thanks are due to my wife, Betty Katzner, for helping with the numerous chores involved in getting the manuscript ready for publication.

The typesetting has been done by Euramerica Translations Inc., Yuri Radzievsky, President.

KENNETH KATZNER

Washington, D.C.
September 1983

On Using the Dictionary

ALPHABETIZATION

All main entries are listed in strict alphabetical order. Derivative words may be run in under a main entry only if they immediately follow or precede the main entry word — that is, no other entry occurs alphabetically in between.

The numerous two-word lexical items that occur in English, such as *blank verse, light year, maiden name,* and *stumbling block,* are most often listed as separate entries in their regular alphabetical position, not run in under either of the two words which comprise them. For example, *light year* is not run in under either "light" or "year," but occurs as a separate entry after the word "lightweight." In the Russian-English section, however, such Russian items are run in under one of their two components.

LABELING OF MEANINGS

If an English word has more than one meaning, each meaning is identified by a label (usually a synonym) inserted in parentheses just before the Russian equivalent that follows. This label (the "contextual gist" label) should make clear which meaning is about to be rendered into Russian. A simple example might be the word "trunk," which is treated as follows: 1, (of a tree) ствол. 2, (of an elephant) хóбот. 3, (torso) тýловище. 4, (large box or case) сундýк. 5, (of an automobile) багáжник. 6, *pl.* (for swimming) плáвки. In some cases the label may be a special field label, such as *physics* or *finance.*

GENDER OF NOUNS

The gender of most Russian nouns is self-evident from their ending. For those ending in a ь, the designation *n.m.* indicates masculine and *n.f.* indicates feminine. The *n.m.* designation is also used with nouns such as дя́дя and слугá, which are masculine despite their -а or -я ending, as well as with many masculine nouns denoting people where the feminine form immediately follows.

The designation *n.m. & f.* is used with a large group of nouns denoting people, which are masculine or feminine depending on the person. The designation *n.m. or f.* is used with a small group of nouns (e.g., коли́бри) that are both masculine and feminine.

Indeclinable nouns ending in -o may be assumed to be neuter unless otherwise indicated. For those with other endings the gender is always given (e.g., кóфе, *n.m. indecl.*).

VERBS

If a Russian verb has both a perfective and imperfective aspect, it is always listed under the imperfective, with the perfective form following immediately in brackets. The perfective verb is also listed separately and cross-referenced to the imperfective verb unless it is alphabetically adjacent to the imperfective verb — that is, no other words occur between. (Even if adjacent it is sometimes included, in order to show an irregularity in its conjugation.)

Reflexive verbs are usually run in under the nonreflexive verb, with only the imperfective aspect given. Unless otherwise indicated, it may be assumed that the perfective of the reflexive verb is formed with the same prefix or ending as the perfective of the nonreflexive verb.

If a prefixed perfective verb is cross-referenced to its nonprefixed imperfective counterpart, it may be assumed that the perfective verb is conjugated like the imperfective verb.

In the treatment of English verbs, intransitive meanings have been set completely apart from transitive meanings, a practice followed by all large dictionaries of English but not, for some reason, by Soviet English-Russian dictionaries.

Abbreviations Used in the Dictionary

abbr.	abbreviation
acc.	accusative
adj.	adjective
aero.	aeronautics
agric.	agriculture
anat.	anatomy
approx.	approximately
archit.	architecture
art.	article
astron.	astronomy
attrib.	attributive
Bib.	Bible, Biblical
biol.	biology
bot.	botany
Brit.	British
cap.	capital, capitalized
chem.	chemistry
colloq.	colloquial
comm.	commerce
comp.	comparative
conj.	conjunction
contr.	contraction
dat.	dative
def.	definite
dem.	demonstrative
dent.	dentistry
dim.	diminutive
dipl.	diplomacy
dir.	direct
eccles.	ecclesiastic
econ.	economics
esp.	especially
fem.	feminine
fig.	figurative
fol.	followed
gen.	genitive
geog.	geography
geol.	geology
geom.	geometry
gram.	grammar
hist.	history
impers.	impersonal
impfv.	imperfective
indecl.	indeclinable
indef.	indefinite
indeterm.	indeterminate
indir.	indirect
inf.	infinitive
infl.	inflected
instr.	instrumental
interj.	interjection
interr.	interrogative
intrans.	intransitive
l.c.	lower case
ling.	linguistics
lit.	literature; literal
loc.	locative
masc.	masculine
math.	mathematics
mech.	mechanics
med.	medicine
metall.	metallurgy
meteorol.	meteorology
mil.	military
myth.	mythology
n.	noun
naut.	nautical
neg.	negative
neut.	neuter
n.f.	feminine noun
n.m.	masculine noun
nom.	nominative
obj.	object
obs.	obsolete
opp.	opposite
Orth. Ch.	Orthodox Church
part.	participle
pers.	personal
pert.	pertaining
pfv.	perfective
philos.	philosophy
phonet.	phonetics
photog.	photography
physiol.	physiology
pl.	plural
polit.	politics, political

poss.	possessive
prep.	preposition
prepl.	prepositional
pre-rev.	prerevolutionary
pres.	present
pron.	pronoun
pros.	prosody
psychol.	psychology
refl.	reflexive
rel.	relative
relig.	religion
R.R.	railroads
sing.	singular
superl.	superlative
theat.	theater
topog.	topography
trans.	transitive
trig.	trigonometry
U.S.	United States
usu.	usually
v.	verb
var.	variant
v. aux.	auxiliary verb
v.i.	intransitive verb
v. impfv.	imperfective verb
v. pfv.	perfective verb
v.r.	reflexive verb
v.t.	transitive verb
vulg.	vulgar
zool.	zoology

REGULAR RUSSIAN DECLENSION PATTERNS

NOUNS

Masculine

Nouns ending in a hard consonant

	Sing.	Pl.
Nom.	билет	билет-ы
Gen.	билет-а	билет-ов
Dat.	билет-у	билет-ам
Acc.	N. or G.	N. or G.
Instr.	билет-ом	билет-ами
Prepl.	билет-е	билет-ах

Nouns ending in ь

	Sing.	Pl.
Nom.	роял-ь	роял-и
Gen.	роял-я	роял-ей
Dat.	роял-ю	роял-ям
Acc.	N. or G.	N. or G.
Instr.	роял-ем	роял-ями
Prepl.	роял-е	роял-ях

Nouns ending in й

	Sing.	Pl.
Nom.	музе-й	музе-и
Gen.	музе-я	музе-ев
Dat.	музе-ю	музе-ям
Acc.	N. or G.	N. or G.
Instr.	музе-ем	музе-ями
Prepl.	музе-е	музе-ях

Feminine

Nouns ending in a

	Sing.	Pl.
Nom.	картин-а	картин-ы
Gen.	картин-ы	картин
Dat.	картин-е	картин-ам
Acc.	картин-у	N. or G.
Instr.	картин-ой	картин-ами
Prepl.	картин-е	картин-ах

Nouns ending in я

	Sing.	Pl.
Nom.	недел-я	недел-и
Gen.	недел-и	недел-ь
Dat.	недел-е	недел-ям
Acc.	недел-ю	N. or G.
Instr.	недел-ей	недел-ями
Prepl.	недел-е	недел-ях

Nouns ending in ь

	Sing.	Pl.
Nom.	цел-ь	цел-и
Gen.	цел-и	цел-ей
Dat.	цел-и	цел-ям
Acc.	цел-ь	N. or G.
Instr.	цел-ью	цел-ями
Prepl.	цел-и	цел-ях

Neuter

Nouns ending in o

	Sing.	Pl.
Nom.	блюд-о	блюд-а
Gen.	блюд-а	блюд
Dat.	блюд-у	блюд-ам
Acc.	блюд-о	блюд-а
Instr.	блюд-ом	блюд-ами
Prepl.	блюд-е	блюд-ах

Nouns ending in ле, ре

	Sing.	Pl.
Nom.	пол-е	пол-я
Gen.	пол-я	пол-ей
Dat.	пол-ю	пол-ям
Acc.	пол-е	пол-я
Instr.	пол-ем	пол-ями
Prepl.	пол-е	пол-ях

Nouns ending in це, ще, же

	Sing.	Pl.
Nom.	чудовищ-е	чудовищ-а
Gen.	чудовищ-а	чудовищ
Dat.	чудовищ-у	чудовищ-ам
Acc.	чудовищ-е	N. or G.
Instr.	чудовищ-ем	чудовищ-ами
Prepl.	чудовищ-е	чудовищ-ах

Nouns ending in ие

	Sing.	Pl.
Nom.	здан-ие	здан-ия
Gen.	здан-ия	здан-ий
Dat.	здан-ию	здан-иям
Acc.	здан-ие	здан-ия
Instr.	здан-ием	здан-иями
Prepl.	здан-ии	здан-иях

Nouns ending in ье, ьё

	Sing.	Pl.
Nom.	ущел-ье	ущел-ья
Gen.	ущел-ья	ущел-ий
Dat.	ущел-ью	ущел-ьям
Acc.	ущел-ье	ущел-ья
Instr.	ущел-ьем	ущел-ьями
Prepl.	ущел-ье	ущел-ьях

The accusative singular of all masculine nouns and the accusative plural of all nouns is the same as the nominative when the noun is inanimate, and the same as the genitive when the noun is animate. Animate nouns include people, animals, birds, fish, insects, and so on.

Special Rules

1 After the consonants г, к, х, ж, ч, ш, щ, the vowel ы is replaced by и (e.g., кни́ги, уро́ки, ножи́, све́чи), and я is replaced by a (e.g., ноча́м, веща́ми).

2 After the consonants ж, ч, ш, щ, ц, the instrumental case endings -ом and -ой become -ем and -ей when unstressed (e.g. му́жем, ты́сячей, ме́сяцем, пти́цей).

3 When stressed, the instrumental case endings -ем and -ей become -ём and -ёй (e.g., рулём, бельём, землёй, статьёй).

4 The prepositional singular ending for nouns ending in -ия is -ии (e.g. а́рмия-а́рмии).

5 The genitive plural of nouns ending in -ая, -ея, -ия, -уя is formed by replacing the я with й (e.g., ста́я-стай, ли́ния-ли́ний).

6 The genitive plural ending for nouns ending in ж, ч, ш, щ is -ей (e.g. ноже́й, ключе́й).

7 The genitive plural ending for nouns ending in ц is -ев when unstressed (e.g. ме́сяцев).

Note. All individual exceptions to the above tables and rules are indicated in the body of the dictionary under the entry for the given word. If only the genitive singular is indicated (e.g., рот – *gen.* рта; лёд – *gen.* льда; за́яц – *gen.* за́йца; руче́й – *gen.* ручья́) the irregularity occurs throughout the singular and plural declension of the noun. This also applies to shifts of stress — e.g., щит – *gen.* щита́; язы́к – *gen.* языка́; руль – *gen.* руля́ mean that the stress shifts to the ending throughout the singular and plural declension. If only the nominative plural is indicated (e.g., дуб – *pl.* дубы́; дом – *pl.* дома́; страна́ – *pl.* стра́ны; лицо́ – *pl.* ли́ца; колесо́ – *pl.* колёса) the irregularity or shift of stress occurs throughout the plural (but not the singular) declension of the noun.

ADJECTIVES

Adjectives ending in -óй

	Masc.	Fem.	Neut.	Pl.
Nom.	прям-óй	-áя	-óе	-ы́е
Gen.	прям-óго	-óй	-óго	-ы́х
Dat.	прям-óму	-óй	-óму	-ы́м
Acc.	N. or G.	-у́ю	-óе	N. or G.
Instr.	прям-ы́м	-óй	-ы́м	-ы́ми
Prepl.	прям-óм	-óй	-óм	-ы́х

Adjectives ending in -ый

	Masc.	Fem.	Neut.	Pl.
Nom.	нóв-ый	-ая	-ое	-ые
Gen.	нóв-ого	-ой	-ого	-ых
Dat.	нóв-ому	-ой	-ому	-ым
Acc.	N. or G.	-ую	-ое	N. or G.
Instr.	нóвым	-ой	-ым	-ыми
Prepl.	нóв-ом	-ой	-ом	-ых

Adjectives ending in -гóй, -кóй, -хóй

	Masc.	Fem.	Neut.	Pl.
Nom.	плох-óй	-áя	-óе	-и́е
Gen.	плох-óго	-óй	-óго	-и́х
Dat.	плох-óму	-óй	-óму	-и́м
Acc.	N. or G.	-у́ю	-óе	N. or G.
Instr.	плох-и́м	-óй	-и́м	-и́ми
Prepl.	плох-óм	-óй	-óм	-и́х

Adjectives ending in -гий, -кий, -хий

	Masc.	Fem.	Neut.	Pl.
Nom.	ти́х-ий	-ая	-ое	-ие
Gen.	ти́х-ого	-ой	-ого	-их
Dat.	ти́х-ому	-ой	-ому	-им
Acc.	N. or G.	-ую	-ое	N. or G.
Instr.	ти́х-им	-ой	-им	-ими
Prepl.	ти́х-ом	-ой	-ом	-их

Adjectives ending in -жóй, -шóй

	Masc.	Fem.	Neut.	Pl.
Nom.	больш-óй	-áя	-óе	-и́е
Gen.	больш-óго	-óй	-óго	-и́х
Dat.	больш-óму	-óй	-óму	-и́м
Acc.	N. or G.	-у́ю	-óе	N. or G.
Instr.	больш-и́м	-óй	-и́м	-и́ми
Prepl.	больш-óм	-óй	-óм	-и́х

Adjectives ending in -жий, -чий, -ший, -щий

	Masc.	Fem.	Neut.	Pl.
Nom.	свéж-ий	-ая	-ее	-ие
Gen.	свéж-его	-ей	-его	-их
Dat.	свéж-ему	-ей	-ему	-им
Acc.	N. or G.	-ую	-ее	N. or G.
Instr.	свéж-им	-ей	-им	-ими
Prepl.	свéж-ем	-ей	-ем	-их

Adjectives ending in -ний

	Masc.	Fem.	Neut.	Pl.
Nom.	си́н-ий	-яя	-ее	-ие
Gen.	си́н-его	-ей	-его	-их
Dat.	си́н-ему	-ей	-ему	-им
Acc.	N. or G.	-юю	-ее	N. or G.
Instr.	си́н-им	-ей	-им	-ими
Prepl.	си́н-ем	-ей	-ем	-их

Adjectives ending in -бий, -вий, -зий, -лий, -сий*

	Masc.	Fem.	Neut.	Pl.
Nom.	ры́б-ий	-ья	-ье	-ьи
Gen.	ры́б-ьего	-ьей	-ьего	-ьих
Dat.	ры́б-ьему	-ьей	-ьему	-ьим
Acc.	N. or G.	-ью	-ье	N. or G.
Instr.	ры́б-ьим	-ьей	-ьим	-ьими
Prepl.	ры́б-ьем	-ьей	-ьем	-ьих

*Adjectives with these endings are derived mainly from the words for animals and other living creatures (e.g., корóвий from корóва, кóзий from козá, собóлий from сóболь, ли́сий from лисá), and include some ending in -ний (олéний), -жий (медвéжий), -чий (пти́чий), and -ший (пету́ший).

Regular Verb Conjugation Patterns

I. Verbs ending in -ать

желáть: желáю, желáешь, желáет, желáем, желáете, желáют
дéлать: дéлаю, дéлаешь, дéлает, дéлаем, дéлаете, дéлают

II. Verbs ending in -ять

менять: меня́ю, меня́ешь, меня́ет, меня́ем, меня́ете, меня́ют

III. Verbs ending in -еть

имéть: имéю, имéешь, имéет, имéем, имéете, имéют

IV. Verbs ending in -ить

говори́ть: говорю́, говори́шь, говори́т, говори́м, говори́те, говоря́т
вéрить: вéрю, вéришь, вéрит, вéрим, вéрите, вéрят

V. Verbs ending in -уть

верну́ть: верну́, вернёшь, вернёт, вернём, вернёте, верну́т
трóнуть: трóну, трóнешь, трóнет, трóнем, трóнете, трóнут

After the letters ж, ч, ш, щ, the endings -ю and -ят are replaced by -у and -ат.

реши́ть: решу́, реши́шь, реши́т, реши́м, реши́те, решáт

The conjugation of verbs with the infinitive endings -оть, -ыть, -сть, -сти, -зти, -зть, -чь, as well as of all irregular verbs and those with shifts of stress, is given in the body of the dictionary under the entry for the given word.

Past Tense

Verbs ending in -ть

	Masculine	Feminine	Neuter	Plural
петь:	пел	пéла	пéло	пéли
мыть:	мыл	мы́ла	мы́ло	мы́ли

In the case of reflexive verbs -ся is added to those forms ending in consonant or ь, and -сь to those forms ending in a vowel.

одевáться: одевáюсь, одевáешься,одевáется, одевáемся, одевáетесь, одевáются

верну́ться: верну́сь, вернёшься, вернётся, вернёмся, вернётесь, верну́тся

Past tense: одевáлся, одевáлась, одевáлось, одевáлись

English-Russian Section

A

A,a пе́рвая бу́ква англи́йского алфави́та. —*n.* **1,** (musical note) ля. **2,** (school grade) пятёрка. Get an A, получи́ть пятёрку; получи́ть "отли́чно". Get straight A's, учи́ться на кру́глые пятёрки. —**from A to Z,** от А до Я.

a *indef. art. Generally not rendered in Russian: a young man,* молодо́й челове́к; *a box of matches,* коро́бка спи́чек; *a story about a little girl,* расска́з о ма́ленькой де́вочке. ♦ *Special uses:* **1,** (one) оди́н: *in a word,* одни́м сло́вом; *just a minute,* одну́ мину́тку. *He didn't say a word,* он ни сло́ва не сказа́л. *I didn't hear a thing,* я ничего́ не слы́шал(а). **2,** (a certain) оди́н: *an old friend of mine,* оди́н мой ста́рый друг. **3,** (of someone unknown) не́кий: *a Mr. Smith called,* вас спра́шивал не́кий ми́стер Смит. **4,** (such a) тако́й: *we live at a time when...,* мы живём в тако́е вре́мя, когда́... **5,** (per) в: *twice a week,* два ра́за в неде́лю. **6,** (for the amount specified) за (+ *acc.*): *two dollars a dozen,* два до́ллара за дю́жину.

aardvark *n.* трубкозу́б.

aback *adv., in* **take aback,** озада́чить; огоро́шить. *I was taken aback,* я был озада́чен.

abacus *n.* счёты.

abandon *v.t.* **1,** (leave; desert) покида́ть; оставля́ть; броса́ть. *Abandon a child,* подбра́сывать ребёнка. **2,** (give up, as an attempt) отка́зываться от. *Abandon hope,* оставля́ть наде́жду. —*n.* беззабо́тность. *With abandon,* беззабо́тно. —**abandoned,** *adj.* поки́нутый.

abase *v.t.* унижа́ть. —**abasement,** *n.* униже́ние.

abash *v.t.* смуща́ть; конфу́зить.

abate *v.t.* ослабля́ть. —*v.i.* затиха́ть; утиха́ть; стиха́ть; спада́ть. —**abatement,** *n.* ослабле́ние. *Without abatement,* неосла́бно.

abbess *n.* аббати́са; игу́менья.

abbey *n.* абба́тство: *Westminster Abbey,* Вестми́нстерское абба́тство.

abbot *n.* абба́т; игу́мен; настоя́тель.

abbreviate *v.t.* сокраща́ть. —**abbreviation,** *n.* сокраще́ние.

ABC *n.* а́збука: *learn the ABC's,* вы́учиться а́збуке. *The ABC's of chemistry,* а́збука хи́мии. —**as simple as ABC,** как два́жды два четы́ре.

abdicate *v.t.* отрека́ться от. —*v.i.* отрека́ться от престо́ла. —**abdication,** *n.* отрече́ние от престо́ла.

abdomen *n.* живо́т. —**abdominal,** *adj.* брюшно́й.

abduct *v.t.* похища́ть. —**abduction,** *n.* похище́ние. —**abductor,** *n.* похити́тель.

aberrant *adj.* ненорма́льный.

aberration *n.* аберра́ция.

abet *v.t.* подстрека́ть. *Abet a crime,* соде́йствовать соверше́нию преступле́ния. —**abetment,** *n.* подстрека́тельство. —**abetter; abettor,** *n.* подстрека́тель.

abeyance *n.* (вре́менное) прекраще́ние. *Hold in abeyance,* откла́дывать.

abhor *v.t.* ненави́деть. —**abhorrence,** *n.* отвраще́ние. —**abhorrent,** *adj.* ненави́стный; отврати́тельный.

abide *v.t.* **1,** (await) ждать. **2,** (tolerate) терпе́ть. —*v.i.* **1,** (remain) остава́ться. **2,** (dwell) жить; пребыва́ть. —**abide by, 1,** (live up to, as an agreement) соблюда́ть; приде́рживаться. **2,** (acquiesce in, as a decision) подчиня́ться (+ *dat.*).

abiding *adj.* постоя́нный; неизме́нный.

ability *n.* спосо́бность; уме́ние.

abject *adj.* **1,** (wretched) уни́женный. *Abject poverty,* кра́йняя нищета́. **2,** (despicable) презре́нный.

abjure *v.t.* **1,** (renounce) отрека́ться от. **2,** (retract) отка́зываться от.

ablaze *adj.* в огне́. *Set ablaze,* воспламеня́ть.

able *adj.* уме́лый; спосо́бный. *Be able,* мочь; уме́ть.

able-bodied *adj.* трудоспосо́бный; работоспосо́бный.

abloom *adj.* в цвету́.

ablution *n.* омове́ние.

ably *adv.* уме́ло.

abnegate *v.t.* отка́зываться от; отрека́ться от. —**abnegation,** *n.* отка́з; отрече́ние.

abnormal *adj.* ненорма́льный; анорма́льный. —**abnormality,** *n.* ненорма́льность. —**abnormally,** *adv.* ненорма́льно.

aboard *adv.* **1,** (position) на борту́; на корабле́. **2,** (motion) на́ борт; на кора́бль. *Go aboard,* сесть на кора́бль. *Take aboard,* брать на́ борт. —**all aboard!,** по ваго́нам!

abode *n.* жили́ще.

abolish *v.t.* отменя́ть; упраздня́ть. —**abolition,** *n.* отме́на; упраздне́ние.

abominable *adj.* отврати́тельный; проти́вный; гну́сный.

abominate *v.t.* ненави́деть; пита́ть отвраще́ние к.

abomination *n.* **1,** (loathing) омерзе́ние. **2,** (loathsome thing) ме́рзость.

aboriginal *adj.* коренно́й; тузе́мный. —**aborigine,** *n.* абориге́н; тузе́мец.

abort *v.t.* **1,** (terminate the pregnancy of) сде́лать або́рт (+ *dat.*). **2,** *fig.* (terminate prematurely) прекраща́ть.

abortion *n.* абóрт. *Have an abortion,* сдéлать абóрт. *Perform an abortion upon,* сдéлать абóрт (+ *dat.*).

abortive *adj.* **1,** *med.* абортúвный. **2,** *fig.* (unsuccessful) безрезультáтный; бесплóдный.

abound *v.i.* **1,** (exist in great numbers) имéться в изобúлии. **2,** *fol. by* **in** *or* **with** (have in great abundance) изобúловать (+ *instr.*).

about *adv.* **1,** (approximately) óколо: *about an hour,* óколо чáса. **2,** (nearly) почтú: about ready, почтú готóв. **3,** (at hand) кругóм; вокрýг: *there was no one about,* кругóм/вокрýг никогó нé было. —*prep.* **1,** (here and there in) по: *walk about town,* ходúть по гóроду. *Her things lay all about the room,* её вéщи валя́лись по всей кóмнате. **2,** (concerning) о: *what are you talking about?,* о чём вы говорúте? —**be about to**, собирáться (+ *inf.*): *I was just about to call you,* я как раз собирáлся вам звонúть. *The train is about to leave,* пóезд вот-вóт отойдёт. *I was about to ask, but...,* я спросúл было, но... —**up and about,** на ногáх. —**what about; how about...?,** как насчёт (+ *gen.*)?

about-face *n.* **1,** *mil.* поворóт кругóм. *About face!,* кругóм! **2,** *fig.* (reversal) поворóт на сто вóсемьдесят грáдусов.

above *prep.* **1,** (over) над: *above sea level,* над ýровнем мóря. **2,** (in excess of) вы́ше: *above average,* вы́ше срéднего. *Five degrees above zero,* пять грáдусов вы́ше нуля́. **3,** (superior to) вы́ше: *head and shoulders above the others,* нá голову вы́ше другúх. **4,** (beyond the reach of) вне: *above suspicion,* вне подозрéний. **5,** (too honorable to engage in) вы́ше: *be above prejudice,* быть вы́ше предрассýдков. —*adv.* наверхý; вы́ше. *From above,* свéрху; свы́ше. —*n., preceded by* **the** вышеупомя́нутое. —**above all, 1,** (most of all) бóльше всегó. **2,** (most importantly) прéжде всегó.

aboveboard *adj.* откры́тый; откровéнный. —*adv.* откры́то; откровéнно.

abracadabra *n.* абракадáбра.

abrade *v.t.* сдирáть (кóжу).

abrasion *n.* **1,** (wearing away) истирáние. **2,** (abraded area, as on the skin) ссáдина.

abrasive *n.* абразúв. —*adj.* **1,** (causing abrasion) абразúвный. **2,** *fig.* (causing friction or resentment) раздражáющий.

abreast *adv.* в рядý; в ряд. *Sit three abreast,* сидéть по трóе в рядý. *March three abreast,* маршировáть по трóе в ряд/рядý. —**keep abreast of, 1,** (keep up with) идтú в нóгу с. *Keep abreast of the times,* идтú в нóгу с жúзнью *or* со врéменем. **2,** (keep well-posted on) следúть за.

abridge *v.t.* **1,** (shorten) сокращáть. **2,** (curtail, as rights) урéзывать.

abridgment *also,* **abridgement** *n.* **1,** (act of abridging) сокращéние. **2,** (abridged edition) сокращённое издáние.

abroad *adv.* **1,** (location) за гранúцей; за рубежóм. **2,** (direction) за гранúцу. *From abroad,* из-за гранúцы.

abrogate *v.t.* отменя́ть; аннулúровать.—**abrogation,** *n.* отмéна; аннулúрование.

abrupt *adj.* **1,** (sudden) внезáпный; рéзкий; крутóй. *Abrupt departure,* внезáпный отъéзд. **2,** (steep) крутóй; обры́вистый. **3,** (brusque) рéзкий. —**abruptly,** *adv.* рéзко. —**abruptness,** *n.* рéзкость.

abscess *n.* абсцéсс; нары́в; гнойнúк.

abscissa *n.* абсцúсса.

abscond *v.i.* скрывáться; бежáть.

absence *n.* отсýтствие. *Absence from class,* прóпуск занятий *or* урóков. *In the absence of,* в отсýтствие *or* за отсýтствием (+*gen.*). *In my absence,* в моё отсýтствие. —**absence without leave,** самовóльная отлýчка.

absent *adj.* отсýтствующий. *Be absent,* отсýтствовать. —*v.t.* [*usu.* **absent oneself**] отлучáться.

absentee *n.* отсýтствующий. —**absenteeism,** *n.* (систематúческие) прогýлы.

absentia *see* **in absentia.**

absently *adv.* отсýтствующим взгля́дом; рассéянно.

absent-minded *adj.* рассéянный.—**absent-mindedly,** *adv.* рассéянно. —**absent-mindedness,** *n.* рассéянность.

absinthe *n.* абсéнт; полы́нная вóдка.

absolute *adj.* **1,** (complete; total) абсолю́тный; совершéнный; пóлный. **2,** (unlimited; unqualified) абсолю́тный; безуслóвный. **3,** (sheer; utter) сплошнóй; сýщий. —*n.* абсолю́т.—**absolute majority,** абсолю́тное большинствó голосóв. —**absolute monarchy,** абсолю́тная монáрхия. —**absolute pitch,** абсолю́тный слух. —**absolute zero,** абсолю́тный нуль.

absolutely *adv.* **1,** (perfectly; entirely; utterly) совершéнно: *absolutely correct/certain,* совершéнно прáвильно/увéрен(а). *Absolutely impossible,* совершéнно *or* абсолю́тно невозмóжно. **2,** (positively) абсолю́тно; решúтельно. *Absolutely everything,* решúтельно всё. *Absolutely nothing,* совершéнно/абсолю́тно/решúтельно/положúтельно ничегó. **3,** *as an exclamation* безуслóвно!

absolution *n.* **1,** (forgiveness) прощéние. **2,** (remission of sin) отпущéние грехóв.

absolutism *n.* абсолютúзм. —**absolutist,** *n.* абсолютúст. —*adj.* абсолютúстский.

absolve *v.t.* **1,** (acquit) опрáвдывать. **2,** (release) освобождáть. *Absolve of responsibility,* снимáть отвéтственность с (+*gen.*). **3,** (remit, as a sin) прощáть; отпускáть.

absorb *v.t.* **1,** (take in; suck up) всáсывать; впúтывать; поглощáть. **2,** (engross) поглощáть: *absorbed in one's work,* поглощён своéй рабóтой; погружён в свою́ рабóту. *Become absorbed in,* погружáться *or* углубля́ться в (+*acc.*). **3,** (take up completely) поглощáть. **4,** (mentally assimilate) воспринимáть; усвáивать.

absorbent *adj.* всáсывающий; поглощáющий. —**absorbent cotton,** вáта.

absorbing *adj.* увлекáтельный; захвáтывающий.

absorption *n.* всáсывание; поглощéние; абсóрбция.

abstain *v.i.* воздéрживаться: *abstain from the voting,* воздéрживаться от голосовáния.

abstemious *adj.* воздéржанный.

abstention *n.* **1,** (act of abstaining) воздержáние. **2,** (failure to vote) воздержáвшийся: *ten in favor, six against, five abstentions,* дéсять за, шесть прóтив, пять воздержáвшихся.

abstinence *n.* воздержáние.

abstract *adj.* отвлечённый; абстрáктный. *Abstract art,* абстракционúзм. —*n.* **1,** (synopsis) реферáт; конспéкт. **2,** (something abstract) абстрáкция. —*v.t.* **1,** (consider separately) абстрагúровать. **2,** (make an abstract of) реферúровать; конспектúровать. —**in the abstract,** абстрáктно; отвлечённо.

abstraction *n.* **1,** (abstract idea or concept) абстра́кция; отвлече́ние. **2,** (absent-mindedness) рассе́янность.

abstruse *adj.* мудрёный; замыслова́тый; зау́мный.

absurd *adj.* неле́пый; абсу́рдный. —**absurdity,** *n.* неле́пость; абсу́рд; абсу́рдность.

abundance *n.* оби́лие; изоби́лие. *In abundance,* в изоби́лии; в избы́тке.

abundant *adj.* оби́льный: *abundant harvest,* оби́льный урожа́й.

abundantly *adv.* **1,** (in abundance) оби́льно. **2,** (extremely) преде́льно: *abundantly clear,* преде́льно я́сно.

abuse *v.t.* **1,** (misuse) злоупотребля́ть: *abuse power,* злоупотребля́ть вла́стью. **2,** (revile) руга́ть; обруга́ть. —*n.* **1,** (misuse; corrupt practice) злоупотребле́ние. **2,** (abusive language) ру́гань; брань.

abusive *adj.* руга́тельный; оскорби́тельный.

abut *v.t.* & *i.* примыка́ть (к).

abutment *n.* **1,** (point of contact) стык. **2,** (support for an arch) пята́. **3,** (support for a bridge) усто́й.

abysmal *adj.* жа́лкий. *Abysmal ignorance,* кра́йнее неве́жество. *Abysmal failure,* по́лный прова́л. *Fail abysmally,* по́лностью провали́ться.

abyss *n.* про́пасть; бе́здна.

acacia *n.* ака́ция.

academic *adj.* академи́ческий.

academician *n.* акаде́мик.

academy *n.* **1,** (learned institution) акаде́мия: *academy of sciences,* акаде́мия нау́к. **2,** (specialized school) шко́ла; учи́лище: *academy of music,* музыка́льная шко́ла; *military academy,* вое́нное учи́лище; *riding academy,* шко́ла верхово́й езды́.

acanthus *n.* ака́нт.

accede *v.i.* [*usu.* **accede to**] **1,** (consent to) соглаша́ться (на). **2,** (assume, as an office) вступа́ть (в). *Accede to the throne,* вступи́ть на престо́л.

accelerate *v.t.* ускоря́ть. *Accelerated course,* ускоре́нный курс. —*v.i.* ускоря́ться. —**acceleration,** *n.* ускоре́ние. —**accelerator,** *n.* ускори́тель; акселера́тор.

accent *n.* **1,** (stress) ударе́ние. **2,** (regional or national manner of speech) акце́нт. **3,** (accent mark) ударе́ние. —*v.t.* =**accentuate.**

accentuate *v.t.* **1,** (pronounce with heavy stress) акценти́ровать; де́лать ударе́ние на. **2,** (emphasize) акценти́ровать; де́лать акце́нт на.

accept *v.t.* **1,** (say yes to) принима́ть: *accept an offer/invitation,* принима́ть предложе́ние/приглаше́ние. **2,** (reconcile oneself to) мири́ться: *accept one's fate,* мири́ться со свое́й судьбо́й. **3,** (admit formally) принима́ть: *he was accepted at X college,* он был при́нят в университе́т икс.

acceptable *adj.* прие́млемый.

acceptance *n.* **1,** (act of accepting) приня́тие. **2,** (condition of being accepted) призна́ние: *gain acceptance,* получи́ть призна́ние.

access *n.* до́ступ: *gain access* to, получи́ть до́ступ к. —**access road,** подъездна́я доро́га.

accessible *adj.* досту́пный. —**accessibility,** *n.* досту́пность.

accession *n.* **1,** (to the throne) вступле́ние; восше́ствие (на престо́л); (to office) вступле́ние (в до́лжность). **2,** (something newly acquired) приобрете́ние. **3,** (agreement; assent) согла́сие.

accessory *n.* **1,** (extra piece of equipment) приста́вка. **2,** *pl.* (items of equipment) принадле́жности. **3,** *pl.* (extra items of dress) принадле́жности костю́ма. **4,** *law* соуча́стник. —*adj.* **1,** (extra) подсо́бный. **2,** *law* соуча́ствующий.

accident *n.* **1,** (mishap) несча́стный слу́чай; катастро́фа; ава́рия. **2,** (chance occurrence) случа́йность. *It is no accident that...,* не случа́йно, что... **3,** (chance) слу́чай. *By accident,* случа́йно.

accidental *adj.* случа́йный; нечаянный. —**accidentally,** *adv.* случа́йно; неча́янно.

acclaim *v.t.* **1,** (welcome with applause) приве́тствовать. **2,** (praise; extol) расхва́ливать. **3,** (proclaim approvingly) провозглаша́ть. —*n.* **1,** (welcoming) шу́мное приве́тствие. **2,** (praise) восхвале́ние.

acclamation *n.* шу́мное одобре́ние. —**by acclamation,** единоду́шно; без голосова́ния.

acclimate *also,* **acclimatize** *v.t.* акклиматизи́ровать. *Become acclimated,* прижива́ться; акклиматизи́роваться. —**acclimation; acclimatization,** *n.* акклимматиза́ция.

accommodate *v.t.* **1,** (oblige; help) услу́живать. **2,** (lodge) помеща́ть. **3,** (have space for) вмеща́ть. **4,** (adapt) приспособля́ть. —**accommodating,** *adj.* услу́жливый; сгово́рчивый.

accommodation *n.* **1,** (a favor) услу́га. **2,** (convenience) удо́бство: *for the accommodation of,* для удо́бства (+*gen.*). **3,** (adaptation; adjustment) приспособле́ние. **4,** (reconciliation) соглаше́ние: *reach an accommodation,* достига́ть соглаше́ния. **5,** *pl.* (lodgings) помеще́ние; жильё. **6,** *pl.* (traveling space) ме́сто.

accompaniment *n.* **1,** (something added) добавле́ние. **2,** *music* аккомпанеме́нт; сопровожде́ние. —**accompanist,** *n.* аккомпаниа́тор.

accompany *v.t.* **1,** (go along with) сопровожда́ть. *Accompanied by,* в сопровожде́нии (+*gen.*). **2,** (escort up to a point) провожа́ть. **3,** *music* аккомпани́ровать.

accomplice *n.* соо́бщник; соуча́стник.

accomplish *v.t.* соверша́ть; осуществля́ть; выполня́ть. *Accomplish a feat/miracle,* соверша́ть по́двиг/чу́до. *Accomplish a task,* выполня́ть зада́чу. *Accomplish a great deal,* доби́ться мно́гого.

accomplished *adj.* **1,** (done) совершённый. *Accomplished fact,* соверши́вшийся факт. **2,** (proficient) зако́нченный.

accomplishment *n.* **1,** (completion) выполне́ние; осуществле́ние. **2,** (an achievement) достиже́ние.

accord *v.t.* **1,** (give; extend) ока́зывать. **2,** (grant; bestow) предоставля́ть. —*v.i.* [*usu.* **accord with**] совпада́ть (с); сходи́ться (с); вяза́ться (с). —*n.* **1,** (an agreement) соглаше́ние. **2,** (harmony) согла́сие. —**of one's own accord,** по до́брой во́ле.

accordance *n.* соотве́тствие. *In accordance with,* в соотве́тствии с; согла́сно.

accordingly *adv.* **1,** (correspondingly) соотве́тственно; соотве́тствующим о́бразом. **2,** (consequently) таки́м о́бразом.

according to **1,** (as stated by) по слова́м (+*gen.*). **2,** (in accordance with) по; согла́сно; в соотве́тствии с. **3,** (in proportion to) по: *each according to his ability,* ка́ждый по его́ спосо́бностям.

accordion *n.* гармо́ника; аккордео́н. —**accordion pleats,** плиссе́.

accordionist *n.* гармони́ст; аккордеони́ст.

accost *v.t.* подходи́ть к; привя́зываться к.
account *n.* **1,** (business record) счёт: *open an account,* открыва́ть счёт. **2,** (report; description) отчёт; расска́з: *an account of events,* отчёт/расска́з о собы́тиях. **3,** (importance; worth) значе́ние; ва́жность. *Of no account,* не име́ющий значе́ния. **4,** (reason; basis) основа́ние; причи́на: *on that account,* на э́том основа́нии; по э́той причи́не. —*v.i.* [*usu.* **account for**] **1,** (explain) объясня́ть: *how do you account for the fact that...?,* чем вы объясня́ете то, что...? *This accounts for his strange behavior,* э́тим объясня́ется его́ стра́нное поведе́ние. **2,** (represent numerically) *inverted in Russian: copper accounts for a third of all exports,* треть всего́ э́кспорта прихо́дится на медь. **3,** (give a statement of) отчи́тываться в: *account for one's expenses,* отчи́тываться в расхо́дах. **4,** in *all present and accounted for,* все налицо́. —**bring to account,** привлека́ть к отве́тственности. —**by all accounts,** по о́бщему мне́нию; по слова́м всех. —**call to account,** призыва́ть к отве́ту. —**give a good account of oneself,** хорошо́ себя́ зарекомендова́ть. —**on account of,** из-за; всле́дствие (+*gen.*). —**on no account,** ни в ко́ем слу́чае. —**on (someone's) account,** ра́ди: *on my account,* ра́ди меня́. —**take into account; take account of,** принима́ть во внима́ние/к све́дению/в расчёт; учи́тывать.
accountable *adj.* отве́тственный; подотчётный. —**accountability,** *n.* подотчётность.
accountant *n.* бухга́лтер; счетово́д.
accounting *n.* бухгалте́рия; счетово́дство. *Accounting department,* бухгалте́рия.
accouterment *also,* **accoutrement** *n., usu. pl.* снаряже́ние.
accredit *v.t., dipl.* аккредитова́ть.
accretion *n.* **1,** (growth in size) приро́ст. **2,** (accumulated matter) наро́ст.
accrue *v.i.* **1,** *fol. by* **to** (fall to) достава́ться (+*dat.*). **2,** (accumulate, as of interest) нараста́ть.
accumulate *v.t.* копи́ть; накопля́ть. —*v.i.* копи́ться; накопля́ться; ска́пливаться.
accumulation *n.* **1,** (act of accumulating) накопле́ние. **2,** (that which has accumulated) скопле́ние.
accuracy *n.* **1,** (freedom from error) то́чность. **2,** (precision, as with a weapon) ме́ткость.
accurate *adj.* **1,** (free from error; correct) то́чный. **2,** (always hitting one's target) ме́ткий. —**accurately,** *adv.* то́чно.
accursed *adj.* прокля́тый.
accusation *n.* обвине́ние.
accusative *adj.* вини́тельный: *accusative case,* вини́тельный паде́ж.
accusatory *adj.* обвини́тельный.
accuse *v.t.* обвиня́ть: *accuse someone of lying,* обвиня́ть кого́-нибудь во лжи. —**accused,** *n., law* обвиня́емый. —**accuser,** *n.* обвини́тель.
accustom *v.t.* приуча́ть.
accustomed *adj.* **1,** (habitual) привы́чный. **2,** *fol. by* **to** (used to) привы́кший (к).
ace *n.* **1,** *cards* туз. **2,** (pilot) ас. —*adj., colloq.* первокла́ссный.
acerbic *adj.* **1,** (astringent) те́рпкий. **2,** *fig.* (caustic) е́дкий. —**acerbity,** *n.* те́рпкость; е́дкость.
acetate *n.* соль у́ксусной кислоты́; уксуснoки́слая соль.
acetic *adj.* у́ксусный. —**acetic acid,** у́ксусная кислота́.
acetone *n.* ацето́н.
acetylene *n.* ацетиле́н. —*adj.* ацетиле́новый.
ache *n.* боль. —*v.i.* боле́ть.
achieve *v.t.* достига́ть; доби́ться. —**achievement,** *n.* достиже́ние.
Achilles' heel ахилле́сова пята́.
acid *n.* кислота́: *sulfuric acid,* се́рная кислота́. —*adj.* **1,** (containing acid) кисло́тный. **2,** (sour) ки́слый. **3,** (caustic, as of a remark) е́дкий.
acidity *n.* кислота́; кисло́тность.
acknowledge *v.t.* **1,** (admit) признава́ть: *acknowledge one's mistakes,* признава́ть свои́ оши́бки. **2,** (recognize and reply to) отвеча́ть на: *acknowledge a letter,* отвеча́ть на письмо́. *Acknowledge receipt of,* подтвержда́ть получе́ние (+*gen.*).
acknowledgment *also,* **acknowledgement** *n.* **1,** (act of admitting) призна́ние. **2,** (document confirming receipt) распи́ска.
acme *n.* вы́сшая то́чка; верх; верши́на. *The acme of perfection,* верх соверше́нства.
acne *n.* угри́.
aconite *n.* акони́т.
acorn *n.* жёлудь.
acoustic *also,* **acoustical** *adj.* акусти́ческий. —**acoustics,** *n.* аку́стика.
acquaint *v.t.* знако́мить; ознакомля́ть. *Acquaint oneself with,* ознакомля́ться с.
acquaintance *n.* **1,** (state of being acquainted) знако́мство. *Make someone's acquaintance,* знако́миться с. **2,** (person known to one) знако́мый.
acquainted *adj.* знако́мый. *Get acquainted,* знако́миться.
acquiesce *v.i.* соглаша́ться. —**acquiescence,** *n.* согла́сие. —**acquiescent,** *adj.* усту́пчивый.
acquire *v.t.* приобрета́ть. —**acquisition,** *n.* приобрете́ние. —**acquisitive,** *adj.* со́бственнический.
acquit *v.t.* опра́вдывать: *he was acquitted,* он был опра́вдан. —**acquit oneself,** вести́ себя́; держа́ться. *Acquit oneself well,* хорошо́ себя́ зарекомендова́ть.
acquittal *n.* оправда́ние.
acre *n.* акр.
acrid *adj.* е́дкий; те́рпкий.
acrimonious *adj.* е́дкий; зло́бный. —**acrimony,** *n.* е́дкость; зло́ба.
acrobat *n.* акроба́т. —**acrobatic,** *adj.* акробати́ческий. —**acrobatics,** *n.* акроба́тика.
acropolis *n.* акро́поль.
across *prep.* **1,** (to the other side of) че́рез: *walk across the street,* перейти́ че́рез у́лицу. **2,** (on the other side of) по ту сто́рону (+*gen.*). *They live across the street,* они́ живу́т напро́тив. **3,** (athwart) поперёк: *lie across the road,* лежа́ть поперёк доро́ги. —*adv.* **1,** (to the other side) *usu. rendered by the prefix* пере-: *walk across,* переходи́ть; *swim across,* переплыва́ть. **2,** (in width) в ширину́: *the river is two miles across,* река́ име́ет две ми́ли в ширину́. —**across from,** напро́тив.
acrostic *n.* акрости́х.
act *v.i.* **1,** (take action) де́йствовать; поступа́ть: *act decisively,* де́йствовать/поступа́ть реши́тельно. *We must act at once,* мы должны́ де́йствовать неме́дленно. **2,** (behave) вести́ себя́: *act foolishly,* вести́ себя́ глу́по; *act like a child,* вести́ себя́ как ребёнок. **3,** (pretend) притворя́ться. **4,** (be an actor)

игра́ть (на сце́не). **5,** *fol. by* **as** (serve as) служи́ть (+*instr.*). —*v.t.* игра́ть. *The play was well acted,* актёры игра́ли хорошо́. —*n.* **1,** (deed) посту́пок; акт. *Catch in the act,* пойма́ть с поли́чным. **2,** (law) акт. **3,** (part of a play or opera) де́йствие; акт. **4,** (item on a variety program) но́мер. **5,** (false show) коме́дия: *put on an act,* разыгра́ть коме́дию. —**act on, 1,** (act according to) сле́довать (*e.g.*сове́ту). **2,** (have an effect on) де́йствовать на. —**act out,** разы́грывать. —**act up,** *colloq.* шали́ть.

acting *n.* **1,** (performance) игра́. **2,** (profession) актёрство. —*adj.* исполня́ющий обя́занности (+*gen.*): *acting manager,* исполня́ющий обя́занности заве́дующего.

actinium *n.* акти́ний.

action *n.* **1,** (doing something) де́йствие. *Plan of action,* план де́йствий. *Freedom of action,* свобо́да де́йствий. *Take action,* де́йствовать. *Put out of action,* выводи́ть из стро́я. **2,** *pl.* (acts; deeds) де́йствия; дела́. *Judge someone by his actions,* суди́ть кого́-нибу́дь по его́ дела́м. *Be responsible for one's actions,* отвеча́ть за свои́ посту́пки. **3,** (of a play or narrative) де́йствие. **4,** *mil.* (combat) бой: *be killed in action,* пасть в бою́. *See action,* воева́ть. **5,** *law* иск; проце́сс. *Bring legal action,* начина́ть суде́бный проце́сс; подава́ть в суд.

activate *v.t.* **1,** (set in motion) приводи́ть в де́йствие. **2,** *mil.* (place on active status) призыва́ть на действи́тельную слу́жбу.

active *adj.* **1,** (energetic; busy) акти́вный; де́ятельный. **2,** (lively; agile) живо́й. **3,** (functioning; in operation) де́йствующий. *Active volcano,* де́йствующий вулка́н. **4,** *gram.* действи́тельный: *active voice,* действи́тельный зало́г. **5,** *mil.* действи́тельный: *active duty,* действи́тельная слу́жба. —**actively,** *adv.* акти́вно.

activist *n.* активи́ст.

activity *n.* **1,** (action) де́ятельность. **2,** (vigorous action) акти́вность. **3,** *pl.* (organized pursuits) мероприя́тия: *extracurricular activities,* внекла́ссные мероприя́тия.

actor *n.* актёр. —**actress,** *n.* актри́са.

actual *adj.* действи́тельный; факти́ческий. —**actuality,** *n.* действи́тельность. —**actually,** *adv.* действи́тельно; факти́чески; на са́мом де́ле.

actuate *v.t.* **1,** (put into action) приводи́ть в де́йствие. **2,** (impel) побужда́ть.

acuity *n.* острота́.

acumen *n.* проница́тельность; зо́ркость.

acupuncture *n.* акупункту́ра; иглотерапи́я; иглоука́лывание.

acute *adj.* о́стрый. —**accute accent,** о́строе ударе́ние. —**acute angle,** о́стрый у́гол.

ad *n.* объявле́ние; рекла́ма.

A.D. на́шей э́ры: *in 200 A.D.,* в двухсо́том году́ на́шей э́ры.

adage *n.* изрече́ние.

adagio *adv. & n.* ада́жио.

adamant *adj.* непрекло́нный.

Adam's apple ада́мово я́блоко; кады́к.

adapt *v.t.* **1,** (adjust) приспособля́ть. **2,** (convert to a new medium) переде́лывать. *Adapt for the stage,* инсцени́ровать. —*v.i.* приспособля́ться.

adaptability *n.* приспособля́емость. —**adaptable,** *adj.* легко́ приспособля́ющийся.

adaptation *n.* **1,** (act of adapting) приспособле́ние. **2,** (of a story, play, etc.) переде́лка. **3,** *biol.* адапта́ция.

adapter *n.* ада́птер.

add *v.t.* **1,** (put additionally) прибавля́ть; добавля́ть: *add two cups of sugar,* прибавля́ть/добавля́ть две ча́шки са́хара. *Add a line to a letter,* прибавля́ть стро́чку к письму́. *Add wood to the fire,* подкла́дывать дров в ого́нь. **2,** (state additionally) добавля́ть: *he added that...,* он доба́вил, что... **3,** *math.* скла́дывать: *add two and two,* скла́дывать два и два. **4,** (join) присоединя́ть: *add one's voice to,* присоединя́ть свой го́лос к. —*v.i.* **1,** (do addition) скла́дывать чи́сла. **2,** *fol. by* **to** (augment) увели́чивать; уси́ливать. —**add on, 1,** (add additionally) прибавля́ть: *add on the interest,* прибавля́ть проце́нты. **2,** (build on) пристра́ивать. —**add up, 1,** (figure the total of) сумми́ровать; подыто́живать. **2,** *usu. neg.* (seem consistent) (не) сходи́ться; (не) выде́рживать кри́тики. —**add up to, 1,** (amount to) составля́ть; равня́ться (+*dat.*). **2,** (signify; come down to) своди́ться (к).

added *adj.* дополни́тельный; доба́вочный.

addendum *n.* приложе́ние; дополне́ние.

adder *n.* (snake) гадю́ка.

addict *n.* **1,** (drug addict) наркома́н; морфини́ст. **2,** (enthusiast) люби́тель. *Chess addict,* стра́стный шахмати́ст. —**addicted,** *adj.* пристрасти́вшийся.

addiction *n.* влече́ние. *Drug addiction,* наркома́ния.

adding machine счётная маши́на.

addition *n.* **1,** (act of adding; something added) прибавле́ние; добавле́ние; дополне́ние. **2,** *math.* сложе́ние. —**in addition,** вдоба́вок; кро́ме того́; к тому́ же. —**in addition to,** кро́ме; в дополне́ние к; в добавле́ние к.

additional *adj.* дополни́тельный; доба́вочный. —**additionally,** *adv.* к тому́ же.

additive *n.* доба́вка; приса́дка.

addle *v.t.* **1,** (spoil) по́ртить. **2,** (confuse) пу́тать.

addled *adj.* **1,** (rotten, as of an egg) ту́хлый. **2,** (confused; mixed up) пу́таный.

address *n.* **1,** (dwelling or mailing place) а́дрес. **2,** (formal speech) выступле́ние. —*v.t.* **1,** (speak to) обраща́ться к; адресова́ться к. **2,** (deliver a speech to) выступа́ть на *or* пе́ред. **3,** (write the address on) адресова́ть. *A letter addressed to the president,* письмо́ на и́мя президе́нта. **4,** (direct, as a remark or question) адресова́ть. **5,** *in* **address oneself to** (turn to; take up) бра́ться за; принима́ться за.

addressee *n.* адреса́т.

adduce *v.t.* приводи́ть.

adenoid *n.* адено́ид.

adept *adj.* иску́сный.

adequacy *n.* доста́точность.

adequate *adj.* доста́точный. —**adequately,** *adv.* доста́точно.

adhere *v.i.* **1,** (stick fast) прилипа́ть; пристава́ть. **2,** *fol. by* **to** (follow consistently) приде́рживаться (+*gen.*); держа́ться (+*gen.*).

adherence *n.* приве́рженность.

adherent *n.* приве́рженец.

adhesion *n.* прилипа́ние.

adhesive *adj.* ли́пкий. —*n.* ли́пкое вещество́. —**adhesive tape,** ли́пкий пла́стырь.

ad hoc специа́льный: *ad hoc committee,* специа́льный комите́т.

adieu *interj.* проща́й! —*n.* проща́ние.

ad infinitum до бесконе́чности.

adipose *adj.* жи́рный.

adjacent *adj.* сме́жный; сосе́дний. —**adjacent angles,** сме́жные углы́.

adjective *n.* и́мя прилага́тельное. —**adjectival,** *adj. Adjectival endings,* оконча́ния имён прилага́тельных.

adjoin *v.t.* прилега́ть к; примыка́ть к. —**adjoining,** *adj.* сме́жный; прилега́ющий.

adjourn *v.t.* закрыва́ть: *declare the meeting adjourned,* объяви́ть заседа́ние закры́тым. *Adjourn a game,* отложи́ть па́ртию. —*v.i.* **1,** (suspend or end proceedings) закрыва́ться; закрыва́ть заседа́ние; объявля́ть переры́в. **2,** *colloq.* (move) переходи́ть. —**adjournment,** *n.* переры́в.

adjudge *v.t.* признава́ть: *he was adjudged insane,* его́ призна́ли душевнобольны́м.

adjudicate *v.t.* суди́ть; выноси́ть реше́ние по.

adjunct *n.* прида́ток.

adjure *v.t.* **1,** (command solemnly) повелева́ть. **2,** (entreat) заклина́ть.

adjust *v.t.* **1,** (make accurate; set right) регули́ровать. *Adjust a clock,* подводи́ть часы́. **2,** (move into the proper position) поправля́ть. **3,** (alter so as to make fit) подгоня́ть. **4,** (compose, as differences) ула́живать. —*v.i.* приспособля́ться. —**adjustable,** *adj.* передвижно́й. —**adjuster,** *n.* нала́дчик.

adjustment *n.* **1,** (adaptation) приспособле́ние. **2,** (regulating; setting) устано́вка; регулиро́вка. **3,** (fixing; setting right) попра́вка: *a slight adjustment,* небольша́я попра́вка. **4,** (composing, as differences) ула́живание.

adjutant *n.* адъюта́нт.

ad-lib *v.t. & i., colloq.* импровизи́ровать.

administer *v.t.* **1,** (manage) управля́ть. **2,** (inflict, as a beating, defeat, etc.) наноси́ть. **3,** (give remedially) дава́ть. *Administer first aid,* ока́зывать пе́рвую по́мощь. *Administer an injection,* сде́лать уко́л. **4,** (give; conduct, as a test) проводи́ть (экза́мен). **5,** (tender, as an oath): *administer the oath to someone,* приводи́ть кого́-нибудь к прися́ге. **6,** (dispense, as justice) отправля́ть (правосу́дие). —*v.i.* [*usu.* **administer to**] ока́зывать по́мощь (кому́-нибудь); удовлетворя́ть (чьи́-нибудь) ну́жды.

administration *n.* **1,** (managing) управле́ние. **2,** (managing officials) администра́ция. **3,** (government) администра́ция. **4,** (government bureau) управле́ние.

administrative *adj.* администрати́вный.

administrator *n.* администра́тор.

admirable *adj.* похва́льный; отли́чный.

admiral *n.* адмира́л. —**Admiral of the Fleet,** адмира́л фло́та.

admiralty *n.* адмиралте́йство.

admiration *n.* преклоне́ние; восхище́ние.

admire *v.t.* **1,** (esteem highly) преклоня́ться пе́ред. **2,** (watch with pleasure) любова́ться.

admirer *n.* покло́нник; почита́тель.

admissible *adj.* допусти́мый; прие́млемый.

admission *n.* **1,** (act of admitting or letting in) впуск; до́пуск; приём; приня́тие. **2,** (entry) до́ступ: *gain admission to,* получи́ть до́ступ в *or* на. **3,** (entrance fee) входна́я пла́та. **4,** (acknowledgment) призна́ние: *admission of guilt,* призна́ние вины́. —**admission charge,** входна́я пла́та.

admit *v.t.* **1,** (allow to enter) впуска́ть; допуска́ть; принима́ть. **2,** (acknowledge; confess) признава́ть. **3,** (concede; grant) допуска́ть.

admittance *n.* **1,** (act of admitting) впуск; до́пуск; приём. **2,** (entry) вход: *no admittance!,* вход воспрещён!

admittedly *adv.* пра́вда; призна́ться.

admix *v.t.* приме́шивать.

admixture *n.* при́месь.

admonish *v.t.* **1,** (chide) жури́ть. **2,** (advise; urge) увещева́ть.

admonition *n.* **1,** (mild rebuke) замеча́ние. **2,** (advice; warning) наставле́ние; нравоуче́ние; увеща́ние.

ad nauseam до тошноты́.

ado *n.* суета́. *Without further ado,* без дальне́йших церемо́ний; без да́льних слов. —**much ado about nothing,** мно́го шу́ма из ничего́.

adobe *n.* кирпи́ч-сыре́ц; сама́н. —*adj.* сама́нный; глинобитный.

adolescence *n.* о́трочество.

adolescent *n.* подро́сток. —*adj.* о́троческий.

adopt *v.t.* **1,** (take into one's family) усыновля́ть; удочеря́ть. **2,** (vote to accept) принима́ть. **3,** (take up and follow) принима́ть; усва́ивать; перенима́ть; заи́мствовать. —**adopted,** *adj.* приёмный.

adoption *n.* **1,** (taking into one's family) усыновле́ние. **2,** (acceptance and use; vote to accept) приня́тие.

adoptive *adj.* приёмный.

adorable *adj.* преле́стный; восхити́тельный.

adore *v.t.* обожа́ть. —**adoration,** *n.* обожа́ние.

adorn *v.t.* украша́ть. —**adornment,** *n.* украше́ние.

adrenal *adj.* надпо́чечный. —**adrenal gland,** надпо́чечная железа́; надпо́чечник.

adrenalin *also,* **adrenaline** *n.* адренали́н.

adrift *adv.* по тече́нию: *set adrift,* пуска́ть по тече́нию.

adroit *adj.* ло́вкий; прово́рный. —**adroitly,** *adv.* ло́вко. —**adroitness,** *n.* ло́вкость; прово́рство.

adsorb *v.t.* адсорби́ровать. —**adsorption,** *n.* адсо́рбция.

adulation *n.* **1,** (excessive praise) восхвале́ние. **2,** (intense admiration) преклоне́ние.

adult *n. & adj.* взро́слый. *Adult education,* обуче́ние взро́слых.

adulterate *v.t.* фальсифици́ровать; разбавля́ть. —**adulteration,** *n.* фальсифика́ция.

adulterer *n.* прелюбоде́й. —**adulteress,** *n.* прелюбоде́йка. —**adulterous,** *adj.* прелюбоде́йский.

adultery *n.* прелюбодея́ние. *Commit adultery,* соверша́ть прелюбодея́ние; прелюбоде́йствовать.

adulthood *n.* зре́лость; возмужа́лость.

advance *v.t.* **1,** (move forward; further; promote) продвига́ть. **2,** (put forward, as a theory) выдвига́ть. **3,** (lend) ссужа́ть. —*v.i.* продвига́ться; выдвига́ться. *Troops are advancing on the capital,* войска́ продвига́ются к столи́це. —*n.* **1,** (move forward) продвиже́ние. **2,** *fig.* (important step forward) достиже́ние. **3,** (loan) ссу́да; ава́нс. **4,** *pl.* (overtures) заи́грывания; уха́живания. —*adj.* **1,** (prior) предвари́тельный: *advance sale,* предвари́тельная прода́жа (биле́тов). **2,** (going ahead) передово́й: *advance*

guard, передовóй отря́д. —**in advance,** зара́нее; предвари́тельно; вперёд; ава́нсом.
advanced *adj.* **1,** (far along) продви́нутый: *advanced student,* продви́нутый учени́к *or* студе́нт. *Advanced course,* курс повы́шенного ти́па. **2,** (modern; progressive) передово́й: *advanced methods,* передовы́е ме́тоды. **3,** (old) преклóнный: *advanced age,* преклóнный вóзраст. *Advanced in years,* преклóнного вóзраста.
advancement *n.* продвиже́ние.
advantage *n.* **1,** (edge; superiority) преиму́щество: *enjoy a clear advantage over,* пóльзоваться я́вным преиму́ществом пе́ред. **2,** (factor giving an edge) преиму́щество; достóинство. *Advantages and disadvantages,* достóинства и недоста́тки. *Have a number of advantages over,* име́ть ряд преиму́ществ пе́ред. **3,** (benefit; profit) вы́года; пóльза. *Turn to one's advantage,* обраща́ть в свою́ пóльзу. —**take advantage of, 1,** (avail oneself of) пóльзоваться (+*instr.*). **2,** (abuse; exploit) злоупотребля́ть; эксплуати́ровать. —**to advantage,** вы́годно; в вы́годном све́те. —**to the best advantage, 1,** (in the best way) наилу́чшим óбразом. **2,** (in the best light) в са́мом вы́годном све́те.
advantageous *adj.* вы́годный.
advent *n.* наступле́ние; прише́ствие.
adventure *n.* приключе́ние; авантю́ра. *Thirst for adventure,* жа́жда приключе́ний. —*adj.* приключе́нческий; авантю́рный: *adventure story,* приключе́нческий/авантю́рный рома́н.
adventurer *n.* иска́тель приключе́ний.
adventuresome *adj.* сме́лый; предприи́мчивый.
adventurism *n.* авантюри́зм. —**adventurist,** *n.* авантюри́ст. —**adventuristic,** *adj.* авантюристи́ческий.
adventurous *adj.* сме́лый; предприи́мчивый.
adverb *n.* наре́чие. —**adverbial,** *adj.* наре́чный.
adversary *n.* проти́вник.
adverse *adj.* неблагоприя́тный. *Adverse wind,* встре́чный ве́тер. —**adversely,** *adv.* отрица́тельно.
adversity *n.* несча́стье; невзгóда.
advertise *v.t. & i.* реклами́ровать. —**advertisement,** *n.* объявле́ние; рекла́ма.
advertising *n.* рекла́ма. —*adj.* рекла́мный.
advice *n.* сове́т.
advisable *adj.* целесообра́зный. —**advisability,** *n.* целесообра́зность.
advise *v.t.* **1,** (give advice to) сове́товать: *What do you advise me to do?,* что вы мне сове́туете де́лать? *He advised against it,* он сове́товал не де́лать э́того. **2,** (notify) сообща́ть; извеща́ть; уведомля́ть; дать знать.
advised *adj.* осведомлённый. *Keep someone advised,* держа́ть когó-нибудь в ку́рсе дел. —**advisedly,** *adv.* наме́ренно; обду́манно. *I say this advisedly,* я наме́ренно э́то говорю́.
advisement *n.* рассмотре́ние. —**take under advisement,** рассма́тривать.
adviser *n.* сове́тник.
advisory *adj.* консультати́вный.
advocacy *n.* защи́та; поддéржка.
advocate *v.t.* стоя́ть за; выступа́ть за. —*n.* **1,** (one who favors a cause) сторóнник: *an advocate of reform,* сторóнник рефóрмы. **2,** *law* защи́тник; засту́пник.
adz *also,* **adze** *n.* теслó.
aegis *n.* эги́да: *under the aegis of,* под эги́дой (+*gen.*).
aerate *v.t.* прове́тривать. —**aeration,** *n.* аэра́ция.
aerial *adj.* возду́шный. *Aerial photograph,* аэросни́мок. —*n.* анте́нна.
aerodrome *n.* = **airdrome.**
aerodynamics *n.* аэродина́мика. —**aerodynamic,** *adj.* аэродинами́ческий.
aeronaut *n.* воздухопла́ватель; аэрона́вт. —**aeronautical,** *adj.* авиациóнный; воздухопла́вательный. *Aeronautical engineer,* авиациóнный инжене́р. —**aeronautics,** *n.* воздухопла́вание; аэрона́втика.
aerosol *n.* аэрозóль.
aerospace *n.* возду́шно-косми́ческое простра́нство. —*adj.* возду́шно-косми́ческий; авиакосми́ческий.
aerostat *n.* аэроста́т. —**aerostatics,** *n.* аэроста́тика.
aesthete *n.* = **esthete.** —**aesthetic,** *adj.* = **esthetic.** —**aesthetics,** *n.* = **esthetics.**
afar *adv., in* **from afar,** издалека́.
affable *adj.* приве́тливый. —**affability,** *n.* приве́тливость.
affair *n.* **1,** (event; matter) де́ло. *Foreign affairs,* иностра́нные дела́. **2,** (amorous relationship) связь; рома́н.
affect *v.t.* **1,** (have an effect upon) де́йствовать на; влия́ть на. **2,** (harm; hurt) затра́гивать; задева́ть; поража́ть. **3,** (touch emotionally) затра́гивать; задева́ть. **4,** (feign) притворя́ться; прики́дываться.
affectation *n.* де́ланность; жема́нство; аффекта́ция.
affected *adj.* **1,** (feigned) наи́гранный; напускнóй; аффекти́рованный. **2,** (artificial in manner) жема́нный; мане́рный. **3,** (moved by emotion) трóнут; растрóганный. **4,** (afflicted) затрóнутый; заде́тый.
affection *n.* привя́занность. —**affectionate,** *adj.* ла́сковый.
affiance *v.t.* обруча́ть.
affidavit *n.* пи́сьменное показа́ние под прися́гой.
affiliate *v.i.* присоединя́ться. *Be affiliated with,* име́ть связь с. —*n.* филиа́л. —**affiliation,** *n.* принадле́жность.
affinity *n.* **1,** (natural attraction; liking) влече́ние. **2,** (similarity implying common origin) родствó; сродствó.
affirm *v.t.* **1,** (assert positively) заявля́ть о: *affirm one's loyalty,* заяви́ть о свое́й лоя́льности. **2,** (confirm) подтвержда́ть; утвержда́ть.
affirmation *n.* **1,** (firm statement) заявле́ние. **2,** (confirmation) подтвержде́ние.
affirmative *adj.* утверди́тельный. *Answer in the affirmative,* отвеча́ть утверди́тельно. —**affirmatively,** *adv.* утверди́тельно.
affix *v.t.* **1,** (attach) прикрепля́ть. **2,** (stick on) накле́ивать; прикле́ивать. **3,** (write; stamp; imprint) накла́дывать; ста́вить: *affix a seal,* накла́дывать/ста́вить печа́ть. *Affix one's signature,* ста́вить свою́ пóдпись.
afflict *v.t.* поража́ть. *Be afflicted with,* страда́ть (+*instr.*).
affliction *n.* **1,** (distress) несча́стье. **2,** (ailment) боле́знь.
affluence *n.* оби́лие; богáтство. —**affluent,** *adj.* богáтый; состоя́тельный.

afford *v.t.* **1,** (have the means for) позво́лить себе́: *I can't afford it,* не могу́ э́того себе́ позво́лить; э́то мне не по сре́дствам (*or* не по карма́ну). *I can't afford the time,* мне не́когда. **2,** (give; provide) доставля́ть; предоставля́ть: *afford pleasure,* доставля́ть удово́льствие; *afford an opportunity,* предоставля́ть возмо́жность. *The balcony affords an excellent view of the lake,* с балко́на открыва́ется прекра́сный вид на о́зеро.

affront *v.t.* оскорбля́ть. —*n.* оскорбле́ние.

Afghan *adj.* [*also,* **Afghanistani**] афга́нский. —*n.* **1,** (native of Afghanistan) афга́нец; афга́нка. **2,** *l.c.* (woolen blanket) шерстяно́е одея́ло.

afield *adv.* от те́мы: *go rather far afield,* отклоня́ться от те́мы. *That would take us far afield,* э́то завело́ бы нас далеко́.

afire *adj.* в огне́. *Set afire,* поджига́ть.

aflame *adj.* в огне́. *Be aflame,* быть в огне́; пыла́ть. *Set aflame,* воспламеня́ть.

afloat *adj. & adv.* на воде́; на плаву́. *Remain afloat,* держа́ться на воде́. *Rumors are afloat,* хо́дят слу́хи.

afoot *adv. & adj., obs.* пешко́м. —**be afoot,** гото́виться; затева́ться.

aforementioned *adj.* вышеупомя́нутый.

aforesaid *adj.* вышеска́занный.

afraid *adj., used predicatively: I am afraid,* мне стра́шно. *Be afraid of,* боя́ться (+ *gen.*). *Be afraid that...,* боя́ться, что...

afresh *adv.* сно́ва: *start afresh,* начина́ть сно́ва.

African *adj.* африка́нский. —*n.* африка́нец.

aft *adv.* на корме́; на корму́.

after *prep.* **1,** (subsequent to) по́сле: *after dinner,* по́сле обе́да. ♦*With expressions of time* че́рез: *after a year,* че́рез год; *after a while,* че́рез не́которое вре́мя. *Ten years after the war,* че́рез де́сять лет по́сле войны́. **2,** (following; behind; in pursuit of) за (+*instr.*): *summer comes after spring,* ле́то идёт за весно́й. *Time after time,* раз за ра́зом. *One after the other,* оди́н за други́м. *Run/look/clean up/after someone,* бежа́ть/присма́тривать/убира́ть за ке́м-нибудь. **3,** (in telling time): *ten after two,* де́сять мину́т тре́тьего. *It is already after six,* уже́ седьмо́й час. **4,** (for; in honor of) в честь: *he was named after his grandfather,* его́ назва́ли в честь де́да. **5,** (in view of) по́сле: *after what went on yesterday,* по́сле того́, что произошло́ вчера́. *After all she has been through,* по́сле всего́, что она́ пережила́. **6,** (in spite of) несмотря́ на: *after all he has done for you,* несмотря́ на всё, что он сде́лал для вас. —*adv.* **1,** (behind) сза́ди; позади́. **2,** (subsequently) поздне́е; пото́м. —*conj.* по́сле того́, как: *after he left,* по́сле того как он ушёл. *After you have read the book,* по́сле того́, как вы прочтёте кни́гу. *After learning about what happened,* узна́в о случи́вшемся. —**after all, 1,** (despite all; in the end) всё-таки: *I was right after all,* всё-таки я был прав. **2,** (when all is said and done) же; ведь: *after all, she is your sister!,* она́ же твоя́ сестра́; ведь она́ твоя́ сестра́. —**after that,** вслед за тем. —**after you!,** прошу́ вас!

afterbirth *n.* де́тское ме́сто.

after-dinner *adj.* послеобе́денный.

aftereffect *n.* после́дствие; отголо́сок.

afterglow *n.* вече́рняя заря́.

afterlife *n.* загро́бная жизнь.

aftermath *n.* отголо́ски.

afternoon *n.* вре́мя по́сле полу́дня; втора́я полови́на дня. —**in the afternoon,** днём; по́сле обе́да; во второ́й полови́не дня. *At three o'clock in the afternoon,* в три часа́ пополу́дни.

aftertaste *n.* при́вкус; оса́док.

afterward *also,* **afterwards** *adv.* по́сле; пото́м; впосле́дствии. *Soon afterward,* вско́ре.

again *adv.* опя́ть; сно́ва; ещё раз. *What, again?,* что, опя́ть? *Try again,* попро́бовать ещё раз. *Meet again,* сно́ва встре́титься. *Happen again,* повторя́ться. —**again and again,** сно́ва и сно́ва. —**but then again,** впро́чем. —**now and again,** вре́мя от вре́мени. —**time and again,** то и де́ло; неоднокра́тно.

against *prep.* **1,** (in opposition to; contrary to; compared to) про́тив: *against the wind,* про́тив ве́тра; *against one's will,* про́тив во́ли. *Compete/struggle against,* состяза́ться/боро́ться с. *Six in favor, three against,* шесть за, три про́тив. **2,** (so as to strike) о (+*acc.*): *beat against the shore,* би́ться о бе́рег. **3,** (so as to touch) к: *lean against a wall,* прислоня́ться к стене́. *Place the table up against the wall,* поста́вить стол вплотну́ю к стене́. **4,** (as a protection from) от: *insurance against breakage,* страхова́ние от поло́мки. *Protection against the cold,* защи́та от хо́лода. **5,** (in anticipation of) на: *against a rainy day,* на чёрный день. **6,** (in contrast to the background of) на фо́не (+*gen.*): *stand out against the sky,* выделя́ться на фо́не не́ба. **7,** (as a debit on) под: *borrow money against an insurance policy,* занима́ть де́ньги под страхово́й по́лис.

agape *adj. & adv.* рази́нув рот.

agate *n.* ага́т. —*adj.* ага́товый.

agave *n.* ага́ва.

age *n.* **1,** (years since birth) во́зраст. *At my age,* в мои́ го́ды. *Be the same age,* быть одни́х лет. *Not to look one's age,* вы́глядеть моло́же свои́х лет. **2,** (old age) ста́рость: *live to a ripe old age,* дожи́ть до ста́рости. **3,** (adulthood) совершенноле́тие: *come of age,* достига́ть совершенноле́тия. *Be of age,* быть совершенноле́тним. **4,** (period in history) век; эпо́ха. *The Stone Age,* ка́менный век. *The space age,* косми́ческий век. **5,** *often pl., colloq.* (a long time) це́лую ве́чность: *I haven't seen you for ages,* не ви́дел вас це́лую ве́чность. —*adj.* возрастно́й: *age group,* возрастна́я гру́ппа. —*v.t.* **1,** (make old) ста́рить. **2,** (mature, as wine) выде́рживать. —*v.i.* **1,** (grow old) старе́ть. **2,** (mature, as of wine) созрева́ть. —**at the age of,** в во́зрасте (+*gen.*): *at the age of twenty-five,* в во́зрасте двадцати́ пяти́ лет; в двадцатипятиле́тнем во́зрасте; в два́дцать пять лет.

aged *adj.* **1,** (old) ста́рый; престаре́лый. **2,** (of a certain age): *a girl aged five,* де́вочка пяти́ лет. **3,** (mature, as of wine) вы́держанный. —**the aged,** старики́.

ageing *adj. & n.* = **aging.**

ageless *adj.* **1,** (seeming not to grow old) ве́чно молодо́й. **2,** (eternal) ве́чный.

agency *n.* **1,** (bureau; department) аге́нство; бюро́; управле́ние; учрежде́ние: *telegraph agency,* телегра́фное аге́нство; *travel agency,* бюро́ путеше́ствий; *specialized agency,* специализи́рованное учрежде́ние. *Central Intelligence Agency,* Центра́льное разве́дывательное управле́ние. **2,** (means; instrumentality) сре́дство. *Through the agency of,* посре́дством (+*gen.*); че́рез посре́дство (+*gen.*).

agenda *n.* повéстка дня.

agent *n.* **1,** (person) агéнт: *insurance agent,* страховóй агéнт; *intelligence agent,* агéнт развéдки. **2,** (substance) веществó; срéдство; агéнт. —**agent provocateur,** провокáтор.

age-old *adj.* вековóй.

agglutination *n.* агглютинáция. —**agglutinative,** *adj.* агглютинатúвный.

aggrandize *v.t.* увелúчивать; расширя́ть. —**aggrandizement,** *n.* увеличéние; расширéние.

aggravate *v.t.* **1,** (make worse) ухудшáть; обостря́ть. **2,** *colloq.* (vex) раздражáть; досаждáть.

aggravating *adj.* досáдный. —**aggravating circumstances,** отягчáющие винý обстоя́тельства.

aggravation *n.* **1,** (making worse) ухудшéние; обострéние. **2,** (vexation) раздражéние; досáда.

aggregate *adj.* совокýпный. —*n.* совокýпность.

aggression *n.* агрéссия. *Act of aggression,* акт агрéссии.

aggressive *adj.* **1,** (militant; hostile) агрессúвный. **2,** (assertive; pushy) напóристый.

aggressor *n.* агрéссор.

aggrieve *v.t.* **1,** (distress) огорчáть. **2,** (wrong) обижáть.

aghast *adj.* в ýжасе.

agile *adj.* проворный. —**agility,** *n.* провóрство.

aging *also,* **ageing** *adj.* старéющий. —*n.* старéние.

agitate *v.t.* **1,** (disturb, as the sea) волновáть. **2,** (shake briskly) взбáлтывать. **3,** (perturb) волновáть. —*v.i.* агитúровать. —**agitated,** *adj.* взволнóванный.

agitation *n.* **1,** (agitated state) волнéние. **2,** *polit.* агитáция.

agitator *n.* агитáтор.

aglet *n.* **1,** (tip at the end of a lace) наконéчник. **2,** (braid on a uniform) аксельбáнт.

aglow *adj., used predicatively: be aglow,* сия́ть.

agnostic *n.* агнóстик. —*adj.* агностúческий. —**agnosticism,** *n.* агностицúзм.

ago *adj.* томý назáд: *two years ago,* два гóда томý назáд. —*adv., in* **long ago,** давнó; **not long ago,** недáвно.

agonize *v.i.* мýчиться. —**agonizing,** *adj.* мучúтельный.

agony *n.* **1,** (intense suffering) мýка; мучéние. **2,** (throes of death) (предсмéртная) агóния.

agrarian *adj.* агрáрный.

agree *v.i.* **1,** (be of the same opinion) быть соглáсным; соглашáться: *I agree with you,* я с вáми соглáсен (соглáсна). **2,** *fol. by* **to** (consent to) соглашáться (+*inf.*) *or with* на (+*acc.*): *agree to a draw,* согласúться на ничью́. **3,** (reach agreement; make arrangements) договорúться. **4,** (be in harmony; coincide) сходúться. **5,** *fol. by* **with** (be suitable or good for): *married life agrees with him,* брáчная жизнь емý по душé. *Turnips don't agree with me,* мой желýдок не вынóсит рéпы. **6,** *gram.* согласовáться.

agreeable *adj.* **1,** (pleasing) приятный. **2,** (ready to consent) соглáсный. **3,** (amenable) сговóрчивый.

agreed *adj.* установленный; полóженный; услóвный; услóвленный. *Also,* **agreed-upon.**

agreement *n.* **1,** (harmony of opinion) соглáсие: *complete agreement,* пóлное соглáсие. **2,** (arrangement; understanding) соглашéние: *come to an agreement,* приходúть к соглашéнию. **3,** *gram.* согласовáние.

agriculture *n.* сéльское хозя́йство. —**agricultural,** *adj.* сельскохозя́йственный.

agronomy *n.* агронóмия. —**agronomic,** *adj.* агронóмический. —**agronomist,** *n.* агронóм.

aground *adj.* на мелú. —*adv.* на мель: *run aground,* сесть на мель.

ah *interj.* а!; ах!

aha *interj.* агá!

ahead *adv.* **1,** (forward) вперёд: *full speed ahead!,* пóлный ход вперёд! *Set a clock ahead,* постáвить часы́ вперёд. **2,** (in front of one) впередú: *ahead lay a river,* впередú былá рекá. *There is danger ahead,* впередú опáсность. **3,** (into or for the future) вперёд: *look ahead,* заглянýть вперёд. *Plan ahead,* планúровать зарáнее. *What lies ahead for him?,* что егó ждёт впередú? —*adj.* впередú: *who is ahead?,* кто впередú? —**ahead of, 1,** (in front of) впередú (+*gen.*): *walk ahead of the others,* идтú впередú остальны́х. *You have your whole life ahead of you,* у вас цéлая жизнь впередú. **2,** (in advance of) прéжде (+*gen.*); рáньше (+*gen.*). *Ahead of time,* рáньше врéмени; рáньше срóка. —**get ahead,** продвигáться (вперёд). —**get ahead of,** опережáть. —**go ahead!,** давáйте! —**straight ahead,** пря́мо.

ahem *interj.* гм!

aid *v.t.* помогáть. —*n.* **1,** (assistance) пóмощь: *first aid,* скóрая пóмощь. *Come to the aid of,* прийтú на пóмощь (+*dat.*). **2,** (helpful device) аппарáт: *hearing aid,* слуховóй аппарáт. **3,** *pl.* (teaching devices) посóбия: *visual aids,* нагля́дные посóбия.

aide *n.* **1,** *mil.* адъютáнт. **2,** (assistant) помóщник.

aide-de-camp *n.* адъютáнт.

aide-mémoire *n.* пáмятная запúска.

aiguillette *n.* аксельбáнт.

ail *v.i.* недомогáть; хворáть. —*v.t. What ails you?,* что вас беспокóит?

aileron *n.* элерóн.

ailment *n.* болéзнь; недомогáние; недýг.

aim *n.* **1,** (objective) цель: *the aim of the experiment,* цель эксперимéнта. **2,** (act of aiming) прицéливание. *Take aim at,* прицéливаться в; взять прицéл на. —*v.t.* направля́ть; наводúть; нацéливать. —*v.i.* **1,** (take aim) прицéливаться; мéтить. **2,** (aspire) стремúться (к); мéтить. *Aim higher,* мéтить вы́ше. **3,** *fol. by* **to** (have as one's goal) имéть цéлью (+*inf.*).

aimless *adj.* бесцéльный. —**aimlessly,** *adv.* бесцéльно.

air *n.* **1,** (atmosphere) вóздух. *Out in the open air,* на откры́том вóздухе. **2,** (appearance) вид. *Assume an air of importance,* напускáть на себя́ вáжность. **3,** *pl.* (affected manners) *usu. in* **put on airs; give oneself airs,** вáжничать; кривля́ться; ломáться; задавáться; зазнавáться. **4,** *radio* эфúр: *on the air,* в эфúре. **5,** (tune; melody) пéсня; напéв. —*adj.* воздýшный: *air filter,* воздýшный фильтр. *Air travel,* поéздки на самолёте. *Air pollution,* загрязнéние вóздуха. —*v.t.* **1,** [*usu.* **air out**] (ventilate) провéтривать. **2,** (express publicly; bring out into the open) разглашáть. —**be in the air,** вéять: *spring is in the air,* вéет веснóй. —**be up in the air,** висéть *or* повúснуть в вóздухе. —**be walking on air,** ног под собóй не чýять. —**by air,** на самолёте; самолётом. —**clear the air,**

разрядить атмосферу. —**take the air,** подышать свежим воздухом. —**vanish into thin air,** как сквозь землю провалиться; как в воду кануть.
air base авиабаза.
airborne *adj.* **1,** (aloft) в воздухе. **2,** *mil.* (transported by air) воздушнодесантный.
air-condition *v.t.* кондиционировать. —**air-conditioned,** *adj.* кондиционированный; с кондиционером. —**air conditioner,** кондиционер. —**air conditioning,** кондиционирование воздуха.
air-cooled *adj.* с воздушным охлаждением.
aircraft *n.* **1,** (airplane) самолёт. **2,** (airplanes collectively) авиация. —**aircraft carrier,** авианосец.
air defense противовоздушная оборона.
airdrome *also,* **aerodrome** *n.* аэродром.
airfield *n.* лётное поле; аэродром.
air force военно-воздушные силы.
air gun духовое ружьё.
air hole отдушина.
airily *adv.* весело; беззаботно.
airing *n.* проветривание.
airless *adj.* душный: *airless room,* душная комната.
airlift *n.* воздушная перевозка; "воздушный мост".
airline *n.* авиакомпания.
airliner *n.* воздушный лайнер.
air mail авиапочта. "*(By) air mail*", авиа; авиапочтой.
airman *n.* лётчик.
airplane *n.* самолёт.
air pocket воздушная яма.
airport *n.* аэропорт.
air pressure давление воздуха.
air raid воздушный налёт. —**air-raid shelter,** бомбоубежище. —**air-raid siren,** сирена воздушной тревоги.
air route авиатрасса.
airship *n.* дирижабль.
airsick *adj.* страдающий воздушной болезнью. *I became airsick,* меня укачало на самолёте. —**airsickness,** *n.* воздушная болезнь.
air space воздушное пространство.
airspeed *n.* воздушная скорость.
airstrip *n.* взлётно-посадочная полоса.
airtight *adj.* герметический.
airwaves *n.pl.* эфир.
airway *n.* авиатрасса.
airworthy *adj.* годный к полёту.
airy *adj.* **1,** (with plenty of air) полный воздуха. **2,** (light; thin) воздушный.
aisle *n.* проход.
ajar *adj. & adv.* приоткрытый; полуоткрытый; полуотворенный; неприкрытый. *Leave the door ajar,* оставлять дверь неприкрытой.
akimbo *adj. & adv.* подбоченившись. *Stand with arms akimbo,* подбочениться.
akin *adj.* родственный. *Be akin to,* быть сродни (+*dat.*).
alabaster *n.* алебастр. —*adj.* алебастровый.
à la carte **1,** *used adjectivally* порционный. **2,** *used adverbially* по порциям.
alacrity *n.* быстрота. *With alacrity,* быстро; живо.
alarm *n.* **1,** (sudden fear) тревога. **2,** (signal of danger) тревога; набат. *Fire alarm,* пожарная тревога. *Sound the alarm,* бить/забить/ударять тревогу; бить /забить/ударять (в) набат. —*adj.* тревожный; набатный: *alarm signal,* тревожный сигнал; *alarm bell,* набатный колокол. *Alarm system,* сигнализация. —*v.t.* тревожить. —**alarm clock,** будильник.
alarmed *adj.* встревоженный.
alarming *adj.* тревожный.
alarmist *n.* паникёр.
alas *interj.* увы!
Albanian *adj.* албанский. —*n.* **1,** (person) албанец; албанка. **2,** (language) албанский язык.
albatross *n.* альбатрос.
albeit *conj.* хотя.
albino *n.* альбинос. —**albinism,** *n.* альбинизм.
album *n.* альбом.
albumen *n.* белок.
albumin *n.* альбумин.
alburnum *n.* заболонь.
alchemy *n.* алхимия. —**alchemist,** *n.* алхимик.
alcohol *n.* **1,** (liquid) спирт; алкоголь. **2,** (intoxicating beverages) алкоголь; спиртные напитки.
alcoholic *adj.* спиртной; алкогольный. —*n.* алкоголик. —**alcoholism,** *n.* алкоголизм.
alcove *n.* альков; ниша.
alder *n.* ольха.
alderman *n.* член городского совета.
ale *n.* эль.
alert *n.* тревога. *Place on alert,* поднимать по тревоге. —*adj.* **1,** (watchful) настороженный; бдительный. **2,** (mentally quick) бойкий. —*v.t.* настораживать. —**on the alert,** настороже.
alexandrite *n.* александрит.
alfalfa *n.* люцерна.
algae *n.pl.* водоросль.
algebra *n.* алгебра. —**algebraic,** *adj.* алгебраический.
Algerian *adj.* алжирский. —*n.* алжирец; алжирка.
algorithm *n.* алгоритм.
alias *n.* вымышленное имя. —*adv.* иначе называемый.
alibi *n.* **1,** *law* алиби. **2,** *colloq.* (excuse) отговорка.
alien *n.* иностранец. —*adj.* **1,** (foreign; strange) чужой: *alien customs,* чужие обычаи. **2,** (adverse; hostile) чуждый: *alien ideology,* чуждая идеология. *It is alien to his nature,* это ему чуждо по духу.
alienate *v.t.* отчуждать; отдалять; отталкивать. —**alienation,** *n.* отчуждение; отдаление.
alight *v.i.* **1,** (dismount) сходить. **2,** (settle) садиться.
align *v.t.* **1,** (arrange in a straight line) выравнивать. **2,** *fol. by* **oneself** (ally oneself) присоединяться.
alignment *n.* **1,** (act of aligning) выравнивание. **2,** *mil.* равнение.
alike *adj.* **1,** (similar) похожий. *They look alike,* (внешне) они похожи (друг на друга). **2,** (identical) одинаковый. —*adv.* одинаково.
alimentary canal пищеварительный канал; желудочно-кишечный тракт.
alimony *n.* алименты.
alive *adj.* **1,** (living) живой: *he is still alive,* он ещё жив. *Remain alive,* оставаться в живых. *Take alive,* брать живьём. *Buried alive,* заживо погребённый. *Keep alive,* поддерживать жизнь (+*gen.*). **2,** (lively; animated) живой. *Come alive,* оживать; оживляться. **3,** *fol. by* **to** (aware of; responsive to) чувствительный (к). *Be alive to,* ясно понимать. **4,** *fol. by* **with** (swarming) кишащий: *be alive with bees,* кишеть пчёлами.
alkali *n.* щёлочь. —**alkaline,** *adj.* щелочной. —**alka-**

linity, *n.* щёлочность.

alkaloid *n.* алкало́ид.

all *adj.* весь (вся, всё, все): *all day,* весь день; *all the time,* всё вре́мя; *all nations,* все стра́ны. —*pron.* **1,** (everything) всё: *that's all,* э́то всё. *All is well,* всё хорошо́. **2,** (everyone) все: *all agree,* все согла́сны. —*n.* [*usu.* **one's all**] *Give one's all,* отдава́ть все си́лы. *Stake one's all,* поста́вить всё на ка́рту. —*adv.* **1,** (completely) весь; соверше́нно; совсе́м. *I got all wet,* я весь промо́к; я вся промо́кла. *All alone,* соверше́нно *or* совсе́м оди́н/одна́. **2,** *sports: the score was two-all,* счёт был два-два. —**all along,** *see* **along.** —**all at once,** *see* **once.** —**all but,** *see* **but.**—**all for,** целико́м за то, что́бы (+*inf.*). —**all in,** *colloq.* без ног. —**all in all, 1,** (in general) в о́бщем и це́лом. **2,** (altogether) всего́.—**all over,** *see* **over.** —**all the same,** *see* **same.** —**all told,** в о́бщей сло́жности. —**at all, 1,** (whatsoever) никако́й: *no difference at all,* никако́й ра́зницы. *For no reason at all,* без вся́кой причи́ны. **2,** (in no way) ника́к: *That won't help at all,* э́то ника́к не помо́жет. **3,** (in any event) вообще́: *I doubt whether he'll come at all,* я сомнева́юсь, придёт ли он вообще́. *See also* **not at all.** —**in all,** всего́; в о́бщей сло́жности. —**not all there,** *colloq.* не в своём уме́; не все до́ма. —**not at all,** *see* **not.** —**of all,** всего́: *most of all,* бо́льше всего́.

Allah *n.* алла́х.

all-around *adj.* всесторо́нний.

allay *v.t.* **1,** (lessen; relieve) смягча́ть; облегча́ть. **2,** (set to rest) успока́ивать: *allay suspicion,* успока́ивать подозре́ние.

all clear отбо́й (возду́шной трево́ги). *Also,* **all-clear signal.**

allegation *n.* (голосло́вное) утвержде́ние.

allege *v.t.* **1,** (assert) утвержда́ть. **2,** (offer as an excuse) ссыла́ться на. —**alleged,** *adj.* предполага́емый: *the alleged murderer,* предполага́емый уби́йца. *For alleged improprieties,* я́кобы за наруше́ние прили́чий. —**allegedly,** *adv.* я́кобы.

allegiance *n.* ве́рность. *Pledge allegiance,* кля́сться в ве́рности.

allegory *n.* аллего́рия; иносказа́ние. —**allegorical,** *adj.* аллегори́ческий; иносказа́тельный.

allegretto *adv.* & *n.* аллегре́тто.

allegro *adv.* & *n.* алле́гро.

all-embracing *adj.* всеобъе́млющий.

allergic *adj.* аллерги́ческий. *Be allergic to,* име́ть аллерги́ю к; не выноси́ть.

allergy *n.* аллерги́я.

alleviate *v.t.* облегча́ть; смягча́ть. —**alleviation,** *n.* облегче́ние; смягче́ние.

alley *n.* у́зкий переу́лок; у́зкий прохо́д. —**alley cat,** бродя́чий кот.

alliance *n.* сою́з.

allied *adj.* **1,** (united) сою́зный. *Be allied with,* быть сою́зником (+*gen.*). **2,** (similar; related) сме́жный; ро́дственный.

alligator *n.* аллига́тор.

alliteration *n.* аллитера́ция.

allocate *v.t.* **1,** (allot; appropriate) выделя́ть; ассигнова́ть; отводи́ть. **2,** (apportion; distribute) распределя́ть. —**allocation,** *n.* ассигнова́ние; распределе́ние.

allopath *n.* аллопа́т. —**allopathic,** *adj.* аллопати́ческий. —**allopathy,** *n.* аллопа́тия.

allot *v.t.* **1,** (parcel out) распределя́ть; наделя́ть. **2,** (allocate) выделя́ть; отводи́ть.

allotment *n.* **1,** (parceling out) распределе́ние; наделе́ние. **2,** (allocating) выделе́ние. **3,** (portion allotted) до́ля.

all-out *adj.* развёрнутый; тота́льный. —**go all out,** *colloq.* напряга́ть все си́лы; лезть из ко́жи вон.

allow *v.t.* **1,** (give permission to) позволя́ть; разреша́ть. *He is not allowed to...,* ему́ не разреша́ется (+*inf.*). **2,** (permit to happen) допуска́ть. *Allow a goal,* пропусти́ть гол. **3,** *fol. by* **in** (permit to enter) допуска́ть; впуска́ть; пропуска́ть. **4,** (concede) допуска́ть. **5,** (acknowledge as valid) признава́ть справедли́вым. **6,** (provide; allot, as time) отводи́ть. **7,** *fol. by* **for** (make allowance for) учи́тывать. **8,** *comm.* де́лать ски́дку (+*dat.*): *allow someone 10%,* де́лать кому́-нибудь ски́дку на де́сять проце́нтов.

allowance *n.* **1,** (deduction) ски́дка. **2,** (money paid or given out) посо́бие. **3,** *mil.* (де́нежное) дово́льствие. *Housing allowance,* кварти́рные де́ньги. *Travel allowance,* командиро́вочные де́ньги. **4,** (consideration) ски́дка: *make allowance for,* де́лать ски́дку на.

alloy *n.* сплав. —*v.t.* сплавля́ть.

all-powerful *adj.* всемогу́щий.

all-purpose *adj.* универса́льный.

all right 1, (expression of assent) ла́дно; хорошо́. **2,** (O.K.) хорошо́. *It's all right with me,* я согла́сен; я не возража́ю. **3,** (so-so) так себе́. **4,** (unhurt) невреди́м. *Are you all right?,* вы не ушиблись? **5,** (recovered) здоро́в. **6,** *preceded by* **it's** *or* **that's** (it doesn't matter) ничего́. **7,** (without a doubt) бу́дьте уве́рены: *that's him all right!,* бу́дьте уве́рены, э́то он!

all-round *adj.* всесторо́нний; универса́льный. *All-round education,* разносторо́ннее образова́ние.

allspice *n.* души́стый пе́рец; гвозди́чный пе́рец.

all-star *adj.* сбо́рный: *all-star team,* сбо́рная кома́нда.

all-time *adj.* непревзойдённый: *all-time record,* непревзойдённый реко́рд. *Prices reached an all-time high,* це́ны дости́гли небыва́ло высо́кого у́ровня.

allude *v.i.* [*usu.* **allude to**] ссыла́ться на; упомина́ть; намека́ть на.

allure *v.t.* зама́нивать; завлека́ть. —*n.* [*also,* **allurement**] прима́нка; обольще́ние. —**alluring,** *adj.* зама́нчивый; маня́щий.

allusion *n.* ссы́лка; упомина́ние; намёк.

alluvium *n.* нано́с; аллю́вий. —**alluvial,** *adj.* нано́сный; аллювиа́льный.

ally *n.* сою́зник. —*v.t. Ally oneself with,* вступа́ть в сою́з с. *Be allied with,* быть сою́зником (+*gen.*).

almanac *n.* альмана́х.

almighty *adj.* всемогу́щий. —**the Almighty,** бог.

almond *n.* **1,** (tree) минда́ль. **2,** (nut) минда́льный оре́х; (*collectively*) минда́ль. —*adj.* минда́льный: *almond oil,* минда́льное ма́сло.

almost *adv.* почти́: *almost never,* почти́ никогда́. ♦*Of something that nearly happened, but did not* едва́ не; чуть не: *I almost fell,* я едва́ не/чуть не/упа́л.

alms *n.* ми́лостыня. —**almshouse,** *n.* богаде́льня.

aloe *n.* ало́э. —**aloes,** *n.* ало́э.

aloft *adj.* & *adv.* **1,** (on high) наверху́; в высоте́. **2,** (airborne) в во́здухе.

alone *adj.* & *adv.* **1,** (without company) оди́н: *are you alone?,* вы оди́н (одна́)? *Be alone with,* быть наедине́

c. **2,** (only) оди́н: *God alone knows,* одному́ бо́гу изве́стно. *Man does not live by bread alone,* не хле́бом еди́ным жив челове́к. **3,** (with nothing else added) (оди́н) то́лько: *this year alone,* то́лько в э́том году́. *Moscow alone has a population of...,* в одно́й то́лько Москве́ живёт... —**go it alone,** *colloq.* де́йствовать в одино́чку. —**leave alone, 1,** *literally* оставля́ть одного́ (одну́, одни́х). **2,** (not bother) оставля́ть в поко́е. —**let alone, 1,** (leave alone) оставля́ть в поко́е. **2,** (not to mention) не говоря́ уже́ о.

along *prep.* **1,** (over the length of) по: *walk along the street,* идти́ по у́лице. *Stop along the way,* останови́ться по пути́. **2,** (along the side of) вдоль: *houses along the road,* дома́ вдоль доро́ги. —*adv.* **1,** (onward) да́льше; вперёд. *Move along!,* проходи́те вперёд! **2,** (with one) с собо́й: *take along,* взять с собо́й. —**all along, 1,** (all the time) всё вре́мя; с са́мого нача́ла. **2,** (along the entire) на всём протяже́нии (+*gen.*). *All along the way,* всю доро́гу; на протяже́нии всего́ пути́. —**along with,** вме́сте с. —**get along,** *see* **get.**

alongside *adv.* ря́дом. —*prep.* ря́дом с; во́зле. *Draw (up) alongside,* поравня́ться с.

aloof *adv.* в стороне́; особняко́м: *remain aloof,* держа́ться в стороне́/особняко́м. —*adj.* отчуждённый. —**aloofness,** *n.* отчуждённость.

aloud *adv.* вслух.

alpaca *n.* альпака́.

alpha *n.* а́льфа. —**alpha particle,** а́льфа-части́ца. —**alpha rays,** а́льфа-лучи́.

alphabet *n.* а́збука; алфави́т. —**alphabetic; alphabetical,** *adj.* алфави́тный. —**alphabetize,** *v.t.* располага́ть в алфави́тном поря́дке.

Alpine *adj.* альпи́йский.

already *adv.* уже́: *it is late already,* уже́ по́здно. *I have already eaten,* я уже́ пое́л(а). *This complicates an already tense situation,* э́то усложня́ет и без того́ напряжённое положе́ние.

also *adv.* то́же; та́кже.

Altaic *adj.* алта́йский.

altar *n.* алта́рь.

alter *v.t.* **1,** (modify) изменя́ть. **2,** (adjust, as a garment) переде́лывать. —*v.i.* изменя́ться.

alteration *n.* **1,** (change) измене́ние. **2,** (adjustment, as of a garment) переде́лка.

altercation *n.* перебра́нка.

alternate *v.t.* чередова́ть; перемежа́ть. —*v.i.* чередова́ться; перемежа́ться. —*n.* замести́тель. —*adj.* **1,** (alternating) череду́ющийся. **2,** (every other) ка́ждый второ́й. *On alternate days,* че́рез день. **3,** (alternative; substitute) запасно́й; альтернати́вный. **4,** *math.* (of an angle) противолежа́щий.

alternately *adv.* попереме́нно; вперемежку.

alternating current переме́нный ток.

alternation *n.* чередова́ние.

alternative *n.* вы́бор; альтернати́ва. *We have no alternative,* у нас нет вы́бора. —*adj.* альтернати́вный.

alternator *n.* альтерна́тор.

although *conj.* хотя́.

altimeter *n.* альтиме́тр; высотоме́р.

altitude *n.* высота́. *At an altitude of,* на высоте́ в (+*acc.*).

alto *n.* альт. —*adj.* альто́вый.

altogether *adv.* **1,** (completely) совсе́м; вполне́. **2,** (in all; all told) всего́; в о́бщей сло́жности.

altruism *n.* альтруи́зм. —**altruist,** *n.* альтруи́ст. —**altruistic,** *adj.* альтруисти́ческий.

alum *n.* квасцы́.

aluminum *also, Brit.,* **aluminium** *n.* алюми́ний. —*adj.* алюми́ниевый.

alumnus *n.* пито́мец; воспи́танник.

alveolus *n.* лу́нка; альвео́ла. —**alveolar,** *adj.* альвеоля́рный.

always *adv.* всегда́.

amalgam *n.* амальга́ма.

amalgamate *v.t.* **1,** *chem.* амальгами́ровать. **2,** (merge) объединя́ть; слива́ть. —*v.i.* объединя́ться; слива́ться.

amalgamation *n.* **1,** *chem.* амальгама́ция. **2,** (mixture; blend) амальга́ма. **3,** (merger) слия́ние; объедине́ние.

amaranth *n.* амара́нт.

amaryllis *n.* амари́ллис.

amass *v.t.* накопля́ть.

amateur *n.* люби́тель; дилета́нт. —*adj.* люби́тельский; самоде́ятельный. *Amateur photographer,* фото́граф-люби́тель. *Amateur status,* ста́тус люби́теля. —**amateurish,** *adj.* дилета́нтский.

amaze *v.t.* изумля́ть. —**amazement,** *n.* изумле́ние. —**amazing,** *adj.* изуми́тельный. —**amazingly,** *adv.* изуми́тельно.

Amazon *n., myth.* амазо́нка.

ambassador *n.* посо́л. —**ambassadorial,** *adj.* посо́льский. *At the ambassadorial level,* на у́ровне посло́в.

amber *n.* янта́рь. —*adj.* янта́рный.

ambergris *n.* а́мбра.

ambiance *also,* **ambience** *n.* среда́.

ambidextrous *adj.* владе́ющий одина́ково свобо́дно обе́ими рука́ми.

ambience *n.* = **ambiance.**

ambiguous *adj.* двусмы́сленный. —**ambiguity,** *n.* двусмы́сленность.

ambition *n.* **1,** (strong desire to succeed) честолю́бие. **2,** (object of one's aspirations) стремле́ние; мечта́. —**ambitious,** *adj.* честолюби́вый.

ambivalent *adj.* двойственный: *ambivalent feelings,* дво́йственное чу́вство. —**ambivalence,** *n.* дво́йственность.

amble *n.* и́ноходь. —*v.i.* **1,** (of a horse) идти́ и́ноходью. **2,** (of a person) идти́ нога́ за́ ногу.

ambrosia *n.* амбро́зия.

ambulance *n.* маши́на ско́рой по́мощи.

ambulatory *adj.* ходя́чий: *ambulatory patient,* ходя́чий больно́й. *He is ambulatory,* он мо́жет ходи́ть.

ambush *n.* заса́да. *Lie in ambush,* быть в заса́де. —*v.t.* напада́ть на (кого́-нибудь) из заса́ды.

ameba *also,* **amoeba** *n.* амёба.

ameliorate *v.t.* улучша́ть. —*v.i.* улучша́ться. —**amelioration,** *n.* улучше́ние.

amen *interj.* ами́нь.

amenable *adj.* сгово́рчивый; покла́дистый; усту́пчивый; пода́тливый.

amend *v.t.* **1,** (revise) исправля́ть. **2,** (add amendments to) вноси́ть попра́вки в.

amendment *n.* попра́вка: *amendment to a bill,* попра́вка к законопрое́кту.

amends *n.pl.* компенсáция; возмещéние. —**make amends for,** искупáть; заглáживать.
amenity *n.* **1,** (pleasantness) приятность. **2,** *pl.* (conveniences) удóбства. **3,** *pl.* (social courtesies) прилúчия.
American *adj.* америкáнский. —*n.* америкáнец; америкáнка.
americium *n.* америций.
amethyst *n.* аметúст. —*adj.* аметúстовый.
amiable *adj.* привéтливый. —**amiability,** *n.* привéтливость.
amicability *n.* дружелю́бие.
amicable *adj.* **1,** (of personal relations) дрýжный; дрýжеский; дружелю́бный. **2,** (of an agreement, settlement, etc.) полюбóвный. —**amicably,** *adv.* дрýжно; полюбóвно.
amid *prep.* средú; посредú. *Also,* **amidst.**
amidships *adv.* в серединé корабля́.
amidst *prep.* = **amid.**
amino acid аминокислотá.
amiss *adj.* нелáдный: *something is amiss,* чтó-то нелáдно. —**take amiss,** обижáться на; толковáть в дурнýю стóрону.
amity *n.* дрýжба; соглáсие; дрýжеские отношéния.
ammeter *n.* ампермéтр.
ammonia *n.* аммиáк. *Liquid ammonia,* нашатырный спирт.
ammonium *n.* аммóний. —**ammonium chloride,** нашатырь; хлóристый аммóний. —**ammonium nitrate,** аммиáчная *or* аммóниевая селúтра. —**ammonium sulfate,** сернокúслый аммóний.
ammunition *n.* боеприпáсы. —**ammunition belt,** патрóнная лéнта; патронтáш. —**ammunition dump,** склад боеприпáсов.
amnesia *n.* потéря пáмяти.
amnesty *n.* амнúстия. *Grant amnesty to,* амнистúровать.
amoeba *n.* = **ameba.**
amok *adv.* = **amuck.**
among *prep.* **1,** (in between; surrounded by) средú: *be among friends,* быть средú друзéй. *First among equals,* пéрвый средú рáвных. **2,** (with one another) мéжду (собóй): *They quarreled among themselves,* онú поссóрились мéжду собóй. **3,** (in the opinion of many) у: *very popular among young people,* óчень популя́рен у молодёжи. *Also,* **amongst.**
amoral *adj.* аморáльный. —**amorality,** *n.* аморáльность.
amorous *adj.* любóвный; влюбчивый. —**amorousness,** *n.* влюбчивость.
amorphous *adj.* бесфóрменный; амóрфный.
amortize *v.t.* амортизúровать. —**amortization,** *n.* амортизáция.
amount *n.* **1,** (sum) сýмма: *the total amount,* óбщая сýмма. **2,** (quantity) колúчество: *a huge amount,* огрóмное колúчество. —*v.i.* [*usu.* **amount to**] **1,** (equal in total) составля́ть; выражáться в сýмме (+*gen.*). **2,** (be equivalent to) равня́ться (+ *dat.*); быть равносúльным (+*dat.*). *It amounts to the same thing,* всё равнó; э́то то же сáмое. **3,** *fol. by* **something, anything,** *etc.* (achieve success): *he'll never amount to anything,* из негó никогдá ничегó не вы́йдет; из негó ничегó пýтного не вы́йдет.
ampere *n.* ампéр.
ampersand *n.* знак &.
amphibian *n.* земновóдное живóтное; амфúбия.
amphibious *adj.* **1,** (of an animal) земновóдный. **2,** (of a vehicle) плáвающий. **3,** *mil.* морскóй десáнтный. *Amphibious landing,* вы́садка морскóго десáнта.
amphitheater *also,* **amphitheatre** *n.* амфитеáтр.
ample *adj.* **1,** (abundant) обúльный. **2,** (sufficient) достáточный. **3,** (spacious) простóрный.
amplification *n.* **1,** (enlargement) расширéние. **2,** (fuller statement) уточнéние. **3,** *electronics* усилéние; звукоусилéние. *Amplification system,* систéма звукоусилéния.
amplifier *n.* усилúтель.
amplify *v.t.* **1,** (enlarge) расширя́ть. **2,** (enlarge upon, as a statement) уточня́ть. **3,** *electronics* усúливать.
amplitude *n.* **1,** (extent) широтá. **2,** *physics* амплитýда.
amply *adv.* щéдро: *amply rewarded,* щéдро награждён.
ampule *also,* **ampoule** *n.* áмпула.
amputate *v.t.* ампутúровать; отнимáть. —**amputation,** *n.* ампутáция.
amuck *adv., in* **run amuck,** бýйствовать; буя́нить.
amulet *n.* амулéт; лáданка.
amuse *v.t.* развлекáть; забавля́ть. *He is not amused,* емý не смешнó. —**amuse oneself,** развлекáться; забавля́ться.
amusement *n.* **1,** (entertainment) развлечéние; забáва. **2,** (state of being amused) весéлье. —**amusement park,** парк с аттракциóнами; увеселúтельный сад; лýна-пáрк.
amusing *adj.* смешнóй; забáвный; занимáтельный.
an *indef. art., var. of* **a.**
Anabaptism *n.* анабаптúзм. —**Anabaptist,** *n.* анабаптúст.
anachronism *n.* анахронúзм. —**anachronistic,** *adj.* анахронúческий.
anaconda *n.* анакóнда.
anaemia *n.* = **anemia.** —**anaemic,** *adj.* = **anemic.**
anaerobe *n.* анаэрóб. —**anaerobic,** *adj.* анаэрóбный.
anaesthesia *n.* = **anesthesia.** —**anaesthetic,** *adj.* & *n.* = **anesthetic.** —**anaesthetize,** *v.* = **anesthetize.**
anagram *n.* анагрáмма.
anal *adj.* заднепрохóдный; анáльный.
analgesic *adj.* болеутоля́ющий. —*n.* болеутоля́ющее срéдство.
analogous *adj.* аналогúчный.
analogy *n.* аналóгия. *By analogy with,* по аналóгии с.
analyse *v.* = **analyze.**
analysis *n.* анáлиз; разбóр. —**in the final analysis,** в конéчном итóге; в конéчном счёте.
analyst *n.* аналúтик.
analytic *also,* **analytical** *adj.* аналитúческий. —**analytic geometry,** аналитúческая геомéтрия.
analyze *also,* **analyse** *v.t.* разбирáть; анализúровать.
anapest *n.* анáпест.
anarchic *adj.* анархúчный.
anarchism *n.* анархúзм. —**anarchist,** *n.* анархúст. —**anarchistic,** *adj.* анархúческий.

anarchy *n.* ана́рхия.
anathema *n.* ана́фема. —**anathematize,** *v.t.* предава́ть ана́феме.
anatomy *n.* анато́мия. —**anatomical,** *adj.* анатоми́ческий. —**anatomist,** *n.* ана́том. —**anatomize,** *v.t.* анатоми́ровать.
ancestor *n.* пре́док. —**ancestral,** *adj.* родово́й. —**ancestry,** *n.* происхожде́ние.
anchor *n.* я́корь. *At anchor,* на я́коре. —*v.t.* ста́вить на я́корь. —*v.i.* станови́ться на я́корь.
anchorage *n.* я́корная стоя́нка.
anchorite *n.* отше́льник; затво́рник.
anchovy *n.* анчо́ус.
ancient *adj.* дре́вний; стари́нный; анти́чный. —**the ancients,** дре́вние.
ancillary *adj.* вспомога́тельный; подсо́бный.
and *conj.* и: *cause and effect,* причи́на и сле́дствие. ♦*Sometimes rendered by* с: *you and I,* мы с ва́ми; *bread and butter,* хлеб с ма́слом. ♦*When in contrast* а: *he is Russian and she is French,* он ру́сский, а она́ францу́женка.
andante *adv. & n.* анда́нте.
andiron *n.* подста́вка для дров.
anecdote *n.* анекдо́т. —**anecdotal,** *adj.* анекдоти́ческий.
anemia *also,* **anaemia** *n.* малокро́вие; анеми́я. —**anemic; anaemic,** *adj.* малокро́вный; анеми́чный.
anemometer *n.* анемо́метр; ветроме́р.
anemone *n.* анемо́н; ве́треница. —**sea anemone,** акти́ния.
anent *prep., archaic* относи́тельно.
aneroid barometer анеро́ид.
anesthesia *also,* **anaesthesia** *n.* анестези́я; нарко́з. —**anesthesiologist,** *n.* анестезио́лог.
anesthetic *also,* **anaesthetic** *adj.* анестези́рующий; обезбо́ливающий. —*n.* анестези́рующее/обезбо́ливающее сре́дство.
anesthetize *also,* **anaesthetize** *v.t.* анестези́ровать; обезбо́ливать. —**anesthetization,** *n.* обезбо́ливание.
anew *adv.* сно́ва; за́ново.
angel *n.* а́нгел. —**angelic,** *adj.* а́нгельский.
angelica *n.* дя́гиль; ду́дник.
anger *n.* гнев. *In anger,* в гне́ве. —*v.t.* серди́ть.
angina *n.* анги́на. —**angina pectoris,** грудна́я жа́ба; стенокарди́я.
angle *n.* **1,** *geom.* у́гол: *right angle,* прямо́й у́гол. **2,** (aspect; point of view) то́чка зре́ния; у́гол зре́ния. *Consider a question from all angles,* рассма́тривать вопро́с со всех сторо́н (*or* на все лады́).—*v.i.* **1,** (fish) уди́ть ры́бу. **2,** *fol. by* **for** (slyly try to obtain) напра́шиваться на.
angler *n.* уди́льщик.
Anglican *adj.* англика́нский.
Anglicism *n.* англици́зм.
Anglicize *v.t.* англизи́ровать.
angling *n.* уже́ние.
Anglophile *n.* англофи́л.
Anglo-Saxon *adj.* англосаксо́нский.
angrily *adv.* серди́то.
angry *adj.* серди́тый. *Be angry,* серди́ться. *Don't be angry with him,* не серди́тесь на него́. *Become/get angry,* рассерди́ться. *Make someone angry,* рассерди́ть кого́-нибудь.
anguish *n.* му́ка; страда́ние. —**anguished,** *adj.* мучи́тельный: *anguished cry,* мучи́тельный крик.
angular *adj.* **1,** (having many angles) углова́тый: *angular features,* углова́тые черты́. **2,** (measured by an angle) углово́й: *angular velocity,* углова́я ско́рость. **3,** (gaunt) костля́вый. **4,** (lacking grace; stiff) углова́тый.
aniline *n.* анили́н. —**aniline dye,** анили́новая кра́ска.
animal *n.* живо́тное. —*adj.* живо́тный: *animal fat,* живо́тный жир. —**animal husbandry,** животново́дство.
animate *v.t.* оживля́ть. —*adj.* одушевлённый: *animate creature,* одушевлённое существо́.
animated *adj.* оживлённый. —**animated cartoon,** мультипликацио́нный фильм.
animation *n.* оживле́ние. *With* (*great*) *animation,* оживлённо; живо.
animism *n.* аними́зм. —**animist,** *n.* аними́ст. —**animistic,** *adj.* анимисти́ческий.
animosity *n.* вражде́бность; вражда́.
anise *n.* ани́с. —*adj.* ани́совый.
anisette *n.* ани́совка.
ankle *n.* лоды́жка; щи́колотка. *Sprain one's ankle,* подверну́ть себе́ но́гу.
annals *n.pl.* анна́лы.
anneal *v.t.* **1,** (heat) отжига́ть. **2,** *fig.* (temper) закаля́ть.
annex *v.t.* присоединя́ть; аннекси́ровать. —*n.* **1,** (subsidiary building) пристро́йка. **2,** (supplement) приложе́ние (к догово́ру). —**annexation,** *n.* присоедине́ние; анне́ксия.
annihilate *v.t.* уничтожа́ть; истребля́ть. —**annihilation,** *n.* уничтоже́ние; истребле́ние.
anniversary *n.* годовщи́на; юбиле́й. ♦*Specific anniversaries are rendered with the suffix* -ле́тие: *tenth anniversary,* десятиле́тие. *The fiftieth anniversary of his death,* пятидесятиле́тие со дня его́ сме́рти. —*adj.* юбиле́йный: *anniversary year,* юбиле́йный год.
annotate *v.t.* комменти́ровать. —**annotation,** *n.* коммента́рий.
announce *v.t.* **1,** (declare publicly) заявля́ть; объявля́ть; сообща́ть. **2,** (state the arrival or presence of) докла́дывать о: *announce a visitor,* докла́дывать о посети́теле.
announcement *n.* **1,** (statement) заявле́ние: *make an announcement,* сде́лать заявле́ние. **2,** (public notice) объявле́ние.
announcer *n.* ди́ктор.
annoy *v.t.* досажда́ть; раздража́ть. —**annoyance,** *n.* доса́да. —**annoyed,** *adj.* раздражён. —**annoying,** *adj.* доса́дный. *How annoying*!, кака́я доса́да!
annual *adj.* **1,** (occurring once a year) ежего́дный. **2,** (pertaining to a given year) годово́й. **3,** *bot.* одноле́тний. —*n.* **1,** (publication) ежего́дник. **2,** (plant) одноле́тнее расте́ние. —**annually,** *adv.* ежего́дно.
annuity *n.* ежего́дная ре́нта.
annul *v.t.* аннули́ровать; отменя́ть. —**annulment,** *n.* аннули́рование; отме́на.
Annunciation *n., relig.* благове́щение.
anode *n.* ано́д.
anoint *v.t.* пома́зывать. —**anointment,** *n.* пома́зание.
anomaly *n.* анома́лия. —**anomalous,** *adj.* анома́льный.

anonymity *n.* анони́мность.
anonymous *adj.* анони́мный. —**anonymously,** *adv.* анони́мно.
anopheles *n.* ано́фелес.
another *adj. & pron.* **1,** (one more) ещё (оди́н): *another glass of milk,* ещё стака́н молока́. **2,** (a different) друго́й: *that's quite another matter,* э́то совсе́м друго́е де́ло. —**one another,** друг дру́га. —**one way or another,** так и́ли ина́че.
answer *v.t. & i.* отвеча́ть. *Answer someone,* отвеча́ть кому́-нибудь. *Answer a question,* отвеча́ть на вопро́с. *Answer the telephone,* подходи́ть к телефо́ну. *Answer the door,* открыва́ть дверь. *Answer the purpose,* отвеча́ть це́ли. *Answer for one's actions,* отвеча́ть за свои́ посту́пки. —*n.* **1,** (reply) отве́т. *In answer to,* в отве́т на (+*acc.*). **2,** (solution) реше́ние: *answer to a problem,* реше́ние зада́чи. —**answer back,** груби́ть; дерзи́ть.
answerable *adj.* отве́тственный. *Be answerable for,* отвеча́ть за.
ant *n.* мураве́й.
antagonism *n.* антагони́зм; вражда́. —**antagonist,** *n.* антагони́ст. —**antagonistic,** *adj.* антагонисти́ческий; вражде́бный.
antagonize *v.t.* восстана́вливать про́тив себя́; отта́лкивать.
antarctic *adj.* антаркти́ческий. —**Antarctic Circle,** Ю́жный поля́рный круг.
ante *n.* ста́вка. *Raise the ante,* повы́сить ста́вку.
anteater *n.* муравье́д. —**spiny anteater,** ехи́дна.
antecedent *n.* **1,** (something that goes before) предше́ствующее собы́тие. **2,** *pl.* (ancestors) пре́дки.
antechamber *n.* пере́дняя; прихо́жая; аванза́л.
antedate *v.t.* **1,** (come before) предше́ствовать. **2,** (put an earlier date on) поме́тить за́дним число́м.
antediluvian *adj.* допото́пный.
antelope *n.* антило́па.
antenna *n.* анте́нна.
anterior *adj.* **1,** (forward; front) пере́дний. **2,** (coming earlier) предше́ствующий.
anteroom *n.* пере́дняя; приёмная; аванза́л.
anthem *n.* гимн: *national anthem,* госуда́рственный гимн.
anther *n.* пы́льник.
anthill *n.* мураве́йник.
anthology *n.* антоло́гия; сбо́рник.
anthracite *n.* антраци́т. —*adj.* антраци́тный; антраци́товый.
anthrax *n.* сиби́рская я́зва.
anthropoid *n.* антропо́ид. —*adj.* человекообра́зный.
anthropology *n.* антрополо́гия. —**anthropological,** *adj.* антропологи́ческий. —**anthropologist,** *n.* антропо́лог.
anthropomorphism *n.* антропоморфи́зм. —**anthropomorphic,** *adj.* антропоморфи́ческий. —**anthropomorphous,** *adj.* человекообра́зный.
antiaircraft *adj.* зени́тный.
anti-American *adj.* антиамерика́нский. —**anti-Americanism,** *n.* антиамерикани́зм.
anti-ballistic missile антираке́та.
antibiotic *n.* антибио́тик.
antibody *n.* антите́ло.
antic *n., usu. pl.* ша́лости; вы́ходки.
Antichrist *n.* анти́христ.
anticipate *v.t.* **1,** (foresee) предви́деть. **2,** (expect) ожида́ть. **3,** (foresee and deal with in advance) предупрежда́ть; предвосхища́ть.
anticipation *n.* **1,** (expectation) ожида́ние; предви́дение: *in anticipation of,* в ожида́нии/предви́дении (+ *gen.*). **2,** (dealing with in advance) предвосхище́ние. **3,** (eagerness) нетерпе́ние.
anticommunism *n.* антикоммуни́зм.
anticommunist *n.* антикоммуни́ст. —*adj.* антикоммунисти́ческий.
antidote *n.* противоя́дие.
antifreeze *n.* антифри́з.
antigen *n.* антиге́н.
antimatter *n.* антивещество́.
antimony *n.* сурьма́.
anti-party *adj.* антиparти́йный.
antipathetic *adj.* **1,** *fol. by* **to** (averse) настро́ен про́тив. **2,** (causing antipathy) антипати́чный.
antipathy *n.* антипа́тия.
anti-personnel *adj., mil.* оско́лочный; противопехо́тный.
antiquary *n.* антиква́р. *Also,* **antiquarian.**
antiquated *adj.* устаре́лый; устаре́вший.
antique *adj.* стари́нный; антиква́рный. —*n.* антиква́рная вещь. *Antique dealer,* антиква́р. *Antique shop,* антиква́рный магази́н.
antiquity *n.* **1,** (ancient times; great age) дре́вность; анти́чность. **2,** *pl.* (ancient relics) дре́вности.
antireligious *adj.* антирелигио́зный.
anti-Semite *n.* антисеми́т. —**anti-Semitic,** *adj.* антисеми́тский. —**anti-Semitism,** *n.* антисемити́зм.
antisepsis *n.* антисе́птика.
antiseptic *adj.* антисепти́ческий. —*n.* антисепти́ческое сре́дство.
antisocial *adj.* **1,** (harmful to society) антиобще́ственный. **2,** (unsociable) необщи́тельный.
anti-Soviet *adj.* антисове́тский.
antitank *adj.* противота́нковый.
antithesis *n.* **1,** (opposite) антите́за. **2,** *logic* антите́зис. —**antithetical,** *adj.* антитети́ческий.
antitoxin *n.* антитокси́н. —**antitoxic,** *adj.* антитокси́ческий.
antiwar *adj.* антивое́нный.
antler *n.* (оле́ний) рог.
antonym *n.* анто́ним.
anus *n.* за́дний прохо́д.
anvil *n.* накова́льня.
anxiety *n.* беспоко́йство; озабо́ченность.
anxious *adj.* **1,** (worried) озабо́ченный; неспоко́йный; трево́жный. *Anxious moment,* трево́жный моме́нт. **2,** (eager): *be anxious to,* о́чень хоте́ться (+ *dat.*). *We are very anxious to see you,* мы вас о́чень ждём.
anxiously *adv.* с нетерпе́нием: *anxiously await,* ждать с нетерпе́нием.
any *adj. & pron.* **1,** (no matter which; every) любо́й; вся́кий: *any time,* в любо́е вре́мя; *in any case,* во вся́ком слу́чае; *at any price,* любо́й ceно́й; *any of you,* любо́й из вас. **2,** (some) како́й-нибудь: *have you any questions?,* у вас есть каки́е-нибудь вопро́сы? *Have you any money?,* у вас есть де́ньги? ♦*In neg. sentences* никако́й: *I didn't buy any books,* я не покупа́л(а) никаки́х книг. *We haven't any flour today,* у нас сего́дня нет муки́. *I don't see any,* не ви́жу ни одного́. **3,** *Any minute,* с мину́ты на ми-

ну́ту; *any day* (*now*), со дня на́ день. —*adv. Not rendered in Russian: is he any better today?*, ему́ лу́чше сего́дня? ♦*In neg. sentences* ниско́лько: *he is not any better today,* ему́ сего́дня ниско́лько не лу́чше. —**any more, 1,** (some more) ещё: *have you any more questions?*, у вас есть ещё вопро́сы? **2,** (no more) бо́льше: *I haven't any more money,* у меня́ нет бо́льше де́нег. *See also* **anymore.**

anybody *pron.* = **anyone.**

anyhow *adv.* **1,** (in any case) во вся́ком слу́чае. **2,** (just the same) всё-таки; всё же.

anymore *adv.* бо́льше: *I don't go there anymore,* я бо́льше не хожу́ туда́.

anyone *pron.* **1,** *in affirmative sentences* любо́й; вся́кий; ка́ждый; кто уго́дно: *anyone can do it,* любо́й/вся́кий/ка́ждый мо́жет э́то сде́лать. *Ask anyone,* спроси́те кого́ уго́дно. **2,** *in interr. and hypothetical sentences* кто́-нибудь: *did you see anyone?*, вы ви́дели кого́-нибудь? **3,** *in neg. sentences* никого́: *I didn't see anyone,* я никого́ не ви́дел(а). *Neither he nor anyone else,* ни он и никто́ друго́й.

anyplace *adv., colloq.* = **anywhere.**

anything *pron.* **1,** *in affirmative sentences* всё; вся́кое; всё, что уго́дно. *Anything is possible,* всё возмо́жно; вся́кое быва́ет. *I would give anything to...*, всё отда́м, что́бы... **2,** *in interr. and hypothetical sentences* что́-нибудь: *do you want anything to drink?*, вы хоти́те что́-нибудь вы́пить? **3,** *in neg. sentences* ничего́: *I don't know anything,* я ничего́ не зна́ю. —**anything but,** совсе́м не: *anything but cheap,* совсе́м не дешёвый.

anytime *adv.* **1,** (at any time) в любо́е вре́мя; когда́ уго́дно. **2,** (whenever) когда́ бы ни; вся́кий раз, когда́.

anyway *adv.* = **anyhow.**

anywhere *adv.* **1,** *in affirmative sentences* где *or* куда́ уго́дно; где *or* куда́ бы то ни́ было. **2,** *in interr. and hypothetical sentences* где́-нибудь; куда́-нибудь. **3,** *in neg. sentences* нигде́; никуда́.

aorta *n.* ао́рта.

apace *adv.* по́лным хо́дом: *proceed apace,* идти́ по́лным хо́дом.

apart *adv.* **1,** (separately) врозь; по́рознь; отде́льно. **2,** (into pieces) на ча́сти. *Take apart,* разбира́ть. —**apart from,** поми́мо. —**tell apart,** различа́ть.

apartheid *n.* апартеид.

apartment *n.* кварти́ра. —**apartment house,** жило́й дом.

apathetic *adj.* апати́чный.

apathy *n.* апа́тия.

ape *n.* обезья́на. —*v.t.* обезья́нничать. —**ape-like,** *adj.* обезья́ний; обезьяноподо́бный. —**ape-man,** *n.* обезьяночелове́к.

aperture *n.* отве́рстие; аперту́ра.

apex *n.* верши́на.

aphasia *n.* афа́зия.

aphelion *n.* афе́лий.

aphorism *n.* афори́зм. —**aphoristic,** *adj.* афористи́ческий; афористи́чный.

apiary *n.* па́сека; пче́льник.

apiece *adv.* **1,** (per item) за шту́ку. **2,** (per person) за *or* на ка́ждого.

aplomb *n.* апло́мб.

apocalypse *n.* апока́липсис. —**apocalyptic,** *adj.* апокалипси́ческий.

Apocrypha *n.pl.* апо́крифы.

Apocryphal *adj.* **1,** (pert. to the Apocrypha) апокрифи́ческий. **2,** *l.c.* (of doubtful authenticity) недостове́рный.

apogee *n.* апоге́й.

apolitical *adj.* аполити́чный.

Apollo *n.* Аполло́н.

apologetic *adj.* извиня́ющийся. *He was very apologetic,* он о́чень извиня́лся. —**apologetically,** *adv.* извиня́ющимся то́ном.

apologetics *n.* апологе́тика.

apologia *n.* аполо́гия.

apologist *n.* апологе́т.

apologize *v.i.* извиня́ться.

apology *n.* извине́ние.

apoplexy *n.* апопле́ксия. —**apoplectic,** *adj.* апоплекси́ческий.

apostasy *n.* отсту́пничество. —**apostate,** *n.* отсту́пник. —*adj.* отсту́пнический.

a posteriori **1,** *used adverbially* апостерио́ри. **2,** *used adjectivally* апостерио́рный.

apostle *n.* апо́стол. —**apostolic,** *adj.* апо́стольский.

apostrophe *n.* апостро́ф.

apothecary *n.* апте́карь.

apotheosis *n.* апофео́з.

appall *also,* **appal** *v.t.* ужаса́ть; приводи́ть в у́жас. *Be appalled,* ужаса́ться; быть в у́жасе; приходи́ть в у́жас. —**appalling,** *adj.* у́жасный; вопию́щий.

apparatus *n.* **1,** (device) аппара́т; прибо́р. **2,** (group of instruments) аппарату́ра. **3,** *sports* гимнасти́ческие снаря́ды. **4,** (system of organization) аппара́т: *spy apparatus,* шпио́нский аппара́т.

apparel *n.* оде́жда; наря́д. *Apparel shop,* магази́н гото́вого пла́тья.

apparent *adj.* ви́димый: *for no apparent reason,* без ви́димой причи́ны. *It is apparent that...*, ви́дно, что...

apparently *adv.* ви́димо; по-ви́димому.

apparition *n.* виде́ние; при́зрак; привиде́ние.

appeal *v.i.* **1,** (earnestly request) обраща́ться; призыва́ть. *Appeal to someone for help,* обраща́ться к кому́-нибудь за по́мощью. *Appeal for unity,* призыва́ть к еди́нству. **2,** *fol. by* **to** (strike favorably) нра́виться. *It doesn't appeal to me,* э́то мне не улыба́ется. **3,** *law* апелли́ровать; подава́ть кассацио́нную жа́лобу. —*v.t.* обжа́ловать: *appeal a verdict,* обжа́ловать пригово́р. —*n.* **1,** (call for aid or support) обраще́ние; призы́в; воззва́ние. **2,** (attraction) привлека́тельность. **3,** *law* (general procedure) обжа́лование: *right of appeal,* пра́во обжа́лования; (request so made) апелля́ция; кассацио́нная жа́лоба. —**appealing,** *adj.* привлека́тельный.

appear *v.i.* **1,** (come into view) появля́ться. **2,** (present oneself; show up) явля́ться; предста́ть: *appear in/before the/court,* яви́ться в суд; предста́ть пе́ред судо́м. **3,** (perform) выступа́ть (на сце́не). **4,** (be published) выходи́ть (в свет). **5,** (seem) каза́ться; представля́ться. *The rain appears to have stopped,* дождь как бу́дто ко́нчился.

appearance *n.* **1,** (coming into sight) появле́ние. *Put in an appearance,* появля́ться. **2,** (coming into public view) выступле́ние: *television appearance,* выступле́ние по телеви́дению. **3,** (outward aspect) вид; о́блик. *External appearance,* вне́шность; нару́жность. *For appearance's sake,* для ви́да. —**from**

appointment *n.* **1,** (act of appointing or being appointed) назначе́ние. **2,** (scheduled meeting) свида́ние; (делова́я) встре́ча. *I have an appointment,* мне назна́чена делова́я встре́ча. *Make an appointment with the doctor,* записа́ться к врачу́. *I have a doctor's appointment,* мне назна́чено прийти́ к врачу́. **3,** *pl.* (furnishings) обстано́вка.

apportion *v.t.* распределя́ть; выделя́ть. —**apportionment,** *n.* распределе́ние; выделе́ние.

apposition *n., gram.* приложе́ние.

appraisal *n.* оце́нка.

appraise *v.t.* оце́нивать. —**appraiser,** *n.* оце́нщик.

appreciable *adj.* заме́тный; ощути́мый.

appreciate *v.t.* **1,** (see the value of; recognize gratefully) цени́ть. **2,** (realize; be aware of) понима́ть; отдава́ть себе́ отчёт в. —*v.i.* повыша́ться в цене́.

appreciation *n.* **1,** (gratitude) призна́тельность. **2,** (sensitive awareness) понима́ние. **3,** (rise in value) повыше́ние сто́имости.

appreciative *adj.* призна́тельный.

apprehend *v.t.* **1,** (take into custody) арестова́ть; брать под стра́жу. **2,** (comprehend; grasp) постига́ть.

apprehension *n.* **1,** (arrest) задержа́ние; аре́ст. **2,** (intuitive understanding) восприя́тие. **3,** (fear; dread) опасе́ние.

apprehensive *adj.* озабо́ченный; беспоко́йный. —**apprehensiveness,** *n.* озабо́ченность; беспоко́йство.

apprentice *n.* учени́к; подмасте́рье. —*v.t.* отдава́ть в уче́ние. —**apprenticeship,** *n.* уче́ние; учени́чество.

apprise *v.t.* извеща́ть; осведомля́ть; уведомля́ть; информи́ровать.

approach *v.i.* подходи́ть; приближа́ться. —*v.t.* **1,** (walk up to; draw near to) подходи́ть к; приближа́ться к. **2,** (make an appeal or proposal to) обраща́ться к. **3,** (begin to deal with) подходи́ть к. —*n.* **1,** (drawing near) приближе́ние. **2,** (way by which a place is reached) подхо́д. *The approaches to a city,* по́дступы к го́роду. **3,** (method of approach, as to a problem) подхо́д.

approachable *adj.* досту́пный.

approbation *n.* одобре́ние; апроба́ция.

appropriate *v.t.* **1,** (allot; allocate) ассигнова́ть. **2,** (take possession of) присва́ивать. —*adj.* **1,** (what is suitable or needed) соотве́тствующий; подходя́щий; надлежа́щий. **2,** (apt) уме́стный. —**appropriately,** *adv.* уме́стно.

appropriation *n.* **1,** (allotment of funds; funds so allotted) ассигнова́ние. **2,** (taking over; seizure) присвое́ние.

approval *n.* одобре́ние.

approve *v.i.* [*usu.* **approve of**] одобря́ть. —*v.t.* утвержда́ть; одобря́ть: *approve a plan,* утвержда́ть/одобря́ть план.

approving *adj.* одобри́тельный. —**approvingly,** *adv.* одобри́тельно.

approximate *adj.* приблизи́тельный. —*v.t.* приближа́ться к. —**approximately,** *adv.* приблизи́тельно; приме́рно. —**approximation,** *n.* приблизи́тельный подсчёт.

appurtenance *n.* **1,** (adjunct) прида́ток. **2,** *pl.* (accessories) принадле́жности.

apricot *n.* абрико́с. *Dried apricots,* курага́; урю́к. —*adj.* абрико́совый.

April *n.* апре́ль. —*adj.* апре́льский.
a priori 1, *used adverbially* априо́ри. 2, *used adjectivally* априо́рный.
apron *n.* пере́дник; фа́ртук. —**be tied to someone's apron springs,** быть под башмако́м у кого́-нибудь.
apropos *adv.* кста́ти. —*adj.* уме́стный. —**apropos of,** относи́тельно; в свя́зи с.
apse *n.* апси́да. *Also,* **apsis.**
apt *adj.* 1, (pertinent) уда́чный; ме́ткий. 2, (quick to learn) спосо́бный. 3, *fol. by* **to** (inclined; likely) скло́нный (к). *In such weather one is apt to catch cold,* в таку́ю пого́ду мо́жно легко́ простуди́ться.
aptitude *n.* спосо́бности: *an aptitude for languages,* спосо́бности к языка́м.
aptly *adv.* уме́стно; уда́чно.
aqualung *n.* аквала́нг.
aquamarine *n.* аквамари́н. —*adj.* аквамари́новый.
aquarium *n.* аква́риум.
Aquarius *n.* Водоле́й.
aquatic *adj.* водяно́й. *Aquatic sports,* во́дный спорт.
aquatint *n.* аквати́нта.
aqueduct *n.* акведу́к.
aquiline *adj.* орли́ный: *aquiline nose,* орли́ный нос.
Arab *n.* ара́б. —*adj.* ара́бский: *Arab countries,* ара́бские стра́ны.
arabesque *n.* арабе́ска.
Arabian *adj.* арави́йский.
Arabic *adj.* ара́бский. —*n.* ара́бский язы́к. *Speak Arabic,* говори́ть по-ара́бски. —**Arabic numerals,** ара́бские ци́фры.
arable *adj.* па́хотный.
Aramaic *adj.* араме́йский. —*n.* араме́йский язы́к.
arbiter *n.* 1, *law* арби́тр; трете́йский судья́. 2, (one who decides) законода́тель: *arbiter of fashions,* законода́тель мод.
arbitrary *adj.* произво́льный; самоупра́вный; самочи́нный. —**arbitrarily,** *adv.* произво́льно. —**arbitrariness,** *n.* произво́л; самоупра́вство.
arbitrate *v.t.* реша́ть в арбитра́жном поря́дке. —**arbitration,** *n.* арбитра́ж. *Court of arbitration,* трете́йский суд. —**arbitrator,** *n.* арби́тр; трете́йский судья́.
arbor *also,* **arbour** *n.* бесе́дка.
arboretum *n.* дендра́рий.
arc *n.* дуга́.
arcade *n.* 1, *archit.* арка́да. 2, (covered passageway with shops) пасса́ж.
arcane *adj.* зау́мный.
arch *n.* 1, (curved structure) а́рка; свод. 2, (curve of the foot) свод стопы́. *Fallen arches,* плоскосто́пие. —*adj.* 1, (sly) лука́вый. 2, [*usu.* **arch-**] (notorious) архи-: *arch-liar,* архилгу́н. —*v.t.* выгиба́ть: *arch one's back,* выгиба́ть спи́ну.
archaeology *n.* = **archeology.** —**archaeological,** *adj.* = **archeological.** —**archaeologist,** *n.* = **archeologist.**
archaic *adj.* архаи́ческий; устаре́вший. —**archaism,** *n.* архаи́зм.
archangel *n.* арха́нгел.
archbishop *n.* архиепи́скоп.
archdeacon *n.* архидья́кон; *Orth. Ch.* протодья́кон.
archdiocese *n.* епа́рхия архиепи́скопа.
archduke *n.* эрцге́рцог. —**archduchess,** *n.* эрцгерцоги́ня. —**archduchy,** *n.* эрцге́рцогство.
arched *adj.* а́рочный; сво́дчатый; дугообра́зный.

archenemy *n.* закля́тый
archeology *also,* **archa**
—**archeological,** *adj.* архе
logist, *n.* архео́лог.
archer *n.* стрело́к из лу́ка
из лу́ка.
archetype *n.* прототи́п; с
archimandrite *n.* архим
archipelago *n.* архипела́
architect *n.* архите́ктор.
architecture *n.* архитект
tectural, *adj.* архитекту́рн
archives *n.pl.* архи́в. —**ar**
arch support супина́тор
archway *n.* сво́дчатый п
arctic *adj.* аркти́ческий; п
Се́верный поля́рный круг
ный Ледови́тый океа́н.
ardent *adj.* стра́стный; ре́
чий. —**ardently,** *adv.* стра́
ardor *also,* **ardour** *n.* пы
arduous *adj.* тру́дный; тя
area *n.* 1, (two-dimensional
of a circle, пло́щадь кру́г
idential area, жило́й райо́
площа́дка: *loading area,* п
(field, as of study or intere
странове́дение.
arena *n.* аре́на.
Argentinean *adj.* [*also,*
—*n.* аргенти́нец; аргенти́
argon *n.* арго́н.
argot *n.* арго́; жарго́н.
argue *v.i.* (engage in an a
(plead, as a case) вести́ (д
да́ть; дока́зывать.
argument *n.* 1, (quarrel)
спо́рить. 2, (objection) в
ment!, без возраже́ний!
каки́х разгово́ров! 3, (re
аргуме́нт: *strong argum*
ме́нт. —**argumentation,**
mentative, *adj.* лю́бящий
aria *n.* а́рия.
arid *adj.* сухо́й; засу́шли
n. су́хость.
Aries *n.* Ове́н.
arise *v.i.* 1, (get up) в
возника́ть; создава́ться.
aristocracy *n.* аристок
стокра́т. —**aristocratic**
аристократи́чный.
arithmetic *n.* арифме́т
cal] арифмети́ческий.
ark *n.* 1, (boat) ковче́г
2, (receptacle in the syn
covenant, ковче́г заве́та
arm *n.* 1, (part of the bod
нести́ на рука́х. *Under*
(of a chair, sofa, etc.) ру́ч
рука́в. 4, *pl.* (weapons)
—*v.i.* вооружа́ться. —**a**
arm's length, на почти́т
open arms, с распрост
armada *n.* арма́да.

armadillo *n.* броненосец.
armament *n.* **1,** (act of arming) вооружение. **2,** *pl.* (arms) вооружения. *The armaments industry,* военная промышленность.
armature *n.* якорь; арматура.
armband *n.* (нарукавная) повязка.
armchair *n.* кресло. —*adj.* кабинетный: *armchair strategist,* кабинетный стратег.
armed *adj.* вооружённый. —**armed forces,** вооружённые силы.
Armenian *adj.* армянский. —*n.* **1,** (person) армянин; армянка. **2,** (language) армянский язык.
armful *n.* охапка.
armhole *n.* пройма.
armistice *n.* перемирие.
armor *also,* **armour** *n.* **1,** (worn by medieval knights) броня; панцирь; доспехи; латы. *Suit of armor,* латные доспехи. **2,** (for warships, tanks, etc.) броня. **3,** *mil.* (armored vehicles) бронированные машины. —*v.t.* бронировать.
armored *adj.* **1,** (protected by armor) броневой; бронированный. *Armored car,* бронеавтомобиль; броневик. *Armored personnel carrier,* бронетранспортёр. **2,** (equipped with armored vehicles) бронетанковый: *armored division,* бронетанковая дивизия.
armor plate броневая плита; броневой лист. *Also,* **armor plating.**
armory *also,* **armoury** *n.* арсенал; склад оружия.
armour *n.* = **armor.** —**armoury,** *n.* = **armory.**
armpit *n.* подмышка.
armrest *n.* подлокотник.
arms *n.pl.* оружие. *Arms race,* гонка вооружений. —**be up in arms over,** встретить в штыки. —**by force of arms,** силой оружия. —**to arms!,** к оружию! —**under arms,** под ружьём.
army *n.* армия. —*adj.* армейский: *army corps,* армейский корпус.
aroma *n.* аромат. —**aromatic,** *adj.* ароматный; душистый.
around *prep.* **1,** (encircling) вокруг: *travel around the world,* путешествовать вокруг света. **2,** (so as to avoid or get past) *rendered by the prefix* об-: *walk around the puddle,* обходить лужу. **3,** (by turning) за: *around the corner,* за углом. **4,** (here and there in) по: *walk around town,* ходить по городу. **5,** *colloq.* (approximately) около: *around six dollars,* около шести долларов. —*adv.* кругом; вокруг. *Turn around,* поворачиваться (кругом); оборачиваться. *There is no one around,* никого нет кругом. *For miles around,* за много миль.
arouse *v.t.* **1,** (awaken) будить. **2,** (stir to action) возбуждать. **3,** (evoke, as a feeling) возбуждать; вызывать.
arpeggio *n.* арпеджио.
arquebus *n.* пищаль.
arraign *v.t.* привлекать к суду. —**arraignment,** *n.* привлечение к суду.
arrange *v.t.* **1,** (put in correct order) располагать; расставлять. **2,** (organize) устраивать. **3,** *music* аранжировать. —*v.i.* **1,** *fol. by inf.* (agree) договариваться; условливаться; сговариваться. **2,** *fol. by* **for** (see to it that) распоряжаться, чтобы.
arrangement *n.* **1,** (act of arranging; order) расположение; устройство. *A flower arrangement,* композиция цветов; букет. *Table arrangement,* сервировка стола. **2,** (agreement) соглашение; (terms of same) порядок: *I suggest this arrangement,* я предлагаю такой порядок. **3,** (way something is to be done) план; вариант: *I suggest a different arrangement,* я предлагаю другой план/вариант. **4,** *pl.* (plans; preparations) меры; приготовления. **5,** *music* аранжировка; переложение.
arrant *adj.* **1,** (notorious) отъявленный. **2,** (downright) сущий.
array *n.* **1,** (arrangement) расположение. **2,** *mil.* боевой порядок. **3,** (imposing collection or display) коллекция; выставка. —*v.t.* **1,** (arrange) располагать. **2,** *mil.* выстраивать.
arrears *n.pl.* задолженность; недоимка. *Be in arrears,* иметь задолженность.
arrest *v.t.* **1,** (take into custody) арестовать; задерживать. **2,** (check, as growth, a disease, etc.) задерживать; останавливать. **3,** (capture, as one's attention) приковывать. —*n.* **1,** (detention) арест. *Under house arrest,* под домашним арестом. *Place under arrest,* посадить под арест; взять *or* заключить под стражу. **2,** *med.* остановка: *cardiac arrest,* остановка сердца.
arresting *adj.* поражающий; захватывающий.
arrival *n.* **1,** (act of arriving) прибытие; приход; приезд. **2,** (one who has just arrived) новоприбывший.
arrive *v.i.* **1,** (come to a place) приходить; приезжать; прибывать. **2,** (come, as of a time or season) наступать. **3,** *fol. by* **at** (reach, as a conclusion) приходить (к).
arrogant *adj.* высокомерный; надменный; заносчивый. —**arrogance,** *n.* высокомерие; надменность; заносчивость.
arrogate *v.t.* присваивать себе.
arrow *n.* **1,** (projectile fired from a bow) стрела. **2,** (pointer; indicator) стрелка.
arrowhead *n.* наконечник стрелы.
arsenal *n.* арсенал.
arsenic *n.* мышьяк. —*adj.* мышьяковый.
arson *n.* поджог. —**arsonist,** *n.* поджигатель.
art *n.* **1,** (creative work or skill) искусство. *Work of art,* произведение искусства. **2,** *pl.* (liberal arts) гуманитарные науки. —*adj.* художественный. *Art exhibit,* выставка картин. *Art gallery,* картинная галерея.
artel *n.* артель.
arterial *adj.* **1,** *anat.* артериальный. **2,** (of a highway) магистральный.
arteriosclerosis *n.* артериосклероз.
artery *n.* артерия.
artesian well артезианский колодец.
artful *adj.* **1,** (wily) хитрый. **2,** (skillful) ловкий.
arthritis *n.* артрит. —**arthritic,** *adj.* артритический.
artichoke *n.* артишок. *Jerusalem artichoke,* земляная груша.
article *n.* **1,** (item) предмет. *Toilet articles,* туалетные принадлежности. **2,** (composition written for publication) статья. **3,** (paragraph of a treaty, constitution, etc.) статья. **4,** *gram.* артикль; член.
articulate *v.t.* **1,** (enunciate) выговаривать. **2,** (express in words) выражать. —*v.i.* артикулировать. —*adj.* членораздельный. —**articulation,** *n.* артикуляция.

artifact *n.* предмéт человéческого трудá.
artifice *n.* улóвка.
artificial *adj.* искýсственный. —**artificial limb,** протéз. —**artificial respiration,** искýсственное дыхáние. *Give artificial respiration to,* откáчивать.
artificiality *n.* искýсственность.
artificially *adv.* искýсственно.
artillery *n.* артиллéрия. —*adj.* артиллерúйский: *artillery fire,* артиллерúйский огóнь. —**artilleryman,** *n.* артиллерúст.
artisan *n.* ремéсленник.
artist *n.* **1,** (one who draws or paints) худóжник. **2,** (performer) артúст.
artistic *adj.* **1,** (of or pert. to art) худóжественный. **2,** (showing good taste or a talent for art) артистúческий. —**artistry,** *n.* артистúчность; худóжественность.
artless *adj.* **1,** (ingenuous) простодýшный; бесхúтростный. **2,** (done without skill; crude) бездáрный.
Aryan *adj.* арúйский. —*n.* арúец; *pl.* арúйцы.
as *conj.* **1,** (to the same degree that) как: *thin as a rail,* худóй как щéпка. **2,** (according to what) как: *as is known,* как извéстно; *as you can see,* как вúдно. *Do as you are told,* дéлайте как вам вéлено. **3,** (while) когдá; в то врéмя как: *he arrived as I was leaving,* он пришёл, когдá я уходúл. **4,** (because; since) так как: *we must be leaving as it is already late,* нáдо уйтú, так как ужé пóздно. **5,** (to the degree that) по мéре тогó, как: *as it became warmer,* по мéре тогó, как становúлось теплéе. **6,** (though; however) как ни: *as smart as he is, he could not solve the problem,* как он ни умён, он не мог решúть задáчу. —*adv.* **1,** (equally) так же; такóй же: *our house is just as large,* наш дом такóй же большóй. **2,** (for example) как; как напримéр. *Such important people as...,* такúе вáжные лúца, как... *African languages, as Swahili,* африкáнские языкú, как напримéр суахúли. —*prep.* (by way of; in the capacity of) как; в кáчестве (+ *gen.*). *As an example,* в кáчестве примéра. *I give you this advice as a friend,* совéтую э́то вам, как друг. ♦*Also rendered by the instrumental case: work as a salesman,* рабóтать продавцóм; *serve as a pretext,* служúть предлóгом. —**as...as,** так (*or* такóй) же...как (и). *He is as tall as you,* он такóй же высóкий как вы. —**as for...,** что касáется (+ *gen.*). —**as if,** (как) бýдто; как бы; слóвно. *As if you didn't know*!, как бýдто вы не знáете! —**as it were,** так сказáть. —**as of,** на: *as of June 1,* на пéрвое иóня. —**as though,** *see* **though.** —**as well,** *see* **well.** —**as you were!,** *mil.* отстáвить!
asbestos *n.* асбéст. —*adj.* асбéстовый.
ascend *v.i.* поднимáться; всходúть. —*v.t.* поднимáться по; всходúть на. *Ascend the throne,* взойтú *or* вступúть на престóл.
ascendancy *n.* власть; госпóдство.
ascendant *adj.* **1,** (rising) восходя́щий. **2,** (dominant) госпóдствующий.
ascension *n.* **1,** (ascent) восхождéние. **2,** *cap., relig.* вознесéние.
ascent *n.* **1,** (upward movement) восхождéние; подъём. **2,** (slope) крутизнá; подъём.
ascertain *v.t.* выясня́ть; устанáвливать.
ascetic *n.* аскéт; подвúжник. —*adj.* аскетúческий. —**asceticism,** *n.* аскетúзм.
ascorbic acid аскорбúновая кислотá.
ascribe *v.t.* приписывать: *the play is sometimes ascribed to Shakespeare,* пьéсу инoгдá припúсывают Шекспúру.
asepsis *n.* асéптика. —**aseptic,** *adj.* асептúческий.
asexual *adj.* беспóлый.
ash *n.* **1,** (tree) я́сень. *Mountain ash,* рябúна. **2,** *usu. pl.* (residue after burning) пéпел; золá. **3,** (fine lava) пéпел: *volcanic ash,* вулканúческий пéпел. **4,** *pl.* (ruins) пéпел: *rise from the ashes,* поднимáться из пéпла. **5,** *pl.* (human remains) прах.
ashamed *adj., used predicatively: be ashamed,* стыдúться. *I am ashamed,* мне сты́дно. *Aren't you ashamed*!, как вам не сты́дно! *You ought to be ashamed of yourself!,* вам должнó быть сты́дно!
ash can мýсорный я́щик.
ashen *adj.* **1,** (of the color of ashes) пéпельного цвéта. **2,** (extremely pale) помертвéлый.
ashore *adv.* на бéрег; к бéрегу. *Go/put/wash ashore,* сходúть/высáживать/выносúть на бéрег. *Swim ashore,* плыть к бéрегу. *The body was washed ashore,* труп прибúло к бéрегу.
ashtray *n.* пéпельница.
Asian *also,* **Asiatic** *adj.* азиáтский. —*n.* азиáт.
aside *adv.* в стóрону. *Joking aside,* шýтки в стóрону; крóме шýток. *Put/set aside,* отклáдывать (в стóрону); сберегáть. —**all else aside,** помúмо всегó прóчего. —**aside from,** помúмо.
asinine *adj.* дурáцкий; идиóтский.
ask *v.t.* **1,** (put a question to; inquire about) спрáшивать: *I'll ask her,* я её спрошý. *Ask a passer-by,* спросúть у прохóжего. *Ask the way,* спросúть дорóгу. *Ask a question,* задавáть вопрóс. **2,** (request) просúть: *ask someone to do the dishes,* просúть когó-нибудь помы́ть посýду. *Ask him to come in,* попросúте егó войтú. *I have a favor to ask of you,* у меня́ к вам прóсьба. **3,** (invite) приглашáть; звать. **4,** (charge, as an amount of money) просúть; спрáшивать. **5,** (demand; expect) трéбовать. —*v.i.* спрáшивать: *if you don't know, ask,* éсли не знáешь, спросú. *She asked about you,* онá о вас спросúла. —**ask for,** **1,** (request) просúть; спрáшивать: *ask for a book,* просúть/спрáшивать кнúгу: *ask for permission,* просúть/спрáшивать разрешéния. *Ask for help,* просúть (о) пóмощи. **2,** (ask to see) спрáшивать: *someone was asking for you,* вас спрáшивал какóй-то человéк. **3,** (invite, as trouble) напрáшиваться на (неприя́тности). *See also* **asking.**
askance *adv.* кóсо: *look askance,* смотрéть кóсо.
askew *adv.* кóсо; крúво.
asking *n. It's yours for the asking,* стóит тóлько попросúть. —**asking price,** запрáшиваемая ценá.
aslant *adv.* кóсо; нáискось.
asleep *adj., used predicatively* **1,** (sleeping): *be asleep,* спать. *Fall asleep,* засыпáть. **2,** (numb): *my foot is asleep,* я отлежáл нóгу.
asp *n.* áспид.
asparagus *n.* спáржа. —*adj.* спáржевый: *asparagus soup,* спáржевый суп.
aspect *n.* **1,** (appearance) вид. **2,** (part; feature) сторонá; момéнт; аспéкт. *Consider a question in all its aspects,* рассмáтривать вопрóс со всех сторóн. *Negative aspects,* отрицáтельные момéнты. **3,** *gram.* вид: *imperfective aspect,* несовершéнный вид.
aspectual *adj., gram.* видовóй.
aspen *n.* осúна. —*adj.* осúновый.

asperity *n.* ре́зкость; гру́бость.
asperse *v.t.* клевета́ть; черни́ть; поро́чить.
aspersion *n.* клевета́. *Cast aspersions on,* броса́ть тень на.
asphalt *n.* асфа́льт. —*adj.* асфа́льтовый. —*v.t.* асфальти́ровать.
asphyxia *n.* асфи́ксия.
asphyxiate *v.t.* удуша́ть. —**asphyxiation,** *n.* удуше́ние; асфи́ксия.
aspic *n.* заливно́е.
aspirant *n.* претенде́нт.
aspirate *n. & adj.* придыха́тельный. —*v.t.* произноси́ть с придыха́нием.
aspiration *n.* **1,** (ambition) стремле́ние. **2,** *phonet.* придыха́ние.
aspire *v.i.* [*usu.* **aspire to**] стреми́ться (к); претендова́ть (на). *Aspire to the role of,* претендова́ть на роль (+ *gen.*).
aspirin *n.* аспири́н. *Aspirin tablet,* табле́тка аспири́на.
ass *n.* **1,** (donkey) осёл. **2,** *slang* (dope; jerk) болва́н. *Make an ass of oneself,* опростоволо́ситься. **3,** *slang* (buttocks) зад.
assail *v.t.* **1,** (assault) напада́ть на. **2,** (denounce) обру́шиваться на. **3,** *fig.* (beset) му́чить: *be assailed by doubts,* му́читься сомне́ниями.
assailant *n.* налётчик.
assassin *n.* уби́йца.
assassinate *v.t.* убива́ть. *Attempt to assassinate,* покуша́ться на. —**assassination,** *n.* уби́йство. *Assassination attempt,* покуше́ние (на).
assault *n.* нападе́ние; штурм; ата́ка. —*v.t.* напада́ть на; атакова́ть. —**assault and battery,** избие́ние; оскорбле́ние де́йствием.
assay *v.t.* **1,** (attempt) пыта́ться. **2,** (estimate) оце́нивать.
assemblage *n.* **1,** (gathering of persons) собра́ние. **2,** *mech.* сбо́рка; монта́ж.
assemble *v.t.* собира́ть. —*v.i.* собира́ться; сходи́ться; съезжа́ться. —**assembler,** *n.* сбо́рщик.
assembly *n.* **1,** (act of meeting or assembling) собра́ние: *freedom of assembly,* свобо́да собра́ний. **2,** (deliberative body) собра́ние; ассамбле́я. **3,** *mech.* сбо́рка; монта́ж. —**assembly hall,** а́ктовый зал. —**assembly line,** сбо́рочный конве́йер.
assent *v.i.* соглаша́ться. —*n.* согла́сие.
assert *v.t.* **1,** (aver) утвержда́ть. **2,** (claim and forcefully defend) отста́ивать; предъявля́ть: *assert one's rights,* отста́ивать/предъявля́ть свои́ права́.
assertion *n.* утвержде́ние.
assertive *adj.* напо́ристый.
assess *v.t.* **1,** (evaluate) оце́нивать. **2,** (levy, as a fine) налага́ть. **3,** (levy a payment upon) облага́ть.
assessment *n.* **1,** (evaluation) оце́нка. **2,** (amount assessed) обложе́ние.
asset *n.* **1,** (something advantageous) преиму́щество; це́нное ка́чество. **2,** *usu. pl., comm.* акти́в.
assiduous *adj.* приле́жный; стара́тельный; усе́рдный. —**assiduousness; assiduity,** *n.* прилежа́ние; стара́тельность; усе́рдность.
assign *v.t.* **1,** (appoint; designate) назнача́ть. **2,** *mil.* прикомандирова́ть. **3,** (allocate) отводи́ть. **4,** (give out, as a task, lesson, etc.) задава́ть.
assignment *n.* **1,** (appointment) назначе́ние. **2,** (task) поруче́ние; зада́ние. *Homework assignment,* дома́шнее зада́ние.
assimilate *v.t.* **1,** *physiol.* ассимили́ровать; усва́ивать. **2,** (absorb mentally) усва́ивать; воспринима́ть. —*v.i.* ассимили́роваться. —**assimilation,** *n.* ассимиля́ция; усвое́ние.
assist *v.t. & i.* помога́ть; соде́йствовать. —**assistance,** *n.* по́мощь; соде́йствие.
assistant *n. & adj.* помо́щник. *Assistant director,* помо́щник дире́ктора. —**assistant professor,** ассисте́нт.
associate *n.* сотру́дник; колле́га. —*v.t.* соединя́ть; свя́зывать; ассоции́ровать. *The problems associated with it,* свя́занные с э́тим пробле́мы. —*v.i.* обща́ться. —**associate member,** член-корреспонде́нт. —**associate professor,** доце́нт.
association *n.* **1,** (act of associating) обще́ние. **2,** (an organization) о́бщество; объедине́ние; ассоциа́ция. **3,** (connection in the mind) ассоциа́ция.
assonance *n.* созву́чие; ассона́нс. —**assonant,** *adj.* созву́чный.
assort *v.t.* сортирова́ть. —**assorted,** *adj.* ра́зные; ра́зного ро́да.
assortment *n.* вы́бор; подбо́р; ассортиме́нт.
assuage *v.t.* **1,** (allay) смягча́ть; облегча́ть. **2,** (calm) успока́ивать. **3,** (appease, as hunger) утоля́ть.
assume *v.t.* **1,** (suppose) предполага́ть; допуска́ть: *let us assume that...,* предполо́жим/допу́стим, что... **2,** (take on; take over) принима́ть: *assume a pose,* принима́ть по́зу; *assume command,* принима́ть кома́ндование. *Assume responsibility,* принима́ть (*or* брать) на себя́ отве́тственность. *Assume the offensive,* переходи́ть в наступле́ние. *Assume office,* вступи́ть в до́лжность. *Assume an injured look,* принима́ть оби́женный вид. *Assume a threatening character,* принима́ть *or* приобрета́ть угрожа́ющий хара́ктер.
assumed *adj.* **1,** (supposed; presumed) предполага́емый. **2,** (fictitious) вы́мышленный. *Under an assumed name,* под чужи́м и́менем.
assumption *n.* **1,** (supposition) предположе́ние. *Proceed on the assumption that...,* исходи́ть из предположе́ния (*or* из того́), что... **2,** (taking on; taking over) приня́тие (на себя́). **3,** (accession, as to a position) вступле́ние. **4,** *cap., relig.* успе́ние. *Cathedral of the Assumption,* Успе́нский собо́р.
assurance *n.* **1,** (positive statement) увере́ние; завере́ние. *Give assurances,* дава́ть завере́ния. **2,** (certainty) уве́ренность. **3,** (confidence) самоуве́ренность.
assure *v.t.* **1,** (promise confidently) уверя́ть; заверя́ть. **2,** (make certain) обеспе́чивать. —**you may rest assured,** мо́жете быть уве́рены.
assuredly *adv.* несомне́нно.
Assyrian *adj.* ассири́йский. —*n.* ассири́ец.
astatine *n.* астати́н.
aster *n.* а́стра.
asterisk *n.* звёздочка.
astern *adv.* **1,** (behind a ship) за кормо́й. **2,** (at the rear of a ship) на корме́.
asteroid *n.* астеро́ид.
asthma *n.* а́стма. —**asthmatic,** *adj.* астмати́ческий. —*n.* астма́тик.
astigmatism *n.* астигмати́зм. —**astigmatic,** *adj.* астигмати́ческий.

astir *adj.* **1,** (in motion) в движе́нии. **2,** (out of bed) на нога́х. **3,** (excited) взволно́ванный.
astonish *v.t.* изумля́ть. —**astonishing,** *adj.* изуми́тельный. —**astonishment,** *n.* изумле́ние.
astound *v.t.* изумля́ть; поража́ть. —**astounding,** *adj.* изуми́тельный; порази́тельный.
astraddle *prep.* верхо́м на (+ *prepl.*).
astrakhan *n.* кара́куль. —*adj.* кара́кулевый.
astray *adv.* с пути́. *Go astray,* сбива́ться с пути́; заблуди́ться. *Lead astray,* сбива́ть с пути́; вводи́ть в заблужде́ние.
astride *prep.* верхо́м на (+ *prepl.*).
astringent *adj.* **1,** (tending to constrict) вя́жущий. **2,** (harsh) те́рпкий. —*n.* вя́жущее сре́дство. —**astringency,** *n.* те́рпкость.
astrolabe *n.* астроля́бия.
astrology *n.* астроло́гия. —**astrologer,** *n.* астро́лог; звездочёт. —**astrological,** *adj.* астрологи́ческий.
astronaut *n.* космона́вт.
astronomy *n.* астроно́мия. —**astronomer,** *n.* астроно́м. —**astronomic(al),** *adj.* астрономи́ческий.
astrophysics *n.* астрофи́зика. —**astrophysical,** *adj.* астрофизи́ческий. —**astrophysicist,** *n.* астрофи́зик.
astute *adj.* проница́тельный; то́нкий. —**astuteness,** *n.* проница́тельность.
asunder *adv.* на ча́сти; на куски́.
asylum *n.* **1,** (refuge) убе́жище; прию́т. **2,** (institution) сумасше́дший дом.
asymmetric *also,* **asymmetrical** *adj.* асимметри́чный; несимметри́чный. —**asymmetry,** *n.* асимметри́я; несимметри́чность.
at *prep.* **1,** (in; attending) в; на (+ *prepl.*): *at the theater,* в теа́тре; *at work,* на рабо́те. *At home,* до́ма. **2,** (near; by) у: *at the window,* у окна́. **3,** (indicating arrival) в; на (+ *acc.*): *arrive at school,* прийти́ в шко́лу. **4,** (at the home of) у: *at my uncle's,* у моего́ дя́ди. **5,** (seated at) за: *be seated at the table,* сиде́ть за столо́м. **6,** (indicating the target or object of something) в, на (+ *acc.*): *look at one's watch,* посмотре́ть на часы́; *fire at a target,* стреля́ть в мише́нь. **7,** (indicating pace or speed) *rendered by the instrumental case: at a trot,* ры́сью; *at a snail's pace,* черепа́шьим ша́гом. **8,** (indicating a certain time) в (+ *acc.*): *at noon,* в по́лдень; *at three o' clock,* в три часа́; *at that time,* в то вре́мя. ♦ *But notice: at night,* но́чью; *at dawn,* на рассве́те; *at what time?,* в кото́ром часу́? **9,** (indicating a state or condition) на (+ *prepl.*): *at liberty,* на свобо́де; *at anchor,* на я́коре; *at one's leisure,* на досу́ге. **10,** (in accordance with) по: *at the request of,* по про́сьбе (+ *gen.*); *at one's discretion,* по своему́ усмотре́нию. **11,** (in reaction to) при: *at the sight of,* при ви́де (+ *gen.*); *shudder at the thought of,* содрога́ться при мы́сли о. **12,** *in various miscellaneous expressions: at fault,* винова́т; *at large,* на свобо́де; *at rest,* в поко́е. —**at all,** *see* **all.** —**at last,** наконе́ц. —**at once,** *see* **once.** —**at that, 1,** (after all) в конце́ концо́в: *not so bad at that,* в конце́ концо́в не так уж пло́хо. **2,** (besides) причём: *he solved all the problems, and rather quickly at that,* он реши́л все зада́чи, причём дово́льно бы́стро. *Only one tie, and a frayed one at that,* то́лько оди́н га́лстук, да и то поно́шенный.

ataman *n.* атама́н.
atavism *n.* атави́зм. —**atavistic,** *adj.* атависти́ческий.
ataxia *n.* атакси́я.
atheism *n.* атеи́зм; безбо́жие. —**atheist,** *n.* атеи́ст; безбо́жник. —**atheistic,** *adj.* атеисти́ческий.
Athenian *adj.* афи́нский.
athlete *n.* спортсме́н; атле́т.
athletic *adj.* атлети́ческий. —**athletics,** *n. pl.* атле́тика.
athwart *prep.* попере́к.
Atlantic *adj.* атланти́ческий. —**Atlantic Ocean,** Атланти́ческий океа́н.
atlas *n.* а́тлас.
atmosphere *n.* **1,** (air) атмосфе́ра. **2,** *fig.* (setting; surroundings) обстано́вка; атмосфе́ра. —**atmospheric,** *adj.* атмосфе́рный.
atoll *n.* ато́лл.
atom *n.* а́том. *Atom-free zone,* беза́томная зо́на.
atomic *adj.* а́томный. —**atomic bomb,** а́томная бо́мба.
atomize *v.t.* распыля́ть. —**atomizer,** *n.* распыли́тель; пульвериза́тор.
atonal *adj.* атона́льный. —**atonality,** *n.* атона́льность.
atone *v.i.* [*usu.* **atone for**] искупа́ть. —**atonement,** *n.* искупле́ние.
atop *prep.* на верху́ (+ *gen.*).
atrocious *adj.* **1,** (cruel; brutal) зве́рский. **2,** *colloq.* (abominable) отврати́тельный.
atrocity *n.* зве́рство.
atrophy *n.* атрофи́я. —*v.i.* атрофи́роваться.
atropine *n.* атропи́н.
attach *v.t.* **1,** (fasten) прикрепля́ть: *attach an antenna to the roof,* прикрепля́ть анте́нну к кры́ше. **2,** (append) прилага́ть: *attached hereto,* при сём прилага́ется. **3,** (ascribe) придава́ть: *attach great importance to,* придава́ть большо́е значе́ние (+ *dat.*). **4,** *mil.* (assign) придава́ть. **5,** *law* налага́ть аре́ст на. *See also* **attached.**
attaché *n.* атташе́.
attached *adj.* **1,** (fastened) прикреплённый. **2,** (affiliated): *he is attached to the university,* он рабо́тает при университе́те. **3,** *fol. by* **to** (devoted) привя́занный (к).
attachment *n.* **1,** (attaching) прикрепле́ние. **2,** (affection) привя́занность. **3,** (accessory) приста́вка. **4,** *law* наложе́ние аре́ста.
attack *v.t.* **1,** (assault) напада́ть на. **2,** (criticize sharply) обру́шиваться на. **3,** (begin working on) бра́ться за. **4,** *med.* (strike) поража́ть. —*v.i.* наступа́ть; атакова́ть. —*n.* **1,** (assault; offensive) нападе́ние; ата́ка. **2,** (denunciation) вы́пад; *pl.* напа́дки. **3,** *med.* (seizure) припа́док; при́ступ. *Heart attack,* серде́чный припа́док; инфа́ркт.
attain *v.t.* достига́ть; доби́ться. —**attainable,** *adj.* достижи́мый. —**attainment,** *n.* достиже́ние.
attempt *v.t.* пыта́ться. *Attempt suicide,* покуша́ться на самоуби́йство. —*n.* **1,** (endeavor) попы́тка. **2,** (attack) покуше́ние: *attempt on someone's life,* покуше́ние на чью-нибудь жизнь. *Make an attempt on someone's life,* покуша́ться на чью-нибудь жизнь.
attend *v.t.* **1,** (be present at) прису́тствовать на. **2,** (go to regularly, as school) посеща́ть. **3,** (take care of; minister to) уха́живать за. —*v.i.* [*usu.* **attend to**]

де́лать; занима́ться; забо́титься о. *Attend to a customer,* занима́ться покупа́телем. *I have some things to attend to,* у меня́ есть ко́е-каки́е дела́.

attendance *n.* **1,** (act of attending) посеще́ние: *compulsory attendance,* обяза́тельное посеще́ние. **2,** (regularity of or number attending) посеща́емость: *poor attendance,* плоха́я посеща́емость.

attendant *n.* обслу́живающее лицо́; служи́тель. —*adj.* сопу́тствующий: *attendant circumstances,* сопу́тствующие обстоя́тельства.

attention *n.* **1,** (heed; care) внима́ние: *pay attention to,* обраща́ть внима́ние на. *Bring/come to someone's attention,* доводи́ть/доходи́ть до чьего́-нибудь све́дения. **2,** *mil.* сто́йка "сми́рно"; строева́я сто́йка. *Attention!,* сми́рно! *Stand at attention,* стоя́ть по сто́йке "сми́рно"; стоя́ть *or* стать сми́рно; стоя́ть навы́тяжку; стать во фронт; принима́ть строеву́ю сто́йку; вы́тянуться в стру́нку.

attentive *adj.* внима́тельный. —**attentively,** *adv.* внима́тельно. —**attentiveness,** *n.* внима́тельность.

attest *v.t.* удостоверя́ть. —*v.i.* [*usu.* **attest to**] свиде́тельствовать о. —**attestation,** *n.* удостовере́ние.

attic *n.* черда́к.

attire *n.* наря́д; пла́тье. —*v.t., usu. passive,* одева́ть: *smartly attired,* шика́рно оде́тый.

attitude *n.* **1,** (feeling; disposition) отноше́ние: *his attitude toward me,* его́ отноше́ние ко мне. **2,** (position; posture) по́за: *strike an attitude,* принима́ть по́зу.

attorney *n.* адвока́т; пове́ренный. —**power of attorney,** дове́ренность.

attorney general мини́стр юсти́ции.

attract *v.t.* привлека́ть. *Attract attention,* привлека́ть к себе́ внима́ние; обраща́ть на себя́ внима́ние.

attraction *n.* **1,** (power to attract; pull) притяже́ние; тяготе́ние. *Hold no attraction for,* не привлека́ть кого́-нибудь. **2,** (something that attracts) прима́нка. **3,** (public entertainment) аттракцио́н.

attractive *adj.* привлека́тельный. —**attractiveness,** *n.* привлека́тельность.

attribute *v.t.* припи́сывать: *to what do you attribute...?,* чему́ вы припи́сываете...? —*n.* **1,** (characteristic) сво́йство; атрибу́т. **2,** *gram.* определе́ние; атрибу́т.

attribution *n.* ссы́лка: *not for attribution,* без ссы́лки на исто́чник.

attributive *n.* атрибу́т. —*adj.* атрибути́вный.

attrition *n.* у́быль персона́ла. —**war of attrition,** война́ на истоще́ние.

attune *v.t.* **1,** (tune) настра́ивать. **2,** (bring into accord) согласо́вывать.

atypical *adj.* атипи́ческий.

auburn *adj.* ру́сый; кашта́новый.

auction *n.* аукцио́н; торги́. —*v.t.* продава́ть с аукцио́на/с торго́в/с молотка́. —**auctioneer,** *n.* аукциони́ст.

audacious *adj.* **1,** (bold) сме́лый. **2,** (brazen) де́рзкий; на́глый. —**audacity,** *n.* сме́лость; де́рзость; на́глость.

audibility *n.* слы́шимость.

audible *adj.* слы́шный. —**audibly,** *adv.* слы́шно. *Speak audibly,* говори́ть вслух; говори́ть гро́мко.

audience *n.* **1,** (spectators; listeners) аудито́рия; зри́тели; слу́шатели; пу́блика. **2,** (formal interview) аудие́нция.

audio *adj.* звуково́й. —*n.* звук.

audit *n.* прове́рка отчётности; реви́зия. —*v.t.* **1,** (conduct an audit of) ревизова́ть. **2,** (attend, as a course) слу́шать.

audition *n.* **1,** (hearing) слу́шание. **2,** (test performance) про́ба (на роль).

auditor *n.* ревизо́р; контролёр.

auditorium *n.* аудито́рия; зри́тельный зал.

auditory *adj.* слухово́й.

Augean stables а́вгиевы коню́шни.

auger *n.* бура́в.

augment *v.t.* увели́чивать; прибавля́ть. —**augmentation,** *n.* увеличе́ние.

augur *n.* авгу́р. —*v.t.* предвеща́ть. —*v.i.* [*usu.* **augur well**] предвеща́ть хоро́шее.

augury *n.* предзнаменова́ние.

august *adj.* вели́чественный; внуши́тельный.

August *n.* а́вгуст. —*adj.* а́вгустовский.

auk *n.* гага́рка.

aunt *n.* тётя; тётка.

aura *n.* орео́л: *aura of mystery,* орео́л таи́нственности.

aureole *n.* орео́л.

auricle *n.* **1,** (chamber of the heart) предсе́рдие. **2,** (external part of the ear) ушна́я ра́ковина.

aurochs *n.* **1,** (extinct wild ox) тур. **2,** (European bison) зубр.

aurora *n.* **1,** (atmospheric phenomenon) сия́ние: *aurora borealis,* се́верное сия́ние. **2,** *poetic* (dawn) авро́ра.

auscultate *v.t.* выслу́шивать. —**auscultation,** *n.* выслу́шивание.

auspice *n., usu. pl.* покрови́тельство: *under the auspices of,* под покрови́тельством (+ *gen.*).

auspicious *adj.* благоприя́тный.

austere *adj.* стро́гий; суро́вый.

austerity *n.* стро́гая эконо́мия. *Austerity program,* режи́м эконо́мии.

Australian *adj.* австрали́йский. —*n.* австрали́ец; австрали́йка.

Austrian *adj.* австри́йский. —*n.* австри́ец; австри́йка.

authentic *adj.* по́длинный. —**authenticate,** *v.t.* устана́вливать по́длинность (+ *gen.*). —**authenticity,** *n.* по́длинность.

author *n.* а́втор.

authoritarian *adj.* авторита́рный.

authoritative *adj.* авторите́тный.

authority *n.* **1,** (power; jurisdiction) полномо́чие. **2,** *pl.* (those in charge) вла́сти. **3,** (expert) авторите́т. **4,** (source of information) исто́чник: *on good authority,* из достове́рных исто́чников.

authorization *n.* разреше́ние. *By authorization of,* по уполномо́чию (+ *gen.*).

authorize *v.t.* **1,** (empower) уполномо́чивать. **2,** (give permission to publish) авторизова́ть. —**authorized,** *adj.* уполномо́ченный; авторизо́ванный. *Authorized translation,* авторизо́ванный перево́д.

authorship *n.* а́вторство.

auto *n., colloq.* маши́на.

autobiography *n.* автобиогра́фия. —**autobiographical,** *adj.* автобиографи́ческий.

autocracy *n.* самодержа́вие; автокра́тия; единовла́стие. —**autocrat,** *n.* самоде́ржец; автокра́т.

—**autocratic,** *adj.* самодержа́вный; автократи́ческий; единовла́стный.
autogiro *n.* автожи́р.
autograph *n.* авто́граф. —*v.t.* надпи́сывать. *Autographed copy,* именно́й экземпля́р.
automat *n.* рестора́н-автома́т.
automate *v.t.* автоматизи́ровать.
automatic *adj.* автомати́ческий. —**automatically,** *adv.* автомати́чески.
automation *n.* **1,** (science) автома́тика: *the age of automation,* век автома́тики. **2,** (act) автоматиза́ция: *automation of production,* автоматиза́ция произво́дства.
automaton *n.* автома́т.
automobile *n.* автомоби́ль. —*adj.* автомоби́льный.
automotive *adj.* автомоби́льный.
autonomous *adj.* автоно́мный. —**autonomy,** *n.* автоно́мия.
autopsy *n.* вскры́тие.
autosuggestion *n.* самовнуше́ние.
autumn *n.* о́сень. *In autumn,* о́сенью. —*adj.* [*also,* **autumnal**] осе́нний: *autumn sky,* осе́ннее не́бо.
auxiliary *adj.* вспомога́тельный. —**auxiliary verb,** вспомога́тельный глаго́л.
avail *v.t.* приноси́ть по́льзу (+ *dat.*). *His efforts availed him nothing,* его́ уси́лия не принесли́ ему́ по́льзы; его́ уси́лия пропа́ли да́ром. —*n.* по́льза; вы́года. *To no avail,* напра́сно. —**avail oneself of,** воспо́льзоваться (+ *instr.*).
availability *n.* нали́чие; досту́пность.
available *adj.* име́ющийся; нали́чный; досту́пный. *Be available,* име́ться; быть в нали́чии.
avalanche *n.* лави́на.
avant-garde *n.* авангарди́сты. —*adj.* авангарди́стский
avarice *n.* жа́дность. —**avaricious,** *adj.* жа́дный.
avenge *v.t.* мстить (за); вымеща́ть. —**avenger,** *n.* мсти́тель.
avenue *n.* **1,** (wide street) проспе́кт; авеню́. *Fifth Avenue,* Пя́тая авеню́. **2,** *fig.* (means of achieving something) путь: *avenue to success,* путь к успе́ху.
aver *v.t.* утвержда́ть.
average *adj.* сре́дний. —*n.* сре́днее число́. *Above /below average,* вы́ше/ни́же сре́днего. —*v.t.* **1,** (find the average of): *average figures together,* выводи́ть о́бщее число́. **2,** (amount to as an average) составля́ть в сре́днем: *average five percent,* составля́ть в сре́днем пять проце́нтов. —**on the average,** в сре́днем.
averse *adj., used predicatively* не располо́жен. *Not be averse to,* быть не прочь (+ *inf.*).
aversion *n.* отвраще́ние; антипа́тия. *Have an aversion to,* пита́ть отвраще́ние к; испы́тывать антипа́тию к; бре́згать (+ *inf.*).
avert *v.t.* **1,** (turn away) отводи́ть. **2,** (prevent) предотвраща́ть.
aviary *n.* волье́р.
aviation *n.* авиа́ция. —*adj.* авиацио́нный.
aviator *n.* лётчик; авиа́тор.
avid *adj.* **1,** (greatly desirous) жа́дный. *Avid for power,* жа́ждущий вла́сти. **2,** (ardent; enthusiastic) стра́стный. —**avidity,** *n.* жа́дность. —**avidly,** *adv.* жа́дно; с жа́дностью.
avocado *n.* авока́до.
avocation *n.* побо́чное заня́тие.
avocet *n.* шилоклю́вка.
avoid *v.t.* **1,** (keep away from; refrain from) избега́ть. *In order to avoid,* во избежа́ние (+ *gen.*). **2,** (evade, as a blow) уклоня́ться от.
avoidance *n.* уклоне́ние. *Avoidance of military service,* уклоне́ние от вое́нной слу́жбы.
avow *v.t.* откры́то признава́ть. —**avowal,** *n.* призна́ние. —**avowed,** *adj.* при́знанный.
await *v.t.* ждать; ожида́ть.
awake *v.t.* **1,** (wake up) буди́ть. **2,** (stir; arouse, as a feeling) пробужда́ть. —*v.i.* **1,** (wake up) просыпа́ться. **2,** *fol. by* **to** (become aware of) осознава́ть. —*adj. Be awake,* не спать; бо́дрствовать.
awaken *v.t.* & *i.* = **awake.** —**awakening,** *n.* пробужде́ние.
award *n.* награ́да. —*v.t.* награжда́ть; присужда́ть; присва́ивать; удоста́ивать.
aware *adj. Be aware* (*of*), знать; сознава́ть; отдава́ть себе́ отчёт в (+ *prepl.*). —**awareness,** *n.* понима́ние; созна́ние; осозна́ние.
away *adv.* прочь; вон. *Away with you!,* вон отсю́да! ♦*Usually rendered by a prefixed verb: carry away,* уноси́ть; *go away,* уходи́ть; уезжа́ть; *pass away,* сконча́ться; *run away,* убега́ть; *throw away,* выбра́сывать; *waste away,* ча́хнуть. —*adj.* **1,** (absent; gone) в отъе́зде; в отлу́чке. *Be away,* уе́хать; отсу́тствовать; быть в отъе́зде/отлу́чке. **2,** (distant) на расстоя́нии (+ *gen.*): *ten miles away,* на расстоя́нии десяти́ миль. *Christmas is three months away,* до Рождества́ оста́лось три ме́сяца.
awe *n.* страх; благогове́ние. *Hold in awe,* держа́ть в стра́хе. —*v.t.* внуша́ть страх (+ *dat.*).
awesome *adj.* стра́шный; гро́зный.
awful *adj.* **1,** (very bad) ужа́сный; отврати́тельный. **2,** (inspiring awe) гро́зный. *An awful stillness,* гробова́я тишина́. —**an awful lot of,** ма́сса (+ *gen.*).
awfully *adv.* **1,** (very badly) ужа́сно; отврати́тельно. **2,** (very; extremely) ужа́сно; о́чень: *awfully tired,* ужа́сно уста́л; *awfully kind of you,* о́чень любе́зно с ва́шей стороны́.
awhile *adv.* немно́го; не́которое вре́мя. *Wait awhile!,* подожди́те немно́го!
awkward *adj.* **1,** (clumsy) неуклю́жий; нело́вкий. **2,** (embarrassing; embarrassed) нело́вкий: *awkward situation,* нело́вкое положе́ние; *feel awkward,* чу́вствовать себя́ нело́вко. —**awkwardly,** *adv.* неуклю́же; нело́вко. —**awkwardness,** *n.* неуклю́жесть; нело́вкость.
awl *n.* ши́ло.
awning *n.* наве́с; тент; зонт.
awry *adv.* **1,** (askew) ко́со; на́бок. **2,** (amiss) насма́рку: *go awry,* идти́/пойти́ насма́рку.
ax *also,* **axe** *n.* топо́р.
axial *adj.* осево́й.
axil *n.* па́зуха.
axiom *n.* аксио́ма. —**axiomatic,** *adj.* аксиомати́ческий.
axis *n.* ось.
axle *n.* ось.
ayatollah *n.* аято́лла.
aye *adv.* да. —*n.* за: *three ayes, two nays,* три за, два про́тив. *The ayes have it,* большинство́ за. —**aye aye, sir!,** есть!
azalea *n.* аза́лия.
azimuth *n.* а́зимут.
azure *n.* лазу́рь. —*adj.* голубо́й; лазу́рный.

B

B, b вторáя бýква английского алфавúта. —*n.* **1,** (musical note) си. **2,** (school grade) четвёрка.

baba au rhum рóмовая бáба.

babble *v.i.* **1,** (prattle) лепетáть. **2,** (of a brook) журчáть. —*n.* **1,** (prattle) лéпет. **2,** (of a brook) журчáние.

babe *n.* **1,** (baby) младéнец. **2,** *slang* (girl) дéвка.

babel *n.* смешéние языкóв; вавилóнское столпотворéние. —**Tower of Babel,** вавилóнская бáшня.

baboon *n.* павиáн.

babushka *n.* платóк.

baby *n.* **1,** (infant) ребёнок. **2,** (young or newborn animal, bird, etc.) детёныш. *Baby elephant,* детёныш слонá; слонёнок. *Baby bird,* птенéц. —*adj.* дéтский: *baby talk,* дéтский лéпет. *Baby brother,* братúшка. *Baby sister,* сестрёнка. —*v.t.* нянчиться с. —**baby carriage,** дéтская коляска. —**baby grand piano,** кабинéтный роя́ль. —**baby tooth,** молóчный зуб.

babyish *adj.* ребя́ческий.

Babylonian *adj.* вавилóнский.

baby sitter приходя́щая ня́ня.

baccalaureate *n.* стéпень бакалáвра.

baccarat *n.* баккарá.

bachelor *n.* **1,** (unmarried man) холостя́к. **2,** (holder of a bachelor's degree) бакалáвр. *Bachelor's degree,* стéпень бакалáвра. —*adj.* холостóй; холостя́цкий. *Bachelor apartment,* холостя́цкая квартúра. —**bachelorhood,** *n.* холостáя жизнь.

bacillus *n.* бацúлла; пáлочка.

back *n.* **1,** (part of the body) спинá. **2,** (part of a chair, garment, etc.) спúнка. **3,** (rear) зад; зáдняя часть; зáдняя сторонá. *In the back of the book,* в концé кнúги. **4,** (reverse side) оборóт; оборóтная сторонá. *Back of a card,* рубáшка. *Back of the hand,* тыльная сторонá рукú. **5,** *sports* (defenseman) защúтник. —*adj.* **1,** (dorsal) спиннóй. **2,** (rear) зáдний: *back seat,* зáднее сидéнье. *Back door,* чёрный ход. **3,** (remote) глухóй. *Back street,* закоýлок. *Back country,* глушь. **4,** (of a past date) стáрый: *back issue,* стáрый нóмер. —*adv.* **1,** (backward) назáд: *step back,* шагáть назáд. **2,** (to or toward where one began) обрáтно. *On the way back,* на обрáтном путú. *When will he be back?,* когдá он вернётся? **3,** (to the original possessor) назáд; обрáтно: *give back,* отдáть назáд; *get back,* получúть обрáтно. **4,** (ago) томý назáд: *a while back,* нéкоторое врéмя томý назáд. ♦ *Often rendered by a prefixed verb: come back,* возвращáться; *hold back,* удéрживать; *pay back,* отплáчивать. —*v.t.* **1,** *fol. by* **up** (move backward) отодвигáть. **2,** (support) поддéрживать. **3,** *fol. by* **up** (substantiate) подкрепля́ть. **4,** (put money into) финансúровать; субсидúровать. **5,** (bet on) стáвить на. *Back the wrong horse,* стáвить не на ту лóшадь. —*v.i.* [*usu.* **back up**] **1,** (move backward) подвигáться *or* отодвигáться назáд; пя́титься. **2,** (go into reverse) давáть зáдний ход. —**back and forth,** взад и вперёд. —**back down,** отступáть; бить отбóй. —**back off,** отступáть. —**back out (of),** отступáть (от). —**back to back,** спинá (*or* спинóй) к спинé. —**behind someone's back,** за чьéй-нибудь спинóй. —**go back on,** нарушáть; не сдержáть. *Go back on one's word,* нарушáть своё слóво; идтú на попя́тный. —**in back of, 1,** (position) за (+ *instr.*). **2,** (motion) за (+ *acc.*). —**there and back,** тудá и обрáтно. —**turn one's back on,** отворáчиваться от.

backache *n.* боль в спинé.

backboard *n.* **1,** (board supporting the back) doскá. **2,** *basketball* щит.

backbone *n.* **1,** (spine) позвонóчник; спиннóй хребéт. **2,** (fortitude) твёрдость; мýжество. **3,** (mainstay) становóй хребéт; station становáя жúла; костя́к.

backbreaking *adj.* непосúльный; кáторжный.

backdate *v.t.* помéтить зáдним числóм.

backdrop *n.* **1,** *theat.* зáдник. **2,** *fig.* (background) фон.

backer *n.* **1,** (supporter) сторóнник. **2,** (patron) покровúтель.

backfire *v.i.* дать осéчку; возымéть обрáтное дéйствие; обернýться прóтив самогó себя́.

backgammon *n.* триктрáк.

background *n.* **1,** (setting) фон; зáдний план; пóле. **2,** (secondary place or position) зáдний план: *remain in the background,* оставáться на зáднем плáне. **3,** (underlying events) канвá. **4,** (training; experience) подготóвка. **5,** (origin; ancestry) происхождéние; род.

backhand *n., tennis* удáр слéва. —*adj.* & *adv.* слéва.

backhanded *adj.* **1,** = **backhand. 2,** (equivocal) сомнúтельный: *backhanded compliment,* сомнúтельный комплимéнт.

backing *n.* **1,** (supporting material) подклáдка. **2,** (endorsement) поддéржка.

backlog *n.* **1,** (accumulation) скоплéние. **2,** (reserve supply) запáс.

backrest *n.* опóра для спины́.

backside *n., colloq.* зад; я́годицы.

backstage *adv.* **1,** (location) за кулúсами. **2,**

(motion) за кули́сы. —*adj.* закули́сный.

backstroke *n.* пла́вание на спине́.

back talk возраже́ния. *No back talk*!, без возраже́ний!; без разгово́ров!; никаки́х разгово́ров!; не разгова́ривать!

backtrack *v.i.* **1,** (return over the same route) возвраща́ться по свои́м следа́м (*or* стопа́м). **2,** *fig.* (reverse oneself) дава́ть за́дний ход.

backward *adv.* [*also,* **backwards**] **1,** (toward the back) наза́д. **2,** (in reverse order) наоборо́т; в обра́тном поря́дке. **3,** (in the reverse direction) за́дом. *Move backward,* пя́титься. **4,** (with the back foremost) за́дом наперёд: *put one's hat on backwards,* наде́ть ша́пку за́дом наперёд. —*adj.* **1,** (rearward) обра́тный. **2,** (retarded) отста́лый. —**bend/lean over backwards,** вся́чески стара́ться; лезть из ко́жи вон. —**know backwards and forwards,** знать (что́-нибудь) вдоль и поперёк.

backwardness *n.* отста́лость.

backwards *adv.* = **backward.**

backwater *n.* за́водь; зато́н.

backwoods *n.pl.* глушь. —*adj.* глухо́й.

bacon *n.* беко́н; копчёная груди́нка.

bacteria *n., pl. of* **bacterium.** —**bacterial,** *adj.* бактериа́льный.

bacteriology *n.* бактериоло́гия. —**bacteriological,** *adj.* бактериологи́ческий. —**bacteriologist,** *n.* бактерио́лог.

bacterium *n.* бакте́рия.

bad *adj.* **1,** (not good) плохо́й; дурно́й. *Bad weather,* плоха́я пого́да. *Bad habits,* дурны́е привы́чки. *That's bad,* э́то пло́хо. *Smell bad,* пло́хо па́хнуть. **2,** (wicked) злой: *the bad fairy,* зла́я фе́я. **3,** (naughty) озорно́й; непослу́шный. **4,** (harmful) вре́дный: *bad for one's health,* вре́дно для здоро́вья. **5,** (sore; defective) больно́й: *a bad heart,* больно́е се́рдце. **6,** (severe) си́льный: *a bad cold,* си́льный на́сморк. —**get in bad,** *colloq.* впада́ть в неми́лость. —**go bad, 1,** (degenerate) вырожда́ться. **2,** (become tainted) по́ртиться. —**go from bad to worse,** станови́ться всё ху́же и ху́же. —**not a bad** (+ *noun*), неплохо́й. —**not bad,** непло́хо; ничего́. —**too bad,** о́чень жаль. *It's too bad that...,* жаль, что...

badge *n.* значо́к; бля́ха.

badger *n.* (animal) барсу́к. —*v.t.* (pester) пристава́ть к; трави́ть.

badly *adv.* **1,** (poorly) пло́хо; ду́рно; скве́рно. **2,** (very much; greatly) о́чень; си́льно. **3,** (severely) си́льно; тяжело́; бо́льно: *badly damaged,* си́льно повреждён; *badly wounded,* тяжело́ ра́нен; *cut oneself badly,* си́льно поре́заться.

badminton *n.* бадминто́н.

baffle *v.t.* озада́чивать. —**baffled,** *adj.* озада́ченный. —**bafflement,** *n.* озада́ченность. —**baffling,** *adj.* недоуме́нный.

bag *n.* **1,** (for carrying something) су́мка. **2,** (sack) мешо́к. **3,** (paper bag) паке́т; паке́тик. **4,** (suitcase) чемода́н. **5,** (handbag) су́мка; су́мочка. **6,** (game killed in hunting) добы́ча. **7,** *pl.* (pouchlike folds of skin) мешки́ (под глаза́ми). —*v.t.* **1,** (put in a bag) класть в мешо́к. **2,** (capture) схва́тывать. **3,** (kill, as game) убива́ть; настреля́ть. —**bag and baggage,** *colloq.* со все́ми пожи́тками. —**be left holding the bag,** *colloq.* оста́ться с но́сом; оста́ться при пи́ковом интере́се. —**it's in the bag,** *colloq.* де́ло в шля́пе.

bagel *n.* бара́нка; бу́блик.

baggage *n.* бага́ж. —*adj.* бага́жный: *baggage car,* бага́жный ваго́н. —**baggage compartment,** бага́жник. —**baggage room,** ка́мера хране́ния (багажа́).

baggy *adj.* мешкова́тый.

bagpipe *n.* волы́нка. *Also,* **bagpipes.**

bah *interj.* тьфу!

bail *n.* поручи́тельство; пору́ка. *Release on bail,* отпуска́ть на пору́ки. —*v.t.* [*usu.* **bail out**] **1,** (remove, as water; remove the water from) вычёрпывать. **2,** (put up bail for) брать на пору́ки. **3,** (help out of difficulty) выруча́ть. —*v.i.* [*usu.* **bail out**] выбра́сываться с парашю́том.

bailiff *n.* суде́бный исполни́тель; *pre-rev.* суде́бный при́став.

bailiwick *n.* часть: *not in my bailiwick,* не по мое́й ча́сти.

bait *n.* нажи́вка; прима́нка. *Take the bait,* попа́сться на у́дочку. —*v.t.* **1,** (apply bait to) наживля́ть. **2,** (entice) зама́нивать; прима́нивать. **3,** (torment; harass) трави́ть.

baize *n.* ба́йка. —*adj.* ба́йковый.

bake *v.t.* **1,** (cook in an oven) печь. **2,** (treat with heat, as bricks) обжига́ть. —*v.i.* **1,** (do baking) печь. **2,** (become baked) пе́чься. *Bake in the sun,* пе́чься (*or* жа́риться) на со́лнце.

baked *adj.* печёный.

bakelite *n.* бакели́т.

baker *n.* пе́карь; бу́лочник. —**baker's dozen,** чёртова дю́жина.

bakery *n.* **1,** (store) бу́лочная; хле́бный магази́н. **2,** (baking establishment) пека́рня.

baking *n.* пече́ние; вы́печка. —*adj.* пека́рный: *baking powder,* пека́рный порошо́к. —**baking sheet,** про́тивень. —**baking soda,** питьева́я со́да.

balalaika *n.* балала́йка.

balance *n.* **1,** (scale) весы́. **2,** (equilibrium) равнове́сие: *lose one's balance,* потеря́ть равнове́сие. **3,** *bookkeeping* бала́нс; са́льдо. **4,** (remainder) оста́ток. —*v.t.* **1,** (keep in a state of equilibrium) уравнове́шивать. *Balance oneself,* баланси́ровать. *Balance a basket on one's head,* баланси́ровать корзи́ной на голове́. **2,** *bookkeeping* баланси́ровать. *Balance the books,* подводи́ть бала́нс. —*v.i.* **1,** (be in equilibrium) баланси́ровать. **2,** (tally) сходи́ться. —**balance of payments,** платёжный бала́нс. —**balance of power,** равнове́сие сил. —**balance of trade,** торго́вый бала́нс. —**hang in the balance,** зави́сеть от исхо́да де́ла. —**on balance,** в о́бщем и це́лом.

balanced *adj.* сбаланси́рованный. *Balanced budget,* сбаланси́рованный бюдже́т. *Balanced diet,* рациона́льная дие́та.

balancer *n.* **1,** (acrobat) эквилибри́ст; балансёр. **2,** *mech.* стабилиза́тор.

balance sheet бала́нсовый отчёт.

balance wheel ма́ятник; баланси́р.

balcony *n.* балко́н.

bald *adj.* лы́сый; плеши́вый. *Become bald,* лысе́ть; плеши́веть.

bald eagle орла́н.

balderdash *n.* белиберда́; галиматья́.

baldheaded *adj.* лы́сый; плеши́вый.

baldness *n.* плеши́вость.

bald spot лы́сина; плешь.

bale *n.* **1,** (bundle) тюк. **2,** (amount) кипа: *bale of cotton,* кипа хлопка. —*v.t.* укладывать в тюки.
baleful *adj.* **1,** (maleficent) пагубный. **2,** (sinister; ominous) зловещий.
balk *v.i.* (refuse) артачиться; упрямиться. —*v.t.* (thwart) расстраивать; срывать.
Balkan *adj.* балканский.
balky *adj.* упрямый; с норовом.
ball *n.* **1,** (sphere) шар. **2,** (used in games) мяч. *Play ball,* играть в мяч. *Billiard ball,* бильярдный шар. **3,** (of thread, yarn, etc.) клубок. *Curl up into a ball,* свернуться клубком. **4,** (projectile) ядро: *cannon ball,* пушечное ядро. **5,** (formal dance) бал. —*v.t.* [*usu.* **ball up**] *colloq.* перепутывать. —**have a ball,** *colloq.* веселиться. —**on the ball,** *colloq.* расторопный. —**start the ball rolling,** пустить дело в ход.
ballad *n.* баллада.
ballade *n.* баллада.
ball-and-socket joint шаровой шарнир.
ballast *n.* балласт.
ball bearing шарикоподшипник; шариковый подшипник.
ballerina *n.* балерина.
ballet *n.* балет. —*adj.* балетный: *ballet company,* балетная труппа. *Ballet dancer,* артист(ка) балета. —**ballet master,** балетмейстер.
ballistic *adj.* баллистический: *ballistic missile,* баллистическая ракета. —**ballistics,** *n.* баллистика.
balloon *n.* воздушный шар. *Weather balloon,* зонд. —*v.i.* раздуваться. —**balloonist,** *n.* аэронавт; воздухоплаватель.
ballot *n.* **1,** (voting ticket) (избирательный) бюллетень. **2,** (vote; voting) голосование; баллотировка. *Secret ballot,* тайное голосование, —**ballot box,** избирательная урна.
ball park стадион.
ball-point pen шариковая ручка.
ballroom *n.* танцевальный зал.
ballyhoo *n., colloq.* шумиха. —*v.t., colloq.* поднимать шумиху вокруг; трубить о.
balm *n.* **1,** (balsam) бальзам. **2,** *fig.* (something that comforts) бальзам; елей.
balmy *adj.* **1,** (mild) мягкий. **2,** *slang* (daft) сумасбродный.
baloney *n.* **1,** = **bologna. 2,** *slang* (nonsense) вздор.
balsam *n.* бальзам.
Baltic *adj.* балтийский; прибалтийский.
baluster *n.* балясина.
balustrade *n.* балюстрада.
bamboo *n.* бамбук. —*adj.* бамбуковый.
ban *v.t.* запрещать; налагать запрет на. —*n.* **1,** (prohibition) запрет; запрещение. **2,** *eccles.* анафема; отлучение от церкви.
banal *adj.* банальный; избитый. —**banality,** *n.* банальность.
banana *n.* банан. —*adj.* банановый: *banana peel,* банановая корка *or* кожура.
band *n.* **1,** (strip for binding) лента. *Armband,* повязка. *Hatband,* околыш. *Rubber band,* резинка. **2,** (stripe) полоса. **3,** (group) группа. **4,** (gang) банда; шайка. **5,** (orchestra) оркестр. **6,** *radio* диапазон. —*v.t.* связывать. —*v.i.* [*usu.* **band together**] объединяться.
bandage *n.* повязка; бинт. —*v.t.* перевязывать; бинтовать.
bandanna *also,* **bandana** *n.* цветной платок.
bandbox *n.* картонка для шляпы.
bandit *n.* разбойник; бандит. —**banditry,** *n.* разбой; бандитизм.
bandmaster *n.* капельмейстер.
band saw ленточная пила.
bandstand *n.* эстрада для оркестра; (оркестровая) раковина.
bandy *v.t.* **1,** (toss back and forth) перебрасываться (+ *instr.*). **2,** (circulate; spread) распространять. *Rumors are being bandied about,* ходят слухи.
bandy-legged *adj.* кривоногий.
bane *n.* отрава. *The bane of one's existence,* отрава *or* проклятие чьей-нибудь жизни.
baneful *adj.* пагубный; губительный; гибельный.
bang *n.* **1,** (blow) удар. **2,** (sound) хлопок. **3,** *pl.* (of hair) чёлка. —*v.t.* **1,** (strike; pound) ударять; стукать; хлопать: *bang one's fist on the table,* ударять/стукать/хлопать кулаком по столу. **2,** (bump accidentally) ударяться; стукаться: *bang one's head on the door,* удариться/стукнуться головой о дверь. —*v.i.* **1,** (make a loud noise) хлопать. **2,** *fol. by* **on** (pound) бить (по); ударять (по); стучать (в). **3,** *fol. by* **into** *or* **against** (bump) ударяться о. —*interj.* бах!; бац! *Bang bang!,* бах бах! —*adv., colloq.* прямо: *bang on the mark,* прямо в цель.
bangle *n.* браслет.
banish *v.t.* **1,** (exile) изгонять; высылать; ссылать. **2,** (expel) выгонять; прогонять. **3,** *fig.* (dismiss, as a thought) отгонять. —**banishment,** *n.* изгнание; высылка; ссылка.
banister *also,* **bannister** *n.* перила.
banjo *n.* банджо.
bank *n.* **1,** (financial institution) банк. **2,** (river edge) берег. **3,** (long mound) вал. *Sandbank,* песчаная мель. **4,** (of snow) занос. **5,** (of clouds) гряда. **6,** (row; set) ряд. **7,** *aero.* крен. **8,** *games* банк: *break the bank,* сорвать банк. —*adj.* банковый; банковский. —*v.t.* **1,** (deposit in a bank) класть в банк. **2,** (heap up into a bank) сваливать в кучу; наваливать. **3,** (tilt, as an aircraft) накренять. —*v.i.* **1,** (maintain a bank account) держать деньги (в банке). **2,** *fol. by* **on** (count on) рассчитывать (на); делать ставку (на).
bank account счет в банке.
bankbook *n.* банковская книжка; сберегательная книжка.
banker *n.* **1,** (bank executive) банкир. **2,** (in a game) банкомёт.
banking *n.* банковое дело.
bank note банкнот; кредитный билет.
bankroll *n.* денежные средства; финансовые ресурсы.
bankrupt *adj.* обанкротившийся. *Go bankrupt,* обанкротиться. —*v.t.* привести к банкротству. —**bankruptcy,** *n.* банкротство.
bank shot *billiards* дуплет.
banner *n.* знамя. —*adj.* рекордный: *banner year,* рекордный год. *Banner headlines,* аршинные заголовки.
bannister *n.* = **banister.**
banquet *n.* банкет; пир. —*adj.* банкетный: *banquet table,* банкетный стол.
banter *n.* болтовня.
baobab *n.* баобаб.

baptism *n.* крещéние. —**baptism of fire,** боевóе крещéние.
baptismal *adj.* крестúльный.
Baptist *n.* баптúст. —*adj.* баптúстский. —**John the Baptist,** Иоáнн Предтéча.
baptistery *also,* **baptistry** *n.* **1,** (place for baptism) баптистéрий. **2,** (baptismal font) купéль.
baptize *v.t.* крестúть. *Be baptized,* крестúться.
bar *n.* **1,** (of wood, metal, etc.) брусóк. **2,** (of gold) слúток (зóлота); (of soap) кусóк; брусóк (мы́ла); (of chocolate) плúтка (шоколáда). **3,** (bolt) засóв. **4,** (obstacle; barrier) прегрáда; барьéр. **5,** *sports* переклáдина; *pl.* брýсья; (*in high jumping*) плáнка. **6,** (tavern) бар. **7,** (counter) стóйка. **8,** (legal profession) адвокатýра. **9,** *fig.* (place of judgment) суд. **10,** *music* такт. **11,** (unit of pressure) бар. —*v.t.* **1,** (bolt) запирáть на засóв. **2,** (block; obstruct) закрывáть; преграждáть; заграждáть; загорáживать. **3,** (exclude) исключáть. **4,** (forbid) запрещáть. —*prep., in* **bar none,** без исключéния. —**behind bars,** за решёткой.
barb *n.* **1,** (of an arrow, fishhook, etc.) зубéц. **2,** (caustic remark) кóлкость.
barbarian *n.* вáрвар. —*adj.* вáрварский.
barbaric *adj.* вáрварский.
barbarism *n.* **1,** (barbarity) вáрварство. **2,** *ling.* варварúзм.
barbarity *n.* вáрварство.
barbarous *adj.* вáрварский.
barbecue *n.* **1,** (grill) рáшпер. **2,** (roasted meat) зажáренная тýша. —*v.t.* жáрить.
barbed *adj.* **1,** (containing barbs) колю́чий. **2,** *fig.* (cutting) кóлкий. —**barbed wire,** колю́чая прóволока.
barbell *n.* штáнга.
barber *n.* парикмáхер.
barberry *n.* барбарúс.
barbershop *n.* парикмáхерская.
barbiturate *n.* барбитурáт.
barcarole *n.* баркарóла.
bard *n.* бард.
bare *adj.* **1,** (naked; uncovered) гóлый; нагóй. *With one's bare hands,* гóлыми рукáми. *Bare feet,* босы́е нóги. *In one's bare feet,* босикóм. *Sleep on the bare floor,* спать на гóлом полý. **2,** (just sufficient): *the bare/barest necessities,* сáмое необходúмое. *Bare majority,* незначúтельное большинствó. —*v.t.* **1,** (uncover) обнажáть; оголя́ть; раскрывáть. **2,** (reveal) обнажáть; раскрывáть. *Bare one's soul to,* откры́ть *or* раскры́ть дýшу пéред. —**lay bare,** обнажáть; выклáдывать.
bareback *adv.* без седлá.
barefaced *adj.* бессты́дный; неприкры́тый. *Barefaced lie,* нáглая ложь.
barefoot *adj.* босóй; босонóгий; разýтый. —*adv.* босикóм.
barehanded *adj.* & *adv.* гóлыми рукáми.
bareheaded *adj.* & *adv.* с непокры́той головóй; простоволóсый.
barely *adv.* едвá; éле; чуть.
bargain *n.* **1,** (deal) сдéлка. **2,** (advantageous purchase) вы́годная покýпка. —*v.i.* торговáться. —**bargain for,** ожидáть. —**into the bargain,** в придáчу.
barge *n.* бáржа. —*v.i.* [*usu.* **barge into**] ворвáться в. —**bargeman,** *n.* бурлáк.
barite *n.* барúт.
baritone *n.* баритóн. —*adj.* баритóнный.
barium *n.* бáрий. —**barium sulfate,** сернокúслый бáрий.
bark *n.* **1,** (cry of a dog) лай. **2,** (covering of a tree) корá. **3,** (sailing vessel) барк. —*v.i.* **1,** (of a dog) лáять. **2,** (of a person) гáркать. —*v.t.* выкрúкивать: *bark* (*out*) *a command,* вы́крикнуть комáнду. —**bark up the wrong tree,** *colloq.* быть на лóжном путú.
barley *n.* ячмéнь. —*adj.* ячмéнный.
barmaid *n.* буфéтчица.
barman *n.* буфéтчик.
barn *n.* **1,** (for storing crops) амбáр. **2,** (for stabling livestock) хлев; корóвник.
barnacle *n.* усонóгий рак. *Acorn barnacle,* морскóй жёлудь. *Goose barnacle,* морскáя ýточка. —**barnacle goose,** белощёкая казáрка.
barn owl сипýха.
barnstorm *v.i.* гастролúровать (в провúнции).
barn swallow деревéнская лáсточка; касáтка.
barnyard *n.* птúчий двор.
barometer *n.* барóметр. —**barometric,** *adj.* барометрúческий.
baron *n.* **1,** (nobleman) барóн. **2,** (magnate) магнáт. —**baroness,** *n.* баронéсса.
baronet *n.* баронéт.
baronial *adj.* барóнский. —**barony,** *n.* барóнство.
baroque *n.* барóкко. —*adj.* в стúле барóкко; барóчный.
barracks *n.pl.* казáрмы.
barrage *n.* **1,** *mil.* заградúтельный огóнь; огневóй вал. **2,** (torrent) потóк; град.
barrel *n.* **1,** (cask) бóчка. **2,** (unit of measure, esp. of oil) бáррель. **3,** (of a firearm) ствол. —**cash on the barrel,** дéньги на бóчку.
barrel organ шармáнка.
barren *adj.* **1,** (of land) бесплóдный; неплодорóдный. **2,** (of a woman) бесплóдная. —**barrenness,** *n.* бесплóдие; неплодорóдность.
barricade *n.* баррикáда. —*v.t.* баррикадúровать.
barrier *n.* **1,** (obstruction) барьéр. *Police barriers,* полицéйские рогáтки. **2,** (gate at a railroad crossing) шлагбáум. **3,** *fig.* (obstacle) барьéр: *racial/trade barriers,* рáсовые/торгóвые барьéры. —**language barrier,** языковóй барьéр. —**sound barrier,** звуковóй барьéр.
barring *prep.* исключáя.
barrister *n., Brit.* адвокáт.
barroom *n.* бар.
barrow *n.* **1,** (wheelbarrow) тáчка. **2,** (burial mound) кургáн.
bartender *n.* буфéтчик.
barter *n.* товарообмéн; меновáя торгóвля. —*v.t.* обмéнивать; промéнивать.
basal metabolism основнóй обмéн.
basalt *n.* базáльт. —*adj.* базáльтовый.
base *n.* **1,** (foundation) оснóва; основáние; бáза. **2,** (installation) бáза: *naval base,* морскáя бáза. **3,** *chem.; math.* основáние. —*adj.* **1,** (low; mean) нúзкий; нúзменный; пóдлый. *Base motives,* нúзменные побуждéния. **2,** (of a base) бáзовый: *base hospital,* бáзовый гóспиталь. **3,** (used as a starting point) бáзисный: *base period,* бáзисный перúод. *Base pay,* основнóй зáработок. **4,** *in* **base metal,** неблаго-

ро́дный мета́лл. —*v.t.* осно́вывать; стро́ить; бази́ровать. *Based on facts,* осно́ванный на фа́ктах. —**be off base,** *colloq.* заблужда́ться. —**not** (*or* **never) get to first base,** *colloq.* ничего́ не дости́гнуть; не сдви́нуться с ме́ста.

baseball *n.* бейсбо́л.

baseless *adj.* необосно́ванный; неоснова́тельный; безоснова́тельный.

basement *n.* подва́л. —*adj.* подва́льный: *basement window,* подва́льное окно́.

baseness *n.* ни́зость; по́длость.

bash *v.t., colloq.* хло́пать; шлёпать.

bashful *adj.* засте́нчивый; ро́бкий. —**bashfulness,** *n.* засте́нчивость; ро́бость.

basic *adj.* основно́й. —*n., usu. pl.* осно́вы. —**basic training,** основна́я *or* первонача́льная подгото́вка.

basically *adv.* в основно́м; по существу́.

basil *n.* базили́к.

basilica *n.* базили́ка.

basin *n.* **1,** (container) таз. **2,** (lowland) бассе́йн.

basis *n.* осно́ва; основа́ние; ба́зис; ба́за. *On the basis of,* на основа́нии (+ *gen.*); на осно́ве (+ *gen.*).

bask *v.i.* гре́ться; не́житься (на со́лнце).

basket *n.* корзи́на; корзи́нка.

basketball *n.* баскетбо́л. *Basketball player,* баскетболи́ст. —*adj.* баскетбо́льный.

Basque *adj.* ба́скский. —*n.* **1,** (person) баск; баско́нка. **2,** (language) ба́скский язы́к.

bas-relief *n.* барелье́ф. —*adj.* барелье́фный.

bass[1] (beis) *n., music* бас. —*adj.* басо́вый: *bass clef,* басо́вый ключ.

bass[2] (bas) *n.* (fish) о́кунь.

bass baritone барито́нальный бас.

bass drum туре́цкий бараба́н.

basso *n.* бас.

bassoon *n.* фаго́т. —**bassoonist,** *n.* фаготи́ст.

bass viol контраба́с.

bast *n.* лы́ко; луб; моча́ло. —*adj.* лы́ковый; лубяно́й.

bastard *n.* **1,** (illegitimate child) внебра́чный ребёнок. **2,** *slang* (scoundrel) сво́лочь. —*adj.* внебра́чный; незаконнорождённый.

baste *v.t.* **1,** (sew) мета́ть; смётывать; намётывать; замётывать. **2,** (moisten) полива́ть.

bastion *n.* **1,** (fortification) бастио́н. **2,** *fig.* (bulwark) опло́т.

bat *n.* **1,** (cudgel) дуби́на; дуби́нка. **2,** *sports* бита́; лапта́. **3,** (flying mammal) летучая мышь. —*v.t.* **1,** (hit) бить. **2,** (wink) морга́ть: *without batting an eye,* гла́зом не моргну́в. *He didn't bat an eye,* он и бро́вью не повёл. —**go to bat for,** *colloq.* заступа́ться за; хлопота́ть за. —**right off the bat,** *colloq.* с ме́ста в карье́р.

batch *n.* **1,** (of bread) вы́печка. **2,** (of letters, papers, etc.) па́чка. **3,** (lot, as of merchandise) па́ртия.

bated *adj., in* **with bated breath,** не дыша́; затаи́в дыха́ние; с затаённым дыха́нием.

bath *n.* **1,** (bathing) ва́нна. **2,** (bathtub) ва́нна. **3,** (bathroom) ва́нная ко́мната. **4,** (public bath) ба́ня.

bathe *v.t.* **1,** (place in liquid; give a bath to) купа́ть. **2,** (apply liquid to for healing) обмыва́ть; промыва́ть. **3,** *fig.* (cover; flood) залива́ть: *bathed in sunlight,* зали́тый со́лнцем. —*v.i.* купа́ться. —**bather,** *n.* купа́льщик.

bathhouse *n.* купа́льня.

bathing *n.* купа́ние. —**bathing cap,** купа́льная ша́почка. —**bathing suit,** купа́льный костю́м.

bathrobe *n.* хала́т.

bathroom *n.* **1,** (for bathing) ва́нная; ва́нная ко́мната. **2,** (lavatory) убо́рная.

bath towel ба́нное полоте́нце.

bathtub *n.* ва́нна.

batiste *n.* бати́ст.

baton *n.* **1,** (symbolic staff) жезл. **2,** (rod used by a conductor) (дирижёрская) па́лочка. **3,** *sports* эстафе́та; эстафе́тная па́лочка.

battalion *n.* батальо́н; дивизио́н. —*adj.* батальо́нный.

batten *v.t.* [*usu.* **batten down**] задра́ивать.

batter *v.t.* **1,** (pound) би́ться о; колоти́ть. **2,** (damage by repeated blows) измя́ть. **3,** *fol. by* **in** (bash in) вда́вливать. —*n.* взби́тое те́сто.

battering-ram *n.* тара́н.

battery *n.* **1,** (storage battery) батаре́я; аккумуля́тор. **2,** (small, as for a flashlight) батаре́йка. **3,** *mil.* батаре́я. —**assault and battery,** *see* **assault.** —**battery-operated,** *adj.* батаре́йный.

batting *n.* вати́н.

battle *n.* бой; би́тва; сраже́ние. *The battle of Stalingrad,* би́тва под Сталингра́дом. *The battle of Borodino,* би́тва при Бородине́. *He died in battle,* он поги́б в бою́. —*adj.* боево́й: *battle cry,* боево́й клич. —*v.t. & i.* сража́ться (с); боро́ться (с).

battlefield *n.* по́ле бо́я; по́ле би́твы; по́ле сраже́ния. *Also,* **battleground.**

battle-hardened *adj.* закалённый в боя́х; обстре́лянный.

battlement *n.* зу́бчатая крепостна́я стена́.

battleship *n.* лине́йный кора́бль; линко́р.

battleworthy *adj.* боеспосо́бный.

batty *adj., slang* сумасше́дший. *Drive batty,* своди́ть с ума́.

bauble *n.* безделу́шка.

bauxite *n.* бокси́т. —*adj.* бокси́товый.

Bavarian *adj.* бава́рский.

bawdy *adj.* са́льный; поха́бный.

bawl *v.i.* вопи́ть; ора́ть; реве́ть. —**bawl out,** *colloq.* брани́ть; разноси́ть.

bay *n.* **1,** (body of water) зали́в; бу́хта. **2,** *archit.* пролёт. **3,** (bark) лай. **4,** (tree) лавр. —*adj.* (color of a horse) гнедо́й. —*v.i.* (bark) ла́ять. —**at bay,** за́гнанный; затра́вленный. —**bring to bay,** загоня́ть; (за)трави́ть.

bay leaf лавро́вый лист.

bayonet *n.* штык. —*v.t.* коло́ть штыко́м.

bay window фона́рь.

bazaar *n.* база́р.

bazooka *n.* противота́нковый гранатомёт.

B.C. до на́шей э́ры: *in 200 B.C.,* в двухсо́том году́ до на́шей э́ры.

be *v.i.* **1,** (expressing condition, location, etc.) быть: *I was home,* я был (была́) до́ма. *I will be home,* я бу́ду до́ма. ♦*Generally omitted in the present tense: he is ill,* он бо́лен; *she is not here,* её нет. *Sometimes rendered by* есть *or* бу́дет: *an order is an order,* прика́з есть прика́з. *If nothing is done,* е́сли ничего́ не бу́дет сде́лано. **2,** (constitute; represent) явля́ться; составля́ть; представля́ть собо́й. —**be that as it may,** как бы то ни́ было. —**it was not to be,** не ту́т-то бы́ло. —**so be it,** так и быть; пусть бу́дет так. —**there is; there are,** *see* **there.** *See also* **were.**

beach *n.* пляж. —*adj.* пля́жный: *beach umbrella,* пля́жный зонт.
beachhead *n.* (примо́рский) плацда́рм.
beacon *n.* **1,** (signal light) сигна́льный ого́нь. **2,** (radio beacon) радиомая́к.
bead *n.* **1,** (single bead) бу́сина; би́серина. **2,** *pl.* (string of beads) бу́сы; би́сер. **3,** *pl.* (rosary) чётки. **4,** (drop, as of perspiration) ка́пля. —**draw a bead on,** взять на прице́л; взять на му́шку.
beaded *adj.* би́серный.
beagle *n.* го́нчая.
beak *n.* клюв.
beaker *n.* **1,** (laboratory container) мензу́рка. **2,** (goblet) ку́бок.
beam *n.* **1,** (of wood, metal, etc.) ба́лка; брус. **2,** (of light) луч. *Turn up/turn down/the high beams,* включи́ть/притуши́ть да́льний свет. —*v.t.* **1,** (radiate) излуча́ть. **2,** (transmit) передава́ть; направля́ть. —*v.i.* сия́ть; *fig.* сия́ть от ра́дости.
bean *n.* боб. *Kidney bean,* фасо́ль. *String beans,* стручко́вая фасо́ль. *Coffee beans,* зёрна ко́фе. —*adj.* бобо́вый; фасо́левый. *Bean soup,* фасо́левый суп. —**spill the beans,** *colloq.* проговори́ться; проболта́ться.
beanpole *n., colloq.* каланча́.
bear *n.* медве́дь. —*adj.* [*also,* **bear's**] медве́жий: *bear hunt,* медве́жья охо́та. —*v.t.* **1,** (carry) нести́; носи́ть. *Bear arms,* носи́ть ору́жие. **2,** (bring and tell) приноси́ть: *bear glad tidings,* приноси́ть ра́достное изве́стие. **3,** (bring forth; produce) приноси́ть: *bear fruit,* приноси́ть плоды́. **4,** (give birth to) рожа́ть; рожда́ть. **5,** (have; show) носи́ть: *bear traces,* носи́ть следы́; *bear one's name,* носи́ть чьё-нибудь и́мя. *Bear a resemblance,* име́ть схо́дство. *Bear no relation to,* не име́ть никако́го отноше́ния к. **6,** (hold; harbor) (за)таи́ть: *bear a grudge,* (за)таи́ть оби́ду *or* зло́бу. **7,** (support, as weight) выде́рживать. **8,** (shoulder, as expense or responsibility) нести́. **9,** (endure; withstand) выде́рживать; выноси́ть; терпе́ть; переноси́ть. **10,** *fol. by* **oneself** (conduct) вести́ себя́: *bear oneself with dignity,* вести́ себя́ с досто́инством. —*v.i.* забира́ть: *bear right,* забира́ть впра́во. —**bear down,** нату́живаться. —**bear down on,** нажима́ть на. —**bear in mind,** име́ть в виду́. —**bear on** *or* **upon,** име́ть отноше́ние к. —**bear out,** подтвержда́ть. —**bear up,** крепи́ться. —**bring to bear,** ока́зывать (давле́ние); напряга́ть (все си́лы).
bearable *adj.* сно́сный; терпи́мый.
beard *n.* борода́.
bearded *adj.* борода́тый. —**bearded vulture,** борода́ч; ягня́тник.
beardless *adj.* **1,** (having no beard) безборо́дый. **2,** *fig.* (callow) безу́сый.
bearer *n.* **1,** (of news) ве́стник. **2,** (of a check, document, etc.) пода́тель; предъяви́тель.
bearing *n.* **1,** (carrying) ноше́ние. **2,** (carriage) вы́правка; оса́нка. **3,** *mech.* подши́пник: ball bearing, ша́риковый подши́пник. **4,** (relevance) отноше́ние: *have no bearing on,* не име́ть отноше́ния к. **5,** *pl.* (sense of direction) ориента́ция: *lose one's bearings,* потеря́ть ориента́цию. *Get one's bearings,* ориенти́роваться. **6,** *navigation* пе́ленг. *Take a bearing on,* пеленгова́ть.
bearskin *n.* медве́жья шку́ра. —*adj.* медве́жий: *bearskin coat,* медве́жья шу́ба.
beast *n.* зверь; живо́тное. —**beast of burden,** вью́чное живо́тное. —**beast of prey,** хи́щный зверь.
beastly *adj.* **1,** (bestial) зве́рский. **2,** *colloq.* (nasty; awful) скве́рный; зве́рский.
beat *v.t.* **1,** (strike repeatedly) бить. *Beat a carpet,* выбива́ть ковёр. **2,** (thrash; whip) бить; избива́ть. *Beat to death,* заби́ть до́ смерти. **3,** (whip; churn) взбива́ть. **4,** (clear, as a path) пробива́ть (тропу́). **5,** (mark, as time) отбива́ть (такт). **6,** (defeat) (по)би́ть; побежда́ть; вы́игрывать у; обы́грывать. **7,** (get ahead of, reach a goal ahead of) опережа́ть. **8,** *in* **beat a retreat,** бить отбо́й. —*v.i.* **1,** (pulsate, as of the heart) би́ться. **2,** (sound when struck, as of drums) бить. **3,** *fol. by* **against** (dash; strike) би́ться (о); стуча́ть (в); хлеста́ть (в). —*n.* **1,** (beating) бие́ние; бой. *The beat of hoofs,* стук *or* цо́кот копы́т. **2,** (rounds; patrol) обхо́д; дозо́р. **3,** *music* ритм; такт. —*adj., slang* (exhausted) без ног. —**beat back,** отбива́ть. —**beat down, 1,** (flatten) прибива́ть. **2,** (of the sun) пали́ть; припека́ть. —**beat it!,** *slang* вон отсю́да!; пошёл вон! —**beat off,** отбива́ть. —**beat up,** избива́ть.
beaten *adj.* **1,** (whipped up, as of eggs) взби́тый. **2,** (defeated) разби́тый; побеждённый. **3,** (crushed in spirit) уби́тый. **4,** (well-worn; familiar) изби́тый; проторённый: *the beaten track,* изби́тая/проторённая доро́га.
beatific *adj.* блаже́нный.
beatify *v.t.* причисля́ть к ли́ку блаже́нных. —**beatification,** *n.* причисле́ние к ли́ку блаже́нных.
beating *n.* **1,** (pulsation, as of the heart) бие́ние. **2,** (act of whipping or thrashing) избие́ние. **3,** (a whipping or thrashing) побо́и; по́рка. **4,** (defeat) разгро́м.
beatitude *n.* блаже́нство. —**the Beatitudes,** за́поведи блаже́нства.
beat-up *adj., colloq.* **1,** (threadbare) поно́шенный. **2,** (dilapidated) полуразру́шенный.
beau *n.* покло́нник; кавале́р.
beautician *n.* космети́чка.
beautification *n.* украше́ние.
beautiful *adj.* краси́вый; прекра́сный. —**beautifully,** *adv.* краси́во.
beautify *v.t.* украша́ть.
beauty *n.* **1,** (beautifulness) красота́. **2,** (beautiful woman) краса́вица. **3,** (beautiful thing) краса́вец; краса́вица.
beauty parlor космети́ческий кабине́т.
beauty spot 1, (cosmetic patch) му́шка. **2,** (birthmark) ро́динка.
beaver *n.* **1,** (animal) бобр. **2,** (fur) бобёр; бобро́вый мех.
becalm *v.t.* успока́ивать.
because *conj.* потому́ что. —**because of,** из-за. *It's all because of...,* э́то всё из-за...; всему́ вино́й (+ *nom.*).
beck *n.* киво́к. —**be at someone's beck and call,** быть у кого́-нибудь на побегу́шках.
beckon *v.t. & i.* мани́ть; подзыва́ть.
becloud *v.t.* завола́кивать; затума́нивать.
become *v.i.* станови́ться; де́латься. *Become ill,* заболе́ть. *Become angry,* рассерди́ться. —*v.t.* **1,** (show to advantage) идти́ (+ *dat.*); быть к лицу́ (+ *dat.*). **2,** (befit) подоба́ть (+ *dat.*); быть к лицу́

(+ *dat.*). —**become of,** стать с; стáться с: *What's become of him?,* что с ним стáло/стáлось?
becoming *adj.* **1,** (suitable; fitting) подобáющий. **2,** (attractive) к лицý.
bed *n.* **1,** (for sleeping) постéль; кровáть. *Hospital bed,* (больни́чная) кóйка. *Go to bed,* ложи́ться спать. *Put to bed,* уклáдывать. **2,** (quarters): *bed and board,* квартúра и стол; (accommodations): *bed and breakfast,* ночлéг и зáвтрак. **3,** (flower bed) клýмба; грядá; гря́дка. **4,** (riverbed) рýсло. **5,** (roadbed) полотнó. **6,** *geol.* пласт: *lava bed,* пласт лáвы. **7,** in *oyster bed,* ýстричная бáнка. —*adj.* постéльный: *bed linen,* постéльное бельё. —**get up on the wrong side of the bed,** встать с лéвой ноги́. —**take to one's bed,** слечь в постéль.
bedazzle *v.t.* ослепля́ть.
bedbug *n.* клоп.
bedclothes *n.pl.* постéльное бельё.
bedding *n.* **1,** (items for a bed) постéльные принадлéжности. **2,** (material for an animal to sleep on) подсти́лка. **3,** *geol.* напластовáние.
bedeck *v.t.* украшáть.
bedevil *v.t.* мýчить; терзáть.
bedlam *n.* бедлáм; хаóс.
Bedouin *n.* бедуи́н.
bedpan *n.* подкладнóе сýдно.
bedpost *n.* стóлбик кровáти.
bedraggled *adj.* растрёпанный; взъерóшенный.
bedridden *adj.* прикóванный к постéли.
bedrock *n.* **1,** *geol.* материкóвая порóда. **2,** *fig.* (fundamental principles) суть: *get down to bedrock,* добрáться до сýти дéла.
bedroom *n.* спáльня. —**bedroom slippers,** домáшние тýфли; шлёпанцы.
bedside *n. At one's bedside,* у постéли.
bedsore *n.* прóлежень.
bedspread *n.* покрывáло.
bedstead *n.* кровáть.
bedtime *n.* врéмя ложи́ться спать. *It is bedtime,* порá спать.
bee *n.* пчелá. —*adj.* пчели́ный. *Bee sting,* укýс пчелы́.
beech *n.* бук. —*adj.* бýковый.
beechnut *n.* бýковый орéшек.
beechwood *n.* бук. —*adj.* бýковый.
beef *n.* **1,** (meat) говя́дина. *Roast beef,* рóстбиф. **2,** *slang* (complaint) жáлоба. —*adj.* говя́жий; мяснóй. *Beef cattle,* мяснóй скот. —*v.t.* [*usu.* **beef up**] пополня́ть. —*v.i., slang* (complain) ныть.
beefsteak *n.* бифштéкс.
beef stroganoff беф-стрóганов.
beefy *adj.* мяси́стый; мýскулистый.
beehive *n.* ýлей.
beekeeper *n.* пчеловóд; пáсечник. —**beekeeping,** *n.* пчеловóдство.
beep *n.* **1,** (sound of a horn) гудóк. **2,** (short high-pitched note) высóкий звук. —**beeper,** *n.* зýммер.
beer *n.* пи́во. —*adj.* пивнóй: *beer mug,* пивнáя крýжка.
beeswax *n.* пчели́ный воск.
beet *n.* свёкла. —*adj.* свекóльный: *beet soup,* свекóльный суп.
beetle *n.* жук.
beetle-browed *adj.* с нави́сшими бровя́ми.
beet sugar свеклови́чный сáхар.
befall *v.t.* постигáть; выпадáть (+ *dat.*); обрýшиваться на.
befit *v.t.* подобáть. —**befitting,** *adj.* подобáющий.
before *prep.* **1,** (prior to) до; пéред: *before the war,* до войны́; *before dinner,* пéред обéдом. *Two years before his death,* за два гóда до егó смéрти. *That was before my time,* э́то бы́ло ещё до меня́. **2,** (ahead of; sooner than) прéжде (+ *gen.*); рáньше (+ *gen.*). **3,** (in front of) пéред: *appear before the court,* предстáть пéред судóм. —*conj.* прéжде чем; пéред тем, как; до тогó, как. *Before leaving the house,* прéжде чем (*or* пéред тем, как) вы́йти и́з дому. *Before I came to America,* до тогó, как я приéхал в Амéрику. *Before it is too late,* покá не пóздно. —*adv.* рáньше; прéжде. *I have never been here before,* я никогдá рáньше здесь не бывáл. *You should have thought of that before!,* нáдо бы́ло дýмать об э́том рáньше! —**as before,** по-прéжнему. —**before last,** позапрóшлый: *the year before last,* позапрóшлый год. —**before long,** в скóром врéмени. —**long before,** задóлго до. —**never before,** никогдá ещё. —**shortly before,** незадóлго до.
beforehand *adv.* зарáнее; предвари́тельно.
befriend *v.t.* подружи́ться с.
befuddle *v.t.* **1,** (cloud, as the mind) дурмáнить. **2,** (confuse; baffle) озадáчивать.
beg *v.t.* **1,** (ask earnestly; plead with) умоля́ть; упрáшивать. **2,** (ask for earnestly) проси́ть: *beg permission,* проси́ть разрешéния. **3,** (evade; sidestep) обходи́ть (вопрóс) —*v.i.* **1,** (solicit alms) ни́щенствовать; проси́ть ми́лостыню. *Go begging to,* идти́ на поклóн к. **2,** *fol. by* **of** (ask earnestly) óчень проси́ть; умоля́ть: *I beg of you,* я вас óчень прошý; умоля́ю вас. **3,** *fol. by* **for** (plead for) проси́ть: *beg for mercy/forgiveness,* проси́ть пощáды/прощéния. **4,** *fol. by inf.* (used in certain forms of politeness): *I beg to differ,* позвóлю себé не согласи́ться. **5,** (of a dog) служи́ть. —**beg off,** отговáриваться. —**go begging,** не имéть спрóса. —**I beg your pardon, 1,** (please excuse me) извини́те!; прости́те!; прошý прощéния! **2,** (what did you say?) прости́те, что вы сказáли? **3,** (I disagree) извини́те!
beget *v.t.* **1,** (father; sire) роди́ть. **2,** *fig.* (generate) порождáть.
beggar *n.* ни́щий. —*v.t.* не поддавáться: *beggar description,* не поддавáться описáнию. —**beggarly,** *adj.* ни́щенский. —**beggary,** *n.* ни́щенство.
begin *v.t.* **1,** *fol. by a noun* начинáть: *begin work,* начинáть рабóту. **2,** *fol. by inf.* начинáть; стать: *he began to write,* он нáчал/стал писáть. —*v.i.* **1,** (start) начинáть: *let us begin,* начнём. **2,** (commence) начинáться: *The meeting is beginning,* собрáние начинáется. **3,** *preceded by* **can't** (do in the slightest degree): *I can't begin to tell you,* не могý дáже сказáть. *It can't begin to compare with...,* э́то не идёт ни в какóе сравнéние с... —**to begin with,** во-пéрвых.
beginner *n.* начинáющий.
beginning *n.* начáло. *In the beginning,* сначáла; вначáле. *From beginning to end,* с начáла до концá. —*adj.* начинáющий. —*prep.* начинáя с: *beginning July 1,* начинáя с пéрвого ию́ля.
begone *interj.* убирáйся!; прочь!
begonia *n.* бегóния.
begrudge *v.t.* **1,** (envy) зави́довать. **2,** (give reluctantly) жалéть; зави́довать.

beguile *v.t.* **1,** (trick) обольща́ть. **2,** (charm) очаро́вывать.
behalf *n., in* **on/in behalf of, 1,** (speaking for; representing) от и́мени (+ *gen.*). **2,** (in the interest of; for the benefit of) в по́льзу (+ *gen.*).
behave *v.i.* **1,** (conduct oneself) вести́ себя́; держа́ть себя́. **2,** (comport oneself properly) вести́ себя́ хорошо́.
behavior *also,* **behaviour** *n.* поведе́ние. —**behaviorism,** *n.* бихевиори́зм.
behead *v.t.* обезгла́вливать. —**beheading,** *n.* обезгла́вливание.
behemoth *n.* бегемо́т.
behest *n. At the behest of,* под дикто́вку (+ *gen.*).
behind *prep.* **1,** (on the far side of) за (+ *instr.*): *behind the scenes,* за кули́сами. **2,** (to the far side of) за (+ *acc.*): *fall behind the couch,* упа́сть за дива́н. **3,** (lagging behind): *be behind schedule,* отстава́ть. *Be behind the times,* не идти́ в но́гу с ве́ком. **4,** (underlying) за (+ *instr.*): *What's behind all this?,* что за э́тим кро́ется? —*adv.* позади́; сза́ди. *Lag behind,* отстава́ть. —*n., colloq.* (buttocks) зад. —**from behind,** из-за (+ *gen.*). *Sneak up on someone from behind,* подкра́дываться к кому́-нибудь сза́ди. —**leave behind, 1,** (get way ahead of) оставля́ть позади́. **2,** (leave after departure or death) оставля́ть по́сле себя́.
behind-the-scenes *adj.* закули́сный.
behold *v.t.* смотре́ть; созерца́ть; зреть. —*interj.* смотри́(те)!
beholden *adj.* обя́занный.
behoove *v.t.* сле́довать (+ *dat.*); надлежа́ть (+ *dat.*): *it behooves you to...,* вам сле́дует (+ *inf.*).
beige *n.* цвет беж. —*adj.* бе́жевый.
being *n.* **1,** (existence) бытие́. **2,** (creature) существо́. *Human being,* челове́к. —**being as/that,** *colloq.* так как. —**come into being,** возника́ть. —**for the time being,** пока́; до поры́ до вре́мени.
belabor *also,* **belabour** *v.t.* **1,** (pummel) колоти́ть. **2,** (assail verbally) обру́шиваться на. **3,** (harp upon) пережёвывать.
belated *adj.* запозда́лый.
belch *v.i.* рыга́ть. —*v.t.* **1,** *fol. by* **up** (cough up) отры́гивать. **2,** *fol. by* **forth** (eject violently) изрыгивать. —*n.* отры́жка.
beleaguer *v.t.* осажда́ть.
belfry *n.* колоко́льня.
Belgian *adj.* бельги́йский. —*n.* бельги́ец; бельги́йка.
belie *v.t.* опроверга́ть; противоре́чить.
belief *n.* **1,** (faith; trust) ве́ра: *belief in God,* ве́ра в бо́га. **2,** (opinion; conviction) убежде́ние: *suffer for one's beliefs,* страда́ть за свои́ убежде́ния. *It is my belief that...,* я счита́ю, что... —**beyond belief,** невероя́тно.
believable *adj.* правдоподо́бный.
believe *v.t.* **1,** (trust the word of; accept as true) ве́рить: *I believe you,* я вам ве́рю. *I can't believe it,* я не могу́ э́тому пове́рить. *I don't believe a word he says,* я не ве́рю ни одному́ его́ сло́ву. *I couldn't believe my eyes,* я не ве́рил(а) свои́м глаза́м. *Believe it or not,* хоти́те ве́рьте, хоти́те нет. **2,** (be of a certain opinion) счита́ть: *I believe him to be mistaken,* я счита́ю, что он ошиба́ется. **3,** (think; be more or less sure) ду́мать: *I believe he left,* ду́маю, что он ушёл. —*v.i.* **1,** (have religious faith) ве́рить. **2,** *fol. by* **in** (have faith in) ве́рить в: *believe in God,* ве́рить в бо́га. —**make believe,** притворя́ться.
believer *n.* ве́рующий.
belittle *v.t.* умаля́ть; принижа́ть.
bell *n.* **1,** (device to be rung) ко́локол; колоко́льчик. **2,** (electrical device, as a doorbell) звоно́к. **3,** (small sphere, as in sleigh bells) бубене́ц; бубе́нчик. **4,** *pl.* (musical instrument) колокола́. **5,** (flare of a wind instrument) растру́б. **6,** *naut.* (ship's bell) ры́нда; (30-minute period) скля́нка: *four bells,* четы́ре скля́нки. —**ring a bell,** *colloq.* быть знако́мым: *the name rings a bell,* и́мя мне знако́мо. *The name doesn't ring a bell,* э́то и́мя мне ничего́ не говори́т.
belladonna *n.* белладо́нна.
bell-bottom *adj., in* **bell-bottom trousers,** брю́ки клёш.
bellboy *n.* коридо́рный. *Also,* **bellhop.**
belle *n.* краса́вица. —**the belle of the ball,** цари́ца ба́ла.
bellflower *n.* колоко́льчик.
bellicose *adj.* вои́нственный. —**bellicosity,** *n.* вои́нственность.
belligerence *n.* вои́нственность.
belligerency *n.* состоя́ние войны́.
belligerent *adj.* **1,** (waging war) вою́ющий. **2,** (bellicose) вои́нственный. —*n.* вою́ющая сторона́.
bellow *v.i.* мыча́ть; реве́ть. —*n.* мыча́ние.
bellows *n.* мехи́.
bell ringer звона́рь.
bell tower колоко́льня.
belly *n.* **1,** (abdomen) живо́т; брю́хо. **2,** *colloq.* (paunch) брюшко́; пу́зо.
bellyache *n.* боль в животе́. —*v.i., slang* (gripe) ныть.
bellyband *n.* подпру́га.
bellybutton *n., colloq.* пуп; пупо́к.
belong *v.i. Usu. rendered with* ме́сто: *I belong here,* моё ме́сто здесь. *This chair belongs in the basement,* э́тому сту́лу ме́сто в подва́ле. *Where do these things belong?,* где ме́сто э́тим веща́м? —**belong to, 1,** (be the property of) принадлежа́ть (+ *dat.*). **2,** (be a member of) принадлежа́ть к; состоя́ть в. **3,** (be one of; be a part of) принадлежа́ть к; относи́ться к.
belongings *n. pl.* пожи́тки.
beloved *adj. & n.* возлю́бленный.
below *adv.* **1,** (at a lower place or level) ни́же; внизу́. *From below,* сни́зу. *They live a floor below,* они́ живу́т этажо́м ни́же. **2,** (to a lower place or level) вниз. —*prep.* ни́же; под. *Below zero,* ни́же нуля́. *Below average,* ни́же сре́днего. *Sink below the horizon,* скры́ться за горизо́нтом.
belt *n.* **1,** (waistband) по́яс; реме́нь. **2,** (zone) по́яс; полоса́. **3,** *mech.* реме́нь: *fan belt,* реме́нь вентиля́тора.
beluga *n.* **1,** (white whale) белу́ха. **2,** (white sturgeon) белу́га.
bemoan *v.t.* се́товать на.
bemused *adj.* **1,** (dazed; bewildered) ошеломлённый; растерянный. **2,** (lost in thought) заду́мчивый; мечта́тельный.
bench *n.* **1,** (seat) скамья́; скаме́йка; ла́вка. **2,** (work table) верста́к.
bench mark репе́р; пике́т.

bend *v.t.* **1,** (curve) гнуть; сгибáть; изгибáть. *Bend out of shape,* искривлять. **2,** (exert, as efforts) прилагáть; направлять; напрягáть. **3,** (force to submit) подчинять: *bend to one's will,* подчинять своéй вóле. —*v.i.* **1,** (become bent) гнýться; сгибáться. **2,** (curve, as of a road) поворáчивать. **3,** *fol. by* **over** (stoop) наклоняться; склоняться; нагибáться; сгибáться. **4,** (yield) гнýться. —*n.* изгиб; сгиб; извилина; излýчина. *See also* **bent.**

bends *n.* кессóнная болéзнь.

beneath *adv.* внизý; ниже. —*prep.* **1,** (below) под. **2,** (unworthy of) ниже: *beneath someone's dignity,* ниже чьегó-нибудь достóинства. *It is beneath him to lie,* лгать недостóйно егó.

benediction *n.* заключительная молитва.

benefactor *n.* благодéтель.

beneficence *n.* **1,** (generosity; kindness) великодýшие. **2,** (beneficent act) благодеяние.

beneficent *adj.* **1,** (kind; generous) великодýшный. **2,** (beneficial) благотвóрный; благодéтельный.

beneficial *adj.* благотвóрный.

beneficiary *n.* наслéдник.

benefit *n.* **1,** (advantage; good) вы́года; пóльза. *For the benefit of,* рáди. **2,** *pl.* (pecuniary aid) посóбие. **3,** *theat.* бенефис. —*v.t.* приносить пóльзу (+ *dat.*). —*v.i.* извлекáть пóльзу. *Both sides benefit,* óбе стороны́ выи́грывают.

benevolent *adj.* доброжелáтельный; благожелáтельный. —**benevolence,** *n.* доброжелáтельство; благожелáтельность.

Bengali *adj.* бенгáльский. —*n.* **1,** (person) бенгáлец; бенгáлка. **2,** (language) бенгáльский язы́к.

benign *adj.* **1,** (kind; gracious) ми́лостивый. **2,** (mild; favorable) благотвóрный. **3,** *med.* доброкáчественный.

bent *adj.* **1,** (curved) изóгнутый. **2,** *fol. by* **on** (determined) реши́вшийся (на); имéющий твёрдое намéрение. —*n.* склóнность; наклóнность; влечéние; тя́га.

benzene *n.* бензóл.

benzine *n.* бензи́н.

benzoin *n.* рóсный лáдан; бензои́н.

benzol *n.* бензóл.

bequeath *v.t.* завещáть.

bequest *n.* посмéртный дар.

berate *v.t.* ругáть; брани́ть.

bereave *v.t.* лишáть. —**bereavement,** *n.* тяжёлая утрáта. —**bereft,** *adj.* лишённый.

beret *n.* берéт.

beriberi *n.* бéри-бéри.

berkelium *n.* беркéлий.

berry *n.* я́года.

berserk *adj.* бéшеный; обезýмевший; исступлённый. *Go berserk,* взбеси́ться; обезýметь; приходи́ть в исступлéние.

berth *n.* **1,** (on a train) (спáльное) мéсто; пóлка. *Upper berth,* вéрхнее мéсто; вéрхняя пóлка. *Lower berth,* ни́жнее мéсто; ни́жняя пóлка. **2,** (on a ship) мéсто; кóйка. **3,** (place of moorage) я́корная стоя́нка; причáл.

beryl *n.* бери́лл.

beryllium *n.* бери́ллий.

beseech *v.t.* умоля́ть; упрáшивать.

beset *v.t.* **1,** (attack) обрýшиваться на. **2,** (hem in) сти́скивать. **3,** (plague) мýчить: *be beset with doubts,* мýчиться сомнéниями. **4,** (stud) усыпáть.

beside *prep.* **1,** (alongside) ря́дом с; вóзле; пóдле. **2,** (other than) крóме; поми́мо. —**beside oneself,** вне себя́: *beside oneself with joy,* вне себя́ от рáдости. —**beside the point,** не к дéлу; некстáти; не по существý.

besides *prep.* крóме; поми́мо. —*adv.* крóме тогó; к томý же.

besiege *v.t.* **1,** (lay siege to) осаждáть. **2,** (overwhelm, as with offers) засыпáть; осаждáть.

besmirch *v.t.* **1,** (soil) пáчкать. **2,** (tarnish; dishonor) черни́ть; пятнáть.

besom *n.* вéник.

bespatter *v.t.* забры́згивать.

bespeak *v.t.* **1,** (be indicative of) говори́ть о. **2,** (presage) предвещáть.

bespectacled *adj.* в очкáх.

besprinkle *v.t.* обры́згивать; окропля́ть; опры́скивать.

best *adj.* лýчший; сáмый лýчший; наилýчший. *Best wishes,* наилýчшие пожелáния. —*adv.* лýчше всегó; бóльше всегó. *I like this one best,* э́тот мне нрáвится бóльше всегó. —*n.* [*usu.* **the best**] лýчший; лýчшее: *one of the best,* оди́н из лýчших. *It's all for the best,* всё к лýчшему. *Hope for the best,* надéяться на лýчшее. *Turn out for the best,* обернýться к лýчшему. —*v.t.* побеждáть: *best one's rival,* победи́ть сопéрника. —**all the best!,** всегó хорóшего!; всегó дóброго!; всегó лýчшего! —**at best,** в лýчшем слýчае. —**be at one's best,** быть в ударе; быть на высотé. —**do one's best,** сдéлать всё возмóжное. —**get the best of,** брать верх над. —**had best,** бы лýчше (+ *dat.*): *you had best go right away,* вам бы лýчше пойти́ сейчáс же. —**make the best of,** мири́ться с. —**to the best of my ability,** по мéре сил; по мéре спосóбностей. —**to the best of my knowledge/belief,** наскóлько мне извéстно.

bestial *adj.* звéрский; живóтный. —**bestiality,** *n.* звéрство.

best man шáфер.

bestow *v.t.* **1,** (give as a gift) дари́ть; даровáть; жáловать. **2,** (confer; award) присуждáть; присвáивать; награждáть. —**bestowal,** *n.* присуждéние; присвоéние; награждéние.

bestrew *v.t.* **1,** (scatter about) разбрáсывать. **2,** (cover with things scattered) усыпáть.

best seller бестсéллер.

bet *n.* пари́. —*v.i.* держáть пари́: *do you want to bet?,* хоти́те держáть пари́? *Bet on a horse,* дéлать стáвку (*or* стáвить) на лóшадь. —*v.t.* стáвить; спóрить на: *bet ten dollars,* стáвить (*or* спóрить на) дéсять дóлларов. *I'll bet you that...,* держý пари́, что... *I bet him ten dollars that...,* я поспóрил с ним на дéсять дóлларов, что... —**you bet!,** конéчно!; бýдьте увéрены!

beta *n.* бéта. —**beta particle,** бéта-части́ца. —**beta rays,** бéта-лучи́.

betake *v.t.* [*usu.* **betake oneself**] отправля́ться.

betel *n.* бéтель.

betide *v.t.* случáться с; постигáть. *Woe betide...!,* гóре (+ *dat.*)!

betray *v.t.* **1,** (be a traitor to; be disloyal to) изменя́ть; предавáть. **2,** (disappoint, as someone's trust) обмáнывать. **3,** (reveal; give away) выдавáть. —**betrayal,** *n.* предáтельство; измéна.

betroth *v.t.* обручáть; помóлвить. —**betrothal,** *n.* обручéние; помóлвка. —**betrothed,** *adj.* обручённый; помóлвленный.

better *adj.* **1,** *modifier* лýчший. **2,** *predicate* лýчше: *he is (feeling) better today,* емý лýчше сегóдня. *Get better,* стать лýчше; улучшáться. —*adv.* лýчше: *play better when it's warm,* игрáть лýчше, когдá теплó. *I like this one better,* э́тот (э́та, э́то) мне бóльше нрáвится. —*n.* **1,** (something better) лýчшее: *change for the better,* перемéна к лýчшему. *To change for the better,* измени́ться в лýчшую стóрону. **2,** *pl.* (one's superiors) стáршие. —*v.t.* **1,** (improve) улучшáть. *Better oneself,* выдвигáться. **2,** (surpass) улучшáть: *better the world record,* улýчшить мировóй рекóрд. —**get the better of,** брать верх над. —**never better,** как нельзя́ лýчше; как никогдá. —**so much the better,** тем лýчше. —**think better of it,** одýматься. —**you had better...,** вам бы лýчше (+ *inf.*).

betterment *n.* улучшéние.

bettor *n.* держáщий пари́.

between *prep.* мéжду. *In between,* посреди́. —**between you and me,** мéжду нáми.

betwixt *prep., archaic* мéжду. —**betwixt and between,** ни то ни сё.

bevel *n.* **1,** (tool) наугóльник. **2,** (sloping part) скос. —*v.t.* скáшивать.

beverage *n.* напи́ток.

bevy *n.* **1,** (group) грýппа. **2,** (flock) стáя.

bewail *v.t.* сéтовать на.

beware *v.i.* [*usu.* **beware of**] берéчься; остерегáться.

bewilder *v.t.* озадáчивать; сбивáть с тóлку. —**bewildered,** *adj.* озадáченный; недоумéнный; недоумевáющий. —**bewildering,** *adj.* недоумевáющий. —**bewilderment,** *n.* недоумéние; растéрянность.

bewitch *v.t.* **1,** (cast a spell over) заколдóвывать; околодóвывать; заворáживать. **2,** (captivate) очарóвывать; зачарóвывать; обворáживать; заворáживать. —**bewitched,** *adj.* заколдóванный; зачарóванный. —**bewitching,** *adj.* очаровáтельный; обаятельный; обворожи́тельный.

beyond *prep.* **1,** (past) за; дáльше. *Beyond the bounds of,* за предéлами (+ *gen.*). *The matter never got beyond the talking stage,* дáльше разговóров дéло не шло. **2,** (after) пóзже (+ *gen.*). **3,** (in addition to; over and above) крóме. **4,** (surpassing; exceeding) вне; вы́ше; свы́ше; сверх. *Beyond compare,* вне сравнéния. *Beyond any doubt,* вне вся́кого сомнéния. *Beyond belief,* невероя́тно. *Beyond all expectations,* сверх вся́кого ожидáния. *Beyond my comprehension,* вы́ше моегó понимáния. *Live beyond one's means,* жить не по свои́м срéдствам.

bias *n.* **1,** (oblique line) кося́я ли́ния. **2,** (partiality) пристрáстие. **3,** (prejudice) предубеждéние; предвзя́тость.

biased *adj.* **1,** (partial) пристрáстный. **2,** (prejudiced) предубеждённый.

bib *n.* нагрýдник.

Bible *n.* би́блия. —**Biblical,** *adj.* библéйский.

bibliography *n.* библиогрáфия. —**bibliographer,** *n.* библиóграф. —**bibliographic,** *adj.* библиографи́ческий.

bibliophile *n.* библиофи́л; книголю́б; кни́жник.

bicameral *adj.* двухпалáтный.

bicarbonate of soda двууглеки́слая сóда; питьевáя сóда.

bicentennial *adj.* двухсотлéтний. —*n.* двухсотлéтие. *Also,* **bicentenary.**

biceps *n.* двуглáвая мы́шца; би́цепс.

bicker *v.i.* спóрить; вздóрить; пререкáться.

bicuspid *n.* мáлый коренно́й зуб.

bicycle *n.* велосипéд. —*adj.* велосипéдный: *bicycle racing,* велосипéдные гóнки. —*v.i.* éздить на велосипéде. —**bicyclist,** *n.* велосипеди́ст.

bid *v.t.* **1,** (order) велéть. **2,** (ask) проси́ть. **3,** (say): *bid farewell,* прощáться; *bid welcome,* приветствовать. **4,** (offer, as a price) предлагáть. **5,** *cards* объявля́ть. —*v.i.* **1,** (make a bid) предлагáть цéну. **2,** *fol. by inf.* (strive) добивáться тогó, чтóбы (+ *inf.*). —*n.* **1,** (offer) предложéние. **2,** (attempt) попы́тка. **3,** *cards* объявлéние. —**bid fair,** обещáть.

bidding *n.* **1,** (making of bids) предложéние цен. **2,** (ordering; directing) диктóвка: *at someone's bidding,* под чью-нибудь диктóвку. *Do someone's bidding,* выполня́ть чью-нибудь вóлю.

bide *v.t.,* in **bide one's time,** выжидáть удóбный слýчай.

biennial *adj.* двухлéтний. —*n.* двухлéтнее растéние.

bier *n.* катафáлк.

bifocal *adj.* двухфóкусный. —**bifocals,** *n.pl.* очки́ с двухфóкусными стёклами.

bifurcate *v.i.* разветвля́ться. —**bifurcation,** *n.* разветвлéние.

big *adj.* **1,** (large) большóй: *big house,* большóй дом. **2,** (elder) стáрший: *my big sister,* моя́ стáршая сестрá. **3,** (important; prominent) крýпный. **4,** (outstanding in its way) большóй: *big secret/risk/liar,* большóй секрéт/риск/лгун.

bigamist *n.* двоежéнец.

bigamy *n.* двоебрáчие; двоежёнство.

Big Dipper Большáя Медвéдица.

big game крýпный зверь. *Big-game hunting,* охóта на крýпного звéря.

big-hearted *adj.* великодýшный.

bighorn *n.* снéжный барáн.

bigmouth *n.* пустозвóн.

bigot *n.* фанáтик; изувéр. —**bigoted,** *adj.* фанати́ческий; нетерпи́мый. —**bigotry,** *n.* фанати́зм.

big shot *slang* ши́шка.

bigwig *n., colloq.* туз; вороти́ла.

bike *n.* & *v., colloq.* = **bicycle.**

bilateral *adj.* двусторóнний.

bile *n.* жёлчь. —**bile duct,** жёлчный протóк.

bilge *n.* **1,** (bottom of a ship) дни́ще. **2,** *colloq.* (twaddle) пустослóвие.

bilingual *adj.* двуязы́чный. —**bilingualism,** *n.* двуязы́чие.

bilious *adj.* жёлчный.

bilk *v.t.* надувáть; обжýливать.

bill *n.* **1,** (statement of charges) счёт: *water bill,* счёт за вóду. **2,** (bank note) билéт; бумáжка: *ten-dollar bill,* билéт/бумáжка в дéсять дóлларов. **3,** (draft of a proposed law) законопроéкт; билль. **4,** (schedule of theatrical entertainment) прогрáмма. **5,** (poster) афи́ша. **6,** (beak) клюв. —*v.t.* **1,** (present with a bill) подавáть счёт (+ *dat.*). **2,** (advertise) анонси́ровать. —**bill and coo,** воркoвáть. —**fill the**

bill, годи́ться; отвеча́ть тре́бованиям.
billboard *n.* рекла́мный щит.
billet *n.* помеще́ние; кварти́ра. —*v.t.* расквартирова́ть; ста́вить на посто́й. —**billeting,** *n.* расквартирова́ние; посто́й.
billfold *n.* бума́жник.
billiard *adj.* билья́рдный: *billiard table,* билья́рдный стол.
billiards *n.* билья́рд.
billion *n.* миллиа́рд. —**billionth,** *adj.* миллиа́рдный.
bill of exchange ве́ксель.
bill of fare меню́.
bill of lading накладна́я; коносаме́нт.
Bill of Rights билль о права́х.
billow *n.* вал. —*v.i.* вздыма́ться; волнова́ться. —**billlowy,** *adj.* вздыма́ющийся.
billy *n.* дуби́нка. *Also,* **billy club.**
billy goat козёл; ко́злик.
bimetallic *adj.* биметалли́ческий. —**bimetallism,** *n.* биметалли́зм.
bimonthly *adj.* двухме́сячный. —*adv.* раз в два ме́сяца. —*n.* двухме́сячник.
bin *n.* **1,** (for grain) ларь; за́кром. **2,** (for coal) бу́нкер (для угля́).
binary *adj.* **1,** (having two components) двойно́й. **2,** *chem.; math.; astron.* бина́рный.
bind *v.t.* **1,** (tie up) вяза́ть; свя́зывать: *bind sheaves,* вяза́ть снопы́; *bind hand and foot,* связа́ть по рука́м и нога́м. **2,** (link closely) свя́зывать. **3,** *usu. fol. by* **up** (bandage) перевя́зывать. **4,** (obligate) обя́зывать: *this does not bind you to anything,* э́то вас ни к чему́ не обя́зывает. **5,** (fasten together, as a book) переплета́ть. *See also* **bound.**
binder *n.* **1,** (bookbinder) переплётчик. **2,** (holder of loose-leaf sheets) тетра́дь.
bindery *n.* переплётная.
binding *n.* **1,** (tying) вяза́ние. **2,** (covering of a book) переплёт. —*adj.* **1,** (obligatory) обя́зывающий; обяза́тельный. **2,** *med.* крепи́тельный.
bindweed *n.* вьюно́к.
binge *n., colloq.* кутёж; вы́пивка. *Go on a binge,* прокути́ть.
bingo *n.* лото́.
binoculars *n.pl.* бино́кль.
binomial *n.* бино́м; двучле́н. —*adj.* двучле́нный. —**binomial theorum,** бино́м Нью́тона.
biochemistry *n.* биохи́мия. —**biochemical,** *adj.* биохими́ческий. —**biochemist,** *n.* биохи́мик.
biography *n.* биогра́фия. —**biographer,** *n.* био́граф. —**biographical,** *adj.* биографи́ческий.
biology *n.* биоло́гия. —**biological,** *adj.* биологи́ческий. —**biologist,** *n.* био́лог.
bionics *n.* био́ника.
biophysics *n.* биофи́зика.
biopsy *n.* биопси́я.
bipartisan *adj.* двухпарти́йный.
bipartite *adj.* двусторо́нний.
biped *adj.* двуно́гий. —*n.* двуно́гое живо́тное.
biplane *n.* бипла́н.
birch *n.* берёза. —*adj.* берёзовый. *Birch bark,* берёста. *Birch forest,* березня́к.
bird *n.* пти́ца. —*adj.* [*also,* **bird's**] пти́чий: *bird's nest,* пти́чье гнездо́. —**a bird in the hand is worth two in the bush,** не сули́ журавля́ в не́бе, а дай сини́цу в ру́ки. —**birds of a feather,** *see* **feather.** —**kill two birds with one stone,** уби́ть двух за́йцев одни́м уда́ром.
birdcage *n.* пти́чья клетка.
birdie *n.* пти́чка.
birdlime *n.* пти́чий клей.
bird of paradise ра́йская пти́ца.
birdseed *n.* пти́чий корм.
bird's-eye view вид с пти́чьего полёта.
birth *n.* **1,** (being born) рожде́ние. *Blind from birth,* слепо́й от рожде́ния *or* от приро́ды. **2,** (giving birth) ро́ды. **3,** (lineage; descent) происхожде́ние. *He is Italian by birth,* он ро́дом из Ита́лии. —**give birth (to),** рожа́ть. *She gave birth to a son,* у неё роди́лся сын.
birth certificate свиде́тельство о рожде́нии; ме́трика.
birth control контро́ль над рожда́емостью. *Practice birth control,* применя́ть противозача́точные сре́дства.
birthday *n.* день рожде́ния. *Birthday present,* пода́рок ко дню рожде́ния.
birthmark *n.* роди́мое пятно́; ро́динка.
birthplace *n.* ме́сто рожде́ния.
birth rate рожда́емость.
birthright *n.* пра́во перворо́дства.
biscuit *n.* пече́нье; суха́рь; гале́та.
bisect *v.t.* разреза́ть.
bisexual *adj.* двупо́лый.
bishop *n.* **1,** (prelate) епи́скоп. **2,** *chess* слон. —**bishopric,** *n.* сан епи́скопа.
bismuth *n.* ви́смут.
bison *n.* **1,** (American) бизо́н. **2,** (European) зубр.
bit *n.* **1,** (small piece) кусо́чек. *Smash to bits,* разбива́ть вдре́безги. **2,** (small amount) чу́точка. **3,** (mouthpiece of a bridle) удила́. **4,** (boring device) пёрка. —**a bit,** немно́го; немно́жко. *He is a bit of a coward,* он трусова́т. —**bit by bit,** ка́пля за ка́плей; ка́пля по ка́пле. —**bit part,** выходна́я роль. —**do one's bit,** внести́ свою́ ле́пту. —**every bit,** всё без оста́тка. —**not a bit,** нисколько; ничу́ть; ни ка́пли; ни на йо́ту. *You haven't changed a bit!,* вы совсе́м не измени́лись! —**take the bit in one's teeth,** закуси́ть удила́.
bitch *n.* су́ка. —**son of a bitch,** *vulg.* су́кин сын.
bite *v.t.* **1,** (grip or cut with the teeth) куса́ть. *Bite one's nails,* грызть *or* куса́ть но́гти. **2,** (sting) жа́лить. —*v.i.* **1,** (grip something with the teeth) куса́ть. **2,** (tend to bite, as of a dog) куса́ться. **3,** (take the bait, as of a fish) клева́ть. **4,** *fig.* (take the bait; be tricked) попа́сться на у́дочку. —*n.* **1,** (act of biting; wound inflicted by biting) уку́с: *mosquito bite,* комари́ный уку́с. **2,** (snack; morsel) заку́ска. *Have a bite to eat,* закуси́ть. **3,** *dent.* прику́с. —**bite off,** отку́сывать. —**bite one's tongue,** прикуси́ть язы́к.
biting *adj.* **1,** (sharp, as of a wind) ре́зкий; хлёсткий. **2,** (caustic; mordant) е́дкий; ко́лкий; хлёсткий.
bitter *adj.* **1,** (acrid) го́рький: *bitter lemon/taste,* го́рький лимо́н/вкус. **2,** (intense) жесто́кий; лю́тый; ожесточённый. *Bitter cold,* лю́тый хо́лод. *Bitter enemy,* злейший враг. *Bitter hatred,* лю́тая не́нависть. *Bitter struggle,* ожесточённая борьба́. *Bitter disappointment,* го́рькое *or* жесто́кое разочарова́ние. **3,** (hard to accept) го́рький: *the bitter truth,* го́рькая пра́вда. *A bitter lesson,* жесто́кий уро́к. **4,** (embittered) озло́бленный. —*adv.* о́чень; ужа́сно.

Bitter cold, ужа́сно хо́лодно. —**to the bitter end,** до са́мого конца́; до после́днего.
bitterly *adv.* го́рько: *cry/complain bitterly,* го́рько пла́кать/жа́ловаться. *Be bitterly disappointed,* жесто́ко разочарова́ться.
bittern *n.* вы́пь.
bitterness *n.* **1,** (bitter taste) го́речь. **2,** (bitter feeling) го́речь; озлобле́ние; ожесточе́ние.
bitters *n.pl.* го́рькая.
bitumen *n.* биту́м. —**bituminous,** *adj.* битумино́зный; биту́мный.
bivalent *adj.* двухвале́нтный.
bivalve *adj.* двуство́рчатый. —*n.* двуство́рчатый моллю́ск.
bivouac *n.* бива́к. —*v.i.* стоя́ть *or* располага́ться бива́ком.
biweekly *adj.* двухнеде́льный. —*adv.* раз в две неде́ли. —*n.* двухнеде́льник.
bizarre *adj.* стра́нный; дико́винный; экстравага́нтный.
blab *v.i.* (chatter) болта́ть. —*v.t.* (give away, as a secret) разба́лтывать; выба́лтывать.
blabbermouth *n., colloq.* болту́н.
black *adj.* чёрный. *Turn black,* черне́ть. *Paint the door black,* кра́сить дверь в чёрный цвет. —*n.* **1,** (color) чёрный цвет. *Dressed in black,* одет(а) в чёрное. **2,** (negro) негр; чёрный. **3,** *chess* чёрные: *black wins,* чёрные выи́грывают. —**black out, 1,** (extinguish all the lights in) затемня́ть. **2,** (lose consciousness) потеря́ть созна́ние.
black-and-blue *adj.* в синяка́х. *Beat black-and-blue,* избива́ть до синяко́в.
black-and-white *adj.* чёрно-бе́лый. *In black-and-white,* чёрным по бе́лому.
blackball *v.t.* забаллоти́ровать.
blackberry *n.* ежеви́ка. —*adj.* ежеви́чный.
blackbird *n.* чёрный дрозд.
blackboard *n.* доска́.
blacken *v.t.* черни́ть. —*v.i.* черне́ть.
black eye подби́тый глаз. *Give someone a black eye,* подби́ть глаз кому́-нибудь.
black grouse те́терев.
blackguard *n.* подле́ц; негодя́й; мерза́вец.
blackhead *n.* у́горь.
blacking *n.* ва́кса.
blackjack *n.* **1,** (weapon) дуби́на; дуби́нка. **2,** (card game) два́дцать одно́.
blacklist *n.* чёрный спи́сок. —*v.t.* вноси́ть в чёрный спи́сок.
black magic чёрная ма́гия.
blackmail *n.* шанта́ж. —*v.t.* шантажи́ровать. —**blackmailer,** *n.* шантажи́ст.
black market чёрный ры́нок.
blackness *n.* чернота́.
blackout *n.* **1,** (extinguishing of lights) затемне́ние; светомаскиро́вка. **2,** (fainting spell) поте́ря созна́ния; о́бморок.
black sheep парши́вая овца́ (в семье́).
blacksmith *n.* кузне́ц.
blackthorn *n.* тёрн; терно́вник.
bladder *n.* пузы́рь.
blade *n.* **1,** (of a tool) ле́звие. **2,** (of a weapon, esp. a sword) клино́к. **3,** (of an oar, propeller, etc.) ло́пасть. **4,** (of a saw) полотно́. **5,** (of a fan, windmill, etc.) крыло́. **6,** (of an ice skate) по́лоз. **7,** (of a leaf) пласти́нка. **8,** (of grass) трави́нка; были́нка. **9,** *colloq.* (dashing young man) у́харь; хват. —**razor blade,** ле́звие бри́твы. —**shoulder blade,** лопа́тка.
blame *v.t.* вини́ть: *don't blame me!,* не вини́те меня́! *You have only yourself to blame,* вы должны́ вини́ть то́лько самого́ себя́. —*n.* **1,** (responsibility) вина́: *place the blame on,* возлага́ть вину́ на. **2,** (censure) порица́ние: *deserve blame,* заслу́живать порица́ния. —**be to blame,** быть винова́тым: *I am to blame,* я винова́т(а).
blameless *adj.* невино́вный; неви́нный.
blameworthy *adj.* заслу́живающий порица́ния.
blanch *v.t.* (bleach) бели́ть. —*v.i.* (turn pale) бледне́ть.
bland *adj.* **1,** (mild; not irritating) мя́гкий. *Bland diet,* лёгкая дие́та. **2,** (flavorless; dull) пре́сный; бесцве́тный.
blandishment *n.* угово́р.
blank *adj.* **1,** (not written on) чи́стый. *Blank space,* пусто́е ме́сто. **2,** (of a cartridge, shot, etc.) холосто́й. **3,** (solid, as of a wall) глухо́й. **4,** (vacant, as of a look) отсу́тствующий; неви́дящий. —*n.* **1,** (space) пусто́е ме́сто. **2,** (form) бланк; анке́та. **3,** (blank cartridge) холосто́й патро́н. **4,** (loss of memory) прова́л па́мяти: *my mind is a complete blank,* у меня́ по́лный прова́л па́мяти. —**draw a blank,** ничего́ не доби́ться. —**go blank, 1,** *My mind went blank,* у меня́ отши́бло па́мять. **2,** *The screen went blank,* карти́на исче́зла с экра́на.
blanket *n.* **1,** (bed covering) одея́ло. **2,** *fig.* (mantle) покро́в: *blanket of snow,* сне́жный покро́в. —*adj.* о́бщий; огу́льный. —*v.t.* оку́тывать.
blankly *adv.* отсу́тствующим взгля́дом.
blank verse бе́лые стихи́.
blare *v.t.* & *i.* труби́ть. —*n.* тру́бный звук.
blarney *n.* лесть.
blasé *adj.* пресы́щенный.
blaspheme *v.i.* богоху́льствовать; кощу́нствовать. —*v.t.* поноси́ть; хули́ть.
blasphemous *adj.* богоху́льный; кощу́нственный. —**blasphemy,** *n.* богоху́льство; кощу́нство.
blast *n.* **1,** (gust of air) поры́в (ве́тра); струя́ (во́здуха). **2,** (loud sound, as of a trumpet) (тру́бный) звук. **3,** (explosion) взрыв. **4,** *colloq.* (verbal attack) вы́пад. —*v.t.* **1,** (blow up) взрыва́ть: *blast rock,* взрыва́ть скалу́. **2,** *colloq.* (assail) обру́шиваться на. —*v.i.* [*usu.* **blast off**] стартова́ть; отрыва́ться от земли́. —**(at) full blast,** по́лным хо́дом.
blasted *adj., colloq.* проклятый.
blast furnace до́мна; до́менная печь.
blasting *n.* взрывны́е рабо́ты. —**blasting powder,** ми́нный по́рох.
blast-off *n.* старт.
blatant *adj.* **1,** (noisy) крикли́вый. **2,** (obvious) я́вный.
blather *n.* пустосло́вие.
blaze *n.* пла́мя. —*v.i.* **1,** (burn) горе́ть; пыла́ть. **2,** (give off great heat) пали́ть: *the blazing sun,* паля́щее со́лнце. **3,** *fol. by* **away** (fire rapidly) открыва́ть ого́нь. —*v.t., in* **blaze a trail,** прокла́дывать путь. —**like blazes,** *colloq.* со всех ног; сломя́ го́лову.
blazer *n.* спорти́вная ку́ртка.
blazon *n.* герб.
bleach *v.t.* бели́ть; отбе́ливать. —*n.* бели́льное сре́дство. —**bleached,** *adj.* белёный.

bleaching *n.* беле́ние. —*adj.* бели́льный. —**bleaching powder,** хло́рная и́звесть.
bleak *adj.* **1,** (desolate) пусты́нный. **2,** (dismal; unpromising) мра́чный.
bleary-eyed *adj.* осолове́лый; посолове́лый.
bleat *v.i.* бле́ять. —*n.* бле́яние.
bleed *v.i.* кровоточи́ть. *His nose is bleeding,* у него́ кровь течёт и́з носу. *He is bleeding profusely,* он истека́ет кро́вью. *My heart bleeds for you,* моё се́рдце за вас кро́вью облива́ется. —*v.t.* **1,** (take blood from) пуска́ть кровь (+ *dat.*). **2,** *colloq.* (extort money from) обира́ть; обдира́ть. —**bleed white,** обобра́ть до ни́тки.
bleeding *n.* кровотече́ние. —*adj.* истека́ющий кро́вью.
blemish *n.* пятно́. —*v.t.* пятна́ть.
blend *v.t.* сме́шивать. —*v.i.* **1,** (merge; unite) сме́шиваться; слива́ться. **2,** (go well together) гармони́ровать; сочета́ться. —*n.* смесь; смеше́ние.
blender *n.* смеси́тель.
bless *v.t.* **1,** (ask divine favor for) благословля́ть: *God bless you!,* да благослови́т тебя́ Бог. ♦*After a sneeze* будь здоро́в(а)!; бу́дьте здоро́вы! **2,** (endow) наделя́ть: *blessed with outstanding ability,* наделён исключи́тельными спосо́бностями. *Be blessed with good health,* по́льзоваться хоро́шим здоро́вьем.
blessed *adj.* **1,** (holy) свяще́нный. **2,** (blissful) блаже́нный. *Of blessed memory,* блаже́нной па́мяти.
blessing *n.* **1,** (benediction) благослове́ние. **2,** (that which gives happiness) бла́го. **3,** (approval) благослове́ние: *with the blessing of,* с благослове́ния (+ *gen.*).
blight *n.* **1,** (plant disease) ожо́ги расте́ний. **2,** *fig.* (plague) бич. —*v.t.* вреди́ть; губи́ть.
blind *adj.* слепо́й. *Go blind,* сле́пнуть. *Blind in one eye,* слепо́й на оди́н глаз. —*adv.* вслепу́ю. —*v.t.* ослепля́ть. —*n.* што́ра. *Venetian blinds,* подъёмные жалюзи́. —**turn a blind eye to,** закрыва́ть глаза́ на; смотре́ть сквозь па́льцы на.
blind alley тупи́к.
blinders *n.pl.* шо́ры; накла́зники.
blindfold *n.* повя́зка (на глаза́х). —*v.t.* завя́зывать глаза́ (+ *dat.*).
blindfolded *adj.* с завя́занными глаза́ми. —*adv.* вслепу́ю.
blinding *adj.* ослепи́тельный.
blindly *adv.* сле́по; вслепу́ю.
blindman's bluff жму́рки.
blindness *n.* слепота́.
blink *v.i.* **1,** (wink; flash) мига́ть; морга́ть. **2,** *fol. by* **at** (pretend not to see) смотре́ть сквозь па́льцы (на). —*v.t.* мига́ть; моргну́ть (глаза́ми). *Without blinking an eye,* гла́зом не моргну́в. —**on the blink,** *colloq.* не рабо́тает.
blinker *n.* **1,** (flashing light) мига́лка. **2,** *pl.* (shades for a horse's eyes) накла́зники; шо́ры.
bliss *n.* блаже́нство. —**blissful,** *adj.* блаже́нный.
blister *n.* волды́рь; пузы́рь.
blistering *adj.* **1,** (of heat) паля́щий. **2,** (scathing, as of criticism) разно́сный.
blithe *adj.* весёлый; беспе́чный; жизнера́достный.
blitzkrieg *n.* молниено́сная война́.
blizzard *n.* вью́га; пурга́; бура́н.
bloat *v.t.* вздува́ть; раздува́ть. —**bloated,** *adj.* взду́тый; разду́тый.
blob *n.* ка́пля; ша́рик.
bloc *n.* блок.
block *n.* **1,** (solid piece) глы́ба: *block of ice,* глы́ба льда. **2,** (block of wood) чурба́н. **3,** (chopping block) коло́да; (execution block) пла́ха. **4,** *usu. pl.* (children's building blocks) ку́бики. **5,** (city block) кварта́л. **6,** (mold for shaping hats) болва́н. **7,** (large building brick) блок. **8,** (pulley) блок. **9,** (in an engine) блок: *cylinder block,* блок цили́ндров. **10,** (obstruction) прегра́да; зато́р. **11,** *philately* блок. **12,** *slang* (head) башка́. *Knock one's block off,* всы́пать по пе́рвое число́. —*v.t.* **1,** (obstruct) прегражда́ть; загражда́ть; загора́живать; перекрыва́ть. **2,** *fol. by* **up** (clog) забива́ть. **3,** (prevent; thwart) меша́ть; срыва́ть. **4,** *sports* блоки́ровать. **5,** *fol. by* **out** (outline) намеча́ть; набра́сывать.
blockade *n.* блока́да. —*v.t.* блоки́ровать.
blockage *n.* **1,** (act of blocking) преграждение. **2,** (obstruction; jam) прегра́да; зато́р. **3,** *med.* непроходи́мость; заку́порка.
blockhead *n.* болва́н; тупи́ца.
blockhouse *n.* блокга́уз.
block letters печа́тные бу́квы.
blond *n.* [*fem.* **blonde**] блонди́н; блонди́нка. —*adj.* белоку́рый.
blood *n.* кровь. *It's in his blood,* э́то у него́ в крови́. —*adj.* **1,** (pert. to blood) кровяно́й. **2,** (related by blood) кро́вный. —**in cold blood,** хладнокро́вно.
blood bath крова́вая ба́ня.
blood clot сгу́сток кро́ви.
bloodcurdling *adj.* душераздира́ющий.
bloodhound *n.* ище́йка.
bloodless *adj.* бескро́вный.
bloodletting *n.* **1,** (drawing of blood) кровопуска́ние. **2,** (bloodshed) кровопроли́тие.
blood orange королёк.
blood poisoning зараже́ние кро́ви.
blood pressure кровяно́е давле́ние.
bloodshed *n.* кровопроли́тие.
bloodshot *adj.* на́литый кро́вью. *Become bloodshot,* нали́ться кро́вью.
bloodstain *n.* кровяно́е *or* крова́вое пятно́. —**bloodstained,** *adj.* окрова́вленный.
bloodstream *n.* ток кро́ви.
bloodsucker *n.* **1,** (leech) пия́вка. **2,** (extortionist) кровопи́йца.
blood test ана́лиз (*or* иссле́дование) кро́ви.
bloodthirsty *adj.* кровожа́дный.
blood transfusion перелива́ние кро́ви.
blood type гру́ппа кро́ви.
blood vessel кровено́сный сосу́д.
bloody *adj.* крова́вый. —*v.t.* окрова́вить. *Bloody someone's nose,* расква́сить кому́-нибудь нос.
bloom *v.i.* цвести́. —*n.* цвет: *in full bloom,* в по́лном цвету́. *Burst into bloom,* расцвета́ть; зацвести́. *Lose its bloom,* отцвета́ть.
blossom *n.* цвет: *apple blossom,* я́блоневый цвет. —*v.i.* цвести́; расцвета́ть.
blot *n.* пятно́. *Inkblot,* кля́кса. —*v.t.* **1,** (stain) пятна́ть. **2,** (dry; soak up) промока́ть. —**blot out, 1,** (hide; cover; obscure) затмева́ть. **2,** (efface; erase) изгла́живать. **3,** (destroy) уничтожа́ть.
blotch *n.* **1,** (spot) пятно́. **2,** (blemish on the skin) прыщ.
blotter *n.* промока́шка.

blotting paper промока́тельная (*or* пропускна́я) бума́га.
blouse *n.* блу́зка; ко́фточка.
blow *n.* **1,** (hard stroke; shock) уда́р: *with one blow,* одни́м уда́ром. *They came to blows,* у них дошло́ до дра́ки. *A blow to the family,* уда́р для семьи́. **2,** (blast of air) дунове́ние. *Blow out the candles with one blow,* заду́ть све́чи одни́м дунове́нием (*or* вы́дохом). —*v.i.* **1,** (of the wind) дуть. **2,** (of a horn, whistle, etc.) гуде́ть. **3,** (puff) дуть: *blow on one's fingers,* дуть на па́льцы. **4,** (be carried by the wind) лете́ть. *The paper blew away,* бума́жка улете́ла. **5,** (of a fuse) перегоре́ть. —*v.t.* **1,** (drive by blowing) гнать (ли́стья); развева́ть (фла́ги). *Blow dust from the shelf,* сдува́ть пыль с по́лки. *Blow smoke in someone's face,* пуска́ть дым в лицо́ (+ *dat.*). **2,** (make, as glass, bubbles, etc.) выдува́ть (стекло́); пуска́ть (мы́льные пузыри́). **3,** (cause to sound, as a trumpet) труби́ть (в трубу́); (a whistle) дать (свисто́к); (a car horn) гуде́ть. **4,** (clear, as one's nose) сморка́ть (нос); сморка́ться. **5,** *slang* (squander) транжи́рить; спуска́ть. **6,** in *blow a kiss,* посла́ть возду́шный поцелу́й. **7,** *in* **blow a fuse; blow one's top; blow one's stack,** *colloq.* взорва́ться. —**blow down,** сва́ливать. —**blow off, 1,** (blow away) сдува́ть. *My hat blew off,* шля́пу у меня́ сду́ло. **2,** (give off, as steam) выпуска́ть. **3,** in *blow off steam, fig., colloq.* дать вы́ход свои́м чу́вствам. —**blow out, 1,** (extinguish by blowing) задува́ть; туши́ть. **2,** (remove by blowing) выдува́ть. **3,** (clean out by blowing) продува́ть. **4,** (burst, as of a tire) ло́пнуть. **5,** (fail, as of a bulb) перегоре́ть. **6,** in *blow one's brains out,* пусти́ть себе́ пу́лю в лоб. —**blow over, 1,** (topple) сва́ливать. **2,** (be forgotten) проходи́ть; минова́ть. **3,** (subside) затиха́ть; утиха́ть. —**blow up, 1,** (inflate) надува́ть. **2,** (destroy) взрыва́ть; подрыва́ть. **3,** *photog.* (enlarge) увели́чивать. **4,** (exaggerate) раздува́ть. **5,** (of a storm) налете́ть. **6,** *colloq.* (lose one's temper) взорва́ться.
blower *n.* вентиля́тор.
blowgun *n.* духово́е ружьё.
blowout *n.* разры́в (ши́ны).
blowpipe *n.* пая́льная тру́бка.
blowtorch *n.* пая́льная ла́мпа.
blubber *n.* во́рвань.
bludgeon *n.* дуби́на; дуби́нка. —*v.t.* бить дуби́ной; дуба́сить.
blue *adj.* **1,** (color) си́ний (*dark*); голубо́й (*light*). **2,** (depressed) уны́лый; пода́вленный. —*n.* си́ний цвет; синева́. —*v.t.* подси́нивать. —**appear out of the blue,** с не́ба свали́ться. —**from out of the blue,** отку́да ни возьми́сь. —**once in a blue moon,** в ко́и ве́ки.
bluebell *n.* колоко́льчик.
blueberry *n.* черни́ка. —*adj.* черни́чный.
blue-eyed *adj.* синегла́зый.
bluefish *n.* луфа́рь.
blue-gray *adj.* си́зый.
blueprint *n.* си́нька.
blues *n.pl.* **1,** (melancholy) хандра́. **2,** *music* блюз.
bluff *v.t.* обма́нывать; вводи́ть в заблужде́ние. —*v.i.* блефова́ть. —*n.* **1,** (deception) блеф. **2,** (cliff) обры́в; утёс. —**call someone's bluff,** заста́вить (кого́-нибудь) раскры́ть ка́рты.
bluing *n.* си́нька.
bluish *adj.* синева́тый; голубова́тый.
blunder *n.* про́мах; оплóшность. —*v.i.* гру́бо ошиба́ться; оплоша́ть.
blunt *adj.* **1,** (not sharp) тупо́й. **2,** (frank; straightforward) прямо́й. —*v.t.* притупля́ть. —**bluntly,** *adv.* пря́мо; начистоту́.
bluntness *n.* **1,** (dullness) ту́пость. **2,** (frankness) прямота́.
blur *v.t.* **1,** (obscure) затума́нивать. **2,** (make fuzzy, as a photograph) сма́зывать. —**blurry,** *adj.* расплы́вчатый.
blurt *v.t.* [*usu.* **blurt out**] сболтну́ть; вы́палить.
blush *v.i.* красне́ть. —*n.* кра́ска стыда́. —**at first blush,** на пе́рвый взгляд.
bluster *v.i.* **1,** (blow stormily) бушева́ть. **2,** (speak noisily or threateningly) кура́житься. —*n.* пусты́е слова́; пусты́е угро́зы.
boa *n.* **1,** (snake) уда́в. **2,** (scarf) боа́. —**boa constrictor,** боа́.
boar *n.* **1,** (male hog) хряк. **2,** (wild boar) каба́н.
board *n.* **1,** (wooden strip; flat surface) доска́. *Bulletin board,* доска́ объявле́ний. *Ironing board,* глади́льная доска́. **2,** (side of a ship) борт: *on board,* на борту́. **3,** (meals) стол: *room and board,* кварти́ра и стол; пансио́н. **4,** (group of officials) правле́ние; управле́ние; сове́т; коми́ссия. *Board of directors,* сове́т директоро́в. *Board of inquiry,* сле́дственная коми́ссия. *Editorial board,* редакцио́нная колле́гия. —*v.t.* **1,** *fol. by* **up** (cover with boards) забива́ть; заколоти́ть. **2,** (get on) сади́ться в *or* на. **3,** (come alongside, as an enemy ship) брать на аборда́ж. —*v.i.* сесть на самолёт.
boarder *n.* пансионе́р.
boarding *n.* поса́дка. —**boarding pass,** поса́дочный тало́н.
boarding house пансио́н.
boarding school шко́ла-интерна́т.
boardwalk *n.* доща́тый насти́л (на пля́же).
boast *v.i.* (brag) хва́статься; хвали́ться. —*v.t.* (proudly possess) быть счастли́вым облада́телем (+ *gen.*). —*n.* хвастовство́. —**boastful,** *adj.* хвастли́вый.
boat *n.* **1,** (small vessel) ло́дка: *motor boat,* мото́рная ло́дка. **2,** (ship) парохо́д. —*adj.* ло́дочный: *boat races,* ло́дочные го́нки. —**in the same boat,** в тако́м же положе́нии. —**miss the boat,** *colloq.* прозева́ть удо́бный слу́чай.
boathouse *n.* ло́дочный сара́й.
boating *n.* ло́дочный спорт; ката́ние на ло́дке. *Go boating,* ката́ться на ло́дке.
boatman *n.* ло́дочник.
boatswain *n.* бо́цман.
bob *n.* **1,** (quick jerking motion) рыво́к. **2,** (knoblike weight) груз отве́са. **3,** (fishing float) поплаво́к. **4,** (short curl or knob of hair) завито́к. —*v.i. Bob up and down,* подпры́гивать. *Bob on the waves,* пока́чиваться на волна́х. —*v.t.* (cut short) ко́ротко стричь.
bobbin *n.* кату́шка.
bobby *n., Brit., colloq.* полисме́н.
bobby pin зако́лка.
bobcat *n.* америка́нская рысь.
bobsled *n.* бо́бслей.
bode *v.t.* & *i.* предвеща́ть: *bode well,* предвеща́ть хоро́шее.
bodice *n.* лиф; корса́ж.

bodily *adj.* телéсный: *bodily injuries,* телéсные повреждéния. —*adv.* собственной персóной. *Throw someone bodily out of the room,* вышвырнуть когó-нибудь из кóмнаты.

body *n.* **1,** (human form) тéло: *the human body,* человéческое тéло. **2,** (corpse) труп. **3,** (substance) тéло: *foreign body,* посторóннее тéло. **4,** (object in space) тéло: *celestial body,* небéсное тéло. **5,** in *body of water,* вóдное прострáнство. **6,** (of various devices) кóрпус; (of a car) кýзов; (of an airplane) фюзеля́ж. **7,** (central part, as of a book) основнáя часть. **8,** (group of persons) óрган; коллекти́в: *legislative body,* законодáтельный óрган; *student body,* студéнческий коллекти́в. **9,** (density) плóтность; прóчность. **10,** (consistency; strength, as of wine) крéпость. —*adj.: body temperature,* температýра тéла. —**body and soul,** душóй и тéлом. —**keep body and soul together,** поддéрживать существовáние; перебивáться.

bodyguard *n.* телохрани́тель.

Boer *n.* бур. —*adj.* бýрский.

bog *n.* болóто; тряси́на; топь. —*v.t. Become bogged down* (in), увязáть (в); погрязáть (в). —*v.i.* [*usu.* **bog down**] (peter out) захлёбываться.

bogeyman *n.* бýка.

boggle *v.t.* потрясáть: *boggle the mind,* потрясáть ум.

boggy *adj.* болóтистый.

bogus *adj.* поддéльный; фальши́вый.

Bohemian *adj.* **1,** (of or from Bohemia) богéмский. **2,** (unconventional) богéмный.

boil *v.t.* **1,** (bring to a boiling point, as water) кипяти́ть. **2,** (cook, as eggs) вари́ть. —*v.i.* кипéть. —*n.* **1,** (boiling state) кипéние: *bring to a boil,* доводи́ть до кипéния. **2,** (skin sore) нары́в; фурýнкул. —**boil down, 1,** (lessen by boiling) увáривать. **2,** (reduce) своди́ть. **3,** *fol. by* **to** (come down to) своди́ться: *the whole thing boils down to this,* всё дéло сво́дится к э́тому. —**boil over,** перекипáть.

boiled *adj.* варёный; кипячёный.

boiler *n.* (паровóй) котёл; куб. —**boiler plate,** котéльное желéзо. —**boiler room,** котéльная; котéльное отделéние.

boilerman *n.* истопни́к.

boiling *adj.* кипя́щий. *Boiling water,* кипятóк. —**boiling hot,** горя́чий как кипятóк. —**boiling point,** тóчка кипéния.

boisterous *adj.* шумли́вый; бýйный.

bold *adj.* **1,** (daring) смéлый. **2,** (brazen) дéрзкий. **3,** (distinct to the eye) чёткий. **4,** *printing* жи́рный. —**make bold,** осмéливаться.

boldface *n.* жи́рный шрифт. —*adj.* жи́рный.

bold-faced *adj.* **1,** (brazen) нáглый. **2,** *printing* жи́рный.

boldly *adv.* смéло.

boldness *n.* смéлость.

boll *n., bot.* корóбочка. —**boll weevil,** хлóпковый долгонóсик.

bologna *n.* болóнская колбасá.

Bolshevik *n.* большеви́к. —*adj.* большеви́стский.

bolster *n.* вáлик. —*v.t.* поддéрживать; подкреплять. *Bolster someone's spirits,* поднимáть чьё-нибудь настроéние.

bolt *n.* **1,** (metal pin) болт. **2,** (sliding bar that locks) засóв; задви́жка. **3,** (sliding mechanism for a rifle) затвóр. **4,** (roll of material) рулóн. **5,** (of thunder or lightning) удáр (грóма/мóлнии). —*v.t.* **1,** (fasten with bolts) скреплять болтáми. **2,** (lock) закрывáть на засóв *or* на задви́жку; задвигáть. **3,** (break away from, as a political party) порвáть с. —*v.i.* **1,** (dash; dart) брóситься: *bolt from the room,* брóситься вон из кóмнаты. **2,** (of a horse) понести́. —**bolt from the blue,** гром средí я́сного нéба.

bomb *n.* бóмба. —*adj.* бóмбовый: *bomb load,* бóмбовая нагрýзка. —*v.t.* бомбардировáть; бомби́ть. —**bomb out,** разбомби́ть.

bombard *v.t.* **1,** (bomb) бомбардировáть. **2,** (shower, as with questions) забрáсывать (+ *instr.*); засыпáть (+ *instr.*). —**bombardier,** *n.* бомбарди́р. —**bombardment,** *n.* бомбардирóвка.

bombast *n.* напы́щенность; высокопáрность. —**bombastic,** *adj.* напы́щенный; высокопáрный.

bomb bay бóмбовый отсéк.

bomber *n.* бомбардирóвщик.

bombing *n.* бомбардирóвка; бомбометáние.

bomb load бóмбовая нагрýзка.

bomb shelter бомбоубéжище.

bombsight *n.* бомбардирóвочный прицéл.

bona fide 1, (made in good faith) добросóвестный. **2,** (genuine) пóдлинный.

bond *n.* **1,** (tie) связь. *Bonds of friendship,* ýзы дрýжбы. **2,** *pl.* (shackles) пýты; окóвы. **3,** *finance* облигáция. **4,** (bail) порýка: *post bond for,* брать на порýки.

bondage *n.* рáбство.

bondsman *n.* **1,** (guarantor) поручи́тель. **2,** (slave) раб. —**bondwoman,** *n.* рабá; рабы́ня.

bone *n.* кость. —*adj.* кóстный: *bone tissue/disease,* кóстная ткань/болéзнь. —*v.t.* вынимáть кóсти из. —*v.i.* [*usu.* **bone up**] *slang* (cram) зубри́ть. —**bag of bones,** кóжа да кóсти. —**bone of contention,** я́блоко раздóра. —**chilled to the bone,** продрóгший до мóзга костéй. —**feel in one's bones,** чýвствовать всем свои́м существóм, (что...). —**have a bone to pick with,** имéть счёты с. —**make no bones about,** не дéлать секрéта из.

bonehead *n., slang* болвáн, остолóп.

bone meal костянáя мукá.

boner *n., colloq.* прóмах; оплóшность.

bonfire *n.* костёр.

bonnet *n.* **1,** (lady's hat) кáпор. **2,** *Brit.* (hood of a car) капóт.

bonus *n.* прéмия.

bon vivant жуи́р.

bony *adj.* **1,** (having many bones) кости́стый. **2,** (skinny) костля́вый.

boo *v.t.* & *i.* осви́стывать.

booby *n.* болвáн; балбéс.

booby trap ми́на-ловýшка.

book *n.* кни́га. —*adj.* кни́жный: *book learning,* кни́жные знáния. —*v.t.* (reserve) закáзывать; брать; брони́ровать. *We're all booked up,* все местá за́няты; свобóдных мест нет. —**be on the books,** быть на учёте. —**in my book,** *colloq.* на мой взгляд. —**keep the books,** вести́ кни́ги. —**know like a book,** знать как свои́ пять пáльцев.

bookbinder *n.* переплётчик. —**bookbinding,** *n.* переплётное дéло.

bookcase *n.* кни́жный шкаф; этажéрка.

bookend *n.* подстáвка для книг.

bookish *adj.* книжный.
bookkeeper *n.* бухгалтер; счетовод. —**bookkeeping,** *n.* бухгалтерия; счетоводство.
booklet *n.* книжечка; брошюра; буклет.
bookmaker *n.* букмекер.
bookmark *n.* закладка.
bookmobile *n.* библиотека-передвижка.
bookplate *n.* экслибрис; книжный знак.
book review рецензия на книгу.
bookseller *n.* продавец книг. *Secondhand bookseller,* букинист.
bookshelf *n.* книжная полка.
bookstore *n.* книжный магазин.
bookworm *n.* книжный червь.
boom *n.* **1,** (deep rumbling sound) гул; грохот. **2,** (rapid rise) бум. **3,** (arm of a derrick) стрела. —*v.i.* **1,** (make a deep rumbling sound) греметь; грохотать. **2,** (flourish) процветать. —*interj.* бум!
boomerang *n.* бумеранг.
boon *n.* благо; благодеяние. *A boon to the city,* благо для города. *A boon to progress,* толчок к прогрессу.
boondocks *n.pl., slang* глушь; захолустье.
boor *n.* хам; невежа; грубиян. —**boorish,** *adj.* хамский. —**boorishness,** *n.* хамство.
boost *v.t.* **1,** (lift) поднимать. **2,** (raise, as prices) повышать. **3,** (increase) увеличивать. —*n.* **1,** (lift) подъём. **2,** (help) содействие. **3,** (raise) повышение.
booster *n.* **1,** *electricity* усилитель. **2,** *rocketry* ускоритель. **3,** (enthusiastic supporter) патриот. —**booster rocket,** ракетный ускоритель; стартовый ракетный двигатель.
boot *n.* **1,** (shoe) ботинок; сапог. **2,** (kick) пинок. **3,** *Brit.* (trunk of a car) багажник. —*v.t.* **1,** (kick) пинать. **2,** *usu. fol. by* **out,** *slang* (expel) выгнать; вышвырнуть. —**give the boot to,** выгонять с работы. —**lick someone's boots,** лизать пятки (+ *dat.*). —**to boot,** вдобавок; в придачу.
bootblack *n.* чистильщик сапог.
booth *n.* **1,** (small compartment) будка; кабина. *Telephone booth,* телефонная будка. *Voting/polling booth,* кабина для голосования. **2,** (stall; stand) киоск; ларёк; палатка. *Change booth,* разменная касса.
bootlicker *n.* лизоблюд; подлиза.
booty *n.* добыча; трофеи.
booze *n., colloq.* хмельное.
borax *n.* бура.
border *n.* **1,** (boundary) граница. **2,** (trim) кайма; бордюр. —*adj.* пограничный: *border post,* пограничный пост; пограничная застава. —*v.t.* **1,** [*also,* **border on**] (bound; verge on) граничить с. **2,** (put a border or edging on) окаймлять; обшивать. —**border guard,** пограничник.
bore *n.* **1,** (of a firearm) канал. **2,** (tiresome person) скучный *or* нудный человек. —*v.t.* **1,** (drill) сверлить; бурить. **2,** (tire) надоедать.
bored *adj.* скучный. *I am bored,* мне скучно; мне надоело.
boredom *n.* скука.
boric *adj.* борный. —**boric acid,** борная кислота.
boring *adj.* **1,** (used for drilling) буровой; бурильный; сверлильный. **2,** (tiresome) скучный; надоедливый.
born *adj.* **1,** (brought forth by birth) рождённый: *born out of wedlock,* рождённый вне брака. *I was born in France,* я родился (родилась) во Франции. *He was born to fly,* он рождён летать. **2,** (having the natural talent of) прирождённый: *a born poet,* прирождённый поэт. —**in all one's born days,** за всю свою жизнь.
boron *n.* бор.
borough *n.* городок.
borrow *v.t.* **1,** (take temporarily) брать: *borrow a book from the library,* брать книгу из библиотеки. *May I borrow your pen for a moment?,* можно попросить на минуту вашу ручку? **2,** (receive as a loan) занимать; брать взаймы. *Borrow money from someone,* занимать деньги у кого-нибудь. **3,** (adopt; take over) заимствовать. —**borrower,** *n.* заёмщик.
borsch *also,* **borsht, borscht** *n.* борщ.
borzoi *n.* борзая.
bosom *n.* **1,** (breast) грудь. **2,** (space formed by the breast) пазуха: *remove from one's bosom,* вынимать из-за пазухи. **3,** *fig.* (source of feelings) душа. —**bosom friend,** закадычный друг.
boss *n.* **1,** (employer; superior) начальник. **2,** (political chief) босс. —*v.t.* **1,** (manage) управлять. **2,** *fol. by* **around** (order about) командовать над. —**bossy,** *adj.* властный.
botany *n.* ботаника. —**botanical,** *adj.* ботанический. —**botanist,** *n.* ботаник.
botch *v.t.* напутать.
both *adj.* оба; обе: *both boys,* оба мальчика; *with both hands,* обеими руками. *People of both sexes,* лица обоего пола. —*pron.* оба; обе; и тот и другой. —*conj.* и... и; как..., так и: *he speaks both English and Russian,* он говорит и по-английски и по-русски. *Both in London and Paris,* как в Лондоне, так и в Париже.
bother *v.t.* **1,** (disturb; pester) мешать. **2,** (worry; trouble; cause discomfort to) беспокоить. —*v.i.* (take the trouble) дать себе труд. —*n.* **1,** (trouble) беспокойство. **2,** (nuisance; annoyance) досада.
bothersome *adj.* надоедливый.
bottle *n.* бутылка: *bottle of milk,* бутылка молока. *Infant's bottle,* рожок. *Ink bottle,* пузырёк для чернил. *Medicine bottle,* склянка для лекарств. *Perfume bottle,* флакон. —*v.t.* **1,** (put in bottles) разливать по бутылкам. **2,** *fol. by* **up** (stifle) сдерживать. —**hit the bottle,** *slang* выпивать.
bottled *adj.* бутылочный: *bottled beer,* бутылочное пиво.
bottleneck *n.* узкое место.
bottom *n.* дно: *go to the bottom,* идти ко дну. *At the bottom of the page,* внизу страницы. —*adj.* нижний: *the bottom step,* нижняя ступенька. —**at bottom,** в сущности; по существу. —**bottoms up!,** до дна! —**from the bottom of one's heart,** от всего сердца; от всей души. —**from top to bottom,** сверху донизу. —**get to the bottom of,** добраться до сути (+ *gen.*).
bottomless *adj.* бездонный.
boudoir *n.* будуар.
bough *n.* сук.
bouillon *n.* бульон.
boulder *n.* валун.
boulevard *n.* проспект.
bounce *v.i.* **1,** (rebound) прыгать. *Bounce off,* отскакивать от. **2,** (leap; spring) вскакивать: *bounce out of bed,* вскакивать с постели. —*v.t.* **1,** (a ball) бить

(мячóм) о зéмлю. **2,** *slang* (dismiss) выгонять. —*n.* **1,** (rebound) рикошéт. **2,** (resiliency) упрýгость. —**bounce back,** оправляться.

bouncer *n., colloq.* вышибáла.

bound *n.* **1,** (leap) прыжóк; скачóк. **2,** *pl.* (limits) грани́цы; предéлы. *Exceed the bounds of...,* вы́йти за предéлы (+ *gen.*). *Know no bounds,* не знать грани́ц. —*adj.* **1,** (tied) свя́занный. **2,** (having a binding) в переплёте. **3,** (obligated) обя́занный. **4,** (headed for): *the train is bound for Moscow,* пóезд отправля́ется в Москвý; пóезд слéдует до Москвы́. **5,** (certain; sure): *it was bound to happen,* э́то и должнó бы́ло случи́тся. *He is bound to find out about it,* он непремéнно узнáет об э́том. —*v.i.* **1,** (leap) пры́гать. *Bound over the fence,* перескочи́ть чéрез забóр. **2,** *fol. by* **back** *or* **off** (rebound) отскáкивать (от). **3,** *fol. by* **on** (border on) грани́чить с. *Sweden is bounded on the west by Norway,* на зáпаде Швéция грани́чит с Норвéгией. —**out of bounds,** *sports* вне игры́.

boundary *n.* грани́ца. —*adj.* пограни́чный: *boundary marker,* пограни́чный знак.

boundless *adj.* безграни́чный; безбрéжный; необозри́мый.

bounteous *adj.* = **bountiful.**

bountiful *adj.* **1,** (generous) щéдрый. **2,** (abundant) оби́льный.

bounty *n.* **1,** (generosity) щéдрость. **2,** (gift) дар. **3,** (reward) наградá.

bouquet *n.* букéт.

bourgeois *n.* буржуá. —*adj.* буржуáзный. —**bourgeoisie,** *n.* буржуази́я.

bout *n.* **1,** (contest) схвáтка. **2,** (siege, as of illness) при́ступ. —**drinking bout,** запóй; попóйка.

boutonniere *n.* бутоньéрка.

bovine *adj.* бычáчий; бы́чий.

bow[1] (bau) *v.i.* **1,** (bend one's head or body) клáняться. **2,** *fol. by* **down** (kneel) преклоня́ться. **3,** (yield) подчиня́ться; покоря́ться. —*v.t.* склоня́ть; наклоня́ть: *bow one's head,* склоня́ть/наклоня́ть гóлову. —*n.* **1,** (bending of the head or body) поклóн. *Take a bow,* раскláниваться. **2,** (of a ship) нос. —**bow and scrape,** низкопоклóнничать. —**bow out,** выходи́ть; выбывáть.

bow[2] (bo) *n.* **1,** (for shooting arrows) лук. **2,** (for playing the violin) смычóк. **3,** (bowknot) бант.

bowel *n.* **1,** (intestine) кишкá; *pl.* кишки́; кишéчник. *Bowel movement,* испражнéние. *Move one's bowels,* испражня́ться. **2,** *pl.* (innermost part) нéдра: *bowels of the earth,* нéдра земли́.

bower *n.* бесéдка.

bowl *n.* **1,** (deep dish) ми́ска; глубóкая тарéлка. **2,** (vase) вáза. **3,** (of a toilet) унитáз. —*v.i.* (go bowling) игрáть в кéгли. —**bowl over, 1,** (knock down) свали́ть с ног. **2,** (stun) ошеломля́ть.

bowlegged *adj.* кривонóгий.

bowler *n.* **1,** (one who bowls) игрóк в кéгли. **2,** (hat) котелóк.

bowling *n.* (игрá в) кéгли. —**bowling alley,** кегельбáн.

bowls *n.* игрá в шары́.

bowman *n.* стрелóк из лýка.

bowsprit *n.* бушпри́т.

bowstring *n.* тетивá.

bow tie бáбочка.

box *n.* **1,** (container) корóбка; я́щик. **2,** *theat.* лóжа. **3,** (booth) бýдка: *sentry box,* карáульная бýдка. **4,** (blow) пощёчина. **5,** (species of tree) самши́т. —*v.t.* **1,** (put in a box) уклáдывать в я́щик. **2,** (strike) дать пощёчину (+ *dat.*). **3,** *fol. by* **in** (crowd; squeeze) вти́скивать. —*v.i.* бокси́ровать.

boxer *n.* боксёр.

boxing *n.* бокс. —**boxing glove,** боксёрская перчáтка.

box office (театрáльная *or* билéтная) кácса. —**box-office receipts,** сбóры.

box seat мéсто в лóже.

boy *n.* мáльчик.

boyar *n.* боя́рин.

boycott *n.* бойкóт. —*v.t.* бойкоти́ровать.

boyfriend *n.* приятель.

boyhood *n.* дéтство.

boyish *adj.* мальчи́шеский.

boy scout скáут.

bra *n.* бюстгáльтер.

brace *n.* **1,** (clamp) скобá; скрéпа. **2,** (tool holding a bit) коловорóт. **3,** (pair; couple) пáра. **4,** *pl., Brit.* (suspenders) подтя́жки. —*v.t.* **1,** (fasten) скрепля́ть. **2,** (invigorate) бодри́ть. —**brace oneself,** напрягáться; собирáться с си́лами.

bracelet *n.* браслéт.

bracing *adj.* бодря́щий. *The air is bracing,* вóздух бодри́т.

bracket *n.* **1,** (shelf support) кронштéйн. **2,** (staple) скобá. **3,** *pl.* ([ ]) (квадрáтные) скóбки. —*v.t.* **1,** (enclose in brackets) заключáть в скóбки. **2,** (group together) стáвить на однý дóску.

brackish *adj.* солоновáтый.

brad *n.* гвóздик; шпи́лька.

brag *v.i.* хвáстаться.

braggart *n.* хвастýн; бахвáл; фанфарóн.

Brahman *also,* **Brahmin** *n.* брахмáн. —**Brahmanism,** *n.* брахмани́зм.

braid *v.t.* **1,** (plait) заплетáть. **2,** (weave) плести́. —*n.* **1,** (ornamental band) тесьмá. **2,** (of hair) косá.

brain *n.* **1,** *anat.* мозг. **2,** *pl.* (food) мозги́. —*adj.* мозговóй. —**brain drain,** утéчка мозгóв.

brainchild *n., colloq.* дéтище.

brainless *adj., colloq.* безмóзглый; безголóвый.

brainstorm *n.* блестя́щая мысль.

brain trust мозговóй трест.

brain-twister *n.* головолóмка.

brainwash *v.t.* промывáть мозги́ (+ *dat.*).

brainwork *n.* мозговáя рабóта; ýмственный труд.

brainy *adj., colloq.* мозгови́тый; башкови́тый.

braise *v.t.* туши́ть.

brake *n.* тóрмоз. —*adj.* тормознóй: *brake fluid,* тормознáя жи́дкость. —*v.t.* & *i.* тормози́ть.

brakeman *n.* тормознóй кондýктор.

bramble *n.* кумани́ка.

brambling *n.* вьюрóк; юрóк.

bran *n.* óтруби.

branch *n.* **1,** (limb) ветвь; вéтка. **2,** (commercial subdivision) филиáл; отделéние. **3,** (field) óтрасль: *branch of science,* óтрасль наýки. **4,** (arm of a river) рукáв. **5,** *mil.* род войск; слýжба. —*adj.* филиáльный: *branch office,* филиáльное отделéние. —*v.i.* **1,** (divide into branches) разветвля́ться. **2,** *fol. by* **off** (go off in a different direction) ответвля́ться.

brand *n.* **1,** (make; kind) мáрка. **2,** (burning piece of wood) головня́. **3,** (mark made on cattle) клеймо́; тавро́. **4,** (stigma) клеймо́. —*v.t.* клейми́ть. —**branding iron,** клеймо́.

brandish *v.t.* размахивать; потрясать.

brand-new *adj.* совсе́м но́вый; но́венький. *Brand-new suit,* костю́м с иго́лочки.

brandy *n.* конья́к.

brant *n.* (goose) каза́рка.

brash *adj.* на́глый; де́рзкий.

brass *n.* **1,** (alloy) лату́нь. **2,** *slang* (top officials) верху́шка; голо́вка. —*adj.* лату́нный. —**brass band,** духово́й орке́стр. —**brass knuckles,** касте́т.

brassiere *n.* бюстга́льтер.

brat *n.* озорни́к; постре́л.

bravado *n.* брава́да.

brave *adj.* хра́брый. —*v.t.* брави́ровать. —**bravely,** *adv.* хра́бро. —**bravery,** *n.* хра́брость.

bravissimo *interj.* брави́ссимо!

bravo *interj.* бра́во!

bravura *n.* браву́рная му́зыка.

brawl *n.* сва́лка; дебо́ш. —*v.i.* сканда́лить; дебоши́рить. —**brawler,** *n.* драчу́н; зади́ра; забия́ка.

brawn *n.* му́скулы; му́скульная си́ла. —**brawny,** *adj.* му́скулистый.

bray *v.i.* крича́ть; реве́ть.

brazen *adj.* **1,** (resembling brass) ме́дный. **2,** (shameless) бессты́дный; беззасте́нчивый.

brazier *n.* **1,** (worker in brass) ме́дник. **2,** (roasting pan) жаро́вня.

Brazilian *adj.* брази́льский. —*n.* брази́лец; бразилья́нка.

breach *n.* **1,** (break) брешь; проло́м. **2,** (violation; infringement) наруше́ние: *breach of promise,* наруше́ние обеща́ния. —*v.t.* пробива́ть; проло́мывать.

bread *n.* хлеб. —*adj.* хле́бный: *bread crumbs,* хле́бные кро́шки. —**take the bread out of someone's mouth,** отбива́ть хлеб у кого́-нибудь.

breadbasket *n.* **1,** (basket for carrying bread) хле́бница. **2,** (region that supplies much grain) жи́тница.

breadth *n.* **1,** (width) ширина́. **2,** (wide extent; scope) широта́.

breadwinner *n.* корми́лец.

break *v.t.* **1,** (split; fracture; put out of working order) лома́ть. *Break one's watch/one's leg,* слома́ть часы́/себе́ но́гу. *Break one's neck,* сверну́ть себе́ ше́ю. *Break the ice,* слома́ть *or* разби́ть лёд. **2,** (smash; shatter) разбива́ть. *Break a window,* разби́ть окно́. **3,** (fail to keep; violate) наруша́ть: *break a promise/one's word/the law,* наруша́ть обеща́ние/сло́во/зако́н. **4,** (interrupt; disturb) наруша́ть; прерыва́ть: *break the silence,* наруша́ть/прерыва́ть молча́ние. **5,** (sever, as relations) порыва́ть; разрыва́ть. **6,** (wear down, as resistance) сломи́ть. *Break a strike,* сорва́ть забасто́вку. **7,** (divide into smaller units) разро́знивать: *break a set of something,* разро́знивать компле́кт чего́-нибудь. *Break a dollar,* разме́нивать до́ллар. **8,** (surpass, as a record) поби́ть. **9,** (get rid of, as a habit) отучи́ться от. *Break someone of a habit,* отуча́ть кого́-нибудь от привы́чки. **10,** (convey, as bad news) сообща́ть. **11,** *colloq.* (bankrupt) разоря́ть. *Break the bank,* сорва́ть банк. **12,** *electricity* размыка́ть: *break a circuit,* размыка́ть цепь. **13,** *in various miscellaneous expressions: break a code,* разга́дывать код; *break camp,* снима́ться с ла́геря; *break ranks,* расходи́ться; *break someone's heart,* разби́ть чьё-нибудь се́рдце. —*v.i.* **1,** (become smashed, cracked, or useless) лома́ться; разбива́ться. **2,** (snap, as of a rope) рва́ться. **3,** (stop suddenly, as of one's voice) лома́ться; срыва́ться; прерыва́ться. **4,** (make a sudden dash) бро́ситься: *break for the door,* бро́ситься к две́ри. **5,** (dawn): *day is breaking,* (рас)света́ет. **6,** *fol. by* **with** (sever ties with) пор(ы)ва́ть с. *Break with tradition,* порва́ть с тради́цией. —*n.* **1,** (burst; rupture) разры́в; проры́в; проло́м. *Water-main break,* разры́в водопрово́дной магистра́ли. **2,** *fig.* (severing) разры́в: *break in diplomatic relations,* разры́в дипломати́ческих отноше́ний. **3,** (interruption; recess) переры́в: *without a break,* без переры́ва; беспреры́вно. **4,** *in* **the break of day,** рассве́т. **5,** (sudden dash) бросо́к. **6,** (escape, as from prison) бе́гство; побе́г (из тюрьмы́). **7,** *colloq.* (stroke of luck) счастли́вый слу́чай. *He gets all the breaks,* ему́ всегда́ везёт. *The breaks were against us,* нам не везло́. —**break apart,** разла́мываться. —**break away,** вырыва́ться. —**break down, 1,** (smash down, as a door) выла́мывать. **2,** (overcome, as resistance) сломи́ть. **3,** (divide) разбива́ть (на гру́ппы, катего́рии, *etc.*). **4,** (go out of working order) испо́ртиться; вы́йти из стро́я. *Communications broke down,* связь прервала́сь. **5,** (fail) прова́ливаться: *all efforts have broken down,* все попы́тки провали́лись. *Negotiations broke down,* перегово́ры зашли́ в тупи́к. **6,** (lose one's composure) не вы́держать: *she broke down and cried,* она́ не вы́держала и запла́кала. —**break even,** остава́ться при свои́х. —**break in, 1,** (enter by force) вла́мываться. **2,** (interrupt) вме́шиваться. **3,** (a car, motor, etc.) обка́тывать; (a horse) выезжа́ть; объезжа́ть; (shoes) разна́шивать. —**break into, 1,** (enter by force) вла́мываться в. **2,** (interrupt, as a conversation) вме́шиваться в. **3,** (give way to, as laughter) разрази́ться (+ *instr.*). *He broke into a sweat,* его́ бро́сило в пот. *Break into song,* запе́ть (пе́сню). —**break off, 1,** (sever by breaking) отла́мывать; отка́лывать. **2,** (come off) отла́мываться; отка́лываться. **3,** (halt abruptly) прекраща́ть; прерыва́ть. **4,** (sever, as relations) порыва́ть; разрыва́ть. **5,** *fol. by* **from** (split off from, as a group) отка́лываться (от). —**break open,** взла́мывать. —**break out, 1,** (start unexpectedly) вспы́хнуть; разрази́ться. **2,** (appear, as of a rash) появля́ться. **3,** (escape) вы́рваться. *Break out of prison,* бежа́ть из тюрьмы́. —**break through,** прорыва́ть; прорыва́ться сквозь; пробива́ться сквозь. —**break up, 1,** (force to disperse) разгоня́ть. **2,** (disperse; split up) расходи́ться. **3,** (divide into smaller parts) разбива́ть. **4,** (be divided up) разбива́ться. **5,** (cease to exist or function) распада́ться.

breakable *adj.* ло́мкий; хру́пкий.

breakage *n.* ло́мка; поло́мка; бой.

breakdown *n.* **1,** (failure to function) ава́рия; поло́мка. **2,** (total failure) разва́л. **3,** (mental collapse) надры́в; надло́м. *Nervous breakdown,* неврастени́я. **4,** (analysis; classification) разбо́р.

breaker *n.* (wave) буру́н.

breakfast *n.* за́втрак. *Have breakfast,* за́втракать.

breaking point моме́нт разры́ва. *Reach the breaking point* (*fig.*), дойти́ до то́чки; дойти́ до преде́ла.

breakneck *adj., in* **at breakneck speed,** сломя́ го́лову.

breakthrough *n.* проры́в.

breakup *n.* **1,** (splitting into pieces) распа́д; разва́л; ло́мка. **2,** (split between people) разры́в.
breakwater *n.* мол; волноло́м; волноре́з.
bream *n.* (fish) лещ.
breast *n.* **1,** (human) грудь. **2,** (of a coat) борт: *double-breasted,* двубо́ртный. —*adj.* грудно́й; нагру́дный. *Breast pocket,* нагру́дный карма́н. *Breast feeding,* кормле́ние гру́дью. *Breast cancer,* рак моло́чной железы́. —**make a clean breast of it,** всё вы́ложить.
breastbone *n.* груди́на.
breastplate *n.* нагру́дник.
breast stroke брасс.
breastwork *n.* бру́ствер.
breath *n.* **1,** (act of breathing) дыха́ние. *Hold one's breath,* затаи́ть дыха́ние. **2,** (a single breath) вдох. *Take a deep breath,* глубоко́ вдохну́ть. —**be out of breath,** запыха́ться. —**it took my breath away,** у меня́ захвати́ло дух. —**under one's breath,** вполго́лоса; шёпотом.
breathe *v.i.* дыша́ть. *Breathe in,* вдыха́ть. *Breathe out,* выдыха́ть. —*v.t.* **1,** (inhale and exhale) дыша́ть (+ *instr.*). *Breathe new life into,* вдохну́ть жизнь в. **2,** (utter; whisper) оброни́ть; обмо́лвиться. *Not breathe a word,* не пророни́ть ни сло́ва; не обмо́лвиться ни сло́вом. —**breathe down someone's neck,** стоя́ть над чьей-нибудь душо́й. —**breathe one's last,** испусти́ть дух.
breather *n.* (respite) переды́шка.
breathing *n.* дыха́ние. —**breathing space/spell,** переды́шка.
breathless *adj.* запыха́вшийся.
breathtaking *adj.* захва́тывающий.
breech *n.* **1,** (of a gun) казённая часть. **2,** (buttocks) зад.
breeches *n.pl.* бри́джи. *Riding breeches,* рейту́зы; галифе́. *Also,* **britches.**
breed *v.t.* **1,** (mate; raise) разводи́ть. **2,** (produce; generate; give rise to) порожда́ть. —*v.i.* плоди́ться; размножа́ться. —*n.* поро́да.
breeder *n.* (of cattle) скотово́д; (of horses) конево́д. —**breeder reactor,** размножа́ющий реа́ктор.
breeding *n.* **1,** (producing of offspring) размноже́ние. **2,** (raising of animals) разведе́ние. ♦*Usu. rendered by the suffix* -во́дство: *cattle breeding,* скотово́дство. **3,** (improving of strains) селе́кция. **4,** (good manners) воспи́танность. —**breeding ground, 1,** (of animals) ме́сто размноже́ния; (*of sea mammals*) ле́жбище; (*of fish*) нерести́лище. **2,** *fig.* (conducive place) оча́г; расса́дник.
breeze *n.* (лёгкий) ветеро́к. *Sea breeze,* бриз.
breezy *adj.* **1,** (brisk; windy) све́жий; ве́треный. **2,** (lively; sprightly) живо́й; лихо́й.
brethren *n.pl.* бра́тья; собра́тья.
brevity *n.* кра́ткость.
brew *v.t.* **1,** (make, as beer) вари́ть. **2,** (prepare, as tea) зава́ривать. —*v.i.* собира́ться; надвига́ться: *a storm is brewing,* собира́ется/надвига́ется гроза́.
brewer *n.* пивова́р. —**brewery,** *n.* пивова́ренный заво́д. —**brewing,** *n.* пивоваре́ние.
briar *n.* = **brier.**
bribe *n.* взя́тка. —*v.t.* подкупа́ть. —**bribery,** *n.* взя́точничество; по́дкуп.
bric-a-brac *n.* вещи́цы; безделу́шки.
brick *n.* кирпи́ч. —*adj.* кирпи́чный.
bricklayer *n.* ка́менщик.
brick-red *adj.* кирпи́чный; кирпи́чного цве́та.
brickwork *n.* кирпи́чная кла́дка.
bridal *adj.* сва́дебный; подвене́чный.
bride *n.* неве́ста.
bridegroom *n.* жени́х.
bridesmaid *n.* подру́жка неве́сты.
bridge *n.* **1,** (structure) мост. **2,** (on a ship) мо́стик. **3,** (of the nose) перено́сица. **4,** (of a stringed instrument) кобы́лка. **5,** (mounting for false teeth) мост. **6,** (card game) бридж. —*v.t.* **1,** (build a bridge across) наводи́ть мост че́рез. **2,** (overcome) преодолева́ть. *Bridge the gap,* восполня́ть пробе́л. —**burn one's bridges,** сжига́ть свои́ мосты́ *or* корабли́.
bridgehead *n.* плацда́рм; предмо́стное укрепле́ние.
bridle *n.* узда́; узде́чка. —*v.t.* взну́здывать; обу́здывать. —*v.i.* разозли́ться; вскипе́ть. —**bridle path,** вью́чная тропа́.
brief *adj.* **1,** (short in time) коро́ткий. **2,** (concise) кра́ткий. —*n.* сво́дка; резюме́. —*v.t.* инструкти́ровать. —**in brief,** вкра́тце; кра́тко; коро́че говоря́.
briefcase *n.* портфе́ль.
briefing *n.* инструкта́ж.
briefly *adv.* ко́ротко; кра́тко; вкра́тце.
brier *also,* **briar** *n.* **1,** (thorny bush) шипо́вник. **2,** (heath) э́рика.
brig *n.* **1,** (ship) бриг. **2,** (place of confinement) гауптва́хта.
brigade *n.* **1,** *mil.* брига́да. **2,** (organized group) кома́нда; брига́да; дружи́на. *Fire brigade,* пожа́рная кома́нда; пожа́рная дружи́на.
brigadier general генера́л-майо́р.
brigand *n.* разбо́йник. —**brigandage,** *n.* разбо́й.
bright *adj.* **1,** (shining; luminous) я́ркий; све́тлый. *Bright light,* я́ркий свет. *Bright colors,* я́ркие цвета́. *Bright sun,* я́ркое со́лнце. *Bright red,* я́рко-кра́сный; я́рко-кра́сного цве́та. *Bright day,* све́тлый день. *Bright future,* све́тлое бу́дущее. **2,** (clever) смышлёный; сообрази́тельный.
brighten *v.t.* **1,** (make bright) озаря́ть. **2,** (bring color or life to) оживля́ть. —*v.i.* **1,** (become bright) светле́ть; проясня́ться. **2,** (become more cheerful) оживля́ться. **3,** (improve) улучша́ться.
brightly *adv.* я́рко.
brightness *n.* я́ркость; све́тлость.
brilliance *n.* блеск.
brilliant *adj.* **1,** (sparkling) я́ркий. **2,** (outstanding) блестя́щий. —**brilliantly,** *adv.* я́рко; блестя́ще.
brim *n.* **1,** (edge) край. *Filled to the brim,* по́лный до краёв. **2,** (of a hat) поля́. —*v.i.* [*usu.* **brim with**] наполня́ться (+ *instr.*).
brine *n.* рассо́л.
bring *v.t.* **1,** (by carrying) приноси́ть: *bring me my shoes,* принеси́ мне боти́нки. **2,** (on foot) приводи́ть: *bring someone to dinner,* приводи́ть кого́-нибудь к обе́ду. **3,** (by conveyance) привози́ть: *bring something from abroad,* привози́ть что́-нибудь из-за грани́цы. **4,** (cause to happen) приноси́ть: *war brings suffering,* война́ прино́сит страда́ния. *It brought tears to my eyes,* э́то вы́звало у меня́ слёзы. **5,** *in various miscellaneous expressions: bring home to,* внуша́ть; втолкова́ть; *bring charges,* предъявля́ть обвине́ние; *bring suit against,* подава́ть в суд на (+ *acc.*); предъявля́ть иск к; *bring to an end,* по-

ложи́ть коне́ц (+ *dat.*); *bring to mind,* напомина́ть; *bring to one's senses,* наводи́ть на ум. —**bring about,** осуществля́ть; доби́ться. —**bring around,** **1,** (persuade) уговори́ть. **2,** (revive) приводи́ть в себя́. —**bring back,** верну́ть. —**bring down, 1,** (carry down) сноси́ть. **2,** (cause to fall) обру́шивать. **3,** (succeed in lowering) снижа́ть. **4,** (overthrow) сверга́ть. —**bring forth,** производи́ть на свет. —**bring in, 1,** (carry in) вноси́ть. **2,** (import) ввози́ть. **3,** (produce, as revenue) приноси́ть. **4,** (render, as a verdict) выноси́ть. —**bring on,** навлека́ть; вызыва́ть. —**bring oneself,** реша́ться: *I can't bring myself to do it,* не могу́ реши́ться на э́то; не могу́ заста́вить себя́ э́то сде́лать; у меня́ рука́ не поднима́ется сде́лать э́то. —**bring out, 1,** *literally* выноси́ть. **2,** (produce) выпуска́ть. **3,** in *bring out into the open,* выводи́ть на чи́стую во́ду. —**bring up, 1,** (raise; rear) воспи́тывать. **2,** (raise, as a subject) поднима́ть. **3,** *mil.* подводи́ть: *bring up the reserves,* подводи́ть резе́рвы. **4,** in *bring up the rear,* замыка́ть ше́ствие.

brink *n.* край; грань.

briny *adj.* солёный.

briquette *n.* брике́т.

brisk *adj.* **1,** (quick) бы́стрый: *at a brisk pace,* бы́стрым ша́гом. **2,** (lively) бо́йкий; оживлённый: *brisk business,* бо́йкая/оживлённая торго́вля. **3,** (fresh and invigorating) све́жий; бодря́щий.

brisket *n.* груди́нка.

bristle *n.* щети́на. —*v.i.* **1,** (become stiff and erect) щети́ниться. **2,** (show sudden anger) (вс)кипе́ть гне́вом; щети́ниться. —**bristly,** *adj.* щети́нистый.

britches *n.pl.* = **breeches.**

British *adj.* англи́йский; брита́нский. —*n., preceded by* **the** англича́не. —**British thermal unit,** брита́нская теплова́я едини́ца.

brittle *adj.* хру́пкий; ло́мкий.

broach *n.* **1,** (spit) ве́ртел. **2,** = **brooch.** —*v.t.* затра́гивать: *broach a subject,* затра́гивать вопро́с.

broad *adj.* широ́кий. —**it's as broad as it is long,** что в лоб, что по́ лбу.

broadcast *n.* переда́ча; радиопереда́ча. —*v.t.* передава́ть по ра́дио *or* в эфи́р. —*v.i.* вести́ радиопереда́чу; веща́ть.

broadcasting *n.* радиовеща́ние. —*adj.* радиовеща́тельный.

broadcloth *n.* сукно́.

broaden *v.t.* расширя́ть. —*v.i.* расширя́ться.

broad-gauge *adj.* ширококоле́йный.

broad jump прыжо́к в длину́. —**running broad jump,** прыжо́к с разбе́га. —**standing broad jump,** прыжо́к с ме́ста.

broadly *adv.* широ́ко́: *interpret broadly,* широ́ко́ толкова́ть. —**broadly speaking,** вообще́ говоря́.

broad-minded *adj.* терпи́мый; свободомы́слящий; с широ́кими взгля́дами.

broad-shouldered *adj.* широкопле́чий; плечи́стый.

broadside *n.* **1,** (firing of a ship's guns) залп. **2,** (verbal attack) град упрёков.

broadsword *n.* пала́ш.

broadtail *n.* каракульча́.

brocade *n.* парча́. —**brocaded,** *adj.* парчо́вый.

broccoli *n.* спа́ржевая капу́ста; бро́кколи.

brochure *n.* брошю́ра.

broil *v.t.* жа́рить. —*v.i.* жа́риться.

broiled *adj.* жа́реный.

broiler *n.* жаро́вня.

broiling *adj.* паля́щий.

broke *adj., colloq.* без гроша́. —**go broke,** прогора́ть. —**go for broke,** идти́ ва-ба́нк.

broken *adj.* **1,** (fractured) сло́манный. **2,** (shattered) разби́тый. **3,** (not functioning) испо́рченный. **4,** (crushed; weakened) надло́мленный. **5,** (imperfectly spoken) ло́маный: *in broken English,* на ло́маном англи́йском языке́. **6,** (violated, as of promises) несде́ржанный. **7,** (rugged, as of terrain) пересечённый. **8,** *in* **broken heart,** разби́тое се́рдце; **a broken man,** сло́мленный челове́к.

broken-down *adj.* ве́тхий; обветша́лый; полуразру́шенный.

broken-hearted *adj.* с разби́тым се́рдцем; уби́тый го́рем.

broker *n.* **1,** (agent) комиссионе́р. **2,** (stockbroker) ма́клер.

brokerage *n.* **1,** (business of a broker) ма́клерство. **2,** (broker's fee) комиссио́нные. —**brokerage house,** ма́клерская фи́рма.

bromide *n.* **1,** *chem.* броми́д. ♦ *In compounds* бро́мистый: *sodium bromide,* бро́мистый на́трий. **2,** *med.* бром. **3,** *colloq.* (cliché) бана́льность.

bromine *n.* бром.

bronchi *n.pl.* бро́нхи.

bronchial *adj.* бронхиа́льный. —**bronchial tubes,** бро́нхи.

bronchitis *n.* бронхи́т.

brontosaurus *n.* бронтоза́вр.

bronze *n.* бро́нза. —*adj.* бро́нзовый. —*v.t.* бронзирова́ть. —**Bronze Age,** бро́нзовый век.

brooch *n.* брошь; бро́шка.

brood *n.* вы́водок. —*v.i.* **1,** (sit on eggs) сиде́ть на я́йцах; выси́живать. **2,** (think long and moodily) заду́мываться (о).

brood hen насе́дка.

brook *n.* руче́й. —*v.t.* терпе́ть: *brook no delay,* не терпе́ть отлага́тельства. —**brook trout,** ручьева́я форе́ль.

broom *n.* метла́.

broomstick *n.* па́лка (для) метлы́.

broth *n.* бульо́н.

brothel *n.* публи́чный дом; дом терпи́мости.

brother *n.* брат. —**brotherhood,** *n.* бра́тство.

brother-in-law *n.* **1,** (husband's brother) де́верь. **2,** (wife's brother) шу́рин. **3,** (sister's husband; husband's sister's husband) зять. **4,** (wife's sister's husband) своя́к.

brotherly *adj.* бра́тский.

brow *n.* **1,** (eyebrow) бровь. **2,** (forehead) лоб.

browbeat *v.t.* запу́гивать.

brown *adj.* кори́чневый. *Brown eyes,* ка́рие глаза́. *Brown hair,* кашта́новые во́лосы. —*n.* кори́чневый цвет. —*v.t.* подрумя́нивать. —*v.i.* **1,** (become sunburned) загора́ть. **2,** *cooking* подрумя́ниваться.

brown bear бу́рый медве́дь.

brownie *n.* (goblin) домово́й.

browse *v.i.* смотре́ть; осма́триваться; огля́дываться.

bruise *n.* синя́к; уши́б; кровоподтёк. —*v.t.* ушиба́ть.

brunet *n.* брюне́т. —**brunette,** *n.* брюне́тка.

brunt *n.* основна́я тя́жесть: *bear the brunt of,* вы́нести основну́ю тя́жесть (+ *gen.*).

brush *n.* **1,** (implement) щётка: *hairbrush,* щётка для волóс. **2,** (paintbrush) кисть. **3,** (encounter; run-in) стычка. **4,** (underbrush) зáросль. **5,** *electricity* щётка. —*v.t.* **1,** (clean with a brush) чистить щёткой. *Brush one's teeth,* чи́стить зýбы. **2,** (groom with a brush) приглáживать щёткой. **3,** *fol. by* **off** (sweep off) счищáть; смáхивать. —*v.i.* [*usu.* **brush against**] задевáть. —**brush aside,** отмáхиваться от. —**brush away,** отмáхиваться от (*e.g.* от мух). —**brush up,** освежáть: *brush up one's Russian,* освежáть свой рýсский язы́к.

brushwood *n.* **1,** (tree branches) хвóрост. **2,** (underbrush) зáросль.

brushwork *n.* кисть.

brusque *adj.* грýбый; рéзкий; бесцеремóнный. —**brusquely,** *adv.* грýбо; рéзко; бесцеремóнно. —**brusqueness,** *n.* грýбость; рéзкость.

Brussels sprouts брюссéльская капýста.

brutal *adj.* звéрский. —**brutality,** *n.* звéрство. —**brutally,** *adv.* звéрски.

brute *n.* живóтное; зверь. —*adj.* грýбый: *brute force,* грýбая си́ла.

bubble *n.* пузы́рь. —*v.i.* **1,** (give off bubbles) пузы́риться. **2,** (make a bubbling sound) клокотáть.

bubo *n.* бубóн.

bubonic *adj.* бубóнный. —**bubonic plague,** бубóнная чумá.

buccaneer *n.* пирáт.

buck *n.* **1,** (male of various animals) самéц. **2,** *slang* (dollar) дóллар. —*v.t., colloq.* (go against) проти́виться. —**buck up,** *colloq.* не пáдать дýхом. —**pass the buck,** свали́ть отвéтственность на другóго.

bucket *n.* ведрó. —**drop in the bucket,** кáпля в мóре. —**kick the bucket,** *slang* сыгрáть в я́щик.

buckle *n.* пря́жка. —*v.t.* застёгивать (пря́жкой). —*v.i.* **1,** (warp; curl) корóбиться. **2,** (give way, as of one's legs) подлáмываться. —**buckle down,** запрягáться.

buckram *n.* коленкóр.

buckshot *n.* крýпная дробь; картéчь.

buckskin *n.* олéнья шкýра.

buckthorn *n.* круши́на.

bucktooth *n.* торчáщий зуб.

buckwheat *n.* гречи́ха; грéчневая крупá. —*adj.* грéчневый.

bucolic *adj.* деревéнский.

bud *n.* пóчка; бутóн. —*v.i.* давáть пóчки. —**nip in the bud,** *see* **nip.**

Buddhism *n.* будди́зм. —**Buddhist,** *n.* будди́ст. —*adj.* будди́стский.

buddy *n., colloq.* товáрищ.

budge *v.t.* сдви́нуть с мéста. —*v.i.* шевели́ться.

budget *n.* бюджéт. —*adj.* бюджéтный: *budget deficit,* бюджéтный дефици́т. —*v.t.* предусмáтривать в бюджéте. *Budget one's time,* распределя́ть своё врéмя. —**budgetary,** *adj.* бюджéтный.

buff *n.* **1,** (leather) бýйволовая кóжа. **2,** (tan color) беж. **3,** *colloq.* (enthusiast) люби́тель. —*v.t.* лощи́ть; полировáть. —**in the buff,** нагишóм.

buffalo *n.* **1,** (Old World animal) бýйвол. **2,** (bison) бизóн.

buffer *n.* бýфер. —**buffer state,** бýферное госудáрство. —**buffer zone,** бýферная зóна.

buffet[1] (**buf**-it) *v.t.* **1,** (hit; club) ударя́ть; колоти́ть. **2,** (knock about) бросáть (*impers.*): *the waves buffeted the ship,* парохóд бросáло по волнáм.

buffet[2] (bu-**fay**) *n.* буфéт.

buffoon *n.* шут; скоморóх; буффóн. —**buffoonery,** *n.* шутовствó; скоморóшество; буффонáда.

bug *n.* **1,** (insect) козя́вка; букáшка. **2,** *colloq.* (defect) неполáдка. —*v.t., slang* **1,** (install a hidden microphone in) прослýшивать: *this apartment is bugged,* э́та кварти́ра прослýшивается. **2,** (nag) пили́ть: *don't bug me!,* не пили́те меня́!

bugaboo *n.* пýгало; жýпел. *Also,* **bugbear.**

buggy *n.* кабриолéт.

bugle *n.* **1,** (horn) горн. *Bugle call,* сигнáл на гóрне. **2,** *pl.* (beads) стекля́рус. —**bugler,** *n.* горни́ст.

build *v.t.* & *i.* стрóить: *build a house,* стрóить дом. *Build a road,* стрóить *or* проклáдывать дорóгу. *Build a fire,* разводи́ть *or* расклáдывать костёр. *Build a nest,* вить гнездó. —*n.* сложéние: *of sturdy build,* крéпкого сложéния. —**build on,** пристрáивать. —**build up, 1,** (create and add to) создавáть. **2,** (increase; make larger) увели́чивать; нарáщивать. **3,** (develop, as an urban area) застрáивать. **4,** (develop, as endurance or immunity) вырабáтывать. **5,** (increase, as strength or confidence) укрепля́ть. *Build up someone's hopes,* подавáть надéжду (+ *dat.*). **6,** (make better known) реклами́ровать. *Build oneself up,* набивáть себé цéну. **7,** (gradually become greater) накопля́ться.

builder *n.* строи́тель.

building *n.* **1,** (structure) здáние; дом. **2,** (construction) строи́тельство; построéние. —*adj.* строи́тельный: *building materials,* строи́тельные материáлы.

build-up *n.* **1,** (publicity; praise) реклáма. **2,** *mil.* нарáщивание (сил).

built-in *adj.* вдéланный. *Built-in closet,* стеннóй шкаф.

bulb *n.* **1,** (light bulb) лáмпочка. **2,** (of a plant) лýковица.

bulbous *adj.* лýковичный.

Bulgarian *adj.* болгáрский. —*n.* **1,** (person) болгáрин; болгáрка. **2,** (language) болгáрский язы́к.

bulge *v.i.* раздувáться; распухáть; оттопы́риваться. —*n.* вы́пуклость; утолщéние.

bulk *n.* **1,** (mass) объём. **2,** (the major part) основнáя мáсса; бóльшая часть. —**in bulk,** гуртóм.

bulkhead *n.* **1,** (on a ship) перебóрка. **2,** (wall to hold back water) перемы́чка.

bulky *adj.* громóздкий; объёмистый.

bull *n.* **1,** (animal) бык. **2,** (papal edict) бýлла. —**bull in a china shop,** слон в посýдной лáвке. —**take the bull by the horns,** взять быкá за рогá.

bulldog *n.* бульдóг.

bulldozer *n.* бульдóзер.

bullet *n.* пýля. —*adj.* пулевóй: *bullet wound,* пулевáя рáна; *bullet hole,* пулевáя прибóина.

bulletin *n.* бюллетéнь. —**bulletin board,** доскá объявлéний.

bulletproof *adj.* пулестóйкий; пуленепробивáемый; пуленепроницáемый.

bullfight *n.* бой быкóв.

bullfinch *n.* снеги́рь.

bullion *n.* сли́тки: *gold bullion,* зóлото в сли́тках.

bullock *n.* вол.

bull's-eye *n.* я́блоко мишéни. *Hit the bull's-eye,* попáсть в цель.

bully *n.* задира; забияка. —*v.t.* запугивать.
bulrush *n.* камыш.
bulwark *n.* **1,** (rampart) вал. **2,** *fig.* (bastion) оплот.
bum *n., slang* лодырь; бродяга.
bumblebee *n.* шмель.
bumbling *adj.* неумелый.
bump *n.* **1,** (swelling) шишка. **2,** (in a road) ухаб. **3,** (jolt) толчок. —*v.t.* удариться (+ *instr.*); стукнуться (+ *instr.*). *Bump heads,* стукнуться головами. *Bump one's head on the door,* удариться/стукнуться головой о дверь. —**bump into, 1,** (collide with) наталкиваться на; сталкиваться с. **2,** (meet by chance) наталкиваться на; натыкаться на; набрести на. —**bump off,** *slang* уложить.
bumper *n.* буфер; бампер. —*adj., in* **bumper crop; bumper harvest,** невиданный урожай.
bumpiness *n.* тряска; *aero.* болтанка.
bumpkin *n.* деревенщина.
bumpy *adj.* тряский; ухабистый.
bun *n.* **1,** (pastry) сдобная булка/булочка; пышка. **2,** (hair worn in a roll) пучок.
bunch *n.* **1,** (collection of similar things fastened together) связка; пучок. **2,** (cluster, as of grapes) кисть; гроздь. **3,** *colloq.* (group of people) группа.
bundle *n.* **1,** (number of things bound together) связка; узел; свёрток; пачка; вязанка. **2,** (package) пакет. —*v.t.* **1,** (wrap or tie together) связывать в узел. **2,** (wrap snugly) закутывать. **3,** *fol. by* **off** (send away) спроваживать. —*v.i.* [*usu.* **bundle up**] одеваться тепло. —**bundle of energy,** сгусток энергии. —**bundle of nerves,** комок нервов.
bungalow *n.* домик.
bungle *v.t.* напутать.
bunion *n.* мозоль.
bunk *n.* **1,** (bed) койка. **2,** *slang* (nonsense) вздор; чушь.
bunker *n.* **1,** (storage bin) бункер. **2,** *mil.* блиндаж.
bunny *n.* зайчик.
Bunsen burner горелка Бунзена.
bunting *n.* **1,** (fabric) материя (для флагов). **2,** (bird) овсянка. *Snow bunting,* пуночка.
buoy *n.* буй; бакен. —*v.t.* поднимать: *buoy someone's spirits,* поднимать дух (+ *dat.*).
buoyancy *n.* **1,** (ability to keep afloat) плавучесть. **2,** *fig.* (exuberance) бодрость.
buoyant *adj.* **1,** (floating) плавучий. **2,** *fig.* (lighthearted) бодрый; жизнерадостный.
bur *n.* репейник.
burbot *n.* налим.
burden *n.* **1,** (load) ноша. **2,** *fig.* (encumbrance) бремя. *Be a burden to,* быть в тягость (+ *dat.*). —*v.t.* обременять. —**burden of proof,** обязанность доказывать.
burdensome *adj.* обременительный.
burdock *n.* лопух; репейник.
bureau *n.* **1,** (dresser) комод. **2,** (agency) бюро.
bureaucracy *n.* бюрократия. —**bureaucrat,** *n.* бюрократ. —**bureaucratic,** *adj.* бюрократический.
burgeon *v.i.* **1,** (bud) давать почки. **2,** (expand rapidly) разрастаться.
burgher *n.* бюргер.
burglar *n.* взломщик. —**burglarize,** *v.t.* взламывать. —**burglary,** *n.* кража со взломом.
burgomaster *n.* бургомистр.
burial *n.* погребение. —**burial ground,** кладбище. —**burial mound,** курган; могильный холм. —**burial place,** место погребения. —**burial vault,** склеп; усыпальница.
burlap *n.* холст; дерюга. —*adj.* холщовый; дерюжный.
burlesque *n.* бурлеск.
burly *adj.* дородный; рослый.
bur marigold череда.
Burmese *adj.* бирманский. *He is Burmese,* он бирманец. —*n.* **1,** (language) бирманский язык. **2,** *preceded by* **the** (people) бирманцы.
burn *v.t.* **1,** (deliberately) жечь. **2,** (accidentally) обжигать: *burn one's finger,* обжигать себе палец. *Burn oneself,* обжигаться. *Burn a hole in,* прожигать дыру в (+ *prepl.*). **3,** (overcook) сжигать; поджигать. **4,** (cause a burning sensation in) жечь; щипать. **5,** (consume, as gas) потреблять. —*v.i.* **1,** (be on fire) гореть. *Burn to the ground,* сгореть дотла. **2,** (of food) гореть; подгорать; перегорать. **3,** (of light, a lamp, etc.) гореть. **4,** (cause a burning sensation; sting) жечь. **5,** (feel hot; smart) гореть. **6,** *fig.* (be consumed with, as an emotion) гореть: *burn with desire,* гореть желанием. —*n.* **1,** (injury) ожог: *suffer burns,* получить ожоги. **2,** (sunburn) загар. *I got quite a burn,* я сильно загорел(а). —**burn down, 1,** (raze) жечь. **2,** (be burned to the ground) сгореть. —**burn one's fingers** (*fig.*), обжигаться. —**burn out, 1,** (destroy by heat) выжигать. **2,** (go out, as of a bulb) перегореть. **3,** (cause to go out) пережигать. —**burn up, 1,** (burn completely) сгорать. **2,** *colloq.* (infuriate) приводить в ярость. —**he has money to burn,** денег у него – хоть пруд пруди; у него денег куры не клюют. —**smell something burning,** чувствовать, как пахнет гарью.
burner *n.* горелка; конфорка. *Gas burner,* газовый рожок.
burning *n.* сжигание: *burning of trash,* сжигание мусора. —*adj.* **1,** (on fire) горящий; пылающий. **2,** (extremely hot) жгучий; палящий. *Burning sensation,* жжение. *Burning question,* жгучий вопрос.
burnish *v.t.* полировать; воронить.
burnt *adj.* жжёный; горелый. —**burnt offering,** жертвоприношение.
burp *n., colloq.* отрыжка. —*v.i., colloq.* рыгать.
burr *n.* **1,** (rough edge on metal) заусеница. **2,** (guttural pronunciation of the letter R) картавость.
burro *n.* ослик.
burrow *n.* нора. —*v.i.* рыть нору. *Burrowing rodent,* роющий грызун.
bursa *n.* сумка.
bursitis *n.* воспаление сумки.
burst *v.i.* **1,** (break open) лопаться; прорываться. *The bubble burst,* пузырь лопнул. *The dam burst,* плотину прорвало. *The boiler burst,* котёл разорвало. **2,** (go off; explode) взрываться; разрываться; лопаться. **3,** *fol. by* **with** (be filled to overflowing) ломиться (от): *the shelves are bursting with books,* полки ломятся от книг. *He is bursting with energy,* энергия в нём бьёт ключом. *She is bursting with envy,* она лопается от зависти. **4,** *fol. by* **into** (come rushing into) ворваться (в); вломиться (в). **5,** *fol. by* **into** *or* **out** (give sudden expression to) разразиться (+ *instr.*): *burst into tears; burst out crying,* разразиться слезами; расплакаться. *Burst out laughing,* разразиться смехом; рассмеяться; рас-

парáт. —**movie camera,** киноаппарáт. —**television camera,** телевизиóнная кáмера.
cameraman *n.* кинооперáтор.
camomile *also,* **chamomile** *n.* ромáшка; пупáвка.
camouflage *n.* маскирóвка. —*v.t.* маскировáть.
camp *n.* лáгерь: *prisoner-of-war camp,* лáгерь для военнопле́нных. *Split into two camps,* расколóться на два лáгеря. —*v.i.* **1,** (set up camp) располагáться лáгерем. **2,** *fol. by* **out** (sleep outdoors) жить (как) на бивуáках.
campaign *n.* кампáния; похóд. —*v.i.* проводи́ть кампáнию.
campanula *n.* колокóльчик.
campfire *n.* костёр.
camphor *n.* камфарá.
campsite *n.* ке́мпинг.
campus *n.* университе́тский городóк.
camshaft *n.* распредели́тельный вал; кулачкóвый вал.
can[1] *v.aux.* **1,** (be able) мочь: *I cannot come today,* я не могý прийти́ сегóдня. *What can I do for you?,* чем могý быть поле́зен? *Can you see the blackboard?,* вам виднá доскá? *Run as fast as you can,* беги́те как мóжно быстре́е. **2,** (know how) уме́ть. *can you drive a car?,* вы уме́ете води́ть маши́ну?
can[2] *n.* **1,** (small container) бáнка. *Tin can,* жестя́нка; консе́рвная бáнка. *Beer can,* жестя́нка из-под пи́ва. **2,** (large container) бидóн: *milk can,* бидóн для молокá. *Garbage can,* мýсорный я́щик. *Watering can,* ле́йка. —*v.t.* (preserve) консерви́ровать. —**can opener,** консе́рвный нож.
Canadian *adj.* канáдский. —*n.* канáдец; канáдка.
canal *n.* канáл.
canard *n.* ýтка.
canary *n.* канаре́йка. —**canary-yellow,** *adj.* канаре́ечный; канаре́ечного цве́та.
cancan *n.* канкáн.
cancel *v.t.* **1,** (call off) отменя́ть. **2,** (void) отменя́ть; аннули́ровать. **3,** (mark, as a postage stamp) погашáть. **4,** *fol. by* **out** (offset) своди́ть на нет. **5,** *math.* сокращáть.
cancellation *n.* **1,** (calling off) отме́на. **2,** (voiding) отме́на; аннули́рование. **3,** (marking of postage stamps) погаше́ние; (mark so made) гаше́ние. **4,** *math.* сокраще́ние.
cancer *n.* **1,** (disease) рак. **2,** *cap., astron.* Рак. —*adj.* рáковый: *cancer cell,* рáковая кле́тка. —**Tropic of Cancer,** трóпик Рáка.
cancerous *adj.* рáковый.
candelabrum *n.* канделя́бр.
candid *adj.* открове́нный; чистосерде́чный.
candidacy *n.* кандидатýра. —**candidate,** *n.* кандидáт.
candied *adj.* засáхаренный.
candle *n.* свечá. —**burn the candle at both ends,** жечь свечý с двух концóв. —**not hold a candle to,** в подмётки не годи́ться (+ *dat.*). —**the game is not worth the candle,** игрá не стóит свеч.
candlelight *n.* свет свечи́: *by candlelight,* при све́те свечи́; при свечáх. —**candle-lit,** *adj.* освещённый свечáми.
candlepower *n.* свечá: *bulb of forty candlepower,* лáмпочка в сóрок свече́й.
candlestick *n.* подсве́чник.

candor *also,* **candour** *n.* открове́нность; чистосерде́чность. —**in all candor,** со всей открове́нностью.
candy *n.* конфе́ты. *Piece of candy,* конфе́та. —*adj.* конфе́тный: *candy wrapper,* конфе́тная обёртка.
cane *n.* **1,** (walking stick) пáлка; трость. **2,** (plant) тростни́к; камы́ш. *Sugar cane,* сáхарный тростни́к. —*v.t.* бить пáлкой. —**cane sugar,** тростникóвый сáхар.
canine *adj.* собáчий. —**canine tooth,** клык.
canister *n.* **1,** (container for tea or spices) корóбка; бáнка. **2,** (part of a gas mask; device for dispensing tear gas) корóбка. —**canister shot,** карте́чь.
canker *n.* я́зва.
canned *adj.* консерви́рованный. *Canned food,* консе́рвы. *Canned meat,* мясны́е консе́рвы. *Canned vegetables,* овощны́е консе́рвы. *Canned fruit,* консерви́рованные фрýкты.
cannery *n.* консе́рвная фáбрика.
cannibal *n.* людое́д. —**cannibalism,** *n.* людое́дство. —**cannibalistic,** *adj.* людое́дский.
cannon *n.* **1,** (weapon) пýшка. **2,** *Brit.* (carom) карамбóль. —**cannon ball,** пýшечное ядрó. —**cannon fodder,** пýшечное мя́со.
cannonade *n.* пýшечная пальбá; канонáда.
cannot *v.* = **can not.**
canny *adj.* **1,** (cautious) осмотри́тельный. **2,** (shrewd) себе́ на уме́.
canoe *n.* канóэ; чёлн; челнóк; байдáрка. —**canoeist,** *n.* канои́ст.
canon *n.* **1,** (religious law; principle; rule) канóн. **2,** (clergyman) канóник. **3,** *music* канóн. —**canon law,** канони́ческое прáво.
canonical *adj.* канони́ческий.
canonize *v.t.* канонизи́ровать; причисля́ть к ли́ку святы́х.
canopy *n.* балдахи́н; пóлог.
cant *n.* жаргóн; аргó. *Thieves' cant,* воровскóй жаргóн; блат.
cantaloupe *n.* канталýпа.
cantankerous *adj.* сварли́вый; вздóрный.
cantata *n.* кантáта.
canteen *n.* **1,** (flask) фля́га; фля́жка. **2,** *mil.* вое́нный магази́н; клуб-столóвая.
canter *n.* лёгкий галóп. —*v.i.* идти́ лёгким галóпом.
cantilever *n.* консóль. —**cantilever bridge,** консóльный мост.
canto *n.* песнь.
canton *n.* кантóн. —**cantonal,** *adj.* кантонáльный.
cantor *n.* кáнтор.
canvas *n.* **1,** (cloth) паруси́на. **2,** (a piece of such material on which to paint) холст. **3,** (painting on canvas) полотнó. **4,** (loosely woven cloth for needlework) канвá. —*adj.* паруси́новый.
canvass *v.t.* **1,** (travel through) объе́здить. **2,** (poll; survey) опрáшивать.
canyon *n.* каньóн; уще́лье.
cap *n.* **1,** (fur) шáпка; (small) ке́пка; (part of a uniform) фурáжка; (fool's, chef's, etc.) колпáк. **2,** (of a mushroom) шля́пка. **3,** (covering, as for a bottle) колпачóк. *Lens cap,* кры́шка объекти́ва. **4,** (percussion cap) кáпсюль. —*v.t.* **1,** (cover) покрывáть. **2,** (complete) довершáть. **3,** (exceed; top) превосходи́ть. —**to cap all,** в доверше́ние всегó.
capability *n.* **1,** (ability) спосóбность. **2,** *usu. pl.*

хохотáться. *Burst into applause,* разрази́ться аплодисме́нтами. **6,** in *burst into flames,* вспы́хнуть плáменем. —*v.t.* прорывáть: *burst the pipes,* прорывáть трýбы. —*n.* **1,** (explosion) взрыв. *Burst of flame,* вспы́шка огня́. *Burst of thunder,* удáр грóма. *Burst of machine-gun fire,* пулемётная óчередь. **2,** *fig.* (outburst, as of laughter or applause) взрыв. *Burst of anger,* вспы́шка *or* поры́в гне́ва. *Burst of energy,* вспы́шка *or* прили́в эне́ргии. **3,** (spurt) бросóк.
bury *v.t.* **1,** (place in a grave) хорони́ть. **2,** (conceal in the ground) закáпывать; зарывáть. **3,** (cover; hide) закрывáть: *bury one's face in one's hands,* закрывáть лицó рукáми. *Bury one's head in a pillow,* зарывáться головóй в подýшку. —**bury oneself in,** зарывáться в. *Bury oneself in a book,* уткнýть нос в кни́гу.
bus *n.* автóбус. —*adj.* автóбусный: *bus line,* автóбусная ли́ния. *Bus driver,* води́тель автóбуса. *Bus stop,* останóвка автóбуса. —*v.t.* перевози́ть на автóбусе.
bush *n.* куст. —**beat around the bush,** ходи́ть вокрýг да óколо; говори́ть обинякáми.
bushed *adj., colloq.* без ног.
bushel *n.* бýшель.
bushing *n.* втýлка.
bushy *adj.* густóй: *bushy eyebrows,* густы́е брóви. *Bushy tail,* пуши́стый хвост.
business *n.* **1,** (commercial dealings) де́ло: *on business,* по де́лу; по делáм. *Business is business,* де́ло есть де́ло. *Get down to business,* приступи́ть к де́лу. *Talk business,* говори́ть по де́лу. **2,** (establishment) предприя́тие; би́знес. **3,** (one's own affairs) де́ло: *it's none of your business,* э́то не вáше де́ло. *Mind your own business!,* не сýйся не в своё де́ло! *What business is it of yours?,* а вам какóе де́ло? —*adj.* деловóй: *business letter,* деловóе письмó. *Business card,* визи́тная кáрточка. *Business address,* служе́бный áдрес. *Business trip,* командирóвка. —**go about one's business,** занимáться свои́ми делáми. —**have no business** (+ *verb*), не име́ть прáва (+ *inf.*). —**make it one's business to...,** стáвить себе́ це́лью (+ *inf.*). *I'll make it my business to be there,* я бýду там обязáтельно. —**mean business,** не шути́ть. —**mix business with pleasure,** сочетáть поле́зное с прия́тным.
businesslike *adj.* деловóй; делови́тый.
businessman *n.* предпринимáтель; бизнесме́н.
bust *n.* **1,** (bosom; sculpture) бюст. **2,** *slang* (flop) провáл; неудáча. —*v.t., slang* **1,** (break) разбивáть. **2,** (bankrupt) разоря́ть.
bustard *n.* дрофá. —**little bustard,** стре́пет.
bustle *n.* суетá; суматóха. —*v.i.* суети́ться. —**bustling,** *adj.* суетли́вый.
busy *adj.* **1,** (occupied) зáнятый: *I am very busy,* я óчень зáнят. *The line is busy,* ли́ния занятá. **2,** (full of activity, as of a street) оживлённый. —*v.t.* [*usu.* **busy oneself with**] занимáться (+ *instr.*).
busybody *n.* хлопотýн.
but *conj.* но: *slowly but surely,* ме́дленно, но ве́рно. *But on the other hand...,* но с другóй стороны́... ♦*Also rendered by* а *and* да: *not he, but his brother,* не он, а егó брат. *She would like to go, but she can't,* онá и пошлá бы, да не мóжет. —*prep.* крóме: *everyone but me,* все, крóме меня́. *What could I do but agree?,* что мне оставáлось, как не согла-

си́ться? —*adv.* тóлько; лишь; прóсто. *He is but a child,* он лишь ребёнок. *Had I but known!,* е́сли бы я тóлько знал! —*n.* "но": *a slight "but",* мáленькое "но". —**all but,** почти́: *all but certain,* почти́ уве́рен. —**but for,** е́сли бы не. —**but then,** затó; впрóчем.
butane *n.* бутáн.
butcher *n.* **1,** (seller of meat) мясни́к. **2,** *fig.* (murderer) палáч. —*v.t.* **1,** (slaughter) ре́зать; закáлывать. **2,** *fig.* (murder, as a language) кове́ркать (язы́к). —**butcher shop,** мяснáя лáвка.
butchery *n.* бóйня; резня́.
butler *n.* дворе́цкий.
butt *n.* **1,** (thick end) торе́ц; (*of an axe*) óбух; обýх. **2,** (rifle butt) приклáд. **3,** (of a cigarette) окýрок. **4,** *fig.* (target) мише́нь: *butt of jokes,* мише́нь для острóт. —*v.t.* бодáть. —*v.i.* бодáться. —**butt in,** *colloq.* совáться.
butter *n.* мáсло. *Butter knife,* нож для мáсла. *Butter dish,* маслёнка. —*v.t.* **1,** (put butter on) намáзывать мáслом. **2,** *fol. by* **up,** *colloq.* (flatter) умáсливать; замáсливать; подмáзываться к.
buttercup *n.* лю́тик; курослéп.
butterfly *n.* бáбочка.
buttermilk *n.* пáхта.
buttocks *n.pl.* я́годицы.
button *n.* **1,** (for a garment) пýговица. **2,** (push button) кнóпка. —*v.t.* застёгивать. —*v.i.* застёгиваться. —**on the button,** *colloq.* рóвно; тóчно.
buttonhole *n.* **1,** (for a button) пе́тля. **2,** (for a flower, ribbon, etc.) петли́ца.
buttress *n.* **1,** *archit.* контрфóрс. **2,** *fig.* (prop) подпóра. —*v.t.* подде́рживать; подпирáть; подкрепля́ть.
butyl *n.* бути́л.
butylene *n.* бутиле́н.
buxom *adj.* полногрýдый.
buy *v.t.* покупáть (*pfv.* купи́ть). *Buy one's wife a present,* купи́ть подáрок жене́. —*n.* **1,** (purchase) покýпка. *You got a good buy,* вы удáчно купи́ли. **2,** *colloq.* (bargain) вы́годная сде́лка. —**buy up,** скупáть; раскупáть; закупáть.
buyer *n.* **1,** (purchaser) покупáтель. **2,** *comm.* (purchasing agent) закýпщик.
buzz *v.i.* жужжáть. —*n.* **1,** (buzzing) жужжáние. **2,** (hum; rumble) гул. —**give someone a buzz,** *colloq.* позвони́ть комý-нибудь.
buzzard *n.* каню́к; сары́ч.
buzzer *n.* зýммер.
by *prep.* **1,** (near) у; óколо. *Stand by the window,* стоя́ть у окнá. **2,** (beside) пóдле; вóзле; ря́дом с. **3,** (past; beyond) ми́мо: *pass by someone's house,* проходи́ть ми́мо чьегó-нибудь дóма. **4,** (through the action or agency of) *rendered by the instr. case: done by me,* сде́лан мнóю; *by force of arms,* си́лой орýжия. *What do you mean by that?,* что вы хоти́те э́тим сказáть? **5,** (mode of travel) на (+ *prepl.*). ♦*Also rendered by the instr. case: go by train,* е́хать на пóезде *or* пóездом. **6,** (with verbs of holding, seizing, etc.) за (+ *acc.*): *hold by the hand,* держáть зá руку; *seize by the collar,* схвати́ть за ши́ворот. **7,** (means of communication) по: *by telephone,* по телефóну. **8,** *expressing various relationships* по: *by mistake,* по оши́бке; *by nature,* по при́роде; *by profession,* по профе́ссии; *call by name,* называ́ть по

и́мени; *judging by this,* сýдя по э́тому. **9,** (according to) по: *by my watch,* по мои́м часáм. **10,** (before; no later than) к: *by two o'clock,* к двум часáм. **11,** (born of) от: *a child by her first husband,* ребёнок от пéрвого мýжа. **12,** (in units of) на: *sell by the pound,* продавáть на фунт. **13,** (in groups of) по: *one by one,* по одномý; оди́н за други́м; *two by two,* пó двое. **14,** (in succession) за: *step by step,* шаг за шáгом. *Day by day,* изо дня в день. *Little by little,* мáло-помáлу. **15,** (in or to the amount or degree of) на: *older than you by two years,* стáрше вас на два гóда. **16,** *in multiplication and division* на: *multiply/divide ten by five,* помнóжить/раздели́ть дéсять на пять. **17,** *with dimensions* на: *six meters by five,* шесть мéтров на пять. **18,** *in various miscellaneous expressions: by day,* днём; *by night,* нóчью; *by heart,* наизýсть; *by chance,* случáйно; *by sight,* в лицó; *by degrees,* постепéнно; *by candlelight,* при свечáх. —*adv.* **1,** (near) бли́зко; ря́дом. *Be standing by,* стоя́ть ря́дом. **2,** (past) ми́мо: *pass by,* пройти́ ми́мо. —**by and by,** со врéменем. —**by and large,** в цéлом; в основнóм. —**by the way,** мéжду прóчим; кстáти.

bye-bye *interj.* до свидáнья!

bygone *adj.* мину́вший; былóй. —**let bygones be bygones,** что прошлó, то прошлó.

bylaw *n.* прáвило; постановлéние.

bypass *n.* обхóд. —*v.t.* обходи́ть.

by-product *n.* побóчный продýкт.

byroad *n.* просёлок; просёлочная дорóга.

bystander *n.* свидéтель; очеви́дец.

byword *n.* послóвица; поговóрка. *Become a byword,* войти́ в послóвицу.

Byzantine *adj.* византи́йский.

C

C, c трéтья бýква англи́йского алфави́та. —*n.* **1,** (musical note) до. **2,** (school grade) трóйка.

cab *n.* **1,** (taxi) такси́. *Cab driver,* шофёр такси́. **2,** (driver's compartment) каби́на.

cabal *n.* **1,** (group of plotters) кли́ка. **2,** (plot) зáговор.

cabana *n.* купáльная каби́на.

cabaret *n.* кабарé.

cabbage *n.* капýста. *Stuffed cabbage,* голубцы́. —**cabbage butterfly,** капýстница. —**cabbage soup,** щи.

cabin *n.* **1,** (hut; cottage) хи́жина; дóмик. *Log cabin,* бревéнчатый дóмик. **2,** (stateroom on a ship) каю́та. **3,** (of an airplane) каби́на. —**cabin boy,** ю́нга.

cabinet *n.* **1,** (cupboard; case) шкаф. *Medicine cabinet,* аптéчка. **2,** (of a radio, television set, etc.) кóрпус. **3,** (advisory body of a chief executive) кабинéт.

cabinetmaker *n.* столя́р.

cable *n.* **1,** (rope or wire) канáт; трос. **2,** (underwater telegraph line) кáбель. **3,** (cablegram) телегрáмма; каблогрáмма. —*v.t.* & *i.* телеграфи́ровать.

cable car подвеснáя вагонéтка; фуникулёр.

cablegram *n.* каблогрáмма; телегрáмма.

cable television кáбельное телеви́дение.

cabriolet *n.* кабриолéт.

cacao *n.* какáо.

cache *n.* тайни́к. *Cache of weapons,* тáйный склад орýжия.

cackle *v.i.* (of a hen) кудáхтать; (of a goose) гоготáть. —*n.* кудáхтанье; гóгот.

cacophonous *adj.* неблагозвýчный; какофони́ческий. —**cacophony,** *n.* неблагозвýчие; какофóния.

cactus *n.* кáктус.

cad *n.* хам.

cadaver *n.* труп. —**cadaverous,** *adj.* мéртвенный; помертвéлый.

caddish *adj.* хáмский.

caddy *n.* чáйница.

cadence *n.* **1,** (rhythm; beat) ритм; такт. **2,** *music* каде́нция.

cadenza *n.* каде́нция.

cadet *n.* **1,** *mil.* (student) курсáнт. **2,** *cap.* (member of the Russian Constitutional Democrat party) кадéт.

cadmium *n.* кáдмий.

cadre *n.* кáдровый состáв. —**cadres,** *n.pl.* кáдры.

caecum *n.* = **cecum.**

Caesarean section кéсарево сечéние.

café *n.* кафé.

cafeteria *n.* кафетéрий.

caffeine *n.* кофеи́н.

caftan *n.* кафтáн.

cage *n.* клéтка. —*v.t.* сажáть в клéтку. *Feel caged in,* чýвствовать себя́ как в клéтке.

cagey *also,* **cagy** *adj.* осторóжный; себé на умé.

cahoots *n.pl., slang, in* **in cahoots with,** в сгóворе с.

caisson *n.* **1,** (watertight chamber) кессóн. **2,** (ammunition wagon) заря́дный я́щик.

cajole *v.t.* уговáривать; задáбривать. —**cajolery,** *n.* уговóры.

cake *n.* **1,** (pastry) торт; кекс. *Sponge cake,* бискви́т. **2,** (patty of meat or fish) котлéта: *fish cakes,* ры́бные котлéты. **3,** (bar, as of soap) кусóк; брусóк. —*v.i.* спекáться; ссыхáться.

calabash *n.* горля́нка.

calamity *n.* бéдствие. —**calamitous,** *adj.* бéдственный.

calcify *v.t.* & *i.* превращáть(ся) в и́звесть.

calcium *n.* кáльций. —*adj.* кáльциевый. —**calcium carbide,** углерóдистый кáльций. —**calcium carbonate,** углеки́слый кáльций. —**calcium chloride,** хлóристый кáльций. —**calcium oxide,** óкись кáльция.

calculate *v.t.* **1,** (compute) рассчи́тывать; подсчи́тывать; вычисля́ть; исчисля́ть. **2,** (intend; design) рассчи́тывать: *calculated for effect,* рассчи́танный на эффéкт.

calculated *adj.* рассчи́танный: *calculated rudeness,* рассчи́танная грýбость. —**calculated risk,** риск с тóчным расчётом; обдýманный риск.

calculating *adj.* **1,** (designed to calculate) счётный: *calculating machine,* счётная маши́на. **2,** (shrewd; cautious) расчётливый; себé на умé.

calculation *n.* расчёт; подсчёт; вычислéние; исчислéние.

calculator *n.* калькуля́тор; арифмóметр.

calculus *n.* исчислéние.

caldron *also,* **cauldron** *n.* котёл.

calendar *n.* календáрь. —*adj.* календáрный: *calendar year,* календáрный год.

calender *n.* калáндр.

calf *n.* **1,** (young of the cow) телёнок. **2,** (young of other animals) детёныш. **3,** (rear part of the leg below the knee) икрá. —*adj.* [*also,* **calf's**] теля́чий: *calf's liver,* теля́чья печёнка.

calfskin *n.* теля́чья кóжа; опóек.

caliber *also,* **calibre** *n.* **1,** (diameter) кали́бр. **2,** *fig.* (ability) кáчества: *person of high caliber,* человéк высóких кáчеств.

calibrate *v.t.* калибровáть. —**calibration,** *n.* калибровáние.

calibre *n.* = **caliber.**

calico *n.* **1,** *U.S.* (printed cloth) си́тец. **2,** *Brit.* (unprinted) миткáль. —*adj.* си́тцевый; миткáлевый.

californium *n.* калифóрний.

caliper *also,* **calliper** *n., usu. pl.* кронци́ркуль.

caliph *n.* хали́ф; кали́ф. —**caliphate,** *n.* халифáт.

calisthenics *also,* **callisthenics** *n.* гимнáстика; заря́дка.

calk *v.t.* = **caulk.**

call *v.t.* **1,** (shout to) звать. **2,** (utter in a loud voice) назывáть: *who called my name?,* кто назвáл моё и́мя? **3,** (summon) звать; вызывáть. **4,** (telephone) звони́ть; вызывáть. **5,** (name) назывáть: *what is this called?,* как э́то назывáется? *Call it what you will,* назывáйте, как хоти́те. **6,** (describe as specified) назывáть: *call someone a liar,* назвáть когó-нибудь лжецóм. *You could hardly call her beautiful,* её нельзя́ назвáть красáвицей. **7,** (declare) признавáть: *call the game a draw,* признáть пáртию ничьéй. **8,** (convene) созывáть. **9,** *with various nouns: call a strike,* объяви́ть забастóвку; *call* (*someone*) *names,* обругáть; *call the roll,* дéлать перекли́чку; *call attention to,* обращáть (чьё-нибудь) внимáние на. **10,** *in various expressions: call to mind,* напоминáть; *call to order,* призывáть к поря́дку; *call to arms,* призывáть к орýжию; *call in question,* стáвить под вопрóс. —*v.i.* **1,** (shout) звать: *call for help,* звать на пóмощь. **2,** (phone) звони́ть. **3,** (of a ship) заходи́ть: *call at a port,* заходи́ть в порт. —*n.* **1,** (cry; shout) крик: *call for help,* крик о пóмощи. **2,** (phone communication; summons) вы́зов. *Were there any calls for me?,* меня́ никтó не вызывáл? **3,** (appeal) призы́в: *a call to action,* призы́в к дéйствию. **4,** (cry of a bird or animal) крик. *Mating call,* токовáние. **5,** (sound of a horn) сигнáл: *bugle call,* сигнáл на гóрне. **6,** (visit) визи́т: *courtesy call,* визи́т вéжливости. *Pay a call on,* заходи́ть к; приходи́ть с визи́том к. —**call aside,** отводи́ть в стóрону. —**call back, 1,** (summon back; recall) отзывáть. **2,** (telephone again) звони́ть ещё раз. —**call down,** *colloq.* отчитáть. —**call for, 1,** (come and pick up) заходи́ть за; заезжáть за. **2,** (appeal for; advocate) призывáть к *or* на. **3,** (require) трéбовать. —**call forth,** вызывáть. —**call in, 1,** (summon) вызывáть. **2,** (phone in) сообщáть по телефóну. **3,** (retire from circulation) изымáть из обращéния. —**call off, 1,** (summon away) отзывáть. **2,** (read aloud) назывáть. **3,** (cancel) отменя́ть. —**call on, 1,** (ask to recite, as in class) спрáшивать; вызывáть. **2,** (allow to speak) предоставля́ть слóво (+ *dat.*). **3,** (visit briefly) посещáть; заходи́ть к. **4,** (urge) призывáть. **5,** (appeal to, as for help) обращáться к. —**call out, 1,** (shout) кричáть; выкри́кивать. *Call out one's name,* вы́крикнуть своё и́мя. **2,** (summon) вызывáть. —**call up, 1,** (call on the telephone) вызывáть; звони́ть. **2,** (summon for military service) призывáть.

caller *n.* гость; посети́тель.

calligraphy *n.* каллигрáфия. —**calligraphic,** *adj.* каллиграфи́ческий.

calling *n.* призвáние: *follow one's calling,* слéдовать своемý призвáнию. —**calling card,** визи́тная кáрточка.

calliper *n.* = **caliper.**

callisthenics *n.* = **calisthenics.**

call number шифр.

callous *adj.* **1,** [*also,* **calloused**] (hardened) огрубéлый; загрубéлый; мозóлистый. **2,** *fig.* (unfeeling) чёрствый. —**callousness,** *n.* чёрствость.

callow *adj.* зелёный; безýсый.

call sign позывнóй сигнáл; позывны́е.

call-up *n.* призы́в.

callus *n.* мозóль.

calm *adj.* спокóйный: *calm sea,* спокóйное мóре; *calm voice,* спокóйный гóлос. —*n.* **1,** (tranquillity) спокóйствие. **2,** (absence of wind) зати́шье. *The calm before the storm,* зати́шье пéред грозóй. —*v.t.* успокáивать. —*v.i.* [*usu.* **calm down**] успокáиваться. —**calmly,** *adv.* спокóйно.

caloric *adj.* тепловóй. *Caloric content,* калори́йность.

calorie *n.* калóрия.

calorimeter *n.* калори́метр; тепломéр.

calumniate *v.t.* клеветáть на. —**calumnious,** *adj.* клеветни́ческий. —**calumny,** *n.* клеветá.

Calvary *n.* Голгóфа.

calve *v.i.* тели́ться.

calyx *n.* чáшечка.

cam *n.* кулáк; кулачóк; эксцéнтрик.

camaraderie *n.* товáрищество.

cambium *n.* кáмбий.

cambric *n.* бати́ст.

camel *n.* верблю́д.

camellia *n.* камéлия.

camel's hair 1, (hair) верблю́жья шерсть. **2,** (cloth) верблю́жье сукнó. —**camel's-hair,** *adj.* верблю́жий.

cameo *n.* камéя.

camera *n.* фотографи́ческий аппарáт; фотоап-

(potential ability) возмóжности.
capable *adj.* спосóбный. *Capable of anything,* спосóбен на всё. —**capably,** *adv.* умéло.
capacious *adj.* ёмкий; вместúтельный.
capacitator *n.* конденсáтор.
capacity *n.* **1,** (ability to hold; volume) вместúмость; ёмкость. *Filled to capacity,* пóлный до откáза; биткóм набúтый. **2,** (ability) спосóбность: *capacity for learning,* спосóбность к учёбе; *carrying capacity,* пропускнáя спосóбность. **3,** (maximum level of production) мóщность: *operate at full capacity,* рабóтать на пóлную мóщность. **4,** (position; function) кáчество: *in the capacity of,* в кáчестве (+ *gen.*). —*adj.* пóлный: *play to capacity crowds,* дéлать пóлные сбóры; идтú с аншлáгом.
cape *n.* **1,** (point of land) мыс. **2,** (garment) накúдка; пелерúна.
caper *n.* **1,** (playful leap) прыжóк. **2,** (prank) вы́ходка; прокáза. **3,** *pl.* (condiment) кáперсы.
capillary *n.* капиллЯр. —*adj.* капиллЯрный.
capital *n.* **1,** (capital city) столúца. **2,** *econ.* капитáл. —*adj.* **1,** (containing the seat of government) столúчный: *capital city,* столúчный гóрод. **2,** *econ.* капитáльный. *Capital investment,* капиталовложéния. **3,** (punishable by death) наказýемый смéртью. *Capital punishment,* смéртная казнь; вы́сшая мéра наказáния. **4,** (of a letter) прописнóй; заглáвный; большóй. *This word is spelled with a capital letter,* э́то слóво пúшется с большóй бýквы. **5,** *colloq.* (excellent; first-rate) превосхóдный; первоклáссный. —**make capital of,** спекулúровать на; выезжáть на.
capitalism *n.* капиталúзм.
capitalist *n.* капиталúст. —*adj.* [*also,* **capitalistic**] капиталистúческий.
capitalization *n.* **1,** *gram.* употреблéние прописны́х букв: *the rules for capitalization,* прáвила употреблéния прописны́х букв. **2,** *econ.* капитализáция.
capitalize *v.t.* **1,** (write with a capital letter) писáть с большóй бýквы. **2,** (convert into capital) капитализúровать. —*v.i.* [*usu.* **capitalize on**] (use to advantage) испóльзовать; пóльзоваться.
capitol *n.* капитóлий.
capitulate *v.i.* капитулúровать. —**capitulation,** *n.* капитулЯция.
capon *n.* каплýн.
caprice *n.* капрúз; причýда; прúхоть. —**capricious,** *adj.* капрúзный; причýдливый; прихотлúвый.
Capricorn *n.* Козерóг. —**Tropic of Capricorn,** трóпик Козерóга.
capsize *v.t.* опрокúдывать. —*v.i.* опрокúдываться.
capstan *n.* кабестáн; шпиль.
capsule *n.* **1,** (for enclosing a dose of medicine) кáпсула. **2,** (detachable part of a rocket) кáпсула; кабúна. —*adj.* крáткий: *capsule summary,* крáткое изложéние.
captain *n.* **1,** (military rank) капитáн; (naval rank) капитáн пéрвого рáнга. **2,** (ship's commander) капитáн; командúр. **3,** *sports* капитáн.
caption *n.* **1,** (heading) заголóвок. **2,** (of an illustration or cartoon) пóдпись. **3,** *motion pictures* субтúтр.
captious *adj.* придúрчивый.
captivate *v.t.* пленЯть; очарóвывать; восхищáть. —**captivating,** *adj.* пленúтельный; очаровáтельный; восхитúтельный.
captive *n.* плéнник; плéнный. —*adj.* взЯтый в плен; плéнный. —**be taken captive,** попáсть в плен. —**take captive,** взять в плен. —**hold captive,** держáть в плену́.
captivity *n.* **1,** (of people) плен; невóля. **2,** (of animals) невóля: *breed in captivity,* размножáться в невóле.
capture *v.t.* **1,** (take or seize by force) захвáтывать. **2,** (take prisoner) взять в плен. **3,** (win in a contest) завоёвывать. **4,** *chess* брать. **5,** (record for posterity) запечатлевáть: *capture on film,* запечатлевáть на плёнке. —*n.* захвáт; пóимка; взЯтие в плен.
capuchin *n.* **1,** *cap.* (monk) капуцúн. **2,** (cloak) плащ с капюшóном. **3,** (monkey) капуцúн.
capybara *n.* водосвúнка.
car *n.* **1,** (automobile) машúна; автомобúль. **2,** (of a train) вагóн.
caracul *also,* **karakul** *n.* **1,** (sheep) каракýльская овцá. **2,** (fur) карáкуль.
carafe *n.* графúн.
caramel *n.* карамéль. —*adj.* карамéльный.
carat *n.* **1,** (unit of weight for gems) карáт. **2,** = **karat.**
caravan *n.* каравáн.
caravel *n.* каравéлла.
caraway *n.* тмин. —*adj.* тмúнный.
carbide *n.* карбúд.
carbine *n.* карабúн.
carbohydrate *n.* углевóд.
carbolic *adj.* карбóловый. —**carbolic acid,** карбóловая кислотá; карбóлка.
carbon *n.* углерóд.
carbonate *n.* карбонáт; углекúслая соль. —*v.t.* газúровать: *carbonated beverages,* газирóванные напúтки.
carbon copy **1,** (copy made with carbon paper) кóпия. *Make carbon copies,* писáть под копúрку. **2,** *colloq.* (perfect likeness) тóчная кóпия.
carbon dioxide углекúслый газ.
carbonic acid углекислотá; ýгольная кислотá.
carbon monoxide угáрный газ.
carbon paper копировáльная бумáга; копúрка.
carborundum *n.* карборýнд.
carbuncle *n.* карбýнкул.
carburetor *also,* **carburettor** *n.* карбюрáтор.
carcass *n.* тýша.
carcinogen *n.* канцерогéн; карциногéн. —**carcinogenic,** *adj.* канцерогéнный.
card *n.* **1,** (piece of stiff paper used for various purposes) кáрточка: *calling card,* визúтная кáрточка. **2,** (playing card) кáрта: *play cards,* игрáть в кáрты. **3,** (certificate of membership) билéт: *membership card,* члéнский билéт. —*adj.* кáрточный: *card trick/catalogue,* кáрточный фóкус/каталóг. —*v.t.* чесáть: *card wool,* чесáть шерсть. —**house of cards,** кáрточный дóмик. —**it was not in the cards,** вúдно, не судьбá! —**lay one's cards on the table,** вы́ложить кáрты на стол.
cardboard *n.* картóн. —*adj.* картóнный.
card file картотéка.
cardiac *adj.* сердéчный.
cardigan *n.* шерстянáя кóфточка.
cardinal *adj.* основнóй; кардинáльный. *Cardinal principle,* основнóй прúнцип. —*n.* **1,** (prelate) кардинáл. **2,** (bird) кардинáл. —**cardinal number,**

количественное числительное. —**cardinal point,** страна́ све́та.
cardiogram *n.* кардиогра́мма.
cardiograph *n.* кардио́граф.
cardiology *n.* кардиоло́гия. —**cardiologist,** *n.* кардио́лог.
cardiovascular *adj.* серде́чно-сосу́дистый.
cardsharp *n.* шу́лер.
card table ка́рточный стол; ло́мберный стол.
care *n.* **1,** (concern; source of concern) забо́та: *my chief care,* гла́вная моя́ забо́та. *She hasn't a care in the world,* она́ не име́ет никаки́х забо́т. **2,** (close attention) ухо́д: *care of the sick,* ухо́д за больны́ми; *care of one's car,* ухо́д за маши́ной. *Require constant care,* тре́бовать постоя́нного ухо́да. *He received excellent care,* за ним был прекра́сный ухо́д. **3,** (charge; supervision) попече́ние: *he was left in the care of his grandmother,* он оста́лся на попече́нии ба́бушки. *Under the care of a physician,* под наблюде́нием врача́. **4,** (painstaking application) тща́тельность. *With the greatest of care,* са́мым тща́тельным о́бразом. **5,** (caution) осторо́жность: *handle with care,* обраща́ться с осторо́жностью. —*v.i.* забо́титься: *care about someone,* забо́титься о ко́м-нибудь. *I don't care,* мне всё равно́. *What do I care?,* како́е мне де́ло? *I don't care what happens,* мне безразли́чно, что бу́дет. —*v.t.* хоте́ть: *I don't care to go,* мне не хо́чется идти́. —**care for, 1,** (tend) забо́титься о; уха́живать за. **2,** (be fond of) люби́ть. **3,** (like; wish) хоте́ть: *would you care for another cup of tea?,* хоти́те ещё ча́шку ча́ю? —**care of,** по а́дресу (+ *gen.*); че́рез; для переда́чи (+ *dat.*). —**take care,** быть осторо́жным. —**take care of, 1,** (care for) забо́титься о; уха́живать за. **2,** (guard; protect) бере́чь; побере́чь. **3,** (attend to) занима́ться (+ *instr.*); выполня́ть. **4,** in *take care of oneself,* побере́чься. —**take care not to,** смотри́те, не (+ *imperative*).
careen *v.i.* крени́ться. *The car careened from side to side,* маши́ну броса́ло из стороны́ в сто́рону.
career *n.* карье́ра. —**careerist,** *n.* карьери́ст.
carefree *adj.* беззабо́тный; беспе́чный.
careful *adj.* **1,** (cautious) осторо́жный. *Be careful!,* осторо́жно!; бу́дьте осторо́жны! **2,** (painstaking) тща́тельный.
carefully *adv.* **1,** (with caution) осторо́жно. **2,** (with great care) тща́тельно. **3,** (with close attention) внима́тельно.
careless *adj.* **1,** (slipshod) небре́жный. *Make a careless mistake,* допусти́ть оши́бку по небре́жности. **2,** (incautious) неосторо́жный. —**carelessly,** *adv.* небре́жно; неосторо́жно. —**carelessness,** *n.* небре́жность; неосторо́жность.
caress *n.* ла́ска. —*v.t.* ласка́ть.
caretaker *n.* дво́рник.
carfare *n.* проездна́я пла́та.
cargo *n.* груз. —*adj.* грузово́й: *cargo ship,* грузово́е су́дно.
caricature *n.* карикату́ра.
caries *n.* костое́да; ка́риес.
carillon *n.* карилько́н.
carious *adj.* карио́зный.
carmine *n.* карми́н. —*adj.* карми́нный; карми́новый.
carnage *n.* резня́; бо́йня.
carnal *adj.* **1,** (of the flesh) пло́тский. **2,** (sexual) полово́й.
carnation *n.* гвозди́ка.
carnival *n.* карнава́л.
carnivore *n.* плотоя́дное живо́тное. —**carnivorous,** *adj.* плотоя́дный.
carol *n.* рожде́ственская пе́сня; коля́дка.
carom *n.* карамбо́ль. —*v.i.* отска́кивать.
carouse *v.i.* кути́ть; гуля́ть. —**carousal,** *n.* кутёж; попо́йка.
carousel *also,* **carrousel** *n.* карусе́ль.
carouser *n.* кути́ла; гуля́ка.
carp *n.* карп; саза́н; кара́сь. —*v.i.* придира́ться.
carpenter *n.* пло́тник. —**carpentry,** *n.* пло́тничье *or* пло́тничное де́ло; пло́тничество.
carpet *n.* ковёр. —*v.t.* устила́ть ковро́м. —**call on the carpet,** *colloq.* вы́звать на ковёр.
carping *adj.* приди́рчивый.
carriage *n.* **1,** (vehicle) коля́ска; экипа́ж; каре́та. *Baby carriage,* де́тская коля́ска. *Gun carriage,* лафе́т. **2,** *Brit.* (railroad passenger car) ваго́н. **3,** (moving part, as of a typewriter) каре́тка. **4,** (manner of carrying oneself; bearing) оса́нка; вы́правка.
carrier *n.* **1,** (one who carries something) перено́счик. **2,** (person transmitting a disease) носи́тель; (insect doing same) перено́счик. **3,** (aircraft carrier) авиано́сец. —**carrier pigeon,** почто́вый го́лубь.
carrion *n.* па́даль; мертвечи́на.
carrot *n.* морко́вь. —*adj.* морко́вный: *carrot juice,* морко́вный сок. —**carrot and stick,** поли́тика кнута́ и пря́ника.
carrousel *n.* = **carousel.**
carry *v.t.* **1,** (bear) нести́: *carry a child in one's arms,* нести́ ребёнка на рука́х; *carry a pack on one's back,* нести́ ра́нец на спине́. **2,** (have or keep on one's person) носи́ть; держа́ть при себе́. *Carry money in one's pocket,* носи́ть де́ньги в карма́не. **3,** (transport) переноси́ть; (*by vehicle*) везти́; перевози́ть: *carry passengers and freight,* перевози́ть пассажи́ров и това́ры. **4,** (have in stock) держа́ть; торгова́ть. **5,** (be pregnant with) вына́шивать. **6,** (print, as an article) помеща́ть. **7,** (extend) доводи́ть: *carry to an extreme,* доводи́ть до кра́йности. **8,** *in various miscellaneous expressions: carry weight,* име́ть вес; *carry insurance,* быть застрахо́ванным. —*v.i.* **1,** (travel, as of sound) доноси́ться. *His voice doesn't carry,* его́ го́лос пло́хо слы́шен. **2,** (be approved): *the resolution carried,* резолю́ция была́ принята́. —**be/get carried away,** увлека́ться. —**carry forward,** *bookkeeping* транспорти́ровать. —**carry on, 1,** (engage in; conduct) вести́. **2,** (continue; keep up) продолжа́ть. **3,** *colloq.* (behave wildly) беси́ться; рвать и мета́ть. —**carry oneself,** держа́ться. —**carry out, 1,** *literally* выноси́ть. **2,** (fulfill, as an order, promise, etc.) выполня́ть; исполня́ть. **3,** (conduct, as an investigation, experiment, etc.) проводи́ть; производи́ть. **4,** (execute, as a mission or raid) соверша́ть. **5,** (put into practice, as a plan or program) осуществля́ть. **6,** (implement, as a threat or sentence) приводи́ть в исполне́ние.
cart *n.* **1,** (vehicle pulled by an animal) теле́га; подво́да; двуко́лка. **2,** (handcart) (ручна́я) теле́жка. —*v.t.* **1,** (transport) везти́; перевози́ть. **2,** (carry with great effort) тащи́ть. —**put the cart before the horse,** начина́ть не с того́ конца́.

cartel *n.* картéль.
carter *n.* вóзчик; ломовóй; ломовóй извóзчик.
cartilage *n.* хрящ. —**cartilaginous,** *adj.* хрящевáтый.
cartography *n.* картогрáфия. —**cartographer,** *n.* картóграф. —**cartographic,** *adj.* картографи́ческий.
carton *n.* картóнка.
cartoon *n.* **1,** (drawing) карикатýра. **2,** (film) мультипликациóнный фильм; мультипликáция. —**cartoonist,** *n.* карикатури́ст.
cartridge *n.* патрóн. —**cartridge case,** ги́льза. —**cartridge clip,** обóйма. —**cartridge pouch,** подсýмок.
carve *v.t.* & *i.* **1,** (make by cutting) рéзать; (*specifically in wood*) вырезáть; (*specifically in stone*) высекáть. **2,** (slice, as meat) нарезáть. **3,** *fol. by* **up** (divide up) разделя́ть; разбивáть. **4,** *fol. by* **out** (achieve) ковáть: *carve out a victory,* ковáть побéду. —**carved,** *adj.* резнóй; вырезнóй. —**carver,** *n.* рéзчик. —**carving,** *n.* резьбá; резнáя рабóта.
caryatid *n.* кариати́да.
cascade *n.* каскáд. —*v.i.* низвергáться.
case *n.* **1,** (instance) слýчай: *in most cases,* в большинствé слýчаев. *In any case,* во вся́ком слýчае. *In case...,* в том слýчае, éсли...; на слýчай, éсли... *In case of,* в слýчае (+ *gen.*). *Just in case,* на вся́кий слýчай. *Make an exception in someone's case,* сдéлать исключéние для когó-нибудь. **2,** (the actual state of affairs): *that is not the case,* э́то не так; э́то не вéрно. *If that's the case; that being the case,* в такóм слýчае; éсли дéло обстои́т так. *As the case may be,* в зави́симости от обстоя́тельств. *As is often the case,* как э́то чáсто бывáет. **3,** *law* дéло: *hear a case,* слýшать дéло. **4,** (argument in support of) дóводы: *the case for capital punishment,* дóводы в пóльзу смéртной кáзни. **5,** (person being treated) больнóй: *a mental case,* психи́чески больнóй. *It's a hopeless case,* больнóй безнадёжен. **6,** *gram.* падéж: *accusative case,* вини́тельный падéж. **7,** (large box) я́щик: *packing case,* упакóвочный я́щик. **8,** (small box) футля́р: *eyeglass case,* футля́р для очкóв. *Cigarette case,* портсигáр. **9,** (cover) чехóл: *case for a camera,* чехóл для фотоаппарáта. **10,** (showcase) витри́на. **11,** (tray for storing type) кáсса.
caseharden *v.t.* цементи́ровать.
case history истóрия болéзни.
casein *n.* казеи́н.
casemate *n.* каземáт.
casement *n.* ствóрка. —**casement window,** ствóрчатое окнó.
cash *n.* нали́чные (дéньги): *pay cash,* плати́ть нали́чными. *Short of cash,* не при деньгáх. —*adj.* нали́чный: *cash payment,* нали́чный расчёт. —*v.t. Cash a check,* **1,** (of a person) получи́ть дéньги по чéку. **2,** (of a bank) вы́дать дéньги по чéку.
cashbook *n.* кáссовая кни́га.
cash box кáсса.
cashier *n.* касси́р. —*v.t.* увольня́ть со слýжбы.
cashmere *n.* кашеми́р. —*adj.* кашеми́ровый.
cash register кáсса.
casing *n.* кожýх; кóрпус.
casino *n.* казинó.
cask *n.* бóчка; бочóнок.
casket *n.* **1,** (small box) шкатýлка. **2,** (coffin) гроб.
cassava *n.* маниóка.
cassette *n.* кассéта.
cassock *n.* ря́са.
cast *v.t.* **1,** (throw) бросáть; кидáть; метáть. **2,** (cause to fall, drop, or occur) бросáть: *cast anchor,* брóсить я́корь; *cast a glance,* брóсить взгляд. *Cast a shadow,* отбрáсывать тень. *Cast doubt upon,* подвергáть сомнéнию. *Cast a spell over,* заколдóвывать; околдóвывать. *Cast one's lot with,* связáть свою́ судьбý с. **3,** (give, as a vote) подавáть; отдавáть (гóлос). **4,** (draw, as lots) бросáть (жрéбий). *The die is cast,* жрéбий брóшен. **5,** (shape; mold) лить; отливáть. —*n.* **1,** (mold) слéпок. **2,** *med.* гипс. **3,** (actors in a play) состáв исполни́телей. **4,** (tinge; shade) оттéнок. **5,** in *cast of mind,* склад умá. —**cast about for,** изы́скивать. —**cast aside,** отбрáсывать. —**cast off, 1,** (throw off) сбрáсывать. **2,** (sail off, as of a boat) отвáливать; отчáливать.
castanets *n.pl.* кастаньéты.
caste *n.* кáста. —*adj.* кáстовый: *caste system,* кáстовая систéма.
caster *n.* **1,** (founder) литéйщик. **2,** [*also,* **castor**] (small wheel) колёсико; рóлик.
castigate *v.t.* подвергáть сурóвой кри́тике; бичевáть.
casting *n.* **1,** (founding) литьё; отли́вка. **2,** (object cast in a mold) отли́вка; *pl.* литьё. **3,** *theat.* распределéние ролéй.
cast iron чугýн. —**cast-iron,** *adj.* чугýнный. *Cast-iron stomach,* лужёный желýдок.
castle *n.* **1,** (fortress) зáмок. **2,** (chess piece) ладья́; турá. —*v.i., chess* рокировáть(ся); дéлать рокирóвку. —**castles in the air,** воздýшные зáмки.
castor *n.* **1,** (cloth) кастóр; бóбрик. **2,** = **caster.** —**castor oil,** кастóровое мáсло.
castrate *v.t.* кастри́ровать; холости́ть; оскопля́ть. —**castration,** *n.* кастрáция.
casual *adj.* **1,** (chance) случáйный. **2,** (informal; relaxed) непринуждённый; небрéжный. *Casual clothes,* повседнéвное плáтье. **3,** (cursory) бéглый. —**casually,** *adv.* случáйно; мимохóдом; попýтно.
casualty *n.* **1,** (person killed or injured) жéртва. *There were no casualties,* жертв нé было. **2,** *pl., mil.* рáненые; потéри. *Heavy casualties,* тяжёлые потéри.
casuist *n.* казуи́ст. —**casuistic,** *adj.* казуисти́ческий. —**casuistry,** *n.* казуи́стика.
cat *n.* кóшка. *Male cat,* кот. —**let the cat out of the bag,** проговáриваться; пробáлтываться; вы́болтать секрéт.
cataclysm *n.* катаклúзм. —**cataclysmic,** *adj.* катастрофи́ческий.
catacombs *n.pl.* катакóмбы.
catafalque *n.* катафáлк.
Catalan *adj.* каталóнский; каталáнский.
catalepsy *n.* каталéпсия. —**cataleptic,** *adj.* каталепти́ческий; каталепси́ческий.
catalogue *also,* **catalog** *n.* **1,** (source of information) каталóг: *card catalogue,* кáрточный каталóг. **2,** (list of items for sale) прейскурáнт. —*v.t.* каталогизи́ровать. —**cataloguer,** *n.* каталогизáтор.
catalysis *n.* катáлиз. —**catalyst,** *n.* катализáтор. —**catalytic,** *adj.* каталити́ческий.
cat-and-mouse game игрá в кóшки-мы́шки.
catapult *n.* катапýльта. —*v.t.* подбрáсывать в вóздух. —*v.i.* взлетáть; вскáкивать; подскáкивать.

cataract *n.* **1,** (waterfall) водопáд; катарáкт. **2,** (opacity of the eye) катарáкта.
catarrh *n.* катáр.
catastrophe *n.* катастрóфа. —**catastrophic,** *adj.* катастрофи́ческий.
catch *v.t.* **1,** (grab; trap; capture) лови́ть (*pfv.* поймáть): *catch a ball/fish/thief,* поймáть мяч/ры́бу/вóра. **2,** (take by surprise) заставáть: *catch unawares,* застáть враспло́х. *Get caught in the rain,* попáсть под дождь. *Be caught stealing,* попáсться на крáже. **3,** (catch up to; overtake) догоня́ть. **4,** (snag) зацепля́ть: *catch one's sleeve on a nail,* зацепи́ть рукавóм за гвоздь. **5,** (jam, as one's fingers in a door) защемля́ть; прищемля́ть (пáльцы двéрью). **6,** (be in time for, as a train) успéть на; попáсть на. **7,** (contract, as an illness) получáть; наживáть; схвáтывать. *Catch cold,* простужáться. **8,** (understand; grasp) улáвливать. **9,** *colloq.* (hear) расслы́шать. **10,** *in various miscellaneous expressions: catch fire,* загорéться; *catch sight of,* уви́деть; зави́деть; *catch one's breath,* перевести́ дух; отдышáться. —*v.i.* **1,** (become snagged) зацепля́ться; задевáть. **2,** (ignite) разжигáться. —*n.* **1,** (act of catching) пóимка. **2,** (quantity caught) улóв. **3,** (fastener) защёлка; язычóк. **4,** (bolt; latch) задви́жка. **5,** (game) игрá в мяч: *play catch,* игрáть в мяч. **6,** *colloq.* (hitch; rub) зацéпка; загвóздка. —**catch it,** *colloq.* достáться (+ *dat.*); попáсть (+ *dat.*): *I'll catch it,* мне достáнется; мне попадёт. —**catch on, 1,** (become popular) прививáться. **2,** (get the knack) приноráвливаться. **3,** *colloq.* (grasp the meaning) понимáть; смекáть. —**catch oneself,** лови́ть себя́ (*with* на + *prepl.*). —**catch someone's eye, 1,** (get the attention of) лови́ть чéй-нибудь взгляд. **2,** (happen to be seen by) привлекáть чьё-нибудь внимáние; попадáться на глазá (+ *dat.*). —**catch up (with** *or* **to),** догоня́ть. *Catch up on one's sleep,* отсыпáться.
catching *adj.* зарáзный; зарази́тельный.
catchy *adj.* легкó запоминáющийся.
catechism *n.* катехи́зис.
categorical *adj.* категори́ческий; реши́тельный. —**categorically,** *adv.* категори́чески; реши́тельно.
categorize *v.t.* **1,** (classify) относи́ть к (какóй-нибудь) категóрии. **2,** (characterize) характеризовáть.
category *n.* категóрия; разря́д.
cater *v.i.* [*usu.* **cater to**] **1,** (serve) обслу́живать. **2,** (satisfy) удовлетворя́ть. **3,** (indulge) потвóрствовать. —*v.t.* обслу́живать.
caterpillar *n.* гу́сеница. —**caterpillar tractor,** гу́сеничный трáктор. —**caterpillar tread,** гу́сеничная лéнта.
catgut *n.* кетгу́т.
catharsis *n.* очищéние желу́дка. —**cathartic,** *adj.* слаби́тельный. —*n.* слаби́тельное.
cathedral *n.* собóр.
catheter *n.* катéтер.
cathode *n.* катóд. —**cathode rays,** катóдные лучи́. —**cathode-ray tube,** катóдная тру́бка.
Catholic *adj.* католи́ческий. —*n.* катóлик. —**Catholicism,** *n.* католици́зм; католи́чество.
catkin *n.* серёжка.
cat-o'-nine-tails *n.* кóшки.
cattail *n.* рогóз.
cattle *n.* скот. *Herd of cattle,* стáдо корóв. —**cattleman,** *n.* скотовóд.
catty-corner *adv.* нáискось.
Caucasian *adj.* **1,** (of the Caucasus) кавкáзский. **2,** (Caucasoid) европеóидный. —*n.* европеóид.
caucus *n.* парти́йное собрáние.
cauldron *n.* = **caldron.**
cauliflower *n.* цветнáя капу́ста.
caulk *also,* **calk** *v.t.* конопáтить.
causal *adj.* причи́нный. —**causality,** *n.* причи́нность. —**causative,** *adj.* причи́нный.
cause *n.* **1,** (that which produces an effect) причи́на: *cause and effect,* причи́на и слéдствие. *The cause of the fire,* причи́на пожáра. *What is the cause of it?,* чем э́то вы́звано? **2,** (ground; occasion) пóвод; причи́на. *There is no cause for alarm,* нет причи́н беспокóиться. **3,** (principle; movement) дéло: *the cause of peace,* дéло ми́ра. —*v.t.* **1,** (be the cause of; bring about) вызывáть; причиня́ть. *Cause an argument/accident,* вы́звать спор/катастрóфу. *Cause damage/grief,* причиня́ть вред/гóре. **2,** (prompt; induce) побуждáть; заставля́ть: *what caused him to...?,* что побуди́ло/застáвило егó (+ *inf.*). —**make common cause with,** солидаризи́роваться с.
caustic *adj.* **1,** (corrosive) éдкий; каусти́ческий. **2,** (biting; sarcastic) éдкий; кóлкий; язви́тельный. —**causticity,** *n.* éдкость.
caustic soda éдкий натр.
cauterize *v.t.* прижигáть; выжигáть. —**cauterization,** *n.* прижигáние; выжигáние.
caution *n.* **1,** (wariness) осторóжность. **2,** (warning) предостережéние. —*v.t.* предостерегáть.
cautious *adj.* осторóжный. —**cautiously,** *adv.* осторóжно.
cavalcade *n.* кавалькáда.
cavalier *n.* ры́царь. —*adj.* **1,** (haughty) надмéнный. **2,** (offhand) бесцеремóнный.
cavalry *n.* кавалéрия; кóнница. —*adj.* кавалери́йский. —**cavalryman,** *n.* кавалери́ст; кóнник.
cave *n.* пещéра. —*v.i.* [*usu.* **cave in**] обвáливаться; обру́шиваться; ру́хнуть.
cave-in *n.* обвáл.
cave man пещéрный человéк.
cavern *n.* пещéра. —**cavernous,** *adj.* похóжий на пещéру.
caviar *also,* **caviare** *n.* икрá.
cavil *v.i.* придирáться. —*n.* приди́рка.
cavity *n.* **1,** (hole; depression) впáдина. **2,** (natural hollow in the body) пóлость: *abdominal cavity,* брюшнáя пóлость. **3,** (in a tooth) дуплó; (in the lungs) кавéрна.
cavort *v.i.* **1,** (leap about) дéлать прыжки́. **2,** (romp; frolic) резви́ться.
caw *v.i.* кáркать. —*n.* кáрканье.
cease *v.t.* **1,** (stop doing an action) переставáть. **2,** (terminate) прекращáть. —*v.i.* прекращáться.
cease-fire *n.* прекращéние огня́.
ceaseless *adj.* непрестáнный; беспрестáнный.
cecum *also,* **caecum** *n.* слепáя кишкá.
cedar *n.* кедр. —*adj.* кедрóвый.
cede *v.t.* сдавáть; уступáть.
cedilla *n.* седи́ль.
ceiling *n.* потолóк. —**hit the ceiling,** прийти́ в я́рость; лезть (полéзть) нá стену.
celebrate *v.t.* **1,** (observe; commemorate) прáздно-

вать; справля́ть. *Celebrate New Year's Eve,* встреча́ть Но́вый год. **2,** (perform, as a mass) служи́ть (обе́дню). **3,** (extol) прославля́ть. —*v.i.* **1,** (observe a holiday) пра́здновать. **2,** (engage in merrymaking) весели́ться. —**celebrated,** *adj.* знамени́тый; просла́вленный. —**celebration,** *n.* пра́здник; пра́зднование; пра́зднество; торжество́.

celebrity *n.* знамени́тость.

celerity *n.* быстрота́.

celery *n.* сельдере́й. —*adj.* сельдере́йный.

celesta *n.* челе́ста.

celestial *adj.* небе́сный. —**celestial navigation,** астронавига́ция.

celibacy *n.* безбра́чие.

celibate *adj.* безбра́чный; холосто́й. —*n.* холостя́к.

cell *n.* **1,** (in a prison) ка́мера; (in a monastery) ке́лья. **2,** *biol.* кле́тка. **3,** (small group) яче́йка. **4,** *electricity* элеме́нт.

cellar *n.* по́греб. *Wine cellar,* ви́нный по́греб.

cellist *n.* виолончели́ст.

cellmate *n.* нока́мерник.

cello *n.* виолонче́ль.

cellophane *n.* целлофа́н. —*adj.* целлофа́новый.

cellular *adj.* кле́точный.

celluloid *n.* целлуло́ид.

cellulose *n.* клетча́тка; целлюло́за.

Celsius *adj.* Це́льсий: *ten degrees Celsius,* де́сять гра́дусов по Це́льсию.

Celt *n.* кельт. —**Celtic,** *adj.* ке́льтский.

cement *n.* цеме́нт. —*adj.* цеме́нтный. —*v.t.* **1,** (cover with cement) цементи́ровать. **2,** *fig.* (solidify) скрепля́ть.

cemetery *n.* кла́дбище.

censer *n.* кади́ло; кури́льница.

censor *n.* це́нзор. —*v.t.* подверга́ть цензу́ре. —**censorship,** *n.* цензу́ра.

censure *v.t.* порица́ть; осужда́ть. —*n.* порица́ние; осужде́ние.

census *n.* пе́репись.

cent *n.* цент. *Not have a cent to one's name,* не име́ть ни гроша́ за душо́й.

centaur *n.* кента́вр.

centenary *adj.* столе́тний. —*n.* столе́тие.

centennial *adj. & n.* = **centenary.**

center *also,* **centre** *n.* **1,** (middle) центр; середи́на. **2,** (focal point) центр: *shopping center,* торго́вый центр. *Be the center of attention,* быть в це́нтре внима́ния. **3,** *basketball* центрово́й. —*adj.* сре́дний: *center aisle,* сре́дний прохо́д. —*v.t.* **1,** (place in the center) помеща́ть в це́нтре. **2,** (direct toward one place; concentrate) сосредото́чивать. —*v.i.* сосредото́чиваться. *The conversation centered around one subject,* разгово́р верте́лся о́коло одного́ предме́та. —**center of gravity,** центр тя́жести.

centerfold *n.* разворо́т.

Centigrade *adj.* Це́льсий: *ten degrees Centigrade,* де́сять гра́дусов по Це́льсию.

centigram *n.* сантигра́мм.

centime *n.* санти́м.

centimeter *also,* **centimetre** *n.* сантиме́тр.

centipede *n.* многоно́жка; сороконо́жка.

centner *n.* це́нтнер.

central *adj.* центра́льный. —**Central Asia,** Сре́дняя А́зия. —**Central Committee,** центра́льный комите́т.

centralism *n.* централи́зм. —**democratic centralism,** демократи́ческий централи́зм.

centralization *n.* централиза́ция.

centralize *v.t.* централизова́ть. —**centralized,** *adj.* централизо́ванный.

centre *see* **center.**

centrifugal *adj.* центробе́жный: *centrifugal force,* центробе́жная си́ла.

centripetal *adj.* центростреми́тельный.

century *n.* век; столе́тие. *In the 19th century,* в девятна́дцатом ве́ке.

century plant столе́тник.

ceramic *adj.* керами́ческий. —**ceramics,** *n.* кера́мика.

cereal *n.* **1,** (grain) (хле́бные) зла́ки. **2,** (breakfast food) блю́до из хле́бных зла́ков. —*adj.* хле́бный; зла́ковый.

cerebellum *n.* мозжечо́к.

cerebral *adj.* мозгово́й. —**cerebral hemorrhage,** кровоизлия́ние в мозг. —**cerebral palsy,** церебра́льный парали́ч.

cerebrum *n.* головно́й мозг.

ceremonial *adj.* церемониа́льный. —*n.* **1,** (ritual) церемониа́л. **2,** (rite) обря́д.

ceremonious *adj.* церемо́нный.

ceremony *n.* **1,** (formal ritual) церемо́ния. **2,** (formality) церемо́нии. —**stand on ceremony,** церемо́ниться.

cerise *adj.* вишнёвый.

cerium *n.* це́рий.

certain *adj.* **1,** (sure; positive) уве́ренный: *I am certain,* я уве́рен(а). **2,** (sure to happen) ве́рный: *certain death,* ве́рная ги́бель. **3,** (sure; indisputable) несомне́нный: *one thing is certain,* одно́ несомне́нно. *He is certain to be late,* он несомне́нно опозда́ет. *It is by no means certain that...,* совсе́м не я́сно, что... **4,** (known but not specified) определённый: *in certain cases,* в определённых слу́чаях. **5,** (some but not others) не́который: *certain people,* не́которые лю́ди. **6,** (some but not all) не́который; изве́стный: *to a certain extent,* до не́которой/изве́стной сте́пени. **7,** *preceded by* **a** (unidentified) не́кий; не́кто: *a certain Mr. Smith,* не́кий/не́кто ми́стер Смит. —**for certain,** достове́рно; наверняка́: *know for certain,* знать достове́рно/наверняка́. —**make certain,** = **make sure** (*see* **sure**).

certainly *adv.* **1,** (of course) коне́чно. **2,** (without a doubt) несомне́нно. —**certainly not,** ни в ко́ем слу́чае.

certainty *n.* **1,** (assuredness) уве́ренность. **2,** (anything certain) несомне́нный факт. —**know for a certainty,** знать наверняка́.

certificate *n.* удостовере́ние; свиде́тельство; аттеста́т; сертифика́т.

certification *n.* удостовере́ние.

certify *v.t.* удостоверя́ть; заверя́ть.

certitude *n.* уве́ренность.

ceruse *n.* **1,** (white lead) свинцо́вые бели́ла. **2,** (cosmetic) бели́ла.

cervical *adj.* ше́йный; заты́лочный.

cervix *n.* **1,** (neck) ше́я. **2,** (necklike part of the uterus) ше́йка ма́тки.

cesium *n.* це́зий.

cessation *n.* прекраще́ние.

cession *n.* усту́пка; сда́ча.

cesspool *n.* выгребная яма; помойная яма.
chafe *v.t.* тереть; натирать; стирать. —*v.i.* **1,** (rub) тереть. **2,** (be irritated or impatient) гореть от нетерпения; горячиться.
chaff *n.* **1,** (husks) мякина. **2,** (fine-cut straw) сечка.
chaffinch *n.* зяблик.
chagrin *n.* огорчение. —**chagrined,** *adj.* огорчённый.
chain *n.* **1,** (connected links) цепь; цепочка. *Put the chain on the door,* запереть дверь на цепочку. **2,** (for a watch, pendant, etc.) цепочка: *watch chain,* цепочка для часов. **3,** *pl.* (shackles) цепи; оковы. *Put (someone) in chains,* заковать (кого-нибудь) в цепи. **4,** (range of mountains) (горная) цепь. **5,** (series) цепь: *chain of events,* цепь событий. **6,** (network, as of stores) сеть. —*adj.* цепной: *chain link,* цепное звено. —*v.t.* [*often* **chain up**] сажать на цепь. *Chain a dog to a post,* приковывать собаку цепью к столбу. —**chain of command,** командные инстанции. —**chain mail,** кольчуга. —**chain reaction,** цепная реакция. —**chain saw,** цепная пила. —**chain stitch,** тамбур; тамбурный шов; тамбурная строчка; цепной стежок.
chain-smoke *v.i.* курить запоем.
chair *n.* **1,** (piece of furniture) стул. **2,** (presiding officer) председатель. **3,** (professorship) кафедра. —*v.t.* председательствовать на (собрании).
chairman *n.* председатель. —**chairmanship,** *n.* председательство.
chaise longue шезлонг.
chalcedony *n.* халцедон.
chalet *n.* шале.
chalice *n.* чаша.
chalk *n.* мел. —*v.t.* натирать мелом. —**chalk up, 1,** (earn; score) одержать (победу); набирать (очки). **2,** *fol. by* **to** (attribute to) относить на счёт (+ *gen.*).
chalky *adj.* меловой.
challenge *v.t.* **1,** (summon to a contest) вызывать. **2,** (call into question; dispute) оспаривать. **3,** (demand identification from) окликать. —*n.* **1,** (summons to a contest) вызов. **2,** (demand for identification) оклик. **3,** *law* отвод. —**challenge cup,** *sports* переходящий кубок.
challenger *n.* претендент.
chamber *n.* **1,** (large room for a certain purpose) камера: *compression chamber,* камера сжатия. *Torture chamber,* застенок. **2,** (bedroom) спальня. **3,** (unit of a legislature) палата. **4,** (of a firearm) патронник.
chamberlain *n.* камергер.
chambermaid *n.* горничная.
chamber music камерная музыка.
chamber of commerce торговая палата.
chamber pot ночной горшок.
chameleon *n.* хамелеон.
chamois *n.* **1,** (antelope) серна. **2,** (soft leather) замша.
chamomile *n.* = **camomile.**
champ *n., colloq.* = **champion.** —*v.i.* чавкать. —**champ at the bit,** грызть удила.
champagne *n.* шампанское.
champion *n.* **1,** (one who is ranked first) чемпион. **2,** (defender, as of a cause) поборник. —*v.t.* бороться за. —*adj.* *Champion swimmer,* чемпион по плаванию.
championship *n.* **1,** (title) первенство; чемпионство. **2,** (competition) чемпионат; первенство. **3,** (advocacy) борьба; защита.
chance *n.* **1,** (fortune; luck) случай; случайность. *Game of chance,* азартная игра. *Leave to chance,* оставлять на волю случая. **2,** (opportunity) случай; возможность. **3,** (probability) шанс: *one chance in ten,* один шанс из десяти. *Stand a chance,* иметь шансы. **4,** (risk) риск: *take a chance,* идти на риск; рисковать. —*adj.* случайный: *a chance meeting,* случайная встреча. —*v.t.* рисковать: *let's chance it,* рискнём. —*v.i.* *I chanced to be there,* я случайно был (была) там. —**by any chance,** случайно. —**by chance,** случайно. —**chances are,** скорее всего.
chancellery *n.* канцелярия.
chancellor *n.* канцлер.
chancre *n.* шанкр. —**chancroid,** *n.* мягкий шанкр.
chancy *adj.* рискованный.
chandelier *n.* люстра.
change *v.t.* **1,** (switch) менять: *change jobs,* менять работу. *Change clothes,* переодеваться; *change shoes,* переодевать туфли. *Change planes, trains, etc.,* пересаживаться; делать пересадку. *Change sides,* перейти на другую сторону. *Change hands,* перейти в другие руки. **2,** (alter) изменять: *change tactics,* изменять тактику. *Change color,* менять свою окраску. **3,** (replace) сменять: *change a tire,* сменить шину. **4,** (exchange; switch) меняться (+ *instr.*): *change places,* меняться местами. **5,** (convert, as money) разменивать: *change ten dollars,* разменять десять долларов. **6,** (diaper) пеленать (ребёнка). —*v.i.* **1,** (vary; become different) меняться; изменяться; перемениться. **2,** (of a young man's voice) ломаться. **3,** *fol. by* **off** (alternate) чередоваться. **4,** = **change clothes, change planes,** *etc.* —*n.* **1,** (alteration; transformation) изменение; перемена: *change in the weather,* изменение/перемена погоды. *Change for the better,* перемена к лучшему. **2,** (replacement) смена: *oil change,* смена масла. **3,** (of planes, trains, etc.) пересадка. **4,** (variety) разнообразие: *for a change,* для разнообразия. *It's a nice day, for a change,* наконец-то хорошая погода! **5,** (small money; coins) мелочь. **6,** (money given back) сдача: *change of a dollar,* сдача с доллара. —**change of life,** климактерий.
changeable *adj.* изменчивый; непостоянный. —**changeability,** *n.* изменчивость.
changeover *n.* переход; переключение.
change purse кошелёк.
channel *n.* **1,** (waterway) пролив. *The English Channel,* Ла-Манш. **2,** (river bed) русло. **3,** *pl.* (means of communication) каналы. **4,** *television* канал. —*v.t.* направлять.
chant *v.t.* & *i.* **1,** (sing) петь. **2,** (call out rhythmically) скандировать. —*n.* песнопение: *Gregorian chant,* григорианское песнопение.
chaos *n.* хаос. —**chaotic,** *adj.* хаотический; хаотичный.
chap *v.t.* обветрить: *chapped lips,* обветренные губы. —*v.i.* трескаться. —*n., colloq.* (fellow) парень; малый.
chapel *n.* часовня; капелла. *The Sistine Chapel,* Сикстинская капелла.
chaperon *also,* **chaperone** *n.* дуэнья.
chaplain *n.* капеллан.

chapter *n.* **1,** (division of a book) глава́. **2,** (branch of a society) отделе́ние.

char *v.t.* обу́гливать.

character *n.* **1,** (individual nature) хара́ктер. *In character,* характе́рно; сво́йственно. *Out of character,* не характе́рно; не сво́йственно; не в чьём-нибудь хара́ктере. **2,** (moral excellence) хара́ктер: *man of character,* челове́к с хара́ктером. **3,** (person; personage) ли́чность. **4,** (person in a play or novel) де́йствующее лицо́. **5,** *colloq.* (an eccentric) оригина́л; чуда́к. **6,** *pl.* (symbols used in writing) письмена́; иеро́глифы. —**character actor,** характе́рный актёр. —**character reference,** характери́стика.

characteristic *n.* сво́йство; осо́бенность; черта́. —*adj.* характе́рный; сво́йственный.

characterization *n.* характери́стика.

characterize *v.t.* характеризова́ть.

charade *n.* шара́да.

charcoal *n.* древе́сный у́голь.

charge *v.t.* **1,** (replenish, as a battery) заряжа́ть. **2,** (entrust, as with an assignment) поруча́ть. **3,** (accuse) обвиня́ть. **4,** (ask as a price) брать; проси́ть: *how much does he charge for this?,* ско́лько он берёт/про́сит за э́то? *Charge a lot for,* брать до́рого за. *They charged us ten dollars,* с нас взя́ли де́сять до́лларов. **5,** (record as a debt to be paid) запи́сывать: *charge it to my account,* запиши́те э́то на мой счёт. *Do you wish to charge it?,* вам присла́ть счёт? **6,** (attack) атакова́ть. —*v.i.* **1,** (ask payment) брать де́ньги; взима́ть пла́ту. **2,** (rush violently forward) бро́ситься. **3,** (attack vigorously) бро́ситься в ата́ку. —*n.* **1,** (quantity of explosives or electricity) заря́д. **2,** (custody) попече́ние: *I leave them in your charge,* оставля́ю их на ва́ше попече́ние. **3,** (ward) подопе́чный. **4,** (assignment; responsibility) поруче́ние. **5,** (accusation) обвине́ние: *press charges against,* предъяви́ть обвине́ние (+ *dat.*). **6,** (money to be paid) пла́та: *admission charge,* входна́я пла́та. *Free of charge,* беспла́тно. *There is an extra charge for that,* за э́то на́до заплати́ть отде́льно. **7,** (attack) ата́ка. —**be in charge,** распоряжа́ться. —**be in charge of,** ве́дать; заве́довать. —**put in charge of,** поста́вить во главе́ (+ *gen.*). —**take charge of,** взять в свои́ ру́ки.

charged *adj.* **1,** *physics* заряжённый: *charged particles,* заряжённые части́цы. **2,** *fig.* (tense) накалённый: *charged atmosphere,* накалённая атмосфе́ра.

chargé d'affaires пове́ренный в дела́х.

charger *n.* **1,** (for batteries) заря́дный агрега́т. **2,** (warhorse) строева́я ло́шадь; боево́й конь.

chariot *n.* колесни́ца. —**charioteer,** *n.* возни́ца.

charitable *adj.* **1,** (kind; generous) милосе́рдный. **2,** (philanthropic) благотвори́тельный. **3,** (lenient in judging) снисходи́тельный.

charity *n.* **1,** (benevolence) милосе́рдие; ми́лость. **2,** (philanthropy) благотвори́тельность. *Raise money for charity,* собира́ть де́ньги на благотвори́тельные це́ли. **3,** (charitable institution) благотвори́тельное учрежде́ние.

charlatan *n.* шарлата́н. —**charlatanism,** *n.* шарлата́нство.

charm *n.* **1,** (delightful quality) пре́лесть: *lose its charm,* теря́ть свою́ пре́лесть. *The charm of country life,* пре́лести жи́зни в дере́вне. **2,** (ability to captivate) очарова́ние; обая́ние; ча́ры. *I succumbed to her charm,* я подда́лся её очарова́нию. **3,** (ornament) брело́к. —*v.t.* **1,** (captivate) очаро́вывать. **2,** (cast a spell over) заколдо́вывать.

charmed *adj.* очаро́ванный; заколдо́ванный. *Charmed!,* о́чень прия́тно! —**he leads a charmed life,** он как бы заколдо́ван.

charmer *n.* (man) чаро́дей; (woman) чаро́дейка; чаровни́ца. —**snake charmer,** заклина́тель змей.

charming *adj.* очарова́тельный; обая́тельный; преле́стный.

charred *adj.* обгоре́лый; обу́гленный.

chart *n.* гра́фик; схе́ма; диагра́мма. —*v.t.* наноси́ть на гра́фик, схе́му, *etc.*

charter *n.* **1,** (grant of rights) ха́ртия. **2,** (constitution) уста́в. —*v.t.* нанима́ть; взять напрока́т; фрахтова́ть.

chartreuse *adj.* жёлто-зелёный.

charwoman *n.* убо́рщица.

chary *adj.* **1,** (cautious) осторо́жный; осмотри́тельный. **2,** (sparing) скупо́й.

chase *v.t.* **1,** (pursue) гна́ться за: *chase a thief,* гна́ться за во́ром. *Chase up a tree,* загоня́ть на де́рево. **2,** *fol. by* **away** (drive away) отгоня́ть: *chase away a fly,* отогна́ть му́ху. **3,** *fol. by* **out** (drive out) выгоня́ть; прогоня́ть: *chase the children out of the room,* вы́гнать/прогна́ть дете́й из ко́мнаты. —*v.i.* **1,** *fol. by* **after** (run after) гна́ться за; бе́гать за. *Chase after women,* бе́гать за же́нщинами. **2,** *colloq.* (rush) бе́гать. *Chase all over town,* обега́ть весь го́род. —*n.* **1,** (pursuit) пого́ня. *Give chase,* погна́ться; пусти́ться вдого́нку. **2,** *preceded by* **the** (hunting) охо́та.

chasm *n.* про́пасть.

chassis *n.* шасси́.

chaste *adj.* целому́дренный.

chasten *v.t.* **1,** (punish) нака́зывать. **2,** (inhibit) стесня́ть.

chastise *v.t.* нака́зывать; кара́ть; бичева́ть.

chastity *n.* целому́дрие.

chasuble *n.* ри́за.

chat *v.i.* бесе́довать. —*n.* бесе́да.

chattel *n.* дви́жимое иму́щество.

chatter *v.i.* **1,** (click, as of the teeth) стуча́ть. **2,** (jabber; prate) болта́ть; треща́ть. **3,** (utter rapid sounds, as of birds) щебета́ть. —*n.* **1,** (utterance of birds) ще́бет. **2,** (idle talk) болтовня́.

chatterbox *n.* болту́н; говору́н; балабо́лка; трещо́тка.

chatty *adj.* болтли́вый.

chauffeur *n.* шофёр; води́тель.

chauvinism *n.* шовини́зм. —**chauvinist,** *n.* шовини́ст. —**chauvinistic,** *adj.* шовинисти́ческий.

cheap *adj.* **1,** (inexpensive) дешёвый. **2,** (niggardly) скупо́й. —*adv.* дёшево: *buy/sell something cheap,* дёшево купи́ть/прода́ть что́-нибудь. *Get off cheap,* дёшево отде́латься.

cheapen *v.t.* **1,** (lessen the value of) обесце́нивать. **2,** (debase) опошля́ть.

cheaply *adv.* дёшево.

cheapskate *n., colloq.* скря́га; скопидо́м; сквалы́га.

cheat *v.t.* обма́нывать; надува́ть. *Cheat someone out of two dollars,* обману́ть/наду́ть кого́-нибудь на два до́ллара. —*v.i.* **1,** (in a game) плутова́ть; жу́льничать. **2,** (on a test) спи́сывать (на экза́мене). —*n.* [*also,* **cheater**] обма́нщик; плут; жу́лик.

check *n.* **1,** (restraint): *hold/keep in check,* сде́рживать; держа́ть в узде́. **2,** (test for accuracy) прове́рка. **3,** (check mark [✓]) га́лочка; пти́чка. **4,** [*also,* **cheque**] (written order to pay money) чек. **5,** (ticket; slip) номеро́к. **6,** (bill, as in a restaurant) счёт. **7,** (square in a checkered pattern) кле́тка. **8,** *chess* шах. —*v.t.* **1,** (halt) остана́вливать; заде́рживать. **2,** (hold back) сде́рживать; обу́здывать. **3,** (examine for accuracy) проверя́ть. **4,** [*often* **check off**] (mark with a check) отмеча́ть га́лочкой. **5,** (deposit for safekeeping) сдава́ть. —*v.i.* **1,** (make an inquiry) спра́шивать. **2,** (tally) сходи́ться; совпада́ть. —**check in,** регистри́роваться; пропи́сываться. —**check out, 1,** (settle up and leave) выпи́сываться (из гости́ницы). *Are you checking out today?,* вы сего́дня уезжа́ете? **2,** (investigate further) разузнава́ть. **3,** (agree; tally) сходи́ться. —**check (up) on,** проверя́ть.

checkbook *n.* че́ковая кни́жка.

checked *adj.* клётчатый.

checker *n.* **1,** (one who checks) контролёр. **2,** (piece used in the game of checkers) ша́шка.

checkerboard *n.* ша́хматная (*or* ша́шечная) доска́.

checkered *adj.* клётчатый.

checkers *n.* ша́шки.

checkmate *n.* мат. —*v.t.* сде́лать мат (+ *dat.*).

checkpoint *n.* контро́льный пункт.

checkroom *n.* **1,** (for apparel) гардеро́б; раздева́лка. **2,** (for baggage) ка́мера хране́ния.

checkup *n.* осмо́тр; обсле́дование. *Go into the hospital for a checkup,* лечь в больни́цу на обсле́дование.

cheek *n.* **1,** (side of the face) щека́. **2,** *colloq.* (effrontery) на́глость. —**turn the other cheek,** подставля́ть другу́ю щёку. —**with tongue in cheek,** в шу́тку.

cheekbone *n.* скула́.

cheep *v.i.* пища́ть. —*n.* писк.

cheer *n.* **1,** (shout of approval) во́зглас; ура́. **2,** (encouragement; comfort) ободре́ние. *Words of cheer,* ободря́ющие слова́. **3,** *in* **be of good cheer,** быть весёлым; не унывать. —*v.t.* **1,** (acclaim with cheers) приве́тствовать (гро́мкими во́згласами); крича́ть ура́ в честь (+ *gen.*). **2,** *fol. by* **up** (gladden) ободря́ть; подбодря́ть; (раз)весели́ть. —*v.i.* **1,** (shout cheers) крича́ть ура́. **2,** *fol. by* **up** (feel encouraged) ободря́ться; подбодря́ться; развесели́ться; воспря́нуть ду́хом.

cheerful *adj.* бо́дрый; весёлый. —**cheerfulness,** *n.* бо́дрость; весёлость.

cheerio *interj., colloq.* до встре́чи!; пока́!

cheerless *adj.* мра́чный; безра́достный; безотра́дный.

cheery *adj.* бо́дрый. *A cheery smile,* ра́достная улы́бка.

cheese *n.* сыр. —*adj.* сы́рный: *cheese omelet,* сы́рный омле́т.

cheesecloth *n.* ма́рля.

cheetah *n.* гепа́рд.

chef *n.* шеф-по́вар.

chemical *adj.* хими́ческий. —*n.* хими́ческий препара́т; хими́ческий проду́кт. —**chemical engineer,** инжене́р-хи́мик. —**chemical warfare,** хими́ческая война́.

chemise *n.* (же́нская) соро́чка.

chemist *n.* **1,** (specialist in chemistry) хи́мик. **2,** *Brit.* (druggist) апте́карь.

chemistry *n.* хи́мия.

chemotherapy *n.* химиотерапи́я.

chenille *n.* сине́ль.

cheque *n., Brit.* = **check,** *n.* (*in sense* #4).

cherish *v.t.* **1,** (hold dear) дорожи́ть. **2,** (nurture, as hopes) леле́ять.

cherry *n.* ви́шня. —*adj.* вишнёвый: *cherry jam,* вишнёвое варе́нье. —**cherry tree,** ви́шня.

cherub *n.* херуви́м. —**cherubic,** *adj.* херуви́мский.

chess *n.* ша́хматы: *play chess,* игра́ть в ша́хматы. —*adj.* ша́хматный: *chess tournament,* ша́хматный турни́р. —**chessboard,** *n.* ша́хматная доска́. —**chessman,** *n.* ша́хматная фигу́ра. —**chess player,** шахмати́ст.

chest *n.* **1,** (part of the body) грудь. **2,** (box) я́щик; сунду́к. *Medicine chest,* апте́чка. *Chest of drawers,* комо́д. —*adj.* грудно́й: *chest cavity,* грудна́я по́лость. *Chest pain,* боль в груди́.

chestnut *n.* кашта́н. —*adj.* кашта́новый. *Chestnut horse,* ры́жая ло́шадь.

cheviot *n.* шевио́т. —*adj.* шевио́товый.

chevron *n.* шевро́н; наши́вка.

chew *v.t.* & *i.* жева́ть. —**chew out,** *slang* вы́бранить; разруга́ть. —**chew the fat** *or* **rag,** *slang* бесе́довать.

chewing *n.* жева́ние. —*adj.* жева́тельный: *chewing gum,* жева́тельная рези́нка; *chewing tobacco,* жева́тельный таба́к.

chic *adj.* шика́рный; сти́льный.

chicanery *n.* интри́га; ко́зни; ка́верза.

chick *n.* **1,** (small chicken) цыплёнок. **2,** *slang* (girl) девчо́нка.

chickadee *n.* га́ичка.

chicken *n.* **1,** (hen or rooster or its flesh) ку́рица. **2,** (young hen or rooster) цыплёнок. —*adj.* кури́ный: *chicken soup,* кури́ный бульо́н; *chicken livers,* кури́ная печёнка. —**chicken coop,** куря́тник. —**chicken pox,** ве́тряная о́спа; ветря́нка.

chickpea *n.* нут; туре́цкий горо́х.

chicory *n.* цико́рий.

chide *v.t.* побрани́ть; жури́ть.

chief *n.* глава́; нача́льник. *Chief of staff,* нача́льник шта́ба. *Chief of state,* глава́ прави́тельства. —*adj.* гла́вный: *chief question/engineer,* гла́вный вопро́с/инжене́р. —**chiefly,** *adv.* гла́вным о́бразом.

chieftain *n.* вождь.

chiffon *n.* шифо́н. —*adj.* шифо́новый.

chiffonier *n.* шифонье́рка.

chignon *n.* шиньо́н.

child *n.* ребёнок. —*adj.* [*also,* **child's**] де́тский: *child labor,* де́тский труд. —**child's play,** пустяко́вое де́ло; па́ра пустяко́в. *See also* **children.**

childbearing *n.* деторожде́ние.

childbirth *n.* ро́ды. *Die in childbirth,* умере́ть от ро́дов.

childhood *n.* де́тство. *Since childhood,* с де́тства; с ма́лых лет.

childish *adj.* де́тский; ребя́ческий. —**childishly,** *adv.* как ребёнок. —**childishness,** *n.* ребя́чество.

childless *adj.* безде́тный. —**childlessness,** *n.* безде́тность.

childlike *adj.* де́тский; неви́нный.

children *n.pl.* де́ти. —**children's,** *adj.* де́тский.

Chilean *adj.* чилийский. —*n.* чилиец; чилийка.
chill *n.* **1,** (sensation of cold) простýда; озноб. *Catch a chill,* схватить простýду. *He has a chill,* его знобит. **2,** (coldness in the air) холодóк. *There is a chill in the air,* свежó. **3,** (feeling of sudden fear) хóлод: *a chill ran down my spine,* хóлод пробежáл по моéй спинé. **4,** (coolness, as in relations) холодóк (в отношéниях). —*v.t.* охлаждáть. *Chilled to the bone,* продрóгший до костéй.
chilling *adj.* **1,** (freezing) леденя́щий: *chilling wind,* леденя́щий вéтер. **2,** (frightening; shocking) жýткий.
chilly *adj.* прохлáдный; свéжий: *it is chilly in here,* здесь прохлáдно/свежó. *It is getting chilly,* свежéет. *I am chilly,* мне прохлáдно.
chime *n., usu. pl.* курáнты. —*v.i.* бить; звучáть; звонить. —**chime in,** ввернýть словéчко; вступить в разговóр.
chimera *n.* химéра. —**chimerical,** *adj.* химерический.
chimney *n.* (дымовáя) трубá. —**chimney sweep,** трубочист.
chimpanzee *n.* шимпанзé.
chin *n.* подборóдок. —**keep one's chin up,** не пáдать дýхом.
china *n.* **1,** (porcelain) фарфóр. **2,** (dishes) посýда. —*adj.* **1,** (made of china) фарфóровый. **2,** (for china) посýдный: *china closet,* посýдный шкаф.
chinchilla *n.* шиншилла.
Chinese *adj.* китáйский. *He* (*she*) *is Chinese,* он китáец; онá китая́нка. —*n.* **1,** (language) китáйский язы́к. *Speak Chinese,* говорить по-китáйски. **2,** *preceded by* **the** (people) китáйцы.
chink *n.* **1,** (slit) щель; расщéлина; сквáжина. **2,** (sound) звон; звя́канье.
chintz *n.* ситец. —*adj.* ситцевый.
chip *n.* **1,** (fragment) щéпка. **2,** (imperfection caused by chipping) щербина. **3,** (counter used in gambling games) фишка. *Bargaining chip,* предмéт тóрга. —*v.t.* **1,** (damage slightly) надбивáть. **2,** *fol. by* **away** (cut away, as ice) скáлывать. —*v.i.* **1,** (lose a chip) биться. **2,** *fol. by* **off** (break off) отбивáться: *a piece of the cup chipped off,* у чáшки отбился край. —**chip in,** внести свою лéпту. —**chip off the old block,** сын своегó отцá. —**in the chips,** при деньгáх. —**when the chips are down,** в решáющий момéнт.
chipmunk *n.* бурундýк.
chipper *adj., colloq.* бóдрый; живóй.
chiropody *n.* педикю́р. —**chiropodist,** *n.* педикю́рша.
chirp *v.i.* чирикать; щебетáть; стрекотáть. —*n.* щéбет.
chisel *n.* долотó. —*v.t.* **1,** (cut) вырезáть; высекáть. **2,** *slang* (swindle) надувáть; обжýливать. —**chiseled,** *adj.* (of features) точёный. —**chiseler,** *n., slang* рвач.
chit *n.* талóн.
chivalry *n.* ры́царство. —**chivalrous,** *adj.* ры́царский.
chive *n.* шнитт-лýк.
chloric *adj.* хлóрный.
chloride *n.* хлорид. ♦ *In compounds* хлóристый: *hydrogen chloride,* хлóристый водорóд. —**chloride of lime,** хлóрная известь.
chlorinate *v.t.* хлорировать. —**chlorination,** *n.* хлорирование.
chlorine *n.* хлор.
chloroform *n.* хлорофóрм. —*v.t.* хлороформировать.
chlorophyll *n.* хлорофилл.
chlorous *adj.* хлóристый.
chock-full *adj.* биткóм наби́тый; наби́тый до откáза.
chocolate *n.* шоколáд. *Hot chocolate,* горя́чий шоколáд. *Box of chocolates,* шоколáдный набóр. —*adj.* шоколáдный: *chocolate cake,* шоколáдный торт.
choice *n.* вы́бор. *He was offered a book of his choice,* емý предложили книгу на вы́бор. *We have no choice but to...,* нам не остаётся другóго вы́бора (*or* ничегó другóго), как... —*adj.* отбóрный; как на подбóр.
choir *n.* **1,** (group of singers) хор. **2,** (part of a church) клирос. —**choirboy,** *n.* пéвчий. —**choirmaster,** *n.* хормéйстер.
choke *v.t.* **1,** (prevent from breathing) души́ть. **2,** (clog) забивáть. **3,** (of weeds) заглушáть. **4,** *fol. by* **off** *or* **down** (suppress) души́ть; подавля́ть. —*v.i.* **1,** (on something caught in one's throat) дави́ться; поперхнýться. **2,** (with tears, anger, etc.) задыхáться (от). —*n., mech.* дрóссель.
cholera *n.* холéра. —*adj.* холéрный: *cholera epidemic,* холéрная эпидéмия. —**choleric,** *adj.* холерический.
cholesterol *n.* холестерин.
choose *v.t.* **1,** (select) выбирáть. **2,** *fol. by inf.* (elect) решáть; решáться; предпочитáть. —*v.i.* выбирáть; дéлать вы́бор.
choosy *adj., colloq.* привередливый.
chop *v.t.* **1,** (hew) руби́ть; колóть: *chop wood,* руби́ть/колóть дровá. **2,** (mince) руби́ть: *chop meat/onions,* руби́ть мя́со/лук. —*n.* (отбивнáя) котлéта. *Lamb chop,* барáнья котлéта. *Pork chop,* свинáя котлéта; свинáя отбивнáя. —**chop down,** руби́ть; срубáть; вырубáть. —**chop off,** отруби́ть. —**chop up,** руби́ть; кроши́ть.
chopped *adj.* ру́бленый: *chopped meat,* ру́бленое мя́со.
chopper *n.* **1,** (tool) косáрь; секáч. **2,** *colloq.* (helicopter) вертолёт.
choppy *adj.* **1,** (rough, as of the sea) взволнóванный. **2,** (jerky) рéзкий; поры́вистый.
chopsticks *n.pl.* пáлочки для еды́.
choral *adj.* хоровóй.
chorale *n.* хорáл.
chord *n.* **1,** *math.* хóрда. **2,** *music* аккóрд. **3,** *anat.* *See* **cord. 4,** *fig.* (emotional response) струнá: *strike a sensitive chord,* задéть чувстви́тельную струнý.
chore *n., usu. pl.* хлóпоты: *household chores,* хлóпоты по хозя́йству.
chorea *n.* хорéя.
choreography *n.* хореогрáфия. —**choreographer,** *n.* хореóграф. —**choreographic,** *adj.* хореографи́ческий.
chorister *n.* пéвчий; хори́ст.
chorus *n.* **1,** (singing group) хор. **2,** (refrain) припéв. **3,** (simultaneous utterance): *chorus of cheers,* дрýжные вóзгласы. —**in a chorus,** хóром.
chosen *adj.* и́збранный.
Christ *n.* Христóс.
christen *v.t.* **1,** (baptize) крести́ть. **2,** (name) нарекáть.

christening *n.* **1,** (act) крещéние. **2,** (ceremony) крести́ны.
Christian *adj.* христиáнский. —*n.* христиани́н; христиáнка. —**Christian name,** и́мя.
Christianity *n.* христиáнство.
Christmas *n.* рождествó. *Merry Christmas!,* с рождествóм! —*adj.* рождéственский: *Christmas tree,* рождéственская ёлка. —**Christmas Eve,** сочéльник.
chromatic *adj.* хромати́ческий.
chrome *n.* хром. —**chrome alum,** хрóмовые квасцы́. —**chrome plating,** хроми́рование; хрóмовое покры́тие. —**chrome steel,** хрóмистая сталь.
chromic acid хрóмовая кислотá.
chromite *n.* хрóмистый железня́к; хроми́т.
chromium *n.* хром.
chromosome *n.* хромосóма.
chronic *adj.* **1,** (of an illness or patient) хрони́ческий. **2,** (inveterate) застарéлый; закоренéлый. **3,** (constant) вéчный: *chronic complaints,* вéчные жáлобы.
chronicle *n.* лéтопись; хрóника. —*v.t.* заноси́ть в днევни́к, лéтопись, *etc.* —**chronicler,** *n.* летопи́сец.
chronology *n.* хронолóгия. —**chronological,** *adj.* хронологи́ческий.
chronometer *n.* хронóметр.
chrysalis *n.* кýколка.
chrysanthemum *n.* хризантéма.
chubby *adj.* пýхлый.
chuck *n.* **1,** (cut of beef) лопáтка. **2,** (clamp; wedge) патрóн. —*v.t.* **1,** (toss) швыря́ть. **2,** *colloq.* (toss out) вышвы́ривать.
chuckle *n.* смешóк. —*v.i.* посмéиваться.
chum *n.* товáрищ; приятель.
chunk *n.* ломóть.
chunky *adj.* плóтный; коренáстый.
church *n.* цéрковь. —*adj.* церкóвный: *church bells,* церкóвные колоколá. —**churchwarden,** *n.* церкóвный стáроста.
churl *n.* грубия́н. —**churlish,** *adj.* грýбый; злой.
churn *n.* маслобóйка. —*v.t.* **1,** (stir) сбивáть; пáхтать. **2,** *fol. by* **up** (dig up; tear up) изрывáть. **3,** *fol. by* **up** (cause to swirl, as water) взбивáть.
chute *n.* жёлоб; лотóк.
cicada *n.* цикáда.
cider *n.* сидр.
cigar *n.* сигáра. —*adj.* сигáрный: *cigar smoke,* сигáрный дым.
cigarette *n.* папирóса; сигарéта. —*adj.* папирóсный; сигарéтный: *cigarette smoke,* папирóсный/сигарéтный дым. *Cigarette butt,* окýрок папирóсы. —**cigarette case,** портсигáр. —**cigarette holder,** мундштýк. —**cigarette lighter,** зажигáлка.
cinch *n.* **1,** (saddle girth) подпрýга. **2,** *colloq.* (easy thing to do) пустяки́.
cinchona *n.* хи́нное дéрево.
cinder *n.* пéпел; *pl.* золá; гарь. —*adj.* гаревóй: *cinder path,* гаревáя дорóжка.
Cinderella *n.* Зóлушка.
cinema *n.* **1,** *preceded by* **the** (motion pictures collectively) кинó. **2,** (motion-picture theater) кинó; кинотеáтр.
cinematography *n.* кинематогрáфия.
cinnabar *n.* ки́новарь.
cinnamon *n.* кори́ца.

cipher *n.* **1,** (zero) нуль. **2,** (code) шифр.
Circassian *adj.* черкéсский. —*n.* черкéс.
circle *n.* **1,** (round figure; circular movement) круг. **2,** *geog.* круг: *Arctic Circle,* Сéверный поля́рный круг. **3,** (small group) круг: *circle of acquaintances,* круг знакóмых. *Ruling circles,* прáвящие круги́. **4,** (social group) кружóк: *dramatic circle,* драмати́ческий кружóк. —*v.t.* **1,** (draw a circle around) обводи́ть. **2,** (go around) обходи́ть; объезжáть; облетáть; вращáться; (*all with* вокрýг). —*v.i.* кружи́ть(ся); опи́сывать круги́.
circuit *n.* **1,** *aerospace* оборóт: *three circuits of the earth,* три оборóта вокрýг Земли́. **2,** (regular journey) обхóд; объéзд. **3,** *electricity* цепь; кóнтур. *Short circuit,* корóткое замыкáние. **4,** *electronics* схéма: *integrated circuit,* интегрáльная схéма. —**circuit breaker,** прерывáтель. —**circuit court,** окружнóй суд.
circuitous *adj.* окóльный; обхóдный; крýжный.
circular *adj.* **1,** (round) крýглый. **2,** (moving in a circle) круговóй; кругообрáзный. —*n.* циркуля́р.
circulate *v.i.* **1,** (move, as of blood) обращáться; циркули́ровать. **2,** *econ.* (of money) обращáться. **3,** (spread, as of rumors) циркули́ровать; распространя́ться. —*v.t.* рассылáть; распространя́ть.
circulation *n.* **1,** (movement, as of air) циркуля́ция. **2,** (of blood) обращéние (крóви); кровообращéние: *poor circulation,* плохóе кровообращéние. **3,** (use) оборóт; обращéние: *put into circulation,* пусти́ть в оборóт/в обращéние. **4,** *econ.* обращéние: *withdraw from circulation,* изъя́ть из обращéния. **5,** (number of copies sold) тирáж.
circulatory *adj.* кровенóсный: *circulatory system,* кровенóсная систéма.
circumcise *v.t.* обрезáть. —**circumcision,** *n.* обрéзание.
circumference *n.* окрýжность.
circumlocution *n.* околи́чности.
circumnavigate *v.t. Circumnavigate the globe,* совершáть кругосвéтное плáвание.
circumscribe *v.t.* **1,** (limit) ограни́чивать. **2,** *math.* опи́сывать. —**circumscription,** *n.* ограничéние.
circumspect *adj.* осмотри́тельный. —**circumspection,** *n.* осмотри́тельность.
circumstance *n.* **1,** (fact; event) обстоя́тельство. **2,** *pl.* (financial condition) обстоя́тельства: *in straitened circumstances,* в стеснённых обстоя́тельствах. —**under no circumstances,** ни в кóем слýчае; ни под каки́м ви́дом; ни при каки́х обстоя́тельствах; ни при каки́х услóвиях.
circumstantial evidence кóсвенные ули́ки.
circumvent *v.t.* **1,** (surround; encircle) окружáть. **2,** (go around; bypass) обходи́ть.
circus *n.* цирк. —*adj.* цирковóй: *circus performer,* цирковóй арти́ст.
cirrhosis *n.* циррóз: *cirrhosis of the liver,* циррóз пéчени.
cistern *n.* цистéрна.
citadel *n.* цитадéль.
citation *n.* **1,** (act of quoting) цити́рование. **2,** (quote) цитáта; ссы́лка. **3,** (commendation) благодáрность. **4,** (summons) вы́зов.
cite *v.t.* **1,** (quote) ссылáться на; цити́ровать. **2,** (refer to, as an example) приводи́ть. **3,** (commend, as for bravery) отмечáть. **4,** *law* привлекáть к отвéтственности.

citizen *n.* граждани́н. —**citizenship,** *n.* гражда́нство.
citrate *n.* цитра́т.
citric acid лимо́нная кислота́.
citrus *n.* ци́трус. —*adj.* ци́трусовый.
city *n.* го́род. —*adj.* городско́й: *city council,* городско́й сове́т. —**city hall,** ра́туша.
civet *n.* виве́рра.
civic *adj.* гражда́нский: *civic duty,* гражда́нский долг.
civil *adj.* **1,** (pert. to citizens) гражда́нский. **2,** (polite) ве́жливый. —**civil defense,** гражда́нская оборо́на. —**civil engineer,** инжене́р-строи́тель. —**civil marriage,** гражда́нский брак. —**civil rights,** гражда́нские права́. —**civil servant,** госуда́рственный слу́жащий. —**civil service,** госуда́рственная слу́жба. —**civil war,** гражда́нская война́.
civilian *n.* шта́тский (челове́к). —*adj.* шта́тский; гражда́нский.
civility *n.* ве́жливость.
civilization *n.* цивилиза́ция.
civilize *v.t.* цивилизова́ть. —**civilized,** *adj.* цивилизо́ванный.
clabber *n.* простоква́ша.
clack *v.i.* цо́кать. —*n.* цо́кот.
clad *adj.* оде́тый. *Snow-clad,* заснё́женный.
claim *v.t.* **1,** (assert one's right to) тре́бовать: *claim damages,* тре́бовать возмеще́ния убы́тков. **2,** (call for; pick up) востре́бовать. **3,** (maintain; assert) утвержда́ть. —*n.* **1,** (request; demand) прете́нзия; притяза́ние; тре́бование. **2,** (assertion; contention) утвержде́ние. —**lay claim to,** претендова́ть на; предъяви́ть тре́бование *or* пра́во на.
claimant *n.* претенде́нт.
claim check квита́нция.
clairvoyance *n.* ясновиде́ние.
clairvoyant *adj.* ясновидящий. —*n.* ясновидец.
clam *n.* моллю́ск. —*v.i.* [*usu.* **clam up**] *colloq.* замолча́ть.
clamber *v.i.* кара́бкаться.
clamor *also,* **clamour** *n.* **1,** (din) шум; гам. **2,** (public outcry) шум. —*v.i.* крича́ть; шуме́ть.
clamp *n.* зажи́м; скре́па. —*v.t.* скрепля́ть. —**clamp down on,** подтя́гивать; присту́нивать.
clan *n.* клан.
clandestine *adj.* та́йный; скры́тый.
clang *n.* лязг. —*v.t. & i.* ля́згать.
clank *n.* лязг; цо́кот. —*v.t. & i.* ля́згать; бряца́ть; цо́кать.
clannish *adj.* за́мкнутый; обосо́бленный.
clap *v.t.* **1,** (strike together, as one's hands) бить; ударя́ть; хло́пать (в ладо́ши). **2,** (toss, as into jail) упря́тывать; упека́ть. —*v.i.* хло́пать. —*n.* **1,** (act of clapping) хло́панье. **2,** (sound, as of thunder) уда́р; раска́т. *There was a clap of thunder,* уда́рил гром.
clapper *n.* язы́к (ко́локола).
claque *n.* кла́ка. —**claqueur,** *n.* клакёр.
claret *n.* (wine) бордо́. —*adj.* (color) бордо́; цве́та бордо́; бордо́вый.
clarification *n.* разъясне́ние.
clarify *v.t.* разъясня́ть; проясня́ть; выясня́ть.
clarinet *n.* кларне́т. —**clarinetist,** *n.* кларнети́ст.
clarion *n.* фанфа́ра. —*adj.* гро́мкий; зву́чный.
clarity *n.* я́сность.
clash *v.i.* **1,** (come into conflict) ста́лкиваться. **2,** (not go well together) дисгармони́ровать. —*n.* столкнове́ние.
clasp *n.* **1,** (hook) застё́жка. **2,** (grip) объя́тие; пожа́тие. —*v.t.* **1,** (fasten) застё́гивать. **2,** (grasp) обнима́ть; обхва́тывать. **3,** in *clasp one's hands,* всплесну́ть рука́ми.
class *n.* **1,** (in most meanings) класс: *the working class,* рабо́чий класс. *Go to class,* идти́ в класс. *Travel first class,* е́хать пе́рвым кла́ссом. **2,** (alumni graduated in one year) вы́пуск: *the class of 1970,* вы́пуск 1970-го го́да. —*adj.* **1,** (pert. to social classes) кла́ссовый: *class consciousness,* кла́ссовое созна́ние. **2,** (pert. to a class in school) кла́ссный. —*v.t.* классифици́ровать.
classic *n.* **1,** (writer) кла́ссик. **2,** (work) класси́ческое произведе́ние; *pl.* кла́ссика. —*adj.* класси́ческий.
classical *adj.* класси́ческий.
classicism *n.* классици́зм. —**classicist,** *n.* кла́ссик.
classification *n.* **1,** (act of classifying) классифика́ция. **2,** *mil.* гриф секре́тности.
classified *adj.* **1,** (grouped) классифици́рованный. **2,** *mil.* секре́тный; засекре́ченный. —**classified ad,** объявле́ние (в газе́те).
classify *v.t.* **1,** (arrange by class) классифици́ровать. **2,** (declare to be secret) засекре́чивать.
classless *adj.* бескла́ссовый.
classmate *n.* однокла́ссник.
classroom *n.* класс; кла́ссная ко́мната.
classy *adj., colloq.* шика́рный; первокла́ссный.
clatter *n.* стук; то́пот; цо́кот. —*v.i.* греме́ть; громыха́ть; цо́кать; тараба́нить.
clause *n.* **1,** (part of a sentence) предложе́ние. **2,** (article; provision) статья́; пункт.
claustrophobia *n.* боя́знь остава́ться в закры́том помеще́нии; клаустрофо́бия.
clavichord *n.* клавико́рды.
clavicle *n.* ключи́ца.
claw *n.* **1,** (of a bird or animal) ко́готь. **2,** (of a lobster or crab) клешня́. **3,** (of a hammer) ла́па. —*v.t.* терза́ть когтя́ми.
clay *n.* гли́на. —*adj.* гли́няный: *clay tablets,* гли́няные табли́чки. —**clayey,** *adj.* гли́нистый.
clean *adj.* чи́стый: *clean shirt/plate,* чи́стая руба́шка/таре́лка. —*adv.* **1,** (so as to be clean) на́чисто: *sweep the floor clean,* на́чисто вы́мести пол. *Lick the plate clean,* обли́зывать таре́лку. **2,** *colloq.* (completely) соверше́нно: *I clean forgot,* я соверше́нно забы́л(а). —*v.t.* чи́стить: *clean a carpet,* чи́стить ковё́р. —**clean out, 1,** (clear of rubbish) очища́ть. **2,** *colloq.* (of a robber) очища́ть; обокра́сть *or* ограбить до́чиста; (in gambling) обчища́ть; обыгра́ть до́чиста. —**clean up, 1,** (tidy up) убира́ть; прибира́ть. **2,** *colloq.* (finish) зако́нчить. **3,** *slang* (make a lot of money) сорва́ть куш.
clean-cut *adj.* опря́тный; вы́холенный.
cleaner *n.* **1,** (person) чи́стильщик; убо́рщик. **2,** (establishment) химчи́стка: *take to the cleaners,* отдава́ть в химчи́стку.
cleaning *n.* чи́стка. —**cleaning woman,** убо́рщица.
cleanliness *n.* чистота́.
cleanly *adj.* чистопло́тный. —*adv.* чи́сто.
cleanse *v.t.* чи́стить; очища́ть. —**cleanser,** *n.* мо́ющее сре́дство.
clean-shaven *adj.* бри́тый; гла́дко вы́бритый.

clear *adj.* **1,** (bright; easily understood) я́сный: *clear day/answer,* я́сный день/отве́т. *As clear as day,* я́сный как бо́жий день. *Make it clear that...,* дать я́сно поня́ть, что... **2,** (pure; unblemished) чи́стый: *clear water/skin/conscience,* чи́стая вода́/ко́жа/со́весть. **3,** (unobstructed) свобо́дный: *the way is clear,* путь свобо́ден. —*adv.* **1,** (distinctly) я́сно: *loud and clear,* гро́мко и я́сно. **2,** (all the way): *clear to the top,* до са́мой верши́ны. —*v.t.* **1,** (rid of dirt, unwanted objects, etc.) очища́ть: *clear the windshield,* очища́ть пере́днее стекло́. *Clear the air,* очища́ть во́здух; *fig.* разряди́ть атмосфе́ру. *Clear one's throat,* отка́шливаться. *Clear a forest,* очища́ть лес. *Clear a path,* расчища́ть доро́жку. *Clear the table,* убира́ть со стола́. *Clear the way,* открыва́ть путь. **2,** (empty; vacate) освобожда́ть; очища́ть: *clear the premises,* освобожда́ть/очища́ть помеще́ние. **3,** (remove) убира́ть; счища́ть. *Clear the dishes from the table,* убира́ть посу́ду со стола́. *Clear the snow off the sidewalk,* счища́ть снег с тротуа́ра. **4,** (jump over) брать: *clear a hurdle,* брать барье́р. **5,** (acquit) опра́вдывать. **6,** (authorize to see classified information) засекре́чивать. **7,** (earn; net) выруча́ть. **8,** in *clear one's name,* восстанови́ть своё до́брое и́мя. —*v.i.* проясня́ться: *the sky is clearing,* не́бо проясня́ется. —**clear away,** убира́ть; счища́ть. —**clear out, 1,** (empty; clean up) очища́ть. **2,** *colloq.* (depart) убира́ться. —**clear up, 1,** (clean up) очища́ть. **2,** (clarify; solve) разъясня́ть. *The matter was cleared up,* де́ло разъясни́лось. **3,** (grow fair, as of the weather) проясня́ться. **4,** (disappear, as of a cold, rash, etc.) проходи́ть.

clearance *n.* **1,** (space) зазо́р. **2,** (sale) распрода́жа. **3,** = **security clearance.**

clear-cut *adj.* чёткий.

clearing *n.* **1,** (act of making clear) очи́стка; очище́ние; расчи́стка. **2,** (place cleared of trees) вы́рубка; поля́на. **3,** *comm.* кли́ринг; безнали́чный расчёт. —**clearing house,** расчётная пала́та.

clearly *adv.* **1,** (in a clear manner) я́сно. **2,** (without a doubt) несомне́нно. **3,** (obviously) очеви́дно.

cleat *n.* шип: *shoes with cleats,* башмаки́ на шипа́х.

cleavage *n.* раско́л.

cleave *v.t.* раска́лывать; рассека́ть.

cleaver *n.* тя́пка; се́чка.

clef *n.* ключ.

cleft *n.* рассе́лина; расще́лина; тре́щина. —*adj.* раздвое́нный. —**cleft palate,** во́лчья пасть.

clematis *n.* ломоно́с.

clemency *n.* милосе́рдие; поща́да; поми́лование.

clench *v.t.* сжима́ть. *Clenched fists,* сжа́тые кулаки́.

clergy *n.* духове́нство. —**clergyman,** *n.* свяще́нник; духо́вное лицо́.

cleric *n.* духо́вное лицо́.

clerical *adj.* **1,** (pert. to the clergy) духо́вный. **2,** (pert. to office work) канцеля́рский.

clerk *n.* **1,** (office worker) конто́рский слу́жащий; клерк. **2,** (salesperson) продаве́ц; прика́зчик. **3,** (record-keeper) регистра́тор.

clever *adj.* **1,** (bright; intelligent) у́мный; сообрази́тельный; смышлёный. **2,** (showing skill or wit) ло́вкий; остроу́мный. —**cleverly,** *adv.* ло́вко; остроу́мно. —**cleverness,** *n.* ло́вкость; сообрази́тельность.

cliché *n.* клише; штамп.

click *n.* щелчо́к: *the click of a camera,* щелчо́к фотоаппара́та. —*v.t.* щёлкать (+ *instr.*). *Click one's heels,* щёлкать *or* присту́кивать каблука́ми. —*v.i.* щёлкать: *the camera clicked,* фотоаппара́т щёлкнул.

client *n.* **1,** (customer) клие́нт. **2,** (of a lawyer) подзащи́тный. —**clientele,** *n.* клиенту́ра.

cliff *n.* утёс; (отве́сная) скала́. *Fall over a cliff,* упа́сть со скалы́.

climactic *adj.* кульминацио́нный.

climate *n.* **1,** (type of weather) кли́мат. **2,** *fig.* (prevailing conditions) атмосфе́ра. —**climatic,** *adj.* климати́ческий.

climax *n.* **1,** (culmination) кульминацио́нный пункт. **2,** (dénouement) развя́зка.

climb *v.i.* **1,** (clamber) лезть: *climb up on the roof,* лезть на кры́шу. **2,** (increase; rise) расти́. **3,** (gain altitude) набира́ть высоту́. —*v.t.* лезть на; влеза́ть на; взбира́ться на. *Climb a tree,* лезть *or* влеза́ть на де́рево. *Climb (the) stairs,* поднима́ться по ле́стнице. —*n.* **1,** (act of climbing) подъём; восхожде́ние. **2,** *aero.* набо́р высоты́. —**climb down,** слеза́ть. —**climb in,** влеза́ть. —**climb out,** вылеза́ть. —**climb over,** перелеза́ть.

climber *n.* **1,** (mountain climber) альпини́ст. **2,** (plant) вью́щееся расте́ние.

climbing *n.* ла́занье. *Mountain climbing,* альпини́зм. —*adj.* (of a plant) вью́щийся. —**climbing irons,** ко́шки.

clinch *v.t.* **1,** (secure; fasten) заклёпывать. **2,** *fig.* (settle for good) реша́ть. *Clinch a deal,* заключи́ть сде́лку.

cling *v.i.* [*usu.* **cling to**] цепля́ться (за). *Cling to life,* цепля́ться за жизнь. *Cling to a hope,* цепля́ться за наде́жду.

clinic *n.* кли́ника. —**clinical,** *adj.* клини́ческий.

clink *n.* **1,** (sound) звон. **2,** *slang* (jail) куту́зка. —*v.t.* звене́ть (+ *instr.*). *Clink glasses,* чо́каться.

clip *n.* **1,** (metal fastener) скре́пка. **2,** (piece of jewelry) брошь. **3,** (cartridge clip) (патро́нная) обо́йма. **4,** *colloq.* (pace) ход: *at a fast clip,* бы́стрым хо́дом. —*v.t.* **1,** (fasten with a clip) скрепля́ть. **2,** (trim) стричь; обреза́ть; подреза́ть. **3,** *fol. by* **out** (cut out) выреза́ть. **4,** *colloq.* (strike) дать: *clip someone on the ear,* дать кому́-нибудь по́ уху. —**clip someone's wings,** подре́зать кры́лья (+ *dat.*).

clipper *n.* **1,** *usu. pl.* (shears) но́жницы. **2,** *usu. pl.* (device for cutting hair) маши́нка для стри́жки. **3,** (ship) кли́пер.

clipping *n.* вы́резка.

clique *n.* кли́ка.

clitoris *n.* кли́тор; похотни́к.

cloak *n.* **1,** (garment) плащ; ма́нтия. **2,** *fig.* (guise; cover) покро́в; ши́рма; ма́ска. —*v.t.* прикрыва́ть; маскирова́ть.

cloakroom *n.* гардеро́б; раздева́лка. *Cloakroom attendant,* гардеро́бщик.

clock *n.* часы́. *Alarm clock,* буди́льник. —*v.t.* хронометри́ровать. —**round the clock,** кру́глые су́тки.

clockwise *adv.* по часово́й стре́лке.

clockwork *n.,* in **work like clockwork,** рабо́тать как часы́.

clod *n.* **1,** (lump) ком; глы́ба. **2,** (dolt) о́лух; недотёпа.

clog *v.t.* засоря́ть; забива́ть. *Become clogged,* засоря́ться.

cloister *n.* **1,** (monastery) монасты́рь. **2,** (covered walk) (кры́тая) арка́да. —*v.t.* **1,** (confine to a monastery) заточа́ть в монасты́рь. **2,** (seclude) уединя́ть.

close[1] (klos) *adj.* **1,** (near) бли́зкий. *Close relative,* бли́зкий ро́дственник. *Close resemblance,* бли́зкое схо́дство. *Close combat,* бли́жний бой. **2,** (intimate) бли́зкий; те́сный. *Close friend,* бли́зкий друг. *Close connection,* те́сная связь. **3,** (tight; compact; crowded) те́сный. *Close weave,* ча́стое переплете́ние. *Close print,* убо́ристый шрифт. *Close order, mil.* со́мкнутый строй. *In close quarters,* в те́сном сосе́дстве. **4,** (keenly contested) напряжённый. *Close match,* напряжённый матч; упо́рная борьба́. *Close vote,* почти́ ра́вное деле́ние голосо́в. **5,** (rigorous; searching) внима́тельный. *Keep a close watch on,* внима́тельно следи́ть за. **6,** (stuffy) ду́шный: *it is close in here,* здесь ду́шно. —*adv.* бли́зко. *Follow close behind,* идти́ сле́дом за. *Press close to one's bosom,* прижима́ть к груди́. —**close by,** бли́зко; ря́дом. —**close to,** о́коло; бли́зко от; недалеко́ от. *He is close to sixty,* ему́ под шестьдеся́т. —**up close,** вблизи́: *the house looks different up close,* вблизи́ дом вы́глядит ина́че.

close[2] (kloz) *v.t.* **1,** (shut) закрыва́ть: *close the door,* закрыва́ть дверь; *close one's eyes,* закрыва́ть глаза́. **2,** (fill up; stop up) заде́лывать: *close a hole with putty,* заде́лывать дыру́ зама́зкой. **3,** (bring together; join) смыка́ть; спла́чивать: *close ranks,* смыка́ть/спла́чивать ряды́. **4,** (conclude) заключа́ть: *close a deal,* заключи́ть сде́лку. —*v.i.* закрыва́ться: *the window won't close,* окно́ не закрыва́ется. —*n.* закры́тие; коне́ц. *Draw to a close,* приближа́ться к концу́. —**close down,** закрыва́ть; прикрыва́ть. —**close in,** смыка́ть кольцо́ окруже́ния. —**close out,** распродава́ть. —**in closing,** в заключе́ние.

closed *adj.* закры́тый. *The city is closed to foreigners,* го́род закры́т для иностра́нцев.

close-fisted *adj.* прижи́мистый.

close-fitting *adj.* те́сный. *Close-fitting dress,* пла́тье, пло́тно облега́ющее фигу́ру.

close-knit *adj.* спа́янный.

closely *adv.* **1,** (intimately) те́сно: *closely connected,* те́сно свя́занный. **2,** (attentively) внима́тельно; чу́тко.

close-mouthed *adj.* за́мкнутый.

closeness *n.* **1,** (nearness) бли́зость. **2,** (tightness) теснота́. **3,** (stuffiness) духота́.

close-out *n.* распрода́жа.

closet *n.* шкаф. —*v.t.* [*usu.* **closet oneself**] уединя́ться.

close-up *n.* кру́пный план. *Take a close-up of,* снима́ть (кого́-нибудь) кру́пным пла́ном.

closing *n.* **1,** (act of shutting) закры́тие. *Closing time,* вре́мя закры́тия. **2,** (end; conclusion) заключе́ние. —*adj.* заключи́тельный.

closure *n.* закры́тие.

clot *n.* сгу́сток: *blood clot,* сгу́сток кро́ви. —*v.t.* сгуща́ть. —*v.i.* сгуща́ться; запека́ться.

cloth *n.* **1,** (fabric) ткань; сукно́; мате́рия. **2,** (small piece for wiping or dusting) суко́нка; тря́пка. —*adj.* суко́нный: *cloth coat,* суко́нное пальто́.

clothe *v.t.* одева́ть.

clothes *n.pl.* оде́жда; пла́тье. —*adj.* платяно́й: *clothes brush,* платяна́я щётка. —**clothesline,** *n.* верёвка для белья́. —**clothespin,** *n.* прище́пка.

clothier *n.* торго́вец гото́вой оде́ждой.

clothing *n.* оде́жда; пла́тье. —*adj.* вещево́й: *clothing allowance,* вещево́е дово́льствие. *Clothing store,* магази́н гото́вого пла́тья.

cloture *n.* прекраще́ние пре́ний.

cloud *n.* о́блако. *Storm cloud,* ту́ча. *Cloud of dust,* клуб пы́ли. —*adj.* о́блачный: *cloud cover,* о́блачный покро́в. —*v.t.* затемня́ть; омрача́ть; затума́нивать. —*v.i.* [*usu.* **cloud up**] затума́ниваться. —**be up in the clouds,** вита́ть в облака́х.

cloudberry *n.* моро́шка.

cloudburst *n.* ли́вень.

cloudiness *n.* о́блачность.

cloudless *adj.* безо́блачный.

cloudy *adj.* **1,** (full of or covered with clouds) о́блачный. **2,** (murky, as of a liquid) му́тный.

clout *n., colloq.* тума́к.

clove *n.* гвозди́ка.

cloven *adj.* раздво́енный. —**cloven hoof,** раздво́енное копы́то.

clover *n.* кле́вер. —**be in clover,** ката́ться как сыр в ма́сле; жить припева́ючи.

clown *n.* кло́ун. —*v.i.* пая́сничать; дура́читься. —**clownish,** *adj.* кло́унский; шутовско́й.

cloy *v.t.* пресыща́ть. —**cloying,** *adj.* прито́рный; слаща́вый.

club *n.* **1,** (cudgel) дуби́на; дуби́нка. **2,** (golf club) клю́шка. **3,** (association or its headquarters) клуб. **4,** *pl., cards* тре́фы. —*v.t.* избива́ть; дуба́сить.

clubfoot *n.* изуро́дованная ступня́.

club soda со́довая вода́.

cluck *v.i.* клохта́ть. —*n.* клохта́нье.

clue *n.* путево́дная нить. *Leave no clues,* не оставля́ть никаки́х следо́в. *Give someone a clue,* наводи́ть кого́-нибудь на след. *I haven't a clue,* поня́тия не име́ю.

clump *n.* **1,** (cluster) гру́ппа: *clump of trees,* гру́ппа дере́вьев. **2,** (lump) комо́к. **3,** (sound of heavy footsteps) то́пот.

clumsy *adj.* неуклю́жий. —**clumsily,** *adv.* неуклю́же. —**clumsiness,** *n.* неуклю́жесть.

cluster *n.* **1,** (bunch, as of grapes) кисть; гроздь. **2,** (small group) гру́ппа; ку́чка. *Star cluster,* звёздное скопле́ние. —*v.i.* [*usu.* **cluster around**] окружа́ть; обступа́ть.

clutch *v.t.* хвата́ть; схва́тывать. —*v.i.* [*usu.* **clutch at**] хвата́ться за. —*n.* **1,** (grip) хва́тка. **2,** *mech.* му́фта; сцепле́ние. —**fall into the clutches of,** попа́сть в ко́гти к; попа́сть в ла́пы (+ *dat.*).

clutter *v.t.* [*usu.* **clutter up**] загроможда́ть.

coach *n.* **1,** (carriage) каре́та. **2,** (tutor) репети́тор. **3,** *sports* тре́нер. —*v.t.* **1,** (tutor) репети́ровать; ната́скивать. **2,** *sports* тренирова́ть. **3,** (prompt) подска́зывать: *no coaching!,* не подска́зывать!

coach house каре́тный сара́й.

coachman *n.* ку́чер; возни́ца; изво́зчик.

coagulant *n.* сгуща́ющее сре́дство; коагуля́нт.

coagulate *v.t.* сгуща́ть; свёртывать. —*v.i.* сгуща́ться; свёртываться; запека́ться. —**coagulation,** *n.* свёртывание; коагуля́ция.

coal *n.* **1,** (mineral) у́голь. **2,** *pl.* (embers) у́гли. —*adj.* у́гольный; каменноуго́льный. *Coal mine,* у́гольная ша́хта. —**rake over the coals,** зада́ть жа́ру (+ *dat.*); взять под обстре́л.

coalesce *v.i.* **1,** (grow together) сраста́ться. **2,**

(unite; merge) объединя́ться; слива́ться. —**coalescence,** *n.* сраще́ние; соедине́ние.
coalition *n.* коали́ция. —*adj.* коалицио́нный.
coal tar каменноу́гольный дёготь.
coarse *adj.* **1,** (rough; crude; unrefined) гру́бый. **2,** (not fine, as of sand) кру́пный.
coarsen *v.t.* де́лать гру́бым. —*v.i.* грубе́ть.
coarseness *n.* гру́бость.
coast *n.* **1,** (edge of the land facing the sea) бе́рег: *along the coast,* вдоль бе́рега; *rocky coast,* скали́стый бе́рег. **2,** (region next to the sea) побере́жье: *the West Coast,* за́падное побере́жье. —*v.i.* кати́ться (свобо́дным колесо́м). —**the coast is clear,** путь свобо́ден.
coastal *adj.* берегово́й; прибре́жный.
coast guard **1,** (unit guarding a coast) берегова́я охра́на. **2,** *cap.* (U.S. branch of service) морска́я пограни́чная слу́жба.
coastline *n.* берегова́я ли́ния.
coat *n.* **1,** (overcoat) пальто́. *Fur coat,* шу́ба. **2,** (suit jacket) пиджа́к. **3,** (skin; fur) мех; шку́ра. **4,** (layer, as of paint) слой. —*v.t.* покрыва́ть; залива́ть. *My tongue is coated,* у меня́ обложи́ло язы́к. —**coat of arms,** герб. —**coat of mail,** па́нцирь; кольчу́га.
coati *n.* носу́ха.
coating *n.* покры́тие; налёт.
coatroom *n.* гардеро́б; раздева́лка.
coattail *n.* фа́лда.
coauthor *n.* соа́втор. —**coauthorship,** *n.* соа́вторство.
coax *v.t.* **1,** (try to persuade) угова́ривать; убежда́ть. **2,** (obtain by persuasion) выпра́шивать.
coaxial cable коаксиа́льный ка́бель.
cob *n.* поча́ток кукуру́зы.
cobalt *n.* ко́бальт. —*adj.* ко́бальтовый.
cobbled *adj.* булы́жный.
cobbler *n.* сапо́жник.
cobblestone *n.* булы́жник. —*adj.* булы́жный.
cobra *n.* очко́вая змея́; ко́бра.
cobweb *n.* паути́на.
coca *n.* ко́ка.
cocaine *n.* кокаи́н.
coccus *n.* кокк.
coccyx *n.* ко́пчик.
co-chairman *n.* сопредседа́тель.
cochineal *n.* кошени́ль.
cock *n.* **1,** (rooster) пету́х. **2,** (faucet) кран. **3,** (hammer of a firearm) куро́к. —*v.t.* **1,** (tilt) зала́мывать (ша́пку). *Cock one's head to one side,* склони́ть го́лову на́бок. **2,** (set, as a firearm) взводи́ть куро́к (пистоле́та). *The gun is cocked,* куро́к на боево́м взво́де.
cockade *n.* кока́рда.
cock-and-bull story небыли́ца; ро́ссказни.
cockatoo *n.* какаду́.
cockchafer *n.* ма́йский жук; хрущ.
cocked hat треуго́лка.
cockerel *n.* петушо́к.
cockeyed *adj.* **1,** (cross-eyed) косогла́зый. **2,** *colloq.* (askew) косо́й. **3,** *colloq.* (absurd) глу́пый; дура́цкий.
cockfight *n.* петуши́ный бой.
cockle *n.* **1,** (weed) ку́коль; пле́вел. **2,** (mollusk) сердцеви́дка. —**cockles of one's heart,** тайники́ се́рдца.
cockpit *n.* каби́на (самолёта).
cockroach *n.*育 тарака́н.
cockscomb *n.* **1,** (comb of a cock) петуши́ный гре́бень. **2,** (plant) пету́ший гребешо́к.
cocksure *adj.* **1,** (absolutely sure) вполне́ уве́ренный. **2,** (too sure of oneself) самоуве́ренный.
cocktail *n.* кокте́йль.
cocky *adj., colloq.* самоуве́ренный; чванли́вый.
coco *n.* коко́совая па́льма; коко́с. *Also,* **coco palm; coconut palm.**
cocoa *n.* кака́о.
coconut *n.* коко́совый оре́х; коко́с. —*adj.* коко́совый.
cocoon *n.* ко́кон.
cod *n.* треска́.
C.O.D. нало́женным платежо́м.
coddle *v.t.* не́жить; изне́живать.
code *n.* **1,** (body of laws) ко́декс; свод зако́нов. **2,** (system of secret communication) код.
codeine *n.* кодеи́н.
codfish *n.* треска́.
codicil *n.* припи́ска.
codify *v.t.* кодифици́ровать. —**codification,** *n.* кодифика́ция.
cod-liver oil ры́бий жир.
coeducation *n.* совме́стное обуче́ние. —**coeducational,** *adj.* совме́стного обуче́ния.
coefficient *n.* коэффицие́нт.
coerce *v.t.* принужда́ть; заставля́ть. —**coercion,** *n.* принужде́ние. —**coercive,** *adj.* принуди́тельный.
coexist *v.i.* сосуществова́ть. —**coexistence,** *n.* сосуществова́ние.
coffee *n.* ко́фе. —*adj.* кофе́йный: *coffee beans,* кофе́йные бобы́. —**coffee-colored,** *adj.* кофе́йный; кофе́йного цве́та. —**coffee house,** кафе́. —**coffee mill,** кофе́йная ме́льница; кофе́йница. —**coffeepot,** *n.* кофе́йник.
coffer *n.* **1,** (strongbox) (де́нежный) я́щик. **2,** *pl.* (treasury) казна́.
coffin *n.* гроб.
cog *n.* зубе́ц.
cogent *adj.* убеди́тельный. —**cogency,** *n.* убеди́тельность.
cogitate *v.i.* размышля́ть; разду́мывать. —**cogitation,** *n.* размышле́ние.
cognac *n.* конья́к.
cognate *adj.* ро́дственный. —*n.* ро́дственное сло́во.
cognition *n.* позна́ние. —**cognitive,** *adj.* познава́тельный.
cognizance *n.* зна́ние. —**take cognizance of,** обраща́ть внима́ние на.
cognizant *adj. Be cognizant of,* осознава́ть; отдава́ть себе́ отчёт в.
cogwheel *n.* зубча́тое колесо́; шестерня́.
cohabit *v.i.* сожи́тельствовать. —**cohabitation,** *n.* сожи́тельство.
cohere *v.i.* слипа́ться; слепля́ться.
coherent *adj.* свя́зный; стро́йный. —**coherence,** *n.* свя́зность.
cohesion *n.* сплочённость. —**cohesive,** *adj.* сплочённый.
cohort *n.* **1,** (band) отря́д. **2,** (associate) посо́бник.
coil *n.* **1,** (roll) вито́к. **2,** *electricity* кату́шка. —*v.t.* нама́тывать; обма́тывать. —*v.i.* ви́ться; обвива́ться.
coin *n.* моне́та. —*v.t.* **1,** (mint) чека́нить. **2,** (invent,

as a word or expression) создавать. —**the other side of the coin,** оборотная сторона медали.

coinage *n.* **1,** (making of coins) чеканка (монеты). **2,** (newly coined word) новообразование.

coincide *v.i.* совпадать.

coincidence *n.* совпадение: *by a curious coincidence,* по забавному совпадению.

coincidental *adj.* случайный. *It's purely coincidental,* это чистая случайность.

coition *n.* совокупление. *Also,* **coitus.**

coke *n.* кокс. —*adj.* коксовый; коксовальный: *coke oven,* коксовая/коксовальная печь. —**coking coal,** коксующийся уголь.

colander *n.* дуршлаг.

cold *adj.* холодный. *It is cold,* холодно. *It is getting cold,* холодает. *I am cold,* мне холодно. *Get cold (of food),* стыть; стынуть; остывать. *Grow cold toward someone,* охладеть к кому-нибудь. —*adv., colloq.* совершенно: *cold sober,* совершенно трезв. *Know something cold,* знать что-нибудь до точки. *Turn down cold,* отказать наотрез. —*n.* **1,** (low temperature) холод. **2,** (ailment) простуда; насморк. *Catch cold,* простудиться. —**be left out in the cold,** остаться за бортом. —**leave someone cold,** не производить никакого впечатления на. —**throw cold water on,** облить холодной водой.

cold-blooded *adj.* **1,** *zool.* холоднокровный. **2,** (sensitive to cold) зябкий. **3,** (callous; heartless) хладнокровный.

cold cream кольдкрем.

coldly *adv.* холодно.

coldness *n.* холодность.

cold war холодная война.

coleslaw *n.* салат из шинкованной капусты.

colic *n.* колики.

coliseum *n.* колизей.

colitis *n.* воспаление толстых кишок; колит.

collaborate *v.i.* сотрудничать. *Collaborate on a book,* совместно писать книгу. *Collaborate with the enemy,* сотрудничать с врагом. —**collaboration,** *n.* сотрудничество.

collaborator *n.* **1,** (associate) сотрудник. **2,** (one who collaborates with the enemy) коллаборационист.

collapse *v.i.* **1,** (cave in) рушиться; рухнуть; обрушиваться; обваливаться; проваливаться; разваливаться. **2,** (break down completely) рухнуть; разваливаться; потерпеть крах. **3,** (break down physically) свалиться. —*n.* **1,** (caving in) обвал; развал. **2,** (failure) распад; развал; крушение; крах. **3,** (extreme prostration) изнеможение.

collapsible *adj.* складной; раскладной; разборный; откидной.

collar *n.* **1,** (of a coat) воротник; (of a shirt, blouse, etc.) воротничок. **2,** (for a dog) ошейник; (for a horse) хомут. —*v.t., colloq.* схватывать. —**get hot under the collar,** (раз)горячиться. —**seize by the collar,** взять за шиворот.

collarbone *n.* ключица.

collate *v.t.* сличать; сверять.

collateral *n.* гарантия; обеспечение. —*adj.* **1,** (secondary; additional) побочный; второстепенный; дополнительный. **2,** (guaranteed by something pledged) обеспеченный.

colleague *n.* коллега; сослуживец.

collect *v.t.* **1,** (gather) собирать: *collect evidence,* собирать доказательства. *Collect one's thoughts,* собираться с мыслями. **2,** (save as a hobby) собирать; коллекционировать. **3,** (pick up; call for) заезжать за. **4,** (pick up and take with one) брать: *collect one's mail,* брать почту. *Collect the garbage,* брать *or* увозить мусор. **5,** (receive in payment) получать: *collect a pension,* получать пенсию. *Collect taxes,* собирать налоги. **6,** (gather, as dust) покрываться (пылью). —*v.i.* собираться; набираться; скопляться; накопляться. *Dust collected on the shelf,* пыль собралась на полке. —**collect oneself,** овладеть собой.

collected *adj.* **1,** (gathered together) собранный. *Collected works,* собрание сочинений. **2,** (cool; calm; composed) хладнокровный.

collection *n.* **1,** (act of collecting) сбор; собирание. **2,** (assemblage, as of books, stamps, etc.) коллекция; собрание. **3,** (anthology) сборник. **4,** (soliciting of money) денежный сбор. **5,** (pickup of mail) выемка.

collective *adj.* **1,** (joint; common) коллективный. **2,** *gram.* собирательный. —*n.* коллектив. —**collective farm,** колхоз.

collectively *adv.* **1,** (through joint efforts) совместно; сообща. **2,** (taken as a whole) в общем; в совокупности.

collectivism *n.* коллективизм.

collectivize *v.t.* коллективизировать. —**collectivization,** *n.* коллективизация.

collector *n.* **1,** (one who collects for a hobby) коллекционер; собиратель. **2,** (one who collects money due) сборщик: *tax collector,* сборщик налогов. **3,** in *ticket collector,* контролер; *garbage collector,* мусорщик.

college *n.* **1,** (school of higher learning) университет; колледж; вуз. **2,** (body) коллегия: *college of cardinals,* коллегия кардиналов. —*adj.* университетский: *a college education,* университетское образование.

collide *v.i.* сталкиваться.

collie *n.* колли; шотландская овчарка.

collision *n.* столкновение.

collodion *n.* коллодий.

colloid *n.* коллоид. —**colloidal,** *adj.* коллоидный.

colloquial *adj.* разговорный. —**colloquialism,** *n.* разговорное слово *or* выражение.

collusion *n.* сговор: *be in collusion with,* быть в сговоре с.

Colombian *adj.* колумбийский.

colon *n.* **1,** (punctuation mark) двоеточие. **2,** *anat.* ободочная кишка.

colonel *n.* полковник.

colonial *adj.* колониальный. —**colonialism,** *n.* колониализм. —**colonialist,** *n.* колонизатор.

colonist *n.* колонист.

colonize *v.t.* колонизировать. —**colonization,** *n.* колонизация.

colonnade *n.* колоннада.

colony *n.* колония.

color *also,* **colour** *n.* **1,** (hue) цвет; краска. *Local color,* местный колорит. *Color in one's cheeks,* румянец. *Dress in bright colors,* одеваться в яркие цвета. *Paint in bright colors,* писать яркими красками. **2,** *pl.* (flag; banner) знамя. *Trooping of the colors,* развод караула. *Call to the colors,* призывать на вое́нную слу́жбу. —*adj.* цветно́й: *color television,* цветно́е телеви́дение. —*v.t.* **1,** (give color to) раскра́шивать. **2,** (influence to some degree) влия́ть на; ска́зываться на. —**show one's true colors,** показа́ть своё настоя́щее лицо́. —**with flying colors,** с бле́ском.

coloration *n.* окра́ска; раскра́ска.

coloratura *n.* колорату́ра. —*adj.* колорату́рный.

color blindness дальтони́зм.

colored *adj.* цветно́й.

colorful *adj.* кра́сочный.

coloring *n.* окра́ска; раскра́ска.

colorless *adj.* бесцве́тный.

colossal *adj.* колосса́льный.

colossus *n.* коло́сс.

colour *see* **color.**

colt *n.* жеребёнок.

column *n.* **1,** (pillar) коло́нна. **2,** (of smoke) столб (ды́ма); (of mercury) сто́лбик (рту́ти). **3,** (in a book, newspaper, etc.) столбе́ц; коло́нка. **4,** (of figures) коло́нна; коло́нка; столбе́ц. **5,** *mil.* коло́нна.

columnar *adj.* напеча́танный столбца́ми.

columned *adj.* коло́нный.

columnist *n.* обозрева́тель; публици́ст.

colza *n.* суре́пица.

coma *n.* ко́ма. —**comatose,** *adj.* комато́зный.

comb *n.* **1,** (for the hair) гре́бень; гребёнка; расчёска. **2,** (crest of certain fowl) гре́бень; гребешо́к. —*v.t.* **1,** (someone's hair) причёсывать; расчёсывать. *Comb one's hair,* причёсываться. **2,** (card, as flax) чеса́ть. **3,** (search thoroughly) прочёсывать.

combat *n.* бой. *See combat,* уча́ствовать в бою́. —*adj.* боево́й: *combat vehicle,* боева́я маши́на. —*v.t.* боро́ться с *or* про́тив. *Combat crime,* боро́ться с престу́пностью. —**combatant,** *n.* деру́щийся. —**combative,** *adj.* вои́нственный; драчли́вый.

combination *n.* сочета́ние; комбина́ция. —**combination lock,** замо́к с секре́том.

combine *v.t.* **1,** (join; amalgamate) объединя́ть: *combine two positions,* объединя́ть две до́лжности. *Combine efforts,* объединя́ть *or* соединя́ть уси́лия. **2,** (mix) сочета́ть; совмеща́ть; соединя́ть; комбини́ровать. *Combine colors,* сочета́ть/комбини́ровать кра́ски. *Combine business with pleasure,* сочета́ть/совмеща́ть поле́зное с прия́тным. —*v.i.* объединя́ться. —*n.* **1,** (harvesting machine) комба́йн. **2,** (association) комбина́т.

combined *adj.* совме́стный.

combings *n.pl.* очёски.

combustible *adj.* горю́чий. —*n.* горю́чий материа́л. —**combustibility,** *n.* горю́честь.

combustion *n.* сгора́ние; воспламене́ние.

come *v.i.* **1,** (approach) идти́: *Come here!,* иди́ сюда́! *I'm coming!,* иду́! *Here he comes,* вот он идёт. **2,** (arrive) приходи́ть; приезжа́ть. *He did not come,* он не пришёл (*or* не прие́хал). **3,** (of a time or season) наступа́ть; наста́ть; приходи́ть. **4,** (reach) доходи́ть: *the dress comes to her knees,* пла́тье дохо́дит ей до коле́н. **5,** (progress) идти́: *how is your work coming?,* как идёт ва́ша рабо́та? **6,** (occur; fall) выпада́ть; приходи́ться: *New Year's Day comes on a Thursday,* Но́вый год выпада́ет/прихо́дится на четве́рг. *B comes after A,* бу́ква Б сле́дует за бу́квой А. **7,** (be available): *this dress comes in five colors/sizes,* э́то пла́тье (мо́жете найти́) в пяти́ цвета́х/разме́рах. **8,** (be due) причита́ться: *you have two dollars coming to you,* вам причита́ется два до́ллара. *He got what was coming to him,* он получи́л по заслу́гам. —**come about,** происходи́ть; случа́ться. —**come across,** натыка́ться на; ната́лкиваться на. —**come along,** идти́; приходи́ть. *He came along with us,* он пришёл вме́сте с на́ми. *How are things coming along?,* как иду́т дела́? —**come apart,** распада́ться. —**come around, 1,** (revive) приходи́ть в себя́. **2,** (recover) оправля́ться. **3,** (agree in the end) соглаша́ться. **4,** *colloq.* (come and visit) заходи́ть. —**come away with,** выноси́ть. —**come back, 1,** (return) возвраща́ться. **2,** *fol. by* **to** (return to one's memory) вспомина́ться (+ *dat.*). —**come between,** разъединя́ть: *nothing can come between us,* ничто́ нас не разъедини́т. —**come by, 1,** (drop by) заходи́ть. **2,** (obtain) достава́ть. —**come down, 1,** (descend) сходи́ть. **2,** (fall; decline) па́дать. *Come down in price,* па́дать в цене́. **3,** *fol. by* **to** (boil down to) своди́ться к. **4,** *fol. by* **with** (develop, as an illness) получа́ть. *I think I'm coming down with the flu,* ду́маю, что у меня́ начина́ется грипп. —**come from, 1,** *literally* приходи́ть из. **2,** (originate from): *wine comes from grapes,* вино́ де́лают из виногра́да. *He comes from California,* он ро́дом из Калифо́рнии. *She comes from a good family,* она́ из хоро́шей семьи́. *Where did this thing come from?,* отку́да взяла́сь э́та шту́ка? —**come in, 1,** (enter) входи́ть. **2,** (be received, as of letters, complaints, etc.) поступа́ть. **3,** (finish) приходи́ть: *come in second,* приходи́ть вторы́м. **4,** *fol. by* **for** (be subjected to) подверга́ться (+ *dat.*). —**come into, 1,** *literally* входи́ть в. **2,** (inherit) получи́ть (что) в насле́дство; достава́ться (+ *dat.*). **3,** *with various nouns* входи́ть в: *come into use,* входи́ть в употребле́ние; *come into fashion,* входи́ть в мо́ду. *Come into being,* возника́ть. *Come into view,* показа́ться. —**come of,** выходи́ть из: *nothing will come of it,* из э́того ничего́ не вы́йдет. —**come off,** отделя́ться; отрыва́ться; срыва́ться; соска́кивать; отстава́ть. —**come on!, 1,** (hurry up) живе́й! **2,** (don't be silly) ну что вы! —**come out, 1,** (emerge; be issued or released) выходи́ть. *The sun came out,* со́лнце вы́шло *or* вы́глянуло. **2,** (make one's debut) дебюти́ровать. **3,** (turn out; end up) сойти́; вы́йти. *Come out well in a picture,* хорошо́ вы́йти на сни́мке. *The picture came out well,* сни́мок получи́лся хоро́ший. **4,** (of a stain) выводи́ться. **5,** (take a position) выступа́ть: *come out in favor of/against,* выступа́ть за/про́тив. **6,** *fol. by* **with** (utter) выпа́ливать. —**come over, 1,** (visit) заходи́ть. **2,** (seize, as of an emotion) овладева́ть; завладева́ть. *What's come over you?,* что э́то на вас нашло́?; что э́то вы? —**come through, 1,** (seep through) проса́чиваться че́рез. **2,** (endure successfully) переноси́ть: *she came through the operation well,* она́ хорошо́ перенесла́ опера́цию. —**come to, 1,** (reach, as an end, agreement, etc.) приходи́ть к. **2,** (amount to) составля́ть. **3,** (result in) своди́ться: *come to naught,* своди́ться к нулю́. **4,** (regain consciousness) приходи́ть в себя́. **5,** (be learned by) дава́ться: *languages come to her easily,* языки́ даю́тся ей легко́. —**come true,** осуществля́ться; сбыва́ться. —**come under, 1,** (fit into, as a category) относи́ться к. **2,** (be subjected to) попада́ть под: *come under suspicion,* попа́сть под подозре́ние.

—**come up, 1,** (rise) подниматься; всходить. **2,** (sprout) всходить. **3,** (arise, as in discussion) возникать. —**come up to, 1,** (approach) подходить к. **2,** (stand as tall as) доставать до: *he comes up to my shoulder,* он мне достаёт до плеча. **3,** *colloq.* (equal; be as good as) сравниться с. —**come up with,** находить. —**come upon,** набрести на; нападать на; находить на. —**come what may,** будь, что будет. —**how come?,** *see* **how.**
comedian *n.* комик.
comedy *n.* комедия.
comely *adj.* хорошенький; миловидный.
comet *n.* комета.
comfort *v.t.* утешать. —*n.* **1,** (solace) утешение. **2,** (ease) комфорт; уют. **3,** *pl.* (conveniences) удобства.
comfortable *adj.* **1,** (providing comfort) удобный; комфортабельный. **2,** (in a state of comfort; at ease) *rendered by* удобно: *are you comfortable?,* вам удобно? **3,** (fairly well-to-do) безбедный. —**comfortably,** *adv.* удобно. *Live comfortably,* жить безбедно *or* в достатке.
comforter *n.* **1,** (one who comforts) утешитель. **2,** (quilted bedcover) стёганое одеяло.
comforting *adj.* утешительный.
comic *adj.* комический; шуточный. —*n.* **1,** (entertainer) комик. **2,** *pl.* (cartoon strips) комиксы. —**comic opera,** комическая опера.
comical *adj.* комичный; комический; смешной.
coming *n.* **1,** (arrival) приход; приезд. *The Second Coming,* второе пришествие. **2,** (advent, as of a season) наступление. —*adj.* следующий; будущий; наступающий.
Comintern *n.* Коминтерн.
comma *n.* запятая.
command *v.t.* **1,** (order) приказывать. **2,** *mil.* (be in command of) командовать. **3,** (inspire, as respect) внушать. **4,** (bring, as a high price) идти; продаваться (по высокой цене). **5,** (afford, as a view): *the room commands a beautiful view of the ocean,* из комнаты открывается прекрасный вид на океан. —*n.* **1,** (an order) приказ; команда. **2,** (authority to command) командование: *under the command of,* под командованием (+ *gen.*). *Be in command of,* командовать (+ *instr.*). **3,** (mastery): *have an excellent command of English,* отлично владеть английским языком. —*adj.* командный: *command post,* командный пункт.
commandant *n.* комендант.
commandeer *v.t.* реквизировать.
commander *n.* **1,** *mil.* командир; командующий. **2,** *naval* капитан второго ранга. —**commander in chief,** главнокомандующий.
commanding *adj.* **1,** (in command): *commanding officer,* командующий; командир. **2,** (authoritative) властный. **3,** (high up; overlooking) господствующий; доминирующий. *Commanding heights,* командная высота.
commandment *n.* заповедь.
commando *n.* десантник.
commemorate *v.t.* праздновать; ознаменовать. —**commemoration,** *n.* празднование; ознаменование.
commemorative *adj.* памятный; мемориальный. *Commemorative stamp,* юбилейная *or* памятная марка.
commence *v.t.* начинать. —*v.i.* начинаться.
commencement *n.* **1,** (beginning) начало. **2,** (graduation exercises) (выпускной) акт.
commend *v.t.* **1,** (praise) хвалить. **2,** (recommend) рекомендовать.
commendable *adj.* похвальный.
commendation *n.* **1,** (praise) похвала. **2,** (award; citation) объявление благодарности.
commensurable *adj.* соизмеримый.
commensurate *adj.* соразмерный.
comment *n.* **1,** (note of explanation) примечание. **2,** (remark) замечание. —*v.i.* делать замечание. *Comment on something,* комментировать что-нибудь. —**no comment,** никаких комментариев.
commentary *n.* комментарий.
commentator *n.* обозреватель; комментатор.
commerce *n.* торговля; коммерция.
commercial *adj.* торговый; коммерческий. —*n.* реклама.
commingle *v.t.* смешивать. —*v.i.* смешиваться.
commiserate *v.i.* [*usu.* **commiserate with**] соболезновать (+ *dat.*). —**commiseration,** *n.* соболезнование.
commissar *n.* комиссар.
commissariat *n.* **1,** *U.S.S.R.* (ministry) комиссариат. **2,** *mil.* интендантство.
commissary *n.* военный магазин.
commission *n.* **1,** (specially appointed body) комиссия. **2,** (fee) комиссионные. **3,** (authorization to buy or sell) комиссия. **4,** (perpetration, as of a crime) совершение. **5,** *mil.* офицерское звание. —*v.t.* поручать; назначать; уполномочивать. —**out of commission,** в неисправности. *Put out of commission,* выводить из строя; приводить в негодность.
commissioned officer офицер.
commissioner *n.* комиссар.
commit *v.t.* **1,** (perpetrate) совершать: *commit a crime,* совершать преступление. *Commit an error,* допустить ошибку. *Commit perjury,* лжесвидетельствовать. *Commit adultery,* совершать прелюбодеяние. **2,** (obligate) обязывать. **3,** (consign, as to a mental institution) помещать. **4,** (give over) предавать: *commit to the flames,* предавать огню. —**commit oneself, 1,** (pledge oneself) обязываться. **2,** (take a firm position) связывать себя словом. —**commit suicide,** покончить жизнь самоубийством; покончить с собой. —**commit to battle,** вводить в бой. —**commit to memory,** заучивать.
commitment *n.* **1,** (confinement, as to an institution) помещение. **2,** (pledge; obligation) обязательство.
committee *n.* комитет; комиссия.
commode *n.* **1,** (chest of drawers) комод. **2,** (movable washstand) умывальник. **3,** (seat over a chamber pot) стульчак.
commodious *adj.* вместительный; просторный.
commodity *n.* товар; продукт; предмет потребления. —**commodity exchange,** товарная биржа.
common *adj.* **1,** (general; joint; public) общий. *In common use,* употребительный. *It is common knowledge that...,* общеизвестно, что... **2,** (widespread) распространённый. **3,** (of the masses; ordinary) простой; обыкновенный; рядовой. **4,** (vulgar; coarse) пошлый. —**have much in common,** иметь много общего. —**have nothing in common,** не иметь ничего общего.

commonality *n.* óбщность.
common denominator óбщий знаменáтель.
commoner *n.* человéк из нарóда; простóй человéк.
common law обы́чное прáво. —**common-law marriage,** факти́ческий брак. —**common-law wife,** граждáнская женá.
commonly *adv.* обы́чно.
Common Market Óбщий ры́нок.
common noun и́мя нарицáтельное.
commonplace *adj.* банáльный; изби́тый. —*n.* банáльность; óбщее мéсто.
common sense здрáвый смысл.
common stock обыкновéнные áкции.
commonwealth *n.* содрýжество: *the British Commonwealth,* Британское содрýжество.
commotion *n.* суматóха; переполóх.
communal *adj.* общи́нный. *Communal apartment,* коммунáльная кварти́ра.
commune *n.* óбщина; коммýна.
communicable *adj.* зарáзный: *communicable disease,* зарáзная болéзнь.
communicate *v.i.* **1,** (express oneself) объясня́ться. **2,** *fol. by* **with** (get in touch with) сообщáться (с); свя́зываться (с); снóситься (с). —*v.t.* сообщáть; передавáть.
communication *n.* **1,** *often pl.* (act or means of communicating) связь; сообщéние: *telephone communications,* телефóнная связь; телефóнное сообщéние. *Ministry of Communications,* Министéрство свя́зи. *Communications officer, mil.* офицéр свя́зи. **2,** *often pl.* (transportation routes) сообщéние; пути́ сообщéния; *mil.* коммуникáции. *Railway communications,* железнодорóжное сообщéние. **3,** (message) сообщéние: *an urgent communication,* срóчное сообщéние. —**communications satellite,** спýтник свя́зи.
communicative *adj.* откровéнный; разговóрчивый.
communion *n.* **1,** (communication; association) общéние. **2,** *cap.* (Eucharist) причáстие.
communiqué *n.* коммюникé.
communism *n.* коммуни́зм.
communist *n.* коммуни́ст. —*adj.* коммунисти́ческий: *communist party,* коммунисти́ческая пáртия.
community *n.* **1,** (neighborhood) райóн. **2,** (group of people with common ties) óбщина; колóния. **3,** (identity; likeness) óбщность. —**community property,** óбщее имýщество супрýгов.
commutation *n.* смягчéние (наказáния *or* приговóра). —**commutation ticket,** сезóнный билéт.
commute *v.t.* смягчáть (наказáние *or* приговóр). —*v.i.* éздить (ежеднéвно). —**commuter,** *n.* ежеднéвный пассажи́р.
compact *adj.* плóтный; компáктный; сжáтый. —*n.* **1,** (cosmetics container) пýдреница. **2,** (covenant) соглашéние; договóр; конвéнция.
companion *n.* **1,** (comrade) товáрищ. **2,** (paid attendant) компаньóнка. **3,** (other of a pair) пáра.
companionable *adj.* компанéйский.
companionship *n.* компáния.
company *n.* **1,** (business firm) компáния. **2,** (companionship; association) компáния; óбщество: *in the company of,* в óбществе (+ *gen.*). *Male company,* мужскóе óбщество. *Keep company with,* водить компáнию с; води́ться с. *Keep someone company,* составля́ть компáнию (+ *dat.*). *Part company,* расходи́ться. **3,** (visitors; guests) гóсти. **4,** (troupe) трýппа: *touring company,* гастрóльная трýппа. **5,** *mil.* рóта.
comparable *adj.* сравни́мый.
comparative *adj.* сравни́тельный. —**comparatively,** *adv.* сравни́тельно.
compare *v.t.* срáвнивать. *Compared to,* по сравнéнию с. —*v.i.* [*usu.* **compare to** or **with**] сравни́ться (с). —*n.,* *in* **beyond compare,** вне сравнéния. —**compare notes,** обмéниваться впечатлéниями.
comparison *n.* сравнéние. *There is no comparison between them,* их нельзя́ срáвнивать.
compartment *n.* **1,** (space; section) отделéние. **2,** (on a train) купé.
compass *n.* **1,** (instrument for determining direction) кóмпас. *Surveyor's compass,* буссóль. **2,** *often pl.* (instrument for describing circles) ци́ркуль. —**compass point,** странá свéта.
compassion *n.* сострадáние. —**compassionate,** *adj.* сострадáтельный.
compatible *adj.* совмести́мый. —**compatibility,** *n.* совмести́мость.
compatriot *n.* соотéчественник; земля́к.
compel *v.t.* заставля́ть; принуждáть; вынуждáть.
compelling *adj.* **1,** (convincing) убеди́тельный: *compelling evidence,* убеди́тельное доказáтельство. **2,** (holding one's attention) захвáтывающий.
compendium *n.* конспéкт; компéндиум.
compensate *v.t.* **1,** (recompense; remunerate) вознаграждáть. **2,** (indemnify) возмещáть: *compensate someone for damages,* возмещáть комý-нибудь убы́тки. —*v.i.* [*usu.* **compensate for**] (make up for; offset) компенси́ровать.
compensation *n.* **1,** (restitution) компенсáция; возмещéние: *compensation for damages,* компенсáция/возмещéние убы́тков. **2,** (payment for services) вознаграждéние.
compensatory *adj.* компенсациóнный. —**compensatory leave,** отгýл.
compete *v.i.* состязáться; соревновáться.
competence *n.* **1,** (ability) спосóбность; компетéнтность. **2,** (jurisdiction) компетéнция.
competent *adj.* **1,** (qualified; capable) компетéнтный. **2,** (legally qualified) правомóчный. **3,** (responsible for one's actions) дееспосóбный.
competition *n.* **1,** (contest) состязáние; соревновáние; кóнкурс. **2,** (business rivalry) конкурéнция.
competitive *adj.* **1,** (involving competition, as of an examination) кóнкурсный. **2,** (able to compete) конкурентоспосóбный. *Competitive prices,* конкурéнтоспосóбные цéны.
competitor *n.* конкурéнт.
compilation *n.* **1,** (act of compiling) собирáние; составлéние; компиля́ция. **2,** (something compiled) компиля́ция.
compile *v.t.* **1,** (gather) собирáть. **2,** (make up; write, as a list or dictionary) составля́ть.
compiler *n.* состави́тель; компиля́тор.
complacent *adj.* самодовóльный. —**complacency,** *n.* самодовóльство.
complain *v.i.* жáловаться. *Complain about the weather,* жáловаться на погóду. *Complain of a headache,* жáловаться на головнýю боль. *I can't complain,* я не могý пожáловаться.

complaint *n.* **1,** (grievance) жáлоба. **2,** (ailment) недомогáние.
complaisant *adj.* услýжливый; любéзный.
complement *n.* **1,** (that which completes) дополнéние. **2,** (full quota) комплéкт. **3,** *gram.* дополнéние. —*v.t.* дополня́ть.
complementary *adj.* дополня́ющий друг дрýга. *Complementary colors,* дополни́тельные цветá.
complete *adj.* **1,** (entire) пóлный: *complete set,* пóлный набóр. **2,** (finished) закóнченный: *the job is complete,* рабóта закóнчена. **3,** (absolute) пóлный: *complete freedom,* пóлная свобóда. —*v.t.* **1,** (finish) закáнчивать; завершáть; довершáть. **2,** (make whole) укомплектовáть. *To complete the picture,* для полноты́ карти́ны. —**completely,** *adv.* совершéнно; вполнé; пóлностью; целикóм. —**completeness,** *n.* полнотá; закóнченность.
completion *n.* окончáние; завершéние.
complex *adj.* слóжный: *a complex matter,* слóжное дéло. —*n.* **1,** (large system or unit) кóмплекс. **2,** *psychoanalysis* кóмплекс; мáния: *inferiority complex,* кóмплекс неполноцéнности; *persecution complex,* мáния преслéдования. —**complex sentence,** сложноподчинённое предложéние.
complexion *n.* **1,** (skin color) цвет лицá: *dark complexion,* смýглый цвет лицá. **2,** *fig.* (aspect) свет; окрáска. *Put a different complexion on something,* придавáть чемý-нибудь другýю окрáску.
complexity *n.* слóжность.
compliance *n.* **1,** (act of complying) подчинéние: *compliance with the law,* подчинéние закóну. **2,** (acquiescence) соглáсие. **3,** (disposition to comply) устýпчивость. —**in compliance with,** в соотвéтствии с.
compliant *adj.* устýпчивый.
complicate *v.t.* усложня́ть; осложня́ть. —**complicated,** *adj.* слóжный.
complication *n.* **1,** (something that complicates) осложнéние; усложнéние. **2,** *med.* осложнéние.
complicity *n.* соучáстие.
compliment *n.* **1,** (expression of praise) комплимéнт. **2,** *pl.* (greetings) привéт; поклóн. —*v.t.* похвали́ть; сдéлать комплимéнт (+ *dat.*).
complimentary *adj.* **1,** (containing a compliment) лéстный. **2,** (given free) бесплáтный; даровóй. *Complimentary ticket,* контрамáрка.
comply *v.i.* подчиня́ться. *Comply with the rules,* подчиня́ться прáвилам. *Comply with a request,* удовлетвори́ть *or* испóлнить прóсьбу.
component *n.* составнáя часть; детáль; компонéнт. —*adj.* составнóй: *component part,* составнáя часть.
comport *v.t.* [*usu.* **comport oneself**] вести́ себя́; держáть себя́.
comportment *n.* поведéние; манéра держáть себя́.
compose *v.t.* **1,** (write; draft) составля́ть. **2,** (create, as a poem or work of music) сочиня́ть. **3,** (reconcile, as differences) улáживать. **4,** *printing* (set in type) набирáть. —**be composed of,** состоя́ть из. —**compose oneself,** овладéть собóй.
composed *adj.* спокóйный; хладнокрóвный.
composer *n.* компози́тор.
composite *adj.* составнóй; свóдный; кóмплексный. —*n.* смесь; состáв; соединéние.
composition *n.* **1,** (musical or literary work; essay for school) сочинéние. **2,** (make-up; structure) состáв. **3,** (artistic arrangement, as of a photograph) компози́ция. **4,** *printing* набóр.
compositor *n.* набóрщик.
compost *n.* компóст.
composure *n.* спокóйствие; самообладáние; хладнокрóвие. *Regain one's composure,* овладéть собóй.
compote *n.* компóт.
compound *n.* **1,** *chem.* соединéние. **2,** (enclosed area) огорóженное мéсто. —*adj.* составнóй; слóжный. —*v.t.* **1,** (mix; combine) смéшивать; соединя́ть. **2,** (add to; intensify) усугубля́ть; осложня́ть. —**compound fracture,** слóжный перелóм. —**compound interest,** слóжные процéнты. —**compound sentence,** сложносочинённое предложéние.
comprehend *v.t.* **1,** (understand) понимáть; постигáть. **2,** (include) охвáтывать.
comprehensible *adj.* поня́тный; постижи́мый; вразуми́тельный.
comprehension *n.* понимáние.
comprehensive *adj.* всесторóнний; развёрнутый; всеобъéмлющий.
compress *v.t.* сжимáть. —*n.* компрéсс: *hot compress,* согревáющий компрéсс. —**compressed air,** сжáтый вóздух.
compression *n.* сжáтие. —**compression chamber,** кáмера сжáтия. —**compression ratio,** стéпень сжáтия.
compressor *n.* компрéссор.
comprise *v.t.* **1,** (consist of) состоя́ть из; заключáть в себé. **2,** (constitute) составля́ть.
compromise *n.* компроми́сс. —*adj.* компроми́ссный: *compromise decision,* компроми́ссное решéние. —*v.i.* идти́ на компроми́сс. —*v.t.* **1,** (adjust by concessions) улáживать. **2,** (place in a compromising position) компрометúровать. —**compromiser,** *n.* соглашáтель.
comptroller *n.* контролёр.
compulsion *n.* принуждéние.
compulsive *adj.* застарéлый; неисправи́мый. *Compulsive desire,* неудержи́мое желáние.
compulsory *adj.* обязáтельный.
compunction *n.* угрызéния сóвести. *Without compunction,* без зазрéния сóвести.
computation *n.* вычислéние; подсчёт.
compute *v.t.* вычисля́ть; подсчи́тывать.
computer *n.* вычисли́тельная маши́на; вычисли́тель; компью́тер.
comrade *n.* товáрищ. —**comrade in arms,** товáрищ по орýжию; сорáтник.
comradeship *n.* товáрищество.
con *n., in* **the pros and cons,** дóводы за и прóтив.
concave *adj.* вóгнутый.
concavity *n.* **1,** (state of being concave) вóгнутость. **2,** (concave area on a surface) впáдина.
conceal *v.t.* скрывáть; утáивать. —**concealment,** *n.* сокры́тие; скры́тие.
concede *v.t.* допускáть: *I'll concede that...,* допускáю, что... —*v.i.* признáть своё поражéние (на вы́борах).
conceit *n.* самомнéние. —**conceited,** *adj.* большóго мнéния о себé; самовлюблённый.

conceivable *adj.* мы́слимый; возмо́жный; допусти́мый. *It is quite conceivable that...,* вполне́ возмо́жно/допусти́мо, что... *Every conceivable precaution,* всевозмо́жные ме́ры предосторо́жности.

conceivably *adv.* возмо́жно; допусти́мо: *there might conceivably be others,* вполне́ возмо́жно/допусти́мо, что существу́ют и други́е.

conceive *v.t.* **1,** (form in the mind) заду́мывать. **2,** (become pregnant with) зача́ть. —*v.i.* **1,** *fol. by* **of** (form a mental image of) представля́ть себе́. **2,** (become pregnant) забере́менеть.

concentrate *v.t.* сосредото́чивать; концентри́ровать. —*v.i.* сосредото́чиваться; концентри́роваться. —*n.* концентра́т.

concentration *n.* **1,** (act of concentrating) сосредото́чение; концентра́ция. **2,** (complete attention) сосредото́ченность. —**concentration camp,** концентрацио́нный ла́герь; концла́герь.

concentric *adj.* концентри́ческий.

concept *n.* поня́тие.

conception *n.* **1,** (mental picture; idea) поня́тие; представле́ние; конце́пция. **2,** (conceiving in the womb) зача́тие.

concern *n.* **1,** (matter of interest) де́ло. *That is not my concern; that is no concern of mine,* э́то не моё де́ло; э́то меня́ не каса́ется. **2,** (solicitude) забо́та; уча́стие: *show concern,* проявля́ть забо́ту/уча́стие. **3,** (anxiety) беспоко́йство; озабо́ченность. *A matter of great concern,* де́ло большо́й ва́жности. **4,** (business enterprise) предприя́тие; конце́рн. —*v.t.* **1,** (relate to; affect) каса́ться. *As far as I am concerned,* что каса́ется меня́. **2,** (trouble; worry) беспоко́ить; трево́жить. —**concern oneself, 1,** (worry) беспоко́иться. **2,** *fol. by* **with** (busy oneself) занима́ться (+ *instr.*).

concerned *adj.* **1,** (interested; involved) заинтересо́ванный: *the parties concerned,* заинтересо́ванные сто́роны. **2,** (uneasy; troubled) озабо́ченный; обеспоко́енный.

concerning *prep.* относи́тельно; каса́ющийся; по по́воду.

concert *n.* конце́рт. —*adj.* конце́ртный: *concert hall,* конце́ртный зал. —**in concert,** совме́стно; сообща́; дру́жно; заодно́.

concerted *adj.* согласо́ванный; дру́жный.

concertina *n.* концерти́но.

concertmaster *n.* концертме́йстер.

concerto *n.* конце́рт.

concession *n.* **1,** (something conceded) усту́пка: *make concessions,* идти́ на усту́пки. **2,** (commercial privilege) конце́ссия.

concessionaire *n.* концессионе́р.

concessive *adj., gram.* уступи́тельный.

conciliate *v.t.* мири́ть; примиря́ть. —**conciliation,** *n.* примире́ние. —**conciliator,** *n.* примири́тель. —**conciliatory,** *adj.* примири́тельный.

concise *adj.* сжа́тый; кра́ткий. —**conciseness,** *n.* сжа́тость; кра́ткость.

conclave *n.* **1,** (meeting) совеща́ние. **2,** *relig.* конкла́в.

conclude *v.t.* заключа́ть: *conclude a deal,* заключи́ть сде́лку. *Conclude one's speech with a toast,* заключи́ть речь то́стом. *This leads me to conclude that...,* из э́того я заключа́ю, что... —*v.i.* заключа́ться. —**concluding,** *adj.* заключи́тельный.

conclusion *n.* **1,** (close; closing part) заключе́ние. **2,** (final judgment or decision) заключе́ние; вы́вод: *come to a conclusion,* приходи́ть к заключе́нию/вы́воду. —**in conclusion,** в заключе́ние.

conclusive *adj.* реша́ющий. *Conclusive evidence,* неопровержи́мые доказа́тельства. —**conclusively,** *adv.* неопровержи́мо: *prove conclusively,* неопровержи́мо доказа́ть.

concoct *v.t.* **1,** (cook) стря́пать. **2,** (devise) приду́мывать. **3,** (make up) выду́мывать. —**concoction,** *n.* стряпня́.

concomitant *adj.* сопу́тствующий.

concord *n.* согла́сие.

concordat *n.* конкорда́т.

concourse *n.* **1.** (large open space, as in a station) зал. **2,** (thoroughfare) проспе́кт.

concrete *n.* бето́н. —*adj.* **1,** (made of concrete) бето́нный. **2,** (real; specific) конкре́тный. —**concrete number,** имено́ванное число́.

concubine *n.* нало́жница.

concur *v.i.* **1,** (agree) быть согла́сным. **2,** (occur simultaneously) совпада́ть.

concurrence *n.* **1,** (agreement) согла́сие. **2,** (coincidence) совпаде́ние.

concurrent *adj.* совпада́ющий; одновре́менный. —**concurrently,** *adv.* одновре́менно.

concussion *n.* сотрясе́ние.

condemn *v.t.* **1,** (denounce) осужда́ть. **2,** (sentence) осужда́ть; пригова́ривать: *condemn to death,* осужда́ть на смерть; пригова́ривать к сме́ртной ка́зни. **3,** (doom to an unhappy fate) осужда́ть; обрека́ть. **4,** (declare unfit for use) признава́ть него́дным (для жилья́). —**condemnation,** *n.* осужде́ние.

condensation *n.* **1,** (abridgment) сокраще́ние. **2,** (that which is abridged) сокращённое изда́ние. **3,** (reduction of a gas to liquid) конденса́ция.

condense *v.t.* **1,** (change from gas to liquid) конденси́ровать. **2,** (make thicker or more concentrated) сгуща́ть: *condensed milk,* сгущённое молоко́. **3,** (abridge) сокраща́ть; сжима́ть.

condenser *n.* конденса́тор.

condescend *v.i.* снисходи́ть. —**condescending,** *adj.* снисходи́тельный. —**condescension,** *n.* снисхожде́ние; снисходи́тельность.

condiment *n.* припра́ва.

condition *n.* **1,** (state) состоя́ние: *in good condition,* в хоро́шем состоя́нии. **2,** (provision; stipulation) усло́вие. **3,** *pl.* (circumstances) усло́вия: *working conditions,* усло́вия труда́. *Under such conditions,* при таки́х усло́виях. **4,** (state of fitness) фо́рма: *out of condition,* не в фо́рме. **5,** (ailment) боле́знь: *a heart condition,* боле́знь се́рдца. —*v.t.* **1,** (limit by a condition) обусло́вливать. **2,** (train) приуча́ть. —**on condition that...,** при усло́вии, что...

conditional *adj.* усло́вный. —**conditional mood,** усло́вное наклоне́ние.

conditionally *adv.* усло́вно.

conditioned reflex усло́вный рефле́кс.

condole *v.i.* [*usu.* **condole with**] соболе́зновать (+ *dat.*). —**condolence,** *n.* соболе́знование.

condominium *n.* кондоми́ниум.

condone *v.t.* проща́ть.

condor *n.* ко́ндор.

conducive *adj. Be conducive to,* располага́ть к: *the atmosphere is conducive to work,* атмосфе́ра располага́ет к рабо́те.

conduct *v.t.* **1,** (guide; lead) водить; проводить; сопровождать. **2,** (carry out; perform; hold) вести; проводить; производить. *Conduct (i.e. hold) a meeting,* проводить собрание. *Conduct negotiations,* вести переговоры. *Conduct an experiment,* проводить *or* производить опыт. **3,** (direct; run) вести: *conduct (i.e. run) a meeting,* вести собрание; *conduct a lesson,* вести урок. **4,** (direct, as an orchestra) дирижировать. **5,** (convey, as electricity) проводить. —*n.* **1,** (behavior) поведение. **2,** (management) ведение. —**conduct oneself,** вести себя; держать себя.

conductivity *n.* проводимость.

conductor *n.* **1,** (leader; guide) проводник. *Tour conductor,* экскурсовод. **2,** (on a train) проводник; кондуктор; (on a bus or streetcar) кондуктор. **3,** (of an orchestra) дирижёр. **4,** *physics* проводник.

conduit *n.* трубопровод.

cone *n.* **1,** (geometric figure) конус. **2,** (fruit, as of the pine) шишка.

confection *n.* конфета. —**confectioner,** *n.* кондитер. —**confectionery,** *n.* кондитерская.

confederacy *n.* конфедерация.

confederate *n.* сообщник; соучастник. —*adj.* конфедеративный. —*v.i.* объединяться в союз. —**confederation,** *n.* конфедерация; федерация.

confer *v.t.* (award) присваивать; присуждать; удостаивать. —*v.i.* [*usu.* **confer with**] совещаться (с).

conferee *n.* участник конференции.

conference *n.* совещание; конференция. *Conference hall,* конференц-зал. *Conference table,* стол переговоров.

confess *v.t.* **1,** (admit) признавать: *confess one's error,* признавать свою ошибку. **2,** (acknowledge; concede) признаваться: *I must confess I never heard of him,* признаюсь, о нём не слышал. —*v.i.* **1,** (admit one's guilt) сознаваться. **2,** *fol. by* **to** (admit) признаваться в; сознаваться в. **3,** *relig.* исповедоваться.

confession *n.* **1,** (admission of guilt) признание. **2,** *relig.* исповедь. —**confessional,** *n.* исповедальня.

confessor *n.* **1,** (priest who hears confessions) духовник; исповедник. **2,** (person who confesses) исповедник.

confetti *n.* конфетти.

confidant *n.* поверенный.

confide *v.t.* доверять; вверять; поверять. —*v.i.* [*usu.* **confide in**] делиться с: *she has no one she can confide in,* ей не с кем поделиться.

confidence *n.* **1,** (trust) доверие. *Vote of confidence,* вотум доверия. **2,** (assurance; certainty) уверенность. **3,** (self-assurance) самоуверенность. —**in confidence,** по секрету. —**take into one's confidence,** доверять свои тайны (+ *dat.*).

confident *adj.* **1,** (sure) уверенный: *confident of victory,* уверен в победе. **2,** (self-assured) самоуверенный.

confidential *adj.* секретный; конфиденциальный.

confidentially *adv.* **1,** (in confidence) конфиденциально; по секрету. **2,** *as an introductory word* между нами.

configuration *n.* конфигурация; очертание.

confine *v.t.* **1,** (limit; restrict) ограничивать. *Confine oneself to,* ограничиваться (+ *instr.*). **2,** (shut in) заключать. *Confined to bed,* прикованный к постели.

confinement *n.* **1,** (imprisonment) заключение: *solitary confinement,* одиночное заключение. **2,** (lying-in) роды.

confines *n.pl.* пределы: *within the confines of,* в пределах (+ *gen.*).

confirm *v.t.* **1,** (corroborate) подтверждать. **2,** (approve; ratify) утверждать. **3,** *relig.* конфирмовать.

confirmation *n.* **1,** (corroboration) подтверждение. **2,** (approval) утверждение. **3,** *relig.* конфирмация.

confirmed *adj.* **1,** (deeply committed) убеждённый. **2,** (inveterate) закоренелый: *confirmed bachelor,* закоренелый холостяк.

confiscate *v.t.* конфисковать. —**confiscation,** *n.* конфискация.

conflagration *n.* пожар.

conflict *n.* **1,** (battle; war) конфликт. **2,** *fig.* (clash) столкновение. —*v.i.* противоречить друг другу. *Conflict with,* противоречить (+ *dat.*). —**conflicting,** *adj.* противоречивый.

confluence *n.* слияние; впадение.

conform *v.i.* [*usu.* **conform to**] сообразоваться с; согласоваться с; соответствовать (+ *dat.*). *Make something conform to something,* сообразовать что-нибудь с чем-нибудь.

conformism *n.* конформизм.

conformity *n.* соответствие; сообразность. *In conformity with,* сообразно с. *Also,* **conformance.**

confound *v.t.* **1,** (bewilder) озадачивать. **2,** (mistake for another) путать.

confounded *adj.* **1,** (taken aback) озадаченный. **2,** *colloq.* (damned) проклятый.

confront *v.t.* **1,** (face) стоять лицом к; стоять перед. *The task confronting us,* задача, стоящая перед нами. **2,** (meet boldly) смотреть (чему-нибудь) в лицо.

confrontation *n.* конфронтация.

confuse *v.t.* **1,** (mix up; throw off) сбивать с толку; путать. **2,** (mistake) спутывать; смешивать.

confused *adj.* **1,** (perplexed) недоуменный: *confused look,* недоуменный взгляд. *Become confused,* сбиться с толку; спутаться; запутаться. **2,** (muddled) спутанный: *confused thoughts,* спутанные мысли.

confusing *adj.* сбивчивый.

confusion *n.* смятение; замешательство; растерянность.

congeal *v.t.* замораживать. —*v.i.* **1,** (harden) застывать. **2,** (coagulate) свёртываться.

congenial *adj.* **1,** (suited to each other) дружный: *congenial couple,* дружная пара. *Congenial tastes,* сходные вкусы. **2,** (friendly; pleasant) дружеский; тёплый: *congenial atmosphere,* дружеская/тёплая атмосфера. *Congenial host,* приветливый хозяин.

congeniality *n.* **1,** (likeness) сродство. **2,** (affability) дружелюбие.

congenital *adj.* врождённый.

congest *v.t.* переполнять. —**congested,** *adj.* тесный; переполненный; скученный.

congestion *n.* **1,** (overcrowding) скученность; переполнение. **2,** (heavy traffic) затор; пробка. **3,** *med.* застой крови.

conglomerate *n.* конгломерат. —**conglomeration,** *n.* нагромождение; конгломерат.

congratulate *v.t.* поздравлять: *congratulate someone on his victory,* поздравлять кого-нибудь с победой.

congratulation *n.* поздравление. *Congratula-*

tions!, поздравля́ю вас! *Hearty congratulations,* серде́чные поздравле́ния.

congratulatory *adj.* поздрави́тельный.

congregate *v.i.* собира́ться; сходи́ться.

congregation *n.* **1,** (assemblage) собра́ние. **2,** *relig.* прихо́д.

congress *n.* **1,** (assembly) съезд; конгре́сс. **2,** *cap.* (U.S. legislative body) конгре́сс. —**Congress of Vienna,** Ве́нский конгре́сс.

congressional *adj.* относя́щийся к конгре́ссу. *Congressional committee,* коми́ссия конгре́сса.

congressman *n.* конгрессме́н.

congruent *adj., math.* конгруэ́нтный. —**congruence,** *n., math.* конгруэ́нция.

conic *adj.* кони́ческий. *Also,* **conical.**

conifer *n.* хво́йное де́рево. —**coniferous,** *adj.* хво́йный.

conjectural *adj.* предположи́тельный; гада́тельный.

conjecture *n.* дога́дка; предположе́ние; до́мысел. *That is a matter of pure conjecture,* об э́том мо́жно то́лько гада́ть. —*v.t. & i.* гада́ть; стро́ить дога́дки; предполага́ть.

conjugal *adj.* супру́жеский; бра́чный. *Conjugal bed,* бра́чное ло́же.

conjugate *v.t.* спряга́ть. —**conjugation,** *n.* спряже́ние.

conjunction *n.* **1,** (combination) сочета́ние. **2,** (simultaneous occurrence) совпаде́ние. **3,** (part of speech) сою́з. —**in conjunction with,** в связи́ с; в сочета́нии с.

conjunctivitis *n.* конъюнктиви́т.

conjure *v.t.* **1,** (summon by oath or magic spell) заклина́ть. **2,** *fol. by* **up** (evoke) воскреша́ть в па́мяти. —*v.i.* (practice magic) колдова́ть.

conjurer *n.* **1,** (sorcerer) колду́н; чароде́й. **2,** (magician) волше́бник; фо́кусник.

conk *v.t., slang* (bash) тра́хнуть. —*v.i.* [*usu.* **conk out**] *slang* отказа́ться рабо́тать; загло́хнуть.

connect *v.t.* **1,** (link; join) соединя́ть; свя́зывать. **2,** (plug in) включа́ть. —*v.i.* соединя́ться; сообща́ться.

connecting *adj.* соедини́тельный. *Connecting rooms,* проходны́е ко́мнаты. —**connecting rod,** шату́н; соедини́тельная тя́га.

connection *also,* **connexion** *n.* **1,** (act of connecting) соедине́ние. **2,** (link) связь. **3,** (context) отноше́ние; связь: *in this connection,* в э́том отноше́нии; в э́той связи́. *In connection with,* в связи́ с. **4,** (change of planes, trains, etc.) переса́дка. **5,** (on the telephone) слы́шимость: *we have a bad connection,* слы́шимость плоха́я. **6,** *pl.* (influential associates) свя́зи.

connective *adj.* соедини́тельный. —**connective tissue,** соедини́тельная ткань.

connexion *n.* = **connection.**

conning tower боева́я ру́бка.

connivance *n.* попусти́тельство.

connive *v.i.* **1,** *fol. by* **at** (tolerate) попусти́тельствовать (+ *dat.*). **2,** *fol. by* **with** (conspire with) интригова́ть (с).

connoisseur *n.* знато́к; цени́тель.

connotation *n.* дополни́тельное значе́ние; отте́нок.

connote *v.t.* означа́ть; говори́ть о; подразумева́ть.

connubial *adj.* супру́жеский; бра́чный.

conquer *v.t.* **1,** (defeat; vanquish) завоёвывать; побежда́ть; покоря́ть. **2,** *fig.* (overcome) преодолева́ть; побежда́ть. —**conqueror,** *n.* завоева́тель.

conquest *n.* **1,** (act of conquering) завоева́ние; покоре́ние. **2,** *pl.* (territory conquered) завоева́ния.

consanguineous *adj.* единокро́вный; ро́дственный. —**consanguinity,** *n.* родство́.

conscience *n.* со́весть. *Have on one's conscience,* име́ть на свое́й со́вести. —**in all conscience,** по со́вести говоря́.

conscientious *adj.* **1,** (scrupulous; honest) со́вестливый. **2,** (careful; painstaking) добросо́вестный. —**conscientiousness,** *n.* добросо́вестность.

conscious *adj.* **1,** (capable of thought) созна́тельный: *man is a conscious being,* челове́к – созна́тельное существо́. **2,** (mentally awake) в созна́нии: *be conscious,* быть в созна́нии. **3,** *fol. by* **of** (aware of) сознаю́щий: *be conscious of,* сознава́ть (что́-нибудь). **4,** (deliberate) созна́тельный. —**consciously,** *adv.* созна́тельно.

consciousness *n.* **1,** (state of being conscious) созна́ние: *lose consciousness,* потеря́ть созна́ние. *Regain consciousness,* приходи́ть в созна́ние; приходи́ть в себя́; очну́ться. **2,** (awareness) (само) созна́ние; созна́тельность: *class consciousness,* кла́ссовое (само)созна́ние; кла́ссовая созна́тельность.

conscript *n.* призывни́к. —*v.t.* призыва́ть. —**conscription,** *n.* во́инская пови́нность.

consecrate *v.t.* освяща́ть. —**consecration,** *n.* освяще́ние.

consecutive *adj.* после́довательный. *Four consecutive days,* четы́ре дня подря́д. —**consecutively,** *adv.* после́довательно.

consensus *n.* **1,** (agreement) согла́сие. **2,** (opinion of most) о́бщее мне́ние.

consent *v.i.* соглаша́ться. —*n.* согла́сие.

consequence *n.* **1,** (effect) после́дствие; сле́дствие. **2,** (importance) значе́ние: *of no consequence,* не име́ющий значе́ния.

consequent *adj.* вытека́ющий.

consequently *adv.* сле́довательно.

conservation *n.* **1,** (act of conserving) сохране́ние: *energy conservation,* сохране́ние эне́ргии. **2,** (protection of natural resources) охра́на приро́ды. —**conservationist,** *n.* сторо́нник охра́ны приро́ды.

conservatism *n.* консервати́зм.

conservative *adj.* **1,** (tending to oppose change) консервати́вный. **2,** (moderate; cautious) скро́мный: *conservative estimate,* скро́мный подсчёт. —*n.* консерва́тор.

conservatory *n.* **1,** (greenhouse) оранжере́я. **2,** (school of music) консервато́рия.

conserve *v.t.* сохраня́ть; бере́чь; сберега́ть.

consider *v.t.* **1,** (examine; take up) рассма́тривать. **2,** (think over) обду́мывать; сообража́ть. **3,** (look upon; regard) счита́ть; рассма́тривать. *I consider him my friend,* я его́ счита́ю свои́м дру́гом. *I consider it an honor,* счита́ю за честь. *I consider it madness,* я рассма́триваю э́то как безу́мие. **4,** (take into account) учи́тывать; счита́ться с; принима́ть во внима́ние. *All things considered,* принима́я всё во внима́ние. **5,** (show consideration for) счита́ться с. **6,** (believe; feel) счита́ть.

considerable *adj.* значи́тельный. —**considerably,** *adv.* значи́тельно.

considerate *adj.* внима́тельный; предупреди́тельный.

consideration *n.* **1,** (careful thought) рассмотре́ние. *The matter is under consideration,* де́ло сейча́с рассма́тривается. **2,** (factor to be considered) соображе́ние. **3,** (thoughtfulness of others) внима́ние. *Have no consideration for others,* не счита́ться с други́ми. **4,** (recompense) вознагражде́ние: *for a small consideration,* за небольшо́е вознагражде́ние. —**in consideration of, 1,** (in view of) принима́я во внима́ние; с учётом (+ *gen.*). **2,** (in return for) в благода́рность за. —**take into consideration,** принима́ть во внима́ние/в соображе́ние/к све́дению/в расчёт; учи́тывать.

considered *adj.* обду́манный; проду́манный.

considering *prep.* принима́я во внима́ние; учи́тывая; ввиду́.

consign *v.t.* **1,** (entrust to someone's care) поруча́ть. **2,** (relegate) предава́ть: *consign to oblivion,* предава́ть забве́нию. **3,** *comm.* (deliver for sale) отправля́ть.

consignment *n.* **1,** (delivery for sale) отпра́вка. **2,** (something consigned) па́ртия (това́ров); тра́нспорт.

consist *v.i.* [*usu.* **consist of**] **1,** (be made up of) состоя́ть из: *the book consists of ten chapters,* кни́га состои́т из десяти́ глав. **2,** (be; involve) состоя́ть в: *what will my work consist of?,* в чем бу́дет состоя́ть моя́ рабо́та?

consistency *n.* **1,** (adherence to pattern) после́довательность. **2,** (firmness) пло́тность; твёрдость; консисте́нция.

consistent *adj.* **1,** (adhering to a pattern) после́довательный. **2,** *fol. by* **with** (not contradicting) соотве́тствующий: *be consistent with,* соотве́тствовать (+ *dat.*). *Not be consistent with,* противоре́чить.

consistently *adv.* **1,** (without contradicting oneself) после́довательно. **2,** (without exception) всегда́.

consolation *n.* утеше́ние. —**consolation prize,** утеши́тельный приз.

console[1] (kun-**sol**) *v.t.* утеша́ть.

console[2] (**kan**-sol) *n.* **1,** (bracket) консо́ль. **2,** (cabinet) ко́рпус. **3,** (control panel) пульт.

consolidate *v.t.* **1,** (make secure) укрепля́ть; закрепля́ть; упро́чивать. **2,** (combine; merge) слива́ть; объединя́ть.

consolidation *n.* **1,** (making secure) укрепле́ние; закрепле́ние; упро́чение; консолида́ция. **2,** (combining; merging) слия́ние; объедине́ние.

consommé *n.* бульо́н.

consonance *n.* созву́чие; консона́нс.

consonant *n.* **1,** (sound) согла́сный звук. **2,** (letter) согла́сная бу́ква. —*adj.* **1,** (consonantal) согла́сный. **2,** (harmonious in sound) созву́чный. **3,** *fol. by* **with** (in keeping with) согла́сный (с). —**consonantal,** *adj.* согла́сный.

consort *n.* супру́г; супру́га. —*v.i.* [*usu.* **consort with**] обща́ться (с); води́ться (с).

consortium *n.* консо́рциум.

conspicuous *adj.* ви́дный; заме́тный; броса́ющийся в глаза́. *Be conspicuous by one's absence,* блиста́ть свои́м отсу́тствием.

conspiracy *n.* за́говор. —**conspirator,** *n.* загово́рщик; конспира́тор. —**conspiratorial,** *adj.* загово́рщический.

conspire *v.i.* (та́йно) сгова́риваться.

constable *n.* консте́бль.

constancy *n.* постоя́нство.

constant *adj.* постоя́нный. —*n.* постоя́нная величина́; конста́нта. —**constantly,** *adv.* постоя́нно.

constellation *n.* созве́здие.

consternation *n.* у́жас; замеша́тельство; расте́рянность.

constipate *v.t.* крепи́ть. *He is constipated,* его́ крепи́т. —**constipation,** *n.* запо́р.

constituency *n.* избира́тельный о́круг.

constituent *adj.* **1,** (component) составно́й. **2,** (authorized to draw up a constitution) учреди́тельный. —*n.* **1,** (constituent part) составна́я часть. **2,** (voter) избира́тель.

constitute *v.t.* **1,** (make up; form) составля́ть: *constitute a quorum,* составля́ть кво́рум. **2,** (be; represent) представля́ть собо́й: *constitute a violation of the law,* представля́ть собо́й наруше́ние зако́на.

constitution *n.* **1,** (charter) конститу́ция. **2,** (physical make-up) (тело)сложе́ние. *Iron constitution,* желе́зное здоро́вье.

constitutional *adj.* **1,** (of a constitution) конституцио́нный. *Constitutional law,* госуда́рственное пра́во. **2,** (inherent in one's make-up) органи́ческий. —*n.* (walk; exercise) моцио́н; прогу́лка для моцио́на.

constrain *v.t.* **1,** (force) принужда́ть; вынужда́ть. **2,** (inhibit) ско́вывать; стесня́ть.

constraint *n.* **1,** (something that holds back) стесне́ние. **2,** (lack of ease) ско́ванность; стесне́ние; принуждённость. **3,** (compulsion) принужде́ние.

constrict *v.t.* **1,** (make smaller or narrower) су́живать. **2,** (produce a tight feeling in) стесня́ть; сжима́ть; сда́вливать; сти́скивать.

constriction *n.* **1,** (act of constricting) суже́ние. **2,** (feeling of pressure or tightness) стесне́ние; сжа́тие. *I feel a constriction in my chest,* мне тесни́т грудь.

construct *v.t.* стро́ить; конструи́ровать. *Construct a triangle,* стро́ить треуго́льник. *Construct a sentence,* стро́ить предложе́ние.

construction *n.* **1,** (act of building) строи́тельство. *Be under construction,* стро́иться. **2,** (design) констру́кция. **3,** (interpretation) истолкова́ние. **4,** *gram.* констру́кция. —*adj.* строи́тельный: *construction site,* строи́тельная площа́дка.

constructive *adj.* конструкти́вный.

construe *v.t.* толкова́ть; истолко́вывать.

consul *n.* ко́нсул —**consular,** *adj.* ко́нсульский. —**consulate,** *n.* ко́нсульство.

consult *v.t.* **1,** (ask the advice of) сове́товаться с. **2,** (refer to, as a dictionary) справля́ться в; обраща́ться к.

consultant *n.* консульта́нт.

consultation *n.* **1,** (act of consulting) консульта́ция. **2,** (meeting between doctors) конси́лиум.

consultative *adj.* совеща́тельный; консультати́вный.

consulting *adj. Rendered by* -консульта́нт: *consulting engineer,* инжене́р-консульта́нт.

consume *v.t.* **1,** (use, as food, fuel, etc.) потребля́ть. **2,** (eat or drink up) съесть; вы́пить. **3,** (destroy, as by burning) пожира́ть. **4,** (use up, as time, money, etc.) поглощáть. **5,** *fol. by* **with** (fill with, as an emotion) пожирáть; глодáть. *He is consumed with envy,* егó глóжет зáвисть.

consumer *n.* потреби́тель. —**consumer goods,** товáры ширóкого потреблéния; ширпотрéб.

consummate *v.t.* завершáть; доводи́ть до концá. —*adj.* закóнченный: *a consummate artist,* закóнченный арти́ст. —**consummation,** *n.* завершéние.

consumption *n.* **1,** (using up) потреблéние. **2,** (disease) чахóтка. —**consumptive,** *adj.* чахóточный.

contact *n.* **1,** (touching) контáкт; соприкосновéние. **2,** (being in touch) контáкт; связь. *Be in contact with,* быть в контáкте с. *Come into contact with,* стáлкиваться с. **3,** *usu. pl.* (helpful acquaintances) свя́зи. —*v.t.* **1,** (touch) соприкасáться с. **2,** (get in touch with) свя́зываться с.

contact lens контáктная ли́нза.

contagion *n.* зарáза.

contagious *adj.* **1,** *med.* зарáзный. **2,** *fig.* (of a smile, laughter, etc.) заразúтельный.

contain *v.t.* **1,** (hold; include) содержáть: *meat contains protein,* мя́со содéржит белóк. *The proposal contains nothing new,* предложéние не содéржит ничегó нóвого. **2,** (restrain) сдéрживать. —**contain oneself,** сдéрживаться; выдéрживать.

container *n.* **1,** (receptacle) сосýд; вмести́лище. **2,** (for shipping goods) контéйнер. —*adj.* контéйнерный: *container ship,* контéйнерное сýдно.

contaminate *v.t.* загрязня́ть; заражáть. —**contamination,** *n.* загрязнéние; заражéние.

contemplate *v.t.* **1,** (gaze at) созерцáть. **2,** (consider) соображáть. **3,** (intend) замышля́ть. **4,** (expect) ожидáть. —*v.i.* размышля́ть.

contemplation *n.* созерцáние. *Be lost in contemplation of,* засмáтриваться на; загля́дываться на.

contemplative *adj.* созерцáтельный.

contemporary *adj.* совремéнный. —*n.* **1,** (person one's own age) свéрстник; ровéсник. **2,** (person living at the same time) совремéнник.

contempt *n.* презрéние. *Contempt of court,* оскорблéние судá. —**contemptible,** *adj.* презрéнный. —**contemptuous,** *adj.* прези́тельный.

contend *v.i.* **1,** (compete) состязáться. *Contend for,* оспáривать. **2,** *fol. by* **with** (cope with) справля́ться с. —*v.t.* (assert) утверждáть.

contender *n.* претендéнт.

content[1] (**kan**-tent) *n.* **1,** *pl.* (what is in a receptacle) содержи́мое. **2,** (subject matter) содержáние. **3,** (substance) содержáние: *form and content,* фóрма и содержáние. **4,** (amount of a substance contained) содержáние: *the fat content of milk,* содержáние жи́ра в молокé.

content[2] (kun-**tent**) *adj.* довóльный. —*v.t.* [*usu.* **content oneself with**] удовлетворя́ться (+ *instr.*); довóльствоваться (+ *instr.*). —**to one's heart's content,** вдóволь; вволю; скóлько душé угóдно.

contented *adj.* довóльный. —**contentedly,** *adv.* довóльно.

contention *n.* **1,** (competition) соревновáние. *Be in contention,* имéть шáнсы. **2,** (strife) раздóр. **3,** (assertion) утверждéние. —**bone of contention,** я́блоко раздóра.

contentious *adj.* задúристый; занóзистый.

contentment *n.* довóльство.

contest *n.* **1,** (struggle; battle) борьбá. **2,** (competition) состязáние; соревновáние; кóнкурс. —*v.t.* оспáривать.

contestant *n.* учáстник состязáния.

context *n.* контéкст. *Take out of context,* вырывáть из контéкста.

contiguity *n.* смéжность; соприкосновéние. —**contiguous,** *adj.* смéжный; соприкасáющийся; прилегáющий; сопредéльный.

continence *n.* воздержáние.

continent *n.* матери́к; континéнт. —**continental,** *adj.* материкóвый; континентáльный.

contingency *n.* (возмóжный) слýчай.

contingent *adj.* **1,** (possible) возмóжный. **2,** (chance) случáйный. **3,** (dependent): *be contingent on,* зави́сеть от. —*n.* контингéнт.

continual *adj.* непрестáнный; беспрестáнный. —**continually,** *adv.* непрестáнно; беспрестáнно.

continuation *n.* продолжéние.

continue *v.t.* продолжáть. —*v.i.* продолжáть(ся): *continue!,* продолжáйте! *The struggle continues,* борьбá продолжáется. —**to be continued,** продолжéние слéдует.

continuer *n.* продолжáтель.

continuity *n.* непреры́вность; преéмственность.

continuous *adj.* **1,** (uninterrupted) непреры́вный; беспреры́вный. **2,** (unbroken) сплошнóй. —**continuously,** *adv.* непреры́вно; беспреры́вно.

contort *v.t.* искривля́ть. —**contortion,** *n.* искривлéние. —**contortionist,** *n.* человéк-змея́.

contour *n.* кóнтур; очертáние. —**contour map,** кóнтурная кáрта.

contraband *n.* контрабáнда. —*adj.* контрабáндный.

contrabass *n.* контрабáс.

contrabassoon *n.* контрафагóт.

contraception *n.* предотвращéние зачáтия.

contraceptive *adj.* противозачáточный. *Contraceptive device,* презервати́в. —*n.* противозачáточное срéдство.

contract *n.* договóр; контрáкт; подря́д. —*v.t.* **1,** (draw together; reduce in size) сокращáть. **2,** (catch, as a disease) получáть; подхвáтывать; наживáть. **3,** (incur, as debts) дéлать (долги́). —*v.i.* **1,** (draw together) сокращáться; сжимáться. **2,** *fol. by* **for** *or inf.* (enter into a contract) заключи́ть договóр (на).

contraction *n.* **1,** (act of contracting) сокращéние; сужéние. **2,** (condensed form of two words) сокращённое слóво.

contractor *n.* **1,** (one who contracts for anything) подря́дчик; контрагéнт. **2,** (builder) подря́дчик-строи́тель.

contractual *adj.* договóрный.

contradict *v.t.* противорéчить. *Contradict oneself,* впадáть в противорéчие. —**contradiction,** *n.* противорéчие. —**contradictory,** *adj.* противоречи́вый.

contradistinction *n., in* **in contradistinction to,** в отли́чие от; в противоположность (+ *dat.*).

contralto *n.* контрáльто. —*adj.* контрáльтовый.

contraption *n., colloq.* приспособлéние.

contrapuntal *adj.* контрапункти́ческий.

contrary *adj.* **1,** (opposite) противоположный. **2,** *fol. by* **to** (in contradiction with) проти́вный (+ *dat.*). *Be contrary to,* противорéчить (+ *dat.*). **3,** (obstinate) упря́мый; сварли́вый. —*n.* *Quite the contrary,* как раз наоборóт. *Unless I hear to the contrary,* éсли я не услы́шу чего́-нибудь ино́го. —**contrary to,** вопреки́; наперекóр. —**on the contrary,** наоборо́т.

contrast *n.* контра́ст. *In contrast to,* в отли́чие от. —*v.t.* сопоставля́ть; противопоставля́ть. —*v.i.* контрасти́ровать.

contravene *v.t.* **1,** (violate) наруша́ть. **2,** (go against; conflict with) идти́ вразре́з с; противоре́чить. —**contravention,** *n.* наруше́ние.

contribute *v.t.* **1,** (donate) же́ртвовать. *Contribute one's share,* вноси́ть свою́ до́лю. **2,** (offer, as an idea, suggestion, etc.) вноси́ть; выдвига́ть. **3,** (furnish for publication) писа́ть. —*v.i.* **1,** (give money) же́ртвовать. **2,** (write articles) сотру́дничать (в газе́те, журна́ле, *etc.*). **3,** *fol. by* **to** (help bring about) соде́йствовать; спосо́бствовать.

contribution *n.* **1,** (monetary donation) поже́ртвование. *Make a contribution,* поже́ртвовать что́-нибудь. **2,** (that which advances something) вклад: *make a contribution to science,* де́лать *or* вноси́ть вклад в нау́ку.

contributor *n.* **1,** (donor) же́ртвователь. **2,** (writer of articles) сотру́дник (газе́ты, журна́ла, *etc.*).

contrite *adj.* ка́ющийся. —**contrition,** *n.* раская́ние; покая́ние.

contrivance *n.* **1,** (device) приспособле́ние. **2,** (scheme) ухищре́ние.

contrive *v.t.* **1,** (plan; devise) измышля́ть. **2,** *fol. by inf.* (manage) ухитря́ться; умудря́ться; изловчи́ться; (succeed through trickery) ухищря́ться.

control *v.t.* **1,** (regulate the operation of) управля́ть; регули́ровать. *This button controls the heat,* э́то — кно́пка отопле́ния. *Control prices,* регули́ровать це́ны. **2,** (hold sway over; dominate) контроли́ровать; держа́ть под свои́м контро́лем. *Control the straits,* контроли́ровать проли́вы. **3,** (keep in check) сде́рживать; обу́здывать. *Control oneself,* владе́ть собо́й. —*n.* **1,** (operation) управле́ние. *Remote contol,* дистанцио́нное управле́ние. **2,** (domination) контро́ль: *gain control of,* брать под свой контро́ль. **3,** (check) контро́ль: *price controls,* контро́ль над це́нами; *birth control,* контро́ль над рожда́емостью. **4,** *pl.* (instruments) рычаги́ управле́ния. *Be at the controls,* стоя́ть за штурва́лом. —*adj.* контро́льный. *Control experiment,* контро́льный о́пыт. *Control post,* контро́льный пост. *Control panel,* щит управле́ния; пульт. —**be in control of,** владе́ть. —**due to circumstances beyond our control,** по не зави́сящим от нас обстоя́тельствам. —**get control of oneself,** овладе́ть собо́й. —**get out of control,** отбива́ться от рук. —**go out of control,** потеря́ть управле́ние. —**lose control of,** потеря́ть управле́ние (+ *instr.*). —**take control of,** взять под свой контро́ль. —**under control,** в поря́дке; норма́льно: *everything is under control,* всё в поря́дке; всё норма́льно. *The fire has been brought under control,* пожа́р остано́влен.

controller *n.* **1,** *finance* контролёр. **2,** *aero.* диспе́тчер: *air traffic controller,* диспе́тчер возду́шного тра́нспорта.

control tower диспе́тчерская вы́шка; диспе́тчерская.

controversial *adj.* спо́рный; дискуссио́нный; полеми́ческий.

controversy *n.* спор; диску́ссия; поле́мика.

contuse *v.t.* конту́зить. —**contusion,** *n.* конту́зия; ушиб.

convalesce *v.i.* выздора́вливать. —**convalescence,** *n.* выздоровле́ние. —**convalescent,** *n. & adj.* выздора́вливающий.

convene *v.t.* созыва́ть. —*v.i.* собира́ться.

convenience *n.* удо́бство. *For the convenience of,* для удо́бства (+ *gen.*). *At your convenience,* когда́ вам бу́дет удо́бно. *At your earliest convenience,* возмо́жно скоре́е. *With all the conveniences,* со все́ми удо́бствами. —**marriage of convenience,** брак по расчёту.

convenient *adj.* удо́бный.

convent *n.* (же́нский) монасты́рь.

convention *n.* **1,** (assembly) съезд; *hist.* конве́нт. **2,** (agreement between nations) конве́нция. **3,** (custom) усло́вность.

conventional *adj.* **1,** (established by general agreement) усло́вный; общепри́нятый. **2,** *mil.* (non-nuclear) обы́чный: *conventional weapons,* обы́чное ору́жие.

conventionality *n.* усло́вность.

converge *v.i.* сходи́ться; стека́ться; слива́ться. —**convergence,** *n.* стече́ние; слия́ние.

conversant *adj.* осведомлённый, све́дущий.

conversation *n.* разгово́р; бесе́да. —**conversational,** *adj.* разгово́рный.

converse *v.i.* разгова́ривать. —*n.* (opposite) обра́тное. —*adj.* обра́тный; противополо́жный. —**conversely,** *adv.* наоборо́т.

conversion *n.* **1,** (changing to something else) превраще́ние; обраще́ние. **2,** *relig.* обраще́ние; перехо́д: *conversion to Christianity,* обраще́ние/перехо́д в христиа́нство. **3,** (changing, as of money) перево́д.

convert *v.t.* **1,** (transform) превраща́ть. **2,** (cause to change to another religion) обраща́ть (в другу́ю ве́ру). **3,** (change to a different unit of measurement) переводи́ть. **4,** *finance* конверти́ровать. —*v.i.* переходи́ть; обраща́ться (в другу́ю ве́ру). *Convert to Christianity,* переходи́ть/обраща́ться в христиа́нство. —*n.* новообращённый.

converter *n.* конве́ртер.

convertibility *n.* обрати́мость.

convertible *adj.* **1,** (capable of being converted) обрати́мый. **2,** (of an automobile) откры́тый. —*n.* откры́тый автомоби́ль.

convex *adj.* вы́пуклый. —**convexity,** *n.* вы́пуклость.

convey *v.t.* **1,** (carry; transport) вози́ть; перевози́ть. **2,** (impart; communicate) передава́ть.

conveyance *n.* **1,** (act of conveying) перево́зка. **2,** (vehicle) перево́зочное сре́дство.

conveyer *also,* **conveyor** *n.* конве́йер; транспортёр. —**conveyer belt,** конве́йерная ле́нта; ле́нточный транспортёр.

convict *v.t.* осужда́ть. —*n.* осуждённый; заключённый; ка́торжник.

conviction *n.* **1,** (finding guilty) осужде́ние. **2,** (one of a numer of times convicted) суди́мость. **3,** (strong belief) убежде́ние. **4,** (air of certainty) убеждённость. *With conviction,* убеждённо. *Carry conviction,* быть (о́чень) убеди́тельным.

convince *v.t.* убежда́ть: *I am convinced of it,* я убеждён (убеждена́) в э́том. *He convinced me to stay,* он убеди́л меня́ оста́ться. —**convincing,** *adj.* убеди́тельный. —**convincingly,** *adv.* убеди́тельно.

convivial *adj.* **1,** (jovial) весёлый. **2,** (festive) праздничный. **3,** (friendly) дружелю́бный. —**conviviality,** *n.* весёлость.
convocation *n.* **1,** (summoning) созы́в. **2,** (ecclesiastic assembly) собо́р.
convoke *v.t.* созыва́ть.
convoluted *adj.* **1,** (twisted) изо́гнутый; изви́листый. **2,** (complicated; intricate) замыслова́тый.
convoy *n.* карава́н; коло́нна.
convulse *v.t.* вызыва́ть су́дорогу *or* конву́льсии у. *Be convulsed with laughter,* надрыва́ть животы́ со́ смеху.
convulsion *n.* су́дорога; конву́льсия. —**convulsive,** *adj.* су́дорожный; конвульси́вный.
coo *v.i.* воркова́ть.
cook *v.t. & i.* гото́вить; стря́пать. —*v.i.* (of food) вари́ться. —*n.* (man) по́вар; (woman) куха́рка. —**cook up,** *colloq.* стря́пать. —**what's cooking?,** *colloq.* что происхо́дит?
cookbook *n.* пова́ренная кни́га.
cookery *n.* кулина́рия.
cookie *n.* пече́нье.
cooking *n.* ку́хня; стол: *French cooking,* францу́зская ку́хня; *home cooking,* дома́шний стол. —*adj.* ку́хонный: *cooking utensils,* ку́хонные принадле́жности.
cool *adj.* **1,** (moderately cold) прохла́дный. **2,** (calm; collected) споко́йный; хладнокро́вный. **3,** (not cordial) холо́дный. —*v.t.* охлажда́ть. —*v.i.* **1,** (of soup, tea, etc.) остыва́ть. **2,** *fol. by* **off** (of a person) освежа́ться; (of the weather) стать прохла́днее. **3,** (moderate; wane, as of feelings) остыва́ть. *Passions have cooled,* стра́сти улегли́сь. **4,** *fol. by* **to** (become less enthusiastic about) охладева́ть (к); остыва́ть (к). —*n.* прохла́да: *the cool of the evening,* вече́рняя прохла́да.
cooler *n.* холоди́льник.
cool-headed *adj.* невозмути́мый. —**cool-headedness,** *n.* невозмути́мость.
coolie *n.* ку́ли.
cooling *n.* охлажде́ние. —*adj.* прохлади́тельный.
coolly *adv.* прохла́дно: *react coolly,* отнести́сь (к чему́-нибудь) прохла́дно.
coolness *n.* **1,** (relatively low temperature) прохла́да. **2,** (calmness) хладнокро́вие. **3,** (distance, as between people) холодо́к; охлажде́ние.
coop *n.* куря́тник. —*v.t.* [*usu.* **coop up**] заключа́ть. *Be cooped up,* юти́ться; жить в тесноте́. —**fly the coop,** *colloq.* удра́ть; смы́ться.
cooper *n.* бо́ндарь; боча́р.
cooperate *v.i.* сотру́дничать. —**cooperation,** *n.* сотру́дничество.
cooperative *adj.* **1,** (joint) совме́стный. **2,** (collectively owned and operated) кооперати́вный. **3,** (helpful) услу́жливый. —*n.* коопера́ция; кооперати́в.
coordinate *v.t.* согласо́вывать; координи́ровать. —*n., math.* координа́та. —*adj., gram.: coordinate clause,* сочинённое предложе́ние; *coordinate conjunction,* сочини́тельный сою́з.
coordination *n.* **1,** (act of coordinating) согласова́ние; координа́ция. **2,** (harmony of action) согласо́ванность; координа́ция. *Lack of coordination,* несогласо́ванность; разла́д. **3,** *physiol.* координа́ция.
coot *n.* лысу́ха.
co-owner *n.* совладе́лец.
cop *n., colloq.* полице́йский; полисме́н.
copal *n.* копа́л.
cope *v.i.* [*usu.* **cope with**] справля́ться с.
copier *n.* **1,** (person) перепи́счик; копиро́вщик. **2,** (machine) копирова́льная маши́на.
copilot *n.* второ́й пило́т.
copious *adj.* оби́льный; бога́тый.
copper *n.* **1,** (metal) медь. **2,** (coin) медя́к. —*adj.* ме́дный.
copperhead *n.* щитомо́рдник.
coppersmith *n.* ме́дник.
copper sulfate ме́дный купоро́с.
coppice *n.* = **copse.**
copra *n.* ко́пра.
copse *n.* переле́сок. *Also,* **coppice.**
Coptic *adj.* ко́птский.
copulate *v.i.* совокупля́ться. —**copulation,** *n.* совокупле́ние.
copulative *adj., gram.* соедини́тельный.
copy *n.* **1,** (duplicate; facsimile) ко́пия. *Rough copy,* чернови́к. **2,** (any of a number of something printed or written) экземпля́р. **3,** (written matter to be printed) материа́л. —*v.t.* **1,** (transcribe) переписывать; спи́сывать. **2,** (reproduce) копи́ровать; снима́ть ко́пию с. **3,** (imitate) копи́ровать; подража́ть.
copyholder *n.* корре́ктор-подчи́тчик.
copying *n.* копи́рование; копиро́вка. —**copying machine,** копирова́льная маши́на.
copyist *n.* перепи́счик; копиро́вщик.
copyright *n.* а́вторское пра́во.
coquetry *n.* коке́тство.
coquette *n.* коке́тка. —**coquettish,** *adj.* коке́тливый.
coral *n.* кора́лл. —*adj.* кора́лловый. —**coral reef,** кора́лловый риф.
cord *n.* **1,** (string) верёвка. **2,** (electrical wire) шнур. **3,** *anat.: vocal cords,* голосовы́е свя́зки; *spinal cord,* спинно́й мозг; *umbilical cord,* пупови́на. **4,** (rib in fabric) ру́бчик.
cordial *adj.* серде́чный; раду́шный. —*n.* ликёр. —**cordiality,** *n.* серде́чность; раду́шие. —**cordially,** *adv.* серде́чно; раду́шно.
cordon *n.* кордо́н. —*v.t.* [*usu.* **cordon off**] оцепля́ть.
corduroy *n.* ру́бчатый вельве́т.
core *n.* **1,** (central part of a fruit) сердцеви́на. **2,** *fig.* (essence) ядро́. —**to the core,** до конца́ ногте́й; до мо́зга косте́й. *Rotten to the core,* насквозь прогни́вший.
coreligionist *n.* единове́рец.
coriander *n.* кориа́ндр. —*adj.* кориа́ндровый.
Corinthian *adj.* кори́нфский.
cork *n.* про́бка. —*adj.* про́бковый. —*v.t.* заку́поривать. —**cork oak,** про́бковый дуб.
corkscrew *n.* што́пор.
cormorant *n.* бакла́н.
corn *n.* **1,** (cereal plant or its kernels) кукуру́за. **2,** *Brit.* (grain) зерно́. **3,** (callus) мозо́ль. —*adj.* кукуру́зный.
corn crake коросте́ль; дерга́ч.
cornea *n.* рогова́я оболо́чка; рогови́ца.
corned beef солони́на.
corner *n.* **1,** (of a room) у́гол: *in the corner,* в углу́. **2,** (street corner) у́гол: *on the corner,* на углу́. *Around the corner,* за угло́м. *Turn the corner,* заверну́ть за́ угол. **3,** (remote region) уголо́к. —*adj.* углово́й:

corner room, угловáя кóмната. —*v.t.* **1,** (force into a corner) загонять в ýгол. **2,** *comm.* монополизи́ровать. —**cut corners,** урéзывать расхóды; эконóмить. —**just around the corner,** на носý: *spring is just around the corner,* веснá на носý.
cornerstone *n.* краеугóльный кáмень.
cornet *n.* корнéт.
cornfield *n.* кукурýзное пóле.
corn flakes кукурýзные хлóпья.
cornflower *n.* василёк.
cornice *n.* карни́з.
cornmeal *n.* кукурýзная мукá.
corn oil кукурýзное мáсло.
cornstalk *n.* кукурýзный стéбель.
cornucopia *n.* рог изоби́лия.
corny *adj., colloq.* банáльный; изби́тый.
corolla *n.* вéнчик.
corollary *n.* вы́вод.
corona *n.* корóна; венéц.
coronary *adj.* венéчный: *coronary artery,* венéчная артéрия. —*n.* [*also,* **coronary thrombosis**] закýпорка артéрий.
coronation *n.* венчáние (на цáрство); коронáция.
coroner *n.* мéдик судéбной эксперти́зы.
coronet *n.* **1,** (small crown) корóна. **2,** (jeweled headband) диадéма.
corporal *n.* капрáл. —*adj.* телéсный: *corporal punishment,* телéсное наказáние.
corporate *adj.* **1,** (pert. to a corporation) корпорати́вный. **2,** (joint; common) совмéстный.
corporation *n.* **1.** (company) корпорáция. **2.** *colloq.* (paunch) брюшкó; пýзо.
corporative *adj.* корпорати́вный.
corporeal *adj.* телéсный.
corps *n.* **1,** (large army unit) кóрпус. **2,** (specialized branch of the armed forces) слýжба: *signal corps,* слýжба свя́зи. *Marine Corps,* морскáя пехóта. **3,** (body of people) кóрпус: *diplomatic corps,* дипломати́ческий кóрпус. —**corps de ballet,** кордебалéт.
corpse *n.* труп.
corpsman *n.* санитáр.
corpulent *adj.* дорóдный; тýчный; грýзный. —**corpulence,** *n.* полнотá; дорóдность; тýчность.
corpuscle *n., usu. pl.* кровяны́е тельцá; кровяны́е шáрики.
corpus delicti состáв преступлéния.
corral *n.* загóн. —*v.t.* загонять; вгонять; сгонять.
correct *v.t.* исправлять; поправлять. —*adj.* **1,** (right; accurate) прáвильный; вéрный. **2,** (proper, as of behavior) корréктный.
correction *n.* попрáвка; исправлéние. —**house of correction,** исправи́тельный дом.
corrective *adj.* исправи́тельный.
correctly *adv.* прáвильно; вéрно. —**correctness,** *n.* прáвильность.
correlate *v.t.* соотноси́ть. —**correlation,** *n.* соотношéние.
correlative *adj.* соотноси́тельный.
correspond *v.i.* **1,** *fol. by* **to** (match; conform) соотвéтствовать (+ *dat.*). **2,** (write letters) перепи́сываться.
correspondence *n.* **1,** (agreement; similarity) соотвéтствие. **2,** (communication by letters) перепи́ска; корреспондéнция. —**correspondence course,** заóчный курс.
correspondent *n.* корреспондéнт.
corresponding *adj.* соотвéтствующий.
corridor *n.* коридóр. *In the corridors,* в кулуáрах.
corroborate *v.t.* подтверждáть. —**corroboration,** *n.* подтверждéние.
corrode *v.t.* разъедáть; выедáть. —*v.i.* ржáветь.
corrosion *n.* коррóзия.
corrosive *adj.* éдкий. —*n.* éдкое веществó. —**corrosive sublimate,** сулемá.
corrosiveness *n.* éдкость.
corrugate *v.t.* гофрировáть. —**corrugated,** *adj.* гофрирóванный; рифлёный.
corrupt *adj.* продáжный. —*v.t.* развращáть.
corruption *n.* **1,** (act of perverting) развращéние. **2,** (graft) коррýпция.
corsage *n.* букéт.
corsair *n.* корсáр.
corset *n.* корсéт.
cortege *n.* **1,** (procession) кортéж. **2,** (retinue) сви́та.
cortex *n.* **1,** (bark) корá. **2,** (of the brain) корá головнóго мóзга.
cortisone *n.* кортизóн.
corundum *n.* корýнд; алмáзный шпат.
coruscate *v.i.* сверкáть; блистáть.
corvette *n.* корвéт.
cosecant *n.* косéканс.
cosine *n.* кóсинус.
cosmetic *n., usu. pl.* космéтика. —*adj.* космети́ческий.
cosmetology *n.* космéтика.
cosmic *adj.* косми́ческий. —**cosmic dust,** косми́ческая пыль. —**cosmic rays,** косми́ческие лучи́.
cosmogony *n.* космогóния.
cosmology *n.* космолóгия.
cosmonaut *n.* космонáвт.
cosmopolitan *adj.* космополити́ческий. —*n.* [*also,* **cosmopolite**] космополи́т. —**cosmopolitanism,** *n.* космополити́зм.
cosmos *n.* кóсмос.
Cossack *n.* казáк. —*adj.* казáцкий.
cost *n.* стóимость: *cost of living,* стóимость жи́зни. *Sell something at cost,* продáть чтó-нибудь по себестóимости. *At the cost of,* ценóй (+ *gen.*). *To one's cost,* на свою́ бедý; на своё гóре; на свою́ гóлову. —*v.t. & i.* стóить; обходи́ться. *How much does it cost?,* скóлько э́то стóит? *Cost someone dearly,* дóрого обходи́ться (+ *dat.*). *It cost him his life,* э́то стóило емý жи́зни. —**at all costs,** во что бы то ни стáло.
costly *adj.* дорогóй; дорогостóящий.
costume *n.* костю́м. —**costume designer,** костюмéр. —**costume party,** костюмирóванный бал.
cosy *adj.* = **cozy.**
cot *n.* раскладýшка.
cotangent *n.* котáнгенс.
coterie *n.* кружóк.
cotillion *n.* котильóн.
cottage *n.* коттéдж; дóмик; дáча.
cottage cheese творóг.
cottage industry кустáрный прóмысел; кустáрное произвóдство.
cotton *n.* **1,** (cloth) бумáжная ткань; хлопчатобумáжная ткань. **2,** (plant from which it comes) хлопчáтник; хлóпок. **3,** (fibers of this plant) хлóпок. *Pick cotton,* собирáть хлóпок. **4,** (absorbent cotton) вáта.

—*adj.* **1,** (pert. to the plant) хло́пковый: *cotton fiber,* хло́пковое волокно́. **2,** (made of cotton) бума́жный; хлопчатобума́жный; си́тцевый. —**cotton gin,** хлопкоочисти́тельная маши́на. —**cotton picker,** сбо́рщик хло́пка.
cottonseed *n.* хло́пковое се́мя. —**cottonseed oil,** хло́пковое ма́сло.
cotyledon *n.* семядо́ля.
couch *n.* куше́тка; дива́н. —*v.t.* (word) облека́ть: *couch in diplomatic language,* облека́ть в дипломати́ческие выраже́ния.
cougar *n.* кугуа́р.
cough *n.* ка́шель. *Cough medicine,* лека́рство от ка́шля. —*v.i.* ка́шлять. —**cough up,** отха́ркивать.
could *v., past tense of* **can.** *I couldn't have done it without you,* без тебя́ я не мог бы э́того сде́лать. *Could you lend me a dollar?,* не мо́жете ли вы одолжи́ть мне до́ллар?
coulomb *n.* куло́н.
council *n.* **1,** (assembly) сове́т. **2,** *relig.* собо́р. —**councilman,** *n.* член сове́та.
counsel *n.* **1,** (advice) сове́т. **2,** (lawyer) адвока́т. —*v.t.* сове́товать. —**keep one's own counsel,** храни́ть молча́ние. —**take counsel with,** совеща́ться с.
counselor *also,* **counsellor** *n.* **1,** (adviser) сове́тник. **2,** (lawyer) адвока́т.
count *v.t.* **1,** (add up; total) счита́ть [*pfv.* сосчита́ть]. **2,** (regard as; consider) счита́ть [*pfv.* счесть]. —*v.i.* **1,** (name numbers in sequence) счита́ть: *count to ten,* счита́ть до десяти́. **2,** (be of significance) име́ть значе́ние: *count for little/nothing,* име́ть ма́лое значе́ние; не име́ть никако́го значе́ния. *That does not count,* э́то не счита́ется; э́то не в счёт. *Every minute counts,* ка́ждая мину́та на счету́. **3,** (be considered) засчи́тываться: *count as time worked,* засчи́тываться в стаж. **4,** *fol. by* **on** (rely on) рассчи́тывать (на); де́лать ста́вку (на). —*n.* **1,** (act of counting) счёт: *lose count of,* потеря́ть счёт (+ *dat.*). **2,** *law* пункт обвине́ния: *guilty on all counts,* вино́вный по всем пу́нктам обвине́ния. **3,** (nobleman) граф. —**count in,** включа́ть. —**count off,** отсчи́тывать. —**count out, 1,** (count while handing over) отсчи́тывать. **2,** (disregard; exclude) сбра́сывать со счето́в. —**not counting,** не счита́я; е́сли не счита́ть.
countdown *n.* обра́тный отсчёт вре́мени.
countenance *n.* **1,** (facial expression) выраже́ние лица́; ми́на. **2,** (composure) самооблада́ние. **3,** (approval) одобре́ние. —*v.t.* **1,** (approve) одобря́ть. **2,** (tolerate) терпе́ть.
counter *n.* **1,** (one who counts; device that records) счётчик. **2,** (flat surface for selling goods) прила́вок; (for serving food) сто́йка. **3,** (token) фи́шка; жето́н. —*adv. Run counter to,* идти́ вразре́з с. —*v.t.* пари́ровать. —**under the counter,** из-под полы́.
counteract *v.t.* противоде́йствовать (+ *dat.*). —**counteraction,** *n.* противоде́йствие.
counterattack *n.* контрата́ка. —*v.t. & i.* контратакова́ть.
counterbalance *n.* противове́с. —*v.t.* уравнове́шивать.
counterblow *n.* встре́чный уда́р; контруда́р.
countercharge *n.* встре́чное обвине́ние.
counterclockwise *adv.* про́тив часово́й стре́лки.
counterespionage *n.* контрразве́дка.
counterfeit *adj.* подде́льный; подло́жный; фальши́вый. —*v.t.* подде́лывать. —*n.* подде́лка. —**counterfeiter,** *n.* подде́лыватель; фальшивомоне́тчик.
counterfoil *n.* корешо́к.
counterintelligence *n.* контрразве́дка.
counterman *n.* буфе́тчик.
countermand *v.t.* отменя́ть (прика́з).
countermeasure *n.* контрме́ра.
counteroffensive *n.* контрнаступле́ние.
counteroffer *n.* контрпредложе́ние.
counterpane *n.* покрыва́ло.
counterpart *n.* собра́т: *the African elephant is larger than its Asian counterpart,* африка́нский слон крупне́е своего́ азиа́тского собра́та. *The Trade Minister conferred with his Japanese counterpart,* мини́стр торго́вли совеща́лся со свои́м япо́нским колле́гой.
counterpoint *n.* контрапу́нкт.
counterpoise *n.* противове́с.
counterproposal *n.* контрпредложе́ние.
counterrevolution *n.* контрреволю́ция.
counterrevolutionary *adj.* контрреволюцио́нный. —*n.* контрреволюционе́р.
countersign *v.t.* скрепля́ть —*n.* паро́ль; про́пуск.
countersignature *n.* скре́па.
counterweight *n.* противове́с.
countess *n.* графи́ня.
countless *adj.* бесчи́сленный; несчётный; неисчисли́мый.
country *n.* **1,** (nation) страна́. **2,** (land of one's birth or allegiance) ро́дина: *love one's country,* люби́ть свою́ ро́дину. **3,** (rural area) дере́вня: *live in the country,* жить в дере́вне. **4,** (region of a specified character) ме́стность: *hilly country,* холми́стая ме́стность. —*adj.* дереве́нский: *country life,* дереве́нская жизнь.
countryman *n.* соотéчественник; земля́к.
countryside *n.* дере́вня; се́льская ме́стность.
county *n.* (in the U.S.) о́круг; (in Great Britain) гра́фство.
coup *n.* **1,** (brilliant stroke) ло́вкий *or* блестя́щий ход. **2,** (seizure of power) переворо́т: *palace coup,* дворцо́вый переворо́т. —**coup d'état,** госуда́рственный переворо́т.
couple *n.* **1,** (pair) па́ра. **2,** (married couple) супру́жеская па́ра; чета́. **3,** *colloq.* (a few; several) *rendered by* не́сколько: *in a couple of days,* че́рез не́сколько дней. —*v.t.* **1,** (hitch together) сцепля́ть. **2,** *fig.* (link) свя́зывать.
coupling *n.* му́фта; сцепле́ние; связь.
coupon *n.* тало́н; купо́н.
courage *n.* хра́брость; му́жество; отва́га. —**courageous,** *adj.* хра́брый; му́жественный; отва́жный. —**courageously,** *adv.* хра́бро; му́жественно; отва́жно.
courier *n.* курье́р.
course *n.* **1,** (direction) курс: *stray off course,* отклоня́ться от ку́рса. **2,** (curriculum) курс: *history course,* курс исто́рии. **3,** (way of proceeding) курс: *course of treatment,* курс лече́ния. *Course of action,* о́браз де́йствий. **4,** (progress) тече́ние; ход: *in the course of,* в тече́ние (+ *gen.*); в хо́де (+ *gen.*). *Course of events,* ход *or* разви́тие собы́тий. *In the course of time,* с тече́нием вре́мени. *Take its course,* идти́ свои́м чередо́м. **5,** (part of a meal) блю́до: *three-course dinner,* обе́д из трёх блюд. **6,** *sports* площа́дка: *golf course,* площа́дка для го́льфа. *Racecourse,*

скаковáя дорóжка. —**as a matter of course,** как нéчто самó собóй разумéющееся. *Take as a matter of course,* принимáть как дóлжное. —**in due course,** своеврéменно; в своё врéмя. —**of course,** конéчно.

court *n.* **1,** (tribunal) суд: *appear before the court,* предстáть пéред судóм. **2,** (courtyard) двор. **3,** (sovereign and his council) двор. **4,** *sports* плошáдка. *Tennis court,* тéннисный корт. —*adj.* **1,** (pert. to a court of law) судéбный. **2,** (pert. to the court of a sovereign) придвóрный: *court jester,* придвóрный шут.—*v.t.* **1,** (seek the favor of) заискивать пéред. **2,** (woo) ухáживать за. **3,** (invite, as trouble) накликáть (бедý). —**pay court to,** ухáживать за.

courteous *adj.* вéжливый; учтúвый; обходúтельный. —**courteously,** *adv.* вéжливо.

courtesan *n.* куртизáнка.

courtesy *n.* вéжливость; учтúвость. *By courtesy of,* благодарá любéзности (+ *gen.*). —**courtesy call,** визúт вéжливости.

courthouse *n.* здáние судá.

courtier *n.* придвóрный.

courtly *adj.* вéжливый; изы́сканный; галáнтный.

court-martial *n.* воéнный суд. —*v.t.* судúть воéнным судóм.

courtroom *n.* зал судá.

courtship *n.* ухáживание.

courtyard *n.* двор.

cousin *n.* двою́родный брат; двою́родная сестрá. —**second cousin,** трою́родный брат; трою́родная сестрá.

cove *n.* бýхточка.

covenant *n.* **1,** (agreement) соглашéние. **2,** *relig.* завéт.

cover *v.t.* **1,** (place something over) покрывáть; закрывáть. **2,** (upholster) обивáть; обтя́гивать. **3,** (lie over, as of snow, dust, etc.) покрывáть. **4,** *fol. by* **up** (conceal) покрывáть; скрывáть. *Cover up one's tracks,* заметáть следы́. **5,** (include; take in) охвáтывать. **6,** (provide for, as of a law, contract, etc.) предусмáтривать. **7,** (defray, as expenses) покрывáть; окупáть (расхóды). **8,** (traverse, as a distance) проходúть; покрывáть. **9,** *cards* покрывáть. **10,** *in* **cover oneself with glory,** покрывáть себя́ слáвой. —*n.* **1,** (lid) кры́шка. **2,** (anything that covers) чехóл; покрóв. *Under cover of night,* под покрóвом нóчи. **3,** (blanket) одея́ло. **4,** (hard cover of a book) переплёт. *Read from cover to cover,* прочéсть от кóрки до кóрки *or* от доскú до доскú. **5,** (soft cover of a book or magazine) облóжка. **6,** (paper cover to protect a book) обёртка. **7,** (envelope) конвéрт: *under separate cover,* в отдéльном конвéрте. **8,** (shelter) укры́тие; прикры́тие. *Take cover,* укрывáться. **9,** (guise; front) прикры́тие. **10,** *mil.* прикры́тие.

coverage *n.* **1,** (treatment in the media) освещéние: *extensive coverage in the press,* ширóкое освещéние в печáти. **2,** (insurance) (страховóе) покры́тие.

covered *adj.* кры́тый; закры́тый. —**covered wagon,** кры́тая повóзка.

covering *n.* покры́тие; покрóв. —**covering letter,** сопроводúтельное письмó.

coverlet *n.* покрывáло.

covert *adj.* скры́тый.

covet *v.t.* желáть; жáждать. —**covetous,** *adj.* жáдный.

covey *n.* **1,** (flock) стáя. **2,** (bevy) грýппа.

cow *n.* **1,** (farm animal) корóва. **2,** (female of certain other animals) сáмка. —*adj.* [*also,* **cow's**] корóвий: *cow's milk,* корóвье молокó. —*v.t.* (intimidate) запýгивать.

coward *n.* трус. —**cowardice,** *n.* трýсость. —**cowardly,** *adj.* труслúвый.

cowberry *n.* брусникá.

cowboy *n.* ковбóй. —*adj.* ковбóйский: *cowboy hat,* ковбóйская шля́па.

cower *v.i.* приседáть (от стрáха).

cowhide *n.* **1,** (hide of a cow) корóвья шкýра. **2,** (leather) волóвья кóжа.

cowl *n.* **1,** (monk's hood) капюшóн. **2,** *mech.* (cover; hood) колпáк; капóт.

cowpox *n.* корóвья óспа.

cowshed *n.* корóвник.

coy *adj.* **1,** (shy) застéнчивый. **2,** (feigning shyness) жемáнный.

coyote *n.* луговóй волк; койóт.

coypu *n.* нýтрия.

cozy *also,* **cosy** *adj.* ую́тный.

crab *n.* **1,** (shellfish) краб. **2,** *colloq.* (grouch) брюзгá. —*v.i., colloq.* (complain) ворчáть; ныть.

crab apple дúкое я́блоко.

crabby *adj.* злой; брюзглúвый.

crack *v.i.* **1,** (split) дать трéщину; трéснуть; трéскаться. **2,** (make a sharp, snapping sound) трещáть. **3,** (break, as of one's voice) ломáться. **4,** (break down) не вы́держать: *crack under the strain,* не вы́держать напряжéния. —*v.t.* **1,** (break open) колóть; щёлкать (орéхи); разбивáть (я́йца). **2,** (make a crack in) дéлать трéщину в; надлáмывать. **3,** (snap, as a whip) щёлкать (кнутóм). **4,** *colloq.* (utter, as a joke) отпускáть. **5,** (break open, as a safe) взлáмывать. **6,** (break, as a code) разгáдывать. —*n.* **1,** (fissure) трéщина. **2,** (slight opening) щель; щёлка. **3,** (sound) щелчóк; треск. *Crack of a whip,* щелчóк кнутá. **4,** *colloq.* (attempt) попы́тка. *Take a crack at,* попытáться (+ *inf.*); попрóбовать свои сúлы на *or* в. **5,** *colloq.* (remark) острóта. **6,** *in* **at the crack of dawn,** чуть свет. —*adj., colloq.* отбóрный: *crack regiment,* отбóрный полк. —**crack down on,** принимáть круты́е мéры прóтив; пристрýнивать. —**crack up,** **1,** (have a breakdown) надлáмываться. **2,** *colloq.* (become convulsed with laughter) лóпаться от смéха; надрывáть животы́ (сó смеху).

cracked *adj.* **1,** (split) надтрéснутый. **2,** *colloq.* (nutty) трóнутый.

cracker *n.* **1,** (biscuit) галéта; сухáрь. **2,** (party favor) хлопýшка.

crackerjack *adj., colloq.* отлúчный; блестя́щий.

crackle *v.i.* трещáть; потрéскивать. —*n.* треск; трескотня́; трещáние.

crackling *n.* **1,** (sound) треск; трескотня́; трещáние. **2,** *pl.* (crisp remains of fat after rendering) шквáрки.

crackpot *n., slang* сумасбрóд.

cradle *n.* колыбéль.

craft *n.* **1,** (trade) ремеслó. **2,** (boat) сýдно. —**craft union,** цеховóй профсою́з.

craftsman *n.* **1,** (one engaged in a craft) ремéсленник. **2,** (skilled artisan) мáстер. —**craftsmanship,** *n.* мастерствó.

crafty *adj.* хúтрый; лукáвый.

crag *n.* скала́; утёс. —**craggy,** *adj.* скали́стый; утёсистый.
crake *n.* ку́рочка.
cram *v.t.* **1,** (stuff into insufficient space) вти́скивать; впи́хивать. **2,** (fill beyond normal capacity) набива́ть. —*v.i., colloq.* (study) зубри́ть. —**crammer,** *n.* зубри́ла.
cramp *n.* **1,** (muscle spasm) су́дорога. *I have a cramp in my leg,* у меня́ свело́ но́гу. **2,** *pl.* (sharp abdominal pains) схва́тки. —*v.t.* **1,** (cause a cramp in) своди́ть. **2,** (confine; restrict) стесня́ть.
cramped *adj.* те́сный.
cranberry *n.* клю́ква. —*adj.* клю́квенный.
crane *n.* **1,** (bird) жура́вль. **2,** (derrick) подъёмный кран. —*v.t., in* **crane one's neck,** вытя́гивать ше́ю.
crane fly долгоно́жка.
cranium *n.* че́реп; черепна́я коро́бка. —**cranial,** *adj.* черепно́й.
crank *n.* **1,** (device) кривоши́п; *(for starting a car)* заводна́я руко́ятка. **2,** *colloq.* (eccentric) чуда́к. **3,** *colloq.* (grouch) брюзга́. —*v.t.* **1,** *usu. fol. by* **up** (start with a crank) заводи́ть. **2,** *fol. by* **out** (mass-produce) фабрикова́ть.
crankcase *n.* ка́ртер.
crankshaft *n.* коле́нчатый вал.
cranky *adj.* брюзгли́вый.
cranny *n.* закоу́лок: *every nook and cranny,* все закоу́лки.
craps *n.* игра́ в ко́сти.
crash *v.i.* **1,** *fol. by* **into** (smash into) вре́заться (в). **2,** (fall with great noise) ру́шиться. **3,** (of an airplane) разби́ться; потерпе́ть ава́рию. **4,** (of the stock market) потерпе́ть крах. —*v.t.* **1,** (smash) разбива́ть. **2,** *colloq.* (come uninvited to) яви́ться без приглаше́ния на. —*n.* **1,** (sound) гро́хот; треск. **2,** (collision; wreck) ава́рия; круше́ние; катастро́фа. *Plane crash,* авиацио́нная катастро́фа. **3,** (financial collapse) крах. —*adj.* уда́рный: *crash program,* уда́рная програ́мма. *Crash course,* ускóренный курс. —**crash helmet,** защи́тный шлем. —**crash landing,** авари́йная поса́дка.
crass *adj.* гру́бый.
crate *n.* я́щик. —*v.t.* упако́вывать в я́щик.
crater *n.* **1,** (of a volcano or on the moon) кра́тер. **2,** (resulting from a bomb) воро́нка.
crave *v.t.* жа́ждать.
craven *adj.* трусли́вый; малоду́шный.
craving *n.* жа́жда; стра́стное жела́ние.
craw *n.* зоб.
crawfish *n.* рак. *Also,* **crayfish.**
crawl *v.i.* **1,** (creep) ползти́. *Crawl in,* вполза́ть. *Crawl out,* выполза́ть. **2,** *fol. by* **with** (swarm; teem) кише́ть (+ *instr.*). —*n., swimming* кроль. —**at a crawl,** черепа́шьим ша́гом.
crawler *n.* **1,** (one who crawls, esp. a baby) ползу́н; ползуно́к. **2,** *pl.* (baby's garment) ползунки́.
crayfish *n.* = **crawfish.**
crayon *n.* цветно́й каранда́ш.
craze *n.* ма́ния. —*v.t.* доводи́ть до бе́шенства. —**crazed,** *adj.* бе́шеный; озвере́лый.
crazily *adv.* как сумасше́дший.
craziness *n.* глу́пость; безу́мие.
crazy *adj.* сумасше́дший; безу́мный. *Crazy about,* без ума́ от. *Drive crazy,* своди́ть с ума́; выводи́ть из себя́; доводи́ть до безу́мия. —**like crazy,** *colloq.* ужа́сно; безу́мно. *Run like crazy,* бежа́ть во все лопа́тки.
creak *v.i.* скрипе́ть. —*n.* скрип. —**creaky,** *adj.* скрипу́чий.
cream *n.* **1,** (part of milk) сли́вки. *Sour cream,* смета́на. *Whipped cream,* взби́тые сли́вки. **2,** (substance, as for a cake, for the face, etc.) крем. *Shaving cream,* крем для бритья́. *Cold cream,* кольдкре́м. **3,** *fig.* (best part) сли́вки: *the cream of society,* сли́вки о́бщества. —*adj.* **1,** (of or for cream) сли́вочный. **2,** (cream-colored) кре́мовый.
cream cheese сли́вочный сыр.
creamer *n.* сли́вочник.
creamery *n.* маслобо́йня; маслозаво́д.
cream of tartar ви́нный ка́мень.
creamy *adj.* сли́вочный.
crease *n.* скла́дка. —*v.t.* **1,** (wrinkle) мять. **2,** (graze) задева́ть. —*v.i.* мя́ться.
create *v.t.* **1,** (make; produce) создава́ть; твори́ть. *Create a work of art,* создава́ть произведе́ние иску́сства. *Create difficulties,* создава́ть тру́дности. *God created the world,* Бог сотвори́л мир. **2,** (cause; give rise to) вызыва́ть: *create doubts,* вызыва́ть сомне́ния.
creation *n.* созда́ние: *creation of capital,* созда́ние капита́ла. *Creation of the world,* сотворе́ние ми́ра. *A marvelous creation,* замеча́тельное созда́ние.
creative *adj.* тво́рческий; созида́тельный. —**creativity,** *n.* тво́рческая си́ла.
creator *n.* творе́ц; созда́тель.
creature *n.* существо́; созда́ние.
credence *n.* ве́ра. *Give credence to; put/place credence in,* ве́рить; дава́ть ве́ру (+ *dat.*).
credentials *n.pl.* вери́тельные гра́моты. —**credentials committee,** манда́тная коми́ссия.
credibility *n.* **1,** (of a story or account) вероя́тность; правдоподо́бие. **2,** (of a person) надёжность; дове́рие к себе́.
credible *adj.* **1,** (plausible) вероя́тный; правдоподо́бный. **2,** (who can be believed) заслу́живающий дове́рия.
credit *n.* **1,** (credence) ве́ра. *Place credit in,* ве́рить. **2,** (praise; approval) похвала́. *He deserves a lot of credit,* он о́чень досто́ин похвалы́. *Give credit to,* отдава́ть до́лжное *or* справедли́вость (+ *dat.*). *Give credit to someone for something,* ста́вить что́-нибудь в заслу́гу (+ *dat.*). *Take credit for,* ста́вить себе́ (что́-нибудь) в заслу́гу. **3,** (favor; honor; reputation) честь: *to his credit it must be said that...,* к его́ че́сти на́до сказа́ть, что... *He is a credit to his profession,* он де́лает честь свое́й профе́ссии. *Have to one's credit,* име́ть на своём счету́. **4,** *comm.* креди́т: *buy on credit,* купи́ть в креди́т. **5,** *bookkeeping* кре́дит.—*adj.* креди́тный. —*v.t.* **1,** (believe) ве́рить; доверя́ть. **2,** (give credit to for something) ста́вить (что́-нибудь) в заслу́гу (+ *dat.*). **3,** (apply, as to an account) запи́сывать в креди́т (на че́й-нибудь счёт). **4,** *bookkeeping* (enter on the credit side) прихо́довать.
creditable *adj.* похва́льный.
credit card креди́тная ка́рточка.
creditor *n.* кредито́р.
credo *n.* кре́до.
credulity *n.* легкове́рие. —**credulous,** *adj.* легкове́рный.
creed *n.* **1,** (credo) си́мвол ве́ры; кре́до. *The*

Apostles' Creed, апо́стольский си́мвол ве́ры. **2,** (one's religion) вероиспове́дание.
creek *n.* **1,** (brook) руче́й. **2,** (inlet) за́водь; зато́н.
creel *n.* ве́рша.
creep *v.i.* **1,** (crawl) ползти́. **2,** (sneak) кра́сться. **3,** (of plants) ползти́; стла́ться. —**creep in, 1,** (sneak in) вкра́дываться; залеза́ть. **2,** *fig.* (of doubts, errors, etc.) вкра́дываться; закра́дываться. —**creep up,** подкра́дываться. —**make one's flesh creep,** приводи́ть в содрога́ние.
creeper *n.* **1,** (plant) ползу́чее расте́ние. **2,** (bird) пищу́ха.
creeps *n.pl., colloq.* содрога́ние. *It gives me the creeps,* у меня́ мура́шки бе́гают по спине́; у меня́ моро́з по ко́же подира́ет.
cremate *v.t.* сжига́ть; креми́ровать. —**cremation,** *n.* крема́ция. —**crematorium,** *n.* кремато́рий.
crenelated *adj.* зубча́тый.
Creole *n.* крео́л. —*adj.* крео́льский.
creosote *n.* креозо́т.
crepe *n.* креп; флёр.
crescendo *n.* креще́ндо.
crescent *n.* полуме́сяц; серп луны́.
cress *n.* кресс.
crest *n.* **1,** (comb of a bird) гре́бень; (feathered tuft) хохо́л. **2,** (top, as of a wave or hill) гре́бень. —**crested,** *adj.* хохла́тый.
crestfallen *adj.* уби́тый; приши́бленный; как в во́ду опу́щенный.
cretaceous *adj.* мелово́й.
cretin *n.* крети́н. —**cretinism,** *n.* кретини́зм.
cretonne *n.* крето́н. —*adj.* крето́новый; крето́нный.
crevice *n.* расще́лина.
crew *n.* **1,** (of a ship, plane, etc.) экипа́ж; кома́нда. *Train crew,* поездна́я брига́да. **2,** (group of workers) брига́да. **3,** *mil.* расчёт: *gun crew,* ору́дийный расчёт.
crew cut ёжик: *in a crew cut,* ёжиком.
crib *n.* **1,** (child's bed) де́тская крова́ть. **2,** (feeding trough) я́сли. **3,** (bin for storing grain) ларь; за́кром. **4,** *colloq.* (concealed student's notes) шпарга́лка.
crick *n.* су́дорога.
cricket *n.* **1,** (insect) сверчо́к. **2,** (game) кри́кет.
crier *n.* глаша́тай.
crime *n.* **1,** (criminal act) преступле́ние. **2,** (criminality) престу́пность: *the increase in crime,* рост престу́пности.
Crimean *adj.* кры́мский. —**Crimean War,** Кры́мская война́.
criminal *n.* престу́пник. —*adj.* **1,** (constituting a crime) престу́пный: *criminal negligence,* престу́пная небре́жность. **2,** (pert. to the administration of penal law) уголо́вный: *criminal law,* уголо́вное пра́во.
criminology *n.* криминоло́гия. —**criminologist,** *n.* кримино́лог.
crimp *v.t.* **1,** (press into small folds) гофрирова́ть. **2,** (curl, as hair) завива́ть. —*n., in* **put a crimp in,** *colloq.* расстра́ивать (*e.g.* пла́ны).
crimson *adj.* мали́новый; багро́вый. —*n.* мали́новый цвет; багря́нец.
cringe *v.i.* **1,** (cower) съёживаться. **2,** (fawn) лебези́ть; раболе́пствовать.
crinkle *v.t.* мо́рщить.
cripple *n.* кале́ка. —*v.t.* **1,** (make a cripple of) кале́чить. **2,** (deal a crippling blow to) разруша́ть. *Crippling blow,* сокруши́тельный уда́р.
crisis *n.* кри́зис.
crisp *adj.* **1,** (brittle) хрустя́щий. **2,** (invigorating) бодря́щий; живи́тельный. **3,** (terse; pithy) живо́й; пика́нтный. —**burn to a crisp,** сгоре́ть дотла́.
crisscross *v.t.* перекре́щивать. —*v.i.* перекре́щиваться. —*adv.* крест-на́крест.
criterion *n.* крите́рий; мери́ло.
critic *n.* кри́тик. *Film critic,* кинокри́тик.
critical *adj.* **1,** (containing criticism) крити́ческий. **2,** (crucial) крити́ческий; отве́тственный; перело́мный. **3,** (extremely serious) крити́ческий.
critically *adv.* **1,** (gravely) тяжело́: *critically ill/wounded,* тяжело́ бо́лен/ра́нен. **2,** (vitally) жи́зненно: *critically important,* жи́зненно ва́жный.
criticism *n.* кри́тика.
criticize *v.t. & i.* критикова́ть.
critique *n.* реце́нзия; крити́ческий разбо́р.
croak *v.i.* ква́кать. —*n.* ква́канье.
Croat *n.* хорва́т. —**Croatian,** *adj.* хорва́тский.
crochet *v.t. & i.* вяза́ть (крючко́м).
crock *n.* гли́няный сосу́д.
crockery *n.* гли́няная посу́да.
crocodile *n.* крокоди́л. —*adj.* крокоди́ловый. —**crocodile tears,** крокоди́ловы слёзы.
crocus *n.* кро́кус.
crook *n.* **1,** (bend) сгиб: *the crook of one's arm,* сгиб ло́ктя. **2,** (staff) по́сох: *shepherd's crook,* пасту́ший по́сох. **3,** *colloq.* (swindler) плут.
crooked *adj.* **1,** (not straight) криво́й. **2,** *colloq.* (dishonest) нечи́стый. —**crookedness,** *n.* кривизна́.
croon *v.t. & i.* напева́ть.
crop *n.* **1,** (farm product) культу́ра; посе́в. *Winter crops,* ози́мые культу́ры. *The crops are coming up,* посе́вы всхо́дят. *Crop rotation,* севооборо́т. **2,** (yield) урожа́й: *the corn crop,* урожа́й кукуру́зы. *Crop failure,* неурожа́й. **3,** (whip handle) кнутови́ще. **4,** (craw of a bird) зоб. —*v.t.* стричь: *crop someone's hair,* стричь кого́-нибудь под гребёнку. —**crop up,** возника́ть.
croquet *n.* кроке́т.
crosier *also,* **crozier** *n.* по́сох.
cross *n.* **1,** (structure or representation of same) крест. *Sign of the cross,* кре́стное зна́мение; крест. **2,** (hybrid) по́месь: *a mule is a cross between a donkey and a female horse,* мул – по́месь осла́ с кобы́лой. —*adj.* **1,** (transverse) попере́чный: *crossbeam,* попере́чная ба́лка. **2,** (intersecting) пересека́ющийся. **3,** (involving interchange) перекрёстный: *cross-pollination,* перекрёстное опыле́ние. **4,** (ill-tempered) злой. *He is cross with me,* он зол на меня́. —*v.t.* **1,** (traverse) переходи́ть; переезжа́ть; пересека́ть. **2,** (intersect) пересека́ть. **3,** (place crosswise) скре́щивать: *cross swords,* скре́щивать шпа́ги *or* мечи́. *Cross one's legs,* класть но́гу на́ ногу. **4,** (crossbreed) скре́щивать. **5,** (double-cross) обма́нывать: *he doesn't like to be crossed,* он не лю́бит, что́бы его́ обма́нывали. **6,** *in* **cross one's mind,** приходи́ть в го́лову (+ *dat.*). —*v.i.* **1,** (go to the other side) переходи́ть. **2,** (intersect) пересека́ться. **3,** *in* **cross in the mail,** размину́ться. —**cross off,** вычёркивать. —**cross oneself,** крести́ться. —**cross out,** зачёркивать. —**cross up,** подводи́ть.
crossbar *n.* **1,** (crossbeam) попере́чина; перекла-

дина. **2,** *sports* (for high jumping) планка; (between goal posts) штанга.

crossbeam *n.* поперечная балка; поперечина; перекладина.

crossbill *n.* клёст.

crossbow *n.* самострел.

crossbreed *v.t.* скрещивать. —*n.* помесь. —**crossbreeding,** *n.* скрещивание; метизация.

cross-country *adj.* **1,** (across a country) через страну: *a cross-country flight,* перелёт через страну. **2,** (across open country): *cross-country race,* кросс. **3,** (able to operate on any terrain) вездеходный. *Cross-country vehicle,* вездеход.

cross-cut saw поперечная пила.

cross-examination *n.* перекрёстный допрос. —**cross-examine,** *v.t.* подвергать перекрёстному допросу; допрашивать.

cross-eye *n.* косоглазие. —**cross-eyed,** *adj.* косоглазый; косой.

crossfire *n.* перекрёстный огонь.

crossing *n.* **1,** (act of crossing) переход; переезд; переправа. **2,** (place to cross) переход; переезд. **3,** (intersection) перекрёсток; скрещение. **4,** (railroad crossing) переезд.

crosspiece *n.* поперечина; крестовина; перемычка.

cross-purposes *n.pl., in* **at cross-purposes,** наперекор друг другу.

cross-reference *n.* перекрёстная ссылка.

crossroad *n.* **1,** (road that crosses) поперечная дорога. **2,** *pl.* (place of intersection) распутье; перепутье. —**at the crossroads,** на распутье; на перепутье.

cross section поперечное сечение; поперечный разрез.

crosswalk *n.* переход.

crosswise *adv.* крестообразно; крест-накрест.

crossword puzzle кроссворд.

crotch *n.* промежность. *The trousers are tight in the crotch,* брюки узки в шагу.

crotchety *adj.* причудливый; сварливый.

Croton bug прусак.

crouch *v.i.* приседать.

croup *n.* круп.

croupier *n.* крупье.

crouton *n.* гренок.

crow *n.* ворона. —*adj.* [*usu.* **crow's**] вороний: *crow's nest,* воронье гнездо. —*v.i.* **1,** (cry, as of a rooster) кукарекать. **2,** *colloq.* (boast) трубить; прокричать. —**as the crow flies,** по прямой.

crowbar *n.* лом.

crowd *n.* толпа. *Avoid crowds,* избегать толпы. —*v.t.* **1,** (make uncomfortable) теснить; стеснять. *Crowd one's neighbor,* теснить соседа. **2,** (fill to excess) заполнять: *people crowded the stores,* публика заполнила магазины. *Crowd a room with furniture,* загромождать *or* заставлять комнату мебелью. **3,** (squeeze; cram) втискивать. *Crowd six people into a car,* помещать шесть человек в машине. **4,** *fol. by* **out** (displace) вытеснять. —*v.i.* **1,** *fol. by* **into** (squeeze into) набиваться в; втискиваться в. **2,** *fol. by* **around** (cluster around) обступать. **3,** *fol. by* **together** (gather closely together) толпиться; столпиться; тесниться; стесняться.

crowded *adj.* тесный; людный; переполненный. *It is crowded here,* здесь тесно.

crown *n.* **1,** (of a sovereign) корона; венец. **2,** (garland; wreath) венок. **3,** (of the head) темя; макушка; (of a tooth) коронка; (of a hat) тулья; (of a tree) крона. **4,** (monetary unit) крона. —*v.t.* **1,** (enthrone) короновать; венчать на царство. **2,** (endow with honor; surmount; make complete) венчать. *Be crowned with success,* увенчаться успехом. **3,** *dentistry* ставить коронку на (зуб). **4,** *checkers* проводить (шашку) в дамки. **5,** *colloq.* (hit on the head) дать по голове.

crown prince наследный принц.

crow's-feet *n.pl.* гусиные лапки.

crozier *n.* = **crosier.**

crucial *adj.* решающий; критический; ответственный.

crucible *n.* **1,** (vessel) тигель. **2,** *fig.* (ordeal) горнило.

crucifix *n.* распятие.

crucifixion *n.* распятие (на кресте).

cruciform *adj.* крестообразный.

crucify *v.t.* распинать.

crude *adj.* **1,** (raw; unrefined) сырой; необработанный. *Crude oil,* нефть-сырец. **2,** (coarse; unpolished) грубый: *crude remark,* грубое замечание.

crudely *adv.* грубо. *To put it rather crudely,* грубо говоря.

crudeness *n.* грубость. *Also,* **crudity.**

cruel *adj.* жестокий: *cruel person,* жестокий человек; *cruel treatment,* жестокое обращение. —**cruelly,** *adv.* жестоко. —**cruelty,** *n.* жестокость.

cruet *n.* уксусница. *Cruet stand,* судок.

cruise *n.* морское путешествие; круиз. —*v.i.* крейсировать. *Cruising speed,* крейсерская скорость. —**cruise missile,** крылатая ракета.

cruiser *n.* крейсер.

crumb *n.* крошка.

crumble *v.t.* крошить. —*v.i.* **1,** (fall into small pieces) крошиться; рассыпаться. **2,** (decay; disintegrate) распадаться; разрушаться.

crumbly *adj.* рыхлый; рассыпчатый.

crummy *adj., slang* дрянной; паршивый.

crumpet *n.* сдобная пышка; лепёшка.

crumple *v.t.* мять; комкать. —*v.i.* мяться.

crunch *v.t. & i.* хрустеть. —*n.* хруст.

crusade *n.* **1,** *hist.* крестовый поход. **2,** (campaign) поход; кампания.

crusader *n.* **1,** *hist.* крестоносец. **2,** (strong advocate) борец: *crusader for freedom,* борец за свободу.

crush *v.t.* **1,** (mash) давить. *Crush to death,* задавить насмерть. **2,** (grind into small particles) дробить; размельчать. **3,** (crease; rumple) мять. **4,** (put down; suppress) подавлять; раздавить. **5,** (defeat; overwhelm) разбивать. —*n.* **1,** (pressure from a crowd) давка; толчея; толкотня. **2,** *colloq.* (infatuation) увлечение.

crushed *adj.* **1,** (in small bits) дроблёный. **2,** (creased; wrinkled) мятый. **3,** (crestfallen) убитый.

crusher *n.* дробилка. *Rock crusher,* камнедробилка.

crushing *adj.* **1,** (designed to crush) дробильный. **2,** *fig.* (devastating) сокрушительный: *crushing blow,* сокрушительный удар. *Crushing defeat,* жестокое поражение.

crust *n.* **1,** (of bread) корка. **2,** (hard surface) кора: *the earth's crust,* земная кора.

crustacean *n.* ракообра́зное.
crutch *n.* косты́ль.
crux *n.* суть: *the crux of the matter,* суть де́ла.
cry *v.i.* **1,** (weep) пла́кать. *Burst out crying,* распла́каться. **2,** (shout) (за)крича́ть. **3,** *fol. by* **out** (shriek) вскри́кивать. —*v.t.* **1,** *in* **cry one's eyes out,** вы́плакать глаза́. **2,** *in* **cry oneself to sleep,** пла́кать пока́ (он) не засну́л. —*n.* **1,** (shout) крик. **2,** (spell of weeping) плач. *Have a good cry,* вы́плакаться. **3,** (call of an animal or bird) крик. **4,** (rallying call) клич: *battle cry,* боево́й клич.
crybaby *n.* пла́кса.
crying *n.* плач. —*adj.* вопию́щий: *crying injustice,* вопию́щая несправедли́вость. *A crying need,* о́страя необходи́мость. *It's a crying shame!,* стыд и срам!
crypt *n.* склеп.
cryptic *adj.* зага́дочный; немногосло́вный; двусмы́сленный.
cryptogram *n.* криптогра́мма.
cryptographer *n.* шифрова́льщик.
cryptography *n.* криптогра́фия. —**cryptographic,** *adj.* криптографи́ческий.
crystal *n.* **1,** (clear glass) хруста́ль. **2,** (solid body) криста́лл. **3,** (of a watch) (часово́е) стекло́. —*adj.* хруста́льный.
crystal-clear *adj.* **1,** (of water) криста́льный. **2,** *fig.* (obvious) преде́льно я́сный.
crystalline *adj.* кристалли́ческий.
crystallize *v.t.* кристаллизова́ть. —*v.i.* кристаллизова́ться. —**crystallization,** *n.* кристаллиза́ция.
cub *n.* детёныш. ♦*Compounds are rendered by the suffix* -ёнок *or* -о́нок: *lion cub,* львёнок; *bear cub,* медвежо́нок.
Cuban *adj.* куби́нский. —*n.* куби́нец; куби́нка.
cube *n.* **1,** (six-sided figure) куб. **2,** (small piece so shaped) ку́бик: *ice cube,* ку́бик льда. **3,** *math.* (third power) куб: *the cube of two is eight,* два в ку́бе – во́семь; куб двух ра́вен восьми́. —*v.t.* возводи́ть в куб. —**cube root,** куби́ческий ко́рень.
cubic *adj.* куби́ческий.
cubicle *n.* клету́шка.
cubism *n.* куби́зм.
cubit *n.* ло́коть.
cuckold *n.* рогоно́сец. —*v.t.* наставля́ть рога́ (+ *dat.*).
cuckoo *n.* куку́шка. —*v.i.* кукова́ть. —**cuckoo clock,** часы́ с куку́шкой.
cucumber *n.* огуре́ц. —*adj.* огуре́чный.
cud *n.* жва́чка: *chew the cud,* жева́ть жва́чку.
cuddle *v.t.* обнима́ть; прижима́ть к себе́. —*v.i.* [*usu.* **cuddle up**] прижима́ться.
cudgel *n.* дуби́на. —*v.t.* дуба́сить.
cue *n.* **1,** (signal on stage) ре́плика. **2,** *billiards* кий.
cuff *n.* **1,** (of a sleeve) манже́та; обшла́г. **2,** (of trousers) отворо́т. **3,** (slap) пощёчина. —**off the cuff,** *colloq.* экспро́мтом.
cuff link за́понка.
cuirass *n.* кира́са.
cuisine *n.* ку́хня.
culinary *adj.* кулина́рный.
cull *v.t.* **1,** (select) че́рпать. **2,** (pick; gather, as flowers) собира́ть.
culminate *v.i.* [*usu.* **culminate in**] конча́ться (+ *instr.*); вылива́ться в. —**culmination,** *n.* кульмина́ция; кульминацио́нный пункт.
culpable *adj.* вино́вный. —**culpability,** *n.* вино́вность.
culprit *n.* вино́вник.
cult *n.* культ.
cultivate *v.t.* **1,** (till) обраба́тывать; возде́лывать. **2,** (grow, as plants) выра́щивать; разводи́ть. **3,** *fig.* (develop) развива́ть; воспи́тывать; культиви́ровать; утонча́ть. **4,** (seek the good will of) заи́скивать пе́ред; льну́ть к.
cultivated *adj.* **1,** (tilled) обрабо́танный. **2,** (cultured) культу́рный; образо́ванный. **3,** (refined) утончённый.
cultivation *n.* **1,** (tillage) обрабо́тка. **2,** (development) разви́тие; воспита́ние.
cultural *adj.* культу́рный.
culture *n.* культу́ра. —**cultured,** *adj.* культу́рный.
cumbersome *adj.* громо́здкий.
cummerbund *n.* куша́к.
cumulative *adj.* кумуляти́вный.
cumulous *adj.* кучево́й. —**cumulus,** *n.* кучевы́е облака́.
cuneiform *n.* кли́нопись.
cunning *adj.* хи́трый. —*n.* хи́трость.
cup *n.* **1,** (vessel) ча́шка. *Paper cup,* бума́жный стака́нчик. **2,** *sports* (trophy) ку́бок. —*v.t., in* **cup one's hand,** держа́ть ру́ку го́рстью.
cupboard *n.* шкаф.
Cupid *n.* Купидо́н.
cupidity *n.* жа́дность; а́лчность.
cupola *n.* ку́пол.
cupping glass ба́нка.
cur *n.* ублю́док.
curable *adj.* излечи́мый.
curative *adj.* лече́бный; целе́бный; цели́тельный.
curator *n.* храни́тель.
curb *n.* **1,** (check; restraint) узда́. **2,** (edge of a sidewalk) обо́чина. —*v.t.* обу́здывать; укроща́ть.
curd *n., often pl.* творо́г.
curdle *v.t.* створа́живать. —*v.i.* свёртываться; створа́живаться.
cure *v.t.* **1,** (heal; remedy) выле́чивать; изле́чивать: *cure an illness,* выле́чивать/изле́чивать боле́знь. *Cure someone of an illness,* выле́чивать/изле́чивать кого́-нибудь от боле́зни. **2,** (preserve, as meat) вя́лить; соли́ть; копти́ть. —*n.* **1,** (treatment) курс лече́ния; излече́ние. **2,** (recovery of one's health) излече́ние. **3,** (remedy) сре́дство: *a cure for cancer,* сре́дство от ра́ка.
cure-all *n.* панаце́я.
curfew *n.* коменда́нтский час.
curia *n.* ку́рия.
curiosity *n.* **1,** (inquisitiveness) любопы́тство. **2,** (thirst for knowledge) любозна́тельность. **3,** (something that arouses interest) ре́дкость; дико́вина.
curious *adj.* **1,** (eager to find out; inquisitive) любопы́тный. *I am curious to know,* мне любопы́тно знать... *A curious look,* любопы́тный взгляд. **2,** (eager to learn; inquiring) любозна́тельный. **3,** (odd; strange) курьёзный.
curiously *adv.* любопы́тно. *Curiously enough...,* как ни стра́нно...
curium *n.* кю́рий.
curl *n.* ло́кон; завито́к; *pl.* ку́дри. —*v.t.* **1,** (form into ringlets, as hair) завива́ть. **2,** (cause to curve, as

paper) коро́бить. **3,** *in* **curl one's lip,** криви́ть гу́бы. —*v.i.* **1,** (of hair) завива́ться; ви́ться. **2,** (of paper) коро́биться. **3,** (of smoke) клуби́ться. **4,** *fol. by* **up** (sit or lie cozily) свёртываться.

curler *n.* бигуди́; папилько́тка.

curlew *n.* кро́ншнеп.

curlicue *n.* завиту́шка; крючо́к.

curling irons щипцы́ для зави́вки.

curly *adj.* кудря́вый; курча́вый; вью́щийся.

currant *n.* **1,** (fruit or berry) сморо́дина. **2,** (seedless raisin) кори́нка.

currency *n.* **1,** (money) валю́та; де́ньги. *Foreign currency,* иностра́нная валю́та. **2,** (prevalence; vogue) хожде́ние: *enjoy wide currency,* име́ть широ́кое хожде́ние. —*adj.* валю́тный: *currency reform,* валю́тная рефо́рма.

current *n.* **1,** (flow) тече́ние: *against the current,* про́тив тече́ния. *Air current,* возду́шное тече́ние. *A current of air,* струя́ во́здуха. **2,** *electricity* ток. —*adj.* теку́щий; ны́нешний; тепе́решний. *Current events,* теку́щие собы́тия. —**currently,** *adv.* ны́не; в настоя́щее вре́мя.

curriculum *n.* курс обуче́ния; уче́бный план.

currier *n.* коже́вник.

curry *v.t.* выде́лывать (ко́жу). —**curry favor,** заи́скивать.

currycomb *n.* скребни́ца.

curse *n.* **1,** (imprecation) прокля́тие. **2,** (bane) бич. —*v.t.* **1,** (damn) проклина́ть. **2,** *fol. by* **out** (berate) руга́ть; обруга́ть. —*v.i.* (swear) руга́ться. —**curse word,** бра́нное сло́во; руга́тельство.

cursed *adj.* прокля́тый.

cursive *adj.* рукопи́сный. *Cursive writing,* ско́ропись.

cursory *adj.* бе́глый. —**cursorily,** *adv.* бе́гло.

curt *adj.* ре́зкий; отры́вистый.

curtail *v.t.* сокраща́ть; уре́зывать. —**curtailment,** *n.* сокраще́ние.

curtain *n.* **1,** (for a window) занаве́ска. **2,** (on stage) за́навес. —*v.t.* заве́шивать; занаве́шивать. —**curtain call,** вы́зов (на сце́ну). —**curtain rod,** па́лка для гарди́н.

curtsy *also,* **curtsey** *n.* рevера́нс; приседа́ние; кни́ксен. —*v.i.* де́лать рeвера́нс; приседа́ть.

curvature *n.* кривизна́; искривле́ние.

curve *n.* **1,** (arc) крива́я. **2,** (bend) изги́б; изви́лина. **3,** (draftsman's instrument) лека́ло. —*v.t.* изгиба́ть. —*v.i.* изгиба́ться.

curved *adj.* изо́гнутый.

curvilinear *adj.* криволине́йный.

cushion *n.* **1,** (pillow) поду́шка. **2,** (rim of a billiard table) борт. —*v.t.* смягча́ть (уда́р).

cuspid *n.* клык.

cuspidor *n.* плева́тельница.

cuss *v.i., colloq.* руга́ться. —*v.t.* [*usu.* **cuss out**] *colloq.* разруга́ть. —*n., colloq.* ма́лый: *a queer old cuss,* стра́нный ма́лый.

custard *n.* заварно́й крем.

custodian *n.* **1,** (caretaker) храни́тель. **2,** (janitor) дво́рник.

custody *n.* **1,** (guardianship) опе́ка; попече́ние. **2,** (detention) аре́ст. *In custody,* под аре́стом; под стра́жей. *Take into custody,* брать под аре́ст; брать под стра́жу.

custom *n.* обы́чай. *See also* **customs.**

customary *adj.* обы́чный; привы́чный. —**customarily,** *adv.* обы́чно.

customer *n.* зака́зчик; покупа́тель; клие́нт.

custom-made *adj.* сде́ланный на зака́з.

customs *n.pl.* **1,** (agency) тамо́жня. *Pass through customs,* проходи́ть тамо́женный осмо́тр. **2,** (duty) по́шлина. —*adj.* тамо́женный: *customs inspector,* тамо́женный надсмо́трщик.

cut *v.t.* **1,** (divide into parts; slice; carve) ре́зать. **2,** (hurt; gash) поре́зать: *cut one's finger,* поре́зать себе́ па́лец. *Cut oneself,* поре́заться. **3,** (trim) подреза́ть (но́гти); стричь (во́лосы); среза́ть (цветы́). **4,** (mow) коси́ть. **5,** (cut out, as cloth) крои́ть. **6,** (shape, as gems) грани́ть. **7,** (divide in two, as of a road or river) рассека́ть. **8,** (have grown in, as a tooth) прореза́ться: *he is cutting a tooth,* у него́ прореза́ется зуб. **9,** (reduce, as prices, taxes, etc.) снижа́ть. **10,** (shorten, as a book, article, etc.) сокраща́ть; уре́зывать. **11,** *cards* снима́ть (коло́ду). **12,** *colloq.* (fail to attend, as a class) прогу́ливать. —*v.i.* **1,** (act as a sharp edge) ре́зать: *the knife does not cut,* нож не ре́жет. **2,** (admit to being cut) ре́заться: *the meat cuts easily,* мя́со легко́ ре́жется. **3,** *cards* снима́ть коло́ду. —*n.* **1,** (gash) поре́з. **2,** (of meat) кусо́к. **3,** (style of a garment) покро́й. **4,** (deletion) купю́ра. **5,** (reduction) сниже́ние; сокраще́ние. —*adj.* **1,** (gashed) поре́занный. **2,** (trimmed, as of flowers) сре́занный. **3,** (of gems, glass, etc.) гранёный. **4,** (reduced) льго́тный. —**cut across,** пересека́ть. —**cut back,** уре́зывать. —**cut down, 1,** (fell) руби́ть; сруба́ть; выруба́ть. **2,** (kill) среза́ть; сража́ть. **3,** (reduce) уре́зывать. —**cut off, 1,** (sever) отреза́ть. **2,** (isolate) разобща́ть. **3,** (halt) прекраща́ть. **4,** (rudely interrupt) оборва́ть. **5,** (on the telephone) прерыва́ть; разъедини́ть: *we've been cut off,* нас прерва́ли/разъедини́ли. —**cut out, 1,** (remove by cutting) выреза́ть. **2,** (shape by cutting, as material) выкра́ивать. **3,** (remove; delete) вычёркивать. **4,** *colloq.* (discontinue; give up) бро́сить (кури́ть); отказа́ться от (мя́са). **5,** *slang* (cease) переста́ть; бро́сить; прекрати́ть. *Cut it out!,* прекрати́! —**cut out for; cut out to be,** со́зданный для: *he is not cut out for it,* он не со́здан для э́того. *He is not cut out to be a soldier,* он не годи́тся в солда́ты. —**cut short,** оборва́ть. —**cut through, 1,** (cut across) пересека́ть. **2,** (penetrate) рассека́ть. —**cut up,** разреза́ть; ре́зать.

cutaway *n.* визи́тка. *Also,* **cutaway coat.**

cutback *n.* сокраще́ние.

cute *adj., colloq.* **1,** (pretty) хоро́шенький; ми́ленький. **2,** (clever) у́мный; остроу́мный.

cutlass *n.* теса́к.

cutlery *n.* ножево́й това́р.

cutlet *n.* (отбивна́я) котле́та. *Veal cutlet,* теля́чья отбивна́я.

cut-rate *adj.* льго́тный.

cutter *n.* **1,** (one who cuts) ре́зальщик. *Diamond cutter,* грани́льщик. *Wood cutter,* лесору́б. **2,** (of cloth) закро́йщик. **3,** (tool) резе́ц; реза́к. **4,** (boat) ка́тер; те́ндер.

cutthroat *n.* головоре́з. —*adj.* жесто́кий; ожесточённый.

cutting *n.* **1,** (act of cutting) ре́зание. **2,** (work of cutting material) кро́йка. **3,** (plant shoot used for grafting) черено́к. —*adj.* **1,** (that cuts) ре́жущий. **2,** (chilling or piercing) ре́зкий. **3,** (sarcastic) ко́лкий.

cuttlefish *n.* каракатица; сепия.
cyanic *adj.* циановый; цианистый.
cyanide *n.* цианид. —**potassium cyanide,** цианистый калий.
cyanogen *n.* циан.
cyanosis *n.* цианоз; синюха.
cybernetics *n.* кибернетика.
cyclamen *n.* цикламен.
cycle *n.* цикл. —*v.i.* ездить на велосипеде. —**cyclical,** *adj.* циклический.
cyclist *n.* **1,** (rider) велосипедист. **2,** (racer) велогонщик.
cyclone *n.* циклон. —**cyclonic,** *adj.* циклонический.
cyclotron *n.* циклотрон.
cylinder *n.* **1,** (geometric figure; object so shaped) цилиндр. **2,** (rotating part of a revolver) барабан. —**cylindrical,** *adj.* цилиндрический.
cymbals *n.pl.* тарелки.
cynic *n.* циник. —**cynical,** *adj.* циничный. —**cynicism,** *n.* цинизм; циничность.
cypress *n.* кипарис.
Cyrillic alphabet кириллица.
cyst *n.* киста.
cytology *n.* цитология. —**cytological,** *adj.* цитологический.
czar *n.* = **tsar.**
Czech *adj.* чешский. —*n.* **1,** (person) чех; чешка. **2,** (language) чешский язык.
Czechoslovak *adj.* чехословацкий.

D

D, d четвёртая буква английского алфавита. —*n.* **1,** (musical note) ре. **2,** (school grade) двойка.
dab *v.t.* **1,** (pat gently): *dab one's eyes with a handkerchief,* прикладывать платок к глазам. **2,** (apply liquid to) мазать. —*n.* (of paint) мазок; (of rouge) капелька.
dabble *v.i.* [*usu.* **dabble in**] заниматься (поверхностно). —**dabbler,** *n.* любитель; дилетант.
dacha *n.* дача.
dachshund *n.* такса.
dactyl *n.* дактиль. —**dactylic,** *adj.* дактилический.
dad *n., colloq.* папа. *Also,* **daddy.**
daffodil *n.* нарцисс.
daffy *adj., slang* сумасбродный.
daft *adj.* сумасшедший.
dagger *n.* **1,** (knife) кинжал. **2,** *printing* (†) крестик.
dahlia *n.* георгин.
daily *adj.* ежедневный. —*adv.* ежедневно. —*n.* ежедневная газета.
dainty *adj.* **1,** (delicately pretty or graceful) изящный; утончённый. **2,** (delicious and choice) лакомый.
dairy *n.* молочная. —*adj.* молочный: *dairy products,* молочные продукты. – **dairy farm,** молочная ферма; молочное хозяйство. —**dairymaid,** *n.* молочница. —**dairyman,** *n.* молочник.
dais *n.* помост; возвышение.
daisy *n.* **1,** (English daisy) маргаритка. **2,** (oxeye daisy) нивяник; поповник.
dale *n.* долина; ложбина; лощина.
dally *v.i.* **1,** (dawdle) мешкать. **2,** *fol. by* **with** (trifle with; toy with) играть (+ *instr.*).
dam *n.* **1,** (barrier) плотина. **2,** (female parent of an animal) матка. —*v.t.* запруживать; перекрывать.
damage *n.* **1,** (harm; injury) вред; повреждение; ущерб; порча. **2,** *pl.* (compensation for losses) убытки: *suit for damages,* иск за убытки. *Pay damages,* возмещать убытки. —*v.t.* повреждать. *Be damaged,* пострадать. —**damaging,** *adj.* вредный.
damask *n.* штоф. —*adj.* штофный.
dame *n.* **1,** (lady) дама. **2,** *slang* (woman) баба.
damn *v.t.* проклинать. —*adj., colloq.* проклятый. *Damn fool,* набитый дурак. —*adv., colloq.* чертовски. *You're damn right!,* вы совершенно правы. —*interj.* чёрт (возьми)!; проклятие! —**not give a damn,** (на) плевать: *he doesn't give a damn,* ему (на)плевать на это. —**not worth a damn,** гроша медного (*or* выеденного яйца) не стоит.
damnable *adj.* **1,** (meriting damnation) предосудительный. **2,** *colloq.* (accursed) проклятый.
damnation *n.* **1,** (act of damning) проклятие. **2,** (eternal punishment) вечные муки.
damned *adj.* проклятый. *I'll be damned if...,* будь я проклят, если...
damning *adj.* изобличительный.
damp *adj.* сырой; влажный. —*v.t.* [*usu.* **damp down**] тушить.
dampen *v.t.* **1,** (moisten) смачивать. **2,** (cool, as enthusiasm, etc.) омрачать; охлаждать.
damper *n.* заслонка; вьюшка. —**put a damper on,** расхолаживать; омрачать.
dampness *n.* сырость; влажность.
damsel *n.* девица.
dance *v.t. & i.* танцевать. *Ask someone to dance,* пригласить кого-нибудь на танец. —*n.* **1,** (dancing; kind of dance) танец: *folk dance,* народный танец; *modern dance,* танец модерн. **2,** (gathering of people for dancing) танцы; танцевальный вечер; бал. *Invite someone to a dance,* пригласить кого-нибудь на танцы. —*adj.* танцевальный: *dance hall,* танцевальный зал. —**dance attendance on,** ходить на задних лапках перед. —**dance to someone's tune,** плясать под чью-нибудь дудку.

dancer *n.* **1,** (one who dances) танцо́р. **2,** (professional dancer) танцо́вщик; танцо́вщица.
dancing *n.* та́нцы: *folk dancing,* наро́дные та́нцы. —*adj.* танцева́льный. *Dancing lessons,* уро́ки та́нцев.
dandelion *n.* одува́нчик.
dander *n., usu. in* **get one's dander up,** разозли́ться.
dandle *v.t.* кача́ть.
dandruff *n.* пе́рхоть.
dandy *n.* **1,** (fop) щёголь; франт. **2,** *colloq.* (excellent thing) пре́лесть.—*adj., colloq.* преле́стный.
Dane *n.* датча́нин; датча́нка. —**Great Dane,** да́тский дог.
danger *n.* опа́сность. *Danger signal,* сигна́л опа́сности.
dangerous *adj.* опа́сный. —**dangerously,** *adv.* опа́сно. *Dangerously ill,* опа́сно *or* тяжело́ бо́лен.
dangle *v.t.* болта́ть. —*v.i.* болта́ться.
Danish *adj.* да́тский. —*n.* да́тский язы́к
dank *adj.* сыро́й; промо́зглый.
dapper *adj.* вы́холенный; щеголева́тый.
dapple *v.t.* испещря́ть. —*adj.* = **dappled.** —*n.* подпа́лина.
dappled *adj.* **1,** (spotted) пятни́стый. **2,** (of a horse) чуба́рый.
dapple-gray *adj.* се́рый в я́блоках.
dare *v.t. & i.* сметь; осме́ливаться. *How dare you...!,* как ты сме́ешь (+ *inf.*)! *He wouldn't dare to do it,* он не посме́ет э́то сде́лать. —*v.t.* вызыва́ть. *I dare you to...,* а ну (+ *imperative*). —**dare say,** сметь *or* осме́ливаться сказа́ть.
daredevil *n.* смельча́к; лиха́ч; удале́ц; головоре́з; сорвиголова́. —*adj.* опроме́тчивый; безрассу́дный.
daring *adj.* сме́лый. —*n.* сме́лость.
dark *adj.* тёмный. *Dark blue,* тёмно-си́ний. *Dark complexion,* сму́глое лицо́. *Get dark,* темне́ть. —*n.* темнота́; тьма; мрак. *Before dark,* за́светло. *After dark,* по́сле наступле́ния темноты́. —**be/keep in the dark,** быть/держа́ть в неве́дении.
darken *v.t.* затемня́ть —*v.i.* темне́ть.
dark-haired *adj.* темноволо́сый.
darkness *n.* темнота́; тьма; мрак.
darkroom *n.* тёмная ко́мната.
dark-skinned *adj.* темноко́жий.
darling *n.* **1,** (beloved person) ми́лый (ми́лая); дорого́й (дорога́я); ду́шенька; голу́бка. **2,** (someone in great favor) люби́мец; ба́ловень.—*adj.* **1,** (beloved) дорого́й; ми́лый. **2,** *colloq.* (cute; lovely) чуде́сный.
darn *v.t.* што́пать. —*adj., colloq.* [*also,* **darned**] прокля́тый.
darnel *n.* пле́вел.
darning needle **1,** (needle used in darning) што́пальная игла́. **2,** (dragonfly) стрекоза́.
dart *n.* **1,** (missile) стрела́. **2,** (dash; rush) бросо́к. —*v.i.* бро́ситься; ри́нуться; помча́ться. *Dart out from behind a bush,* вы́лететь из-за куста́.
dash *v.i.* **1,** (dart; rush) бро́ситься; ри́нуться; помча́ться. *Dash out of the room,* вы́бежать из ко́мнаты. **2,** (land with great force) би́ться; ударя́ться: *the waves dashed against the shore,* во́лны би́лись/ударя́лись о бе́рег. —*v.t.* **1,** (throw violently) бро́сить (изо всех сил): *dash to the ground,* бро́сить о зе́млю. **2,** (shatter, as hopes) разбива́ть (наде́жды). **3,** *fol. by* **off** (write hastily) набра́сывать. —*n.* **1,** (rush) бросо́к. *Make a dash for the door,* бро́ситься к две́ри. **2,** *sports* бег: *100-meter dash,* бег на сто ме́тров. **3,** (—) тире́. **4,** (bit; touch) при́месь.
dashboard *n.* прибо́рная доска́.
dashing *adj.* лихо́й; бра́вый; молодцева́тый.
dastard *n.* трус; подле́ц. —**dastardly,** *adj.* трусли́вый; по́длый.
data *n.pl.* да́нные. —**data bank/base,** спра́вочно-информацио́нный фонд. —**data processing,** обрабо́тка да́нных.
date *n.* **1,** (day of the month) число́: *what is today's date?,* како́е сего́дня число́? **2,** (statement of calendar time) да́та: *date of birth,* да́та рожде́ния. *Put the date on the letter,* проставля́ть да́ту на письме́. **3,** (day when something is to happen) срок: *by a certain date,* к определённому сро́ку. *Set the date,* назнача́ть срок. *Date of departure,* срок *or* день отъе́зда. **4,** (social engagement) свида́ние: *go out on dates,* ходи́ть на свида́ния. **5,** (fruit) фи́ник. —*v.t.* **1,** (put the date on) дати́ровать; помеча́ть: *the letter was dated May 6th,* письмо́ бы́ло дати́ровано/поме́чено шесты́м ма́я. **2,** (see socially) встреча́ться с. —*v.i.* относи́ться: *this building dates from the 15th century,* э́то зда́ние отно́сится к пятна́дцатому ве́ку. *Date back to ancient times,* восходи́ть к дре́вности. —**to date,** до сих пор. —**up to date,** в ку́рсе де́ла. *Bring up to date,* вводи́ть в курс де́ла. *See also* **out-of-date** *and* **up-to-date.**
dated *adj.* **1,** (marked with a date) дати́рованный. **2,** (outdated) устаре́вший.
date line Ли́ния переме́ны да́ты. *Also,* **International Date Line.**
date palm фи́никовая па́льма.
dative *adj.* да́тельный: *dative case,* да́тельный паде́ж.
daub *v.t. & i.* ма́зать; малева́ть; мара́ть. —*n.* мазня́; пачкотня́.
daughter *n.* дочь. —**daughter-in-law,** *n.* неве́стка; сноха́.
daunt *v.t.* **1,** (make afraid) запу́гивать; устраша́ть. **2,** (dishearten) обескура́живать. —**dauntless,** *adj.* неустраши́мый; бесстра́шный.
dauphin *n.* дофи́н.
davenport *n.* дива́н-крова́ть.
dawdle *v.i.* ме́шкать; ло́дырничать; кани́телиться.
dawn *n.* **1,** (daybreak) рассве́т; у́тренняя заря́. **2,** *fig.* (beginning) заря́. —*v.i.* **1,** (begin to grow light) света́ть; рассвета́ть: *day is dawning,* света́ет; рассвета́ет. **2,** *fol. by* **on** *or* **upon** (begin to be understood) озаря́ть: *it dawned on me,* меня́ озари́ла мысль.
day *n.* день. —*adj.* дневно́й: *the day shift,* дневна́я сме́на. —**any day (now),** со дня на́ день. —**day after day,** изо дня в день. —**day by day,** день ото дня. —**day off,** выходно́й день. —**in those days,** в те времена́. —**one of these days,** на днях. —**some day,** когда́-нибудь. —**the day before,** накану́не. —**the other day,** на днях. —**to this day,** по сей день.
daybed *n.* дива́н-крова́ть.
daybreak *n.* рассве́т.
daydream *n.* мечта́; грёза. —*v.i.* мечта́ть; грёзить. —**daydreaming,** *n.* мечта́ние.
daylight *n.* **1,** (light of day) дневно́й свет. *In broad daylight,* средь бе́ла дня. **2,** (dawn) рассве́т: *before daylight,* до рассве́та; за́темно. **3,** (daytime) дневно́е вре́мя: *two hours of daylight,* два часа́ дневно́го вре́мени. —**scare the daylights out of,** *colloq.* напуга́ть

до́ смерти. —**see daylight,** ви́деть вы́ход из положе́ния.

daytime *n.* дневно́е вре́мя. *In the daytime,* днём. —*adj.* дневно́й: *daytime activities,* дневны́е заня́тия.

day-to-day *adj.* повседне́вный.

daywork *n.* подённая рабо́та; подёнщина. —**day-worker,** *n.* подёнщик; подённый.

daze *n.* отупе́ние. *Be in a daze,* быть (как) в чаду́. —*v.t.* ошеломля́ть. —**dazed,** *adj.* обалде́лый.

dazzle *v.t.* ослепля́ть. —**dazzling,** *adj.* ослепи́тельный.

deacon *n.* дья́кон.

deactivate *v.t.* **1,** (disband) распуска́ть. **2,** (render inoperative) обезвре́живать.

dead *adj.* **1,** (of a person) мёртвый. *He is dead,* он у́мер. *Dead body,* труп. *Play dead,* притворя́ться мёртвым. **2,** (of an animal) до́хлый. **3,** (of trees, leaves, etc.) сухо́й. **4,** (failing to operate) загло́хший: *the motor went dead,* мото́р загло́х. **5,** *with certain nouns* мёртвый: *dead languages,* мёртвые языки́; *dead season,* мёртвый сезо́н; *dead silence,* мёртвая тишина́; *dead weight,* мёртвый груз. —*adv.* соверше́нно: *dead right,* соверше́нно прав. *Dead against,* реши́тельно про́тив. *Dead tired,* до́ смерти уста́лый. *Dead drunk,* мертве́цки пьян. *Stop dead in one's tracks,* останови́ться как вко́панный. —*n.* **1,** *preceded by* **the** (those who have died) мёртвые; уме́ршие. *Rise from the dead,* воскреса́ть. **2,** (coldest or darkest point) *rendered by* глубо́кий: *in the dead of night/winter,* глубо́кой но́чью/зимо́й.

dead center мёртвая то́чка: *move off dead center,* сдви́нуть(ся) с мёртвой то́чки.

deaden *v.t.* **1,** (make less intense) заглуша́ть: *deaden the sound/pain,* заглуша́ть звук/боль. **2,** (make numb) умерщвля́ть: *deaden a tooth,* умерщвля́ть нерв зу́ба.

dead end тупи́к.

dead letter 1, (undelivered letter) недоста́вленное письмо́. **2,** (something no longer valid or enforced) мёртвая бу́ква.

deadline *n.* срок; после́дний срок; кра́йний срок; преде́льный срок. *The deadline for payment,* срок платежа́.

deadlock *n.* мёртвая то́чка; тупи́к. —*v.t.* заводи́ть в тупи́к. *Be deadlocked,* заходи́ть в тупи́к.

deadly *adj.* смерте́льный; смертоно́сный. —*adv., colloq.* смерте́льно: *deadly dull,* смерте́льно ску́чно.

dead reckoning счисле́ние пути́.

deaf *adj.* глухо́й. *Become deaf,* (о)гло́хнуть. *Be deaf to,* быть глухи́м к. —**fall on deaf ears,** оста́ться без внима́ния. —**turn a deaf ear to,** пропусти́ть ми́мо уше́й.

deaf-and-dumb *adj.* глухонемо́й.

deafen *v.t.* оглуша́ть. —**deafening,** *adj.* оглуши́тельный.

deaf-mute *n.* глухонемо́й.

deafness *n.* глухота́.

deal *n.* **1,** (transaction) сде́лка. **2,** *cards* сда́ча. **3,** *in a* **great** (*or* **good**) **deal,** мно́го: *a great deal of money,* мно́го де́нег. *I learned a great deal,* я мно́гому научи́лся. *She is a good deal better today,* ей сего́дня значи́тельно лу́чше. —*v.t.* **1,** *usu. fol. by* **out** (apportion; distribute) раздава́ть; распределя́ть. **2,** *cards* сдава́ть (ка́рты). **3,** (administer, as a blow) наноси́ть (уда́р). —*v.i.* **1,** *cards* сдава́ть ка́рты. *Who deals?,* кто сдаёт? **2,** *fol. by* **in** (sell; trade) торгова́ть (+ *instr.*). —**deal with, 1,** (have dealings with) име́ть де́ло с. **2,** (behave toward) поступа́ть с. **3,** (handle; take care of) справля́ться с. **4,** (take up; treat) рассма́тривать.

dealer *n.* **1,** (merchant; seller) торго́вец. **2,** *cards* тот, кто сдаёт ка́рты: *who is the dealer?,* кто сдаёт?

dealing *n.* **1,** (conduct toward others) поведе́ние: *honest dealing,* че́стное поведе́ние. **2,** *usu. pl.* (transactions) (торго́вые) дела́.

dean *n.* **1,** (university official) дека́н. **2,** (of a cathedral) настоя́тель. **3,** (senior member) старшина́.

dear *adj.* дорого́й. —*n., used in direct address* дорого́й (дорога́я); ми́лый (ми́лая). —**oh dear!; dear me!,** бо́же мой!; о бо́же!; го́споди!

dearly *adv.* до́рого: *pay dearly for,* до́рого заплати́ть за. *It cost him dearly,* э́то ему́ до́рого обошло́сь. *Love someone dearly,* горячо́ люби́ть кого́-нибудь.

dearth *n.* недоста́ток; нехва́тка.

death *n.* смерть. *Be near death,* быть при́ смерти. *Sentence to death,* пригова́ривать к сме́ртной ка́зни. *Put to death,* предава́ть сме́рти. —*adj.* сме́ртный: *death penalty,* сме́ртная казнь; *death sentence,* сме́ртный пригово́р. *Death rate,* сме́ртность. *Death certificate,* свиде́тельство о сме́рти. —**at death's door,** при́ смерти. —**be the death of,** своди́ть в моги́лу; сжива́ть со све́та. —**to death,** до́ смерти: *frighten to death,* напуга́ть до́ смерти. *Be bored to death,* смерте́льно скуча́ть. —**to the death,** на́смерть: *fight to the death,* сража́ться на́смерть; боро́ться (*or* борьба́) не на жизнь, а на смерть.

deathbed *n.* сме́ртное ло́же. *On one's deathbed,* на сме́ртном одре́.

deathblow *n.* смерте́льный уда́р.

deathly *adj.* мёртвенный: *deathly pallor,* мёртвенная бле́дность. *Deathly silence,* гробово́е молча́ние. —*adv.* смерте́льно: *be deathly afraid of,* смерте́льно боя́ться (+ *gen.*).

death mask посме́ртная ма́ска.

debacle *n.* катастро́фа.

debar *v.t.* **1,** (shut out) не допуска́ть. **2,** (prevent) лиша́ть пра́ва: *debar from voting,* лиша́ть пра́ва го́лоса.

debark *v.t.* выса́живать. —*v.i.* выса́живаться. —**debarkation,** *n.* вы́садка.

debase *v.t.* **1,** (cheapen) обесце́нивать: *debase the currency,* обесце́нивать валю́ту. **2,** (lower in dignity) унижа́ть. *Debase oneself,* унижа́ться.

debatable *adj.* спо́рный; оспори́мый; дискуссио́нный. *That's debatable,* э́то спо́рный вопро́с.

debate *v.i.* дебати́ровать. —*v.t.* **1,** (discuss) обсужда́ть; дебати́ровать; дискути́ровать. **2,** (consider; weigh) сообража́ть, взве́шивать. —*n.* **1,** (discussion) деба́ты; пре́ния; диску́ссия. **2,** (formal contest) ди́спут.

debauch *v.t.* развраща́ть; совраща́ть. —**debauchery,** *n.* развра́т; разгу́л.

debenture *n.* облига́ция.

debilitate *v.t.* ослабля́ть; расслабля́ть. —**debilitation,** *n.* ослабле́ние; расслабле́ние.

debility *n.* сла́бость; бесси́лие.

debit *n.* де́бет. —*v.t.* дебетова́ть.

debonair *adj.* **1,** (affable; gracious) любе́зный. **2,** (carefree; gay) весёлый; жизнера́достный.

debris *n.* обло́мки.

debt *n.* долг. *I am in your debt,* я у вас в долгу́.

debtor *n.* должни́к. *Debtor's prison,* долгова́я тюрьма́; долгова́я я́ма.
debut *n.* дебю́т. *Make one's debut,* дебюти́ровать. —**debutante,** *n.* дебюта́нтка.
decade *n.* десятиле́тие.
decadence *n.* упа́дочничество; декаде́нтство.
decadent *adj.* упа́дочный; упа́дочнический; декаде́нтский. —*n.* декаде́нт.
decagon *n.* десятиуго́льник.
decahedron *n.* десятигра́нник. —**decahedral,** *adj.* десятигра́нный.
decal *n.* переводна́я карти́нка.
decamp *v.i.* **1,** (break camp) снима́ться с ла́геря. **2,** (depart) удира́ть; смыва́ться.
decanter *n.* графи́н.
decapitate *v.t.* обезгла́вливать. —**decapitation,** *n.* обезгла́вливание.
decathlon *n.* десятибо́рье.
decay *v.i.* **1,** (rot; decompose) гнить; разлага́ться; (*of teeth*) по́ртится. **2,** (deteriorate physically) ветша́ть. *Decaying building,* обветша́лое зда́ние. **3,** *fig.* (go into a decline) приходи́ть в упа́док. —*n.* **1,** (decomposition) гние́ние; разложе́ние. *Tooth decay,* ка́риес зубо́в. **2,** (decline) упа́док. **3,** *chem.; physics* распа́д.
deceased *adj.* поко́йный. —*n., preceded by* **the** поко́йник; поко́йный; уме́рший.
deceit *n.* обма́н. —**deceitful,** *adj.* обма́нный; лжи́вый.
deceive *v.t. & i.* обма́нывать.
decelerate *v.t.* замедля́ть. —*v.i.* замедля́ть ход. —**deceleration,** *n.* замедле́ние.
December *n.* дека́брь. —*adj.* дека́брьский. —**Decembrist,** *n.* декабри́ст.
decency *n.* прили́чие. *A man without decency,* бессо́вестный челове́к. *He didn't have the decency to apologize,* у него́ хвати́ло со́вести не извини́ться.
decent *adj.* **1,** (proper) прили́чный. **2,** (respectable) поря́дочный. **3,** (adequate; passable) прили́чный. **4,** (kind; thoughtful) любе́зный. —**decently,** *adv.* прили́чно.
decentralize *v.t.* децентрализова́ть. —**decentralization,** *n.* децентрализа́ция.
deception *n.* обма́н. —**deceptive,** *adj.* обма́нчивый.
decibel *n.* децибе́л.
decide *v.t. & i.* реша́ть: *I decided to leave,* я реши́л(а) уе́хать. *Decide the outcome of,* реша́ть исхо́д (+ *gen.*). *Decide on a course of action,* реши́ться на (како́й-нибудь) посту́пок.
decided *adj.* я́вный; бесспо́рный; реши́тельный. —**decidedly,** *adv.* реши́тельно.
deciduous *adj.* листопа́дный.
decigram *also,* **decigramme** *n.* децигра́мм.
deciliter *also,* **decilitre** *n.* децили́тр.
decimal *adj.* десяти́чный. —*n.* десяти́чная дробь.
decimate *v.t.* разоря́ть; коси́ть.
decimeter *also,* **decimetre** *n.* дециме́тр.
decipher *v.t.* **1,** (decode) расшифро́вывать; дешифри́ровать. **2,** (read; make out) разбира́ть. —**decipherment,** *n.* расшифро́вка; дешифро́вка.
decision *n.* реше́ние.
decisive *adj.* **1,** (forceful; conclusive) реши́тельный: *decisive person,* реши́тельный челове́к; *decisive victory,* реши́тельная побе́да. **2,** (determining the final outcome) реша́ющий: *decisive factor,* реша́ющий фа́ктор. —**decisively,** *adv.* реши́тельно. —**decisiveness,** *n.* реши́тельность.
deck *n.* **1,** (of a ship) па́луба. **2,** (pack of cards) коло́да. —*v.t.* [*usu.* **deck out**] принаряжа́ть: *decked out in a new suit,* принаряжённый в но́вый костю́м.
deckhouse *n.* ру́бка.
declaim *v.t. & i.* деклами́ровать.
declamation *n.* деклама́ция. —**declamatory,** *adj.* декламацио́нный.
declaration *n.* объявле́ние; деклара́ция. *Declaration of love,* объясне́ние в любви́. *Customs declaration,* тамо́женная деклара́ция.
declarative *adj.* **1,** (making a statement or assertion) декларати́вный. **2,** *gram.* повествова́тельный.
declare *v.t.* **1,** (announce formally; proclaim) объявля́ть: *declare war on,* объяви́ть войну́ (+ *dat.*). **2,** (assert; avow) заявля́ть. **3,** (pronounce) признава́ть: *declare someone insane,* призна́ть кого́-нибудь душевнобольны́м. **4,** (make a statement of, as taxable goods) называ́ть. *Have you anything to declare?,* у вас есть что́-нибудь, подлежа́щее обложе́нию по́шлиной? —**declare oneself,** выска́зываться.
declassify *v.t.* рассекре́чивать.
declension *n., gram.* склоне́ние.
declinable *adj.* склоня́емый.
declination *n.* **1,** *astron.* склоне́ние. **2,** (magnetic declination) магни́тное отклоне́ние.
decline *v.t.* **1,** (turn down) отклоня́ть; отка́зываться от. **2,** *fol. by inf.* (refuse) отка́зываться. **3,** *gram.* склоня́ть. —*v.i.* **1,** (refuse to accept something) отка́зываться. **2,** (decrease; go down) уменьша́ться; па́дать. **3,** (deteriorate) приходи́ть в упа́док. —*n.* **1,** (downward slope) склон. **2,** (drop; reduction) паде́ние; сниже́ние. **3,** (deterioration) упа́док.
declivity *n.* склон; спуск; отко́с.
decoction *n.* отва́р.
decode *v.t.* расшифро́вывать. —**decoding,** *n.* расшифро́вка.
décolleté *adj.* декольте́; декольтиро́ванный. —**décolletage,** *n.* декольте́.
decompose *v.t.* разлага́ть. —*v.i.* разлага́ться. —**decomposition,** *n.* разложе́ние.
decontaminate *v.t.* **1,** (rid of germs) обеззара́живать. **2,** (rid of poisonous or radioactive substances) дегази́ровать. —**decontamination,** *n.* обеззара́живание; дегаза́ция.
decontrol *v.t.* освобожда́ть от контро́ля.
décor *n.* обстано́вка.
decorate *v.t.* **1,** (adorn) украша́ть; декори́ровать. **2,** (furnish) обставля́ть; отде́лывать. **3,** (award a medal to) награжда́ть.
decoration *n.* **1,** (act of decorating) украше́ние. **2,** (ornament) украше́ние. **3,** (award) о́рден; знак отли́чия.
decorative *adj.* декорати́вный.
decorator *n.* декора́тор.
decorous *adj.* прили́чный; присто́йный; чи́нный.
decorum *n.* прили́чие; деко́рум.
decoy *n.* прима́нка. —*v.t.* зама́нивать; прима́нивать.
decrease *v.t.* уменьша́ть. —*v.i.* уменьша́ться. —*n.* уменьше́ние.
decree *n.* ука́з; декре́т; постановле́ние. —*v.t. & i.* постановля́ть.
decrepit *adj.* дря́хлый. —**decrepitude,** *n.* дря́хлость.

decry *v.t.* осуждáть; порицáть.
dedicate *v.t.* **1,** (devote; inscribe) посвящáть. *Dedicate a book to,* посвятúть кнúгу (+ *dat.*). **2,** (open formally) открывáть. —**dedicated,** *adj.* прéданный.
dedication *n.* **1,** (act of dedicating) посвящéние. **2,** (formal opening) откры́тие. **3,** (devotion) прéданность.
deduce *v.t.* выводúть: *from this I deduced that...,* из э́того я вы́вел, что...
deduct *v.t.* **1,** (subtract) вычитáть. **2,** (withhold) удéрживать; отчислять.
deduction *n.* **1,** (subtraction; withholding) вы́чет; удержáние. **2,** (reasoning) дедýкция. **3,** (conclusion) вы́вод. —**deductive,** *adj.* дедуктúвный.
deed *n.* **1,** (act) постýпок; дéло. *Good deed,* дóброе дéло. **2,** (exploit) пóдвиг. **3,** *pl.* (action, as opposed to words) делá. **4,** (legal document) акт; грáмота.
deem *v.t.* считáть: *deem something necessary,* считáть чтó-нибудь необходúмым.
de-emphasize *v.t.* преуменьшáть.
deep *adj.* **1,** (extending far down, back or into) глубóкий: *deep hole/river,* глубóкая я́ма/рекá. *Deep cut,* глубóкий порéз. **2,** (having a specified depth): глубинóй в: *ten meters deep,* глубинóй в дéсять мéтров. **3,** (profound; intense) глубóкий. **4,** (of sleep) глубóкий; беспробýдный. **5,** (absorbed, as in thought) погружённый (в мы́сли). **6,** (low-pitched) нúзкий; густóй. **7,** (dark, as of a color) тёмный: *deep blue,* тёмно-сúний. —*adv.* глубокó: *dig deep,* ры́ть глубокó. —**deep into,** вглубь (+ *gen.*).
deepen *v.t.* углублять. —*v.i.* углубляться.
deeply *adv.* глубокó.
deep-rooted *adj.* укоренúвшийся; закоренéлый.
deep-sea *adj.* глубоковóдный. *Deep-sea fishing,* лóвля ры́бы в глубóких вóдах. *Deep-sea diving,* водолáзное дéло.
deep-seated *adj.* укоренúвшийся.
deer *n.* олéнь. —*adj.* [*also,* **deer's**] олéний: *deer hide,* олéнья шкýра.
deerskin *n.* олéнья шкýра. —*adj.* олéний: *deerskin coat,* олéнья шýба.
deface *v.t.* **1,** (mar; disfigure) урóдовать; обезобрáживать. **2,** (efface; obliterate) стирáть; изглáживать.
de facto **1,** *used adverbially* де-фáкто. **2,** *used adjectivally* фактúческий: *de facto recognition,* фактúческое признáние.
defamation *n.* диффамáция; поношéние; клеветá. —**defamatory,** *adj.* клеветнúческий.
defame *v.t.* поносúть; клеветáть.
default *n.* **1,** (failure to pay money due) неплатёж. **2,** (failure to appear) неявка. —*v.i.* не выполнять обязáтельств. —**defaulter,** *n.* неплатéльщик.
defeat *n.* поражéние: *suffer a defeat,* потерпéть поражéние. *Admit defeat,* признáть себя побеждённым. —*v.t.* **1,** (vanquish) побеждáть. **2,** (beat in a game) побеждáть; (по)бúть; вы́игрывать у; обы́грывать. **3,** (thwart; frustrate) расстрáивать; срывáть.
defeatism *n.* поражéнчество.
defeatist *n.* поражéнец. —*adj.* поражéнческий.
defecate *v.i.* испражняться. —**defecation,** *n.* испражнéние.
defect *n.* порóк; недостáток; дефéкт; брак; изъян. *Speech defect,* дефéкт рéчи. —*v.i.* перебегáть; переметнýться.
defection *n.* перебéжка.
defective *adj.* **1,** (imperfect; faulty) неисправный; дефéктный; бракóванный. **2,** (subnormal in intelligence) дефектúвный.
defector *n.* невозвращéнец; перебéжчик.
defence *n.* = **defense.**
defend *v.t.* **1,** (protect) защищáть; оборонять. **2,** (uphold) защищáть; отстáивать. **3,** (represent in court) защищáть.
defendant *n., law* подсудúмый; обвиняемый; ответчик.
defender *n.* защúтник.
defense *also,* **defence** *n.* **1,** (protection) защúта: *self-defense,* самозащúта. **2,** *mil.* оборóна: *minister of defense,* минúстр оборóны. *Break through the enemy's defenses,* прорвáть оборóну протúвника. **3,** *law; sports* защúта: *witness for the defense,* свидéтель защúты. —**defense attorney,** защúтник.
defenseless *adj.* беззащúтный.
defenseman *n.* защúтник.
defensive *adj.* оборонúтельный. —*n.* оборóна: *on the defensive,* в оборóне.
defer *v.t.* (put off) отклáдывать; отсрóчивать. —*v.i.* [*usu.* **defer to**] **1,** (show deference toward) относúться с почтéнием к. **2,** (yield to; rely on) полагáться на.
deference *n.* уважéние; почтéние; почтúтельность. *In deference to,* из уважéния к.
deferential *adj.* почтúтельный.
deferment *n.* отсрóчка.
defiance *n.* неповиновéние. *In defiance of,* вопрекú; наперекóр.
defiant *adj.* вызывáющий.
deficiency *n.* недостáток.
deficient *adj.* имéющий недостáтки; недостáточный.
deficit *n.* дефицúт.
defile *v.t.* осквернять; развращáть. —*n.* (narrow passage) теснúна. —**defilement,** *n.* осквернéние; развращéние.
define *v.t.* **1,** (give the definition of) определять. **2,** (specify) определять; устанáвливать; характеризовáть.
definite *adj.* определённый; тóчный. *Make it definite,* договорúться определённо. *Nothing is definite yet,* покá ещё нет ничегó определённого. —**definite article,** *gram.* определённый артúкль *or* член.
definitely *adv.* **1,** (for sure) определённо: *I can't say definitely,* не могý сказáть определённо. **2,** (absolutely) безуслóвно: *this is definitely the last time,* э́то безуслóвно послéдний раз. **3,** (without fail) обязáтельно.
definition *n.* **1,** (of a word) определéние. **2,** (clarity; sharpness) рéзкость.
definitive *adj.* окончáтельный. —**definitively,** *adv.* окончáтельно.
deflate *v.t.* **1,** (release the air from) спускáть. **2,** (puncture the pride of) сбивáть спесь с.
deflation *n., econ.* дефляция.
deflect *v.t.* отводúть; отклонять; отбивáть. —*v.i.* отклоняться. —**deflection,** *n.* отклонéние.
deforest *v.t.* обезлéсить. —**deforestation,** *n.* обезлéсение.
deform *v.t.* урóдовать. —**deformation,** *n.* деформáция. —**deformed,** *adj.* урóдливый. —**deformity,** *n.* урóдство.
defraud *v.t.* обмáнывать.
defray *v.t.* покрывáть (расхóды). —**defrayal,** *n.* покры́тие (расхóдов).

defrock *v.t.* расстригáть; лишáть духóвного сáна.
defrost *v.t.* разморáживать. —*v.i.* разморáживаться. —**defroster,** *n.* обогревáтель.
deft *adj.* лóвкий; провóрный.
defunct *adj.* бóльше не существýющий.
defuse *v.t.* обезврéживать: *defuse a bomb,* обезврéдить бóмбу. *Defuse tension,* смягчáть напряжéние. *Defuse the situation,* разрядúть атмосфéру.
defy *v.t.* **1,** (openly challenge) брóсить вы́зов (+ *dat.*): *defy world opinion,* брóсить вы́зов мировóй общéственности. **2,** (ignore): *defy an order,* пренебрегáть прикáзом; ослýшаться прикáза. *Defy death/danger,* презирáть смерть/опáсность. **3,** (dare): *I defy you to do it,* ручáюсь, что вам э́того не сдéлать. **4,** (be beyond) не поддавáться (+ *dat.*): *defy description,* не поддавáться описáнию. *His actions defy logic,* егó постýпки противорéчат лóгике (*or* лишены́ лóгики).
degeneracy *n.* вырождéние.
degenerate *v.i.* вырождáться. —*n.* дегенерáт. —*adj.* вы́родившийся. —**degeneration,** *n.* вырождéние; дегенерáция. —**degenerative,** *adj.* вырождéнческий.
degradation *n.* унижéние.
degrade *v.t.* унижáть. —**degrading,** *adj.* унизúтельный.
degree *n.* **1,** (extent) стéпень: *to a certain degree,* до извéстной стéпени. *First-degree burns,* ожóги пéрвой стéпени. **2,** (unit of measure for angles; unit of temperature) грáдус: *ten degrees below zero,* дéсять грáдусов нúже нуля́. **3,** *gram.* стéпень: *comparative degree,* сравнúтельная стéпень. **4,** (academic title) (учёная) стéпень: *master's degree,* стéпень магúстра. —**by degrees,** постепéнно.
dehydrate *v.t.* обезвóживать. —**dehydration,** *n.* обезвóживание.
deify *v.t.* обожествля́ть; обоготворя́ть. —**deification,** *n.* обожествлéние; обоготворéние.
deign *v.i.* удостáивать; снисходúть; соизволя́ть; соблаговолúть.
deism *n.* деúзм. —**deist,** *n.* деúст. —**deistic,** *adj.* деистúческий.
deity *n.* божествó.
dejected *adj.* уны́лый; подáвленный; удручённый; угнетённый. —**dejection,** *n.* уны́ние.
de jure де-ю́ре.
delay *v.t.* **1,** (cause to be late) задéрживать; замедля́ть. **2,** (postpone) отклáдывать; отсрóчивать. —*v.i.* задéрживаться; мéдлить. —*n.* **1,** (holdup) задéржка; замедлéние; промедлéние; проволóчка. *Without delay,* немéдленно; без промедлéния; без проволóчек. **2,** (short postponement) отсрóчка.
delayed-action *adj.* замéдленного дéйствия.
delectable *adj.* прелéстный.
delegate *n.* делегáт. —*v.t.* **1,** (assign) поручáть. **2,** (turn over to a subordinate) передавáть.
delegation *n.* **1,** (group of persons) делегáция. **2,** (turning over) передáча.
delete *v.t.* вычёркивать; исключáть.
deleterious *adj.* врéдный; пáгубный; тлетвóрный.
deletion *n.* **1,** (act of deleting) вычёркивание. **2,** (that which is deleted) вы́черкнутое слóво, выражéние, *etc.*
delftware *n.* фая́нс.
deliberate *adj.* **1,** (intentional) нарочúтый; намéренный; умы́шленный. **2,** (careful) осторóжный; осмотрúтельный. **3,** (unhurried) нетороплúвый. —*v.i.* **1,** (think carefully) соображáть. **2,** (consult; confer) совещáться.
deliberately *adv.* нарóчно; умы́шленно.
deliberation *n.* **1,** (careful thought) размышлéние. **2,** (slowness and care) осторóжность; осмотрúтельность. **3,** *pl.* (discussion and debate) совещáние.
deliberative *adj.* совещáтельный: *deliberative body,* совещáтельный óрган.
delicacy *n.* **1,** (need of tactful treatment) деликáтность; щекотлúвость. **2,** (frailty) хрýпкость. **3,** (fineness of quality) утончённость. **4,** (choice item of food) деликатéс; лáкомство.
delicate *adj.* **1,** (gentle; tender; frail) нéжный; хрýпкий; деликáтный. **2,** (tactful; subtle) деликáтный. **3,** (needing tactful handling) щекотлúвый; деликáтный. **4,** (fine; exquisite) тóнкий; утончённый.
delicatessen *n.* **1,** (store) гастрономúческий магазúн; магазúн кулинáрии; гастронóм. **2,** (food) кулинáрия.
delicious *adj.* óчень вкýсный.
delight *n.* **1,** (great pleasure) (большóе) удовóльствие; наслаждéние; отрáда. **2,** (something that gives great pleasure) прéлесть. —*v.t.* восхищáть. —*v.i.* [*usu.* **delight in**] наслаждáться (+ *instr.*).
delighted *adj.* óчень рад.
delightful *adj.* прелéстный; восхитúтельный.
delimit *v.t.* разгранúчивать; размежёвывать; отмежёвывать. —**delimitation,** *n.* разграничéние.
delineate *v.t.* **1,** (outline) очéрчивать. **2,** (describe in detail) обрисóвывать.
delinquency *n.* правонарушéние. *Juvenile delinquency,* дéтская престýпность.
delinquent *adj.* **1,** (having done wrong) винóвный. **2,** (overdue) неоплáченный. —*n.* (ю́ный) правонарушúтель.
delirious *adj.* бредовóй. *Be delirious,* быть в бредý; брéдить.
delirium *n.* бред.
deliver *v.t.* **1,** (take to a place) доставля́ть. **2,** (distribute, as mail) разносúть. **3,** (save; set free) избавля́ть. **4,** (surrender; hand over) сдавáть. **5,** (deal, as a blow) наносúть (удáр). **6,** (give, as a speech, lecture, etc.) произносúть (речь); читáть (лéкцию). **7,** (assist at the birth of) принимáть.
deliverance *n.* избавлéние. —**deliverer,** *n.* избавúтель.
delivery *n.* **1,** (transporting; distributing) достáвка. **2,** (birth) рóды. **3,** (rescue) избавлéние. **4,** (manner of speaking) дúкция. **5,** *sports* подáча. —**delivery boy/man,** рассы́льный. —**delivery room,** *med.* родúльное отделéние. —**delivery system,** *mil.* срéдство достáвки.
dell *n.* ложбúна; лощúна.
delphinium *n.* жúвокость; шпóрник.
delta *n.* дéльта. —**deltoid,** *adj.* дельтовúдный.
delude *v.t.* вводúть в заблуждéние. *Delude oneself,* заблуждáться.
deluge *n.* **1,** (downpour) лúвень. **2,** (flood) потóп. **3,** (overwhelming influx) потóк; град. —*v.t.* **1,** (flood) затопля́ть. **2,** (overwhelm) засыпáть.
delusion *n.* заблуждéние: *be under a delusion,* быть в заблуждéнии. —**delusions of grandeur,** мáния велúчия.

de luxe роскóшный; -люкс: *de luxe hotel,* гости́ница-люкс.
delve *v.i.* [*usu.* **delve into**] углубля́ться (в); вника́ть (в).
demagnetize *v.t.* размагни́чивать.
demagogue *n.* демагóг. —**demagoguery; demagogy,** *n.* демагóгия. —**demagogic,** *adj.* демагоги́ческий.
demand *v.t.* трéбовать: *demand an apology,* трéбовать извинéния. —*n.* **1,** (insistent request) трéбование. **2,** *econ.* спрос: *supply and demand,* спрос и предложéние. *In great demand,* в большóм ходу́. —**on demand,** по предъявлéнии.
demanding *adj.* трéбовательный; взыска́тельный.
demarcate *v.t.* разграни́чивать.
demarcation *n.* демарка́ция. *Line of demarcation,* демаркациóнная ли́ния.
démarche *n.* демáрш.
demean *v.t.* унижа́ть; роня́ть. *Demean oneself,* унижа́ться; роня́ть своё достóинство.
demeanor *also,* **demeanour** *n.* поведéние; манéра держа́ть себя́.
demented *adj.* сумасшéдший; помéшанный. —**dementia,** *n.* сумасшéствие; помеша́тельство.
demerit *n.* **1,** (fault; defect) недостáток. **2,** (mark for bad conduct) взыскáние.
demigod *n.* полубóг.
demilitarization *n.* демилитаризáция.
demilitarize *v.t.* демилитаризовáть. *Demilitarized zone,* демилитаризóванная зóна.
demise *n.* кончи́на.
demitasse *n.* мáленькая чáшка.
demobilize *v.t.* демобилизовáть. —**demobilization,** *n.* демобилизáция.
democracy *n.* демокрáтия.
democrat *n.* демокрáт. —**democratic,** *adj.* демократи́ческий.
democratize *v.t.* демократизи́ровать. —**democratization,** *n.* демократизáция.
demography *n.* демогрáфия. —**demographer,** *n.* демóграф. —**demographic,** *adj.* демографи́ческий.
demolish *v.t.* **1,** (tear down) сноси́ть. **2,** (destroy) разрушáть. **3,** *fig.* (refute, as a theory) разбивáть.
demolition *n.* разрушéние. —*adj.* подрывнóй: *demolition work,* подрывны́е рабóты. —**demolition bomb,** фугáсная бóмба.
demon *n.* дéмон. —**demoniac; demonic,** *adj.* демони́ческий.
demonstrable *adj.* доказу́емый.
demonstrate *v.t.* **1,** (show) демонстри́ровать. **2,** (prove) доказáть. **3,** (reveal, as a quality) проявля́ть: *demonstrate courage,* проявля́ть му́жество. —*v.i.* демонстри́ровать: *demonstrate against something,* демонстри́ровать прóтив чегó-нибудь.
demonstration *n.* **1,** (show, display) демонстрáция: *demonstration of merchandise,* демонстрáция товáров. **2,** (manifestation) проявлéние: *demonstration of affection,* проявлéние нéжности. **3,** (parade; march) демонстрáция; манифестáция.
demonstrative *adj.* **1,** (given to showing one's feelings) экспанси́вный. **2,** (showing clearly; convincing) нагля́дный; доказáтельный. **3,** *gram.* указáтельный: *demonstrative pronoun,* указáтельное местоимéние.
demonstrator *n.* **1,** (one who demonstrates something) демонстрáтор. **2,** (one who participates in a demonstration) демонстрáнт.
demoralize *v.t.* деморализовáть. —**demoralization,** *n.* деморализáция.
demote *v.t.* понижáть (в чи́не, по слу́жбе, *etc.*). —**demotion,** *n.* понижéние.
demur *v.i.* возражáть.
demure *adj.* **1,** (sedate) степéнный. **2,** (retiring; shy) застéнчивый.
demurral *n.* возражéние.
den *n.* **1,** (lair) лóговище; лóгово; берлóга. *Lion's den,* лóгово льва. **2,** (hideout for illegal activity) притóн: *thieves'/gambling den,* воровскóй/игóрный притóн. *Den of iniquity,* притóн разврáта. **3,** (study) кабинéт.
denature *v.t.* денатури́ровать. —**denatured alcohol,** денатури́рованный спирт; денатурáт.
dendrite *n.* дендри́т.
denial *n.* **1,** (act of denying) отрицáние. **2,** (statement of denial) опровержéние. **3,** (refusal to grant something) откáз; отклонéние: *denial of a request,* откáз в прóсьбе; отклонéние прóсьбы. **4,** (repudiation) отречéние.
denigrate *v.t.* порóчить; черни́ть; поноси́ть. —**denigration,** *n.* поношéние.
denizen *n.* жи́тель; обитáтель.
denomination *n.* **1,** (name) наименовáние. **2,** (religious group) вероисповéдание. **3,** (value of a coin or bill) достóинство: *coins of small denomination,* монéты мáлого достóинства.
denominator *n.* знаменáтель. *Least common denominator,* наимéньший óбщий знаменáтель.
denotation *n.* **1,** (act of denoting) обозначéние. **2,** (explicit meaning) значéние.
denote *v.t.* **1,** (mean) знáчить; означáть; обозначáть. **2,** (indicate) обозначáть: *on a map blue denotes water,* си́ний цвет на кáрте обозначáет мóре.
dénouement *n.* развя́зка.
denounce *v.t.* **1,** (condemn) осуждáть. **2,** (inform against) доноси́ть на.
dense *adj.* **1,** (thick) густóй; плóтный: *dense forest,* густóй лес; *dense fog,* густóй *or* плóтный тумáн. **2,** (thickheaded) тупóй; тупоу́мный.
densely *adv.* гу́сто; плóтно. *Densely populated,* густонаселённый; плóтно населённый.
density *n.* **1,** (denseness) густотá; плóтность. *Population density,* плóтность населéния. **2,** *physics* плóтность. **3,** (stupidity) тупоу́мие.
dent *n.* вмя́тина; вы́боина. —*v.t.* вдáвливать; вминáть.
dental *adj.* зубоврачéбный; зубнóй. *Dental school/practice,* зубоврачéбная шкóла/прáктика. *Dental technician,* зубнóй тéхник.
dentifrice *n.* зубнóй порошóк; зубнáя пáста.
dentine *also,* **dentin** *n.* денти́н.
dentist *n.* зубнóй врач; стоматóлог. —**dentistry,** *n.* стоматолóгия.
denture *n.* зубнóй протéз.
denude *v.t.* обнажáть; оголя́ть.
denunciation *n.* **1,** (condemnation) осуждéние. **2,** (informing against) донóс.
denunciatory *adj.* осуждáющий.
deny *v.t.* **1,** (refuse to acknowledge) отрицáть: *deny one's guilt,* отрицáть свою́ вину́. *He denied that...,* он отрицáл, что... *Deny responsibility for,* не брать

на себя́ отве́тственности за. *There is no denying that...,* нельзя́ не призна́ть, что...; слов нет,... **2,** (declare to be untrue) опроверга́ть: *deny a charge,* опрове́ргнуть обвине́ние. **3,** (refuse to grant) отка́зывать в: *deny someone's request,* отка́зывать кому́-нибудь в про́сьбе. *He was denied permission,* ему́ не да́ли разреше́ния. **4,** (deprive) лиша́ть: *denied the right to vote,* лишены́ пра́ва го́лоса. —**deny oneself (something),** отка́зывать себе́ в (+ *prepl.*).

deodorant *n.* дезодора́тор.

depart *v.i.* **1,** (leave) уходи́ть; уезжа́ть; отправля́ться; отбыва́ть. **2,** *fol. by* **from** (deviate from) отклоня́ться (от); отходи́ть (от); отступа́ть (от). —*v.t.* покида́ть. *Depart this world,* поки́нуть свет.

departed *adj.* уме́рший. —*n.* поко́йник.

department *n.* **1,** (section) отде́л; отделе́ние. **2,** (government bureau) ве́домство; департа́мент. **3,** (subdivision of a college) факульте́т; ка́федра.

departmental *adj.* ве́домственный.

department store универса́льный магази́н; универма́г.

departure *n.* **1,** (leaving) отъе́зд; ухо́д; отхо́д; отправле́ние; отбы́тие. **2,** (deviation) отклоне́ние; отступле́ние; отхо́д. —**point of departure,** то́чка отправле́ния.

depend *v.i.* [*usu.* **depend on**] **1,** (be contingent on) зави́сеть (от). *It (all) depends,* смотря́ как. **2,** (rely on; count on) полага́ться (на); рассчи́тывать (на). —**depending on,** в зави́симости от; смотря́ по.

dependable *adj.* надёжный. —**dependability,** *n.* надёжность.

dependant *n.* = **dependent.**

dependence *n.* зави́симость.

dependency *n.* **1,** = **dependence. 2,** (dependent territory) зави́симая страна́.

dependent *adj.* зави́симый: *dependent countries,* зави́симые стра́ны. *Be dependent on someone for support,* быть на иждиве́нии кого́-нибудь. —*n.* [*also,* **dependant**] иждиве́нец. *How many dependents have you?,* ско́лько у вас на иждиве́нии? —**dependent clause,** прида́точное предложе́ние.

depersonalize *v.t.* обезли́чивать.

depict *v.t.* изобража́ть.

deplete *v.t.* истоща́ть. —**depletion,** *n.* истоще́ние.

deplore *v.t.* опла́кивать; сожале́ть о. —**deplorable,** *adj.* приско́рбный; плаче́вный.

deploy *v.t.* развёртывать. —*v.i.* развёртываться. —**deployment,** *n.* развёртывание.

depopulate *v.t.* обезлю́дить. *Become depopulated,* обезлю́деть.

deport *v.t.* высыла́ть; ссыла́ть. —**deport oneself,** вести́ себя́; держа́ть себя́.

deportation *n.* вы́сылка; ссы́лка.

deportment *n.* поведе́ние; мане́ры.

depose *v.t.* сверга́ть; низлага́ть.

deposit *n.* **1,** (money placed in a bank) вклад. **2,** (anything given as security) зало́г; зада́ток. **3,** (accumulation of minerals in the ground) за́лежь; месторожде́ние. **4,** (natural accumulation) отложе́ние: *calcium/lime deposits,* ка́льциевые/известко́вые отложе́ния. —*v.t.* класть; опуска́ть. *Deposit money in a bank,* класть де́ньги в банк. *Deposit a coin in a machine,* опуска́ть моне́ту в автома́т.

deposition *n.* **1,** (act of deposing) низложе́ние. **2,** (written statement used as evidence) показа́ние.

depositor *n.* вкла́дчик.

depository *n.* храни́лище.

depot *n.* **1,** (warehouse) склад. **2,** (train or bus station) вокза́л; ста́нция.

deprave *v.t.* развраща́ть. —**depraved,** *adj.* развращённый; поро́чный. —**depravity,** *n.* развращённость; поро́чность.

deprecate *v.t.* **1,** (express disapproval of) осужда́ть. **2,** (belittle) умаля́ть.

depreciate *v.i.* обесце́ниваться. —*v.t.* **1,** (lessen the value of) обесце́нивать. **2,** (belittle) умаля́ть.

depreciation *n.* **1,** (decline in value) обесце́нение. **2,** (allowance made for this in accounting) амортиза́ция.

depredation *n.* грабёж; ограбле́ние.

depress *v.t.* **1,** (dispirit) подавля́ть; угнета́ть; удруча́ть. **2,** (press down on) нажима́ть на. —**depressed,** *adj.* пода́вленный; удручённый; угнетённый. —**depressing,** *adj.* гнету́щий; тя́гостный; подавля́ющий.

depression *n.* **1,** (sunken place; hollow) впа́дина; углубле́ние. **2,** (melancholy) пода́вленность; упа́док ду́ха; депре́ссия. **3,** (economic crisis) депре́ссия; кри́зис.

deprive *v.t.* лиша́ть: *deprive someone of his rights,* лиша́ть кого́-нибудь прав. —**deprivation,** *n.* лише́ние.

depth *n.* **1,** (distance downward) глубина́. **2,** *pl.* (deepest part) глубь: *the ocean depths,* морска́я глубь. **3,** (intellectual capacity or profundity) глубина́; глубокомы́слие. —**in depth,** глубоко́.

depth charge глуби́нная бо́мба.

deputation *n.* депута́ция.

deputize *v.t.* назнача́ть замести́телем.

deputy *n.* **1,** (one appointed to act for another) замести́тель. **2,** (member of a legislature in certain countries) депута́т. —*adj. Deputy director,* замести́тель дире́ктора.

derail *v.t.* пуска́ть (по́езд) под отко́с. —**derailment,** *n.* сход с ре́льсов.

derange *v.t.* своди́ть с ума́. —**deranged,** *adj.* сумасше́дший; поме́шанный. *Become deranged,* сойти́ с ума́. —**derangement,** *n.* сумасше́ствие; умопомеша́тельство.

derby *n.* **1,** (hat) котело́к. **2,** *cap.* (race) де́рби.

derelict *n.* бродя́га; бося́к. —*adj. Be derelict in one's duty,* измени́ть своему́ до́лгу.

dereliction *n.* наруше́ние: *dereliction of duty,* наруше́ние до́лга.

deride *v.t.* насмеха́ться над; осме́ивать; высме́ивать.

derision *n.* насме́шка; осмея́ние; издева́тельство.

derisive *adj.* насме́шливый; издева́тельский.

derivation *n.* **1,** (obtaining) получе́ние. *Derivation of a formula,* вы́вод фо́рмулы. **2,** (origin, as of a word) происхожде́ние.

derivative *adj.* произво́дный. —*n.* **1,** *chem.* произво́дное; дерива́т. **2,** *ling.* произво́дное сло́во. **3,** *math.* произво́дная.

derive *v.t.* **1,** (receive, as pleasure, benefit, etc.) получа́ть; извлека́ть. **2,** (deduce, as a formula) выводи́ть. —*v.i.* (originate) происходи́ть.

dermatology *n.* дерматоло́гия. —**dermatologist,** *n.* дермато́лог.

derogate *v.i.* [*usu.* **derogate from**] умаля́ть. —**derogation,** *n.* умале́ние.

derogatory *adj.* оскорби́тельный; оби́дный: *derogatory remarks,* оскорби́тельные/оби́дные замеча́ния.

derrick *n.* **1,** (crane) де́ррик; де́ррик-кран. **2,** (oil derrick) бурова́я вы́шка.

dervish *n.* де́рвиш.

desalinize *also,* **desalinate** *v.t.* опресня́ть. —**desalinization; desalination,** *n.* опресне́ние.

descend *v.i.* **1,** (go down) сходи́ть; спуска́ться. **2,** *fol. by* **on** (visit without warning) нагря́нуть к. **3,** *fol. by* **to** (stoop to) унижа́ться (до). **4,** *fol. by* **from** [*also,* **be descended from**] (spring from a stock or source) происходи́ть (из). **5,** (pass by inheritance) переходи́ть. —*v.t.* сходи́ть с; спуска́ться с.

descendant *n.* пото́мок.

descent *n.* **1,** (downward motion) спуск: *descent from a mountain,* спуск с горы́. *Descent of an airplane,* сниже́ние самолёта. **2,** (downward slope) спуск; склон; скат. **3,** (ancestry) происхожде́ние: *of Russian descent,* ру́сский по происхожде́нию.

describe *v.t.* **1,** (give a description of) опи́сывать. **2,** (depict in a certain way) характеризова́ть.

description *n.* описа́ние. *Of every description,* вся́кого ро́да.

descriptive *adj.* описа́тельный. —**descriptive geometry,** начерта́тельная геоме́трия.

descry *v.t.* рассмотре́ть; разгляде́ть.

desecrate *v.t.* оскверня́ть. —**desecration,** *n.* оскверне́ние.

desegregate *v.t.* десегреги́ровать. —**desegregation,** *n.* десегрега́ция.

desert[1] (**dez**-ert) *n.* пусты́ня. —*adj.* пусты́нный. *Desert island,* необита́емый о́стров.

desert[2] (di-**zurt**) *v.t.* броса́ть; покида́ть; оставля́ть. —*v.i., mil.* дезерти́ровать. —*n., often pl.* заслу́га: *get one's just deserts,* получи́ть по заслу́гам.

deserted *adj.* безлю́дный; пусты́нный; опусте́лый. *The streets were deserted,* на у́лицах бы́ло пу́сто.

deserter *n.* дезерти́р.

desertion *n.* **1,** (abandonment) оставле́ние. **2,** *mil.* дезерти́рство.

deserve *v.t.* заслу́живать. *He got what he deserved,* он получи́л по заслу́гам. —**deserved,** *adj.* заслу́женный; досто́йный. —**deservedly,** *adv.* по заслу́гам; по пра́ву. —**deserving,** *adj.* досто́йный.

design *v.t.* **1,** (plan the construction of, as a building) проекти́ровать. *A building designed by...,* зда́ние, постро́енное по прое́кту (+ *gen.*). **2,** (plan the external appearance of, as a book, stage set, etc.) оформля́ть. **3,** (style, as a dress) модели́ровать. **4,** (intend; mean) предназнача́ть: *the dictionary is designed for children,* слова́рь предназна́чен для дете́й. —*n.* **1,** (pattern) узо́р. **2,** (of a building, aircraft, etc.) констру́кция; (of a book) оформле́ние. **3,** (sketch) прое́кт; чертёж. **4,** (purpose; intention) за́мысел; у́мысел. *By design,* с у́мыслом. *Have designs on,* име́ть ви́ды на.

designate *v.t.* **1,** (indicate; mark) обознача́ть. **2,** (appoint) назнача́ть. —*adj.* назна́ченный.

designation *n.* **1,** (name; title) назва́ние. **2,** (appointment) назначе́ние. **3,** (mark; sign) обозначе́ние.

designedly *adv.* умы́шленно; с у́мыслом.

designer *n.* чертёжник; проектиро́вщик; констру́ктор; оформи́тель. *Aircraft designer,* авиаконстру́ктор. *Dress designer,* моделье́р. *Stage designer,* декора́тор; оформи́тель.

designing *adj.* интригу́ющий.

desirable *adj.* жела́тельный. —**desirability,** *n.* жела́тельность.

desire *v.t.* жела́ть. *Leave much to be desired,* оставля́ть жела́ть мно́го лу́чшего. —*n.* жела́ние: *a great desire,* большо́е жела́ние.

desired *adj.* жела́нный; жела́емый. *Produce the desired effect,* дать жела́емый результа́т; име́ть до́лжный эффе́кт.

desirous *adj.* жела́ющий.

desist *v.i.* перестава́ть.

desk *n.* пи́сьменный стол. *School desk,* па́рта. *Information desk,* спра́вочный стол. —*adj.* насто́льный: *desk lamp,* насто́льная ла́мпа. *Desk drawer,* я́щик стола́.

desman *n.* вы́хухоль.

desolate *adj.* **1,** (barren) забро́шенный. **2,** (deserted) пусты́нный; безлю́дный. —*v.t.* **1,** (depopulate) обезлю́дить. **2,** (devastate) опустоша́ть.

desolation *n.* **1,** (laying waste) опустоше́ние. **2,** (emptiness; waste) запусте́ние.

despair *n.* отча́яние. —*v.i.* отча́иваться.

desperado *n.* головоре́з.

desperate *adj.* отча́янный: *desperate attempt,* отча́янная попы́тка. *I am desperate,* я в отча́янном положе́нии.

desperately *adv.* **1,** (with desperation) отча́янно: *fight desperately,* боро́ться отча́янно. *Try desperately,* всеми си́лами стара́ться. **2,** (extremely; frightfully) кра́йне; ужа́сно. *Desperately ill,* тяжело́ бо́лен. **3,** (urgently) до заре́зу: *he needs money desperately,* ему́ нужны́ де́ньги до заре́зу.

desperation *n.* отча́яние.

despicable *adj.* презре́нный; ни́зкий; по́длый. —**despicably,** *adv.* ни́зко; по́дло.

despise *v.t.* презира́ть.

despite *prep.* несмотря́ на. *Despite all,* несмотря́ ни на что.

despoil *v.t.* гра́бить; разоря́ть.

despondent *adj.* уны́лый; пода́вленный. —**despondency,** *n.* уны́ние; пода́вленность.

despot *n.* де́спот. —**despotic,** *adj.* деспоти́ческий. —**despotism,** *n.* деспоти́зм.

dessert *n.* десе́рт. *For dessert,* на сла́дкое; на десе́рт. —*adj.* десе́ртный: *dessert spoon,* десе́ртная ло́жка.

destination *n.* ме́сто назначе́ния.

destine *v.t.* предназнача́ть. *We were not destined to...,* нам не суждено́ (*or* не судьба́) бы́ло (+ *inf.*).

destiny *n.* судьба́.

destitute *adj.* обездо́ленный; обнища́лый. *Be left destitute,* оста́ться ни с чем *or* без средств. —**destitution,** *n.* нищета́; обнища́ние.

destroy *v.t.* разруша́ть; уничтожа́ть.

destroyer *n.* **1,** (one who or that which destroys) разруши́тель. **2,** (ship) эска́дренный миноно́сец; эсми́нец.

destruction *n.* **1,** (act of destroying) разруше́ние. **2,** (heavy damage) разруше́ния. —**destructive,** *adj.* разруши́тельный.

desultory *adj.* несвя́зный; бессвя́зный; отры́вочный.

detach *v.t.* отделя́ть. —**detachable,** *adj.* съёмный; отрезно́й.

detached *adj.* **1,** (separate) отдéльный. **2,** (impartial) беспристрáстный.
detachment *n.* **1,** (removal) отделéние. **2,** (impartiality) беспристрáстие. **3,** *mil.* отря́д.
detail *n.* **1,** (minute element) подрóбность; детáль. *In detail,* подрóбно. *Go into detail,* вдавáться в подрóбности. **2,** *mil.* (small detachment) наря́д. —*v.t.* **1,** (describe minutely) подрóбно расскáзывать. **2,** *mil.* (assign) наряжáть; отряжáть.
detailed *adj.* подрóбный; детáльный.
detain *v.t.* задéрживать: *don't let me detain you!,* не хочу́ вас задéрживать. *He was detained by the police,* егó задержáла поли́ция.
detect *v.t.* обнару́живать. —**detection,** *n.* обнару́жение.
detective *n.* сы́щик; детекти́в. —**detective story,** детекти́в.
detector *n.* детéктор.
détente *n.* разря́дка.
detention *n.* задержáние; содержáние под арéстом. *Be in detention,* быть под стрáжей.
deter *v.t.* удéрживать.
detergent *n.* мóющее срéдство; стирáльный порошóк.
deteriorate *v.i.* ухудшáться; пóртиться. —**deterioration,** *n.* ухудшéние.
determinant *n.* определи́тель.
determinate *adj.* определённый; установленный.
determination *n.* **1,** (act of determining) определéние. **2,** (firm resolve) реши́мость; реши́тельность.
determine *v.t.* определя́ть: *determine the distance between...,* определя́ть расстоя́ние мéжду... *Determine the outcome of,* определя́ть *or* решáть исхóд (+ *gen.*).
determined *adj.* реши́тельный; пóлный реши́мости.
determinism *n.* детермини́зм.
deterrent *adj.* сдéрживающий; удéрживающий. —*n.* сдéрживающий фáктор.
detest *v.t.* ненави́деть. —**detestable,** *adj.* отврати́тельный; мéрзкий. —**detestation,** *n.* нéнависть.
dethrone *v.t.* свергáть с престóла; низлагáть. —**dethronement,** *n.* свержéние с престóла; низложéние.
detonate *v.t.* взрывáть. —*v.i.* взрывáться; детони́ровать. —**detonation,** *n.* детонáция. —**detonator,** *n.* детонáтор.
detour *n.* объéзд; крюк. —*v.i.* сдéлать крюк.
detract *v.i.* [*usu.* **detract from**] умаля́ть. —**detraction,** *n.* умалéние. —**detractor,** *n.* хули́тель.
detriment *n.* вред; ущéрб: *to the detriment of,* во вред *or* в ущéрб (+ *dat.*). —**detrimental,** *adj.* врéдный.
deuce *n.* **1,** (two) двóйка. **2,** *tennis* рáвный счёт. **3,** *colloq.* (devil; dickens) чёрт: *what the deuce is he doing there!,* какóго чёрта он там дéлает!
deuterium *n.* дейтéрий.
Deuteronomy *n.* Второзакóние.
devalue *v.t.* девальви́ровать. —**devaluation,** *n.* девальвáция.
devastate *v.t.* **1,** (lay waste) опустошáть. **2,** *fig.* (shatter; demoralize) потрясáть.
devastating *adj.* **1,** (extremely destructive) опустоши́тельный. *Devastating blow,* сокруши́тельный удáр. **2,** *fig.* (withering; scathing) уничтожáющий.
devastation *n.* опустошéние.
develop *v.t.* **1,** (expand; improve) развивáть: *develop one's muscles,* развивáть мускулату́ру. *Develop new sources of energy,* развивáть нóвые истóчники энéргии. **2,** (work out; perfect) разрабáтывать: *develop a method,* разрабáтывать мéтод; *develop a new aircraft,* разрабáтывать нóвый самолёт. **3,** (acquire gradually) развивáть; приобретáть. *Develop an interest in,* развивáть интерéс к. *Develop a taste for,* приобретáть вкус к. *Develop pneumonia,* получи́ть воспалéние лёгких. *He has developed the habit of...,* у негó вы́работалась привы́чка (+ *inf.*). **4,** (build up) застрáивать. **5,** *photog.* проявля́ть. —*v.i.* **1,** (increase in maturity, scope, etc.) развивáться. *Developing countries,* развивáющиеся стрáны. **2,** (gradually come into being) создавáться; склáдываться. **3,** *fol. by* **into** (gradually become) вырастáть в; выливáться в. **4,** (turn out) вы́ясниться: *it developed that...,* вы́яснилось, что...
developer *n.* **1,** (builder) застрóйщик. **2,** *photog.* прояви́тель.
development *n.* **1,** (act or process of developing) разви́тие. **2,** (working out; designing) разрабóтка. **3,** (building up) застрóйка. **4,** (event; occurrence) собы́тие.
deviant *adj.* ненормáльный; противоестéственный.
deviate *v.i.* [*usu.* **deviate from**] отклоня́ться (от); уклоня́ться (от); отступáть (от). —**deviation,** *n.* отклонéние; уклонéние; отступлéние.
device *n.* **1,** (apparatus) прибóр; устрóйство; приспособлéние. **2,** (something used to achieve an effect) приём. **3,** (scheme) ухищрéние. —**leave to one's own devices,** предоставля́ть самому́ себé.
devil *n.* чёрт; дья́вол. *What the devil are you doing?,* какóго чёрта ты дéлаешь? —*adj.* [*usu.* **devil's**] чёртов. —**between the devil and the deep blue sea,** мéжду двух огнéй; мéжду мóлотом и наковáльней. —**give someone the devil,** дать нагоня́й (+ *dat.*). —**lucky devil,** счастли́вец. —**poor devil,** бедня́га. —**talk of the devil!,** лёгок на поми́не!
devilish *adj.* чертóвский; дья́вольский. —**devilishly,** *adv.* чертóвски.
devil-may-care *adj.* бесшабáшный; залихвáтский.
devious *adj.* **1,** (circuitous) окóльный. **2,** (shifty) увёртливый.
devise *v.t.* приду́мывать.
devoid *adj.* [*usu.* **devoid of**] лишённый (+ *gen.*).
devolve *v.i.* [*usu.* **devolve upon**] переходи́ть (к).
devote *v.t.* **1,** (dedicate) посвящáть. *Devote oneself to,* посвящáть себя́ (+ *dat.*); отдавáться (+ *dat.*). **2,** (give, as time, attention, etc.) уделя́ть. —**devoted,** *adj.* прéданный. —**devotee,** *n.* поклóнник.
devotion *n.* прéданность.
devour *v.t.* **1,** (consume) пожирáть. **2,** *fig.* (read or listen to avidly) поглощáть. *Devour every word (when listening),* лови́ть кáждое слóво.
devout *adj.* **1,** (pious) нáбожный; благочести́вый. **2,** (earnest) и́скренний: *devout wish,* и́скреннее желáние.
dew *n.* росá. —**dewdrop,** *n.* роси́нка; кáпля росы́.
dewlap *n.* подгру́док.
dewy *adj.* роси́стый.
dexterity *n.* лóвкость; провóрство. —**dexterous,** *adj.* лóвкий; провóрный.

dextrose *n.* декстро́за.
diabetes *n.* диабе́т; са́харная боле́знь. —**diabetic,** *adj.* диабети́ческий. —*n.* диабе́тик.
diabolic *adj.* дья́вольский. *Also,* **diabolical.**
diacritical *adj.* диакрити́ческий. —**diacritical mark,** диакрити́ческий знак.
diadem *n.* диаде́ма.
diagnose *v.t.* распознава́ть; определя́ть (боле́знь).
diagnosis *n.* диа́гноз.
diagnostic *adj.* диагности́ческий. —**diagnostician,** *n.* диагно́ст.
diagonal *adj.* диагона́льный. —*n.* диагона́ль. —**diagonally,** *adv.* по диагона́ли; на́искось.
diagram *n.* схе́ма; диагра́мма. —**diagrammatic,** *adj.* схемати́ческий.
dial *n.* **1,** (of a radio, gauge, etc.) шкала́; цифербла́т. **2,** (tuning knob) ру́чка (настро́йки). **3,** (telephone device) диск. —*v.t.* **1,** (a telephone number) набира́ть (но́мер). **2,** *radio* (tune in) настра́ивать.
dialect *n.* диале́кт; наре́чие; го́вор. —**dialectal,** *adj.* диале́ктный.
dialectical *adj.* диалекти́ческий. —**dialectics,** *n.* диале́ктика.
dialogue *n.* диало́г.
diameter *n.* диа́метр.
diametrical *adj.* диаметра́льный. —**diametrically,** *adv.* диаметра́льно: *diametrically opposite,* диаметра́льно противополо́жный.
diamond *n.* **1,** (stone) алма́з. **2,** (gem) бриллиа́нт. **3,** (figure) ромб. **4,** *pl., cards* бу́бны. —*adj.* бриллиа́нтовый; алма́зный.
diaper *n.* пелёнка. —*v.t.* пелена́ть.
diaphragm *n.* **1,** *anat.* грудобрю́шная прегра́да; диафра́гма. **2,** *physics; mech.* мембра́на. **3,** *optics; photog.* диафра́гма.
diarchy *n.* двоевла́стие.
diarrhea *also,* **diarrhoea** *n.* поно́с. *He has diarrhea,* его́ сла́бит.
diary *n.* дневни́к.
diathermy *n.* диатерми́я.
diatonic *adj.* диатони́ческий.
diatribe *n.* бра́нная речь.
dice *n.pl.* игра́льные ко́сти. *Play dice,* игра́ть в ко́сти.
dichotomy *n.* деле́ние.
dickens *n., slang* чёрт: *what the dickens do you want?,* како́го чёрта вам ну́жно? —**give someone the dickens,** дать кому́-нибудь нагоня́й.
dicker *v.i.* торгова́ться.
dickey *also,* **dicky** *n.* **1,** (shirt front) мани́шка. **2,** (bib) нагру́дник.
dicotyledon *n.* двудо́льное расте́ние. —**dicotyledonous,** *adj.* двудо́льный.
dictaphone *n.* диктофо́н.
dictate *v.t. & i.* диктова́ть. —*n.* веле́ние: *the dictates of one's conscience,* веле́ние со́вести.
dictation *n.* **1,** (act of dictating, as a letter) дикто́вка: *take dictation,* писа́ть под дикто́вку. **2,** (classroom exercise) дикта́нт.
dictator *n.* дикта́тор. —**dictatorial,** *adj.* дикта́торский. —**dictatorship,** *n.* диктату́ра.
diction *n.* ди́кция.
dictionary *n.* слова́рь.
dictum *n.* **1,** (authoritative pronouncement) постановле́ние. **2,** (saying) изрече́ние.
didactic *adj.* наставительный; назида́тельный; дидакти́ческий. —**didactics,** *n.* дида́ктика.
die *v.i.* умира́ть; (*of animals*) до́хнуть; (*of plants*) ги́бнуть. —*n.* **1,** (engraving stamp) штамп. **2,** *sing. of* **dice.** *The die is cast,* жре́бий бро́шен. —**be dying to,** жа́ждать; рва́ться: *I am dying to see you,* я жа́жду/рвусь уви́деть вас. *I am dying to tell her,* меня́ так и подмыва́ет сказа́ть ей. —**die away,** замолка́ть; умолка́ть. —**die down,** замира́ть; затиха́ть; утиха́ть; стиха́ть; гло́хнуть. —**die laughing,** умира́ть со́ смеху. —**die out, 1,** (of a fire) угаса́ть. **2,** (go out of use) отмира́ть. **3,** (become extinct) вымира́ть.
dieresis *n.* две то́чки.
diesel *adj.* ди́зельный. *Diesel engine,* ди́зель. *Diesel locomotive,* теплово́з.
diet *n.* дие́та. *Go on a diet,* сесть на дие́ту. *Put on a diet,* посади́ть на дие́ту. —*v.i.* быть на дие́те. —**dietary,** *adj.* диети́ческий.
dietetic *adj.* диетети́ческий. —**dietetics,** *n.* диете́тика.
dietitian *also,* **dietician** *n.* диетвра́ч.
differ *v.i.* **1,** (be dissimilar) отлича́ться; различа́ться. *Differ from the rest,* отлича́ться от остальны́х. **2,** (disagree) расходи́ться. *We differ on this issue,* на́ши мне́ния по э́тому вопро́су расхо́дятся.
difference *n.* **1,** (dissimilarity; variation) ра́зница: *the enormous difference between them,* огро́мная ра́зница ме́жду ни́ми. *Age difference,* ра́зница лет or во́зрастов. *Difference in time,* ра́зница во вре́мени. *A difference of ten dollars,* ра́зница в десяти́ до́лларах. **2,** (disagreement) разногла́сие; расхожде́ние. *Difference of opinion,* разногла́сие/разли́чие/расхожде́ние во мне́ниях. **3,** *math.* ра́зность. —**make a difference:** *it makes a great difference,* больша́я ра́зница. *It makes no difference* (*to me*), (мне) всё равно́. —**what's the difference?,** кака́я ра́зница?
different *adj.* **1,** (dissimilar; various) ра́зный; разли́чный. *Be different from,* отлича́ться от. *In different ways,* по-ра́зному. **2,** (another) друго́й. *That's different,* э́то друго́е де́ло.
differential *n.* **1,** (difference) разли́чие; ра́зница: *price differential,* разли́чие/ра́зница в цене́. **2,** *math.; mech.* дифференциа́л. —*adj.* дифференциа́льный: *differential calculus/equation,* дифференциа́льное исчисле́ние/уравне́ние.
differentiate *v.t. & i.* различа́ть; разграни́чивать.
differentiation *n.* разграниче́ние; дифференциа́ция.
differently *adv.* **1,** (in a different way) ина́че; по-друго́му. **2,** (in various ways) по-ра́зному.
difficult *adj.* **1,** (hard to do, solve, or handle) тру́дный: *difficult work,* тру́дная рабо́та; *a difficult problem,* тру́дная зада́ча; *a difficult child,* тру́дный ребёнок. **2,** (hard to deal or cope with; complex) сло́жный: *difficult matter,* сло́жное де́ло. **3,** (unpleasant; trying; awkward) тру́дный; затрудни́тельный; тяжёлый. *Difficult times,* тяжёлые времена́. *Under difficult conditions,* в тру́дных усло́виях. *In a difficult situation,* в затрудни́тельном положе́нии.
difficulty *n.* **1,** (quality of being difficult) тру́дность. *With difficulty,* с трудо́м. *Without difficulty,* без труда́. **2,** (difficult situation) затрудне́ние: *be in difficulty,* быть в затрудне́нии. **3,** (complication; obstacle) затрудне́ние; тру́дность.

diffidence *n.* застéнчивость; стеснúтельность. —**diffident,** *adj.* застéнчивый; стеснúтельный.
diffuse *v.t.* **1,** (scatter) рассéивать. **2,** (disseminate, as knowledge) распространя́ть. —*adj.* **1,** (scattered) рассéянный. **2,** (verbose) многослóвный.
diffusion *n.* **1,** (dissemination) рассéивание; распространéние. **2,** *physics* диффу́зия. *Diffusion of light,* рассéяние свéта.
dig *v.t.* копáть; рыть: *dig a hole,* копáть/рыть я́му. —*v.i.* копáться; ры́ться: *dig in the sand,* копáться/ры́ться в пескé. —*n., colloq.* **1,** (poke) тычóк. **2,** (gibe) шпúлька. —**dig in,** окáпываться. —**dig up, 1,** (tear up; churn up) искáпывать; изрывáть. **2,** (unearth) выкáпывать; вырывáть; откáпывать; отрывáть. **3,** *colloq.* (find; discover) выкáпывать; откáпывать; раскáпывать.
digest *v.t.* усвáивать; перевáривать. —*n.* **1,** (synopsis) резюмé. **2,** (collection) сбóрник.
digestible *adj.* удобоварúмый. —**digestibility,** *n.* удобоварúмость.
digestion *n.* пищеварéние. —**digestive,** *adj.* пищеварúтельный.
digger *n.* копáтель; землекóп.
digging *n.* копáние; рытьё.
digit *n.* **1,** (finger; toe) пáлец. **2,** (number) знак: *two-digit number,* двузнáчное числó.
digital computer цифровáя вычислúтельная машúна.
digitalis *n.* наперстя́нка.
dignified *adj.* величáвый; степéнный.
dignify *v.t.* придавáть достóинство (+ *dat.*).
dignitary *n.* санóвник; высокопостáвленное лицó.
dignity *n.* достóинство. *Beneath one's dignity,* нúже чегó-нибудь достóинства.
digress *v.i.* отклоня́ться; уклоня́ться; отступáть; отходúть; отвлекáться. —**digression,** *n.* отклонéние; уклонéние; отступлéние.
dihedral *adj.* двугрáнный.
dike *n.* дáмба.
dilapidated *adj.* вéтхий; обветшáлый; полуразру́шенный.
dilate *v.t.* расширя́ть. —**dilation,** *n.* расширéние.
dilatory *adj.* мéдленный; медлúтельный.
dilemma *n.* дилéмма. *Be in a dilemma,* стоя́ть пéред дилéммой.
dilettante *n.* дилетáнт; любúтель. —**dilettantism,** *n.* дилетантúзм; дилетáнтство.
diligence *n.* прилежáние; старáтельность.
diligent *adj.* прилéжный; старáтельный. —**diligently,** *adv.* прилéжно; старáтельно.
dill *n.* укрóп.
dillydally *v.i.* мéшкать; лóдырничать.
dilute *v.t.* разбавля́ть; разжижáть; разводúть. —**dilution,** *n.* разжижéние.
dim *adj.* **1,** (not bright) ту́склый. **2,** (not clear; hazy; vague) сму́тный. —*v.t.* притушúть: *dim the headlights,* притушúть фáры. —*v.i.* тускнéть. —**take a dim view of,** относúться скептúчески к.
dime *n.* монéта в дéсять цéнтов.
dimension *n.* **1,** (measurable extent) измерéние. *Three-dimensional,* трёхмéрный. **2,** *pl.* (extent) размéры.
diminish *v.t.* уменьшáть. —*v.i.* уменьшáться.
diminuendo *n.* диминуэ́ндо.
diminution *n.* уменьшéние.
diminutive *adj.* **1,** (small) мáленький; миниатю́рный. **2,** *gram.* уменьшúтельный. —*n.* уменьшúтельное существúтельное.
dimly *adv.* **1,** (not brightly) ту́скло. **2,** (vaguely) сму́тно.
dimness *n.* ту́склость.
dimple *n.* я́мочка.
dimwit *n., colloq.* тупоу́мный человéк; тупúца; тугоду́м. —**dimwitted,** *adj., colloq.* тупоу́мный; тупоголóвый.
din *n.* грóхот; гвалт. —*v.t.* [*usu.* **din into**] вдáлбливать (чтó-нибудь + *dat.*).
dine *v.i.* обéдать.
diner *n.* **1,** (person dining) обéдающий. **2,** (dining car) вагóн-ресторáн. **3,** (small restaurant) заку́сочная.
dinghy *n.* я́лик.
dingy *adj.* ту́склый; мрáчный.
dining car вагóн-ресторáн.
dining room столóвая.
dinner *n.* обéд. *Have dinner,* обéдать. —*adj.* обéденный: *dinner table,* обéденный стол. —**dinner jacket,** смóкинг. —**dinner party,** звáный обéд.
dinnertime *n.* обéденное врéмя.
dinosaur *n.* динозáвр.
dint *n., in* **by dint of,** посрéдством (+ *gen.*); путём (+ *gen.*).
diocese *n.* епáрхия.
diode *n.* диóд.
dioxide *n.* двуóкись.
dip *v.t.* (immerse) погружáть; окунáть; макáть; обмáкивать. —*v.i.* **1,** (immerse oneself) окунáться. **2,** (descend; drop) спускáться; опускáться. **3,** (decline; go down) пáдать; снижáться; пойтú вниз. —*n.* **1,** (brief swim): *go for a dip,* поплáвать. **2,** (depression, as in a road) впáдина; углублéние. **3,** (drop; decline) падéние; снижéние.
diphtheria *n.* дифтерúя; дифтерúт. —**diphtherial,** *adj.* дифтерúйный.
diphthong *n.* дифтóнг; двуглáсный звук.
diploma *n.* диплóм
diplomacy *n.* **1,** (dealings between nations) дипломáтия. **2,** (tact) дипломатúчность.
diplomat *n.* диплмáт.
diplomatic *adj.* **1,** (pert. to diplomacy) дипломатúческий. **2,** (tactful) дипломатúческий; дипломатúчный.
dipper *n.* **1,** (ladle) ковш; черпáк. **2,** *cap., astron.* Медвéдица. **3,** (bird) оля́пка.
dipstick *n.* щуп.
dire *adj.* **1,** (grave; extreme) крáйний: *dire need,* крáйняя нуждá. **2,** (disastrous) бéдственный: *be in dire straits,* быть в бéдственном положéнии. **3,** (ominous) зловéщий: *dire predictions,* зловéщие предсказáния.
direct *adj.* **1,** (by the shortest way) прямóй: *direct route,* прямóй путь. **2,** (with nothing in between) прямóй; непосрéдственный: *direct connection,* прямáя связь; *direct cause,* непосрéдственная причúна. **3,** (straightforward) прямóй: *direct answer,* прямóй отвéт. —*adv.* пря́мо: *direct from the factory,* пря́мо с завóда. —*v.t.* **1,** (aim) направля́ть; обращáть. **2,** (show the way to) указáть дорóгу (+ *dat.*). **3,** (manage; run) руководúть. *Direct traffic,* регулúровать движéние. **4,** (order) предпúсывать. **5,** *music* дири-

жи́ровать. **6,** *theat.* режисси́ровать. —**direct current,** постоя́нный ток. —**direct object,** *gram.* прямо́е дополне́ние.

direction *n.* **1,** (course) направле́ние; сторона́. *In the direction of,* по направле́нию к; в сто́рону (+ *gen.*). *In all directions,* во всех направле́ниях; врассыпну́ю. *Sense of direction,* чу́вство ориенти́ро́вки. **2,** (supervision) руково́дство. **3,** *usu. pl.* (instructions) указа́ния. **4,** *theat.* режиссу́ра.

directional *adj.* напра́вленный: *directional antenna,* напра́вленная анте́нна. —**directional signal,** указа́тель поворо́та.

direction finder (радио) пеленга́тор.

directive *n.* директи́ва; устано́вка.

directly *adv.* **1,** (without deviating) пря́мо. **2,** (immediately) сра́зу; неме́дленно.

directness *n.* прямота́; прямоду́шие.

director *n.* **1,** (manager) дире́ктор. **2,** *theat.* режиссёр; постано́вщик.

directorate *n.* **1,** (board of directors) директора́т. **2,** (Soviet governmental department) управле́ние.

directorial *adj.* дире́кторский.

directory *n.* спра́вочник; указа́тель; а́дресная кни́га. *Telephone directory,* телефо́нная кни́га; телефо́нный спра́вочник.

dirge *n.* погреба́льное пе́ние.

dirigible *n.* дирижа́бль.

dirt *n.* грязь. —*adj.* грунтово́й: *dirt road,* грунтова́я доро́га.

dirt-cheap *adj.* деше́вле па́реной ре́пы. —*adv.* по дешёвке.

dirty *adj.* **1,** (unclean) гря́зный. **2,** (obscene) са́льный; скабрёзный. **3,** (mean; despicable) по́длый. —*v.t.* па́чкать; загрязня́ть. —**dirty look,** укори́зненный взгляд. *Give someone a dirty look,* посмотре́ть на кого́-нибудь укори́зненно. —**dirty trick,** зла́я шу́тка; по́длость; га́дость. *Play a dirty trick on,* сыгра́ть с (+ *instr.*) злу́ю шу́тку; подложи́ть свинью́ (+ *dat.*).

disability *n.* нетрудоспосо́бность; инвали́дность.

disable *v.t.* де́лать нетрудоспосо́бным; выводи́ть из стро́я.

disabled *adj.* **1,** (incapacitated) нетрудоспосо́бный; неработоспосо́бный; *mil.* небоеспосо́бный. **2,** (of a vehicle) испо́ртившийся.

disabuse *v.t.* [*usu.* **disabuse of**] разубежда́ть (в); разуверя́ть (в).

disadvantage *n.* **1,** (unfavorable position) невы́года. *Be at a disadvantage,* быть в невы́годном положе́нии. **2,** (drawback) недоста́ток: *advantages and disadvantages,* досто́инства и недоста́тки. **3,** (detriment) вред: *work to the disadvantage of,* де́йствовать во вред (+ *dat.*). —**disadvantageous,** *adj.* невы́годный.

disaffect *v.t.* отчужда́ть. —**disaffection,** *n.* отчужде́ние.

disagree *v.i.* **1,** (have different opinions) не соглаша́ться; расходи́ться во мне́ниях. *I disagree with you,* я с ва́ми не согла́сен (согла́сна). **2,** (fail to coincide, as of versions of a story) расходи́ться; не совпада́ть; не сходи́ться. **3,** *fol. by* **with** (upset, as of food) пло́хо де́йствовать (на).

disagreeable *adj.* неприя́тный.

disagreement *n.* **1,** (difference of opinion) разногла́сие; расхожде́ние. **2,** (dispute; quarrel) ссо́ра.

disallow *v.t.* отка́зывать в (+ *prepl.*); отклоня́ть.

disappear *v.i.* **1,** (pass out of sight) исчеза́ть. *Disappear from view,* скры́ться из виду. **2,** (be missing; be lost) пропада́ть. —**disappearance,** *n.* исчезнове́ние.

disappoint *v.t.* разочаро́вывать. —**disappointed,** *adj.* разочаро́ванный. —**disappointing,** *adj.* разочаро́вывающий. —**disappointment,** *n.* разочарова́ние.

disapproval *n.* **1,** (unfavorable attitude) неодобре́ние. *In disapproval,* неодобри́тельно. **2,** (rejection) отклоне́ние.

disapprove *v.i.* [*usu.* **disapprove of**] не одобря́ть. —*v.t.* (reject) отверга́ть; отклоня́ть. —**disapproving,** *adj.* неодобри́тельный.

disarm *v.t.* **1,** (seize a weapon from) обезору́живать; разоружа́ть. **2,** (reduce the armed forces or weapons of) разоружа́ть. **3,** (win over) обезору́живать. —*v.i.* разоружа́ться.

disarmament *n.* разоруже́ние.

disarming *adj.* обезору́живающий.

disarrange *v.t.* расстра́ивать; (пере)пу́тать; приводи́ть в беспоря́док.

disarray *n.* беспоря́док; расстро́йство.

disassemble *v.t.* разбира́ть (на ча́сти).

disassociate *v.t.* = **dissociate.**

disaster *n.* бе́дствие; катастро́фа. *On the brink of disaster,* на краю́ про́пасти. —**disastrous,** *adj.* бе́дственный; катастрофи́ческий; ги́бельный.

disavow *v.t.* **1,** (deny; disown) отрица́ть. **2,** (repudiate; renounce) отрека́ться от; отка́зываться от.

disavowal *n.* **1,** (denial) отрица́ние. **2,** (repudiation) отрече́ние; отка́з.

disband *v.t.* распуска́ть. —*v.i.* расходи́ться; рассе́иваться.

disbar *v.t.* лиша́ть пра́ва адвока́тской пра́ктики.

disbelief *n.* неве́рие. *In disbelief,* не ве́ря свои́м глаза́м *or* уша́м.

disbelieve *v.t.* не ве́рить.

disburse *v.t.* выпла́чивать. —**disbursement,** *n.* вы́плата.

disc *n.* = **disk.**

discard *v.t.* **1,** (throw away) выбра́сывать. **2,** *cards* сбра́сывать; ски́дывать; сноси́ть.

discern *v.t.* различа́ть; рассмотре́ть; разгляде́ть; распознава́ть. —**discernible,** *adj.* различи́мый. —**discerning,** *adj.* проница́тельный. —**discernment,** *n.* проница́тельность.

discharge *v.t.* **1,** (unload) выгружа́ть (груз); выса́живать (пассажи́ров). **2,** (release) освобожда́ть; (*from military service*) увольня́ть; (*from a hospital*) выпи́сывать. **3,** (dismiss from a job) увольня́ть; рассчи́тывать. **4,** (perform, as duties) исполня́ть; выполня́ть. **5,** (pay, as a debt) выпла́чивать. **6,** (emit) выпуска́ть; испуска́ть; выделя́ть. **7,** (fire; shoot) выпуска́ть; пуска́ть. **8,** *electricity* разряжа́ть. —*v.i.* **1,** (go off, as of a cannon) вы́стрелить. **2,** *electricity* разряжа́ться. —*n.* **1,** (from military service) увольне́ние; (from a hospital) вы́писка; (from a job) увольне́ние; расчёт. **2,** (fulfillment; performance) исполне́ние; выполне́ние. **3,** (payment, as of a debt) упла́та; покры́тие. **4,** (firing; shooting off) вы́стрел. **5,** (secretion) выделе́ние. **6,** *electricity* разря́д.

disciple *n.* **1,** *relig.* апо́стол. **2,** (pupil; follower) учени́к; после́дователь.

discipline *n.* дисципли́на. —*v.t.* дисциплини́ровать. —**disciplinary,** *adj.* дисциплина́рный.

disclaim *v.t.* отрица́ть: *he disclaimed any knowledge of the incident,* он отрица́л, что знал о происше́дшем. *Disclaim responsibility for,* не брать на себя́ отве́тственности за. —**disclaimer,** *n.* опроверже́ние.

disclose *v.t.* раскрыва́ть. —**disclosure,** *n.* раскры́тие.

discolor *also,* **discolour** *v.t.* обесцве́чивать. —**discoloration,** *n.* обесцве́чивание.

discomfit *v.t.* **1,** (frustrate; thwart) расстра́ивать. **2,** (disconcert) смуща́ть. —**discomfiture,** *n.* смуще́ние; замеша́тельство.

discomfort *n.* **1,** (lack of comfort) неудо́бство. **2,** (distress; embarrassment) неудо́бство; смуще́ние. **3,** (pain): *she is in great discomfort,* ей тяжело́; ей о́чень бо́льно.

discommode *v.t.* затрудня́ть; причиня́ть неудо́бство (+ *dat.*).

disconcert *v.t.* смуща́ть; сбива́ть; приводи́ть в замеша́тельство.

disconnect *v.t.* разъединя́ть: *we've been disconnected,* нас разъедини́ли. *Disconnect a telephone,* отключи́ть телефо́н.

disconnected *adj.* несвя́зный; бессвя́зный.

disconsolate *adj.* неуте́шный.

discontent *n.* [*also,* **discontentment**] недово́льство. —*adj.* [*also,* **discontented**] недово́льный.

discontinue *v.t.* прекраща́ть. —**discontinuation,** *n.* прекраще́ние.

discord *n.* **1,** (dissension) разногла́сие; раздо́р; разла́д. **2,** *music* диссона́нс.

discordant *adj.* **1,** (not in accord) противоречи́вый. **2,** (not harmonious in sound) нестро́йный; несогла́сный; неблагозву́чный.

discount *n.* ски́дка: *at a discount,* со ски́дкой. —*v.t.* **1,** *comm.* учи́тывать (ве́ксель). **2,** (take no account of) не счита́ться с; не принима́ть в расчёт. —**discount rate,** учётная ста́вка; учётный проце́нт.

discourage *v.t.* **1,** (dishearten) обескура́живать. **2,** *fol. by* **from** (dissuade) отгова́ривать (от). —**discouragement,** *n.* обескура́женность. —**discouraging,** *adj.* обескура́живающий.

discourse *n.* **1,** (conversation) разгово́р. **2,** (lengthy discussion) рассужде́ние. **3,** (treatise) тракта́т. —*v.i.* рассужда́ть.

discourteous *adj.* неве́жливый. —**discourtesy,** *n.* неве́жливость.

discover *v.t.* **1,** (be the first to see) открыва́ть. **2,** (find; detect; realize) обнару́живать. —**discoverer,** *n.* открыва́тель. —**discovery,** *n.* откры́тие.

discredit *v.t.* **1,** (damage in reputation) поро́чить; дискредити́ровать. **2,** (not believe; discount) не ве́рить; не доверя́ть. **3,** (show to be untrue) развéнчивать. —*n. Bring discredit upon,* дискредити́ровать.

discreet *adj.* благоразу́мный; такти́чный; осторо́жный. *Discreet distance,* почти́тельное расстоя́ние.

discrepancy *n.* несоотве́тствие; разногла́сие.

discretion *n.* **1,** (prudence) благоразу́мие. **2,** (power to decide) усмотре́ние: *at (someone's) discretion,* по (чьему́-нибудь) усмотре́нию. *Leave to someone's discretion,* представля́ть на чьё-нибудь усмотре́ние. *Use one's discretion,* де́йствовать по своему́ усмотре́нию.

discretionary *adj.* дискрецио́нный.

discriminate *v.i.* **1,** (act with prejudice) дискримини́ровать. *Discriminate against women,* дискримини́ровать же́нщин. **2,** *fol. by* **between** (distinguish between) различа́ть (ме́жду).

discriminating *adj.* разбо́рчивый. *Discriminating taste,* то́нкий вкус.

discrimination *n.* **1,** (injustice) дискримина́ция. **2,** (discernment) разбо́рчивость. —**discriminatory,** *adj.* дискриминацио́нный.

discus *n.* диск. *Discus throw,* мета́ние ди́ска.

discuss *v.t.* обсужда́ть.

discussion *n.* обсужде́ние; диску́ссия. *Be under discussion,* обсужда́ться.

disdain *v.t.* **1,** (scorn) презира́ть; гнуша́ться. **2,** *fol. by inf.* (refuse scornfully) бре́згать; гнуша́ться. —*n.* презре́ние. —**disdainful,** *adj.* презри́тельный.

disease *n.* боле́знь. —**diseased,** *adj.* больно́й; заболе́вший.

disembark *v.t.* выса́живать. —*v.i.* выса́живаться. —**disembarkation,** *n.* вы́садка.

disembowel *v.t.* потроши́ть.

disenchant *v.t.* разочаро́вывать. —**disenchantment,** *n.* разочарова́ние.

disenfranchise *v.* = **disfranchise.**

disengage *v.t.* разъединя́ть. —*v.i.* разъединя́ться. —**disengagement,** *n.* разъедине́ние.

disentangle *v.t.* распу́тывать; выпу́тывать.

disestablish *v.t.* отделя́ть (це́рковь) от госуда́рства.

disfavor *also,* **disfavour** *n.* неми́лость; опа́ла. *Fall into disfavor,* впасть в неми́лость.

disfigure *v.t.* обезобра́живать; уро́довать. —**disfigured,** *adj.* изуро́дованный. —**disfigurement,** *n.* обезобра́живание.

disfranchise *v.t.* лиша́ть гражда́нских *or* избира́тельных прав.

disgorge *v.t.* изверга́ть; изрыга́ть.

disgrace *n.* **1,** (shame; dishonor) позо́р; бесче́стье. **2,** (disfavor) неми́лость; опа́ла. —*v.t.* позо́рить; бесче́стить. —**disgrace oneself,** позо́риться; покры́ть себя́ позо́ром. *He did not disgrace himself,* он не уда́рил лицо́м в грязь.

disgraceful *adj.* позо́рный. *It's simply disgraceful!,* э́то про́сто безобра́зие!

disgruntle *v.t.* вызыва́ть (чьё-нибудь) недово́льство. —**disgruntled,** *adj.* недово́льный; в дурно́м настрое́нии.

disguise *v.t.* маскирова́ть; переодева́ть. *Disguise one's voice,* меня́ть *or* изменя́ть го́лос. *Disguise oneself as,* переодева́ться (+ *instr.*). —*n.* маскиро́вка. *In disguise,* замаскиро́ванный; переоде́тый.

disgust *n.* отвраще́ние. —*v.t.* внуша́ть отвраще́ние (+ *dat.*).

disgusted *adj. I am/got disgusted,* мне надое́ло; мне опроти́вело; мне осточерте́ло.

disgusting *adj.* отврати́тельный; проти́вный. *It is disgusting to watch,* проти́вно смотре́ть.

dish *n.* **1,** (small plate) таре́лка. **2,** *pl.* (table utensils) посу́да: *do the dishes,* мыть посу́ду. **3,** (particular kind of food) блю́до: *my favorite dish,* моё люби́мое блю́до. —*v.t.* [*usu.* **dish out** *or* **dish up**] подава́ть; сервирова́ть.

disharmony *n.* **1,** (dissonance) дисгармо́ния; неблагозву́чие. **2,** (discord) дисгармо́ния; разногла́сие.

dishcloth *n.* посу́дная тря́пка.
dishearten *v.t.* обескура́живать. *Become disheartened,* унывать; па́дать ду́хом.
disheveled *also,* **dishevelled** *adj.* растрёпанный; взъеро́шенный; взлохма́ченный.
dishonest *adj.* нече́стный. —**dishonestly,** *adv.* нече́стно. —**dishonesty,** *n.* нече́стность.
dishonor *also,* **dishonour** *n.* бесче́стье. —*v.t.* бесче́стить. —**dishonorable,** *adj.* бесче́стный.
dishpan *n.* таз (для мытья́ посу́ды).
dishrag *n.* посу́дная тря́пка.
dishtowel *n.* посу́дное полоте́нце.
dishwasher *n.* **1,** (person) судомо́йка. **2,** (machine) посудомо́ечная маши́на; посудомо́йка.
dishwater *n.* помо́и.
disillusion *v.t.* разочаро́вывать. —**disillusioned,** *adj.* разочаро́ванный. *Become disillusioned,* разочаро́вываться. —**disillusionment,** *n.* разочарова́ние.
disinclination *n.* нерасположе́ние; нежела́ние; неохо́та. —**disinclined,** *adj.* не скло́нен (к); не располо́жен (к).
disinfect *v.t.* дезинфици́ровать; обеззара́живать.
disinfectant *adj.* дезинфици́рующий. —*n.* дезинфици́рующее сре́дство. —**disinfection,** *n.* дезинфе́кция; обеззара́живание.
disinformation *n.* дезинформа́ция.
disingenuous *adj.* нейскренний; непрямо́й.
disinherit *v.t.* лиша́ть насле́дства. —**disinheritance,** *n.* лише́ние насле́дства.
disintegrate *v.i.* распада́ться. —*v.t.* раздробля́ть; измельча́ть. —**disintegration,** *n.* распа́д.
disinter *v.t.* выка́пывать; отка́пывать.
disinterest *n.* **1,** (impartiality) беспристра́стие. **2,** (indifference) равноду́шие. —**disinterested,** *adj.* незаинтересо́ванный; бескоры́стный.
disjoint *v.t.* **1,** (dislocate) вы́вихнуть. **2,** (take apart at the joints) разде́лывать.
disjointed *adj.* **1,** (dislocated) вы́вихнутый. **2,** (disconnected; incoherent) несвя́зный; бессвя́зный; отры́вистый; отры́вочный; обры́вочный.
disjunctive *adj.* раздели́тельный.
disk *also,* **disc** *n.* диск. —**disk brake,** ди́сковый то́рмоз. —**disk harrow,** ди́сковая борона́.
dislikable *adj.* неприя́тный.
dislike *v.t.* не люби́ть. —*n.* [*also,* **disliking**] нелюбо́вь; нерасположе́ние; антипа́тия. *Take a disliking to,* невзлюби́ть; настро́иться про́тив.
dislocate *v.t., med.* вы́вихнуть.
dislocation *n.* **1,** (displacement) перемеще́ние. **2,** *med.* вы́вих.
dislodge *v.t.* выбива́ть; вышиба́ть.
disloyal *adj.* нелоя́льный. —**disloyalty,** *n.* нелоя́льность.
dismal *adj.* мра́чный; тоскли́вый; па́смурный.
dismantle *v.t.* разбира́ть; демонти́ровать.
dismay *v.t.* **1,** (distress) смуща́ть. **2,** (dishearten) обескура́живать. —*n.* **1,** (consternation) смуще́ние. **2,** (alarm) трево́га.
dismember *v.t.* расчленя́ть. —**dismemberment,** *n.* расчлене́ние.
dismiss *v.t.* **1,** (tell to go or disperse) отпуска́ть; распуска́ть. **2,** (remove from office or employment) увольня́ть; рассчи́тывать. **3,** (put out of one's mind) отбра́сывать. **4,** *law* прекраща́ть (де́ло); отклоня́ть (иск).
dismissal *n.* **1,** (ordering or allowing to disperse) ро́спуск. **2,** (discharge; removal) увольне́ние; расчёт. —**dismissal notice,** уведомле́ние об увольне́нии.
dismount *v.i.* сходи́ть *or* слеза́ть с ло́шади; спе́шиваться.
disobedience *n.* непослуша́ние; неповинове́ние. —**disobedient,** *adj.* непослу́шный.
disobey *v.t. & i.* не слу́шаться; ослу́шаться.
disorder *n.* **1,** (disarray) беспоря́док. **2,** *often pl.* (public disturbances) беспоря́дки. **3,** (ailment) расстро́йство. —*v.t.* (пере)пу́тать; приводи́ть в беспоря́док.
disorderly *adj.* **1,** (unsystematic) беспоря́дочный. **2,** (unruly) бу́йный. —**disorderly conduct,** хулига́нство.
disorganize *v.t.* дезорганизова́ть. —**disorganization,** *n.* дезорганиза́ция; неорганизо́ванность. —**disorganized,** *adj.* дезорганизо́ванный; неорганизо́ванный; беспоря́дочный.
disorient *v.t.* дезориенти́ровать. —**disorientation,** *n.* дезориента́ция.
disown *v.t.* отрека́ться от; отка́зываться от.
disparage *v.t.* умаля́ть; принижа́ть; поро́чить; хули́ть. —**disparagement,** *n.* умале́ние; приниже́ние. —**disparaging,** *adj.* оскорби́тельный; оби́дный.
disparate *adj.* разли́чный: *disparate elements,* разли́чные элеме́нты. —**disparity,** *n.* ра́зница; несоотве́тствие.
dispassionate *adj.* беспристра́стный.
dispatch *v.t.* **1,** (send off) отправля́ть. **2,** (kill) добива́ть; прика́нчивать. —*n.* **1,** (sending) отправле́ние; отпра́вка. **2,** (message) донесе́ние; депе́ша. **3,** (alacrity) быстрота́.
dispatcher *n.* диспе́тчер.
dispel *v.t.* рассе́ивать; разгоня́ть.
dispensable *adj.* необяза́тельный; без чего́ мо́жно обойти́сь.
dispensary *n.* амбулато́рия.
dispensation *n.* **1,** (distribution) разда́ча. **2,** (release from an obligation) освобожде́ние (от обяза́тельства).
dispense *v.t.* **1,** (distribute) раздава́ть. **2,** (administer, as justice) отправля́ть (правосу́дие). —*v.i.* [*usu.* **dispense with**] обходи́ться без.
dispenser *n.* автома́т.
dispersal *n.* рассе́ивание; разго́н.
disperse *v.t.* рассе́ивать; разгоня́ть. —*v.i.* рассе́иваться; расходи́ться; разбега́ться. —**dispersion,** *n.* рассе́ивание; рассе́яние; *physics* диспе́рсия.
dispirit *v.t.* удруча́ть; угнета́ть. —**dispirited,** *adj.* удручённый; угнетённый.
displace *v.t.* **1,** (force out; supersede) вытесня́ть. **2,** (remove) смеща́ть. —**displaced person,** перемещённое лицо́.
displacement *n.* **1,** (superseding) вытесне́ние. **2,** (removal) смеще́ние. **3,** (tonnage) водоизмеще́ние.
display *v.t.* **1,** (exhibit) выставля́ть. **2,** (reveal; manifest) проявля́ть; обнару́живать. —*n.* **1,** (showing) пока́з. *Put on display,* выставля́ть напока́з. **2,** (exhibit) вы́ставка. **3,** (manifestation) проявле́ние.
displease *v.t.* не нра́виться. —**displeased,** *adj.* недово́льный. —**displeasure,** *n.* неудово́льствие; недово́льство.
disposable *adj.* одноразо́вого употребле́ния; бро́совый.

disposal *n.* **1,** (arrangement) расположе́ние. **2,** (getting rid of) удале́ние: *waste disposal,* удале́ние отхо́дов. —**at one's disposal,** в чьём-нибудь распоряже́нии. *Have at one's disposal,* располага́ть (+ *instr.*); име́ть в своём распоряже́нии. *Place at someone's disposal,* предоста́вить в чьё-нибудь распоряже́ние. *My room is at your disposal,* моя́ ко́мната к ва́шим услу́гам.

dispose *v.t.* **1,** (place; arrange) располага́ть. **2,** (incline in a certain way) располага́ть; настра́ивать; склоня́ть. —**dispose of, 1,** (get rid of; remove) удаля́ть; убира́ть. **2,** (take care of; finish off) поко́нчить с; разде́латься с; распра́виться с.

disposed *adj.* располо́женный.

disposition *n.* **1,** (arrangement) расположе́ние. **2,** (temperament) нрав; хара́ктер. **3,** (tendency) расположе́ние; скло́нность. **4,** (handling; distribution) распоряже́ние. **5,** *mil.* дислока́ция.

dispossess *v.t.* лиша́ть со́бственности.

disproportion *n.* несоразме́рность; непропорциона́льность; диспропо́рция. —**disproportionate,** *adj.* несоразме́рный; непропорциона́льный. —**disproportionately,** *adv.* несоразме́рно; непропорциона́льно.

disprove *v.t.* опроверга́ть.

disputation *n.* деба́ты; ди́спут. —**disputatious,** *adj.* лю́бящий спо́рить.

dispute *n.* спор: *border dispute,* пограни́чный спор. *Be in dispute,* быть предме́том спо́ра. —*v.t.* оспа́ривать. *Disputed territory,* спо́рная террито́рия.

disqualify *v.t.* дисквалифици́ровать. —**disqualification,** *n.* дисквалифика́ция.

disquiet *v.t.* беспоко́ить; трево́жить. —*n.* [*also,* **disquietude**] беспоко́йство; трево́га. —**disquieting,** *adj.* беспоко́йный; трево́жный.

disquisition *n.* тракта́т.

disregard *v.t.* пренебрега́ть; игнори́ровать. —*n.* пренебреже́ние.

disrepair *n.* неиспра́вность. *Fall into disrepair,* приходи́ть в ве́тхость *or* в него́дность.

disreputable *adj.* по́льзующийся дурно́й сла́вой.

disrepute *n.* дурна́я сла́ва. *Fall into disrepute,* приобрести́ дурну́ю сла́ву.

disrespect *n.* неуваже́ние; непочте́ние; непочти́тельность. —**disrespectful,** *adj.* непочти́тельный.

disrobe *v.t.* раздева́ть; обнажа́ть. —*v.i.* раздева́ться; обнажа́ться.

disrupt *v.t.* наруша́ть; срыва́ть; дезорганизова́ть. —**disruption,** *n.* наруше́ние; дезорганиза́ция.

disruptive *adj.* **1,** (tending to disrupt) подрывно́й. **2,** (unruly) непоко́рный.

dissatisfaction *n.* недово́льство; неудовлетворённость. —**dissatisfied,** *adj.* недово́льный; неудовлетворённый.

dissect *v.t.* **1,** (cut apart) вскрыва́ть; анатоми́ровать. **2,** (analyze closely) разбира́ть.

dissection *n.* **1,** (cutting apart) вскры́тие. **2,** (analysis) разбо́р.

dissemble *v.t.* **1,** (conceal the real nature of) скрыва́ть; маскирова́ть. **2,** (feign) притворя́ться (+ *instr.*). —*v.i.* лицеме́рить; криви́ть душо́й.

disseminate *v.t.* распространя́ть. —**dissemination,** *n.* распростране́ние.

dissension *n.* разла́д; раздо́р.

dissent *v.i.* не соглаша́ться; возража́ть. *Dissenting vote,* го́лос про́тив. —*n.* инакомы́слие. —**dissenter,** *n.* инакомы́слящий.

dissertation *n.* диссерта́ция.

disservice *n.* плоха́я услу́га.

dissidence *n.* инакомы́слие. —**dissident,** *n. & adj.* инакомы́слящий.

dissimilar *adj.* непохо́жий; несхо́дный. —**dissimilarity,** *n.* несхо́дство.

dissipate *v.t.* **1,** (dispel) рассе́ивать; разгоня́ть. **2,** (squander) растра́чивать; расточа́ть. —*v.i.* рассе́иваться.

dissipation *n.* **1,** (dispelling) рассе́ивание. **2,** (squandering) расточе́ние. **3,** (dissoluteness) распу́тство.

dissociate *v.t.* разобща́ть. *Dissociate oneself from,* отмежёвываться от.

dissolute *adj.* распу́тный; распу́щенный; развра́тный; беспу́тный. —**dissoluteness,** *n.* распу́тство; распу́щенность; беспу́тство.

dissolution *n.* **1,** (melting) растворе́ние. **2,** (termination) расторже́ние; ликвида́ция. **3,** (dismissal) ро́спуск. **4,** (breaking up) распа́д.

dissolve *v.t.* **1,** (melt) растворя́ть. **2,** (terminate) расторга́ть (брак); ликвиди́ровать (компа́нию). **3,** (dismiss, as an assembly) распуска́ть. —*v.i.* растворя́ться.

dissonance *n.* диссона́нс; неблагозву́чие. —**dissonant,** *adj.* неблагозву́чный; нестро́йный.

dissuade *v.t.* отгова́ривать; отсове́товать.

distaff *n.* пря́лка. —**distaff side,** же́нская ли́ния.

distance *n.* расстоя́ние. *At a distance,* на не́котором расстоя́нии. *In the distance,* в отдале́нии; вдали́; вдалеке́. *Into the distance,* вдаль. *From a distance,* и́здали; издалека́. *Quite a distance from here,* дово́льно далеко́ отсю́да. *Because of the great distance,* за да́льностью расстоя́ния. —**keep one's distance,** держа́ться вдалеке́; держа́ться на почти́тельном расстоя́нии.

distant *adj.* **1,** (remote) далёкий; да́льний; отдалённый. *Distant relative,* да́льний ро́дственник. *Distant resemblance,* отдалённое схо́дство. **2,** (cold; indifferent) холо́дный; сухо́й.

distaste *n.* отвраще́ние; антипа́тия. —**distasteful,** *adj.* неприя́тный.

distemper *n.* **1,** (ill humor) плохо́е настрое́ние. **2,** (disease of dogs) соба́чья чума́. **3,** *painting* те́мпера.

distend *v.t.* надува́ть. —*v.i.* надува́ться. —**distended,** *adj.* наду́тый; напряжённый.

distill *also,* **distil** *v.t.* **1,** (purify) дистилли́ровать: *distilled water,* дистиллиро́ванная вода́. **2,** (make, as whiskey) перегоня́ть; гнать. —**distillation,** *n.* дистилля́ция; перего́нка; винокуре́ние. —**distiller,** *n.* виноку́р. —**distillery,** *n.* перего́нный *or* виноку́ренный заво́д.

distinct *adj.* **1,** (clear; plain) отчётливый; чёткий. **2,** (evident; marked) я́вный; заме́тный. *Distinct improvement,* заме́тное улучше́ние. *Distinct advantage,* я́вное преиму́щество. **3,** (different) различ́ный: *distinct dialects,* разли́чные диале́кты. —**as distinct from,** в отли́чие от.

distinction *n.* **1,** (differentiation) разли́чие: *make a distinction between,* де́лать разли́чие ме́жду. **2,** (eminence) изве́стность. *Man of distinction,* выдаю́щийся челове́к. **3,** (honor) честь: *dubious distinction,* сомни́тельная честь. *Serve/graduate with distinction,* служи́ть/око́нчить шко́лу/с отли́чием. *He has*

the distinction of being..., на его́ до́лю вы́пала честь быть...
distinctive *adj.* **1,** (distinguishing) отличи́тельный. **2,** (characteristic; peculiar) своеобра́зный.
distinctly *adv.* отчётливо; чётко.
distinguish *v.t.* **1,** (tell apart) различа́ть; отлича́ть. *Distinguish colors,* разли́чать цвета́. *Distinguish good from evil,* отлича́ть добро́ от зла. **2,** (make different; set apart) отлича́ть. *Distinguishing characteristic,* отличи́тельная черта́. **3,** (discern) различа́ть. —*v.i.* [*usu.* **distinguish between**] различа́ть (ме́жду). —**distinguish oneself,** отлича́ться.
distinguishable *adj.* различи́мый.
distinguished *adj.* **1,** (eminent) выдаю́щийся. **2,** *in direct address* уважа́емый: *distinguished guests,* уважа́емые го́сти. **3,** (dignified in appearance) импоза́нтный.
distort *v.t.* **1,** (contort) искажа́ть; искривля́ть. **2,** (misrepresent) искажа́ть; извраща́ть. —**distortion,** *n.* искаже́ние; извраще́ние.
distract *v.t.* отвлека́ть: *distract someone from his/her work,* отвлека́ть кого́-нибудь от рабо́ты.
distraction *n.* **1,** (act of distracting) отвлече́ние. **2,** (something that distracts) поме́ха. **3,** (mental derangement) безу́мие. *love someone to distraction,* люби́ть кого́-нибудь до безу́мия.
distraught *adj.* обезу́мевший (от го́ря).
distress *n.* **1,** (pain; suffering) огорче́ние. **2,** (trouble; danger) бе́дствие. *Distress signal,* сигна́л бе́дствия. *A ship in distress,* су́дно, те́рпящее бе́дствие. —*v.t.* огорча́ть. —**distressed,** *adj.* огорчённый. —**distressing,** *adj.* огорчи́тельный; гнету́щий; тя́гостный.
distribute *v.t.* **1,** (allot; parcel out) распределя́ть. **2,** (hand out) раздава́ть.
distribution *n.* **1,** (parceling out) распределе́ние. **2,** (range of occurrence) распростране́ние. —**distributive,** *adj.* распредели́тельный.
distributor *n.* **1,** (one who distributes) распредели́тель. **2,** *comm.* опто́вая фи́рма; опто́вый торго́вец. **3,** *mech.* распредели́тель.
district *n.* райо́н; о́круг. —*adj.* райо́нный; окружно́й. —**district attorney,** окружно́й прокуро́р.
distrust *n.* недове́рие. —*v.t.* не доверя́ть. —**distrustful,** *adj.* недове́рчивый.
disturb *v.t.* **1,** (bother; interrupt) меша́ть: *I hope I'm not disturbing you,* наде́юсь, что я вам не меша́ю. **2,** (disrupt) наруша́ть: *disturb the balance,* наруша́ть равнове́сие. **3,** (trouble; disquiet) беспоко́ить.
disturbance *n.* **1,** (disruption) наруше́ние. **2,** (interruption; intrusion) беспоко́йство. **3,** (public disorder) волне́ния; беспоря́дки. **4,** *med.* расстро́йство.
disturbed *adj.* **1,** (troubled) обеспоко́енный. **2,** (emotionally unstable) душевнобольно́й.
disturbing *adj.* беспоко́йный; трево́жный.
disunity *n.* отсу́тствие еди́нства; разла́д; разногла́сие.
disuse *n. Fall into disuse,* вы́йти из употребле́ния.
disyllabic *adj.* двусло́жный.
ditch *n.* кана́ва; ров. —*v.t. Ditch a plane over water,* де́лать вы́нужденную поса́дку на́ воду.
ditto *n.* то же. —**ditto marks,** кавы́чки (вме́сто повторе́ния).
ditty *n.* частýшка.
diuretic *adj.* мочего́нный. —*n.* мочего́нное сре́дство.
diurnal *adj.* дневно́й.
divan *n.* тахта́.
dive *v.i.* **1,** (plunge head first into water) ныря́ть. **2,** (leap; plunge) бро́ситься. **3,** *aero.* пики́ровать. —*n.* **1,** (plunge into water) прыжо́к в во́ду; ныро́к. **2,** *aero.* пики́рование; пике́. **3,** *colloq.* (cheap place) кабачо́к.
dive bomber пики́рующий бомбардиро́вщик.
diver *n.* **1,** *sports* ныря́льщик. **2,** (deep-sea diver) водола́з. *Pearl diver,* иска́тель же́мчуга.
diverge *v.i.* расходи́ться. —**divergence,** *n.* расхожде́ние.
divergent *adj.* **1,** (diverging) расходя́щийся. **2,** (different) разли́чный.
diverse *adj.* ра́зный; разнообра́зный.
diversify *v.t.* разнообра́зить. —**diversification,** *n.* диверсифика́ция.
diversion *n.* **1,** (turning aside) отво́д. **2,** (amusement) развлече́ние. **3,** *mil.* диве́рсия; демонстра́ция. —**diversionary,** *adj.* диверсио́нный; демонстрати́вный.
diversity *n.* разнообра́зие.
divert *v.t.* **1,** (draw off in another direction) отвлека́ть: *divert attention from,* отвлека́ть внима́ние от. *Divert a river,* изменя́ть ру́сло реки́. **2,** (entertain) развлека́ть.
divest *v.t.* лиша́ть. —**divest oneself of,** отка́зываться от.
divide *v.t.* **1,** (separate into parts; give out in shares) разделя́ть; дели́ть: *divide something in half,* разделя́ть/дели́ть что́-нибудь попола́м. *Divide up the loot,* дели́ть/разделя́ть добы́чу. **2,** (separate; be a boundary between) отделя́ть. **3,** *math.* дели́ть; разделя́ть. **4,** *fig.* (set apart) разъединя́ть: *the things that divide us,* то, что нас разъединя́ет. *Opinions are divided,* мне́ния расхо́дятся. —*v.i.* разделя́ться; дели́ться: *the road divides,* доро́га разделя́ется/де́лится. *Divide up into two groups,* разделя́ться на две гру́ппы.
dividend *n.* **1,** *finance* дивиде́нд. **2,** *math.* дели́мое.
divider *n.* **1,** (partition) перегоро́дка. **2,** *pl.* (pair of compasses) ци́ркуль.
dividing *adj.* раздели́тельный: *dividing line,* раздели́тельная черта́.
divination *n.* гада́ние; ворожба́.
divine *adj.* боже́ственный. —*n.* богосло́в. —*v.t.* предуга́дывать; разга́дывать.
diving *n.* **1,** *sports* прыжки́ в во́ду. **2,** (deep-sea diving) водола́зное де́ло. —**diving board,** трампли́н. —**diving helmet,** водола́зный шлем. —**diving suit,** водола́зный костю́м; скафа́ндр.
divinity *n.* **1,** (divine nature) боже́ственность. **2,** (deity) божество́. **3,** (study of religion) богосло́вие.
divisible *adj.* **1,** (general term) дели́мый. **2,** *math.* кра́тный: *divisible by two,* кра́тный двум. *Six is divisible by three,* шесть де́лится на три; шесть — кра́тное трём. —**divisibility,** *n.* дели́мость.
division *n.* **1,** (act of dividing) деле́ние; разделе́ние; разде́л. *Division of labor,* разделе́ние труда́. **2,** (section) отде́л. **3,** (military unit) диви́зия. **4,** *math.* деле́ние.
divisional *adj.* дивизио́нный.
divisive *adj.* раско́льнический.
divisor *n., math.* дели́тель.

divorce *n.* разво́д. —*adj.* бракоразво́дный: *divorce case,* бракоразво́дное де́ло. —*v.t.* **1,** (get a divorce from) разводи́ться с. **2,** (separate) отделя́ть; отрыва́ть. —**divorced,** *adj.* разведённый. *They are divorced,* они́ в разво́де. —**divorcée,** *n.* разведённая.
divulge *v.t.* разглаша́ть. —**divulgence,** *n.* разглаше́ние.
dizzy *adj.* **1,** (giddy): *I am dizzy,* у меня́ кру́жится голова́. **2,** (causing dizziness) головокружи́тельный. —**dizziness,** *n.* головокруже́ние.
do[1] (doo) *v.t.* **1,** (perform; attend to) де́лать: *what are you doing?,* что вы де́лаете? *Do one's lessons,* де́лать уро́ки. *Do the dishes,* мыть посу́ду. *Do a lot of reading,* мно́го чита́ть. **2,** (work at) рабо́тать; занима́ться: *what do you do for a living?,* кем вы рабо́таете?; чем вы занима́етесь? **3,** (cause) причиня́ть: *do harm to,* причиня́ть вред *or* зло (+ *dat.*); де́лать зло (+ *dat.*). *Do someone good,* приноси́ть по́льзу (+ *dat.*). **4,** (render; perform) де́лать: *do someone a favor/service,* сде́лать кому́-нибудь одолже́ние. *What can I do for you?,* чем могу́ быть поле́зен (поле́зна)? **5,** *fol. by* **to** (hurt) де́лать: *what did you do to him?,* что вы ему́ сде́лали? *What did he ever do to you?,* что он тако́е вам сде́лал? *What did you do to your leg?,* что случи́лось с ва́шей ного́й? —*v.i.* **1,** (act; behave) де́лать: *do as you are told,* де́лайте, как вам ве́лено. **2,** (fare): *how are you doing?,* как (ва́ши) дела́? *How did he do?,* как у него́ получи́лось? **3,** (be suitable) годи́ться; подходи́ть. *That won't do,* э́то не подойдёт. **4,** (be sufficient) хвата́ть: *that will do,* хва́тит!; э́того хва́тит. —*v.aux.* **1,** *in forming questions: do you speak Russian?,* вы говори́те по-ру́сски? **2,** *in forming neg. sentences: I do not speak Russian,* я не говорю́ по-ру́сски. **3,** *to add emphasis: Do pay us a visit,* пожа́луйста, зайди́те к нам! *Do be quiet!,* да замолчи́те же! **4,** *to replace a verb previously expressed or understood: Do you know how to cook? Yes, I do.,* уме́ете ли вы гото́вить? Да, уме́ю. *You don't know how to cook. Yes, I do.,* вы не уме́ете гото́вить. Непра́вда, уме́ю. —**do away with,** уничтожа́ть; поко́нчить с. —**do not,** *see* **don't.** —**do over,** переде́лывать. —**do with,** дева́ть: *what did I do with my glasses?,* куда́ я дел мои́ очки́? —**do without,** обходи́ться без. *See also* **doing, done, don't.**
do[2] (do) *n., music* до.
docile *adj.* послу́шный; поко́рный. —**docility,** *n.* поко́рность.
dock *n.* **1,** (place where a ship stands) док: *dry dock,* сухо́й док. **2,** (pier) при́стань. **3,** (prisoner's stand) скамья́ подсуди́мых: *in the dock,* на скамье́ подсуди́мых. —*v.i.* **1,** (of a ship) прича́ливать. **2,** (of space vehicles) стыкова́ться. —*v.t.* (deduct from) уре́зывать.
docket *n., law* спи́сок дел.
docking *n., aerospace* стыко́вка.
dockyard *n.* верфь.
doctor *n.* **1,** (physician) врач. **2,** (holder of a doctorate) до́ктор. —*v.t.* **1,** (treat) лечи́ть. **2,** (tamper with) подде́лывать; фальсифици́ровать. —**doctoral,** *adj.* до́кторский. —**doctorate,** *n.* до́кторская сте́пень.
doctrine *n.* доктри́на. —**doctrinaire,** *adj.* доктринёрский.
document *n.* докуме́нт. —*v.t.* документи́ровать.
documentary *adj.* документа́льный. —*n.* документа́льный фильм.
documentation *n.* документа́ция.
dodder *v.i.* **1,** (tremble) трясти́сь. **2,** (wobble along) ковыля́ть; шата́ться. *A doddering old man,* ковыля́ющий стари́к; стари́к, е́ле передвига́ющий но́ги.
dodge *v.t.* уклоня́ться от; увёртываться от; увиливать от. —*n.* увёртка.
doe *n.* **1,** (female deer) олену́ха. **2,** (female of other animals) са́мка.
doeskin *n.* за́мша.
doff *v.t.* снима́ть.
dog *n.* соба́ка. —*adj.* соба́чий: *dog collar,* соба́чий оше́йник. —*v.t.* **1,** (track; pursue) гна́ться по пята́м за; увя́зываться за. *Dog someone's footsteps,* сле́довать по пята́м за. **2,** *fig.* (haunt; hound) пресле́довать: *dogged by misfortune,* пресле́дуемый несча́стьями. —**a dog's age,** це́лая ве́чность. —**a dog's life,** соба́чья жизнь. —**dog tired,** уста́лый как соба́ка. —**go to the dogs,** пойти́ пра́хом. —**it is raining cats and dogs,** дождь льёт как из ведра́. —**let sleeping dogs lie,** не тронь ли́ха, пока́ спит ти́хо.
doge *n.* дож.
dogeared *adj.* захва́танный.
dogfight *n., aero.* возду́шный бой.
dogfish *n.* морска́я соба́ка.
dogged *adj.* упо́рный; насто́йчивый.
doggerel *n.* ви́рши.
doggone *adj., colloq.* прокля́тый.
doggy *n.* соба́чка.
doghouse *n.* конура́.
dogma *n.* до́гма. —**dogmatic,** *adj.* догмати́ческий. —**dogmatism,** *n.* догмати́зм. —**dogmatist,** *n.* догма́тик.
dog sled на́рты.
dogwood *n.* кизи́л.
doily *n.* салфе́точка.
doing *n. Big doings,* больши́е собы́тия. *It is mainly their doing,* э́то в основно́м де́ло их рук. *That will take some doing,* э́то потре́бует нема́ло уси́лий.
doldrums *n.pl.* **1,** *naut.* штилевы́е по́лосы. **2,** *fig.* (low spirits) пода́вленное настрое́ние; уны́ние.
dole *n.* **1,** (handout) пода́чка. **2,** *Brit.* (unemployment insurance) посо́бие (по безрабо́тице). —*v.t.* [*usu.* **dole out**] выдава́ть.
doleful *adj.* ско́рбный; жа́лобный.
doll *n.* ку́кла. *Play with dolls,* игра́ть в ку́клы. —*v.t. & i.* [*usu.* **doll up**] разоде́ть(ся). *All dolled up,* весь разоде́тый; вся разоде́тая.
dollar *n.* до́ллар. *Dollar bill,* биле́т *or* бума́жка в оди́н до́ллар. —**in dollars and cents,** в де́нежном выраже́нии.
dollhouse *n.* ку́кольный до́мик.
dolly *n.* **1,** (doll) ку́колка. **2,** (cart) теле́жка.
dolomite *n.* доломи́т.
dolphin *n.* дельфи́н.
dolt *n.* глупе́ц; болва́н; тупи́ца.
domain *n.* **1,** (territory; realm) владе́ние; террито́рия. **2,** (sphere; field) о́бласть; сфе́ра; круг.
dome *n.* ку́пол.
domestic *adj.* **1,** (of the home) дома́шний. *Domestic animals,* дома́шние живо́тные. **2,** (internal) вну́тренний. **3,** (produced at home; not imported) ме́стный; оте́чественный. —*n.* (servant) слуга́; прислу́га. —**domestic science,** домово́дство.
domesticate *v.t.* приуча́ть; одома́шнивать. —**domesticated,** *adj.* ручно́й; приручённый. —**domestication,** *n.* прируче́ние; одома́шнивание.
domicile *n.* местожи́тельство.
dominance *n.* госпо́дство. —**dominant,** *adj.* госпо́дствующий.

dominate *v.t. & i.* **1,** (control) госпо́дствовать: *dominate the sea/air,* госпо́дствовать на мо́ре/в во́здухе. *Dominate other nations,* госпо́дствовать над други́ми стра́нами. **2,** (tower over) домини́ровать над; госпо́дствовать над. —**domination,** *n.* госпо́дство.

domineer *v.t. & i.* вла́ствовать (над); кома́ндовать (над). —**domineering,** *adj.* вла́стный.

dominion *n.* **1,** (sovereignty; rule) влады́чество. **2,** *pl.* (territory under control) владе́ния. **3,** (self-governing member of the British Commonwealth) доминио́н.

domino *n.* **1,** (masquerade costume) домино́. **2,** *pl.* (game) домино́. **3,** (tile used in this game) кость.

don *v.t.* надева́ть.

donate *v.t.* же́ртвовать. —**donation,** *n.* поже́ртвование.

done *adj.* **1,** (carried out) сде́лан: *the deed is done,* де́ло сде́лано. **2,** (finished) (о)ко́нчен. *Are you done?,* вы ко́нчили? **3,** (adequately cooked) гото́в: *is the meat done yet?,* мя́со уже́ гото́во? **4,** (socially acceptable) при́нят: *that is not done,* э́то не при́нято. —**done for,** пропа́вший; поги́бший: *we are done for,* мы пропа́ли; мы поги́бли.

donkey *n.* осёл.

donor *n.* же́ртвователь. *Blood donor,* до́нор.

don't *contr. of* **do not,** *rendered by* не *plus the imperative: don't cry!,* не плачь!; не пла́чьте! *Don't forget!,* не забу́дь!; не забу́дьте!

doom *n.* ги́бель. *Sense of doom,* чу́вство обречённости. —*v.t.* обрека́ть: *doomed to failure,* обречённый на прова́л.

doomsday *n.* день Стра́шного суда́. —**till doomsday,** до второ́го прише́ствия.

door *n.* дверь. —*adj.* дверно́й: *door lock,* дверно́й замо́к. —**behind closed doors,** при закры́тых дверя́х. —**next door,** ря́дом. —**out of doors,** на дворе́. —**show someone the door,** показа́ть кому́-нибудь на дверь.

doorbell *n.* (дверно́й) звоно́к.

doorkeeper *n.* привра́тник.

doorknob *n.* дверна́я ру́чка.

doorman *n.* швейца́р.

doormat *n.* полови́к.

doorpost *n.* (дверно́й) créва: кося́к.

doorstep *n.* поро́г. —**camp on someone's doorstep,** обива́ть поро́ги у кого́-нибудь. —**lay the blame on someone's doorstep,** возлага́ть вину́ на кого́-нибудь.

doorway *n.* дверно́й проём. *In the doorway,* в дверя́х.

dope *n., slang* **1,** (drug) нарко́тик; дурма́н. **2,** (dumbbell) глупе́ц. **3,** (information) све́дения; информа́ция. —*v.t., colloq.* **1,** (drug) дурма́нить. **2,** *fol. by* **out** (figure out) разга́дывать. —**dope addict; dope fiend,** наркома́н.

dopey *adj., colloq.* **1,** (in a stupor) одурма́ненный. **2,** (dumb) глу́пый.

dormant *adj.* **1,** (sleeping) спя́щий. **2,** (inactive) усну́вший: *dormant volcano,* усну́вший вулка́н. —**lie dormant,** быть забы́тым; быть отло́женным (в сто́рону).

dormer window слухово́е окно́.

dormitory *n.* общежи́тие.

dormouse *n.* со́ня.

dorsal *adj.* спинно́й.

dosage *n.* дозиро́вка.

dose *n.* до́за.

dossier *n.* досье́.

dot *n.* то́чка. *Dots and dashes,* то́чки и тире́. *Polka dots,* горо́шек. —*v.t.* **1,** (mark with a dot) ста́вить то́чку на. **2,** (stud) усе́ивать: *the fields are dotted with flowers,* поля́ усе́яны цвета́ми. —**on the dot, 1,** *with the time of day,* ро́вно. **2,** (exactly on time) мину́та в мину́ту.

dotage *n.* ста́рческое слабоу́мие. *Be in one's dotage,* впада́ть в де́тство.

dote *v.i.* [*usu.* **dote on** *or* **upon**] души́ не ча́ять в; носи́ть на рука́х.

dotted *adj.* в кра́пинку; в горо́шек. —**dotted line,** пункти́рная ли́ния; пункти́р.

dotterel *n.* си́вка глу́пая; хруста́н.

double *adj.* **1,** (dual; twofold) двойно́й; двоя́кий. *Double portion,* двойна́я по́рция. *Double bed,* двуспа́льная крова́ть. *Double room,* ко́мната *or* но́мер на двои́х. *Double chin,* двойно́й подборо́док. *Double exposure,* двойна́я *or* двукра́тная экспози́ция. *Double pneumonia,* двусторо́ннее воспале́ние лёгких. *Double standard,* двойна́я ме́рка. **2,** *bot.* махро́вый: *double rose,* махро́вая ро́за. —*adv.* вдво́е бо́льше; вдвойне́. *Double the price,* вдво́е доро́же. —*n.* **1,** (perfect likeness) двойни́к. **2,** *pl., tennis* па́рная игра́. —*v.t.* удва́ивать. —*v.i.* удва́иваться. —**double back,** возвраща́ться по свои́м следа́м. —**double up,** скрю́чивать(ся): *he was doubled up in pain,* он скрю́чился (*or* его́ скрю́чило) от бо́ли. —**on the double,** бего́м; на бегу́. —**see double,** двои́ться в глаза́х: *I am seeing double,* у меня́ двои́тся в глаза́х.

double-barreled *adj.* двуство́льный.

double bass контраба́с.

double bassoon контрафаго́т.

double-breasted *adj.* двубо́ртный.

double-cross *v.t., colloq.* обма́нывать; надува́ть.

double-dealer *n.* двуру́шник. —**double-dealing,** *adj.* двуру́шнический. —*n.* двуру́шничество.

double-edged *adj.* обоюдоо́стрый. —**double-edged sword,** па́лка о двух конца́х.

double entendre двусмы́сленность.

double-space *v.t.* печа́тать че́рез два интерва́ла.

doubly *adv.* вдвойне́.

doubt *n.* сомне́ние: *without a doubt,* без вся́кого сомне́ния. *Have doubts about someone,* сомнева́ться в ко́м-нибудь. —*v.t.* сомнева́ться в: *I doubt that,* я в э́том сомнева́юсь. *Doubt someone's honesty,* сомнева́ться в чье́й-нибудь че́стности. *I doubt if he'll agree,* я сомнева́юсь (в том), что он согласи́тся. —**be in doubt,** не знать: *when in doubt — ask,* е́сли не зна́ешь, спроси́. *The outcome is still in doubt,* исхо́д де́ла ещё не я́сен. —**no doubt, 1,** (undoubtedly) без сомне́ния; несомне́нно. **2,** (probably) наве́рно.

doubtful *adj.* **1,** (uncertain): *be doubtful,* сомнева́ться. *It is doubtful,* вряд ли. **2,** (questionable; dubious) сомни́тельный.

doubtless *adv.* **1,** (undoubtedly) несомне́нно. **2,** (probably) наве́рно. *Also,* **doubtlessly.**

douche *n.* душ; облива́ние.

dough *n.* **1,** (flour paste) те́сто. **2,** *slang* (money) моне́та.

doughnut *n.* по́нчик.

doughty *adj.* сто́йкий; отва́жный.

dour *adj.* мра́чный; угрю́мый.

douse *v.t.* **1,** (immerse) погружа́ть; окуна́ть. **2,** (drench) обдава́ть; облива́ть; ока́чивать. **3,** (extinguish) туши́ть; гаси́ть. *Douse a fire,* залива́ть костёр.

dove *n.* го́лубь. —**dovecote,** *n.* голубя́тня.
dovetail *n.* ла́сточкин хвост.
dowager *n.* **1,** (widow) вдова́. *Dowager queen,* вдо́вствующая короле́ва. **2,** *colloq.* (elderly woman) матро́на.
dowdy *adj.* немо́дный; неэлега́нтный.
dowel *n.* шпо́нка; штифт; штырь.
down *adv.* **1,** (to a lower position; toward the ground) вниз: *look down,* смотреть вниз. ♦*Usu. rendered by a single verb: sit down,* сесть; *lie down,* лечь; *go* (or *come*) *down,* сойти́; *climb down,* слезть; *fall down,* упа́сть; *knock down,* повали́ть; сбить с ног; *tear down,* снести́; *burn down,* сгоре́ть; *write down,* записа́ть; *calm down,* успоко́ить(ся). **2,** (as a down payment) нали́чными: *forty dollars down and the rest in monthly installments,* со́рок до́лларов нали́чными, а остально́е ежеме́сячными взно́сами. —*adj. The sun is down,* со́лнце зашло́. *Her temperature is down,* её температу́ра пони́зилась. *Strike a man when he is down,* бить лежа́чего. *He is down with the grippe,* он лежи́т с гри́ппом. —*prep.* с: *fall down the stairs,* упа́сть с ле́стницы. *Sail down the river,* плыть вниз по реке́. —*n.* пух: *eider down,* гага́чий пух. —*v.t.* **1,** (shoot down) сбива́ть. **2,** (drink) вы́пить за́лпом. —**down and out,** разорённый; в нищете́. —**down to,** вплоть до. —**down with...!,** доло́й...!
downcast *adj.* уны́лый; поню́рый.
downfall *n.* паде́ние; круше́ние.
downgrade *n.* склон; укло́н. —*v.t.* **1,** (demote) понижа́ть. **2,** (minimize) умаля́ть. —**on the downgrade,** в состоя́нии упа́дка.
downhearted *adj.* па́вший ду́хом; уны́лый. *Don't be downhearted!,* не унывай́!
downhill *adv.* по́д гору.
down payment зада́ток.
downpour *n.* ли́вень.
downright *adj.* я́вный; сплошно́й; су́щий. —*adv.* про́сто; пря́мо: *it's downright amazing!,* э́то про́сто/пря́мо удиви́тельно!
downstairs *adv.* **1,** (location) внизу́. **2,** (motion) вниз. —*n.* ни́жний эта́ж.
downstream *adv.* вниз по тече́нию.
downtime *n.* просто́й.
downtown *n.* центр го́рода; делова́я часть го́рода.—*adj.* центра́льный. —*adv.* в це́нтр(е) го́рода.
downtrodden *adj.* заби́тый; за́гнанный.
downward *adv.* [*also,* **downwards**] вниз; книзу; под укло́н. —*adj.* под укло́н: *downward movement,* движе́ние под укло́н.
downy *adj.* пуши́стый; пухо́вый.
dowry *n.* прида́ное.
doze *v.i.* дрема́ть. *Doze off,* задрема́ть; вздремну́ть; забыва́ться.
dozen *n.* дю́жина.
drab *adj.* бесцве́тный; се́рый; однообра́зный. —**drabness,** *n.* бесцве́тность; однообра́зие.
drachma *n.* дра́хма.
draconian *adj.* драко́новский.
draft *n.* **1,** (preliminary version) набро́сок; эски́з. *First draft,* черновик. *Final draft,* оконча́тельная реда́кция. *Draft resolution,* прое́кт резолю́ции. **2,** (current of air) сквозня́к. **3,** (device to regulate air intake) тя́га. **4,** (conscription) во́инская пови́нность. **5,** *finance* чек. **6,** *naut.* (depth of a vessel below the water) оса́дка. —*adj.* **1,** (for hauling) тя́гловый. *Draft animals,* (живо́е) тя́гло; рабо́чий скот. **2,** (drawn from a cask) разливно́й: *draft beer,* разливно́е пи́во. —*v.t.* **1,** (conscript) призыва́ть (на вое́нную слу́жбу). **2,** (compose in preliminary form) составля́ть; разраба́тывать. *Also, chiefly Brit.,* **draught.**
draft board призывно́й пункт.
draftee *n.* призывни́к.
draftsman *also,* **draughtsman** *n.* чертёжник.
drafty *adj. It is drafty in here,* здесь сквози́т.
drag *v.t.* **1,** (pull along the ground) тащи́ть; волочи́ть. *Drag one's feet,* волочи́ть но́ги. **2,** (dredge, as a river) очища́ть (дно реки́). **3,** (force to go against one's will) тащи́ть. **4,** *fol. by* **out** (prolong) тяну́ть; затя́гивать; растя́гивать. —*v.i.* **1,** (trail along) тащи́ться; волочи́ться. **2,** *fol. by* **on** *or* **out** (progress slowly; last a long time) тяну́ться; затя́гиваться. —*n.* **1,** (hindrance) то́рмоз; обу́за. **2,** *colloq.* (draw, as on a cigarette) затя́жка.
dragnet *n.* **1,** (net) бре́день. **2,** (network for catching a criminal) обла́ва.
dragon *n.* драко́н.
dragonfly *n.* стрекоза́.
dragoon *n.* драгу́н.
drain *v.t.* **1,** (draw off, as water) отводи́ть. **2,** (draw water from) отводи́ть во́ду из; осуша́ть; дрени́ровать. **3,** (drink all the contents of) осуша́ть. **4,** *surgery* дрени́ровать. **5,** *fig.* (exhaust; consume totally) истоща́ть. —*v.i.* впада́ть: *the river drains into the ocean,* река́ впада́ет в океа́н. —*n.* **1,** (channel; pipe) водосто́к; (водо)сто́чная труба́. **2,** *fig.* (continuous outflow) уте́чка. —**go down the drain,** пойти́ насма́рку.
drainage *n.* дрена́ж; осуше́ние.— *adj.* дрена́жный; осуши́тельный; отво́дный; водоотво́дный.
drainpipe *n.* водосто́чная труба́.
drake *n.* се́лезень.
drama *n.* дра́ма. *Drama critic,* театра́льный кри́тик.
dramatic *adj.* **1,** (of drama; stirring) драмати́ческий. **2,** (striking; drastic) ре́зкий: *dramatic change,* ре́зкая переме́на. —**dramatically,** *adv.* ре́зко; кру́то: *change dramatically,* ре́зко/кру́то измени́ться.
dramatics *n.* драмати́ческое иску́сство. —**dramatist,** *n.* драмату́рг. —**dramatize,** *v.t.* драматизи́ровать. —**dramaturgy,** *n.* драматурги́я.
drape *v.t.* драпирова́ть. *The coffin was draped in black,* гроб был обтя́нут чёрным. —*n.* = **drapery.**
drapery *n., usu. pl.* драпиро́вка.
drastic *adj.* круто́й; ре́зкий.
draught *n.* = **draft.**
draughts *n.pl., Brit.* = **checkers.**
draughtsman *n.* = **draftsman.**
draw *v.t.* **1,** (pull) тащи́ть: *the horse draws the carriage,* ло́шадь та́щит каре́ту. *Draw the curtain/blind,* задёргивать занаве́ску/што́ру. **2,** (pull tight) натя́гивать: *draw the bow,* натя́гивать лук. **3,** (move in a given direction) отводи́ть: *draw someone aside,* отводи́ть кого́-нибудь в сто́рону. **4,** (take out; withdraw) вынима́ть; выхва́тывать. *Draw one's sword,* вынима́ть шпа́гу из но́жен. *Draw a knife/gun,* выхва́тывать нож/пистоле́т. *Draw a card from the deck,* тяну́ть ка́рту из коло́ды. **5,** (cause to flow) че́рпать: *draw water from a well,* че́рпать во́ду из коло́дца. *Draw blood,* пуска́ть кровь. *Draw a bath,* напо́лнить ва́нну. **6,** (attract) привлека́ть; обраща́ть на себя́. *Draw someone's attention to,* обраща́ть чьё-нибудь внима́ние на. **7,** (elicit) вызыва́ть: *draw enemy fire,* вызыва́ть ого́нь проти́вника. *Draw criticism,* подверга́ться кри́тике. **8,** (sketch) рисова́ть: *draw a picture,* рисова́ть карти́ну. *Draw a line,* проводи́ть ли-

нию *or* черту́. *Draw a map,* черти́ть ка́рту. **9,** (get or receive by chance) *rendered by* выпада́ть (+ *dat.*): *he drew a tough assignment,* ему́ вы́пало тру́дное зада́ние. **10,** (get or pick at random) тяну́ть: *draw lots,* тяну́ть жре́бий. **11,** (derive, as a conclusion) де́лать (вы́вод). **12,** (make, as a comparison) проводи́ть (сравне́ние). **13,** (earn, as a salary, interest, etc.) зараба́тывать. *Draw a good salary,* хорошо́ зараба́тывать. **14,** (issue, as a check) выпи́сывать. **15,** (inhale) вдыха́ть: *draw fresh air into one's lungs,* вдыха́ть све́жий во́здух. *Draw a breath,* передохну́ть. **16,** *naut.* име́ть оса́дку в: *the ship draws 15 feet,* парохо́д име́ет оса́дку в пятна́дцать фу́тов. —*v.i.* **1,** (sketch) рисова́ть. **2,** (move in a certain direction): *draw near,* приближа́ться; *draw to a close,* подходи́ть к концу́. **3,** (draw lots) тяну́ть жре́бий. *Draw for partners,* выбира́ть партнёров по жре́бию. **4,** (play to a tie) сыгра́ть вничью́; сде́лать ничью́. **5,** (take in air) тяну́ть: *the chimney isn't drawing,* труба́ не тя́нет. —*n.* **1,** (act of pulling, attracting, etc.) тя́га. **2,** (tie) ничья́. —**draw aside,** отводи́ть в сто́рону. *Draw aside the curtain,* отдёрнуть занаве́ску. —**draw back, 1,** (pull back) отдёргивать. **2,** (step back) отпря́нуть. —**draw in,** втя́гивать. —**draw off, 1,** (siphon off) отводи́ть. **2,** *mil.* отводи́ть; оття́гивать (войска́). —**draw out,** вытя́гивать. —**draw up, 1,** (compose; draft) составля́ть; разраба́тывать. **2,** *fol. by* **to** (pull up to) подъезжа́ть (к).

drawback *n.* недоста́ток.

drawbridge *n.* подъёмный мост; разводно́й мост.

draw curtain раздвижно́й за́навес.

drawer *n.* **1,** (sliding box) я́щик. *Chest of drawers,* комо́д. **2,** *comm.* трасса́нт. **3,** *pl.* (undergarment) кальсо́ны.

drawing *n.* **1,** (art) рисова́ние; черче́ние. *Mechanical drawing,* механи́ческое черче́ние. **2,** (picture) рису́нок. **3,** (sketch; design) чертёж. **4,** (selection of tickets in a lottery) ро́зыгрыш.

drawing board чертёжная доска́.

drawing pin *Brit.* (thumbtack) кно́пка.

drawing room 1, (living room) гости́ная. **2,** (private compartment on a train) купе́.

drawl *n.* протя́жное произноше́ние. —*v.i.* говори́ть врастя́жку; растя́гивать слова́.

drawn *adj.* **1,** (haggard) измождённый. **2,** (tied, as of a game) ниче́йный.

dray *n.* ломова́я теле́га. —**dray horse,** ломова́я ло́шадь. —**drayman,** *n.* ломово́й изво́зчик.

dread *v.t.* боя́ться; страши́ться. —*n.* страх; боя́знь. —*adj.* стра́шный; гро́зный.

dreadful *adj.* стра́шный; ужа́сный.

dreadnought *n.* дредно́ут.

dream *n.* **1,** (thoughts while asleep) сон; сновиде́ние. *Bad dream,* дурно́й сон. *I had a dream,* я ви́дел(а) сон. *Walk around in a dream,* ходи́ть, как во сне. **2,** (cherished hope) мечта́; грёза. —*v.i.* **1,** (have a dream; have dreams) ви́деть *or* сни́ться сон/сны. *Am I dreaming?,* э́то мне сни́тся? *I dreamt about you,* вы мне сни́лись; я вас ви́дел(а) во сне. **2,** *fol. by* **of** (envision, as in a dream) мечта́ть: *dream of a trip abroad,* мечта́ть о пое́здке за грани́цу. *Dream of becoming an actress,* мечта́ть стать актри́сой. **3,** *fol. by* **of** (consider doing) сни́ться: *I never even dreamt of it,* э́то мне да́же и не сни́лось. *I wouldn't dream of it!,* и не поду́маю!; об э́том не мо́жет быть и ре́чи. —*v.t.* сни́ться: *I dreamt that...,* мне сни́лось, что... *I never dreamt that...,* мне не приходи́ло в го́лову, что... —**dream up, 1,** (devise) приду́мывать. **2,** (concoct) выду́мывать.

dreamer *n.* мечта́тель.

dreamland *n.* **1,** (sleep) сон. **2,** = **dreamworld.**

dreamworld *n.* мир грёз; ца́рство грёз.

dreamy *adj.* мечта́тельный.

dreary *adj.* мра́чный; па́смурный; хму́рый. —**dreariness,** *n.* мра́чность.

dredge *n.* драга́. —*v.t.* очища́ть (дно реки́).

dregs *n.pl.* **1,** (residue) подо́нки; гу́ща. **2,** *fig.* (worst portion) подо́нки: *the dregs of society,* подо́нки о́бщества.

drench *v.t.* прома́чивать; выма́чивать. *Get drenched,* промока́ть; вымока́ть.

dress *n.* **1,** (woman's garment) пла́тье. **2,** (apparel) оде́жда; пла́тье. —*adj.* **1,** (for a dress): *dress fabric,* мате́рия на пла́тье. **2,** *mil.* пара́дный: *dress uniform,* пара́дная фо́рма. —*v.t.* **1,** (clothe) одева́ть. *Get dressed,* одева́ться. **2,** (adorn) украша́ть; убира́ть. **3,** (bandage) перевя́зывавть. **4,** (prepare for cooking) чи́стить; разде́лывать; свежева́ть. **5,** *mil.* выра́внивать. —*v.i.* **1,** (put on one's clothes) одева́ться. **2,** *mil.* (come into alignment) равня́ться: *dress right!,* напра́во - равня́йся! —**dress down,** *colloq.* дать нагоня́й *or* взбу́чку (+ *dat.*). —**dress up,** наряжа́ться; приоде́ться. *Dress up as,* переодева́ться (+ *instr.*).

dress circle бельэта́ж.

dresser *n.* **1,** (one who dresses in a certain way): *she is a good dresser,* она́ хорошо́ одева́ется. **2,** (chest of drawers) комо́д.

dressing *n.* **1,** (act of clothing) одева́ние. **2,** (bandage) перевя́зка. **3,** (sauce) припра́ва. **4,** (stuffing) начи́нка; фарш. —**dressing gown,** хала́т. —**dressing room, 1,** (of an actor or performer) убо́рная. **2,** (in a gymnasium, public bath, etc.) раздева́льня. **3,** (for trying on clothes) приме́рочная. —**dressing table,** туале́тный сто́лик; туале́т.

dressing-down *n.* нагоня́й; взбу́чка.

dressmaker *n.* портни́ха.

dress rehearsal генера́льная репети́ция.

drib *n., in* **in dribs and drabs,** че́рез час по ча́йной ло́жке.

dribble *v.i.* **1,** (drip) ка́пать. **2,** (drool) пуска́ть слю́ни. —*v.t. & i., basketball* вести́ (мяч).

dried *adj.* сушёный.

drier *n.* = **dryer.**

drift *n.* **1,** *naut.; aero.* дрейф; снос. **2,** (snowdrift) зано́с; сугро́б. **3,** (meaning) смысл: *get the drift of the conversation,* улови́ть смысл разгово́ра. —*v.i.* **1,** (move with the current) плыть; дрейфова́ть. *Drift downstream,* плыть вниз по тече́нию. **2,** (move aimlessly) идти́ самотёком. *Let things drift,* пусти́ть де́ло на самотёк. *Drift from place to place,* переходи́ть с ме́ста на ме́сто. *We drifted apart,* на́ши пути́ разошли́сь. **3,** (stray) отклоня́ться: *drift off course,* отклоня́ться от ку́рса. **4,** (pile up, as of snow) намета́ть; нава́ливать (*both impers.*).

drifter *n.* бродя́га.

driftwood *n.* плавни́к.

drill *n.* **1,** (tool for making holes) сверло́; дрель. **2,** (dentist's drill) бормаши́на. **3,** (training exercise) трениро́вка. **4,** *mil.* строева́я подгото́вка; муштра́; муштро́вка. —*v.t.* **1,** (make, as a hole) пробива́ть; просве́рливать (отве́рстие). **2,** (make a hole in) сверли́ть; просве́рливать. **3,** (bore, as rock) бури́ть. **4,** (teach; train) обуча́ть; тренирова́ть. **5,** *mil.* муштрова́ть. —*v.i.* **1,** (practice) упражня́ться; тренирова́ться. **2,** *mil.* проводи́ть строеву́ю подгото́вку.

drillmaster *n.* инстру́ктор строево́й подгото́вки.

drink *v.t. & i.* пить. *Drink to someone's health,* пить за чьё-нибудь здоро́вье. *Would you like something to drink?,* хоти́те что́-нибудь вы́пить? —*n.* напи́ток: *food and drinks,* еда́ и напи́тки. *Would you like a drink of water?,* хоти́те воды́? —**drink in,** впи́тывать. —**take to drink,** спива́ться.

drinkable *adj.* го́дный для питья́.

drinker *n.* пью́щий.

drinking *n.* питьё. —*adj.* питьево́й: *drinking water,* питьева́я вода́. —**drinking bout,** запо́й; попо́йка. —**drinking companion,** собуты́льник. —**drinking fountain,** фонта́нчик. —**drinking song,** засто́льная пе́сня.

drip *v.i.* **1,** (of a liquid) ка́пать: *water was dripping from the faucet,* вода́ ка́пала из кра́на. *His hands were dripping with blood,* кровь стека́ла с его́ рук. **2,** (of a candle) оплыва́ть; отека́ть. —*v.t.* ка́пать (+ *instr.*). —*n.* ка́панье.

dripping *adj.* ка́пающий: *dripping faucet,* ка́пающий кран. —*adv., in* **dripping wet,** мо́крый, хоть вы́жми. —*n., usu. pl.* вы́текший сок.

drive *v.t.* **1,** (propel) дви́гать: *steam drives the mechanism,* пар дви́жет механи́зм. **2,** (operate, as a car) вести́; води́ть (маши́ну); управля́ть; пра́вить (маши́ной). **3,** (transport in a vehicle) отвози́ть: *drive someone to the airport,* отвози́ть кого́-нибудь в аэропо́рт. **4,** (lead; herd, as cattle) гнать. **5,** (force; chase; press) загоня́ть: *drive into a corner,* загоня́ть в у́гол. *Drive the invaders from the country,* прогоня́ть захва́тчиков из страны́. **6,** (hammer) вбива́ть; забива́ть: *drive a nail into a wall,* вбива́ть/забива́ть гвоздь в стену. *Drive a wedge between,* вбива́ть клин ме́жду. **7,** (bring to a certain state) доводи́ть (до): *drive to despair,* доводи́ть до отча́яния. *Drive mad,* своди́ть с ума́. —*v.i.* **1,** (go in a vehicle) е́хать (на маши́не). **2,** (operate a vehicle) вести́/води́ть маши́ну; пра́вить/управля́ть маши́ной. **3,** *fol. by* **at** (mean; intend) гнуть; клони́ть: *what are you driving at?,* куда́ ты гнёшь?; к чему́ ты кло́нишь? —*n.* **1,** (ride in a car) езда́; прогу́лка. *A two-hour drive,* два часа́ езды́. *Go for a drive,* е́здить на прогу́лку; ката́ться на маши́не; прокати́ться; прое́хаться. *Take for a drive,* ката́ть; прокати́ть. **2,** (street; avenue) у́лица; проспе́кт. **3,** (campaign) похо́д: *economy drive,* похо́д за эконо́мию. **4,** (energy; ambition) эне́ргия. *Sexual drive,* полово́е влече́ние. **5,** *mech.* переда́ча; приво́д. —**drive away, 1,** (repel) прогоня́ть; отгоня́ть. **2,** (depart in a vehicle) укати́ть; (of a vehicle) укати́ться. —**drive back,** оттесня́ть. —**drive home, 1,** *literally* отвози́ть домо́й. **2,** (make someone understand) внуша́ть. —**drive off,** = **drive away.** —**drive out, 1,** (chase out; expel) выгоня́ть. **2,** (exit in a vehicle) выезжа́ть. —**drive up to,** подъезжа́ть к.

drivel *v.i.* **1,** (drool) пуска́ть слю́ни. **2,** (talk foolishly) поро́ть чушь; нести́ вздор. —*n.* **1,** (saliva) слю́ни. **2,** (foolish talk) чушь; вздор. —**driveling,** *adj.* слюня́вый.

driver *n.* **1,** (of a car or truck) води́тель; шофёр. **2,** (of a carriage) ку́чер; изво́зчик. **3,** (of cattle) пого́нщик; гуртовщи́к. —**driver's license,** води́тельские права́.

drive shaft приводно́й вал.

driveway *n.* подъе́зд (к до́му).

driving *n.* вожде́ние. —*adj.* **1,** *mech.* приводно́й: *driving wheel,* приводно́е колесо́. **2,** (violent, as of rain) проливно́й.

drizzle *n.* и́зморось. —*v.i.* мороси́ть: *it is drizzling,* мороси́т.

droll *adj.* заба́вный. —**drollery,** *n.* шу́тки; ю́мор.

dromedary *n.* дромадёр.

drone *n.* **1,** (hum) гул. **2,** (bee; *also fig.* idler) тру́тень. —*v.i.* **1,** (hum) гуде́ть; жужжа́ть. **2,** *fol. by* **on** (speak in a monotonous tone) бубни́ть; дуде́ть.

drool *v.i.* пуска́ть слю́ни.

droop *v.i.* свиса́ть; отвиса́ть; обвиса́ть; поника́ть; ни́кнуть.

drop *n.* **1,** (liquid globule) ка́пля: *drop of water,* ка́пля воды́. *Not touch a drop,* ка́пли в рот не брать. **2,** *pl.* (liquid medicine) ка́пли: *eye drops,* глазны́е ка́пли. *Cough drops,* табле́тки от ка́шля. **3,** *pl.* (small pieces of candy) драже́. **4,** (fall; decrease) паде́ние; пониже́ние. —*v.t.* **1,** (accidentally let drop) роня́ть: *you dropped your comb,* вы урони́ли гре́бень. **2,** (deposit) опуска́ть: *drop a letter in the mailbox,* опуска́ть письмо́ в почто́вый я́щик. *Drop one's ballot in the box,* опуска́ть бюллете́нь в избира́тельную у́рну. **3,** (let fall from an airplane) сбра́сывать: *drop bombs,* сбра́сывать бо́мбы. *Drop by parachute,* сбра́сывать на парашю́те. **4,** (let off, as from a conveyance) выса́живать. **5,** (omit; delete) исключа́ть; опуска́ть. **6,** (give up; abandon) бро́сить. *Drop the subject,* оста́вить те́му. **7,** (send, as a note) присыла́ть; черкну́ть: *drop me a line,* пришли́те мне ве́сточку; черкни́те мне не́сколько строк. **8,** *colloq.* (utter casually) оброни́ть. *Drop a hint,* сде́лать намёк. **9,** *in* **drop anchor,** бро́сить я́корь. **10,** *in* **drop a stitch,** спусти́ть пе́тлю. —*v.i.* **1,** (fall) па́дать. *Drop out of one's hands,* вы́пасть из рук. *Be ready to drop,* вали́ться с ног от уста́лости. *You could have heard a pin drop,* слы́шно бы́ло, как му́ха пролети́т. **2,** (decline) па́дать; снижа́ться; пойти́ вниз. —**at the drop of a hat,** по мале́йшему по́воду. —**drop back,** отступа́ть. —**drop by/in/over,** заходи́ть. —**drop in the bucket,** ка́пля в мо́ре. —**drop off, 1,** (let off, as from a vehicle) выса́живать. **2,** (fall asleep) засыпа́ть. **3,** (decrease) па́дать; снижа́ться. —**drop out, 1,** (fall from) выпада́ть (из). **2,** (withdraw) выходи́ть; выбыва́ть; отсе́иваться. **3,** *Drop out of sight,* вы́пасть из по́ля зре́ния.

droplet *n.* ка́пелька.

dropout *n.* тот, кто отсе́ялся из шко́лы. *Dropout rate,* проце́нт отсе́ва.

dropper *n.* ка́пельница; пипе́тка.

droppings *n.pl.* помёт.

dropsy *n.* водя́нка.

droshky *n.* дро́жки.

dross *n.* ока́лина.

drought *n.* за́суха.

drove *n.* ста́до; гурт. —**in droves,** то́лпами.

drover *n.* гуртовщи́к; пого́нщик.

drown *v.i.* тону́ть. *Drowning man,* утопа́ющий. —*v.t.* **1,** (cause to drown) топи́ть. *Drown oneself,* (у)топи́ться. *Drown one's sorrows in drink,* топи́ть го́ре в вине́. **2,** *fol. by* **out** (muffle, as sound) заглуша́ть; глуши́ть; подавля́ть; покрыва́ть. —**drowning,** *n.* утопле́ние.

drowse *v.i.* дрема́ть.

drowsy *adj.* со́нный; сонли́вый; дремо́тный. *I feel*

drowsy, меня́ кло́нит ко сну. —**drowsiness,** *n.* сонли́вость; дремо́та; забытьё.

drub *v.t.* **1,** (beat) дуба́сить. **2,** (defeat) разбива́ть.

drubbing *n.* **1,** (beating) побои. **2,** (defeat) разгро́м.

drudgery *n.* кропотли́вая рабо́та.

drug *n.* **1,** (medication) лека́рство; медикаме́нт. **2,** (narcotic) нарко́тик. —*v.t.* наркотизи́ровать. —**drug addict,** наркома́н.

druggist *n.* апте́карь.

drugstore *n.* апте́ка.

drum *n.* бараба́н. —*v.i.* **1,** (beat a drum) бить в бараба́н. **2,** (tap) бараба́нить па́льцами (*e.g.* по́ столу). —*v.t.* **1,** *fol. by* **into** (instill) вда́лбливать. **2,** *fol. by* **out** (expel) изгоня́ть.

drumbeat *n.* бараба́нный бой.

drummer *n.* бараба́нщик.

drumstick *n.* **1,** (stick for beating a drum) бараба́нная па́лочка. **2,** (leg of a fowl) но́жка.

drunk *adj. & n.* пья́ный. *Get drunk,* напи́ться; опьяне́ть.

drunkard *n.* пья́ница.

drunken *adj.* пья́ный: *in a drunken state,* в пья́ном ви́де. *Drunken revelry,* пья́ный кутёж. —**drunkenness,** *n.* пья́нство.

dry *adj.* сухо́й. *Dry land,* су́ша. —*v.t.* **1,** (make dry) суши́ть; осуша́ть. **2,** (wipe) вытира́ть: *dry the dishes,* вытира́ть посу́ду. *Dry one's eyes,* осуша́ть глаза́. —*v.i.* со́хнуть; суши́ться. —**dry up; run dry,** высыха́ть; иссыха́ть; пересыха́ть; иссяка́ть.

dry cleaning хими́ческая чи́стка.

dry dock сухо́й док.

dryer *also,* **drier** *n.* суши́лка. *Hair dryer,* фен.

dry goods галантере́я.

dry ice сухо́й лёд.

dryly *adv.* су́хо.

dry measure ме́ра сыпу́чих тел.

dryness *n.* су́хость.

dry run испыта́тельный пробе́г.

dual *adj.* **1,** (double) двойно́й; двоя́кий; дво́йственный. *Dual purpose,* двоя́кая цель. **2,** (joint) совме́стный. —**dualism,** *n.* дуали́зм. —**dualistic,** *adj.* дуалисти́ческий. —**duality,** *n.* дво́йственность.

dub *v.t.* **1,** (knight) посвяща́ть (в ры́цари). **2,** (nickname) прозыва́ть; окрести́ть. **3,** *motion pictures* дубли́ровать.

dubious *adj.* **1,** (doubtful): *be dubious,* сомнева́ться. **2,** (of doubtful worth) сомни́тельный: *a dubious honor,* сомни́тельная честь.

ducal *adj.* ге́рцогский.

ducat *n.* **1,** (old coin) дука́т. **2,** *slang* (ticket) биле́т.

duchess *n.* герцоги́ня.

duchy *n.* ге́рцогство. *Grand duchy,* вели́кое кня́жество.

duck *n.* у́тка. —*adj.* [*also,* **duck's**] ути́ный: *duck feathers,* ути́ные пе́рья. —*v.t.* **1,** (immerse) окуна́ть. **2,** (dodge) уверну́ться от. —*v.i.* **1,** (so as to avoid a blow) нырну́ть. **2,** (in order to pass under something) нагну́ть го́лову. **3,** *fol. by* **out** (leave suddenly) улизну́ть. —**like water off a duck's back,** как с гу́ся вода́.

duckbill *n.* утконо́с.

duckling *n.* утёнок. —**ugly duckling,** га́дкий утёнок.

duckweed *n.* ря́ска.

duct *n.* прото́к; кана́л. *Bile duct,* же́лчный прото́к.

ductile *adj.* ко́вкий; тягу́чий.

ductless gland железа́ вну́тренней секре́ции.

due *adj.* **1,** (owed; payable) сле́дуемый: *the amount due me,* сле́дуемая мне су́мма. *Five rubles are due you,* вам причита́ется пять рубле́й. *The bill is/falls due on May 1,* счёт подлежи́т упла́те пе́рвого ма́я. **2,** (proper) до́лжный: *with due regard for,* с до́лжным внима́нием к. *With all due respect to,* при всём (моём) уваже́нии к. *Give credit where it is due,* отдава́ть до́лжное. **3,** (expected) до́лжен: *he is due here at noon,* он до́лжен прийти́ в по́лдень. —*adv.* пря́мо на: *due north,* пря́мо на се́вер. —*n.* **1,** (that which one deserves) до́лжное: *give someone his due,* отда́ть до́лжное (+ *dat.*). **2,** *pl.* (fee) взно́сы: *membership dues,* чле́нские взно́сы. —**due to,** по: *due to illness,* по боле́зни. *Due to circumstances beyond our control,* по не зави́сящим от нас обстоя́тельствам. *Death was due to asphyxiation,* смерть была́ вы́звана удуше́нием. —**in due course; in due time,** своевре́менно; в своё вре́мя.

duel *n.* дуэ́ль; поеди́нок. —*v.i.* дра́ться на дуэ́ли. —**duelist,** *n.* дуэли́ст.

duet *n.* дуэ́т.

dugout *n.* **1,** (boat) челно́к. **2,** (shelter) земля́нка; *mil.* блинда́ж.

duke *n.* ге́рцог. *Grand duke,* вели́кий князь. —**dukedom,** *n.* ге́рцогство.

dulcet *adj.* сла́дкий; благозву́чный; мелоди́чный

dulcimer *n.* цимба́лы.

dull *adj.* **1,** (blunt) тупо́й. **2,** (not bright; not shiny) ту́склый. **3,** (gloomy; cloudy) мра́чный; па́смурный. **4,** (boring) ску́чный. **5,** (mentally slow; obtuse) тупо́й. **6,** (not distinct, as of a sound) глухо́й; тупо́й. **7,** (not acute, as of pain) тупо́й. —*v.t.* **1,** (make less sharp) тупи́ть; притупля́ть. **2,** (cloud, as the senses) мути́ть; притупля́ть. —*v.i.* тупи́ться.

dullard *n.* тупи́ца.

dullness *n.* ту́пость.

duly *adv.* **1,** (properly) до́лжным о́бразом; надлежа́щим о́бразом. **2,** (at the proper time) своевре́менно.

dumb *adj.* **1,** (mute) немо́й. **2,** (of animals) бесслове́сный. **3,** *colloq.* (stupid) глу́пый.

dumbbell *n.* **1,** (weight for exercise) ги́ря; ганте́ль. **2,** *slang* (dolt) болва́н; глупе́ц.

dumfound *also,* **dumbfound** *v.t.* ошара́шивать.

dummy *n.* **1,** (mannequin) манеке́н. **2,** *printing* маке́т. **3,** *cards* болва́н. **4,** *slang* (dolt) болва́н; тупи́ца. —*adj.* ло́жный; фальши́вый.

dump *v.t.* **1,** (drop heavily) вали́ть; сва́ливать. **2,** (throw out) выбра́сывать; выва́ливать. **3,** *comm.* выбра́сывать: *dump goods on the market,* выбра́сывать това́р на ры́нок. *Dump shares of stock,* сбра́сывать а́кции. —*n.* **1,** (field for rubbish) сва́лка. **2,** *mil.* (storage place) склад: *ammunition dump,* склад боеприпа́сов. —**in the dumps,** в уны́нии.

dumpling *n.* клёцка; галу́шка.

dump truck самосва́л.

dunce *n.* глупе́ц; тупи́ца. —**dunce cap,** дура́цкий колпа́к.

dunderhead *n.* о́лух; остоло́п; растя́па.

dune *n.* дю́на; песча́ный холм.

dung *n.* помёт; наво́з.

dungarees *n.pl.* рабо́чие брю́ки.

dung beetle наво́зный жук; наво́зник.

dungeon *n.* темница.
dunghill *n.* навóзная кýча.
dunk *v.t.* **1,** (immerse) погружáть; окунáть. **2,** (dip, as a doughnut) макáть.
duo *n.* пáра; дуэ́т.
duodenal *adj.* двенадцатипéрстный. —**duodenum,** *n.* двенадцатипéрстная кишкá.
dupe *n.* простáк. —*v.t.* надувáть; наставля́ть нос (+ *dat.*).
duplex *adj.* двойнóй. —*n.* **1,** (house) двухквартúрный дом. **2,** (apartment) двухэтáжная квартúра.
duplicate *n.* дубликáт; дублёт; кóпия. *In duplicate,* в двух экземпля́рах. —*adj.* дубликáтный. —*v.t.* дублúровать. —**duplication,** *n.* дублúрование. —**duplicator,** *n.* копировáльная машúна.
duplicity *n.* двулúчие; двулúчность.
durable *adj.* прóчный. —**durability,** *n.* прóчность.
duralumin *n.* дюралюмúний.
duration *n.* продолжúтельность; длúтельность. *For the duration of,* на врéмя (+ *gen.*). *Of short duration,* непродолжúтельный; недолговéчный.
duress *n.* принуждéние. *Under duress,* по принуждéнию.
during *prep.* во врéмя (+ *gen.*); за (+ *acc.*); в течéние (+ *gen.*). *During the war/lesson,* во врéмя войны́/урóка. *During that time,* за э́то врéмя. *During the last year,* за послéдний год. *During the winter,* в течéние зимы́. *I'm home during the day,* днём я дóма. *It rained during the night,* нóчью шёл дождь. *During the last two weeks,* в течéние послéдних двух недéль.
durum *n.* твёрдая пшенúца. *Also,* **durum wheat.**
dusk *n.* сýмерки. *From dawn till dusk,* от зарú до зарú.
dust *n.* **1,** (tiny bits, as of earth) пыль. **2,** (mortal remains) прах. —*v.t.* **1,** (wipe the dust from) стирáть пыль с. **2,** (sprinkle with a powdery substance) опы́ливать: *dust crops,* опы́ливать посéвы. —*v.i.* стирáть пыль. —**bite the dust,** упáсть. —**shake the dust from one's feet,** отрястú прах от своúх ног. —**throw dust in someone's eyes,** втирáть очкú (+ *dat.*); пускáть пыль в глазá (+ *dat.*).
dustbin *n., Brit.* мýсорный я́щик.
duster *n.* **1,** (cloth for dusting) пы́льная тря́пка. **2,** (protective smock) пы́льник.
dust jacket суперoблóжка.
dustman *n., Brit.* мýсорщик.
dustpan *n.* совóк (для мýсора).
dust storm пы́льная бýря.
dusty *adj.* пы́льный.
Dutch *adj.* голлáндский. —*n.* **1,** (language) голлáндский язы́к. **2,** *preceded by* **the** (people) голлáндцы. —**Dutchman,** *n.* голлáндец.
duteous *adj.* послýшный. *Also,* **dutiful.**
duty *n.* **1,** (obligation) долг; обя́занность. **2,** *pl.* (work required) обя́занности. **3,** (service; watch) дежýрство; слýжба. *Be on duty,* дежýрить. *Guard duty,* караýльная слýжба. **4,** (tariff) пóшлина: *pay duty,* (у)платúть пóшлину. —*adj.* дежýрный: *duty officer,* дежýрный офицéр. *Duty roster,* расписáние дежýрств. —**in line of duty,** при исполнéнии служéбных обя́занностей.
duty-free *adj.* беспóшлинный.
dwarf *n.* кáрлик. —**dwarfish,** *adj.* кáрликовый.
dwell *v.i.* **1,** (reside) жить. **2,** *fol. by* **on** (linger) останáвливаться: *dwell on a subject,* останáвливаться на вопрóсе. —**dweller,** *n.* жúтель; обитáтель. —**dwelling,** *n.* жилúще.
dwindle *v.i.* уменьшáться; истощáться.
dye *n.* крáска; красúтель. —*v.t.* крáсить.
dyed *adj.* крáшеный. —**dyed-in-the-wool,** *adj.* твердолóбый.
dyeing *n.* крáшение. —**dyer,** *n.* красúльщик.
dyestuff *n.* крáсящее веществó.
dye works красúльня.
dying *n.* умирáние. —*adj.* **1,** (about to die) умирáющий. **2,** (uttered just before death) предсмéртный. —**till one's dying day,** до сáмой смéрти.
dynamic *adj.* динамúческий. —**dynamics,** *n.* динáмика. —**dynamism,** *n.* динамúзм.
dynamite *n.* динамúт. —*adj.* динамúтный. —*v.t.* взрывáть динамúтом.
dynamo *n.* динáмо.
dynamometer *n.* динамóметр; силомéр.
dynasty *n.* динáстия. —**dynastic,** *adj.* династúческий.
dyne *n., physics* дúна.
dysentery *n.* дизентерúя.
dyspepsia *n.* диспепсúя.
dysprosium *n.* диспрóзий.
dystrophy *n.* дистрофúя.

E

E, e пятая буква английского алфавита. —*n.* (musical note) ми.

each *adj. & pron.* каждый: *each participant,* каждый участник. *Each of them,* каждый из них. *To each his own,* каждому своё. —*adv.* (apiece) за штуку: *ten cents each,* десять центов за штуку. *They received five rubles each,* каждый получил по пять рублей. —**each other,** друг друга: *love each other,* любить друг друга. *Write to each other,* писать друг другу. *They resemble each other,* они похожи друг на друга. ♦ *Also with the refl. verb: see each other,* видеться; *scratch each other,* царапаться.

eager *adj.* **1,** (ardent) усердный: *eager pupil,* усердный ученик. *Eager fans,* страстные болельщики. **2,** *fol. by* **for** (earnestly seeking; impatiently awaiting) жаждущий (+ *gen.*): *eager for fame,* жаждущий славы. **3,** (anxious): *I am eager to see him,* мне очень хочется увидеть его. *I am eager to begin,* мне не терпится начать.

eagerly *adv.* жадно; с жадностью; с нетерпением.

eagerness *n.* пыл; рвение; задор.

eagle *n.* орёл. *Bald eagle,* орлан. *Golden eagle,* беркут. —*adj.* орлиный: *eagle eye,* орлиный взгляд. —**eagle owl,** филин.

eaglet *n.* орлёнок.

ear *n.* **1,** (organ of hearing) ухо. *Whisper in someone's ear,* говорить на ухо (+ *dat.*). **2,** (sense of hearing) слух: *ear for music,* музыкальный слух. *Play by ear,* играть по слуху. **3,** (of corn) початок. **4,** (of wheat, oats, etc.) колос. —*adj.* ушной: *ear drops,* ушные капли. —**be all ears,** во все уши слушать; превращаться в слух; быть весь (вся) внимание. —**in one ear and out the other,** в одно ухо вошло, в другое вышло. —**up to one's ears,** по уши (в работе, в долгах, *etc.*).

earache *n.* боль в ухе; ушная боль.

eardrum *n.* барабанная перепонка.

earflap *n.* наушник.

earl *n.* граф.

early *adj.* ранний: *in early autumn,* ранней осенью. *Since early childhood,* с раннего детства. *It is still early,* ещё рано. *He is an early riser,* он рано встаёт. *In the early 1960s,* в начале шестидесятых годов. *He is in his early forties,* ему лет сорок с небольшим. *Early release from prison,* досрочное освобождение из тюрьмы. —*adv.* рано: *go to bed early,* ложиться рано. —**early bird,** ранняя пташка.

earmark *v.t.* предназначать; выделять.

earmuff *n.* наушник.

earn *v.t.* **1,** (receive in payment for labor) зарабатывать. *Earn a living,* зарабатывать на жизнь. *Earned income,* трудовые доходы. **2,** (gain; deserve) заслужить: *earn the right,* заслужить право.

earnest *adj.* **1,** (intent in purpose) серьёзный; добросовестный; исправный. **2,** (marked by deep feeling) искренний. —**in earnest, 1,** (not joking) всерьёз. *Are you in earnest?,* вы это всерьёз? **2,** (with determination) вплотную.

earnings *n.pl.* **1,** (wages) заработок. **2,** (profit) выручка.

earphone *n.* наушник.

earring *n.* серьга.

earshot *n.* предел слышимости: *within earshot,* в пределах слышимости.

earth *n.* **1,** *often cap.* (the planet) Земля: *revolve around the earth,* вращаться вокруг Земли. *The earth's axis/crust,* земная ось/кора. **2,** (land; ground; this world) земля: *fall to earth,* упасть на землю. *Peace on earth,* мир на земле. —**on earth,** *rendered variously in Russian: why on earth did he say that?,* почему же он это сказал? *Why on earth should I do that?,* с какой стати мне сделать это? *How on earth did you find out?,* как вы смогли узнать это?

earthen *adj.* **1,** (made of earth) земляной. **2,** (made of baked clay) глиняный.

earthenware *n.* глиняная посуда; гончарные изделия. —*adj.* глиняный.

earthly *adj.* **1,** (worldly) земной. **2,** (possible; conceivable): *of no earthly use,* совершенно бесполезный. *For no earthly reason,* безо всякой причины.

earthquake *n.* землетрясение.

earthwork *n.* **1,** *usu. pl.* (embankment; fortification) земляное укрепление. **2,** (excavation) земляные работы.

earthworm *n.* земляной червь.

earthy *adj.* **1,** (of or like earth) землистый. **2,** (hearty; spicy) солёный.

ear trumpet слуховая трубка; слуховой рожок.

earwax *n.* ушная сера.

ease *n.* **1,** (freedom from pain, worry, or trouble) покой. *A life of ease,* спокойная жизнь; привольная жизнь. **2,** (facility) лёгкость: *with ease,* с лёгкостью. —*v.t.* **1,** (facilitate; alleviate) облегчать. **2,** (move slowly and carefully) (осторожно) подвигать. **3,** *fol. by* **out** (oust gently) вытеснять. —*v.i.* смягчаться; успокаиваться. —**at ease, 1,** (relaxed) спокойный. *Set someone's mind at ease,* успокаивать кого-нибудь. *My mind is at ease,* у меня на душе спокойно.

Feel ill at ease, чу́вствовать себя́ нело́вко. **2,** *mil.* во́льно. *At ease!,* во́льно!
easel *n.* мольбе́рт.
easily *adv.* **1,** (with ease) легко́; без труда́. **2,** (beyond question) несомне́нно; бесспо́рно. **3,** (very possibly) вполне́ вероя́тно: *you may easily be right,* вполне́ вероя́тно, что вы пра́вы.
east *n.* восто́к. *The East,* Восто́к. —*adj.* восто́чный: *east wind,* восто́чный ве́тер. —*adv.* на восто́к; к восто́ку. *East of,* к восто́ку от; восто́чнее (+ *gen.*).
Easter *n.* па́сха. —*adj.* пасха́льный.
easterly *adj.* восто́чный.
eastern *adj.* восто́чный. —**easternmost,** *adj.* са́мый восто́чный.
eastward *adv.* к восто́ку. —*adj.* восто́чный.
easy *adj.* лёгкий: *easy lesson/test/way,* лёгкий уро́к/экза́мен/спо́соб. —**be on easy street,** жить в доста́тке *or* в дово́льстве. —**come easy to,** дава́ться легко́ (+ *dat.*). —**easier said than done,** ле́гче сказа́ть, чем сде́лать. —**easy come, easy go,** как на́жито, так и про́жито. —**take it easy, 1,** (remain calm) не волнова́ться. **2,** (not hurry) не торопи́ться. **3,** (relax; rest) отдыха́ть.
easy chair кре́сло.
easygoing *adj.* **1,** (good-natured) ужи́вчивый. **2,** (leisurely) неторопли́вый.
eat *v.t. & i.* есть; ку́шать. *Have you already eaten?,* вы уже́ пое́ли? *I do not eat meat,* я не ем мя́са. —**eat away,** разъеда́ть; изъеда́ть. —**eat into,** въеда́ться в; изъеда́ть. —**eat one's heart out,** изводи́ться. —**eat one's words,** брать наза́д свои́ слова́. —**eat out,** обе́дать вне до́ма. —**eat up,** съесть; пожира́ть. —**what's eating you?,** кака́я му́ха вас укуси́ла?
eatable *adj.* съедо́бный.
eater *n.* едо́к.
eau de Cologne одеколо́н.
eaves *n.* стреха́.
eavesdrop *v.i.* подслу́шивать.
ebb *n.* отли́в. *Ebb and flow,* прили́в и отли́в. —*v.i.* убыва́ть; угаса́ть. —**ebb tide,** отли́в.
ebonite *n.* эбони́т.
ebony *n.* чёрное де́рево; эбе́новое де́рево. —*adj.* эбе́новый.
ebullient *adj.* кипу́чий.
eccentric *adj.* **1,** (odd) эксцентри́чный. **2,** *math.* эксцентри́ческий. —*n.* чуда́к; оригина́л.
eccentricity *n.* **1,** (eccentric nature) эксцентри́чность. **2,** (peculiarity; quirk) стра́нность.
ecclesiastic *adj.* церко́вный; духо́вный. *Also,* **ecclesiastical.**
echelon *n.* **1,** (step-like formation) эшело́н; ступе́нчатое расположе́ние. **2,** (section of a military force) эшело́н: *rear echelon,* второ́й *or* тылово́й эшело́н. **3,** (level of authority) инста́нция; звено́.
echidna *n.* ехи́дна.
echo *n.* э́хо; о́тзвук; отголо́сок. —*v.i.* отклика́ться *or* отдава́ться э́хом. —*v.t.* вто́рить.
éclair *n.* экле́р.
eclectic *adj.* эклекти́ческий; эклекти́чный. —*n.* экле́ктик. —**eclecticism,** *n.* эклекти́зм.
eclipse *n.* затме́ние. —*v.t.* затмева́ть.
ecliptic *n.* эклипти́ка.
ecology *n.* эколо́гия. —**ecological,** *adj.* экологи́ческий.
economic *adj.* экономи́ческий.
economical *adj.* **1,** (thrifty) эконо́мный. **2,** (efficient; avoiding waste) экономи́чный.
economics *n.* эконо́мика. —**economist,** *n.* экономи́ст.
economize *v.i.* эконо́мить; соблюда́ть эконо́мию.
economy *n.* **1,** (thrift) эконо́мия; эконо́мность; бережли́вость. **2,** (economic system or condition) эконо́мика; хозя́йство.
ecstasy *n.* восто́рг; экста́з. —**ecstatic,** *adj.* восто́рженный; экстати́ческий. *She was ecstatic,* она́ была́ в восто́рге.
ectoplasm *n.* эктопла́зма.
ecumenical *adj.* вселе́нский. —**ecumenical council,** вселе́нский собо́р.
eczema *n.* экзе́ма.
eddy *n.* водоворо́т.
edelweiss *n.* эдельве́йс.
edema *n., med.* отёк.
Eden *n.* Эде́м.
edge *n.* **1,** (border; brink) край: *edge of a table/cliff/city,* край стола́/обры́ва/го́рода. *Edge of a forest,* опу́шка. *At the water's edge,* на са́мом берегу́; у са́мой воды́. **2,** (cutting part of a blade) остриё. **3,** *colloq.* (advantage) преиму́щество; переве́с. —*v.t.* **1,** (trim) окаймля́ть. **2,** *Edge one's way,* пробира́ться; проти́скиваться. —*v.i.* подвига́ться: *edge forward,* подвига́ться вперёд. —**on edge,** в не́рвном состоя́нии. —**take the edge off,** притупля́ть.
edgewise *adv.* бо́ком; бочко́м. —**get a word in edgewise,** ввернУ́ть слове́чко.
edging *n.* кайма́; кант; бордю́р; обши́вка; оторо́чка; вы́пушка.
edgy *adj.* не́рвный; раздражи́тельный.
edible *adj.* съедо́бный. —**edibles,** *n.pl.* съестно́е.
edict *n.* ука́з.
edification *n.* назида́ние: *for the edification of,* в назида́ние (+ *dat.*).
edifice *n.* зда́ние; сооруже́ние.
edify *v.t.* поуча́ть; просвеща́ть. —**edifying,** *adj.* поучи́тельный; назида́тельный.
edit *v.t.* редакти́ровать. *Edit a film,* монти́ровать фильм.
edition *n.* **1,** (of a book) изда́ние. **2,** (of a newspaper) вы́пуск: *the morning edition,* у́тренний вы́пуск.
editor *n.* реда́ктор. *Editor's note,* "от реда́кции." *Letter to the editor,* письмо́ в реда́кцию. —**editor in chief,** гла́вный реда́ктор.
editorial *adj.* редакцио́нный; реда́кторский. *Editorial board,* редакцио́нная колле́гия. —*n.* редакцио́нная статья́.
educate *v.t.* воспи́тывать. —**educated,** *adj.* образо́ванный.
education *n.* образова́ние; просвеще́ние.
educational *adj.* **1,** (pert. to education) образова́тельный; воспита́тельный. **2,** (providing instruction) уче́бный: *educational film,* уче́бный фильм; *educational institution,* уче́бное заведе́ние. **3,** (instructive) поучи́тельный.
educator *n.* воспита́тель; педаго́г.
eel *n.* у́горь.
eerie *adj.* таи́нственный; при́зрачный; жу́ткий.
efface *v.t.* **1,** (erase) стира́ть. **2,** (blot out; obliterate) изгла́живать.

effect *n.* **1,** (result) слéдствие: *cause and effect,* причи́на и слéдствие. **2,** (influence) влия́ние; дéйствие; воздéйствие. *Have an effect (on),* окáзывать влия́ние/(воз)дéйствие (на); (по)дéйствовать (на); возымéть дéйствие. *Have a harmful effect on,* врéдно дéйствовать на. *The medicine has taken effect,* лекáрство подéйствовало. **3,** (force) си́ла; дéйствие: *go into effect,* вступáть в си́лу/дéйствие. *Put a law into effect,* вводи́ть закóн в дéйствие. **4,** (impression purposely produced) эффéкт: *done for effect,* рассчи́танный на эффéкт. *Sound effects,* шумовы́е эффéкты. **5,** (meaning) смысл. *To the effect that,* о том, что. *Something to that effect,* чтó-то в э́том дýхе. **6,** (specific scientific phenomenon) эффéкт: *Doppler effect,* эффéкт Дóплера. **7,** *pl.* (belongings) имýщество; пожи́тки. *Personal effects,* ли́чные вéщи. —*v.t.* производи́ть; совершáть; осуществля́ть. —**in effect, 1,** (in force) в си́ле. **2,** (in essence) факти́чески; по существý.

effective *adj.* **1,** (producing the desired result) дéйственный; эффекти́вный. **2,** (in force) дéйствующий; в си́ле. *Become effective,* вступáть в си́лу.

effectively *adv.* **1,** (in an effective manner) эффекти́вно. **2,** (in effect) факти́чески.

effectiveness *n.* дéйственность; эффекти́вность.

effectual *adj.* эффекти́вный; дéйственный.

effectuate *v.t.* совершáть; осуществля́ть.

effeminate *adj.* женоподóбный.

effervesce *v.i.* **1,** (give off bubbles of gas) шипéть. **2,** *fig.* (show exhilaration) кипéть.

effervescence *n.* **1,** (bubbling state) шипýчесть. **2,** (vivacity) кипýчесть.

effervescent *adj.* **1,** (sparkling) игри́стый; шипýчий. **2,** (exuberant) кипýчий.

effete *adj.* **1,** (exhausted) истощённый. **2,** (barren) бесплóдный.

efficacious *adj.* дéйственный; эффекти́вный. —**efficacy,** *n.* дéйственность; эффекти́вность.

efficiency *n.* эффекти́вность.

efficient *adj.* **1,** (systematic; not wasteful) эффекти́вный. **2,** (competent; thorough) дéльный; аккурáтный; расторóпный; исполни́тельный. —**efficiently,** *adv.* эффекти́вно; аккурáтно.

effigy *n.* чýчело. —**burn/hang in effigy,** сжечь/повéсить чýчело (когó-нибудь).

effort *n.* уси́лие: *without effort,* без уси́лия; без уси́лий. *Make an effort to,* дéлать уси́лия для. *Make every effort,* прилагáть все уси́лия.

effortless *adj.* сдéланный без уси́лий; глáдкий. —**effortlessly,** *adv.* без уси́лий; игрáючи.

effrontery *n.* нáглость; нахáльство.

effulgent *adj.* лучезáрный.

effusion *n.* излия́ние.

effusive *adj.* экспанси́вный.

egalitarian *adj.* уравни́тельный; эгалитáрный.

egg *n.* яйцó. —*adj.* я́ичный: *egg yoke,* я́ичный желтóк. —*v.t.* [*usu.* **egg on**] подстрекáть; подбивáть; наýськивать. —**put all one's eggs in one basket,** постáвить всё на однý кáрту.

egghead *n., slang* интеллигéнт.

eggplant *n.* баклажáн.

eggshell *n.* я́ичная скорлупá.

egg white белóк.

ego *n.* **1,** (the self) ли́чность. **2,** (conceit) самомнéние. **3,** (self-esteem) самолю́бие.

egoism *n.* эгои́зм; себялю́бие. —**egoist,** *n.* эгои́ст. —**egoistic,** *adj.* эгоисти́ческий.

egotism *n.* эготи́зм. —**egotist,** *n.* эгои́ст. —**egotistical,** *adj.* эгоисти́ческий; эгоисти́чный.

egregious *adj.* вопию́щий.

egress *n.* вы́ход.

egret *n.* бéлая цáпля.

Egyptian *adj.* еги́петский. —*n.* египтя́нин. —**Egyptian vulture,** стервя́тник.

Egyptology *n.* египтолóгия. —**Egyptologist,** *n.* египтóлог.

eider *n.* гáга. —*adj.* гагáчий. —**eiderdown,** *n.* гагáчий пух.

eight *adj.* вóсемь. —*n.* **1,** (cardinal number) вóсемь. **2,** *cards* восьмёрка. —**figure (of) eight,** восьмёрка.

eighteen *n. & adj.* восемнáдцать. —**eighteenth,** *adj.* восемнáдцатый.

eighth *adj.* восьмóй. —*n.* **1,** (eighth part) восьмáя часть. **2,** (fraction) восьмáя: *one-eighth,* однá восьмáя.

eight hundred восемьсóт. —**eight-hundredth,** *adj.* восьмисóтый.

eighty *n. & adj.* вóсемьдесят. —**eightieth,** *adj.* восьмидеся́тый.

einsteinium *n.* эйнштéйний.

either *adj.* **1.** (one or the other of two) любóй: *in either case,* в любóм слýчае. **2,** (each of two; one and the other) óба: *on either side of the street,* по обéим сторонáм ýлицы. —*pron.* **1,** (either one) любóй; и тот и другóй. **2,** (neither one) ни тот ни другóй: *I don't like either one,* мне не нрáвится ни тот ни другóй. —*adv.* тóже: *I don't know either,* я тóже не знáю. —**either...or,** и́ли...и́ли.

ejaculate *v.t.* извергáть. —**ejaculation,** *n.* семяизлия́ние.

eject *v.t.* **1,** (emit; discharge) выбрáсывать; извергáть. **2,** (expel; evict) исключáть; выгоня́ть.

ejection *n.* **1,** (discharging) выбрáсывание. **2,** (expulsion) исключéние. —**ejection seat,** катапýльта.

eke *v.t.* [*usu.* **eke out**] *Eke out a living,* перебивáться кóе-как. *Eke out a narrow victory,* с трудóм вы́рвать побéду.

elaborate *adj.* **1,** (worked out carefully and thoroughly) тщáтельно разрабóтанный. **2,** (intricate; ornate) замысловáтый; затéйливый. **3,** (lavish; plush) пы́шный; роскóшный. —*v.t.* разрабáтывать. —*v.i.* вдавáться в подрóбности. *Elaborate on a subject,* развивáть тéму.

elaboration *n.* уточнéние: *require no further elaboration,* не трéбовать уточнéния.

eland *n.* оленебы́к.

elapse *v.i.* **1,** (pass) проходи́ть; протекáть. **2,** (expire) истекáть.

elastic *adj.* **1,** (resilient) упрýгий; эласти́чный. **2,** (flexible; adaptable) ги́бкий. —*n.* рези́нка; лáстик.

elasticity *n.* **1,** (resiliency) упрýгость; эласти́чность. **2,** (flexibility) ги́бкость.

elate *v.t.* óчень обрáдовать. —**elated,** *adj.* обрáдованный. —**elation,** *n.* востóрг; ликовáние.

elbow *n.* лóкоть. —*v.t.* толкáть лóктем. *Elbow one's way,* протáлкиваться. —**at one's elbow,** под рукóй. —**rub elbows with,** якшáться с.

elbowroom *n.* простóр.

elder *adj.* стáрший. —*n.* **1,** (elder person; senior member) стáрший. **2,** (shrub) бузинá.

elderberry *n.* я́года бузины́.
elderly *adj.* пожило́й.
eldest *adj.* ста́рший.
elect *v.t.* **1,** (vote into office) избира́ть; выбира́ть. **2,** *fol. by inf.* (choose; decide) реши́ть.
election *n.* **1,** (act of choosing) избра́ние. **2,** (popular vote) вы́боры. —*adj.* избира́тельный; предвы́борный: *election campaign,* избира́тельная/предвы́борная кампа́ния.
elective *adj.* **1,** (chosen by election) вы́борный: *elective office,* вы́борная до́лжность. **2,** (optional) факультати́вный.
elector *n.* вы́борщик. —**electoral,** *adj.* избира́тельный. —**electorate,** *n.* избира́тели.
electric *adj.* электри́ческий. *Electric power,* электроэне́ргия. *Electric shock,* уда́р электри́ческим то́ком. *Electric train,* электропо́езд.
electrical *adj.* электри́ческий. —**electrical engineer,** инжене́р-эле́ктрик; электроте́хник. —**electrical engineering,** электроте́хника.
electric chair электри́ческий стул.
electric eye фотоэлеме́нт.
electrician *n.* (электро)монтёр; эле́ктрик.
electricity *n.* электри́чество.
electrification *n.* электрифика́ция.
electrify *v.t.* **1,** (charge with electricity) электризова́ть. **2,** (provide with electric power) электрифици́ровать. **3,** *fig.* (charge with excitement) электризова́ть.
electrocardiogram *n.* электрокардиогра́мма. —**electrocardiograph,** *n.* электрокардио́граф.
electrocute *v.t.* **1,** (execute) казни́ть на электри́ческом сту́ле. **2,** (kill accidentally by electricity) убива́ть электри́ческим то́ком.
electrocution *n.* казнь на электри́ческом сту́ле.
electrode *n.* электро́д.
electrolysis *n.* электро́лиз.
electrolyte *n.* электроли́т.
electromagnet *n.* электромагни́т. —**electromagnetic,** *adj.* электромагни́тный. —**electromagnetism,** *n.* электромагнети́зм.
electron *n.* электро́н. —*adj.* электро́нный: *electron microscope,* электро́нный микроско́п.
electronic *adj.* электро́нный. —**electronically,** *adv.* с по́мощью электро́нной аппарату́ры.
electronics *n.* электро́ника.
electrostatics *n.* электроста́тика. —**electrostatic,** *adj.* электростати́ческий.
elegance *n.* элега́нтность; изя́щество.
elegant *adj.* элега́нтный; изя́щный. —**elegantly,** *adv.* элега́нтно; изя́щно.
elegiac *adj.* элеги́ческий. —**elegiacs,** *n.pl.* элеги́ческие стихи́.
elegy *n.* эле́гия.
element *n.* **1,** (in most meanings) элеме́нт: *chemical element,* хими́ческий элеме́нт. *Consist of a number of elements,* состоя́ть из ря́да элеме́нтов. *The criminal element,* престу́пный элеме́нт. *The element of surprise,* внеза́пность. **2,** (customary environment) стихи́я: *be in one's element,* быть в свое́й стихи́и. **3,** (trace) до́ля: *element of truth,* до́ля и́стины. *Element of doubt,* тень сомне́ния. **4,** *pl.* (fundamentals) осно́вы; элеме́нты. **5,** *pl.* (weather conditions) стихи́и: *withstand the elements,* противостоя́ть стихи́ям.
elemental *adj.* стихи́йный: *elemental force,* стихи́йная си́ла.
elementary *adj.* **1,** (fundamental) элемента́рный. **2,** (pert. to the first years of schooling) нача́льный: *elementary school,* нача́льная шко́ла.
elephant *n.* слон.
elephantiasis *n.* слоно́вая боле́знь; слоно́вость.
elephant seal морско́й слон.
elevate *v.t.* поднима́ть; повыша́ть; возвыша́ть.
elevated *adj.* **1,** (raised, as of a railroad) надзе́мный. **2,** *fig.* (lofty) возвы́шенный; припо́днятый.
elevation *n.* **1,** (act of elevating) подня́тие. **2,** (height; altitude) высота́. **3,** (raised area) возвы́шенность.
elevator *n.* лифт. *Grain elevator,* элева́тор. —**elevator operator,** лифтёр; лифтёрша.
eleven *n. & adj.* оди́ннадцать. —**eleventh,** *adj.* оди́ннадцатый.
elf *n.* эльф.
elicit *v.t.* **1,** (draw out; obtain) выявля́ть: *elicit the facts,* выявля́ть фа́кты. *Elicit information,* выве́дывать информа́цию. **2,** (evoke) вызыва́ть: *elicit applause,* вызыва́ть аплодисме́нты. *Elicit no reply,* не принести́ отве́та.
eligibility *n.* пра́во: *eligibility for a position,* пра́во на заня́тие до́лжности.
eligible *adj.* **1,** (qualified) име́ющий пра́во. **2,** (desirable for marriage) вы́годный: *eligible bachelor,* вы́годный жени́х.
eliminate *v.t.* **1,** (get rid of) устраня́ть. **2,** (rule out, as a possibility) исключа́ть. **3,** *sports* выводи́ть. *Be eliminated,* выбыва́ть. **4,** *physiol.* (excrete) выделя́ть.
elimination *n.* **1,** (getting rid of) устране́ние. **2,** *physiol.* (secretion) выделе́ние. —**process of elimination,** ме́тод исключе́ния.
elite *n.* эли́та. *Social elite,* сли́вки *or* цвет о́бщества.
elixir *n.* эликси́р.
elk *n.* лось.
ellipse *n.* э́ллипс.
ellipsis *n.* э́ллипсис; э́ллипс.
ellipsoid *n.* эллипсо́ид.
elliptical *adj.* эллипти́ческий.
elm *n.* вяз; ильм.
elocution *n.* ора́торское иску́сство.
elongate *v.t.* удлиня́ть. —**elongated,** *adj.* удлинённый; продолгова́тый.
elope *v.i.* бежа́ть (с возлю́бленным).
eloquence *n.* красноре́чие. —**eloquent,** *adj.* красноречи́вый.
else *adj.* **1,** (different) друго́й: *something else,* что́-то друго́е; *someone else,* кто́-то друго́й; *no one else,* никто́ друго́й. *Everything else,* всё остально́е. *Everyone else,* все други́е; все остальны́е. **2,** (additional) ещё: *what else do you need?,* что ещё вам ну́жно? ♦ *With negatives* бо́льше: *nothing else,* бо́льше ничего́. *Nothing else happened,* ничего́ бо́льше не случи́лось. *No one else knows about it,* никто́ бо́льше об э́том не зна́ет. *There was no one else there,* никого́ бо́льше не́ было там. —*adv.* ещё: *where else did you go?,* куда́ ещё вы е́здили? *Somewhere else,* где́-то в друго́м ме́сте. *Nowhere else in the world,* бо́льше нигде́ в ми́ре. —**or else,** а то; а не то; ина́че. —**someone else's,** чужо́й.
elsewhere *adv.* (где́-нибудь) в друго́м ме́сте; (куда́-нибудь) в друго́е ме́сто.
elucidate *v.t.* разъясня́ть; освеща́ть. —**elucidation,** *n.* разъясне́ние; освеще́ние.
elude *v.t.* избега́ть; увёртываться от; ускольза́ть от.

elusive *adj.* неуловимый. —**elusiveness,** *n.* неуловимость.
emaciate *v.t.* истощать. —**emaciated,** *adj.* истощённый; измождённый; исхудалый; тощий.
emanate *v.i.* **1,** (of heat, light, etc.) излучаться. **2,** (originate) исходить; истекать.
emanation *n.* эманация.
emancipate *v.t.* освобождать; эмансипировать; раскрепощать. —**emancipation,** *n.* освобождение; эмансипация; раскрепощение. —**emancipator,** *n.* освободитель; эмансипатор.
emasculate *v.t.* выхолащивать (*lit. & fig.*).
embalm *v.t.* бальзамировать. —**embalmer,** *n.* бальзамировщик.
embankment *n.* **1,** (to hold back water) набережная. **2,** (to support a roadway) насыпь.
embargo *n.* эмбарго.
embark *v.i.* **1,** (go aboard a vessel) садиться на корабль. **2,** *fol. by* **on** *or* **upon** (start out on) начинать; пускаться в. —**embarkation,** *n.* посадка (на корабль).
embarrass *v.t.* смущать. *Be embarrassed,* смущаться. —**embarrassment,** *n.* смущение.
embassy *n.* посольство.
embed *v.t.* **1,** (implant firmly) вделывать. **2,** (fix, as in one's memory) врезать; запечатлевать (в памяти).
embellish *v.t.* **1,** (beautify) украшать. **2,** (embroider; exaggerate) приукрашивать; прикрашивать.
embellishment *n.* **1,** (decoration) украшение. **2,** (fictitious details) прикрасы.
ember *n.* тлеющий уголь. *Live embers,* горячие угли.
embezzle *v.t.* растрачивать. —**embezzlement,** *n.* растрата. —**embezzler,** *n.* растратчик.
embitter *v.t.* озлоблять; ожесточать.
emblem *n.* эмблема. —**emblematic,** *adj.* эмблематический.
embody *v.t.* воплощать; олицетворять. —**embodiment,** *n.* воплощение; олицетворение.
embolism *n.* эмболия; закупорка.
emboss *v.t.* **1,** (cover with raised figures, as a surface) украшать *or* лепить (что-нибудь) рельефом. **2,** (raise upon a surface, as a design) чеканить; гофрировать.
embossed *adj.* **1,** (of a surface) рельефный. **2,** (of a design) тиснёный. —**embossing,** *n.* тиснение.
embrace *v.t.* **1,** (hug) обнимать. **2,** (include; encompass) охватывать. **3,** (take up; adopt) принимать. —*v.i.* обниматься. —*n.* объятие.
embrasure *n.* **1,** (opening for a door or window) проём. **2,** (opening through which a gun may be fired) амбразура; бойница.
embroider *v.t.* **1,** (decorate with needlework) вышивать. **2,** *fig.* (embellish, as a story) приукрашивать; прикрашивать. —*v.i.* вышивать.
embroidery *n.* **1,** (needlework) вышивание; вышивка. **2,** (embroidered design) вышивка.
embroil *v.t.* впутывать; втягивать.
embryo *n.* зародыш; зачаток; эмбрион.
embryology *n.* эмбриология. —**embryologist,** *n.* эмбриолог.
embryonic *adj.* зародышевый; эмбриональный. *In an embryonic state,* в зачаточном состоянии.
emerald *n.* изумруд. —*adj.* изумрудный.
emerge *v.i.* **1,** (come out) выходить. **2,** (come into being) возникать. **3,** (come to light) всплывать; выплывать. —**emergence,** *n.* выход; возникновение.
emergency *n.* крайняя необходимость. *In case of emergency,* в случае крайней необходимости. *State of emergency,* чрезвычайное положение. —*adj.* **1,** (used in an emergency) аварийный: *emergency brake/signal,* аварийный тормоз/сигнал. *Emergency exit,* запасный выход. **2,** (occurring or invoked in an emergency) чрезвычайный: *emergency meeting,* чрезвычайное собрание. *Emergency powers,* чрезвычайные полномочия. *Emergency landing,* вынужденная *or* аварийная посадка.
emeritus *adj.* в отставке. *Professor emeritus,* заслуженный профессор в отставке.
emery *n.* наждак. —*adj.* наждачный.
emetic *adj.* рвотный. —*n.* рвотное; рвотное средство.
emigrant *n.* эмигрант.
emigrate *v.i.* эмигрировать. —**emigration,** *n.* эмиграция.
émigré *n.* эмигрант.
eminence *n.* **1,** (exalted position) знаменитость. **2,** (elevation; hill) возвышенность.
eminent *adj.* выдающийся; знаменитый. —**eminently,** *adv.* весьма; вполне.
emir *n.* эмир. —**emirate,** *n.* эмират.
emissary *n.* эмиссар.
emission *n.* испускание.
emit *v.t.* испускать; издавать.
emotion *n.* чувство; эмоция.
emotional *adj.* **1,** (pert. to the emotions) душевный: *emotional state,* душевное состояние. **2,** (easily aroused to emotion; appealing to emotions) эмоциональный.
empathize *v.i.* [*usu.* **empathize with**] входить в (чьё-нибудь) положение.
empathy *n.* сочувствие.
emperor *n.* император.
emphasis *n.* ударение; акцент. *Lay/place (the) emphasis on,* делать упор/ударение/акцент на. *Pronounce with emphasis,* произносить подчёркнуто.
emphasize *v.t.* подчёркивать.
emphatic *adj.* подчёркнутый; решительный. —**emphatically,** *adv.* решительно; категорически.
emphysema *n.* эмфизема.
empire *n.* империя.
empirical *adj.* эмпирический. —**empiricism,** *n.* эмпиризм. —**empiricist,** *n.* эмпирик.
emplacement *n., mil.* площадка: *machine-gun emplacement,* пулемётная площадка.
employ *v.t.* **1,** (use) использовать; применять. **2,** (hire) нанимать. —*n.* служба: *be in the employ of the government,* быть на государственной службе.
employee *n.* служащий. —**employer,** *n.* наниматель; работодатель.
employment *n.* **1,** (use) использование; применение. **2,** (hiring) наём: *opportunities for employment,* возможности найма. **3,** (work; occupation) работа. **4,** *econ.* занятость: *full employment,* полная занятость.
empower *v.t.* уполномочивать.
empress *n.* императрица.
emptiness *n.* пустота.
empty *adj.* пустой: *empty glass/bus/hall,* пустой стакан/автобус/зал. *Empty seat,* свободное место.

Empty words/promises, пусты́е слова́/обеща́ния. —*v.t.* **1,** (remove the contents of) опора́жнивать. **2,** (toss out) выбра́сывать: *empty the trash from the wastebasket,* выбра́сывать сор из корзи́ны. **3,** *fol. by* **into** (pour into) вылива́ть (в); высыпа́ть (в). —*v.i.* **1,** (become empty) опора́жниваться. **2,** *fol. by* **into** (flow into, as of a river) впада́ть (в); нести́ свои́ во́ды (в).

empty-handed *adj.* ни с чем; с пусты́ми рука́ми.

empty-headed *adj.* пустоголо́вый.

emu *n.* э́му.

emulate *v.t.* равня́ться по: *emulate one's predecessors,* равня́ться по свои́м предше́ственникам. *Emulate one's father's success,* доби́ться того́ же успе́ха, что и оте́ц.

emulsion *n.* эму́льсия.

enable *v.t.* позволя́ть; дава́ть возмо́жность (+ *dat.*).

enact *v.t.* **1,** (make into law) принима́ть. **2,** (act out) разы́грывать. —**enactment,** *n.* приня́тие.

enamel *n.* эма́ль. —*adj.* эма́левый; эмалиро́ванный. —*v.t.* покрыва́ть эма́лью; эмалирова́ть. —**enamelware,** *n.* эмалиро́ванная посу́да.

enamored *also,* **enamoured** *adj.* влюблён. *Be enamored of,* увлека́ться (+ *instr.*).

encamp *v.i.* располага́ться ла́герем.

encampment *n.* **1,** (setting up a camp) расположе́ние ла́герем. **2,** (camp; campsite) стоя́нка.

encase *v.t.* вде́лывать.

encephalitis *n.* энцефали́т.

enchant *v.t.* очаро́вывать; восхища́ть; пленя́ть; обвора́живать.

enchanted *adj.* **1,** (captivated) зачаро́ванный; очаро́ванный. **2,** (having a seemingly magical quality) заколдо́ванный; зачаро́ванный.

enchanting *adj.* очарова́тельный; обая́тельный; обворожи́тельный; восхити́тельный. —**enchantment,** *n.* очарова́ние; восхище́ние; обая́ние. —**enchantress,** *n.* чаровни́ца; чароде́йка.

encipher *v.t.* шифрова́ть.

encircle *v.t.* окружа́ть. —**encirclement,** *n.* окруже́ние.

enclave *n.* анкла́в.

enclose *v.t.* **1,** (fence in) огора́живать; загора́живать. **2,** (insert) вкла́дывать (в конве́рт); прилага́ть (к письму́). **3,** (place between, as in parentheses) заключа́ть (в ско́бки).

enclosure *n.* **1,** (act of enclosing) огора́живание. **2,** (enclosed area) огоро́женное ме́сто. **3,** (fence) огра́да. **4,** (something enclosed with a letter) вложе́ние; приложе́ние.

encode *v.t.* шифрова́ть; коди́ровать.

encomium *n.* панеги́рик.

encompass *v.t.* **1,** (encircle) окружа́ть. **2,** (take in; include) охва́тывать.

encore *interj.* бис. —*n. Give an encore,* испо́лнить что́-нибудь на бис; биси́ровать.

encounter *n.* **1,** (meeting) встре́ча. **2,** (contact; clash) столкнове́ние. —*v.t.* встреча́ть; ста́лкиваться с. *Encounter difficulties,* ста́лкиваться с тру́дностями. *Encounter resistance,* встреча́ть сопротивле́ние.

encourage *v.t.* **1,** (hearten) ободря́ть; подбодря́ть; обнадёживать. **2,** (stimulate) поощря́ть. **3,** (help bring about) спосо́бствовать. —**encouragement,** *n.* ободре́ние; поощре́ние. —**encouraging,** *adj.* ободри́тельный; поощри́тельный; обнадёживающий. *Initial results are encouraging,* пе́рвые результа́ты обнадёживают.

encroach *v.i.* [*usu.* **encroach on** *or* **upon**] посяга́ть (на); покуша́ться (на). —**encroachment,** *n.* посяга́тельство.

encrust *v.t.* инкрусти́ровать.

encumber *v.t.* **1,** (hinder; hamper) стесня́ть. **2,** (clutter; obstruct) загромозжда́ть.

encumbrance *n.* **1,** (hindrance) препя́тствие; поме́ха. **2,** (burden) бре́мя; обу́за.

encyclical *n.* энци́клика.

encyclopedia *n.* энциклопе́дия. —**encyclopedic,** *adj.* энциклопеди́ческий. —**encyclopedist,** *n.* энциклопеди́ст.

end *n.* **1,** (extremity; conclusion) коне́ц: *the end of the street,* коне́ц у́лицы. *Come to an end,* приходи́ть к концу́. *Put an end to,* положи́ть коне́ц (+ *dat.*). *To the bitter end,* до са́мого конца́; до после́дней ка́пли кро́ви. **2,** (goal; purpose) цель: *toward this end,* с э́той це́лью. *The end justifies the means,* цель опра́вдывает сре́дства. **3,** (death) смерть; кончи́на: *meet one's end,* найти́ свою́ смерть. —*adj.* коне́чный: *end product,* коне́чный проду́кт. *End result,* исхо́д де́ла. —*v.t.* **1,** (conclude) конча́ть; зака́нчивать; заключа́ть. **2,** (halt; put a stop to) прекраща́ть. —*v.i.* конча́ться: *all's well that ends well,* всё хорошо́, что хорошо́ конча́ется. *End in disaster,* ко́нчиться катастро́фой. —**at loose ends,** без де́ла; не у дел. —**be the end of,** своди́ть в моги́лу. —**end up,** очути́ться. —**in the end,** в конце́ концо́в. —**make ends meet,** своди́ть концы́ с конца́ми. —**no end of,** отбо́ю нет от; хоть отбавля́й. —**on end,** по це́лым: *for weeks on end,* по це́лым неде́лям. —**stand on end, 1,** (set upright) ста́вить стоймя́; ста́вить на ребро́. **2,** (bristle, as of one's hair) встава́ть *or* станови́ться ды́бом. —**to the ends of the earth,** на край све́та (*or* земли́).

endanger *v.t.* подверга́ть опа́сности; ста́вить под угро́зу.

endear *v.t.* сде́лать дороги́м се́рдцу. *Endear oneself to,* покоря́ть се́рдце (+ *gen.*). —**endearing,** *adj.* подкупа́ющий; обезору́живающий.

endearment *n.* ла́ска. —**term of endearment,** ласка́тельное и́мя.

endeavor *also,* **endeavour** *v.t.* пыта́ться; стара́ться. —*n.* **1,** (attempt) попы́тка. **2,** (undertaking) предприя́тие; зате́я.

endemic *adj.* эндеми́ческий.

end game *chess* э́ндшпиль.

ending *n.* оконча́ние: *verb/chess/nerve endings,* глаго́льные/ша́хматные/не́рвные оконча́ния. *The story has a happy ending,* расска́з име́ет счастли́вый коне́ц.

endless *adj.* бесконе́чный; нескончаемый. —**endlessly,** *adv.* без конца́; бесконе́чно.

endocrine *adj.* эндокри́нный. —**endocrine glands,** эндокри́нные же́лезы; же́лезы вну́тренней секре́ции.

endocrinology *n.* эндокриноло́гия.

endorse *v.t.* **1,** *finance* индосси́ровать. **2,** (support, as a candidate) подде́рживать кандидату́ру (+ *gen.*). **3,** (express one's agreement with) присоединя́ться к.

endorsement *n.* **1,** (support) подде́ржка. **2,** (signature on the back of a check) переда́точная на́дпись; индоссаме́нт; жи́ро.

endow *v.t.* **1,** (provide with funds) обеспе́чивать. **2,** (invest with, as certain qualities) наделя́ть; одаря́ть.
endowment *n.* **1,** (bequest) дар; поже́ртвование. **2,** (natural gift) дарова́ние; одарённость.
endurance *n.* выно́сливость; вы́держка.
endure *v.t.* терпе́ть; выноси́ть; переноси́ть; выде́рживать. —*v.i.* дли́ться; продолжа́ться. —**enduring,** *adj.* про́чный: *enduring peace,* про́чный мир.
endwise *adv.* **1,** (on end) стоймя́. **2,** (lengthwise) в длину́. **3,** (with the end foremost) концо́м вперёд.
enema *n.* кли́зма.
enemy *n.* враг; неприя́тель; проти́вник. —*adj.* вра́жеский; неприя́тельский.
energetic *adj.* энерги́чный. —**energetically,** *adv.* энерги́чно.
energy *n.* **1,** (general term) эне́ргия. **2,** *pl.* (efforts) си́лы: *direct one's energies to,* направля́ть свои́ си́лы на (+ *acc.*).
enervate *v.t.* обесси́ливать; расслабля́ть.
enfeeble *v.t.* ослабля́ть; обесси́ливать. —**enfeebled,** *adj.* одряхле́вший.
enfold *v.t.* **1,** (surround with a covering) заку́тывать. **2,** (embrace) обнима́ть.
enforce *v.t.* осуществля́ть; проводи́ть в жизнь. —**enforceable,** *adj.* осуществи́мый. —**enforcement,** *n.* осуществле́ние.
enfranchise *v.t.* предоставля́ть избира́тельные права́ (+ *dat.*)
engage *v.t.* **1,** (hire) нанима́ть. **2,** (occupy; absorb) занима́ть; поглоща́ть. *Engage someone in conversation,* занима́ть кого́-нибудь разгово́ром. *Engage someone's attention,* поглоща́ть чьё-нибудь внима́ние. *The work engages much of my time,* рабо́та поглоща́ет у меня́ мно́го вре́мени. **3,** (meet in battle) вступа́ть в бой с. —*v.i.* **1,** *fol. by* **in** (involve oneself; take part) занима́ться (+ *instr.*). **2,** (mesh) сцепля́ться.
engaged *adj.* **1,** (occupied) за́нятый. *Be engaged in,* быть за́нятым (+ *instr.*); занима́ться (+ *instr.*). **2,** (betrothed) помо́лвленный; обручённый. *Become engaged to,* обруча́ться с.
engagement *n.* **1,** (betrothal) помо́лвка; обруче́ние. **2,** (appointment) свида́ние. **3,** (battle) бой. —*adj.* обруча́льный: *engagement ring,* обруча́льное кольцо́.
engaging *adj.* привлека́тельный; подкупа́ющий.
engender *v.t.* порожда́ть; зарожда́ть.
engine *n.* **1,** (motor) дви́гатель; мото́р; маши́на. **2,** (locomotive) парово́з; локомоти́в. —**engine room,** маши́нное отделе́ние.
engineer *n.* **1,** (one trained in a branch of engineering) инжене́р. **2,** (locomotive operator) машини́ст. —*v.t.* соверша́ть: *engineer an escape,* соверши́ть побе́г. *Engineer a victory,* кова́ть побе́ду.
engineering *n.* инжене́рное де́ло; те́хника.
English *adj.* англи́йский. —*n.* **1,** (language) англи́йский язы́к. *Speak English,* говори́ть по-англи́йски. **2,** *preceded by* **the** (people) англича́не.
English horn англи́йский рожо́к.
Englishman *n.* англича́нин. —**Englishwoman,** *n.* англича́нка.
engrain *v.* = **ingrain.**
engrave *v.t.* гравирова́ть. —**engraver,** *n.* граве́р.
engraving *n.* **1,** (art) гравирова́ние; гравиро́вка. **2,** (engraved plate) гравю́ра.
engross *v.t.* поглоща́ть. *Be engrossed in,* быть поглощённым в; углубля́ться в; погружа́ться в. —**engrossing,** *adj.* увлека́тельный; захва́тывающий.
engulf *v.t.* **1,** (of flames, darkness, etc.) охва́тывать. **2,** (of waves, the sea, etc.) поглоща́ть.
enhance *v.t.* увели́чивать; повыша́ть.
enigma *n.* зага́дка. —**enigmatic,** *adj.* зага́дочный.
enjoin *v.t.* **1,** (order; direct) предпи́сывать. **2,** (forbid; prohibit) запреща́ть.
enjoy *v.t.* **1,** (have a good time at): *did you enjoy the play?,* пье́са вам понра́вилась? **2,** (relish; admire) наслажда́ться. **3,** (have, as an advantage, good health, etc.) по́льзоваться; облада́ть. —**enjoy oneself,** хорошо́ проводи́ть вре́мя; получи́ть (большо́е) удово́льствие.
enjoyable *adj.* прия́тный.
enjoyment *n.* **1,** (pleasure) удово́льствие; наслажде́ние. **2,** (possession) облада́ние.
enlarge *v.t.* **1,** (make larger) расширя́ть. **2,** *photog.* увели́чивать. —*v.i.* **1,** (become larger) расширя́ться; увели́чиваться. **2,** *fol. by* **upon** (treat in greater detail) распространя́ться о.
enlargement *n.* **1,** (act of enlarging) увеличе́ние; расшире́ние. **2,** (enlarged copy) увеличе́ние.
enlarger *n., photog.* увеличи́тель; увеличи́тельный аппара́т.
enlighten *v.t.* **1,** (bring knowledge to) просвеща́ть. **2,** (inform) осведомля́ть. —**enlightened,** *adj.* просвещённый. —**enlightening,** *adj.* поучи́тельный. —**enlightenment,** *n.* просвеще́ние.
enlist *v.i.* (доброво́льно) поступа́ть (*e.g.* на вое́нную слу́жбу). —*v.t.* **1,** (recruit) вербова́ть. **2,** (secure, as services) заруча́ться. —**enlisted man,** военнослу́жащий рядово́го соста́ва.
enlistment *n.* **1,** (act of enlisting) поступле́ние (на вое́нную слу́жбу). **2,** (term) срок слу́жбы.
enliven *v.t.* оживля́ть.
en masse в ма́ссе.
enmity *n.* вражда́; неприя́знь.
ennoble *v.t.* облагора́живать.
ennui *n.* ску́ка; тоска́.
enormity *n.* **1,** (heinousness) чудо́вищность. **2,** (heinous crime) злодея́ние.
enormous *adj.* огро́мный; грома́дный. —**enormously,** *adv.* в огро́мной сте́пени; чрезвыча́йно.
enough *adj.* доста́точно (+ *gen.*): *enough money,* доста́точно де́нег. *Be enough,* хвата́ть: *that will be enough for today,* э́того хва́тит на сего́дня. *There is enough room for everyone,* на всех хвата́ет ме́ста. —*adv.* **1,** (sufficiently) доста́точно: *old enough to understand,* доста́точно взро́слый, что́бы поня́ть. **2,** (adequately) дово́льно: *he plays well enough,* он игра́ет дово́льно хорошо́. **3,** *in* **oddly enough,** как ни стра́нно; **sure enough,** *see* **sure.** —*n.* доста́точно: *I've had enough,* мне уже́ доста́точно. —*interj.* доста́точно!; хва́тит!
en passant **1,** (in passing) мимохо́дом. **2,** *chess* на прохо́д.
enrage *v.t.* беси́ть; разъяря́ть; приводи́ть в я́рость. —**enraged,** *adj.* разъярённый. *Become enraged,* приходи́ть в я́рость.
enrapture *v.t.* восхища́ть; восторга́ть.
enrich *v.t.* обогаща́ть. *Enriched uranium,* обогащённый ура́н. —**enrichment,** *n.* обогаще́ние.

enroll *also,* **enrol** *v.t.* зачисля́ть. —*v.i.* запи́сываться; зачисля́ться.

enrollment *also,* **enrolment** *n.* **1,** (act of enrolling) зачисле́ние. **2,** (number of students enrolled) число́ уча́щихся.

en route по (*or* в) пути́; по (*or* в) доро́ге.

ensconce *v.t.* устра́ивать. *Ensconce oneself,* устра́иваться; засе́сть.

ensemble *n.* **1,** (group) анса́мбль. **2,** (attire) наря́д.

enshrine *v.t.* храни́ть; сохраня́ть. *Enshrined in our hearts forever,* наве́чно сохранён в на́ших сердца́х.

enshroud *v.t.* оку́тывать.

ensign *n.* **1,** (flag) зна́мя; флаг. **2,** (emblem) значо́к; эмбле́ма. **3,** (rank) мла́дший лейтена́нт.

enslave *v.t.* порабоща́ть. —**enslavement,** *n.* порабоще́ние. —**enslaver,** *n.* поработи́тель.

ensnare *v.t.* пойма́ть в лову́шку.

ensue *v.i.* **1,** (follow) сле́довать. **2,** (result) вытека́ть. —**ensuing,** *adj.* после́дующий; вытека́ющий.

ensure *v.t.* обеспе́чивать.

entail *v.t.* влечь за собо́й; быть свя́занным с.

entangle *v.t.* запу́тывать. *Become entangled,* запу́тываться.

enter *v.t.* **1,** (go into; come into) входи́ть в: *enter the hall,* входи́ть в зал. *Enter the hospital,* лечь в больни́цу. *Enter one's head,* приходи́ть в го́лову (+ *dat.*). **2,** (join; enroll in) вступа́ть в; поступа́ть в. **3,** (pierce; penetrate) вонза́ться в; проника́ть в. **4,** (begin, as a new era) вступа́ть в. **5,** (place, as on a list) вноси́ть; заноси́ть; впи́сывать; зачисля́ть. **6,** (place; register, as in school) запи́сывать. **7,** (submit formally) заявля́ть: *enter a protest,* заявля́ть проте́ст. —*v.i.* входи́ть. —**enter into,** вступа́ть в; входи́ть в. *Enter into an agreement,* заключа́ть соглаше́ние.

enteritis *n.* энтери́т.

enterprise *n.* **1,** (undertaking; business operation) предприя́тие. **2,** (economic activity) предпринима́тельство: *private enterprise,* ча́стное предпринима́тельство. **3,** (initiative) предприи́мчивость.

enterprising *adj.* предприи́мчивый.

entertain *v.t.* **1,** (amuse) развлека́ть; забавля́ть; занима́ть. **2,** (extend hospitality to) принима́ть; угоща́ть. **3,** (consider) обду́мывать. *Entertain a motion,* принима́ть предложе́ние к рассмотре́нию. **4,** (harbor) пита́ть. —*v.i.* принима́ть госте́й.

entertaining *adj.* занима́тельный.

entertainment *n.* **1,** (entertaining of guests) приём (госте́й); угоще́ние. **2,** (diversion) развлече́ние. **3,** (show; performance) варьете́.

enthrall *v.t.* **1,** (captivate) увлека́ть; захва́тывать; завлека́ть. **2,** *obs.* (enslave) порабоща́ть. —**enthralling,** *adj.* увлека́тельный; захва́тывающий; завлека́тельный.

enthrone *v.t.* возводи́ть на престо́л.

enthusiasm *n.* энтузиа́зм; увлече́ние; воодушевле́ние; подъём. —**enthusiast,** *n.* энтузиа́ст; охо́тник. —**enthusiastic,** *adj.* восто́рженный; по́лный энтузиа́зма.

entice *v.t.* зама́нивать; завлека́ть; прельща́ть.

enticement *n.* **1,** (act of enticing) зама́нивание. **2,** (that which entices) прима́нка.

enticing *adj.* зама́нчивый; завлека́тельный.

entire *adj.* **1,** (whole) це́лый; весь: *an entire day,* це́лый день; *the entire day,* весь день. **2,** (complete) по́лный.

entirely *adv.* соверше́нно; совсе́м; вполне́; целико́м; всеце́ло.

entirety *n.* полнота́. *In its entirety,* во всей полноте́; со всей полното́й.

entitle *v.t.* **1,** (qualify; authorize) дава́ть пра́во (+ *dat.*). *Be entitled to,* име́ть пра́во на. **2,** (name) озагла́вливать. *The book is entitled...,* кни́га называ́ется...

entity *n.* вещь: *separate entities,* ра́зные ве́щи.

entomb *v.t.* погреба́ть.

entomology *n.* энтомоло́гия. —**entomological,** *adj.* энтомологи́ческий. —**entomologist,** *n.* энтомо́лог.

entourage *n.* окруже́ние.

entrails *n.pl.* вну́тренности; требуха́.

entrance[1] (**en**-trens) *n.* **1,** (act of entering) вход. **2,** (place to enter) вход; ход. *Back entrance,* чёрный ход. **3,** *theat.* вы́ход (на сце́ну). —*adj.* входно́й; вступи́тельный. *Entrance examination,* вступи́тельный экза́мен.

entrance[2] (en-**trans**) *v.t.* очаро́вывать; завора́живать.

entrant *n.* уча́стник (состяза́ния).

entrap *v.t.* пойма́ть в лову́шку.

entreat *v.t.* умоля́ть; упра́шивать. —**entreaty,** *n.* мольба́.

entrée *n.* **1,** (right of entry) пра́во вхо́да. *Have entrée,* быть вхо́жим. **2,** (main course) второ́е (блю́до).

entrench *v.t.* **1,** (fortify with a trench) ока́пывать. **2,** (establish firmly) укореня́ть. *Become entrenched,* укореня́ться.

entrepreneur *n.* предпринима́тель.

entrust *v.t.* доверя́ть; вверя́ть; поруча́ть.

entry *n.* **1,** (act of entering) вход. **2,** (opening; passage) вход; прохо́д. **3,** (notation) за́пись; отме́тка. **4,** (item in a reference book) статья́.

entwine *v.t.* **1,** (intertwine) вплета́ть; сплета́ть. *Become entwined,* переплета́ться. **2,** (twine around) обвива́ть. —*v.i.* [*usu.* **entwine around**] обвива́ться вокру́г.

enumerate *v.t.* перечисля́ть.

enumeration *n.* **1,** (act of enumerating) перечисле́ние. **2,** (list; catalogue) пе́речень.

enunciate *v.t.* **1,** (articulate) выгова́ривать. **2,** (state systematically) излага́ть. **3,** (announce; proclaim) провозглаша́ть. —*v.i.* произноси́ть.

enunciation *n.* **1,** (pronunciation) вы́говор. **2,** (formal statement) изложе́ние; провозглаше́ние.

envelop *v.t.* охва́тывать; оку́тывать; обвола́кивать.

envelope *n.* конве́рт.

envelopment *n.* охва́т.

envenom *v.t.* отравля́ть.

enviable *adj.* зави́дный.

envious *adj.* зави́стливый. *Be envious of,* зави́довать (+ *dat.*).

environment *n.* окруже́ние; среда́. *The environment,* окружа́ющая среда́. —**environmental,** *adj.* свя́занный с окружа́ющей средо́й. —**environmentalist,** *n.* сторо́нник охра́ны окружа́ющей среды́.

environs *n.pl.* окре́стности.

envisage *v.t.* предусма́тривать.

envision *v.t.* **1,** (picture in the mind) представля́ть. **2,** (provide for in the future) предусма́тривать.

envoy *n.* **1,** (messenger) посла́нец; по́сланный. **2,** (diplomat) посла́нник.

envy *n.* зáвисть. —*v.t.* завúдовать: *I don't envy him,* я не завúдую емý.
enzyme *n.* фермéнт.
eon *n.* вéчность.
epaulet *also,* **epaulette** *n.* эполéт; эполéта.
ephemeral *adj.* недолговéчный; преходя́щий; эфемéрный.
epic *n.* эпúческая поэ́ма; эпопéя. —*adj.* эпúческий.
epicenter *also,* **epicentre** *n.* эпицéнтр.
epicure *n.* эпикурéец. —**epicurean,** *adj.* эпикурéйский.
epidemic *n.* эпидéмия. —*adj.* эпидемúческий.
epidermis *n.* эпидéрмис.
epiglottis *n.* надгортáнник.
epigram *n.* эпигрáмма. —**epigrammatic,** *adj.* эпиграмматúческий.
epigraph *n.* **1,** (inscription) нáдпись; эпúграф. **2,** (opening quotation) эпúграф.
epilepsy *n.* эпилéпсия. —**epileptic,** *adj.* эпилептúческий. —*n.* эпилéптик.
epilogue *n.* эпилóг; послеслóвие.
Epiphany *n.* крещéние; богоявлéние.
episcopal *adj.* епúскопский.
Episcopalian *adj.* епископáльный. —*n.* член епископáльной цéркви.
episode *n.* эпизóд. —**episodic,** *adj.* эпизодúческий.
epistemology *n.* теóрия познáния.
epistle *n.* эпúстола. —**epistolary,** *adj.* эпистоля́рный.
epitaph *n.* надгрóбная нáдпись; эпитáфия.
epithelium *n.* эпитéлий. —**epithelial,** *adj.* эпителиáльный.
epithet *n.* **1,** (descriptive word or phrase) эпúтет. **2,** (disparaging word or phrase) ругáтельство. *Hurl epithets at,* осыпáть (когó-нибудь) брáнью.
epitome *n.* **1,** (perfect example; embodiment) воплощéние. **2,** (summary) конспéкт.
epitomize *v.t.* **1,** (typify) воплощáть. **2,** (summarize) конспектúровать.
epoch *n.* эпóха. —**epochal,** *adj.* эпохáльный.
Epsom salt *also,* **Epsom salts** англúйская соль.
equable *adj.* **1,** (not fluctuating) рóвный; равномéрный. **2,** (tranquil; serene) рóвный; уравновéшенный.
equal *adj.* рáвный: *equal parts,* рáвные чáсти. *Equal rights,* равнопрáвие. *In equal measure,* в рáвной мéре. *Other things being equal,* при прóчих рáвных услóвиях. —*v.t.* **1,** (be equal to) равня́ться (+ *dat.*): *six plus three equals nine,* шесть плюс три равня́ется (*or* равнó) девятú. *Let x equal y,* пусть икс рáвен úгреку. **2,** (duplicate; tie) повторя́ть: *equal a record,* повторя́ть рекóрд. —*n.* рáвный: *he has no equal,* емý нет рáвного; он не имéет себé рáвного. *Treat someone as an equal,* относúться к комý-нибудь как к рáвному. —**equal to,** на высотé (+ *gen.*): *equal to the occasion,* на высотé положéния. *He is not equal to the task,* э́та задáча емý не под сúлу.
equality *n.* рáвенство.
equalize *v.t.* урáвнивать. —**equalization,** *n.* уравнéние.
equally *adv.* **1,** (in equal parts) пóровну. **2,** (uniformly) одинáково; в рáвной мéре; в одинáковой мéре. **3,** (by the same token) рáвным óбразом.
equal sign знак равéнства.
equanimity *n.* спокóйствие; самообладáние; хладнокрóвие.
equate *v.t.* равня́ть; прирáвнивать.
equation *n.* уравнéние.
equator *n.* эквáтор. —**equatorial,** *adj.* экваториáльный.
equestrian *adj.* кóнный.
equiangular *adj.* равноугóльный.
equidistant *adj.* на рáвном расстоя́нии.
equilateral *adj.* равносторóнний.
equilibrium *n.* равновéсие.
equine *adj.* лошадúный.
equinox *n.* равнодéнствие.
equip *v.t.* оборýдовать; снаряжáть; оснащáть. —**equipment,** *n.* оборýдование; снаряжéние.
equitable *adj.* справедлúвый; беспристрáстный.
equity *n.* **1,** (fairness) справедлúвость. **2,** *finance* актúвы.
equivalent *adj.* равносúльный; равнознáчный; эквивалéнтный. —*n.* эквивалéнт. —**equivalence,** *n.* эквивалéнтность.
equivocal *adj.* двусмы́сленный.
equivocate *v.i.* увúливать; виля́ть. —**equivocation,** *n.* двусмы́сленность; уклóнчивость. *Without equivocation,* недвусмы́сленно.
era *n.* э́ра; эпóха.
eradicate *v.t.* **1,** (destroy; wipe out) уничтожáть: *eradicate pests,* уничтожáть вредúтелей. **2,** *fig.* (eliminate; put an end to) искореня́ть, уничтожáть, ликвидúровать. —**eradication,** *n.* искоренéние; уничтожéние; ликвидáция.
erase *v.t.* **1,** (rub out) стирáть. *Erase the blackboard,* стирáть с доскú. **2,** (obliterate, as from one's mind) изглáживать (из пáмяти).
eraser *n.* **1,** (for something written in pencil) резúнка; лáстик. **2,** (for blackboards) тря́пка.
erasure *n.* подчúстка.
erbium *n.* э́рбий.
ere *prep., poetic* до; пéред. —*conj., poetic* прéжде чем.
erect *adj.* стоя́чий: *erect position,* стоя́чее положéние. *Stand erect,* держáться пря́мо. *With one's head erect,* с пóднятой головóй. —*v.t.* (build) сооружáть; возводúть; воздвигáть.
erection *n.* **1,** (construction) сооружéние; возведéние. **2,** *physiol.* эрéкция.
erg *n.* эрг.
ergo *adv.* слéдовательно.
ergot *n.* спорынья́.
ermine *n.* горностáй. —*adj.* горностáевый.
erode *v.t.* **1,** (wear away, as of the wind) вывéтривать. **2,** (wash away, as of water) размывáть. **3,** (eat into, as of acid) разъедáть. —*v.i.* вывéтриваться.
erosion *n.* эрóзия; вывéтривание; размы́в.
erotic *adj.* эротúческий. —**eroticism,** *n.* эротúзм.
err *v.i.* ошибáться; заблуждáться.
errand *n.* поручéние. *Run errands for,* быть у когó-нибудь на посы́лках *or* на побегýшках. —**errand boy,** рассы́льный.
errant *adj.* **1,** (wandering) стрáнствующий; блуждáющий. **2,** (having gone astray) заблýдший; сбúвшийся с путú.
erratic *adj.* неустóйчивый; нерóвный.
erratum *n.* опечáтка.
erroneous *adj.* ошúбочный; невéрный; лóжный. —**erroneously,** *adv.* ошúбочно; по ошúбке.

error *n.* ошибка. *Be in error,* ошибáться; заблуждáться.
ersatz *adj.* суррогáтный.
erstwhile *adj.* прéжний.
erudite *adj.* учёный; знáющий; эрудúрованный. —**erudition,** *n.* эрудúция; учёность; начúтанность.
erupt *v.i.* **1,** (of a volcano) извергáться. **2,** (of a rash) высыпáть; выступáть. **3,** *fig.* (of an argument, fight, etc.) вспы́хивать.
eruption *n.* **1,** (of a volcano) извержéние. **2,** (rash) сыпь.
erysipelas *n.* рóжа.
escalate *v.i.* перерастáть. —**escalation,** *n.* перерастáние; эскалáция.
escalator *n.* эскалáтор.
escapade *n.* вы́ходка; продéлка.
escape *v.i.* **1,** (get free) бежáть; убегáть. *Escape from prison,* бежáть из тюрьмы́. **2,** (avoid injury, danger, etc.) спасáться. *He barely escaped,* он едвá спáсся; он едвá нóги унёс. *Escape with minor injuries,* отдéлаться лёгкими ранéниями. **3,** (leak out; seep out) утекáть; вытекáть. *Gas escaped from the pipe,* газ утекáл из трубы́. —*v.t.* **1,** (manage to avoid) спасáться от: *escape death,* спасáться от смéрти. *There is no escaping the fact that...,* никудá не уйтú от тогó, что... **2,** (be unnoticed or forgotten by) ускользáть от: *escape someone's notice,* ускользáть от чьегó-нибудь внимáния. *Nothing escapes him,* от негó ничтó не укрóется. *His name escapes me,* не могу́ припóмнить егó úмени. **3,** (slip out inadvertently, as from one's lips) срывáться (с языкá). —*n.* **1,** (breaking out) побéг; бéгство. **2,** (avoidance of near disaster) спасéние: *miraculous escape,* чудéсное спасéние. *Have a narrow escape,* едвá спастúсь.
escarpment *n.* откóс; *mil.* эскáрп.
eschew *v.t.* сторонúться; чуждáться.
escort *n.* **1,** (one who accompanies) провожáтый. **2,** (for a lady) кавалéр. **3,** (armed guard) конвóир. *Under police escort,* под конвóем полицéйских. **4,** *mil.* (single ship or plane) конвóир; конвóйный; (a number of ships or planes) конвóй; эскóрт. —*v.t.* **1,** (accompany) сопровождáть; провожáть. **2,** *mil.* конвоúровать; эскортúровать.
escutcheon *n.* щит гербá.
Eskimo *n.* эскимóс. —*adj.* эскимóсский.
esophagus *also,* **oesophagus** *n.* пищевóд.
esoteric *adj.* малодосту́пный; зау́мный.
espalier *n.* шпалéра.
especial *adj.* осóбенный; осóбый.
especially *adv.* **1,** (to a particularly large degree) осóбенно: *especially pleased,* осóбенно рад. *What especially struck me,* что меня́ осóбенно поразúло. **2,** (specifically) специáльно: *especially for you,* специáльно для вас. *I came especially to...,* я пришёл специáльно для тогó, чтóбы... **3,** (the more so) осóбенно: *especially now/if/when,* осóбенно тепéрь/éсли/когдá. *Especially since...,* тем бóлее, что...
Esperanto *n.* эсперáнто.
espionage *n.* шпионáж. —*adj.* шпиóнский: *espionage activity,* шпиóнская дéятельность.
esplanade *n.* эспланáда.
espouse *v.t.* выступáть за; поддéрживать; отстáивать. —**espousal,** *n.* поддéржка.
espy *v.t.* рассмотрéть; разглядéть.
esquire *n.* эсквáйр.
essay *n.* óчерк. —*v.t.* **1,** (try out) прóбовать. **2,** (attempt) пытáться. —**essayist,** *n.* очеркúст.
essence *n.* **1,** (fundamental nature; heart; crux) су́щность; существó; суть. **2,** (extract) эссéнция. —**in essence,** в су́щности; по существу́; по су́ти дéла.
essential *adj.* **1,** (absolutely necessary) необходúмый. **2,** (fundamental) существéнный: *an essential difference,* существéнная рáзница. —*n., usu. pl.* **1,** (necessities) необходúмое: *the barest essentials,* сáмое необходúмое. **2,** (heart; crux) суть: *get down to the essentials,* добрáться до су́ти дéла. **3,** (fundamentals) оснóвы; элемéнты.
essentially *adv.* в су́щности; по существу́.
essential oil эфúрное мáсло.
establish *v.t.* **1,** (found) оснóвывать: *establish a museum/newspaper,* основáть музéй/газéту. **2,** (bring about; set up) устанáвливать: *establish order/relations/a dictatorship/,* установúть порядок/отношéния/диктату́ру. **3,** (ascertain; prove) устанáвливать: *establish a fact/the cause of something/one's innocence/,* установúть факт/причúну чегó-нибудь /свою́ невинóвность/. —**establish oneself,** устрáиваться.
establishment *n.* **1,** (act of establishing) установлéние; основáние. **2,** (institution) учреждéние; заведéние.
estate *n.* **1,** (piece of landed property) имéние; помéстье; усáдьба. **2,** (possessions of a deceased person) иму́щество; состоя́ние. **3,** (social class in feudal times) сослóвие.
esteem *v.t.* **1,** (respect) уважáть; ценúть. **2,** (regard; deem) считáть. —*n.* уважéние; почёт. *Hold in high esteem,* высокó ценúть. *Be held in high esteem,* пóльзоваться почётом.
esthete *also,* **aesthete** *n.* эстéт. —**esthetic,** *adj.* эстетúческий. —**esthetics,** *n.* эстéтика.
estimable *adj.* достóйный уважéния; уважáемый; многоуважáемый.
estimate *v.t.* оцéнивать; исчислять. *Estimate the distance,* определя́ть расстоя́ние глазомéром. *Estimated cost,* смéтная стóимость. —*n.* оцéнка; смéта.
estimation *n.* мнéние; суждéние. *Go up in someone's estimation,* вы́играть в чьём-нибудь мнéнии; вы́расти в чьúх-нибудь глазáх. *Go down in someone's estimation,* терять *or* проигрáть в чьём-нибудь мнéнии.
Estonian *adj.* эстóнский. —*n.* **1,** (person) эстóнец; эстóнка. **2,** (language) эстóнский язы́к.
estrange *v.t.* отдаля́ть; отчуждáть; разобщáть. —**estrangement,** *n.* отдалéние; отчуждéние.
estuary *n.* лимáн.
et cetera и так дáлее; и тому́ подóбное.
etch *v.t.* гравировáть; травúть.
etcher *n.* гравёр.
etching *n.* **1,** (process) гравировáние; травлéние. **2,** (figure so made) гравю́ра; офóрт.
eternal *adj.* вéчный. —**eternally,** *adv.* вéчно.
eternity *n.* вéчность. *Seem like an eternity,* казáться вéчностью.
ether *n.* эфúр. —**ethereal,** *adj.* эфúрный.
ethical *adj.* этúческий; этúчный.
ethics *n.pl.* э́тика.
Ethiopian *adj.* эфиóпский. —*n.* эфиóп; эфиóпка.
ethnic *adj.* этнúческий.
ethnography *n.* этногрáфия. —**ethnographer,** *n.*

этно́граф. —**ethnographic,** *adj.* этнографи́ческий.
ethnology *n.* этноло́гия. —**ethnological,** *adj.* этнологи́ческий. —**ethnologist,** *n.* этно́лог.
ethyl *n.* эти́л. —*adj.* эти́ловый. —**ethyl alcohol,** эти́ловый *or* ви́нный спирт.
ethylene *n.* этиле́н.
etiquette *n.* этике́т.
Etruscan *adj.* этру́сский.
étude *n.* этю́д.
etymology *n.* этимоло́гия. —**etymological,** *adj.* этимологи́ческий. —**etymologist,** *n.* этимо́лог.
eucalyptus *n.* эвкали́пт. —*adj.* эвкали́птовый.
Eucharist *n.* прича́стие; евхари́стия.
eugenics *n.* евге́ника. —**eugenic,** *adj.* евгени́ческий.
eulogize *v.t.* восхваля́ть. —**eulogy,** *n.* надгро́бная речь; надгро́бное сло́во; панеги́рик.
eunuch *n.* е́внух.
euphemism *n.* эвфеми́зм. —**euphemistic,** *adj.* эвфемисти́ческий. —**euphemistically,** *adv.* для прили́чия: *euphemistically called...,* для прили́чия называ́емый...
euphonic *adj.* благозву́чный.
euphonious *adj.* благозву́чный. —**euphoniousness,** *n.* благозву́чность.
euphony *n.* благозву́чие.
euphoria *n.* эйфори́я.
Eurasian *adj.* еврази́йский.
eureka *interj.* э́врика!
European *adj.* европе́йский. —*n.* европе́ец. *The Europeans,* европе́йцы.
europium *n.* евро́пий.
Eustachian tube евста́хиева труба́.
evacuate *v.t.* **1,** (remove) эвакуи́ровать. **2,** (vacate) освобожда́ть. **3,** (excrete) выделя́ть. —**evacuation,** *n.* эвакуа́ция. —**evacuee,** *n.* эвакуи́рованный.
evade *v.t.* избега́ть; уклоня́ться от; ускольза́ть от.
evaluate *v.t.* оце́нивать. —**evaluation,** *n.* оце́нка.
evanescent *adj.* мимолётный; мину́тный.
evangelical *adj.* евангели́ческий.
evangelist *n.* **1,** *cap., Bib.* евангели́ст. **2,** (preacher) пропове́дник.
evaporate *v.t.* испаря́ть. —*v.i.* испаря́ться; улету́чиваться. —**evaporated milk,** сгущённое молоко́.
evaporation *n.* испаре́ние.
evasion *n.* **1,** (avoidance) уклоне́ние: *evasion of military service,* уклоне́ние от вое́нной слу́жбы. *Tax evasion,* уклоне́ние от упла́ты нало́гов. **2,** (subterfuge) уло́вка; увёртка.
evasive *adj.* укло́нчивый. —**evasiveness,** *n.* укло́нчивость.
eve *n.* кану́н. *On the eve of,* в кану́н (+ *gen.*); накану́не (+ *gen.*). —**Christmas Eve,** соче́льник. —**New Year's Eve,** кану́н Но́вого го́да.
even *adj.* **1,** (level) ро́вный: *even ground,* ро́вная земля́. **2,** (uniform) ро́вный; равноме́рный. **3,** (calm; tranquil) ро́вный; уравнове́шенный. **4,** *fol. by* **with** (flush with) вро́вень с. **5,** (divisible by 2) чётный: *even number,* чётное число́. **6,** (exact) *rendered by* то́чно: *an even dozen,* то́чно дю́жина. **7,** (having settled debts, scores, etc.) кви́ты; в расчёте: *now we are even,* тепе́рь мы с ва́ми кви́ты/в расчёте/. —*adv.* да́же: *even in winter,* да́же зимо́й. *What is even worse...,* что ещё ху́же... —*v.t.* **1,** (smooth; level) выра́внивать; ровня́ть. **2,** (equalize) равня́ть. *Even the score,* сравня́ть счёт. —*v.i.* [*usu.* **even out**] выра́вниваться. —**break even,** оста́ться при свои́х. —**even if,** да́же е́сли; хотя́ бы. —**even so,** всё равно́; хоть бы и так. —**even though,** хотя́ и. —**get even with,** распла́чиваться с; рассчи́тываться с; расквита́ться с.
even-handed *adj.* беспристра́стный.
evening *n.* ве́чер. *In the evening,* ве́чером. *This evening,* сего́дня ве́чером. *Good evening!,* до́брый ве́чер! —*adj.* вече́рний: *evening dress,* вече́рнее пла́тье.
evenly *adv.* ро́вно. *Divide evenly,* дели́ть по́ровну. *Evenly matched teams,* равноси́льные кома́нды.
evenness *n.* ро́вность.
event *n.* **1,** (occurrence) собы́тие. **2,** (item on a sports program) но́мер. —**in any event,** во вся́ком слу́чае. —**in the event of,** в слу́чае (+ *gen.*). —**in the event that,** в том слу́чае, е́сли...
even-tempered *adj.* уравнове́шенный.
eventful *adj.* по́лный собы́тий.
eventual *adj.* коне́чный: *the eventual outcome,* коне́чный исхо́д.
eventuality *n.* (возмо́жный) слу́чай; случа́йность.
eventually *adv.* в конце́ концо́в.
eventuate *v.i.* **1,** *fol. by* **in** (result in) ко́нчиться (+ *instr.*). **2,** (develop; happen) получи́ться; случи́ться.
ever *adv.* **1,** (at any time) когда́-нибудь; когда́-либо: *have you ever been there?,* вы когда́-нибудь быва́ли там? *The best film I ever saw,* са́мый лу́чший фильм, кото́рый я когда́-либо ви́дел. *More than ever before,* бо́льше чем когда́-либо ра́ньше. ♦ *In neg. constructions* никогда́: *no one has ever been there,* никто́ никогда́ не́ был там. **2,** (at all times) всегда́: *as ever,* как всегда́. —*particle: thank you ever so much!,* большо́е вам спаси́бо! *What ever do you mean by that?,* что же, со́бственно, вы хоти́те э́тим сказа́ть? —**ever since,** с тех пор (как). —**hardly ever,** почти́ никогда́.
evergreen *adj.* вечнозелёный. —*n.* вечнозелёное расте́ние.
everlasting *adj.* ве́чный.
ever-present *adj.* безотлу́чный.
every *adj.* **1,** (each) ка́ждый: *every day,* ка́ждый день. **2,** (all possible) все: *have every reason to suppose,* име́ть все основа́ния предполага́ть. **3,** (each sequentially) ка́ждый: *every three hours,* ка́ждые три часа́; *every few minutes,* ка́ждые не́сколько мину́т. —**every now and then; every once in a while; every so often,** вре́мя от вре́мени. —**every one,** все без исключе́ния. —**every other,** че́рез; ка́ждый второ́й; ка́ждые два: *every other day,* че́рез день. —**every time,** вся́кий раз. *Every time he speaks,* вся́кий раз, когда́ он говори́т. —**every which way,** *colloq.* врассыпну́ю; врозь. —**in every way, 1,** (in every respect) во всех отноше́ниях. **2,** (using every method) вся́чески.
everybody *pron.* все.
everyday *adj.* повседне́вный; жите́йский; бу́дничный. *Everyday occurrence,* обы́чное явле́ние.
everyone *pron.* все.
everything *pron.* всё: *everything is all right,* всё в поря́дке. *There is a time for everything,* всему́ своё вре́мя.
everywhere *adv.* везде́; всю́ду; повсю́ду. *Every-*

where we went, всю́ду, куда́ мы приезжа́ли. *From everywhere,* отовсю́ду.

evict *v.t.* выселя́ть. —**eviction,** *n.* выселе́ние.

evidence *n.* **1,** (something that tends to prove) свиде́тельство; доказа́тельство. **2,** (testimony) показа́ние; свиде́тельство: *give evidence,* дава́ть показа́ние; свиде́тельствовать. **3,** (incriminating information) ули́ки: *there is no evidence against him,* про́тив него́ нет никаки́х ули́к. —*v.t.* **1,** (indicate) свиде́тельствовать о. **2,** (evince) проявля́ть. —**in evidence,** заме́тный; на виду́.

evident *adj.* очеви́дный. —**evidently,** *adv.* очеви́дно; по-ви́димому.

evil *n.* зло: *good and evil,* добро́ и зло. *Choose the lesser of two evils,* из двух зол вы́брать ме́ньшее. —*adj.* злой; дурно́й: *evil spirit,* злой дух; *evil thoughts,* дурны́е мы́сли.

evildoer *n.* злоде́й.

evil eye дурно́й глаз.

evince *v.t.* проявля́ть; выка́зывать.

eviscerate *v.t.* потроши́ть.

evoke *v.t.* вызыва́ть.

evolution *n.* эволю́ция. —**evolutionary,** *adj.* эволюцио́нный.

evolve *v.t.* развива́ть; разраба́тывать. —*v.i.* развива́ться; эволюциони́ровать.

ewe *n.* овца́.

ex- *prefix* бы́вший: *ex-president,* бы́вший президе́нт.

exacerbate *v.t.* обостря́ть. —**exacerbation,** *n.* обостре́ние.

exact *adj.* то́чный: *exact copy,* то́чная ко́пия; *exact meaning,* то́чный смысл. —*v.t.* взы́скивать. *Exact payment,* взима́ть пла́ту. *Exact tribute,* налага́ть дань.

exacting *adj.* тре́бовательный; взыска́тельный.

exactitude *n.* то́чность.

exactly *adv.* **1,** (in an exact manner) то́чно. **2,** (just) как раз: *exactly what I need,* как раз то, что мне ну́жно. **3,** (specifically) и́менно: *where exactly does he live?,* где и́менно он живёт? **4,** (quite so) вот и́менно; соверше́нно ве́рно. —**not exactly,** не совсе́м; (э́то) не совсе́м так.

exactness *n.* то́чность.

exaggerate *v.t. & i.* преувели́чивать. —**exaggeration,** *n.* преувеличе́ние.

exalt *v.t.* **1,** (raise in status) возвыша́ть. **2,** (glorify) возвели́чивать. **3,** (extol) восхваля́ть.

exaltation *n.* восто́рг; упое́ние; экзальта́ция.

exalted *adj.* высо́кий; возвы́шенный.

examination *n.* **1,** (scrutiny) осмо́тр; рассмотре́ние. *Physical examination,* медици́нский осмо́тр. **2,** (test of knowledge) экза́мен. —**examination paper,** экзаменацио́нная рабо́та.

examine *v.t.* **1,** (scrutinize) осма́тривать; рассма́тривать. *Examine a patient,* осма́тривать больно́го. **2,** (give a test to) экзаменова́ть.

examiner *n.* **1,** (inspector) контролёр. **2,** (one who gives an examination) экзамена́тор.

example *n.* приме́р. —**for example,** наприме́р.

exasperate *v.t.* выводи́ть из себя́; изводи́ть; донима́ть. —**exasperating,** *adj.* доса́дный. —**exasperation,** *n.* доса́да; раздраже́ние.

excavate *v.t.* раска́пывать. —**excavation,** *n.* раско́пка; *pl.* раско́пки.

exceed *v.t.* **1,** (be more than; go beyond) превыша́ть: *exceed ten dollars,* превыша́ть де́сять до́лларов; *exceed the speed limit,* превыша́ть дозво́ленную ско́рость. **2,** (surpass) превосходи́ть: *exceed all expectations,* превосходи́ть все ожида́ния. —**exceedingly,** *adv.* чрезвыча́йно.

excel *v.t.* превосходи́ть. —*v.i.* выдава́ться; выделя́ться; отлича́ться.

exellence *n.* высо́кое ка́чество. *For excellence in studies,* за отли́чную учёбу.

Excellency *n.* превосходи́тельство: *Your Excellency,* ва́ше превосходи́тельство.

excellent *adj.* отли́чный; прекра́сный; превосхо́дный. —**excellently,** *adv.* отли́чно.

excelsior *n.* стру́жка.

except *prep.* кро́ме; за исключе́нием (+ *gen.*). *Every day except Sunday,* ка́ждый день, кро́ме воскресе́нья. —*conj.* кро́ме как; ра́зве то́лько: *except in the summertime,* кро́ме как (*or* ра́зве то́лько) в ле́тнее вре́мя. —*v.t.* исключа́ть. *Present company excepted,* исключа́я прису́тствующих. —**except for,** за исключе́нием (+ *gen.*); е́сли не счита́ть.

excepting *prep.* исключа́я; за исключе́нием (+ *gen.*).

exception *n.* исключе́ние. *With the exception of,* за исключе́нием (+ *gen.*). *Make an exception in your case,* де́лать исключе́ние для вас. —**take exception to, 1,** (take issue with) возража́ть про́тив. **2,** (take offense at) обижа́ться на.

exceptional *adj.* исключи́тельный. —**exceptionally,** *adv.* исключи́тельно.

excerpt *n.* вы́держка; отры́вок; вы́писка. —*v.t.* выпи́сывать; выбира́ть (отры́вки).

excess *n.* **1,** (surplus) изли́шек; избы́ток. **2,** *usu. pl.* (instances of immoderation) изли́шества; переги́бы; эксце́ссы. —*adj.* ли́шний: *excess weight,* ли́шний вес. *Excess profits,* сверхпри́быль. *Pay for excess baggage,* доплати́ть за ли́шний вес. —**in excess of,** сверх (+ *gen*); свы́ше (+ *gen.*). —**to excess,** до изли́шества. *Drink to excess,* перепива́ть.

excessive *adj.* чрезме́рный; непоме́рный; изли́шний. —**excessively,** *adv.* чрезме́рно.

exchange *v.t.* **1,** (trade for another) меня́ть; обме́нивать: *exchange one book for another,* меня́ть/обме́нивать одну́ кни́гу на другу́ю. **2,** (interchange) меня́ться; обме́ниваться (+ *instr.*): *exchange gifts,* меня́ться/обме́ниваться пода́рками. **3,** (change, as money) разме́нивать. —*n.* **1,** (swap) обме́н: *exchange of views,* обме́н мне́ниями *or* взгля́дами. *In exchange for,* в обме́н на. **2,** (central place for brokers, merchants, etc.) би́ржа: *stock exchange,* фо́ндовая би́ржа. **3,** *finance* валю́та: *foreign exchange,* иностра́нная валю́та. *Bill of exchange,* ве́ксель. *Rate of exchange,* валю́тный курс.

exchequer *n.* казначе́йство; казна́.

excise *n.* [*also,* **excise tax**] акци́з. —*v.t.* **1,** *med.* выреза́ть; иссека́ть. **2,** (delete) исключа́ть; вычёркивать. —**excision,** *n., med.* иссече́ние,

excitable *adj.* возбуди́мый. —**excitability,** *n.* возбуди́мость.

excitation *n.* возбужде́ние.

excite *v.t.* **1,** (rouse; stir up) возбужда́ть; волнова́ть. **2,** (evoke) возбужда́ть; вызыва́ть.

excited *adj.* возбуждённый; взволно́ванный. *Get excited,* волнова́ться.

excitement *n.* возбуждéние; волнéние.
exciting *adj.* волнýющий; захвáтывающий.
exclaim *v.t. & i.* восклицáть.
exclamation *n.* восклицáние. —**exclamation point,** восклицáтельный знак.
exclamatory *adj.* восклицáтельный.
exclude *v.t.* исключáть. —**excluding,** *prep.* исключáя. —**exclusion,** *n.* исключéние.
exclusive *adj.* **1,** (sole) исключúтельный: *exclusive right,* исключúтельное прáво. **2,** (admitting only a select group) для úзбранных. —**exclusive of,** не считáя; исключáя.
exclusively *adv.* исключúтельно.
excommunicate *v.t.* отлучáть от цéркви. —**excommunication,** *n.* отлучéние (от цéркви).
excoriate *v.t.* осуждáть; разносúть.
excrement *n.* испражнéния; кал.
excrescence *n.* нарóст; (*on trees*) наплы́в.
excrete *v.t.* выделя́ть. —**excretion,** *n.* выделéние. —**excretory,** *adj.* выделúтельный; выводнóй.
excruciating *adj.* мучúтельный.
exculpate *v.t.* оправдывать.
excursion *n.* экскýрсия. —*adj.* экскурсиóнный.
excusable *adj.* простúтельный; извинúтельный.
excuse *v.t.* **1,** (forgive; pardon) извиня́ть; прощáть. *Excuse me!,* извинúте!; простúте! *Excuse the interruption!,* извинúте/простúте за беспокóйство! **2,** (justify; make all right) опрáвдывать. **3,** (release; let off) освобождáть: *excuse from classes,* освобождáть от заня́тий. —*n.* **1,** (pretext) отговóрка; предлóг. **2,** (valid reason) извинéние; оправдáние. —**excuse oneself,** извиня́ться; просúть прощéния.
execrable *adj.* отвратúтельный; гнýсный.
execrate *v.t.* **1,** (denounce) проклинáть. **2,** (detest) ненавúдеть.
execute *v.t.* **1,** (carry out; perform) выполня́ть; исполня́ть. **2,** (put to death) казнúть.
execution *n.* **1,** (carrying out; performance) выполнéние; исполнéние. **2,** (putting to death) казнь.
executioner *n.* палáч.
executive *adj.* **1,** (exercising authority) исполнúтельный: *executive committee,* исполнúтельный комитéт. **2,** (of an executive) административный: *executive duties,* администратúвные обя́занности. —*n.* руководя́щий рабóтник.
executor *n.* душеприкáзчик.
exemplary *adj.* примéрный; образцóвый.
exemplify *v.t.* служúть примéром (+ *gen.*).
exempt *v.t.* освобождáть. —*adj.* [*usu.* **exempt from**] освобождённый (от); не подлежáщий (+ *dat.*).
exemption *n.* **1,** (act of exempting) освобождéние. **2,** (tax deduction) льгóта (по налóгу).
exercise *n.* **1,** (physical activity) физúческие упражнéния; заря́дка; моциóн. *Do one's exercises,* дéлать заря́дку. *You should get more exercise,* вам нýжно бóльше физúческих упражнéний. **2,** (that which develops proficiency) упражнéние: *exercises for the piano,* упражнéния для фортепья́но. **3,** (performance, as of duties) исполнéние; отправлéние. **4,** (act of using or exerting) осуществлéние; применéние. **5,** *pl.* (ceremonies) торжествá. *Graduation exercises,* выпускнóй акт. **6,** *mil.* учéние. —*v.t.* **1,** (drill; train) упражня́ть. **2,** (execute; discharge, as duties) исполня́ть; выполня́ть. **3,** (use; put into play) осуществля́ть; применя́ть: *exercise a right,* осуществля́ть прáво; *exercise authority,* применя́ть власть. **4,** (display, as caution, patience, etc.) проявля́ть. **5,** (exert, as influence) окáзывать. **6,** (worry; upset) расстрáивать. —*v.i.* дéлать моциóн; дéлать заря́дку.
exert *v.t.* **1,** (strain) напрягáть. *Exert oneself,* напрягáться. *Exert every effort,* прилагáть все усúлия; напрягáть все сúлы. **2,** (exercise; bring to bear) окáзывать: *exert pressure,* окáзывать давлéние.
exertion *n.* напряжéние.
exhale *v.t. & i.* выдыхáть. —**exhalation,** *n.* вы́дох; выдыхáние.
exhaust *v.t.* **1,** (tire out) изнуря́ть; истощáть. **2,** (use up; deplete) исчéрпывать; истощáть: *exhaust supplies,* исчéрпывать/истощáть запáсы. *My patience is exhausted,* моё терпéние кóнчилось *or* лóпнуло. **3,** (deal with completely) исчéрпывать: *exhaust a subject,* исчéрпывать тéму. —*n., mech.* вы́хлоп. —*adj.* выхлопнóй; вытяжнóй: *exhaust pipe,* выхлопнáя трубá; *exhaust fan,* вытяжнóй вентиля́тор.
exhausted *adj.* **1,** (tired out) изнурённый; измýченный. *Be exhausted,* замýчиться; вы́биться из сил; быть без ног. **2,** (depleted) исчéрпанный; истощённый.
exhausting *adj.* утомúтельный; изнурúтельный.
exhaustion *n.* **1,** (extreme fatigue) изнурéние; истощéние; изнеможéние. **2,** (depletion) истощéние.
exhaustive *adj.* исчéрпывающий.
exhibit *v.t.* **1,** (put on show) выставля́ть; экспонúровать. **2,** (manifest; give evidence of) проявля́ть. —*n.* экспонáт.
exhibition *n.* **1,** (display; manifestation) проявлéние. **2,** (public display) вы́ставка: *exhibition of paintings,* вы́ставка картúн.
exhibitor *n.* экспонéнт.
exhilarate *v.t.* развеселúть; оживля́ть. —**exhilaration,** *n.* весёлость; припóднятое настроéние.
exhort *v.t.* призывáть; увещевáть. —**exhortation,** *n.* увещáние.
exhume *v.t.* выкáпывать; вырывáть.
exigency *n.* **1,** (urgency) неотлóжность. **2,** (urgent situation) (крáйний) слýчай. **3,** *pl.* (requirements) потрéбности.
exile *n.* **1,** (banishment) изгнáние; ссы́лка. **2,** (one who is exiled) изгнáнник; ссы́льный. —*v.t.* изгоня́ть; ссылáть.
exist *v.i.* существовáть.
existence *n.* существовáние. *Come into existence,* возникáть; появля́ться. *Go out of existence,* перестáть существовáть. *The best plane in existence,* сáмый лýчший самолёт из всех существýющих. *Lead a miserable existence,* влачúть жáлкое существовáние.
existent *adj.* существýющий.
existential *adj.* экзистенциáльный. —**existentialism,** *n.* экзистенциалúзм. —**existentialist,** *adj.* экзистенциáльный. —*n.* экзистенциалúст.
exit *n.* вы́ход. *Exit visa,* выезднáя вúза. —*v.i.* **1,** (go out) выходúть. **2,** (stage direction) "он/онá ухóдит"
exodus *n.* **1,** (outpouring of people) (мáссовый) отъéзд. **2,** *cap., Bib.* исхóд; (*book*) Исхóд.
exonerate *v.t.* оправдывать. —**exoneration,** *n.* оправдáние.
exorbitant *adj.* непомéрный.

exorcise *also,* **exorcize** *v.t.* изгоня́ть (злых ду́хов). —**exorcism,** *n.* изгна́ние злых ду́хов.

exotic *adj.* экзоти́ческий.

expand *v.t.* **1,** (enlarge; extend) расширя́ть. **2,** *math.* разлага́ть. —*v.i.* **1,** (become larger) расширя́ться. **2,** *fol. by* **on** (discuss more fully) распространя́ться на (те́му).

expanse *n.* простра́нство; просто́р; ширь.

expansion *n.* **1,** (enlargement) расшире́ние. **2,** (extension of one's territory) экспа́нсия.

expansionism *n.* экспансиони́зм. —**expansionist,** *adj.* экспансиони́стский; захва́тнический.

expansive *adj.* экспанси́вный.

expatiate *v.i.* распространя́ться (о).

expatriate *n.* экспатриа́нт. —*v.t.* экспатрии́ровать. —**expatriation,** *n.* экспатриа́ция.

expect *v.t.* **1,** (anticipate) ожида́ть; ждать: *be expecting company,* ожида́ть *or* ждать госте́й. *It was to be expected,* э́того сле́довало ожида́ть. **2,** *fol. by inf.* (plan; intend) ду́мать; предполага́ть; рассчи́тывать. **3,** (consider due or obligated) тре́бовать: *expect too much of,* тре́бовать сли́шком мно́го от. —**be expecting,** ждать *or* ожида́ть ребёнка; быть в положе́нии.

expectancy *n.* ожида́ние; предвкуше́ние. —**life expectancy,** продолжи́тельность жи́зни.

expectant *adj.* ожида́ющий. *Expectant mother,* бере́менная же́нщина.

expectation *n.* ожида́ние: *contrary to all expectations,* вопреки́ всем ожида́ниям.

expectorate *v.i.* **1,** (cough up phlegm) отха́ркиваться. **2,** (spit) ха́ркать. —*v.t.* отха́ркивать.

expedient *adj.* целесообра́зный; вы́годный. —**expediency,** *n.* целесообра́зность.

expedite *v.t.* **1,** (speed up) ускоря́ть. *Expedite a matter,* продви́нуть де́ло. **2,** (do quickly) (бы́стро) выполня́ть.

expedition *n.* экспеди́ция. —**expeditionary,** *adj.* экспедицио́нный.

expeditious *adj.* бы́стрый; ско́рый.

expel *v.t.* **1,** (discharge; eject) выбра́сывать; изверга́ть. *Expel air from the lungs,* выпуска́ть во́здух из лёгких. **2,** (dismiss) исключа́ть; выгоня́ть.

expend *v.t.* тра́тить; затра́чивать; расхо́довать.

expenditure *n.* **1,** (act of expending) затра́та; расхо́дование. **2,** (that which is expended) тра́та; затра́та; расхо́д.

expense *n.* **1,** (financial outlay) расхо́д. *Go to expense,* тра́тить де́ньги; тра́титься. *Put to expense,* вводи́ть в расхо́д. *At one's own expense,* на свои́ сре́дства. **2,** *pl.* (costs) расхо́ды; изде́ржки; затра́ты. —**at the expense of,** за *or* на счёт (+ *gen.*): *at government expense,* за казённый счёт. *Jokes at my expense,* шу́тки на мой счёт *or* по моему́ а́дресу.

expensive *adj.* дорого́й.

experience *n.* **1,** (accumulated knowledge) о́пыт. **2,** (something lived through) пережива́ние. —*v.t.* испы́тывать; пережива́ть. —**experienced,** *adj.* о́пытный.

experiment *n.* о́пыт; экспериме́нт. —*v. i.* производи́ть о́пыты; эксперименти́ровать.

experimental *adj.* эксперимента́льный; о́пытный. —**experimentation,** *n.* эксперименти́рование.

expert *n.* экспе́рт; специали́ст; знато́к. —*adj.* иску́сный; о́пытный. *Expert advice,* экспе́ртный сове́т.

expertise *n.* специа́льные зна́ния.

expiate *v.t.* искупа́ть. —**expiation,** *n.* искупле́ние. —**expiatory,** *adj.* искупи́тельный.

expiration *n.* **1,** (termination) истече́ние. **2,** (exhalation) выдыха́ние.

expire *v.i.* **1,** (elapse, as of a time period) истека́ть. **2,** (become invalid) теря́ть си́лу. **3,** (exhale) выдыха́ть. **4,** (breathe one's last) испусти́ть дух.

explain *v.t. & i.* объясня́ть. —**explain oneself,** объясня́ть своё поведе́ние.

explainable *adj.* объясни́мый.

explanation *n.* объясне́ние.

explanatory *adj.* объясни́тельный; разъясни́тельный; поясни́тельный. —**explanatory note,** примеча́ние.

expletive *n.* **1,** (imprecation) бра́нное сло́во; руга́тельство. **2,** (word used to fill out a sentence) вставно́е сло́во.

explicable *adj.* объясни́мый.

explicit *adj.* я́сный; то́чный; определённый. —**explicitly,** *adv.* я́сно; недвусмы́сленно.

explode *v.i.* взрыва́ться. —*v.t.* **1,** (set off) взрыва́ть. **2,** *fig.* (refute, as a theory) разбива́ть; уничтожа́ть; опроверга́ть. *Explode a myth,* разве́ять миф.

exploit *v.t.* **1,** (capitalize on; take advantage of) испо́льзовать; по́льзоваться. **2,** (use selfishly for one's own ends) эксплуати́ровать. —*n.* по́двиг. —**exploitation,** *n.* эксплуата́ция. —**exploiter,** *n.* эксплуата́тор.

exploration *n.* **1,** (traveling and studying) иссле́дование. **2,** (prospecting) разве́дка: *exploration for oil,* разве́дка не́фти; нефтеразве́дка.

exploratory *adj.* **1,** (involving research or exploration) иссле́довательский. **2,** *geol.* разве́дочный. **3,** *med.* про́бный: *exploratory operation,* про́бная опера́ция. **4,** *fig.* (sounding out the possibilities) зонди́рующий.

explore *v.t.* **1,** (travel into and study) иссле́довать. **2,** (look into; investigate) изуча́ть; рассма́тривать. —*v.i.* [*usu.* **explore for**] разве́дывать на. —**explorer,** *n.* иссле́дователь.

explosion *n.* взрыв. —**population explosion,** демографи́ческий взрыв.

explosive *adj.* **1,** (liable to explode) взры́вчатый. *Explosive bullet,* разрывна́я пу́ля. **2,** *fig.* (highly volatile) опа́сный; угрожа́ющий. —*n.* взры́вчатое вещество́.

exponent *n.* **1,** (advocate) сторо́нник; пропове́дник. **2,** *math.* показа́тель; экспоне́нт.

export *v.t.* вывози́ть; экспорти́ровать. —*n., often pl.* вы́воз; э́кспорт. —*adj.* вывозно́й; э́кспортный.

exportation *n.* вы́воз.

exporter *n.* экспортёр.

expose *v.t.* **1,** (bare) раскрыва́ть. **2,** (deprive of protection) подставля́ть. **3,** (bring to light; unmask) разоблача́ть. **4,** *fol. by* **to** (subject to) подверга́ть (+ *dat.*). *Be exposed to danger,* подверга́ться опа́сности. **5,** *photog.* экспони́ровать.

exposer *n.* обличи́тель; изобличи́тель.

exposition *n.* **1,** (presentation of subject matter) изложе́ние. **2,** (large exhibition) вы́ставка.

expository *adj.* объясни́тельный; разъясни́тельный.

expostulate *v.i.* [*usu.* **expostulate with**] увещева́ть. —**expostulation,** *n.* увеща́ние.

exposure *n.* **1,** (act of exposing) раскры́тие; разоблаче́ние. **2,** (condition of being exposed): *die from exposure,* поги́бнуть от хо́лода. *Avoid excessive exposure to the sun,* возде́рживаться от чрезме́рного пребыва́ния на со́лнце. **3,** (direction faced): *the room has a southern exposure,* ко́мната выхо́дит на юг. **4,** *photog.* вы́держка; экспози́ция. —**exposure meter,** экспози́метр; экспоно́метр.

expound *v.t.* **1,** (set forth) излага́ть. **2,** (interpret) разъясня́ть. —*v.i.* [*usu.* **expound on**] распространя́ться (о).

express *v.t.* выража́ть; выска́зывать. *Express one's opinion,* вы́разить/вы́сказать своё мне́ние. —*adj.* **1,** (explicit) я́сный; то́чный. **2,** (specific) специа́льный: *for the express purpose of,* специа́льно для того́, что́бы. **3,** (rapid) сро́чный: *express telegram,* сро́чная телегра́мма. *Express train,* курье́рский по́езд; экспре́сс. —*adv.* экспре́ссом. —*n.* (train) экспре́сс. —**express oneself, 1,** (make oneself understood) объясня́ться. **2,** (state one's opinion) выража́ться; выска́зываться.

expression *n.* выраже́ние. *Idiomatic expression,* идиомати́ческое выраже́ние. *Expression on one's face,* выраже́ние лица́. *Read with expression,* чита́ть с выраже́нием.

expressive *adj.* вырази́тельный. —**expressiveness,** *n.* вырази́тельность.

expressly *adv.* **1,** (explicitly) я́сно. **2,** (specifically) специа́льно.

expressway *n.* автостра́да; автомагистра́ль.

expropriate *v.t.* экспроприи́ровать. —**expropriation,** *n.* экспроприа́ция.

expulsion *n.* изгна́ние; исключе́ние.

expunge *v.t.* вычёркивать.

expurgate *v.t.* вычёркивать нежела́тельные места́ в (кни́ге).

exquisite *adj.* **1,** (extremely beautiful) прекра́сный. **2,** (delicate; refined) изы́сканный; утончённый.

extant *adj.* сохрани́вшийся; существу́ющий.

extemporaneous *adj.* импровизи́рованный. —**extemporaneously,** *adv.* без подгото́вки; экспро́мтом.

extemporize *v.t.* & *i.* импровизи́ровать.

extend *v.t.* **1,** (stretch out; hold out) протя́гивать. *Extend one's hand,* протя́гивать *or* подава́ть ру́ку. **2,** (enlarge) расширя́ть; удлиня́ть. **3,** (expand, as influence) распространя́ть. **4,** (prolong in time) продлева́ть. **5,** (give; grant; accord) ока́зывать: *extend aid to,* ока́зывать по́мощь (+ *dat.*). *Extend credit to,* открыва́ть креди́т (+ *dat.*). **6,** (give; convey) передава́ть; выража́ть. *Extend regards/an invitation,* передава́ть приве́т/приглаше́ние. *Extend thanks/sympathy,* выража́ть благода́рность/сочу́вствие. —*v.i.* (stretch) тяну́ться; простира́ться. —**extend oneself,** утружда́ть себя́.

extended *adj.* **1,** (stretched out) протя́нутый; распростёртый. **2,** (lengthy; prolonged) дли́тельный; продолжи́тельный. **3,** (enlarged in scope) расши́ренный.

extensible *adj.* раздвижно́й.

extension *n.* **1,** (extending; expanding) удлине́ние; расшире́ние. **2,** (addition, as to a house) пристро́йка. **3,** (extra time allowed a debtor) отсро́чка; продле́ние сро́ка. **4,** (internal telephone number) доба́вочный: *extension five,* доба́вочный пять. —**extension cord,** удлини́тельный шнур; удлини́тель. —**extension ladder,** раздвижна́я ле́стница.

extensive *adj.* **1,** (vast) обши́рный. **2,** (broad in scope) широ́кий; обши́рный. *Extensive knowledge,* обши́рные зна́ния. *Extensive damage,* больши́е поврежде́ния. *Extensive repairs,* кру́пный ремо́нт.

extensively *adv.* мно́го: *read/travel extensively,* мно́го чита́ть/путеше́ствовать.

extent *n.* **1,** (length) протяже́ние; протяжённость. **2,** (degree) сте́пень; ме́ра: *to a certain extent,* до не́которой *or* до изве́стной сте́пени; в изве́стной ме́ре. **3,** (scope) сте́пень; разме́р: *extent of the damage,* сте́пень поврежде́ния; разме́р уще́рба. *To the full extent of the law,* по всей стро́гости зако́на.

extenuate *v.t.* смягча́ть. —**extenuating circumstances,** смягча́ющие вину́ обстоя́тельства.

exterior *adj.* нару́жный; вне́шний. —*n.* нару́жность; вне́шность.

exterminate *v.t.* уничтожа́ть; истребля́ть; выводи́ть; мори́ть; трави́ть. —**extermination,** *n.* уничтоже́ние; истребле́ние.

external *adj.* вне́шний; нару́жный.

extinct *adj.* **1,** (of an animal, bird, etc.) вы́мерший. *Become extinct,* вымира́ть. **2,** (of a volcano) поту́хший.

extinction *n.* **1,** (extinguishing) гаше́ние; туше́ние. **2,** (dying out) вымира́ние.

extinguish *v.t.* гаси́ть; туши́ть.

extirpate *v.t.* искореня́ть; выкорчёвывать; вырыва́ть с ко́рнем. —**extirpation,** *n.* искорене́ние.

extol *v.t.* превозноси́ть; расхва́ливать; восхваля́ть.

extort *v.t.* вымога́ть (де́ньги); вы́рвать (призна́ние); исто́ргнуть (обеща́ние). —**extortion,** *n.* вымога́тельство. —**extortionate,** *adj.* граби́тельский. —**extortionist,** *n.* вымога́тель.

extra *adj.* **1,** (additional) дополни́тельный: *extra expenses,* дополни́тельные расхо́ды. *Postage is extra,* за пересы́лку берётся осо́бая пла́та. *Pay two dollars extra,* припла́чивать два до́ллара. **2,** (spare) ли́шний: *have you an extra pencil?,* есть ли у вас ли́шний каранда́ш? —*adv.* осо́бенно; осо́бо. *Of extra fine quality,* осо́бенно высо́кого ка́чества. —*n.* **1,** *theat.* (supernumerary) стати́ст. **2,** (special edition) э́кстренный вы́пуск.

extract *v.t.* **1,** (draw out; remove) извлека́ть; удаля́ть; выта́скивать; вырыва́ть. **2,** (remove from the ground) добыва́ть. **3,** (obtain by pressing or squeezing) выжима́ть. **4,** (copy out; choose for quotation) выпи́сывать; выбира́ть. **5,** (obtain, as a promise, confession, etc.) вырыва́ть; вынужда́ть; исторга́ть. **6,** *math.* извлека́ть. —*n.* **1,** (excerpt) извлече́ние; вы́держка; вы́писка; вы́борка. **2,** (concentrate) вы́тяжка; экстра́кт; насто́й.

extraction *n.* **1,** (act of extracting) извлече́ние; удале́ние; добы́ча. **2,** (origin; descent) происхожде́ние.

extracurricular *adj.* внекла́ссный.

extradite *v.t.* выдава́ть. —**extradition,** *n.* вы́дача.

extramarital *adj.* внебра́чный.

extraneous *adj.* **1,** (coming from outside; foreign) посторо́нний. **2,** (irrelevant) не име́ющий отноше́ния (к чему́-нибудь).

extraordinarily *adv.* чрезвыча́йно; в вы́сшей сте́пени.

extraordinary *adj.* **1,** (remarkable; exceptional) чрезвыча́йный; необыча́йный. **2,** (special, as of a

meeting) чрезвыча́йный; внеочередно́й. **3,** (of an envoy) чрезвыча́йный.
extrapolate *v.t. & i.* экстраполи́ровать. —**extrapolation,** *n.* экстраполя́ция.
extraterritorial *adj.* экстерриториа́льный.
extravagance *n.* расточи́тельность.
extravagant *adj.* **1,** (wasteful) расточи́тельный. **2,** (excessive) непоме́рный.
extreme *adj.* кра́йний: *extreme caution/poverty,* кра́йняя осторо́жность/нищета́. *Extreme measures/views,* кра́йние ме́ры/взгля́ды. *Extreme old age,* глубо́кая ста́рость. —*n.* кра́йность: *to an extreme,* до кра́йности. *Go to extremes,* вдава́ться в кра́йности. *Go from one extreme to the other,* впада́ть из одно́й кра́йности в другу́ю.
extremely *adv.* кра́йне; чрезвыча́йно.
extremism *n.* экстреми́зм.
extremist *n.* экстреми́ст. —*adj.* экстреми́стский.
extremity *n.* **1,** (end; edge) коне́ц; край. **2,** *pl.* (appendages of the body) коне́чности.
extricate *v.t.* выпу́тывать; вытáскивать. *Extricate oneself,* выпу́тываться; выкара́бкиваться.
exuberance *n.* жизнера́достность.
exuberant *adj.* кипу́чий; жизнера́достный.
exude *v.t.* **1,** (discharge) выделя́ть. **2,** *fig.* (radiate) пы́хать (+ *instr.*); сия́ть (+ *instr.*). —*v.i.* выделя́ться; проступа́ть.
exult *v.i.* ликова́ть; торжествова́ть.—**exultant,** *adj.* лику́ющий; торжеству́ющий. —**exultation,** *n.* ликова́ние; торжество́.
eye *n.* **1,** (organ of sight) глаз. **2,** (of a needle) ушко́. —*adj.* глазно́й: *eye doctor,* глазно́й врач. —*v.t.* разгля́дывать; загля́дываться на; засма́триваться на. —**an eye for an eye,** о́ко за о́ко. —**be all eyes,** смотре́ть во все глаза́. —**before one's very eyes,** на чьи́х-нибудь глаза́х; на глаза́х у кого́-нибудь. —**close one's eyes to,** закрыва́ть глаза́ на. —**give someone the eye; make eyes at,** де́лать *or* стро́ить гла́зки (+ *dat.*). —**have an (*or* one's) eye on,** име́ть на приме́те. —**in the eyes of,** в глаза́х (+ *gen.*). —**keep an eye on,** присма́тривать за. —**see eye to eye,** сходи́ться во взгля́дах; быть одного́ мне́ния.
eyeball *n.* глазно́е я́блоко.
eyebrow *n.* бровь.
eyecup *n.* глазна́я ва́нночка.
eyeglasses *n. pl.* очки́.
eyelash *n.* ресни́ца.
eyelet *n.* пе́телька.
eyelid *n.* ве́ко.
eyepiece *n.* окуля́р.
eyeshade *n.* нагла́зник.
eyesight *n.* зре́ние.
eye socket глазна́я впа́дина; глазни́ца.
eyesore *n.* безобра́зие.
eyestrain *n.* напряже́ние гла́з.
eyetooth *n.* глазно́й зуб.
eyewash *n.* примо́чка для глаз.
eyewitness *n.* очеви́дец.

F

F, f шеста́я бу́ква англи́йского алфави́та. —*n.* **1,** (musical note) фа. **2,** (failing grade) едини́ца.
fa *n., music* фа.
fable *n.* ба́сня. —**fabled,** *adj.* баснosло́вный; ска́зочный.
fabric *n.* **1,** (cloth) ткань; мате́рия; материа́л. **2,** *fig.* (basic structure) стро́й; строе́ние. *The social fabric,* обще́ственный строй.
fabricate *v.t.* **1,** (manufacture) производи́ть; фабрикова́ть. **2,** (make up; invent) фабрикова́ть; выду́мывать.
fabrication *n.* **1,** (manufacture) произво́дство; фабрика́ция. **2,** (falsehood) вы́думка; вы́мысел.
fabulist *n.* баснопи́сец.
fabulous *adj.* баснoсло́вный; ска́зочный.
façade *n.* фаса́д.
face *n.* **1,** (of a human being) лицо́. **2,** (of a clock) цифербла́т. **3,** (surface) лицо́; лик. *Face of the moon,* лик луны́. *Vanish from the face of the earth,* исче́знуть с лица́ земли́. **4,** (expression; countenance) лицо́; ми́на; физионо́мия. *Long face,* вы́тянутое лицо́. **5,** (exaggerated expression) грима́са. *Make faces,* грима́сничать; де́лать *or* стро́ить грима́сы. **6,** (front; main side) лицева́я сторона́; лицо́. **7,** (dignity) лицо́: *loss of face,* поте́ря лица́. —*v.t.* **1,** (front; look out on) смотре́ть; выходи́ть (*with* в *or* на). **2,** (stand facing) стоя́ть лицо́м к. **3,** (confront) стоя́ть пе́ред: *the problems facing us,* пробле́мы, стоя́щие пе́ред на́ми. *We are faced with a difficult task,* нам предстои́т тру́дная зада́ча. *He faces life imprisonment,* ему́ грози́т пожи́зненное тюре́мное заключе́ние. **4,** (confront squarely) смотре́ть в лицо́ (+ *dat.*): *face death/the truth/,* смотре́ть сме́рти/пра́вде в лицо́. **5,** (cover with a layer of something else) облицо́вывать; обкла́дывать. —**face down,** лицо́м вниз; ничко́м. —**face to face,** лицо́м к лицу́; оди́н на оди́н. —**face up,** лицо́м кве́рху. —**face up to,** смотре́ть в лицо́ (+ *dat.*). —**in the face of,** пе́ред лицо́м (+ *gen.*). —**on the face of it,** на пе́рвый взгляд. —**to one's face,** в лицо́ (+ *dat.*).
face card фигу́ра.
face cream крем для лица́.
faceless *adj.* безли́кий; безли́чный.
face powder пу́дра для лица́.

facet *n.* **1,** (of a gem) грань; фасе́т(ка). **2,** *fig.* (aspect) сторона́.

facetious *adj.* шутли́вый; шу́точный.

face towel полоте́нце для лица́.

face value номина́льная сто́имость. —**take at face value,** принима́ть за чи́стую моне́ту.

facial *adj.* лицево́й. *Facial features,* черты́ лица́. *Facial expression,* выраже́ние лица́. —*n.* масса́ж лица́.

facile *adj.* бе́глый; бо́йкий.

facilitate *v.t.* **1,** (make easier) облегча́ть. **2,** (promote; stimulate) спосо́бствовать.

facility *n.* **1,** (ease) лёгкость. *With facility,* легко́; бе́гло; с лёгкостью. **2,** (aptitude) спосо́бности. **3,** *pl.* (conveniences; services) сре́дства; удо́бства; услу́ги.

facing *n.* **1,** (outer covering) облицо́вка. **2,** (trim) кант; отде́лка.

facsimile *n.* факси́миле.

fact *n.* факт. *It is a fact that...,* факт, что... *The fact that...,* то, что... *The fact is...,* де́ло в том, что... —**after the fact,** за́дним число́м. —**as a matter of fact,** *see* **matter.** —**in fact,** факти́чески; на са́мом де́ле. —**know for a fact,** знать то́чно; знать наверняка́.

faction *n.* фра́кция. —**factional,** *adj.* фракцио́нный.

factious *adj.* фракцио́нный.

factor *n.* **1,** (contributing element) фа́ктор; обстоя́тельство. *You forgot one important factor,* вы забы́ли об одно́м ва́жном обстоя́тельстве. **2,** (agent) комиссионе́р. **3,** *math.* мно́житель; сомно́житель; коэффицие́нт. —*v.t.* разлага́ть на мно́жители.

factory *n.* фа́брика; заво́д. —*adj.* фабри́чный: *factory worker,* фабри́чный рабо́чий.

factual *adj.* факти́ческий.

faculty *n.* **1,** *usu. pl.* (power of the mind) спосо́бности: *mental faculties,* у́мственные спосо́бности. *The faculty of speech,* дар ре́чи. *In full possession of one's faculties,* в по́лном рассу́дке. *Lose possession of one's faculties,* вы́жить из ума́. **2,** (knack) спосо́бности: *a faculty for languages,* спосо́бности к языка́м. **3,** (department of a university) факульте́т. **4,** (teaching staff) преподава́тельский соста́в.

fad *n.* пове́трие.

fade *v.i.* **1,** (lose color) линя́ть; выцвета́ть. **2,** (wither) вя́нуть; блёкнуть. **3,** (grow dim) блёкнуть. **4,** (grow inaudible) замира́ть. **5,** (lessen; wane) га́снуть; угаса́ть: *hopes are fading,* наде́жды га́снут/угаса́ют. **6,** (disappear gradually) исчеза́ть: *fade into the distance,* исчеза́ть вдали́. *Fade from view,* скрыва́ться из виду. *Fade from memory,* стере́ться в па́мяти. —*v.t.* обесцве́чивать: *sunlight fades the fabric,* со́лнце обесцве́чивает ткань.

faded *adj.* вы́цветший.

faeces *n.* = **feces.**

fag *v.t.* утомля́ть. *Be fagged out,* заму́читься.

fagot *also,* **faggot** *n.* вяза́нка хво́роста.

Fahrenheit *adj.* Фаренге́йт: *forty degrees Fahrenheit,* со́рок гра́дусов по Фаренге́йту.

fail *v.i.* **1,** (be unsuccessful) не удава́ться; терпе́ть неуда́чу; прова́ливаться. **2,** (stop working; cease to function) отказа́ть; отказа́ться рабо́тать. **3,** (decline; deteriorate) слабе́ть; сдава́ть. *His eyesight is failing,* его́ зре́ние слабе́ет; зре́ние ему́ изменя́ет. **4,** (become insolvent) прогора́ть. **5,** (receive a failing grade) прова́ливаться. —*v.t.* **1,** (be of no help to) изменя́ть: *his strength failed him,* си́лы ему́ измени́ли. *Words fail me,* не нахожу́ слов. **2,** (disappoint; let down) подводи́ть: *don't fail me,* не подведи́те меня́. **3,** *fol. by inf.* (not do): *he failed to answer,* он не отве́тил. *I fail to see the difference,* не ви́жу ра́зницы. **4,** (not pass) прова́ливаться на (*e.g.* экза́мене) *or* по (*e.g.* хи́мии). **5,** (not give a passing grade to) прова́ливать. —**without fail,** обяза́тельно; в обяза́тельном поря́дке.

failing *n.* недоста́ток; сла́бость. —*adj.* **1,** (not passing, as of a mark) неудовлетвори́тельный. **2,** (deteriorating, as of eyesight) слабе́ющий. *She is in failing health,* у неё сла́бое здоро́вье. —*prep.* за неиме́нием (+ *gen.*). *Failing which,* ина́че; в проти́вном слу́чае.

failure *n.* **1,** (lack of success) неуда́ча; прова́л. *Doomed to failure,* обречён на прова́л. *Crop failure,* неурожа́й. **2,** (one who is unsuccessful) неуда́чник. **3,** (non-perfomance) неисполне́ние: *failure to carry out an order,* неисполне́ние распоряже́ния. **4,** (malfunctioning) ава́рия; отка́з; неиспра́вность. *Mechanical failure,* механи́ческая неиспра́вность. *Power failure,* отка́з электропита́ния. **5,** (a becoming bankrupt) крах; банкро́тство.

faint *adj.* **1,** (weak; dim; slight) сла́бый: *faint mark,* сла́бый след; *faint hope,* сла́бая наде́жда. *Faint resemblance,* отдалённое схо́дство. **2,** (ready to faint): *feel faint,* чу́вствовать дурноту́. *I feel faint,* мне ду́рно. —*n.* о́бморок: *in a dead faint,* в глубо́ком о́бмороке. —*v.i.* упа́сть в о́бморок.

fainthearted *adj.* малоду́шный. —**faintheartedness,** *n.* малоду́шие.

faintly *adv.* **1,** (dimly) сла́бо; нея́сно. **2,** (slightly) слегка́.

faintness *n.* **1,** (dimness) сла́бость. **2,** (weak feeling) дурнота́.

fair *adj.* **1,** (beautiful; lovely) прекра́сный. **2,** (light, as of skin) све́тлый. **3,** (blond) белоку́рый. **4,** (clear; sunny) я́сный. **5,** (just and honest) справедли́вый; че́стный. **6,** (fairly large) изря́дный: *a fair amount,* изря́дное коли́чество. **7,** (average; so-so) неплохо́й; посре́дственный; сно́сный. —*adv.* че́стно; поря́дочно; по пра́вилам. —*n.* **1,** (market) я́рмарка. **2,** (exposition) вы́ставка: *world's fair,* всеми́рная вы́ставка. —**bid fair,** обеща́ть. —**fair copy,** чистово́й экземпля́р; чистови́к. —**fair enough!,** согла́сен!; согла́сна! —**fair sex,** прекра́сный пол. —**fair to middling,** так себе́; сно́сно; ни ша́тко ни ва́лко.

fair-haired *adj.* **1,** (light-haired) белоку́рый; ру́сый; светловоло́сый. **2,** (favorite) излю́бленный.

fairly *adv.* **1,** (justly) справедли́во; че́стно. **2,** (rather) дово́льно: *fairly well,* дово́льно хорошо́.

fairness *n.* справедли́вость. —**in all fairness,** справедли́вости ра́ди.

fairy *n.* фе́я. —**fairyland,** *n.* ска́зочная страна́; волше́бное ца́рство. —**fairy tale,** (волше́бная) ска́зка.

fait accompli соверши́вшийся факт. *Present someone with a fait accompli,* поста́вить кого́-нибудь пе́ред фа́ктом.

faith *n.* **1,** (trust; confidence) ве́ра; дове́рие. *Put one's faith in,* полага́ться на. **2,** (belief in God) ве́ра: *faith in God,* ве́ра в бо́га. *Man of faith,* ве́рующий. **3,** (religious denomination) ве́ра; вероиспове́дание. —**bad faith,** недобросо́вестность. *In bad faith,* недобросо́вестно. —**good faith,** и́скренность. *In good faith,* и́скренне; по чи́стой со́вести. —**keep faith with,** остава́ться ве́рным (+ *dat.*). —**take on faith,** принима́ть на ве́ру.

faithful *adj.* ве́рный. —**faithfully,** *adv.* ве́рно. —**faithfulness,** *n.* ве́рность.

faithless *adj.* неве́рный.

fake *v.t.* **1,** (feign) притворя́ться (+ *instr.*). **2,** (forge) подде́лывать. —*v.i.* притворя́ться. —*adj.* подде́льный; подло́жный; фальши́вый. —*n.* подде́лка; фальши́вка.

faker *n.* обма́нщик; притво́рщик. —**fakery,** *n.* обма́н.

falcon *n.* со́кол. —**falconry,** *n.* соколи́ная охо́та.

fall *v.i.* **1,** (lose one's footing; drop) па́дать. *Fall down the stairs,* упа́сть с ле́стницы. *Fall in battle,* пасть в бою́. *Prices fell,* це́ны упа́ли. *Rain fell during the night,* но́чью шёл дождь. *Dusk is falling,* спуска́ются су́мерки. *Shadows are falling,* те́ни ложа́тся. *His face fell,* его́ лицо́ вы́тянулось. **2,** (be caught or captured) попада́ть: *fall into a trap,* попа́сть в лову́шку. *Fall into the hands of,* попа́сть в ру́ки (+ *gen.*). *Fall victim to,* пасть же́ртвой (+ *gen.*). **3,** (be conquered or overthrown) пасть: *the fortress fell,* кре́пость па́ла. *Fall from power,* лиши́ться вла́сти. **4,** (occur) наступа́ть: *night fell,* наступи́ла ночь. *New Year's Day falls on a Wednesday,* Но́вый год выпада́ет *or* прихо́дится на сре́ду. *The stress falls on the first syllable,* ударе́ние па́дает на пе́рвый слог. **5,** (come by lot or chance) па́дать; выпада́ть: *the lot fell upon him,* ему́ вы́пал жре́бий; жре́бий пал на него́. **6,** (pass into a particular state): *fall asleep,* засыпа́ть; *fall ill,* заболева́ть; *fall silent,* замолка́ть; умолка́ть; *fall in love,* влюбля́ться. **7,** (be classified; belong) относи́ться: *fall into a certain category,* относи́ться к тако́й-то катего́рии. *Fall into three categories,* дели́ться на три катего́рии. *Fall within one's jurisdiction,* входи́ть в чью́-нибудь компете́нцию. **8,** *fol. by inf.* (begin; set about) *rendered variously in Russian: they fell to work immediately,* они́ сра́зу взя́лись за рабо́ту. *They fell to quarreling among themselves,* они́ поссо́рились ме́жду собо́й. —*n.* **1,** (loss of footing; drop; collapse) паде́ние. *Take a bad fall,* си́льно разби́ться. *Fall in prices,* паде́ние цен. *The fall of the Roman Empire,* паде́ние Ри́мской Импе́рии. **2,** *pl.* (waterfall) водопа́д. **3,** (autumn) о́сень. *In the fall,* о́сенью. —*adj.* осе́нний: *fall weather,* осе́нняя пого́да. —**fall apart,** распада́ться; разва́ливаться. —**fall back,** отступа́ть. —**fall back on,** прибега́ть к. —**fall behind, 1,** *literally* зава́ливаться за (+ *acc.*). **2,** (lag) отстава́ть. —**fall down,** па́дать. —**fall flat,** прова́ливаться. —**fall for, 1,** (be tricked by, as bait) попада́ться на (у́дочку). **2,** (be captivated by) влюбля́ться в; увлека́ться (+ *instr.*). —**fall in, 1,** (cave in) обва́ливаться; прова́ливаться. **2,** *mil.* стро́иться. *Fall in!,* станови́сь! —**fall in with,** попа́сть в: *fall in with a bad crowd,* попа́сть в плоху́ю компа́нию. —**fall off, 1,** (tumble from) упа́сть с; свали́ться с. **2,** (decline) уме́ньшиться; упа́сть. —**fall out, 1,** *literally* выпада́ть; выва́ливаться. **2,** *mil.* выходи́ть из стро́я. —**fall over,** опроки́дываться. —**fall short of,** не достига́ть. *Fall short of expectations,* обма́нывать ожида́ния. —**fall through,** прова́ливаться; срыва́ться.

fallacious *adj.* оши́бочный; ло́жный. —**fallaciousness,** *n.* оши́бочность.

fallacy *n.* **1,** (false notion; error) оши́бка. **2,** (fallaciousness) оши́бочность.

fallen *adj.* па́вший; па́дший. —**fallen arches,** плоскосто́пие. —**fallen woman,** па́дшая же́нщина.

fallible *adj.* подве́рженный оши́бкам.

falling *adj.* па́дающий.

falling-out *n.* ссо́ра. *They have had a falling-out,* они́ в ссо́ре; они́ рассо́рились; ме́жду ни́ми пробежа́ла чёрная ко́шка.

Fallopian tubes фалло́пиевы тру́бы.

fallout *n.* **1,** (particles) радиоакти́вные оса́дки. **2,** (descent of same) выпаде́ние радиоакти́вных оса́дков.

fallow *adj.* парово́й. *Fallow land,* земля́ под па́ром. *Lie fallow,* лежа́ть под па́ром. —**fallow deer,** лань.

false *adj.* **1,** (incorrect; insincere) ло́жный: *false rumor,* ло́жный слух; *false modesty,* ло́жная скро́мность. *False advertising,* лжи́вая рекла́ма. **2,** (forged) фальши́вый: *false passport,* фальши́вый па́спорт. —**false alarm,** ло́жная трево́га.— **false note,** фальши́вая *or* неве́рная но́та. —**false start,** неве́рный старт. —**false step,** ло́жный шаг. —**false teeth,** вставны́е зу́бы. —**under a false name,** под чужи́м и́менем.

falsehood *n.* ложь; вы́мысел.

falsely *adv.* ло́жно.

falsetto *n.* фальце́т; фи́стула. —*adj.* фальце́тный.

falsification *n.* фальсифика́ция.

falsifier *n.* фальсифика́тор.

falsify *v.t.* фальсифици́ровать.

falsity *n.* **1,** (falseness) ло́жность. **2,** (falsehood) ложь.

falter *v.i.* **1,** (hesitate; waver) дро́гнуть. **2,** (lose strength or momentum) слабе́ть.

fame *n.* сла́ва; изве́стность. —**famed,** *adj.* просла́вленный.

familiar *adj.* **1,** (well-known) знако́мый: *a familiar voice,* знако́мый го́лос. *His face is familiar to me,* его́ лицо́ мне знако́мо. **2,** *fol. by* **with** (having knowledge of) знако́мый с; в ку́рсе (+ *gen.*). *Become familiar with,* знако́миться с; ознакомля́ться с. **3,** (unduly intimate) фамилья́рный; развя́зный; бесцеремо́нный.

familiarity *n.* **1,** (knowledge) знако́мство. **2,** (undue intimacy) фамилья́рность; бесцеремо́нность.

familiarization *n.* ознакомле́ние.

familiarize *v.t.* знако́мить; ознакомля́ть. *Familiarize oneself with,* знако́миться с; ознакомля́ться с.

family *n.* **1,** (parents and children) семья́. **2,** *biol.* семе́йство. **3,** (of languages) семья́. —*adj.* семе́йный; фами́льный. *Family ties,* ро́дственные свя́зи. —**family man,** семе́йный челове́к. —**family name,** фами́лия. —**family planning,** плани́рование семьи́. —**family tree,** родосло́вное де́рево. —**in the family way,** в интере́сном положе́нии.

famine *n.* го́лод. —**feast or famine,** то гу́сто, то пу́сто.

famished *adj.* голо́дный как соба́ка; умира́ющий от го́лода.

famous *adj.* знамени́тый. *Be famous for,* сла́виться (+ *instr.*).

fan *n.* **1,** (manual device) ве́ер. **2,** (machine) вентиля́тор. **3,** *colloq.* (devotee) боле́льщик; люби́тель; покло́нник. —*v.t.* **1,** (cool with a fan) обма́хивать. *Fan* *oneself,* обма́хиваться. **2,** (direct air on, as a fire) раздува́ть. **3,** *fig.* (stir up; foment) раздува́ть. —*v.i.* [*usu.* **fan out**] развёртываться ве́ером.

fanatic *n.* фана́тик. —*adj.* [*also,* **fanatical**] фанати́ческий; фанати́чный. —**fanaticism,** *n.* фанати́зм.

fan belt реме́нь вентиля́тора.

fanciful *adj.* **1,** (imaginary; unreal) фантасти́ческий. **2,** (whimsical) каприз́ный.

fancy *n.* **1,** (imagination) фанта́зия: *flight of fancy,* полёт фанта́зии. **2,** (whim) при́хоть; причу́да; фанта́зия. **3,** (liking) увлече́ние. *Take a fancy to,* увлека́ться (+ *instr.*). *Catch the fancy of,* пригляну́ться (+ *dat.*). —*adj.* **1,** (not plain) замыслова́тый; зате́йливый. **2,** *colloq.* (high, as of prices) ду́тый. —*v.t.* **1,** (imagine) вообража́ть. *Fancy oneself as a writer,* вообража́ть себя́ писа́телем. **2,** (suppose; surmise) предполага́ть; вообража́ть. **3,** (like): *what do you fancy?,* что вам нра́вится? **4,** (feel like): *I don't fancy...,* у меня́ нет охо́ты (+ *inf. or* на+ *acc.*).

fanfare *n.* **1,** (flourish of trumpets) фанфа́ра. **2,** (ballyhoo) шуми́ха. *Without fanfare,* без зате́й.

fang *n.* клык.

fantastic *adj.* фантасти́ческий.

fantasy *n.* **1,** (creative imagination) фанта́зия. **2,** (something existing only in the imagination) фанта́стика; фанта́зия.

far *adj.* **1,** (distant) A, *used predicatively* далеко́: *Moscow is far away,* Москва́ далеко́. *Not far from here,* недалеко́ отсю́да. B, *used as a modifier* далёкий: *the far north,* далёкий се́вер. **2,** (more distant) да́льний: *in the far corner,* в да́льнем углу́. —*adv.* **1,** (a long way) далеко́: *go too far,* зайти́ сли́шком далеко́. **2,** *in comparisons* (by a great deal) гора́здо; намно́го: *far better,* гора́здо/намно́го лу́чше. —**as far as, 1,** (up to) до: *we drove as far as Boston,* мы доéхали до Бо́стона. **2,** (to the extent that) наско́лько: *as far as I know,* наско́лько я зна́ю. *As far as I am concerned,* что каса́ется меня́. —**by far; far and away,** несомне́нно; бесспо́рно. —**far and wide,** повсю́ду; вдоль и поперёк. —**far be it from me to...,** я далёк от того́, что́бы... —**far from, 1,** *literally* далеко́ от. **2,** (by no means) далеко́ не: *far from dumb,* далеко́ не глуп. —**far from it,** далеко́ не так; ничего́ подо́бного. —**go far,** далеко́ пойти́: *he will go far,* он далеко́ пойдёт. —**far into,** вглубь (+ *gen.*): *far into the woods,* вглубь ле́са. *Far into the night,* до глубо́кой но́чи. *Look far into the future,* загля́дывать в далёкое бу́дущее. —**how far?,** ско́лько на́до е́хать?; ско́лько киломе́тров? —**so far,** пока́ что; пока́ ещё; до сих пор. —**so far, so good,** пока́ всё хорошо́.

faraway *adj.* **1,** (distant) далёкий; отдалённый. **2,** (dreamy, as of a look) отсу́тствующий.

farce *n.* фарс. —**farcical,** *adj.* фа́рсовый.

fare *v.i.* пожива́ть: *how are you faring?,* как вы пожива́ете? —*n.* **1,** (price of a trip) пла́та за прое́зд; сто́имость прое́зда. *What is the fare to Washington?,* ско́лько сто́ит прое́зд *or* биле́т в Вашингто́н? **2,** (paying passenger) пассажи́р. **3,** (food) пи́ща; пита́ние; стол.

Far East да́льний восто́к. —**Far Eastern,** дальневосто́чный.

farewell *n.* проща́ние. *Bid farewell to,* проща́ться с. —*adj.* проща́льный; напу́тственный. —*interj.* проща́й(те)!

farfetched *adj.* наду́манный; притя́нутый за́ волосы.

far-flung *adj.* обши́рный; раздо́льный.

farina *n.* ма́нная крупа́. —**farinaceous,** *adj.* мучни́стый.

farm *n.* фе́рма. *Collective farm,* колхо́з. —*adj.* сельскохозя́йственный: *farm products/machinery,* сельскохозя́йственные проду́кты/маши́ны. —*v.t.* **1,** (cultivate) обраба́тывать. **2,** *fol. by* **out** (let out) отдава́ть на о́ткуп. —*v.i.* занима́ться се́льским хозя́йством.

farmer *n.* фе́рмер.

farm hand сельскохозя́йственный рабо́чий; батра́к.

farmhouse *n.* дом на фе́рме.

farming *n.* земледе́лие.

farmland *n.* па́хотная земля́.

farmstead *n.* уса́дьба.

farmyard *n.* ско́тный двор.

faro *n.* фарао́н; банк.

far-off *adj.* далёкий; да́льний.

far-reaching *adj.* далеко́ иду́щий.

farrow *n.* опоро́с.

farsighted *adj.* **1,** *med.* дальнозо́ркий. **2,** (having or showing foresight) дальнови́дный. —**farsightedness,** *n.* дальнозо́ркость.

farther *adv.* да́льше. *Not a step farther!,* ни ша́гу да́льше!

farthing *n.* фа́ртинг.

fascinate *v.t.* увлека́ть. —**fascinating,** *adj.* увлека́тельный.

fascination *n.* **1,** (state of being fascinated) увлече́ние. **2,** (charm; attraction) очарова́ние.

fascism *n.* фаши́зм.

fascist *n.* фаши́ст. —*adj.* фаши́стский.

fashion *n.* **1,** (current style; vogue) мо́да: *be in fashion,* быть в мо́де. *The latest fashion,* после́дняя мо́да. *Fashion magazine,* журна́л мод. *Fashion show,* пока́з моде́лей оде́жды. **2,** (way; manner) о́браз; спо́соб; мане́ра. —*v.t.* выде́лывать. *Fashion out of clay,* вы́лепить из гли́ны. —**after a fashion,** не́которым о́бразом; в своём ро́де.

fashionable *adj.* **1,** (in style) мо́дный. **2,** (high-class) фешене́бельный. —**become fashionable, 1,** (of clothes) входи́ть в мо́ду. **2,** (of a practice) стать мо́дно.

fashionably *adv.* мо́дно.

fashion plate мо́дник; мо́дная карти́нка.

fast *adj.* **1,** (swift) бы́стрый; ско́рый. *Fast horse,* бы́страя ло́шадь. *Fast train,* ско́рый по́езд. **2,** (of a timepiece): *my watch is (ten minutes) fast,* мои́ часы́ спеша́т (на де́сять мину́т). **3,** (loyal; close, as of friends) ве́рный. **4,** (not fading) про́чный: *fast colors,* про́чные кра́ски. **5,** (dissolute) беспу́тный; разгу́льный. —*adv.* **1,** (rapidly) бы́стро: *run fast,* бежа́ть бы́стро. **2,** (firmly) кре́пко. *Stand fast,* сто́йко держа́ться. **3,** *He is fast asleep,* он кре́пко спит. —*n.* пост: *observe a fast,* соблюда́ть пост. —*v.i.* пости́ться.

fasten *v.t.* **1,** (attach) прикрепля́ть: *fasten a mirror to the wall,* прикрепля́ть зе́ркало к стене́. **2,** (secure) закрепля́ть; скрепля́ть. **3,** (draw and pull tight) застёгивать: *fasten one's seat belt,* застегну́ть привязно́й реме́нь. —*v.i.* **1,** *fol. by* **to** *or* **onto** (attach to) прикрепля́ться (к). **2,** (button; hook; clasp) застёгиваться. —**fastener,** *n.* застёжка.

fastidious *adj.* **1,** (neat) чистоплóтный. **2,** (discriminating) разбóрчивый.
fast-moving *adj.* быстрохóдный.
fastness *n.* **1,** (remote and secure place) тверды́ня. **2,** (firmness) прóчность.
fat *adj.* **1,** (obese) пóлный; тóлстый; тýчный. *Get fat,* полнéть; толстéть. **2,** (fatty) жи́рный. —*n.* жир; сáло.
fatal *adj.* **1,** (mortal; lethal) смертéльный. **2,** (causing ruin; disastrous) роковóй: *fatal mistake,* роковáя оши́бка. *Fatal consequences,* ги́бельные послéдствия.
fatalism *n.* фатали́зм. —**fatalist,** *n.* фатали́ст. —**fatalistic,** *adj.* фаталисти́ческий.
fatality *n.* смертéльный слýчай: *no fatalities,* никаки́х смертéльных слýчаев.
fatally *adv.* смертéльно.
fate *n.* **1,** (invisible force) судьбá; рок. **2,** (what happens to someone) судьбá; ýчасть.
fated *adj.* суждено́: *we were not fated to...,* нам не суждено́ бы́ло (+ *inf.*).
fateful *adj.* **1,** (momentous) роковóй. **2,** (telltale) пророческий.
father *n.* **1,** (male parent) отéц. **2,** *pl.* (ancestors) прéдки. —*v.t.* роди́ть; производи́ть. —**fatherhood,** *n.* отцóвство.
father-in-law *n.* **1,** (husband's father) свёкор. **2,** (wife's father) тесть.
fatherland *n.* отéчество.
fatherly *adj.* отéческий.
fathom *n.* морскáя сáжень. —*v.t.* проникáть в; разгáдывать; разбирáть.
fatigue *n.* утомлéние; устáлость. —*v.t.* утомля́ть. —*v.i.* уставáть. —**fatiguing,** *adj.* утоми́тельный.
fatten *v.t.* корми́ть на убóй; откáрмливать; раскáрмливать.
fattening *adj.* жи́рный. *Avoid fattening foods,* избегáть жирóв.
fatty *adj.* жи́рный; жировóй. —**fatty acid,** жи́рная кислотá.
fatuous *adj.* глýпый; дурáцкий.
faucet *n.* (водопровóдный) кран.
fault *n.* **1,** (responsibility; blame) винá. *It's my fault,* я виновáт(а). *It's all your fault,* э́то всё вы виновáты. **2,** (flaw; defect) недостáток. **3,** *geol.* сдвиг. —*v.t.* придирáться к; критиковáть. —**at fault,** виновáт. —**find fault with,** придирáться к. —**to a fault,** чрезмéрно.
faultfinder *n.* приди́ра; критикáн.
faultless *adj.* безупрéчный; безукори́зненный.
faulty *adj.* неисправный; дефéктный.
faun *n.* фавн.
fauna *n.* фáуна.
faux pas лóжный шаг.
favor *also,* **favour** *n.* **1,** (good turn) одолжéние; любéзность; ми́лость; услýга. *Do someone a favor,* сдéлать одолжéние (+ *dat.*). *I have a favor to ask of you,* у меня́ к вам прóсьба. **2,** (friendly regard; approval) ми́лость; благосклóнность; расположéние. *Out of favor,* в неми́лости. *Find favor in someone's eyes,* снискáть чьё-нибудь расположéние. *Look upon with favor,* относи́ться благосклóнно к. *Gain favor among,* находи́ть поддéржку у. —*v.t.* **1,** (oblige) благоволи́ть. **2,** (show partiality toward; prefer) окáзывать предпочтéние (+ *dat.*). **3,** (be in favor of; advocate) быть за; стоя́ть за; выступáть за. **4,** (facilitate; aid) благоприя́тствовать. **5,** (resemble) уроди́ться в. —**in favor of, 1,** (for; supporting) за: *be in favor of,* быть/стоя́ть/выступáть за. **2,** (to the advantage of) в пóльзу (+ *gen.*): 3-2 *in favor of...,* три-два в пóльзу (+ *gen.*). *The matter was settled in our favor,* дéло реши́лось в нáшу пóльзу.
favorable *also,* **favourable** *adj.* благоприя́тный. *Favorable balance of trade,* акти́вный торгóвый балáнс.
favorably *also,* **favourably** *adv.* благосклóнно: *be favorably disposed toward,* относи́ться благосклóнно к. *Compare favorably with,* выи́грывать в сравнéнии с.
favorite *adj.* люби́мый; излю́бленный. —*n.* **1,** (that best liked) люби́мец; фавори́т. **2,** *sports* фавори́т. —**favoritism** *n.* фаворити́зм.
favour *n.&v.* = **favor.**—**favourable,** *adj.* = **favorable.**
fawn *n.* молодóй олéнь. —*v.i.* [*usu.* **fawn on** *or* **upon**] раболéпствовать (пéред); пресмыкáться (пéред); лебези́ть (пéред).
faze *v.t., colloq.* смущáть; расстрáивать.
fealty *n.* вéрность.
fear *n.* **1,** (fright) страх. **2,** (concern) опасéние: *arouse fears,* вызывáть опасéния. —*v.t. & i.* боя́ться: *fear trouble,* боя́ться неприя́тностей; *fear for one's life,* боя́ться за свою́ жизнь. —**for fear of/that,** из стрáха, что; боя́сь, что; из боя́зни, что.
fearful *adj.* **1,** (dreadful) стрáшный. **2,** (apprehensive): *be fearful that...,* боя́ться, что...
fearless *adj.* бесстрáшный; неустраши́мый. —**fearlessness,** *n.* бесстрáшие; неустраши́мость.
fearsome *adj.* стрáшный; грóзный.
feasible *adj.* выполни́мый; исполни́мый; осуществи́мый. —**feasibility,** *n.* осуществи́мость.
feast *n.* **1,** (sumptuous meal) пир. **2,** (religious festival) прáздник. —*v.i.* **1,** (have a feast) пировáть. **2,** *fol. by* **on** (eat) лáкомиться (+ *instr.*). —*v.t.* чéствовать. —**feast one's eyes on,** любовáться (+ *instr.*); упивáться (+ *instr.*).
feat *n.* пóдвиг.
feather *n.* перó. *Light as a feather,* лёгкий, как пёрышко. —**birds of a feather,** одногó пóля я́года. *Birds of a feather flock together,* моря́к моря́кá (*or* рыбáк рыбакá) ви́дит издалекá. —**feather in one's cap,** большóе достижéние; предмéт гóрдости. —**feather one's nest,** нагрéть рýки; наби́ть себé кармáн; свить себé тёплое гнёздышко.
feather bed пери́на; пухови́к.
feathered *adj.* оперённый; пернáтый.
feather grass ковы́ль.
feathery *adj.* **1,** (covered with feathers) пернáтый. **2,** (light; soft) пуши́стый.
feature *n.* **1,** (characteristic) чертá; осóбенность. *Distinguishing feature,* отличи́тельная чертá. **2,** *pl.* (facial appearance) черты́ лицá. **3,** (highlight) гвоздь. —*v.t.* отводи́ть важнéйшее мéсто (+ *dat.*); помещáть на ви́дном мéсте; выводи́ть в глáвной рóли.
febrile *adj.* лихорáдочный.
February *n.* феврáль. —*adj.* феврáльский.
feces *also,* **faeces** *n.pl.* кал; испражнéния.
feckless *adj.* **1,** (careless; irresponsible) неради́вый. **2,** (ineffectual) слáбый: *feckless attempt,* слáбая попы́тка.

fecund *adj.* плодовитый. —**fecundity**, *n.* плодовитость.
federal *adj.* федеральный; федеративный; союзный. —**federalism**, *n.* федерализм. —**federalist**, *n.* федералист.
federate *v.t.* & *i.* объединять(ся) в союз. —**federated**, *adj.* федеративный. —**federation**, *n.* федерация; союз.
fee *n.* **1**, (for professional services) гонорар. **2**, (for admission, membership, etc.) плата; взнос.
feeble *adj.* **1**, (infirm) немощный; хилый. **2**, *fig.* (ineffective) слабый: *feeble attempt*, слабая попытка.
feeble-minded *adj.* слабоумный. —**feeble-mindedness**, *n.* слабоумие.
feed *v.t.* **1**, (give food to; help to eat) кормить: *feed the baby*, кормить ребёнка; *feed oats to the horses*, кормить лошадей овсом. **2**, (keep nourished; sustain) кормить; питать. **3**, *in* **feed oneself**, есть самостоятельно. *Be able to feed oneself*, мочь сам (сама) есть. —*v.i.* **1**, (of animals) кормиться. **2**, *fol. by* **on** (use as food) питаться (+ *instr.*). —*n.* корм. —**be fed up**, надоесть; осточертеть: *I am fed up with it*, это мне надоело/осточертело.
feedbag *n.* торба.
feeder *n.* **1**, (branch line) ветка. **2**, *electricity* фидер.
feeding *n.* кормление. —**feeding bottle**, детский рожок. —**feeding trough**, кормушка.
feel *v.t.* **1**, (sense; experience) чувствовать; ощущать: *feel pain*, чувствовать/ощущать боль. **2**, (touch) щупать, ощупывать, потрогать. *Feel someone's pulse*, (по)щупать пульс у кого-нибудь. **3**, *in* **feel one's way**, пробираться ощупью. **4**, (think; consider) считать. —*v.i.* **1**, (be in a certain physical condition) чувствовать себя: *how do you feel?*, как вы себя чувствуете? *Feel ill*, плохо себя чувствовать. **2**, (experience some emotion): *feel sorry for*, жалеть. *Feel bad about*, сожалеть о. **3**, (seem, as to the touch) казаться: *the water feels warm*, вода кажется тёплой. —*n.* ощущение; осязание. *Get the feel of*, освоиться с. —**feel for**, **1**, (grope for) искать ощупью; нащупывать. **2**, (sympathize with) сочувствовать (+ *dat.*); страдать за; болеть за. —**feel like**, хотеться (+ *dat.*); иметь охоту; быть не прочь. —**make itself felt**, давать себя знать; давать себя чувствовать.
feeler *n.* **1**, *zool.* усик. **2**, *fig.* (hint) пробный шар. *Put out a feeler*, закинуть удочку.
feeling *n.* **1**, (emotion; sense) чувство: *feeling of pride*, чувство гордости. *Play with feeling*, играть с чувством; играть с душой., **2**, (sensation) ощущение. *I have no feeling in my arm*, у меня рука онемела. **3**, *pl.* (sensibilities) самолюбие: *hurt someone's feelings*, задевать чьё-нибудь самолюбие. **4**, (impression; opinion) впечатление; мнение. **5**, (presentiment) предчувствие.
feign *v.t.* & *i.* притворяться. —**feigned**, *adj.* притворный.
feint *n.* финт. —*v.i.* сделать финт.
feldspar *n.* полевой шпат.
felicitate *v.t.* поздравлять. —**felicitation**, *n.* поздравление.
felicitous *adj.* удачный; меткий.
felicity *n.* **1**, (great happiness) счастье; блаженство. **2**, (aptness) меткость.
feline *adj.* кошачий.
fell *v.t.* **1**, (cut down) рубить; срубать; вырубать. **2**, (knock down) валить; сбивать с ног.
fellow *n.* человек; парень; малый. —*adj.* товарищ по; со-: *fellow worker*, товарищ по работе; *fellow citizen*, согражданин. *Fellow countryman*, соотечественник.
fellowship *n.* **1**, (comradeship) товарищество. **2**, (grant) стипендия.
fellow traveler попутчик.
felon *n.* преступник. —**felonious**, *adj.* преступный. —**felony**, *n.* уголовное преступление.
felt *n.* войлок; фетр. —*adj.* войлочный; фетровый.
female *adj.* женский; женского пола. —*n.* **1**, (woman) женщина. **2**, (female animal) самка; матка.
feminine *adj.* **1**, (female) женский. **2**, (womanly) женственный. **3**, *gram.* женского рода. *Feminine gender*, женский род. —**femininity**, *n.* женственность.
feminism *n.* феминизм. —**feminist**, *n.* феминист; феминистка. —*adj.* феминистский; феминистический.
femur *n.* бедренная кость.
fence *n.* забор; ограда. —*v.t.* **1**, *fol. by* **in** (enclose) загораживать; огораживать. **2**, *fol. by* **off** (separate) отгораживать; выгораживать. —*v.i.* фехтовать.
fencer *n.* фехтовальщик. —**fencing**, *n.* фехтование.
fend *v.t.* [*usu.* **fend off**] отражать; отбивать. —**fend for oneself**, заботиться о себе. *He was left to fend for himself*, он был предоставлен самому себе.
fender *n.* крыло.
fennel *n.* фенхель.
ferment *n.* **1**, (substance producing fermentation) фермент; закваска. **2**, *fig.* (agitation) брожение. —*v.i.* бродить. —*v.t.* вызывать брожение в; заквашивать.
fermentation *n.* брожение.
fermented *adj.* перебродивший.
fermium *n.* фермий.
fern *n.* папоротник.
ferocious *adj.* свирепый; лютый. —**ferocity**, *n.* свирепость; лютость.
ferret *n.* хорёк. —*v.t.* [*usu.* **ferret out**] выведывать; выпытывать.
ferric oxide окись железа.
Ferris wheel чёртово колесо.
ferrotype *n.* ферротипия.
ferrous *adj.* железистый. —**ferrous metals**, чёрные металлы. —**ferrous oxide**, закись железа. —**ferrous sulfate**, железный купорос.
ferrule *n.* наконечник.
ferry *n.* [*also*, **ferryboat**] паром. —*v.t.* перевозить; переправлять. —**ferryman**, *n.* паромщик; перевозчик.
fertile *adj.* плодородный: *fertile soil*, плодородная почва. *Fertile imagination*, богатое/живое/пылкое воображение.
fertility *n.* **1**, (of the soil) плодородие. **2**, *biol.* плодовитость.
fertilization *n.* **1**, (of the soil) удобрение. **2**, *biol.* оплодотворение.
fertilize *v.t.* **1**, (spread fertilizer on) удобрять. **2**, *biol.* оплодотворять. *Fertilized egg*, оплодотворённое яйцо.
fertilizer *n.* удобрение.

ferule *n.* ферýла.
fervent *adj.* горячий; страстный; пылкий. —**fervently,** *adv.* горячо́.
fervid *adj.* горячий; пылкий; пламенный.
fervor *also,* **fervour** *n.* жар; пыл; задо́р.
fester *v.i.* гноиться.
festering *n.* гное́ние; нагное́ние. —*adj.* гно́йный.
festival *n.* **1,** (holiday) празднество. **2,** (music, film, youth, etc.) фестива́ль.
festive *adj.* праздничный; торжественный.
festivity *n.* **1,** (gaiety; mirth) весе́лье. **2,** *pl.* (festive proceedings) празднества; торжества́.
festoon *n.* **1,** (hanging decoration) гирлянда. **2,** (ornamental carving) фесто́н. —*v.t.* украша́ть.
fetal *adj.* пло́дный.
fetch *v.t.* идти́ за; сходи́ть за; приноси́ть; приводи́ть.
fetching *adj.* привлека́тельный; хоро́шенький; коке́тливый.
fete *n.* празднество. —*v.t.* че́ствовать.
fetid *adj.* злово́нный; воню́чий.
fetish *n.* фети́ш.
fetlock *n.* щётка.
fetter *n., usu. pl.* **1,** (chains) пу́ты; кандалы́. **2,** *fig.* (shackles) око́вы; у́зы; пу́ты. —*v.t.* спу́тывать (ло́шадь).
fettle *n.* состоя́ние; настрое́ние.
fetus *also,* **foetus** *n.* плод; заро́дыш.
feud *n.* вражда́. —*v.i.* враждова́ть.
feudal *adj.* феода́льный. —**feudalism,** *n.* феодали́зм.
fever *n.* **1,** (high temperature) жар. **2,** (disease) лихора́дка: *yellow fever,* жёлтая лихора́дка. **3,** (excitement) лихора́дка; горя́чка: *speculative fever,* биржева́я лихора́дка/горя́чка.
feverish *adj.* лихора́дочный. *I feel feverish,* меня́ зноби́т; меня́ лихора́дит.
few *adj.* **1,** (not many) ма́ло; немно́гие. *There were very few people there,* там бы́ло ма́ло наро́ду. *Few people know about it,* ма́ло кто зна́ет об э́том. *With few exceptions,* за немно́гими исключе́ниями. **2,** *usu. preceded by* **a** (a certain small number of) не́сколько: *in a few minutes,* че́рез не́сколько мину́т; *in a few words,* в не́скольких слова́х. *Every few days,* ка́ждые не́сколько дней. *Quite a few,* дово́льно мно́го. —*pron.* немно́гие: *one of the few who...,* оди́н из тех немно́гих, кото́рые... —**few and far between,** о́чень ре́дкие; наперечёт.
fez *n.* фе́ска.
fiancé *n.* жени́х. —**fiancée,** *n.* неве́ста.
fiasco *n.* фиа́ско.
fiat *n.* декре́т; ука́з.
fib *n.* вы́думка; непра́вда. —*v.i.* врать; привира́ть. —**fibber,** *n.* вы́думщик.
fiber *also,* **fibre** *n.* **1,** (filament) волокно́. **2,** *fig.* (inner strength) хара́ктер. —**fiberglass,** *n.* стекловолокно́.
fibrous *adj.* волокни́стый.
fibula *n.* ма́лая берцо́вая кость.
fickle *adj.* непостоя́нный; изме́нчивый.
fiction *n.* **1,** (literature) беллетри́стика; худо́жественная литерату́ра. **2,** (fabrication) фи́кция; вы́мысел. —**fictional,** *adj.* беллетристи́ческий.
fictitious *adj.* **1,** = **fictional. 2,** (false) вы́думанный; вы́мышленный; фикти́вный.
fiddle *n.* скри́пка. —*v.i.* **1,** *colloq.* (play the violin) игра́ть на скри́пке. **2,** *fol. by* **with** (fidget with) вози́ться с; игра́ть (+ *instr.*). —*v.t.* [*usu.* **fiddle away**] растра́чивать. —**fit as a fiddle,** совсе́м здоро́в; как нельзя́ лу́чше. —**play second fiddle,** игра́ть втору́ю скри́пку.
fiddler *n.* скрипа́ч.
fiddlesticks *interj.* вздор!; чепуха́!
fidelity *n.* **1,** (faithfulness) ве́рность. **2,** (accuracy) то́чность.
fidget *v.i.* **1,** (move restlessly) ёрзать; егози́ть; суети́ться. **2,** *fol. by* **with** (fuss with) игра́ть (+ *instr.*). —*n.* непосе́да; егоза́; юла́. —**fidgety,** *adj.* суетли́вый; егозли́вый; непосе́дливый.
fie *interj.* фи!
fief *n.* фео́д.
field *n.* **1,** (piece of open land) по́ле: *cornfield,* кукуру́зное по́ле. *Playing field,* спорти́вное по́ле. *Landing field,* поса́дочная площа́дка. **2,** (place containing a natural resource) месторожде́ние; про́мысел: *oil fields,* месторожде́ния не́фти; нефтяны́е про́мыслы. **3,** *fig.* (sphere, as of knowledge) о́бласть; о́трасль. —*adj.* полево́й: *field gun,* полево́е ору́дие. —**field of vision,** по́ле зре́ния.
field glasses полево́й бино́кль.
field goal гол с игры́.
field hockey хокке́й на траве́.
field marshal фельдма́ршал.
field mouse полева́я мышь.
fiend *n.* и́зверг; изуве́р. *Dope fiend,* наркома́н.
fiendish *adj.* зве́рский; изуве́рский.
fierce *adj.* **1,** (ferocious) свире́пый; лю́тый. **2,** (violent, as of a storm) неи́стовый. **3,** (bitter; intense, as of a struggle) жесто́кий; ожесточённый.
fiery *adj.* **1,** (ablaze) о́гненный. **2,** (impassioned) о́гненный; огнево́й; горя́чий; пла́менный. **3,** (easily provoked) горя́чий; вспы́льчивый.
fife *n.* ду́дка.
fifteen *n. & adj.* пятна́дцать.
fifteenth *adj.* пятна́дцатый. —*n.* **1,** (fifteenth part) пятна́дцатая часть. **2,** (fraction) пятна́дцатая: *one-fifteenth,* одна́ пятна́дцатая.
fifth *adj.* пя́тый. —*n.* **1,** (fifth part) пя́тая часть. **2,** (fraction) пя́тая: *one-fifth,* одна́ пя́тая. —**fifth column,** пя́тая коло́нна. —**fifth wheel,** пя́тое колесо́ в теле́ге; пя́тая спи́ца в колесни́це.
fiftieth *adj.* пятидеся́тый. —*n.* **1,** (fiftieth part) пятидеся́тая часть. **2,** (fraction) пятидеся́тая: *one-fiftieth,* одна́ пятидеся́тая.
fifty *n. & adj.* пятьдеся́т.
fig *n.* **1,** (tree) инжи́р; фи́га; фи́говое де́рево; смоко́вница. **2,** (fruit) инжи́р; фи́га; ви́нная я́года; смо́ква. **3,** (insulting gesture) шиш; ку́киш; фи́га. —**fig leaf,** фи́говый листо́к.
fight *v.i.* **1,** (engage in fisticuffs) дра́ться. **2,** (take part in combat) сража́ться: *fight bravely,* сража́ться хра́бро. **3,** (wage war) воева́ть: *England fought against Germany,* А́нглия воева́ла с Герма́нией. **4,** (wage a campaign) боро́ться: *fight for an idea,* боро́ться за иде́ю; *fight against injustice,* боро́ться про́тив несправедли́вости. —*v.t.* **1,** (combat physically) дра́ться с. **2,** (combat in war) сража́ться с; боро́ться с: *fight the enemy,* сража́ться/боро́ться с враго́м. **3,** (wage; carry on, as a war or battle) вести́. *Fight a duel,* дра́ться на дуэ́ли. **4,** (try to do away with) боро́ться с: *fight crime/poverty,* боро́ться с престу́пностью/ни-

щетóй. **5,** *Fight one's way,* пробивáть себé дорóгу. —*n.* **1,** (fistfight) дрáка: *start a fight,* затéять дрáку. *Get into a fight with,* подрáться с. **2,** (fighting) бой: *surrender without a fight,* сдáться без бóя. **3,** *fig.* (battle; campaign) борьбá: *the fight against crime,* борьбá с престýпностью. —**fight back, 1,** (not yield) окáзывать сопротивлéние. **2,** (try to suppress, as tears) борóться с. —**fight off,** отбивáться от.

fighter *n.* **1,** (combatant) боéц. **2,** (pugilist) боксёр. **3,** (strong advocate, as of a cause) борéц. **4,** (fighter plane) истребúтель. —**fighter-bomber,** *n.* истребúтель-бомбардирóвщик. —**fighter-pilot,** *n.* лётчик-истребúтель.

fighting *n.* бой. *Heavy fighting,* тяжёлые *or* упóрные бои. —*adj.* **1,** (pert. to combat) боевóй. **2,** (militant, as of a speech) вои́нственный.

figment *n.* вы́мысел; вы́думка. *Figment of the imagination,* плод *or* игрá воображéния.

figurative *adj.* перенóсный. —**figuratively,** *adv.* óбразно: *figuratively speaking,* óбразно говоря́.

figure *n.* **1,** (form; shape; anything visible by its outline) фигýра. **2,** (number) ци́фра: *exact figures,* тóчные ци́фры. *Figure eight,* восьмёрка. *Bad at figures,* слаб в арифмéтике. **3,** (representation; picture; design) фигýра. **4,** (diagram in a textbook) рисýнок. **5,** (personage) фигýра; лицó; персóна; дéятель. **6,** *geom.* фигýра. —*v.t.* **1,** *often fol. by* **out** (calculate) рассчи́тывать; подсчи́тывать. **2,** *colloq.* (think; reckon) полагáть; считáть. **3,** *fol. by* **out** (solve) разгáдывать. **4,** *fol. by* **out** (understand) сообрази́ть. —*v.i.* **1,** (appear prominently) фигури́ровать. **2,** *fol. by* **on** (count on) рассчи́тывать на. —**figure of speech,** оборóт рéчи.

figured *adj.* фигýрный; узóрчатый.

figurehead *n.* номинáльный главá.

figure skating фигýрное катáние. —**figure skater,** фигури́ст.

figurine *n.* фигýрка; статуэ́тка.

filament *n.* **1,** (fine thread or fiber) волокнó. **2,** (of a bulb) нить; волосóк.

filbert *n.* фундýк.

filch *v.t.* стащи́ть; стянýть.

file *n.* **1,** (cabinet) шкаф; (folder) пáпка; скоросшивáтель. **2,** (record) дéло; досьé. *Card file,* картотéка. *Newspaper file,* газéтная подши́вка. **3,** (line) ряд; шерéнга; колóнна; верени́ца. *Single file,* гуськóм. **4,** *chess* вертикáль. **5,** (tool) напи́льник. *Nail file,* пи́лка для ногтéй. —*v.t.* **1,** (smooth with a file) подпи́ливать. **2,** (store in a file) подшивáть (к дéлу). **3,** (submit; lodge; register) подавáть: *file an application/complaint,* подавáть заявлéние/жáлобу. *File suit against,* подавáть в суд на (+ *acc.*). *File a claim/protest,* заяви́ть претéнзию/протéст. —*v.i.* **1,** (march in file) идти́ колóнной; идти́ гуськóм. *File in,* входи́ть гуськóм. *File out,* выходи́ть гуськóм. **2,** (make application) подавáть заявлéние. *File for divorce,* возбуждáть дéло о развóде.

filet *n.* филé.

filial *adj.* сынóвний; дочéрний.

filigree *n.* филигрáнь. —*adj.* филигрáнный.

filing cabinet шкаф (для хранéния докумéнтов).

filings *n.pl.* опи́лки.

fill *v.t.* **1,** (make full) наполня́ть: *fill the pail with water,* напóлнить ведрó водóй. *The room was filled with smoke,* кóмната напóлнилась ды́мом. **2,** (occupy the whole of) заполня́ть. **3,** (plug up; close) затыкáть: *fill the cracks,* затыкáть щéли. **4,** (complete, as an order for merchandise) выполня́ть (закáз). **5,** (satisfy, as a need) удовлетворя́ть. **6,** (occupy, as an office) занимáть. **7,** (put a filling in, as a tooth) пломбировáть. —*v.i.* [*usu.* **fill up**] наполня́ться. —**eat one's fill,** наéсться дóсыта *or* ввóлю. —**fill in, 1,** (fill, as cracks) затыкáть. **2,** (fill up, as a hole) засыпáть; закáпывать. **3,** (write in) впи́сывать. **4,** *fol. by* **for** (be a substitute for) заменя́ть. **5,** *fol. by* **on** (provide with information about) вводи́ть в курс (+ *gen.*). —**fill out, 1,** (complete, as a questionnaire) заполня́ть. **2,** (become fuller or more rounded) полнéть; округля́ться. —**fill up, 1,** (make full) наполня́ть. **2,** (become full) наполня́ться.

filler *n.* **1,** (substance to increase bulk) наполни́тель. **2,** (substance to fill cracks) шпаклёвка. **3,** (filling, as for pies) начи́нка.

fillet *n.* **1,** (band) лéнта. **2,** (of meat) филé; вы́резка.

filling *n.* **1,** (act of filling) наполнéние. **2,** (for pastry, cake, etc.) фарш; начи́нка. **3,** (for a tooth) плóмба. **4,** *textiles* (weft; woof) утóк. —*adj.* (of food) сы́тный. —**filling station,** бензозапрáвочная стáнция; автозапрáвочная стáнция.

fillip *n.* **1,** (snap of the fingers) щелчóк. **2,** *fig.* (stimulus) толчóк.

filly *n.* кобы́лка.

film *n.* **1,** (thin layer) плёнка. **2,** *photog.* плёнка; фотоплёнка. **3,** (movie) фильм; карти́на. —*v.t.* **1,** (photograph) снимáть; засня́ть. **2,** (make a movie of) экранизи́ровать.

filmy *adj.* похóжий на плёнку; вя́зкий.

filter *n.* фильтр. —*v.t.* фильтровáть; процéживать. —*v.i.* просáчиваться.

filth *n.* грязь. —**filthy,** *adj.* гря́зный.

filtration *n.* фильтрáция.

fin *n.* плавни́к.

final *adj.* **1,** (last) послéдний; конéчный; заключи́тельный. *Final examination,* курсовóй экзáмен. **2,** (definitive) окончáтельный: *the decision of the court is final,* решéние судá — окончáтельное. —*n., often pl., sports* финáл.

finale *n.* финáл.

finalist *n.* финали́ст.

finality *n.* окончáтельность. *With an air of finality,* повели́тельным тóном.

finally *adv.* наконéц.

finance *n., often pl.* финáнсы. —*v.t.* финанси́ровать. —**financial,** *adj.* финáнсовый. —**financier,** *n.* финанси́ст.

finch *n.* вьюрóк. *Bullfinch,* снеги́рь. *Chaffinch,* зя́блик. *Goldfinch,* щегóл.

find *v.t.* **1,** (locate; discover) находи́ть. **2,** (discover by chance) заставáть: *find someone at home,* застáть когó-нибудь дóма. **3,** (discover on arrival) находи́ть: *find the door open,* находи́ть дверь откры́той. **4,** (consider; think) находи́ть: *find the book interesting,* находи́ть кни́гу интерéсной. **5,** (receive, as pleasure, application, etc.) находи́ть. **6,** (reach; attain) попадáть в: *find its mark,* попадáть в цель. **7,** (adjudge) признавáть: *find someone guilty,* признáть когó-нибудь винóвным. **8,** (recover the use of): *he has found his tongue,* у негó язы́к развязáлся. **9,** *in* **find fault with,** придирáться к. **10,** *in* **find (the) time,** находи́ть врéмя. —*n.* нахóдка: *a real find,* настоя́щая нахóдка. —**be found,** находи́ться. *Kangaroos are* *found only in Australia,* кенгуру́ во́дятся то́лько в Австра́лии. *He is nowhere to be found,* его́ нигде́ нет. —**find oneself, 1,** (perceive oneself to be somewhere) оказа́ться; очути́ться. **2,** (become aware) лови́ть себя́: *find oneself doing something,* лови́ть себя́ на том, что (+ *verb*). **3,** (discover one's special abilities) найти́ себя́. —**find out,** узнава́ть.

finding *n.* **1,** (verdict) реше́ние. **2,** *usu. pl.* (results of an inquiry) вы́воды. **3,** *pl.* (accessories used in dressmaking) прикла́д.

fine *adj.* **1,** (excellent) хоро́ший; прекра́сный. **2,** (clear; cloudless) я́сный; пого́жий. **3,** (very small, as of print; not coarse, as of sand) ме́лкий. **4,** (very thin, as of thread) то́нкий. **5,** (subtle) то́нкий. *Fine point,* то́нкость. —*adv.* **1,** (into small particles) ме́лко. **2,** (O.K.; swell) хорошо́. —*n.* штраф: *a ten-dollar fine,* штраф в де́сять до́лларов. —*v.t.* штрафова́ть: *he was fined 100 dollars,* его́ оштрафова́ли (*or* он был оштрафо́ван) на сто до́лларов. —**fine arts,** изя́щные *or* изобрази́тельные иску́сства.

finely *adv.* то́нко.

fineness *n.* то́нкость.

finery *n.* наря́ды.

finesse *n.* то́нкость.

finger *n.* па́лец. —*v.t.* перебира́ть. —**not lay a finger on,** па́льцем не тро́гать. —**not lift a finger,** па́лец о па́лец не уда́рить. —**point one's finger at,** пока́зывать *or* ука́зывать па́льцем на (+ *acc.*). —**put the finger on,** *slang* доноси́ть на.

finger board гриф.

fingering *n., music* аппликату́ра.

finger mark пятно́ от па́льца.

fingernail *n.* но́готь.

fingerprint *n.* отпеча́ток па́льца. —*v.t.* снима́ть отпеча́тки па́льцев с (+ *gen.*).

fingertip *n.* ко́нчик па́льца. —**have at one's fingertips,** знать как свои́ пять па́льцев.

finical *adj.* привере́дливый. *Also,* **finicky.**

finish *v.t.* **1,** (complete) конча́ть; зака́нчивать. **2,** (ruin) дока́нчивать; доконáть. **3,** (give a desired surface to) отде́лывать. —*v.i.* **1,** (complete something being done) конча́ть: *have you finished?,* вы ко́нчили? **2,** (come to an end) конча́ться. —*n.* **1,** (end) коне́ц. *Fight to the finish,* борьба́ не на жизнь, а на смерть. **2,** *sports* фи́ниш. *Finish line,* фи́ниш. **3,** (surface texture) полиро́вка: *dull finish,* ту́склая полиро́вка. —**finish off, 1,** (complete) зака́нчивать. **2,** (eat or drink) прика́нчивать. **3,** (kill; destroy) добива́ть; прика́нчивать; дока́нчивать.

finished *adj.* **1,** (completed) зако́нченный. **2,** (completely processed) гото́вый: *finished goods,* гото́вые изде́лия. **3,** (highly skilled; polished) зако́нченный. **4,** (done for) пропа́вший; поги́бший: *we're finished,* мы пропа́ли; мы поги́бли.

finite *adj.* коне́чный.

Finn *n.* финн; фи́нка. —**Finnish,** *adj.* фи́нский. —*n.* фи́нский язы́к.

Finno-Ugric *adj.* фи́нно-уго́рский.

fiord *n.* фио́рд.

fir *n.* пи́хта. —*adj.* пи́хтовый.

fire *n.* **1,** (flames) ого́нь. *Be on fire,* быть в огне́; горе́ть. **2,** (campfire) костёр: *sit around the fire,* сиде́ть вокру́г костра́. **3,** (conflagration) пожа́р: *forest fire,* лесно́й пожа́р. **4,** (shooting) ого́нь; обстре́л. *Open fire,* откры́ть ого́нь. *Be under fire,* быть под обстре́лом. —*adj.* пожа́рный: *fire hydrant,* пожа́рный кран. —*v.t.* **1,** (shoot, as a gun) стреля́ть из. **2,** (propel) пуска́ть: *fire a bullet,* пуска́ть пу́лю. *Fire a shot,* производи́ть вы́стрел. **3,** (feed the fire of) топи́ть. **4,** (bake in a kiln) обжига́ть. **5,** *fol. by* **up** (rouse; excite) зажига́ть; воспламеня́ть. **6,** *colloq.* (discharge) увольня́ть; прогоня́ть; выгоня́ть с рабо́ты. —*v.i.* **1,** (shoot) стреля́ть. *Fire on,* стреля́ть в; вести́ ого́нь по. *Fire into a crowd,* стреля́ть в толпу́. **2,** (go off) вы́стрелить. —**be on fire,** горе́ть; быть в огне́. —**catch fire,** загоре́ться. —**come under fire, 1,** (come under gunfire) попа́сть под обстре́л. **2,** (come under criticism) попа́сть под обстре́л кри́тики. —**hang fire,** дать осе́чку. —**play with fire,** игра́ть с огнём. —**set fire to; set on fire,** поджига́ть.

fire alarm пожа́рная трево́га.

firearm *n.* огнестре́льное ору́жие.

fireball *n.* **1,** (large meteor) боли́д. **2,** (cloud formed by a nuclear blast) о́гненный шар.

firebird *n.* жар-пти́ца.

fire bomb зажига́тельная бо́мба.

firebrand *n.* **1,** (piece of smoldering wood) голове́шка. **2,** (one who inflames passions) пла́менный ора́тор.

firecracker *n.* петáрда.

fire engine пожа́рная маши́на.

fire escape пожа́рная ле́стница.

fire extinguisher огнетуши́тель.

firefighter *n.* пожа́рный.

firefly *n.* светля́к; светлячо́к.

firehouse *n.* пожа́рное депо́.

fire irons ками́нные щипцы́.

fireman *n.* **1,** (firefighter) пожа́рный. **2,** (stoker) кочега́р.

fireplace *n.* ками́н.

fireplug *n.* пожа́рный кран; гидра́нт.

firepower *n.* огнева́я мощь.

fireproof *adj.* огнесто́йкий; несгора́емый.

fire screen ками́нная решётка.

fireside *n.* оча́г.

fire station пожа́рное депо́.

firewood *n.* дрова́.

fireworks *n.* фейерве́рк.

firing *n.* **1,** (shooting) стрельба́. **2,** (laying off) увольне́ние. —**firing line,** огнево́й рубе́ж; ли́ния огня́. —**firing pin,** уда́рник. —**firing range,** стре́льбище; полиго́н.

firm *adj.* твёрдый; про́чный. *Firm ground,* твёрдая по́чва. *Firm foundation,* про́чный фунда́мент. *Firm tone,* твёрдый тон. *Firm belief,* твёрдое убежде́ние. —*adv.* твёрдо: *stand firm,* держа́ться твёрдо; твёрдо стоя́ть на своём. —*n.* фи́рма: *law firm,* юриди́ческая фи́рма.

firmament *n.* небе́сный свод; небосво́д.

firmly *adv.* твёрдо; про́чно; кре́пко.

firmness *n.* твёрдость.

first *adj.* пе́рвый: *the first time,* пе́рвый раз. *The first thing that comes to mind,* пе́рвое, что прихо́дит в го́лову. —*adv.* **1,** (before all others) пе́рвым: *come in first,* прийти́ пе́рвым. **2,** (before doing something else) снача́ла: *Think first!,* снача́ла поду́майте! **3,** (for the first time) впервы́е: *when I first saw her,* когда́ я впервы́е уви́дел(а) её. **4,** (sooner; preferably) скоре́е: *I'd die first,* я скоре́е умру́. —*n.* пе́рвый. (*On*) *the first of the month,* пе́рвого числа́. *It's the first I've heard* *of it,* пéрвый раз слы́шу. —**at first,** сначáла. —**first of all,** прéжде всегó. —**in the first place,** во-пéрвых.

first aid скóрая пóмощь; пéрвая пóмощь. —**first-aid kit,** аптéчка; *mil.* санитáрная сýмка. —**first-aid station,** медпýнкт.

first-born *n.* пéрвенец.

first-class *adj.* **1,** (first-rate) первоклáссный. **2,** (most expensive, as of accommodations) пéрвого клáсса. —*adv.* пéрвым клáссом.

first cousin двоюрóдный брат; двоюрóдная сестрá.

firsthand *adj. & adv.* из пéрвых рук.

firstly *adv.* во-пéрвых.

first name и́мя.

first-rate *adj.* первоклáссный.

fiscal *adj.* финáнсовый. —**fiscal year,** финáнсовый год.

fish *n.* ры́ба. —*adj.* ры́бный: *fish soup,* ры́бный суп. —*v.i.* **1,** (go fishing) лови́ть *or* уди́ть ры́бу; рыбáчить. **2,** *fol. by* **for** (attempt to catch) уди́ть. **3,** *fol. by* **for** (seek indirectly) напрáшиваться на: *fish for compliments,* напрáшиваться на комплимéнты. —*v.t.* [*usu.* **fish out**] вылáвливать. —**drink like a fish,** пить как бóчка; пить запóем. —**fish in troubled waters,** лови́ть ры́бу в мýтной водé. —**neither fish nor fowl,** ни ры́ба ни мя́со.

fishbone *n.* ры́бья кость.

fishbowl *n.* аквáриум.

fish cake ры́бная котлéта.

fisher *n.* (animal) и́лька.

fisherman *n.* рыбáк; рыболóв.

fishery *n.* **1,** (business of fishing) ры́бный прóмысел. **2,** (fishing ground) ры́бные местá.

fishhook *n.* (рыболóвный) крючóк.

fishing *n.* ры́бная лóвля. —*adj.* рыболóвный. —**fishing boat,** рыбáчья лóдка. —**fishing line,** лесá. —**fishing rod,** ýдочка; уди́лище. —**fishing tackle,** рыболóвная снасть.

fish story охóтничий расскáз.

fish tank аквáриум.

fishy *adj.* **1,** (suggestive of fish) ры́бный. **2,** (expressionless) ры́бий: *fishy eyes,* ры́бьи глазá. **3,** *colloq.* (questionable; suspicious) сомни́тельный. *Something is fishy here,* тут чтó-то нелáдно.

fission *n.* **1,** *physics* расщеплéние; делéние. *Nuclear fission,* я́дерное делéние. **2,** *biol.* делéние (клéток). —**fissionable,** *adj.* расщепля́ющийся.

fissure *n.* трéщина; рассéлина; расщéлина.

fist *n.* кулáк. —**fistfight,** *n.* кулáчный бой.

fisticuffs *n.pl.* **1,** (fistfight) кулáчный бой. **2,** (pugilism) бокс.

fistula *n.* фи́стула; свищ.

fit *v.t.* **1,** (be the right size for) быть впóру (+ *dat.*); быть в сáмый раз (+ *dat.*). *The key fits the lock,* ключ подхóдит к замкý. **2,** (be appropriate to) подходи́ть (+ *dat.*); быть подходя́щим для; соотвéтствовать (+ *dat.*). **3,** (find room for; squeeze into) умещáть. **4,** (tailor; adjust) пригоня́ть. **5,** *fol. by* **out** (equip) снаряжáть; оснащáть. —*v.i.* **1,** (be the right size) быть впóру; подходи́ть. **2,** (be able to go into something) входи́ть; вмещáться; помещáться; умещáться; уклáдываться. *Fit through the door,* проходи́ть в дверь. *Fit around the table,* умести́ться за столóм. **3,** *fol. by* **in** (be suitable) подходи́ть. *That fits in with my plans,* э́то совпадáет с мои́ми плáнами. —*adj.* **1,** (suitable) гóдный; пригóдный. *Fit to drink,* гóдный для питья́. *Fit for military service,* гóдный к воéнной слýжбе. *Not fit for anything,* ни на что не спосóбен. **2,** (in good physical condition) здорóвый; в хорóшем состоя́нии. **3,** *fol. by passive inf.* (in suitable condition) в состоя́нии (+ *inf.*). *I am not fit to be seen,* я не могý показáться. —*n.* **1,** (seizure; spell) припáдок; при́ступ. *Epileptic fit,* эпилепти́ческий припáдок. *Fit of coughing,* при́ступ кáшля. **2,** (outburst) поры́в: *fit of rage,* поры́в гнéва. **3,** (manner of fitting): *be a good fit,* хорошó сидéть. —**by fits and starts,** уры́вками. —**fit to be tied,** вне себя́ от гнéва.—**see fit,** считáть нýжным (+ *inf.*). *Do as you see fit,* дéлайте, как вы считáете нýжным. *He will do as he sees fit,* он постýпит так, как емý заблагорассýдится.

fitch *n.* хорёк. *Also,* **fitchew.**

fitful *adj.* поры́вистый; преры́вистый.

fitness *n.* гóдность; пригóдность. —**physical fitness,** физи́ческая подготóвка.

fitter *n.* **1,** (of machinery) монтёр; слéсарь. **2,** (of clothes) портнóй.

fitting *adj.* достóйный: *fitting reward/rebuke,* достóйная наградá/óтповедь. —*n.* **1,** (trying on) примéрка: *have a fitting,* сдéлать примéрку. **2,** *pl.* (fixtures) арматýра. —**fittingly,** *adv.* достóйно.

five *adj.* пять. —*n.* **1,** (cardinal number) пять. **2,** (written numeral; school grade) пятёрка. **3,** *cards* пятёрка.

fivefold *adj.* пятикрáтный. —*adv.* впя́теро.

five hundred пятьсóт. —**five-hundredth,** *adj.* пятисóтый.

Five-Year Plan пятилéтка; пятилéтний план.

fix *v.t.* **1,** (repair) чини́ть; налáживать. **2,** *fol. by* **up** (decorate, as a room) обставля́ть; отдéлывать. **3,** (fasten securely) укрепля́ть; закрепля́ть. **4,** (direct steadily, as one's gaze) устремля́ть; прикóвывать; фикси́ровать. **5,** (set, as a date) назначáть; определя́ть; фикси́ровать. **6,** (prepare, as a meal) готóвить. **7,** (determine, as blame) устанáвливать (винóвность). **8,** *photog.* закрепля́ть; фикси́ровать. **9,** *colloq.* (get even with) раздéлываться с. *I'll fix him!,* я емý задáм! —*n., colloq.* передéлка: *get into a fix,* попáсть в передéлку; сесть в лýжу.

fixation *n.* навя́зчивая идéя.

fixed *adj.* **1,** (stationary; immobile) неподви́жный: *fixed point,* неподви́жная тóчка. **2,** (not fluctuating) фикси́рованный. **3,** (provided for) обеспéченный: *well fixed,* хорошó обеспéченный. *She is well fixed,* онá живёт в достáтке. *How are you fixed for money?,* как у вас с деньгáми? —**fixed bayonets,** при́мкнутые штыки́. —**fixed idea,** навя́зчивая идéя.

fixture *n.* прибóр; детáль; *pl.* арматýра.

fizz *v.i.* шипéть. —*n.* шипéние.

fizzle *v.i.* **1,** (hiss) шипéть. **2,** *colloq.* (peter out) вы́дыхáться.

flabbergast *v.t., colloq.* ошарáшивать.

flabby *adj.* дря́блый; вя́лый; обрю́згший; обрю́зглый. *Become flabby,* обрю́згнуть. —**flabbiness,** *n.* дря́блость.

flaccid *adj.* дря́блый; отви́слый.

flag *n.* флаг. —*v.t.* [*usu.* **flag down**] (hail; signal to stop) окликáть. —*v.i.* (slacken; wane) слабéть; ослабевáть. *The conversation flagged,* разговóр (чáсто) замолкáл.

flagellate *v.t.* бичева́ть. —**flagellation,** *n.* бичева́ние.
flagman *n.* сигна́льщик.
flag officer фла́гман.
flagpole *n.* флагшто́к.
flagrant *adj.* гру́бый; вопию́щий.
flagship *n.* фла́гманский кора́бль; фла́гман.
flagstaff *n.* флагшто́к.
flagstone *n.* плита́; плитня́к. —*adj.* плитняко́вый.
flail *n.* цеп. —*v.t.* **1,** (thresh) молоти́ть. **2,** (beat) колоти́ть.
flair *n.* спосо́бности: *a flair for music/languages,* спосо́бности к му́зыке/языка́м.
flak *n.* зени́тная артилле́рия.
flake *n., usu. pl.* хло́пья. *Corn flakes,* кукуру́зные хло́пья. *Soap flakes,* мы́льная стру́жка. —*v.i.* [*usu.* **flake off**] лупи́ться; шелуши́ться. —**flaky,** *adj.* слоёный.
flamboyant *adj.* цвети́стый; пы́шный; показно́й.
flame *n.* **1,** (fire) пла́мя: *burst into flame,* вспы́хнуть пла́менем. *Be in flames,* быть в огне́. **2,** (passion) увлече́ние. **3,** *colloq.* (sweetheart) зазно́ба. —*v.i.* пыла́ть. —**flame thrower,** огнемёт.
flaming *adj.* **1,** (ablaze) пыла́ющий. **2,** (intense; ardent) пла́менный.
flamingo *n.* флами́нго.
flammable *adj.* огнеопа́сный.
flange *n.* **1,** (for a pipe) фла́нец. **2,** (for a wheel) ребо́рда.
flank *n.* фланг. —*v.t.* фланки́ровать. *He was flanked by two bodyguards,* у него́ по бока́м стоя́ли два телохрани́теля. —**flanking,** *adj.* флангóвый.
flannel *n.* флане́ль. —*adj.* флане́левый.
flap *v.t.* взма́хивать (кры́льями). —*v.i.* развева́ться. —*n.* **1,** (flapping, as of wings) взмах. **2,** (of a garment or tent) пола́; (of a pocket) кла́пан. **3,** *aero.* закры́лок.
flare *n.* **1,** (burst of flame) вспы́шка. **2,** (signal light) фа́кел; сигна́льная раке́та. **3,** (expanding part) растру́б; клёш. *Flared skirt,* ю́бка клёш. —*v.i.* [*usu.* **flare up**] **1,** (flame up brightly) возгора́ться. **2,** (suddenly become angry) вспыли́ть. **3,** *fig.* (break out; erupt) разгора́ться; вспы́хивать. *Tempers flared,* стра́сти разгоре́лись.
flash *n.* **1,** (of light) вспы́шка; про́блеск. *Flash of lightning,* вспы́шка мо́лнии. **2,** (instant) миг: *in a flash,* ми́гом; в оди́н миг. **3,** *pl.* (sudden manifestations, as of wit) блёстки (остроу́мия). —*v.i.* **1,** (shine brightly or suddenly) сверка́ть: *lightning flashed,* сверкну́ла мо́лния. *A flashing light,* мига́ющий свет. *His eyes flashed with anger,* его́ глаза́ сверка́ли гне́вом. **2,** *fol. by* **by, past, across** (pass suddenly and swiftly) мелькну́ть; промелькну́ть. *An idea flashed across my mind,* у меня́ (про)мелькну́ла *or* блесну́ла мысль; меня́ осени́ла мысль. —*v.t.* **1,** (shine) свети́ть: *flash a light in someone's eyes,* свети́ть кому́-нибудь в глаза́. **2,** (send at great speed) сообщи́ть (с быстрото́й мо́лнии). *Flash a signal,* подава́ть сигна́л. **3,** *colloq.* (display ostentatiously) выставля́ть; демонстри́ровать.
flash bulb ла́мпа-вспы́шка; блиц.
flasher *n.* мига́лка.
flash gun вспы́шка.
flashlight *n.* карма́нный фона́рь.
flashy *adj.* крича́щий; крикли́вый.
flask *n.* **1,** (for carrying liquids) фля́га; фля́жка. **2,** (for use in a laboratory) ко́лба.
flat *adj.* **1,** (level) пло́ский: *flat surface,* пло́ская пове́рхность. **2,** (lacking zest, as of a drink) вы́дохшийся. **3,** (dull; insipid) пло́ский; пре́сный. **4,** (absolute; pointblank) категори́ческий. —*adv.* **1,** (prostrate) плашмя́; врастя́жку. *Lie flat,* ложи́ться плашмя́; распласта́ться. *Flat on one's back,* на́взничь; пласто́м. **2,** (in full contact) вплотну́ю: *flat against the wall,* вплотну́ю к стене́. **3,** (completely) соверше́нно: *flat broke,* соверше́нно разорённый. **4,** (exactly) ро́вно: *in two minutes flat,* ро́вно за две мину́ты. **5,** *music* не в лад. *Sing flat,* фальши́вить. —*n.* **1,** (apartment) кварти́ра. **2,** *music* бемо́ль: *E-flat,* ми-бемо́ль. **3,** (low-lying area) бассе́йн: *salt flats,* соляны́е бассе́йны. **4,** *pl.* (flat-heeled shoes) ту́фли без каблука́. **5,** = **flat tire.** —**fall flat,** прова́ливаться. —**flat tire,** спу́щенная ши́на *or* покры́шка: *we had a flat tire,* у нас спусти́ла ши́на/покры́шка.
flat-bottomed *adj.* плоскодо́нный.
flatcar *n.* платфо́рма; ваго́н-платфо́рма.
flat-chested *adj.* плоскогру́дый.
flatfoot *n.* пло́ская стопа́; плоскосто́пие.
flatfooted *adj.* страда́ющий плоскосто́пием. —**catch flatfooted,** *colloq.* заста́ть врасплох.
flatiron *n.* утю́г.
flatly *adv.* (categorically) наотре́з.
flatness *n.* пло́скость.
flatten *v.t.* сплю́щивать; расплю́щивать. —*v.i.* [*usu.* **flatten out**] **1,** (become flat) сплю́щиваться. **2,** *aero.* (resume a horizontal line of flight) выра́вниваться.
flatter *v.t.* льстить. *I am flattered,* мне ле́стно; я польщён. —**flatterer,** *n.* льстец.
flattering *adj.* **1,** (intended to flatter) льсти́вый. **2,** (complimentary) ле́стный.
flattery *n.* лесть.
flatulence *n.* скопле́ние га́зов; метеори́зм.
flatware *n.* столо́вые прибо́ры.
flatworm *n.* пло́ский червь.
flaunt *v.t.* выставля́ть; козыря́ть; коке́тничать; щеголя́ть (*last three with instr.*).
flavor *also,* **flavour** *n.* **1,** (distinctive taste) вкус. **2,** (distinctive quality) при́вкус. —*v.t.* приправля́ть.
flavoring *also,* **flavouring** *n.* припра́ва.
flavour *n. & v.* = **flavor.** —**flavouring,** *n.* = **flavoring.**
flaw *n.* поро́к; брак; изъя́н —*v.t.* по́ртить. —**flawed,** *adj.* с изъя́ном.
flawless *adj.* безупре́чный; безукори́зненный. —**flawlessly,** *adv.* безупре́чно; безукори́зненно.
flax *n.* лён. —**flaxen,** *adj.* льняно́й. *Flaxen hair,* льняны́е во́лосы.
flay *v.t.* **1,** (strip off the skin of) сдира́ть ко́жу с; обдира́ть. **2,** *fig.* (criticize severely) хлеста́ть.
flea *n.* блоха́. —**fleabite,** *n.* блоши́ный уку́с. —**flea market,** толку́чка.
fleck *n.* пятно́; кра́пинка. —*v.t.* испещря́ть. *Hair flecked with gray,* во́лосы с про́седью.
fledged *adj.* опери́вшийся. *Become fully fledged,* оперя́ться.
fledgling *n.* птене́ц.
flee *v.i.* бежа́ть; убега́ть; спаса́ться бе́гством. —*v.t.* бежа́ть из; убега́ть из.
fleece *n.* руно́. —*v.t.* (swindle) обира́ть; обдира́ть.
fleecy *adj.* **1,** (soft and light) пуши́стый. **2,** (of clouds) пе́ристый.
fleet *n.* **1,** (of warships) флот. **2,** (of boats) флоти́лия:

whaling fleet, китобойная флотилия. **3,** (of vehicles) парк. —*adj.* быстрый; быстроногий. —*v.i.* бежать; лететь.

fleeting *adj.* **1,** (momentary) мимолётный. **2,** *phonet.* (of a vowel) беглый.

Fleming *n.* фламандец. —**Flemish,** *adj.* фламандский. —*n.* фламандский язык.

flesh *n.* **1,** (soft substance of the body) мякоть; мясо. *Flesh wound,* поверхностная рана. **2,** (the body as distinguished from the soul) плоть. —**in the flesh,** во плоти. —**it makes my flesh creep,** у меня мурашки бегают по спине. —**one's own flesh and blood,** чья-нибудь плоть и кровь.

flesh-colored *adj.* телесный; телесного цвета.

fleshy *adj.* мясистый.

flex *v.t.* гнуть; сгибать.

flexible *adj.* гибкий. —**flexibility,** *n.* гибкость.

flick *n.* щелчок. —*v.t.* **1,** (strike deftly) щёлкать. **2,** (remove with a quick snap) смахивать.

flicker *v.i.* **1,** (glimmer) мерцать; мигать; трепетать. **2,** *fol. by* **out** (go out) гаснуть; угасать. —*n.* **1,** (wavering light) мерцание; мигание; трепет. **2,** (ray, as of hope) искра (надежды).

flier *also,* **flyer** *n.* лётчик.

flight *n.* **1,** (act of flying) полёт. *Be in flight,* быть в полёте. **2,** (trip made by air) полёт; перелет. **3,** (scheduled trip of an airplane) рейс. **4,** (abrupt departure) бегство: *put to flight,* обращать в бегство; *take flight,* обращаться в бегство. **5,** (set of stairs) марш. **6,** (flock of birds) стая. **7,** (group of airplanes) звено. **8,** (soaring beyond normal limits) полет: *flight of fantasy,* полёт фантазии. —**flight deck,** полётная палуба (авианосца). —**flight engineer,** бортмеханик. —**flight path,** траектория полёта. —**flight recorder,** бортовой самописец.

flighty *adj.* легкомысленный; ветреный.

flimsy *adj.* **1,** (lacking solidity) непрочный. **2,** (poor, as of an excuse) слабый. —**flimsiness,** *n.* непрочность.

flinch *v.i.* **1,** (wince, as from pain) вздрагивать. **2,** (draw back; shrink, as from fear) дрогнуть.

fling *v.t.* кидать; метать; швырять. *Fling open,* распахивать. —*n.* **1,** (toss) бросок. **2,** *colloq.* (try) попытка. *Have a fling at,* попробовать.

flint *n.* кремень.

flip *v.t.* **1,** (toss) бросать. **2,** (toss into the air, as a coin) подбрасывать. **3,** (flick) смахивать. **4,** (turn rapidly, as a dial) вертеть; крутить. **5,** *fol. by* **over** (invert) перевёртывать. —*v.i.* **1,** *fol. by* **over** (turn over) перевёртываться. **2,** *fol. by* **through** (leaf through) перелистывать.

flippant *adj.* дерзкий. —**flippancy,** *n.* дерзость.

flipper *n.* ласт.

flirt *v.i.* кокетничать; флиртовать. —*n.* кокетка. —**flirtation,** *n.* кокетство; флирт. —**flirtatious,** *adj.* кокетливый.

flit *v.i.* порхать.

float *v.i.* **1,** (not sink) плавать; не тонуть; держаться на воде. **2,** (drift) плыть; нестись. *Float to the surface,* всплывать *or* выплывать на поверхность. —*v.t.* **1,** (ship by water, as logs) сплавлять. **2,** (arrange for, as a loan) размещать (заём). —*n.* поплавок.

floating *adj.* **1,** (on water) плавающий; плавучий. **2,** *finance* оборотный: *floating capital,* оборотный капитал. **3,** *med.* блуждающий: *floating kidney,* блуждающая почка.

flock *n.* **1,** (of sheep, goats, etc.) стадо. **2,** (of birds) стая. **3,** (congregation) паства. **4,** (crowd) толпа. —*v.i.* толпиться; стекаться.

floe *n.* плавучая льдина.

flog *v.t.* сечь; пороть; хлестать; стегать.

flood *n.* **1,** (deluge) наводнение. *The Flood,* всемирный потоп. **2,** *fig.* (huge flow or influx) поток. —*v.t.* **1,** (fill with water) затоплять; заливать. **2,** *fig.* (overwhelm) наводнять.

floodgate *n.* шлюз; шлюзные ворота.

floodlight *n.* прожектор.

flood plain (заливная) пойма.

flood tide прилив.

floodwaters *n.pl.* полая вода. *The floodwaters are receding,* воды убывают.

floor *n.* **1,** (in a room) пол. **2,** (story of a building) этаж: *on the sixth floor,* на шестом этаже. **3,** (bottom) дно: *ocean floor,* морское дно. **4,** (right to speak) слово: *ask for the floor,* просить слова. *Questions from the floor,* вопросы с места. —*v.t.* **1,** (knock to the ground) валить на пол. **2,** *colloq.* (stun) оглушить.

floorboard *n.* половица.

flooring *n.* настил.

floor lamp торшер.

floor show варьете.

floorspace *n.* жилая площадь; жилплощадь.

flop *v.i.* **1,** (fall) плюхаться; бухаться; хлопаться. **2,** *slang* (fail) проваливаться. —*n., colloq.* неудача; фиаско.

flophouse *n., colloq.* ночлежка.

flora *n.* флора.

floral *adj.* цветочный.

floriculture *n.* цветоводство.

florid *adj.* цветистый; витиеватый.

florin *n.* флорин.

florist *n.* торговец цветами. *Florist's shop,* цветочный магазин.

flotilla *n.* флотилия.

flounce *n.* оборка.

flounder *n.* (fish) камбала. —*v.i.* **1,** (move with great difficulty) барахтаться. **2,** *fig.* (fare badly) хромать на обе ноги.

flour *n.* мука. —*adj.* мучной: *flour sack,* мучной мешок.

flourish *v.i.* процветать. —*n.* **1,** (embellishment in writing) росчерк; завиток; завитушка. **2,** (use of ornate language) завиток; завитушка: *rhetorical flourishes,* риторические завитушки. **3,** (sound of trumpets) фанфара; туш.

flout *v.t.* бросить вызов (+ *dat.*); попирать.

flow *v.i.* течь; литься. *Flow out to sea,* вытекать в море. *The Volga flows into the Caspian Sea,* Волга впадает в Каспийское море. *The Danube flows through eight countries,* Дунай течёт *or* протекает через восемь стран. —*n.* **1,** (of a fluid) течение. *Flow of blood,* кровотечение. **2,** *fig.* (steady movement) поток; течение; ход. —**a lot of water has flown under the bridge since then,** много воды утекло с тех пор.

flower *n.* цветок (*pl.* цветы). —*adj.* цветочный: *flower show,* цветочная выставка. —*v.i.* цвести; расцветать. —**flower bed,** клумба; цветник. —**flower girl,** цветочница.

flowering *adj.* цветущий; цветковый.

flowerpot *n.* цветочный горшок; вазон.

flowery *adj.* цвети́стый; кра́сочный; витиева́тый.
flowing *adj.* **1,** (smooth and continuous) пла́вный. **2,** (hanging loosely at full length) свиса́ющий.
flu *n.* грипп.
fluctuate *v.i.* колеба́ться. —**fluctuation,** *n.* колеба́ние.
flue *n.* дымохо́д.
fluency *n.* пла́вность; бе́глость.
fluent *adj.* пла́вный; бе́глый; свобо́дный. —**fluently,** *adv.* свобо́дно; бе́гло.
fluff *n.* пух; пушо́к. —*v.t.* [*usu.* **fluff up**] взбива́ть; (рас)пуши́ть. —**fluffy,** *adj.* пуши́стый; пы́шный.
fluid *n.* жи́дкость. —*adj.* жи́дкий; теку́чий. —**fluidity,** *n.* теку́честь.
fluke *n.* **1,** (fish) ка́мбала. **2,** (part of an anchor) ла́па. **3,** *slang* (lucky chance) игра́ слу́чая.
flunk *v.t., colloq.* **1,** (fail, as an exam) сре́заться на (экза́мене). **2,** (fail, as a student) сре́зать. —*v.i., colloq.* сре́заться.
flunky *also,* **flunkey** *n.* лаке́й.
fluoresce *v.i.* флуоресци́ровать.
fluorescence *n.* свече́ние; флуоресце́нция.
fluorescent *adj.* флуоресци́рующий. —**fluorescent lamp,** люминесце́нтная ла́мпа.
fluoride *n.* фтори́д. ♦ *In combinations* фто́ристый: *sodium fluoride,* фто́ристый на́трий.
fluorine *n.* фтор.
fluorite *n.* плавико́вый шпат. *Also,* **fluorspar.**
flurry *n.* **1,** *pl.* (of snow) снежи́нки. **2,** (sudden burst) поры́в.
flush *v.t.* **1,** (purge) промыва́ть; очища́ть. *Flush the toilet,* спусти́ть во́ду в убо́рной. **2,** (drive from cover) выку́ривать. **3,** (redden) румя́нить. —*v.i.* красне́ть; багрове́ть; румя́ниться; але́ть. —*n.* кра́ска: *flush of anger,* кра́ска гне́ва. —*adj.* [*usu.* **flush with** *or* **against**] вро́вень (с); вприты́к (к).
fluster *v.t.* конфу́зить. *Become flustered,* теря́ться; растеря́ться; конфу́зиться.
flute *n.* фле́йта.
fluted *adj.* рифлёный.
flutist *n.* флейти́ст.
flutter *v.i.* развева́ться; трепета́ть.
flux *n.* **1,** (continual change): *in a state of flux,* в состоя́нии измене́ния; в состоя́нии неопределённости. **2,** *metall.* флюс; пла́вень.
fly *v.i.* **1,** (general term) лете́ть; лета́ть. *The little bird cannot fly,* пти́чка не мо́жет лета́ть. *Fly across the ocean,* лете́ть че́рез океа́н. *Sparks flew in all directions,* и́скры лете́ли во все сто́роны. *Time flies,* вре́мя лети́т. **2,** (wave, as of a flag) развева́ться. **3,** *fol. by* **into** (burst into) приходи́ть в: *fly into a rage,* приходи́ть в я́рость. —*v.t.* **1,** (operate, as an aircraft) вести́; управля́ть. **2,** (float, as a kite) пуска́ть (змея́). **3,** (transport by aircraft) перевози́ть (по во́здуху); перебра́сывать. **4,** (complete, as a sortie or mission) соверша́ть (вы́лет). —*n.* **1,** (insect) му́ха. *He wouldn't hurt a fly,* он и му́хи не оби́дит. **2,** (on trousers) шири́нка. —**fly across,** перелета́ть. —**fly away,** улета́ть —**fly by,** пролета́ть. —**fly in, 1,** (arrive by plane) прилета́ть. **2,** (deliver by air) доставля́ть (самолётом). —**fly in the face of,** идти́ вразре́з с; противоре́чить. —**fly in the ointment,** ло́жка дёгтя в бо́чке мёда. —**fly off,** улета́ть. —**fly open,** распахну́ться. —**fly past,** пролета́ть ми́мо. —**let fly,** пуска́ть. —**on the fly,** на лету́.

flycatcher *n.* мухоло́вка.
flyer *n.* = **flier.**
flying *n.* лета́ние; лётное де́ло. —*adj.* **1,** (that flies) лета́ющий; лету́чий. *Flying fish,* лету́чая ры́ба. *Flying saucer,* лета́ющая таре́лка. **2,** (used for flying) лета́тельный: *flying machine,* лета́тельный аппара́т. **3,** (suitable for flying) лётный: *flying weather,* лётная пого́да. —**with flying colors,** с бле́ском.
flying squirrel летя́га.
flyleaf *n.* фо́рзац.
flypaper *n.* липу́чая бума́га от мух; липу́чка от мух.
fly swatter хлопу́шка.
flytrap *n.* мухоло́вка.
flywheel *n.* махово́е колесо́; махови́к.
foal *n.* жеребёнок. —*v.t.* рожа́ть. —*v.i.* жереби́ться.
foam *n.* пе́на. —*v.i.* пе́ниться. —**foam rubber,** гу́бчатая рези́на.
foamy *adj.* пе́нистый.
focal *adj.* фо́кусный: *focal length,* фо́кусное расстоя́ние. *Focal point,* фо́кус; центр; средото́чие.
focus *n.* фо́кус: *be in focus,* быть в фо́кусе. *Be the focus of attention,* быть в це́нтре внима́ния. —*v.t.* **1,** (adjust the focus of) фокуси́ровать. **2,** (concentrate) сосредото́чивать.
fodder *n.* корм; фура́ж.
foe *n.* враг.
foetus *n.* = **fetus.**
fog *n.* тума́н. —*v.t.* тума́нить; затума́нивать. —*v.i.* [*usu.* **fog up**] вспоте́ть; запотева́ть.
foggy *adj.* тума́нный. *It is foggy today,* сего́дня тума́н; сего́дня тума́нно. —**fogginess,** *n.* тума́нность.
foghorn *n.* наутофо́н.
foible *n.* сла́бое ме́сто; сла́бая сторона́; сла́бость.
foil *v.t.* расстра́ивать; срыва́ть. —*n.* **1,** (thin sheet of metal) фо́льга. *Tin foil,* станио́ль. **2,** (sword) рапи́ра.
foist *v.t.* навя́зывать; всуча́ть.
fold *v.t.* [*often* **fold up**] скла́дывать. *Fold one's hands,* скла́дывать ру́ки. *Fold up a map,* скла́дывать ка́рту. —*v.i.* **1,** [*often* **fold up**] (be folded) скла́дываться. *A bed that folds up,* складна́я крова́ть. **2,** *colloq.* (fail and close down) прогоре́ть. —*n.* **1,** (in paper or cloth; of skin) скла́дка. **2,** (of a tent) пола́; (of a screen) ство́рка. **3,** (pen) заго́н. **4,** (flock; group) па́ства.
folder *n.* па́пка; скоросшива́тель.
folding *adj.* **1,** (of a chair, table, etc.) складно́й; раскладно́й; откидно́й. **2,** (of doors) (дву)ство́рчатый.
foliage *n.* листва́.
folio *n.* **1,** (sheet) лист. **2,** (book) фолиа́нт; фо́лио.
folk *n.* лю́ди: *simple folk,* просты́е лю́ди. —*adj.* наро́дный: *folk song,* наро́дная пе́сня.
folklore *n.* фолькло́р.
follicle *n.* фолли́кул.
follow *v.t.* **1,** (go after; come after) сле́довать за. *Follow me!,* иди́те за мной! **2,** (watch; trail; keep track of) следи́ть за. **3,** (proceed along, as a road) идти́ по; е́хать по. **4,** (heed; obey) сле́довать (+ *dat.*): *follow advice,* сле́довать сове́ту. *Follow orders,* выполня́ть приказа́ния. **5,** (understand the logic of) понима́ть. —*v.i.* (come next or as a result) сле́довать. *From this it follows that...,* из э́того сле́дует, что... —**as follows,** сле́дующее: *the telegram reads as follows,* телегра́мма гласи́т сле́дующее. *Your duties are as follows,* ва́ши обя́занности заключа́ются в сле́дующем.
follower *n.* после́дователь.

following *adj.* слéдующий. *The following day,* на другóй день. *The following morning,* наýтро. —*n.* **1,** (group of followers or fans) послéдователи; поклóнники. **2,** *preceded by* **the** (what follows) слéдующее. —*prep.* пóсле: *following the meeting,* пóсле собрáния.

folly *n.* глýпость; безýмие.

foment *v.t.* раздувáть; разжигáть.

fond *adj.* **1,** *fol. by* **of** (liking): *be fond of,* любить. **2,** (affectionate) лáсковый; нéжный. **3,** (cherished, as of a wish) завéтный.

fondle *v.t.* ласкáть.

fondness *n.* любóвь; увлечéние.

font *n.* **1,** (receptacle for holy water) купéль. **2,** *printing* комплéкт шрифта.

food *n.* пища. —*adj.* пищевóй: *food poisoning,* пищевóе отравлéние. —**food for thought,** пища для умá; пища для размышлéния.

foodstuff *n., usu. pl.* пищевые продýкты; продовóльственные товáры.

fool *n.* **1,** (stupid person) дурáк. **2,** (court jester) шут. —*adj.* [*usu.* **fool's**] дурáцкий; шутовскóй: *fool's cap,* дурáцкий/шутовскóй колпáк. —*v.t.* дурáчить; обмáнывать. —*v.i.* **1,** (jest) шутить: *I'm not fooling,* я не шучý. *Don't fool with him!* с ним не шути! **2,** *fol. by* **with** (play with carelessly) игрáть (+ *instr.*). —**fool around,** дурáчиться. —**make a fool of,** остáвить в дуракáх; дурáчить. —**make a fool of oneself,** остáться в дуракáх; опростоволóситься. —**nobody's fool,** мáлый не прóмах. —**play the fool,** валя́ть дуракá.

foolhardy *adj.* безрассýдный. —**foolhardiness,** *n.* безрассýдство.

foolish *adj.* глýпый. —**foolishly,** *adv.* глýпо. —**foolishness,** *n.* глýпость.

foot *n.* **1,** (of humans) ногá. **2,** (of animals) лáпа. **3,** (base) поднóжие. **4,** (lower end; bottom) конéц. *At the foot of the stairs,* внизý лéстницы. *At the foot of the bed,* в ногáх кровáти. **5,** (of a mountain, hill, etc.) поднóжие; подóшва. **6,** (measure of length) фут. **7,** *pros.* стопá. —*adj.* ножнóй: *foot brake,* ножнóй тóрмоз. —**get cold feet,** струсить. —**get to one's feet,** вставáть нá ноги. —**get on one's feet** (*fig.*), стать нá ноги. —**on foot,** пешкóм. —**put one's best foot forward,** показáть товáр лицóм. —**put one's foot in it,** попáсть впросáк; сесть в лýжу. —**set foot on,** ступить на: *set foot on the moon,* ступить на Лунý. *I never set foot in there,* ногá моя́ тудá не ступáет.

footage *n.* **1,** (length expressed in feet) длинá (в фýтах). **2,** *motion pictures* метрáж.

foot-and-mouth-disease я́щур.

football *n.* **1,** (game) футбóл. **2,** (ball) футбóльный мяч.

footbridge *n.* мóстик; пешехóдный мост.

foothill *n.* предгóрье.

foothold *n.* тóчка опóры: *gain a foothold,* найти тóчку опóры.

footing *n.* **1,** (firm placing of the feet): *keep one's footing,* удержáться на ногáх; *lose one's footing,* поскользнýться. **2,** (position; standing): *on an equal footing,* на рáвных услóвиях; на рáвной ногé. *Place on a war footing,* перестрóить на воéнный лад.

footlights *n.pl.* рáмпа.

footman *n.* лакéй; скорохóд.

footnote *n.* примечáние; снóска.

footprint *n.* след; отпечáток ноги.

foot soldier пехотинец.

footstep *n., usu. pl.* **1,** (footprints) следы́. **2,** (sound of someone walking) шаги. —**follow in the footsteps of,** идти по стопáм (+ *gen.*).

footstool *n.* скамéйка для ног.

footwear *n.* óбувь.

fop *n.* фат; франт; щёголь; хлыщ. —**foppery,** *n.* фатовствó; щегольствó. —**foppish,** *adj.* фатовáтый; франтовáтый.

for *prep.* **1,** (used for; intended for; as regards) для: *a book for children,* книга для детéй; *bad for one's health,* врéдно для здорóвья. ♦ *Less commonly* на: *the lesson for tomorrow,* урóк на зáвтра; *plans for the summer,* плáны на лéто; *a room for two,* кóмната на двоих. **2,** (in favor of; in exchange for; in recognition of) за (+ *acc.*): *vote for,* голосовáть за; *pay for,* платить за; *fight for,* борóться за. *An award for bravery,* наградá за мýжество. *Thanks for your help,* спасибо за пóмощь. **3,** (to fetch) за (+ *instr.*): *send for the doctor,* послáть за врачóм. **4,** (indicating destination) в (+ *acc.*): *leave for Washington,* уезжáть в Вашингтóн. **5,** (indicating duration of time) *usu. omitted in Russian: wait for two hours,* ждать два чacá. *I haven't seen you for ages,* не видел вас цéлую вéчность. ♦ *Also* в течéние: *for the last two weeks,* в течéние послéдних двух недéль. **6,** (for a period of time begun as action is completed) на (+ *acc.*): *lie down for an hour,* прилéчь на час. *Come in for a minute!,* зайдите на минýту! **7,** (in view of the normal character of) для: *very warm for May,* óчень теплó для мáя. *Not bad for a beginner,* неплóхо для начинáющего. **8,** (in place of) за (+ *acc.*); вмéсто. *To sign for the chairman,* расписáться за председáтеля. *A substitute for sugar,* суррогáт сáхара. **9,** (from; because of) от: *jump for joy,* пры́гать от рáдости. **10,** (owing to) за (+ *instr.*): *for lack of evidence,* за неимéнием улик. *For many reasons,* по мнóгим причинам. **11,** (as a cure for) от: *have you anything for a headache?,* у вас есть чтó-нибудь от головнóй бóли? **12,** (despite) при: *for all his knowledge,* при всех егó знáниях. *For all that,* при всём том. —*conj.* (because; inasmuch as) ибо; поскóльку.

forage *n.* фурáж; корм. —*adj.* кормовóй: *forage crops,* кормовы́е культýры. —*v.i.* [*usu.* **forage for**] разы́скивать.

foray *n.* набéг; налёт.

forbear *v.t.* (refrain from) удéрживаться от; воздéрживаться от. —*v.i.* (have patience) терпéть. —*n.* = **forebear.**

forbearance *n.* **1,** (abstinence) воздержáние. **2,** (patient endurance) терпели́вость.

forbid *v.t.* запрещáть; воспрещáть. —**God forbid!,** не дай бог!; бóже упаси!

forbidden *adj.* **1,** *used predicatively* запрещенó: *it is forbidden,* э́то запрещенó. **2,** *modifier* запрéтный: *forbidden fruit,* запрéтный плод.

forbidding *adj.* непристýпный; непривéтливый.

force *n.* **1,** (strength; power) сила: *the force of a blow,* сила удáра. **2,** (physical pressure or coercion) сила: *by force,* силой; насильно. *The use of force,* применéние силы. **3,** (validity) сила: *remain in force,* оставáться в силе. **4,** *pl., mil.* силы: *armed forces,* вооружённые силы. —*v.t.* **1,** (compel) заставля́ть;

вынуждáть; принуждáть. *Force oneself,* дéлать над собóй усúлие. **2,** (cause to move against resistance) втáлкивать; вгонять. *Force out of power,* вытеснять из правлéния. *Force the crowd back,* осáживать толпý. *Force the enemy back,* оттеснять протúвника. *Force one's way into/through,* влáмываться в; пробивáться сквозь. **3,** (break open, as a lock or door) взлáмывать. **4,** (impose, as one's opinions) навязывать. **5,** (produce by effort) вы́давить: *force a smile,* вы́давить улы́бку. **6,** (make grow faster, as plants) выгонять. —**by force of arms,** сúлой орýжия. —**by force of habit,** в сúлу привы́чки.

forced *adj.* **1,** (compulsory) принудúтельный: *forced labor,* принудúтельный труд. **2,** (emergency, as of a landing) вы́нужденный. **3,** (unnatural, as of a smile) натянутый. —**forced march,** *mil.* форсúрованный марш.

forceful *adj.* решúтельный: *forceful measures,* решúтельные мéры.

forceps *n.* хирургúческие щипцы́.

forcible *adj.* насúльственный. —**forcibly,** *adv.* насúльно.

ford *n.* брод. —*v.t.* переходúть вброд.

fore *n.* перéдний план: *come to the fore,* выдвигáться на перéдний план.

fore-and-aft *adj.* продóльный. *Fore-and-aft sail,* косóй пáрус.

forearm *n.* предплéчье.

forebear *also,* **forbear** *n.* прéдок.

forebode *v.t.* предвещáть. —**foreboding,** *n.* дурнóе предчýвствие.

forecast *n.* прогнóз; предсказáние. *Weather forecast,* прогнóз *or* свóдка погóды. —*v.t.* предскáзывать. —**forecaster,** *n.* предсказáтель.

forecastle *n.* бак.

forefather *n.* прéдок.

forefinger *n.* указáтельный пáлец.

forefront *n.* авангáрд. *In the forefront,* в авангáрде; в пéрвых рядáх.

forego *v.* = **forgo.**

foregoing *adj.* предшéствующий; вышеукáзанный. —**the foregoing,** предыдýщее.

foregone *adj.* прошéдший. —**foregone conclusion,** зарáнее извéстный результáт. *The result was a foregone conclusion,* в исхóде нé было сомнéний.

foreground *n.* перéдний план.

forehand *n., tennis* удáр спрáва. —*adj.* спрáва.

forehead *n.* лоб.

foreign *adj.* **1,** (of another country) инострáнный; чужóй: *foreign language,* инострáнный язы́к; *foreign country,* чужáя странá. **2,** (conducted with other nations) внéшний: *foreign policy,* внéшняя полúтика; *foreign trade,* внéшняя торгóвля. *Foreign aid,* пóмощь инострáнным государствам. **3,** (extraneous) посторóнний: *foreign body,* посторóннее тéло. **4,** (alien; strange) чýждый: *jealousy is foreign to his nature,* рéвность емý чуждá.

foreigner *n.* инострáнец.

foreign minister минúстр инострáнных дел.

foreleg *n.* перéдняяногá; перéдняя лáпа.

forelock *n.* чуб; чёлка; вихóр.

foreman *n.* мáстер; бригадúр.

foremast *n.* фок-мáчта.

foremost *adj.* **1,** (in front) перéдний; передовóй. **2,** (leading; outstanding) выдаю́щийся. —**first and foremost,** прéжде всегó.

forenoon *n.* врéмя до полýдня; ýтро.

forensic *adj.* судéбный.

foreordain *v.t.* предопределять.

forerunner *n.* предшéственник; предвéстник.

foresail *n.* фок.

foresee *v.t.* предвúдеть. —**in the foreseeable future,** в обозрúмом бýдущем.

foreshadow *v.t.* предвещáть.

foreshorten *v.t.* взять в ракýрсе. —**foreshortened,** *adj.* в ракýрсе.

foresight *n.* предусмотрúтельность.

foreskin *n.* крáйняя плоть.

forest *n.* лес. —*adj.* леснóй: *forest fire,* леснóй пожáр. —**not see the forest for the trees,** за дерéвьями лéса не вúдно.

forestall *v.t.* предупреждáть; предвосхищáть.

forester *n.* леснúчий. —**forestry,** *n.* леснóе хозяйство; лесовóдство.

foretaste *n.* предвкушéние.

foretell *v.t.* предскáзывать.

forethought *n.* предусмотрúтельность.

forever *adv.* **1,** (for all time) вéчно; навсегдá; навéк(и). *Live forever,* жить вéчно. **2,** (constantly) вéчно: *they are forever arguing,* онú вéчно спóрят.

forewarn *v.t.* предостерегáть.

foreword *n.* предислóвие.

forfeit *n.* **1,** (penalty) неустóйка. **2,** *pl.* (game) фáнты. —*v.t.* лишáться; утрáчивать. —**forfeiture,** *n.* потéря; утрáта.

forge *n.* **1,** (smithy) кýзница. **2,** (furnace) горн. —*v.t.* **1,** (shape; fashion) ковáть. **2,** (counterfeit) поддéлывать. —*v.i.* [*usu.* **forge ahead**] продвигáться вперёд; вы́скочить вперёд. —**forged,** *adj.* поддéльный; подлóжный. —**forger,** *n.* фальшивомонéтчик.

forgery *n.* **1,** (act of forging) подлóг; поддéлка. **2,** (something forged) поддéлка.

forget *v.t. & i.* забывáть: *don't forget!,* не забýдьте! *I completely forgot about it,* я совершéнно забы́л(а) об э́том. *I forgot to lock the door,* я забы́л(а) заперéть дверь.

forgetful *adj.* забы́вчивый. —**forgetfulness,** *n.* забы́вчивость.

forget-me-not *n.* незабýдка.

forgivable *adj.* простúтельный.

forgive *v.t.* прощáть: *forgive me for being late,* простúте меня за опоздáние. *I shall never forgive you for this,* я вам э́того никогдá не прощý. —**forgiveness,** *n.* прощéние.

forgo *also,* **forego** *v.t.* откáзываться от; воздéрживаться от; поступáться (+ *instr.*).

forgotten *adj.* забы́тый.

fork *n.* **1,** (eating utensil) вúлка. **2,** (in a road) разветвлéние; развúлка. —*v.i.* разветвляться; раздвáиваться.

forked *adj.* раздвóенный; разветвлённый. *Forked lightning,* зигзагообрáзная мóлния.

forlorn *adj.* жáлкий: *forlorn appearance,* жáлкий вид. —**forlorn hope,** (óчень) слáбая надéжда.

form *n.* **1,** (outward appearance) фóрма: *form and content,* фóрма и содержáние. **2,** (type; variety) фóрма: *form of energy,* фóрма энéргии. *Form of government,* óбраз правлéния. *Low forms of life,* нúзшие фóрмы жúзни. *Familiar form of address,* обращéние на "ты". **3,** (character) фóрма: *take the form of,* принимáть фóрму (+ *gen.*). *In the form of,* в вúде (+ *gen.*). **4,** (blank document) анкéта. **5,** (fitness) фóрма: *be in good form,* быть в фóрме. **6,** (correct social behavior) фóрма; тон: *for form's sake; as a matter of form,* для фóрмы; для профóрмы. *A sign of poor form,* прúзнак дурнóго тóна. **7,** *gram.* фóрма: *short form of adjectives,* крáткая фóрма прилагáтельных. **8,** (mold; dummy) фóрма: *form for hats,* фóрма для шляп. —*v.t.* **1,** (make; put together; organize) образóвывать; составлять; формировáть. *Form a circle,* образовáть круг. *Form a group,* образовáть/составлять грýппу. *Form a government,* образовáть/формировáть правúтельство. *Form an alliance with,* заключúть союз с. **2,** (develop in one's mind) составлять: *form an opinion,* состáвить себé мнéние. **3,** (develop, as a habit) вырабáтывать (в себé привы́чку). **4,** (make up; constitute) составлять: *form a single whole,* составлять едúное цéлое. *Form the boundary between,* образовáть грáницу мéжду. *Form the basis of,* лежáть в оснóве (+ *gen.*). —*v.i.* образóвываться; формировáться. *Puddles formed from the rain,* от дождя образовáлись лýжи. *Long lines formed,* вы́строились длúнные óчереди.

formal *adj.* **1,** (in various meanings) формáльный: *formal logic,* формáльная лóгика. **2,** (official) официáльный: *formal protest,* официáльный протéст. **3,** (of clothes) парáдный: *formal attire,* парáдное плáтье. **4,** (stiff; constrained) церемóнный.

formaldehyde *n.* формальдегúд.

formalism *n.* формалúзм. —**formalist,** *n.* формалúст —**formalistic,** *adj.* формалистúческий.

formality *n.* формáльность. *It's a mere formality,* это пустáя формáльность.

formalize *v.t.* оформлять.

formally *adv.* формáльно.

format *n.* формáт.

formation *n.* **1,** (process of forming) образовáние; формировáние. **2,** *mil.* строй; построéние. **3,** *geol.* формáция.

former *adj.* **1,** (earlier) прéжний: *in former times,* в прéжнее врéмя. **2,** (ex-) бы́вший. **3,** (opp. of latter) пéрвый. —**formerly,** *adv.* рáньше; прéжде.

formic *adj.* муравьúный: *formic acid,* муравьúная кислотá.

formidable *adj.* **1,** (awesome) грóзный. **2,** (hard to accomplish, as of a task) тяжёлый. **3,** (strikingly impressive) внушúтельный.

formless *adj.* бесфóрменный.

formula *n.* фóрмула.

formulate *v.t.* формулúровать. —**formulation,** *n.* формулирóвка.

fornication *n.* внебрáчная связь.

forsake *v.t.* **1,** (leave; abandon) бросáть; покидáть. **2,** (give up; renounce) откáзываться от; отрекáться от.

forswear *v.t.* зарекáться от.

fort *n.* форт.

forte *adj. & adv., music* фóрте. —*n.* (strong point) сúльная сторонá.

forth *adv.* **1,** (forward) вперёд. *Step forth,* выступáть. **2,** (outward) нарýжу. *Spew forth,* извергáть. —**and so forth,** и так дáлее; и томý подóбное; и прóчее. —**back and forth,** взад и вперёд.

forthcoming *adj.* **1,** (impending) предстоящий. **2,** (available when needed): *be forthcoming,* поступáть; имéться налицó.

forthright *adj.* прямодýшный; прямолинéйный. —**forthrightness,** *n.* прямодýшие; прямотá.

forthwith *adv.* немéдленно.

fortieth *adj.* сороковóй. —*n.* **1,** (fortieth part) сороковáя часть. **2,** (fraction) сороковáя: *one-fortieth,* однá сороковáя.

fortification *n.* укреплéние; фортификáция.

fortify *v.t.* **1,** (strengthen; provide with defenses) укреплять. **2,** (reinforce; invigorate) подкреплять.

fortissimo *adj. & adv.* фортúссимо.

fortitude *n.* стóйкость.

fortnight *n.* две недéли. —**fortnighty,** *adj.* происходящий раз в две недéли; *(of a publication)* двухнедéльный. —*adv.* раз в две недéли.

fortress *n.* крéпость.

fortuitous *adj.* случáйный, нечáянный. —**fortuitousness; fortuity,** *n.* случáйность.

fortunate *adj.* счастлúвый: *fortunate occurrence,* счастлúвый слýчай. *It was fortunate that...,* хорошó, что... —**fortunately,** *adv.* к счáстью.

fortune *n.* **1,** (fate; lot; destiny) судьбá. **2,** (luck) счáстье; удáча. *Have the good fortune to...,* имéть счáстье (+ *inf.*). **3,** (great amount of wealth) состояние: *make a fortune,* наживáть состояние. —**tell fortunes,** гадáть; ворожúть.

fortuneteller *n.* гадáлка; ворожея. —**fortunetelling,** *n.* гадáние; ворожбá.

forty *n. & adj.* сóрок.

forum *n.* фóрум.

forward *adv.* вперёд. *Step/come forward,* выступáть. —*adj.* **1,** (toward the front) поступáтельный: *forward motion,* поступáтельный ход; движéние вперёд. **2,** (in the front) пéредний; передовóй. **3,** (presumptuous) развязный. —*v.t.* **1,** (send) отправлять. **2,** (send to a further destination) пересылáть; переправлять; переадресóвывать. **3,** (promote; advance) продвигáть. —*n., sports* нападáющий. —**forward march!,** шáгом марш!

fossil *n.* окаменéлость; ископáемое. —*adj.* ископáемый: *fossil remains,* ископáемые остáтки; *fossil fuel,* ископáемое тóпливо. —**fossilized,** *adj.* ископáемый.

foster *v.t.* **1,** (promote; stimulate) спосóбствовать. **2,** (cultivate; instill) воспúтывать. **3,** (cherish) лелéять. —*adj.* приёмный: *foster father,* приёмный отéц.

foul *adj.* гáдкий; сквéрный; мéрзкий. *Foul air,* нечúстый вóздух. *Foul language,* сквернослóвие. —*v.t.* **1,** (soil; defile) загрязнять; загáживать. **2,** *fol. by* **up** (bungle) напýтать. —*n., sports* фол: *personal foul,* персонáльный фол. —**foul the trail,** запýтывать следы́.

found *v.t.* оснóвывать.

foundation *n.* **1,** (supporting part of a building) фундáмент. **2,** (basis) основáние. *Be without foundation,* не имéть основáния; не имéть под собóй пóчвы. **3,** (endowed institution) фонд.

founder *n.* **1,** (one who founds or establishes) оснoвáтель. **2,** (caster of metals) литéйщик. —*v.i.* **1,** (sink) тонýть. **2,** (fail) срывáться.

foundling *n.* подкúдыш; найдёныш. *Foundling home,* приют; детдóм.

foundry *n.* литéйный завóд. *Iron foundry,* чугунолитéйный завóд *or* цех.

fount *n.* кла́дезь.
fountain *n.* **1,** (large) фонта́н. **2,** (drinking fountain) фонта́нчик. —**fountain pen,** автору́чка.
four *adj.* четы́ре. —*n.* **1,** (cardinal number) четы́ре. **2,** (written numeral; school grade) четвёрка. **3,** *cards* четвёрка. —**on all fours,** ползко́м; на четвере́ньках.
fourfold *adj.* четырёхкра́тный. —*adv.* вче́тверо.
four hundred четы́реста. —**four-hundredth,** *adj.* четырёхсо́тый.
four-legged *adj.* четвероно́гий.
fourteen *n. & adj.* четы́рнадцать. —**fourteenth,** *adj.* четы́рнадцатый.
fourth *adj.* четвёртый. —*n.* **1,** (quarter) че́тверть: *three-fourths,* три че́тверти. **2,** *music* ква́рта. —**in the fourth place,** в-четвёртых.
four-wheel *adj.* четырёхколёсный. *Also,* **four-wheeled.**
fowl *n.* дома́шняя пти́ца. —**fowler,** *n.* птицело́в. —**fowling,** *n.* птицело́вство.
fox *n.* лиса́; лиси́ца. —*adj.* ли́сий: *fox fur,* ли́сий мех.
foxglove *n.* наперстя́нка.
foxhole *n., mil.* яче́йка.
fox terrier фокстерье́р.
fox trot фокстро́т.
foxy *adj.* ли́сий; хи́трый.
foyer *n.* фойе́; вестибю́ль.
fracas *n.* шу́мная ссо́ра; дебо́ш.
fraction *n.* **1,** *math.* дробь. **2,** *fol. by* **of** (small portion) деся́тая до́ля (+ *gen.*). —**fractional,** *adj.* дро́бный.
fractious *adj.* **1,** (cross) злой. **2,** (unruly) непоко́рный.
fracture *n.* перело́м. —*v.t.* лома́ть; перела́мывать.
fragile *adj.* хру́пкий; ло́мкий. —**fragility,** *n.* хру́пкость; ло́мкость.
fragment *n.* обло́мок; оско́лок. —*v.t.* дроби́ть; раздробля́ть. —**fragmentary,** *adj.* отры́вочный.
fragmentation *n.* **1,** (splitting up) дробле́ние. **2,** (state of being divided) раздро́бленность. —**fragmentation bomb,** оско́лочная бо́мба.
fragrance *n.* арома́т; благоуха́ние.
fragrant *adj.* души́стый; арома́тный; благоуха́нный.
frail *adj.* хру́пкий; тщеду́шный. —**frailty,** *n.* хру́пкость; тщеду́шие.
frame *n.* **1,** (for a picture) ра́ма; ра́мка. **2,** (of a window or door) ра́ма. **3,** (for eyeglasses) опра́ва. **4,** (of a building) карка́с; о́стов; сруб. **5,** (build, as of the human body) (тело)сложе́ние. **6,** *motion pictures* кадр. —*v.t.* **1,** (put into a frame) вставля́ть в ра́му; обрамля́ть. **2,** (devise; formulate) составля́ть; формули́ровать. **3,** *colloq.* (falsely incriminate) ло́жно обвиня́ть. —**frame of mind,** настрое́ние; расположе́ние ду́ха.
frame house карка́сный дом.
framework *n.* **1,** (skeleton; structure) карка́с; о́стов; сруб. **2,** *fig.* (basic structure) ра́мки: *within the framework of,* в ра́мках (+ *gen.*).
franc *n.* франк.
franchise *n.* **1,** (suffrage) пра́во го́лоса. **2,** (concession granted by a government) привиле́гия.
francium *n.* фра́нций.
frank *adj.* открове́нный.
frankfurter *n.* соси́ска.
frankincense *n.* ла́дан.
frankly *adv.* **1,** (in a frank manner) открове́нно. **2,** (to be frank; in truth) открове́нно говоря́.
frankness *n.* открове́нность.
frantic *adj.* **1,** (beside oneself with worry) отча́янный. **2,** (hectic; frenetic) лихора́дочный.
fraternal *adj.* бра́тский. —**fraternal twins,** двуяйцевы́е близнецы́.
fraternity *n.* **1,** (brotherhood) бра́тство. **2,** (fraternal organization) бра́тия.
fraternize *v.i.* брата́ться. —**fraternization,** *n.* брата́ние.
fratricide *n.* братоуби́йство. —**fratricidal,** *adj.* братоуби́йственный.
fraud *n.* **1,** (criminal deception) обма́н; моше́нничество. **2,** (a cheat) обма́нщик; самозва́нец.
fraudulent *adj.* обма́нный; жу́льнический; моше́ннический. —**fraudulently,** *adv.* обма́ном; обма́нным путём.
fraught *adj.* [*usu.* **fraught with**] чрева́тый (+ *instr.*).
fray *n.* **1,** (brawl) дра́ка. **2,** (battle) бой. —*v.t.* обтрепа́ть. —*v.i.* обтрепа́ться. —**frayed,** *adj.* обтрёпанный.
freak *n.* уро́д. *Freak of nature,* чу́до *or* игра́ приро́ды. —**freakish,** *adj.* капри́зный; чудакова́тый.
freckle *n.* весну́шка. —**freckled; freckle-faced,** *adj.* весну́шчатый.
free *adj.* **1,** (independent; unrestricted; unburdened; not occupied) свобо́дный: *free country/press,* свобо́дная страна́/печа́ть. *Free from worry,* свобо́дный от забо́т. *Are you free this evening?,* вы свобо́дны сего́дня ве́чером? **2,** *fol. by inf.* (at liberty) во́лен (вольна́): *you are free to leave,* ты во́лен/вольна́ уйти́. **3,** (not costing anything) беспла́тный. —*adv.* беспла́тно; да́ром. —*v.t.* освобожда́ть. *Free oneself,* освобожда́ться. —**free city,** во́льный го́род. —**free enterprise,** свобо́дное предпринима́тельство. —**free fall,** свобо́дное паде́ние. —**free hand,** свобо́да де́йствий: *give someone a free hand,* дать кому́-нибудь по́лную свобо́ду де́йствий. —**free love,** свобо́дная любо́вь. —**free port,** откры́тый порт. —**free speech,** свобо́да сло́ва. —**free thought,** вольноду́мство. —**free throw,** *basketball,* штрафно́й бросо́к. —**free trade,** свобо́дная торго́вля. —**free translation,** во́льный перево́д. —**free verse,** во́льный стих. —**set free,** выпуска́ть *or* отпуска́ть на свобо́ду *or* на во́лю.
freedom *n.* свобо́да. —**freedom-loving,** *adj.* свободолюби́вый.
free-for-all *n.* о́бщая сва́лка.
free-lance *adj.* внешта́тный.
freely *adv.* свобо́дно.
Freemason *n.* франкмасо́н. —**Freemasonry,** *n.* франкмасо́нство.
freestyle *n., swimming* во́льный стиль.
freethinker *n.* вольноду́мец; свободомы́слящий. —**freethinking,** *adj.* вольноду́мный; свободомы́слящий.
freeze *v.i.* **1,** (from the cold) мёрзнуть: *I am freezing,* я мёрзну. *The river froze over,* река́ замёрзла. *The pipes froze,* тру́бы замёрзли. *Freeze to death,* поги́бнуть от хо́лода; замёрзнуть. **2,** (from fear, shock, etc.) цепене́ть; ледене́ть; замира́ть: *freeze in horror,* цепене́ть/ледене́ть/замира́ть от у́жаса. *Freeze in one's tracks,* останови́ться как вко́панный. **3,** *impers.* (be very cold) моро́зить: *it is freezing,* мо-

рóзит. **4,** *fol. by* **to** (become attached by freezing) примерзáть (к). —*v.t.* заморáживать; морóзить. —*n.* **1,** (freezing weather) морóз. **2,** (of prices, wages, etc.) заморáживание: *price freeze,* заморáживание цен.

freezer *n.* морóзилка.

freezing *adj.* морóзный: *freezing weather,* морóзная погóда. *Freezing cold,* жестóкий хóлод. *Freezing temperature,* температýра нúже нулá (по Цéльсию). *I am freezing,* я мёрзну. —**freezing point,** тóчка замерзáния.

freight *n.* **1,** (goods being transported) товáр; груз. **2,** (transportation of goods) перевóзка. **3,** (charge for such transportation) плáта за провóз. *What will be the freight charges?,* скóлько бýдет стóить перевóзка? —*adj.* товáрный; грузовóй: *freight train,* товáрный пóезд; *freight traffic,* грузовóе движéние.

freighter *n.* грузовóе сýдно.

French *adj.* францýзский. —*n.* **1,** (language) францýзский язы́к. *Speak French,* говорúть по-францýзски. **2,** *preceded by* **the** (people) францýзы.

French curve лекáло.

French horn валтóрна.

Frenchman *n.* францýз.

frenetic *adj.* лихорáдочный; кипýчий.

frenzy *n.* исступлéние. —**frenzied,** *adj.* исступлённый.

frequency *n.* частотá. —*adj.* частóтный. —**frequency modulation,** частóтная модулáция.

frequent *adj.* чáстый. —*v.t.* чáсто посещáть.

frequentative *adj., gram.* многокрáтный.

frequently *adv.* чáсто.

fresco *n.* фрéска.

fresh *adj.* **1,** (not used, treated, or spoiled) свéжий: *fresh air,* свéжий вóздух; *fresh linen,* свéжее·бельё; *fresh eggs/vegetables,* свéжие я́йца/óвощи. *Fresh in one's memory,* свеж (свежó) в пáмяти. **2,** (not salt, as of water) прéсный. **3,** *colloq.* (impudent) нахáльный.

freshen *v.t.* освежáть. —*v.i.* [*usu.* **freshen up**] **1,** (become fresh) свежéть. **2,** (make oneself clean and fresh) освежáться.

freshly *adv.* недáвно; тóлько что: *freshly baked,* тóлько что вы́печенный.

freshman *n.* первокýрсник; нóвенький.

freshness *n.* **1,** (newness) свéжесть. **2,** (insolence) дéрзость.

fresh-water *adj.* пресновóдный.

fret *v.i.* мýчиться. —*n., music* лад. —**fretful,** *adj.* раздражúтельный; капрúзный.

fret saw лóбзик.

fretwork *n.* резнáя рабóта.

friable *adj.* ры́хлый; рассы́пчатый.

friar *n.* монáх; úнок.

fricassee *n.* фрикасé.

fricative *adj.* фрикатúвный.

friction *n.* **1,** (rubbing together; resistance) трéние. **2,** (conflict; disagreement) трéния.

Friday *n.* пя́тница. —**Good Friday,** страстнáя пя́тница.

fried *adj.* жáреный. *Fried eggs,* я́ичница-глазýнья.

friend *n.* друг. *Be friends,* дружúть. *Become friends,* дружúться.

friendly *adj.* **1,** (outgoing) привéтливый. **2,** (amicable) дрýжеский; дружелю́бный. *Friendly countries,* дрýжественные стрáны. —**friendliness,** *n.* привéтливость; дружелю́бие.

friendship *n.* дрýжба.

frieze *n.* фриз.

frigate *n.* фрегáт.

fright *n.* **1,** (sudden fear) испýг. *Give someone (quite) a fright,* напугáть когó-нибудь. **2,** *colloq.* (grotesque person or thing) страшúлище.

frighten *v.t.* пугáть. *Be frightened,* пугáться. —**frighten away** *or* **off,** спýгивать.

frightening *adj.* тревóжный: *frightening rumors,* тревóжные слýхи. *It is frightening,* жýтко.

frightful *adj.* ужáсный; стрáшный. —**frightfully,** *adv.* ужáсно: *frightfully expensive,* ужáсно дорогóй.

frigid *adj.* холóдный; ледянóй.

frigidity *n., physiol.* половáя хóлодность.

frill *n.* обóрка.

fringe *n.* **1,** (trimming) бахромá. **2,** (edge; margin) край; окрáина. —**fringe benefits,** дополнúтельные льгóты.

frisk *v.i.* (frolic) резвúться. —*v.t., colloq.* (search) обы́скивать.

frisky *adj.* рéзвый; игрúвый.

fritter *n.* олáдья. —*v.t.* [*usu.* **fritter away**] растрáчивать.

frivolity *n.* легкомы́слие.

frivolous *adj.* легкомы́сленный.

fro *adv., in* **to and fro,** вперёд и назáд.

frock *n.* **1,** (dress) плáтье. **2,** (monk's habit) ря́са. —**frock coat,** сюртýк.

frog *n.* лягýшка. —**frog in one's throat,** хрипотá. —**frogs' legs,** лягýшечьи лáпки.

frogman *n.* водолáз-подрывнúк.

frolic *v.i.* резвúться; возúться. —**frolicsome,** *adj.* рéзвый; шаловлúвый.

from *prep.* **1,** (away from; a certain distance from) от: *move away from the window,* отходúть от окнá. *Get up from the table,* вставáть из-за столá. *Far from home,* далекó от дóма. *Three miles from the airport,* в трёх мúлях от аэропóрта. **2,** (from a place) из: *arrive from Paris,* приéхать из Парúжа; *news from America,* нóвости из Амéрики. ♦*With certain nouns* с: *from work,* с рабóты; *from the post office,* с пóчты; *from the south,* с ю́га. *From head to toe,* с головы́ до ног. *From all over the world,* со всегó мúра. **3,** (from a person) A, (where the subject initiates the action) у: *buy from,* покупáть у; *take from,* брать у; *find out from,* узнáть у; *get from,* получúть у. B, (where the subject is the recipient of the action) от: *learn/hear from,* узнáть от; *receive a letter from a friend,* получúть письмó от дрýга. **4,** (from out of) из: *drink from a glass,* пить из стакáна; *remove from one's pocket,* вынимáть из кармáна. **5,** (off of; down from) с: *dismount from a horse,* сойтú с лóшади; *take a book from the shelf,* достáть кнúгу с пóлки; *fall from the sky,* пáдать с нéба. *Hang from the ceiling,* висéть на потолкé. **6,** *with numbers, time, etc.* от; с: *from four to six,* от четырёх до шестú; *from morning till evening,* с утрá до вéчера; *from Monday till Friday,* с понедéльника до пя́тницы. *From this moment onward,* с э́того момéнта. **7,** (from a source or origin) из: *from the newspapers,* из газéт; *from a good family,* из хорóшей семьи́. *Wine is made from grapes,* винó дéлают из виногрáда. *From this it follows that...,* из э́того слéдует, что... **8,** (because of) от:

suffer from insomnia, страда́ть от бессо́нницы; *shiver from the cold,* дрожа́ть от хо́лода. **9,** *with various verbs* от: *differ from,* отлича́ться от; *keep from laughing,* удержа́ться от сме́ха; *hide from the police,* пря́таться от поли́ции; *save from disaster,* избавля́ть от катастро́фы; *protect one's eyes from the sun,* защища́ть глаза́ от со́лнца. **10,** *with various verbs* из: *disappear from view,* скрыва́ться из виду; *return from a vacation,* верну́ться из о́тпуска; *strike from the list,* вы́черкнуть из спи́ска; *expel from the party,* исключи́ть из па́ртии; *subtract three from eight,* вычита́ть три из восьми́.

front *n.* **1,** (foremost part or side) пере́дняя часть; пере́дняя сторона́; фаса́д; перёд. *In the front of the book,* в нача́ле кни́ги. **2,** *mil.* фронт: *at the front,* на фро́нте. **3,** *meteorol.* фронт: *cold front,* холо́дный фронт. **4,** (coalition) фронт: *united front,* еди́ный фронт. **5,** *colloq.* (person used as a decoy) подставно́е лицо́. —*adj.* пере́дний: *front wheel,* пере́днее колесо́. *Front door,* пара́дный ход. *Front view,* вид спе́реди. *Front row,* пе́рвый ряд. *Front page,* пе́рвая страни́ца. *Front sight,* му́шка. —*v.t.* (face) выходи́ть в *or* на —**in front,** впереди́. —**in front of,** пе́ред.

frontal *adj.* **1,** (from the front) спе́реди: *frontal view,* вид спе́реди. **2,** *mil.* лобово́й; фронта́льный: *frontal assault,* лобова́я/фронта́льная ата́ка; ата́ка в лоб. **3,** (of the forehead) ло́бный.

frontier *n.* грани́ца.

frontispiece *n.* фронтиспи́с.

frost *n.* **1,** (freezing temperature) моро́з: *ten degrees of frost,* де́сять гра́дусов моро́за. **2,** (hoarfrost) и́ней; и́зморозь.

frostbite *n.* отморо́жение; обморо́жение. *Suffer frostbite,* обмора́живаться. —**frostbitten,** *adj.* отморо́женный; обморо́женный. *My ears are frostbitten,* я отморо́зил/обморо́зил себе́ у́ши.

frosted *adj.* покры́тый и́неем. —**frosted glass,** ма́товое стекло́.

frosting *n.* глазу́рь.

frosty *adj.* **1,** (freezing) моро́зный. **2,** (cold and unfriendly) ледяно́й.

froth *n.* пе́на. —*v.t.* пе́нить. —*v.i.* пе́ниться. —**frothy,** *adj.* пе́нистый.

frown *v.i.* **1,** (contract the brows) хму́риться; хму́рить бро́ви; хму́рить лицо́. **2,** *fol. by* **on** (disapprove of) смотре́ть ко́со (на). —*n.* хму́рое лицо́.

frozen *adj.* **1,** (cold; numb; icebound) замёрзший: *my hands are frozen,* у меня́ замёрзли ру́ки. **2,** (preserved through freezing) моро́женый; заморо́женный.

frugal *adj.* **1,** (thrifty) бережли́вый. **2,** (meager) ску́дный. —**frugality,** *n.* бережли́вость.

fruit *n.* **1,** (juicy edible thing to eat) фрукт; (*in the collective sense*) фру́кты: *I like fruit,* я люблю́ фру́кты. **2,** (yield of a plant or tree) плод: *the acorn is the fruit of the oak tree,* жёлудь – плод ду́ба. **3,** *fig.* (result) плоды́: *bear fruit,* приноси́ть плоды́. *The fruits of one's labor,* плоды́ свои́х трудо́в. —*adj.* фрукто́вый: *fruit juice,* фрукто́вый сок.

fruitful *adj.* плодотво́рный.

fruition *n.* осуществле́ние. *Reach fruition,* осуществля́ться.

fruitless *adj.* беспло́дный.

frustrate *v.t.* расстра́ивать; срыва́ть.

frustration *n.* **1,** (act of frustrating) расстро́йство; срыв. **2,** (feeling of being frustrated) фрустра́ция.

fry *v.t.* жа́рить. —*v.i.* жа́риться. —*n.,* in **small fry,** мелюзга́; мелкота́.

frying pan сковорода́; сковоро́дка. —**out of the frying pan into the fire,** из огня́ да в по́лымя.

fuchsia *n.* фу́ксия.

fuchsin *also,* **fuchsine** *n.* фукси́н.

fudge *n.* мя́гкая шокола́дная конфе́та.

fuel *n.* то́пливо; горю́чее. —**add fuel to the fire,** подлива́ть ма́сла в ого́нь.

fuel-efficient *adj.* малолитра́жный.

fuel gauge бензиноме́р.

fuel pump то́пливный насо́с.

fuel tank то́пливный бак; бак горю́чего.

fugitive *n.* бегле́ц. —*adj.* бе́глый.

fugue *n., music* фу́га.

fulcrum *n.* то́чка опо́ры.

fulfill *also,* **fulfil** *v.t.* выполня́ть; исполня́ть. —**fulfillment,** *n.* выполне́ние; исполне́ние.

full *adj.* **1,** (filled; complete; rounded out) по́лный. *Full of water,* по́лон воды́. **2,** (sated) сы́тый. —*v.t.* валя́ть: *to full cloth,* валя́ть сукно́. —**full brother** *or* **sister**), родно́й брат; родна́я сестра́. —**full house,** по́лный зал; по́лный сбор; аншла́г. —**full member,** полнопра́вный член. —**full moon,** по́лная луна́; полнолу́ние.—**full of oneself,** поглощён собо́й. —**full professor,** профе́ссор. —**full speed ahead!,** по́лный ход! —**full stop, 1,** (halt; standstill) по́лная остано́вка. **2,** (period) то́чка. —**full well,** прекра́сно: *I know full well,* я прекра́сно зна́ю. —**in full,** по́лностью; сполна́: *paid in full,* по́лностью опла́чено. *Write your name in full,* напиши́те ва́ше и́мя по́лностью.—**to the full** *or* **fullest,** в по́лной ме́ре. *Develop to the full,* разверну́ться во всю ширь.

full-blooded *adj.* полнокро́вный.

fuller *n.* валя́льщик.

full-fledged *adj.* полноце́нный.

full-length *adj.* **1,** (of a portrait) во весь рост. **2,** (unabridged) по́лный. *Full-length film,* полнометра́жный фильм.

fullness *n.* полнота́.

full-scale *adj.* **1,** (the same size as the original) в натура́льную величину́. **2,** (all-out) развёрнутый.

fully *adv.* вполне́; по́лностью; в по́лной ме́ре.

fulmar *n.* глупы́ш.

fulminate *v.i.* мета́ть гро́мы и мо́лнии. *Fulminate against,* громи́ть. —**fulminate of mercury,** гриму́чая ртуть.

fulsome *adj.* гру́бый; слаща́вый. *Fulsome flattery,* гру́бая лесть.

fumble *v.i.* **1,** *fol. by* **for** (grope for) нащу́пывать. **2,** *fol. by* **with** (handle clumsily) вози́ться с. —*v.t.* (fail to hold) роня́ть; теря́ть.

fume *n., usu. pl.* чад; испаре́ния. *Exhaust fumes,* выхлопны́е га́зы. —*v.i.* **1,** (emit fumes) чади́ть. **2,** (fret; rage) кипяти́ть.

fumigate *v.t.* оку́ривать. —**fumigation,** *n.* оку́ривание.

fun *n.* заба́ва; поте́ха. —**for the fun of it,** из спорти́вного интере́са. —**have fun, 1,** (live it up) весели́ться. **2,** (have a good time) хорошо́ проводи́ть вре́мя. —**in** (*or* **for**) **fun,** в шу́тку. —**make fun of; poke fun at,** шути́ть над; смея́ться над; подшу́чивать над; подсме́иваться над.

function *n.* **1,** (role) фу́нкция. **2,** (social affair) ве́чер;

приём. **3,** *math.* фу́нкция. —*v.i.* де́йствовать; функциони́ровать. —**functional,** *adj.* фунциона́льный.
functionary *n.* чино́вник.
fund *n.* **1,** (money reserved for a specific purpose) фонд. **2,** *pl.* (money available) сре́дства. **3,** (store; supply) запа́с.
fundamental *adj.* основно́й; коренно́й. —**fundamentally,** *adv.* коренны́м о́бразом. —**fundamentals,** *n.pl.* осно́вы.
funeral *n.* по́хороны. *At the funeral,* на похорона́х. —*adj.* похоро́нный; погреба́льный. *Funeral service,* заупоко́йная слу́жба.
funereal *adj.* гробово́й; тра́урный.
fungous *adj.* грибко́вый. —**fungus,** *n.* грибо́к.
funicular *adj.* кана́тный. *Funicular railway,* фуникулёр.
funnel *n.* **1,** (conical device) воро́нка. **2,** (smokestack) дымова́я труба́.
funny *adj.* **1,** (amusing) смешно́й; заба́вный. **2,** *colloq.* (strange; odd) стра́нный. —**funny bone,** локтева́я кость.
fur *n.* мех; *pl.* пушни́на; меха́. —*adj.* **1,** (made of fur) мехово́й. **2,** (pert. to fur) пушно́й: *fur auction,* пушно́й аукцио́н. —**fur-bearing,** *adj.* пушно́й. —**fur-lined,** *adj.* на меху́; подби́тый ме́хом.
furious *adj.* **1,** (extremely angry): *be furious,* быть в я́рости; о́чень разозли́ться. **2,** (violent; intense; fierce) неи́стовый; я́ростный.
furlough *n.* о́тпуск.
furnace *n.* печь; горн.
furnish *v.t.* **1,** (fit out with furniture) обставля́ть; меблирова́ть. **2,** (provide; give) ока́зывать (по́мощь); дава́ть (информа́цию); представля́ть (доказа́тельства). **3,** (supply) снабжа́ть: *furnish the guests with linen,* снабжа́ть госте́й бельём. —**furnished,** *adj.* меблиро́ванный.
furnishings *n.pl.* меблиро́вка; убра́нство.
furniture *n.* ме́бель; обстано́вка. —*adj.* ме́бельный: *furniture store,* ме́бельный магази́н.
furor *n.* шуми́ха; фуро́р.
furrier *n.* меховщи́к; скорня́к.
furrow *n.* борозда́. —*v.t.* борозди́ть. *Furrowed brow,* изборождённый лоб.
furry *adj.* пуши́стый.
fur seal (морско́й) ко́тик.
further *adj.* дальне́йший. *For further information,* за дальне́йшими све́дениями. *Until further notice,* впредь до распоряже́ния; до осо́бого распоряже́ния. *Without further ado,* без дальне́йших церемо́ний. *I have nothing further to say,* бо́льше мне не́чего сказа́ть. —*adv.* да́льше: *not a step further!,* ни ша́гу да́льше! —*v.t.* спосо́бствовать; продвига́ть.
furtherance *n.* продвиже́ние.
furthermore *adv.* кро́ме того́; сверх того́; к тому́ же.
furthermost *adj.* са́мый да́льний.
furtive *adj.* сде́ланный укра́дкой; borова́тый; кра́дущийся. —**furtively,** *adv.* укра́дкой; кра́дучись.
furuncle *n.* фуру́нкул.
fury *n.* **1,** (rage) я́рость; бе́шенство. **2,** (violence, as of a storm) неистовство. **3,** *cap., myth.* фу́рия.
furze *n.* дрок.
fuse *n.* **1,** *electricity* про́бка: *a fuse blew,* про́бка перегоре́ла. **2,** (powder wick) запа́л; шнур. **3,** [*also,* **fuze**] (detonating device) взрыва́тель; тру́бка. —*v.t.* **1,** (melt) пла́вить; сплавля́ть. **2,** (blend) слива́ть. —*v.i.* **1,** (melt) пла́виться. **2,** (merge; blend) слива́ться.
fuselage *n.* фюзеля́ж.
fusible *adj.* пла́вкий.
fusillade *n.* стрельба́; обстре́л.
fusion *n.* **1,** (act of fusing; state of being fused) пла́вка. **2,** (union; merger) слия́ние. **3,** *physics* си́нтез. —**fusion bomb,** термоя́дерная бо́мба.
fuss *n.* **1,** (bustle) суета́; возня́; хлопотня́. **2,** (stir; row) шум; сканда́л. *Make/raise a fuss,* поднима́ть шум; сканда́лить. —*v.i.* **1,** (bustle) суети́ться. **2,** *fol. by* **with** (fiddle with) вози́ться с. **3,** *fol. by* **over** (show excessive care or concern) носи́ться с. **4,** *colloq.* (complain) хны́кать.
fussy *adj.* **1,** (exacting) взыска́тельный. **2,** (finicky) привере́дливый.
futile *adj.* тще́тный; напра́сный; бесполе́зный. —**futility,** *n.* тще́тность.
future *adj.* бу́дущий. —*n.* [*usu.* **the future**] бу́дущее. *In the future,* в бу́дущем; в дальне́йшем.
futurism *n.* футури́зм. —**futuristic,** *adj.* футуристи́ческий.
fuze *n.* = **fuse** (*in sense #3*).
fuzz *n.* пух.
fuzzy *adj.* **1,** (having fuzz) пуши́стый. **2,** (blurred; vague) сму́тный.

G

G, g седьмáя бýква английского алфавита. —*n.* (musical note) соль.
gab *n., colloq.* болтовня́. —*v.i., colloq.* болтáть; трепáть языкóм. —**gift of gab,** дар слóва.
gabardine *n.* габарди́н. —*adj.* габарди́новый.
gabby *adj., colloq.* болтли́вый; разговóрчивый.
gable *n.* щипéц. —**gable roof,** двускáтная кры́ша.
gad *v.i.* [*usu.* **gad about**] шля́ться; слоня́ться.
gadfly *n.* **1,** (insect) óвод. **2,** (annoying person) надоéда.
gadget *n.* приспособлéние.
gadolinium *n.* гадоли́ний.
Gaelic *adj.* гэ́льский. —*n.* гэ́льский язы́к.
gaff *n.* рыболóвный багóр.
gaffe *n.* оплóшность. *Commit a gaffe,* допусти́ть оплóшность; попáсть впросáк.
gag *n.* **1,** (silencer) кляп. **2,** *slang* (joke) шýтка. —*v.t.* засýнуть кляп в рот (+ *dat.*). —*v.i.* (choke) дави́ться.
gaiety *n.* весéлье; весёлость.
gaily *adv.* вéсело.
gain *v.t.* **1,** (get; win; acquire) получáть; завоёвывать. *Gain recognition,* получáть признáние. *Gain one's freedom,* завоёвывать свобóду. *Gain experience,* приобретáть óпыт. *Gain an advantage,* получи́ть преимýщество. **2,** (achieve) доби́ться: *gain one's end,* доби́ться своéй цéли. *What did you gain by that?,* что вы вы́гадали на э́том? **3,** (increase in) набирáть: *gain altitude,* набирáть высотý. *Gain weight,* прибавля́ть в вéсе. *Gain ten pounds,* прибáвить дéсять фýнтов. **4,** (receive, as an impression) выноси́ть (впечатлéние). *I gained the impression that...,* у меня́ создалóсь впечатлéние, что... —*v.i.* **1,** (benefit) выигрывать. *Stand to gain,* быть в вы́игрыше. *Gain in someone's estimation,* выигрывать в чьём-нибудь мнéнии. **2,** *fol. by* **on** (draw nearer to) догоня́ть; нагоня́ть. —*n.* **1,** (benefit) вы́года; вы́игрыш. **2,** *pl.* (that which is gained) вы́игрыш; завоевáния. **3,** (increase) увеличéние; прирóст. —**gain ground, 1,** (make progress) дéлать успéхи. **2,** *fol. by* **on** (draw nearer to) догоня́ть; нагоня́ть. —**gain time, 1,** (of a timepiece) идти́ вперёд. **2,** (obtain a delay to one's advantage) вы́играть врéмя.
gainer *n.* тот, кто выигрывает. *Be the gainer,* быть в вы́игрыше.
gainful *adj.* **1,** (profitable) дохóдный; при́быльный. **2,** (paid) оплáчиваемый. —**gainfully,** *adv.* с оплáтой. *Be gainfully employed,* имéть оплáчиваемую рабóту; рабóтать за дéньги.
gainsay *v.t.* отрицáть; опровергáть.
gait *n.* **1,** (walk; step) похóдка; пóступь. **2,** (of a horse) аллю́р.
gaiters *n.pl.* гéтры.
gal *n., colloq.* дéвушка.
gala *adj.* прáздничный; торжéственный; парáдный.
galactic *adj.* галакти́ческий.
galaxy *n.* **1,** *astron.* галáктика. **2,** (brilliant assemblage) плеяда.
gale *n.* **1,** (strong wind) шторм. *Winds of gale force,* вéтры штормовóй си́лы. **2,** (outburst) раскáт: *gales of laughter,* раскáты смéха.
galena *n.* галени́т; свинцóвый блеск.
gall *n.* **1,** (bile) жёлчь. **2,** (rancor) жёлчь. **3,** *colloq.* (effrontery) нáглость. **4,** *bot.* галл. —*v.t.* раздражáть; обижáть. *It galls me,* мне оби́дно.
gallant *adj.* **1,** (brave; daring) хрáбрый; дóблестный. **2,** (chivalrous) галáнтный.
gallantry *n.* **1,** (valor) дóблесть. **2,** (courtly manner) галáнтность.
gall bladder жёлчный пузы́рь.
gallery *n.* галерéя. *Shooting gallery,* тир.
galley *n.* **1,** (ship) галéра. **2,** (ship's kitchen) кáмбуз. **3,** *printing* (proof) грáнка.
Gallic *adj.* гáлльский. —**Gallicism,** *n.* галлици́зм.
galling *adj.* оби́дный. *It is galling,* оби́дно.
gallinule *n.* водянáя кýрочка.
gallium *n.* гáллий.
gallivant *v.i.* шля́ться.
gallnut *n.* черни́льный орéшек.
gallon *n.* галлóн.
galloon *n.* галýн; позумéнт.
gallop *n.* галóп. *At a gallop,* галóпом; вскачь. *Full gallop,* карьéр. —*v.i.* галопи́ровать. *Gallop off,* ускакáть. —*v.t.* пускáть галóпом.
gallows *n.* ви́селица.
gallstone *n.* жёлчный кáмень.
galore *adv.* хоть отбавля́й.
galosh *n.* галóша.
galvanic *adj.* гальвани́ческий.
galvanize *v.t.* **1,** *electricity; metall.* гальванизи́ровать. **2,** *fig.* (rouse to action) возбуждáть; побуждáть.
gambit *n.* гамби́т.
gamble *v.i.* **1,** (play for stakes) игрáть в азáртные и́гры. **2,** (take a chance) рисковáть. —*v.t.* **1,** (risk) рисковáть. **2,** *fol. by* **away** (squander by gambling) проигрывать. —*n.* рискóванная игрá.
gambler *n.* игрóк; картёжник.
gambling *n.* азáртная игрá. —*adj.* игóрный: *gambling house/parlor/casino,* игóрный дом.

gambol *v.i.* резвиться.
game *n.* **1,** (play; sport) игра́: *children's games,* де́тские и́гры. *Join in the game,* включи́ться в игру́. **2,** (single contest) па́ртия: *win three games,* вы́играть три па́ртии. **3,** (scheme) игра́: *play a double game,* вести́ двойну́ю игру́. *See through someone's game,* ви́деть кого́-нибудь насквозь. **4,** (animals or birds hunted for food) дичь. *Big game,* кру́пная дичь; кру́пный зверь. —*adj.* **1,** (of animals or birds) промысло́вый. *Game laws,* зако́ны об охо́те. **2,** (plucky; courageous) сме́лый; сто́йкий. **3,** *colloq.* (ready; willing) гото́вый. **4,** (lame) хромо́й. —**game bag,** ягдта́ш.
gamely *adv.* сто́йко; отва́жно.
gamete *n.* гаме́та.
gaming *adj.* иго́рный: *gaming table,* иго́рный стол.
gamma globulin га́мма-глобули́н.
gamma rays га́мма-лучи́.
gamut *n.* га́мма: *the whole gamut of emotions,* це́лая га́мма ощуще́ний. —**run the gamut,** быть/быва́ть са́мые ра́зные.
gander *n.* гуса́к. —**take a gander,** *slang* взгляну́ть.
gang *n.* **1,** (band, as of thieves) ба́нда; ша́йка. **2,** (crew of workers) брига́да. —*v.i.* [*usu.* **gang up on**] обру́шиваться на.
gangling *adj.* долговя́зый.
ganglion *n.* не́рвный у́зел; га́нглий.
gangplank *n.* схо́дни.
gangrene *n.* гангре́на. —**gangrenous,** *adj.* гангрено́зный.
gangster *n.* га́нгстер.
gangway *n.* **1,** (passageway) прохо́д. **2,** (gangplank) схо́дни. —*interj.* посторони́тесь!
gannet *n.* о́луша.
gantlet *n.* = **gauntlet** (in sense #3).
gaol *n.* = **jail.**
gap *n.* **1,** (opening; breach) брешь; проло́м. **2,** (break; lacuna) пробе́л: *fill a gap,* восполня́ть пробе́л. **3,** (disparity) разры́в: *the generation gap,* разры́в поколе́ний. **4,** (mountain pass) го́рный прохо́д.
gape *v.i.* **1,** (stare open-mouthed) глазе́ть; зева́ть. **2,** (open wide) зия́ть: *gaping wound,* зия́ющая ра́на.
garage *n.* гара́ж. *Public garage,* автоба́за.
garb *n.* наря́д; одея́ние.
garbage *n.* му́сор; отбро́сы. —**garbage can,** му́сорный я́щик. —**garbage collector,** му́сорщик.
garble *v.t.* **1,** (make unintelligible) искажа́ть. **2,** (misrepresent) перевира́ть. **3,** (pronounce indistinctly) глота́ть.
garden *n.* сад. *Vegetable garden,* огоро́д. —*adj.* садо́вый; огоро́дный.
gardener *n.* садо́вник; садово́д.
gardenia *n.* гарде́ния.
gardening *n.* садово́дство.
gargantuan *adj.* гига́нтский.
gargle *v.i.* полоска́ть го́рло.
garish *adj.* крича́щий; крикли́вый; бро́ский.
garland *n.* гирля́нда; вено́к. —*v.t.* украша́ть гирля́ндами.
garlic *n.* чесно́к.
garment *n.* **1,** (article of clothing) предме́т оде́жды. **2,** *pl.* (clothing) оде́жда. —**garment factory,** шве́йная фа́брика.
garner *v.t.* **1,** (store) скла́дывать в амба́р. **2,** (win; obtain) получа́ть: *garner first prize,* получи́ть пе́рвую пре́мию.
garnet *n.* грана́т.
garnish *v.t.* **1,** (embellish) приукра́шивать. **2,** *cooking* гарни́ровать. —*n.* гарни́р.
garret *n.* черда́к; манса́рда.
garrison *n.* гарнизо́н.
garrulous *adj.* болтли́вый; говорли́вый; разгово́рчивый.
garter *n.* подвя́зка.
gas *n.* **1,** (vapor) газ: *natural gas,* приро́дный газ. *Turn on the gas,* включи́ть газ. **2,** (gasoline) бензи́н. **3,** *physiol.* га́зы. —*adj.* **1,** (pert. to gas) га́зовый. **2,** (pert. to gasoline) бензи́новый. —**step on the gas,** дать газ.
gas burner га́зовый рожо́к.
gas chamber га́зовая ка́мера.
gaseous *adj.* газообра́зный.
gash *n.* глубо́кий поре́з. —*v.t.* си́льно поре́зать.
gasket *n.* прокла́дка. —**blow a gasket,** *slang* вы́йти из себя́.
gaslight *n.* **1,** (light) га́зовое освеще́ние. **2,** (lamp) га́зовая ла́мпа.
gas main га́зовая магистра́ль.
gas mask противога́з.
gas meter га́зовый счётчик; газоме́р.
gasoline *n.* бензи́н. —*adj.* бензи́новый.
gasp *v.i.* задыха́ться. —*v.t.* [*usu.* **gasp out**] говори́ть задыха́ющимся го́лосом. —*n.* вздох. —**to the last gasp,** до после́днего издыха́ния.
gas station бензозапра́вочная ста́нция; автозапра́вочная ста́нция.
gas tank бензоба́к.
gastric *adj.* желу́дочный. —**gastric juice,** желу́дочный сок. —**gastric ulcer,** я́зва желу́дка.
gastritis *n.* гастри́т.
gastrointestinal *adj.* желу́дочно-кише́чный.
gastronome *n.* гастроно́м. —**gastronomic,** *adj.* гастрономи́ческий. —**gastronomy,** *n.* гастроно́мия.
gate *n.* **1,** (entrance) воро́та. **2,** (swinging door in a picket fence) кали́тка. **3,** *pl.* (entrance to a city) заста́ва. **4,** (movable barrier) шлагба́ум. **5,** (box-office receipts) сбо́ры.
gatehouse *n.* сторо́жка (у воро́т).
gatekeeper *n.* привра́тник.
gateway *n.* воро́та; вход.
gather *v.t.* **1,** (pick; collect) собира́ть: *gather firewood,* собира́ть дрова́; *gather data,* собира́ть да́нные. *Gather in the harvest,* собира́ть урожа́й. *Gather dust,* пыли́ться. **2,** (infer) заключа́ть. **3,** (draw into folds) собира́ть. **4,** (gain, as speed) набира́ть (ско́рость). *Gather momentum,* разгоня́ться. —*v.i.* собира́ться; сходи́ться; съезжа́ться. —*n., usu. pl.* сбо́рки.
gathering *n.* **1,** (collecting) сбор; собира́ние. *Hunting and gathering,* охо́та и собира́тельство. **2,** (an assemblage) собра́ние; сбор; сбо́рище.
gaudy *adj.* крича́щий; пёстрый.
gauge *n.* **1,** (instrument for measuring) измери́тель. *Pressure gauge,* мано́метр. *Fuel gauge,* бензиноме́р. **2,** *R.R.* колея́: *broad gauge,* широ́кая колея́. **3,** (standard of measurement) кали́бр. **4,** *fig.* (standard; yardstick) мери́ло. —*v.t.* **1,** (measure) измеря́ть. **2,** (estimate; assess) оце́нивать; суди́ть о.
gaunt *adj.* исхуда́лый; измождённый.
gauntlet *n.* **1,** (glove) (ла́тная) перча́тка. **2,** *fig.* (challenge): *throw down/take up/the gauntlet,* бро-

са́ть/поднима́ть перча́тку. **3,** [*also,* **gantlet**] (form of punishment): *make someone run the gauntlet,* прогоня́ть кого́-нибудь сквозь строй.

gauze *n.* ма́рля. —**gauzy,** *adj.* прозра́чный.

gavel *n.* молото́к.

gawk *v.i.* глазе́ть; зева́ть.

gay *adj.* весёлый.

gaze *n.* при́стальный взгляд. —*v.i.* смотре́ть; вгля́дываться.

gazelle *n.* газе́ль.

gazette *n.* (официа́льная) газе́та.

gazetteer *n.* географи́ческий спра́вочник.

gear *n.* **1,** (toothed wheel) шестерня́. **2,** (adjustment relative to speed) ско́рость; переда́ча. *First/second gear,* пе́рвая/втора́я ско́рость. *High gear,* вы́сшая ско́рость *or* переда́ча. *Low gear,* ни́зшая переда́ча. *Reverse gear,* за́дний ход. *Shift gears,* переключи́ть ско́рость. **3,** (device; mechanism) устро́йство: *landing gear,* поса́дочное устро́йство; шасси́. **4,** (equipment) принадле́жности. —*v.t.* (adjust; adapt) приводи́ть в соотве́тствие (с).

gearbox *n.* коро́бка переда́ч; коро́бка скоросте́й.

gearshift *n.* переключе́ние переда́ч.

Geiger counter счётчик Ге́йгера.

geisha *n.* ге́йша.

gelatin *n.* желати́н. —**gelatinous,** *adj.* желати́новый.

geld *v.t.* холости́ть; кастри́ровать.

gelding *n.* ме́рин.

gem *n.* драгоце́нный ка́мень.

Gemini *n.* Близнецы́.

gemstone *n.* драгоце́нный ка́мень.

gendarme *n.* жанда́рм. —**gendarmerie,** *n.* жандарме́рия.

gender *n.* род: *feminine gender,* же́нский род.

gene *n.* ген.

genealogy *n.* генеало́гия; родосло́вие; родосло́вная. —**genealogical,** *adj.* генеалоги́ческий; родосло́вный.

general *n.* **1,** (military officer) генера́л. **2,** *preceded by* **the** (that which is applicable to the whole) о́бщее. —*adj.* **1,** (not specific or restricted) о́бщий. *General anesthetic,* о́бщий нарко́з. *General practitioner,* врач о́бщей пра́ктики. **2,** (widespread; nationwide) всео́бщий: *general strike,* всео́бщая забасто́вка. *The general public,* широ́кая пу́блика. **3,** (chief; highest-ranking) генера́льный: *general staff,* генера́льный штаб. *Secretary-general,* генера́льный секрета́рь. —**in general,** вообще́.

General Assembly Генера́льная Ассамбле́я.

general delivery до востре́бования.

generalissimo *n.* генерали́ссимус.

generality *n.* обобще́ние. *Talk in generalities,* говори́ть о́бщими слова́ми.

generalization *n.* обобще́ние.

generalize *v.i.* говори́ть о́бщими слова́ми; де́лать о́бщий вы́вод.

generally *adv.* **1,** (usually) обы́чно; как пра́вило. **2,** (in general) вообще́: *generally speaking,* вообще́ говоря́. **3,** (popularly; commonly) обще-: *generally known,* общеизве́стный; *generally accepted,* общепри́нятый.

generate *v.t.* порожда́ть.

generation *n.* **1,** (stage in natural descent) поколе́ние. **2,** (production, as of electricity) генера́ция.

generator *n.* генера́тор.

generic *adj.* **1,** (general) о́бщий: *generic term,* о́бщее обозначе́ние. **2,** *biol.* родово́й.

generosity *n.* ще́дрость.

generous *adj.* ще́дрый. —**generously,** *adv.* ще́дро.

genesis *n.* **1,** (origin) происхожде́ние; возникнове́ние; ге́незис. **2,** *cap.* (book of the Bible) Бытие́; Кни́га Бытия́.

genetic *adj.* генети́ческий. —**genetic code,** генети́ческий код.

genetics *n.* гене́тика. —**geneticist,** *n.* гене́тик.

genial *adj.* серде́чный; доброду́шный. —**geniality,** *n.* серде́чность; доброду́шие.

genie *n.* джин. —**let the genie out of the bottle,** вы́пустить джи́на из буты́лки.

genital *adj.* полово́й; детоpо́дный. —**genitals,** *n.pl.* половы́е *or* детоpо́дные о́рганы.

genitive *adj.* роди́тельный: *genitive case,* роди́тельный паде́ж.

genius *n.* **1,** (person) ге́ний. **2,** (extraordinary talent) гениа́льность. *Man of genius,* гениа́льный челове́к.

genocide *n.* геноци́д.

genre *n.* жанр. —**genre painting,** жа́нровая жи́вопись; жанр.

genteel *adj.* **1,** (well-bred) благовоспи́танный. **2,** (elegant; polished) изя́щный.

gentian *n.* гореча́вка.

gentile *n.* не евре́й. —*adj.* не евре́йский.

gentility *n.* **1,** (noble birth) родови́тость. **2,** (delicacy; refinement) изя́щество.

gentle *adj.* **1,** (tender) не́жный. **2,** (mild; not severe) мя́гкий: *gentle voice,* мя́гкий го́лос. **3,** (not violent) лёгкий: *gentle nudge,* лёгкий толчо́к; *gentle breeze,* лёгкий ветеро́к. **4,** (docile) сми́рный. **5,** (not steep) отло́гий.

gentlefolk *n.* дворя́нство.

gentleman *n.* джентльме́н; господи́н. *Ladies and gentlemen!,* да́мы и господа́! —**gentlemen's agreement,** джентльме́нское соглаше́ние.

gentlemanly *adj.* джентльме́нский.

gentleness *n.* мя́гкость; не́жность.

gently *adv.* мя́гко; не́жно.

gentry *n.* дворя́нство.

genuflect *v.i.* преклоня́ть коле́на (коле́ни).

genuine *adj.* **1,** (authentic) по́длинный; настоя́щий. **2,** (sincere) и́скренний. —**genuinely,** *adv.* и́скренне.

genus *n.* род.

geocentric *adj.* геоцентри́ческий.

geodesy *n.* геоде́зия. —**geodetic,** *adj.* геодези́ческий.

geography *n.* геогра́фия. —**geographer,** *n.* гео́граф. —**geographic; geographical,** *adj.* географи́ческий.

geology *n.* геоло́гия. —**geological,** *adj.* геологи́ческий. —**geologist,** *n.* гео́лог.

geometry *n.* геоме́трия. —**geometric; geometrical,** *adj.* геометри́ческий.

geophysics *n.* геофи́зика. —**geophysical,** *adj.* геофизи́ческий.

geopolitics *n.* геополи́тика.

Georgian *adj.* грузи́нский. —*n.* **1,** (person) грузи́н; грузи́нка. **2,** (language) грузи́нский язы́к.

geothermal *adj.* геотерма́льный; геотерми́ческий.

geranium *n.* гера́нь.

gerbil *n.* песча́нка.
geriatrics *n.* гериатри́я. —**geriatric,** *adj.* гериатри́ческий.
germ *n.* микро́б. —**germ warfare,** бактериологи́ческая война́.
German *adj.* герма́нский; неме́цкий. —*n.* **1,** (person) не́мец; не́мка. **2,** (language) неме́цкий язы́к. *Speak German,* говори́ть по-неме́цки.
germane *adj.* относя́щийся к де́лу.
Germanic *adj.* герма́нский.
germanium *n.* герма́ний.
German measles красну́ха.
German shepherd неме́цкая овча́рка.
germinal *adj.* заро́дышевый; зача́точный.
germinate *v.i.* пуска́ть ростки́; прораста́ть. —**germination,** *n.* прораста́ние.
gerontology *n.* геронтоло́гия.
gerund *n.* геру́ндий.
gestation *n.* бере́менность.
gesticulate *v.i.* жестикули́ровать. —**gesticulation,** *n.* жестикуля́ция.
gesture *n.* жест. —*v.i.* де́лать жест.
get *v.t.* **1,** (receive) получа́ть: *get a letter,* получи́ть письмо́. **2,** (obtain) достава́ть; получа́ть: *get tickets,* доста́ть биле́ты; *get permission,* получи́ть разреше́ние. *Where can I get...?,* где я могу́ доста́ть/получи́ть...? **3,** (fetch; bring) приноси́ть; сходи́ть за. *Get my shoes,* принеси́ мне боти́нки. *Get some cigarettes,* сходи́ть за папиро́сами. **4,** (deliver quickly or on time) доставля́ть: *get the manuscript to the printer,* доста́вить ру́копись в типогра́фию. **5,** (catch, as an illness) получа́ть: *get pneumonia,* получи́ть воспале́ние лёгких. **6,** (make; prepare, as a meal) гото́вить. **7,** (cause to happen): *get the work done,* зако́нчить рабо́ту. *Get something fixed,* отдава́ть что́-нибудь в почи́нку. *Get one's feet wet,* промочи́ть но́ги. *I can't get the door (to) open,* не могу́ сде́лать, что́бы дверь откры́лась. **8,** (induce; prevail upon) заста́вить; убеди́ть; уговори́ть. **9,** (apprehend; nab) пойма́ть; схвати́ть. **10,** (succeed in shooting or swatting) попа́сть в. *I got him!,* попа́л! **11,** (be sentenced to): *he got ten years,* ему́ да́ли де́сять лет. **12,** *colloq.* (hear) расслы́шать. **13,** *colloq.* (understand) понима́ть. **14,** *colloq.* (stump) озада́чить. —*v.i.* **1,** (arrive) приходи́ть; приезжа́ть: *when I got home,* когда́ я пришёл/прие́хал домо́й. **2,** (reach) попа́сть; добра́ться до. *How do I get there?,* как мне туда́ попа́сть? *Get to the end/truth,* добра́ться до конца́/и́стины. **3,** (become) станови́ться: *get better,* стать лу́чше. ♦ *Usu. rendered by individual verbs: get dressed,* одева́ться; *get tired,* устава́ть; *get sick,* заболева́ть; *get well,* оправля́ться; поправля́ться; *get lost,* заблуди́ться; *get wet,* промока́ть; *get angry,* серди́ться; *get dark,* темне́ть; *get married,* жени́ться; вы́йти за́муж; *get ready,* гото́виться; *get stuck,* застрева́ть; *get used to,* привыка́ть к; *get caught in the rain,* попа́сть под дождь. **4,** *fol. by* **to** (begin) принима́ться за: *get to work,* принима́ться за рабо́ту. *We got to talking,* мы разговори́лись; у нас завяза́лся разгово́р. **5,** *fol. by* **to** (have the opportunity) приходи́ться (+ *dat.*): *I don't get to see her often,* мне ре́дко прихо́дится встреча́ться с ней. —**get about,** передвига́ться. —**get across, 1,** (reach the opposite side of) перебира́ться (че́рез). **2,** (transmit; convey) передава́ть. —**get along, 1,** (fare; progress) пожива́ть. **2,** (manage) обходи́ться; устра́иваться. *Get along without,* обходи́ться без. *Get along on 100 rubles a month,* существова́ть на сто рубле́й в ме́сяц. **3,** (be compatible) ла́дить; ужива́ться. *They could not get along,* они́ не ла́дили; они́ не могли́ ужи́ться; они́ не сошли́сь хара́ктерами. —**get around, 1,** (travel, as of news) распространя́ться. **2,** (circumvent) обходи́ть. **3,** (walk) передвига́ться. **4,** *fol. by* **to** (find time to) успе́ть; удосу́житься. —**get at, 1,** (reach) добира́ться до. **2,** (imply) клони́ть: *what are you getting at?,* к чему́ ты кло́нишь? —**get away, 1,** (go away) уходи́ть; уезжа́ть. *Get away from me!,* прочь от меня́! *Get away for a few days,* уезжа́ть на не́сколько дней. **2,** (escape) убега́ть; уходи́ть. *The fish got away,* ры́ба ускользну́ла. —**get away with, 1,** (make off with) утащи́ть. **2,** (escape unpunished) сходи́ть с рук. *he got away with it,* э́то сошло́ ему́ с рук. —**get back, 1,** (recover) получи́ть обра́тно. **2,** (return) возвраща́ться. **3,** (step back) отступа́ть наза́д. —**get behind, 1,** (fall behind) отстава́ть. **2,** (give support to) подде́рживать. —**get by, 1,** (pass) проходи́ть. **2,** (sneak past) проскользну́ть ми́мо. **3,** *colloq.* (manage) устра́иваться. —**get down,** сходи́ть; спуска́ться. —**get down to,** бра́ться за; засе́сть за. *Get down to business,* приступи́ть к де́лу. —**get in, 1,** (enter) входи́ть; влеза́ть. **2,** (arrive) приходи́ть; приезжа́ть. **3,** (manage to say) вверну́ть. **4,** (receive, as a supply of merchandise) получи́ть. —**get into, 1,** (enter, as a vehicle) сади́ться в; влеза́ть в. **2,** (manage to enter) попа́сть в: *get into the house,* попа́сть в дом. **3,** (arrive in) приезжа́ть в; прибыва́ть в. **4,** (put into with difficulty) попа́сть (+ *instr.*): *get the key into the lock,* попа́сть ключо́м в замо́к. **5,** (squeeze into) умеща́ть: *get everything into the suitcase,* умеща́ть всё в чемода́не. **6,** (fit into) умеща́ться в; влеза́ть в. **7,** (penetrate) проника́ть в. *Water got into the basement,* вода́ затекла́ в подва́л. *Sand got into my shoes,* песо́к засы́пался мне в ту́фли. **8,** (become involved in) попа́сть в: *get into trouble,* попа́сть в беду́. *Get into a fight,* подра́ться. *Get into an argument,* поспо́рить. **9,** (put on) напя́ливать. **10,** *Get into debt,* влезть в долги́; *get into the habit of,* привыка́ть (+ *inf.*). —**get it,** *colloq.* **1,** (understand) понима́ть. **2,** (be punished) доста́ться (+ *dat.*); попа́сть (+ *dat.*): *he'll get it for doing that,* ему́ доста́нется/попадёт за э́то. —**get off, 1,** (debark) выходи́ть; сходи́ть. **2,** (dismount) сходи́ть; слеза́ть. **3,** (remove; take off) снима́ть. **4,** (send off) отправля́ть. **5,** (escape) отде́лываться: *get off cheap,* дёшево отде́латься. **6,** (help to escape punishment) спасти́ от наказа́ния. —**get on, 1,** (mount; board) сади́ться в *or* на. **2,** (put on) надева́ть. **3,** = **get along. 4,** *Get on one's nerves,* де́йствовать на не́рвы (+ *dat.*). **5,** *Get on in years,* быть в года́х *or* в лета́х. —**get out, 1,** (leave) уйти́. *Get out!,* вон отсю́да! **2,** (become known) вы́йти нару́жу. —**get out of, 1,** (escape from) выбира́ться из. **2,** (depart from) убира́ться: *get out of here!,* убира́йтесь!; прочь отсю́да! *Get out of the way!,* прочь с доро́ги! *Get out of my sight!,* прочь с глаз мои́х! **3,** (remove) вынима́ть: *get the key out of the lock,* вынима́ть ключ из замка́. **4,** (evade doing something) избега́ть (+ *inf.*). **5,** (elicit from) вырыва́ть; выве́дывать. **6,** *Get out of bed,* встава́ть с посте́ли. **7,** *Get out of debt,* выхо-

ди́ть из долго́в. **8,** *Get out of the habit of,* отвыка́ть (+ *inf.*). —**get over, 1,** (surmount) преодолева́ть. **2,** (recover from) оправля́ться от. **3,** *with* **can't** *or* **couldn't** (not but wonder) (не мочь) надиви́ться. **4,** = **get across.** —**get through, 1,** (manage to complete) оси́ливать. **2,** (manage to survive) пережива́ть. **3,** *fol. by* **to** (make oneself understood) доходи́ть до. —**get together,** встреча́ться. —**get up, 1,** (stand up) встава́ть. **2,** *fol. by* **to** (read as far as) доходи́ть до. *See also* **got.**
get-together *n.* сбо́рище.
getup *n., colloq.* наря́д.
geyser *n.* ге́йзер.
ghastly *adj.* стра́шный; жу́ткий.
gherkin *n.* корнишо́н.
ghetto *n.* ге́тто.
ghost *n.* привиде́ние; при́зрак. —**give up the ghost,** испусти́ть дух. —**not a ghost of a chance,** ни мале́йшего ша́нса.
ghostly *adj.* при́зрачный.
ghoul *n.* вампи́р. —**ghoulish,** *adj.* жу́ткий; чудо́вищный.
giant *n.* гига́нт; велика́н; исполи́н. —*adj.* гига́нтский; исполи́нский.
gibberish *n.* набо́р слов; тараба́рщина.
gibbet *n.* ви́селица.
gibbon *n.* гиббо́н.
gibe *v.t. & i.* издева́ться (над); насмеха́ться (над). —*n.* издёвка; насме́шка.
giblets *n.pl.* потроха́; ли́вер.
giddap *interj.* гей!
giddiness *n.* головокруже́ние.
giddy *adj.* **1,** (dizzy) чу́вствующий головокруже́ние. **2,** (causing giddiness, as of a height) головокружи́тельный. **3,** (frivolous) ве́треный; легкомы́сленный.
giddyap *interj.* гей!
gift *n.* **1,** (present) пода́рок. **2,** (talent) дар; спосо́бности. —**gift shop,** магази́н пода́рков.
gifted *adj.* дарови́тый; одарённый.
gig *n.* **1,** (carriage) кабриоле́т; одноко́лка; шараба́н. **2,** (boat) ги́чка.
gigantic *adj.* гига́нтский; исполи́нский.
giggle *v.i.* хихи́кать.
gigolo *n.* сутенёр.
gild *v.t.* золоти́ть.
gilded *adj.* золочёный; позоло́ченный; вы́золоченный. —**gilded cage,** золочёная кле́тка.
gilding *n.* **1,** (process) золоче́ние. **2,** (substance) позоло́та.
gills *n.pl.* жа́бры. —**stuffed to the gills,** сыт по го́рло.
gillyflower *n.* левко́й.
gilt *adj.* золочёный; позоло́ченный; вы́золоченный. —*n.* позоло́та.
gimlet *n.* бура́в; бура́вчик.
gimmick *n., colloq.* уло́вка; трюк; приём.
gin *n.* (liquor) джин. —**cotton gin,** хлопкоочисти́тельная маши́на.
ginger *n.* имби́рь. —*adj.* имби́рный.
gingerbread *n.* имби́рный пря́ник; коври́жка.
gingerly *adj.* осмотри́тельный; осторо́жный. —*adv.* осмотри́тельно; осторо́жно.
gingivitis *n.* воспале́ние дёсен.
ginseng *n.* женьше́нь.
Gipsy *n. & adj.* = **Gypsy.**
giraffe *n.* жира́ф.
gird *v.t.* опоя́сывать; подпоя́сывать.
girder *n.* ба́лка; прого́н.
girdle *n.* по́яс; корсе́т.
girl *n.* **1,** (female child) де́вочка. **2,** (young woman) де́вушка. **3,** (female servant) служа́нка.
girlfriend *n.* **1,** (female friend) подру́га. **2,** (man's steady companion) прия́тельница.
girlhood *n.* дева́чество.
girlish *adj.* де́вичий; деви́ческий.
girth *n.* **1,** (circumference) обхва́т. **2,** (band) подпру́га; чересседе́льник.
gist *n.* суть; су́щность.
give *v.t.* **1,** (hand over; provide; administer) дава́ть: *give me a cigarette,* да́йте мне сигаре́ту. *Give advice/evidence,* дава́ть сове́т/показа́ния. *Give a concert,* дава́ть конце́рт. *Give a signal,* дава́ть *or* подава́ть сигна́л. **2,** (make a present of) дари́ть; преподноси́ть. *Give someone a present,* де́лать кому́-нибудь пода́рок. **3,** (convey) передава́ть: *give him my regards,* переда́йте ему́ приве́т. **4,** (issue, as an order) отдава́ть. **5,** (deliver, as a lecture; teach, as a course) чита́ть. **6,** (impart) придава́ть (си́лу); доставля́ть (удово́льствие). *He gave us hope,* он всели́л в нас наде́жду. **7,** (hold, as a party) устра́ивать. **8,** (sacrifice, as one's life) отдава́ть (свою́ жизнь). *I'd give anything to...,* всё отда́м, что́бы... **9,** (care to the extent of): *I don't give a damn,* мне наплева́ть на э́то. **10,** *used with various nouns: give one's word,* дава́ть че́стное сло́во; *give birth,* рожа́ть; *give thanks,* благодари́ть; *give a hint,* сде́лать намёк; *give rise to,* порожда́ть. —*v.i.* **1,** (give donations) же́ртвовать. **2,** (yield to physical pressure) подава́ться. —**give away, 1,** (give freely) отдава́ть. **2,** (reveal; betray) выдава́ть. —**give back,** возвраща́ть; отдава́ть. —**give in (to),** уступа́ть (+ *dat.*); поддава́ться (+ *dat.*); склоня́ться (пе́ред). —**give off,** испуска́ть; выделя́ть. —**give out, 1,** (distribute) выдава́ть; раздава́ть. **2,** (be exhausted, as of supplies) иссяка́ть; истоща́ться. —**give to understand,** дать поня́ть. —**give up, 1,** (yield; relinquish) уступа́ть; сдава́ть. **2,** (surrender) сдава́ться. **3,** (abandon, as hope) оставля́ть (наде́жду). **4,** (abandon, as an idea, attempt, etc.) отка́зываться от. **5,** (cease; drop; quit) бро́сить. —**give way,** *see* **way.**
given *adj.* **1,** [*usu.* **the given**] (present) да́нный: *under the given circumstances,* при да́нных обстоя́тельствах. **2,** [*usu.* **a given**] (stated; specified) устано́вленный: *in a given amount of time,* в устано́вленный срок. *At a given signal,* по сигна́лу. **3,** *fol. by* **to** (prone to) скло́нный (к): *given to exaggeration,* скло́нен к преувеличе́ниям. —*prep.* при: *given the situation,* при тако́м положе́нии дел. —**given name,** и́мя.
glacial *adj.* леднико́вый. —**glacial epoch,** леднико́вый пери́од.
glacier *n.* ледни́к; гле́тчер.
glad *adj.* **1,** (happy; pleased) рад: *I am glad to see you,* я рад (ра́да) вас ви́деть. **2,** (bringing joy) ра́достный: *glad tidings,* ра́достное изве́стие.
gladden *v.t.* ра́довать.
glade *n.* поля́на.
gladiator *n.* гладиа́тор.
gladiolus *n.* гладио́лус.
gladly *adv.* охо́тно; с удово́льствием.

gladness *n.* рáдость.
glamorous *also,* **glamourous** *adj.* чарýющий; очаровáтельный.
glamour *also,* **glamor** *n.* чáры; очаровáние.
glance *n.* (бы́стрый) взгляд. *Passing glance,* мимолётный взгляд. —*v.i.* **1,** *fol. by* **at** (give a quick look at) взгля́дывать (на). **2,** *fol. by* **over** *or* **through** (look over quickly) просмáтривать. **3,** *fol. by* **off** (strike and be deflected) скользнýть по; отскочи́ть от. *Glancing blow,* скользя́щий удáр. —**at a glance,** с пéрвого взгля́да. —**at first glance,** на пéрвый взгляд; с пéрвого взгля́да.
gland *n.* железá.
glanders *n.* сап.
glandular *adj.* желéзистый.
glandule *n.* желёзка.
glare *n.* **1,** (dazzling light) сверкáние. **2,** (angry stare) свирéпый взгляд. —*v.i.* **1,** (shine very brightly) сверкáть. **2,** (stare fiercely) свирéпо смотрéть.
glaring *adj.* **1,** (dazzlingly bright) я́ркий; ослепи́тельный. **2,** (flagrant) грýбый; вопию́щий.
glass *n.* **1,** (substance) стеклó. **2,** (container) стакáн: *a glass of water,* стакáн воды́. *Wineglass,* бокáл. *Raise one's glass to,* поднимáть бокáл за (+ *acc.*). —*adj.* стекля́нный: *glass vase/door,* стекля́нная вáза/дверь.
glass blower стеклодýв.
glassful *n.* стакáн.
glassware *n.* стекля́нные издéлия.
glassworks *n.* стекóльный завóд.
glassy *adj.* **1,** (smooth, as of the surface of a lake) зеркáльный. **2,** (blank, as of a stare) стекля́нный.
glaucoma *n.* глаукóма.
glaze *n.* глазýрь. —*v.t.* **1,** (fit with glass) застекля́ть. **2,** (apply a glaze to) глазировáть.
glazed *adj.* глазирóванный. *Glazed paper,* лощёная бумáга.
glazier *n.* стекóльщик.
gleam *n.* прóблеск. *Gleam in one's eye,* огонёк в глазáх. —*v.i.* свети́ться.
glean *v.t.* **1,** (collect, as grain) подбирáть (колóсья). **2,** (gather, as information) чéрпать; почерпáть.
glee *n.* рáдость; ликовáние. —**glee club,** хоровóй кружóк.
gleeful *adj.* рáдостный; ликýющий.
glen *n.* лощи́на; ложби́на.
glib *adj.* бóйкий.
glide *v.i.* **1,** (move smoothly) скользи́ть. **2,** *aero.* плани́ровать. —*n.* **1,** (smooth easy movement) скольжéние. **2,** (powerless flight) плани́рование.
glider *n.* планёр. *Glider pilot,* планери́ст.
glimmer *v.i.* мерцáть. —*n.* **1,** (faint light) мерцáние. **2,** *Glimmer of hope,* и́скра надéжды; прóблеск надéжды.
glimpse *n.* мимолётный взгляд. —*v.t.* увидеть мéльком.
glint *n.* вспы́шка; блеск.
glisten *v.i.* блестéть.
glitter *v.i.* блестéть; сверкáть. —*n.* блеск. —**glittering,** *adj.* блестя́щий; блистáтельный.
gloaming *n.* сýмерки.
gloat *v.i.* злорáдствовать.
global *adj.* мировóй; всеми́рный; глобáльный.
globe *n.* **1,** (sphere) шар. **2,** (the earth) земнóй шар. **3,** (spherical model of the earth) глóбус.
globular *adj.* шаровóй; шарови́дный.
globule *n.* **1,** (tiny sphere) шáрик. **2,** (drop) кáпля.
gloom *n.* **1,** (darkness) мрак. **2,** (melancholy feeling) мрáчность; уны́ние.
gloomy *adj.* **1,** (dark; dismal) мрáчный; хмýрый. **2,** (melancholy; morose) мрáчный; угрю́мый; хмýрый; пáсмурный. —**gloominess,** *n.* мрáчность; угрю́мость.
glorify *v.t.* прославля́ть. —**glorification,** *n.* прославлéние.
glorious *adj.* **1,** (possessing or deserving glory) слáвный. **2,** *colloq.* (delightful) чудéсный.
glory *n.* слáва. —*v.i.* [*usu.* **glory in**] наслаждáться (+ *instr.*); упивáться (+ *instr.*).
gloss *n.* **1,** (luster) лоск; гля́нец. **2,** (commentary) глóсса. —*v.t.* [*usu.* **gloss over**] смáзывать; замáзывать.
glossary *n.* глоссáрий.
glossy *adj.* лощёный; глянцеви́тый; гля́нцевый.
glottis *n.* голосовáя щель.
glove *n.* перчáтка.
glow *v.i.* **1,** (shine; beam) свети́ться. **2,** (smolder) тлеть. **3,** *fig.* (radiate, as with emotion) сия́ть. —*n.* **1,** (luminosity) зáрево. **2,** (flush; redness) румя́нец.
glower *v.i.* смотрéть исподлóбья; смотрéть вóлком; смотрéть звéрем.
glowing *adj.* **1,** (burning) тлéющий. **2,** (rich and warm, as of colors) я́ркий. **3,** (ruddy; healthy) румя́ный. **4,** (highly enthusiastic) востóрженный.
glowworm *n.* светля́к.
gloxinia *n.* глокси́ния.
glucose *n.* глюкóза.
glue *n.* клей. —*v.t.* клéить; приклéивать. *Glue together,* склéивать. *We sat glued to the TV set,* мы не могли́ оторвáться от телеви́зора.
glum *adj.* мрáчный; угрю́мый; хмýрый.
glut *n.* избы́ток. —*v.t.* пресыщáть. *Glut the market,* наводня́ть ры́нок товáрами.
glutton *n.* обжóра. —**gluttonous,** *adj.* прожóрливый. —**gluttony,** *n.* обжóрство.
glycerin *also,* **glycerine** *n.* глицери́н.
glycogen *n.* гликогéн.
gnarl *n.* сучóк.
gnarled *adj.* **1,** (knotty) сучковáтый. **2,** (twisted, as of fingers) сучковáтый; коря́вый.
gnash *v.t.* скрежетáть (зубáми).
gnat *n.* мóшка.
gnaw *v.t. & i.* грызть; глодáть. *Gnaw a hole,* выгрызáть дырý. —**gnawing,** *adj.* (of a pain) сверля́щий.
gneiss *n.* гнейс.
gnome *n.* гном.
gnu *n.* гну.
go *v.i.* **1,** (proceed on foot) идти́. *Go for a walk,* идти́ гуля́ть. *Who goes there?,* кто идёт? **2,** (travel by vehicle) éхать. *Go for a ride,* éздить на прогýлку; катáться на маши́не. *Go by plane,* летéть на самолёте. **3,** (leave; depart) уходи́ть. *It's time to go,* порá идти́ *or* уходи́ть. **4,** (proceed; progress) идти́; проходи́ть; сходи́ть. *Things are going well,* делá идýт хорошó. *Everything went well,* всё сошлó хорошó. **5,** (function; work) идти́; рабóтать. *The car won't go,* маши́на отказáла. **6,** (be phrased; read) гласи́ть. *As the saying goes,* как говори́тся. **7,** (engage in an activity): *go swimming,* купáться; *go skiing,* ходи́ть

на лы́жах; *go shopping,* идти́ за поку́пками. **8,** *used with various adjectives: go mad,* сходи́ть с ума́; *go broke,* прогора́ть; *go blind,* осле́пнуть; *go bad,* испо́ртиться; *go hungry,* голода́ть; *go free,* остава́ться на свобо́де. **9,** (fail) пропада́ть; слабе́ть. *His eyesight is going,* он теря́ет зре́ние. **10,** *fol. by* **with** (be in harmony) гармони́ровать (с); сочета́ться (с). —*v.t. Used mainly in set expressions: go shares with,* войти́ в до́лю с. *We are going the same way,* нам с ва́ми по пути́. —*n. Used mainly in set colloquial expressions: on the go,* на нога́х; в движе́нии. *Have a go at,* попыта́ться. *From the word "go",* с са́мого нача́ла. —**be going to,** собира́ться: *what are you going to do?,* что вы собира́етесь де́лать? —**go about, 1,** (circulate, as of rumors) ходи́ть. **2,** (proceed with) принима́ться за: *I don't know how to go about it,* я не зна́ю, как приня́ться за э́то. —**go against, 1,** (oppose) идти́ про́тив. **2,** (be contrary to) противоре́чить; идти́ вразре́з с. —**go ahead!,** дава́йте! —**go along, 1,** (proceed) идти́. **2,** *fol. by* **with** (accompany) сопровожда́ть. **3,** (consent) соглаша́ться. **4,** *fol. by* **with** (agree with) быть согла́сным с. —**go around, 1,** (walk around) обходи́ть. **2,** (revolve around) враща́ться вокру́г. **3,** (enclose; surround) окружа́ть. **4,** (fit around) сходи́ться на (+ *prepl.*). **5,** (suffice for all) хвата́ть: *there is not enough to go around,* на всех не хва́тит. —**go away,** уходи́ть; уезжа́ть. —**go back,** возвраща́ться. —**go back on,** *see* **back.** —**go by, 1,** (pass) проходи́ть. **2,** (be guided by) руководствоваться (+ *instr.*). **3,** (be known as): *he goes by the name of...,* он изве́стен под и́менем... —**go down, 1,** (descend) сходи́ть; спуска́ться. **2,** (set, as of the sun) сади́ться; заходи́ть. **3,** (sink, as of a ship) идти́ ко дну. **4,** (subside, as of swelling) опада́ть. **5,** (fall, as of prices) снижа́ться. **6,** *Go down in history,* войти́ в исто́рию. —**go for, 1,** (fetch) идти́ за (+ *instr.*). **2,** (be used for a purpose) идти́ на (+ *acc.*). **3,** (be sold for) продава́ться за (+ *acc.*). **4,** *slang* (take a fancy to) увлека́ться (+ *instr.*). —**go in, 1,** (enter) входи́ть. **2,** (fit) вмеща́ться; умеща́ться. —**go in for,** занима́ться (+ *instr.*). —**go into, 1,** (enter) входи́ть в. *Go into detail,* вдава́ться в подро́бности. *Go into effect,* вступа́ть в си́лу. **2,** (fit into) вмеща́ться в; умеща́ться в; укла́дываться в. **3,** (be invested in) уйти́ на: *a lot of work went into that,* мно́го рабо́ты ушло́ на э́то. —**go off, 1,** (stray) отклоня́ться: *go off course,* отклоня́ться от ку́рса. *The train went off the tracks,* по́езд сошёл с ре́льсов. **2,** (depart) уходи́ть: *go off to war,* уходи́ть на войну́. **3,** (detonate, as of a bomb) взрыва́ться; (discharge, as of a gun) вы́стрелить. —**go on, 1,** (continue) продолжа́ть. *Life goes on,* жизнь продолжа́ется. **2,** (happen) происходи́ть; де́латься. **3,** (appear, as on stage) выходи́ть (на сце́ну). **4,** (be turned on, as of light) зажига́ться. —**go out, 1,** (go outside) выходи́ть на у́лицу. **2,** (stop burning) га́снуть; ту́хнуть. —**go out of, 1,** (leave) выходи́ть из. **2,** *Go out of style,* выходи́ть из мо́ды. **3,** *Go out of control,* потеря́ть управле́ние. —**go over, 1,** (cross over) переходи́ть. **2,** (tumble over) сва́ливаться: *the car went over the cliff,* маши́на свали́лась со скалы́. **3,** (examine) просма́тривать. **4,** (repeat) повторя́ть. —**go round,** враща́ться. —**go through, 1,** (fit through) проходи́ть в; пролеза́ть в. **2,** (pass, as a red light) проскочи́ть. **3,** (search) обша́ривать. **4,** (endure) пережива́ть. **5,** (repeat) повторя́ть. **6,** (be completed, as of a deal) состоя́ться. **7,** (spend; squander) промота́ть. —**go under, 1,** (sink) тону́ть. **2,** (go bankrupt) прогоре́ть. —**go up, 1,** (ascend) поднима́ться. **2,** (increase) расти́; повыша́ться. —**go without,** обходи́ться без. *See also* **going** *and* **gone.**

goad *v.t.* **1,** (prod, as cattle) подгоня́ть. **2,** (incite) подстрека́ть.

go-ahead *n., colloq.* разреше́ние (сде́лать что́-нибудь). *Give (someone) the go-ahead to...,* дать (кому́-нибудь) добро́ на (+ *acc.*).

goal *n.* **1,** (aim; objective) цель. **2,** *sports* (scoring area) воро́та. **3,** *sports* (point scored) гол.

goalie *n.* врата́рь. *Also,* **goalkeeper.**

goal line ли́ния воро́т.

goal post сто́йка воро́т.

goat *n.* (female) коза́; (male) козёл. —*adj.* [*also,* **goat's**] ко́зий: *goat's milk,* ко́зье молоко́. —**get someone's goat,** *colloq.* разозли́ть; вы́вести из себя́.

goatee *n.* козли́ная боро́дка.

goatskin *n.* ко́зья шку́ра. —*adj.* козло́вый; козли́ный.

goatsucker *n.* козодо́й.

gobble *v.t.* пожира́ть.

go-between *n.* посре́дник.

goblet *n.* бока́л.

goblin *n.* эльф; гном; ле́ший; домово́й.

goby *n.* бычо́к.

god *also,* **God** *n.* бог. —**by God,** кляну́сь бо́гом. —**for God's sake!,** ра́ди бо́га! —**God bless you!** *(after a sneeze),* бу́дьте здоро́вы! —**God forbid!,** не дай бог!; бо́же упаси́! —**God knows!,** бог его́ зна́ет! —**God willing,** е́сли бог даст. —**good God!; my God!,** бо́же мой! —**thank God!,** сла́ва бо́гу!

godchild *n.* кре́стник; кре́стница.

goddaughter *n.* кре́стница; крёстная дочь.

goddess *n.* боги́ня.

godfather *n.* крёстный; крёстный оте́ц.

god-fearing *adj.* богобоя́зненный.

godforsaken *adj.* захолу́стный. *Godforsaken place,* захолу́стье; трущо́ба.

godless *adj.* безбо́жный. —**godlessness,** *n.* безбо́жие.

godly *adj.* на́божный; благочести́вый.

godmother *n.* крёстная; крёстная мать.

godsend *n.* дар бо́жий.

godson *n.* кре́стник; крёстный сын.

goggle *v.i.* тара́щить глаза́; де́лать кру́глые глаза́. —**goggle-eyed,** *adj.* пучегла́зый. —**goggles,** *n.pl.* защи́тные очки́.

going *n.* **1,** (act of going) хожде́ние. **2,** (departure) отъе́зд. —*adj.* **1,** (present) теку́щий: *at the going rate,* по теку́щим тари́фам. **2,** (operating and doing well) соли́дный; рента́бельный: *a going concern,* соли́дная компа́ния; рента́бельное предприя́тие.

goiter *also,* **goitre** *n.* зоб. *Exophthalmic goiter,* базе́дова боле́знь.

gold *n.* зо́лото. —*adj.* золото́й. —**be worth its weight in gold,** быть на вес зо́лота. —**have a heart of gold,** име́ть золото́е се́рдце.

gold dust золото́й песо́к.

golden *adj.* золото́й; золоти́стый. —**golden age,** золото́й век. —**golden eagle,** бе́ркут. —**Golden**

Fleece, золотóе рунó. —**golden mean,** золотáя середѝна.
goldeneye *n.* гóголь.
goldenrod *n.* золотáрник.
goldfinch *n.* щегóл.
goldfish *n.* золотáя рыбка. *Goldfish bowl,* аквáриум с золотыми рыбками.
gold leaf сусáльное зóлото.
gold mine 1, *often pl.* (mine producing gold ore) золотые прѝиски. **2,** *fig.* (source of great wealth) золотóе дно.
gold plate накладнóе зóлото. —**gold-plate,** *v.t.* золотѝть. —**gold-plated,** *adj.* накладнóго зóлота.
goldsmith *n.* золотых дел мáстер.
gold standard золотóй стандáрт.
golf *n.* гольф. —**golf club,** клюшка. —**golf course,** площáдка для гóльфа.
gonad *n.* **1,** (testicle) яѝчко. **2,** (ovary) яѝчник.
gondola *n.* гондóла. —**gondolier,** *n.* гондольéр.
gone *adj.* **1,** (departed; away) ушéдший; в отъéзде. **2,** (missing) пропáвший. **3,** (dead) умéрший.
gong *n.* гонг.
gonococcus *n.* гонокóкк.
gonorrhea *n.* гонорéя; трѝппер.
good *adj.* **1,** (general term) хорóший: *good manners,* хорóшие манéры. *That's good,* э́то хорошó. *Smell good,* хорошó пáхнуть. *Have a good time,* хорошó провестѝ врéмя. ♦ *In certain set expressions* дóбрый: *good morning!,* дóброе у́тро! *Good evening!,* дóбрый вéчер! *Good will,* дóбрая вóля. *The good fairy,* дóбрая фéя. **2,** *fol. by* **at** (having a knack for) спосóбный (к); сѝлен (в). **3,** *fol. by* **for** (of use; helpful) полéзный. *This medicine is good for a cough,* э́то лекáрство полéзно (*or* помогáет) от кáшля. *Not be good for anything,* ни на что не годѝться. **4,** (honorable) дóбрый. *Good intentions,* дóбрые *or* благѝе намéрения. *One's good name,* своё дóброе ѝмя. **5,** (sound) уважѝтельный: *a good reason/excuse,* уважѝтельная причѝна. **6,** (valid) действѝтельный: *good for six months,* действѝтелен на шесть мéсяцев. **7,** (considerable) изря́дный: *a good distance,* изря́дное расстоя́ние. *A good while,* довóльно дóлго. **8,** (not less than) дóбрый: *a good hour,* дóбрый час. —*n.* **1,** (something good; what is right) добрó: *good and evil,* добрó и зло. *Do good,* дéлать добрó. **2,** (benefit; welfare) блáго: *for the good of mankind,* на блáго человéчества. **3,** (gain; advantage) пóльза: *what's the good of it?,* какáя от э́того пóльза? *Do (someone) good,* быть *or* идтѝ на пóльзу (+ *dat.*). —**as good as...,** всё равнó, что... —**be up to no good,** замышля́ть недóброе. —**come to no good,** плóхо кóнчить. —**for good,** навсегдá; окончáтельно. —**good and...,** *colloq.* здóрово: *good and tired,* здóрово устáл. —**make good,** преуспевáть. —**to the good,** в вы́игрыше.
goodbye *interj.* до свидáния! —*n.* прощáние. *Say goodbye (to),* прощáться (с).
good-for-nothing *adj.* никчёмный. —*n.* шалопáй.
Good Friday страстнáя пя́тница.
good-hearted *adj.* добросердéчный.
good-looking *adj.* красѝвый; хорóш собóй; хорóшенький; миловѝдный.
goodly *adj.* (rather large) поря́дочный; изря́дный.
good-natured *adj.* доброду́шный.
good-neighbor *adj.* добрососéдский.
goodness *n.* добротá. —*interj.* гóсподи! —**for goodness' sake!,** рáди бóга! —**thank goodness!,** слáва бóгу!
goods *n.* **1,** (merchandise) издéлия; товáр(ы). *Leather goods,* кóжаные издéлия. *Canned goods,* консéрвы. *Consumer goods,* ширпотрéб. *Goods and services,* товáры и услу́ги. **2,** (personal possessions) вéщи; иму́щество. **3,** (fabric) матéрия.
good will дóбрая вóля: *people of good will,* лю́ди дóброй вóли. —**goodwill,** *adj.* дóброй вóли: *goodwill mission,* мѝссия дóброй вóли.
goose *n.* гусь. —*adj.* гусѝный: *goose feathers,* гусѝные пéрья.
gooseberry *n.* крыжóвник.
goose flesh гусѝная кóжа. *Also,* **goose pimples.**
goose step гусѝный шаг.
gopher *n.* **1,** (burrowing rodent) гóфер. **2,** (ground squirrel) су́слик.
Gordian knot гóрдиев у́зел.
gore *n.* **1,** (blood) кровь. **2,** (gusset) клин. —*v.t.* забодáть.
gorge *n.* ущéлье. —*v.t.* обкáрмливать. *Gorge oneself,* наéсться дóсыта.
gorgeous *adj.* великолéпный; прекрáсный.
gorilla *n.* горѝлла.
gory *adj.* **1,** (covered with blood) окровáвленный. **2,** (involving bloodshed) кровáвый.
goshawk *n.* тетеревя́тник.
gosling *n.* гусёнок.
gospel *n.* евáнгелие. —**gospel truth,** святáя прáвда.
gossamer *n.* **1,** (cobweb) паутѝна. **2,** (fabric) газ.
gossip *n.* **1,** (talk) сплéтня; пересу́ды. **2,** (person) сплéтник; сплéтница. —*v.i.* сплéтничать.
got *v., past tense of* **get.** —**have got, 1,** (having): *have you got a match?,* у вас есть спѝчка? **2,** *fol. by* **to** (must) нáдо: *I've got to go,* мне нáдо идтѝ.
Goth *n.* гот.
Gothic *adj.* **1,** (of architecture, script, etc.) готѝческий. **2,** (of the language) гóтский. —*n.* **1,** (architecture) гóтика. **2,** (language) гóтский язы́к.
gouache *n.* гуáшь.
gouge *v.t.* **1,** (make grooves or holes in) долбѝть. **2,** *fol. by* **out** (cut out) выдáлбливать. **3,** *fol. by* **out** (put out, as an eye) выкáлывать. **4,** *colloq.* (cheat; overcharge) обжу́ливать. —*n.* **1,** (tool) долотó. **2,** (groove) вы́емка.
goulash *n.* гуля́ш.
gourd *n.* **1,** (calabash) горля́нка. **2,** (pumpkin) ты́ква.
gourmand *n.* **1,** (glutton) обжóра. **2,** = **gourmet.**
gourmet *n.* гурмáн; гастронóм.
gout *n.* подáгра.
govern *v.t.* **1,** (rule over) прáвить; управля́ть: *govern a country,* прáвить/управля́ть странóй. **2,** (determine) определя́ть. **3,** *gram.* управля́ть. —*v.i.* прáвить.
governess *n.* гувернáнтка; воспитáтельница.
government *n.* **1,** (governing body of a nation) прáвительство. *Work for the government,* быть на госудáрственной слу́жбе. **2,** (administration; rule) правлéние; управлéние. *Form of government,* óбраз правлéния. *Organs of local government,* óрганы мéстного управлéния.
governmental *adj.* правѝтельственный.
governor *n.* **1,** *polit.* губернáтор. **2,** *mech.* регуля-

тор. —**governorship,** *n.* губернáторство.

gown *n.* **1,** (long dress) плáтье: *evening gown,* вечéрнее плáтье. **2,** (long robe) мáнтия.

grab *v.t.* **1,** (grasp; snatch) хватáть; схвáтывать; выхвáтывать. **2,** (seize; take possession of) захвáтывать.

grace *n.* **1,** (beauty; elegance) грáция; изя́щество: *grace of movement,* грáция/изя́щество движéний. **2,** (proper behavior; sense of what is right): *social graces,* прáвила хорóшего тóна. *He conceded defeat with good grace,* он признáл своё поражéние с достóинством. *At least he had the grace to apologize,* по крáйней мéре, он набрáлся смéлости извини́ться. **3,** (favor) ми́лость: *by God's grace,* бóжьей ми́лостью. *Be in someone's good graces,* быть в ми́лости у когó-нибудь; быть у когó-нибудь на хорóшем счету́. *Fall from grace,* впасть в неми́лость. **4,** (extension) отсрóчка: *receive a month's grace,* получи́ть мéсячную отсрóчку. **5,** (prayer at meals) моли́тва: *say grace,* читáть моли́тву. **6,** *cap.* (title of respect) свéтлость: *Your Grace,* вáша свéтлость. —*v.t.* украшáть: *flowers graced the table,* цветы́ украшáли стол.

graceful *adj.* **1,** (moving with grace) грацио́зный: *graceful dancer,* грацио́зный танцóр. *Graceful movements,* грацио́зные *or* изя́щные движéния. **2,** (well-proportioned) изя́щный; стрóйный.

gracefully *adv.* **1,** (with grace of movement) грацио́зно. **2,** (with good grace) с достóинством.

grace note форшлáг.

grace period льгóтный срок.

gracious *adj.* любéзный. —*interj.* бóже мой! —**graciously,** *adv.* любéзно. —**graciousness,** *n.* любéзность.

gradation *n.* градáция.

grade *n.* **1,** (rank) звáние; чин. **2,** (quality) сорт; кáчество. **3,** (school class or year) класс. **4,** (mark in school) отмéтка; оцéнка; балл. **5,** (slope) склон; уклóн. —*v.t.* **1,** (classify) сортировáть. **2,** (give a grade to) стáвить отмéтку *or* оцéнку (+ *dat.*). **3,** (level) укáтывать; нивели́ровать. —**make the grade,** быть на дóлжной высотé.

grader *n.* **1,** (machine for grading) грéйдер. **2,** (pupil): *third grader,* учени́к трéтьего клáсса.

grade school начáльная шкóла.

gradient *n.* **1,** (slope) склон; уклóн. **2,** *physics* (rate of change) градиéнт.

gradual *adj.* постепéнный. —**gradually,** *adv.* постепéнно.

graduate *v.t. & i.* кóнчить; окóнчить (шкóлу *or* университéт). *Graduating class,* выпускнóй класс; вы́пуск. —*n.* выпускни́к. —**graduate school,** аспирантýра: *go to graduate school,* пойти́ в аспирантýру. —**graduate student,** аспирáнт.

graduated *adj.* **1,** (containing gradations) градуи́рованный. **2,** (of a tax) прогресси́вный.

graduation *n.* **1,** (completion of studies) окончáние. **2,** (commencement exercises) выпускнóй акт.

graft *v.t.* **1,** *horticulture* прививáть. **2,** *surgery* пересáживать. —*n.* **1,** *horticulture* черенóк. **2,** *surgery* пересáженная ткань. **3,** (corruption) пóдкуп.

grain *n.* **1,** (seed; crops) зернó; хлеб. **2,** (particle) зернó; крупи́нка; крупи́ца. *Grain of sand,* песчи́нка. *Grain of truth,* зернó *or* крупи́ца и́стины. **3,** (arrangement of fibers or layers) волокнó. **4,** (unit of weight) гран. —**against the grain,** прóтив шéрсти.

grain elevator элевáтор.

grainy *adj.* зерни́стый; крупчáтый.

gram *also,* **gramme** *n.* грамм.

grammar *n.* **1,** (structure of a language) граммáтика. **2,** (book on grammar) учéбник граммáтики. —**grammarian,** *n.* граммати́ст. —**grammatical,** *adj.* граммати́ческий.

gramme *n.* = **gram.**

gramophone *n.* граммофóн.

granary *n.* **1,** (storehouse for grain) амбáр; зернохрани́лище. **2,** (grain-producing region) жи́тница.

grand *adj.* **1,** (magnificent; luxurious) великолéпный. *Live in grand style,* жить широкó; жить на ширóкую нóгу. **2,** *colloq.* (fine; splendid) чудéсный. **3,** (overall) óбщий: *grand total,* óбщий итóг.

grandchild *n.* внук; вну́чка. —**grandchildren,** *n.pl.* вну́ки.

granddaughter *n.* вну́чка.

grand duke вели́кий князь. —**grand duchy,** вели́кое кня́жество.

grandeur *n.* **1,** (splendor) великолéпие. **2,** (greatness) грандио́зность. —**delusions of grandeur,** мáния вели́чия.

grandfather *n.* дéдушка; дед.

grandiloquent *adj.* высокопáрный; напы́щенный. —**grandiloquence,** *n.* высокопáрность; напы́щенность.

grandiose *adj.* грандио́зный. —**grandiosity,** *n.* грандио́зность.

grand jury большóе жюри́.

grandmaster *n.* **1,** (of a monastic order) маги́стр. **2,** *chess* гроссмéйстер.

grandmother *n.* бáбушка.

grandnephew *n.* внучáтый племя́нник.

grandniece *n.* внучáтая племя́нница.

grandparent *n.* дéдушка; бáбушка.

grand piano роя́ль.

grand slam большóй шлем.

grandson *n.* внук.

grandstand *n.* трибу́на.

grange *n.* усáдьба.

granite *n.* грани́т. —*adj.* грани́тный.

grant *v.t.* **1,** (give; bestow) предоставля́ть; давáть: *grant credit,* предоставля́ть креди́т; *grant a delay,* давáть отсрóчку. **2,** (agree to fulfill, as a wish or request) исполня́ть; удовлетворя́ть. **3,** (concede; allow) допускáть. *Granted she is no beauty,* пусть онá не красáвица. —*n.* дотáция. —**take for granted, 1,** (assume as obvious) считáть самó собóй разумéющимся. **2,** (fail to appreciate) принимáть как дóлжное.

granular *adj.* зерни́стый.

granulate *v.t.* грануляи́ровать. —**granulated sugar,** сáхарный песóк.

granulation *n.* грануля́ция.

granule *n.* зёрнышко.

grape *n.* виногрáдина; *pl.* виногрáд. —*adj.* виногрáдный: *grape wine,* виногрáдное винó.

grapefruit *n.* грéйпфрут.

grape sugar виногрáдный сáхар.

grapevine *n.* **1,** (plant) виногрáдная лозá. **2,** (rumors) слу́хи; тóлки: *the grapevine has it that...,* иду́т тóлки о том, что...

graph *n.* грáфик; диагрáмма.

graphic *adj.* **1,** (illustrated by graphs) графический.

2, (vivid) óбразный; нагля́дный: *graphic description,* óбразное описáние; *graphic example,* нагля́дный примéр. —**graphic arts,** грáфика; графи́ческое иску́сство.
graphically *adv.* нагля́дно; воóчию.
graphite *n.* графи́т. —*adj.* графи́товый.
graph paper бумáга в клéтку.
grapnel *n.* кóшка.
grapple *v.t.* зацепля́ть. —*v.i.* **1,** (fight; wrestle) схвáтываться; сцепля́ться. **2,** *fol. by* **with** (contend with, as a problem) би́ться (над); схвáтываться (с).
grappling iron кóшка.
grasp *v.t.* **1,** (seize; grab) хватáть; схвáтывать. **2,** (understand) схвáтывать; воспринимáть; постигáть. —*v.i.* [*usu.* **grasp at**] хватáться за; ухвати́ться за: *grasp at a straw,* хватáться за солóминку; *grasp at an opportunity,* ухвати́ться за слу́чай. —*n.* **1,** (firm hold; grip) хвáтка. **2,** (comprehension) понимáние: *beyond one's grasp,* вы́ше чьегó-нибудь понимáния.
grasping *adj.* **1,** (prehensile) цéпкий. **2,** (avaricious) жáдный; áлчный.
grass *n.* травá. —*adj.* травянóй.
grasshopper *n.* кузнéчик.
grassland *n.* травянóе угóдье.
grass widow солóменная вдовá.
grassy *adj.* травянóй; травяни́стый.
grate *n.* решётка. —*v.t.* терéть: *grate carrots,* терéть моркóвь. —*v.i.* **1,** (make a harsh grinding sound) скрежетáть. **2,** *fol. by* **on** (irritate) корóбить. *Grate on one's ear,* рéзать у́хо *or* слух (+ *dat.*).
grateful *adj.* благодáрный; признáтельный.
grater *n.* тёрка.
gratification *n.* **1,** (act of gratifying) удовлетворéние. **2,** (sense of satisfaction) удовлетворéние; удовóльствие.
gratify *v.t.* **1,** (give satisfaction to) доставля́ть удовóльствие (+ *dat.*); рáдовать. **2,** (satisfy; indulge, as a desire) удовлетворя́ть. —**gratifying,** *adj.* отрáдный.
grating *n.* решётка. —*adj.* рéзкий; скрипу́чий.
gratis *adv.* бесплáтно; дáром.
gratitude *n.* благодáрность; признáтельность.
gratuitous *adj.* **1,** (freely given) безвозмéздный. **2,** (uncalled-for) неумéстный: *gratuitous remarks,* неумéстные замечáния. *Gratuitous insult,* ничéм не вы́званное оскорблéние.
gratuity *n.* чаевы́е.
grave *n.* моги́ла. —*adj.* **1,** (serious) серьёзный: *grave matter,* серьёзное дéло; *grave appearance,* серьёзный вид; *in grave danger,* в серьёзной опáсности. **2,** (critical) тяжёлый; тя́жкий: *a grave illness,* тяжёлая/тя́жкая болéзнь. *In grave condition,* в тяжёлом состоя́нии. **3,** *phonet.* тупóй: *grave accent,* тупóе ударéние. —**dig one's own grave,** самому́ себé рыть моги́лу. —**have one foot in the grave,** стоя́ть однóй ногóй в моги́ле. —**turn over in one's grave,** переверну́ться в гробу́.
gravedigger *n.* моги́льщик.
gravel *n.* **1,** (mixture of pebbles and sand) грáвий. **2,** *med.* мочевóй песóк.
gravely *adv.* тяжелó: *gravely ill,* тяжелó бóлен.
graven *adj.* вы́сеченный. —**graven image,** и́дол; куми́р.
gravestone *n.* моги́льная плитá; моги́льный кáмень.
graveyard *n.* клáдбище; погóст.
gravitate *v.i.* тяготéть. —**gravitation,** *n.* тяготéние; гравитáция.
gravity *n.* **1,** (seriousness) серьёзность; тя́жесть. **2,** *physics* тя́жесть; тяготéние. *Center of gravity,* центр тя́жести. *The law of gravity,* закóн (всеми́рного) тяготéния.
gravy *n.* сóус; подли́вка. —**gravy boat,** сóусник; судóк.
gray *also,* **grey** *adj.* сéрый; *(of hair)* седóй; *(of a horse)* си́вый. —*n.* сéрый цвет. *Hair flecked with gray,* вóлосы с прóседью. —**gray matter,** сéрое веществó (мóзга). —**turn gray,** серéть; *(of hair)* седéть.
gray-haired *adj.* седóй; седоволóсый.
graze *v.t.* **1,** (brush lightly, as of a bullet) задевáть; скользну́ть по. **2,** (put to pasture) пáсти. —*v.i.* пасти́сь. —**grazing land,** пáстбищные угóдья.
grease *n.* **1,** (melted fat) топлёное сáло; жир. *Grease spot,* жи́рное пятнó. **2,** (lubricant) смáзка. **3,** (ointment) мазь. —*v.t.* смáзывать. —**grease the palm of,** подмáзывать.
grease monkey *slang* смáзчик.
grease paint грим.
greasy *adj.* **1,** (smeared with grease) сáльный; жи́рный. **2,** (containing grease, as of food) жи́рный.
great *adj.* **1,** (eminent; outstanding) вели́кий: *a great writer,* вели́кий писáтель. *Peter the Great,* Пётр Вели́кий. **2,** (large) большóй: *a great distance,* большóе расстоя́ние. **3,** (far beyond the ordinary) большóй; кру́пный: *a great victory,* большáя/кру́пная побéда. *A great honor,* большáя честь. *Great friends,* больши́е друзья́. *With great pleasure,* с больши́м удовóльствием. **4,** *colloq.* (splendid) чудéсный: *have a great time,* чудéсно провести́ врéмя. —*adv., colloq.* прекрáсно; чу́дно. *Feel great,* прекрáсно чу́вствовать себя́.
great-aunt *n.* сестрá дéдушки; сестрá бáбушки.
great circle большóй круг.
Great Dane дáтский дог.
great-granddaughter *n.* прáвнучка.
great-grandfather *n.* прáдед.
great-grandmother *n.* прабáбка; прабáбушка.
great-grandson *n.* прáвнук.
great-great-granddaughter *n.* прапрáвнучка.
great-great-grandfather *n.* прапрáдед.
great-great-grandmother *n.* прапрабáбка; прапрабáбушка.
great-great-grandson *n.* прапрáвнук.
greatly *adv.* óчень; си́льно.
greatness *n.* вели́чие.
great-uncle *n.* брат дéдушки; брат бáбушки.
grebe *n.* погáнка.
greed *n.* жáдность; áлчность. —**greedily,** *adv.* жáдно. —**greediness,** *n.* = **greed.** —**greedy,** *adj.* жáдный; áлчный.
Greek *adj.* грéческий. —*n.* **1,** (person) грек; гречáнка. **2,** (language) грéческий язы́к.
green *adj.* зелёный. *Be green with envy,* лóпаться от зáвисти. —*n.* **1,** (color) зелёный цвет. **2,** *pl.* (leafy vegetables) зéлень. **3,** (grassy lawn) лужáйка.
greenery *n.* зéлень.
green-eyed *adj.* зеленоглáзый.
greengrocer *n.* зеленщи́к.
greenhorn *n.* новичóк; молокосóс.
greenhouse *n.* тепли́ца; оранжерéя.

greenish *adj.* зеленова́тый.
green light зелёный свет. —**give someone the green light,** дать кому́-нибудь зелёную у́лицу.
greet *v.t.* **1,** (say hello to) здоро́ваться с. **2,** (welcome) приве́тствовать. **3,** (meet in a specified manner) встреча́ть: *he was greeted with applause,* его́ встре́тили аплодисме́нтами.
greeting *n.* **1,** (salutation) приве́тствие. **2,** *pl.* (regards) приве́т.
gregarious *adj.* **1,** (living in herds) ста́дный. **2,** (fond of company) общи́тельный.
Gregorian *adj.* григориа́нский. —**Gregorian calendar,** григориа́нский календа́рь.
gremlin *n.* чертёнок.
grenade *n.* грана́та. —**grenade launcher,** гранатомёт.
grenadier *n.* гренаде́р.
grey *adj. & n.* = **gray.**
greyhound *n.* борза́я.
grid *n.* **1,** (grating) решётка. **2,** (lines dividing a map) се́тка. **3,** *electricity* се́тка.
griddle *n.* сковоро́дка.
gridiron *n.* **1,** (cooking utensil) ра́шпер. **2,** (football field) футбо́льное по́ле.
grief *n.* го́ре. —**come to grief,** потерпе́ть неуда́чу. —**good grief!,** бо́же мой!
grief-stricken *adj.* уби́тый го́рем.
grievance *n.* **1,** (wrong; injustice) оби́да. **2,** (complaint) прете́нзия.
grieve *v.t.* огорча́ть; печа́лить. —*v.i.* горева́ть; скорбе́ть; печа́литься; сокруша́ться.
grievous *adj.* **1,** (distressing) мучи́тельный. **2,** (severe; serious) тяжёлый; тя́жкий. *Grievous insult,* кро́вная *or* смерте́льная оби́да.
griffin *n.* гриф; грифо́н.
griffon *n.* **1,** (dog) грифо́н. **2,** (griffon vulture) сип.
grill *n.* **1,** (gridiron) ра́шпер. **2,** (grilled meat) жа́реное (на ра́шпере) мя́со. —*v.t.* **1,** (broil) жа́рить. **2,** *colloq.* (interrogate) допра́шивать.
grille *n.* решётка.
grilled *adj.* жа́реный.
grim *adj.* **1,** (ghastly) жу́ткий. **2,** (forbidding; stern) суро́вый. **3,** (resolute; relentless) непоколеби́мый.
grimace *n.* грима́са; ужи́мка. —*v.i.* де́лать грима́су; грима́сничать.
grime *n.* грязь; са́жа. —**grimy,** *adj.* гря́зный; запа́чканный.
grin *v.i.* ухмыля́ться; ска́лить зу́бы; расплыва́ться в улы́бке. —*n.* усме́шка. —**grin and bear it,** де́лать хоро́шую ми́ну при плохо́й игре́.
grind *v.t.* **1,** (pulverize) моло́ть; разма́лывать; растира́ть. **2,** (shape by friction) шлифова́ть. **3,** (sharpen) точи́ть. **4,** (grate, as one's teeth) скрежета́ть (зуба́ми). **5,** (press; force) вда́вливать (в зе́млю). —*v.i.* (grate) скрежета́ть. —*n.* **1,** (degree of fineness) помо́л. **2,** *colloq.* (monotonous routine) колея́. **3,** *colloq.* (laborious study) зубрёжка. **4,** *colloq.* (one who so studies) зубри́ла. —**grind away,** *colloq.* **1,** (work steadily) рабо́тать без у́стали. **2,** (study hard) зубри́ть. —**grind down, 1,** (make smooth) шлифова́ть. **2,** (oppress) заму́чить. —**grind out,** *colloq.* штампова́ть. —**grind up,** дроби́ть; измельча́ть.
grinder *n.* **1,** (person)точи́льщик. *Organ grinder,* шарма́нщик. **2,** (machine for crushing) дроби́лка. *Meat grinder,* мясору́бка. **3,** (grindstone) точи́льный стано́к.
grinding *n.* **1,** (pulverizing) растира́ние. **2,** (sharpening) точе́ние. **3,** (grating, as of wheels) скре́жет. —*adj.* мучи́тельный. *Grinding poverty,* кра́йняя нищета́.
grindstone *n.* точи́льный ка́мень. —**keep one's nose to the grindstone,** рабо́тать, не поклада́я рук.
grip *v.t.* **1,** (hold tenaciously) зажима́ть. **2,** *fig.* (seize; engross) завладева́ть; овладева́ть; захва́тывать. —*n.* **1,** (firm hold) сжа́тие; хва́тка. **2,** *colloq.* (valise) чемода́н. —**come to grips with,** схва́тываться с.
gripe *v.t., colloq.* (annoy) раздража́ть. —*v.i., colloq.* (grouse) ворча́ть. —*n., colloq.* жа́лоба. —**griper,** *n.* ворчу́н.
grippe *n.* грипп.
grisly *adj.* стра́шный; жу́ткий.
grist *n.* зерно́ для помо́ла. —**be grist for** (*or* **bring grist to**) **someone's mill,** лить во́ду на чью́-нибудь ме́льницу.
gristle *n.* хрящ. —**gristly,** *adj.* хрящева́тый.
grit *v.t.* сти́скивать: *grit one's teeth,* сти́скивать зу́бы. —*n.* (pluck) вы́держка.
grizzly bear гри́зли.
groan *n.* стон. —*v.i.* стона́ть.
groats *n.pl.* крупа́.
grocer *n.* бакале́йщик.
groceries *n.pl.* проду́кты; бакале́я; гастроно́мия.
grocery store продукто́вый/продово́льственный/бакале́йный магази́н; гастроно́м.
grog *n.* грог.
groggy *adj.* обалде́лый; одуре́лый.
groin *n.* пах.
groom *n.* **1,** (stableboy) ко́нюх. **2,** (bridegroom) жени́х. —*v.t.* хо́лить; вы́холить: *well-groomed,* хо́леный; вы́холенный.
groove *n.* желобо́к.
grope *v.i.* **1,** (feel one's way) идти́ о́щупью. **2,** *fol. by* **for** (search for clumsily) нащу́пывать; иска́ть о́щупью.
grosbeak *n.* дубоно́с.
gross *adj.* **1,** (fat; heavy) то́лстый; ту́чный. **2,** (crude; flagrant) гру́бый. **3,** (total; without deductions) валово́й: *gross national product,* валово́й национа́льный проду́кт. *Gross weight,* вес бру́тто. —*n.* (144) гросс.
grotesque *adj.* **1,** *art* гроте́скный. **2,** (outlandish) абсу́рдный; карикату́рный.
grotto *n.* грот.
grouch *n., colloq.* брюзга́. —*v.i.* брюзжа́ть. —**grouchy,** *adj.* брюзгли́вый.
ground *n.* **1,** (surface of the earth) земля́: *lie on the ground,* лежа́ть на земле́. **2,** (soil) по́чва: *soft ground,* мя́гкая по́чва. **3,** (area used for a specific purpose) площа́дка. *Parade ground,* плац. **4,** *pl.* (basis; valid reason) основа́ние; по́вод: *on what grounds?,* на како́м основа́нии? *Grounds for divorce,* по́вод для разво́да. **5,** *pl.* (dregs; sediment) гу́ща: *coffee grounds,* кофе́йная гу́ща. **6,** *painting* грунт. —*adj.* **1,** (made fine by grinding) мо́лотый; толчёный. **2,** *mil.* (operating on the ground) назе́мный: *ground troops,* назе́мные войска́. —*v.t.* **1,** (cause to run aground) посади́ть на мель. **2,** (teach; instruct) подко́вывать: *well-grounded in mathematics,* хорошо́ подко́ван по матема́тике. **3,** (cancel, as a flight) отменя́ть; запреща́ть. **4,** *electricity* заземля́ть. —**be on firm ground,** стоя́ть на твёрдой по́чве. —**burn to the**

ground, сжечь *or* сгоре́ть дотла́. —**cut the ground from under one's feet,** выбива́ть по́чву из-под ног у кого́-нибудь. —**gain ground,** *see* **gain.** —**give ground, 1,** (retreat) отступа́ть. **2,** (yield) уступа́ть. —**shift one's ground,** перемени́ть пози́цию. —**stand one's ground,** усто́ять; сто́ять на своём.
ground floor пе́рвый эта́ж; ни́жний эта́ж.
ground glass притёртое стекло́.
ground hog суро́к.
grounding *n.* подгото́вка: *a good grounding in chemistry,* хоро́шая подгото́вка по хи́мии.
groundless *adj.* необосно́ванный; неоснова́тельный; беспричи́нный; беспо́чвенный; не име́ющий под собо́й по́чвы. *Groundless fears,* беспричи́нные опасе́ния.
ground speed путева́я ско́рость.
ground squirrel су́слик.
groundswell *n.* мёртвая зыбь.
ground water грунтовы́е во́ды.
groundwork *n.* фунда́мент. *Lay the groundwork,* закла́дывать фунда́мент; подгота́вливать по́чву.
group *n.* гру́ппа. *Literary group,* литерату́рный кружо́к. —*adj.* группово́й: *group portrait,* группово́й портре́т. —*v.t.* группирова́ть. —*v.i.* группирова́ться.
grouping *n.* группиро́вка.
grouse *n. Black grouse,* те́терев. *Hazel grouse,* ря́бчик. *Wood grouse,* глуха́рь. —*v.i., colloq.* (grumble) ворча́ть.
grove *n.* ро́ща: *orange grove,* апельси́новая ро́ща.
grovel *v.i.* пресмыка́ться; низкопокло́нничать.
grow *v.i.* **1,** (increase in size) расти́. **2,** (increase) расти́; увели́чиваться; уси́ливаться. **3,** (become) станови́ться. *Grow old,* старе́ть. *Grow tired,* устава́ть. —*v.t.* **1,** (cultivate) выра́щивать. **2,** (develop, as a beard) отра́щивать. —**grow into, 1,** *literally* враста́ть в: *grow into the soil,* враста́ть в по́чву. **2,** (develop into) выраста́ть в. —**grow out of, 1,** (outgrow) выраста́ть из. **2,** (develop from) выраста́ть из. **3,** (result from) вытека́ть из. —**grow up,** расти́; выраста́ть; подраста́ть. *He is quite grown up,* он совсе́м вы́рос.
grower *n. Rendered by the suffix* –во́д: *tobacco grower,* табаково́д; *cotton grower,* хлопково́д.
growing *adj.* расту́щий. —**growing pains,** боле́зни ро́ста.
growl *v.i.* рыча́ть; ворча́ть. —*n.* рыча́ние; ворча́ние.
grown *adj.* взро́слый.
grownup *n.* взро́слый; большо́й.
growth *n.* **1,** (development; increase; expansion) рост: *slow growth,* ме́дленный рост. *Economic growth,* экономи́ческий рост. *Population growth,* рост *or* приро́ст населе́ния. **2,** (tumor) наро́ст; о́пухоль.
grub *n.* **1,** (larva) личи́нка. **2,** *slang* (food) харчи́. —*v.t.* (clear of roots; root out) выкорчёвывать. —*v.i.* **1,** (rummage) ры́ться. **2,** (toil) труди́ться.
grubby *adj.* неря́шливый; гря́зный.
grudge *n.* зло́ба. *Have/bear a grudge against,* пита́ть *or* (за)таи́ть зло́бу к *or* про́тив; (за)таи́ть оби́ду на; *colloq.* име́ть зуб про́тив. —*v.t.* = **begrudge.**
grudging *adj.* неохо́тный. —**grudgingly,** *adv.* неохо́тно; не́хотя; с неохо́той; скрепя́ се́рдце.
gruel *n.* каши́ца; размазня́.
grueling *also,* **gruelling** *adj.* изнури́тельный.
gruesome *adj.* ужа́сный; жу́ткий.
gruff *adj.* гру́бый: *gruff voice,* гру́бый го́лос.
grumble *v.i.* брюзжа́ть; ропта́ть; ворча́ть. —**grumbler,** *n.* брюзга́; ворчу́н.
grumpy *adj.* брюзгли́вый; ворчли́вый.
grunt *v.i.* хрю́кать. —*n.* хрю́канье.
guano *n.* гуа́но.
guarantee *n.* гара́нтия; руча́тельство; поручи́тельство. —*v.t.* гаранти́ровать; руча́ться за.
guarantor *n.* поручи́тель.
guard *v.t.* охраня́ть; стере́чь; сторожи́ть; карау́лить. —*v.i.* [*usu.* **guard against**] бере́чься (+ *gen.*). —*n.* **1,** (one who guards) сто́рож; часово́й. *Prison guard,* надзира́тель. **2,** (unit that guards) карау́л; стра́жа; охра́на. *Guard of honor,* почётный карау́л. *Changing of the guard,* сме́на карау́ла. **3,** *often pl.* (special unit of troops) гва́рдия: *red guards,* кра́сная гва́рдия. **4,** (device that protects) щит: *mudguard,* щит от гря́зи. **5,** *sports* защи́тник. —*adj.* карау́льный: *guard duty,* карау́льная слу́жба. —**be on one's guard,** быть настороже́. —**catch off one's guard,** заста́ть врасплох. —**put on one's guard,** насторáживать. —**stand guard,** сто́ять на часа́х/на карау́ле/на стра́же/. —**under guard,** под охра́ной; под конво́ем.
guarded *adj.* **1,** (watched; protected) охраня́емый. **2,** (cautious; restrained) осторо́жный.
guardhouse *n.* **1,** (house used by a guard) карау́льная. **2,** (military prison) гауптва́хта.
guardian *n.* **1,** (protector) блюсти́тель; страж. *Guardian of the law,* блюсти́тель поря́дка. **2,** (one assigned to care for a minor) опеку́н; попечи́тель. —**guardian angel,** а́нгел-храни́тель.
guardianship *n.* опе́ка; опеку́нство; попечи́тельство.
guardsman *n.* гварде́ец.
gubernatorial *adj.* губерна́торский.
gudgeon *n.* песка́рь.
guerrilla *n.* партиза́н. —*adj.* партиза́нский: *guerrilla warfare,* партиза́нская война́.
guess *v.t.* & *i.* **1,** (make a guess) дога́дываться; уга́дывать; отга́дывать. **2,** *colloq.* (think; suppose) полага́ть. —*n.* дога́дка. —**guesser,** *n.* отга́дчик.
guesswork *n.* дога́дки; гада́ние. *By guesswork,* наугад.
guest *n.* гость. —**guest conductor,** приглашённый дирижёр. —**guest of honor,** почётный гость. —**guest room,** ко́мната для госте́й.
guffaw *v.i.* хохота́ть. —*n.* хо́хот.
guidance *n.* **1,** (direction) руково́дство. **2,** (advice) консульта́ция. **3,** *aerospace* наведе́ние.
guide *v.t.* **1,** (lead; conduct) вести́. **2,** (direct; manage; govern) руководи́ть. *Be guided by,* руково́дствоваться (+ *instr.*). —*n.* **1,** (person) гид; проводни́к. **2,** (guidebook) путеводи́тель. **3,** (manual; handbook) руково́дство. **4,** (guiding principle) руково́дство.
guidebook *n.* путеводи́тель.
guided missile управля́емая раке́та; управля́емый реакти́вный снаря́д.
guideline *n.* руково́дство.
guidepost *n.* указа́тельный столб.
guild *n.* ги́льдия; цех.
guilder *n.* гу́льден.
guile *n.* хи́трость; кова́рство.
guillemot *n.* чи́стик.

guillotine *n.* гильоти́на. —*v.t.* гильотини́ровать.
guilt *n.* вина́; вино́вность.
guiltless *adj.* неви́нный; невино́вный.
guilty *adj.* **1,** (having done wrong) винова́тый. **2,** (having committed a crime) вино́вный. *Guilty party,* вино́вник. **3,** (showing or feeling guilt) винова́тый: *guilty look,* винова́тый вид. *Guilty conscience,* нечи́стая со́весть. —**plead guilty,** признава́ть свою́ вину́; признава́ть себя́ вино́вным. —**plead not guilty,** отрица́ть свою́ вину́; не признава́ть себя́ вино́вным. —**verdict of "guilty",** обвини́тельный пригово́р. —**verdict of "not guilty",** оправда́тельный пригово́р.
guinea *n.* гине́я.
guinea fowl цеса́рка. *Also,* **guinea hen.**
guinea pig 1, (rodent) морска́я сви́нка. **2,** (person used in experiments) подо́пытный кро́лик.
guise *n.* вид: *in the guise of,* под ви́дом (+ *gen.*).
guitar *n.* гита́ра. —**guitarist,** *n.* гитари́ст.
gulf *n.* **1,** (body of water) зали́в. **2,** (chasm) про́пасть.
gull *n.* ча́йка.
gullet *n.* **1,** (esophagus) пищево́д. **2,** (throat) гло́тка.
gullible *adj.* легкове́рный. —**gullibility,** *n.* легкове́рие.
gully *n.* овра́г.
gulp *v.t.* & *i.* хлеба́ть. —*n.* глото́к. *In one gulp,* одни́м глотко́м; за́лпом.
gum *n.* **1,** (substance) каме́дь; гу́мми. **2,** (chewing gum) жева́тельная рези́нка. **3,** (flesh in which the teeth are set) десна́. —*v.t.* **1,** (glue in place) накле́ивать. **2,** *fol. by* **up,** *slang* (botch up) напу́тать. —**gum arabic,** гуммиара́бик.
gumbo *n.* ба́мия; о́кра.
gumboil *n.* флюс.
gummy *adj.* кле́йкий; ли́пкий.
gumption *n., colloq.* сме́лость.
gun *n.* **1,** (portable firearm) ружьё. **2,** (pistol) пистоле́т. **3,** (heavy weapon) ору́дие; пу́шка. *Machine gun,* пулемёт. —*adj.* ору́дийный: *gun sight,* ору́дийный прице́л. —*v.t.* **1,** (race, as an engine) дава́ть по́лный газ (+ *dat.*). **2,** *fol. by* **down** (shoot; kill) застрели́ть. **3,** *fol. by* **for** (seek to catch) охо́титься за; (seek to obtain) стреми́ться к. —**stick to one's guns,** стоя́ть на своём. —**under the gun,** под уда́ром.
gunboat *n.* каноне́рская ло́дка; каноне́рка. —**gunboat diplomacy,** "диплома́тия каноне́рок".
gun carriage лафе́т.
gunfire *n.* ору́дийный ого́нь. *Exchange of gunfire,* перестре́лка.
gunman *n.* банди́т.
gunner *n.* артиллери́ст; пулемётчик; стрело́к.
gunnery *n.* артиллери́йское де́ло. *Gunnery school,* артиллери́йская шко́ла.
gunpoint *n., in* **at gunpoint,** под ду́лом пистоле́та.
gunpowder *n.* по́рох.
gunshot *n.* вы́стрел. *Gunshot wound,* огнестре́льная ра́на.
gunsmith *n.* оруже́йный ма́стер; оруже́йник; руже́йник.
gunwale *n.* планши́р.
gurgle *v.i.* бу́лькать. —*n.* бу́льканье.
gush *v.i.* хлы́нуть; бры́згать; бить.
gusset *n.* клин.
gust *n.* поры́в: *gust of wind,* поры́в ве́тра.
gustatory *adj.* вкусово́й.
gusto *n.* смак: *with gusto,* со сма́ком.
gusty *adj.* **1,** (of wind) поры́вистый. **2,** (of weather conditions) ве́треный.
gut *n.* **1,** (intestine) кишка́. **2,** *pl., slang* (courage) дух: *he hasn't got the guts to...,* у него́ не хвата́ет ду́ха (+ *inf.*). —*adj., colloq.* **1,** (instinctive, as of a reaction) инстинкти́вный. **2,** (basic, as of an issue) жи́зненно ва́жный. —*v.t.* **1,** (remove the intestines from) потроши́ть. **2,** (destroy) опустоша́ть. —**hate someone's guts,** *colloq.* смерте́льно ненави́деть (кого́-нибудь).
gutta-percha *n.* гуттапе́рча.
gutter *n.* **1,** (of a road) сто́чная кана́ва. **2,** (of a roof) водосто́чный жёлоб; водосто́чная кана́ва.
guttersnipe *n.* беспризо́рник; у́личный мальчи́шка.
guttural *adj.* горта́нный; горлово́й.
guy *n., colloq.* па́рень; ма́лый. *Nice guy,* сла́вный ма́лый.
guzzle *v.t.* лака́ть.
gym *n., colloq.* = **gymnasium.**
gymnasium *n.* гимнасти́ческий зал.
gymnast *n.* гимна́ст. —**gymnastic,** *adj.* гимнасти́ческий. —**gymnastics,** *n.pl.* гимна́стика.
gym suit физкульту́рный костю́м.
gynecology *n.* гинеколо́гия. —**gynecological,** *adj.* гинекологи́ческий. —**gynecologist,** *n.* гинеко́лог.
gyp *n., slang* **1,** (swindler) жу́лик; плут. **2,** (swindle) афе́ра. —*v.t., colloq.* обжу́ливать.
gypsum *n.* гипс.
Gypsy *also,* **Gipsy** *n.* цыга́н; цыга́нка. —*adj.* цыга́нский. —**gypsy moth,** непа́рный шелкопря́д.
gyrate *v.i.* враща́ться (по кру́гу); крути́ться. —**gyration,** *n.* враще́ние.
gyrfalcon *n.* кре́чет.
gyrocompass *n.* гироко́мпас.
gyroscope *n.* гироско́п.

H

H, h восьмáя бýква английского алфавита.
haberdasher *n.* галантерéйщик.
haberdashery *n.* **1,** (goods) галантерéя. **2,** (shop) галантерéйный магазин.
habit *n.* **1,** (customary practice) привычка: *bad habit,* дурнáя привычка. *Drug habit,* наркомáния. *Be in the habit of,* имéть привычку *or* обыкновéние (+ *inf.*). **2,** *pl.* (mannerisms) повáдки: *study the habits of a wolf,* изучáть повáдки вóлка. **3,** (garb): *riding habit,* амазóнка; *monk's habit,* монáшеская ря́са.
habitable *adj.* гóдный для жилья́.
habitat *n.* средá; стихия.
habitation *n.* жильё: *unfit for human habitation,* непригóдный для жилья́.
habitual *adj.* **1,** (customary) привычный; обычный. **2,** (inveterate) закоренéлый; отъя́вленный.
habituate *v.t.* приучáть.
habitué *n.* завсегдáтай.
hack *n.* **1,** (tool) кайлó. **2,** (banal writer) халтýрщик. —*adj.* халтýрный. —*v.t.* (chop) рубить; разрубáть.
hackneyed *adj.* избитый; затáсканный.
hacksaw *n.* ножóвка.
hackwork *n.* халтýра.
haddock *n.* пикша.
Hades *n.* ад; преиспóдняя.
haematite *n.* = **hematite.**
haemoglobin *n.* = **hemoglobin.** —**haemophilia,** *n.* = **hemophilia.** —**haemorrhage,** *n.* = **hemorrhage.** —**haemorrhoid,** *n.* = **hemorrhoid.**
hafnium *n.* гáфний.
haft *n.* черенóк.
hag *n.* вéдьма; каргá.
haggard *adj.* измождённый; исхудáлый.
haggle *v.i.* торговáться.
hagiography *n.* агиогрáфия.
hail *n.* град. *Hail of bullets,* град пуль. —*v.t.* **1,** (call) окликáть. *Hail a taxi,* подозвáть такси. **2,** (greet; welcome) привéтствовать. **3,** (acclaim) расхвáливать.—*v.i.* **1,** (be hailing) идти: *it is hailing,* град идёт. **2,** *fol. by* **from** (be from) быть рóдом из: *he hails from California,* он рóдом из Калифóрнии.
hailstone *n.* грáдина.
hailstorm *n.* грозá с грáдом.
hair *n.* **1,** (a single hair) вóлос. **2,** (hair collectively) вóлосы: *red hair,* ры́жие вóлосы. —*adj.* волосянóй. *Hair net,* сéтка для волóс. —**split hairs,** спóрить о мелочáх; вдавáться в тóнкости. —**tear one's hair,** рвать на себé вóлосы.
hairbreadth *also,* **hairsbreadth** *n., in* **within a hairbreadth of,** на волосóк (*or* на волоскé) от.
hairbrush *n.* щётка для волóс.
haircut *n.* стрижка. *Get a haircut,* стричься; постригáться.
hairdo *n.* причёска.
hairdresser *n.* парикмáхер.
hair dryer фен.
hairpiece *n.* парик; наклáдка.
hairpin *n.* шпилька.
hair-raising *adj.* душераздирáющий.
hair shirt власяница.
hairspring *n.* волосóк (в часáх).
hairstyle *n.* причёска.
hairy *adj.* волосáтый.
Haitian *adj.* гаитя́нский. —*n.* гаитя́нин; гаитя́нка.
halberd *n.* алебáрда.
halcyon *n.* зиморóдок. —*adj.* спокóйный; блáгостный.
hale *adj.* крéпкий; здорóвый. —**hale and hearty,** бóдрый; ядрёный.
half *n.* половина: *half of the money,* половина дéнег. *One and a half,* полторá. *Two and a half,* два с половиной. *Half past four,* половина пя́того. *At half past twelve,* в половинe пéрвого. ♦ *Often rendered by the prefixes* пол- *and* полу-: *half an hour,* полчасá; *a half-turn,* полуоборóт. —*adj.* половинный: *a half share,* половинная дóля. *At half strength,* в половинном состáве. —*adv.* наполовину: *half done,* наполовину сдéлано. ♦ *Also with* вдвóе *and comp. adj. of opp. meaning: half as much,* вдвóе мéньше. *He is half my age,* он вдвóе молóже меня́. *Be half the price of,* быть вдвóе дешéвле (+ *gen.*). —**at half price,** за полцены́. —**go halves with,** войти в дóлю с. —**half again as much,** в полторá рáза бóльше. —**in half,** пополáм: *divide in half,* делить пополáм. —**listen with half an ear,** слýшать крáем ýха. —**that's not the half of it,** э́то далекó не всё.
half-asleep *adj. Be half-asleep,* быть в полуснé.
halfback *n.* полузащитник.
half-baked *adj.* **1,** (incompletely baked) недопечённый. **2,** *fig.* (crude; not well planned) доморóщенный.
half-blooded *adj.* полукрóвный; нечистокрóвный.
half-breed *n.* полукрóвка.
half brother свóдный брат.
half-dead *adj.* полумёртвый.
half-dozen *n.* полдю́жины.
halfhearted *adj.* нерешительный; неохóтный.
half-hour *n.* полчасá.
half-life *n.* перúод полураспáда.

half-mast *n.* приспу́щенный флаг. *Lower a flag to half-mast,* приспуска́ть флаг.
half-moon *n.* полуме́сяц.
half note полови́нная но́та.
half sister сво́дная сестра́.
half slip ни́жняя ю́бка.
half-staff *n.* = **half-mast.**
half tone *music* полуто́н.
halftone *n., art* полуто́н.
half-turn *n.* полуоборо́т.
halfway *adv.* на полпути́: *stop halfway,* остана́вливаться на полпути́. *Turn back halfway,* возвраща́ться с полпути́. *Meet someone halfway,* идти́ навстре́чу (+ *dat.*). *Fly halfway around the world,* лете́ть че́рез полови́ну земно́го ша́ра. —*adj.* **1,** (midway): *the halfway point,* полпути́. **2,** (inadequate; indecisive) полови́нчатый.
half-wit *n.* дура́к; болва́н. —**half-witted,** *adj.* слабоу́мный.
halibut *n.* па́лтус.
hall *n.* **1,** (large public building or room) зал. *Town/city hall,* ра́туша. **2,** (vestibule) пере́дняя; прихо́жая. **3,** (corridor) коридо́р.
hallelujah *interj.* аллилу́йя.
hallmark *n.* **1,** (of precious metals) про́ба. **2,** (indication of excellence) при́знак; крите́рий.
halloo *interj.* ату́!; улюлю́! —*v.i.* улюлю́кать.
hallow *v.t.* освяща́ть.
Halloween *n.* кану́н дня всех святы́х (= *Allhallows eve*).
hallucination *n.* галлюцина́ция.
hallway *n.* **1,** (vestibule) пере́дняя; прихо́жая. **2,** (corridor) коридо́р.
halo *n.* орео́л.
halogen *n.* гало́ге́н.
halt *v.t.* **1,** (bring to a stop) остана́вливать. **2,** (cease) прекраща́ть. —*v.i.* остана́вливаться. —*n.* **1,** (stop) остано́вка. **2,** (cessation) прекраще́ние. —**call a halt to,** прекрати́ть; положи́ть коне́ц (+ *dat.*). —**come to a halt, 1,** (stop moving) остана́вливаться. **2,** (end) прекраща́ться.
halter *n.* **1,** (strap for confining an animal) недоу́здок. **2,** (woman's garment) лиф.
halting *adj.* свя́занный: *halting speech,* свя́занная речь.
halve *v.t.* **1,** (divide in two) дели́ть попола́м. **2,** (reduce by half) уменьша́ть вдво́е *or* наполови́ну.
halyard *n.* фал.
ham *n.* **1,** (meat) ветчина́. *Ham sandwich,* бутербро́д с ветчино́й. **2,** *slang* (one who overacts) позёр. **3,** *colloq.* (amateur radio operator) радиолюби́тель.
hamburger *n.* ру́бленая котле́та.
Hamitic *adj.* хами́тский.
hamlet *n.* дереву́шка.
hammer *n.* **1,** (tool) молото́к. *Large hammer,* мо́лот. **2,** (of a gun) куро́к. **3,** *sports* мо́лот: *hammer throw,* мета́ние мо́лота. —*v.t.* **1,** (drive in with a hammer) вбива́ть; забива́ть: *hammer a nail into a wall,* вбива́ть/забива́ть гвоздь в сте́ну. **2,** (drum in) вбива́ть в го́лову. **3,** *fol. by* **out** (shape with a hammer) выбива́ть. **4,** *fol. by* **out** (work out, as an agreement) выраба́тывать. —*v.i.* **1,** (use a hammer) рабо́тать молотко́м. **2,** (knock; pound) стуча́ть.
hammerhead *n.* мо́лот-ры́ба.
hammock *n.* гама́к; подвесна́я ко́йка.
hamper *v.t.* меша́ть; затрудня́ть; препя́тствовать. —*n.* корзи́на.
hamster *n.* хомя́к.
hand *n.* **1,** (part of the body) рука́: *right hand,* пра́вая рука́. **2,** (of a clock) стре́лка: *minute hand,* мину́тная стре́лка. **3,** *pl.* (workers) (рабо́чие) ру́ки. **4,** *pl.* (ship's crew) экипа́ж; кома́нда. *All hands on deck!,* все наве́рх! **5,** (help; assistance) по́мощь: *give/lend someone a helping hand,* подава́ть ру́ку по́мощи (+ *dat.*). **6,** (handwriting) по́черк; рука́. **7,** (permission to marry) рука́: *ask for the hand of,* проси́ть руки́ кого́-нибудь. **8,** *colloq.* (round of applause) аплодисме́нты. **9,** *cards* ка́рты: *a bad hand,* плохи́е ка́рты. —*adj.* ручно́й: *hand luggage,* ручно́й бага́ж. —*v.t.* передава́ть: *hand me my hat,* переда́йте мне шля́пу. —**at hand, 1,** (nearby) под руко́й. **2,** (about to occur) на носу́. —**at the hands of,** от рук (+ *gen.*). —**by hand, 1,** (manually) ручны́м спо́собом. *This is made by hand,* э́то ручно́й рабо́ты. *Copy by hand,* писа́ть от руки́. **2,** (in person) вручну́ю: *deliver by hand,* доставля́ть вручну́ю. —**first hand,** из пе́рвых рук. —**from hand to hand,** из рук в ру́ки. —**get off one's hands,** сбыва́ть с рук. —**get one's hands on,** добира́ться до: *wait till I get my hands on him!,* я ещё до него́ доберу́сь! *Everything they could get their hands on,* всё, что им попада́лось по́д руку. —**get out of hand,** отбива́ться от рук. —**hand down, 1,** (pass on) передава́ть: *the legend was handed down from generation to generation,* леге́нда передава́лась из поколе́ния в поколе́ние. **2,** (deliver; render, as a verdict) выноси́ть (пригово́р). —**hand in,** подава́ть; сдава́ть. —**hand in hand,** рука́ в ру́ку; рука́ о́б руку. —**hand it to,** *colloq.* отдава́ть до́лжное (+ *dat.*). —**hand out,** выдава́ть; раздава́ть. —**hand over,** передава́ть; отдава́ть; сдава́ть. —**hands down,** легко́; без труда́. —**hands off!,** ру́ки прочь! —**hands up!,** ру́ки вверх! —**have a hand in,** приложи́ть ру́ку к; уча́ствовать в; игра́ть роль в. —**have one's hands full,** име́ть рабо́ты по го́рло. *I have my hands full,* у меня́ хлопо́т по́лон рот. —**live from hand to mouth,** жить сего́дняшним днём; жить на пти́чьих права́х; перебива́ться с хле́ба на квас. —**on hand, 1,** (available) под руко́й. **2,** (present) налицо́. —**on one's hands,** на рука́х. —**on the one hand,** с одно́й стороны́. —**on the other hand,** с друго́й стороны́. —**play into the hands of,** игра́ть на́ руку (+ *dat.*). —**reveal** *or* **tip one's hand,** раскры́ть свои́ ка́рты. —**take in hand,** взять в свои́ ру́ки.
handbag *n.* су́мка; су́мочка.
handball *n.* гандбо́л; ручно́й мяч.
handbill *n.* рекла́мный листо́к.
handbook *n.* руково́дство.
handcar *n.* дрези́на.
handcart *n.* ручна́я теле́жка.
handcuff *v.t.* надева́ть нару́чники на. —**handcuffs,** *n.pl.* нару́чники.
handful *n.* горсть; при́горшня.
hand grenade ручна́я грана́та.
handgun *n.* ручно́е огнестре́льное ору́жие.
handicap *n.* **1,** *sports* гандика́п. **2,** (disadvantage) недоста́ток. **3,** (disability) физи́ческий недоста́ток. —*v.t.* **1,** (put a handicap on) дава́ть гандика́п (+ *dat.*). **2,** (put at a disadvantage) препя́тствовать; затрудня́ть.
handicapped *adj.* с физи́ческими недоста́тками; дефекти́вный.

handicraft *n.* **1,** (craft) ремесло́. **2,** *pl.* (products so made) куста́рные изде́лия. —**handicraftsman,** *n.* реме́сленник; куста́рь.
handily *adv.* **1,** (deftly) ло́вко. **2,** (easily) без труда́.
handiwork *n.* **1,** (manual work) ручна́я рабо́та. **2,** (work; creation) де́ло рук. *It's his handiwork,* э́то его́ рук де́ло.
handkerchief *n.* носово́й плато́к.
handle *n.* ру́чка; рукоя́тка. —*v.t.* **1,** (touch) тро́гать. **2,** (manipulate; treat) обраща́ться с: *handle with care,* обраща́ться с осторо́жностью. **3,** (operate) управля́ть; обраща́ться с. **4,** (deal with) справля́ться с. **5,** (deal in) торгова́ть (+ *instr.*). —*v.i. This car handles easily,* э́той маши́ной легко́ управля́ть. —**fly off the handle,** *colloq.* лезть на́ стену.
handlebar *n.* руль (велосипе́да).
handling *n.* обраще́ние.
handmade *adj.* ручно́й рабо́ты: *this is handmade,* э́то ручно́й рабо́ты.
hand organ шарма́нка.
handout *n.* пода́чка.
handrail *n.* пери́ла; по́ручни.
handsaw *n.* ручна́я пила́; ножо́вка.
handshake *n.* пожа́тие (руки́); рукопожа́тие.
handsome *adj.* **1,** (good looking) краси́вый. **2,** (considerable) изря́дный: *a handsome sum,* изря́дная су́мма.
handstand *n.* сто́йка. *Do a handstand,* стать на́ руки; де́лать сто́йку на рука́х.
hand-to-hand *adj.* рукопа́шный: *hand-to-hand combat,* рукопа́шный бой.
handwriting *n.* по́черк.
handwritten *adj.* от руки́; руко́й напи́санный; рукопи́сный; собственнору́чный.
handy *adj.* **1,** (dexterous) ло́вкий; иску́сный. **2,** (within easy reach) под руко́й. **3,** (convenient; useful) удо́бный; поле́зный. —**come in handy,** приходи́ться кста́ти; пригоди́ться.
hang *v.t.* **1,** (fasten from above) ве́шать: *hang a picture,* ве́шать карти́ну. *Hang a door,* наве́шивать дверь. *Hang wallpaper,* клеи́ть обо́и. **2,** (execute) ве́шать. *Hang oneself,* ве́шаться. **3,** (let droop, as one's head) ве́шать; поника́ть; пону́рить. **4,** (decorate with hanging things) уве́шивать; обве́шивать; заве́шивать. **5,** *in* **hang fire,** дать осе́чку. —*v.i.* висе́ть. *Hang from the ceiling,* висе́ть на потолке́. *Hang by a thread,* висе́ть на волоске́. —*n.* сноро́вку. *Get the hang of,* напрактикова́ться в; наловчи́ться (+ *inf.*); наби́ть ру́ку на. —**hang around, 1,** (spend time idly) слоня́ться; окола́чиваться. **2,** *fol. by* **with** (keep company with) якша́ться с. —**hang down,** свиса́ть. —**hang on, 1,** (hold on) повиса́ть. **2,** (hold the line) не ве́шать тру́бку. **3,** (persist, as of a cold) упо́рствовать. **4,** *Hang on every word,* лови́ть ка́ждое сло́во. —**hang onto,** повиса́ть на. —**hang out, 1,** (hang up, as wash) выве́шивать. **2,** (lean out) высо́вываться. **3,** *colloq.* (spend one's time) крути́ться. —**hang over,** висе́ть на; нависа́ть над. —**hang up, 1,** (place on a hanger or hook) ве́шать. **2,** (a telephone receiver) ве́шать (тру́бку).
hangar *n.* анга́р.
hanger *n.* ве́шалка.
hanger-on *n.* прихлеба́тель; приживáльщик.
hanging *n.* **1,** (execution) пове́шение: *death by hanging,* казнь че́рез пове́шение. **2,** *usu. pl.* (something hung on a wall) драпиро́вки. —*adj.* вися́чий.
hangman *n.* пала́ч.
hangnail *n.* заусе́ница.
hangover *n.* **1,** (remnant) пережи́ток. **2,** (aftereffect of intoxication) похме́лье.
hank *n.* мото́к.
hanker *v.i.* жа́ждать. —**hankering,** *n.* жела́ние; жа́жда.
haphazard *adj.* беспоря́дочный; бессисте́мный. —**haphazardly,** *adv.* беспоря́дочно; как попа́ло.
hapless *adj.* несча́стный; злополу́чный.
happen *v.i.* **1,** (take place) случа́ться; происходи́ть. *What happened?,* что случи́лось? *Nothing happened,* ничего́ не случи́лось. *As if nothing happened,* как ни в чём не быва́ло. *As often happens,* как э́то ча́сто быва́ет. *It so happens that...,* случи́лось так, что... **2,** *fol. by* **to** (become of; befall) случа́ться с: *what happened to him?,* что случи́лось с ним? **3,** *fol. by inf.* (chance) случи́ться *(impers.)*: *I happened to notice that...,* мне случи́лось заме́тить, что... *I (just) happened to be home,* я случа́йно был (была́) до́ма. *He happens to be my friend,* он, ока́зывается, мой друг. **4,** *fol. by* **on** *or* **upon** (run into) натыка́ться на; ната́лкиваться на.
happening *n.* слу́чай; собы́тие.
happenstance *n.* слу́чай; случа́йность.
happily *adv.* **1,** (in happiness) счастли́во: *live happily,* жить счастли́во. **2,** (gladly) с ра́достью. **3,** (luckily) к сча́стью.
happiness *n.* сча́стье.
happy *adj.* **1,** (joyous; contented) счастли́вый. *Make happy,* ра́довать. **2,** (satisfactory, as of an outcome) благополу́чный. **3,** (well-chosen) уда́чный. —**Happy Birthday!,** поздравля́ю вас с днём рожде́ния! —**happy medium,** золота́я середи́на. —**Happy New Year!,** с Но́вым го́дом!
happy-go-lucky *adj.* беззабо́тный; беспе́чный.
hara-kiri *n.* харaки́ри.
harass *v.t.* **1,** (harry) беспоко́ить; пресле́довать; дёргать. **2,** *mil.* беспоко́ить; изма́тывать. —**harassment,** *n.* беспоко́йство; пресле́дование.
harbinger *n.* предве́стник.
harbor *also,* **harbour** *n.* га́вань; порт. —*v.t.* **1,** (shelter) укрыва́ть; приюти́ть. **2,** (entertain in the mind) пита́ть; (за)таи́ть. —**harbor pilot,** ло́цман.
hard *adj.* **1,** (not soft) твёрдый; жёсткий: *hard surface,* твёрдая пове́рхность; *hard seat,* жёсткое сиде́нье. **2,** (difficult) тру́дный: *hard problem,* тру́дная зада́ча. *It is hard to say,* тру́дно сказа́ть. **3,** (rigorous; trying) тяжёлый: *hard work/life,* тяжёлая рабо́та/жизнь. *Hard times,* тяжёлые времена́. **4,** (industrious) трудолюби́вый: *hard worker,* трудолюби́вый рабо́тник. **5,** (of or with great force) си́льный: *hard blow,* си́льный уда́р. **6,** (stern; strict) жёсткий; стро́гий. —*adv.* **1,** (with great effort) тяжело́; уси́ленно. *Work/breathe hard,* тяжело́ рабо́тать/дыша́ть. *Study hard,* приле́жно учи́ться; уси́ленно занима́ться. *Try hard,* о́чень стара́ться. *Try hard to persuade someone,* уси́ленно угова́ривать кого́-нибудь. **2,** (with great force) си́льно: *hit hard,* си́льно уда́рить. *It is raining hard,* идёт си́льный дождь. **3,** (with sorrow or distress) тяжело́: *take something hard,* тяжело́ переноси́ть *or* пережива́ть что́-нибудь. —**hard and fast,** жёсткий: *hard and fast rules,* жёсткие пра́вила. —**hard cash,** нали́чные де́ньги. —**hard labor,** ка́торга; ка-

торжные работы. —**hard line,** жёсткая линия. —**hard liquor,** спиртные напитки. —**hard luck,** невезение. —**hard of hearing,** тугой на ухо. —**hard palate,** твёрдое нёбо. —**hard up,** не при деньгах; стеснённый в деньгах. —**hard water,** жёсткая вода.

hard-boiled *adj.* **1,** (of eggs) крутой: *hard-boiled egg,* крутое яйцо; яйцо вкрутую. **2,** *colloq.* (unsentimental) чёрствый; твердокаменный.

hardbound *adj.* в твёрдой обложке; в переплёте. *Also,* **hard-cover.**

harden *v.t.* **1,** (make hard) делать (более) твёрдым; закалять. **2,** (toughen) закалять; ожесточать. —*v.i.* твердеть; затвердевать; (*of metals*) закаляться.

hardened *adj.* **1,** (having become hard) затвердéлый; закалённый. *Hardened steel,* закалённая сталь. **2,** (inveterate) закоренелый: *hardened criminal,* закоренелый преступник.

hardening *n.* затвердение. —**hardening of the arteries,** артериосклероз.

hardheaded *adj.* **1,** (practical; realistic) практичный; трезвый. **2,** (stubborn) упрямый.

hardhearted *adj.* жестокосердный. —**hardheartedness,** *n.* жестокосердие.

hardiness *n.* выносливость.

hardly *adv.* **1,** (scarcely) едва; еле: *we could hardly keep up with him,* мы едва/еле поспевали за ним. **2,** (almost not at all) *rendered by* мало: *hardly anyone,* мало кто; *hardly ever,* мало когда; *hardly anywhere,* мало где. **3,** (almost surely not) едва ли; вряд ли: *that is hardly possible,* едва ли это возможно. *He will hardly come now,* вряд ли он уже придёт.

hardness *n.* твёрдость; жёсткость.

hardship *n.* лишение: *suffer hardships,* терпеть лишения.

hardware *n.* **1,** (tools and household items) скобяной товар; скобяные изделия. *Hardware store,* скобяной магазин. **2,** (of a computer) техническое обеспечение.

hard-working *adj.* трудолюбивый.

hardy *adj.* **1,** (robust) крепкий; выносливый; живучий. **2,** (adventuresome) смелый. **3,** (frost-resistant) морозостойкий.

hare *n.* заяц.

harebrained *adj.* легкомысленный; безрассудный.

harelip *n.* заячья губа.

harem *n.* гарем.

hark *v.i.* слушать. —*interj.* слушай! —**hark back, 1,** (return) возвращаться. **2,** (date back) восходить.

harken *v.* = **hearken.**

harlequin *n.* арлекин; шут.

harlot *n.* проститутка.

harm *n.* вред; зло; ущерб. *She meant no harm,* она не хотела никого обидеть. *He wishes you no harm,* он не желает вам зла. *I see no harm in it,* я не вижу в этом ничего плохого. *It won't do any harm,* вреда от этого не будет. *It won't do any harm to...,* не повредит, если... *What harm is there in asking?,* что страшного в том, если мы спросим? *Do more harm than good,* принести больше вреда, чем пользы. —*v.t.* вредить; наносить *or* причинять вред (+ *dat.*). *No one was harmed,* никто не пострадал. *Don't harm her!,* не трогайте её! —**out of harm's way,** от греха подальше.

harmful *adj.* вредный.

harmless *adj.* безвредный; безобидный.

harmonic *adj.* гармонический. —*n., music* обертон.

harmonica *n.* губная гармоника.

harmonious *adj.* гармоничный; согласный.

harmonium *n.* фисгармония.

harmonize *v.t.* гармонизировать. —*v.i.* гармонировать.

harmony *n.* **1,** *music* гармония. **2,** (accord) гармония; согласие. *Harmony of interests,* гармония интересов. *Live in harmony,* жить в согласии.

harness *n.* упряжь; сбруя. —*v.t.* **1,** (put a harness on) запрягать. **2,** *fig.* (utilize the potential of) использовать. —**harness races,** бега.

harp *n.* арфа. —*v.i.* [*usu.* **harp on**] твердить (о). —**harp on the same string,** тянуть всё ту же песню; заладить одно и то же.

harpist *n.* арфист; арфистка.

harpoon *n.* острога; гарпун. —*v.t.* бить острогой/гарпуном; гарпунить.

harpsichord *n.* клавесин.

harquebus *n.* пищаль.

harridan *n.* старая карга.

harrier *n.* (bird) лунь.

harrow *n.* борона. —*v.t.* боронить. —**harrowing,** *adj.* душераздирающий.

harry *v.t.* мучить; травить; изводить. *A harried look,* измученный вид.

harsh *adj.* **1,** (grating) резкий; жёсткий. **2,** (severe; grim; cruel) резкий; суровый; жестокий. —**harshly,** *adv.* резко; жестоко. —**harshness,** *n.* резкость; суровость.

hart *n.* рогач.

harum-scarum *adv.* как попало; очертя голову.

harvest *n.* **1,** (crop) урожай. *Poor harvest,* неурожай; недород. **2,** (gathering in of a crop) жатва; сбор *or* уборка урожая. *Harvest time,* время жатвы. —*v.t.* собирать: *harvest the crops,* собирать урожай.

harvester *n.* уборочная машина; жатвенная машина; жнейка; жатка.

hash *n.* **1,** (food) рубленое мясо. **2,** (mishmash) мешанина.

hashish *n.* гашиш.

hasp *n.* пробой.

hassle *n., colloq.* перебранка; препирательство.

hassock *n.* пуф.

haste *n.* поспешность; торопливость. *In haste,* поспешно; наспех; второпях. *In my haste,* второпях; впопыхах. —**haste makes waste,** поспешишь – людей насмешишь. —**make haste,** спешить; торопиться.

hasten *v.i.* спешить; торопиться. *He hastened to add that...,* он поспешил добавить, что... —*v.t.* торопить; ускорять.

hastily *adv.* поспешно; наскоро; наспех; второпях.

hasty *adj.* поспешный; торопливый.

hat *n.* шляпа. —*adj.* шляпный: *hat shop,* шляпный магазин. —**at the drop of a hat,** по малейшему поводу; чуть что. —**keep under one's hat,** помалкивать о. —**take off one's hat to,** снимать шляпу перед; преклоняться перед. —**talk through one's hat,** нести чушь.

hatband *n.* околыш.

hatbox *n.* картонка для шляпы.

hatch *v.t.* **1,** (bring forth, as young) выси́живать; выводи́ть. **2,** (incubate, as an egg) наси́живать. **3,** (devise, as plans) вына́шивать. **4,** (mark with lines) штрихова́ть.—*v.i.* выводи́ться; вылупля́ться. —*n.* люк: *escape hatch,* спаса́тельный люк.

hatchet *n.* топо́рик.

hate *v.t.* **1,** (detest) ненави́деть: *hate onions/liars/war,* ненави́деть лук/лгуно́в/войну́. **2,** (dislike doing) о́чень не люби́ть *or* хоте́ть. *Hate writing letters,* о́чень не люби́ть (*or* ненави́деть) писа́ть пи́сьма. *I hate to interrupt, but...,* о́чень не хочу́ переби́ть, но... *I hate to spend money for that,* мне жаль тра́тить де́ньги на э́то. —*n.* не́нависть.

hated *adj.* ненави́стный.

hateful *adj.* ненави́стный.

hatpin *n.* була́вка для шля́пы; шля́пная була́вка.

hatrack *n.* ве́шалка для шляп.

hatred *n.* не́нависть.

hatter *n.* шля́пный ма́стер; шля́пник; ша́почник.

haughty *adj.* надме́нный; высокоме́рный. —**haughtiness,** *n.* надме́нность; высокоме́рие.

haul *v.t.* **1,** (drag) тяну́ть; тащи́ть. **2,** (transport) перевози́ть. **3,** *fol. by* **in** (pull in, as a fish) выта́скивать. **4,** *fol. by* **down** (pull down) спуска́ть. —*n.* **1,** (distance covered) рейс. **2,** (of fish) уло́в. **3,** (of loot) добы́ча. —**haul off,** *colloq.* размахну́ться: *haul off and strike,* размахну́ться и уда́рить. —**over the long haul,** в долгосро́чном пла́не.

haulage *n.* перево́зка.

haunch *n.* бедро́; ля́жка.

haunt *v.t.* **1,** (dwell in, as of a ghost) обита́ть. *Haunted house,* заколдо́ванный дом. **2,** (obsess, as of a thought) пресле́довать. *Haunting melody,* навя́зчивый моти́в. —*n.* люби́мое ме́сто.

have *v.t.* **1,** (possess) име́ть: *have the right/opportunity/misfortune,* име́ть пра́во/возмо́жность/несча́стье. ♦ *Most commonly rendered, however, by* у: *do you have a match?,* у вас есть спи́чка? *I have no time,* у меня́ нет вре́мени. **2,** (receive) получа́ть: *I've had no news from him,* я не получа́л о нём изве́стий. **3,** (do; perform; carry on) *rendered by various verbs: have a look,* посмотре́ть; *have a talk with,* поговори́ть с; *have an argument,* поспо́рить. **4,** (cause to do or be done): *have him come in,* попроси́те его́ войти́. *Have one's picture taken,* снима́ться. **5,** (cause to be treated) отдава́ть: *have fixed,* отдава́ть в ремо́нт; *have cleaned,* отдава́ть в чи́стку; *have washed,* отдава́ть в сти́рку. **6,** (experience) *rendered by* у: *she has a cold,* у неё на́сморк; *he had a heart attack,* у него́ был серде́чный припа́док. *Have a dream,* ви́деть сон. *Have a good time,* хорошо́ проводи́ть вре́мя. **7,** (harbor) пита́ть: *have an aversion to,* пита́ть отвраще́ние к. **8,** (feel and show): *have mercy on,* щади́ть; *have pity on,* сжа́литься над. **9,** (eat; drink): *have tea,* пить чай. *Have supper,* у́жинать. *What will you have?,* что вы бу́дете пить? **10,** (bear; beget) роди́ть: *she had a son,* у неё роди́лся сын. **11,** (permit; tolerate) потерпе́ть: *I won't have such conduct,* я не потерплю́ тако́го поведе́ния. **12,** (declare; state) гласи́ть: *legend has it that...,* леге́нда гласи́т, что... *Rumor has it,* хо́дят слу́хи, что... —*v.aux.* **1,** *used to form perfect tenses: I have already eaten,* я уже́ пое́л. **2,** *in contrary-to-fact sentences* е́сли бы: *had I only known!,* е́сли бы я то́лько знал! ♦ *Also rendered by the imperative: had the blast occurred ten minutes earlier,* произойди́ взрыв на де́сять мину́т ра́ньше. **3,** (*fol. by inf.*) *expressing obligation* на́до; ну́жно; до́лжен: *I have to go,* мне на́до/ну́жно идти́; я до́лжен (должна́) идти́. —**have it in for,** име́ть зуб на. —**have it out with,** объясня́ться с. —**have on,** быть в (+ *prepl.*); быть оде́тым в (+ *acc.*): *have a raincoat on,* быть в плаще́. *What else did she have on?,* что ещё на ней бы́ло наде́то? —**have to do with, 1,** (have a connection with) име́ть отноше́ние к: *what has this to do with me?,* како́е э́то име́ет отноше́ние ко мне?; при чём я тут? *Money has nothing to do with it,* де́ньги тут ни при чём. **2,** (associate with) име́ть де́ло с: *he refused to have anything to do with me,* он отказа́лся име́ть де́ло со мной.

haven *n.* **1,** (harbor) га́вань. **2,** (shelter) убе́жище; прию́т.

haversack *n.* вещево́й мешо́к; ра́нец.

havoc *n.* опустоше́ние. —**play havoc with,** приводи́ть в расстро́йство.

hawk *n.* я́стреб. —*v.t. & i.* (peddle) торгова́ть вразно́с. —*v.i.* (clear one's throat) отха́ркиваться. —**hawker,** *n.* разно́счик.

hawk-eyed *adj.* зо́ркий.

hawser *n* пе́рлинь.

hawthorn *n.* боя́рышник.

hay *n.* се́но. —*adj.* сенно́й. —**hit the hay,** *colloq.* отпра́виться на бокову́ю. —**make hay while the sun shines,** куй желе́зо, пока́ горячо́.

haycock *n.* копна́.

hay fever сенна́я лихора́дка.

hayfield *n.* сеноко́с.

hayloft *n.* сенова́л.

haystack *n.* стог се́на; скирд; скирда́.

hazard *n.* опа́сность; риск. —*v.t.* **1,** (risk) рискова́ть. **2,** (venture) осме́ливаться: *hazard a guess,* осме́литься догада́ться. —**hazardous,** *adj.* опа́сный; риско́ванный.

haze *n.* ды́мка; мгла; ма́рево.

hazel *n.* **1,** (tree) оре́шник; лещи́на. **2,** (nut) лесно́й оре́х. —*adj.* све́тло-кори́чневый.

hazel grouse ря́бчик. *Also,* **hazel hen.**

hazelnut *n.* лесно́й оре́х.

hazy *adj.* **1,** (misty) тума́нный; мгли́стый. **2,** (vague) сму́тный; тума́нный.

he *pers.pron.* он: *he is ill,* он бо́лен; *he left,* он ушёл. *He is not here,* его́ нет. *He who,* тот, кто... *See also* **him.**

head *n.* **1,** (part of the body) голова́. **2,** (top part; head end) глава́: *at the head of the table,* во главе́ стола́. **3,** (of a pin, match, etc.) голо́вка; (of a nail) шля́пка. **4,** (of cabbage) коча́н. **5,** (of a bed) изголо́вье. **6,** (unit, as of cattle) голова́. **7,** (chief) глава́: *head of the family,* глава́ семьи́. **8,** (mind; brain) голова́; ум: *clear head,* я́сная голова́; я́сный ум. *Do figures in one's head,* счита́ть в уме́. **9,** *Ten dollars a/per head,* де́сять до́лларов с головы́ *or* с но́са. —*adj.* **1,** (of or for the head) головно́й. **2,** (chief) гла́вный; ста́рший: *head physician,* гла́вный/ста́рший врач. —*v.t.* **1,** (set the course of) направля́ть. **2,** (be the head of) возглавля́ть. **3,** *fol. by* **off** (intercept; avert) пресека́ть. —*v.i.* (move in a specified direction) направля́ться. *Head north,* направля́ться (*or* брать курс) на се́вер. —**come into one's head,** взбрести́ в го́лову. —**come to a head,** назре́ть.

—**from head to toe,** с головы́ до ног. —**get it into one's head,** вбива́ть/забива́ть/забира́ть себе́ в го́лову. —**get it through someone's head,** вбива́ть в го́лову (+ *dat.*). —**go to one's head, 1,** (intoxicate) ударя́ть в го́лову (+ *dat.*). **2,** (make vain) вскружи́ть го́лову (+ *dat.*). —**head and shoulders above,** на́ голову вы́ше (+ *gen.*). —**head over heels, 1,** (tumbling) ку́барем; кувырко́м; вверх торма́шками. **2,** (completely) по́ уши (влюблён, в долга́х, *etc.*). —**heads or tails?,** орёл и́ли ре́шка? —**lose one's head,** потеря́ть го́лову. —**make head or tail of,** разбира́ться в. —**over one's head, 1,** (too difficult for) вы́ше (чьего́-нибудь) понима́ния. **2,** (bypassing) че́рез (чью́-нибудь) го́лову. —**take it into one's head,** взду́мать (+ *inf.*). —**talk someone's head off,** загова́ривать. —**turn one's head,** вскружи́ть го́лову (+ *dat.*). —**two heads are better than one,** ум хорошо́, а два лу́чше. —**use one's head,** шевели́ть мозга́ми.

headache *n.* головна́я боль. *I have a headache,* у меня́ боли́т голова́.

head cold на́сморк.

headdress *n.* головно́й убо́р.

headfirst *adv.* голово́й вперёд.

heading *n.* ру́брика.

headland *n.* мыс.

headless *adj.* безголо́вый.

headlight *n.* фа́ра.

headline *n.* заголо́вок.

headlong *adv.* **1,** (headfirst) голово́й вперёд. **2,** (at breakneck speed) о́прометью; стремгла́в. **3,** (rashly) очертя́ го́лову; напропалу́ю. —*adj.* стреми́тельный; безогля́дный.

headmaster *n.* дире́ктор (шко́лы).

head-on *adv.* в лоб; но́сом. —*adj.* прямо́й: *head-on collision,* прямо́е столкнове́ние.

headphone *n.* нау́шник.

headquarters *n.pl.* **1,** (place of command) штаб. **2,** (main building) штаб-кварти́ра.

headset *n.* головно́й телефо́н.

head start фо́ра.

headstone *n.* **1,** (tombstone) надгро́бный ка́мень. **2,** *obs.* (cornerstone) краеуго́льный ка́мень.

headstrong *adj.* упря́мый; своево́льный.

headwaiter *n.* метрдоте́ль.

headwaters *n.pl.* исто́ки; верхо́вье.

headway *n.* **1,** (motion forward) продвиже́ние. **2,** (progress) прогре́сс. *Make headway,* сдвига́ться с ме́ста.

head wind встре́чный ве́тер.

heady *adj.* опьяня́ющий.

heal *v.t.* зале́чивать. —*v.i.* залива́ть. —**healer,** *n.* исцели́тель.

health *n.* здоро́вье. *Public health,* здравоохране́ние. *He is in good health,* он здоро́в; он облада́ет хоро́шим здоро́вьем. *She is in poor health,* у неё сла́бое здоро́вье. —**to your health!,** за ва́ше здоро́вье!

healthful *adj.* здоро́вый; целе́бный.

healthy *adj.* здоро́вый.

heap *n.* ку́ча; гру́да. —*v.t.* **1,** *often fol. by* **up** (pile up) нагроможда́ть. **2,** (shower) осыпа́ть: *heap ridicule on,* осыпа́ть (кого́-нибудь) насме́шками.

hear *v.t.* **1,** (perceive; learn) слы́шать: *hear the music/news,* слы́шать му́зыку/но́вость. *I can't hear you,* не слы́шу вас. *I can't hear a thing,* мне ничего́ не слы́шно. *You can hear the sound of the waves,* слы́шен шум волн. *I heard someone approaching from behind,* я слы́шал, как кто́-то подходи́л сза́ди. **2,** *law* слу́шать: *hear a case,* слу́шать де́ло. —*v.i.* **1,** (be able to perceive sound) слы́шать: *he can't hear,* он не слы́шит. **2,** *fol. by* **of** *or* **about** (learn of) слы́шать (о). *It's the first I've heard of it,* пе́рвый раз слы́шу. **3,** *fol. by* **from** (get mail or a call from) получи́ть изве́стие от. *Let us hear from you,* да́йте нам знать о вас. **4,** *fol. by* **of** (consider; consent) слы́шать (о): *I won't hear of it,* я об э́том и слы́шать не хочу́. —**hear out,** выслу́шивать.

hearing *n.* **1,** (sense) слух. *Hard of hearing,* туго́й на́ ухо. *Lose one's hearing,* (о)гло́хнуть. **2,** *law* слу́шание. **3,** (earshot) слы́шимость: *within hearing,* в преде́лах слы́шимости. —**hearing aid,** слухово́й аппара́т.

hearken *also,* **harken** *v.i.* слу́шать. *Hearken to,* внима́ть (+ *dat.*).

hearsay *n.* слу́хи; молва́. *Through hearsay,* по слу́хам; понаслы́шке.

hearse *n.* похоро́нные дро́ги; погреба́льная колесни́ца; катафа́лк.

heart *n.* **1,** (organ of the body) се́рдце. **2,** (center) центр; се́рдце. *In the heart of Europe,* в са́мом це́нтре (*or* в се́рдце) Евро́пы. **3,** (essence; crux) суть; су́щность: *get to the heart of the matter,* добра́ться до су́ти де́ла. **4,** *pl., cards* че́рви. —*adj.* серде́чный: *heart muscle,* серде́чная мы́шца. —**at heart,** в глубине́ души́. —**by heart,** наизу́сть. —**lose heart,** па́дать ду́хом; уныва́ть. —**not have the heart to,** не хвата́ть ду́ху (*with* у): *I haven't the heart to...,* у меня́ не хвата́ет ду́ху (+ *inf.*). —**take heart,** ободря́ться; воспря́нуть ду́хом. —**take to heart,** принима́ть бли́зко к се́рдцу. —**with a heavy heart,** с тяжёлым се́рдцем; с бо́лью на душе́. —**with all one's heart,** всем се́рдцем; всей душо́й. —**with one's heart in one's mouth,** с замира́нием се́рдца.

heartache *n.* душе́вная боль.

heart attack серде́чный приа́док; инфа́ркт.

heartbeat *n.* бие́ние се́рдца; сердцебие́ние.

heartbreaking *adj.* (душе)раздира́ющий.

heartbroken *adj.* уби́тый го́рем.

heartburn *n.* изжо́га.

heart disease заболева́ние се́рдца.

hearten *v.t.* ободря́ть; подбодря́ть.

heart failure парали́ч се́рдца.

heartfelt *adj.* серде́чный; душе́вный; задуше́вный.

hearth *n.* оча́г.

heartily *adv.* **1,** (warmly; cordially) серде́чно. **2,** (with a hearty appetite) с аппети́том; пло́тно. **3,** (completely) вполне́: *I heartily agree/approve,* я вполне́ согла́сен/одобря́ю.

heartless *adj.* бессерде́чный; безду́шный. —**heartlessness,** *n.* бессерде́чие; бессерде́чность; безду́шие.

heart-rending *adj.* (душе)раздира́ющий.

heart-shaped *adj.* сердцеви́дный.

heartsick *adj.* (о́чень) огорчён; (о́чень) расстро́ен.

heart-to-heart *adj.* инти́мный; серде́чный. *Heart-to-heart talk,* разгово́р по душа́м.

heartwarming *adj.* ра́достный.

hearty *adj.* **1,** (cordial, as of a welcome) серде́чный; раду́шный. **2,** (solid, as of a meal) пло́тный; сы́тный. **3,** (big, as of one's appetite) хоро́ший; отли́чный.

heat *n.* **1,** (hotness) жара́. **2,** *physics* теплота́; тепло́. **3,** (heating system) отопле́ние: *steam heat,* парово́е отопле́ние. **4,** (excitement; strong feelings) жар; пыл. *In the heat of battle,* в пылу́ сраже́ния. **5,** (sexual excitement) те́чка: *be in heat,* быть в те́чке. **6,** *sports* забе́г; *swimming* заплы́в. —*v.t.* **1,** (provide with heat) топи́ть. **2,** (make warm) нагрева́ть; согрева́ть. —*v.i.* [*usu.* **heat up**] нагрева́ться; согрева́ться.

heated *adj.* **1,** (warmed) нагре́тый. **2,** (vehement, as of an argument) горя́чий. —**heatedly,** *adv.* горячо́.

heater *n.* нагрева́тельный прибо́р; нагрева́тель. *Electric heater,* электри́ческийками́н.

heath *n.* **1,** (uncultivated land) пу́стошь. **2,** (shrub) э́рика.

heathen *n.* язы́чник. —*adj.* язы́ческий.

heather *n.* ве́реск.

heating *n.* **1,** (providing with heat) отопле́ние. **2,** (making warm) нагрева́ние. —*adj.* отопи́тельный; нагрева́тельный. —**heating oil,** отопи́тельная нефть. —**heating pad,** электри́ческая гре́лка.

heat lightning зарни́ца.

heat rash потни́ца.

heat-resistant *adj.* теплосто́йкий.

heat shield теплово́й экра́н.

heatstroke *n.* теплово́й уда́р.

heat wave полоса́ си́льной жары́.

heave *v.t.* **1,** (hurl) броса́ть; швыря́ть. **2,** *Heave a sigh,* испусти́ть вздох. —*v.i.* **1,** (rise and fall rhythmically) вздыма́ться. **2,** *colloq.* (retch) рвать.—*n.* бросо́к. —**heave ho!,** раз, два, дру́жно!

heaven *n.* не́бо. —**be in seventh heaven,** быть на седьмо́м не́бе. —**for heaven's sake!,** ра́ди бо́га! —**heaven forbid!,** не дай бог!; бо́же упаси́! —**heavens!,** бо́же мой! —**thank heaven!,** сла́ва бо́гу! —**move heaven and earth,** пусти́ть в ход все сре́дства.

heavenly *adj.* **1,** (of the heavens) небе́сный: *heavenly body,* небе́сное те́ло. **2,** (divine; sublime) боже́ственный.

heaves *n.pl.* запа́л.

heavily *adv.* тяжело́. *Heavily armed,* си́льно вооруже́нный. *Heavily in debt,* в большо́м долгу́; кругом в долгу́.

heaviness *n.* тя́жесть.

heavy *adj.* **1,** (weighty) тяжёлый. **2,** (difficult; arduous) тяжёлый: *heavy work,* тяжёлая рабо́та; *heavy breathing,* тяжёлое дыха́ние. **3,** (intense) си́льный: *heavy rain,* си́льный дождь; *a heavy cold,* си́льный на́сморк. *Under heavy guard,* под си́льной охра́ной. *Heavy traffic,* интенси́вное движе́ние. *Heavy fighting,* тяжёлые *or* упо́рные бои́. *Heavy drinker,* го́рький пья́ница. **4,** (severe, as of losses) тяжёлый; большо́й; кру́пный; серьёзный. *Pay a heavy price for,* заплати́ть дорого́й цено́й за. **5,** (large, as of industry, artillery, etc.) тяжёлый. **6,** (ponderous, as of writing) тяжёлый; тяжелове́сный. **7,** (hard to digest) тяжёлый. **8,** (choppy, as of the sea) бу́рный. **9,** (gloomy, as of the sky) мра́чный; хму́рый. —*adv.* тяжело́. —**hang heavy,** ме́дленно тяну́ться.

heavy-handed *adj.* неуклю́жий; нело́вкий.

heavyset *adj.* призе́мистый; корена́стый.

heavy water тяжёлая вода́.

heavyweight *n.* тяжелове́с. —*adj.* тяжёлого ве́са.

Hebrew *adj.* (древне)евре́йский. —*n.* **1,** (person) евре́й. **2,** (ancient language) древнееврейский язы́к. **3,** (modern language) иври́т.

heckle *v.t.* прерыва́ть кри́ками.

hectare *n.* гекта́р.

hectic *adj.* сумато́шный; бу́рный; горя́чий.

hedge *n.* жива́я и́згородь. —*v.t.* [*usu.* **hedge in**] обноси́ть и́згородью. —*v.i.* (equivocate) виля́ть.

hedgehog *n.* ёж.

hedonism *n.* гедони́зм. —**hedonist,** *n.* гедони́ст. —**hedonistic,** *adj.* гедонисти́ческий.

heed *v.t.* слу́шать; прислу́шиваться к. *Heed someone's advice,* прислу́шиваться к чьему́-нибудь сове́ту. *Heed a warning,* обрати́ть внима́ние на предупрежде́ние. —*n.* внима́ние: *pay no need to,* не обраща́ть (никако́го) внима́ния на. —**heedful,** *adj.* обраща́ющий внима́ние. —**heedless,** *adj.* не обраща́ющий внима́ния.

heel *n.* **1,** (part of the foot) пя́тка; пята́. **2,** (part of a shoe) каблу́к. **3,** (part of a stocking) пя́тка. —**head over heels,** *see* **head.** —**on the heels of,** вслед за. —**take to one's heels,** показа́ть пя́тки; улепётывать; дать тя́гу; пусти́ться наутёк; смота́ть у́дочки. —**under the heel of,** под пято́й (+ *gen.*).

hefty *adj.* **1,** (burly) ро́слый; дю́жий. **2,** (substantial) поря́дочный; изря́дный.

hegemony *n.* гегемо́ния.

heifer *n.* тёлка.

height *n.* **1,** (size; altitude) высота́. **2,** (of a person) рост. **3,** *often pl.* (high point) высь. **4,** *fol. by* **of** (greatest degree) верх: *the height of folly,* верх глу́пости. *At the height of its glory,* на верши́не его́ сла́вы. **5,** (time of greatest activity) разга́р: *at the height of the season,* в разга́ре сезо́на. *Be at its height,* быть в разга́ре.

heighten *v.t.* **1,** (raise) повыша́ть. **2,** (intensify) повыша́ть; уси́ливать. —*v.i.* повыша́ться; уси́ливаться.

heinous *adj.* гну́сный. —**heinousness,** *n.* гну́сность.

heir *n.* насле́дник. *Heir to the throne,* насле́дник престо́ла. —**heiress,** *n.* насле́дница.

heirloom *n.* фами́льное сокро́вище.

helicopter *n.* вертолёт.

heliograph *n.* гелио́граф

heliotrope *n.* гелиотро́п.

heliport *n.* площа́дка для вертолётов.

helium *n.* ге́лий.

hell *n.* ад. —*interj.* чёрт возьми́! —**a hell of a...,** а́дский; черто́вский. *A hell of a long way,* черто́вски далеко́. —**as hell,** черто́вски: *mad as hell,* черто́вски серди́т. —**catch hell,** *slang* получи́ть по ша́пке. —**come hell or high water,** во что бы то ни ста́ло. —**for the hell of it,** про́сто так. —**give someone hell,** *colloq.* распека́ть. —**go through hell,** переноси́ть му́ки а́да. —**go to hell!,** иди́те к чёрту! —**like hell, 1,** (with all one's might) как чёрт: *work like hell,* рабо́тать как чёрт. **2,** *as an exclamation* чёрта с два!; как бы не так! —**raise hell,** *colloq.* поднима́ть шум. —**to hell with,** а ну (+ *gen.*): *to hell with him!,* а ну его́! *To hell with it!,* к чёрту! —**what the hell...?,** како́го чёрта: *what the hell is he doing there?,* како́го чёрта он там де́лает?

hellebore *n.* чемери́ца.

Hellenic *adj.* э́ллинский.

hellish *adj.* а́дский.

hello *interj.* здра́вствуйте! ♦*When answering the telephone* алло́!; слу́шаю!

helm *n.* руль; штурва́л. *Be at the helm,* стоя́ть у руля́.
helmet *n.* шлем; ка́ска.
helmsman *n.* рулево́й; штурва́льный.
help *v.t.* **1,** (aid; assist) помога́ть. *Help someone up,* помо́чь кому́-нибудь встать. *Help someone on with his coat,* подава́ть кому́-нибудь пальто́. **2,** (assist in accomplishing) спосо́бствовать: *help to achieve our goal,* спосо́бствовать достиже́нию на́шей це́ли. **3,** (wait on) обслу́живать. **4,** (serve) класть: *help oneself to,* класть себе́ на таре́лку (+ *gen.*). *May I help you to some meat?,* мо́жно вам положи́ть мя́са? *Help yourself!,* угоща́йтесь, пожа́луйста! **5,** (prevent; change): *I can't help it,* ничего́ не могу́ поде́лать. *It can't be helped,* ничего́ не поде́лаешь. —*v.i.* помога́ть. —*n.* **1,** (aid; assistance) по́мощь. *You were a big help,* вы нам о́чень помогли́. **2,** (workers) рабо́чие ру́ки. **3,** (household help) слу́ги. —*interj.* на по́мощь! —**not help** (**doing something**), не мочь не (+ *inf.*): *I could not help noticing that...,* я не мог не заме́тить, что... *I couldn't help laughing,* я не мог удержа́ться от сме́ха. *I can't help thinking that...,* я не могу́ освободи́ться от мы́сли, что... —**so help me God,** да помо́жет мне бог.
helper *n.* помо́щник.
helpful *adj.* **1,** (useful) поле́зный. **2,** (accommodating) услу́жливый.
helping *n.* по́рция. —*adj., in* **lend a helping hand,** подава́ть ру́ку по́мощи.
helpless *adj.* беспо́мощный; бесси́льный. —**helplessness,** *n.* беспо́мощность; бесси́лие.
helter-skelter *adv.* как попа́ло; врассыпну́ю.
hem *n.* рубе́ц. —*v.t.* **1,** (sew a hem in) подруба́ть. **2,** *fol. by* **in** (encircle) сти́скивать. —*v.i., in* **hem and haw,** тяну́ть и мя́млить; ни шьёт ни по́рет.
he-man *n., colloq.* настоя́щий мужчи́на.
hematite *also,* **haematite** *n.* кра́сный железня́к; желе́зный блеск.
hemisphere *n.* полуша́рие.
hemlock *n.* **1,** (poisonous plant) болиголо́в. *Water hemlock,* цику́та. **2,** (evergreen tree) тсу́га.
hemoglobin *also,* **haemoglobin** *n.* гемоглоби́н.
hemophilia *also,* **haemophilia** *n.* гемофили́я; кровоточи́вость.
hemorrhage *also,* **haemorrhage** *n.* кровоизлия́ние. —*v.i.* кровоточи́ть.
hemorrhoid *also,* **haemorrhoid** *n., usu. pl.* геморро́й.
hemp *n.* **1,** (plant) конопля́. **2,** (fiber) пенька́. —*adj.* конопля́ный; пенько́вый.
hemstitch *n.* ажу́рная стро́чка.
hen *n.* ку́рица.
henbane *n.* белена́.
hence *adv.* **1,** (therefore) сле́довательно; отсю́да. **2,** (from now) че́рез: *a week hence,* че́рез неде́лю.
henceforth *adv.* впредь; отны́не; с э́того вре́мени. *Also,* **henceforward.**
henchman *n.* приспе́шник.
henhouse *n.* куря́тник.
henna *n.* хна.
henpecked *adj.* под башмако́м (у жены́).
hepatic *adj.* печёночный.
hepatica *n.* печёночница; переле́ска.
hepatitis *n.* воспале́ние пе́чени; гепати́т.
heptagon *n.* семиуго́льник. —**heptagonal,** *adj.* семиуго́льный.
her *pers.pron.* **1,** *used as dir. obj. of a verb* её: *ask her,* спроси́ её. **2,** *used as indir. obj. of a verb* ей: *give her the keys,* дай ей ключи́. **3,** *used as obj. of a prep.* неё; ней: *from her,* от неё; *with her,* с ней. —*poss.adj.* её: *her brother,* её брат. ♦*When the possessor is the subject of the sentence* свой: *she took her purse with her,* она́ взяла́ с собо́й свою́ су́мку.
herald *n.* **1,** *hist.* геро́льд. **2,** (messenger) ве́стник. —*v.t.* возвеща́ть. —**heraldic,** *adj.* геральди́ческий. —**heraldry,** *n.* гера́льдика.
herb *n.* трава́. —**herbaceous,** *adj.* травяно́й; травяни́стый. —**herbarium,** *n.* герба́рий. —**herbicide,** *n.* гербици́д. —**herbivorous,** *adj.* травоя́дный.
Hercules *n.* геркуле́с.
herd *n.* ста́до: *herd of elephants,* ста́до слоно́в. —*v.t.* **1,** (tend) пасти́. **2,** (drive as if in a herd) гнать. *Herd into a pen,* загоня́ть в заго́н. *Herd together,* сгоня́ть. —**herd instinct,** ста́дный инсти́нкт.
herdsman *n.* гуртовщи́к.
here *adv.* **1,** (in this place) здесь; тут. *From here,* отсю́да. **2,** (to this place) сюда́: *come here!,* иди́ сюда́! **3,** *used in presenting something* вот: *here are your glasses,* вот ва́ши очки́. —**here and now,** сейча́с же. —**here and there,** ко́е-где; места́ми; там и тут. —**here's to...,** за (+ *acc.*): *here's to our hosts!,* за на́ших хозя́ев!
hereabout *also,* **hereabouts** *adv.* побли́зости.
hereafter *adv.* впредь; отны́не; в дальне́йшем.
hereby *adv.* сим; настоя́щим.
hereditary *adj.* насле́дственный.
heredity *n.* насле́дственность.
herein *adv.* в э́том; здесь.
hereinafter *adv.* в дальне́йшем: *hereinafter referred to as...,* в дальне́йшем имену́емый...
heresy *n.* е́ресь.
heretic *n.* ерети́к. —**heretical,** *adj.* ерети́ческий.
hereto *adv.* при сём: *attached hereto,* при сём прилага́ется.
heretofore *adv.* до э́того; до сих пор; до сего́ вре́мени.
herewith *adv.* при сём: *enclosed herewith,* при сём прилага́ется.
heritage *n.* насле́дие.
hermaphrodite *n.* гермафроди́т.
hermetic *adj.* гермети́ческий. —**hermetically,** *adv.* гермети́чески.
hermit *n.* отше́льник; затво́рник; пусты́нник.
hernia *n.* гры́жа. —**hernial,** *adj.* грыжево́й.
hero *n.* геро́й. *He received a hero's welcome,* его́ приве́тствовали как геро́я.
heroic *adj.* герои́ческий; геро́йский. —**heroically,** *adv.* герои́чески; геро́йски.
heroin *n.* герои́н.
heroine *n.* герои́ня.
heroism *n.* герои́зм; геро́йство.
heron *n.* ца́пля.
herpes *n.* лиша́й.
herring *n.* сельдь; селёдка.
herringbone *n.* ёлочка: *in herringbone style,* ёлочкой; в ёлочку.
hers *poss.pron.* её: *this umbrella is hers,* э́тот зо́нтик её. *An uncle of hers,* оди́н её дя́дя. *My dress is red, hers is blue,* моё пла́тье кра́сное, её – си́нее.
herself *pers.pron.* **1,** *used for emphasis* (она́) сама́: *she did it herself,* она́ сама́ э́то сде́лала. **2,** *used*

reflexively себя́: *she bought it for herself,* она́ купи́ла э́то для себя́. *She hurt herself,* она́ уши́блась. —**by herself,** одна́. —**she is not herself,** она́ сама́ не своя́.

hesitancy *n.* колеба́ние.

hesitant *adj.* колеблющийся. *She is hesitant to ask,* она́ стесня́ется попроси́ть.

hesitate *v.i.* **1,** (waver) колеба́ться. **2,** (be reluctant) стесня́ться.

hesitation *n.* колеба́ние. *Without (a moment's) hesitation,* без колеба́ний; не разду́мывая; недо́лго ду́мая.

heterodox *adj.* не ортодокса́льный; ерети́ческий.

heterogeneous *adj.* разноро́дный. —**heterogeneity,** *n.* разноро́дность.

hew *v.t.* **1,** (chop) руби́ть; теса́ть. **2,** (carve) высека́ть; вытёсывать.

hex *n.* дурно́й глаз. —*v.t.* сгла́зить.

hexagon *n.* шестиуго́льник. —**hexagonal,** *adj.* шестиуго́льный.

hey *interj.* эй!; гей!

heyday *n.* зени́т; расцве́т.

hi *interj.* приве́т!

hiatus *n.* **1,** (gap) пробе́л. **2,** (break) переры́в. **3,** *ling.* зия́ние.

hibernate *v.i.* залега́ть в зи́мнюю спя́чку. —**hibernation,** *n.* зи́мняя спя́чка.

hibiscus *n.* гиби́скус.

hiccup *also,* **hiccough** *v.i.* ика́ть. —**hiccups,** *n.pl.* ико́та.

hick *n.* провинциа́л; дереве́нщина. —*adj., colloq.* провинциа́льный.

hickory *n.* гико́ри.

hidden *adj.* скры́тый; та́йный.

hide *v.t.* пря́тать; скрыва́ть. *Hide something in the drawer,* пря́тать что́-нибудь в я́щик(е) стола́. —*v.i.* пря́таться; скрыва́ться: *hide in the basement/under the bed/behind a tree/,* пря́таться/скрыва́ться в подва́л(е)/под крова́ть(ю)/за де́рево(м)/. —*n.* шку́ра: *cowhide,* коро́вья шку́ра.

hide-and-seek *n.* пря́тки.

hideaway *n.* тайни́к.

hidebound *adj.* ограни́ченный; узколо́бый.

hideous *adj.* отврати́тельный; уро́дливый. —**hideousness,** *n.* уро́дство; безобра́зие.

hideout *n.* тайни́к.

hiding *n.* скры́тие. *In hiding,* в бега́х. *Go into hiding,* скрыва́ться. —**hiding place,** тайни́к.

hierarchy *n.* иера́рхия. —**hierarchical,** *adj.* иерархи́ческий.

hieroglyph *also,* **hieroglyphic** *n.* иеро́глиф. —**hieroglyphic,** *adj.* иероглифи́ческий.

high *adj.* **1,** (lofty) высо́кий: *a high mountain,* высо́кая гора́. *On a high level,* на высо́ком у́ровне. **2,** (having a specified height): *that building is 100 meters high,* э́то зда́ние в сто ме́тров высото́й. **3,** (above average) высо́кий: *high temperature,* высо́кая температу́ра; *high quality,* высо́кое ка́чество. *High prices,* высо́кие *or* дороги́е це́ны. *High speed,* больша́я ско́рость. *High hopes,* ра́дужные наде́жды. *A high honor,* высо́кая честь. *Have a high opinion of,* быть высо́кого мне́ния о. *Play for high stakes,* игра́ть по большо́й. **4,** (high-pitched) высо́кий: *high notes,* высо́кие но́ты. **5,** (of high rank) высокопоста́вленный; ста́рший. **6,** (gay) весёлый: *high spirits,* весёлое настрое́ние. **7,** *colloq.* (tipsy) под хмелько́м. **8,** *High winds,* си́льный ве́тер. **9,** *The high seas,* откры́тое мо́ре. **10,** *High crimes,* госуда́рственные преступле́ния. —*adv.* высоко́: *aim high,* ме́тить высоко́. —*n.* вы́сшая то́чка. *Prices reached a new high,* це́ны повы́сились до но́вого преде́ла. —**high and dry,** на мели́. *Leave high and dry,* оста́вить с но́сом. —**high and mighty,** высоко́мерный. —**it is high time,** давно́ уже́ пора́. —**look high and low,** иска́ть всю́ду и везде́. —**on high,** в высоте́; в вышине́. *From on high,* с высоты́. *See also* **higher.**

highbrow *n.* интеллиге́нт.

highchair *n.* высо́кий де́тский сту́льчик.

high-class *adj.* фешене́бельный.

high command верхо́вное *or* гла́вное кома́ндование.

higher *adj., comp. of* **high.** —**higher education,** вы́сшее образова́ние. —**higher mathematics,** вы́сшая матема́тика.

high-flown *adj.* высокопа́рный; напы́щенный.

high-handed *adj.* самово́льный; вла́стный. —**high-handedness,** *n.* своево́лие; самово́лие; саму́рство.

high-heeled *adj.* на высо́ких каблука́х.

high jump прыжо́к в высоту́.

highland *n.* наго́рье. —**highlander,** *n.* го́рец.

highlight *n.* **1,** *art; photog.* светово́й эффе́кт. **2,** *fig.* (high point; feature) гвоздь. —*v.t.* обрисо́вывать; обознача́ть.

highly *adv.* **1,** (to a high degree) высоко́. *Highly developed,* высокора́звитый. *Highly seasoned,* о́стро припра́вленный. **2,** (extremely) весьма́: *highly probable/successful,* весьма́ вероя́тно/успе́шный. **3,** (with admiration) высоко́: *value highly,* высоко́ ценить. *Think highly of,* быть высо́кого мне́ния о. **4,** (with praise) ле́стно: *speak highly of,* ле́стно отозва́ться о.

high-minded *adj.* иде́йный. —**high-mindedness,** *n.* иде́йность.

Highness *n.* высо́чество: *Your Highness,* ва́ше высо́чество.

high-paid *adj.* высокоопла́чиваемый.

high-pitched *adj.* высо́кий.

high-powered *adj.* (of a weapon) кру́пного кали́бра; (of a telescope or microscope) си́льный.

high-priced *adj.* дорогосто́ящий.

high priest первосвяще́нник.

high-ranking *adj.* высокопоста́вленный.

high-rise *adj.* многоэта́жный; высо́тный.

high school сре́дняя шко́ла.

high sign усло́вленный знак.

high society вы́сшее о́бщество; вы́сший свет.

high-sounding *adj.* гро́мкий; высокопа́рный.

high-speed *adj.* быстрохо́дный; скоростно́й.

high-strung *adj.* не́рвный; нерво́зный.

high-tension *adj.* высо́кого напряже́ния.

high tide по́лная вода́.

high treason госуда́рственная изме́на.

highway *n.* шоссе́; магистра́ль.

highwayman *n.* разбо́йник.

hijack *v.t.* угоня́ть; похища́ть (самолёт). —**hijacker,** *n.* похити́тель (самолёта). —**hijacking,** *n.* уго́н (самолёта); похище́ние (самолёта); нападе́ние (на самолёт).

hike *v.i.* ходи́ть пешко́м. —*v.t., colloq.* (raise) повыша́ть. —*n.* **1,** (long walk) похо́д. **2,** (increase) повыше́ние: *price/wage hike,* повыше́ние цен/зарпла́ты.

hilarious *adj.* **1,** (gay) весёлый. **2,** (screamingly funny) умори́тельный. —**hilarity,** *n.* весе́лье.

hill *n.* холм.

hillock *n.* хо́лмик; го́рка; буго́р.

hillside *n.* склон горы́; склон холма́; косого́р.

hilltop *n.* верши́на холма́.

hilly *adj.* холми́стый.

hilt *n.* рукоя́тка; эфе́с. —**to the hilt,** по́лностью; до конца́.

him *pers.pron.* **1,** *used as dir. obj. of a verb* его́: *ask him,* спроси́те его́. **2,** *used as indir. obj. of a verb* ему́: *give him a dollar,* дай ему́ до́ллар. **3,** *used as obj. of a prep.* него́; нему́; нём; ним.

himself *pers.pron.* **1,** *used for emphasis* (он) сам: *he did it himself,* он сам э́то сде́лал. **2,** *used reflexively* себя́: *he bought himself a coat,* он купи́л себе́ пальто́. *He hurt himself,* он уши́бся. —**by himself,** оди́н. —**he is not himself,** он сам не свой.

hind *adj.* за́дний.

hinder *v.t.* меша́ть; препя́тствовать.

Hindi *n.* хи́нди.

hindrance *n.* препя́тствие; поме́ха.

hindsight *n.* ретроспе́кция.

Hindu *n.* инду́с. —*adj.* инду́сский. —**Hinduism,** *n.* индуи́зм.

hinge *n.* **1,** (joint) пе́тля; шарни́р. **2,** (for a postage stamp) накле́йка. —*v.i.* [*usu.* **hinge on**] (depend on) зави́сеть (от).

hinny *n.* лоша́к.

hint *n.* намёк. —*v.t.* намека́ть. —*v.i.* [*usu.* **hint at**] намека́ть (на).

hinterland *n.* глушь; захолу́стье.

hip *n.* бедро́. —**shoot from the hip,** *colloq.* руби́ть сплеча́.

hipbone *n.* та́зовая кость.

hippopotamus *n.* бегемо́т; гиппопота́м.

hire *v.t.* **1,** (employ) нанима́ть. **2,** (rent) брать напрока́т. —*n.* наём. *Be for hire,* сдава́ться напрока́т.

hired *adj.* наёмный. *Hired hand,* наёмный рабо́чий.

hireling *n.* наёмник; найми́т.

his *poss.adj. & pron.* его́: *his aunt,* его́ тётя. *An aunt of his,* одна́ его́ тётя. ♦*When the possessor is the subject of the sentence* свой: *he sold his house,* он про́дал свой дом.

hiss *v.i.* **1,** (give off a hissing sound) шипе́ть. **2,** (whistle disapproval) свисте́ть; ши́кать. —*v.t.* осви́стывать (+ *acc.*); ши́кать (+ *dat.*). —*n.* = **hissing.**

hissing *n.* **1,** (sound of escaping air) шипе́ние. **2,** (sound of disapproval) свист. —*adj.* шипя́щий.

histology *n.* гистоло́гия.

historian *n.* исто́рик.

historic *adj.* истори́ческий.

historical *adj.* истори́ческий. —**historically,** *adv.* истори́чески.

historiography *n.* историогра́фия. —**historiographer,** *n.* историо́граф.

history *n.* исто́рия. *History lesson,* уро́к исто́рии. *History teacher,* учи́тель исто́рии.

histrionic *adj.* театра́льный. —**histrionics,** *n.pl.* театра́льность.

hit *v.t.* **1,** (deal a blow to) ударя́ть. **2,** (strike against) ударя́ться о *or* в. *The car hit a tree,* маши́на наскочи́ла *or* налете́ла на де́рево. **3,** (strike, as a target) попада́ть в. **4,** (reach; attain) достига́ть: *the temperature hit 100°,* температу́ра дости́гла ста гра́дусов. *Hit a high note,* взять высо́кую но́ту. **5,** *usu. passive* (affect severely): *be hard hit by the flood,* си́льно пострада́ть от наводне́ния. —*v.i.* **1,** (strike, as of a storm) обру́шиваться. **2,** *fol. by* **on** *or* **upon** (come up with, as an idea) напада́ть (на); набрести́ (на); доду́маться (до). —*n.* **1,** (blow) уда́р. **2,** (striking of a target) попада́ние: *direct hit,* прямо́е попада́ние. **3,** (success) успе́х: *be a big hit,* име́ть большо́й успе́х. **4,** (film) боеви́к. —**hit back,** дава́ть сда́чи (+ *dat.*). —**hit it off,** сойти́сь хара́ктерами. *Hit it off with,* ла́дить с. —**hit or miss,** как попа́ло; наudáчу; наобу́м. —**hit the road,** *slang* отпра́виться в путь.

hitch *v.t.* **1,** (tie; fasten) привя́зывать; прикрепля́ть. *Hitch a horse to a wagon,* запряга́ть *or* впряга́ть ло́шадь в теле́гу. *Hitch a car onto a train,* прицепля́ть ваго́н к по́езду. **2,** (pull up with a jerk) подтя́гивать: *hitch up one's trousers,* подтя́гивать брю́ки. —*n.* **1,** (tug; jerk) рыво́к. **2,** (delay; complication) зами́нка: *without a hitch,* без зами́нки. **3,** *colloq.* (period of service) срок (слу́жбы).

hitchhike *v.i.* е́хать на попу́тной маши́не; "голосова́ть" на доро́ге.

hitching post ко́новязь.

hither *adv.* сюда́.

hitherto *adv.* до сих пор.

Hittite *adj.* хе́ттский. —**Hittites,** *n.pl.* хе́тты.

hive *n.* **1,** (beehive) у́лей. **2,** *pl.* (skin condition) крапи́вница.

hoard *n.* запа́с. —*v.t.* запаса́ть; накопля́ть; припря́тывать.

hoarfrost *n.* и́ней; и́зморозь.

hoarse *adj.* хри́плый; си́плый. *Be hoarse,* хрипе́ть. *Become hoarse,* (о)хри́пнуть. *Talk oneself hoarse,* договори́ться до хрипоты́. —**hoarsely,** *adv.* хри́пло.

hoarseness *n.* хрипота́.

hoary *adj.* **1,** (gray or white with age) седо́й. **2,** (ancient; venerable) почте́нный.

hoax *n.* шу́тка; мистифика́ция.

hobble *v.i.* ковыля́ть. *Hobble along,* идти́ прихра́мывая. —*v.t.* (fetter) трено́жить; спу́тывать.

hobby *n.* хо́бби.

hobbyhorse *n.* конь-кача́лка.

hobgoblin *n.* **1,** (elf) домово́й. **2,** (bugaboo) жу́пел.

hobnob *v.i.* води́ть компа́нию; якша́ться.

hobo *n.* бродя́га; бося́к.

hock *v.t., colloq.* закла́дывать. —*n., colloq., usu. in* **in hock,** в закла́де.

hockey *n.* хокке́й. —*adj.* хокке́йный: *hockey match,* хокке́йный матч. —**hockey player,** хокке́ист. —**hockey stick,** клю́шка.

hockshop *n.* ломба́рд.

hocus-pocus *n.* фо́кус-по́кус.

hodgepodge *n.* мешани́на; ерала́ш.

hoe *n.* моты́га. —*v.t.* моты́жить.

hog *n.* бо́ров; свинья́.

hogwash *n.* **1,** (swill) по́йло (для свине́й). **2,** (nonsense) чепуха́.

hoi polloi плебс; простонаро́дье.

hoist *v.t.* поднима́ть. *Hoist a flag,* поднима́ть/выбро́сить/вы́кинуть флаг. —*n.* **1,** (act of hoisting) подъём. **2,** (hoisting device) подъёмник.

hold *v.t.* **1,** (grip) держа́ть: *hold in one's hand,* держа́ть в руке́. *Hold hands,* бра́ться за́ руки. *Hold* *one's nose,* зажима́ть нос. **2,** (keep in a certain position) держа́ть: *hold one's head high,* держа́ть го́лову высоко́. **3,** (bear the weight of) уде́рживать: *the hook will not hold the mirror,* крючо́к не уде́ржит зе́ркала. **4,** (detain) держа́ть: *hold prisoner,* держа́ть в плену́. **5,** (delay the departure of, as a train) заде́рживать. **6,** (set aside until needed or requested) оставля́ть. **7,** (prevent from being captured) уде́рживать. **8,** (have; organize; carry on) проводи́ть; устра́ивать. *Hold a meeting,* проводи́ть собра́ние. *Hold elections,* проводи́ть вы́боры. **9,** (occupy, as a job or office) занима́ть. **10,** (have room for; accommodate) вмеща́ть. **11,** (own) владе́ть. **12,** (maintain, as an opinion) приде́рживаться. **13,** (command, as attention) владе́ть. **14,** (consider; regard): *hold in high esteem,* высоко́ цени́ть; *hold sacred,* свя́то чтить; *hold in contempt,* относи́ться с презре́нием к. **15,** (believe; maintain) утвержда́ть. **16,** (rule) постановля́ть: *the court held that...,* суд постанови́л, что... —*v.i.* **1,** (retain a hold) держа́ться: *hold tight,* держа́ться кре́пко. **2,** (not break or collapse) выде́рживать: *the rope held,* верёвка вы́держала. **3,** (be true or valid) остава́ться в си́ле. —*n.* **1,** (grip) сжа́тие; хва́тка. *Take/catch/grab hold of,* ухвати́ться за. *Lose hold of,* упуска́ть. **2,** (of a ship) трюм. **3,** (sway; control) власть; влия́ние. —**get (a) hold of, 1,** (get a grip on) ухвати́ться за. **2,** *colloq.* (obtain) раздобы́ть. **3,** *colloq.* (reach, as by telephone) связа́ться с; дозвони́ться к. **4,** *Get hold of oneself,* взять себя́ в ру́ки. —**hold against,** ста́вить в упрёк (+ *dat.*). —**hold back, 1,**(restrain) уде́рживать; сде́рживать. **2,** (withhold) уде́рживать; заде́рживать. **3,** (not reveal)ута́ивать. **4,** (retard) заде́рживать. —**hold down, 1,** (pin down) прижима́ть к земле́. **2,** (keep down, as prices) уде́рживать. **3,** *colloq.* (have; keep, as a job) уде́рживаться на (рабо́те). *Hold down two jobs,* рабо́тать на двух рабо́тах; рабо́тать по совмести́тельству. —**hold forth,** разглаго́льствовать. —**hold good,** остава́ться в си́ле. —**hold it!,** стой!; стоп! —**hold off, 1,** (check the advance of) уде́рживать. **2,** (delay in doing something) повремени́ть. —**hold on,** держа́ться. —**hold on to, 1,** (hold so as not to fall) держа́ться за: *hold on to the banister,* держа́ться за пери́ла. **2,** (hold in place) приде́рживать: *hold on to one's hat,* приде́рживать шля́пу. —**hold out, 1,** (proffer) протя́гивать. **2,** (offer, as hope) подава́ть (наде́жду). **3,** (stand firm) держа́ться; продержа́ться; устоя́ть; вы́стоять. **4,** (last; suffice) хвата́ть. —**hold still,** не шевели́ться. —**hold up, 1,** (raise) подноси́ть: *hold up to the light,* подноси́ть к све́ту. **2,** (support; keep from falling) подде́рживать; уде́рживать. **3,** (delay) заде́рживать. **4,** (expose; exhibit): *hold up as an example,* ста́вить в приме́р. *Hold up to ridicule,* поднима́ть на́ смех. **5,** (last; continue to function) выде́рживать. **6,** (rob) гра́бить.

holder *n.* **1,** (possessor) держа́тель; облада́тель. *Holder of an order,* кавале́р о́рдена. **2,** (device) держа́тель. *Cigarette holder,* мундшту́к.

holding *n.* **1,** (having, as elections) проведе́ние. **2,** *usu. pl.* (property) владе́ния; (money) вкла́ды. —**holding pattern,** маршру́т ожида́ния.

holdover *n.* пережи́ток.

holdup *n., colloq.* **1,** (delay) заде́ржка. **2,** (robbery) налёт.

hole *n.* **1,** (opening; tear) дыра́; ды́рка. **2,** (in the ground) я́ма. **3,** (animal's burrow) нора́; но́рка. **4,** *golf* лу́нка. **5,** *colloq.* (small dingy quarters) конура́. —*v.i.* [*usu.* **hole up**] скрыва́ться.

holiday *n.* **1,** (commemorative day) пра́здник. **2,** *Brit.* (vacation) о́тпуск. —*adj.* пра́здничный.

holiness *n.* **1,** (sanctity) свя́тость. **2,** *cap.* (papal title) святе́йшество: *His Holiness,* его́ святе́йшество.

holler *v.i., colloq.* ора́ть.

hollow *adj.* **1,** (having a cavity within) по́лый. **2,** (sunken, as of cheeks) впа́лый. **3,** (muffled, as of a sound) глухо́й. **4,** (meaningless; shallow) пусто́й. —*n.* **1,** (cavity) дупло́. **2,** (depression) углубле́ние; впа́дина; вы́емка. —*v.t.* [*usu.* **hollow out**] долби́ть; выда́лбливать.

holly *n.* па́дуб; остроли́ст.

hollyhock *n.* штокро́за.

holmium *n.* го́льмий.

holocaust *n.* катастро́фа; уничтоже́ние.

holography *n.* голографи́я.

holster *n.* кобура́.

holy *adj.* свято́й; свяще́нный. —**Holy Alliance,** Свяще́нный сою́з. —**Holy Ghost,** свято́й дух. —**holy of holies,** свята́я святы́х. —**Holy Scripture,** свяще́нное писа́ние. —**Holy Thursday,** страстно́й четве́рг. —**holy water,** свята́я вода́. —**Holy Week,** свята́я *or* страстна́я неде́ля.

homage *n.* по́чести: *pay homage to,* ока́зывать *or* воздава́ть по́чести (+ *dat.*).

home *n.* дом. —*adj.* дома́шний: *home address,* дома́шний а́дрес. *The home team,* хозя́ева по́ля. —*adv.* **1,** (to one's home) домо́й: *go home,* идти́ домо́й. **2,** (at one's home) до́ма: *he is not home,* его́ нет до́ма. —**at home, 1,** (in one's house) до́ма. **2,** *sports* на своём по́ле. **3,** (comfortable; at ease) как до́ма: *feel at home,* чу́вствовать себя́ как до́ма. *Make yourself at home!,* бу́дьте как дома! —**bring home to,** внуша́ть; втолкова́ть. —**from home,** из до́ма; от до́ма: *mail from home,* пи́сьма из до́ма; *far from home,* далеко́ от до́ма. *I'm calling from home,* я звоню́ из до́ма. —**strike home,** попа́сть не в бровь, а в глаз.

homebody *n.* домосе́д.

homebred *adj.* доморо́щенный.

home-brew *n.* самого́н.

homecoming *n.* возвраще́ние домо́й.

home economics домово́дство.

home front вну́тренний фронт.

homeland *n.* ро́дина; оте́чество.

homeless *adj.* бездо́мный; бесприю́тный; беспризо́рный.

homely *adj.* **1,** (unpretentious) просто́й. **2,** (unattractive) некраси́вый; невзра́чный.

homemade *adj.* дома́шний; самоде́льный.

homemaker *n.* дома́шняя хозя́йка.

homeopathy *n.* гомеопа́тия. —**homeopath,** *n.* гомеопа́т. —**homeopathic,** *adj.* гомеопати́ческий.

homeowner *n.* домовладе́лец.

home rule самоуправле́ние.

homesick *adj.* тоску́ющий по до́му *or* по ро́дине. *Be homesick,* тоскова́ть по до́му/по ро́дине/.

homespun *adj.* **1,** (woven at home) домотка́ный. **2,** (simple; unpretentious) доморо́щенный.

homestead *n.* уса́дьба.

home town родно́й го́род.

homeward *adv.* домо́й; к до́му. —**homeward-bound,** *adj.* возвраща́ющийся домо́й.

homework *n.* дома́шнее зада́ние; дома́шняя ра-

бо́та. *Do one's homework,* (при)гото́вить уро́ки *or* дома́шние зада́ния.
homicide *n.* уби́йство.
homily *n.* поуче́ние.
homing pigeon почто́вый го́лубь.
hominy *n.* мамалы́га.
homogeneous *adj.* одноро́дный. —**homogeneity,** *n.* одноро́дность.
homogenize *v.t.* гомогенизи́ровать.
homonym *n.* омо́ним.
homosexual *n.* гомосексуали́ст. —*adj.* гомосексуа́льный. —**homosexuality,** *n.* гомосексуали́зм.
hone *v.t.* точи́ть. —*n.* точи́льный ка́мень.
honest *adj.* че́стный. *To be honest...,* че́стно говоря́... —**honest to goodness!,** че́стное сло́во!
honestly *adv.* **1,** (in an honest manner) че́стно. **2,** (really; truly) че́стное сло́во.
honesty *n.* че́стность. —**in all honesty,** че́стно говоря́; по со́вести (говоря́).
honey *n.* **1,** (sweet substance) мёд. **2,** *colloq.* (term of endearment) ми́лый; голу́бчик. —*adj.* медо́вый.
honeybee *n.* медоно́сная пчела́.
honeycomb *n.* со́ты.
honeydew *n.* медвя́ная роса́. —**honeydew melon,** зи́мняя ды́ня.
honeyed *adj.* медо́вый; слаща́вый; при́торный.
honeymoon *n.* медо́вый ме́сяц.
honeysuckle *n.* жи́молость.
honk *n.* **1,** (call of the goose) клик. **2,** (sound of an automobile horn) гудо́к. —*v.i.* **1,** (of a goose) кли́кать. **2,** (blow the horn) гуде́ть. —*v.t.* дать (гудо́к).
honor *also,* **honour** *n.* **1,** (integrity; reputation; privilege) честь. *Consider it an honor,* счита́ть за честь. **2,** (esteem) почёт. *Place of honor,* почётное ме́сто. **3,** *pl.* (ceremonies of respect) по́чести: *with military honors,* с во́инскими по́честями. **4,** *cap.* (title of respect) честь: *Your Honor,* ва́ша честь. **5,** *pl.* (credit awarded to outstanding students) отли́чие: *graduate with honors,* око́нчить с отли́чием. **6,** *pl., cards* онёры. —*v.t.* **1,** (show special respect for) почита́ть. **2,** (bring honor or distinction to) ока́зывать честь (+ *dat.*). **3,** (pay tribute to) че́ствовать. **4,** (observe, as one's commitments) выполня́ть. —**do honor to,** де́лать честь (+ *dat.*). —**in honor of,** в честь (+ *gen.*). —**on my honor; word of honor,** че́стное сло́во.
honorable *also,* **honourable** *adj.* **1,** (honest; upright) че́стный. **2,** (deserving of respect) почётный.
honorarium *n.* гонора́р.
honorary *adj.* почётный.
honored *also,* **honoured** *adj.* почётный: *honored guest,* почётный гость. *I am honored to...,* счита́ю за честь (+ *inf.*).
honor guard почётный карау́л.
honor roll кра́сная доска́.
honour *n.* & *v.* = **honor.** —**honourable,** *adj.* = **honorable.** —**honoured,** *adj.* = **honored.**
hood *n.* **1,** (head covering) капюшо́н. **2,** (cover of an engine) капо́т.
hooded *adj.* **1,** (wearing a hood) в капюшо́не. **2,** (containing a hood) с капюшо́ном. —**hooded seal,** хохла́ч.
hoodlum *n.* хулига́н.
hoodwink *v.t.* обма́нывать; провести́; обжу́ливать.
hoof *n.* копы́то. —**hoofed,** *adj.* копы́тный.
hook *n.* крюк; крючо́к. —*v.t.* **1,** (fasten) застёгивать (на крючо́к). **2,** (attach; hitch) прицепля́ть. **3,** *fol. by* **up** (connect) подключа́ть. **4,** (catch, as a fish) выу́живать. —*v.i.* **1,** (fasten) застёгиваться: *the dress hooks in back,* пла́тье застёгивается сза́ди. **2,** *fol. by* **onto** (be attached to) пристёгиваться к; прицепля́ться к. —**by hook or by crook,** каки́м бы то ни́ было спо́собом; все́ми пра́вдами и непра́вдами; не мытьём, так ка́таньем. —**hook, line, and sinker,** по́лностью; целико́м.
hooked *adj.* **1,** (curved like a hook) крючкова́тый. *Hooked nose,* горба́тый нос; нос с горби́нкой. **2,** *fol. by* **on,** *slang* (addicted to) поме́шанный (на).
hookup *n.* **1,** (network) сеть. **2,** *colloq.* (connection) связь.
hookworm *n.* глист.
hooky *n., in* **play hooky,** прогу́ливать уро́ки.
hooligan *n.* хулига́н. —**hooliganism,** *n.* хулига́нство.
hoop *n.* о́бруч.
hoopla *n.* шум; шуми́ха.
hoopoe *n.* удо́д.
hoop skirt криноли́н.
hooray *interj.* ура́!
hoosegow *n., colloq.* куту́зка.
hoot *n.* **1,** (cry of an owl) крик (совы́). **2,** (toot) гудо́к. —*v.i.* (of an owl) у́хать. —*v.t.* (jeer) осви́стывать.
hop *v.i.* **1,** (leap, as of a frog) пры́гать. **2,** (jump on one foot) пры́гать *or* скака́ть на одно́й ноге́. —*v.t.* вска́кивать: *hop a train,* вскочи́ть на по́езд. —*n.* **1,** (jump) прыжо́к; скачо́к. **2,** *colloq.* (short flight) рейс. **3,** (plant) хмель. **4,** *pl.* (flavoring for beer) хмель.
hope *n.* наде́жда. —*v.t.* & *i.* наде́яться: *I hope so,* наде́юсь, что да; *I hope not,* наде́юсь, что нет. *Hope for the best,* наде́яться на лу́чшее. *I hope to see you again soon,* наде́юсь ско́ро вас сно́ва уви́деть.
hopeful *adj.* **1,** (having hope): *be hopeful,* наде́яться; пита́ть наде́жды. **2,** (giving hope) обнадёживающий; пода́ющий наде́жды.
hopefully *adv.* **1,** (with hope) с наде́ждой. **2,** (if all goes well) на́до наде́яться, что...
hopeless *adj.* **1,** (offering no hope) безнадёжный; безвы́ходный. **2,** *colloq.* (worthless; without merit) беспо́мощный. —**hopelessness,** *n.* безнадёжность.
hopper *n.* бу́нкер.
hopscotch *n.* кла́ссы.
horde *n.* по́лчище; орда́.
horizon *n.* **1,** (line between earth and sky) горизо́нт. **2,** *fig.* (intellect) кругозо́р; горизо́нт.
horizontal *adj.* горизонта́льный. —*n.* горизонта́ль. —**horizontal bar,** *sports* перекла́дина; турни́к.
horizontally *adv.* горизонта́льно.
hormone *n.* гормо́н.
horn *n.* **1,** (bonelike growth) рог. **2,** (instrument sounded by blowing) рог. **3,** (brass-wind instrument) рожо́к. **4,** (of an automobile) гудо́к. —*v.i.* [*usu.* **horn in**] *slang* вме́шиваться; сова́ться. —**blow one's own horn,** труби́ть о себе́. —**draw/pull in one's horns,** бить отбо́й. —**horn of plenty,** рог изоби́лия. —**take the bull by the horns,** брать быка́ за рога́.
hornbeam *n.* граб.
hornblende *n.* рогова́я обма́нка.
horned *adj.* рога́тый.

hornet *n.* шершень. —**hornets' nest,** осиное гнездо́.
hornless *adj.* безро́гий; комо́лый.
horn-rimmed *adj.* рогово́й: *horn-rimmed glasses,* роговы́е очки́.
horny *adj.* **1,** (having horns) рога́тый. **2,** (calloused; tough) мозо́листый.
horoscope *n.* гороско́п.
horrendous *adj.* = **horrible.**
horrible *adj.* стра́шный; ужа́сный.
horrid *adj.* ужа́сный; проти́вный.
horrify *v.t.* ужаса́ть; приводи́ть в у́жас. *Be horrified,* ужаса́ться; приходи́ть в у́жас. —**horrifying,** *adj.* ужаса́ющий.
horror *n.* **1,** (terror) у́жас. **2,** *pl.* (that which horrifies) у́жасы: *the horrors of war,* у́жасы войны́. —**horror movie,** фильм у́жасов.
hors d'oeuvre заку́ска.
horse *n.* **1,** (animal) ло́шадь; конь. **2,** (frame) ра́ма. *Sawhorse,* ко́злы. **3,** *gymnastics* конь; кобы́ла. —*adj.* лошади́ный; ко́нный. —*v.i.* [*usu.* **horse around**] *colloq.* озорнича́ть; прока́зничать; дури́ть. —**back the wrong horse,** поста́вить не на ту ло́шадь. —**change horses in midstream,** меня́ть лошаде́й во вре́мя перепра́вы. —**horse of a different color,** совсе́м друго́й коленко́р. —**look a gift horse in the mouth,** смотре́ть в зу́бы дарёному коню́. —**play the horses,** игра́ть на ска́чках. —**work like a horse,** рабо́тать как вол.
horseback *adv.* верхо́м: *ride horseback,* е́здить верхо́м. *Be on horseback,* быть верхо́м. —**horseback riding,** верхова́я езда́. *Go horseback riding,* ката́ться верхо́м.
horse breeder конево́д. —**horse breeding,** коневодство; коннозаво́дство.
horsecar *n.* ко́нка.
horse chestnut ко́нский кашта́н.
horsecloth *n.* попо́на.
horse doctor конова́л.
horse-drawn *adj.* ко́нный.
horseflesh *n.* кони́на.
horsefly *n.* слепе́нь.
horsehair *n.* ко́нский во́лос. —*adj.* волосяно́й: *horsehair mattress,* волосяно́й матра́ц.
horsehide *n.* ко́нская шку́ра.
horselaugh *n.* хо́хот.
horseman *n.* вса́дник; нае́здник. —**horsemanship,** *n.* иску́сство верхово́й езды́; нае́здничество.
horsemeat *n.* кони́на.
horseplay *n.* баловство́; озорство́.
horsepower *n.* лошади́ная си́ла.
horse racing ска́чки.
horseradish *n.* хрен.
horseshoe *n.* подко́ва.
horsetail *n.* (plant) хвощ.
horse thief конокра́д.
horsetrader *n.* бары́шник.
horsewhip *n.* хлыст. —*v.t.* отхлеста́ть.
horsewoman *n.* вса́дница; нае́здница; амазо́нка.
horticulture *n.* садово́дство. —**horticultural,** *adj.* садово́дческий. —**horticulturist,** *n.* садово́д.
hosanna *n.* оса́нна.
hose *n.* **1,** (device for squirting water) шланг; кишка́; рука́в. **2,** (stockings) чулки́. —*v.t.* полива́ть из шла́нга.
hosiery *n.* чуло́чные изде́лия.
hospitable *adj.* гостеприи́мный.
hospital *n.* больни́ца; *mil.* го́спиталь. —*adj.* больни́чный; госпита́льный. —**hospital ship,** госпита́льное *or* санита́рное су́дно.
hospitality *n.* гостеприи́мство.
hospitalization *n.* **1,** (being hospitalized) госпитализа́ция. **2,** (insurance) страхова́ние на слу́чай госпитализа́ции.
hospitalize *v.t.* помеща́ть в больни́цу; госпитализи́ровать.
host *n.* **1,** (one who entertains) хозя́ин. **2,** (multitude) мно́жество; тьма. —**play host to,** *sports* принима́ть на своём по́ле.
hostage *n.* зало́жник.
hostel *n.* турба́за. *Youth hostel,* молодёждая турба́за.
hostelry *n.* постоя́лый двор.
hostess *n.* хозя́йка.
hostile *adj.* **1,** (antagonistic) вражде́бный; неприя́зненный. **2,** (being or belonging to an enemy) вра́жеский.
hostility *n.* **1,** (antagonism) вражда́; вражде́бность; неприя́знь. *With hostility,* вражде́бно. **2,** *pl.* (warfare) вое́нные де́йствия.
hot *adj.* **1,** (of the weather, temperature, etc.) жа́ркий: *a hot day,* жа́ркий день. *I am hot,* мне жа́рко. **2,** (of an object, liquid, etc.) горя́чий. **3,** (highly spiced) о́стрый. **4,** (impassioned; fiery) горя́чий. —**get into hot water,** попа́сть в беду́; попа́сть как кур во́ щи. —**hot on the trail of,** по горя́чим следа́м (+ *gen.*). —**not so hot,** так себе́.
hot air 1, *literally* нагре́тый во́здух. **2,** *colloq.* (empty talk) пустосло́вие.
hotbed *n.* **1,** (glass-covered bed of soil) парни́к. **2,** *fig.* (breeding ground) оча́г.
hot-blooded *adj.* горя́чий; пы́лкий; стра́стный.
hot cake блин. —**sell like hot cakes,** продава́ться нарасхва́т.
hot dog *colloq.* соси́ска.
hotel *n.* гости́ница. *Hotel room,* но́мер гости́ницы.
hothead *n.* горя́чая голова́; кипято́к. —**hotheaded,** *adj.* горя́чий; вспы́льчивый.
hothouse *n.* тепли́ца; оранжере́я. —*adj.* тепли́чный; оранжере́йный; парнико́вый.
hotly *adv.* горячо́.
hot-tempered *adj.* горя́чий; вспы́льчивый; запа́льчивый.
hot-water bottle гре́лка.
hound *n.* охо́тничья соба́ка; го́нчая. —*v.t.* **1,** (pursue relentlessly) пресле́довать; трави́ть. **2,** *colloq.* (nag; pester) пристава́ть к.
hour *n.* час: *two hours,* два часа́. *Hour after hour,* час за ча́сом. *Hour by hour,* час о́т часу.
hourglass *n.* песо́чные часы́.
hour hand часова́я стре́лка.
hourly *adj.* **1,** (occurring every hour) ежеча́сный. **2,** (per hour) часово́й. —*adv.* ежеча́сно.
house *n.* **1,** (dwelling place) дом. *At my house,* у меня́. *To my house,* ко мне. **2,** (building) зда́ние; дом. *Schoolhouse,* шко́льное зда́ние. *Rooming house,* пансио́н. *Movie house,* кино́. *Opera house,* о́перный теа́тр. *House of worship,* моли́твенный дом. **3,** (institution) дом: *house of correction,* исправи́тельный дом. **4,** (business establishment) фи́рма. *Publishing*

house, издáтельство. **5,** (theater; audience) зал: *full house,* пóлный зал. **6,** (legislative body) палáта: *House of Representatives,* палáта представи́телей. *House of Commons,* палáта óбщин. *House of Lords,* палáта лóрдов. **7,** (dynasty) дом: *House of Tudor,* дом Тюдóров. —*adj.* домáшний: *house arrest,* домáшний арéст. *House plant,* кóмнатное растéние. —*v.t.* **1,** (provide quarters for) помещáть. **2,** (serve as the home of) вмещáть. —**house of cards,** кáрточный дóмик. —**keep house,** вести́ (домáшнее) хозя́йство. —**on the house,** за счёт предприя́тия.

houseboat *n.* плавýчий дом.

housebreaker *n.* взлóмщик.

housecoat *n.* капóт.

household *n.* семья́; домочáдцы. —*adj.* домáшний; хозя́йственный. *Household goods,* хозя́йственные товáры. *Household items,* предмéты домáшнего обихóда. *Household appliances,* бытовы́е прибóры. *Household chores,* хлóпоты по хозя́йству.

housekeeper *n.* **1,** (housewife) хозя́йка. **2,** (woman hired to run a house) экономка.

housekeeping *n.* ведéние хозя́йства; домáшнее хозя́йство; домовóдство.

housemaid *n.* гóрничная; домрабóтница.

housetop *n., in* **from the housetops,** во всеуслы́шание; на всех перекрёстках.

housewarming *n.* новосéлье.

housewife *n.* домáшняя хозя́йка.

housework *n.* рабóта по хозя́йству. *Help with the housework,* помогáть по хозя́йству.

housing *n.* **1,** (living quarters) жили́ще; жилóе помещéние. *Poor housing,* неудовлетвори́тельные жили́щные услóвия. *Provide with housing,* обеспéчивать жили́щем. *Shortage of housing,* нехвáтка жилплóщади. **2,** (casing) кожýх. —*adj.* жили́щный: *housing conditions,* жили́щные услóвия. *Housing allowance,* кварти́рное довóльствие.

hovel *n.* лачýга; хибáрка.

hover *v.i.* **1,** (remain suspended in the air) рéять. **2,** *fol. by* **over** (stick close to) стоя́ть над (чьéй-нибудь) душóй. **3,** (waver) колебáться. *Hover between life and death,* быть мéжду жи́знью и смéртью.

hovercraft *n.* сýдно на воздýшной подýшке.

how *adv.* **1,** (in what manner; in what state) как: *how is this done?,* как э́то дéлается? *How are you?,* как вы поживáете? *How does the story end?,* чем кончáется расскáз? **2,** (to what extent) наскóлько: *how true is this?,* наскóлько э́то вéрно? *How tall are you?,* какóго вы рóста? *How high is this building?,* какóй высоты́ э́то здáние? **3,** *in exclamations* как: *how strange!,* как стрáнно! —**and how!,** ещё бы! —**how about...?,** как насчёт...? —**how come?,** почемý же? *How come you're not asleep?,* что же ты не спишь? —**how do you do?, 1,** (hello) здрáвствуйте! **2,** *on being introduced* óчень прия́тно! —**how far?,** *see* **far.** —**how long?,** *see* **long.** —**how many?; how much?,** скóлько? —**how so?,** как же так?

however *conj.* однáко. —*adv.* как (бы) ни: *however hard he tried,* как он ни старáлся.

howitzer *n.* гáубица.

howl *v.i.* **1,** (of an animal or the wind) выть; завывáть. **2,** (cry out) ревéть; вопи́ть. **3,** (laugh loudly) хохотáть. —*n.* вой; рёв. —**howling monkey,** ревýн.

hub *n.* **1,** (of a wheel) ступи́ца. **2,** (center; focal point) ýзел; средотóчие.

hubbub *n.* гам; гвалт; галдёж.

hubcap *n.* колпáк (ступи́цы).

huckleberry *n.* черни́ка.

huckster *n.* торгáш; бары́шник.

huddle *v.i.* **1,** (crowd together) жáться; тесни́ться; юти́ться. **2,** *fol. by* **up** (hunch up, as from the cold) ёжиться; жáться.

hue *n.* **1,** (color) цвет; крáска. **2,** (shade) оттéнок. —**hue and cry,** шум: *raise a hue and cry,* поднимáть шум.

huff *n.* вспы́шка гнéва. *Get into a huff,* удáриться в амби́цию. —*v.i.* (blow) дуть; фýкать. *Huff and puff,* задыхáться.

huffy *adj.* оби́дчивый.

hug *v.t.* **1,** (embrace) обнимáть. **2,** (stick close to) держáться (+ *gen.*): *hug the shore,* держáться бéрега. —*v.i.* обнимáться. —*n.* объя́тие.

huge *adj.* огрóмный; громáдный.

Huguenot *n.* гугенóт.

hulk *n.* **1,** (remains of an old ship) кóрпус корабля́. **2,** (huge bulky thing) громáда. —**hulking,** *adj.* неуклю́жий; медвéжий.

hull *n.* **1,** (shell; husk) шелухá. **2,** (body of a ship) кóрпус (корабля́). —*v.t.* шелуши́ть; лущи́ть.

hullabaloo *n.* шуми́ха; тарарáм.

hum *v.i.* **1,** (sing without words) напевáть. **2,** (buzz) жужжáть. **3,** *colloq.* (be full of activity) кипéть. —*v.t.* напевáть. —*n.* **1,** (of insects) жужжáние. **2,** (of voices) гул; гóмон.

human *adj.* человéческий; людскóй. —**human being,** человéк. —**human nature,** человéческая прирóда. —**human race,** человéческий род. —**human rights,** правá человéка.

humane *adj.* гумáнный; человéчный. —**humanely,** *adv.* гумáнно. —**humaneness,** *n.* гумáнность; человéчность.

humanism *n.* гумани́зм.

humanist *n.* гумани́ст. —**humanistic,** *adj.* гуманисти́ческий.

humanitarian *adj.* гумáнный; гуманитáрный. —*n.* благотвори́тель; филантрóп.

humanity *n.* **1,** (mankind) человéчество. **2,** (humaneness) гумáнность; человéчность. **3,** *pl.* (literature, fine arts, etc.) гуманитáрные наýки.

humanize *v.t.* очеловéчивать.

humankind *n.* человéчество.

humanly *adv. Everything that is/was humanly possible,* всё, что в человéческих си́лах. *Not humanly possible,* вы́ше человéческих сил.

humble *adj.* **1,** (not proud or self-assertive) смирéнный; покóрный. *Your humble servant,* ваш покóрный слугá. *Humble request,* покóрная прóсьба. **2,** (of low social rank) ни́зкий: *of humble origin,* ни́зкого происхождéния. **3,** (unpretentious) скрóмный: *humble abode,* скрóмное жили́ще. —*v.t.* унижáть; принижáть. *Humble oneself,* унижáться. —**humbly,** *adv.* смирéнно; покóрно.

humdrum *adj.* однообрáзный; бýдничный.

humid *adj.* влáжный.

humidify *v.t.* увлажня́ть.

humidity *n.* влáжность.

humiliate *v.t.* унижáть. —**humiliating,** *adj.* унизи́тельный. —**humiliation,** *n.* унижéние.

humility *n.* смирéние; смирéнность.

hummingbird *n.* коли́бри.

hummock *n.* **1,** (low mound) ко́чка. **2,** (ridge in an ice field) торо́с.
humor *also,* **humour** *n.* **1,** (drollery; sense or use of same) ю́мор: *sense of humor,* чу́вство ю́мора. **2,** (mood) настрое́ние: *in good humor,* в хоро́шем настрое́нии. *Out of humor,* не в ду́хе. *—v.t.* ублажа́ть; ува́жить.
humoresque *n.* юморе́ска.
humorist *n.* юмори́ст.
humorous *adj.* **1,** (amusing) заба́вный; смешно́й. **2,** (containing humor) юмористи́ческий.
humour *n. & v.* = **humor.**
hump *n.* горб.
humpback *n.* **1,** (hump) горб. **2,** (person so afflicted) горбу́н; горба́тый. —**humpbacked,** *adj.* горба́тый.
humus *n.* перегно́й; гу́мус.
Hun *n.* гунн.
hunch *n.* **1,** (hump) горб. **2,** *colloq.* (feeling) предчу́вствие. *—v.t.* го́рбить; суту́лить. *—v.i.* го́рбиться.
hunchback *n.* = **humpback.** —**hunchbacked,** *adj.* = **humpbacked.**
hundred *adj.* сто. *—n.* **1,** (cardinal number) сто. **2,** *pl.* (groups of 100) со́тни (+ *gen.*): *hundreds of people,* со́тни люде́й.
hundredfold *adj.* стокра́тный. *—adv.* во́ сто крат.
hundredth *adj.* со́тый. *See also* **one-hundredth.**
Hungarian *adj.* венге́рский. *—n.* **1,** (person) венгр; венге́рка. **2,** (language) венге́рский язы́к.
hunger *n.* **1,** (craving for food) го́лод. **2,** *fig.* (craving) жа́жда. *—adj.* голо́дный: *hunger pangs,* голо́дные бо́ли. *—v.i.* [*usu.* **hunger for**] жа́ждать (+ *gen.*). —**die of hunger,** умира́ть с го́лоду; умира́ть голо́дной сме́ртью. *I am dying of hunger (i.e. very hungry),* я умира́ю от го́лода; я стра́шно проголода́лся.
hunger strike голодо́вка.
hungry *adj.* **1,** (wanting or needing food) голо́дный. *I am hungry,* я го́лоден (голодна́); мне хо́чется есть. *Go hungry,* голода́ть. **2,** *fol. by* **for** (craving) жа́ждущий: *be hungry for,* жа́ждать (+ *gen.*).
hunk *n.* ломо́ть.
hunky-dory *adj., slang, in* **everything is hunky-dory,** всё идёт как по ма́слу.
hunt *v.t.* **1,** (try to kill, as game) охо́титься на. **2,** (chase; pursue) пресле́довать. **3,** *fol. by* **down** (track down) затрави́ть; вы́следить. *—v.i.* **1,** (go hunting) охо́титься. **2,** *fol. by* **for** (search for) разы́скивать. *—n.* **1,** (hunting) охо́та. **2,** (search) по́иски.
hunter *n.* охо́тник.
hunting *n.* охо́та: *duck hunting,* охо́та на у́ток. *Go hunting,* идти́ на охо́ту. *—adj.* охо́тничий: *hunting season,* охо́тничий сезо́н.
huntsman *n.* = **hunter.**
hurdle *n.* **1,** (barrier) барье́р; препя́тствие. **2,** *pl.* (hurdle race) барье́рный бег; бег с препя́тствиями. *—v.t.* **1,** (clear, as a barrier) брать (барье́р). **2,** (overcome) преодолева́ть.
hurl *v.t.* **1,** (throw; fling) мета́ть; швыря́ть. **2,** (utter vehemently) осыпа́ть: *hurl insults at,* осыпа́ть (кого́-нибудь) оскорбле́ниями. —**hurl back,** отбива́ть.
hurly-burly *n.* сумато́ха; переполо́х.
hurrah *interj.* ура́! *Also,* **hurray.**
hurricane *n.* урага́н.
hurried *adj.* торопли́вый; поспе́шный. —**hurriedly,** *adv.* торопли́во; поспе́шно; на́скоро; на́спех; второпя́х.
hurry *v.i.* [*also,* **hurry up**] спеши́ть; торопи́ться. *Hurry up!,* скоре́й!; быстре́е!; потора́пливайтесь! *—v.t.* торопи́ть. *—n.* спе́шка; торопли́вость; поспе́шность. *Be in a hurry,* спеши́ть; торопи́ться. *There is no hurry,* не на́до спеши́ть; э́то не к спе́ху.
hurt *v.t.* **1,** (cause pain or discomfort to) причиня́ть боль (+ *dat.*). *It hurts me to walk,* мне бо́льно ходи́ть. *The sun hurts my eyes,* от со́лнца глаза́м бо́льно. **2,** (injure) поврежда́ть; ушиба́ть. *Hurt oneself,* ушиба́ться. **3,** (be detrimental to; damage) вреди́ть; по́ртить. *It wouldn't hurt you to...,* вам не меша́ло бы (+ *inf.*). **4,** (wound the feelings of) задева́ть; обижа́ть. *—v.i.* **1,** (be painful) боле́ть: *my stomach hurts,* у меня́ боли́т живо́т. *Does it hurt?,* вам бо́льно? *It hurts to lie on my back,* бо́льно лечь на́ спину. **2,** (cause harm) меша́ть: *excessive caution never hurts,* чрезме́рная осторо́жность никогда́ не меша́ет.
hurtle *v.i.* **1,** (rush violently) нести́сь; мча́ться. **2,** *fol. by* **against** (collide with) вреза́ться в.
husband *n.* муж. *—v.t.* (conserve) эконо́мить.
husbandry *n.* земледе́лие. —**animal husbandry,** животново́дство.
hush *v.i.* молча́ть. *—v.t.* **1,** (call upon to be silent) ши́кать на. **2,** [*usu.* **hush up**] (suppress) зама́лчивать; замя́ть. *—n.* тишина́; молча́ние. *—interj.* ти́ше!; тсс!; шш!
husk *n.* шелуха́. *—v.t.* шелуши́ть; лущи́ть.
husky *adj.* **1,** (hoarse) си́плый; хри́плый. **2,** (burly) ро́слый; дю́жий. *—n.* (dog) ла́йка.
hussar *n.* гуса́р.
hussy *n.* же́нщина лёгкого поведе́ния.
hustle *v.t.* затолка́ть. *—v.i.* торопи́ться; суети́ться. *—n.* [*often* **hustle and bustle**] суета́; сумато́ха.
hustler *n.* **1,** (petty racketeer) живодёр. **2,** (go-getter) хлопоту́н.
hut *n.* хи́жина.
hyacinth *n.* гиаци́нт.
hybrid *n.* по́месь; гибри́д. *—adj.* гибри́дный; разноро́дный; сме́шанный.
hydra *n.* ги́дра.
hydrangea *n.* горте́нзия.
hydrant *n.* водоразбо́рный кран; водоразбо́рная коло́нка; гидра́нт. *Fire hydrant,* пожа́рный кран/гидра́нт.
hydrate *n.* гидра́т.
hydraulic *adj.* гидравли́ческий. —**hydraulics,** *n.* гидра́влика.
hydrocarbon *n.* углеводоро́д.
hydrochloric acid соля́ная кислота́.
hydrodynamics *n.* гидродина́мика.
hydroelectric *adj.* гидроэлектри́ческий. *Hydroelectric station,* гидроэлектроста́нция.
hydrofluoric acid плавико́вая кислота́.
hydrofoil *n.* **1,** (winglike structure) подво́дное крыло́. **2,** (craft) су́дно на подво́дных кры́льях.
hydrogen *n.* водоро́д. *—adj.* водоро́дный. —**hydrogen bomb,** водоро́дная бо́мба. —**hydrogen peroxide,** пе́рекись водоро́да. —**hydrogen sulfide,** сероводоро́д.
hydrology *n.* гидроло́гия.
hydrolysis *n.* гидро́лиз.
hydrometer *n.* гидро́метр.
hydrophobia *n.* водобоя́знь; бе́шенство.

hydroplane *n.* **1,** (boat) гли́ссер. **2,** (seaplane) гидросамолёт.
hydrostatics *n.* гидроста́тика.
hydroxide *n.* гидро́окись.
hyena *n.* гие́на.
hygiene *n.* гигие́на.
hygienic *adj.* **1,** (pert. to hygiene) гигиени́ческий. **2,** (clean; sanitary) гигиени́чный.
hymen *n.* де́вственная плева́.
hymn *n.* гимн. —**hymnal,** *n.* сбо́рник ги́мнов.
hyperbola *n.* гипе́рбола.
hyperbole *n.* гипе́рбола.
hyperbolic *adj.* гиперболи́ческий.
hypercritical *adj.* приди́рчивый.
hypertension *n.* гипертони́я.
hyphen *n.* дефи́с; чёрточка.
hyphenate *v.t.* писа́ть че́рез дефи́с *or* че́рез чёрточку.
hypnosis *n.* гипно́з. —**hypnotic,** *adj.* гипноти́ческий. —**hypnotism,** *n.* гипноти́зм. —**hypnotist,** *n.* гипнотизёр. —**hypnotize,** *v.t.* гипнотизи́ровать.
hypo *n., photog.* фикса́ж.
hypochondria *n.* ипохо́ндрия. —**hypochondriac,** *n.* ипохо́ндрик.
hypocrisy *n.* лицеме́рие.
hypocrite *n.* лицеме́р. —**hypocritical,** *adj.* лицеме́рный.
hypodermic *adj.* подко́жный. *Hypodermic needle,* игла́ для подко́жных впры́скиваний.
hypotenuse *n.* гипотену́за.
hypothesis *n.* гипо́теза.
hypothesize *v.i.* стро́ить гипо́тезу. —*v.t.* предполага́ть.
hypothetical *adj.* предположи́тельный; гада́тельный; гипотети́ческий.
hyrax *n.* дама́н.
hyssop *n.* иссо́п.
hysterectomy *n.* удале́ние ма́тки.
hysteria *n.* истери́я. —**hysterical,** *adj.* истери́ческий. *Become hysterical,* впада́ть в исте́рику. —**hysterics,** *n.pl.* исте́рика.

I

I, i девя́тая бу́ква англи́йского алфави́та. —**dot the "i's" and cross the "t's",** ста́вить то́чки над "и".
I *pers.pron.* я: *I don't know,* я не зна́ю. *You and I,* мы с ва́ми. *See also* **me.**
iamb *n.* ямб. —**iambic,** *adj.* ямби́ческий. *Iambic pentameter,* пятисто́пный ямб. *Iambic tetrameter,* четырёхсто́пный ямб.
ibex *n.* **1,** (alpine) козеро́г. **2,** (Asiatic) сиби́рский го́рный козёл.
ibidem *adv.* [*usu. abbreviated to* **ibid.**] там же.
ibis *n.* и́бис.
ice *n.* лёд. —*adj.* ледяно́й. —*v.t.* замора́живать. —*v.i.* [*usu.* **ice up**] обледене́ть. —**break the ice,** разби́ть *or* слома́ть лёд.
ice age леднико́вый пери́од.
ice bag пузы́рь со льдом.
iceberg *n.* а́йсберг.
iceboat *n.* бу́ер.
icebound *adj.* **1,** (held fast by ice) затёртый льда́ми: *the ship is icebound,* су́дно затёрло льда́ми. **2,** (blocked by ice, as of a river) ско́ванный льда́ми.
icebox *n.* холоди́льник.
icebreaker *n.* ледоко́л.
icecap *n.* леднико́вый покро́в.
ice-cold *adj.* ледяно́й; холо́дный как лёд.
ice cream моро́женое.
iced tea чай со льдом.
ice field плаву́чая льди́на. *Also,* **ice floe.**
ice hockey хокке́й с ша́йбой.
Icelander *n.* исла́ндец. —**Icelandic,** *adj.* исла́ндский. —*n.* исла́ндский язы́к.
ice skate конёк. —**ice-skate,** *v.i.* ката́ться на конька́х.
ice water вода́ со льдом.
ichneumon *n.* ихневмо́н.
ichthyology *n.* ихтиоло́гия.
icicle *n.* сосу́лька.
icing *n.* **1,** (frosting, as for a cake) глазу́рь. **2,** *aero.* обледене́ние.
icon *n.* ико́на. —*adj.* ико́нный. —**icon case,** кио́т. —**icon lamp,** лампа́да.
iconoclasm *n.* иконобо́р(че)ство. —**iconoclast,** *n.* иконобо́рец. —**iconoclastic,** *adj.* иконобо́рческий.
iconostasis *n.* иконоста́с.
icy *adj.* ледяно́й.
idea *n.* иде́я; мысль. *Not have the slightest idea,* не име́ть ни мале́йшего поня́тия *or* представле́ния.
ideal *n.* идеа́л. —*adj.* идеа́льный.
idealism *n.* идеали́зм. —**idealist,** *n.* идеали́ст. —**idealistic,** *adj.* идеалисти́ческий.
idealize *v.t.* идеализи́ровать.
identical *adj.* одина́ковый; тожде́ственный; иденти́чный. —**identically,** *adv.* одина́ково.
identification *n.* **1,** (act of identifying) опозна́ние. **2,** (that which serves to identify) удостовере́ние ли́чности.
identify *v.t.* опознава́ть. *Identify oneself,* назва́ть себя́; назва́ться. —**identifying,** *adj.* опознава́тельный.
identity *n.* **1,** (sameness) то́ждество; тожде́ственность. **2,** (fact of being someone) ли́чность. —**identity card,** удостовере́ние ли́чности.

ideogram *n.* идеогра́мма. *Also,* **ideograph.**
ideology *n.* идеоло́гия. —**ideological,** *adj.* идеологи́ческий; иде́йный. —**ideologist,** *n.* идео́лог.
ides *n.pl.* и́ды: *the ides of March,* и́ды ма́рта.
idiocy *n.* **1,** (mental deficiency) идиоти́зм. **2,** (extreme foolishness) идио́тство.
idiom *n.* **1,** (idiomatic expression) идиомати́ческое выраже́ние; идио́ма. **2,** (language; dialect) язы́к; го́вор; наре́чие. —**idiomatic,** *adj.* идиомати́ческий.
idiosyncrasy *n.* стра́нность; причу́да; вы́верт; заско́к.
idiot *n.* идио́т. —**idiotic,** *adj.* идио́тский; дура́цкий.
idle *adj.* **1,** (doing nothing; not occupied) без де́ла; пра́здный. **2,** (not in operation) безде́йствующий. *Stand idle,* проста́ивать. **3,** (casual) пра́здный: *idle curiosity,* пра́здное любопы́тство. *Idle fantasy,* досу́жая фанта́зия. **4,** (meaningless) пусто́й: *idle chatter,* пуста́я болтовня́. —*v.i.* **1,** (loaf) безде́льничать. **2,** (of a motor) рабо́тать вхолосту́ю. —*v.t.* **1,** (make idle) оставля́ть без рабо́ты. **2,** *fol. by* **away** (while away) корота́ть.
idleness *n.* безде́лье; пра́здность.
idler *n.* безде́льник.
idly *adv.* пра́здно.
idol *n.* **1,** (image of a god) и́дол; истука́н **2,** (object of infatuation) и́дол; куми́р.
idolater *n.* идолопокло́нник. —**idolatrous,** *adj.* идолопокло́ннический. —**idolatry,** *n.* идолопокло́нство.
idolize *v.t.* обожа́ть; боготвори́ть.
idyll *also,* **idyl** *n.* иди́ллия. —**idyllic,** *adj.* идилли́ческий.
if *conj.* **1,** (in the event that; on condition that) е́сли: *if I had known,* е́сли бы я знал. **2,** (whether) ли: *I don't know if she's coming,* я не зна́ю, придёт ли она́ (и́ли нет). —**as if,** *see* **as.** —**even if,** да́же е́сли; хотя́ бы. —**if it were not for...,** е́сли бы не (+ *nom.*). —**if not, 1,** (if that is not the case) е́сли нет. **2,** (not to say) е́сли не сказа́ть: *difficult if not impossible,* тру́дно, е́сли не сказа́ть невозмо́жно. —**if only, 1,** (be it only) хотя́ бы: *if only for a few minutes,* хотя́ бы на не́сколько мину́т. **2,** *to express a profound wish* е́сли (бы) то́лько; о, е́сли бы; лишь бы.
igloo *n.* иглу́.
igneous *adj.* **1,** (of fire) о́гненный. **2,** *geol.* изве́рженный.
ignite *v.t.* зажига́ть; воспламеня́ть. —*v.i.* загора́ться; воспламеня́ться.
ignition *n.* зажига́ние; воспламене́ние. *Turn on the ignition,* включи́ть зажига́ние. —**ignition key,** ключ от зажига́ния. —**ignition switch,** выключа́тель зажига́ния.
ignoble *adj.* неблагоро́дный.
ignominious *adj.* позо́рный; бессла́вный. —**ignominy,** *n.* позо́р; бессла́вие.
ignoramus *n.* неве́жда; не́уч.
ignorance *n.* **1,** (lack of education) неве́жество. **2,** (lack of knowledge or information) незна́ние; неве́дение.
ignorant *adj.* **1,** (knowing very little; uninformed) неве́жественный. **2,** (lacking knowledge of a certain field) несве́дущий: *ignorant of physics,* несве́дущий в фи́зике. **3,** (unaware) неосведомлённый.
ignore *v.t.* не обраща́ть внима́ния на; игнори́ровать.
iguana *n.* игуа́на.
ilk *n.* род: *of that ilk,* тако́го ро́да.
ill *adj.* **1,** (sick) больно́й. *Become ill,* заболева́ть. **2,** (bad) дурно́й. *Ill health,* сла́бое здоро́вье. *Ill will,* недоброжела́тельство. —*adv.* **1,** (badly) ду́рно: *speak ill of,* ду́рно говори́ть о. **2,** (hardly) едва́ ли: *we can ill afford to lose him,* едва́ ли мы обойдёмся без него́. —*n.* **1,** (evil; harm) зло; вред. **2,** (malady) неду́г. —**ill at ease,** нело́вко: *feel ill at ease,* чу́вствовать себя́ нело́вко.
ill-advised *adj.* неблагоразу́мный.
ill-bred *adj.* невоспи́танный.
ill-considered *adj.* неблагоразу́мный; неразу́мный.
ill-disposed *adj.* не располо́жен (к).
illegal *adj.* незако́нный; нелега́льный; противозако́нный. —**illegality,** *n.* незако́нность; нелега́льность; противозако́нность. —**illegally,** *adv.* незако́нно; нелега́льно.
illegible *adj.* неразбо́рчивый. —**illegibility,** *n.* неразбо́рчивость.
illegitimate *adj.* **1,** (unlawful) незако́нный. **2,** (born out of wedlock) внебра́чный; незаконнорождённый. —**illegitimacy,** *n.* незако́нность.
ill-fated *adj.* злополу́чный.
illicit *adj.* незако́нный; недозво́ленный.
illiteracy *n.* негра́мотность. —**illiterate,** *adj.* негра́мотный; безгра́мотный.
ill-mannered *adj.* невоспи́танный.
illness *n.* боле́знь.
illogical *adj.* нелоги́чный.
ill-starred *adj.* злополу́чный.
ill-tempered *adj.* злой; раздражи́тельный.
ill-timed *adj.* несвоевре́менный.
illuminate *v.t.* освеща́ть. —**illuminated manuscript,** лицева́я ру́копись.
illuminating *adj.* **1,** (providing light) освети́тельный. **2,** *fig.* (enlightening) поучи́тельный.
illumination *n.* освеще́ние.
illusion *n.* иллю́зия.
illusory *adj.* иллюзо́рный; обма́нчивый; при́зрачный. *Also,* **illusive.**
illustrate *v.t.* иллюстри́ровать. —**illustration,** *n.* иллюстра́ция. —**illustrative,** *adj.* иллюстрати́вный. —**illustrator,** *n.* иллюстра́тор.
illustrious *adj.* знамени́тый; выдаю́щийся; просла́вленный.
image *n.* о́браз; изображе́ние. *He is the image of his father,* он вы́литый оте́ц; он весь в отца́.
imagery *n.* о́бразность.
imaginary *adj.* вообража́емый; мни́мый. *Imaginary line,* вообража́емая *or* усло́вная ли́ния.
imagination *n.* воображе́ние. *It's just your imagination,* э́то вам то́лько показа́лось.
imaginative *adj.* име́ющий большу́ю си́лу воображе́ния.
imagine *v.t. & i.* **1,** (visualize in the mind) вообража́ть; представля́ть себе́. **2,** (suppose) ду́мать; полага́ть.
imbalance *n.* несоотве́тствие.
imbecile *n.* слабоу́мный; идио́т; глупе́ц. —**imbecilic,** *adj.* идио́тский; дура́цкий. —**imbecility,** *n.* слабоу́мие; идиоти́зм.
imbed *v.* = **embed.**
imbibe *v.t.* **1,** (drink) пить. **2,** (absorb) впи́тывать.
imbue *v.t.* внуша́ть; всели́ть; привива́ть.

imitate *v.t.* подражáть; имитúровать.
imitation *n.* **1,** (act of imitating) подражáние; имитáция. **2,** (fake) имитáция. —*adj.* искýсственный. *Imitation pearl,* имитáция жéмчуга. —**imitative,** *adj.* подражáтельный. —**imitator,** *n.* подражáтель; имитáтор.
immaculate *adj.* безукорúзненно чúстый. —**Immaculate Conception,** непорóчное зачáтие.
immaterial *adj.* **1,** (not consisting of matter) невещéственный. **2,** (inconsequential) безразлúчный. *It's immaterial to me,* мне э́то безразлúчно.
immature *adj.* незрéлый. —**immaturity,** *n.* незрéлость.
immeasurable *adj.* неизмерúмый. —**immeasurably,** *adv.* неизмерúмо.
immediacy *n.* неотлóжность.
immediate *adj.* **1,** (instant) немéдленный: *an immediate reply,* немéдленный отвéт. **2,** (nearest; next) ближáйший: *in the immediate future,* в ближáйшем бýдущем. **3,** (direct) непосрéдственный: *immediate threat,* непосрéдственная угрóза.
immediately *adv.* **1,** (right away) немéдленно; срáзу; сейчáс же; тóтчас же. **2,** (right now) сейчáс; тóтчас; немéдленно.
immemorial *adj.* незапáмятный. —**from time immemorial,** с незапáмятных времён.
immense *adj.* огрóмный. —**immensity,** *n.* огрóмность.
immerse *v.t.* погружáть. —**immersion,** *n.* погружéние.
immigrant *n.* иммигрáнт. —**immigrate,** *v.i.* иммигрúровать.
immigration *n.* иммигрáция. —*adj.* иммиграциóнный.
imminent *adj.* надвигáющийся. *Be imminent,* надвигáться.
immobile *adj.* неподвúжный. —**immobility,** *n.* неподвúжность. —**immobilize,** *v.t.* дéлать неподвúжным; лишáть подвúжности.
immoderate *adj.* неумéренный. —**immoderation,** *n.* неумéренность; невоздéржанность.
immodest *adj.* нескрóмный. —**immodesty,** *n.* нескрóмность.
immolate *v.t.* приносúть в жéртву. —**immolation,** *n.* жертвоприношéние.
immoral *adj.* безнрáвственный. —**immorality,** *n.* безнрáвственность.
immortal *adj.* бессмéртный. —**immortality,** *n.* бессмéртие.
immortalize *v.t.* обессмéртить; увековéчивать. —**immortalization,** *n.* увековéчение.
immovable *adj.* неподвúжный; недвúжимый.
immune *adj.* **1,** (protected from a certain disease) невосприúмчивый. *She is immune to the mumps,* у неё иммунитéт прóтив свúнки. **2,** (exempt) свобóдный.
immunity *n.* иммунитéт; невосприúмчивость. —**diplomatic immunity,** дипломатúческая неприкосновéнность; дипломатúческий иммунитéт.
immunize *v.t.* иммунизúровать. —**immunization,** *n.* иммунизáция.
immutable *adj.* непрелóжный.
imp *n.* чертёнок; бесёнок; пострéл.
impact *n.* **1,** (force of a collision) удáр; толчóк. **2,** *fig.* (effect) влия́ние; воздéйствие; эффéкт. *Have a deep impact upon,* оказáть глубóкое влия́ние на.
impair *v.t.* пóртить; вредúть. —**impairment,** *n.* пóрча; вред.
impale *v.t.* **1,** (pierce) пронзáть. **2,** (kill or torture) сажáть нá кол.
impart *v.t.* **1,** (transmit, as a quality) придавáть. **2,** (reveal; pass along) сообщáть.
impartial *adj.* беспристрáстный. —**impartiality,** *n.* беспристрáстие.
impassable *adj.* непроходúмый; непроéзжий. —**impassability,** *n.* непроходúмость.
impasse *n.* тупúк.
impassioned *adj.* стрáстный; пылкий; горя́чий.
impassive *adj.* бесстрáстный. —**impassivity,** *n.* бесстрáстие.
impatience *n.* нетерпéние. —**impatient,** *adj.* нетерпелúвый. —**impatiently,** *adv.* нетерпелúво.
impeachment *n.* импúчмент.
impeccable *adj.* безупрéчный; безукорúзненный.
impecunious *adj.* бездéнежный.
impede *v.t.* препя́тствовать; мешáть.
impediment *n.* **1,** (obstruction) препя́тствие. **2,** (defect) дефéкт: *speech impediment,* дефéкт рéчи.
impel *v.t.* побуждáть; заставля́ть.
impending *adj.* предстоя́щий; надвигáющийся.
impenetrability *n.* непроницáемость; непроходúмость.
impenetrable *adj.* **1,** (impossible to pierce or break through) непроницáемый; непробивáемый. **2,** (impossible to walk or travel across) непроходúмый. **3,** (impossible to see through) непрогля́дный.
impenitent *adj.* нераскáянный.
imperative *adj.* **1,** (essential) необходúмый: *it is imperative that we be on time,* нам необходúмо приéхать вóвремя. **2,** *gram.* повелúтельный. —*n., gram.* повелúтельное наклонéние.
imperceptible *adj.* незамéтный; неощутúмый. —**imperceptibly,** *adv.* незамéтно.
imperfect *adj.* несовершéнный.
imperfection *n.* **1,** (state of being imperfect) несовершéнство. **2,** (defect; flaw) недостáток; дефéкт; несовершéнство.
imperfective *adj., gram.* несовершéнный: *imperfective aspect,* несовершéнный вид.
imperforate *adj.* беззубцóвый.
imperial *adj.* импéрский; императóрский. —**imperialism,** *n.* империалúзм. —**imperialist,** *n.* империалúст. —**imperialistic,** *adj.* империалистúческий.
imperil *v.t.* подвергáть опáсности; стáвить под угрóзу.
imperious *adj.* повелúтельный; влáстный; императúвный.
imperishable *adj.* **1,** (not subject to decay) непóртящийся. **2,** (enduring; everlasting) нерушúмый; нетлéнный.
impermanent *adj.* непостоя́нный. —**impermanence,** *n.* непостоя́нство.
impermeable *adj.* непроницáемый. —**impermeability,** *n.* непроницáемость.
impermissible *adj.* недопустúмый; непозволúтельный.
impersonal *adj.* безлúчный.
impersonate *v.t.* подражáть; выдавáть себя́ за.
impertinent *adj.* дéрзкий; нáглый; нахáльный. —**impertinence,** *n.* дéрзость; нáглость; нахáльство.

imperturbable *adj.* невозмути́мый. —**imperturbability,** *n.* невозмути́мость.
impervious *adj.* **1,** (impenetrable) непроница́емый. **2,** *fol. by* **to** (not open to; not influenced by) глух (к).
impetuosity *n.* опроме́тчивость.
impetuous *adj.* опроме́тчивый; поры́вистый. —**impetuously,** *adv.* опроме́тчиво.
impetus *n.* **1,** (motive force) и́мпульс. **2,** (stimulus) толчо́к; побужде́ние.
impiety *n.* непочти́тельность.
impinge *v.i.* [*usu.* **impinge upon**] посяга́ть на; покуша́ться на.
impish *adj.* прока́зливый; шаловли́вый.
implacable *adj.* неумоли́мый.
implant *v.t.* **1,** (set firmly in the ground) вка́пывать. **2,** *med.* вживля́ть. **3,** *fig.* (instill; inculcate) привива́ть; укореня́ть; насажда́ть.
implausible *adj.* невероя́тный; неправдоподо́бный.
implement *n.* ору́дие; инструме́нт. —*v.t.* осуществля́ть. —**implementation,** *n.* осуществле́ние.
implicate *v.t.* вовлека́ть; заме́шивать; впу́тывать.
implication *n.* **1,** (act of involving) вовлече́ние. **2,** (inference) намёк. **3,** (application; significance) значе́ние.
implicit *adj.* **1,** (understood; implied) подразумева́емый. *Be implicit,* подразумева́ться. *Implicit agreement,* молчали́вое соглаше́ние. **2,** (unreserved; absolute) беспрекосло́вный. *Implicit faith,* слепа́я ве́ра.
implore *v.t.* умоля́ть.
imply *v.t.* **1,** (intimate; suggest) намека́ть. **2,** (presuppose) предполага́ть.
impolite *adj.* неве́жливый. —**impoliteness,** *n.* неве́жливость.
impolitic *adj.* неблагоразу́мный; нетакти́чный; беста́ктный.
imponderable *adj.* нея́сный; неопределённый; неизве́стный.
import *v.t.* ввози́ть; импорти́ровать. —*n.* **1,** *pl.* (goods imported) ввоз; и́мпорт. **2,** (significance; importance) значе́ние; ва́жность. —*adj.* и́мпортный; вво́зный: *import duty,* и́мпортная/вво́зная по́шлина.
importance *n.* ва́жность: *of particular importance,* осо́бой ва́жности. *Assume an air of importance,* напуска́ть на себя́ ва́жность.
important *adj.* ва́жный: *important person/event/discovery,* ва́жное лицо́/собы́тие/откры́тие. *It's not important,* э́то не ва́жно.
importation *n.* ввоз; и́мпорт.
imported *adj.* вво́зный; и́мпортный.
importer *n.* импортёр.
importunate *adj.* навя́зчивый; назо́йливый; неотвя́зный.
importune *v.t.* докуча́ть; надоеда́ть.
impose *v.t.* **1,** (place; levy) налага́ть; облага́ть. *Impose sanctions,* применя́ть са́нкции. **2,** (force) навя́зывать: *impose one's will on someone,* навя́зывать кому́-нибудь свою́ во́лю. —*v.i.* [*usu.* **impose on** *or* **upon**] эксплуати́ровать.
imposing *adj.* внуши́тельный; представи́тельный; импоза́нтный.
imposition *n.* **1,** (levying) наложе́ние; обложе́ние. **2,** (taking advantage) эксплуата́ция.
impossibility *n.* невозмо́жность.
impossible *adj.* невозмо́жный: *it/that is impossible,* э́то невозмо́жно. *It is impossible to...,* нельзя́ (+ *inf.*). *Impossible task,* невыполни́мая зада́ча. *Impossible dream,* неисполни́мая мечта́. —*n., preceded by* **the** невозмо́жное.
impost *n.* нало́г; по́дать.
impostor *n.* самозва́нец.
impotence *n.* **1,** (helplessness) бесси́лие. **2,** *med.* импоте́нция; полово́е бесси́лие.
impotent *adj.* **1,** (helpless) бесси́льный. **2,** *med.* импоте́нтный.
impound *v.t.* **1,** (shut up in a pound) загоня́ть. **2,** (take into legal custody) конфискова́ть.
impoverish *v.t.* **1,** (reduce to poverty) доводи́ть до нищеты́. **2,** (exhaust, as soil) истоща́ть. —**impoverished,** *adj.* обедне́вший; обнища́лый. —**impoverishment,** *n.* обедне́ние; обнища́ние.
impracticable *adj.* невыполни́мый; неисполни́мый; неосуществи́мый. —**impracticability,** *n.* невыполни́мость; неисполни́мость; неосуществи́мость.
impractical *adj.* непракти́чный. —**impracticality,** *n.* непракти́чность.
imprecate *v.t.* призыва́ть на чью-нибудь го́лову. —**imprecation,** *n.* прокля́тие.
imprecise *adj.* нето́чный. —**imprecision,** *n.* нето́чность.
impregnable *adj.* непристу́пный.
impregnate *v.t.* **1,** (make pregnant) оплодотворя́ть. **2,** (saturate) пропи́тывать. —**impregnation,** *n.* оплодотворе́ние.
impresario *n.* антрепренёр; импреса́рио.
impress *v.t.* **1,** (imprint) отпеча́тывать. **2,** (produce a marked effect upon) производи́ть впечатле́ние на; импони́ровать. **3,** (establish firmly in one's mind) внуша́ть: *impress upon someone the fact that...,* внуша́ть кому́-нибудь, что... **4,** (force into military service) наси́льно вербова́ть.
impression *n.* **1,** (imprint) о́ттиск; отпеча́ток. **2,** (effect produced on the mind) впечатле́ние: *what are your impressions?,* каки́е у вас впечатле́ния? *Make a good/deep impression on,* производи́ть хоро́шее/глубо́кое впечатле́ние на (+ *acc.*). *I was under the impression that...,* я ду́мал(а), что... —**impressionable,** *adj.* впечатли́тельный.
impressionism *n.* импрессиони́зм. —**impressionist,** *n.* импрессиони́ст. —*adj.* [*also,* **impressionistic**] импрессионисти́ческий; импрессиони́стский.
impressive *adj.* впечатля́ющий; внуши́тельный; представи́тельный.
impressment *n.* наси́льственная вербо́вка.
imprint *n.* отпеча́ток. —*v.t.* отпеча́тывать.
imprison *v.t.* заключа́ть (в тюрьму́); сажа́ть (в тюрьму́). —**imprisonment,** *n.* (тюре́мное) заключе́ние. *Life imprisonment,* пожи́зненное заключе́ние.
improbable *adj.* маловероя́тный; неправдоподо́бный. —**improbability,** *n.* невероя́тность; неправдоподо́бие.
impromptu *adj.* импровизи́рованный. —*adv.* экспро́мтом.
improper *adj.* **1,** (incorrect) непра́вильный: *improper use of a word,* непра́вильное употребле́ние сло́ва. **2,** (unseemly) неприли́чный: *improper behavior,* неприли́чное поведе́ние. **3,** (inappropriate) не-

подходя́щий: *improper dress,* неподходя́щая оде́жда. —**improper fraction,** непра́вильная дробь.

improperly *adv.* **1,** (incorrectly) непра́вильно. **2,** (in an unseemly manner) неприли́чно.

impropriety *n.* **1,** (being improper or inappropriate) неприли́чие; неуме́стность. **2,** (improper act) просту́пок.

improve *v.t.* улучша́ть. —*v.i.* улучша́ться.

improvement *n.* улучше́ние. *Land improvement,* мелиора́ция.

improvident *adj.* непредусмотри́тельный; нерасчётливый. —**improvidence,** *n.* непредусмотри́тельность; нерасчётливость.

improvise *v.t. & i.* импровизи́ровать. —**improvisation,** *n.* импровиза́ция. —**improviser,** *n.* импровиза́тор.

imprudent *adj.* неблагоразу́мный; неосмотри́тельный. —**imprudence,** *n.* неблагоразу́мие; неосмотри́тельность.

impudent *adj.* де́рзкий; на́глый. —**impudence,** *n.* де́рзость; на́глость.

impugn *v.t.* оспа́ривать; подверга́ть сомне́нию.

impulse *n.* **1,** (impelling force; impetus) толчо́к; и́мпульс. **2,** (sudden inclination) поры́в; и́мпульс. *Yield to a sudden impulse,* подчиня́ться внеза́пному и́мпульсу.

impulsive *adj.* импульси́вный.

impunity *n.* безнака́занность. *With impunity,* безнака́занно.

impure *adj.* нечи́стый.

impurity *n.* **1,** (state of being impure) нечистота́. **2,** *pl.* (foreign matter) нечисто́ты.

impute *v.t.* **1,** (charge, as a crime) вменя́ть (что́-нибудь) в вину́ (+ *dat.*). **2,** (attribute) приписывать.

in *prep.* **1,** (in a certain place or condition) в (+ *prepl.*): *in Moscow,* в Москве́; *in the room,* в ко́мнате; *in the car,* в маши́не; *in one's hand,* в руке́; *in order,* в поря́дке; *in good condition,* в хоро́шем состоя́нии. ♦*With certain nouns* на: *in one's arms,* на рука́х; *in the sun,* на со́лнце; *in the sky,* на не́бе; *in the south,* на ю́ге; *in orbit,* на орби́те. **2,** (into; arriving in) в (+ *acc.*): *arrive in Moscow,* прие́хать в Москву́. *Dip a pen in ink,* обмакну́ть перо́ в черни́ла. *Put something in a box,* положи́ть что́-нибудь в я́щик. *Put someone in prison,* посади́ть кого́-нибудь в тюрьму́. **3,** (with months, years, centuries) в (+ *prepl.*): *in August,* в а́вгусте; *in 1900,* в ты́сяча девятисо́том году́. **4,** (with seasons, parts of the day) *rendered by the instr. case: in the morning,* у́тром; *in the evening,* ве́чером; *in the fall,* о́сенью. **5,** (with expressions of time, indicating how long it takes or took to complete a task) в; за: *read a book in two days,* прочёсть кни́гу в/за два дня. **6,** (indicating a certain amount of time from now) че́рез: *he will be here in ten minutes,* он придёт че́рез де́сять мину́т. **7,** (with languages) по-; на (+ *prepl.*): *in Russian,* по-ру́сски; на ру́сском языке́. **8,** (with weather conditions) в (+ *acc.*): *in such weather/heat,* в таку́ю пого́ду/жару́. **9,** (in the person of) в лице́ (+ *gen.*): *a true friend in him,* ве́рный друг в его́ лице́. **10,** *expressing various relationships* в (+ *prepl.*): *in any case,* во вся́ком слу́чае; *in the light of,* в све́те (+ *gen.*); *poor in arithmetic,* слаб в арифме́тике; *fall in battle,* пасть в бою́. **11,** *expressing various relationships, rendered by the instr. case: rich in vitamins,* бога́т витами́нами; *paint in oils,* писа́ть ма́слом; *end in disaster,* ко́нчиться катастро́фой. **12,** *in various miscellaneous expressions: in fact,* факти́чески; на са́мом де́ле; *in jest,* в шу́тку; *in passing,* мимохо́дом; вскользь; *in short,* коро́че говоря́. —*adj.* **1,** (at home) до́ма. **2,** (in one's office) у себя́. **3,** (having arrived) прибы́вший: *the train is in,* по́езд при́был *or* пришёл. —*adv. Usu. rendered by a prefixed verb: come in,* входи́ть; *drop in,* заходи́ть; *cave in,* обвали́ться. —**in for,** *rendered by* ждать *or* предстоя́ть: *I know what I'm in for,* я зна́ю, что меня́ ждёт. *We are in for a cold winter,* нам предстои́т холо́дная зима́. —**in on, 1,** (having a part in) прича́стный к. **2,** (having knowledge of) посвящён в: *in on the secret,* посвящён в та́йну. —**in that,** тем, что... —**know all the ins and outs,** знать все ходы́ и вы́ходы.

inability *n.* неспосо́бность; неуме́ние.

in absentia зао́чно: *be tried in absentia,* суди́ться зао́чно.

inaccessible *adj.* недосту́пный. —**inaccessibility,** *n.* недосту́пность.

inaccurate *adj.* нето́чный. —**inaccuracy,** *n.* нето́чность.

inaction *n.* безде́йствие.

inactive *adj.* безде́йственный; безде́ятельный. —**inactivity,** *n.* безде́йствие; безде́ятельность.

inadequacy *n.* **1,** (state of being inadequate) недоста́точность. **2,** (failing; lack) недоста́ток.

inadequate *adj.* недоста́точный; не отвеча́ющий тре́бованиям.

inadmissible *adj.* недопусти́мый.

inadvertence *n.* **1,** (carelessness) невнима́тельность; небре́жность. **2,** (oversight) недосмо́тр; опло́шность.

inadvertent *adj.* **1,** (not duly attentive) невнима́тельный; небре́жный. **2,** (unintentional) нечаянный. —**inadvertently,** *adv.* нечаянно; не́хотя.

inadvisable *adj.* нецелесообра́зный.

inalienable *adj.* неотъе́млемый.

inane *adj.* глу́пый; ну́дный.

inanimate *adj.* неодушевлённый.

inanity *n.* глу́пость.

inapplicable *adj.* неприменимый.

inappropriate *adj.* неуме́стный; неподходя́щий.

inarticulate *adj.* нечленоразде́льный; невня́тный.

inasmuch as так как; поско́льку; ввиду́ того́, что.

inattention *n.* невнима́ние. —**inattentive,** *adj.* невнима́тельный.

inaudible *adj.* неслы́шный.

inaugural *adj.* вступи́тельный. *Inaugural address,* речь при вступле́нии в до́лжность.

inaugurate *v.t.* **1,** (induct into office) вводи́ть в до́лжность. **2,** (introduce; launch) вводи́ть. —**inauguration,** *n.* инаугура́ция.

inauspicious *adj.* неблагоприя́тный; неутеши́тельный.

inborn *adj.* врождённый; прирождённый. *Also,* **inbred.**

incalculable *adj.* несме́тный; неисчисли́мый.

incandescence *n.* нака́л; кале́ние.

incandescent *adj.* накалённый. —**incandescent lamp,** ла́мпа нака́ливания.

incantation *n.* заклина́ние; за́говор.

incapable *adj.* неспосо́бный: *incapable of telling a lie,* неспосо́бный на ложь.

incapacitate *v.t.* де́лать нетрудоспосо́бным. —**in-**

capacitated, *adj.* нетрудоспосóбный. —**incapacity,** *n.* нетрудоспосóбность.
incarcerate *v.t.* заключáть (в тюрьмý); заточáть (в тюрьмý). —**incarceration,** *n.* (тюрéмное) заключéние; заточéние.
incarnate *adj.* воплощённый. —*v.t.* воплощáть. —**incarnation,** *n.* воплощéние.
incautious *adj.* неосторóжный.
incendiary *adj.* зажигáтельный: *incendiary bomb,* зажигáтельная бóмба. *Incendiary speeches,* зажигáтельные рéчи.
incense *n.* фимиáм; лáдан. —*v.t.* приводи́ть в я́рость; разгневáть. —**incensed,** *adj.* разгнéванный. *Become incensed,* приходи́ть в я́рость.
incentive *n.* побуждéние; толчóк; сти́мул.
inception *n.* начáло.
inceptive *adj.* начáльный. —**inceptive verb,** начинáтельный глагóл.
incertitude *n.* неувéренность.
incessant *adj.* беспрестáнный; бесконéчный; непрестáнный. —**incessantly,** *adv.* беспрестáнно; бесконéчно.
incest *n.* кровосмешéние. —**incestuous,** *adj.* кровосмеси́тельный.
inch *n.* дюйм. —*v.i.* ползти́: *inch forward,* ползти́ вперёд. —**every inch a...,** с головы́ до ног; до мóзга костéй. —**inch by inch,** пядь за пя́дью. —**not yield** (or **budge**) **an inch,** не уступи́ть ни пя́ди *or* ни на йóту. —**with an inch of,** на волосóк (*or* на волоскé) от. *Beat within an inch of one's life,* избивáть до полусмéрти; бить смéртным бóем.
inchoate *adj.* **1,** (in a rudimentary stage) зачáточный. **2,** (lacking order; shapeless) бесфóрменный.
incidence *n.* **1,** (prevalence) распространéние. *Incidence of a disease,* заболевáемость. **2,** *physics* падéние: *angle of incidence,* ýгол падéния.
incident *n.* происшéствие; инцидéнт. *Without incident,* без происшéствий. *Border incident,* пограни́чный инцидéнт. —*adj.* [*usu.* **incident to**] свя́занный с.
incidental *adj.* **1,** *fol. by* **to** (associated with) свя́занный (с). **2,** (minor; secondary) побóчный. *Incidental expenses,* случáйные расхóды.
incidentally *adv.* мéжду прóчим; кстáти.
incinerate *v.t.* испепеля́ть; сжигáть дотлá. —**incinerator,** *n.* мусоросжигáтельная печь.
incipient *adj.* начáльный.
incise *v.t.* **1,** (cut into) надрезáть. **2,** (carve; engrave) вырезáть; насекáть.
incision *n.* разрéз; надрéз.
incisive *adj.* **1,** (trenchant) тóнкий. **2,** (keen; penetrating) проницáтельный.
incisor *n.* резéц.
incite *v.t.* возбуждáть; подстрекáть. —**incitement,** *n.* подстрекáтельство.
inclement *adj.* ненáстный. *Inclement weather,* ненáстье; непогóда.
inclination *n.* **1,** (slant; slope) наклóн; наклонéние. *Angle of inclination,* ýгол наклóна. **2,** (tendency; disposition) склóнность; наклóнность.
incline *v.t.* наклоня́ть; склоня́ть. —*v.i.* наклоня́ться; склоня́ться. —*n.* наклóн; склон; уклóн; скат.
inclined *adj.* **1,** (sloping) наклóнный. **2,** *fol. by* **to** (tending toward) склóнный (к). *I am inclined to think that...,* я склóнен дýмать, что...
include *v.t.* включáть. —**including,** *prep.* включáя; в том числé.
inclusion *n.* включéние.
inclusive *adj.* **1,** *fol. by* **of** (including) включáя. **2,** (within the limits mentioned) включи́тельно.
incognito *adv.* инкóгнито.
incoherent *adj.* бессвя́зный; несвя́зный. —**incoherence,** *n.* бессвя́зность; несвя́зность.
incombustible *adj.* невоспламеня́емый.
income *n.* дохóд. —**income tax,** подохóдный налóг.
incoming *adj.* входя́щий; вступáющий.
incommensurable *adj.* несоизмери́мый. —**incommensurability,** *n.* несоизмери́мость.
incommensurate *adj.* несоразмéрный.
incommode *v.t.* затрудня́ть; мешáть; беспокóить. —**incommodious,** *adj.* неудóбный.
incommunicado *adj. & adv.* лишённый прáва сообщéния.
incomparable *adj.* **1,** (not comparable) несравни́мый. **2,** (matchless; unsurpassed) несравнéнный. —**incomparably,** *adv.* несравнéнно.
incompatible *adj.* несовмести́мый. —**incompatibility,** *n.* несовмести́мость.
incompetence *n.* **1,** (lack of ability) некомпетéнтность. **2,** *law* неправомóчность; недееспосóбность.
incompetent *adj.* **1,** (lacking ability) некомпетéнтный. **2,** *law* неправомóчный; недееспосóбный.
incomplete *adj.* непóлный; незакóнченный. —**incompleteness,** *n.* неполнотá.
incomprehensible *adj.* непоня́тный; непостижи́мый. —**incomprehensibility,** *n.* непоня́тность; непостижи́мость. —**incomprehensibly,** *adv.* непоня́тно.
incomprehension *n.* непонимáние.
inconceivable *adj.* невообрази́мый.
inconclusive *adj.* неокончáтельный.
incongruous *adj.* несообрáзный. —**incongruity,** *n.* несообрáзность.
inconsequential *adj.* несущéственный; не имéющий значéния.
inconsiderate *adj.* невнимáтельный.
inconsistent *adj.* непослéдовательный. —**inconsistency,** *n.* непослéдовательность.
inconsolable *adj.* безутéшный; неутéшный.
inconspicuous *adj.* незамéтный; неприметный.
inconstant *adj.* непостоя́нный. —**inconstancy,** *n.* непостоя́нство.
incontestable *adj.* неоспори́мый; бесспóрный.
incontinence *n.* **1,** (immoderate behavior) невоздéржанность. **2,** *med.* недержáние (мочи́). —**incontinent,** *adj.* невоздéржанный.
incontrovertible *adj.* неопровержи́мый.
inconvenience *n.* неудóбство. —*v.t.* затрудня́ть. —**inconvenient,** *adj.* неудóбный.
incorporate *v.t.* **1,** (combine) объединя́ть. **2,** *fol. by* **into** (make part of) включáть (в); вводи́ть (в); своди́ть (в). **3,** (form into a corporation) инкорпори́ровать. —*v.i.* объединя́ться. —**incorporation,** *n.* инкорпорáция.
incorporeal *adj.* бестелéсный.
incorrect *adj.* непрáвильный; невéрный. —**incorrectly,** *adv.* непрáвильно; невéрно.
incorrigible *adj.* неисправи́мый.

incorruptible *adj.* неподку́пный. —**incorruptibility,** *n.* неподку́пность.
increase *v.t.* увели́чивать. —*v.i.* увели́чиваться; возраста́ть. —*n.* увеличе́ние; приро́ст.
increasing *adj.* возраста́ющий. *An ever increasing number of people,* всё бо́льшее коли́чество люде́й.
increasingly *adv.* всё бо́лее: *the work is becoming increasingly difficult,* рабо́та стано́вится всё бо́лее тру́дной.
incredible *adj.* невероя́тный. —**incredibly,** *adv.* невероя́тно; до невероя́тности.
incredulity *n.* недове́рие. —**incredulous,** *adj.* недове́рчивый.
increment *n.* прираще́ние.
incriminate *v.t.* изоблича́ть. —**incriminating,** *adj.* изобличи́тельный.
incubate *v.t.* сиде́ть на (я́йцах). —**incubation,** *n.* инкуба́ция. —**incubator,** *n.* инкуба́тор.
inculcate *v.t.* внуша́ть; вселя́ть; внедря́ть.
incumbent *adj.* **1,** *fol. by* **on** *or* **upon** (obligatory) надлежа́щий: *it is incumbent on us to help,* нам надлежи́т помо́чь. **2,** (in office) стоя́щий у вла́сти. —*n.* тот, кто стои́т у вла́сти.
incur *v.t.* **1,** (bring on oneself) навлека́ть на себя́: *incur suspicion,* навлека́ть на себя́ подозре́ние. **2,** (suffer, as losses) нести́ (убы́тки). **3,** (contract, as debts) де́лать (долги́).
incurable *adj.* неизлечи́мый.
incursion *n.* вторже́ние; наше́ствие; набе́г.
indebted *adj.* [*usu.* **indebted to**] в долгу́ (у *or* пе́ред); обя́зан (+ *dat.*). —**indebtedness,** *n.* задо́лженность.
indecency *n.* неприли́чие.
indecent *adj.* неприли́чный. —**indecently,** *adv.* неприли́чно.
indecipherable *adj.* **1,** (of a coded message) не поддаю́щийся расшифро́вке. **2,** (of handwriting) неразбо́рчивый.
indecision *n.* нереши́тельность; нереши́мость.
indecisive *adj.* нереши́тельный. —**indecisi ene s,v** *n.* нереши́тельность.
indeclinable *adj.* несклоня́емый.
indecorous *adj.* некорре́ктный; неприли́чный.
indeed *adv.* в са́мом де́ле; действи́тельно. *I am very glad indeed,* я действи́тельно о́чень рад. *Yes, indeed!,* о да!; да, да! —*interj.* да ну!; вот ещё!
indefatigable *adj.* неутоми́мый. —**indefatigability,** *n.* неутоми́мость.
indefensible *adj.* **1,** *mil.* неприго́дный для оборо́ны. **2,** (inexcusable) непрости́тельный.
indefinable *adj.* неопредели́мый.
indefinite *adj.* неопределённый: *for an indefinite period,* на неопределённый срок. *Indefinite leave of absence,* бессро́чный о́тпуск. —**indefinite article,** неопределённый арти́кль *or* член.
indefinitely *adv.* на неопределённое вре́мя.
indelible *adj.* **1,** (unable to be erased) несмыва́емый: *indelible ink,* несмыва́емые черни́ла. *Indelible pencil,* хими́ческий каранда́ш. **2,** (permanent; lasting) неизглади́мый.
indelicate *adj.* неделика́тный; некорре́ктный; нескро́мный. —**indelicacy,** *n.* неделика́тность.
indemnify *v.t.* возмеща́ть; компенси́ровать. —**indemnification,** *n.* возмеще́ние.
indemnity *n.* **1,** (compensation) возмеще́ние. **2,** (protection) гара́нтия.
indent *v.t.* **1,** (space in from the margin) писа́ть с абза́ца; писа́ть с о́тступом. **2,** (notch) зазу́бривать. —*v.i.* отступа́ть: *indent slightly,* отступа́ть немно́го.
indentation *n.* **1,** (notch) зазу́брина. **2,** [*also,* **indention**] (spacing in from the margin) абза́ц; о́тступ.
independence *n.* **1,** (freedom from foreign rule) незави́симость. **2,** (self-sufficiency) самостоя́тельность.
independent *adj.* **1,** (autonomous) незави́симый. **2,** (self-sufficient; done on one's own) самостоя́тельный. —**independently,** *adv.* незави́симо; самостоя́тельно.
in-depth *adj.* глубо́кий; углублённый.
indescribable *adj.* неопису́емый.
indestructible *adj.* неразруши́мый.
indeterminate *adj.* неопределённый.
index *n.* **1,** (alphabetical list) указа́тель. **2,** *math.; econ.* показа́тель; и́ндекс: *price index,* и́ндекс цен. —*v.t.* **1,** (provide with an index) снабжа́ть указа́телем. **2,** (make an index of) заноси́ть в указа́тель. —**index finger,** указа́тельный па́лец.
India ink тушь.
Indian *n.* **1,** (American) инде́ец. **2,** (of India) инди́ец. —*adj.* **1,** (of America) инде́йский. **2,** (of India) инди́йский. —**Indian Ocean,** Инди́йский океа́н. —**Indian summer,** ба́бье ле́то.
indicate *v.t.* **1,** (point out) ука́зывать. **2,** (be a sign of) ука́зывать на; означа́ть.
indication *n.* указа́ние; при́знак.
indicative *adj.* **1,** (revealing) показа́тельный. *Be indicative of,* ука́зывать на; говори́ть о. **2,** *gram.* изъяви́тельный: *indicative mood,* изъяви́тельное наклоне́ние.
indicator *n.* **1,** (needle, dial, etc.) указа́тель; индика́тор. **2,** *fig.* (general indication) показа́тель.
indict *v.t.* обвиня́ть; предъявля́ть обвине́ние (+ *dat.*); привлека́ть к уголо́вной отве́тственности.
indictment *n.* **1,** (act of indicting) обвине́ние. **2,** (formal written accusation) обвини́тельный акт; обвини́тельное заключе́ние.
indifference *n.* равноду́шие; безразли́чие. *With indifference,* равноду́шно; безразли́чно.
indifferent *adj.* **1,** (unconcerned; apathetic) безразли́чный; равноду́шный. **2,** (mediocre) посре́дственный.
indigence *n.* нужда́; нищета́.
indigenous *adj.* коренно́й; тузе́мный.
indigent *adj.* неиму́щий; обездо́ленный.
indigestible *adj.* неудобовари́мый.
indigestion *n.* несваре́ние желу́дка; расстро́йство пищеваре́ния.
indignant *adj.* негоду́ющий; возмущённый. *Be indignant,* негодова́ть; возмуща́ться.
indignation *n.* негодова́ние; возмуще́ние.
indignity *n.* оскорбле́ние; униже́ние: *suffer indignities,* подверга́ться оскорбле́ниям/униже́ниям.
indigo *n.* инди́го. —*adj.* цве́та инди́го.
indirect *adj.* **1,** (roundabout) непрямо́й. **2,** (not pertaining to or following directly) ко́свенный; побо́чный. *Indirect evidence,* ко́свенные ули́ки. —**indirect object,** ко́свенное дополне́ние.
indirectly *adv.* ко́свенно.
indiscernible *adj.* неразличи́мый.
indiscreet *adj.* нескро́мный; беста́ктный. —**indis-**

cretion, *n.* бестáктность: *commit an indiscretion,* совершúть бестáктность.
indiscriminate *adj.* **1,** (not discriminating) неразбóрчивый. **2,** (random; haphazard) огýльный. —**indiscriminately,** *adv.* без разбóра; без вы́бора.
indispensable *adj.* незаменúмый.
indisposed *adj.* **1,** (unwell) нездорóвый. **2,** (disinclined) нерасполóженный.
indisposition *n.* **1,** (ailment) недомогáние. **2,** (disinclination) нерасположéние.
indisputable *adj.* неоспорúмый; бесспóрный.
indissoluble *adj.* **1,** (incapable of being dissolved) нерастворúмый. **2,** (lasting; permanent) неразры́вный; нерасторжúмый; нерушúмый.
indistinct *adj.* неотчётливый; нея́сный.
indistinguishable *adj.* неразличúмый.
indium *n.* úндий.
individual *adj.* отдéльный; индивидуáльный. —*n.* индивúдуум; лицó; осóба; óсобь.
individualism *n.* индивидуалúзм. —**individualist,** *n.* индивидуалúст. —**individuality,** *n.* индивидýальность.
individually *adv.* отдéльно; в отдéльности.
indivisible *adj.* неделúмый; неразделúмый; нераздéльный. —**indivisibility,** *n.* неделúмость.
indoctrinate *v.t.* обрабáтывать. —**indoctrination,** *n.* обрабóтка.
Indo-European *adj.* индоевропéйский.
indolent *adj.* ленúвый; вя́лый. —**indolence,** *n.* лень; вя́лость.
indomitable *adj.* неукротúмый.
Indonesian *adj.* индонезúйский. —*n.* индонезúец.
indoor *adj.* **1,** (situated inside) внýтренний. *Indoor pool,* закры́тый бассéйн. **2,** (taking place inside) кóмнатный: *indoor games,* кóмнатные úгры.
indoors *adv.* в дóме; внутрú дóма; в закры́том помещéнии. *Stay indoors,* не выходúть на ýлицу.
indorse *v.* = **endorse.**
indubitable *adj.* несомнéнный. —**indubitably,** *adv.* несомнéнно.
induce *v.t.* **1,** (cause; prompt) побуждáть. **2,** (persuade; prevail upon) уговорúть. **3,** (cause; bring on) вызывáть.
inducement *n.* побуждéние; примáнка.
induct *v.t.* **1,** (install in office) вводúть в дóлжность. **2,** *mil.* зачислять на воéнную слýжбу.
inductee *n.* призывнúк.
induction *n.* **1,** (installation in office) введéние в дóлжность. **2,** *mil.* зачислéние на воéнную слýжбу. **3,** *electricity; logic* индýкция. —**induction center,** призывнóй пункт. —**induction coil,** индукциóнная катýшка.
inductive *adj.* индуктúвный.
indulge *v.t.* потвóрствовать; потакáть. —*v.i.* [*usu.* **indulge in**] предавáться (+ *dat.*); баловáться (+ *instr.*). *Indulge in a cigar,* баловáться сигáрой. *Indulge in fantasy,* предавáться фантáзиям.
indulgence *n.* потвóрство; потакáние; поблáжка; снисходúтельность.
indulgent *adj.* снисходúтельный.
industrial *adj.* промы́шленный; индустриáльный.
industrialist *n.* промы́шленник.
industrialize *v.t.* индустриализúровать. —**industrialization,** *n.* индустриализáция.
industrious *adj.* трудолюбúвый; прилéжный. —**industriousness,** *n.* трудолю́бие; прилежáние.
industry *n.* **1,** (branch of the economy) промы́шленность; индýстрия. **2,** (diligence) трудолю́бие.
inebriate *v.t.* опьяня́ть. —**inebriated,** *adj.* пья́ный; опьянéвший.
inedible *adj.* несъедóбный.
ineffable *adj.* невыразúмый; несказáнный; неописýемый.
ineffective *adj.* неэффектúвный; безрезультáтный. *Also,* **ineffectual.**
inefficacy *n.* неэффектúвность.
inefficient *adj.* неэффектúвный. —**inefficiency,** *n.* неэффектúвность.
ineligible *adj.* не имéющий прáва; не могýщий быть úзбранным.
inept *adj.* **1,** (incompetent) неумéлый; бездáрный. **2,** (inappropriate) неумéстный. —**ineptitude,** *n.* неумéние; бездáрность.
inequality *n.* нерáвенство.
inequitable *adj.* несправедлúвый. —**inequity,** *n.* несправедлúвость.
ineradicable *adj.* **1,** (indelible, as of ink) несмывáемый. **2,** (ingrained) неискоренúмый.
inert *adj.* **1,** *chem.* инéртный: *inert gases,* инéртные гáзы. **2,** (sluggish) инéртный.
inertia *n.* **1,** *physics* инéрция. **2,** *fig.* (disinclination to move or act) инéрция; инéртность.
inescapable *adj.* неизбéжный; неминýемый.
inestimable *adj.* неоценúмый.
inevitable *adj.* неизбéжный. —**inevitability,** *n.* неизбéжность. —**inevitably,** *adv.* неизбéжно.
inexact *adj.* нетóчный. —**inexactness; inexactitude,** *n.* нетóчность.
inexcusable *adj.* непростúтельный.
inexhaustible *adj.* неистощúмый; неисчерпáемый; неиссякáемый.
inexorable *adj.* неумолúмый; непреклóнный.
inexpensive *adj.* дешёвый; недорогóй. —**inexpensively,** *adv.* дёшево; недóрого.
inexperience *n.* неóпытность. —**inexperienced,** *adj.* неóпытный.
inexplicable *adj.* необъяснúмый.
inexpressible *adj.* невыразúмый.
inexpressive *adj.* невыразúтельный.
infallible *adj.* непогрешúмый. —**infallibility,** *n.* непогрешúмость.
infamous *adj.* позóрный; гнýсный.
infamy *n.* **1,** (shame) позóр. **2,** (infamous character) гнýсность.
infancy *n.* младéнчество. *Since infancy,* с рáннего дéтства.
infant *n.* младéнец. —*adj.* дéтский: *infant mortality,* дéтская смéртность.
infanticide *n.* детоубúйство.
infantile *adj.* дéтский; младéнческий. —**infantile paralysis,** дéтский паралúч.
infantry *n.* пехóта. —*adj.* пехóтный: *infantry regiment,* пехóтный полк. —**infantryman,** *n.* пехотúнец.
infatuated *adj. Be infatuated with,* безýмно увлéчься (+ *instr.*). —**infatuation,** *n.* увлечéние.
infeasible *adj.* невыполнúмый; неисполнúмый; неосуществúмый.
infect *v.t.* заражáть. —**infection,** *n.* зарáза; заражéние; инфéкция.

infectious *adj.* **1,** *med.* заразный; инфекционный. **2,** *fig.* (of a smile, laughter, etc.) заразительный.
infer *v.t.* **1,** (deduce) заключать; выводить. **2,** (imply) намекать. —**inference,** *n.* вывод; заключение.
inferior *adj.* **1,** (lower in rank) низший. **2,** (of poor or poorer quality) неполноценный; недоброкачественный. —*n.* подчинённый.
inferiority *n.* неполноценность; недоброкачественность. —**inferiority complex,** комплекс неполноценности.
infernal *adj.* **1,** (hellish) адский. **2,** *colloq.* (damnable) проклятый.
inferno *n.* ад.
infertile *adj.* **1,** (unable to produce offspring) бесплодный. **2,** (barren, as of soil) неплодородный; бесплодный. —**infertility,** *n.* бесплодие; неплодородность.
infest *v.t.* наводнять. *Be infested with,* кишеть (+ *instr.*). *Lice-infested,* вшивый.
infidel *n.* неверный.
infidelity *n.* неверность; измена.
infighting *n.* ближний бой.
infiltrate *v.t.* просачиваться в; проникать в. —**infiltration,** *n.* просачивание; проникновение.
infinite *adj.* бесконечный; безграничный. —**infinitely,** *adv.* бесконечно; *(with comp. adjectives)* неизмеримо.
infinitesimal *adj.* бесконечно малый.
infinitive *n.* неопределённая форма глагола; инфинитив.
infinity *n.* бесконечность.
infirm *adj.* немощный.
infirmary *n.* небольшая больница; лазарет.
infirmity *n.* немощь.
inflame *v.t.* **1,** (fire up) зажигать. **2,** (arouse, as passions) разжигать. —**inflamed,** *adj.* воспалённый. *Become inflamed,* воспаляться.
inflammable *adj.* горючий; огнеопасный. —**inflammability,** *n.* воспламеняемость.
inflammation *n.* воспаление.
inflammatory *adj.* **1,** *med.* воспалительный. **2,** (tending to incite) зажигательный.
inflatable *adj.* надувной.
inflate *v.t.* **1,** (fill with air) надувать; накачивать. **2,** (raise or increase unduly) вздувать; раздувать. *Inflated figures/prices,* дутые цифры/цены.
inflation *n.* **1,** (act of inflating) надувание. **2,** *econ.* инфляция. —**inflationary,** *adj.* инфляционный.
inflect *v.t.* **1,** (change the pitch of, as one's voice) модулировать. **2,** *gram.* склонять; спрягать. *Inflected language,* флективный язык.
inflection *also,* **inflexion** *n.* **1,** (of the voice) модуляция. **2,** *gram.* флексия.
inflexible *adj.* **1,** (stiff; rigid) негибкий; несгибаемый. **2,** (intransigent) непреклонный; несгибаемый. —**inflexibility,** *n.* непреклонность.
inflexion *n.* = **inflection.**
inflict *v.t.* наносить: *inflict losses on,* наносить потери (+ *dat.*). *Inflict punishment on,* подвергать (кого-нибудь) наказанию.
inflow *n.* приток; наплыв.
influence *n.* **1,** (impact; effect) влияние; воздействие. **2,** (connections; pull) блат. —*v.t.* влиять на; воздействовать на. —**influential,** *adj.* влиятельный.
influenza *n.* грипп.
influx *n.* наплыв; прилив.
inform *v.t.* сообщать; извещать; осведомлять; уведомлять; информировать. —*v.i.* [*usu.* **inform on** *or* **against**] доносить (на).
informal *adj.* **1,** (casual) без формальностей. **2,** (unofficial) неофициальный. —**informality,** *n.* отсутствие формальностей.
informant *n.* осведомитель; информатор.
information *n.* сведения; информация. *For your information,* к вашему сведению. —*adj.* справочный: *information bureau,* справочное бюро.
informative *adj.* поучительный; содержательный.
informed *adj.* осведомлённый. *Keep someone informed,* держать кого-нибудь в курсе.
informer *n.* осведомитель; доносчик.
infraction *n.* нарушение.
infrared *adj.* инфракрасный.
infrequent *adj.* редкий. —**infrequently,** *adv.* редко.
infringe *v.t.* нарушать. —*v.i.* [*usu.* **infringe on** *or* **upon**] посягать (на); вторгаться (в).
infringement *n.* **1,** (violation) нарушение. **2,** (encroachment) посягательство.
infuriate *v.t.* приводить в ярость; разъярять; бесить.
infuse *v.t.* вливать; вселять; внушать. —**infusion,** *n.* вливание.
ingenious *adj.* **1,** (of an idea, solution, etc.) остроумный; блестящий. **2,** (of a device) замысловатый; затейливый. **3,** (of a person) изобретательный; хитроумный. —**ingenuity,** *n.* изобретательность.
ingenuous *adj.* бесхитростный; простодушный.
ingest *v.t.* глотать; проглатывать.
inglorious *adj.* бесславный.
ingot *n.* слиток.
ingrain *v.t.* укоренять. —**ingrained,** *adj.* укоренившийся; закоренелый; закоснелый. *Become ingrained,* закоренеть; укореняться. *Become ingrained in one's memory,* запечатлеться в памяти.
ingratiate *v.t. Ingratiate oneself with,* заискивать перед; снискать (чью-нибудь) милость.
ingratiating *adj.* **1,** (pleasing) подкупающий. **2,** (meant to gain favor) заискивающий; вкрадчивый; льстивый.
ingratitude *n.* неблагодарность.
ingredient *n.* составная часть; ингредиент.
ingrown *adj.* **1,** (grown into the flesh) вросший. **2,** (inborn) врождённый.
inhabit *v.t.* обитать в *or* на. —**inhabitant,** *n.* житель; обитатель. —**inhabited,** *adj.* обитаемый.
inhalation *n.* вдыхание.
inhalator *n.* ингалятор.
inhale *v.t. & i.* вдыхать. —*v.i.* (draw in tobacco smoke) затягиваться.
inhaler *n.* ингалятор.
inherent *adj.* **1,** (intrinsic) присущий. **2,** (inborn) врождённый. —**inherently,** *adv.* по своему существу.
inherit *v.t.* наследовать; получить в наследство.
inheritance *n.* **1,** (act of inheriting) наследование. **2,** (something inherited) наследство. —**inheritance tax,** налог на наследство.
inherited *adj.* унаследованный.
inhibit *v.t.* стеснять; тормозить. —**inhibited,** *adj.* стеснительный. —**inhibition,** *n.* стеснение.

inhospitable *adj.* негостеприи́мный; неприве́тливый.
inhuman *adj.* бесчелове́чный. —**inhumanity,** *n.* бесчелове́чность.
inimical *adj.* **1,** *fol. by* **to** (detrimental) вре́дный (для). **2,** (hostile) вражде́бный.
inimitable *adj.* неподража́емый; неповтори́мый.
iniquitous *adj.* гну́сный; поро́чный.
iniquity *n.* **1,** (wickedness) гну́сность; поро́чность. **2,** *usu. pl.* (transgression) грех; просту́пок; прегреше́ние. —**den of iniquity,** прито́н развра́та.
initial *adj.* нача́льный; первонача́льный. —*n.* инициа́л. —*v.t.* **1,** (place one's initials on) ста́вить инициа́лы на; подпи́сывать инициа́лами. **2,** (tentatively approve, as a treaty or document) парафи́ровать.
initially *adv.* снача́ла; вначáле.
initiate *v.t.* **1,** (begin; launch) вводи́ть; быть инициа́тором (+ *gen.*). **2,** (introduce to a subject) знако́мить. **3,** (admit; induct) вводи́ть; посвяща́ть.
initiation *n.* посвяще́ние. *Initiation fee,* вступи́тельный взнос.
initiative *n.* инициати́ва; почи́н. *Take the initiative,* взять инициати́ву в свои́ ру́ки.
initiator *n.* инициа́тор; зачина́тель.
inject *v.t.* **1,** *med.* впры́скивать, вводи́ть. **2,** (introduce, as a new element) вводи́ть. **3,** (interject) вставля́ть.
injection *n.* инъе́кция; впры́скивание; влива́ние; уко́л. *Give an injection to,* сде́лать инъе́кцию/уко́л (+ *dat.*).
injector *n.* форсу́нка. *fuel injector,* форсу́нка горю́чего.
injudicious *adj.* неблагоразу́мный; неразу́мный.
injunction *n.* **1,** (order) предписа́ние. **2,** *law* суде́бный запре́т.
injure *v.t.* **1,** (cause physical harm to) поврежда́ть; ушиба́ть. *Be injured,* пострада́ть; получи́ть поврежде́ние *or* ране́ние. *No one was injured,* никто́ не пострада́л. **2,** (be injurious to) вреди́ть.
injured *adj.* **1,** (damaged; hurt) уши́бленный; ра́неный; повреждённый. **2,** (offended) оби́женный.
injurious *adj.* вре́дный. *Smoking is injurious to health,* куре́ние вреди́т здоро́вью.
injury *n.* **1,** (physical harm) поврежде́ние; ране́ние; тра́вма. **2,** (damage) вред.
injustice *n.* несправедли́вость. *Do someone an injustice,* быть несправедли́вым к кому́-нибудь.
ink *n.* черни́ла: *write in ink,* писа́ть черни́лами. *Printer's ink,* типогра́фская кра́ска. —*adj.* черни́льный: *ink spot,* черни́льное пятно́.
inkblot *n.* кля́кса.
inkling *n.* **1,** (hint; suggestion) намёк. **2,** (vague idea) представле́ние.
ink pad поду́шка для штемпеле́й; ште́мпельная поду́шка.
inkstand *n.* черни́льный прибо́р.
inkwell *n.* черни́льница.
inky *adj.* покры́тый черни́лами; в черни́лах.
inlaid *adj.* инкрусти́рованный; мозаи́чный. *Inlaid table,* сто́лик с инкруста́цией.
inland *adj.* вну́тренний: *inland waterways,* вну́тренние во́дные пути́. *Inland sea,* вну́треннее *or* закры́тое мо́ре. —*adv.* внутрь страны́; в глубь страны́.
in-law *n.* сво́йственник.
inlay *v.t.* **1,** (set flush into a surface) вкла́дывать. **2,** (decorate by inserting such designs) инкрусти́ровать. —*n.* **1,** (inlaid work) моза́ика; инкруста́ция. **2,** *dent.* пло́мба.
inlet *n.* **1,** (bay) бу́хта. **2,** (creek) за́водь; зато́н.
inmate *n.* **1,** (in a prison) заключённый. **2,** (in an asylum) больно́й.
inn *n.* посто́ялый двор; тракти́р.
innards *n.pl.* вну́тренности.
innate *adj.* врождённый; прирождённый; приро́дный.
inner *adj.* вну́тренний. —**inner ear,** вну́треннее у́хо. —**inner sole,** сте́лька. —**inner tube,** ка́мера.
innermost *adj.* **1,** (farthest in) са́мый глубо́кий. **2,** (most intimate, as of feelings) сокрове́нный.
innkeeper *n.* тракти́рщик.
innocence *n.* **1,** (absence of guilt) невино́вность. **2,** (lack of sophistication) неви́нность.
innocent *adj.* **1,** (not guilty) невино́вный. **2,** (naive; harmless) неви́нный.
innocuous *adj.* безвре́дный; безоби́дный.
innovate *v.i.* вводи́ть но́вшества. —**innovation,** *n.* но́вшество; нововведе́ние. —**innovative,** *adj.* нова́торский. —**innovator,** *n.* нова́тор.
innuendo *n.* инсинуа́ция.
innumerable *adj.* бесчи́сленный; несчётный.
inoculate *v.t.* привива́ть: *inoculate someone for typhus,* привива́ть кому́-нибудь тиф. —**inoculation,** *n.* приви́вка.
inoffensive *adj.* безоби́дный.
inoperable *adj.* неопера́бельный.
inoperative *adj.* безде́йствующий.
inopportune *adj.* несвоевре́менный.
inordinate *adj.* чрезме́рный; непоме́рный.
inorganic *adj.* неоргани́ческий.
input *n.* ввод.
inquest *n.* сле́дствие; дозна́ние.
inquire *v.i.* **1,** (ask; seek information) спра́шивать; справля́ться; осведомля́ться. **2,** *fol. by* **into** (investigate; study) рассле́довать; иссле́довать.
inquiry *n.* **1,** (request for information) запро́с. *Make inquiries about,* наводи́ть спра́вки о. **2,** (investigation) рассле́дование; сле́дствие. *Committee of inquiry,* сле́дственная коми́ссия.
inquisition *n.* инквизи́ция.
inquisitive *adj.* пытли́вый; любозна́тельный. —**inquisitiveness,** *n.* пытли́вость; любозна́тельность.
inquisitor *n.* инквизи́тор.
inroad *n.* **1,** (incursion) набе́г. **2,** *usu. pl.* (encroachment) посяга́тельство.
insane *adj.* сумасше́дший; душевнобольно́й; умалишённый. —**insane asylum,** сумасше́дший дом; дом умалишённых; психиатри́ческая больни́ца.
insanity *n.* **1,** (mental condition) сумасше́ствие; умопомеша́тельство. **2,** (folly) безу́мие.
insatiable *adj.* ненасы́тный.
inscribe *v.t.* **1,** (write) надпи́сывать. **2,** (engrave; carve) выреза́ть. **3,** *geom.* впи́сывать.
inscription *n.* на́дпись.
inscrutable *adj.* непостижи́мый; неисповеди́мый.
insect *n.* насеко́мое.
insecticide *n.* сре́дство от насеко́мых; инсектици́д.
insecure *adj.* **1,** (not safe) небезопа́сный. **2,** (lacking confidence or assurance) неуве́ренный в себе́. —**insecurity,** *n.* неуве́ренность в себе́.

insemination *n.* оплодотворе́ние; осемене́ние. *Artificial insemination,* иску́сственное оплодотворе́ние/осемене́ние.
insensate *adj.* бесчу́вственный.
insensible *adj.* бесчу́вственный; нечувстви́тельный. —**insensibility,** *n.* бесчу́вствие; нечувстви́тельность.
insensitive *adj.* нечувстви́тельный; бесчу́вственный; нечу́ткий. —**insensitivity,** *n.* нечувстви́тельность; бесчу́вствие.
inseparable *adj.* **1,** (of two people) неразлу́чный. **2,** (of objects, concepts, etc.) неотдели́мый. —**inseparability,** *n.* неразлу́чность; неотдели́мость.
insert *v.t.* **1,** (place inside) вкла́дывать; вставля́ть; опуска́ть. **2,** (add; enter) вноси́ть. —*n.* вкла́дка.
insertion *n.* **1,** (act of inserting) вкла́дывание; внесе́ние. **2,** (something inserted) вста́вка.
inset *n.* **1,** (in a book) вкле́йка. **2,** (in a dress) вста́вка.
inside *prep.* внутри́: *inside the house,* внутри́ до́ма. —*adv.* **1,** (motion) внутрь. **2,** (location) внутри́. —*adj.* **1,** (interior) вну́тренний. **2,** *colloq.* (known to only a few) секре́тный: *inside information,* секре́тные све́дения. —*n.* **1,** (interior) вну́тренняя часть; вну́тренность. *From/on the inside,* изнутри́. **2,** *pl., colloq.* (innards) вну́тренности. —**inside out, 1,** (reversed) наизна́нку. *Turn inside out,* вы́вернуть (наизна́нку). **2,** *colloq.* (thoroughly) вдоль и поперёк.
insidious *adj.* кова́рный. —**insidiousness,** *n.* кова́рство.
insight *n.* **1,** (discernment) зо́ркость; проница́тельность. **2,** (illuminating glimpse) понима́ние.
insignia *n.pl.* зна́ки разли́чия.
insignificant *adj.* незначи́тельный. —**insignificance,** *n.* незначи́тельность.
insincere *adj.* нei̇скренний. —**insincerity,** *n.* нei̇скренность.
insinuate *v.t.* **1,** (introduce gradually) незаме́тно внуша́ть. *Insinuate oneself into someone's confidence,* втира́ться в чьё-нибудь дове́рие. **2,** (hint; suggest) намека́ть; подразумева́ть.
insinuation *n.* намёк; инсинуа́ция.
insipid *adj.* **1,** (tasteless) невку́сный. **2,** (dull) бесцве́тный; пре́сный.
insist *v.t. & i.* наста́ивать. —**insistence,** *n.* настоя́ние. —**insistent,** *adj.* насто́йчивый; настоя́тельный.
insofar as 1, (as far as) наско́лько. **2,** (to the full extent that) посто́льку, поско́льку.
insole *n.* сте́лька.
insolent *adj.* на́глый; де́рзкий. —**insolence,** *n.* на́глость; наха́льство; де́рзость.
insoluble *adj.* **1,** (not soluble) нераствори́мый. **2,** (not solvable) неразреши́мый.
insolvent *adj.* несостоя́тельный; неплатёжеспосо́бный. —**insolvency,** *n.* несостоя́тельность; неплатёжеспосо́бность.
insomnia *n.* бессо́нница.
inspect *v.t.* **1,** (examine) осма́тривать; обсле́довать. **2,** (conduct an inspection of) обсле́довать; инспекти́ровать. **3,** (review, as troops) производи́ть смотр (+ *dat.*).
inspection *n.* **1,** (examination) обсле́дование; осмо́тр; досмо́тр; инспе́кция; реви́зия. **2,** *mil.* смотр.
inspector *n.* инспе́ктор; контролёр; ревизо́р; обсле́дователь.
inspiration *n.* **1,** (feeling of being inspired) вдохнове́ние; воодушевле́ние. **2,** (one who inspires) вдохнови́тель. **3,** (inspired idea) блестя́щая мысль.
inspire *v.t.* **1,** (animate; stir) вдохновля́ть; воодушевля́ть. **2,** (arouse; produce, as an emotion) внуша́ть; вселя́ть. —**inspired,** *adj.* вдохнове́нный.
instability *n.* неусто́йчивость.
install *v.t.* **1,** (fix in position for use) устана́вливать; ста́вить; проводи́ть. **2,** (induct) вводи́ть в до́лжность.
installation *n.* **1,** (act of installing) устано́вка; проведе́ние. **2,** (something installed) устано́вка. **3,** (induction) введе́ние в до́лжность. **4,** *mil.* ба́за; объе́кт.
installment *also,* **instalment** *n.* **1,** (payment) взнос. *On the installment plan,* в рассро́чку. **2,** (of a published article) вы́пуск.
instance *n.* **1,** (example) приме́р: *for instance,* наприме́р. **2,** (case) слу́чай: *in this instance,* в да́нном слу́чае. **3,** *law* инста́нция: *court of first instance,* суд пе́рвой инста́нции.
instant *n.* мгнове́ние; миг; мину́та; моме́нт. *This instant,* сию́ мину́ту. —*adj.* момента́льный; мгнове́нный. —**instant coffee,** быстрораствори́мый ко́фе.
instantaneous *adj.* момента́льный; мгнове́нный.
instantly *adv.* момента́льно; мгнове́нно.
instead *adv.* вме́сто *(must be followed by a word in the genitive case): he is ill, so I came instead,* он заболе́л, и я пришёл вме́сто него́. —**instead of,** вме́сто (+ *gen.*): *drink beer instead of wine,* пить пи́во вме́сто вина́. ♦*When followed by -ing form of a verb* вме́сто того́, что́бы (+ *inf.*): *instead of going to the theater,* вме́сто того́, что́бы пойти́ в теа́тр.
instep *n.* подъём.
instigate *v.t.* **1,** (foment; provoke) провоци́ровать. **2,** (spur; goad) подстрека́ть. —**instigation,** *n.* подстрека́тельство. —**instigator,** *n.* подстрека́тель; зачи́нщик.
instill *also,* **instil** *v.t.* внуша́ть; вселя́ть; влива́ть.
instinct *n.* инсти́нкт.
instinctive *adj.* инстинкти́вный. —**instinctively,** *adv.* инстинкти́вно.
institute *n.* институ́т. —*v.t.* **1,** (establish) устана́вливать; учрежда́ть. **2,** (initiate) вводи́ть; заводи́ть. *Institute reforms,* проводи́ть рефо́рмы.
institution *n.* **1,** (organization) учрежде́ние; заведе́ние. *Institution of higher learning,* вы́сшее уче́бное заведе́ние. **2,** (established custom) учрежде́ние; институ́т: *The institution of marriage,* учрежде́ние/институ́т бра́ка. **3,** (place of confinement) дом: *mental institution,* дом умалишённых.
instruct *v.t.* **1,** (teach) обуча́ть. **2,** (order; direct) поруча́ть.
instruction *n.* **1,** (teaching) обуче́ние. **2,** *pl.* (directions) указа́ния; наставле́ние; инстру́кция. —**instructional,** *adj.* уче́бный; инструкти́вный.
instructive *adj.* поучи́тельный.
instructor *n.* инстру́ктор.
instrument *n.* **1,** (implement) инструме́нт; ору́дие: *surgical instruments,* хирурги́ческие инструме́нты; *instrument of torture,* ору́дие пы́тки. **2,** (means; agency) ору́дие. **3,** (musical instrument) инструме́нт. **4,** (gauge) прибо́р: *instrument landing,* поса́дка по прибо́рам. *Instrument panel,* прибо́рная доска́. **5,** (legal document) гра́мота: *instruments of ratification,* ратификацио́нные гра́моты.

instrumental *adj.* **1,** (serving to achieve an end): *be instrumental in,* сыгра́ть реша́ющую роль в. **2,** *music* инструмента́льный. **3,** *gram.* твори́тельный: *instrumental case,* твори́тельный паде́ж.

instrumentalist *n.* инструментали́ст.

instrumentality *n. Through the instrumentality of,* при посре́дстве (+ *gen.*); че́рез посре́дство (+ *gen.*).

insubordinate *adj.* самово́льный. —**insubordination,** *n.* неподчине́ние; неповинове́ние.

insufferable *adj.* невыноси́мый; нестерпи́мый; несно́сный.

insufficiency *n.* недоста́точность.

insufficient *adj.* недоста́точный. —**insufficiently,** *adv.* недоста́точно.

insular *adj.* островно́й.

insulate *v.t.* изоли́ровать. —**insulation,** *n.* изоля́ция. —**insulator,** *n.* изоля́тор.

insulin *n.* инсули́н.

insult *v.t.* оскорбля́ть. —*n.* оскорбле́ние; оби́да. —**insulting,** *adj.* оскорби́тельный; оби́дный.

insuperable *adj.* непреодоли́мый.

insurance *n.* страхова́ние. —*adj.* страхово́й: *insurance company,* страхова́я компа́ния. *Insurance policy/agent,* страхово́й по́лис/аге́нт.

insure *v.t.* **1,** (guarantee) обеспе́чивать. **2,** (take out insurance for) страхова́ть. —**insurer,** *n.* страхо́вщик.

insurgency *n.* восста́ние; мяте́ж.

insurgent *n.* повста́нец; мяте́жник. —*adj.* повста́нческий; мяте́жный.

insurmountable *adj.* непреодоли́мый.

insurrection *n.* восста́ние; мяте́ж.

intact *adj.* це́лый; в це́лости; в сохра́нности.

intake *n.* впуск.

intangible *adj.* неосяза́емый.

integer *n.* це́лое число́; це́лое.

integral *adj.* **1,** (essential) неотъе́млемый: *integral part,* неотъе́млемая часть. **2,** *math.* интегра́льный: *integral calculus,* интегра́льное исчисле́ние. —*n., math.* интегра́л.

integrate *v.t.* **1,** (combine into a whole) интегри́ровать. **2,** (desegregate) десегреги́ровать. —**integrated circuit,** интегра́льная схе́ма.

integration *n.* **1,** (combining into a whole) интегра́ция. **2,** (desegregation) десегрега́ция.

integrity *n.* **1,** (uprightness; honesty) че́стность. **2,** (entirety) це́лостность: *territorial integrity,* территориа́льная це́лостность.

integument *n.* покро́в.

intellect *n.* ум; ра́зум; интелле́кт.

intellectual *adj.* у́мственный; интеллектуа́льный. —*n.* интеллиге́нт; интеллектуа́л.

intelligence *n.* **1,** (mental ability) ум; у́мственные спосо́бности. **2,** (collection of secret information; organization engaged in same) разве́дка. **3,** (information so collected) разве́дывательные да́нные. —*adj.* разве́дывательный; разве́дочный. —**intelligence quotient,** показа́тель у́мственных спосо́бностей. —**intelligence test,** испыта́ние у́мственных спосо́бностей.

intelligent *adj.* **1,** (endowed with intellect) разу́мный. **2,** (smart; clever) у́мный.

intelligentsia *n.* интеллиге́нция.

intelligible *adj.* поня́тный; толко́вый; вразуми́тельный. —**intelligibility,** *n.* поня́тность.

intemperance *n.* невозде́ржанность; невоздержа́ние.

intemperate *adj.* **1,** (given to excesses; excessive) неуме́ренный; невозде́ржанный. **2,** (improper; rude) невозде́ржанный: *intemperate language,* невозде́ржанный язы́к.

intend *v.t.* **1,** (have in mind; plan) собира́ться; намерева́ться. *What do you intend to do?,* что вы наме́рены де́лать? **2,** (design for a specific purpose) предназнача́ть: *intended for children,* предназна́чен для дете́й.

intense *adj.* **1,** (keenly felt) си́льный; о́стрый. *Intense heat/hatred,* си́льная жара́/не́нависть. *Intense pain,* си́льная *or* о́страя боль. **2,** (strenuous; heated) напряжённый.

intensify *v.t.* **1,** (increase; step up) уси́ливать; усугубля́ть. *Intensify one's efforts,* усугубля́ть уси́лия. **2,** (make more acute) обостря́ть. —*v.i.* обостря́ться. —**intensification,** *n.* усиле́ние; обостре́ние.

intensity *n.* интенси́вность.

intensive *adj.* интенси́вный. —**intensive care,** интенси́вная терапи́я.

intent *n.* **1,** (intention) наме́рение. **2,** *law* у́мысел: *malicious intent,* злой у́мысел. —*adj.* **1,** (firmly fixed or directed) при́стальный. **2,** *fol. by* **on** (determined) по́лный реши́мости. —**to all intents and purposes,** факти́чески.

intention *n.* наме́рение. *Have no intention of,* отню́дь не собира́ться (+ *inf.*).

intentional *adj.* наме́ренный; преднаме́ренный; умы́шленный. —**intentionally,** *adv.* наме́ренно; наро́чно.

intently *adv.* при́стально.

inter *v.t.* хорони́ть; погреба́ть.

interact *v.i.* взаимоде́йствовать. —**interaction,** *n.* взаимоде́йствие.

intercede *v.i.* **1,** (plead in behalf of another) хлопота́ть; хода́тайствовать; вступа́ться; заступа́ться. **2,** (mediate) посре́дничать.

intercept *v.t.* перехва́тывать. —**interception,** *n.* перехва́т. —**interceptor,** *n.* истреби́тель-перехва́тчик.

intercession *n.* засту́пничество; хода́тайство. —**intercessor,** *n.* засту́пник; хода́тай.

interchange *v.t.* меня́ться (+ *instr.*); обме́ниваться (+ *instr.*). —*v.i.* меня́ться места́ми. —*n.* (взаи́мный) обме́н.

interchangeable *adj.* взаимозаменя́емый.

intercity *adj.* междугоро́дный.

interconnect *v.i.* соединя́ться. *The bedrooms interconnect,* спа́льни соединены́ ме́жду собо́й. —**interconnected,** *adj.* взаимосвя́занный.

intercontinental *adj.* межконтинента́льный.

intercourse *n.* **1,** (dealings) обще́ние; сноше́ния. **2,** (copulation) полова́я связь.

interdependence *n.* взаимозави́симость. —**interdependent,** *adj.* взаимозави́симый.

interdict *v.t.* **1,** (forbid) запреща́ть. **2,** *mil.* воспреща́ть.

interdiction *n.* **1,** (act of forbidding) запре́т; запреще́ние. **2,** *mil.* воспреще́ние.

interest *n.* **1,** (curiosity) интере́с: *interest in music,* интере́с к му́зыке. *Be of interest,* представля́ть интере́с. **2,** (advantage; benefit) интере́сы: *it is in your interest,* э́то в ва́ших интере́сах. *In the public interest,* в общéственных интерéсах. *Protect one's interests,* защищáть свои́ интерéсы. **3,** (payment for the use of money) процéнты. **4,** (legal share) дóля: *a half interest,* полови́нная дóля. —*v.t.* интересовáть. —**in the interest of,** в интерéсах (+ *gen.*); рáди. —**with interest,** с лихвóй: *repay with interest,* отплати́ть с лихвóй.

interested *adj.* заинтересóванный. *Be interested in,* интересовáться (+ *instr.*); быть заинтересóванным в (+ *prepl.*). *He is not interested,* емý не интерéсно.

interest-free *adj.* беспроцéнтный.

interesting *adj.* интерéсный.

interfere *v.i.* **1,** (meddle; intervene) вмéшиваться. **2,** *fol. by* **with** (hinder; obstruct) мешáть.

interference *n.* **1,** (act of interfering) вмешáтельство. **2,** (static) помéхи.

interim *n.* промежýток. *In the interim,* тем врéменем. —*adj.* врéменный; предвари́тельный; промежýточный.

interior *adj.* внýтренний. —*n.* внýтренность; внýтренняя часть. —**interior decorator,** декорáтор.

interject *v.t.* вставля́ть; ввёртывать.

interjection *n.* междомéтие.

interlace *v.t.* **1,** (intertwine) сплетáть; переплетáть. **2,** (intersperse) уснащáть; пересыпáть.

interlard *v.t.* уснащáть; пересыпáть.

interlay *v.t.* переклáдывать; проклáдывать.

interlock *v.t.* сцепля́ть. —*v.i.* сцепля́ться.

interloper *n.* незвáный гость; при́шлый человéк.

interlude *n.* **1,** (interval) промежýток. **2,** *music* интерлю́дия.

intermarriage *n.* смéшанный брак; брак мéжду людьми́ различ́ной рáсы. —**intermarry,** *v.i.* вступи́ть в смéшанный брак.

intermediary *n.* посрéдник. —*adj.* **1,** (intermediate) промежýточный. **2,** (acting as a mediator) посрéднический.

intermediate *adj.* **1,** (situated in between) промежýточный. **2,** (between elementary and advanced) срéдний.

interment *n.* погребéние.

intermezzo *n.* интермéццо.

interminable *adj.* бесконéчный; нескончáемый.

intermingle *v.t.* смéшивать; перемéшивать. —*v.i.* смéшиваться.

intermission *n.* **1,** (recess) переры́в. **2,** *theat.* антрáкт.

intermittent *adj.* перемежáющийся; преры́вистый. —**intermittently,** *adv.* с переры́вами.

intern *n.* интéрн. —*v.i.* служи́ть интéрном. —*v.t.* (confine) интерни́ровать.

internal *adj.* внýтренний. —**internal-combustion engine,** дви́гатель внýтреннего сгорáния. —**internal medicine,** терапи́я.

internally *adv.* внýтренне. *Take medicine internally,* принимáть лекáрство внутрь.

international *adj.* международный. —**International Date Line,** Ли́ния перемéны дáты.

Internationale *n.* Интернационáл.

internationalism *n.* интернационали́зм.

internecine *adj.* **1,** (marked by great slaughter) истреби́тельный. **2,** (internal) междоусóбный.

internist *n.* терапéвт.

internment *n.* интерни́рование. —**internment camp,** лáгерь для интерни́рованных.

interplanetary *adj.* межпланéтный.

interplay *n.* взаимодéйствие.

interpolate *v.t.* **1,** (interject; interpose) вставля́ть. **2,** *math.* интерполи́ровать. —**interpolation,** *n.* интерполя́ция.

interpose *v.t.* **1,** (place between) стáвить (мéжду). **2,** (inject, as a comment) вставля́ть.

interpret *v.t.* **1,** (translate orally) переводи́ть. **2,** (explain; construe) толковáть; истолкóвывать; трактовáть; интерпрети́ровать.

interpretation *n.* **1,** (translation) перевóд. **2,** (explanation) толковáние; истолковáние; трактóвка; интерпретáция.

interpreter *n.* **1,** (translator) перевóдчик. **2,** (commentator) толковáтель; истолковáтель; интерпретáтор.

interregnum *n.* междуцáрствие.

interrelated *adj.* взаимодéйствующий; взаимосвя́занный.

interrelation *n.* взаимоотношéние. —**interrelationship,** *n.* взаи́мная связь.

interrogate *v.t.* допрáшивать. —**interrogation,** *n.* допрóс.

interrogative *adj.* вопроси́тельный.

interrupt *v.t.* прерывáть; перебивáть; обрывáть. —*v.i.* перебивáть: *don't interrupt!,* не перебивáй(те)!

interruption *n.* **1,** (act of interrupting) прерывáние. *Interruption of telephone service,* нарушéние телефóнной свя́зи. *Interruption of pregnancy,* прерывáние берéменности. **2,** (instance of interrupting) помéха: *without any interruptions,* без вся́ких помéх. *Excuse the interruption!,* извини́те за беспокóйство! **3,** (break) переры́в: *without interruption,* без переры́ва.

intersect *v.t.* пересекáть. —*v.i.* пересекáться.

intersection *n.* **1,** (of lines) пересечéние. **2,** (of streets, roads, etc.) перекрёсток.

intersperse *v.t.* **1,** (scatter) разбрáсывать; рассыпáть. **2,** (interlace, as with comments) уснащáть; пересыпáть.

interstellar *adj.* межзвёздный.

intertwine *v.t.* сплетáть; переплетáть. —*v.i.* сплетáться; переплетáться.

interval *n.* **1,** (space; gap; break) промежýток; интервáл. **2,** *Brit.* (intermission) антрáкт.

intervene *v.i.* **1,** (intercede) вмéшиваться. **2,** (occur in the meantime) происходи́ть (тем врéменем). *In the intervening period,* тем врéменем.

intervention *n.* вмешáтельство; интервéнция.

interview *n.* **1,** (meeting to evaluate) встрéча. **2,** (for a publication, on TV, etc.) интервью́. —*v.t.* брать интервью́ у; интервьюи́ровать. —**interviewer,** *n.* интервьюéр.

interweave *v.t.* сплетáть; переплетáть *(lit. & fig.).*

intestate *adj.* без завещáния; не остáвив завещáния.

intestine *n.* кишкá; *pl.* кишки́; кишéчник. —**intestinal,** *adj.* кишéчный.

intimacy *n.* инти́мность; бли́зость.

intimate[1] (**in**-ti-mit) *adj.* инти́мный: *intimate friend/circle,* инти́мный друг/круг. *Become intimate with,* сойти́сь с.

intimate[2] (**in**-ti-mate) *v.t.* намекáть.

intimately *adv.* инти́мно. *Intimately connected with,* те́сно свя́занный с.
intimation *n.* намёк.
intimidate *v.t.* запу́гивать. —**intimidation,** *n.* запу́гивание.
into *prep.* в (+ *acc.*): *walk into a room,* входи́ть в ко́мнату; *fall into a trap,* попа́сть в лову́шку. *Put into operation,* вводи́ть в де́йствие. *Get into trouble,* попа́сть в беду́. ♦ *With certain verbs* на: *divide into parts,* дели́ть на ча́сти. *Run into an acquaintance,* ната́лкиваться на дру́га. *Translate into Russian,* переводи́ть на ру́сский язы́к.
intolerable *adj.* нетерпи́мый.
intolerant *adj.* нетерпи́мый. —**intolerance,** *n.* нетерпи́мость.
intonation *n.* интона́ция.
intone *v.i.* говори́ть нараспе́в *or* речитати́вом. —*v.t.* чита́ть *or* произноси́ть нараспе́в/речитати́вом.
intoxicate *v.t.* пьяни́ть; опьяня́ть. —**intoxicated,** *adj.* пья́ный; хмельно́й; опьяне́вший. —**intoxicating,** *adj.* опьяня́ющий; хмельно́й. —**intoxication,** *n.* опьяне́ние.
intractable *adj.* несгово́рчивый; непода́тливый.
intransigent *adj.* непреклонный. —**intransigence,** *n.* непрекло́нность.
intransitive *adj.* неперехо́дный.
intravenous *adj.* внутриве́нный.
intrepid *adj.* неустраши́мый; бесстра́шный. —**intrepidity,** *n.* неустраши́мость.
intricacy *n.* **1,** (complexity) запу́танность; сло́жность. **2,** *pl.* (intricate details) сло́жности.
intricate *adj.* запу́танный; замыслова́тый; сло́жный.
intrigue *n.* интри́га; *pl.* интри́ги; про́иски. —*v.t.* (fascinate) интригова́ть. —*v.i.* (engage in intrigue) интригова́ть.
intrinsic *adj.* суще́ственный. *Intrinsic value,* вну́тренняя *or* действи́тельная це́нность. —**intrinsically,** *adv.* в су́щности свое́й; по своему́ существу́.
introduce *v.t.* **1,** (present so as to make acquainted) знако́мить; представля́ть. *Introduce someone to someone,* (по)знако́мить кого́-нибудь с ке́м-нибудь. *Allow me to introduce...,* разреши́те мне предста́вить... **2,** (present to an audience) представля́ть. **3,** (institute) вводи́ть; заводи́ть. **4,** (offer, as a bill) вноси́ть. —**introduce oneself,** представля́ться; (от)рекомендова́ться.
introduction *n.* **1,** (presentation) представле́ние: *introduction of a speaker,* представле́ние ора́тора. *A flowery introduction,* кра́сочное представле́ние. **2,** (opening portion, as of a book) введе́ние; вступле́ние. **3,** (instituting) введе́ние. **4,** (elementary phase of study) введе́ние: *introduction to philosophy,* введе́ние в филосо́фию. **5,** *music* интроду́кция.
introductory *adj.* вступи́тельный; вво́дный.
introspection *n.* самонаблюде́ние; самоана́лиз; интроспе́кция. —**introspective,** *adj.* интроспекти́вный.
intrude *v.i.* вме́шиваться; навя́зываться. —*v.t.* навя́зывать.
intruder *n.* **1,** (interloper) незва́ный гость. **2,** (housebreaker) взло́мщик.
intrusion *n.* **1,** (encroachment) вторже́ние: *intrusion of (a country's) airspace,* вторже́ние в возду́шное простра́нство. **2,** (interruption) беспоко́йство: *pardon the intrusion,* прости́те за беспоко́йство.
intrusive *adj.* навя́зчивый.
intuition *n.* интуи́ция.
intuitive *adj.* интуити́вный. —**intuitively,** *adv.* интуити́вно; по наи́тию.
inundate *v.t.* **1,** (flood) затопля́ть. **2,** *fig.* (overwhelm) наводня́ть. —**inundation,** *n.* наводне́ние.
inure *v.t.* приуча́ть; закаля́ть.
invade *v.t. & i.* вторга́ться (в) —**invader,** *n.* захва́тчик.
invalid[1] (**in**-va-lid) *n.* инвали́д.
invalid[2] (in-**val**-id) *adj.* **1,** (null; void) недействи́тельный. **2,** (unsound, as of an argument) необосно́ванный. **3,** (illegitimate, as of an excuse) неуважи́тельный.
invalidate *v.t.* де́лать недействи́тельным; аннули́ровать.
invaluable *adj.* неоцени́мый; бесце́нный.
invariable *adj.* неизме́нный. —**invariably,** *adv.* неизме́нно.
invasion *n.* вторже́ние; наше́ствие. *Invasion of,* вторже́ние в (+ *acc.*); наше́ствие на (+ *acc.*).
invective *n.* брань; ру́гань.
inveigh *v.i.* [*usu.* **inveigh against**] ра́товать (про́тив).
inveigle *v.t.* **1,** (talk into) ула́мывать. **2,** (wangle) выпра́шивать.
invent *v.t.* **1,** (devise, create) изобрета́ть. **2,** (fabricate; concoct) выду́мывать; сочиня́ть; измышля́ть.
invention *n.* **1,** (device conceived by original effort) изобрете́ние. **2,** (fabrication) вы́думка, измышле́ние.
inventive *adj.* изобрета́тельный. —**inventiveness,** *n.* изобрета́тельность.
inventor *n.* изобрета́тель.
inventory *n.* **1,** (stock-taking) о́пись; инвента́рь; учёт; переучёт. *Take inventory,* де́лать о́пись; составля́ть инвента́рь. *Closed for inventory,* закры́т на учёт. **2,** (stock on hand) инвента́рь; запа́с. —*v.t.* опи́сывать; инвентаризи́ровать.
inverse *adj.* обра́тный; противополо́жный. —*n.* противополо́жность. —**inversely,** *adv.* обра́тно: *inversely proportional to,* обра́тно пропорциона́льный (+ *dat.*).
inversion *n.* **1,** (act of inverting) перевёртывание. **2,** (reversal of order) перестано́вка. **3,** *gram.; chem.; meteorol.* инве́рсия.
invert *v.t.* **1,** (turn upside down) перевёртывать. **2,** (reverse the order of) переставля́ть. *Inverted order,* обра́тный поря́док.
invertebrate *adj.* беспозвоно́чный. —*n.* беспозвоно́чное. *The invertebrates,* беспозвоно́чные.
invest *v.t.* **1,** (put, as money, effort, etc.) вкла́дывать. **2,** (give power to) облека́ть. —*v.i.* [*usu.* **invest in**] вкла́дывать де́ньги в (+ *acc.*).
investigate *v.t.* **1,** (subject to an official probe) рассле́довать. **2,** (explore scientifically) иссле́довать.
investigation *n.* **1,** (official probe) рассле́дование; сле́дствие. *Federal Bureau of Investigation,* Федера́льное бюро́ рассле́дований. **2,** (scientific study) иссле́дование.
investigator *n.* сле́дователь. —**investigatory,** *adj.* сле́дственный.
investiture *n.* инвеститу́ра.

investment *n.* вложе́ние; капиталовложе́ние. —**investor,** *n.* вкла́дчик.
inveterate *adj.* закоренелый; застарелый; зая́длый.
invidious *adj.* **1,** (odious) гну́сный. **2,** (giving offense) оскорби́тельный.
invigorate *v.t.* бодри́ть; оживля́ть. —**invigorating,** *adj.* бодря́щий; живи́тельный.
invincible *adj.* непобеди́мый. —**invincibility,** *n.* непобеди́мость.
inviolable *adj.* неруши́мый; неприкоснове́нный. —**inviolability,** *n.* неруши́мость; неприкоснове́нность.
inviolate *adj.* **1,** (not violated) не нару́шенный. *Keep inviolate,* свя́то храни́ть. **2,** (not profaned) нетро́нутый.
invisible *adj.* неви́димый. —**invisible ink,** симпати́ческие черни́ла.
invitation *n.* приглаше́ние.
invite *v.t.* **1,** (request the presence of) приглаша́ть. **2,** (tend to bring on; lay oneself open to) наклика́ть.
inviting *adj.* привлека́тельный; зама́нчивый; соблазни́тельный.
invocation *n.* **1,** (appeal to a higher power) обраще́ние. **2,** (opening prayer) моли́тва.
invoice *n.* факту́ра; накладна́я.
invoke *v.t.* **1,** (call on for help) обраща́ться к. **2,** (resort to; put into force) вводи́ть в де́йствие. **3,** (summon by incantation) заклина́ть.
involuntary *adj.* нево́льный; непроизво́льный.
involve *v.t.* **1,** (entail) влечь за собо́й; быть свя́занным с. **2,** (implicate; embroil) вовлека́ть. **3,** (absorb; engross) поглоща́ть.
involved *adj.* **1,** (concerned) заинтересо́ванный. **2,** *fol. by* **in** (a party to) прича́стный (к). **3,** (complex) запу́танный.
involvement *n.* **1,** (act of involving) вовлече́ние. **2,** (state of being involved) уча́стие; прича́стность.
invulnerable *adj.* неуязви́мый. —**invulnerability,** *n.* неуязви́мость.
inward *adj.* вну́тренний. —*adv.* [*also,* **inwards**] внутрь. —**inwardly,** *adv.* вну́тренне; в душе́.
iodine *n.* йод.
ion *n.* ио́н. —**ionic,** *adj.* ио́нный.
ionize *v.t.* ионизи́ровать. —**ionization,** *n.* ионизáция.
ionosphere *n.* ионосфе́ра.
iota *n.* йо́та. *Not one iota,* ни на йо́ту.
Iranian *adj.* ира́нский. —*n.* ира́нец; ира́нка.
Iraqi *adj.* ира́кский.
irascible *adj.* вспы́льчивый.
irate *adj.* гне́вный; разгне́ванный.
ire *n.* гнев.
iridescent *adj.* ра́дужный; перели́вчатый. —**iridescence,** *n.* ра́дужность.
iridium *n.* ири́дий.
iris *n.* **1,** (of the eye) ра́дужная оболо́чка. **2,** (flower) и́рис; каса́тик.
Irish *adj.* ирла́ндский. —*n., preceded by* **the** ирла́ндцы. —**Irishman,** *n.* ирла́ндец.
irk *v.t.* раздража́ть; досажда́ть; надоеда́ть. —**irksome,** *adj.* доса́дный; надое́дливый.
iron *n.* **1,** (metal) желе́зо. **2,** (flatiron) утю́г. **3,** (instrument of iron): *soldering iron,* пая́льник. *Fire irons,* ками́нные щипцы́. **4,** *pl.* (shackles) кандалы́: *in irons,* в кандала́х. —*adj.* желе́зный: *iron ore,* желе́зная руда́. —*v.t.* **1,** (press) утю́жить; гла́дить. **2,** *fol. by* **out** (smooth over, as differences) сгла́живать, ула́живать. —**Iron Age,** желе́зный век. —**iron curtain,** желе́зный за́навес.
ironic *also,* **ironical** *adj.* ирони́ческий. —**ironically,** *adv.* ирони́чески; по иро́нии судьбы́.
ironing *n.* утю́жка; гла́женье. —**ironing board,** глади́льная доска́.
ironworks *n.* чугунолите́йный заво́д.
irony *n.* иро́ния.
irradiate *v.t.* **1,** (illuminate) освеща́ть; озаря́ть. **2,** (expose to rays or radiation) облуча́ть. —**irradiation,** *n.* иррадиа́ция; облуче́ние.
irrational *adj.* **1,** (not reasoning; senseless) неразу́мный; нерассуди́тельный. **2,** *math.* иррациона́льный. —**irrationality,** *n.* неразу́мность; нерассуди́тельность.
irreconcilable *adj.* непримири́мый. —**irreconcilability,** *n.* непримири́мость.
irrecoverable *adj.* непоправи́мый; невозвра́тный.
irrefutable *adj.* неопровержи́мый.
irregular *adj.* **1,** (not symmetrical) непра́вильный: *irregular features,* непра́вильные черты́. **2,** (uneven in occurrence) нерегуля́рный. **3,** (spasmodic) неро́вный: *irregular heartbeat,* неро́вное бие́ние се́рдца. **4,** *gram.* неправи́льный: *irregular verb,* непра́вильный глаго́л. **5,** *mil.* нерегуля́рный.
irregularity *n.* непра́вильность; нерегуля́рность.
irrelevance *also,* **irrelevancy** *n.* неуме́стность. *That is an irrelevance,* э́то не отно́сится к де́лу.
irrelevant *adj.* неуме́стный; не относя́щийся к де́лу.
irreligious *adj.* неве́рующий.
irremovable *adj.* неустрани́мый.
irreparable *adj.* непоправи́мый; невозвра́тный; невознагради́мый. *Irreparable damage,* непоправи́мый уще́рб. *Irreparable loss,* невозвра́тная/невознагради́мая поте́ря *or* утра́та.
irreplaceable *adj.* незамени́мый.
irrepressible *adj.* **1,** (impossible to hold back) неудержи́мый. **2,** (impossible to discourage) неугомо́нный.
irreproachable *adj.* безукори́зненный; безупре́чный.
irresistible *adj.* неотрази́мый; непреодоли́мый. —**irresistibility,** *n.* неотрази́мость.
irresolute *adj.* нереши́тельный.
irrespective *adj., in* **irrespective of,** незави́симо от; безотноси́тельно к.
irresponsible *adj.* безотве́тственный. —**irresponsibility,** *n.* безотве́тственность.
irretrievable *adj.* непоправи́мый; невозвра́тный.
irreverence *n.* непочте́ние. —**irreverent,** *adj.* непочти́тельный.
irreversible *adj.* необрати́мый.
irrevocable *adj.* бесповоро́тный.
irrigate *v.t.* ороша́ть. —**irrigation,** *n.* ороше́ние; ирригáция.
irritable *adj.* раздражи́тельный. —**irritability,** *n.* раздражи́тельность.
irritant *n.* раздражи́тель.
irritate *v.t.* раздража́ть. —**irritation,** *n.* раздраже́ние.

is *v. see* **be.**
isinglass *n.* **1,** (gelatin) рыбий клей. **2,** (mica) слюда́.
Islam *n.* исла́м. —**Islamic,** *adj.* мусульма́нский.
island *n.* о́стров. —**islander,** *n.* островитя́нин.
isle *n.* острово́к.
isobar *n.* изоба́ра.
isolate *v.t.* изоли́ровать; обособля́ть. —**isolated,** *adj.* изоли́рованный; обосо́бленный. *Isolated cases,* едини́чные слу́чаи.
isolation *n.* изоля́ция; обособле́ние. —**isolation ward,** изоля́тор.
isolationism *n.* изоляциони́зм.
isolationist *n.* изоляциони́ст. —*adj.* изоляциони́стский.
isomer *n.* изоме́р.
isosceles *adj.* равнобе́дренный.
isotope *n.* изото́п.
Israeli *adj.* изра́ильский. —*n.* израильтя́нин; израильтя́нка.
issuance *n.* **1,** (handing out) вы́дача. **2,** (putting out) вы́пуск. **3,** (promulgation) изда́ние.
issue *n.* **1,** = **issuance. 2,** (something issued, as of bonds, stamps, etc.) вы́пуск. **3,** (single number of a periodical) но́мер. **4,** (point in question) вопро́с. *At issue,* под вопро́сом. **5,** (progeny) пото́мки; пото́мство. —*v.t.* **1,** (give; grant; hand out) выдава́ть: *issue a visa,* выдава́ть ви́зу. **2,** (put out, as stamps, money, etc.) выпуска́ть. **3,** (promulgate, as an order) издава́ть. *Issue an ultimatum,* предъяви́ть ультима́тум. —*v.i.* исходи́ть; вытека́ть. —**take issue with,** оспа́ривать.
isthmus *n.* переше́ек.
it *pron.* **1,** *pers.* он; она́; оно́: *I don't know how good it is,* я не зна́ю наско́лько он хоро́ш. *Where did you put it?,* куда́ вы его́ положи́ли? ♦ *Frequently omitted in Russian: give it to me,* да́йте мне. *Did you find it?,* нашли́? *Would you like to see it?,* хоти́те посмотре́ть? **2,** *indef.* э́то: *it is I,* э́то я. *I already knew about it,* я уже́ знал об э́том. **3,** *impers.: it seems,* ка́жется. *It is raining,* идёт дождь. *It is cold,* хо́лодно. *It's hard to say,* тру́дно сказа́ть. *It's time to go,* пора́ идти́.
Italian *adj.* италья́нский. —*n.* **1,** (person) италья́нец; италья́нка. **2,** (language) италья́нский язы́к. *Speak Italian,* говори́ть по-италья́нски.
italic *n., usu. pl.* курси́в; курси́вный шрифт. *In italics,* курси́вом. —*adj.* курси́вный. —**italicize,** *v.t.* выделя́ть курси́вом.
itch *n.* зуд. —*v.i.* **1,** (have or produce an itch) чеса́ться; зуде́ть. **2,** (cause itching, as of rough material) шерсти́ть. **3,** (have an urge): *I am itching to* (+ *inf.*), у меня́ ру́ки че́шутся *or* зудя́т; мне не те́рпится; меня́ так и подмыва́ет.
itchy *adj.* зудя́щий; колю́чий.
item *n.* **1,** (article) предме́т. **2,** (unit) статья́: *item of export/expense,* статья́ э́кспорта/расхо́да. **3,** (on an agenda) пункт; вопро́с. **4,** (in a newspaper) заме́тка; сообще́ние. **5,** (on a program) но́мер.
itemize *v.t.* перечисля́ть по пу́нктам; ука́зывать в отде́льности.
itinerant *adj.* стра́нствующий; бродя́чий
itinerary *n.* маршру́т.
its *poss.adj.* **1,** (its own) свой. **2,** (something else's) его́; её.
itself *pron.* **1,** *used for emphasis* сам: *the room itself was not large,* сама́ ко́мната была́ небольша́я. **2,** *used reflexively* себя́; сам себя́: *it speaks for itself,* э́то говори́т само́ за себя́. *Right itself,* поправля́ться. *Reveal itself,* обнару́живаться.
ivory *n.* слоно́вая кость.
ivy *n.* плющ.

J

J, j деся́тая бу́ква англи́йского алфави́та.
jab *v.t. & i.* ты́кать. —*n.* тычо́к.
jabber *v.i.* болта́ть; тарато́рить.
jack *n.* **1,** (lever) домкра́т. **2,** (socket) гнездо́. **3,** *cards* вале́т. —*v.t.* [*usu.* **jack up**] **1,** (hoist with a jack) поднима́ть домкра́том. **2,** (raise, as prices) набива́ть; взви́нчивать.
jackal *n.* шака́л.
jackass *n.* осёл.
jackdaw *n.* га́лка.
jacket *n.* **1,** (man's sport coat) пиджа́к. **2,** (man's outer garment, as a lumberjacket) ку́ртка. **3,** (woman's garment) жаке́т; ко́фта. **4,** (casing; covering) кожу́х. **5,** (dust jacket) супероблóжка. **6,** (skin of a potato) кожура́. *Potatoes boiled in their jackets,* карто́фель в мунди́ре.
jackhammer *n.* пневмати́ческий отбо́йный молото́к.
jack-of-all-trades *n.* ма́стер на все ру́ки.
jackpot *n.* банк. —**hit the jackpot,** сорва́ть банк.
jack rabbit за́яц.
jacksnipe *n.* га́ршнеп.
jackstraws *n. pl.* бирю́льки.
jade *n.* **1,** (mineral) нефри́т. **2,** (old horse) кля́ча; одёр.
jaded *adj.* **1,** (worn out) изму́ченный. **2,** (satiated) пресы́щенный.
jag *n.* зубе́ц.
jagged *adj.* зубча́тый; зазу́бренный. *Jagged coastline,* изре́занный бе́рег.
jaguar *n.* ягуа́р.
jail *n.* тюрьма́. —*adj.* тюре́мный: *jail term,* срок

тюре́много заключе́ния. —*v.t.* посади́ть в тюрьму́.
jailbreak *n.* побе́г *or* бе́гство из тюрьмы́.
jailer *also,* **jailor** *n.* тюре́мщик.
jalopy *n.* драндуле́т; колыма́га.
jalousie *n.* жалюзи́.
jam *v.t.* **1,** (force; wedge) впи́хивать; вкли́нивать. **2,** (catch, as one's fingers in a door) защемля́ть; ущемля́ть; прищемля́ть. **3,** (cause to become unworkable) заклинивать. **4,** (crowd; pack) запру́живать: *people jammed the streets,* лю́ди запруди́ли у́лицы. *The aisles were jammed,* прохо́ды бы́ли заби́ты. *The place was jammed,* наро́ду бы́ло битко́м наби́то. **5,** (interfere with, as a broadcast) глуши́ть; заглуша́ть. **6,** *Jam on the brakes,* ре́зко затормози́ть. —*v.i.* **1,** (fail to operate; stick) заеда́ть *(impers.): the wheels jammed,* колёса зае́ло. **2,** (crowd) набива́ться: *jam into the elevator,* набива́ться в ли́фте. —*n.* **1,** (congestion) зато́р: *traffic jam,* зато́р у́личного движе́ния; про́бка. **2,** (fruit preserve) варе́нье; джем; пови́дло. **3,** *colloq.* (predicament) переде́лка; переплёт.
jamb *n.* костя́к.
jangle *v.i.* звя́кать. —*v.t.* **1,** (cause to jangle) звя́кать (+ *instr.*). **2,** (irritate, as nerves) трепа́ть (не́рвы). —*n.* звя́канье.
janitor *n.* убо́рщик.
January *n.* янва́рь. —*adj.* янва́рский.
Japanese *adj.* япо́нский. *He (she) is Japanese,* он япо́нец; она́ япо́нка. —*n.* **1,** (language) япо́нский язы́к. *Speak Japanese,* говори́ть по-япо́нски. **2,** *preceded by* **the** (people) япо́нцы.
jar *n.* **1,** (container) ба́нка. **2,** (jolt) толчо́к. —*v.t.* потряса́ть. —*v.i.* **1,** *fol. by* **on** (grate on) коро́бить. **2,** *fol. by* **with** (clash) дисгармони́ровать (с).
jargon *n.* жарго́н.
jasmine *n.* жасми́н. —*adj.* жасми́нный; жасми́новый.
jasper *n.* я́шма. —*adj.* я́шмовый.
jaundice *n.* желту́ха.
jaundiced *adj.* **1,** (having jaundice) поражённый желту́хой. **2,** (prejudiced) предвзя́тый; предубеждённый.
jaunt *n.* прогу́лка.
jaunty *adj.* **1,** (sprightly) бо́йкий; задо́рный. **2,** (stylish) мо́дный; шика́рный.
javelin *n.* копьё; дро́тик. —**javelin throw,** мета́ние копья́.
jaw *n.* че́люсть. *In the jaws of death,* в когтя́х сме́рти.
jawbone *n.* че́люсть; челюстна́я кость.
jay *n.* со́йка.
jazz *n.* джаз. —*adj.* джа́зовый.
jealous *adj.* ревни́вый. *Be jealous of,* ревнова́ть; зави́довать. —**jealously,** *adv.* ревни́во.
jealousy *n.* ре́вность.
jeans *n.pl.* джи́нсы.
jeep *n.* джип; ви́ллис.
jeer *v.t.* издева́ться над; насмеха́ться над. —*v.i.* издева́тельски крича́ть. —*n.* издёвка.
jejune *adj.* сухо́й; бесцве́тный.
jell *v.i.* **1,** (congeal) застыва́ть. **2,** *fig.* (take definite form) определя́ться.
jelly *n.* желе́.
jellyfish *n.* меду́за.
jeopardize *v.t.* ста́вить под угро́зу.
jeopardy *n.* опа́сность. *Be in jeopardy,* находи́ться под угро́зой. *Place in jeopardy,* ста́вить под угро́зу.
jerboa *n.* тушка́нчик.
jerk *v.t.* дёргать. —*v.i.* дёрнуться. —*n.* **1,** (tug) рыво́к. **2,** *slang* (dope) болва́н.
jerky *adj.* поры́вистый.
jersey *n.* фуфа́йка.
jest *n.* шу́тка: *in jest,* в шу́тку. —*v.i.* шути́ть.
jester *n.* шут: *court jester,* придво́рный шут.
Jesuit *n.* иезуи́т. —*adj.* иезуи́тский.
Jesus *n.* Иису́с.
jet *n.* **1,** (spurt; gush) струя́. **2,** (spout; nozzle) жиклёр. **3,** (mineral) гага́т. **4,** (plane) реакти́вный самолёт. —*adj.* реакти́вный: *jet propulsion,* реакти́вное движе́ние. —*v.i.* бить струёй.
jet-black *adj.* чёрный как смоль.
jet-propelled *adj.* реакти́вный.
jet stream стру́йное тече́ние.
jettison *v.t.* выбра́сывать за́ борт.
jetty *n.* **1,** (breakwater) мол. **2,** (wharf) при́стань.
Jew *n.* евре́й.
jewel *n.* драгоце́нный ка́мень; драгоце́нность.
jeweler *also,* **jeweller** *n.* ювели́р.
jewelry *also.* **jewellery** *n.* драгоце́нности. *Jewelry store,* ювели́рный магази́н.
Jewish *adj.* евре́йский. —**Jewry,** *n.* евре́йство.
jib *n.* **1,** (sail) кли́вер. **2,** (boom of a derrick) стрела́.
jib boom утле́гарь.
jibe *v.i.* **1,** = **gibe. 2,** *colloq.* (agree; square) сходи́ться.
jiffy *n., colloq.* миг; мгнове́ние. *In a jiffy,* ми́гом; в два счёта.
jig *n.* джи́га: *dance a jig,* танцева́ть джи́гу. —**in jig time,** *colloq.* в два счёта. —**the jig is up,** *colloq.* игра́ ко́нчена.
jigger *n.* рю́мочка.
jiggle *v.t.* шевели́ть.
jigsaw puzzle составна́я карти́нка.
jilt *v.t.* броса́ть; оставля́ть.
jimmy *n.* отмы́чка; воровско́й лом. —*v.t.* [*usu.* **jimmy open**] взла́мывать.
jimsonweed *n.* дурма́н.
jingle *v.t. & i.* звене́ть. —*n.* **1,** (sound) звон. **2,** (humorous verse) частушка.
jinks *n.pl.* [*usu.* **high jinks**] шу́мное весе́лье.
jinx *n., colloq.* дурно́й глаз. —*v.t.* сгла́зить.
jitters *n.pl., colloq.* не́рвность. *Have the jitters,* не́рвничать. —**jittery,** *adj., colloq.* не́рвный.
job *n.* **1,** (piece of work) рабо́та; труд. *Odd jobs,* случа́йная рабо́та. *By the job,* сде́льно; поуро́чно. **2,** (position of employment) рабо́та; слу́жба; ме́сто. *Change jobs,* меня́ть рабо́ту. *Soft job,* тёплое месте́чко. **3,** (task; chore) рабо́та; зада́ние. —**give up as a bad job,** *colloq.* махну́ть руко́й на (+ *acc.*); поста́вить крест на (+ *acc. or prepl.*). —**lie down on the job,** *colloq.* рабо́тать спустя́ рукава́. —**on the job, 1,** (at work) на слу́жбе. **2,** (while at work) в рабо́чем поря́дке.
jobber *n.* оптови́к; торго́вый посре́дник.
jobless *adj.* безрабо́тный.
jockey *n.* жоке́й.
jocose *adj.* шутли́вый; игри́вый.
jocular *adj.* шутли́вый; шу́точный.
jocund *adj.* весёлый.
jog *v.i.* **1,** (of a person) бе́гать. **2,** (of a horse) идти́

трусцóй; трусить. —*v.t.* (nudge) подтáлкивать. —**jogger**, *n.* бегýн.

join *v.t.* **1,** (bring together; link; unite) соединя́ть; свя́зывать. *Join hands,* брáться зá руки. *Join forces,* соединя́ть *or* объединя́ть си́лы. **2,** (attach) присоединя́ть. **3,** (meet and accompany) присоединя́ться к. *Join the crowd,* присоединя́ться *or* примыкáть к толпé. **4,** (become a member of) вступáть в: *join the party,* вступи́ть в пáртию. **5,** (enlist in, as a branch of military service) поступáть в *or* на. **6,** (enroll in, as a library) запи́сываться в. **7,** (connect with) соединя́ться с. —*v.i.* **1,** (come together) соединя́ться; сходи́ться. **2,** (become a member) присоединя́ться. **3,** *fol. by* **in** (take part with others) присоединя́ться. *Join in the conversation,* вступи́ть в разговóр. *Join in singing,* подхвáтывать пéсню; подпевáть. **4,** *fol. by* **up** (enlist) поступáть на воéнную слýжбу.

joiner *n.* (carpenter) столя́р.

joint *n.* **1,** *anat.* сустáв. **2,** (juncture, as of two pipes) стык. **3,** (coupling) шарни́р: *universal joint,* универсáльный шарни́р. **4,** *slang* (cheap restaurant) кабачóк. —*adj.* **1,** (done or executed in common) совмéстный. **2,** (shared with another) óбщий; со—: *joint account,* óбщий счёт; *joint owner,* совладéлец. —**out of joint,** вы́вихнутый.

jointly *adv.* совмéстно; сообщá.

joint-stock company акционéрное óбщество.

joke *n.* шýтка; острóта. *Practical joke,* мистификáция. —*v.i.* шути́ть: *you're joking!,* вы шýтите! *Joking aside,* шýтки в стóрону.

joker *n.* **1,** (one who jokes) шутни́к. **2,** *cards* джóкер.

jokester *n.* шутни́к.

jokingly *adv.* шутя́; в шýтку.

jolly *adj.* весёлый. —*adv., Brit., colloq.* óчень.

jolt *n.* толчóк. —*v.t.* трясти́; встря́хивать.

jonquil *n.* жонки́ль.

Jordanian *adj.* иордáнский.

josh *v.i., colloq.* шути́ть.

jostle *v.t.* толкáть; пихáть. —*v.i.* толкáться.

jot *v.t.* [*usu.* **jot down**] запи́сывать; набрáсывать.

joule *n.* джóуль.

journal *n.* **1,** (daily record) дневни́к. **2,** (publication) газéта; журнáл.

journalism *n.* журнали́стика. —**journalist,** *n.* журнали́ст. —**journalistic,** *adj.* журнали́стский.

journey *n.* поéздка; путешéствие. —*v.i.* путешéствовать.

joust *n.* ры́царский поеди́нок. —*v.i.* би́ться на поеди́нке.

jovial *adj.* весёлый. —**joviality,** *n.* весёлость.

jowl *n.* **1,** (jaw) чéлюсть. **2,** (cheek) щекá. **3,** (dewlap of cattle) подгрýдок.

joy *n.* рáдость; отрáда. —**joyful,** *adj.* рáдостный. —**joyless,** *adj.* безрáдостный. —**joyous,** *adj.* рáдостный.

jubilant *adj.* ликýющий. —**jubilation,** *n.* ликовáние.

jubilee *n.* юбилéй.

Judaic *adj.* иудéйский.

Judaism *n.* иудаи́зм; иудéйство.

Judas *n.* Иýда.

judge *n.* **1,** (one who judges; magistrate) судья́. **2,** (connoisseur) цени́тель; знатóк. *Be a good judge of,* быть знатокóм (+ *gen.*); знать толк в. *I am no judge of such matters,* я не судья́ в э́том дéле. —*v.t. & i.* суди́ть. *Judging by,* сýдя по. *Judge for yourself,* посуди́те сáми.

judgment *n.* **1,** (legal decision) решéние: *pronounce judgment,* выноси́ть решéние; *defer judgment,* откла́дывать решéние. *Pass judgment on,* суди́ть. **2,** (faculty of judging wisely) рассуди́тельность; благоразýмие. *Show good judgment,* суди́ть здрáво. **3,** (opinion) мнéние; взгляд; суждéние. *In my judgment,* на мой взгляд. —**Judgment Day,** Сýдный день; Стрáшный суд.

judicial *adj.* судéбный; юриди́ческий.

judiciary *adj.* судéбный; юриди́ческий. —*n.* судоустрóйство.

judicious *adj.* благоразýмный; рассуди́тельный. —**judiciously,** *adv.* благоразýмно.

judo *n.* дзюдó.

jug *n.* **1,** (vessel) кувши́н; жбан. **2,** *slang* (jail) кутýзка.

juggle *v.t.* **1,** (toss and catch) жонгли́ровать. **2,** *fig.* (manipulate, as facts) подтасóвывать; жонгли́ровать; передёргивать. —**juggler,** *n.* жонглёр. —**juggling,** *n.* жонглёрство.

jugular vein ярéмная вéна.

juice *n.* сок. —**juicer,** *n.* соковыжимáлка.

juicy *adj.* сóчный. —**juiciness,** *n.* сóчность.

jujitsu *n.* джи́у-джи́тсу; япóнская борьбá.

Julian calendar юлиáнский календáрь.

July *n.* ию́ль. —*adj.* ию́льский.

jumble *v.t.* пýтать; перепýтывать. —*n.* пýтаница.

jumbo *adj.* большóй; гигáнтский.

jump *v.i.* **1,** (leap) пры́гать; скакáть. *Jump to one's feet,* вскочи́ть нá ноги. **2,** (start in astonishment) вздрáгивать. **3,** (rise abruptly in amount) подскáкивать. **4,** *in* **jump to a conclusion,** поспеши́ть с вы́водом. —*v.t.* **1,** (jump over) перепры́гивать. *Jump rope,* пры́гать чéрез скакáлку. **2,** (leave, as a track) сходи́ть с (рéльсов). **3,** *colloq.* (attack suddenly) набрáсываться на. —*n.* прыжóк; скачóк. —**jump at,** ухвати́ться за. —**jump into,** впры́гивать в; вскáкивать в. —**jump off,** спры́гивать; соскáкивать. —**jump on, 1,** (board quickly) вскочи́ть в. **2,** *colloq.* (rebuke; assail) набрáсываться на. —**jump out of,** выпры́гивать из; выбрáсываться из; выскáкивать из. *Jump out of bed,* вскочи́ть *or* соскочи́ть с постéли. —**jump over,** перепры́гивать; перескáкивать. —**jump up,** вскáкивать.

jumper *n.* **1,** (one who jumps) прыгýн. **2,** (dress) плáтье (без рукавóв). **3,** (loose smock) блýза.

jump rope скакáлка.

jumpy *adj.* нéрвный.

junction *n.* **1,** (of roads) ýзел; перекрёсток. *Railway junction,* железнодорóжный ýзел. **2,** (of rivers) слия́ние.

juncture *n.* **1,** (joint) соединéние. **2,** (point in time) момéнт: *at this juncture,* в э́тот момéнт.

June *n.* ию́нь. —*adj.* ию́ньский.

jungle *n.* джýнгли. —**jungle fever,** тропи́ческая лихорáдка; тропи́ческая маляри́я.

junior *adj.* млáдший: *junior partner,* млáдший партнёр. *John Smith, Jr.,* Джон Смит млáдший. —*n.* **1,** (younger person): *he is ten years my junior,* он molóже меня́ на дéсять лет. **2,** (third-year student) студéнт трéтьего кýрса.

juniper *n.* можжевéльник.

junk *n.* **1,** (rubbish; trash) старьё; ру́хлядь. *Junk dealer,* старьёвщик. **2,** (boat) джо́нка.
Junker *n.* ю́нкер.
junket *n.* моло́чный кисе́ль.
junkman *n.* старьёвщик.
junta *n.* ху́нта.
Jupiter *n.* Юпи́тер.
Jurassic *adj.* ю́рский.
juridical *adj.* юриди́ческий.
jurisdiction *n.* **1,** (right to exercise official authority) юрисди́кция. **2,** (domain over which such authority extends) ве́дение; компете́нция.
jurisprudence *n.* юриспруде́нция; законове́дение.
jurist *n.* юри́ст.
juror *n.* прися́жный.
jury *n.* **1,** (in a court of law) прися́жные. **2,** (in a contest) жюри́.
just *adj.* **1,** (fair; right; proper) справедли́вый: *just decision,* справедли́вое реше́ние; *just war,* справедли́вая война́. *Just cause,* пра́вое де́ло. **2,** (deserved) заслу́женный: *just reward,* заслу́женная награ́да. *Get one's just reward/deserts,* получи́ть по заслу́гам. **3,** (upright; righteous) пра́ведный. —*adv.* **1,** (precisely) как раз; и́менно. *Just in time,* как раз во́время. *Just what I need,* как раз то, что мне ну́жно. **2,** (barely) едва́. **3,** (merely) про́сто. **4,** (only a moment ago) то́лько что: *he just left,* он то́лько что ушёл. —*particle* то́лько: *just think!,* поду́мать то́лько! *Just you try!,* то́лько попро́буйте! *Just look at him!,* вы то́лько посмотри́те на него́! *Just what do you mean by that?,* что вы, со́бственно, хоти́те э́тим сказа́ть? —**just about, 1,** (almost; very nearly) почти́: *just about everything,* почти́ всё. **2,** (on the point of) вот–вот: *he is just about to leave,* он вот–вот уйдёт. *I was just about to call you,* я как раз собира́лся вам звони́ть. —**just a minute!,** одну́ мину́тку! —**just as, 1,** *with adjectives* сто́лько же. **2,** (at the moment when) в тот моме́нт, когда́... **3,** (in the same way that) подо́бно тому́, как... —**just as soon,** скоре́е. —**just as well,** с тем же успе́хом. *It's just as well,* ну что же. —**just in case,** на вся́кий слу́чай. —**just now, 1,** (at this instant) сейча́с. **2,** (a moment ago) то́лько сейча́с. —**just the same,** всё равно́.
justice *n.* **1,** (administration of law) правосу́дие; юсти́ция. **2,** (fairness) справедли́вость. **3,** (judge) судья́: *justice of the peace,* мирово́й судья́. *Supreme Court justice,* член верхо́вного суда́. —**bring to justice,** привлека́ть к отве́тственности. —**do justice (to),** отдава́ть до́лжное (+ *dat.*). *The picture doesn't do her justice,* фотогра́фия не де́лает ей комплиме́нта.
justifiable *adj.* зако́нный; позволи́тельный. —**justifiably,** *adv.* по пра́ву.
justification *n.* оправда́ние.
justify *v.t.* опра́вдывать.
justly *adv.* **1,** (fairly) справедли́во. **2,** (rightly; deservedly) по пра́ву.
jut *v.i.* [*usu.* **jut out**] выдава́ться; выступа́ть; торча́ть.
jute *n.* джут.
juvenile *adj.* ю́ный; ю́ношеский. —*n.* ю́ноша; подро́сток; малоле́тний. —**juvenile delinquency,** де́тская престу́пность.
juxtapose *v.t.* **1,** (place side by side) помеща́ть бок о́ бок. **2,** (contrast) сопоставля́ть.

K

K, k оди́ннадцатая бу́ква англи́йского алфави́та.
Kaiser *n.* ка́йзер.
kaleidoscope *n.* калейдоско́п. —**kaleidoscopic,** *adj.* калейдоскопи́ческий.
kangaroo *n.* кенгуру́.
kaolin *n.* каоли́н.
kapok *n.* капо́к.
karakul *n.* = **caracul.**
karat *n.* **1,** (24th part of pure gold) про́ба. ♦ *The Russian system, however, is based on 96: 18-karat gold,* зо́лото се́мьдесят второ́й про́бы. **2,** = **carat.**
kasha *n.* ка́ша.
kayak *n.* байда́рка; кая́к.
keel *n.* киль. —*v.i.* [*usu.* **keel over**] **1,** (capsize) опроки́дываться. **2,** (faint away) упа́сть без чувств. —**be on an even keel,** идти́ ро́вным ку́рсом; приде́рживаться ро́вного ку́рса.
keen *adj.* **1,** (sharp; acute) о́стрый. **2,** (sensitive; perceptive) о́стрый; чу́ткий; ме́ткий; то́нкий. **3,** (avid; enthusiastic) стра́стный. *Be keen on,* увлека́ться (+ *instr.*). —**keenness,** *n.* острота́; чу́ткость; ме́ткость; то́нкость.
keep *v.t.* **1,** (hold in a specified place or state) держа́ть; храни́ть. *Keep one's hands in one's pockets,* держа́ть ру́ки в карма́нах. *Keep money in the bank,* держа́ть/храни́ть де́ньги в ба́нке. *Keep something secret,* храни́ть/держа́ть что́-нибудь в секре́те *or* в та́йне. **2,** (retain for oneself) сохраня́ть; оставля́ть; уде́рживать. **3,** (maintain; preserve) сохраня́ть: *keep order,* сохраня́ть поря́док. *Keep watch,* сторожи́ть. *Keep a secret,* храни́ть/сохраня́ть секре́т *or* та́йну. *Keep in mind,* име́ть в виду́. *Keep one's seat,* остава́ться сиде́ть. *Keep one's feet,* уде́рживаться на нога́х. **4,** (maintain at home) держа́ть: *keep a dog,* держа́ть соба́ку; *keep servants,* держа́ть прислу́гу. **5,** (carry out; fulfill) сдержа́ть: *keep one's word,* сдержа́ть

своё сло́во; *keep a promise,* сдержа́ть обеща́ние. **6,** (observe) соблюда́ть: *keep the laws,* соблюда́ть зако́н. *Keep an appointment,* прийти́ на свида́ние. **7,** (maintain; perform) вести́: *keep score,* вести́ счёт; *keep a diary,* вести́ дневни́к; *keep the books,* вести́ кни́ги; *keep count of,* вести́ счёт (+ *dat.*); *keep house,* вести́ (дома́шнее) хозя́йство. *Keep company with,* води́ть компа́нию с. **8,** (delay) заде́рживать. *Keep someone waiting,* заставля́ть кого́-нибудь ждать. **9,** *fol. by* **from** (prevent) уде́рживать (от). *Keep from laughing,* удержа́ться от сме́ха. *—v.i.* **1,** (persist; continue) продолжа́ть. *Prices keep going up,* це́ны всё расту́т. *I kept imagining that...,* мне всё каза́лось, что... **2,** (remain) держа́ться: *keep to the right,* держа́ться пра́вой стороны́. *Keep to oneself,* держа́ться особняко́м. *Keep away,* держа́ться на расстоя́нии; не подходи́ть. *Keep off the grass!,* по траве́ не ходи́ть! *Keep quiet,* молча́ть. *Keep warm,* гре́ться. **3,** (not spoil) сохраня́ться. *—n.* **1,** (livelihood; support) содержа́ние. **2,** (stronghold of a castle) гла́вная ба́шня (за́мка). —**for keeps,** навсегда́. —**keep back, 1,** (hold back) уде́рживать. **2,** (not move forward) держа́ться сза́ди. *Keep back!,* наза́д! —**keep on, 1,** (continue) продолжа́ть; не перестава́ть. **2,** (not remove) не снима́ть. —**keep out, 1,** (not let in) не пуска́ть; не пропуска́ть. **2,** (stay outside) не входи́ть. *Keep out!,* вход воспрещён! **3,** *fol. by* **of** (steer clear of) держа́ться в стороне́ (от). —**keep up, 1,** (maintain) подде́рживать: *keep up a correspondence,* подде́рживать перепи́ску. **2,** (maintain the pace) идти́ в но́гу; не отстава́ть. **3,** (continue; not cease) продолжа́ться. **4,** (prevent from sleeping) не дава́ть спать. —**keep up with,** идти́ в но́гу с; не отстава́ть от; поспева́ть за; угна́ться за.

keeper *n.* храни́тель. *Lighthouse keeper,* смотри́тель маяка́.

keeping *n.* хране́ние. —**in keeping with,** соотве́тствующий (+ *dat.*); сообра́зный с.

keepsake *n.* пода́рок на па́мять.

keg *n.* бочо́нок. —**powder keg,** порохова́я бо́чка; порохово́й по́греб.

ken *n.* круг позна́ний. *Beyond one's ken,* вы́ше чьего́-либо понима́ния.

kennel *n.* конура́.

kept woman содержа́нка; коко́тка.

kerchief *n.* плато́к; косы́нка.

kernel *n.* **1,** (grain or seed) зерно́. **2,** (edible part of a nut) ядро́. **3,** *in* **kernel of truth,** зерно́ и́стины.

kerosene *n.* кероси́н. *—adj.* кероси́новый.

kestrel *n.* пустельга́.

ketchup *n.* тома́тный со́ус.

kettle *n.* **1,** (teakettle) ча́йник. **2,** (pot) котело́к. —**kettle of fish,** исто́рия: *that's a pretty kettle of fish!,* вот так исто́рия!

kettledrum *n.* лита́вра.

key *n.* **1,** (for a lock) ключ. **2,** (of a piano, typewriter, etc.) кла́виша. **3,** (code; solution) ключ. **4,** (explanatory table) ключ. **5,** *fig.* (vital element) зало́г: *the key to his success,* зало́г его́ успе́хов. **6,** *music* тона́льность; лад. *Key of B flat,* тона́льность си бемо́ль. *Sing off key,* петь не в тон *or* фальши́во; фальши́вить. **7,** (tone; style; mood) тон. *—adj.* ключево́й; веду́щий. *Key role,* важне́йшая роль. *Key question,* узлово́й *or* стержнево́й вопро́с. *—v.t.* **1,** (adapt) приспособля́ть. **2,** *fol. by* **up** (arouse) взви́нчивать: *keyed up,* взви́нченный.

keyboard *n.* клавиату́ра.

keyhole *n.* замо́чная сква́жина.

key ring кольцо́ для ключе́й.

khaki *n.* защи́тный цвет; ха́ки. —**khaki-colored,** *adj.* защи́тного цве́та; цве́та ха́ки.

khan *n.* хан. —**khanate,** *n.* ха́нство.

kibitzer *n.* непро́шеный зри́тель.

kick *v.t.* **1,** (strike with the foot) ударя́ть ного́й; дава́ть пинка́ (+ *dat.*); пина́ть. **2,** (propel with the foot, as a ball) поддава́ть (ного́й). **3,** *sports* (score, as a goal) забива́ть (гол). **4,** *slang* (overcome, as a habit) избавля́ться от (привы́чки). *—v.i.* **1,** (of a person, esp. a child) дры́гать нога́ми. **2,** (of a horse) брыка́ть(ся); ляга́ть(ся). **3,** *colloq.* (complain; grumble) ворча́ть. *—n.* **1,** (blow with the foot) пино́к. **2,** *sports* уда́р: *free kick,* свобо́дный уда́р. **3,** (recoil of a firearm) отда́ча. **4,** *colloq.* (complaint) жа́лоба. —**kick out,** выгоня́ть; вышиба́ть. —**kick up,** поднима́ть: *kick up dust,* поднима́ть пыль; *kick up a fuss,* поднима́ть шум.

kid *n.* **1,** (young goat) козлёнок. **2,** (leather) ла́йка; шевро́. **3,** *colloq.* (child) ребёнок; малы́ш. *—adj.* **1,** (made of kidskin) ла́йковый; шевро́вый. **2,** *colloq.* (younger) мла́дший. *—v.t., colloq.* **1,** (try to fool) шути́ть с. **2,** (tease) дразни́ть. *—v.i., colloq.* шути́ть: *you're kidding!,* вы шу́тите! —**treat with kid gloves,** делика́тничать с.

kidder *n.* зубоска́л.

kidnap *v.t.* похища́ть. —**kidnaper,** *n.* похити́тель. —**kidnaping,** *n.* похище́ние.

kidney *n.* по́чка. —**kidney bean,** фасо́ль. —**kidney stones,** по́чечные ка́мни.

kidskin *n.* ла́йка; шевро́. *—adj.* ла́йковый; шевро́вый.

kill *v.t.* убива́ть. *Be killed,* поги́бнуть. *Thou shalt not kill,* не убий. *Kill cockroaches,* трави́ть телака́нов. *Kill time,* убива́ть вре́мя. *Kill a bill,* провали́ть законопрое́кт. *Kill one's hopes,* убива́ть наде́жды. *Frost killed the flowers,* моро́з погуби́л цветы́. *My feet are killing me,* у меня́ стра́шно боля́т но́ги. —**kill two birds with one stone,** уби́ть двух за́йцев одни́м уда́ром.

killer *n.* уби́йца. —**killer whale,** коса́тка.

killing *n.* **1,** (murder) уби́йство. **2,** *colloq.* (sudden large profit) куш. *—adj.* уби́йственный.

kiln *n.* обжига́тельная печь.

kilocycle *n.* килоге́рц.

kilogram *also,* **kilogramme** *n.* килогра́мм.

kilometer *also,* **kilometre** *n.* киломе́тр.

kiloton *n.* килото́нна.

kilowatt *n.* килова́тт. —**kilowatt-hour,** *n.* килова́тт-ча́с.

kilt *n.* шотла́ндская ю́бочка.

kilter *n., in* **out of kilter,** не в поря́дке.

kimono *n.* кимоно́.

kin *n.* родня́; родны́е; ро́дственники. —**next of kin,** ближа́йшие ро́дственники.

kind *n.* род; вид; сорт. *All kinds of,* вся́кого ро́да (+ *nom.*). *A mandarin is a kind of orange,* мандари́н — вид апельси́на. *The first such book of its kind,* пе́рвая тако́го ро́да кни́га. *What kind of books do you like best?,* каки́е кни́ги вы лю́бите бо́льше всего́? *What kind of person is he?,* что он за челове́к? *Something of the kind,* что́-то вро́де э́того. *Nothing of the kind,* ничего́ подо́бного. *—adj.* **1,** (kindly) до́брый: *kind* *man,* добрый человек. *Kind heart/face,* доброе сердце/лицо. **2,** (considerate) любезный; милый: *very kind of you,* очень любезно/мило с вашей стороны. **3,** (cordial) сердечный: *(with) kind regards,* с сердечным приветом. —**be so kind as to...,** будьте добры *or* любезны (+ *imperative*). —**in kind, 1,** (in goods) натурой. **2,** (in like manner) той же монетой. —**kind of,** *colloq.* как-то: *he is acting kind of strange,* он ведёт себя как-то странно.

kindergarten *n.* детский сад.

kindhearted *adj.* добросердечный; отзывчивый. —**kindheartedness,** *n.* добросердечие; отзывчивость.

kindle *v.t.* разжигать; зажигать.

kindling *n.* **1,** (act of kindling) разжигание. **2,** (kindling wood) растопка.

kindly *adj.* добрый; добродушный. —*adv.* **1,** (out of kindness) любезно. **2,** (cordially; warmly) добродушно. **3,** (please) будьте добры. —**take kindly to,** относиться благосклонно к.

kindness *n.* **1,** (quality of being kind) доброта. **2,** (kind act; favor) любезность. **3,** (solicitude) внимание.

kindred *adj.* родственный.

kinescope *n.* кинескоп.

kinetic *adj.* кинетический. —**kinetic energy,** кинетическая энергия; живая сила.

kinetics *n.* кинетика.

kinfolk *n.pl.* родные; родня.

king *n.* **1,** (sovereign) король. **2,** (most powerful creature) царь: *the king of beasts/birds,* царь зверей/птиц. **3,** (tycoon) король: *oil king,* нефтяной король. **4,** *cards; chess* король. **5,** *checkers* дамка. —*adj.* [*usu.* **king's**] королевский. *King's bishop, chess* королевский слон. —**live like a king,** жить барином.

kingbolt *n.* шкворень.

kingdom *n.* **1,** (monarchy) королевство: *United Kingdom,* Соединённое Королевство. **2,** *fig.* (realm) царство: *animal kingdom,* животное царство.

kingfisher *n.* зимородок.

kinglet *n.* (bird) королёк.

kingly *adj.* королевский; царственный.

kingpin *n.* **1,** = **kingbolt. 2,** *colloq.* (key figure) главарь.

kink *n.* **1,** (bend; loop; knot) загиб; петля; узел. **2,** (cramp; crick) судорога. —**kinky,** *adj.* кудрявый; курчавый.

kinsfolk *n.pl.* родные; родня.

kinship *n.* родство.

kinsman *n.* родственник.

kiosk *n.* киоск.

kipper *n.* копчёная селёдка.

kiss *v.t.* целовать. —*v.i.* (of two people) целоваться. —*n.* поцелуй.

kisser *n., slang* морда; рыло; харя.

kit *n.* **1,** (set of equipment) набор; комплект. *First-aid kit,* аптечка; *mil.* санитарная сумка. **2,** (container for same; case) сумка; ящик.

kitchen *n.* кухня. —*adj.* кухонный: *kitchen table,* кухонный стол.

kite *n.* **1,** (device that flies) змей. **2,** (bird) коршун.

kitten *n.* котёнок.

kittiwake *n.* моёвка.

kitty *n.* **1,** (kitten) котёнок; киска. **2,** *cards* банк.

kiwi *n.* киви-киви.

kleptomania *n.* клептомания. —**kleptomaniac,** *n.* клептоман.

knack *n.* сноровка. *Get the knack of,* приноравливаться к; наловчиться (+ *inf.*).

knapsack *n.* рюкзак; ранец; котомка; вещевой мешок.

knave *n.* **1,** (rascal) плут; мошенник. **2,** *cards* валет.

knead *v.t.* месить; замешивать.

knee *n.* колено. *On one's hands and knees,* на четвереньках. —*adj.* коленный: *knee joint,* коленный сустав. —**bring to one's knees,** ставить (кого-нибудь) на колени.

kneecap *n.* коленная чашка; коленная чашечка.

knee-deep *adj.* по колено; по колени.

kneel *v.i.* **1,** (assume a kneeling position) становиться на колени. **2,** (be in a kneeling position) стоять на коленях.

kneepad *n.* наколенник.

knell *n.* похоронный звон. —**sound the death knell for,** предвещать конец (+ *gen.*).

knickers *n.pl.* бриджи.

knickknack *n.* безделушка; вещица; финтифлюшка.

knife *n.* нож. —*adj.* ножевой: *knife wound,* ножевая рана. —*v.t.* резать *or* колоть ножом.

knight *n.* **1,** (medieval warrior) рыцарь. **2,** *chess* конь. —*v.t.* посвящать в рыцари. —**knight-errant,** *n.* странствующий рыцарь. —**knighthood,** *n.* рыцарство. —**knightly,** *adj.* рыцарский.

knit *v.t.* **1,** (weave) вязать. **2,** (contract, as one's eyebrows) хмурить; сдвинуть. —*v.i.* (grow together, as of bones) срастаться.

knitted *adj.* вязаный; трикотажный. *Knitted fabric,* трикотаж.

knitting *n.* вязание. —*adj.* вязальный. —**knitting kneedle,** (вязальная) спица; вязальная игла.

knob *n.* **1,** (handle of a door) (дверная) ручка. **2,** (lump; protuberance) шишка; бугор.

knock *v.i.* стучать (в дверь). —*v.t.* **1,** (hit; strike) ударять; бить; колотить. *Knock someone to the ground,* повалить кого-нибудь на землю. *Be knocked unconscious,* лишиться сознания. **2,** (bang) ударяться; стукаться: *knock heads,* стукнуться головами. *Knock one's head on the door,* удариться головой о дверь. **3,** (make by striking) пробивать: *knock a hole in the wall,* пробивать отверстие в стене. **4,** *colloq.* (criticize) придираться к. —*n.* **1,** (rap, as on a door) стук. **2,** (blow) удар. —**knock about,** *colloq.* слоняться; шататься. —**knock down,** сбивать с ног; валить; сваливать. —**knock loose,** расшатывать. —**knock off, 1,** (dislodge; topple) сбивать. **2,** *colloq.* (deduct) скидывать. **3,** *colloq.* (compose quickly; dash off) (на)строчить. **4,** *slang* (quit work) шабашить. —**knock out, 1,** (dislodge) выбивать. **2,** (exhaust completely) истомлять. **3,** *boxing* нокаутировать. **4,** *mil.* (destroy) выводить из строя; подбивать. —**knock over,** опрокидывать. —**knock together,** сколачивать; сбивать.

knockdown *n., boxing* нокдаун.

knocker *n.* дверной молоток.

knock-kneed *adj.* кривоногий.

knockout *n., boxing* нокаут.

knoll *n.* холмик; бугор; пригорок.

knot *n.* **1,** (in rope) узел. **2,** (in wood) сук; сучок. **3,** (nautical mile per hour) узел. —*v.t.* завязывать узлом.

knothole *n.* свищ.
knotted *adj.* **1,** (tied with a knot) завя́занный узло́м. **2,** (full of knots) узлова́тый.
knotty *adj.* **1,** (full of knots, as of wood) сучкова́тый. **2,** *fig.* (difficult; intricate) запу́танный.
knout *n.* кнут.
know *v.t. & i.* знать: *I don't know,* я не зна́ю. *Know what's what,* знать что к чему́. *As far as I know,* наско́лько я зна́ю. *For all one knows,* чего́ до́брого. *How should I know?,* отку́да же я зна́ю? *—n., in* **in the know,** в ку́рсе де́ла. **—know better,** знать: *I should have known better than to do that,* я до́лжен был знать, что не сле́дует де́лать э́того. **—know how,** уме́ть.
knowing *adj.* **1,** (knowledgeable; astute) зна́ющий; то́нкий. **2,** (of a smile, glance, etc.) многозначи́тельный.
knowingly *adv.* **1,** (deliberately) созна́тельно; наме́ренно; заве́домо. **2,** (as if having secret information) значи́тельно.
know-it-all *n., colloq.* всезна́йка.
knowledge *n.* зна́ние. *With/without the knowledge of,* с/без ве́дома (+ *gen.*). **—to (the best of) my knowledge,** наско́лько мне изве́стно.
knowledgeable *adj.* зна́ющий; све́дущий; гра́мотный; осведомлённый. **—knowledgeability,** *n.* зна́ния; гра́мотность; осведомлённость.
known *adj.* изве́стный: *a known fact,* изве́стный факт. *As is known,* как изве́стно. *It is known that...,* изве́стно, что... **—make known,** раскрыва́ть; разглаша́ть.
knuckle *n.* **1,** (joint of the finger) костя́шка. **2,** (animal joint used as food) но́жка. *—v.i.* **1,** *fol. by* **down** (apply oneself vigorously) запряга́ться. **2,** *fol. by* **under** (give in; yield) идти́ на пово́ду (у).
kohlrabi *n.* кольра́би.
kolinsky *n.* колоно́к.
kopeck *n.* копе́йка.
Koran *n.* кора́н.
Korean *adj.* коре́йский. *—n.* **1,** (person) коре́ец; корея́нка. **2,** (language) коре́йский язы́к.
kosher *adj.* коше́рный.
kowtow *v.i.* низкопокло́нничать; раболе́пствовать.
Kremlin *n.* кремль. *—adj.* кремлёвский. **—Kremlinologist,** *n.* советолог.
krypton *n.* крипто́н.
kulak *n.* кула́к.
Kurd *n.* курд. *The Kurds,* ку́рды. **—Kurdish,** *adj.* ку́рдский. *—n.* ку́рдский язы́к.

L

L, l двена́дцатая бу́ква англи́йского алфави́та.
la *n., music* ля.
label *n.* ярлы́к; этике́тка; би́рка. *—v.t.* накле́ивать ярлы́к на (*also fig.*).
labial *adj.* губно́й.
labor *also,* **labour** *n.* **1,** (work; toil) труд: *manual/child labor,* ручно́й/де́тский труд. *Capital and labor,* капита́л и труд. *Department of Labor,* министе́рство труда́. **2,** (trade unions) профсою́зы. **3,** (childbirth) ро́ды; родовы́е поту́ги. *Be in labor,* быть в ро́дах. *—v.i.* **1,** (toil) труди́ться. **2,** *fol. by* **under** (be afflicted with): *labor under a delusion,* быть в заблужде́нии. *—adj.* **1,** (pert. to work or workers) трудово́й: *labor laws,* трудово́е законода́тельство. **2,** (pert. to trade unions) профсою́зный: *the labor movement,* профсою́зное движе́ние. **3,** (pert. to childbirth) родово́й: *labor pains,* родовы́е поту́ги/схва́тки/му́ки.
laboratory *n.* лаборато́рия. *Language laboratory,* кабине́т иностра́нных языко́в. *—adj.* лаборато́рный: *laboratory experiments,* лаборато́рные о́пыты.
labored *also,* **laboured** *adj.* **1,** (done with difficulty) затруднённый. **2,** (ponderous) вы́мученный.
laborer *also,* **labourer** *n.* рабо́чий.
laborious *adj.* кропотли́вый.
labor union профсою́з.
labour *n. & v.* = **labor. —Labour,** *adj.* лейбори́стский: *Labour Party,* лейбори́стская па́ртия. **—Labourite,** *n.* лейбори́ст.
labyrinth *n.* лабири́нт.
lace *n.* **1,** (fabric) кру́жево. **2,** (cord, as for shoes) шнуро́к. *—adj.* кружевно́й. *—v.t.* шнурова́ть. *—v.i.* [*usu.* **lace into**] *colloq.* обру́шиваться на.
lacerate *v.t.* разрыва́ть; раздира́ть. **—laceration,** *n.* разры́в; рва́ная ра́на.
lachrymal *adj.* слёзный. **—lachrymose,** *adj.* слезли́вый.
lack *n.* **1,** (shortage) недоста́ток: *for lack of money,* за недоста́тком де́нег. **2,** (absence) отсу́тствие: *lack of ability,* отсу́тствие спосо́бностей. *For lack of evidence,* за неиме́нием ули́к. *—v.t.* **1,** (be without) не име́ть. *The building lacks an elevator,* в до́ме нет ли́фта. *Lacking the most basic conveniences,* лишённый элемента́рных удо́бств. **2,** (not have enough of) не хвата́ть (*impers.*); недостава́ть (*impers.*). *He lacks the strength to...,* ему́ не хвата́ет сил, что́бы... *—v.i.* не хвата́ть: *there is only one thing lacking,* одного́ то́лько не хвата́ет.
lackadaisical *adj.* хала́тный; неради́вый.
lackey *n.* лаке́й.
lackluster *also,* **lacklustre** *adj.* **1,** (lacking brightness) ту́склый. **2,** *fig.* (uninspired) пре́сный.
laconic *adj.* лакони́ческий; немногосло́вный.

lacquer *n.* лак. —*v.t.* лакировáть. —**lacquerware,** *n.* лакирóванные издéлия.
lacrosse *n.* лякрóсс.
lactation *n.* лактáция.
lacteal *adj.* молóчный.
lactic *adj.* молóчный. —**lactic acid,** молóчная кислотá.
lactose *n.* молóчный сáхар; лактóза.
lacuna *n.* пробéл; прóпуск.
lad *n.* пáрень; ю́ноша.
ladder *n.* лéстница.
laden *adj.* нагрýженный; перегрýженный.
ladies' man волокúта; ловелáс; бáбник. *Also,* **lady's man.**
ladies' room дáмская убóрная; дáмский туалéт.
ladle *n.* разливáтельная лóжка. —*v.t.* разливáть.
lady *n.* **1,** (woman) дáма. *Ladies and gentlemen,* дáмы и господá. **2,** (woman of rank or nobility) лéди. *The First Lady,* пéрвая лéди. —**lady of the house,** хозя́йка дóма.
ladybug *n.* бóжья корóвка. *Also,* **ladybird.**
lady in waiting фрéйлина.
lady-killer *n., colloq.* покорúтель сердéц; сердцеéд.
ladylike *adj.* жéнственный; воспúтанный; прилúчный.
ladylove *n.* дáма сéрдца; differentзазнóба.
lag *v.i.* отставáть: *lag behind the others,* отставáть от остальны́х. —*n.* отставáние; запáздывание.
lager *n.* лёгкое пúво.
laggard *n. & adj.* отстаю́щий.
lagoon *n.* лагýна.
lair *n.* лóговище; берлóга.
laity *n.* миря́не.
lake *n.* óзеро.
lama *n.* лáма. —**Lamaism,** *n.* ламаúзм. —**lamasery,** *n.* ламаúстский монасты́рь.
lamb *n.* **1,** (animal) ягнёнок; барáшек. **2,** (meat) (молодáя) барáнина. —**lamb chop,** барáнья отбивнáя.
lambaste *v.t., colloq.* **1,** (beat) колотúть. **2,** (berate) хлестáть.
lambskin *n.* барáшек; мерлýшка. —*adj.* барáшковый; мерлýшковый.
lame *adj.* **1,** (crippled) хромóй. **2,** (poor, as of an excuse) слáбый. —**lameness,** *n.* хромотá.
lament *v.t. & i.* сокрушáться (о); сéтовать (на). —**lamentable,** *adj.* плачéвный; прискóрбный. —**lamentation,** *n.* причитáние; сéтование.
laminated *adj.* слоúстый.
lamp *n.* лáмпа.
lamplighter *n.* фонáрщик.
lampoon *n.* шарж; пáсквиль. —*v.t.* шаржúровать.
lamppost *n.* фонáрный столб.
lamprey *n.* минóга.
lampshade *n.* абажýр.
lance *n.* **1,** (weapon) пúка. **2,** (surgical knife) ланцéт. —*v.t.* вскрывáть; разрезáть.
lancet *n.* (knife) ланцéт. —**lancet arch,** стрéльчатая áрка. —**lancet window,** стрéльчатое окнó.
land *n.* **1,** (earth; ground) земля́. *Dry land,* сýша. **2,** (country) странá; край. *Native land,* рóдина. —*adj.* земéльный: *land reform,* земéльная реф́орма. —*v.t.* **1,** (set down, as an aircraft) посадúть. **2,** (catch, as a fish) вы́тащить (ры́бу). **3,** (deliver, as a blow) наносúть (удáр). **4,** *colloq.* (obtain) получúть. *Land a job,* попáсть на рабóту. —*v.i.* **1,** (put into port) высáживаться. **2,** (touch down, as of an aircraft) приземля́ться. **3,** (fall; strike) попáсть; прийтúсь. **4,** *colloq.* (end up; wind up) попáсть; угодúть: *land in jail,* попáсть/угодúть в тюрьмý.
landed *adj.* **1,** (owning land) помéстный: *the landed gentry,* помéстное дворя́нство. **2,** (consisting of land) земéльный.
landing *n.* **1,** (of an aircraft) посáдка. **2,** (debarkation) вы́садка. **3,** *mil.* вы́садка; десáнт; вы́садка десáнта. **4,** (platform, as on stairs) площáдка. —**landing craft,** десáнтное сýдно. —**landing field,** посáдочная площáдка. —**landing gear,** шассú. —**landing strip,** взлётно-посáдочная полосá.
landlady *n.* хозя́йка.
landless *adj.* безземéльный.
landlocked *adj.* не имéющий вы́хода к мóрю.
landlord *n.* хозя́ин.
landmark *n.* **1,** (prominent object to go by) ориентúр. **2,** (major event) вéха.
land mine фугáс.
landowner *n.* помéщик; землевладéлец.
landscape *n.* пейзáж; ландшáфт. —**landscape architecture,** садóво-пáрковое искýсство.
landslide *n.* обвáл; óползень.
lane *n.* **1,** (narrow path) дорóжка. **2,** (narrow street) ýличка. **3,** (marked division on a highway) ряд; полосá. **4,** (on a running track or swimming pool) дорóжка. **5,** *naut.* (морскóй) путь.
language *n.* язы́к: *foreign language,* инострáнный язы́к. *Bad language,* брань; рýгань. *Strong language,* сúльные выражéния. —*adj.* языковóй: *language barrier,* языковóй барьéр.
languid *adj.* вя́лый; тóмный.
languish *v.i.* **1,** (lose vigor; droop) вя́нуть; чáхнуть. **2,** (live under dispiriting conditions) томúться; изнывáть.
languor *n.* вя́лость. —**languorous,** *adj.* вя́лый.
lanky *adj.* долговя́зый.
lanolin *n.* ланолúн.
lantern *n.* фонáрь.
lanthanum *n.* лантáн.
lap *n.* **1,** (area between the waist and knees) колéни: *sit on one's mother's lap,* сидéть у мáтери на колéнях. **2,** (secure place) лóно: *in the lap of nature,* на лóне прирóды. *Live in the lap of luxury,* утопáть в рóскоши. **3,** (front part of skirt for carrying things) подóл. **4,** (one circuit of a racecourse) круг. **5,** *swimming* заплы́в. —*v.t.* [*usu.* **lap up**] (lick up) лакáть. —*v.i.* (of waves) плескáть.
lap dog кóмнатная собáчка.
lapel *n.* отворóт; лáцкан.
lapidary *n.* гранúльщик. —*adj.* гранúльный.
lapis lazuli ля́пис-лазýрь.
Lapp *n.* [*also,* **Laplander**] саáм. —*adj.* [*also,* **Lappish**] саáмский.
lap robe пóлость.
lapse *n.* **1,** (slip; failure) ля́псус. *Lapse of the tongue,* обмóлвка; оговóрка. *Lapse of memory,* провáл пáмяти. **2,** (interval, as of time) промежýток. —*v.i.* **1,** *fol. by* **into** (slip into; sink into) впадáть (в). **2,** (expire) теря́ть сúлу.
lapwing *n.* чúбис; пúгалица.
larceny *n.* крáжа; воровствó. —**larcenous,** *adj.* воровскóй.
larch *n.* лúственница.

lard *n.* (топлёное свинóе) сáло; шпик. —*v.t.* **1,** (apply lard to) шпиговáть. **2,** *fig.* (sprinkle; intersperse) уснащáть; пересыпáть.
larder *n.* кладовáя.
large *adj.* большóй; крýпный. —**at large,** на свобóде. —**by and large,** в цéлом; в основнóм. —**in large part,** во мнóгом.
large intestine тóлстая кишкá.
largely *adv.* **1,** (to a great extent) во мнóгом. **2,** (for the most part) в основнóм.
large-scale *adj.* в большóм масштáбе. *Large-scale map,* крупномасштáбная кáрта.
largess *also,* **largesse** *n.* щéдрость.
largo *adj. & adv.* лáрго.
lariat *n.* аркáн; лассó.
lark *n.* жáворонок.
larkspur *n.* живокость; шпóрник.
larva *n.* личúнка. —**larval,** *adj.* личúночный.
laryngeal *adj.* гортáнный. —**laryngitis,** *n.* ларингúт.
larynx *n.* гортáнь.
lascivious *adj.* похотлúвый. —**lasciviousness,** *n.* похотлúвость.
laser *n.* лáзер. —*adj.* лáзерный: *laser beam,* лáзерный луч.
lash *n.* **1,** (whip) плеть; бич. **2,** (stroke of a whip) удáр плетью. **3,** (eyelash) ресница. —*v.t.* **1,** (flog) хлестáть; стегáть. **2,** (dash against) хлестáть в *or* о (+ *acc.*) **3,** (shake violently, as the tail) махáть. **4,** (tie) привя́зывать. —**lash out against,** обрýшиваться на.
lashing *n.* пóрка.
lass *n.* дéвушка; девúца.
lassitude *n.* вя́лость; истóма.
lasso *n.* лассó; аркáн. —*v.t.* аркáнить.
last *adj.* **1,** (final) послéдний. *At the last moment,* в сáмый послéдний момéнт. *The last time I was in England,* в послéдний раз, когдá я был (былá) в Áнглии. **2,** (just past) прóшлый: *last week,* на прóшлой недéле; *last month,* в прóшлом мéсяце; *last year,* в прóшлом годý; *last Sunday,* в прóшлое воскресéнье; *last summer,* прóшлым лéтом. *Last night,* вчерá вéчером. —*adv.* **1,** (after all others) послéдним: *come in last,* прийтú послéдним. *He spoke last,* он вы́ступил пóсле всех. **2,** (for the last time) в послéдний раз. **3,** (finally; lastly) наконéц. —*n.* **1,** (final one) послéдний: *the last of the Mohicans,* послéдний из могикáн. *He was the last to leave,* он ушёл послéдним; он ушёл пóсле всех. *See the last of someone,* вúдеть когó-нибудь в послéдний раз. *Breathe one's last,* испустúть дух. **2,** (shoe mold) колóдка. —*v.i.* **1,** (continue; remain in existence) продолжáться; длúться. **2,** (remain in good condition) сохраня́ться. **3,** (hold out) вы́держать. **4,** (be enough; suffice) хватáть. —**at last,** наконéц. —**at long last,** наконéц-то. —**before last,** позапрóшлый: *the year before last,* в позапрóшлом годý. —**last but not least,** послéднее по поря́дку, но не по вáжности. —**last name,** фамúлия. —**last straw,** послéдняя кáпля. —**last word,** послéднее слóво: *have the last word,* сказáть послéднее слóво. —**next to last,** предпослéдний. —**to the last,** до послéднего: *fight to the last,* бúться до послéднего.
lasting *adj.* прóчный: *lasting peace,* прóчный мир. —*n.* (cloth) лáстик.
lastly *adv.* наконéц.
latch *n.* щекóлда; защёлка. —*v.t.* запирáть на щекóлду.
late *adj.* **1,** (tardy; at an advanced time) пóздний: *late hour/arrival,* пóздний час/прихóд. *In late autumn,* пóздней óсенью. *In late October,* в концé октября́. *Be late,* опáздывать. *You're late,* вы опоздáли. **2,** *preceded by* **the** (deceased) покóйный. —*adv.* пóздно. —**of late,** в *or* за послéднее врéмя. *See also* **later** *and* **latest.**
latecomer *n.* опоздáвший.
lately *adv.* в *or* за послéднее врéмя.
lateness *n.* опоздáние; запоздáние; запáздывание.
latent *adj.* скры́тый; латéнтный.
later *adv.* **1,** (comp. degree of late) пóзже. *A little later,* попóзже. **2,** (later on) потóм. *A little while later,* немнóго погодя́. —**sooner or later,** рáно или пóздно.
lateral *adj.* боковóй.
latest *adj.* новéйший; послéдний. *The latest news,* послéдние извéстия. —**at the latest,** сáмое пóзднее.
latex *n.* лáтекс.
lath *n.* дрáнка; плáнка; рéйка.
lathe *n.* токáрный станóк.
lather *n.* (мы́льная) пéна. —*v.t.* мы́лить; намы́ливать.
Latin *adj.* латúнский. —*n.* латúнский язы́к; латы́нь.
latitude *n.* **1,** *geog.* широтá. **2,** (freedom to maneuver) свобóда дéйствий.
latrine *n.* отхóжее мéсто.
latter *adj.* **1,** (second of two) послéдний (из двух). **2,** (nearer the end) послéдний: *in the latter part of the year,* в послéдней чáсти гóда.
lattice *n.* решётка. —**latticed,** *adj.* решётчатый. —**latticework,** *n.* решётчатая конструкция.
Latvian *adj.* латвúйский; латы́шский. —*n.* **1,** (person) латвúец; латы́ш. **2,** (language) латы́шский язы́к.
laud *v.t.* восхваля́ть; превозносúть. —**laudable,** *adj.* похвáльный. —**laudatory,** *adj.* хвалéбный.
laugh *v.i.* смея́ться. *What are you laughing at?,* чемý вы смеётесь? —*n.* смех. —**laugh off,** смея́ться над.
laughable *adj.* смехотвóрный.
laughing *n.* смех. —*adj.* шýточный: *no laughing matter,* не шýточное дéло. —**laughing gas,** веселя́щий газ.
laughingstock *n.* посмéшище. *Make a laughingstock of,* выставля́ть на посмéшище; выставля́ть в смешнóм вúде.
laughter *n.* смех.
launch *v.t.* **1,** (set afloat) спускáть (нá воду). **2,** (set in flight) запускáть. **3,** (initiate) открывáть; предпринимáть; пускáть в ход. *Launch a campaign,* развернýть кампáнию. *Launch an offensive,* повестú наступлéние. —*v.i.* [*usu.* **launch into**] пускáться в: *launch into an explanation,* пускáться в объяснéния. —*n.* **1,** (act of launching) зáпуск. **2,** (boat) кáтер.
launcher *n.* (пусковáя) установка. *Rocket launcher,* ракéтная *or* реактúвная установка. *Grenade launcher,* гранатомёт.
launching *n.* зáпуск. —**launching pad,** пусковáя *or* стáртовая площáдка.

launder *v.t.* стира́ть. —**laundress,** *n.* пра́чка.

laundry *n.* **1,** (items to be laundered) бельё. *Take in laundry,* брать бельё в сти́рку. **2,** (business establishment) пра́чечная.

laureate *n.* лауреа́т.

laurel *n.* **1,** (tree) лавр. **2,** *pl.* (fame; honor) ла́вры. —*adj.* ла́вровый; лавро́вый. *Laurel wreath,* лавро́вый вено́к. —**rest on one's laurels,** почива́ть на ла́врах.

lava *n.* ла́ва.

lavaliere *n.* подве́ска.

lavatory *n.* убо́рная.

lavender *n.* лава́нда. —*adj.* **1,** (pert. to the shrub) лава́ндовый. **2,** (pale purple) бле́дно-лило́вый.

lavish *adj.* **1,** (very generous) ще́дрый: *lavish in one's praise,* ще́дрый на похвалы́. **2,** (sumptuous; grand) пы́шный. —*v.t.* расточа́ть: *lavish praise upon,* расточа́ть похвалы́ (+ *dat.*). *Lavish care upon,* окружа́ть (кого́-нибудь) забо́той.

law *n.* **1,** (rule of conduct; scientific principle) зако́н: *break the law,* наруша́ть зако́н. *The law of gravity,* зако́н (всеми́рного) тяготе́ния. **2,** (jurisprudence) пра́во: *criminal law,* уголо́вное пра́во. *Study law,* изуча́ть пра́во. *Practice law,* занима́ться адвокату́рой. —**take the law into one's own hands,** распра́виться без суда́.

law-abiding *adj.* законопослу́шный.

lawbreaker *n.* правонаруши́тель.

lawful *adj.* зако́нный.

lawless *adj.* беззако́нный. —**lawlessness,** *n.* беззако́ние.

lawmaker *n.* законода́тель.

lawn *n.* лужа́йка; газо́н. —**lawn mower,** газонокоси́лка.

law school юриди́ческий факульте́т.

lawsuit *n.* суде́бный проце́сс; иск.

lawyer *n.* юри́ст; адвока́т.

lax *adj.* расхля́банный; распу́щенный. *Lax morals,* лёгкие нра́вы.

laxative *n.* слаби́тельное.

laxity *n.* расхля́банность; распу́щенность. *Also,* **laxness.**

lay *v.t.* **1,** (put or place horizontally) класть: *lay the wounded man on a stretcher,* класть ра́неного на носи́лки. **2,** (install; place in position) прокла́дывать: *lay a pipeline,* прокла́дывать трубопрово́д. *Lay bricks,* класть кирпичи́. *Lay mines,* ста́вить *or* закла́дывать ми́ны. *Lay a foundation,* закла́дывать фунда́мент. **3,** (spread, as a tablecloth, carpet, etc.) стлать. **4,** (produce, as eggs) класть; нести́. **5,** (locate): *the scene is laid in France,* де́йствие происхо́дит во Фра́нции. **6,** *with various abstract nouns: lay plans,* стро́ить пла́ны; *lay the blame on,* возлага́ть *or* вали́ть вину́ на; *lay emphasis on,* де́лать упо́р на; *lay claim to, see* **claim. 7,** *in fig. expressions involving parts of the body: lay (one's) hands on,* распра́виться с; *lay eyes on,* (у)ви́деть; *lay a finger on,* па́льцем тро́нуть. **8,** (bet) держа́ть пари́ на. —*v.i.* (of a hen) нести́сь. —*adj.* (secular) мирско́й; све́тский. —*n.* (ballad) песнь. *The Lay of Igor's Host,* Сло́во о полку́ И́гореве. —**lay aside/away/by,** откла́дывать в сто́рону. —**lay bare,** обнажа́ть; выкла́дывать. —**lay down, 1,** (place in a horizontal position) класть; укла́дывать. **2,** (give up; surrender) сложи́ть: *lay down one's arms/life,* сложи́ть ору́жие/го́лову. **3,** (state authoritatively, as rules) устана́вливать. *Lay down the law,* установи́ть твёрдое пра́вило. —**lay low,** свали́ть; повали́ть; срази́ть. —**lay off, 1,** (discharge) увольня́ть; рассчи́тывать. **2,** *colloq.* (stop; give up) бро́сить. —**lay of the land,** положе́ние веще́й. —**lay oneself open to,** подверга́ться (+ *dat.*). —**lay out, 1,** (spread out) раскла́дывать; выкла́дывать. **2,** (design) планирова́ть; разбива́ть. **3,** (spend, as money) тра́тить. —**lay to rest,** хорони́ть. —**lay up, 1,** (store) заготовля́ть впрок. **2,** (confine to bed) укла́дывать. —**lay waste,** опустоша́ть.

layer *n.* **1,** (covering) слой; пласт. *Layer of dust/fat,* слой пы́ли/жи́ра. *Layer of snow,* пласт сне́га. **2,** (workman who lays something) укла́дчик: *track layer,* укла́дчик путе́й. **3,** (hen as an egg producer) несу́шка. *Good layer,* но́ская ку́рица.

layette *n.* прида́ное.

layman *n.* миря́нин.

layoff *n.* **1,** (dismissal) увольне́ние. **2,** (period of inactivity) переры́в.

layout *n.* **1,** (arrangement) расположе́ние; устро́йство; планиро́вка. **2,** (design; format, as of a newspaper) оформле́ние.

layover *n.* остано́вка (в пути́).

laze *v.i.* не́житься; лентя́йничать.

laziness *n.* лень; ле́ность.

lazy *adj.* лени́вый. —**lazybones,** *n., colloq.* лентя́й; лежебо́ка.

lead[1] (led) *n.* **1,** (heavy metal) свине́ц. **2,** (graphite, as used in pencils) графи́т. —*adj.* свинцо́вый. —**lead pencil,** просто́й *or* графи́товый каранда́ш. —**lead poisoning,** отравле́ние свинцо́м.

lead[2] (leed) *v.t.* **1,** (guide) вести́: *lead a blind man,* вести́ слепо́го. *Lead troops into battle,* вести́ войска́ в бой. **2,** (direct) руководи́ть: *lead an expedition,* руководи́ть экспеди́цией. **3,** (induce; prompt) побужда́ть. **4,** (be first among) быть впереди́ (+ *gen.*). **5,** *Lead the way,* идти́ впереди́. **6,** (live, as a certain kind of life) вести́. **7,** *cards* идти́ с: *lead an ace,* идти́ с туза́. —*v.i.* **1,** (serve as a route) вести́: *this road leads to town,* э́та доро́га ведёт к го́роду. **2,** *fol. by* **to** (tend toward a certain result) вести́ (к); привести́ (к): *lead to nothing,* ни к чему́ не вести́ *or* привести́. **3,** (be in the lead) лиди́ровать. **4,** *cards: who leads?,* чей ход? —*n.* **1,** (first place in a contest) ли́дерство. *Be in the lead,* лиди́ровать. **2,** (distance in front): *have a long lead,* быть далеко́ впереди́. **3,** (role of leader) инициати́ва: *take the lead,* взять инициати́ву в свои́ ру́ки. **4,** (example) приме́р: *follow someone's lead,* сле́довать чьему́-нибудь приме́ру. **5,** *theat.* гла́вная роль. **6,** *cards* ход. **7,** *electricity* про́вод. —*adj.* веду́щий: *lead aircraft,* веду́щий самолёт. *Lead role,* гла́вная роль. *Lead article,* передова́я статья́. —**lead away,** уводи́ть. —**lead in,** вводи́ть. —**lead on,** води́ть за́ нос. —**lead out,** выводи́ть.

leaded *adj.* (of gasoline) этили́рованный.

leaden *adj.* свинцо́вый: *leaden skies,* свинцо́вое не́бо.

leader *n.* руководи́тель; вождь; ли́дер. —**leadership,** *n.* руково́дство.

lead-in *n.* ввод.

leading *adj.* веду́щий. —**leading lady,** премье́рша. —**leading light,** свети́ло; све́точ; корифе́й. —**leading man,** премье́р. —**leading question,** наводя́щий вопро́с.

leaf *n.* **1,** (of a tree or plant) лист: *the leaves are falling,* ли́стья па́дают. *Tea/tobacco leaf,* ча́йный/таба́чный лист. **2,** (of a book) лист. **3,** (of a table) доска́. **4,** (of a door or gate) ство́рка; поло́тнище. **5,** *in* **gold/silver leaf,** суса́льное зо́лото/серебро́. —*v.t.* [*usu.* **leaf through**] перели́стывать. —**take a leaf from someone's book,** брать приме́р с. —**turn over a new leaf,** испра́виться.
leaflet *n.* листо́вка.
leafy *adj.* ли́ственный.
league *n.* ли́га; сою́з. *In league with,* в сою́зе с; в сго́воре с. —**League of Nations,** Ли́га на́ций.
leak *n.* течь: *spring a leak,* дать течь. —*v.i.* **1,** (admit water) течь; протека́ть. **2,** *fol. by* **into** (seep into) затека́ть (в); протека́ть (в). —**leak out, 1,** (seep out) вытека́ть. **2,** *fig.* (become known) вы́йти нару́жу; проса́чиваться.
leakage *n.* уте́чка.
leaky *adj.* име́ющий течь.
lean *v.i.* **1,** (incline one's body) наклоня́ться: *lean over the cradle,* наклоня́ться над колыбе́лью. *Lean over the railing,* перегиба́ться че́рез пери́ла. *Lean out of the window,* высо́вываться из окна́. *Lean back in the chair,* отки́дываться в кре́сле. **2,** (not be erect; slant) наклоня́ться. **3,** *fol. by* **against** (rest against) прислоня́ться (к). **4,** *fol. by* **on** (support oneself on; depend on) опира́ться (на). **5,** *fol. by* **toward** (favor slightly) склоня́ться (к). —*v.t.* **1,** (tilt) наклоня́ть. **2,** (prop) прислоня́ть; опира́ть. —*adj.* **1,** (thin) худо́й. **2,** (not fatty, as of meat) не жи́рный; по́стный. **3,** *Lean years,* неурожа́йные го́ды.
leaning *n.* скло́нность; накло́нность. —*adj.* накло́нный.
leanness *n.* худоба́.
leap *v.i.* пры́гать; скака́ть. —*n.* прыжо́к; скачо́к. —**by leaps and bounds,** скачка́ми.
leapfrog *n.* чехарда́.
leap year високо́сный год.
learn *v.t.* **1,** (gain knowledge or mastery of) (на)учи́ться: *learn a great deal,* научи́ться мно́гому; *learn how to swim,* научи́ться пла́вать. **2,** (memorize) зау́чивать. **3,** (find out) узнава́ть. —*v.i.* **1,** (gain knowledge) учи́ться: *learn from one's mistakes,* учи́ться на оши́бках. **2,** *fol. by* **of** *or* **about** (find out about) узнава́ть (о). —**learned,** *adj.* зна́ющий; учёный. —**learner,** *n.* учени́к: *slow learner,* сла́бый учени́к.
learning *n.* **1,** (acquiring knowledge) уче́ние. **2,** (erudition) учёность; эруди́ция.
lease *v.t.* **1,** (rent) брать в аре́нду. **2,** (let) сдава́ть в аре́нду. —*n.* аре́ндный догово́р. —**new lease on life,** втора́я мо́лодость.
leaseholder *n.* аренда́тор.
leash *n.* при́вязь; поводо́к.
least *adj.* мале́йший; наиме́ньший: *not the least doubt,* ни мале́йшего сомне́ния; *the line of least resistance,* ли́ния наиме́ньшего сопротивле́ния. —*adv.* **1,** *before adjectives* наиме́нее: *the least important question,* наиме́нее ва́жный вопро́с. **2,** *with verbs* ме́ньше всего́: *what I like least,* что мне нра́вится ме́ньше всего́. —*n.* [*usu.* **the least**] са́мое ме́ньшее; са́мое ма́лое. *That's the least of my worries,* э́то меня́ ме́ньше всего́ беспоко́ит. —**at least,** по кра́йней ме́ре; хоть; хотя́ бы. —**at the least,** са́мое ме́ньшее; са́мое ма́лое. —**not in the least,** ниско́лько; ни в мале́йшей сте́пени. —**not the least bit** (+ *adj.*), ниско́лько не; совсе́м не —**to say the least,** е́сли (*or* что́бы) не сказа́ть бо́льше.
leather *n.* ко́жа. —*adj.* ко́жаный.
leave *v.i.* уходи́ть; уезжа́ть: *he left,* он ушёл; *she left for Florida,* она́ уе́хала во Флори́ду. *The train leaves at eight,* по́езд отхо́дит в во́семь часо́в. —*v.t.* **1,** (go out of) выходи́ть из: *leave the room/house,* выходи́ть из ко́мнаты/и́з дому/. **2,** (depart from) уходи́ть из; уезжа́ть из: *leave home,* уходи́ть/уезжа́ть из до́ма. **3,** (go without taking; let remain) оставля́ть: *leave the children at home,* оставля́ть дете́й до́ма. *Leave far behind,* оставля́ть далеко́ позади́. *Leave the door open,* оставля́ть дверь откры́той. *Leave in peace,* оставля́ть в поко́е. **4,** (forget) забы́ть; оста́вить: *leave one's notebook home,* забы́ть/оста́вить тетра́дь до́ма. **5,** (forsake) покида́ть; оставля́ть; бро́сить. *Don't leave me!,* не покида́йте меня́! **6,** (entrust) предоставля́ть: *leave it to me to decide,* предоста́вьте реша́ть э́то мне. **7,** (be survived by): *he leaves a wife and two children,* по́сле него́ оста́лись жена́ и дво́е дете́й. **8,** (bequeath) завеща́ть. **9,** *in subtraction: seven minus three leaves four,* семь ми́нус три равня́ется четырём. —*n.* **1,** (permission) разреше́ние. **2,** *mil.* (furlough) о́тпуск; побы́вка. *Sick leave,* о́тпуск по боле́зни. *Absence without leave,* самово́льная отлу́чка. **3,** *in* **take leave of,** проща́ться с; **take one's leave,** уходи́ть. —**be left,** оста́ться: *be left homeless,* оста́ться без кро́ва. *How much time is left?,* ско́лько вре́мени оста́лось? *I have only one pencil left,* у меня́ оста́лся то́лько оди́н каранда́ш. —**leave alone,** *see* **alone.** —**leave aside,** оставля́ть в стороне́: *leaving aside the question of...,* оставля́я в стороне́ вопро́с о... —**leave back,** оста́вить на второ́й год (в шко́ле). —**leave behind,** *see* **behind.** —**leave off, 1,** (omit at the end) пропуска́ть. **2,** (stop) остана́вливаться: *where did we leave off?,* где мы останови́лись? —**leave out,** пропуска́ть.
leaven *n.* заква́ска; опа́ра. —*v.t.* заква́шивать.
leavings *n.pl.* оста́тки.
Lebanese *adj.* лива́нский.
lecher *n.* развра́тник; распу́тник. —**lecherous,** *adj.* развра́тный; распу́тный. —**lechery,** *n.* развра́т; распу́тство.
lectern *n.* **1,** (speaker's stand) пюпи́тр. **2,** (reading desk in a church) анало́й.
lecture *n.* **1,** (discourse) ле́кция. **2,** (reprimand) нота́ция. —*v.i.* чита́ть ле́кции. —*v.t.* поуча́ть. —**lecture hall,** лекцио́нный зал.
lecturer *n.* ле́ктор.
ledge *n.* **1,** (small shelf) по́лочка. **2,** (on the side of a cliff) вы́ступ; усту́п.
ledger *n.* гла́вная кни́га; гроссбу́х.
leech *n.* пия́вка.
leek *n.* поре́й; лук-поре́й.
leer *v.i.* смотре́ть и́скоса. —*n.* косо́й взгляд.
leery *adj., colloq.* подозри́тельный; скепти́ческий. *Be leery of,* относи́ться подозри́тельно/скепти́чески к.
lees *n.pl.* гу́ща; муть.
leeward *adj.* подве́тренный.
leeway *n.* свобо́да де́йствий.
left[1] *adj.* ле́вый: *left hand,* ле́вая рука́. —*adv.* нале́во: *turn left,* повора́чивать нале́во. —*n.* **1,** (side opp. from the right) ле́вая сторона́. *To the left; on the*

left, налéво; слéва. **2,** *polit.* [*usu.* **the Left**] лéвые.
left² *past tense and past part. of* **leave.** *See* **leave.**
left-hand *adj.* лéвый.
left-handed *adj.* **1,** (favoring the left hand): *I am left-handed,* я левшá. **2,** (backhanded) сомни́тельный: *left-handed compliment,* сомни́тельный комплимéнт.
leftist *n. & adj.* лéвый.
leftovers *n.pl.* объéдки.
left-wing *adj.* лéвый.
leg *n.* **1,** (part of the body) ногá. **2,** (of a piece of furniture) нóжка. **3,** (of a pair of trousers) штани́на. **4,** (piece of meat) ногá: *leg of mutton,* барáнья ногá. **5,** (stage of a journey) этáп. —**be on one's last legs,** доживáть послéдние дни. —**not have a leg to stand on,** не имéть под собóй пóчвы. —**pull someone's leg,** шути́ть над кéм-нибудь.
legacy *n.* наслéдие.
legal *adj.* **1,** (pert. to law) правовóй; юриди́ческий: *legal question,* юриди́ческий вопрóс; *legal norms,* правовы́е нóрмы. **2,** (pert. to lawyers or lawsuits) судéбный: *legal costs,* судéбные издéржки. *Take legal action,* начинáть судéбный процéсс. **3,** (lawful; legitimate) закóнный; легáльный. —**legal tender,** закóнное платёжное срéдство.
legality *n.* закóнность; легáльность.
legalize *v.t.* узакóнивать; легализи́ровать. —**legalization,** *n.* узаконéние; легализáция.
legation *n.* ми́ссия.
legato *adj. & adv.* легáто.
legend *n.* легéнда; предáние. —**legendary,** *adj.* легендáрный.
legerdemain *n.* лóвкость рук.
leggings *n.pl.* гамáши; крáги.
legibility *n.* разбóрчивость.
legible *adj.* разбóрчивый. —**legibly,** *adv.* разбóрчиво.
legion *n.* легиóн. —**legionnaire,** *n.* легионéр.
legislation *n.* законодáтельство. —**legislative,** *adj.* законодáтельный. —**legislator,** *n.* законодáтель. —**legislature,** *n.* законодáтельное учреждéние.
legitimate *adj.* **1,** (lawful) закóнный. **2,** (valid, as of an excuse) уважи́тельный. **3,** (born in wedlock) законнорождённый. —**legitimacy,** *n.* закóнность.
legitimize *v.t.* узакóнивать.
legless *adj.* безнóгий.
legroom *n.* мéсто для ног.
leguminous *adj.* бобóвый; стручкóвый.
leisure *n.* досýг: *at one's leisure,* на досýге. —*adj.* свобóдный: *leisure time,* свобóдное врéмя. *The leisure class,* прáздный класс.
leisurely *adj.* неторопли́вый. —*adv.* неторопли́во.
leitmotif *n.* лейтмоти́в.
lemming *n.* лéмминг.
lemon *n.* лимóн. —*adj.* лимóнный. —**lemonade,** *n.* лимонáд.
lemur *n.* лемýр.
lend *v.t.* **1,** (let have temporarily) одолжáть; давáть: *could you lend me a pencil?,* вы не мóжете одолжи́ть/дать мне карандáш? **2,** (give as a loan) одолжáть; давáть взаймы́. **3,** (give; impart) придавáть. **4,** (give; contribute) подавáть: *lend a helping hand,* подавáть рýку пóмощи. **5,** *fol. by* **itself** (be suitable) поддавáться (+ *dat.*): *not lend itself to translation,* не поддавáться перевóду.
lender *n.* кредитóр.
length *n.* **1,** (distance from end to end) длинá. **2,** (extent) протяжéние. *Walk the length of the street,* проходи́ть (всю) ýлицу. **3,** (duration) продолжи́тельность. **4,** (piece, as of cloth) отрéз; отрéзок. **5,** *horse racing* кóрпус: *win by two lengths,* опереди́ть други́х на два кóрпуса. —**at length,** подрóбно. —**go to any length,** идти́ на всё. —**keep at arm's length,** держáть на почти́тельном расстоя́нии.
lengthen *v.t.* удлиня́ть. —*v.i.* удлиня́ться.
lengthwise *adv.* в длинý; вдоль.
lengthy *adj.* дли́тельный; продолжи́тельный.
lenient *adj.* снисходи́тельный. —**leniency,** *n.* снисходи́тельность.
Leninism *n.* ленини́зм. —**Leninist,** *n.* лéнинец. —*adj.* лéнинский.
lens *n.* **1,** (glass) ли́нза; объекти́в. **2,** (of the eye) хрустáлик. —**lens cap,** кры́шка объекти́ва.
Lent *n.* вели́кий пост. —**Lenten,** *adj.* великопóстный.
lentil *n.* чечеви́ца. —*adj.* чечеви́чный.
lento *adj. & adv.* лéнто.
Leo *n.* Лев.
leopard *n.* леопáрд.
leotard *n.* трикó.
leper *n.* прокажённый. —**leper colony,** колóния прокажённых.
leprosy *n.* прокáза. —**leprous,** *adj.* прокажённый.
lesbian *n.* лесбия́нка. —*adj.* лесби́йский.
lesion *n.* поврежд́ение.
less *adj.* мéньше (+ *gen.*): *less time,* мéньше врéмени. —*adv.* **1,** *before adjectives* мéнее: *less likely,* мéнее вероя́тно. **2,** *with verbs* мéньше: *smoke less,* мéньше кури́ть. —*n.* мéньше: *eat less,* мéньше есть. *Less than I expected,* мéньше, чем я ожидáл(а). —*prep.* за вы́четом (+ *gen.*). —**less and less,** всё мéньше и мéньше; *(with adjectives)* всё мéнее (+ *adj.*). —**more or less,** бóлее и́ли мéнее. —**much less, 1,** *literally* горáздо мéньше. **2,** *before adjectives* горáздо мéнее. **3,** (especially not) тем бóлее.
lessee *n.* арендáтор.
lessen *v.t.* уменьшáть. *Lessen international tension,* уменьшáть/ослабля́ть/разряжáть междунарóдную напряжённость. —*v.i.* уменьшáться.
lesser *adj.* мéньший: *a lesser offense,* мéньший простýпок. *An official of lesser rank,* сотрýдник мéньшего рáнга. —**the lesser of two evils,** мéньшее из двух зол.
lesson *n.* урóк. *Learn one's lesson (fig.),* получи́ть хорóший урóк. *Learn a lesson from,* извлéчь урóк из. *Teach someone a lesson,* проучи́ть когó-нибудь; дать комý-нибудь урóк. *Let this be a lesson to you,* э́то бýдет тебé урóком.
lest *conj.* **1,** (so that...not) чтóбы не: *lest any doubts remain,* чтóбы не оставáлось сомнéний. **2,** (for fear that) как бы не: *lest something worse should happen,* как бы хýже нé было.
let *v.t.* **1,** (allow) разрешáть; позволя́ть; давáть. *Let him speak,* дай емý говори́ть. *Let me think,* дáйте мне подýмать. *Let me help you,* давáйте я вам помогý. *Let an opportunity slip by,* упусти́ть возмóжность. *Don't let this happen again!,* чтóбы э́того бóльше нé было! ♦*Also with* пусть: *let him go,* пусть

он идёт. **2,** (rent; give out) сдава́ть внаём *or* в аре́нду. *Let a contract,* сдава́ть подря́д. *House to let,* сдаётся дом. *—v.aux.* **1,** [*usu.* **let's**] *in suggestions, rendered by the 1st person pl.: let's go!,* пойдём(те)! ♦*Also by* дава́й *or* дава́йте: *let's take the bus,* дава́й(те) ся́дем на авто́бус. **2,** *acquiescence* пусть: *let it rain!,* пусть бу́дет дождь. **3,** *assumption* пусть: *let x equal y,* пусть икс ра́вен и́греку. **—let alone,** *see* **alone.** **—let down, 1,** (lower) опуска́ть; спуска́ть. **2,** (undo, as one's hair) распуска́ть. **3,** (fail to keep one's word to) подводи́ть. **—let go (of),** отпуска́ть. **—let in,** пуска́ть; допуска́ть; впуска́ть; пропуска́ть. **—let in on,** посвяща́ть в: *let someone in on a secret,* посвяща́ть кого́-нибудь в та́йну. **—let know,** дать знать. **—let off, 1,** (emit) испуска́ть. **2,** (release; dismiss) отпуска́ть. **—let on,** *colloq. (usu. neg.)* (никому́ не) говори́ть; (не) подава́ть ви́ду. **—let out, 1,** (release) выпуска́ть: *let a bird out of a cage,* выпуска́ть пти́цу из кле́тки. *Let the water out of the bathtub,* спуска́ть во́ду из ва́нны. *Let the air out of a tire,* спуска́ть ши́ну. **2,** (loosen) распуска́ть. **3,** (make longer) выпуска́ть. **4,** (emit) испуска́ть. **5,** (be over) конча́ться. **—let through,** пропуска́ть. **—let up, 1,** (slacken) ослабева́ть. **2,** (abate, as of a storm) затиха́ть.

letdown *n.* разочарова́ние.

lethal *adj.* смертоно́сный; смерте́льный. *Lethal weapon,* смертоно́сное ору́жие. *Lethal dose,* смерте́льная до́за.

lethargic *adj.* летарги́ческий; вя́лый. **—lethargy,** *n.* летарги́я; вя́лость.

Lett *n.* латы́ш.

letter *n.* **1,** (of the alphabet) бу́ква. **2,** (message sent by mail) письмо́. *—v.t.* помеча́ть бу́квами. **—letter of the law,** бу́ква зако́на. **—man of letters,** литера́тор. **—to the letter,** то́чка в то́чку; в то́чности.

letter carrier почтальо́н.

letterhead *n.* на́дпись (на почто́вой бума́ге).

lettering *n.* на́дпись: *hand lettering,* на́дпись от руки́.

letter of credit аккредити́в.

letter-perfect *adj.* соверше́нно то́чный.

Lettish *adj.* латы́шский. *—n.* латы́шский язы́к.

lettuce *n.* сала́т.

letup *n.* переры́в; остано́вка. *Without letup,* безостано́вочно.

leucocyte *n.* = **leukocyte.**

leukemia *n.* белокро́вие; лейкеми́я.

leukocyte *also,* **leucocyte** *n.* лейкоци́т.

levee *n.* да́мба.

level *n.* **1,** (elevation; standard) у́ровень: *water level,* у́ровень воды́. *On/at a high level,* на высо́ком у́ровне. *On a level with,* наравне́ с; наряду́ с; вро́вень с. **2,** (instrument) ватерпа́с; ниве́ли́р; у́ровень. *—adj.* ро́вный: *level ground,* ро́вная ме́стность. *—v.t.* **1,** (make level) выра́внивать; сра́внивать (*pfv.* сровня́ть). **2,** (knock down; raze) сра́внивать/сровня́ть с землёй. **3,** (aim) наводи́ть. **4,** (direct, as an accusation) выдвига́ть (про́тив); возводи́ть (на); броса́ть (+ *dat.*). **5,** *surveying* нивели́ровать. **—do one's level best,** сде́лать всё, что в чьи́х-нибудь си́лах. **—on the level,** *colloq.* че́стно; правди́во.

levelheaded *adj.* уравнове́шенный; здравомы́слящий.

lever *n.* рыча́г.

leverage *n.* **1,** (action of a lever) де́йствие рычага́. **2,** *fig.* (power to influence) рычаги́: *use leverage,* испо́льзовать рычаги́.

leviathan *n.* левиафа́н.

Leviticus *n.* Леви́т.

levity *n.* легкомы́слие.

levy *v.t.* **1,** (impose) облага́ть (нало́гом); налага́ть (штраф). **2,** (collect) взима́ть; взы́скивать. *—n.* сбор; нало́г.

lewd *adj.* **1,** (lascivious) похотли́вый. **2,** (obscene) са́льный. **—lewdness,** *n.* похотли́вость.

lexical *adj.* лекси́ческий; слова́рный.

lexicography *n.* лексикогра́фия. **—lexicographer,** *n.* лексико́граф. **—lexicographic.** *adj.* лексикографи́ческий.

lexicon *n.* **1,** (wordbook; dictionary) лексико́н. **2,** (vocabulary) ле́ксика; лексико́н.

liability *n.* **1,** (state of being liable) отве́тственность. **2,** *pl.* (debts; obligations) пасси́в.

liable *adj.* **1,** (legally obligated): *be liable for damages,* нести́ материа́льную отве́тственность за убы́тки. **2,** *fol. by* **to** (subject to) подлежа́щий (+ *dat.*); подве́рженный (+ *dat.*). *Be liable to,* подлежа́ть (+ *dat.*). **3,** (likely) *rendered by* мочь: *you're liable to catch cold,* ты мо́жешь простуди́ться. *He is liable to come at any moment,* он мо́жет прийти́ в любо́й моме́нт. *He is liable to do anything,* он спосо́бен на всё.

liaison *n.* **1,** (means of contact) связь. **2,** (adulterous relationship) (любо́вная) связь. **3,** *phonet.* слия́ние зву́ков.

liar *n.* лгун; лжец.

libation *n.* возлия́ние.

libel *n.* клевета́. *Libel suit,* иск за клевету́. *—v.t.* клевета́ть на. **—libelous,** *adj.* клеветни́ческий.

liberal *adj.* **1,** *polit.* либера́льный. **2,** (generous; ample) ще́дрый. **3,** (of an education) гуманита́рный. *Liberal arts,* гуманита́рные нау́ки. *—n.* либера́л. **—liberalism,** *n.* либерали́зм. **—liberality,** *n.* ще́дрость.

liberalize *v.t.* де́лать бо́лее либера́льным.

liberate *v.t.* освобожда́ть. **—liberation,** *n.* освобожде́ние. **—liberator,** *n.* освободи́тель.

libertine *n.* распу́тник; развра́тник.

liberty *n.* свобо́да. **—at liberty,** на свобо́де. *At liberty to,* во́лен (+ *inf.*). **—take liberties,** позво́лить себе́ во́льности. **—take liberties with,** фамилья́рничать с. **—take the liberty of,** позво́лить себе́ (+ *inf.*); брать на себя́ сме́лость (+ *inf.*).

Libra *n.* Весы́.

librarian *n.* библиоте́карь. **—librarianship,** *n.* библиоте́чное де́ло.

library *n.* библиоте́ка. *Record library,* фоноте́ка. *Film library,* фильмоте́ка. *—adj.* библиоте́чный: *library book,* библиоте́чная кни́га. **—library science,** библиотекове́дение.

libretto *n.* либре́тто. **—librettist,** *n.* либретти́ст.

Libyan *adj.* ливи́йский.

license *n.* **1,** (official permit) разреше́ние; свиде́тельство; лице́нзия. *Marriage license,* бра́чное свиде́тельство. *Driver's license,* води́тельские права́. **2,** (freedom) во́льность: *poetic license,* поэти́ческая во́льность. *—v.t.* разреша́ть; санкциони́ровать. **—license plate,** номерно́й знак.

licentious *adj.* распу́тный; распу́щенный. **—licentiousness,** *n.* распу́тство; распу́щенность.

lichen *n.* лиша́йник; лиша́й.
lick *v.t.* **1,** (pass the tongue over) лиза́ть; obли́зывать. *Lick off,* сли́зывать. **2,** (touch lightly, as of flames) лиза́ть. **3,** *colloq.* (defeat soundly) поби́ть. —**lick one's chops,** obли́зываться. —**lick one's wounds,** зали́зывать ра́ны. —**lick someone's boots,** лиза́ть пя́тки (+ *dat.*).
licking *n.* **1,** (act of licking) лиза́ние. **2,** *colloq.* (thrashing) по́рка; взбу́чка.
lickspittle *n.* лизоблю́д; подхали́м.
licorice *also,* **liquorice** *n.* лакри́ца. —*adj.* лакри́чный.
lid *n.* кры́шка.
lie *v.i.* **1,** (be in a recumbent position) лежа́ть: *she was lying on the ground,* она́ лежа́ла на земле́. **2,** *fol. by* **down** (assume a recumbent position) ложи́ться: *lie down on the ground,* ложи́ться на зе́млю. **3,** (be situated) лежа́ть. **4,** (be in a certain condition) лежа́ть: *lie idle,* лежа́ть без употребле́ния; *lie fallow,* лежа́ть под па́ром. *Lie at anchor,* стоя́ть на я́коре. **5,** (be buried) поко́иться: *here lies...,* здесь поко́ится... **6,** *fol. by* **in** (be) состоя́ть в; заключа́ться в: *the difficulty lies in the fact that...,* тру́дность состои́т/заключа́ется в том, что... **7,** (make false statements) лгать; врать. *You're lying!,* лжёшь! —*n.* ложь: *it's all a lie,* э́то всё ложь. —**lie ahead,** предстоя́ть. —**lie around/about,** валя́ться. —**lie in wait for,** подстерега́ть. —**lie low,** залега́ть; отлёживаться; прита́иться. —**take lying down,** прогла́тывать (оскорбле́ние).
lie detector дете́ктор лжи.
lien *n.* пра́во аре́ста: *obtain a lien on someone's property,* получи́ть пра́во аре́ста чьего́-нибудь иму́щества.
lieu *n., in* **in lieu of,** вме́сто (+ *gen.*).
lieutenant *n.* лейтена́нт. *First lieutenant,* ста́рший лейтена́нт. *Second lieutenant,* мла́дший лейтена́нт. —**lieutenant colonel,** подполко́вник. —**lieutenant commander,** капита́н тре́тьего ра́нга. —**lieutenant general,** генера́л-полко́вник. —**lieutenant governor,** ви́це-губерна́тор.
life *n.* жизнь: *all one's life,* всю жизнь. —*adj.* пожи́зненный: *life imprisonment,* пожи́зненное заключе́ние. —**come to life,** ожива́ть; оживля́ться. —**for dear life,** изо всех сил. —**for life,** на всю жизнь. *Be appointed for life,* назнача́ться пожи́зненно. —**for the life of me,** хоть убе́й. —**life-and-death struggle,** борьба́ не на жизнь, а на смерть. —**life of the party,** душа́ о́бщества. —**matter of life and death,** вопро́с жи́зни и сме́рти. —**not on your life,** ни за что на све́те. —**take one's own life,** лиши́ть себя́ жи́зни. —**true to life,** как живо́й.
life belt спаса́тельный по́яс; про́бковый по́яс.
lifeboat *n.* спаса́тельная ло́дка *or* шлю́пка.
life buoy спаса́тельный круг.
lifeguard *n.* спаса́тель.
life insurance страхова́ние жи́зни.
life jacket спаса́тельный жиле́т.
lifeless *adj.* мёртвый; мёртвенный; безжи́зненный; бездыха́нный.
lifelike *adj.* жи́зненный.
lifelong *adj.* на всю жизнь: *lifelong friend,* друг на всю жизнь. *Lifelong desire,* заве́тное жела́ние.
life preserver спаса́тельный по́яс.
life raft спаса́тельный плот.
lifesaver *n.* спаси́тель.
life-size *also,* **life-sized** *adj.* в натура́льную величину́.
lifetime *n.* жизнь: *in one's lifetime,* в тече́ние чьей-нибудь жи́зни. *It's the chance of a lifetime,* тако́й слу́чай представля́ется раз в жи́зни.
lifework *n.* де́ло (чьей-нибудь) жи́зни.
lift *v.t.* **1,** (raise) поднима́ть. *Lift someone's spirits,* поднима́ть дух *or* настрое́ние кого́-нибудь. **2,** (remove; withdraw, as a siege, ban, etc.) снима́ть. *Lift sanctions,* отменя́ть са́нкции. **3,** *Lift out of context,* вы́рвать из конте́кста. —*v.i.* (of fog) рассе́иваться. —*n.* **1,** (instance of lifting): *give something a lift,* поднима́ть что́-нибудь. **2,** (free ride): *give a lift to,* подвози́ть. **3,** (machine for lifting) подъёмная маши́на; подъёмник. **4,** *Brit.* (elevator) лифт. **5,** (part of the heel of a shoe) набо́йка. **6,** (elevation of one's spirits): *give someone a lift,* подбодря́ть кого́-нибудь.
liftoff *n.* отры́в от земли́.
ligament *n.* свя́зка.
ligature *n.* лигату́ра.
light *n.* **1,** (illumination) свет: *dim light,* ту́склый свет. *Turn out the light,* (по)туши́ть свет. *Read in good light,* чита́ть при хоро́шем све́те. **2,** (source of illumination) фона́рь: *street light,* у́личный фона́рь. *The lights of a city,* огни́ го́рода. **3,** (traffic light) светофо́р. *Red light,* кра́сный свет. **4,** (for a cigarette): *can you give me a light?,* разреши́те прикури́ть! **5,** (aspect) свет: *see something in its true light,* ви́деть что́-нибудь в и́стинном све́те. —*adj.* **1,** (not dark; bright) све́тлый: *light hair/colors,* све́тлые во́лосы/кра́ски. *It is getting light,* света́ет; светле́ет. ♦ *With colors* светло-: *light gray,* светло-се́рый. **2,** (of or pert. to light) светово́й: *light wave,* светова́я волна́. **3,** (not heavy; not serious) лёгкий: *light suitcase/breakfast/breeze,* лёгкий чемода́н/за́втрак/ветеро́к. *Light reading,* лёгкое чте́ние. *Light sentence,* мя́гкий пригово́р. *Be a light sleeper,* чу́тко спать. —*adv.* легко́. *Travel light,* путеше́ствовать налегке́. —*v.t.* **1,** (ignite; turn on, as a lamp, match, etc.) зажига́ть. *Light a fire,* разжига́ть ого́нь *or* костёр. *Light a stove,* зата́пливать плиту́. *Light (up) a cigarette,* заку́ривать папиро́су. **2,** *often fol. by* **up** (illuminate) освеща́ть; озаря́ть. —*v.i.* **1,** (ignite) зажига́ться. **2,** *fol. by* **up** (brighten, as of one's face) освеща́ться; озаря́ться; (of one's eyes) загоре́ться; засвети́ться. **3,** (dismount) сходи́ть; слеза́ть. **4,** (come to rest; perch) сади́ться. **5,** *fol. by* **on** *or* **upon** (come upon) ната́лкиваться на. **6,** *fol. by* **into** (attack violently) обру́шиваться на. —**bring to light,** выявля́ть. —**come to light,** обнару́живаться; вскрыва́ться; всплыва́ть. —**in (the) light of,** в све́те (+ *gen.*). —**make light of,** относи́ться легко́ к. —**see the light,** прозре́ть.
light bulb ла́мпочка.
lighted *adj.* зажжённый: *lighted candles,* зажжённые све́чи.
lighten *v.t.* **1,** (make less heavy) облегча́ть. **2,** (make lighter, as colors) де́лать светле́е. —*v.i.* облегча́ться.
lighter *n.* **1,** (igniting device) зажига́лка. **2,** (boat) ли́хтер.
light-fingered *adj.* на́ руку нечи́ст.
light-haired *adj.* светловоло́сый.
lightheaded *adj.* **1,** (giddy; dizzy): *I feel lightheaded,*

у меня́ кру́жится голова́. **2,** (frivolous; silly) легкомы́сленный.

lighthearted *adj.* беззабо́тный; весёлый.

lighthouse *n.* мая́к.

lighting *n.* **1,** (act of lighting) зажига́ние: *lighting of candles,* зажига́ние свеч. **2,** (illumination) освеще́ние. —*adj.* освети́тельный: *lighting system,* освети́тельная сеть.

lightly *adv.* **1,** (gently) легко́. **2,** (slightly) слегка́. **3,** (not as a serious matter) несерьёзно. *Take lightly,* не принима́ть всерьёз. **4,** (with little or no penalty) дёшево: *get off lightly,* дёшево отде́латься.

light meter экспози́метр; экспоно́метр.

lightness *n.* **1,** (brightness) све́тлость. **2,** (not being heavy) лёгкость.

lightning *n.* мо́лния. —*adj.* молниено́сный: *with lightning speed,* с молниено́сной быстрото́й. —*v.i. It is lightning,* мо́лния сверка́ет. —**lightning bug,** светля́к. —**lightning rod,** громоотво́д; молниеотво́д.

lightproof *adj.* светонепроница́емый.

lightweight *adj.* лёгкий; легкове́сный. —*n., sports* легкове́с.

light year светово́й год.

lignite *n.* лигни́т.

likable *also,* **likeable** *adj.* ми́лый; симпати́чный.

like *v.t.* **1,** (be fond of) люби́ть. **2,** (enjoy) *rendered by* нра́виться: *how did you like the movie?,* как вам понра́вился э́тот фильм? **3,** (wish) хоте́ть: *I would like a cup of tea,* я бы хоте́л ча́шку ча́ю. —*v.i.* хоте́ть: *do as you like,* де́лайте, как хоти́те. *Ask any questions you like,* задава́йте каки́е уго́дно вопро́сы. —*prep.* **1,** (similar to) похо́жий на: *she is like her mother,* она́ похо́жа на свою́ мать. *What is he like?,* что он собо́й представля́ет?; что он за челове́к? **2,** (in a manner similar to) как: *act like a madman,* поступа́ть как безу́мец. *Don't talk like that!,* не говори́те так! *All Russians are like that,* все ру́сские таковы́. **3,** (characteristic of) похо́же; типи́чно: *that's just* (or *not*) *like him,* э́то на него́ (не) похо́же; э́то (не) типи́чно для него́. —*adj.* **1,** (similar) подо́бный: *in like manner,* подо́бным (же) о́бразом. **2,** (equal) ра́вный: *a like amount,* ра́вная су́мма. —*n.* **1,** (anything similar): *and the like,* и тому́ подо́бное. *I have never seen the like of it,* я никогда́ не ви́дел ничего́ подо́бного. **2,** *pl.* (preferences): *likes and dislikes,* симпа́тии и антипа́тии. —**like it or not,** хо́чешь не хо́чешь.

likeable *adj.* = **likable.**

likelihood *n.* вероя́тность. *In all likelihood,* по всей вероя́тности.

likely *adj.* **1,** (probable; credible) вероя́тный; правдоподо́бный. *A likely story,* правдоподо́бный расска́з. *He is likely to be late,* он, вероя́тно, опозда́ет. **2,** (suitable) подходя́щий. —*adv.* вероя́тно. *Quite likely,* вполне́ вероя́тно. *More likely,* скоре́е. *Most likely,* скоре́е всего́.

liken *v.t.* уподобля́ть.

likeness *n.* **1,** (similarity) схо́дство; подо́бие. **2,** (image) ко́пия: *a perfect likeness,* то́чная ко́пия. **3,** (guise) личи́на: *in the likeness of,* под личи́ной (+ *gen.*).

likewise *adv.* **1,** (in the same manner) подо́бным о́бразом. **2,** (by the same token) ра́вным о́бразом. **3,** (too; also) та́кже.

liking *n.* симпа́тия; расположе́ние. *Take a liking to,* полюби́ть. *Be to one's liking,* быть по душе́ (+ *dat.*).

lilac *n.* сире́нь. —*adj.* сире́невый.

lilt *n.* ритм. —**lilting,** *adj.* перели́вчатый.

lily *n.* ли́лия. —**lily of the valley,** ла́ндыш.

lima bean фасо́ль ли́мская.

limb *n.* **1,** (branch) сук; ветвь. **2,** (arm; leg) член. —**out on a limb,** *colloq.* в ша́тком (*or* в ско́льзком) положе́нии. —**tear from limb to limb,** разорва́ть (*or* растерза́ть) на ча́сти.

limber *adj.* **1,** (flexible; pliant) ги́бкий. **2,** (agile; nimble) прово́рный. —*v.t. & i.* [*usu.* **limber up**] размина́ть(ся).

limbo *n.* неопределённость: *in a state of limbo,* в состоя́нии неопределённости.

lime *n.* **1,** (citrus fruit; tree that bears it) лайм. **2,** (European linden tree) ли́па. **3,** (calcium oxide, used in cement) и́звесть.

limelight *n.* свет ра́мпы. —**in the limelight,** в це́нтре внима́ния.

limerick *n.* стихотворе́ние из пяти́ строк.

limestone *n.* известня́к. —*adj.* известняко́вый.

limewater *n.* известко́вая вода́.

limit *n.* преде́л; грани́ца. *Speed limit,* преде́льная ско́рость. *Time limit,* преде́льный срок. *City limits,* преде́лы *or* черта́ го́рода. *That's the limit!,* э́то уж сли́шком!; э́то уже́ после́днее де́ло! —*v.t.* ограни́чивать. —**off limits,** закры́т: *off limits to foreigners,* закры́т для иностра́нцев.

limitation *n.* **1,** (restriction) ограниче́ние. **2,** (drawback) недоста́ток.

limited *adj.* ограни́ченный. —**limited edition,** малотира́жное изда́ние. —**limited monarchy,** конституцио́нная мона́рхия.

limitless *adj.* безграни́чный; беспреде́льный.

limonite *n.* бу́рый железня́к.

limousine *n.* лимузи́н.

limp *v.i.* хрома́ть. —*n.* хромота́. *Have a limp; walk with a limp,* хрома́ть. —*adj.* дря́блый; вя́лый.

limpid *adj.* прозра́чный.

linage *n.* число́ строк.

linchpin *n.* **1,** *mech.* чека́. **2,** *fig.* (mainstay) станово́й хребе́т.

linden *n.* ли́па.

line *n.* **1,** (thin, continuous mark) ли́ния; черта́. *Draw a line,* провести́ черту́. **2,** (line of writing) строка́: *read between the lines,* чита́ть ме́жду строк. **3,** (row; file) ли́ния; ряд. **4,** (queue) о́чередь: *stand in line,* стоя́ть в о́череди. **5,** (border) грани́ца: *the state line,* грани́ца шта́та. **6,** *sports* ли́ния: *starting line,* ста́ртовая ли́ния. **7,** *pl.* (contour) ли́нии; очерта́ния. **8,** *pl.* (wrinkles) морщи́ны. **9,** (rope; string) верёвка: *hang the clothes on the line,* ве́шать бельё на верёвку. **10,** (course of movement or action) ли́ния: *line of flight,* ли́ния полёта; *line of fire,* ли́ния огня́. **11,** (system of transportation) ли́ния: *bus line,* авто́бусная ли́ния. **12,** (wires to conduct electricity) про́вод: *telephone line,* телефо́нный про́вод. **13,** (telephone connection) ли́ния; про́вод. *The line is busy,* ли́ния занята́. *Direct line,* прямо́й про́вод. *The chief is on the line,* нача́льник на про́воде. *The voice on the other end of the line,* го́лос на друго́м конце́ про́вода. **14,** *pl.* (actor's part) роль: *memorize one's lines,* зау́чивать роль. **15,** (attitude; policy) ли́ния: *take a hard line,* занима́ть жёсткую ли́нию. **16,** (succession of descendants) ли́ния: *the male line,* мужска́я ли́ния. —*v.t.* **1,** (mark with lines) линова́ть. **2,** *fol. by* **up** (arrange in a line) выстра́ивать. **3,** (put a lining in) де́лать *or* подшива́ть подкла́дку к; подбива́ть. **4,** (fill; cram) заставля́ть: *the shelves are lined with books,* по́лки заста́влены кни́гами. **5,** (form a line along) вы́строиться вдоль. —*v.i.* [*usu.* **line up**] выстра́иваться. —**all along the line,** во всех отноше́ниях; во всём. —**bring into line,** приводи́ть в соотве́тствие. —**draw the line,** проводи́ть чёткую черту́ (*or* грань). —**drop me a line,** пришли́те мне ве́сточку; черкни́те мне не́сколько слов. —**get a line on,** разузна́ть о. —**hold the line, 1,** *mil.* держа́ть оборо́ну. **2,** (stand firm) держа́ться. **3,** (not hang up the telephone) не ве́шать тру́бку. —**in line of duty,** при исполне́нии служе́бных обя́занностей. —**in line with,** в соотве́тствии с. —**lay it on the line,** *colloq.* говори́ть напрями́к. —**line of work,** род заня́тий. —**not in/out of/my line,** не по моей ча́сти. —**out of line, 1,** (not aligned) не в ряд. **2,** (improper; uncalled-for) неуме́стный.

lineage *n.* родосло́вная; происхожде́ние.

lineal *adj.* прямо́й: *lineal descendant,* прямо́й пото́мок.

linear *adj.* лине́йный. —**linear equation,** лине́йное уравне́ние. —**linear measure,** лине́йная ме́ра; ме́ра длины́.

lined *adj.* **1,** (ruled) лино́ванный; в лине́йку. **2,** (wrinkled) морщи́нистый. **3,** (having a lining) на подкла́дке.

lineman *n.* лине́йный монтёр.

linen *n.* **1,** (fabric) полотно́; холст. **2,** (articles made of linen or other cloth) бельё: *bed linen,* посте́льное бельё. —*adj.* **1,** (made of linen) льняно́й; полотня́ный; холщёвый. **2,** (for linen) бельево́й: *linen closet,* бельево́й шкаф.

liner *n.* **1,** (ship) ла́йнер. **2,** (plane) возду́шный ла́йнер. **3,** (lining) подкла́дка.

linesman *n.* **1,** *sports* судья́ на ли́нии. **2,** = **lineman.**

line-up *n.* соста́в (кома́нды). *Starting line-up,* ста́ртовый соста́в.

linger *v.i.* **1,** (tarry) заде́рживаться. **2,** (continue to exist; remain alive) протяну́ть.

lingerie *n.* да́мское бельё.

lingo *n.* жарго́н.

linguist *n.* языкове́д; лингви́ст. —**linguistic,** *adj.* языково́й; лингвисти́ческий. —**linguistics,** *n.* языкозна́ние; лингви́стика.

liniment *n.* втира́ние.

lining *n.* подкла́дка: *silk lining,* шёлковая подкла́дка. *Brake lining,* тормозна́я накла́дка. —**every cloud has a silver lining,** нет ху́да без добра́.

link *n.* **1,** (part of a chain) звено́. **2,** (tie; connection) связь. —*v.t.* соединя́ть; свя́зывать. —*v.i.* [*usu.* **link up**] соединя́ться; смыка́ться. —**linking verb,** глаго́л-свя́зка.

linkage *n.* **1,** (act of linking; coupling) сцепле́ние. *Genetic linkage,* сцепле́ние ге́нов. **2,** (connection) связь. **3,** (linking of two issues) увя́зка.

linnet *n.* коноплю́нка; реполо́в.

linoleum *n.* лино́леум.

linotype *n.* линоти́п.

linseed *n.* льняно́е се́мя. —**linseed oil,** льняно́е ма́сло.

lint *n.* **1,** (fluff) пушо́к. **2,** (substance formerly used for dressing wounds) ко́рпия.

lintel *n.* перемы́чка; при́толока.

lion *n.* лев. —*adj.* [*also,* **lion's**] льви́ный: *lion skin,* льви́ная шку́ра. —**lion's share,** льви́ная до́ля.

lioness *n.* льви́ца.

lionize *v.t.* поднима́ть на щит.

lip *n.* губа́. —**be on everyone's lips,** быть у всех на уста́х. —**keep a stiff upper lip,** храбри́ться. —**none of your lip!,** без де́рзостей! —**pay lip service to,** признава́ть то́лько на слова́х.

lip reading чте́ние с губ.

lipstick *n.* губна́я пома́да.

liquefy *v.t.* сжижа́ть. *Liquefied gas,* сжи́женный газ. —**liquefaction,** *n.* сжиже́ние.

liqueur *n.* ликёр.

liquid *n.* жи́дкость. —*adj.* **1,** (fluid) жи́дкий. **2,** *finance* ликви́дный: *liquid assets,* ликви́дные сре́дства. —**liquid measure,** ме́ра жи́дкости.

liquidate *v.t.* ликвиди́ровать. —**liquidation,** *n.* ликвида́ция.

liquidity *n.* ликви́дность.

liquor *n.* спиртны́е напи́тки.

liquorice *n.* = **licorice.**

lira *n.* ли́ра.

lisp *n.* шепеля́вость; сюсю́канье. —*v.i.* шепеля́вить; сюсю́кать.

lissome *adj.* **1,** (supple) ги́бкий. **2,** (agile) прово́рный.

list *n.* **1,** (enumeration) спи́сок. *Price list,* прейскура́нт. **2,** (tilt, as of a ship) крен. —*v.t.* составля́ть спи́сок (+ *gen.*); перечисля́ть. —*v.i.* (of a ship) крени́ться.

listen *v.i.* слу́шать. —**listener,** *n.* слу́шатель.

listening post пункт *or* пост подслу́шивания.

listless *adj.* вя́лый; апати́чный. —**listlessly,** *adv.* вя́ло. —**listlessness,** *n.* вя́лость.

list price прейскура́нтная цена́.

litany *n.* лита́ния.

liter *also,* **litre,** *n.* литр.

literacy *n.* гра́мотность.

literal *adj.* **1,** (reflecting the exact meaning) буква́льный. **2,** (word for word) досло́вный. —**literally,** *adv.* буква́льно; досло́вно.

literary *adj.* литерату́рный.

literate *adj.* гра́мотный.

literature *n.* литерату́ра.

lithe *adj.* **1,** (supple) ги́бкий. **2,** (graceful) стро́йный.

lithium *n.* ли́тий.

lithograph *n.* литогра́фия; литогра́фский о́ттиск. —*v.t.* литографи́ровать. —**lithographer,** *n.* лито́граф. —**lithographic,** *adj.* литогра́фский. —**lithography,** *n.* литогра́фия.

lithosphere *n.* литосфе́ра.

Lithuanian *adj.* лито́вский. —*n.* **1,** (person) лито́вец; лито́вка. **2,** (language) лито́вский язы́к.

litigate *v.i.* суди́ться. —**litigation,** *n.* иск; суде́бное де́ло.

litmus *n.* ла́кмус. —**litmus paper,** ла́кмусовая бума́га.

litre *n.* = **liter.**

litter *n.* **1,** (trash) сор; хлам. **2,** (stretcher) носи́лки. **3,** (animals born at one time) помёт; вы́водок. —*v.t.* **1,** (make untidy) засоря́ть. **2,** (scatter about) сори́ть. —*v.i.* сори́ть.

little *adj.* **1,** (small in size) ма́ленький; небольшо́й.

2, (small in amount) мало: *little time/hope,* мало времени/надежды. *Little cause for alarm,* мало оснований для тревоги. *Have little effect on,* мало повлиять на. —*adv.* мало: *too little,* слишком мало. *Things have changed very little,* дело очень мало изменилось. *Little did he suspect that...,* он совсем не подозревал, что... —*n.* мало; малое; мало что. *I ate very little,* я ел очень мало. *Be satisfied with little,* довольствоваться малым. *Little has changed,* мало что изменилось. *We see very little of them,* мы редко видимся с ними. *I have little to add,* мне почти нечего добавить. —**a little,** немного: *a little water,* немного воды; *a little tired,* немного устал; *a little better,* немного лучше. —**little by little,** понемногу; мало-помалу. —**make little of,** не придавать значения (+ *dat.*). —**think little of,** быть плохого мнения о. —**what little,** то немногое, что: *I did what little I could,* я сделал то немногое, что мог.

little finger мизинец.

liturgy *n.* литургия. —**liturgical,** *adj.* литургический.

livable *also,* **liveable** *adj.* **1,** (habitable) годный для жилья. **2,** (endurable, as of life) сносный.

live[1] (liv) *v.i. & t.* жить: *live next door,* жить рядом. *Live forever,* жить вечно. *Live to a ripe old age,* дожить до старости. *Live a normal life,* жить нормальной жизнью. *Live a long life,* прожить долгую жизнь. —**live down,** искупать; заглаживать. —**live for,** жить (+ *instr.*): *live for one's son,* жить своим сыном. —**live it up,** *colloq.* разгуливаться. —**live off, 1,** (use to live on) жить на (+ *acc.*): *live off one's savings,* жить на свои сбережения. **2,** (sponge off) жить за счёт (кого-нибудь). —**live on, 1,** (support oneself on) жить на (+ *acc.*): *what are they living on?,* на какие средства они живут? *It's hardly enough to live on,* этого едва хватает на жизнь. **2,** (subsist on) питаться (+ *instr.*): *live on fruit,* питаться фруктами. **3,** (not fade from memory) жить. *His name will live on,* его имя не умрёт. —**live out,** доживать: *live out one's last days,* доживать последние дни. —**live through,** переживать. —**live up to, 1,** (live in accordance with) жить согласно (+ *dat.*). **2,** (satisfy, as expectations) оправдывать. **3,** (fulfill, as a bargain) выполнять. —**live with, 1,** (cohabit with) жить с. **2,** (learn to accept) мириться с.

live[2] (laiv) *adj.* **1,** (alive) живой: *live fish,* живая рыба. **2,** (burning) горячий: *live coals,* горячие угли. **3,** (active, as of a volcano) действующий. **4,** (charged with electricity) под напряжением. **5,** (not exploded) боевой: *live ammunition,* боевые патроны. **6,** (broadcast while being performed) прямой: *live broadcasting,* прямой эфир.

liveable *adj.* = **livable.**

livelihood *n.* средства к жизни. *Earn one's livelihood,* зарабатывать на жизнь.

liveliness *n.* живость; оживлённость.

lively *adj.* живой; оживлённый. —*adv., in* **step lively!,** живей!; скорей!; побыстрее!

liven *v.t.* [*usu.* **liven up**] оживлять —*v.i.* [*usu.* **liven up**] оживляться.

liver *n.* **1,** (organ) печень. **2,** (meat) печёнка. —*adj.* печёночный: *liver extract,* печёночный экстракт.

liveried *adj.* в ливрее; ливрейный.

liverwort *n.* печёночник.

liverwurst *n.* ливерная колбаса.

livery *n.* ливрея. —**livery stable,** платная конюшня.

livestock *n.* (домашний) скот; живой инвентарь.

livid *adj.* **1,** (pale) (мертвенно) бледный. **2,** (incensed) разъярённый; вне себя от ярости.

living *n.* **1,** (manner or means of living) жизнь: *cost of living,* стоимость жизни; *standard of living,* уровень жизни. *Earn a living,* зарабатывать на жизнь. **2,** *preceded by* **the** (those that are alive) живые. —*adj.* **1,** (alive; in use) живой. **2,** (pert. to living) жилищный: *living conditions,* жилищные условия. *Living quarters,* жилые помещения.

living room гостиная.

lizard *n.* ящерица.

llama *n.* лама.

lo *interj.* вот! —**lo and behold!,** и вот!; и вдруг!

load *n.* **1,** (something carried) груз; тяжесть. *Heavy load,* тяжёлый груз. *Carry a load on one's back,* нести груз/тяжесть на спине. **2,** (work performed) нагрузка: *teaching load,* преподавательская нагрузка; *peak load,* максимальная нагрузка. **3,** *fig.* (burden) бремя; тяжесть. *Load off one's shoulders* (or *mind*), тяжесть *or* гора с плеч. **4,** *pl., fol. by* **of,** *colloq.* (a great deal of) масса (+ *gen.*): *we have loads of time,* у нас масса времени. —*v.t.* **1,** (place on a conveyance; place cargo on) грузить; нагружать. **2,** (put ammunition or film into) заряжать. **3,** *often fol. by* **down** (fill; cover; weigh down) заваливать. —*v.i.* **1,** (take on cargo) грузиться. **2,** *fol. by* **into** (board in large numbers) погружаться (в): *load into a bus,* погружаться в автобус.

loaded *adj.* **1,** (carrying a load) загруженный; нагруженный; гружёный. **2,** (filled to capacity) переполненный. **3,** (ready to fire) заряжённый: *loaded gun,* заряжённый пистолет. **4,** (overburdened) заваленный: *loaded with work,* завален работой. **5,** *slang* (rich) при деньгах. *He is loaded,* он купается в золоте. **6,** *slang* (drunk) пьяный. *Get loaded,* напиваться.

loading *n.* погрузка. —*adj.* погрузочный: *loading machine,* погрузочная машина.

loaf *n.* буханка. *Long loaf,* батон. *Round loaf,* каравай. —*v.i.* бездельничать; лодырничать.

loafer *n.* **1,** (idler) бездельник; лодырь. **2,** (casual shoe) спортивная туфля.

loam *n.* суглинок; супесь. —**loamy,** *adj.* суглинистый.

loan *n.* заём; ссуда. —*v.t.* одолжать; давать взаймы. —**loan translation,** калька. —**loanword,** *n.* заимствованное слово.

loath *adj.* неохотный. *Be loath to,* не хотеть (+ *inf.*).

loathe *v.t.* ненавидеть. —**loathing,** *n.* отвращение; омерзение. —**loathsome,** *adj.* отвратительный; омерзительный.

lob *v.t.* высоко подбрасывать (мяч).

lobby *n.* **1,** (hall) вестибюль; фойе; холл. **2,** *polit.* лобби. —**lobbyist,** *n.* лоббист.

lobe *n.* доля. *Ear lobe,* мочка.

lobster *n.* омар.

lobule *n.* долька.

local *adj.* местный. —*n.* **1,** (local resident) местный житель. **2,** (local train) пригородный поезд. —**local anesthetic,** местный наркоз. —**local color,** местный колорит.

locale *n.* место действия.

locality *n.* местность; район.

localize *v.t.* локализовáть. —**localization,** *n.* локализáция.
locate *v.t.* **1,** (place; situate) располагáть: *locate a factory near a river,* располагáть фáбрику у реки́. *Be located,* быть; находи́ться; быть располóженным (гдé-нибудь). **2,** (find; discover) найти́; разыскáть. *Locate a town on a map,* найти́ городóк на кáрте.
location *n.* **1,** (place where something is) местонахождéние. **2,** (site) местоположéние. *Move to a new location,* переходи́ть на нóвое мéсто. **3,** *motion pictures* натýра: *on location,* на натýре.
locative *adj., in* **locative case,** мéстный падéж.
locator *n.* локáтор: *sound locator,* звуковóй локáтор.
lock *n.* **1,** (on a door or box) замóк. **2,** (of a canal) шлюз. **3,** (curl of hair) лóкон. —*v.t.* **1,** [*also,* **lock up**] (secure with a lock; confine) запирáть; закрывáть: *lock the door,* запирáть/закрывáть дверь. *Lock something in the desk,* запирáть чтó-нибудь в стол. **2,** (interlock) сцепля́ться (+ *instr.*): *lock horns*/bumpers, сцепля́ться рогáми/буферáми. *Be locked in mortal combat,* сцепи́ться в смертéльной схвáтке. —*v.i.* запирáться. —**lock, stock and barrel,** целикóм; пóлностью; "со всéми потрохáми". —**under lock and key,** под замкóм.
locker *n.* (запирáющийся) шкáфчик. —**locker room,** раздевáльня.
locket *n.* медальóн.
lockjaw *n.* тризм; столбня́к.
lockout *n.* локáут.
locksmith *n.* слéсарь.
locomotion *n.* передвижéние.
locomotive *n.* локомоти́в; паровóз. —*adj.* движущий.
locus *n.* геометри́ческое мéсто тóчек.
locust *n.* саранчá.
locution *n.* оборóт рéчи; речéние.
lode *n.* (рýдная) жи́ла.
lodestar *n.* путевóдная звездá.
lodge *n.* **1,** (hut; cabin) дóмик; сторóжка. *Hunting lodge,* охóтничий дóмик. **2,** (base for outdoor activity) бáза: *skiing lodge,* лы́жная бáза. **3,** (fraternal society) лóжа. —*v.t.* **1,** (house) помещáть; вселя́ть. **2,** (file, as a complaint) подавáть. —*v.i.* **1,** (be housed) помещáться. **2,** (become embedded, as of a bullet) засéсть.
lodger *n.* жилéц.
lodging *n.* помещéние; жильё. *Lodging for the night,* ночлéг.
loft *n.* **1,** (attic) чердáк. **2,** (hayloft) сеновáл. **3,** (balcony, as for a choir) хóры.
lofty *adj.* высóкий; возвы́шенный. —**loftiness,** *n.* возвы́шенность.
log *n.* **1,** (piece of timber) бревнó. **2,** (same used for burning) полéно. **3,** *pl.* (timber floated down a river) лес. **4,** (daily record) формуля́р. *Ship's log,* вáхтенный/бортовóй/судовóй журнáл. —*adj.* бревéнчатый. *Log cabin,* бревéнчатый дóмик; избá. —*v.t.* **1,** (enter in a log) вноси́ть в журнáл. **2,** (cover, as a certain distance) пройти́; проéхать. *Log 2000 flying hours,* налетáть две ты́сячи часóв. —**sleep like a log,** спать как сурóк.
logarithm *n.* логари́фм. —**logarithmic,** *adj.* логарифми́ческий.
loge *n.* лóжа.
logger *n.* лесорýб.
loggerheads *n.pl.,in* **at loggerheads,** не в ладáх; на ножáх.
logic *n.* лóгика. —**logical,** *adj.* логи́ческий; логи́чный. —**logically,** *adv.* логи́чески; логи́чно. —**logician,** *n.* лóгик.
logistics *n.* тыл и снабжéние; тыловóе обеспéчение; материáльно-техни́ческое обеспéчение. —**logistical,** *adj.* тыловóй.
loin *n.* **1,** (part of the back) поясни́ца. **2,** *pl.* (region of the thigh and groin) пах. —**loincloth,** *n.* набéдренная повя́зка.
loiter *v.i.* **1,** (drift about) слоня́ться. **2,** (dawdle) мéшкать. —**loiterer,** *n.* лóдырь.
loll *v.i.* валя́ться; нéжиться.
lollipop *n.* леденéц (на пáлочке).
lone *adj.* одинóкий.
loneliness *n.* одинóчество.
lonely *adj.* **1,** (lonesome) одинóкий. **2,** (solitary) уединённый. **3,** (remote) глухóй: *a lonely street,* глухáя ýлица.
loner *n., colloq.* дикáрь; бирю́к.
lonesome *adj.* одинóкий.
lone wolf одинóчка; бирю́к.
long *adj.* **1,** (of considerable length) дли́нный: *long hair,* дли́нные вóлосы. *A long distance,* большóе расстоя́ние. *We (still) have a long way to go,* нам ещё далекó éхать. **2,** (having a specified length): длинóй в: *two meters long,* длинóй в два мéтра. **3,** (of considerable duration) дóлгий: *long life,* дóлгая жизнь; *a long silence,* дóлгое молчáние. *(For) a long time,* давнó; дóлго. **4,** (taking a long time): *I won't be long,* я не дóлго; я не надóлго. *He was not long in answering,* он не замéдлил с отвéтом. **5,** *Long face,* вы́тянутое лицó. —*adv.* **1,** (for a long time in the past or future) дóлго: *did you have to wait long?,* вам пришлóсь дóлго ждать? *He hasn't long to live,* емý остáлось недóлго жить. **2,** (for a long time up to and including the present) давнó: *have you been waiting long?,* вы давнó ждёте? **3,** (for the duration of) напролёт: *all night long,* всю ночь напролёт. —*n.* мнóго врéмени: *it won't take long,* э́то не займёт мнóго врéмени. —*v.i.* **1,** *fol. by* **for** (miss; yearn for) тосковáть по. **2,** *fol. by inf.* (earnestly desire) óчень хотéть; стреми́ться. —**any longer; no longer,** бóльше не; ужé не. *It's no longer a joke,* э́то ужé не шýтка. —**as long as, 1,** (for all the time that) покá: *as long as I live,* покá я бýду жив (живá). *As long as you like,* скóлько хоти́те. **2,** (inasmuch as) так как; ввидý тогó, что. **3,** (provided that) éсли тóлько; лишь бы. —**at long last,** наконéц-то. —**before long,** в скóром врéмени. —**how long?, 1,** (in time) скóлько врéмени?; как дóлго? **2,** (in length): *how long is this carpet?,* каковá длинá э́того коврá?; какóй длины́ э́тот ковёр? —**in the long run,** *see* **run.** —**long after,** дóлгое врéмя пóсле. —**long ago,** давнó. —**long before,** задóлго до. —**long live...,** да здрáвствует... —**so long, 1,** (for such a long time) так дóлго. **2,** (goodbye) до свидáния!; покá! —**the long and the short of it,** корóче говоря́.
long-awaited *adj.* долгождáнный.
long-distance *adj.* на дáльнее расстоя́ние: *long-distance flight,* полёт на дáльнее расстоя́ние. *Long-distance train,* пóезд дáльнего слéдования. *Long-distance call,* междугорóдный телефóнный разговóр. *Long-distance race,* бег на дли́нную дистáнцию.

longevity *n.* долгове́чность; долголе́тие.
long-haired *adj.* длинноволо́сый.
longhand *n.* по́черк. *Written in longhand,* напи́санный от руки́.
longing *n.* стремле́ние; жа́жда. —*adj.* тоску́ющий: *a longing look,* тоску́ющий взгляд. —**longingly,** *adv.* с тоско́й; тоскли́во.
longitude *n.* долгота́. —**longitudinal,** *adj.* продо́льный.
long-lasting *adj.* про́чный; сто́йкий.
long-legged *adj.* длинноно́гий.
long-lived *adj.* долгове́чный; многоле́тний.
long-playing *adj.* долгоигра́ющий.
long-range *adj.* **1,** (of a weapon or aircraft) да́льнего де́йствия; дальнобо́йный. **2,** (long-term, as of plans) перспекти́вный.
longshoreman *n.* (порто́вый) гру́зчик; до́кер.
long shot 1, *horse racing* аутса́йдер. **2,** (unpromising venture) риско́ванное де́ло. —**not by a long shot,** нико́им о́бразом; далеко́ не. *Not everyone by a long shot,* далеко́ не все.
long-standing *adj.* да́вний; давни́шний.
long-suffering *adj.* многострада́льный.
long-term *adj.* долгосро́чный.
long wave дли́нная волна́. —**long-wave,** *adj.* длинново́лновый.
long-winded *adj.* многосло́вный.
look *v.i.* **1,** (use one's sense of sight) смотре́ть: *look at one's watch,* (по)смотре́ть на часы́. **2,** (search) иска́ть: *I don't know but I'll look,* не зна́ю, но поищу́. **3,** (appear; seem) вы́глядеть; име́ть (како́й-нибудь) вид: *she looks well,* она́ вы́глядит хорошо́; у неё хоро́ший вид. —*v.t.* **1,** (face squarely) смотре́ть (+ *dat.*): *look someone in the face,* смотре́ть кому́-нибудь в лицо́. **2,** (appear to be a certain age): *he looks about forty,* ему́ на вид лет со́рок. *She doesn't look her age,* она́ вы́глядит моло́же свои́х лет. —*n.* **1,** (glance) взгляд. **2,** (expression) выраже́ние лица́. **3,** (appearance) вид; о́блик; нару́жность; вне́шность. —**look after,** присма́тривать за; уха́живать за; следи́ть за; смотре́ть за. —**look ahead,** смотре́ть *or* загляну́ть вперёд. —**look around, 1,** (turn around and look back) обора́чиваться. **2,** (look all around) смотре́ть круго́м; осма́триваться; огля́дываться. —**look back,** огля́дываться наза́д. —**look down on,** смотре́ть свысока́ на. —**look for, 1,** (search for) иска́ть. **2,** (expect) ожида́ть. —**look forward to,** о́чень ждать; ждать с нетерпе́нием; предвкуша́ть. —**look here!,** послу́шайте! —**look in on,** загляну́ть к. —**look into,** рассма́тривать; рассле́довать. —**look like, 1,** (resemble) быть похо́жим на. **2,** (be of a certain appearance): *what does he look like?,* како́в он собо́й? **3,** *colloq.* (seem as if): *it looks like rain,* похо́же, что бу́дет дождь. —**look out, 1,** *literally* выгля́дывать. *Look out the window,* смотре́ть *or* выгля́дывать в окно́ *or* из окна́. **2,** (be careful) быть осторо́жным; гляде́ть в о́ба. *Look out!,* осторо́жно! **3,** *fol. by* **for** (beware of) бере́чься (+ *gen.*). **4,** *fol. by* **for** (protect) бере́чь. **5,** *fol. by* **on** (face) выходи́ть; смотре́ть (*with* в *or* на). —**look over,** просма́тривать. —**look through, 1,** = **look over. 2,** (peep through) загля́дывать в. —**look to,** рассчи́тывать на. —**look up, 1,** *literally* поднима́ть глаза́. **2,** (seek in a reference book) иска́ть: *look up a word in the dictionary,* иска́ть сло́во в словаре́. **3,** *fol. by* **to** (admire; respect) смотре́ть на (+ *acc.*) сни́зу вверх. **4,** *colloq.* (call on; visit) заходи́ть к; загляну́ть к. **5,** *colloq.* (get better) поправля́ться: *things are looking up,* дела́ поправля́ются. —**look upon,** счита́ть; рассма́тривать.
looking glass зе́ркало.
lookout *n.* **1,** (act of watching) наблюде́ние: *keep a lookout,* вести́ наблюде́ние. *Be on the lookout,* быть настороже́. **2,** (place for keeping watch) наблюда́тельный пункт.
loom *n.* тка́цкий стано́к. —*v.i.* **1,** (appear) видне́ться; вырисо́вываться. **2,** (impend) надвига́ться.
loon *n.* гага́ра.
loop *n.* **1,** (doubled cord) пе́тля. **2,** *aero.* мёртвая пе́тля: *loop the loop,* де́лать мёртвую пе́тлю. —*v.t.* обма́тывать.
loophole *n.* **1,** (embrasure) бойни́ца; амбразу́ра. **2,** *fig.* (avenue of escape) лазе́йка.
loose *adj.* **1,** (not tight or taut) сла́бый. **2,** (loose-fitting) свобо́дный. **3,** (not firmly fastened; not firmly in place) шата́ющийся: *I have a loose tooth,* у меня́ зуб шата́ется. **4,** (dissolute) распу́тный. *Loose morals,* лёгкие нра́вы. —*adv.* свобо́дно. —*v.t.* **1,** (loosen) ослабля́ть. **2,** (shoot; let fly) стреля́ть; пуска́ть. —**at loose ends,** без де́ла; не у дел. —**break loose,** вырыва́ться. —**come loose, 1,** (come untied) развя́зываться; отвя́зываться. **2,** (be dislodged from a fixed position) расша́тываться. —**loose bowels,** поно́с. —**loose soil,** ры́хлая по́чва. —**lose talk,** кривото́лки. —**loose tongue,** язы́к без косте́й. —**loose translation,** нето́чный перево́д. —**on the loose,** на свобо́де. —**set/let/turn loose,** отпуска́ть. —**work loose,** выпу́тываться; вывёртываться.
loose-leaf *adj.* с вкладны́ми листа́ми.
loosely *adv.* **1,** (not tightly) свобо́дно: *fit loosely,* сиде́ть свобо́дно. **2,** (not strictly) широко́: *interpret loosely,* широко́ толкова́ть.
loosen *v.t.* **1,** (make less tight) ослабля́ть; отпуска́ть; распуска́ть. *Loosen someone's tongue,* развяза́ть кому́-нибудь язы́к. **2,** (make less dense, as soil) рыхли́ть; разрыхля́ть. —*v.i.* ослабе́ть.
loot *n.* добы́ча. —*v.t.* гра́бить. —**looter,** *n.* граби́тель. —**looting,** *n.* грабёж.
lop *v.t.* [*usu.* **lop off**] отруба́ть; обруба́ть.
lope *v.i.* бежа́ть вприпры́жку.
lop-eared *adj.* лопоу́хий; вислоу́хий.
lopsided *adj.* кривобо́кий; однобо́кий.
loquacious *adj.* болтли́вый; говорли́вый; разгово́рчивый. —**loquaciousness,** *n.* болтли́вость; говорли́вость; разгово́рчивость.
lord *n.* **1,** (ruler; master) влады́ка; господи́н; ба́рин. **2,** (British title) лорд. *House of Lords,* пала́та ло́рдов. **3,** *cap.* (God) бог; госпо́дь: *oh Lord!; Good Lord!,* го́споди!; бо́же мой! —*v.i., usu. in* **lord it over,** кома́ндовать над; вла́ствовать над.
lordly *adj.* ба́рственный.
lordship *n.* све́тлость: *Your Lordship,* ва́ша све́тлость.
lore *n.* зна́ния.
lorgnette *n.* лорне́т.
lorry *n.* грузови́к.
lose *v.t.* **1,** (misplace) теря́ть. **2,** (be unable to maintain) теря́ть: *lose one's balance,* теря́ть равнове́сие. **3,** (fail to win; gamble away) прои́грывать. **4,** (suffer the loss of) теря́ть; утра́чивать; лиша́ться. **5,** (miss,

as an opportunity) упускать; пропускать. **6,** *colloq.* (elude; shake off) ускользать от. —*v.i.* проигрывать. —**lose heart,** падать духом; унывать. —**lose one's head,** потерять голову. —**lose one's mind,** сходить с ума. —**lose one's temper,** выходить из себя. —**lose one's way,** заблудиться; сбиваться с пути *or* с дороги. —**lose patience,** терять терпение; выходить из терпения. —**lose sight of,** *see* **sight.** —**lose weight,** терять в весе; убавлять в весе. *See also* **lost.**

loser *n.* проигравший. *He is a poor loser,* он не умеет достойно проигрывать.

losing *adj.* проигрышный.

loss *n.* **1,** (act of losing; that which is lost) потеря; утрата. **2,** (money lost; opp. of profit) убыток. *Sell at a loss,* продавать в убыток/с убытком/невыгодно. **3,** (defeat in a game) проигрыш; поражение. **4,** *pl.* (casualties) потери. **5,** *pl.* (what is lost in gambling) проигрыш. —**be at a loss,** теряться в догадках. *I am at a loss for words,* не нахожу слов. *He is never at a loss for words,* он не лезет за словом в карман. *I was at a loss as to how to answer,* я не нашёлся, что ответить. —**throw for a loss,** озадачивать.

lost *adj.* **1,** (missing; misplaced; gone) потерянный. *The letter was lost,* письмо потерялось. *Make up for lost time,* наверстать потерянное время. **2,** (having lost one's way) заблудший. *Be/get lost,* заблудиться. *Get lost in a crowd,* потеряться *or* замешаться в толпе. **3,** (killed, drowned, sunk, etc.) погибший. *Give up for lost,* считать погибшим. **4,** (engrossed) погружённый: *lost in thought,* погружённый в размышления. **5,** (missed, as of an opportunity) пропущенный; упущенный. **6,** *fol. by* **on** *or* **upon** (unheeded): *the lesson was not lost upon him,* урок не прошёл для него даром. —**lost cause,** гиблое дело. —**lost sheep,** заблудшая овца.

lot *n.* **1,** (object used to determine something by chance) жребий: *cast lots,* бросать жребий. *Decide something by lot,* решить что-нибудь по жребию. *The lot fell upon him,* жребий пал на него. **2,** (fate; portion) судьба; участь: *cast one's lot with,* связать свою судьбу с. *Fall to someone's lot,* выпасть на чью-нибудь долю. **3,** (plot of land) участок. *Parking lot,* стоянка (автомобилей). **4,** (batch; quantity) партия. **5,** *colloq.* [*also pl.* **lots**] много: *a lot of money,* много денег. *Read a lot,* много читать. *Have lots to do,* иметь много дел. *I've heard a lot about you,* я много о вас слышал(а). *Your have quite a lot to be proud of,* вам есть чем гордиться. —*adv.* гораздо; намного: *a lot easier,* гораздо/намного легче.

lotion *n.* (косметическая) жидкость. *Hand lotion,* жидкость для рук. *Face lotion,* лосьон.

lottery *n.* лотерея. —*adj.* лотерейный: *lottery ticket,* лотерейный билет.

lotto *n.* лото.

lotus *n.* лотос.

loud *adj.* **1,** (strongly audible) громкий. *Loud noise,* сильный шум. **2,** *colloq.* (garish) кричащий; крикливый; броский. —*adv.* громко. *Out loud,* вслух. —**loudly,** *adv.* громко.

loudmouth *n.* крикун. —**loudmouthed,** *adj.* крикливый.

loudness *n.* громкость.

loudspeaker *n.* громкоговоритель; репродуктор.

lounge *n.* **1,** (public room) салон. **2,** (sofa) кушетка. —*v.i.* [*often* **lounge around**] нежиться; валяться.

lour *v.* = **lower**[2].

louse *n.* **1,** (insect) вошь. **2,** *slang* (contemptible person) подлец. —**louse up,** *slang* напутать.

lousy *adj.* **1,** (infested with lice) вшивый. **2,** *slang* (rotten; miserable) паршивый; дрянной.

lout *n.* хам; невежа; увалень.

lovable *adj.* милый; славный.

love *n.* любовь. *Love of/for music,* любовь к музыке. *In love,* влюблён. *Fall in love (with),* влюбиться (в). *Marry for love,* жениться *or* выйти замуж по любви. —*adj.* любовный: *love letter,* любовное письмо; *love song,* любовная песнь. *Love story,* история о любви. *Love affair,* роман. —*v.t. & i.* любить: *I love you,* я тебя люблю.

lovely *adj.* прекрасный; прелестный; чудесный. —**loveliness,** *n.* красота; прелесть.

lover *n.* **1,** (person in love) влюблённый. **2,** (enthusiast) любитель. **3,** (paramour) любовник.

love seat диван на двоих.

loving *adj.* **1,** (feeling love) любящий. **2,** (tender) любовный. —**loving cup,** круговая чаша.

lovingly *adv.* любовно; с любовью.

low *adj.* **1,** (not high) низкий: *low ceiling,* низкий потолок. *Low prices,* низкие цены. *Low pressure,* низкое давление. *Low gear,* первая передача. *Low tide,* низшая точка отлива. **2,** (poor; inferior) низкий; плохой: *low quality,* низкое качество; *low mark,* плохая отметка. *Have a low opinion of,* быть невысокого *or* плохого мнения о. **3,** (not loud) негромкий; тихий. **4,** (low-pitched; deep) низкий. **5,** (humble in origin) низкий: *of low station,* низкого происхождения. **6,** (base; mean) подлый; низкий. **7,** (dejected) унылый. *Low spirits,* уныние. **8,** *fol. by* **on** (not well supplied with): *we're low on gas,* бензин кончается. —*adv.* **1,** (at a low level) низко. **2,** (softly) тихо. —*n.* низшая точка. *Prices reached a new low,* цены понизились до нового предела. —*v.i.* (bellow) мычать. —**lay low,** свалить; повалить; сразить. —**lie low,** залегать; отлёживаться; притаиться. —**run low,** кончаться; истощаться.

low-cut *adj.* с низким вырезом.

lower[1] (**lo**-er) *v.t.* **1,** (let down) спускать; опускать. **2,** (reduce) снижать; понижать. **3,** (weaken, as one's resistance) ослаблять. **4,** (reduce the volume of) понижать. **5,** *in* **lower oneself,** унижаться. —*adj.* нижний: *lower berth,* нижняя полка; *lower deck,* нижняя палуба. *Lower House,* нижняя палата. *Lower class,* низший класс.

lower[2] (**lau**-er) *also,* **lour** *v.i.* смотреть волком; смотреть зверем.

lower case строчные буквы.

low-grade *adj.* недоброкачественный; низкосортный; низкопробный.

lowland *n.* низменность.

lowly *adj.* **1,** (of low rank) низкий. **2,** (humble; meek) скромный; смиренный.

low-lying *adj.* низменный; низинный.

low-necked *adj.* с низким вырезом.

low-paid *adj.* низкооплачиваемый.

low-powered *adj.* маломощный; слабосильный.

low-priced *adj.* дешёвый.

lox *n.* сёмга.

loyal *adj.* верный; лояльный. —**loyalty,** *n.* верность; лояльность.

lozenge *n.* лепёшка, таблетка.

lubricant *n.* смáзочный материáл; смáзка.
lubricate *v.t.* смáзывать. —**lubrication,** *n.* смáзка; смáзывание. —**lubricator,** *n.* маслёнка.
lucid *adj.* я́сный: *lucid exposition,* я́сное изложéние. *Lucid mind,* свéтлый ум. *Lucid intervals,* свéтлые минýты. —**lucidity,** *n.* я́сность.
luck *n.* счáстье; удáча. *Good luck!,* желáю вам счáстья. —**as luck would have it,** как нарóчно; как назлó; как на бедý; как на грех. —**bad luck,** несчáстье: *I had the bad luck to...,* я имéл(а) несчáстье (+ *inf.*). —**be in luck,** повезти́ (+ *dat.*): *you are in/out of/luck,* вам (не) повезлó. —**for (good) luck,** на счáстье.
luckily *adv.* к счáстью. *Luckily for me,* на моё счáстье.
luckless *adj.* несчастли́вый; незадáчливый.
lucky *adj.* счастли́вый; удáчливый. —**be lucky,** везти́ (+ *dat.*): *he is lucky at cards,* емý везёт в кáртах. *It is lucky for you that...,* вам повезлó, что...
lucrative *adj.* при́быльный; дохóдный.
lucre *n.* нажи́ва. —**filthy lucre,** презрéнный метáлл.
ludicrous *adj.* смешнóй; нелéпый; смехотвóрный.
lug *v.t.* тащи́ть; волочи́ть.
luggage *n.* багáж.
lugubrious *adj.* печáльный; грýстный; мрáчный.
lukewarm *adj.* тепловáтый.
lull *v.t.* усыпля́ть; убаю́кивать. —*n.* зати́шье.
lullaby *n.* колыбéльная пéсня.
lumbago *n.* прострéл; люмбáго.
lumbar *adj.* поясни́чный.
lumber *n.* лес; лесоматериáл. —*adj.* леснóй. —*v.i.* (move heavily) громыхáть. —**lumberjack,** *n.* лесорýб. —**lumber jacket,** кýртка. —**lumberyard,** *n.* леснóй склад.
luminary *n.* свети́ло.
luminescence *n.* свечéние; люминесцéнция. —**luminescent,** *adj.* светя́щийся; люминесцéнтный.
luminosity *n.* освещённость.
luminous *adj.* светя́щийся; световóй.
lummox *n., colloq.* ýвалень; простофи́ля.
lump *n.* **1,** (shapeless mass) ком; комóк: *lump of dirt,* ком гря́зи. **2,** (piece, as of sugar) кусóк. **3,** (swelling; bump) ши́шка. —*v.t.* [*usu.* **lump together**] вали́ть в однý кýчу; стричь под однý гребёнку. —**lump in one's throat,** ком/комóк/клубóк в гóрле. *I felt a lump in my throat,* ком подступи́л к гóрлу. —**lump sugar,** кусковóй *or* пилёный сáхар; рафинáд. —**lump sum,** единоврéменно выплáчиваемая сýмма. *Pay (out) in a lump sum,* заплати́ть всё срáзу; выплáчивать единоврéменно.
lumpy *adj.* с комкáми.
lunacy *n.* безýмие.
lunar *adj.* лýнный.
lunatic *n.* душевнобольнóй; сумасшéдший. *Lunatic asylum,* сумасшéдший дом.
lunch *n.* обéд; ленч. *Have lunch,* обéдать. —*adj.* обéденный: *lunch break,* обéденный переры́в.
luncheon *n.* обéд. —**luncheonette,** *n.* закýсочная.
lung *n.* лёгкое. —*adj.* лёгочный. *Lung cancer,* рак лёгких. —**at the top of one's lungs,** во весь гóлос; во всё гóрло; во всю глóтку.
lunge *v.i.* дёрнуться. —*n.* наскóк; вы́пад.
lupus *n.* волчáнка.
lurch *v.i.* покачнýться. —*n.* толчóк. —**leave in the lurch,** поки́нуть в бедé.
lure *n.* примáнка. —*v.t.* завлекáть; замáнивать; примáнивать.
lurid *adj.* **1,** (glowing) óгненный. **2,** (shocking) жýткий.
lurk *v.i.* таи́ться; притаи́ться.
luscious *adj.* лáкомый; сóчный.
lush *adj.* **1,** (luxuriant, as of foliage) бýйный; пы́шный; тýчный. **2,** (succulent) сóчный. —*n., slang* (drunkard) пья́ница.
lust *n.* **1,** (sexual desire) пóхоть; вожделéние. **2,** (any overwhelming desire) жáжда; страсть. —*v.i.* [*usu.* **lust for** *or* **after**] жáждать (+ *gen.*).
luster *also,* **lustre** *n.* блеск; лоск; гля́нец. *Lose its luster,* тускнéть.
lustful *adj.* похотли́вый.
lustre *n.* = **luster.**
lustrous *adj.* глянцеви́тый; гля́нцевый.
lusty *adj.* крéпкий; дю́жий.
lute *n.* лю́тня.
lutetium *n.* лютéций.
Lutheran *adj.* лютерáнский. —*n.* лютерáнин. —**Lutheranism,** *n.* лютерáнство.
luxuriant *adj.* пы́шный; бýйный.
luxuriate *v.i.* [*usu.* **luxuriate in**] нéжиться (в *or* на); наслаждáться (+ *instr.*).
luxurious *adj.* роскóшный.
luxury *n.* рóскошь. —*adj.* люкс: *luxury hotel,* гости́ница-люкс. *Luxury item,* предмéт рóскоши.
lycée *n.* лицéй.
lye *n.* щёлок.
lying *adj.* **1,** (recumbent) лежáщий; лежáчий. **2,** (false) лжи́вый; лóжный. —*n.* лганьё; враньё.
lymph *n.* ли́мфа. *Lymph nodes,* лимфати́ческие узлы́. —**lymphatic,** *adj.* лимфати́ческий.
lynch *v.t.* линчевáть. —**lynching,** *n.* линчевáние; самосýд.
lynx *n.* рысь.
lyre *n.* ли́ра.
lyric *n.* **1,** (lyric poem) ли́рика. **2,** *pl.* (words of a song) текст. —*adj.* [*also,* **lyrical**] лири́ческий.
lyricism *n.* лири́зм.

M

M, m трина́дцатая бу́ква англи́йского алфави́та.
ma *n., colloq.* ма́ма
macabre *adj.* жу́ткий.
macadam *n.* щёбень. *—adj.* щебёночный. *—v.t.* мости́ть щёбнем.
macaque *n.* мака́ка.
macaroni *n.* макаро́ны.
macaroon *n.* минда́льное печёнье.
macaw *n.* а́ра; ара́ра.
mace *n.* **1,** (club) булава́. **2,** (staff of office) жезл. **3,** (spice) муска́тный цвет.
Macedonian *adj.* македо́нский.
Machiavellian *adj.* макиавёллевский.
machination *n., usu. pl.* махина́ции; ко́зни.
machine *n.* маши́на; стано́к. *—adj.* маши́нный. *Machine shop,* механи́ческий цех; механи́ческая мастерска́я. *Machine tool,* стано́к. *Machine translation,* маши́нный перево́д.
machine gun пулемёт. **—machine-gun,** *v.t.* обстрёливать пулемётным огнём. **—machine gunner,** пулемётчик.
machinery *n.* **1,** (machines collectively) маши́ны. **2,** (system; organization) аппара́т.
machinist *n.* машини́ст.
mackerel *n.* ску́мбрия; макрёль.
mackintosh *n.* макинто́ш; плащ.
macrocosm *n.* макроко́см.
mad *adj.* **1,** (insane) сумасшёдший. *Drive mad,* своди́ть с ума́. *Go mad,* сходи́ть с ума́. **2,** (reckless; foolish) безу́мный. **3,** (rabid) бёшеный. **4,** *fol. by* **about** (infatuated) без ума́ (от). **5,** *colloq.* (angry) серди́тый. *Get mad,* серди́ться. **—like mad,** сломя́ го́лову.
madam *n.* мада́м; суда́рыня; госпожа́.
madcap *n.* сумасбро́д; сорване́ц; сорвиголова́.
madden *v.t.* **1,** (drive mad) своди́ть с ума́. **2,** (make furious) беси́ть. **—maddening,** *adj.* доса́дный.
madder *n.* (plant) марёна.
Madeira *n.* (wine) мадёра.
mademoiselle *n.* мадемуазёль.
made-to-order *adj.* сдёланный на зака́з.
madhouse *n.* сумасшёдший дом.
madly *adv.* безу́мно. *Madly in love with,* безу́мно влюблён (влюблена́) в; без ума́ от.
madman *n.* сумасшёдший; безу́мец.
madness *n.* **1,** (insanity) сумасшёствие. **2,** (folly) безу́мие.
Madonna *n.* мадо́нна.
madrigal *n.* мадрига́л.
maelstrom *n.* водоворо́т; вихрь.
maestro *n.* маэ́стро.
magazine *n.* **1,** (publication) журна́л. **2,** (of a firearm) магази́н. **3,** (storage place) по́греб: *powder magazine,* порохово́й по́греб. *—adj.* журна́льный: *magazine article,* журна́льная статья́.
magenta *n.* фукси́н. *—adj.* кра́сно-лило́вый.
maggot *n.* личи́нка.
Magi *n.pl.* волхвы́.
magic *n.* ма́гия; волшебство́. *As if by magic,* как бу́дто по волшебству́. *—adj.* [*also,* **magical**] маги́ческий; волшёбный. *Magic lantern,* волшёбный фона́рь. *Magic wand,* волшёбная па́лочка.
magician *n.* **1,** (sorcerer; wizard) волшёбник; чаро-дёй. **2,** (entertainer who performs magic tricks) фо́кусник; иллюзиони́ст.
magisterial *adj.* **1,** (of or pert. to a magistrate) судёбный. **2,** (imperious) повели́тельный.
magistracy *n.* магистрату́ра.
magistrate *n.* мирово́й судья́.
Magna Carta *also,* **Magna Charta** Вели́кая ха́ртия во́льностей.
magnanimity *n.* великоду́шие. **—magnanimous,** *adj.* великоду́шный.
magnate *n.* магна́т.
magnesia *n.* магнёзия.
magnesium *n.* ма́гний.
magnet *n.* магни́т.
magnetic *adj.* **1,** *physics* магни́тный: *magnetic field,* магни́тное по́ле. *Magnetic tape,* магни́тная лёнта. **2,** *fig.* (powerfully attractive) магнети́ческий. **—magnetics,** *n.* магнети́зм. **—magnetism,** *n.* магнети́зм.
magnetite *n.* магнети́т.
magnetize *v.t.* намагни́чивать.
magneto *n.* магнёто.
magnetron *n.* магнетро́н.
magnification *n.* увеличёние.
magnificence *n.* великолёпие.
magnificent *adj.* великолёпный. **—magnificently,** *adv.* великолёпно.
magnify *v.t.* **1,** (enlarge) увели́чивать. **2,** (exaggerate) преувели́чивать. **—magnifying glass,** увеличи́тельное стекло́; лу́па.
magnitude *n.* **1,** (size; brightness) величина́. **2,** (significance) ва́жность.
magnolia *n.* магно́лия.
magpie *n.* соро́ка.
Magyar *n.* мадья́р. *—adj.* мадья́рский.
maharajah *n.* магара́джа.
mahogany *n.* кра́сное дёрево. *—adj.* кра́сного дёрева.

maid *n.* **1,** (young woman) де́ва; деви́ца; де́вушка. **2,** (housemaid) го́рничная; домрабо́тница; (chambermaid) го́рничная; убо́рщица. —**old maid,** ста́рая де́ва.
maiden *n.* де́ва; деви́ца; де́вушка. —*adj.* **1,** (unmarried) незаму́жняя. **2,** (initial) пе́рвый: *maiden voyage,* пе́рвый рейс.
maidenhead *n.* де́вственная плева́.
maidenhood *n.* деви́чество.
maidenly *adj.* деви́чий.
maiden name де́вичья фами́лия.
mail *n.* **1,** (post; letters) по́чта: *by mail,* по по́чте. **2,** (armor) кольчу́га. —*adj.* почто́вый: *mail train,* почто́вый по́езд. —*v.t.* **1,** (deposit in a mailbox) опуска́ть (в почто́вый я́щик). **2,** (send by mail) посыла́ть по по́чте.
mailbag *n.* почто́вый мешо́к. *Also,* **mail pouch.**
mailbox *n.* почто́вый я́щик.
mailed fist брониро́ванный кула́к.
mailman *n.* почтальо́н.
mail-order *adj.* посы́лочный: *mail-order house,* посы́лочная фи́рма.
maim *v.t.* кале́чить; уве́чить.
main *adj.* гла́вный; основно́й. *The main thing,* (са́мое) гла́вное. *Main floor,* пе́рвый эта́ж. *Main course,* второ́е (блю́до). —*n.* магистра́ль: *water main,* водопрово́дная магистра́ль. —**in the main,** в основно́м. —**with might and main,** изо всех сил; во всю мочь.
mainland *n.* матери́к.
mainly *adv.* в основно́м; гла́вным о́бразом; бо́льшей ча́стью.
mainmast *n.* грот-ма́чта.
mainsail *n.* грот.
mainspring *n.* **1,** (of a watch) ходова́я пружи́на. **2,** *fig.* (chief source or motive) гла́вная пружи́на.
mainstay *n.* станово́й хребе́т.
mainstream *n.* гла́вное ру́сло: *outside the mainstream,* в стороне́ от гла́вного ру́сла.
maintain *v.t.* **1,** (assert; claim) утвержда́ть. **2,** (carry on; keep up) подде́рживать. **3,** (preserve; retain) сохраня́ть. **4,** (have; own; keep) держа́ть. **5,** (support; provide for) содержа́ть. **6,** (keep in good repair) содержа́ть в испра́вности.
maintenance *n.* **1,** (support) содержа́ние. **2,** (servicing) ухо́д.
maître d'hôtel метрдоте́ль.
maize *n.* маис.
majestic *adj.* вели́чественный.
majesty *n.* **1,** (grandeur) вели́чие. **2,** *cap.* (title) вели́чество: *Your Majesty,* ва́ше вели́чество.
major *n.* **1,** (military officer) майо́р. **2,** *music* мажо́р: *key of F major,* тона́льность фа мажо́р. **3,** (main field of study) предме́т специализа́ции. —*adj.* **1,** (greater) бо́льший: *the major part,* бо́льшая часть. **2,** (important; significant) ва́жный; значи́тельный. **3,** (prominent) кру́пный: *a major writer,* кру́пный писа́тель. **4,** (broad in scope) капита́льный: *major repairs,* капита́льный ремо́нт. **5,** *music* мажо́рный. —*v.i.* специализи́роваться.
majordomo *n.* мажордо́м.
major general генера́л-лейтена́нт.
majority *n.* **1,** (more than half of a total) большинство́. **2,** (full legal age) совершенноле́тие.
make *v.t.* **1,** (accomplish; carry out; commit) де́лать; соверша́ть: *make a mistake,* де́лать/соверша́ть оши́бку; *make an attempt,* де́лать попы́тку; *make an offer,* де́лать предложе́ние; *make progress,* де́лать успе́хи; *make a deal,* соверша́ть сде́лку. **2,** (produce; manufacture) дела́ть; производи́ть; выраба́тывать; изготовля́ть. *What is this made of?,* из чего́ э́то сде́лано? **3,** (produce; cause) производи́ть: *make an impression,* производи́ть впечатле́ние. *Make a noise,* поднима́ть шум. *Make a scene,* устра́ивать сце́ну. **4,** (produce as a result) де́лать: *make no secret of,* не де́лать секре́та из. *Make an example of,* ста́вить в приме́р. *Make a mess of,* напу́тать. **5,** (cause to be) *usu. rendered by a single verb: make happy,* ра́довать; *make shorter,* укора́чивать. *Make public,* предава́ть гла́сности. **6,** (cause to; force to) заставля́ть: *make someone wait,* заставля́ть кого́-нибудь ждать. *Make someone promise,* брать сло́во с. **7,** (prompt to; impel to) побужда́ть: *what made you do it?,* что вас побуди́ло э́то сде́лать? **8,** (amount to; constitute) составля́ть. *Two and two make four,* два и два равно́ четырём. **9,** (turn out to be; become) ока́зываться. *He will make a good teacher,* из него́ вы́йдет хоро́ший учи́тель. **10,** (establish; enact, as laws or rules) устана́вливать. **11,** (appoint) назнача́ть. **12,** (earn) зараба́тывать: *make a living,* зараба́тывать на жизнь. *Make a fortune,* нажи́ть состоя́ние. **13,** (arrive in time for; catch) успева́ть на *or* к. **14,** (cook) гото́вить: *make dinner,* гото́вить обе́д. *Make tea,* зава́ривать чай. **15,** *with certain nouns* дава́ть: *make a promise,* дава́ть обеща́ние; *make a recommendation,* дава́ть рекоменда́цию. *Make room for,* дава́ть ме́сто (+ *dat.*). **16,** *with certain nouns* идти́ на: *make concessions,* идти́ на усту́пки; *make sacrifices,* идти́ на же́ртвы. **17,** *used with various other nouns: make a bed,* убира́ть посте́ль; *make a speech,* говори́ть *or* произноси́ть речь; *make a request,* обраща́ться с про́сьбой; *make a decision,* принима́ть реше́ние; *make a date,* назнача́ть свида́ние; *make changes,* вноси́ть измене́ния; *make sense,* име́ть смысл. **18,** *Make oneself understood,* объясня́ться; *make oneself at home,* быть как до́ма; *make oneself comfortable,* устро́иться поудо́бнее. —*n.* **1,** (brand) ма́рка. **2,** (manufacture) изде́лие; произво́дство. *Of foreign make,* иностра́нного произво́дства. —**make as if; make as though,** де́лать вид; притворя́ться. —**make do,** обходи́ться: *make do with what we have on hand,* обходи́ться име́ющимися запа́сами. —**make for, 1,** (head for) направля́ться к. **2,** (make a dash for) бро́ситься к. **3,** (tend to create) спосо́бствовать; соде́йствовать. **4,** *Made for each other,* со́зданы друг для дру́га. —**make good,** преуспева́ть. —**make it, 1,** (achieve a certain thing) попа́сть. **2,** (be on time) успе́ть. **3,** (judge; estimate): *I make it twenty miles,* по-мо́ему здесь два́дцать миль. **4,** *Make it a rule to,* взять себе́ за пра́вило (+ *inf.*). —**make of,** понима́ть: *what do you make of his action?,* как вы понима́ете его́ посту́пок? *I don't know what to make of it,* я не зна́ю, что об э́том и ду́мать. —**make off with,** уноси́ть; утащи́ть. —**make out, 1,** (discern) различа́ть; разбира́ть; распознава́ть. **2,** (be able to read) разбира́ть. **3,** (comprehend) понима́ть. **4,** (draw up) составля́ть. **5,** (fill out) заполня́ть. **6,** (write out, as a check) выпи́сывать. **7,** *colloq.* (manage; get along) обходи́ться. *How are you making out?,* как у вас дела́? —**make over, 1,** (re-

make) передéлывать. **2,** (transfer; sign over) передавáть. —**make up, 1,** (put together; compose; constitute) составлять. **2,** (invent; concoct) выдýмывать. **3,** (be reconciled) мирúться. **4,** *theat.* гримировáть. **5,** *printing* верстáть. **6,** *Make up the difference,* доплáчивать рáзницу. —**make up for,** восполнять; возмещáть; навёрстывать. *Make up for lost time,* возместúть/наверстáть потéрянное врéмя. —**make way,** *see* **way.**

maker *n.* **1,** (manufacturer) фабрикáнт: *weapons maker,* фабрикáнт орýжия. ♦*Usu. in combinations: dressmaker,* портнúха; *peacemaker,* миротвóрец. **2,** *cap.* (God) творéц; создáтель.

makeshift *adj.* врéменный; подрýчный.

make-up *n.* **1,** (composition) состáв. **2,** (nature; disposition) натýра; харáктер. **3,** (cosmetics) космéтика. *Put on/use/wear make-up,* крáситься; мáзаться. **4,** *theat.* грим. *Make-up artist,* гримёр. **5,** *printing* вёрстка.

makeweight *n.* довéсок.

making *n.* **1,** (creation) создáние. **2,** (manufacture) произвóдство. **3,** *pl.* (potential ability) задáтки; дáнные: *he has the makings of a fine writer,* у негó задáтки хорóшего писáтеля; у негó все дáнные, чтóбы стать хорóшим писáтелем.

malachite *n.* малахúт. —*adj.* малахúтовый.

maladjusted *adj.* неприспосóбленный. —**maladjustment,** *n.* неприспосóбленность.

maladroit *adj.* неуклю́жий; нелóвкий.

malady *n.* болéзнь.

Malaga *n.* (wine) малáга.

malaise *n.* недомогáние.

malapropos *adj.* неумéстный. —*adv.* некстáти.

malaria *n.* малярúя. —**malarial,** *adj.* малярúйный.

Malay *adj.* малáйский. —*n.* **1,** (person) малáец; малáйка. **2,** (language) малáйский язы́к.

malcontent *n. & adj.* недовóльный.

male *adj.* мужскóй; мужскóго пóла. —*n.* **1,** (man) мужчúна. **2,** (male animal) самéц.

malediction *n.* проклятие.

malefactor *n.* престýпник; правонарушúтель; злодéй.

maleficent *adj.* врéдный; зловрéдный.

malevolent *adj.* злóбный; недоброжелáтельный. —**malevolence,** *n.* злóба; недоброжелáтельство.

malfeasance *n.* должностнóе преступлéние.

malformation *n.* урóдство. —**malformed,** *adj.* урóдливый.

malfunction *n.* неисправность; откáз. —*v.i.* откáзывать.

malice *n.* злóба; злость.

malicious *adj.* **1,** (spiteful) злóбный; злóстный. **2,** *law* злой; злонамéренный. *Malicious act,* злонамéренный постýпок. *Malicious intent,* злой ýмысел. —**maliciously,** *adv.* злóбно; зло; со злóбой.

malign *v.t.* клеветáть на; порóчить.

malignancy *n.* злокáчественная óпухоль.

malignant *adj.* **1,** (malicious) злóбный. **2,** (pernicious) пáгубный. **3,** *med.* злокáчественный.

malinger *v.i.* притворяться больны́м; симулúровать болéзнь. —**malingerer,** *n.* симулянт.

mall *n.* аллéя; бульвáр.

mallard *n.* кряква.

malleable *adj.* кóвкий. —**malleability,** *n.* кóвкость.

mallet *n.* колотýшка.

mallow *n.* мáльва.

malnutrition *n.* недоедáние.

malodorous *adj.* зловóнный; воню́чий.

malpractice *n.* небрéжное лечéние.

malt *n.* сóлод.

maltose *n.* мальтóза; солодóвый сáхар.

maltreat *v.t.* дýрно *or* плóхо обращáться с. —**maltreatment,** *n.* дурнóе *or* плохóе обращéние.

mama *also,* **mamma** *n.* мáма. —**mama's boy,** мáменькин сынóк.

mammal *n.* млекопитáющее.

mammary *adj.* груднóй; молóчный.

mammoth *n.* мáмонт. —*adj.* огрóмный; гигáнтский; колоссáльный.

man *n.* **1,** (person) человéк: *a nice man,* симпатúчный человéк. *Man in the street,* "человéк с ýлицы". *Man of letters,* литерáтор. *All men are mortal,* все лю́ди смéртны. **2,** (male human being) мужчúна: *for men only,* тóлько для мужчúн. **3,** (mankind) человéк: *primitive man,* первобы́тный человéк. *Man is a rational being,* человéк – существó разýмное. —*adj.* [*usu.* **man's** *or* **men's**] мужскóй: *men's clothes,* мужскóе плáтье. —*v.t.* **1,** (furnish with men) (у)комплектовáть. **2,** (take stations at) становúться к *or* на. —**as one man,** все как одúн. —**my good man!,** мúлый мой. —**to a man,** все до одногó.

manacle *n.* нарýчник. —*v.t.* надевáть нарýчники на; скóвывать.

manage *v.t.* **1,** (direct; administer) управлять; завéдовать; руководúть. **2,** *fol. by inf.* (contrive; succeed) сумéть; ухитряться; умудряться; изловчúться. —*v.i.* (make out; get along) обходúться; устрáиваться.

management *n.* **1,** (act of managing) управлéние; завéдование. **2,** (those who manage) правлéние; дирéкция; администрáция.

manager *n.* завéдующий; управляющий; дирéктор.

managerial *adj.* дирéкторский; администратúвный. *Managerial abilities,* организáторские спосóбности.

manatee *n.* ламантúн.

Manchu *adj.* маньчжýрский. —*n.* **1,** (person) маньчжýр. **2,** (language) маньчжýрский язы́к.

mandarin *n.* **1,** (Chinese official) мандарúн. **2,** *cap.* (language) мандарúнский язы́к. **3,** (tangerine) мандарúн.

mandate *n.* **1,** (instruction from constituents) накáз (избирáтелей). **2,** (charge to administer a territory) мандáт.

mandatory *adj.* обязáтельный.

mandible *n.* нúжняя чéлюсть.

mandolin *n.* мандолúна.

mandrake *n.* мандрагóра.

mandrel *also,* **mandril** *n.* опрáвка.

mandrill *n.* мандрúл.

mane *n.* грúва.

maneuver *also,* **manoeuvre** *n.* манёвр. —*v.t. & i.* маневрúровать. —**maneuverable,** *adj.* манёвренный. —**maneuverability,** *n.* манёвренность.

manganese *n.* мáрганец.

manganite *n.* манганúт.

mange *n.* чесóтка; паршá.

manger *n.* ясли. —**dog in the manger,** собáка на сéне.

mangle *v.t.* **1,** (mutilate; disfigure) калéчить. **2,** (spoil; ruin) ковéркать. **3,** (press in a mangle) катáть. —*n.* катóк (для бельá).
mango *n.* мáнго.
mangy *adj.* парши́вый; шелуди́вый; облéзлый.
manhandle *v.t.* грýбо обращáться с.
manhole *n.* люк; лаз.
manhood *n.* возмужáлость; зрéлость.
man-hour *n.* человéко-чáс.
manhunt *n.* полицéйская облáва.
mania *n.* мáния. —**maniac,** *n.* маньáк. —**maniacal,** *adj.* маниакáльный.
manic *adj.* маниакáльный. —**manic-depressive,** *adj.* маниакáльно-депресси́вный.
manicure *n.* маникю́р. —*v.t.* дéлать маникю́р (+ *dat.*). —**manicurist,** *n.* маникю́рша.
manifest *v.t.* проявля́ть. *Manifest itself,* проявля́ться; выражáться. —*adj.* очеви́дный; я́вный. —**manifestation,** *n.* проявлéние.
manifesto *n.* манифéст.
manifold *adj.* разнообрáзный; разносторóнний. —*n.* (pipe) трубопровóд.
manikin *n.* манекéн.
manioc *n.* маниóка.
manipulate *v.t.* манипули́ровать. —**manipulation,** *n.* манипуля́ция. —**manipulator,** *n.* манипуля́тор.
mankind *n.* человéчество.
manlike *adj.* человекоподóбный.
manly *adj.* мýжественный. —**manliness,** *n.* мýжественность.
man-made *adj.* искýсственный.
manna *n.* мáнна. *Manna from heaven,* мáнна небéсная.
manned *adj.* пилоти́руемый; с человéком на бортý.
mannequin *n.* манекéн.
manner *n.* **1,** (way) спóсоб. *In this manner,* таки́м óбразом; *in like manner,* подóбным óбразом. **2,** (mode of behavior) манéра. **3,** *pl.* (social ways) манéры: *good manners,* хорóшие манéры. *Table manners,* этикéт. —**all manner of,** всевозмóжные. —**by no manner of means,** отню́дь не. —**in a manner of speaking,** так сказáть; éсли мóжно так вы́разиться. —**in the manner of,** на манéр (+ *gen.*).
mannered *adj.* манéрный.
mannerism *n.* **1,** (excessive use of an affected style) манéрность. **2,** (peculiarity of manner) манéра.
mannerly *adj.* вéжливый; воспи́танный.
mannish *adj.* мужеподóбный.
manoeuvre *n.* & *v.* = **maneuver.**
man-of-war *n.* воéнный корáбль.
manometer *n.* манóметр. —**manometric,** *adj.* манометри́ческий.
manor *n.* помéстье. —**manor house,** помéщичий дом.
manorial *adj.* помéщичий.
manpower *n.* **1,** (power supplied by human physical effort) рабóчая си́ла. **2,** (people available for work) живáя си́ла.
mansard *n.* мансáрдная кры́ша. *Also,* **mansard roof.**
manservant *n.* слугá.
mansion *n.* особня́к.
manslaughter *n.* непредумы́шленное убийство; убийство по неосторóжности.
mantel *n.* ками́нная пóлка. *Also,* **mantelpiece.**
mantilla *n.* манти́лья.
mantis *n.* богомóл.
mantle *n.* **1,** (cloak) мáнтия. **2,** (incandescent hood) кали́льная сéтка. **3,** *fig.* (cover) покрóв.
manual *adj.* ручнóй: *manual labor,* ручнóй труд. *Manual training,* урóки по трудý. —*n.* **1,** (book of instructions) руковóдство. **2,** *mil.* наставлéние. *Field manual,* боевóй устáв. —**manually,** *adv.* вручнýю.
manufacture *v.t.* производи́ть; изготовля́ть; вырабáтывать; вы́делывать; фабриковáть. *Manufactured goods,* промы́шленные товáры.—*n.* произвóдство; изготовлéние; вы́работка; вы́делка; фабрикáция. —**manufacturer,** *n.* фабрикáнт; промы́шленник.
manure *n.* навóз; удобрéние.
manuscript *n.* рýкопись. —*adj.* рукопи́сный.
many *adj.* мнóго: *many times,* мнóго раз; *in many cases,* во мнóгих слýчаях. —*pron.* мнóгие: *many of them,* мнóгие из них. *Many believe that...,* мнóгие считáют, что... —**a great many,** óчень мнóго. —**as many,** стóлько же. *Twice as many,* в два рáза (*or* вдвóе) бóльше. —**as many as, 1,** (the same quantity) стóлько же..., скóлько и...: *as many adults as children,* стóлько же взрóслых, скóлько и детéй. *Take as many as you like,* бери́те (стóлько), скóлько вам угóдно. **2,** (before numbers, emphasizing a large amount) цéлые; цéлых; до. —**how many?,** скóлько? —**so many,** так мнóго; стóлько. *I told him in so many words that...,* я так и сказáл емý, что... —**the many,** большинствó. —**too many,** слишком мнóго.
many-sided *adj.* многосторóнний.
map *n.* кáрта. —*v.t.* **1,** (make a map of) наноси́ть на кáрту; картографи́ровать. **2,** *fol. by* **out** (plan) намечáть. —**map maker,** картóграф. —**map making,** картогрáфия.
maple *n.* клён. —*adj.* кленóвый. —**maple sugar,** кленóвый сáхар. —**maple syrup,** кленóвый сирóп.
mar *v.t.* **1,** (spoil) пóртить; отравля́ть. **2,** (damage) повреждáть. *Mar the appearance of,* урóдовать; безобрáзить.
marabou *n.* марабý.
maraschino *n.* мараски́н.
marasmus *n.* марáзм.
marathon *n.* марафóнский бег.
maraud *v.i.* мародёрствовать. —**marauder,** *n.* мародёр. —**marauding,** *n.* мародёрство. —*adj.* мародёрский.
marble *n.* **1,** (mineral) мрáмор. **2,** (little ball) шáрик: *play marbles,* игрáть в шáрики. —*adj.* мрáморный.
march *v.i.* маршировáть. —*n.* **1,** *mil.* марш; похóд; перехóд. *A two-day march,* двухднёвный перехóд. **2,** (demonstration) марш: *protest march,* марш протéста. **3,** *music* марш. **4,** (progress) ход: *march of events,* ход собы́тий. —**on the march,** на мáрше.
March *n.* март. —*adj.* мáртовский.
marching *n.* марширóвка. —*adj.* похóдный; марширóвочный.
marchioness *n.* марки́за.
marchpane *n.* марципáн.
Mardi gras мáсленица.
mare *n.* кобы́ла.
margarine *n.* маргари́н.
margin *n.* **1,** (edge of a page) поля́ (страни́цы): *write in the margin,* писáть на поля́х. **2,** (border; edge)

край. **3,** (reserve) запа́с: *margin of safety,* запа́с безопа́сности; запа́с про́чности. **4,** (difference, as in votes) переве́с: *by a narrow margin,* с незначи́тельным переве́сом.

marginal *adj.* **1,** (written in the margin) напи́санный на поля́х: *marginal note,* заме́тка на поля́х. **2,** (border-line) сре́дний. **3,** (barely profitable) малоприбыльный.

marginalia *n.pl.* маргина́лии.

marigold *n.* **1,** (African or French marigold) ба́рхатцы. **2,** (pot marigold) ноготки́.

marijuana *n.* марихуа́на.

marinade *n.* марина́д.

marinate *v.t.* маринова́ть. —**marinated,** *adj.* марино́ванный.

marine *adj.* морско́й. —*n.* **1,** (seagoing soldier) морско́й пехоти́нец. **2,** *pl.* (Marine Corps) морска́я пехо́та. —**merchant marine,** торго́вый флот.

mariner *n.* моря́к; матро́с.

marionette *n.* марионе́тка.

marital *adj.* супру́жеский; бра́чный. *Marital status,* семе́йное положе́ние.

maritime *adj.* морско́й; примо́рский.

marjoram *n.* майора́н.

mark *n.* **1,** (written line or symbol) ме́тка; поме́тка. **2,** (scratch, scar, etc.) след. **3,** (grade) отме́тка; оце́нка; балл. **4,** (sign in lieu of a signature) крест. **5,** (impression) отпеча́ток: *leave its mark,* накла́дывать свой отпеча́ток. **6,** (token; indication) знак: *mark of respect,* знак внима́ния. **7,** (standard): *up to the mark,* на до́лжной высоте́. **8,** (target) цель: *hit the mark,* попа́сть *or* бить в цель. *Be wide of the mark,* бить ми́мо це́ли; *fig.* попа́сть па́льцем в не́бо. **9,** (starting line in a race) старт: *on your mark!,* на старт! **10,** (monetary unit) ма́рка. —*v.t.* **1,** (place a mark on; indicate with a mark) ме́тить; отмеча́ть; помеча́ть; обознача́ть. *Mark the place in a book,* отмеча́ть/помеча́ть ме́сто в кни́ге. *The roads are poorly marked,* доро́ги пло́хо обозна́чены. **2,** (grade) ста́вить отме́тку (отме́тки) на. **3,** (celebrate; commemorate) отмеча́ть. *To mark the anniversary,* в ознаменова́ние юбиле́я. **4,** (signify; represent) знаменова́ть (собо́й). *Mark the beginning of a new era,* знаменова́ть нача́ло но́вой эпо́хи. —**mark down,** уце́нивать. —**mark my words,** попо́мните моё сло́во. —**mark off,** отсчи́тывать: *mark off ten paces,* отсчи́тывать де́сять шаго́в. —**mark time,** топта́ться на ме́сте. —**mark up, 1,** (cover with markings) испещря́ть. **2,** (raise the price of) наце́нивать.

marked *adj.* **1,** (having a mark or marks) ме́ченый. *Marked cards,* краплёные ка́рты. **2,** (strikingly evident) заме́тный: *a marked improvement,* заме́тное улучше́ние.

marker *n.* **1,** (one who marks) ме́тчик. **2,** (device for marking) флома́стер. **3,** (indicator) знак: *boundary marker,* пограни́чный знак. **4,** (chip; counter) фи́шка.

market *n.* ры́нок. *Black market,* чёрный ры́нок. —*adj.* ры́ночный: *market price,* ры́ночная цена́. *Market basket,* корзи́на для прови́зии. —*v.t.* продава́ть; сбыва́ть.

marketplace *n.* база́рная пло́щадь.

marking *n.* **1,** (mark) ме́тка. **2,** (coloration) окра́ска; расцве́тка.

marksman *n.* (ме́ткий) стрело́к. —**marksmanship,** *n.* ме́ткость.

markup *n.* наце́нка.

marl *n.* ме́ргель.

marmalade *n.* джем; пови́дло.

marmoset *n.* марты́шка.

marmot *n.* суро́к.

maroon *adj.* бордо́; цве́та бордо́; бордо́вый. —*v.t.* выса́живать (на необита́емом о́строве).

marquee *n.* театра́льный наве́с.

marquis *n.* марки́з. —**marquise,** *n.* марки́за.

marriage *n.* брак; жени́тьба; заму́жество.

married *adj.* **1,** (of a man) жена́т; *modifier* жена́тый. **2,** (of a woman) за́мужем; *modifier* заму́жняя. **3,** (of two or many people) жена́ты. *Married people,* жена́тые. *Married couple,* супру́жеская чета́ *or* па́ра. *Married life,* бра́чная жизнь; супру́жеская жизнь. —**get married,** *see* **marry.**

marrow *n.* ко́стный мозг. —**to the marrow,** до мо́зга косте́й.

marry *v.t.* **1,** (get married to) A, (of a man) жени́ться на (+ *prepl.*). B, (of a woman) выходи́ть за́муж за (+ *acc.*). **2,** *usu. fol. by* **off** (give in marriage) A, (a son) жени́ть. B, (a daughter) выдава́ть за́муж. **3,** (perform the marriage ceremony for) венча́ть. —*v.i.* вступа́ть в брак; жени́ться; выходи́ть за́муж; *(of two people)* пожени́ться.

Mars *n.* Марс.

Marsala *n.* (wine) марсала́.

Marseillaise *n.* Марселье́за.

marsh *n.* боло́то; топь.

marshal *n.* **1,** *mil.* ма́ршал. **2,** (law-enforcement officer) суде́бный исполни́тель. —*v.t.* **1,** (array, as for battle) выстра́ивать. **2,** (assemble, as thoughts, facts, etc.) собира́ть.

marsh gas боло́тный газ.

marshland *n.* боло́тистая ме́стность.

marshmallow *n.* (candy) зефи́р. —**marsh mallow,** (plant) просви́рник; просвирня́к; проскурня́к.

marsh marigold калу́жница.

marshy *adj.* боло́тистый; то́пкий.

marsupial *n.* & *adj.* су́мчатый.

marten *n.* куни́ца.

martial *adj.* вое́нный; во́инский. —**martial law,** вое́нное положе́ние.

Martian *n.* марсиа́нин. —*adj.* марсиа́нский.

martyr *n.* му́ченик. —*v.t.* подверга́ть му́ченической сме́рти. —**martyrdom,** *n.* му́ченичество.

marvel *n.* чу́до; ди́во. —*v.i.* диви́ться; изумля́ться.

marvelous *also,* **marvellous** *adj.* удиви́тельный; изуми́тельный; чу́дный; чуде́сный. —**marvelously,** *adv.* удиви́тельно; изуми́тельно; чу́дно; чуде́сно.

Marxism *n.* маркси́зм. —**Marxian,** *adj.* маркси́стский. —**Marxist,** *n.* маркси́ст. —*adj.* маркси́стский.

marzipan *n.* марципа́н.

mascara *n.* тушь.

mascot *n.* талисма́н.

masculine *adj.* **1,** (male) мужско́й. **2,** (manly) му́жественный. **3,** *gram.* мужско́го ро́да. *Masculine gender,* мужско́й род. —**masculinity,** *n.* му́жественность.

mash *n.* **1,** (brewing mixture) су́сло. **2,** (feed for livestock) по́йло; ме́сиво. —*v.t.* размина́ть. *Mashed potatoes,* карто́фельное пюре́.

mask *n.* ма́ска; личи́на. —*v.t.* маскирова́ть. —**masked,** *adj.* замаскиро́ванный.
masochism *n.* мазохи́зм. —**masochist,** *n.* мазохи́ст. —**masochistic,** *adj.* мазохи́стский.
mason *n.* **1,** (worker in stone) ка́менщик. **2,** *cap.* (Freemason) масо́н.
Masonic *adj.* масо́нский.
masonry *n.* **1,** (work in stone) ка́менная кла́дка. **2,** *cap.* (Freemasonry) масо́нство.
masquerade *n.* маскара́д. —*v.i.* выдава́ть себя́ (за).
mass *n.* **1,** (body of matter) ма́сса: *a mass of clay,* гли́няная ма́сса. **2,** (great amount) ма́сса: *a mass of information,* ма́сса информа́ции. **3,** *physics* ма́сса: *critical mass,* крити́ческая ма́сса. **4,** *pl., preceded by* **the** (the common people) ма́ссы. **5,** *cap.* (church service) ме́сса; обе́дня. —*adj.* ма́ссовый: *mass production,* ма́ссовое произво́дство; *mass media,* сре́дства ма́ссовой информа́ции. —*v.t.* масси́ровать: *troops massed on the border,* войска́, масси́рованные на грани́це. —*v.i.* масси́роваться.
massacre *n.* резня́; бо́йня; избие́ние. —*v.t.* выреза́ть; изруби́ть.
massage *n.* масса́ж —*v.t.* масси́ровать; растира́ть.
masseur *n.* массажи́ст. —**masseuse,** *n.* массажи́стка.
massive *adj.* **1,** (huge; heavy and solid) масси́вный. **2,** (enormous in scope) огро́мный.
mast *n.* ма́чта.
master *n.* **1,** (one having control over another) хозя́ин; господи́н. *The dog's master,* хозя́ин соба́ки. *Serve two masters,* служи́ть двум господа́м. **2,** (skilled workman or practitioner) ма́стер. *Past master,* иску́сник. **3,** (holder of a master's degree) маги́стр. *Master's degree,* сте́пень маги́стра. **4,** (captain of a merchant ship) капита́н. —*adj.* **1,** (being master) госпо́дствующий. *Master race,* ра́са госпо́д. **2,** (comprehensive): *master plan,* генера́льный план. **3,** (brilliantly executed) мастерско́й: *master stroke,* мастерско́й уда́р. **4,** (original, as of a copy) по́длинный. **5,** *mech.* (of a switch, cylinder, etc.) гла́вный. —*v.t.* **1,** (bring under control) одолева́ть; оси́лить. **2,** (learn thoroughly) усва́ивать; овладева́ть.
masterful *adj.* **1,** (expert) мастерско́й. **2,** (domineering) вла́стный. —**masterfully,** *adv.* мастерски́.
master key отмы́чка.
masterly *adj.* мастерско́й.
mastermind *v.t.* заду́мать; замышля́ть.
master of ceremonies конферансье́.
masterpiece *n.* шеде́вр.
master sergeant старшина́.
mastery *n.* **1,** (control; dominion) госпо́дство. **2,** (command, as of a subject) овладе́ние.
masthead *n.* **1,** *naut.* топ ма́чты. **2,** (of a newspaper) ша́пка.
mastic *n.* масти́ка. —*adj.* масти́ковый.
masticate *v.t. & i.* жева́ть. —**mastication,** *n.* жева́ние.
mastiff *n.* дог.
mastitis *n.* грудни́ца; масти́т.
mastodon *n.* мастодо́нт.
masturbate *v.i.* онани́ровать. —**masturbation,** *n.* онани́зм.
mat *n.* **1,** (small rug) ко́врик; цино́вка. *Doormat,* полови́к. **2,** (something placed under a dish or vase) подсти́лка. **3,** *sports* ковёр. **4,** (dull surface) ма́товая пове́рхность. —*adj.* ма́товый. —*v.t.* (tangle) спу́тывать. —*v.i.* спу́тываться.
match *n.* **1,** (device for igniting) спи́чка. **2,** (equal; peer) ро́вня; ровня́. *No match for,* не чета́ (+ *dat.*). *Meet one's match,* найти́ ра́вного проти́вника. **3,** (suitable or possible mate) па́ра; па́ртия: *she is not a good match for him,* она́ ему́ не па́ра/па́ртия. **4,** (combination; marriage) па́ртия: *a good match,* хоро́шая па́ртия. **5,** (contest) состяза́ние; матч. —*v.t.* **1,** (be equal to; rival) равня́ться с. **2,** (correspond to) быть под стать (+ *dat.*). **3,** (go well with) гармони́ровать с; сочета́ться с; подходи́ть к. **4,** (make a match of; choose to suit) сочета́ть. *Choose a tie to match one's suit,* подбира́ть га́лстук под цвет костю́ма. **5,** *fol. by* **up** (pair; mate) сва́тать. **6,** (pit; place in opposition) противопоставля́ть. *Match wits,* состяза́ться в остро́умии. —*v.i.* гармони́ровать.
matchbox *n.* спи́чечная коро́бка.
matchless *adj.* несравне́нный; бесподо́бный.
matchmaker *n.* сват; сва́ха. —**matchmaking,** *n.* сватовство́.
mate *n.* **1,** (one of a pair) па́ра. **2,** (spouse) супру́г; супру́га. **3,** (associate; buddy) това́рищ; напа́рник. **4,** *naut.* помо́щник капита́на. **5,** *chess* мат. —*v.t.* **1,** (pair for breeding) спа́ривать; случа́ть. **2,** *chess* де́лать мат (+ *dat.*). —*v.i.* спа́риваться.
material *n.* **1,** (that of which something is made) материа́л. *Raw materials,* сырьё. **2,** (textile fabric) мате́рия; материа́л. **3,** *pl.* (implements) принадле́жности: *writing materials,* пи́сьменные принадле́жности. **4,** (data to be worked up) материа́л. —*adj.* **1,** (physical) материа́льный; веще́ственный. *Material well-being,* материа́льное благополу́чие. *Material evidence,* веще́ственные доказа́тельства. **2,** (significant; substantial) суще́ственный. *Material witness,* ва́жный свиде́тель.
materialism *n.* материали́зм. —**materialist,** *n.* материали́ст. —**materialistic,** *adj.* материалисти́ческий.
materialize *v.i.* осуществля́ться; реализова́ться.
materially *adv.* **1,** (in a material sense) материа́льно: *materially well-off,* материа́льно обеспе́ченный. **2,** (significantly) суще́ственным о́бразом.
matériel *n.* материа́льная часть.
maternal *adj.* **1,** (motherly) матери́нский. **2,** (on one's mother's side of the family) со стороны́ ма́тери; с матери́нской стороны́.
maternity *n.* матери́нство. —**maternity clothes,** оде́жда для бере́менной же́нщины. —**maternity leave,** о́тпуск по бере́менности и ро́дам; декре́тный о́тпуск. —**maternity ward,** роди́льное отделе́ние.
mathematics *n.* матема́тика. —**mathematical,** *adj.* математи́ческий. —**mathematician,** *n.* матема́тик.
matin *n., usu. pl.* у́треня; зау́треня.
matinee *n.* дневно́й спекта́кль.
mating *n.* спа́ривание. —**mating call,** токова́ние. —**mating season,** бра́чный пери́од.
matins *n., pl. of* **matin.**
matriarch *n.* мать. —**matriarchal,** *adj.* матриарха́льный. —**matriarchy,** *n.* матриарха́т.
matricide *n.* матереуби́йство.
matriculate *v.i.* зачисля́ться (в вы́сшее уче́бное

заведе́ние). —**matriculation,** *n.* зачисле́ние (в вы́сшее учёбное заведе́ние).
matrimony *n.* супру́жество; брак. —**matrimonial,** *adj.* супру́жеский; бра́чный; матримониа́льный.
matrix *n.* ма́трица.
matron *n.* матро́на.
matted *adj.* спу́танный.
matter *n.* **1,** (substance) мате́рия; вещество́. **2,** (something printed) материа́л: *reading matter,* материа́л для чте́ния. **3,** (affair; question) вопро́с; де́ло. *A matter of taste,* де́ло вку́са. *A matter of life and death,* вопро́с жи́зни и сме́рти. *As matters stand,* при да́нном положе́нии дел. *It is no laughing matter,* э́то не шу́точное де́ло. —*v.i.* име́ть значе́ние. *It doesn't matter,* ничего́; нева́жно; не име́ет значе́ния. —**as a matter of fact, 1,** (in point of fact) на са́мом де́ле; факти́чески. **2,** (now that you mention it) предста́вьте себе́: *as a matter of fact, yes,* предста́вьте себе́, да. **3,** (in this connection) ме́жду про́чим. —**for that matter,** что каса́ется э́того; в э́том отноше́нии. —**no matter how/what/when** *etc.,* как бы ни/что бы ни/когда́ бы ни, *etc.* —**something is the matter,** что́-то не так. —**to make matters worse,** в доверше́ние всего́. —**what is the matter?,** в чём де́ло?; что тако́е? —**what is the matter with you?,** что с ва́ми?
matter-of-fact *adj.* сухо́й; прозаи́чный.
matting *n.* рого́жа.
mattock *n.* моты́га.
mattress *n.* матра́с; матра́ц.
maturation *n.* созрева́ние.
mature *adj.* зре́лый. —*v.i.* созрева́ть. —*v.t.* доводи́ть до зре́лости. —**maturity,** *n.* зре́лость.
matutinal *adj.* у́тренний.
matzo *n.* маца́.
maudlin *adj.* слезли́вый.
maul *n.* колоту́шка; кува́лда. —*v.t.* терза́ть; растерза́ть.
Maundy Thursday страстно́й четве́рг.
Mauser *n.* ма́узер.
mausoleum *n.* мавзоле́й.
mauve *adj.* лило́вый.
maverick *n.* **1,** (unbranded calf) телёнок без клейма́. **2,** (independent person) индивидуали́ст.
mawkish *adj.* при́торный; слаща́вый.
maxim *n.* изрече́ние; сенте́нция.
maximal *adj.* максима́льный.
maximize *v.t.* доводи́ть до ма́ксимума.
maximum *n.* ма́ксимум. —*adj.* максима́льный; преде́льный.
may *v.aux.* **1,** *expressing possibility or contingency* мочь: *they may have gone home already,* они́ могли́ уже́ уйти́ домо́й. ♦*Also rendered by* возмо́жно: *it may be true,* возмо́жно, э́то пра́вда. **2,** *requesting or granting permission* мочь; мо́жно: *may I come in?,* мо́жно войти́? *You may go now,* вы мо́жете идти́ тепе́рь. **3,** *expressing wish, hope, or prayer* пусть; да: *may all your dreams come true!,* пусть/да сбу́дутся все ва́ши мечты́! *May he rest in peace,* мир пра́ху его́. —**be that as it may,** как бы то ни́ было. —**come what may,** будь, что бу́дет.
May *n.* май. —*adj.* ма́йский.
maybe *adv.* мо́жет быть.
May Day Пе́рвое ма́я; пра́здник Пе́рвого ма́я. —**May-Day,** *adj.* первома́йский.
mayfly *n.* подёнка.
mayhem *n.* **1,** *law* нанесе́ние уве́чья. **2,** (havoc) хао́с.
mayonnaise *n.* майоне́з.
mayor *n.* мэр.
maze *n.* лабири́нт.
mazurka *n.* мазу́рка.
me *pers.pron.* **1,** *used as dir. obj. of a verb* меня́: *he loves me,* он лю́бит меня́. **2,** *used as indir. obj. of a verb* мне: *show me!,* покажи́те мне. **3,** *used as obj. of a prep.* меня́; мне; мной.
mead *n.* мёд.
meadow *n.* луг.
meadowsweet *n.* та́волга.
meager *also,* **meagre** *adj.* **1,** (scanty) ску́дный. **2,** (lean) худо́й; то́щий.
meal *n.* **1,** (repast) еда́. *Eat three meals a day,* есть три ра́за в день. **2,** (ground grain) мука́: *corn meal,* кукуру́зная мука́.
mealy *adj.* мучни́стый.
mean *v.t.* **1,** (signify; denote) зна́чить: *what does this mean?,* что э́то зна́чит? **2,** *fol. by inf.* (intend) предполага́ть. **3,** (intentionally plan or wish) хоте́ть: *I didn't mean to offend you,* я не хоте́л вас оби́деть. *He means you no harm,* он не жела́ет вам зла. **4,** (intend to express) хоте́ть сказа́ть: *what do you mean by that?,* что вы хоти́те э́тим сказа́ть? **5,** (have in mind) име́ть в виду́: *whom do you mean?,* кого́ вы име́ете в виду́? **6,** *fol. by* **it** (be serious): *do you really mean it?,* вы э́то серьёзно? *I mean it,* я говорю́ серьёзно. *You don't mean it!,* вы шу́тите! **7,** (intend; design) предназнача́ть. *They were meant for each other,* они́ со́зданы друг для дру́га. **8,** (matter) зна́чить: *mean a great deal to,* мно́го зна́чить для. —*v.i. Mean well,* име́ть до́брые наме́рения. —*adj.* **1,** (nasty) злой: *a mean old man,* злой стари́к. *Be mean to someone,* пло́хо *or* гру́бо обраща́ться с ке́м-нибудь. **2,** (malicious) ни́зкий; по́длый; злой: *mean trick,* ни́зкий/по́длый посту́пок; зла́я шу́тка. **3,** (average) сре́дний: *mean distance,* сре́днее расстоя́ние. —*n.* **1,** (something between extremes) середи́на: *golden mean,* золота́я середи́на. **2,** *math.* сре́днее число́. **3,** *pl.* (method; instrument) сре́дства: *means of production,* сре́дства произво́дства. *The end justifies the means,* цель опра́вдывает сре́дства. **4,** *pl.* (money; wealth) сре́дства: *man of means,* челове́к со сре́дствами. *Live beyond one's means,* жить не по сре́дствам. —**by all means, 1,** (without fail) обяза́тельно. **2,** (of course) коне́чно; пожа́луйста. —**by means of,** посре́дством (+ *gen.*); путём (+ *gen.*); при по́мощи (+ *gen.*). —**by no means, 1,** *fol. by an adj.* (not the least bit) совсе́м не. **2,** *as an exclamation* (not at all) нет, что вы! —**not...by any means,** совсе́м не: *not cheap by any means,* совсе́м не дёшево.
meander *v.i.* **1,** (follow a winding course) извива́ться. **2,** (ramble; wander) броди́ть. —**meandering,** *adj.* изви́листый.
meaning *n.* значе́ние.
meaningful *adj.* **1,** (having meaning) зна́чащий. **2,** (significant) многозначи́тельный.
meaningless *adj.* бессмы́сленный; не име́ющий смы́сла; ничего́ не зна́чащий.
meanness *n.* зло́ба; ни́зость; по́длость.
meantime *n., usu. in* **in the meantime,** тем вре́ме-

нем; мéжду тем. —*adv.* = **in the meantime.** *Also,* **meanwhile.**

measles *n.* корь. *German measles,* краснýха.

measly *adj., colloq.* ничтóжный; нúщенский.

measurable *adj.* **1,** (allowing of measurement) измерúмый. **2,** (appreciable) замéтный; ощутúмый.

measure *n.* **1,** (unit or system of measurement) мéра: *measure of length,* мéра длины́; *dry measure,* мéра сыпýчих тел. **2,** (action; step) мéра: *drastic measures,* круты́е мéры. **3,** (degree; extent) мéра; стéпень: *in full measure,* в пóлной мéре. *In some measure,* до нéкоторой стéпени; в извéстной мéре. *In great measure,* в большóй *or* значúтельной мéре. **4,** *pros.* (meter) размéр; метр. **5,** *music* размéр; такт. —*v.t.* **1,** (determine the size of) измеря́ть. **2,** (appraise; gauge) оцéнивать. **3,** (bring into comparison) мéриться: *measure one's strength against,* мéриться сúлами с. **4,** *fol. by* **off** (mark off) отмеря́ть. —*v.i.* имéть (размéры): *the room measures ten feet in length,* кóмната имéет дéсять фýтов в длинý. —**beyond measure,** неизмерúмо; чрезвычáйно. —**for good measure,** в придáчу. —**measure one's length,** растянýться во всю длинý. —**measure up,** быть на высотé. *Measure up to expectations,* оправдывать ожидáния. —**take one's measure, 1,** (take someone's measurements) снимáть мéрку с (+ *gen.*). **2,** (size up) присмáтриваться к. —**to measure,** по мéрке: *made to measure,* сшúтый по мéрке.

measured *adj.* **1,** (ascertained by measurement) измéренный. **2,** (regular; steady; deliberate) мéрный; размéренный.

measurement *n.* **1,** (measuring) измерéние. **2,** *usu. pl.* (size found by measuring) мéрка: *take someone's measurements,* снимáть мéрку с (+ *gen.*).

meat *n.* мя́со. —*adj.* мяснóй. —**meatballs,** *n.pl.* тéфтели; биткú. —**meat grinder,** мясорýбка. —**meat loaf,** мяснóй рулéт. —**meat pie,** пирóг с мя́сом.

meaty *adj.* **1,** (fleshy) мясúстый. **2,** (full of substance) содержáтельный.

mechanic *n.* механик.

mechanical *adj.* **1,** (pert. to machinery) механúческий: *mechanical failure,* механúческая неисправность. *Mechanical toy,* заводнáя игрýшка. *Mechanical aptitude,* техни́ческие спосóбности. **2,** *fig.* (automatic; done without thinking) машинáльный; механúческий. —**mechanical drawing,** техни́ческое черчéние. —**mechanical engineer,** механик; инженéр-механик.

mechanics *n.* механика.

mechanism *n.* механúзм.

mechanize *v.t.* механизúровать; машинизúровать. —**mechanization,** *n.* механизáция; машинизáция.

medal *n.* медáль. —**medalist,** *n.* медалúст.

medallion *n.* медальóн.

medallist *n.* = **medalist.**

meddle *v.i.* вмéшиваться. —**meddlesome,** *adj.* вмéшивающийся не в свои́ делá. —**meddling,** *n.* вмешáтельство.

media *n.pl.* срéдства мáссовой информáции.

mediaeval *adj.* = **medieval.**

median *adj.* срéдний. —*n.* медиáна.

mediate *v.i.* посрéдничать. —*v.t.* улáживать. —**mediation,** *n.* посрéдничество. —**mediator,** *n.* посрéдник.

medical *adj.* медицúнский.

medication *n.* медикамéнты; лекáрство.

medicinal *adj.* лекáрственный; целéбный.

medicine *n.* **1,** (the science) медицúна. **2,** (something taken when ill) лекáрство. —**medicine chest/cabinet,** (домáшняя) аптéчка; аптéчный шкаф. —**medicine man,** знáхарь; шамáн.

medieval *also,* **mediaeval** *adj.* средневекóвый.

mediocre *adj.* посрéдственный; заурядный. —**mediocrity,** *n.* посрéдственность.

meditate *v.i.* размышля́ть; раздýмывать; задýмываться. —**meditation,** *n.* размышлéние; раздýмье. —**meditative,** *adj.* задýмчивый.

medium *n.* **1,** (mean) серединá: *happy medium,* золотáя серединá. **2,** (means) срéдство: *medium of exchange,* срéдство обмéна. *Through the medium of,* посрéдством (+ *gen.*); чéрез посрéдство (+ *gen.*). **3,** *physics* средá. **4,** (culture medium) питáтельная средá. **5,** (spiritualist) мéдиум. —*adj.* срéдний: *of medium height,* срéднего рóста. *Medium bomber,* срéдний бомбардирóвщик. —**medium-range,** *adj.* срéднего рáдиуса дéйствия. —**medium-sized,** *adj.* срéдней величины́; срéднего размéра. *See also* **media.**

medlar *n.* мушмулá.

medley *n.* **1,** (hodgepodge) мешанúна; мéсиво. **2,** *music* попуррú.

medulla *n.* **1,** (marrow) кóстный мозг. **2,** (inner part of an organ) мозговóй слой. —**medulla oblongata,** продолговáтый мозг.

medusa *n.* медýза.

meek *adj.* крóткий; смирéнный. —**meekness,** *n.* крóтость; смирéние.

meerschaum *n.* (морскáя) пéнка. —*adj.* пéнковый.

meet *v.t.* **1,** (come upon; join) встречáть: *meet a friend/a train/resistance,* встречáть дрýга/пóезд/сопротивлéние. **2,** (make the acquaintance of) знакóмиться с. *I would like you to meet my wife,* позвóльте познакóмить вас с моéй женóй. **3,** (conform to; satisfy) отвечáть; удовлетворя́ть: *meet the requirements,* отвечáть/удовлетворя́ть трéбованиям. *Meet a demand,* удовлетворúть трéбование. —*v.i.* **1,** (come upon or join each other) встречáться. **2,** (become acquainted) знакóмиться. *Have you met?,* вы знакóмы? **3,** *fol. by* **with** (confer with) встречáться с; совещáться с. **4,** *fol. by* **with** (encounter) встречáть; стáлкиваться с. **5,** (gather; assemble) собирáться; сходúться. **6,** (intersect) сходúться. **7,** (compete) встречáться; сходúться. —*n.* соревновáние: *track meet,* легкоатлетúческие соревновáния.

meeting *n.* **1,** (encounter) встрéча. **2,** (scheduled appointment) встрéча; свидáние. **3,** (gathering; assembly; conference) собрáние.

megacycle *n.* мегагéрц.

megalomania *n.* мáния велúчия.

megaphone *n.* рýпор; мегафóн.

megaton *n.* мегатóнна.

melancholia *n.* меланхóлия. —**melancholic,** *adj.* меланхолúческий.

melancholy *n.* уны́ние; тоскá; грусть; меланхóлия. —*adj.* уны́лый; тосклúвый; меланхолúческий.

mélange *n.* смешéние; смесь.

melee *n.* свáлка.

meliorate *v.t.* улучшáть. —*v.i.* улучшáться. —**melioration,** *n.* улучшéние.

mellifluous *adj.* медоточи́вый; сладкозву́чный.

mellow *adj.* **1,** (fully-flavored; full-bodied) со́чный: *mellow voice,* со́чный го́лос. **2,** *colloq.* (genial) доброду́шный. *Become mellow with age,* подобре́ть с года́ми. —*v.t.* смягча́ть. —*v.i.* добре́ть.

melodic *adj.* мелоди́ческий. —**melodics,** *n.* мело́дика.

melodious *adj.* мелоди́чный; певу́чий. —**melodiousness,** *n.* мелоди́чность; певу́честь.

melodrama *n.* мелодра́ма. —**melodramatic,** *adj.* мелодрамати́ческий; театра́льный.

melody *n.* мело́дия.

melon *n.* ды́ня. *Melon field,* бахча́.

melt *v.t.* **1,** (reduce to a liquid state) *A,* (butter, ice, etc.) топи́ть; растá пливать. *B,* (metals) пла́вить; расплавля́ть. **2,** (dissolve) растворя́ть. —*v.i.* **1,** (turn to liquid) *A,* (of snow, ice cream, etc.) та́ять. *B,* (of metals) пла́виться. **2,** (dissolve) растворя́ться. **3,** (fade away; dwindle) улету́чиваться. *Melt into the background,* слива́ться с фо́ном. —**melt in one's mouth,** та́ять во рту.

melted *adj.* (of snow) та́лый; (of butter) топлёный; (of metals) распла́вленный.

melting *n.* плавле́ние; пла́вка. *Melting point,* то́чка плавле́ния. —**melting pot,** плави́льный котёл.

member *n.* член.

membership *n.* **1,** (status of a member) чле́нство. **2,** (members collectively) чле́ны. **3,** (number of members) коли́чество чле́нов. —*adj.* чле́нский: *membership dues,* чле́нские взно́сы.

membrane *n.* плева́; перепо́нка; оболо́чка. —**membranous,** *adj.* перепо́нчатый.

memento *n.* па́мятный пода́рок; сувени́р.

memo *n., colloq.* = **memorandum.**

memoirs *n.pl.* мему́ары.

memorable *adj.* па́мятный; знамена́тельный.

memorandum *n.* **1,** (reminder) па́мятная запи́ска; мемора́ндум. **2,** (informal communication) делова́я *or* докладна́я запи́ска; мемора́ндум. **3,** *dipl.* мемора́ндум.

memorial *n.* па́мятник. —*adj.* мемориа́льный. *Memorial plaque,* па́мятная доска́. *Memorial service,* заупоко́йная слу́жба.

memorialize *v.t.* увекове́чивать.

memorize *v.t.* запомина́ть; зау́чивать (наизу́сть).

memory *n.* **1,** (capacity to remember) па́мять. *From memory,* на па́мять; по па́мяти. *Within my memory,* на мое́й па́мяти. **2,** (recollection) воспомина́ние: *memories of childhood,* воспомина́ния де́тства. **3,** (commemoration) па́мять: *in memory of,* в па́мять (+ *gen.*). **4,** *computer science* запомина́ющее устро́йство.

menace *n.* угро́за. —*v.t.* угрожа́ть; грози́ть. —**menacing,** *adj.* гро́зный; угрожа́ющий.

menagerie *n.* звери́нец.

mend *v.t.* **1,** (repair) чини́ть. **2,** (darn) што́пать. **3,** *in* **mend one's ways,** исправля́ться. —*v.i.* (of bones) сраста́ться. —**be on the mend,** выздора́вливать. *He is on the mend,* у него́ де́ло идёт на popра́вку.

mendacious *adj.* лжи́вый; ло́жный. —**mendacity,** *n.* лжи́вость.

mendelevium *n.* менделе́вий.

mendicant *n.* ни́щий. —*adj.* ни́щенствующий. —**mendicancy,** *n.* ни́щенство.

menial *adj.* чёрный: *menial tasks,* чёрная рабо́та.

meningitis *n.* менинги́т.

menopause *n.* климакте́рий.

Menshevik *n.* меньшеви́к. —*adj.* меньшеви́стский.

men's room мужска́я убо́рная; мужско́й туале́т.

menstrual *adj.* менструа́льный.

menstruate *v.i.* менструи́ровать. —**menstruation,** *n.* менструа́ция.

mensuration *n.* измере́ние.

mental *adj.* **1,** (pert. to the mind) у́мственный: *mental faculties,* у́мственные спосо́бности. **2,** (taking place in the mind) мы́сленный: *mental image,* мы́сленный о́браз. **3,** (pert. to the mentally ill) душе́вный; психи́ческий: *mental illness,* душе́вная/психи́ческая боле́знь. *Mental case; mental patient,* душевнобольно́й; психи́чески больно́й. *Mental hospital,* психиатри́ческая больни́ца.

mentality *n.* **1,** (intelligence) ум; у́мственные спосо́бности. **2,** (state of mind) склад ума́.

mentally *adv.* **1,** (in one's mind) мы́сленно. **2,** (as regards one's mental faculties) у́мственно; психи́чески. *Mentally ill,* душевнобольно́й; психи́чески больно́й. *Mentally retarded,* у́мственно отста́лый.

menthol *n.* менто́л. —**mentholated,** *adj.* менто́ловый.

mention *v.t.* упомина́ть. —*n.* упомина́ние: *at the mention of,* при упомина́нии (+ *gen.*). —**don't mention it!,** пожа́луйста; не сто́ит благода́рности. —**not to mention,** не говоря́ уже́ о.

mentor *n.* наста́вник; воспита́тель.

menu *n.* меню́.

meow *v.i.* мяу́кать. —*n.* мяу́канье.

mercantile *adj.* **1,** (commercial) торго́вый; комме́рческий. **2,** (pert. to mercantilism) мерканти́льный. —**mercantilism,** *n.* меркантили́зм.

mercenary *adj.* **1,** (selfish) коры́стный. **2,** (serving for pay) наёмный. —*n.* наёмник.

merchandise *n.* това́р.

merchant *n.* купе́ц; торго́вец. —**merchant marine,** торго́вый флот. —**merchant ship,** торго́вое су́дно.

merciful *adj.* милосе́рдный; сострада́тельный.

merciless *adj.* безжа́лостный; беспоща́дный; неща́дный. —**mercilessly,** *adv.* безжа́лостно; беспоща́дно; неща́дно.

mercurial *adj.* **1,** [*also,* **mercuric**] (of mercury) рту́тный. **2,** (volatile) изме́нчивый; переме́нчивый. —**mercuric chloride,** сулема́. —**mercuric oxide,** о́кись рту́ти. —**mercuric sulfide,** серни́стая ртуть.

mercury *n.* **1,** (element) ртуть. **2,** *cap.* (god; planet) Мерку́рий. —*adj.* рту́тный: *mercury barometer,* рту́тный баро́метр.

mercy *n.* милосе́рдие; ми́лость; поща́да. *Show mercy toward,* проявля́ть милосе́рдие к. *Have/take mercy on,* щади́ть. —*interj.* го́споди! —**at the mercy of,** во вла́сти (+ *gen.*). *Throw oneself at the mercy of,* отда́ться на ми́лость (+ *gen.*).

mere *adj.* просто́й: *mere mortals,* просты́е сме́ртные. *He is a mere child,* да он ещё ребёнок. *At the mere thought of,* при одно́й мы́сли о.

merely *adv.* то́лько; про́сто.

meretricious *adj.* показно́й; мишу́рный.

merganser *n.* кроха́ль.

merge *v.t.* объединя́ть. —*v.i.* слива́ться; объединя́ться.

merger *n.* слия́ние; объедине́ние.

meridian *n.* меридиа́н.
meringue *n.* мере́нга.
merino *n.* мерино́с. —*adj.* мерино́совый.
merit *n.* **1,** (positive quality; virtue) заслу́га; досто́инство. **2,** *pl.* (intrinsic rights and wrongs) существо́: *the merits of a case,* существо́ де́ла. —*v.t.* заслу́живать.
meritorious *adj.* похва́льный. *Award for meritorious service,* награ́да за заслу́ги.
merlin *n.* (bird) де́рбник.
mermaid *n.* руса́лка.
merrily *adv.* ве́село.
merriment *n.* весе́лье.
merry *adj.* весёлый. *Merry Christmas!,* с Рождество́м христо́вым. —**make merry,** весели́ться. —**the more the merrier,** чем бо́льше, тем лу́чше.
merry-go-round *n.* карусе́ль.
merrymaker *n.* весельча́к. —**merrymaking,** *n.* весе́лье.
mesa *n.* столо́вая гора́; плоского́рье.
mesh *n.* очко́; яче́йка. —*v.i.* (engage) сцепля́ться.
mesmerism *n.* гипно́з; гипноти́зм. —**mesmerist,** *n.* гипнотизёр. —**mesmerize,** *v.t.* гипнотизи́ровать.
meson *n.* мезо́н.
Mesozoic *adj.* мезозо́йский.
mess *n.* **1,** (dirty or untidy condition) грязь: *what a mess!,* кака́я грязь! **2,** (confused state) пу́таница; неразбери́ха. *Make a mess of,* напу́тать. **3,** (trouble) беда́. *Get into a mess,* попа́сть в беду́/переплет/переде́лку. **4,** (group taking meals together; a meal so taken) о́бщий стол. —*v.t.* [*usu.* **mess up**] **1,** (soil) (за)па́чкать. **2,** (disarrange) приводи́ть в беспоря́док. **3,** (bungle; botch) напу́тать. —*v.i.* **1,** (take meals together) столова́ться. **2,** *fol. by* **around** *or* **about** (putter) вози́ться.
message *n.* **1,** (communication) сообще́ние; донесе́ние. **2,** (written note) запи́ска. **3,** (verbal communication to be passed on) *rendered idiomatically: is there any message?,* что ему́ (*or* ей) переда́ть? *Did he leave a message?,* он проси́л что́-нибудь переда́ть? **4,** (formal address) посла́ние.
messenger *n.* **1,** (one bringing a message or news) ве́стник. **2,** (errand boy) посы́льный; курье́р. *Send something by messenger,* посыла́ть что́-нибудь с посы́льным.
mess hall столо́вая.
Messiah *n.* месси́я. —**Messianic,** *adj.* мессиа́нский.
messy *adj.* **1,** (untidy; disorderly) неопря́тный. **2,** *fig.* (complicated; unpleasant) неприя́тный.
mestizo *n.* мети́с.
metabolism *n.* обме́н веще́ств. —**metabolic,** *adj.* относя́щийся к обме́ну веще́ств: *metabolic disease,* боле́знь обме́на веще́ств.
metacarpus *n.* пясть.
metal *n.* мета́лл. —*adj.* металли́ческий. —**metallic,** *adj.* металли́ческий.
metalliferous *adj.* металлоно́сный.
metalloid *n.* металло́ид.
metallurgy *n.* металлу́ргия. —**metallurgic,** *adj.* металлурги́ческий. —**metallurgist,** *n.* металлу́рг.
metalworker *n.* сле́сарь; металли́ст.
metamorphosis *n.* **1,** *biol.* метаморфо́з. **2,** *fig.* (complete transformation) метаморфо́за.
metaphor *n.* мета́фора. —**metaphorical,** *adj.* метафори́ческий.
metaphysics *n.* метафи́зика. —**metaphysical,** *adj.* метафизи́ческий. —**metaphysician; metaphysicist,** *n.* метафи́зик.
metastasis *n.* метаста́з.
metatarsus *n.* плюсна́. —**metatarsal,** *adj.* плюснево́й.
mete *v.t.* [*usu.* **mete out**] выделя́ть; распределя́ть. *Mete out punishment,* определя́ть наказа́ние.
meteor *n.* метео́р.
meteoric *adj.* **1,** (of a meteor) метео́рный. **2,** *fig.* (dazzlingly fast) головокружи́тельный.
meteorite *n.* метеори́т.
meteorology *n.* метеороло́гия. —**meteorological,** *adj.* метеорологи́ческий. —**meteorologist,** *n.* метео́ролог.
meter *also,* **metre** *n.* **1,** (unit of length) метр. **2,** (measuring instrument) счётчик: *gas meter,* га́зовый счётчик. *Water meter,* водоме́р. **3,** *pros.* разме́р; метр. **4,** *music* ритм.
methane *n.* мета́н.
method *n.* ме́тод; спо́соб. —**methodical,** *adj.* методи́ческий; методи́чный.
Methodist *n.* методи́ст. —*adj.* методи́стский. —**Methodism,** *n.* методи́зм.
methodology *n.* методоло́гия. —**methodological,** *adj.* методологи́ческий.
methyl *n.* мети́л. —**methyl alcohol,** мети́ловый спирт.
methylene *n.* метиле́н.
meticulous *adj.* аккура́тный; дото́шный. —**meticulousness,** *n.* аккура́тность.
metre *n.* = **meter.**
metric *adj.* метри́ческий.
metrics *n.* ме́трика.
metronome *n.* метроно́м.
metropolis *n.* кру́пный го́род.
metropolitan *adj.* столи́чный. —*n.* (archbishop) митрополи́т.
mettle *n.* зака́лка; вы́держка. *Prove one's mettle,* прояви́ть себя́.
Mexican *adj.* мексика́нский. —*n.* мексика́нец; мексика́нка.
mezzanine *n.* бельэта́ж.
mezzo-soprano *n.* ме́ццо-сопра́но.
mi *n., music* ми.
miasma *n.* миа́змы.
mica *n.* слюда́. —*adj.* слюдяно́й.
microbe *n.* микро́б.
microbiology *n.* микробиоло́гия. —**microbiologist,** *n.* микробио́лог.
microcircuit *n.* микросхе́ма.
microcosm *n.* микроко́см.
microfilm *n.* микрофи́льм.
micrometer *n.* микро́метр.
micron *n.* микро́н.
microorganism *n.* микрооргани́зм.
microphone *n.* микрофо́н.
microscope *n.* микроско́п. —**microscopic,** *adj.* микроскопи́ческий.
mid- *prefix* в середи́не (+ *gen.*): *in mid-June,* в середи́не ию́ня.
midair *n., in* **in midair,** на лету́. *Midair collision,* столкнове́ние в во́здухе.

midday *n.* по́лдень. —*adj.* полу́денный; полдне́вный.
middle *n.* середи́на. —*adj.* сре́дний: *the middle window,* сре́днее окно́; *the middle class,* сре́дний класс. —**in the middle of,** в середи́не (+ *gen.*); посреди́ (+ *gen.*); посереди́не (+ *gen.*). *In the middle of May,* в середи́не (*or* в полови́не) ма́я. *In the middle of the night,* среди́ но́чи.
middle age сре́дний во́зраст. —**middle-aged,** *adj.* сре́дних лет.
Middle Ages сре́дние века́; средневеко́вье.
middle ear сре́днее у́хо.
Middle East Бли́жний Восто́к. *Middle East countries,* ближневосто́чные стра́ны.
Middle English среднеангли́йский язы́к.
middle finger сре́дний па́лец.
middleman *n.* посре́дник.
middle name второ́е и́мя.
middling *adj.* сре́дний; посре́дственный. —**fair to middling,** так себе́; сно́сно; ни ша́тко ни ва́лко.
midge *n.* мо́шка.
midget *n.* ка́рлик. —*adj.* ка́рликовый.
midnight *n.* по́лночь. *Stay up till midnight,* сиде́ть до по́лночи. —*adj.* полно́чный; полу́ночный; полуно́чный. —**burn the midnight oil,** по́здно заси́живаться за рабо́той.
midshipman *n.* курса́нт вое́нно-морско́го учи́лища.
midst *n.* середи́на. *In the midst of,* в середи́не (+ *gen.*); среди́ (+ *gen.*). *In our midst,* среди́ нас.
midway *adj., in* **the midway point,** полпути́; полдоро́ги. —*adv.* на полпути́; на полдоро́ге.
midwife *n.* акуше́рка. —**midwifery,** *n.* акуше́рство.
mien *n.* вид; ми́на.
miff *v.t., colloq.* обижа́ть: *somewhat miffed,* не́сколько оби́жен.
might[1] *v.aux.* мочь: *who might that be?,* кто бы э́то мог быть? *I might have guessed it,* я мог бы об э́том догада́ться. *You might have offered to help,* вы могли́ бы предложи́ть свою́ по́мощь. *You might at least have said something about it,* вы хоть сказа́ли бы об э́том. *I might (just) as well have stayed home,* с тем же успе́хом я мог бы сиде́ть до́ма.
might[2] *n.* мощь; могу́щество. —**with all one's might,** изо всех сил; во всю мочь; со всего́ разма́ху.
mightily *adv.* усе́рдно; изо всех сил.
mighty *adj.* **1,** (powerful) мо́щный; могу́чий; могу́щественный. **2,** (great; huge) грома́дный; колосса́льный. —*adv., colloq.* о́чень.
mignonette *n.* резеда́.
migraine *n.* мигре́нь.
migrant *n.* переселе́нец. —*adj.* кочу́ющий.
migrate *v.i.* **1,** (of people) мигри́ровать; переселя́ться. **2,** (of birds) соверша́ть перелёт; перелета́ть; кочева́ть.
migration *n.* **1,** (of people) мигра́ция; переселе́ние. **2,** (of birds) перелёт.
migratory *adj.* **1,** (of people) кочу́ющий. **2,** (of birds) перелётный.
milch *adj.* моло́чный; до́йный.
mild *adj.* **1,** (gentle in disposition) мя́гкий: *a mild man,* мя́гкий челове́к. **2,** (moderate; temperate) мя́гкий: *mild weather,* мя́гкая пого́да. **3,** (not severe) мя́гкий; лёгкий: *a mild reproach,* мя́гкий упрёк; *a mild case,* лёгкий слу́чай (заболева́ния). **4,** (not strong, as of tobacco) лёгкий; некре́пкий.
mildew *n.* **1,** (plant disease) мучни́стая роса́. **2,** (mold) пле́сень. —**mildewed,** *adj.* запле́сневелый.
mildly *adv.* мя́гко. —**to put it mildly,** мя́гко выража́ясь.
mild-mannered *adj.* сми́рный; безро́потный.
mildness *n.* мя́гкость.
mile *n.* ми́ля.
mileage *n.* расстоя́ние в ми́лях.
milepost *n.* верстово́й столб.
milestone *n.* **1,** = **milepost. 2,** (important event) ве́ха.
milieu *n.* среда́; окруже́ние.
militancy *n.* во́инственность.
militant *adj.* во́инственный; во́инствующий. —*n.* активи́ст.
militarily *adv.* с вое́нной то́чки зре́ния; в вое́нном отноше́нии.
militarism *n.* милитари́зм. —**militarist,** *n.* милитари́ст. —**militaristic,** *adj.* милитаристи́ческий.
militarize *v.t.* милитаризи́ровать. —**militarization,** *n.* милитариза́ция.
military *adj.* вое́нный. —*n., preceded by* **the** вое́нные.
militate *v.i.* [*usu.* **militate in favor of** *or* **against**] **1,** (work in one's favor or against) спосо́бствовать (+ *dat.*); быть поме́хой (+ *dat.*). **2,** (be an argument for or against) (не) говори́ть в по́льзу (+ *gen.*).
militia *n.* мили́ция; ополче́ние. —**militiaman,** *n.* милиционе́р; ополче́нец.
milk *n.* молоко́. —*adj.* моло́чный: *milk diet,* моло́чная дие́та. —*v.t.* дои́ть: *milk a cow,* дои́ть коро́ву. —**there's no use crying over spilt milk,** что с во́зу упа́ло, то пропа́ло.
milking *n.* дое́ние; до́йка. —**milking machine,** до́йльная маши́на.
milkmaid *n.* доя́рка.
milkman *n.* моло́чник.
milk shake моло́чный кокте́йль.
milksop *n.* ба́ба; тря́пка; мо́края ку́рица.
milky *adj.* моло́чный. —**Milky Way,** Мле́чный Путь.
mill *n.* **1,** (machine or building for grinding) ме́льница. *Coffee mill,* кофе́йница. **2,** (factory) фа́брика; заво́д: *paper mill,* бума́жная фа́брика; *steel mill,* сталелите́йный заво́д. **3,** (machine for rolling metal) (прока́тный) стан. —*v.t.* **1,** (grind) моло́ть. **2,** (roll, as metal) прока́тывать. **3,** (shape, as metal) фрезерова́ть. —*v.i.* [*usu.* **mill around** *or* **about**] толо́чься.
millennium *n.* тысячеле́тие.
millepede *n.* = **millipede.**
miller *n.* ме́льник.
millet *n.* **1,** (cereal grass) про́со. **2,** (food grain) пшено́.
milliard *n., Brit.* миллиа́рд.
milligram *also,* **milligramme** *n.* миллигра́мм.
millimeter *also,* **millimetre** *n.* миллиме́тр.
milliner *n.* моди́стка.
millinery *n.* да́мские шля́пы. —**millinery shop,** шля́пный магази́н.
milling *n.* **1,** (grinding) размо́л. **2,** (shaping, as of metal) фрезерова́ние. —**milling cutter,** фре́за. —**milling machine,** фре́зерный стано́к.
million *n.* миллио́н.
millionaire *n.* миллионе́р.

millionth *adj.* миллио́нный. —*n.* миллио́нная часть.
millipede *also,* **millepede** *n.* многоно́жка.
millrace *n.* ме́льничный лото́к.
millstone *n.* жёрнов. *Millstone about one's neck,* ка́мень на шее́.
milquetoast *n., slang* тихо́ня.
milt *n.* моло́ки.
mime *n.* **1,** (pantomime) пантоми́ма. **2,** (farce performed in ancient times) мим. **3,** (mimic) мими́ст.
mimeograph *n.* рота́тор. —*v.t.* размножа́ть на рота́торе.
mimic *v.t.* передра́знивать. —*n.* **1,** (one adept at mimicking) имита́тор. **2,** (stage performer) мими́ст.
mimicry *n.* **1,** (imitating) ми́мика. **2,** *biol.* мимикри́я.
mimosa *n.* мимо́за.
minaret *n.* минаре́т.
mince *v.t.* **1,** (chop) кроши́ть; руби́ть. **2,** (lessen the force of): *not mince words,* не стесня́ться в выраже́ниях. —*v.i.* **1,** (speak or behave daintily) жема́ниться. **2,** (walk daintily or affectedly) семени́ть нога́ми.
mincemeat *n.* **1,** *obs.* (chopped meat) ру́бленое мя́со. **2,** (pie filling) фарш. —**make mincemeat of,** стере́ть в порошо́к.
mind *n.* ум. *On one's mind,* на уме́. *To my mind,* по-мо́ему; на мой взгляд. —*v.t.* **1,** (pay attention to) обраща́ть внима́ние на. *Mind one's own business,* не вме́шиваться в чужи́е дела́. **2,** (obey) слу́шаться. **3,** (look after) присма́тривать за (+ *instr.*). **4,** (object to) возража́ть про́тив. *I wouldn't mind a cup of tea,* не откажу́сь от ча́шки ча́я. **5,** (take care not to): *mind you don't slip,* осторо́жно, не оступи́тесь. *Mind you're not late,* смотри́те, не опозда́йте. —*v.i.* **1,** (be obedient) слу́шаться. **2,** (object) возража́ть; име́ть что́-нибудь про́тив: *if you don't mind,* е́сли вы не возража́ете; е́сли вы не име́ете ничего́ про́тив. —**bear, have, keep in mind,** име́ть в виду́. —**be in one's right mind,** быть в своём (*or* в здра́вом) уме́. —**be of one mind,** быть одного́ мне́ния. —**bring, call, recall to mind,** напомина́ть; воскреша́ть в па́мяти. —**change one's mind,** переду́мать; разду́мать. —**come to mind; cross one's mind,** приходи́ть в го́лову (+ *dat.*). —**give someone a piece of one's mind,** сказа́ть кому́-нибудь па́ру тёплых слов. —**go out of** (*or* **lose**) **one's mind,** сходи́ть с ума́. —**keep one's mind on,** сосредото́чиваться на. —**make up one's mind,** реши́ть; реши́ться; собра́ться. *I can't make up my mind,* я не могу́ реши́ть. —**never mind!,** ничего́; нева́жно; всё равно́. —**out of one's mind,** сумасше́дший. *Are you out of your mind?,* вы с ума́ сошли́? —**read someone's mind,** чита́ть чьи́-нибудь мы́сли. —**slip one's mind,** вы́скочить из головы́. —**speak one's mind,** выска́зываться.
mindful *adj.* [*usu.* **mindful of**] име́я в виду́; отдава́я себе́ отчёт (в).
mindless *adj.* **1,** (senseless) бессмы́сленный. **2,** *fol. by* **of** (heedless; unmindful) не обраща́я внима́ния (на).
mind's eye духо́вное о́ко.
mine[1] *poss.pron.* мой. *A friend of mine,* оди́н мой друг; оди́н из мои́х друзе́й.
mine[2] *n.* **1,** (pit) рудни́к; ша́хта; при́иск. *Coal mine,* у́гольная ша́хта; *gold mines,* золоты́е при́иски; *copper mine,* ме́дный рудни́к. **2,** (charge of explosives) ми́на. *Land mine,* фуга́с. —*v.t.* **1,** (extract, as ore) добыва́ть (руду́). **2,** (lay explosives under) мини́ровать; закла́дывать ми́ны под. —*v.i.* производи́ть го́рные рабо́ты.
mine detector миноиска́тель.
minefield *n.* ми́нное по́ле.
minelayer *n.* (ми́нный) загради́тель.
miner *n.* шахтёр; горня́к.
mineral *n.* минера́л; *pl.* минера́лы; поле́зные ископа́емые. *Rich in minerals,* бога́т поле́зными ископа́емыми. —*adj.* минера́льный: *mineral oil,* минера́льное ма́сло.
mineralogy *n.* минерало́гия. —**mineralogical,** *adj.* минералоги́ческий. —**mineralogist,** *n.* минерало́г.
minesweeper *n.* тра́льщик.
mingle *v.i.* **1,** (become mixed) сме́шиваться. **2,** (associate) обща́ться; враща́ться.
miniature *n.* миниатю́ра. —*adj.* миниатю́рный.
minimal *adj.* минима́льный.
minimize *v.t.* **1,** (reduce to a minimum) доводи́ть до ми́нимума. **2,** (belittle) умаля́ть.
minimum *n.* ми́нимум. —*adj.* минима́льный. —**minimum wage,** ми́нимум за́работной пла́ты.
mining *n.* го́рное де́ло. —*adj.* го́рный: *mining engineer,* го́рный инжене́р.
minion *n.* **1,** (servile follower) приспе́шник; клевре́т. **2,** (favorite) ба́ловень: *minion of fortune,* ба́ловень судьбы́.
minister *n.* **1,** (officer of state) мини́стр. **2,** (envoy) посла́нник. **3,** (clergyman) па́стор. —*v.i.* [*usu.* **minister to**] служи́ть; помога́ть.
ministerial *adj.* министе́рский. *On the ministerial level,* на у́ровне мини́стров.
ministration *n.* оказа́ние по́мощи.
ministry *n.* **1,** (governmental department) министе́рство. **2,** (clergy) духове́нство.
mink *n.* но́рка. —*adj.* но́рковый.
minnow *n.* голья́н.
minor *adj.* **1,** (unimportant) незначи́тельный: *minor defects,* незначи́тельные недоста́тки. **2,** (of lesser importance) ме́лкий; второстепе́нный. *Minor role,* второстепе́нная роль; *minor repairs,* ме́лкий ремо́нт. **3,** (under legal age) несовершенноле́тний. **4,** *music* мино́рный. —*n.* **1,** (one under legal age) несовершенноле́тний. **2,** *music* мино́р: *key of G-sharp minor,* тона́льность соль-дие́з мино́р. —**minor piece,** *chess* лёгкая фигу́ра.
minority *n.* **1,** (less than half of a total) меньшинство́. **2,** (period of being under legal age) несовершенноле́тие.
minstrel *n.* менестре́ль.
mint *n.* **1,** (plant) мя́та. **2,** (confection) мя́тная конфе́та. **3,** (place where money is coined) моне́тный двор. —*adj.* **1,** (containing mint) мя́тный. **2,** (of a postage stamp) негашёный. —*v.t.* чека́нить: *mint coins,* чека́нить моне́ты.
mintage *n.* чека́нка.
minuend *n.* уменьша́емое.
minuet *n.* менуэ́т.
minus *prep.* **1,** (less) ми́нус. **2,** (lacking) без. —*n.* (drawback) ми́нус. —*adj.* отрица́тельный. —**minus sign,** ми́нус; знак ми́нуса.
minuscule *adj.* кро́хотный; малю́сенький.
minute[1] (**min**-it) *n.* **1,** (60th part of an hour or degree)

минýта. *Any minute,* с минýты на минýту. **2,** *pl.* (record) протокóл. —**minute hand,** минýтная стрéлка.
minute[2] (mai-**noot**) *adj.* **1,** (tiny) мéлкий. **2,** (pains taking; detailed) подрóбный. —**minutely,** *adv.* подрóбно; до тóнкостей.
minutiae *n.pl.* мéлочи.
miracle *n.* чýдо. *He escaped by a miracle,* он спáсся каки́м-то чýдом.
miraculous *adj.* **1,** (as if by a miracle) чудéсный: *miraculous escape,* чудéсное спасéние. **2,** (seeming to work miracles) чудотвóрный; чудодéйственный. —**miraculously,** *adv.* чудéсно; чýдом.
mirage *n.* мирáж; мáрево.
mire *n.* **1,** (bog) тряси́на. **2,** (mud) грязь. —*v.t. Become mired in,* завязáть в; увязáть в; погрязáть в.
mirror *n.* зéркало. —*v.t.* отражáть.
mirth *n.* весéлье. —**mirthful,** *adj.* весёлый.
misadventure *n.* злоключéние.
misanthrope *n.* человеконенави́стник; мизантрóп. —**misanthropic,** *adj.* человеконенави́стнический; мизантропи́ческий. —**misanthropy,** *n.* человеконенави́стничество; мизантрóпия.
misapply *v.t.* непрáвильно применя́ть.
misapprehension *n.* заблуждéние. *Be under a misapprehension,* заблуждáться; быть в заблуждéнии.
misappropriate *v.t.* растрáчивать; расхищáть. —**misappropriation,** *n.* растрáта; хищéние; расхищéние.
misbegotten *adj.* внебрáчный; незаконнорождённый.
misbehave *v.i.* дýрно вести́ себя́. —**misbehavior,** *n.* дурнóе поведéние.
miscalculate *v.t.* непрáвильно подсчи́тывать. —*v.i.* просчи́тываться. —**miscalculation,** *n.* просчёт.
miscarriage *n.* вы́кидыш. *Have a miscarriage,* вы́кинуть. —**miscarriage of justice,** судéбная оши́бка.
miscarry *v.i.* **1,** (go wrong; fail) давáть осéчку. **2,** (have a miscarriage) вы́кинуть.
miscast *v.t.* дать (актёру) неподходя́щую роль.
miscegenation *n.* рáсовое смешéние.
miscellaneous *adj.* **1,** (not falling into a single category) рáзные; *(as a heading)* рáзное. **2,** (made up of different elements) разнорóдный.
miscellany *n.* **1,** (miscellaneous collection) смесь. **2,** (collection of writings) сбóрник.
mischance *n.* несчáстье; несчáстный слýчай. *If by some mischance...,* éсли по несчáстной случáйности...
mischief *n.* озорствó; баловствó; шáлости. —**mischief-maker,** *n.* озорни́к; шалýн; прокáзник; бедокýр. —**mischievous,** *adj.* озорнóй; шаловли́вый.
misconception *n.* заблуждéние.
misconduct *n.* дурнóе поведéние.
misconstrue *v.t.* превráтно истолкóвывать; перетолкóвывать.
miscount *v.t.* просчи́тывать. —*v.i.* просчи́тываться; обсчи́тываться. —*n.* просчёт.
miscreant *n.* злодéй; негодя́й.
misdeal *v.t. & i.* ошибáться при сдáче (карт). —*n.* непрáвильная сдáча.
misdeed *n.* простýпок.
misdemeanor *also,* **misdemeanour** *n.* простýпок.
misdirect *v.t.* **1,** (give wrong directions to) сбивáть с дорóги. **2,** (address to the wrong person) отправля́ть не по áдресу. *Your remarks are misdirected,* вáши замечáния направлены не по áдресу.
miser *n.* скупéц; скря́га.
miserable *adj.* **1,** (unhappy; wretched) жáлкий; несчáстный. **2,** (awful; rotten) сквéрный; отврати́тельный. **3,** (despicable) жáлкий; презрéнный. **4,** (squalid) жáлкий; убóгий.
miserly *adj.* скупóй. —**miserliness,** *n.* скýпость.
misery *n.* **1,** (suffering; distress) страдáние. **2,** (poverty) нищетá. —**put out of one's misery,** положи́ть конéц чьи́м-нибудь страдáниям.
misfire *v.i.* давáть осéчку. —*n.* осéчка.
misfortune *n.* несчáстье.
misgiving *n.* **1,** (doubt) сомнéние. **2,** (apprehensions) опасéние.
misguided *adj.* **1,** (mistaken) оши́бочный. **2,** (deluded) заблуждáющийся.
mishandle *v.t.* **1,** (treat roughly) плóхо обращáться с. **2,** (manage badly) напýтать.
mishap *n.* злоключéние; авáрия. *Without mishap,* без происшéствий.
mishmash *n.* мешани́на.
misinform *v.t.* непрáвильно информи́ровать. —**misinformation,** *n.* непрáвильная информáция.
misinterpret *v.t.* превráтно истолкóвывать; перетолкóвывать. —**misinterpretation,** *n.* невéрное истолковáние.
misjudge *v.t.* непрáвильно оцéнивать. —**misjudgment,** *n.* оши́бка; просчёт.
mislay *v.t.* затеря́ть; заложи́ть.
mislead *v.t.* вводи́ть в заблуждéние. —**misleading,** *adj.* вводя́щий в заблуждéние; обмáнчивый.
mismanage *v.t.* плóхо вести́ *or* управля́ть. —**mismanagement,** *n.* бесхозя́йственное ведéние дел; бесхозя́йственность.
mismatch *n.* плохáя пáртия.
misnomer *n.* непрáвильное названиé.
misogynist *n.* женоненави́стник. —**misogyny,** *n.* женоненави́стничество.
misplace *v.t.* **1,** (put in the wrong place) класть не на мéсто. **2,** (mislay; lose) затеря́ть; заложи́ть.
misprint *n.* опечáтка.
mispronounce *v.t.* непрáвильно произноси́ть. —**mispronunciation,** *n.* непрáвильное произношéние.
misquote *v.t.* непрáвильно цити́ровать. —**misquotation,** *n.* непрáвильная цитáта.
misread *v.t.* **1,** (read incorrectly) непрáвильно прочéсть. **2,** (interpret incorrectly) непрáвильно истолкóвывать.
misrepresent *v.t.* искажáть; извращáть. —**misrepresentation,** *n.* искажéние; извращéние.
misrule *n.* плохóе правлéние.
miss *v.t.* **1,** (fail to hit) не попáсть в (цель). **2,** (fail to catch) не поймáть. **3,** (fail to attend) пропускáть. **4,** (fail to meet) не застáть. **5,** (fail to understand or appreciate) не понимáть. **6,** (fail to hear) прослýшать. **7,** (let slip by) упускáть; пропускáть. **8,** (be late for, as a train) опáздывать на. **9,** (escape; avoid, as a mishap): *he narrowly missed being killed,* он чуть не поги́б. **10,** (overlook) проглядéть; не замéтить. **11,** (feel the absence of) не хватáть *(impers.)*; скучáть по. *I miss you,* мне вас не хватáет. *We shall miss you,* мы бýдем скучáть по вас. **12,** (lack) не хватáть *(impers.)*; не-

доставáть *(impers.). The book is missing a few pages,* в кни́ге не хватáет нéсколько страни́ц. —*v.i.* промахну́ться; не попáсть в цель. —*n.* **1,** (failure to hit) прóмах; непопадáние. **2,** (young lady) мисс.

misshapen *adj.* урóдливый.

missile *n.* **1,** (any projectile) снаря́д. **2,** *mil.* (rocket) ракéта; реакти́вный снаря́д. —*adj.* ракéтный: *missile strike,* ракéтный удáр.

missing *adj.* отсу́тствующий; недостаю́щий. *Be missing,* отсу́тствовать; не хватáть; недоставáть; не оказáться. *Missing in action,* пропáвший без вести. —**missing link,** недостаю́щее звенó.

mission *n.* **1,** (assignment; trip) ми́ссия: *rescue mission,* спасáтельная ми́ссия. *Goodwill mission,* ми́ссия дóброй вóли. **2,** (combat operation) боевáя задáча. **3,** (military flight) (боевóй) вы́лет. **4,** (legation) ми́ссия. **5,** (delegation) ми́ссия: *trade mission,* торгóвая ми́ссия. **6,** *relig.* ми́ссия.

missionary *n.* миссионéр. —*adj.* миссионéрский.

missive *n.* послáние.

misspell *v.t.* непрáвильно писáть. —**misspelling,** *n.* орфографи́ческая оши́бка. —**misspelt,** *adj.* непрáвильно напи́санный.

misspend *v.t.* растрáчивать; расточáть. *Misspent youth,* растрáченная мóлодость.

misstate *v.t.* лóжно излагáть; искажáть. —**misstatement,** *n.* лóжное заявлéние.

misstep *n.* лóжный шаг.

mist *n.* лёгкий тумáн; ды́мка.

mistake *n.* оши́бка. *By mistake,* по оши́бке. *Make a mistake,* ошибáться; дéлать оши́бку. —*v.t.* **1,** (misinterpret) непрáвильно понимáть. **2,** *fol. by* **for** (take for someone else) принимáть за (+ *acc.*).

mistaken *adj.* **1,** (in error): *you are mistaken,* вы ошибáетесь. **2,** (erroneous) оши́бочный: *mistaken identity,* оши́бочное опознáние. —**mistakenly,** *adv.* оши́бочно; по оши́бке.

mister *n.* ми́стер; господи́н.

mistletoe *n.* омéла.

mistranslate *v.t.* непрáвильно переводи́ть. —**mistranslation,** *n.* непрáвильный перевóд.

mistreat *v.t.* ду́рно обращáться с. —**mistreatment,** *n.* дурнóе обращéние.

mistress *n.* **1,** (lady of the house; owner) хозя́йка. **2,** (paramour) любóвница.

mistrial *n.* непрáвильное судéбное разбирáтельство.

mistrust *n.* недовéрие. —*v.t.* не доверя́ть. —**mistrustful,** *adj.* недовéрчивый.

misty *adj.* **1,** (marked by mist) тумáнный. **2,** (obscured by mist) затумáненный.

misunderstand *v.t.* непрáвильно поня́ть. —**misunderstanding,** *n.* недоразумéние.

misuse *v.t.* **1,** (use incorrectly) непрáвильно употребля́ть. **2,** (abuse) злоупотребля́ть. —*n.* **1,** (incorrect use) непрáвильное употреблéние. **2,** (abuse) злоупотреблéние.

mite *n.* **1,** (parasite) клещ. **2,** (tiny person) крóшка. **3,** (small contribution) лéпта. —**a mite,** чу́точку: *a mite better,* чу́точку лу́чше.

miter *also,* **mitre** *n.* **1,** (headdress) ми́тра. **2,** (beveled joint) скос. —*v.t.* скáшивать.

mitigate *v.t.* смягчáть. *Mitigating circumstances,* смягчáющие вину́ обстоя́тельства.

mitosis *n.* митóз.

mitre *n.* & *v.* = **miter.**

mitten *n.* рукави́ца; вáрежка.

mix *v.t.* **1,** (blend into a single mass) мешáть; смéшивать: *mix paints,* мешáть/смéшивать крáски. *Rain mixed with snow,* дождь, смéшанный со снéгом. **2,** (make by mixing) готóвить: *mix a salad,* (при)готóвить салáт. **3,** (combine) сочетáть; совмещáть. *Mix business with pleasure,* сочетáть полéзное с прия́тным. —*v.i.* **1,** (become mixed) смéшиваться; соединя́ться. **2,** (associate; mingle) общáться; вращáться. —*n.* смесь. —**mix up, 1,** (mix thoroughly) смéшивать. **2,** (confuse; jumble) пу́тать; спу́тывать; смéшивать. *Get mixed up,* пу́таться. **3,** (involve) замéшивать; впу́тывать. *Get mixed up in,* замéшиваться в; впу́тываться в.

mixed *adj.* смéшанный. —**mixed marriage,** смéшанный брак. —**mixed number,** смéшанное числó.

mixer *n.* мешáлка; смеси́тель.

mixture *n.* смесь.

mix-up *n.* недоразумéние; неувя́зка.

mizzen *n.* бизáнь. —**mizzenmast,** *n.* бизáнь-мáчта.

mnemonic *adj.* мнемони́ческий. —**mnemonics,** *n.* мнемóника.

moan *n.* стон. —*v.i.* стонáть.

moat *n.* крепостнóй ров.

mob *n.* толпá. —*v.t.* **1,** (crowd around) нападáть толпóй на. **2,** (jam) набивáться в. *The place was mobbed,* нарóду бы́ло биткóм наби́то.

mobile *adj.* подвижнóй; моби́льный; передвижнóй. *Mobile warfare,* манёвренная войнá. —**mobility,** *n.* подви́жность; моби́льность.

mobilize *v.t.* мобилизовáть. —*v.i.* мобилизовáться. —**mobilization,** *n.* мобилизáция.

mobster *n., colloq.* гáнгстер.

moccasin *n.* **1,** (shoe) мокаси́н. **2,** (snake) мокаси́новая змея́.

mocha *n.* мóкко.

mock *v.t.* издевáться над; насмехáться над; высмéивать; осмéивать. —*adj.* инсцени́рованный: *mock trial,* инсцени́рованный судéбный процéсс. —**mocker,** *n.* насмéшник.

mockery *n.* **1,** (ridicule; derision) издевáтельство; насмéшка; осмея́ние. **2,** (travesty) парóдия.

mocking *adj.* издевáтельский; насмéшливый.

mockingbird *n.* пересмéшник.

mock-up *n.* макéт.

modal *adj.* модáльный.

mode *n.* **1,** (way; manner) спóсоб. *Mode of living,* óбраз жи́зни. **2,** (style; fashion) мóда: *dress in the latest mode,* одевáться по послéдней мóде.

model *n.* **1,** (small-scale reproduction) образéц; модéль; макéт. **2,** (make; design) модéль. **3,** (standard; ideal) образéц. **4,** (one who poses) нату́рщик; нату́рщица. **5,** (one who displays clothes by wearing them) манекéнщик; манекéнщица. —*adj.* образцóвый; примéрный. *Model airplane,* модéль самолёта. —*v.t.* **1,** (make figures of) лепи́ть. **2,** (pattern after) дéлать по образцу́ (+ *gen.*). —*v.i.* рабóтать манекéнщиком (-щицей).

modeler *also,* **modeller** *n.* модéльщик.

modeling *also,* **modelling** *n.* **1,** (making of figures) лéпка. **2,** (working as a model): *do modeling,* рабóтать манекéнщиком (-щицей). —**modeling clay,** гли́на для лéпки.

modeller *n.* = **modeler.**

moderate *adj.* **1,** (not extreme) уме́ренный. **2,** (medium) сре́дний. **3,** (reasonable, as of prices) досту́пный. —*v.t.* смягча́ть; умеря́ть. —*v.i.* **1,** (become less extreme or severe) смягча́ться; умеря́ться. **2,** (act as moderator) председа́тельствовать.
moderately *adv.* **1,** (in moderation) уме́ренно. **2,** (fairly; more or less) дово́льно: *moderately well,* дово́льно хорошо́.
moderation *n.* **1,** (act of moderating) смягче́ние. **2,** (moderateness) уме́ренность. —**in moderation,** уме́ренно.
moderator *n.* председа́тель.
modern *adj.* совреме́нный: *modern art,* совреме́нное иску́сство; *modern methods of treatment,* совреме́нные ме́тоды лече́ния. *Modern history,* но́вая исто́рия. *Modern languages,* но́вые языки́. *Modern dance,* та́нец моде́рн.
modernism *n.* модерни́зм. —**modernist,** *n.* модерни́ст. —**modernistic,** *adj.* модерни́стский. —**modernity,** *n.* совреме́нность.
modernize *v.t.* модернизи́ровать. —**modernization,** *n.* модерниза́ция.
modest *adj.* скро́мный. —**modestly,** *adv.* скро́мно. —**modesty,** *n.* скро́мность.
modicum *n.* чу́точка; ка́пелька.
modification *n.* видоизмене́ние; модифика́ция. *Make modifications in the design,* вноси́ть измене́ния в констру́кцию.
modifier *n., gram.* определе́ние; атрибу́т.
modify *v.t.* **1,** (alter) видоизменя́ть; модифици́ровать. **2,** (moderate) смягча́ть. **3,** *gram.* определя́ть.
modulate *v.t.* модули́ровать. —*v.i.* перелива́ться. —**modulation,** *n.* модуля́ция. —**modulator,** *n.* модуля́тор.
module *n.* **1,** (unit of measurement) мо́дуль. **2,** (space vehicle) отсе́к.
modulus *n.* мо́дуль.
Mogul *n.* **1,** *hist.* мого́л. **2,** *l.c.* (powerful person) магна́т.
mohair *n.* мохе́р. —*adj.* мохе́ровый.
Mohammedan *n.* магомета́нин. —*adj.* магомета́нский. —**Mohammedanism,** *n.* магомета́нство; мусульма́нство.
moire *n.* муа́р. —**moiré,** *adj.* муа́ровый.
moist *adj.* вла́жный.
moisten *v.t.* сма́чивать.
moisture *n.* вла́жность; вла́га.
molar *n.* коренно́й зуб.
molasses *n.* па́тока.
mold *also,* **mould** *n.* **1,** (fungus) пле́сень; гниль. **2,** (matrix) фо́рма. **3,** (cast; model) сле́пок. **4,** *fig.* (distinctive character) заква́ска. **5,** *fig.* (fixed pattern) шабло́н. —*v.t.* **1,** (make) формова́ть. **2,** *fig.* (shape) формирова́ть.
molder *also,* **moulder** *v.i.* рассыпа́ться (в пыль).
molding *also,* **moulding** *n.* лепно́е украше́ние.
moldy *also,* **mouldy** *adj.* запле́сневелый.
mole *n.* **1,** (blemish) ро́динка. **2,** (rodent) крот.
molecule *n.* моле́кула. —**molecular,** *adj.* молекуля́рный.
molehill *n.* крото́вая нора́. —**make a mountain out of a molehill,** де́лать из му́хи слона́.
mole rat слепы́ш.
moleskin *n.* **1,** (fur) крото́вый мех; крот. **2,** (cloth) молески́н. —*adj.* крото́вый; молески́новый.
molest *v.t.* пристава́ть к; беспоко́ить.
mollify *v.t.* **1,** (placate) уми́лостивить. **2,** (make less intense) смягча́ть.
mollusk *also,* **mollusc** *n.* моллю́ск.
mollycoddle *v.t., colloq.* изне́живать. —*n., colloq.* не́женка.
molt *also,* **moult** *v.i.* линя́ть.
molten *adj.* распла́вленный; жи́дкий. *Molten lava,* жи́дкая ла́ва.
molybdenum *n.* молибде́н. —**molybdic,** *adj.* молибде́новый.
mom *n., colloq.* ма́ма.
moment *n.* **1,** (instant; point in time) моме́нт. *At the moment,* в да́нный моме́нт. *At any moment,* в любо́й моме́нт. *For the moment,* пока́. **2,** (importance) ва́жность; значе́ние.
momentarily *adv.* **1,** (for a moment) на мину́ту. **2,** (very soon) че́рез не́сколько мину́т. **3,** (any moment) с мину́ты на мину́ту.
momentary *adj.* мгнове́нный. *Catch a momentary glimpse of,* уви́деть ме́льком.
momentous *adj.* знамена́тельный.
momentum *n.* ине́рция; разго́н. *Gather momentum,* разгоня́ться.
mommy *n.* ма́ма; мама́ша.
monarch *n.* мона́рх. —**monarchical,** *adj.* монархи́ческий. —**monarchism,** *n.* монархи́зм.
monarchist *n.* монархи́ст. —*adj.* монархи́ческий.
monarchy *n.* мона́рхия.
monastery *n.* монасты́рь. —**monasterial,** *adj.* монасты́рский.
monastic *adj.* мона́шеский. *Monastic vows,* мона́шеские обе́ты. —**monasticism,** *n.* мона́шество.
Monday *n.* понеде́льник.
monetary *adj.* де́нежный; моне́тный.
money *n.* де́ньги: *a lot of money,* мно́го де́нег. *Cost a lot of money,* сто́ить больши́х де́нег. *Play for money,* игра́ть на де́ньги. —*adj.* де́нежный: *money market,* де́нежный ры́нок.
moneybag *n.* **1,** (sack for money) мешо́к для де́нег. **2,** *pl., colloq.* (rich man) золото́й *or* де́нежный мешо́к; толстосу́м.
money box копи́лка; кубы́шка.
moneychanger *n.* меня́ла.
moneylender *n.* ростовщи́к.
moneymaking *adj.* дохо́дный; при́быльный.
money order де́нежный перево́д.
Mongol *n.* монго́л. —*adj.* монго́льский. *Also,* **Mongolian.**
mongoose *n.* мангу́ста.
mongrel *n.* **1,** (plant or animal of mixed breed) по́месь. **2,** (dog of mixed breed) дворня́га; дворня́жка. —*adj.* нечистокро́вный.
moniker *also,* **monicker** *n., slang* про́звище; кли́чка.
monism *n.* мони́зм. —**monistic,** *adj.* монисти́ческий.
monitor *n.* **1,** (in school) кла́ссный руководи́тель; ста́роста. **2,** (TV monitor) контро́льный кинеско́п. —*v.t.* проверя́ть; контроли́ровать. —**monitor lizard,** вара́н.
monk *n.* мона́х.
monkey *n.* обезья́на. —*v.i.* [*usu.* **monkey with**] *slang* вози́ться с. —**make a monkey out of,** *slang* оста́вить в дурака́х.
monkey business *slang* чуда́чества.

monkey wrench францу́зский ключ. —**throw a monkey wrench into the works,** вставля́ть па́лки в колёса.
monkhood *n.* мона́шество.
monkshood *n.* (plant) акони́т.
monochromatic *adj.* одноцве́тный; монохрома́тический.
monocle *n.* моно́кль.
monogamy *n.* единобра́чие; монога́мия. —**monogamous,** *adj.* единобра́чный; монога́мный.
monogram *n.* ве́нзель; моногра́мма.
monograph *n.* моногра́фия. —**monographic,** *adj.* монографи́ческий.
monolith *n.* моноли́т. —**monolithic,** *adj.* моноли́тный.
monologue *n.* моноло́г.
mononucleosis *n.* мононуклео́з.
monoplane *n.* монопла́н.
monopolist *n.* монополи́ст. —**monopolistic,** *adj.* монополисти́ческий.
monopolize *v.t.* монополизи́ровать. —**monopolization,** *n.* монополиза́ция.
monopoly *n.* монопо́лия.
monorail *n.* однорéльсовая желе́зная доро́га.
monosyllabic *adj.* односло́жный. —**monosyllable,** *n.* односло́жное сло́во.
monotheism *n.* монотеи́зм; единобо́жие. —**monotheistic,** *adj.* монотеисти́ческий.
monotone *n.* моното́нная речь; моното́нное пе́ние. *In a monotone,* моното́нно. —*adj.* моното́нный; одното́нный.
monotonous *adj.* **1,** (unchanging in tone) моното́нный. **2,** (tedious; repetitious) однообра́зный. —**monotony,** *n.* однообра́зие.
monotype *n.* моноти́п.
monsieur *n.* мосье́.
Monsignor *n.* монсеньёр.
monsoon *n.* муссо́н.
monster *n.* **1,** (fantastic creature) чудо́вище. **2,** (ugly or grotesque creature) чудо́вище; уро́д. **3,** (vicious or depraved person) чудо́вище; и́зверг.
monstrosity *n.* **1,** (state of being monstrous) чудо́вищность. **2,** (very ugly thing) уро́д.
monstrous *adj.* чудо́вищный; зве́рский.
montage *n.* монта́ж.
month *n.* ме́сяц. *A month's vacation,* ме́сячный о́тпуск.
monthly *adj.* ежеме́сячный. —*adv.* ежеме́сячно. —*n.* ежеме́сячник.
monument *n.* па́мятник. —**monumental,** *adj.* монумента́льный.
moo *v.i.* мыча́ть. —*n.* мыча́ние.
mood *n.* **1,** (frame of mind) настрое́ние: *in a bad mood,* в плохо́м настрое́нии. **2,** *gram.* наклоне́ние. —**in the mood,** располо́жен: *I am not in the mood for work today,* я не располо́жен (*or* у меня́ нет расположе́ния) сего́дня рабо́тать. *He is not in the mood for jokes,* ему́ не до шу́ток.
moody *adj.* **1,** (gloomy; sullen) угрю́мый. **2,** (subject to changes of mood) капри́зный.
moon *n.* луна́. *To the moon,* на Луну́. —**once in a blue moon,** в кои ве́ки.
moonbeam *n.* луч луны́.
moon landing прилуне́ние.
moonlight *n.* лу́нный свет. —**moonlit,** *adj.* лу́нный: *moonlit night,* лу́нная ночь.
moonstone *n.* лу́нный ка́мень.
moor *n.* (tract of land) пу́стошь. —*v.t., naut.* прича́ливать; швартова́ть. —*v.i., naut.* прича́ливать; швартова́ться.
Moor *n.* мавр.
moorage *n.* прича́л.
mooring *n.* **1,** (tying up) прича́л. **2,** *often pl.* (lines, cables, etc.) шварто́вы. —**mooring line,** шварто́в; чал; ча́лка; прича́л; прича́льный кана́т.
Moorish *adj.* маврита́нский.
moose *n.* лось.
moot *adj.* спо́рный.
mop *n.* **1,** (cleaning tool) шва́бра. **2,** (mass of hair) копна́ (воло́с). —*v.t.* **1,** (clean) мыть шва́брой. **2,** (wipe) вытира́ть. **3,** *fol. by* **up,** *mil.* очища́ть от проти́вника.
mope *v.i.* хандри́ть.
moped *n.* мопе́д.
moraine *n.* море́на.
moral *adj.* мора́льный; нра́вственный. *Moral code,* мора́льный ко́декс. *Moral support/victory/duty,* мора́льная подде́ржка/побе́да/обя́занность. —*n.* **1,** *pl.* (standards of behavior) мора́ль; нра́вственность. *Loose morals,* лёгкие нра́вы. **2,** (lesson) мора́ль.
morale *n.* мора́льное состоя́ние.
moralist *n.* морали́ст. —**moralistic,** *adj.* нравоучи́тельный.
morality *n.* мора́ль; нра́вственность.
moralize *v.i.* морализи́ровать.
morally *adv.* **1,** (from a moral point of view) мора́льно. **2,** (virtuously) мора́льно; нра́вственно. **3,** (virtually) практи́чески: *morally certain,* практи́чески уве́рен.
morass *n.* боло́то; тряси́на.
moratorium *n.* морато́рий.
moray *n.* муре́на. *Also,* **moray eel.**
morbid *adj.* **1,** (unhealthy) боле́зненный. **2,** (gruesome) жу́ткий. —**morbidity,** *n.* боле́зненность.
mordant *adj.* ко́лкий; язви́тельный. —*n.* протра́ва.
more *adj.* **1,** (greater in quantity) бо́льше: *it will take more time,* э́то займёт бо́льше вре́мени. **2,** (additional) ещё: *would you like some more tea?,* хоти́те ещё ча́ю? —*n.* **1,** (a greater quantity) бо́льше: *it's more than we need,* э́то бо́льше, чем нам ну́жно. *More than meets the eye,* бо́льше, чем ка́жется на пе́рвый взгляд. **2,** (an additional quantity) ещё: *would you like some more?,* хоти́те ещё? ♦*In neg. sentences* бо́льше: *I will have no more of this,* я бо́льше не бу́ду терпе́ть. *I have nothing more to say,* мне бо́льше не́чего сказа́ть. —*adv.* **1,** *used to form the comp. degree of adjectives and adverbs* бо́лее: *more interesting,* бо́лее интере́сный. **2,** (greater in amount or degree) бо́льше: *more than enough,* бо́льше чем доста́точно. *More than a hundred people,* бо́льше ста челове́к. *More than ever before,* бо́льше, чем когда́-либо ра́ньше. —**all the more,** всё бо́лее (+ *adj.*). —**(all) the more so because...,** тем бо́лее, что... —**any more,** *see* **any.** —**more and more,** всё бо́льше и бо́льше; *(with adjectives)* всё бо́лее (+ *adj.*). —**more or less,** бо́лее и́ли ме́нее. —**once more,** ещё раз. —**the more..., the more...,** чем бо́льше..., тем бо́льше... —**what's more,** бо́лее того́; бо́льше того́.
morel *n.* сморчо́к.

moreover *adv.* кро́ме того́; сверх того́; к тому́ же.
mores *n.pl.* нра́вы.
morganatic *adj.* морганати́ческий.
morgue *n.* морг; поко́йницкая; мертве́цкая.
moribund *adj.* умира́ющий.
Mormon *n.* мормо́н. —*adj.* мормо́нский.
morning *n.* у́тро. *This morning,* сего́дня у́тром. *Tomorrow morning,* за́втра у́тром. *The next morning,* нау́тро. *Monday morning,* в понеде́льник у́тром. —*adj.* у́тренний: *morning newspaper,* у́тренняя газе́та. —**good morning!,** до́брое у́тро! —**in the morning,** у́тром. *Two o'clock in the morning,* два часа́ но́чи. *Eight o'clock in the morning,* во́семь часо́в утра́.
morning coat визи́тка.
morning-glory *n.* ипоме́я.
morocco *n.* сафья́н. —*adj.* сафья́нный; сафья́новый.
moron *n.* слабоу́мный; идио́т. —**moronic,** *adj.* слабоу́мный; идио́тский.
morose *adj.* мра́чный; угрю́мый; па́смурный. —**moroseness,** *n.* мра́чность; угрю́мость.
morpheme *n.* морфе́ма.
morphine *n.* мо́рфий. *Morphine addict,* морфини́ст.
morphology *n.* морфоло́гия. —**morphological,** *adj.* морфологи́ческий.
Morse code а́збука Мо́рзе.
morsel *n.* кусо́чек.
mortal *adj.* **1,** (subject to death) сме́ртный: *man is mortal,* челове́к – сме́ртен. **2,** (fatal) смерте́льный: *mortal blow,* смерте́льный уда́р. **3,** (fought to the death) сме́ртный: *mortal combat,* сме́ртный бой. **4,** (bitter; grievous) смерте́льный: *mortal fear/enemy,* смерте́льный страх/враг. —*n.* сме́ртный: *mere mortal,* просто́й сме́ртный. —**mortal remains,** бре́нные оста́нки. —**mortal sin,** сме́ртный грех.
mortality *n.* сме́ртность: *infant mortality,* де́тская сме́ртность.
mortally *adv.* смерте́льно; на́смерть.
mortar *n.* **1,** (mixing bowl) сту́пка; сту́па. **2,** (cement) строи́тельный раство́р. **3,** (military weapon) миномёт; морти́ра. —*adj., mil.* миномётный: *mortar fire,* миномётный ого́нь.
mortgage *n.* закладна́я; ипоте́ка. —*v.t.* закла́дывать. —**mortgagee,** *n.* залогодержа́тель. —**mortgagor,** *n.* закла́дчик.
mortician *n.* дире́ктор похоро́нного бюро́.
mortification *n.* **1,** (humiliation) униже́ние. **2,** (self-denial) умерщвле́ние (пло́ти).
mortify *v.t.* **1,** (humiliate) унижа́ть. **2,** (discipline, as the body) умерщвля́ть (плоть). —**mortifying,** *adj.* унизи́тельный.
mortise *n.* паз; гнездо́.
mortuary *n.* морг; поко́йницкая; мертве́цкая. —*adj.* похоро́нный; погреба́льный.
mosaic *n.* моза́ика. —*adj.* мозаи́чный.
Moslem *n.* мусульма́нин. —*adj.* мусульма́нский.
mosque *n.* мече́ть.
mosquito *n.* кома́р. —**mosquito bite,** уку́с комара́.
moss *n.* мох. —**moss-grown,** *adj.* замше́лый; обомше́лый. —**mossy,** *adj.* мши́стый.
most *adj.* **1,** (in the greatest amount) наибо́льшее коли́чество: *receive the most votes,* получи́ть наибо́льшее коли́чество голосо́в. **2,** (in the majority of instances) большинство́ (+ *gen.*): *in most cases,* в большинстве́ слу́чаев. —*n.* **1,** (the majority) большинство́; бо́льшая часть: *most of them,* большинство́ из них; *most of the time,* бо́льшая часть вре́мени. **2,** *preceded by* **the** (the greatest amount) са́мое бо́льшее: *the most I can do,* са́мое бо́льшее, что я могу́ сде́лать. —*adv.* **1,** (in or to the greatest extent) бо́льше всего́: *what I need most,* что мне бо́льше всего́ ну́жно. **2,** *used to form the superl. degree of adjectives* са́мый: *the most difficult part,* са́мая тру́дная часть. *Most likely,* скоре́е всего́. **3,** (very; highly) весьма́; в вы́сшей сте́пени. —**at (the) most,** са́мое бо́льшее; от си́лы; ма́ксимум. —**for the most part,** гла́вным о́бразом; бо́льшей ча́стью; в большинстве́ (своём). —**make the most of,** максима́льно испо́льзовать.
mostly *adv.* гла́вным о́бразом; бо́льшей ча́стью; в основно́м.
mote *n.* пыли́нка; сори́нка.
motel *n.* моте́ль.
moth *n.* **1,** (night-flying insect) ба́бочка; мотылёк. **2,** (clothes moth) моль.
mothball *n.* **1,** *pl.* (substance) нафтали́н. **2,** (single ball of same) ша́рик нафтали́на.
moth-eaten *adj.* изъе́денный мо́лью.
mother *n.* мать. —*adj.* **1,** (maternal) матери́нский. **2,** (native) родно́й. —**mother country,** ро́дина; оте́чество. —**mother tongue,** родно́й язы́к.
motherhood *n.* матери́нство.
mother-in-law *n.* **1,** (husband's mother) свекро́вь. **2,** (wife's mother) тёща.
motherland *n.* ро́дина; оте́чество.
motherless *adj.* лишённый ма́тери.
motherly *adj.* матери́нский.
mother-of-pearl *n.* перламу́тр. —*adj.* перламу́тровый.
mother superior игу́менья.
motif *n.* моти́в.
motion *n.* **1,** (movement) движе́ние; ход. *Set in motion,* приводи́ть в движе́ние; дать ход (+ *dat.*). **2,** (gesture) жест. **3,** (proposal to be put to a vote) предложе́ние. **4,** *law* хода́тайство. —*v.t.* пока́зывать же́стом. *He motioned me to a chair,* он указа́л мне на стул. —*v.i.* жестикули́ровать. *He motioned to me to sit down,* он же́стом пригласи́л меня́ сесть.
motionless *adj.* неподви́жный; без движе́ния. *Stand motionless,* стоя́ть неподви́жно.
motion picture **1,** (movie) кинофи́льм; кинокарти́на. **2,** *pl.* (the art or field of movie-making) кино́; кинематогра́фия.
motivate *v.t.* побужда́ть. —**motivation,** *n.* побужде́ние.
motive *n.* моти́в; побужде́ние. —*adj.* дви́жущий; дви́гательный.
motley *adj.* пёстрый.
motor *n.* мото́р; дви́гатель. —*adj.* мото́рный. —*v.i.* е́хать *or* ката́ться на маши́не.
motorbike *n.* мопе́д.
motorboat *n.* мото́рная ло́дка.
motorbus *n.* авто́бус.
motorcade *n.* корте́ж.
motorcar *n.* автомоби́ль.
motorcycle *n.* мотоци́кл. *Motorcycle races,* мото-го́нки. —**motorcyclist,** *n.* мотоцикли́ст.
motorist *n.* автомобили́ст.

motorized *adj.* моторизо́ванный.
motorman *n.* **1,** (tram driver) вагоновожа́тый. **2,** (engineer on a train) машини́ст.
motor nerve дви́гательный нерв.
motor scooter моторо́ллер.
motor ship теплохо́д.
motor vehicle автомаши́на.
mottle *v.t.* испещря́ть. —**mottled,** *adj.* кра́пчатый.
motto *n.* деви́з.
mould *n. & v.* = **mold.** —**moulder,** *v.* = **molder.** —**moulding,** *n.* = **molding.** —**mouldy,** *adj.* = **moldy.**
moult *v.* = **molt.**
mound *n.* буго́р. *Burial mound,* курга́н; моги́льный холм.
mount *v.t.* **1,** (go up; climb up) поднима́ться на; взбира́ться на. **2,** (get up on; get on) сади́ться на. **3,** (set, as a jewel) вставля́ть *or* вде́лывать в опра́ву; оправля́ть. **4,** (display, as a picture) вкле́ивать в альбо́м; накле́ивать на карто́н. **5,** (set in position, as a gun) устана́вливать. **6,** (launch, as an attack) предпринима́ть. —*v.i.* **1,** (ascend; climb) поднима́ться. **2,** (increase) возраста́ть. —*n.* **1,** (used in names of mountain peaks) гора́: *Mount Everest,* гора́ Эвере́ст. **2,** (horse) верхова́я ло́шадь; ло́шадь под седло́м. **3,** (setting, as for a jewel) опра́ва. **4,** (stand, as for a weapon) устано́вка. **5,** (supporting structure) крепле́ние. *Engine mount,* у́зел крепле́ния дви́гателя.
mountain *n.* гора́. —*adj.* го́рный: *mountain air,* го́рный во́здух.
mountain ash ряби́на.
mountain climbing альпини́зм. —**mountain climber,** альпини́ст.
mountaineer *n.* **1,** (highlander) го́рец. **2,** (mountain climber) альпини́ст. —**mountaineering,** *n.* альпини́зм.
mountain lion пу́ма; кугуа́р.
mountainous *adj.* гори́стый; го́рный.
mountaintop *n.* верши́на (горы́).
mountebank *n.* зна́харь; шарлата́н.
mounted *adj.* ко́нный: *mounted police,* ко́нная поли́ция.
mounting *n.* устано́вка; крепле́ние.
mourn *v.t.* опла́кивать. —*v.i.* **1,** (grieve) горева́ть; скорбе́ть. **2,** (be in mourning) быть в тра́уре; носи́ть тра́ур.
mourner *n.* горю́ющий; скорбя́щий.
mournful *adj.* ско́рбный; тра́урный; жа́лобный; плаче́вный.
mourning *n.* тра́ур: *in mourning,* в тра́уре. *Be in mourning for,* носи́ть тра́ур по. *Go into mourning,* наде́ть тра́ур. —*adj.* тра́урный.
mourning cloak (butterfly) тра́урница.
mouse *n.* мышь.
mousetrap *n.* мышело́вка.
mousse *n.* мусс.
moustache *n.* = **mustache.**
mousy *adj.* мыши́ный.
mouth *n.* **1,** *anat.* рот. *Have five mouths to feed,* име́ть пять ртов в семье́. **2,** (opening) жерло́; у́стье. **3,** (of a river) у́стье. —*v.t.* произноси́ть. —**by word of mouth,** из уст в уста́. —**down at the mouth,** па́вший ду́хом; в уны́нии. —**live from hand to mouth,** *see* **hand.** —**put words in someone's mouth,** вложи́ть слова́ в чьи-нибудь уста́. —**you took the words right out of my mouth,** и́менно э́то я хоте́л сказа́ть.
mouthful *n.* глото́к. *You said a mouthful,* э́тим вы мно́гое сказа́ли.
mouthpiece *n.* **1,** (part that goes in the mouth) мундшту́к. **2,** *colloq.* (spokesman) ру́пор.
mouthwash *n.* полоска́ние.
movable *adj.* **1,** (that can be moved) подвижно́й; передвижно́й. **2,** *law* (of property) дви́жимый. —**movables,** *n.pl., law* дви́жимость.
move *v.t.* **1,** (change the location of) дви́гать: *move furniture,* дви́гать ме́бель. **2,** (move from a certain place) сдвига́ть. **3,** (move from one place to another) передвига́ть; перемеща́ть. **4,** (transfer) переноси́ть; переводи́ть. **5,** (prompt; cause) побужда́ть. **6,** (touch the feelings of) тро́гать; растро́гать. *Move to tears,* тро́гать (кого́-нибудь) до слёз. **7,** (propose) предлага́ть. **8,** *chess* игра́ть (+ *instr.*); идти́ (+ *instr.*). **9,** (evacuate, as the bowels) очища́ть. —*v.i.* **1,** (change location or position) дви́гаться; сдвига́ться; передвига́ться. *Don't move!,* не дви́гайтесь!; не шевели́тесь! **2,** (change residence) переезжа́ть: *move to Chicago,* переезжа́ть в Чика́го. —*n.* **1,** (movement) движе́ние: *the slightest move,* мале́йшее движе́ние. *One (false) move and I'll shoot!,* одно́ движе́ние и я бу́ду стреля́ть! **2,** (step; maneuver) ход; шаг. **3,** (change of residence) перее́зд. **4,** (play, as in games) ход. —**get a move on!,** *colloq.* потора́пливайтесь! —**move aside,** отодвига́ть(ся) наза́д. —**move in/into,** въезжа́ть (в). —**move in on,** переезжа́ть к. —**move out,** съезжа́ть; выезжа́ть. —**move over,** подвига́ться. —**move up, 1,** (advance in rank or status) продвига́ться. **2,** (schedule earlier) переноси́ть на бо́лее ра́нний срок. —**on the move,** в разъе́здах.
movement *n.* **1,** (motion) движе́ние. **2,** (organized campaign) движе́ние: *the trade union movement,* профсою́зное движе́ние. **3,** *music* (portion of a work) часть. **4,** (emptying of the bowels) испражне́ние.
mover *n.* перево́зчик.
movie *n.* **1,** (motion picture) фильм; кинофи́льм. **2,** *pl.* (showing) кино́: *go to the movies,* ходи́ть в кино́. —**movie camera,** киноаппара́т; кинока́мера. —**movie star,** кинозвезда́.
moving *adj.* **1,** (that moves; in motion) дви́жущийся: *moving parts,* дви́жущиеся ча́сти. **2,** (stirring the emotions) тро́гательный.
mow *v.t.* коси́ть. —**mow down,** коси́ть.
mower *n.* **1,** (person) коса́рь; косе́ц. **2,** (machine) коси́лка.
Mr. *abbr.* ми́стер; господи́н.
Mrs. *abbr.* ми́ссис; госпожа́.
much *adj.* мно́го: *much time,* мно́го вре́мени. —*adv.* **1,** (to a great extent or degree) о́чень: *much obliged,* о́чень обя́зан. *I want very much to go,* я о́чень хочу́ пойти́. **2,** (by far) гора́здо; намно́го: *much better,* гора́здо/намно́го лу́чше. **3,** (nearly; about) почти́: *much the same,* почти́ тако́й же. —*n.* мно́го; мно́гое: *leave much to be desired,* оставля́ть жела́ть мно́го лу́чшего. *There is much we still don't know,* мы мно́гого не зна́ем ещё. —**as much... as,** сто́лько же... ско́лько и. —**how much?,** ско́лько? —**make much of, 1,** (consider important) придава́ть большо́е значе́ние (+ *dat.*). **2,** (fuss over) носи́ть на рука́х. —**much**

as, как ни: *much as I hate to,* как э́то ни оби́дно. —**much less,** *see* **less.** —**much to my surprise,** к моему́ вели́кому удивле́нию. —**not much,** ма́ло. —**not much of a...,** нева́жный: *he is not much of a swimmer,* он нева́жно пла́вает. —**so much,** *see* **so.** —**so much the better/worse,** тем лу́чше/ху́же. —**too much,** сли́шком мно́го; сли́шком. —**too much for,** не под си́лу (+ *dat.*).

mucilage *n.* **1,** (gummy secretion) (расти́тельная) слизь. **2,** (glue) (расти́тельный) клей.

muck *n.* **1,** (filth) грязь. **2,** (manure) наво́з.

mucous *adj.* сли́зистый. —**mucous membrane,** сли́зистая оболо́чка.

mucus *n.* слизь.

mud *n.* грязь. —*adj.* грязево́й: *mud bath,* грязева́я ва́нна. *Mud hut,* глиноби́тная земля́нка. —**drag through the mud,** втопта́ть в грязь. —**sling mud at,** забра́сывать (кого́-нибудь) гря́зью.

muddle *v.t.* **1,** (mix up; confuse) пу́тать; спу́тывать. **2,** (bungle) напу́тать. —*v.i.* [*usu.* **muddle through**] ко́е-как перебива́ться. —*n.* пу́таница; неразбери́ха.

muddy *adj.* гря́зный. —*v.t.* **1,** (soil with mud) испа́чкать гря́зью. **2,** (make turbid) мути́ть. —**muddy the waters,** мути́ть во́ду.

mudguard *n.* брызгови́к; щит от гря́зи.

mudslide *n.* о́ползень.

mudslinger *n.* клеветни́к; злопыха́тель.

muezzin *n.* муэдзи́н.

muff *n.* му́фта. —*v.t.* **1,** (fail to catch) пропусти́ть. **2,** (bungle) упусти́ть: *muff a chance,* упусти́ть слу́чай. *Muff one's lines,* смаза́ть свою́ ре́плику.

muffin *n.* сдо́бная бу́лка.

muffle *v.t.* **1,** (cover up; wrap) заку́тывать. **2,** (deaden, as sound) глуши́ть; заглуша́ть.

muffler *n.* **1,** (scarf) кашне́. **2,** (silencing device) глуши́тель.

mufti *n.* **1,** (civilian garb) шта́тское пла́тье. **2,** (Moslem jurist) му́фтий.

mug *n.* **1,** (vessel) кру́жка. **2,** *slang* (face) мо́рда; ро́жа; ры́ло; ха́ря. —*v.t., colloq.* гра́бить. —**mugger,** *n., colloq.* налётчик.

muggy *adj.* сыро́й; гнило́й.

mulatto *n.* мула́т.

mulberry *n.* **1,** (tree) ту́товое де́рево; шелкови́ца. **2,** (fruit) ту́товая я́года.

mulch *n.* му́льча.

mule *n.* мул. *Mule team,* упря́жка му́лов. *Stubborn as a mule,* упря́мый как осёл. —**muleteer,** *n.* пого́нщик му́лов.

mull *v.i.* [*usu.* **mull over**] обду́мывать.

mullah *n.* мулла́.

mullet *n.* **1,** (gray mullet) кефа́ль. **2,** (red mullet) бараобу́лька; султа́нка.

multicolored *also,* **multicoloured** *adj.* многоцве́тный; многокра́сочный.

multifaceted *adj.* разносторо́нний.

multifarious *adj.* разнообра́зный.

multiform *adj.* многообра́зный.

multilateral *adj.* многосторо́нний.

multilingual *adj.* многоязы́чный.

multimillionaire *n.* мультимиллионе́р; миллиарде́р.

multinational *adj.* многонациона́льный.

multiple *adj.* **1,** (numerous) многочи́сленный. *Receive multiple injuries,* получи́ть мно́го поврежде́ний. **2,** (involving more than one element) сло́жный: *a multiple process,* сло́жный проце́сс. —*n.* кра́тное: *least common multiple,* о́бщее наиме́ньшее кра́тное. —**multiple sclerosis,** рассе́янный склеро́з.

multiplicand *n.* мно́жимое.

multiplication *n.* умноже́ние. —**multiplication table,** табли́ца умноже́ния.

multiplicity *n.* мно́жество: *a multiplicity of cases,* мно́жество слу́чаев; многочи́сленные слу́чаи.

multiplier *n., math.* мно́житель.

multiply *v.t.* мно́жить; умножа́ть: *multiply six by eight,* мно́жить/умножа́ть шесть на во́семь. —*v.i.* **1,** (perform multiplication) мно́жить; умножа́ть. **2,** (increase) мно́житься; умножа́ться. **3,** (propagate) размножа́ться.

multipurpose *adj.* универса́льный.

multistage *adj.* многоступе́нчатый.

multistoried *adj.* многоэта́жный. *Also,* **multistory.**

multitude *n.* мно́жество. —**multitudinous,** *adj.* многочи́сленный.

mum *adj., colloq.* ни гугу́. *Keep mum,* пома́лкивать. —**mum's the word,** (об э́том) ни гугу́.

mumble *v.t. & i.* бормота́ть. —*n.* бормота́ние.

mummy *n.* **1,** (embalmed body) му́мия. **2,** *colloq.* (mother) ма́мочка.

mumps *n.* сви́нка.

munch *v.t. & i.* ча́вкать.

mundane *adj.* земно́й; мирско́й; жите́йский.

municipal *adj.* городско́й; муниципа́льный. —**municipality,** *n.* муниципалите́т.

munificent *adj.* ще́дрый. —**munificence,** *n.* ще́дрость.

munition *n., usu. pl.* вое́нные припа́сы; вое́нное иму́щество. *Munitions factory,* вое́нный заво́д.

mural *n.* (стенна́я) ро́спись. —*adj.* стенно́й.

murder *n.* уби́йство. —*v.t.* **1,** (kill) убива́ть. **2,** (butcher) кове́ркать: *murder the English language,* кове́ркать англи́йский язы́к. —**murderer,** *n.* уби́йца. —**murderous,** *adj.* уби́йственный.

murky *adj.* **1,** (dark; gloomy) мра́чный. **2,** (turbid) му́тный.

murmur *n.* **1,** (sound) ро́пот: *murmur of voices,* ро́пот голосо́в. *Without a murmur,* безро́потно. **2,** *med.* шум (в се́рдце). —*v.i.* ропта́ть.

murrain *n.* падёж.

murre *n.* ка́йра.

muscat *n.* муска́т. —*adj.* муска́тный.

muscatel *n.* муска́т.

muscle *n.* мы́шца; му́скул. —*adj.* мы́шечный: *muscle tone,* мы́шечный то́нус. —*v.i.* [*usu.* **muscle in**] *colloq.* пробива́ться.

Muscovite *n.* москви́ч.

muscular *adj.* **1,** (of or done by the muscles) мы́шечный; му́скульный. **2,** (brawny) му́скулистый. —**muscular dystrophy,** мы́шечная дистрофи́я.

musculature *n.* мускулату́ра.

muse *v.i.* размышля́ть; заду́мываться. —*n.* му́за.

museum *n.* музе́й. —**museum piece,** музе́йная ре́дкость.

mush *n.* ка́ша.

mushroom *n.* гриб. —*v.i.* разраста́ться. —**mushroom cloud,** грибови́дное о́блако.

mushy *adj.* **1,** (soft; pulpy) мя́гкий. **2,** *colloq.* (excessively sentimental) слаща́вый.

music *n.* **1,** (general term) му́зыка. *Set words to* *music,* положи́ть слова́ на му́зыку. **2,** (written score) но́ты: *play from/without music,* игра́ть по но́там/без нот/. —*adj.* музыка́льный; но́тный. *Music stand,* но́тный пюпи́тр.

musical *adj.* музыка́льный: *musical instrument,* музыка́льный инструме́нт. —*n.* мю́зикл. —**musical comedy,** музыка́льная коме́дия.

musicale *n.* музыка́льный ве́чер.

music box музыка́льная шкату́лка; музыка́льный я́щик.

music hall мю́зик-хо́лл.

musician *n.* музыка́нт.

musicology *n.* музыкове́дение. —**musicologist,** *n.* музыкове́д.

musk *n.* му́скус.

musk deer кабарга́.

musket *n.* мушке́т. —**musketeer,** *n.* мушкетёр.

musketry *n.* стрелко́вое де́ло.

musk ox овцебы́к.

muskrat *n.* онда́тра.

Muslim *n. & adj.* = **Moslem.**

muslin *n.* мусли́н; кисея́. —*adj.* мусли́новый; кисе́йный.

muss *v.t.* растрепа́ть; еро́шить; взлохма́чивать.

mussel *n.* ми́дия.

must *v.aux.* **1,** *expressing necessity* до́лжен; на́до: *I must go,* мне на́до идти́; я до́лжен идти́. **2,** *expressing strong probability* должно́ быть: *he must be here,* он, должно́ быть, здесь. *You must have heard about it,* вы, должно́ быть, слы́шали об э́том. **3,** *used negatively, expressing prohibition* нельзя́; не на́до; не до́лжен: *you mustn't say such things,* таки́х веще́й нельзя́ говори́ть. *We must not be seen together,* нас не должны́ ви́деть вме́сте. *This must not happen again!,* что́бы э́того бо́льше не́ было!

mustache *also,* **moustache** *n.* усы́.

mustang *n.* муста́нг.

mustard *n.* горчи́ца. —**mustard gas,** горчи́чный газ; ипри́т. —**mustard oil,** горчи́чное ма́сло. —**mustard plaster,** горчи́чник.

muster *v.t.* **1,** (assemble) собира́ть. **2,** (summon, as strength, courage, etc.) набира́ться (+ *gen.*); собира́ться с. **3,** *fol. by* **out** (discharge) увольня́ть (с вое́нной слу́жбы); демобилизова́ть. —*v.i.* собира́ться. —*n.* **1,** (assemblage, as of troops) сбор; смотр. **2,** (list; roll) именно́й спи́сок. —**pass muster,** оказа́ться на высоте́.

musty *adj.* за́тхлый.

mutate *v.t.* видоизменя́ть. —*v.i.* видоизменя́ться.

mutation *n.* **1,** *biol.* мута́ция. **2,** *phonet.* перегласо́вка.

mute *adj.* немо́й. —*n.* **1,** (one incapable of speech) немо́й. **2,** *music* сурди́нка. —*v.t.* **1,** *music* надева́ть сурди́нку на. **2,** (muffle) приглуша́ть.

muted *adj.* приглушённый.

muteness *n.* немота́; онеме́ние.

mutilate *v.t.* уве́чить; кале́чить. —**mutilation,** *n.* уве́чье.

mutineer *n.* мятéжник; бунтовщи́к.

mutinous *adj.* мяте́жный; бунта́рский.

mutiny *n.* мяте́ж; бунт. —*v.i.* подня́ть мяте́ж; бунтова́ть.

mutter *v.t. & i.* бормота́ть.

mutton *n.* бара́нина. —*adj.* бара́ний: *mutton chop,* бара́нья отбивна́я.

mutual *adj.* **1,** (given and received in kind) взаи́мный; обою́дный. *Mutual assistance,* взаимопо́мощь. **2,** (possessed in common) о́бщий: *mutual acquaintances,* о́бщие знако́мые. —**mutuality,** *n.* взаи́мность; обою́дность. —**mutually,** *adv.* взаи́мно; обою́дно. *Mutually advantageous/beneficial,* взаимовы́годный.

muzhik *n.* мужи́к.

muzzle *n.* **1,** (of a firearm) ду́ло; жерло́. **2,** (snout) мо́рда; ры́ло. **3,** (covering for an animal's mouth) намо́рдник. —*v.t.* **1,** (put a muzzle on) надева́ть намо́рдник на. **2,** (silence; gag) затыка́ть рот (+ *dat.*).

my *poss. adj.* мой (моя́, моё, мои́). *my mother,* моя́ мать. ♦*When the possessor is the subject of the sentence* свой: *I finished my work,* я зако́нчил свою́ рабо́ту. —*interj.* бо́же мой!; ну и ну!

myopia *n.* близору́кость. —**myopic,** *adj.* близору́кий.

myriad *n.* мириа́ды. —*adj.* бесчи́сленный; несме́тный.

myriapod *n.* многоно́жка.

myrrh *n.* ми́рра.

myrtle *n.* мирт. —*adj.* ми́ртовый.

myself *pers. pron.* **1,** *used for emphasis* (я) сам: *I don't know myself,* я сам (сама́) не зна́ю. **2,** *used reflexively* себя́: *I bought it for myself,* я купи́л(а) э́то для себя́. *I hurt myself,* я ушибся (ушиблась). —**by myself,** оди́н (одна́). —**to myself,** себе́; про себя́.

mysterious *adj.* та́инственный; зага́дочный.

mystery *n.* **1,** (enigma) та́йна; зага́дка. **2,** (mysteriousness) та́йна; таи́нственность. **3,** (mystery story) детекти́вный рома́н.

mystic *adj.* мисти́ческий. —*n.* ми́стик. —**mystical,** *adj.* мисти́ческий.

mysticism *n.* ми́стика; мистици́зм.

mystify *v.t.* озада́чивать. —**mystification,** *n.* озада́ченность.

mystique *n.* таи́нственность.

myth *n.* миф. —**mythical,** *adj.* мифи́ческий.

mythology *n.* мифоло́гия. —**mythological,** *adj.* мифологи́ческий.

N

N, n четы́рнадцатая бу́ква англи́йского алфави́та.
nab *v.t., colloq.* схвати́ть.
nadir *n.* **1,** *astron.* нади́р. **2,** *fig.* (low point) ни́зшая то́чка.
nag *v.t.* придира́ться к; пристава́ть к; пили́ть. —*n.* **1,** (person who nags) приди́ра. **2,** (old horse) кля́ча.
nagging *n.* пристава́ние. —*adj.* **1,** (of a person) надое́дливый. **2,** (of a pain) но́ющий. **3,** (of a thought, question, etc.) назо́йливый; неотвя́зный. *Nagging fear,* тупо́й страх.
naiad *n.* наяда.
nail *n.* **1,** (of a finger or toe) но́готь. **2,** (metal fastener) гвоздь. —*v.t.* **1,** (fasten with a nail or nails) прибива́ть: *nail a notice to the wall,* приби́ть объявле́ние к стене́. **2,** *fol. by* **up** (board up) закола́чивать. **3,** *fol. by* **down** (fasten down with nails) прибива́ть. **4,** (fix firmly; rivet) пригвожда́ть. **5,** *fol. by* **down** (clinch) заключи́ть: *nail down an agreement,* заключи́ть соглаше́ние. —**hit the nail on the head,** попа́сть в (са́мую) то́чку; попа́сть не в бровь, а в глаз.
nail file пи́лка.
nail polish лак для ногте́й.
naïve *adj.* наи́вный. —**naïveté,** *n.* наи́вность.
naked *adj.* го́лый; наго́й; обнажённый. *Run around naked,* пробега́ть в го́лом ви́де *or* нагишо́м. *The naked truth,* го́лая и́стина. *Naked aggression,* неприкры́тая агре́ссия. —**with the naked eye,** просты́м гла́зом; невооружённым гла́зом.
nakedness *n.* нагота́.
name *n.* **1,** (first name; Christian name) и́мя. *What is your name?,* как вас зову́т? *My name is...,* меня́ зову́т... **2,** (last name; surname) фами́лия: *a man by the name of Smith,* челове́к по фами́лии Смит. *He goes by the name of Sokolov,* он изве́стен под и́менем Соколо́ва. **3,** (appellation) назва́ние: *the name of the city,* назва́ние го́рода. **4,** (reputation) и́мя: *make a name for oneself,* сде́лать себе́ и́мя. **5,** *colloq.* (celebrity) и́мя: *big names,* кру́пные имена́. —*v.t.* **1,** (give a name to; call) называ́ть. **2,** (state) называ́ть: *name your price,* назови́те ва́шу це́ну. **3,** (appoint; designate) назнача́ть. —**by name,** поимённо: *mention by name,* называ́ть поимённо. —**call (someone) names,** руга́ть; обруга́ть. —**in name only,** то́лько номина́льно. —**in the name of,** во и́мя (+ *gen.*). *In the name of the law,* и́менем зако́на. —**name names,** называ́ть имена́: *I don't want to name names,* я не хочу́ называ́ть имён. —**to one's name,** за душо́й: *he hasn't a penny to his name,* у него́ за душо́й ни гроша́.
name day имени́ны.
nameless *adj.* безымя́нный.
namely *adv.* а и́менно.
nameplate *n.* доще́чка.
namesake *n.* тёзка.
nanny *n.* ня́ня. —**nanny goat,** коза́.
nap *n.* **1,** (brief sleep) сон. *Take a nap,* поспа́ть; вздремну́ть. **2,** (fuzzy surface) ворс; начёс. —*v.i.* **1,** (be asleep) спать. **2,** (be off one's guard) дрема́ть. *Catch someone napping,* заста́ть кого́-нибудь врасплóх.
napalm *n.* напа́лм. —*adj.* напа́лмовый.
nape *n.* загри́вок.
naphtha *n.* лигрои́н.
naphthalene *n.* нафтали́н.
naphthol *n.* нафто́л.
napkin *n.* салфе́тка.
narcissus *n.* нарци́сс.
narcotic *n.* нарко́тик. —*adj.* наркоти́ческий.
nard *n.* нард.
narrate *v.t.* расска́зывать.
narration *n.* **1,** (act of narrating) расска́зывание. **2,** (a narrative) повествова́ние. **3,** (running commentary for a film) коммента́рий.
narrative *n.* повествова́ние. —*adj.* повествова́тельный.
narrator *n.* **1,** (storyteller) расска́зчик. **2,** (of a film) ди́ктор; коммента́тор.
narrow *adj.* **1,** (not wide) у́зкий: *narrow street/bridge/passageway,* у́зкий переу́лок/мост/прохо́д. **2,** (tight) у́зкий; те́сный: *narrow in the waist,* у́зок/те́сен в та́лии. **3,** (limited in scope) у́зкий: *narrow subject,* у́зкая те́ма. *Narrow circle of friends,* у́зкий *or* те́сный круг друзе́й. **4,** (uncomfortably close) незначи́тельный: *score a narrow victory,* победи́ть с незначи́тельным переве́сом. *Have a narrow escape,* едва́ спасти́сь; едва́ но́ги унести́. —*v.t.* су́живать. —*v.i.* су́живаться. —**narrow down to,** своди́ть(ся) к.
narrow-gauge *adj.* узкоколе́йный.
narrowly *adv.* чуть; е́ле-е́ле. *He narrowly missed being killed,* он чуть не поги́б.
narrow-minded *adj.* у́зкий; ограни́ченный; узколо́бый.
narrowness *n.* у́зость.
narwhal *n.* нарва́л.
nary *adj., colloq.* ни оди́н: *nary a person,* ни одного́ челове́ка.

nasal *adj.* **1,** (pert. to the nose; pronounced through the nose) носовóй. **2,** (having a nasal quality) гнусáвый.
nascent *adj.* молодóй: *a nascent republic,* молодáя респýблика.
nasturtium *n.* настýрция.
nasty *adj.* **1,** (nauseating; disgusting) протѝвный; отвратѝтельный: *nasty odor,* протѝвный/отвратѝтельный зáпах. **2,** (very unpleasant) сквéрный; отвратѝтельный: *nasty weather,* сквéрная/отвратѝтельная погóда. *He is in for a nasty surprise,* его ждёт большáя неприя́тность. **3,** (malicious; mean) злой: *nasty trick,* злáя шýтка. **4,** (causing harm or discomfort) серьёзный; досáдный: *nasty accident,* серьёзная авáрия; *nasty cough,* досáдный кáшель.
natal *adj.* относя́щийся к рождéнию.
nation *n.* странá. *The United Nations,* Объединённые Нáции.
national *adj.* национáльный; государственный. —*n.* граждани́н; пóдданный.
nationalism *n.* национали́зм.
nationalist *n.* национали́ст. —*adj.* националисти́ческий. —**nationalistic,** *adj.* националисти́ческий.
nationality *n.* **1,** (national origin) национáльность. **2,** (body of people) национáльность; нарóдность. *The nationality question,* национáльный вопрóс.
nationalize *v.t.* национализи́ровать. —**nationalization,** *n.* национализáция.
nationwide *adj.* всенарóдный.
native *adj.* **1,** (of the land of one's birth) роднóй: *one's native land,* роднáя странá; роднóй край; рóдина. **2,** (indigenous) тузéмный; коренной. *Native New Yorker,* урожéнец Нью-Йóрка. **3,** (inborn; innate) врождённый. —*n.* **1,** (one born in a particular place) урожéнец. **2,** (original inhabitant; aborigine) тузéмец.
nativity *n.* **1,** (birth) рождéние. **2,** *cap.* (birth of Christ) рождествó Христóво.
natty *adj.* наря́дный; щеголевáтый.
natural *adj.* естéственный; прирóдный. *Natural disaster,* стихи́йное бéдствие. *Die a natural death,* умерéть своéй смéртью. —*n., music* бекáр. —**natural gas,** прирóдный газ. —**natural resources,** естéственные *or* прирóдные богáтства. —**natural selection,** естéственный отбóр.
naturalism *n.* натурали́зм.
naturalist *n.* естествоиспытáтель; натурали́ст.
naturalize *v.t.* натурализовáть. —**naturalization,** *n.* натурализáция.
naturally *adv.* **1,** (in a natural manner) естéственно. **2,** (by nature) по прирóде; по натýре; натурáльно. **3,** (as one might expect; of course) конéчно; разумéется; естéственно.
nature *n.* **1,** (universe) прирóда: *the beauties of nature,* красóты прирóды. **2,** (temperament; disposition) натýра: *by nature,* по натýре; по прирóде. **3,** (essential characteristics) харáктер: *the nature of the work,* харáктер рабóты. *By its very nature,* по сáмой своéй сýщности. **4,** (sort; kind) род: *things of that nature,* такóго рóда вéщи. —**in the nature of things,** в поря́дке вещéй; в прирóде вещéй.
naught *n.* нуль. *All for naught,* всё напрáсно. *Go for naught,* пропáсть дáром. *Come to naught,* сводѝться к нулю́ *or* на нет.
naughty *adj.* **1,** (mischievous) шаловли́вый. *Be naughty,* шали́ть. *Naughty child,* шалýн. **2,** (indecent) рискóванный; двусмы́сленный.
nausea *n.* тошнотá. —**nauseate,** *v.t.* вызывáть тошнотý у. —**nauseating,** *adj.* тошнотвóрный.
nauseous *adj.* **1,** (nauseating) тошнотвóрный. **2,** (nauseated): *I feel nauseous,* меня́ тошни́т.
nautical *adj.* морскóй. —**nautical mile,** морскáя ми́ля.
nautilus *n.* корáблик.
naval *adj.* морскóй; воéнно-морскóй. *Naval academy,* воéнно-морскóе учи́лище. *Naval warfare,* войнá на мóре.
nave *n.* корáбль.
navel *n.* пупóк.
navigable *adj.* судохóдный. —**navigability,** *n.* судохóдность.
navigate *v.t.* **1,** (sail through) переплывáть. **2,** (steer; operate) управля́ть. —*v.i.* **1,** (sail) плáвать (на сýдне). **2,** *colloq.* (walk) передвигáться.
navigation *n.* **1,** (sailing; shipping) судохóдство; навигáция; мореплáвание. **2,** (the science) навигáция; кораблевождéние. —**navigational,** *adj.* навигациóнный.
navigator *n.* **1,** (on a ship or aircraft) штýрман. **2,** (explorer) мореплáватель.
navy *n.* (воéнно-морскóй) флот.
navy blue тёмно-си́ний цвет. —**navy-blue,** *adj.* темно-си́ний.
navy yard воéнно-морскáя верфь.
nay *adv.* нет. —*n.* прóтив: *three ayes, two nays,* три за, два прóтив. *The nays have it,* большинствó прóтив.
Nazi *n.* наци́ст. —*adj.* наци́стский. —**Nazism,** *n.* наци́зм.
Neanderthal *adj.* неандертáльский. —**Neanderthal man,** неандертáлец.
near *adj.* бли́зкий: *the end is near,* конéц бли́зок. *It's quite near,* э́то совсéм бли́зко. *In the near future,* в скóром *or* в ближáйшем бýдущем. *The nearest way to town,* кратчáйший путь в гóрод. —*adv.* бли́зко. *Draw near,* бли́зиться; приближáться. —*prep.* óколо; у; вóзле; бли́зко от *or* к; недалекó от. *Near here,* недалекó отсю́да; побли́зости. *Sit near me,* сядь óколо меня́. *Sit near each other,* сидéть бли́зко друг к дрýгу. *The post office is near the station,* пóчта недалекó от вокзáла. *Be near death,* быть при́ смéрти. —*v.t. & i.* бли́зиться (к); приближáться (к): *be nearing an end,* бли́зиться/приближáться к концý. —**near at hand,** бли́зко; под рукóй; на носý. —**near miss,** попадáние близ цéли.
nearby *adj.* бли́зкий; сосéдний. *Their house is right nearby,* их дом совсéм бли́зко *or* совсéм ря́дом. —*adv.* бли́зко; вблизи́; побли́зости.
Near East Бли́жний Востóк.
nearly *adv.* почти́; едвá ли не; чуть ли не. ♦*With verbs* едвá не; чуть не: *he nearly drowned,* он едвá не *or* чуть не утонýл. —**not nearly,** совсéм не: *not nearly ready,* совсéм не готóв.
nearness *n.* бли́зость.
nearsighted *adj.* близорýкий. —**nearsightedness,** *n.* близорýкость.
neat *adj.* **1,** (tidy) опря́тный; аккурáтный; чистоплóтный. **2,** *colloq.* (adroit) лóвкий. —**neatly,** *adv.*

опря́тно; аккура́тно. —**neatness,** *n.* опря́тность; аккура́тность.

nebula *n.* тума́нность.

nebulous *adj.* сму́тный; нея́сный; тума́нный.

necessarily *adv.* обяза́тельно.

necessary *adj.* необходи́мый; ну́жный. *If necessary,* е́сли ну́жно. *That is not necessary,* э́то не ну́жно (*or* не на́до). *It will be necessary to...,* придётся (+ *inf.).*

necessitate *v.t.* де́лать необходи́мым; тре́бовать.

necessity *n.* **1,** (the fact of being necessary) необходи́мость; на́добность. *Out of necessity,* по необходи́мости. **2,** (something that is necessary) необходи́мая вещь. *The barest necessities,* са́мое необходи́мое; предме́ты пе́рвой необходи́мости.

neck *n.* **1,** (part of the body) ше́я. **2,** (of a garment) вы́рез: *V-neck,* треуго́льный вы́рез. **3,** (of a bottle) го́рлышко; го́рло. **4,** (of a violin; of the uterus) ше́йка. **5,** (of land) переше́ек. —*adj.* ше́йный. —**get it in the neck,** получи́ть по ше́е. —**neck and neck,** голова́ в го́лову. —**risk one's neck,** лезть в пе́тлю. —**stick one's neck out,** ста́вить себя́ под уда́р.

neckerchief *n.* ше́йный плато́к.

necklace *n.* ожере́лье.

neckline *n.* вы́рез: *low neckline,* глубо́кий вы́рез.

necktie *n.* га́лстук.

necrosis *n.* некро́з.

nectar *n.* некта́р.

née *adj.* урождённая.

need *n.* **1,** (poverty) нужда́: *live in dire need,* жить в нужде́. **2,** (necessity) на́добность; нужда́: *no need to,* нет на́добности/нужды́ (+ *inf.*). *In case of dire need,* в слу́чае кра́йней нужды́. **3,** *pl.* (wants; requirements) ну́жды; потре́бности. —*v.t.* **1,** (have need of) нужда́ться в. ♦*More commonly rendered by* ну́жно: *what do you need that for?,* для чего́ э́то вам ну́жно? *I need a pencil,* мне ну́жен каранда́ш. *I need money,* мне нужны́ де́ньги. **2,** (require) тре́бовать. —*v.aux.* (have to) *rendered by* на́до *or* ну́жно: *you need to rest more,* вам на́до бо́льше отдыха́ть. *You need not be afraid,* вам не ну́жно боя́ться. —**be in need of,** нужда́ться в; тре́бовать. —**if need be,** е́сли ну́жно; в слу́чае нужды́.

needle *n.* **1,** (sewing implement) игла́; иго́лка. **2,** (knitting needle) (вяза́льная) спи́ца. **3,** (of a compass) стре́лка. **4,** (hypodermic needle) игла́ (для подко́жных впры́скиваний). **5,** (for a phonograph) (граммофо́нная) игла́. **6,** (used in engraving) (гравирова́льная) игла́. **7,** (needle-shaped leaf) игла́. —*v.t., colloq.* придира́ться к; грызть; подпуска́ть шпи́льки (+ *dat.*). —**be on pins and needles,** быть *or* сиде́ть как на иго́лках. —**needle in a haystack,** иго́лка в сто́ге се́на.

needless *adj.* нену́жный; бесполе́зный. —**needless to say,** разуме́ется; не́чего и говори́ть.

needlessly *adv.* бесполе́зно.

needlework *n.* шитьё; вышива́ние; рукоде́лие. —**needleworker,** *n.* рукоде́льница.

needy *adj.* нужда́ющийся.

ne'er-do-well *n.* никчёмный челове́к; него́дник; шалопа́й.

nefarious *adj.* гну́сный.

negate *v.t.* **1,** (nullify) своди́ть на нет *or* к нулю́. **2,** (contradict; refute) опроверга́ть. —**negation,** *n.* отрица́ние.

negative *adj.* отрица́тельный. —*n.* **1,** *gram.* отрица́ние. **2,** *photog.* негати́в. —**in the negative,** отрица́тельно: *answer in the negative,* отве́тить отрица́тельно.

neglect *v.t.* **1,** (fail to give proper attention to) пренебрега́ть; запуска́ть; забра́сывать. **2,** *fol. by inf.* (fail to) забыва́ть: *neglect to mention,* забы́ть упомяну́ть; не упомяну́ть. —*n.* **1,** (act of neglecting) пренебреже́ние. **2,** (state of neglect) запу́щенность; запусте́ние. *In a state of neglect,* в запу́щенном состоя́нии; в заго́не; в забро́се.

neglectful *adj.* небре́жный; невнима́тельный.

negligee *n.* неглиже́.

negligence *n.* небре́жность. *Criminal negligence,* престу́пная небре́жность *or* хала́тность. —**negligent,** *adj.* небре́жный.

negligible *adj.* незначи́тельный; ничто́жный.

negotiable *adj.* **1,** (capable of being negotiated) подлежа́щий обсужде́нию: *this question is not negotiable,* э́тот вопро́с не подлежи́т обсужде́нию. **2,** *finance* оборо́тный: *negotiable instrument,* оборо́тный докуме́нт.

negotiate *v.i.* вести́ перегово́ры. —*v.t.* **1,** (conclude through negotiations) заключа́ть. **2,** *colloq.* (traverse; surmount) преодолева́ть.

negotiation *n., usu. pl.* перегово́ры. —**negotiator,** *n.* лицо́, веду́щее перегово́ры.

Negro *n.* негр. —*adj.* негритя́нский.

Negroid *adj.* негро́идный.

neigh *v.i.* ржать.

neighbor *also,* **neighbour** *n.* **1,** (person living nearby) сосе́д. **2,** (fellow being) бли́жний.

neighborhood *also,* **neighbourhood** *n.* райо́н; окру́га. —**in the neighborhood of, 1,** (near) по сосе́дству с. **2,** (approximately) о́коло; приблизи́тельно.

neighboring *adj.* сосе́дний.

neighborly *adj.* добрососе́дский.

neither *adj.* ни тот, ни друго́й: *in neither case,* ни в том, ни в друго́м слу́чае. —*pron.* **1,** *when standing alone* ни тот, ни друго́й. **2,** *fol. by* **of** ни оди́н из; никто́ из. —*conj.* **1,** *used with* **nor** ни..., ни...: *neither for nor against,* ни за, ни про́тив. **2,** (nor) то́же не: *neither do I,* я то́же не (хочу́, зна́ю, *etc.*). —**neither here nor there,** ни к селу́, ни к го́роду.

nemesis *n.* Немези́да.

neoclassic *adj.* неокласси́ческий. —**neoclassicism,** *n.* неоклассици́зм.

neodymium *n.* ниоди́мий.

neolithic *adj.* неолити́ческий.

neologism *n.* неологи́зм.

neon *n.* нео́н. —*adj.* нео́новый.

neophyte *n.* **1,** *eccles.* неофи́т; новообращённый. **2,** (novice) новичо́к; неофи́т.

neoplasm *n.* новообразова́ние.

nephew *n.* племя́нник.

nephrite *n.* нефри́т.

nephritis *n.* нефри́т.

nepotism *n.* кумовство́; семе́йственность; непоти́зм.

Neptune *n.* Непту́н.

neptunium *n.* непту́ний.

nerve *n.* **1,** *physiol.* нерв. *Get on one's nerves,* де́йствовать на не́рвы (+ *dat.*). *Calm one's nerves,* успока́ивать не́рвы. **2,** (courage; daring) му́жество.

Lose one's nerve, стру́сить. **3,** *Strain every nerve,* напряга́ть все си́лы. **4,** *colloq.* (audacity) на́глость; наха́льство. —*adj.* не́рвный: *nerve centers,* не́рвные це́нтры.

nerve-racking *adj.* мучи́тельный.

nervous *adj.* не́рвный. *Be nervous,* волнова́ться; не́рвничать. —**nervous breakdown,** неврастени́я. —**nervous system,** не́рвная систе́ма.

nervousness *n.* не́рвность.

nest *n.* гнездо́. —*v.i.* гнезди́ться. —**nest egg,** сбереже́ния на чёрный день.

nestle *v.i.* **1,** (cuddle) прижима́ться; льну́ть. **2,** (lie sheltered) юти́ться.

nestling *n.* птене́ц.

net *n.* **1,** (for fishing, hunting, etc.) сеть. **2,** (for catching butterflies) сачо́к. **3,** (for the hair) се́тка. **4,** (for tennis, badminton, etc.) се́тка. **5,** (for hockey, soccer, etc.) воро́та. —*adj.* чи́стый: *net profit,* чи́стая при́быль. *The net result,* коне́чный результа́т. —*v.t.* **1,** (ensnare) пойма́ть (се́тью). **2,** (earn) выруча́ть.

nether *adj.* ни́жний. —**nethermost,** *adj.* са́мый ни́жний. —**nether world,** преиспо́дняя.

netting *n.* се́тка.

nettle *n.* крапи́ва. —*v.t.* уязвля́ть; уколо́ть.

network *n.* сеть.

neural *adj.* не́рвный.

neuralgia *n.* невралги́я. —**neuralgic,** *adj.* невралги́ческий.

neuritis *n.* воспале́ние не́рва; неври́т.

neurology *n.* невроло́гия. —**neurological,** *adj.* неврологи́ческий. —**neurologist,** *n.* невро́лог; невропато́лог.

neuron *n.* нейро́н.

neurosis *n.* невро́з.

neurosurgery *n.* нейрохирурги́я. —**neurosurgeon,** *n.* нейрохиру́рг.

neurotic *adj.* невроти́ческий.

neuter *adj.* сре́дний; сре́днего ро́да. —*n.* сре́дний род.

neutral *adj.* нейтра́льный. —*n.* **1,** (country) нейтра́льное госуда́рство. **2,** (gear) нейтра́льная ско́рость. —**neutrality,** *n.* нейтралите́т.

neutralize *v.t.* нейтрализова́ть. —**neutralization,** *n.* нейтрализа́ция.

neutron *n.* нейтро́н. —*adj.* нейтро́нный. —**neutron bomb,** нейтро́нная бо́мба.

never *adv.* никогда́: *he is never at home,* он никогда́ не быва́ет до́ма. ♦*Also rendered by* так и не: *I never found out,* я так и не узна́л(а). *He never regained consciousness,* он так и не пришёл в созна́ние. —**better late than never,** лу́чше по́здно, чем никогда́. —**never again,** никогда́ бо́льше: *I never saw him again,* я его́ никогда́ бо́льше не ви́дел(а). —**never before,** никогда́ ещё. —**never mind,** *see* **mind.** —**now or never,** тепе́рь и́ли никогда́.

never-ending *adj.* несконча́емый; непрекраща́ющийся.

nevermore *adv.* никогда́ бо́льше.

nevertheless *adv.* тем не ме́нее.

new *adj.* но́вый. *What's new?,* что но́вого?; что слы́шно? —**New Deal,** Но́вый курс. —**new moon,** новолу́ние; молодо́й ме́сяц. —**new potatoes,** молодо́й карто́фель. —**New Testament,** Но́вый заве́т. —**new wine,** молодо́е вино́. —**New World,** Но́вый свет. —**New Year,** Но́вый год. *Happy New Year!,* с Но́вым го́дом!

newborn *adj.* новорождённый.

newcomer *n.* прише́лец; прие́зжий; новоприбы́вший.

Newfoundland *n.* (dog) водола́з.

newly *adv.* вновь: *the newly elected president,* вновь и́збранный президе́нт.

newlyweds *n.pl.* новобра́чные; молодожёны.

newness *n.* новизна́.

news *n.* но́вости; изве́стия; ве́сти. *Piece of news,* но́вость; изве́стие; весть. *It's news to me,* э́то для меня́ но́вость. —**news agency,** телегра́фное аге́нство.

newsboy *n.* газе́тчик.

newscast *n.* переда́ча после́дних изве́стий.

newsletter *n.* информацио́нный бюллете́нь.

newsman *n.* **1,** (reporter) репортёр; корреспонде́нт. **2,** (dealer) газе́тчик.

newspaper *n.* газе́та. —*adj.* газе́тный: *newspaper clipping,* газе́тная вы́резка. —**newspaperman,** *n.* журнали́ст.

newsprint *n.* газе́тная бума́га.

newsreel *n.* кинохро́ника.

newsstand *n.* газе́тный кио́ск.

newt *n.* трито́н.

next *adj.* **1,** (coming after the present one) сле́дующий: *who is next?,* кто сле́дующий? *The next stop,* сле́дующая остано́вка. *Next time,* в сле́дующий раз. **2,** *with intervals or periods of time* сле́дующий; бу́дущий: *next week,* на сле́дующей/бу́дущей неде́ле; *next year,* в сле́дующем (бу́дущем) году́. *Next summer,* сле́дующим ле́том. *The next day,* на сле́дующий (*or* на друго́й) день. *The next morning,* нау́тро. **3,** (adjacent) сосе́дний: *in the next room,* в сосе́дней ко́мнате. —*adv.* **1,** (after that) пото́м; да́льше: *what happened next?,* что случи́лось пото́м? *What next?,* (a) что же да́льше? **2,** (again) в сле́дующий раз; сно́ва: *when next we meet,* когда́ мы сно́ва встре́тимся. —**next to, 1,** (beside; alongside) у; ря́дом с; по́дле. **2,** (almost; nearly) почти́: *next to impossible,* почти́ невозмо́жно. **3,** (after; indicating that something is second best) по́сле. —**next to last,** предпосле́дний. —**next to nothing,** почти́ ничего́. *I bought it for next to nothing,* я купи́л э́то за гроши́. —**than the next,** оди́н друго́го (+ *comp. adj.*): *one taller than the next,* оди́н друго́го вы́ше.

next door ря́дом; в сосе́днем до́ме. *Next door to,* ря́дом с. *Next-door neighbor,* ближа́йший сосе́д. *The girl next door,* сосе́дская де́вушка.

nib *n.* ко́нчик; остриё.

nibble *v.t. & i.* **1,** (eat in small bites) грызть; обгрыза́ть. **2,** (bite, as of a fish) клева́ть. —*n.* **1,** (little bit) кусо́чек. **2,** (bite, in fishing): *not a nibble,* ни одна́ ры́ба не клю́нула.

nice *adj.* **1,** (fine; pleasant) хоро́ший; прия́тный: *nice weather,* хоро́шая/прия́тная пого́да. *Have a nice time,* хорошо́ провести́ вре́мя. **2,** (kind; gracious) ми́лый; любе́зный: *very nice of you,* о́чень ми́ло/любе́зно с ва́шей стороны́. **3,** (proper) прили́чный; поря́дочный. *A nice girl,* прили́чная де́вушка. *That's not nice,* э́то некраси́во. **4,** (well-executed) ло́вкий; уда́чный. **5,** (subtle) то́нкий: *a nice distinction,* то́нкое разли́чие. —**nice and...,** и краси́во: *it's nice and warm in here!,* здесь так тепло́ и краси́во!

nice-looking *adj.* мило́ви́дный; хоро́шенький.
nicely *adv.* хорошо́; прили́чно.
nicety *n.* **1,** (fine point) то́нкость. **2,** *pl.* (proprieties) прили́чия.
niche *n.* ни́ша.
nick *n.* щерби́на; цара́пина. —*v.t.* цара́пать. —**in the nick of time,** как раз во́время; в са́мый после́дний моме́нт.
nickel *n.* **1,** (element) ни́кель. **2,** (five-cent coin) пята́к. —*adj.* ни́келевый.
nickel plate никелиро́вка. —**nickel-plate,** *v.t.* никелирова́ть.
nickname *n.* про́звище; кли́чка. —*v.t.* прозыва́ть; окрести́ть.
nicotine *n.* никоти́н.
niece *n.* племя́нница.
nifty *adj., colloq.* **1,** (splendid; first-rate) чу́дный. **2,** (stylish) шика́рный.
niggardly *adj.* **1,** (stingy) скупо́й; ска́редный. **2,** (meager) ску́дный.
niggling *adj.* ме́лочный.
nigh *adv.* **1,** (near) бли́зко. *Draw nigh,* приближа́ться. **2,** *fol. by* **onto** (nearly) чуть ли не.
night *n.* ночь. *At night,* но́чью; по ноча́м. *Last night,* вчера́ ве́чером; вчера́ но́чью. *Tomorrow night,* за́втра ве́чером. *Saturday night,* в суббо́ту ве́чером. *Spend the night,* ночева́ть. —*adj.* ночно́й: *night train,* ночно́й по́езд. —**good night!,** споко́йной но́чи!
night blindness кури́ная слепота́.
nightcap *n.* **1,** (cap worn in bed) ночно́й колпа́к. **2,** *colloq.* (drink before retiring) стака́нчик спиртно́го на́ ночь.
nightclothes *n.pl.* ночно́е бельё.
night club ночно́й клуб.
nightfall *n.* наступле́ние но́чи; наступле́ние темноты́. *Before nightfall,* за́светло.
nightgown *n.* ночна́я руба́шка; ночна́я соро́чка.
nightingale *n.* солове́й.
night light ночни́к.
nightly *adj.* ежено́щный. —*adv.* ежено́щно; ка́ждую ночь.
nightmare *n.* кошма́р. *I had a nightmare,* мне присни́лся кошма́р; я ви́дел во сне кошма́р. —**nightmarish,** *adj.* кошма́рный.
night owl полуно́чник.
night school вече́рняя шко́ла.
nightshade *n.* паслён.
nightshirt *n.* ночна́я руба́шка; ночна́я соро́чка.
nightstick *n.* дуби́нка.
night table ночно́й сто́лик; ту́мбочка.
nighttime *n.* ночно́е вре́мя; ночь.
night watch ночно́й дозо́р; *naval* ночна́я ва́хта. —**night watchman,** ночно́й сто́рож.
nihilism *n.* нигили́зм. —**nihilist,** *n.* нигили́ст. —**nihilistic,** *adj.* нигилисти́ческий.
nil *n.* нуль; ничего́.
nimble *adj.* прово́рный.
nimbus *n.* нимб.
nincompoop *n.* простофи́ля; дурале́й; растя́па.
nine *adj.* де́вять. —*n.* **1,** (cardinal number) де́вять. **2,** *cards* девя́тка.
nine hundred девятьсо́т. —**nine-hundredth,** *adj.* девятисо́тый.
nineteen *n. & adj.* девятна́дцать. —**nineteenth,** *adj.* девятна́дцатый.
ninety *n. & adj.* девяно́сто. —**ninetieth,** *adj.* девяно́стый.
ninny *n.* простофи́ля; дурале́й.
ninth *adj.* девя́тый. —*n.* **1,** (ninth part) девя́тая часть. **2,** (fraction) девя́тая: *one-ninth,* одна́ девя́тая.
niobium *n.* нио́бий.
nip *v.t.* **1,** (pinch) щипа́ть; ущипну́ть. **2,** *fol. by* **off** (snip; cut off) отщи́пывать. **3,** (damage, as of frost) поби́ть; тро́нуть. **4,** (check; head off) пресека́ть. *Nip in the bud,* подавля́ть в заро́дыше; пресека́ть в ко́рне. —*n.* **1,** (pinch) щипо́к. **2,** (cold) моро́зец: *there is a nip in the air,* во́здух па́хнет моро́зцем. **3,** *colloq.* (small drink) рю́мочка. —**nip and tuck,** голова́ в го́лову.
nipper *n.* **1,** (claw) клешня́. **2,** *pl.* (pincers) клещи.
nipple *n.* **1,** (on the breast) сосо́к. **2,** (for a nursing bottle) со́ска. **3,** (threaded pipe) ни́ппель.
nippy *adj.* холо́дненький.
nirvana *n.* нирва́на.
nit *n.* гни́да.
niter *also,* **nitre** *n.* сели́тра.
nitrate *n.* соль азо́тной кислоты́; нитра́т. ♦*In compounds* сели́тра: *sodium nitrate,* на́триевая сели́тра. *Silver nitrate,* ля́пис.
nitre *n.* = **niter.**
nitric *adj.* азо́тный. —**nitric acid,** азо́тная кислота́. —**nitric oxide,** о́кись азо́та.
nitrite *n.* соль азо́тистой кислоты́; нитри́т.
nitrogen *n.* азо́т.
nitroglycerin *also,* **nitroglycerine** *n.* нитроглицери́н.
nitrous *adj.* азо́тистый. —**nitrous acid,** азо́тистая кислота́. —**nitrous oxide,** за́кись азо́та.
nitwit *n., slang* простофи́ля; балда́; балбе́с.
no *adv.* **1,** (opp. of yes) нет: *yes or no,* да и́ли нет. *No, thank you,* спаси́бо, нет. *Not take no for an answer,* не принима́ть отка́за. *He doesn't know how to say no,* он не уме́ет отка́зывать. **2,** *with comp. adjectives* (not at all) не: *no bigger than a postage stamp,* не бо́льше почто́вой ма́рки. *She is no better today,* ей сего́дня (нисколько) не лу́чше. —*adj.* никако́й: *no comment,* никаки́х коммента́риев. *There can be no doubt,* не мо́жет быть никако́го сомне́ния. *She is no beauty,* никака́я она́ не краса́вица. ♦*Often rendered by* не *or* нет: *spare no effort,* не щади́ть уси́лий. *I have no time,* у меня́ нет вре́мени. *No smoking!,* не кури́ть! —*n.* отка́з: *an emphatic "no",* реши́тельный отка́з. *The noes have it,* большинство́ про́тив.
nobelium *n.* нобе́лий.
Nobel Prize Нобелевская пре́мия.
nobility *n.* **1,** (aristocracy) дворя́нство. **2,** (quality of being noble) благоро́дство.
noble *adj.* благоро́дный: *a noble act,* благоро́дный посту́пок. *Of noble birth,* благоро́дного происхожде́ния. —*n.* дворяни́н.
nobleman *n.* дворяни́н.
nobody *pron.* никто́: *nobody knows,* никто́ не зна́ет. ♦*With infinitives* не́кого: *there was nobody to send to the store,* посла́ть в магази́н бы́ло не́кого. *He has nobody to play with,* ему́ не́ с кем игра́ть. *There is nobody to replace him,* не́кому его́ замени́ть. —*n.* ничто́жество; пусто́е ме́сто.
nocturnal *adj.* ночно́й.
nocturne *n.* ноктю́рн.

nod *n.* кивóк. —*v.t.* кивáть; качáть (головóй). *Nod assent,* утвердúтельно кивнýть головóй. —*v.i.* **1,** (nod one's head) кивáть; качáть головóй. **2,** (drowse) клевáть нóсом. —**nodding acquaintance,** шáпочное знакóмство.
node *n.* ýзел. *Lymph nodes,* лимфатúческие узлы́.
nodule *n.* узелóк.
Noel *n.* рождествó.
noggin *n., colloq.* башкá.
noise *n.* шум. *Make noise,* шумéть. —**noiseless,** *adj.* бесшýмный. —**noisily,** *adv.* шýмно.
noisome *adj.* **1,** (foul) протúвный. **2,** (harmful) врéдный.
noisy *adj.* шýмный; шумлúвый. *It is very noisy in here,* здесь óчень шýмно.
nomad *n.* кочéвник. —**nomadic,** *adj.* кочевóй; кочýющий.
no man's land ничья́ землья́.
nomenclature *n.* номенклатýра.
nominal *adj.* номинáльный.
nominate *v.t.* выдвигáть (на дóлжность; на прéмию, etc.); выставля́ть (чью-нибудь) кандидатýру.
nomination *n.* кандидатýра; выдвижéние кандидáтом. *Second the nomination,* поддéрживать кандидатýру (когó-нибудь). *Decline the nomination,* откáзывать в выдвижéнии кандидáтом. *Seek the Presidential nomination,* добивáться выдвижéния кандидáтом на пост президéнта.
nominative *adj.*именúтельный: *nominative case,* именúтельный падéж.
nominee *n.* кандидáт.
nonaggression *n.* ненападéние. *Nonaggression pact,* пакт о ненападéнии.
nonalcoholic *adj.* безалкогóльный.
nonaligned *adj.* неприсоединúвшийся. —**nonalignment,** *n.* неприсоединéние.
nonbeliever *n.* невéрующий.
nonbelligerent *adj.* невоюющий.
nonbreakable *adj.* небьющийся.
nonchalance *n.* беззабóтность; непринуждённость. —**nonchalant,** *adj.* беззабóтный; непринуждённый.
noncombatant *n. & adj.* нестроевóй.
noncommissioned officer сержáнт; ýнтерофицéр.
noncommittal *adj.* уклóнчивый.
nonconductor *n.* непроводнúк.
noncontagious *adj.* незарáзный.
nondescript *adj.* неприметный; ни то ни сё.
nondrinker *n.* непьющий.
none *pron.* **1,** (no one) никтó: *none of them answered,* никтó из них не отвéтил. *None of us wanted to go,* никтó из нас не хотéл пойтú. **2,** (not any) ни оди́н: *none of them were any good,* ни оди́н из них нé был хорóш. *None of this concerns me,* всё э́то меня́ не касáется. *He would have none of it,* он об э́том и слы́шать не хотéл. —*adv.* нискóлько; ничýть: *he is none the worse for it,* емý от э́того нискóлько не хýже. —**none other than,** не кто инóй, как.
nonentity *n.* ничтóжество; пустóе мéсто.
nonessential *adj. Nonessential items,* вéщи, в которых нет абсолютной необходúмости.
nonetheless *adv.* тем не мéнее.
nonexistence *n.* небытиé. —**nonexistent,** *adj.* несуществýющий.
nonferrous *adj.* цветнóй.
nonflammable *adj.* несгорáемый; невоспламеня́емый.
nonfulfillment *n.* невыполнéние.
noninterference *n.* невмешáтельство.
nonintervention *n.* невмешáтельство.
nonpayment *n.* неуплáта; неплатёж.
nonperishable *adj.* непóртящийся.
nonplus *v.t.* стáвить в тупúк; озадáчивать.
nonproductive *adj.* непроизводúтельный.
nonproliferation *n.* нераспространéние.
nonrecognition *n.* непризнáние.
non-Russian *adj.* нерýсский.
nonsense *n.* ерундá; чепухá; глýпости; вздор. —**nonsensical,** *adj.* глýпый; вздóрный.
nonsmoker *n.* некуря́щий.
nonstop *adj.* безостанóвочный; беспосáдочный. —*adv.* безостанóвочно.
nonvoting *adj. Nonvoting member,* член с совещáтельным гóлосом.
nonworking *adj.* нерабóчий.
noodle *n.* **1,** (food) лапшá. *Noodle pudding,* лапшéвник. *Noodle soup,* лапшá. **2,** *slang* (head) башкá.
nook *n.* уголóк; закоýлок.
noon *n.* пóлдень. —*adj.* [*also,* **noonday**] полýденный; полднéвный.
no one никтó. *See* **nobody.**
noose *n.* пéтля.
nor *conj.* **1,** (neither) тóже: *nor do I; nor am I,* я тóже. *Nor is there any doubt that...,* нет сомнéния и в том, что... **2,** (and besides) да и (вообщé): *I have not seen him, nor do I wish to,* я егó не вúдел(а), да и вообщé не хочý. —**neither... nor,** ни..., ни...: *neither for nor against,* ни за, ни прóтив.
norm *n.* нóрма; норматúв.
normal *adj.* нормáльный. —*n.* **1,** (natural condition) нормáльное состоя́ние. *Return to normal,* войтú в нормáльную колею; снóва налáживаться. **2,** *math.* нормáль.
normalcy *n.* нормáльность.
normalize *v.t.* нормализовáть. —**normalization,** *n.* нормализáция.
normally *adv.* **1,** (in a normal manner) нормáльно. **2,** (ordinarily) обы́чно.
Norman *adj.* нормáндский: *Norman Conquest,* Нормáндское завоевáние Áнглии.
normative *adj.* нормативный.
Norse *adj.* нормáнский. —**Norseman,** *n.* номáнн.
north *n.* сéвер. —*adj.* сéверный: *north wind,* сéверный вéтер. —*adv.* на сéвер; к сéверу. *North of,* к сéверу от; сéвернее (+ *gen.*).
northeast *n.* сéверо-востóк. —*adj.* сéверо-востóчный. —*adv.* к сéверо-востóку; на сéверо-востóк.
northeaster *n.* норд-óст.
northeasterly *adj.* сéверо-востóчный.
northeastern *adj.* сéверо-востóчный.
northerly *adj.* сéверный.
northern *adj.* сéверный.
northerner *n.* северя́нин.
northern lights сéверное сия́ние.
northernmost *adj.* сáмый сéверный.
North Pole Сéверный пóлюс.
North Star Поля́рная звездá.
northward *adv.* к сéверу. —*adj.* сéверный.
northwest *n.* сéверо-зáпад. —*adj.* сéверо-зáпад-

ный. —*adv.* к се́веро-за́паду; на се́веро-за́пад.
northwester *n.* норд-ве́ст.
northwesterly *adj.* се́веро-за́падный.
northwestern *adj.* се́веро-за́падный.
Norwegian *adj.* норве́жский. —*n.* **1,** (person) норве́жец; норве́жка. **2,** (language) норве́жский язы́к.
nose *n.* **1,** (of a person) нос. *Speak through one's nose,* говори́ть в нос. **2,** (of a ship or aircraft) нос. —*v.i.* [*usu.* **nose about** *or* **around**] разню́хивать. —**as plain as the nose on your face,** я́сный как бо́жий день. —**follow one's nose,** идти́ куда́ глаза́ глядя́т. —**have a nose for,** име́ть нюх на. —**lead by the nose,** вести́ на поводу́. —**look down one's nose at,** смотре́ть свысока́ на. —**not see farther than the end of one's nose,** не ви́деть да́льше своего́ но́са. —**on the nose,** в (са́мую) то́чку. —**pay through the nose,** плати́ть бе́шеные де́ньги; плати́ть втри́дорога. —**poke one's nose into someone else's affairs,** сова́ть нос в чужи́е дела́. —**turn up one's nose,** задира́ть нос. —**under one's (very) nose,** под са́мым но́сом; по́д носом. *From under one's very nose,* из-под са́мого но́са.
nosebleed *n.* кровотече́ние и́з носу.
nose cone носово́й ко́нус.
nose dive **1,** *aero.* пики́рование. **2,** (sharp drop) ре́зкое паде́ние.
nose drops ка́пли от на́сморка.
nosegay *n.* буке́тик цвето́в.
nosey *adj.* = **nosy.**
nostalgia *n.* ностальги́я. —**nostalgic,** *adj.* ностальги́ческий. *Feel nostalgic,* испы́тывать ностальги́ю.
nostril *n.* ноздря́.
nosy *also,* **nosey** *adj.* (не в ме́ру) любопы́тный.
not *adv.* **1,** *expressing negation* не: *not today,* не сего́дня. *He did not come,* он не пришёл. *I am not angry,* я не серди́т. **2,** *expressing the absence of something* нет: *he is not here,* его́ нет. **3,** *in replies* нет: *why not?,* почему́ нет? *Not yet,* нет ещё. *I hope not,* наде́юсь, что нет. —**not a ...,** ни; ни оди́н: *not a word,* ни (одного́) сло́ва. —**not at all, 1,** (not in the least) совсе́м не; ниско́лько не: *not at all tired,* совсе́м/ниско́лько не уста́л. *Am I disturbing you?, No, not at all,* я вам не меша́ю? Нет, что вы! **2,** *in reply to an expression of thanks* пожа́луйста!; не́ за что! —**not that,** не то, что́бы: *it's not that I'm ill, I'm just tired,* я не то, что бо́лен, а про́сто уста́л. *Not that I know of,* наско́лько мне изве́стно, нет. —**or not,** и́ли нет: *are you going or not?,* вы идёте и́ли нет? *Like it or not,* хо́чешь не хо́чешь.
notable *adj.* **1,** (noteworthy) примеча́тельный. **2,** (distinguished) зна́тный. —*n., usu. pl.* зна́тные лю́ди.
notably *adv.* **1,** (strikingly) удиви́тельно. **2,** (particularly) осо́бенно.
notarize *v.t.* засвиде́тельствовать.
notary *n.* нота́риус. *Also,* **notary public.**
notation *n.* **1,** (note) заме́тка; за́пись. **2,** (system of signs or symbols) нота́ция: *chess notation,* ша́хматная нота́ция.
notch *n.* **1,** (on a flat surface) зару́бка. **2,** (on a cutting edge) зазу́брина. **3,** (defile) тесни́на. —*v.t.* заруба́ть; зазу́бривать.
note *n.* **1,** (short informal letter) запи́ска. **2,** (official communication between governments) но́та. **3,** *usu. pl.* (something written down for future reference) запи́ска; заме́тка; за́пись: *take/make notes,* де́лать заме́тки/за́писи. *Lecture from notes,* чита́ть ле́кцию по за́писям. *Take notes of a lecture,* запи́сывать ле́кцию. **4,** *pl.* (record of impressions) заме́тки: *travel notes,* путевы́е заме́тки. **5,** (explanatory comment) заме́тка: *note in the margin,* заме́тка на поля́х. *Explanatory note,* примеча́ние. **6,** *music* но́та: *high note,* высо́кая но́та. **7,** (negotiable instrument) биле́т: *bank note,* креди́тный биле́т; *treasury note,* казначе́йский биле́т. *Promissory note,* ве́ксель; долгово́е обяза́тельство. **8,** (trace; touch) но́тка: *note of anxiety,* но́тка беспоко́йства. **9,** (notice; attention) внима́ние: *worthy of note,* досто́йный внима́ния. **10,** (distinction) изве́стность. *A writer of note,* небезызве́стный писа́тель. —*v.t.* **1,** (notice) замеча́ть. **2,** (make mention of; point out) отмеча́ть. **3,** *fol. by* **down** (record) запи́сывать. —**compare notes,** обме́ниваться впечатле́ниями. —**make a note of,** запи́сывать; отме́ча́ть. —**take note of, 1,** (make a mental note of) брать на заме́тку. **2,** (notice; pay attention to) обраща́ть внима́ние на.
notebook *n.* тетра́дь; записна́я кни́жка.
noted *adj.* изве́стный; знамени́тый.
notepaper *n.* почто́вая бума́га.
noteworthy *adj.* примеча́тельный; достопримеча́тельный.
nothing *n.* **1,** (not anything) ничего́: *what did you do? Nothing,* что ты сде́лал? Ничего́. *Nothing of the kind,* ничего́ подо́бного. *He said nothing,* он ничего́ не сказа́л. *Be left with nothing,* оста́ться ни с чем. ♦*Less commonly* ничто́: *nothing bothers him,* ничто́ не беспоко́ит его́. *That's nothing compared to...,* э́то ничто́ по сравне́нию с... ♦*Before infinitives* не́чего: *I have nothing to say,* мне не́чего сказа́ть. *You have nothing to fear,* вам не́чего боя́ться. **2,** *preceded by* **a** (nonentity) ничто́; ничто́жество. —*adv.* совсе́м не: *nothing like it used to be,* совсе́м не похо́ж на то, что бы́ло. —**for nothing, 1,** (free; at no cost) беспла́тно; да́ром. **2,** (to no avail) напра́сно; да́ром; зря. **3,** (for no reason) зря. —**have nothing to do with, 1,** (bear no relation to) не име́ть никако́го отноше́ния к; совсе́м не каса́ться. **2,** (refuse to associate with) не жела́ть име́ть ничего́ о́бщего с. —**to say nothing of,** не говоря́ уже́ о.
notice *v.t.* замеча́ть. —*n.* **1,** (attention) внима́ние: *take notice of,* обраща́ть внима́ние на. *Take no notice of,* оста́вить без внима́ния. *Bring to someone's notice,* доводи́ть до чьего́-нибудь све́дения. **2,** (notification) извеще́ние; уведомле́ние; предупрежде́ние. *Dismissal notice,* уведомле́ние об увольне́нии. *Give notice to,* ста́вить (кого́-нибудь) в изве́стность. *Give notice of,* сде́лать предупрежде́ние о. *Until further notice,* впредь до дальне́йшего уведомле́ния; до осо́бого распоряже́ния. *I realize this is very short notice,* я понима́ю, что даю́ вам ма́ло вре́мени. **3,** (announcement) объявле́ние. **4,** (review) о́тзыв: *receive favorable notices,* получи́ть благоприя́тные о́тзывы. —**at a moment's notice,** по пе́рвому тре́бованию; в любо́й моме́нт.
noticeable *adj.* заме́тный. —**noticeably,** *adv.* заме́тно.
notification *n.* **1,** (act of notifying) извеще́ние; уведомле́ние; осведомле́ние; оповеще́ние. **2,** (notice given or received) извеще́ние; уведомле́ние.

notify *v.t.* извещáть; уведомлять; осведомлять; оповещáть.
notion *n.* **1,** (general idea) понятие; представлéние. **2,** *pl.* (small miscellaneous articles) галантерéя.
notoriety *n.* извéстность.
notorious *adj.* завéдомый; пресловýтый.
notwithstanding *adv.* тем не мéнее. —*prep.* несмотря на.
nougat *n.* нугá.
nought *n.* = **naught.**
noun *n.* существи́тельное; и́мя существи́тельное. *Common noun,* и́мя нарицáтельное. *Proper noun,* и́мя сóбственное.
nourish *v.t.* питáть. —**nourishing,** *adj.* питáтельный. —**nourishment,** *n.* питáние.
nova *n.* нóвая звездá.
novel *n.* ромáн. —*adj.* нóвый; необыкновéнный. —**novelist,** *n.* романи́ст.
novella *n.* новéлла.
novelty *n.* **1,** (quality of being new) новизнá; нóвость. **2,** (something new) нóвость; нови́нка; нóвшество.
November *n.* ноябрь. —*adj.* ноябрьский.
novice *n.* **1,** (beginner) новичóк. **2,** *eccles.* пóслушник
novocaine *n.* новокаи́н.
now *adv.* **1,** (at the present time) тепéрь; сейчáс. **2,** (at once) сейчáс; сейчáс же. —*particle* ну: *come now!,* ну вот ещё! —**by now,** ужé: *he should have been here by now,* он ужé дóлжен быть здесь. —**for now,** покá. —**from now on,** впредь; отны́не. —**now and then,** врéмя от врéмени; кóе-когдá. —**now that...,** тепéрь, когдá... —**until now,** до сих пор.
nowadays *adv.* в нáше врéмя; в тепéрешнее врéмя; ны́нче.
nowhere *adv.* **1,** (in no place) нигдé. **2,** (to no place) никудá. ♦ *With infinitives* нéгде; нéкуда: *nowhere to sit,* нéгде сесть; *nowhere to go,* нéкуда поéхать. —**from out of nowhere,** откýда ни возьми́сь. —**get nowhere,** ничегó не доби́ться. —**in the middle of nowhere,** у чёрта на кули́чках. —**lead nowhere,** ни к чемý не привести́. —**nowhere near,** отню́дь не: *nowhere near as big as you think,* отню́дь не такóй большóй, как вы дýмаете.
noxious *adj.* врéдный; пáгубный.
nozzle *n.* соплó; брандспóйт.
nth *adj.* э́нный: *to the nth degree,* в э́нной стéпени.
nuance *n.* оттéнок; нюáнс.
nub *n.* **1,** (knob; lump) ши́шка. **2,** *colloq.* (gist; point) суть.
nuclear *adj.* я́дерный: *nuclear energy/war,* я́дерная энéргия/войнá. *Nuclear-free zone,* безъя́дерная зóна.
nucleus *n.* ядрó.
nude *adj.* нагóй; гóлый; обнажённый. —*n.* обнажённая фигýра. —**in the nude,** в гóлом ви́де.
nudge *v.t.* подтáлкивать лóктем. —*n.* толчóк лóктем.
nudity *n.* наготá.
nugget *n.* саморóдок.
nuisance *n.* **1,** (annoying thing) досáда: *what a nuisance!,* какáя досáда! **2,** (pest) надоéда. *Make a nuisance of oneself,* прокáзничать; озорничáть.
null *adj.* [*often* **null and void**] недействи́тельный; не имéющий закóнной си́лы.
nullification *n.* аннули́рование.
nullify *v.t.* **1,** (make null and void) аннули́ровать. **2,** (negate) своди́ть на нет *or* к нулю́.
numb *adj.* **1,** (from the cold) окоченéлый; окоченéвший. **2,** (from paralysis) онемéлый. **3,** (from emotion) оцепенéлый. *Become numb,* (о)коченéть; (о)немéть; (о)цепенéть. —*v.t.* скóвывать: *the cold numbed our hands,* хóлод сковáл нам рýки.
number *n.* **1,** (numeral) числó: *even number,* чётное числó. *Theory of numbers,* теóрия чи́сел. **2,** (numeral used to identify something) нóмер: *telephone number,* нóмер телефóна. **3,** (quantity) числó; коли́чество. **4,** (indefinite quantity) ряд: *in a number of cases,* в ря́де слýчаев. **5,** (item on a musical program) нóмер. **6,** *gram.* (singular or plural) числó. —*v.t.* **1,** (assign numbers to) нумеровáть. **2,** (amount to; contain) насчи́тывать: *the garrison numbered 300 men,* гарнизóн насчи́тывал три́ста человéк. **3,** *fol. by* **among** (count among) причисля́ть (к); относи́ть к числý (+ *gen.*). **4,** *His days are numbered,* егó дни сочтены́. —*v.i.* **1,** (reach an amount) исчисля́ться: *number in the thousands,* исчисля́ться ты́сячами. **2,** *fol. by* **among** (be one of) принадлежáть к числý (+ *gen.*). —**without number,** без числá; без счёта.
numbered *adj.* нумеровáнный; номернóй.
numbering *n.* нумерáция. *Numbering machine,* нумерáтор.
numberless *adj.* бесчи́сленный.
Numbers *n., Bib.* Чи́сла.
numbness *n.* онемéние.
numeral *n.* **1,** (number) ци́фра. *Roman numerals,* ри́мские ци́фры. **2,** *gram.* (Russian part of speech) (и́мя) числи́тельное.
numeration *n.* нумерáция.
numerator *n.* числи́тель.
numerical *adj.* числовóй; чи́сленный; цифровóй. *Numerical superiority,* чи́сленное превосхóдство. *Numerical data,* цифровы́е дáнные. —**numerically,** *adv.* чи́сленно.
numerous *adj.* многочи́слеиный.
numismatics *n.* нумизмáтика. —**numismatic,** *adj.* нумизмати́ческий. —**numismatist,** *n.* нумизмáт.
numskull *n.* óлух; тупи́ца; болвáн.
nun *n.* монáхиня.
nuncio *n.* нýнций.
nunnery *n.* жéнский монасты́рь.
nuptial *adj.* брáчный; свáдебный. —**nuptials,** *n.pl.* свáдьба.
nurse *n.* **1,** (one who tends the sick) медсестрá; сидéлка. *Male nurse,* брат милосéрдия. **2,** (nursemaid) ня́ня. —*v.t.* **1,** (suckle) корми́ть. *Nursing mother,* кормя́щая мать. **2,** (take care of) ухáживать за; ня́нчить. **3,** (treat gently) берéчь. **4,** (take steps to cure, as a cold) лечи́ть. **5,** (harbor, as a grudge) питáть; таи́ть.
nursemaid *n.* ня́ня; ня́нька.
nursery *n.* **1,** (children's room) дéтская. **2,** (day nursery) я́сли. **3,** (place where plants are raised) питóмник. —**nursery rhymes,** дéтские пéсенки; дéтские стишки́. —**nursery school,** дéтский сад.
nursing *n.* **1,** (suckling) кормлéние (грýдью). **2,** (profession) ухóд за больны́ми. *Study nursing,* учи́ться на медсестрý. *School of nursing,* шкóла медсестёр. —**nursing bottle,** рожóк. —**nursing home,** лечéбница.

nurture *v.t.* лелéять: *nurture a child/hope,* лелéять ребёнка/надéжду.
nut *n.* **1,** (fruit) орéх. **2,** (what goes with a bolt) гáйка. **3,** *slang* (crazy person) чудáк; сумасбрóд; псих.
nutcracker *n.* щипцы́ для орéхов.
nuthatch *n.* пóползень.
nutmeg *n.* **1,** (seed) мускáтный орéх; мускáт. **2,** (tree) мускáтник; мускáтное дéрево. —*adj.* мускáтный.
nutria *n.* нýтрия.
nutrient *n.* питáтельное веществó.
nutrition *n.* **1,** (nourishment) питáние. **2,** (study of proper diet) диетéтика. —**nutritional,** *adj.* пищевóй; питáтельный. —**nutritious,** *adj.* питáтельный.
nuts *adj., slang* **1,** (crazy) обалдéлый. **2,** *fol. by* **about** (mad about) без умá (от). —*interj., slang* тьфу!
nutshell *n., in* **in a nutshell,** вкрáтце; в двух словáх; в крáтких словáх.
nutty *adj.* **1,** (having or made with nuts) орéховый. **2,** *slang* (silly) глýпый.
nuzzle *v.t.* терéться нóсом о.
nylon *n.* **1,** (fabric) нейлóн. **2,** *pl.* (stockings) нейлóновые чулки́. —*adj.* нейлóновый.
nymph *n.* ни́мфа.
nymphomania *n.* нимфомáния. —**nymphomaniac,** *n.* нимфомáнка.

O

O, o пятнáдцатая бýква англи́йского алфави́та. —*n.* (zero) нуль. —*interj.* о!; ах!
oaf *n.* дýрень; тупи́ца; óлух. —**oafish,** *adj.* придурковáтый.
oak *n.* дуб. —*adj.* дубóвый.
oakum *n.* пáкля.
oar *n.* веслó. —**oarlock,** *n.* уклю́чина.
oarsman *n.* гребéц.
oasis *n.* оáзис.
oat *n., usu. pl.* овёс. —*adj.* овся́ный.
oath *n.* **1,** (solemn promise) прися́га; кля́тва. *Take the oath,* приноси́ть *or* принимáть прися́гу. **2,** (swearword) прокля́тие.
oatmeal *n.* овся́ная кáша; овся́ная крупá; овся́нка; толокнó; геркулéс.
obdurate *adj.* **1,** (obstinate) упря́мый. **2,** (hardhearted) чёрствый. —**obduracy,** *n.* упря́мство.
obedient *adj.* послýшный. —**obedience,** *n.* послушáние; повиновéние.
obeisance *n.* **1,** (bow) поклóн. **2,** (deference) почтéние.
obelisk *n.* обели́ск.
obese *adj.* пóлный; тýчный; грýзный. —**obesity,** *n.* тýчность; ожирéние; полнотá.
obey *v.t.* **1,** (mind; heed) слýшаться (+ *gen.*); повиновáться (+ *dat.*). **2,** (observe; carry out) подчиня́ться (+ *dat.*): *obey an order/the law/,* подчиня́ться прикáзу/закóну. —*v.i.* слýшаться.
obfuscate *v.t.* затемня́ть. —**obfuscation,** *n.* затемнéние.
obituary *n.* некролóг.
object[1] (**ob**-jekt) *n.* **1,** (material thing) предмéт. **2,** (that to which something is directed) объéкт; предмéт. **3,** (goal; purpose) цель. **4,** *gram.* дополнéние.
object[2] (ub-**jekt**) *v.i.* возражáть: *no one objected,* никтó не возражáл.
objection *n.* возражéние. *Have no objection,* не возражáть; не имéть возражéний; ничегó не имéть прóтив.
objectionable *adj.* нежелáтельный; неприя́тный.
objective *n.* **1,** (goal; purpose) цель. **2,** *mil.* объéкт. —*adj.* объекти́вный. —**objective case,** объéктный падéж.
objectivity *n.* объекти́вность.
object lesson нагля́дный урóк.
obligate *v.t.* обя́зывать. —**obligated,** *adj.* обя́занный.
obligation *n.* обязáтельство. *Under an obligation,* обя́зан. *Under no obligation,* нискóлько не обя́зан.
obligatory *adj.* обязáтельный.
oblige *v.t.* **1,** (compel) обя́зывать. **2,** (place under a debt of gratitude) обя́зывать: *you will oblige me greatly,* вы меня́ óчень обя́жете. **3,** (do a favor for): *could you oblige me with an answer?,* вы не могли́ бы дать мне отвéт? —**obliged,** *adj.* обя́занный.
obliging *adj.* услýжливый; предупреди́тельный.
oblique *adj.* **1,** (slanting) косóй. **2,** (indirect) кóсвенный.
obliquely *adv.* **1,** (at an angle) кóсо; нáискось; вкось. **2,** (indirectly) кóсвенно.
obliterate *v.t.* **1,** (efface) изглáживать. **2,** (wipe out) уничтожáть. —**obliteration,** *n.* уничтожéние.
oblivion *n.* забвéние. *Sink into oblivion,* кáнуть в вéчность.
oblivious *adj.* [*usu.* **oblivious of** *or* **to**] не имéющий поня́тия о; в пóлном невéдении (относи́тельно).
oblong *adj.* продолговáтый. —*n.* продолговáтая фигýра.
obloquy *n.* **1,** (abusive language) злослóвие. **2,** (disgrace) позóр.
obnoxious *adj.* неприя́тный; проти́вный.
oboe *n.* гобóй. —**oboist,** *n.* гобои́ст.
obscene *adj.* непристóйный. —**obscenity,** *n.* непристóйность.
obscurant *n.* мракобéс; обскурáнт. —**obscuran-**

tism, *n.* мракобе́сие; обскуранти́зм.
obscure *adj.* **1,** (dark) тёмный. **2,** (unclear; vague) нея́сный; сму́тный. **3,** (hardly known) безве́стный. —*v.t.* затемня́ть.
obscurity *n.* **1,** (lack of clarity) нея́сность. **2,** (state of being unknown) неизве́стность; безве́стность.
obsequious *adj.* уго́дливый; раболе́пный; подобостра́стный. —**obsequiousness,** *n.* уго́дливость; раболе́пие; подобостра́стие.
observable *adj.* заме́тный.
observance *n.* **1,** (compliance) соблюде́ние. **2,** (celebration) пра́зднование.
observant *adj.* **1,** (perceptive) наблюда́тельный. **2,** (religious) благочести́вый. **3,** *fol. by* **of** (strict in observing something) соблюда́ющий.
observation *n.* **1,** (act of observing) наблюде́ние: *keep under observation,* держа́ть под наблюде́нием. **2,** *usu. pl.* (result of observing) наблюде́ния: *personal observations,* ли́чные наблюде́ния. **3,** (remark) замеча́ние. —**observation post,** наблюда́тельный пункт.
observatory *n.* обсервато́рия.
observe *v.t.* **1,** (watch) наблюда́ть: *observe the sunrise,* наблюда́ть восхо́д со́лнца. **2,** (notice) замеча́ть. **3,** (comply with; obey) соблюда́ть: *observe the law,* соблюда́ть зако́н. *Observe neutrality,* подде́рживать нейтрали́тет. **4,** (remark) замеча́ть. **5,** (celebrate) отмеча́ть; пра́здновать.
observer *n.* наблюда́тель.
obsess *v.t.* пресле́довать. *Obsessed by,* одержи́мый (+ *instr.*).
obsession *n.* одержи́мость. —**obsessive,** *adj.* навя́зчивый.
obsolescent *adj.* устарева́ющий; отжива́ющий. —**obsolescence,** *n.* мора́льный изно́с.
obsolete *adj.* устаре́лый; устаре́вший.
obstacle *n.* препя́тствие. —**obstacle course,** полоса́ препя́тствий.
obstetrics *n.* акуше́рство. —**obstetric,** *adj.* акуше́рский. —**obstetrician,** *n.* акуше́р.
obstinate *adj.* упря́мый. —**obstinacy,** *n.* упря́мство.
obstreperous *adj.* шу́мный; бу́йный; непоко́рный.
obstruct *v.t.* **1,** (bar; block) прегражда́ть; загражда́ть; загора́живать. **2,** (hinder; impede) препя́тствовать. **3,** (cut off from sight) заслоня́ть.
obstruction *n.* **1,** (blocking) прегражде́ние. **2,** (impediment) прегра́да; загражде́ние. **3,** (delaying tactics) обстру́кция. **4,** *med.* непроходи́мость; закупорка.
obstructionism *n.* обструкциони́зм.
obstructionist *n.* обструкциони́ст. —*adj.* обструкцио́нный.
obtain *v.t.* получа́ть; достава́ть; добыва́ть. —*v.i.* (be in effect) существова́ть.
obtrude *v.t.* **1,** (thrust forward) высо́вывать. **2,** (thrust forward unasked) навя́зывать. —*v.i.* навя́зываться; вторга́ться. —**obtrusive,** *adj.* навя́зчивый.
obtuse *adj.* тупо́й. *Obtuse angle,* тупо́й у́гол. —**obtuseness,** *n.* ту́пость.
obverse *adj.* лицево́й. —*n.* лицева́я сторона́.
obviate *v.t.* устраня́ть; предупрежда́ть.
obvious *adj.* очеви́дный; я́вный. —**obviously,** *adv.* очеви́дно; я́вно.
ocarina *n.* окари́на.
occasion *n.* **1,** (event) собы́тие: *this happy occasion,* э́то ра́достное собы́тие. **2,** (time when something occurs) слу́чай: *on the occasion of,* по слу́чаю (+ *gen.*). **3,** (particular time) раз: *on several occasions,* не́сколько раз. **4,** (opportunity) слу́чай: *take the occasion,* по́льзоваться слу́чаем. **5,** (cause; grounds) по́вод: *occasion for a quarrel,* по́вод для ссо́ры. —*v.t.* вызыва́ть; обусло́вливать. —**have occasion to,** приходи́ться (+ *dat.*): *I frequently had occasion to...,* мне ча́сто приходи́лось (+ *inf.*). —**on occasion,** от слу́чая к слу́чаю. —**rise to the occasion,** быть на высоте́ положе́ния.
occasional *adj.* быва́ющий вре́мя от вре́мени. *I receive an occasional letter from her,* вре́мя от вре́мени я получа́ю от неё письмо́. —**occasionally,** *adv.* иногда́; вре́мя от вре́мени.
occident *n., often cap.* За́пад. —**occidental,** *adj.* за́падный.
occlude *v.t.* заку́поривать. —**occlusion,** *n.* заку́порка.
occult *adj.* таи́нственный; окку́льтный. —**occultism,** *n.* оккульти́зм.
occupancy *n.* заня́тие; заселе́ние.
occupant *n.* жиле́ц.
occupation *n.* **1,** (act of occupying) заня́тие. **2,** *mil.* оккупа́ция. *Army of occupation,* оккупацио́нная а́рмия. **3,** (what one does with one's time) заня́тие. **4,** (type of work) заня́тие; профе́ссия. *What is your occupation?,* чем вы занима́етесь?; кем вы рабо́таете?
occupational *adj.* профессиона́льный. —**occupational therapy,** трудова́я терапи́я.
occupy *v.t.* **1,** (fill; take up; inhabit) занима́ть: *occupy a seat/house/post,* занима́ть ме́сто/дом/пост. *Be occupied with,* занима́ться (+ *instr.*); быть за́нятым (+ *instr.*). **2,** *mil.* оккупи́ровать; занима́ть.
occur *v.i.* **1,** (happen) случа́ться; происходи́ть. **2,** (exist; be found) встреча́ться; води́ться. **3,** *fol. by* **to** (come to mind) приходи́ть в го́лову (+ *dat.*).
occurrence *n.* слу́чай; происше́ствие; явле́ние.
ocean *n.* океа́н. —*adj.* океа́нский: *ocean liner,* океа́нский парохо́д. —**oceanic,** *adj.* океа́нский.
oceanography *n.* океаногра́фия. —**oceanographer,** *n.* океано́граф. —**oceanographic,** *adj.* океанографи́ческий.
ocelot *n.* оцело́т.
ocher *also,* **ochre** *n.* о́хра.
o'clock *adv., in* **one o'clock,** час; **two o'clock,** два часа́; **five o'clock,** пять часо́в, *etc.*
octagon *n.* восьмиуго́льник. —**octagonal,** *adj.* восьмиуго́льный.
octahedron *n.* восьмигра́нник. —**octahedral,** *adj.* восьмигра́нный.
octane *n.* окта́н.
octave *n.* окта́ва.
octavo *n.* восьму́шка.
octet *n.* окте́т.
October *n.* октя́брь. —*adj.* октя́брьский.
octopus *n.* осьмино́г; восьмино́г; спрут.
ocular *adj.* глазно́й.
oculist *n.* окули́ст.
odd *adj.* **1,** (strange; queer) стра́нный: *odd name/behavior,* стра́нное и́мя/поведе́ние. **2,** (not even) нечётный: *odd number,* нечётное число́. **3,** (not paired) непа́рный. **4,** (one of an incomplete set) разро́знен-

ный. **5,** (about; some) с ли́шним: *forty odd years ago,* со́рок с ли́шним лет тому́ наза́д. **6,** (occasional) случа́йный: *odd jobs,* случа́йная рабо́та.

oddity *n.* **1,** (strangeness) стра́нность. **2,** (strange person or thing) стра́нный челове́к; стра́нное де́ло; чуда́к.

oddly *adv.* стра́нно. *Oddly enough,* как ни стра́нно.

odds *n.pl.* ша́нсы: *the odds are in your favor,* ша́нсы на ва́шей стороне́. *The odds are that...,* скоре́е всего́... *Against overwhelming odds,* про́тив значи́тельно превосходя́щих сил. —**at odds,** в ссо́ре; не в лада́х. —**by all odds,** несомне́нно; бесспо́рно. —**give odds,** дать не́сколько очко́в вперёд. —**odds and ends,** ме́лкие ве́щи; ме́лочь.

ode *n.* о́да.

odious *adj.* гну́сный; ненави́стный; одио́зный.

odometer *n.* одо́метр.

odontology *n.* одонтоло́гия.

odor *also,* **odour** *n.* за́пах.

odoriferous *adj.* души́стый; паху́чий.

odorless *also,* **odourless** *adj.* не име́ющий за́паха.

odorous *adj.* души́стый; паху́чий.

odour *n.* = **odor.** —**odourless,** *adj.* = **odorless.**

odyssey *n.* одиссе́я.

oesophagus *n.* = **esophagus.**

of *prep.* **1,** (denoting possession, relation, a part of something, the contents of something) *rendered by the gen. case: the name of the book,* назва́ние кни́ги; *a glass of water,* стака́н воды́; *a pound of sugar,* фунт са́хару. **2,** (with the names of cities or countries) *not rendered in Russian (nom. case follows): the city of Moscow,* го́род Москва́; *the State of Israel,* Госуда́рство Изра́иль; *the Kingdom of Denmark,* Короле́вство Да́ния; *in the Republic of India,* в Респу́блике И́ндия. **3,** (from; denoting origin or material) из: *a statue of bronze,* ста́туя из бро́нзы. **4,** (out of; out of a total of) из: *some of us,* не́которые из нас. **5,** (on one's part) с (чьей-нибудь) стороны́: *very kind of you,* о́чень любе́зно с ва́шей стороны́. **6,** (indicating direction from) от: *south of the city,* к ю́гу от го́рода. **7,** (indicating cause) от: *die of cancer,* умира́ть от ра́ка. **8,** (about; concerning) о: *news of his arrival,* весть о его́ прие́зде. *Think a great deal of oneself,* мно́го ду́мать о себе́. **9,** (in telling time) без: *twenty of two,* без двадцати́ два. **10,** (with dates) от: *my letter of May 5th,* моё письмо́ от пя́того ма́я. **11,** *with various miscellaneous verbs: smell of onions,* па́хнуть лу́ком; *accuse someone of stealing,* обвиня́ть кого́-нибудь в кра́же. *He was cured of tuberculosis,* он вы́лечился от туберкулёза. *She was robbed of her purse and glasses,* у неё укра́ли су́мку и очки́.

off *adv. Usu. rendered by a prefixed verb: take off,* снима́ть; *cut off,* отреза́ть; *jump off,* спры́гивать; *see off,* провожа́ть. —*adj.* **1,** (not turned on) вы́ключенный: *the light is off,* свет вы́ключен. **2,** (canceled): *The wedding is off,* сва́дьба не состои́тся. *The deal is off,* де́ло расстро́илось. **3,** (free from one's job): *I'm off on Friday,* пя́тница у меня́ выходно́й. **4,** (in error): *be off in one's calculations,* ошиби́ться в расчётах. **5,** (away; into the future): *Christmas is two months off,* до рождества́ оста́лось два ме́сяца. **6,** (in a certain state): *well off,* обеспе́ченный. *You'd be better off if you stayed home,* вам бы лу́чше оста́ться до́ма. **7,** (about to go somewhere): *well, I'm off to town,* ну, пошёл (пошла́) в го́род. **8,** (declining): *production is off,* произво́дство упа́ло. —*prep.* **1,** (away from) с: *the train went off the tracks,* по́езд сошёл с ре́льсов. *Keep off the grass!,* по траве́ не ходи́ть! **2,** (distant from) от: *100 miles off the coast,* в ста ми́лях от бе́рега. *Just off the main square,* в двух шага́х от гла́вной пло́щади. **3,** (deviating from) от: *stray off course,* отклоня́ться от ку́рса. **4,** (below) ни́же: *ten dollars off the usual price,* де́сять до́лларов ни́же обы́чной цены́. **5,** *with various nouns: off duty,* не дежу́рит; *off balance,* потеря́вший равнове́сие; *off limits,* закры́т; *off one's game,* не в фо́рме. —*interj.* вон; прочь! *Off with you!,* убира́йтесь вон! —**off and on,** с переры́вами.

offal *n.* требуха́.

off-color *also,* **off-colour** *adj.* **1,** (imperfect, as of a gem) нечи́стой воды́. **2,** (risqué) риско́ванный; сомни́тельный.

offence *n.* = **offense.**

offend *v.t.* обижа́ть; оскорбля́ть.

offender *n.* **1,** (one who offends) оби́дчик. **2,** (wrongdoer) правонаруши́тель.

offense *also,* **offence** *n.* **1,** (affront) оби́да. *No offense meant,* не в оби́ду будь ска́зано. **2,** (attack) нападе́ние. **3,** (misdeed; transgression) просту́пок. **4,** *law* преступле́ние; правонаруше́ние. —**give offense (to),** обижа́ть кого́-нибудь. —**take offense,** обижа́ться.

offensive *adj.* **1,** (disagreeable) неприя́тный; проти́вный. **2,** (insulting) оби́дный; оскорби́тельный. **3,** *mil.* наступа́тельный: *offensive weapons,* наступа́тельное ору́жие. —*n.* наступле́ние: *take the offensive,* переходи́ть в наступле́ние.

offer *v.t.* **1,** (present; put forward) предлага́ть: *offer one's services,* предлага́ть свои́ услу́ги. *Offer one's apologies,* приноси́ть свои́ извине́ния. *Offer one's condolences,* выража́ть своё соболе́знование. **2,** (provide) предоставля́ть: *offer opportunities,* предоставля́ть возмо́жности. *Offer hope,* подава́ть наде́жду. **3,** *fol. by inf.* (volunteer) предлага́ть; вызыва́ться. **4,** (put up, as resistance) ока́зывать. —*n.* предложе́ние: *make an offer,* де́лать предложе́ние.

offering *n.* **1,** (gift; contribution) приноше́ние. **2,** (sacrifice) жертвоприноше́ние.

offhand *adv.* без подгото́вки; экспро́мтом. —*adj.* **1,** (impromptu) импровизи́рованный. **2,** (casual) случа́йный.

office *n.* **1,** (place of business) конто́ра; канцеля́рия. **2,** (private room for work) кабине́т. **3,** (high position) до́лжность. *Term of office,* срок полномо́чий. **4,** (administrative body) бюро́. **5,** (government department) министе́рство; ве́домство; управле́ние. **6,** *pl.* (services) услу́ги: *good offices,* до́брые услу́ги. —*adj.* служе́бный. *Office hours,* служе́бные *or* приёмные часы́. *Office worker,* канцеляри́ст.

office boy рассы́льный; посы́льный.

officeholder *n.* должностно́е лицо́.

officer *n.* **1,** *mil.* офице́р. **2,** (person in authority) должностно́е лицо́. **3,** (policeman) полице́йский. —*adj.* [*also,* **officer's** *or* **officers'**] офице́рский.

official *adj.* **1,** (authorized; formal) официа́льный. *Official language,* госуда́рственный язы́к. **2,** (connected with one's work) служе́бный: *official duties,* служе́бные обя́занности. —*n.* чино́вник; должностно́е лицо́.

officialdom *n.* чино́вничество.

officially *adv.* официа́льно.
officiate *v.i.* **1,** (preside) председа́тельствовать (на собра́нии). **2,** (conduct a service) соверша́ть богослуже́ние.
officious *adj.* назо́йливый; навя́зчивый.
offing *n., in* **be in the offing,** предстоя́ть; гото́виться.
off-season *adj. & adv.* не в сезо́нное вре́мя.
offset *v.t.* возмеща́ть; компенси́ровать. —*n., printing* офсе́т. —**offset printing,** офсе́тная печа́ть.
offshoot *n.* отро́сток; о́тпрыск; ответвле́ние.
offshore *adj.* прибре́жный. —*adj.* недалеко́ от бе́рега.
offside *adj., sports* вне игры́.
offspring *n.* пото́мок; о́тпрыск.
offstage *adj.* закули́сный. —*adv.* за кули́сами; за кули́сы.
off-white *adj.* беле́сый; белова́тый.
off-year *adj. Off-year elections,* промежу́точные вы́боры.
often *adv.* ча́сто. *How often?,* как ча́сто? —**every so often,** вре́мя от вре́мени. —**more often than not,** ча́ще всего́.
ogle *v.i.* де́лать гла́зки; игра́ть глаза́ми.
ogre *n.* велика́н-людое́д.
oh *interj.* о!; ах!; ох!
ohm *n.* ом.
oho *interj.* ого́!
oil *n.* **1,** (viscous substance) ма́сло. **2,** (petroleum) нефть. **3,** *art* ма́сло: *paint in oils,* писа́ть ма́слом. —*adj.* ма́сляный; нефтяно́й. —*v.t.* сма́зывать.
oilcan *n.* маслёнка.
oilcloth *n.* клеёнка.
oil color ма́сляная кра́ска.
oiler *n.* **1,** (device for oiling) маслёнка. **2,** (ship) нефтеналивно́е су́дно.
oil filter ма́сляный фильтр.
oil painting карти́на, напи́санная ма́сляными кра́сками.
oilseed *n.* ма́сличное се́мя.
oil shale нефтено́сный сла́нец.
oil well нефтяна́я сква́жина.
oily *adj.* ма́сленый; масляни́стый. *Oily skin,* жи́рная ко́жа.
ointment *n.* мазь.
O.K. *interj.* хорошо́!; ла́дно!
okapi *n.* ока́пи.
okra *n.* ба́мия; о́кра.
old *adj.* ста́рый. *Old man,* стари́к. *Old woman,* стару́ха. *Get/grow old,* старе́ть; ста́риться. *How old are you?,* ско́лько вам лет? *I am ten years old,* мне де́сять лет. —**in days of old,** в старину́; в бы́лые времена́.
old age ста́рость. *Old age pension,* пе́нсия по ста́рости. —**old age home,** дом для престаре́лых.
Old Believer старове́р; старообря́дец.
olden *adj.* было́й; да́вний. *In olden times,* в старину́.
old-fashioned *adj.* старомо́дный.
old hand тёртый кала́ч; стре́ляный воробе́й.
old maid ста́рая де́ва.
oldster *n., colloq.* стари́к.
Old Testament Ве́тхий заве́т. *Old Testament prophet,* ветхозаве́тный проро́к.
old-time *adj.* стари́нный; ста́рых времён.
old-timer *n.* старожи́л.
old wives' tale ба́бья ска́зка.
Old World Ста́рый свет.
oleaginous *adj.* масляни́стый.
oleander *n.* олеа́ндр.
oleomargarine *n.* маргари́н.
olfactory *adj.* обоня́тельный.
oligarchy *n.* олига́рхия. —**oligarch,** *n.* олига́рх. —**oligarchic,** *adj.* олигархи́ческий.
olive *n.* оли́ва; оли́вка; масли́на. —*adj.* оли́вковый; масли́чный. —**olive branch,** оли́вковая *or* масли́чная ветвь. —**olive-green,** *adj.* оли́вковый. —**olive oil,** оли́вковое *or* прова́нское ма́сло. —**olive tree,** оли́ва; масли́на.
Olympiad *n.* олимпиа́да.
Olympian *adj.* олимпи́йский.
Olympic *adj.* олимпи́йский. —**Olympic Games,** Олимпи́йские и́гры.
Olympics *n.pl.* олимпиа́да.
omega *n.* оме́га.
omelet *also,* **omelette** *n.* омле́т.
omen *n.* предзнаменова́ние.
ominous *adj.* злове́щий.
omission *n.* упуще́ние; про́пуск.
omit *v.t.* пропуска́ть.
omnibus *n.* **1,** *obs.* (bus) авто́бус. **2,** (anthology) антоло́гия; сбо́рник. —*adj.* о́бщий; всеобъе́млющий.
omnipotent *adj.* всемогу́щий. —**omnipotence,** *n.* всемогу́щество.
omnipresent *adj.* вездесу́щий.
omniscient *adj.* всеве́дущий. —**omniscience,** *n.* всеве́дение.
omnivorous *adj.* всея́дный.
on *prep.* **1,** (indicating position upon) на (+ *prepl.*): *your keys are on the dresser,* ва́ши ключи́ (лежа́т) на комо́де. *The picture is hanging on the wall,* карти́на виси́т на стене́. **2,** (onto) на (+ *acc.*): *put the books on the shelf,* положи́ть кни́ги на по́лку. *Lie down on the floor,* лечь на́ пол. *Set foot on the moon,* ступи́ть на Луну́. **3,** *with various abstract nouns* на: *based on facts,* осно́ванный на фа́ктах; *on the following conditions,* на сле́дующих усло́виях. *Pin one's hopes on,* возлага́ть наде́жды на (+ *acc.*). *Live on one's earnings,* жить на свой за́работок. *Spend money on books,* тра́тить де́ньги на кни́ги. **4,** (on coming in contact with) о (+ *acc.*): *stumble on a stone,* споткну́ться о ка́мень. *Wipe one's hands on one's apron,* вытира́ть ру́ки о пере́дник. *Cut one's finger on a piece of glass,* поре́зать себе́ па́лец о стекло́. **5,** (in one's possession) при: *I have no money on me,* у меня́ при себе́ нет де́нег. **6,** (through the medium of) по: *appear on television,* выступа́ть по телеви́дению. **7,** (about; concerning) о: *an essay on war,* о́черк о войне́. *A book on art,* кни́га по иску́сству. *My opinion on this subject,* моё мне́ние по э́тому вопро́су. **8,** (at the time of) по (+ *prepl.*); при: *on his arrival,* по прие́зде; *on entering the room,* при вхо́де в ко́мнату. **9,** (with dates) *expressed by the gen. case: on July 4th,* четвёртого ию́ля. **10,** (with days of the week) в (+ *acc.*): *on Wednesday,* в сре́ду. ♦*In the meaning "each" or "every"* по (+ *dat.pl.*): *on Wednesday(s),* по среда́м. **11,** *colloq.* (at the expense of): *this is on me,* я угоща́ю. *Drinks are on the house,* все напи́тки за счёт заведе́ния. **12,** *in various miscellaneous expressions: on board,* на борту́; *on fire,* в огне́; *on purpose,* наро́чно;

on time, вóвремя; *on trial,* под судóм. —*adv.* дáльше: *go on,* идтú дáльше. *Read on!,* читáйте дáльше! ♦*Usu. rendered by a prefixed verb: put on,* надевáть; *turn on,* включáть. —*adj.* **1,** (being worn) надéтый: *your hat is on backwards,* у вас шля́па надéта зáдом напéрёд. **2,** (turned on) включён: *the light is on,* свет включён. **3,** (in progress) *expressed by the verb* идтú: *the exam is on,* идёт экзáмен. **4,** (not canceled) в сúле. —**on and off,** попеременно; то..., то... —**on and on,** без концá.

onager *n.* онáгр.

on-board *adj.* бортовóй.

once *adv.* **1,** (one time) раз; одúн раз. *Once a month,* раз в мéсяц. *Once is enough,* одúн раз – достáточно. *More than once,* не раз. *Not once,* ни рáзу. **2,** (on a certain occasion in the past) однáжды; кáк-то раз. **3,** (formerly) нéкогда; когдá-то. *The ruins of a once great city,* руúны нéкогда большóго гóрода. —*conj.* как тóлько; раз. *Once he finds out about it,* как тóлько он узнáет об э́том. —**all at once, 1,** (all simultaneously) все *or* всё вмéсте; срáзу. **2,** (suddenly) вдруг. —**at once, 1,** (right now) сейчáс; немéдленно. **2,** (just then; immediately) срáзу; немéдленно. —**for once,** на э́тот раз. —**just this once,** хотя́ бы на э́тот раз. —**once again; once more,** ещё раз. —**once and for all,** раз (и) навсегдá. —**once in a while,** врéмя от врéмени. —**once or twice,** раз-другóй; рáза два. —**once upon a time,** однáжды; жил-был.

oncoming *adj.* встрéчный; надвигáющийся.

one *n.* одúн. ♦*In counting* раз: *one, two, three,* раз, два, три. —*adj.* **1,** (a single) одúн (однá, однó): *one time,* одúн раз; *one portion,* однá пóрция; *one summer,* однó лéто. *One o'clock,* час. *Act One,* дéйствие пéрвое. **2,** (only) едúнственный: *the one man who can do it,* едúнственный, кто мóжет э́то сдéлать. **3,** (united) едúный. —*indef.pron.* **1,** (single element in a group) одúн (однá): *one of them,* одúн/однá из них. **2,** (a person) *Rendered variously in Russian: one must observe the rules,* нáдо соблюдáть прáвила. *One is never too old to learn,* век живú – век учúсь. **3,** (item) *Omitted in Russian: the red one,* крáсный (крáсная, крáсное). *Buy a new one,* купúть нóвый (нóвую, нóвое). **4,** *preceded by* **the** (specific person or thing) тот: *not the one I wanted,* не тот, котóрый я хотéл. **5,** (the kind of person) такóй: *he is not one to back down,* он не такóй, чтóбы отступáть. —**at one with,** заоднó с; солидáрный с. —**one and all,** все до однoгó. —**one another,** друг дрýга. —**one by one, 1,** (one at a time) по одномý. **2,** (one after the other) одúн за другúм.

one-armed *adj.* однорýкий.

one-celled *adj.* одноклéточный.

one-eyed *adj.* одноглáзый.

one hundred сто. —**one-hundredth,** *adj.* сóтый. —*n.* сóтая: *one one-hundredth,* однá сóтая.

one-legged *adj.* однонóгий.

oneness *n.* **1,** (unity) едúнство. **2,** (sameness) тóждество.

one-room *adj.* однокóмнатный.

onerous *adj.* тя́гостный; обременúтельный.

oneself *pers.pron.* **1,** *used reflexively* себя́: *underestimate oneself,* недооцéнивать себя́. *Kill oneself,* покóнчить с собóй. ♦*Often rendered by the reflexive verb: hurt oneself,* ушибúться; *shoot oneself,* застрелúться. **2,** *used for emphasis* сам: *I don't know myself,* я сам (самá) не знáю. —**be oneself,** быть самúм собóй. —**by oneself,** одúн. —**not oneself,** не по себé (+ *dat.*); сам не свой. —**to oneself,** себé; про себя́.

one-sided *adj.* односторóнний.

one-story *adj.* одноэтáжный.

one-time *adj.* **1,** (former) бы́вший. **2,** (done only once) рáзовый.

one-volume *adj.* однотóмный.

one-way *adj.* **1,** (moving in one direction) односторóнний. *One-way street,* ýлица с односторóнним движéнием. **2,** (not providing for a return, as of a trip or ticket) в одúн конéц.

onion *n.* лýковица; голóвка лýка; *pl.* лук.

onlooker *n.* зрúтель.

only *adv.* **1,** (merely; exclusively) тóлько; лишь. **2,** (as recently as) ещё: *only last year,* ещё в прóшлом годý. —*adj.* едúнственный: *the only way out,* едúнственный вы́ход. *Only child,* едúнственный ребёнок. *The only one of its kind,* едúнственный в своём рóде. *The only thing I can say,* едúнственно, что я могý сказáть. —*conj.* тóлько; но. *Only be careful!,* тóлько бýдьте осторóжны! —**have only to,** стóит тóлько: *one has only to ask,* стóит тóлько попросúть. —**if only,** *see* **if.** —**not only,** не тóлько. —**only too,** тóлько: *I would be only too happy to do it,* мне бýдет тóлько приятно э́то сдéлать.

onomatopoeia *n.* звукоподражáние.

onrush *n.* напл́ыв; притóк.

onset *n.* начáло; наступлéние.

onslaught *n.* нáтиск.

onstage *adv.* на сцéну: *walk onstage,* выходúть на сцéну.

onto *prep.* на (+ *acc.*): *climb onto the roof,* влезть на кры́шу.

ontology *n.* онтолóгия. —**ontological,** *adj.* онтологúческий.

onus *n.* брéмя; ответственность.

onward *adv.* вперёд. —*adj.* поступáтельный.

onyx *n.* óникс. —*adj.* óниксовый.

oodles *n.pl., colloq.* ýйма.

ooze *v.i.* сочúться.

opacity *n.* непрозрáчность.

opal *n.* опáл. —*adj.* опáловый.

opalescent *adj.* рáдужный.

opaline *adj.* опáловый.

opaque *adj.* непрозрáчный; светонепроницáемый. —**opaqueness,** *n.* непрозрáчность.

open *v.t.* открывáть: *open the window/one's eyes,* открывáть окнó/глазá. *Open fire,* откры́ть огóнь. —*v.i.* **1,** (become open) открывáться. **2,** (spread apart, as of buds) распускáться. **3,** *fol. by* **on** *or* **onto** (give access to) выходúть в *or* на. —*adj.* откры́тый: *the door is open,* дверь откры́та. *Open wound,* откры́тая рáна. *Open question,* откры́тый вопрóс.—*n.* [*usu.* **the open**]. *Out in the open,* на откры́том вóздухе. *Come out/bring out/into the open,* вы́йти/вы́вести нарýжу.

open-air *adj.* откры́тый; на откры́том вóздухе; под откры́тым нéбом.

opener *n. Can opener,* консéрвный нож. —**for openers,** *colloq.* для начáла.

open-hearted *adj.* чистосердéчный. —**open-heartedness,** *n.* чистосердéчие.

open-hearth *adj.* мартеновский: *open-hearth furnace,* мартеновская печь; мартен.
opening *n.* **1,** (act of opening) открытие. **2,** (hole; gap) отверстие. **3,** (vacancy) вакансия. **4,** *theat.* премьера. **5,** *chess* дебют. —*adj.* **1,** (first; initial) первый; начальный. **2,** (introductory) вступительный.
openly *adv.* открыто; в открытую.
open-minded *adj.* непредубеждённый.
open-mouthed *adj.* разинув рот.
openness *n.* прямота; откровенность.
openwork *n.* ажурная работа; ажур; мережка.
opera *n.* опера. —*adj.* оперный. —**opera glasses,** театральный бинокль. —**opera house,** оперный театр.
operate *v.i.* **1,** (function) работать; действовать. **2,** (carry on certain activities) действовать; орудовать. **3,** (perform surgery) оперировать. *Operate on someone,* оперировать кого-нибудь. —*v.t.* **1,** (manage, as an enterprise) управлять; заведовать. **2,** (handle, as a machine) управлять; обращаться с; обслуживать.
operatic *adj.* оперный.
operating *adj.* **1,** *med.* операционный: *operating table,* операционный стол. *Operating room,* операционная. **2,** *econ.* эксплуатационный: *operating costs/expenses,* эксплуатационные расходы.
operation *n.* **1,** (functioning) действие. *Put into operation,* вводить в действие; вводить в строй. *Be in operation,* работать; действовать. *Be out of operation,* не работать; не действовать. **2,** *med.* операция: *heart operation,* операция на сердце. **3,** (handling) управление: *operation of a motor vehicle,* управление автомашиной. **4,** *finance* операция. **5,** *mil.* операция; *pl.* действия.
operational *adj.* **1,** (in use; operating) действующий. **2,** *mil.* оперативный.
operative *adj.* **1,** (in operation) действующий. **2,** (in force; valid) действующий; действительный. **3,** *med.* оперативный. —*n.* агент; сыщик.
operator *n.* **1,** (one who works a machine) оператор. *Lathe operator,* токарь. *Radio operator,* радист. **2,** (telephone operator) телефонистка. **3,** (owner; director) владелец; управляющий.
operetta *n.* оперетта.
ophthalmology *n.* офтальмология. —**ophthalmologist,** *n.* офтальмолог.
opiate *n.* **1,** (drug) наркотик. **2,** (that which dulls the senses) опиум: *the opiate of the masses,* опиум народных масс.
opinion *n.* мнение. *In my opinion,* по моему мнению; по-моему. *Have a high opinion of,* быть высокого мнения о.
opinionated *adj.* упрямый; своевольный.
opium *n.* опиум; опий. *Opium den,* курильня опиума.
opossum *n.* опоссум.
opponent *n.* противник.
opportune *adj.* **1,** (appropriate; suitable) подходящий. **2,** (timely) своевременный.
opportunism *n.* оппортунизм. —**opportunist,** *n.* оппортунист. —**opportunistic,** *adj.* оппортунистический.
opportunity *n.* возможность; (удобный) случай. *At the first convenient opportunity,* при первом удобном случае.
oppose *v.t.* **1,** (resist) противиться. **2,** (be against) выступать против. **3,** (compete against) состязаться с. **4,** (set in opposition) противопоставлять.
opposed *adj.* против: *be strongly opposed to something,* быть решительно против чего-нибудь. *Nine in favor, five opposed,* девять за, пять против. —**as opposed to,** в отличие от.
opposing *adj.* противный: *opposing sides,* противные стороны. *Opposing views,* противоположные взгляды.
opposite *adj.* **1,** (facing) противоположный: *the opposite shore,* противоположный берег. **2,** (reverse) обратный: *in the opposite direction,* в обратном направлении. **3,** (contrary) противоположный: *opposite views,* противоположные взгляды. *The opposite sex,* противоположный пол. —*n.* противоположность; обратное. *He is the exact opposite of his brother,* он полная противоположность своему брату. *Yesterday you were saying the opposite,* вчера вы утверждали обратное. —*adv.* напротив: *sit opposite,* сидеть напротив. —*prep.* против; напротив. *Sit opposite each other,* сидеть друг против друга.
opposition *n.* **1,** (state of being opposed) возражение: *my opposition to this bill,* моё возражение против этого законопроекта. *Announce one's opposition to,* выступить против. **2,** (resistance) противодействие; сопротивление: *meet with opposition,* встретить противодействие/сопротивление. **3,** *polit.* оппозиция. **4,** *astron.* противостояние. —*adj.* оппозиционный.
oppress *v.t.* угнетать; притеснять. —**oppression,** *n.* угнетение; притеснение; гнет.
oppressive *adj.* **1,** (causing distress) гнетущий; угнетающий; томительный. *Oppressive heat,* томительная жара. *Oppressive thoughts,* гнетущие мысли. **2,** (tyrannical) деспотический.
oppressor *n.* угнетатель; притеснитель; насильник.
opprobrious *adj.* **1,** (scurrilous) оскорбительный. **2,** (shameful) позорный. —**opprobrium,** *n.* позор.
opt *v.i.* [*usu.* **opt for**] выбирать; останавливать свой выбор на.
optic *adj.* глазной; зрительный. —**optic nerve,** глазной/зрительный нерв.
optical *adj.* зрительный; оптический. —**optical illusion,** оптический обман; обман зрения.
optician *n.* оптик.
optics *n.* оптика.
optimism *n.* оптимизм. —**optimist,** *n.* оптимист. —**optimistic,** *adj.* оптимистический. *I am optimistic,* я настроен оптимистически.
optimum *adj.* наилучший; оптимальный. —*n.* оптимум.
option *n.* выбор. —**optional,** *adj.* необязательный; факультативный.
optometrist *n.* оптик.
opulent *adj.* пышный; роскошный; богатый. —**opulence,** *n.* пышность.
opus *n.* опус.
or *conj.* **1,** (introducing an alternative) или: *yes or no,* да или нет. **2,** (otherwise; lest) а то; иначе. *Careful, or you'll fall,* осторожно, а то упадёте. —**or so,** около: *an hour or so,* около часа. *In a month or so,* приблизительно через месяц.
oracle *n.* оракул.

oral *adj.* **1,** (spoken) у́стный. **2,** (of the mouth) ротово́й.
orally *adv.* **1,** (verbally) у́стно. **2,** (by mouth) в рот.
orange *n.* апельси́н. —*adj.* **1,** (of or pert. to oranges) апельси́новый; апельси́нный. **2,** (color) ора́нжевый. —**orange blossom,** помера́нцевый цвет. —**orange grove,** апельси́новая ро́ща. —**orange juice,** апельси́новый сок. —**orange tree,** апельси́новое де́рево.
orangutan *also,* **orangutang** *n.* орангута́нг.
orate *v.i.* ора́торствовать; разглаго́льствовать.
oration *n.* речь.
orator *n.* ора́тор. —**oratorical,** *adj.* ора́торский.
oratorio *n.* орато́рия.
oratory *n.* **1,** (art of public speaking) ора́торское иску́сство. **2,** (eloquence) красноре́чие.
orb *n.* шар; сфе́ра.
orbit *n.* орби́та. *Be in orbit,* быть на орби́те. *Go into orbit,* вы́йти на орби́ту. —*v.t. & i.* дви́гаться по орби́те (вокру́г). —**orbital,** *adj.* орбита́льный.
orchard *n.* фрукто́вый сад. *Apple orchard,* я́блоневый сад.
orchestra *n.* **1,** (large group of musicians) орке́стр. **2,** (main floor of a theater) парте́р. —**orchestral,** *adj.* оркестро́вый.
orchestrate *v.t.* оркестрова́ть; инструментова́ть. —**orchestration,** *n.* оркестро́вка; инструменто́вка.
orchid *n.* орхиде́я.
ordain *v.t.* **1,** (decree) предпи́сывать. **2,** (predestine) предопределя́ть. **3,** (confer holy orders upon) посвяща́ть (в духо́вный сан).
ordeal *n.* тяжёлое испыта́ние; мыта́рство; иску́с.
order *n.* **1,** (sequence; methodical arrangement; proper condition) поря́док: *in alphabetical order,* в алфави́тном поря́дке. *Everything is in order,* всё в поря́дке. **2,** (command) прика́з; распоряже́ние. *By order of,* по прика́зу (+ *gen.*). **3,** (direction to buy or sell) зака́з: *rush order,* сро́чный зака́з. **4,** (restaurant portion) по́рция: *two orders of peas,* две по́рции горо́ха. **5,** (warrant; writ) о́рдер. **6,** (scientific classification) отря́д. **7,** (medal) о́рден: *the Order of Lenin,* о́рден Ле́нина. **8,** (regime) поря́док; строй. *The old order,* ста́рый поря́док. **9,** *mil.* поря́док; строй. **10,** (society; brotherhood) о́рден. —*v.t.* **1,** (command; direct) прика́зывать: *order the driver to stop,* приказа́ть води́телю останови́ться. *The doctor ordered me to rest,* врач веле́л мне отдыха́ть. **2,** (place an order for) зака́зывать: *order dinner,* зака́зывать обе́д. *Order something by mail,* вы́писать что́-нибудь по по́чте. **3,** (arrange; manage) устра́ивать: *order one's life,* устра́ивать жизнь. —**call to order,** призыва́ть к поря́дку. —**in order that/to,** для того́, что́бы. —**in short order,** в спе́шном поря́дке. —**on order,** зака́зан(ный). —**on the order of, 1,** (resembling) вро́де (+ *gen.*); наподо́бие (+ *gen.*). **2,** (approximately) поря́дка (+ *gen.*). —**order about,** кома́ндовать над; помыка́ть (+ *instr.*). —**order arms!,** *mil.* к ноге́! —**order out,** показа́ть на дверь; вы́ставить за дверь. —**out of order,** не в поря́дке. *The elevator is out of order,* лифт не рабо́тает. —**to order,** на зака́з: *made to order,* сде́ланный на зака́з.
orderly *adj.* **1,** (tidy) аккура́тный. **2,** (without disruption) организо́ванный; упоря́доченный. *Orderly demonstration,* ми́рная демонстра́ция. —*n.* **1,** *mil.* ордина́рец. **2,** (hospital aide) санита́р.
ordinal number поря́дковое числи́тельное.
ordinance *n.* ука́з; постановле́ние.
ordinarily *adv.* обы́чно.
ordinary *adj.* **1,** (not exceptional) обы́чный; обыкнове́нный. **2,** (somewhat inferior) зауря́дный; посре́дственный. —**out of the ordinary,** из ря́да вон выходя́щий.
ordinate *n., math.* ордина́та.
ordination *n.* посвяще́ние (в духо́вный сан); рукоположе́ние.
ordnance *n.* артилле́рия. *Piece of ordnance,* артиллери́йское ору́дие.
ore *n.* руда́: *iron ore,* желе́зная руда́.
organ *n.* **1,** (musical instrument) орга́н. *Barrel organ,* шарма́нка. **2,** (part of the body) о́рган: *organs of speech,* о́рганы ре́чи. **3,** (organization; body) о́рган. **4,** (publication) о́рган: *press organ,* о́рган печа́ти. *House organ,* многотира́жка. —*adj.* орга́нный: *organ music,* орга́нная му́зыка.
organdy *n.* то́нкая кисея́.
organ grinder шарма́нщик.
organic *adj.* органи́ческий.
organism *n.* органи́зм.
organist *n.* органи́ст.
organization *n.* организа́ция. —**organizational,** *adj.* организацио́нный; организа́торский.
organize *v.t.* устра́ивать; организова́ть. —*v.i.* организова́ться. —**organizer,** *n.* организа́тор.
orgasm *n.* орга́зм.
orgy *n.* о́ргия; разгу́л. —**orgiastic,** *adj.* разгу́льный.
orient *v.t.* ориенти́ровать.
Orient *n.* Восто́к.
Oriental *adj.* восто́чный. —*n.* уроже́нец Восто́ка. —**Orientalist,** *n.* востокове́д.
orientation *n.* **1,** (bearings) ориента́ция; ориенти́ровка. **2,** (leaning) ориента́ция.
orifice *n.* отве́рстие.
origin *n.* **1,** (beginning; original source) происхожде́ние; возникнове́ние. *Have its origin in,* вести́ своё нача́ло от. **2,** (ancestry) происхожде́ние: *of Russian origin,* ру́сского происхожде́ния; ру́сский, по происхожде́нию.
original *adj.* **1,** (first; earliest) первонача́льный: *lose its original shape,* теря́ть первонача́льную фо́рму. **2,** (not imitated; creative) оригина́льный. **3,** (being that from which a copy is made) по́длинный. —*n.* по́длинник; оригина́л: *read in the original,* чита́ть в по́длиннике *or* в оригина́ле. —**original sin,** первоpо́дный грех.
originality *n.* оригина́льность.
originally *adv.* **1,** (at first) снача́ла; первонача́льно. **2,** (by origin) ро́дом.
originate *v.t.* создава́ть; порожда́ть. —*v.i.* зарожда́ться; брать нача́ло. *The idea originated with him,* э́то у него́ зароди́лась така́я мысль. —**originator,** *n.* а́втор; созда́тель.
oriole *n.* **1,** (European bird) и́волга. **2,** (American bird) трупиа́л.
Orion *n.* Орио́н.
ornament *n.* украше́ние. —*v.t.* украша́ть. —**ornamental,** *adj.* декорати́вный. —**ornamentation,** *n.* украше́ние.
ornate *adj.* витиева́тый; вы́чурный.
ornery *adj., colloq.* злой; упря́мый; сварли́вый.
ornithology *n.* орнитоло́гия. —**ornithological,**

adj. орнитологи́ческий. —**ornithologist,** *n.* орнито́лог.

orotund *adj.* **1,** (sonorous) зву́чный. **2,** (pompous) напы́щенный.

orphan *n.* сирота́. —*adj.* **1,** (for orphans) сиро́тский. **2,** (orphaned) осироте́лый. —*v.t.* де́лать сирото́й. *Be orphaned,* (о)сироте́ть.

orphanage *n.* сиро́тский дом; сиро́тский прию́т.

orphanhood *n.* сиро́тство.

orthodontia *n.* ортодонти́я.

orthodox *adj.* **1,** (pert. to the Orthodox Church) правосла́вный. **2,** (adhering to traditional practice) правове́рный; ортодокса́льный. —**Orthodox Church,** правосла́вная це́рковь.

orthodoxy *n.* **1,** (religion of the Orthodox Church) правосла́вие. **2,** (conformity) ортодо́ксия.

orthography *n.* орфогра́фия; правописа́ние. —**orthographic,** *adj.* орфографи́ческий.

orthopedic *adj.* ортопеди́ческий. —**orthopedics,** *n.* ортопе́дия. —**orthopedist,** *n.* ортопе́д.

ortolan *n.* садо́вая овся́нка.

oryx *n.* сернобы́к.

oscillate *v.i.* кача́ться; колеба́ться. —**oscillation,** *n.* кача́ние; колеба́ние. —**oscillator,** *n.* генера́тор; осцилля́тор; вибра́тор.

oscillograph *n.* осцилло́граф.

oscilloscope *n.* осциллоско́п.

osier *n.* и́ва.

osmium *n.* о́смий.

osmosis *n.* о́смос.

osprey *n.* скопа́.

osseous *adj.* ко́стный; кости́стый.

ossify *v.i.* костене́ть. —**ossification,** *n.* окостене́ние. —**ossified,** *adj.* окостене́лый.

ostensible *adj.* **1,** (apparent) ви́димый. **2,** (professed) официа́льный. —**ostensibly,** *adv.* я́кобы.

ostentation *n.* мишура́. —**ostentatious,** *adj.* показно́й; мишу́рный.

osteology *n.* остеоло́гия. —**osteologist,** *n.* остео́лог.

ostracize *v.t.* изгоня́ть. —**ostracism,** *n.* изгна́ние; остраки́зм.

ostrich *n.* стра́ус. —*adj.* стра́усовый: *ostrich egg/feather,* стра́усовое яйцо́/перо́.

other *adj.* **1,** *preceded by* **the,** A (being the remaining one of two) друго́й: *the other hand/room/car,* друга́я рука́/ко́мната/маши́на. B, (being the remaining ones of many) остальны́е: *the other children,* остальны́е де́ти. **2,** (different) друго́й; ино́й. *In other countries,* в други́х стра́нах. *In other words,* други́ми слова́ми; ины́ми слова́ми. *Somehow or other,* так и́ли ина́че. *For some reason or other,* по той и́ли ино́й причи́не. **3,** (additional) *rendered by* ещё: *have you any other brothers?,* у вас есть ещё бра́тья? **4,** (opposite; reverse) обра́тный; друго́й. *The other side of the coin,* обра́тная сторона́ моне́ты. *On the other side of the river,* по ту сто́рону (*or* на друго́й стороне́) реки́. —*n. & pron.* [*usu.* **the others**] други́е; остальны́е. —**each other,** *see* **each.** —**none other than,** не кто ино́й, как. —**other than,** кро́ме. —**other things being equal,** при про́чих ра́вных усло́виях. —**some other time,** ка́к-нибудь в друго́й раз. —**the other day,** на днях. —**the other way round,** как раз наоборо́т.

otherwise *adv.* **1,** (differently) ина́че; по-друго́му. **2,** (if not) ина́че; а то; в проти́вном слу́чае. **3,** (in all other respects) в остально́м.

otter *n.* вы́дра. *Sea otter,* морска́я вы́дра; кала́н.

ottoman *n.* **1,** (divan) оттома́нка; тахта́. **2,** (footstool) скаме́йка для ног.

ouch *interj.* ай!; ой!

ought *v.aux. Generally rendered by* до́лжен, сле́довать, *or the subjunctive mood. He ought to be grateful to you,* он до́лжен быть вам благода́рен. *She ought to be here at any moment,* она́ должна́ прийти́ в любо́й моме́нт. *You ought to see a doctor,* вам сле́дует (*or* вам бы) пойти́ к врачу́.

ounce *n.* **1,** (unit of weight) у́нция. **2,** (small amount; bit) ка́пля; чу́точка.

our *poss. adj.* наш: *our house,* наш дом; *our street,* на́ша у́лица; *our friends,* на́ши друзья́.

ours *poss. pron.* наш. *A friend of ours,* оди́н наш друг; оди́н из на́ших друзе́й. *Their room is on the first floor and ours is on the second,* их ко́мната на пе́рвом этаже́, а на́ша – на второ́м.

ourselves *pers. pron.* **1,** *used for emphasis* (мы) са́ми: *we don't know ourselves,* мы са́ми не зна́ем. **2,** *used reflexively* себя́: *we underestimated ourselves,* мы недооцени́ли себя́. —**by ourselves,** одни́.

oust *v.t.* вытесня́ть; выгоня́ть. —**ouster,** *n.* вытесне́ние.

out *adj.* **1,** (not in; away): *he is out,* он вы́шел; его́ нет. *Out to lunch,* ушёл обе́дать. **2,** (not turned on) вы́ключен: *the light is out,* свет вы́ключен. **3,** (ended): *before the week is out,* до конца́ неде́ли. **4,** (not to be considered) исключён: *London is out,* Ло́ндон исключен. **5,** (no longer in style): *narrow ties are out,* у́зкие га́лстуки вы́шли из мо́ды. **6,** (known) раскры́т: *the secret is out,* секре́т раскры́т; секре́т стал всем изве́стен. **7,** (unconscious) без созна́ния. **8,** *colloq.* (having lost) в про́игрыше: *I am out 100 dollars,* у меня́ про́игрыш в сто до́лларов. —*adv.* нару́жу. ♦*Usu. rendered by a prefixed verb: go out,* выходи́ть; *take out,* вынима́ть; *throw out,* выбра́сывать; *leave out,* пропуска́ть; *start out,* отправля́ться; *break out,* вспы́хивать; *fill out,* заполня́ть. —*prep.* в; из: *look out the window,* смотре́ть в окно́; выгля́дывать из окна́. *Throw something out the window,* вы́бросить что́-нибудь в окно́. *Walk out the door,* выходи́ть в дверь. —*interj.* вон! —**on the outs,** в ссо́ре; в ко́нтрах. —**out for,** жа́ждущий (+ *gen.*): *he is out for blood/revenge,* он жа́ждет кро́ви/ме́сти. —**out of, 1,** (from within) из: *walk out of the room,* вы́йти из ко́мнаты; *drink out of a glass,* пить из стака́на. **2,** (through) из: *lean out of the window,* высо́вываться из окна́. **3,** (beyond the limits of) за; вне: *out of town,* за́ городом; в отъе́зде. *Out of danger,* вне опа́сности. *Out of turn,* вне о́череди. *Pass out of sight,* скрыва́ться и́з виду. **4,** (from; made of) из: *made out of wood,* сде́ланный из де́рева. **5,** (from; as a result of) из: *out of curiosity,* из любопы́тства. *Out of spite,* назло́; со зла. **6,** (from among) из: *in 99 cases out of 100,* в девяно́сто девяти́ слу́чаях из ста. **7,** (not having) без: *out of work,* без рабо́ты. *We are out of gas,* у нас вы́шел *or* ко́нчился бензи́н. **8,** (not in a condition of) не в: *out of order,* не в поря́дке; *out of step,* не в но́гу; *out of sorts,* не в ду́хе.

out-and-out *adj.* отъя́вленный: *an out-and-out liar,* отъя́вленный лгун. *Out-and-out lie,* я́вная ложь.

outargue *v.t.* переспóрить.
outboard motor подвеснóй мотóр.
outbound *adj.* уходя́щий; отбывáющий.
outbreak *n.* вспы́шка. *Outbreak of war,* начáло *or* возникновéние войны́.
outbuilding *n.* надвóрная пострóйка.
outburst *n.* взрыв; вспы́шка.
outcast *n.* изгнáнник; пáрия; отвéрженный. —*adj.* отвéрженный.
outclass *v.t.* превосходи́ть; оставля́ть далекó позади́.
outcome *n.* исхóд; результáт.
outcry *n.* **1,** (shout) крик; вы́крик. **2,** (public protest) шум.
outdated *adj.* устарéлый; устарéвший.
outdistance *v.t.* обгоня́ть; перегоня́ть; опережáть.
outdo *v.t.* превосходи́ть. *He was not to be outdone,* он не остáлся в долгу́. —**outdo oneself,** превосходи́ть (самогó) себя́.
outdoor *adj.* на откры́том вóздухе. —**outdoors,** *adv.* **1,** (location) на дворé; на (откры́том) вóздухе. **2,** (motion) на у́лицу; нару́жу; на вóздух.
outdrink *v.t.* перепивáть.
outer *adj.* **1,** (external) внéшний; нару́жный: *outer covering,* внéшняя/нару́жная оболóчка. *Outer garments,* вéрхняя одéжда. *Outer Mongolia,* Внéшняя Монгóлия. **2,** (farther from the center) дáльний; крáйний. *Outer limits,* крáйние предéлы. —**outer space,** кóсмос.
outermost *adj.* сáмый дáльний от середи́ны; крáйний.
outfit *n.* **1,** (set of equipment) снаряжéние. **2,** (set of clothing) наря́д. **3,** *colloq.* (group) гру́ппа; пáртия; компáния. —*v.t.* снаряжáть; экипировáть.
outflank *v.t.* обходи́ть.
outflow *n.* истечéние; утéчка.
outfox *v.t.* перехитри́ть.
outgoing *adj.* **1,** (going out; leaving) уходя́щий; исходя́щий. **2,** (extroverted) общи́тельный; компанéйский.
outgrow *v.t.* **1,** (surpass in growth) перерастáть. **2,** (grow too big to wear) вырастáть из. **3,** (grow too old for) стать сли́шком больши́м для. **4,** (get rid of in the course of growing up) избавля́ться от; отдéлываться от.
outgrowth *n.* **1,** (excrescence) отрóсток; óтпрыск. **2,** (consequence) продýкт; результáт.
outguess *v.t.* перехитри́ть.
outhouse *n.* отхóжее мéсто.
outing *n.* прогу́лка; похóд; экску́рсия.
outlandish *adj.* дикóвинный.
outlast *v.t.* **1,** (remain in existence longer than) переживáть. **2,** (overcome after a long struggle) переси́ливать.
outlaw *n.* банди́т; разбóйник. —*v.t.* запрещáть; объявля́ть вне закóна.
outlay *n.* расхóд; трáта.
outlet *n.* **1,** (passage for letting something out) выходнóе *or* выпускнóе отвéрстие. *Outlet to the sea,* вы́ход к мóрю. **2,** (means of release or expression) вы́ход; отду́шина. **3,** (electrical outlet) (штéпсельная) розéтка. **4,** (commercial market) ры́нок.
outline *n.* **1,** (line forming the outer edge) очертáния; кóнтур. **2,** (sketch) наброćок; эски́з. **3,** (short summary) схéма. —*v.t.* **1,** (sketch) очéрчивать. **2,** (describe in general terms) намечáть. —**in broad outline,** в óбщих чертáх.
outlive *v.t.* переживáть.
outlook *n.* **1,** (prospect) ви́ды; перспекти́вы. **2,** (mental attitude) кругозóр; воззрéние.
outlying *adj.* окрáинный; перифери́йный.
outmoded *adj.* устарéлый; устарéвший.
outnumber *v.t.* превосходи́ть чи́сленностью.
out-of-date *adj.* устарéлый.
out-of-the-way *adj.* отдалённый; захолу́стный.
outpace *v.t.* опережáть; обгоня́ть.
outpatient *n.* амбулатóрный (*or* приходя́щий) больнóй.
outplay *v.t.* переигрывать.
outpost *n.* **1,** *mil.* аванпóст; форпóст. **2,** (outlying settlement) форпóст; окрáина.
outpouring *n.* излия́ние.
output *n.* продýкция; вы́пуск; вы́работка.
outrage *n.* **1,** (vicious act) безобрáзие; бесчи́нство; надругáтельство. *It's an outrage!,* (э́то) безобрáзие!; (э́то) возмути́тельно! **2,** (resentful anger) возмущéние; негодовáние. —*v.t.* **1,** (offend) оскорбля́ть. **2,** (infuriate) возмущáть. *Be outraged,* возмущáться.
outrageous *adj.* **1,** (grossly offensive) возмути́тельный; вопию́щий. **2,** (exorbitant) непомéрный: *outrageous demands,* непомéрные трéбования. *Outrageous prices,* бéшеные цéны. —**outrageously,** *adv.* возмути́тельно.
outrank *v.t.* быть стáрше чем (по звáнию).
outrigger *n.* утлéгарь.
outright *adj.* **1,** (unqualified) безоговóрочный. *Outright refusal,* прямóй откáз. *Outright grant,* безвозврáтная ссу́да. **2,** (total) пóлный: *an outright loss,* пóлная ги́бель. **3,** (out-and-out) отъя́вленный. *An outright lie,* я́вная ложь. —*adv.* **1,** (straight to one's face) прямо (в лицó). **2,** (on the spot) на мéсте; наповáл.
outrun *v.t.* **1,** (run faster than) обгоня́ть; перегоня́ть; опережáть. **2,** (elude by running) убежáть от. **3,** (exceed) превышáть.
outsell *v.t.* продавáться лу́чше чем.
outset *n.* начáло. *At the outset,* сначáла. *From the outset,* с сáмого начáла.
outshine *v.t.* затмевáть.
outside *adv.* **1,** (location) на у́лице; на дворé: *it's cold outside,* на у́лице *or* на дворé хóлодно. **2,** (motion) на у́лицу; нару́жу. *Let's go outside,* пойдём на у́лицу; давáйте вы́йдем на у́лицу. *Come in from outside,* войти́ с у́лицы. —*adj.* **1,** (external) внéшний; нару́жный. **2,** (coming from without) посторóнний: *outside help,* посторóнняя пóмощь. —*n.* нару́жная сторонá. *On the outside,* снару́жи. —*prep.* вне; за предéлами (+ *gen.*). —**at the outside,** сáмое бóльшее. —**outside of,** крóме.
outsider *n.* **1,** (one not part of a group) посторóнний. **2,** *sports* аутсáйдер.
outskirts *n.pl.* окрáина.
outsmart *v.t.* перехитри́ть. *Outsmart oneself,* перехитри́ть самогó себя́.
outspoken *adj.* прямóй; откровéнный.
outspread *adj.* распростёртый.
outstanding *adj.* **1,** (distinguished; extraordinary) выдаю́щийся. **2,** (unsettled, as of an issue) спóрный. **3,** (unpaid) неуплáченный.

outstretched *adj.* распростёртый.
outstrip *v.t.* обгонять; опережать.
outtalk *v.t.* переговорить.
outward *adj.* внешний; наружный. —*adv.* [*also,* **outwards**] наружу. —**outwardly,** *adv.* внешне; снаружи; на вид.
outwear *v.t.* изнашивать.
outweigh *v.t.* перевешивать.
outwit *v.t.* перехитрить.
ouzel *n.* **1,** (water ouzel) оляпка. **2,** (ring ouzel) белозобый дрозд.
oval *adj.* овальный. —*n.* овал.
ovary *n.* **1,** *anat.* яичник. **2,** *bot.* завязь.
ovate *adj.* яйцевидный.
ovation *n.* овация. *Give an ovation to,* устроить овацию (+ *dat.*).
oven *n.* духовка; печь.
over *prep.* **1,** (above) над: *fly over the city,* пролететь над городом; *lean over the cradle,* наклоняться над колыбелью. *Appear over the horizon,* показаться из-за горизонта. **2,** (higher than) выше: *the water was over our heads,* вода была выше головы. **3,** (above and across) через: *jump over the fence,* перепрыгнуть через забор; *lean over the railing,* перегибаться через перила; *look over the edge,* заглянуть через край. **4,** (along the surface of) по: *run one's fingers over the keyboard,* пробежать пальцами по клавиатуре. **5,** (so as to cover) поверх; на. *Wear a sweater over one's shirt,* надеть свитер поверх рубашки. *Pull the blanket over oneself,* натянуть на себя одеяло. *Pull one's hat down over one's eyes,* надвинуть шляпу на глаза. **6,** (more than) больше; свыше: *over an hour,* больше часа; *over 2000 dollars,* свыше двух тысяч долларов. *People over forty,* те, кому за сорок. **7,** (on; through the medium of) по: *over the radio,* по радио. **8,** (about) о: *argue over something,* спорить о чём-нибудь. *Fight over a girl,* драться из-за девушки. **9,** (while engaged in or partaking of something) за (+ *instr.*): *discuss the question over dinner,* обсуждать вопрос за обедом. **10,** (during) в течение: *over the next ten years,* в течение ближайших десяти лет. **11,** *Victory over someone,* победа над кем-нибудь; *advantage over someone,* преимущество перед кем-нибудь. —*adv. Usu. rendered by a prefixed verb.* **1,** (once more; again) пере-: *do over,* переделывать. **2,** (across; transferring) пере-: *cross over,* переходить; *hand over,* передавать. *Walk over to the window,* переходить к окну. *Come over and see us,* зайдите к нам. **3,** (inverting; overturning) пере-: *turn over,* перевёртывать(ся); *roll over,* переваливаться. *Knock over,* опрокидывать. **4,** (thoroughly; through) об-; про-: *talk over,* обсуждать; *think over,* обдумывать; продумывать; *read over,* прочитать. **5,** (cursorily) про-: *look/glance over,* просматривать. **6,** *after numbers* больше; выше. *Children five and over,* дети от пяти лет и больше. —*adj.* оконченный: *the meeting is over,* собрание окончено. *The war is over,* война окончилась. —**all over, 1,** (everywhere) всюду. *All over the world,* по всему миру. *From all over the world,* со всех концов мира. *I ache all over,* у меня всё тело болит. **2,** (finished) кончен: *it's all over,* всё кончено. *It's all over between them,* между ними всё кончено. **3,** *often fol. by* **again** (again completely) заново. *Start all over (again),* начинать всё сначала. —**over again,** сначала; снова. —**over against,** против. —**over and above,** сверх; не считая. —**over and over,** снова и снова. —**over here,** здесь; тут. —**over there,** вон там.
overabundance *n.* избыток. —**overabundant,** *adj.* избыточный.
overact *v.i.* переигрывать.
overage[1] (**o**-ve-rij) *n.* избыток; излишек.
overage[2] (o-ver-**ayj**) *adj.* вышедший из возраста: *he is overage,* он вышел из возраста.
overall *adj.* общий: *overall length,* общая длина. *Overall impression,* общее впечатление.
overalls *n.pl.* рабочий халат; комбинезон; спецодежда; роба.
overbearing *adj.* властный.
overblown *adj.* раздутый.
overboard *adv.* за борт; за бортом. *Toss overboard,* выбросить за борт. —**go overboard,** *colloq.* перегнуть палку. —**man overboard!,** человек за бортом! —**wash overboard,** смывать (*impers.*): *he was washed overboard,* его смыло волной (с судна).
overburden *v.t.* перегружать; переобременять.
overcast *adj.* облачный; хмурый; пасмурный. —*n.* облачность. —*v.t., sewing* обмётывать.
overcharge *v.t.* **1,** (charge too high a price) брать лишнее с. **2,** (overload, as a battery) перезаряжать.
overcoat *n.* пальто.
overcome *v.t.* **1,** (surmount; get over) преодолевать; превозмогать. **2,** (defeat) одолевать; побороть. **3,** (seize, as of an emotion) одолевать; охватывать.
overconfident *adj.* чрезмерно уверенный. —**overconfidence,** *n.* чрезмерная уверенность.
overcook *v.t.* переваривать; пережаривать.
overcritical *adj.* придирчивый.
overcrowd *v.t.* переполнять. —**overcrowded,** *adj.* тесный; переполненный; скученный. —**overcrowding,** *n.* теснота; переполнение; скученность.
overdo *v.t.* **1,** (carry too far) утрировать. **2,** = **overcook.** —**overdo it, 1,** (overexert oneself) переутомляться. **2,** (go too far) перебарщивать; зарываться; перестараться; пересаливать.
overdone *adj.* **1,** (done to excess) утрированный. **2,** (overcooked) пережаренный.
overdose *n.* слишком большая доза; чрезмерная доза.
overdraft *n.* превышение кредита (в банке).
overdraw *v.t.* превышать остаток (счёта в банке).
overdress *v.t.* одевать слишком нарядно.
overdue *adj.* **1,** *comm.* просроченный. **2,** (late): *the train is overdue,* поезд опаздывает *or* запаздывает.
overeat *v.i.* переедать; объедаться.
overemphasize *v.t.* преувеличивать.
overestimate *v.t.* переоценивать. —**overestimation,** *n.* переоценка.
overexert *v.t.* перенапрягать. —**overexertion,** *n.* перенапряжение.
overexpenditure *n.* перерасход.
overexpose *v.t., photog.* передерживать. —**overexposure,** *n., photog.* передержка.
overfeed *v.t.* перекармливать; обкармливать; закармливать.
overfill *v.t.* переполнять.
overflow *v.i.* литься через край; переливаться

чéрез край. *The bathtub overflowed,* водá в вáнне перелилáсь чéрез край. —*v.t.* вы́ступить из: *overflow its banks,* вы́ступить из берегóв. —*n.* **1,** (overflowing) разли́в. **2,** (that which overflows) изли́шек воды́. —*adj. An overflow crowd,* пóлный зал. —**filled to overflowing,** перепóлненный.

overfulfill *v.t.* перевыполня́ть. —**overfulfillment,** *n.* перевыполнéние.

overgrown *adj.* **1,** (covered, as with vegetation) зарóсший: *the field is overgrown with weeds,* пóле заросло́ сóрной травóй. **2,** (grown excessively) перерóсший.

overhand *adj. & adv., sports* свéрху.

overhang *v.t.* нависáть над; висéть над.

overhaul *v.t.* **1,** (examine for possible revision) пересмáтривать. **2,** (renovate) ремонти́ровать. **3,** (overtake) догоня́ть. —*n.* ремóнт.

overhead *adv.* наверху́; над головóй. *Directly overhead,* над сáмой головóй. —*adj.* **1,** (elevated) возду́шный; надзéмный. **2,** (suspended) подвеснóй. **3,** *comm.* (of costs) накладны́е. —*n.* накладны́е расхóды.

overhear *v.t.* подслу́шать; услы́шать.

overheat *v.t.* перегревáть. —*v.i.* перегревáться.

overindulge *v.t.* баловáть; потвóрствовать. —*v.i.* переедáть; объедáться.

overindulgence *n.* **1,** (excessive leniency) баловствó. **2,** (immoderation) неумéренность.

overindulgent *adj.* **1,** (too lenient) сли́шком снисходи́тельный. **2,** (immoderate) неумéренный.

overjoyed *adj.* вне себя́ от рáдости.

overkill *n.* многокрáтное уничтожéние.

overland *adj.* сухопу́тный; назéмный. —*adv.* по су́ше; на су́ше.

overlap *v.i.* части́чно совпадáть.

overlay *v.t.* **1,** (place over) наклáдывать. **2,** (coat; cover) покрывáть. —*n.* покры́шка.

overload *v.t.* перегружáть. —*n.* перегру́зка.

overlook *v.t.* **1,** (fail to notice) просмотрéть. **2,** (lose sight of) упускáть и́з виду. **3,** (ignore) смотрéть сквозь пáльцы на. **4,** (afford a view of) выходи́ть в *or* на. **5,** (rise above) возвышáться над.

overly *adv.* чрезмéрно; сли́шком.

overnight *adv.* **1,** (for the night) нá ночь: *stay overnight,* остáться нá ночь. **2,** (very quickly; suddenly) моментáльно. —*adj.* **1,** (lasting or staying through the night): *overnight stop,* ночлéг. *Overnight guests,* гóсти, остаю́щиеся нá ночь. **2,** (very rapid; instant) моментáльный.

overpass *n.* путепровóд; эстакáда.

overpay *v.t.* переплáчивать. —**overpayment,** *n.* переплáта.

overplay *v.t.* **1,** (overact) переи́грывать. **2,** (exaggerate) преувели́чивать. —**overplay one's hand,** перестарáться; зайти́ сли́шком далекó.

overpopulate *v.t.* перенаселя́ть. —**overpopulated,** *adj.* перенаселённый. —**overpopulation,** *n.* перенаселéние; перенаселённость.

overpower *v.t.* переси́ливать. —**overpowering,** *adj.* подавля́ющий; неотрази́мый.

overproduction *n.* перепроизвóдство.

overrate *v.t.* переоцéнивать.

override *v.t.* **1,** (disregard; wave aside) отмáхиваться от. **2,** (nullify, as a Presidential veto) аннули́ровать.

overriding *adj.* глáвный; важнéйший; решáющий.

overripe *adj.* перезрéлый.

overrule *v.t.* **1,** (set aside) отменя́ть; аннули́ровать. **2,** (disallow) отклоня́ть; отвергáть.

overrun *v.t.* **1,** (invade and conquer) завоёвывать: *overrun a country,* завоевáть странý. *Overrun the enemy's defenses,* прорвáть оборóну проти́вника. **2,** (swarm over) наводня́ть. *Be overrun with mice,* кишéть мышáми. —*n.* превышéние: *cost overrun,* превышéние стóимости.

overseas *adj.* замóрский; заграни́чный. —*adv.* **1,** (location) зá морем; за грани́цей. **2,** (motion) зá море; за грани́цу. —**overseas cap,** *mil.* пилóтка.

oversee *v.t.* надзирáть за; наблюдáть за. —**overseer,** *n.* надзирáтель; надсмóтрщик.

overshadow *v.t.* затмевáть; заслоня́ть.

overshoe *n.* галóша.

overshoot *v.t. Overshoot one's target; overshoot a landing field,* давáть перелёт.

oversight *n.* **1,** (failure to notice something) недосмóтр; просмóтр; упущéние. **2,** (supervision) надзóр.

oversimplify *v.t.* упрощáть. —**oversimplification,** *n.* упрощéн(че)ство.

oversize *adj.* бóльше обы́чного размéра. *Also,* **oversized.**

oversleep *v.i.* просыпáть.

overstate *v.t.* преувели́чивать. —**overstatement,** *n.* преувеличéние.

overstay *v.t., in* **overstay one's welcome,** загости́ться.

overstep *v.t.* переступáть.

oversupply *n.* избы́ток.

overt *adj.* откры́тый; неприкры́тый; я́вный.

overtake *v.t.* **1,** (catch up with) догоня́ть. **2,** (befall) постигáть.

overtax *v.t.* **1,** (tax too heavily) обременя́ть сли́шком высóкими налóгами. **2,** (overexert) надрывáть; надлáмывать.

overthrow *v.t.* свергáть. —*n.* сверж́ение.

overtime *n.* **1,** (extra time worked) сверхурóчное врéмя. **2,** (extra work) сверхурóчная рабóта. **3,** (payment for same) сверхурóчные. **4,** *sports* дополни́тельное врéмя. —*adj.* сверхурóчный. —*adv.* сверхурóчно.

overtone *n.* **1,** *music* обертóн. **2,** *usu. pl.* (implications) скры́тые намёки.

overture *n.* **1,** *music* увертю́ра. **2,** *usu. pl.* (offer to negotiate) предложéние: *peace overtures,* ми́рные предложéния. **3,** *usu. pl.* (flirtatious advances) заи́грывания; ухáживания.

overturn *v.t.* опроки́дывать. —*v.i.* опроки́дываться; перевёртываться.

overview *n.* обзóр.

overweening *adj.* **1,** (arrogant) высокомéрный. **2,** (excessive) чрезмéрный.

overweight *adj.* вéсящий бóльше (*or* вы́ше) полóженного вéса. *I am ten pounds overweight,* я вéшу на дéсять фу́нтов бóльше/вы́ше полóженного.

overwhelm *v.t.* **1,** (overpower; crush) разбивáть; (раз)громи́ть; сокрушáть. **2,** (swamp) завáливать: *overwhelmed with work,* завáлен рабóтой. **3,** (overcome, as with emotion) охвáтывать. *Overwhelmed with grief,* уби́тый гóрем.

overwhelming *adj.* подавля́ющий. *Overwhelming*

majority, подавляющее большинство.
overwind *v.t.* перевёртывать (часы).
overwork *v.t.* переутомлять. —*v.i.* переутомляться; перерабатывать. —*n.* переутомление.
oviduct *n.* яйцевод.
oviparous *adj.* яйцекладущий; яйцеродный.
ovulation *n.* овуляция.
ovule *n.* **1,** *biol.* яйцеклетка. **2,** *bot.* семяпочка.
ovum *n.* яйцо.
owe *v.t.* **1,** (be indebted in the sum of) *rendered by* должен: *he owes me five dollars,* он мне должен пять долларов. *You owe ten rubles,* с вас (приходиться) десять рублей. *I owe you an apology,* я должен извиниться перед вами. **2,** (be obligated for) *rendered by* обязан: *I owe everything to my teacher,* я всем обязан моему учителю.
owing to из-за; благодаря (+ *dat.*); вследствие (+ *gen.*); по причине (+ *gen.*).
owl *n.* сова. —**owlish,** *adj.* совиный.
own *v.t.* владеть: *own a house/car,* владеть домом/машиной. —*v.i.* [*usu.* **own up**] признаться (во всём). —*adj.* собственный: *see with one's own eyes,* видеть (что-нибудь) собственными глазами. *A house of one's own,* свой собственный дом. *Go one's own way,* идти своей дорогой. *She makes all her own clothes,* она шьёт себе всё сама. —**come into one's own,** вступить в свой права. —**hold one's own,** держаться. *He can hold his own against the best players,* он может поспорить с лучшими игроками. —**on one's own, 1,** (alone; independently) в одиночку; самостоятельно. *Leave on one's own,* предоставлять самому себе. **2,** (on one's own initiative) по собственному почину *or* побуждению. —**to each his own,** каждому своё.
owner *n.* владелец; собственник; хозяин. —**ownerless,** *adj.* бесхозяйный. —**ownership,** *n.* владение; собственность.
ox *n.* вол.
oxalic acid щавелевая кислота.
oxeye daisy нивяник.
oxford *n.* полуботинок. *Also,* **oxford shoe.**
oxidation *n.* окисление.
oxide *n.* окись; окисел. *Ferric oxide,* окись железа. *Ferrous oxide,* закись железа.
oxidize *v.t.* окислять. —*v.i.* окисляться.
oxygen *n.* кислород. —*adj.* кислородный. —**oxygen mask,** кислородная маска. —**oxygen tent,** кислородная палатка.
oyster *n.* устрица. —*adj.* устричный: *oyster shell,* устричная раковина.
ozocerite *n.* озокерит.
ozone *n.* озон.

P

P, p шестнадцатая буква английского алфавита.
pa *n., colloq.* папа.
pace *n.* **1,** (step) шаг: *step off twenty paces,* отсчитывать двадцать шагов. **2,** (rate of speed or progress) темп. *At a brisk/snail's pace,* быстрым/черепашьим шагом. **3,** (gait of a horse) иноходь. —*v.t.* **1,** (walk back and forth across) расхаживать по; прохаживаться по. **2,** *fol. by* **off** (measure by paces) отмерять. **3,** *fol. by* **oneself** (set a pace for oneself) задавать себе темп. —*v.i.* шагать; расхаживать. —**keep pace with,** идти в ногу с; идти наравне с; поспевать за. —**off the pace,** позади: *keep off the pace,* держаться позади. —**put through one's paces,** подвергать испытаниям. —**set the pace,** задавать темп.
pacemaker *n., med.* стимулятор сердца.
pacer *n.* иноходец.
pachyderm *n.* толстокожее животное.
pacific *adj.* **1,** (peaceful; calm) спокойный; тихий. **2,** (not warlike) мирный; миролюбивый. —**Pacific Ocean,** Тихий океан.
pacification *n.* умиротворение.
pacifier *n.* **1,** (one who pacifies) миротворец. **2,** (for a baby to suck on) соска.
pacifism *n.* пацифизм. —**pacifist,** *n.* пацифист. —*adj.* пацифистский.
pacify *v.t.* **1,** (quiet; calm) усмирять. **2,** (establish peace in) умиротворять.
pack *n.* **1,** (carried by a person) котомка; ранец. **2,** (carried by an animal) вьюк. **3,** (of cigarettes) пачка. **4,** (of cards) колода. **5,** (of dogs, wolves, etc.) стая; свора. **6,** (gang; band) шайка; свора. **7,** *med.* обёртывание. **8,** *in* **pack of lies,** сплошная ложь. —*v.t.* **1,** (put in a suitcase; fill, as a suitcase) укладывать; упаковывать. **2,** (put in a box, bag, etc.) упаковывать; запаковывать. **3,** (cram) заполнять; набивать. *The hall was packed,* зал был битком набит. *Play to packed houses,* делать полные сборы; идти с аншлагом. **4,** *fol. by* **down** (press down firmly) уплотнять. **5,** *fol. by* **off** (send off) отсылать. —*v.i.* **1,** *often fol. by* **up** (pack one's things) укладываться; упаковываться. **2,** (form into a solid mass) уплотняться. —**send packing,** спроваживать; выпроваживать.
package *n.* **1,** (bundle) пакет. **2,** (parcel) посылка. —*v.t.* фасовать.
packaging *n.* фасовка; расфасовка.
pack animal вьючное животное.
packer *n.* упаковщик.
packet *n.* **1,** (small package) пакет; пачка. **2,** (ship) пакетбот.

packing *n.* **1,** (act) упакóвка. **2,** (material) набивка. —*adj.* упакóвочный. —**packing case,** упакóвочный я́щик. —**packing house,** консéрвная фáбрика.
packsaddle *n.* вью́чное седлó.
pact *n.* пакт; договóр.
pad *n.* **1,** (cushionlike object) подýшечка. **2,** (writing tablet) блокнóт. **3,** (floating leaf, as of a lily) лист. **4,** (stamp pad) подýшечка для штемпелéй. —*v.t.* **1,** (line with padding) подбивáть вáтой *or* волосáми. **2,** (expand unduly) раздувáть; размáзывать.
padding *n.* набивка; проклáдка.
paddle *n.* **1,** (oar) веслó; гребóк. **2,** (stick for administering punishment) пáлка. **3,** *sports* (racket) ракéтка. —*v.t.* **1,** (row) грести́. **2,** (spank) бить пáлкой. —**paddle boat,** колёсный парохóд. —**paddle wheel,** гребнóе колесó.
paddock *n.* загóн.
paddy *n.* [*usu.* **rice paddy**] ри́совое пóле.
padlock *n.* ви́сячий замóк. —*v.t.* запирáть на ви́сячий замóк.
paean *n.* хвалéбная песнь.
pagan *n.* язы́чник. —*adj.* язы́ческий. —**paganism,** *n.* язы́чество.
page *n.* **1,** (of a book, newspaper, etc.) страни́ца. **2,** (attendant) паж. —*v.t.* (call; summon) вызывáть.
pageant *n.* **1,** (dramatic presentation) спектáкль. **2,** (costumed procession) шéствие; парáд. —**pageantry,** *n.* пóмпа; блеск; великолéпие.
page proofs вёрстка; корректýра в листáх.
pagination *n.* пагинáция.
pagoda *n.* пáгода.
paid *adj.* оплáчиваемый; плáтный. *Paid vacation,* оплáчиваемый óтпуск. *Paid worker,* плáтный рабóтник. *Well paid,* хорошó оплáчиваемый.
pail *n.* ведрó. *Milk pail,* подóйник.
pain *n.* **1,** (feeling of discomfort) боль: *pain in one's chest,* боль в груди́. *Cry out in pain,* вскри́кнуть от бóли. *Are you in much pain?,* вам óчень бóльно? **2,** *pl.* (efforts) старáния. *Take pains,* прилагáть старáния; óчень старáться. —*v.t.* огорчáть. *It pains me to think about it,* мне бóльно дýмать об э́том. —**on pain of,** под стрáхом (+ *gen.*): *on pain of death,* под стрáхом смéрти.
pained *adj.* огорчённый: *pained look,* огорчённый вид.
painful *adj.* **1,** (hurting) больнóй. *Is it painful?,* вам бóльно? **2,** (causing pain) болéзненный: *painful bite,* болéзненный укýс. **3,** (unpleasant; agonizing) мучи́тельный. *It is painful to watch,* бóльно смотрéть на э́то. —**painfully,** *adv.* болéзненно; мучи́тельно.
painkiller *n.* болеутоля́ющее срéдство.
painless *adj.* безболéзненный. —**painlessly,** *adv.* безболéзненно.
painstaking *adj.* тщáтельный; старáтельный. —**painstakingly,** *adv.* тщáтельно; старáтельно.
paint *n.* крáска. —*v.t.* **1,** (coat with paint) крáсить. **2,** (make, as a picture; make a picture of) писáть. **3,** (apply cosmetics to) крáсить. **4,** (swab) смáзывать. **5,** *fig.* (describe; depict) рисовáть; изображáть. —*v.i.* писáть крáсками. *Paint in oils,* писáть мáслом.
paintbrush *n.* кисть.
painted *adj.* крáшеный.
painter *n.* **1,** (house painter) маля́р. **2,** (artist) худóжник.
painting *n.* **1,** (the art) жи́вопись. **2,** (a painted picture) рóспись; карти́на.
pair *n.* пáра: *pair of shoes/pants,* пáра сапóг/брюк. *Pair of scissors,* нóжницы. *In pairs,* пáрами; попáрно. —*v.t.* спáривать; случáть. —*v.i.* [*usu.* **pair off**] разделя́ться попáрно.
pajamas *also,* **pyjamas** *n.* пижáма.
Pakistani *adj.* пакистáнский. —*n.* пакистáнец; пакистáнка.
pal *n., colloq.* прия́тель; товáрищ. —*v.i.,* [*usu.* **pal around**] дружи́ть (с).
palace *n.* дворéц. —*adj.* дворцóвый: *palace guard,* дворцóвая стрáжа; *palace coup,* дворцóвый переворóт.
palatable *adj.* **1,** (fit to be eaten) вкýсный. **2,** (agreeable; acceptable) прия́тный.
palatal *adj.* **1,** (pert. to the palate) нёбный. **2,** *phonet.* палатáльный.
palatalize *v.t.* палатализовáть. —**palatalization,** *n.* палатализáция.
palate *n.* **1,** (roof of the mouth) нёбо. **2,** (sense of taste) вкус.
palatial *adj.* роскóшный; великолéпный.
palaver *n.* пустáя болтовня́.
pale *adj.* **1,** (pallid; not bright) блéдный: *pale cheeks/colors,* блéдные щёки/крáски. *Pale moon,* блéдная лунá. **2,** (denoting a light shade) бледно-: *pale blue,* бледно-голубóй. —*n.* **1,** (stake) кол. **2,** (boundary) грани́ца; предéлы. *The Pale of Settlement,* чертá осéдлости. —*v.i.* **1,** (turn pale) бледнéть. **2,** *fol. by* **before** (suffer in comparison with) бледнéть (пéред); тускнéть (пéред).
Paleo-Asiatic *adj.* палеоазиáтский.
paleography *n.* палеогрáфия. —**paleographer,** *n.* палеóграф. —**paleographic,** *adj.* палеографи́ческий.
paleolithic *adj.* палеолити́ческий.
paleontology *n.* палеонтолóгия. —**paleontologist,** *n.* палеонтóлог. —**paleontological,** *adj.* палеонтологи́ческий.
Paleozoic *adj.* палеозóйский.
Palestinian *adj.* палести́нский. —*n.* палести́нец; палести́нка.
palette *n.* пали́тра. —**palette knife,** шпáтель.
paling *n.* частокóл; тын.
palisade *n.* палисáд.
pall *n.* **1,** (covering for a coffin) покрóв. **2,** (gloom) мрáчность. *Cast a pall over,* омрачáть. —*v.i.* [*usu.* **pall on**] приедáться (+ *dat.*); пригля́дываться (+ *dat.*).
palladium *n.* паллáдий.
pallbearer *n.* человéк, несýщий гроб.
pallet *n.* **1,** (straw mattress) тюфя́к. **2,** (pawl) собáчка.
palliate *v.t.* облегчáть; смягчáть. —**palliative,** *n.* паллиати́в. —*adj.* паллиати́вный.
pallid *adj.* блéдный. —**pallor,** *n.* блéдность.
palm *n.* **1,** (of the hand) ладóнь. **2,** (tree) пáльма. —*adj.* пáльмовый. —*v.t.* [*usu.* **palm off**] всучáть; подсóвывать. —**know like the palm of one's hand,** знать как свой пять пáльцев.
palmist *n.* хиромáнт. —**palmistry,** *n.* хиромáнтия.
palm oil пáльмовое мáсло.
Palm Sunday вéрбное воскресéнье.

palpable *adj.* **1,** (tangible) осяза́емый; ощути́мый. **2,** (obvious) очеви́дный; я́вный.
palpitate *v.i.* трепета́ть. —**palpitation,** *n.* тре́пет; трепета́ние.
palsy *n.* парали́ч.
paltry *adj.* ничто́жный; пустяко́вый.
pampas *n.pl.* пампа́сы.
pamper *v.t.* балова́ть; не́жить; изне́живать.
pamphlet *n.* **1,** (small unbound book) брошю́ра. **2,** (political article published in same) памфле́т. —**pamphleteer,** *n.* памфлети́ст.
pan *n.* **1,** (frying pan) сковорода́; (roasting pan) жаро́вня; (baking pan) про́тивень. **2,** (dishpan) таз для мытья́ посу́ды; (dustpan) сово́к. —*v.t.* **1,** (separate, as gold) промыва́ть. **2,** *colloq.* (criticize unfavorably) раскритикова́ть; разруга́ть. —**pan out,** *colloq.* вы́гореть.
panacea *n.* панаце́я; универса́льное сре́дство.
Panama hat пана́ма.
pancake *n.* блин; ола́дья.
panchromatic *adj.* панхромати́ческий.
pancreas *n.* поджелу́дочная железа́. —**pancreatic,** *adj.* поджелу́дочный.
panda *n.* па́нда.
pandemic *n.* пандеми́я.
pandemonium *n.* гвалт; хао́с; бедла́м.
pander *v.i.* **1,** (act as a pander) сво́дничать. **2,** *fol. by* **to** (cater to) потво́рствовать. —*n.* [*also,* **panderer**] сво́дник.
pane *n.* (око́нное) стекло́.
panegyric *n.* панеги́рик. —**panegyrist,** *n.* панегири́ст.
panel *n.* **1,** (section of a wall, door, etc.) пане́ль; филёнка. **2,** (board with instruments or controls) щит; щито́к. *Instrument panel,* прибо́рная доска́. *Control panel,* щит управле́ния; пульт. **3,** (committee) коми́ссия. *Panel of judges,* суде́йская колле́гия. —*v.t.* обшива́ть пане́лями *or* филёнками. —**paneled,** *adj.* филёночный; филёнчатый. —**paneling,** *n.* пане́ль.
pang *n., usu. pl.* му́ки; бо́ли: *hunger pangs,* му́ки го́лода; голо́дные бо́ли. *Pangs of childbirth,* родовы́е му́ки *or* поту́ги. —**pangs of conscience,** угрызе́ния со́вести.
pangolin *n.* я́щер.
panhandler *n.* попроша́йка.
panic *n.* па́ника. —*v.t.* наводи́ть па́нику на. —*v.i.* впада́ть в па́нику; поддава́ться па́нике.
panicky *adj.* пани́ческий. *Get panicky,* впада́ть в па́нику.
panicle *n.* метёлка.
panic-stricken *adj.* пани́ческий; охва́ченный па́никой.
panoply *n.* **1,** (suit of armor) доспе́хи. **2,** (magnificent array) блеск.
panorama *n.* панора́ма. —**panoramic,** *adj.* панора́мный.
pansy *n.* аню́тины гла́зки.
pant *v.i.* пыхте́ть; задыха́ться; запыха́ться; отдува́ться. —*n.* вздох.
pantheism *n.* пантеи́зм. —**pantheist,** *n.* пантеи́ст. —**pantheistic,** *adj.* пантеисти́ческий.
pantheon *n.* пантео́н.
panther *n.* панте́ра.
panties *n.pl.* тру́сики.
pantomime *n.* пантоми́ма. —*adj.* пантомими́ческий; пантоми́мный.
pantry *n.* кладова́я.
pants *n.pl.* брю́ки; штаны́.
panty hose колго́тки.
pap *n.* ка́шка.
papa *n.* па́па.
papacy *n.* па́пство. —**papal,** *adj.* па́пский.
papaya *n.* ды́нное де́рево.
paper *n.* **1,** (material) бума́га. **2,** (newspaper) газе́та. **3,** (treatise) докла́д: *deliver a paper,* чита́ть докла́д. **4,** (written work for school) сочине́ние. *Term paper,* курсова́я рабо́та. **5,** (document) бума́га; докуме́нт. —*adj.* бума́жный. —*v.t.* **1,** (cover with wallpaper) окле́ивать (обо́ями). **2,** *fol. by* **over** (cover up) зама́зывать. —**on paper, 1,** (in writing) в пи́сьменной фо́рме. **2,** (in theory) в тео́рии.
paperback *n.* кни́га в бума́жной обло́жке.
paper clip скре́пка.
paperhanger *n.* обо́йщик.
paperweight *n.* пресс-папье́.
paper work делопроизво́дство.
papier-mâché *n.* папье́-маше́.
papoose *n.* инде́йский ребёнок.
paprika *n.* кра́сный пе́рец; па́прика.
papule *n.* па́пула.
papyrus *n.* папи́рус.
par *n.* **1,** (equal status): *be/rank on a par with,* быть наравне́ с; стоя́ть в одно́м ряду́ с. **2,** (normal state or level): *up to par,* на до́лжной высоте́; *below par,* не на высоте́. **3,** *finance* номина́л. —*adj.* **1,** *finance* номина́льный: *par value,* номина́льная цена́. **2,** (normal; up to par) норма́льный.
parable *n.* при́тча.
parabola *n.* пара́бола. —**parabolic,** *adj.* параболи́ческий.
parachute *n.* парашю́т. —*v.i.* пры́гать *or* вы́броситься с парашю́том. —**parachutist,** *n.* парашюти́ст.
parade *n.* пара́д. —*v.i.* ше́ствовать. —*v.t.* (flaunt) щеголя́ть. —**parade ground,** плац.
paradigm *n.* паради́гма.
paradise *n.* рай.
paradox *n.* парадо́кс. —**paradoxical,** *adj.* парадокса́льный.
paraffin *n.* парафи́н.
paragon *n.* образе́ц.
paragraph *n.* абза́ц; пара́граф. *Begin a new paragraph,* начина́ть с но́вой (*or* с кра́сной) строки́.
parakeet *n.* ма́ленький попуга́й.
parallax *n.* паралла́кс.
parallel *adj.* паралле́льный. —*adv.* паралле́льно. —*n.* паралле́ль: *the 40th parallel,* сорокова́я паралле́ль. *Draw a parallel,* проводи́ть паралле́ль. *Without parallel,* не име́ющий себе́ ра́вного. —*v.t.* **1,** (run parallel to) идти́ паралле́льно (+ *dat.*). **2,** (be analogous to) соотве́тствовать (+ *dat.*). —**parallel bars,** паралле́льные бру́сья.
parallelepiped *n.* параллелепи́пед.
parallelism *n.* параллели́зм.
parallelogram *n.* параллелогра́мм.
paralyse *v.t.* = **paralyze.**
paralysis *n.* парали́ч. —**paralytic,** *adj.* паралити́ческий; парали́чный. —*n.* парали́тик.

paralyze *also,* **paralyse** *v.t.* парализова́ть. —**paralyzed,** *adj.* парализо́ван(ный).
paramecium *n.* ту́фелька; параме́ция.
parameter *n.* пара́метр.
paramilitary *adj.* полувое́нный.
paramount *adj.* **1,** (first in rank or title) верхо́вный. **2,** (overriding) первостепе́нный. *Of paramount importance,* велича́йшей *or* первостепе́нной ва́жности.
paramour *n.* любо́вник; любо́вница.
paranoia *n.* парано́йя. —**paranoiac,** *n.* парано́ик. —**paranoid,** *adj.* паранои́ческий.
parapet *n.* **1,** (low wall or railing) парапе́т. **2,** *mil.* (embankment) бру́ствер.
paraphernalia *n.* принадле́жности.
paraphrase *n.* перефразиро́вка. —*v.t.* перефрази́ровать.
paraplegia *n.* параплеги́я. —**paraplegic,** *n.* больно́й параплеги́ей.
parasite *n.* **1,** *biol.* парази́т. **2,** (sponger) тунея́дец; дармое́д; прихлеба́тель; парази́т. —**parasitic,** *adj.* паразити́ческий; парази́тный. —**parasitism,** *n.* паразити́зм.
parasol *n.* со́лнечный зо́нтик.
parathyroid gland околощитови́дная железа́; паращитови́дная железа́.
paratrooper *n.* парашюти́ст.
paratyphoid *n.* парати́ф. *Also,* **paratyphoid fever.**
parcel *n.* **1,** (package sent through the mail) посы́лка. **2,** (package; bundle) паке́т. **3,** (plot of land) уча́сток (земли́). —*v.t.* [*usu.* **parcel out**] выделя́ть; распределя́ть. —**part and parcel,** неотъе́млемая часть.
parch *v.t.* иссуша́ть. *My throat is parched,* у меня́ в го́рле пересо́хло. *My lips are parched,* мои́ гу́бы запекли́сь.
parchment *n.* перга́мент. —*adj.* перга́ментный.
pardon *v.t.* **1,** (forgive) проща́ть; извиня́ть. **2,** (release from punishment) поми́ловать. —*n.* **1,** (forgiveness) проще́ние. *I beg your pardon, see* **beg. 2,** (release from punishment) поми́лование. —**pardonable,** *adj.* прости́тельный.
pare *v.t.* **1,** (peel) чи́стить. **2,** (reduce) уре́зывать.
parent *n., usu. pl.* роди́тели. —**parentage,** *n.* происхожде́ние. —**parental,** *adj.* роди́тельский.
parentheses *n.pl.* ско́бки. —**parenthesize,** *v.t.* заключа́ть в ско́бки. —**parenthetic(al),** *adj.* вво́дный. —**parenthetically,** *adv.* в ско́бках.
parenthood *n.* отцо́вство; матери́нство.
paresis *n.* паре́з.
par excellence превосхо́дный; замеча́тельный.
pariah *n.* па́рия.
pari-mutuel *n., usu. pl.* тотализа́тор.
paring knife нож для чи́стки фру́ктов и овоще́й; фрукто́вый нож.
parish *n.* (церко́вный) прихо́д. —*adj.* прихо́дский: *parish priest,* прихо́дский свяще́нник. —**parishioner,** *n.* прихожа́нин.
Parisian *adj.* пари́жский. —*n.* парижа́нин.
parity *n.* парите́т.
park *n.* парк. —*v.t.* **1,** (a car) ста́вить (маши́ну). **2,** *colloq.* (place) оставля́ть; положи́ть. *Park oneself somewhere,* располо́жи́ться; усе́сться.
parka *n.* па́рка.
parking *n.* стоя́нка. *No parking!,* стоя́нка запрещена́! —**parking lights,** подфа́рники. —**parking lot,** стоя́нка (для автомоби́лей). —**parking place/space,** ме́сто (стоя́нки автомоби́ля).
parkway *n.* шоссе́.
parlance *n.* язы́к: *legal parlance,* юриди́ческий язы́к. *In common parlance,* в просторе́чии.
parley *n.* перегово́ры. —*v.i.* вести́ перегово́ры.
parliament *n.* парла́мент. —**parliamentarianism,** *n.* парламентари́зм. —**parliamentary,** *adj.* парла́ментский; парламента́рный.
parlor *also,* **parlour** *n.* **1,** (sitting room) гости́ная. **2,** (establishment): *beauty parlor,* космети́ческий кабине́т; *ice-cream parlor,* кафе́-моро́женое. —**parlor car,** сало́н-ваго́н. —**parlor games,** ко́мнатные и́гры.
parochial *adj.* **1,** (of a parish) прихо́дский. **2,** (narrow; provincial) у́зкий; ограни́ченный. —**parochial school,** прихо́дская шко́ла.
parody *n.* паро́дия. —*v.t.* пароди́ровать. —**parodist,** *n.* пароди́ст.
parole *n.* усло́вно-досро́чное освобожде́ние. —*v.t.* освобожда́ть под че́стное сло́во.
paroxysm *n.* пароксизм.
parquet *n.* парке́т. —*adj.* парке́тный. —**parquetry,** *n.* парке́т.
parrot *n.* попуга́й. —*v.t.* **1,** (repeat) повторя́ть как попуга́й. **2,** (say the same thing as) подпева́ть.
parry *v.t.* **1,** (ward off) отража́ть; отбива́ть; пари́ровать. **2,** (evade) уклоня́ться от: *parry a question,* уклоня́ться от отве́та.
parse *v.t.* разбира́ть.
parsimonious *adj.* скупо́й. —**parsimony,** *n.* ску́пость.
parsley *n.* петру́шка.
parsnip *n.* пастерна́к.
parson *n.* прихо́дский свяще́нник.
part *n.* **1,** (portion; element) часть: *part of the whole,* часть це́лого. *Parts of the body,* ча́сти те́ла. *Spare parts,* запасны́е ча́сти. *Part of speech,* часть ре́чи. **2,** (role) роль: *bit part,* выходна́я роль. **3,** *pl.* (locality) края́: *in these parts,* в э́тих края́х. **4,** (in one's hair) пробо́р. **5,** *music* па́ртия. —*adj.* части́чный: *a part interest in,* части́чная до́ля (+ *gen.*). *Part owner,* совладе́лец. —*adv.* части́чно: *she is part Russian and part French,* она́ части́чно ру́сская и части́чно францу́женка. —*v.t.* **1,** (separate) разлуча́ть. *Till death do us part,* пока́ смерть нас не разлучи́т. **2,** (comb with a part): *part one's hair,* де́лать себе́ пробо́р. *Part one's hair in the middle/on the side/,* носи́ть во́лосы на прямо́й/косо́й пробо́р. —*v.i.* **1,** (divide) разделя́ться; расступа́ться; раздвига́ться. **2,** (part company) расстава́ться; разлуча́ться. *We parted friends,* мы расста́лись *or* разошли́сь друзья́ми. **3,** *fol. by* **with** (relinquish) расстава́ться с. —**do one's part,** де́лать своё де́ло. —**for my part,** я, со свое́й стороны́; что каса́ется меня́. —**for the most part,** *see* **most.** —**in large part,** во мно́гом. —**in part,** ча́стью; части́чно; отча́сти. —**in parts,** по частя́м. —**on the part of,** со стороны́ (+ *gen.*). —**take part in,** принима́ть уча́стие в; уча́ствовать в.
partake *v.i.* **1,** *fol. by* **in** (take part in) принима́ть уча́стие (в). **2,** *fol. by* **of** (take, as food) пое́сть. —**partake oneself,** угоща́ться.
parthenogenesis *n.* партеногене́з.
Parthenon *n.* Парфено́н.
partial *adj.* **1,** (involving only a part) части́чный. **2,**

(biased) пристрáстный. **3,** *fol. by* **to** (particularly fond of) пристрáстный (к).

partiality *n.* пристрáстие; пристрáстность.

partially *adv.* частúчно; отчáсти.

participant *n.* учáстник.

paticipate *v.i.* учáствовать. —**participation,** *n.* учáстие.

participle *n.* причáстие. —**participial,** *adj.* причáстный.

particle *n.* **1,** (speck) частúца: *particle of dust,* частúца пы́ли. **2,** (tiny amount) частúца; крупúнка; крупúца. *Not a particle of difference,* ни малéйшей рáзницы. **3,** *physics* частúца: *elementary particle,* элементáрная частúца. **4,** *gram.* частúца.

particular *adj.* **1,** (special; unusual) осóбенный; осóбый. *Nothing in particular,* ничегó осóбенного. *For no particular reason,* без осóбой причúны. **2,** (specific; individual) чáстный. *At this particular time,* в дáнный момéнт. *Why did you choose this particular color?,* почемý вы вы́брали úменно э́тот цвет? **3,** (fussy) разбóрчивый; привередливый. —*n.* подрóбность. —**in particular,** в чáстности; в осóбенности.

particularity *n.* осóбенность.

particularly *adv.* осóбенно.

parting *n.* расставáние; разлýка; прощáние. *At parting,* на прощáние. —*adj.* прощáльный.

partisan *n.* **1,** (adherent) сторóнник. **2,** (guerrilla) партизáн. —*adj.* **1,** (biased) пристрáстный. **2,** (of guerrillas) партизáнский. —**partisanship,** *n.* пристрáстие.

partition *n.* **1,** (dividing up) разделéние; раздéл. **2,** (something that divides) перегорóдка. —*v.t.* **1,** (divide into parts) разделя́ть. **2,** *fol. by* **off** (separate by a partition) отгорáживать; перегорáживать.

partitive *adj., gram.* раздели́тельный.

partly *adv.* чáстью; частúчно; отчáсти.

partner *n.* **1,** (in business) компаньóн; товáрищ; партнёр. **2,** (in a game) партнёр. **3,** (in dancing) кавалéр; дáма. —**partnership,** *n.* товáрищество.

partridge *n.* куропáтка.

part-time *adj.* рабóтающий непóлный день. *She works part-time,* онá рабóтает непóлный день.

partway *adv.* полпутú: *I'll walk you partway,* я пройдý с вáми полпутú.

party *n.* **1,** (social gathering) вечерúнка; вéчер. **2,** (political party) пáртия. **3,** *law* сторонá: *interested party,* заинтересóванная сторонá. *Through a third party,* чéрез трéтье лицó. **4,** (participant) учáстник. *Be a party to,* быть причáстным к. **5,** (group of people organized for a purpose) грýппа: *search party,* поискóвая грýппа. **6,** *mil.* (detachment; detail) комáнда; пáртия. *Rescue party,* спасáтельная комáнда. —*adj.* партúйный: *party congress,* партúйный съезд. —**party line, 1,** (of telephones) телефóн смéшанного пóльзования. **2,** *polit.* партúйная лúния.

paschal *adj.* пасхáльный. —**paschal lamb,** пасхáльный áгнец.

pasha *n.* пашá.

pass *v.t.* **1,** (go by; go past) проходúть мúмо; проезжáть мúмо; миновáть. **2,** (go beyond) проходúть; проезжáть. **3,** (overtake) обгоня́ть. *No passing!,* не обгоня́ть!; обгóн воспрещён! **4,** (hand over, as at the table) передавáть. **5,** (move in a certain way) проводúть: *pass one's hand through one's hair,* проводúть рукóй по волосáм. *Pass something through a filter,* пропускáть чтó-нибудь чéрез фильтр. **6,** (complete successfully, as a test) сдать; вы́держать. **7,** (enact, as a bill) принимáть. **8,** (while away, as time) коротáть. **9,** (pronounce, as a sentence) выносúть. **10,** (excrete; void) испускáть. **11,** *sports* пасовáть. —*v.i.* **1,** (move ahead; move past; extend) проходúть. *Let pass,* пропускáть. **2,** (go by; be over) проходúть; миновáть: *a whole year passed,* прошёл цéлый год; *the danger has passed,* опáсность миновáла. **3,** (be transferred or communicated) переходúть. **4,** (be approved or adopted) быть при́нятым. **5,** *cards* пасовáть. —*n.* **1,** (passage between mountains) перевáл. **2,** (permit) прóпуск; путёвка. **3,** (free ticket) контрамáрка. **4,** *mil.* (leave) óтпуск; побы́вка. **5,** *sports* пас; передáча. **6,** *cards* пас. —**come to pass,** произойтú; случúться. —**pass away,** скончáться. —**pass by,** проходúть мúмо; проходúть сторонóй. —**pass for,** сходúть за. —**pass off,** выдавáть: *pass oneself off as a physician,* выдавáть себя́ за врачá. —**pass on, 1,** (give to the next person) передавáть. **2,** (die) умирáть. —**pass out, 1,** (hand out) раздавáть. **2,** *colloq.* (faint) потеря́ть сознáние; упáсть в óбморок. —**pass over, 1,** (skip; disregard) пропускáть; обходúть. *Pass over in silence,* обходúть молчáнием. **2,** (fail to promote) обходúть. —**pass through,** проезжáть чéрез. *I am just passing through,* я здесь проéздом. —**pass up,** *colloq.* пропускáть.

passable *adj.* **1,** (traversable) проходúмый. **2,** (barely satisfactory) снóсный.

passage *n.* **1,** (passing) перехóд; прохождéние; прохóд; проéзд. **2,** (passageway) прохóд; перехóд; проéзд. **3,** (voyage) переéзд. *To book passage,* брать билéт на пароxóд. **4,** (lapse, as of time) течéние (врéмени). **5,** (enactment, as of a law) приня́тие. **6,** (portion of something written) отры́вок. **7,** *music* пассáж.

passageway *n.* прохóд; перехóд; коридóр.

passbook *n.* сберегáтельная книжка.

passed pawn *chess* проходнáя пéшка.

passenger *n.* пассажúр. —*adj.* пассажúрский. *Passenger car,* легковóй автомобúль. —**passenger pigeon,** стрáнствующий гóлубь.

passer-by *n.* прохóжий; встрéчный.

passing *adj.* **1,** (going by) проходя́щий. *With each passing year,* с кáждым гóдом; год óт году. **2,** (quick; cursory) бéглый: *passing glance,* бéглый взгляд. **3,** (transitory) мимолётный: *passing fancy,* мимолётная прúхоть. **4,** (casual, as of a remark) попýтный. **5,** (satisfactory, as of a grade) перехóдный. —*n.* **1,** (act of passing) прохождéние. **2,** (death) кончúна. —**in passing,** мимохóдом; вскользь.

passion *n.* страсть: *a passion for music,* страсть к мýзыке. *Passions flared,* стрáсти разгорéлись. *Fit of passion,* поры́в *or* вспы́шка гнéва.

passionate *adj.* стрáстный. —**passionately,** *adv.* стрáстно.

passive *adj.* **1,** (not active) пассúвный: *passive role,* пассúвная роль. *Passive vocabulary,* пассúвный словáрь; пассúвный запáс слов. **2,** *gram.* страдáтельный: *passive voice,* страдáтельный залóг. —**passivity,** *n.* пассúвность.

passkey *n.* отмы́чка.

Passover *n.* пáсха.

passport *n.* пáспорт. —*adj.* пáспортный: *passport department,* пáспортный отдéл.

password *n.* паро́ль; про́пуск.
past *adj.* **1,** (of a former time) про́шлый: *past wars,* про́шлые во́йны. **2,** *preceded by* **the** (just gone by) после́дний; мину́вший; исте́кший. *During the past year,* за после́дний/исте́кший год. **3,** (former) бы́вший: *past president,* бы́вший президе́нт. **4,** *gram.* проше́дший: *past tense,* проше́дшее вре́мя. —*n.* **1,** (past time) про́шлое. *In the past,* в про́шлом; ра́ньше. *A thing of the past,* де́ло про́шлое. **2,** *gram.* проше́дшее вре́мя. —*prep.* **1,** (by) ми́мо: *slip past the guard,* проскользну́ть ми́мо сто́рожа. **2,** (beyond) за: *past the city limits,* за преде́лами го́рода. *Just past the station,* сра́зу по́сле вокза́ла. *Well past midnight,* далеко́ за́ полночь. **3,** *in telling time: half-past six,* полови́на седьмо́го; *twenty past one,* два́дцать мину́т второ́го. —*adv.* ми́мо. ♦*Often with the prefix* про-: *fly past,* пролета́ть; *dart past,* промча́ться.
paste *n.* **1,** (soft, creamy substance) па́ста: *toothpaste,* зубна́я па́ста; *tomato paste,* тома́т-па́ста. **2,** (adhesive) (мучно́й) клей; кле́йстер. **3,** (dough) те́сто: *puff paste,* слоёное те́сто. —*v.t.* **1,** (affix) накле́ивать. *Paste together,* скле́ивать. *Paste stamps in an album,* вкле́ивать ма́рки в альбо́м. **2,** (cover with pasted material) окле́ивать. **3,** *slang* (smack) тре́снуть.
pasteboard *n.* карто́н.
pastel *n.* пасте́ль. —*adj.* пасте́льный.
pastern *n.* ба́бка.
pasteurize *v.t.* пастеризова́ть. —**pasteurization,** *n.* пастериза́ция.
pastime *n.* времяпрепровожде́ние.
past master иску́сник.
pastor *n.* па́стор; па́стырь.
pastoral *adj.* пастора́льный. —*n.* пастора́ль.
pastorale *n.* пастора́ль.
pastry *n.* конди́терские изде́лия; пиро́жное. —**pastry cook; pastry chef,** конди́тер. —**pastry shop,** конди́терская.
pasturage *n.* **1,** (grass) подно́жный корм. **2,** (land) па́стбище. **3,** (grazing) пастьба́.
pasture *n.* па́стбище. —*v.i.* пасти́сь. —**put out to pasture, 1,** *literally* (вы)пуска́ть на подно́жный корм. **2,** (allow or compel to retire) увольня́ть в отста́вку.
pat *v.t.* похло́пывать; трепа́ть. *Pat someone on the back,* похло́пывать кого́-нибудь по плечу́. —*n.* **1,** (tap) хлопо́к. **2,** (small piece, as of butter) кусо́чек; комо́к. —*adj.* гото́вый: *a pat answer for everything,* гото́вый отве́т на всё. —**give (someone) a pat on the back,** гла́дить по голо́вке. —**have down** (*or* **know) pat,** знать назубо́к. —**stand pat,** стоя́ть на своём.
patch *n.* **1,** (covering, as for mending) запла́та. **2,** (bandage) повя́зка: *eye patch,* повя́зка на глазу́. **3,** (small plot) уча́сток; клочо́к. **4,** (small piece or area) клочо́к: *patch of fog,* клочо́к тума́на; *patch of blue,* клочо́к лазу́ри. *Patch of sunlight,* со́лнечный блик. —*v.t.* **1,** (mend) лата́ть; накла́дывать запла́ту на. **2,** *fol. by* **up** (settle) ула́живать.
patch pocket накладно́й карма́н.
patchwork *n.* **1,** (fabric made of patches) лоску́тная рабо́та: *patchwork quilt,* лоску́тное одея́ло. **2,** (jumble) мешани́на; ерала́ш.
pate *n.* башка́.
pâté *n.* паште́т.
patent *n.* пате́нт. —*adj.* **1,** (of or pert. to patents) пате́нтный. **2,** (patented) патенто́ванный. **3,** (obvious) я́вный: *a patent lie,* я́вная ложь. —*v.t.* патентова́ть. —**patent leather,** лакиро́ванная ко́жа. —**patent medicine,** патенто́ванное лека́рство.
paternal *adj.* **1,** (of one's father) отцо́вский. **2,** (fatherly) оте́ческий.
paternalistic *adj.* оте́ческий.
paternity *n.* отцо́вство.
path *n.* **1,** (footway) тропи́нка; тропа́; доро́жка. **2,** (course) путь.
pathetic *adj.* жа́лкий.
pathology *n.* патоло́гия. —**pathological,** *adj.* патологи́ческий. —**pathologist,** *n.* пато́лог.
pathos *n.* тро́гательность.
pathway *n.* тропи́нка; тропа́; доро́жка.
patience *n.* терпе́ние.
patient *adj.* терпели́вый. *Be patient!,* име́йте терпе́ние! —*n.* больно́й; пацие́нт. —**patiently,** *adv.* терпели́во.
patio *n.* па́тио.
patois *n.* ме́стный го́вор.
patriarch *n.* патриа́рх. —**patriarchal,** *adj.* патриарха́льный. —**patriarchate,** *n.* патриа́ршество. —**patriarchy,** *n.* патриарха́т.
patrician *n.* патри́ций.
patricide *n.* отцеуби́йство.
patrimony *n.* отцо́вское насле́дие.
patriot *n.* патрио́т. —**patriotic,** *adj.* патриоти́ческий. —**patriotism,** *n.* патриоти́зм.
patrol *v.t.* патрули́ровать. —*n.* дозо́р; патру́ль. *Be on patrol,* быть в дозо́ре. —*adj.* дозо́рный; патру́льный. *Patrol boat,* дозо́рное су́дно; сторожево́й ка́тер. —**patrolman,** *n.* полице́йский.
patron *n.* **1,** (benefactor) покрови́тель. *Patron of the arts,* мецена́т. **2,** (customer) клие́нт.
patronage *n.* покрови́тельство; проте́кция.
patronize *v.t.* **1,** (sponsor) покрови́тельствовать. **2,** (be a regular customer of) покупа́ть в. —**patronizing,** *adj.* покрови́тельственный.
patronymic *n.* о́тчество. *Also,* **patronymic name.**
patter *n.* **1,** (drumming sound) стук; шум. *The patter of rain,* шум дождя́. *The patter of feet,* то́пот ног. **2,** (rapid-fire speech) скорогово́рка. **3,** (cant; jargon) жарго́н. —*v.i.* бараба́нить.
pattern *n.* **1,** (decorative design) узо́р. **2,** (diagram used in making garments) вы́кройка. **3,** (model; example) образе́ц: *on the pattern of,* по образцу́ (+*gen.*). *Set the pattern for,* стать образцо́м для. **4,** *aero.* маршру́т: *holding pattern,* маршру́т ожида́ния; *landing pattern,* маршру́т захо́да на поса́дку. —*v.t.* [*usu.* **pattern after**] де́лать (что́-нибудь) по образцу́ (+ *gen.*). *Pattern oneself after,* брать приме́р с.
patty *n.* **1,** (flat piece of chopped meat) котле́та. **2,** (small pie) пирожо́к.
paucity *n.* ску́дность.
paunch *n.* **1,** (potbelly) брюшко́; пу́зо. **2,** (rumen) рубе́ц. —**paunchy,** *adj.* пуза́тый.
pauper *n.* бедня́к; ни́щий. *He died a pauper,* он у́мер в нищете́.
pause *n.* па́уза; переры́в; переды́шка. —*v.i.* де́лать па́узу; остана́вливаться. —**give one pause,** наводи́ть на размышле́ния.
pave *v.t.* мости́ть. —**pave the way,** прокла́дывать путь; подгота́вливать по́чву.

paved *adj.* мощёный.
pavement *n.* тротуа́р; пане́ль.
pavilion *n.* павильо́н.
paving *n.* моще́ние. —**paving block/stone,** торе́ц; *pl.* брусча́тка.
paw *n.* ла́па. —*v.t.* обла́пить.
pawl *n.* соба́чка.
pawn *n., chess* пе́шка. —*v.t.* закла́дывать; отдава́ть в зало́г. —**pawnbroker,** *n.* залогодержа́тель. —**pawnshop,** *n.* ломба́рд. —**pawn ticket,** ломба́рдная квита́нция.
pay *v.t.* **1,** (give in payment; settle) плати́ть: *pay ten dollars,* плати́ть де́сять до́лларов; *pay (in) cash,* плати́ть нали́чными. *Pay a fine,* плати́ть штраф. *Pay a debt,* выпла́чивать/упла́чивать/отдава́ть долг. **2,** (give money to; remunerate) плати́ть (+ *dat.*): *pay the doctor,* плати́ть врачу́. *Pay the cashier,* плати́ть касси́ру; плати́ть в ка́ссу. **3,** *fol. by inf.* (be worthwhile) сто́ить: *it doesn't pay to argue with him,* не сто́ит с ним спо́рить. **4,** (offer in wages): *the job pays 10,000 a year,* зарпла́та – де́сять ты́сяч в год. **5,** *used with certain nouns: pay a visit on,* нанести́ визи́т (+ *dat.*); *pay attention to,* обраща́ть внима́ние на; *pay someone a compliment,* сде́лать кому́-нибудь комплиме́нт. —*v.i.* **1,** (make payment) плати́ть. **2,** (offer wages): *the job pays well,* рабо́та хорошо́ опла́чивается. **3,** (be worthwhile) сто́ить. **4,** (be profitable) окупа́ться. —*n.* пла́та; зарпла́та; жа́лованье, окла́д. *Receive no pay,* не получа́ть зарпла́ты. *Base pay,* основно́й окла́д. *In the pay of,* на жа́лованье у. —**pay back, 1,** (a person) отпла́чивать (+ *dat.*). **2,** (money) возвраща́ть. *Pay back a loan,* выпла́чивать *or* возвраща́ть заём. —**pay for, 1,** *literally* плати́ть за. **2,** (suffer the consequences of) плати́ться за; отве́тить за; распла́чиваться за. **3,** *Pay for itself,* окупа́ться. —**pay off, 1,** (pay in full) выпла́чивать; распла́чиваться с; рассчи́тываться с; погаша́ть. **2,** *colloq.* (succeed) увенча́ться успе́хом. **3,** *slang* (bribe) подкупа́ть. —**pay out, 1,** (disburse, as money) выпла́чивать. **2,** *naut.* (let out, as a rope) трави́ть. —**pay up,** выпла́чивать. *See also* **paid.**
payable *adj. Be payable,* подлежа́ть упла́те.
paycheck *n.* получка.
payday *n.* платёжный день.
payee *n.* получа́тель (де́нег).
payer *n.* плате́льщик.
paying *adj.* **1,** (who pays) пла́тный. **2,** (profitable) рента́бельный.
payload *n.* **1,** *comm.* поле́зный груз. **2,** *aero.* поле́зная нагру́зка.
paymaster *n.* касси́р; казначе́й.
payment *n.* **1,** (act of paying) пла́та; опла́та; упла́та; платёж. **2,** (something paid) платёж. *Down payment,* зада́ток. *Balance of payments,* платёжный бала́нс.
payoff *n., colloq.* **1,** (bribe) взя́тка. **2,** (climax) развя́зка.
pay phone телефо́н-автома́т.
payroll *n.* платёжная ве́домость.
pea *n.* горо́шина; *pl.* горо́х; горо́шек. —*adj.* горо́ховый: *pea soup,* горо́ховый суп.
peace *n.* **1,** (absence of war) мир: *at peace,* в ми́ре. *Live in peace,* жить в ми́ре. *Make peace with,* заключи́ть мир с. **2,** (peace of mind) поко́й: *leave in peace,* оставля́ть в поко́е. *May he rest in peace,* мир пра́ху его́. **3,** (public order) поря́док: *keep/disturb the peace,* блюсти́/наруша́ть поря́док. —*adj.* ми́рный: *peace treaty,* ми́рный догово́р. —**hold** (*or* **keep**) **one's peace,** придержа́ть язы́к.
peaceable *adj.* ми́рный.
peaceful *adj.* **1,** (not involving war) ми́рный: *for peaceful purposes,* в ми́рных це́лях. **2,** (tranquil) споко́йный. —**peacefully,** *adv.* ми́рно; споко́йно.
peacekeeping *n.* поддержа́ние *or* сохране́ние ми́ра. *Peacekeeping force,* войска́ по поддержа́нию ми́ра.
peace-loving *adj.* миролюби́вый.
peacemaker *n.* миротво́рец.
peacetime *n.* ми́рное вре́мя.
peach *n.* пе́рсик. —*adj.* пе́рсиковый. —**peach tree,** пе́рсик; пе́рсиковое де́рево.
peacock *n.* павли́н. *Peacock feathers,* павли́ньи пе́рья.
peahen *n.* па́ва.
pea jacket бушла́т.
peak *n.* **1,** (of a cap) козырёк. **2,** (of a mountain) пик; верши́на. **3,** *fig.* (high point; zenith) вы́сшая то́чка; верши́на. *At the peak of one's powers,* в расцве́те (тво́рческих) сил. —*adj.* максима́льный: *peak load,* максима́льная нагру́зка.
peal *n.* **1,** (of a bell) звон; трезво́н. **2,** (of thunder, laughter, etc.) раска́т. —*v.i.* греме́ть; трезво́нить.
peanut *n.* ара́хис; земляно́й оре́х. —**peanut butter,** па́ста из тёртого арахиса.
pear *n.* гру́ша. —*adj.* гру́шевый.
pearl *n.* же́мчуг. *A single pearl,* жемчу́жина. —*adj.* жемчу́жный. —**pearl barley,** перло́вая крупа́. —**pearl oyster,** жемчу́жница.
pearly *adj.* жемчу́жный.
peasant *n.* крестья́нин. —*adj.* крестья́нский. —**peasantry,** *n.* крестья́нство.
peat *n.* торф. —*adj.* торфяно́й. —**peat moss,** торфяно́й мох.
pebble *n.* ка́мешек; голы́ш; га́лька.
pecan *n.* пека́н.
peccadillo *n.* грешо́к.
peccary *n.* пе́кари.
peck *v.t.* & *i.* клева́ть. —*n.* клево́к.
pectoral *adj.* грудно́й: *pectoral muscles,* грудны́е мы́шцы. *Pectoral cross,* напе́рсный крест.
peculiar *adj.* **1,** (unique; particular) осо́бенный; своеобра́зный. **2,** (odd) стра́нный. —**peculiarity,** *n.* стра́нность.
pecuniary *adj.* де́нежный.
pedagogue *n.* педаго́г. —**pedagogic(al),** *adj.* педагоги́ческий. —**pedagogy,** *n.* педаго́гика.
pedal *n.* педа́ль. —*v.t.* вести́ (велосипе́д). —*v.i.* **1,** (work a pedal) нажима́ть педа́ль. **2,** (ride a bicycle) е́хать на велосипе́де.
pedant *n.* педа́нт. —**pedantic,** *adj.* педанти́чный. —**pedantry,** *n.* педанти́зм.
peddle *v.t.* & *i.* торгова́ть вразно́с. —**peddler,** *n.* коробе́йник; разно́счик.
pederast *n.* педера́ст. —**pederasty,** *n.* педера́стия.
pedestal *n.* пьедеста́л; постаме́нт; подно́жие.
pedestrian *n.* пешехо́д. —*adj.* **1,** (of or for pedestrians) пешехо́дный. **2,** (commonplace; dull) прозаи́ческий.
pediatrics *n.* педиатри́я. —**pediatric,** *adj.* педиатри́ческий. —**pediatrician,** *n.* педиа́тр.

pedicel *n.* цветоно́жка.
pedicure *n.* педикю́р.
pedigree *n.* **1,** (lineage) происхожде́ние. **2,** (list of ancestors) родосло́вная. —**pedigreed,** *adj.* поро́дистый; племенно́й; чистокро́вный.
pediment *n.* фронто́н.
pedlar *n.* = **peddler.**
pedometer *n.* шагоме́р; педо́метр.
peek *n.* бы́стрый взгляд; взгляд укра́дкой. —*v.i.* загля́дывать.
peel *n.* ко́рка; кожура́; ко́жица; шелуха́. —*v.t.* **1,** (pare, as potatoes, fruit, etc.) чи́стить. **2,** *fol. by* **off** (remove) снима́ть (ко́рку); откле́ивать (ма́рку). —*v.i.* **1,** (shed skin) лупи́ться: *my face is peeling,* у меня́ лу́пится лицо́. **2,** *often fol. by* **off** (come off) сходи́ть; шелуши́ться; осыпа́ться; лупи́ться; облу́пливаться. —**keep an eye peeled,** смотре́ть в о́ба.
peelings *n.pl.* очи́стки.
peep *v.i.* **1,** (look furtively) загля́дывать; подгля́дывать. **2,** (come partly into view) выгля́дывать; прогля́дывать. **3,** (chirp) пища́ть. —*n.* **1,** (glimpse) бы́стрый взгляд. **2,** (chirp) писк. **3,** (sound) звук.
peephole *n.* глазо́к.
peer *n.* **1,** (equal) ра́вный. **2,** (person one's own age) све́рстник. **3,** (nobleman) пэр. —*v.i.* всма́триваться; вгля́дываться. *Peer into a telescope,* смотре́ть в телеско́п. *Peer out the window,* выгля́дывать из окна́.
peerage *n.* **1,** (rank) пэ́рство. **2,** (peers collectively) сосло́вие пэ́ров.
peerless *adj.* несравне́нный; бесподо́бный.
peeve *v.t.* раздража́ть. —*n., usu. in* **pet peeve,** люби́мая мозо́ль; больно́е ме́сто. —**peeved,** *adj.* раздражённый. —**peevish,** *adj.* сварли́вый.
peg *n.* **1,** (conical pin) ко́лышек. **2,** (such a pin on a stringed instrument) коло́к. —**take (someone) down a peg,** сбива́ть спесь с.
peg leg деревя́нная нога́; деревя́шка.
peg top куба́рь.
peignoir *n.* пеньюа́р.
pejorative *adj.* уничижи́тельный.
pelican *n.* пелика́н.
pellagra *n.* пелла́гра.
pellet *n.* **1,** (small round ball) ша́рик. **2,** (small lead shot) дроби́н(к)а.
pellicle *n.* ко́жица; плёнка.
pell-mell *adv.* **1,** (in total disorder) вперемё́шку. **2,** (in wild haste) сломя́ го́лову.
pellucid *adj.* прозра́чный.
pelt *n.* шку́ра. —*v.t.* (bombard) забра́сывать; засыпа́ть. —*v.i.* (beat down) бараба́нить.
pelvis *n.* таз. —**pelvic,** *adj.* та́зовый.
pen *n.* **1,** (quill pen) перо́; (fountain pen, ball-point, etc.) ру́чка. *Fountain pen,* автору́чка. **2,** (enclosure for animals) заго́н. *Pigpen,* свина́рник. —*v.t.* **1,** (write; compose) писа́ть; сочиня́ть. **2,** (confine in a pen) загоня́ть в заго́н. —**pen name,** псевдони́м.
penal *adj.* **1,** (prescribing punishment) уголо́вный: *penal code,* уголо́вный ко́декс. **2,** (of or for prisoners) штрафно́й: *penal colony,* штрафна́я коло́ния. *Penal battalion,* штрафно́й батальо́н. —**penal servitude,** ка́торга; ка́торжные рабо́ты.
penalize *v.t.* штрафова́ть.
penalty *n.* **1,** (punishment) наказа́ние; взыска́ние; штраф; пе́ня. *Death penalty,* сме́ртная казнь. *Pay the penalty,* поплати́ться. **2,** *sports* штраф. —*adj.* штрафно́й: *penalty kick,* штрафно́й уда́р.
penance *n.* покая́ние.
pence *n.pl.* пенс: *six pence,* шесть пе́нсов.
penchant *n.* скло́нность; накло́нность. *Have a penchant for neatness,* отлича́ться аккура́тностью.
pencil *n.* каранда́ш. —*adj.* каранда́шный: *pencil drawing,* каранда́шный рису́нок. —*v.t.* писа́ть (карандашо́м). *Pencil one's eyebrows,* подводи́ть бро́ви. —**pencil case,** пена́л. —**pencil sharpener,** точи́лка.
pendant *n.* куло́н; подве́ска.
pending *adj.* ожида́ющий реше́ния. —*prep.* в ожида́нии (+ *gen.*).
pendulum *n.* ма́ятник.
penetrate *v.t.* & *i.* проника́ть (в).
penetrating *adj.* **1,** (of cold, wind, etc.) прони́зывающий. **2,** (keen; discerning) проница́тельный.
penetration *n.* проникнове́ние.
penguin *n.* пингви́н.
penholder *n.* ру́чка (для пера́).
penicillin *n.* пеницилли́н.
peninsula *n.* полуо́стров. —**peninsular,** *adj.* полуостровно́й.
penis *n.* мужско́й полово́й член.
penitence *n.* покая́ние.
penitent *adj.* **1,** (of a person) ка́ющийся. **2,** (of a look, expression, etc.) покая́нный.
penitentiary *n.* ка́торжная тюрьма́.
penknife *n.* перочи́нный но́ж(ик).
penmanship *n.* каллигра́фия; чистописа́ние.
pennant *n.* вы́мпел.
penniless *adj.* безде́нежный; без копе́йки; без гроша́.
penny *n.* (American coin) моне́та в оди́н цент; (British coin) пе́нни; пенс. —**a penny for your thoughts,** о чём ты заду́мался? —**cost a pretty penny,** обойти́сь в копе́ечку; бить по карма́ну. —**not have a penny to one's name,** не име́ть ни копе́йки (*or* ни гроша́) за душо́й.
penny pincher скопидо́м; скупердя́й.
pension *n.* пе́нсия. —*v.t.* [*usu.* **pension off**] увольня́ть на пе́нсию. —**pensioner,** *n.* пенсионе́р.
pensive *adj.* заду́мчивый; вду́мчивый. —**pensiveness,** *n.* заду́мчивость.
pentagon *n.* **1,** (geometric figure) пятиуго́льник. **2,** *cap.* (headquarters of U.S. Defense Dept.) Пентаго́н. —**pentagonal,** *adj.* пятиуго́льный.
pentahedron *n.* пятигра́нник.
pentameter *n.* пятисто́пный стих; пента́метр. *Iambic pentameter,* пятисто́пный ямб. —*adj.* пятисто́пный.
Pentateuch *n.* пятикни́жие.
pentathlon *n.* пятибо́рье.
Pentecost *n.* пятидеся́тница.
penthouse *n.* кварти́ра на ве́рхнем этаже́.
pent-up *adj.* затаённый.
penultimate *adj.* предпосле́дний.
penumbra *n.* полуте́нь.
penurious *adj.* **1,** (stingy) скупо́й. **2,** (poor) бе́дный.
penury *n.* нужда́; нищета́.
peon *n.* пео́н. —**peonage,** *n.* пеона́ж.
peony *n.* пио́н.
people *n.* **1,** (persons) лю́ди. **2,** (nation) наро́д.

—*v.t.* населя́ть. —**people's,** *adj.* наро́дный: *people's republic,* наро́дная респу́блика.
pep *n., colloq.* эне́ргия; прыть. —*v.t.* [*usu.* **pep up**] оживля́ть.
pepper *n.* пе́рец. —*v.t.* **1,** (season) пе́рчить. **2,** (pelt) осыпа́ть. —**pepper shaker,** пе́речница.
peppermint *n.* **1,** (herb) пе́речная мя́та. **2,** (candy) мя́тный леденéц.
pepsin *n.* пепси́н.
peptic ulcer я́звенная боле́знь.
peptone *n.* пепто́н.
per *prep.* **1,** (for each) в; за: *ten miles per hour,* де́сять миль в час; *ten cents per item,* де́сять це́нтов за шту́ку. *Ten dollars per person,* де́сять до́лларов с челове́ка. **2,** [*often,* **as per**] (according to) в соотве́тствии с.
peradventure *adv., archaic* мо́жет быть; возмо́жно.
perambulator *n.* де́тская коля́ска.
per annum в год.
percale *n.* перка́ль.
per capita на ду́шу населе́ния.
perceive *v.t.* **1,** (become aware of through the senses) воспринима́ть; ощуща́ть. **2,** (come to understand) понима́ть; осознава́ть.
percent *n.* проце́нт: *fifty percent,* пятьдеся́т проце́нтов.
percentage *n.* **1,** (percent) проце́нт. **2,** (part; proportion) часть; до́ля. **3,** (fee; commission) проце́нты: *work on percentage,* рабо́тать на проце́нтах.
perceptible *adj.* заме́тный; ощути́мый.
perception *n.* **1,** (act of perceiving) восприя́тие. **2,** (keenness of mind) проница́тельность.
perceptive *adj.* проница́тельный; то́нкий; зо́ркий. *Perceptive comment,* то́нкое замеча́ние.
perch *n.* **1,** (fish) о́кунь. **2,** (roost) насе́ст. —*v.i.* уса́живаться.
perchance *adv.* случа́йно.
perchloric acid хло́рная кислота́.
percolate *v.t.* проце́живать. —*v.i.* **1,** (seep; ooze) проса́чиваться. **2,** (start bubbling up) кипе́ть. —**percolator,** *n.* кофе́йник с си́течком.
percussion *n.* столкнове́ние; уда́р. —**percussion cap,** ка́псюль; писто́н. —**percussion instrument,** уда́рный инструме́нт.
per diem 1, (per day) за день. **2,** (daily allowance) су́точные де́ньги.
perdition *n.* прокля́тие: *condemn to perdition,* предава́ть прокля́тию.
peregrination *n.* стра́нствие.
peregrine falcon сапса́н.
peremptory *adj.* **1,** (barring further action) безапелляцио́нный. **2,** (allowing no room for disagreement) повели́тельный.
perennial *adj.* **1,** (perpetual) ве́чный. **2,** *bot.* многоле́тний. —*n., bot.* многоле́тнее расте́ние.
perfect *adj.* **1,** (complete; exact; utter) соверше́нный. **2,** (flawless) безупре́чный. **3,** (ideal) идеа́льный; образцо́вый; превосхо́дный. —*v.t.* соверше́нствовать; доводи́ть до соверше́нства. —*n., gram.* перфе́кт.
perfection *n.* **1,** (state of being perfect) соверше́нство. *To perfection,* в соверше́нстве. **2,** (act of perfecting) соверше́нствование.
perfective *adj., gram.* соверше́нный. —*n., gram.* соверше́нный вид.
perfectly *adv.* **1,** (to perfection) в соверше́нстве. **2,** (completely; fully) соверше́нно: *perfectly obvious,* соверше́нно очеви́дно. *I know perfectly well that...,* я прекра́сно зна́ю, что... **3,** (without a hitch) безотка́зно: *work perfectly,* рабо́тать безотка́зно.
perfidious *adj.* вероло́мный. —**perfidy,** *n.* вероло́мство.
perforate *v.t.* **1,** (drill a hole or holes through) просве́рливать. **2,** (pierce with holes in rows, as stamps) перфори́ровать. —*adj.* = **perforated.**
perforated *adj.* **1,** (pierced with holes) перфори́рованный. **2,** (of stamps) зубцо́вый. —**perforated ulcer,** прободна́я я́зва.
perforation *n.* **1,** *med.* прободе́ние; перфора́ция. **2,** (on stamps) перфора́ция; зубцо́вка.
perforce *adv.* во́лей-нево́лей.
perform *v.t.* **1,** (execute; carry out) выполня́ть; исполня́ть. *Perform an operation,* сде́лать опера́цию. *Perform an experiment,* проводи́ть о́пыт. *Perform a trick,* показа́ть фо́кус. **2,** (give a performance of) исполня́ть. —*v.i.* **1,** (give a performance) игра́ть; выступа́ть. **2,** (function; operate) рабо́тать.
performance *n.* **1,** (carrying out) выполне́ние; исполне́ние. **2,** (rendition) исполне́ние; игра́. **3,** (show) представле́ние; спекта́кль; сеа́нс. **4,** (efficiency of operation) ходовы́е ка́чества. *Performance tests,* ходовы́е испыта́ния.
performer *n.* исполни́тель.
perfume *n.* духи́. *Perfume bottle,* флако́н для духо́в. —*v.t.* души́ть. —**perfumer,** *n.* парфюме́р. —**perfumery,** *n.* парфюме́рия.
perfunctory *adj.* пове́рхностный; механи́ческий. —**perfunctorily,** *adv.* пове́рхностно; ме́льком.
perhaps *adv.* мо́жет быть.
pericardium *n.* околосерде́чная су́мка.
pericarp *n.* околопло́дник.
perigee *n.* периге́й.
perihelion *n.* периге́лий.
peril *n.* опа́сность; риск. *At one's own peril,* на свой страх и риск. —*v.t.* ста́вить под угро́зу. —**perilous,** *adj.* опа́сный; риско́ванный.
perimeter *n.* пери́метр.
period *n.* **1,** (in history) пери́од; эпо́ха. **2,** (interval of time) срок; пери́од. **3,** (dot placed at end of a sentence) то́чка. **4,** (division of a school day) уро́к. **5,** (division of a game) пери́од; тайм. —*adj.* сти́льный: *period furniture,* сти́льная ме́бель.
periodic *adj.* периоди́ческий.
periodical *adj.* периоди́ческий. —*n.* периоди́ческое изда́ние.
periodically *adv.* **1,** (at regular intervals) периоди́чески. **2,** (from time to time) вре́мя от вре́мени.
peripatetic *adj.* стра́нствующий.
peripheral *adj.* **1,** (away from the center) перифери́ческий. **2,** *fig.* (incidental; tangential) несуще́ственный; второстепе́нный.
periphery *n.* перифери́я.
periphrasis *n.* перифра́за; парафра́за.
periscope *n.* перisко́п.
perish *v.i.* ги́бнуть; погиба́ть. —**perish the thought!,** упаси́ Бог!; Бо́же упаси́!
perishable *adj.* скоропо́ртящийся. —*n., usu. pl.* скоропо́ртящиеся проду́кты.

peristalsis *n.* перистáльтика. —**peristaltic,** *adj.* перистальтúческий.
peristyle *n.* перистúль.
peritoneum *n.* брюшúна. —**peritonitis,** *n.* воспалéние брюшúны; перитонúт.
periwinkle *n.* **1,** (plant) барвúнок. **2,** (mollusk) litopúна.
perjure *v.t.* [*usu.* **perjure oneself**] лжесвидéтельствовать. —**perjurer,** *n.* лжесвидéтель; клятвопрестýпник. —**perjury,** *n.* лжесвидéтельство; клятвопреступлéние.
perk *v.t.* [*usu.* **perk up**] оживлять; ободрять. —*v.i.* [*usu.* **perk up**] оживáть; оживлятьcя; воспрянуть дýхом. —**perky,** *adj.* бóйкий; задóрный.
permafrost *n.* вéчная мерзлотá.
permanence *n.* постоянство.
permanent *adj.* постоянный. —*n.* = **permanent wave.**
permanently *adv.* на дóлгое врéмя; навсегдá. *Permanently damaged,* непоправúмо повреждeн.
permanent wave перманéнт; шестимéсячная завúвка.
permeable *adj.* проницáемый. —**permeability,** *n.* проницáемость.
permeate *v.t.* проникáть в; пронúзывать.
permissible *adj.* позволúтельный; допустúмый; дозвóленный.
permission *n.* разрешéние; позволéние.
permissive *adj.* не стрóгий; снисходúтельный.
permit *v.t.* **1,** (give permission to) разрешáть; позволять: *permit me to...,* разрешúте/позвóльте мне (+ *inf.*). **2,** (allow to happen) допускáть. **3,** (enable) позволять: *this will permit me to...,* э́то позвóлит мне (+ *inf.*). —*v.i.* позволять: *if time permits,* éсли врéмя позволяет; *weather permitting,* éсли погóда позвóлит. —*n.* прóпуск; разрешéние.
permutation *n.* перестанóвка.
pernicious *adj.* пáгубный. —**pernicious anemia,** злокáчественное малокрóвие.
perorate *v.i.* орáторствовать; разглагóльствовать.
peroxide *n.* **1,** (chemical) пéрекись. **2,** (antiseptic) пéрекись водорóда.
perpendicular *adj.* перпендикулярный. —*n.* перпендикуляр.
perpetrate *v.t.* совершáть: *perpetrate a crime,* совершúть преступлéние. —**perpetration,** *n.* совершéние (преступлéния). —**perpetrator,** *n.* винóвник (преступлéния).
perpetual *adj.* вéчный. *Perpetual motion,* вéчное движéние. —**perpetually,** *adv.* вéчно.
perpetuate *v.t.* увековéчивать. —**perpetuation,** *n.* увековéчение.
perpetuity *n.* вéчность. —**in perpetuity,** навéчно.
perplex *v.t.* приводúть в недоумéние; озадáчивать. —**perplexed,** *adj.* недоумéнный; недоумевáющий; озадáченный. —**perplexing,** *adj.* недоумéнный. —**perplexity,** *n.* недоумéние; озадáченность.
perquisite *n.* прúработок.
per se сам по себé.
persecute *v.t.* преслéдовать. —**persecution,** *n.* преслéдование; гонéние. —**persecutor,** *n.* преслéдователь; гонúтель.
persevere *v.i.* упóрствовать. —**perseverance,** *n.* упóрство; настóйчивость.
Persian *adj.* персúдский. —*n.* **1,** (person) перс; персиянка. **2,** (language) персúдский язы́к. —**Persian cat,** сибúрская кóшка. —**Persian lamb,** карáкуль.
persiflage *n.* беззлóбная насмéшка.
persimmon *n.* хурмá.
persist *v.i.* **1,** (refuse to give up) упóрствовать. **2,** (continue to exist) сохранятьcя.
persistence *n.* упóрство; настóйчивость; настоятельность.
persistent *adj.* **1,** (refusing to relent) упóрный; настóйчивый; настоятельный. *Persistent cough,* упóрный кáшель. **2,** (repeated; continuous) бесконéчный.
person *n.* **1,** (human being) человéк. **2,** *gram.* лицó: *first person,* пéрвое лицó. —**in person,** лúчно; сóбственной персóной. —**in the person of,** в лицé (+ *gen.*). —**on one's person,** при себé.
personable *adj.* симпатúчный; располагáющий.
personage *n.* **1,** (person) лицó: *historic personage,* истори́ческое лицó. **2,** (character in a play, history, etc.) персонáж.
personal *adj.* лúчный: *my personal opinion,* мое лúчное мнéние. *Get personal,* переходúть на лúчности. —**personal pronoun,** лúчное местоимéние.
personality *n.* лúчность.
personally *adv.* лúчно. *Take something personally,* принимáть чтó-нибудь на свой счет.
persona non grata персóна нон грáта.
personify *v.t.* олицетворять. —**personification,** *n.* олицетворéние.
personnel *n.* кáдры; персонáл; лúчный состáв. *Personnel department,* отдéл кáдров.
perspective *n.* **1,** *art* перспектúва. **2,** (viewpoint) свет: *in a different perspective,* в другóм свéте. *Keep things in perspective,* ширóкó смотрéть на вéщи. —*adj.* перспектúвный.
perspicacious *adj.* проницáтельный. —**perspicacity,** *n.* проницáтельность.
perspiration *n.* пот; испáрина.
perspire *v.i.* потéть.
persuade *v.t.* **1,** (induce) уговáривать. **2,** (convince) убеждáть.
persuasion *n.* **1,** (act of persuading) убеждéние. *After considerable persuasion,* пóсле дóлгих уговóров. **2,** (religious belief) вероисповéдание.
persuasive *adj.* убедúтельный. —**persuasively,** *adv.* убедúтельно. —**persuasiveness,** *n.* убедúтельность.
pert *adj.* **1,** (impudent) развязный. **2,** (lively) задóрный.
pertain *v.i.* [*usu.* **pertain to**] относúться (к).
pertinacious *adj.* **1,** (stubborn) упрямый. **2,** (persistent) упóрный. —**pertinacity,** *n.* упрямство; упóрство.
pertinent *adj.* умéстный; относящийся к дéлу. —**pertinence,** *n.* умéстность.
perturb *v.t.* смущáть; волновáть.
perturbation *n., astron.* пертурбáция.
peruse *v.t.* **1,** (read carefully) внимáтельно прочитáть. **2,** (read casually; scan) просмáтривать. —**perusal,** *n.* прочтéние.
Peruvian *adj.* перуáнский.
pervade *v.t.* наполнять; насыщáть; пропúтывать; пронúзывать; распространятьcя по. —**pervasive,** *adj.* распространяющийся повсю́ду.
perverse *adj.* **1,** (contrary) упрямый. **2,** (perverted) порóчный.

perversion *n.* извращéние.
perversity *n.* **1,** (contrariness) упря́мство. **2,** (depravity) извращённость; поро́чность.
pervert *v.t.* **1,** (distort; twist) извраща́ть. **2,** (lead astray; corrupt) соврaща́ть. —*n.* извращённый челове́к.
perverted *adj.* поро́чный; извращённый; противоесте́ственный.
peseta *n.* песе́та; пезе́та.
pesky *adj., colloq.* надое́дливый; доку́чливый.
peso *n.* пе́со; пе́зо.
pessimism *n.* пессими́зм. —**pessimist,** *n.* пессими́ст. —**pessimistic,** *adj.* пессимисти́ческий. *I am pessimistic,* я настро́ен пессимисти́чески.
pest *n.* **1,** (annoying person) надое́да. **2,** (destructive insect) вреди́тель.
pester *v.t.* надоеда́ть; докуча́ть; пристава́ть к.
pesticide *n.* ядохимика́т.
pestilence *n.* чума́.
pestle *n.* пест; пе́стик.
pet *n.* **1,** (animal) дома́шнее живо́тное. **2,** (favorite) люби́мец; ба́ловень. —*adj.* люби́мый. —*v.t.* гла́дить. —**pet name,** уменьши́тельное *or* ласка́тельное и́мя.
petal *n.* лепесто́к.
petard *n.* пета́рда.
petcock *n.* спускно́й кран.
peter *v.i.* [*usu.* **peter out**] выдыха́ться.
petiole *n.* черешо́к.
petition *n.* пети́ция. —*v.t.* обраща́ться с пети́цией к. —**petitioner,** *n.* проси́тель.
petrel *n.* буреве́стник; качу́рка.
petrified *adj.* **1,** (having turned to stone) окамене́лый. **2,** (terrified) оцепене́вший. *We were petrified,* мы дрожа́ли от стра́ха.
petrify *v.t.* превраща́ть в ка́мень. —*v.i.* (о)камене́ть.
petrochemical *n.* нефтехими́ческий проду́кт. —*adj.* нефтехими́ческий.
petrol *n., Brit.* бензи́н.
petroleum *n.* нефть. —*adj.* нефтяно́й.
petticoat *n.* ни́жняя ю́бка.
pettifoggery *n.* крючкотво́рство.
pettiness *n.* ме́лочность.
petty *adj.* **1,** (minor; trivial) ме́лкий. **2,** (picayune; niggling) ме́лочный. —**petty larceny,** ме́лкая кра́жа. —**petty officer,** старшина́.
petulant *adj.* раздражи́тельный; сварли́вый. —**petulance,** *n.* раздражи́тельность.
petunia *n.* пету́ния.
pew *n.* (церко́вная) скамья́.
pewit *n.* чи́бис; пи́галица.
pewter *n.* сплав на оловя́нной осно́ве. —*adj.* оловя́нный.
phaeton *n.* фаэто́н.
phagocyte *n.* фагоци́т.
phalanx *n.* фала́нга.
phalarope *n.* плаву́нчик.
phallus *n.* фа́ллос. —**phallic,** *adj.* фалли́ческий.
phantasmagoria *n.* фантасмаго́рия. —**phantasmagoric,** *adj.* фантасмагори́ческий.
phantom *n.* при́зрак; виде́ние; фанто́м.
Pharaoh *n.* фарао́н.
pharisee *n.* фарисе́й. —**pharisaic,** *adj.* фарисе́йский.
pharmaceutical *adj.* апте́карский; фармацевти́ческий. —**pharmaceutics,** *n.* фармаце́втика.
pharmacist *n.* фармаце́вт; апте́карь; прови́зор.
pharmacology *n.* фармаколо́гия. —**pharmacological,** *adj.* фармакологи́ческий. —**pharmacologist,** *n.* фармако́лог.
pharmacopeia *n.* фармакопе́я.
pharmacy *n.* **1,** (the science) фармаце́втика; фарма́ция. **2,** (drugstore) апте́ка.
pharynx *n.* зев.
phase *n.* фа́за; фа́зис. —*v.t.* [*usu.* **phase in** *or* **phase out**] постепе́нно вводи́ть *or* упраздня́ть. —**phased,** *adj.* постепе́нный; по эта́пам.
pheasant *n.* фаза́н.
phenobarbital *n.* люмина́л; фенобарбита́л.
phenol *n.* фено́л.
phenomenal *adj.* феномена́льный.
phenomenon *n.* **1,** (observable fact) явле́ние. **2,** (marvel; wonder) фено́мен.
phial *n.* пузырёк; флако́н; скля́нка.
philander *v.i.* флиртова́ть. —**philanderer,** *n.* волоки́та; ухажёр.
philanthropy *n.* филантро́пия. —**philanthropic,** *adj.* филантропи́ческий. —**philanthropist,** *n.* филантро́п.
philately *n.* филатели́я. —**philatelic,** *adj.* филателисти́ческий. —**philatelist,** *n.* филатели́ст.
philharmonic *adj.* филармони́ческий. —*n.* **1,** (orchestra) симфони́ческий орке́стр. **2,** (group supporting same) филармо́ния.
philippic *n.* фили́ппика.
Philippine *adj.* филиппи́нский.
philodendron *n.* филоде́ндрон.
philology *n.* филоло́гия. —**philological,** *adj.* филологи́ческий. —**philologist,** *n.* фило́лог.
philosopher *n.* фило́соф. —**philosophic(al),** *adj.* филосо́фский. —**philosophize,** *v.i.* филосо́фствовать.
philosophy *n.* филосо́фия.
phlebitis *n.* флеби́т.
phlebotomy *n.* кровопуска́ние.
phlegm *n.* **1,** (mucus) мокро́та. **2,** (apathy) фле́гма. —**phlegmatic,** *adj.* флегмати́чный.
phloem *n.* фло́эма.
phlox *n.* флокс.
phobia *n.* фо́бия.
Phoenician *adj.* финики́йский.
phoenix *n.* фе́никс.
phone *n., colloq.* телефо́н. *Phone call,* вы́зов (по телефо́ну); телефо́нный звоно́к. *Phone number,* но́мер телефо́на. *Pick up the phone!,* возьми́те тру́бку! —*v.t., colloq.* звони́ть.
phoneme *n.* фоне́ма. —**phonemic,** *adj.* фонемати́ческий.
phonetic *adj.* фонети́ческий. —**phonetics,** *n.* фоне́тика.
phoney *adj.* = **phony.**
phonograph *n.* граммофо́н; патефо́н; проигрыватель. *Phonograph record,* грампласти́нка.
phonology *n.* фоноло́гия.
phony *also,* **phoney** *adj., slang* подде́льный; ли́повый.
phooey *interj.* тьфу!
phosgene *n.* фосге́н.
phosphate *n.* фосфа́т.

phosphorescence *n.* свече́ние; фосфоресце́нция. —**phosphorescent,** *adj.* фосфоресци́рующий.
phosphorus *n.* фо́сфор. —**phosphoric; phosphorous,** *adj.* фо́сфорный.
photo *n., colloq.* фотогра́фия; фо́то.
photocopier *n.* копирова́льная маши́на; фотоста́т. —**photocopy,** *n.* фотоко́пия.
photoelectric *adj.* фотоэлектри́ческий. —**photoelectric cell,** фотоэлеме́нт.
photoengraving *n.* фотогравю́ра.
photogenic *adj.* фотогени́чный.
photograph *n.* фотогра́фия; фотосни́мок. —*v.t.* фотографи́ровать. —*v.i. I do not photograph well,* я пло́хо выхожу́ на фотогра́фии.
photographer *n.* фото́граф.
photography *n.* фотогра́фия. —**photographic,** *adj.* фотографи́ческий.
photogravure *n.* фотогравю́ра.
photometer *n.* фото́метр.
photon *n.* фото́н.
photosphere *n.* фотосфе́ра.
photostat *n.* фотоко́пия.
photosynthesis *n.* фотоси́нтез.
phrase *n.* фра́за; оборо́т. —*v.t.* формули́ровать. —**phrase book,** разгово́рник.
phraseology *n.* фразеоло́гия. —**phraseological,** *adj.* фразеологи́ческий.
phrenology *n.* френоло́гия.
phylactery *n.* филакте́рия.
phylum *n.* тип.
physical *adj.* физи́ческий. —*n., colloq.* медици́нский осмо́тр. —**physical education,** физи́ческое воспита́ние; физи́ческая культу́ра; физкульту́ра. —**physical examination,** медици́нский осмо́тр. —**physical exercise,** физи́ческие упражне́ния. —**physical science,** физи́ческие нау́ки. —**physical training** = **physical education.**
physically *adv.* физи́чески.
physician *n.* врач.
physicist *n.* фи́зик.
physics *n.* фи́зика.
physiognomy *n.* физионо́мия.
physiology *n.* физиоло́гия. —**physiological,** *adj.* физиологи́ческий. —**physiologist,** *n.* физио́лог.
physiotherapy *n.* физиотерапи́я. —**physiotherapist,** *n.* физиотерапе́вт.
physique *n.* телосложе́ние.
pianissimo *adj. & adv.* пиани́ссимо.
pianist *n.* пиани́ст.
piano *n.* роя́ль; фортепья́но. *Upright piano,* пиани́но. —*adj.* фортепья́нный: *piano concerto,* фортепья́нный конце́рт. *Piano bench,* скаме́йка для роя́ля. *Piano lessons,* уро́ки игры́ на роя́ле. —*adv.* пиа́но.
pianoforte *n.* фортепья́но.
piaster *also,* **piastre** *n.* пиа́стр.
pica *n.* ци́церо.
picaresque *adj.* плутовско́й.
picayune *adj.* пустяко́вый; ерундо́вый; ме́лочный.
piccolo *n.* пи́кколо.
pick *n.* **1,** (tool) кирка́. **2,** (choice) вы́бор. *Take your pick,* выбира́йте. **3,** (choicest part) лу́чшая часть; цвет. —*v.t.* **1,** (select) выбира́ть; подбира́ть. **2,** (gather, as berries) собира́ть. **3,** (pluck) срыва́ть. **4,** (remove the feathers of, as a chicken) щипа́ть; ощи́пывать. **5,** (pry open, as a lock) взла́мывать. **6,** (provoke, as a fight or quarrel) лезть в (дра́ку); иска́ть (ссо́ры). **7,** *Pick one's nose/teeth,* ковыря́ть в носу́/зуба́х. **8,** *Pick someone's pocket,* залеза́ть в карма́н (+ *dat.*). —*v.i.* (select) выбира́ть. —**pick on,** придира́ться к. —**pick out, 1,** (select) выбира́ть. **2,** (distinguish; discern) различа́ть. **3,** (play by ear) подбира́ть: *pick out a tune on the piano,* подбира́ть моти́в на роя́ле. —**pick up, 1,** (take up from the ground or floor) поднима́ть; подбира́ть. **2,** (call for) заходи́ть за; заезжа́ть за. **3,** (go and collect) идти́ за. **4,** (give a lift to on the road) подвози́ть. **5,** (take on, as a passenger or freight) забира́ть. **6,** (acquire casually) приобрета́ть; подцепля́ть. **7,** (learn superficially) нахвата́ться. **8,** (gain, as speed) набира́ть (ско́рость). **9,** (find, as a trail or scent) напада́ть на (след). **10,** (receive, as a radio signal) лови́ть; ула́вливать. **11,** (give added energy to) подбодря́ть. **12,** (take into custody) заде́рживать. **13,** *colloq.* (improve) поправля́ться.
pickax *also,* **pickaxe** *n.* кирка́.
picker *n.* сбо́рщик.
pickerel *n.* щу́ка.
picket *n.* **1,** (stake) кол. **2,** (protester) пике́тчик. **3,** *mil.* пике́т. —*v.t. & i.* пикети́ровать. —**picket fence,** частоко́л. —**picket line,** пике́т.
pickle *n.* (солёный) огуре́ц. —*v.t.* соли́ть; заса́ливать; маринова́ть. —**pickled,** *adj.* солёный. *Pickled herring,* сельдь в рассо́ле.
pickpocket *n.* карма́нный вор.
pickup *n.* **1,** (acceleration): *the car has good pickup,* маши́на хорошо́ (*or* бы́стро) набира́ет ско́рость. **2,** (collection of mail) вы́емка. **3,** *colloq.* (improvement) оживле́ние. —**pickup truck,** пика́п.
picky *adj., colloq.* привере́дливый.
picnic *n.* пикни́к.
pictograph *n.* пиктогра́мма. —**pictographic,** *adj.* пиктографи́ческий. —**pictography,** *n.* пиктогра́фия.
pictorial *adj.* **1,** (graphic) живопи́сный; изобрази́тельный; о́бразный. **2,** (containing pictures) иллюстри́рованный.
picture *n.* **1,** (drawing or painting) карти́на. **2,** (photograph) фотогра́фия; сни́мок; ка́рточка. *Take a picture of,* фотографи́ровать; снима́ть. *Take pictures,* фотографи́ровать. *Have one's picture taken,* снима́ться. **3,** (movie) фильм. **4,** (image on a TV screen) изображе́ние. **5,** (vivid description) карти́на: *a picture of life in Ancient Rome,* карти́на жи́зни в дре́внем Ри́ме. **6,** (mental image) представле́ние: *have a clear picture of,* име́ть я́сное представле́ние о. **7,** (general situation) карти́на: *a gloomy picture,* мра́чная карти́на. *Be out of the picture,* не фигури́ровать. *I get the picture,* я понима́ю в чём де́ло. **8,** (embodiment) воплоще́ние: *the picture of health,* воплоще́ние здоро́вья. —*adj.* карти́нный: *picture gallery,* карти́нная галере́я. —*v.t.* **1,** (visualize) представля́ть себе́. **2,** (depict) изобража́ть.
picture postcard откры́тка с ви́дом.
picturesque *adj.* живопи́сный.
picture tube кинеско́п.
piddling *adj.* ничто́жный; пустяко́вый.
pie *n.* пиро́г; пирожо́к.
piebald *adj.* пе́гий.
piece *n.* **1,** (portion) кусо́к: *piece of bread/meat,* кусо́к хле́ба/мя́са. *Piece of paper,* бума́жка. *Piece of candy,*

конфе́та. *Piece of advice,* сове́т. **2,** *pl.* (fragments) куски́; клочки́: *tear to pieces,* рвать на куски́ *or* в клочки́. *Smash to pieces,* разбива́ть вдре́безги. **3,** (item) шту́ка. *Piece of furniture,* ме́бель. *Five pieces of luggage,* пять мест. *Three-piece suit,* костю́м-тро́йка. *Sell by the piece,* продава́ть пошту́чно. **4,** (artistic creation) произведе́ние: *piece of art,* произведе́ние иску́сства. *Museum piece,* музе́йная ре́дкость. **5,** (coin) моне́та. **6,** (firearm) ору́дие: *artillery piece,* артиллери́йское ору́дие. **7,** *chess* фигу́ра. —*v.t.* [*usu.* **piece together**] составля́ть по кусо́чкам. —**give someone a piece of one's mind,** сказа́ть кому́-нибудь па́ру тёплых слов. —**go to pieces,** потеря́ть го́лову. —**speak one's piece,** вы́сказать своё мне́ние.

piecemeal *adv.* по частя́м.

piecework *n.* сде́льная рабо́та. —**pieceworker,** *n.* сде́льщик.

pier *n.* **1,** (wharf) при́стань. **2,** (of a bridge) бык. **3,** (between windows) просте́нок.

pierce *v.t.* пронза́ть; прока́лывать; протыка́ть. *Have one's ears pierced,* проколо́ть у́ши. —**piercing,** *adj.* пронзи́тельный.

pier glass трюмо́.

pier table подзерка́льник.

piety *n.* на́божность; благоче́стие.

pig *n.* свинья́. *Baby pig,* поросёнок.

pigeon *n.* го́лубь.

pigeonhole *v.t.* класть под сукно́.

pigeon-toed *adj.* косола́пый.

piggyback *adv.* на спине́; на закорках.

piggy bank копи́лка (в ви́де поросёнка).

pigheaded *adj.* крепколо́бый.

pig iron чугу́н в чу́шках.

piglet *n.* поросёнок.

pigment *n.* пигме́нт. —**pigmentation,** *n.* пигмента́ция.

pigpen *n.* свина́рник.

pigskin *n.* **1,** (leather) свина́я ко́жа. **2,** *colloq.* (football) футбо́льный мяч.

pigsty *n.* **1,** (pigpen) свина́рник. **2,** (filthy place) хлев.

pigtail *n.* коси́чка; крыси́ный хво́стик.

pika *n.* пищу́ха.

pike *n.* **1,** (fish) щу́ка. **2,** (spear) пи́ка.

pilaf *n.* пила́в.

pilaster *n.* пиля́стра.

pile *n.* **1,** (heap) ку́ча; гру́да; ки́па. *A pile of money,* ку́ча де́нег. **2,** (foundation for a pier) сва́я. **3,** (soft nap) ворс. —*v.t.* **1,** [*usu.* **pile up**] (make a pile of) скла́дывать; нагроможда́ть. **2,** (load) нава́ливать. **3,** (cover) зава́ливать: *the table is piled with books,* стол зава́лен кни́гами. —*v.i.* [*usu.* **pile up**] **1,** (form a pile) нагроможда́ться. **2,** (accumulate) накопля́ться.

pile driver копёр.

piles *n.pl.* геморро́й.

pilfer *v.t.* красть; тащи́ть; стяну́ть. —**pilferage,** *n.* ме́лкая кра́жа.

pilgrim *n.* пало́мник; пилигри́м. —**pilgrimage,** *n.* пало́мничество.

pill *n.* пилю́ля.

pillage *v.t.* гра́бить. —*v.i.* мародёрствовать. —*n.* грабёж; мародёрство.

pillar *n.* **1,** (column) столб. *Pillar of smoke,* столб ды́ма. **2,** *fig.* (mainstay) столп: *the pillars of society,* столпы́ о́бщества.

pillbox *n.* **1,** (box for pills) коро́бочка для пилю́ль. **2,** *mil.* дот.

pillory *n.* позо́рный столб. —*v.t.* пригвожда́ть/ста́вить/выставля́ть к позо́рному столбу́.

pillow *n.* поду́шка. —**pillowcase,** *n.* на́волочка.

pilot *n.* **1,** (of an aircraft) пило́т; лётчик. **2,** (harbor pilot) ло́цман. —*v.t.* вести́; управля́ть; пилоти́ровать. —*adj.* о́пытный; про́бный; эксперимента́льный. *Pilot program,* эксперимента́льная програ́мма.

pilot fish ло́цман.

pilothouse *n.* рулева́я ру́бка.

pimento *n.* **1,** [*also,* **pimiento**] (variety of pepper) стручко́вый пе́рец. **2,** = **allspice.**

pimp *n.* сво́дник.

pimpernel *n.* о́чный цвет.

pimple *n.* прыщ. —**pimply,** *adj.* прыща́вый; угрева́тый.

pin *n.* **1,** (small metal fastener) була́вка: *safety pin,* англи́йская була́вка. **2,** (bar or rod that fastens) штифт; шпи́лька. **3,** (broach) бро́шка. **4,** (badge) значо́к. **5,** *bowling* ке́гля. —*v.t.* **1,** (fasten with a pin) прика́лывать. *Pin up,* подка́лывать. **2,** (immobilize) прижима́ть: *pin to the ground/ropes,* прижима́ть к земле́/кана́там. *Pinned under the wreckage,* зажа́т под обло́мками. **3,** (place, as hopes, blame, etc.) возлага́ть. —**be on pins and needles,** быть *or* сиде́ть как на иго́лках. —**you could have heard a pin drop,** слы́шно бы́ло, как му́ха пролети́т.

pinafore *n.* пере́дник; фа́ртук.

pince-nez *n.* пенсне́.

pincers *n.pl.* **1,** (tool) клещи; пинце́т. **2,** (claw) клешня́. —**pincers movement,** клещи́.

pinch *v.t.* **1,** (nip) щипа́ть; ущипну́ть. **2,** *colloq.* (steal) красть; тащи́ть. —*v.i.* (of a shoe) жать. —*n.* **1,** (nip) щипо́к. **2,** (bit, as of salt) щепо́ть; щепо́тка. **3,** (emergency) кра́йний слу́чай: *in a pinch,* в кра́йнем слу́чае. —**pinch pennies,** жа́ться; стесня́ть себя́ в сре́дствах.

pincushion *n.* поду́шечка для була́вок.

pine *n.* сосна́. —*adj.* сосно́вый; хво́йный: *pine cone,* сосно́вая ши́шка; *pine tar,* хво́йный дёготь. —*v.i.* **1,** *fol. by* **away** (waste away) ча́хнуть; томи́ться. **2,** *fol. by* **for** (long for) тоскова́ть по; томи́ться по.

pineal *adj.* шишкови́дный.

pineapple *n.* анана́с. —*adj.* анана́сный: *pineapple juice,* анана́сный сок.

ping *n.* звон.

ping-pong *n.* пинг-по́нг.

pinhole *n.* була́вочная ды́рка.

pinion *n.* шестерня́.

pink *adj.* ро́зовый. —*n.* **1,** (flower) гвозди́ка. **2,** (color) ро́зовый цвет. —**in the pink,** в расцве́те сил.

pinkeye *n.* о́стрый зара́зный конъюнктиви́т.

pinkie *also,* **pinky** *n.* мизи́нец.

pin money де́ньги на була́вки.

pinnacle *n.* верши́на. *The pinnacle of power,* верши́на вла́сти.

pinnate *adj.* пе́ристый.

pinpoint *n.* остриё була́вки. —*v.t* то́чно определя́ть.

pinprick *n.* була́вочный уко́л.

pint *n.* пи́нта.

pintail *n.* шилохво́сть.

pinto *n.* пе́гая ло́шадь.

pioneer *n.* пионе́р. —*adj.* пионе́рский.

pious *adj.* **1,** (devout) на́божный; благочести́вый. **2,** (sanctimonious) ха́нжеский.

pip *n.* **1,** (bird disease) типу́н. **2,** (spot on a playing card) очко́.

pipe *n.* **1,** (tube) труба́. **2,** (for smoking) тру́бка. **3,** (musical instrument) свире́ль. —*adj.* тру́бочный: *pipe tobacco,* тру́бочный таба́к. —*v.t.* передава́ть че́рез трубу́ *or* че́рез трубопрово́д. —**pipe down,** сба́вить тон. *Pipe down!,* молчи́! —**pipe up,** заговори́ть.

pipe dream несбы́точная мечта́.

pipeline *n.* трубопрово́д. *Oil pipeline,* нефтепрово́д. *Gas pipeline,* газопрово́д.

pipe organ орга́н.

piper *n.* волы́нщик.

piping *n.* **1,** (tubing) тру́бы; систе́ма труб. **2,** (edging for dresses) кант; вы́пушка. —**piping hot,** с пы́лу, с жа́ру.

pipistrelle *n.* нетопы́рь.

pipsqueak *n., colloq.* ме́лкая со́шка.

piquant *adj.* пика́нтный. —**piquancy,** *n.* пика́нтность.

pique *n.* оби́да; доса́да. —*v.t.* **1,** (cause resentment in) уязвля́ть; уколо́ть. **2,** (arouse; stimulate) возбужда́ть.

piqué *n.* пике́. —*adj.* пике́йный.

piquet *n.* (card game) пике́т.

piracy *n.* пира́тство.

pirate *n.* пира́т. —*adj.* пира́тский: *pirate ship,* пира́тский кора́бль. —**piratical,** *adj.* пира́тский.

pirouette *n.* пиру́эт.

piscatorial *adj.* рыболо́вный; рыба́цкий.

Pisces *n.* ры́бы.

pistachio *n.* фиста́шка. —*adj.* фиста́шковый.

pistil *n.* пе́стик.

pistol *n.* пистоле́т. *Toy pistol,* пуга́ч.

piston *n.* **1,** (of an engine) по́ршень. **2,** (of a wind instrument) писто́н. —*adj.* поршнево́й: *piston engine,* поршнево́й дви́гатель; *piston ring,* поршнево́е кольцо́; *piston rod,* поршнево́й шток.

pit *n.* **1,** (stone of a fruit) ко́сточка. **2,** (hole) я́ма. **3,** (mine) ша́хта. **4,** *anat.* впа́дина. *Armpit,* подмы́шка. *In the pit of the stomach,* под ло́жечкой. **5,** (place where an orchestra sits) орке́стр; оркестро́вая я́ма. —*v.t.* **1,** (remove the pit from) вынима́ть ко́сточку из. **2,** (set in competition) противопоставля́ть.

pitch *v.t.* **1,** (throw) броса́ть; кида́ть. *Pitch hay,* вороши́ть се́но. **2,** (erect, as a tent) разбива́ть; раски́дывать. **3,** (cover or treat with pitch) смоли́ть. —*v.i.* **1,** (fall headlong) сва́ливаться. **2,** (toss, as of a ship) кача́ть; кача́ться. —*n.* **1,** (resin) смола́. **2,** (slope) скат; укло́н; накло́н. **3,** (tossing of a ship) ка́чка. **4,** *music* высота́. *Absolute pitch,* абсолю́тный слух. **5,** (degree of intensity) нака́л: *reach a fever pitch,* дойти́ до нака́ла. —**pitch in,** внести́ свою́ ле́пту.

pitchblende *n.* смоляна́я обма́нка.

pitch-dark *adj.* непрогля́дный. *It is pitch-dark in here,* здесь ни зги не ви́дно.

pitched battle генера́льное сраже́ние.

pitcher *n.* **1,** (vessel) кувши́н. **2,** *sports* подаю́щий.

pitchfork *n.* ви́лы.

piteous *adj.* жа́лкий.

pitfall *n.* подво́дный ка́мень.

pith *n.* сердцеви́на. —**pithy,** *adj.* вырази́тельный; содержа́тельный.

pitiable *adj.* = **pitiful.**

pitiful *adj.* жа́лкий.

pitiless *adj.* безжа́лостный.

pittance *n.* жа́лкие гроши́.

pituitary gland гипо́физ.

pity *n.* **1,** (compassion) жа́лость. *Have/take pity on,* сжа́литься над. **2,** (cause for sorrow) *rendered by* жаль: *It's a pity that...,* жаль, что... *What a pity!,* как жаль! —*v.t.* жале́ть. *I pity him,* я жале́ю его́; мне жаль его́.

pivot *n.* сте́ржень; шкво́рень. —*v.i.* враща́ться. —**pivotal,** *adj.* центра́льный; стержнево́й.

pizzicato *adj.* щипко́вый. —*adv.* щипко́м; пиццика́то; пиччика́то.

placard *n.* плака́т; афи́ша.

placate *v.t.* умиротворя́ть; уми́лостивить.

place *n.* ме́сто: *from place to place,* с ме́ста на ме́сто. *Come over to my place,* заходи́те ко мне. *Set a place for Nina,* поста́вить прибо́р для Ни́ны. *What would you do in my place?,* что вы сде́лаете на моём ме́сте? —*v.t.* **1,** (put; set) класть; ста́вить. **2,** (put in a certain situation or position) помеща́ть: *place a child in school,* помеща́ть ребёнка в шко́лу. **3,** (order; list) помеща́ть: *place an ad,* помеща́ть рекла́му; *place an order,* помеща́ть зака́з. *Place orders,* размеща́ть зака́зы. *Place a telephone call,* зака́зывать разгово́р по телефо́ну. **4,** (name; identify): *I can't place him,* не могу́ вспо́мнить, кто он тако́й. **5,** (repose; pin) возлага́ть (наде́жду); ока́зывать (дове́рие). —*v.i.* занима́ть (како́е-нибудь ме́сто): *place third,* заня́ть тре́тье ме́сто. —**in place of,** вме́сто (+ *gen.*). —**in places,** места́ми. —**in the first place,** во-пе́рвых. —**in the second place,** во-вторы́х. —**know one's place,** знать своё ме́сто. —**no place,** нигде́; никуда́. —**out of place, 1,** (not in the proper place) не на (своём) ме́сте; не на тех места́х. **2,** (inappropriate) не к ме́сту; неуме́стный. —**put someone in his place,** поста́вить кого́-нибудь на ме́сто. —**take place,** име́ть ме́сто; происходи́ть; состоя́ться. —**take the place of,** заменя́ть.

placebo *n.* безоби́дное сре́дство.

placement *n.* **1,** (act of placing) помеще́ние; размеще́ние. **2,** (placing persons in jobs) расстано́вка.

place name географи́ческое назва́ние.

placenta *n.* плаце́нта; после́д; де́тское ме́сто.

place setting прибо́р.

placid *adj.* споко́йный; безмяте́жный; невозмути́мый.

plagiarism *n.* литерату́рное воровство́; плагиа́т. —**plagiarist,** *n.* плагиа́тор.

plagiarize *v.t.* заимствовать (чужо́е произведе́ние).

plague *n.* **1,** (disease) чума́. **2,** (calamity; scourge) бич. —*v.t.* му́чить. *Be plagued by doubts,* му́читься сомне́ниями.

plaice *n.* ка́мбала.

plaid *n.* шотла́ндка. —*adj.* клётчатый; в клётку.

plain *n.* равни́на. —*adj.* **1,** (clear; unambiguous) я́сный; поня́тный. *In plain English,* поня́тным англи́йским языко́м. *In plain view of everyone,* у всех на виду́. *As plain as the nose on your face,* ясне́е я́сного. **2,** (simple; unpretentious) просто́й: *plain folk,* просты́е лю́ди; *plain food,* проста́я пи́ща. **3,** (downright) чи́стый; су́щий: *plain nonsense,* чи́стый/су́щий вздор. **4,** (having no design) одноцве́тный; гла́дкий. **5,** (unattractive) некраси́вый; невзра́чный. **6,** (not encoded) откры́тый: *plain text,* откры́тый текст.

plainclothesman *n.* сыщик в штатском платье.
plainly *adv.* **1,** (clearly) ясно. **2,** (simply) просто: *dress plainly,* одеваться просто.
plain-spoken *adj.* откровенный; прямодушный.
plaintiff *n.* истец; предъявитель иска.
plaintive *adj.* жалобный.
plait *n.* коса. —*v.t.* плести; заплетать.
plan *n.* план. —*v.t.* **1,** (draw up plans for) намечать; планировать. **2,** *fol. by inf.* (intend; expect) собираться; намереваться; предполагать. *We stayed longer than planned,* мы остались дольше, чем предполагали. —*v.i.* строить планы.
plane *n.* **1,** (flat surface) плоскость. **2,** (tool) рубанок. **3,** (airplane) самолёт. *Plane ticket,* билет на самолёт. *Plane fare,* стоимость полёта самолётом. *Plane crash,* авиационная катастрофа. **4,** *fig.* (level) уровень: *on a high moral plane,* на высоком нравственном уровне. —*adj.* плоский. —*v.t.* строгать.
plane geometry планиметрия.
planer *n.* строгальщик.
planet *n.* планета. —**planetarium,** *n.* планетарий. —**planetary,** *adj.* планетный.
plane tree платан; чинар(а).
plank *n.* доска; планка. —*v.t.* настилать. —**planking,** *n.* доски; обшивка.
plankton *n.* планктон.
planned *adj.* запланированный. *Planned economy,* плановое хозяйство.
planner *n.* **1,** (economic planner) плановик. **2,** (designer) планировщик: *town planner,* планировщик городов.
planning *n.* планирование; планировка. *Planning department,* плановый отдел.
plant *n.* **1,** (living organism) растение. **2,** (factory) завод. **3,** (complete apparatus) установка: *power plant,* силовая установка. —*v.t.* **1,** (place in the ground) сажать: *plant a tree,* сажать дерево. **2,** (furnish with plants, as a field) засаживать; усаживать. **3,** (place firmly) упираться (+ *instr.*). **4,** (place surreptitiously) подкладывать; подбрасывать. *Plant a bomb,* подложить бомбу.
plantain *n.* подорожник.
plantation *n.* плантация.
planter *n.* **1,** (plantation owner) плантатор. **2,** (machine for planting) сажалка.
plant louse тля.
plaque *n.* доска; дощечка; табличка.
plasma *n.* плазма.
plaster *n.* **1,** (substance for coating walls) штукатурка. **2,** (substance applied to the body) пластырь. **3,** (plaster of Paris) гипс. —*adj.* штукатурный; гипсовый. —*v.t.* **1,** (cover with plaster) штукатурить. **2,** (cover all over) облеплять. —**plaster cast, 1,** (copy of a statue) гипсовый слепок. **2,** *med.* гипс.
plasterer *n.* штукатур.
plastic *n.* пластмасса; пластик. —*adj.* **1,** (made of plastic) пластмассовый. **2,** (pert. to modeling) пластический. **3,** (capable of being molded) пластичный. —**plastic arts,** пластика. —**plastic bomb,** пластиковая бомба. —**plastic surgery,** пластическая хирургия.
plat du jour дежурное блюдо.
plate *n.* **1,** (dish) тарелка. **2,** (sheet of metal) пластинка.
plateau *n.* плоскогорье; плато.
plate glass зеркальное стекло.
platelet *n., usu. pl.* кровяная пластинка.
platen *n.* валик.
platform *n.* **1,** (landing alongside railway tracks) платформа; перрон. **2,** (stage; rostrum) помост. **3,** (of a railway car or streetcar) площадка. **4,** (of a political party) платформа.
platinum *n.* платина. —*adj.* платиновый.
platitude *n.* общее место; банальность.
platonic *adj.* платонический.
platoon *n.* взвод. *Platoon leader,* взводный.
platter *n.* блюдо.
platypus *n.* утконос.
plaudit *n., usu. pl.* **1,** (applause) аплодисменты. **2,** (praise) восторженные отзывы.
plausible *adj.* правдоподобный. *Plausible excuse,* благовидный предлог. —**plausibility,** *n.* правдоподобие.
play *v.i.* **1,** (engage in recreation or a game) играть: *play with a doll/with dolls/,* играть с куклой/в куклы/. *Play with blocks,* играть кубиками *or* в кубики. *Play with matches/fire,* играть со спичками/с огнём/. **2,** *fol. by* **with** (fiddle with) играть (+ *instr.*): *play with one's keys,* играть ключами. **3,** (of a film, show, etc.) идти. **4,** (pretend to be) притворяться (+ *instr.*): *play dead,* притворяться мёртвым. **5,** *in* **play for time,** оттягивать время; стараться выиграть время. **6,** *in* **play into the hands of,** играть на руку (+ *dat.*). —*v.t.* **1,** (engage in, as a game) играть в (+ *acc.*): *play ball/chess/cards,* играть в мяч/шахматы/карты. **2,** (perform on, as a musical instrument) играть на (+ *prepl.*): *play the violin,* играть на скрипке. **3,** (compete against) играть с. **4,** (perform) играть: *play a role,* играть роль; *play Hamlet,* играть Гамлета. *Play the fool,* валять дурака. **5,** (gamble at) играть на (+ *prepl.*): *play the horses,* играть на скачках; *play the stock market,* играть на бирже. **6,** (lead, as a card) идти с (+ *gen.*); (move, as a chess piece) играть (+ *instr.*); идти (+ *instr.*). **7,** *Play a record,* (по)ставить пластинку. **8,** *Play tricks,* шалить. **9,** *Play a joke/trick on,* сыграть шутку с. —*n.* **1,** (recreation) игра: *at play,* за игрой. **2,** (drama) пьеса. **3,** (maneuver in a game) комбинация. **4,** *in* **out of play,** вне игры; **in play,** в игре. **5,** *in* **play on words,** игра слов. —**bring into play,** пускать в ход. —**come into play,** вступать в действие. —**play around,** шалить. —**play down,** преуменьшать. —**play on** *or* **upon,** играть на: *play on someone's emotions,* играть на чьих-нибудь чувствах. —**play up,** подчёркивать; выпячивать. —**play up to,** заигрывать с; угодничать перед; подмазываться к.
play-acting *n.* актёрство; позёрство. —**play-actor,** *n.* позёр.
playbill *n.* **1,** (poster) афиша. **2,** (printed program) программа.
playboy *n.* повеса; гуляка; жуир.
player *n.* **1,** (contestant) игрок. *Basketball player,* баскетболист. *Chess player,* шахматист. **2,** (actor) актёр. **3,** (musician) музыкант.
player piano пианола.
playful *adj.* игривый; резвый; шаловливый. —**playfulness,** *n.* игривость; резвость; шаловливость.
playgoer *n.* театрал.
playground *n.* площадка для игр.
playhouse *n.* театр.

playing *adj.* игрáющий. —**playing card,** игрáльная кáрта. —**playing field,** спортúвное пóле; спортúвная площáдка. —**playing time,** *sports* игровóе врéмя.
playmate *n.* друг дéтства.
playoff *n., sports* рóзыгрыш.
playpen *n.* манéж.
plaything *n.* игрýшка.
playwright *n.* драматýрг.
plaza *n.* плóщадь.
plea *n.* **1,** (entreaty) мольбá: *a plea for help,* мольбá о пóмощи. **2,** *law* заявлéние: *plea of not guilty,* заявлéние о своéй невинóвности.
plead *v.i.* **1,** (beg) умолять; упрáшивать: *plead with someone for help,* умолять/упрáшивать когó-нибудь о пóмощи. **2,** *law* (put forward a plea): *plead guilty,* признáть себя винóвным. *Plead not guilty,* заявлять о своéй невинóвности. —*v.t.* **1,** (argue; present, as a case) вестú (дéло). **2,** (offer as justification) ссылáться на; отговáриваться (+ *instr.*).
pleasant *adj.* приятный.
pleasantly *adv.* приятно: *I was pleasantly surprised,* я был приятно удивлён.
pleasantry *n.* шутлúвое замечáние; шýтка. *Exchange pleasantries,* обмéниваться комплимéнтами.
please *v.t.* нрáвиться; угождáть. *You can't please everybody,* на всех не угодúшь. —*v.i.* **1,** (give satisfaction) давáть удовлетворéние. **2,** (wish) хотéть: *do as you please,* дéлайте как хотúте. —*imperative* **1,** *in polite requests* пожáлуйста; бýдьте добры́; бýдьте любéзны. **2,** *in earnest entreaties* я вас óчень прошý! —**if you please, 1,** (if you would be so kind) пожалýйста; с вáшего разрешéния. **2,** *used ironically* представьте себé!; подýмайте тóлько! —**please God,** дай Бог.
pleased *adj.* рад; довóлен. *Pleased to meet you!,* óчень рад познакóмиться с вáми!
pleasing *adj.* приятный; привлекáтельный.
pleasurable *adj.* приятный.
pleasure *n.* **1,** (satisfaction) удовóльствие: *with pleasure,* с удовóльствием. **2,** (wish; choice; perference) желáние. *What is your pleasure?,* что вам угóдно? —*adj.* увеселúтельный: *pleasure trip,* увеселúтельная поéздка.
pleat *n.* склáдка. —*v.t.* плиссировáть. —**pleated,** *adj.* склáдчатый; в склáдку; плиссирóванный.
plebeian *adj.* плебéйский. —*n.* плебéй.
plebiscite *n.* плебисцúт.
plectrum *n.* плектр.
pledge *n.* **1,** (vow) зарóк. *Pledge of allegiance,* клятва вéрности. **2,** (security) залóг. —*v.t.* **1,** (solemnly promise) обязываться (+ *inf.*); клясться в (+ *prepl.*). *Pledge allegiance,* клясться в вéрности. **2,** (leave as security) заклáдывать; отдавáть в залóг.
Pleiades *n.pl.* плеяды.
plenary *adj.* **1,** (complete; absolute) пóлный. **2,** (fully attended) пленáрный: *plenary session,* пленáрное заседáние.
plenipotentiary *adj.* полномóчный. —*n.* полномóчный представúтель; уполномóченный.
plentiful *adj.* обúльный; изобúльный.
plenty *n.* изобúлие: *the horn of plenty,* рог изобúлия. —*adj., colloq.* óчень; изрядно. —**plenty of,** мнóго; мнóжество (+ *gen.*).
plenum *n.* плéнум.
plethora *n.* **1,** *med.* полнокрóвие. **2,** (superabundance) изобúлие.
pleura *n.* плéвра. —**pleural,** *adj.* плеврáльный.
pleurisy *n.* плеврúт.
plexiglass *n.* плексиглáс.
plexus *n., anat.* сплетéние: *solar plexus,* сóлнечное сплетéние.
pliable *adj.* гúбкий. —**pliability,** *n.* гúбкость.
pliant *adj.* = **pliable.**
pliers *n.pl.* клéщи; плоскогýбцы.
plight *n.* плачéвное состояние.
plinth *n.* плúнтус.
plod *v.i.* брестú; тащúться; плестúсь.
plop *v.i.* бултыхáться. —*adv.* бултых.
plot *n.* **1,** (piece of ground) учáсток. **2,** (conspiracy) зáговор. **3,** (story line) фáбула; сюжéт; интрúга. —*v.t.* **1,** (trace) наносúть (на кáрту). **2,** (make secret plans for) замышлять. —**plotter,** *n.* заговóрщик.
plough *v. & n.* = **plow.** —**ploughing,** *n.* = **plowing.** —**ploughman,** *n.* = **plowman.** —**ploughshare,** *n.* = **plowshare.**
plover *n.* ржáнка; зуёк. *Golden plover,* сúвка.
plow *also,* **plough** *n.* плуг. —*v.t.* **1,** (use a plow on) пахáть. **2,** *fol. by* **up** (turn up) распáхивать. —*v.i.* **1,** (use a plow) пахáть. **2,** *fol. by* **into** (run into) врéзаться в. **3,** *fol. by* **through** (work one's way through) осúливать: *plow through a book,* осúлить кнúгу.
plowing *also,* **ploughing** *n.* пáхота; вспáшка.
plowman *also,* **ploughman** *n.* пáхарь.
plowshare *also,* **ploughshare** *n.* лéмех; сошнúк. —**beat swords into plowshares,** перековáть мечú на орáла.
ploy *n.* приём.
pluck *v.t.* **1,** (pick) срывáть. **2,** (snatch) выдёргивать. **3,** (pull out the feathers of) щипáть; ощúпывать; общúпывать. **4,** (pull at, as the strings of a musical instrument) щипáть. —*n.* (courage; fortitude) смéлость; стóйкость. —**plucky,** *adj.* смéлый.
plug *n.* **1,** (stopper) прóбка; заты́чка; втýлка. **2,** (two-pronged electrical device) штéпсель; вúлка. **3,** = **fireplug.** —*v.t.* **1,** [*often* **plug up**] (stop up) затыкáть; закýпоривать. **2,** *fol. by* **in** (connect) вставлять (в розéтку); включáть (в сеть).
plum *n.* слúва. —*adj.* слúвовый: *plum brandy,* слúвовая настóйка.
plumage *n.* оперéние.
plumb *n.* **1,** (device for finding the exact perpendicular) отвéс. **2,** (device for determining the depth of water) лот. —*adj.* отвéсный; вертикáльный. —*adv.* **1,** (vertically) отвéсно; по отвéсу. **2,** *slang* (utterly) совершéнно; абсолютно. *I plumb forgot,* я так и забы́л. —*v.t.* **1,** (test the depth of) измерять глубинý (+ *gen.*). **2,** *fig.* (go deep into) проникáть в.
plumber *n.* водопровóдчик. —**plumbing,** *n.* водопровóд.
plume *n.* **1,** (feather) перó. **2,** (ornament for a hat or helmet) плюмáж; султáн.
plummet *v.i.* пáдать (как кáмень); летéть вниз.
plump *adj.* пóлный; пýхлый. —*v.i.* бýхаться.
plunder *v.t.* грáбить. —*n.* **1,** (robbery) грабёж. **2,** (booty) добы́ча.
plunge *v.t.* **1,** (thrust, as a dagger) вонзáть. **2,** (throw into, as darkness, despair, etc.) погружáть; ввергáть; повергáть. *The city was plunged into darkness,* гóрод

погрузился (*or* был погружён) в темноту́. *Plunge a country into war,* ввергать страну́ в войну́. —*v.i.* **1,** (dive; dash headlong) бро́ситься: *plunge into the water,* бро́ситься в во́ду. *Plunge down an embankment,* свали́ться под отко́с. *The car plunged into the crowd,* маши́на вре́залась в толпу́. **2,** *fig.* (plummet) лете́ть вниз. —*n.* **1,** (dive) ныро́к. **2,** (sudden decline) ре́зкое паде́ние.

plunger *n.* плу́нжер.

plunk *v.t.* **1,** (strum) бренча́ть. **2,** *fol. by* **down** (toss down) бро́сить: *plunk down a dollar on the counter,* бро́сить до́ллар на прила́вок.

pluperfect *adj.* давнопроше́дший. —*n.* давнопроше́дшее вре́мя.

plural *adj.* мно́жественный. *Plural noun,* существи́тельное мно́жественного числа́. —*n.* мно́жественное число́.

plurality *n.* **1,** (largest number of votes but less than 50%) относи́тельное большинство́. **2,** (excess of votes over nearest competitor) переве́с.

plus *prep. & n.* плюс. —**plus sign,** знак плю́са; плюс.

plush *n.* (fabric) плюш. —*adj.* **1,** (of this fabric) плю́шевый. **2,** [*also,* **plushy**] *colloq.* (luxurious) роско́шный.

Pluto *n.* Плуто́н.

plutocracy *n.* плутокра́тия. —**plutocrat,** *n.* плутокра́т. —**plutocratic,** *adj.* плутократи́ческий.

plutonium *n.* плуто́ний.

ply *v.t.* **1,** (do work with; wield) рабо́тать (+ *instr.*). *Ply the oars,* налега́ть на весла. **2,** (practice, as a trade) подвиза́ться на (како́м-нибудь по́прище). **3,** (address constantly with, as questions) засыпа́ть (вопро́сами). **4,** (keep supplying with) по́тчевать: *ply with wine,* по́тчевать вино́м. **5,** (traverse regularly) борозди́ть: *ply the seas,* борозди́ть моря́. —*v.i.* (travel back and forth) курси́ровать; снова́ть. —*n.* слой: *three-ply wood,* трёхсло́йная фане́ра.

plywood *n.* фане́ра. —*adj.* фане́рный.

pneumatic *adj.* пневмати́ческий. —**pneumatic drill,** пневмати́ческое сверло́.

pneumonia *n.* воспале́ние лёгких.

poach *v.t.* вари́ть (без скорлупы́). *Poached egg,* яйцо́-пашо́т. —*v.i.* занима́ться браконье́рством. *Poach on,* вторга́ться в.

poacher *n.* браконье́р. —**poaching,** *n.* браконье́рство.

pochard *n.* ныро́к.

pocket *n.* **1,** (of a garment) карма́н. **2,** *billiards* лу́за. **3,** (small area) у́зел; оча́г. *Pocket of resistance,* оча́г сопротивле́ния. **4,** *in* **air pocket,** возду́шная я́ма. —*adj.* карма́нный: *pocket comb,* карма́нная расчёска.—*v.t.* **1,** (put in one's pocket) класть в карма́н. **2,** (take dishonestly) класть (себе́) в карма́н; прикарма́нивать. **3,** (endure, as an insult) проглоти́ть. —**out of pocket,** в убы́тке; в про́игрыше.

pocket billiards лу́зный билья́рд.

pocketbook *n.* **1,** (lady's handbag) су́мка; су́мочка. **2,** = **paperback.** —**put a hole in one's pocketbook,** бить *or* ударя́ть по карма́ну.

pocketknife *n.* карма́нный нож.

pocket money карма́нные де́ньги.

pockmark *n.* о́спина; ряби́на. —**pockmarked,** *adj.* в о́спинах; изры́тый о́спой; рябо́й.

pod *n.* стручо́к. *Peas in the pod,* стручко́вый горо́х. —**like two peas in a pod,** как две ка́пли воды́.

podiatrist *n.* специали́ст по лече́нию ног. —**podiatry,** *n.* лече́ние заболева́ний ног.

podium *n.* помо́ст.

podzol *n.* подзо́л.

poem *n.* стихотворе́ние; поэ́ма.

poet *n.* поэ́т. —**poetess,** *n.* поэте́сса.

poetic *adj.* поэти́ческий. —**poetic license,** поэти́ческая во́льность.

poetical *adj.* поэти́ческий.

poetry *n.* поэ́зия; стихи́.

pogrom *n.* погро́м.

poignancy *n.* тро́гательность.

poignant *adj.* **1,** (cutting; harsh) о́стрый. **2,** (touching) тро́гательный.

point *n.* **1,** (sharp end) ко́нчик; остриё. **2,** (point in space) пункт; то́чка. *The furthermost point,* са́мый да́льний пункт. *The shortest distance between two points,* наиме́ньшее расстоя́ние ме́жду двумя́ то́чками. **3,** (stage; juncture) то́чка; пункт: *starting point,* нача́льный пункт; *boiling point,* то́чка кипе́ния; *turning point,* поворо́тный пункт. *Reach the point where,* дойти́ до того́, что... **4,** (specific moment in time) моме́нт. *At this point I should like to...,* здесь я хоте́л бы (+ *inf.*). **5,** (item; element) пункт: *the main points of the plan,* основны́е пу́нкты пла́на. *Fine point,* тонкость. *Point of interest,* достопримеча́тельность. **6,** (essence; gist) суть; существо́: *come to the point,* доходи́ть до су́ти де́ла. *Speak to the point,* говори́ть по существу́ *or* напрями́к. *Miss the point,* не ви́деть са́мого гла́вного. *The point is...,* де́ло в том, что... *That's just the point,* в то́м-то и де́ло. *That's not the point,* не в э́том де́ло. **7,** (idea advanced, esp. a valid one): *I don't get your point,* я не понима́ю, что вы хоти́те сказа́ть *or* куда́ вы гнёте. *He has a point there!,* в э́том он прав. **8,** (purpose; use; advantage) смысл: *there is no point in arguing with him,* нет смы́сла (*or* не сто́ит) с ним спо́рить. *There is no point in even trying,* не́чего и пыта́ться. **9,** (unit of scoring) очко́. *Win on points,* победи́ть по очка́м. **10,** (characteristic) сторона́; ме́сто: *weak points,* сла́бые сто́роны/места́. *Have one's good points,* име́ть свои́ хоро́шие сто́роны. **11,** (promontory; cape) мыс; нос. **12,** *printing* пункт. —*v.t.* **1,** (direct, as a weapon) направля́ть; наводи́ть; наставля́ть. **2,** (show by pointing) ука́зывать: *point the way to someone,* ука́зывать путь кому́-нибудь. **3,** *fol. by* **out** (indicate; explain) ука́зывать (на). **4,** *fol. by* **up** (emphasize; make clear) заостря́ть. —*v.i.* **1,** *fol. by* **to** (motion toward) пока́зываать на; ука́зывать на. **2,** (be turned in a given direction) ука́зывать на: *the needle points south,* стре́лка ука́зывает на юг. **3,** *fol. by* **to** (indicate; suggest) говори́ть о: *everything points to the fact that...,* всё говори́т о том, что... —**be on the point of,** как раз собира́ться (+ *inf.*). —**beside the point,** не к де́лу; некста́ти; не по существу́. —**case in point,** хоро́ший приме́р э́того. —**in point of,** в отноше́нии (+ *gen.*); с то́чки зре́ния (+ *gen.*). —**in point of fact,** факти́чески; на са́мом де́ле. —**make a point of; make it a point to,** взять себе́ за пра́вило (+ *inf.*). —**point of view,** то́чка зре́ния.

pointblank *adj.* **1,** (fired straight at the mark) прямо́й. **2,** (explicit) категори́ческий. —*adv.* **1,** (straight at the mark) в упо́р. **2,** (without hesitation or equivocation) наотре́з; напрями́к.

pointed *adj.* **1,** (coming to a point) заострённый; ос-

троконе́чный. **2,** (sharp; incisive) о́стрый; ме́ткий. **3,** (deliberately emphasized) демонстрати́вный.
pointer *n.* **1,** (indicator) стре́лка; указа́тель. **2,** (rod used in classrooms) па́лочка; ука́зка. **3,** (dog) лега́вая соба́ка; по́йнтер. **4,** *colloq.* (tip; advice) сове́т.
pointless *adj.* бессмы́сленный; бесце́льный; беспредме́тный. *It is pointless to...,* нет смы́сла (+ *inf.*).
poise *n.* **1,** (equilibrium) равнове́сие. **2,** (composure) уравнове́шенность. —*v.t.* уравнове́шивать.
poised *adj.* **1,** (composed) уравнове́шенный. **2,** *fol. by* **to** (suspended in readiness) гото́вый (к).
poison *n.* яд; отра́ва. —*adj.* ядови́тый: *poison gas,* ядови́тый газ. —*v.t.* отравля́ть. —**poisoning,** *n.* отравле́ние: *food poisoning,* пищево́е отравле́ние. —**poisonous,** *adj.* ядови́тый.
poke *v.t.* **1,** (jab) ты́кать; толка́ть. *Poke someone in the ribs,* толкну́ть кого́-нибудь в бок. *Poke one's finger at someone,* ты́кать па́льцем на кого́-нибудь. **2,** (thrust) сова́ть: *poke one's nose into,* сова́ть нос в. **3,** (stir, as a fire) меша́ть; переме́шивать (у́гли). **4,** (make, as a hole) протыка́ть. —*v.i.* **1,** *fol. by* **around** *or* **about** (search leisurely) ры́ться. **2,** *fol. by* **along** (plod along) таска́ться. **3,** *fol. by* **out** (protrude) торча́ть. —*n.* тычо́к. —**buy a pig in a poke,** купи́ть кота́ в мешке́. —**poke fun at,** *see* **fun.**
poker *n.* **1,** (rod for stirring a fire) кочерга́. **2,** (card game) по́кер.
poky *also,* **pokey** *adj.* те́сный. —*n., slang* (jail) куту́зка.
polar *adj.* поля́рный. —**polar bear,** бе́лый *or* поля́рный медве́дь. —**polar fox,** песе́ц.
polarity *n.* поля́рность.
polarize *v.t.* поляризова́ть. —**polarization,** *n.* поляриза́ция.
pole *n.* **1,** (long stick) шест; жердь. **2,** (upright post) столб. **3,** (of the earth) по́люс: *North Pole,* Се́верный по́люс.
Pole *n.* поля́к; по́лька. *The Poles,* поля́ки.
poleax *also,* **poleaxe** *n.* секи́ра.
polecat *n.* хорёк.
polemic *n.* поле́мика. —*adj.* [*also,* **polemical**] полеми́ческий. —**polemicist,** *n.* полеми́ст. —**polemics,** *n.* поле́мика.
pole vault прыжо́к с шесто́м. —**pole-vault,** *v.i.* пры́гать с шесто́м.
police *n.* поли́ция; мили́ция. —*adj.* полице́йский: *police station,* полице́йский уча́сток. —*v.t.* **1,** (keep order in) охраня́ть; патрули́ровать. **2,** (clean up) чи́стить; убира́ть.
policeman *n.* **1,** (in the USSR) милиционе́р. **2,** (elsewhere) полице́йский; полисме́н.
police state полице́йское госуда́рство.
policy *n.* **1,** (course of action) поли́тика. **2,** (contract of insurance) по́лис.
poliomyelitis *n.* полиомиели́т.
polish *v.t.* **1,** (shine) полирова́ть; шлифова́ть. *Polish one's shoes,* чи́стить боти́нки. **2,** (refine; perfect) шлифова́ть. —*n.* **1,** (glossy finish) поли́ровка. **2,** (polishing substance) лак: *nail polish,* лак для ногте́й. *Shoe polish,* гутали́н; ва́кса. **3,** *fig.* (elegance; refinement) лоск. —**polish off,** поко́нчить с.
Polish *adj.* по́льский. —*n.* по́льский язы́к. *Speak Polish,* говори́ть по-по́льски.
polished *adj.* **1,** (shiny) полиро́ванный. **2,** (elegant) изы́сканный; лощёный. **3,** (finished; flawless) зако́нченный.
polisher *n.* полиро́вщик; шлифова́льщик.
Politburo *n.* политбюро́.
polite *adj.* **1,** (courteous) ве́жливый. **2,** (refined) изы́сканный: *polite society,* изы́сканное о́бщество. —**politely,** *adv.* ве́жливо. —**politeness,** *n.* ве́жливость.
politic *adj.* полити́чный.
political *adj.* полити́ческий. —**political prisoner,** политзаключённый.
politician *n.* **1,** (one engaged in politics) полити́ческий де́ятель; поли́тик. **2,** (political opportunist) политика́н.
politics *n.* поли́тика.
polity *n.* о́браз правле́ния.
polka *n.* по́лька.
polka dots горо́шек: *polka-dot necktie,* га́лстук в горо́шек.
poll *n.* **1,** (vote) голосова́ние. **2,** *pl.* (voting place) избира́тельный уча́сток. *Go to the polls,* (идти́) голосова́ть. **3,** (survey of opinion) опро́с. —*v.t.* **1,** (receive, as votes) получа́ть; собира́ть. **2,** (survey; canvass) опра́шивать.
pollen *n.* пыльца́.
pollinate *v.t.* опыля́ть. —**pollination,** *n.* опыле́ние.
polling booth каби́на для голосова́ния.
polling place избира́тельный уча́сток.
polliwog *n.* голова́стик.
poll tax поду́шный нало́г; избира́тельный нало́г.
pollute *v.t.* загрязня́ть. —**pollutant,** *n.* загрязня́ющее вещество́. —**pollution,** *n.* загрязне́ние.
polo *n.* по́ло.
polonaise *n.* полоне́з.
polonium *n.* поло́ний.
polo shirt те́нниска.
poltroon *n.* трус.
polyandry *n.* полиа́ндрия.
polychromatic *adj.* многоцве́тный; многокра́сочный.
polyclinic *n.* поликли́ника.
polyester *n.* полиэфи́р. —*adj.* полиэфи́рный.
polyethylene *n.* полиэтиле́н. —*adj.* полиэтиле́новый.
polygamy *n.* многобра́чие; многожёнство; полига́мия. —**polygamist,** *n.* многоже́нец. —**polygamous,** *adj.* многобра́чный; полига́мный; полигами́ческий.
polyglot *adj.* многоязы́чный. —*n.* полигло́т.
polygon *n.* многоуго́льник. —**polygonal,** *adj.* многоуго́льный.
polyhedron *n.* многогра́нник. —**polyhedral,** *adj.* многогра́нный.
polymer *n.* полиме́р. —**polymeric,** *adj.* полиме́рный.
Polynesian *adj.* полинези́йский. —*n.* полинези́ец.
polynomial *n.* многочле́н. —*adj.* многочле́нный.
polyp *n.* поли́п.
polystyrene *n.* полистиро́л.
polysyllabic *adj.* многосло́жный.
polytechnic *adj.* политехни́ческий.
polytheism *n.* политеи́зм; многобо́жие. —**polytheist,** *n.* политеи́ст. —**polytheistic,** *adj.* политеисти́ческий.
pomade *n.* пома́да. —*v.t.* пома́дить.
pomegranate *n.* грана́т.
pommel *n.* (of a saddle) лука́. —*v.t.* (beat) колоти́ть.

pomp *n.* пышность; пóмпа.

pompon *n.* помпóн.

pompous *adj.* напыщенный; надýтый. —**pomposity,** *n.* напыщенность.

poncho *n.* пóнчо.

pond *n.* пруд.

ponder *v.t.* обдýмывать; соображáть. —*v.i.* размышлять; задýмываться; раздýмывать.

ponderous *adj.* тяжёлый; тяжеловéсный.

pond scum тина.

pondweed *n.* рдест.

pontiff *n.* **1,** (Pope) пáпа. **2,** (bishop) епи́скоп. —**pontifical,** *adj.* пáпский; епи́скопский.

pontificate *n.* понтификáт. —*v.i.* орáторствовать.

pontoon *n.* (boat) понтóн. —**pontoon bridge,** понтóнный мост.

pony *n.* пóни.

pooch *n., colloq.* собáчка.

poodle *n.* пýдель.

pool *n.* **1,** (puddle) лýжа. **2,** (swimming pool) бассéйн для плáвания. **3,** (billiards) (лýзный) бильярд. **4,** (combination of resources) фонд. —*v.t.* объединять: *pool one's resources,* объединять ресýрсы.

pool table бильярд.

poop *n., naut.* ют; полуют. —**poop deck,** пáлуба юта.

poor *adj.* **1,** (needy) бéдный: *poor family/country,* бéдная семья/странá. **2,** (unfortunate) бéдный: *poor Nina!,* бéдная Ни́на! *Poor man/woman/creature!,* бедняга! **3,** (bad) плохóй; слáбый: *poor memory,* плохáя/слáбая пáмять. *Poor grades,* плохи́е отмéтки. *Poor student,* слáбый учени́к. *Poor quality,* ни́зкое кáчество. *Poor harvest,* плохóй урожáй; неурожáй. *Read in poor light,* читáть при плохóм свéте. *She is in poor health,* у неё слáбое здорóвье. —*n., preceded by* **the** бéдные; беднотá.

poorbox *n.* крýжка.

poorhouse *n.* богадéльня; рабóтный дом.

poorly *adv.* плóхо; слáбо; невáжно.

pop *n.* **1,** (sound) хлопóк. **2,** (drink) гази́рованная водá. **3,** *colloq.* (dad) пáпа; папáша. —*v.i.* **1,** (make a short explosive sound) хлóпать; трéснуть. **2,** *fol. by* **up** *or* **out** (appear suddenly) покáзываться. **3,** *fol. by* **in** (drop in for a moment) заглянýть. **4,** (of one's eyes) широкó раскрывáться. *His eyes nearly popped out of his head,* у негó глазá полезли́ на лоб. —*v.t.* **1,** (put quickly or suddenly) совáть; всóвывать. *Pop one's head out the window,* высóвывать гóлову из окнá. **2,** *in* **pop the question** (propose) сдéлать предложéние.

popcorn *n.* воздýшная кукурýза.

Pope *n.* пáпа.

popgun *n.* пугáч.

poplar *n.* тóполь. —*adj.* тóполевый.

poplin *n.* попли́н. —*adj.* попли́новый.

poppy *n.* мак. *Poppy seeds,* мак.

poppycock *n., colloq.* чушь; галиматья; белибердá.

populace *n.* населéние.

popular *adj.* **1,** (well-liked; enjoyed by many) популярный. **2,** (of the people) нарóдный. *By popular demand,* по трéбованию пýблики. **3,** (within the means of most people) достýпный.

popularity *n.* популярность.

popularize *v.t.* популяризи́ровать. —**popularization,** *n.* популяризáция.

populate *v.t.* населять; заселять. *Densely/sparsely populated,* гýсто/рéдко населённый.

population *n.* населéние. —**population explosion,** демографи́ческий взрыв.

Populist *n.* нарóдник. —*adj.* нарóднический. —**Populism,** *n.* нарóдничество.

populous *adj.* лю́дный; многолю́дный; густонаселённый.

porcelain *n.* фарфóр. —*adj.* фарфóровый.

porch *n.* крыльцó.

porcupine *n.* дикобрáз.

pore *n.* пóра. —*v.i.* [*usu.* **pore over**] корпéть (над); коптéть (над).

pork *n.* свини́на. —*adj.* свинóй: *pork chop,* свинáя котлéта; свинáя отбивнáя.

pornography *n.* порногрáфия. —**pornographic,** *adj.* порнографи́ческий.

porous *adj.* пóристый; ноздревáтый. —**porosity,** *n.* пóристость.

porphyry *n.* порфи́р.

porpoise *n.* морскáя свинья.

porridge *n.* кáша.

port *n.* **1,** (harbor; seaport) порт. **2,** (left side of a vessel) лéвый борт. **3,** (wine) портвéйн. —**port of call,** порт захóда.

portable *adj.* перенóсный; портати́вный.

portage *n.* **1,** (act of carrying) перенóска. **2,** (route over which boats are carried) вóлок.

portal *n.* портáл.

portend *v.t.* предвещáть.

portent *n.* **1,** (omen) предзнаменовáние; предвéстие. **2,** (significance) значéние.

portentous *adj.* **1,** (ominous) зловéщий. **2,** (momentous) знаменáтельный.

porter *n.* **1,** (baggage carrier)носи́льщик. **2,** (handyman) убóрщик.

portfolio *n.* портфéль. *Minister without portfolio,* мини́стр без портфéля.

porthole *n.* иллюминáтор.

portico *n.* пóртик.

portion *n.* **1,** (part of a whole) часть; дóля. **2,** (serving of food) пóрция. —*v.t.* [*usu.* **portion out**] распределять; выделять.

portly *adj.* пóлный; дорóдный.

portrait *n.* портрéт. *Portrait gallery,* портрéтная галерéя. *Portrait painter,* портрети́ст.

portray *v.t.* изображáть. —**portrayal,** *n.* изображéние.

Portuguese *adj.* португáльский. *He (she) is Portuguese,* он португáлец; онá португáлка. —*n.* **1,** (language) португáльский язы́к. *Speak Portuguese,* говори́ть по-португáльски. **2,** *preceded by* **the** (people) португáльцы.

portulaca *n.* портулáк.

pose *n.* пóза. —*v.i.* **1,** (assume a position, as for a portrait) пози́ровать. **2,** *fol. by* **as** (represent oneself as) выдавáть себя (за). —*v.t.* **1,** (put, as a question) стáвить; задавáть; предлагáть. **2,** (present) представлять: *pose difficulties/a threat/,* представлять трýдности/угрóзу.

posh *adj., colloq.* роскóшный; шикáрный.

position *n.* **1,** (location; posture; situation; status) положéние: *in a sitting/awkward position,* в сидячем/нелóвком положéнии. *Be in a position to,* быть в состоянии (+ *inf.*). *What would you do in my position?,* что бы вы сде́лали на моём ме́сте? **2,** *mil.* пози́ция. **3,** (job) ме́сто. **4,** (point of view; stand) пози́ция. —*v.t.* ста́вить; помеща́ть.

positional *adj.* позицио́нный.

positive *adj.* **1,** (affirmative; favorable) положи́тельный. **2,** (certain) уве́ренный: *I am positive that...,* я (абсолю́тно) уве́рен, что... **3,** *math.; electricity* положи́тельный. **4,** *photog.* позити́вный. —*n., photog.* позити́в. —**positively,** *adv.* положи́тельно.

positivism *n.* позитиви́зм.

positron *n.* позитро́н.

possess *v.t.* **1,** (have; own) облада́ть: *possess talent,* облада́ть тала́нтом. **2,** (come over) овладева́ть: *fear possessed him,* им овладе́л страх. *What possessed you to do that?,* что вас заста́вило сде́лать э́то?

possessed *adj.* **1,** *fol. by* **of** (having) облада́ющий. **2,** (obsessed) одержи́мый.

possession *n.* **1,** (fact of possessing) облада́ние; владе́ние. *Be in someone's possession,* быть в чьём-нибудь распоряже́нии. *Take possession of,* вступи́ть во владе́ние (+ *instr.*). **2,** (territory belonging to an outside country) владе́ние. **3,** *pl.* (belongings) иму́щество.

possessive *adj.* **1,** (desiring to possess) со́бственнический. **2,** *gram.* притяжа́тельный.

possessor *n.* облада́тель.

possibility *n.* возмо́жность: *the possibility of error,* возмо́жность оши́бки. *There is little possibility of that,* ша́нсов на э́то ма́ло. *There are two possibilities,* существу́ют два вариа́нта.

possible *adj.* возмо́жный. *If possible,* е́сли возмо́жно. *That is not possible,* э́то невозмо́жно. *That's entirely possible,* э́то вполне́ возмо́жно. *Do everything possible,* сде́лать, всё возмо́жное. *Make it possible to,* позволя́ть (+ *inf.*). —**as...as possible,** как мо́жно (+ *comparative*): *as soon as possible,* как мо́жно скоре́е.

possibly *adv.* возмо́жно: *I may possibly be late,* я, возмо́жно, опозда́ю. *As soon as I possibly can,* как то́лько я смогу́. *He could not possibly have done it,* не мо́жет быть, что́бы он сде́лал э́то.

possum *n., colloq.* = **opossum.** —**play possum,** притворя́ться мёртвым.

post *n.* **1,** (upright pole) столб. **2,** (station) пункт; пост: *observation post,* наблюда́тельный пункт; *control post,* контро́льный пост. **3,** (assigned position) пост: *remain at one's post,* остава́ться на своём посту́. **4,** (camp; base) городо́к: *military post,* вое́нный городо́к. **5,** (appointed public office) пост; до́лжность. **6,** (mail) по́чта. —*v.t.* **1,** (put up; hang up) выве́шивать; раскле́ивать. **2,** (announce) объявля́ть: *post a reward,* объяви́ть пре́мию. **3,** (station, as a sentry) ста́вить; выставля́ть (часово́го); расставля́ть; разводи́ть (часовы́х). **4,** (assign) назнача́ть. **5,** (keep informed) держа́ть в ку́рсе. *Well posted on politics,* в ку́рсе поли́тики. **6,** *comm.* (transfer to a ledger) переноси́ть в гроссбу́х. **7,** *chiefly Brit.* (mail) отправля́ть; опуска́ть (в почто́вый я́щик). **8,** *in* **post bond for,** брать на пору́ки.

postage *n.* почто́вые расхо́ды; сто́имость пересы́лки. *Pay the postage,* (у)плати́ть за пересы́лку. —**postage stamp,** почто́вая ма́рка.

postal *adj.* почто́вый: *postal rates,* почто́вый тари́ф.

postcard *n.* почто́вая ка́рточка; откры́тка.

poster *n.* плака́т; афи́ша.

posterior *adj.* **1,** (rear) за́дний. **2,** (subsequent) после́дующий. —*n.* зад.

posterity *n.* пото́мство: *the verdict of posterity,* суд пото́мства.

postgraduate *n.* аспира́нт. *Postgraduate studies,* аспиранту́ра.

posthaste *adv.* сломя́ го́лову; момента́льно.

posthumous *adj.* посме́ртный. —**posthumously,** *adv.* посме́ртно.

postilion *also,* **postillion** *n.* форе́йтор.

postman *n.* почтальо́н.

postmark *n.* почто́вый ште́мпель. —*v.t.* штемпелева́ть.

postmaster *n.* почтме́йстер. —**postmaster general,** мини́стр почт.

post-mortem *n.* **1,** (autopsy) вскры́тие. **2,** *colloq.* (post-game analysis) ана́лиз игры́.

postnatal *adj.* послеродово́й.

post office по́чта.

postoperative *adj.* послеоперацио́нный.

postpaid *adj. & adv.* с опла́ченными почто́выми расхо́дами.

postpone *v.t.* откла́дывать. —**postponement,** *n.* отсро́чка.

postscript *n.* **1,** (to a letter) припи́ска; постскри́птум. **2,** (to a book or article) послесло́вие.

postulate *n.* постула́т. —*v.t.* постули́ровать.

posture *n.* **1,** (position) положе́ние. **2,** (way of standing) оса́нка: *poor posture,* плоха́я оса́нка. **3,** *fig.* (stance) пози́ция.

postwar *adj.* послевое́нный.

posy *n.* **1,** (flower) цвето́к. **2,** (bouquet) буке́т.

pot *n.* **1,** (for cooking) кастрю́ля; котело́к. *Coffeepot,* кофе́йник. **2,** (for plants) горшо́к: *flowerpot,* цвето́чный горшо́к. —**go to pot,** вы́лететь в трубу́.

potable *adj.* го́дный для питья́.

potash *n.* пота́ш.

potassium *n.* ка́лий. —**potassium bromide,** бро́мистый ка́лий. —**potassium carbonate,** углеки́слый ка́лий. —**potassium chloride,** хло́ристый ка́лий. —**potassium cyanide,** циа́нистый ка́лий. —**potassium iodide,** йо́дистый ка́лий. —**potassium nitrate,** ка́лиевая *or* кали́йная сели́тра.

potato *n.* карто́фелина; *pl.* карто́фель. —*adj.* карто́фельный. —**potato beetle** (*or* **bug**), (колора́дский) карто́фельный жук. —**potato chips,** чи́псы.

potbelly *n., colloq.* пу́зо; брю́хо. — **potbellied,** *adj., colloq.* пуза́тый.

pot cheese творо́г.

Potemkin village потёмкинская дере́вня.

potency *n.* си́ла.

potent *adj.* **1,** (powerful, as of a weapon) мо́щный. **2,** (convincing; cogent) си́льный; убеди́тельный. **3,** (effective, as of a drug or drink) си́льный; кре́пкий.

potentate *n.* властели́н.

potential *adj.* потенциа́льный. —*n.* потенциа́л. —**potentiality,** *n.* возмо́жности.

pothole *n.* уха́б; ры́твина; вы́боина.

potion *n.* зе́лье. *Love potion,* любо́вный напи́ток.

potpourri *n.* мешани́на; винегре́т.

pot shot вы́стрел в упо́р. *Take a pot shot at,* вы́стрелить в (кого́-нибудь) в упо́р.

pottage *n.* похлёбка.

potted *adj.* **1,** (kept in a pot, as of plants) горше́чный. **2,** *slang* (drunk) пья́ный.

potter *n.* гончáр. —*v.i.* = **putter.** —**potter's wheel,** гончáрный круг.

pottery *n.* гончáрные (*or* глиняные) издéлия.

pouch *n.* **1,** (small bag) сýмка; мешóчек. *Tobacco pouch,* кисéт. **2,** (of a kangaroo) сýмка. —**diplomatic pouch,** дипломатическая пóчта.

poultice *n.* припáрка.

poultry *n.* домáшняя птица.

pounce *v.i.* [*usu.* **pounce on** *or* **upon**] набрáсываться (на); обрýшиваться (на); налетáть (на).

pound *n.* **1,** (measure of weight; monetary unit) фунт. **2,** (enclosure for stray animals) загóн. —*v.t.* **1,** (bang) ударя́ть; колоти́ть: *pound one's fist on the table,* ударя́ть/колоти́ть кулакóм пó столу. **2,** [*also intrans.* **pound on**] (strike heavily) ударя́ть (по); колоти́ть (по); стучáть (о). **3,** (crush; pulverize) толóчь; дроби́ть; размельчáть. —*v.i.* колоти́ться: *my heart was pounding,* у меня́ сéрдце колоти́лось.

poundage *n.* вес (в фýнтах).

pour *v.t.* **1,** (a liquid) наливáть; лить. *Pour oneself a glass of milk,* наливáть себé стакáн молокá. *Pour tea for the guests,* разливáть гостя́м чай. **2,** (a dry substance) сы́пать: *pour salt in the soup,* сы́пать соль в суп. —*v.i.* ли́ться; лить. *It is pouring,* идёт си́льный дождь; дождь так и льёт; дождь ливмя́ льёт. *Tears were pouring down her cheeks,* слёзы кати́лись у неё по щекáм. —**pour in, 1,** (stream into a place) вали́ть. **2,** (arrive in great numbers) сы́паться. —**pour out, 1,** *literally* вывивáть. **2,** (give vent to, as one's feelings) изливáть. **3,** (come streaming out) выливáться; вали́ть.

pout *v.i.* дýться; надувáть гýбы.

poverty *n.* бéдность; нищетá. —**poverty-stricken,** *adj.* обеднéвший; обнищáлый.

powder *n.* **1,** (substance of fine particles) порошóк: *tooth powder,* зубнóй порошóк. **2,** (talcum) пýдра: *face powder,* пýдра для лицá. *Baby powder,* дéтская присы́пка. **3,** (gunpowder) пóрох. —*adj.* пороховóй: *powder keg,* порохова́я бóчка. —*v.t.* пýдрить. *Powder one's nose,* пýдриться. —**keep one's powder dry,** держáть пóрох сухи́м.

powdered *adj.* напýдренный: *powdered wig,* напýдренный пари́к. —**powdered eggs,** яи́чный порошóк. —**powdered milk,** молóчный порошóк. —**powdered sugar,** сáхарная пýдра.

powder puff пухóвка.

powder room дáмская убóрная; дáмский туалéт.

powdery *adj.* порошкообрáзный.

power *n.* **1,** (strength; might) мощь; могýщество. *Military/air power,* вóенная/воздýшная мощь. *The power of the printed word,* власть печáтного слóва. **2,** (political control) власть: *be in power,* быть у влáсти. *Seize power,* захвати́ть власть. **3,** (form of energy) си́ла; мóщность; энéргия. *Horsepower,* лошади́ная си́ла. *Electric power,* электроэнéргия. *Power failure,* откáз электропитáния. *The power is out,* нет электри́чества. **4,** (large nation) держáва. **5,** *pl.* (faculties) си́лы: *mental powers,* ýмственные си́лы. **6,** *pl.* (authority) полномóчия: *broad powers,* ширóкие полномóчия. **7,** *math.* стéпень: *ten to the sixth power,* дéсять в шестóй стéпени. —*adj.* **1,** (generating or transmitting power) силовóй: *power lines,* силовы́е проводá. *Power station,* электростáнция. **2,** (driven by a motor) механи́ческий: *power tool,* механи́ческий инструмéнт. *Power saw,* мотопилá. —*v.t.* дви́гать: *the plane is powered by two large engines,* два больши́х мотóра дви́жут самолёт. —**do everything in one's power,** сдéлать всё, что в чьи́х-нибудь си́лах. —**the powers that be,** власть имýщие. —**under one's own power,** сóбственными си́лами; свои́м хóдом.

powerful *adj.* си́льный; мóщный; могýчий. *Powerful engine/weapon,* мóщный дви́гатель; мóщное орýжие. *Powerful army,* си́льная *or* могýчая áрмия. *Powerful nation,* могýчая *or* могýщественная странá. *Powerful argument,* си́льный дóвод. —**powerfully,** *adv.* си́льно.

powerless *adj.* бесси́льный.

power of attorney довéренность.

power pack блок питáния.

power plant 1, (source of power) силовáя установка. **2,** (power station) электростáнция.

pox *n.* óспа.

practicable *adj.* осуществи́мый; реáльный. —**practicability,** *n.* осуществи́мость.

practical *adj.* практи́ческий; практи́чный: *practical person/advice,* практи́ческий *or* практи́чный человéк/совéт. *Practical application,* практи́ческое применéние. *Practical method,* практи́чный мéтод. —**practical joke,** мистификáция.

practicality *n.* практи́чность.

practically *adv.* **1,** (in a practical way) практи́чески. **2,** (virtually; in effect) практи́чески: *practically impossible,* практи́чески невозмóжно. **3,** (almost) почти́: *practically all week,* почти́ всю недéлю. —**practically speaking,** факти́чески.

practice *also,* **practise** *n.* **1,** (repeated performance; proficiency) прáктика. *In practice,* на прáктике; на дéле. *Be out of practice,* не имéть прáктики. *Put into practice,* проводи́ть *or* претворя́ть в жизнь. **2,** (habitual way of doing things) привы́чка; обы́чай. *Make it a practice to; make a practice of,* взять себé за прáвило (+ *inf.*). **3,** (professional activity or clientele) прáктика: *legal practice,* адвокáтская прáктика. *He has a large practice,* у негó большáя прáктика. **4,** *pl.* (questionable activities) делá: *shady practices,* тёмные делá. —*adj.* прóбный: *practice shot/jump,* прóбный вы́стрел/прыжóк. —*v.t.* **1,** (observe; exercise) соблюдáть. *Practice thrift,* соблюдáть эконóмию. *Practice one's religion,* исповéдовать свою́ рели́гию. **2,** (drill oneself in) упражня́ться в *or* на; практиковáться в. *Practice the piano,* упражня́ться на роя́ле. **3,** (pursue, as a profession): *practice law,* быть адвокáтом. —*v.i.* **1,** (drill) упражня́ться; практиковáться. **2,** (pursue a certain profession) практиковáть.

practiced *adj.* óпытный; умéлый.

practitioner *n. General practitioner,* врач óбщей прáктики.

praetor *n.* прéтор.

pragmatic *adj.* прагмати́ческий. —**pragmatism,** *n.* прагмати́зм. —**pragmatist,** *n.* прагмати́ст.

prairie *n.* прéрия; степь.

praise *v.t.* хвали́ть. —*n.* похвалá. *In praise of,* в похвалý (+ *dat.*). —**praise to the skies,** превозноси́ть до небéс. —**sing the praises of,** петь дифирáмбы (+ *dat.*).

praiseworthy *adj.* похвáльный.

pram *n., colloq.* = **perambulator.**

prance *v.i.* **1,** (on a horse) гарцевáть. **2,** (swagger; strut) вáжничать; ходи́ть гóголем.

prank *n.* выходка; проказа; проделка; шалость. *Play pranks,* проказничать. —**prankish,** *adj.* проказливый. —**prankster,** *n.* проказник.

praseodymium *n.* празеодим.

prate *v.i.* болтать; трещать.

prattle *v.i.* лепетать. —*n.* лепет.

prawn *n.* креветка.

pray *v.i.* (offer prayers) молиться: *pray to God,* молиться богу. —*v.t. & i.* (beg; beseech) умолять. *Pray tell me,* да скажите пожалуйста!

prayer *n.* молитва: *say a prayer,* читать молитву. *Call to prayer,* звать к молитве. *Kneel in prayer,* молиться на коленях. —**prayer book,** молитвенник. —**prayer service,** моление.

praying mantis богомол.

preach *v.t.* **1,** (espouse) проповедовать. **2,** (deliver, as a sermon) произносить. —*v.i.* (deliver a sermon) проповедовать. —**preacher,** *n.* проповедник.

preamble *n.* преамбула.

prearranged *adj.* заранее условленный; условный.

precarious *adj.* опасный; шаткий: *precarious position,* опасное/шаткое положение.

precaution *n.* предосторожность. *Take precautions,* принимать (меры) предосторожности. —**precautionary,** *adj., in* **precautionary measures,** меры предосторожности.

precede *v.t.* предшествовать.

precedence *n.* предпочтение: *give precedence to,* отдавать предпочтение (+ *dat.*). *This task takes precedence over all others,* эту задачу надо решить в первую очередь.

precedent *n.* прецедент: *set a precedent,* создавать прецедент.

preceding *adj.* предшествующий; предыдущий.

precept *n.* завет; наставление.

precinct *n.* участок; округ.

precious *adj.* **1,** (highly valuable) драгоценный: *precious stones,* драгоценные камни. **2,** (held dear) дорогой: *precious memories,* дорогие воспоминания. **3,** (vitally important) драгоценный; дорогой. *Waste precious time,* терять драгоценное время. *Time was precious,* время было дорого. **4,** (delightful) прелестный: *a precious child,* прелестный ребёнок. **5,** (affected, as of a style) манерный.

precipice *n.* обрыв.

precipitate *v.t.* приводить к; вызывать. —*adj.* = **precipitous.**

precipitation *n.* осадки.

precipitous *adj.* **1,** (steep) крутой; обрывистый. **2,** (hasty; rash) опрометчивый.

precise *adj.* **1,** (accurate; exact) точный. **2,** (punctilious) аккуратный. **3,** (particular) как раз: *at that precise moment,* как раз в тот момент.

precisely *adv.* **1,** (in a precise manner) точно. **2,** (just; exactly) именно: *precisely for this reason,* именно по этой причине.

precision *n.* точность. —*adj.* точный: *precision instruments,* точные приборы.

preclude *v.t.* исключать возможность (+ *gen.*): *preclude escape,* исключать возможность побега. *Preclude someone's attending the meeting,* мешать кому-нибудь присутствовать на собрании.

precocious *adj.* развитой; развит не по годам.

preconceived *adj.* предвзятый.

preconception *n.* предвзятое мнение.

precondition *n.* **1,** (prerequisite) предпосылка. **2,** (prior stipulation) предварительное условие.

precursor *n.* **1,** (predecessor) предшественник. **2,** (harbinger) предвестник.

predate *v.t.* **1,** (come before) предшествовать. **2,** (put an earlier date on) пометить задним числом.

predator *n.* хищник.

predatory *adj.* **1,** (characterized by plundering) грабительский. **2,** (rapacious, as of a bird) хищный.

predecessor *n.* предшественник.

predestine *v.t.* предопределять. —**predestination,** *n.* предопределение.

predetermine *v.t.* предопределять; предрешать. —**predetermination,** *n.* предопределение.

predicament *n.* затруднительное положение.

predicate *n.* сказуемое; предикат. —*v.t.* основывать: *on what is this predicated?,* на чём это основано? —**predicative,** *adj.* предикативный.

predict *v.t. & i.* предсказывать. —**predictable,** *adj.* предсказуемый. —**prediction,** *n.* предсказание.

predilection *n.* пристрастие; склонность.

predispose *v.t.* предрасполагать. —**predisposed,** *adj.* предрасположенный. —**predisposition,** *n.* предрасположение.

predominance *n.* преобладание. —**predominant,** *adj.* преобладающий. —**predominantly,** *adv.* преимущественно. *The population is predominantly Catholic,* основная часть населения – католики.

predominate *v.i.* преобладать; господствовать.

preeminent *adj.* выдающийся. —**preeminence,** *n.* превосходство.

preempt *v.t.* захватывать (прежде других). —**preemptive,** *adj.* упреждающий: *preemptive strike,* упреждающий удар.

preen *v.t.* **1,** (smooth with the beak) чистить клювом. **2,** (primp) прихорашивать.

prefabricated *adj.* сборный.

preface *n.* предисловие. —*v.t.* предпосылать: *preface one's report with a story,* предпослать докладу рассказ. —**prefatory,** *adj.* вступительный; вводный.

prefect *n.* префект. —**prefecture,** *n.* префектура.

prefer *v.t.* **1,** (like better) предпочитать: *prefer spring to summer,* предпочитать весну лету. **2,** (file) предъявлять: *prefer charges against,* предъявить обвинение (+ *dat.*). *See also* **preferred.**

preferable *adj.* предпочтительный. *Plastic is preferable to wood,* пластмасса предпочтительнее дерева. —**preferably,** *adv.* лучше; скорее.

preference *n.* предпочтение: *give preference to,* отдавать *or* оказываать предпочтение (+ *dat.*). *What is your preference?,* что вы предпочитаете?

preferential *adj.* льготный. *Preferential tariff,* предпочтительный тариф.

preferred *adj.* предпочтительный. —**preferred stock,** привилегированные акции.

prefix *n.* приставка; префикс. —*v.t.* присоединять приставку к (слову). —**prefixed,** *adj.* приставочный. —**prefixion,** *n.* префиксация.

pregnancy *n.* беременность.

pregnant *adj.* беременная. *She is pregnant,* она беременна; она в положении. *Become pregnant,* стать беременной; (за)беременеть.

prehensile *adj.* цепкий.

prehistoric *adj.* доистори́ческий.
prejudge *v.t.* предреша́ть.
prejudice *n.* **1,** (bias) предрассу́док; предубежде́ние; предвзя́тость. **2,** (detriment) уще́рб. —*v.t.* **1,** (bias) предубежда́ть. **2,** (damage) наноси́ть уще́рб (+ *dat.*). —**prejudiced,** *adj.* предубежённый. *I am prejudiced against him,* к нему́ я отношу́сь предубеждённо; про́тив него́ я настро́ен предубеждённо. —**prejudicial,** *adj.* вре́дный.
prelate *n.* прела́т.
preliminary *adj.* предвари́тельный.
prelude *n.* прелю́дия.
premarital *adj.* добра́чный.
premature *adj.* **1,** (occurring earlier than expected) преждевре́менный: *premature birth/death,* преждевре́менные ро́ды; преждевре́менная смерть. *Premature child,* недоно́шенный ребёнок; недоно́сок. **2,** (too hasty) поспе́шный: *premature conclusion,* поспе́шный вы́вод. —**prematurely,** *adv.* преждевре́менно.
premeditated *adj.* преднаме́ренный; умы́шленный. —**premeditation,** *n.* преднаме́ренность.
premier *adj.* пе́рвый. —*n.* премье́р-мини́стр; премье́р.
première *n.* премье́ра.
premise *n.* **1,** (assumption) предпосы́лка. **2,** *pl.* (building and grounds) помеще́ние.
premium *n.* пре́мия. *At a premium,* нарасхва́т. *Put a premium on,* высоко́ цени́ть.
premonition *n.* предчу́вствие: *a premonition of disaster,* предчу́вствие несча́стья.
prenatal *adj.* предродово́й. *Prenatal care,* гигие́на бере́менной.
preoccupation *n.* **1,** (absorption) одержи́мость. **2,** (something that preoccupies) забо́та.
preoccupied *adj.* **1,** (lost in thought) погружённый в мы́сли. **2,** (totally involved) поглощённый.
preoccupy *v.t.* поглоща́ть.
preordain *v.t.* предопределя́ть.
prepaid *adj.* упла́ченный *or* опла́ченный зара́нее.
preparation *n.* **1,** (act of preparing something or getting ready) приготовле́ние; подгото́вка. **2,** *pl.* (steps taken to prepare) приготовле́ния. *Make preparations for,* гото́виться к. **3,** (substance) препара́т.
preparatory *adj.* приготови́тельный; подготови́тельный. —**preparatory to,** пре́жде чем.
prepare *v.t.* гото́вить; приготовля́ть; подгота́вливать. —*v.i.* гото́виться; приготовля́ться; подгота́вливаться. *Prepare for an exam,* гото́виться к экза́мену. *Prepare to depart,* гото́виться к отъе́зду.
prepared *adj.* гото́вый. —**preparedness,** *n.* гото́вность; подгото́вленность.
prepay *v.t.* упла́чивать *or* опла́чивать зара́нее.
preponderance *n.* переве́с; преоблада́ние. —**preponderant,** *adj.* преоблада́ющий.
preposition *n.* предло́г. —**prepositional,** *adj.* предло́жный.
prepossessing *adj.* располага́ющий; прия́тный; привлека́тельный.
preposterous *adj.* неле́пый; абсу́рдный; ди́кий.
prerequisite *n.* предпосы́лка.
prerevolutionary *adj.* дореволюцио́нный.
prerogative *n.* прерогати́ва; привиле́гия.
presage *v.t.* предвеща́ть.
presbyter *n.* пресви́тер.
Presbyterian *n.* пресвитериа́нин; пресвитериа́нец. —*adj.* пресвитериа́нсикй.
preschool *adj.* дошко́льный.
prescience *n.* предви́дение. —**prescient,** *adj.* проница́тельный.
prescribe *v.t.* **1,** (set down to be followed) предпи́сывать: *prescribe rules,* предпи́сывать пра́вила. **2,** (order the use of, as medicine) пропи́сывать.
prescription *n.* **1,** (instruction; directive) предписа́ние. **2,** *med.* реце́пт. **3,** *law* да́вность.
presence *n.* прису́тствие; нали́чие. *In the presence of,* при; в прису́тствии (+ *gen.*). —**presence of mind,** прису́тствие ду́ха.
present *adj.* **1,** (now going on; current) настоя́щий; тепе́решний; ны́нешний. **2,** (here; on hand) прису́тствующий. *Be present,* прису́тствовать; быть нали́цо́. **3,** (this; now being discussed) да́нный; настоя́щий. **4,** *gram.* настоя́щий: *the present tense,* настоя́щее вре́мя. —*n.* **1,** *preceded by* **the** (present time) настоя́щее. *At present,* сейча́с; в настоя́щее вре́мя. *For the present,* пока́. **2,** (gift) пода́рок. —*v.t.* **1,** (give; offer) представля́ть: *present facts/evidence/a report/,* представля́ть фа́кты/свиде́тельство/отчёт. **2,** (produce; show) предъявля́ть; представля́ть. **3,** (hand over; submit) вруча́ть: *present one's credentials,* вручи́ть свой вери́тельные гра́моты. **4,** (give or award formally) вруча́ть; преподноси́ть. *Present an award,* вручи́ть награ́ду. *She was presented with a bouquet of roses,* ей преподнесли́ буке́т роз. **5,** (introduce) представля́ть. **6,** (offer, as problems or difficulties) представля́ть. **7,** (give, as a play) пока́зывать; ста́вить. —**present arms,** взять на карау́л. —**present itself,** явля́ться; представля́ться.
presentable *adj.* прили́чный; презента́бельный.
presentation *n.* **1,** (submitting; introducing) представле́ние. **2,** (producing; showing) предъявле́ние. **3,** (awarding; bestowing) вруче́ние. **4,** (a performance) представле́ние.
present-day *adj.* совреме́нный. *By present-day standards,* по ме́ркам на́шего вре́мени.
presentiment *n.* предчу́вствие.
presently *adv.* **1,** (soon) ско́ро; вско́ре. **2,** (at present) сейча́с; в настоя́щее вре́мя.
preservation *n.* **1,** (act of preserving) сохране́ние. **2,** (state of being preserved) сохра́нность.
preservative *n.* консерва́нт.
preserve *v.t.* **1,** (keep; maintain) сохраня́ть. **2,** (prepare, as food, for future use) консерви́ровать. —*n.* **1,** (restricted area) запове́дник. **2,** *pl.* (confection) варе́нье.
preside *v.i.* председа́тельствовать.
president *n.* **1,** (chief executive) президе́нт. **2,** (presiding officer) председа́тель. **3,** (of a university) ре́ктор. —**presidency,** *n.* президе́нтство. —**presidential,** *adj.* президе́нтский.
presidium *n.* прези́диум.
press *v.t.* **1,** (push, as a button) нажима́ть на (кно́пку). **2,** (squeeze out the juice from) дави́ть; жать. **3,** (work in a press) прессова́ть: *press cotton,* прессова́ть хло́пок. **4,** (iron) гла́дить. **5,** *fol. by* **to** *or* **against** (embrace closely) прижима́ть: *press to one's bosom,* прижима́ть к груди́. **6,** (urge persistently) угова́ривать. *Press someone for an answer,* торопи́ть кого́-нибудь с отве́том. **7,** (be insistent about) наста́ивать на: *press a matter,* наста́ивать на чём-нибудь. *I will*

not press the point, я не бу́ду наста́ивать на э́том. **8,** (bring, as charges) предъявля́ть (обвине́ние). **9,** (straiten) стесня́ть: *pressed for money,* стеснённый в деньга́х. *I am pressed for time,* у меня́ вре́мени в обре́з. **10,** *in* **press one's luck,** искуша́ть *or* испы́тывать судьбу́. —*v.i.* **1,** (push hard) нажима́ть; нада́вливать; прида́вливать. *Press hard!,* нажми́ кре́пко! **2,** *fol. by* **against** (lean hard against) прижима́ться (к); приника́ть (к). **3,** (advance forcibly) пробира́ться; прота́лкиваться. *Press forward,* протолкну́ться вперёд. —*n.* **1,** (device for pressing or crushing) пресс: *hydraulic press,* гидравли́ческий пресс; *wine press,* дави́льный пресс. *Printing press,* печа́тный стано́к. **2,** (newspapers collectively) печа́ть; пре́сса. *Freedom of the press,* свобо́да печа́ти. **3,** (publishing company) изда́тельство. **4,** (printing) печа́ть: *go to press,* поступи́ть в печа́ть. **5,** (crush) да́вка. **6,** *weightlifting* жим. —*adj.* корреспонде́нтский: *press card/corps,* корреспонде́нтский биле́т/ко́рпус.

press conference пресс-конфере́нция.

presser *n.* прессовщи́к.

pressing *n.* гла́женье. —*adj.* неотло́жный; сро́чный.

pressman *n.* **1,** (one who works a press) прессовщи́к. **2,** (operator of a printing press) печа́тник.

pressmark *n., Brit.* шифр.

pressure *n.* давле́ние. —*v.t.* ока́зывать давле́ние на. —**pressure gauge,** мано́метр.

pressurized *adj.* гермети́ческий: *pressurized cabin,* гермети́ческая каби́на.

prestidigitation *n.* ло́вкость рук. —**prestidigitator,** *n.* фо́кусник.

prestige *n.* прести́ж; авторите́т. —**prestigious,** *adj.* прести́жный.

presto *adv., music* пре́сто.

presumably *adv.* предположи́тельно.

presume *v.t.* **1,** (assume) предполага́ть. **2,** *fol. by inf.* (dare; venture) осме́ливаться; бра́ться. *I do not presume to judge,* не беру́сь суди́ть. —*v.i.* [*usu.* **presume on** *or* **upon**] злоупотребля́ть.

presumption *n.* **1,** (supposition) предположе́ние. **2,** *law* презу́мпция: *presumption of innocence,* презу́мпция невино́вности. **3,** (effrontery) самонаде́янность.

presumptive *adj.* предположи́тельный. —**heir presumptive,** вероя́тный насле́дник.

presumptuous *adj.* самонаде́янный.

presuppose *v.t.* предполага́ть.

pretence *n.* = **pretense.**

pretend *v.t. & i.* притворя́ться; де́лать вид. —**pretended,** *adj.* притво́рный.

pretender *n.* претенде́нт.

pretense *also,* **pretence** *n.* **1,** (sham) притво́рство; по́за. **2,** (claim) прете́нзия. *Make no pretense of,* не претендова́ть на. **3,** (pretext) предло́г. *Under false pretenses,* обма́нным путём.

pretension *n.* прете́нзия. *Have pretensions of,* претендова́ть на.

pretentious *adj.* претенцио́зный; с прете́нзиями. —**pretentiousness,** *n.* претенцио́зность.

pretext *n.* предло́г.

prettily *adv.* краси́во; ми́ло.

pretty *adj.* **1,** (pleasing to the eye) хоро́шенький; милови́дный. **2,** (pleasing to the ear, as of a song or voice) прия́тный; краси́вый. **3,** *colloq.* (quite a large) изря́дный: *a pretty sum,* изря́дная су́мма. **4,** *ironic* (fine; nice) хоро́шенький: *a pretty mess,* хоро́шенькая исто́рия. —*adv.* дово́льно; доста́точно. *Pretty good,* неду́рно; так себе́. —*v.t.* [*usu.* **pretty up**] прикра́шивать.

pretzel *n.* кре́ндель.

prevail *v.i.* **1,** *often fol. by* **over** (triumph; win out) (вос)торжествова́ть (над); брать верх (над); преоблада́ть (над). **2,** (be in use; be current) существова́ть. **3,** *fol. by* **upon** (persuade) убеди́ть; уговори́ть; упроси́ть; умоли́ть. —**prevailing,** *adj.* преоблада́ющий; госпо́дствующий.

prevalent *adj.* распространённый. —**prevalence,** *n.* распростране́ние.

prevaricate *v.i.* **1,** (speak evasively) уви́ливать. **2,** (lie) привира́ть.

prevent *v.t.* **1,** (keep from happening) предупрежда́ть; предотвраща́ть. **2,** (stop from doing something) меша́ть: *illness prevented me from coming,* боле́знь помеша́ла мне прийти́.

prevention *n.* предупрежде́ние; предотвраще́ние.

preventive *adj.* предупреди́тельный; предохрани́тельный. —**preventive medicine,** предупреди́тельная медици́на. —**preventive war,** превенти́вная война́.

preview *n.* **1,** (of a film) предвари́тельный просмо́тр. **2,** (advance view) предвари́тельный взгляд (на бу́дущее).

previous *adj.* предыду́щий: *the previous day/issue,* предыду́щий день/но́мер. —**previous to,** до; пре́жде.

previously *adv.* ра́ньше.

prewar *adj.* довое́нный; предвое́нный.

prey *n.* **1,** (animal killed by another) добы́ча. **2,** (victim) же́ртва: *fall prey to,* пасть же́ртвой (+ *gen.*). **3,** *in* **bird of prey,** хи́щная пти́ца; хи́щник. —*v.i.* [*usu.* **prey on** *or* **upon**] **1,** (seek and take for food) охо́титься на; лови́ть; пита́ться (+ *instr.*). **2,** (plunder) гра́бить. **3,** (victimize) эксплуати́ровать. **4,** *Prey on one's mind,* пресле́довать.

price *n.* цена́. *The price of bread,* цена́ хле́ба *or* цена́ на хлеб. *At any price,* любо́й ценой. —*v.t.* **1,** (set a price on) расце́нивать. **2,** *colloq.* (ask the price of) прице́ниваться к.

priceless *adj.* бесце́нный. *This ring is priceless,* цены́ э́тому кольцу́ нет.

price list прейскура́нт.

price tag ярлы́к с указа́нием цены́.

prick *v.t.* **1,** (pierce accidentally) уколо́ть: *prick one's finger,* уколо́ть себе́ па́лец. **2,** (puncture, as a bubble or balloon) прока́лывать. —*n.* уко́л. —**prick up one's ears,** насторожи́ть *or* навостри́ть у́ши; насторожи́ться.

prickle *n.* шип; колю́чка.

prickly *adj.* колю́чий; ко́лкий. —**prickly heat,** потни́ца. —**prickly pear,** опу́нция.

pride *n.* **1,** (pleasure; satisfaction) го́рдость. *Take pride in,* горди́ться (+ *instr.*). **2,** (conceit; self-esteem) самолю́бие; го́рдость. *Hurt someone's pride,* заде́ть чьё-нибудь самолю́бие. **3,** (that of which one is proud) го́рдость. —*v.t.* [*usu.* **pride oneself on**] горди́ться (+ *instr.*).

priest *n.* свяще́нник. *Pagan priest,* жрец. —**priest-**

hood, *n.* священство; духовенство. —**priestly,** *adj.* священнический.
prim *adj.* чопорный.
primacy *n.* первенство; примат.
prima donna примадонна.
primarily *adv.* преимущественно; в основном; прежде всего.
primary *adj.* **1,** (first) первичный. **2,** (chief; basic) основной: *the primary purpose,* основная цель. —*n.* первичные выборы. —**primary color,** основной цвет. —**primary school,** начальная школа. —**primary source,** первоисточник.
primate *n.* **1,** *eccles.* примас. **2,** *zool.* примат.
prime *adj.* **1,** (chief; paramount) основной: *prime requisite,* основное требование. *A prime example,* яркий пример. *Of prime concern,* величайшей важности. **2,** (of the finest quality) первосортный. —*n.* расцвет. *In one's prime; in the prime of life,* во цвете лет; в расцвете сил. —*v.t.* **1,** (make ready) подготавливать. **2,** (set, as a gun) вставлять запал в. **3,** (fill, as a pump) наполнять (водой). —**prime cost,** себестоимость. —**prime minister,** премьер-министр. —**prime number,** простое число; неделимое число.
primer[1] (**prim**-er) *n.* (beginning reading book) букварь.
primer[2] (**prai**-mer) *n.* (detonating device) запал; капсюль.
primeval *adj.* первобытный.
priming *n., painting* грунт.
primitive *adj.* **1,** (earliest) первобытный: *primitive man,* первобытный человек. **2,** (plain, crude) примитивный.
primogeniture *n.* первородство.
primordial *adj.* исконный; изначальный.
primp *v.i.* прихорашиваться.
primrose *n.* первоцвет; примула.
prince *n.* **1,** (in prerevolutionary Russia) князь. **2,** (in other countries) принц.
princely *adj.* княжеский. *A princely sum,* огромная сумма.
princess *n.* **1,** *pre-rev.* (prince's wife) княгиня; (prince's daughter) княжна. **2,** (outside Russia) принцесса.
principal *adj.* главный; основной: *principal reason,* главная/основная причина. —*n.* **1,** (head of a school) директор. **2,** *finance* капитал: *principal and interest,* капитал и проценты.
principality *n.* княжество.
principally *adv.* главным образом; преимущественно.
principle *n.* принцип. *A man of principle,* принципиальный человек. —**in principle,** в принципе. —**on principle,** из принципа.
print *n.* **1,** (impression) отпечаток: *footprint,* отпечаток ноги. **2,** (type) шрифт; печать. *Large print,* крупный шрифт. **3,** *photog.* отпечаток. **4,** (engraving, woodcut, etc.) гравюра. **5,** (fabric with a printed design) набивной ситец. —*adj.* ситцевый: *a print dress,* ситцевое платье. —*v.t.* **1,** (produce from type; publish in print) печатать. **2,** (produce from a negative) отпечатывать. **3,** (write in block letters) писать печатными буквами. **4,** *textiles* набивать. —**in print,** печатается. *See one's name in print,* видеть своё имя в печати. —**out of print,** больше не печатается.
printed *adj.* печатный; напечатанный; отпечатанный. —**printed matter,** бандероль. —**the printed word,** печатное слово.
printer *n.* печатник; типограф. *Send a manuscript to the printer,* послать рукопись в типографию.
printing *n.* **1,** (act) печатание. **2,** (art) печатное дело; полиграфия. **3,** (quantity printed at one time) тираж. **4,** *textiles* набивка. —**printing press,** печатный станок.
prior *adj.* предварительный: *prior condition,* предварительное условие. *By prior agreement,* по предварительному соглашению. *We have a prior engagement,* у нас другие планы; нас уже пригласили. —*n.* (of a monastery) приор; настоятель. —**prior to,** до.
priority *n.* приоритет.
priory *n.* монастырь.
prism *n.* призма. —**prismatic,** *adj.* призматический.
prison *n.* тюрьма: *put in prison,* сажать в тюрьму. *Two years in prison,* два года тюремного заключения. —*adj.* тюремный: *prison cell,* тюремная камера.
prisoner *n.* заключенный. *Take prisoner,* взять в плен. *Be taken prisoner,* попасть в плен. *Hold prisoner,* держать в плену. —**prisoner of war,** военнопленный.
pristine *adj.* первобытный.
privacy *n.* уединение. *Invasion of privacy,* вторжение в личную жизнь.
private *adj.* частный. —*n., mil.* рядовой. —**in private,** наедине.
privately *adv.* наедине; частным образом; в частном порядке.
privation *n.* лишение: *suffer privations,* терпеть лишения.
privilege *n.* привилегия; льгота. —**privileged,** *adj.* привилегированный. *I am privileged to...,* имею честь (+ *inf.*).
privy *adj.* [*usu.* **privy to**] посвященный (в). —*n.* отхожее место. —**privy council,** тайный совет.
prize *n.* премия; приз. —*adj.* **1,** (given as a prize) призовой. **2,** (having won a prize) премированный. —*v.t.* ценить; дорожить.
prize fight боксерское состязание. —**prize fighter,** боксер.
prizewinner *n.* призер.
pro *n.* **1,** (argument in favor): *the pros and cons,* доводы за и против. **2,** *colloq.* (professional) профессионал.
pro- *prefix* про-: *pro-American,* проамериканский.
probability *n.* вероятность. *In all probability,* по всей вероятности.
probable *adj.* вероятный. *Highly probable,* весьма вероятно.
probably *adv.* вероятно; наверно; пожалуй. *Most probably,* скорее всего.
probate *n.* утверждение (завещания).
probation *n.* условное освобождение. *He was given a year on probation,* он получил год условно.
probe *n.* **1,** (instrument) зонд; щуп. **2,** (investigation) расследование. —*v.t.* **1,** *med.* зондировать. **2,** (investigate) вникать в; расследовать.
probity *n.* честность; порядочность.
problem *n.* **1,** (difficult question or matter) проблема. **2,** (arithmetical problem) задача. —**problem child,** трудный ребенок.

problematic *adj.* проблемати́ческий; проблема-ти́чный. *Also,* **problematical.**

proboscis *n.* хо́бот.

procedure *n.* процеду́ра; поря́док. —**procedural,** *adj.* процеду́рный.

proceed *v.i.* **1,** (go forward) идти́; е́хать: *proceed with caution,* идти́ *or* е́хать осторо́жно. **2,** (begin) приступа́ть: *proceed with the vote,* приступи́ть к голосова́нию. *I don't know how to proceed,* не зна́ю, как приступи́ть к э́тому де́лу. **3,** (continue) продолжа́ть: *please proceed,* продолжа́йте, пожа́луйста. **4,** *fol. by* **on** *or* **from** (begin in one's reasoning) исходи́ть из: *proceed on the assumption that...,* исходи́ть из того́, что...

proceedings *n.pl.* **1,** (action taking place) происходя́щее. **2,** (legal action) судопроизво́дство. **3,** (records; minutes) протоко́л.

proceeds *n.pl.* вы́ручка.

process *n.* проце́сс. *In the process of,* в проце́ссе (+ *gen.*). —*v.t.* **1,** (treat) обраба́тывать; перераба́тывать. **2,** (handle, as a document) оформля́ть.

procession *n.* ше́ствие; проце́ссия.

proclaim *v.t.* провозглаша́ть. —**proclamation,** *n.* объявле́ние; провозглаше́ние.

proclivity *n.* скло́нность; накло́нность; тенде́нция.

proconsul *n.* проко́нсул.

procrastinate *v.i.* ме́длить; ме́шкать. —**procrastination,** *n.* промедле́ние; проволо́чка. —**procrastinator,** *n.* медли́тель.

procreate *v.i.* производи́ть пото́мство. —**procreation,** *n.* деторожде́ние.

proctor *n.* **1,** (for supervising an examination) надзира́тель. **2,** *law* (agent; representative) пове́ренный.

procure *v.t.* достава́ть; добыва́ть.

procurement *n.* **1,** (acquisition) приобрете́ние. **2,** (purchase by the government) загото́вка.

procurer *n.* сво́дник.

prod *v.t.* **1,** (poke) ты́кать. **2,** (urge; goad) подгоня́ть. —*n.* тычо́к.

prodigal *adj.* расточи́тельный. —**prodigal son,** блу́дный сын.

prodigality *n.* расточи́тельность; мотовство́.

prodigious *adj.* огро́мный; колосса́льный.

prodigy *n.* чу́до. *Child prodigy,* вундерки́нд.

produce *v.t.* **1,** (manufacture; bring into being) производи́ть. **2,** (show; offer for inspection) предъявля́ть; пока́зывать. **3,** (bring about) приноси́ть; дава́ть: *produce income,* приноси́ть дохо́д; *produce results,* дава́ть результа́ты. **4,** (bring to the stage or screen) ста́вить; режисси́ровать. —*n.* сельскохозя́йственные проду́кты.

producer *n.* **1,** (one who produces) производи́тель. **2,** *theat.* дире́ктор. **3,** (of a film) продю́сер.

product *n.* **1,** (something produced) проду́кт. **2,** *fig.* (result; outgrowth) плод. **3,** *math.* произведе́ние.

production *n.* **1,** (act of producing) произво́дство: *go into production,* поступи́ть в произво́дство. **2,** *theat.* постано́вка: *a new production of Swan Lake,* Лебеди́ное о́зеро в но́вой постано́вке. —*adj.* произво́дственный: *production plan,* произво́дственный план. —**production line,** пото́чная ли́ния.

productive *adj.* **1,** (producing) производи́тельный; продукти́вный. **2,** (fruitful) плодотво́рный. —**productivity,** *n.* производи́тельность; продукти́вность.

profanation *n.* оскверне́ние; профана́ция.

profane *adj.* **1,** (irreverent; blasphemous) нечести́вый; богоху́льный. **2,** (vulgar; coarse) вульга́рный; гру́бый. **3,** (secular) све́тский. —*v.t.* оскверня́ть.

profanity *n.* брань; ру́гань; *pl.* са́льности.

profess *v.t.* **1,** (openly declare or admit) заявля́ть о; (откры́то) признава́ть. *Profess one's love,* призна́ться в любви́. **2,** (avow, as a religion) испове́довать.

profession *n.* **1,** (occupation) профе́ссия: *a lawyer by profession,* юри́ст по профе́ссии. *The medical profession,* врачи́. **2,** (open declaration) заявле́ние. **3,** (avowal of a religion) испове́дание.

professional *adj.* профессиона́льный. *Professional man,* челове́к свобо́дной профе́ссии. —*n.* профессиона́л.

professor *n.* профе́ссор. —**professorial,** *adj.* профе́ссорский. —**professorship,** *n.* профе́ссорство; профессу́ра.

proffer *v.t.* предлага́ть.

proficiency *n.* уме́ние; на́вык; сноро́вка. *Proficiency in a language,* зна́ние языка́.

proficient *adj.* иску́сный; уме́лый.

profile *n.* про́филь.

profit *n.* **1,** (monetary gain) при́быль: *sell at a profit,* продава́ть с при́былью. **2,** (benefit) по́льза; вы́года. —*v.t.* приноси́ть по́льзу (+ *dat.*). —*v.i.* [*usu.* **profit from**] извлека́ть по́льзу (из).

profitable *adj.* **1,** (yielding a profit) при́быльный; вы́годный; дохо́дный. **2,** (beneficial) поле́зный.

profiteer *n.* спекуля́нт. —*v.i.* спекули́ровать.

profligacy *n.* **1,** (dissoluteness) распу́тство. **2,** (reckless extravagance) расточи́тельность.

profligate *adj.* **1,** (dissolute) распу́тный; развра́тный. **2,** (recklessly extravagant) расточи́тельный. —*n.* распу́тник; развра́тник.

profound *adj.* глубо́кий: *profound knowledge/grief,* глубо́кие зна́ния; глубо́кое го́ре. *Profound difference,* огро́мная ра́зница. *Profound consequences,* далеко́ иду́щие после́дствия. *Undergo a profound change,* о́чень измени́ться. —**profoundly,** *adv.* глубоко́.

profundity *n.* глубина́.

profuse *adj.* **1,** (abundant) оби́льный. **2,** (lavish): *be profuse in one's praise,* рассыпа́ться в похвала́х. *Apologize profusely,* рассыпа́ться в извине́ниях. —**profusion,** *n.* изоби́лие.

progenitor *n.* родонача́льник.

progeny *n.* пото́мство.

prognosis *n.* прогно́з.

prognosticate *v.t. & i.* предска́зывать. —**prognostication,** *n.* предсказа́ние. —**prognosticator,** *n.* предсказа́тель.

program *also,* **programme** *n.* програ́мма. —*v.t.* программи́ровать. —**programmed,** *adj.* програ́ммный; программи́рованный. —**programmer,** *n.* программи́ст. —**programming,** *n.* программи́рование.

progress *n.* прогре́сс; успе́хи. *Make progress,* де́лать успе́хи. —*v.i.* **1,** (make progress) прогресси́ровать; продвига́ться. **2,** (get along) идти́: *how is your work progressing?,* как идёт ва́ша рабо́та? —**be in progress,** идти́.

progression *n.* **1,** (advancement) продвиже́ние. **2,** *math.* прогре́ссия: *geometric progression,* геометри́ческая прогре́ссия.

progressive *adj.* прогрессивный.
prohibit *v.t.* запрещáть. *Be prohibited,* запрещáться; воспрещáться. —**prohibition,** *n.* запрещéние.
prohibitive *adj.* запретительный. *Prohibitive prices,* недостýпные цéны.
project *n.* проéкт. —*v.t.* **1,** (plan) проектировать. **2,** (estimate into the future) исчислять. **3,** (convey; get across) передавáть; внушáть. **4,** (cause to appear on a surface) отбрáсывать. —*v.i.* (protrude) выдавáться; выступáть.
projectile *n.* снаряд.
projection *n.* **1,** (something jutting out) вы́ступ. **2,** (system used in mapmaking) проéкция. **3,** (screening) проéкция. **4,** (advance estimate) оцéнка; прогнóз; исчислéние. —**projection booth,** проекциóнная бýдка.
projectionist *n.* киномехáник.
projector *n.* проекциóнный аппарáт *or* фонáрь; проéктор. *Movie projector,* киноустанóвка.
prolapse *n.* выпадéние; опущéние.
proletarian *n.* пролетáрий. —*adj.* пролетáрский. —**proletariat,** *n.* пролетариáт.
proliferate *v.i.* размножáться; распространяться. —**proliferation,** *n.* распространéние.
prolific *adj.* плодовитый.
prolix *adj.* многослóвный; пространный.
prologue *n.* прологг.
prolong *v.t.* продлевáть. —**prolongation,** *n.* продлéние. —**prolonged,** *adj.* длительный; продолжительный.
promenade *n.* **1,** (stroll) прогýлка. **2,** (mall) бульвáр. —*v.i.* прогýливаться. —**promenade deck,** прогýлочная пáлуба.
Prometheus *n.* Прометéй.
promethium *n.* промéтий.
prominence *n.* **1,** (fame) извéстность: *come into prominence,* приобретáть извéстность. **2,** (bulge) вы́ступ.
prominent *adj.* **1,** (leading; well-known) ви́дный; извéстный. **2,** (protruding) выступáющий вперёд.
promiscuous *adj.* лёгкого поведéния; распýтный. —**promiscuity,** *n.* лёгкое поведéние.
promise *v.t. & i.* обещáть: *I promise you I won't be late,* обещáю вам, что не опоздáю. *The movie promises to be interesting,* фильм обещáет быть интерéсным. *Make someone promise,* брать слóво с. —*n.* **1,** (pledge) обещáние. **2,** (basis for expectation): *show great promise,* подавáть большие надéжды. *A violinist of great promise,* многообещáющий скрипáч. —**Promised Land,** обетовáнная землá.
promising *adj.* многообещáющий; перспективный.
promissory note вéксель; долговóе обязáтельство.
promontory *n.* мыс.
promote *v.t.* **1,** (foster; further) способствовать; содéйствовать. **2,** (raise in rank) продвигáть; повышáть в чи́не. *He was promoted at work,* он получил повышéние по слýжбе. *He was promoted to captain,* емý присвóили звáние капитáна; егó произвели в капитáны. **3,** (move forward a grade in school) переводить в слéдующий класс. **4,** (publicize) рекламировать. **5,** *chess* превращáть (пéшку).
promotion *n.* **1,** (advancement in rank) повышéние *or* продвижéние по слýжбе; *mil.* присвоéние звáния; произвóдство. **2,** (furtherance) продвижéние; поощрéние. **3,** (publicity) реклáма. **4,** *chess* превращéние (пéшки).
promotional *adj.* реклáмный.
prompt *adj.* **1,** (done without delay) бы́стрый; срóчный. *Prompt reply,* бы́стрый отвéт. *Take prompt measures,* принимáть срóчные мéры. **2,** (punctual) аккурáтный. —*v.t.* **1,** (induce) побуждáть. **2,** (give rise to; occasion) вызывáть. **3,** (assist with a reminder) подскáзывать. **4,** *theat.* суфлировать. —*v.i.* подскáзывать: *no prompting!,* не подскáзывать! —**prompter,** *n.* суфлёр. —**promptly,** *adv.* бы́стро; срáзу.
promptness *n.* **1,** (speed) быстротá. **2,** (punctuality) аккурáтность.
promulgate *v.t.* издавáть; опубликовáть; обнарóдовать. —**promulgation,** *n.* издáние; опубликовáние; обнарóдование.
prone *adj.* **1,** (prostrate) лежáщий ничкóм. *Prone position,* положéние лёжа. **2,** *fol. by* **to** (inclined) склóнный (к); подвéрженный (+ *dat.*). *Prone to error,* подвéрженный оши́бкам. *Prone to violence,* склóнный к наси́лию.
prong *n.* зубéц.
pronoun *n.* местоимéние. —**pronominal,** *adj.* местоимéнный.
pronounce *v.t.* **1,** (articulate) произноси́ть. **2,** (declare to be) объявлять; признавáть. *I pronounce you man and wife,* объявляю вас мýжем и женóй. *Pronounce someone guilty/insane,* признáть когó-нибудь винóвным/душевнобольны́м. **3,** (announce, as a sentence) объявлять; зачи́тывать (приговóр). *Pronounce judgment,* выноси́ть решéние.
pronounced *adj.* замéтный; ярко вы́раженный.
pronouncement *n.* **1,** (act of announcing) объявлéние. **2,** (formal declaration) (официáльное) заявлéние.
pronunciation *n.* произношéние.
proof *n.* **1,** (conclusive evidence) доказáтельство. **2,** *printing* корректýра; грáнка; óттиск. *Page proofs,* вёрстка; корректýра в листáх.
proofread *v.t.* корректировать. —*v.i.* держáть *or* прáвить корректýру. —**proofreader,** *n.* коррéктор. —**proofreading,** *n.* корректýра; прáвка корректýры.
prop *v.t.* **1,** *fol. by* **up** (hold up; support) подпирáть. **2,** *fol. by* **against** (lean against) прислонять (к). —*n.* **1,** (support) подпóра; подпóрка. **2,** *pl., theat.* реквизи́т; бутафóрия.
propaganda *n.* пропагáнда. —**propagandist,** *n.* пропаганди́ст. —**propagandistic,** *adj.* пропаганди́стский. —**propagandize,** *v.t.* пропагандировать.
propagate *v.t.* **1,** (breed) размножáть. **2,** (disseminate) распространять; проповéдовать. —*v.i.* размножáться.
propagation *n.* **1,** (reproduction) размножéние. **2,** (dissemination) распространéние; прóповедь.
propane *n.* пропáн.
propel *v.t.* двигать; приводи́ть в дéйствие.
propellant *also,* **propellent** *n.* **1,** (explosive charge) метáтельное взры́вчатое веществó. **2,** (fuel for a rocket) ракéтное тóпливо.
propeller *n.* **1,** (of an aircraft) (воздýшный) винт; пропéллер. **2,** (of a boat) гребнóй винт. —**propeller-driven,** *adj.* винтовóй.
propensity *n.* склóнность; наклóнность; предрасположéние.

proper *adj.* **1,** (appropriate) подходя́щий. **2,** (correct) пра́вильный. **3,** (seemly) прили́чный; присто́йный. **4,** (in the narrow sense) со́бственно: *the city proper,* со́бственно го́род. **5,** *gram.* со́бственный: *proper noun,* и́мя со́бственное. **6,** *math.* пра́вильный: *proper fraction,* пра́вильная дробь.

properly *adv.* как сле́дует; до́лжным о́бразом.

propertied *adj.* иму́щий.

property *n.* **1,** (that which is owned) со́бственность; иму́щество. **2,** (attribute) сво́йство. **3,** *pl., theat.* рекви́зит; бутафо́рия. —**property man,** бутафо́р. —**property tax,** нало́г на недви́жимость.

prophecy *n.* проро́чество; прорица́ние. —**prophesy,** *v.t. & i.* проро́чить; прорица́ть.

prophet *n.* проро́к. —**prophetic,** *adj.* проро́ческий.

prophylactic *adj.* профилакти́ческий. —*n.* профилакти́ческое сре́дство. —**prophylaxis,** *n.* профила́ктика.

propinquity *n.* **1,** (nearness) бли́зость. **2,** (kinship) родство́.

propitiate *v.t.* уми́лостивить.

propitious *adj.* благоприя́тный; подходя́щий.

proponent *n.* сторо́нник; пропове́дник.

proportion *n.* **1,** *math.* пропо́рция. *Direct/inverse proportion,* пряма́я/обра́тная пропорциона́льность. **2,** (balance; symmetry) соразме́рность. *Sense of proportion,* чу́вство ме́ры. **3,** *pl.* (size; scope) разме́ры. —*v.t.* соразмеря́ть. —**in proportion to,** соразме́рно (+ *dat.*); пропорциона́льно (+ *dat.*). —**out of proportion,** чрезме́рно; че́рез ме́ру. *Out of proportion to,* несоразме́рно с.

proportional *also,* **proportionate** *adj.* пропорциона́льный; соразме́рный. —**proportionally; proportionately,** *adv.* пропорциона́льно.

proposal *n.* предложе́ние.

propose *v.t.* **1,** (suggest) предлага́ть. *Propose a toast,* предложи́ть тост. **2,** *fol. by inf.* (intend) предполага́ть. —*v.i.* сде́лать предложе́ние (о бра́ке).

proposition *n.* **1,** (proposal) предложе́ние. **2,** (thesis) положе́ние. **3,** *logic* выска́зывание.

propound *v.t.* выдвига́ть: *propound a theory,* выдвига́ть тео́рию.

proprietary *adj.* со́бственнический; хозя́йский.

proprietor *n.* со́бственник; владе́лец; хозя́ин.

propriety *n.* прили́чие. *Observe the proprieties,* соблюда́ть прили́чия.

propulsion *n.* движе́ние вперёд; приведе́ние в движе́ние. *Jet propulsion,* реакти́вное движе́ние.

pro rata пропорциона́льно.

prorate *v.t.* распределя́ть пропорциона́льно.

prorogue *v.t.* распуска́ть (парла́мент).

prosaic *adj.* прозаи́ческий; прозаи́чный.

proscenium *n.* просце́ниум; авансце́на.

proscribe *v.t.* **1,** (prohibit) запреща́ть. **2,** (outlaw) объявля́ть вне зако́на. **3,** (banish) изгоня́ть. —**proscription,** *n.* запре́т; запреще́ние.

prose *n.* про́за. *Work of prose,* произведе́ние про́зы. —*adj.* прозаи́ческий. *Prose writer,* проза́ик.

prosecute *v.t.* **1,** *law* отдава́ть под суд; предава́ть суду́; пресле́довать (кого́-нибудь) суде́бным поря́дком. **2,** (conduct, as a war) вести́. —*v.i.* возбужда́ть иск *or* де́ло.

prosecution *n.* **1,** (conducting) веде́ние. **2,** *law* (prosecuting) пресле́дование. **3,** (party initiating criminal proceedings) обвине́ние. *Witness for the prosecution,* свиде́тель обвине́ния.

prosecutor *n.* обвини́тель. *Public prosecutor,* прокуро́р.

proselyte *n.* новообращённый; прозели́т. —**proselytize,** *v.t.* обраща́ть (в свою́ ве́ру). —*v.i.* иска́ть прозели́тов.

prosody *n.* просо́дия. —**prosodic,** *adj.* просоди́ческий.

prospect *n.* **1,** (outlook; chance) перспекти́ва; *pl.* ви́ды; перспекти́вы. **2,** (likely candidate) кандида́т. —*v.t.* разве́дывать. —*v.i.* [*usu.* **prospect for**] иска́ть: *prospect for gold,* иска́ть зо́лото. —**be in prospect,** быть в перспекти́ве.

prospective *adj.* **1,** (future) бу́дущий. **2,** (potential) возмо́жный.

prospector *n.* разве́дчик; изыска́тель. *Prospector for gold,* золотоиска́тель; стара́тель.

prospectus *n.* проспе́кт.

prosper *v.i.* процвета́ть. —**prosperity,** *n.* процвета́ние. —**prosperous,** *adj.* зажи́точный; состоя́тельный; обеспе́ченный.

prostate *n.* предста́тельная железа́; проста́та.

prosthetic *adj.* проте́зный. *Prosthetic device,* проте́з.

prostitute *n.* проститу́тка. —**prostitution,** *n.* проститу́ция.

prostrate *adj.* **1,** (flat; prone) распростёртый. *Lie prostrate,* лежа́ть ничко́м. **2,** (exhausted) истощённый. —*v.t.* **1,** *fol. by* **oneself** (lie face down in humility) па́дать ниц. **2,** (exhaust) истоща́ть. —**prostration,** *n.* изнеможе́ние; простра́ция.

protactinium *n.* протакти́ний.

protagonist *n.* протагони́ст.

protect *v.t.* защища́ть; охраня́ть; предохраня́ть; огражда́ть; оберега́ть; убере́чь.

protection *n.* защи́та; охра́на; предохране́ние; огражде́ние.

protectionism *n.* протекциони́зм.

protective *adj.* **1,** (serving to protect) защи́тный: *protective helmet,* защи́тный шлем. **2,** (carefully protecting) забо́тливый: *an overly protective mother,* сли́шком забо́тливая мать. *Be protective of,* бе́режно забо́титься о. —**protective coloration,** защи́тная *or* покрови́тельственная окра́ска. —**protective tariff,** покрови́тельственный тари́ф.

protector *n.* защи́тник.

protectorate *n.* протектора́т.

protégé *n.* протеже́; ста́вленник.

protein *n.* бело́к; протеи́н. —*adj.* белко́вый.

protest *n.* проте́ст. —*v.i.* протестова́ть. —*v.t.* протестова́ть про́тив.

Protestant *n.* протеста́нт. —*adj.* протеста́нтский. —**Protestantism,** *n.* протестанти́зм; протеста́нтство.

protestation *n.* (торже́ственное) заявле́ние. *Protestations of one's innocence,* заявле́ния о свое́й невино́вности.

protester *n.* протеста́нт.

protocol *n.* **1,** (etiquette) пра́вила (дипломати́ческого) этике́та. **2,** (agreement between states) протоко́л.

proton *n.* прото́н.

protoplasm *n.* протопла́зма.

prototype *n.* прототи́п; про́образ; перво́образ.

protoxide *n.* за́кись.
protozoa *n.pl.* просте́йшие.
protract *v.t.* тяну́ть; затя́гивать. —**protracted,** *adj.* дли́тельный; затяжно́й.
protractor *n.* транспорти́р.
protrude *v.i.* выдава́ться; торча́ть. —*v.t.* высо́вывать.
protrusion *n.* вы́ступ.
protuberance *n.* бугоро́к; вы́пуклость. —**protuberant,** *adj.* вы́пуклый.
proud *adj.* го́рдый: *proud man,* го́рдый челове́к. *Proud father,* счастли́вый оте́ц. *Be proud of,* горди́ться (+ *instr.*). *He is too proud to...,* он сли́шком горд, что́бы... —**do someone proud,** де́лать честь (+ *dat.*).
proud flesh ди́кое мя́со.
proudly *adv.* го́рдо; с го́рдостью.
prove *v.t.* дока́зывать. —*v.i.* (turn out to be) оказа́ться (+ *instr.*); показа́ть *or* прояви́ть себя́ (+ *instr.*). —**prove itself,** оправда́ть себя́ (на пра́ктике). —**prove oneself,** показа́ть себя́; прояви́ть себя́.
proven *adj.* **1,** (demonstrated) дока́занный. **2,** (tested and found valid) испы́танный: *proven method,* испы́танный ме́тод.
provenance *n.* происхожде́ние.
provender *n.* корм; фура́ж.
proverb *n.* посло́вица. —**Book of Proverbs,** Кни́га при́тчей Соломо́новых.
proverbial *adj.* воше́дший в посло́вицу.
provide *v.t.* **1,** (supply with something useful) снабжа́ть; обеспе́чивать. **2,** (give; furnish) дава́ть; ока́зывать. *Provide assistance,* ока́зывать по́мощь. **3,** (give; afford, as pleasure) доставля́ть. **4,** (stipulate) предусма́тривать. —*v.i.* [*usu.* **provide for**] **1,** (furnish with means of subsistence) содержа́ть; обеспе́чивать. **2,** (allow for; stipulate) предусма́тривать.
provided *conj.* при усло́вии, что; е́сли то́лько.
providence *n.* **1,** (foresight) предусмотри́тельность. **2,** *cap.* (divine care) провиде́ние.
provident *adj.* предусмотри́тельный; запа́сливый.
providential *adj.* провиденциа́льный.
providing *conj.* = **provided.**
province *n.* **1,** (division of a country) прови́нция. **2,** *pl.* (rural areas) прови́нция; перифери́я. **3,** *fig.* (sphere of knowledge or activity) о́бласть зна́ний; сфе́ра; компете́нция.
provincial *adj.* провинциа́льный. —*n.* провинциа́л. —**provincialism,** *n.* провинциали́зм.
proving ground испыта́тельный полиго́н.
provision *n.* **1,** (supplying) снабже́ние. **2,** (clause in a legal document) положе́ние. **3,** (stipulation; proviso) усло́вие. **4,** *pl.* (victuals) прови́зия. —**make provision for,** предусма́тривать.
provisional *adj.* вре́менный.
proviso *n.* усло́вие; огово́рка.
provocation *n.* провока́ция. *Without provocation,* без вся́кого по́вода. *At the slightest provocation,* по мале́йшему по́воду.
provocative *adj.* вызыва́ющий; провокацио́нный.
provoke *v.t.* **1,** (excite to a certain action; cause; bring about) провоци́ровать. **2,** (evoke, as an emotion) вызыва́ть; возбужда́ть. **3,** (vex) раздража́ть.
provost *n.* ре́ктор; дека́н. —**provost marshal,** нача́льник вое́нной поли́ции.
prow *n.* нос (су́дна).
prowess *n.* **1,** (bravery) до́блесть; у́даль. **2,** (skill) мастерство́.
prowl *v.i.* ры́скать; кра́сться. —**prowl car,** маши́на полице́йского патруля́.
prowler *n.* взло́мщик.
proximity *n.* бли́зость.
proxy *n.* **1,** (person authorized to act for another) дове́ренный. **2,** (authority) полномо́чие. —**by proxy,** по дове́ренности.
prude *n.* челове́к стро́гих нра́вов.
prudence *n.* благоразу́мие.
prudent *adj.* благоразу́мный; расчётливый. —**prudently,** *adv.* благоразу́мно.
prudish *adj.* чо́порный; пурита́нский.
prune *n.* (dried plum) чернosли́в. —*v.t.* (trim) обреза́ть; подреза́ть.
prurient *adj.* похотли́вый.
Prussian *adj.* пру́сский. —*n.* прусса́к. —**Prussian blue,** берли́нская лазу́рь.
prussic acid сини́льная кислота́.
pry *v.t.* **1,** (open; loosen) открыва́ть; взла́мывать (при по́мощи рычага́). **2,** (worm out, as a secret) выве́дывать; выпы́тывать. —*v.i.* **1,** (snoop) подгля́дывать. **2,** *fol. by* **into** (meddle) сова́ть нос (в). —**prying,** *adj.* пытли́вый.
psalm *n.* псало́м.
Psalter *n.* псалты́рь.
pseudonym *n.* псевдони́м.
pseudoscience *n.* лженау́ка. —**pseudoscientific,** *adj.* лженау́чный.
pshaw *interj.* фи!
psoriasis *n.* псориа́з.
psyche *n.* пси́хика.
psychiatry *n.* психиатри́я. —**psychiatric,** *adj.* психиатри́ческий. —**psychiatrist,** *n.* психиа́тр.
psychic *adj.* психи́ческий; душе́вный.
psychoanalysis *n.* психоана́лиз. —**psychoanalyst,** *n.* специали́ст по психоана́лизу. —**psychoanalytic(al),** *adj.* психоаналити́ческий. —**psychoanalyze,** *v.t.* подверга́ть психоана́лизу.
psychology *n.* психоло́гия. —**psychological,** *adj.* психологи́ческий. —**psychologist,** *n.* психо́лог.
psychopath *n.* психопа́т. —**psychopathic,** *adj.* психопати́ческий. —**psychopathy,** *n.* психопа́тия.
psychosis *n.* психо́з.
psychosomatic *adj.* психосомати́ческий.
psychotherapy *n.* психотерапи́я. —**psychotherapist,** *n.* психотерапе́вт.
psychotic *adj.* психоти́ческий.
ptarmigan *n.* бе́лая куропа́тка.
PT boat торпе́дный ка́тер.
pterodactyl *n.* птерода́ктиль.
ptomaine *n.* тру́пный яд. —**ptomaine poisoning,** отравле́ние тру́пным я́дом.
pub *n., Brit.* пивна́я; каба́к.
puberty *n.* полова́я зре́лость.
public *adj.* **1,** (of or for the community at large) обще́ственный; публи́чный. *Public opinion,* обще́ственное мне́ние. *Public library,* публи́чная библиоте́ка. *Public health,* здравоохране́ние. **2,** (done or made in public; open) публи́чный. *Public speaking,* ора́торское иску́сство. **3,** (of the government) госуда́рственный; казённый. —*n.* пу́блика: *the general public,* широ́кая пу́блика. —**in public,** публи́чно; на лю́дях. —**make public,** предава́ть гла́сности.

public-address system система́ звукоусиле́ния.

publication *n.* **1,** (act of publishing) изда́ние; опублико́вание; публика́ция. *Year of publication,* год изда́ния. **2,** (something published) изда́ние; публика́ция.

publicist *n.* публици́ст.

publicity *n.* **1,** (public notice) гла́сность; огла́ска. **2,** (advertising) рекла́ма.

publicize *v.t.* предава́ть гла́сности; реклами́ровать.

publicly *adv.* публи́чно.

publish *v.t.* **1,** (print and issue) издава́ть. **2,** (print in a certain publication) публикова́ть. —**publisher,** *n.* изда́тель.

publishing *n.* изда́тельское де́ло. —**publishing house,** изда́тельство.

puck *n., hockey* ша́йба.

pucker *v.t.* мо́рщить. —*v.i.* мо́рщиться. —*n.* **1,** (pleat) скла́дка. **2,** (wrinkle) морщи́на.

pudding *n.* пу́динг.

puddle *n.* лу́жа.

pudgy *adj.* пу́хлый.

puerile *adj.* ребя́ческий. —**puerility,** *n.* ребя́чество.

puerperal *adj.* роди́льный. —**puerperal fever,** роди́льная горя́чка.

Puerto Rican 1, *used adjectivally* пуэрторика́нский. **2,** *used as a noun* пуэрторика́нец; пуэрторика́нка.

puff *n.* **1,** (of air, wind, etc.) дунове́ние. **2,** (of smoke) клуб. **3,** (draw at a cigarette) затя́жка. **4,** (powder puff) пухо́вка. **5,** (pastry) сло́йка. —*v.t.* **1,** (emit forcibly) пуска́ть. **2,** *fol. by* **up** (swell) надува́ть; раздува́ть. —*v.i.* **1,** (pant) пыхте́ть; отдува́ться. **2,** *fol. by* **on** (smoke) попы́хивать (+ *instr.*). **3,** *fol. by* **up** (swell up) вздува́ться.

puffin *n.* ту́пик.

puff paste слоёное те́сто. —**puff pastry,** слоёный пиро́г.

puffy *adj.* одутлова́тый. *Become puffy,* отека́ть.

pug *n.* (dog) мопс; мо́ська.

pugilism *n.* бокс. —**pugilist,** *n.* боксёр.

pugnacious *adj.* драчли́вый. —**pugnacity,** *n.* драчли́вость.

pug nose курно́сый нос. —**pug-nosed,** *adj.* курно́сый.

pulchritude *n.* красота́.

pull *v.t.* **1,** (draw; drag) тащи́ть: *the horse is pulling the cart,* ло́шадь та́щит теле́гу. **2,** (tug; yank) тяну́ть: *pull the rope,* тяну́ть верёвку. *Pull someone's hair,* дёргать кого́-нибудь за́ волосы. **3,** (draw into a certain position) натя́гивать: *pull a blanket over oneself,* натяну́ть на себя́ одея́ло. *Pull one's cap down over one's ears,* надви́нуть ша́пку на́ уши. **4,** (remove) вырыва́ть: *pull a tooth,* вы́рвать зуб. *Six bodies were pulled from the water,* из воды́ извлечены́ шесть тру́пов. **5,** (strain, as a muscle) растя́гивать. —*v.i.* тяну́ть. *Pull at someone's sleeve,* дёргать кого́-нибудь за рука́в. *Pull at one's beard,* теребить бо́роду. —*n.* **1,** (tug; jerk) рыво́к. **2,** (drawing) тя́га; натяже́ние. **3,** *slang* (influence) блат; зару́чка. —**pull apart,** разнима́ть; раста́скивать. —**pull back, 1,** (draw back suddenly) отдёргивать. **2,** (step back) отступа́ть. —**pull down, 1,** (lower, as a shade) опуска́ть. **2,** (take down; remove) снима́ть. **3,** (tear down, as a building) сноси́ть. —**pull in, 1,** (draw in) втя́гивать. **2,** (arrive) прибыва́ть. —**pull into, 1,** *literally* вта́скивать. **2,** (arrive in *or* at) прибыва́ть в *or* на. **3,** (drive into) въезжа́ть в. —**pull off, 1,** (remove) стя́гивать; ста́скивать; сдёргивать. **2,** (turn off, as from a road) свора́чивать с (доро́ги). **3,** *colloq.* (accomplish; engineer) соверша́ть. —**pull on,** натя́гивать: *pull on one's shoes,* натяну́ть сапоги́. —**pull oneself together,** взять себя́ в ру́ки. —**pull out, 1,** (remove) выта́скивать; выдёргивать. **2,** (depart) отходи́ть; уходи́ть. **3,** (withdraw) выходи́ть. **4,** *fol. by* **of** (drive out of in a car) выезжа́ть (из). —**pull over,** подъезжа́ть: *pull over to the curb,* подъе́хать к тротуа́ру. —**pull together,** де́йствовать сообща́. —**pull through,** выжива́ть; выкара́бкиваться (из). —**pull up, 1,** (uproot) вырыва́ть. **2,** (move closer) подставля́ть: *pull up a chair for someone,* подставля́ть стул кому́-нибудь. **3,** *fol. by* **to** (drive up to) подъезжа́ть (к). **4,** *Pull up stakes,* сня́ться с ме́ста.

pullet *n.* ку́рочка; молода́я ку́рица.

pulley *n.* шкив; блок.

pullover *n.* пуло́вер; дже́мпер.

pulmonary *adj.* лёгочный.

pulp *n.* **1,** (juicy part of a fruit) мя́коть. **2,** (material used in making paper) древе́сная ма́сса. **3,** (part of a tooth) пу́льпа. —**beat to a pulp,** не оста́вить живо́го ме́ста на (+ *prepl.*).

pulpit *n.* ка́федра.

pulpy *adj.* мяси́стый.

pulsar *n.* пульса́р.

pulsate *v.i.* пульси́ровать. —**pulsation,** *n.* пульса́ция.

pulse *n.* пульс. *Pulse rate,* частота́ пу́льса.

pulverize *v.t.* измельча́ть *or* превраща́ть в порошо́к.

puma *n.* пу́ма.

pumice *n.* пе́мза.

pummel *v.t.* колоти́ть; дуба́сить.

pump *n.* **1,** (device) насо́с. *Gasoline pump,* бензоколо́нка. *Stomach pump,* желу́дочный зонд. **2,** (shoe) ло́дочка. —*v.t.* **1,** (propel by means of a pump) кача́ть: *pump water/oil,* кача́ть во́ду/нефть. *Pump air,* нагнета́ть во́здух. **2,** *fol. by* **out** (remove by means of a pump) выка́чивать; отка́чивать. **3,** *fol. by* **up** (inflate) нака́чивать. **4,** (shake vigorously) трясти́. **5,** (fire, as bullets) пуска́ть (пу́ли в кого́-нибудь). **6,** *colloq.* (question closely) выспра́шивать.

pumpernickel *n.* чёрный хлеб.

pumping *n.* кача́ние. —**pumping station,** насо́сная ста́нция; водока́чка.

pumpkin *n.* ты́ква.

pun *n.* каламбу́р; игра́ слов. —*v.i.* каламбу́рить.

punch *n.* **1,** (blow) уда́р (кулако́м). **2,** (hole puncher) дыроко́л; (for punching a ticket) компо́стер. **3,** (beverage) пунш. —*v.t.* **1,** (strike) ударя́ть кулако́м. *Punch someone in the nose,* дать (+ *dat.*) по́ носу. **2,** (make, as a hole) пробива́ть. **3,** (validate, as a ticket) компости́ровать. **4,** (form with a machine that punches) штампова́ть. —**punch card,** перфока́рта. —**punch press,** штампова́льный *or* штампо́вочный пресс.

punching bag боксёрский мешо́к.

punctilious *adj.* щепети́льный.

punctual *adj.* аккура́тный; пунктуа́льный. —**punctuality,** *n.* аккура́тность; пунктуа́льность. —**punctually,** *adv.* аккура́тно.

punctuate *v.t.* **1,** (insert punctuation marks in) ста́-

вить зна́ки препина́ния в. **2,** (intersperse) пересыпа́ть.

punctuation *n.* пунктуа́ция. —**punctuation marks,** зна́ки препина́ния.

puncture *v.t.* прока́лывать. —*n.* проко́л.

pundit *n.* учёный; мудре́ц.

pungent *adj.* о́стрый; пика́нтный. *Pungent odor,* о́стрый *or* ре́зкий за́пах. —**pungency,** *n.* острота́.

punish *v.t.* нака́зывать: *punish a child for disobedience,* наказа́ть ребёнка за непослуша́ние.

punishable *adj.* наказу́емый. *Be punishable by death,* кара́ться сме́ртной ка́знью.

punishment *n.* наказа́ние. *In/as punishment for,* в наказа́ние за (+ *acc.*).

punitive *adj.* кара́тельный.

punk *n., slang* хулига́н. —*adj., slang* дрянно́й; парши́вый.

punster *n.* каламбури́ст.

puny *adj.* **1,** (frail; sickly) щу́плый. **2,** (insignificant) ничто́жный.

pup *n.* **1,** (puppy) щено́к. **2,** (young of certain animals) детёныш.

pupa *n.* ку́колка.

pupil *n.* **1,** (student) учени́к; уча́щийся. **2,** (of the eye) зрачо́к.

puppet *n.* **1,** (animated figure) ку́кла; марионе́тка. **2,** *fig.* (person controlled by another) марионе́тка. —*adj.* **1,** (pert. to puppets) ку́кольный: *puppet show,* ку́кольный теа́тр. **2,** *fig.* (controlled by someone else) марионе́точный.

puppy *n.* щено́к.

purblind *adj.* подслепова́тый.

purchase *v.t.* покупа́ть. —*n.* **1,** (act of purchasing) ку́пля; поку́пка. **2,** (something purchased) поку́пка. —**purchase price,** покупна́я цена́. —**purchasing power,** покупа́тельная спосо́бность.

purchaser *n.* покупа́тель.

pure *adj.* чи́стый: *pure gold,* чи́стое зо́лото; *pure chance,* чи́стая случа́йность; *pure nonsense,* чи́стый вздор.

purée *n.* пюре́.

purely *adv.* чи́сто: *purely by chance,* чи́сто случа́йно.

purgative *adj.* слаби́тельный. —*n.* слаби́тельное.

purgatory *n.* чисти́лище.

purge *v.t.* **1,** (evacuate, as the bowels) очища́ть. **2,** *fig.* (rid of undesirable elements) чи́стить. **3,** (remove and do away with) ликвиди́ровать. —*n.* чи́стка.

purify *v.t.* очища́ть. —**purification,** *n.* очи́стка; очище́ние.

purism *n.* пури́зм. —**purist,** *n.* пури́ст.

Puritan *n.* пурита́нин. —*adj.* пурита́нский. —**puritanical,** *adj.* пурита́нский.

purity *n.* чистота́.

purl *v.i.* журча́ть.

purloin *v.t.* красть; ута́скивать.

purple *adj.* фиоле́товый; лило́вый.

purport *v.t.* претендова́ть (на). —*n.* смысл.

purpose *n.* цель. *Answer/serve the purpose,* отвеча́ть це́ли. —**on purpose,** наро́чно. —**to all intents and purposes,** факти́чески. —**to no purpose,** напра́сно.

purposeful *adj.* целеустремлённый.

purposely *adv.* наро́чно; наме́ренно; умы́шленно.

purr *v.i.* мурлы́кать. —*n.* мурлы́канье.

purse *n.* **1,** (change purse) кошелёк. **2,** (handbag) су́мка; су́мочка. **3,** (prize money) приз; пре́мия. —*v.t.,* *in* **purse one's lips,** поджима́ть *or* мо́рщить гу́бы.

purser *n.* казначе́й.

purslane *n.* портула́к.

pursuance *n.* выполне́ние; исполне́ние. —**in pursuance of,** во исполне́ние (+ *gen.*).

pursuant *adj. & adv.* [*usu.* **pursuant to**] соотве́тственно (+ *dat.*).

pursue *v.t.* **1,** (chase; seek) пресле́довать: *pursue a fugitive/goal,* пресле́довать беглеца́/цель. **2,** (proceed along; follow) идти́ по. *Pursue a policy,* проводи́ть поли́тику. **3,** (take up; engage in) занима́ться (+ *instr.*). *Pursue a career,* де́лать *or* составля́ть карье́ру. **4,** (continue) продолжа́ть: *pursue one's studies,* продолжа́ть учёбу.

pursuer *n.* пресле́дователь: *elude one's pursuers,* ускользну́ть от пресле́дователей.

pursuit *n.* **1,** (act of pursuing) пресле́дование; пого́ня. *Set out in pursuit of,* пусти́ться в пого́ню за. **2,** (act of seeking) пого́ня; стремле́ние: *the pursuit of happiness,* пого́ня за сча́стьем; стремле́ние к сча́стью. **3,** (activity; avocation) заня́тие.

purvey *v.t.* поставля́ть. —**purveyor,** *n.* поставщи́к.

purview *n.* сфе́ра; компете́нция.

pus *n.* гной.

push *v.t.* **1,** (propel; shove) толка́ть: *push a baby carriage,* толка́ть де́тскую коля́ску. *Push one's way through a crowd,* прота́лкиваться че́рез толпу́. **2,** (press, as a button) нажима́ть на. **3,** (urge on) подта́лкивать. **4,** (prosecute vigorously) прота́лкивать: *push a matter,* протолкну́ть де́ло. **5,** *colloq.* (be approaching) *rendered by* сту́кнуть: *he is pushing fifty,* ему́ ско́ро сту́кнет пятьдеся́т. —*v.i.* **1,** (exert force on something) толка́ть: *push harder!,* толкни́те поси́льнее! **2,** (shove) толка́ться: *don't push!,* не толка́йтесь! —*n.* толчо́к. —**push away,** отта́лкивать. —**push back,** отбра́сывать; оттесня́ть. —**push off,** **1,** (force off) ста́лкивать. **2,** *colloq.* (leave; depart) уходи́ть; убира́ться. —**push on,** продолжа́ть путь. —**push out,** выта́лкивать. —**push through,** **1,** (shove through) прота́лкивать. **2,** *fig.* (force through, as a resolution) прота́скивать.

push button кно́пка.

pushcart *n.* ручна́я теле́жка.

pushy *adj., colloq.* пробивно́й; напо́ристый.

pusillanimous *adj.* малоду́шный. —**pusillanimity,** *n.* малоду́шие.

puss *n.* **1,** (cat) ко́шечка; ки́с(к)а. **2,** *slang* (face) ха́ря.

pussy *n.* ко́шечка; ки́с(к)а. *Also,* **pussy cat.**

pussy willow ве́рба.

pustule *n.* гнойничо́к.

put *v.t.* **1,** (lay) класть: *put the book on the table,* класть кни́гу на стол. **2,** (stand) ста́вить: *put the flowers in water,* ста́вить цветы́ в во́ду. **3,** (place) помеща́ть; ста́вить. *Put a child in kindergarten,* помеща́ть ребёнка в де́тский сад. *Put an ad in a newspaper,* помеща́ть объявле́ние в газе́те. *Put someone in prison,* посади́ть кого́-нибудь в тюрьму́. *Put one's signature on,* ста́вить свою́ по́дпись на (+ *prepl.*). *Put a period at the end of a sentence,* ста́вить то́чку в конце́ предложе́ния. *Put in an awkward position,* ста́вить в нело́вкое положе́ние. *Put yourself in my place,* поста́вьте себя́ на моё ме́сто. **4,** (bring to a certain state): *put at ease,* успока́ивать. *Put in order,* приводи́ть в поря́док. *Put to bed,* укла́дывать. *Put to death,* предава́ть сме́рти. *Put to flight,*обрати́ть в бе́гство. *Put to shame,* пристыди́ть. *Put to sleep,* усыпля́ть. *Put to work,* уса́живать за рабо́ту. **5,** (cause to take effect): *put an end to,* положи́ть коне́ц (+ *dat.*). *Put into effect/operation,* вводи́ть в де́йствие. **6,** (apply; expend) вкла́дывать: *put a lot of work into,* вкла́дывать мно́го труда́ в. *Put one's heart and soul into,* вкла́дывать всю ду́шу в. **7,** (cause to undergo) подверга́ть: *put to the test,* подверга́ть испыта́нию. *Put on trial,* предава́ть суду́. *Put to expense,* вводи́ть в расхо́д. *Put to a vote,* поста́вить на голосова́ние. **8,** (exert) ока́зывать: *put pressure on,* ока́зывать давле́ние на. **9,** (express) выража́ть: *put into words,* выража́ть (что́-нибудь) слова́ми. *To put it mildly,* мя́гко выража́ясь. *I don't know how to put it,* я не зна́ю, как э́то сказа́ть. **10,** (pose, as a question) ста́вить; задава́ть. **11,** (render; set): *put words to music,* положи́ть слова́ на му́зыку. **12,** (attach; attribute): *put the blame on,* вали́ть вину́ на. *Put a wrong interpretation on,* дава́ть непра́вильное толкова́ние (+ *dat.*). **13,** (invest; deposit) вкла́дывать; помеща́ть. *Put money in a savings account,* помеща́ть де́ньги в сберка́ссу. **14,** (estimate at a certain figure) оце́нивать. **15,** (bet) ста́вить. **16,** *sports: put the shot,* толка́ть ядро́. —**put aside,** откла́дывать (в сто́рону); сберега́ть. —**put away, 1,** (remove from sight) убира́ть. **2,** (save; reserve) откла́дывать. **3,** *colloq.* (commit, as to jail) сажа́ть. **4,** *colloq.* (consume) съесть; вы́пить. —**put back, 1,** (restore to its place) ста́вить на ме́сто. **2,** (turn back, as a clock) переводи́ть. —**put down, 1,** (lay down) положи́ть. **2,** (write down) запи́сывать. **3,** (suppress, as a revolt) подавля́ть. **4,** *fol. by* **to** (attribute to) относи́ть на счёт (+ *gen.*). **5,** (pay in a lump sum) дать в зада́ток. **6,** (land) приземля́ться. **7,** *Put down roots,* пуска́ть ко́рни. —**put forth, 1,** (sprout) пуска́ть. **2,** (exert, as effort) напряга́ть. **3,** (advance, as a proposal) выдвига́ть. —**put in, 1,** (insert) вкла́дывать; вставля́ть. *Put in a good word for,* замо́лвить слове́чко за. **2,** (enter, as a claim) предъявля́ть. **3,** *fol. by* **for** (apply for) подава́ть заявле́ние о. **4,** *colloq.* (expend, as time) уделя́ть. —**put into, 1,** (insert) вкла́дывать (в); вставля́ть (в). **2,** *naut.* заходи́ть: *put into port,* заходи́ть в га́вань. —**put off, 1,** (make get off) выса́живать; сса́живать. **2,** (postpone) откла́дывать. **3,** *colloq.* (repel) отта́лкивать. —**put on, 1,** (don) надева́ть. **2,** (apply) накла́дывать. *Put on make-up,* кра́ситься. *Put on the brakes,* тормози́ть. **3,** (turn on, as a light) включа́ть. **4,** (stage, as a play) ста́вить. **5,** (assume; affect) напуска́ть на себя́. **6,** (gain, as weight) прибавля́ть в (ве́се). *Put on ten pounds,* прибавля́ть де́сять фу́нтов. **7,** *Put on a record,* (по)ста́вить пласти́нку. **8,** *Put on some tea,* (по)ста́вить ча́йник. —**put out, 1,** (extend) протя́гивать. **2,** (lay out) выкла́дывать. **3,** (stick out) высо́вывать. **4,** (extinguish) туши́ть. **5,** (gouge out, as an eye) выка́лывать. **6,** (eject; dismiss) выгоня́ть. **7,** (manufacture; publish) выпуска́ть. **8,** (inconvenience) затрудня́ть. *Put oneself out,* дать себе́ нема́ло труда́. **9,** (vex) обижа́ть. *Be put out,* быть оби́женным. **10,** *Put out of action,* выводи́ть из стро́я; *put out of one's head,* выбра́сывать из головы́. **11,** *Put out to sea,* выходи́ть в мо́ре. —**put over,** (postpone) переноси́ть. —**put right,** нала́живать; поправля́ть. —**put through, 1,** (implement) проводи́ть. **2,** (cause to undergo) подверга́ть (+ *dat.*). —**put together, 1,** (assemble) собира́ть. **2,** (place together) составля́ть. **3,** (amass) накопля́ть. **4,** (combined) взя́тые вме́сте: *more than all the rest put together,* бо́льше чем все остальны́е взя́тые вме́сте. —**put up, 1,** (erect) стро́ить; воздвига́ть. **2,** (hang; post) ве́шать; взве́шивать. **3,** (preserve; can) консерви́ровать. **4,** (advance; invest, as money) вкла́дывавть. **5,** (give lodging to) устра́ивать (на́ ночь *or* на ночле́г). **6,** (offer): *put up for sale,* пуска́ть в прода́жу. *Put up resistance,* ока́зывать сопротивле́ние. **7,** *fol. by* **with** (endure; tolerate) терпе́ть; выноси́ть. **8,** *fol. by* **to** (incite; goad) подбива́ть; поду́чивать; подгова́ривать.

putative *adj.* предполага́емый.

putrefaction *n.* гние́ние; разложе́ние.

putrefy *v.i.* гнить. —*v.t.* гнои́ть.

putrid *adj.* **1,** (rotten) гнило́й. **2,** (stinking) воню́чий.

putsch *n.* путч.

puttee *n., usu. pl.* кра́ги; обмо́тки.

putter *v.i.* вози́ться.

putty *n.* зама́зка; шпаклёвка. —*v.t.* зама́зывать; шпаклева́ть. —**putty knife,** шпа́тель.

puzzle *n.* зага́дка; головоло́мка. *Jigsaw puzzle,* составна́я карти́нка. *Crossword puzzle,* кроссво́рд. —*v.t.* **1,** (perplex) приводи́ть в недоуме́ние; озада́чивать. **2,** *fol. by* **out** (solve) разга́дывать; распу́тывать. —*v.i.* [*usu.* **puzzle over**] би́ться над; лома́ть себе́ го́лову над.

puzzled *adj.* недоуме́нный; недоумева́ющий. *Be puzzled,* недоумева́ть.

puzzlement *n.* недоуме́ние. —**puzzling,** *adj.* недоуме́нный.

pygmy *n.* пигме́й.

pyjamas *n.* = **pajamas.**

pylon *n.* пило́н.

pyorrhea *also,* **pyorrhoea** *n.* пиоре́я.

pyramid *n.* пирами́да. —**pyramidal,** *adj.* пирамида́льный.

pyre *n.* погреба́льный костёр.

pyrite *n.* пири́т.

pyrites *n.* колчеда́н.

pyrography *n.* выжига́ние.

pyromania *n.* пирома́ния.

pyrotechnics *n.* пироте́хника.

Pyrrhic victory пи́ррова побе́да.

Pythagorean theorum пифаго́рова теоре́ма.

python *n.* пито́н.

Q

Q, q семна́дцатая бу́ква англи́йского алфави́та.

quack *n.* **1,** (duck's cry) кря́канье. **2,** (false doctor) зна́харь; шарлата́н. —*adj.* шарлата́нский. —*v.i.* кря́кать.

quackery *n.* зна́харство; шарлата́нство.

quadrangle *n.* четырёхуго́льник. —**quadrangular,** *adj.* четырёхуго́льный.

quadrant *n.* квадра́нт.

quadratic *adj.* квадра́тный.

quadrennial *adj.* происходя́щий раз в четы́ре го́да.

quadrilateral *n.* четырёхуго́льник. —*adj.* четырёхсторо́нний.

quadrille *n.* кадри́ль.

quadrillion *n.* квадрильо́н.

quadruped *n.* четвероно́гое.

quadruple *adj.* четверно́й; четырёхкра́тный. —*v.t.* учетверя́ть. —*v.i.* увели́чиваться в четы́ре ра́за; учетверя́ться.

quadruplets *n.pl.* четверня́.

quadruplicate *n. In quadruplicate,* в четырёх экземпля́рах.

quaff *v.t.* пить за́лпом.

quagmire *n.* трясина.

quail *n.* пе́репел. —*v.i.* (lose courage) дро́гнуть.

quaint *adj.* причу́дливый; прихотли́вый.

quake *v.i.* дрожа́ть; трясти́сь. —*n.* = **earthquake.**

Quaker *n.* ква́кер. —*adj.* ква́керский.

qualification *n.* **1,** (ability; competence) квалифика́ция. *He has all the necessary qualifications,* он подхо́дит по всем статья́м. **2,** (limitation; reservation) огово́рка.

qualified *adj.* **1,** (able; fit) компете́нтный. *Qualified for a position,* приго́дный для до́лжности. **2,** (limited; with reservations) ограни́ченный; с огово́рками.

qualifier *n., gram.* определе́ние; атрибу́т.

qualify *v.t.* **1,** (make eligible) дава́ть пра́во (+ *dat.*). **2,** (make less categorical): *qualify a statement,* сде́лать огово́рку. **3,** *gram.* (modify) определя́ть. —*v.i.* выслу́живать: *qualify for a pension,* выслу́живать пе́нсию. *Qualify for the finals,* вы́йти в фина́л. *He qualifies on all counts,* он подхо́дит по всем статья́м.

qualitative *adj.* ка́чественный. —**qualitative analysis,** ка́чественный ана́лиз.

quality *n.* ка́чество. —*adj., colloq.* доброка́чественный; добро́тный; высокока́чественный.

qualm *n., usu. pl.* **1,** (misgivings) сомне́ние. **2,** (compunctions) угрызе́ния со́вести.

quandary *n.* затрудни́тельное положе́ние; затрудне́ние.

quantitative *adj.* коли́чественный. —**quantitative analysis,** коли́чественный ана́лиз.

quantity *n.* **1,** (amount) коли́чество: *enormous quantity,* огро́мное коли́чество. *Buy in quantity,* покупа́ть в большо́м коли́честве. **2,** *math.* величина́: *unknown quantity,* неизве́стная величина́.

quantum *n., physics* квант. —*adj.* ква́нтовый: *quantum mechanics/theory,* ква́нтовая меха́ника/тео́рия.

quarantine *n.* каранти́н; изоля́ция. —*v.t.* подверга́ть каранти́ну; изоли́ровать.

quarrel *n.* ссо́ра. —*v.i.* ссо́риться. —**quarrelsome,** *adj.* вздо́рный; сварли́вый.

quarry *n.* **1,** (place of excavation) каменоло́мня; карье́р. **2,** (prey) добы́ча. —*v.t.* добыва́ть. *Quarry stone,* лома́ть ка́мень.

quart *n.* ква́рта.

quarter *n.* **1,** (one-fourth) че́тверть: *three-quarters,* три че́тверти. **2,** (25-cent piece) четверта́к. **3,** (period of three months) кварта́л. **4,** (part of an academic year) че́тверть. **5,** (fifteen minutes) че́тверть: *a quarter of two,* без че́тверти два; *a quarter past seven,* че́тверть восьмо́го. **6,** (district of a city) кварта́л. **7,** (direction) сторона́: *from every quarter,* со всех сторо́н. **8,** *pl.* (place of lodging) помеще́ние; *mil.* кварти́ры. **9,** (part of an animal) часть: *hind quarters,* за́дняя часть. **10,** (mercy) поща́да. *Give someone no quarter,* не дава́ть спу́ска (+ *dat.*). —*v.t.* **1,** (divide in four) дели́ть на четы́ре ча́сти. **2,** (billet) расквартирова́ть. **3,** *hist.* (execute) четвертова́ть.

quarterdeck *n.* шка́нцы; ют.

quarterfinal *n.* четвертьфина́л. —*adj.* четвертьфина́льный.

quarterly *adj.* кварта́льный. —*adv.* покварта́льно. —*n.* журна́л, выходя́щий покварта́льно.

quartermaster *n.* интенда́нт; квартирме́йстер. —**quartermaster corps,** интенда́нтство.

quarter note *music* четвертная но́та.

quartet *n.* кварте́т.

quartz *n.* кварц. —*adj.* ква́рцевый.

quartzite *n.* кварци́т.

quasar *n.* кваза́р.

quash *v.t.* **1,** (suppress) подавля́ть. **2,** *law* (set aside) аннули́ровать.

quasi- *prefix* полу-: *quasi-official,* полуофициа́льный.

quatrain *n.* четверости́шие.

quaver *v.i.* **1,** (tremble; quake) дрожа́ть. **2,** (be tremulous, as of the voice) дро́гнуть. —*n.* трель.
quay *n.* при́стань.
queasiness *n.* **1,** (nausea) тошнота́. **2,** (squeamishness) брезгли́вость.
queasy *adj.* **1,** (sick to one's stomach): *I felt queasy,* меня́ тошни́ло. **2,** (squeamish) брезгли́вый.
queen *n.* **1,** (sovereign) короле́ва. **2,** *cards* да́ма. **3,** *chess* ферзь. —*adj.* [*usu.* **queen's**] **1,** (of a queen) короле́вский. **2,** *chess* фе́рзевый: *queen's bishop/gambit,* фе́рзевый слон/гамби́т. —**queen bee,** (пчели́ная) ма́тка. —**queen dowager,** вдо́вствующая короле́ва.
queer *adj.* стра́нный; чудакова́тый; эксцентри́чный. —**queerly,** *adv.* стра́нно.
quell *v.t.* **1,** (suppress) подавля́ть. **2,** (allay) успока́ивать.
quench *v.t.* **1,** (extinguish; put out) гаси́ть; туши́ть. **2,** (slake, as thirst) утоля́ть.
querulous *adj.* ворчли́вый; сварли́вый.
query *n.* вопро́с. —*v.t.* **1,** (ask questions of) расспра́шивать. **2,** (express doubt about) сомнева́ться в; ста́вить под вопро́с.
quest *n.* по́иски. *In quest of,* в по́исках (+ *gen.*).
question *n.* **1,** (query) вопро́с. **2,** (subject; problem; issue) вопро́с; пробле́ма. **3,** (doubt) сомне́ние. *Without question,* бесспо́рно. *Beyond question,* вне сомне́ния. *Open to question,* под вопро́сом. *Call into question,* ста́вить под вопро́с. —*v.t.* **1,** (ask questions of) расспра́шивать. **2,** (interrogate) допра́шивать. **3,** (express uncertainty about) сомнева́ться в; ста́вить под вопро́с. **4,** (challenge; dispute) оспа́ривать. —**in question, 1,** (under consideration) о кото́ром идёт речь: *the case in question,* слу́чай, о кото́ром идёт речь. **2,** (in dispute) под вопро́сом. —**it is a question of...,** речь идёт о... —**that is out of the question,** об э́том не мо́жет быть и ре́чи.
questionable *adj.* сомни́тельный.
question mark вопроси́тельный знак.
questionnaire *n.* анке́та; вопро́сник; опро́сный лист.
queue *n.* о́чередь. —*v.i.* [*usu.* **queue up**] стоя́ть в о́череди; станови́ться в о́чередь.
quibble *n.* **1,** (evasion of a point) увёртка. **2,** (minor criticism) приди́рка. —*v.i.* **1,** (cavil) придира́ться. **2,** (bicker) спо́рить. —**quibbler,** *n.* приди́ра.
quick *adj.* **1,** (rapid; swift) бы́стрый; ско́рый. *Be quick!,* скоре́е! **2,** (bright; alert) поня́тливый. *Quick to grasp things,* сообрази́тельный. **3,** (easily aroused) вспы́льчивый: *quick temper,* вспы́льчивый хара́ктер. —*adv.* бы́стро. *Come quick!,* иди́ скоре́й! —*n.,* *in* **cut to the quick,** заде́ть за живо́е.
quick-change artist трансформа́тор.
quicken *v.t.* **1,** (accelerate) ускоря́ть. *Quickened pulse,* учащённый пульс. **2,** (arouse; stir) оживля́ть. —*v.i.* ускоря́ться.
quicklime *n.* негашёная и́звесть.
quickly *adv.* бы́стро. *Come quickly!,* иди́ скоре́й!
quickness *n.* **1,** (rapidity) быстрота́. **2,** (keenness of mind) сообрази́тельность.
quicksand *n.* сыпу́чий песо́к.
quicksilver *n.* ртуть.
quick-tempered *adj.* вспы́льчивый.
quick-witted *adj.* сообрази́тельный; сме́тливый; дога́дливый.
quiescent *adj.* неподви́жный; споко́йный. —**quiescence,** *n.* поко́й; неподви́жность.
quiet *adj.* **1,** (making no noise) ти́хий. *Be/keep quiet,* молча́ть. *Keep something quiet,* зама́лчивать что́-нибудь. **2,** (calm; tranquil) споко́йный. —*n.* тишина́; споко́йствие. —*v.t.* успока́ивать. —*v.i.* [*usu.* **quiet down**] успока́иваться. —*interj.* ти́ше!; не шуме́ть! —**quietly,** *adv.* ти́хо.
quietude *n.* поко́й; споко́йствие.
quill *n.* **1,** (feather) перо́. **2,** (spine, as of a porcupine) игла́. **3,** (quill pen) перо́.
quilt *n.* стёганое одея́ло. —*v.t.* стега́ть. —**quilted,** *adj.* стёганый.
quince *n.* айва́.
quinine *n.* хини́н.
quintessence *n.* квинтэссе́нция.
quintet *n.* квинте́т.
quintuplets *n.pl.* пя́теро близнецо́в.
quip *n.* остро́та. —*v.i.* остри́ть.
quire *n.* (ру́сская) десть.
quirk *n.* причу́да; вы́верт; заско́к. *Quirk of fate,* игра́ судьбы́; игра́ слу́чая.
quit *v.t.* **1,** (cease) перестава́ть. **2,** (give up) бро́сить: *quit smoking,* бро́сить кури́ть. **3,** (leave) покида́ть. **4,** (resign from) уходи́ть от *or* с. —*v.i.* **1,** (resign) уходи́ть. **2,** (give up; stop trying) сдава́ться.
quite *adv.* **1,** (entirely) совсе́м; вполне́. *Not quite,* не совсе́м. **2,** (rather) дово́льно: *quite far from here,* дово́льно далеко́ отсю́да. *Quite a few,* дово́льно мно́го. *Quite a while,* дово́льно до́лго. **3,** *fol. by* **a** (considerable) изря́дный: *quite a distance,* изря́дное расстоя́ние. *It was quite a surprise,* э́то бы́ло большо́й неожи́данностью.
quits *adj.* кви́ты. —**call it quits, 1,** (stop work) ко́нчить рабо́ту; шаба́шить. **2,** (retire) вы́йти на пе́нсию; сойти́ со сце́ны.
quiver *v.i.* трепета́ть; дро́гнуть. —*n.* **1,** (tremor) тре́пет. **2,** (case for arrows) колча́н.
quixotic *adj.* донкихо́тский.
quiz *n.* **1,** (short test) опро́с; контро́льная рабо́та. **2,** (game) виктори́на. —*v.t.* **1,** (interrogate) допра́шивать. **2,** (give a short test to) проверя́ть зна́ния (+ *gen.*).
quizzical *adj.* недоуме́нный; недоумева́ющий.
quorum *n.* кво́рум.
quota *n.* кво́та; но́рма.
quotation *n.* **1,** (words or passage quoted) цита́та. **2,** *finance* котиро́вка. —**quotation marks,** кавы́чки.
quote *v.t.* **1,** (cite) ссыла́ться на; цити́ровать. **2,** *finance* коти́ровать. —*n.* **1,** *colloq.* = **quotation. 2,** *pl.* = **quotation marks.**
quotient *n.* ча́стное.

R

R, r восемна́дцатая бу́ква англи́йского алфави́та. —**the three R's,** чте́ние, письмо́, арифме́тика.
rabbi *n.* равви́н. —**rabbinical,** *adj.* равви́нский.
rabbit *n.* кро́лик. —*adj.* кро́личий: *rabbit hole,* кро́личья нора́.
rabble *n.* толпа́. —**the rabble,** сброд; чернь; отре́бье.
rabid *adj.* **1,** (having rabies) бе́шеный. **2,** (fanatical) я́рый; оголте́лый; махро́вый.
rabies *n.* бе́шенство; водобоя́знь.
raccoon *n.* ено́т. —*adj.* ено́товый.
race *n.* **1,** (contest of speed) бег; пробе́г; го́нки. *Horse race,* зае́зд. *The races,* ска́чки; бега́. **2,** (any contest) го́нка: *the arms race,* го́нка вооруже́ний. **3,** (ethnic group) ра́са. **4,** *in* **the human race,** челове́ческий род. —*adj.* ра́совый: *race relations,* ра́совые отноше́ния. —*v.i.* **1,** (compete in a race) бежа́ть; *(of a horse)* скака́ть. **2,** (dash) мча́ться. *Race by,* промча́ться. —*v.t.* **1,** (run against) бежа́ть наперего́нки с. **2,** (run at high speed, as an engine) дава́ть по́лный газ (+ *dat.*).
racecourse *n.* скакова́я доро́жка.
racehorse *n.* бегова́я ло́шадь; скакова́я ло́шадь.
raceme *n.* кисть; соцве́тие.
racer *n.* **1,** (racing driver) го́нщик. **2,** (horse) скакова́я ло́шадь; скаку́н. **3,** (auto) го́ночный автомоби́ль.
racetrack *n.* ипподро́м.
racial *adj.* ра́совый.
racing *n.* бега́; ска́чки. —*adj.* **1,** (of racing) бегово́й; скаково́й. **2,** (used in racing) го́ночный: *racing car,* го́ночный автомоби́ль.
racism *n.* раси́зм. —**racist,** *n.* раси́ст. —*adj.* раси́стский.
rack *n.* **1,** (for coats, hats, etc.) ве́шалка. **2,** (for books or other standing objects) стелла́ж. **3,** (for bombs) бомбодержа́тель. **4,** (instrument of torture) ды́ба. **5,** (toothed bar) зубча́тая ре́йка. —*v.t.* **1,** [*also,* **wrack**] (afflict) изму́чить; (ис)терза́ть. *Racked with disease,* изму́ченный боле́знью. **2,** *fol. by* **up** (score) набира́ть (...очко́в); одержа́ть (побе́ду). **3,** *in* **rack one's brains,** лома́ть себе́ го́лову. —**go to rack and ruin,** пойти́ пра́хом.
racket *n.* **1,** (din) гам; гвалт. **2,** *sports* (webbed bat) раке́тка. **3,** (fraud) рэ́кет. —**racketeer,** *n.* га́нгстер; рэкети́р.
raconteur *n.* расска́зчик.
racy *adj.* **1,** (lively) колори́тный. **2,** (risqué) солёный.
radar *n.* **1,** (system) радиолока́ция. **2,** (device) радиолока́тор. —*adj.* радиолокацио́нный.
radial *adj.* лучево́й; радиа́льный.
radiance *n.* сия́ние; блеск.
radiant *adj.* **1,** (sending out or transmitted by rays) лучи́стый: *radiant heat/energy,* лучи́стая теплота́/эне́ргия. **2,** (beaming, as with joy) сия́ющий; лучеза́рный.
radiate *v.t.* **1,** (emit) излуча́ть. **2,** (manifest in a glowing manner) сия́ть; лучи́ться: *radiate happiness,* сия́ть/лучи́ться сча́стьем. —*v.i.* **1,** (spread out in rays) излуча́ться. **2,** (branch out) расходи́ться.
radiation *n.* излуче́ние; радиа́ция; лучеиспуска́ние. *Radiation treatment,* облуче́ние. —**radiation sickness,** лучева́я боле́знь.
radiator *n.* батаре́я отопле́ния; радиа́тор.
radical *adj.* **1,** *polit.* радика́льный. **2,** (drastic) коренно́й; радика́льный. —*n.* **1,** *polit.* радика́л. **2,** *math.* ко́рень. *Radical sign,* знак ко́рня; радика́л. **3,** *chem.* радика́л. —**radicalism,** *n.* радикали́зм. —**radically,** *adv.* коренны́м о́бразом; радика́льно.
radio *n.* **1,** (receiving set) радиоприёмник. **2,** (small portable receiver and transmitter) ра́ция. **3,** (broadcasting medium) ра́дио. —*v.t. & i.* ради́ровать. —**radio operator,** ради́ст. —**radio station,** радиоста́нция.
radioactive *adj.* радиоакти́вный. —**radioactivity,** *n.* радиоакти́вность.
radiogram *n.* радиогра́мма.
radiology *n.* **1,** (use of X-rays) рентгеноло́гия. **2,** (use of radiation) радиоло́гия. —**radiologist,** *n.* рентгено́лог; радио́лог.
radio-phonograph *n.* радио́ла.
radiotelegraphy *n.* радиотелеграфи́я.
radiotelephone *n.* радиотелефо́н. —**radiotelephony,** *n.* радиотелефони́я.
radiotherapy *n.* радиотерапи́я.
radish *n.* реди́ска; ре́дька; *pl.* реди́с; реди́ски.
radium *n.* ра́дий. —*adj.* ра́диевый.
radius *n.* ра́диус. *Within a radius of,* в ра́диусе (+ *gen.*).
radon *n.* радо́н.
raffle *n.* лотере́я. *Raffle ticket,* лотере́йный биле́т. —*v.t.* разы́грывать.
raft *n.* **1,** (float) плот. **2,** *colloq.* (large amout) у́йма; ку́ча.
rafter *n.* стропи́ло.
rag *n.* **1,** (piece of cloth) тря́пка: *dust rag,* пы́льная тря́пка. **2,** *pl.* (scraps of cloth) тряпьё; ве́тошь. **3,** *pl.* (shabby clothes; tatters) лохмо́тья; тряпьё; ру́бище; отре́пья. —*adj.* тряпи́чный: *rag paper,* тряпи́чная бума́га.

ragamuffin *n.* обо́рвыш.
rag doll тряпи́чная ку́кла.
rage *n.* **1,** (fury) я́рость; бе́шенство. *Fly into a rage,* приходи́ть в я́рость. **2,** *colloq.* (fad; craze) после́дний крик мо́ды. —*v.i.* **1,** (be furious) беси́ться. **2,** (of a storm, fire, etc.) бушева́ть; свире́пствовать.
ragged *adj.* **1,** (tattered) поно́шенный; изо́рванный; обо́рванный. **2,** (rough; jagged) шерохова́тый; зазу́бренный. —**run oneself ragged,** избе́гаться; забе́гаться.
raglan *n.* регла́н.
ragman *n.* тряпи́чник.
ragout *n.* рагу́.
ragweed *n.* амбро́зия.
raid *n.* **1,** *mil.* налёт; набе́г; рейд. *Air raid,* возду́шный налёт. **2,** (by the police) обла́ва. —*v.t.* соверша́ть налёт/набе́г на.
rail *n.* **1,** (horizontal bar) попере́чина; перекла́дина. **2,** (handrail; railing) пери́ла; по́ручни. **3,** (railroad track) рельс. **4,** (railroad) желе́зная доро́га: *by rail,* по желе́зной доро́ге. **5,** (bird) пастушо́к. —*adj.* железнодоро́жный: *rail junction,* железнодоро́жный у́зел. —*v.i.* [*usu.* **rail at** *or* **against**] брани́ть. —**thin as a rail,** худо́й как ще́пка.
railing *n.* **1,** (fence) огра́да. **2,** (banister) пери́ла.
raillery *n.* беззло́бная насме́шка.
railroad *n.* желе́зная доро́га. —*adj.* железнодоро́жный.
railway *n.* = **railroad.**
raiment *n.* одея́ние.
rain *n.* дождь. —*adj.* дождево́й: *rain water,* дожева́я вода́. —*v.i.* **1,** (be raining) идти́: *it is raining,* идёт дождь. **2,** *fig.* (fall like rain) сы́паться. —*v.t.* обру́шивать. *Rain blows on,* обру́шивать уда́ры на; осыпа́ть (кого́-нибудь) уда́рами. —**it is raining cats and dogs,** дождь льёт как из ведра́. —**rain or shine,** в любу́ю пого́ду; кака́я бы ни была́ пого́да.
rainbow *n.* ра́дуга.
raincoat *n.* плащ; дождеви́к.
raindrop *n.* дождева́я ка́пля.
rainfall *n.* коли́чество оса́дков.
rain hat шля́па от дождя́.
rainstorm *n.* ли́вень.
rainy *adj.* дождли́вый. —**put aside for a rainy day,** сбере́чь на че́рный день.
raise *v.t.* **1,** (lift) поднима́ть. **2,** (increase) повыша́ть. **3,** (rear) воспи́тывать. **4,** (cultivate) выра́щивать. **5,** (breed) разводи́ть. **6,** (make louder, as one's voice) повыша́ть. **7,** (collect, as money) собира́ть. **8,** (bring up, as a question) поднима́ть; ста́вить; возбужда́ть. **9,** (evoke, as doubts) вызыва́ть. **10,** (start; cause, as a clamor) поднима́ть. **11,** (cause to form, as a blister) натира́ть. **12,** *math.* возводи́ть (в сте́пень). **13,** *in* **raise from the dead,** оживля́ть; воскреша́ть. —*n., colloq.* повыше́ние зарпла́ты; приба́вка; надба́вка.
raised *adj.* релье́фный: *raised design,* релье́фный узо́р.
raisin *n.* изю́мина; изю́минка; *pl.* изю́м.
rajah *n.* ра́джа.
rake *n.* **1,** (garden tool) гра́бли. **2,** (roué) пове́са; распу́тник. —*v.t.* **1,** (gather or smooth with a rake) грести́; сгреба́ть. *Rake leaves,* сгреба́ть ли́стья. **2,** (cover with gunfire) простре́ливать. **3,** *fol. by* **in** (amass in large quantities) загреба́ть: *rake in money,* загреба́ть де́ньги лопа́той. **4,** *fol. by* **up** (dig up from the past) отка́пывать. —**rake over the coals,** зада́ть жа́ру (+ *dat.*); взять под обстре́л.
rakish *adj.* **1,** (jaunty) лихо́й. **2,** (dissolute) распу́тный.
rally *v.t.* **1,** (bring together for a common purpose) спла́чивать. **2,** (summon; muster) набира́ться: *rally one's forces,* набра́ться сил. —*v.i.* **1,** (unite) спла́чиваться. **2,** (show a sudden improvement) оправля́ться. —*n.* **1,** (mass meeting) ми́тинг; слёт. **2,** (sudden improvement) улучше́ние; попра́вка.
ram *n.* **1,** (male sheep) бара́н. **2,** (battering-ram) тара́н. —*v.t.* **1,** (force into a narrow space; jam) забива́ть; вти́скивать. **2,** [*also intrans.* **ram into**] (crash or smash into) наскочи́ть на; налете́ть на.
ramble *v.i.* **1,** (wander) броди́ть. **2,** (speak aimlessly) загова́риваться. *He tends to ramble,* он ча́сто уклоня́ется от тё́мы.
rambling *adj.* **1,** (wandering) бродя́чий. **2,** (disconnected) бессвя́зный. **3,** (spread out) разбро́санный.
rambunctious *adj., colloq.* бу́йный; непоко́рный.
ramification *n.* **1,** (branch) разветвле́ние. **2,** *pl.* (consequences) после́дствия.
ramp *n.* **1,** (inclined passageway) скат. **2,** (boarding ramp) трап.
rampage *n.* бу́йство. —*v.i.* [*also,* **go on a rampage**] бу́йствовать; буя́нить.
rampant *adj.* **1,** (growing unchecked, as of plants) бу́йный. **2,** (spreading unchecked) безу́держный: *rampant inflation,* безу́держная инфля́ция.
rampart *n.* крепостно́й вал.
ramrod *n.* шо́мпол. —**ramrod straight,** как арши́н проглоти́л.
ramshackle *adj.* ве́тхий; обветша́лый.
ranch *n.* ра́нчо.
rancid *adj.* прого́ркпый. *Turn rancid,* (про)го́ркнуть.
rancor *also,* **rancour** *n.* зло́ба; озлобле́ние. —**rancorous,** *adj.* зло́бный; злопа́мятный.
random *adj.* случа́йный. —**at random,** науда́чу; науга́д; набо́м.
random access произво́льная вы́борка.
range *n.* **1,** (scope; extent) разма́х. *Range of interests,* круг интере́сов. **2,** (of a weapon, transmitter, etc.) да́льность; досяга́емость. *Within range,* в преде́лах досяга́емости. *Out of range,* вне досяга́емости. *The gun has a range of 500 meters,* ору́дие бьёт на пятьсо́т ме́тров. **3,** (of an aircraft, missile, etc.) ра́диус де́йствия; да́льность полёта. **4,** (distance) расстоя́ние: *at close range,* на бли́зком расстоя́нии. *Fire at close range,* стреля́ть в упо́р. **5,** (variety) круг: *a broad range of questions,* широ́кий круг вопро́сов. **6,** (limits of variation) преде́лы: *fluctuate within a narrow range,* колеба́ться в у́зких преде́лах. **7,** *music* диапазо́н. **8,** (of mountains) хребе́т; го́рная цепь. **9,** (place for shooting practice) стре́льбище; полиго́н. **10,** (large stove) плита́. **11,** (grazing land) па́стбище.—*v.t.* выстра́ивать в ряд. *They ranged themselves along the sidewalk,* они́ вы́строились вдоль тротуа́ра. *Various groups were ranged against us,* разли́чные гру́ппы выступа́ли про́тив нас. —*v.i.* **1,** (wander) ры́скать. **2,** (vary within stated limits) колеба́ться. *The children's ages range from two to six,* во́зраст дете́й – от двух до шести́. **3,** *fol. by* **over** (cover; take in) охва́тывать: *range over many topics,* охва́тывать мно́го предме́тов.
range finder дальноме́р.

ranger *n.* **1,** (forest guard) лесни́к; объе́здчик. **2,** *mil.* диверса́нт.

rangy *adj.* долговя́зый.

rank *n.* **1,** (grade; position) зва́ние; чин; ранг. *The rank of admiral,* адмира́льское зва́ние; адмира́льский чин. *An official of lesser rank,* сотру́дник ме́ньшего ра́нга. *Persons of rank,* зна́тные лю́ди. **2,** (category): *a writer of the first rank,* первокла́ссный писа́тель. **3,** (column) шере́нга; ряд. *Close ranks,* смыка́ть *or* спла́чивать ряды́. *Break ranks,* расходи́ться. **4,** *pl.* (armed forces) ряды́: *serve in the ranks of the army,* служи́ть в ряда́х а́рмии. **5,** *pl.* (enlisted men) рядовы́е: *rise from the ranks,* выдвига́ться (из рядовы́х в офице́ры). **6,** *pl.* (body of people) ряды́: *the ranks of the unemployed,* ряды́ безрабо́тных. *Take into their ranks,* принима́ть в свои́ ряды́. —*v.t.* **1,** (evaluate relative to each other) дава́ть оце́нку (+ *dat.).* **2,** (consider; number) относи́ть к числу́ (+ *gen.*); причисля́ть. —*v.i. Rank first,* занима́ть пе́рвое ме́сто. *Rank on a par with,* стоя́ть в одно́м ряду́ с; быть наравне́ с. *Rank among the finest,* принадлежа́ть к числу́ са́мых лу́чших. —*adj.* **1,** (luxuriant) роско́шный; бу́йный. **2,** (rancid) прого́рклый. **3,** (utter; gross) я́вный; сущий. *Rank ingratitude,* черная неблагода́рность. *Rank injustice,* вопию́щая несправедли́вость. —**rank and file,** *mil.* рядово́й соста́в.

ranking *adj.* ста́рший.

rankle *v.i.* му́чить; глода́ть: *the memory still rankles,* воспомина́ние об э́том ещё му́чит/гло́жет меня́.

ransack *v.t.* **1,** (search thoroughly) ры́ться в; обша́ривать. **2,** (rob and leave in disarray) разгра́бить.

ransom *n.* вы́куп: *hold for ransom,* тре́бовать вы́купа за (+ *acc.*). —*v.t.* выкупа́ть.

rant *v.i.* неистовствовать; беснова́ться; безу́мствовать. —**rant and rave,** рвать и мета́ть; мета́ть гро́мы и мо́лнии.

rap *n.* **1,** (quick, sharp blow) уда́р. **2,** (tapping sound) стук. **3,** *slang* (blame; punishment) наказа́ние: *beat the rap,* избежа́ть наказа́ния. *Take the rap for,* отдува́ться за (кого́-нибудь). —*v.t. & i.* ударя́ть (по); стуча́ть (в). —**not give/care a rap,** *colloq.* наплева́ть: *I don't give a rap,* мне наплева́ть на э́то.

rapacious *adj.* хи́щный.

rape *n.* **1,** (sexual violation) изнаси́лование. **2,** (plant) рапс; суре́пица. —*v.t.* наси́ловать. —**rape oil,** ра́псовое ма́сло; суре́пное ма́сло.

rapid *adj.* бы́стрый; стреми́тельный. *Rapid growth,* бу́рный рост. —**rapidity,** *n.* быстрота́. —**rapidly,** *adv.* бы́стро.

rapids *n.pl.* поро́ги; стремни́на; быстрина́.

rapier *n.* рапи́ра.

rapist *n.* наси́льник.

rapport *n.* взаимопонима́ние; согла́сие.

rapprochement *n.* сближе́ние.

rapt *adj.* **1,** (enraptured) восхищенный. **2,** (engrossed) поглощённый. *Rapt attention,* напряжённое внима́ние.

rapture *n.* восто́рг; упое́ние. —**rapturous,** *adj.* восто́рженный.

rara avis бе́лая воро́на.

rare *adj.* **1,** (uncommon) ре́дкий. **2,** (lightly cooked) крова́вый.

rarefy *v.t.* разрежа́ть. —**rarified,** *adj.* разрежённый.

rarely *adv.* ре́дко.

rareness *n.* ре́дкость.

rarity *n.* ре́дкость.

rascal *n.* **1,** (scoundrel) подле́ц. **2,** (imp) постре́л.

rash *adj.* опроме́тчивый; необду́манный; безрассу́дный. —*n.* сыпь. *Heat rash,* потни́ца.

rasher *n.* ло́мтик бекона.

rashly *adv.* опроме́тчиво; безрассу́дно.

rashness *n.* опроме́тчивость; безрассу́дство.

rasp *v.t.* скрести́. —*v.i.* скрипе́ть. —*n.* **1,** (sound) скре́жет. **2,** (tool) ра́шпиль.

raspberry *n.* мали́на. —*adj.* мали́новый: *raspberry jam,* мали́новое варе́нье.

rasping *adj.* скрипу́чий.

rat *n.* **1,** (rodent) кры́са. **2,** (contemptible person) гад. —*adj.* кры́синый: *rat poison,* кры́синый яд. —**smell a rat,** чу́ять недо́брое.

ratchet *n.* храпови́к; трещо́тка. —**ratchet wheel,** храпово́е колесо́.

rate *n.* **1,** (measurement relative to a standard) ста́вка. *rate of interest,* ста́вка проце́нта; *wage rate,* ста́вка зарпла́ты. *Rate of exchange,* валю́тный курс. *Rate of return,* но́рма при́были. *Birth rate,* рожда́емость. *Death rate,* сме́ртность. **2,** *often pl.* (price; cost) тари́ф; расце́нка. *Postal rates,* почто́вый тари́ф. *Advertising rates,* расце́нка объявле́ний. **3,** (pace) темп: *rate of growth,* темп ро́ста. *Pulse rate,* частота́ пу́льса. *At this rate we'll never get there,* при тако́м те́мпе мы никогда́ не доберёмся. —*v.t.* **1,** (evaluate) оце́нивать. **2,** (consider; regard) счита́ть. **3,** *colloq.* (deserve) заслу́живать. —*v.i.* счита́ться: *he rates among the best,* он счита́ется одни́м из са́мых лу́чших. —**at any rate,** во вся́ком слу́чае.

rather *adv.* **1,** (somewhat) дово́льно. **2,** (preferably) скоре́е. *I would rather...,* я предпочёл бы (+ *inf.*). *Which would you rather have?,* что вы предпочита́ете?; чего́ вам бо́льше хо́чется? **3,** (more correctly) верне́е. —**rather than,** вме́сто того́, что́бы...

rathole *n.* кры́синая нора́.

ratify *v.t.* ратифици́ровать. —**ratification,** *n.* ратифика́ция.

rating *n.* **1,** (evaluation) оце́нка. **2,** (scolding) нагоня́й.

ratio *n.* отноше́ние; соотноше́ние; коэффицие́нт. *The ratio of women to men,* соотноше́ние же́нщин и мужчи́н.

ration *n.* **1,** (share; portion) паек; рацио́н. **2,** *pl.* (food) продово́льствие. —*v.t.* нормирова́ть. *Bread is rationed,* хлеб выдаётся по ка́рточкам. —**ration card,** продово́льственная ка́рточка.

rational *adj.* **1,** (able to reason; reasonable) разу́мный; рассу́дочный; рациона́льный. *Man is a rational being,* челове́к – разу́мное существо́. **2,** *math.* рациона́льный.

rationale *n.* моти́в: *the rationale behind a decision,* моти́в для реше́ния.

rationalism *n.* рационали́зм. —**rationalist,** *n.* рационали́ст. —**rationalistic,** *adj.* рационалисти́ческий.

rationality *n.* рациона́льность.

rationalize *v.t.* **1,** (give plausible excuses for) опра́вдывать. **2,** (apply modern methods of efficiency to) рационализи́ровать.

rationally *adv.* разу́мно.

rationing *n.* ка́рточная систе́ма; нормирова́ние. *Introduce rationing,* вводи́ть ка́рточную систе́му.

rattan *n.* рота́нг. —*adj.* рота́нговый.

rattle *v.i.* **1,** (shake with quick sharp sounds) дребезжа́ть. **2,** (move with such sounds) грохота́ть: *rattle along the road,* грохота́ть по доро́ге. —*v.t.* **1,** (shake noisily) греме́ть: *rattle the dishes,* греме́ть посу́дой. *The wind rattled the windows,* стёкла дребезжа́ли от ве́тра. **2,** *colloq.* (fluster) сбива́ть с то́лку. *Get rattled,* (рас)теря́ться. **3,** *fol. by* **off** (recite rapidly) отбараба́нить. —*n.* **1,** (sound) дребезжа́ние. **2,** (sound in one's throat) хрип: *death rattle,* предсме́ртный хрип. **3,** (baby's toy) погрему́шка. **4,** (noisemaker) трещо́тка.
rattlesnake *n.* грему́чая змея́.
rattletrap *n.* колыма́га.
rattrap *n.* крысоло́вка.
raucous *adj.* **1,** (loud and harsh) хри́плый; ре́зкий. **2,** (rowdy; disorderly) шумли́вый; бу́йный.
ravage *v.t.* разоря́ть; опустоша́ть. —*n., usu. pl.* опустоши́тельное де́йствие: *the ravages of time,* опустоши́тельное де́йствие вре́мени.
rave *v.i.* **1,** (speak incoherently) бре́дить. **2,** *fol. by* **about** (praise enthusiastically) быть в восто́рге от; расхва́ливать. —*adj., colloq.* восто́рженный. —*n., colloq.* восто́рженный о́тзыв.
ravel *v.t.* **1,** (fray) обтрепа́ть. **2,** (disentangle) распу́тывать. —*v.i.* обтрепа́ться.
raven *n.* во́рон. —*adj.* чёрный как смоль.
ravenous *adj.* **1,** (voracious; gluttonous) прожо́рливый. *Ravenous appetite,* во́лчий аппети́т. **2,** (rapacious) хи́щный.
ravine *n.* уще́лье; овра́г.
raving *adj.* **1,** (wild) бу́йный: *raving maniac,* бу́йный сумасше́дший. **2,** (ravishing) восхити́тельный. —*n., often pl.* бред; бре́дни.
ravish *v.t.* **1,** (enrapture) восхища́ть. **2,** (rape) растлева́ть. —**ravishing,** *adj.* восхити́тельный.
raw *adj.* **1,** (uncooked) сыро́й. **2,** (untreated; unprocessed) необрабо́танный. *Raw data,* необрабо́танные да́нные. ♦ *Often rendered by* -сыре́ц: *raw silk,* шёлк-сыре́ц; *raw whiskey,* спирт-сыре́ц. **3,** (cold and damp) сыро́й. **4,** (exposed; irritated) обо́дранный. *Raw wound,* жива́я ра́на. **5,** (untrained) необу́ченный. **6,** (bawdy) са́льный. —**in the raw,** нагишо́м.
rawboned *adj.* костля́вый.
rawhide *n.* сыромять. —*adj.* сыромя́тный.
raw material сырьё.
ray *n.* **1,** (beam, as of light) луч. **2,** (glimmer, as of hope) луч; и́скра; про́блеск (наде́жды). **3,** (fish) скат.
rayon *n.* иску́сственный шёлк; виско́за.
raze *v.t.* сноси́ть; срыва́ть (*pfv.* срыть); сровня́ть с землёй; разруша́ть до основа́ния.
razor *n.* бри́тва. —**razor blade,** ле́звие бри́твы.
re *n., music* ре.
reach *v.t.* **1,** (get to) достига́ть; доходи́ть до; доезжа́ть до; *(with difficulty)* добира́ться до. *The letter/news did not reach me,* письмо́/изве́стие до меня́ не дошло́. **2,** (extend as far as) доходи́ть до: *her dress reaches the floor,* её пла́тье дохо́дит до по́ла. **3,** *fol. by* **out** (extend, as one's hand) протя́гивать. **4,** (be able to touch) достава́ть до; дотя́гиваться до. **5,** (obtain and hand over) передава́ть: *reach me the salt,* переда́йте, пожа́луйста, соль. **6,** (attain) достига́ть: *reach one's goal,* достига́ть свое́й це́ли. *Reach supersonic speed,* достига́ть сверхзвуково́й ско́рости. **7,** (come to, as a conclusion or agreement) приходи́ть к. **8,** (get in touch with, as by phone) связа́ться с; дозвони́ться к. —*v.i.* **1,** *often fol. by* **out** (extend one's hand) протя́гивать ру́ку. *Reach into one's pocket,* тяну́ться *or* лезть в карма́н. *A hand reached out from the crowd,* из толпы́ протяну́лась рука́. **2,** *fol. by* **for** (attempt to grasp) тяну́ться за *or* к. —*n.* **1,** (range) досяга́емость: *within reach,* в преде́лах досяга́емости; *out of reach,* вне досяга́емости. **2,** *pl.* (of a river) тече́ние: *the upper reaches of the Volga,* ве́рхнее тече́ние Во́лги; верхо́вье Во́лги.
react *v.i.* реаги́ровать. —**reaction,** *n.* реа́кция.
reactionary *adj.* реакцио́нный. —*n.* реакционе́р.
reactive *adj.* реакти́вный.
reactor *n.* реа́ктор.
read *v.t. & i.* чита́ть. *Read someone's lips,* чита́ть с чьи́х-нибудь губ. *Read someone's mind,* чита́ть чьи́-нибудь мы́сли. —*v.t.* **1,** (make out) разбира́ть. **2,** (interpret) толкова́ть; понима́ть. **3,** (indicate; register) пока́зывать. **4,** *Brit.* (study) изуча́ть: *read law,* изуча́ть пра́во. —*v.i.* **1,** (have a particular wording) гласи́ть: *the telegram reads as follows,* телегра́мма гласи́т сле́дующее. **2,** (admit of being read) чита́ться: *the book reads easily,* кни́га легко́ чита́ется. —**read between the lines,** чита́ть ме́жду строк. —**read out of,** исключа́ть из. —**read through,** прочита́ть.
readable *adj.* удобочита́емый. *The book is very readable,* кни́га легко́ чита́ется.
readdress *v.t.* переадресо́вывать.
reader *n.* **1,** (person who reads) чита́тель. **2,** (professional reciter) чтец. **3,** *Brit.* (lecturer) ле́ктор. **4,** (textbook) хрестома́тия.
readership *n.* круг чита́тетей.
readily *adv.* **1,** (willingly; promptly) охо́тно. **2,** (easily) легко́; без труда́.
readiness *n.* гото́вность. *All is in readiness,* всё гото́во. *Hold in readiness,* держа́ть нагото́ве.
reading *n.* **1,** (act of reading; recital) чте́ние. **2,** (interpretation) толкова́ние. **3,** (indication on a meter) показа́ние; отсчёт. —**reading desk,** пюпи́тр. —**reading glasses,** очки́ для чте́ния. —**reading room,** чита́льный зал; чита́льня.
readjust *v.t.* (сно́ва) регули́ровать. —*v.i.* приспособля́ться (к). —**readjustment,** *n.* приспособле́ние.
readout *n.* счи́тывание информа́ции.
ready *adj.* гото́вый: *are you ready?,* вы гото́вы? *Ready for takeoff,* гото́вый к вы́лету. *Ready for use,* гото́вый для употребле́ния. *Get ready,* гото́виться. *Ready cash,* нали́чные де́ньги. —*v.t.* гото́вить. —**at the ready,** на изгото́вку.
ready-made *adj.* гото́вый: *ready-made clothes,* гото́вая оде́жда.
reaffirm *v.t.* вновь подтвержда́ть.
reagent *n.* реакти́в; реаге́нт.
real *adj.* **1,** (actual; existing) действи́тельный; реа́льный. **2,** (genuine) настоя́щий; натура́льный. **3,** (true, as of a friend) настоя́щий; и́стинный. —*adv., colloq.* о́чень: *get up real early,* встава́ть о́чень ра́но. —**real estate,** недви́жимое иму́щество; недви́жимость. —**real number,** действи́тельное число́. —**real wages,** реа́льная за́работная пла́та.
realign *v.t.* перестра́ивать. —**realignment,** *n.* перестро́йка; перестано́вка.
realism *n.* реали́зм. —**realist,** *n.* реали́ст. —**realistic,** *adj.* реалисти́ческий; ре́альный.
reality *n.* действи́тельность; реа́льность. —**in reality,** в действи́тельности; на са́мом де́ле.

realization *n.* **1,** (recognition; awareness) понима́ние; осозна́ние. **2,** (becoming a reality) осуществле́ние; созна́ние; реализа́ция.

realize *v.t.* **1,** (be or become aware of) понима́ть; сознава́ть; осознава́ть; отдава́ть себе́ отчёт в. **2,** (achieve; bring about) осуществля́ть; реализова́ть. **3,** (gain; obtain, as a profit) получа́ть.

really *adv.* **1,** (actually; in actual fact) действи́тельно; на са́мом де́ле. *Better than it really is,* лу́чше чем оно́ есть на са́мом де́ле. **2,** (truly; indeed) действи́тельно; в са́мом де́ле. *The meal really turned out well,* еда́ в са́мом де́ле оказа́лась хоро́шей. —**really?,** неуже́ли? *Did I really say that?,* неуже́ли я э́то говори́л(а)?

realm *n.* **1,** (kingdom) короле́вство; ца́рство. **2,** (sphere) о́бласть; сфе́ра.

realtor *n.* аге́нт по прода́же недви́жимости. —**realty,** *n.* недви́жимое иму́щество.

ream *n.* **1,** (quantity of paper) стопа́. **2,** *usu. pl., colloq.* (large amount) ма́сса; ку́ча; у́йма.

reamer *n.* развёртка.

reanimation *n.* реанима́ция.

reap *v.t.* **1,** (cut; gather) жать. **2,** *fig.* (gain as a reward) пожина́ть.

reaper *n.* **1,** (one who reaps) жнец. **2,** (reaping machine) жа́твенная маши́на; жа́тка; жне́йка.

reappear *v.i.* сно́ва появля́ться.

reapportion *v.t.* перераспределя́ть. —**reapportionment,** *n.* перераспределе́ние.

reappraise *v.t.* переоце́нивать; пересма́тривать. —**reappraisal,** *n.* переоце́нка; пересмо́тр.

rear *n.* **1,** (back part) за́дняя часть; зад. **2,** (tail end) хвост. **3,** *mil.* тыл. —*adj.* **1,** (back) за́дний: *rear wheel,* за́днее колесо́. **2,** (from the back): *rear view,* вид сза́ди. **3,** (located in the back part of a house) чёрный: *rear door,* чёрный ход. **4,** *mil.* тылово́й. —*v.t.* **1,** (elevate) поднима́ть: *rear one's head,* поднима́ть го́лову. **2,** (raise; bring up) воспи́тывать. —*v.i.* (of a horse) станови́ться на дыбы́. —**at/in the rear of, 1,** (behind) позади́; сза́ди. **2,** (in the back part of) в за́дней ча́сти (+ *gen.*). **3,** (at the tail end of) в хвосте́ (+ *gen.*). —**bring up the rear,** замыка́ть ше́ствие. —**rear end, 1,** (tail end) хвост. **2,** (buttocks) зад.

rear admiral контр-адмира́л.

rear guard арьерга́рд. —**rearguard,** *adj.* арьерга́рдный.

rearm *v.t.* перевооружа́ть. —*v.i.* перевооружа́ться. —**rearmament,** *n.* перевооруже́ние.

rearrange *v.t.* **1,** (move around) переставля́ть: *rearrange the furniture,* переставля́ть ме́бель. **2,** *music* перекла́дывать. —**rearrangment,** *n.* перестано́вка.

rear-view mirror зе́ркало за́днего ви́да.

reason *n.* **1,** (cause; motive) причи́на. *By reason of,* по причи́не (+ *gen.*). *For the reason that...,* по той причи́не, что... *For some reason or other,* по той и́ли ино́й причи́не. *For no reason whatsoever,* безо вся́кой причи́ны. **2,** (justification) основа́ние: *with good reason,* с по́лным основа́нием. **3,** (ability to think) ра́зум; рассу́док. **4,** (common sense; sanity) рассу́док: *devoid of reason,* лишён рассу́дка. —*v.i.* **1,** (think logically) рассужда́ть. **2,** *fol. by* **with** (persuade) урезо́нивать. —*v.t.* [*usu.* **reason out**] проду́мывать. —**bring to reason,** образу́мить; урезо́нить; наводи́ть на ум. —**listen to reason,** прислу́шиваться к го́лосу рассу́дка. —**stand to reason,** само́ собо́й разуме́ться. —**within reason,** разу́мный: *any offer within reason,* вся́кое разу́мное предложе́ние.

reasonable *adj.* **1,** (amenable to reason) разу́мный; рассуди́тельный; благоразу́мный. **2,** (fair) разу́мный: *a reasonable offer,* разу́мное предложе́ние. **3,** (not excessive) досту́пный: *reasonable prices,* досту́пные це́ны. **4,** (not expensive) недорого́й.

reasonably *adv.* **1,** (sensibly) разу́мно. **2,** (fairly) дово́льно: *reasonably good,* дово́льно хорошо́. *Reasonably certain,* бо́лее и́ли ме́нее уве́рен.

reasoning *n.* рассужде́ние: *sound reasoning,* здра́вое рассужде́ние. *Line of reasoning,* аргумента́ция.

reassess *v.t.* переоце́нивать; пересма́тривать. —**reassessment,** *n.* переоце́нка; пересмо́тр.

reassign *v.t.* назнача́ть (*or* переводи́ть) на другу́ю до́лжность.

reassure *v.t.* ободря́ть; обнадёживать. —**reassurance,** *n.* ободре́ние. —**reassuring,** *adj.* ободри́тельный; ободря́ющий; успокои́тельный.

rebandage *v.t.* перебинтова́ть.

rebate *n.* **1,** (discount) ски́дка. **2,** (refund) возвра́т.

rebel *v.i.* восстава́ть; бунтова́ть. —*n.* повста́нец; бунтовщи́к, мяте́жник. —*adj.* повста́нческий; мяте́жный: *rebel troops,* повста́нческие/мяте́жные войска́.

rebellion *n.* восста́ние; бунт; мяте́ж.

rebellious *adj.* **1,** (inclined to rebel) мяте́жный. **2,** (opposing any control) непоко́рный. —**rebelliousness,** *n.* непоко́рность.

rebirth *n.* возрожде́ние.

reborn *adj. Be reborn,* возрожда́ться.

rebound *v.i.* отска́кивать. —*n.* рикоше́т. *On the rebound,* рикоше́том.

rebuff *n.* отпо́р. —*v.t.* дать отпо́р (+ *dat.*).

rebuild *v.t.* перестра́ивать.

rebuke *n.* упрёк; вы́говор; замеча́ние; о́тповедь. —*v.t.* упрека́ть.

rebus *n.* ре́бус.

rebut *v.t.* опроверга́ть. —**rebuttal,** *n.* опроверже́ние.

recalcitrant *adj.* непоко́рный. —**recalcitrance,** *n.* непоко́рность.

recall *v.t.* **1,** (call back) отзыва́ть. **2,** (remember) по́мнить; вспо́мнить. **3,** (reminisce about) вспомина́ть. **4,** (bring back to mind) напомина́ть. —*n.* **1,** (summons to return) о́тзыв. **2,** (ability to remember) па́мять.

recant *v.t.* отрека́ться от. —*v.i.* (публи́чно) ка́яться.

recapitulate *v.t. & i.* сумми́ровать; резюми́ровать. —**recapitulation,** *n.* сумми́рование; резюме́.

recapture *v.t.* брать обра́тно; сно́ва захва́тывать; отбива́ть.

recast *v.t.* **1,** (remold) перелива́ть. **2,** (rework) переде́лывать.

recede *v.i.* **1,** (move back) отступа́ть: *recede into the background,* отступа́ть на за́дний план. **2,** (subside, as of floodwaters) убыва́ть; сбыва́ть; идти́ на у́быль. —**receding forehead,** пока́тый лоб.

receipt *n.* **1,** (act of receiving) получе́ние: *upon receipt of,* по получе́нии (+ *gen.*). *Acknowledge receipt of,* подтверди́ть получе́ние (+ *gen.*). **2,** (note acknowledging payment) распи́ска; квита́нция. **3,** *pl.* (proceeds; income) вы́ручка; поступле́ния. *Box-office receipts,* сбо́ры.

receivable *adj.* подлежа́щий упла́те.

receive *v.t.* **1,** (get; have inflicted on one) получáть: *receive permission,* получи́ть разрешéние; *receive a blow,* получи́ть удáр. **2,** (admit; greet) принимáть: *receive guests,* принимáть гостéй. **3,** (pick up, as a signal) принимáть. **4,** (deal in, as stolen goods) укрывáть.

receiver *n.* **1,** (part of a telephone) трýбка. **2,** (instrument for receiving signals) приёмник.

recent *adj.* **1,** (having just occurred) недáвний: *recent trip/attempt,* недáвняя поéздка/попы́тка. **2,** (just past) послéдний: *in recent years,* в *or* за послéдние гóды. *The events of recent weeks,* собы́тия послéдних недéль.

recently *adv.* недáвно; в *or* за послéднее врéмя. *Until recently,* до недáвнего врéмени. —**as recently as,** ещё: *as recently as last year,* ещё в прóшлом годý.

receptacle *n.* **1,** (container) вмести́лище. **2,** *bot.* цветолóже.

reception *n.* **1,** (social gathering; manner of being received) приём. **2,** *radio; television* приём. —**reception room,** приёмная.

receptionist *n.* секретáрша (в приёмной).

receptive *adj.* восприи́мчивый. —**receptivity; receptiveness,** *n.* восприи́мчивость.

recess *n.* **1,** (short break between sessions) переры́в. *Parliament is in recess,* парлáмент распýщен. **2,** (break between school terms) кани́кулы. **3,** (hollow place) углублéние. **4,** *usu. pl.* (inner place, as of the heart) тайни́к. —*v.t.* **1,** (set back into a recess) отодвигáть назáд. **2,** (adjourn) закрывáть. —*v.i.* дéлать переры́в.

recession *n.* спад.

recessive *adj.* рецесси́вный.

recharge *v.t.* перезаряжáть.

rechristen *v.t.* перекрéщивать.

recidivism *n.* рецидиви́зм. —**recidivist,** *n.* рецидиви́ст.

recipe *n.* рецéпт.

recipient *n.* получáтель.

reciprocal *adj.* взаи́мный; обою́дный. —*n., math.* обрáтная величинá.

reciprocate *v.t.* отвечáть. *Reciprocate someone's feelings,* отвечáть на чьи́-нибудь чýвства; отвечáть комý-нибудь взаи́мностью. —*v.i.* отплáчивать: *we would like to reciprocate somehow,* нам бы хотéлось вам чéм-то отплати́ть. —**reciprocating engine,** поршневóй дви́гатель.

reciprocity *n.* взаи́мность; обою́дность.

recital *n.* **1,** (narration) изложéние. **2,** *music* концéрт.

recitation *n.* **1,** (public reading) декламáция. **2,** (school exercise) ответ (урóка).

recitative *n., music* речитати́в.

recite *v.t.* читáть; деклами́ровать. *Recite poetry/one's prayers/,* читáть стихи́/моли́твы. *Recite one's lesson,* отвечáть урóк. —**reciter,** *n.* декламáтор.

reckless *adj.* безрассýдный. —**recklessly,** *adv.* безрассýдно. —**recklessness,** *n.* безрассýдство.

reckon *v.t.* **1,** (figure; compute) считáть; подсчи́тывать. **2,** (regard) считáть; рассмáтривать. **3,** *colloq.* (think; suppose) дýмать; полагáть. —**reckon on,** рассчи́тывать на. —**reckon with, 1,** (settle accounts with) расплáчиваться с. **2,** (take into account) считáться с.

reckoning *n.* расчёт; счёт. —**day of reckoning,** день (*or* час) расплáты. —**dead reckoning,** счислéние пути́.

reclaim *v.t.* **1,** (claim back) трéбовать обрáтно. **2,** (cultivate, as land) поднимáть; осваивать.

reclamation *n.* мелиорáция.

recline *v.i.* полулежáть.

recluse *n.* затвóрник; отшéльник.

recognition *n.* **1,** (identification) узнавáние. *Beyond recognition,* до неузнавáемости. **2,** (acknowledgment; acclaim) признáние: *gain recognition,* получи́ть признáние. *In recognition of his services,* в знак признáния егó заслýг.

recognize *v.t.* **1,** (identify from previous knowledge) узнавáть: *I hardly recognize you,* я едвá узнáл(а) вас. **2,** (formally acknowledge) признавáть: *recognize a new nation,* признавáть нóвую странý. **3,** (realize; be aware of) сознавáть: *recognize the danger,* сознавáть опáсность. **4,** (give the floor to) предоставля́ть слóво (+ *dat.*).

recoil *v.i.* **1,** (shrink back) отскáкивать; отпря́нуть; отшатнýться. **2,** (of a firearm) отдавáть; откáтываться. —*n.* отдáча; откáт. —**recoilless,** *adj.* безоткáтный.

recollect *v.t. & i.* вспоминáть; припоминáть.

recollection *n.* **1,** (capacity to remember) пáмять: *within my recollection,* на моéй пáмяти. *To the best of my recollection,* наскóлько я пóмню. **2,** (something remembered) воспоминáние.

recommend *v.t.* рекомендовáть: *can you recommend a good doctor?,* мóжете ли вы порекомендовáть мне хорóшего врачá? *You were recommended to me by...,* вас мне рекомендовáл(а)... *That is not recommended,* э́то не рекомендýется.

recommendation *n.* рекомендáция. —**letter of recommendation,** рекомендáтельное письмó.

recompense *v.t.* вознаграждáть; компенси́ровать. —*n.* вознаграждéние; компенсáция.

reconcile *v.t.* **1,** (restore to good terms; make content) мири́ть; примиря́ть. *Become reconciled to; reconcile oneself to,* мири́ться с; примиря́ться с. **2,** (adjust; resolve) улáживать: *reconcile differences,* улáживать разноглáсия. *Reconcile contradictions,* примиря́ть противорéчия.

reconciliation *n.* **1,** (bringing or coming together) примирéние. **2,** (adjustment, as of differences) улáживание.

recondite *adj.* замысловáтый; мудрёный.

recondition *v.t.* ремонти́ровать.

reconnaissance *n.* развéдка; рекогносцирóвка. —*adj.* развéдывательный.

reconnoiter *also,* **reconnoitre** *v.t.* развéдывать; рекогносци́ровать. —*v.i.* вести́ развéдку.

reconsider *v.t.* пересмáтривать. —**reconsideration,** *n.* пересмóтр.

reconstruct *v.t.* **1,** (rebuild) перестрáивать; реконструи́ровать. **2,** (put together from clues) восстанáвливать; воссоздавáть. —**reconstruction,** *n.* перестрóйка; реконстрýкция.

reconvene *v.i.* снóва собирáться.

recook *v.t.* перевáривать.

record *n.* **1,** (written account) зáпись; учёт: *keep record of,* вести́ зáпись/учёт (+ *gen.*). **2,** (official account of proceedings) протокóл. **3,** (recorded facts about someone) спи́сок: *work record,* трудовóй спи́сок. *Attendance record,* посещáемость. *Criminal rec-*

ord, уголо́вное про́шлое; суди́мости. **4,** (best achievement) реко́рд: *break/set a record,* поби́ть/поста́вить реко́рд. **5,** (phonograph record) пласти́нка; грампласти́нка. —*adj.* реко́рдный: *in record time,* с реко́рдным вре́менем; в реко́рдный срок. —*v.t.* **1,** (set down in writing; keep a record of) запи́сывать; регистри́ровать. **2,** (transcribe, as sound) запи́сывать на плёнку *or* на пласти́нку. *Record one's voice,* нагова́ривать пласти́нку. —**a matter of record,** неоспори́мый факт. —**off the record,** неофициа́льно; не для печа́ти. —**on the record,** официа́льно: *go on the record,* заяви́ть официа́льно. —**on record,** зарегистри́рованный: *the worst earthquake on record,* са́мое си́льное из когда́-либо зарегистри́рованных землетрясе́ний.

recorder *n.* **1,** (recording device) самопи́сец: *flight recorder,* бортово́й самопи́сец. *Tape recorder,* магнитофо́н. **2,** (person who takes notes or minutes) протоколи́ст.

record holder рекордсме́н; рекорди́ст.

recording *n.* **1,** (taking down) за́пись; запи́сывание. **2,** (entering) занесе́ние. **3,** (something on a record or tape) за́пись. *Sound recording,* звукоза́пись.

record player граммофо́н; прои́грыватель.

recount *v.t.* **1,** (relate) расска́зывать. **2,** (count again) пересчи́тывать. —*n.* пересчёт.

recoup *v.t.* оты́грывать. *Recoup one's losses,* оты́грываться.

recourse *n. Have recourse to,* прибега́ть к. *Have no other recourse but to...,* не име́ть никако́го друго́го вы́хода, кро́ме...

recover *v.t.* **1,** (get back) получа́ть обра́тно; возвраща́ть. **2,** (cover again) перекрыва́ть. —*v.i.* **1,** (regain one's health) выздора́вливать; оправля́ться; поправля́ться. **2,** (regain one's composure) овладе́ть собо́й.

recovery *n.* **1,** (getting back) возвраще́ние. **2,** (getting well) выздоровле́ние. *He is on the road to recovery,* у него́ де́ло идёт на попра́вку. —**recovery room,** послеоперацио́нная пала́та.

re-create *v.t.* воссоздава́ть; пересоздава́ть; воспроизводи́ть.

recreation *n.* развлече́ние.

recrimination *n.* взаи́мное обвине́ние.

recruit *v.t.* вербова́ть; набира́ть. —*n.* новобра́нец. —**recruiter,** *n.* вербо́вщик. —**recruiting; recruitment,** *n.* вербо́вка.

rectal *adj.* относя́щийся к прямо́й кишке́.

rectangle *n.* прямоуго́льник. —**rectangular,** *adj.* прямоуго́льный.

rectify *v.t.* исправля́ть. —**rectifiable,** *adj.* исправи́мый. —**rectification,** *n.* исправле́ние.

rectilinear *adj.* прямолине́йный.

rectitude *n.* пра́ведность.

rector *n.* **1,** (clergyman) прихо́дский свяще́нник. **2,** (university head) ре́ктор.

rectum *n.* пряма́я кишка́.

recumbent *adj.* лежа́чий; лежа́щий.

recuperate *v.i.* восстана́вливать си́лы; поправля́ться; выздора́вливать. —**recuperation,** *n.* выздоровле́ние.

recur *v.i.* возвраща́ться; повторя́ться; происходи́ть вновь. —**recurrence,** *n.* возвра́т; повторе́ние; рециди́в.

recurrent *adj.* повто́рный; повторя́ющийся; периоди́ческий.

recycle *v.t.* втори́чно испо́льзовать; возвраща́ть в оборо́т.

red *adj.* кра́сный: *red banner,* кра́сное зна́мя. *Red hair,* ры́жие во́лосы. *Turn red,* красне́ть. *Paint something red,* кра́сить что́-нибудь в кра́сный цвет. —*n.* **1,** (color) кра́сный цвет. *Red is my favorite color,* мой люби́мый цвет – кра́сный. **2,** *pl.* (communists) кра́сные. —**in the red, 1,** (showing a loss) с убы́тком. **2,** (in debt) в долгу́. —**paint the town red,** *colloq.* кути́ть; гуля́ть —**see red,** *colloq.* приходи́ть в я́рость.

red-blooded *adj.* полнокро́вный.

Red Cross Кра́сный Крест.

red deer благоро́дный оле́нь.

redden *v.t.* румя́нить. —*v.i.* красне́ть.

reddish *adj.* краснова́тый.

redeem *v.t.* **1,** (buy back; pay off) выкупа́ть. **2,** (cash in) реализова́ть. **3,** (rescue; liberate) избавля́ть. **4,** (make amends for) искупа́ть. *Redeem oneself,* оправда́ть себя́. —**redeemer,** *n.* избави́тель.

redemption *n.* **1,** (paying off) вы́куп. **2,** (deliverance) спасе́ние; избавле́ние.

redesign *v.t.* переконструи́ровать.

red-handed *adj.* с поли́чным: *catch red-handed,* пойма́ть с поли́чным.

redhead *n.* ры́жий. —**redheaded,** *adj.* ры́жий; рыжеволо́сый.

red-hot *adj.* накалённый *or* раскалённый докрасна́; калёный.

redistribute *v.t.* перераспределя́ть; передели́ть. —**redistribution,** *n.* перераспределе́ние; переде́л.

red lead (свинцо́вый) су́рик.

red light кра́сный свет. *Go through a red light,* проскочи́ть светофо́р.

redness *n.* краснота́. *Redness in one's cheeks,* румя́нец.

redo *v.t.* переде́лывать.

redolent *adj.* **1,** (fragrant) души́стый; благоуха́нный. **2,** *fol. by* **of** (smelling of) па́хнущий (+ *instr.*). —**redolence,** *n.* благоуха́ние.

redouble *v.t.* **1,** (double again) втори́чно удва́ивать. **2,** (increase greatly) удва́ивать; усугубля́ть.

redoubt *n.* **1,** (small defensive fortification) реду́т. **2,** (earthwork within a fortification) редюи́т.

redoubtable *adj.* **1,** (fearsome) гро́зный. **2,** (estimable) почте́нный.

redound *v.i. Redound to the credit of,* де́лать честь (+ *dat.*). *Redound to the advantage of,* благоприя́тствовать (+ *dat.*).

red pepper кра́сный пе́рец; стручко́вый пе́рец.

redpoll *n.* чечётка.

redress *v.t.* **1,** (set right, as a wrong) загла́живать (вину́). **2,** (restore, as a balance) восстана́вливать (равнове́сие). —*n.* возмеще́ние. *Demand redress,* тре́бовать возмеще́ния убы́тков.

redskin *n.* красноко́жий.

redstart *n.* горихво́стка.

red tape волоки́та.

reduce *v.t.* **1,** (lessen) уменьша́ть; сокраща́ть. *Reduce to the minimum,* доводи́ть до ми́нимума. **2,** (lower, as a price) понижа́ть; снижа́ть. **3,** (put in a simpler form) своди́ть: *reduce to a simple formula,* своди́ть к просто́й фо́рмуле. *Reduce to a common denominator,* приводи́ть к о́бщему знамена́телю. **4,** (bring to an extreme state) *rendered by various verbs: reduce to dust,* обрати́ть в прах; *reduce to rubble,*

превращáть в развáлины; *reduce to poverty,* доводи́ть до нищеты́; *reduce to naught,* своди́ть на нет *or* к нулю́. —*v.i.* убавля́ть в вéсе.
reduction *n.* **1,** (lessening) уменьшéние; сокращéние. **2,** (lowering) понижéние; снижéние. **3,** (discount) ски́дка. **4,** *math.* приведéние (к óбщему знаменáтелю). **5,** *in various technical senses* редýкция.
redundancy *n.* **1,** (state of being redundant) ненýжность. **2,** (redundant word or phrase) тавтолóгия.
redundant *adj.* **1,** (superfluous) изли́шний; ли́шний. **2,** (wordy; verbose) многослóвный. **3,** (needlessly repeating something) тавтологи́ческий.
reduplicate *v.t.* удвáивать. —**reduplication,** *n.* удвоéние.
redwood *n.* секвóйя.
reed *n.* **1,** (plant) тростни́к; камы́ш. **2,** (primitive musical instrument) свирéль. **3,** *music* (vibrating piece) язычóк. —*adj.* тростникóвый; камышóвый. —**reed instrument,** язычкóвый инструмéнт.
re-educate *v.t.* перевоспи́тывать. —**re-education,** *n.* перевоспитáние.
reedy *adj.* **1,** (full of reeds) тростникóвый. **2,** (of thin, sharp tone) тóнкий.
reef *n.* риф; подвóдный кáмень; подвóдная скалá.
reek *v.i.* воня́ть. —**reek of/with,** воня́ть (+ *instr.*); рази́ть; нести́ *(both impers. with instr.). He reeks of vodka,* от негó рази́т/несёт вóдкой.
reel *n.* **1,** (for thread, rope, etc.) катýшка. **2,** (for movie film) рóлик. **3,** (for fishing) катýшка. *Rod and reel,* ýдочка со спи́ннингом. —*v.t.* **1,** (wind) намáтывать. **2,** *fol. by* **in** (pull in, as a fish) вытя́гивать. **3,** *fol. by* **off** (recite fluently) отбарабáнить. —*v.i.* **1,** (stagger) шатáться. **2,** (whirl) кружи́ться.
re-elect *v.t.* переизбирáть. —**re-election,** *n.* переизбрáние.
re-enlist *v.i.* поступáть на сверхсрóчную слýжбу.
re-enter *v.t.* снóва входи́ть в.
re-equip *v.t.* переоборýдовать.
re-establish *v.t.* восстанáвливать. —**re-establishment,** *n.* восстановлéние.
re-evaluate *v.t.* переоцéнивать.
re-examine *v.t.* **1,** (scrutinize again) снóва осмáтривать *or* рассмáтривать. **2,** (review; reconsider) пересмáтривать.
refashion *v.t.* преобразóвывать; перекрáивать.
refectory *n.* **1,** (in a school) столóвая. **2,** (in a monastery) трáпезная.
refer *v.t.* **1,** (send; direct) посылáть; отсылáть; направля́ть. *Refer a patient to a specialist,* направля́ть больнóго к специали́сту. **2,** (submit for consideration) передавáть. —*v.i.* [*usu.* **refer to**] **1,** (pertain to) относи́ться к. **2,** (allude to) ссылáться на. *To whom are you referring?,* когó вы имéете в видý? **3,** (consult, as a dictionary) обращáться к.
referee *n.* судья́. —*v.t. & i.* суди́ть.
reference *n.* **1,** (act of referring to or consulting) спрáвка: *for reference only,* тóлько для спрáвок. **2,** (allusion) ссы́лка; упоминáние. *Make reference to,* ссылáться на; упоми́нать. **3,** (note) ссы́лка: *cross-reference,* перекрёстная ссы́лка. **4,** (recommendation) óтзыв; рекомендáция. *Character reference,* характери́стика; аттестáция. —*adj.* спрáвочный: *reference material,* спрáвочный материáл. —**with reference to,** в связи́ с; в отношéнии (+*gen.*).
reference book спрáвочник.
reference point ориенти́р; ориентирóвочный пункт; тóчка отсчёта.
referendum *n.* референдум; всенарóдный опрóс.
refill *v.t.* снóва наполня́ть.
refine *v.t.* **1,** (purify) очищáть. *Refine oil,* перерабáтывать нефть. **2,** (polish, as one's manners) утончáть. **3,** (perfect) совершéнствовать.
refined *adj.* **1,** (purified) очи́щенный. **2,** (cultivated; polished) утончённый; изя́щный; изы́сканный.
refinement *n.* **1,** (elegance of manner) утончённость; изя́щество; изы́сканность. *Lack of refinement,* некультýрность. **2,** (small improvement) усовершéнствование.
refinery *n.* очисти́тельный завóд. *Oil refinery,* нефтеперегóнный завóд. *Sugar refinery,* сáхарный завóд.
reflect *v.t.* отражáть: *reflect light,* отражáть свет. *Reflect someone's views,* отражáть чьи́-нибудь взгля́ды. —*v.i.* **1,** (be reflected) отражáться. **2,** (meditate) размышля́ть. **3,** *fol. by* **on** *or* **upon** (tend to discredit) бросáть тень (на). —**reflecting telescope,** зеркáльный телескóп; рефлéктор.
reflection *n.* **1,** (act of reflecting; image reflected) отражéние. **2,** (meditation) размышлéние. **3,** (something that discredits) тень.
reflective *adj.* **1,** (reflecting) отражáющий. **2,** (thoughtful) вдýмчивый.
reflector *n.* рефлéктор; отражáтель.
reflex *n.* рефлéкс. —*adj.* рефлектóрный: *reflex reaction,* рефлектóрная реáкция. —**reflex camera,** зеркáльный фотоаппарáт.
reflexive *adj.* возврáтный: *reflexive verb,* возврáтный глагóл.
reforge *v.t.* перекóвывать.
re-form *v.t.* **1,** (form again) вновь формировáть. **2,** *mil.* перестрáивать. —*v.i., mil.* перестрáиваться.
reform *v.t.* **1,** (introduce changes in) реформи́ровать; преобразóвывать. **2,** (cause to mend one's ways) исправля́ть. —*v.i.* исправля́ться. —*n.* редóрма; преобразовáние. *Land reform,* земéльная рефóрма. *Calendar/spelling reform,* рефóрма календаря́/правописáния.
reformation *n.* **1,** (change; reshaping) преобразовáние. **2,** *cap., hist.* реформáция.
reformatory *n.* исправи́тельный дом; исправи́тельная колóния.
reformed *adj.* испрáвленный. —**Reformed Church,** реформáтская цéрковь.
reformer *n.* реформáтор; преобразовáтель.
reform school = **reformatory.**
refract *v.t.* преломля́ть. —**refracting,** *adj.* преломля́ющий. *Refracting telescope,* рефрáктор. —**refraction,** *n.* преломлéние; рефрáкция. —**refractor,** *n.* рефрáктор.
refractory *adj.* **1,** (obstinate) упря́мый; непокóрный. **2,** (heat-resistant) огнеупóрный.
refrain *v.i.* [*usu.* **refrain from**] воздéрживаться (от); удéрживаться (от). —*n.* припéв; рефрéн.
refresh *v.t.* освежáть. —**refresher course,** повтори́тельный курс; переподготóвка. —**refreshing,** *adj.* освежáющий; освежи́тельный.
refreshment *n.* **1,** (act of refreshing) освежéние. **2,** *pl.* (food, drink, etc.) угощéние.
refrigerate *v.t.* охлаждáть; заморáживать. —**re-**

frigeration, *n.* охлаждéние; заморáживание. —**refrigerator,** *n.* холоди́льник.

refuel *v.t.* дозаправля́ть. —*v.i.* дозаправля́ться. *Without refueling,* без дозапрáвки.

refuge *n.* убéжище; прию́т; пристáнище. *Take refuge in,* найти́ убéжище в.

refugee *n.* бéженец. *Refugee camp,* лáгерь для бéженцев.

refund *v.t.* возвращáть (дéньги). —*n.* возврáт (дéнег).

refurbish *v.t.* обновля́ть; ремонти́ровать.

refusal *n.* откáз.

refuse[1] (ri-**fyooz**) *v.t.* **1,** *fol. by inf.* (decline to) откáзываться (+ *inf.*). **2,** (decline to accept) откáзываться от: *refuse help,* отказáться от пóмощи. **3,** (decline to give) откáзывать: *refuse help to someone,* откáзывать комý-нибудь в пóмощи. **4,** (turn down the request of) откáзывать (+ *dat.*): *she refused him,* онá емý отказáла. —*v.i.* откáзываться: *he flatly refused,* он отказáлся наотрéз.

refuse[2] (**ref**-yoos) *n.* мýсор; сор; отбрóсы; хлам.

refute *v.t.* опровергáть. —**refutation,** *n.* опровержéние.

regain *v.t.* возвращáть; вернýть. *Regain consciousness,* приходи́ть в сознáние (*or* в себя́), очнýться. *Regain one's composure,* овладéть собóй. *Regain one's health,* восстанáвливать своё здорóвье. *Regain one's balance,* сбаланси́ровать. *Regain one's eyesight,* прозрéть. *Regain the use of one's legs,* снóва владéть ногáми. *Regain the world championship title,* возврати́ть/вернýть себé звáние чемпиóна ми́ра.

regal *adj.* **1,** (of a king) королéвский. **2,** *fig.* (magnificent; stately) цáрственный; цáрский.

regale *v.t.* угощáть; пóтчевать.

regalia *n.pl.* регáлии. *In full regalia,* во всех регáлиях.

regard *v.t.* **1,** (contemplate) смотрéть на; разгля́дывать. **2,** (look upon; consider) считáть; рассмáтривать. *I regard it as nonsense,* я считáю э́то ерундóй. *I regard it as madness,* я рассмáтриваю э́то как безýмие. *Regard someone highly,* быть высóкого мнéния о. *Regard something with favor,* относи́ться к чемý-нибудь благосклóнно. **3,** (concern) касáться. *As regards...,* что касáется (+ *gen.*).—*n.* **1,** (consideration; esteem) уважéние: *out of regard for,* из уважéния к. *Have no regard for others,* не считáться с другáми. *Without regard to,* безотноси́тельно к. *Have a high regard for,* быть высóкого мнéния о. **2,** (attention) внимáние: *pay no regard to,* не обращáть (никакóго) внимáния на. **3,** *pl.* (greetings) привéт: *best regards,* сердéчный привéт. *Give one's regards to,* клáняться (+ *dat.*); передавáть привéт (+ *dat.*). **4,** (relation; connection) отношéние: *in this regard,* в э́том отнóшении. *You need not worry in that regard,* на э́тот счёт мóжете быть спокóйны. —**in/with regard to,** в отношéнии (+ *gen.*); относи́тельно; в свя́зи с; что касáется.

regarding *prep.* относи́тельно; касáющийся; по пóводу.

regardless *adv., colloq.* невзирáя ни на что. —**regardless of,** незави́симо от; вне зави́симости от; невзирáя на.

regatta *n.* регáта.

regency *n.* рéгентство.

regenerate *v.t.* перерождáть. —*v.i.* перерождáться.

regeneration *n.* **1,** (renewal) перерождéние. **2,** *mech.; biol.* регенерáция. —**regenerative,** *adj.* регенерати́вный.

regent *n.* рéгент.

regicide *n.* цареубúйство.

regime *n.* режи́м.

regimen *n.* режи́м.

regiment *n.* полк. —*v.t.* дисциплини́ровать. —**regimental,** *adj.* полковóй. —**regimentation,** *n.* стрóгая дисципли́на.

region *n.* мéстность; óбласть; райóн. —**regional,** *adj.* областнóй; региональный.

register *n.* **1,** (record) вéдомость; реги́стр; реéстр. **2,** (book containing such a record) журнáл; реги́стр; реéстр. *Guest register,* кни́га для посети́телей. **3,** *music* (range) реги́стр. —*v.t.* **1,** (record; enroll) регистри́ровать. **2,** (indicate, as by a mechanical device) покáзывать. **3,** (show, as emotion) проявля́ть; обнарýживать. **4,** (insure delivery of, as a letter) посылáть (письмó) заказны́м. *Registered letter,* заказнóе письмó. —*v.i.* **1,** (sign up) регистри́роваться; отмечáться. **2,** (make an impression): *the name doesn't register with me,* э́то и́мя мне ничегó не говори́т. —**cash register,** кáсса.

registrar *n.* регистрáтор.

registration *n.* регистрáция. —*adj.* регистрациóнный.

registry *n.* **1,** = **registration. 2,** (place of registration) регистратýра.

regress *v.i.* регресси́ровать. —**regression,** *n.* регрéсс. —**regressive,** *adj.* регресси́вный.

regret *v.t.* сожалéть; жалéть: *regret one's decision,* сожалéть/жалéть о своём решéнии. —*n.* **1,** (troubled feeling) сожалéние. *I have no regrets,* я не сожалéю об э́том. **2,** *pl.* (polite refusal) извинéния.

regretful *adj.* пóлный сожалéния. *Be regretful,* сожалéть.

regrettable *adj.* досáдный: *regrettable incident,* досáдный слýчай. —**regrettably,** *adv.* к сожалéнию.

regroup *v.t.* перегруппирóвывать. —*v.i.* перегруппирóвываться. —**regrouping,** *n.* перегруппирóвка.

regular *adj.* **1,** (recurring at set times) регуля́рный. **2,** (even, as of one's pulse or heartbeat) прáвильный. **3,** (steady) постоя́нный: *regular customer,* постоя́нный клиéнт. **4,** (customary) обы́чный: *one's regular place,* чьё-нибудь обы́чное мéсто. **5,** (regularly scheduled) очереднóй. **6,** (symmetrical, as of features) прáвильный. **7,** *gram.* прáвильный: *regular verb,* прáвильный глагóл. **8,** *mil.* регуля́рный; кáдровый. **9,** *colloq.* (out-and-out) настоя́щий. **10,** *slang* (likable) слáвный: *a regular guy,* слáвный мáлый. —**regularity,** *n.* регуля́рность; прáвильность. —**regularly,** *adv.* регуля́рно.

regulate *v.t.* регули́ровать.

regulation *n.* **1,** (act of regulating) регули́рование. **2,** (rule) прáвило. **3,** *pl.* (set of rules) прáвила; устáв. —*adj.* устáвный; устанóвленный.

regulator *n.* регуля́тор.

regurgitate *v.t.* изрыгáть; отры́гивать.

rehabilitate *v.t.* реабилити́ровать. —**rehabilitation,** *n.* реабилитáция.

rehash *n.* повторéние; перепéв.

rehearsal *n.* репети́ция. *Dress rehearsal,* генера́льная репети́ция.

rehearse *v.t. & i.* репети́ровать.

reheat *v.t.* разогрева́ть; подогрева́ть.

reign *n.* **1,** (period of rule) ца́рствование. *During the reign of Peter I,* в ца́рствование Петра́ Пе́рвого; при Петре́ Пе́рвом. **2,** (rule) власть: *reign of law,* власть зако́на. —*v.i.* **1,** (of a monarch) ца́рствовать. **2,** *fig.* (of silence, etc.) цари́ть; воцаря́ться. —**reigning,** *adj.* ца́рствующий.

reimburse *v.t.* возмеща́ть. —**reimbursement,** *n.* возмеще́ние.

rein *n.* **1,** (for a horse) по́вод (*pl.* пово́дья); вожжа́ (*pl.* во́жжи). **2,** *The reins of government,* бразды́ правле́ния. —*v.t.* [*usu.* **rein in**] оса́живать (ло́шадь). —**give free rein to,** дава́ть во́лю (+ *dat.*). —**keep a tight rein on,** держа́ть в узде́.

reincarnate *v.t.* перевоплоща́ть. —**reincarnation,** *n.* перевоплоще́ние.

reindeer *n.* се́верный оле́нь. —**reindeer moss,** оле́ний мох; я́гель.

reinforce *v.t.* уси́ливать; укрепля́ть; подкрепля́ть. —**reinforced concrete,** железобето́н.

reinforcement *n.* **1,** (strengthening) усиле́ние; укрепле́ние; подкрепле́ние. **2,** *pl., mil.* подкрепле́ния.

reinstate *v.t.* восстана́вливать в (пре́жней) до́лжности. —**reinstatement,** *n.* восстановле́ние в до́лжности.

reinsure *v.t.* перестрахо́вывать. —**reinsurance,** *n.* перестрахо́вка.

reinvest *v.t.* сно́ва вкла́дывать (де́ньги).

reissue *v.t.* переиздава́ть. —*n.* переизда́ние.

reiterate *v.t.* повторя́ть; тверди́ть. —**reiteration,** *n.* повторе́ние.

reject *v.t.* **1,** (turn down) отклоня́ть; отверга́ть. **2,** (discard because of defects) бракова́ть. —*n.* брак; брако́ванное изде́лие. —**rejection,** *n.* отка́з; отклоне́ние.

rejoice *v.i.* ра́доваться; ликова́ть. —**rejoicing,** *n.* ликова́ние.

rejoin *v.t.* **1,** (meet again after an interval) присоединя́ться к. **2,** (come back to) возвраща́ться к. **3,** (resume membership in) сно́ва присоединя́ться к.

rejoinder *n.* возраже́ние; ре́плика.

rejuvenate *v.t.* омола́живать. —**rejuvenation,** *n.* омоложе́ние.

relapse *v.i.* [*usu.* **relapse into**] (сно́ва) впада́ть в; (сно́ва) предава́ться (+ *dat.*). —*n.* рециди́в —**relapsing fever,** возвра́тный тиф.

relate *v.t.* **1,** (narrate) расска́зывать. **2,** (connect) свя́зывать. —*v.i.* [*usu.* **relate to**] относи́ться к.

related *adj.* **1,** (connected) свя́занный. **2,** (kindred) ро́дственный. *Be related to,* быть в родстве́ с; быть сродни́ (+ *dat.*). *How is he related to you?,* кем он вам прихо́дится?

relation *n.* **1,** (connection) отноше́ние; связь. **2,** (relative; kin) ро́дственник. **3,** *pl.* (dealings; intercourse) отноше́ния: *friendly/international/diplomatic relations,* дру́жеские/междунаро́дные/дипломати́ческие отноше́ния. *Sexual relations,* полова́я связь. —**in relation to,** в отноше́нии (+ *gen.*).

relationship *n.* **1,** (connection) отноше́ние; связь. **2,** (kinship) родство́.

relative *n.* ро́дственник: *distant relative,* да́льний ро́дственник. —*adj.* **1,** (comparative; not absolute) относи́тельный: *relative quiet,* относи́тельная тишина́. *Everything is relative,* всё относи́тельно. **2,** *fol. by* **to** (pertaining; relevant) относя́щийся (к). **3,** *gram.* относи́тельный: *relative pronoun,* относи́тельное местоиме́ние.

relatively *adv.* относи́тельно: *relatively happy,* относи́тельно сча́стлив. *Relatively speaking,* вообще́ говоря́.

relativity *n.* относи́тельность: *theory of relativity,* тео́рия относи́тельности.

relax *v.t.* **1,** (make less tight or strict) ослабля́ть. *Relax the muscles,* расслабля́ть мы́шцы. **2,** *fig.* (make less tense) разряжа́ть. —*v.i.* **1,** (become less tight) ослабева́ть. **2,** (take one's ease) отдыха́ть.

relaxation *n.* **1,** (making less tight or strict) ослабле́ние. **2,** (making less tense) разря́дка: *relaxation of tension,* разря́дка напряжённости. **3,** (rest) о́тдых. **4,** (recreation) развлече́ние.

relaxed *adj.* непринуждённый.

re-lay *v.t.* перекла́дывать. *Re-lay a floor,* перестила́ть пол.

relay *n.* **1,** (shift) сме́на. *Work in relays,* рабо́тать посме́нно. **2,** (race) эстафе́та. **3,** *electricity* реле́. —*v.t.* передава́ть. —**relay race,** эстафе́та; эстафе́тный бег.

relearn *v.t.* переу́чиваться (+ *dat.*).

release *v.t.* **1,** (let out; set free) выпуска́ть; освобожда́ть: *release from prison,* выпуска́ть/освобожда́ть из тюрьмы́. *Release a bird from a cage,* выпуска́ть *or* отпуска́ть пти́цу из кле́тки. **2,** (let go of) отпуска́ть; пуска́ть. **3,** (let loose against a target) выпуска́ть; пуска́ть: *release bombs,* выпуска́ть бо́мбы; *release an arrow,* пусти́ть стрелу́ из лу́ка. **4,** (disengage, as a brake) отпуска́ть (то́рмоз); (cause to snap, as a shutter) спуска́ть (затво́р). **5,** (relieve, as from an obligation) освобожда́ть. **6,** (allow to be known or published) выпуска́ть. —*n.* **1,** (act of releasing) освобожде́ние. **2,** (something issued or produced) вы́пуск.

relegate *v.t.* **1,** (consign) отсыла́ть. *Relegate to the background,* отодвига́ть на за́дний план. **2,** (refer; delegate) передава́ть.

relent *v.i.* смягча́ться.

relentless *adj.* неотсту́пный: *relentless pursuit,* неотсту́пное пресле́дование. —**relentlessness,** *n.* неотсту́пность.

relevance *n.* **1,** (relation) отноше́ние (к де́лу). **2,** (timeliness) актуа́льность.

relevant *adj.* **1,** (pertinent) относя́щийся к де́лу. **2,** (timely) актуа́льный.

reliable *adj.* **1,** (of a person) надёжный. **2,** (of information, a source, etc.) достове́рный. —**reliability,** *n.* надёжность; достове́рность.

reliance *n.* **1,** (dependence) зави́симость. *Place one's reliance on,* наде́яться на. **2,** (trust) дове́рие. **3,** (something relied on) наде́жда; опо́ра.

reliant *adj. Be reliant on,* полага́ться на; рассчи́тывать на.

relic *n.* **1,** (ancient object) рели́кт. **2,** (memento of the past) рели́квия: *relics of the past,* рели́квии про́шлого. **3,** (object of religious worship) рели́квия.

relief *n.* **1,** (easing of pain or anxiety) облегче́ние. *Sigh with relief,* вздохну́ть с облегче́нием (*or* облегчённо). **2,** (replacement) сме́на. **3,** (emergency aid) по́мощь. **4,** (financial assistance) посо́бие. **5,** (raised

decoration) рельéф. *In relief,* рельéфно. —**relief map,** рельéфная кáрта.
relieve *v.t.* **1,** (alleviate) облегчáть: *relieve pain,* облегчáть боль. *Relieve boredom,* развéять скýку. *Relieve the monotony,* вносить разнообрáзие. **2,** (reduce, as tension or pressure) ослаблять. **3,** (free from anxiety) успокáивать. *Feel relieved,* облегчáться. **4,** (free, as from a burden) освобождáть. **5,** (furnish aid to) окáзывать пóмощь (+ *dat.*). **6,** (remove; release) смещáть (с дóлжности); снимáть (с рабóты); отстранять; освобождáть (от дóлжности). **7,** (replace) сменять. —**relieve oneself,** "облегчáться".
religion *n.* религия. *Freedom of religion,* свобóда религии.
religiosity *n.* религиóзность.
religious *adj.* религиóзный: *religious man/custom,* религиóзный человéк/обычай. *Religious persecution,* преслéдование религии.
religiously *adv.* свято: *observe one's diet religiously,* свято соблюдáть диéту.
relinquish *v.t.* **1,** (give up) откáзываться от: *relinquish one's rights,* откáзываться от своих прав. *Relinquish one's seat/place to someone,* уступить мéсто (+ *dat.*). **2,** (let go): *relinquish one's hold on,* выпускáть из рук.
relish *n.* **1,** (enjoyment; zest) смак. **2,** (condiment) приправа. —*v.t.* наслаждáться; смаковáть. *I don't relish the prospect,* перспектива мне не улыбáется.
relive *v.t.* снóва пережи**вá**ть.
reload *v.t.* **1,** (transfer to another vehicle) перегружáть. **2,** (load again, as a vehicle) снóва грузить. **3,** (refill, as a camera or gun) перезаряжáть.
relocate *v.t.* перемещáть; переселять. —*v.i.* переселяться.
reluctance *n.* неохóта; нежелáние. —**reluctant,** *adj.* неохóтный. —**reluctantly,** *adv.* неохóтно; с неохóтой; нéхотя.
rely *v.i.* [*usu.* **rely on** *or* **upon**] полагáться на.
remain *v.i.* оставáться: *remain at home,* оставáться дóма. *Nothing remained,* ничегó не остáлось. *Remain silent,* хранить молчáние. *He remained faithful to his principles,* он остáлся вéрен своим принципам.
remainder *n.* остáток.
remaining *adj.* остальнóй.
remains *n.pl.* **1,** (remnants) остáтки. **2,** (dead body) остáнки; прах. *Mortal remains,* брéнные остáнки.
remake *v.t.* передéлывать.
remand *v.t.* возвращáть: *remand to custody,* возвращáть под стрáжу.
remark *n.* замечáние. —*v.t.* замечáть: *he remarked to me that...,* он замéтил мне, что... —*v.i.* [*usu.* **remark on**] (comment on) дéлать замечáние (о).
remarkable *adj.* замечáтельный; удивительный. —**remarkably,** *adv.* удивительно.
remarry *v.i.* вступáть в нóвый брак.
rematch *n.* ревáнш.
remeasure *v.t.* перемéривать.
remediable *adj.* исправимый.
remedial *adj.* коррективный: *remedial reading,* коррективное чтéние.
remedy *n.* срéдство: *remedy for a cough,* срéдство от кáшля. —*v.t.* **1,** (cure) вылéчивать. **2,** (correct) исправлять.
remember *v.t.* **1,** (recall) пóмнить: *what do you remember about him?,* что вы пóмните о нём? *Remember what I told you,* запóмните то, что я вам сказáл(а). *I can't remember his name,* я не могý вспóмнить егó имени. **2,** (mention in sending regards) клáняться: *remember me to your sister,* клáняйтесь вáшей сестрé. —*v.i.* пóмнить: *I don't remember,* я не пóмню. *I'll remember,* я бýду пóмнить. *Try to remember,* постарáйтесь вспóмнить.
remembrance *n.* **1,** (memory) пáмять: *in remembrance of,* в пáмять (+ *gen.*). **2,** (memento) сувенир: *a remembrance of our trip,* сувенир от нáшей поéздки.
remind *v.t.* напоминáть: *remind someone about a promise,* напóмнить комý-нибудь об обещáнии. *He reminds me of my brother,* он напоминáет мне моегó брáта. —**which reminds me,** а кстáти...
reminder *n.* напоминáние: *after repeated reminders,* пóсле неоднокрáтных напоминáний.
reminisce *v.i.* вспоминáть. —**reminiscence,** *n.* воспоминáние. —**reminiscent,** *adj.* напоминáющий: *be reminiscent of,* напоминáть.
remiss *adj.* небрéжный; невнимáтельный. *Be remiss in one's duties,* пренебрегáть своими обязанностями.
remission *n.* **1,** (pardon) отпущéние: *remission of sins,* отпущéние грехóв. **2,** *med.* ремиссия.
remit *v.t.* **1,** (send, as payment) переводить; пересылáть. **2,** (pardon; forgive) прощáть; отпускáть. **3,** (slacken) ослаблять. **4,** (refrain from exacting) прощáть; снимáть.
remittance *n.* перевóд (дéнег); пересылка.
remnant *n.* **1,** (remainder) остáток. **2,** (vestige) пережиток. **3,** (leftover piece of cloth) остáток.
remodel *v.t.* передéлывать.
remold *v.t.* перекóвывать.
remonstrance *n.* увещáние.
remonstrate *v.i.* **1,** *fol. by* **with** (exhort) увещевáть. **2,** *fol. by* **against** (protest; object) возражáть; протестовáть (прóтив).
remorse *n.* раскáяние. —**remorseful,** *adj.* пóлный раскáяния. —**remorseless,** *adj.* безжáлостный.
remote *adj.* отдалённый: *remote place/past/resemblance,* отдалённое мéсто/прóшлое/схóдство. *The chances of that are remote,* шáнсы на э́то незначительные. —**not the remotest,** ни малéйшего (понятия, представлéния, *etc.*). —**remote control,** дистанциóнное управлéние.
remoteness *n.* отдалённость.
remount *v.t. & i.* снóва сесть (на лóшадь).
removable *adj.* съёмный; сменяемый.
removal *n.* **1,** (taking out; taking away) удалéние. **2,** (taking down) съёмка. **3,** (moving to another place) перемещéние. **4,** (dismissal, as from office) смещéние (с дóлжности).
remove *v.t.* **1,** (take away) убирáть; удалять. **2,** (take out; draw out) вынимáть. **3,** (take out; extract) удалять. **4,** (take off; take down) снимáть. **5,** (move to another place) перемещáть. **6,** (eradicate, as a stain) выводить. **7,** (eliminate; get rid of) устранять. **8,** (dismiss, as from office) смещáть (с дóлжности). —*v.i.* переезжáть; переселяться. —**cousin twice removed,** брат (сестрá) во вторóм колéне.
remunerate *v.t.* вознаграждáть. —**remuneration,** *n.* вознаграждéние. —**remunerative,** *adj.* выгодный; дохóдный.

renaissance *n.* **1,** (rebirth) возрождéние. **2,** *cap., hist.* Возрождéние.

renal *adj.* пóчечный.

rename *v.t.* переименóвать. *The city was renamed in honor of Lenin,* гóроду бы́ло присвóено и́мя Лéнина.

renascence *n.* возрождéние. —**renascent,** *adj.* возрождáющийся.

rend *v.t.* рвать; разрывáть; раздирáть. *Rend the air,* сотрясáть вóздух.

render *v.t.* **1,** (give; provide) окáзывать: *render assistance,* окáзывать содéйствие. *Render homage,* окáзывать *or* воздавáть пóчести. *For services rendered,* за услу́ги. **2,** (submit, as a bill) предъявля́ть. **3,** (hand down, as a verdict) выноси́ть (пригóвор). **4,** (cause to be or become) *rendered by various verbs: render harmless,* обезврéживать; *render lifeless,* обескрóвливать. **5,** (translate) переводи́ть. **6,** (depict) изображáть. **7,** (perform) исполня́ть. **8,** (melt, as fat) топи́ть.

rendezvous *n.* **1,** (meeting) свидáние. **2,** (meeting place) мéсто свидáния. —*v.i.* встречáться.

rendition *n.* **1,** (performance) исполнéние. **2,** (translation) перевóд.

renegade *n.* отщепéнец; ренегáт.

renege *v.i.* **1,** *fol. by* **on** (go back on) нарушáть; не сдержáть. **2,** *cards* (revoke) дéлать ренóнс. —*n., cards* ренóнс.

renew *v.t.* **1,** (resume; extend) возобновля́ть. **2,** (make new again) обновля́ть. —**renewal,** *n.* возобновлéние; обновлéние.

rennet *n.* сычу́г.

rennin *n.* сычу́жный фермéнт; сычу́жина.

renounce *v.t.* отрекáться от; откáзываться от.

renovate *v.t.* обновля́ть; ремонти́ровать. —**renovation,** *n.* обновлéние; ремóнт.

renown *n.* слáва; извéстность. —**renowned,** *adj.* знамени́тый; прослáвленный.

rent *n.* **1,** (payment for lodgings) кварти́рная плáта. *Pay the rent,* плати́ть за кварти́ру. *How much rent do you pay?,* скóлько у вас кварти́рная плáта? **2,** *econ.* рéнта. —*v.t.* **1,** (obtain the use of, as an apartment) снимáть; брать внаём; (a car, equipment, etc.) брать напрокáт. **2,** (give the use of, as an apartment) сдавáть; давáть внаём; (a car, equipment, etc.) давáть напрокáт. —**for rent,** сдаётся внаём.

rental *n.* **1,** (of an apartment) арéнда; (of a car, equipment, etc.) прокáт. **2,** (money paid for use) арéндная плáта; плáта за прокáт.

renter *n.* арендáтор.

renumber *v.t.* перенумеровáть.

renunciation *n.* отречéние; откáз.

reoccur *v.i.* повторя́ться.

reopen *v.t.* вновь открывáть: *reopen the discussion,* вновь открывáть диску́ссию. *Reopen old wounds,* береди́ть стáрые рáны. —*v.i.* вновь открывáться.

reorder *v.t.* **1,** (order again) снóва закáзывать. **2,** (restructure) перестрáивать. —*v.i.* сдéлать повтóрный закáз. —*n.* повтóрный закáз.

reorganize *v.t.* реорганизовáть; перестрáивать; переустрáивать; преобразóвывать. —**reorganization,** *n.* реорганизáция; перестрóйка; переустрóйство; преобразовáние.

repaint *v.t.* перекрáшивать.

repair *v.t.* чини́ть; исправля́ть; ремонти́ровать. *Repair the damage,* исправля́ть повреждéние. —*v.i.* (go) направля́ться. —*n.* **1,** (act of repairing) ремóнт; почи́нка. *Closed for repairs,* закры́то на ремóнт. **2,** (working condition) исправность: *in good repair,* в испрáвности. —*adj.* ремóнтный: *repair shop,* ремóнтная мастерскáя.

repairable *adj.* исправи́мый. *Is it repairable?,* мóжно э́то испрáвить?

repairman *n.* мáстер: *TV repairman,* мáстер по ремóнту телеви́зоров.

reparable *adj.* исправи́мый.

reparations *n.pl.* репарáции.

repast *n.* едá.

repatriate *v.t.* репатрии́ровать. —*n.* репатриáнт. —**repatriation,** *n.* репатриáция.

repay *v.t.* **1,** (pay off, as a debt, loan, etc.) возвращáть; отдавáть; выплáчивать. **2,** (return a favor on the part of) отплáчивать (+ *dat.*): *how can I ever repay you?,* как я могу́ отплати́ть вам?

repayment *n.* **1,** (of money) вы́плата: *repayment of a loan,* вы́плата зáйма. **2,** (returning a favor or ill turn) отплáта.

repeal *v.t.* отменя́ть; аннули́ровать. —*n.* отмéна; аннули́рование.

repeat *v.t.* повторя́ть. *Repeat oneself/itself,* повторя́ться. —*n.* повторéние. —*adj.* повтóрный: *repeat order,* повтóрный закáз.

repeated *adj.* неоднокрáтный; многокрáтный. —**repeatedly,** *adv.* неоднокрáтно; многокрáтно.

repeater *n.* **1,** (pupil not promoted) второгóдник. **2,** (person more than once in jail) рецидиви́ст.

repeating *adj.* (of a firearm) магази́нный. —**repeating decimal,** периоди́ческая дробь.

repel *v.t.* **1,** (ward off) отражáть; отбивáть. **2,** (arouse repulsion in) оттáлкивать.

repellent *adj.* оттáлкивающий. —*n. Insect repellent,* срéдство от насекóмых.

repent *v.t. & i.* раскáиваться (в); кáяться (в). —**repentance,** *n.* раскáяние; покая́ние.

repentant *adj.* **1,** (feeling repentance) кáющийся: *repentant sinner,* кáющийся грéшник. **2,** (showing repentance) покая́нный: *repentant look,* покая́нный вид.

repercussion *n., usu. pl.* послéдствия.

repertoire *n.* репертуáр.

repertory *n.* **1,** (repertoire) репертуáр. **2,** (repository) храни́лище. —*adj.* репертуáрный.

repetition *n.* повторéние.

repetitious *adj.* повторя́ющийся. *Become repetitious,* начáть повторя́ться. *Also,* **repetitive.**

rephrase *v.t.* перефрази́ровать.

replace *v.t.* **1,** (put back) класть *or* стáвить обрáтно. **2,** (find a substitute for) заменя́ть: *replace old furniture,* заменя́ть стáрую мéбель. *Replace a window pane,* постáвить нóвое стеклó. *He will be hard to replace,* тру́дно бу́дет егó замени́ть. **3,** (take the place of) заменя́ть; сменя́ть; вытесня́ть. *There is no one to replace him,* нéкому егó замени́ть. *A replaced B as prime minister,* А смени́л Б на посту́ премьéр-мини́стра. *Electricity replaced gas as a means of illumination,* электри́чество замени́ло/вы́теснило газ как срéдство освещéния.

replaceable *adj.* замени́мый.

replacement *n.* **1,** (act of replacing; one who replaces) замéна. **2,** *mil.* пополнéние; *pl.* пополнéния.

replay *v.t.* переигрывать.

replenish *v.t.* пополня́ть; обновля́ть. —**replenishment,** *n.* пополне́ние; обновле́ние.
replete *adj.* изоби́лующий: *be replete with,* изоби́ловать (+ *instr.*).
replica *n.* ко́пия.
reply *v.t. & i.* отвеча́ть: *reply to an invitation,* отвеча́ть на приглаше́ние. —*n.* отве́т. *In reply to,* в отве́т на.
report *n.* **1,** (formal account) докла́д; отчёт. **2,** (message; communication) сообще́ние. **3,** (assessment) о́тзыв: *a favorable report,* благоприя́тный о́тзыв. **4,** (rumor) слух; молва́. —*v.t.* **1,** (convey; relate) сообща́ть (о): *report the latest news,* сообща́ть после́дние изве́стия. *Report an incident to the police,* сообща́ть о происше́ствии в мили́цию. **2,** (denounce to a person in authority) доноси́ть на. —*v.i.* **1,** (give a report) докла́дывать: *report on the situation,* докла́дывать обстано́вку. **2,** (present oneself; appear) явля́ться: *report for work,* явля́ться на рабо́ту.
report card та́бель (успева́емости).
reportedly *adv.* по слу́хам.
reporter *n.* репортёр.
repose *n.* **1,** (rest) о́тдых; отдохнове́ние. **2,** (tranquillity) поко́й; споко́йствие. —*v.t.* (place, as trust) возлага́ть. —*v.i.* **1,** (lie at rest) лежа́ть. **2,** (rest; relax) отдыха́ть. **3,** (rest in death) поко́иться.
repository *n.* храни́лище.
reprehensible *adj.* предосуди́тельный.
represent *v.t.* **1,** (symbolize; stand for) представля́ть; изобража́ть. *This figure represents good and this one evil,* э́та фигу́ра представля́ет добро́, а э́та — зло. *Phonetic symbols represent sounds,* фонети́ческие зна́ки изобража́ют зву́ки. **2,** (serve as the agent or representative of) представля́ть. **3,** (be; constitute) представля́ть (собо́й). *Represent nothing new,* не представля́ть собо́й ничего́ но́вого. —**répresent oneself as,** изобража́ть из себя́ (+ *acc.*); выдава́ть себя́ за.
representation *n.* **1,** (being represented) представи́тельство: *proportional representation,* пропорциона́льное представи́тельство. **2,** (picture; image) изображе́ние. **3,** (formal statement or protest) представле́ние: *make representations to,* де́лать представле́ния (+ *dat.*).
representative *n.* представи́тель. —*adj.* **1,** (based on the principle of representation) представи́тельный. **2,** (typical) характе́рный. —**House of Representatives,** пала́та представи́телей.
repress *v.t.* подавля́ть; сде́рживать.
repression *n.* **1,** (suppression) подавле́ние. **2,** (practice of repressing) репре́ссия. *Political repression,* полити́ческие репре́ссии.
repressive *adj.* репресси́вный.
reprieve *n.* отсро́чка приведе́ния в исполне́ние (сме́ртного) пригово́ра.
reprimand *n.* вы́говор. —*v.t.* де́лать вы́говор (+ *dat.*).
reprint *v.t.* перепеча́тывать. —*n.* перепеча́тка; о́ттиск.
reprisal *n., often pl.* отве́тная ме́ра: *economic reprisals,* отве́тные экономи́ческие ме́ры.
reprise *n.* репри́за.
reproach *v.t.* упрека́ть; укоря́ть. —*n.* упрёк; уко́р. *Beyond reproach,* безупре́чный. —**reproachful,** *adj.* укори́зненный.
reprobate *n.* распу́тник. —*adj.* распу́тный.
reprobation *n.* порица́ние; осужде́ние.
reproduce *v.t.* воспроизводи́ть: *reproduce a picture,* воспроизводи́ть карти́ну. —*v.i.* размножа́ться: *reproduce by cellular division,* размножа́ться клéточным деле́нием.
reproduction *n.* **1,** (act of reproducing) воспроизведе́ние. **2,** (copy; facsimile) репроду́кция. **3,** (propagation) размноже́ние.
reproductive *adj.* воспроизводи́тельный. *Reproductive organs,* о́рганы размноже́ния.
reproof *n.* вы́говор; замеча́ние; упрёк; о́тповедь.
reprove *v.t.* упрека́ть; сде́лать вы́говор *or* замеча́ние (+ *dat.*).
reptile *n.* пресмыка́ющееся.
republic *n.* респу́блика.
republican *n.* республика́нец. —*adj.* республика́нский.
republish *v.t.* переиздава́ть. —**republication,** *n.* переизда́ние.
repudiate *v.t.* **1,** (renounce; disavow) отрека́ться от; отка́зываться от. **2,** (reject as untrue) отрица́ть. **3,** (reject with disapproval) отверга́ть.
repudiation *n.* **1,** (disavowal) отрече́ние; отка́з. **2,** (rejection; rebuff) отпо́р.
repugnance *n.* отвраще́ние.
repugnant *adj.* отта́лкивающий; отврати́тельный. *Be repugnant to,* отта́лкивать.
repulse *v.t.* **1,** (repel) отража́ть; отбива́ть. **2,** (rebuff) дать отпо́р (+ *dat.*). —*n.* отпо́р.
repulsion *n.* **1,** (repulsing) отраже́ние. **2,** (repugnance) отвраще́ние.
repulsive *adj.* отта́лкивающий; отврати́тельный.
repurchase *v.t.* перекупа́ть.
reputable *adj.* соли́дный; по́льзующийся хоро́шей репута́цией.
reputation *n.* репута́ция.
repute *n.* репута́ция.
reputed *adj.* предполага́емый. —**be reputed to be,** слыть (+ *instr.*): *he is reputed to be an expert,* он слывёт знатоко́м.
request *n.* про́сьба. *At the request of,* по про́сьбе (+ *gen.*). —*v.t.* проси́ть: *request permission,* проси́ть разреше́ния. —**on/by request,** по про́сьбе; по тре́бованию.
requiem *n.* панихи́да; ре́квием.
require *v.t.* тре́бовать: *require constant care,* тре́бовать постоя́нного ухо́да.
required *adj.* **1,** (needed; necessary) потре́бный. **2,** (compulsory, as of a subject) обяза́тельный. **3,** *fol. by* **to** (obliged) обя́зан (+ *inf.*).
requirement *n.* **1,** (condition; prerequisite) тре́бование: *meet the requirements,* отвеча́ть тре́бованиям. **2,** (need) потре́бность.
requisite *adj.* необходи́мый; потре́бный.
requisition *v.t.* реквизи́ровать. —*n.* тре́бование; зая́вка.
requital *n.* взаи́мность: *without requital,* без взаи́мности.
requite *v.t.* **1,** (return) отпла́чивать. *Requite someone's love,* отвеча́ть кому́-нибудь взаи́мностью. **2,** (avenge) вымеща́ть (оби́ду).
reread *v.t.* перечи́тывать.
resale *n.* перепрода́жа.

rescind *v.t.* отменя́ть; аннули́ровать. —**rescission,** *n.* отме́на; аннули́рование.
rescue *v.t.* спаса́ть; избавля́ть. —*n.* спасе́ние. *Come to the rescue of,* приходи́ть на по́мощь (+ *dat.*). —*adj.* спаса́тельный: *rescue operations,* спаса́тельные опера́ции; *rescue party,* спаса́тельная кома́нда.
rescuer *n.* спаси́тель.
research *n.* иссле́дование. —*adj.* иссле́довательский: *research work,* иссле́довательская рабо́та. —*v.t.* иссле́довать. —**researcher,** *n.* иссле́дователь.
resection *n., med.* резе́кция.
resell *v.t.* перепродава́ть.
resemblance *n.* схо́дство.
resemble *v.t.* быть похо́жим на: *he resembles his father,* он похо́ж на отца́.
resent *v.t.* обижа́ться на; негодова́ть на. —**resentful,** *adj.* оби́женный. —**resentment,** *n.* оби́да.
reservation *n.* **1,** (limiting condition) огово́рка: *without reservation,* без огово́рок; безогово́рочно. **2,** (advance order) бро́ня: *I have a reservation,* у меня́ бро́ня. *Make a reservation,* брони́ровать ме́сто; сде́лать предвари́тельный зака́з. **3,** (reserve for Indians) резерва́ция.
reserve *v.t.* **1,** (set aside) откла́дывать: *reserve one copy for me,* отложи́те оди́н экземпля́р для меня́. *Reserve a book in the library,* откла́дывать кни́гу в библиоте́ке. *These seats are reserved for tourists,* э́ти места́ предназна́чены для тури́стов. **2,** (secure in advance) брони́ровать; зака́зывать. *Reserve a room in a hotel,* брони́ровать но́мер в гости́нице. *Reserve a table for two,* заказа́ть стол на двои́х. **3,** (retain for oneself, as a right) сохраня́ть *or* оставля́ть за собо́й. **4,** (defer) откла́дывать. *Reserve judgment,* воздержа́ться от сужде́ния. —*n.* **1,** (something kept for future use) запа́с; резе́рв. *Hold in reserve,* держа́ть про запа́с. **2,** (reservation of public land) запове́дник: *forest reserve,* лесно́й запове́дник. **3,** (qualification; reservation) огово́рка: *without reserve,* без огово́рок. **4,** (reticence) сде́ржанность. **5,** *often pl., mil.* запа́с; резе́рв. **6,** *finance* резе́рвный фонд. **7,** *sports* запасно́й игро́к. —*adj.* запасно́й. *Reserve officer,* офице́р запа́са.
reserved *adj.* **1,** (secured in advance) заброни́рованный. *Reserved seat,* нумеро́ванное ме́сто. **2,** (reticent) сде́ржанный.
reservist *n.* резерви́ст; запасно́й.
reservoir *n.* водохрани́лище; резервуа́р.
reset *v.t.* **1,** *med.* вправля́ть. **2,** *printing* перебира́ть.
resettle *v.t.* переселя́ть. —*v.i.* переселя́ться. —**resettlement,** *n.* переселе́ние.
reshoot *v.t.* переснима́ть.
reshuffle *v.t.* перетасо́вывать. —*n.* перетасо́вка. *Cabinet reshuffle,* перемеще́ния в кабине́те.
reside *v.i.* прожива́ть; жить.
residence *n.* **1,** (act of residing) прожива́ние. *Residence permit,* пропи́ска. **2,** (dwelling place) местожи́тельство; местопребыва́ние; резиде́нция.
resident *n.* жи́тель. —**residential,** *adj.* жило́й: *residential area,* жило́й райо́н.
residue *n.* оста́ток. —**residual,** *adj.* оста́точный.
resign *v.i.* **1,** (give up one's office or position) уходи́ть *or* выходи́ть в отста́вку. **2,** *chess* сдава́ться. —*v.t.* отка́зываться от (до́лжности). —**resign oneself to; become resigned to,** покоря́ться (+ *dat.*); мири́ться с.
resignation *n.* **1,** (act of resigning) отста́вка: *submit one's resignation,* подава́ть в отста́вку. **2,** (being resigned to something) смире́ние.
resilient *adj.* упру́гий. —**resilience,** *n.* упру́гость.
resin *n.* смола́. —**resinous,** *adj.* смоли́стый.
resist *v.t.* **1,** (try to stop) сопротивля́ться: *resist the invaders,* сопротивля́ться захва́тчикам. *Resist someone's advances,* отверга́ть чьи́-нибудь уха́живания. **2,** (withstand, as temptation) усто́ять про́тив *or* пе́ред; удержа́ться от. *The offer is hard to resist,* от э́того предложе́ния тру́дно отказа́ться. **3,** (restrain oneself) выде́рживать: *I couldn't resist teasing him,* я не вы́держал (*or* я не мог удержа́ться от собла́зна), что́бы не подразни́ть его́. —*v.i.* сопротивля́ться; ока́зывать сопротивле́ние.
resistance *n.* **1,** (act of resisting) сопротивле́ние. *Resistance movement,* движе́ние сопротивле́ния. **2,** *med.* сопротивля́емость. —**follow the line of least resistance,** идти́ по ли́нии наиме́ньшего сопротивле́ния.
resistant *adj.* сто́йкий. *Heat-resistant,* теплосто́йкий. *Rust-resistant,* нержаве́ющий.
resolute *adj.* реши́тельный; твёрдый. —**resoluteness,** *n.* реши́тельность; реши́мость; твёрдость.
resolution *n.* **1,** (act of solving or resolving) разреше́ние. **2,** (formal expression of opinion) резолю́ция. **3,** (vow; pledge) заро́к.
resolve *v.t.* **1,** (decide) реша́ть; реша́ться. **2,** (express by resolution) постановля́ть. **3,** (solve; settle) разреша́ть. *Resolve doubts,* разреша́ть сомне́ния. —*n.* **1,** (determination) реши́мость. **2,** (decision; resolution) твёрдое реше́ние.
resonance *n.* резона́нс. —**resonant,** *adj.* зву́чный; гу́лкий.
resonator *n.* резона́тор.
resort *v.i.* [*usu.* **resort to**] прибега́ть к. —*n.* **1,** (vacation spot) куро́рт. **2,** (recourse) ресу́рс: *last resort,* после́дний ресу́рс. *As a last resort,* в кра́йнем слу́чае. *Have resort to,* прибега́ть к. *Without resort to,* не прибега́я к. —*adj.* куро́ртный: *resort area,* куро́ртный райо́н.
resound *v.i.* **1,** (sound; be heard) раздава́ться; резони́ровать. **2,** (be filled with the sound of) оглаша́ться (+ *instr.*).
resounding *adj.* **1,** (reverberating) зво́нкий; зву́чный; зы́чный; гу́лкий. **2,** (decisive) реши́тельный.
resource *n.* **1,** (source of help) ресу́рс. **2,** *pl.* (assets; wealth) ресу́рсы; бога́тства: *natural resources,* приро́дные ресу́рсы; есте́ственные бога́тства. *Pool one's resources,* объединя́ть ресу́рсы.
resourceful *adj.* нахо́дчивый. —**resourcefulness,** *n.* нахо́дчивость.
respect *v.t.* уважа́ть. —*n.* **1,** (esteem) уваже́ние. **2,** *pl.* (expressions of esteem) почте́ние: *pay one's respects to,* (за)свиде́тельствовать почте́ние (+ *dat.*). *Pay one's last respects to,* отдава́ть после́дний долг (+ *dat.*). **3,** (aspect) отноше́ние: *in many respects,* во мно́гих отноше́ниях. —**in/with respect to,** в отноше́нии (+ *gen.*).
respectable *adj.* **1,** (proper; presentable) приличный; респекта́бельный. **2,** (fairly good or large) прили́чный; поря́дочный. —**respectability,** *n.* респекта́бельность.

respected *adj.* уважа́емый.
respectful *adj.* почти́тельный; уважи́тельный.
respectfully *adv.* почти́тельно. —**respectfully yours,** с почте́нием.
respecting *prep.* относи́тельно; по отноше́нию к.
respective *adj.* свой: *in their respective places,* ка́ждый на своём ме́сте.
respectively *adv.* соотве́тственно.
respiration *n.* дыха́ние. —**respirator,** *n.* респира́тор. —**respiratory,** *adj.* дыха́тельный.
respire *v.i. & t.* дыша́ть.
respite *n.* переды́шка. *Without respite,* без переды́шки.
resplendent *adj.* блиста́тельный. —**resplendence,** *n.* блеск.
respond *v.i.* [*usu.* **respond to**] отвеча́ть (на); отзыва́ться (на); отклика́ться (на). *Respond to treatment,* поддава́ться лече́нию.
response *n.* **1,** (answer) отве́т. **2,** (reaction) о́тклик.
responsibility *n.* **1,** (accountability) отве́тственность. *Position of responsibility,* отве́тственный пост. **2,** (duty) обя́занность.
responsible *adj.* **1,** (accountable) отве́тственный. *Be responsible for,* отвеча́ть за; нести́ отве́тственность за. **2,** (being the cause of): *the person responsible for a crime,* вино́вник преступле́ния. *He is responsible for my being here,* благодаря́ емý я здесь. **3,** (reliable) надёжный. **4,** (entailing great responsibility) отве́тственный.
responsive *adj.* отзы́вчивый.
rest *n.* **1,** (relaxation) о́тдых. **2,** (peace and quiet) поко́й. **3,** (absence of motion) поко́й: *at rest,* в поко́е. *Come to rest,* сади́ться. **4,** *music* па́уза. **5,** (the remainder) оста́ток; остально́е. *The rest of the time,* остально́е вре́мя. **6,** (the remaining ones) остальны́е. —*v.i.* **1,** (relax) отдыха́ть. **2,** (lean; be supported) опира́ться. **3,** (fall, as of blame, a duty, etc.) лежа́ть. **4,** *fol. by* **upon** (be based upon) осно́вываться (на). —*v.t.* **1,** (place) класть; ста́вить. **2,** (lean) опира́ть. **3,** (allow to rest) дать отдохну́ть (+ *dat.*). —**eternal rest,** ве́чный поко́й. *Go to one's eternal rest,* засну́ть ве́чным сном. —**lay to rest,** хорони́ть. —**may he rest in peace,** мир пра́ху его́. —**put to rest,** рассе́ивать (сомне́ния). —**rest!** *(mil. command),* во́льно!
restate *v.t.* вновь заяви́ть.
restaurant *n.* рестора́н.
restful *adj.* споко́йный. *Restful color,* споко́йный цвет.
rest home дом о́тдыха.
restitution *n.* **1,** (restoration) восстановле́ние. **2,** (reimbursement) возмеще́ние убы́тков. *Make restitution,* возмеща́ть убы́тки.
restive *adj.* **1,** (restless) беспоко́йный; непосе́дливый. **2,** (balky, as of a horse) норови́стый.
restless *adj.* беспоко́йный; непосе́дливый. —**restlessness,** *n.* беспоко́йство; непосе́дливость.
restoration *n.* **1,** (bringing back) восстановле́ние. **2,** (repair; rebuilding; restoring of a monarchy) реставра́ция.
restore *v.t.* **1,** (bring back; re-establish) восстана́вливать: *restore order,* восстанови́ть поря́док. *Be restored to health,* восстанови́ть своё здоро́вье. *The king was restored to the throne,* коро́ль был возвращён на престо́л. **2,** (bring back to its original state) реставри́ровать. **3,** (return; give back) возвраща́ть.
restrain *v.t.* сде́рживать; уде́рживать; обу́здывать.
restraint *n.* **1,** (act of restraining) обузда́ние. **2,** (limitation) ограниче́ние: *wage restraints,* ограниче́ния за́работной пла́ты. **3,** (reserve; moderation) сде́ржанность.
restrict *v.t.* ограни́чивать. *Restricted area,* запре́тная зо́на. —**restriction,** *n.* ограниче́ние. —**restrictive,** *adj.* ограничи́тельный.
rest room туале́т; убо́рная.
result *n.* результа́т; сле́дствие. *As a result (of),* в результа́те (+ *gen.*). —*v.i.* **1,** (happen) вытека́ть; происходи́ть; проистека́ть. **2,** *fol. by* **in** (lead to) приводи́ть (к); конча́ться (+ *instr.*).
resultant *adj.* вытека́ющий.
resume *v.t.* **1,** (start again after a break) возобновля́ть. **2,** (assume again) сно́ва принима́ть. *Resume one's seat,* сно́ва сесть. —*v.i.* возобновля́ться.
résumé *n.* резюме́.
resumption *n.* возобновле́ние.
resurgence *n.* возрожде́ние. —**resurgent,** *adj.* возрожда́ющийся.
resurrect *v.t.* воскреша́ть.
resurrection *n.* **1,** (returning to life) воскресе́ние. **2,** *fig.* (revival) возрожде́ние; воскреше́ние.
resuscitate *v.t.* оживля́ть; приводи́ть в созна́ние. —**resuscitation,** *n.* оживле́ние.
retail *n.* ро́зничная прода́жа. —*adj.* ро́зничный: *retail store,* ро́зничный магази́н. —*adv.* в ро́зницу. —*v.t. & i.* продава́ть(ся) в ро́зницу. —**retailer,** *n.* ро́зничный торго́вец.
retain *v.t.* **1,** (keep possession of) уде́рживать: *retain power,* уде́рживать власть. **2,** (maintain; keep) сохраня́ть: *retain control over,* сохраня́ть контро́ль над. **3,** (hold within) заде́рживать: *retain moisture,* заде́рживать вла́гу. **4,** (remember) уде́рживать в па́мяти; запомина́ть. **5,** (hire) нанима́ть.
retainer *n.* **1,** (servant) приближённый. **2,** (fee) (предвари́тельный) гонора́р.
retaining wall подпо́рная сте́нка.
retake *v.t.* **1,** (recapture) отбива́ть; отвоёвывать. **2,** (photograph again) переснима́ть. **3,** (take again, as an examination) пересдава́ть; переде́рживать.
retaliate *v.i.* **1,** (repay in kind) отпла́чивать тем же. **2,** *mil.* наноси́ть отве́тный уда́р. —**retaliation,** *n.* отпла́та; отве́тный уда́р. —**retaliatory,** *adj.* отве́тный.
retard *v.t.* заде́рживать; замедля́ть; тормози́ть.
retardation *n.* **1,** (act of retarding) торможе́ние. **2,** (mental deficiency) у́мственная отста́лость *or* нера́звитость.
retarded *adj.* отста́лый.
retch *v.i.* рвать. —**retching,** *n.* рво́та.
retell *v.t.* переска́зывать.
retention *n.* **1,** (keeping for oneself) удержа́ние. **2,** (maintaining; keeping) сохране́ние. **3,** (holding within) задержа́ние. **4,** (ability to remember) па́мять.
retentive *adj.* це́пкий: *retentive memory,* це́пкая па́мять.
reticent *adj.* сде́ржанный; молчали́вый. —**reticence,** *n.* сде́ржанность; молчали́вость.
retie *v.t.* перевя́зывать.
retighten *v.t.* перетя́гивать.
retina *n.* сетча́тка; се́тчатая оболо́чка; рети́на. —**detached retina,** отсло́йка сетча́тки; отсло́йка се́тчатой оболо́чки.
retinue *n.* сви́та.

retire *v.i.* **1,** (withdraw) удаля́ться. **2,** (give up one's work or career) вы́йти *or* уйти́ в отста́вку *or* на пе́нсию. **3,** (go to bed) ложи́ться спать. —*v.t.* **1,** (relieve of duty) увольня́ть в отста́вку. **2,** (withdraw from circulation) изыма́ть из обраще́ния. —**retired,** *adj.* в отста́вке; отставно́й.

retiree *n.* пенсионе́р.

retirement *n.* **1,** (act of retiring) отста́вка. **2,** (seclusion) уедине́ние.

retiring *adj.* скро́мный; засте́нчивый.

retort *v.i.* (ре́зко) отве́тить. —*n.* **1,** (quick, sharp reply) возраже́ние; ре́плика. **2,** (vessel) ко́лба; рето́рта.

retouch *v.t.* **1,** (touch up) подправля́ть. **2,** *photog.* ретуши́ровать. —**retoucher,** *n.* ретуше́р. —**retouching,** *n.* ре́тушь.

retrace *v.t.* **1,** (go back over, as one's steps) возвраща́ться по (свои́м следа́м). **2,** (trace the history of) просле́живать.

retract *v.t.* **1,** (pull in) втя́гивать. *Retract the landing gear,* убира́ть шасси́. **2,** (take back; disavow) отка́зываться от; брать наза́д. —**retraction,** *n.* опроверже́ние: *print a retraction,* печа́тать опроверже́ние.

retrain *v.t.* переу́чивать; переквалифици́ровать. —**retraining,** *n.* переквалифика́ция.

retreat *v.i.* отступа́ть: *retreat from danger,* отступа́ть пе́ред опа́сностью. *Retreat a few steps,* отступи́ть на не́сколько шаго́в. —*n.* **1,** (withdrawal) отступле́ние. *Beat a retreat,* бить отбо́й. **2,** (signal to retreat; bugle call at sunset) отбо́й. *Sound retreat,* дава́ть *or* бить отбо́й. **3,** (secluded place) прию́т; приста́нище.

retrench *v.i.* сокраща́ть расхо́ды; эконо́мить.

retrial *n.* повто́рное слу́шание де́ла.

retribution *n.* возме́здие.

retrieval *n.* возвраще́ние. *Retrieval of information,* по́иск информа́ции.

retrieve *v.t.* взять обра́тно. —**retriever,** *n.* охо́тничья соба́ка.

retroactive *adj.* име́ющий обра́тную си́лу (*or* обра́тное де́йствие). *Make retroactive to January 1,* счита́ть вступи́вшим в си́лу с пе́рвого января́.

retrograde *adj.* обра́тный: *retrograde motion,* обра́тное движе́ние.

retrogress *v.i.* регресси́ровать. —**retrogression,** *n.* регре́сс. —**retrogressive,** *adj.* регресси́вный.

retro-rocket *n.* тормозна́я раке́та.

retrospect *n., in* **in retrospect,** огля́дываясь наза́д.

retrospection *n.* ретроспе́кция. —**retrospective,** *adj.* ретроспекти́вный.

retry *v.t.* сно́ва слу́шать (де́ло); сно́ва суди́ть (обвиня́емого).

return *v.i.* возвраща́ться: *return home,* возвраща́ться домо́й. —*v.t.* **1,** (give back) отдава́ть; возвраща́ть. **2,** (put back) класть обра́тно. **3,** (reciprocate) отвеча́ть на: *return the enemy's fire,* отвеча́ть на ого́нь проти́вника. *Return a favor,* отвеча́ть услу́гой за услу́гу. *Return a visit,* нанести́ отве́тный визи́т; прийти́ с отве́тным визи́том. *Have him return my call,* пусть он мне позвони́т; попроси́те его́ мне позвони́ть. **4,** (yield, as a profit) приноси́ть. **5,** (render, as a verdict) выноси́ть. **6,** (elect) избира́ть; (re-elect) переизбира́ть. **7,** *sports* отбива́ть (мяч). —*n.* **1,** (act of returning) возвраще́ние; возвра́т. **2,** (profit; yield) дохо́д. **3,** (report, as on taxes) деклара́ция. **4,** *pl.* (election returns) результа́ты вы́боров. —*adj.* **1,** (in the opposite direction) обра́тный: *return ticket/address,* обра́тный биле́т/а́дрес. *By return mail,* с обра́тной по́чтой. **2,** (done or held in return) отве́тный: *return visit,* отве́тный визи́т. *Return match,* рева́нш; матч-рева́нш. —**in return,** взаме́н: *receive nothing in return,* ничего́ не получи́ть взаме́н. —**in return for,** в отве́т на; в обме́н на; в отпла́ту за. —**many happy returns of the day,** поздравля́ю вас с днём рожде́ния; жела́ю вам до́лгих лет жи́зни.

retype *v.t.* перепеча́тывать.

reunification *n.* воссоедине́ние.

reunion *n.* встре́ча; сбор.

reunite *v.t.* воссоединя́ть. —*v.i.* воссоединя́ться.

reupholster *v.t.* перебива́ть.

reuse *v.t.* повто́рно испо́льзовать.

revamp *v.t.* переде́лывать; перекра́ивать.

revanchism *n.* реванши́зм. —**revanchist,** *n.* реванши́ст. —*adj.* реванши́стский.

reveal *v.t.* **1,** (show; uncover; display) пока́зывать; обнару́живать: *reveal one's face/feelings,* пока́зывать/обнару́живать своё лицо́/свои́ чу́вства/. **2,** (disclose; divulge) раскрыва́ть. *Reveal a secret,* раскры́ть *or* откры́ть секре́т. —**revealing,** *adj.* показа́тельный; знамена́тельный.

reveille *n.* побу́дка; подъём; (у́тренняя) заря́.

revel *v.i.* **1,** (carouse) пирова́ть; кути́ть. **2,** *fol. by* **in** (delight in) наслажда́ться (+ *instr.*); упива́ться (+ *instr.*).

revelation *n.* **1,** (act of revealing) раскры́тие. **2,** (something revealed): *new revelations have come to light,* но́вые све́дения всплы́ли нару́жу. **3,** (striking discovery) открове́ние: *it was quite a revelation to me,* для меня́ э́то бы́ло настоя́щим открове́нием. **4,** *cap., Bib.* апока́липсис.

reveler *also,* **reveller** *n.* кути́ла; гуля́ка.

revelry *n.* весе́лье.

revenge *n.* **1,** (vengeance) месть; мще́ние. *In revenge for,* в отме́стку за. *Take revenge,* мстить. **2,** (reversal of a defeat) рева́нш: *gain revenge,* взять рева́нш. —*v.t.* мстить за; вымеща́ть.

revengeful *adj.* мсти́тельный.

revenue *n.* дохо́д.

reverberate *v.i.* отража́ться; отдава́ться. —**reverberation,** *n.* ревербера́ция.

revere *v.t.* почита́ть; благогове́ть.

reverence *n.* **1,** (veneration) почте́ние; благогове́ние. **2,** *cap.* (title) преподо́бие.

reverend *adj., usu. cap.* его́ преподо́бие (+ *name*).

reverent *adj.* почти́тельный; благогове́йный.

reverie *n.* мечта́ние; мечта́тельность. *Indulge in reverie,* предава́ться мечта́м.

reversal *n.* **1,** (complete change) измене́ние; пере-ме́на. **2,** *law* отме́на; аннули́рование.

reverse *adj.* обра́тный: *in reverse order,* в обра́тном поря́дке. *Reverse gear,* за́дний ход. —*n.* **1,** *preceded by* **the** (opposite) обра́тное; противополо́жное. *Quite the reverse,* совсе́м наоборо́т. **2,** (setback) неуда́ча. **3,** (backward motion) за́дний ход: *put a car in reverse,* дать за́дний ход. —*v.t.* **1,** (turn about) повора́чивать круго́м. **2,** (turn inside out) вывёртывать. **3,** (turn upside down) перевёртывать. **4,** (change completely) по́лностью изменя́ть: *reverse one's opinion,* по́лностью измени́ть своё мне́ние. **5,** (transpose) переставля́ть: *reverse two chapters in a book,* переставля́ть две главы́ в кни́ге. *Reverse the* *order of something,* изменить порядок чего-нибудь на обратный. **6,** *law* (set aside; overturn) отменять; аннулировать. —**reverse oneself,** давать задний ход.

reversible *adj.* **1,** (that can be reversed) обратимый. **2,** (worn on either side) двусторонний. —**reversibility,** *n.* обратимость.

reversion *n.* возвращение.

revert *v.i.* возвращаться: *revert to one's old habits,* возвращаться к старым привычкам.

revet *v.t.* облицовывать. —**revetment,** *n.* облицовка.

review *n.* **1,** (re-examination) рассмотрение; пересмотр. *The matter is under review,* дело сейчас рассматривается. **2,** (critique) рецензия; отзыв. *Book review,* рецензия на книгу. *Get rave reviews,* получить восторженные отзывы. **3,** (survey) обзор. **4,** (restudying, as of lessons) повторение. **5,** *mil.* смотр: *review of the troops,* смотр войскам. **6,** (journal) обозрение. —*v.t.* **1,** (reconsider) рассматривать; пересматривать. **2,** (go over, as a lesson) повторять. **3,** (write a review of) рецензировать. **4,** *mil.* принимать (парад); производить смотр (войскам).

reviewer *n.* рецензент.

reviewing stand трибуна.

revile *v.t.* поносить; ругать.

revise *v.t.* **1,** (alter; change) пересматривать. **2,** (reedit; rework) перерабатывать. *Revised edition,* исправленное издание.

revision *n.* **1,** (act of revising) пересмотр (программы); переработка (книги). **2,** (change; correction) изменение; поправка. **3,** (revised edition) переработка.

revisionism *n.* ревизионизм. —**revisionist,** *n.* ревизионист. —*adj.* ревизионистский.

revisit *v.t.* вновь посетить.

revitalize *v.t.* оживлять; обновлять.

revival *n.* **1,** (resuscitation) оживление. **2,** (restoration; renascence) оживление; возрождение. **3,** (restaging) возобновление (постановки).

revive *v.t.* **1,** (resuscitate) оживлять; приводить в себя *or* в сознание. **2,** (bring back; restore) возрождать; воскрешать. **3,** (bring back to mind) воскрешать в памяти. **4,** (produce or exhibit again) возобновлять. —*v.i.* **1,** (regain consciousness) очнуться. **2,** (regain vigor) оживать: *the flowers revived in water,* цветы в воде ожили. **3,** (come back into existence) воскресать; возрождаться. *Hope revived,* надежда воскресла.

revocation *n.* отмена; аннулирование.

revoke *v.t.* отменять; аннулировать. —*v.i., cards* делать ренонс. —*n., cards* ренонс.

revolt *v.i.* (rebel) восставать. —*v.t.* (disgust) вызывать отвращение у; отталкивать. —*n.* восстание; мятеж. —**revolting,** *adj.* отвратительный; отталкивающий.

revolution *n.* **1,** (political upheaval; momentous change) революция. **2,** (rotation) оборот: *70 revolutions per minute,* семьдесят оборотов в минуту.

revolutionary *adj.* революционный. —*n.* [*also,* **revolutionist**] революционер.

revolutionize *v.t.* революционизировать.

revolve *v.i.* вращаться; вертеться: *revolve around the sun,* вращаться/вертеться вокруг Солнца.

revolver *n.* револьвер.

revolving *adj.* вращающийся. —**revolving door,** вращающаяся дверь; вертушка.

revue *n.* обозрение; ревю.

revulsion *n.* отвращение.

reward *n.* награда. *Get one's just reward,* получить по заслугам. —*v.t.* награждать; вознаграждать. *Our patience has been rewarded,* наше терпение вознаграждено. —**rewarding,** *adj.* выгодный; полезный.

rewind *v.t.* перематывать.

reword *v.t.* переделывать; переписывать; перефразировать.

rework *v.t.* перерабатывать.

rewrite *v.t.* **1,** (write again) переписывать. **2,** (revise) перерабатывать.

rhapsody *n.* рапсодия.

rhenium *n.* рений.

rheostat *n.* реостат.

rhetoric *n.* риторика. —**rhetorical,** *adj.* риторический.

rheumatic *adj.* ревматический. —*n.* ревматик. —**rheumatic fever,** суставной ревматизм.

rheumatism *n.* ревматизм.

rhinestone *n.* искусственный бриллиант.

rhinoceros *n.* носорог.

rhizome *n.* корневище.

rhodium *n.* родий.

rhododendron *n.* рододендрон.

rhombic *adj.* ромбический.

rhomboid *n.* ромбоид.

rhombus *n.* ромб.

rhubarb *n.* ревень. —*adj.* ревенный.

rhyme *n.* рифма. —*v.t.* рифмовать. —*v.i.* рифмоваться. —**without rhyme or reason,** ни с того ни с сего.

rhymer *n.* рифмач; рифмоплёт. *Also,* **rhymester.**

rhythm *n.* ритм. —**rhythmic; rhythmical,** *adj.* ритмический; ритмичный. —**rhythmics,** *n.* ритмика.

rib *n.* **1,** *anat.* ребро. *Poke someone in the ribs,* толкнуть кого-нибудь в бок. **2,** (raised stripe in cloth) рубчик. —*v.t., colloq.* (tease) поддразнивать.

ribald *adj.* скабрёзный; неприличный. —**ribaldry,** *n.* скабрёзность.

ribbed *adj.* **1,** (lined with ridges) ребристый; рубчатый. **2,** (fluted; corrugated) рифлёный.

ribbon *n.* **1,** (ornamental band; military decoration) лента. **2,** *pl.* (shreds) клочья.

rice *n.* рис. —*adj.* рисовый: *rice pudding,* рисовый пудинг.

rich *adj.* **1,** (wealthy) богатый: *rich widow/country,* богатая вдова/страна. *Rich in iron/vitamins,* богат железом/витаминами. *Get rich,* (раз)богатеть. **2,** (fertile) плодородный. **3,** (fattening) жирный. **4,** (deep; vivid; mellow) сочный; густой. —*n., preceded by* **the** богатые; богачи.

riches *n.pl.* богатства.

richly *adv.* **1,** (lavishly) богато. **2,** (fully) вполне: *richly deserved,* вполне заслуженный.

richness *n.* **1,** (wealth) богатство. **2,** (fertility) плодородие. **3,** (vividness, as of sound or color) густота.

rick *n.* стог; скирд; скирда.

rickets *n.* рахит.

rickety *adj.* шаткий; расшатанный.

rickshaw *n.* рикша.

ricochet *n.* рикошет. —*v.i.* рикошетировать.

rid *v.t.* избавля́ть; освобожда́ть; очища́ть. *Rid the house of mice,* очища́ть дом от мыше́й. —**get rid of,** отде́лываться от; избавля́ться от.

riddance *n.* избавле́ние. —**good riddance!,** ска́тертью доро́га!

riddle *n.* зага́дка. —*v.t.* **1,** (pierce with holes or bullets) изреше́чивать. **2,** *fig.* (affect every part of) проника́ть: *riddled with graft,* прони́кнут корру́пцией.

ride *v.i.* **1,** (be conveyed in a vehicle) е́хать; е́здить. **2,** (be borne on horseback) е́здить верхо́м. **3,** (handle, as of a car) идти́; ходи́ть: *the car rides well,* маши́на хорошо́ идёт/хо́дит. **4,** *fol. by* **on** (depend on) зави́сеть от. —*v.t.* **1,** (be transported by or on) е́хать на; е́здить на; ката́ться на: *ride a bicycle,* е́хать/е́здить на велосипе́де; *ride a horse,* е́здить верхо́м; *ride a camel,* е́здить верхо́м на верблю́де; *ride a merry-go-round,* ката́ться на карусе́ли; *ride the waves,* ката́ться на волна́х. **2,** *usu. passive* (beset) му́чить: *be ridden by doubts,* му́читься сомне́ниями. **3,** *colloq.* (tease) высме́ивать. **4,** *fol. by* **out** (weather, as a storm) вы́держивать. —*n.* **1,** (act of riding) езда́: *a ten-minute ride,* де́сять мину́т езды́. **2,** (leisurely drive) прогу́лка: *go for a ride,* е́здить на прогу́лку; ката́ться на маши́не; прокати́ться; прое́хаться. *Take for a ride,* ката́ть; прокати́ть. —**ride at anchor,** стоя́ть на я́коре. —**ride away; ride off,** отъезжа́ть.

rider *n.* **1,** (one who rides horseback) вса́дник; нае́здник; верхово́й; седо́к; ездо́к. **2,** (passenger) седо́к. **3,** (clause added to a document) дополне́ние; добавле́ние.

ridge *n.* **1,** (range of hills) гряда́; кряж. **2,** (strip of earth raised by a plow) гре́бень. **3,** (rib on material) ру́бчик. **4,** (apex of a roof) конёк; гре́бень.

ridicule *n.* осмея́ние; насме́шка. *Hold up to ridicule,* поднима́ть на́ смех. —*v.t.* насмеха́ться над; осме́ивать; высме́ивать.

ridiculous *adj.* смешно́й; неле́пый. *Don't be ridiculous!,* не глупи́те! —**ridiculously,** *adv.* до смешно́го.

riding *n.* езда́: *horseback riding,* верхова́я езда́. —**riding breeches,** рейту́зы; галифе́. —**riding habit,** амазо́нка. —**riding master,** бере́йтор. —**riding school,** мане́ж.

rife *adj.* **1,** (widespread) распространённый. **2,** *fol. by* **with** (full; abounding) по́лный; изоби́лующий. *The country is rife with rumors,* страна́ полна́ слу́хов (*or* слу́хами).

riffraff *n.* сброд; чернь; подо́нки.

rifle *n.* винто́вка. —*adj.* винто́вочный; ружéйный. —*v.t.* (force open) взла́мывать. —**rifleman,** *n.* стрело́к.

rift *n.* **1,** (crack) тре́щина; рассе́лина. **2,** *fig.* (disagreement) тре́щина; раско́л.

rig *v.t.* **1,** (fit out, as a ship) оснаща́ть. **2,** *fol. by* **up** (construct hastily) скола́чивать. **3,** (control fraudulently) манипули́ровать; фальсифици́ровать. —*n.* **1,** (arrangement of sails) осна́стка. **2,** (device) устано́вка: *drilling rig,* бурова́я устано́вка.

rigging *n.* такела́ж; осна́стка.

right *adj.* **1,** (correct) пра́вильный; пра́вый; ве́рный. *You are right,* вы пра́вы. *Quite right,* соверше́нно пра́вильно. **2,** (opposite of left) пра́вый. **3,** (the one wanted or needed) тот: *is this the right train?,* э́то тот по́езд? **4,** (appropriate) подходя́щий: *the right moment,* подходя́щий моме́нт. **5,** (designating the side to be seen, as of cloth) пра́вый; лицево́й. *Right side up,* лицо́м кве́рху. **6,** *math.* (of an angle) прямо́й; (of a triangle) прямоуго́льный. —*adv.* **1,** (correctly) пра́вильно. **2,** (to the right) напра́во: *turn right,* поверну́ть напра́во. **3,** (immediately) сейча́с: *I'll be right back,* я сейча́с верну́сь. **4,** (directly) пря́мо. **5,** (exactly; just) как раз: *right in the middle,* как раз в середи́не. *He is standing right over there,* вот он там стои́т. **6,** *used for emphasis: come right in!,* войди́те, пожа́луйста! *Right to the end,* до са́мого конца́. *The bullet went right through him,* пу́ля прошла́ навы́лет. **7,** *colloq.* (very) о́чень; здо́рово: *right happy,* о́чень рад. *He was right angry,* он здо́рово рассерди́лся. —*n.* **1,** (that which is right) справедли́вость. *Tell right from wrong,* различа́ть ме́жду добро́м и злом. **2,** (just claim) пра́во: *civil rights,* гражда́нские права́. *Have the right to,* име́ть пра́во (+ *inf.*). **3,** (side opp. the left) пра́вая сторона́. *To the right; on the right,* напра́во; спра́ва. **4,** *polit.* [*usu.* **the right**] пра́вые. —*v.t.* **1,** (set straight) выпрямля́ть. **2,** (redress, as a wrong) исправля́ть (зло). —**all right,** *see* **all right.** —**be in one's right mind,** быть в своём (*or* в здра́вом) уме́. —**be in the right,** быть пра́вым. —**by rights,** по справедли́вости. —**in one's own right,** сам; сам по себе́. —**might makes right,** кто си́лён, тот и прав. —**put right,** нала́живать; поправля́ть. —**right after,** сра́зу по́сле (+ *gen.*). —**right away, 1,** (right now) сейча́с; сейча́с же. **2,** (right then) сра́зу. —**right itself, 1,** (regain a vertical position) встава́ть. **2,** (correct itself; return to normal) нала́живаться. —**right now, 1,** (at present) сейча́с. **2,** (immediately) сейча́с; сейча́с же. —**right you are!,** соверше́нно ве́рно!

righteous *adj.* пра́ведный. —**righteousness,** *n.* пра́ведность.

rightful *adj.* зако́нный. —**rightfully,** *adv.* по пра́ву.

right-hand *adj.* пра́вый. —**right-hand man,** пра́вая рука́.

right-handed *adj.* по́льзующийся пра́вой руко́й.

rightist *n.* & *adj.* пра́вый.

rightly *adv.* **1,** (correctly) пра́вильно. **2,** (fairly) справедли́во. **3,** (justly; deservedly) по пра́ву. —**and rightly so,** да и соверше́нно справедли́во.

rightness *n.* пра́вильность; правота́.

right of way пра́во прохо́да; пра́во прое́зда.

right-wing *adj.* пра́вый.

rigid *adj.* **1,** (stiff; not bending) жёсткий; негну́щийся; неги́бкий. **2,** *fig.* (strict; not deviating) жёсткий; стро́гий; неги́бкий.

rigidity *n.* **1,** (immobility) жёсткость. **2,** (inflexibility) непреклонность.

rigor *also,* **rigour** *n.* **1,** (strictness) стро́гость. **2,** (severity) суро́вость. **3,** *usu. pl.* (hardships) тя́готы.

rigor mortis тру́пное окочене́ние.

rigorous *adj.* **1,** (rigidly precise) стро́гий. **2,** (full of rigors; harsh) суро́вый.

rigour *n.* = **rigor.**

rile *v.t., colloq.* раздража́ть; досажда́ть.

rill *n.* ручеёк.

rim *n.* **1,** (edge) край: *the rim of a canyon,* край уще́лья. **2,** (of glasses) опра́ва. **3,** (outer part of a wheel) о́бод. **4,** *basketball* кольцо́ (корзи́ны).

rime *n.* **1,** = **rhyme. 2,** (hoarfrost) и́ней.

rind *n.* кожура́; ко́жица; ко́рка.

ring *n.* **1,** (circular band) кольцо́: *engagement ring,* обручáльное кольцó. *Diamond ring,* бриллиáнтовый пéрстень. *The rings of Saturn,* кóльца Сатýрна. **2,** (circle) круг; кольцó: *form a ring,* стать в круг. *Rings under one's eyes,* круги́ под глазáми. *Blow smoke rings,* пускáть кóльца ды́ма. **3,** (arena, as for a circus) арéна; манéж. **4,** (boxing ring) ринг. **5,** (illegal band) шáйка; бáнда. *Smuggling ring,* шáйка контрабанди́стов. **6,** (sound of a bell) звон; звонóк. *Give someone a ring,* позвони́ть комý-нибудь. —*v.t.* **1,** (cause to sound, as a bell) звони́ть в (кóлокол); давáть (звонóк). **2,** [*also, Brit.* **ring up**] (call on the telephone) звони́ть (+ *dat.*). **3,** (encircle) окружáть. —*v.i.* **1,** (of a bell or telephone) звони́ть. **2,** (ring a bell) давáть звонóк. **3,** *Ring in one's ears,* звучáть в ушáх. *My ears are ringing,* у меня́ звени́т в ушáх. —**ring a bell,** *see* **bell.** —**ring for,** вызывáть. —**ring in,** встречáть (Нóвый год). —**ring off,** дать отбóй. —**ring out,** раздавáться; гря́нуть: *a shot rang out,* раздáлся/гря́нул вы́стрел. —**ring true,** звучáть и́скренне.

ringer *n.* **1,** (person who rings a bell) звонáрь. **2,** *slang* (person who greatly resembles another) двойни́к.

ring finger безымя́нный пáлец.

ringing *n.* звон. —*adj.* звóнкий.

ringleader *n.* зачи́нщик; главáрь.

ringlet *n.* **1,** (small ring) колéчко. **2,** (of hair) кудря́шка.

ringworm *n.* стригýщий лишáй.

rink *n.* катóк.

rinse *v.t.* полоскáть. *Rinse out,* выполáскивать. —*n.* полоскáние.

riot *n.* **1,** (wild disturbance) бунт. **2,** *colloq.* (something extremely funny) умóра. **3,** *A riot of color,* всевозмóжные цветá. —*v.i.* бунтовáть. —**read the riot act to,** читáть нотáцию (+ *dat.*). —**run riot,** бýйствовать; буя́нить.

rioter *n.* бунтовщи́к.

riotous *adj.* **1,** (rioting) бунтýющий. **2,** (boisterous) бýйный.

rip *v.t.* рвать; разрывáть. *Rip open,* распáрывать. —*v.i.* рвáться; разрывáться. —*n.* разры́в. —**rip into,** обрýшиваться на. —**rip off, 1,** (tear off) срывáть. **2,** *slang* (cheat) содрáть. —**rip up,** разрывáть.

ripcord *n.* вытяжнóй трос (парашю́та).

ripe *adj.* спéлый; зрéлый. —**ripen,** *v.i.* спеть; зреть; поспевáть; созревáть. —**ripeness,** *n.* спéлость; зрéлость.

riposte *n.* **1,** *fencing* ответный вы́пад. **2,** (quick rejoinder) рéплика.

ripple *n.* **1,** (small wave) рябь; зыбь. *Ripples on the water,* круги́ на водé. **2,** (slight sound): *ripple of laughter/applause,* небольшáя (*or* крáткая) вспы́шка аплодисмéнтов. —*v.t. & i.* ряби́ть.

ripsaw *n.* продóльная пилá.

rise *v.i.* **1,** (ascend) поднимáться. **2,** (stand up; get up) вставáть. **3,** (extend upward) возвышáться. **4,** (of the sun, moon, etc.) всходи́ть; восходи́ть; вставáть. **5,** (originate, as of a river) брать начáло. **6,** (increase, as of prices, temperature, etc.) поднимáться; повышáться; расти́; возрастáть. **7,** [*usu.* **rise up**] (rebel) восставáть. **8,** (return to life) воскресáть. —*n.* **1,** (ascent) восхóд; подъём. **2,** (raised ground) возвы́шенность. **3,** (increase) повышéние; рост. **4,** (emergence, as of an empire) возвышéние. —**give rise to,** порождáть; вызывáть к жи́зни. —**rise above,** быть вы́ше (+ *gen.*).

rising *adj.* **1,** (ascending) восходя́щий. **2,** (growing, as of a generation) подрастáющий.

risk *n.* риск. *Take a risk,* идти́ на риск. *At one's own risk,* на свой страх и риск. —*v.t.* рисковáть (+ *instr. or inf.*): *risk one's life,* рисковáть жи́знью; *risk being killed,* рисковáть поги́бнуть.

risky *adj.* рискóванный.

risqué *adj.* рискóванный.

rite *n.* обря́д.

ritual *n.* ритуáл. —*adj.* ритуáльный; обря́довый.

rival *n.* сопéрник. —*adj.* сопéрничающий. —*v.t.* сопéрничать с. —**rivalry,** *n.* сопéрничество.

river *n.* рекá. —*adj.* речнóй. —**riverbank; riverside,** *n.* речнóй бéрег; бéрег реки́. —**riverboat,** *n.* речнóе сýдно; речнóй пароxóд.

rivet *n.* заклёпка. —*v.t.* **1,** (fasten with rivets) клепáть. **2,** *fig.* (fix rigidly in place) прикóвывать; пригвождáть: *riveted to the spot,* прикóванный/пригвождённый к мéсту. —**riveter,** *n.* клепáльщик.

rivulet *n.* ручéй.

roach *n.* **1,** (cockroach) таракáн. **2,** (fish) плотвá; тарáнь.

road *n.* **1,** (path; highway) дорóга. **2,** *fig.* (avenue) путь: *the road to success,* путь к успéху. —*adj.* дорóжный: *road surface,* дорóжное покры́тие. —**be on the road, 1,** (be traveling) разъезжáть. **2,** (be on tour) гастроли́ровать. **3,** *sports* быть на вы́езде.

roadbed *n.* полотнó.

roadblock *n.* **1,** (barrier) заграждéние *or* засáда на дорóге. *Set up roadblocks,* перекры́ть дорóги. **2,** *fig.* (obstacle) завáл на пути́.

road map путевáя кáрта.

roadside *adj.* придорóжный.

road sign дорóжный знак.

roadstead *n., naut.* рейд.

roadway *n.* мостовáя.

roam *v.i. & t.* **1,** (walk around aimlessly) броди́ть; блуждáть: *roam (about) the streets,* броди́ть/блуждáть по ýлицам. **2,** (wander far and wide) стрáнствовать; скитáться: *roam the world,* стрáнствовать/скитáться по свéту *or* пó миру. —*n.* прогýлка: *a roam around town,* прогýлка по гóроду.

roan *adj.* чáлый.

roar *v.i.* ревéть. *Roar with laughter,* покати́ться *or* покáтываться сó смеху. —*v.t.* выкри́кивать: *the crowd roared its approval,* толпá выкри́кивала одобрéние. —*n.* рёв.

roast *v.t.* жáрить. —*v.i.* жáриться. —*adj.* жáреный: *roast lamb,* жáреная барáнина. *Roast beef,* рóстбиф. —*n.* жаркóе.

roasted *adj.* жáреный: *roasted coffee,* жáреный кóфе. *Roasted nuts,* калёные орéхи.

roasting pan жарóвня.

rob *v.t.* **1,** (steal from) грáбить; обкрáдывать: *rob a house,* грáбить/обкрáдывать дом. *He was robbed of $200,* у негó укрáли двéсти дóлларов. **2,** (deprive of something) лишáть; отнимáть. *Rob someone of sleep,* отнимáть сон у когó-нибудь.

robber *n.* грабитель. —**robbery,** *n.* грабёж; ограблéние.

robe *n.* **1,** (long, loose garment) мáнтия. **2,** (bathrobe) халáт. —*v.t.* облачáть.

robin *n.* мали́новка; заря́нка.

robot *n.* рóбот; автомáт.

robust *adj.* крéпкий; дю́жий.

rock *n.* **1,** (large stone) ка́мень. **2,** (cliff) скала́. **3,** (reef) (подво́дная) скала́: *strike a rock,* наскочи́ть на скалу́. **4,** (substance) го́рная поро́да. —*v.t.* **1,** (move gently) кача́ть. *Rock to sleep,* ука́чивать; баю́кать. **2,** (shake violently) потряса́ть; сотряса́ть. —*v.i.* кача́ться. —**on the rocks, 1,** (in difficulty) на мели́. **2,** (of drinks) со льдом. —**rock crusher,** камнедроби́лка. —**rock crystal,** го́рный хруста́ль. —**rock salt,** ка́менная соль.

rocker *n.* **1,** (rocking chair) кача́лка. **2,** (runner of a rocking chair) по́лоз. —**off one's rocker,** *slang* сумасше́дший. *Are you off your rocker?,* ты с ума́ сошёл?

rocket *n.* **1,** (projectile; space vehicle) раке́та. **2,** (firework) шути́ха. —*adj.* раке́тный: *rocket launcher,* раке́тная устано́вка. —*v.i.* взмыва́ть. —**rocketry,** *n.* раке́тная те́хника.

rocking chair кача́лка.

rocking horse конь-кача́лка.

rocky *adj.* **1,** (stony) скали́стый. **2,** (shaky) ша́ткий.

rococo *n.* рококо́. —*adj.* в сти́ле рококо́.

rod *n.* **1,** (slender, straight stick) прут. **2,** (bar) сте́ржень. **3,** (whip; switch) ро́зга. —**curtain rod,** па́лка для гарди́н. —**fishing rod,** у́дочка; уди́лище. —**lightning rod,** громоотво́д; молниеотво́д. —**piston rod,** поршнево́й шток.

rodent *n.* грызу́н.

roe *n.* **1,** (fish eggs; hard roe) икра́. **2,** (milt; soft roe) моло́ки. **3,** (roe deer) косу́ля.

roebuck *n.* саме́ц косу́ли.

roe deer косу́ля.

rogue *n.* плут; жу́лик; моше́нник. —**roguish,** *adj.* жуликова́тый.

roil *v.t.* **1,** (make turbid) мути́ть. **2,** (annoy) раздража́ть.

role *n.* роль.

roll *v.t.* **1,** (cause to roll; move by rolling) кати́ть: *roll the ball,* кати́ть мяч. **2,** (flatten; shape, as dough) ката́ть; раска́тывать. **3,** (smooth the surface of, as a road) ука́тывать. **4,** (turn, as in bread crumbs) валя́ть (в сухаря́х). **5,** (make, as a cigarette) крути́ть; скру́чивать. **6,** (flatten into a sheet, as metal) прока́тывать; вальцева́ть. **7,** (throw, as dice) броса́ть. **8,** (move in circles, as one's eyes) враща́ть (глаза́ми). —*v.i.* **1,** (move by turning over and over) кати́ться. *The ball rolled under the bed,* мяч покати́лся (*or* закати́лся) под крова́ть. *He is rolling in money,* он купа́ется в зо́лоте. **2,** (toss, as of a ship) кача́ть. **3,** (sound, as of a drum) грохота́ть. —*n.* **1,** (anything rolled up) сви́ток; свёрток; руло́н; *(of film)* кату́шка. **2,** (small bread or biscuit) бу́лка; бу́лочка. **3,** (list of names) ве́домость; рее́стр. *Call the roll,* де́лать перекли́чку. **4,** (swaying of a ship) ка́чка. **5,** (sound of drums) гро́хот. —**roll down, 1,** (move downward by rolling) ска́тывать. *Roll down one's sleeves,* рассучи́ть рукава́. **2,** (slide down) ска́тываться. —**roll out,** расстила́ть: *roll out the red carpet for,* расстила́ть кра́сный ковёр пе́ред. —**roll over,** перева́ливаться. —**roll up, 1,** (form into a roll) свёртывать; ска́тывать. **2,** (turn up, as one's sleeves) засу́чивать. **3,** (arrive by vehicle) подъезжа́ть.

roll call перекли́чка. —**roll-call vote,** поимённое голосова́ние.

roller *n.* **1,** (caster) колёсико; ро́лик. **2,** (heavy cylinder for smoothing roads) като́к. —**roller bearing,** ро́ликовый подши́пник. —**roller coaster,** америка́нские го́ры.

roller skate ро́лик; конёк на ро́ликах; ро́ликовый конёк. —**roller-skate,** *v.i.* ката́ться на ро́ликах.

rollick *v.i.* резви́ться; вози́ться.

rolling *n.* **1,** (moving by turning over and over) ката́ние. **2,** (swaying of a ship or vehicle) ка́чка. **3,** (flattening of metal) прока́тка. —*adj.* **1,** (moving on wheels or rollers) на колёсах. **2,** (pert. to the rolling of metal) прока́тный. **3,** (undulating) волни́стый. —**rolling mill,** прока́тный стан; вальцо́вая ме́льница. —**rolling pin,** ска́лка. —**rolling stock,** подвижно́й соста́в.

roly-poly *adj.* пу́хлый.

Roman *adj.* ри́мский. *Roman numerals,* ри́мские ци́фры. —*n.* ри́млянин.

Roman Catholic 1, *used as a noun* като́лик. **2,** *used adjectivally* ри́мско-католи́ческий.

romance *n.* **1,** (romantic tale) рома́н. **2,** (love affair) рома́н. **3,** (fascination; appeal) рома́нтика. **4,** *music* рома́нс. —*adj., cap.* рома́нский: *Romance languages,* рома́нские языки́.

Romanesque *adj.* рома́нский. —*n.* рома́нский стиль.

Romanian *also,* **Rumanian** *adj.* румы́нский. —*n.* **1,** (person) румы́н; румы́нка. **2,** (language) румы́нский язы́к.

romantic *adj.* романти́ческий; романти́чный. —**romanticism,** *n.* романти́зм; рома́нтика. —**romanticist,** *n.* рома́нтик. —**romanticize,** *v.t.* романтизи́ровать.

romp *v.i.* вози́ться; резви́ться.

rondo *n.* ро́ндо.

roof *n.* кры́ша. *Roof of the mouth,* нёбо. —**roofer,** *n.* кро́вельщик. —**roofing,** *n.* кро́вля.

rook *n.* **1,** (bird) грач. **2,** *chess* ладья́. —*v.t., colloq.* (cheat; swindle) обсчи́тывать.

rookery *n.* ле́жбище.

rookie *n.* новичо́к.

room *n.* **1,** (part of a house or building) ко́мната. *Three-room apartment,* трёхко́мнатная кварти́ра. **2,** (in a hotel) но́мер. **3,** (space) ме́сто: *make room for,* дава́ть ме́сто (+ *dat.*). *Take up too much room,* занима́ть сли́шком мно́го ме́ста. **4,** *pl.* (living quarters) помеще́ние. —*adj.* ко́мнатный: *room temperature,* ко́мнатная температу́ра. —*v.i.* жить. —**room and board,** стол и кварти́ра; по́лный пансио́н.

roomer *n.* пансионе́р.

roominess *n.* вмести́тельность.

rooming house пансио́н.

roommate *n.* това́рищ по ко́мнате; сожи́тель. *They are roommates,* они́ живу́т в одно́й ко́мнате.

roomy *adj.* просто́рный; вмести́тельный.

roost *n.* насе́ст. —*v.i.* сади́ться на насе́ст; сиде́ть на насе́сте. —**rule the roost,** верте́ть всем до́мом.

rooster *n.* пету́х.

root *n.* ко́рень: *root of a tree/tooth/word,* ко́рень де́рева/зу́ба/сло́ва. *Square root,* квадра́тный ко́рень. *Pull up by the roots,* вы́рвать (что́-нибудь) с ко́рнем. —*adj.* основно́й: *root cause,* основна́я причи́на. —*v.t.* **1,** (implant deeply) укореня́ть. *Be rooted in,* корени́ться в; (быть) укоренён в (+ *prepl.*). *Rooted to the spot,* прико́ванный к ме́сту. **2,** *fol. by* **out** (eliminate completely) вырыва́ть с ко́рнем; искореня́ть. —*v.i.* [*usu.* **root for**] боле́ть (за). —**root and**

branch, в кóрне; коренны́м óбразом. —**root of all evil,** кóрень зла. —**take root,** укореня́ться.

rooter *n.* болéльщик.

rootlet *n.* корешóк.

rope *n.* верёвка; канáт. *Jump rope,* скакáлка. —*adj.* верёвочный: *rope ladder,* верёвочная лéстница. —*v.t.* **1,** (fasten by a rope) привя́зывать *or* свя́зывать верёвкой. **2,** (lasso) лови́ть аркáном. **3,** *fol. by* **off** (fence off) оцепля́ть. **4,** *fol. by* **in** (entice) втя́гивать. —**know the ropes,** знать все ходы́ и вы́ходы. —**learn the ropes,** ориенти́роваться. —**reach the end of one's rope,** дойти́ до тóчки.

rorqual *n.* полосáтик.

rosary *n.* чётки.

rose *n.* **1,** (flower) рóза. **2,** (color) рóзовый цвет. —*adj.* рóзовый.

roseate *adj.* рóзовый.

rosebud *n.* бутóн рóзы.

rosebush *n.* рóза; рóзовый куст.

rose-colored *adj.* рóзовый. —**see through rose-colored glasses,** смотрéть сквозь рóзовые очки́.

rosemary *n.* розмари́н.

rosette *n.* розéтка.

rose water рóзовая водá.

rosewood *n.* рóзовое дéрево; палисáндр. —*adj.* палисáндровый.

rosin *n.* канифóль.

roster *n.* **1,** (list of names) спи́сок; реéстр. **2,** (duty schedule) расписáние дежу́рств; расписáние нарядов.

rostrum *n.* трибу́на; кáфедра.

rosy *adj.* **1,** (rose-colored) рóзовый; румя́ный. **2,** *fig.* (bright; cheerful; optimistic) рóзовый; рáдужный. *Paint a rosy picture of,* представля́ть в рóзовом/рáдужном свéте. —**rosy-cheeked,** *adj.* розовощёкий.

rot *v.i.* гнить; ту́хнуть. —*v.t.* гнои́ть —*n.* **1,** (decay) гниéние. **2,** (anything rotten) гниль; прель. **3,** (plant disease) гниль. **4,** *slang* (nonsense) вздор.

rotary *adj.* вращáтельный; поворóтный; ротациóнный. —**rotary engine,** ротациóнный дви́гатель. —**rotary press,** ротациóнная (печáтная) маши́на.

rotate *v.i.* **1,** (turn) вращáться. **2,** (alternate) чередовáться. —*v.t.* **1,** (cause to turn) вращáть. **2,** (alternate) чередовáть. *Rotate crops,* чередовáть *or* сменя́ть культу́ры. **3,** (interchange, as tires) переставля́ть (ши́ны).

rotation *n.* **1,** (rotary motion) вращéние. **2,** (alternation) чередовáние. *In rotation,* по óчереди. —**rotation of crops,** севооборóт. —**rotation of the seasons,** круговорóт времён гóда.

rote *adj.* зазу́бренный. *Rote learning,* зубрёжка. —**by rote,** машинáльно. *Learn by rote,* зубри́ть.

rotor *n.* рóтор.

rotten *adj.* **1,** (decayed) гнилóй; ту́хлый. **2,** *colloq.* (miserable) парши́вый; дряннóй; отврати́тельный.

rottenness *n.* гни́лость.

rotund *adj.* **1,** (round; plump) пу́хлый. **2,** (sonorous) зву́чный.

rotunda *n.* ротóнда.

roué *n.* распу́тник.

rouge *n.* румя́на. —*v.t.* румя́нить.

rough *adj.* **1,** (not smooth; coarse) гру́бый; шершáвый; шероховáтый. *Rough skin/material,* гру́бая/шершáвая кóжа/ткань. *Rough surface,* шероховáтая повéрхность. *Rough road,* нерóвная дорóга. *Rough terrain,* пересечённая мéстность. **2,** (not gentle) гру́бый: *rough handling/treatment,* гру́бое обращéние. **3,** (preliminary, as of something written) черновóй. *Rough draft/copy,* чернови́к. **4,** (choppy, as of the sea) бу́рный. **5,** (approximate) гру́бый: *a rough estimate,* гру́бый подсчёт. *A rough idea of,* óбщее представлéние о. **6,** *colloq.* (difficult; unpleasant) тру́дный; тяжёлый; неприя́тный. —*adv.* гру́бо. —*v.t.* **1,** *fol. by* **up** (beat up) поби́ть. **2,** *fol. by* **out** (sketch) набрáсывать. —**in the rough,** вчернé; нáчерно. —**rough it,** жить без удóбств.

roughage *n.* гру́бая пи́ща.

roughen *v.t.* дéлать гру́бым. —*v.i.* грубéть.

rough-hew *v.t.* обтёсывать. —**rough-hewn,** *adj.* гру́бо обтёсанный.

roughly *adv.* **1,** (not gently) гру́бо. **2,** (approximately) приблизи́тельно: *roughly forty miles,* приблизи́тельно сóрок миль. —**roughly speaking,** гру́бо говоря́.

roughneck *n.* буя́н.

roughness *n.* гру́бость; шероховáтость.

roughshod *adj.* подкóванный на шипы́. —**ride roughshod over,** попирáть.

roulade *n.* **1,** *music* рулáда. **2,** (meat pie) пирожóк.

roulette *n.* рулéтка. —**roulette wheel,** рулéтка.

round *adj.* кру́глый: *round table,* кру́глый стол. *In round figures,* кру́глым счётом; в кру́глых ци́фрах. —*n.* **1,** (unit of ammunition) вы́стрел; патрóн. **2,** *often pl.* (tour) обхóд: *make one's rounds,* идти́ в обхóд. *Make the round of all the stores,* обходи́ть все магази́ны. **3,** (of a tournament, negotiations, etc.) тур. **4,** *boxing* рáунд. **5,** (burst, as of applause) взрыв. —*v.t.* **1,** (make round) округля́ть; закругля́ть. **2,** (go round, as a bend, turn, etc.) огибáть (поворóт). —*adv.* **1,** (around) вокру́г; кругóм. *Go round,* вращáться. **2,** (throughout): *the year round,* кру́глый год. —*prep.* вокру́г. —**round off, 1,** (finish into rounded form) округля́ть; закругля́ть. **2,** (state as a round number) округля́ть. —**round out, 1,** (fill out; become round) округля́ться. **2,** (complete) завершáть. *Round out a collection,* (у)комплектовáть коллéкцию. —**round the clock,** кру́глые су́тки. —**round up, 1,** (assemble) собирáть. **2,** (herd together) сгоня́ть. **3,** (seize and arrest) производи́ть облáву на.

roundabout *adj.* окóльный; обхóдный; кружнóй.

rounded *adj.* закруглённый; округленный.

roundhouse *n.* паровóзное депó.

roundish *adj.* кругловáтый.

roundly *adv.* **1,** (sharply; severely) рéзко. **2,** (thoroughly; soundly) здóрово.

round robin кругов́ая систéма.

round-shouldered *adj.* суту́лый.

round-the-clock *adj.* круглосу́точный.

round trip поéздка тудá и обрáтно. *Round-trip ticket,* билéт тудá и обрáтно.

roundup *n.* **1,** (of cattle) загóн. **2,** (raid) облáва. **3,** (summary) обзóр; обозрéние.

rouse *v.t.* **1,** (waken) буди́ть. **2,** (excite; stimulate) возбуждáть: *rouse the populace/one's curiosity/,* возбуждáть населéние/любопы́тство.

rousing *adj.* **1,** (stirring) волну́ющий. **2,** (enthusiastic) востóрженный: *rousing welcome,* востóрженный приём.

rout *v.t.* **1,** (put to flight) обращáть в бéгство. **2,** (defeat overwhelmingly) громи́ть; разби́ть нáголову.

3, (drive out) выгонять. *Rout out of bed,* поднимать с постели. —*n.* разгром.

route *n.* **1,** (road; way) путь: *the shortest route to town,* кратчайший путь в город. **2,** (itinerary) маршрут: *the route of a trip,* маршрут путешествия. *Bus route,* маршрут автобуса. —*v.t.* направлять: *route the traffic through the park,* направлять движение через парк. —**en route,** по (*or* в) пути; по (*or* в) дороге.

routine *n.* режим; распорядок; колея. *Daily routine,* распорядок дня. *Settle into a routine,* войти в колею. —*adj.* обычный; установленный.

rove *v.i.* бродить; скитаться; странствовать.

rover *n.* скиталец. —**land rover,** вездеход.

roving *adj.* бродячий. —**roving ambassador,** посол по особым поручениям.

row[1] (ro) *n.* ряд: *row of houses,* ряд домов. *In the third row,* в третьем ряду. —*v.t. & i.* грести. *Row a boat,* грести на лодке. —**in a row, 1,** (in a line) в ряд; в ряду. **2,** (consecutively) подряд.

row[2] (rau) *n.* шумная ссора; скандал; дебош.

rowan *n.* рябина. —**rowanberry,** *n.* рябина.

rowboat *n.* гребная лодка; гребная шлюпка.

rowdy *n.* буян; хулиган; скандалист; безобразник. —*adj.* буйный. —**rowdiness,** *n.* хулиганство.

rower *n.* гребец.

rowing *n.* гребля; гребной спорт. —*adj.* гребной.

rowlock *n.* уключина.

royal *adj.* королевский.

royalism *n.* роялизм. —**royalist,** *n.* роялист. —*adj.* роялистский.

royalty *n.* **1,** (royal persons) члены королевской семьи. **2,** *pl.* (fees) авторский гонорар.

rub *v.t.* **1,** (stroke hard) тереть; потирать: *rub one's eyes,* тереть глаза; *rub one's hands,* потирать руки. *Rub one's injured knee,* потирать ушибленное колено. *Rub two sticks together,* тереть две палки друг о друга. *Rub one's back with alcohol,* натирать спину спиртом. **2,** (apply with pressure) растирать. *Rub cream into one's face,* натирать лицо кремом. **3,** (chafe) тереть; натирать; стирать. *The collar is rubbing my neck,* воротник натирает мне шею. —*v.i.* **1,** (apply repeated pressure) тереть: *keep rubbing!,* продолжайте тереть! **2,** (chafe) тереть: *the shoe rubs,* сапог трёт. **3,** *fol. by* **against** (scrape) тереться о (+ *acc.*). —*n.* **1,** (vigorous stroking): *give something a good rub,* хорошенько потереть что-нибудь. **2,** (difficulty; catch) загвоздка: *that's the rub,* вот в чём загвоздка. —**rub down,** обтирать. —**rub in,** втирать. —**rub it in,** растравлять рану; пилить кого-нибудь. —**rub off,** стираться. —**rub off on,** передаваться (+ *dat.*). —**rub out,** стирать. —**rub the wrong way,** гладить (кого-нибудь) против шерсти.

rubber *n.* **1,** (raw rubber) каучук. **2,** (processed rubber) резина. **3,** (overshoe) галоша. **4,** *cards* роббер. —*adj.* резиновый. —**rubber band,** резинка.

rubberize *v.t.* прорезинивать.

rubber plant 1, (plant yielding crude rubber) каучуконос. **2,** (ornamental house plant) фикус.

rubber stamp штамп; штемпель; гриф.

rubbish *n.* **1,** (refuse) хлам; мусор; сор. **2,** (nonsense) вздор; чепуха; глупости.

rubble *n.* **1,** (rough broken stones) рваный камень. **2,** (ruins) развалины: *reduce to rubble,* превращать в развалины.

rubdown *n.* обтирание; массаж.

rube *n., slang* деревенщина.

rubella *n.* краснуха.

Rubicon *n., in* **cross the Rubicon,** перейти Рубикон.

rubicund *adj.* румяный.

rubidium *n.* рубидий.

ruble *n.* рубль.

rubric *n.* рубрика.

ruby *n.* рубин. —*adj.* рубиновый.

rucksack *n.* рюкзак.

ruckus *n., colloq.* шум; гвалт; баталия.

rudder *n.* руль.

ruddy *adj.* румяный.

rude *adj.* грубый; невежливый. —**rudeness,** *n.* грубость; невежливость.

rudiment *n.* **1,** *pl.* (fundamentals) основы; элементы; начатки. **2,** (incompletely developed organ) рудиментарный орган; рудимент.

rudimentary *adj.* **1,** (elementary) элементарный. **2,** (incompletely developed) рудиментарный; зачаточный.

rue *v.t.* **1,** (feel remorse for) раскаиваться в. **2,** (regret) сожалеть о. —**rue the day,** проклинать тот день, когда...

rueful *adj.* печальный; унылый; скорбный.

ruff *n.* **1,** (frilled collar) брыжи. **2,** (bird) турухтан. **3,** (fish) ёрш. —*v.t. & i.* = **trump.**

ruffian *n.* хулиган; буян.

ruffle *n.* оборка. —*v.t.* **1,** (disturb) рябить: *ruffle the surface of the lake,* рябить поверхность озера. **2,** (fluster) смущать; конфузить. **3,** (erect, as feathers) ерошить. *The hen ruffled its feathers,* курица нахохлилась.

rug *n.* ковёр.

rugby *n.* регби.

rugged *adj.* **1,** (rough, as of terrain) пересечённый; изрезанный. **2,** (wrinkled; furrowed) грубый: *rugged features,* грубые черты лица. **3,** (trying; severe) тяжёлый; суровый. **4,** (robust; sturdy) крепкий; дюжий.

ruin *n.* **1,** (destruction; downfall) гибель; крушение. **2,** (financial collapse) разорение. **3,** *pl.* (remains of something destroyed) развалины; руины. *Lie in ruins,* лежать в развалинах. —*v.t.* **1,** (destroy) губить. **2,** (bankrupt) разорять. —**ruination,** *n.* гибель. —**ruinous,** *adj.* гибельный; губительный; пагубный; разорительный.

rule *n.* **1,** (regulation) правило: *the rules of the game,* правила игры. **2,** (act of governing) правление; управление. *Self-rule,* самоуправление. **3,** (domination; sway) власть: *under colonial rule,* под колониальной властью. **4,** (measuring stick) линейка. —*v.t.* **1,** (govern) править; управлять. **2,** (decide authoritatively) постановлять: *the court ruled that...,* суд постановил, что... **3,** (mark with lines) линовать; графить. **4,** *fol. by* **out** (eliminate from consideration) исключать; сбрасывать со счетов. —*v.i.* править. —**as a rule,** как правило. —**make it a rule,** взять себе за правило.

ruled *adj.* линованный; в линейку; графлёный; разграфлённый.

ruler *n.* **1,** (one who governs) правитель. **2,** (measuring stick) линейка.

ruling *n.* постановление. —*adj.* правящий. —**ruling circles,** правящие круги.

rum *n.* ром.
Rumanian *adj. & n.* = **Romanian.**
rumba *n.* ру́мба.
rumble *v.i.* **1,** (roar) громыха́ть; грохота́ть; греме́ть; рокота́ть. **2,** (gurgle, as of the stomach) урча́ть; бурча́ть. **3,** (move with such a sound) громыха́ть; грохота́ть. —*n.* гро́хот; ро́кот. —**rumble seat,** откидно́е сиде́нье.
rumen *n.* рубе́ц.
ruminant *n.* жва́чное живо́тное. —*adj.* жва́чный.
ruminate *v.i.* **1,** (chew the cud) жева́ть жва́чку. **2,** (ponder) разду́мывать; размышля́ть.
rummage *v.t. & i.* ры́ться в; обша́ривать.
rumor *also,* **rumour** *n.* слух. —*v.t. It is rumored that...,* хо́дят слу́хи, что...
rump *n.* **1,** (hind part of an animal) кресте́ц. **2,** (buttocks) зад; я́годицы.
rumple *v.t.* мять. —*v.i.* мя́ться.
rump steak ромште́кс.
rumpus *n.* шум; гам; гвалт.
run *v.i.* **1,** (move swiftly) бежа́ть: *run fast,* бежа́ть бы́стро. *Run home/upstairs,* побежа́ть домо́й/наве́рх. **2,** (go; operate; function) ходи́ть: *the trains aren't running,* поезда́ не хо́дят. *The elevator isn't running,* лифт не рабо́тает. *Leave the motor running,* не выключа́ть мото́ра. **3,** (extend) идти́; тяну́ться. *The road runs along the coast,* доро́га идёт вдоль бе́рега. **4,** (stream; flow) течь; ли́ться. *My nose is running,* у меня́ из носу течёт. **5,** (spread, as of colors or dyes) линя́ть; (of ink) растека́ться; расплыва́ться. **6,** (be in force) быть действи́тельным; остава́ться в си́ле. **7,** (be on, as of a play) идти́. **8,** (be a candidate) баллоти́роваться. **9,** (come in; finish) приходи́ть: *run last,* приходи́ть после́дним. **10,** *used with various adjectives: run dry,* высыха́ть; *run low,* истоща́ться. *Feelings ran high,* стра́сти разгоре́лись *or* разыгра́лись. *Run short, see* **short.** —*v.t.* **1,** (cover by running) пробега́ть: *run five miles,* пробега́ть пять миль. **2,** (take; drive) отвози́ть: *I'll run you to the station,* я вас отвезу́ на вокза́л. **3,** (chase) прогоня́ть: *run someone out of town,* прогна́ть кого́-нибудь из го́рода. **4,** (cause to move quickly) пробега́ть: *run one's fingers over the keyboard,* пробега́ть па́льцами по клавиату́ре. **5,** (manage; govern; conduct) вести́; руководи́ть; управля́ть. *Run a meeting,* вести́ собра́ние. *Run the country,* руководи́ть *or* управля́ть страно́й. **6,** (print; carry, as a story) печа́тать; помеща́ть. **7,** *used with various nouns: run a risk,* рискова́ть; *run errands,* быть на посы́лках; *run a blockade,* прорва́ть блока́ду; *run a red light,* проскочи́ть светофо́р. *He is running a temperature,* у него́ жар. —*n.* **1,** (rapid movement) бег; пробе́г. **2,** (single trip) рейс: *maiden run,* пе́рвый рейс. **3,** (streak, as of luck; spell, as of weather) полоса́. **4,** (tear in one's stocking) спусти́вшаяся пе́тля: *I have a run in my stocking,* у меня́ на чулке́ спусти́лась пе́тля. **5,** *music* рула́да. —**in the long run,** в коне́чном счёте; в коне́чном ито́ге. —**on the run, 1,** (while in motion) на ходу́. **2,** (hurriedly) второпя́х. **3,** (fleeing from justice) в бега́х. —**run across, 1,** *literally* перебега́ть. **2,** (encounter) ната́лкиваться на. —**run after,** бежа́ть за. —**run along,** побежа́ть: *I'll be running along,* ну, я побегу́. —**run around with,** води́ться с; пу́таться с. —**run away,** убега́ть. —**run down, 1,** *literally* сбега́ть с: *run down the stairs,* сбега́ть с ле́стницы. **2,** (run along; run through) пробега́ть по: *run down the street,* пробега́ть по у́лице. *A chill ran down her back,* дрожь пробежа́ла по её спине́. **3,** *fol. by* **to** (make a short trip to) сходи́ть (в); сбе́гать (в); съе́здить (в). **4,** (of a clock) стать; (of a battery) разряжа́ться. **5,** (pursue and catch) настига́ть. **6,** (knock over with a vehicle) нае́хать на. **7,** (read over rapidly) пробега́ть. **8,** (disparage) поро́чить. —**run into, 1,** *literally* вбега́ть в. **2,** (encounter by chance) ната́лкиваться на. **3,** (collide with) ста́лкиваться с; нае́хать на; налете́ть на. **4,** (add up to) составля́ть. —**run off, 1,** (run away) убега́ть. **2,** (flow off; drain) стека́ть. **3,** (print) печа́тать; отпеча́тывать. —**run out, 1,** *literally* выбега́ть. **2,** (expire) истека́ть. **3,** (be used up) выходи́ть; конча́ться; истоща́ться. *We ran out of gas,* у нас вышел/ко́нчился бензи́н. *His luck ran out,* сча́стье ему́ измени́ло. —**run over, 1,** (overflow) перелива́ться че́рез. *My cup runneth over,* моя́ ча́ша перепо́лнена. **2,** (exceed) превыша́ть. **3,** (knock down with a vehicle) задави́ть. *He was run over by a car,* он попа́л под маши́ну. **4,** (review again quickly) повторя́ть. —**run through, 1,** *literally* пробега́ть че́рез. **2,** (review again quickly) повторя́ть. **3,** (pierce) прока́лывать. **4,** (squander) прома́тывать. —**run up, 1,** *literally* взбега́ть на *or* по. **2,** (hoist, as a flag) вы́кинуть. **3,** (pile up, as debts) наде́лать (долго́в).
runaway *adj.* бежа́вший; бе́глый. *Runaway victory,* лёгкая побе́да. *Runaway inflation,* безу́держная инфля́ция.
rundown *n.* кра́ткое изложе́ние; сво́дка.
run-down *adj.* **1,** (tired; worn out) переутомлённый. **2,** (in poor condition) обветша́лый.
rune *n.* ру́на.
rung *n.* ступе́нька.
runic *adj.* руни́ческий.
run-in *n.* скло́ка; перебра́нка.
runner *n.* **1,** (one who runs) бегу́н. **2,** (messenger) посы́льный. **3,** (smuggler) контрабанди́ст. **4,** (blade, as of a sled) по́лоз. **5,** (strip of carpet) доро́жка. **6,** (trailing plant stem) ус.
running *n.* **1,** (act of running; jogging) бег. *Take up running,* бе́гать; нача́ть бе́гать. **2,** (chances of winning) ша́нсы: *be in the running,* име́ть ша́нсы; *be out of the running,* потеря́ть все ша́нсы. —*adj.* **1,** (moving fast) бегу́щий. **2,** (used for running) бегово́й: *running track,* бегова́я доро́жка. **3,** (continuous) непреры́вный. —*adv.* подря́д: *three years running,* три го́да подря́д. —**running board,** подно́жка. —**running broad jump,** прыжо́к с разбе́га. —**running head,** колонти́тул. —**running water,** водопрово́д.
run-of-the-mill *adj.* зауря́дный.
runt *n.* недоро́сток; коро́тыш(ка).
runway *n.* лётная доро́жка; взлётно-поса́дочная полоса́.
rupee *n.* ру́пия.
rupture *n.* **1,** (break) разры́в. **2,** (hernia) гры́жа. —*v.t.* прорыва́ть. —*v.i.* прорыва́ться.
rural *adj.* се́льский; деревенский.
ruse *n.* уло́вка.
rush *v.i.* **1,** (hurry) спеши́ть. **2,** (dash) бро́ситься; ри́нуться. **3,** (flow rapidly) хлы́нуть. *A rushing river,* стреми́тельная река́. *Blood rushed to her cheeks,* кровь бро́силась ей в щёки; кровь прилила́ к её щека́м. —*v.t.* **1,** (force to move hastily) торопи́ть:

don't rush me!, не торопи́те меня́! **2,** (whisk) мчать. *He was rushed to the hospital,* его́ сро́чно доста́вили в больни́цу. —*n.* **1,** (hurry) спе́шка: *what's the rush?,* к чему́ така́я спе́шка? *There is no rush,* не на́до спеши́ть. *I'm in a big rush,* я о́чень тороплю́сь. **2,** (dash) бросо́к. *Gold rush,* золота́я лихора́дка. **3,** (heavy flow, as of air) поры́в. **4,** (grasslike plant) тростни́к; камы́ш; си́тник. —*adj.* **1,** (urgent) сро́чный. **2,** (made of rush) тростнико́вый; камышо́вый. —**rush hours,** часы́-пик.

rusk *n.* сла́дкий суха́рь.

russet *adj.* кра́сно-бу́рый.

Russia leather юфть.

Russian *adj.* ру́сский. —*n.* **1,** (person) ру́сский; ру́сская. **2,** (language) ру́сский язы́к. *Do you speak Russian?,* вы говори́те (*or* разгова́риваете) по-ру́сски?

Russify *v.t.* русифици́ровать. *Become Russified,* обрусе́ть. —**Russification,** *n.* русифика́ция.

Russophile *n.* русофи́л.

Russophobe *n.* русофо́б —**Russophobia,** *n.* русофо́бство.

rust *n.* ржа́вчина. —*adj.* (rust-colored) ржа́вый. —*v.i.* ржа́веть.

rustic *adj.* дереве́нский.

rustle *v.i.* шелесте́ть; шурша́ть. —*v.t.* шелесте́ть (+ *instr.*). —*n.* ше́лест; шо́рох.

rusty *adj.* ржа́вый; заржа́вленный. *My French is a bit rusty,* я немно́го забы́л(а) свой францу́зский.

rut *n.* колея́.

rutabaga *n.* брю́ква.

ruthenium *n.* руте́ний.

ruthless *adj.* безжа́лостный. —**ruthlessly,** *adv.* безжа́лостно. —**ruthlessness,** *n.* безжа́лостность.

rye *n.* рожь. —*adj.* ржано́й: *rye bread,* ржано́й хлеб.

S

S, s девятна́дцатая бу́ква англи́йского алфа́вита.

Sabbath *n.* суббо́та: *observe the Sabbath,* соблюда́ть суббо́ту.

sabbatical *n.* годи́чный о́тпуск.

saber *also,* **sabre** *n.* са́бля; ша́шка. —**saber rattling,** бряца́ние ору́жием.

sable *n.* со́боль. —*adj.* со́болий; соболи́ный.

sabotage *n.* сабота́ж; диве́рсия; вреди́тельство. —*v.t.* саботи́ровать. —**saboteur,** *n.* сабота́жник; диверса́нт; вреди́тель.

sabre *n.* = **saber.**

sac *n.* мешо́чек.

saccharin *n.* сахари́н.

saccharine *adj.* **1,** (of or like sugar) са́харистый. **2,** (cloyingly sweet) са́харный; слаща́вый.

sacerdotal *adj.* свяще́ннический.

sack *n.* мешо́к. —*v.t.* **1,** (plunder) гра́бить; разгра́бить; громи́ть. **2,** *slang* (fire) выгоня́ть с рабо́ты. —**get the sack,** *slang* вы́лететь с рабо́ты.

sackcloth *n.* **1,** (sacking) мешкови́на; дерю́га; холст. **2,** (symbol of penitence) власяни́ца.

sacking *n.* мешкови́на; дерю́га.

sacrament *n.* та́инство. —**sacramental,** *adj.* относя́щийся к та́инству; свяще́нный.

sacred *adj.* свяще́нный; свято́й.

sacrifice *n.* **1,** (religious offering) жертвоприноше́ние. **2,** (giving up of something) же́ртва: *make sacrifices,* идти́ на же́ртвы. —*v.t.* же́ртвовать; приноси́ть в же́ртву. —**sacrificial,** *adj.* же́ртвенный.

sacrilege *n.* святота́тство; кощу́нство. —**sacrilegious,** *adj.* святота́тственный; кощу́нственный.

sacristy *n.* ри́зница.

sacrosanct *adj.* свяще́нный; неприкоснове́нный.

sacrum *n.* кресте́ц.

sad *adj.* печа́льный; гру́стный. *Why are you so sad?,* почему́ вам так гру́стно?

sadden *v.t.* печа́лить.

saddle *n.* седло́. —*v.t.* **1,** (put a saddle on) седла́ть. **2,** (burden) обременя́ть: *saddled with debts,* обременён долга́ми. *Saddle someone with a job,* взва́ливать рабо́ту на кого́-нибудь. —**saddlebag,** *n.* седе́льная *or* переме́тная сума́. —**saddlecloth,** *n.* потни́к. —**saddler,** *n.* седе́льный ма́стер; седе́льник; шо́рник.

sadism *n.* сади́зм. —**sadist,** *n.* сади́ст. —**sadistic,** *adj.* сади́стский.

sadly *adv.* печа́льно; гру́стно. *Be sadly lacking in,* о́чень *or* о́стро нужда́ться в (+ *prepl.*). ♦*As an introductory word* к несча́стью.

sadness *n.* печа́ль; грусть.

safari *n.* охо́тничья экспеди́ция.

safe *adj.* **1,** (free from danger) безопа́сный: *safe place,* безопа́сное ме́сто. *It is safe here,* здесь безопа́сно. **2,** (dependable) надёжный: *in safe hands,* в надёжных рука́х. **3,** (cautious) осторо́жный: *a safe driver,* осторо́жный води́тель. **4,** (without mishap) благополу́чный: *safe return,* благополу́чное возвраще́ние. **5,** (unharmed) невреди́мый: *the boy is safe,* ма́льчик невреди́м. —*n.* сейф. —**play safe,** де́йствовать наверняка́. —**safe and sound,** цел и невреди́м; в це́лости и сохра́нности. —**to be on the safe side,** для бо́льшей ве́рности; для перестрахо́вки; на вся́кий слу́чай.

safe-conduct *n.* осо́бая охра́на. *Safe-conduct pass,* охра́нная гра́мота; охра́нный лист.

safeguard *n.* гара́нтия; ме́ра предосторо́жности. —*v.t.* охраня́ть; защища́ть.

safekeeping *n.* хране́ние; сохране́ние: *turn over*

for safekeeping, отдава́ть на хране́ние/сохране́ние.
safely *adv.* **1,** (without mishap) благополу́чно. **2,** (without fear of being wrong) с уве́ренностью; сме́ло.
safety *n.* безопа́сность. —**safety catch,** предохрани́тель. —**safety pin,** англи́йская була́вка. —**safety razor,** безопа́сная бри́тва. —**safety valve,** предохрани́тельный кла́пан.
safflower *n.* сафло́р.
saffron *n.* шафра́н.
sag *v.i.* прогиба́ться; провиса́ть. —*n.* проги́б.
saga *n.* са́га.
sagacious *adj.* проница́тельный; прозорли́вый. —**sagacity,** *n.* проница́тельность; прозорли́вость.
sage *n.* **1,** (wise man) мудре́ц. **2,** (shrub) шалфе́й. —*adj.* му́дрый.
sagebrush *n.* полы́нь.
Sagittarius *n.* Стреле́ц.
sail *n.* **1,** (piece of canvas to propel a ship) па́рус. **2,** (ride on a sailing vessel) прогу́лка под паруса́ми. *Go for a sail,* идти́ ката́ться на па́русной ло́дке. —*v.i.* **1,** (travel by ship or boat) пла́вать; плыть. *Sail around the world,* соверши́ть кругосве́тное пла́вание. **2,** (set sail) отплыва́ть; отходи́ть. **3,** (soar; glide) плыть; пари́ть. —*v.t.* **1,** (handle; steer) вести́; управля́ть. **2,** (travel on or over) пла́вать по *or* в. —**sail into, 1,** *literally* входи́ть в; вплыва́ть в. **2,** (assail) обру́шиваться на. —**set sail,** отплыва́ть; отходи́ть.
sailboat *n.* па́русная ло́дка.
sailfish *n.* па́русник.
sailing *n.* **1,** (the sport) па́русный спорт. **2,** (riding in a sailboat) пла́вание; ката́ние на (па́русной) ло́дке. **3,** (departure from port) отплы́тие. —**sailing vessel,** па́русное су́дно; па́русник.
sailor *n.* моря́к; матро́с. —*adj.* [*also,* **sailor's**] матро́сский: *sailor suit,* матро́сский костю́м.
saint *n.* свято́й. *St. Peter,* св. Пётр. *St. Patrick's Day,* день св. Па́трика. *St. Petersburg,* Санкт-Петербу́рг. *St. Louis,* Сент-Лу́ис. *St. Lawrence River,* река́ Свято́го Лавре́нтия. *St. Basil's Cathedral,* храм Васи́лия Блаже́нного.
Saint Bernard сенберна́р.
sainthood *n.* лик святы́х: *confer sainthood upon,* причи́слить к ли́ку святы́х.
saintly *adj.* свято́й; подоба́ющий свято́му.
Saint Vitus' dance пля́ска свято́го Ви́тта; ви́ттова пля́ска.
sake *n., in* **for the sake of,** ра́ди (+ *gen.*). —**for goodness' sake!,** ра́ди бо́га!
salacious *adj.* са́льный; скабрёзный.
salad *n.* сала́т. —**salad bowl,** сала́тник. —**salad dressing,** припра́ва к сала́ту.
salamander *n.* салама́ндра.
salami *n.* колбаса́ твёрдого копче́ния; саля́ми.
salary *n.* жа́лованье; зарпла́та.
sale *n.* **1,** (selling) прода́жа; сбыт. **2,** (clearance sale) распрода́жа. **3,** *pl.* (volume of business) объём прода́ж: *sales are off/down,* объём прода́ж упа́л. —**for sale,** продаётся.
saleslady *n.* продавщи́ца. *Also,* **salesgirl; saleswoman.**
salesman *n.* **1,** [*also,* **salesclerk**] (seller in a store) продаве́ц. **2,** (traveling agent) коммивояжёр.
sales slip квита́нция.
sales tax нало́г на поку́пки.
salient *adj.* **1,** (protruding) выдаю́щийся. **2,** (noteworthy) примеча́тельный. *The salient points of the plan,* основны́е пу́нкты пла́на. —*n., mil.* вы́ступ; клин.
saline *adj.* соляно́й; солево́й. —**salinity,** *n.* солёность.
saliva *n.* слюна́. —**salivary,** *adj.* слю́нный. —**salivate,** *v.i.* выделя́ть слюну́.
sallow *adj.* желтова́тый; земли́стый.
sally *n.* **1,** *mil.* вы́лазка. **2,** (witticism) остро́та; ре́плика. —*v.i.* [*usu.* **sally forth**] отправля́ться.
salmon *n.* **1,** (fish) ло́со́сь. **2,** (food) лососи́на. *Smoked salmon,* сёмга. —*adj.* **1,** (of salmon) лососёвый. **2,** (pinkish orange) ора́нжево-ро́зового цве́та.
salon *n.* сало́н.
saloon *n.* бар; пивна́я.
salt *n.* соль. *Smelling salts,* ню́хательная соль. —*adj.* соляно́й: *salt mines,* соляны́е ко́пи. *Salt water,* солёная вода́. *Salt marsh,* солонча́к. —*v.t.* соли́ть; заса́ливать. —**rub salt on a wound,** растравля́ть ра́ну. —**salt away,** откла́дывать; накопля́ть. —**salt of the earth,** соль земли́. —**take with a grain of salt,** относи́ться скепти́чески к.
saltcellar *n.* соло́нка.
salted *adj.* солёный.
saltiness *n.* солёность.
saltpeter *also,* **saltpetre** *n.* сели́тра.
salt shaker соло́нка.
saltworks *n.* солева́рня; солева́ренный заво́д.
saltwort *n.* соля́нка.
salty *adj.* солёный.
salubrious *adj.* здоро́вый; целе́бный.
salutary *adj.* благотво́рный.
salutation *n.* приве́тствие. —**salutatory,** *adj.* приве́тственный.
salute *n.* **1,** (with the hand) отда́ча че́сти; во́инское приве́тствие. **2,** (with guns) салю́т. —*v.t.* **1,** *mil.* отдава́ть честь (+ *dat.*). **2,** (hail) приве́тствовать. —*v.i.* отдава́ть честь.
salvage *n.* **1,** (act of saving) спасе́ние. **2,** (property saved from danger) спасённое иму́щество. —*adj.* спаса́тельный: *salvage ship,* спаса́тельное су́дно. —*v.t.* спаса́ть.
salvation *n.* спасе́ние.
salve *n.* (целе́бная) мазь.
salvo *n.* залп.
samarium *n.* сама́рий.
same *adj.* **1,** (the one just mentioned) тот же; тот са́мый; тот же са́мый: *the same day,* в тот же день; *in the same place,* в *or* на том же са́мом ме́сте. *The same thing,* то же са́мое. **2,** (one; applying to both or all) оди́н: *live under the same roof,* жить под одно́й кры́шей. *They are the same age,* они́ одного́ во́зраста (*or* одни́х лет). **3,** (alike; identical) одина́ковый: *all politicians are the same,* все поли́тики одина́ковы. **4,** (unchanged) тако́й же: *remain the same,* оста́ться таки́м же (каки́м был). —*pron.* [*usu.* **the same**] то же са́мое; одно́ и то же. *The same to you!,* и вам того́ же!; и вас та́кже! —*adv.* [*usu.* **the same**] так же. *They are pronounced the same,* они́ произно́сятся одина́ково. —**all the same, 1,** [*also,* **just the same**] (nevertheless) всё же; всё ещё; всё равно́. *Thank you just the same,* всё же благодарю́ вас. **2,** *fol. by* **to** (making no difference) всё равно́; безразли́чно: *it's all the same to me,* мне всё равно́; мне безразли́чно. —**at the same time,** *see* **time.**

sameness *n.* **1,** (identity) тóждество. **2,** (monotony) однообрáзие.
samovar *n.* самовáр.
sample *n.* **1,** (typical example) образéц; обрáзчик; прóба. **2,** *statistics* вы́борка: *random sample,* случáйная вы́борка. —*adj.* прóбный: *sample copy,* прóбный экземпля́р. —*v.t.* прóбовать.
samurai *n.* самурáй.
sanatorium *n.* санатóрий.
sanctify *v.t.* освящáть. —**sanctification,** *n.* освящéние.
sanctimony *n.* хáнжество. —**sanctimonious,** *adj.* хáнжеский.
sanction *n.* **1,** (official permission) сáнкция. **2,** *usu. pl.* (punitive measures) сáнкции: *impose sanctions,* применя́ть сáнкции. —*v.t.* санкциони́ровать.
sanctity *n.* свя́тость.
sanctuary *n.* **1,** (sacred place) святи́лище. **2,** (place of refuge) убéжище.
sanctum *n.* убéжище.
sand *n.* песóк. —*adj.* песóчный; песчáный. —*v.t.* **1,** (sprinkle with sand) посыпáть пескóм. **2,** (sandpaper) натирáть наждáчной бумáгой.
sandal *n.* сандáлия.
sandalwood *n.* сандáл.
sandbag *n.* мешóк с пескóм.
sandbank *n.* песчáная мель *or* óтмель, перекáт; бáнка. *Also,* **sand bar.**
sandbox *n.* песóчница.
sanderling *n.* песчáнка.
sand fly моски́т.
sandpaper *n.* наждáчная бумáга; шкýрка.
sandpiper *n.* песóчник; перевóзчик.
sandstone *n.* песчáник.
sandstorm *n.* песчáная бýря.
sandwich *n.* бутербрóд.
sandy *adj.* **1,** (consisting of sand) песчáный. **2,** (of the color of sand) песóчный.
sane *adj.* **1,** (of sound mind) в здрáвом умé; нормáльный. **2,** (sensible) разýмный.
sanguinary *adj.* **1,** (bloody) кровáвый. **2,** (bloodthirsty) кровожáдный.
sanguine *adj.* **1,** (ruddy) румя́ный. **2,** (optimistic) оптимисти́ческий.
sanitarium *n.* санатóрий.
sanitary *adj.* санитáрный; гигиени́ческий; оздорови́тельный.
sanitation *n.* санитари́я.
sanity *n.* рассýдок.
Sanskrit *n.* санскри́т. —*adj.* санскри́тский.
Santa Claus дед-морóз.
sap *n.* **1,** (juice of a plant) сок. **2,** *slang* (fool) простофи́ля. **3,** *mil.* (trench) сáпа. —*v.t.* подтáчивать: *sap someone's strength,* подтáчивать чьй-нибудь си́лы.
sapling *n.* дéревце; деревцó.
sapper *n., mil.* сапёр.
sapphire *n.* сапфи́р. —*adj.* сапфи́рный; сапфи́ровый.
sapwood *n.* зáболонь.
sarcasm *n.* саркáзм. —**sarcastic,** *adj.* саркасти́ческий; язви́тельный. —**sarcastically,** *adv.* саркасти́чески.
sarcophagus *n.* саркофáг.
sardine *n.* сарди́на; сарди́нка. —**like sardines,** как сéльди в бóчке.
sardonic *adj.* сардони́ческий.
sartorial *adj.* портня́жный.
sash *n.* **1,** (band worn around the waist) кушáк. **2,** (window frame) окóнная рáма; окóнный переплёт.
sassy *adj., colloq.* нахáльный.
Satan *n.* сатанá. —**satanic,** *adj.* сатани́нский.
satchel *n.* рáнец; сýмка.
sate *v.t.* пресыщáть.
sateen *n.* сати́н. —*adj.* сати́новый.
satellite *n.* **1,** (moon) спýтник. **2,** *fig.* (nation dominated by another) сателли́т.
satiate *v.t.* **1,** (satisfy) насыщáть. **2,** (surfeit) пресыщáть. —**satiation; satiety,** *n.* насыщéние; пресыщéние; сы́тость.
satin *n.* атлáс. —*adj.* атлáсный.
satire *n.* сати́ра. —**satirical,** *adj.* сатири́ческий. —**satirist,** *n.* сати́рик. —**satirize,** *v.t.* высмéивать; осмéивать.
satisfaction *n.* удовлетворéние; удовлетворённость.
satisfactory *adj.* удовлетвори́тельный. —**satisfactorily,** *adv.* удовлетвори́тельно.
satisfied *adj.* довóльный: *I am satisfied,* я довóлен; я довóльна.
satisfy *v.t.* удовлетворя́ть: *satisfy the teacher,* удовлетворя́ть учи́теля; *satisfy someone's needs,* удовлетворя́ть чьй-нибудь потрéбности.
satrap *n.* сатрáп. —**satrapy,** *n.* сатрáпия.
saturate *v.t.* насыщáть; пропи́тывать.
saturation *n.* насыщéние. —**saturation point,** тóчка насыщéния.
Saturday *n.* суббóта.
Saturn *n.* Сатýрн.
saturnine *adj.* мрáчный; молчали́вый.
satyr *n.* сати́р.
sauce *n.* сóус; подли́вка.
saucepan *n.* кастрю́ля.
saucer *n.* блю́дце; блю́дечко. —**flying saucer,** летáющая тарéлка.
saucy *adj.* дéрзкий; нахáльный.
sauerkraut *n.* ки́слая капýста.
saunter *v.i.* прогýливаться; прохáживаться.
sausage *n.* колбасá.
sauterne *n.* сотéрн.
savage *adj.* **1,** (uncivilized) ди́кий: *savage tribes,* ди́кие племенá. **2,** (ferocious; vicious) свирéпый: *savage beast,* свирéпый зверь. *Savage attack,* я́ростная атáка. —*n.* дикáрь. —**savagery,** *n.* ди́кость.
savanna *also,* **savannah** *n.* савáнна.
savant *n.* учёный.
save *v.t.* **1,** (rescue) спасáть: *save someone's life,* спасáть чью-нибудь жизнь. **2,** (retain; not throw away) храни́ть; берéчь. **3,** (lay aside for future use) берéчь; сберегáть. **4,** (conserve) берéчь: *save one's strength,* берéчь свои́ си́лы. **5,** (reduce the expenditure of, as time or money) эконóмить. *Save ten dollars,* эконóмить дéсять дóлларов. **6,** (spare) избавля́ть: *that will save me a lot of trouble,* э́то избáвит меня́ от мнóгих хлопóт. **7,** (collect as a hobby) собирáть. **8,** *fol. by* **up** (keep and gradually amass) копи́ть. —*v.i.* **1,** (economize) эконóмить: *save on fuel,* эконóмить на тóпливе. **2,** *often fol. by* **up** (put money aside) копи́ть дéньги. —*prep.* крóме; за исключéнием (+ *gen.*).
saving *n.* **1,** (rescuing) спасéние. **2,** (reduction in cost)

экономия. **3,** *pl.* (money saved up) сбережения. —*adj.* спасительный.
savings bank сберегательная касса.
savior *also,* **saviour** *n.* спаситель.
savor *also,* **savour** *n.* вкус; смак. —*v.t.* смаковать; наслаждаться.
savory *also,* **savoury** *adj.* **1,** (appetizing) вкусный. **2,** (piquant) пикантный. **3,** *fig.* (respectable) порядочный. —*n.* (plant) чабёр.
savvy *n., slang* смётка. —*v.t. & i., slang* понимать; смекать.
saw *n.* **1,** (cutting tool) пила. **2,** (maxim; saying) изречение. —*v.t. & i.* пилить. *Saw in half,* распиливать пополам. —**saw off,** отпиливать. *Sawed-off rifle,* обрез.
sawdust *n.* опилки.
sawfish *n.* рыба-пила.
sawhorse *n.* козлы.
sawmill *n.* лесопильный завод; лесопилка.
sawyer *n.* пильщик.
saxifrage *n.* камнеломка.
Saxon *n.* сакс. —*adj.* саксонский.
saxophone *n.* саксофон.
say *v.t.* **1,** (utter; state) говорить (*pfv.* сказать). *They say he's leaving,* говорят, что он уезжает. *I have nothing to say,* мне нечего сказать. **2,** (recite) читать: *say one's prayers,* читать молитвы. **3,** (assert) утверждать: *he says he's innocent,* он утверждает, что он невиновен. **4,** (assume) допускать: *let's say it's true,* допустим, что это так. **5,** (read; go, as of a law or proverb) гласить. —*n.* слово. *Have one's say,* сказать своё слово; высказывать своё мнение; высказываться. —**as they say,** как говорят; что называется. —**if I (one) may say so,** с позволения сказать; если можно так выразиться. —**I should say so!,** ещё бы! —**it goes without saying,** само собой разумеется. —**that is to say,** то есть. —**when all is said and done,** в конце концов; в конечном счёте. —**you don't say!,** да что вы говорите! —**you might say,** можно сказать.
saying *n.* поговорка; изречение. *As the saying goes,* как говорится.
scab *n.* струп.
scabbard *n.* ножны.
scabies *n.* чесотка.
scads *n.pl., colloq.* масса; уйма.
scaffold *n.* **1,** (platform for a gallows) эшафот. **2,** (raised wooden framework) подмостки. —**scaffolding,** *n.* (строительные) леса.
scald *v.t.* обваривать; ошпаривать. *Scald oneself,* обвариваться; ошпариваться.
scale *n.* **1,** (instrument for weighing) весы. **2,** (scope) масштаб: *on a large scale,* в большом масштабе. **3,** (series of marks for measuring) шкала. **4,** (projection on a map) масштаб: *large-scale map,* карта крупного масштаба. **5,** (graded system of classification) шкала; лестница: *wage scale,* шкала заработной платы; *social scale,* общественная лестница. **6,** *music* гамма. **7,** *pl.* (of fish and reptiles) чешуя. —*v.t.* **1,** (have a weight of) весить. **2,** (climb to the top of) взбираться на. **3,** *fol. by* **down** (reduce) понижать; снижать. **4,** (remove the scales from) снимать чешую с; чистить. —**tip the scales,** склонить чашу весов (*e.g.* в чью-нибудь пользу).
scalene *adj., math.* разносторонний.
scallion *n.* зелёный лук.
scallop *n.* **1,** (mollusk) гребешок. **2,** *pl.* (decorative curves forming an edge) фестоны. —**scalloped,** *adj.* фестонный; фестончатый.
scalp *n.* **1,** (skin on the top of the head) кожа головы. **2,** (portion of this taken in battle) скальп. —*v.t.* скальпировать.
scalpel *n.* скальпель.
scaly *adj.* чешуйчатый.
scamp *n.* негодяй; мерзавец.
scamper *v.i.* **1,** (race; dash) мчаться. **2,** (frolic) резвиться.
scan *v.t.* **1,** (scrutinize) рассматривать. **2,** (glance over) просматривать. **3,** *pros.* скандировать.
scandal *n.* скандал. —**scandalize,** *v.t.* скандализировать. —**scandalous,** *adj.* скандальный.
Scandinavian *adj.* скандинавский. —*n.* скандинав.
scandium *n.* скандий.
scant *adj.* **1,** (hardly any) почти никакой. *Pay scant attention,* еле обращать внимание. **2,** (just short of) всего на: *miss by a few scant inches,* промахнуться всего на несколько дюймов.
scanty *adj.* скудный: *scanty supplies/information,* скудные запасы/сведения. *Scantily attired,* едва одетый.
scapegoat *n.* козёл отпущения.
scar *n.* **1,** (mark) рубец; шрам. **2,** *fig.* (lasting effect) след. —*v.t.* оставлять рубцы *or* шрамы на; обезображивать. —*v.i.* рубцеваться.
scarab *n.* скарабей.
scarce *adj.* **1,** (in short supply) дефицитный. **2,** (rarely seen) редкий. —**make oneself scarce,** не показываться; не попадаться на глаза.
scarcely *adv.* едва; еле; с трудом. *Scarcely enough,* едва достаточно. *He is scarcely breathing,* он еле дышит. *I could scarcely make out the road,* я с трудом различал дорогу.
scarcity *n.* **1,** (dearth) нехватка; дефицит. **2,** (rarity) редкость.
scare *v.t.* **1,** (frighten) пугать. *I'm scared,* мне страшно. *Be scared to death,* испугаться до смерти. **2,** *fol. by* **away** *or* **off** (drive away) спугивать. —*v.i.* пугаться. *He doesn't scare easily,* его не так легко испугать. —*n.* *Give someone a scare,* напугать кого-нибудь. *Have quite a scare,* очень перепугаться.
scarecrow *n.* пугало; чучело.
scarf *n.* шарф.
scarlet *adj.* алый. —*n.* алый цвет. —**scarlet fever,** скарлатина.
scary *adj., colloq.* пугающий; страшный.
scat *interj.* прочь!; поди прочь!; прочь отсюда!
scathing *adj.* хлёсткий; разносный; уничтожающий.
scatter *v.t.* **1,** (strew) разбрасывать; рассыпать. **2,** (disperse; rout) рассеивать; разгонять. —*v.i.* рассеиваться; рассыпаться; разбегаться.
scatterbrain *n.* ветреник; разиня. —**scatterbrained,** *adj.* ветреный; безголовый.
scavenge *v.i.* искать отбросы; рыться в мусоре. —**scavenger,** *n.* животное, питающееся падалью.
scenario *n.* сценарий.
scene *n.* **1,** (place where something occurs) место: *scene of the crime,* место преступления. *Appear on the scene,* явиться на сцену. *Pass from the scene,*

сойти́ со сце́ны. **2,** (division of an act of a play) сце́на; явле́ние; карти́на. *Act One, Scene Two,* де́йствие пе́рвое, сце́на втора́я. **3,** (part or setting of a play, movie or story) сце́на: *love scenes,* любо́вные сце́ны. *Scenes from a movie,* ка́дры из фи́льма. *The scene is laid in Ancient Rome,* де́йствие происхо́дит в дре́внем Ри́ме. **4,** (sight; spectacle) сце́на; зре́лище. **5,** (view) вид: *the scene from the window,* вид из окна́. **6,** (display of temper) сце́на: *make a scene,* устро́ить сце́ну. —**behind the scenes,** за кули́сами.

scenery *n.* **1,** (landscape) пейза́ж. **2,** *theat.* декора́ции. —**change of scenery, 1,** *theat.* переме́на декора́ций. **2,** *fig.* (change of surroundings) переме́на обстано́вки.

scenic *adj.* **1,** (pert. to stage effects) сцени́ческий: *scenic effects,* сцени́ческие эффе́кты. **2,** (having beautiful scenery) живопи́сный.

scent *n.* **1,** (odor) за́пах; арома́т. **2,** (trail of an animal) след: *pick up the scent,* напа́сть на след. **3,** (sense of smell) чутьё. **4,** (perfume) духи́. —*v.t.* **1,** (smell) обоня́ть. **2,** (sense; suspect) чу́ять. **3,** (perfume) души́ть.

scepter *also,* **sceptre** *n.* ски́петр.

sceptic *n.* = **skeptic.** —**sceptical,** *adj.* = **skeptical.** —**scepticism,** *n.* = **skepticism.**

sceptre *n.* = **scepter.**

schedule *n.* расписа́ние. *On schedule,* по расписа́нию; в срок. *Ahead of schedule,* до сро́ка; ра́ньше сро́ка. —*v.t.* назнача́ть; намеча́ть: *the meeting is scheduled for May 5th,* собра́ние назна́чено/назнача́ется/намеча́ется на пя́тое ма́я.

schematic *adj.* схемати́ческий.

scheme *n.* **1,** (plan of action) план. **2,** (underhanded plot) махина́ция; интри́га. **3,** (diagram) схе́ма. **4,** (orderly combination) сочета́ние: *color scheme,* сочета́ние цвето́в. —*v.i.* интригова́ть; вести́ интри́гу. —**schemer,** *n.* интрига́н.

scherzo *n.* ске́рцо.

schism *n.* раско́л; схи́зма. —**schismatic,** *adj.* раско́льнический.

schist *n.* сла́нец.

schizophrenia *n.* шизофрени́я. —**schizophrenic,** *adj.* шизофрени́ческий. —*n.* шизофре́ник.

schnitzel *n.* шни́цель.

scholar *n.* учёный. —**scholarly,** *adj.* учёный.

scholarship *n.* **1,** (learning) учёность. **2,** (grant) стипе́ндия.

scholastic *adj.* шко́льный; уче́бный.

school *n.* **1,** (place of learning) шко́ла: *go to school,* ходи́ть в шко́лу. *Law school,* юриди́ческий факульте́т. **2,** (classes) заня́тия; уро́ки: *miss school,* пропусти́ть заня́тия. *Keep in after school,* оставля́ть по́сле уро́ков. **3,** (trend in the arts) шко́ла: *the impressionist school,* импрессиони́стская шко́ла. **4,** (large group of fish) кося́к. —*adj.* шко́льный; уче́бный. *School age,* шко́льный во́зраст. *School year,* уче́бный год. —*v.t.* **1,** (educate) воспи́тывать. *He was schooled in England,* он получи́л образова́ние в А́нглии. **2,** (train; discipline) приуча́ть. —**a man of the old school,** челове́к ста́рого зака́ла. —**school of thought,** то́чка зре́ния: *there are two schools of thought on this question,* на э́тот счёт существу́ют две разли́чных то́чки зре́ния. —**tell tales out of school,** выноси́ть сор из избы́.

schoolbook *n.* уче́бник.

schoolboy *n.* шко́льник. —**schoolchildren,** *n.pl.* шко́льники. —**schoolgirl,** *n.* шко́льница.

schoolhouse *n.* шко́льное зда́ние.

schooling *n.* образова́ние.

schoolteacher *n.* учи́тель; учи́тельница.

schooner *n.* шху́на.

sciatic *adj.* седа́лищный: *sciatic nerve,* седа́лищный нерв.

sciatica *n.* и́шиас.

science *n.* нау́ка. —**science fiction,** нау́чная фанта́стика.

scientific *adj.* нау́чный. —**scientifically,** *adv.* нау́чно.

scientist *n.* **1,** (eminent scientist) учёный. **2,** (person engaged in scientific research) нау́чный рабо́тник.

scimitar *n.* ятага́н.

scintilla *n.* ка́пелька; крупи́ца; тень. *Not a scintilla of evidence,* ни мале́йших доказа́тельств.

scintillate *v.i.* и́скриться. —**scintillating,** *adj.* блестя́щий.

scion *n.* о́тпрыск.

scissors *n.* но́жницы.

sclerosis *n.* склеро́з. —**sclerotic,** *adj.* склероти́ческий.

scoff *v.i.* [*usu.* **scoff at**] осме́ивать; высме́ивать.

scold *v.t.* брани́ть. —**scolding,** *n.* вы́говор; нагоня́й.

scoop *n.* сово́к; ковш; черпа́к. —*v.t.* **1,** *fol. by* **up** (gather up) че́рпать; заче́рпывать. **2,** *fol. by* **out** (remove) вычё́рпывать.

scoot *v.i., colloq.* бежа́ть; удира́ть.

scooter *n.* самока́т. —**motor scooter,** моторо́ллер.

scope *n.* **1,** (range; extent) разма́х; масшта́б. **2,** (outlook; intellect) кругозо́р: *broaden one's scope,* расширя́ть кругозо́р.

scorch *v.t.* опа́ливать; подпа́ливать. —**scorched-earth policy,** страте́гия вы́жженной земли́.

scorching *adj.* паля́щий.

score *n.* **1,** (in sports and games) счёт: *keep score,* вести́ счёт. *What's the score?,* како́й счёт? *By a score of 2-0,* со счётом два-ноль. **2,** (achievement in a test or competition) результа́т: *achieve the highest score,* показа́ть лу́чший результа́т. **3,** (account) счёт: *have no fear on that score,* на э́тот счёт мо́жете быть споко́йны. **4,** *pl.* (grievance demanding satisfaction) счёты: *settle scores with,* своди́ть счёты с. **5,** (twenty) два́дцать; два деся́тка; *pl.* деся́тки; не́сколько деся́тков; мно́жество. **6,** *music* партиту́ра. **7,** (mark; incision) след; зару́бка. —*v.t.* **1,** *sports: score a goal,* заби́ть гол. *Score a point,* получи́ть *or* вы́играть очко́. *Score ten points,* набра́ть де́сять очко́в. **2,** (achieve) получи́ть; доби́ться. *Score a victory,* одержа́ть побе́ду. **3,** (denounce) осужда́ть. **4,** *music* оркестрова́ть. —*v.i.* получи́ть очко́; заби́ть гол. *Score first; be the first to score,* откры́ть счёт. —**know the score,** знать что к чему́.

scoreboard *n.* табло́.

scorekeeper *n.* судья́.

scoreless *adj.* нулево́й: *scoreless tie,* нулева́я ничья́.

scorn *n.* презре́ние. —*v.t.* презира́ть. —**scornful,** *adj.* презри́тельный.

Scorpio *n.* Скорпио́н.

scorpion *n.* скорпио́н.

Scotch *adj.* шотла́ндский. —*n.* **1,** *preceded by* **the**

(people) шотла́ндцы. **2,** (whiskey) (шотла́ндское) ви́ски.

scotch *v.t.* опроверга́ть: *scotch a rumor,* опрове́ргнуть слух.

Scotchman *n.* шотла́ндец.

scot-free *adj.* безнака́занный.

Scotsman *n.* шотла́ндец.

Scottish *adj.* шотла́ндский. —**Scottish terrier,** шотла́ндский терье́р.

scoundrel *n.* подле́ц; негодя́й; мерза́вец; прохво́ст.

scour *v.t.* **1,** (clean thoroughly) чи́стить; отчища́ть. **2,** (range over in search of something) ры́скать по: *scour the woods,* ры́скать по ле́су.

scourge *n.* бич. *The scourge of war,* бич войны́.

scout *n.* **1,** (agent) разве́дчик; лазу́тчик. **2,** (boy scout) ска́ут. —*v.t.* разве́дывать.

scow *n.* шала́нда.

scowl *v.i.* хму́риться. —*n.* серди́тый взгляд.

scraggly *adj.* нечёсаный; взъеро́шенный.

scram *v.i., slang* убира́ться.

scramble *v.i.* **1,** (climb hurriedly) кара́бкаться: *scramble up a tree,* кара́бкаться на де́рево. **2,** (dash) бро́ситься: *scramble for cover/safety,* бро́ситься в укры́тие/в безопа́сное ме́сто/. *The boys scrambled for the coins,* ма́льчики бро́сились за моне́тами. —*v.t.* (mix up; jumble) переме́шивать. —*n.* сва́лка. —**scrambled eggs,** яи́чница-болту́нья.

scrap *n.* **1,** (fragment) обры́вок; обре́зок, (of paper) клочо́к; (of material) лоску́т; (of bread) кусо́чек. **2,** *pl.* (bits of food) объе́дки. **3,** (waste metal) лом; ути́ль. **4,** *slang* (fight; quarrel) дра́ка; потасо́вка. —*adj.* ути́льный. *Scrap iron,* желе́зный лом; ути́льное желе́зо. *Scrap metal,* металлоло́м. *Scrap heap,* сва́лка. —*v.t.* **1,** (junk) сдава́ть на слом. *Be scrapped,* идти́ на слом. **2,** (drop, as a project) бро́сить. —*v.i., slang* (quarrel) вздо́рить.

scrapbook *n.* альбо́м для вы́резок.

scrape *v.t.* **1,** (rub the surface of) скрести́; скобли́ть. **2,** (injure; abrade) сдира́ть; сса́живать. —*n.* **1,** (abrasion) сса́дина. **2,** (predicament) переде́лка; передря́га. —**scrape along,** ко́е-как перебива́ться. —**scrape off,** соска́бливать; отска́бливать. —**scrape up; scrape together,** наскрести́; скола́чивать; выкра́ивать.

scraper *n.* скребо́к.

scrapper *n., colloq.* драчу́н; зади́ра; забия́ка.

scrappy *adj., slang* драчли́вый.

scratch *n.* цара́пина. —*v.t.* **1,** (tear the skin slightly) цара́пать. **2,** (rub to relieve itching) чеса́ть. **3,** *fol. by* **out** (cross out) вычёркивать. **4,** (withdraw from a contest) снима́ть с состяза́ний. —*v.i.* **1,** (have a tendency to scratch) цара́паться. **2,** (rub to relieve itching) чеса́ться. **3,** (produce a grating sound) скрипе́ть. —**scratch the surface,** скользи́ть по пове́рхности. —**start from scratch,** нача́ть с азо́в. —**up to scratch,** на до́лжной высоте́.

scratch pad блокно́т.

scratch paper бума́га для заме́ток.

scratchy *adj.* скрипу́чий.

scrawl *n.* кара́кули; мара́нье. —*v.t.* (на)цара́пать. *Slogans were scrawled all over the wall,* стена́ была́ испи́сана ло́зунгами.

scrawny *adj.* костля́вый; сухопа́рый.

scream *v.i.* **1,** (yell) крича́ть: *scream from the pain,* крича́ть от бо́ли; *scream with delight,* крича́ть от восто́рга. **2,** (whistle; roar) реве́ть: *sirens screamed,* сире́ны реве́ли. —*n.* **1,** (shriek) (пронзи́тельный) крик. **2,** *colloq.* (very funny person or thing) умо́ра.

screech *n.* визг; клёкот. —*v.i.* визжа́ть; клекота́ть.

screen *n.* **1,** (partition; anything that covers or protects) ши́рма. *Smoke screen,* дымова́я заве́са. **2,** (mesh for a window to keep out insects) се́тка. **3,** (surface for projecting pictures) экра́н. **4,** (motion pictures collectively) кино́; экра́н. *Adapt for the screen,* экранизи́ровать. —*v.t.* **1,** (shield) прикрыва́ть. **2,** *fol. by* **off** (separate by a screen) отгора́живать ши́рмой. **3,** (separate and select) фильтрова́ть.

screw *n.* винт. —*v.t.* **1,** *fol. by* **on** *or* **in** (turn tight, as a lid) нави́нчивать; зави́нчивать; приви́нчивать. *Screw in a bulb,* вви́нчивать *or* вверты́вать ла́мпочку. **2,** (attach with a screw) приви́нчивать: *screw a lock onto a door,* приви́нчивать замо́к к две́ри. *Screw something into a wall,* вви́нчивать что́-нибудь в сте́ну. **3,** *fol. by* **up** (contort) мо́рщить. *Screw up one's eyes,* щу́рить глаза́; щу́риться. **4,** *fol. by* **up,** *slang* (botch) напу́тать. —*v.i.* [*usu.* **screw on** *or* **onto**] нави́нчиваться; вви́нчиваться. —**he has a screw loose,** *slang* у него́ ви́нтика не хвата́ет. —**put the screws on,** нажима́ть на. —**tighten the screws,** зави́нчивать га́йки.

screwball *n., slang* сумасбро́д; чуда́к.

screwdriver *n.* отвёртка.

screw propeller гребно́й винт.

screwy *adj., slang* **1,** (crazy) сумасбро́дный. **2,** (odd) чудакова́тый.

scribble *v.t. & i.* строчи́ть; цара́пать; мара́ть. —*n.* кара́кули; мара́нье. —**scribbler,** *n.* писа́ка.

scribe *n.* **1,** (copier of manuscripts) писе́ц. **2,** *Bib.* кни́жник.

scrimmage *n.* **1,** (tussle) сва́лка. **2,** *football* сва́лка вокру́г мяча́.

scrimp *v.i.* скупи́ться.

scrip *n.* бума́жные де́ньги.

script *n.* **1,** (copy of something to be read) текст. **2,** (system of writing) письмо́: *the Arabic script,* ара́бское письмо́.

scriptural *adj.* библе́йский.

Scripture *n., usu. pl.* свяще́нное писа́ние.

scrofula *n.* золоту́ха.

scroll *n.* сви́ток.

scrotum *n.* мошо́нка.

scrub *v.t.* мыть.(щёткой с мы́лом).

scruff *n.* загри́вок. —**by the scruff of the neck,** за ши́ворот.

scruffy *adj.* неря́шливый.

scrumptious *adj., colloq.* великоле́пный; о́чень вку́сный.

scruple *n., often pl.* угрызе́ния со́вести. *Have no scruples,* не стесня́ться в сре́дствах. —*v.i.* стесня́ться; со́веститься.

scrupulous *adj.* **1,** (honest) со́вестливый. **2,** (meticulous) добросо́вестный; скрупулёзный. —**scrupulously,** *adv.* свя́то: *scrupulously observe,* свя́то соблюда́ть (что́-нибудь).

scrutinize *v.t.* (при́стально) рассма́тривать. —**scrutiny,** *n.* рассмотре́ние.

scuffle *n.* дра́ка; сва́лка; потасо́вка. —*v.i.* дра́ться.

scull *n.* **1,** (single long oar) кормово́е весло́. **2,** (one

of a pair of short oars) па́рное весло́. **3,** (boat) гребна́я ло́дка. —*v.t. & i.* грести́.
scullery *n.* судомо́йня.
sculpt *v.t.* вая́ть; лепи́ть.
sculptor *n.* ску́льптор; вая́тель.
sculptural *adj.* скульпту́рный.
sculpture *n.* **1,** (art) скульпту́ра; вая́ние. **2,** (piece of sculptured work) скульпту́ра; извая́ние. —*v.t.* вая́ть.
scum *n.* **1,** (extraneous matter on liquid) на́кипь. **2,** (riffraff) подо́нки.
scurrilous *adj.* гру́бый; оскорби́тельный; непристо́йный.
scurry *v.i.* бежа́ть; мча́ться.
scurvy *n.* цинга́; скорбу́т.
scutch *v.t.* трепа́ть. —*n.* трепа́ло.
scuttle *v.t.* затопля́ть (кора́бль).
scythe *n.* коса́.
Scythian *adj.* ски́фский. —*n.* скиф.
sea *n.* мо́ре. *Put (out) to sea,* выходи́ть в мо́ре. —*adj.* морско́й: *sea water,* морска́я вода́. —**be all at sea,** быть как в лесу́.
sea anemone акти́ния.
seabed *n.* морско́е дно.
seaboard *n.* побере́жье.
sea breeze морско́й бриз; примо́рский ве́тер.
seacoast *n.* побере́жье.
sea cow морска́я коро́ва.
sea dog морско́й волк.
sea elephant морско́й слон.
seafarer *n.* морепла́ватель; морехо́д.
seafood *n.* морски́е проду́кты.
seagoing *adj.* океа́нский; да́льнего пла́вания.
sea gull ча́йка.
sea horse морско́й конёк.
sea kale морска́я капу́ста.
seal *n.* **1,** (imprint; stamp for making same) печа́ть: *affix a seal to,* ста́вить печа́ть на (+ *acc.*). *The Great Seal of the United States,* госуда́рственная печа́ть США. **2,** (wax to secure an envelope) печа́ть: *break the seal,* взлома́ть печа́ть. **3,** (something that closes tightly) уплотни́тель: *rubber seal,* рези́новый уплотни́тель. **4,** (sign; token) знак: *seal of approval,* знак одобре́ния. **5,** (marine animal) тюле́нь. *Fur seal,* ко́тик. —*v.t.* **1,** (close, as an envelope) закле́ивать; запеча́тывать. **2,** *often fol. by* **up** (close tightly) заде́лывать; забива́ть; зама́зывать; залепля́ть. **3,** *fol. by* **off** (cordon off) оцепля́ть. **4,** (affix a seal to) скрепля́ть печа́тью: *signed, sealed and delivered,* подпи́сано, скреплено́ печа́тью и вручено́. **5,** (settle finally) реши́ть: *his fate is sealed,* его́ судьба́ решена́.
sealed move *chess* запи́санный ход.
sea level у́ровень мо́ря.
sealing wax сургу́ч.
sea lion морско́й лев.
sealskin *n.* ко́тик. —*adj.* ко́тиковый; тюле́невый.
seam *n.* шов. —*v.t.* сшива́ть. —**come apart at the seams,** треща́ть по всем швам.
seaman *n.* матро́с; моря́к.
seamless *adj.* **1,** (of stockings) без шва. **2,** (of pipes) бесшо́вный.
seamstress *n.* швея́; белошве́йка.
seamy *adj., in* **the seamy side,** изна́нка: *the seamy side of life,* изна́нка жи́зни.
séance *n.* спирити́ческий сеа́нс.
seaplane *n.* гидропла́н; гидросамолёт.
seaport *n.* **1,** (harbor) морско́й порт. **2,** (city) порто́вый го́род.
sear *v.t.* опа́ливать. *Searing heat,* паля́щая жара́.
search *v.i.* [*usu.* **search for**] иска́ть: *search for one's keys,* иска́ть свои́ ключи́. *I've searched everywhere,* я всю́ду иска́л(а). —*v.t.* обы́скивать: *search a house/suspect,* обы́скивать дом/подозрева́емого. *Search the woods,* обы́скивать лес. —*n.* **1,** (for something missing or desired) по́иски: *in search of,* в по́исках (+ *gen.*). *Set out in search of,* отпра́виться на по́иски (+ *gen.*). **2,** (of a suspect person or place) о́быск. —**search party,** поиско́вая гру́ппа. —**search warrant,** о́рдер на о́быск.
searching *adj.* **1,** (extremely thorough) тща́тельный. **2,** (penetrating, as of a look) испыту́ющий.
searchlight *n.* проже́ктор.
seascape *n.* морско́й пейза́ж; мари́на.
sea shell раку́шка.
seashore *n.* морско́й бе́рег.
seasick *adj.* *Be seasick,* укача́ть (*impers.*): *I got seasick,* меня́ укача́ло. —**seasickness,** *n.* морска́я боле́знь.
seaside *n.* бе́рег мо́ря; примо́рье. —*adj.* примо́рский: *seaside resort,* примо́рский куро́рт. *Seaside cottage,* да́ча на мо́ре.
season *n.* **1,** (quarter of the year) вре́мя го́да: *the four seasons,* четы́ре вре́мени го́да. **2,** (period of the year, as for business, sports, etc.) сезо́н. *Strawberries are out of season,* сейча́с не сезо́н для клубни́ки. —*adj.* сезо́нный: *season ticket,* сезо́нный биле́т. —*v.t.* **1,** (flavor) приправля́ть; заправля́ть; сдабривать. **2,** (inure; harden) закаля́ть. —*v.i.* (become seasoned) созрева́ть.
seasonal *adj.* сезо́нный.
seasoning *n.* припра́ва.
seat *n.* **1,** (place to sit) ме́сто: *reserved seat,* нумеро́ванное ме́сто. *Take a seat,* сади́ться. *Take your seats,* занима́йте свои́ места́. *Have a seat!,* приса́живайтесь! *Seat in parliament,* ме́сто в парла́менте. *We sat in the cheap seats,* мы сиде́ли на дешёвых места́х. **2,** (that on which one sits) сиде́нье: *seat of a chair,* сиде́нье сту́ла. *Back seat,* за́днее сиде́нье. **3,** (back part of trousers) зад; сиде́нье. *Tight in the seat,* у́зки в шагу́. **4,** (center; site) местопребыва́ние: *seat of government,* местопребыва́ние прави́тельства. *Seat of learning,* расса́дник просвеще́ния. —*v.t.* **1,** (place on a seat) сажа́ть; уса́живать. **2,** (hold; accommodate) вмеща́ть. —**be seated, 1,** (sit down) сади́ться. *Please be seated,* прошу́ сади́ться. **2,** (be sitting down) сиде́ть.
seat belt привязно́й реме́нь; реме́нь безопа́сности.
seating *n.* сидя́чие места́. —**seating capacity,** число́ мест. *The stadium has a seating capacity of 100,000,* стадио́н вмеща́ет сто ты́сяч челове́к.
sea urchin морско́й ёж.
sea wall волноре́з; волноло́м.
seaway *n.* фарва́тер.
seaweed *n.* (морска́я) во́доросль.
seaworthy *adj.* го́дный для пла́вания; морехо́дный.
sebaceous glands са́льные же́лезы.
secant *n.* **1,** *geom.* секу́щая. **2,** *trig.* се́канс.
secede *v.i.* выходи́ть (из сою́за). —**secession,** *n.* вы́ход.

seclude *v.t.* уединя́ть. —**secluded,** *adj.* уединённый; укро́мный. —**seclusion,** *n.* уедине́ние.
second *adj.* второ́й. *Come in second,* прийти́ вторы́м. *She married for a second time,* она́ вы́шла за́муж втори́чно. *He is second to none,* он никому́ не уступа́ет. —*n.* **1,** (unit of time or angular measure) секу́нда. *Just a second!,* одну́ мину́т(к)у!; одну́ секу́нд(очк)у! **2,** (attendant in boxing, a duel, etc.) секунда́нт. **3,** *music* секу́нда. **4,** *pl.* (imperfect merchandise) (за)брако́ванный това́р. —*v.t.* подде́рживать: *second the motion,* подде́рживать предложе́ние. —**in the second place,** во-вторы́х.
secondary *adj.* **1,** (of less importance) второстепе́нный. **2,** (of education, school, etc.) сре́дний. —**secondary sex characteristics,** втори́чные полов́ые при́знаки.
second-class *adj.* второкла́ссный; второразря́дный. *Second-class passengers,* пассажи́ры второ́го кла́сса. *Second-class coach,* жёсткий ваго́н. —*adv.* вторы́м кла́ссом: *travel second-class,* е́хать вторы́м кла́ссом.
second cousin *see* **cousin.**
second hand секу́ндная стре́лка.
secondhand *adj.* (not new) подде́ржанный. *Secondhand bookstore,* букинисти́ческий магази́н. —*adv.* (not from the original source) из вторы́х рук.
second lieutenant мла́дший лейтена́нт.
secondly *adv.* во-вторы́х.
second nature втора́я нату́ра.
second-rate *adj.* второсо́ртный; второразря́дный.
second thought разду́ме: *he had second thoughts,* его́ взя́ло разду́мье. —**on second thought,** по зре́лом размышле́нии; пораски́нув умо́м.
second wind второ́е дыха́ние.
secrecy *n.* секре́тность. *In great secrecy,* под больши́м секре́том.
secret *n.* секре́т; та́йна. *In secret,* та́йно; вта́йне; тайко́м. —*adj.* **1,** (done or operating in secret) секре́тный; та́йный. *Secret agent,* та́йный аге́нт. *Keep (something) secret,* держа́ть *or* храни́ть в секре́те (*or* в та́йне). **2,** (hidden) потайно́й: *secret passage,* потайно́й ход.
secretarial *adj.* секрета́рский.
secretariat *n.* секретариа́т.
secretary *n.* **1,** (clerical assistant) секрета́рь; секрета́рша. **2,** (official; officer) секрета́рь. **3,** (cabinet officer) мини́стр; секрета́рь. *Secretary of state,* госуда́рственный секрета́рь. *Secretary of the treasury,* мини́стр фина́нсов. *Foreign secretary,* мини́стр иностра́нных дел. —**secretary general,** генера́льный секрета́рь.
secrete *v.t.* **1,** (conceal) укрыва́ть; пря́тать. **2,** *physiol.* выделя́ть. —**secretion,** *n.* секре́ция; выделе́ние.
secretive *adj.* скры́тный. —**secretiveness,** *n.* скры́тность.
secretly *adv.* та́йно; вта́йне; тайко́м.
secretory *adj.* выдели́тельный.
sect *n.* се́кта.
sectarian *adj.* секта́нтский. —*n.* секта́нт. —**sectarianism,** *n.* секта́нтство.
section *n.* **1,** (portion, as of a road) отре́зок. **2,** (part, as of a fence or bookcase) се́кция. **3,** (view in a given plane) сече́ние; разре́з: *cross section,* попере́чное сече́ние; попере́чный разре́з. *Conic section,* кони́ческое сече́ние. **4,** (district; neighborhood) райо́н. **5,** (division of an organization) отде́л; се́кция. **6,** (division of a book or newspaper) отде́л; разде́л; (of a law) пара́граф. **7,** (slice, as of an orange) до́лька. **8,** (slice of something used for microscopic study) срез. **9,** (incision) сече́ние: *Caesarean section,* ке́сарево сече́ние.
sectional *adj.* **1,** (made up of sections) секцио́нный; составно́й. **2,** (regional) ме́стный.
sector *n.* **1,** (part of a circle) се́ктор. **2,** *mil.* уча́сток. **3,** (division) се́ктор: *the private sector,* ча́стный се́ктор.
secular *adj.* све́тский; мирско́й.
secularize *v.t.* секуляризи́ровать. —**secularization,** *n.* секуляриза́ция.
secure *adj.* **1,** (safe) безопа́сный: *secure place,* безопа́сное ме́сто. *Feel secure,* чу́вствовать себя́ в безопа́сности. **2,** (firm) про́чный; кре́пкий: *secure foothold,* про́чная опо́ра; *secure grip,* кре́пкая хва́тка. —*v.t.* **1,** (firmly fasten) закрепля́ть. **2,** (make safe) обезопа́сить. **3,** (make certain; ensure) обеспе́чивать. **4,** (gain; obtain) получи́ть; доста́ть. —**securely,** *adv.* про́чно: *tie securely,* про́чно привя́зывать.
security *n.* **1,** (safety; protection) безопа́сность: *national security,* госуда́рственная безопа́сность. *Provide security,* обеспе́чивать безопа́сность. **2,** (material well-being) обеспе́чение; обеспе́ченность. *Financial security,* материа́льное обеспе́чение. **3,** (pledge; deposit) зало́г: *leave something as security,* оста́вить что́-нибудь под зало́г. **4,** *pl.* (stocks, bonds, etc.) це́нные бума́ги. —*adj. Security guard,* сто́рож; охра́нник. *Security measures,* ме́ры безопа́сности. —**security clearance, 1,** (check) прове́рка благонадёжности. **2,** (access) до́пуск.
Security Council Сове́т Безопа́сности.
sedan *n.* легково́й автомоби́ль. —**sedan chair,** портше́з.
sedate *adj.* степе́нный; чи́нный. —*v.t.* дава́ть успокои́тельное сре́дство (+ *dat.*).
sedation *n.* успокое́ние. *Place under sedation,* дава́ть успокои́тельное сре́дство (+ *dat.*). —**sedative,** *n.* успокои́тельное *or* успока́ивающее сре́дство; успокои́тельное.
sedentary *adj.* сидя́чий.
sedge *n.* осо́ка.
sediment *n.* **1,** (matter that settles at the bottom) оса́док. **2,** *geol.* отложе́ние. —**sedimentary,** *adj.* оса́дочный.
sedition *n.* подстрека́тельство к мятежу́. —**seditious,** *adj.* мятёжный; бунта́рский.
seduce *v.t.* соблазня́ть; обольща́ть. —**seducer,** *n.* соблазни́тель; обольсти́тель. —**seduction,** *n.* обольще́ние. —**seductive,** *adj.* соблазни́тельный; обольсти́тельный.
sedulous *adj.* прилёжный; стара́тельный.
see *v.t. & i.* **1,** (perceive visually; have the power of sight) ви́деть: *see a man/car/difference,* ви́деть челове́ка/маши́ну/ра́зницу. *Can you see?,* вам ви́дно? *See in the dark,* ви́деть в темноте́. *I saw him come in,* я ви́дел, как он вошёл. **2,** (view) смотре́ть: *see a play,* смотре́ть пье́су. *Would you like to see it?,* хоти́те посмотре́ть? *I'll go see,* я пойду́ посмотре́ть. **3,** (understand) понима́ть: *I see,* я понима́ю. *I see what you mean,* я понима́ю, что вы име́ете в виду́. —*v.t.* **1,** (consult) обраща́ться к: *see a doctor,* обраща́ться к

врачу́. **2,** (receive) принима́ть: *he refused to see me,* он отказа́лся приня́ть меня́. **3,** (visit; meet) ви́деть; встреча́ть: *we rarely see each other,* мы ре́дко ви́димся/встреча́емся. *He came to see me last night,* он пришёл ко мне вчера́ ве́чером. **4,** (escort) провожа́ть: *see someone to the door,* провожа́ть кого́-нибудь до двере́й. **5,** (find out; ascertain) смотре́ть; узнава́ть: *see who is at the door,* посмотри́те, кто стучи́т *or* звони́т (в дверь). **6,** (visualize) представля́ть (себе́). *I can't see myself doing that,* не могу́ предста́вить себя́ в э́той ро́ли. **7,** (interpret) рассма́тривать: *his hesitancy is seen as a sign of weakness,* его́ колеба́ние рассма́тривается как при́знак сла́бости. **8,** (admire) находи́ть: *what does she see in him?,* что она́ в нём нашла́? *—n.* престо́л: *holy see,* па́пский престо́л. **—let me see!,** да́йте мне поду́мать. **—see fit,** *see* **fit. —see for oneself,** воо́чию убеди́ться. *I want to see for myself,* я хочу́ убеди́ться сам (сама́). **—see here!,** послу́шайте! **—see off,** провожа́ть: *see someone off on the train,* провожа́ть кого́-нибудь на по́езд. **—see things,** каза́ться (+ *dat.*); чу́диться (+ *dat.*): *you're seeing things!,* вам то́лько ка́жется/чу́дится. **—see through, 1,** (not be fooled by) ви́деть насквóзь. **2,** (carry through to the end) доводи́ть до конца́. **3,** (carry through a difficult time) хвата́ть: *this money should see you through the week,* де́нег должно́ вам хвати́ть до конца́ неде́ли. **—see to,** забо́титься о. **—see (to it) that...,** забо́титься о том, что́бы; доби́ться того́, что́бы.

seed *n.* **1,** (that which can grow into a new plant) се́мя. **2,** (of fruits, sunflowers, etc.) се́мечко. **3,** *fig.* (source) се́мя: *seeds of rebellion,* семена́ бу́нта. *—adj.* семенно́й: *seed coat,* семенна́я оболо́чка. *—v.t.* засева́ть (*e.g.* сад) семена́ми. **—go to seed, 1,** (shed seeds) пойти́ в семена́. **2,** (deteriorate) опуска́ться.

seeder *n.* се́ялка.

seedless *adj.* бессемя́нный.

seedling *n.* се́янец; *pl.* расса́да.

seedy *adj.* потрёпанный; потёртый.

seeing *conj.* [*usu.* **seeing that**] поско́льку; ввиду́ того́, что...

Seeing Eye dog соба́ка-поводы́рь.

seek *v.t.* **1,** (try to find) иска́ть: *seek one's long-lost sister,* иска́ть свою́ давно́ пропа́вшую сестру́. **2,** (try to obtain) иска́ть; добива́ться. *Seek work/help/advice/the cause/,* иска́ть рабо́ту/по́мощи/сове́та/причи́ну. *Seek recognition/an advantage/,* добива́ться призна́ния/преиму́щества. **3,** *fol. by inf.* (endeavor) пыта́ться; стреми́ться.

seeker *n.* иска́тель.

seem *v.i.* каза́ться: *he seems ill,* он ка́жется больны́м. *It seems to me that...,* мне ка́жется, что... *It may seem strange to you,* вам э́то мо́жет показа́ться стра́нным. *I can't seem to get used to it,* я ника́к не могу́ привы́кнуть к э́тому.

seeming *adj.* ви́димый. **—seemingly,** *adv.* каза́лось бы: *a seemingly small amount,* каза́лось бы небольша́я су́мма.

seemly *adj.* прили́чный; присто́йный.

seep *v.i.* проса́чиваться. **—seepage,** *n.* проса́чивание.

seer *n.* проро́к; прови́дец.

seesaw *n.* каче́ли.

seethe *v.i.* кипе́ть; бурли́ть.

segment *n.* **1,** (section) отре́зок. **2,** *geom.* сегме́нт.

segregate *v.t.* отделя́ть. **—segregation,** *n.* сегрега́ция.

seismic *adj.* сейсми́ческий.

seismograph *n.* сейсмо́граф.

seismology *n.* сейсмоло́гия. **—seismological,** *adj.* сейсмологи́ческий. **—seismologist,** *n.* сейсмо́лог.

seize *v.t.* **1,** (grasp) хвата́ть; схва́тывать. **2,** (take by force) захва́тывать; завладева́ть. **3,** (confiscate) конфискова́ть. **4,** (take prompt advantage of) ухвати́ться за. **5,** (overwhelm, as of fear) овладева́ть; охва́тывать; обуя́ть.

seizure *n.* **1,** (act of seizing) захва́т. **2,** (confiscation) конфиска́ция. **3,** (fit; attack) припа́док; при́ступ; уда́р.

seldom *adv.* ре́дко.

select *v.t.* отбира́ть; подбира́ть; избира́ть. *Selected works,* и́збранные сочине́ния. *—adj.* отбо́рный; и́збранный.

selection *n.* **1,** (act of selecting) отбо́р; подбо́р. **2,** (assortment) вы́бор; ассортиме́нт. **3,** *biol.* отбо́р: *natural selection,* есте́ственный отбо́р. **—selection committee,** отбо́рочная коми́ссия.

selective *adj.* **1,** (covering only selected items) вы́борочный. **2,** (choosy) разбо́рчивый. **—selective service,** во́инская пови́нность.

selectivity *n.* разбо́рчивость.

selenite *n.* селени́т.

selenium *n.* селе́н.

self *n.* *One's own self,* со́бственная персо́на. *My other self,* моё второ́е я. *He is only a shadow of his former self,* от него́ оста́лась одна́ тень.

self-addressed *adj.* адресо́ванный самому́ себе́.

self-assurance *n.* самоуве́ренность; самонаде́янность. **—self-assured,** *adj.* самоуве́ренный; самонаде́янный.

self-centered *also,* **self-centred** *adj.* себялюби́вый.

self-complacent *adj.* самодово́льный. **—self-complacency,** *n.* самодово́льство.

self-confidence *n.* самоуве́ренность. **—self-confident,** *adj.* самоуве́ренный.

self-conscious *adj.* засте́нчивый; стесни́тельный; стыдли́вый.

self-contained *adj.* **1,** (existing on its own) самодовле́ющий. **2,** *mech.* автоно́мный: *self-contained equipment,* автоно́мное обору́дование.

self-control *n.* самооблада́ние. **—self-controlled,** *adj.* вы́держанный.

self-criticism *n.* самокри́тика. **—self-critical,** *adj.* самокрити́чный.

self-deception *n.* самообма́н.

self-defense *also,* **self-defence** *n.* самозащи́та; самооборо́на.

self-denial *n.* самоотрече́ние.

self-designation *n.* самоназва́ние.

self-destruction *n.* самоуничтоже́ние.

self-determination *n.* самоопределе́ние.

self-discipline *n.* самодисципли́на.

self-employed *adj.* самостоя́тельно за́нятый; за́нятый со́бственным де́лом.

self-esteem *n.* самоуваже́ние.

self-evident *adj.* самоочеви́дный.

self-governing *adj.* самоуправля́ющийся. **—self-government,** *n.* самоуправле́ние.

self-immolation *n.* самосожже́ние.

self-importance *n.* ва́жность: *assume an air of self-importance,* напуска́ть на себя́ ва́жность. —**self-important,** *adj.* ва́жный.

self-interest *n.* коры́сть; корыстолю́бие; своекоры́стие.

selfish *adj.* **1,** (of a person) эгоисти́ческий; эгоисти́чный. **2,** (of interests, motives, etc.) коры́стный. —**selfishness,** *n.* эгои́зм.

selfless *adj.* самоотве́рженный. —**selflessness,** *n.* самоотве́рженность.

self-portrait *n.* автопортре́т.

self-possessed *adj.* вы́держанный.

self-preservation *n.* самосохране́ние.

self-propelled *adj.* самохо́дный; самодви́жущийся.

self-reliant *adj.* самостоя́тельный. —**self-reliance,** *n.* самостоя́тельность.

self-respect *n.* чу́вство со́бственного досто́инства; самолю́бие; самоуваже́ние.

self-restraint *n.* сде́ржанность.

self-righteous *adj.* ха́нжеский. —**self-righteousness,** *n.* ха́нжество.

self-sacrifice *n.* самопоже́ртвование.

selfsame *adj.* тот же са́мый.

self-satisfaction *n.* самодово́льство. —**self-satisfied,** *adj.* самодово́льный.

self-seeking *adj.* своекоры́стный.

self-service *n.* самообслу́живание. *Self-service store,* магази́н самообслу́живания.

self-starter *n.* самопу́ск.

self-styled *adj.* самозва́н(н)ый.

self-sufficient *adj.* самостоя́тельный. —**self-sufficiency,** *n.* (экономи́ческая) самостоя́тельность.

self-supporting *adj.* самостоя́тельный.

self-taught *adj.* *Rendered by* самоу́чка: *self-taught engineer,* инжене́р-самоу́чка.

self-willed *adj.* самово́льный.

sell *v.t.* **1,** (transfer for money) продава́ть: *she was selling flowers,* она́ продава́ла цветы́. *I sold my house,* я про́дал свой дом. **2,** (deal in; carry) торгова́ть (+ *instr.*). *The store sells bicycles,* в магази́не продаю́тся велосипе́ды; магази́н торгу́ет велосипе́дами. —*v.i.* **1,** (engage in selling) продава́ть. **2,** (be sold) продава́ться; расходи́ться: *be selling well,* хорошо́ продава́ться/расходи́ться. *These ties sell for a dollar,* э́ти га́лстуки мо́жно купи́ть за до́ллар. —**sell oneself, 1,** (sell one's services) продава́ться; продава́ть себя́. **2,** *colloq.* (convince others of one's worth) набива́ть себе́ це́ну. —**sell out, 1,** (sell completely) распрода́ть: *the book is sold out,* кни́га распро́дана. *The book sold out immediately,* кни́га разошла́сь момента́льно; кни́гу неме́дленно раскупи́ли. **2,** *colloq.* (betray one's cause) продава́ться: *sell out to the enemy,* продава́ться врагу́.

seller *n.* продаве́ц.

selling *n.* прода́жа. —**selling price,** прода́жная цена́.

sellout *n.* *The show is a complete sellout,* пье́са де́лает по́лные сбо́ры.

seltzer *n.* [*usu.* **seltzer water**] се́льтерская вода́.

selvage *n.* кро́мка.

semantic *adj.* семанти́ческий; смыслово́й. —**semantics,** *n.* сема́нтика.

semaphore *n.* семафо́р.

semblance *n.* **1,** (likeness; copy) подо́бие. **2,** (outward appearance) ви́димость: *a semblance of order,* ви́димость поря́дка.

semen *n.* се́мя; спе́рма.

semester *n.* семе́стр.

semiannual *adj.* полугодово́й.

semiautomatic *adj.* полуавтомати́ческий.

semicircle *n.* полукру́г. —**semicircular,** *adj.* полукру́глый.

semicolon *n.* то́чка с запято́й.

semiconductor *n.* полупроводни́к.

semiconscious *adj.* полусозна́тельный; полубессозна́тельный; в полу(бес)созна́тельном состоя́нии.

semidarkness *n.* полумра́к; полутьма́; су́мрак.

semifinal *n.* [*also,* **semifinals**] полуфина́л. —*adj.* полуфина́льный. —**semifinalist,** *n.* полуфинали́ст.

semiliterate *adj.* полугра́мотный; малогра́мотный.

seminal *adj.* **1,** *biol.* семенно́й: *seminal fluid,* семенна́я жи́дкость. **2,** *fig.* (breaking new ground) основополага́ющий.

seminar *n.* семина́р.

seminary *n.* семина́рия.

semiprecious *adj.* самоцве́тный. *Semiprecious stone,* самоцве́т.

Semitic *adj.* семи́тский; семити́ческий.

semitrailer *n.* полуприце́п.

senate *n.* сена́т. —**senator,** *n.* сена́тор. —**senatorial,** *adj.* сена́торский.

send *v.t.* посыла́ть; присыла́ть; отправля́ть: *send a package/messenger,* посыла́ть/присыла́ть/отправля́ть посы́лку/курье́ра. *Send a telegram,* дать/посла́ть/отпра́вить телегра́мму. *Send regards,* посыла́ть *or* передава́ть приве́т. *Send a pupil from the room,* выгоня́ть ученика́ из кла́сса. —**send away,** усыла́ть. —**send away for,** выпи́сывать. —**send for,** посыла́ть за (+ *instr.*). —**send off,** отсыла́ть. —**send out, 1,** (mail out) высыла́ть; рассыла́ть: *send out a package,* высыла́ть посы́лку; *send out invitations,* рассыла́ть приглаше́ния. **2,** (assign; dispatch) засыла́ть: *send out spies,* засыла́ть шпио́нов. **3,** (transmit, as a signal) передава́ть. —**send word,** сообща́ть; передава́ть.

sender *n.* отправи́тель.

send-off *n.* про́воды.

senile *adj.* ста́рческий. —**senility,** *n.* ста́рость.

senior *adj.* ста́рший: *senior member,* ста́рший член. *John Smith, Sr.,* Джон Смит ста́рший. —*n.* **1,** (elder) ста́рший. *Three years my senior,* ста́рше меня́ на три го́да. **2,** (student) старшеку́рсник. —**seniority,** *n.* старшинство́.

sensation *n.* **1,** (feeling) чу́вство; ощуще́ние. **2,** (great excitement; that which causes it) сенса́ция.

sensational *adj.* **1,** (causing great excitement) сенсацио́нный. **2,** (extraordinary; phenomenal) потряса́ющий.

sense *n.* **1,** (faculty) чу́вство: *the five senses,* пять чувств. *Sense of smell,* обоня́ние. *Sense of touch,* осяза́ние. *Sense of humor,* чу́вство ю́мора. *Sense organs,* о́рганы чувств. **2,** (good judgment; logic; point) смысл: *common sense,* здра́вый смысл. *There is no sense in...,* нет смы́сла (+ *inf.*). *Make no sense at all,* не име́ть никако́го смы́сла. *Talk sense,* говори́ть де́ло. **3,** *pl.* (rationality) ум: *take leave of one's senses,* сойти́ с ума́; *come to one's senses,* бра́ться за ум;

bring to one's senses, наводи́ть на ум. **4,** (meaning) смысл: *in the literal sense of the word,* в буква́льном смы́сле э́того сло́ва. —*v.t.* чу́вствовать; ощуща́ть; чу́ять. *Sense danger,* чу́вствовать опа́сность. *I sensed that something was wrong,* я почу́вствовал что́-то недо́брое. —**in a sense,** в изве́стном смы́сле.

senseless *adj.* **1,** (making no sense) бессмы́сленный. **2,** (unconscious) без созна́ния. *Knock senseless,* бить до бесчу́вствия. —**senselessly,** *adv.* бессмы́сленно.

senselessness *n.* **1,** (irrationality) бессмы́сленность. **2,** (unconsciousness) бесчу́вствие.

sensibility *n.* **1,** (ability to perceive) чувстви́тельность. **2,** *pl.* (feelings; pride) чу́вства (прили́чия); самолю́бие.

sensible *adj.* разу́мный; благоразу́мный. —**sensibly,** *adv.* разу́мно.

sensitive *adj.* **1,** (perceptive; responsive; tender) чувстви́тельный: *sensitive skin/film,* чувстви́тельная ко́жа/плёнка. *Sensitive to light,* чувстви́тельный к све́ту. **2,** (easily offended) оби́дчивый. **3,** (involving secret matters) секре́тный; засекре́ченный. —**sensitivity,** *n.* чувстви́тельность.

sensor *n.* да́тчик.

sensory *adj.* сенсо́рный. *Sensory nerve,* чувстви́тельный нерв.

sensual *adj.* чу́вственный; сладостра́стный. —**sensuality,** *n.* чу́вственность; сладостра́стие.

sensuous *adj.* чу́вственный.

sentence *n.* **1,** (group of words) предложе́ние; фра́за. **2,** (penalty pronounced) пригово́р. *Death sentence,* сме́ртный пригово́р. *Serve out a sentence,* отбыва́ть срок наказа́ния. —*v.t.* пригова́ривать: *sentence to prison,* пригова́ривать к тюре́мному заключе́нию.

sententious *adj.* сентенцио́зный.

sentiment *n.* **1,** *usu. pl.* (feelings) чу́вства: *lofty sentiments,* высо́кие чу́вства. *Pacifist sentiments,* пацифи́стские настрое́ния. **2,** (opinion) мне́ние: *public sentiment,* обще́ственное мне́ние. **3,** (sentimentality) сентимента́льность.

sentimental *adj.* сентимента́льный. —**sentimentality,** *n.* сентимента́льность.

sentinel *n.* часово́й.

sentry *n.* часово́й; карау́льный. —**sentry box,** карау́льная *or* постова́я бу́дка.

sepal *n.* чашели́стик.

separate *v.t.* **1,** (set apart) отделя́ть: *separate the boys from the girls,* отделя́ть ма́льчиков от де́вочек. **2,** (form a barrier or boundary between) разделя́ть. **3,** (pull apart, as two combatants) разнима́ть. **4,** (force to part company) разъединя́ть; разлуча́ть. *Be separated from the group,* отстава́ть от гру́ппы. *Become separated in a crowd,* потеря́ть друг дру́га в толпе́. —*v.i.* **1,** (become divided) отделя́ться. **2,** (part company) разлуча́ться. **3,** (break up without a divorce) расходи́ться; разъезжа́ться. —*adj.* отде́льный: *separate entrance,* отде́льный вход. *Conclude a separate peace,* заключи́ть сепара́тный мир. —**separately,** *adv.* отде́льно.

separation *n.* **1,** (dividing) отделе́ние. **2,** (parting company) разлу́ка. —**separation of powers,** разделе́ние вла́сти.

separatism *n.* сепарати́зм. —**separatist,** *n.* сепарати́ст. —*adj.* сепарати́стский.

separator *n.* сепара́тор.

sepia *n.* се́пия. —*adj.* кори́чневый.

sepsis *n.* се́псис.

September *n.* сентя́брь. —*adj.* сентя́брьский.

septic *adj.* септи́ческий.

sepulcher *also,* **sepulchre** *n.* моги́ла; склеп. —**sepulchral,** *adj.* моги́льный; замоги́льный.

sequel *n.* продолже́ние.

sequence *n.* поря́док. *In sequence,* по поря́дку. *Sequence of events,* ход собы́тий. *Sequence of tenses, gram.* согласова́ние времён.

sequester *v.t.* налага́ть секве́стр на; секвестрова́ть. —**sequestration,** *n.* секве́стр.

sequin *n.* блёстка.

sequoia *n.* секво́йя.

seraglio *n.* сера́ль.

seraph *n.* серафи́м.

Serb *n.* серб. —**Serbian,** *adj.* се́рбский. —*n.* се́рбский язы́к.

Serbo-Croatian *adj.* сербохорва́тский; сербскохорва́тский.

serenade *n.* серена́да.

serene *adj.* **1,** (unclouded) безо́блачный. **2,** (tranquil) споко́йный; безмяте́жный. —**serenity,** *n.* споко́йствие; безмяте́жность.

serf *n.* крепостно́й. —**serfdom,** *n.* крепостно́е пра́во; крепостни́чество.

serge *n.* са́ржа. —*adj.* са́ржевый.

sergeant *n.* сержа́нт.

serial *adj.* сери́йный. —*n.* по́весть в не́скольких частя́х; фильм в не́скольких се́риях.

serialize *v.t.* издава́ть се́риями.

serial number 1, (of a serviceman) ли́чный но́мер. **2,** (of a manufactured product) поря́дковый но́мер.

sericulture *n.* шелково́дство.

series *n.* **1,** (set) се́рия: *series of experiments,* се́рия о́пытов. **2,** (number of; succession of) ряд: *a whole series of disasters,* це́лый ряд катастро́ф. **3,** *math.* ряд.

serious *adj.* серьёзный: *serious tone/step/student,* серьёзный тон/шаг/студе́нт; *serious error/illness,* серьёзная оши́бка/боле́знь. *Are you serious?,* вы э́то серьёзно? *I'm serious,* я говорю́ серьёзно.

seriously *adv.* **1,** (in earnest) серьёзно: *talk seriously,* говори́ть серьёзно. *Take seriously,* принима́ть всерьёз. **2,** (gravely) тяжело́: *seriously ill/injured,* тяжело́ бо́лен/ра́нен.

seriousness *n.* серьёзность. *In all seriousness,* серьёзно; со всей серьёзностью.

sermon *n.* про́поведь. *Sermon on the Mount,* Наго́рная про́поведь.

sermonize *v.i.* пропове́довать. —**sermonizer,** *n.* пропове́дник; резонёр.

serology *n.* сероло́гия.

serpent *n.* змея́. —**serpentine,** *adj.* змееви́дный.

serrate *adj.* зубча́тый; зазу́бренный. *Also,* **serrated.**

serum *n.* сы́воротка.

servant *n.* (man) слуга́; (woman) служа́нка; прислу́га. *Servants,* слу́ги; прислу́га. —**civil servant,** госуда́рственный слу́жащий.

serve *v.t.* **1,** (work for; be in the service of) служи́ть (+ *dat.*): *serve one's country,* служи́ть свое́й ро́дине. *If memory serves me correctly,* е́сли па́мять мне не изменя́ет. **2,** (provide with goods or services) обслу́живать: *serve a customer/district,* обслу́живать покупа́теля/райо́н. **3,** (prepare and offer, as food or a meal) подава́ть; сервирова́ть. *Dinner is served!,* обе́д по́дан! **4,** (set food before): *may I serve you?,* мо́жно вам положи́ть на таре́лку? **5,** (present; deliver, as a legal document) вруча́ть. **6,** (complete, as a prison term) отбыва́ть: *serve one's sentence,* отбыва́ть срок наказа́ния. *Serve five years in prison,* (от)сиде́ть пять лет в тюрьме́. **7,** *sports* подава́ть (мяч). **8,** *Serve the purpose,* отвеча́ть це́ли. —*v.i.* **1,** (perform service) служи́ть: *serve in the navy,* служи́ть во фло́те. **2,** *fol. by* **as** (function as) служи́ть (+ *instr.*): *serve as a judge/bedroom/pretext,* служи́ть судьёй/спа́льней/предло́гом. **3,** (be suitable or usable) годи́ться. **4,** *sports* подава́ть. —*n., sports* пода́ча. —**it serves him right,** так ему́ и на́до; туда́ ему́ и доро́га.

server *n.* **1,** (waiter) подава́льщик. **2,** (tray) подно́с; (utensil) лопа́тка. **3,** *sports* игро́к, подаю́щий мяч.

service *n.* **1,** (act of serving) слу́жба: *military service,* вое́нная слу́жба. **2,** (work professionally performed) обслу́живание: *medical service,* медици́нское обслу́живание. *Poor service,* плохо́е обслу́живание. **3,** (public institution or facility) слу́жба: *weather service,* слу́жба пого́ды. *Rail service,* железнодоро́жное сообще́ние *or* движе́ние. *Telephone service,* телефо́нная связь. **4,** (help given another) услу́га: *offer one's services,* предлага́ть свои́ услу́ги. **5,** *pl.* (deeds performed) заслу́ги: *in recognition of one's services,* в знак призна́ния чьи́х-нибудь заслу́г. **6,** (armed forces) вое́нная слу́жба. *drafted into the service,* при́зван на вое́нную слу́жбу. **7,** (set of dishes) серви́з: *tea service,* ча́йный серви́з. **8,** (public worship) слу́жба; богослуже́ние. **9,** (religious ceremony) слу́жба. *funeral service(s),* заупоко́йная слу́жба. **10,** *sports* пода́ча. —*adj.* обслу́живающий: *service personnel,* обслу́живающий персона́л. *Service elevator,* грузово́й лифт. *Service record,* послужно́й спи́сок. —*v.t.* обслу́живать: *service a car,* обслу́живать автомоби́ль. —**at your service,** к ва́шим услу́гам. —**be in service,** рабо́тать; де́йствовать. —**be of service,** быть поле́зным. —**"out of service",** "не рабо́тает".

serviceable *adj.* поле́зный; приго́дный.

service cap фура́жка.

service charge допла́та за обслу́живание.

serviceman *n.* **1,** (member of the armed forces) военнослу́жащий. **2,** (repairman) ма́стер.

service station бензозапра́вочная ста́нция; автозапра́вочная ста́нция.

servile *adj.* раболе́пный; подобостра́стный. —**servility,** *n.* раболе́пие; подобостра́стие.

serving *n.* по́рция.

servitude *n.* ра́бство. —**penal servitude,** ка́торга; ка́торжные рабо́ты.

sesame *n.* кунжу́т; сеза́м. —*adj.* кунжу́тный; сеза́мовый. —**open sesame!,** сеза́м, откро́йся!

session *n.* **1,** (meeting) заседа́ние; се́ссия. *Joint session,* совме́стное заседа́ние. *Be in session,* заседа́ть. **2,** (sitting; appointment) сеа́нс. **3,** (school term): *summer session,* ле́тние ку́рсы.

set *v.t.* **1,** (put; place) ста́вить; класть: *set the package on the table,* ста́вить/класть посы́лку на стол. **2,** (arrange, as a table) накрыва́ть. *Set the table for six,* накры́ть стол на шесть прибо́ров. **3,** (adjust to a certain setting) ста́вить: *set the alarm for 6:00,* ста́вить буди́льник на шесть часо́в. *Set one's watch by the radio,* ста́вить *or* установи́ть часы́ по ра́дио. **4,** (mount, as a gem) оправля́ть; обде́лывать. **5,** (arrange, as one's hair) укла́дывать. **6,** (lay, as a trap) ста́вить. **7,** *med.* вправля́ть: *set a bone,* вправля́ть кость. **8,** (fix, as a date) назнача́ть; намеча́ть (срок); (a price) устана́вливать (це́ну). **9,** (establish) устана́вливать: *set a limit,* устана́вливать преде́л. *Set a record,* устана́вливать *or* ста́вить реко́рд. *Set a precedent,* создава́ть прецеде́нт. *Set an example,* подава́ть приме́р. *Set the tone,* задава́ть тон. **10,** (assign; lay down) ста́вить: *set a task for oneself,* ста́вить себе́ зада́чу. **11,** *printing* набира́ть. **12,** (bring to a certain state) *rendered by various verbs: set free,* освобожда́ть; *set in motion,* приводи́ть в движе́ние; *set at ease,* успока́ивать; *set on fire,* поджига́ть; *set to music,* положи́ть на му́зыку. —*v.i.* **1,** (sink below the horizon) заходи́ть; сади́ться. **2,** (solidify; congeal) затвердева́ть; застыва́ть. —*n.* **1,** (group of matching things) набо́р; компле́кт; гарниту́р; прибо́р. *Set of tools,* набо́р/компле́кт инструме́нтов. *Desk set,* пи́сьменный прибо́р. *Set of china,* фарфо́ровый серви́з. *Set of underwear,* гарниту́р белья́. *Chess set,* ша́хматы. *Set of stamps,* се́рия ма́рок. **2,** (transmitting or receiving device) устро́йство. *Television set,* телеви́зор. **3,** (group of people) о́бщество; свет. *The smart set,* мо́дный свет. **4,** *theat.* обстано́вка. **5,** *motion pictures* съёмочная площа́дка. **6,** *tennis* сет. **7,** *math.* мно́жество: *theory of sets,* тео́рия мно́жеств. —*adj.* **1,** (fixed) устано́вленный; определённый. **2,** (rigid, unchanging) неизме́нный. *Set pattern,* шабло́н. *Set expression,* усто́йчивое словосочета́ние. **3,** *colloq.* (ready) гото́вый. *Get set,* гото́виться. **4,** *in* **dead set against,** категори́чески про́тив. —**set about,** начина́ть; приступа́ть к. —**set against, 1,** (balance; compare) противопоставля́ть. **2,** (prejudice against) восстана́вливать про́тив; настра́ивать про́тив; вооружа́ть про́тив. —**set apart,** выделя́ть. —**set aside, 1,** (lay aside) откла́дывать (в сто́рону); сберега́ть. **2,** (annul) отменя́ть. —**set back, 1,** (move back, as a clock) ста́вить наза́д. **2,** (hinder the progress of) заде́рживать: *the fire set us back six months,* пожа́р задержа́л на́шу рабо́ту на шесть ме́сяцев. **3,** *The house is set back from the road,* дом стои́т в стороне́ от доро́ги. **4,** *colloq.* (cost) сто́ить; обходи́ться. *How much did it set you back?,* ско́лько вы за э́то заплати́ли? —**set down, 1,** (put down) ста́вить; класть. **2,** (land, as an aircraft) посади́ть. **3,** (put in writing) запи́сывать; пи́сьменно излага́ть. —**set forth, 1,** (state; express) излага́ть. **2,** (start out) отправля́ться. —**set in,** устана́вливаться; водворя́ться; воцаря́ться. *Winter has set in,* установи́лась зима́. —**set off, 1,** (start; touch off) вызыва́ть; порожда́ть. *Set off a chain reaction,* вызыва́ть цепну́ю реа́кцию. **2,** (cause to go off or explode) взрыва́ть. **3,** (set in relief; make prominent) оттеня́ть. **4,** (start out) отправля́ться. —**set out, 1,** (display) выставля́ть. **2,** (start out) отправля́ться; дви́гаться в путь. —**set up,** устра́ивать; создава́ть; организова́ть. *Set up house,* обзавести́сь хозя́йством. *Set up camp,* располага́ться ла́герем. —**set upon, 1,** (attack) напада́ть на. **2,** (cause to attack) натра́вливать (соба́ку) на.

setback *n.* неуда́ча.

settee *n.* небольшо́й дива́н.

setter *n.* лега́вая соба́ка; се́ттер.

setting *n.* **1,** (surroundings; background) окруже́ние; обстано́вка. **2,** (mount, as for a jewel) опра́ва. **3,** (position, as on a dial) установка. **4,** (place setting) прибор. **5,** *Setting of the sun,* заход солнца.

settle *v.t.* **1,** (resolve, as a dispute, issue, etc.) решать; разрешать; улаживать; урегулировать. *The matter is settled,* вопрос исчерпан. **2,** (populate; colonize) заселять; осваивать. **3,** (cause to come to rest) прибивать: *the rain settled the dust,* дождь прибил пыль. **4,** (calm, as one's nerves or stomach) успокаивать. **5,** (dispose of; pay) оплачивать; уплачивать: *settle an account,* оплатить счёт; уплатить по счёту. *Settle one's debts,* расплачиваться с долгами. *Settle scores with,* сводить счёты с. —*v.i.* **1,** (establish residence) поселяться; обосновываться. **2,** (come to rest) садиться; оседать. *The dust settled,* пыль улеглась. **3,** (become clear, as of liquids) отстаиваться; устояться. —**settle down, 1,** (calm down; quiet down) успокаиваться. **2,** (lead a more settled life) остепениться. **3,** *fol. by* **to** (sit down and begin) усаживаться за (+ *acc.*); располагаться (+ *inf.*). —**settle for,** довольствоваться (+ *instr.*): *settle for a draw,* довольствоваться ничьёй. —**settle on/upon, 1,** (decide upon) останавливаться на. **2,** (agree upon) договариваться о. —**settle up,** рассчитываться; расплачиваться.

settlement *n.* **1,** (resolution, as of a dispute) урегулирование; разрешение. **2,** (agreement) соглашение. **3,** (settling of a new region) заселение. **4,** (small settled area) поселение; селение; посёлок. **5,** (payment) расчёт.

settler *n.* поселенец.

setup *n.* организация; структура; устройство.

seven *adj.* семь. —*n.* **1,** (cardinal number) семь. **2,** *cards* семёрка.

sevenfold *adj.* семикратный. —*adv.* в семь раз.

seven hundred семьсот. —**seven-hundredth,** *adj.* семисотый.

seventeen *n. & adj.* семнадцать. —**seventeenth,** *adj.* семнадцатый.

seventh *adj.* седьмой. —*n.* **1,** (seventh part) седьмая часть. **2,** (fraction) седьмая: *one-seventh,* одна седьмая. **3,** *music* септима. —**be in seventh heaven,** быть на седьмом небе.

seventy *n. & adj.* семьдесят. —**seventieth,** *adj.* семидесятый.

sever *v.t.* **1,** (cut off) отрезать; отрубать; откалывать. **2,** (break off, as ties) порывать; разрывать; прерывать.

several *adj.* несколько: *several times,* несколько раз. —*n.* некоторые: *several of them,* некоторые из них.

severance *n.* разрыв. —**severance pay,** выходное пособие.

severe *adj.* **1,** (harsh) суровый; строгий. *Severe winter,* суровая зима. *Severe sentence,* суровый/строгий приговор. **2,** (very great; intense) сильный: *severe pain,* сильная боль. *Severe frost,* сильный *or* жестокий мороз. *Suffer severe damage,* сильно пострадать.

severely *adv.* **1,** (harshly) сурово; строго. **2,** (seriously) сильно: *severely damaged,* сильно повреждён.

severity *n.* суровость; строгость.

sew *v.t. & i.* шить. —**sew on,** пришивать. —**sew up,** зашивать.

sewage *n.* нечистоты; сточные воды.

sewer *n.* сточная труба. —**sewerage,** *n.* канализация.

sewing *n.* шитьё. —**sewing machine,** швейная машина.

sex *n.* **1,** (male or female) пол: *the opposite sex,* противоположный пол. **2,** (sexual activity, feelings, etc.) секс: *a book about sex,* книга о сексе. *Have sex with,* вступить в половую связь с. —*adj.* половой: *the sex act,* половой акт; *sex education,* половое воспитание.

sexless *adj.* бесполый.

sextant *n.* секстант.

sextet *also,* **sextette** *n.* секстет.

sexton *n.* церковный сторож; пономарь.

sexual *adj.* половой; сексуальный. —**sexuality,** *n.* сексуальность.

shabbily *adv.* **1,** (poorly) бедно: *shabbily dressed,* бедно одетый. **2,** (meanly) подло.

shabbiness *n.* убогость.

shabby *adj.* **1,** (threadbare) поношенный; потёртый; потрёпанный. **2,** (run-down; dilapidated) ветхий; убогий. **3,** (mean; unfair) подлый; низкий.

shack *n.* хижина.

shackle *n., usu. pl.* кандалы; оковы. —*v.t.* заковывать в кандалы; сковывать.

shade *n.* **1,** (darkness; dark area) тень: *in the shade,* в тени. **2,** (gradation of color) оттенок. **3,** (nuance) оттенок: *shade of meaning,* оттенок значения. **4,** (blind) штора. **5,** (small amount): *she is a shade better today,* ей немного лучше сегодня. —*v.t.* **1,** (screen from light) затенять; заслонять. *Shade one's eyes from the sun,* защищать глаза от солнца. **2,** (add shading to) оттенять; тушевать; штриховать.

shading *n.* **1,** (small variation) различие. **2,** *drawing* тушёвка; штриховка.

shadow *n.* тень: *cast a shadow,* отбрасывать тень. *Shadows are falling,* тени ложатся. *Not a shadow of doubt,* ни тени сомнения. *He is only a shadow of his former self,* от него осталась одна тень. —*v.t.* (trail) следить за; выслеживать; прослеживать. —**shadow boxing,** бой с тенью.

shadowy *adj.* тёмный; смутный.

shady *adj.* **1,** (in the shade at a given time) теневой; (generally in the shade) тенистый. **2,** *colloq.* (dubious; underhanded) тёмный.

shaft *n.* **1,** (long body, as of a spear) древко. **2,** (beam, as of light) луч (света). **3,** (bar transmitting motion) вал: *drive shaft,* приводной вал. **4,** (pole to which an animal is hitched) оглобля; дышло. **5,** (passage, as in a mine or for an elevator) шахта.

shaggy *adj.* косматый; лохматый; мохнатый.

shah *n.* шах.

shake *v.t.* **1,** (agitate) трясти: *shake a tree,* трясти дерево. *Shake one's watch,* встряхивать часы. *Shake well before using,* взбалтывать перед употреблением. **2,** (rock; jolt) потрясать; сотрясать. **3,** (brandish) потрясать: *shake one's fists,* потрясать кулаками. *Shake one's fist at,* грозить кулаком (+ *dat.*). **4,** (shock; unnerve) потрясать. **5,** (weaken; undermine) колебать; пошатнуть: *shake one's faith in,* колебать/пошатнуть чью-нибудь веру в (+ *acc.*). **6,** *in* **shake hands,** пожимать руки. *Shake hands with,* пожимать руку (+ *dat.*). **7,** *in* **shake one's head,** качать головой. —*v.i.* дрожать; трястись; сотрясаться. —*n.* **1,** (an act of shaking) встряска. **2,** *pl.* [*usu.* **the shakes**] (trembling) дрожь. **3,** (drink) коктейль: *milk shake,* молочный коктейль. **4,** *colloq.* (jiffy) миг. *In two* *shakes,* в два счёта. —**shake down,** стря́хивать: *shake down a thermometer,* стря́хивать термо́метр. —**shake off, 1,** (brush off) отря́хивать; стря́хивать. **2,** (get rid of, as a feeling) избавля́ться от; отде́лываться от; сбра́сывать; стря́хивать. *Shake off a cold,* изба́виться от просту́ды. **3,** (elude) отрыва́ться от. —**shake out,** вытря́хивать; вытряса́ть. —**shake up, 1,** (shake hard) встря́хивать; взба́лтывать. **2,** (unnerve) потрясти́. **3,** (shuffle) перетасо́вывать.

shake-up *n.* перетасо́вка.

shaky *adj.* ша́ткий; нетвёрдый; зы́бкий.

shale *n.* (гли́нистый) сла́нец. *Oil shale,* нефтено́сный сла́нец. —**shale oil,** сла́нцевое ма́сло.

shall *v.aux.* **1,** *used to form the future tense: What shall we do?,* что мы бу́дем де́лать? **2,** *used to make a suggestion: Shall we dance?,* потанцу́ем?

shallot *n.* шало́т.

shallow *adj.* **1,** (not deep) ме́лкий. **2,** *fig.* (lacking depth) пове́рхностный.

sham *n.* **1,** (fraudulent imitation) подде́лка. **2,** (pretense) притво́рство.

shaman *n.* шама́н. —**shamanism,** *n.* шама́нство.

shambles *n.* разгро́м: *the room was a shambles,* в ко́мнате был по́лный разгро́м.

shame *n.* **1,** (feeling of guilt) стыд. *Shame on you!,* сты́дно!; как вам не сты́дно! **2,** (disgrace, dishonor) позо́р. *Bring shame upon,* (о)позо́рить. **3,** (a pity) жаль: *what a shame!,* как жаль! *It's a shame that...,* жаль, что... —*v.t.* **1,** (make ashamed) стыди́ть. **2,** (disgrace) позо́рить. —**put to shame, 1,** (make ashamed) пристыди́ть; устыди́ть. **2,** (excel; outshine) затмева́ть; заткну́ть за́ пояс.

shameful *adj.* позо́рный; посты́дный.

shameless *adj.* бессты́дный. —**shamelessness,** *n.* бессты́дство.

shampoo *n.* **1,** (act of washing) мытьё. *Give oneself a shampoo,* помы́ть го́лову. **2,** (soaplike preparation) шампу́нь. —*v.t.* мыть (го́лову).

shamrock *n.* трили́стник.

shank *n., anat.* го́лень.

shanty *n.* хиба́рка; лачу́га.

shape *n.* **1,** (physical form) фо́рма: *oval shape,* ова́льная фо́рма. **2,** *colloq.* (condition) состоя́ние: *in bad shape,* в плохо́м состоя́нии. **3,** *colloq.* (good physical condition) фо́рма: *out of shape,* не в фо́рме. —*v.t.* **1,** (give shape to) формова́ть. **2,** (cause to develop in a certain way) определя́ть. **3,** (adjust; adapt) приспособля́ть. —**shape up,** *colloq.* **1,** (turn out; develop) скла́дываться. **2,** (start behaving or performing properly) исправля́ться. —**take shape,** скла́дываться; оформля́ться; определя́ться.

shapeless *adj.* бесфо́рменный.

shapely *adj.* стро́йный; ста́тный.

share *n.* **1,** (portion) до́ля. *Do one's share,* вноси́ть свою́ до́лю. **2,** (unit of corporate stock) а́кция; пай. —*v.t.* **1,** (use jointly) дели́ть; дели́ться; разделя́ть. *Share a room with,* дели́ть ко́мнату с. *Share everything with,* дели́ть всё (*or* дели́ться всем) с. *Share thoughts,* дели́ться мы́слями. **2,** (hold or experience jointly) разделя́ть: *share someone's opinion/fate,* разделя́ть чьё-нибудь мне́ние (чью-нибудь судьбу́). —*v.i.* [*usu.* **share in**] уча́ствовать в: *share in the expenses,* уча́ствовать в расхо́дах. —**go shares with,** войти́ в до́лю с.

sharecropper *n.* испо́льщик; издо́льщик.

shareholder *n.* акционе́р; па́йщик.

shark *n.* аку́ла.

sharp *adj.* **1,** (having a fine cutting edge) о́стрый: *sharp knife,* о́стрый нож. **2,** (acute; pungent) о́стрый: *sharp pain,* о́страя боль; *sharp cheese,* о́стрый сыр. *He has a sharp tongue,* у него́ о́стрый язы́к. **3,** (keen; acute) зо́ркий: *sharp eyes,* зо́ркие глаза́. **4,** (harsh; biting) ре́зкий: *sharp wind,* ре́зкий ве́тер; *sharp retort,* ре́зкий отве́т. **5,** (abrupt) круто́й: *sharp turn,* круто́й поворо́т. **6,** (sudden; precipitous) ре́зкий: *a sharp drop in prices,* ре́зкое паде́ние цен. **7,** (clever; astute) бо́йкий; шу́стрый. —*adv.* то́чно; ро́вно: *at six o'clock sharp,* ро́вно в шесть часо́в. —*n., music* дие́з: *F sharp,* фа дие́з.

sharpen *v.t.* точи́ть; заостря́ть. *Sharpen a pencil,* точи́ть *or* чини́ть каранда́ш.

sharpener *n.* точи́лка.

sharp-eyed *adj.* зо́ркий; остроглá́зый; глаза́стый.

sharply *adv.* о́стро; ре́зко.

sharpness *n.* **1,** (cutting quality) острота́. **2,** (clarity; definition) ре́зкость; чёткость.

sharpshooter *n.* иску́сный стрело́к.

shashlik *n.* шашлы́к.

shatter *v.t.* **1,** (smash) разбива́ть (вдре́безги). **2,** (ruin, as one's health) разруша́ть; расша́тывать. **3,** (dash, as hopes) разбива́ть; разруша́ть. —*v.i.* разбива́ться (вдре́безги).

shattering *adj.* сокруши́тельный: *shattering blow,* сокруши́тельный уда́р.

shatterproof *adj.* небью́щийся.

shave *v.t.* **1,** (cut, as a beard; cut the beard of) брить. *Shave off,* сбрива́ть. **2,** (plane) строга́ть. —*v.i.* бри́ться: *I haven't shaved for three days,* я три дня не бри́лся. —*n.* бритьё. *I need a shave,* мне на́до побри́ться. —**have a close shave,** едва́ спасти́сь; быть на волосо́к от ги́бели.

shaver *n.* **1,** (razor) (электри́ческая) бри́тва. **2,** *colloq.* (youngster) юне́ц.

shaving *n.* **1,** (act of one who shaves) бритьё. **2,** *pl.* (pieces of thinly sliced wood) стру́жка. —**shaving brush,** помазо́к; ки́сточка для бритья́. —**shaving cream,** крем для бритья́.

shawl *n.* шаль.

she *pers.pron.* она́: *she left,* она́ ушла́. *She is not here,* её нет. *See also* **her.**

she- *combining form, denoting the female of animals* -и́ца; -и́ха: *she-lion,* льви́ца; *she-elephant,* слони́ха.

sheaf *n.* **1,** (of hay, grain, etc.) сноп. **2,** (of papers) свя́зка.

shear *v.t.* **1,** (cut off; cut the fleece from) стричь. **2,** *fol. by* **off** (slice off) отсека́ть. —**shears,** *n.pl.* но́жницы.

sheatfish *n.* сом.

sheath *n.* но́жны. —**sheathe,** *v.t.* вкла́дывать в но́жны.

shed *v.t.* **1,** (pour forth, as blood, tears, light, etc.) пролива́ть. **2,** (cast off, as leaves, feathers, skin, etc.) сбра́сывать; роня́ть; теря́ть. —*v.i.* линя́ть. —*n.* сара́й: *woodshed,* дровяно́й сара́й.

sheen *n.* блеск; лоск.

sheep *n.* **1,** (domesticated) овца́. **2,** (wild) бара́н. —*adj.* ове́чий; бара́ний. —**black sheep,** парши́вая овца́ (в семье́). —**lost sheep,** заблу́дшая овца́.

sheep dog овча́рка.

sheepfold *n.* овча́рня.

sheepish *adj.* застéнчивый; стыдли́вый.
sheepskin *n.* овчи́на. —*adj.* овчи́нный; бара́ний.
sheer *adj.* **1,** (extremely thin) прозра́чный; сквозно́й. **2,** (precipitous) отвéсный. **3,** (utter; absolute) сплошно́й; чи́стый; су́щий.
sheet *n.* **1,** (for a bed) простыня́. **2,** (of paper, metal, etc.) лист. **3,** (list) вéдомость: *expense sheet,* вéдомость расхо́дов. **4,** (continuous expanse) пелена́: *sheet of fog,* пелена́ тума́на. *Sheet of ice,* сплошно́й лёд.
sheeting *n.* **1,** (material for bedsheets) просты́нное полотно́. **2,** (thin plates, as of metal) обши́вка.
sheet metal листово́й метáлл.
sheik *n.* шейх.
sheldrake *n.* пега́нка.
shelf *n.* **1,** (horizontal support) по́лка. **2,** (ledge jutting out from a cliff) усту́п; вы́ступ.
shell *n.* **1,** (hard covering of a mollusk) ра́ковина. **2,** (of a turtle) па́нцирь; щит. **3,** (of a fruit or seed) оболо́чка. **4,** (of a nut or egg) скорлупа́. **5,** (sea shell) ра́ковина; раку́шка. **6,** (framework) о́стов; сруб. **7,** (projectile) снаря́д. **8,** (cartridge) ги́льза. —*v.t.* **1,** (remove from a shell) лущи́ть; шелуши́ть. *Shell peas,* лущи́ть горо́х. **2,** (bombard) обстрéливать. **3,** *fol. by* **out,** *colloq.* (spend) тра́тить. —**come out of one's shell,** вы́йти из своéй скорлупы́. —**withdraw into one's shell,** уйти́ в свою́ скорлупу́.
shellac *n.* шелла́к. —*v.t.* покрыва́ть шелла́ком.
shellfish *n.* моллю́ск.
shelter *n.* **1,** (refuge) убéжище; прию́т; приста́нище; кров. *Take shelter,* укры́ться. **2,** (something affording protection) убéжище; укры́тие. *Bomb shelter,* бомбоубéжище. —*v.t.* **1,** (protect) укрыва́ть. **2,** (give refuge to) приюти́ть.
shelve *v.t.* **1,** (put on a shelf) ста́вить *or* класть на по́лку. **2,** (put off) откла́дывать; класть под сукно́; откла́дывать в до́лгий я́щик.
shelving *n.* стелла́ж.
shenanigans *n.pl., colloq.* чуда́чества.
shepherd *n.* пасту́х. —*v.t.* проводи́ть: *shepherd tourists around town,* проводи́ть тури́стов по го́роду.
sherbet *n.* шербéт.
sheriff *n.* шери́ф.
sherry *n.* хéрес.
shh *interj.* шш!
shield *n.* щит. —*v.t.* защища́ть; заслоня́ть.
shift *v.t.* **1,** (move; transfer) передвига́ть; перемеща́ть; перекла́дывать. *Shift the furniture,* передвига́ть мéбель. *Shift the blame,* свали́ть вину́. **2,** (change; switch) перемени́ть; переключа́ть. *Shift gears,* переключи́ть ско́рость. *Shift one's ground,* перемени́ть пози́цию. —*v.i.* **1,** (move) передвига́ться; перемеща́ться. *Shift from foot to foot,* перемина́ться с ноги́ на́ ногу. **2,** (switch) переходи́ть; переключа́ться. *Shift to the offensive,* переходи́ть в наступлéние. *The wind shifted,* вéтер перемени́лся. *The scene shifts to London,* дéйствие перехо́дит в Ло́ндон. **3,** (get along) обходи́ться: *shift for oneself,* обходи́ться без посторо́нней по́мощи. —*n.* **1,** (movement) перемещéние. **2,** (change; switch) сдвиг. **3,** (work period) смéна. *Work in shifts,* рабо́тать посмéнно. **4,** (gearshift) переда́ча: *automatic shift,* автомати́ческая переда́ча. —**shift work,** смéнная *or* посмéнная рабо́та.
shiftless *adj.* лени́вый; неради́вый.
shifty *adj.* увёртливый; изворо́тливый.
shillelagh *n.* дуби́нка.
shilling *n.* ши́ллинг.
shimmer *v.i.* мерца́ть.
shin *n.* го́лень. —**shinbone,** *n.* больша́я берцо́вая кость.
shine *v.i.* **1,** (emit light) свети́ть; свети́ться. *The sun is shining,* со́лнце свéтит. **2,** (gleam) блестéть; сия́ть. **3,** (excel) блиста́ть. —*v.t.* **1,** (polish) полирова́ть. *Shine shoes,* чи́стить боти́нки. **2,** (point; direct, as light) свети́ть (+ *instr.*): *shine the light in the corner,* свети́ть фонарём в углу́. *Don't shine the light in my eyes,* не свети́те мне в глаза́. —*n.* **1,** (luster) лоск; блеск; гля́нец. **2,** (shoeshine): *get a shine,* почи́стить боти́нки. —**take a shine to,** *colloq.* полюби́ть.
shiner *n.* **1,** (fish) голья́н. **2,** *slang* (black eye) фона́рь.
shingle *n.* **1,** (wood tile) дра́нка; *pl.* гонт. **2,** (small sign) вы́веска.
shingles *n., med.* опоя́сывающий лиша́й.
shinguard *n.* щито́к.
shining *adj.* сия́ющий; блестя́щий.
Shinto *n.* синтои́зм. *Also,* **Shintoism.**
shiny *adj.* лосня́щийся.
ship *n.* **1,** (large vessel) парохо́д; су́дно. *Go by ship,* éхать на парохо́де. *Cargo ship,* грузово́е су́дно. **2,** (naval vessel) кора́бль. *Warship,* воéнный кора́бль. —*v.t.* **1,** (transport) отправля́ть; перевози́ть; отгружа́ть. **2,** *fol. by* **off** (send away) отсыла́ть. —*v.i.* [*usu.* **ship out**] отправля́ться; отплыва́ть.
shipbuilder *n.* кораблестрои́тель; судострои́тель.
shipbuilding *n.* кораблестроéние; судостроéние.
shipment *n.* **1,** (shipping of goods) отпра́вка; отгру́зка. **2,** (a consignment of goods) па́ртия.
shipowner *n.* судовладéлец.
shipper *n.* грузоотправи́тель.
shipping *n.* **1,** (shipment) отгру́зка; отпра́вка. **2,** (movement of ships carrying cargo) судохо́дство: *closed to shipping,* закры́т для судохо́дства. **3,** (ships collectively) суда́. —*adj.* судохо́дный: *shipping company,* судохо́дная компа́ния.
shipshape *adj.* в по́лном поря́дке.
shipwreck *n.* кораблекрушéние. *Be shipwrecked,* потерпéть кораблекрушéние.
shipyard *n.* верфь; судовéрфь.
shire *n.* гра́фство.
shirk *v.t.* уклоня́ться от; уви́ливать от. —**shirker,** *n.* прогу́льщик.
shirt *n.* руба́шка; соро́чка. —**keep one's shirt on,** *slang* не горячи́ться; не кипяти́ться. —**lose one's shirt,** *slang* проигра́ться.
shirtsleeves *n.pl.,* *in* **in one's shirtsleeves,** без пиджака́.
shirttail *n.* низ руба́шки. *Your shirttail is hanging out,* у вас вы́лезла руба́шка.
shish kebab шашлы́к.
shiver *v.i.* дрожа́ть; трясти́сь. —*n.* дрожь. *It gives one the shivers,* моро́з по ко́же подира́ет.
shoal *n.* мель; о́тмель.
shock *n.* **1,** (sudden jolt) уда́р; толчо́к; сотрясéние. **2,** (sudden emotional disturbance) потрясéние. **3,** *med.* шок. **4,** (jolt of electricity) (электри́ческий) уда́р. **5,** (mass, as of hair) копна́; ша́пка (воло́с). —*v.t.* потряса́ть; шоки́ровать.
shock absorber амортиза́тор.

shocking *adj.* **1,** (extremely upsetting) стра́шный; ужаса́ющий. **2,** (outrageous) возмути́тельный; сканда́льный.
shock troops уда́рные войска́.
shock wave уда́рная волна́.
shoddy *adj.* недоброка́чественный.
shoe *n.* **1,** (general term) боти́нок. **2,** (lady's) ту́фля. **3,** (for a horse) подко́ва. **4,** *mech.* башма́к; коло́дка: *brake shoe,* тормозно́й башма́к; тормозна́я коло́дка. —*adj.* обувно́й: *shoe store,* обувно́й магази́н. —*v.t.* обува́ть: *well shod,* хорошо́ обу́тый. *Shoe a horse,* подкова́ть ло́шадь. —**be in someone's shoes,** быть на чьём-нибудь ме́сте; быть в чьей-нибудь шку́ре. —**fill someone's shoes,** занима́ть чьё-нибудь ме́сто.
shoehorn *n.* рожо́к.
shoelace *n.* шнуро́к (для боти́нок).
shoemaker *n.* сапо́жник.
shoe polish гутали́н; ва́кса; сапо́жный крем; сапо́жная мазь.
shoeshine *n.* чи́стка сапо́г. —**shoeshine boy,** чисти́льщик сапо́г.
shoetree *n.* коло́дка.
shoo *interj.* кш!; вон! —*v.t.* [*usu.* **shoo away**] ши́кать на.
shoot *v.t.* **1,** (let forth; discharge) пуска́ть: *shoot an arrow,* пуска́ть стрелу́. **2,** (fire at and hit) стреля́ть в (и ра́нить): *shoot a burglar,* стреля́ть во взло́мщика (и ра́нить его́). *Shoot someone in the leg,* ра́нить кого́-нибудь в но́гу. **3,** (fire at and kill) застрели́ть. *Shoot oneself,* застрели́ться. **4,** (hunt and kill) стреля́ть: *shoot deer,* стреля́ть оле́ней. **5,** (execute) расстре́ливать. **6,** *fol. by* **down** (bring down by shooting) сбива́ть. **7,** (fire, as a gun) стреля́ть из (ружья́). **8,** (propel with great force) запуска́ть. *Shoot forth lava,* изверга́ть ла́ву. **9,** (photograph) снима́ть; засня́ть. **10,** *sports* посыла́ть (мяч). **11,** *games* игра́ть в: *shoot dice/pool/marbles,* игра́ть в ко́сти/в билья́рд/в ша́рики/. **12,** *Shoot rapids,* переправля́ться че́рез поро́ги. —*v.i.* **1,** (fire a weapon) стреля́ть: *don't shoot!,* не стреля́йте! **2,** (flash; dart) мча́ться; нести́сь. *Shoot past,* промча́ться; проноси́ться; промелькну́ть. *Shoot ahead,* вы́рваться вперёд. *The horse shot out of the gate,* ло́шадь вы́летела из-за барье́ра. *Flames shot up into the air,* пла́мя взвило́сь в во́здух. **3,** *fol. by* **up** (soar, as of prices, temperature, etc.) подска́кивать. **4,** *fol. by* **up** (grow rapidly) вы́расти; вы́тянуться. **5,** *fol. by* **for** (aim for; strive for) ме́тить в. —*n.* отро́сток; росто́к; побе́г. —**shoot back, 1,** (return fire) отвеча́ть огнём. **2,** *colloq.* (retort) найти́сь. —**shoot off one's mouth,** *slang* проболта́ться. —**shoot the breeze,** *colloq.* болта́ть. —**shoot the works,** *slang* идти́ ва-ба́нк.
shooting *n.* **1,** (firing of weapons) стрельба́. **2,** (filming) съёмка. —*adj.* **1,** (pert. to shooting) стрелко́вый. **2,** (stabbing, as of pain) стреля́ющий; ко́лющий. —**shooting gallery,** тир. —**shooting star,** па́дающая звезда́.
shop *n.* **1,** (small store) магази́н; ла́вка. **2,** (place where work is done) мастерска́я: *repair shop,* ремо́нтная мастерска́я. **3,** (factory division) цех; мастерска́я: *machine shop,* механи́ческий цех; механи́ческая мастерска́я. —*adj.* цехово́й: *shop foreman,* цехово́й ма́стер. —*v.i.* [*also,* **go shopping**] ходи́ть по магази́нам; де́лать поку́пки. —**talk shop,** говори́ть о служе́бных дела́х.
shopkeeper *n.* ла́вочник.
shoplifter *n.* магази́нный вор.
shopper *n.* покупа́тель.
shopping bag су́мка для поку́пок; хозя́йственная су́мка.
shopping center торго́вый центр.
shore *n.* бе́рег. —*v.t.* [*usu.* **shore up**] подпира́ть.
shoreline *n.* берегова́я ли́ния.
short *adj.* **1,** (not long) коро́ткий: *a short distance,* коро́ткое расстоя́ние; коро́ткая диста́нция. *Short hair/sleeves,* коро́ткие во́лосы/рукава́. *The shortest distance between two points,* наиме́ньшее расстоя́ние ме́жду двумя́ то́чками. **2,** (not tall) ни́зкого ро́ста; ма́ленького ро́ста: *a short man,* челове́к ни́зкого/ма́ленького ро́ста. **3,** (not of long duration) коро́ткий: *short winter/memory,* коро́ткая зима́/па́мять. *A short time ago,* неда́вно. **4,** (brief; concise) коро́ткий; кра́ткий. **5,** (insufficient) недоста́точный. *Be in short supply,* име́ться в недоста́точном коли́честве; быть дефици́тным. **6,** *fol. by* **of** (not having enough of): *we are short of milk,* у нас не хвата́ет молока́. **7,** (brusque; curt) ре́зкий. —*adv.* ко́ротко: *cut one's hair short,* ко́ротко постри́чь во́лосы. —*n.* **1,** (short film) короткометра́жный фильм. **2,** *pl.* (short pants) *see* **shorts. 3,** = **short circuit.** —**cut short,** обрыва́ть. —**fall short of,** не достига́ть: *fall short of the mark,* не достига́ть це́ли. —**for short,** сокращённо; для кра́ткости. —**in short,** коро́че говоря́. —**in short order,** в спе́шном поря́дке. —**run short,** иссяка́ть; истоща́ться: *our supplies are running short,* на́ши запа́сы иссяка́ют/истоща́ются. *Time is running short,* вре́мя истека́ет. —**short of,** кро́ме; поми́мо. —**stop short,** внеза́пно останови́ться; *(in speaking)* останови́ться на полусло́ве. —**to make a long story short,** коро́че говоря́.
shortage *n.* недоста́ток; нехва́тка; дефици́т.
shortbread *n.* песо́чное пече́нье; рассы́пчатое пече́нье.
shortcake *n.* песо́чный торт.
shortchange *v.t., colloq.* обсчи́тывать.
short circuit коро́ткое замыка́ние.
shortcoming *n.* недоста́ток.
shortcut *n.* коро́ткий путь. *Take a shortcut,* сре́зать у́гол.
shorten *v.t.* укора́чивать; сокраща́ть.
shortening *n.* сдо́ба.
shortfall *n.* дефици́т; недобо́р.
shorthand *n.* стеногра́фия. *Take down in shorthand,* стенографи́ровать.
short-lived *adj.* недолгове́чный.
shortly *adv.* ско́ро; вско́ре. *Shortly before,* незадо́лго до. *Shortly after,* вско́ре по́сле. *Shortly thereafter,* вско́ре.
shortness *n.* коро́ткость. —**shortness of breath,** оды́шка.
short-range *adj.* бли́жнего де́йствия; с ма́лым ра́диусом де́йствия.
shorts *n.pl.* трусы́; тру́сики; шо́рты.
shortsighted *adj.* близору́кий; недальнови́дный. —**shortsightedness,** *n.* близору́кость; недальнови́дность.
short story расска́з; нове́лла.
short-tempered *adj.* вспы́льчивый.

short-term *adj.* краткосро́чный.

short wave коро́ткая волна́. —**short-wave,** *adj.* коротково́лновый.

shot *n.* **1,** (discharge of a firearm) вы́стрел: *I heard a shot,* я услы́шал вы́стрел. **2,** (one who shoots) стрело́к: *a good shot,* хоро́ший стрело́к. **3,** (small pellets) дробь. **4,** (picture) сни́мок. **5,** *sports* бросо́к; уда́р. *Penalty shot,* штрафно́й уда́р. *Take a shot,* де́лать бросо́к. *Put the shot,* толка́ть ядро́. **6,** (inoculation) приви́вка: *rabies shot,* приви́вка от (*or* про́тив) бе́шенства. **7,** *colloq.* (drink of liquor) глото́к (спиртно́го). **8,** *colloq.* (attempt) попы́тка. —*adj.* **1,** (streaked): *shot with gold,* с золоты́м отли́вом. **2,** *colloq.* (worn out) изно́шенный. *These pants are shot,* э́ти брю́ки совсе́м износи́лись. —**big shot,** (ва́жная) ши́шка. —**call the shots,** распоряжа́ться. —**like a shot,** пу́лей: *take off like a shot,* понести́сь пу́лей. —**not by a long shot,** отню́дь нет; далеко́ не.

shotgun *n.* дробови́к. *Sawed-off shotgun,* обре́з.

shot-put *n.* толка́ние ядра́.

should *v.aux.* **1,** *expressing mild obligation or advisability: you should write a book about it,* вы бы об э́том кни́гу написа́ли. *You shouldn't have done it,* вы не должны́ бы́ли де́лать э́того. *It should be borne in mind that...,* сле́дует име́ть в виду́, что... **2,** *expressing expectation* до́лжен: *he should be here soon,* он до́лжен ско́ро прийти́. **3,** *expressing condition or assumption* е́сли: *should the need arise,* е́сли возни́кнет необходи́мость. *Should I be late,* (в слу́чае) е́сли я опозда́ю. **4,** *used in polite requests* бы: *I should like to ask...,* я бы хоте́л(а) спроси́ть...

shoulder *n.* **1,** (part of the body) плечо́. *Wear a coat over one's shoulders,* носи́ть пальто́ внаки́дку. **2,** (side of a road) обо́чина. —*v.t.* **1,** (place on one's shoulders) взва́ливать на пле́чи. **2,** (assume; bear) брать на себя́; брать на пле́чи. **3,** *in* **shoulder one's way,** прота́лкиваться. —**give someone the cold shoulder,** хо́лодно встре́тить. —**have a good head on one's shoulders,** име́ть го́лову на плеча́х. —**shoulder to shoulder,** плечо́м к плечу́. —**straight from the shoulder,** начистоту́.

shoulder blade лопа́тка.

shoulder strap пого́н.

shout *v.t. & i.* крича́ть: *don't shout!,* не кричи́(те)! *Shout hurrah,* крича́ть ура́. *Shout someone's name,* вы́крикнуть чьё-нибудь и́мя. *Shout slogans,* выкри́кивать ло́зунги. —*n.* крик; вы́крик; во́зглас. —**shout down,** перекрича́ть.

shove *v.t.* толка́ть; пиха́ть. —*v.i.* толка́ться: *don't shove!,* не толка́йтесь! —*n.* толчо́к. —**shove off, 1,** (push off from shore) отта́лкиваться от бе́рега. **2,** *colloq.* (depart) уходи́ть; отправля́ться.

shovel *n.* лопа́та. —*v.t.* сгреба́ть: *shovel snow from the sidewalk,* сгреба́ть снег с тротуа́ра.

show *v.t.* **1,** (make visible; point out; demonstrate) пока́зывать: *show one's ticket,* пока́зывать биле́т; *show someone the way,* показа́ть кому́-нибудь доро́гу. *I'll show you how to do it,* я вам покажу́ как э́то де́лается. **2,** (display publicly) выставля́ть. **3,** (reveal; evince) проявля́ть; обнару́живать. *Show courage,* проявля́ть му́жество. *Show no signs of life,* не подава́ть при́знаков жи́зни. **4,** (prove; demonstrate) пока́зывать; дока́зывать; устана́вливать. **5,** (guide; escort) провожа́ть: *show someone to the door,* провожа́ть кого́-нибудь до двере́й. **6,** (extend) ока́зывать: *show kindness to,* ока́зывать любе́зность (+ *dat.*). **7,** (indicate; register) пока́зывать: *the clock shows 3:00,* часы́ пока́зывают три часа́. **8,** *colloq.* (teach a lesson to) показа́ть: *I'll show him!,* я ему́ покажу́! **9,** *Show one's face,* показа́ться. **10,** *Show oneself to be...,* показа́ть себя́ (+ *instr.*). —*v.i.* быть ви́дным; быть заме́тным; видне́ться. *Your slip is showing,* у вас видна́ ни́жняя ю́бка. —*n.* **1,** (piece of entertainment) спекта́кль. **2,** (single performance or presentation) сеа́нс. **3,** (exhibition) вы́ставка: *dog show,* вы́ставка соба́к. **4,** (pointed display) демонстра́ция: *show of strength/force,* демонстра́ция си́лы. **5,** (that which is intended to impress) эффе́кт. *Done for show,* сде́ланный напока́з; рассчи́танный на эффе́кт. **6,** *Show of hands,* подня́тие руки́. —**show in,** вводи́ть. —**show off, 1,** (flaunt) щеголя́ть (+ *instr.*); выставля́ть напока́з. **2,** (make a great display of oneself) рисова́ться; красова́ться. —**show out,** провожа́ть до двере́й. —**show up, 1,** (arrive) явля́ться. **2,** *colloq.* (prove superior to) затмева́ть.

showcase *n.* витри́на.

showdown *n.* развя́зка.

shower *n.* **1,** (shower bath) душ: *take a shower,* принима́ть душ. **2,** (light rain) дождь; до́ждик. **3,** (torrent; profusion) град. —*v.t.* **1,** (cover; pelt) забра́сывать: *shower someone with leaflets,* заброса́ть кого́-нибудь листо́вками. **2,** (spray) обры́згивать. **3,** *fig.* (deluge) засыпа́ть; осыпа́ть; забра́сывать (*e.g.* пода́рками). *Shower with praise,* осыпа́ть похвала́ми. —*v.i.* принима́ть душ. —**shower room,** душева́я.

showing *n.* **1,** (act of showing) пока́з. **2,** (overall performance) результа́т: *make a good showing,* показа́ть хоро́ший результа́т.

showman *n.* антрепренёр.

showroom *n.* вы́ставочный зал; демонстрацио́нный зал; сало́н.

show trial показа́тельный суд.

showy *adj.* показно́й; эффе́ктный.

shrapnel *n.* шрапне́ль. *Shrapnel wound,* оско́лочная ра́на.

shred *n.* клок; клочо́к; лоску́т. *Tear to shreds,* разрыва́ть в кло́чья *or* в клочки́. *Not a shred of evidence,* ни мале́йших доказа́тельств. —*v.t.* измельча́ть; кромса́ть. *Shred cabbage,* шинкова́ть капу́сту. *Shred documents,* уничтожа́ть докуме́нты.

shrew *n.* **1,** (animal) землеро́йка. **2,** (scolding woman) меге́ра; фу́рия.

shrewd *adj.* **1,** (of a person) проница́тельный; расчётливый. **2,** (of an action) ло́вкий. —**shrewdness,** *n.* проница́тельность.

shriek *n.* пронзи́тельный крик. —*v.i.* пронзи́тельно крича́ть.

shrift *n., in* **make short shrift of,** (бы́стро) распра́виться с.

shrike *n.* сорокопу́т.

shrill *adj.* ре́зкий; пронзи́тельный.

shrimp *n.* **1,** (crustacean) креве́тка. **2,** *colloq.* (small person) коро́ты́ш(ка); недоро́сток.

shrine *n.* **1,** (tomb of a saint) ра́ка. **2,** (revered site) святы́ня.

shrink *v.i.* **1,** (of fabric) сади́ться. **2,** (become smaller) сжима́ться. **3,** (draw back; recoil) отпря́нуть. **4,** *fol. by* **from** (avoid) уклоня́ться от. —*v.t.* **1,** (cause shrinkage in) вызыва́ть уса́дку (+ *gen.*). **2,** (reduce in size) сжима́ть.

shrinkage *n.* усáдка.

shrivel *v.i.* смóрщиваться; съёживаться.

shroud *n.* **1,** (burial cloth) сáван. **2,** (that which covers or envelops) пеленá. —*v.t.* окýтывать: *shrouded in secrecy,* окýтанный тáйной.

Shrovetide *n.* мáсленица.

shrub *n.* куст; кустáрник. —**shrubbery,** *n.* кустáрник.

shrug *v.t. & i.* пожимáть (плечáми). —*n.* пожимáние (плеч). —**shrug off,** не обращáть внимáния на.

shuck *n.* **1,** (husk) шелухá. **2,** (shell) скорлупá. —*v.t.* лущи́ть; шелуши́ть.

shucks *interj.* чёрт побери́!

shudder *v.i.* содрогáться. —*n.* содрогáние.

shuffle *v.t.* **1,** (drag, as one's feet) шáркать (ногáми); волочи́ть (нóги). **2,** (mix, as cards) тасовáть. —*v.i.* **1,** *fol. by* **along** (walk by dragging one's feet) волочи́ться. **2,** (mix the cards) тасовáть. —*n.* **1,** (of feet) шáрканье. **2,** (mixing of cards) тасóвка.

shun *v.t.* избегáть; сторони́ться.

shunt *v.t.* **1,** (turn aside) отводи́ть. **2,** *R.R.* переводи́ть на запáсный путь.

shut *v.t.* закрывáть. —*v.i.* закрывáться. —**shut down,** закрывáть(ся). —**shut off, 1,** (turn off) отключáть. **2,** (halt, as debate) прекращáть. **3,** (isolate) отгорáживать. —**shut out, 1,** (keep out) не допускáть. **2,** *sports* сдéлать сухýю (+ *dat.*). —**shut up, 1,** (incarcerate) заточáть. **2,** *colloq.* (stop talking) замолчáть. *Shut up!,* заткни́сь!

shutout *n., sports* сухáя.

shutter *n.* **1,** (for a window) стáвень; стáвня. **2,** (of a camera) затвóр. —*v.t.* закрывáть стáвнями.

shuttle *n.* челнóк. *Space shuttle,* косми́ческий челнóк. —**shuttle diplomacy,** "челнóчная" диломáтия.

shuttlecock *n.* волáн.

shy *adj.* **1,** (timid) рóбкий; застéнчивый. **2,** *colloq.* (lacking; short): *we are shy a few dollars,* нам не хватáет нéсколько дóлларов. —*v.i.* **1,** (rear, as of a horse) отпря́нуть. **2,** [*usu.* **shy away from**] (avoid) уклоня́ться от. —*v.t.* (throw) бросáть.

shyness *n.* рóбость; застéнчивость.

si *n., music* си.

Siamese *adj.* сиáмский. —**Siamese twins,** сиáмские близнецы́.

Siberian *adj.* сиби́рский. —*n.* сибиря́к.

sibilant *n. & adj.* **1,** (ж,ч,ш,щ) шипя́щий. **2,** (с,з) свистя́щий.

sibling *n.* роднóй брат; роднáя сестрá.

sic *also,* **sick** *v.t.* натрáвливать. —**sic 'im!,** атý егó!

sick *adj.* **1,** (ill) больнóй: *sick child,* больнóй ребёнок. *I was sick,* я был бóлен; я былá больнá. **2,** (nauseous): *I feel sick to my stomach,* меня́ тошни́т. **3,** (mentally ill) душевнобольнóй. **4,** (perverted) извращённый: *sick mind,* извращённый ум. **5,** (extremely upset) óчень огорчён. *I am sick at heart,* у меня́ боли́т душá. **6,** *fol. by* **of** (fed up with): *I am sick of staying home,* мне надоéло сидéть дóма. —*n., preceded by* **the** больны́е. —**take sick,** заболевáть.

sick bay лазарéт.

sicken *v.t.* прети́ть. *It sickens me,* мне прети́т (*or* меня́ тошни́т) от э́того.

sickening *adj.* тошнотвóрный; отврати́тельный.

sickle *n.* серп.

sick leave óтпуск по болéзни.

sickly *adj.* болéзненный; хи́лый. —**sickliness,** *n.* болéзненность.

sickness *n.* болéзнь.

side *n.* **1,** (in most meanings) сторонá: *the right side of the road,* прáвая сторонá дорóги. *The two sides of a coin,* óбе стороны́ монéты. *On the other side of the river,* по ту стóрону реки́. *Whose side are you on?,* вы на чьей сторонé? *A relative on his mother's side,* рóдственник со стороны́ мáтери. **2,** (either half of the human body) бок: *lie on one's side,* лежáть на бокý. **3,** (area immediately adjacent) край: *along the side of the road,* по крáю дорóги. *Stand at someone's side,* стоя́ть ря́дом с кéм-нибудь. **4,** (of a geometric figure) грань: *a cube has six sides,* куб имéет шесть грáней. **5,** (vertical surface) стéнка; стенá: *the side of a box/canyon,* стéнка я́щика; стенá каньóна. **6,** *naut.* борт: *starboard side,* прáвый борт. **7,** (of beef) бок: *side of mutton,* барáний бок. —*adj.* **1,** (located on one side) боковóй: *side door,* боковáя дверь. **2,** (from one side) сбóку: *side view,* вид сбóку. **3,** (incidental) побóчный: *side effects,* побóчные эффéкты. —*v.i.* [*usu.* **side with**] станови́ться *or* вставáть на стóрону (+ *gen.*). —**from side to side,** из стороны́ в стóрону; с бóку нá бок. —**on all sides,** со всех сторóн. —**on the side,** на сторонé: *do work on the side,* подрабáтывать на сторонé. —**side by side,** бок ó бок. —**take sides,** стать на чью-нибудь стóрону.

sideboard *n.* буфéт; сервáнт.

sideburns *n.pl.* бакенбáрды.

sidecar *n.* коля́ска (мотоци́кла).

sideline *n.* **1,** (additional work) побóчная рабóта. *He does this as a sideline,* он занимáется э́тим мéжду дéлом. **2,** *sports* боковáя ли́ния. —**on the sidelines,** в сторонé.

sidelong *adj.* косóй: *sidelong glance,* косóй взгляд.

sidestep *v.t.* обходи́ть (сторонóй); уклоня́ться от.

side street переýлок; боковáя ýлица.

sidetrack *n.* запáсный путь. —*v.t.* **1,** *R.R.* переводи́ть на запáсный путь. **2,** (divert; shunt aside): *I got sidetracked on the way,* я задержáлся в дорóге. *The bill got sidetracked in Congress,* обсуждéние законопроéкта в конгрéссе бы́ло отлóжено.

sidewalk *n.* тротуáр.

sideways *adv.* бóком; бочкóм.

siding *n.* запáсный путь.

sidle *v.i.* ходи́ть бóком; пробирáться бочкóм. *Sidle up to,* пробрáться бочкóм к.

siege *n.* осáда; блокáда. *Under siege,* в осáде. —**lay siege to,** осаждáть. —**state of siege,** осáдное положéние.

sienna *n.* сиéна.

sieve *n.* решетó; си́то.

sift *v.t.* **1,** (pass through a sieve) просéивать. **2,** (consider carefully) взвéшивать. —*v.i.* [*usu.* **sift through**] ры́ться в.

sigh *v.i.* вздыхáть. —*n.* вздох.

sight *n.* **1,** (vision; eyesight) зрéние: *lose one's sight,* лиши́ться зрéния. *Lose the sight of one eye,* ослéпнуть на оди́н глаз. **2,** (act of seeing) вид: *at the sight of,* при ви́де (+ *gen.*). *I can't stand the sight of blood,* я не выношý ви́да крóви. **3,** (field of vision) пóле зрéния: *come within sight,* попáсть в пóле зрéния. *The end is in sight,* конéц ужé ви́ден. *There was not a house in sight,* нé было ви́дно ни одногó дóма.

Pass out of sight, скрыва́ться из ви́ду. *Out of my sight!,* с глаз мои́х доло́й! **4,** (something seen) зре́лище: *a horrible sight,* ужа́сное зре́лище. **5,** *pl.* (places worth seeing) достопримеча́тельности: *see the sights,* осма́тривать достопримеча́тельности. **6,** (mechanism on a gun) прице́л. —*v.t.* уви́деть: *sight land,* уви́деть зе́млю. —**a darned sight,** *colloq.* гора́здо; несравне́нно (+ *comp.*). —**catch sight of,** уви́деть; зави́деть. —**from sight,** с листа́: *play from sight,* игра́ть с листа́. —**know by sight,** знать в лицо́. —**lose sight of, 1,** (see no longer) (по)теря́ть и́з виду. **2,** (fail to realize) упуска́ть и́з виду; (по)теря́ть и́з виду. —**love at first sight,** любо́вь с пе́рвого взгля́да. —**out of sight, out of mind,** с глаз доло́й, из се́рдца вон. —**shoot on sight,** стреля́ть без предупрежде́ния. —**sight unseen,** загла́зно; за глаза́.

sighted *adj.* ви́дящий; зря́чий.

sightless *adj.* неви́дящий; незря́чий.

sight-read *v.t. & i.* чита́ть с листа́.

sightseeing *n.* осмо́тр достопримеча́тельностей. *Go sightseeing,* осма́тривать достопримеча́тельности. *Sightseeing tour of the city,* экску́рсия по го́роду. —**sightseer,** *n.* тури́ст; экскурса́нт.

sign *n.* **1,** (mark; symbol; gesture; token; omen) знак: *minus sign,* знак ми́нус. *A sign of respect,* знак уваже́ния. *A good sign,* до́брый знак. *The signs of the zodiac,* зна́ки зодиа́ка. **2,** (display board) вы́веска. *Road sign,* доро́жный знак. *Neon sign,* нео́новая рекла́ма. **3,** (evidence; trace; indication) при́знак: *signs of life,* при́знаки жи́зни. *Sign of the times,* зна́мение вре́мени. —*v.t.* подпи́сывать: *sign a petition,* подпи́сывать пети́цию. *Sign one's name,* подпи́сываться; распи́сываться. —*v.i.* распи́сываться. *Sign for a parcel,* распи́сываться в получе́нии посы́лки. —**sign off,** зака́нчивать радиопереда́чу. —**sign out,** отмеча́ться. —**sign up (for),** запи́сываться (в *or* на).

signal *n.* сигна́л: *distress signal,* сигна́л бе́дствия. *Hand signal,* знак руко́й. *At a given signal,* по сигна́лу; по зна́ку. —*adj.* знамена́тельный: *a signal achievement,* знамена́тельное достиже́ние. —*v.t.* **1,** (make a signal to) подава́ть сигна́л *or* знак (+ *dat.*). **2,** (indicate) сигнализи́ровать. —*v.i.* подава́ть сигна́л; сигнализи́ровать.

signalman *n.* сигна́льщик; *mil.* связи́ст.

signatory *n.* подписа́вший.

signature *n.* **1,** (name written by oneself) по́дпись. **2,** *printing* печа́тный лист.

signboard *n.* вы́веска.

signer *n.* подписа́вший.

signet *n.* печа́тка.

significance *n.* значе́ние: *be of great significance,* име́ть большо́е значе́ние.

significant *adj.* значи́тельный: *significant discovery/increase,* значи́тельное откры́тие/увеличе́ние. *Be significant,* име́ть значе́ние. *It is significant that...,* характе́рно, что...; знамена́тельно, что... —**significantly,** *adv.* значи́тельно.

signify *v.t.* **1,** (mean; denote) зна́чить; означа́ть. **2,** (make known; indicate) ука́зывать: *signify by raising one's hand,* ука́зывать подня́тием руки́.

sign language нема́я а́збука; жестикуля́ция.

sign painter ма́стер по вы́вескам; оформи́тель *or* изготови́тель вы́весок.

signpost *n.* указа́тельный столб.

silage *n.* си́лос.

silence *n.* **1,** (absence of sound) тишина́. **2,** (failure to speak) молча́ние. *In silence,* мо́лча. —*interj.* помолчи́те! —*v.t.* **1,** (make silent) заста́вить замолча́ть. **2,** (suppress; still) заглуша́ть.

silencer *n.* глуши́тель.

silent *adj.* **1,** (making no sound; tacit; taciturn) молчали́вый; безмо́лвный. *Keep silent,* молча́ть. *Fall silent,* замолка́ть; умолка́ть. *Remain silent,* храни́ть молча́ние. **2,** (not pronounced): *the "k" is silent,* бу́ква "k" не произно́сится. **3,** (of a film) немо́й.

silently *adv.* мо́лча.

silhouette *n.* силуэ́т.

silica *n.* кремнезём.

silica gel силикаге́ль.

silicate *n.* силика́т.

siliceous *adj.* кремни́стый.

silicic *adj.* кре́мниевый: *silicic acid,* кре́мниевая кислота́.

silicon *n.* кре́мний.

silicone *n.* силико́н.

silk *n.* шёлк. *Raw silk,* шёлк-сыре́ц. —*adj.* шёлковый.

silken *adj.* шелкови́стый.

silkworm *n.* (ту́товый) шелкопря́д; шелкови́чный червь.

silky *adj.* шелкови́стый.

sill *n.* подоко́нник.

silliness *n.* глу́пость.

silly *adj.* глу́пый. *Don't be silly!,* не говори́те глу́пости! *Laugh oneself silly,* смея́ться до упа́ду.

silo *n.* си́лос.

silt *n.* ил. —*v.i.* [*usu.* **silt up**] засоря́ться и́лом. —**silty,** *adj.* и́листый.

silver *n.* серебро́. —*adj.* сере́бряный. —*v.t.* серебри́ть. —**be born with a silver spoon in one's mouth,** роди́ться в соро́чке *or* в руба́шке.

silver fox черно-бу́рая лиси́ца.

silver nitrate ля́пис.

silver plate 1, (coating of silver) серебро́. **2,** (silverware) столо́вое серебро́; сере́бряная посу́да. —**silver-plate,** *v.t.* серебри́ть. —**silver-plated,** *adj.* посеребрённый.

silversmith *n.* сере́бряных дел ма́стер.

silverware *n.* столо́вое серебро́.

silvery *adj.* серебри́стый.

similar *adj.* **1,** (alike) подо́бный; похо́жий; схо́дный. *A rabbit is similar to a hare,* кро́лик подо́бен за́йцу; кро́лик похо́ж на за́йца; кро́лик схо́ден с за́йцем. **2,** *geom.* подо́бный.

similarity *n.* схо́дство: *a great similarity between them,* большо́е схо́дство ме́жду ни́ми. *The similarity between Victor and his father,* схо́дство Ви́ктора с отцо́м.

similarly *adv.* подо́бным о́бразом.

simile *n.* сравне́ние.

simmer *v.i.* закипа́ть. —**simmer down,** успока́иваться.

simper *v.i.* ухмыля́ться.

simple *adj.* просто́й: *simple woman/task/food/life,* проста́я же́нщина/зада́ча/пи́ща/жизнь. *It's not so simple,* э́то не так про́сто. —**simple fracture,** просто́й перело́м. —**simple sentence,** просто́е предложе́ние.

simple-hearted *adj.* простоду́шный; простосердéчный. —**simple-heartedness,** *n.* простодýшие; простосердéчие.

simple-minded *adj.* слабоýмный.

simpleton *n.* простáк.

simplicity *n.* простотá.

simplify *v.t.* упрощáть. —**simplification,** *n.* упрощéние. —**simplified,** *adj.* упрощённый.

simplistic *adj.* упрощéнческий.

simply *adv.* прóсто: *write/live simply,* писáть/жить прóсто. *It's simply outrageous,* э́то прóсто безобрáзие.

simulate *v.t.* симули́ровать; притворя́ться. —**simulation,** *n.* симуля́ция. —**simulator,** *n.* симуля́нт.

simultaneity *n.* одновремéнность.

simultaneous *adj.* одновремéнный. *Simultaneous translation,* синхрóнный перевóд. —**simultaneously,** *adv.* одновремéнно.

sin *n.* грех. —*v.i.* греши́ть.

since *adv.* **1,** (between then and now) с тех пор: *I have lived here ever since,* я живý здесь с тех пор. *He has since changed his mind,* он потóм передýмал. **2,** (ago) ужé: *long since forgotten,* давнó ужé забы́т. —*prep.* с (+ *gen.*); со врéмени (+ *gen.*): *since childhood,* с дéтства; *since yesterday,* со вчерáшнего дня; *since the war,* со врéмени войны́. ♦*Also* пóсле: *since his return,* пóсле егó возвращéния. *For the first time since last year,* впервы́е пóсле прóшлого гóда. —*conj.* **1,** (during the time after) с тех пор, как: *since he arrived,* с тех пор, как он приéхал. **2,** (because; inasmuch as) так как; поскóльку. —**since then,** с тех пор. —**since when?,** с каки́х пор?

sincere *adj.* и́скренний.

sincerely *adv.* и́скренне; и́скренно. *I mean that sincerely,* я говорю́ и́скренне; я действи́тельно так дýмаю. —**sincerely yours,** и́скренне ваш.

sincerity *n.* и́скренность. —**in all sincerity,** от чи́стого сéрдца.

sine *n., math.* си́нус.

sinecure *n.* синекýра.

sinew *n.* сухожи́лие. —**sinewy,** *adj.* жи́листый.

sinful *adj.* грéшный.

sing *v.t. & i.* петь: *can you sing?,* вы поёте? *Sing us a song,* спóйте нам пéсню.

singe *v.t.* **1,** (burn slightly) подпáливать. **2,** (burn off the feathers of) опáливать: *singe a goose,* опáливать гýся.

singer *n.* певéц; певи́ца.

singing *n.* пéние.

single *adj.* **1,** (only one) оди́н; еди́ный: *a single purpose,* еди́ная цель. *Made from a single piece of material,* сдéланный из одногó кускá матéрии. *Every single one,* все до одногó; все до еди́ного. *Not a single word,* ни одногó (*or* ни еди́ного) слóва. **2,** (unmarried) A, (of a man) неженáтый; холостóй. B, (of a woman) незамýжняя. *Single mother,* мать-одинóчка. **3,** (for use by one person) одинóчный. *Single room,* кóмната *or* нóмер на одногó. *Single bed,* односпáльная кровáть. —*v.t.* [*usu.* **single out**] выделя́ть; отличáть. —*n.* **1,** = **single room. 2,** *pl., tennis* и́гры в одинóчном разря́де.

single-breasted *adj.* однобóртный.

single combat одинóчный бой; единобóрство.

single file колóнна по одномý. *Proceed single file,* идти́ гуськóм.

single-handed *adj. & adv.* без посторóнней пóмощи.

single-minded *adj.* целеустремлённый.

single-track *adj.* одноколéйный.

singly *adv.* **1,** (separately; alone) оди́н; в одинóчку. **2,** (one at a time) поодинóчке.

singsong *adj.* монотóнный. *In a singsong voice,* нараспéв.

singular *adj.* **1,** (unique) исключи́тельный. **2,** (peculiar; distinctive) своеобрáзный. **3,** *gram.* еди́нственный. —*n., gram.* еди́нственное числó. —**singularity,** *n.* своеобрáзие. —**singularly,** *adv.* необычáйно.

sinister *adj.* зловéщий.

sink *v.i.* **1,** (go beneath the surface) погружáться: *sink into quicksand,* погружáться в сыпýчий песóк. **2,** (go down in water) тонýть: *the ship sank,* корáбль потонýл *or* затонýл. *Sink to the bottom,* идти́ ко дну. **3,** (descend slowly) опускáться; сади́ться; оседáть: *sink into a chair,* опускáться в крéсло; *sink below the horizon,* сади́ться за горизóнт. *The foundation is sinking,* фундáмент оседáет. **4,** (pass gradually into a given condition) впадáть; погружáться: *sink into despair,* впадáть/погружáться в отчáяние. **5,** (fall; drop) пáдать. **6,** (be near death) гáснуть. **7,** *My heart sank,* у меня́ сéрдце замерло, у меня́ душá ушлá в пя́тки. **8,** *fol. by* **in** (penetrate the mind) запечатлевáться. —*v.t.* **1,** (cause to sink) топи́ть: *the ship was sunk,* корáбль был потóплен. **2,** (drive into something) вонзáть; втыкáть; всáживать. *Sink one's teeth into,* впивáться зубáми в (+ *acc.*). **3,** (dig, as a well) рыть. **4,** *basketball* забрáсывать: *sink a shot,* забрóсить мяч в корзи́ну. **5,** *colloq.* (invest) всáживать. —*n.* рáковина: *kitchen sink,* кýхонная рáковина.

sinker *n., fishing* грузи́ло.

sinking fund амортизациóнный фонд.

sinner *n.* грéшник.

sinuous *adj.* изви́листый.

sinus *n.* пáзуха; си́нус. —**sinusitis,** *n.* синуси́т; синуи́т.

sip *v.t.* потя́гивать; отпивáть; прихлёбывать. *Sip lemonade through a straw,* сосáть лимонáд чéрез солóминку. —*n.* мáленький глотóк. *Take a sip of,* отпи́ть; прихлебнýть; пригýбить.

siphon *n.* сифóн. —*v.t.* сливáть *or* спускáть сифóном.

sir *n.* сэр; сýдарь.

sire *n.* **1,** (progenitor) производи́тель. **2,** (form of address for a sovereign) госудáрь. —*v.t.* производи́ть.

siren *n.* сирéна.

sirloin *n.* филé.

sirocco *n.* сирóкко.

sisal *n.* сизáль.

siskin *n.* чиж.

sissy *n., colloq.* нéженка.

sister *n.* сестрá.

sister-in-law *n.* **1,** (husband's sister) золóвка. **2,** (wife's sister) свояченица. **3,** (brother's wife or spouse's brother's wife) невéстка.

sit *v.i.* **1,** [*usu.* **sit down**] (take a seat) сади́ться: *sit down!,* сади́тесь! *Sit down to dinner,* сади́ться за обéд. **2,** (be in a sitting position) сидéть: *he was sitting on the floor,* он сидéл на полý. **3,** (be located) стоять: *the house sits on a hill,* дом стоит на холму. **4,** (remain inactive or unused) сидеть: *sit home all day,* весь день сидеть дома. *Sit idle,* простаивать. **5,** (pose) позировать. **6,** (be in session) заседать. —*v.t.* сажать; усаживать: *sit someone down to work,* сажать/усаживать кого-нибудь за работу. —**sit back,** откидываться. —**sit out,** высидеть до конца. —**sit through,** просидеть. —**sit up, 1,** (rise to a sitting position) приподниматься. *Sit up in bed,* сесть в постели. **2,** (stay up late) не ложиться спать; засиживаться до поздней ночи. *Sit up all night,* просидеть всю ночь. —**sit well with,** устраивать.

sit-down strike сидячая забастовка; итальянская забастовка.

site *n.* **1,** (place where something is) местоположение. **2,** (place where something takes place) место: *crash site,* место аварии. *Building site,* строительная площадка.

sitting *n.* **1,** (act of sitting) сидение. **2,** (session) сеанс. *At one sitting,* в один присест. —*adj.* сидячий: *sitting position,* сидячее положение. —**sitting room,** гостиная.

situate *v.t.* располагать. —**situated,** *adj.* расположенный.

situation *n.* **1,** (state of affairs) положение; обстановка; ситуация. **2,** (position of employment) место; работа.

six *adj.* шесть. —*n.* **1,** (cardinal number) шесть. **2,** *cards* шестерка.

sixfold *adj.* шестикратный. —*adv.* в шесть раз.

six hundred шестьсот. —**six-hundredth,** *adj.* шестисотый.

six-shooter *n., colloq.* шестизарядный револьвер.

sixteen *n. & adj.* шестнадцать. —**sixteenth,** *adj.* шестнадцатый.

sixth *adj.* шестой. —*n.* **1,** (sixth part) шестая часть. **2,** (fraction) шестая: *one-sixth,* одна шестая. **3,** *music* секста. —**sixth sense,** шестое чувство.

sixty *n. & adj.* шестьдесят. —**sixtieth,** *adj.* шестидесятый.

sizable *also,* **sizeable** *adj.* значительный; порядочный.

size *n.* **1,** (largeness) величина; размер. *Hailstones the size of one's fist,* град величиной/размером с (*or* в) кулак. *Be twice/half the size of,* быть в два раза (*or* вдвое) больше/меньше (+ *gen.*). **2,** (standard measure for shoes, clothes, etc.) размер; номер: *what size shoe do you wear?,* какой размер/номер ботинок вы носите? **3,** *colloq.* (state of affairs): *that's about the size of it,* вот как обстоит дело. —*v.t.* [*usu.* **size up**] оценивать. *Size up the situation,* уяснить себе положение.

sizeable *adj.* = **sizable.**

sizzle *v.i.* шипеть.

skate *n.* **1,** (ice skate) конёк; (roller skate) ролик; конёк на роликах. **2,** (fish) скат. —*v.i.* [*also,* **go skating**] кататься на коньках *or* на роликах. —**skater,** *n.* конькобежец.

skating *n.* катание на коньках; конькобежный спорт. *Speed skating,* скоростной бег на коньках. —**skating rink,** каток.

skedaddle *v.i., slang* улепётывать.

skein *n.* моток.

skeletal *adj.* скелетный.

skeleton *n.* **1,** *anat.* скелет; костяк. **2,** (inner framework) остов; каркас. —**skeleton key,** отмычка.

skeptic *also,* **sceptic** *n.* скептик. —**skeptical,** *adj.* скептический. —**skepticism,** *n.* скептицизм.

sketch *n.* **1,** (rough drawing) набросок; эскиз; зарисовка. **2,** (short essay or outline) очерк. **3,** (short play; skit) скетч. —*v.t.* **1,** (draw in rough outline) набрасывать; зарисовывать. **2,** *fig.* (outline; describe) обрисовывать; очерчивать.

sketchy *adj.* схематический; поверхностный.

skewer *n.* вертел.

ski *n.* лыжа. —*adj.* лыжный: *ski suit,* лыжный костюм. —*v.i.* ходить на лыжах. *Go skiing,* идти/пойти на лыжах.

skid *v.i.* **1,** (slip because of lack of traction) заносить (*impers.*): *the car skidded,* машину занесло. **2,** (slide instead of revolving) идти юзом.

skier *n.* лыжник.

skiff *n.* скиф; ялик.

skiing *n.* лыжный спорт.

ski jump лыжный трамплин.

skilful *adj.* = **skillful.**

skill *n.* **1,** (expertness) мастерство; умение; искусство. *Chess is a game of skill,* шахматы требуют мастерства. **2,** (a specific ability) навык; квалификация. *Reading skills,* навыки чтения.

skilled *adj.* квалифицированный.

skillet *n.* сковорода; сковородка.

skillful *also,* **skilful** *adj.* искусный; умелый. —**skillfully,** *adv.* искусно; умело.

skim *v.t.* **1,** (remove from the top of a liquid) снимать: *skim the cream from the milk,* снимать сливки с молока. **2,** (read superficially) (бегло) просматривать. **3,** (glide lightly over) скользить по: *skim the surface,* скользить по верхам *or* по поверхности. —*v.i.* **1,** (glide) скользить. **2,** *fol. by* **through** *or* **over** (read superficially) (бегло) просматривать.

skimmer *n.* шумовка.

skim milk снятое (*or* обезжиренное) молоко.

skimp *v.i.* скупиться; экономничать.

skimpy *adj.* **1,** (meager) скудный. **2,** (not quite large enough) куцый.

skin *n.* **1,** (tissue covering the body) кожа. **2,** (hide; pelt) кожа; шкура. **3,** (thin skin, as of a sausage) кожица. **4,** (rind; peel) кожура; кожица; корка. **5,** (vessel for holding liquids) мех. —*adj.* кожный: *skin disease,* кожная болезнь. *Skin rash,* накожная сыпь. *Skin cancer,* рак кожи. —*v.t.* **1,** (remove the skin from) сдирать кожу с; обдирать; свежевать. **2,** (scrape; abrade) ссаживать: *skin one's knee,* ссаживать себе колено. —**by the skin of one's teeth,** с грехом пополам. —**save one's skin,** спасти свою шкуру. —**skin and bones,** кожа да кости. —**soaked to the skin,** промокший до костей.

skin-deep *adj.* поверхностный.

skin diver аквалангист. —**skin diving,** подводное плавание (с аквалангом).

skinflint *n., colloq.* скряга; скопидом; сквалыга.

skinny *adj.* тощий; худой; сухощавый; сухопарый.

skip *v.i.* **1,** (move with light springing steps) бежать вприпрыжку. **2,** (move quickly from point to point) перескакивать: *skip from place to place,* перескакивать с одного места на другое. **3,** *fol. by* **over** (jump over; omit) перескакивать: *skip over a puddle/page,* перескакивать лужу/страницу. —*v.t.* **1,** (jump over) перескакивать. *Skip rope,* прыгать через скакалку.

2, (omit; bypass; fail to attend) пропуска́ть: *skip a line,* пропуска́ть стро́чку. *Skip a grade,* перескаќивать че́рез класс. *My heart skipped a beat,* у меня́ се́рдце ёкнуло. 3, *colloq.* (depart hurriedly from) удра́ть от: *skip town,* удра́ть от го́рода. —*n.* прыжо́к; скачо́к.
skipper *n.* шки́пер.
skirmish *n.* сты́чка; схва́тка; перестре́лка. —*v.i.* перестре́ливаться.
skirt *n.* ю́бка. —*v.t.* (go around; avoid) огиба́ть; обходи́ть (что́-нибудь) стороно́й.
skit *n.* скетч.
skittish *adj.* норови́стый.
skittles *n.* ке́гли.
skulduggery *also,* **skullduggery** *n.* надува́тельство.
skulk *v.i.* кра́сться.
skull *n.* че́реп. *Fracture one's skull,* разби́ть го́лову. —**skull and crossbones,** че́реп и ко́сти.
skullcap *n.* ермо́лка; тюбете́йка; скуфья́.
skullduggery *n.* = **skulduggery.**
skunk *n.* 1, (animal) скунс; воню́чка. 2, *colloq.* (vile person) гад.
sky *n.* не́бо. *In the sky,* на не́бе. *Fall from the sky,* па́дать с не́ба. —**out of a clear blue sky,** ни с того́ ни с сего́; как снег на́ голову. —**praise to the skies,** превозноси́ть до небе́с.
sky-high *adv.* до небе́с; высоко́-высоко́.
skylark *n.* жа́воронок.
skylight *n.* застеклённая крыша; светово́й люк; фона́рь.
skyline *n.* очерта́ние небоскрёбов на фо́не не́ба.
skyrocket *v.i.* подска́кивать.
skyscraper *n.* небоскрёб.
skyward *adv.* к не́бу; в не́бо.
slab *n.* плита́.
slack *adj.* 1, (not taut) сла́бый; свобо́дный. 2, (slow; sluggish) ме́дленный: *slack pace,* ме́дленный темп. 3, (marked by a slowdown in activity) вя́лый. *Slack period,* глуха́я пора́. —*n.* слабина́: *take up the slack,* выбира́ть слабину́. —*v.i.* [*usu.* **slack off**] ослабева́ть; спада́ть.
slacken *v.t.* 1, (loosen; relax) ослабля́ть. 2, (slow down) замедля́ть. —*v.i.* ослабева́ть.
slacker *n.* лентя́й; прогу́льщик.
slacks *n.pl.* брю́ки.
slag *n.* шлак.
slake *v.t.* 1, (quench, as thirst) утоля́ть. 2, (treat with water, as lime) гаси́ть.
slalom *n.* сла́лом.
slam *v.t.* 1, (shut with force) захло́пывать (дверь). 2, (throw or apply with force) хло́пать: *slam the book on the table,* хло́пать кни́гой по́ столу. *Slam down the telephone,* бро́сить тру́бку. *Slam on the brakes,* ре́зко тормози́ть. —*v.i.* 1, (shut noisily) захло́пываться. 2, *fol. by* **into** (run into) вре́заться в; налета́ть на. —*n.* 1, (act of slamming) хло́панье. 2, *cards* шлем.
slander *n.* клевета́. —*v.t.* клевета́ть на. —**slanderer,** *n.* клеветни́к. —**slanderous,** *adj.* клеветни́ческий.
slang *n.* жарго́н. —*adj.* жарго́нный.
slant *v.t.* 1, (set at an angle) наклоня́ть. 2, *colloq.* (write so as to express a bias) искажа́ть. —*v.i.* коси́ться. —*n.* накло́н; укло́н; склон. *On a slant,* ко́со.
slanted *adj.* (biased) пристра́стный; тенденцио́зный.
slanting *adj.* 1, (oblique) косо́й; накло́нный. 2, (of eyes) раско́сый.
slap *v.t.* шлёпать; хло́пать. *Slap someone's face,* уда́рить кого́-нибудь по лицу́. —*n.* шлепо́к. *Slap in the face,* пощёчина.
slapdash *adj.* безала́берный; неря́шливый. —*adv.* ко́е-как; на ско́рую ру́ку; спустя́ рукава́.
slapstick *n.* фарс. —*adj.* фа́рсовый.
slash *v.t.* 1, (cut severely) поре́зать; руби́ть. *Slash tires,* вспа́рывать ши́ны. *Slash one's wrists,* вскры́ть себе́ на рука́х ве́ны. 2, (reduce drastically) уре́зывать. —*n.* 1, (sweeping stroke) взмах. 2, (sign [/]) дробь: *8/10,* во́семь дробь де́сять. —**slashing,** *adj.* ре́зкий; хлёсткий.
slat *n.* пла́нка; пласти́нка.
slate *n.* 1, (mineral) сла́нец; ши́фер. 2, (writing plate) гри́фельная доска́. 3, (list of candidates) спи́сок кандида́тов. —*adj.* 1, (of slate) сла́нцевый; ши́ферный. 2, (slate-colored) цве́та сла́нца. —**wipe the slate clean,** всё прости́ть.
slattern *n.* 1, (slob) неря́ха; грязну́ля. 2, (slut) шлю́ха.
slaughter *n.* 1, (of animals) убо́й: *lead to the slaughter,* вести́ на убо́й. 2, (massacre) резня́; бо́йня; избие́ние. *The slaughter of thousands of people,* уби́йство ты́сяч люде́й. —*v.t.* 1, (kill, as animals) ре́зать. 2, (massacre) уничтожа́ть.
slaughterhouse *n.* бо́йня; скотобо́йня.
Slav *n.* славяни́н.
slave *n.* раб. —*adj.* ра́бский; нево́льничий. *Slave labor,* ра́бский труд. *Slave market,* нево́льничий ры́нок. *Slave trade,* работорго́вля. —*v.i.* труди́ться. —**slaveowner,** *n.* рабовладе́лец.
slaver *n.* слю́ни. —*v.i.* пуска́ть слю́ни.
slavery *n.* ра́бство.
Slavic *adj.* славя́нский. —**Slavicist,** *n.* слави́ст.
slavish *adj.* ра́бский.
Slavonic *adj.* славя́нский.
Slavophile *n.* славянофи́л.
slaw *n.* = **coleslaw.**
slay *v.t.* убива́ть. —**slayer,** *n.* уби́йца.
sleazy *adj.* 1, (flimsy) непро́чный. 2, (run-down) убо́гий.
sled *n.* 1, (for traveling over distances) са́ни. *Dog sled,* на́рты. 2, (for children) са́нки. —*v.i.* [*usu.* **go sledding**] ката́ться на са́нках.
sledge *n.* са́ни; са́нки.
sledgehammer *n.* мо́лот; кува́лда.
sleek *adj.* прили́занный.
sleep *v.i.* спать. *Go to sleep,* ложи́ться спать. —*n.* сон. —**put to sleep,** 1, (put to bed) укла́дывать (в посте́ль). 2, (make drowsy) усыпля́ть; нагоня́ть сон на. 3, (put to death, as a sick animal) усыпля́ть. —**sleep it off,** проспа́ться. —**sleep through,** просыпа́ть. —**sleep with,** спать с.
sleeper *n.* 1, (one who sleeps): *he is a light/heavy sleeper,* он чу́тко/кре́пко спит. 2, (sleeping car) спа́льный ваго́н. 3, *Brit.* (railroad tie) шпа́ла.
sleepiness *n.* сонли́вость.
sleeping *adj.* 1, (asleep) спя́щий. 2, (of or for sleep) спа́льный. —**sleeping bag,** спа́льный мешо́к. —**sleeping car,** спа́льный ваго́н. —**sleeping pill,** снотво́рная табле́тка. —**sleeping sickness,** со́нная боле́знь.

sleepless *adj.* бессо́нный. *Spend a sleepless night,* провести́ ночь без сна.
sleepwalker *n.* луна́тик. —**sleepwalking,** *n.* лунати́зм.
sleepy *adj.* со́нный; сонли́вый. —**be sleepy,** хоте́ть спать: *I am sleepy,* я хочу́ спать.
sleepy-eyed *adj.* за́спанный.
sleepyhead *n.* со́ня; со́нная тетёря.
sleet *n.* дождь со сне́гом.
sleeve *n.* рука́в: *short sleeves,* коро́ткие рукава́. —**have something up one's sleeve,** име́ть что́-то на уме́; замышля́ть что́-то.
sleeveless *adj.* без рукаво́в; безрука́вный. *Sleeveless jacket,* безрука́вка.
sleigh *n.* са́ни. —*v.i.* [*usu.* **go sleighing** *or* **sleigh riding**] ката́ться на саня́х. —**sleigh bells,** бубе́нчики.
sleight of hand ло́вкость рук.
slender *adj.* **1,** (thin) то́нкий. **2,** (gracefully slim) стро́йный. **3,** (meager) ску́дный. **4,** (slight; feeble, as of hope) сла́бый.
sleuth *n.* **1,** (detective) сы́щик; шпик; ище́йка. **2,** (bloodhound) ище́йка.
slew *n., colloq.* ма́сса; у́йма.
slice *n.* ло́мтик. *Slice of bread,* кусо́к хле́ба. —*v.t.* **1,** (divide into slices) ре́зать; нареза́ть. **2,** *fol. by* **off** (cut off) отреза́ть. **3,** *sports* ре́зать; сре́зать (мяч).
slick *adj.* **1,** (slippery) ско́льзкий. **2,** (sleek, as of hair) прили́занный. **3,** *colloq.* (clever; tricky) хи́трый. —*v.t.* [*usu.* **slick down**] пригла́живать. —*n.* покрыва́ло: *oil slick,* нефтяно́е покрыва́ло.
slide *v.i.* **1,** (slip; glide) скользи́ть: *slide on the ice,* скользи́ть по льду. *Slide down a pole,* соска́льзывать по шесту́. **2,** (move easily, as of a drawer) задвига́ться; выдвига́ться. **3,** *fol. by* **off** (slip off) соска́льзывать. —*v.t.* задвига́ть: *slide the suitcase under the bed,* задвига́ть чемода́н под крова́ть. —*n.* **1,** (act of sliding) скольже́ние. **2,** (inclined track) скат. **3,** (avalanche) обва́л; о́ползень. **4,** (transparency) диапозити́в. **5,** (specimen holder) предме́тное стекло́.
slide rule логарифми́ческая лине́йка.
sliding *adj.* скользя́щий; задвижно́й; выдвижно́й; раздвижно́й. *Sliding door,* раздвижна́я дверь. *Sliding scale,* скользя́щая шкала́. —**sliding board,** го́рка.
slight *adj.* **1,** (not great) небольшо́й: *a slight increase,* небольшо́е увеличе́ние. **2,** (not severe or heavy) лёгкий: *a slight cold,* лёгкий на́сморк. *A slight accent,* лёгкий акце́нт. *A slight temperature,* повы́шенная температу́ра. **3,** (short; brief) небольшо́й: *a slight pause,* небольшо́й переры́в. **4,** (slender; slim) то́нкий. —*v.t.* **1,** (neglect) пренебрега́ть. **2,** (treat discourteously) обижа́ть; трети́ровать. —*n.* оби́да; щелчо́к.
slightest *adj.* мале́йший: *I haven't the slightest idea,* я не име́ю ни мале́йшего представле́ния. *Not in the slightest,* ничу́ть; ни на йо́ту.
slighting *adj.* оби́дный: *slighting remark,* оби́дное замеча́ние.
slightly *adv.* слегка́; немно́го. *Slightly wounded,* легко́ ра́неный.
slim *adj.* **1,** (thin; slender) то́нкий; стро́йный. **2,** (meager) ску́дный. **3,** (poor, as of a chance) сла́бый. —*v.i.* [*usu.* **slim down**] худе́ть.
slime *n.* **1,** (mud) грязь. **2,** (animal secretion) слизь.
slimy *adj.* **1,** (covered with slime) сли́зистый. **2,** (repulsive) га́дкий.
sling *n.* **1,** (support for an injured arm) пе́ревязь. **2,** (rifle strap) (руже́йный) реме́нь. **3,** (device for shooting stones) праща́. **4,** = **slingshot.** —*v.t.* броса́ть; швыря́ть. *Sling a gun over one's shoulder,* заки́нуть ружьё за плечо́. *Sling mud at,* забра́сывать (кого́-нибудь) гря́зью.
slingshot *n.* рога́тка.
slink *v.i.* кра́сться; идти́ кра́дучись. *Slink away,* ускольза́ть.
slip *v.i.* **1,** (lose one's footing) поскользну́ться: *slip on the ice,* поскользну́ться на льду. **2,** (slide out of place) скользи́ть. *Slip off,* соска́льзывать; сбива́ться. **3,** (slide from one's grasp) выска́льзывать (из). **4,** (move quickly or furtively) скользну́ть. *Slip in/into,* вкра́дываться (в); прокра́дываться (в). *Slip out (of),* выска́льзывать (из). *Slip away (from),* ускольза́ть (от); улизну́ть (из). *Slip by/past,* скользну́ть (ми́мо); проска́льзывать (ми́мо). **5,** *fol. by* **over to, down to,** *etc.* (run a quick errand) сбе́гать (в). **6,** *fol. by* **into** (put on quickly) наки́нуть. **7,** *fol. by* **by** (pass imperceptibly, as of time) проноси́ться; промелькну́ть. **8,** (decline in vigor) сдава́ть. —*v.t.* **1,** *fol. by* **on** (put on quickly) наки́нуть. **2,** *fol. by* **off** (take off quickly) сбро́сить. **3,** (thrust quickly) засо́вывать. **4,** (convey stealthily) подбра́сывать; подкла́дывать; подсо́вывать. **5,** (escape, as one's mind) вы́скочить (из головы́). —*n.* **1,** (mistake; lapse) оши́бка. *Slip of the tongue,* обмо́лвка; огово́рка. **2,** (woman's undergarment) комбина́ция. *Your slip is showing,* у вас видна́ ни́жняя ю́бка. **3,** (pillowcase) на́волочка. **4,** (piece, as of paper) листо́к (бума́ги). *Order slip,* бланк зака́за. *Sales slip,* квита́нция. **5,** (plant cutting) черено́к. **6,** (docking place) прича́л. —**give someone the slip,** ускольза́ть от кого́-нибудь. —**let slip, 1,** (miss, as an opportunity) упуска́ть. **2,** (utter unintentionally) отпуска́ть. —**slip through someone's fingers,** проскочи́ть (*or* проскользну́ть) у кого́-нибудь ме́жду па́льцами (па́льцев). —**slip up,** *colloq.* оплоша́ть.
slip cover чехо́л.
slipknot *n.* скользя́щий у́зел.
slippage *n.* скольже́ние; проска́льзывание.
slipper *n.* (дома́шняя) ту́фля; шлёпанец.
slippery *adj.* **1,** (smooth; slick) ско́льзкий. **2,** (shifty; elusive) увёртливый; изворо́тливый.
slipshod *adj.* небре́жный; неря́шливый. *In a slipshod manner,* спустя́ рукава́.
slip-up *n., colloq.* неувя́зка.
slit *n.* щель; разре́з; проре́з; про́резь. —*v.t.* разреза́ть. *Slit someone's throat,* перере́зать го́рло (+ *dat.*). *Slit open an envelope,* вскрыть конве́рт. —**slit trench,** щель.
slither *v.i.* **1,** (slide) скользи́ть. **2,** (move like a snake) ползти́.
sliver *n.* ще́пка.
slob *n., slang* неря́ха; грязну́ля; растрёпа.
slobber *v.i.* пуска́ть слю́ни. —*n.* слю́ни.
sloe *n.* тёрн.
slogan *n.* ло́зунг.
sloop *n.* шлюп.
slop *n.* помо́и. —*v.t.* расплёскивать. —**slop basin,** полоска́тельница.
slope *n.* склон; накло́н; укло́н; отко́с; скат; спуск.

—*v.i.* иметь наклон. *Slope downward,* идти *or* спускаться под уклон. *Slope forty degrees,* иметь наклон в сорок градусов. —**sloping,** *adj.* наклонный; покатый; пологий; отлогий.

sloppy *adj.* **1,** (muddy) грязный. **2,** (untidy; slipshod) неряшливый. —**sloppiness,** *n.* неряшливость.

slosh *v.i.* шлёпать (по грязи).

slot *n.* **1,** (long opening) щель. **2,** (round opening for a coin) отверстие.

sloth *n.* **1,** (animal) ленивец. **2,** (indolence) леность. —**slothful,** *adj.* ленивый; инертный.

slot machine игорный автомат.

slouch *v.i.* сутулиться; горбиться. —*n.* **1,** (bent posture) сутулость. **2,** (incompetent person): *he is no slouch,* он не лыком шит.

slough *v.t.* **1,** (shed) сбрасывать. **2,** *cards* сбрасывать. —*v.i.* сходить; шелушиться.

Slovak *n.* **1,** (person) словак. **2,** (language) словацкий язык. —*adj.* словацкий.

Slovene *n.* словенец. —**Slovenian,** *adj.* словенский. —*n.* словенский язык.

slovenly *adj.* неряшливый. —**slovenliness,** *n.* неряшливость; неряшество.

slow *adj.* **1,** (not fast) медленный: *slow pace,* медленный ход. *On a slow fire,* на медленном огне. *Be slow in replying,* замедлить с ответом. **2,** (behind time, as of a clock): *my watch is slow,* мои часы отстают. **3,** (dull-witted) тупой. —*adv.* медленно. —*v.t.* [*usu.* **slow down**] замедлять. —*v.i.* [*usu.* **slow down**] замедлять ход; замедляться.

slowdown *n.* замедление.

slowly *adv.* медленно.

slow motion замедленная съёмка.

slowness *n.* медленность.

slowpoke *n., colloq.* медлительный человек.

sludge *n.* грязь; ил.

slug *n.* **1,** (bullet) пуля. **2,** (object used in place of a coin) жетон. **3,** *printing* шпон. **4,** (mollusk) слизняк; слизень. —*v.t.* (punch) тузить.

sluggard *n.* лентяй; лежебока.

sluggish *adj.* вялый; инертный. —**sluggishly,** *adv.* вяло. —**sluggishness,** *n.* вялость.

sluice *n.* шлюз. —**sluice gate,** шлюзные ворота.

slum *n.* трущоба.

slumber *n.* сон. —*v.i.* спать; дремать.

slump *n.* спад. —*v.i.* **1,** (fall heavily) валиться. *Slump into a chair,* опуститься в кресло. **2,** (decline suddenly) резко падать.

slung shot кистень.

slur *v.t.* **1,** (pronounce indistinctly) глотать (слова). *His speech is slurred,* у него язык заплетается. **2,** [*usu.* **slur over**] (pass over lightly) смазывать. **3,** (disparage) порочить. —*n.* **1,** (stain) пятно (на репутации). *Cast slurs on someone's reputation,* чернить чью-нибудь репутацию. **2,** (disparaging remark) инсинуация. **3,** *music* лига.

slush *n.* слякоть; талый снег. —**slushy,** *adj.* слякотный.

slut *n.* **1,** (slovenly woman) неряха. **2,** (loose woman) шлюха.

sly *adj.* хитрый. —**on the sly,** тайком; потихоньку.

slyly *adv.* хитро.

smack *v.t.* **1,** (slap) хлопать; шлёпать. **2,** *Smack one's lips,* чмокать губами. —*v.i.* отдавать (+ *instr.*): *smack of dishonesty,* отдавать нечестностью. —*n.* **1,** (slap) шлепок. **2,** (trace; suggestion) привкус. —*adv., colloq.* прямо: *run smack into a tree,* врезаться прямо в дерево.

small *adj.* **1,** (little; not large) маленький; небольшой; мелкий. *Small child/house/town,* маленький ребенок/дом/городок. *Small print,* мелкий шрифт. *Small income,* небольшой доход. *On a small scale,* в небольшом масштабе. *She is a small eater,* она мало ест. *These shoes are too small,* эти ботинки (мне) малы. **2,** (operating on a limited scale) мелкий: *a small business,* мелкое предприятие; *small depositor,* мелкий вкладчик. **3,** (petty) мелкий; мелочный. **4,** *in* **small letter,** маленькая *or* строчная буква. —*n., in* **small of the back,** поясница.

small arms стрелковое оружие.

small change мелкие деньги; мелочь.

small fry *colloq.* мелкая сошка; *collective* мелюзга; мелкота.

small intestine тонкая кишка.

small-minded *adj.* мелкий; мелочный.

smallpox *n.* (чёрная) оспа.

small talk салонный разговор.

smart *adj.* **1,** (bright; clever) умный; способный. **2,** (brisk; vigorous) быстрый: *at a smart pace,* быстрым ходом. **3,** (stylish) шикарный; нарядный. —*v.i.* **1,** (sting; burn) саднить. **2,** (suffer keenly) мучиться. —**smart aleck,** *colloq.* умник.

smarten *v.t.* [*usu.* **smarten up**] **1,** (improve in appearance) прихорашивать. **2,** (make more aware) вразумлять. —*v.i.* [*usu.* **smarten up**] образумиться.

smartly *adv.* **1,** (stylishly) шикарно. **2,** (with brisk and precise movements) четко.

smash *v.t.* **1,** (break to pieces) разбивать: *smash a vase,* разбить вазу. *Smash up a car,* разбить машину. *Smash down a door,* выломать дверь. *Smash something to the ground,* разбить что-нибудь о землю. **2,** (defeat utterly) разбивать; громить. —*v.i.* **1,** (break into pieces) разбиваться. **2,** *fol. by* **into** (run into) врезаться в; налететь на. —*n.* грохот.

smashing *adj., colloq.* потрясающий.

smattering *n.* поверхностное знание.

smear *v.t.* **1,** (cover with grease, paint, etc.) мазать. **2,** (spread on; apply) намазывать; размазывать. **3,** (soil) мазать; пачкать. **4,** (smudge, as ink) размазывать. **5,** (defame) чернить. —*v.i.* размазываться. —*n.* **1,** (spot; smudge) пятно. **2,** *med.* мазок. **3,** (slander) клевета.

smell *v.i.* **1,** (have a certain odor) пахнуть: *smell good,* хорошо пахнуть; *smell of fish,* пахнуть рыбой. **2,** (be malodorous) вонять. —*v.t.* **1,** (catch the smell of) чувствовать запах (+ *gen.*). *I don't smell anything,* я не чувствую никакого запаха. **2,** (test by smelling; sniff) нюхать. **3,** (sense the presence of) чуять: *smell a rat,* чуять недоброе. —*n.* **1,** (sense of smell) обоняние. **2,** (odor; aroma) запах. *There is a smell of smoke,* пахнет дымом.

smelling salts нюхательная соль.

smelly *adj.* дурно пахнущий; зловонный.

smelt *n.* (fish) корюшка. —*v.t.* (fuse; melt) плавить; выплавлять. —**smelter,** *n.* плавильщик. —**smelting,** *n.* плавка.

smidgen *also,* **smidgeon** *n., colloq.* чуточка.

smile *v.i.* улыбаться. *Fortune smiled on him,* счастье ему улыбнулось. —*n.* улыбка.

smirch *v.t.* пятнать; марать. —*n.* пятно.

smirk *n.* усмéшка. —*v.i.* ухмыля́ться.
smite *v.t.* **1,** (strike; kill; afflict) поража́ть. **2,** (affect strongly) охва́тывать: *smitten with love,* охва́ченный любо́вью. **3,** (captivate) увлека́ть; восхища́ть.
smith *n.* кузне́ц.
smithereens *n.pl., in* **smash to smithereens,** разбива́ть вдре́безги.
smithy *n.* ку́зница.
smock *n.* блу́за; хала́т.
smog *n.* ды́мная мгла́; "смог".
smoke *n.* **1,** (vapor) дым. **2,** (an act of smoking): *have a smoke,* покури́ть. —*adj.* дымово́й: *smoke signal,* дымово́й сигна́л. —*v.i.* **1,** (indulge in smoking) кури́ть. *No smoking!,* не кури́ть! **2,** (give off smoke) дыми́ть; дыми́ться. —*v.t.* **1,** (a cigarette, pipe, opium, etc.) кури́ть. **2,** (treat or preserve with smoke) копти́ть. **3,** *fol. by* **out** (drive out) выку́ривать. —**go up in smoke,** взлете́ть на во́здух.
smoked *adj.* копчёный: *smoked fish,* копчёная ры́ба. *Smoked salmon,* сёмга.
smokehouse *n.* копти́льня.
smoker *n.* куря́щий; кури́льщик.
smoke screen дымова́я заве́са.
smokestack *n.* дымова́я труба́.
smoking *n.* **1,** (of a cigarette, cigar, etc.) куре́ние. **2,** (treatment with smoke) копче́ние. —**smoking car,** ваго́н для куря́щих.
smoky *adj.* ды́мный.
smolder *also,* **smoulder** *v.i.* **1,** (burn) тлеть. **2,** (exist in a suppressed state) таи́ться. *Smoldering resentment,* затаённая зло́ба.
smooth *adj.* **1,** (not rough) гла́дкий: *smooth surface/skin,* гла́дкая пове́рхность/ко́жа. **2,** (not jerky) пла́вный; споко́йный. *Smooth gait,* пла́вная похо́дка. *Smooth trip/flight,* споко́йный рейс. —*v.t.* **1,** (make smooth) сгла́живать; пригла́живать. **2,** *fol. by* **out** (remove the wrinkles from) разгла́живать; расправля́ть. **3,** *fol. by* **over** (mitigate) сгла́живать.
smoothbore *adj.* гладкостволь́ный.
smoothly *adv.* гла́дко: *go smoothly,* проходи́ть гла́дко.
smoothness *n.* гла́дкость.
smooth-spoken *adj.* сладкоречи́вый.
smorgasbord *n.* шве́дская заку́ска.
smother *v.t.* души́ть; удуша́ть. —*v.i.* задыха́ться.
smoulder *v.* = **smolder.**
smudge *n.* пятно́. —*v.t.* разма́зывать. —*v.i.* разма́зываться. —**smudge pot,** дымова́я ша́шка.
smug *adj.* самодово́льный.
smuggle *v.t.* **1,** (bring into a country illegally) провози́ть. **2,** (convey surreptitiously) проноси́ть: *smuggle a gun into prison,* проноси́ть пистоле́т в тюрьму́. —**smuggler,** *n.* контрабанди́ст. —**smuggling,** *n.* контраба́нда.
smugness *n.* самодово́льство.
smut *n.* **1,** (sooty matter) са́жа. **2,** (plant disease) головня́. **3,** (obscene writing) непристо́йность.
snack *n.* заку́ска. *Have a snack,* закуси́ть. —**snack bar,** заку́сочная; буфе́т.
snaffle *n.* тре́нзель.
snafu *n., slang* пу́таница.
snag *n.* **1,** (tree stump sticking out of the water) коря́га. **2,** *fig.* (hitch) зацéпка; запи́нка; загво́здка. *Hit a snag,* наскочи́ть на мель. —*v.t.* зацепля́ть. —*v.i.* зацепля́ться; задева́ть: *snag on a nail,* зацепля́ться/задева́ть за гвоздь.
snail *n.* ули́тка. —**at a snail's pace,** черепа́шьим ша́гом.
snake *n.* змея́. —*v.i.* змеи́ться. —**snake in the grass,** змея́ подколо́дная.
snakebite *n.* уку́с змеи́.
snake charmer заклина́тель змей.
snap *v.i.* **1,** (break suddenly) ло́пнуть; порва́ться. **2,** [*usu.* **snap shut**] (close with a sudden sharp sound) защёлкиваться. **3,** *fol. by* **at** (bite suddenly) ца́пать (за); (lunge at menacingly) огрыза́ться (на). **4,** (speak or retort sharply) отре́зать; отруби́ть; огрыза́ться. *Snap at someone,* огрыза́ться на кого́-нибудь. **5,** *Snap to attention,* вы́тянуться в сто́йке "сми́рно". —*v.t.* **1,** (cause to make a sharp sound) щёлкать: *snap one's fingers,* щёлкать па́льцами. **2,** [*usu.* **snap shut**] (fasten with a sharp sound) защёлкивать. **3,** (release, as a shutter) щёлкать (затво́ром *or* затво́р). **4,** (take, as a picture) сде́лать (сни́мок). **5,** (break) порва́ть. **6,** *fol. by* **up** (buy quickly) расхва́тывать. —*n.* **1,** (sharp sound) щёлканье; щёлк. **2,** (fastening device) застёжка; кно́пка. **3,** (brief spell) полоса́. *Cold snap,* похолода́ние. **4,** (cookie) пря́ник: *ginger snap,* имби́рный пря́ник. **5,** *slang* (easy task) пустяки́; ерунда́. —*adj.* скоропали́тельный: *snap judgment,* скоропали́тельное сужде́ние. —**snap back,** оправля́ться. —**snap out of,** избавля́ться от.
snapdragon *n.* льви́ный зев; льви́ная пасть.
snappy *adj.* **1,** (brisk) бы́стрый; живо́й. **2,** (cold and invigorating) холо́дненький. **3,** *colloq.* (stylish) бро́ский. —**make it snappy!,** жи́во!; поскоре́е!
snapshot *n.* сни́мок; фотосни́мок.
snare *n.* сило́к; тенёта. —*v.t.* **1,** (catch; trap) пойма́ть в лову́шку. **2,** (entice; inveigle) зама́нивать; завлека́ть.
snarl *v.i.* **1,** (growl) рыча́ть; огрыза́ться **2,** (become entangled) спу́тываться; запу́тываться. —*v.t.* спу́тывать; запу́тывать. —*n.* **1,** (growl) рыча́ние. **2,** (tangle) пу́таница.
snatch *v.t.* **1,** (grab) хвата́ть; выхва́тывать; урыва́ть. **2,** *fol. by* **up** (buy quickly) расхва́тывать. —*v.i.* [*usu.* **snatch at**] хвата́ться за; ухвати́ться за. —*n.* **1,** (act of snatching) хва́тка. **2,** *weightlifting* рыво́к. **3,** (bit) обры́вок; отры́вок. *Snatches of a conversation,* отры́вки разгово́ра. **4,** (brief period of time): *work in snatches,* рабо́тать уры́вками.
snazzy *adj., slang* бро́ский; шика́рный.
sneak *v.i.* кра́сться. *Sneak into,* вкра́дываться в; лезть в. *Sneak out of,* вы́скользнуть из. *Sneak up to,* подкра́дываться к. —*v.t.* проноси́ть; прота́скивать. —*adj.* внеза́пный: *sneak attack,* внеза́пное нападе́ние. —*n.* пройдо́ха.
sneakers *n.pl.* та́почки; ке́ды.
sneaky *adj.* лука́вый; проны́рливый.
sneer *n.* усме́шка. —*v.i.* **1,** (make a sneer) насмеха́ться; насме́шничать. **2,** *fol. by* **at** (scoff at) насмеха́ться (над).
sneeze *v.i.* чиха́ть. —*n.* чих.
snicker *v.i.* хихи́кать. —*n.* хихи́канье.
snide *adj.* язви́тельный; ехи́дный.
sniff *v.i.* сопе́ть. —*v.t.* **1,** (breathe in forcibly) вдыха́ть. **2,** (try to smell by sniffing) ню́хать. —*n.* вдох но́сом.
sniffle *v.i.* **1,** (breathe with difficulty) сопе́ть. **2,**

(cry intermittently) всхлипывать. —**sniffles**, *n.pl.* насморк.

snip *v.t.* **1,** (cut; clip) резать. **2,** *fol. by* **off** (cut off) отрезать; отхватывать.

snipe *n.* кулик; бекас.

sniper *n.* снайпер.

snitch *v.t., slang* (swipe) стащить. —*v.i.* [*usu.* **snitch on**] *slang* (tell on) ябедничать (на).

snivel *v.i.* **1,** (run at the nose) распускать сопли. **2,** (complain; whine) хныкать; распускать нюни.

snob *n.* сноб. —**snobbery**, *n.* снобизм. —**snobbish**, *adj.* чванный; спесивый. —**snobbishness**, *n.* снобизм.

snoop *v.i., colloq.* подглядывать; подслушивать. —**snoop around**, рыскать; шнырять.

snooty *adj., colloq.* чванный; спесивый.

snooze *v.i., colloq.* вздремнуть. —*n., colloq.* короткий сон.

snore *v.i.* храпеть. —*n.* храп. —**snorer**, *n.* храпун.

snorkel *n.* шноркель.

snort *v.i.* фыркать. —*n.* **1,** (snorting sound) фырканье. **2,** *slang* (short drink) глоток (спиртного); рюмочка.

snot *n.* сопли.

snotty *adj.* **1,** (covered with snot) сопливый. **2,** *slang* (saucy) нахальный.

snout *n.* рыло; морда.

snow *n.* снег. —*adj.* снежный. —*v.i.* снежить. *It is snowing,* идёт снег. —*v.t.* **1,** *fol. by* **in** *or* **under** (cover or obstruct with snow) заваливать снегом. **2,** *fol. by* **under** (overwhelm, as with work) заваливать (работой).

snowball *n.* снежок; снежный ком. *Throw snowballs,* играть в снежки.

snowbank *n.* снежный занос.

snowbound *adj.* заваленный снегом.

snow bunting пуночка.

snow-clad *adj.* заснеженный. *Also,* **snow-covered.**

snowdrift *n.* сугроб; снежный занос; снежный завал.

snowdrop *n.* подснежник.

snowfall *n.* снегопад.

snowflake *n.* снежинка; *pl.* хлопья снега.

snow leopard барс.

snow line снеговая линия.

snow maiden снегурка; снегурочка.

snowman *n.* снежная баба.

snowmobile *n.* снегоход.

snowplow *also,* **snowplough** *n.* снегоочиститель; снеговой плуг.

snowshoe *n.* снегоступ.

snowstorm *n.* метель.

snow-white *adj.* белоснежный.

snowy *adj.* снежный. —**snowy owl**, белая сова.

snub *v.t.* третировать. —*n.* щелчок. —*adj.* (of the nose) вздёрнутый.

snub-nosed *adj.* курносый.

snuff *n.* **1,** (powdered tobacco) нюхательный табак. **2,** (charred end of a candle) нагар. —*v.t.* нюхать. —**snuff out**, **1,** (extinguish) тушить. **2,** (suppress; destroy) разрушать. *Snuff out human lives,* погубить человеческие жизни. —**up to snuff**, *colloq.* на должной высоте.

snuffbox *n.* табакерка.

snug *adj.* **1,** (cozy) уютный. **2,** (compact; tight-fitting) тесный.

snuggle *v.i.* [*usu.* **snuggle up to**] прижиматься (к).

so *adv.* **1,** (to the extent indicated; to a high degree) так: *so soon,* так скоро; *so long,* так долго. *I am so sorry!,* мне так жаль! ♦*Before long-form adjectives* такой: *she is so beautiful!,* она такая красивая! **2,** (thus; in the manner indicated) так. *He said so,* он так сказал. *I think/hope so,* думаю/надеюсь, что да. *I don't think so,* думаю, что нет. *Let us hope so,* будем надеяться. *It so happened that...,* случилось так, что... **3,** (then; it turns out) так; так что; значит. *So you know her!,* так вы её знаете! *So if you want to go...,* так что, если вам хочется пойти... *So you've come after all!,* значит, вы всё равно пришли! **4,** (also; likewise) тоже: *so do I,* я тоже. **5,** *expressing disagreement with a neg. statement: you don't know how to cook. I do so,* вы не умеете готовить. Неправда, умею. —*adj.* так: *isn't that so?,* не так ли? *That is not so,* это не верно. *Is that so!,* да что вы говорите! —*conj.* поэтому: *it was raining, so we stayed home,* шёл дождь, и поэтому мы остались дома. —**and so**, итак. —**and so on; and so forth**, и так далее. —**or so**, *see* **or**. —**so as to**, с тем, чтобы. —**so be it**, так и быть; пусть будет так. —**so far**, *see* **far**. —**so long!**, пока!; до свиданья! —**so long as**, если только; лишь бы. —**so many; so much**, **1,** (such a large amount or number) так много; столько. **2,** (a specific amount or number) столько-то. —**so much for...**, вот тебе и...: *so much for our trip to Europe!,* вот тебе и поездка в Европу! —**so much the better/worse**, тем лучше/хуже. —**so that**, с тем, чтобы. —**so what?**, ну и что?

soak *v.t.* **1,** (keep in water) мочить; замачивать; вымачивать. **2,** (drench) промачивать. *Get soaked,* промокать. **3,** *fol. by* **up** (absorb) впитывать; всасывать. **4,** *fol. by* **off** (remove, as a stamp) отмачивать. —*v.i.* **1,** (stay immersed in water) пролежать в воде; мокнуть. **2,** *fol. by* **through** (seep through) просачиваться (сквозь). —**soaking wet**, мокрый, хоть выжми.

so-and-so *n.* такой-то: *Mr. So-and-so,* господин такой-то.

soap *n.* мыло. —*adj.* мыльный: *soap bubble,* мыльный пузырь. —*v.t.* мылить; намыливать.

soap dish мыльница.

soap flakes мыльная стружка.

soap powder стиральный порошок.

soapstone *n.* мыльный камень.

soapsuds *n.pl.* мыльная пена.

soapwort *n.* мыльнянка.

soapy *adj.* мыльный.

soar *v.i.* **1,** (fly high into the air) взлетать; взвиваться; взмывать. **2,** (glide) парить; реять. **3,** (shoot up, as of prices) подскакивать.

sob *v.i.* рыдать. —*n.* рыдание.

sober *adj.* трезвый. —*v.t.* отрезвлять; вытрезвлять. *Have a sobering effect upon,* действовать (на кого-нибудь) отрезвляюще. —*v.i.* [*usu.* **sober up**] трезветь; отрезвляться; вытрезвляться. —**sobering-up station**, вытрезвитель.

sobriety *n.* трезвость.

sobriquet *n.* прозвище; кличка.

so-called *adj.* так называемый.

soccer *n.* футбо́л.
sociable *adj.* общи́тельный. —**sociability,** *n.* общи́тельность.
social *adj.* **1,** (pert. to society) обще́ственный; социа́льный: *social status,* обще́ственное/социа́льное положе́ние. *Social strata,* слои́ о́бщества. **2,** (involving relations between people) дру́жеский: *social visit,* дру́жеский визи́т. *Social gathering,* встре́ча друзе́й. —**social security,** социа́льное обеспе́чение.
socialism *n.* социали́зм. —**socialist,** *n.* социали́ст. —*adj.* [*also,* **socialistic**] социалисти́ческий.
socialize *v.t.* социализи́ровать; обобществля́ть. *Socialized medicine,* госуда́рственное медици́нское обслу́живание. —*v.i.* (associate; consort) обща́ться. —**socialization,** *n.* социализа́ция; обобществле́ние.
society *n.* о́бщество: *feudal society,* феода́льное о́бщество. *High society,* вы́сшее о́бщество; вы́сший свет. *A scientific society,* нау́чное о́бщество.
sociology *n.* социоло́гия. —**sociological,** *adj.* социологи́ческий. —**sociologist,** *n.* социо́лог.
sock *n.* **1,** (short stocking) носо́к. **2,** *slang* (a punch) тума́к. —*v.t., slang* тра́хнуть.
socket *n.* **1,** (electric outlet) розе́тка; гнездо́. **2,** (for an electric bulb) патро́н. **3,** *anat.* впа́дина. *Eye socket,* глазна́я впа́дина; глазни́ца. *Socket of a tooth,* яче́йка.
socle *n.* цо́коль.
sod *n.* дёрн. —*v.t.* обкла́дывать дёрном.
soda *n.* **1,** (sodium or sodium compound) со́да. **2,** = **soda water.** —**soda fountain,** сто́йка. —**soda water,** со́довая вода́; газиро́ванная вода́.
sodden *adj.* промо́кший; пропи́танный вла́гой.
sodium *n.* на́трий. —**sodium bicarbonate,** двууглеки́слый на́трий. —**sodium carbonate,** углеки́слый на́трий. —**sodium chloride,** хло́ристый на́трий. —**sodium fluoride,** фто́ристый на́трий. —**sodium hydroxide,** е́дкий натр. —**sodium nitrate,** на́триевая seли́тра. —**sodium phosphate,** фосфа́т на́трия. —**sodium sulfate,** сернокислый на́трий. —**sodium-vapor lamp,** на́триевая ла́мпа.
sodomy *n.* педера́стия; скотоло́жство.
sofa *n.* дива́н; софа́.
soft *adj.* **1,** (not hard) мя́гкий: *soft pillow,* мя́гкая поду́шка. **2,** (not loud) ти́хий: *soft voice,* ти́хий го́лос. **3,** (not bright; subdued) мя́гкий: *soft colors,* мя́гкие тона́. **4,** (out of condition; flabby) дря́блый; не в фо́рме. **5,** (easy to digest) лёгкий: *soft foods,* лёгкая пи́ща. **6,** (nonalcoholic) безалкого́льный. **7,** *colloq.* (easy): *soft job,* тёплое месте́чко. —*adv.* мя́гко; ти́хо. —**have a soft spot in one's heart for,** пита́ть сла́бость к.
soft-boiled egg яйцо́ всмя́тку.
soft coal битумино́зный у́голь.
soften *v.t.* смягча́ть. —*v.i.* смягча́ться.
softhearted *adj.* мягкосерде́чный. —**softheartedness,** *n.* мягкосерде́чие; мягкосерде́чность.
soft landing мя́гкая поса́дка.
softly *adv.* **1,** (gently) мя́гко. **2,** (quietly) ти́хо.
softness *n.* мя́гкость.
soft palate мя́гкое нёбо.
soft-spoken *adj.* ти́хий; кро́ткий.
software *n.* математи́ческое обеспе́чение (цифрово́й вычисли́тельной маши́ны).
soggy *adj.* сыро́й; отсыре́лый.
soil *n.* **1,** (top layer of the earth's surface) по́чва. **2,** *fig.* (country; land) земля́: *on foreign soil,* на чужо́й земле́. —*v.t.* (dirty) па́чкать. —*v.i.* па́чкаться. —**soil science,** почвове́дение. —**soil scientist,** почвове́д.
soirée *n.* ве́чер; вечери́нка.
sojourn *v.i.* жить. —*n.* пребыва́ние.
sol *n., music* соль.
solace *n.* утеше́ние.
solar *adj.* со́лнечный. *Solar system,* со́лнечная систе́ма. *Solar energy,* со́лнечная эне́ргия.
solarium *n.* соля́рий.
solar plexus со́лнечное сплете́ние.
solder *n.* припо́й. —*v.t.* пая́ть. *Solder together,* спа́ивать. —**solderer,** *n.* пая́льщик. —**soldering iron,** пая́льник.
soldier *n.* солда́т. *Play soldier,* игра́ть в солда́тики. —**soldier of fortune,** кондотье́р.
soldierly *adj.* вое́нный; во́инский.
sole *n.* **1,** (of the foot) ступня́; подо́шва. **2,** (of a shoe) подмётка; подо́шва. *Inner sole,* сте́лька. **3,** (fish) ка́мбала. —*v.t.* ста́вить подмётку на; подшива́ть. —*adj.* **1,** (only) еди́нственный: *the sole reason,* еди́нственная причи́на. **2,** (exclusive) исключи́тельный: *sole right,* исключи́тельное пра́во. *Sole owner,* еди́нственный владе́лец.
solecism *n.* солеци́зм.
solely *adv.* еди́нственно; то́лько; исключи́тельно.
solemn *adj.* торже́ственный: *solemn occasion/oath,* торже́ственный слу́чай; торже́ственная кля́тва.
solemnity *n.* торже́ственность. *With great solemnity,* торже́ственно.
solemnly *adv.* торже́ственно: *I solemnly swear,* торже́ственно кляну́сь.
solenoid *n.* солено́ид.
solfeggio *n.* сольфе́джио.
solicit *v.t.* проси́ть; выпра́шивать; хода́тайствовать о. *Solicit alms,* проси́ть ми́лостыню. —**solicitation,** *n.* хода́тайство.
solicitor *n.* **1,** (one who solicits) проси́тель. **2,** (lawyer) адвока́т.
solicitous *adj.* забо́тливый. —**solicitude,** *n.* забо́тливость.
solid *adj.* **1,** (of firm structure) твёрдый: *solid body/state,* твёрдое те́ло/состоя́ние. *Solid food,* твёрдая пи́ща. **2,** (sturdily built) соли́дный; про́чный: *solid building,* соли́дное/про́чное зда́ние. **3,** (upstanding; reliable) соли́дный: *solid person,* соли́дный челове́к; *solid company,* соли́дная компа́ния. **4,** (unbroken) сплошно́й: *solid line/wall,* сплошна́я ли́ния/стена́. **5,** (pure; unalloyed) чи́стый: *of solid gold,* из чи́стого зо́лота. **6,** (plain; without a design) однотóнный: *solid color,* однотóнная кра́ска. **7,** (three-dimensional) куби́ческий; трёхме́рный. **8,** (uninterrupted) це́лый. *A solid hour,* би́тый час. —*n.* твёрдое те́ло.
solidarity *n.* солида́рность; сплочённость.
solid geometry стереоме́трия.
solidify *v.i.* затвердева́ть; отвердева́ть. —*v.t.* **1,** (harden) де́лать твёрдым. **2,** (consolidate) закрепля́ть.
solidity *n.* твёрдость.
solidly *adv.* про́чно; соли́дно.
soliloquize *v.i.* произноси́ть моноло́г.
soliloquy *n.* моноло́г.

solitaire *n.* **1,** (gem) солитéр. **2,** (card game) пасьянс.
solitary *adj.* **1,** (lone) одинóчный; одинóкий. **2,** (single; sole) еди́нственный. **3,** (secluded; remote) уединённый; обосóбленный. —**solitary confinement,** одинóчное заключéние.
solitude *n.* одинóчество; уединéние.
solo *n.* сóло. —*adj.* сóльный. —**soloist,** *n.* соли́ст; соли́стка.
solstice *n.* солнцестоя́ние.
soluble *adj.* раствори́мый. —**solubility,** *n.* раствори́мость.
solution *n.* **1,** (answer to a problem or puzzle) решéние. **2,** (resolution of a question or issue) разрешéние. **3,** (dissolving) растворéние. **4,** (mixture of various substances) раствóр.
solvable *adj.* разреши́мый.
solve *v.t.* **1,** (find the answer to) решáть; разгáдывать. **2,** (resolve; settle) разрешáть.
solvency *n.* платёжеспосóбность.
solvent *adj.* **1,** (able to pay one's debts) платёжеспосóбный. **2,** (dissolving another substance) растворя́ющий. —*n.* раствори́тель.
somatic *adj.* соматúческий.
somber *also,* **sombre** *adj.* **1,** (gloomy) мрáчный; хмýрый; пáсмурный. **2,** (morose) мрáчный; угрю́мый.
some *adj.* **1,** (of an unspecified quantity) *rendered by the gen. case: would you like some tea?,* хоти́те чáю? ♦ *With abstract nouns* нéкоторый: *some time/doubt,* нéкоторое врéмя/сомнéние; *to some extent,* в нéкоторой стéпени. **2,** (a few) нéсколько: *some apples,* нéсколько я́блок. **3,** (rather a lot of) немáло: *it took some effort,* понáдобилось немáло уси́лий. **4,** (certain ones) нéкоторые: *some people,* нéкоторые лю́ди. **5,** (unspecified one of ones) какóй-то; какóй-нибудь. *Some man was asking for you,* вас спрáшивал какóй-то человéк. **6,** *slang* (quite a) вот э́то; ну и: *some singer!,* вот э́то певéц! *Some weather!,* ну и погóда! —*pron.* **1,** (a certain amount) *not rendered in Russian: would you like some?,* хоти́те?; хоти́те попрóбовать? **2,** (certain ones) нéкоторые: *some of my friends,* нéкоторые из мои́х друзéй. *Some believe that...,* нéкоторые считáют, что... **3,** (certain ones as opposed to others) одни́: *some want to go, others do not,* одни́ хотя́т пойти́, други́е нет. —*adv.* (approximately) óколо; до; какóй-нибудь. *Some forty miles,* каки́е-нибудь сóрок миль. —**and then some,** *colloq.* и ещё сверх тогó. —**some other time,** кáк-нибудь в другóй раз.
somebody *pron.* ктó-то; ктó-нибудь. *Somebody else,* ктó-то другóй; ктó-нибудь другóй. *Somebody's,* чéй-то; чéй-нибудь. —*n., colloq.* вáжная персóна; вáжная осóба.
someday *adv.* когдá-то; когдá-нибудь.
somehow *adv.* кáк-то; кáк-нибудь. —**somehow or other,** так и́ли инáче.
someone *pron.* ктó-то; ктó-нибудь. *Someone else,* ктó-то другóй; ктó-нибудь другóй. *Someone else's,* чужóй. *Someone's,* чéй-то; чéй-нибудь.
someplace *adv.* = **somewhere.**
somersault *n.* сáльто; сáльто-мортáле. —*v.i.* кувыркáться.
something *pron.* чтó-то; чтó-нибудь; кóе-что. *Something is happening,* чтó-то происхóдит. *Would you like something to drink?,* хоти́те чтó-нибудь вы́пить? *I want to ask you something,* я хочý вас кóе-что спроси́ть. *Something else,* чтó-то другóе; чтó-нибудь другóе. *Something like that,* чтó-то в э́том рóде. *Or something,* и́ли чтó-то в э́том рóде.
sometime *adv.* когдá-то; когдá-нибудь.
sometimes *adv.* иногдá.
somewhat *adv.* немнóго; нéсколько; слегкá.
somewhere *adv.* гдé-то; гдé-нибудь; кудá-то; кудá-нибудь. *Somewhere else,* гдé-то в другóм мéсте.
somnambulate *v.i.* ходи́ть во сне. —**somnambulism,** *n.* лунати́зм. —**somnambulist,** *n.* лунáтик.
somnolent *adj.* **1,** (sleepy) сóнный; сонли́вый. **2,** (causing drowsiness) снотвóрный. —**somnolence,** *n.* сонли́вость; дремóта.
son *n.* сын.
sonar *n.* **1,** (method) гидролокáция. **2,** (device) гидролокáтор.
sonata *n.* сонáта.
song *n.* пéсня. *Break/burst into song,* запéть. —**for a song,** за бесцéнок; за грош.
songbird *n.* пéвчая пти́ца.
songbook *n.* пéсенник.
songster *n.* певéц. —**songstress,** *n.* певи́ца.
songwriter *n.* пéсенник.
sonic *adj.* звуковóй. —**sonic boom,** звуковóй удáр, сверхзвуковóй хлопóк.
son-in-law *n.* зять.
sonnet *n.* сонéт.
sonny *n.* сынóк.
sonorous *adj.* звýчный; звóнкий.
soon *adv.* скóро. *Soon after,* вскóре пóсле. *Too soon,* сли́шком рáно. —**as soon as,** как тóлько. —**just as soon,** скорéе; лýчше. *I'd just as soon stay home,* я предпочёл бы остáться дóма.
sooner *adv.* **1,** (earlier) скорéе; рáньше. **2,** (preferably) скорéе: *I would sooner die,* я скорéе умрý. —**no sooner,** едвá: *no sooner did we start out than the car broke down,* едвá мы отпрáвились в путь, как маши́на испóртилась. —**no sooner said than done,** скáзано – сдéлано. —**sooner or later,** рáно и́ли пóздно. —**the sooner the better,** чем рáньше, тем лýчше.
soot *n.* сáжа; кóпоть.
soothe *v.t.* **1,** (calm; mollify) успокáивать. **2,** (alleviate; ease) облегчáть.
soothsayer *n.* предсказáтель; прорицáтель.
sooty *adj.* в сáже; закоптéлый.
sop *v.t.* **1,** (soak) намáчивать. **2,** *fol. by* **up** (absorb) впи́тывать. —*n.* подáчка.
sophism *n.* софи́зм. —**sophist,** *n.* софи́ст. —**sophistic,** *adj.* софисти́ческий.
sophisticated *adj.* **1,** (urbane) искушённый; утончённый; изы́сканный. **2,** (technologically advanced) слóжный. —**sophistication,** *n.* утончённость; изы́сканность.
sophistry *n.* софи́стика.
sophomore *n.* студéнт-второкýрсник.
soporific *adj.* **1,** *med.* снотвóрный; усыпля́ющий. **2,** (boring) усыпи́тельный.
sopping *adj.* промóкший. —**sopping wet,** мóкрый, хоть вы́жми.
soprano *n.* сопрáно. —*adj.* сопрáновый; сопрáнный.
sorcerer *n.* колдýн; чародéй. —**sorceress,** *n.* кол-

ду́нья; чароде́йка. —**sorcery,** *n.* колдовство́; чароде́йство.

sordid *adj.* гря́зный. *A sordid affair,* гря́зное де́ло; гря́зная исто́рия.

sore *adj.* **1,** (hurting) больно́й: *sore finger,* больно́й па́лец. *I have a sore throat,* у меня́ боли́т го́рло. **2,** *fig.* (painful; irritating) больно́й: *sore point; sore subject,* больно́й вопро́с. **3,** *colloq.* (offended; angry) оби́женный; серди́тый. —*n.* боля́чка; я́зва.

sorely *adv.* **1,** (grievously) до бо́ли: *sorely distressed,* до бо́ли огорчён. **2,** (greatly) о́чень: *you were sorely missed,* вас о́чень не хвата́ло. *I am sorely tempted,* э́то о́чень соблазни́тельно.

soreness *n.* боле́зненное ощуще́ние; боль.

sorghum *n.* со́рго.

sorrel *n.* **1,** (plant) щаве́ль. *Wood sorrel,* кисли́ца. **2,** (color) кра́сно-кори́чневый цвет.

sorrow *n.* печа́ль; скорбь. *To my sorrow,* на своё го́ре.

sorrowful *adj.* печа́льный; ско́рбный. —**sorrowfully,** *adv.* ско́рбно; сокрушённо.

sorry *adj.* **1,** (feeling sympathy) жаль: *I am sorry,* мне жаль. *I feel sorry for her,* мне её жаль. **2,** (feeling regret): *be sorry,* сожале́ть; жале́ть: *I am sorry now that I did it,* тепе́рь я сожале́ю, что сде́лал э́то. **3,** (expressing one's apologies): *I'm sorry!,* прости́те!; прошу́ извине́ния. **4,** (pitiful) жа́лкий; плаче́вный: *a sorry sight,* жа́лкое зре́лище; *in a sorry state,* в плаче́вном состоя́нии.

sort *n.* род; сорт; вид. *A sort of,* вро́де (+ *gen.*); не́что вро́де (+ *gen.*). *All sorts of,* всевозмо́жные; вся́кого ро́да (+ *nom.*). *Something of the sort,* что́-то вро́де э́того; что́-то в э́том ро́де. *Nothing of the sort,* ничего́ подо́бного. *What sort of person is he?,* что он за челове́к? —*v.t.* [*also,* **sort out**] разбира́ть; сортирова́ть; перебира́ть. —**after a sort; of sorts,** не́которым о́бразом. —**out of sorts,** не в ду́хе. —**sort of,** ка́к-то: *I'm sort of glad,* я ка́к-то рад.

sorter *n.* **1,** (person) сортиро́вщик. **2,** (machine) сортиро́вочная маши́на.

sortie *n.* вы́лазка.

so-so *adj.* нева́жный; сно́сный. —*adv.* так себе́; сно́сно.

sot *n.* го́рький пья́ница.

soufflé *n.* суфле́.

soul *n.* душа́. *A simple soul,* проста́я душа́. *There was not a soul present,* там не́ было ни души́. *Put one's heart and soul into,* вкла́дывать всю ду́шу в (+ *acc.*). *Don't tell a soul!,* никому́ не говори́те!; об э́том ни гугу́!

sound *n.* **1,** (what can be heard) звук: *not a sound,* ни зву́ка. *The sound of footsteps,* звук *or* шум шаго́в. **2,** (inlet) зали́в. **3,** (strait) проли́в. —*adj.* **1,** (healthy) здоро́вый. *Of sound mind,* в здра́вом уме́; *law* вменя́емый. **2,** (free from defect or harm) испра́вный. *In sound condition,* в хоро́шем состоя́нии; в испра́вности. *Safe and sound,* цел и невреди́м. **3,** (solid; firm; stable) про́чный; основа́тельный. *Sound basis,* про́чная осно́ва. **4,** (sensible; logical) здра́вый; разу́мный; благоразу́мный; основа́тельный. *Sound advice,* у́мный *or* де́льный сове́т; *sound arguments,* основа́тельные до́воды. **5,** (of sleep) кре́пкий. **6,** (thorough) здоро́вый: *sound thrashing,* здоро́вая по́рка. **7,** (pert. to sound) звуково́й: *sound barrier,* звуково́й барье́р. —*adv.* *She is sound asleep,* она́ кре́пко спит. —*v.i.* звуча́ть; раздава́ться. *The whistle sounded,* разда́лся гудо́к. *It sounds strange somehow,* э́то звучи́т ка́к-то стра́нно. —*v.t.* **1,** (cause to sound) труби́ть в: *sound the trumpets,* труби́ть в тру́бы. *Sound the bells,* звони́ть в колокола́. *Sound the alarm,* бить/заби́ть/ударя́ть трево́гу *or* (в) наба́т. *Sound retreat,* дава́ть *or* бить отбо́й. **2,** (pronounce; articulate) произноси́ть. **3,** (fathom; probe) зонди́ровать. **4,** *fol. by* **out** (solicit the opinion of) зонди́ровать; расспра́шивать. —**sound off, 1,** *mil.* отклика́ться. **2,** *colloq.* (express one's views) выска́зываться.

sound effects шумовы́е эффе́кты.

sounding board де́ка.

soundless *adj.* беззву́чный.

soundly *adv.* **1,** (logically) разу́мно; толко́во. **2,** (so as not to be awakened) кре́пко: *sleep soundly,* кре́пко спать. **3,** (thoroughly; decisively) здо́рово: *our team was soundly beaten,* на́ша кома́нда была́ здо́рово разби́та.

soundness *n.* **1,** (solidity) про́чность. **2,** (logic; validity) основа́тельность.

soundproof *adj.* звуконепроница́емый.

sound track звукова́я доро́жка.

soup *n.* суп. —*adj.* супово́й: *soup tureen,* супова́я ми́ска. —**soupspoon,** *n.* столо́вая ло́жка.

sour *adj.* **1,** (having a sharp acid taste) ки́слый. **2,** (cross; peevish) злой. *In a sour mood,* в дурно́м настрое́нии. —*v.i.* **1,** (turn sour) ки́снуть; скиса́ть; прокиса́ть. **2,** *fol. by* **on** (become disenchanted with) разочарова́ться в. —*v.t.* (disenchant) отта́лкивать. —**sour grapes!,** зе́лен виногра́д!

source *n.* **1,** (beginning of a stream or river) исто́к. **2,** (that from which something comes) исто́чник: *source of energy,* исто́чник эне́ргии. **3,** (something that provides information) исто́чник: *reliable source,* достове́рный исто́чник.

sour cream смета́на.

souse *v.t.* **1,** (pickle) маринова́ть. **2,** (plunge in a liquid) погружа́ть; окуна́ть. **3,** (drench; soak) прома́чивать. **4,** *slang* (intoxicate) опьяня́ть. —*n., slang* (drunkard) пья́ница.

south *n.* юг. —*adj.* ю́жный: *the south bank,* ю́жный бе́рег. —*adv.* на юг; к ю́гу. *South of,* к ю́гу от; южне́е (+ *gen.*).

southeast *n.* ю́го-восто́к. —*adj.* ю́го-восто́чный. —*adv.* на ю́го-восто́к.

southeaster *n.* зюйд-о́ст.

southeasterly *adj.* ю́го-восто́чный. —*adv.* к ю́го-восто́ку; с ю́го-восто́ка.

southeastern *adj.* ю́го-восто́чный.

southerly *adj.* ю́жный.

southern *adj.* ю́жный. —**southerner,** *n.* южа́нин. —**southernmost,** *adj.* са́мый ю́жный.

southpaw *n., slang* левша́.

South Pole Ю́жный по́люс.

southward *adv.* к ю́гу. —*adj.* ю́жный.

southwest *n.* ю́го-за́пад. —*adj.* ю́го-за́падный. —*adv.* на ю́го-за́пад.

southwester *n.* зюйд-ве́ст.

southwesterly *adj.* ю́го-за́падный. —*adv.* к ю́го-за́паду; с ю́го-за́пада.

southwestern *adj.* ю́го-за́падный.

souvenir *n.* сувени́р. *Souvenir shop,* магази́н сувени́ров.

sovereign *n.* **1,** (ruler) госуда́рь; суверéн. **2,** (British coin) соверéн. —*adj.* суверéнный. —**sovereignty,** *n.* суверенитéт.

soviet *n.* совéт. *The Supreme Soviet,* Верхо́вный Совéт. —**Soviet,** *adj.* совéтский: *the Soviet government,* совéтское прави́тельство. —**Soviet Union,** Совéтский Сою́з.

sow[1] (so) *v.t.* **1,** (scatter) сéять: *sow wheat,* сéять пшени́цу. **2,** (plant seed in) засева́ть: *sow a field with rye,* засева́ть по́ле ро́жью. **3,** *fig.* (implant) сéять: *sow suspicion,* сéять подозрéние. —*v.i.* сéять: *as you sow so you shall reap,* что посéешь, то и пожнёшь.

sow[2] (sau) *n.* свинома́тка.

sower *n.* сéятель.

sowing *n.* сев; посéв; засéв.

soy *n.* со́я. *Also,* **soya.**

soybean *n.* со́я; со́евый боб. —*adj.* со́евый: *soybean oil,* со́евое ма́сло.

soy sauce со́я.

spa *n.* куро́рт с минера́льными во́дами.

space *n.* **1,** (infinite expanse) простра́нство: *time and space,* врéмя и простра́нство. **2,** (place; room) мéсто. *Parking space,* мéсто для стоя́нки маши́ны. *Living space,* жила́я пло́щадь. *Take up a lot of space,* занима́ть мно́го мéста. **3,** (interval) промежу́ток; интерва́л. *Leave a space between,* оставля́ть промежу́ток мéжду. *Within the space of five years,* в течéние пяти́ лет. **4,** (outer space) ко́смос. —*adj.* косми́ческий: *space flight,* косми́ческий полёт. —*v.t.* **1,** (arrange with spaces between) расставля́ть с промежу́тками. **2,** *printing* разбива́ть на шпа́ции. —**spacecraft,** *n.* косми́ческий аппара́т. —**spaceman,** *n.* космона́вт. —**spaceship,** *n.* косми́ческий кора́бль. —**space suit,** скафа́ндр.

spacious *adj.* просто́рный; вмести́тельный. —**spaciousness,** *n.* просто́р; вмести́тельность.

spade *n.* **1,** (tool) лопа́та; за́ступ. **2,** *pl., cards* пи́ки. —**call a spade a spade,** называ́ть вéщи свои́ми имена́ми. —**spade work,** подготови́тельная рабо́та.

spaghetti *n.* то́нкие макаро́ны; спагéтти.

span *n.* **1,** (distance from thumb to little finger) пядь. **2,** (distance between vertical supports) пролёт. **3,** (spread) разма́х: *wingspan,* разма́х кры́льев. **4,** (period of time) отрéзок: *a short span of time,* небольшо́й отрéзок врéмени. —*v.t.* **1,** (extend across) протя́гиваться чéрез. *The bridge spans the river,* мост соединя́ет берега́ реки́. **2,** *fig.* (encompass, as a period of time) охва́тывать.

spangle *n.* блёстка.

Spaniard *n.* испа́нец; испа́нка.

spaniel *n.* спаниéль.

Spanish *adj.* испа́нский. —*n.* испа́нский язы́к. *Speak Spanish,* говори́ть по-испа́нски. —**Spanish fly,** шпа́нская му́шка; шпа́нка. —**Spanish moss,** испа́нский *or* луизиа́нский мох.

spank *v.t.* шлёпать.

spanking *n.* шлёпка. —*adv., colloq.* совершéнно: *spanking new,* совершéнно но́вый.

spanner *n., Brit.* га́ечный ключ.

spar *n.* **1,** *naut.* рангоу́тное дéрево. **2,** *aero.* лонжеро́н. **3,** (mineral) шпат. —*v.i.* **1,** (box) дра́ться на кула́чках. **2,** (argue) препира́ться; пререка́ться.

spare *v.t.* **1,** (show mercy toward) щади́ть: *spare the women and children,* щади́ть жéнщин и детéй. *Spare someone's life/feelings,* щади́ть чью-нибудь жизнь/чьи-нибудь чу́вства/. **2,** (use sparingly) щади́ть; жалéть. *Spare no expense/effort,* не жалéть расхо́дов/уси́лий. **3,** (give up conveniently) обходи́ться без: *I can't spare him,* без него́ не могу́ обходи́ться. *Spare time for something,* уделя́ть врéмя чему́-нибудь. *Can you spare a dollar?,* вы мо́жете дать мне до́ллар?; нет ли у вас ли́шнего до́ллара? *We haven't a moment to spare,* у нас нет ни одно́й свобо́дной мину́ты. **4,** (save) избавля́ть: *spare someone trouble,* избавля́ть кого́-нибудь от хлопо́т. —*adj.* **1,** (extra) ли́шний. *Spare time,* свобо́дное врéмя. **2,** (in reserve) запасно́й: *spare parts,* запасны́е ча́сти. *Spare tire,* запасна́я ши́на *or* покры́шка. **3,** (lean) худо́й; худоща́вый. **4,** (meager; frugal) ску́дный.

spareribs *n.pl.* свины́е рёбра.

sparing *adj.* скупо́й. *sparing with words,* скупо́й на слова́.

spark *n.* и́скра. —*v.i.* и́скриться. —*v.t.* вызыва́ть; порожда́ть. *Spark interest,* вызыва́ть интерéс.

sparkle *v.i.* **1,** (glitter) сверка́ть. **2,** (effervesce) игра́ть. —*n.* про́блеск.

sparkler *n.* **1,** (firecracker) шути́ха. **2,** *colloq.* (diamond) солитéр.

sparkling *adj.* **1,** (glittering) искря́щийся; искри́стый. **2,** (effervescent) игри́стый; шипу́чий.

spark plug запа́льная свеча́.

sparrow *n.* воробéй. —*adj.* [*also,* **sparrow's**] воробьи́ный: *sparrow's nest,* воробьи́ное гнездо́. —**sparrow hawk,** перепеля́тник.

sparse *adj.* рéдкий. —**sparseness; sparsity,** *n.* рéдкость.

Spartan *adj.* спарта́нский. —*n.* спарта́нец.

spasm *n.* спазм; спа́зма.

spasmodic *adj.* **1,** (convulsive) спазмати́ческий. **2,** (uneven; irregular) скачкообра́зный.

spastic *adj.* спасти́ческий.

spat *n.* **1,** (petty quarrel) перебра́нка; размо́лвка. **2,** *usu. pl.* (short cloth gaiters) гéтры. —*v.i.* (squabble) препира́ться.

spate *n.* пото́к.

spatial *adj.* простра́нственный.

spatter *v.t.* **1,** (scatter in drops) бры́згать; разбры́згивать. **2,** (splash; spot; soil) бры́згать; забры́згивать; обры́згивать. —*v.i.* разбры́згиваться.

spatula *n.* шпа́тель.

spawn *v.i.* мета́ть икру́. —*v.t.* (give rise to) порожда́ть.

spawning *n.* мета́ние икры́; нéрест. —**spawning ground,** нерести́лище.

spay *v.t.* удаля́ть яи́чники у.

speak *v.t. & i.* говори́ть: *speak to someone,* говори́ть с кéм-нибудь. *Speak the truth,* говори́ть пра́вду. *Speak Russian,* говори́ть *or* разгова́ривать по-ру́сски. *Frankly speaking,* откровéнно говоря́. *Speak at a meeting,* выступа́ть на собра́нии. —**it speaks for itself,** э́то говори́т само́ за себя́. —**so to speak,** так сказа́ть. —**speak one's mind,** вы́сказать своё мнéние. —**speak out,** выска́зываться. —**speak up,** говори́ть гро́мче. —**speak up for,** заступа́ться за. —**speak well for,** говори́ть в по́льзу (+ *gen.*). —**speak well of,** хорошо́ отзыва́ться о. —**to speak of,** осо́бенный: *nothing to speak of,* ничего́ осо́бенного.

speaker *n.* **1,** (person speaking) тот, кто говори́т; говоря́щий. **2,** (person giving a speech) выступа́ющий. **3,** (one who speaks a certain language) носи́тель. **4,** (orator) ора́тор. **5,** (presiding officer) спи́кер. **6,** (loudspeaker) громкоговори́тель.

speaking *n.* разгово́р. *Public speaking,* ора́торское иску́сство. —**in a manner of speaking,** *see* **manner.** —**not be on speaking terms,** не говори́ть (*or* не разгова́ривать) друг с дру́гом.

spear *n.* **1,** (weapon) копьё. **2,** (for spearing fish) острога́. —*v.t.* пронза́ть копьём; бить (ры́бу) острого́й.

spearhead *n.* **1,** (head of a spear) остриё. **2,** *fig.* (that which leads) передово́й отря́д. —*v.t.* возглавля́ть; стоя́ть во главе́ (+ *gen.*).

special *adj.* **1,** (distinctive; particular) осо́бенный; осо́бый: *special case,* осо́бенный/осо́бый слу́чай. *Special assignment,* осо́бое зада́ние. *Require special effort,* тре́бовать осо́бых уси́лий. *Nothing special,* ничего́ осо́бенного. **2,** (separate) осо́бый: *special section,* осо́бый разде́л. **3,** (having a particular purpose) специа́льный: *special course/flight/correspondent,* специа́льный курс/рейс/корреспонде́нт. **4,** (extra) э́кстренный: *special edition,* э́кстренный вы́пуск. —**special delivery,** спе́шная по́чта.

specialist *n.* специали́ст.

speciality *n.* = **specialty.**

specialization *n.* специализа́ция.

specialize *v.i.* специализи́роваться. —**specialized,** *adj.* специа́льный: *specialized terms,* специа́льные те́рмины.

specialty *also,* **speciality** *n.* специа́льность. —**specialty of the house,** фи́рменное блю́до.

specie *n.* зво́нкая моне́та.

species *n.* вид.

specific *adj.* **1,** (explicit) конкре́тный: *specific purpose,* конкре́тная цель; *specific proposal,* конкре́тное предложе́ние. **2,** (individual; particular) отде́льный: *in each specific case,* в ка́ждом отде́льном слу́чае. **3,** *physics* уде́льный: *specific gravity,* уде́льный вес. —*n., usu. pl.* подро́бности.

specifically *adv.* в ча́стности.

specification *n.* **1,** (act of specifying) специфика́ция. **2,** *pl.* (detailed description) техни́ческие усло́вия.

specify *v.t.* **1,** (indicate clearly) ука́зывать: *specify the time,* ука́зывать вре́мя. **2,** (stipulate) предусма́тривать: *the law specifies that...,* зако́н предусма́тривает, что...

specimen *n.* образе́ц; экземпля́р.

specious *adj.* благови́дный.

speck *n.* **1,** (spot) пя́тнышко; кра́пинка. **2,** (small particle) части́ца. *Speck of dust,* пыли́нка; сори́нка.

speckle *n.* кра́пинка. —*v.t.* испещря́ть. —**speckled,** *adj.* (of material) в кра́пинку; кра́пчатый; (of an animal) ряб́ой.

spectacle *n.* **1,** (sight) зре́лище. **2,** *pl.* (glasses) очки́. —**make a spectacle of oneself,** обраща́ть на себя́ внима́ние.

spectacular *adj.* грандио́зный; потряса́ющий.

spectator *n.* зри́тель.

specter *also,* **spectre** *n.* при́зрак.

spectral *adj.* **1,** (ghostly) при́зрачный. **2,** (produced by a spectrum) спектра́льный.

spectre *n.* = **specter.**

spectroscope *n.* спектроско́п. —**spectroscopic,** *adj.* спектроскопи́ческий.

spectrum *n.* спектр.

speculate *v.i.* **1,** (ponder) размышля́ть. **2,** (conjecture) стро́ить дога́дки. **3,** *comm.* спекули́ровать.

speculation *n.* **1,** (conjecture) дога́дка: *a matter of sheer speculation,* чи́стая дога́дка. **2,** *comm.* спекуля́ция.

speculative *adj.* **1,** (based on an assumption) гипотети́ческий. **2,** (involving risk) спекуляти́вный.

speculator *n.* спекуля́нт.

speech *n.* речь: *organs of speech,* о́рганы ре́чи. *Make a speech,* говори́ть *or* произноси́ть речь. *Freedom of speech,* свобо́да сло́ва. —*adj.* речево́й. *Speech defect,* дефе́кт ре́чи.

speechless *adj.* **1,** (incapable of speech) немо́й. **2,** (at a loss for words) онеме́вший: *we were left speechless,* мы онеме́ли от изумле́ния.

speed *n.* ско́рость. *At full speed,* по́лным хо́дом; во весь опо́р. —*v.t.* [*usu.* **speed up**] ускоря́ть. —*v.i.* **1,** (move rapidly; race) мча́ться. *Speed by,* промча́ться. *Speed away/off,* умча́ться; унести́сь. **2,** (go too fast) превыша́ть дозво́ленную ско́рость. **3,** *fol. by* **up** (go faster) ускоря́ть ход. —**speed limit,** дозво́ленная ско́рость.

speedboat *n.* быстрохо́дный ка́тер.

speedometer *n.* спидо́метр.

speed skating скоростно́й бег на конька́х.

speedway *n.* **1,** (racing strip) автодро́м. **2,** (superhighway) автостра́да.

speedy *adj.* бы́стрый; ско́рый.

spell *v.t.* **1,** (write using certain letters) писа́ть: *how is this word spelled?,* как пи́шется э́то сло́во? **2,** (name the letters of) называ́ть по бу́квам: *spell the word* "воскресе́нье", назови́те по бу́квам сло́во "воскресе́нье". **3,** (be the letters of) образо́вывать. **4,** (signify; mean) означа́ть. **5,** (replace temporarily; relieve) сменя́ть. —*v.i. He spells poorly,* у него́ хрома́ет орфогра́фия. —*n.* **1,** (compelling attraction) ча́ры. *Cast a spell over,* заколдо́вывать; околдо́вывать. **2,** (short period) полоса́: *spell of good weather,* полоса́ хоро́шей пого́ды. *Cold spell,* похолода́ние. **3,** (attack; fit) при́ступ: *coughing spell,* при́ступ ка́шля. *Fainting spell,* о́бморок. —**spell out,** уточня́ть; подро́бно излага́ть.

spellbound *adj.* очаро́ванный; зачаро́ванный; заворожённый.

spelling *n.* орфогра́фия; правописа́ние. *Correct spelling,* пра́вильная орфогра́фия. *Correct spelling of a word,* пра́вильное написа́ние сло́ва. —*adj.* орфографи́ческий: *spelling error,* орфографи́ческая оши́бка. *Spelling rules,* пра́вила правописа́ния. *Spelling reform,* орфографи́ческая рефо́рма; рефо́рма правописа́ния.

spend *v.t.* **1,** (expend) тра́тить: *spend money,* тра́тить де́ньги. *Spend two hours fixing something,* тра́тить два часа́ на почи́нку чего́-нибудь. **2,** (pass) проводи́ть: *spend the summer at the seashore,* проводи́ть ле́то на мо́ре. **3,** (use up; exhaust) истоща́ть; исче́рпывать.

spending *n.* расхо́ды: *military spending,* вое́нные расхо́ды. —**spending money,** де́ньги на ме́лкие расхо́ды.

spendthrift *n.* расточи́тель; транжи́ра; мот.

spent *adj.* **1,** (physically exhausted) изнурённый;

измученный. **2,** (used up) истощённый; исчерпанный. **3,** (fired) стреляный: *spent shell,* стреляная гильза. *Spent bullet,* пуля на излёте.

sperm *n.* сперма. —**sperm whale,** кашалот.

spew *v.t.* извергать. —*v.i.* извергаться: *lava spewed forth from the volcano,* лава извергалась из вулкана.

sphere *n.* **1,** (round body) шар; сфера. **2,** *fig.* (area) сфера: *sphere of influence,* сфера влияния. *Out of my sphere,* не в моей сфере; вне моей сферы. —**spherical,** *adj.* шарообразный; сферический.

spheroid *n.* сфероид. —**spheroidal,** *adj.* сфероидальный.

sphinx *n.* сфинкс.

spice *n.* **1,** (seasoning) пряность; специя. **2,** (zest; piquancy) острота; пикантность. —*v.t.* приправлять. *Spice a story with jokes,* приправлять рассказ остротами.

spick-and-span *adj.* чисто-начисто; безукоризненно чистый.

spicy *adj.* **1,** (highly seasoned) пряный. **2,** *fig.* (titillating) солёный; пикантный.

spider *n.* паук. —**spider web,** паутина.

spigot *n.* **1,** (faucet) кран. **2,** (plug) пробка; затычка.

spike *n.* **1,** (sharp-pointed projection) остриё. **2,** (large nail) костыль. **3,** (for athletic shoes) шип. **4,** (ear of grain) колос. —*v.t.* **1,** (pierce with a spike) пронзать; прокалывать. **2,** (squash, as a rumor) опровергать.

spikenard *n.* нард.

spill *v.t.* **1,** (a liquid) проливать; разливать. **2,** (a dry substance) просыпать; рассыпать. —*v.i.* **1,** (of a liquid) проливаться; разливаться. *Spill over the top,* переливаться через край. **2,** (of a dry substance) сыпаться; просыпаться; рассыпаться. **3,** *fol. by* **over** (spread) перекидываться. —**spill the beans,** *see* **bean.**

spillway *n.* водослив.

spin *v.t.* **1,** (make into thread) прясть: *spin flax,* прясть лён. *Spin a web,* плести *or* ткать паутину. **2,** (twirl) кружить; вертеть. *Spin a top,* вертеть *or* пускать волчок. **3,** (relate; tell) плести: *spin tales,* плести небылицы. —*v.i.* **1,** (spin thread) прясть. **2,** (whirl) кружиться; вертеться. *My head is spinning,* у меня кружится голова. **3,** (move along smoothly) катиться. —*n.* **1,** (spinning motion) кружение. **2,** (short ride) прогулка. *Go for a spin,* проехаться; прокатиться. **3,** *aero.* штопор: *go into a spin,* входить в штопор.

spinach *n.* шпинат.

spinal *adj.* спинной; спинномозговой. —**spinal column,** спинной хребет; позвоночный столб; позвоночник. —**spinal cord,** спинной мозг. —**spinal fluid,** спинномозговая жидкость.

spindle *n.* **1,** (rod used in spinning) веретено. **2,** (axle; shaft) шпиндель.

spindlelegs *n.pl.* журавлиные ноги.

spine *n.* **1,** (backbone) позвоночник; спинной хребет. **2,** (quill) игла. **3,** (thorn) шип. **4,** (stiff backing, as of a book) корешок. —**spineless,** *adj.* бесхребетный; бесхарактерный.

spinet *n.* пианино.

spinner *n.* прядильщик; прядильщица; пряха.

spinning *n.* прядение. —*adj.* прядильный. —**spinning machine,** прядильная машина. —**spinning wheel,** прялка.

spinoff *n.* побочный продукт.

spinster *n.* старая дева.

spiny *adj.* иглистый. —**spiny anteater,** ехидна. —**spiny lobster,** лангуст.

spiral *n.* спираль. —*adj.* спиральный. *Spiral staircase,* витая *or* винтовая лестница.

spire *n.* шпиль.

spirit *n.* **1,** (vital principle in man) дух. **2,** *often pl.* (frame of mind) настроение: *in low spirits,* в дурном настроении. **3,** (supernatural being) дух: *evil spirit,* злой дух. **4,** (real meaning or intent) дух: *the spirit of the law,* дух закона. **5,** *pl.* (alcohol) спиртные напитки; спиртное. **6,** *pl.* (distillate) спирт: *spirits of camphor,* камфарный спирт. —*v.t.* [*usu.* **spirit away** *or* **off**] умчать.

spirited *adj.* живой; оживлённый.

spirit lamp спиртовая лампа; спиртовка.

spirit level ватерпас.

spiritual *adj.* духовный. —*n.* негритянская религиозная песнь.

spiritualism *n.* **1,** (belief in communication with the dead) спиритизм. **2,** *philos.* спиритуализм.

spiritualist *n.* **1,** (medium) спирит. **2,** *philos.* спиритуалист.

spit *v.i.* плевать: *no spitting!,* не плевать! *Spit on the floor,* наплевать на пол. *Spit in someone's face,* плюнуть кому-нибудь в лицо. —*v.t.* плевать (+ *instr.*) *Spit blood,* плевать *or* харкать кровью. *Spit out the pits,* выплёвывать косточки. —*n.* **1,** (saliva) плевок. **2,** (rack for roasting meat) вертел. **3,** (narrow point of land) коса; стрелка. —**the spit and** (*or* **spitting**) **image of,** живой портрет (+ *gen.*).

spite *n.* злоба. *For/out of/spite,* назло; со зла. —*v.t.* делать назло (+ *dat.*). *Do something in order to spite someone,* делать что-нибудь назло (*or* в пику) кому-нибудь. —**in spite of,** несмотря на.

spiteful *adj.* злобный.

spittle *n.* плевок.

spittoon *n.* плевательница.

spitz *n.* шпиц.

splash *v.t.* **1,** (scatter about, as a liquid or mud) брызгать; плескать. **2,** (spatter, as with water or mud) забрызгивать. —*v.i.* **1,** (fall or strike with a splash) плескать; плескаться. **2,** (move about with splashes) плескаться; полоскаться. —*n.* **1,** (act or sound of splashing) плеск; всплеск. **2,** (that which is splashed) брызги.

splashdown *n.* приводнение.

splatter *v.t. & i.* = **spatter.**

splay *n.* скос. —*v.t.* скашивать.

spleen *n.* **1,** *anat.* селезёнка. **2,** (ill will) злоба. —**vent one's spleen,** сорвать злобу.

splendid *adj.* **1,** (magnificent) великолепный; пышный; роскошный. **2,** *colloq.* (fine; excellent) великолепный; чудный; чудесный.

splendor *also,* **splendour** *n.* великолепие; пышность; блеск. *In all its splendor,* во всём (своём) блеске.

splenetic *adj.* **1,** *anat.* селезёночный. **2,** (peevish) жёлчный.

splice *v.t.* сращивать: *splice wires,* сращивать провода.

splint *n.* лубок; шина.

splinter *n.* **1,** (fragment) осколок. **2,** (that which gets under the skin) заноза. —*v.t.* раздроблять. —*v.i.* раздробляться.

split *v.t.* **1,** (cleave) раска́лывать; расщепля́ть: *split logs,* раска́лывать/расщепля́ть поле́нья. *Split the atom,* расщепля́ть а́том. **2,** (disunite) раска́лывать. **3,** (divide up and share) дели́ть. **4,** *fol. by* **up** (divide into smaller units) разбива́ть. —*v.i.* **1,** (break in two) раска́лываться; расщепля́ться. *The ship split in two,* кора́бль расколо́лся на́двое. **2,** (burst; rip apart) ло́паться; распа́рываться. **3,** (divide into two or more groups or factions) разбива́ться; раска́лываться. **4,** *fol. by* **up** (separate; part company) расходи́ться. **5,** *fol. by* **off** (break off or away) отка́лываться. **6,** *in* **my head is splitting,** у меня́ трещи́т голова́. —*n.* **1,** (break; tear) тре́щина. **2,** (division; schism) раско́л. **3,** *gymnastics* шпага́т. —*adj.* раско́лотый; расщеплённый. —**split decision,** *boxing* неединогла́сное реше́ние. —**split hairs,** спо́рить о мелоча́х; вдава́ться в то́нкости. —**split personality,** раздвое́ние ли́чности. —**split second,** мгнове́ние о́ка. *Split-second timing,* синхрониза́ция с то́чностью до секу́нды. —**split the difference,** подели́ть ра́зницу попола́м.

splitting *n.* расщепле́ние: *splitting of the atom,* расщепле́ние а́тома. —*adj.* мучи́тельный: *splitting headache,* мучи́тельная головна́я боль.

splotch *n.* пятно́; кля́кса.

splurge *v.i.* раскоше́ливаться.

splutter *v.i.* **1,** (make hissing sounds) шипе́ть. **2,** (speak hurriedly or confusedly) лопота́ть.

spoil *v.t.* **1,** (damage; mar) по́ртить. **2,** (pamper) балова́ть. —*v.i.* по́ртиться. —*n., usu. pl.* добы́ча; трофе́и. —**be spoiling for a fight,** лезть в дра́ку.

spoilage *n.* по́рча.

spoiled *adj.* **1,** (damaged) испо́рченный. **2,** (pampered) избало́ванный; бало́ванный.

spoke *n.* спи́ца. —**put a spoke in someone's wheel,** вставля́ть па́лки в колёса (+ *dat.*).

spoken *adj.* у́стный.

spokesman *n.* представи́тель.

sponge *n.* гу́бка. —*v.t.* вытира́ть гу́бкой. —*v.i., colloq.* жить на чужо́й счёт. *Sponge off someone,* жить за счёт кого́-нибудь. —**throw/toss in the sponge,** *colloq.* призна́ть себя́ побеждённым.

sponge cake бискви́т.

sponger *n., colloq.* тунея́дец; дармое́д; прихлеба́тель; прижива́льщик.

spongy *adj.* гу́бчатый.

sponsor *n.* **1,** (guarantor) поручи́тель. **2,** (patron; benefactor) покрови́тель. —*v.t.* **1,** (act as a sponsor for) руча́ться за. **2,** (pay for) финанси́ровать. **3,** (introduce, as a bill or resolution) вноси́ть.

sponsorship *n.* покрови́тельство; поручи́тельство.

spontaneity *n.* стихи́йность; непосре́дственность; самопроизво́льность.

spontaneous *adj.* **1,** (resulting from a natural impulse) стихи́йный; непосре́дственный. *Spontaneous uprising,* стихи́йное восста́ние. *Spontaneous laughter,* непосре́дственный смех. **2,** (self-generated) самопроизво́льный; сponта́нный. —**spontaneous combustion,** самовоспламене́ние; самовозгора́ние. —**spontaneous generation,** самозарожде́ние.

spoof *n.* паро́дия; сати́ра. —*v.i.* шути́ть. —*v.t.* высме́ивать.

spook *n., colloq.* **1,** (ghost) привиде́ние; при́зрак. **2,** (secret agent) шпик. —**spooky,** *adj.* при́зрачный; пуга́ющий.

spool *n.* шпу́лька; кату́шка.

spoon *n.* ло́жка. —*v.t.* че́рпать ло́жкой.

spoon bait блесна́.

spoonbill *n.* ко́лпица.

spoonful *n.* ло́жка.

sporadic *adj.* спораdи́ческий. —**sporadically,** *adv.* споради́чески; вре́мя от вре́мени.

spore *n.* спо́ра.

sport *n.* **1,** *usu. pl.* (athletic activity) спорт. **2,** (particular game) вид спо́рта: *my favorite sport,* мой люби́мый вид спо́рта. **3,** (fun; diversion) заба́ва; поте́ха. **4,** (jest) шу́тка: *say something in sport,* сказа́ть что́-нибудь в шу́тку. **5,** *colloq.* (good fellow) молоде́ц. *Be a sport!,* будь челове́ком! —*adj.* [*also,* **sports**] спорти́вный: *sport shirt,* спорти́вная руба́шка; *sports car,* спорти́вный автомоби́ль. —*v.t.* щеголя́ть в: *sport a new suit,* щеголя́ть в но́вом костю́ме. —**make sport of,** подшу́чивать над.

sporting *adj.* **1,** (used in sports) спорти́вный: *sporting gear,* спорти́вное обору́дование. **2,** (fair) неплохо́й: *a sporting chance,* неплохи́е ша́нсы.

sportscaster *n.* спорти́вный коммента́тор.

sportsman *n.* спортсме́н. —**sportsmanlike,** *adj.* спортсме́нский. —**sportsmanship,** *n.* поведе́ние, подоба́ющее спортсме́ну.

sportswear *n.* спорти́вная оде́жда.

spot *n.* **1,** (stain; blemish) пятно́: *grease spot,* жи́рное пятно́. *Spots on one's face,* пя́тна на лице́. **2,** *usu. pl.* (marking on an animal or bird) пятно́; кра́пинка. **3,** (place; location) ме́сто: *a convenient spot,* удо́бное ме́сто. *Sore spot,* больно́е ме́сто. *Weak spot,* сла́бое ме́сто. *Nailed to the spot,* пригвождённый к ме́сту. *Have a soft spot in one's heart for,* пита́ть сла́бость к. **4,** (set of circumstances) положе́ние: *in a tight spot,* в затрудни́тельном положе́нии. —*v.t.* **1,** (stain) пятна́ть. **2,** (catch sight of; detect) заме́тить; уви́деть; рассмотре́ть; разгляде́ть. **3,** (give, as a certain number of points) дава́ть (не́сколько очко́в) вперёд. —*v.i.* па́чкаться. —**in spots,** места́ми. —**on the spot, 1,** (at once) сра́зу. **2,** (at the scene of action) на ме́сте. **3,** (in a difficult position) в тупике́. *Put on the spot,* ста́вить в тупи́к.

spot check вы́борочная прове́рка.

spotless *adj.* незапя́тнанный. *Spotlessly clean,* чи́сто-на́чисто; безукори́зненно чи́стый.

spotlight *n.* проже́ктор. —**be in the spotlight,** быть в це́нтре внима́ния.

spotted *adj.* пятни́стый; кра́пчатый; рябо́й.

spotter *n., mil.* корректиро́вщик. —**spotter plane,** самолёт-корректиро́вщик.

spouse *n.* супру́г; супру́га.

spout *v.t.* **1,** (discharge with force) изверга́ть. **2,** (utter profusely) сы́пать. —*v.i.* **1,** (shoot out with force) хлы́нуть; бить струёй. **2,** (speak pompously) разглаго́льствовать. —*n.* **1,** (projection for pouring a liquid) но́сик. **2,** (stream of liquid) струя́.

sprain *n.* растяже́ние. —*v.t.* растя́гивать; подвёртывать. *Sprain one's ankle,* подверну́ть себе́ но́гу.

sprat *n.* ки́лька; шпро́та.

sprawl *v.i.* растя́гиваться; разва́ливаться. *Send someone sprawling,* повали́ть кого́-нибудь с ног.

spray *n.* **1,** (fine liquid particles) бры́зги. **2,** (atomizer) распыли́тель; пульвериза́тор. **3,** (liquid discharged from an atomizer) жи́дкость: *hair spray,* жи́дкость для воло́с. **4,** (branch) ве́точка. —*v.t.* **1,** (direct a spray of) обры́згивать; разбры́згивать. **2,** (treat with a spray) опры́скивать; распыля́ть.

sprayer *n.* распыли́тель; пульвериза́тор.

spray gun краскопу́льт.

spread *v.t.* **1,** (lay; unfurl) расстила́ть: *spread a tablecloth,* расстила́ть ска́терть. *Spread one's wings,* расправля́ть кры́лья. **2,** (lay out in display) выкла́дывать; раскла́дывать; раски́дывать. **3,** (draw or move apart) раздвига́ть; расставля́ть; раски́дывать. **4,** (diffuse; disseminate) распространя́ть: *spread rumors,* распространя́ть слу́хи. *Flies spread disease,* му́хи распространя́ют боле́зни. **5,** (scatter; strew) рассыпа́ть; разбра́сывать. *Spread manure,* разбра́сывать наво́з. **6,** (smear) нама́зывать: *spread butter on bread,* нама́зывать ма́сло на хлеб. **7,** (extend over a period of time, as payments) рассро́чивать. —*v.i.* распространя́ться: *the fire spread quickly,* пожа́р бы́стро распространя́лся. *The news spread all over town,* но́вость обошла́ весь го́род. —*n.* **1,** (diffusion; dissemination) распростране́ние. **2,** (expanse) разма́х: *wingspread,* разма́х кры́льев. **3,** (bedspread) покрыва́ло. **4,** (soft food) па́ста: *cheese spread,* сы́рная па́ста. **5,** (difference, as between prices) разры́в. —**spread oneself thin,** разбра́сываться.

spreading *n.* распростране́ние. —*adj.* **1,** (expanding its range) бы́стро распространя́ющийся. **2,** (of a tree) разве́систый; раски́дистый.

spree *n.* кутёж. *Go on a spree,* кути́ть; устра́ивать кутёж.

sprig *n.* ве́точка; побе́г.

sprightly *adj.* живо́й; оживлённый.

spring *v.i.* **1,** (leap) пры́гать; вска́кивать. *Spring to one's feet,* вскочи́ть на́ ноги. **2,** *fol. by* **up** (come into being) возника́ть; появля́ться. *New towns are springing up everywhere,* но́вые города́ возника́ют повсю́ду. **3,** *fol. by* **from** (stem from; be due to) происходи́ть (от). **4,** *in* **spring open,** распахну́ться; **spring shut,** захло́пнуться. —*v.t.* **1,** (release; actuate) пуска́ть в ход. **2,** (present or make known suddenly) преподноси́ть: *spring a surprise on,* преподноси́ть сюрпри́з (+ *dat.*). **3,** *in* **spring a leak,** дать течь. —*n.* **1,** (leap) прыжо́к. **2,** (season) весна́. *In spring,* весно́й. **3,** (device for applying tension) пружи́на; *(on vehicles)* рессо́ра. **4,** (elasticity) упру́гость. **5,** (water rising from the ground) исто́чник; ключ; родни́к. —*adj.* **1,** (of springtime) весе́нний: *spring vacation,* весе́нние кани́кулы. **2,** (motivated by tension) пружи́нный: *spring mattress,* пружи́нный матра́с. **3,** (flowing up from the ground) ключево́й; родниково́й.

springboard *n.* **1,** (used by athletes and acrobats) трампли́н. **2,** *fig.* (avenue to success) трампли́н; плацда́рм.

springtime *n.* весна́; весе́нняя пора́; весе́ннее вре́мя.

springy *adj.* упру́гий; пружи́нистый.

sprinkle *v.t.* **1,** (scatter in drops) бры́згать: *sprinkle water on,* бры́згать водо́й на (+ *acc.*). **2,** (scatter drops of something on) обры́згивать; кропи́ть; окропля́ть; опры́скивать (*e.g.* что́-нибудь водо́й). **3,** (scatter in particles) сы́пать: *sprinkle salt in the soup,* сы́пать соль в суп. **4,** (scatter particles of something on) посыпа́ть: *sprinkle the road with sand,* посыпа́ть доро́гу песко́м. —*v.i.* (rain lightly) мороси́ть; накра́пывать. —*n.* до́ждик; и́зморось.

sprinkler *n.* пульвериза́тор. —**sprinkler system,** дождева́льная устано́вка.

sprinkling *n.* **1,** (spraying of water) дождева́ние. **2,** (small admixture) при́месь. —**sprinkling can,** ле́йка.

sprint *n.* **1,** (short race) спринт. **2,** (extra burst of speed) рыво́к; бросо́к. —*v.i.* бро́ситься; помча́ться; бежа́ть во весь опо́р. —**sprinter,** *n.* спри́нтер.

sprite *n.* эльф. *Water sprite,* водяно́й.

sprocket *n.* зуб; зубе́ц. —**sprocket wheel,** цепно́е колесо́.

sprout *v.i.* пуска́ть ростки́; прораста́ть. —*v.t.* отра́щивать. —*n.* отро́сток; росто́к; побе́г.

spruce *n.* (tree) ель. —*v.t. & i.* [*usu.* **spruce up**] наряжа́ть(ся); прихора́шивать(ся).

spry *adj.* живо́й; бо́йкий; ю́ркий. —**spryness,** *n.* жи́вость; бо́йкость.

spud *n., colloq.* карто́фелина.

spume *n.* пе́на; на́кипь.

spun *adj.* пря́деный.

spunk *n., colloq.* сме́лость. —**spunky,** *adj., colloq.* сме́лый.

spur *n.* **1,** (of a horseman) шпо́ра. **2,** (of a gamecock) (петуши́ная) шпо́ра. **3,** (of a mountain) отро́г. **4,** (branch line) подъездно́й путь. **5,** *fig.* (stimulus) толчо́к. —*v.t.* **1,** (urge on with spurs) пришпо́ривать. **2,** (goad; impel) побужда́ть; подстрека́ть. —**on the spur of the moment,** под влия́нием мину́ты. —**win one's spurs,** сде́лать себе́ и́мя.

spurious *adj.* **1,** (counterfeit) подло́жный; подде́льный. **2,** (false; not true) ло́жный: *spurious charges,* ло́жные обвине́ния.

spurn *v.t.* отверга́ть; отта́лкивать.

spurt *n.* **1,** (gush of liquid) струя́. **2,** (sudden burst of speed) рыво́к; бросо́к. —*v.i.* **1,** (gush) бить струёй; бры́згать. **2,** (put on a burst of speed) сде́лать рыво́к *or* бросо́к.

sputter *v.i.* **1,** (make hissing sounds) шипе́ть. **2,** (speak hurriedly or confusedly) лопота́ть.

sputum *n.* плево́к.

spy *n.* шпио́н. —*adj.* шпио́нский: *spy ring,* шпио́нская организа́ция *or* сеть. —*v.i.* **1,** (engage in espionage) шпио́нить. **2,** *fol. by* **on** (watch furtively) подсма́тривать за. —*v.t.* (see; catch sight of) рассмотре́ть; разгляде́ть.

spyglass *n.* подзо́рная труба́.

squab *n.* (неопери́вшийся) го́лубь.

squabble *n.* перебра́нка; пререка́ния. —*v.i.* вздо́рить; пререка́ться; препира́ться.

squad *n.* **1,** (smallest army unit) отделе́ние. **2,** (small organized group) отря́д; наря́д; кома́нда; брига́да. *Rescue squad,* спаса́тельная кома́нда.

squadron *n.* **1,** *naval* эска́дра. **2,** (of cavalry) эскадро́н. **3,** *aero.* эскадри́лья.

squalid *adj.* убо́гий.

squall *n.* **1,** (yell) вопль. **2,** (storm) шквал. —*v.i.* ора́ть; вопи́ть.

squalor *n.* убо́жество; убо́гость. *Live in squalor,* жить в убо́жестве.

squander *v.t.* растра́чивать; расточа́ть; прома́тывать. —**squanderer,** *n.* расточи́тель.

square *n.* **1,** (equilateral rectangle) квадра́т. **2,** (open area in a city) пло́щадь: *Red Square,* Кра́сная пло́щадь. **3,** *math.* квадра́т: *the square of three is nine,* три в квадра́те равно́ девяти́. **4,** (T-shaped or L-shaped instrument) уго́льник; науго́льник; рейсши́на. **5,** (space on a checkerboard) кле́тка. —*adj.* **1,** (square in shape) квадра́тный. **2,** (expressing surface measures) квадра́тный: *square meter,* квадра́тный метр. *Ten meters square,* де́сять ме́тров в длину́ и в ширину́. **3,** (honest; fair; equitable) че́стный: *square deal,* че́стная сде́лка. **4,** (paid-up; even) в расчёте; кви́ты: *we're all square,* мы с ва́ми в расчёте; мы с ва́ми кви́ты. **5,** *Square meal,* пло́тный обе́д. —*v.t.* **1,** (cut into a square shape) обтёсывать. **2,** (straighten, as one's shoulders) расправля́ть; распрямля́ть. **3,** (multiply by itself) возводи́ть в квадра́т. *Ten squared equals 100,* де́сять в квадра́те равня́ется ста. **4,** (settle, as accounts) своди́ть (счёты). **5,** (reconcile, as one statement with another) увя́зывать. —*v.i.* (conform) соотве́тствовать; вяза́ться. —*adv.* **1,** (at right angles) под прямы́м угло́м. **2,** (fairly) че́стно. **3,** (directly) пря́мо.

squarely *adv.* пря́мо. *Face the facts squarely,* смотре́ть фа́ктам пря́мо в лицо́.

square root квадра́тный ко́рень.

squash *n.* **1,** (vegetable) кабачо́к. **2,** (beverage) лимона́д. —*v.t.* **1,** (crush) расплю́щивать; (раз)дави́ть. **2,** (suppress) подавля́ть.

squat *v.i.* приседа́ть; сиде́ть на ко́рточках; сесть на ко́рточки. —*n.* приседа́ние. —*adj.* призе́мистый. —**squatter,** *n.* сква́ттер.

squaw *n.* индиа́нка.

squawk *v.i.* **1,** (cry hoarsely) клекота́ть. **2,** *slang* (complain) ворча́ть. —*n.* **1,** (hoarse cry) клёкот. **2,** *slang* (complaint) жа́лоба.

squeak *v.i.* скрипе́ть. —*n.* скрип. —**squeaky,** *adj.* скрипу́чий.

squeal *v.i.* **1,** (utter a loud, sharp sound) визжа́ть. **2,** *slang* (inform) доноси́ть. —*n.* визг. —**squealer,** *n., slang* (informer) доно́счик; стука́ч.

squeamish *adj.* брезгли́вый. —**squeamishness,** *n.* брезгли́вость.

squeeze *v.t.* **1,** (compress) сжима́ть; сда́вливать; сти́скивать. *Squeeze a lemon,* дави́ть *or* жать лимо́н. **2,** (extract by squeezing) выжима́ть. **3,** (cram) вти́скивать. —*v.i.* **1,** (apply pressure) жать; сжима́ть. **2,** *fol. by* **in, into** *or* **through** (force one's way) вти́скиваться (в); проти́скиваться (в). —*n.* **1,** (act of squeezing) сжа́тие. *Give someone's hand a squeeze,* кре́пко пожа́ть ру́ку (+ *dat.*). **2,** (embrace) объя́тие. **3,** (cramming; crowding) да́вка. *It was something of a squeeze,* бы́ло тесновато.

squeezer *n.* соковыжима́лка.

squelch *v.t.* пресека́ть; подавля́ть. *Squelch a rumor,* разве́ять слух.

squid *n.* кальма́р.

squiggle *n.* закорю́чка.

squint *v.i.* **1,** (screw up one's eyes) жму́риться; щу́риться. **2,** (be cross-eyed) коси́ть. **3,** (look sideways) коси́ть глаза́ми. —*n.* косогла́зие.

squire *n.* **1,** (title) сква́йр. **2,** (lady's escort) кавале́р. —*v.t.* сопровожда́ть.

squirm *v.i.* **1,** (wriggle) извива́ться; ко́рчиться. *Squirm out of,* вывёртываться из. **2,** (fret; worry) му́читься.

squirrel *n.* бе́лка. —*adj.* бе́личий: *squirrel coat,* бе́личья шу́ба.

squirt *v.t.* пуска́ть струёй. *Squirt water in someone's face,* пуска́ть стру́йку воды́ в лицо́ (+ *dat.*). —*v.i.* бить струёй. —*n.* струя́; стру́йка.

stab *v.t.* коло́ть. *Stab to death,* заколо́ть. *Stab in the back,* наноси́ть (+ *dat.*) преда́тельский уда́р. —*n.* уда́р (ножо́м). *Stab in the back,* нож в спи́ну. —**stabbing pain,** ко́лющая боль.

stability *n.* усто́йчивость; стаби́льность.

stabilize *v.t.* стабилизи́ровать. —*v.i.* стабилизи́роваться. —**stabilization,** *n.* стабилиза́ция. —**stabilizer,** *n.* стабилиза́тор.

stable *adj.* **1,** (steady; firm) усто́йчивый; стаби́льный. *Stable currency,* усто́йчивая валю́та. *Stable prices,* усто́йчивые *or* стаби́льные це́ны. **2,** *chem.* сто́йкий. —*n.* коню́шня. —*v.t.* ста́вить в коню́шню; держа́ть в коню́шне. —**stable hand,** ко́нюх.

staccato *adj.* отры́вистый. —*adv.* стакка́то.

stack *n.* **1,** (orderly pile) ки́па: *stack of papers,* ки́па бума́г. *Stack of logs,* поле́нница. **2,** (pile of hay or straw) стог; скирд; скирда́. **3,** (chimney) дымова́я труба́. **4,** (set of shelves) стелла́ж. —*v.t.* [*often* **stack up**] скла́дывать. —**stack the cards** *or* **deck,** подтасо́вывать ка́рты.

stadium *n.* стадио́н.

staff *n.* **1,** (long stick) по́сох. **2,** (flagpole) дре́вко. **3,** (rod as a symbol of authority) жезл. **4,** (personnel) штат; соста́в. *Be on the staff,* быть *or* состоя́ть в шта́те. *Teaching staff,* преподава́тельский соста́в. *Staff reduction,* сокраще́ние шта́тов. **5,** *mil.* штаб: *the general staff,* генера́льный штаб. *Chief of staff,* нача́льник шта́ба. **6,** *music* но́тный стан; нотоно́сец. —*adj.* **1,** (permanent) шта́тный: *staff position,* шта́тная до́лжность. **2,** *mil.* штабно́й: *staff officer,* штабно́й офице́р. —*v.t.* обеспе́чивать персона́лом; *mil.* укомплектова́ть ли́чным соста́вом.

stag *n.* (male deer) рога́ч. —*adj., colloq.* (for men only) холостя́цкий. —**stag beetle,** рога́ч.

stage *n.* **1,** (theater platform) сце́на: *appear on the stage,* выступа́ть на сце́не. **2,** (dais) помо́ст. **3,** (theatrical profession) сце́на: *retire from the stage,* уходи́ть со сце́ны. **4,** (step; phase) ста́дия; эта́п. *In stages,* по ста́диям. **5,** (leg of a journey) перего́н. —*v.t.* **1,** (put on) ста́вить: *stage a play,* ста́вить пье́су. **2,** (adapt for the stage) инсцени́ровать. **3,** (carry out; hold) устра́ивать; проводи́ть; организова́ть. **4,** (make appear spontaneous) инсцени́ровать. —**set the stage for,** подгота́вливать по́чву для.

stagecoach *n.* дилижа́нс.

stage fright стесне́ние пе́ред пу́бликой. *Suffer from stage fright,* стесня́ться пу́блики.

stagehand *n.* рабо́чий сце́ны.

stage manager режиссёр.

stage props реквизи́т; бутафо́рия.

stagger *v.i.* шата́ться; пошатну́ться. —*v.t.* **1,** (overwhelm; stun) потряса́ть; ошеломля́ть. **2,** (alternate) чередова́ть. —**staggering,** *adj.* потряса́ющий; ошеломля́ющий.

staging *n.* постано́вка (пье́сы). —**staging area,** *mil.* плацда́рм.

stagnant *adj.* **1,** (foul; polluted) стоя́чий; засто́йный. *Become stagnant,* заста́иваться. **2,** *fig.* (sluggish) вя́лый; ко́сный.

stagnate *v.i.* **1,** (become foul) заста́иваться. **2,** (become sluggish) коснéть. —**stagnation,** *n.* застóй.

staid *adj.* степéнный; положи́тельный.

stain *n.* **1,** (spot; blemish) пятнó. **2,** (coloring substance) мори́лка. —*v.t.* **1,** (spot; soil) пятнáть; пáчкать. **2,** (color; tint) мори́ть: *stain wood,* мори́ть дéрево. —*v.i.* пáчкаться.

stained *adj.* морёный: *stained oak,* морёный дуб. —**stained glass,** цветнóе стеклó. *Stained-glass window,* витрáж.

stainless steel нержавéющая сталь.

stair *n.* **1,** (step) ступéнька. **2,** [*usu.* **stairs**] (staircase) лéстница.

staircase *n.* лéстница. *Also,* **stairway.**

stairwell *n.* лéстничная клéтка; пролёт; прогóн.

stake *n.* **1,** (pointed stick) кол. **2,** (boundary mark) вéха. **3,** (post for execution): *be burned at the stake,* поги́бнуть на кострé. **4,** (money wagered) стáвка. *Play for high stakes,* игрáть по большóй. **5,** (share; interest) дóля. *Have a stake in the outcome,* быть заинтересóванным в исхóде дéла. —*v.t.* **1,** *fol. by* **out** *or* **off** (delineate) отмечáть вéхами. *Stake out a claim,* заявля́ть претéнзию. **2,** *fol. by* **out** (put under surveillance) установи́ть слéжку за. **3,** (bet; risk) стáвить; стáвить на кáрту. *Stake one's all,* постáвить всё на кáрту. *Stake one's life on it,* ручáться за чтó-нибудь головóй; давáть рýку (*or* гóлову) на отсечéние. **4,** (provide with money or resources) финанси́ровать. —**at stake,** постáвлен на кáрту. *The fate of the country was at stake,* решáлась судьбá нарóда. —**pull up stakes,** сня́ться с мéста.

Stakhanovite *n.* стахáновец.

stalactite *n.* сталакти́т.

stalagmite *n.* сталагми́т.

stale *adj.* **1,** (no longer fresh) чёрствый: *stale bread,* чёрствый хлеб. *Stale air,* спёртый вóздух. *Become stale,* черствéть. **2,** (trite; hackneyed) изби́тый. *Stale news,* устарéвшие нóвости.

stalemate *n.* **1,** *chess* пат. **2,** (deadlock) мёртвая тóчка; тупи́к. —*v.t.* заводи́ть в тупи́к. *Be stalemated,* заходи́ть в тупи́к.

stalk *n.* стéбель. —*v.i.* шагáть. *Stalk out of the room,* демонстрати́вно уйти́ из кóмнаты. —*v.t.* **1,** (pursue stealthily) выслéживать. **2,** (advance grimly across) броди́ть по: *hunger stalked the land,* гóлод броди́л по странé.

stall *n.* **1,** (for an animal) стóйло. **2,** (market booth) ларёк; палáтка. **3,** *Brit.* (orchestra seat) крéсло в партéре. —*v.t.* **1,** (put or lodge in a stall) стáвить в стóйло. **2,** (delay; check) задéрживать; тормози́ть. *Negotiations are stalled,* переговóры зашли́ в тупи́к. **3,** *fol. by* **off** (delay; divert) задéрживать. —*v.i.* **1,** (stop running, as of an engine) глóхнуть; захлёбываться. **2,** (get stuck) застревáть. **3,** (use delaying tactics) уви́ливать. *Stall for time,* оття́гивать врéмя.

stallion *n.* жеребéц.

stalwart *adj.* **1,** (robust) дю́жий; рóслый. **2,** (loyal; staunch) вéрный; стóйкий. **3,** (brave; valiant) отвáжный; дóблестный. —*n.* стóйкий сторóнник.

stamen *n.* тычи́нка.

stamina *n.* выносливость.

stammer *v.i.* заикáться. —*n.* заикáние. —**stammerer,** *n.* заи́ка. —**stammering,** *n.* заикáние.

stamp *n.* **1,** (marking device; impression so made) печáть; штамп; штéмпель. **2,** (postage stamp) мáрка. **3,** (a stamping of the foot) тóпот. **4,** *fig.* (mark) печáть: *the stamp of genius,* печáть гéния. **5,** (kind; ilk) склад: *people of that stamp,* лю́ди такóго склáда. —*v.t.* **1,** (bring down forcibly) тóпать: *stamp one's feet,* тóпать ногáми. **2,** (impress with a mark) штамповáть; штемпелевáть. *Stamp a passport,* штамповáть пáспорт; стáвить штамп на пáспорт. **3,** (imprint permanently, as in one's memory) запечатлевáть. **4,** *fol. by* **out** (extinguish by stamping on) затáптывать. **5,** *fol. by* **out** (eradicate) искореня́ть. —*v.i.* тóпать ногáми. —**stamp album,** альбóм для мáрок. —**stamp collecting,** собирáние мáрок. —**stamp collection,** коллéкция мáрок. —**stamp collector,** филатели́ст. —**stamp pad,** подýшка для штемпелéй; штéмпельная подýшка.

stampede *n.* пани́ческое бéгство. —*v.i.* бросáться врассыпнýю; обращáться в пани́ческое бéгство.

stance *n.* пóза; положéние.

stanch *v.t.* останáвливать (кровотечéние). —*adj.* = **staunch.**

stanchion *n.* стóйка; *naut.* пи́ллерс.

stand *v.i.* **1,** (be in an upright position) стоя́ть: *she was standing in the doorway,* онá стоя́ла в дверя́х. *Stand (i.e. wait) in line,* стоя́ть в óчереди. **2,** (station oneself somewhere standing) станови́ться (*pfv.* стать): *stand in the corner,* стать в ýгол. *Stand (i.e. get) in line,* стать в óчередь. **3,** *often fol. by* **up** (get up; rise) вставáть. **4,** (be placed or situated) стоя́ть: *the house stands on a hill,* дом стои́т на холмé. **5,** (be a certain height) быть рóстом: *he stands six feet tall,* он рóстом шесть фýтов. **6,** (be; remain) стоя́ть. *The door stood open,* дверь былá нáстежь. *That is how matters stand,* вот как обстои́т дéло. *Stand accused of,* обвиня́ться в. *The thermometer stands at zero,* термóметр покáзывает нуль. **7,** (remain in effect) оставáться в си́ле: *the decision stands,* решéние остаётся в си́ле. *The record did not stand for long,* рекóрд продержáлся недóлго. **8,** *Brit.* (be a candidate) баллоти́роваться. —*v.t.* **1,** (set upright) стáвить: *stand the vase on the table,* стáвить вáзу на стол. **2,** (endure) терпéть; выноси́ть. *I can't stand it,* я э́того терпéть не могý. **3,** *Stand guard,* стоя́ть на часáх/на карáуле/на стрáже/. **4,** *Stand trial,* идти́ под суд. **5,** *Stand a chance,* имéть шáнсы. —*n.* **1,** (instance of standing) стоя́ние: *a long stand in line,* дóлгое стоя́ние в óчереди. **2,** (small table, rack, etc.) стенд; стóлик; этажéрка. **3,** (support; base) подстáвка. **4,** (platform) эстрáда. **5,** (market stall) ларёк; киóск. **6,** (parking place for taxis) стоя́нка. **7,** *pl.* (grandstand) трибýна. **8,** (defensive effort) сопротивлéние: *make a stand,* окáзывать сопротивлéние. **9,** (view; opinion; position) пози́ция. *Take a stand,* занимáть определённую пози́цию. **10,** *One-night stand,* однонéвные гастрóли. —**stand aside, 1,** (of a person) отходи́ть в стóрону. **2,** (of a crowd) расступáться. —**stand back,** отступáть; держáться на расстоя́нии. —**stand by, 1,** (remain aloof) держáться в сторонé. **2,** (stand ready) быть наготóве. **3,** (stand firmly behind) оставáться вéрным (+ *dat.*). **4,** (not depart from) придéрживаться (+ *gen.*). —**stand for, 1,** (represent; signify) означáть. **2,** (tolerate) терпéть. **3,** (advocate; favor) стоя́ть за. —**stand in for,** замещáть. —**stand out,** выделя́ться: *stand out in a crowd,* выделя́ться в толпé. —**stand over,** стоя́ть над (чьéй-нибудь) душóй. —**stand up, 1,** (rise) вставáть. *Stand up straight,* держáться пря́мо. **2,** (set upright) стáвить стоймя́. **3,** *slang* (disappoint) подводи́ть. **—stand up for,** стоя́ть за; заступа́ться за. **—stand up to,** вы́стоять про́тив. **—stand up under,** выде́рживать.

standard *n.* **1,** (norm) станда́рт; но́рма; мери́ло; ме́рка. *Double standard,* двойна́я ме́рка. **2,** (degree; level) у́ровень: *standard of living,* жи́зненный у́ровень. **3,** (basis of a monetary system) станда́рт: *gold standard,* золото́й станда́рт. **4,** (banner) зна́мя; штанда́рт. *—adj.* станда́ртный; типово́й. **—standard-bearer,** *n.* знамено́сец.

standardize *v.t.* стандартизи́ровать; нормирова́ть; унифици́ровать. **—standardization,** *n.* стандартиза́ция; нормирова́ние; унифика́ция.

standee *n., colloq.* стоя́щий зри́тель; стоя́щий пассажи́р.

stand-in *n.* дублёр.

standing *n.* **1,** (act of standing) стоя́ние. **2,** (status) положе́ние. *Be in good standing,* быть на хоро́шем счету́. **3,** *pl., sports* положе́ние: *team standings,* положе́ние кома́нд. *—adj.* **1,** (upright; on one's feet) стоя́чий; стоя́щий. *Standing position,* стоя́чее положе́ние. **2,** *sports* (from a standing position) с ме́ста: *standing broad jump,* прыжо́к с ме́ста. **3,** (permanent) постоя́нный: *standing army,* постоя́нная а́рмия; *standing invitation,* постоя́нное приглаше́ние. **—of long standing,** да́вний: *a friendship of long standing,* да́вняя дру́жба.

standing room стоя́чие места́: *standing room only,* биле́ты то́лько на стоя́чие места́.

stand-off *n.* ничья́. **—standoffish,** *adj.* необщи́тельный; холо́дный.

standpoint *n.* то́чка зре́ния.

standstill *n.* мёртвая то́чка. *Be at a standstill,* прост́аивать; быть на мёртвой то́чке. *Come to a standstill,* замира́ть.

stanza *n.* строфа́.

staple *n.* **1,** (wire clamp) скоба́; ско́бка. **2,** (clip) скре́пка. **3,** (principal commodity) основно́й проду́кт. **4,** (raw material) сырьё. *—adj.* основно́й; гла́вный. *—v.t.* скрепля́ть.

star *n.* звезда́. *Movie star,* кинозвезда́. *—adj.* **1,** (of stars) звёздный: *star map,* звёздная ка́рта. **2,** (outstanding) выдаю́щийся. *—v.t.* **1,** (mark with an asterisk) помеча́ть звёздочкой. **2,** (feature): *the film stars...,* в фи́льме...игра́ет гла́вную роль. **—see stars,** *colloq.* све́та невзви́деть. *He saw stars,* у него́ и́скры из глаз посы́пались. **—thank one's lucky stars,** благодари́ть судьбу́.

starboard *adj.* пра́вый. *—n.* пра́вый борт.

starch *n.* крахма́л. *—v.t.* крахма́лить. **—starched,** *adj.* накрахма́ленный; крахма́льный.

starchy *adj.* **1,** (containing starch) крахма́листый. **2,** (stiffened with starch) накрахма́ленный.

stare *v.i.* смотре́ть при́стально. *Stare at,* уста́виться на. *—n.* при́стальный взгляд.

starfish *n.* морска́я звезда́.

stark *adj.* **1,** (bleak; desolate) пусты́нный. **2,** (blunt; grim) жесто́кий. **3,** (pure; sheer; utter) сплошно́й. *Stark contrast,* ре́зкий контра́ст. *—adv.* соверше́нно: *stark naked,* соверше́нно го́лый; *stark raving mad,* соверше́нно сумасше́дший.

starless *adj.* беззвёздный.

starlight *n.* свет звёзд.

starling *n.* скворе́ц.

starry *adj.* звёздный.

start *v.t.* **1,** (begin) начина́ть: *start work,* начина́ть рабо́ту. *She started to cry,* она́ начала́ пла́кать; она́ запла́кала. **2,** (initiate) заводи́ть; завя́зывать; зате́ять. *Start an argument,* зате́ять спор. *Start a fight,* завяза́ть бой. *Start a rumor,* пусти́ть слух. *Start a war,* развяза́ть войну́. **3,** (organize, as a business) заводи́ть (де́ло). **4,** (set going, as an engine) запуска́ть (мото́р). *Start the car,* заводи́ть маши́ну. *—v.i.* **1,** (begin) начина́ть: *start from the beginning,* начина́ть снача́ла. *Starting 1 April,* начина́я с пе́рвого апре́ля. **2,** (commence) начина́ться: *the meeting starts at 10:00,* собра́ние начина́ется в де́сять часо́в. **3,** (begin to move) тро́нуться: *the train started,* по́езд тро́нулся. **4,** (begin to function, as of an engine) заводи́ться. **5,** *fol. by* **out** (set out) отправля́ться в путь. **6,** (be a starter in a race) стартова́ть. **7,** (jump from fright) вздра́гивать. *—n.* **1,** (beginning) нача́ло. *From start to finish,* снача́ла до конца́. **2,** (beginning of a race) старт: *false start,* неве́рный старт. **3,** (edge; advantage) фо́ра. **4,** (sudden movement): *give a start,* вздра́гивать. *Give someone a start,* испуга́ть *or* напуга́ть кого́-нибудь. **5,** *in* **by fits and starts,** уры́вками.

starter *n.* **1,** *mech.* ста́ртер. **2,** (one who starts in a race) уча́стник (состяза́ния). **3,** (one who gives the signal to start in a race) ста́ртер. **4,** (dispatcher) диспе́тчер. **—for starters,** *colloq.* для нача́ла.

starting line старт; ста́ртовая ли́ния.

starting point нача́льный пункт; отправно́й пункт; исхо́дная то́чка.

startle *v.t.* **1,** (frighten) испуга́ть. **2,** (shock) поража́ть. **—startling,** *adj.* порази́тельный; потряса́ющий.

starvation *n.* го́лод; голода́ние. *Die of starvation,* умира́ть с го́лоду; умира́ть голо́дной сме́ртью.

starve *v.i.* **1,** (go continually hungry) голода́ть. *Starve to death,* умира́ть с го́лоду; умира́ть голо́дной сме́ртью. **2,** *colloq.* (be very hungry) быть о́чень голо́дным. *I'm starving,* я умира́ю от го́лода; я стра́шно проголода́лся. *—v.t.* мори́ть го́лодом: *starve oneself,* мори́ть себя́ го́лодом. *Starve into submission,* взять измо́ром.

starveling *n.* замо́рыш.

starving *adj.* голода́ющий.

stash *v.t., colloq.* [*usu.* **stash away**] припря́тывать.

state *n.* **1,** (condition) состоя́ние; положе́ние. *State of affairs,* положе́ние дел *or* веще́й. *State of mind,* душе́вное состоя́ние. *State of emergency,* чрезвыча́йное положе́ние. *State of siege,* оса́дное положе́ние. *In a drunken state,* в пья́ном ви́де. **2,** (nation; government) госуда́рство: *sovereign state,* суверéнное госуда́рство. *The State of Israel,* Госуда́рство Изра́иль. *Affairs of state,* госуда́рственные дела́. *Separation of church and state,* отделе́ние це́ркви от госуда́рства. **3,** (unit of a republic) штат: *United States,* Соединённые Шта́ты. *—adj.* **1,** (of a nation) госуда́рственный: *state secret,* госуда́рственная та́йна. *(The U.S.) State Department,* госуда́рственный департа́мент. **2,** (of a U.S. state) *rendered by* шта́та: *state law,* зако́н шта́та. **3,** (marked by ceremony) торже́ственный: *state dinner,* торже́ственный обе́д. *—v.t.* **1,** (set forth) излага́ть: *state one's case,* излага́ть своё де́ло. *State one's opinion,* вы́сказать своё мне́ние. **2,** (announce; assert) заявля́ть: *he stated that...,* он заяви́л, что... —**lie in state,** поко́иться в откры́том гробу́.

stated *adj.* **1,** (announced) изло́женный; вы́сказанный. **2,** (fixed) устано́вленный; определённый.

stateless *adj.* не име́ющий гражда́нства.

stately *adj.* вели́чественный; велича́вый.

statement *n.* **1,** (act of stating) изложе́ние. **2,** (something stated; a declaration) заявле́ние. **3,** *comm.* отчёт.

stateroom *n.* каю́та.

statesman *n.* госуда́рственный де́ятель.

static *adj.* **1,** *physics* стати́ческий: *static pressure,* стати́ческое давле́ние. **2,** (not moving or progressing) стати́чный. —*n.* поме́хи. —**static electricity,** стати́ческое электри́чество.

statics *n.* ста́тика.

station *n.* **1,** (terminal) вокза́л; ста́нция. **2,** (establishment) ста́нция: *gas station,* бензозапра́вочная ста́нция; *tracking station,* ста́нция слеже́ния. *Fire station,* пожа́рное депо́. *Police station,* полице́йский уча́сток; отделе́ние мили́ции. *First-aid station,* меди́цинский пункт. **3,** (duty post) пост: *battle station,* боево́й пост. **4,** (status) обще́ственное положе́ние. **5,** *radio* радиоста́нция. **6,** *mil.; naval* ба́за. —*v.t.* размеща́ть; дислоци́ровать (войска́). *Station a guard at the door,* ста́вить часово́го у две́ри. *Station oneself at the window,* стать у окна́. *He is stationed in Texas,* он слу́жит в Теха́се.

stationary *adj.* неподви́жный.

stationer *n.* торго́вец канцеля́рскими принадле́жностями.

stationery *n.* **1,** (paper) почто́вая бума́га. **2,** (supplies) канцеля́рские *or* писчебума́жные принадле́жности. —**stationery store,** писчебума́жный магази́н.

station house полице́йский уча́сток.

stationmaster *n.* нача́льник ста́нции.

statistical *adj.* статисти́ческий.

statistician *n.* стати́стик.

statistics *n.* **1,** (science) стати́стика. **2,** (figures) статисти́ческие да́нные.

statue *n.* ста́туя.

statuesque *adj.* скульпту́рный; ста́тный.

statuette *n.* статуэ́тка.

stature *n.* **1,** (height) рост. **2,** *fig.* (reputation) прести́ж.

status *n.* состоя́ние; положе́ние; ста́тус. —**status quo,** ста́тус-кво́.

statute *n.* стату́т; зако́н. —**statute law,** пи́саный зако́н. —**statute mile,** англи́йская ми́ля. —**statute of limitations,** срок да́вности.

statutory *adj.* устано́вленный зако́ном.

staunch *adj.* ве́рный; сто́йкий.

stave *n.* клёпка. —*v.t.* [*usu.* **stave off**] предотвраща́ть.

stay *v.i.* **1,** (remain) остава́ться: *stay home,* остава́ться до́ма. **2,** (reside temporarily) остана́вливаться: *stay at a hotel,* остана́вливаться в гости́нице. *Stay with friends,* остана́вливаться *or* гости́ть у друзе́й. *Where are you staying?,* где вы останови́лись? —*v.t.* **1,** (stop; halt) остана́вливать; приостана́вливать. *Stay the hand of,* останови́ть ру́ку (+ *gen.*). **2,** (appease, as hunger) утоля́ть. —*n.* **1,** (sojourn) пребыва́ние. **2,** (delay) приостановле́ние: *stay of execution,* приостановле́ние исполне́ния пригово́ра. **3,** (collar support) ко́сточка. —**stay away,** отсу́тствовать; не приходи́ть. —**stay in,** остава́ться до́ма. —**stay out,** прогу́ливать: *stay out all night,* прогу́ливать всю ночь. —**stay put,** *colloq.* остава́ться на ме́сте. —**stay up,** не ложи́ться спать. *Stay up all night,* просиде́ть всю ночь.

stay-at-home *n.* домосе́д.

staying power выно́сливость.

staysail *n.* ста́ксель.

stead *n.* ме́сто. *In someone's stead,* вме́сто (+ *gen.*). —**stand (someone) in good stead,** пригоди́ться (+ *dat.*); сослужи́ть (+ *dat.*) хоро́шую слу́жбу.

steadfast *adj.* сто́йкий; непоколеби́мый. —**steadfastness,** *n.* сто́йкость; непоколеби́мость.

steady *adj.* **1,** (stable; firm) усто́йчивый: *steady ladder,* усто́йчивая ле́стница. *Steady on one's feet,* твёрдый на нога́х. *Sew with a steady hand,* шить твёрдой руко́й. **2,** (regular) постоя́нный: *steady job,* постоя́нная рабо́та; *steady customer,* постоя́нный клие́нт. **3,** (uninterrupted) непреры́вный; неукло́нный. *Steady downpour,* беспреры́вные дожди́. *Steady growth,* неукло́нный рост. **4,** (even) равноме́рный: *steady speed,* равноме́рная ско́рость. **5,** (reliable; not frivolous) степе́нный. —*v.t.* **1,** (prevent from rocking) приводи́ть в равнове́сие. **2,** (calm) успока́ивать: *steady one's nerves,* успока́ивать не́рвы. —*v.i.* приходи́ть в равнове́сие.

steak *n.* бифште́кс; антреко́т.

steal *v.t.* **1,** (rob) красть. *His bicycle was stolen,* у него́ укра́ли велосипе́д. **2,** *fig.* (take furtively): *steal a glance at,* укра́дкой посмотре́ть на; *steal a kiss,* сорва́ть поцелу́й. —*v.i.* **1,** (commit theft) красть. **2,** (move furtively) кра́сться; подкра́дываться. *Steal into,* вкра́дываться в; прокра́дываться в. *Steal away,* ускольза́ть.

stealth *n., usu. in* **by stealth,** укра́дкой. —**stealthily,** *adv.* укра́дкой; кра́дучись. —**stealthy,** *adj.* сде́ланный укра́дкой: *stealthy glance,* взгляд укра́дкой.

steam *n.* пар. —*adj.* парово́й: *steam heat,* парово́е отопле́ние. —*v.t.* па́рить. *Steamed oysters,* паровы́е у́стрицы. —*v.i.* **1,** (emit vapor) выпуска́ть пар. **2,** *fol. by* **up** (become covered with vapor) запотева́ть. **3,** (move by steam) плыть. *The ship steamed into port,* парохо́д вошёл в га́вань. —**let/blow off steam,** дава́ть вы́ход свои́м чу́вствам. —**under a full head of steam,** на всех пара́х. —**under one's own steam,** со́бственными си́лами; свои́м хо́дом.

steamboat *n.* парохо́д.

steam engine парова́я маши́на.

steamer *n.* (steamship) парохо́д. —**steamer rug,** плед. —**steamer trunk,** бау́л.

steamroller *n.* парово́й като́к.

steam room пари́льня.

steamship *n.* парохо́д.

steam shovel землеро́йная маши́на; экскава́тор.

steamy *adj.* **1,** (filled with steam) напо́лненный па́ром. **2,** (hot and humid) зно́йный; вла́жный. *Steamy jungle,* вла́жные джу́нгли.

stearin *n.* стеари́н.

steatite *n.* стеати́т.

steed *n.* конь.

steel *n.* сталь. —*adj.* стально́й. *Steel mill,* сталелите́йный заво́д. —*v.t.* **1,** (plate with steel) покрыва́ть ста́лью. **2,** *fig.* (harden; make tough) закаля́ть.

steelworker *n.* сталелите́йщик; сталева́р. —**steelworks,** *n.* сталелите́йный заво́д.

steelyard *n.* безме́н.

steep *adj.* **1,** (precipitous) круто́й. **2,** *colloq.* (high, as of a price) высо́кий; (expensive) дорого́й. —*v.t.* **1,** (soak) выма́чивать; зама́чивать. **2,** *fig.* (immerse; saturate): *steep oneself in a subject,* глубоко́ изуча́ть како́й-нибудь предме́т. *Be steeped in ignorance,* погряза́ть в неве́жестве.

steepen *v.t.* де́лать бо́лее круты́м.

steeple *n.* шпиль.

steeplechase *n.* ска́чки с препя́тствиями.

steeplejack *n.* верхола́з.

steeply *adv.* кру́то.

steepness *n.* кру́тость; крутизна́.

steer *v.t.* **1,** (guide) пра́вить; управля́ть. **2,** (set and follow) держа́ться: *steer a middle course,* держа́ться сре́днего ку́рса. —*v.i.,* *in* **steer clear of,** избега́ть; сторони́ться. —*n.* (ox) вол.

steerage *n.* **1,** (part of a ship) ни́зший класс. **2,** (steering) управле́ние.

steering *n.* рулево́е управле́ние. —**steering column,** рулева́я коло́нка. —**steering committee,** руководя́щий комите́т. —**steering wheel,** руль; рулево́е колесо́; штурва́л.

stein *n.* пивна́я кру́жка.

stellar *adj.* **1,** (consisting of stars) звёздный. **2,** (outstanding) превосхо́дный.

stem *n.* **1,** (of a plant) сте́бель. **2,** (of a glass) но́жка. **3,** (of a pipe) черено́к. **4,** (of a ship) форште́вень. **5,** *ling.* осно́ва. —*v.t.* остана́вливать. —*v.i.* [*usu.* **stem from**] вытека́ть из; происходи́ть от; проистека́ть из.

stench *n.* вонь; смрад; злово́ние.

stencil *n.* шабло́н; трафаре́т. —*v.t.* наноси́ть по трафаре́ту.

stenography *n.* стеногра́фия. —**stenographer,** *n.* стено́граф; стенографи́ст; стенографи́стка. —**stenographic,** *adj.* стенографи́ческий.

stentorian *adj.* громово́й; зы́чный.

step *n.* **1,** (movement of the foot) шаг: *take a step,* сде́лать шаг. **2,** (gait) шаг; похо́дка; по́ступь. *Smooth step,* пла́вный шаг; пла́вная похо́дка. **3,** (in dancing) па. **4,** (stair) ступе́нь; ступе́нька. *Flight of steps,* марш. **5,** (action) шаг; мероприя́тие. *Take steps,* предпринима́ть шаги́. *In taking this step,* пойдя́ на тако́й шаг. **6,** (degree of progress or retrogression) шаг: *a big step forward,* большо́й шаг вперёд; *a step backward,* шаг наза́д. —*v.i.* шага́ть; ступа́ть. *Step this way please!,* сюда́, пожа́луйста! —**in step,** в но́гу. —**keep in step,** идти́ в но́гу. —**out of step,** не в но́гу. —**step aside,** сторони́ться. *Step aside for,* уступа́ть доро́гу (+ *dat.*). —**step back,** отступа́ть. —**step by step,** шаг за ша́гом. —**step down,** уйти́ с поста́. —**step in, 1,** (enter) входи́ть. *Won't you step in?,* зайди́те, пожа́луйста! **2,** (step into) ступа́ть в: *step in a puddle,* ступи́ть в лу́жу. —**step off, 1,** *literally* сходи́ть с. **2,** (mark off) отсчи́тывать: *step off ten paces,* отсчи́тывать де́сять шаго́в. —**step on,** наступа́ть на. *Step on the gas,* дать газ. —**step on it,** поторапливаться. *Step on it!,* живе́й!; скоре́й! —**step out,** выходи́ть. —**step over,** переступа́ть; переша́гивать. —**step up, 1,** (step forward) проходи́ть. **2,** (increase) повыша́ть; нара́щивать.

stepbrother *n.* сво́дный брат.

stepchild *n.* па́сынок.

stepdaughter *n.* па́дчерица.

stepfather *n.* о́тчим.

stepladder *n.* стремя́нка.

stepmother *n.* ма́чеха.

stepparent *n.* о́тчим; ма́чеха.

steppe *n.* степь.

stepping stone ступе́нька на пути́: *stepping stone to success,* ступе́нька на пути́ к успе́ху.

stepsister *n.* сво́дная сестра́.

stepson *n.* па́сынок.

stereophonic *adj.* стереофони́ческий.

stereoscope *n.* стереоско́п. —**stereoscopic,** *adj.* стереоскопи́ческий. —**stereoscopy,** *n.* стереоскопи́я.

stereotype *n.* **1,** *printing* стереоти́п. **2,** (conventional notion) шабло́н; трафаре́т; станда́рт; стереоти́п. —*v.t.* **1,** *printing* стереотипи́ровать. **2,** (represent in a conventional way) превраща́ть в станда́рт. —**stereotyped,** *adj.* шабло́нный; трафаре́тный.

sterile *adj.* **1,** (germ-free) стери́льный. **2,** (incapable of producing offspring) беспло́дный. **3,** *fig.* (devoid of substance) пусто́й.

sterility *n.* **1,** (absence of germs) стери́льность. **2,** (inability to produce offspring) беспло́дие.

sterilize *v.t.* стерилизова́ть. —**sterilization,** *n.* стерилиза́ция. —**sterilizer,** *n.* стерилиза́тор.

sterlet *n.* сте́рлядь.

sterling *n.* **1,** (standard for British coins) сте́рлинг. *Pound sterling,* фунт сте́рлингов. **2,** (silver) серебро́. —*adj.* **1,** (pert. to the pound sterling) сте́рлинговый. **2,** (silver) сере́бряный. **3,** (excellent; outstanding) превосхо́дный.

stern *adj.* стро́гий; суро́вый. *Stern judge,* стро́гий судья́. *Stern look,* стро́гий *or* суро́вый взгляд. *Stern measures,* стро́гие *or* суро́вые ме́ры. —*n.* (of a ship) корма́. —**sternness,** *n.* стро́гость; суро́вость.

sternpost *n.* ахтерште́вень.

sternum *n.* груди́на.

steroid *n.* стеро́ид.

stethoscope *n.* стетоско́п.

stevedore *n.* гру́зчик.

stew *n.* тушёное мя́со; рагу́. —*v.t.* туши́ть; па́рить. —*v.i.* туши́ться; па́риться.

steward *n.* **1,** (manager of a household) завхо́з; эконо́м. **2,** (on a ship or plane) бортпроводни́к; стю́ард. —**stewardess,** *n.* бортпроводни́ца; стюарде́сса.

stewed *adj.* **1,** (cooked by stewing) тушёный; па́реный. **2,** *slang* (drunk) под хмелько́м. —**stewed fruit,** компо́т.

stewpan *n.* кастрю́ля.

stick *n.* **1,** (long slender piece of wood) па́лка; па́лочка. *Walking stick,* трость; па́лка. *Hockey stick,* клю́шка. **2,** (sticklike piece, as of chewing gum) пли́тка. *Stick of dynamite,* ша́шка динами́та. **3,** *aero.* рыча́г. **4,** *pl., colloq.* (rural districts) глушь. —*v.t.* **1,** (prick) коло́ть. **2,** (insert; pin) втыка́ть; вка́лывать. *Stick a pin into something,* воткну́ть була́вку во что́-нибудь. *Stick a flower in one's lapel,* воткну́ть цвето́к в петли́цу. **3,** (thrust) сова́ть: *stick a pie in the oven,* су́нуть пиро́г в духо́вку. *Stick one's head in the door,* просу́нуть го́лову в дверь. *Stick one's head out the window,* вы́сунуться из окна́. **4,** (glue) прикле́ивать; накле́ивать. —*v.i.* **1,** (adhere) кле́иться; заклеиваться; пристава́ть. *The envelope doesn't stick,* конвéрт не заклéивается. **2,** *fol. by* **to** (adhere to) ли́пнуть (к); прилипáть (к); приставáть (к). **3,** (become embedded) застревáть. *The words stuck in her throat,* словá застря́ли у неё в гóрле. **4,** (fail to operate; jam) заедáть *(impers.): the door stuck,* дверь заéло. **5,** (become permanent, as of a nickname) приставáть; приклéиваться. **6,** *fol. by* **to** (not deviate from) не отклоня́ться от; придéрживаться. **7,** *fol. by* **to** (persevere in) упóрствовать в. —**stick around,** *colloq.* оставáться поблúзости. —**stick by,** оставáться вéрным (+ *dat.*); не покидáть. —**stick out, 1,** (protrude) торчáть. **2,** (put out) высóвывать; выставля́ть. *Stick out one's tongue,* вы́сунуть язы́к. **3,** (be conspicuous) отличáться; выдавáться. —**stick together, 1,** (adhere) склéиваться; слипáться. **2,** (remain united) держáться вмéсте. —**stick up, 1,** (protrude upward) торчáть; выдавáться. **2,** *slang* (rob) грáбить. **3,** *Stick 'em up!,* рýки вверх! —**stick up for,** заступáться за. *See also* **stuck.**

sticker *n.* наклéйка.

stickiness *n.* клéйкость.

sticking plaster ли́пкий плáстырь.

sticking point загвóздка; зацéпка.

stickleback *n.* кóлюшка.

stickup *n., slang* налёт; грабёж; ограблéние.

sticky *adj.* **1,** (adhesive; gummy) ли́пкий; клéйкий. **2,** (humid) влáжный. **3,** *colloq.* (ticklish) щекотли́вый.

stiff *adj.* **1,** (rigid, unbending) жёсткий, негнýщийся. *Stiff brush,* жёсткая щётка. *Stiff cardboard,* твёрдый *or* негнýщийся картóн. **2,** (sore and not moving easily) онемéвший: *stiff joints,* онемéвшие сустáвы. *I have a stiff neck,* мне надýло (в) шéю; у меня́ шéя не поворáчивается. *My hands are stiff from the cold,* рýки мои́ окоченéли от хóлода. **3,** (hard to move or operate) тугóй: *stiff door,* тугáя дверь. **4,** (awkward; constrained) натя́нутый; принуждённый. **5,** (moving with great force) си́льный. *Stiff wind,* си́льный/жестóкий вéтер. *Stiff current,* бы́строе течéние. **6,** (stout; resolute) упóрный. *Stiff resistance,* упóрное *or* жестóкое сопротивлéние. **7,** (harsh; severe) сурóвый: *stiff sentence,* сурóвый приговóр. **8,** (difficult; demanding) трýдный: *stiff exam,* трýдный экзáмен. *Stiff requirements,* высóкие трéбования. *Stiff competition,* óстрая конкурéнция. **9,** (potent) крéпкий: *stiff drink,* крéпкий напи́ток. **10,** *colloq.* (high, as of a price) дýтый. —*adv.* **1,** (so as to be stiff): *be frozen stiff,* окоченéть от хóлода. **2,** *colloq.* (to an extreme degree) дó смерти: *be scared stiff,* перепугáться дó смерти.

stiffen *v.t.* **1,** (make stiff) дéлать жёстким. **2,** (make more resolute) укрепля́ть: *stiffen someone's will,* укрепля́ть чью-нибудь вóлю. —*v.i.* станови́ться неподви́жным; коченéть.

stiffness *n.* **1,** (firmness) жёсткость. **2,** *med.* неподви́жность. **3,** (awkwardness) натя́нутость; принуждённость.

stifle *v.t.* **1,** (suffocate; smother) души́ть; удушáть. **2,** (suppress, as a yawn) подавля́ть. **3,** (suppress, as criticism or initiative) подавля́ть; глуши́ть; души́ть; зажимáть. —**stifling,** *adj.* удýшливый.

stigma *n.* **1,** (mark of shame) клеймó. **2,** *bot.* ры́льце. —**stigmatize,** *v.t.* клейми́ть.

stiletto *n.* стилéт.

still *adj.* **1,** (motionless) неподви́жный. **2,** (tranquil) ти́хий: *still water,* ти́хая водá. **3,** (silent) безмóлвный. *Be still!,* молчи́! —*n.* **1,** (distilling apparatus) перегóнный куб. **2,** (distillery) винокýренный завóд. **3,** (silence; quiet) тишинá. *In the still of the night,* в ночнóй тиши́. —*adv.* **1,** (yet) ещё; всё ещё: *she is still young,* онá (всё) ещё молодáя. **2,** (all the same) всё же; всё-таки; всё равнó: *I still love him,* я всё же/всё-таки/всё равнó/люблю́ егó. **3,** *with comp. adjectives* ещё: *still further,* ещё дáльше. **4,** (motionless) неподви́жно. *Sit still!,* сиди́те сми́рно! —*v.t.* **1,** (silence) унимáть. **2,** (calm) успокáивать. —*v.i.* успокáиваться. —*conj.* всё же; всё-таки; тем не мéнее. *Still, you ought to go,* всё же/тем не мéнее/вам слéдует пойти́. —**still and all,** несмотря́ на всё э́то; тем не мéнее.

stillborn *adj.* мертворождённый.

still life натюрмóрт.

stillness *n.* **1,** (motionlessness) неподви́жность. **2,** (calm; quiet) тишинá.

stilt *n.* **1,** (tall pole) ходýля: *walk on stilts,* ходи́ть на ходýлях. **2,** (post; support) свáя. **3,** (wading bird) ходýлочник.

stilted *adj.* ходýльный: *stilted phrases,* ходýльные фрáзы.

stimulant *adj.* возбуждáющий. —*n.* возбуждáющее срéдство.

stimulate *v.t.* возбуждáть; поощря́ть; стимули́ровать. —**stimulation,** *n.* возбуждéние; поощрéние; стимули́рование.

stimulus *n.* сти́мул; побуждéние; толчóк.

sting *v.t.* **1,** (wound, as of a bee) жáлить. **2,** (cause severe pain to; burn) щипáть; жечь. **3,** *fig.* (hurt; distress) уязвля́ть. —*v.i.* **1,** (of a bee) жáлить. **2,** (hurt) жечь. —*n.* **1,** (wound caused by stinging) укýс. **2,** (stinger) жáло.

stinger *n.* (stinging organ) жáло.

stingily *adv.* скýпо.

stinginess *n.* скýпость.

stinging *adj.* язви́тельный: *stinging rebuke,* язви́тельный упрёк.

stingray *n.* морскóй кот.

stingy *adj.* скупóй. *Don't be (so) stingy!,* не скупи́тесь!

stink *v.i.* воня́ть; смердéть. —*v.t.* [*usu.* **stink up**] провоня́ть. —*n.* зловóние; вонь; смрад.

stinking *adj.* воню́чий; зловóнный; смрáдный.

stint *v.t. & i.* скупи́ться (на); урéзывать себя́ (в). *Not stint one's praise,* не скупи́ться на похвалы́. *He does not stint himself,* он не стесня́ет себя́ в срéдствах. *She stints herself in everything,* онá урéзывает себя́ во всём. —*n.* **1,** (limitation; restriction) ограничéние. **2,** (short period of service) срок.

stipend *n.* **1,** (salary) жáлованье. **2,** (scholarship) стипéндия.

stipple *v.t.* рисовáть *or* гравировáть пункти́ром.

stipulate *v.t.* обуслóвливать; оговáривать; предусмáтривать. —**stipulation,** *n.* услóвие; оговóрка.

stir *v.t.* **1,** (agitate) мешáть: *stir the coffee/fire,* мешáть кóфе/ýгли. **2,** (move slightly) шевели́ть: *the wind stirred the leaves,* вéтер шевели́л ли́стья. **3,** (arouse, as an emotion) возбуждáть; вызывáть. **4,** *fol. by* **up** (incite; foment) возбуждáть; разжигáть: *stir up the crowd,* возбуждáть толпý; *stir up hatred,* разжигáть нéнависть. *Stir up trouble,* мути́ть вóду. **5,** (affect strongly) волновáть. —*v.i.* двигаться; сдвига́ться; шевели́ться. —*n.* **1,** (act of stirring): *give the soup a stir,* помеша́ть суп. **2,** (movement) движе́ние. **3,** (excited reaction) резона́нс: *create quite a stir,* вы́звать широ́кий резона́нс.

stirring *adj.* волну́ющий.

stirrup *n.* стре́мя. —**stirrup cup,** проща́льный ку́бок.

stitch *n.* **1,** *sewing* стежо́к. **2,** *knitting* пе́тля. **3,** *surgery* шов. **4,** (sudden sharp pain) резь. *I have a stitch in my side,* у меня́ ко́лет в боку́. **5,** (article of clothing): *without a stitch of clothing,* в чём мать родила́. —*v.t.* **1,** *sewing* строчи́ть; простра́чивать. **2,** *surgery* накла́дывать швы на (ра́ну). —**be in stitches,** *colloq.* надрыва́ть животы́ (со́ смеху).

St.-John's-wort *n.* зверобо́й.

stock *n.* **1,** (supply of merchandise) инвента́рь; ассортиме́нт. *In stock,* в нали́чии. *Out of stock,* нет в прода́же; распро́дан. **2,** (reserve supply) запа́с. **3,** (corporate shares) а́кции; фо́нды. **4,** (lineage) род: *of good stock,* хоро́шего ро́да. **5,** (part of a firearm) ло́жа. **6,** (raw material) сырьё: *paper stock,* бума́жное сырьё. **7,** (broth from boiled meat) мясно́й отва́р. **8,** (livestock) скот. **9,** *Summer stock,* ле́тний теа́тр. **10,** *pl.* (instrument of punishment) коло́дки. —*adj.* **1,** (of the stock market) биржево́й. *Stock prices,* курс а́кций. **2,** (regularly on sale) основно́й. *Stock sizes,* станда́ртные разме́ры. **3,** (regularly used) шабло́нный: *stock phrases,* шабло́нные фра́зы. —*v.t.* **1,** (supply with merchandise) снабжа́ть (това́рами). *Well-stocked stores,* хорошо́ снабжа́емые магази́ны. **2,** (have on hand) держа́ть. **3,** *Stock a pond with fish,* запусти́ть ры́бу в пруд. —*v.i.* [*usu.* **stock up**] запаса́ться. *Stock up on food,* запаса́ться продово́льствием; запаса́ть продово́льствие. —**take stock, 1,** (take inventory) составля́ть инвента́рь. **2,** *fol. by* **of** (inventory) инвентаризова́ть; переучи́тывать. **3,** *fig.* (evaluate a situation) подводи́ть ито́ги.

stockade *n.* **1,** (fence) частоко́л. **2,** (fort) форт. **3,** (prison) гауптва́хта.

stockbroker *n.* (биржево́й) ма́клер.

stock car го́ночный автомоби́ль.

stock company 1, *comm.* акционе́рная компа́ния. **2,** *theat.* театра́льная тру́ппа.

stock exchange фо́ндовая би́ржа.

stockfish *n.* вя́леная ры́ба.

stockholder *n.* акционе́р.

stocking *n.* чуло́к. *In one's stocking feet,* в одни́х чулка́х.

stock market фо́ндовая би́ржа.

stockpile *n.* запа́с; резе́рв. —*v.t.* накопля́ть; запаса́ть.

stocky *adj.* призе́мистый; корена́стый.

stockyard *n.* ско́тный двор; скотоприго́нный двор.

stodgy *adj.* ску́чный; ну́дный.

stoic *n.* сто́ик. —**stoical,** *adj.* стои́ческий. —**stoically,** *adv.* стои́чески; сто́йко. —**stoicism,** *n.* стоици́зм.

stoke *v.t.* **1,** (stir, as a fire) расшевели́ть (у́гли). **2,** (tend, as a furnace) топи́ть.

stoker *n.* **1,** (person) кочега́р; истопни́к. **2,** (device) сто́кер.

stole *n.* паланти́н.

stolen *adj.* кра́деный.

stolid *adj.* бесстра́стный.

stomach *n.* **1,** (digestive organ) желу́док. *On an empty stomach,* натоща́к. **2,** (abdomen; belly) живо́т. —*v.t.* (tolerate) перева́ривать. —**stomach ache,** боль в животе́. *I have a stomach ache,* у меня́ боли́т живо́т. —**stomach pump,** желу́дочный зонд.

stomatology *n.* стоматоло́гия. —**stomatologist,** *n.* стомато́лог.

stomp *v.t.* & *i.* то́пать (нога́ми). *Stomp on,* топта́ть.

stone *n.* **1,** (substance) ка́мень: *pave with stone,* мости́ть ка́мнем. *Heart of stone,* ка́менное се́рдце. **2,** (small rock) ка́мень. *Precious stone,* драгоце́нный ка́мень. *Throw stones at,* заброса́ть (кого́-нибудь) камня́ми. **3,** (pit of fruits) ко́сточка. **4,** *med.* ка́мень: *kidney stone,* по́чечный ка́мень. —*adj.* ка́менный: *stone wall,* ка́менная стена́. —*v.t.* забива́ть камня́ми. —**leave no stone unturned,** сде́лать всё возмо́жное; пусти́ть в ход все сре́дства. —**not to leave a stone standing,** ка́мня на ка́мне не оста́вить. —**within a stone's throw,** в двух шага́х; руко́й пода́ть.

Stone Age ка́менный век.

stone-broke *adj.* без гроша́.

stonecutter *n.* камнере́з.

stone-deaf *adj.* соверше́нно глухо́й.

stonemason *n.* ка́менщик; каменотёс.

stonework *n.* ка́менная кла́дка.

stony *adj.* **1,** (of or like stone) ка́менный. **2,** (full of stones) камени́стый. **3,** *fig.* (unfeeling) ка́менный; окамене́лый. *Stony gaze,* ка́менный взгляд. **4,** *Stony silence,* гробово́е молча́ние.

stooge *n., colloq.* **1,** *theat.* посме́шище. **2,** (underling) приспе́шник.

stool *n.* **1,** (seat) табуре́тка; табуре́т. **2,** (excrement) стул. —**fall between two stools,** сиде́ть ме́жду двух сту́льев.

stool pigeon стука́ч.

stoop *v.i.* **1,** (bend the body) наклоня́ться; нагиба́ться. **2,** (slouch) суту́литься. **3,** *fol. by* **to** (lower or degrade oneself) унижа́ться до; снисходи́ть до. —*n.* **1,** (slouch) суту́лость. **2,** (front steps) крыльцо́. —**stooped,** *adj.* суту́лый.

stop *v.t.* **1,** (bring to a halt) остана́вливать: *stop a car/traffic/pain,* останови́ть маши́ну/у́личное движе́ние/боль. **2,** (terminate) прекраща́ть: *stop a war/payments/assistance,* прекрати́ть войну́/платежи́/по́мощь. *Stop that noise!,* прекрати́ э́тот шум! **3,** (cease) перестава́ть: *stop crying,* переста́ть пла́кать. **4,** (prevent) меша́ть; уде́рживать. *Stop someone from speaking,* меша́ть кому́-нибудь говори́ть. *Stop someone from committing suicide,* удержа́ть кого́-нибудь от самоуби́йства. **5,** *fol. by* **up** (block; plug) затыка́ть; заку́поривать. —*v.i.* **1,** (come to a halt) остана́вливаться. *My watch has stopped,* у меня́ часы́ ста́ли *or* останови́лись. **2,** (cease) прекраща́ться; перестава́ть. *The rain has stopped,* дождь ко́нчился/переста́л/прошёл/прекрати́лся. **3,** (stay, as at a hotel) остана́вливаться. —*n.* **1,** (halt; place to stop) остано́вка: *bus stop,* авто́бусная остано́вка. *Get off at the next stop,* сойти́ на сле́дующей остано́вке. **2,** *music* (of a fretted instrument) лад; (of an organ) реги́стр. —**pull out all the stops,** нажа́ть на все пружи́ны. —**put a stop to,** положи́ть коне́ц (+ *dat.*). —**stop at nothing,** ни пе́ред чем не остана́вливаться. —**stop by; stop in,** зайти́; загляну́ть. —**stop off,** останови́ться в пути́. —**stop short,** *see* **short.**

stopgap *n.* паллиати́в. —*adj.* паллиати́вный.

stoplight *n.* **1,** (traffic light) светофо́р. **2,** (brake light) стоп-сигна́л.
stopover *n.* остано́вка в пути́.
stoppage *n.* прекраще́ние: *work stoppage,* прекраще́ние рабо́ты.
stopper *n.* про́бка.
stopwatch *n.* секундоме́р.
storage *n.* хране́ние: *put in storage,* отдава́ть *or* сдава́ть на хране́ние. —**storage battery,** аккумуля́торная батаре́я.
store *n.* **1,** (shop) магази́н: *shoe/furniture store,* обувно́й/ме́бельный магази́н. **2,** (supply) запа́с: *stores of food,* запа́сы продово́льствия; *store of knowledge,* запа́с зна́ний. —*v.t.* **1,** *often fol. by* **up** (put aside for future use) запаса́ть; заготовля́ть (впрок). **2,** (put away for safekeeping) отдава́ть *or* сдава́ть на хране́ние. —**be in store,** предстоя́ть; ждать впереди́. *What is in store for him?,* что его́ ждёт? —**hold in store,** держа́ть про запа́с. *Who knows what the future holds in store?,* кто зна́ет, что ждёт нас впереди́? —**set store by,** придава́ть значе́ние (+ *dat.*).
storehouse *n.* **1,** (warehouse) склад. **2,** *fig.* (abundant source) сокро́вищница: *storehouse of knowledge,* сокро́вищница зна́ний.
storekeeper *n.* **1,** (shopkeeper) ла́вочник. **2,** (keeper of supplies) кладовщи́к.
storeroom *n.* кладова́я; чула́н.
storey *n.* = **story** *(in sense* #5).
storied *adj.* легенда́рный; басносло́вный.
stork *n.* а́ист.
storm *n.* **1,** (windstorm) бу́ря; (thunderstorm) гроза́. **2,** *naut.* шторм. **3,** *fig.* (outburst) бу́ря; взрыв. **4,** *mil.* штурм: *take by storm,* взять шту́рмом. —*v.i.* **1,** (rage) бушева́ть: *it is storming,* бушу́ет гроза́. **2,** (move with great force) проноси́ться. *Storm into the room,* ворва́ться в ко́мнату. —*v.t.* штурмова́ть: *storm the town,* штурмова́ть го́род. —**take by storm,** *fig.* захвати́ть; увле́чь; покори́ть.
storm cloud (грозова́я) ту́ча.
storm trooper штурмови́к.
storm windows двойны́е ра́мы; вставны́е ра́мы.
stormy *adj.* бу́рный.
story *n.* **1,** (short literary work) расска́з; по́весть. *Short story,* но́велла. *Detective story,* детекти́в. **2,** (something related; account) исто́рия; расска́з. *Tell someone a story,* рассказа́ть кому́-нибудь исто́рию. *The story of one's life,* исто́рия свое́й жи́зни. *Get ahead of one's story,* забега́ть вперёд в расска́зе. **3,** (news event) собы́тие; (report on same) сообще́ние. **4,** *colloq.* (lie) ска́зка: *don't tell me stories!,* ска́зки мне не расска́зывай! **5,** [*also,* **storey**] (floor of a building) эта́ж. —**a long story,** до́лгая пе́сня. —**to make a long story short,** коро́че говоря́. —**that's a different story,** э́то друго́е де́ло.
storyteller *n.* **1,** (narrator) расска́зчик. **2,** *colloq.* (fibber) вы́думщик.
stout *adj.* **1,** (corpulent) по́лный; ту́чный. **2,** (sturdy) кре́пкий; про́чный. *On his stout back,* на его́ кре́пкой спине́. **3,** (resolute) сто́йкий: *stout defense,* сто́йкая оборо́на. *Stout resistance,* упо́рное сопротивле́ние.
stouthearted *adj.* сто́йкий; отва́жный.
stove *n.* **1,** (coal or wood stove) печь. **2,** (electric or gas range) плита́.
stovepipe *n.* дымохо́д.
stow *v.t.* укла́дывать. —**stow away, 1,** (store) убира́ть; пря́тать. **2,** (hide aboard a ship) е́хать за́йцем.
stowaway *n.* безбиле́тный пассажи́р; "за́яц".
strabismus *n.* косогла́зие.
straddle *v.t.* сиде́ть верхо́м на.
strafe *v.t.* обстре́ливать.
straggle *v.i.* **1,** (move along separately) идти́ враздро́д. **2,** (fall behind) отстава́ть. **3,** (stray) отбива́ться. —**straggler,** *n.* отста́вший.
straight *adj.* **1,** (not crooked; not curly) прямо́й: *straight line,* пряма́я ли́ния; *straight hair,* прямы́е во́лосы. **2,** (properly arranged) в поря́дке. *Put things straight,* приводи́ть дела́ в поря́док. **3,** (direct and candid) прямо́й; открове́нный. **4,** (consecutive) подря́д: *five straight days,* пять дней подря́д. **5,** *colloq.* (undiluted) чи́стый: *straight alcohol,* чи́стый спирт. **6,** *in* **straight razor,** опа́сная бри́тва. —*adv.* пря́мо: *straight to the airport,* пря́мо в аэропо́рт. *Go straight home,* пойти́ домо́й пря́мо. *Stand up straight,* держа́ться пря́мо. *Is my hat on straight?,* у меня́ шля́па пра́вильно наде́та? —**get (something) straight,** вспо́мнить: *I can't get their names straight,* не могу́ вспо́мнить их имена́. *Get this straight!,* заруби́те э́то на носу́. —**set (someone) straight,** наставля́ть на путь и́стинный. —**straight ahead,** пря́мо. —**straight face,** бесстра́стное лицо́. *With a straight face,* не рассмея́вшись. —**straight away; straight off,** сра́зу.
straightedge *n.* лине́йка.
straighten *v.t.* **1,** (make straight) выпрямля́ть; распрямля́ть; расправля́ть. **2,** (adjust, as one's tie) поправля́ть. **3,** *fol. by* **up** (tidy up) убира́ть. **4,** *fol. by* **out** (set right) нала́живать. —*v.i.* **1,** *fol. by* **up** (stand up straight) выпрямля́ться; распрямля́ться; разгиба́ться. **2,** *fol. by* **out** (become straight) распрямля́ться. **3,** *fol. by* **out** (return to normal) нала́живаться; образова́ться.
straightforward *adj.* прямо́й; прямоду́шный. —**straightforwardness,** *n.* прямота́; прямоду́шие.
straightness *n.* прямизна́.
strain *v.t.* **1,** (exert to the utmost) напряга́ть: *strain every nerve,* напряга́ть все си́лы. **2,** (overtax) надрыва́ть. *Strain one's voice,* сорва́ть го́лос. *Strain one's eyes,* по́ртить себе́ глаза́; по́ртить зре́ние. **3,** (injure; sprain) растя́гивать. **4,** (filter) цеди́ть; проце́живать. —*v.i.* напряга́ться. *Strain at the leash,* рва́ться с привя́зи. —*n.* **1,** (tension; pressure) напряже́ние: *nervous strain,* не́рвное напряже́ние. *Withstand the strain,* выде́рживать напряже́ние. **2,** (sprain) растяже́ние. **3,** (species) поро́да: *a new strain of cattle,* но́вая поро́да скота́. **4,** *pl.* (sounds of music) зву́ки: *the strains of a waltz,* зву́ки ва́льса.
strained *adj.* **1,** (aggravated) натя́нутый; напряжённый. **2,** (passed through a strainer) проце́женный.
strainer *n.* си́то; решето́.
strait *n.* **1,** (channel) проли́в. **2,** *pl.* (difficulty) затрудни́тельное положе́ние; стеснённые обстоя́тельства.
straiten *v.t.* стесня́ть. *In straitened circumstances,* в стеснённых обстоя́тельствах.
strait jacket смири́тельная руба́шка.
strait-laced *adj.* чо́порный; пурита́нский.
strand *v.t.* **1,** (drive or run aground) посади́ть на мель. **2,** (leave in a helpless position) поки́нуть в

бедé. —*n.* **1,** (of hair, rope, etc.) прядь. **2,** (string, as of beads) нитка.

strange *adj.* **1,** (queer; odd) стрáнный: *strange man,* стрáнный человéк; *strange occurrence,* стрáнное явлéние. *It is strange,* стрáнно. *Strange as it seems,* как ни стрáнно. **2,** (unfamiliar) незнакóмый: *strange place,* незнакóмое мéсто. **3,** (foreign) чужóй: *in a strange country,* в чужóй странé. —**strangely,** *adv.* стрáнно. —**strangeness,** *n.* стрáнность.

stranger *n.* **1,** (person not known) незнакóмец. **2,** (outsider) посторóнний. **3,** (newcomer) приéзжий.

strangle *v.t.* души́ть; удави́ть. —*v.i.* задыхáться.

stranglehold *n. Have a stranglehold on,* держáть в тискáх.

strangulation *n.* **1,** (strangling) удавлéние. **2,** *med.* ущемлéние.

strap *n.* **1,** (general term) ремéнь. **2,** (of an undergarment) бретéль(ка). —*v.t.* свя́зывать *or* скрепля́ть ремнём.

strapped *adj., colloq.* стеснённый в деньгáх.

strapping *adj.* рóслый; дю́жий.

stratagem *n.* воéнная хи́трость; улóвка.

strategy *n.* стратéгия. —**strategic,** *adj.* стратеги́ческий. —**strategist,** *n.* стратéг.

stratification *n.* **1,** *geol.* наслоéние; напластовáние; стратификáция. **2,** *fig.* (division into strata) расслоéние: *stratification of society,* расслоéние óбщества.

stratified *adj.* слои́стый. *Stratified society,* расслоёное óбщество.

stratify *v.t.* расслáивать.

stratosphere *n.* стратосфéра.

stratum *n.* **1,** (layer) слой; пласт; прослóйка. **2,** *fig.* (class; division) слой; прослóйка.

stratus *n.* слои́стое óблако.

straw *n.* **1,** (stalk of grain) солóма. **2,** (sipping tube) солóминка. —*adj.* солóменный: *straw hat,* солóменная шля́па. —**grasp at a straw,** хватáться за солóминку. —**the last straw,** послéдняя кáпля; предéл терпéния.

strawberry *n.* (wild) земляни́ка; (cultivated) клубни́ка. —*adj.* земляни́чный; клубни́чный.

stray *v.i.* **1,** (wander off) отбивáться: *stray from the flock,* отбивáться от стáда. **2,** (deviate) отклоня́ться; уклоня́ться: *stray off course,* отклоня́ться/уклоня́ться от кýрса. —*adj.* **1,** (lost) заблуди́вшийся; бездóмный. *Stray dog,* бродя́чая *or* бездóмная собáка. **2,** (random; chance) случáйный. *Stray bullet,* шальнáя пýля.

streak *n.* **1,** (thin line, as in marble) прожи́лка. **2,** (mark; smear) потёк; подтёк; *pl.* развóды. **3,** (trace of a certain characteristic) жи́лка. *Person with a lazy streak,* человéк с ленцóй. **4,** (spell; run) полосá. **5,** *sports* шéствие: *winning streak,* побéдное шéствие. —*v.t., usu. passive: hair streaked with gray,* вóлосы с прóседью. *The wallpaper is all streaked,* обóи все в потёках. —*v.i.* **1,** (form streaks) растекáться. **2,** (dash; flash) проноси́ться; промелькнýть. —**talk a blue streak,** *colloq.* говори́ть без ýмолку.

stream *n.* **1,** (small river) ручéй. **2,** (current) течéние. **3,** (steady flow) потóк. —*v.i.* **1,** (flow rapidly) течь; ли́ться; хлы́нуть; струи́ться. *Tears were streaming down her cheeks,* слёзы кати́лись у неё по щекáм. **2,** (move in large numbers) вали́ть.

streamer *n.* серпанти́н.

streamline *v.t.* **1,** (shape so as to offer little wind resistance) придавáть (+ *dat.*) обтекáемую фóрму. **2,** (modernize) рационализи́ровать. —**streamlined,** *adj.* обтекáемый.

street *n.* ýлица. *Gorky Street,* ýлица Гóрького. —*adj.* ýличный: *street scene,* ýличная сцéна. —**man in the street,** рядовóй человéк; "человéк с ýлицы".

streetcar *n.* трамвáй.

street lamp ýличный фонáрь. *Also,* **street light.**

streetwalker *n.* ýличная дéвка/деви́ца/жéнщина.

strength *n.* **1,** (force; power) си́ла: *physical strength,* физи́ческая си́ла. **2,** (durability) прóчность: *tensile strength,* прóчность на разры́в. **3,** (potency) крéпость. **4,** (complement of personnel) чи́сленность. *At full strength,* в пóлном состáве. —**on the strength of,** в си́лу (+ *gen.*); на основáнии (+ *gen.*).

strengthen *v.t.* уси́ливать; укрепля́ть.

strenuous *adj.* **1,** (requiring great exertion) напряжённый. **2,** (emphatic) реши́тельный: *strenuous objection,* реши́тельное возражéние.

streptococcus *n.* стрептокóкк.

streptomycin *n.* стрептомици́н.

stress *n.* **1,** (physical pressure exerted) напряжéние. **2,** (mental strain) стресс: *be under great stress,* быть под больши́м стрéссом. **3,** (accent) ударéние: *the stress is on the first syllable,* ударéние пáдает на пéрвый слог. **4,** (emphasis) ударéние. *Lay stress on,* дéлать ударéние/акцéнт/упóр на. —*v.t.* **1,** (emphasize) подчёркивать. **2,** (pronounce with emphasis) дéлать ударéние на. *Stressed syllable,* удáрный слог.

stretch *v.t.* **1,** (expand; extend) растя́гивать; вытя́гивать. *Stretch one's legs,* размин́ать нóги. *Stretch a canvas over a frame,* натя́гивать холст на рáмку. *Stretch a rope across the yard,* протя́гивать верёвку чéрез двор. *Have one's shoes stretched,* отдáть тýфли на растя́жку. **2,** *fol. by* **out** (put forth; hold out) протя́гивать. **3,** *in* **stretch one's luck,** искушáть судьбý; **stretch a point,** допусти́ть натя́жку. —*v.i.* **1,** (be capable of being stretched) тянýться; растя́гиваться. **2,** (take a stretch) потя́гиваться. **3,** *fol. by* **out** (lie flat) растя́гиваться; вытя́гиваться. **4,** (extend) тянýться; простирáться. *Stretch for many miles,* тянýться на мнóго миль. —*n.* **1,** (act of stretching): *take a stretch,* потя́гиваться. **2,** (expanse) отрéзок: *stretch of land,* отрéзок земли́. **3,** (interval of time) срок: *three-month stretch,* трёхмéсячный срок. —*adj.* эласти́чный; безразмéрный: *stretch socks,* эласти́чные/безразмéрные носки́. —**at a stretch,** подря́д; за оди́н присéст.

stretchable *adj.* растяжи́мый; тягýчий. —**stretchability,** *n.* растяжи́мость; тягýчесть.

stretcher *n.* носи́лки: *carry on a stretcher,* нести́ (когó-нибудь) на носи́лках. —**stretcher-bearer,** *n.* санитáр; санитáр-носи́льщик.

strew *v.t.* **1,** (scatter) разбрáсывать; рассыпáть. *Papers were strewn all over the floor,* бумáги бы́ли разбрóсаны по всемý пóлу. **2,** (cover with scattered things) засыпáть; усыпáть.

stricken *adj.* поражённый; пострадáвший. ♦*Often as a combining form: grief-stricken,* уби́тый гóрем; *poverty-stricken,* обеднéвший; обнищáлый.

strict *adj.* стрóгий: *strict teacher/diet,* стрóгая учи́тельница/диéта; *strict rules,* стрóгие прáвила. *In strict confidence,* под больши́м секрéтом.

strictly *adv.* стрóго: *strictly forbidden,* стрóго запрещáется. —**strictly speaking,** стрóго говоря́; сóбственно говоря́.

strictness *n.* стрóгость.

stricture *n.* стрóгая крúтика; осуждéние.

stride *v.i.* шагáть. —*n.* **1,** (long step) большóй шаг. **2,** *pl.* (progress) успéхи: *make great strides,* дéлать большúе успéхи; далекó шагнýть вперёд.

strident *adj.* рéзкий. *Strident criticism,* рéзкая крúтика.

strife *n.* рáспря; раздóр.

strike *v.t.* **1,** (deal a blow to; hit) ударя́ть: *strike someone in the face,* удáрить когó-нибудь по лицý *or* в лицó. **2,** (deliver, as a blow) наносúть (удáр). **3,** (bang; knock) ударя́ться: *strike one's head on the door,* удáриться головóй о дверь. **4,** (make impact against) удáриться о; попáсть в (+ *acc.*). *The boat struck a rock,* лóдка удáрилась о скалý. *The bullet struck him in the shoulder,* пýля попáла емý в плечó. *Two bullets struck the general,* две пýли попáли в генерáла. *He was struck by a car,* егó сбил автомобúль. *A hurricane struck the island,* ургáн обрýшился на óстров. **5,** (cause to ignite, as a match) чúркнуть (спúчкой). **6,** (mint, as a coin or medal) чекáнить. **7,** (announce by striking) бить; пробúть; ударя́ть. *The clock struck ten,* часы́ пробúли дéсять часóв. **8,** (discover) находúть: *strike oil,* найтú нефть. **9,** (attack; afflict) поражáть. *Strike dead,* сражáть нáсмерть. *Be struck dumb,* онемéть. *The disease strikes mainly young people,* болéзнь поражáет в основнóм молодёжь. **10,** (impress; appear to; seem to) казáться: *he strikes me as an honest man,* он мне кáжется чéстным человéком. *How does this strike you?,* как вам э́то нрáвится? **11,** (impress strongly) поражáть; бросáться в глазá (+ *dat.*). **12,** (implant, as an emotion) нагоня́ть: *strike fear into the heart of,* нагоня́ть страх на. **13,** (occur to; come to mind) приходúть (+ *dat.*) в гóлову; осенúть; озаря́ть. **14,** *often fol. by* **off** *or* **from** (delete; drop) исключáть; вычёркивать. **15,** (assume, as a pose or attitude) стать (в пóзу). **16,** (sound, as a note) взять (нóту). **17,** (conclude, as an agreement) заключáть. *Strike a bargain,* пойтú на сдéлку; удáрить по рукáм. **18,** (achieve, as a balance) подводúть (балáнс). —*v.i.* **1,** (deliver a blow) наносúть удáр. *Strike while the iron is hot,* куй железó, покá горячó. **2,** (attack) ударя́ть. *The enemy struck at dawn,* враг удáрил на рассвéте. **3,** (refuse to work) бастовáть. —*n.* **1,** (attack) удáр: *air strike,* удáр с вóздуха. **2,** (work stoppage) забастóвка: *go (out) on strike,* объявúть забастóвку. —*adj.* забастóвочный: *strike fund,* забастóвочный фонд. —**strike down, 1,** (knock down; afflict) сражáть. **2,** (overrule; annul) отменя́ть. —**strike home,** *see* **home.** —**strike it rich,** напáсть на золотýю жúлу. —**strike off,** вычёркивать (из спúска). —**strike out, 1,** (cross out) зачёркивать. **2,** (fail) потерпéть неудáчу. —**strike up, 1,** (initiate, as a conversation) завя́зывать; заводúть. **2,** (begin to play) заигрáть.

strikebreaker *n.* штрейкбрéхер.

striker *n.* забастóвщик; бастýющий.

striking *adj.* **1,** (remarkable) поразúтельный. **2,** (refusing to work) бастýющий. —**within striking distance,** в предéлах досягáемости.

strikingly *adv.* поразúтельно.

string *n.* **1,** (cord) верёвка; бечёвка. **2,** (on clothes) завя́зка: *apron string,* завя́зка пéредника. **3,** (of pearls, beads, etc.) нúтка. **4,** (of a musical instrument) струнá. **5,** *pl.* (musical instruments) стрýнные инструмéнты. **6,** (of a tennis racket) струнá. **7,** (bowstring) тетивá. **8,** (succession; series) ряд. **9,** *sports* состáв: *first string,* пéрвый состáв. **10,** *pl.* (limiting condition) услóвия: *with no strings attached,* без какúх-либо услóвий. —*adj.* стрýнный: *string quartet,* стрýнный квартéт. —*v.t.* **1,** (provide with strings) снабжáть стрýнами. **2,** (arrange on a string) нанúзывать. **3,** (extend; stretch) протя́гивать: *string a rope across the yard,* протя́гивать верёвку чéрез двор. **4,** *fol. by* **up,** *colloq.* (hang) вéшать; вздёргивать. —**pull strings,** нажимáть на тáйные пружúны. —**string (someone) along,** водúть зá нос.

string bean стручкóвая фасóль; фасóль в стручкáх.

stringed instrument стрýнный инструмéнт.

stringent *adj.* стрóгий. —**stringency,** *n.* стрóгость.

stringy *adj.* волокнúстый; жúлистый.

strip *n.* **1,** (undress) раздевáть. **2,** *fol. by* **off** (take off; remove) снимáть; срывáть (с себя́). **3,** (tear off) сдирáть: *strip the bark from a tree,* сдирáть корý с дéрева. **4,** (deprive; divest) лишáть. **5,** (dismantle) разбирáть. —*v.i.* раздевáться; обнажáться. —*n.* **1,** (long narrow piece or area) полосá; полóска. **2,** (airstrip) (взлётно-посáдочная) полосá.

stripe *n.* **1,** (band of different color) полосá. **2,** (insignia) нашúвка. **3,** (kind; ilk) род; тип. *Of every stripe,* всех мастéй. —**striped,** *adj.* полосáтый; в полóску.

stripling *n.* ю́ноша; подрóсток.

strip mining открúтая добы́ча угля́.

striptease *n.* стриптúз.

strive *v.i.* стремúться: *strive for success,* стремúться к успéху. *Strive to become independent,* стремúться стать самостоя́тельным.

stroboscope *n.* стробоскóп.

stroke *n.* **1,** (single movement) удáр; взмах; мах: *with one stroke,* однúм удáром/взмáхом/мáхом. *Deft stroke,* лóвкий удáр. **2,** (of a brush in painting) штрих. *With a stroke of the pen,* однúм рóсчерком перá. **3,** (of an oar) гребóк; взмах веслá. **4,** *swimming* стиль. **5,** (gentle caress) лáска. **6,** *mech.* ход: *stroke of a piston,* ход пóршня. **7,** (sounding of a bell or chime) удáр. *At the stroke of ten,* рóвно в дéсять часóв. **8,** *med.* удáр; инсýльт. **9,** *in* **stroke of luck,** удáча; **stroke of bad luck,** удáр судьбы́. **10,** (effective or inspired action) ход; приём. *Master stroke,* мастерскóй удáр. *Stroke of genius,* гениáльная идéя. —*v.t.* глáдить: *stroke one's beard,* глáдить бóроду.

stroll *v.i.* прогýливаться. —*n.* прогýлка. *Go for a stroll,* идтú гуля́ть; погуля́ть.

strong *adj.* **1,** (powerful; intense; forceful) сúльный: *strong swimmer,* сúльный пловéц; *strong medicine,* сúльное лекáрство. *Strong language,* сúльные выражéния. *Strong measures,* жёсткие *or* круты́е мéры. **2,** (capable of enduring stress) крéпкий; прóчный. *Strong rope,* крéпкая верёвка. **3,** (concentrated, as of coffee) крéпкий. **4,** (deeply held) твёрдый; глубóкий: *strong beliefs,* твёрдые/глубóкие убеждéния. **5,** (clearly noticeable) сúльный: *a strong accent,* сúльный акцéнт. *Strong resemblance,* большóе схóдство. **6,** (numbering): *one hundred strong,* числéнностью в сто человéк; в колúчестве ста человéк.

strongbox *n.* несгора́емый я́щик.
stronghold *n.* кре́пость; тверды́ня.
strongly *adv.* реши́тельно: *strongly condemn,* реши́тельно осужда́ть. *Be strongly opposed to,* быть реши́тельно про́тив. *He feels very strongly about it,* он твёрдо убеждён в э́том.
strong point *n.* **1,** *mil.* опо́рный пункт. **2,** *fig.* (asset) си́льная сторона́.
strong-willed *adj.* волево́й; своево́льный.
strontium *n.* стро́нций.
strop *n.* точи́льный реме́нь.
structural *adj.* структу́рный. *Structural changes,* измене́ния в констру́кции. —**structural engineer,** инжене́р-строи́тель. —**structural linguistics,** структу́рная лингви́стика. —**structural steel,** строи́тельная сталь.
structure *n.* **1,** (arrangement of parts) структу́ра; строе́ние; устро́йство. **2,** (something built) строе́ние; сооруже́ние.
struggle *n.* борьба́: *the struggle for survival,* борьба́ за существова́ние. —*v.i.* боро́ться: *struggle with an assailant,* боро́ться с налётчиком. *Struggle to one's feet,* с трудо́м подня́ться на́ ноги. *Struggle to break loose,* вырыва́ться.
strum *v.t. & i.* тре́нькать; бренча́ть.
strumpet *n.* потаску́ха.
strut *v.i.* выступа́ть; ходи́ть го́голем. —*n.* **1,** (swagger) ва́жная похо́дка. **2,** (brace) сто́йка; подко́с.
strychnine *n.* стрихни́н.
stub *n.* **1,** (fragment; end) огры́зок; *(of a cigar)* оку́рок. **2,** (counterfoil) корешо́к. —*v.t.* расшиба́ть: *stub one's toe,* расшиби́ть па́лец ноги́.
stubble *n.* **1,** (stubs of grain) жнивьё; стерня́. **2,** (rough growth, as of beard) щети́на.
stubborn *adj.* **1,** (obstinate) упря́мый: *stubborn as a mule,* упря́мый как осёл. **2,** (persistent) упо́рный: *stubborn cough,* упо́рный ка́шель; *stubborn resistance,* упо́рное сопротивле́ние.
stubbornness *n.* **1,** (obstinacy) упря́мство. **2,** (persistence) упо́рство.
stubby *adj.* **1,** (short and thickset) то́лстый. **2,** (bristly, as of a beard) щети́нистый.
stucco *n.* штукату́рка. —*adj.* штукату́рный. —*v.t.* штукату́рить.
stuck *adj.* **1,** (mired): *get stuck in the mud,* застря́ть *or* завя́знуть в грязи́. **2,** (jammed): *the door is stuck,* дверь зае́ло. **3,** *colloq.* (stumped) в тупике́.
stud *n.* **1,** (shirt front ornament) за́понка. **2,** (projecting pin or spike) штифт. **3,** (breeding) разво́д; заво́д. *Purchase for stud,* купи́ть на разво́д. —*v.t.* усыпа́ть; усе́ивать; уни́зывать. *Studded with diamonds,* усы́пан алма́зами.
student *n.* **1,** (pupil) учени́к; уча́щийся. **2,** (university student) студе́нт. —*adj.* студе́нческий: *student unrest,* студе́нческие волне́ния.
stud farm ко́нный заво́д; конево́дческая фе́рма.
stud horse заво́дская ло́шадь; жеребе́ц-производи́тель.
studied *adj.* **1,** (not natural; affected) зау́ченный. **2,** (carefully considered) обду́манный.
studio *n.* **1,** (workroom) сту́дия; мастерска́я; ателье́. **2,** *motion pictures* киносту́дия; павильо́н. **3,** (for broadcasting) сту́дия; радиосту́дия; телесту́дия.
studious *adj.* приле́жный; стара́тельный. —**studiously,** *adv.* стара́тельно: *studiously avoid,* стара́тельно избега́ть.
study *n.* **1,** (studying) изуче́ние: *the study of history,* изуче́ние исто́рии. *Make a study of,* тща́тельно изуча́ть. **2,** *pl.* (academic pursuits) заня́тия; уче́ние; учёба. *Continue one's studies,* продолжа́ть учёбу. **3,** (a work on a particular subject) иссле́дование. **4,** (deep thought) разду́мье. **5,** (room reserved for study) кабине́т. —*v.t.* **1,** (take a course in) изуча́ть; учи́ться (+ *dat.*): *study Russian,* изуча́ть ру́сский язы́к; учи́ться ру́сскому языку́. *Study music/drawing,* учи́ться му́зыке/рисова́нию. **2,** (make a study of) изуча́ть: *study a problem,* изуча́ть пробле́му. *Study the origin/behavior of,* изуча́ть происхожде́ние/поведе́ние (+ *gen.*). —*v.i.* **1,** (take courses) учи́ться: *he is studying to be a doctor,* он у́чится что́бы быть врачо́м; он у́чится на врача́. **2,** (do one's lessons) занима́ться. **3,** *fol. by* **for** (prepare for) гото́виться (к).
stuff *n.* **1,** (material) материа́л. **2,** *colloq.* (things; effects) ве́щи. **3,** (basic elements; character) заква́ска. *He is made of different stuff,* он из друго́го те́ста. **4,** (anything eaten or drunk): *sweet stuff,* сла́сти. *I don't touch the stuff,* ка́пли в рот не беру́. **5,** (rubbish; junk) хлам; дрянь. **6,** (nonsense) дрянь. **7,** *in* **kid stuff,** пустяко́вое де́ло; **rough stuff,** чуда́чества. **8,** *in* **know/do one's stuff,** *colloq.* знать/де́лать своё де́ло. —*v.t.* **1,** (fill; pack) набива́ть: *stuff one's briefcase with papers,* набива́ть портфе́ль бума́гами. **2,** (cram in) вти́скивать; запи́хивать: *stuff one's things in a suitcase,* вти́скивать/запи́хивать ве́щи в чемода́н. **3,** (thrust in) засо́вывать. **4,** *cookery* начиня́ть; фарширова́ть. **5,** (glut with food) зака́рмливать; корми́ть как на убо́й. *I'm stuffed,* я сыт по го́рло. *Stuff oneself,* объеда́ться. **6,** (plug; block) затыка́ть. *My nose is stuffed up,* мне заложи́ло нос.
stuffed *adj.* фарширо́ванный: *stuffed peppers,* фарширо́ванный пе́рец. *Stuffed animal,* чу́чело.
stuffiness *n.* духота́.
stuffing *n.* **1,** (act of stuffing) наби́вка. **2,** (material for stuffing) ва́та; наби́вка. **3,** *cookery* начи́нка; фарш.
stuffy *adj.* ду́шный; спёртый.
stultify *v.t.* ско́вывать; стесня́ть.
stumble *v.i.* **1,** (trip) спотыка́ться; оступа́ться. **2,** (stagger) шата́ться; пошатну́ться. **3,** (falter in speech) запина́ться. **4,** *fol. by* **on, upon,** *or* **across** (chance to meet) ната́лкиваться на; натыка́ться на; набрести́ на.
stumbling block ка́мень преткнове́ния.
stump *n.* **1,** (tree trunk) пень. **2,** (remaining part; stub) обру́бок; *(of an amputated limb)* культя́. —*v.t.* (baffle) ста́вить в тупи́к.
stun *v.t.* ошеломля́ть; оглуша́ть; потряса́ть.
stunning *adj.* **1,** (staggering, as of a blow) сокруши́тельный. **2,** (shocking, as of news) ошеломля́ющий; сногсшиба́тельный. **3,** *colloq.* (gorgeous) великоле́пный.
stunt *n.* трюк: *acrobatic stunt,* акробати́ческий трюк. —*v.t.* остана́вливать: *stunt the growth of,* остана́вливать рост (+ *gen.*).
stupefaction *n.* отупе́ние; оцепене́ние; остолбене́ние.
stupefy *v.t.* **1,** (dull the senses of) дурма́нить. **2,** (astound) ошеломля́ть.

stupendous *adj.* колоссáльный; потрясáющий.

stupid *adj.* глýпый. —**stupidity,** *n.* глýпость. —**stupidly,** *adv.* глýпо.

stupor *n.* отупéние; оцепенéние; остолбенéние; стýпор. *In a stupor,* в состоя́нии отупéния/оцепенéния.

sturdy *adj.* **1,** (strong; stout) крéпкий: *of sturdy build,* крéпкого сложéния. **2,** (firm; steady) прóчный: *sturdy table/foundation,* прóчный стол/фундáмент.

sturgeon *n.* **1,** (fish) осётр. *White sturgeon,* белýга. **2,** (food) осетри́на.

stutter *v.i.* заикáться. —*n.* заикáние. —**stutterer,** *n.* заи́ка.

sty *n.* **1,** (pigpen) свинáрник. **2,** (inflammation of the eyelid) ячмéнь.

style *n.* **1,** (fashion) мóда; фасóн. *Be in style,* быть в мóде. *The latest style,* послéдняя мóда. **2,** (manner of expression or design) стиль: *writing style,* стиль письмá. *Lofty style,* возвы́шенный стиль. *Byzantine style,* византи́йский стиль. **3,** (way of doing things) стиль: *that's not my style,* э́то не в моём сти́ле. **4,** (way of reckoning dates) стиль: *Old/New Style,* по стáрому/нóвому сти́лю. **5,** (elegance; grace) шик: *do something with style,* дéлать чтó-нибудь с ши́ком. *Live in style,* жить на ширóкую нóгу. **6,** *bot.* стóлбик. —*v.t.* модели́ровать. *style dresses,* модели́ровать плáтья.

stylish *adj.* мóдный. —**stylishly,** *adv.* мóдно.

stylist *n.* **1,** (master of literary style) стили́ст. **2,** (designer) модельéр. **3,** *Hair stylist,* парикмáхер.

stylistic *adj.* стилисти́ческий. —**stylistics,** *n.* стили́стика.

stylize *v.t.* стилизовáть. —**stylization,** *n.* стилизáция.

stylus *n.* гравировáльная иглá.

stymie *v.t.* срывáть. *Be stymied,* зайти́ в тупи́к.

styptic *adj.* кровоостанáвливающий.

styrene *n.* стирóл.

suave *adj.* обходи́тельный. —**suavity,** *n.* обходи́тельность.

subclass *n.* подклáсс.

subcommittee *n.* подкоми́ссия; подкомитéт.

subconscious *adj.* подсознáтельный. —*n., preceded by* **the** подсознáние.

subcontinent *n.* субконтинéнт.

subcontract *n.* субподря́д. —**subcontractor,** *n.* субподря́дчик.

subdivide *v.t.* подразделя́ть. —*v.i.* подразделя́ться. —**subdivision,** *n.* подразделéние.

subdue *v.t.* покоря́ть; подчиня́ть.

subdued *adj.* **1,** (less noisy or aggressive) подáвленный. **2,** (less bright) мя́гкий; нея́ркий.

subgroup *n.* подгрýппа.

subheading *n.* подзаголóвок. *Also,* **subhead.**

subject *n.* **1,** (topic) тéма; предмéт. *Change the subject,* перемени́ть разговóр. **2,** (academic course) предмéт. **3,** (recipient of treatment, examination, etc.) субъéкт. **4,** (one who owes allegiance) пóдданный: *British subject,* британский пóдданный. **5,** *gram.* подлежáщее. —*adj.* **1,** (under the power of another) подчинённый. **2,** *fol. by* **to** (open to) подлежáщий (+ *dat.*); подвéрженный (+ *dat.*). *Be subject to arrest,* подлежáть арéсту. *The treaty is subject to revision,* договóр подлежи́т пересмóтру. **3,** *fol. by* **to** (prone to) подвéрженный (+ *dat.*); предрасполóженный (+ *dat.*). *He is subject to nervous fits,* он подвéржен нéрвным припáдкам. **4,** *fol. by* **to** (contingent on) зави́сящий (от). *All this is subject to the chief's approval,* всё э́то зави́сит от одобрéния начáльника. —*v.t.* **1,** (expose) подвергáть. *He was subjected to harsh criticism,* он подвéргся рéзкой кри́тике. **2,** (subjugate) подчиня́ть; покоря́ть. —**subject matter,** содержáние; сюжéт.

subjection *n.* подчинéние.

subjective *adj.* субъекти́вный. —**subjectivism,** *n.* субъективи́зм. —**subjectivity,** *n.* субъекти́вность.

subjugate *v.t.* покоря́ть; подчиня́ть. —**subjugation,** *n.* покорéние; подчинéние.

subjunctive *adj.* сослагáтельный. —*n.* сослагáтельное наклонéние.

sublease *n.* субарéнда. —*v.t.* [*also,* **sublet**] передавáть.

sublimate *v.t., chem.* возгоня́ть; сублими́ровать. —*n.* сублимáт. —**corrosive sublimate,** сулемá.

sublimation *n.* возгóнка; сублимáция.

sublime *adj.* вели́чественный; возвы́шенный. —**from the sublime to the ridiculous,** от вели́кого до смешнóго.

submachine gun пистолéт-пулемёт; автомáт.

submarine *n.* подвóдная лóдка. —*adj.* подвóдный. *submarine warfare,* подвóдная война.

submerge *v.t.* погружáть (в вóду). —*v.i.* погружáться (в вóду).

submersion *n.* погружéние (в вóду).

submission *n.* **1,** (presentation) представлéние; подáча: *submission of evidence,* представлéние доказáтельств; *submission of an application,* подáча заявлéния. **2,** (yielding) подчинéние. *Starve into submission,* взять измóром.

submissive *adj.* покóрный. —**submissiveness,** *n.* покóрность.

submit *v.t.* **1,** (present for consideration) представля́ть; выдвигáть; вноси́ть; подавáть. *Submit a list of names,* представля́ть спи́сок имён. *Submit a proposal,* вноси́ть *or* выдвигáть предложéние. *Submit an application,* подавáть заявлéние. **2,** (contend) утверждáть: *I submit that...,* смéю утверждáть, что... —*v.i.* уступáть; подчиня́ться; покоря́ться. *Submit to someone's demands,* уступáть чьим-нибудь трéбованиям.

subnormal *adj.* **1,** (below normal) ни́же нормáльного. **2,** (of low intelligence) слабоýмный.

subordinate *adj.* **1,** (lower-ranking) подчинённый. *Be subordinate to,* быть в подчинéнии у. **2,** *gram.* придáточный: *subordinate clause,* придáточное предложéние. —*n.* подчинённый. —*v.t.* подчиня́ть.

subordination *n.* подчинённость; подчинéние.

suborn *v.t.* подкупáть.

subpoena *n.* повéстка в суд. —*v.t.* вызывáть в суд.

subscribe *v.i.* [*usu.* **subscribe to**] **1,** (take out a subscription to) подпи́сываться на. **2,** (receive regularly by subscription) выпи́сывать. **3,** (endorse; support) присоединя́ться к.

subscriber *n.* подпи́счик.

subscription *n.* (to a magazine or newspaper) подпи́ска; (to a series of cultural events) абонемéнт.

subsequent *adj.* послéдующий; дальнéйший. —**subsequently,** *adv.* впослéдствии.

subservience *n.* подчинéние. *Position of subservience,* подчинённое положéние.

subservient *adj.* **1,** (subordinate) подчинённый. **2,** (servile) раболе́пный.
subside *v.i.* **1,** (abate; wane) утиха́ть; затиха́ть; стиха́ть; уле́чься. **2,** (ease, as of pain) стиха́ть; смягча́ться; успока́иваться. **3,** (go down, as of fever or swelling) спада́ть. **4,** (recede, as of floodwaters) спада́ть; убыва́ть; идти́ на у́быль.
subsidiary *adj.* вспомога́тельный; подсо́бный. —*n.* доче́рняя компа́ния; филиа́л.
subsidize *v.t.* субсиди́ровать.
subsidy *n.* субси́дия; дота́ция.
subsist *v.i.* **1,** (continue to exist) просуществова́ть. **2,** *fol. by* **on** (sustain oneself) пита́ться (+ *instr.*); корми́ться (+ *instr.*).
subsistence *n.* существова́ние; пропита́ние. *Means of subsistence,* сре́дства к существова́нию; сре́дства пропита́ния.
subsoil *n.* подпо́чва; матери́к.
subsonic *adj.* дозвуково́й.
subspecies *n.* подви́д.
substance *n.* **1,** (material) вещество́: *a hard substance,* твёрдое вещество́. **2,** (essence; gist) су́щность; существо́; суть. *In substance,* в су́щности. **3,** (wealth): *a man of substance,* состоя́тельный челове́к. **4,** (density; body) твёрдость; пло́тность. **5,** *fig.* (solid quality) содержа́ние: *lacking substance,* бе́ден содержа́нием. *A report lacking in substance,* бессодержа́тельный докла́д. **6,** *philos.* субста́нция.
substandard *adj.* ни́зкого ка́чества; ни́же устано́вленного станда́рта.
substantial *adj.* **1,** (firm; solid) соли́дный: *a substantial building,* соли́дное зда́ние. *A substantial breakfast,* пло́тный за́втрак. **2,** (considerable; significant) суще́ственный; значи́тельный: *substantial improvement,* суще́ственное/значи́тельное улучше́ние. *A substantial difference,* суще́ственная ра́зница. *Substantial income,* соли́дный дохо́д. **3,** (in essentials) основно́й. *We are in substantial agreement,* в основно́м мы схо́димся во взгля́дах; в основно́м мы договори́лись. —**substantially,** *adv.* суще́ственно; значи́тельно.
substantiate *v.t.* обосно́вывать. —**substantiation,** *n.* обоснова́ние.
substantative *adj.* суще́ственный. —*n., gram.* и́мя существи́тельное.
substation *n.* подста́нция.
substitute *n.* **1,** (replacement) заме́на; замести́тель. **2,** *sports* запасно́й (игро́к). **3,** (synthetic product) замени́тель; суррога́т. —*adj.* **1,** (of a product) суррога́тный. **2,** (of a person): *substitute teacher,* замести́тель. —*v.t.* подставля́ть: *substitute one word for another,* подставля́ть одно́ сло́во вме́сто друго́го. —*v.i.* [*usu.* **substitute for**] заменя́ть; замеща́ть.
substitution *n.* **1,** (act of substituting) заме́на; замеще́ние. **2,** *math.* подстано́вка.
substratum *n.* субстра́т.
subsume *v.t.* подводи́ть: *subsume under a certain category,* подводи́ть под катего́рию.
subterfuge *n.* увёртка; уло́вка.
subterranean *adj.* подзе́мный.
subtitle *n.* **1,** (secondary title) подзаголо́вок. **2,** *motion pictures* субти́тр.
subtle *adj.* то́нкий: *subtle hint,* то́нкий намёк; *subtle distinction,* то́нкое разли́чие. —**subtlety,** *n.* то́нкость. —**subtly,** *adv.* то́нко.
subtotal *n.* ча́стный ито́г.
subtract *v.t. & i.* вычита́ть. —**subtraction,** *n.* вычита́ние.
subtrahend *n.* вычита́емое.
subtropics *n. pl.* субтро́пики. —**subtropical,** *adj.* субтропи́ческий.
subunit *n., mil.* подразделе́ние.
suburb *n.* при́город; предме́стье; *pl.* при́городы; предме́стья; окре́стности. —**suburban,** *adj.* при́городный; да́чный. —**suburbanite,** *n.* жи́тель при́города.
subversion *n.* **1,** (subversive activities) подрывна́я де́ятельность. **2,** (overthrow) сверже́ние; ниспроверже́ние. —**subversive,** *adj.* подрывно́й.
subvert *v.t.* **1,** (destroy; overthrow) сверга́ть; ниспроверга́ть. **2,** (corrupt) развраща́ть.
subway *n.* метро́; метрополите́н.
subzero *adj.* ни́же нуля́.
succeed *v.i.* **1,** (achieve one's purpose) доби́ться успе́ха. **2,** (achieve a specified purpose) удава́ться (*impers., with dat.*): *he succeeded in obtaining a loan,* ему́ удало́сь получи́ть заём. **3,** (achieve success) преуспева́ть: *succeed in life,* преуспева́ть в жи́зни. **4,** (turn out successfully) удава́ться; увенча́ться успе́хом. **5,** *fol. by* **to** (inherit) насле́довать: *succeed to the throne,* насле́довать престо́л. —*v.t.* **1,** (come after) сле́довать за; сменя́ть. **2,** (take the place of) приходи́ть на сме́ну (+ *dat.*).
succeeding *adj.* после́дующий.
success *n.* успе́х: *achieve success,* доби́ться успе́ха. —**be a success, 1,** (succeed in life) преуспева́ть. **2,** (turn out well) удава́ться: *the experiment was a success,* о́пыт уда́лся. *The play was a huge success,* пье́са име́ла огро́мный успе́х.
successful *adj.* успе́шный; уда́чный. —**be successful, 1,** (achieve one's purpose) доби́ться успе́ха. **2,** (turn out successfully) удава́ться: *the operation was successful,* опера́ция удала́сь.
successfully *adv.* успе́шно; уда́чно.
succession *n.* **1,** (following in order) преéмственность. **2,** (transfer of power) преéмственность; перехо́д вла́сти. **3,** (succeeding by descent) пра́во насле́дования. *Succession to the throne,* престолонасле́дие. *War of the Austrian Succession,* война́ за Австри́йское насле́дство. **4,** (series) ряд; цепь. —**in succession, 1,** (one after another) по поря́дку. **2,** (in a row; consecutively) подря́д.
successive *adj.* после́довательный. *Three successive years,* три го́да подря́д.
successor *n.* преéмник.
succinct *adj.* сжа́тый; кра́ткий.
succor *also,* **succour** *n.* по́мощь; соде́йствие.
succotash *n.* блю́до из кукуру́зы и бобо́в.
succour *n.* = **succor.**
succulent *adj.* со́чный. —**succulence,** *n.* со́чность.
succumb *v.i.* **1,** (yield) уступа́ть; поддава́ться. *Succumb to pressure,* уступа́ть давле́нию. *Succumb to temptation,* поддава́ться собла́зну *or* искуше́нию. **2,** (die) умере́ть.
such *adj. & adv.* тако́й: *in such cases,* в таки́х слу́чаях; *such a large house,* тако́й большо́й дом; *such tall buildings,* таки́е высо́кие зда́ния. *Such a long time ago,* так давно́. *In such a way that,* так, что... —*pron.* тако́в: *such is life,* такова́ жизнь. —**and such,** и тому́ подо́бное. —**as such,** как таково́й; сам по себе́. —**no such thing,** ничего́ тако́го; ничего́ по-

до́бного. *I said no such thing,* я не сказа́л(а) ничего́ тако́го/подо́бного. —**such a thing,** тако́е: *how could you say such a thing?,* как вы могли́ сказа́ть тако́е? —**such and such,** тако́й-то. —**such as,** как наприме́р.

suck *v.t.* соса́ть. —**give suck,** корми́ть гру́дью. —**suck in,** вса́сывать; заса́сывать.

sucker *n.* **1,** (person or thing that sucks) сосу́н; сосуно́к. **2,** *bot.; zool.* присо́сок. **3,** *slang* (dupe) проста́к.

suckle *v.t.* корми́ть (гру́дью). —*v.i.* соса́ть.

suckling *n.* сосу́н; сосуно́к. —*adj.* грудно́й; моло́чный. *Suckling pig,* поросёнок.

sucrose *n.* сахаро́за.

suction *n.* вса́сывание. —**suction pump,** вса́сывающий насо́с.

sudden *adj.* внеза́пный; неожи́данный. *Sudden departure/downpour,* внеза́пный отъе́зд/ли́вень. *Sudden death,* внеза́пная *or* скоропости́жная смерть. *This is so sudden,* э́то так неожи́данно. —**all of a sudden,** вдруг; внеза́пно; ни с того́ ни с сего́.

suddenly *adv.* вдруг; внеза́пно. —**suddenness,** *n.* внеза́пность.

suds *n. pl.* **1,** (soapy water) мы́льная вода́. **2,** (lather) мы́льная пе́на.

sue *v.t. & i.* подава́ть в суд (на); предъявля́ть иск (к); возбужда́ть де́ло *or* иск (о *or* про́тив). *Sue for damages,* предъявля́ть иск о возмеще́нии убы́тков. *Sue for libel,* возбужда́ть де́ло о клевете́. *Sue for peace,* добива́ться ми́ра. *He sued to get his job back,* он по́дал в суд, что́бы его́ восстанови́ли на рабо́ту.

suede *n.* за́мша. —*adj.* за́мшевый.

suffer *v.i.* страда́ть: *suffer from the cold,* страда́ть от хо́лода; *suffer from a rare disease,* страда́ть ре́дкой боле́знью. *Suffer in translation,* теря́ть в перево́де. —*v.t.* **1,** (sustain) потерпе́ть; понести́; получи́ть. *Suffer a defeat,* потерпе́ть пораже́ние. *Suffer losses,* понести́ поте́ри. *Suffer an injury,* получи́ть поврежде́ние. *He suffered the same fate,* его́ пости́гла та же у́часть. **2,** (put up with) терпе́ть; выноси́ть. *Suffer fools,* терпе́ть дурако́в.

sufferance *n.* **1,** (passive permission) ми́лость: *at the sufferance of,* по ми́лости (+ *gen.*). **2,** (endurance) терпе́ние; терпели́вость.

sufferer *n.* страда́лец.

suffering *n.* страда́ние. —*adj.* страда́ющий.

suffice *v.i.* быть доста́точным; хвата́ть. —**suffice (it) to say,** доста́точно сказа́ть.

sufficiency *n.* доста́точность.

sufficient *adj.* доста́точно: *sufficient fuel,* доста́точно то́плива. *Three gallons are sufficient,* три галло́на – доста́точно. —**sufficiently,** *adv.* доста́точно.

suffix *n.* су́ффикс.

suffocate *v.t.* души́ть; удуша́ть. —*v.i.* задыха́ться. —**suffocation,** *n.* удуше́ние.

suffrage *n.* пра́во го́лоса; избира́тельное пра́во.

suffragette *n.* суфражи́стка.

suffuse *v.t.* залива́ть: *the room is suffused with light,* ко́мната залита́ све́том.

sugar *n.* са́хар. —*adj.* са́харный. —**sugar beet,** са́харная свёкла. —**sugar bowl,** са́харница. —**sugar cane,** са́харный тростни́к. —**sugar loaf,** голова́ (*or* голо́вка) са́хару. —**sugar refinery,** са́харный заво́д.

sugar-coat *v.t.* покрыва́ть са́харом; *fig.* подсла́щивать.

sugary *adj.* **1,** (of or containing sugar) са́харный; са́харистый. **2,** *fig.* (cloyingly sweet) слаща́вый; са́харный; при́торный.

suggest *v.t.* **1,** (advise; recommend) предлага́ть: *he suggested that I see a doctor,* он предложи́л мне обрати́ться к врачу́. **2,** (offer, as an idea) подава́ть; наводи́ть на (мысль). **3,** (indicate; lead to believe) говори́ть о: *the evidence suggests that...,* ули́ки говоря́т о том, что... **4,** (imply) намека́ть: *are you suggesting that...?,* вы намека́ете, что...?

suggestion *n.* **1,** (something suggested) предложе́ние. **2,** (faint hint; trace) намёк; но́тка. **3,** *psychol.* внуше́ние.

suggestive *adj.* **1,** *fol. by* **of** (recalling; resembling) напомина́ющий. **2,** (suggesting something indecent) двусмы́сленный.

suicidal *adj.* самоуби́йственный.

suicide *n.* самоуби́йство. —**commit suicide,** поко́нчить жизнь самоуби́йством; поко́нчить с собо́й.

suit *n.* **1,** (outfit) костю́м: *three-piece suit,* костю́м-тро́йка. *Bathing suit,* купа́льный костю́м. *Space suit,* косми́ческий костю́м. *Suit of armor,* ла́тные доспе́хи. **2,** *law* иск; де́ло; проце́сс. *Divorce suit,* бракоразво́дный проце́сс. *Bring/file suit against,* подава́ть в суд на (+ *acc.*); предъявля́ть иск к. **3,** *cards* масть. *Follow suit,* ходи́ть в масть. —*v.t.* **1,** (be right for) подходи́ть: *the job doesn't suit him,* рабо́та ему́ не подхо́дит. **2,** (please; be to one's liking) устра́ивать: *it suits me fine,* э́то меня́ вполне́ устра́ивает. *Nothing suits him,* на него́ (*or* ему́) не угоди́шь. **3,** (adapt) приспособля́ть. —**suit yourself,** де́лайте как хоти́те. *See also* **suited.**

suitability *n.* го́дность; приго́дность.

suitable *adj.* **1,** (appropriate) подходя́щий. **2,** (usable) го́дный; приго́дный: *suitable for drinking,* го́дный для питья́. —**suitably,** *adv.* как сле́дует; до́лжным о́бразом.

suitcase *n.* чемода́н.

suite *n.* **1,** (of rooms) анфила́да. **2,** (of furniture) гарниту́р. **3,** (retinue) сви́та. **4,** *music* сюи́та.

suited *adj.* *Be suited for/to,* годи́ться в: *he is not suited to be a teacher,* он не годи́тся в учителя́. *He is not suited for this type of work,* така́я рабо́та ему́ не подхо́дит.

suiting *n.* костю́мный материа́л.

suitor *n.* покло́нник.

sulfa drugs *also,* **sulpha drugs** сульфанилами́дные препара́ты.

sulfate *also,* **sulphate** *n.* сульфа́т; сернoки́слая соль. *See also* **ammonium/barium/copper/sodium sulfate.**

sulfide *also,* **sulphide** *n.* сульфи́д. ♦*In compounds* серни́стый: *hydrogen sulfide,* серни́стый водоро́д.

sulfur *also,* **sulphur** *n.* се́ра. —*adj.* се́рный: *sulfur springs,* се́рные исто́чники. —**sulfur dioxide,** дву́окись се́ры.

sulfuric *also,* **sulphuric** *adj.* се́рный. —**sulfuric acid,** се́рная кислота́.

sulfurous *also,* **sulphurous** *adj.* серни́стый.

sulk *v.i.* ду́ться.

sulky *adj.* наду́тый. —*n.* (carriage) одноме́стная дву́колка.

sullen *adj.* угрю́мый; хму́рый; па́смурный. —**sullenness,** *n.* угрю́мость.
sully *v.t.* **1,** (soil) па́чкать; пятна́ть. **2,** (tarnish, as someone's reputation) пятна́ть.
sulphate *n.* = **sulfate.** —**sulphide,** *n.* = **sulfide.** —**sulphur,** *n.* = **sulfur.** —**sulphuric,** *adj.* = **sulfuric.** —**sulphurous,** *adj.* = **sulfurous.**
sultan *n.* султа́н. —**sultanate,** *n.* султана́т.
sultry *adj.* зно́йный. *It is sultry,* па́рит.
sum *n.* **1,** (total) су́мма; ито́г. **2,** (amount) су́мма: *a healthy sum of money,* изря́дная су́мма де́нег. —*v.t.* [*usu.* **sum up**] сумми́ровать; резюми́ровать; поды-то́живать; подводи́ть ито́г (+ *dat.*). —*v.i.* [*usu.* **sum up**] подводи́ть ито́ги. *To sum up,* в ито́ге; коро́че говоря́. —**sum total,** о́бщий ито́г. —**the sum and substance of,** са́мая суть (+ *gen.*).
sumac *n.* сума́х.
summarily *adv.* бесцеремо́нно.
summarize *v.t.* сумми́ровать; резюми́ровать.
summary *n.* сво́дка; резюме́; конспе́кт. —*adj.* **1,** (brief; general) сумма́рный. **2,** (without observing the formalities) бесцеремо́нный.
summation *n.* резюме́. —**in summation,** в ито́ге; подводя́ ито́ги.
summer *n.* ле́то. *In summer,* ле́том. —*adj.* ле́тний: *summer day,* ле́тний день. —*v.i.* проводи́ть ле́то.
summerhouse *n.* бесе́дка.
summer lightning зарни́ца.
summertime *n.* ле́то; ле́тнее вре́мя.
summery *adj.* ле́тний.
summit *n.* верши́на. —**summit conference,** сове-ща́ние на вы́сшем у́ровне; совеща́ние в (*or* на) верха́х.
summon *v.t.* **1,** (order to appear) вызыва́ть. **2,** (convene) созыва́ть. **3,** *fol. by* **up** (muster) собра́ться с; набра́ться (+ *gen.*): *summon up courage,* собра́ться с ду́хом; набра́ться хра́брости.
summons *n.* вы́зов; пове́стка (в суд).
sumptuous *adj.* роско́шный; пы́шный. —**sumptuousness,** *n.* пы́шность.
sun *n.* со́лнце. —*adj.* со́лнечный. —*v.t.* [*usu.* **sun oneself**] гре́ться на со́лнце. —**sun bath,** со́лнечная ва́нна.
sun-bathe *v.i.* принима́ть со́лнечную ва́нну; за-гора́ть.
sunbeam *n.* со́лнечный луч.
sunburn *n.* зага́р. —**sunburned; sunburnt,** *adj.* загоре́лый. *Get/become sunburned,* загора́ть.
sundae *n.* пломби́р.
Sunday *n.* воскресе́нье. —*adj.* воскре́сный: *Sunday issue,* воскре́сный но́мер.
sunder *v.t.* раска́лывать; разбива́ть.
sundew *n.* producá́нка.
sundial *n.* со́лнечные часы́.
sundown *n.* зака́т. *At sundown,* на зака́те.
sundries *n. pl.* ра́зное; вся́кая вся́чина.
sundry *adj.* разли́чный; ра́зный.
sunfish *n.* луна́-ры́ба.
sunflower *n.* подсо́лнечник. *Sunflower oil,* под-со́лнечное ма́сло. *Sunflower seeds,* се́мечки.
sunglasses *n.* очки́ от со́лнца.
sunken *adj.* **1,** (under water) зато́пленный; затону́в-ший. **2,** (hollow, as of cheeks, eyes, etc.) впа́лый; запа́вший; углублённый.
sun lamp ла́мпа со́лнечного све́та.
sunlight *n.* со́лнечный свет.
sunlit *adj.* освещённый со́лнцем.
sunny *adj.* **1,** (bright with sunshine) со́лнечный. *It is sunny,* со́лнечно. **2,** *fig.* (cheerful) весёлый; ра́-достный.
sunrise *n.* восхо́д со́лнца. *At sunrise,* на заре́.
sunset *n.* захо́д со́лнца; зака́т. *At sunset,* на за-ка́те.
sunshade *n.* **1,** (parasol) зо́нтик. **2,** (awning) на-ве́с. **3,** (visor) козырёк.
sunshine *n.* **1,** (sunlight) со́лнечный свет. *In the sunshine,* на со́лнце. **2,** *fig.* (good cheer) весе́лье.
sunspot *n.* со́лнечное пятно́.
sunstroke *n.* со́лнечный уда́р.
sun tan зага́р. —**suntanned,** *adj.* загоре́лый.
super *n., colloq.* = **superintendent** *(in sense #1).* —*adj., colloq.* чу́дный; превосхо́дный.
superabundance *n.* чрезме́рный избы́ток.
superannuated *adj.* **1,** (retired) в отста́вке. **2,** (past one's point of usefulness) отжи́вший свой век.
superb *adj.* превосхо́дный; великоле́пный.
supercharger *n.* нагнета́тель.
supercilious *adj.* высокоме́рный; надме́нный.
superficial *adj.* пове́рхностный. —**superficiality,** *n.* пове́рхностность. —**superficially,** *adv.* пове́рх-ностно.
superfluous *adj.* изли́шний; ли́шний.
superhighway *n.* автостра́да; автомагистра́ль.
superhuman *adj.* сверхчелове́ческий. *Superhuman efforts,* нечелове́ческие уси́лия.
superimpose *v.t.* накла́дывать.
superintend *v.t.* надзира́ть (за); заве́довать; управля́ть.
superintendent *n.* **1,** (of a building) смотри́тель; коменда́нт. **2,** (of a military academy) нача́льник.
superior *adj.* **1,** (higher in quality) лу́чший: *far superior to,** намно́го лу́чше (+ *gen.*). **2,** (higher in rank) ста́рший. **3,** (greater; preponderant) превосходя́-щий: *superior forces,* превосходя́щие си́лы. **4,** (excellent) отли́чный; отме́нный. *Of superior quality,* вы́сшего ка́чества. **5,** (haughty) высокоме́рный; надме́нный. —*n.* **1,** (one superior in rank) ста́рший; нача́льник. **2,** (head of a monastery) настоя́тель. *Mother superior,* игу́менья; настоя́тельница.
superiority *n.* превосхо́дство.
superlative *adj.* превосхо́дный. —*n., gram.* пре-восхо́дная сте́пень.
superman *n.* сверхчелове́к.
supermarket *n.* суперма́ркет.
supernatural *adj.* сверхъесте́ственный.
supernumerary *adj.* сверхшта́тный. —*n., theat.* стати́ст.
superpower *n.* сверхдержа́ва.
superscript *n.* надстро́чный знак.
supersede *v.t.* заменя́ть; идти́ на сме́ну (+ *dat.*).
supersensitive *adj.* сверхчувстви́тельный.
supersonic *adj.* сверхзвуково́й.
superstition *n.* суеве́рие. —**superstitious,** *adj.* суеве́рный.
superstructure *n.* надстро́йка.
supertanker *n.* суперта́нкер.
supervise *v.t.* наблюда́ть за; надзира́ть за. —**supervision,** *n.* наблюде́ние; надзо́р; присмо́тр; надсмо́тр.
supervisor *n.* **1,** (overseer) надзира́тель; над-

смóтрщик. **2,** (immediate superior) начáльник. —**supervisory,** *adj.* руководя́щий: *supervisory personnel,* руководя́щие рабóтники.

supine *adj.* **1,** (on one's back) лежáщий нáвзничь. **2,** (inactive; passive) безучáстный.

supper *n.* у́жин. *Have supper,* у́жинать. —**the Last Supper,** тáйная вéчеря.

suppertime *n.* врéмя у́жина.

supplant *v.t.* вытесня́ть; идти́ на смéну (+ *dat.*).

supple *adj.* ги́бкий.

supplement *n.* **1,** (anything added) дополнéние. **2,** (addition to a publication) приложéние. —*v.t.* дополня́ть. —**supplemental; supplementary,** *adj.* дополни́тельный; добáвочный.

suppliant *n.* проси́тель. —*adj.* умоля́ющий; проси́тельный. *Also,* **supplicant.**

supplicate *v.t.* моли́ть; умоля́ть. —**supplication,** *n.* мольбá.

supplier *n.* поставщи́к.

supply *v.t.* **1,** (provide with what is needed) снабжáть; обеспéчивать. *Supply a factory with raw materials,* снабжáть фáбрику сырьём. **2,** (make available) поставля́ть. *Supply merchandise to a store,* поставля́ть товáр магази́ну; снабжáть магази́н товáром. —*n.* **1,** (act of supplying) снабжéние. **2,** (stock) запáс. **3,** *econ.* предложéние: *supply and demand,* спрос и предложéние. **4,** *pl.* (provisions) запáсы; припáсы.

support *v.t.* **1,** (hold up) поддéрживать; держáть: *beams support the ceiling,* бáлки поддéрживают/дéржат потолóк. **2,** (back) поддéрживать: *support a proposal/candidate,* поддéрживать предложéние/кандидáта. **3,** (provide for) содержáть: *support a family,* содержáть семью́. **4,** (confirm, as a theory) подтверждáть. **5,** (tolerate) терпéть; выноси́ть. —*n.* **1,** (backing) поддéржка: *moral support,* морáльная поддéржка. **2,** (base; prop) опóра; подпóрка; подстáвка. **3,** (maintenance) содержáние. *Child support,* дéньги на содержáние ребёнка. *Be left without visible means of support,* остáться без поддéржки. **4,** *mil.* обеспéчение; поддéржка: *air support,* авиациóнное обеспéчение; авиациóнная поддéржка.

supporter *n.* сторóнник.

supporting *adj.* опóрный: *supporting beam,* опóрная бáлка. —**supporting cast,** исполни́тели второстепéнных ролéй.

supportive *adj.* отзы́вчивый; учáстливый.

suppose *v.t.* **1,** (think; imagine) полагáть: *I suppose so,* полагáю, что да. *What do you suppose this means?,* что э́то, по-вáшему, знáчит? **2,** (assume) предполагáть. **3,** *used to make a suggestion: suppose we do it this way,* давáйте сдéлаем э́то так.

supposed *adj.* **1,** (assumed) предполагáемый: *the supposed cause of the crash,* предполагáемая причи́на aváрии. **2,** (expected) дóлжен; полóжено. *He is supposed to be here at noon,* он дóлжен прийти́ в пóлдень. *You are supposed to obey,* тебé полóжено слу́шаться. *I am not supposed to drink,* мне пить не полагáется.

supposedly *adv.* предположи́тельно; я́кобы. *The money which he supposedly took,* дéньги, котóрые он я́кобы забрáл. *Supposedly, he will be there already,* предполагáется, что он ужé бу́дет там.

supposition *n.* предположéние.

suppository *n.* свечá; свéчка.

suppress *v.t.* **1,** (quell; crush) подавля́ть; усмиря́ть. **2,** (repress, as a yawn, one's feelings, etc.) подавля́ть; сдéрживать. **3,** (hush up) замáлчивать; замя́ть. **4,** (keep from being published) запрещáть. —**suppression,** *n.* подавлéние.

suppurate *v.i.* гнои́ться. —**suppuration,** *n.* нагноéние.

supremacy *n.* **1,** (supreme power) госпóдство; главéнство. **2,** (superiority) превосхóдство: *military supremacy,* воéнное превосхóдство.

supreme *adj.* верхóвный. *The Supreme Court,* верхóвный суд. *The supreme penalty,* вы́сшая мéра наказáния. *Make the supreme sacrifice,* жéртвовать жи́знью.

supremely *adv.* в вы́сшей стéпени. *Supremely confident of victory,* совершéнно увéренный в побéде.

surcease *n.* прекращéние; остановка.

surcharge *n.* приплáта; доплáта.

surcingle *n.* подпру́га.

sure *adj.* **1,** (certain; confident) увéренный: *you may be sure,* бу́дьте увéрены. *You may be sure of that,* вы мóжете не сомневáться в э́том. **2,** (reliable; unfailing; inevitable) вéрный: *sure sign,* вéрный при́знак; *sure death,* вéрная смерть. **3,** (not disputed) несомнéнный: *one thing is sure,* однó несомнéнно. **4,** *fol. by inf.* (bound to) обязáтельно: *he is sure to be there,* он обязáтельно там бу́дет. **5,** (confident; steady) увéренный: *sure hand,* увéренная рукá; *sure step,* увéренный шаг. —*adv., colloq.* конéчно! —**be sure to,** не забы́ть (+ *inf.*). *Be sure not to...,* смотри́(те), не (+ *inf.*). —**for sure, 1,** (without fail) обязáтельно. **2,** (for a certainty) навернякá: *no one knows for sure,* никтó не знáет навернякá. —**make sure, 1,** (see to it) постарáться (чтóбы); доби́ться (чтóбы). **2,** (ascertain for certain) убеди́ться. —**sure enough,** действи́тельно; на сáмом дéле. —**to be sure, 1,** (certainly) что и говори́ть. **2,** (admittedly) прáвда.

sure-footed *adj.* твёрдо стоя́щий на ногáх.

surely *adv.* несомнéнно; навернякá; конéчно. *Surely you don't believe that,* вы, конéчно, э́тому не вéрите. —**slowly but surely,** мéдленно, но вéрно.

sureness *n.* увéренность.

surety *n.* **1,** (certainty) увéренность. **2,** (guarantee) порýка. **3,** (guarantor) поручи́тель.

surf *n.* прибóй; буруны́.

surface *n.* повéрхность. *smooth surface,* глáдкая повéрхность. *Road surface,* дорóжное покры́тие. *Float to the surface,* всплывáть на повéрхность. —*adj.* **1,** (moving over land or water) назéмный; надвóдный: *surface forces,* назéмные си́лы; *surface ship,* надвóдный корáбль. **2,** (superficial) повéрхностный: *surface judgments,* повéрхностные суждéния. —*v.t.* (pave) мости́ть; замáщивать. —*v.i.* (come to the surface) всплывáть. —**on the surface,** внéшне.

surfeit *n.* **1,** (overindulgence) пресыщéние. **2,** (excess) изли́шек. —*v.t.* пресыщáть.

surge *n.* волнá; притóк; прили́в. —*v.i.* **1,** (billow) вздымáться. **2,** (move in large numbers) хлы́нуть; нахлы́нуть. *The crowd surged forward,* толпá подалáсь вперёд.

surgeon *n.* хиру́рг.

surgery *n.* хирурги́я. *Undergo surgery,* подвéргнуться оперáции. —**surgical,** *adj.* хирурги́ческий.

surly *adj.* злой; ворчли́вый.

surmise *v.t. & i.* предполага́ть. —*n.* предположе́ние; дога́дка.
surmount *v.t.* **1,** (overcome) преодолева́ть: *surmount difficulties,* преодолева́ть тру́дности. **2,** *usu. passive* (place on top of) уве́нчивать: *surmounted by a dome,* уве́нчан ку́полом. —**surmountable,** *adj.* преодоли́мый.
surname *n.* фами́лия.
surpass *v.t.* **1,** (exceed) превосходи́ть: *surpass all expectations,* превосходи́ть все ожида́ния. **2,** (overtake and pass) перегоня́ть. —**surpassing,** *adj.* исключи́тельный; несравне́нный.
surplice *n.* стиха́рь.
surplus *n.* избы́ток; изли́шек. —*adj.* избы́точный. —**surplus value,** приба́вочная сто́имость.
surprise *v.t.* **1,** (astonish) удивля́ть. *Be surprised,* удивля́ться. *I'm surprised at you,* я тебе́ удивля́юсь. **2,** (catch unawares) заста́ть врасплóх. —*n.* **1,** (astonishment) удивле́ние. *In surprise,* удивлённо. **2,** (unexpected development) неожи́данность; сюрпри́з. —*adj.* неожи́данный; внеза́пный. *Surprise attack,* внеза́пное нападе́ние. —**take by surprise,** заста́ть врасплóх.
surprising *adj.* удиви́тельный. —**surprisingly,** *adv.* удиви́тельно; на удивле́ние.
surrealism *n.* сюрреали́зм. —**surrealist,** *n.* сюрреали́ст. —**surrealistic,** *adj.* сюрреалисти́ческий.
surrender *v.t.* **1,** (yield; give up) сдава́ть: *surrender a fortress,* сдава́ть кре́пость. **2,** (relinquish) отка́зываться: *surrender a right,* отказа́ться от пра́ва. —*v.i.* сдава́ться: *I surrender!,* я сдаю́сь! *Surrender to the enemy,* сдава́ться врагу́. —*n.* сда́ча; капитуля́ция.
surreptitious *adj.* та́йный. —**surreptitiously,** *adv.* тайко́м; исподтишка́.
surrey *n.* пролётка.
surrogate *n.* **1,** (substitute; deputy) замести́тель. **2,** *law* судья́ по насле́дственным дела́м. —**surrogate court,** суд по насле́дственным дела́м.
surround *v.t.* окружа́ть. *Surrounded on all sides,* окружён со всех сторо́н. *Surround oneself with,* окружа́ть себя́ (+ *instr.*).
surrounding *adj.* окружа́ющий. —**surroundings,** *n. pl.* окруже́ние; среда́; окружа́ющая обстано́вка.
surtax *n.* доба́вочный нало́г.
surveillance *n.* надзо́р; наблюде́ние; сле́жка.
survey *v.t.* **1,** (view; review) обозрева́ть. *Survey the situation,* уясни́ть себе́ положе́ние. **2,** (poll) опра́шивать. **3,** (measure, as land) межева́ть. —*n.* **1,** (review) обзо́р; обозре́ние. **2,** (poll) опро́с. **3,** (measurement) съёмка. —**surveying,** *n.* межева́ние. —**surveyor,** *n.* землеме́р.
survival *n.* **1,** (fact of surviving) выжива́ние. *Survival of the fittest,* выжива́ние наибо́лее приспосо́бленных. **2,** (vestige) пережи́ток.
survive *v.i.* **1,** (remain alive) выжива́ть; уцеле́ть; остава́ться в живы́х. **2,** (continue in existence) сохраня́ться. —*v.t.* **1,** (come through alive) уцеле́ть от; пережива́ть. **2,** (outlive) пережива́ть.
survivor *n.* оста́вшийся в живы́х; уцеле́вший. *There were no survivors,* никто́ не уцеле́л.
susceptibility *n.* подве́рженность; восприи́мчивость.
susceptible *adj.* [*usu.* **susceptible to**] подве́рженный (+ *dat.*); восприи́мчивый (к). *Susceptible to colds,* подве́рженный просту́де. *Susceptible to flattery,* па́дкий на лесть.
suspect *v.t.* **1,** (believe possibly guilty; sense the existence of) подозрева́ть: *he is suspected of murder,* его́ подозрева́ют в уби́йстве. *Suspect arson/cancer,* подозрева́ть поджо́г/рак. **2,** (believe to be the case; surmise) полага́ть. —*n.* подозрева́емый. —*adj.* вызыва́ющий подозре́ние.
suspend *v.t.* **1,** (hang from above) подве́шивать. **2,** (halt temporarily) приостана́вливать; прекраща́ть. **3,** (debar temporarily) вре́менно отстраня́ть (от до́лжности, заня́тий, *etc.*). **4,** (revoke temporarily, as a rule) вре́менно отменя́ть. *His driver's licence was suspended,* он был вре́менно лишён води́тельских прав. **5,** (defer) откла́дывать. *Suspend judgment,* воздержа́ться от сужде́ний.
suspended *adj.* подвесно́й. *Be suspended from the ceiling,* висе́ть на потолке́. —**suspended animation,** бесчу́вствие. —**suspended sentence,** усло́вный пригово́р.
suspenders *n. pl.* подтя́жки; по́мочи.
suspense *n.* неизве́стность; неопределённость. *Keep in suspense,* держа́ть в неизве́стности. *The suspense is killing me,* неопределённость му́чит меня́.
suspension *n.* **1,** (temporary halt) приостано́вка; прекраще́ние. **2,** (temporary debarment) вре́менное отстране́ние (от до́лжности). **3,** (temporary revocation) вре́менная отме́на. **4,** *mech.* подве́ска. —**suspension bridge,** вися́чий мост. —**suspension points,** многото́чие.
suspicion *n.* подозре́ние.
suspicious *adj.* подозри́тельный: *suspicious person/noise/look,* подозри́тельный челове́к/шум/взгляд. *Be suspicious of,* относи́ться подозри́тельно к. —**suspiciously,** *adv.* подозри́тельно.
sustain *v.t.* **1,** (hold up; support) подде́рживать; держа́ть. **2,** (support; maintain) подде́рживать: *sustain life,* подде́рживать жизнь. **3,** (experience; suffer) потерпе́ть; понести́. *Sustain losses,* понести́ поте́ри. *Sustain injuries,* получи́ть уве́чье. **4,** (strengthen the spirits of) подкрепля́ть. **5,** (uphold, as an objection) принима́ть: *objection sustained,* возраже́ние принима́ется. **6,** (prolong, as a note) тяну́ть; протя́гивать.
sustenance *n.* пропита́ние.
suture *n.* шов; нить. —*v.t.* сшива́ть.
suzerain *n.* сюзере́н. —*adj.* сюзере́нный. —**suzerainty,** *n.* сюзерените́т.
svelte *adj.* стро́йный; ги́бкий.
swab *v.t.* **1,** (mop; scrub) дра́ить. **2,** *med.* (paint) сма́зывать: *swab with iodine,* сма́зывать йо́дом.
swaddle *v.t.* свива́ть; пелена́ть. —**swaddling clothes,** свива́льник.
swag *n., slang* добы́ча.
swagger *v.i.* идти́ ва́жной по́ступью; выступа́ть. —*n.* ва́жная по́ступь.
Swahili *n.* суахи́ли.
swallow *v.i.* глота́ть. —*v.t.* **1,** (pass into the stomach) глота́ть; прогла́тывать. **2,** (pronounce indistinctly) глота́ть; прогла́тывать (слова́). **3,** (endure, as an insult) прогла́тывать (оби́ду). **4,** (suppress) подавля́ть: *swallow one's pride,* подави́ть самолю́бие. **5,** *fol. by* **up** (engulf) поглоща́ть; заса́сывать. **6,** *colloq.* (believe credulously) ве́рить; принима́ть на ве́ру. *Swallow the bait,* попа́сться на у́дочку. —*n.* **1,** (gulp) глото́к. **2,** (bird) ла́сточка.

swallowtail *n.* (butterfly) па́русник; махао́н. —**swallow-tailed coat,** фрак.
swamp *n.* боло́то. —*v.t.* завали́ть: *swamped with work,* зава́лен рабо́той.
swampland *n.* боло́то.
swampy *adj.* боло́тистый; то́пкий.
swan *n.* ле́бедь. —*adj.* [*also,* **swan's**] лебя́жий; лебеди́ный. *Swan's-down,* лебя́жий пух. *Swan's neck,* лебеди́ная ше́я. —**swan dive,** прыжо́к в во́ду ла́сточкой. —**swan song,** лебеди́ная пе́сня.
swank *n., slang* шик; форс. —*adj.* [*also,* **swanky**] *colloq.* шика́рный; роско́шный.
swap *v.t.* **1,** (exchange for something different) обме́нивать; меня́ть (что на что). **2,** (exchange like things) меня́ться; обме́ниваться (+ *instr.*). —*v.i.* обме́ниваться. —*n.* обме́н.
swarm *n.* рой: *swarm of bees,* рой пчёл. —*v.i.* **1,** (move about in great numbers) рои́ться; кише́ть; копоши́ться. **2,** *fol. by* **with** (teem with) кише́ть (+ *instr.*).
swarthy *adj.* сму́глый.
swashbuckler *n.* сорвиголова́.
swastika *n.* сва́стика.
swat *v.t., colloq.* **1,** (slap) шлёпать. **2,** (crush, as a fly) раздави́ть. —*n., colloq.* шлепо́к.
swatch *n.* обра́зчик.
swath *n.* прокос. —**cut a wide swath, 1,** *mil.* де́йствовать на широ́ком фро́нте. **2,** *fig.* (attract notice) наде́лать мно́го шу́ма; привлека́ть всео́бщее внима́ние.
swathe *v.t.* заку́тывать; обма́тывать. *Swathed in bandages,* обмо́танный бинта́ми.
sway *v.i.* кача́ться; колеба́ться; колыха́ться. *Sway in the breeze,* колыха́ться на ветру́ *or* от ве́тра. —*v.t.* **1,** (cause to sway) кача́ть; колыха́ть. **2,** (influence; persuade) склоня́ть. —*n.* **1,** (swaying movement) кача́ние; колеба́ние; колыха́ние. **2,** (power; dominion) власть. *Hold sway over,* властвовать над; госпо́дствовать над.
swear *v.i.* **1,** (make an oath) кля́сться; присяга́ть; дава́ть кля́тву *or* прися́гу. *I swear to God!,* кляну́сь бо́гом! *Make someone swear that...,* взять с кого́-нибудь кля́тву, что... **2,** (use profanity) руга́ться. *Swear at someone,* обруга́ть кого́-нибудь. —*v.t.* кля́сться. *Swear an oath,* дава́ть кля́тву *or* прися́гу. *Swear allegiance to,* кля́сться *or* присяга́ть в ве́рности (+ *dat.*). *Swear someone to secrecy,* взять с кого́-нибудь кля́тву молча́ть. —**swear by, 1,** (name in taking an oath) кля́сться (+ *instr.*). **2,** (have great faith in) пита́ть по́лное дове́рие к. —**swear in,** приводи́ть к прися́ге. —**swear off,** зарека́ться (+ *instr.*); дать заро́к не (+ *inf.*). *See also* **sworn.**
swearword *n.* бра́нное сло́во; руга́тельство.
sweat *v.i.* поте́ть. —*v.t.* [*usu.* **sweat up**] *My shirt is all sweated up,* моя́ руба́шка намо́кла (*or* промо́кла) от по́та; моя́ руба́шка пропита́лась по́том. —*n.* пот: *in a sweat,* в поту́. —**by the sweat of one's brow,** в по́те лица́.
sweater *n.* сви́тер.
sweat gland потова́я железа́.
sweat shirt фуфа́йка.
sweatshop *n.* потого́нная фа́брика.
sweaty *adj.* по́тный.
Swede *n.* швед; шве́дка.
Swedish *adj.* шве́дский. —*n.* шве́дский язы́к.
sweep *v.t.* **1,** (clean or remove with a broom) мести́; подмета́ть. **2,** (carry with force) мчать; проноси́ть. **3,** (move quickly throughout) охва́тывать: *flames swept the building,* пла́мя охвати́ло зда́ние. *A wave of strikes swept the country,* волна́ забасто́вок прокати́лась по стране́. —*v.i.* **1,** (use a broom) мести́. **2,** (move swiftly) мча́ться; проноси́ться. *A murmur swept through the crowd,* ро́пот пронёсся по толпе́. —*n.* **1,** (motion; stroke) взмах; разма́х. **2,** (scope; extent) разма́х; охва́т. —**sweep away,** уноси́ть: *the boat was swept away by the current,* ло́дку унесло́ тече́нием. —**sweep off,** смета́ть. —**sweep out,** вымета́ть. *Sweep out the basement,* вымета́ть *or* подмета́ть подва́л.
sweeper *n.* подмета́льщик.
sweeping *adj.* **1,** (extending in a wide curve) широ́кий; разма́шистый. **2,** (wide-ranging) огу́льный. *Sweeping generalization,* широ́кое обобще́ние. *Sweeping changes,* радика́льные измене́ния. —*n.* **1,** (act of sweeping) подмета́ние. **2,** *pl.* (litter) му́сор; сор.
sweepstakes *n.* лотере́я.
sweet *adj.* **1,** (having a sugary taste) сла́дкий: *sweet wine,* сла́дкое вино́. **2,** (pleasant) сла́дкий, прия́тный. *Smell sweet,* прия́тно па́хнуть. **3,** (likable; kind) ми́лый: *sweet girl,* ми́лая де́вушка. *Very sweet of you,* о́чень ми́ло с ва́шей стороны́. **4,** (not saline) пре́сный. —*n.* **1,** *pl.* (confections) сла́сти; сла́дости; сла́дкое. **2,** *Brit.* (piece of candy) конфе́та. **3,** *Brit.* (dessert) сла́дкое. **4,** (beloved person) дорого́й.
sweet-and-sour *adj.* ки́сло-сла́дкий.
sweetbread *n.* сла́дкое мя́со.
sweeten *v.t.* подсла́щивать. —**sweeten the pill,** золоти́ть *or* подсла́щивать пилю́лю.
sweetener *n.* сла́дкое вещество́. *Also,* **sweetening.**
sweetheart *n.* возлю́бленный; возлю́бленная.
sweetly *adv.* сла́дко.
sweetmeat *n.* конфе́та; сласть.
sweetness *n.* сла́дость.
sweet pea души́стый горо́шек.
sweet potato сла́дкий карто́фель; бата́т.
sweet-smelling *adj.* души́стый; арома́тный.
sweet tooth *colloq.* пристра́стие к сластя́м. *Have a sweet tooth,* быть па́дким до сла́дкого. *Person with a sweet tooth,* сластёна; ла́комка.
sweet william туре́цкая (*or* борода́тая) гвозди́ка.
swell *v.i.* пу́хнуть; набуха́ть; вздува́ться. —*v.t.* наду́вать; раздува́ть. *Swell the ranks,* увели́чивать ряды́. —*n.* **1,** (bulge in the ground) возвыше́ние. **2,** (rise of the sea) зыбь. **3,** *colloq.* (dandy) франт; щёголь. —*adj., colloq.* **1,** (fine; excellent) чу́дный. **2,** (stylish) щегольско́й. —**get a swelled head,** зазнава́ться; надува́ться; заноси́ться; возомни́ть о себе́. *See also* **swollen.**
swelling *n.* о́пухоль; припу́хлость; взду́тие.
swelter *v.i.* изнемога́ть от жары́. —**sweltering,** *adj.* зно́йный; ду́шный.
sweptback *adj.* стрелови́дный.
swerve *v.t. & i.* свора́чивать (в сто́рону).
swift *adj.* бы́стрый: *swift current,* бы́строе тече́ние. —*n.* (bird) стриж. —**swiftly,** *adv.* бы́стро. —**swiftness,** *n.* быстрота́.
swig *n., colloq.* большо́й глото́к.

swill *n.* **1,** (garbage; slop) помо́и. **2,** (food for animals) по́йло. —*v.t.* жа́дно пить; лака́ть.
swim *v.i.* пла́вать; плыть. *Go swimming,* купа́ться. —*v.t.* переплыва́ть: *swim the English Channel,* переплы́ть Ла-Ма́нш. —*n. Go for a swim,* попла́вать.
swimmer *n.* плове́ц; пловчи́ха.
swimming *n.* пла́вание. —*adj.* **1,** (that swims) пла́вающий. **2,** (of or for swimming) пла́вательный. —**swimming pool,** бассе́йн для пла́вания.
swimsuit *n.* купа́льный костю́м.
swindle *v.t.* обжу́ливать. —*n.* афе́ра. —**swindler,** *n.* моше́нник; плут; жу́лик; афери́ст.
swine *n.* свинья́.
swineherd *n.* свинопа́с.
swing *v.i.* **1,** (move back and forth) кача́ться. **2,** (turn on a pivot) верте́ться. *Swing open,* распа́хиваться. **3,** *fol. by* **around** (turn around quickly) повора́чиваться. **4,** (move laterally) свора́чивать: *swing over to the right,* сверну́ть напра́во. **5,** (shift) переходи́ть: *swing over to our side,* переходи́ть на на́шу сто́рону. **6,** (aim or deliver a blow) разма́хиваться. **7,** *colloq.* (be executed by hanging) быть пове́шенным: *he'll swing for it,* его́ пове́сят за э́то. —*v.t.* **1,** (cause to oscillate) кача́ть; раска́чивать. **2,** (wave; brandish) разма́хивать. **3,** (turn) развора́чивать: *swing the car around,* развора́чивать маши́ну. **4,** *Swing an election,* реши́ть исхо́д вы́боров. —*n.* **1,** (movement back and forth) кача́ние: *swing of the pendulum,* кача́ние ма́ятника. **2,** (stroke; sweep) разма́х; взмах. **3,** (shift) сдвиг. **4,** (playground device) каче́ли. **5,** (short trip) пое́здка; объе́зд. —**in full swing,** в (по́лном) разга́ре; в по́лном ходу́.
swingle *n.* трепа́ло; трепа́лка.
swingletree *n.* валёк.
swinish *adj.* сви́нский.
swipe *v.t., slang* (steal) стяну́ть; стащи́ть —*n., colloq.* (blow) тума́к.
swirl *v.t.* крути́ть; кружи́ть; клуби́ть; взвива́ть. —*v.i.* кружи́ться; клуби́ться. —*n.* вихрь: *swirl of dust,* вихрь пы́ли.
swish *v.t.* разма́хивать. *Swish one's tail,* пома́хивать *or* бить хвосто́м. —*v.i.* рассека́ть во́здух (со сви́стом). —*n.* **1,** (whistling sound) свист. **2,** (movement producing such a sound) взмах.
Swiss *adj.* швейца́рский. —*n., preceded by* **the,** швейца́рцы. —**Swiss cheese,** швейца́рский сыр.
switch *n.* **1,** (flexible rod) прут. **2,** *electricity* выключа́тель; переключа́тель. **3,** *R.R.* стре́лка. **4,** (change; shift) поворо́т; переме́на. —*v.t.* **1,** (change; shift) перемени́ть; переключа́ть. **2,** (exchange) меня́ться: *switch places,* меня́ться места́ми. —*v.i.* переключа́ться. —**switch off,** выключа́ть. —**switch on,** включа́ть.
switchboard *n.* коммута́тор; распредели́тельный щит.
switchman *n.* стре́лочник.
switchyard *n.* сортиро́вочная ста́нция.
swivel *n.* вертлю́г. —*v.i.* враща́ться. —**swivel chair,** стул с враща́ющимся сиде́ньем.
swollen *adj.* **1,** (of a part of one's body) взду́тый; разду́тый; опу́хший; вспу́хший. **2,** (of a river or stream) взду́тый; разду́тый; набу́хший; взбу́хший.
swoon *n.* о́бморок. —*v.i.* па́дать в о́бморок.
swoop *v.i.* [*usu.* **swoop down upon**] устремля́ться (на); налете́ть (на); броса́ться (на). —*n.* налёт. —**in one fell swoop,** одни́м уда́ром; одни́м ма́хом.
sword *n.* меч; шпа́га. —**at swords' points,** на ножа́х. —**cross swords,** скрести́ть мечи́ *or* шпа́ги. —**put to the sword,** предава́ть мечу́. —**sword of Damocles,** дамо́клов меч.
swordfish *n.* меч-ры́ба.
swordplay *n.* фехтова́ние.
swordsman *n.* фехтова́льщик.
sworn *adj.* под прися́гой: *sworn testimony,* показа́ния под прися́гой. *Sworn enemy,* закля́тый враг.
sybarite *n.* сибари́т. —**sybaritic,** *adj.* сибари́тский.
sycamore *n.* **1,** (fig tree of the Middle East) сикомо́р. **2,** (maple tree of Eurasia) я́вор. **3,** (plane tree of America) за́падный плата́н; сикомо́р.
sycophant *n.* льстец; подхали́м.
syllable *n.* слог. —**syllabic,** *adj.* слогово́й.
syllabus *n.* програ́мма (ку́рса).
syllogism *n.* силлоги́зм. —**syllogistic,** *adj.* силлогисти́ческий.
sylph *n.* сильф. —**sylphid,** *n.* сильфи́да.
sylvan *adj.* лесно́й; леси́стый.
symbiosis *n.* симбио́з.
symbol *n.* си́мвол. —**symbolic,** *adj.* символи́ческий; символи́чный.
symbolism *n.* символи́зм.
symbolize *v.t.* символизи́ровать.
symmetry *n.* симметри́я. —**symmetrical,** *adj.* симметри́чный; симметри́ческий.
sympathetic *adj.* сочу́вственный; отзы́вчивый; чу́ткий. *Be sympathetic to,* сочу́вствовать (+ *dat.*). —**sympathetic nervous system,** симпати́ческая не́рвная систе́ма.
sympathetically *adv.* сочу́вственно; чу́тко.
sympathize *v.i.* [*usu.* **sympathize with**] сочу́вствовать (+ *dat.*).
sympathy *n.* **1,** (pity; compassion) сочу́вствие; сострада́ние. *My sincere sympathy,* моё и́скреннее соболе́знование. **2,** (sameness of feeling) симпа́тия: *the sympathies of the crowd,* симпа́тии толпы́. *Be in sympathy with,* симпатизи́ровать (+ *dat.*). —**sympathy strike,** ста́чка солида́рности.
symphonic *adj.* симфони́ческий.
symphony *n.* симфо́ния. *Symphony orchestra,* симфони́ческий орке́стр.
symposium *n.* симпо́зиум.
symptom *n.* симпто́м; при́знак.
symptomatic *adj.* **1,** *med.* симптомати́ческий. **2,** (indicative of something) симптомати́чный.
synagogue *n.* синаго́га.
synchronic *adj.* синхрони́ческий.
synchronize *v.t.* синхронизи́ровать. —**synchronization,** *n.* синхрониза́ция.
synchronous *adj.* синхро́нный.
syncopate *v.t.* синкопи́ровать. —**syncopation,** *n.* синко́па.
syncope *n.* **1,** *med.* о́бморок. **2,** *gram.* синко́па.
syndicate *n.* синдика́т —*v.t.* объединя́ть в синдика́т.
syndrome *n.* синдро́м.
synod *n.* сино́д. —**synodal,** *adj.* синода́льный.
synonym *n.* сино́ним. —**synonymous,** *adj.* синоними́ческий; однозна́чный.
synopsis *n.* конспе́кт; аннота́ция.

syntax *n.* си́нтаксис. —**syntactical,** *adj.* синтакси́ческий.
synthesis *n.* си́нтез.
synthesize *v.t.* обобща́ть; синтези́ровать.
synthetic *adj.* синтети́ческий.
syphilis *n.* си́филис. —**syphilitic,** *adj.* сифилити́ческий. —*n.* сифили́тик.
Syrian *adj.* сири́йский. —*n.* сири́ец; сири́йка.
syringe *n.* **1,** (bulb-shaped device) спринцо́вка. **2,** (hypodermic syringe) шприц. —*v.t.* спринцева́ть.
syrup *n.* сиро́п.
system *n.* **1,** (set arrangement or method) систе́ма. *The solar system,* со́лнечная систе́ма. *The nervous system,* не́рвная систе́ма. **2,** (political, social, economic) систе́ма; строй; устро́йство. **3,** (the human body) органи́зм: *bad for one's system,* вре́дно для органи́зма. **4,** *mech.* систе́ма: *ignition system,* систе́ма зажига́ния. **5,** *aerospace* систе́ма; ко́мплекс. *Missile system,* ракéтный ко́мплекс. *Delivery system,* сре́дство доста́вки. **6,** (network) систе́ма; сеть. *Highway system,* доро́жная сеть. *Early-warning system,* систе́ма да́льнего обнару́жения.
systematic *adj.* системати́ческий. —**systematically,** *adv.* системати́чески.
systematize *v.t.* систематизи́ровать.
systole *n.* си́стола. —**systolic,** *adj.* систоли́ческий.

T

T, t двадца́тая бу́ква англи́йского алфави́та. —**to a T,** вполне́; точь-в-точь.
tab *n.* **1,** (flap to aid in handling) ушко́. **2,** *colloq.* (bill) счёт. —**keep tab (***or* **tabs) on,** следи́ть за.
tabernacle *n.* **1,** (portable sanctuary) ски́ния. **2,** (house of worship) моле́льня.
table *n.* **1,** (article of furniture) стол. *Night table,* ночно́й сто́лик; ту́мбочка. *Operating table,* операцио́нный стол. **2,** (chart with rows and columns) табли́ца. *Multiplication table,* табли́ца умноже́ния. **3,** (list; roster) та́бель. *Table of contents,* оглавле́ние. —*adj.* столо́вый: *table linen,* столо́вое бельё. —*v.t.* **1,** (postpone) откла́дывать. **2,** *Brit.* (submit for discussion) ста́вить на обсужде́ние. —**turn the tables on,** бить (кого́-нибудь) его́ же ору́жием. —**under the table,** из-под полы́.
tableau *n.* **1,** (dramatic scene) карти́на. **2,** (tableau vivant) жива́я карти́на.
tablecloth *n.* ска́терть.
table d'hôte табльдо́т.
tableland *n.* плоского́рье; столо́вая гора́.
tablespoon *n.* столо́вая ло́жка.
tablet *n.* **1,** (writing pad) блокно́т. **2,** (pill) табле́тка. **3,** (slab with writing) табли́чка.
table tennis насто́льный те́ннис.
tableware *n.* столо́вые прибо́ры.
taboo *also,* **tabu** *n.* табу́. —*adj.* запрещённый.
tabular *adj.* табли́чный. *In tabular form,* в ви́де табли́цы.
tabulate *v.t.* своди́ть в табли́цу. —**tabulator,** *n.* табуля́тор.
tachometer *n.* тахо́метр.
tacit *adj.* молчали́вый: *tacit consent,* молчали́вое согла́сие.
taciturn *adj.* молчали́вый; неразгово́рчивый. —**taciturnity,** *n.* молчали́вость; неразгово́рчивость.
tack *n.* **1,** (nail) гво́здик; кно́пка. **2,** *naut.* галс. **3,** (course of action) путь; курс. —*v.t.* **1,** (fasten) прикрепля́ть (гво́здиками). **2,** *fol. by* **on** (add on) прибавля́ть. —*v.i., naut.* лави́ровать. —**get down to brass tacks,** добра́ться до су́ти де́ла.
tackle *n.* снасть: *fishing tackle,* рыболо́вная снасть. —*v.t.* **1,** (jump on and pin down) схва́тывать. **2,** (undertake) бра́ться за.
tacky *adj.* **1,** (sticky) кле́йкий; ли́пкий. **2,** *colloq.* (gaudy; showy) мишу́рный.
tact *n.* такт; такти́чность. —**tactful,** *adj.* такти́чный. —**tactfully,** *adv.* такти́чно; с та́ктом.
tactic *n.* та́ктика. —**tactical,** *adj.* такти́ческий. —**tactician,** *n.* та́ктик.
tactics *n.* та́ктика.
tactile *adj.* осяза́тельный.
tactless *adj.* беста́ктный; нетакти́чный. —**tactlessness,** *n.* беста́ктность; нетакти́чность.
tadpole *n.* голова́стик.
taffeta *n.* тафта́. —*adj.* тафтяно́й.
taffy *n.* тяну́чка; ири́с.
tag *n.* **1,** (label) ярлы́к; ярлычо́к; этике́тка; би́рка. **2,** (game) пятна́шки; са́лки. —*v.t.* накле́ивать ярлычо́к на. —*v.i.* [*usu.* **tag along**] идти́ вслед. —**tag end,** са́мый коне́ц.
taiga *n.* тайга́.
tail *n.* **1,** (of an animal or bird) хвост. **2,** (of an aircraft, kite, comet, etc.) хвост. **3,** (of a coat) фа́лда. **4,** *pl.* (tailcoat) фрак. **5,** *pl.* (reverse side of a coin) ре́шка: *heads or tails?,* орёл и́ли ре́шка? —*adj.* хвостово́й: *tail section,* хвостова́я часть. —*v.t., colloq.* (shadow) выслéживать. —*v.i.* [*usu.* **tail along**] идти́ вслед. —**tail end,** са́мый коне́ц. —**turn tail,** пусти́ться наутёк.
tailcoat *n.* фрак.
taillight *n.* за́дний фона́рь.
tailor *n.* портно́й. —*v.t.* **1,** (fit) подгоня́ть. **2,** *fig.* (adapt) приспособля́ть. —**tailor-made,** *adj.* сши́тый на зака́з.
tailpipe *n.* выхлопна́я труба́.

tailspin *n., aero.* што́пор на хвост.
tail wind попу́тный ве́тер.
taint *v.t.* **1,** (infect; contaminate) по́ртить. **2,** (tarnish, as one's reputation) пятна́ть. —*n.* **1,** (blemish) пятно́. **2,** (trace of decay) душо́к. —**tainted,** *adj.* ту́хлый; испо́рченный; с душко́м.
take *v.t.* **1,** (grasp; get possession of) брать (*pfv.* взять): *who took my umbrella?,* кто взял мой зо́нтик? *Take by the hand,* брать за́ руку. *Take a book from the shelf,* доста́ть кни́гу с по́лки. **2,** (seize; capture) брать; захва́тывать. **3,** (bring along) брать с собо́й. **4,** (carry; deliver) относи́ть: *take a letter to the post office,* относи́ть письмо́ на по́чту. **5,** (escort) отводи́ть: *take a child to school,* отводи́ть ребёнка в шко́лу. **6,** (drive) отвози́ть: *take to the airport,* отвози́ть в аэропо́рт. **7,** (require) тре́бовать. **8,** (use up, as time) занима́ть; отнима́ть. **9,** (travel by means of) брать; пое́хать на; сесть в *or* на. **10,** (follow, as a street or road) идти́ по; е́хать по. **11,** (follow, as advice) сле́довать; слу́шаться. *Take the hint,* поня́ть намёк. **12,** (win) получа́ть: *take first prize,* получи́ть пе́рвую пре́мию. **13,** (rent temporarily) снима́ть. **14,** (choose) выбира́ть. **15,** (measure, as temperature, pulse, etc.) измеря́ть. *Take someone's measurements,* снима́ть ме́рку с. **16,** (subtract) вычита́ть. **17,** (study) изуча́ть: *take French,* изуча́ть францу́зский язы́к. **18,** (be subjected to; absorb) подверга́ться (+ *dat.*). **19,** (endure, as a joke, criticism, etc.) терпе́ть. **20,** (assume) принима́ть; брать на себя́. *Take command,* принима́ть кома́ндование. *Take the offensive,* переходи́ть в наступле́ние. *Take the blame,* брать на себя́ вину́. *Take the name Smith,* принима́ть фами́лию Смит. **21,** (charm) увлека́ть: *be taken with,* увлека́ться (+ *instr.*). **22,** (receive or regard in a certain way) принима́ть; восприннима́ть. *Take seriously,* принима́ть всерьёз. *Take something hard,* тяжело́ перенести́ что́-нибудь. *Take life as it is,* восприннима́ть жизнь тако́й, кака́я она́ есть. **23,** *gram.* тре́бовать: *take the dative case,* тре́бовать да́тельного падежа́. **24,** *chess* (capture) брать; взять. **25,** *colloq.* (cheat; dupe) надува́ть: *I was taken for ten rubles,* меня́ наду́ли на де́сять рубле́й. **26,** *with certain nouns* брать: *take lessons,* брать уро́ки; *take a vacation,* брать о́тпуск; *take a bribe,* брать взя́тку; *take prisoner,* взять в плен. **27,** *with certain nouns* принима́ть: *take food,* принима́ть пи́щу; *take medicine,* принима́ть лека́рство; *take poison,* принима́ть яд; *take a bath,* принима́ть ва́нну; *take measures,* принима́ть ме́ры; *take part,* принима́ть уча́стие; *take someone's side,* принима́ть чью́-нибудь сто́рону. **28,** *with certain nouns* де́лать: *take a step,* де́лать шаг; *take a picture,* де́лать фотогра́фию; *take notes,* де́лать заме́тки. **29,** *used with various other nouns: take aim,* прице́ливаться; *take a course,* (про)слу́шать курс; *take an examination,* сдава́ть экза́мен; *take a look,* посмотре́ть; *take a nap,* поспа́ть; вздремну́ть; *take a poll,* производи́ть опро́с; *take a seat,* приса́живаться; *take a certain size,* носи́ть (како́й-нибудь) разме́р; *take a trip,* соверша́ть пое́здку; *take a walk,* погуля́ть; *take cover/shelter,* укры́ться; *take offense,* обижа́ться; *take office,* вступи́ть в до́лжность; *take pity,* сжа́литься; *take pride in,* горди́ться (+ *instr.*); *take revenge,* мстить; *take turns,* чередова́ться. **30,** *used in various set expressions: take place,* происходи́ть; состоя́ться; име́ть ме́сто; *take the trouble to,* дать себе́ труд (+ *inf.*); *take by surprise,* заста́ть враспло́х; *take one's own life,* лиши́ть себя́ жи́зни. —*v.i.* **1,** (have the intended effect) де́йствовать. *The vaccination didn't take,* о́спа не привила́сь *or* не приняла́сь. **2,** (become): *take sick/ill,* заболе́ть. **3,** *fol. by* **to** (go to; leave for) отправля́ться в: *take to the road,* отправля́ться в путь. *Take to one's bed,* слечь в посте́ль. **4,** *Take to drink,* спи́ться. **5,** *Take to one's heels,* показа́ть пя́тки. —**take aback,** озада́чить; огоро́шить. —**take after, 1,** (pursue) погна́ться за. **2,** (resemble) быть похо́жим на; уроди́ться в. —**take along,** брать с собо́й. —**take apart,** разбира́ть. —**take aside,** отводи́ть в сто́рону; отзыва́ть. —**take away, 1,** (carry off) уноси́ть; увози́ть. **2,** (remove) убира́ть. **3,** (seize) отбира́ть; отнима́ть. —**take back, 1,** (return) возвраща́ть. **2,** (retract) брать наза́д. —**take down, 1,** (carry down) сноси́ть. **2,** (pull down) снима́ть. **3,** (write down) запи́сывать. —**take for,** принима́ть за: *I took him for a German,* я его́ при́нял за не́мца. —**take in, 1,** (accept) брать. *Take in lodgers,* брать *or* пуска́ть жильцо́в. *Take in laundry,* брать бельё в сти́рку. **2,** (shorten; narrow) собира́ть; забира́ть; ушива́ть; су́живать. **3,** (include) охва́тывать. **4,** (trick) надува́ть. **5,** (visit; tour) осма́тривать. *Take in a movie,* пойти́ в кино́. —**take it, 1,** (assume) полага́ть. **2,** (withstand difficulty) терпе́ть. —**take it out on,** сорва́ть зло́бу на. —**take off, 1,** (remove) снима́ть. **2,** (lose, as weight or so many pounds) сгоня́ть. **3,** (deduct) вычита́ть. **4,** (of an airplane) взлета́ть. **5,** *colloq.* (depart) уходи́ть; уезжа́ть. —**take on, 1,** (take on board) нагружа́ться (+ *instr.*). **2,** (undertake; assume) брать *or* принима́ть на себя́. **3,** (hire) нанима́ть. **4,** (compete with) состяза́ться с. —**take out, 1,** (remove) вынима́ть. *Take out a tooth,* удаля́ть зуб. *Take out stains,* выводи́ть пя́тна. **2,** (escort) повести́: *take out to dinner,* повести́ (в рестора́н) обе́дать. **3,** (obtain by application) получа́ть: *take out a patent,* получи́ть пате́нт. *Take out insurance,* застрахо́вываться. **4,** (vent) сорва́ть; вымеща́ть: *take out one's anger on,* сорва́ть/вымеща́ть зло́бу на (+ *prepl.*). —**take over, 1,** (assume direction) принима́ть дела́. *Take over someone's duties,* принима́ть дела́ от. **2,** (assume direction of) принима́ть: *take over the class,* принима́ть класс. —**take up, 1,** (carry up) поднима́ть. **2,** (occupy, as space) занима́ть. **3,** (consume, as time) занима́ть; отнима́ть. **4,** (go in for) занима́ться (+ *instr.*). **5,** (assume; begin, as an assignment) принима́ть. **6,** (discuss) рассма́тривать. **7,** (quickly accept or adopt) подхва́тывать. **8,** (remove the slack from) натя́гивать. **9,** *Take up arms,* бра́ться за ору́жие. —**take upon oneself,** брать на себя́. —**take up with,** гуля́ть с.
takeoff *n.* **1,** *aero.* взлёт; вы́лет; отры́в от земли́. **2,** *colloq.* (imitation) подража́ние; карикату́ра.
taking *n.* **1,** (act of taking) взя́тие. **2,** *pl.* вы́ручка; сбор.
talc *n.* тальк.
talcum *n.* тальк. —*adj.* та́льковый. —**talcum powder,** та́льковый порошо́к; тальк.
tale *n.* **1,** (story) расска́з; по́весть. **2,** (folk tale; fairy tale) ска́зка. **3,** (falsehood) ска́зка.
talebearer *n.* спле́тник; я́бедник.
talent *n.* тала́нт. —**talented,** *adj.* тала́нтливый.
talisman *n.* талисма́н.

talk *v.i.* **1,** (speak) говори́ть. **2,** (converse) разгова́ривать. *What is there to talk about?,* како́й мо́жет быть разгово́р? **3,** (chat) бесе́довать. **4,** (gossip) погова́ривать. *People are starting to talk,* уже́ пошли́ то́лки. **5,** (yield information under stress) заговори́ть. —*v.t.* говори́ть; болта́ть. *Talk nonsense,* говори́ть чепуху́; болта́ть глу́пости; нести́ вздор. *Talk oneself hoarse,* договори́ться до хрипоты́. —*n.* **1,** (conversation) разгово́р. *Have a talk with,* поговори́ть с. *Small talk,* сало́нный разгово́р. **2,** (chat) бесе́да. **3,** *pl.* (high-level discussions) перегово́ры. **4,** (informal speech or lecture) бесе́да; ле́кция. **5,** (type of speech) речь. *Baby talk,* де́тский ле́пет. **6,** (meaningless conversation) пусто́й разгово́р. *It's just talk,* э́то одни́ слова́. **7,** (rumors) разгово́ры; то́лки; молва́. *There is talk that...,* погова́ривают, что... —**talk back,** груби́ть; дерзи́ть. —**talk into,** уговори́ть. —**talk out of,** отговори́ть от. —**talk over,** обсужда́ть.

talkative *adj.* болтли́вый; разгово́рчивый; говорли́вый. —**talkativenes,** *n.* разгово́рчивость; говорли́вость.

talking-to *n., colloq.* взбу́чка; нагоня́й.

tall *adj.* **1,** (of considerable height) высо́кий: *a tall man,* высо́кий челове́к. *He is tall,* он высо́кого ро́ста. **2,** (having a specified height) ро́стом в: *six feet tall,* ро́стом в шесть фу́тов. *I am six feet tall,* мой рост шесть фу́тов. *How tall are you?,* како́й ваш рост?; како́го вы ро́ста? —**tall story,** небыли́ца.

tallow *n.* са́ло. —*adj.* са́льный: *tallow candle,* са́льная свеча́.

tally *n.* **1,** *obs.* (notched stick) би́рка. **2,** (score) счёт. —*v.t.* (calculate) подсчи́тывать. —*v.i.* (agree) совпада́ть; сходи́ться; вяза́ться.

tallyho *interj.* ату́!

Talmud *n.* талму́д. —**Talmudic,** *adj.* талмуди́ческий.

talon *n.* ко́готь.

tamarind *n.* тамари́нд.

tamarisk *n.* тамари́ск.

tambour *n.* пя́льцы.

tambourine *n.* бу́бен; тамбури́н.

tame *adj.* **1,** (domesticated) ручно́й; приручённый. **2,** (docile) поко́рный. **3,** (lacking excitement) пре́сный. —*v.t.* **1,** (domesticate) прируча́ть; укроща́ть. **2,** (control, as passions) укроща́ть; смиря́ть.

tamer *n.* укроти́тель.

tamper *v.i.* [*usu.* **tamper with**] **1,** (meddle with) тро́гать. **2,** (fraudulently alter) фальсифици́ровать. **3,** (bribe) подкупа́ть.

tampon *n.* тампо́н.

tan *adj.* **1,** (light brown) светло-кори́чневый. **2,** (bronzed by the sun) загоре́лый. —*n.* **1,** (color) светло-кори́чневый цвет. **2,** (sun tan) зага́р. —*v.t.* **1,** (cure, as leather) дуби́ть. **2,** *usu. passive* (give a sun tan to): *well tanned,* загоре́лый. **3,** *in* **tan one's hide,** сечь; драть.

tanager *n.* тана́гра.

tandem *n.* та́ндем. —**in tandem,** цу́гом.

tang *n.* при́вкус.

tangent *n.* **1,** *geom.* каса́тельная. **2,** *trig.* та́нгенс. —**go off on a tangent,** отклоня́ться от те́мы.

tangential *adj.* **1,** *math.* тангенциа́льный. **2,** (not directly related) не име́ющий прямо́го отноше́ния.

tangerine *n.* мандари́н.

tangible *adj.* осяза́емый; осяза́тельный; ощути́мый.

tangle *v.t.* запу́тывать. —*v.i.* **1,** (become entangled) запу́тываться. **2,** *fol. by* **with** (come into conflict with) ста́лкиваться (с). —*n.* **1,** (snarled or intricate mass) сплете́ние. **2,** (confused state) пу́таница. —**tangled,** *adj.* запу́танный.

tango *n.* та́нго.

tangy *adj.* о́стрый; с ре́зким при́вкусом.

tank *n.* **1,** (container) бак. *Gas tank,* бензоба́к. *Fish tank,* садо́к. *Oil storage tank,* нефтехрани́лище. **2,** (military vehicle) танк. —*adj.* та́нковый: *tank army,* та́нковая а́рмия.

tankard *n.* кру́жка.

tank car цисте́рна.

tanker *n.* наливно́е су́дно; та́нкер. *Oil tanker,* нефтеналивно́е су́дно.

tanned *adj.* **1,** (treated by tanning) дублёный. **2,** (sunburned) загоре́лый.

tanner *n.* дуби́льщик. —**tannery,** *n.* коже́венный заво́д; дуби́льня.

tannic *adj.* тани́нный. —**tannic acid,** дуби́льная кислота́.

tannin *n.* тани́н.

tanning *n.* **1,** (process of tanning hides) дубле́ние. **2,** *colloq.* (thrashing) взбу́чка.

tantalize *v.t.* му́чить; дразни́ть.

tantalum *n.* танта́л.

tantamount *adj.* [*usu.* **tantamount to**] равноси́льный (+ *dat.*).

tantrum *n.* при́ступ гне́ва.

tap *v.t.* **1,** (strike gently) сту́кнуть: *tap someone on the shoulder,* сту́кнуть кого́-нибудь по плечу́. **2,** (strike repeatedly against something) посту́кивать: *tap a pencil on the table,* посту́кивать карандашо́м по́ столу. **3,** *fol. by* **out** (produce by tapping, as a message) высту́кивать. **4,** (wiretap) перехва́тывать. **5,** (draw upon, as resources) испо́льзовать. —*v.i.* **1,** (make repeated sounds by striking something) посту́кивать. **2,** *fol. by* **on** (rap gently) ти́хо сту́кать в. —*n.* **1,** (light blow) стук. **2,** (faucet) кран. *Tap water,* вода́ из-под кра́на; водопрово́дная вода́. **3,** (leather affixed to a shoe) набо́йка. —**on tap, 1,** (served from a tap) разливно́й. **2,** *colloq.* (ready for action or use) гото́вый; под руко́й.

tap dance чечётка. —**tap-dance,** *v.i.* отбива́ть чечётку.

tape *n.* **1,** (strip of material) ле́нта. *Adhesive tape,* ли́пкий пла́стырь. **2,** (material used for recording) плёнка. *Magnetic tape,* магнитофо́нная ле́нта. **3,** (strip across the finish line) фи́нишная ле́нта. —*v.t.* **1,** (fasten with tape) прикрепля́ть: *tape something to the wall,* прикрепля́ть что́-нибудь к стене́. **2,** *fol. by* **up** (bind with tape) перевя́зывать. **3,** (record on tape) запи́сывать на плёнку.

tape deck магнитофо́нная приста́вка.

tape measure руле́тка; сантиме́тр.

taper *n.* то́нкая свеча́. —*v.t.* заостря́ть. —*v.i.* [*usu.* **taper off**] **1,** (narrow toward one end) заостря́ться. **2,** *fig.* (diminish; subside) убыва́ть.

tape-record *v.t.* запи́сывать на плёнку. —**tape recorder,** магнитофо́н. —**tape recording,** магнитофо́нная за́пись.

tapestry *n.* гобеле́н.

tapeworm *n.* ле́нточный червь; солитёр.

tapioca *n.* тапио́ка.

tapir *n.* тапи́р.

taproom *n.* пивная́.
taproot *n.* стержнево́й ко́рень.
taps *n.* (вече́рняя) заря́.
tar *n.* дёготь; смола́. —*v.t.* смоли́ть.
tarantula *n.* тара́нтул.
tardy *adj.* **1,** (late) запозда́лый. **2,** (slow) медли́тельный. —**tardiness,** *n.* опозда́ние; запозда́ние; запа́здывание.
tare *n.* **1,** (vetch) ви́ка. **2,** *comm.* та́ра.
target *n.* **1,** (object fired at in practice) мише́нь. **2,** (something aimed or fired at) цель: *moving target,* дви́жущаяся цель. **3,** *mil.* цель; объе́кт. *Hit the target,* поража́ть цель. **4,** *fig.* (object, as of criticism or ridicule) мише́нь; предме́т. **5,** (goal) цель; план. —**target date,** наме́ченная да́та. —**target practice,** уче́бная стрельба́.
tariff *n.* тари́ф. —*adj.* тари́фный: *tariff barriers,* тари́фные барье́ры.
tarnish *v.t.* **1,** (dim the luster of) лиша́ть бле́ска. **2,** (detract from, as one's reputation) пятна́ть. —*v.i.* тускне́ть. —*n.* ту́склость.
tarpaulin *n.* брезе́нт.
tarragon *n.* эстраго́н.
tarred *adj.* смолёный.
tarry *v.i.* **1,** (delay) ме́длить. **2,** (stay) остава́ться.
tarsus *n.* предплюсна́. —**tarsal,** *adj.* предплюснево́й.
tart *adj.* **1,** (sour) ки́слый; те́рпкий. **2,** *fig.* (caustic) е́дкий; ко́лкий. —*n.* **1,** (pie) пиро́г. **2,** (loose woman) потаску́ха.
tartan *n.* шотла́ндка.
tartar *n.* ви́нный ка́мень. —**tartaric,** *adj.* виннока́менный.
Tartar *n.* тата́рин. —*adj.* тата́рский.
task *n.* зада́ча; зада́ние. —**take to task,** взять в рабо́ту; взять в оборо́т.
task force операти́вная гру́ппа.
taskmaster *n.* надсмо́трщик. *Hard taskmaster,* стро́гий нача́льник.
tassel *n.* кисть; ки́сточка.
taste *n.* вкус. *A matter of taste,* де́ло вку́са. *Take a taste of,* попро́бовать (что́-нибудь) на вкус. —*v.t.* **1,** (test the flavor of) про́бовать. **2,** (detect the flavor of) чу́вствовать вкус (+ *gen.*). **3,** (experience) вкуша́ть; изве́дывать; отве́дывать. —*v.i.* име́ть (како́й-нибудь) вкус: *taste sour,* име́ть ки́слый вкус. —**in bad taste,** безвку́сно; беста́ктно. —**in good taste,** со вку́сом. —**to one's taste,** по вку́су (+ *dat.*); в чьём-нибудь вку́се.
taste bud вкусова́я по́чка.
tasteful *adj.* сде́ланный со вку́сом. —**tastefully,** *adv.* со вку́сом.
tasteless *adj.* безвку́сный. —**tastelessness,** *n.* безвку́сие.
taster *n.* дегуста́тор.
tasty *adj.* вку́сный.
Tatar *n.* тата́рин. —*adj.* тата́рский.
tatter *n., usu. pl.* лохмо́тья; тряпьё; ру́бище; отре́пья.
tatterdemalion *n.* оборва́нец; обо́рвыш.
tattered *adj.* разо́рванный; обо́рванный; потрёпанный; растрёпанный.
tattle *v.i.* [*often* **tattle on**] я́бедничать (на).
tattler *n.* я́бедник; фиска́л. *Also,* **tattletale.**
tattoo *n.* татуиро́вка. —*v.t.* татуи́ровать.
taunt *v.t.* насмеха́ться над; издева́ться над. —*n.* насме́шка.
Taurus *n.* Телёц.
taut *adj.* туго́й; ту́го натя́нутый.
tautology *n.* тавтоло́гия. —**tautological,** *adj.* тавтологи́ческий.
tavern *n.* тракти́р; каба́к; бар. —**tavern keeper,** тракти́рщик.
tawdry *adj.* мишу́рный.
tawny *adj.* светло-кори́чневый. —**tawny owl,** нея́сыть.
tax *n.* нало́г. —*adj.* нало́говый: *tax revenues,* нало́говые дохо́ды. —*v.t.* **1,** (impose a tax on) облага́ть (+ *acc.*) нало́гом. **2,** (put a strain on) надрыва́ть. **3,** (try, as someone's patience) испы́тывать. —**tax collector,** сбо́рщик нало́гов.
taxable *adj.* облага́емый нало́гом; подлежа́щий обложе́нию нало́гом.
taxation *n.* обложе́ние (нало́гом); налогообложе́ние.
tax-exempt *adj.* освобождённый от нало́гов.
taxi *n.* такси́. —*v.i.* **1,** (travel by taxi) е́хать на такси́. **2,** *aero.* рули́ть. *Taxi up to,* подру́ливать к.
taxicab *n.* такси́.
taxidermy *n.* наби́вка чу́чел. —**taxidermist,** *n.* наби́вщик чу́чел.
taxi driver шофёр такси́.
taximeter *n.* таксо́метр.
taxonomy *n.* таксоно́мия. —**taxonomic,** *adj.* таксономи́ческий.
taxpayer *n.* налогоплате́льщик.
tea *n.* чай: *a cup of tea,* ча́шка ча́ю. *I'll put on some tea,* я поста́влю ча́йник. —*adj.* ча́йный: *tea service,* ча́йный серви́з.
tea bag мешо́чек *or* паке́тик с ча́ем.
tea caddy ча́йница.
teach *v.t.* **1,** (be a teacher of or in) преподава́ть: *teach Russian,* преподава́ть ру́сский язы́к. *Teach a course,* чита́ть курс. *Teach school,* преподава́ть в шко́ле. *Teach first grade,* преподава́ть в пе́рвом кла́ссе. **2,** (give instruction to) учи́ть; обуча́ть: *teach someone Russian,* учи́ть/обуча́ть кого́-нибудь ру́сскому языку́. *Teach someone how to swim,* (на)учи́ть кого́-нибудь пла́вать. **3,** (show by experience) учи́ть: *history teaches that...,* исто́рия у́чит, что... *Teach someone a lesson,* проучи́ть кого́-нибудь. —*v.i.* преподава́ть.
teacher *n.* учи́тель; учи́тельница.
teaching *n.* **1,** (act of teaching) преподава́ние. **2,** (profession of teaching) учи́тельство. **3,** *usu. pl.* (precepts) уче́ние: *the teachings of Christ,* уче́ние Христа́. —*adj.* преподава́тельский; педагоги́ческий: *teaching experience,* преподава́тельский о́пыт; *teaching load,* педагоги́ческая нагру́зка.
teacup *n.* ча́йная ча́шка.
teahouse *n.* ча́йный до́мик.
teak *n.* тик. —*adj.* ти́ковый.
teakettle *n.* ча́йник.
teal *n.* чиро́к.
tea leaf ча́йный лист.
team *n.* **1,** *sports* кома́нда. **2,** (working group) брига́да. **3,** (horses harnessed to a vehicle) упря́жка. —*v.i.* [*usu.* **team up**] объединя́ться.
teammate *n.* член той же кома́нды.
teamster *n.* **1,** *obs.* (driver of a team) пого́нщик. **2,** (truck driver) води́тель грузовика́.

teamwork *n.* сыгранность.
teapot *n.* чайник.
tear[1] (teer) *n.* слеза́. *Be in tears,* быть в слеза́х. *Tears of joy,* слёзы ра́дости. —*v.i.* слези́ться: *my eyes are tearing,* мои́ глаза́ слезя́тся.
tear[2] (tayr) *v.t.* **1,** (rip accidentally) рвать; разрыва́ть: *tear one's stocking,* рвать/разрыва́ть чуло́к. *Tear one's dress on a nail,* порва́ть/разорва́ть пла́тье о гвоздь. *Your trousers are torn in the back,* брю́ки у вас по́рваны/разо́рваны сза́ди. **2,** *fol. by* **up** (rip up) разрыва́ть; рвать: *tear up a letter,* разрыва́ть/рвать письмо́. **3,** (make; open, as a hole) пробива́ть (отве́рстие). *Tear a hole in the wall,* проби́ть сте́ну. *Tear a hole in one's stocking,* протира́ть ды́рку в чулке́. **4,** (snatch) вырыва́ть; выхва́тывать: *tear something out of someone's hands,* вы́рвать/вы́хватить что́-нибудь из чьи́х-нибудь рук. **5,** (plague; rack) му́чить; терза́ть. **6,** *in* **tear one's hair,** рвать на себе́ во́лосы. —*v.i.* **1,** (rip) рва́ться: *this material tears easily,* э́та мате́рия легко́ рвётся. **2,** (move swiftly) нести́сь; мча́ться: *tear along the road,* нести́сь/мча́ться по доро́ге. —*n.* проре́ха; дыра́; ды́рка. —**tear apart, 1,** (tear to pieces; kill) растерза́ть. **2,** *colloq.* (criticize severely) разруга́ть. —**tear away,** отрыва́ть: *I couldn't tear myself away from the book,* я не мог оторва́ться от кни́ги. —**tear down,** снести́ть. —**tear off,** отрыва́ть; срыва́ть. —**tear open,** разрыва́ть. —**tear out,** вырыва́ть. —**tear to pieces, 1,** (rip up) рвать *or* разрыва́ть на куски́ *or* на клочки́. **2,** (kill) терза́ть; растерза́ть.
teardrop *n.* слеза́; слези́нка.
tear duct слёзный прото́к.
tearful *adj.* слезли́вый.
tear gas слезоточи́вый газ.
tearoom *n.* ча́йная.
tear-stained *adj.* запла́канный.
teary *adj.* слезоточи́вый.
tease *v.t.* дразни́ть; поддра́знивать.
teaspoon *n.* ча́йная ло́жка.
teat *n.* сосо́к.
technetium *n.* техне́ций.
technical *adj.* техни́ческий.
technicality *n.* **1,** (technical term) техни́ческая дета́ль. **2,** (minute point) форма́льность.
technically *adv.* **1,** (from a technical point of view) техни́чески. **2,** (strictly speaking) форма́льно: *technically you're correct,* форма́льно вы пра́вы.
technician *n.* те́хник.
technique *n.* **1,** (sophisticated method) приём. **2,** (technical skill) те́хника.
technology *n.* техноло́гия; те́хника. —**technological,** *adj.* технологи́ческий. —**technologist,** *n.* техно́лог.
teddy bear ми́шка.
tedious *adj.* ску́чный; утоми́тельный; кропотли́вый.
tedium *n.* ску́ка.
teem *v.i.* **1,** *fol. by* **with** (swarm; abound) кише́ть (+ *instr.*). **2,** (of rain) ливмя́ лить.
teen-age *adj.* о́троческий. —**teenager,** *n.* подро́сток.
teeny *adj., colloq.* кро́хотный; кро́шечный.
teeter *v.i.* кача́ться; колеба́ться.
teethe *v.i. The child is teething,* у ребёнка проре́заются зу́бы.
teetotaler *also,* **teetotaller** *n.* тре́звенник; непью́щий.
telecast *n.* телепереда́ча. —*v.t.* передава́ть по телеви́дению.
telegram *n.* телегра́мма.
telegraph *n.* телегра́ф. —*adj.* телегра́фный. *Telegraph office,* телегра́ф. *Telegraph operator,* телеграфи́ст. —*v.t.* телеграфи́ровать.
telegrapher *n.* телеграфи́ст.
telegraphic *adj.* телегра́фный.
telegraphy *n.* телеграфи́я.
telemeter *n.* телеме́тр. —**telemetry,** *n.* телеметри́я.
teleology *n.* телеоло́гия. —**teleological,** *adj.* телеологи́ческий.
telepathy *n.* телепа́тия. —**telepathic,** *adj.* телепати́ческий.
telephone *n.* телефо́н. *Just a minute, I'm on the telephone!,* одну́ мину́ту, я разгова́риваю по телефо́ну. —*adj.* телефо́нный: *telephone book,* телефо́нная кни́га. *Telephone number,* но́мер телефо́на. *Telephone call,* вы́зов по телефо́ну. *Telephone bill,* счёт за телефо́н. *Telephone operator,* телефони́ст(ка). —*v.t.* звони́ть по телефо́ну; телефони́ровать.
telephonic *adj.* телефо́нный.
telephony *n.* телефони́я.
telephoto lens телеобъекти́в.
telescope *n.* телеско́п. —**telescopic,** *adj.* телескопи́ческий.
teletype *n.* телета́йп.
televise *v.t.* пока́зывать по телеви́дению.
television *n.* телеви́дение. *Watch television,* смотре́ть телеви́зор. *What's on television?,* что идёт по телеви́зору? —*adj.* телевизио́нный. —**television set,** телеви́зор.
tell *v.t.* **1,** (utter) говори́ть (*pfv.* сказа́ть): *tell the truth,* говори́ть пра́вду; *tell a lie,* сказа́ть непра́вду. **2,** (relate) расска́зывать: *tell a story,* рассказа́ть исто́рию. **3,** (inform) говори́ть; сказа́ть (+ *dat.*): *can you tell me how to...?,* вы не ска́жете, как...? *I told you so!,* я тебе́ и говори́л. *I can't tell you how sorry I am,* не могу́ да́же сказа́ть, наско́лько мне жаль. **4,** (order) сказа́ть; веле́ть. *Tell him to go away,* скажи́те ему́, что́бы он ушёл. *Do as you are told,* де́лайте, как вам ве́лено. **5,** (determine; decide; know) сказа́ть: *know how to tell time,* уме́ть сказа́ть, кото́рый час. *Tell the difference,* различа́ть. **6,** (distinguish) отлича́ть: *tell one from the other,* отлича́ть оди́н от друго́го. **7,** (indicate) ука́зывать. *The clock tells time,* часы́ пока́зывают вре́мя. —*v.i.* **1,** (say) сказа́ть: *it's hard to tell,* тру́дно сказа́ть. *Time will tell,* вре́мя пока́жет. **2,** *fol. by* **of** (give an account of) расска́зывать (о). **3,** (have force or effect) ска́зываться. —**tell apart,** различа́ть. —**tell off,** *colloq.* брани́ть; отчи́тывать. —**tell on, 1,** [*also,* **tell upon**] (have an effect upon) ска́зываться на. **2,** *colloq.* (tattle on) я́бедничать на.
teller *n.* **1,** (narrator) расска́зчик. **2,** (bank clerk) касси́р. **3,** (one who counts votes) счётчик.
telling *adj.* **1,** (having great force) си́льный. *A telling blow,* тяжёлый уда́р. **2,** (revealing) многозначи́тельный.
telltale *adj.* показа́тельный: *telltale sign,* показа́тельный при́знак.
tellurium *n.* теллу́р.
temerity *n.* сме́лость.

temper *n.* **1,** (composure; equanimity): *keep one's temper,* владе́ть собо́й; *lose one's temper,* выходи́ть из себя́. **2,** (disposition) нрав; хара́ктер: *bad temper,* дурно́й нрав/хара́ктер. *Hot temper,* вспы́льчивость. **3,** (mood) настрое́ние. **4,** (anger; rage) гнев: *fit of temper,* при́ступ гне́ва. *Tempers flared,* стра́сти разгоре́лись. —*v.t.* **1,** *metall.* закаля́ть. **2,** *fig.* (moderate) умеря́ть; смягча́ть.

tempera *n.* те́мпера. *In tempera,* те́мперой.

temperament *n.* темпера́мент; нрав.

temperamental *adj.* капри́зный; темпера́ментный.

temperance *n.* **1,** (moderation) уме́ренность. **2,** (abstinence) возде́ржанность.

temperate *adj.* уме́ренный. *Temperate Zone,* уме́ренный по́яс.

temperature *n.* **1,** (degree of heat or cold) температу́ра. **2,** (fever) температу́ра; жар. *He has a temperature,* у него́ повы́шенная температу́ра; у него́ жар.

tempest *n.* бу́ря. —**tempest in a teapot,** бу́ря в стака́не воды́.

tempestuous *adj.* бу́рный.

template *n.* шабло́н.

temple *n.* **1,** (church) храм. **2,** (side of the head) висо́к.

templet *n.* = **template.**

tempo *n.* темп.

temporal *adj.* **1,** (pert. to time) временно́й. **2,** (temporary; transient) вре́менный; преходя́щий. **3,** (worldly; secular) мирско́й; све́тский.

temporary *adj.* вре́менный. *Be temporary,* носи́ть вре́менный хара́ктер. —**temporarily,** *adv.* вре́менно.

temporize *v.i.* оття́гивать вре́мя.

tempt *v.t.* соблазня́ть; искуша́ть. *I am tempted,* меня́ э́то соблазня́ет. *Tempt fate,* искуша́ть *or* испы́тывать судьбу́. —**temptation,** *n.* собла́зн; искуше́ние. —**tempter,** *n.* соблазни́тель; искуси́тель. —**tempting,** *adj.* соблазни́тельный; зама́нчивый.

ten *adj.* де́сять. —*n.* **1,** (cardinal number) де́сять. **2,** (written numeral) деся́тка. **3,** *cards* деся́тка. **4,** *pl.* (quantities of 10) деся́тки (+ *gen.*): *tens of thousands,* деся́тки ты́сяч.

tenacious *adj.* це́пкий.

tanacity *n.* **1,** (firmness of hold) це́пкость. **2,** (persistence) упо́рство.

tenant *n.* **1,** (one who rents) нанима́тель; аренда́тор; квартира́нт. **2,** (occupant) жиле́ц. —**tenant farmer,** фе́рмер-аренда́тор.

tend *v.t.* **1,** (care for) уха́живать за: *tend the sick,* уха́живать за больны́ми. **2,** (look after) присма́тривать за. *Tend sheep,* пасти́ ове́ц. *Tend the fire,* подде́рживать ого́нь. —*v.i.* **1,** (lead in a certain direction) направля́ться. **2,** *fol. by* **to** (have a tendency) име́ть тенде́нцию (к). *He tends to exaggerate,* он скло́нен преувели́чивать. **3,** *fol. by* **to** (mind) обраща́ть внима́ние на.

tendency *n.* тенде́нция; скло́нность; накло́нность.

tendentious *adj.* тенденцио́зный. —**tendentiousness,** *n.* тенденцио́зность.

tender *adj.* **1,** (gentle; delicate) не́жный: *tender caress,* не́жная ла́ска; *tender skin,* не́жная ко́жа. *Tender age,* не́жный во́зраст. **2,** (sensitive; painful) чувстви́тельный: *tender spot,* чувстви́тельное ме́сто. **3,** (soft, as of meat) мя́гкий. —*n.* **1,** (offer) предложе́ние. **2,** (money) платёжное сре́дство: *legal tender,* зако́нное платёжное сре́дство. **3,** *R.R.* те́ндер. **4,** *naut.* плаву́чая ба́за. —*v.t.* предлага́ть. *Tender one's resignation,* подава́ть в отста́вку.

tenderhearted *adj.* мягкосерде́чный. —**tenderheartedness,** *n.* мягкосерде́чие; мягкосерде́чность.

tenderloin *n.* вы́резка.

tenderly *adv.* не́жно.

tenderness *n.* не́жность.

tendon *n.* сухожи́лие.

tendril *n.* у́сик.

tenement *n.* (убо́гий) жило́й дом.

tenet *n.* положе́ние; устано́вка.

tenfold *adj.* десятикра́тный. —*adv.* в де́сять раз; вде́сятеро.

tennis *n.* те́ннис. —*adj.* те́ннисный: *tennis court,* те́ннисный корт; *tennis racket,* те́ннисная раке́тка. *Tennis player,* теннеси́ст; теннеси́стка. —**tennis shoes,** та́почки.

tenon *n.* шип.

tenor *n.* **1,** *music* те́нор. **2,** (purport; thrust) смысл. —*adj.* теноро́вый. —**tenor clef,** теноро́вый ключ.

tenpins *n.* ке́гли.

tense *adj.* напряжённый: *tense atmosphere,* напряжённая атмосфе́ра. —*v.t.* напряга́ть. —*v.i.* напряга́ться. —*n., gram.* вре́мя: *present tense,* настоя́щее вре́мя.

tensile *adj.* растяжи́мый. —**tensile strength,** растяжи́мость; про́чность на разры́в.

tension *n.* **1,** (strain; strained relations) напряже́ние; напряжённость. *International tension,* междунаро́дная напряжённость. **2,** *electricity* напряже́ние.

tent *n.* пала́тка; шатёр.

tentacle *n.* щу́пальце.

tentative *adj.* предвари́тельный; усло́вный. —**tentatively,** *adv.* усло́вно.

tenterhook *n., in* **be on tenterhooks,** быть *or* сиде́ть как на иго́лках *or* как на у́гольях.

tenth *adj.* деся́тый. —*n.* **1,** (tenth part) деся́тая часть. **2,** (fraction) деся́тая: *one-tenth,* одна́ деся́тая.

tenuous *adj.* **1,** (thin) то́нкий. **2,** (not firm or strong) непро́чный.

tenure *n.* **1,** (holding of a position) пребыва́ние: *one's tenure in office,* пребыва́ние у вла́сти (*or* в до́лжности). **2,** (permanence of a position) несменя́емость.

tepid *adj.* теплова́тый.

terbium *n.* те́рбий.

tercentenary *adj.* трёхсотле́тний. —*n.* трёхсотле́тие.

term *n.* **1,** (period of time) срок: *term of office,* срок полномо́чий. *Prison term,* срок тюре́много заключе́ния. *Be elected for a four-year term,* избира́ться сро́ком на четы́ре го́да. **2,** (semester) семе́стр. **3,** (word or phrase) те́рмин: *technical term,* техни́ческий те́рмин. **4,** *pl.* (manner of expression) выраже́ния: *in flattering terms,* в ле́стных выраже́ниях. **5,** *pl.* (provisions, as of a contract) усло́вия. **6,** *pl.* (relations) отноше́ния. *Be on good terms with,* быть в хоро́ших отноше́ниях с; быть на дру́жеской (*or* на коро́ткой) ноге́ с. **7,** *math.* член. —*v.t.* называ́ть; характеризова́ть. —**come to terms,** прийти́ к заключе́нию; догова́риваться. —**come to terms with,** мири́ться с (че́м-нибудь). —**in terms of,** с то́чки зре́ния (+ *gen.*).

termagant *n.* мегéра; фу́рия.

terminal *n.* **1,** (terminus; station) вокза́л. *Air terminal,* аэровокза́л. **2,** *electricity* зажи́м. **3,** (for a computer) термина́л. —*adj.* **1,** (last; final) коне́чный. **2,** *med.* смерте́льный: *terminal illness,* смерте́льная боле́знь.

terminate *v.t.* прекраща́ть. —*v.i.* конча́ться; ока́нчиваться. —**termination,** *n.* прекраще́ние.

terminology *n.* терминоло́гия.

terminus *n.* коне́чная ста́нция.

termite *n.* терми́т.

term paper курсова́я рабо́та.

tern *n.* кра́чка.

terrace *n.* терра́са. —**terraced,** *adj.* терра́сный.

terra cotta террако́та. —**terra-cotta,** *adj.* террако́товый.

terrain *n.* ме́стность.

terrapin *n.* черепа́ха.

terrestrial *adj.* земно́й.

terrible *adj.* ужа́сный; стра́шный. —**terribly,** *adv.* ужа́сно; стра́шно.

terrier *n.* терье́р.

terrific *adj.* **1,** (very great; tremendous) огро́мный: *terrific speed,* огро́мная ско́рость. *Terrific noise,* стра́шный шум. **2,** *colloq.* (marvelous) чу́дный; потряса́ющий.

terrified *adj. Be terrified,* ужаса́ться. *Be terrified of,* ужа́сно *or* безу́мно боя́ться (+ *gen.*). *Terrified look,* выраже́ние у́жаса.

terrify *v.t.* ужаса́ть; приводи́ть в у́жас. —**terrifying,** *adj.* ужаса́ющий.

territorial *adj.* территориа́льный. —**territorial waters,** территориа́льные во́ды.

territory *n.* террито́рия.

terror *n.* **1,** (intense fear) у́жас. **2,** (use of violence as a political weapon) терро́р.

terrorism *n.* террори́зм. —**terrorist,** *n.* террори́ст. —*adj.* террористи́ческий.

terrorize *v.t.* терроризи́ровать.

terror-stricken *adj.* объя́тый *or* охва́ченный у́жасом.

terry cloth махро́вая ткань.

terse *adj.* кра́ткий; сжа́тый. —**terseness,** *n.* кра́ткость; сжа́тость.

tertiary *adj.* трети́чный.

test *n.* **1,** (trial) испыта́ние; про́ба. *Test of strength,* про́ба сил. *Put to the test,* подверга́ть испыта́нию. **2,** (school examination) зачёт; экза́мен. **3,** *med.* ана́лиз: *blood test,* ана́лиз кро́ви. —*adj.* испыта́тельный; про́бный: *test flight,* испыта́тельный/про́бный полёт. —*v.t.* испы́тывать; проверя́ть; испро́бовать.

testament *n.* завеща́ние. *Last will and testament,* духо́вное завеща́ние; после́дняя во́ля. —**New Testament,** Но́вый заве́т. —**Old Testament,** Ве́тхий заве́т.

testator *n.* завеща́тель. —**testatrix,** *n.* завеща́тельница.

tester *n.* испыта́тель.

testes *n. pl.* яички.

testicle *n.* яичко.

testify *v.t. & i.* дава́ть показа́ния; пока́зывать; свиде́тельствовать. *He testified that...,* он показа́л, что...

testimonial *n.* рекоменда́ция; характери́стика. —*adj.* рекоменда́тельный. *Testimonial dinner,* обе́д в честь кого́-нибудь.

testimony *n.* **1,** (statement made under oath) показа́ние; свиде́тельство. **2,** (proof) свиде́тельство.

test pilot лётчик-испыта́тель.

test tube проби́рка.

testy *adj.* раздражи́тельный; брюзгли́вый.

tetanus *n.* столбня́к.

tête-à-tête *n.* бесе́да с гла́зу на глаз.

tether *n.* при́вязь. —*v.t.* привя́зывать. —**reach the end of one's tether,** дойти́ до то́чки.

tetragon *n.* четырёхуго́льник. —**tetragonal,** *adj.* четырёхуго́льный.

tetrahedron *n.* четырёхгра́нник. —**tetrahedral,** *adj.* четырёхгра́нный.

tetrameter *n.* четырёхсто́пный стих. *Iambic tetrameter,* четырёхсто́пный ямб. —*adj.* четырёхсто́пный.

Teuton *n.* тевто́н. —**Teutonic,** *adj.* тевто́нский.

text *n.* текст.

textbook *n.* уче́бник.

textile *n., usu. pl.* тексти́ль. —*adj.* тексти́льный.

textual *adj.* **1,** (pert. to a text) текстово́й; тексту́альный. **2,** (literal) тексту́альный.

texture *n.* строе́ние; переплете́ние (тка́ни).

Thai *adj.* та́йский. —*n.* та́йский язы́к.

thallium *n.* та́ллий.

than *conj.* чем: *less strict than you,* ме́нее стро́гий (стро́гая), чем вы. *More than ever before,* бо́льше чем когда́ либо ра́ньше. ♦*Also rendered by the genitive case: he is taller than you,* он вы́ше вас.

thank *v.t.* благодари́ть. —**thank God!,** сла́ва бо́гу! —**thank you,** спаси́бо; благодарю́ вас. *Thank you very much!,* большо́е (вам) спаси́бо!

thankful *adj.* благода́рный. —**thankfulness,** *n.* благода́рность.

thankless *adj.* неблагода́рный.

thanks *n.pl.* благода́рность. —*interj.* спаси́бо. —**thanks to,** благодаря́ (+ *dat.*).

thanksgiving *n.* **1,** (giving of thanks) благодаре́ние. *A prayer of thanksgiving,* благода́рственная моли́тва. **2,** *cap.* (American holiday) День Благодаре́ния.

that *adj.* тот: *that house,* тот дом; *at that time,* в то вре́мя. —*dem.pron.* э́то: *that's all,* э́то всё; *that's not the point,* де́ло не в э́том. *Is that you, Nina?,* э́то ты, Ни́на? —*rel.pron.* кото́рый; что: *the book that was lying on the table,* кни́га, кото́рая лежа́ла на столе́. *Everything that happened,* всё, что случи́лось. —*conj.* что: *I admit that I was wrong,* я признаю́, что был непра́в. *He demanded that we apologize,* он потре́бовал, что́бы мы извини́лись. —*adv.* так; тако́й. *I can't walk that far,* я не могу́ идти́ так далеко́. —**and all that,** и всё тако́е. —**at that,** *see* **at.** —**by that,** э́тим. —**for all that,** при всём том. —**in that,** тем, что. —**like that,** так. —**so that,** с тем, что́бы. —**that is,** то есть. —**that much,** так мно́го; сто́лько. —**that which,** то, что... —**this and that,** *see* **this.**

thatch *n.* кро́вельная соло́ма. —*v.t.* крыть соло́мой. *Thatched roof,* соло́менная кры́ша.

thaw *n.* о́ттепель. —*v.i.* та́ять; отта́ивать. —*v.t.* раста́пливать; отта́ивать.

the *def.art. Not rendered in Russian: the end of the road,* коне́ц доро́ги; *the 20th century,* двадца́тый век. —**the..., the...,** чем..., тем...: *the sooner the better,* чем ра́ньше, тем лу́чше.

theater *n.* **1,** (playhouse) теáтр. *Theater tickets,* билéты в теáтр. **2,** *mil.* теáтр: *theater of operations,* теáтр воéнных дéйствий. *Theater nuclear weapons,* я́дерное orúжие срéдней дáльности. —**theatergoer,** *n.* театрáл. —**theatrical,** *adj.* театрáльный.

theatrics *n.pl.* **1,** (art of the theater) театрáльное искýсство. **2,** (histrionics) театрáльность.

thee *pers.pron., archaic* тебя́; тебé; тобóй.

theft *n.* воровствó; крáжа.

their *poss.adj.* их: *their mother,* их мать. ♦*When the possessor is the subject of the sentence* свой: *they sold their house,* они́ прóдали свой дом.

theirs *poss.pron.* их: *a friend of theirs,* оди́н из их друзéй. *Is this our luggage or theirs?,* э́тот багáж наш и́ли их?

theism *n.* теи́зм. —**theist,** *n.* теи́ст. —**theistic,** *adj.* теисти́ческий.

them *pers.pron.* **1,** *used as dir. obj. of a verb* их: *I saw them,* я ви́дел их. **2,** *used as indir. obj. of a verb* им: *give them the money,* дáйте им дéньги. **3,** *used as obj. of a prep.* них; ним; ни́ми.

thematic *adj.* темати́ческий.

theme *n.* тéма.

themselves *pers.pron.* **1,** *used for emphasis* (они́) сáми: *they don't know themselves,* они́ сáми не знáют. **2,** *used reflexively* себя́: *they behaved themselves badly,* они́ плóхо вели́ себя́. *They hurt themselves,* они́ ушиблись. —**by themselves,** одни́.

then *adv.* **1,** (at that time) тогдá; в то врéмя. *We were young then,* тогдá мы бы́ли молоды́ми. *Where were you living then?,* где вы жи́ли в то врéмя? **2,** (afterward; next) потóм; затéм: *first we go to London, and then to Paris,* сначáла мы поéдем в Лóндон, а потóм/затéм в Пари́ж. **3,** (in that case) тогдá; то. *What will you do then?,* что вы бýдете дéлать тогдá? *If he is ill, then we shouldn't go there,* éсли он бóлен, то не нáдо идти́ тудá. **4,** (so) знáчит: *then you're not going,* знáчит, вы не идёте. —*adj., preceded by* **the** тогдáшний. —**but then,** затó; впрóчем. —**by then,** к томý врéмени. —**now and then,** врéмя от врéмени; кóе-когдá. —**since then,** с тех пор. —**then and there,** тут же. —**till then,** до тех пор.

thence *adv.* **1,** (from there) оттýда. **2,** (from that time) с тех пор. **3,** (therefore) отсю́да; поэ́тому.

thenceforth *adv.* с тех пор; с тогó врéмени. *Also,* **thenceforward.**

theocracy *n.* теокрáтия. —**theocratic,** *adj.* теократи́ческий.

theologian *n.* богослóв.

theological *adj.* богослóвский; теологи́ческий. *Theological seminary,* духóвная семинáрия.

theology *n.* богослóвие; теолóгия.

theorem *n.* теорéма.

theoretical *adj.* теорети́ческий. —**theoretically,** *adv.* теорети́чески; в теóрии.

theoretician *n.* теорéтик. *Also,* **theorist.**

theorize *v.i.* теоретизи́ровать.

theory *n.* теóрия.

theosophy *n.* теосóфия. —**theosophical,** *adj.* теосóфский; теософи́ческий. —**theosophist,** *n.* теосóф.

therapeutic *adj.* терапевти́ческий.

therapist *n.* физиотерапéвт. *Speech therapist,* логопéд.

therapy *n.* терапи́я. *Physical therapy,* физиотерапи́я. *Speech therapy,* логопéдия.

there *adv.* **1,** (in that place) там. *From there,* оттýда. **2,** (to that place) тудá: *there and back,* тудá и обрáтно. **3,** (from that place) оттýда: *he left there,* он уéхал оттýда. **4,** *used to call attention* вон: *there he goes!,* вон он идёт! **5,** (in that matter) здесь: *I disagree with you there,* здесь я с вáми не соглáсен. *You've got me there!,* здесь я попáлся. **6,** (at that point) в (*or* на) э́том; э́тим. *He didn't stop there,* он на э́том не останови́лся. *The matter didn't end there,* э́тим дéло не кóнчилось. —*interj.* **1,** *to express satisfaction* ну вот! **2,** *to express sympathy* ну ну! —**not all there,** *colloq.* (у негó/неё) не все дóма. —**over there,** вон там. —**there and then,** тут же. —**there is; there are,** есть; имéется (имéются). *There is reason to believe that...,* есть основáние полагáть, что... *There is nothing/no one/here,* здесь ничегó/никогó нет. *There is no telling when...,* нельзя́ сказáть, когдá... *There is no stopping him,* егó не останóвишь. *There is nothing you can do about it,* ничегó не подéлаешь. —**there was; there were,** был; бы́ло: *there was no one there,* там никогó нé было. *There were three of them,* их бы́ло трóе.

thereabout *adv.* **1,** (near that place) побли́зости. **2,** (approximately) óколо э́того: *ten miles or thereabout,* дéсять миль и́ли чтó-нибудь óколо э́того. *Also,* **thereabouts.**

thereafter *adv.* с э́того (*or* с тогó) врéмени.

thereby *adv.* тем сáмым.

therefore *adv.* поэ́тому.

therein *adv.* в э́том.

thereupon *adv.* **1,** (following that) вслед за тем. **2,** (because of that) вслéдствие тогó.

thermal *adj.* теплвóй; терми́ческий.

Thermit *also,* **Thermite** *n.* терми́т.

thermocouple *n.* термопáра.

thermodynamics *n.* термодинáмика. —**thermodynamic,** *adj.* термодинами́ческий.

thermometer *n.* термóметр; грáдусник.

thermonuclear *adj.* термоя́дерный.

thermos *n.* тéрмос. *Also,* **thermos bottle.**

thermostat *n.* термостáт.

thesaurus *n.* тезáурус.

these *dem.adj. & pron.* э́ти: *these houses,* э́ти домá. *I'll take these,* я возьмý э́ти. *These are my children,* э́то мои́ дéти. *One of these days,* на днях.

thesis *n.* **1,** (proposition) тéзис; положéние. **2,** (dissertation) диссертáция.

Thespian *adj.* траги́ческий; драмати́ческий. —*n.* траги́ческий актёр.

they *pers.pron.* они́. *They say that...,* говоря́т, что... *See also* **them.**

thick *adj.* **1,** (not thin) тóлстый: *thick book/board/neck,* тóлстая кни́га/доскá/шéя. **2,** (having a specified thickness) толщинóй в: *six inches thick,* толщинóй в шесть дю́ймов. **3,** (dense; not watery) густóй: *thick fog/soup/syrup,* густóй тумáн/суп/сирóп. **4,** (heavy, as of an accent) си́льный. —*adv. Slice the bread thick,* нарезáть хлеб тóлстыми ломтя́ми. —**lay it on thick,** сгущáть крáски. —**thick and fast,** грáдом.

thicken *v.t.* **1,** (make thicker or broader) утолщáть. **2,** (make more dense) сгущáть: *thicken a solution,* сгущáть раствóр. —*v.i.* густéть; сгущáться. *The plot*

thickens, интрига становится всё сложнее.
thicket *n.* чаща; чащоба.
thickheaded *adj.* тупоголовый; тупоумный; твердолобый.
thick-lipped *adj.* толстогубый; губастый.
thickness *n.* **1,** (size) толщина. **2,** (density) густота. **3,** (layer) слой.
thickset *adj.* коренастый; приземистый; кряжистый.
thick-skinned *adj.* толстокожий.
thief *n.* вор.
thieve *v.i.* воровать. —**thievery,** *n.* воровство. —**thievish,** *adj.* вороватый.
thigh *n.* бедро. —**thighbone,** *n.* бедренная кость.
thimble *n.* напёрсток.
thin *adj.* **1,** (not thick) тонкий: *thin line/waist/shirt,* тонкая линия/талия/рубашка. **2,** (not fat) худой. *She has gotten very thin,* она очень похудела. **3,** (not dense) редкий. *His hair is getting thin,* волосы у него редеют. **4,** (watery) жидкий: *thin soup,* жидкий суп. —*adv. Slice the bread thin,* нарезать хлеб тонкими ломтями. —*v.t.* **1,** *often fol. by* **down** (make thinner) утончать. **2,** *fol. by* **out** (make less dense) разрежать. —*v.i.* **1,** *fol. by* **out** (become less dense) редеть. **2,** *fol. by* **down** (slim down) худеть. —**wear thin, 1,** (become worn) изнашиваться; стираться. **2,** *fig.* (of patience) истощаться; иссякать.
thine *poss.pron. & adj., archaic* твой.
thing *n.* **1,** (object) вещь. *The same thing,* то же самое. *I haven't a thing to wear,* мне нечего надеть. **2,** *pl.* (clothes; belongings) вещи. **3,** (matter; factor; circumstance) дело: *it's a strange thing,* странное дело! *Other things being equal,* при прочих равных условиях. ♦*Often omitted in Russian: the first thing (that)...,* первое, что... *The main thing is to...,* самое главное, чтобы... *It's a good thing (that)...,* хорошо, что... *Only one thing bothers me,* меня беспокоит лишь одно. *Such a thing could not happen here,* такое не может случиться здесь. *It comes to the same thing,* это всё равно. **4,** (act; task) дело: *I have a number of things to do,* у меня много дел; мне многое надо сделать. *You did the right thing,* вы правильно поступили. **5,** *pl.* (state of affairs) дела: *how are things?,* как дела? **6,** (creature) существо. *Poor thing!,* бедняжка! —**a thing or two,** кое-что.
think *v.i.* **1,** (exercise one's mind) думать: *let me think,* дайте мне подумать. *I don't think so,* думаю, что нет. **2,** (reason) мыслить: *think logically,* логически мыслить. *The ability to think,* способность мыслить. —*v.t.* **1,** (have in mind; imagine): *who would have thought it?,* кто бы мог подумать? *How could you think such things?,* как у вас могли появиться такие мысли? **2,** (believe; suppose) полагать; считать. *I think he's wrong,* я считаю, что он неправ. *There is no reason to think that...,* нет оснований полагать, что... —**think better of it,** одуматься. —**think nothing of,** *rendered by* хоть бы что (+ *dat.*): *he thinks nothing of running five miles,* ему хоть бы что пробежать пять миль. *He thinks nothing of hurting a person's feelings,* ему ничего не стоит обидеть человека. —**think of, 1,** (have an opinion about) думать о. **2,** (choose) задумать: *think of a number,* задумать какое-нибудь число. **3,** (be concerned about) думать о: *she thinks only of herself,* она думает только о себе. **4,** (recall) припомнить. **5,** (intend) думать: *she is thinking of getting married,* она думает выйти замуж. —**think out** *or* **through,** продумывать. —**think over,** обдумывать. —**think twice (before),** подумать хорошенько (прежде чем...). —**think up, 1,** (devise) придумывать. **2,** (concoct) выдумывать.
thinkable *adj.* мыслимый.
thinker *n.* мыслитель.
thinking *adj.* мыслящий. —*n.* мышление. —**to my way of thinking,** по моему мнению; на мой взгляд.
thinly *adv.* тонко. *Thinly veiled threat,* едва скрываемая угроза.
thinness *n.* тонкость; худоба.
thin-skinned *adj.* **1,** (having a thin skin) тонкокожий. **2,** (sensitive) обидчивый; чувствительный.
third *adj.* третий. *The third world,* третий мир. —*n.* **1,** (fraction) треть: *two-thirds,* две трети. **2,** *music* терция. —**in the third place,** в третьих.
third-rate *adj.* третьесортный; третьестепенный.
thirst *n.* жажда. —*v.i.* [*usu.* **thirst for**] жаждать (+ *gen.*).
thirsty *adj.* жаждущий. *I am thirsty,* я хочу пить.
thirteen *n. & adj.* тринадцать. —**thirteenth,** *adj.* тринадцатый.
thirty *n. & adj.* тридцать. —**thirtieth,** *adj.* тридцатый.
this *adj.* этот: *this house,* этот дом; *this book,* эта книга; *this place,* это место; *this one,* этот; *this time,* на этот раз; *this week,* на этой неделе; *this month,* в этом месяце; *this year,* в этом году.—*dem.pron.* это: *what does this mean?,* что это значит? —*adv.* так: *this quiet,* так тихо; *this soon,* так скоро. —**like this,** так. —**this and that,** то и сё; то да сё. *Talk about this and that,* поговорить о том, о сём. —**this is,** это: *this is my sister,* это моя сестра. —**this is how, where,** *etc.*, вот как; вот где, *etc.*
thistle *n.* чертополох.
thither *adv.* туда.
thong *n.* **1,** (strap) ремень. **2,** (lash of a whip) плеть.
thoracic *adj.* грудной. —**thoracic duct,** грудной проток.
thorax *n.* грудная клетка.
thorium *n.* торий.
thorn *n.* шип; колючка. —**thorn in one's flesh** (*or* **side**), бельмо на глазу.
thorn apple дурман.
thorny *adj.* **1,** (full of thorns) колючий. **2,** (controversial) спорный: *thorny question,* спорный вопрос. **3,** *fig.* (full of pitfalls) тернистый: *thorny path,* тернистый путь.
thorough *adj.* **1,** (painstaking; complete) основательный; доскональный. **2,** (utter; out-and-out) совершенный; отъявленный.
thoroughbred *adj.* чистокровный; породистый. —*n.* чистокровная/породистая лошадь.
thoroughfare *n.* **1,** (main road) магистраль. **2,** (passage) проезд: *no thoroughfare,* нет проезда.
thoroughgoing *adj.* = **thorough.**
thoroughly *adv.* **1,** (carefully) основательно. **2,** (completely; utterly) совершенно.
thoroughness *n.* основательность; доскональность.
those *dem.adj. & pron.* те: *those buildings,* те здания. *Those wishing to go,* те, кто желает идти. *Those were my children,* то были мои дети.

thou *pers.pron., archaic* ты.
though *conj.* **1,** (in spite of the fact that) хотя́: *though it is late,* хотя́ уже́ по́здно. **2,** (while) хотя́ и; хоть и: *our house, though small, is very cozy,* наш дом, хотя́/хоть небольшо́й, но о́чень ую́тный. —*adv.* всё же; всё-таки; впро́чем. *Do as you like, though,* впро́чем, де́лайте как хоти́те. —**as though,** бу́дто; как бу́дто; сло́вно.
thought *n.* **1,** (idea) мысль. *At the thought of,* при мы́сли о. **2,** (thinking) мышле́ние. **3,** (reflection; meditation) размышле́ние. *Lost in thought,* погружён в размышле́ния. **4,** (intention) наме́рение. *Have no thought of,* отню́дь не собира́ться (+ *inf.*). —**give thought to,** обду́мывать. —**on second thought,** по зре́лом размышле́нии; пораски́нув умо́м.
thoughtful *adj.* **1,** (pensive) заду́мчивый; вду́мчивый. **2,** (considerate) забо́тливый; внима́тельный. —**thoughtfulness,** *n.* забо́тливость; внима́тельность.
thoughtless *adj.* **1,** (ill-considered) необду́манный. **2,** (inconsiderate) невнима́тельный.
thousand *n.* & *adj.* ты́сяча.
thousandfold *adj.* тысячекра́тный. —*adv.* в ты́сячу раз.
thousandth *adj.* ты́сячный. —*n.* **1,** (thousandth part) ты́сячная часть. **2,** (fraction) ты́сячная: *one thousandth,* одна́ ты́сячная.
Thracian *adj.* фраки́йский.
thrash *v.t.* поро́ть; колоти́ть. —*v.i.* [*usu.* **thrash about**] мета́ться; бара́хтаться. —**thrash out,** подро́бно обсужда́ть.
thrashing *n.* трёпка; взбу́чка; по́рка.
thread *n.* **1,** (thin cord; fiber) ни́тка. **2,** (spiral ridge of a screw) наре́зка; резьба́. **3,** *fig.* (sequence) нить: *lose the thread of the conversation,* потеря́ть нить разгово́ра. —*v.t.* **1,** (pass through the eye of a needle) продева́ть; вдева́ть (ни́тку в иго́лку). **2,** (string) нани́зывать. **3,** (cut grooves in, as a screw) нареза́ть. **4,** *in* **thread one's way,** пробира́ться (сквозь). —**hang by a thread,** висе́ть на волоске́.
threadbare *adj.* потёртый; потрёпанный; изно́шенный.
threat *n.* угро́за. *The threat of war,* угро́за войны́. *A threat to peace,* угро́за ми́ру. *He is always making threats,* он всегда́ угрожа́ет.
threaten *v.t.* грози́ть; угрожа́ть. *Don't threaten me!,* вы мне не грози́те! *Threaten to resign,* грози́ть вы́йти в отста́вку. *He threatened to kill me,* он грози́л уби́ть меня́. *Threaten the very existence of,* грози́ть са́мому существова́нию (+ *gen.*).
threatening *adj.* угрожа́ющий: *threatening gesture,* угрожа́ющий жест. *Threatening weather,* мра́чная пого́да.
three *adj.* три. —*n.* **1,** (cardinal number) три. **2,** (written number; school grade) тро́йка. **3,** *cards* тро́йка.
three-colored *adj.* трёхцве́тный.
three-dimensional *adj.* трёхме́рный; *(optics; photog.)* объёмный.
threefold *adj.* тройно́й. —*adv.* втро́е; втройне́.
three hundred три́ста. —**three-hundredth,** *adj.* трёхсо́тый.
three-legged *adj.* трено́гий.
three-quarter time трёхдо́льный разме́р.
three-room *adj.* трёхко́мнатный.
three-sided *adj.* трёхсторо́нний.
three-story *adj.* трёхэта́жный.
three-time *adj.* троекра́тный: *three-time champion,* троекра́тный чемпио́н.
three-way *adj.* тройно́й: *three-way exchange,* тройно́й обме́н.
three-wheel *adj.* трёхколёсный. *Also,* **three-wheeled.**
thresh *v.t.* молоти́ть.
thresher *n.* **1,** (one who threshes) молоти́льщик. **2,** (threshing machine) молоти́лка. **3,** (variety of shark) морска́я лиси́ца.
threshing *n.* молотьба́. *Threshing floor,* гумно́; ток.
threshold *n.* **1,** (doorstep) поро́г. **2,** *fig.* (beginning) поро́г; преддве́рие.
thrice *adv.* три́жды.
thrift *n.* бережли́вость; расчётливость; эконо́мность. —**thrifty,** *adj.* бережли́вый; расчётливый; эконо́мный.
thrill *v.t.* захва́тывать. —*n.* о́строе ощуще́ние. —**thriller,** *n.* захва́тывающий рома́н, фильм, *etc.* —**thrilling,** *adj.* захва́тывающий.
thrive *v.i.* процвета́ть.
throat *n.* го́рло. *Clear one's throat,* отка́шливаться. *Cut someone's throat,* перере́зать го́рло (+ *dat.*). —**cut one's own throat,** рыть самому́ себе́ я́му. —**jump down someone's throat,** набра́сываться на кого́-нибудь.
throaty *adj.* горлово́й; горта́нный.
throb *v.i.* си́льно би́ться; стуча́ть; пульси́ровать. *Throbbing pain,* ко́лющая боль. —*n.* бие́ние; стук; пульса́ция.
throe *n., usu. pl.* му́ки. *Throes of death,* (предсме́ртная) аго́ния.
thrombosis *n.* тромбо́з.
throne *n.* престо́л; трон. —*adj.* тро́нный: *throne room,* тро́нный зал.
throng *n.* толпа́. —*v.i.* толпи́ться; стека́ться. —*v.t.* заполня́ть: *people thronged the square,* лю́ди запо́лнили пло́щадь.
throttle *n.* дро́ссель. —*v.t.* души́ть.
through *prep.* **1,** (in and out of) че́рез; сквозь: *through a tunnel,* че́рез тунне́ль; *through the crowd,* сквозь толпу́. *Breathe through one's mouth,* дыша́ть ртом. ♦*With certain nouns* в: *through a window,* в окно́; *look through a telescope,* смотре́ть в телеско́п; *speak through one's nose,* говори́ть в нос. **2,** (in the midst of) по: *walk through the mud,* идти́ по грязи́; *fly through the air,* лете́ть по во́здуху. **3,** (to various places in) по: *travel through France,* е́здить по Фра́нции. **4,** (up to and including) по (+ *acc.*): *from May through September,* с ма́я по сентя́брь. *I'm staying through Sunday,* я бу́ду здесь по воскресе́нье. **5,** [*usu.* **all through**] (throughout) в тече́ние всего́: *all through dinner,* в тече́ние всего́ обе́да. *All through the night,* всю ночь напролёт. **6,** (because of) по: *through no fault of mine,* не по мое́й вине́. **7,** (through the medium of) че́рез: *speak through an interpreter,* говори́ть че́рез перево́дчика. **8,** (by means of) путём; посре́дством. *Achieve one's goals through revolution,* дости́гнуть це́лей путём револю́ции. ♦*Often with the prefix* про-: *look through a report,* просмотре́ть докла́д; *go through a red light,* проскочи́ть кра́сный свет. *Pass through three stages of development,* проходи́ть три ста́дии разви́тия. *Less commonly* пере-: *leaf through a book,* перели́стывать

кни́гу; *live through a crisis,* пережи́ть кри́зис. —*adj.* **1,** (direct) беспереса́дочный: *through flight,* беспереса́дочный полёт. **2,** (finished): *are you through?,* вы ко́нчили? —*adv.* **1,** (in space) насквозь: *soaked through,* промо́кший насквозь. *Let him through,* пропусти́те его́. **2,** (in time) напролёт: *the whole night through,* всю ночь напролёт. —**through and through, 1,** (thoroughly; throughout) насквозь: *soaked through and through,* промо́кший насквозь. **2,** (completely; in every respect) соверше́нно; до конца́.

throughout *prep.* **1,** (in every part of) по всему́; по всей (+ *dat*): *throughout the country,* по всей стране́. **2,** (from the beginning to the end of) в тече́ние всего́/всей (+ *gen.*); в продолже́ние всего́/всей (+ *gen.*); на протяже́нии всего́/всей (+ *gen.*). —*adv.* повсю́ду; во всех отноше́ниях.

throw *v.t.* **1,** (toss) броса́ть; кида́ть. *Throw stones at,* забра́сывать камня́ми (+ *acc.*). *Throw into prison,* бро́сить в тюрьму́. *Throw troops into battle,* броса́ть войска́ в бой. **2,** *fol. by* **oneself** (lunge) бро́ситься; набро́ситься. *Throw oneself at,* набро́ситься на (+ *acc.*). *Throw oneself into someone's arms,* бро́ситься в чьи-нибудь объя́тия. **3,** (put on; lay over) набро́сить; наки́нуть: *throw a shawl over one's shoulders,* набро́сить/наки́нуть шаль на пле́чи. **4,** (unseat, as a rider) сбра́сывать. **5,** (put into a certain condition) приводи́ть: *throw into confusion,* приводи́ть в замеша́тельство. **6,** *colloq.* (give, as a big party) задава́ть. —*v.i.* броса́ть; кида́ть. —*n.* **1,** (single act) бросо́к. **2,** (general act) мета́ние: *discus throw,* мета́ние ди́ска. —**throw away, 1,** (discard) выбра́сывать. **2,** (waste) расточа́ть. **3,** (lose; miss) пропуска́ть. —**throw back,** отбра́сывать; отки́дывать. —**throw off, 1,** (cast off) сбра́сывать. **2,** (disconcert) сбива́ть. **3,** (shake off; elude) отрыва́ться от. **4,** (emit) испуска́ть. —**throw open,** распа́хивать. —**throw out, 1,** (discard) выбра́сывать. **2,** (evict; eject) выгоня́ть. **3,** (put forth) предлага́ть. —**throw up, 1,** (construct) стро́ить; возводи́ть. *Throw up a bridge,* наводи́ть мост. **2,** (vomit) рвать: *he threw up,* его́ вы́рвало. **3,** *Throw up one's hands,* развести́ рука́ми.

throwaway *adj.* бро́совый.

thrower *n.* мета́тель.

throw-weight *n.* забра́сываемый вес.

thru *prep., adj. & adv.* = **through.**

thrush *n.* **1,** (bird) дрозд. **2,** (disease) моло́чница.

thrust *v.t.* **1,** (stick, as one's hands in one's pockets) сова́ть; засо́вывать. **2,** (plunge, as a dagger) вонза́ть. —*n.* **1,** (shove) толчо́к. **2,** (lunge) вы́пад. **3,** (of an engine, propeller, etc.) тя́га. **4,** *mil.* уда́р.

thruway *n.* автостра́да.

thud *n.* глухо́й звук. —*v.i.* па́дать с глухи́м зву́ком.

thug *n.* громи́ла; головоре́з.

thulium *n.* ту́лий.

thumb *n.* большо́й па́лец. —*v.t.* **1,** (soil by handling) захва́тывать (*pfv.* захвата́ть). **2,** *fol. by* **through** (leaf through) перели́стывать. **3,** *in* **thumb a ride,** *colloq.* "голосова́ть" на доро́ге. —**he is all thumbs,** у него́ всё из рук ва́лится. —**thumb one's nose at,** показа́ть нос (+ *dat.*). —**turn thumbs down on,** реши́тельно отклоня́ть. —**under the thumb of,** под башмако́м *or* под каблуко́м у.

thumbnail *n.* но́готь большо́го па́льца. —**thumbnail sketch,** кра́ткое описа́ние.

thumbscrew *n.* **1,** (screw turned by hand) бара́шек. **2,** (instrument of torture) тиски́ для больши́х па́льцев.

thumbtack *n.* кно́пка.

thump *n.* тяжёлый уда́р; тума́к. —*v.t.* колоти́ть. —*v.i.* колоти́ться: *my heart was thumping,* у меня́ се́рдце колоти́лось.

thunder *n.* гром. —*v.i.* **1,** (produce thunder) греме́ть. *It is thundering,* гром греми́т. **2,** (make or move with a loud noise) грохота́ть.

thunderbolt *n.* уда́р мо́лнии.

thunderclap *n.* уда́р гро́ма.

thundercloud *n.* грозова́я ту́ча.

thunderous *adj.* громово́й.

thundershower *n.* ли́вень.

thunderstorm *n.* гроза́.

thunderstruck *adj.* как гро́мом поражённый.

Thursday *n.* четве́рг.

thus *adv.* **1,** (in this manner) так; таки́м о́бразом. **2,** (hence) так; поэ́тому. **3,** (thereby) тем са́мым. —**thus far,** пока́ что; пока́ ещё.

thwart *v.t.* расстра́ивать; срыва́ть.

thy *poss.adj., archaic* твой.

thyme *n.* тимья́н; чабре́ц.

thymus *n.* зо́бная железа́.

thyroid *n.* [*also,* **thyroid gland**] щитови́дная железа́. —*adj.* щитови́дный.

ti *n., music* си.

tiara *n.* тиа́ра.

Tibetan *adj.* тибе́тский. —*n.* тибе́тский язы́к.

tibia *n.* больша́я берцо́вая кость.

tic *n.* тик: *nervous tic,* не́рвный тик.

tick *n.* **1,** (sound) ти́канье. **2,** (parasite) клещ. **3,** (mark) пти́чка; га́лочка. —*v.i.* ти́кать. —*v.t.* [*usu.* **tick off**] **1,** (check off) отмеча́ть пти́чкой/га́лочкой. **2,** (rattle off) отбараба́нить. **3,** *slang* (anger; annoy) разозли́ть.

ticker *n.* ти́ккер.

ticket *n.* **1,** (token of admission) биле́т: *theater tickets,* биле́ты в теа́тр. *Plane ticket,* биле́т на самолёт. *Tickets to a show/match,* биле́ты на спекта́кль/матч. **2,** (check; receipt) номеро́к; квита́нция. *Pawn ticket,* зало́говая квита́нция. **3,** (label; tag) этике́тка; ярлы́к. **4,** (notification of a violation) штраф. **5,** (electoral slate) спи́сок кандида́тов (како́й-нибудь па́ртии). —*v.t.* приkле́ивать этике́тку *or* ярлы́к к. —**ticket collector,** билетёр; контролёр. —**ticket office; ticket window,** биле́тная ка́сса.

ticking *n.* **1,** (sound) ти́канье. **2,** (material) тик.

tickle *v.t. & i.* щекота́ть: *don't tickle!,* не щекочи́! *My throat tickles,* у меня́ в го́рле перши́т. —*n.* щеко́тка; щекота́ние. —**be tickled to death,** захлёбываться от удово́льствия.

ticklish *adj.* **1,** (sensitive to tickling): *be ticklish,* боя́ться щеко́тки. **2,** (delicate; tricky) щекотли́вый. —**ticklishness,** *n.* щекотли́вость.

tick-tack-toe *n.* (игра́ в) кре́стики и но́лики.

tidal *adj.* прили́вный. —**tidal wave,** прили́вная волна́; волна́ прили́ва.

tidbit *n.* ла́комый кусо́чек.

tiddlywinks *n.* бло́шки.

tide *n.* **1,** (rise and fall of waters) прили́вы и отли́вы. *Flood tide,* прили́в. *Ebb tide,* отли́в. *High tide,* вы́сшая то́чка прили́ва. *Low tide,* ни́зшая то́чка отли́ва. *The tide is in/out,* сейча́с прили́в/отли́в. **2,** (drift of events) дела́; ход собы́тий. *The tide has turned,* дела́ при́няли ино́й оборо́т. *Turn the tide,* измени́ть ход собы́тий. *Go against the tide,* идти́ про́тив тече́ния. —*v.t.* [*usu.* **tide over**] подкрепля́ть. *This will tide us over till spring,* э́того нам хва́тит до весны́.

tidewater *n.* прили́вная вода́.

tidiness *n.* опря́тность; аккура́тность.

tidings *n.pl.* ве́сти; но́вости; изве́стия.

tidy *adj.* **1,** (neat) опря́тный; аккура́тный. **2,** *colloq.* (considerable) поря́дочный; изря́дный; кру́гленький. —*v.t.* [*usu.* **tidy up**] убира́ть; прибира́ть; приводи́ть в поря́док.

tie *v.t.* **1,** (fasten) завя́зывать: *tie one's shoelaces,* завя́зывать шнурки́. *Tie one's shoes,* шнурова́ть боти́нки. *Tie one's tie,* повя́зывать га́лстук. *Tie a knot,* завя́зывать у́зел. *Tie a horse to a post,* привяза́ть ло́шадь к столбу́. *Tie a rope around something,* обвяза́ть что́-нибудь верёвкой. *Tie someone's hands (fig.),* связа́ть кому́-нибудь ру́ки. **2,** *fol. by* **to** (confine; restrict) привя́зывать (к): *she is tied to the kitchen,* она́ привя́зана к ку́хне. **3,** (link) связывать: *closely tied to,* те́сно свя́занный с. **4,** *sports* сыгра́ть вничью́ с; сде́лать ничью́ с. *Tie the score,* сравня́ть счёт. *Tie a record,* повторя́ть реко́рд. —*v.i.* **1,** (be tied) завя́зываться: *the apron ties in front,* пере́дник завя́зывается спе́реди. **2,** *sports: tie for first place,* подели́ть пе́рвое и второ́е ме́сто. —*n.* **1,** (necktie) га́лстук. **2,** (bond) связь; *pl.* у́зы. *Ties of friendship,* у́зы дру́жбы. **3,** (draw; stalemate) ничья́. **4,** *R.R.* шпа́ла. —**tie down,** привя́зывать. —**tie up, 1,** (tie securely) привя́зывать: *the dog is tied up,* соба́ка привя́зана. **2,** (tie with a string) перевя́зывать. **3,** (bind hand and foot) связа́ть по рука́м и нога́м. **4,** (moor) прича́ливать; швартова́ться. **5,** (obstruct; halt) тормози́ть: *tie up traffic,* тормози́ть у́личное движе́ние. **6,** (keep busy) занима́ть: *I'm tied up right now,* я сейча́с за́нят.

tiepin *n.* зако́лка. *Also,* **tie clasp.**

tier *n.* я́рус. —**tiered,** *adj.* я́русный.

tie-up *n.* **1,** (stoppage) остано́вка. **2,** (jam, as of traffic) зато́р (у́личного движе́ния); про́бка.

tiff *n.* размо́лвка; перебра́нка.

tiger *n.* тигр. —*adj.* тигро́вый: *tiger skin,* тигро́вая шку́ра.

tiger lily тигро́вая ли́лия.

tight *adj.* **1,** (taut; fast) туго́й: *tight spring,* тугая пружи́на. **2,** (fitting closely) те́сный; у́зкий. *These shoes are tight,* э́ти ту́фли жмут. **3,** (crowded; cramped) те́сный: *tight quarters,* те́сное помеще́ние. **4,** (strict; rigid) стро́гий: *tight control,* стро́гий контро́ль. **5,** (affording little leeway) жёсткий: *tight schedule,* жёсткий гра́фик; жёсткое расписа́ние. **6,** (difficult) пи́ковый: *a tight spot,* пи́ковое положе́ние. **7,** *colloq.* (stingy) скупо́й. **8,** *slang* (drunk) подвы́пивший. —*adv.* **1,** (taut) ту́го. **2,** (firmly) кре́пко: *hold tight!,* держи́тесь кре́пко! **3,** (with no openings) на́глухо: *sealed up tight,* на́глухо закры́т. —**sit tight,** выжида́ть. —**sleep tight!,** спи́те споко́йно!

tighten *v.t.* **1,** (pull tight; make taut) натя́гивать; затя́гивать; стя́гивать. *Tighten a rope/spring,* натя́гивать верёвку/пружи́ну. *Tighten the strings on a violin,* натя́гивать стру́ны на скри́пке. *Tighten a knot,* затя́гивать *or* стя́гивать у́зел. **2,** (turn to a tight position) зави́нчивать; завёртывать: *tighten a screw,* зави́нчивать/завёртывать га́йку. *Tighten a faucet,* завёртывать кран. **3,** (compress; close) сжима́ть; смыка́ть: *tighten the ring around,* сжима́ть/смыка́ть кольцо́ вокру́г. *Tighten one's grip,* сжима́ть кре́пче. —*v.i.* **1,** (become taut) натя́гиваться. **2,** (tense up) напряга́ться. **3,** (become smaller; close in) сжима́ться; смыка́ться. —**tighten one's belt, 1,** *literally* затяну́ться по́ясом. **2,** (be more frugal) класть зу́бы на по́лку. —**tighten the screws,** зави́нчивать га́йки.

tight-fisted *adj.* скупо́й; ска́редный; прижи́мистый.

tight-lipped *adj.* за́мкнутый.

tightly *adv.* **1,** (tight) ту́го. **2,** (firmly) про́чно. **3,** (with no openings) на́глухо.

tightness *n.* теснота́. *I feel a tightness in my chest,* мне тесни́т грудь.

tightrope *n.* кана́т. —**tightrope walker,** ка̀натохо́дец; эквилибри́ст.

tights *n.pl.* трико́.

tightwad *n., slang* скопидо́м; скуперд́яй.

tigress *n.* тигри́ца.

tilde *n.* ти́льда.

tile *n.* **1,** (glazed slab) ка́фель; изразе́ц. **2,** (roof tile) черепи́ца; (floor tile) пли́тка. —*v.t.* крыть черепи́цей.

tiled *adj.* (of a stove) ка́фельный; изразцо́вый; (of a roof) черепи́чный; (of a floor) пли́точный.

till *prep.* до: *till now,* до сих пор; *till then,* до тех пор; *till tomorrow,* до за́втра. *From morning till night,* с утра́ до ве́чера. *Till then!,* пока́! *Till we meet again!,* до сле́дующей встре́чи. —*conj.* пока́ не: *till he arrives,* пока́ он не придёт. *She is not coming till Sunday,* она́ придёт то́лько в воскресе́нье. —*n.* (cash box) ка́сса. —*v.t.* обраба́тывать; возде́лывать (зе́млю).

tillage *n.* обрабо́тка.

tiller *n.* земледе́лец.

tilt *v.t.* наклоня́ть: *tilt one's head to one side,* наклоня́ть го́лову на́бок. *Tilt a chair backward,* наклоня́ть стул наза́д. —*v.i.* **1,** (slant) наклоня́ться. **2,** *fol. by* **over** (tip over) опроки́дываться. —*n.* **1,** (slant) накло́н. **2,** (joust) поеди́нок. —**at full tilt,** по́лным хо́дом; во весь опо́р.

timber *n.* лес; лесоматериа́л; древеси́на. —**timber line,** грани́ца распростране́ния ле́са.

timbre *n.* тембр.

time *n.* **1,** (general term) вре́мя: *all the time,* всё вре́мя; *at the time,* в то вре́мя; *any time,* в любо́е вре́мя. *Dinner time,* обе́денное вре́мя. *I have no time,* у меня́ нет вре́мени; мне не́когда. **2,** (occasion) раз: *three times,* три ра́за; *this time,* на э́тот раз. **3,** (period; interval) срок: *in a short time,* в коро́ткий срок. **4,** *often pl.* (historical period or conditions) времена́: *hard times,* тяжёлые времена́. *In Dante's time,* во времена́ Да́нте. *Since ancient times,* с да́вних времён. *Times have changed,* времена́ измени́лись. **5,** *music* такт: *keep time,* отбива́ть такт. *Three-quarter time,* трёхдо́льный разме́р. **6,** *pl., in multiplication, rendered by* два́жды, три́жды, пя́тью, ше́стью, *etc.*: *three times seven is twenty-one,* три́жды семь – два́дцать оди́н. —*v.t.* **1,** (set for a certain time; set to coincide with) приуро́чивать (к). **2,** (measure the time of) хронометри́ровать. —**ahead of time,** заблаговре́менно. —**at no time,** никогда́; ни ра́зу. —**at one time, 1,** (simultaneously) одновре́менно; ра́зом. **2,** (at a certain time in the past) одно́ вре́мя. —**at the same time, 1,** (simultaneously) в то же вре́мя; одновре́менно. **2,** (besides) вме́сте с тем. —**at times,** иногда́; времена́ми. —**do time,** *colloq.* отбыва́ть срок. —**for the time being,** пока́; до поры́ до вре́мени. —**from time to time,** вре́мя от вре́мени; по времена́м. —**have a good time,** хорошо́ провести́ вре́мя. —**in due time,** в своё вре́мя. —**in good time,** своевре́менно. —**in no time,** в два счёта. —**in one's time,** в своё вре́мя. *I have seen a lot in my time,* я мно́го повида́л на своём веку́. —**in time, 1,** (on time) во́время. **2,** (eventually) со вре́менем. —**it is time,** пора́: *it is time to go,* пора́ идти́. —**many a time,** мно́го раз. —**once upon a time,** одна́жды; жил-был. —**one at a time,** по одному́; поодино́чке. —**on time, 1,** (punctually) во́время. **2,** (on installment) в рассро́чку. —**take one's time,** не спеши́ть; не торопи́ться. —**time after time; time and time again,** раз за ра́зом. —**what time is it?,** кото́рый тепе́рь час?; ско́лько вре́мени сейча́с?

time bomb бо́мба заме́дленного де́йствия.

time clock та́бельные часы́.

time-consuming *adj.* отнима́ющий мно́го вре́мени.

time exposure больша́я вы́держка.

time-honored *adj.* освящённый века́ми.

timekeeper *n.* **1,** (one who records the hours worked by employees) та́бельщик. **2,** *sports* хронометри́ст.

timeless *adj.* вневре́менный.

timely *adj.* своевре́менный; уме́стный. —**timeliness,** *n.* своевре́менность; уме́стность.

time-out *n.* переры́в.

timepiece *n.* часы́; хроно́метр.

timer *n.* **1,** (timepiece) хроно́метр. **2,** (timekeeper) хронометри́ст.

time study хронометра́ж.

timetable *n.* расписа́ние; гра́фик.

time trouble *chess* цейтно́т.

time zone часово́й по́яс.

timid *adj.* ро́бкий; засте́нчивый; боязли́вый. —**timidity,** *n.* ро́бость; засте́нчивость. —**timidly,** *adv.* ро́бко.

timing *n.* расчёт вре́мени; синхрониза́ция.

timorous *adj.* боязли́вый; пугли́вый.

timothy *n., bot.* тимофе́евка. *Also,* **timothy grass.**

timpani *also,* **tympani** *n. pl.* тимпа́н.

tin *n.* **1,** (metal) о́лово. **2,** (tin plate) жесть. **3,** [*also,* **tin can**] (container) ба́нка; жестя́нка. —*adj.* оловя́нный; жестяно́й. —*v.t.* луди́ть.

tincture *n.* тинкту́ра; насто́йка.

tinder *n.* трут. —**tinderbox,** *n.* порохова́я бо́чка (*fig.*).

tine *n.* зубе́ц.

tin foil стanио́ль.

tinge *n.* отте́нок; при́месь; налёт. —*v.t.* **1,** (tint) подкра́шивать. *Tinged with blue,* с голубова́тым отте́нком. **2,** (give a slight trace to) придава́ть отте́нок: *her voice was tinged with sadness,* в её го́лосе чу́вствовался отте́нок гру́сти. *Admiration tinged with envy,* восхище́ние с при́месью за́висти.

tingle *v.i.* пощи́пывать *(impers.)*: *my cheeks are tingling,* щёки у меня́ пощи́пывает. *Tingle with excitement,* трепета́ть от возбужде́ния.

tinker *n.* ме́дник. —*v.i.* (putter) вози́ться.

tinkle *v.i.* звя́кать. —*v.t.* звя́кать (+ *instr.*). —*n.* звя́канье.

tinny *adj.* оловя́нный. *Tinny sound,* металли́ческий звук.

tin plate жесть. —**tin-plate,** *v.t.* луди́ть. —**tin-plated,** *adj.* лужёный.

tinsel *n.* **1,** (thin strips of something shiny) блёстки. **2,** (something superficially showy) мишура́.

tinsmith *n.* луди́льщик; жестя́нщик.

tint *n.* отте́нок. —*v.t.* подкра́шивать.

tintype *n.* ферроти́пия.

tiny *adj.* кро́хотный; кро́шечный; малю́сенький.

tip *n.* **1,** (point; end) ко́нчик. **2,** (piece attached to the end of something) наконе́чник. **3,** (gratuity) чаевы́е. *Give someone a tip,* дава́ть (+ *dat.*) на чай. **4,** (piece of advice) сове́т. —*v.t.* **1,** (tilt) наклоня́ть. **2,** *fol. by* **over** (overturn) опроки́дывать. **3,** (give a gratuity to) дава́ть (+ *dat.*) на чай. **4,** *fol. by* **off** (notify; warn) сообща́ть; предупрежда́ть. —*v.i.* **1,** (tilt) наклоня́ться. **2,** *fol. by* **over** (overturn) опроки́дываться. —**it is on the tip of my tongue,** э́то ве́ртится у меня́ на языке́. —**tip one's hand,** раскры́ть свои́ ка́рты. —**tip the scales (at),** ве́сить.

tipoff *n., colloq.* намёк; предупрежде́ние.

tipple *v.i.* выпива́ть. —**tippler,** *n.* пья́ница.

tipsy *adj.* подвы́пивший; под хмелько́м; навеселе́.

tiptoe *n.* цы́почки: *on tiptoe; on one's tiptoes,* на цы́почках; на цы́почки. —*v.i.* ходи́ть на цы́почках.

tiptop *adj.* отли́чный: *in tiptop shape,* в отли́чном состоя́нии.

tirade *n.* тира́да.

tire[1] *v.i.* **1,** (become weary) устава́ть; утомля́ться: *tire easily,* бы́стро устава́ть/утомля́ться. **2,** *fol. by* **of** (lose interest in) устава́ть (+ *inf.*). *I never tire of looking at...,* не могу́ насмотре́ться *or* налюбова́ться на (+ *acc.*). —*v.t.* утомля́ть.

tire[2] *also,* **tyre** *n.* ши́на; покры́шка.

tired *adj.* **1,** (fatigued) уста́лый. *I am tired,* я уста́л(а). *Get tired,* устава́ть. **2,** *fol. by* **of** (impatient; no longer willing): *I am tired of always waiting for him,* мне надое́ло всегда́ ждать его́.

tireless *adj.* неутоми́мый. —**tirelessly,** *adv.* не устава́я; без у́стали.

tiresome *adj.* **1,** (tiring) утоми́тельный. **2,** (annoying) надое́дливый.

tiring *adj.* утоми́тельный.

tissue *n.* **1,** (structural material) ткань: *nerve tissue,* не́рвная ткань. **2,** (piece of soft absorbent paper) бума́га: *toilet tissue,* туале́тная бума́га. **3,** *fig.* (web, as of lies) сплете́ние (лжи). —**tissue paper,** папиро́сная бума́га.

tit *n.* (titmouse) сини́ца. —**tit for tat,** той же моне́той.

titan *n.* тита́н. —**titanic,** *adj.* титани́ческий.

titanium *n.* тита́н.

tithe *n.* десяти́на.

titillate *v.t.* щекота́ть. —**titillation,** *n.* щекота́ние; щеко́тка.

title *n.* **1,** (name, as of a book) загла́вие; назва́ние. **2,** (designation of rank or profession) зва́ние. **3,** (designation of nobility) ти́тул. **4,** *law* пра́во. **5,** *sports* чемпио́нское зва́ние. *The heavyweight title,* зва́ние чемпио́на по тяжёлому ве́су. **6,** (subtitle) титр. —*v.t.* озагла́вливать. —**title page,** загла́вный лист; ти́тульный лист. —**title role,** загла́вная роль.

titled *adj.* титуло́ванный.

titmouse *n.* сини́ца.

titter *v.i.* хихи́кать. —*n.* хихи́канье.

tittle-tattle *n.* тáры-бáры.
titular *adj.* номинáльный.
TNT тол; тротúл; тринитротолуóл.
to *prep.* **1,** (indicating destination) в (+ *acc.*): *go to the store/theater,* идтú в магазúн/теáтр; *go to London/England,* поéхать в Лóндон/Áнглию. ♦*With certain nouns* на: *go to the post office,* идтú на пóчту; *go to work,* éхать на рабóту. **2,** (toward) к: *come to me,* идú ко мне; *walk to the river,* идтú к рекé. **3,** (as far as; till) до: *to the end of the street,* до концá ýлицы; *soaked to the skin,* промóкший до костéй; *to a certain extent,* до нéкоторой стéпени; *from four to six o'clock,* от четырёх до шестú часóв. *To this day,* по сей день. **4,** *introducing the indirect object, rendered by the dative case: it seems to me,* мне кáжется; *I gave the letter to him,* я дал емý письмó. **5,** *used to form the infinitive: to read,* читáть; *to dance,* танцевáть. *An operation to remove a bullet,* оперáция по удалéнию пýли. **6,** (in one's behavior toward) к: *he is very kind to her,* он óчень добр к ней. *Polite to one's relatives,* вéжлив со своúми рóдственниками. **7,** (producing or resulting in) к: *to my surprise,* к моемý удивлéнию. **8,** (belonging to) от: *the key to the room,* ключ от кóмнаты. **9,** *in toasts* за (+ *acc.*): *drink to someone's health,* пить за здорóвье когó-нибудь. **10,** (to the accompaniment of) под (+ *acc.*): *dance to the music,* танцевáть под мýзыку. **11,** *used in telling time: a quarter to three,* без чéтверти три. **12,** *with various nouns and verbs* в: *introduction to physics,* введéние в фúзику; *shift to the offensive,* переходúть в наступлéние. **13,** *with various nouns and verbs* на: *spring to one's feet,* вскочúть нá ноги; *tear to pieces,* разорвáть на кускú; *come to someone's aid,* прийтú на пóмощь (+ *dat.*); *from Russian to English,* с рýсского на англúйский. **14,** *in various constructions* к: *face to face,* лицóм к лицý; *deaf to our pleas,* глух к нáшим прóсьбам; *come to an end,* приходúть к концý; *tie to a post,* привязáть к столбý; *sentence to death,* приговорúть к смéртной кáзни. **15,** *in certain combinations* для: *open to the public,* открыт для пýблики; *be of interest to all,* представлять интерéс для всех; *mean a great deal to,* мнóго знáчить для. —**as to,** что касáется. —**to and fro,** взад и вперёд.
toad *n.* жáба.
toadstool *n.* погáнка.
toady *n.* подхалúм. —*v.i.* подхалúмничать (пéред). —**toadyism,** *n.* подхалúмство.
toast *n.* **1,** (toasted bread) поджáренный хлеб. **2,** (drink in honor of someone) тост. —*v.t.* **1,** (brown) поджáривать. **2,** (pay tribute to) провозглашáть тост за (+ *acc.*).
toaster *n.* тóстер.
toastmaster *n.* тамадá.
tobacco *n.* табáк. —*adj.* табáчный: *tobacco leaves,* табáчные лúстья. —**tobacco grower,** табаковóд. —**tobacco pouch,** кисéт.
toboggan *n.* салáзки. —*v.i.* катáться на салáзках.
tocsin *n.* набáт.
today *n. & adv.* сегóдня. *What is today's date?,* какóе сегóдня числó? *Today's lesson,* сегóдняшний урóк.
toddle *v.i.* ковылять. —**toddler,** *n.* ребёнок, начинáющий ходúть.
toe *n.* **1,** (digit of the foot) пáлец ногú; пáлец на ногé. **2,** (tip of a stocking or shoe) носóк. —**on one's toes,** начекý; настороже́. —**toe the line** (*or* **mark**), **1,** *sports* встать на стáртовую лúнию. **2,** (conform to the rules) ходúть по стрýнке.
toenail *n.* нóготь на пáльце ногú.
toffee *also,* **toffy** *n.* тянýчка; ирúс.
toga *n.* тóга.
together *adv.* вмéсте: *go together,* идтú вмéсте. *Tie together,* связывать. *Paste together,* склéивать. *Rub two sticks together,* терéть две пáлки друг о дрýга. —**together with,** вмéсте с.
toil *n.* (тяжёлый) труд. —*v.i.* трудúться. —**toiler,** *n.* трýженик.
toilet *n.* **1,** (receptacle) унитáз. **2,** (washroom) убóрная; туалéт. **3,** (personal appearance) туалéт. —*adj.* туалéтный. —**toilet paper,** туалéтная бумáга. —**toilet seat,** стульчáк. —**toilet water,** туалéтная водá.
toiletries *n. pl.* туалéтные принадлéжности.
token *n.* **1,** (sign; symbol) знак; залóг: *as a token of,* в знак *or* в залóг (+ *gen.*). **2,** (keepsake) сувенúр. **3,** (coin; counter) жетóн. —*adj.* символúческий: *token payment,* символúческий взнос. —**by the same token,** рáвным óбразом.
tolerable *adj.* **1,** (endurable) терпúмый; снóсный. **2,** (passable) снóсный; прилúчный. —**tolerably,** *adv.* [*also,* **tolerably well**] снóсно.
tolerance *n.* **1,** (toleration) терпúмость. **2,** *mech.* дóпуск.
tolerant *adj.* терпúмый. *Be tolerant of,* относúться терпúмо к.
tolerate *v.t.* **1,** (bear; endure) терпéть. **2,** (allow; permit) допускáть. —**toleration,** *n.* терпúмость.
toll *n.* **1,** (fee) сбор. **2,** (peal of a bell) звон. **3,** (extent of losses) потéри. *The hurricane took a heavy toll of lives,* ураган унёс мнóго человéческих жизней. —*adj.* плáтный: *toll bridge,* плáтный мост. *Toll call,* междугорóдный телефóнный разговóр. *Toll collector,* сбóрщик. —*v.t.* звонúть в. —*v.i.* звонúть: *for whom the bell tolls,* по ком звонúт кóлокол. —**take its toll,** брать своё: *time had taken its toll,* врéмя брáло своё.
tollgate *n.* застáва (где взимáется сбор).
toluene *n.* толуóл.
tomahawk *n.* томагáвк.
tomato *n.* помидóр; томáт. —*adj.* томáтный: *tomato juice,* томáтный сок. *Tomato paste,* томáт-пáста.
tomb *n.* гробнúца. —**Tomb of the Unknown Soldier,** могúла Неизвéстного солдáта.
tomboy *n.* сорванéц.
tombstone *n.* надгрóбный кáмень; надгрóбная плитá.
tomcat *n.* кот.
tome *n.* том.
tomfoolery *n.* **1,** (foolish behavior) дурáчества. **2,** (nonsense) чепухá.
Tommy gun автомáт.
tommyrot *n., slang* вздор; галиматья́.
tomorrow *n. & adv.* зáвтра. *Beginning tomorrow,* начинáя с зáвтрашнего дня. —*adj.* [*usu.* **tomorrow's**] зáвтрашний: *tomorrow's date,* зáвтрашнее числó. —**the day after tomorrow,** послезáвтра. —**tomorrow morning,** зáвтра ýтром. —**tomorrow evening; tomorrow night,** зáвтра вéчером.
tomtit *n.* синúца.
tom-tom *n.* тамтáм.

ton *n.* тóнна.
tonal *adj.* тонáльный. —**tonality,** *n.* тонáльность.
tone *n.* **1,** (quality of sound or color) тон: *light tones,* свéтлые тонá. *Tone of voice,* тон гóлоса. **2,** *physiol.* тóнус: *muscle tone,* мы́шечный тóнус. **3,** *fig.* (general tenor) тон: *set the tone,* задáть тон. —*v.t.* **1,** *fol. by* **down** (moderate; soften) смягчáть; тушевáть. **2,** *fol. by* **up,** *physiol.* тонизи́ровать.
tone poem симфони́ческая поэ́ма.
tongs *n. pl.* щипцы́; клéщи.
tongue *n.* язы́к. *Loose tongue,* язы́к без костéй. *Mother tongue,* роднóй язы́к. *Smoked tongue,* копчёный язы́к. *Tongue of a shoe,* язычóк боти́нка. *Tongues of flame,* языки́ плáмени. —**hold one's tongue,** придержáть язы́к; проглоти́ть язы́к; держáть язы́к за зубáми. —**with tongue in cheek,** в шýтку.
tongue-lashing *n.* нагоня́й; разнóс.
tongue-tie *n.* косноязы́чие. —*v.t.* связáть язы́к (+ *dat.*). —**tongue-tied,** *adj.* косноязы́чный.
tongue twister скороговóрка.
tonic *n.* укрепля́ющее срéдство. —*adj.* тони́ческий.
tonight *n. & adv.* сегóдня вéчером.
tonnage *n.* тоннáж.
tonsil *n.* миндáлина; миндалеви́дная железá; глáнда.
tonsillectomy *n.* удалéние миндáлин.
tonsillitis *n.* воспалéние миндáлин.
tonsorial *adj.* парикмáхерский.
tonsure *n.* тонзýра.
too *adv.* **1,** (also; as well) тóже; тáкже. *I'm sorry too,* мне тóже жаль. **2,** (excessively) сли́шком: *too far,* сли́шком далекó. —**not too,** не óчень: *not too clever,* не óчень умён. —**only too,** тóлько: *I will be only too happy to...,* я бýду тóлько рад (+ *inf.*). —**too bad,** *see* **bad.** —**too much,** сли́шком мнóго; сли́шком. —**too much for,** не под си́лу (+ *dat.*).
tool *n.* **1,** (hand-held implement) инструмéнт: *carpenter's tools,* плóтничные инструмéнты. **2,** (anything that serves as a tool) орýдие: *tools of production,* орýдия произвóдства. **3,** (stooge) орýдие; марионéтка. —*v.t.* **1,** (shape with a tool) обрабáтывать. **2,** *fol. by* **up** (provide with tools) оборýдовать инструмéнтами. —*v.i.* [*usu.* **tool along**] (ride; drive) éхать; кати́ться. —**toolbox,** *n.* я́щик для инструмéнтов. —**toolmaker,** *n.* инструментáльщик.
toot *n.* гудóк. —*v.t. & i.* гудéть.
tooth *n.* **1,** (in the mouth) зуб (*pl.* зýбы). **2,** (projecting point, as of a saw) зуб (*pl.* зýбья); зубéц. —**armed to the teeth,** вооружённый до зубóв. —**in the teeth of,** вопреки́; наперекóр. *In the teeth of the wind,* пря́мо прóтив вéтра. —**show one's teeth,** покáзывать кóгти. —**tooth and nail,** изо всех сил; всéми си́лами.
toothache *n.* зубнáя боль. *I have a toothache,* у меня́ боля́т зýбы.
toothbrush *n.* зубнáя щётка.
toothed *adj.* зубчáтый.
toothless *adj.* беззýбый.
toothpaste *n.* зубнáя пáста.
toothpick *n.* зубочи́стка.
tooth powder зубнóй порошóк.
toothy *adj.* зубáстый.
top *n.* **1,** (highest part) верхýшка; верши́на; верх; макýшка. *At the top of,* на верхý (+ *gen.*). *At the top of the page,* вверхý страни́цы. *From the top,* свéрху. **2,** (lid; cover) кры́шка. **3,** (toy) волчóк. **4,** *pl.* (above-ground part of a plant) ботвá. —*adj.* **1,** (highest) вéрхний: *on the top shelf,* на вéрхней пóлке. **2,** (best) лýчший; пéрвый: *top pupil,* лýчший/пéрвый учени́к. —*v.t.* **1,** (be at the top of): *top the list,* стоя́ть пéрвым в спи́ске. **2,** (place something on top of) покрывáть. *Top fruit with whipped cream,* покрывáть фрýкты взби́тыми сли́вками. **3,** (exceed; surpass) превышáть; превосходи́ть. **4,** *fol. by* **off** (climax) закáнчивать. —**at top speed,** во весь опóр. —**blow one's top,** *colloq.* взорвáться. —**from top to bottom,** свéрху дóнизу. —**on top,** наверхý. *Come out on top,* прийти́ пéрвым; взять верх. —**on top of, 1,** (on) на. **2,** (in addition to) крóме; сверх. *On top of everything (else),* сверх всегó. **3,** (following upon) вслед за. **4,** (in control of) на высотé (+ *gen.*): *on top of the situation,* на высотé положéния. —**on top of the world,** *colloq.* на седьмóм нéбе; на верхý блажéнства. —**sleep like a top,** спать как сурóк. —**to top it off,** в довершéние всегó.
topaz *n.* топáз. —*adj.* топáзовый.
topcoat *n.* пальтó.
topflight *adj.* первоклáссный; превосхóдный.
topgallant *n.* [*also,* **topgallant sail**] брáмсель. —**topgallant mast,** брам-стéньга.
top hat цили́ндр.
topic *n.* тéма; предмéт.
topical *adj.* **1,** (pert. to a topic) темати́ческий. **2,** (of current interest) актуáльный.
topknot *n.* хохóл.
topmast *n.* стéньга.
topnotch *adj., colloq.* первоклáссный.
topography *n.* топогрáфия. —**topographer,** *n.* топóграф. —**topographical,** *adj.* топографи́ческий.
topology *n.* тополóгия.
topple *v.t.* **1,** (overturn) вали́ть; опроки́дывать. **2,** (overthrow) свергáть. —*v.i.* [*usu.* **topple over**] вали́ться; опроки́дываться.
topsail *n.* тóпсель; мáрсель.
top-secret *adj.* совершéнно секрéтный.
topside *adv.* на пáлубе. —**topsides,** *n. pl.* надвóдная часть.
topsoil *n.* вéрхний слой пóчвы; пóчвенный покрóв.
topsy-turvy *adv.* вверх дном; ши́ворот-навы́ворот.
toque *n.* ток.
Torah *n.* тóра.
torch *n.* **1,** (flaming light) фáкел. **2,** (device used in welding and soldering) горéлка: *acetylene torch,* ацетилéновая горéлка. **3,** *Brit.* (flashlight) кармáнный фонáрь. **4,** *fig.* (source of enlightenment) фáкел; свéточ: *the torch of knowledge,* фáкел/свéточ знáния. —**torchbearer,** *n.* фáкельщик.
torchlight *n.* свет фáкела. *Torchlight procession,* фáкельное шéствие.
toreador *n.* тореадóр.
torment *v.t.* мýчить. —*n.* мýка; мучéние. —**tormentor,** *n.* мучи́тель.
tornado *n.* смерч.
torpedo *n.* торпéда. —*v.t.* торпеди́ровать. —**torpedo boat,** минонóсец.
torpid *adj.* **1,** (sluggish) вя́лый. **2,** (numb) онемéлый.
torpor *n.* оцепенéние; отупéние.
torrent *n.* потóк. —**torrential,** *adj.* проливнóй.
torrid *adj.* **1,** (scorching) паля́щий. **2,** *fig.* (heated; ardent) горя́чий. —**Torrid Zone,** тропи́ческий пóяс.

torsion *n.* кручéние.
torso *n.* **1,** (of the human body) тýловище. **2,** (statue) торс.
tort *n.* правонарушéние.
tortoise *n.* черепáха.
tortoise shell черепáха. —**tortoise-shell,** *adj.* черепáховый.
tortuous *adj.* извúлистый.
torture *n.* **1,** (inflicting of pain) пы́тка; истязáние. **2,** *fig.* (agony) мýка: *sheer/pure torture,* настоя́щая мýка. —*v.t.* подвергáть пы́тке; пытáть; истязáть. —**torture chamber,** застéнок.
torturer *n.* истязáтель.
Tory *n.* тóри.
toss *v.t.* **1,** (throw) бросáть; кидáть; метáть. *Toss one's hat in the air,* брóсить шля́пу в вóздух. **2,** (flip, as a coin) подбрáсывать (монéту). **3,** (jerk upward, as the head) вскúдывать. **4,** (fling about) подбрáсывать: *the waves tossed the ship,* вóлны подбрáсывали сýдно. **5,** *fol. by* **off** (drink down) вы́пить зáлпом. —*v.i.* **1,** (be thrown about) качáть; бросáть; швыря́ть *(impers): the boat is tossing,* лóдку качáет/бросáет/швыря́ет. **2,** (shift about restlessly) метáться: *toss in one's sleep,* метáться во сне. —*n.* бросóк. *Toss of a coin,* жеребьёвка. —**toss aside,** отбрáсывать. —**toss out,** выбрáсывать; вышвы́ривать.
tot *n.* малы́ш.
total *n.* сýмма; итóг; *(at the bottom of a column of figures)* итогó. *A total of...,* в óбщей слóжности. —*adj.* **1,** (overall) óбщий: *the total amount/cost,* óбщая сýмма/стóимость. **2,** (complete; utter) пóлный: *total victory,* пóлная побéда. *Total eclipse,* пóлное затмéние. *The house is a total loss,* от дóма ничегó не остáлось. **3,** (all-out, as of war) тотáльный. —*v.t.* **1,** (add up) суммúровать; подытóживать; подводúть итóг (+ *dat.*). **2,** (amount to) составля́ть. **3,** *slang* (demolish) разбúть вдрéбезги.
totalitarian *adj.* тоталитáрный. —**totalitarianism,** *n.* тоталитарúзм.
totality *n.* совокýпность.
totalizator *n.* тотализáтор.
totally *adv.* пóлностью; целикóм; совершéнно.
tote *v.t., colloq.* нестú; тащúть. *Tote a gun,* имéть при себé орýжие.
totem *n.* тотéм. —**totemism,** *n.* тотемúзм.
totter *v.i.* шатáться; ковыля́ть.
toucan *n.* тукáн.
touch *v.t.* **1,** (place one's hand on) трóгать: *don't touch me!,* не трóгай меня́! **2,** (come into contact with) касáться: *touch bottom,* коснýться дна. **3,** *usu. neg.* (eat some of) притрáгиваться к; прикасáться к. **4,** (border) соприкасáться с. **5,** (injure slightly) трóнуть *(impers.): frost touched the plants,* морóзом трóнуло растéния. **6,** (move emotionally) трóгать; растрóгать. *Touch someone's heart,* брать зá сердце *or* зá душу. —*v.i.* трóгать: *"do not touch",* не трóгать! —*n.* **1,** (act of touching; feeling of being touched) прикосновéние. **2,** (sense of touch) осязáние. *To the touch,* на óщупь. **3,** (tinge; dash) прúмесь; налёт. **4,** (slight attack, as of illness) лёгкий прúступ. **5,** *music* тушé. **6,** *in* **finishing touches,** послéдние штрихú. —**in touch with, 1,** (in communication with) в контáкте с. *Get in touch with,* связáться с. *Keep in touch with,* поддéрживать связь с. **2,** (informed about) в кýрсе (+ *gen.*). —**lose touch with,** потеря́ть связь с; оторвáться от. —**touch down,** приземля́ться. —**touch off, 1,** (detonate) взрывáть. **2,** (initiate; trigger) вызывáть. —**touch on** *or* **upon,** затрáгивать; касáться. —**touch up,** подкрáшивать.
touched *adj.* **1,** (affected with emotion) трóнут; растрóганный. **2,** *colloq.* (unbalanced) трóнутый.
touchiness *n.* обúдчивость.
touching *adj.* трóгательный.
touch-me-not *n.* недотрóга.
touchstone *n.* **1,** (testing stone) пробúрный кáмень; оселóк. **2,** *fig.* (criterion; standard) прóбный кáмень; оселóк.
touch-type *v.i.* печáтать на машúнке вслепýю. —**touch-typing,** *n.* слепóй мéтод печáтания на машúнке.
touchy *adj.* **1,** (easily offended) обúдчивый. **2,** (delicate) щекотлúвый.
tough *adj.* **1,** (firm; durable) прóчный: *tough leather,* прóчная кóжа. **2,** (hard to chew) жёсткий: *tough meat,* жёсткое мя́со. **3,** (difficult) трýдный: *tough job,* трýдная задáча. **4,** (robust; rugged) вынóсливый. **5,** *colloq.* (unfortunate): *tough luck; a tough break,* незадáча; невезéние.
toughen *v.t.* закаля́ть.
toughness *n.* **1,** (durability) прóчность. **2,** (strength of character) закáл; закáлка.
toupee *n.* парúк.
tour *n.* **1,** (organized trip) турнé; поéздка. *Sightseeing tour of the city,* экскýрсия по гóроду. **2,** (round of public appearances) гастрóли. *Be on tour,* гастролúровать. **3,** *mil.* срок: *tour of duty,* срок слýжбы. —*v.i.* **1,** (travel) путешéствовать. **2,** (give public appearances) гастролúровать. —*v.t.* совершáть турнé по; объезжáть.
touring *adj.* гастрóльный: *touring company,* гастрóльная трýппа.
tourism *n.* турúзм.
tourist *n.* турúст. —*adj.* турúстский. —**tourist class,** трéтий класс.
tourmaline *n.* турмалúн.
tournament *n.* турнúр.
tourniquet *n.* жгут.
tousle *v.t.* ерóшить; взлохмáчивать.
tow *v.t.* тянýть (на буксúре); тащúть; буксúровать. —*n.* **1,** (act of towing) буксирóвка. **2,** (fiber) пáкля; кудéль. —**take in tow,** брать на буксúр.
towage *n.* буксирóвка.
toward *prep.* **1,** (in the direction of) к: *walk toward the house,* идтú к дóму. **2,** (with respect to) к: *animosity toward someone,* враждá к комý-нибудь. *America's policy toward the USSR,* полúтика США в отношéнии СССР. **3,** (near in point of time) к; под: *toward evening,* к вéчеру; под вéчер. *Toward the end of his life,* подконéц жúзни. **4,** (in furtherance of) для: *money toward one's education,* дéньги для получéния образовáния. *Also,* **towards.**
towboat *n.* буксúр.
towel *n.* полотéнце.
tower *n.* бáшня; вы́шка. —*v.i.* [*usu.* **tower over** *or* **above**] вы́ситься (над); возвышáться (над). —**tower of strength,** надёжная опóра.
towering *adj.* **1,** (very high) высóкий; возвышáющийся. **2,** (outstanding) выдаю́щийся. **3,** (intense, as of rage) неúстовый.
towheaded *adj.* белобры́сый.

towing *n.* буксиро́вка.
towline *n.* букси́р; бечева́.
town *n.* го́род. *Small town,* (ма́ленький) городо́к. *Out of town,* в отъе́зде. —**town crier,** глаша́тай. —**town hall,** ра́туша. —**town planning,** плани́рование го́рода; градострои́тельство.
townsfolk *n. pl.* горожа́не; городски́е жи́тели.
townsman *n.* горожа́нин.
towpath *n.* бечевни́к.
towrope *n.* букси́р; бечева́.
tow truck авари́йная маши́на.
toxemia *n.* токсеми́я.
toxic *adj.* токси́ческий; ядови́тый; отравля́ющий.
toxicology *n.* токсиколо́гия. —**toxicological,** *adj.* токсикологи́ческий. —**toxicologist,** *n.* токсико́лог.
toxin *n.* токси́н.
toy *n.* игру́шка. —*adj.* игру́шечный: *toy pistol,* игру́шечный пистоле́т. —*v.i.* [*usu.* **toy with**] игра́ть (+ *instr.*). *Toy with the idea of,* носи́ться с иде́ей (+ *inf.*).
trace *n.* **1,** (mark; track) след. *Disappear without a trace,* исче́знуть бессле́дно. **2,** (barely perceptible display) тень: *a trace of sadness,* тень печа́ли. *Not a trace of evidence,* ни мале́йших доказа́тельств. **3,** (part of a harness) постро́мка. —*v.t.* **1,** (sketch) черти́ть. **2,** (make a tracing of) калькиро́вать. **3,** (track down) высле́живать. **4,** (outline the development of) просле́живать. *Trace one's ancestry back to...,* вести́ свой род от...
tracer *n.* запро́с (о пропа́вшей посы́лке). —**tracer bullet,** трасси́рующая пу́ля.
trachea *n.* трахе́я. —**tracheal,** *adj.* трахе́йный.
trachoma *n.* трахо́ма.
tracing *n.* ка́лька. —**tracing paper,** бума́жная ка́лька.
track *n.* **1,** (mark; trace) след: *tracks in the snow,* следы́ на снегу́. **2,** *R.R.* (single rail) рельс: *go off the tracks,* сходи́ть с ре́льсов. **3,** *R.R.* (set of rails) путь; колея́. *Sidetrack,* запа́сный путь. *What track does the train leave on?,* с како́й платфо́рмы отхо́дит по́езд? **4,** *sports* доро́жка; трек. *Running track,* бегова́я доро́жка. **5,** (track and field) лёгкая атле́тика. **6,** (method of proceeding) путь: *on the right/wrong track,* на ве́рном/ло́жном пути́. —*v.t.* **1,** (follow the tracks of) высле́живать. **2,** *fol. by* **down** (pursue and capture) вы́следить. **3,** (monitor the course of) следи́ть за. **4,** *fol. by* **up** (leave footprints in or on) следи́ть (*pfv.* наследи́ть) в *or* на (+ *prepl.*). —**in one's tracks,** на ме́сте. *Stop dead in one's tracks,* останови́ться, как вко́панный. —**keep track of, 1,** (keep a record of) запи́сывать. **2,** (remain informed about) быть в ку́рсе (+ *gen.*); следи́ть за. —**lose track of, 1,** (lose touch with) (по)теря́ть и́з виду. *We lost track of each other,* мы потеря́ли друг дру́га и́з виду. **2,** (lose count of) (по)теря́ть счёт (+ *dat.*). —**make tracks,** *colloq.* дать тя́гу. —**throw (someone) off the track,** сбива́ть (кого́-нибудь) с пути́.
tracking station ста́нция слеже́ния.
trackman *n.* укла́дчик путе́й. *Also,* **track layer.**
track meet состяза́ние по лёгкой атле́тике.
tract *n.* **1,** (expanse) масси́в. **2,** *anat.* тракт; пути́: *digestive tract,* пищевари́тельный тракт; *respiratory tract,* дыха́тельные пути́. **3,** (brief treatise) тракта́т.
tractable *adj.* **1,** (docile) сгово́рчивый. **2,** (malleable) ко́вкий.
tractile *adj.* тягу́чий; ко́вкий.
traction *n.* **1,** (pulling power) тя́га. **2,** (friction that prevents skidding) сцепле́ние (с гру́нтом). **3,** *med.* вытяже́ние.
tractive *adj.* тя́говый.
tractor *n.* **1,** (farm vehicle) тра́ктор. **2,** (truck for pulling trailers) тяга́ч. —**tractor-trailer,** *n.* тяга́ч с прице́пом.
trackwalker *n.* путево́й обхо́дчик.
trade *n.* **1,** (commerce) торго́вля: *foreign trade,* вне́шняя торго́вля. **2,** (craft) ремесло́: *learn a trade,* учи́ться ремеслу́. **3,** (exchange) обме́н. *Make a trade,* соверши́ть обме́н; обменя́ться. —*adj.* торго́вый: *trade relations,* торго́вые отноше́ния. —*v.t.* **1,** (swap) меня́ться: *trade places,* меня́ться места́ми. **2,** (give in exchange for) обме́нивать: *trade cigarettes for vodka,* обме́нивать папиро́сы на во́дку. —*v.i.* **1,** (swap) обме́ниваться: *let's trade,* дава́йте обменя́емся. **2,** (engage in trade) торгова́ть: *trade with other countries,* торгова́ть с други́ми стра́нами.
trademark *n.* фабри́чная ма́рка.
trader *n.* торго́вец.
trade school реме́сленное учи́лище.
tradesman *n.* торго́вец.
trade union профсою́з.
trade wind écca...

trading *n.* торго́вля. —*adj.* торго́вый; торгу́ющий. —**trading post,** факто́рия.
tradition *n.* традиция. —**traditional,** *adj.* традицио́нный.
traduce *v.t.* клевета́ть на; черни́ть; поро́чить.
traffic *n.* **1,** (movement of vehicles) движе́ние: *heavy traffic,* интенси́вное движе́ние. **2,** (trade) торго́вля: *drug traffic,* торго́вля нарко́тиками. —*v.i.* [*usu.* **traffic in**] торгова́ть (+ *instr.*). —**traffic circle,** пло́щадь с кругово́ым движе́нием. —**traffic jam,** зато́р у́личного движе́ния; про́бка. —**traffic light,** светофо́р. —**traffic manager,** диспе́тчер. —**traffic sign,** доро́жный знак. —**traffic signal,** доро́жный сигна́л.
tragedian *n.* тра́гик. —**tragedienne,** *n.* траги́ческая актри́са.
tragedy *n.* **1,** (form of drama; calamity) траге́дия. **2,** (tragic nature) траги́чность; траги́зм.
tragic *adj.* траги́ческий; траги́чный. —**tragically,** *adv.* траги́чески; траги́чно.
tragicomedy *n.* трагикоме́дия. —**tragicomic,** *adj.* трагикоми́ческий.
trail *n.* **1,** (tracks) след: *pick up the trail,* найти́ след. *Leave a trail behind,* оставля́ть за собо́й след. *Be hot on the trail of,* идти́ по горя́чим следа́м (+ *gen.*). **2,** (stream) след: *trail of blood,* крова́вый след. *Leave behind a trail of dust,* оставля́ть за собо́й столб пы́ли. **3,** (path) тропа́; тропи́нка. *Blaze a trail,* прокла́дывать путь. —*v.t.* **1,** (drag loosely) тащи́ть; волочи́ть. **2,** (follow; shadow) высле́живать; просле́живать. **3,** (lag behind, as in a contest) отстава́ть от. —*v.i.* **1,** (be dragged) тащи́ться; волочи́ться. **2,** (move slowly along) тащи́ться; плести́сь. **3,** *sports* (be behind) прои́грывать: *trail by a score of 3-2,* прои́грывать со счётом три-два. **4,** *fol. by* **off** (fade away) замира́ть.
trailblazer *n.* пионе́р; нова́тор; следопы́т.
trailer *n.* прице́п.
train *n.* **1,** *R.R.* по́езд. **2,** (long line of vehicles) цепь; верени́ца. *Wagon train,* обо́з. **3,** (sequence) ход: *train*

of thought, ход мы́слей. **4,** (of a dress) шлейф. —*adj.* поездно́й: *train crew,* поездна́я брига́да. *Train service,* железнодоро́жное сообще́ние. *Train schedule,* расписа́ние поездо́в. *Train wreck,* круше́ние по́езда. —*v.t.* **1,** (instruct systematically) обуча́ть; гото́вить. **2,** (teach to act properly or in a certain way) воспи́тывать; приуча́ть. **3,** (make physically sound; prepare for an athletic contest) тренирова́ть. *Train one's ear,* тренирова́ть слух. **4,** (teach to perform tricks, as an animal) дрессирова́ть. **5,** (aim) наводи́ть. —*v.i.* тренирова́ться.

trained *adj.* **1,** (of a person) подгото́вленный; трениро́ванный. *Trained nurse,* медсестра́. **2,** (of an animal) дрессиро́ванный.

trainee *n.* практика́нт.

trainer *n.* **1,** (of athletes) тре́нер. **2,** (of animals) дрессиро́вщик.

training *n.* **1,** (of people) обуче́ние; подгото́вка; трениро́вка. *Voice training,* постано́вка го́лоса. **2,** (of animals) дрессиро́вка. —*adj.* уче́бный; трениро́вочный. *Training program,* курс обуче́ния/подгото́вки.

trait *n.* черта́.

traitor *n.* преда́тель; изме́нник. —**traitorous,** *adj.* преда́тельский; изме́ннический.

trajectory *n.* траекто́рия.

tram *n.* трамва́й.

trammel *n., usu. pl.* **1,** (shackles) пу́ты. **2,** (hindrance) око́вы. —*v.t.* ско́вывать.

tramp *v.i.* то́пать; топота́ть. *Tramp all over town,* исходи́ть весь го́род. —*n.* (vagabond) бродя́га;턱 craving: бося́к.

trample *v.t. & i.* **1,** [*also,* **trample on** *or* **down**] (press down; mash) топта́ть; раста́птывать; выта́птывать. **2,** (crush and injure severely) зата́птывать: *trample to death,* зата́птывать на́смерть. **3,** *fig.* (flout, as someone's rights) попира́ть.

trampoline *n.* бату́т.

trance *n.* транс: *in a trance,* в тра́нсе.

tranquil *adj.* споко́йный. —**tranquilize,** *v.t.* успока́ивать. —**tranquilizer,** *n.* успокои́тельное сре́дство. —**tranquillity,** *n.* споко́йствие.

transact *v.t.* **1,** (carry on) вести́: *transact business,* вести́ дела́. **2,** (complete) заключа́ть: *transact a deal,* заключи́ть сде́лку.

transaction *n.* **1,** (act of transacting) веде́ние (дел). **2,** (business deal) сде́лка.

transatlantic *adj.* трансатланти́ческий.

transcend *v.t.* **1,** (go beyond the range of) выходи́ть за преде́лы (+ *gen.*). **2,** (rise above; excel) превосходи́ть.

transcendent *adj.* **1,** (surpassing) исключи́тельный; непревзойдённый. **2,** *philos.* трансценде́нтный.

transcendental *adj.* **1,** *philos.* трансцендента́льный. **2,** *math.* трансценде́нтный.

transcontinental *adj.* трансконтинента́льный.

transcribe *v.t.* **1,** (make a written copy of) перепи́сывать. **2,** (record) запи́сывать на плёнку.

transcript *n.* ко́пия. *Stenographic transcript,* стеногра́мма. *Academic transcript,* академи́ческая спра́вка.

transcription *n.* **1,** *ling.* транскри́пция: *phonetic transcription,* фонети́ческая транскри́пция. **2,** (recording) звукоза́пись. **3,** *music* транскри́пция.

transfer *v.t.* **1,** (move to another place) переноси́ть; перемеща́ть. **2,** (move to a different job, school, etc.) переводи́ть; перемеща́ть. **3,** (shift; remit, as funds) переводи́ть. **4,** (make over possession of) передава́ть. —*v.i.* **1,** (change affiliation) переходи́ть. **2,** (change trains, buses, etc.) переса́живаться. —*n.* **1,** (carrying; conveying) перено́с; перенесе́ние; перемеще́ние. **2,** (change of jobs or affiliation) перево́д; перемеще́ние. **3,** (shift or remittal of funds) перево́д. **4,** (making over possession) переда́ча. **5,** (change of trains, buses, etc.) переса́дка. **6,** (ticket for same) переса́дочный *or* транзи́тный биле́т.

transferable *adj.* могу́щий быть пе́реданным. —**"not transferable",** без пра́ва переда́чи.

transference *n.* перенесе́ние; перемеще́ние. *Thought transference,* переда́ча мы́слей.

Transfiguration *n., relig.* преображе́ние.

transfigure *v.t.* преобража́ть.

transfix *v.t.* **1,** (impale) пронза́ть. **2,** (make motionless) прико́вывать к ме́сту.

transform *v.t.* **1,** (change the appearance of) преобража́ть. **2,** (change the basic nature of) преобразо́вывать. **3,** (turn into something else) превраща́ть. **4,** *electricity; physics* преобразо́вывать.

transformation *n.* превраще́ние; преобразова́ние; преображе́ние.

transformer *n.* преобразова́тель; трансформа́тор.

transfuse *v.t.* перелива́ть. —**transfusion,** *n.* перелива́ние: *blood transfusion,* перелива́ние кро́ви.

transgress *v.t.* наруша́ть; переступа́ть. —*v.i.* греши́ть. —**transgression,** *n.* грех; прегреше́ние; правонаруше́ние. —**transgressor,** *n.* гре́шник; правонаруши́тель.

transient *adj.* **1,** (fleeting) преходя́щий; мимолётный; скороте́чный. **2,** (staying for a short time) прое́зжий. —*n.* прое́зжий.

transistor *n.* транзи́стор.

transit *n.* **1,** (passage) перее́зд. *Be in transit,* быть в пути́. **2,** (conveyance) транзи́т; перево́зка. *Damaged in transit,* испо́рчен при перево́зке. —*adj.* транзи́тный.

transition *n.* перехо́д. —*adj.* [*also,* **transitional**] перехо́дный: *transition period,* перехо́дный пери́од.

transitive *adj.* перехо́дный: *transitive verb,* перехо́дный глаго́л.

transitory *adj.* преходя́щий; мимолётный; скороте́чный.

translate *v.t. & i.* переводи́ть: *translate from Russian to English,* переводи́ть с ру́сского (языка́) на англи́йский.

translation *n.* перево́д. *Read something in translation,* чита́ть что́-нибудь в перево́де.

translator *n.* перево́дчик.

transliterate *v.t.* транслитери́ровать. —**transliteration,** *n.* транслитера́ция.

translucent *adj.* полупрозра́чный. *Be translucent,* просве́чивать.

transmigration *n.* **1,** (migration) переселе́ние. **2,** *relig.* переселе́ние душ.

transmission *n.* переда́ча.

transmit *v.t.* передава́ть. —**transmittal,** *n.* переда́ча. —**transmitter,** *n.* (радио)переда́тчик.

transoceanic *adj.* трансокеа́нский; заокеа́нский.

transom *n.* **1,** (small window above a door) фраму́га. **2,** (crossbeam) перекла́дина.

transparency *n.* **1,** (quality of being transparent) прозра́чность. **2,** (slide) диапозити́в.
transparent *adj.* **1,** (not opaque) прозра́чный. **2,** (easily detected) я́вный.
transpire *v.i.* **1,** (become known) обнару́живаться. **2,** (occur) происходи́ть.
transplant *v.t.* переса́живать. —*n.* переса́дка. —**transplantation,** *n.* переса́дка.
transport *v.t.* **1,** (convey) перевози́ть; транспорти́ровать. **2,** (carry away with emotion) охва́тывать: *transported with joy,* охва́чен ра́достью; вне себя́ (*or* не по́мня себя́) от ра́дости. —*n.* **1,** (act of transporting) тра́нспорт; перево́зка. *Public transport,* обще́ственный тра́нспорт. **2,** (ship) тра́нспорт: *troop transport,* войсково́й тра́нспорт.
transportable *adj.* транспорта́бельный.
transportation *n.* перево́зка; тра́нспорт.
transporter *n.* транспортёр: *tank transporter,* та́нковый транспортёр.
transpose *v.t.* **1,** (interchange) переставля́ть. **2,** *music* транспони́ровать.
transposition *n.* **1,** (act of transposing) переста́новка. **2,** *music* транспониро́вка. **3,** *chess* переста́новка ходо́в.
transship *v.t.* перегружа́ть; перева́ливать. —**transshipment,** *n.* перегру́зка; перева́лка. *Transshipment point,* перегру́зочный *or* перева́лочный пункт; перева́лка.
trans-Siberian *adj.* транссиби́рский.
transverse *adj.* попере́чный.
trap *n.* западня́; лову́шка. —*v.t.* пойма́ть в западню́. *People were trapped in the building,* лю́ди, находя́щиеся в до́ме, оказа́лись в лову́шке.
trap door люк.
trapeze *n.* трапе́ция.
trapezoid *n.* трапе́ция.
trapper *n.* зверoло́в.
trappings *n. pl.* **1,** (adornments) украше́ния; декора́ции. **2,** (items associated with something) си́мволы: *the trappings of monarchy,* си́мволы мона́рхии.
trapshooting *n.* стрельба́ по таре́лочкам; сте́ндовая стрельба́.
trash *n.* **1,** (refuse) отбро́сы; му́сор; хлам; сор. **2,** (worthless literature) макулату́ра. —**trash can,** му́сорный я́щик.
trashy *adj.* **1,** (like junk) дрянно́й. **2,** (of literature) бульва́рный.
trauma *n.* **1,** (bodily injury) тра́вма. **2,** (emotional shock) психи́ческая тра́вма. —**traumatic,** *adj.* травмати́ческий. —**traumatize,** *v.t.* травми́ровать. —**traumatology,** *n.* травматоло́гия.
travail *n.* **1,** (hard work) тяжёлый труд. **2,** (anguish) му́ка.
travel *v.i.* путеше́ствовать; разъезжа́ть. *Travel abroad,* е́хать за грани́цу; путеше́ствовать за грани́цей. *The news traveled fast,* но́вость бы́стро распространя́лась. *Light travels at 186,000 miles per second,* ско́рость све́та – 186,000 миль в секу́нду. —*n.* **1,** (traveling) путеше́ствие. **2,** *pl.* (series of trips) разъе́зды. —*adj.* доро́жный: *travel expenses,* доро́жные расхо́ды. *Travel allowance,* командиро́вочные де́ньги. —**travel agency,** бюро́ путеше́ствий.
traveler *also,* **traveller** *n.* путеше́ственник; пу́тник. —**traveler's check,** доро́жный чек.
traveling *also,* **travelling** *adj.* **1,** (journeying) путеше́ствующий. **2,** (of or for travel) доро́жный: *traveling clothes,* доро́жный костю́м. —**traveling bag,** саквоя́ж. —**traveling companion,** спу́тник; попу́тчик. —**traveling salesman,** коммивояжёр.
traverse *v.t.* пересека́ть. —*n.* попере́чина. —*adj.* попере́чный.
travesty *n.* паро́дия.
trawl *n.* трал. —*v.t.* тра́лить. —**trawler,** *n.* тра́улер.
tray *n.* **1,** (for food or utensils) подно́с. **2,** (of a street peddler) лото́к.
treacherous *adj.* **1,** (perfidious) преда́тельский; вероло́мный; кова́рный. **2,** (unsafe) опа́сный; ненадёжный. —**treachery,** *n.* преда́тельство; вероло́мство; кова́рство.
treacle *n.* па́тока.
tread *v.i.* **1,** (step; walk) ступа́ть: *tread lightly,* ступа́ть легко́. **2,** *fol. by* **on** (step on) наступа́ть на. —*v.t.* идти́ по (како́му-нибудь) пути́. —*n.* **1,** (stepping; footsteps) шаги́. **2,** (surface of a tire) проте́ктор. —**tread water,** плыть сто́я.
treadle *n.* педа́ль.
treadmill *n.* топча́к. *Be on a treadmill,* верте́ться, как бе́лка в колесе́.
treason *n.* изме́на.
treasonable *adj.* изме́ннический; преда́тельский. *Also,* **treasonous.**
treasure *n.* сокро́вище. *Buried treasure,* клад. —*v.t.* дорожи́ть.
treasure house сокро́вищница.
treasurer *n.* казначе́й.
treasury *n.* казначе́йство. *Secretary of the Treasury,* мини́стр фина́нсов. —*adj.* казначе́йский: *treasury note,* казначе́йский биле́т.
treat *v.t.* **1,** (behave in a certain manner toward) обраща́ться с; обходи́ться с; поступа́ть с. **2,** (deal with, as a subject) тракто́вать. **3,** (regard and act accordingly) относи́ться к: *treat as a joke,* относи́ться (к чему́-нибудь) как к шу́тке. **4,** (subject to a process) обраба́тывать. **5,** (give medical attention to) лечи́ть. **6,** (entertain at one's own expense) угоща́ть. —*v.i.* угоща́ть. —*n.* **1,** (something paid for by someone else): *it's my treat; the treat's on me,* я угоща́ю. **2,** *colloq.* (something very enjoyable) удово́льствие.
treatise *n.* тракта́т.
treatment *n.* **1,** (way in which one treats another) обраще́ние; обхожде́ние. **2,** (medical treatment) лече́ние. *Undergo treatment,* лечи́ться; проходи́ть курс лече́ния. **3,** (processing) обрабо́тка. **4,** (handling of a subject) тракто́вка.
treaty *n.* догово́р. *Treaty obligations,* догово́рные обяза́тельства.
treble *adj.* **1,** (threefold) тройно́й. **2,** *music* диска́нтовый. —*n., music* ди́скант. —*v.t.* утра́ивать. —*v.i.* утра́иваться. —**treble clef,** скрипи́чный ключ.
tree *n.* де́рево. *Christmas tree,* рожде́ственская ёлка. *Family tree,* родосло́вное де́рево.
tree frog древе́сница; ква́кша.
treeless *adj.* безле́сный.
treetops *n. pl.* верху́шки дере́вьев.
trefoil *n.* трили́стник.
trek *v.i.* тащи́ться; переселя́ться. —*n.* путеше́ствие; переселе́ние.
trellis *n.* шпале́ры; трелья́ж.
tremble *v.i.* дрожа́ть: *tremble with fear,* дрожа́ть от стра́ха. —*n.* дрожь.

tremendous *adj.* огрóмный; громáдный.
tremolo *n.* трéмоло; вибрáция.
tremor *n.* дрожь; трéпет. *Earth tremor,* подзéмный толчóк.
tremulous *adj.* дрожáщий; трéпетный.
trench *n.* **1,** (ditch) ров; канáва. **2,** *mil.* окóп; траншéя. —**trench coat,** плащ. —**trench fever,** траншéйная лихорáдка. —**trench foot,** траншéйная стопá. —**trench warfare,** окóпная войнá.
trenchant *adj.* óстрый; кóлкий.
trend *n.* направлéние; тендéнция; течéние. *Trend of thought,* ход мыслей.
trepak *n.* трепáк.
trepidation *n.* трéпет: *fear and trepidation,* страх и трéпет.
trespass *v.i.* **1,** (enter another's property unlawfully) нарушáть грани́цу. **2,** *fol. by* **on** (encroach upon) посягáть (на). —**trespasser,** *n.* наруши́тель.
tress *n.* **1,** (lock; ringlet) лóкон. **2,** *pl.* (hair) вóлосы.
trestle *n.* **1,** (wooden frame) кóзлы. **2,** (bridge) эстакáда.
trey *n.* трóйка.
triad *n.* **1,** (group of three) триáда. **2,** *music* трезвýчие.
trial *n.* **1,** *law* суд; (судéбный) процéсс. *The trial of...,* суд над... *Be on trial,* быть под судóм. *Put on trial,* предавáть судý. **2,** (test) прóба; испытáние. *Take on trial,* взять (чтó-нибудь) на прóбу. *Method of trial and error,* мéтод проб и оши́бок. **3,** (hardship) испытáние. —*adj.* прóбный; испытáтельный. *Trial period/run,* испытáтельный срок/пробéг. —**trial balance,** прóбный балáнс. —**trial balloon,** прóбный шар.
triangle *n.* **1,** (figure) треугóльник. **2,** (drawing instrument) угóльник. —**triangular,** *adj.* треугóльный.
triangulation *n.* триангуля́ция.
Triassic *adj.* триáсовый.
tribal *adj.* племеннóй; родовóй.
tribe *n.* плéмя. *The ten lost tribes of Israel,* дéсять исчéзнувших колéн Изрáилевых.
tribesman *n.* член плéмени.
tribulation *n.* **1,** (suffering) страдáние. **2,** (misfortune) несчáстье.
tribunal *n.* трибунáл.
tribune *n.* трибýн.
tributary *n.* притóк.
tribute *n.* **1,** (enforced payment) дань. **2,** (testimonial) дань; дóлжное: *pay tribute to,* отдáть дань/дóлжное (+ *dat.*).
tricentennial *adj. & n.* = **tercentenary.**
triceps *n.* трёхглáвая мышца.
trichina *n.* трихи́на.
trichinosis *n.* трихинеллёз.
trick *n.* **1,** (ruse) обмáн; хи́трость; подвóх. *I suspect a trick,* мне кáжется, здесь какóй-то подвóх (*or* чтó-то нечи́сто). **2,** (prank; practical joke) шýтка; продéлка; прокáза; вы́ходка. *Play a trick on,* сыгрáть шýтку с. *Dirty/mean trick,* зля́я шýтка; пóдлость. *Play a dirty trick on,* подложи́ть свинью́ (+ *dat.*). *None of your tricks!,* без фóкусов! **3,** (stunt; feat) трюк; фóкус. *Card trick,* кáрточный фóкус. **4,** (knack) сноровка: *there's a trick to it,* тут сноровка нужнá. **5,** *cards* взя́тка. —*adj.* трю́ковый: *trick photography,* трю́ковая съёмка. *Trick lock,* замóк с секрéтом. —*v.t.* обмáнывать; надувáть. —**he doesn't miss a trick,** от негó ничтó не укрóется. —**that'll do the trick,** вот так э́то полýчится.
trickery *n.* обмáн; надувáтельство.
trickle *v.i.* сочи́ться: *blood trickled from the wound,* кровь сочи́лась из рáны. *Tears trickled down her cheeks,* слёзы ползли́ у неё по щекáм. —*n.* стрýйка: *a trickle of perspiration,* стрýйка пóта.
trickster *n.* обмáнщик; плут.
tricky *adj.* **1,** (deceptive; sly) хи́трый: *tricky methods,* хи́трые приёмы. **2,** (intricate) хи́трый; слóжный; мудрёный. *A tricky game,* хи́трая игрá. **3,** (delicate) щекотли́вый: *a tricky situation,* щекотли́вое положéние.
tricolor *also,* **tricolour** *adj.* трёхцвéтный. —*n.* трёхцвéтный флаг.
tricot *n.* трикó.
tricycle *n.* трёхколёсный велосипéд.
trident *n.* трезýбец.
tried *adj.* испы́танный.
trifle *n.* пустя́к; мéлочь. —*v.i.* [*usu.* **trifle with**] шути́ть с. *He is not to be trifled with,* с ним шýтки плóхи. —*v.t.* [*usu.* **trifle away**] растрáчивать. —**a trifle,** немнóжко: *a trifle annoyed,* немнóжко раздражён.
trifler *n.* бездéльник; лени́вец.
trifling *adj.* ничтóжный; пустякóвый. *A trifling amount,* ничтóжная сýмма. *No trifling matter,* не шýточное дéло.
trigger *n.* собáчка; гашéтка; спусковóй крючóк. *Pull the trigger,* спускáть курóк. —*v.t.* порождáть; пусти́ть в ход.
trigonometry *n.* тригонометри́я. —**trigonometric,** *adj.* тригонометри́ческий.
trihedron *n.* трёхгрáнник. —**trihedral,** *adj.* трёхгрáнный.
trilateral *adj.* трёхсторóнний.
trill *n.* трель. —*v.i.* пускáть *or* выводи́ть трель.
trillion *n.* *(U.S.)* триллиóн; *(Brit.)* миллиóн триллиóнов.
trilogy *n.* трилóгия.
trim *v.t.* **1,** (clip; prune) подстригáть; подрезáть; обрезáть; подрáвнивать. **2,** (adorn) отдéлывать: *trim with lace,* отдéлывать кружевáми. **3,** (reduce; pare) урéзывать. —*n.* **1,** (haircut): *give someone a trim,* подрáвнивать вóлосы (+ *dat.*). **2,** (trimming) отдéлка: *lace trim,* кружевнáя отдéлка. **3,** (proper condition) готóвность; фóрма. *In fighting trim,* в боевóй готóвности. —*adj.* **1,** (neat; tidy) опря́тный; аккурáтный. **2,** (well-proportioned) стрóйный.
trimester *n.* тримéстр.
trimming *n.* **1,** (decoration; ornament) отдéлка; обши́вка; бордю́р. **2,** *pl.* (side dishes) гарни́р.
trinitrotoluene *n.* тринитротолуóл; троти́л.
Trinity *n.* трóица.
trinket *n.* безделýшка.
trinomial *n.* трёхчлéн. —*adj.* трёхчлéнный.
trio *n.* три́о.
triode *n.* триóд.
trip *n.* поéздка; путешéствие. *Go on a trip,* соверши́ть поéздку. —*v.i.* **1,** (stumble) спотыкáться; оступáться. **2,** (run lightly; skip) семени́ть ногáми; бежáть вприпры́жку. —*v.t.* **1,** (release, as a mechanism) спускáть. **2,** (cause to stumble) подставля́ть нóжку (*dat.*); давáть поднóжку (+ *dat.*). **3,** *fol. by* **up** (cause to make a mistake) запýтывать.
tripartite *adj.* трёхсторóнний; трóйственный.

tripe *n.* **1,** (food) рубе́ц. **2,** *colloq.* (rubbish) чушь.
triphammer *n.* па́дающий мо́лот.
triple *adj.* тройно́й; троя́кий; тро́йственный. —*v.t.* утра́ивать. —*v.i.* утра́иваться.
triplet *n.* **1,** *pl.* (three offspring born together) тро́йня. **2,** *music* трио́ль.
triplicate *n. In triplicate,* в трёх экземпля́рах.
tripod *n.* трено́га; трено́жник; штати́в.
triptych *n.* три́птих.
trisect *v.t.* дели́ть на три ра́вные ча́сти.
trisyllabic *adj.* трёхсло́жный.
trite *adj.* бана́льный; изби́тый.
tritium *n.* три́тий.
triton *n.* трито́н.
triumph *n.* **1,** (victory) побе́да; торжество́; триу́мф. **2,** (exultation over victory) торжество́; ликова́ние. —*v.i.* побежда́ть; торжествова́ть. —**triumphal,** *adj.* торже́ственный; триумфа́льный.
triumphant *adj.* **1,** (victorious) победоно́сный. **2,** (exultant in triumph) торжеству́ющий.
triumvir *n.* триумви́р. —**triumvirate,** *n.* триумвира́т.
trivalent *adj.* трёхвале́нтный.
trivet *n.* **1,** (for holding pots over a fire) тага́н. **2,** (for holding hot dishes) подста́вка.
trivia *n.pl.* ме́лочи. —**trivial,** *adj.* ничто́жный; пустяко́вый. —**triviality,** *n.* ме́лочь.
trochaic *adj.* хоре́ический; трохеи́ческий.
troche *n.* табле́тка.
trochee *n.* хоре́й; трохе́й.
troika *n.* тро́йка.
Trojan *adj.* троя́нский. —**Trojan horse,** троя́нский конь. —**Trojan War,** Троя́нская война́.
troll *n., folklore* тролль. —*v.t. & i.* (sing) распева́ть.
trolley *n.* **1,** (streetcar) трамва́й. **2,** (small truck) вагоне́тка. **3,** (device for conducting current) токоприёмник. —**trolley bus,** тролле́йбус. —**trolley car,** трамва́й.
trollop *n.* **1,** (slovenly woman) неря́ха; грязну́ля. **2,** (prostitute) потаску́ха.
trombone *n.* тромбо́н. —**trombonist,** *n.* тромбони́ст.
troop *n.* **1,** (group) гру́ппа; отря́д. **2,** *pl.* (soldiers collectively) войска́. —*adj.* войсково́й. *Troop train,* во́инский эшело́н. —*v.i.* идти́ стро́ем.
trooper *n.* **1,** (cavalryman) кавалери́ст. **2,** (policeman) полице́йский. —**swear like a trooper,** руга́ться как изво́зчик.
troopship *n.* войсково́й тра́нспорт.
trope *n.* троп.
trophy *n.* **1,** (prize) приз; ку́бок. **2,** (memento of war) трофе́й.
tropic *n.* тро́пик. —**Tropic of Cancer,** тро́пик Ра́ка. —**Tropic of Capricorn,** тро́пик Козеро́га.
tropical *adj.* тропи́ческий.
tropics *n.pl.* тро́пики.
troposphere *n.* тропосфе́ра.
trot *n.* **1,** (gait of a horse) рысь. *At a trot,* ры́сью; на ры́ся́х. **2,** (jogging gait of a person) рысца́. —*v.i.* **1,** (of a horse) идти́ ры́сью. **2,** (of a person) труси́ть.
trotter *n.* рыси́стая ло́шадь; рыса́к.
trotting races рыси́стые бега́.
troubadour *n.* трубаду́р; менестре́ль.
trouble *n.* **1,** (difficult or distressing situation) беда́; неприя́тности. *Get into trouble,* попа́сть в беду́. *Ask for trouble,* напра́шиваться на неприя́тности. **2,** (problem) беда́: *the trouble is...,* беда́ в том, что... *What's the trouble?,* в чём де́ло? *That's just the trouble!,* в то́м-то и беда́. **3,** (difficulty) труд: *without any trouble,* без труда́. *I'm having trouble opening the safe,* я ника́к не могу́ откры́ть сейф. **4,** (extra effort; bother) труд; хло́поты. *Take the trouble to,* дать себе́ *or* взять на себя́ труд (+ *inf.*); потруди́ться (+ *inf.*). *Will it be much trouble?,* э́то вас не затрудни́т? *It will be no trouble,* э́то не соста́вит труда́. *It's not worth the trouble,* не сто́ит труда́. *Give someone a lot of trouble,* доставля́ть кому́-нибудь мно́го хлопо́т. **5,** (malfunction) неиспра́вность: *engine trouble,* неиспра́вность дви́гателя. *Stomach trouble,* расстро́йство желу́дка. *Heart trouble,* больно́е се́рдце. —*v.t.* **1,** (worry; bother; upset) беспоко́ить: *what's troubling you?,* что вас беспоко́ит? **2,** (bother; inconvenience) беспоко́ить; затрудня́ть. *Don't trouble yourself!,* не беспоко́йтесь! *May I trouble you for a match?,* мо́жно попроси́ть у вас спи́чку?
troubled *adj.* беспоко́йный; обеспоко́енный.
troublemaker *n.* смутья́н.
troublesome *adj.* беспоко́йный.
trough *n.* **1,** (container) коры́то. *Feeding trough,* корму́шка. *Kneading trough,* квашня́. **2,** (long narrow depression) впа́дина; котлови́на.
trounce *v.t.* **1,** (thrash) колоти́ть. **2,** *colloq.* (defeat decisively) разбива́ть.
troupe *n.* тру́ппа.
trousers *n.pl.* брю́ки; штаны́.
trousseau *n.* прида́ное.
trout *n.* форе́ль.
trowel *n.* лопа́тка; садо́вый сово́к.
truancy *n.* прогу́л.
truant *n.* прогу́льщик. —**play truant,** прогу́ливать уро́ки; стать прогу́льщиком.
truce *n.* переми́рие.
truck *n.* **1,** (motor vehicle) грузови́к. **2,** (cart) теле́жка; вагоне́тка. —*v.t.* перевози́ть на грузовике́. —**trucker,** *n.* води́тель грузовика́.
truck farm огоро́дное хозя́йство. —**truck farmer,** огоро́дник. —**truck farming,** огоро́дничество.
truckle *v.i.* [*usu.* **truckle to**] раболе́пствовать (пе́ред); уго́дничать (пе́ред).
truculent *adj.* **1,** (fierce) свире́пый. **2,** (pugnacious) драчли́вый. **3,** (scathing) хлёсткий.
trudge *v.i.* брести́; тащи́ться; плести́сь.
true *adj.* **1,** (accurate; correct) и́стинный. *It/that is true,* э́то пра́вда; э́то ве́рно. *Is it true that...?,* пра́вда ли, что...? **2,** (factual) правди́вый: *a true story,* правди́вая исто́рия; правди́вый расска́з. **3,** (actual) действи́тельный: *the true state of affairs,* действи́тельное положе́ние веще́й. **4,** (genuine) настоя́щий: *true gold,* настоя́щее зо́лото. **5,** (rightful) зако́нный: *its true owner,* зако́нный владе́лец. **6,** (faithful) ве́рный: *remain true to,* остава́ться ве́рным (+ *dat.*). **7,** *astron.* и́стинный: *true north,* и́стинный се́вер. —**come true,** осуществля́ться; сбыва́ться.
truffle *n.* трю́фель.
truism *n.* изби́тая/прописна́я/а́збучная и́стина; трюи́зм.
truly *adv.* **1,** (indeed) и́стинно; пои́стине. **2,** (sincerely) и́скренне. —**yours truly,** пре́данный вам.
trump *n.* ко́зырь. *Play one's trump card,* пусти́ть в ход после́дний ко́зырь. —*v.i.* козыря́ть. —*v.t.* бить

or крыть ко́зырем. —**trump up,** фабрикова́ть: *trumped-up charges,* сфабрико́ванные обвине́ния.

trumpet *n.* труба́. —*v.i.* (of an elephant) реве́ть. —*v.t.* (proclaim loudly) труби́ть о. —**trumpeter,** *n.* труба́ч.

truncate *v.t.* усека́ть. —**truncated,** *adj.* усечённый.

truncheon *n.* **1,** (cudgel) дуби́на. **2,** (staff) жезл.

trundle *n.* колёсико. —*v.t.* кати́ть. —*v.i.* кати́ться. —**trundle bed,** крова́ть на колёсиках.

trunk *n.* **1,** (of a tree) ствол. **2,** (of an elephant) хо́бот. **3,** (torso) ту́ловище. **4,** (large box or case) сунду́к. **5,** (of an automobile) бага́жник. **6,** *pl.* (for swimming) пла́вки.

truss *n.* **1,** (support, as for a bridge) фе́рма. **2,** (device worn to support a hernia) грыжево́й банда́ж.

trust *n.* **1,** (confidence in another's honesty) дове́рие. **2,** (monopoly) трест. —*v.t.* **1,** (have confidence in) доверя́ть: *he is not to be trusted,* ему́ нельзя́ доверя́ть. **2,** (rely on) полага́ться на. *Trust one's memory,* полага́ться на свою́ па́мять. *Trust someone's judgment,* полага́ться на чьё-нибудь мне́ние. **3,** (assume confidently) наде́яться. —*v.i., in* **trust to luck,** полага́ться на слу́чай.

trustee *n.* опеку́н; попечи́тель. —**trusteeship,** *n.* опе́ка; попечи́тельство.

trustful *adj.* дове́рчивый. *Also,* **trusting.**

trust territory подопе́чная террито́рия.

trustworthy *adj.* заслу́живающий дове́рия; надёжный. —**trustworthiness,** *n.* надёжность.

trusty *adj.* ве́рный.

truth *n.* пра́вда. —**in truth,** на са́мом де́ле. —**to tell the truth...,** по пра́вде говоря́; по пра́вде сказа́ть...

truthful *adj.* правди́вый. —**truthfulness,** *n.* правди́вость.

try *v.t.* **1,** *fol. by inf.* (attempt) пыта́ться; стара́ться. **2,** (taste) про́бовать. **3,** (test) про́бовать: *try a new remedy,* про́бовать но́вое сре́дство. *Try one's luck,* попыта́ть сча́стья. *Try one's hand at,* про́бовать си́лы в (+ *prepl.*). **4,** (strain) испы́тывать: *try one's patience,* испы́тывать чьё-нибудь терпе́ние. **5,** (put on trial) суди́ть: *he was tried for murder,* его́ суди́ли за уби́йство. *He was tried and executed,* он был суди́м и казнён. **6,** (hear, as a case) слу́шать (де́ло). —*v.i.* стара́ться: *I'll try,* я постара́юсь. —*n.* попы́тка: *on the first try,* с перво́й попы́тки. —**try on,** примеря́ть. —**try out,** испы́тывать; про́бовать.

trying *adj.* тру́дный; тяжёлый.

tryout *n.* про́ба (на роль).

try square уго́льник.

tryst *n.* любо́вное свида́ние.

tsar *n.* царь. —**tsarevitch,** *n.* царе́вич. —**tsarevna,** *n.* царе́вна. —**tsarina,** *n.* цари́ца. —**tsarism,** *n.* цари́зм. —**tsarist,** *adj.* ца́рский.

tsetse fly (му́ха) цеце́.

T-shirt *n.* ма́йка.

T square рейсши́на.

tub *n.* **1,** (large container) ка́дка; лоха́нь; уша́т. **2,** (bathtub) ва́нна. **3,** *colloq.* (old boat) посу́дина.

tuba *n.* ту́ба.

tubby *adj.* пу́хлый; ту́чный.

tube *n.* **1,** (hollow cylinder) тру́бка. **2,** (inner tube for a tire) ка́мера. **3,** (radio component) ла́мпа. **4,** (container for glue, toothpaste, etc.) тю́бик. **5,** *anat.* труба́.

tubeless *adj.* беска́мерный.

tuber *n.* клу́бень.

tubercle *n.* бугоро́к. —**tubercle bacillus,** туберкулёзная па́лочка.

tubercular *adj.* туберкулёзный.

tuberculosis *n.* туберкулёз. —**tuberculous,** *adj.* туберкулёзный.

tuberose *n.* туберо́за.

tuberous *adj.* клубнево́й; бugо́рчатый.

tubing *n.* тю́бинг.

tubular *adj.* тру́бчатый.

tuck *v.t.* **1,** (place so as to be held firmly) заправля́ть: *tuck one's shirt into one's trousers,* заправля́ть руба́шку в штаны́. **2,** (fold under something) подбира́ть; подгиба́ть; подвёртывать; подтыка́ть. *Tuck in a blanket,* подвёртывать *or* подтыка́ть одея́ло. **3,** (place snugly) засо́вывать: *tuck something into one's pocket,* засо́вывать что́-нибудь в карма́н. *Tuck a child into bed,* уложи́ть ребёнка в посте́ль. —*n.* вы́тачка.

tucker *v.t., colloq.* [*usu.* **tucker out**] изнуря́ть. *Be tuckered out,* измá́яться; быть без ног.

Tuesday *n.* вто́рник.

tuft *n.* **1,** (of hair) вихо́р; клок воло́с. **2,** (of grass) пук; пучо́к.

tug *v.t. & i.* тяну́ть; дёргать. —*n.* **1,** (strong pull): *give a tug,* потяну́ть; дёрнуть. **2,** (tugboat) букси́р.

tugboat *n.* букси́р.

tuition *n.* **1,** (fee) пла́та за обуче́ние. **2,** (teaching) обуче́ние: *free tuition,* беспла́тное обуче́ние.

tulip *n.* тюльпа́н. —*adj.* тюльпа́нный.

tulle *n.* тюль. —*adj.* тю́левый.

tumble *v.i.* **1,** (fall; drop) па́дать; вали́ться. *Tumble down the stairs,* упа́сть с ле́стницы. *Tumble over a cliff,* свали́ться со скалы́. *Come tumbling down,* ру́хнуть; обру́шиваться; сва́ливаться; обва́ливаться. *Prices tumbled,* це́ны упа́ли. **2,** (do somersaults) кувырка́ться. —*n.* паде́ние.

tumble-down *adj.* ве́тхий; обветша́лый; полуразру́шенный.

tumbler *n.* **1,** (glass) стака́н. **2,** (of a lock) сува́льда. **3,** (gymnast) акроба́т. **4,** (pigeon) ту́рман.

tumbleweed *n.* перекати́-по́ле.

tumid *adj.* распу́хший.

tummy *n., colloq.* живо́тик.

tumor *also,* **tumour** *n.* о́пухоль.

tumult *n.* сумато́ха. —**tumultuous,** *adj.* шу́мный; бу́йный.

tuna *n.* туне́ц.

tundra *n.* ту́ндра.

tune *n.* **1,** (melody) моти́в; напе́в. **2,** (proper pitch or key) лад: *sing in tune,* петь в лад. *The piano is out of tune,* роя́ль расстро́ен. —*v.t.* **1,** (a musical instrument) настра́ивать. **2,** (an engine) (от)регули́ровать. **3,** *fol. by* **in** (adjust a radio to receive) настра́иваться на. —**be in tune with the times,** идти́ в но́гу со вре́менем. —**call the tune,** распоряжа́ться. —**change one's tune,** запе́ть друго́е; запе́ть на друго́й лад. —**dance to someone's tune,** пляса́ть под чью́-нибудь ду́дку. —**to the tune of,** на су́мму (+ *gen.*).

tuneful *adj.* мелоди́чный.

tuner *n.* настро́йщик: *piano tuner,* настро́йщик роя́лей.

tune-up *n.* регулиро́вка: *engine tune-up,* регулиро́вка двигателя.

tung oil ту́нговое ма́сло.

tungsten *n.* вольфра́м. —*adj.* вольфра́мовый.

tung tree тунг; ту́нговое де́рево.

tunic *n.* **1,** (garment worn in ancient times) туника. **2,** (uniform coat) китель.
tuning fork камертон.
tunnel *n.* туннель. —*v.i.* **1,** (build a tunnel) прокладывать туннель: *tunnel through a mountain,* прокладывать туннель через гору. **2,** *fol. by* **under** (dig one's way) подкапывать; подкапываться под.
tunny *n., Brit.* = **tuna.**
turban *n.* тюрбан; чалма.
turbid *adj.* мутный. —**turbidity,** *n.* мутность.
turbine *n.* турбина.
turbojet *adj.* турбореактивный. —*n.* турбореактивный самолёт.
turboprop *adj.* турбовинтовой. —*n.* турбовинтовой самолёт.
turbot *n.* тюрбо.
turbulent *adj.* бурный; буйный; бурливый. —**turbulence,** *n.* волнение; *aero.* болтанка.
tureen *n.* миска. *Soup tureen,* суповая миска; супник.
turf *n.* **1,** (matted grass) дёрн. **2,** (grass part of a racetrack) трава. **3,** (horse racing) скачки.
turgid *adj.* **1,** (swollen) опухший. **2,** (bombastic) напыщенный.
Turk *n.* турок. *The Turks,* турки.
turkey *n.* индейка. —**talk turkey,** *colloq.* говорить без обиняков.
Turkic *adj.* тюркский.
Turkish *adj.* турецкий. —*n.* турецкий язык. —**Turkish bath,** турецкая баня. —**Turkish delight,** рахатлукум. —**Turkish towel,** мохнатое полотенце.
turmeric *n.* куркума.
turmoil *n.* беспорядок; суматоха.
turn *v.t.* **1,** (change the position or direction of) поворачивать: *turn one's head,* поворачивать голову; *turn a key in a lock,* поворачивать ключ в замке. **2,** (cause to revolve) вращать: *turn a wheel,* вращать колесо. **3,** (aim; direct) направлять; обращать. *Turn a hose on someone,* направить струю на кого-нибудь. *Turn a gun on oneself,* обратить оружие против себя. *Turn one's attention to,* направлять внимание на. **4,** (shape in a lathe) точить. **5,** *in various combinations: turn the page,* перевёртывать страницу; *turn the corner,* завернуть за угол; *turn one's back on,* отворачиваться от; *turn somersaults,* кувыркаться; *turn one's ankle,* подвернуть себе ногу. **6,** *in various idiomatic expressions: turn a deaf ear to,* пропускать мимо ушей; *turn one's stomach,* претить; *turn the other cheek,* подставлять другую щёку; *turn someone's head,* кружить голову (+ *dat.*); *turn to one's advantage,* обращать в свою пользу. *He turned forty,* ему исполнилось сорок лет. —*v.i.* **1,** (change direction) поворачивать: *turn (to the) right,* поворачивать направо. **2,** (face in a different direction) поворачиваться: *turn toward someone,* поворачиваться к кому-нибудь. **3,** (be able to be turned) поворачиваться: *the key won't turn,* ключ не поворачивается. **4,** (rotate) вращаться. **5,** (become) становиться: *turn cold,* становиться холодно. *Turn traitor,* стать предателем. ♦*Also rendered by various verbs: turn sour,* киснуть; *turn gray,* седеть; *turn pale,* побледнеть. **6,** (shift) переходить: *the conversation turned to politics,* разговор перешёл к политике. **7,** (change color) желтеть: *the leaves are turning,* листья желтеют. **8,** (become sour or rancid) прокисать. —*n.* **1,** (change of direction) поворот: *turn to the right,* поворот направо. *Make a turn,* делать поворот. **2,** (revolution) оборот: *turn of a wheel,* оборот колеса. **3,** (turning, as in a road) поворот. **4,** (occasion; chance) очередь: *wait one's turn,* ждать своей очереди. *In turn,* по очереди; поочерёдно; попеременно. *Out of turn,* вне очереди. *Take turns,* чередоваться. **5,** (action; deed) услуга: *ill turn,* плохая услуга. *One good turn deserves another,* долг платежом красен. **6,** (change in trend) поворот; оборот. *Turn of events,* поворот дела. *Take a turn for the worse,* принимать дурной оборот. *Things took a turn for the better,* дело повернулось к лучшему. **7,** *in various expressions: turn of mind,* склад ума; *turn of speech,* оборот речи; *turn of the century,* начало века. —**at every turn,** на каждом шагу. —**to a turn,** как раз в меру. —**turn against, 1,** (set against) восстанавливать *or* настраивать против. **2,** (rise up against) восставать против. —**turn around, 1,** (face in the opposite direction) поворачиваться (кругом); оборачиваться. **2,** (reverse the direction of) разворачивать. —**turn aside, 1,** (turn to one side) разворачивать. **2,** (turn and face a different way) свернуть в сторону. **3,** (reject) отклонять. —**turn away, 1,** (turn so as not to be visible) отворачивать. *Turn away one's eyes,* отворачивать *or* отводить (свои) глаза. **2,** (send away) прогонять. **3,** (turn one's back) отворачиваться. —**turn back, 1,** (fold back) отгибать. **2,** (set back, as a clock) повернуть *or* перевести назад. **3,** (turn around and return) повернуть назад *or* обратно. **4,** (force to turn around and return) заворачивать. **5,** (repulse) отражать. —**turn down, 1,** (fold down) отворачивать; загибать. **2,** (turn into, as a narrow street) сворачивать в *or* на; поворачивать в. *Turn down a path,* сворачивать на тропинку. **3,** (reject) отклонять; отвергать; отказываться от. *Turn down an invitation,* отклонить приглашение; отказаться от приглашения. *Turn down a part,* отказаться от роли. *Turn down someone's request,* отказать кому-нибудь в просьбе. *They turned him down,* ему отказали. **4,** (reduce) уменьшать: *turn down the volume,* уменьшать звук. —**turn in, 1,** (hand in) сдавать; предъявлять. **2,** (inform on) доносить на. **3,** *colloq.* (go to bed) ложиться спать. —**turn into, 1,** (make a turn into) сворачивать в; поворачивать в. **2,** (transform into) превращать в; обращать в. **3,** (be transformed into) превращаться в; обращаться в. —**turn loose,** отпускать; выпускать. —**turn off, 1,** (leave, as a road) сворачивать с. **2,** (extinguish) тушить; выключать. **3,** (switch off) выключать. *Turn off the water,* закрывать кран. —**turn on, 1,** (switch on) включать; зажигать. *Turn on the water,* открывать кран. **2,** (attack) наброситься на. —**turn out, 1,** (extinguish) тушить; выключать. **2,** (eject) выгонять. **3,** (produce) выпускать. **4,** (come; appear) приходить; являться. **5,** (prove to be) оказываться (+*instr.*). **6,** (end up) обернуться. *It turned out that...,* оказалось *or* выяснилось, что... *Turn out well,* кончиться благополучно. —**turn over, 1,** (invert) перевёртывать. **2,** (topple) опрокидывать. **3,** (roll over, as when lying down) перевёртываться. **4,** (capsize) перевёртываться. **5,** (start, as of an engine) заводиться. **6,** (hand over) передавать; отдавать; сдавать. **7,** *comm.* иметь оборот в. **8,** *Turn over in one's mind,* перебирать. —**turn to, 1,** (appeal to; refer to) обращаться к. **2,** (open to a certain page) откры-

ва́ть на (како́й-нибудь страни́це). **3,** (begin; take up) бра́ться за; принима́ться за. **4,** (change into) превраща́ться в. —**turn up, 1,** (fold up) подвёртывать. **2,** (loosen, as soil) взрыхля́ть. **3,** (uncover; discover) раскрыва́ть; обнару́живать. **4,** (increase) увели́чивать: *turn up the volume,* увели́чивать звук. **5,** (arrive; appear) явля́ться; пока́зываться; ока́зываться; подверну́ться. **6,** *Turn up one's nose,* задира́ть нос. —**turn upon, 1,** (attack) набро́ситься на. **2,** (hinge on) зави́сеть от.

turnabout *n.* **1,** (turn) поворо́т круго́м. **2,** *fig.* (reversal) поворо́т на сто во́семьдесят гра́дусов.

turncoat *n.* перебе́жчик; ренега́т.

turndown *adj. (of a collar)* отложно́й.

turner *n.* то́карь.

turning *n.* поворо́т. —*adj.* враща́ющийся. —**turning point,** поворо́тный пункт; перело́м.

turnip *n.* ре́па.

turnout *n.* **1,** (gathering) собра́ние. **2,** (number of people assembled): *a large turnout,* мно́го наро́ду.

turnover *n.* оборо́т. *Turnover of personnel,* теку́честь ка́дров.

turnpike *n.* автомагистра́ль; автостра́да.

turnstile *n.* турнике́т.

turntable *n.* **1,** *R.R.* поворо́тный круг. **2,** (of a phonograph) диск.

turpentine *n.* скипида́р.

turpitude *n.* развра́т; развращённость: *moral turpitude,* нра́вственный развра́т; нра́вственная развращённость.

turquoise *n.* бирюза́. —*adj.* бирюзо́вый.

turret *n.* **1,** (small tower) ба́шенка. **2,** (revolving structure for a gun) оруди́йная ба́шня. —**turret lathe,** револьве́рный стано́к.

turtle *n.* черепа́ха. —*adj.* черепа́ховый: *turtle soup,* черепа́ховый суп.

turtledove *n.* го́рлица.

tusk *n.* клык; би́вень.

tussle *n.* дра́ка; сва́лка. —*v.i.* дра́ться.

tut *interj.* фи!; цыц!

tutelage *n.* **1,** (guardianship) опе́ка. **2,** (instruction) обуче́ние.

tutelary *adj.* опеку́нский.

tutor *n.* репети́тор; гувернёр. —*v.t.* репети́ровать. —*v.i.* дава́ть ча́стные уро́ки. —**tutorial,** *adj.* репети́торский.

tutu *n.* па́чка.

tuxedo *n.* смо́кинг.

twaddle *v.i.* пустословить. —*n.* пустосло́вие. —**twaddler,** *n.* пустосло́в; пустоме́ля.

twang *n.* гнуса́вость. *Nasal twang,* гнуса́вый го́лос.

tweak *v.t.* ущипну́ть. —*n.* щипо́к.

tweed *n.* твид.

tweet *n.* щёбет. —*v.i.* щебета́ть; чири́кать.

tweezers *n.pl.* пинце́т; щи́пчики.

twelfth *adj.* двена́дцатый. —*n.* **1,** (twelfth part) двена́дцатая часть. **2,** (fraction) двена́дцатая: *one-twelfth,* одна́ двена́дцатая.

twelve *n. & adj.* двена́дцать.

twentieth *adj.* двадца́тый. —*n.* **1,** (twentieth part) двадца́тая часть. **2,** (fraction) двадца́тая: *one-twentieth,* одна́ двадца́тая.

twenty *n. & adj.* два́дцать.

twice *adv.* **1,** (two times) два́жды; два ра́за. **2,** (doubly) вдво́е; в два ра́за: *twice as much,* вдво́е *or* в два ра́за бо́льше. *He is twice her age,* он вдво́е ста́рше её. —**once or twice,** раз-друго́й; ра́за два.

twiddle *v.t.* игра́ть (+ *Instr.*); верте́ть. —**twiddle one's thumbs,** бить баклу́ши.

twig *n.* прут; ве́тка; ве́точка.

twilight *n.* су́мерки.

twin *n.* близне́ц; *pl.* близнецы́; дво́йня. —*adj.* **1,** (being a twin or twins): *twin brothers,* бра́тья-близнецы́. **2,** (forming an identical pair) спа́ренный: *twin engines,* спа́ренные мото́ры. *Twin beds,* две односпа́льные крова́ти.

twine *n.* бечёвка; шпага́т. —*v.t.* обвива́ть. —*v.i.* ви́ться. *Twine around,* обвива́ться вокру́г.

twin-engine *adj.* двухмото́рный. *Also,* **twin-engined.**

twinge *n.* при́ступ бо́ли. *Twinge of conscience,* угрызе́ние со́вести.

twinkle *v.i.* мерца́ть; мига́ть. —*n.* мерца́ние; мига́ние.

twinkling *n.* **1,** (gleam) мерца́ние; мига́ние. **2,** (instant) мгнове́ние. —**in the twinkling of an eye,** в мгнове́ние о́ка.

twirl *v.t.* кружи́ть; верте́ть. *Twirl a baton,* верте́ть па́лочкой. *Twirl one's mustache,* крути́ть усы́.

twist *v.t.* **1,** (turn; wind) крути́ть; закру́чивать: *twist the handle,* крути́ть рукоя́тку. *The rope became twisted,* верёвка закрути́лась. **2,** (make by twisting) вить; крути́ть; скру́чивать; сучи́ть. **3,** (wrench; sprain) подверну́ть; вы́вернуть. **4,** (warp; distort) искажа́ть. —*v.i.* **1,** (squirm; writhe) ко́рчиться. **2,** (wind, as of a road) ви́ться; извива́ться. **3,** *fol. by* **around** (twine around) ви́ться; обвива́ться (вокру́г). —*n.* **1,** (twisting motion) круче́ние. *Give something a twist,* закрути́ть что́-нибудь. **2,** (bend; curve) поворо́т; изги́б. **3,** *fig.* unexpected turn or change) поворо́т; оборо́т. **4,** (loaf of bread) вито́й хлеб; вита́я бу́лка; плетёнка. —**twist around one's little finger,** обвести́ вокру́г па́льца; вить верёвки из. —**twist someone's arm,** вы́вернуть *or* вы́крутить кому́-нибудь ру́ку. *Twist someone's arms behind his back,* закрути́ть кому́-нибудь ру́ки.

twit *v.t.* язви́ть.

twitch *v.t.* дёргать; подёргивать. —*v.i.* дёргаться; подёргиваться. —*n.* подёргивание.

twitter *v.i.* щебета́ть; чири́кать. —*n.* щёбет; чири́канье.

two *adj.* два; две. —*n.* **1,** (cardinal number) два. **2,** (written number; school grade) дво́йка. **3,** *cards* дво́йка. —**in two,** на́двое; попола́м. —**two by two,** по́ два; по́ двое; попа́рно.

two-faced *adj.* двули́чный; двули́кий.

twofold *adj.* двойно́й; двоя́кий; двукра́тный. —*adv.* вдво́е; вдвойне́.

two-headed *adj.* двугла́вый.

two hundred две́сти. —**two-hundredth,** *adj.* двухсо́тый.

two-legged *adj.* двуно́гий.

two-party *adj.* двухпарти́йный.

two-room *adj.* двухко́мнатный.

two-sided *adj.* двусторо́нний.

twosome *n.* па́ра.

two-story *adj.* двухэта́жный.

two-syllable *adj.* дву(х)сло́жный.

two-time *adj.* двукра́тный: *two-time champion,* двукра́тный чемпио́н.

two-way *adj.* двусторо́нний. *Two-way street,* у́лица с двусторо́нним движе́нием.
two-wheel *adj.* двухколёсный. *Also,* **two-wheeled.**
tycoon *n., colloq.* магна́т.
tyke *n.* малы́ш.
tympani *n.pl.* = **timpani.**
type *n.* **1,** (kind; class) тип; род. **2,** (print) печа́ть; шрифт. *Set in type,* набира́ть. —*v.t.* (categorize) классифици́ровать. —*v.t. & i.* (typewrite) писа́ть на маши́нке.
typeface *n.* шрифт.
typescript *n.* машинопи́сный текст.
typesetter *n.* набо́рщик.
typewriter *n.* пи́шущая маши́нка.
typewritten *adj.* машинопи́сный. *Eight typewritten pages,* во́семь страни́ц маши́нописи.
typhoid *n.* (брюшно́й) тиф. —*adj.* тифо́зный. —**typhoid fever,** тифо́зная лихора́дка; брюшно́й тиф.
typhoon *n.* тайфу́н.
typhus *n.* (сыпно́й) тиф.
typical *adj.* типи́чный; характе́рный. *Typical of,* типи́чно для; характе́рно для. —**typically,** *adv.* типи́чно.
typify *v.t.* служи́ть типи́чным приме́ром (+ *gen.*).
typing *n.* маши́нопись.
typist *n.* машини́стка.
typographer *n.* типо́граф; печа́тник. —**typographic; typographical,** *adj.* типогра́фский.
typography *n.* типогра́фское де́ло; типогра́фское иску́сство.
tyrannical *adj.* тирани́ческий. —**tyrannize,** *v.t.* тира́нить.
tyranny *n.* терани́я; тира́нство.
tyrant *n.* тира́н; наси́льник.
tyre *n.* = **tire**[2].
tyro *n.* новичо́к.

U

U, u два́дцать пе́рвая бу́ква англи́йского алфави́та.
ubiquitous *adj.* вездесу́щий.
udder *n.* вы́мя.
ugh *interj.* фу!
ugliness *n.* уро́дство; уро́дливость; безобра́зие.
ugly *adj.* **1,** (unsightly) некраси́вый; безобра́зный. **2,** (nasty; unpleasant) неприя́тный; скве́рный; ме́рзкий. —**ugly duckling,** га́дкий утёнок.
ukase *n.* ука́з.
Ukrainian *adj.* украи́нский. —*n.* **1,** (person) украи́нец; украи́нка. **2,** (language) украи́нский язы́к.
ukulele *n.* гава́йская гита́ра.
ulcer *n.* я́зва.
ulcerate *v.t.* изъязвля́ть. —*v.i.* изъязвля́ться.
ulcerous *adj.* я́звенный.
ulterior *adj.* скры́тый. —**ulterior motive,** за́дняя мысль; скры́тый моти́в.
ultimate *adj.* коне́чный; оконча́тельный. *The ultimate purpose of something,* коне́чная цель чего́-нибудь. *The ultimate weapon,* абсолю́тное ору́жие. —*n.* [*usu.* **the ultimate in**] вы́сшая сте́пень (+ *gen.*). —**ultimately,** *adv.* в конце́ концо́в; в коне́чном ито́ге; в коне́чном счёте.
ultimatum *n.* ультима́тум.
ultra- *prefix* ультра-.
ultramarine *n.* ультрамари́н. —*adj.* ультрамари́новый.
ultramodern *adj.* ультрасовреме́нный.
ultrasonic *adj.* ультразвуково́й.
ultraviolet *adj.* ультрафиоле́товый.
umber *n.* у́мбра.
umbilical *adj.* пупо́чный. —**umbilical cord,** пупови́на.
umbilicus *n.* пупо́к.
umbra *n.* тень.
umbrage *n.* оби́да. *Take umbrage,* обижа́ться; уда́риться в амби́цию.
umbrella *n.* зо́нтик; зонт.
umlaut *n.* умля́ут.
umpire *n.* **1,** *sports* судья́. **2,** (one empowered to settle a dispute) арби́тр. —*v.t.* суди́ть.
umpteen *adj., colloq.* мно́го; бесчи́сленные. *Umpteen reasons,* ты́сяча причи́н. —**umpteenth,** *adj., colloq. For the umpteenth time,* в кото́рый раз.
unable *adj.* не в состоя́нии. *I am unable to come today,* не могу́ прийти́ сего́дня.
unabridged *adj.* по́лный; несокращённый.
unaccented *adj.* безуда́рный.
unacceptable *adj.* неприе́млемый. —**unacceptability,** *n.* неприе́млемость.
unaccompanied *adj.* без сопровожде́ния.
unaccountable *adj.* **1,** (inexplicable) необъясни́мый. **2,** (not responsible) безотве́тственный.
unaccounted-for *adj.* пропа́вший бе́з вести.
unaccustomed *adj.* **1,** *fol. by* **to** (unused to): *be/become unaccustomed to,* не привыка́ть к; отвыка́ть от. **2,** (unfamiliar) непривы́чный.
unacquainted *adj.* незнако́мый.
unadorned *adj.* неприкра́шенный: *the unadorned truth,* неприкра́шенная и́стина.
unadulterated *adj.* **1,** (undiluted) чи́стый; це́льный. **2,** *fig.* (sheer; utter) чи́стый; сплошно́й.
unaffected *adj.* **1,** (not affected): *I am unaffected by the decision,* реше́ние меня́ не каса́ется. **2,** (without affectation) непринуждённый; есте́ственный.

unafraid *adj.* *Be unafraid,* не боя́ться; не страши́ться.
unaided *adj.* без (посторо́нней) по́мощи. *With the unaided eye,* невооружённым гла́зом.
unalike *adj.* непохо́жий; несхо́дный.
unalterable *adj.* неизме́нный; неизменя́емый. —**unalterably,** *adv.* категори́чески: *unalterably opposed,* категори́чески про́тив.
unambiguous *adj.* недвусмы́сленный.
unanimity *n.* единоду́шие; единогла́сие.
unanimous *adj.* единоду́шный; единогла́сный. —**unanimously,** *adv.* единоду́шно; единогла́сно.
unannounced *adj.* без докла́да: *walk in unannounced,* входи́ть без докла́да.
unanswered *adj.* без отве́та: *go unanswered,* остава́ться без отве́та.
unappealing *adj.* непривлека́тельный; неаппети́тный.
unappetizing *adj.* неаппети́тный.
unapproachable *adj.* недосту́пный.
unarmed *adj.* невооружённый; безору́жный.
unassailable *adj.* **1,** (impregnable) непристу́пный. **2,** (incontrovertible) неоспори́мый; неопровержи́мый.
unassisted *adj.* без (посторо́нней) по́мощи.
unassuming *adj.* непритяза́тельный; скро́мный.
unattached *adj.* **1,** (not connected) неприкреплённый. **2,** (unmarried) нежена́тый; незаму́жняя.
unattainable *adj.* недостижи́мый.
unattended *adj.* без ухо́да; без присмо́тра.
unattractive *adj.* непривлека́тельный; некраси́вый.
unauthorized *adj.* самово́льный; недозво́ленный.
unavailable *adj.* не име́ющийся в нали́чии. *Further information is unavailable at this time,* никаки́х бо́льше све́дений сейча́с нет.
unavailing *adj.* тщётный; напра́сный; бесполе́зный; безрезульта́тный; безуспе́шный.
unavoidable *adj.* неизбе́жный; немину́емый. —**unavoidably,** *adv.* неизбе́жно; немину́емо.
unaware *adj.* *Be unaware (of),* не знать (о); не отдава́ть себе́ отчёта (в).
unawares *adv.* врасплóх: *catch unawares,* заста́ть врасплóх.
unbalanced *adj.* неуравнове́шенный.
unbandage *v.t.* разбинто́вывать.
unbearable *adj.* невыноси́мый; непереноси́мый; нестерпи́мый; несно́сный. —**unbearably,** *adv.* невыноси́мо.
unbeaten *adj.* не потерпе́вший пораже́ния.
unbecoming *adj.* **1,** (not attractive or flattering) не к лицу́. **2,** (unseemly; indecorous) неприли́чный; неподоба́ющий.
unbeknown *adj.* неве́домый. *Unbeknown to me,* без моего́ ве́дома. *Also,* **unbeknownst.**
unbelievability *n.* невероя́тность.
unbelievable *adj.* невероя́тный. —**unbelievably,** *adv.* невероя́тно; до невероя́тности.
unbeliever *n.* неве́рующий. —**unbelieving,** *adj.* неве́рующий.
unbend *v.t.* распрямля́ть; выпрямля́ть; разгиба́ть; отгиба́ть. —**unbending,** *adj.* несгиба́емый; непрекло́нный.
unbiased *adj.* беспристра́стный.
unbind *v.t.* развя́зывать; отвя́зывать.
unbleached *adj.* небелёный; суро́вый.
unblemished *adj.* незапя́тнанный.
unboiled *adj.* сыро́й: *drink unboiled water,* пить сыру́ю во́ду.
unborn *adj.* (ещё) не рождённый (*or* роди́вшийся).
unbosom *v.t.* *Unbosom oneself,* излива́ть ду́шу.
unbound *adj.* без переплёта.
unbounded *adj.* неограни́ченный; безме́рный.
unbraid *v.t.* расплета́ть.
unbreakable *adj.* небью́щийся.
unbridle *v.t.* разну́здывать.
unbridled *adj.* **1,** (having no bridle) разну́зданный. **2,** *fig.* (unrestrained) необу́зданный.
unbroken *adj.* **1,** (intact) це́лый. **2,** (continuous) сплошно́й.
unbuckle *v.t.* расстёгивать.
unburden *v.t.* снима́ть бре́мя с. —**unburden oneself,** отводи́ть ду́шу.
unbutton *v.t.* расстёгивать.
uncalled-for *adj.* **1,** (unnecessary) нену́жный. **2,** (out of place) неуме́стный.
uncanceled *also,* **uncancelled** *adj.* (of stamps) негашёный.
uncanny *adj.* необъясни́мый.
uncared-for *adj.* безнадзо́рный; забро́шенный.
unceasing *adj.* непреста́нный; беспреста́нный.
unceremonious *adj.* бесцеремо́нный. —**unceremoniously,** *adv.* бесцеремо́нно.
uncertain *adj.* **1,** (unsure) неуве́ренный. **2,** (indefinite) неопределённый. —**in no uncertain terms,** недвусмы́сленно.
uncertainty *n.* **1,** (lack of confidence) неуве́ренность. **2,** (lack of definite information) неизве́стность; неопределённость.
unchain *v.t.* **1,** (release from a chain) спуска́ть с це́пи. **2,** *fig.* (set free) раско́вывать.
unchallengeable *adj.* неоспори́мый.
unchallenged *adj.* **1,** (having no rivals) не име́ющий сопе́рников. **2,** (not answered or disputed) без возраже́ний: *allow to go unchallenged,* пропуска́ть без возраже́ний; ничего́ не говори́ть в отве́т.
unchanging *adj.* неизме́нный; неизменя́емый.
uncharted *adj.* неиссле́дованный.
unchecked *adj.* беспрепя́тственный.
uncivil *adj.* неве́жливый; неучти́вый.
uncivilized *adj.* **1,** (barbarous) нецивилизо́ванный. **2,** (crude) некульту́рный.
unclaimed *adj.* невостре́бованный.
unclassified *adj.* несекре́тный.
uncle *n.* дя́дя.
unclean *adj.* нечи́стый. —**uncleanliness,** *n.* нечистота́. —**uncleanly,** *adj.* нечи́стый.
unclear *adj.* нея́сный.
unclench *v.t.* размина́ть.
uncoil *v.t.* разма́тывать; раскру́чивать.
uncomfortable *adj.* неудо́бный: *uncomfortable chair,* неудо́бный стул; *uncomfortable situation,* неудо́бное положе́ние. *I am uncomfortable,* мне неудо́бно. —**uncomfortably,** *adv.* неудо́бно.
uncommitted *adj.* неприсоедини́вшийся.
uncommon *adj.* ре́дкий; необыкнове́нный. —**uncommonly,** *adv.* необыкнове́нно.
uncommunicative *adj.* молчали́вый; неразгово́рчивый.

uncomplaining *adj.* безро́потный.
uncompleted *adj.* незако́нченный; незавершённый.
uncomplicated *adj.* несло́жный.
uncomplimentary *adj.* нele̒стный.
uncompromising *adj.* бескомпроми́ссный.
unconcealed *adj.* нескрыва́емый.
unconcern *n.* **1,** (lack of worry) беззабо́тность; беспе́чность. **2,** (indifference) безразли́чие; равноду́шие.
unconcerned *adj.* **1,** (unworried) беззабо́тный; беспе́чный. **2,** (indifferent) безразли́чный; равноду́шный.
unconditional *adj.* безогово́рочный; безусло́вный. —**unconditional surrender,** безогово́рочная капитуля́ция.
unconfirmed *adj.* неподтверждённый.
unconnected *adj.* **1,** (not related) не свя́занный: *the two events are unconnected,* э́ти два собы́тия не свя́заны друг с дру́гом. **2,** (incoherent) бессвя́зный.
unconquerable *adj.* непобеди́мый.
unconscientious *adj.* недобросо́вестный.
unconscionable *adj.* бессо́вестный.
unconscious *adj.* **1,** (having lost consciousness): *he is unconscious,* он без созна́ния; он в бессозна́тельном состоя́нии. *The blow knocked him unconscious,* уда́р лиши́л его́ созна́ния. **2,** (involuntary) бессозна́тельный; безотчётный. —**unconsciousness,** *n.* бессозна́тельное состоя́ние; беспа́мятство; бесчу́вствие.
unconstitutional *adj.* неконституцио́нный.
uncontrollable *adj.* неукроти́мый; неудержи́мый; безу́держный. *Uncontrollable anger,* неукроти́мый гнев. *Uncontrollable desire,* неудержи́мое жела́ние. *Uncontrollable laughter,* безу́держный смех.
uncontrolled *adj.* бесконтро́льный.
unconventional *adj.* необы́чный; оригина́льный.
unconvinced *adj.* не убеждён. *I remain unconvinced,* я остаю́сь при своём мне́нии.
unconvincing *adj.* неубеди́тельный.
uncooked *adj.* сыро́й.
uncooperative *adj.* несгово́рчивый.
uncoordinated *adj.* несогласо́ванный.
uncork *v.t.* отку́поривать; раску́поривать.
uncountable *adj.* неисчисли́мый. —**uncounted,** *adj.* несчётный; бесчи́сленный.
uncouple *v.t.* расцепля́ть; отцепля́ть.
uncouth *adj.* гру́бый; неотёсанный.
uncover *v.t.* раскрыва́ть; открыва́ть. —**uncovered,** *adj.* непокры́тый; неприкры́тый.
uncritical *adj.* некрити́ческий.
uncrowned *adj.* некороно́ванный.
unction *n.* **1,** (act of anointing) миропома́зание. *Extreme unction,* собо́рование. **2,** (oil; ointment) еле́й; мазь.
unctuous *adj.* еле́йный.
uncultivated *adj.* **1,** (untilled) необрабо́танный; невозде́ланный. **2,** (unrefined) некульту́рный.
uncultured *adj.* некульту́рный.
uncut *adj.* **1,** (not sliced) неразре́занный. **2,** (not abridged) по́лный; несокращённый. **3,** (not ground or polished) неотшлифо́ванный.
undamaged *adj.* невреди́мый.
undaunted *adj.* неустраши́мый; бесстра́шный.
undecided *adj.* **1,** (not settled) под вопро́сом. **2,** (not having reached a decision) в нереши́тельности; в нереши́мости. *I am still undecided as to what to do,* я ещё не реши́л(а), что сде́лать.
undecipherable *adj.* неразбо́рчивый.
undeclared *adj.* необъя́вленный: *undeclared war,* необъя́вленная война́.
undefeated *adj.* не потерпе́вший пораже́ния.
undefended *adj.* незащищённый.
undemanding *adj.* нетре́бовательный; невзыска́тельный.
undemocratic *adj.* антидемократи́ческий.
undeniable *adj.* неоспори́мый; бесспо́рный.
undependable *adj.* ненадёжный.
under *prep.* **1,** (below) под (+ *instr.*): *under the table/tree,* под столо́м/де́ревом. *Under water,* под водо́й. *From under the table,* из-под стола́. *Live under the same roof,* жить под одно́й кры́шей. ♦*With verbs of motion* под (+ *acc.*): *the ball rolled under the bed,* мяч закати́лся под крова́ть. *Slip something under the door,* подсу́нуть что́-нибудь под дверь. **2,** (less than) ме́ньше чем: *under two dollars,* ме́ньше чем два до́ллара; ме́ньше двух до́лларов. *Children under five,* де́ти до пяти́ лет. **3,** (according to) по; согла́сно: *under the terms of the treaty,* по усло́виям догово́ра. **4,** (in view of) при: *under the circumstances,* при таки́х обстоя́тельствах. **5,** (in the time of) при: *under the old regime,* при ста́ром режи́ме. **6,** *with various nouns* под: *under oath,* под прися́гой; *under arrest,* под аре́стом; *under arms,* под ружьём; *under lock and key,* под замко́м; *under the leadership of,* под руково́дством (+ *gen.*), *under an assumed name,* под чужи́м и́менем. *Be under repair/siege,* быть в ремо́нте/оса́де. ♦*Also with the refl. verb: be under construction,* стро́иться; *be under discussion,* обсужда́ться; *be under consideration,* рассма́триваться. —*adv.* **1,** (to a place below) вниз. *The swimmer went under,* плове́ц утону́л. *The business went under,* де́ло прогоре́ло. **2,** (less) ме́ньше: *five dollars or under,* пять до́лларов и́ли (да́же) ме́ньше. *Children six and under,* де́ти от шести́ лет и моло́же. —**under way,** *see* **way.**
underage *adj.* несовершенноле́тний; малоле́тний.
underbodice *n.* ли́фчик.
underbrush *n.* подле́сок.
undercarriage *n.* шасси́.
undercharge *v.t.* брать сли́шком дёшево с.
underclothes *n.pl.* ни́жнее бельё.
undercook *v.t.* недовари́ть; недожа́рить.
undercover *adj.* та́йный; секре́тный.
undercurrent *n.* **1,** (lower current) подво́дное тече́ние. **2,** (latent manifestation): *undercurrent of discontent,* скры́тое недово́льство.
undercut *v.t.* **1,** = **undersell. 2,** (undermine) подрыва́ть.
underdeveloped *adj.* недора́звитый. *Underdeveloped countries,* слабора́звитые стра́ны.
underdone *adj.* недожа́ренный; крова́вый.
underdrawers *n.pl.* кальсо́ны.
underestimate *v.t.* недооце́нивать; преуменьша́ть. —**underestimation,** *n.* недооце́нка; преуменьше́ние.
underexpose *v.t., photog.* недоде́рживать. —**underexposure,** *n.* недоде́ржка.

underfed *adj. Be underfed,* недоеда́ть.
underfoot *adv.* под нога́ми. *Trample underfoot,* зата́птывать.
undergarment *n.* предме́т ни́жнего белья́.
undergo *v.t.* проходи́ть: *undergo tests/training,* проходи́ть испыта́ния/подгото́вку. *Undergo changes,* претерпе́ть измене́ния. *Undergo an operation,* подве́ргнуться опера́ции.
undergraduate *n.* студе́нт университе́та.
underground *n.* **1,** (clandestine movement) подпо́лье. *Go underground,* уйти́ в подпо́лье. **2,** *Brit.* = **subway.** —*adj.* **1,** (subterranean) подзе́мный. **2,** (clandestine) подпо́льный. —*adv.* под землёй.
undergrowth *n.* подле́сок; за́росли.
underhand *adj.* = **underhanded.** —*adj. & adv., sports* сни́зу.
underhanded *adj.* та́йный; надува́тельский.
underlie *v.t.* **1,** (lie under) лежа́ть под. **2,** (be the basis of) лежа́ть в осно́ве (+ *gen.*).
underline *v.t.* подчёркивать.
underling *n.* прислу́жник.
underlying *adj.* лежа́щий в осно́ве; основно́й.
undermine *v.t.* подрыва́ть.
underneath *adv.* внизу́; ни́же. —*prep.* под: *underneath the rug,* под ковро́м.
undernourished *adj. Be undernourished,* недоеда́ть.
underpaid *adj.* низкоопла́чиваемый.
underpants *n.pl.* **1,** (shorts; panties) трусы́; тру́сики. **2,** (long drawers) кальсо́ны.
underpass *n.* подзе́мный перехо́д.
underpay *v.t.* опла́чивать (кого́-нибудь) сли́шком ни́зко. —*v.i.* недопла́чивать: *underpay by ten dollars,* недопла́чивать де́сять до́лларов.
underpopulated *adj.* малонаселённый.
underprivileged *adj.* неиму́щий.
underproduction *n.* недопроизво́дство.
underrate *v.t.* недооце́нивать; преуменьша́ть.
underripe *adj.* недоспе́лый; недозре́лый.
underscore *v.t.* подчёркивать.
undersea *adj.* подво́дный.
undersecretary *n.* замести́тель мини́стра.
undersell *v.t.* продава́ть деше́вле чем.
undershirt *n.* ни́жняя руба́шка.
undershorts *n.pl.* трусы́.
underside *n.* изна́нка.
undersigned *n., preceded by* **the** нижеподписа́вшийся.
undersized *adj.* малоро́слый; низкоро́слый.
underskirt *n.* ни́жняя ю́бка.
understand *v.t. & i.* понима́ть: *understand Russian,* понима́ть по-ру́сски. *I don't understand,* я не понима́ю. —*v.t.* **1,** (hear) слы́шать: *I understand that...,* я слы́шал(а), что... **2,** (assume without stating) подразумева́ть: *the subject (of the sentence) is understood,* подлежа́щее подразумева́ется. —**give to understand,** дать поня́ть. —**make oneself understood,** объясня́ться.
understandable *adj.* поня́тный. —**understandably,** *adv.* поня́тно; поня́тное де́ло.
understanding *n.* **1,** (comprehension) понима́ние. **2,** (an agreement) договорённость; соглаше́ние. —*adj.* **1,** (comprehending) понима́ющий. **2,** (sympathetic) отзы́вчивый.
understate *v.t.* преуменьша́ть. —**understatement,** *n.* преуменьше́ние. *That's an understatement!,* э́то сли́шком мя́гкое выраже́ние; так сказа́ть – ничего́ не сказа́ть.
understudy *n.* дублёр. —*v.t.* дубли́ровать.
undertake *v.t.* **1,** (take upon oneself; agree to do) предпринима́ть; бра́ться за. *Undertake a trip,* предпринима́ть пое́здку. *Undertake a job/an assignment/,* бра́ться за рабо́ту/поруче́ние. **2,** *fol. by inf.* (pledge) обя́зываться.
undertaker *n.* владе́лец похоро́нного бюро́.
undertaking *n.* предприя́тие.
undertone *n. In an undertone,* вполго́лоса.
undertow *n.* подво́дное тече́ние.
undervalue *v.t.* недооце́нива́ть.
underwater *adj.* подво́дный.
underwear *n.* ни́жнее бельё.
underweight *adj.* ве́сящий ме́ньше (*or* ни́же) поло́женного ве́са. *I am ten pounds underweight,* я ве́шу на де́сять фу́нтов ме́ньше/ни́же поло́женного.
underworld *n.* **1,** (criminal element) престу́пный мир; уголо́вщина. **2,** (hell) преиспо́дняя.
underwrite *v.t.* гаранти́ровать: *underwrite a loan,* гаранти́ровать размеще́ние за́йма.
underwriter *n.* страхо́вщик.
undeserved *adj.* незаслу́женный.
undesirable *adj.* нежела́тельный. —*n., usu.pl.* сомни́тельные элеме́нты.
undetermined *adj.* неопределённый.
undeveloped *adj.* неразвито́й.
undignified *adj.* недосто́йный.
undisciplined *adj.* недисциплини́рованный.
undiscriminating *adj.* неразбо́рчивый.
undisguised *adj.* неприкры́тый; нескрыва́емый.
undismayed *adj.* необескура́женный.
undisputed *adj.* неоспори́мый.
undistinguished *adj.* заура́дный; непримеча́тельный.
undisturbed *adj.* споко́йный; необеспоко́енный.
undivided *adj.* безразде́льный. *One's undivided attention,* по́лное внима́ние.
undo *v.t.* **1,** (reverse the doing of) своди́ть на нет. *Undo an error,* исправля́ть оши́бку. *Undo what has been done,* уничтожа́ть сде́ланное. **2,** (unfasten) расстёгивать; отстёгивать; развя́зывать.
undoing *n. Be (or prove) the undoing of,* (по)губи́ть кого́-нибудь.
undone *adj.* **1,** (not done) незако́нченный. **2,** (unfastened): *come undone,* расстёгиваться; отстёгиваться; развя́зываться.
undoubted *adj.* несомне́нный; бесспо́рный. —**undoubtedly,** *adv.* несомне́нно; бесспо́рно.
undreamed-of *adj.* во сне не сни́вшийся; невообрази́мый.
undress *v.t.* раздева́ть. —*v.i.* раздева́ться. —**undressed,** *adj.* разде́тый.
undue *adj.* чрезме́рный: *undue haste,* чрезме́рная поспе́шность.
undulate *v.i.* **1,** (ripple) ряби́ть. **2,** (flutter) колыха́ться. —**undulating,** *adj.* волни́стый; волнообра́зный.
unduly *adv.* чрезме́рно.
undying *adj.* неугаси́мый; неувяда́емый; неме́ркнущий.
unearned *adj.* **1,** (not earned) нетрудово́й: *unearned*

income, нетрудовы́е дохо́ды. **2,** (not deserved) незаслу́женный.
unearth *v.t.* **1,** (dig up from the earth) выка́пывать; вырыва́ть; отка́пывать; отрыва́ть. **2,** (find; discover) выка́пывать; отка́пывать; раска́пывать.
unearthly *adj.* неземно́й; незде́шний. *At this unearthly hour,* в таку́ю рань.
uneasy *adj.* беспоко́йный; неспоко́йный. —**uneasiness,** *n.* беспоко́йство.
uneatable *adj.* несъедо́бный.
uneconomical *adj.* неэконо́мный; бесхозя́йственный.
uneducated *adj.* необразо́ванный.
unemployed *adj.* безрабо́тный. —*n., preceded by* **the** безрабо́тные.
unemployment *n.* безрабо́тица. *Unemployment insurance/benefits,* посо́бие по безрабо́тице.
unencouraging *adj.* неутеши́тельный.
unending *adj.* несконча́емый.
unendurable *adj.* невыноси́мый; непереноси́мый; несно́сный; нестерпи́мый.
unenforceable *adj.* неосуществи́мый.
unenlightened *adj.* непросвещённый.
unenterprising *adj.* непредприи́мчивый; безынициати́вный.
unenthusiastic *adj.* лишённый энтузиа́зма. *The critics were unenthusiastic,* критики не́ были в восто́рге; кри́тики относи́лись хо́лодно (к чему́-нибудь)
unenviable *adj.* незави́дный.
unequal *adj.* **1,** (not equal in amount; not equitable) нера́вный. *Unequal battle,* нера́вный бой. *Unequal treaty,* неравнопра́вный догово́р. **2,** *fol. by* **to** (not up to): *he proved unequal to the task,* зада́ча оказа́лась ему́ не под си́лу.
unequaled *also,* **unequalled** *adj.* непревзойдённый.
unequivocal *adj.* недвусмы́сленный. —**unequivocally,** *adv.* недвусмы́сленно.
unerring *adj.* безоши́бочный.
unethical *adj.* неэти́чный.
uneven *adj.* **1,** (not level or straight) неро́вный. **2,** (not uniform or consistent) неравноме́рный. **3,** (odd, as of a number) нечётный. —**unevenly,** *adv.* неро́вно; неравноме́рно. —**unevenness,** *n.* неро́вность; неравноме́рность.
uneventful *adj.* без происше́ствий: *the trip was uneventful,* путь прошёл без происше́ствий.
unexampled *adj.* бесприме́рный.
unexcelled *adj.* непревзойдённый.
unexceptionable *adj.* безупре́чный.
unexceptional *adj.* ничем не выделя́ющийся; зауря́дный.
unexpected *adj.* неожи́данный. —**unexpectedly,** *adv.* неожи́данно.
unexplainable *adj.* необъясни́мый.
unexplored *adj.* неиссле́дованный; неизве́данный; неразве́данный.
unexposed *adj., photog.* неэкспони́рованый.
unexpressed *adj.* невы́сказанный.
unexpressive *adj.* невырази́тельный.
unfailing *adj.* **1,** (constant; unflagging) неосла́бный. **2,** (devoted; staunch) неизме́нный. —**unfailingly,** *adv.* неукосни́тельно.
unfair *adj.* **1,** (inequitable) несправедли́вый. **2,** (unethical) нече́стный. —**unfairly,** *adv.* несправедли́во. —**unfairness,** *n.* несправедли́вость.
unfaithful *adj.* неве́рный. *Be unfaithful to,* изменя́ть; обма́нывать.
unfamiliar *adj.* незнако́мый.—**unfamiliarity,** *n.* незнако́мство.
unfasten *v.t.* **1,** (detach) открепля́ть. **2,** (unbutton; untie) расстёгивать; отстёгивать; отвя́зывать.
unfathomable *adj.* **1,** (impossible to measure) неизмери́мый. **2,** (impossible to understand) непостижи́мый.
unfavorable *also,* **unfavourable** *adj.* неблагоприя́тный. *Unfavorable balance of trade,* пасси́вный торго́вый бала́нс.
unfeasible *adj.* невыполни́мый; неосуществи́мый.
unfeeling *adj.* бесчу́вственный.
unfeigned *adj.* непритво́рный; неподде́льный.
unfetter *v.t.* раско́вывать.
unfilled *adj.* **1,** (vacant) вака́нтный. *Unfilled position,* вака́нсия. **2,** (not executed) невы́полненный: *unfilled orders,* невы́полненные зака́зы.
unfinished *adj.* незако́нченный.
unfit *adj.* него́дный; неприго́дный.
unflagging *adj.* неосла́бный.
unflappable *adj., colloq.* невозмути́мый.
unflattering *adj.* неле́стный.
unfledged *adj.* неопери́вшийся.
unflinching *adj.* непоколеби́мый; неукло́нный.
unfold *v.t.* развёртывать. —*v.i.* **1,** (open out) развёртываться. **2,** (gradually become known) раскрыва́ться; развёртываться.
unforeseen *adj.* непредви́денный.
unforgettable *adj.* незабыва́емый; незабве́нный.
unforgivable *adj.* непрости́тельный.
unfortunate *adj.* **1,** (unlucky; hapless) несча́стный. **2,** (regrettable; inappropriate) неуда́чный. —**unfortunately,** *adv.* к сожале́нию; к несча́стью.
unfounded *adj.* необосно́ванный; неоснова́тельный; беспо́чвенный.
unfreeze *v.t.* размора́живать.
unfriendly *adj.* недружелю́бный; неприве́тливый. —**unfriendliness,** *n.* недружелю́бие; неприве́тливость.
unfrock *v.t.* расстрига́ть; лиша́ть духо́вного са́на.
unfulfilled *adj.* **1,** (not realized) невы́полненный. **2,** (broken; unkept) несде́ржанный.
unfurl *v.t.* развёртывать; распуска́ть.
unfurnished *adj.* немеблиро́ванный.
ungainly *adj.* неуклю́жий; нескла́дный.
ungird *v.t.* распоя́сывать.
unglue *v.t.* откле́ивать; раскле́ивать. *Come unglued,* откле́иваться; раскле́иваться.
ungodly *adj.* **1,** (not believing in God) безбо́жный. **2,** *colloq.* (horrible) ди́кий. *At this ungodly hour,* в таку́ю рань.
ungraceful *adj.* нестро́йный; нескла́дный.
ungracious *adj.* нелюбе́зный; неприве́тливый. —**ungraciousness,** *n.* неприве́тливость.
ungrammatical *adj.* негра́мотный; безгра́мотный.
ungrateful *adj.* неблагода́рный.
ungrounded *adj.* **1,** (unfounded) необосно́ванный; неоснова́тельный; беспо́чвенный. **2,** (unversed) несве́дущий.

unguarded *adj.* **1,** (unprotected) незащищённый. **2,** (indiscreet) неосторóжный; неосмотри́тельный.
unguent *n.* мазь.
ungulate *adj.* копы́тный. —*n.* копы́тное живóтное.
unhampered *adj.* беспрепя́тственный.
unhand *v.t.* отнимáть рýки от.
unhandy *adj.* **1,** (inconvenient) неудóбный. **2,** (clumsy) безрýкий.
unhappiness *n.* недовóльство; неудовóльствие.
unhappy *adj.* **1,** (sad) грýстный: *why are you so unhappy?,* почемý вам так грýстно? *You look unhappy,* у вас несчáстный вид. **2,** (unfortunate; miserable) несчастли́вый; несчáстный: *unhappy life,* несчастли́вая/несчáстная жизнь. **3,** (not successful; unsatisfactory) несчастли́вый; неблагополýчный. *Unhappy ending,* несчастли́вый конéц. *Unhappy outcome,* неблагополýчный исхóд. **4,** (dissatisfied) недовóлен: *unhappy with the results,* недовóлен результáтами. **5,** (inappropriate) неудáчный: *an unhappy choice,* неудáчный вы́бор.
unharmed *adj.* невреди́мый.
unharness *v.t.* распрягáть; отпрягáть; выпрягáть.
unhealthy *adj.* нездорóвый.
unheard-of *adj.* несльı́ханный.
unheated *adj.* не имéющий отоплéния; холóдный.
unheeded *adj. His advice went unheeded,* егó совéты остáлись без внимáния.
unhelpful *adj.* бесполéзный: *unhelpful advice,* бесполéзный совéт. *He was completely unhelpful,* он совсéм не помóг.
unhesitatingly *adv.* без колебáний.
unhindered *adj.* беспрепя́тственный.
unhinge *v.t.* **1,** (remove from its hinges) снимáть с пéтель. **2,** (unbalance; upset) расшáтывать. *His mind became unhinged,* он трóнулся умóм.
unhitch *v.t.* отцепля́ть; расцепля́ть.
unholy *adj.* **1,** (wicked) нечести́вый. **2,** *colloq.* (dreadful) сýщий: *unholy hell,* сýщий ад.
unhook *v.t.* **1,** (detach) отцепля́ть; расцепля́ть. **2,** (unbutton) расстёгивать.
unhurried *adj.* неторопли́вый.
unhurt *adj.* невреди́мый.
Uniat *n.* униáт. —*adj.* униáтский.
unicameral *adj.* однопалáтный.
unicorn *n.* единорóг.
unidentified *adj.* неопóзнанный.
unification *n.* объединéние.
uniform *n.* фóрма; обмундировáние. *In uniform,* в фóрме. —*adj.* **1,** (of a uniform) фóрменный: *uniform dress,* фóрменная одéжда. **2,** (regular; unchanging) рóвный; равномéрный. *Uniform temperature,* рóвная температýра. **3,** (the same everywhere) единообрáзный: *a uniform system,* единообрáзная систéма. —**uniformed,** *adj.* одéтый в фóрму.
uniformity *n.* единообрáзие.
unify *v.t.* объединя́ть.
unilateral *adj.* односторóнний.
unimaginable *adj.* невообрази́мый.
unimpeachable *adj.* безукори́зненный; безупрéчный.
unimpeded *adj.* беспрепя́тственный.
unimportant *adj.* невáжный.
unimpressed *adj. I was unimpressed,* э́то на меня́ не произвелó никакóго впечатлéния.
uninformed *adj.* неосведомлённый; несвéдущий.
uninhabitable *adj.* непригóдный для жилья́.
uninhabited *adj.* необитáемый; безлю́дный.
uninhibited *adj.* нестеснённый; раскóванный.
uninitiated *adj.* непосвящённый.
uninjured *adj.* невреди́мый.
uninspired *adj.* бездýшный; бескры́лый.
unintelligent *adj.* неýмный.
unintelligible *adj.* непоня́тный; невразуми́тельный. —**unintelligibility,** *n.* непоня́тность.
unintentional *adj.* ненамéренный; невóльный; неумы́шленный. —**unintentionally,** *adv.* ненамéренно; невóльно.
uninteresting *adj.* неинтерéсный.
uninterrupted *adj.* непреры́вный; беспреры́вный; бесперебóйный.
uninvited *adj.* незвáный; непрóшеный.
uninviting *adj.* непривéтливый.
union *n.* **1,** (joining together) соединéние; объединéние; слия́ние. *Marital union,* брáчный сою́з. **2,** (a confederation) сою́з; объединéние. *Universal Postal Union,* Всеми́рный почтóвый сою́з. **3,** (labor union) профсою́з. —*adj.* **1,** *USSR* сою́зный: *union republic,* сою́зная респýблика. **2,** (pert. to a trade union) профсою́зный.
unionize *v.t. & i.* объединя́ть(ся) в профсою́з.
unique *adj.* еди́нственный в своём рóде; уникáльный; исключи́тельный; неповтори́мый. *Unique opportunity,* исключи́тельная возмóжность.
unisexual *adj.* однопóлый.
unison *n.* унисóн. —**in unison,** в унисóн.
unit *n.* **1,** (basic element or amount) едини́ца: *monetary unit,* дéнежная едини́ца. **2,** *mil.* часть. **3,** (apparatus) установка; блок; ýзел.
unite *v.t.* соединя́ть; объединя́ть. —*v.i.* соединя́ться; объединя́ться. *"Workers of the world unite!",* Пролетáрии всех стран, соединя́йтесь!
united *adj.* соединённый; объединённый. *United front,* еди́ный фронт. —**United Kingdom,** Соединённое Королéвство. —**United Nations,** Объединённые Нáции. —**United States,** Соединённые Штáты.
unity *n.* **1,** (oneness; sameness) еди́нство. **2,** (quality of being united) еди́нство; единéние; сплочённость.
universal *adj.* **1,** (worldwide) всеóбщий; всеми́рный. *Universal suffrage,* всеóбщее избирáтельное прáво. *Universal language,* всеми́рный язы́к. **2,** (touching everything) универсáльный. —**universal joint,** универсáльный шарни́р.
universality *n.* универсáльность.
universally *adv.* во всём ми́ре; всéми. *Universally recognized,* всéми при́знанный.
universe *n.* вселéнная.
university *n.* университéт. —*adj.* университéтский.
unjust *adj.* несправедли́вый.
unjustified *adj.* неопрáвданный.
unjustly *adv.* несправедли́во.
unkempt *adj.* **1,** (uncombed) нечёсаный. **2,** (untidy) неопря́тный; неря́шливый; нечистоплóтный.
unkept *adj.* несдéржанный.
unkind *adj.* недóбрый.
unknown *adj.* **1,** (not known) неизвéстный; безвéстный. **2,** *math.* неизвéстный. —*n., math.* неизвéстное; искóмое. —**fear of the unknown,** страх пéред неизвéстностью.

unlace *v.t.* расшнуро́вывать.
unlawful *adj.* незако́нный; противозако́нный. —**unlawfully,** *adv.* незако́нно.
unleaded *adj.* (of gasoline) неэтили́рованный.
unleash *v.t.* спуска́ть с при́вязи. *Unleash a war,* развяза́ть *or* разжига́ть войну́.
unleavened *adj.* пре́сный. *Unleavened bread,* пре́сный хлеб; маца́.
unless *conj.* е́сли не: *unless I am mistaken,* е́сли я не ошиба́юсь. *Unless I hear to the contrary,* е́сли я не услы́шу чего́-нибудь ино́го.
unlighted *adj.* неосвещённый.
unlike *adj.* непохо́жий; несхо́дный. —*prep.* **1,** (differing from) непохо́жий на. ♦*When introducing a contrasting situation* в отли́чие от; не в приме́р (+ *dat.*). **2,** (not typical of) нетипи́чно (для); нехарактéрно (для).
unlikelihood *n.* маловероя́тность.
unlikely *adj.* маловероя́тный. *It is unlikely that he will come,* вряд ли он придет.
unlikeness *n.* несхо́дство.
unlimited *adj.* неограни́ченный.
unlisted *adj.* не включённый в спи́сок. *We have an unlisted number,* наш но́мер не внесен в телефо́нную кни́гу.
unlit *adj.* неосвещённый
unload *v.t.* **1,** (remove cargo from, as a ship) разгружа́ть. **2,** (remove, as cargo) выгружа́ть. **3,** (remove the ammunition from) разряжа́ть. **4,** *colloq.* (sell; get rid of) спуска́ть. —*v.i.* разгружа́ться. —**unloaded,** *adj.* незаря́женный. —**unloading,** *n.* разгру́зка; вы́грузка.
unlock *v.t.* отпира́ть. —*v.i.* отпира́ться. —**unlocked,** *adj.* неза́пертый.
unloose *v.t.* **1,** (relax, as a grip) ослабля́ть. **2,** (release) выпуска́ть. *Also,* **unloosen.**
unloved *adj.* нелюби́мый.
unlucky *adj.* **1,** (having no luck) неуда́чливый; незада́чливый. **2,** (bringing bad luck) несчастли́вый: *unlucky number,* несчастли́вая ци́фра.
unmanned *adj.* беспило́тный.
unmannerly *adj.* невоспи́танный; некульту́рный
unmarried *adj.* (of a man) нежена́тый; (of a woman) незаму́жняя.
unmask *v.t.* разоблача́ть.
unmentionable *adj.* нецензу́рный. —**unmentionables,** *n.pl., colloq.* "невырази́мые".
unmerciful *adj.* немилосе́рдный; беспоща́дный.
unmindful *adj.* [*usu.* **unmindful of**] не обраща́я внима́ния на.
unmistakable *adj.* **1,** (that cannot be confused) ве́рный: *unmistakable sign,* ве́рный при́знак. **2,** (allowing no misunderstanding) недвусмы́сленный.
unmitigated *adj.* **1,** (thoroughgoing; out-and-out) отъя́вленный. **2,** (total; utter) по́лный.
unmoved *adj.* нетро́нутый; нерастро́ганный.
unnamed *adj.* нена́званный.
unnatural *adj.* неесте́ственный.
unnavigable *adj.* несудохо́дный.
unnecessary *adj.* нену́жный.
unnerve *v.t.* нерви́ровать; расстра́ивать; лиша́ть прису́тствия ду́ха. —**unnerved,** *adj.* расстро́енный; разви́нченный.
unnoticed *adj.* незаме́ченный: *go unnoticed,* пройти́ незаме́ченным.
unobservant *adj.* ненаблюда́тельный.
unobtainable *adj.* недосту́пный.
unoccupied *adj.* неза́нятый.
unofficial *adj.* неофициа́льный.
unorganized *adj.* неорганизо́ванный.
unorthodox *adj.* необы́чный; оригина́льный.
unpack *v.t.* распако́вывать. —*v.i.* распако́вываться.
unpaid *adj.* **1,** (not yet paid) неопла́ченный; неупла́ченный. **2,** (receiving no pay) не получа́ющий пла́ты.
unpainted *adj.* некра́шеный.
unpalatable *adj.* невку́сный.
unparalleled *adj.* бесприме́рный; беспрецеде́нтный.
unpardonable *adj.* непрости́тельный.
unpaved *adj.* немощёный.
unpin *v.t.* отка́лывать.
unplanned *adj.* беспла́новый.
unpleasant *adj.* неприя́тный. —**unpleasantness,** *n.* неприя́тность.
unplug *v.t.* отключа́ть.
unpolished *adj.* неотполиро́ванный; неотшлифо́ванный.
unpopular *adj.* непопуля́рный. —**unpopularity,** *n.* непопуля́рность.
unprecedented *adj.* беспрецеде́нтный; небыва́лый.
unpredictable *adj.* непредсказу́емый.
unprejudiced *adj.* непредубежденный.
unpremeditated *adj.* непреднаме́ренный; непредумы́шленный.
unprepared *adj.* неподготовленный. *Catch unprepared,* заста́ть враспло́х.
unpretentious *adj.* непритяза́тельный; неприхотли́вый.
unpreventable *adj.* неотврати́мый; неизбе́жный; немину́емый.
unprincipled *adj.* беспринци́пный.
unprintable *adj.* непеча́тный; нецензу́рный.
unproductive *adj.* непродукти́вный; непроизводи́тельный. —**unproductiveness,** *n.* непродукти́вность; непроизводи́тельность.
unprofitable *adj.* **1,** (not yielding a profit) невы́годный; беспри́быльный; нерента́бельный. **2,** (not accomplishing anything) безрезульта́тный.
unpromising *adj.* не подающий наде́жды; неперспекти́вный.
unpronounceable *adj.* не(удобо)произноси́мый.
unpropitious *adj.* неблагоприя́тный.
unprotected *adj.* незащищенный; беззащи́тный.
unproved *adj.* недока́занный. *Also,* **unproven.**
unprovoked *adj.* неспровоци́рованный.
unpublished *adj.* неопублико́ванный; неи́зданный.
unpunished *adj.* безнака́занный. *Go unpunished,* оста́ться безнака́занным.
unqualified *adj.* **1,** (not fit) не име́ющий (соотве́тствующей) квалифика́ции. **2,** (unreserved) безогово́рочный: *unqualified support,* безогово́рочная подде́ржка.
unquenchable *adj.* **1,** (inextinguishable) неугаси́мый. **2,** (insatiable) неутоли́мый.
unquestionable *adj.* неоспори́мый; бесспо́рный. —**unquestionably,** *adv.* бесспо́рно.
unquestioned *adj.* несомне́нный; неоспори́мый.

unquestioning *adj.* беспрекосло́вный.
unravel *v.t.* **1,** (untangle) распу́тывать. **2,** (solve) распу́тывать; разга́дывать.
unreadable *adj.* неудобочита́емый.
unready *adj.* негото́вый.
unreal *adj.* нереа́льный.
unrealistic *adj.* нереа́льный.
unrealizable *adj.* неосуществи́мый; несбы́точный.
unreasonable *adj.* **1,** (impossible to reason with) неразу́мный. **2,** (excessive; unfair) непоме́рный. —**unreasonableness,** *n.* неразу́мность.
unreasoning *adj.* неразу́мный; нерассуди́тельный.
unreceptive *adj.* невосприи́мчивый.
unrecognizable *adj.* неузнава́емый.
unrecognized *adj.* непри́знанный.
unreel *v.t.* разма́тывать.
unrefined *adj.* **1,** (raw) неочи́щенный. **2,** (lacking refinement) невоспи́танный.
unrehearsed *adj.* неподгото́вленный.
unrelated *adj.* [*usu.* **unrelated to**] не име́ющий отноше́ния к.
unrelenting *adj.* **1,** (relentless) неотсту́пный. **2,** (not relaxing or slackening) неосла́бный.
unreliable *adj.* ненадёжный. —**unreliability,** *n.* ненадёжность.
unrelieved *adj.* беспросве́тный: *unrelieved misery,* беспросве́тная тоска́.
unremitting *adj.* неосла́бный.
unremunerative *adj.* невы́годный; беспри́быльный.
unrepentant *adj.* нераска́янный.
unrequited *adj.* без взаи́мности; безотве́тный.
unreserved *adj.* **1,** (not reserved, as of a seat) незаброни́рованный; (of a car on a train) бесплацка́ртный. **2,** (unqualified; unconditional) безогово́рочный.
unresolved *adj.* неразрешённый; нерешённый.
unresponsive *adj.* неотзы́вчивый.
unrest *n.* **1,** (worry; concern) беспоко́йство; волне́ние. **2,** (disturbances; agitation) волне́ния; беспоря́дки.
unrestrained *adj.* несде́ржанный; необу́зданный; безу́держный.
unrestricted *adj.* неограни́ченный.
unripe *adj.* незре́лый; неспе́лый.
unrivaled *also,* **unrivalled** *adj.* не име́ющий себе́ ра́вных; непревзойдённый.
unroll *v.t.* развёртывать; раска́тывать.
unruffled *adj.* безмяте́жный.
unruly *adj.* непоко́рный; бу́йный.
unsaddle *v.t.* рассёдлывать.
unsafe *adj.* опа́сный. *Unsafe bridge,* ненадёжный мост.
unsanitary *adj.* антисанита́рный.
unsatisfactory *adj.* неудовлетвори́тельный. —**unsatisfactorily,** *adv.* неудовлетвори́тельно.
unsaturated *adj.* ненасы́щенный.
unsavory *also,* **unsavoury** *adj.* **1,** (having an unpleasant taste) невку́сный. **2,** (disreputable) сомни́тельный; тёмный.
unscathed *adj.* невреди́мый. *Emerge unscathed,* вы́йти сухи́м из воды́.
unscientific *adj.* ненау́чный.
unscramble *v.t.* **1,** (unravel) распу́тывать. **2,** (decipher) расшифро́вывать.
unscrew *v.t.* отви́нчивать; разви́нчивать; выви́нчивать; вывёртывать; отвёртывать.
unscrupulous *adj.* бессо́вестный; недобросо́вестный; беспринци́пный; неразбо́рчивый в сре́дствах. —**unscrupulousness,** *n.* неразбо́рчивость в сре́дствах.
unseal *v.t.* распеча́тывать; вскрыва́ть.
unseat *v.t.* **1,** (throw from the saddle) сбра́сывать с седла́. **2,** (remove from office) смеща́ть с до́лжности.
unseeing *adj.* неви́дящий; незря́чий.
unseemly *adj.* неподоба́ющий; неблагови́дный.
unseen *adj.* неви́димый. —**sight unseen,** за глаза́; загла́зно.
unselfish *adj.* бескоры́стный. —**unselfishness,** *n.* бескоры́стие.
unsettle *v.t.* **1,** (make unstable) подрыва́ть; расша́тывать. **2,** (disconcert) расстра́ивать; смуща́ть.
unsettled *adj.* **1,** (disordered) неустро́енный. **2,** (unresolved) неразрешённый; неурегули́рованный. **3,** (unpaid) неопла́ченный. **4,** (not populated) незаселённый.
unshackle *v.t.* раско́вывать.
unshakable *also,* **unshakeable** *adj.* непоколеби́мый.
unshaven *adj.* небри́тый.
unsheathe *v.t.* обнажа́ть; вынима́ть из но́жен.
unshoe *v.t.* раско́вывать (ло́шадь).
unsightly *adj.* некраси́вый; неприглядный.
unsinkable *adj.* непотопля́емый.
unskilled *adj.* неквалифици́рованный.
unskillful *also,* **unskilful** *adj.* неиску́сный; неуме́лый.
unsnarl *v.t.* распу́тывать.
unsociable *adj.* необщи́тельный; нелюди́мый. —**unsociability,** *n.* необщи́тельность; нелюди́мость.
unsold *adj.* залежа́лый: *unsold merchandise,* залежа́лый това́р. *Remain unsold,* не находи́ть сбы́та.
unsolder *v.t.* распа́ивать.
unsolicited *adj.* непро́шеный.
unsolved *adj.* нерешённый; неразрешённый; неразга́данный.
unsophisticated *adj.* неискушённый; бесхи́тростный; безыску́сственный.
unsought *adj.* непро́шеный.
unsound *adj.* **1,** (not healthy) нездоро́вый. **2,** (not solid or firm) непро́чный. **3,** (not valid; fallacious) необосно́ванный.
unspeakable *adj.* невырази́мый; несказа́нный.
unspecified *adj.* неука́занный.
unspoiled *adj.* неиспо́рченный.
unspoken *adj.* невы́сказанный.
unsportsmanlike *adj.* недосто́йный спортсме́на; неспорти́вный.
unstable *adj.* **1,** (not stable) неусто́йчивый; непро́чный. **2,** *chem.* несто́йкий.
unstained *adj.* незапя́тнанный.
unsteady *adj.* неусто́йчивый; нетвёрдый; ша́ткий. *Be unsteady on one's feet,* нетвёрдо держа́ться на нога́х.
unstinting *adj.* *Be unstinting in,* не скупи́ться на (+ *acc.*).
unstitch *v.t.* распа́рывать; поро́ть.
unstressed *adj.* безуда́рный.

unstuck *adj., in* **come unstuck, 1,** (come loose) отклéиваться; расклéиваться. **2,** *colloq.* (go awry) расклéиваться.
unsubstantiated *adj.* бездоказáтельный; беспóчвенный.
unsuccessful *adj.* неудáчный; безуспéшный. *Be unsuccessful,* не удáться. —**unsuccessfully,** *adv.* безуспéшно.
unsuitable *adj.* неподходя́щий.
unsuited *adj.* непригóдный: *unsuited for this type of work,* непригóдный к э́той рабóте.
unsullied *adj.* незапя́тнанный.
unsung *adj.* невоспéтый: *unsung hero,* невоспéтый герóй.
unsupervised *adj.* безнадзóрный; бесконтрóльный.
unsupported *adj.* **1,** (not buttressed) не имéющий опóры. **2,** (unsubstantiated) бездоказáтельный.
unsure *adj.* неувéренный.
unsurpassed *adj.* непревзойдённый.
unsuspecting *adj.* ни о чём не подозревáющий.
unsympathetic *adj.* несочýвствующий. *Be unsympathetic to,* не сочýвствовать (+ *dat.*).
unsystematic *adj.* бессистéмный; беспоря́дочный.
untalented *adj.* неталáнтливый; бесталáнный; бездáрный.
untamable *adj.* неукроти́мый.
untangle *v.t.* распýтывать.
untapped *adj.* нетрóнутый.
untarnished *adj.* незапя́тнанный.
untenable *adj.* **1,** (unsound, as of an argument) несостоя́тельный. **2,** (that cannot be defended or saved) безвы́ходный: *in an untenable position,* в безвы́ходном положéнии.
untested *adj.* неиспы́танный.
unthinkable *adj.* немы́слимый.
unthinking *adj.* бездýмный.
untidy *adj.* неопря́тный; неаккурáтный. —**untidiness,** *n.* неопря́тность.
untie *v.t.* развя́зывать; отвя́зывать.
until *prep.* до: *until spring,* до весны́. *Until tomorrow!,* до зáвтра! —*conj.* покá не: *wait until he comes,* подождите, покá он не придёт. —**not until,** тóлько: *not until ten o'clock,* тóлько в дéсять часóв. *He did not return until the next morning,* он вернýлся тóлько на слéдующее ýтро.
untilled *adj.* невоздéланный; необрабóтанный.
untimely *adj.* **1,** (ill-timed) несвоеврéменный; неумéстный. **2,** (premature, as of a death) преждеврéменный; безврéменный.
untiring *adj.* неустáнный; неутоми́мый.
unto *prep., poetic & archaic* = **to.**
untold *adj.* **1,** (not told) нерасскáзанный. **2,** (incalculable) несчётный; несмéтный.
untouchable *n., usu. pl.* неприкасáемые.
untouched *adj.* нетрóнутый.
untoward *adj.* **1,** (unfavorable) неблагоприя́тный. **2,** (unfortunate) несчáстный: *untoward incident,* несчáстный слýчай. **3,** (improper; inappropriate) неподходя́щий; неумéстный.
untrained *adj.* неподготóвленный.
untranslatable *adj.* непереводи́мый.
untried *adj.* неиспы́танный.
untroubled *adj.* безмятéжный.
untrue *adj.* невéрный. *That is untrue,* э́то невéрно. *Be untrue to,* быть невéрным (+ *dat.*).
untrustworthy *adj.* ненадёжный.
untruth *n.* неprávда. —**untruthful,** *adj.* лóжный; лжи́вый.
untwist *v.t.* раскрýчивать; открýчивать.
unusable *adj.* непригóдный.
unused *adj.* **1,** (not made use of) неиспóльзованный. **2,** *fol. by* **to** (unaccustomed) не привы́кший (к). **3,** *philately* негашёный.
unusual *adj.* необы́чный; необыкновéнный.
unusually *adv.* необыкновéнно: *unusually large,* необыкновéнно большóй.
unutterable *adj.* невырази́мый; несказáнный.
unvarnished *adj.* **1,** (not varnished) нелакирóванный. **2,** (undisguised) неприкрáшенный: *the unvarnished truth,* неприкрáшенная и́стина.
unvarying *adj.* неизмéнный.
unveil *v.t.* открывáть; раскрывáть.
unverified *adj.* непровéренный.
unversed *adj.* несвéдущий.
unvoiced *adj., phonet.* глухóй.
unwanted *adj.* нежелáтельный.
unwarranted *adj.* неопрáвданный.
unwary *adj.* неосторóжный.
unwavering *adj.* непоколеби́мый; незы́блемый.
unwed *adj.* незамýжняя. —**unwed mother,** мать-одинóчка.
unwelcome *adj.* нежелáтельный.
unwell *adj.* нездорóвый. *He is unwell,* емý нездорóвится.
unwholesome *adj.* нездорóвый.
unwieldy *adj.* громóздкий.
unwilling *adj.* неохóтный. *Be unwilling to,* не хотéть (+ *inf.*). —**unwillingly,** *adv.* неохóтно; нéхотя. —**unwillingness,** *n.* неохóта; нежелáние.
unwind *v.t.* размáтывать. —*v.i.* размáтываться.
unwise *adj.* неýмный; неразýмный; неблагоразýмный.
unwitting *adj.* невóльный; ненамéренный. —**unwittingly,** *adv.* невóльно; ненамéренно.
unworkable *adj.* непракти́чный; неосуществи́мый.
unworried *adj.* необеспокóенный.
unworthy *adj.* недостóйный. *Unworthy of respect,* недостóин уважéния. *He is unworthy of her,* он её недостóин.
unwrap *v.t.* развёртывать.
unwritten *adj.* неписаный: *unwritten law,* неписаный закóн.
unyielding *adj.* неустýпчивый; неподáтливый.
up *adv.* **1,** (to a higher level) вверх; навéрх: *hands up!,* рýки вверх! ♦*Usu. rendered by a prefixed verb: go up,* поднимáться; *stand up,* вставáть; *climb up,* влезáть. **2,** (at a high or higher level) наверхý: *what are you doing up there?,* что ты дéлаешь там наверхý? *They live three floors up,* они́ живýт тремя́ этажáми вы́ше. **3,** *used as an intensifier: eat up,* съесть; *tear up,* разорвáть; *dry up,* вы́сохнуть. —*adj.* **1,** (having risen): *prices are up,* цéны подняли́сь; *the sun is up,* сóлнце ужé встáло. **2,** (awake; out of bed) на ногáх. *The children are already up,* дéти ужé встáли. *I was up all night,* я не спал всю ночь. **3,** (over; finished) кóнчено: *your time is up,* врéмя кóнчилось *or* истеклó. *The game (or jig) is up,* игрá кóнчена. **4,** *colloq.* (going on): *what's*

up?, в чём де́ло? *Something is up,* что́-то происхо́дит. —*prep.* **1,** (to a high or higher place on) вверх по: *up the stairs,* вверх по ле́стнице. *The dog chased the cat up a tree,* соба́ка загнала́ ко́шку на де́рево. **2,** (farther along) да́льше по: *just up the road,* чуть да́льше по э́той доро́ге. —*v.t.* повыша́ть: *up the price,* повыша́ть це́ну. —*v.i.* взять: *he up and left,* он взял и ушёл. —*n., in* **ups and downs,** превра́тности судьбы́. —**up against,** лицо́м к лицу́ с (+ *instr.*). —**up against it,** *colloq.* ту́го: *he is up against it,* ему́ ту́го прихо́дится. —**up and about,** на нога́х. —**up and down, 1,** *literally* вверх и вниз. *Jump up and down,* подпры́гивать. **2,** (back and forth) взад и вперёд: *walk up and down the room,* ходи́ть взад и вперёд по ко́мнате. —**up on,** в ку́рсе (+ *gen.*). —**up to, 1,** (to; as far as) по (+ *acc.*); до: *up to one's waist,* по по́яс; *up to the ceiling,* до потолка́. *Up to one's ears in debt,* по́ уши в долга́х. **2,** (until) до: *up to now,* до сих пор. **3,** (approaching) к: *walk up to someone,* подходи́ть к кому́-нибудь. **4,** (incumbent upon) за: *it's up to you,* де́ло за ва́ми. **5,** (equal to): *up to the mark,* на до́лжной высоте́. *I am not up to the task,* э́та зада́ча мне не под си́лу. **6,** *colloq.* (plotting): *what is he up to?,* что он замышля́ет/выде́лывает/вытворя́ет? *He is up to something,* он что́-то затева́ет.

up-and-coming *adj., colloq.* многообеща́ющий.

upas *n.* анча́р.

upbraid *v.t.* упрека́ть; порица́ть.

upbringing *n.* воспита́ние.

upcoming *adj.* предстоя́щий.

update *v.t.* дополня́ть; включи́ть (са́мые) после́дние да́нные в.

upend *v.t.* опроки́дывать.

upgrade *n.* подъём. —*v.t.* **1,** (raise to a higher rank) возводи́ть. **2,** (raise to a higher standard) повыша́ть ка́чество (+ *gen.*).

upheaval *n.* переворо́т; потрясе́ние.

uphill *adv.* в го́ру. —*adj.* **1,** (upward) иду́щий в го́ру. **2,** (difficult) тру́дный; тяжёлый.

uphold *v.t.* **1,** (maintain; defend) отста́ивать: *uphold one's opinion,* отста́ивать своё мне́ние. **2,** (approve) утвержда́ть: *uphold a sentence,* утвержда́ть пригово́р.

upholster *v.t.* обива́ть. *Upholstered chair,* оби́тый стул. —**upholsterer,** *n.* обо́йщик; драпиро́вщик. —**upholstery,** *n.* оби́вка.

upkeep *n.* содержа́ние.

upland *n.* наго́рье.

uplift *v.t.* поднима́ть. *Uplift someone's spirits,* поднима́ть чьё-нибудь настрое́ние.

upon *prep.* **1,** (resting on) на: *high upon the hill,* высоко́ на холме́. **2,** (at the time of) по: *upon (his/her) arrival,* по прие́зде. **3,** (after) за: *row upon row,* ряд за ря́дом. **4,** *fol. by* **us** (having arrived): *winter is upon us,* наступи́ла зима́. **5,** *in verbal combinations: come upon,* набрести́ на; *look upon,* рассма́тривать; *rely upon,* полага́ться на. —**once upon a time,** одна́жды; жил-был. —**upon my word!,** че́стное сло́во!

upper *adj.* ве́рхний: *upper berth,* ве́рхняя по́лка; *upper house,* ве́рхняя пала́та. *Upper class,* вы́сший класс. *Upper Volta,* Ве́рхняя Во́льта. —**gain the upper hand,** брать *or* одержа́ть верх.

upper case прописны́е бу́квы.

upper crust верху́шка о́бщества.

uppermost *adj.* са́мый ве́рхний. *Uppermost in one's mind,* в це́нтре чьего́-нибудь внима́ния.

upright *adj.* **1,** (erect) прямо́й; стоя́чий. **2,** (honorable) че́стный; пра́ведный. —*adv.* пря́мо; стоймя́. —*n.* сто́йка. —**upright piano,** пиани́но.

uprising *n.* восста́ние.

uproar *n.* шум; гам; гвалт.

uproarious *adj.* шу́мный; бу́рный; бу́йный.

uproot *v.t.* **1,** (remove from the ground) вырыва́ть с ко́рнем; корчева́ть; выкорчёвывать. **2,** (force to leave a familiar place) срыва́ть с ме́ста. *Uproot oneself,* снима́ться с ме́ста. *Uproot people from their homes,* выгоня́ть люде́й из свои́х домо́в.

upset *v.t.* **1,** (tip over) опроки́дывать. **2,** (distress; unnerve) расстра́ивать; смуща́ть. **3,** (disrupt) наруша́ть; расстра́ивать: *upset the balance,* наруша́ть равнове́сие; *upset someone's plans,* расстра́ивать чьи́-нибудь пла́ны. **4,** *Upset one's stomach,* расстра́ивать желу́док. —*adj.* **1,** (overturned) опроки́нутый. **2,** (distressed) расстро́енный: *she is very upset,* она́ о́чень расстро́ена. —*n., sports* неожи́данный результа́т. —**upset stomach,** расстро́йство желу́дка.

upsetting *adj.* трево́жный: *upsetting news,* трево́жные ве́сти.

upshot *n.* исхо́д; развя́зка.

upside down вверх дном; вверх нога́ми. *Turn upside down,* переверну́ть вверх дном/нога́ми.

upstage *v.t.* затмева́ть.

upstairs *adv.* **1,** (location) наверху́. **2,** (direction) наве́рх. —*n.* ве́рхняя часть (до́ма).

upstanding *adj.* **1,** (erect) прямо́й; стоя́чий. **2,** (honorable) че́стный; прямо́й.

upstart *n.* вы́скочка.

upstream *adv.* вверх по тече́нию; про́тив тече́ния.

upsurge *n.* рост; подъём.

up-to-date *adj.* совреме́нный.

upturn *n.* оживле́ние.

upward *also,* **upwards** *adv.* наве́рх; вверх. —**upwards of,** свы́ше (+ *gen.*).

uranium *n.* ура́н. —*adj.* ура́новый.

Uranus *n.* Ура́н.

urban *adj.* городско́й. *Urban planning/development,* градострои́тельство. *Urban renewal,* перестро́йка городо́в.

urbane *adj.* ве́жливый; обходи́тельный.

urchin *n.* мальчи́шка. —**sea urchin,** морско́й ёж.

Urdu *n.* урду́.

urea *n.* мочеви́на.

uremia *n.* уреми́я. —**uremic,** *adj.* уреми́ческий.

urethra *n.* мочеиспуска́тельный кана́л; уре́тра.

urge *v.t.* **1,** (try hard to persuade) убежда́ть. **2,** *usu. fol. by* **on** (drive onward) подгоня́ть; погоня́ть; понука́ть. **3,** (advocate strongly) призыва́ть к. —*n.* побужде́ние; стремле́ние; позы́в.

urgency *n.* сро́чность; неотло́жность. *A matter of great urgency,* сро́чное *or* неотло́жное де́ло.

urgent *adj.* **1,** (requiring immediate action) сро́чный; неотло́жный; спе́шный; настоя́тельный; безотлага́тельный. **2,** (conveying a sense of urgency) настоя́тельный: *urgent request,* настоя́тельная про́сьба.

urgently *adv.* сро́чно; безотлага́тельно. *Urgently request,* настоя́тельно проси́ть.

uric *adj.* мочево́й. —**uric acid,** мочева́я кислота́.

urinal *n.* писсуа́р.

urinalysis *n.* ана́лиз мочи́.

urinary *adj.* мочевóй.
urinate *v.i.* мочи́ться. —**urination,** *n.* мочеиспускáние.
urine *n.* мочá.
urn *n.* **1,** (vase) ýрна. **2,** (container for brewing coffee or tea) самовáр.
urology *n.* урóлогия. —**urological,** *adj.* урологи́ческий. —**urologist,** *n.* урóлог.
Ursa Major Большáя Медвéдица. —**Ursa Minor,** Мáлая Медвéдица.
us *pers.pron.* **1,** *used as dir. obj. of a verb* нас: *they drove us home,* нас отвезли́ домóй. **2,** *used as indir. obj. of a verb* нам: *tell us a story,* расскажи́ нам истóрию. **3,** *used as obj. of a prep.* нас; нам; нáми.
usable *also,* **useable** *adj.* гóдный к употреблéнию.
usage *n.* употреблéние. *Proper usage,* прáвильное употреблéние слов.
use *v.t.* **1,** (employ; utilize) употребля́ть; пóльзоваться; испóльзовать; применя́ть. *Use an expression,* употребля́ть выражéние. *Use salt in one's food,* употребля́ть соль в пи́щу. *Use a pencil/dictionary,* пóльзоваться карандашóм/словарём. *Use a method,* испóльзовать *or* применя́ть мéтод. *Use force,* применя́ть си́лу. **2,** (consume) испóльзовать; потребля́ть; расхóдовать. *Use raw materials,* испóльзовать сырьё. **3,** *fol. by* **up** (consume completely; exhaust) расхóдовать; трáтить. —*v.i., fol. by* **to 1,** (do customarily) *rendered by the imperfective aspect in Russian: we used to visit them every week,* мы их посещáли кáждую недéлю. **2,** (formerly) рáньше: *they used to live in Kiev,* рáньше они́ жи́ли в Ки́еве. —*n.* **1,** (employment; utilization) употреблéние; испóльзование; применéние. *Be in use,* быть в употреблéнии; употребля́ться. *Go out of use,* вы́йти из употреблéния. *Have many uses,* применя́ться для разли́чных цéлей. **2,** (control, as of one's limbs): *have the use of one's legs,* владéть ногáми. *He has lost the use of his right arm,* у негó не дéйствует прáвая рукá. **3,** (benefit; advantage) пóльза: *be of use,* приноси́ть пóльзу. *Be of no use,* быть бесполéзным. *There is no use asking him,* нет смы́сла (*or* не стóит) егó спрáшивать. *What's the use of arguing?,* какóй смысл (*or* к чемý) спóрить? —**have no use for, 1,** (have no need for) не нуждáться в. *I have no use for it,* э́то мне совершéнно не нýжно. **2,** (dislike strongly) не выноси́ть: *I have no use for him,* я не выношý егó. —**make use of,** пóльзоваться; испóльзовать. —**put to use,** применя́ть.
useable *adj.* = **usable.**
used *adj.* **1,** (having been used) испóльзованный. **2,** (secondhand) подéржанный. **3,** (cancelled, as of a stamp) гашёный. **4,** *fol. by* **to** (accustomed) привы́кший (к). *Get used to,* привыкáть к.
useful *adj.* полéзный. *Be useful to,* пригоди́ться (+ *dat.*). —**usefulness,** *n.* полéзность.
useless *adj.* бесполéзный. —**uselessly,** *adv.* бесполéзно; дáром. —**uselessness,** *n.* бесполéзность.
user *n.* потреби́тель.
usher *n.* билетёр. —*v.t.* **1,** (escort) провожáть. *Usher someone into a room,* вводи́ть когó-нибудь в кóмнату. **2,** *fol. by* **in** (herald) возвещáть: *usher in a new era,* возвещáть нóвую э́ру.
usherette *n.* билетёрша.
usual *adj.* обыкновéнный; обы́чный. —**as usual,** как обы́чно. —**than usual,** чем обы́чно; обы́чного.
usually *adv.* обы́чно; обыкновéнно.
usurer *n.* ростовщи́к. —**usurious,** *adj.* ростовщи́ческий.
usurp *v.t.* узурпи́ровать. —**usurpation,** *n.* узурпáция. —**usurper,** *n.* узурпáтор.
usury *n.* ростовщи́чество.
utensil *n.* посýда; *pl.* ýтварь; посýда. *Kitchen utensils,* кýхонная посýда/ýтварь.
uterus *n.* мáтка. —**uterine,** *adj.* мáточный; утрóбный.
utilitarian *adj.* утилитáрный. —**utilitarianism,** *n.* утилитари́зм.
utility *n.* **1,** (usefulness) полéзность. **2,** (public service company) предприя́тие обществéнного пóльзования. **3,** *pl.* (gas, electricity, etc.) (домáшние) удóбства.
utilize *v.t.* испóльзовать; утилизи́ровать. —**utilization,** *n.* испóльзование; утилизáция.
utmost *adj.* крáйний; предéльный; максимáльный; величáйший. *Of the utmost importance,* величáйшей вáжности. —*n.* **1,** (greatest possible degree) вы́сшая стéпень. *To the utmost,* до послéднего. **2,** (best of one's abilities) всё возмóжное: *do one's utmost,* дéлать всё возмóжное.
utopia *n.* утóпия. —**utopian,** *adj.* утопи́ческий. —**utopianism,** *n.* утопи́зм.
utter *v.t.* **1,** (make, as a sound) издавáть (звук). **2,** (say, as a word) произноси́ть. *Not utter a word,* не пророни́ть ни слóва. —*adj.* пóлный; чи́стый; сплошнóй. *Utter nonsense,* сплошнáя ерундá; чи́стый вздор.
utterance *n.* выскáзывание. *Give utterance to,* выскáзывать; дать вы́ход (+ *dat.*).
utterly *adv.* совершéнно.
uttermost *adj.* **1,** (outermost) сáмый отдалённый. **2,** (extreme; utmost) крáйний; предéльный.
U-turn *n.* разворóт.
uvula *n.* язычóк; нёбная занавéска. —**uvular,** *adj.* язычкóвый.
Uzbek *n.* **1,** (person) узбéк. **2,** (language) узбéкский язы́к. —*adj.* узбéкский.

V

V, v двáдцать вторáя бýква англи́йского алфави́та.
vacancy *n.* **1,** (emptiness) пустотá. **2,** (unfilled position) вакáнсия. **3,** (untenanted quarters) свобóдная кóмната *or* кварти́ра; (in a hotel) свобóдный нóмер.
vacant *adj.* **1,** (empty) пустóй. **2,** (unoccupied) свобóдный. **3,** (not filled, as of a position) вакáнтный. **4,** (blank, as of a stare) отсýтствующий.
vacate *v.t.* освобождáть.
vacation *n.* óтпуск; *(from school)* канúкулы. *Be on vacation,* быть в óтпуске. *—adj.* отпускнóй: *vacation time,* отпускнóе врéмя. *—v.i.* отдыхáть.
vaccinate *v.t.* прививáть óспу (+ *dat.*); вакцини́ровать. **—vaccination,** *n.* приви́вка óспы; оспопрививáние; вакцинáция.
vaccine *n.* вакци́на.
vacillate *v.i.* колебáться. **—vacillation,** *n.* колебáние.
vacuity *n.* пустотá.
vacuole *n.* вакýоля.
vacuous *adj.* пустóй.
vacuum *n.* безвоздýшное прострáнство; вáкуум; пустотá. *—v.t.* чи́стить пылесóсом. **—vacuum cleaner,** пылесóс. **—vacuum pump,** вáкуум-насóс. **—vacuum tube,** электрóнная лáмпа.
vagabond *n.* бродя́га; бося́к.
vagary *n.* капри́з; причýда.
vagina *n.* влагáлище. **—vaginal,** *adj.* влагáлищный.
vagrant *n.* бродя́га. *—adj.* бродя́чий. **—vagrancy,** *n.* бродя́жничество.
vague *adj.* смýтный; нея́сный; тумáнный; неопределённый. *Vague resemblance,* отдалённое схóдство. *I haven't the vaguest notion,* не имéю ни малéйшего поня́титя. **—vaguely,** *adv.* смýтно: *I vaguely remember,* я смýтно пóмню. **—vagueness,** *n.* нея́сность; неопределённость.
vain *adj.* **1,** (futile) тщéтный; напрáсный. **2,** (conceited) тщеслáвный. **—in vain,** напрáсно; тщéтно; дáром. *It was all in vain,* всё бы́ло напрáсно.
vainglorious *adj.* тщеслáвный; хвастли́вый. —**vainglory,** *n.* тщеслáвие; хвастли́вость.
vainly *adv.* напрáсно; тщéтно.
valance *n.* **1,** (for a bed) пóлог. **2,** (across the top of a window) карни́з.
vale *n.* доли́на; дол.
valedictory *adj.* прощáльный. *—n.* прощáльная речь.
valence *n.* валéнтность.
valerian *n.* валерья́на.
valet *n.* камерди́нер.
valiant *adj.* хрáбрый; дóблестный.
valid *adj.* **1,** (having legal force) действи́тельный. **2,** (sound; well-founded) обоснóванный. **3,** (legitimate, as of a reason or excuse) уважи́тельный.
validate *v.t.* оформля́ть: *validate a passport,* офóрмить пáспорт.
validity *n.* **1,** (legal force) действи́тельность; закóнная си́ла. **2,** (sound basis) обоснóванность. *Have no validity,* не имéть под собóй пóчвы.
valise *n.* чемодáн.
valley *n.* доли́на.
valor *also,* **valour** *n.* дóблесть. **—valorous,** *adj.* дóблестный.
valuable *adj.* цéнный. **—valuables,** *n.pl.* цéнные вéщи; цéнности; драгоцéнности.
valuation *n.* оцéнка.
value *n.* **1,** (worth) цéнность. *Be of great value,* представля́ть большýю цéнность. **2,** *econ.* стóимость: *surplus value,* прибáвочная стóимость. **3,** (numerical quantity) величинá; значéние. **4,** *pl.* (principles; standards) цéнности. *—v.t.* **1,** (estimate the value of) оцéнивать. **2,** (prize; treasure) цени́ть; дорожи́ть.
valued *adj.* цéнный.
valve *n.* **1,** *mech.; anat.* клáпан. **2,** (of a mollusk) ствóрка.
vamoose *v.i., slang* убирáться; удирáть.
vamp *n.* передóк (боти́нка).
vampire *n.* **1,** *folklore* вампи́р; упы́рь; вурдалáк. **2,** = **vampire bat.**
vampire bat (true bloodsucker) кровосóс; (non-bloodsucker) вампи́р.
van *n.* фургóн: *moving van,* мéбельный фургóн.
vanadium *n.* ванáдий.
vandal *n.* хулигáн. **—vandalism,** *n.* хулигáнство. **—vandalize,** *v.t.* наноси́ть ущéрб (+ *dat.*).
vane *n.* **1,** (weathercock) флю́гер. **2,** (revolving blade of a windmill) крылó.
vanguard *n.* авангáрд; передовóй отря́д.
vanilla *n.* вани́ль. *—adj.* вани́льный.
vanish *v.i.* исчезáть. *All hope vanished,* все надéжды разлетéлись. *Vanish into thin air,* как в вóду кáнуть.
vanity *n.* **1,** (pride; conceit) тщеслáвие. **2,** (triviality) суетá: *vanity of vanities,* суетá сyéт. **3,** (dressing table) туалéтный стóлик; туалéт. **—vanity case,** несессéр.
vanquish *v.t.* побеждáть.
vantage point 1, (position with a commanding view) комáндная пози́ция; комáндная высотá. **2,** *fig.* (perspective; viewpoint) тóчка зрéния.
vapid *adj.* пустóй; прéсный; бессодержáтельный; бесцвéтный.

vapor *also,* **vapour** *n.* пар. —**vapor trail,** конденсационный след.
vaporize *v.t.* испаря́ть. —*v.i.* испаря́ться. —**vaporization,** *n.* парообразова́ние. —**vaporizer,** *n.* испари́тель.
vaporous *adj.* парообра́зный.
vapour *n.* = **vapor.**
variable *adj.* переме́нный. —*n.* переме́нная величина́.
variance *n.* **1,** (difference) расхожде́ние. *Be at variance with,* противоре́чить. **2,** (variation; fluctuation) измене́ние.
variant *n.* вариа́нт. —*adj.* ра́зный; разли́чный.
variation *n.* **1,** (change; fluctuation) измене́ние; колеба́ние. **2,** (anything somewhat different) вариа́нт; вариа́ция. **3,** *music* вариа́ция.
varicolored *also,* **varicoloured** *adj.* разноцве́тный.
varicose *adj.* варико́зный. —**varicose veins,** расшире́ние вен.
varied *adj.* **1,** (assorted) разли́чный. **2,** (diverse) разнообра́зный.
variegate *v.t.* **1,** (mark with different colors) испестря́ть. **2,** (diversify) разнообра́зить.
variegated *adj.* **1,** (having diverse colors) пёстрый. **2,** (having different forms) разнообра́зный.
variety *n.* **1,** (diversity) разнообра́зие. **2,** (number) ряд: *for a variety of reasons,* по (це́лому) ря́ду причи́н. **3,** (type) род; сорт: *items of every variety,* вся́кого ро́да това́ры. **4,** (subspecies) разнови́дность: *varieties of wheat,* разнови́дности пшени́цы. —**variety show,** варьете́. —**variety store,** галантере́йный магази́н.
various *adj.* ра́зный; разли́чный: *various kinds of,* ра́зного/разли́чного ро́да (+ *nom.*). *For various reasons,* по ра́зным причи́нам.
varnish *n.* лак. —*v.t.* лакирова́ть.
vary *v.t.* **1,** (modify) изменя́ть. **2,** (make diverse) разнообра́зить. —*v.i.* **1,** (change) меня́ться; изменя́ться. **2,** (fluctuate) колеба́ться. *With varying (degrees of) success,* с переме́нным успе́хом. **3,** (differ) расходи́ться: *opinions vary,* мне́ния расхо́дятся.
vascular *adj.* сосу́дистый.
vase *n.* ва́за.
vaseline *n.* вазели́н.
vassal *n.* васса́л. —*adj.* васса́льный.
vast *adj.* **1,** (of great extent or size) обши́рный; грома́дный; необозри́мый. **2,** (great in number or degree) огро́мный. —**vastly,** *adv.* значи́тельно; в огро́мной сте́пени. —**vastness,** *n.* необозри́мость.
vat *n.* чан.
Vatican *n.* Ватика́н.
vaudeville *n.* эстра́да; варьете́; водеви́ль. —*adj.* эстра́дный.
vault *n.* **1,** (arched roof or chamber) свод. **2,** (safe storage place) храни́лище; сейф. **3,** (burial vault) склеп. **4,** (leap) прыжо́к. *Pole vault,* прыжо́к с шесто́м. —*v.i.* пры́гать. *Vault over a fence,* перепры́гнуть (че́рез) забо́р. —**vaulted,** *adj.* сво́дчатый.
vaunted *adj.* хвалёный.
veal *n.* теля́тина. —*adj.* теля́чий: *veal cutlet,* теля́чья отбивна́я.
vector *n.* ве́ктор. —*adj.* ве́кторный: *vector analysis,* ве́кторный ана́лиз.
veer *v.t. & i.* свора́чивать (в сто́рону). *Veer around,* ре́зко повора́чиваться круго́м.
vegetable *n.* о́вощ. —*adj.* овощно́й; расти́тельный. *Vegetable garden,* огоро́д. —**vegetable kingdom,** расти́тельный мир. —**vegetable oil,** расти́тельное ма́сло.
vegetarian *n.* вегетариа́нец. —*adj.* вегетариа́нский.
vegetate *v.i.* **1,** (grow) расти́. **2,** (live an inactive life) прозяба́ть.
vegetation *n.* **1,** (plant life) расти́тельность. **2,** (process of vegetating) вегета́ция.
vehement *adj.* бу́рный; горя́чий: *vehement argument/protest,* бу́рный/горя́чий спор/проте́ст. —**vehemence,** *n.* горя́чность.
vehicle *n.* **1,** (conveyance) маши́на. *Motor vehicle,* автомаши́на. *Space vehicle,* косми́ческий кора́бль. **2,** *fig.* (means) сре́дство: *vehicle to success,* сре́дство (для) достиже́ния успе́ха.
veil *n.* **1,** (light fabric worn over the face) вуаль. **2,** (bridal veil) фата́. **3,** (face-covering worn by Moslem women) чадра́. **4,** (anything that covers or conceals) заве́са. —*v.t.* **1,** (cover with a veil) закрыва́ть вуа́лью *or* чадро́й. **2,** *fig.* (conceal; hold back) скрыва́ть; завуали́ровать: *veiled threat,* скры́тая/завуали́рованная угро́за. —**take the veil,** постри́чься в мона́хини.
vein *n.* **1,** (blood vessel) ве́на; жи́ла; жи́лка. **2,** (when showing through the skin) прожи́лка. **3,** (of a leaf) жи́лка. **4,** (in marble) жи́лка; прожи́лка. **5,** (lode) жи́ла. **6,** *fig.* (mood; tone; style) дух, тон, стиль. *In the same vein,* в том же ду́хе. **7,** *fig.* (streak; tendency) жи́лка.
velar *adj.* веля́рный, задненёбный.
vellum *n.* **1,** (parchment) (то́нкий) перга́мент. **2,** (paper) веле́невая бума́га.
velocity *n.* ско́рость.
velodrome *n.* велодро́м.
velour *also,* **velours** *n.* велю́р. —*adj.* велю́ровый.
velvet *n.* ба́рхат. —*adj.* ба́рхатный.
velveteen *n.* вельве́т. —*adj.* вельве́товый.
velvety *adj.* бархати́стый.
venal *adj.* прода́жный. —**venality,** *n.* прода́жность.
vend *v.t. & i.* продава́ть.
vender *n.* = **vendor.**
vendetta *n.* кро́вная месть.
vending machine автома́т.
vendor *also,* **vender** *n.* продаве́ц; торго́вец. *Street vendor,* у́личный торго́вец.
veneer *n.* **1,** (thin layer of wood) фане́ра. **2,** *fig.* (superficial display) (вне́шний) лоск.
venerable *adj.* почте́нный.
venerate *v.t.* благогове́ть. —**veneration,** *n.* благогове́ние.
venereal *adj.* венери́ческий: *venereal disease,* венери́ческая боле́знь.
Venetian *adj.* венециа́нский. —**Venetian blind,** подъёмные жалюзи́.
Venezuelan *adj.* венесуэ́льский.
vengeance *n.* месть; мще́ние. *Take vengeance,* мстить. —**with a vengeance,** с лихво́й.
vengeful *adj.* мсти́тельный.
venial *adj.* прости́тельный.
venison *n.* оле́нина.
venom *n.* яд. —**venomous,** *adj.* ядови́тый.
venous *adj.* вено́зный.
vent *n.* отду́шина. —*v.t.* [*also,* **give vent to**] изли-

ва́ть; срыва́ть; вымеща́ть; дать вы́ход (+ *dat.*).
ventilate *v.t.* прове́тривать; вентили́ровать. —**ventilation**, *n.* прове́тривание; вентиля́ция. —**ventilator**, *n.* вентиля́тор.
ventral *adj.* брюшно́й.
ventricle *n.* желу́дочек.
ventriloquism *n.* чревовеща́ние. —**ventriloquist**, *n.* чревовеща́тель.
venture *n.* затея́; предприя́тие. —*v.t.* **1**, (risk) рискова́ть. **2**, (bet; stake) ста́вить. **3**, (express at the risk of criticism) выска́зывать (мне́ние). **4**, *fol. by inf.* (dare) сметь; осме́ливаться; отва́живаться; позво́лить себе́. —*v.i.* осме́ливаться: *venture out on the street at night*, осме́ливаться выходи́ть на у́лицу но́чью.
venturesome *adj.* сме́лый; отва́жный.
Venus *n.* Вене́ра.
veracious *adj.* правди́вый. —**veracity**, *n.* правди́вость.
veranda *n.* вера́нда.
verb *n.* глаго́л. —*adj.* глаго́льный: *verb endings*, глаго́льные оконча́ния.
verbal *adj.* **1**, (oral) у́стный: *verbal agreement*, у́стное соглаше́ние. **2**, (pert. to words) слове́сный: *verbal battle*, слове́сная война́. **3**, *gram.* глаго́льный; отглаго́льный. —**verbal adverb**, дееприча́стие. —**verbal noun**, отглаго́льное существи́тельное.
verbalize *v.t.* выража́ть слова́ми.
verbally *adv.* у́стно.
verbatim *adj.* досло́вный. —*adv.* досло́вно; сло́во в сло́во.
verbena *n.* вербе́на.
verbiage *n.* пусты́е слова́; пустосло́вие.
verbose *adj.* многосло́вный. —**verbosity**, *n.* многосло́вие.
verdant *adj.* зелёный.
verdict *n.* пригово́р; верди́кт. *Verdict of "guilty"*, обвини́тельный пригово́р. *Verdict of "not guilty"*, оправда́тельный пригово́р. *The verdict of history*, суд исто́рии.
verdigris *n.* медя́нка; ярь-медя́нка.
verdure *n.* зе́лень.
verge *n.* грань: *on the verge of*, на гра́ни (+ *gen.*). —*v.i.* [*usu.* **verge on**] грани́чить с.
verify *v.t.* проверя́ть. —**verification**, *n.* прове́рка; контро́ль.
verily *adv., archaic* пои́стине; вои́стину.
verisimilitude *n.* правдоподо́бие.
veritable *adj.* настоя́щий; и́стинный.
vermicelli *n.* вермише́ль.
vermiform *adj.* червеобра́зный. —**vermiform appendix**, червеобра́зный отро́сток.
vermilion *n.* **1**, (pigment) ки́новарь. **2**, (color) ярко-кра́сный цвет. —*adj.* ярко-кра́сный.
vermin *n.* вреди́тели; парази́ты.
vermouth *n.* ве́рмут.
vernacular *n.* просторе́чие. —*adj.* просторе́чный.
vernal *adj.* весе́нний. —**vernal equinox**, весе́ннее равноде́нствие.
vernalize *v.t.* яровизи́ровать. —**vernalization**, *n.* яровиза́ция.
versatile *adj.* многосторо́нний; разносторо́нний. —**versatility**, *n.* многосторо́нность; разносторо́нность.
verse *n.* **1**, (line of poetry) стих. **2**, (stanza) строфа́. **3**, (poetry) стихи́: *in verse*, в стиха́х.
versed *adj.* [*usu.* **versed in**] све́дущий (в).
versification *n.* стихосложе́ние.
version *n.* ве́рсия; вариа́нт.
versus *prep.* про́тив.
vertebra *n.* позвоно́к. —**vertebral**, *adj.* позвоно́чный.
vertebrate *adj.* позвоно́чный. —*n.* позвоно́чное живо́тное.
vertex *n.* верши́на.
vertical *adj.* вертика́льный. —*n.* вертика́ль. —**vertically**, *adv.* вертика́льно.
vertigo *n.* головокруже́ние. —**vertiginous**, *adj.* головокружи́тельный.
verve *n.* жи́вость; подъём; огонёк.
very *adv.* **1**, (to a high degree) о́чень: *very glad*, о́чень рад. **2**, (precisely) же: *the very same day*, на сле́дующий же день; *the very same place*, то же са́мое ме́сто. **3**, *before superlatives* са́мый: *the very best*, са́мый лу́чший. —*adj.* **1**, (absolute) са́мый: *from the very beginning*, с са́мого нача́ла; *in the very center of town*, в са́мом це́нтре го́рода. **2**, (precise) тот са́мый: *at that very moment*, в тот са́мый моме́нт. *This very minute*, сию́ же мину́ту. **3**, (identical) тот са́мый: *the very man we read about*, тот са́мый челове́к, о кото́ром мы чита́ли. **4**, (precisely) и́менно тот: *you're the very person I wanted to see*, вы и́менно тот, кого́ я хоте́л ви́деть. **5**, (mere) оди́н: *at the very thought of it*, при одно́й мы́сли об э́том. —**very much**, о́чень: *want very much to go*, о́чень хоте́ть идти́. *Thank you very much!*, большо́е (вам) спаси́бо! —**very well!**, хорошо́!; ла́дно!
vespers *n.pl.* вече́рня; все́нощная.
vessel *n.* **1**, (container) сосу́д. **2**, *anat.* сосу́д: *blood vessel*, кровено́сный сосу́д. **3**, (ship) су́дно; кора́бль. *Fishing vessel*, рыболо́вное су́дно.
vest *n.* жиле́т; жиле́тка. —*adj.* жиле́тный: *vest pocket*, жиле́тный карма́н. —*v.t.* **1**, (clothe) облача́ть. **2**, (endow, as with power) облека́ть.
vestibule *n.* пере́дняя; прихо́жая.
vestige *n.* оста́ток; пережи́ток. —**vestigial**, *adj.* оста́точный; рудимента́рный.
vestment *n.* облаче́ние.
vestry *n.* ри́зница.
vetch *n.* ви́ка.
veteran *n.* ветера́н. —*adj.* ста́рый; быва́лый; матёрый.
veterinarian *n.* ветерина́р.
veterinary *adj.* ветерина́рный. —**veterinary medicine**, ветерина́рия.
veto *n.* ве́то. *Veto power*, пра́во ве́то. —*v.t.* наложи́ть ве́то на.
vex *v.t.* досажда́ть; раздража́ть. —**vexation**, *n.* доса́да; раздраже́ние. —**vexatious**, *adj.* доса́дный.
via *prep.* че́рез.
viable *adj.* жизнеспосо́бный. —**viability**, *n.* жизнеспосо́бность.
viaduct *n.* виаду́к.
vial *n.* пузырёк; флако́н; скля́нка.
vibrant *adj.* **1**, (vibrating) вибри́рующий. **2**, (lively; pulsating) живо́й; оживлённый.
vibrate *v.i.* вибри́ровать. —**vibration**, *n.* вибра́ция. —**vibrator**, *n.* вибра́тор.
viburnum *n.* кали́на.
vicar *n.* вика́рий.
vicarious *adj.* чужо́й.

vice *n.* **1,** (immoral behavior; personal failing) поро́к. **2,** (vise) тиски́.
vice-admiral *n.* ви́це-адмира́л.
vice-consul *n.* ви́це-ко́нсул.
vice-president *n.* ви́це-президе́нт.
viceroy *n.* ви́це-коро́ль.
vice versa наоборо́т; обра́тно.
vicinity *n.* **1,** (proximity) сосе́дство; бли́зость. *In the vicinity of,* по сосе́дству с. **2,** (neighborhood) окру́га; райо́н.
vicious *adj.* **1,** (malicious) зло́стный: *vicious remark,* зло́стное замеча́ние. **2,** (heinous; depraved) гну́сный: *vicious act/criminal,* гну́сный посту́пок/престу́пник. **3,** (savage; fierce) злой; свире́пый: *vicious dog,* зла́я соба́ка; *vicious shark,* свире́пая аку́ла.
vicissitude *n.* превра́тность; перипети́я.
victim *n.* же́ртва; пострада́вший. *Flood victims,* пострада́вшие от наводне́ния. *Fall victim to,* пасть *or* стать же́ртвой (+ *gen.*).
victimize *v.t.* надува́ть; обдира́ть.
victor *n.* победи́тель. —**victorious,** *adj.* победоно́сный.
victory *n.* побе́да.
victuals *n. pl.* пи́ща; я́ства; съестны́е припа́сы.
vicuna *n.* виго́нь. —*adj.* виго́невый.
video *n.* телеви́дение. —*adj.* телевизио́нный. —**video tape,** видеоза́пись.
vie *v.i.* сопе́рничать; тяга́ться. *Vie with one another,* сопе́рничать друг с дру́гом. *Vie for the championship,* соревнова́ться за (*or* оспа́ривать) зва́ние чемпио́на. *Vie for the honor of...,* добива́ться че́сти (+ *inf.*).
Viennese *adj.* ве́нский.
Vietnamese *adj.* вьетна́мский.
view *n.* **1,** (sight) вид: *disappear from view,* скры́ться из виду. *Come into view,* показа́ться. **2,** (scene; vista) вид: *room with a view of the mountains,* ко́мната с ви́дом на го́ры. **3,** (opinion) взгляд; мне́ние: *exchange of views,* обме́н взгля́дами/мне́ниями. —*v.t.* **1,** (look at; examine) осма́тривать. **2,** (regard) смотре́ть на: *how do you view the situation?,* как вы смо́трите на положе́ние дел? —**in view,** ви́дно. —**in view of,** ввиду́ (+ *gen.*). —**on view,** у всех на виду́. —**with a view to,** с це́лью (+ *inf. or gen.*); в це́лях (+ *gen.*).
viewer *n.* телезри́тель.
view finder видоиска́тель; визи́р.
viewpoint *n.* то́чка зре́ния.
vigil *n.* бде́ние. *Keep vigil,* дежу́рить; бо́дрствовать.
vigilant *adj.* бди́тельный. —**vigilance,** *n.* бди́тельность.
vignette *n.* **1,** (ornamental design) виньe̋тка. **2,** (literary piece) о́черк.
vigor *also,* **vigour** *n.* си́ла; бо́дрость. —**vigorous,** *adj.* бо́дрый; энерги́чный. —**vigorously,** *adv.* энерги́чно.
Viking *n.* ви́кинг.
vile *adj.* га́дкий; ме́рзкий; проти́вный; гну́сный.
vilify *v.t.* поноси́ть; поро́чить; черни́ть. —**vilification,** *n.* поноше́ние.
villa *n.* ви́лла.
village *n.* дере́вня; село́. —*adj.* дереве́нский; се́льский. —**villager,** *n.* се́льский жи́тель.
villain *n.* злоде́й. —**villainous,** *adj.* злоде́йский. —**villainy,** *n.* злоде́йство.
vim *n.* прыть.
vindicate *v.t.* опра́вдывать. —**vindication,** *n.* оправда́ние.
vindictive *adj.* мсти́тельный. —**vindictiveness,** *n.* мсти́тельность.
vine *n.* **1,** (climbing or trailing plant) вью́щееся *or* ползу́чее расте́ние. **2,** (grapevine) лоза́.
vinegar *n.* у́ксус. —*adj.* у́ксусный.
vineyard *n.* виногра́дник.
viniculture *n.* виногра́дарство.
vintage *n.* урожа́й: *this wine is vintage 1960,* э́то вино́ урожа́я 1960-го го́да. —*adj.* вы́сшего ка́чества. *Vintage wine,* ма́рочное вино́.
vinyl *n.* вини́л.
viol *n.* вио́ла. —**bass viol,** контраба́с.
viola *n.* альт; вио́ла.
violate *v.t.* **1,** (break) наруша́ть: *violate a law/an oath/,* наруша́ть зако́н/кля́тву. **2,** (rape) наси́ловать.
violation *n.* **1,** (breaking) наруше́ние. **2,** (rape) изнаси́лование. —**violator,** *n.* наруши́тель.
violence *n.* **1,** (physical force intended to harm) наси́лие: *resort to violence,* прибега́ть к наси́лию. **2,** (great force; intensity) си́ла. —**do violence to,** искажа́ть; кове́ркать.
violent *adj.* **1,** (fierce; powerful) неи́стовый; я́ростный; свире́пый, бу́рный. *Violent storm,* неи́стовая/я́ростная/свире́пая бу́ря. *Violent argument,* я́ростный/бу́рный спор. *Violent passions,* неи́стовые/бу́рные стра́сти. **2,** (marked or caused by violence) наси́льственный: *violent death,* наси́льственная смерть.
violet *n.* фиа́лка. —*adj.* фиоле́товый.
violin *n.* скри́пка. —*adj.* скрипи́чный: *violin concerto,* скрипи́чный конце́рт. —**violinist,** *n.* скрипа́ч.
violoncello *n.* виолонче́ль.
VIP *colloq.* ва́жное лицо́; ва́жная персо́на; высокопоста́вленное лицо́.
viper *n.* **1,** (snake) гадю́ка. **2,** (vicious person) гадю́ка; ехи́дна.
virago *n.* меге́ра.
viral *adj.* ви́русный.
virgin *n.* де́вственница. *The Virgin Mary,* богоро́дица. —*adj.* **1,** (chaste) де́вственный. **2,** *fig.* (unexploited) де́вственный; цели́нный. *Virgin forest,* де́вственный лес. *Virgin lands,* цели́нные зе́мли. *Virgin soil,* целина́.
virginal *adj.* де́вственный; непоро́чный.
virginity *n.* де́вственность.
Virgo *n.* Де́ва.
virile *adj.* возмужа́лый. —**virility,** *n.* возмужа́лость.
virtual *adj.* факти́ческий. —**virtually,** *adv.* практи́чески; почти́.
virtue *n.* **1,** (moral excellence; admirable quality) доброде́тель. **2,** (merit; advantage) досто́инство. —**by virtue of,** в си́лу (+ *gen.*).
virtuoso *n.* виртуо́з. —**virtuosity,** *n.* виртуо́зность.
virtuous *adj.* доброде́тельный.
virulence *n.* **1,** *med.* вируле́нтность. **2,** (bitterness) я́рость.
virulent *adj.* **1,** (noxious; deadly) вируле́нтный. **2,** (bitterly hostile) я́ростный; зло́стный: *virulent attacks,* я́ростные/зло́стные напа́дки.
virus *n.* ви́рус.
visa *n.* ви́за.

visage *n.* **1,** (face) лицо́. **2,** (countenance) вид; выраже́ние лица́.
vis-à-vis *prep.* по отноше́нию к; в отноше́нии (+ *gen.*).
viscera *n.pl.* вну́тренности.
viscose *n.* виско́за.
viscosity *n.* вя́зкость; тягу́честь.
viscount *n.* вико́нт.
viscous *adj.* вя́зкий; тягу́чий.
vise *n.* тиски́: *grip in a vise,* зажима́ть в тиски́.
visibility *n.* ви́димость.
visible *adj.* **1,** (in sight) ви́димый; ви́дный. *The lake is not visible from here,* отсю́да о́зера не ви́дно. *The moon is hardly visible behind the clouds,* луна́ чуть видна́ из-за туч. **2,** (noticeable; marked) ви́димый; заме́тный: *visible improvement,* ви́димое/заме́тное улучше́ние. *With no visible means of support,* без определённых средств к существова́нию.
visibly *adv.* заме́тно; я́вно: *he was visibly shaken,* он был заме́тно/я́вно потрясён.
vision *n.* **1,** (sense of sight) зре́ние. *Field of vision,* по́ле зре́ния. **2,** (foresight) проница́тельность. *A man of vision,* дальнови́дный челове́к. **3,** (mental image) мечта́: *visions of glory,* мечты́ о сла́ве. **4,** (revelation) виде́ние.
visionary *adj.* несбы́точный; непракти́чный. —*n.* мечта́тель; фантазёр.
visit *v.t.* **1,** (call on) навеща́ть; посеща́ть. **2,** (go to) посеща́ть: *visit a museum,* посеща́ть музе́й. —*n.* посеще́ние; визи́т. *Pay a visit on,* наноси́ть визи́т (+ *dat.*).
visitation *n.* посеще́ние.
visiting *adj.* прие́зжий. —**visiting hours,** часы́ посеще́ния. —**visiting professor,** приглашённый профе́ссор.
visitor *n.* посети́тель.
visor *also,* **vizor** *n.* **1,** (of a cap) козырёк. **2,** (of a helmet) забра́ло.
vista *n.* вид; перспекти́ва.
visual *adj.* **1,** (produced by sight) зри́тельный: *visual impressions,* зри́тельные впечатле́ния. **2,** (serving to instruct) нагля́дный: *visual aids,* нагля́дные посо́бия.
visualize *v.t.* представля́ть себе́.
vital *adj.* **1,** (basic to survival) жи́зненный; насу́щный: *vital interests,* жи́зненные/насу́щные интере́сы. *Vital necessity,* жи́зненная необходи́мость. *Vital organs,* жи́зненно ва́жные о́рганы. **2,** *fol. by* **to** (essential) необходи́мый (для): *vital to the success of,* абсолю́тно необходи́м для успе́ха (+ *gen.*). **3,** (utmost) первостепе́нный: *of vital importance,* первостепе́нной ва́жности.
vitality *n.* **1,** (ability to sustain life) жи́зненность. **2,** (vigor; energy) эне́ргия; энерги́чность.
vitally *adv.* жи́зненно: *vitally important,* жи́зненно ва́жный. *Vitally interested,* кро́вно заинтересо́ванный.
vitamin *n.* витами́н. —**vitamin B**¹, витами́н В¹ (*pronouced* бэ оди́н). —**vitamin C,** витами́н С (*pronounced* цэ).
vitiate *v.t.* **1,** (spoil) по́ртить. **2,** (invalidate) де́лать недействи́тельным.
viticulture *n.* виногра́дарство.
vitreous *adj.* стекля́нный; стекo´льный.
vitriol *n.* купоро́с. *Blue/green/white vitriol,* ме́дный/желе́зный/ци́нковый купоро́с. —**oil of vitriol,** се́рная кислота́.
vitriolic *adj.* е́дкий; exи́дный.
vituperation *n.* брань; ру́гань. —**vituperative,** *adj.* бра́нный; руга́тельный.
vivacious *adj.* живо́й; оживлённый. —**vivaciousness; vivacity,** *n.* жи́вость; оживлённость.
vivid *adj.* **1,** (intense, as of a color) я́ркий. **2,** (lively; striking) живо́й; я́ркий. *Vivid description,* я́ркое описа́ние. *Vivid memories,* живы́е/я́ркие воспомина́ния. *Vivid imagination,* живо́е *or* пы́лкое воображе́ние.
vividly *adv.* я́рко; жи́во. *Vividly remember,* жи́во по́мнить.
vividness *n.* я́ркость; жи́вость.
viviparous *adj.* живородя́щий.
vivisection *n.* вивисе́кция.
vixen *n.* **1,** (female fox) са́мка лиси́цы. **2,** (ill-tempered woman) мегера.
vizier *n.* визи́рь.
vizor *n.* = **visor.**
V-neck *n.* треуго́льный вы́рез.
vocabulary *n.* слова́рь; запа́с слов. *Vocabulary building,* накопле́ние словаря́.
vocal *adj.* **1,** (pert. to the voice) голосово́й. **2,** (meant to be sung) вока́льный. **3,** (vociferous) гро́мкий; шу́мный. —**vocal cords,** голосовы́е свя́зки.
vocalist *n.* певе́ц; певи́ца.
vocation *n.* призва́ние.
vocational *adj.* профессиона́льный: *vocational training,* профессиона́льное образова́ние. *Vocational school,* реме́сленное учи́лище.
vocative *adj.* зва́тельный: *vocative case,* зва́тельный паде́ж.
vociferous *adj.* гро́мкий; шу́мный.
vodka *n.* во́дка.
vogue *n.* мо́да. *Be in vogue,* быть в мо́де.
voice *n.* **1,** (sound made when speaking) го́лос: *in a loud voice,* гро́мким го́лосом. *Be in good voice,* быть в го́лосе. **2,** *gram.* зало́г: *passive voice,* страда́тельный зало́г. —*v.t.* выска́зывать: *voice one's opinion,* вы́сказать своё мне́ние. —**give voice to,** выража́ть. —**with one voice,** в оди́н го́лос.
voice box горта́нь.
voiced *adj., phonet.* зво́нкий.
voiceless *adj.* **1,** (having no voice) безголо́сый. **2,** *phonet.* глухо́й.
void *adj.* **1,** (invalid) недействи́тельный: *declare null and void,* объяви́ть недействи́тельным. **2,** *fol. by* **of** (utterly lacking) лишённый (+ *gen.*): *void of sense,* лишён смы́сла. **3,** (empty) пусто́й. —*n.* пустота́: *a void in one's life,* пустота́ в жи́зни. *Fill a void,* запо́лнить пустоту́. —*v.t.* (nullify) де́лать недействи́тельным; аннули́ровать. —*v.i., physiol.* опорожня́ть мочево́й пузы́рь; мочи́ться.
voile *n.* газ.
volatile *adj.* **1,** (evaporating rapidly) летý́чий. **2,** (changeable; fickle) изме́нчивый. **3,** (unstable; explosive) неусто́йчивый.
volatility *n.* **1,** *chem.* лету́честь. **2,** (changeability) изме́нчивость.
volcanic *adj.* вулкани́ческий.
volcano *n.* вулка́н.
vole *n.* полёвка.
volition *n.* во́ля. *Of one own's volition,* по со́бственному жела́нию; по до́брой во́ле. —**volitional,** *adj.* волево́й.

volley *n.* **1,** (salvo) залп. **2,** *fig.* (torrent) град.
volleyball *n.* волейбо́л.
volt *n.* вольт. —**voltage,** *n.* напряже́ние; вольта́ж. —**voltmeter,** *n.* вольтме́тр.
voluble *adj.* говорли́вый; разгово́рчивый. —**volubility,** *n.* говорли́вость; разгово́рчивость.
volume *n.* **1,** (size; amount) объём: *the volume of a sphere,* объём ша́ра; *volume of trade,* объём торго́вли. **2,** (book) том: *in two volumes,* в двух тома́х. **3,** (loudness) си́ла зву́ка; гро́мкость. *Turn down the volume,* уменьши́ть звук. —**speak volumes,** говори́ть о мно́гом.
volumetric *adj.* объёмный.
voluminous *adj.* обши́рный: *voluminous correspondence,* обши́рная перепи́ска.
voluntary *adj.* **1,** (done by free choice) доброво́льный. **2,** *physiol.* произво́льный. —**voluntarily,** *adv.* доброво́льно.
volunteer *n.* доброво́лец. *Are there any volunteers?,* есть жела́ющие?; есть охо́тники? —*adj.* доброво́льческий: *volunteer army,* доброво́льческая а́рмия. —*v.t.* предлага́ть: *volunteer one's services,* предлага́ть свои́ услу́ги. —*v.i.* вызыва́ться: *volunteer to help,* вы́зваться помо́чь.
voluptuous *adj.* чу́вственный.
vomit *v.i.* рвать *(impers.): he is vomiting,* его́ рвёт; *she vomited,* её вы́рвало. —*n.* рво́тная ма́сса. —**vomiting,** *n.* рво́та.
voodoo *n.* колдовство́.
voracious *adj.* прожо́рливый. *Voracious appetite,* во́лчий аппети́т. *He is a voracious reader,* он чита́ет запо́ем.
vortex *n.* вихрь; водоворо́т.
vote *n.* **1,** (choice expressed) го́лос: *win by ten votes,* вы́играть с переве́сом в де́сять голосо́в. **2,** (act of voting) голосова́ние: *put to a vote,* поста́вить на голосова́ние. *Vote of confidence,* во́тум дове́рия. *By a majority vote,* большинство́м голосо́в. *By a 5-4 vote,* пятью́ голоса́ми про́тив четырёх. —*v.i.* голосова́ть: *vote for a candidate,* голосова́ть за кандида́та. *The right to vote,* пра́во го́лоса. —*v.t.* **1,** (authorize by vote) одобря́ть; ассигнова́ть. **2,** *fol. by* **in** (elect) избира́ть. **3,** *fol. by* **down** (defeat; reject) прова́ливать.
voter *n.* избира́тель.
voting *n.* голосова́ние. —**voting booth,** каби́на для голосова́ния. —**voting member,** член с реша́ющим го́лосом.
vouch *v.i.* [*usu.* **vouch for**] руча́ться (за).
voucher *n.* о́рдер: *expense voucher,* расхо́дный о́рдер.
vouchsafe *v.t.* удоста́ивать; соизволя́ть.
vow *n.* обе́т; кля́тва; заро́к. —*v.t. & i.* кля́сться (в). *Vow loyalty,* кля́сться в ве́рности.
vowel *n.* **1,** (sound) гла́сный звук. **2,** (letter) гла́сная бу́ква.
voyage *n.* путеше́ствие; пла́вание. —*v.i.* путеше́ствовать.
vulcanite *n.* эбони́т.
vulcanize *v.t.* вулканизи́ровать. —**vulcanization,** *n.* вулканиза́ция.
vulgar *adj.* гру́бый; по́шлый; вульга́рный. —**vulgarism,** *n.* вульгари́зм. —**vulgarity,** *n.* вульга́рность.
vulgarize *v.t.* опошля́ть; вульгаризи́ровать.
vulnerable *adj.* уязви́мый. —**vulnerability,** *n.* уязви́мость.
vulture *n.* гриф.

W, w два́дцать тре́тья бу́ква англи́йского алфави́та.
wacky *adj., slang* чудакова́тый; эксцентри́чный.
wad *n.* **1,** (small lump or mass) комо́к; кусо́чек. *Wad of cotton,* комо́к ва́ты. **2,** (bunch; roll) па́чка: *wad of money,* па́чка де́нег. **3,** (for a firearm) пыж.
wadding *n.* ва́та; наби́вка.
waddle *v.i.* перева́ливаться (с бо́ку на́ бок); ходи́ть вперева́лку; ходи́ть вразва́лку; ходи́ть у́точкой. —*n.* перева́лка.
wade *v.i.* идти́ вброд. *Wade into the water,* входи́ть в во́ду. *Wade across a river,* переходи́ть ре́ку вброд. —**wade through, 1,** (walk through) пробира́ться сквозь. **2,** *fig.* (plow through; work one's way through) оси́ливать (*e.g.* кни́гу).
wading bird боло́тная пти́ца.
wafer *n.* **1,** (biscuit) сухо́е пече́нье. **2,** (bread used in the Eucharist) обла́тка.
waffle *n.* ва́фля. —**waffle iron,** ва́фельница.
waft *v.t.* навева́ть. —*v.i.* тяну́ть *(impers.): cool air wafted in from the sea,* с мо́ря тяну́ло све́жим во́здухом. —*n.* дунове́ние (во́здуха).
wag *v.t.* виля́ть; маха́ть (хвосто́м). *Wag one's tongue,* болта́ть языко́м; чеса́ть язы́к. —*v.i.* виля́ть. —*n.* шутни́к; остря́к; балагу́р.
wage *n., often pl.* за́работная пла́та; жа́лованье. —*v.t.* вести́ (войну́); проводи́ть (кампа́нию). —**wage earner,** рабо́чий. —**wage scale,** шкала́ за́работной пла́ты.
wager *n.* пари́. —*v.i.* держа́ть пари́; би́ться об закла́д. —*v.t.* ста́вить.
wagon *also,* **waggon** *n.* пово́зка; теле́га; подво́да. *Covered wagon,* фурго́н.
wagtail *n.* трясогу́зка.
waif *n.* у́личный мальчи́шка; беспризо́рник.
wail *v.i.* выть; вопи́ть. —*n.* вой; вопль.

wainscot *n.* панéль.
waist *n.* тáлия. ♦*In idioms* пóяс: *bow from the waist,* клáняться в пóяс. *Strip to the waist,* раздéться до пóяса. *In water up to one's waist,* по пóяс в водé.
waistband *n.* пóяс.
waistcoat *n.* жилéт.
waistline *n.* тáлия.
wait *v.i.* ждать. *Wait for the train,* ждать пóезда. *Wait for the rain to stop,* ждать, когдá (*or* покá) перестáнет дождь. *I can't wait!,* жду не дождýсь!; я не могý дождáться! —*n.* **1,** (time spent waiting) ожидáние: *a long wait,* дóлгое ожидáние. **2,** *in* **lie in wait for,** подстерегáть. —**wait on,** обслýживать. *Wait on a table,* обслýживать стол. —**wait out,** выжидáть; пережидáть.
waiter *n.* официáнт.
waiting *n.* ожидáние. *Waiting period,* срок ожидáния. —*adj.* выжидáтельный: *play a waiting game,* занимáть выжидáтельную позúцию.
waiting list óчередь: *a long waiting list,* большáя óчередь. *Be on the waiting list,* быть *or* стоя́ть на óчереди. *Put someone on the waiting list,* постáвить когó-нибудь на óчередь.
waiting room 1, (in a railroad station) зал ожидáния. **2,** (in a doctor's office) приёмная.
waitress *n.* официáнтка.
waive *v.t.* **1,** (give up; forgo) откáзываться от; поступáться (+ *instr.*). **2,** (set aside; dispense with) воздéрживаться от. *Waive a rule,* не применя́ть прáвила.
waiver *n.* откáз.
wake *v.t.* будúть: *wake me at seven o'clock,* разбудúте меня́ в семь часóв. —*v.i.* [*usu.* **wake up**] просыпáться. —*n.* **1,** (for a dead person) помúнки. **2,** (track of a ship) кильвáтер. **3,** (route passed over): *leave in its wake,* оставля́ть за собóй. *Bring in its wake,* влечь за собóй. —**in the wake of,** по следáм (+ *gen.*); по пятáм (+ *gen.*).
waken *v.t.* будúть. —*v.i.* просыпáться.
walk *v.i.* **1,** (take steps; proceed on foot) ходúть; идтú (пешкóм). *Walk slowly,* ходúть/идтú мéдленно. *Learn to walk,* учúться ходúть. *Don't run, walk!,* не бегúте, идúте шáгом! *It's not far — I'll walk,* э́то недалекó – я пойдý пешкóм. **2,** (stroll) ходúть; гуля́ть; прогýливаться; прохáживаться. *Walk in the park,* ходúть/гуля́ть в пáрке *or* по пáрку. —*v.t.* **1,** (pace) расхáживать по: *walk the floors,* расхáживать по кóмнате. **2,** (take for a walk) прогýливать: *walk the dog,* прогýливать собáку. **3,** (accompany) провожáть: *walk someone home,* провожáть когó-нибудь домóй. —*n.* **1,** (act of walking; distance walked) ходьбá: *ten minute walk,* дéсять минýт ходьбы́. *20-km. walk, sports* ходьбá на двáдцать киломéтров. **2,** (stroll) прогýлка. *Go for a walk,* идтú гуля́ть. *Take for a walk,* водúть гуля́ть. **3,** (manner of walking; gait) похóдка. **4,** (slow pace) шаг: *slow a horse to a walk,* сводúть лóшадь на шаг. **5,** (path; promenade) аллéя; дорóжка. **6,** *in* **from all walks of life,** всех слоёв óбщества. —**walk off,** уходúть. *Walk off the job,* объявúть забастóвку. —**walk off with, 1,** (steal) утащúть. **2,** (win) взять; завоевáть. —**walk out,** выходúть. *Walk out of a meeting,* (демонстратúвно) уйтú с собрáния. —**walk out on,** брóсить; уйтú от. —**walk up to,** подходúть к.
walker *n.* **1,** (person) ходóк. **2,** (device to aid in walking) ходункú.
walkie-talkie *n.* (портатúвная) рáция.
walking *adj.* ходя́чий. *It is within walking distance,* тудá мóжно дойтú пешкóм. —*n.* ходьбá. —**get one's walking papers,** быть увóленным; вы́лететь.
walking stick пáлка; трость.
walkout *n.* **1,** (abrupt departure) демонстратúвный ухóд. **2,** (strike) забастóвка.
wall *n.* стенá. —*adj.* стеннóй; настéнный. *Wall newspaper,* стенная газéта. —*v.t.* **1,** *fol. by* **in** (enclose) обносúть стенóй. **2,** *fol. by* **up** (board up) задéлывать; замурóвывать. **3,** *fol. by* **off** (partition off) отгорáживать. —**drive up a wall,** *colloq.* сводúть с умá; доводúть до сумасшéствия. —**up against (*or* with one's back to) the wall,** припёртый к стенé.
wallet *n.* бумáжник.
walleye *n.* бельмó.
wallflower *n.* **1,** (plant) лакфиóль; желтофиóль. **2,** *colloq.* (girl without a partner at a dance) дéвушка без кавалéра.
wallop *n.* тумáк. —*v.t.* дать тумакá (+ *dat.*).
wallow *v.i.* [*usu.* **wallow in**] **1,** (roll about in) валя́ться (в). **2,** *fig.* (indulge oneself to excess) погря́знуть (в); утопáть (в).
wallpaper *n.* обóи. —*v.t.* оклéивать (кóмнату) обóями.
walnut *n.* **1,** (tree; wood) орéх; орéховое дéрево. **2,** (nut) грéцкий орéх. —*adj.* орéховый.
walrus *n.* морж.
waltz *n.* вальс. —*v.i.* вальсúровать.
wan *adj.* блéдный.
wand *n.* пáлочка: *magic wand,* волшéбная пáлочка.
wander *v.i.* **1,** (walk or stroll aimlessly) бродúть; блуждáть. **2,** (roam about the world) стрáнствовать; скитáться. **3,** (fail to concentrate) блуждáть: *his mind tends to wander,* егó мы́сли чáсто блуждáют. —**wander into,** забрестú в. —**wander off, 1,** [*also,* **wander away**] (stray) забрестú. *Wander off/away from the group,* отставáть от грýппы. **2,** [*also,* **wander from**] (digress) отходúть от.
wanderer *n.* стрáнник; скитáлец.
wandering *n.* стрáнствие; скитáние. —*adj.* бродя́чий; блуждáющий.
wanderlust *n.* страсть к путешéствиям.
wane *v.i.* **1,** (of the moon) убывáть. **2,** *fig.* (fade; ebb) угасáть; идтú на ýбыль. —*n., in* **on the wane,** на ущéрбе.
wangle *v.t.* выпрáшивать; раздобывáть. *Wangle a ticket/an invitation/,* вы́просить/раздобы́ть билéт/приглашéние. *Wangle a secret from someone,* вывéдывать секрéт у когó-нибудь.
want *v.t.* хотéть: *what do you want?,* что вы хотúте? *What do you want me to do?,* что вы хотúте, чтóбы я сдéлал(а)? *You are wanted on the phone,* вас прóсят к телефóну. *He is wanted by the authorities,* он разы́скивается властя́ми. —*n.* **1,** (lack) недостáток. *For want of something better,* за неимéнием лýчшего. **2,** (poverty; need) нуждá: *freedom from want,* свобóда от нужды́. *Be in want of,* нуждáться в. **3,** *pl.* (needs) потрéбности.
want ad *colloq.* объявлéние (в газéте).
wanton *adj.* **1,** (vicious; unprovoked) бессмы́сленный. **2,** (dissolute) распýтный.
war *n.* войнá. *Be at war,* быть в состоя́нии войны́; воевáть. —*adj.* воéнный: *war game,* воéнная игрá. —*v.i.* воевáть: *warring parties,* вою́ющие стóроны.

warble *v.i.* щёлкать. —*n.* трель.
warbler *n.* сла́вка.
war crime вое́нное преступле́ние. —**war criminal,** вое́нный престу́пник.
war cry боево́й клич.
ward *n.* **1,** (dependent) опека́емый; подопе́чный. **2,** (of a hospital) пала́та. *Maternity ward,* роди́льное отделе́ние. **3,** (district) райо́н. —*v.t.* [*usu.* **ward off**] отража́ть; отводи́ть.
warden *n.* сто́рож; объе́здчик: *forest warden,* лесно́й сто́рож/объе́здчик. *Prison warden,* тюре́мщик. *Game warden,* инспе́ктор по охра́не ди́чи.
warder *n.* **1,** (guard; watchman) сто́рож. **2,** *Brit.* = **prison warden.**
wardrobe *n.* **1,** (clothes closet) гардеро́б; платяно́й шкаф. **2,** (supply of clothes) гардеро́б.
ware *n.* **1,** *pl.* (merchandise) това́ры. **2,** *used in compounds* изде́лия; посу́да: *hardware,* скобяны́е изде́лия; *earthenware,* гли́няная посу́да.
warehouse *n.* склад.
warfare *n.* война́: *guerrilla warfare,* партиза́нская война́.
warhead *n.* **1,** (section of a missile) боева́я часть; боева́я голо́вка. **2,** (explosive charge contained therein) заря́д; боеприпа́с: *nuclear warhead,* я́дерный заря́д/боеприпа́с.
warhorse *n.* боево́й конь.
warily *adv.* осторо́жно.
wariness *n.* осторо́жность.
warlike *adj.* войнственный.
warm *adj.* тёплый: *warm milk/summer/coat/letter,* тёплое молоко́/ле́то/пальто́/письмо́. *It is warm,* тепло́. *Are you warm?,* вам тепло́? *The sun is warm,* со́лнце гре́ет. *Get warm,* согрева́ться. —*v.t.* [*also,* **warm up**] греть; нагрева́ть; согрева́ть: *warm up the food,* греть/нагрева́ть/согрева́ть пи́щу. *Warm one's feet by the fire,* греть но́ги у огня́. *Warm one's heart,* ра́довать се́рдце; согрева́ть ду́шу. —*v.i.* **1,** *fol. by* **up** (of the weather, temperature, etc.) тепле́ть. **2,** *fol. by* **up** (of a heating device, food on the stove, etc.) согрева́ться; нагрева́ться; (of an engine) прогрева́ться. **3,** *fol. by* **to** (get into the swing of) войти́ во вкус (+ *gen.*). *Warm to one's subject,* разговори́ться. —**warm oneself,** гре́ться. —**warm over,** разогрева́ть; подогрева́ть: *warmed-over dinner,* разогре́тый обе́д. —**warm up,** (exercise; limber up) де́лать разми́нку; размина́ться. —**warm up to,** (бо́лее) тепло́ относи́ться к.
warm-blooded *adj.* теплокро́вный.
warmhearted *adj.* тёплый; серде́чный.
warmly *adv.* **1,** (so as to be warm) тепло́: *dress warmly,* тепло́ одева́ться. **2,** (cordially) тепло́; серде́чно.
warmonger *n.* поджига́тель войны́.
warmth *n.* тепло́; теплота́. *Give off warmth,* излуча́ть тепло́. *Warmth of feeling,* теплота́ чу́вства. *With great warmth,* с большо́й теплото́й.
warm-up *n.* разми́нка.
warn *v.t.* предупрежда́ть: *I'm warning you!,* предупрежда́ю (вас)! *I warned you not to do it,* я предупрежда́л(а) вас не де́лать э́того. *Don't say I didn't warn you!,* не говори́те, что я вас не предупрежда́л(а).
warning *n.* предупрежде́ние; предостереже́ние. *Fire without warning,* стреля́ть без предупрежде́ния. *Get off with a warning,* отде́латься предупрежде́нием. —*adj.* предупреди́тельный: *warning shot,* предупреди́тельный вы́стрел.
warp *v.t.* **1,** (twist; bend) коро́бить. **2,** (pervert) извраща́ть; кове́ркать. *Warped mind,* извращённый ум. —*v.i.* коро́биться. —*n.* **1,** (bend) коро́бление. **2,** *textiles* осно́ва.
warplane *n.* вое́нный самолёт.
warrant *n.* о́рдер; манда́т; наря́д. *Search warrant,* о́рдер на о́быск. —*v.t.* **1,** (justify) опра́вдывать. **2,** (merit) заслу́живать.
warrant officer (in the army) пра́порщик; (in the navy) ми́чман.
warranty *n.* гара́нтия; руча́тельство.
warren *n.* кро́личья нора́; кро́личий садо́к.
warrior *n.* бое́ц; во́ин.
warship *n.* вое́нный кора́бль.
wart *n.* борода́вка.
wart hog борода́вочник.
wartime *n.* вое́нное вре́мя.
wary *adj.* осторо́жный; осмотри́тельный. *Be wary of,* остерега́ться (+ *gen.*).
wash *v.t.* **1,** (clean; scrub) мыть; умыва́ть. *Wash one's hands,* мыть ру́ки. *Wash the dishes,* мыть посу́ду. **2,** (launder) стира́ть: *wash clothes,* стира́ть бельё. **3,** (flow over) омыва́ть: *waves wash the shore,* во́лны омыва́ют бе́рег. —*v.i.* **1,** [*often* **wash up**] (get washed) мы́ться; умыва́ться. **2,** (do laundry) стира́ть. **3,** (be capable of being washed) стира́ться. **4,** *colloq.* (stand up to scrutiny): *the story won't wash,* э́та исто́рия никого́ не убеди́т. —*n.* **1,** (act of washing) мытьё. **2,** (laundering) сти́рка: *fade in the wash,* линя́ть от сти́рки. *The stains came out in the wash,* пя́тна вы́велись при сти́рке. **3,** (things to be washed) бельё: *hang out the wash,* выве́шивать бельё. **4,** (liquid refuse) жи́жа. **5,** (liquid used for cleansing) примо́чка: *eyewash,* примо́чка для глаз. —**wash away,** размыва́ть; сноси́ть *(impers.)*: *the road was washed away,* доро́гу размы́ло. *The bridge was washed away by the flood,* мост снесло́ водо́й. —**wash down,** запива́ть: *wash down medicine with water,* запива́ть лека́рство водо́й. —**wash off,** смыва́ть. —**wash one's hands of something,** умыва́ть ру́ки. —**wash out, 1,** (wash) стира́ть (*pfv.* вы́стирать). *Wash out one's socks,* вы́стирать носки́. **2,** (rinse out) спола́скивать. **3,** (remove) смыва́ть: *wash out a stain,* смыва́ть пятно́. **4,** (wash away) размыва́ть: *the flood washed out the road,* вода́ размы́ла доро́гу. —**wash overboard,** *see* **overboard.** —**wash up, 1,** (wash one's hands and face) умыва́ться. **2,** (deposit on the shore) наноси́ть на бе́рег.
washbasin *n.* умыва́льник.
washboard *n.* стира́льная доска́.
washbowl *n.* умыва́льник.
washcloth *n.* тря́пка для мытья́.
washed-out *adj.* **1,** (faded) полиня́вший. **2,** *colloq.* (tired; weak) лишён сил. **3,** *colloq.* (wan) бле́дный.
washer *n.* **1,** (person who washes) мо́йщик: *window washer,* мо́йщик о́кон. **2,** (washing machine) стира́льная маши́на. **3,** *mech.* ша́йба; прокла́дка.
washerwoman *n.* пра́чка.
washing *n.* мытьё; мо́йка; умыва́ние; *(of clothes)* сти́рка. —**washing machine,** стира́льная маши́на.
washrag *n.* = **washcloth.**
washroom *n.* убо́рная; туалёт.
washstand *n.* умыва́льник.

washtub *n.* лоха́нь: коры́то.
wasp *n.* оса́.
waste *v.t.* **1,** (spend needlessly) тра́тить; да́ром/по́пусту/зря тра́тить. *Waste time,* теря́ть вре́мя. *Waste one's breath,* тра́тить слова́ да́ром. *His efforts were wasted,* его́ уси́лия пропа́ли да́ром. **2,** (fail to take advantage of) упуска́ть; прозева́ть (удо́бный слу́чай). —*v.i.* [*usu.* **waste away**] ча́хнуть. —*n.* **1,** (unnecessary expenditure) растра́та. *Waste of time,* поте́ря *or* растра́та вре́мени; пуста́я тра́та вре́мени. **2,** (superfluous matter) отхо́ды; отбро́сы. *Industrial wastes,* отхо́ды произво́дства. **3,** *physiol.* выделе́ния. —**go to waste,** пропада́ть да́ром. —**lay waste,** опустоша́ть. —**waste products,** отхо́ды. *See also* **wasted.**
wastebasket *n.* корзи́на для бума́ги.
wasted *adj.* **1,** (squandered) растра́ченный. **2,** (fruitless; gone for naught) напра́сный; пропа́вший да́ром. **3,** (emaciated) истощённый: *wasted by disease,* истощённый боле́знью.
wasteful *adj.* расточи́тельный. —**wastefulness,** *n.* расточи́тельность.
wasteland *n.* пусты́ня.
wastrel *n.* **1,** (spendthrift) транжи́р. **2,** (good-for-nothing) шалопа́й.
watch *v.t.* **1,** (look at; observe) смотре́ть; наблюда́ть. *Watch television,* смотре́ть телеви́зор. *Watch the sun rise,* наблюда́ть восхо́д со́лнца. **2,** (guard; keep an eye on; look after) смотре́ть за; следи́ть за; наблюда́ть за. —*v.i.* смотре́ть: *watch how it's done,* посмотри́те, как э́то де́лается. *Watch that he doesn't fall,* смотри́те, что́бы он не упа́л. —*n.* **1,** (timepiece) часы́. **2,** (observation) наблюде́ние. *Keep watch over,* наблюда́ть за. *Be on the watch for,* подстерега́ть. **3,** (guarding) стра́жа; *naval* ва́хта: *stand watch,* стоя́ть на стра́же *or* на ва́хте. **4,** (those who guard) стра́жа; дозо́р. *Night watch,* ночно́й дозо́р. —*adj.* часово́й: *watch spring,* часова́я пружи́на. —**watch for,** ждать; стере́чь; подстерега́ть. —**watch it!,** осторо́жно! —**watch oneself,** бере́чься. —**watch one's step, 1,** (be careful not to fall) стара́ться не оступи́ться: *watch your step!,* осторо́жно, не оступи́тесь! **2,** (be prudent) бере́чься; быть осторо́жным; соблюда́ть осторо́жность. —**watch out,** бере́чься. *Watch out!,* осторо́жно! —**watch out for,** бере́чься (+ *gen.*); остерега́ться (+ *gen.*).
watchband *n.* ремешо́к для часо́в.
watch chain цепо́чка для часо́в.
watchdog *n.* дворо́вая соба́ка; сторожево́й пёс.
watchful *adj.* насторо́женный. *Keep a watchful eye on,* внима́тельно следи́ть за.
watchmaker *n.* часовщи́к.
watchman *n.* сто́рож.
watchtower *n.* сторожева́я ба́шня/вы́шка.
watchword *n.* **1,** (password) паро́ль. **2,** (motto) ло́зунг; деви́з.
water *n.* вода́: *be under water,* быть под водо́й. *Mineral/territorial waters,* минера́льные/территориа́льные во́ды. *Ship something by water,* отправля́ть что́-нибудь во́дным путём. *Land a plane on the water,* посади́ть самолёт на́ воду. —*adj.* во́дный; водяно́й: *water sports,* во́дный спорт; *water vapor,* водяно́й пар. *Water glass,* стака́н для воды́. —*v.t.* **1,** (pour water on) полива́ть: *water the flowers,* полива́ть цветы́. **2,** (provide with water, as animals) пои́ть. **3,** *fol. by* **down** (dilute; weaken) разбавля́ть; разжижа́ть; *fig.* смягча́ть. —*v.i.* **1,** (of one's eyes) слези́ться. **2,** (of one's mouth): *my mouth is watering,* у меня́ слю́нки теку́т.—**of the first water,** чи́стой *or* чисте́йшей воды́. —**not hold water,** не выде́рживать кри́тики. —**throw cold water on,** облива́ть (+ *acc.*) холо́дной водо́й.
water buffalo инди́йский (*or* водяно́й) бу́йвол.
water carrier водоно́с; водово́з.
water closet убо́рная.
watercolor *also,* **watercolour** *n., often pl.* акваре́ль. —*adj.* акваре́льный. —**watercolorist,** *n.* акварели́ст.
water-cooled *adj.* с водяны́м охлажде́нием.
watercress *n.* водяно́й кресс.
waterfall *n.* водопа́д.
waterfowl *n.* водопла́вающая пти́ца.
waterfront *n.* по́рт; райо́н по́рта.
watering *n.* **1,** (of plants) поли́вка. **2,** (of livestock) водопо́й. —**watering can,** ле́йка. —**watering place,** водопо́й.
waterless *adj.* безво́дный.
water lily водяна́я ли́лия; кувши́нка.
waterline *n.* ватерли́ния.
waterlogged *adj.* пропи́танный водо́й.
water main водопрово́дная магистра́ль.
watermark *n.* водяно́й знак.
watermelon *n.* арбу́з. —*adj.* арбу́зный: *watermelon seeds,* арбу́зные ко́сточки.
water meter водоме́р.
water pipe водопрово́дная труба́.
water polo во́дное по́ло; ватерпо́ло.
water power во́дная эне́ргия.
waterproof *adj.* непромока́емый; водонепроница́емый. *Be waterproof,* не пропуска́ть воды́.
watershed *n.* водоразде́л.
water ski во́дная лы́жа. —**water-ski,** *v.i.* ката́ться на во́дных лы́жах. —**water-skiing,** *n.* воднолы́жный спорт.
waterspout *n.* **1,** (outlet for water) водосто́чная труба́. **2,** (tornado) смерч.
water sprite водяно́й.
water table у́ровень грунтовы́х вод.
watertight *adj.* **1,** (waterproof) водонепроница́емый; непромока́емый. **2,** (impossible to refute) неопровержи́мый.
water tower водонапо́рная ба́шня.
waterway *n.* во́дный путь; во́дная арте́рия.
water wheel водяно́е колесо́.
watery *adj.* водяни́стый; жи́дкий.
watt *n.* ватт: *100-watt bulb,* ла́мпочка в сто ватт. —**wattage,** *n.* мо́щность (в ва́ттах).
wattle *n.* **1,** (interlaced twigs forming a fence) плете́нь. **2,** (fleshy skin hanging from the throat of certain fowl) борода́; серёжка. —**wattled,** *adj.* плетёный.
wave *n.* **1,** (of water) волна́. **2,** (in one's hair) зави́вка. **3,** *physics* волна́: *sound wave,* звукова́я волна́. **4,** (motion with the hand) взмах. **5,** *fig.* (surge) волна́: *a wave of discontent,* волна́ недово́льства. **6,** (period of cold or heat) полоса́. —*v.t.* **1,** (move back and forth; swing) маха́ть; помаха́ть. *Wave goodbye,* маха́ть/помаха́ть на проща́ние. *Wave a flag,* разма́хивать фла́гом. **2,** (curl, as hair) завива́ть. —*v.i.* **1,** (flutter) развева́ться. **2,** (wave one's hand) маха́ть/помаха́ть

рукóй. *Wave to someone,* махáть рукóй (+ *dat.*). —**wave aside,** отмáхиваться от.

wavelength *n.* длинá волны́.

waver *v.i.* **1,** (sway; flutter) колыхáться; развевáться. **2,** (show hesitation) дрóгнуть; колебáться.

wavy *adj.* волни́стый.

wax *n.* воск. —*adj.* восковóй. —*v.t.* вощи́ть. *Wax the floor,* натирáть пол. —*v.i.* **1,** (of the moon) прибывáть; прибавля́ться. **2,** (become): *wax angry,* рассерди́ться; *wax calm,* успокóиться.

waxen *adj.* восковóй.

wax museum панóптикум.

wax paper вощёная бумáга; вощáнка.

waxwing *n.* свиристéль.

waxy *adj.* восковóй.

way *n.* **1,** (route) путь; дорóга: *on the way home,* по пути́/по дорóге/домóй. *All the way,* всю дорóгу. *Part of the way,* часть пути́. *The shortest way to town,* кратчáйший путь в гóрод. *Lose one's way,* заблуди́ться; сби́ться с пути́/с дорóги. *Are you going my way?,* нам по пути́?; вам со мной по пути́? **2,** (direction) сторонá: *he went that way,* он пошёл в ту стóрону. *Which way are you going?,* вам в какýю стóрону? *This way, please!,* сюдá, пожáлуйста! **3,** (position such as to be an obstacle): *be in the way,* мешáть. *Get out of the way!,* не мешáйте!; прочь с дорóги! *Keep out of the way,* держáться в сторонé. *Stand in someone's way,* стоя́ть на чьём-нибудь пути́; стоя́ть у когó-нибудь поперёк дорóги. **4,** (manner; method) спóсоб; путь: *this way,* таки́м спóсобом; таки́м óбразом. *The same way,* так же. *In what way?,* каки́м óбразом?, каки́м путём? *One's own way,* на свой лад; по-своéму. *Don't do it that way,* не дéлайте так. *There is no other way to do it,* э́то нельзя́ сдéлать инáче. *Try in every way,* всéми си́лами старáться. **5,** (respect) отношéние: *in a way,* в нéкотором отношéнии; в нéкотором рóде; в извéстном смы́сле. *In many ways,* во мнóгих отношéниях. **6,** (distance): *a long way from here,* далекó отсю́да. *We have a long way to go,* нам ещё далекó éхать. *We've come a long way,* мы приéхали издалекá; мы продéлали большóй путь; *fig.* мы доби́лись мнóгого. **7,** (wish; will): *have one's way,* настоя́ть на своём. *Get one's way,* доби́ться своегó. *Have it your way,* пусть бýдет по-вáшему. **8,** *colloq.* (condition) положéние: *in a bad way,* в плохóм положéнии. **9,** *colloq.* (locality; region) райóн: *out our way,* в нáшем райóне. **10,** *pl.* (customs; manners) нрáвы. *Mend one's ways,* исправля́ться. —*adv.* далекó: *way behind,* далекó позади́. —**by the way,** мéжду прóчим; кстáти. —**by way of, 1,** (via) чéрез. **2,** (as) в кáчестве (+ *gen.*): *by way of example,* в кáчестве примéра. *By way of proof,* в ви́де доказáтельства. —**come one's way,** попадáться (+ *dat.*). —**give way, 1,** (yield to physical pressure) поддавáться: *the door gave way,* дверь поддалáсь. *The rope gave way,* верёвка порвалáсь. *The roof gave way,* кры́ша обвали́лась. *His legs gave way under him,* у негó нóги подкоси́лись. **2,** *fol. by* **to** (succumb to) поддавáться (+ *dat.*); предавáться (+ *dat.*). *Give way to despair,* предавáться отчáянию. **3,** *fol. by* **to** (be replaced or succeeded by) сменя́ться (+ *instr.*); уступáть мéсто (+ *dat.*). —**go out of one's way, 1,** (make a detour) сдéлать крюк. **2,** (put oneself out) прилагáть осóбые уси́лия. —**have a way with,** умéть обращáться с. —**in one's way; in its way,** в своём рóде. —**in the way of, 1,** (hindering): *stand in the way of progress,* тормози́ть прогрéсс. **2,** (in; by way of) в кáчестве (+ *gen.*). *What have you got in the way of fabrics?,* что у вас есть из материáлов? —**lead the way,** идти́ вперéди́. —**make one's way,** пробирáться. —**make way,** сторони́ться; расступáться. *Make way for,* дать *or* уступи́ть дорóгу (+ *dat.*). —**out of the way, 1,** (not on one's route) не по пути́. **2,** (not blocking anything; aside) в сторонé. **3,** (finished; disposed of) закóнчен. **4,** *Put (someone) out of the way, colloq.* (kill) ликвиди́ровать; уложи́ть. —**under way,** *rendered by various verbs: talks are under way,* переговóры начали́сь/идýт/ведýтся. *Get under way,* начинáть(ся); отправля́ться в путь. —**way of life,** óбраз *or* уклáд жи́зни. —**ways and means,** пути́ и срéдства. —**way out,** вы́ход.

waybill *n.* накладнáя.

wayfarer *n.* пýтник. —**wayfaring,** *adj.* стрáнствующий.

waylay *v.t.* нападáть на; устрáивать засáду на.

wayside *adj.* придорóжный. *Wayside inn,* постоя́лый двор. —**fall by the wayside,** выбывáть из стрóя.

way station попýтная стáнция; полустáнок.

wayward *adj.* заблýдший; беспýтный. *Wayward son,* заблýдший сын. *Wayward existence,* беспýтная жизнь.

we *pers.pron.* мы. *See also* **us.**

weak *adj.* слáбый: *weak from hunger,* слáбый от гóлода. *Weak link,* слáбое звенó. *Weak tea,* слáбый чай. *Weak point,* слáбое мéсто. *Grow weak,* слабéть; ослабевáть. *Feel weak,* чýвствовать какýю-то слáбость. *Have a weak spot in one's heart for,* имéть *or* питáть слáбость к.

weaken *v.t.* ослабля́ть. —*v.i.* слабéть.

weakling *n.* тря́пка.

weakly *adj.* хи́лый. —*adv.* слáбо.

weakness *n.* слáбость. *Have a weakness for,* имéть *or* питáть слáбость к.

weak-willed *adj.* безвóльный; слабовóльный; бесхарáктерный.

weal *n.* **1,** (welt) рубéц; полосá. **2,** *archaic* (welfare) бл́аго; благосостоя́ние.

wealth *n.* **1,** (riches; prosperity) богáтство. **2,** *fol. by* **of** (abundance) богáтство; оби́лие (+ *gen.*). *A wealth of information,* мáсса информáции. *A wealth of material,* богáтый материáл.

wealthy *adj.* богáтый; зажи́точный; состоя́тельный.

wean *v.t.* **1,** (a child) отнимáть от груди́. **2,** (break, as of a habit) отучáть (от).

weapon *n.* орýжие *(always sing.): secret weapon,* секрéтное орýжие; *nuclear weapons,* я́дерное орýжие. *Weapons of mass destruction,* орýжие мáссового уничтожéния. —**weaponry,** *n.* вооружéние.

wear *v.t.* **1,** (have on) надевáть: *what are you going to wear to the party?,* что ты собирáешься надéть на вéчер? *I have nothing to wear,* мне нéчего надéть. *He is wearing a new suit,* на нём нóвый костю́м. **2,** (wear habitually) носи́ть: *wear glasses/a beard/,* носи́ть очки́/бóроду. *Wear one's hair short,* носи́ть корóткие вóлосы. *He always wears a tie,* он всегдá нóсит гáлстук. *What size shoe do you wear?,* какóй нóмер боти́нок вы нóсите? **3,** (bring to a state by wearing) изнáшивать: *wear a coat to shreds,* изнáшивать пальто́ до дыр. *Wear a hole in one's pocket,* продыря́вить карма́н. **4,** (have; exhibit) име́ть: *wear a dejected look,* име́ть мра́чный вид. —*v.i.* **1,** (hold up) носи́ться: *this skirt wears well,* э́та ю́бка хорошо́ но́сится. **2,** (show the effects of wear) изна́шиваться. —*n.* **1,** (act of wearing) но́ска: *from long wear,* от до́лгой но́ски. **2,** (effect of wearing) изно́с. *Show signs of wear,* обтрепа́ться. **3,** (clothes) оде́жда: *men's wear,* мужска́я оде́жда. —**wear and tear,** изно́с. —**wear away,** стира́ть. *The inscription is worn away,* на́дпись стёрлась. —**wear down, 1,** (wear out, as footwear) ста́птывать. **2,** (overcome, as resistance) преодолева́ть; сломи́ть. —**wear off,** проходи́ть: *the pain wore off,* боль прошла́. —**wear out, 1,** (wear until no longer usable) изна́шивать. **2,** (be no longer usable) изна́шиваться. **3,** (exhaust) изнуря́ть; изму́чить. —**wear thin,** *see* **thin.**

weariness *n.* уста́лость; утомле́ние.

wearing *adj.* утоми́тельный. —**wearing apparel,** оде́жда.

wearisome *adj.* томи́тельный.

weary *adj.* уста́лый; утомлённый. —*v.t.* утомля́ть. —*v.i.* устава́ть; утомля́ться.

weasel *n.* ла́ска.

weather *n.* пого́да. *Weather forecast,* прогно́з пого́ды. —*v.t.* **1,** (wear away by exposure to the elements) выве́тривать. **2,** (survive) выде́рживать: *weather a storm,* вы́держать бу́рю. —**keep one's weather eye open,** держа́ть у́хо востро́. —**under the weather, 1,** (ill) нездоро́в. **2,** (drunk) под хмелько́м.

weather-beaten *adj.* обве́тренный.

weathercock *n.* флю́гер.

weatherman *n.* сино́птик; метеоро́лог.

weather map синопти́ческая ка́рта.

weather satellite метеорологи́ческий спу́тник; метеоспу́тник.

weather vane флю́гер.

weave *v.t.* **1,** (form into fabric) ткать: *weave cloth,* ткать сукно́. **2,** (make by weaving) плести́: *weave a basket,* плести́ корзи́ну. **3,** (spin, as a tale) плести́. —*v.i.* **1,** (do weaving) ткать. **2,** (zigzag) петля́ть; виля́ть. —*n.* переплете́ние: *close weave,* ча́стое переплете́ние.

weaver *n.* ткач.

weaving *n.* тканьё.

web *n.* **1,** (spider's web) паути́на. **2,** *fig.* (tangle) сплете́ние; паути́на: *web of lies,* сплете́ние/паути́на лжи. **3,** *zool.* (membrane) перепо́нка.

webbed *adj.* перепо́нчатый: *webbed feet,* перепо́нчатые ла́пы.

web-footed *adj.* с перепо́нчатыми ла́пами.

wed *v.t.* жени́ться на; выходи́ть за́муж за. —*v.i.* жени́ться; выходи́ть за́муж; вступи́ть в брак.

wedded *adj.* **1,** (married): *my lawfully wedded wife,* моя́ зако́нная супру́га. **2,** *fol. by* **to** (bound) привя́занный: *I am not wedded to this job,* я не привя́зан(а) к э́той рабо́те.

wedding *n.* сва́дьба. —*adj.* сва́дебный: *wedding cake/present,* сва́дебный торт/пода́рок. *Wedding day,* день сва́дьбы. *Wedding dress,* сва́дебное *or* подвене́чное пла́тье. *Wedding palace,* дворе́ц бракосочета́ния. *Wedding ring,* обруча́льное кольцо́.

wedge *n.* клин. —*v.t.* закли́нивать. *Become wedged,* закли́ниваться. —**wedge-shaped,** *adj.* клинови́дный; клинообра́зный.

wedlock *n.* брак. *Born out of wedlock,* рождённый вне бра́ка.

Wednesday *n.* среда́.

wee *adj.* кро́шечный; малю́сенький. —**a wee bit,** чуть-чуть.

weed *n.* со́рная трава́; сорня́к. —*v.t.* **1,** (clear of weeds) поло́ть; пропа́лывать. **2,** *fol. by out* (eliminate) отсе́ивать. —**weed-killer,** *n.* гербици́д.

week *n.* неде́ля. *A week's vacation,* неде́льный о́тпуск. *A week from Wednesday,* в сре́ду на сле́дующей неде́ле; че́рез неде́лю в сре́ду.

weekday *n.* бу́дний *or* бу́дничный день.

weekend *n.* суббо́та и воскресе́нье.

weekly *adj.* еженеде́льный. —*adv.* еженеде́льно —*n.* еженеде́льник.

weep *v.i.* **1,** (cry) пла́кать. **2,** *fol. by* **for** (mourn) опла́кивать. —*v.t.* (shed, as tears) пролива́ть.

weeping *n.* плач. —**weeping willow,** плаку́чая и́ва.

weevil *n.* долгоно́сик.

weft *n., textiles* уто́к.

weigh *v.t.* взве́шивать. *Weigh oneself,* взве́шиваться. *Weigh one's words,* взве́шивать свои́ слова́. —*v.i.* **1,** (have a certain weight) ве́сить. *How much do you weigh?,* како́й у вас вес?; ско́лько вы ве́сите? *I weigh 140 pounds,* мой вес (*or* я ве́шу) сто со́рок фу́нтов. **2,** (carry weight) име́ть вес: *weigh heavily,* име́ть большо́й вес. **3,** *Weigh on one's mind,* тяготи́ть (кого́-нибудь). —**weigh anchor,** снима́ться с я́коря. —**weigh down,** отягоща́ть; оття́гивать. —**weigh out,** отве́шивать; разве́шивать.

weight *n.* **1,** (heaviness) вес. *Gain/lose weight,* прибавля́ть/теря́ть в ве́се. **2,** *fig.* (influence; importance) вес: *carry weight,* име́ть вес. *Attach great weight to,* придава́ть большо́е значе́ние (+ *dat.*). **3,** *fig.* (burden) тя́жесть: *the weight of cares,* тя́жесть забо́т. *The weight of evidence,* тя́жесть ули́к. **4,** (anything heavy, used for its weight) ги́ря. *Paperweight,* пресс-папье́. **5,** *sports* ги́ря; шта́нга; тя́жесть: *lift weights,* поднима́ть ги́ри/тя́жести. —*v.t.* утяжеля́ть: *weight sacks with lead,* утяжеля́ть мешки́ свинцо́м. —**throw one's weight around,** распоряжа́ться; хозя́йничать. —**worth its weight in gold,** на вес зо́лота.

weightless *adj.* невесо́мый. —**weightlessness,** *n.* невесо́мость.

weightlifter *n.* гиреви́к; штанги́ст; тяжелоатле́т. —**weightlifting,** *n.* подня́тие тя́жестей; тяжёлая атле́тика.

weighty *adj.* ве́ский; весо́мый.

weir *n.* запру́да.

weird *adj.* **1,** (eerie) таи́нственный. **2,** (odd) стра́нный.

welcome *adj.* **1,** (gladly received) прия́тный: *welcome news,* прия́тное изве́стие. *A welcome guest,* жела́нный гость. **2,** *fol. by* **to** (gladly invited): *you are always welcome to come,* ми́лости про́сим. *You are welcome to use my car,* моя́ маши́на к ва́шим услу́гам. —*n.* приём; встре́ча: *hearty welcome,* раду́шный приём; раду́шная встре́ча. *Speech of welcome,* приве́тственная речь. —*v.t.* приве́тствовать: *welcome a delegation/proposal,* приве́тствовать делега́цию/предложе́ние. —*interj.* добро́ пожа́ловать!: *welcome to Moscow!,* добро́ пожа́ловать в Москву́! —**you are welcome!,** пожа́луйста!

weld *v.t.* **1,** (join by heating and fusing) сва́ривать. **2,**

fig. (bring into close union) спла́чивать. —**welder,** *n.* сва́рщик.

welding *n.* сва́рка. —*adj.* сва́рочный: *welding torch,* сва́рочная горе́лка.

welfare *n.* **1,** (well-being) благосостоя́ние; благополу́чие. **2,** (support of the needy) социа́льное обеспе́чение. *Be on welfare,* получа́ть посо́бие.

well[1] *n.* коло́дец. *Oil well,* нефтяна́я сква́жина. —*adj.* коло́дезный: *well water,* коло́дезная вода́. —*v.i.* [*usu.* **well up**] (of emotions) вскипа́ть. *Tears welled up in her eyes,* слёзы наверну́лись на её глаза́.

well[2] *adv.* **1,** (satisfactorily; properly; excellently) хорошо́: *well said!,* хорошо́ ска́зано! *Turn out well,* ко́нчиться благополу́чно. *Shake well before using,* взба́лтывать пе́ред употребле́нием. *All's well that ends well,* всё хорошо́, что хорошо́ конча́ется. **2,** (fully; entirely) вполне́: *it may well be that...,* вполне́ возмо́жно, что... *Be well aware of,* отдава́ть себе́ по́лный отчёт в. **3,** (considerably; far) далеко́: *well past midnight,* далеко́ за́ полночь. —*adj.* **1,** (in good health) здоро́вый. *Get well,* выздора́вливать. *He looks well,* он хорошо́ вы́глядит. **2,** (satisfactory) хорошо́; в поря́дке: *all is well,* всё в поря́дке. —*interj.* **1,** *used to introduce a statement* ну. **2,** *expressing surprise* вот как; вот тебе́ и на. —**as well,** а та́кже: *and in Paris as well,* а та́кже в Пари́же. —**as well as, 1,** (in addition) а та́кже: *as well as in a number of other countries,* а та́кже в ря́де други́х стран. **2,** (equally with) как..., так...: *women as well as men,* как же́нщины, так и мужчи́ны. —**wish someone well,** жела́ть кому́-нибудь добра́.

well-behaved *adj.* благовоспи́танный. *The children were well-behaved,* де́ти вели́ себя́ хорошо́.

well-being *n.* благополу́чие; благосостоя́ние.

well-bred *adj.* (благо)воспи́танный.

well-done *adj.* **1,** (capably done) хорошо́ сде́ланный. **2,** (thoroughly cooked) (хорошо́) прожа́ренный.

well-dressed *adj.* хорошо́ оде́тый; наря́дный.

well-earned *adj.* заслу́женный.

well-fed *adj.* отко́рмленный; упи́танный.

well-founded *adj.* обосно́ванный; состоя́тельный.

well-groomed *adj.* хо́леный.

well-grounded *adj.* **1,** (well-founded) обосно́ванный. **2,** (knowledgeable) хорошо́ подко́ван (*e.g.* в хи́мии).

well-informed *adj.* (хорошо́) осведомлённый.

well-intentioned *adj.* име́ющий до́брые наме́рения; благонаме́ренный.

well-known *adj.* изве́стный.

well-mannered *adj.* (благо)воспи́танный.

well-meaning *adj.* име́ющий до́брые наме́рения; благонаме́ренный.

well-nigh *adv.* почти́; чуть ли не.

well-off *adj.* зажи́точный; состоя́тельный; обеспе́ченный.

well-paid *adj.* хорошо́ опла́чиваемый.

well-preserved *adj.* хорошо́ сохрани́вшийся.

well-read *adj.* начи́танный.

well sweep жура́вль.

well-to-do *adj.* зажи́точный; состоя́тельный; обеспе́ченный.

well-versed *adj.* све́дущий.

well-wisher *n.* доброжела́тель. —**well-wishing,** *adj.* доброжела́тельный.

Welsh *adj.* уэ́льский; валли́йский. —*n.* уэ́льский/валли́йский язы́к. —**Welshman,** *n.* валли́ец.

welt *n.* **1,** (part of a shoe) рант. **2,** (cord trimming) обши́вка. **3,** (mark left by a whip or stick) полоса́.

welter *n.* пу́таница: *welter of ideas,* пу́таница мы́слей.

welting *n.* обши́вка.

wench *n.* де́вка.

wend *v.t., in* **wend one's way,** направля́ть свой шаги́ *or* стопы́.

were *v., past tense of* **be.** —*subjunctive* будь: *were he alive today,* будь он сейча́с жив. —**as it were,** так сказа́ть.

werewolf *n.* о́боротень.

west *n.* за́пад. *The West,* За́пад. —*adj.* за́падный: *the West Coast,* за́падное побере́жье. —*adv.* на за́пад; к за́паду. *West of,* к за́паду от; за́паднее (+ *gen.*).

westerly *adj.* за́падный.

western *adj.* за́падный. —*n.* ковбо́йский фильм. —**westernmost,** *adj.* са́мый за́падный.

westward *adv.* к за́паду. —*adj.* за́падный.

wet *adj.* мо́крый: *wet hands//shoes,* мо́крые ру́ки/ту́фли. *Wet pavement,* мо́крый тротуа́р. *"Wet paint!",* осторо́жно! окра́шено! *Get wet,* промока́ть. *Get one's feet wet,* промочи́ть но́ги. —*v.t.* мочи́ть; сма́чивать. *Wet one's bed,* де́лать под себя́. —**he is still wet behind the ears,** у него́ молоко́ на губа́х не обсо́хло.

wet nurse кормилица.

whack *n., colloq.* тума́к. —*v.t., colloq.* тра́хнуть; тре́снуть. —**out of whack,** *slang* не в поря́дке.

whale *n.* кит. —*adj.* кито́вый: *whale oil,* кито́вый жир.

whalebone *n.* кито́вый ус.

whaler *n.* **1,** (person) китобо́й. **2,** (ship) китобо́й; китобо́ец; китобо́йное су́дно.

whaling *n.* китобо́йный про́мысел. —*adj.* китобо́йный. —**whaling ship,** китобо́йное су́дно; китобо́й; китобо́ец.

whammy *n., slang* дурно́й глаз. *Put the whammy on,* сгла́зить (кого́-нибудь).

wharf *n.* при́стань.

what *pron.* **1,** *interr.* что?: *what is this?,* что э́то тако́е? *What do you want?,* что вы хоти́те? *What else do you need?,* что ещё вам ну́жно? *What is that building?,* что э́то за зда́ние? ♦*Often rendered by* как *and* како́й: *what is your name?,* как вас зову́т? *What is this called?,* как э́то называ́ется? *What's the score?,* како́й счёт? *What is your phone number?,* како́й у вас но́мер телефо́на? *What's the difference between...?,* кака́я ра́зница ме́жду...? **2,** *rel.* то, что: *just what I need,* как раз то, что мне ну́жно. *What he says is true,* то, что он говори́т – пра́вда. *Say what you will,* что ни говори́те. *And what is worse,* а что ещё ху́же. *Come what may,* будь, что бу́дет. *Did you find what you were looking for?,* вы нашли́, что иска́ли? —*adj.* **1,** *interr.* како́й: *what clothes should I take?,* каку́ю оде́жду мне с собо́й взять? *What good will it do?,* кака́я от э́того по́льза? *What time is it?,* кото́рый тепе́рь час? **2,** *used in exclamations* како́й: *what nonsense!,* кака́я чепуха́! *What a surprise!,* како́й сюрпри́з! **3,** (as much; whatever) тот: *I forgot what little I knew,* я забы́л то немно́гое, что знал. *I gave him what money I had,* я дал ему́ все де́ньги, каки́е у меня́ бы́ли. —*adv.* **1,** *interr.: what does it matter?,* како́е э́то име́ет значе́ние? **2,** *used in exclamations* како́й: *what lovely weather!,* кака́я чу́дная пого́да! —**what about...?,** а что с...?; как насчёт...? —**what for?,** заче́м? —**what if...?,** а что е́сли...? —**what of it?,** ну, что?; ма́ло ли что! —**what's more,** *see* **more.** —**what's what,** что к чему́. —**what with,** из-за; ввиду́.

whatever *pron.* **1,** (no matter what) что ни; что бы ни: *whatever happens,* что бы ни случи́лось. *Whatever the outcome,* незави́симо от исхо́да. **2,** (anything) что уго́дно: *take whatever you like,* возьми́те что вам уго́дно. **3,** *expressing perplexity or wonderment* что же: *whatever can he want?,* что же он хо́чет? —*adj.* **1,** (no matter which) како́й бы ни: *whatever city you come to,* в како́й бы го́род вы ни прие́хали. **2,** (absolutely) абсолю́тно; реши́тельно. *No doubt whatever,* абсолю́тно никако́го сомне́ния. *I know nothing whatever about it,* я реши́тельно ничего́ не зна́ю об э́том.

whatsoever *adv.* абсолю́тно; реши́тельно. *No plans whatsoever,* абсолю́тно никаки́х пла́нов.

wheat *n.* пшени́ца. —*adj.* пшени́чный: *wheat flour,* пшени́чная мука́. *Wheat crop,* урожа́й пшени́цы.

wheedle *v.t.* **1,** (cajole; coax) обха́живать. **2,** (get by cajolery) выпра́шивать; выма́нивать; выкля́нчивать.

wheel *n.* **1,** (circular device) колесо́: *rear wheel,* за́днее колесо́. *Potter's wheel,* гонча́рный круг. *Spinning wheel,* пря́лка. **2,** (steering wheel) руль: *be at the wheel,* быть за рулём. **3,** *slang* (big shot) ши́шка; туз. —*v.t.* кати́ть: *wheel a baby carriage,* кати́ть де́тскую коля́ску. —*v.i.* [*usu.* **wheel around** *or* **about**] кру́то поверну́ться. —**break on the wheel,** колесова́ть.

wheelbarrow *n.* та́чка.

wheelbase *n.* колёсная ба́за.

wheelchair *n.* инвали́дное кре́сло.

wheeled *adj.* колёсный.

wheel horse коренни́к; коренна́я ло́шадь.

wheeze *v.i.* дыша́ть с при́свистом; сопе́ть. —*n.* свистя́щее дыха́ние.

whelp *n.* щено́к. —*v.i.* щени́ться.

when *adv. & conj.* когда́: *when will you be ready?,* когда́ вы бу́дете гото́вы? *When she comes I'll ask her,* когда́ она́ придёт, я её спрошу́. ♦*With the -ing form of the verb* при: *when crossing the border,* при перее́зде че́рез грани́цу. —*conj.* (considering that; since) е́сли: *why ask him when he's bound to say no?,* заче́м его́ проси́ть, е́сли он обяза́тельно отка́жет? —**since when?,** с каки́х пор?

whence *adv.* отку́да. *From whence he came,* отку́да он пришёл.

whenever *adv. & conj.* когда́ (бы) ни; вся́кий раз, когда́. *Whenever you like,* когда́ хоти́те; когда́ вам уго́дно.

where *adv. & conj.* **1,** (in what or that place) где: *where is he right now?,* где он сейча́с? *This is where I live,* вот где я живу́. *Stay where you are!,* остава́йтесь там, где вы сейча́с! *There have been cases where...,* быва́ли слу́чаи, когда́... **2,** (to what or that place) куда́: *where are you going?,* куда́ вы идёте? *Let's go where there are not so many people,* пойдём туда́, где не так мно́го наро́ду. **3,** (from what place) отку́да: *where are you from?,* отку́да вы? *Where shall we begin?,* с чего́ мы начнём?

whereabouts *n.* местонахожде́ние. —*adv.* где?; о́коло како́го ме́ста?

whereas *conj.* **1,** (in view of the fact that) поско́льку; ввиду́ того́, что. **2,** (while on the one hand) в то вре́мя как; е́сли. **3,** (while on the other hand) тогда́ как; в то вре́мя как; ме́жду тем как.

whereby *adv.* при кото́ром: *a new method whereby...,* но́вый ме́тод, при кото́ром...

wherefore *adv., archaic* почему́? —*conj., archaic* почему́.

wherein *adv.* (in what way) в чём? —*conj.* (in which) в кото́ром.

whereof *adv. & conj.* о кото́ром; о чём. *In witness whereof,* в удостовере́ние чего́.

whereupon *conj.* по́сле чего́.

wherever *adv. & conj.* где бы ни; куда́ бы ни; везде́, где. *Wherever possible,* везде́, где мо́жно. *Wherever you like,* где *or* куда́ хоти́те; где *or* куда́ вам уго́дно.

wherewithal *n.* необходи́мые сре́дства.

wherry *n.* я́лик.

whet *v.t.* **1,** (sharpen) точи́ть; отта́чивать. **2,** (stimulate, as the appetite) возбужда́ть; дразни́ть.

whether *conj.* ли: *tell me whether you like it,* скажи́те мне, нра́вится ли э́то вам. *Whether you want to or not,* хо́чешь ты и́ли нет; хо́чешь не хо́чешь.

whetstone *n.* точи́льный ка́мень; осело́к; бруса́к.

whew *interj.* фу!

whey *n.* сы́воротка.

which *pron. & adj.* **1,** *interr.* како́й?: *which newspapers do you read?,* каки́е газе́ты вы чита́ете? *Which way did he go?,* в каку́ю сто́рону он пошёл? *Which is your house?,* како́й дом ваш? *Which (one) of you?,* кто из вас? *Which one of these umbrellas is yours?,* кото́рый из э́тих зо́нтиков ваш? *Which is worse — drugs or alcohol?,* что ху́же – нарко́тики или алкого́ль? **2,** *rel.* кото́рый: *the book which you lent me,* кни́га, кото́рую вы мне одолжи́ли. *The play which you told me about,* пье́са, о кото́рой вы мне говори́ли. *The first case in which...,* пе́рвый слу́чай, когда́... ♦*When referring to a fact or circumstance* что: *I did not answer, which made him even angrier,* я не отве́тил, что рассерди́ло его́ ещё бо́льше. **3,** (just mentioned) *rendered by* чего́: *in which case,* в слу́чае чего́; *after which,* по́сле чего́.

whichever *pron. & adj.* како́й бы ни: *whichever country you go to,* в каку́ю бы страну́ вы ни пое́хали. *Take whichever one you want,* возьми́те како́й вам уго́дно.

whiff *n.* **1,** (puff; gust) дунове́ние. **2,** (slight odor) лёгкий за́пах: *a whiff of onions,* лёгкий за́пах лу́ка. **3,** (inhalation): *take a whiff of,* поню́хать (что́-нибудь).

while *conj.* **1,** (at the time that) пока́; когда́; в то вре́мя как. *While I was waiting for her,* пока́/когда́ я её ждал. *While in London,* бу́дучи в Ло́ндоне. *While on vacation,* во вре́мя о́тпуска. *While sitting by the fireplace,* си́дя у ками́на. **2,** (during all the time that; as long as) пока́: *while she is here,* пока́ она́ здесь. *Make hay while the sun shines,* куй желе́зо, пока́ горячо́. **3,** (whereas by contrast) тогда́ как. **4,** (whereas on the one hand) в то вре́мя как: *while most are in favor, some are opposed,* в то вре́мя как большинство́ за, не́которые выступа́ют про́тив. **5,** (although) хотя́: *while many disagree...,* хотя́ мно́гие несогла́сны... —*n.* не́которое вре́мя: *a while ago,* не́которое вре́мя наза́д. *For a while,* не́которое вре́-

мя. *A short while,* недолго. *In a little while,* скоро. *After a while,* через некоторое время. *All the while,* всё время. —*v.t.* [*usu.* **while away**] коротать (время). —**be worth one's while,** стоить труда. —**once in a while,** время от времени.

whilst *conj.* = **while.**

whim *n.* прихоть; причуда; каприз.

whimper *v.i.* **1,** (of a person, esp. a child) хныкать. **2,** (of a dog) скулить. —*n.* хныканье.

whimsical *adj.* причудливый; прихотливый.

whimsy *n.* прихоть; причуда.

whine *v.i.* хныкать; ныть. —*n.* хныканье. —**whiner,** *n.* нытик.

whinny *v.i.* ржать. —*n.* ржание.

whip *n.* кнут; хлыст. —*v.t.* **1,** (thrash; flog) хлестать; сечь; пороть; стегать. **2,** (beat, as eggs, cream, etc.) сбивать; взбивать. **3,** *fol. by* **out** (take out suddenly) выхватывать. —**whip up, 1,** (stir up; foment) раздувать. **2,** *colloq.* (cook in a hurry) состряпать.

whipped cream взбитые сливки.

whippet *n.* борзая.

whipping *n.* порка; трёпка. —**whipping boy,** козёл отпущения.

whippoorwill *n.* козодой.

whipsaw *n.* лучковая пила.

whir *also,* **whirr** *v.i.* жужжать. —*n.* жужжание.

whirl *v.i.* **1,** (spin) кружиться. **2,** *fol. by* **around** (turn quickly around) круто повернуться. —*v.t.* **1,** (spin) вертеть; кружить. **2,** (swirl, as dust) крутить. —*n.* **1,** (rapid gyration) кружение. *My head is in a whirl,* у меня кружится голова. **2,** *colloq.* (brief try): *give it a whirl,* попробовать.

whirligig *n.* юла.

whirlpool *n.* водоворот.

whirlwind *n.* вихрь; смерч.

whirr *v.* & *n.* = **whir.**

whisk *v.t.* **1,** (carry swiftly) мчать; нести; проносить. *Whisk away,* уносить. **2,** *fol. by* **off** (brush away) смахивать.

whisk broom метёлка.

whisker *n., usu. pl.* **1,** (on a man's face) бакенбарды. **2,** (of an animal) усы.

whiskey *also,* **whisky** *n.* виски.

whisper *v.t.* & *i.* шептать. —*n.* шёпот. *In a whisper,* шёпотом. —**whisperer,** *n.* шептун.

whist *n.* вист.

whistle *v.i.* свистеть. *Whistle for a taxi,* свистом подозвать такси. *The wind whistled through the trees,* ветер свистел в деревьях. *Bullets whistled past our ears,* пули просвистывали мимо наших ушей. —*v.t.* насвистывать: *whistle a tune,* насвистывать мотив. —*n.* **1,** (sound) свист. **2,** (device to be blown) свисток. **3,** (of a factory, train, etc.) гудок. —**wet one's whistle,** промочить горло.

whistler *n.* свистун.

whit *n.* йота: *not a whit,* ни на йоту.

white *adj.* белый. *White meat/wine,* белое мясо/вино. *White hair,* седые волосы. *The White House,* Белый дом. —*n.* **1,** (color) белый цвет. *All in white,* весь (вся) в белом. **2,** (of an egg; of the eye) белок. **3,** (Caucasian) белый. **4,** *chess* белые: *white resigned,* белые сдались. —**turn white, 1,** (become white) белеть. **2,** (turn pale) побледнеть; побелеть.

white bread белый хлеб.

whitecap *n., usu. pl.* барашки; беляки.

whitefish *n.* сиг.

white-haired *adj.* белоголовый.

white heat белое каление; белый накал.

white-hot *adj.* раскалённый добела.

white lead свинцовые белила.

white lie невинная ложь.

whiten *v.t.* белить.

whiteness *n.* белизна.

whitewash *v.t.* **1,** (whiten with whitewash) белить. **2,** *fig.* (gloss over) смазывать. —*n.* известковый раствор. —**whitewashing,** *n.* побелка.

white whale белуха.

whither *adv.* куда.

whiting *n.* белила.

whitish *adj.* белёсый; беловатый.

Whitmonday *n.* духов день.

Whitsunday *n.* троицын день; троица.

whittle *v.t.* **1,** (carve) строгать. **2,** *fol. by* **down** (reduce) урезывать.

whiz *also,* **whizz** *v.i.* **1,** (whir; hiss) свистеть. **2,** (rush past) промчаться. —*n., slang* (marvel) феномен.

who *pron.* **1,** *interr.* кто?: *who are you?,* кто вы? *Who is there?,* кто там? *Who knows?,* кто знает? *Do you know who he is?,* вы знаете, кто он? **2,** *rel.* который: *the man who was just here,* человек, который только сейчас был здесь. ♦*After* тот (та, те) *and* все — кто: *those who came late,* те, кто опоздал. *Everyone who was at the meeting,* все, кто был на собрании. *See also* **whom.**

whoa *interj.* тпру!

whoever *pron.* **1,** (no matter who) кто ни; кто бы ни: *whoever you are,* кто бы вы ни были. **2,** (whatever person) кто; тот, кто. *Whoever says that is mistaken,* кто говорит это, ошибается. **3,** *expressing perplexity or bewilderment* кто?: *whoever heard of such a thing?,* кто слыхал подобное? *See also* **whomever.**

whole *adj.* **1,** (entire; complete) целый: *a whole piece,* целый кусок; *a whole year,* целый год. *A whole series of,* целый ряд (+ *gen.*). *Swallow something whole,* проглотить что-нибудь целиком. **2,** *preceded by* **the** (all) весь: *the whole world,* весь мир. **3,** (with none of the elements removed) цельный: *whole milk,* цельное молоко; *whole blood,* цельная кровь. —*n.* целое: *into a single whole,* в единое целое. —**as a whole,** в целом. —**on the whole,** в общем; в общем и целом.

wholehearted *adj.* беззаветный. *Wholehearted support,* горячая поддержка.

wholeness *n.* цельность; целость.

whole note *music* целая нота.

whole number целое число; целое.

wholesale *adj.* **1,** *comm.* оптовый. **2,** *fig.* (blanket; sweeping) огульный. —*adv.* оптом. —**wholesaler,** *n.* оптовик.

wholesome *adj.* здоровый; полезный: *wholesome food,* здоровая/полезная пища. *Wholesome influence,* благотворное влияние.

wholly *adv.* целиком; полностью.

whom *pron., objective case of* **who,** кого; кому; кем; ком: *whom do you have in mind?,* кого вы имеете в виду? *To whom did you give the money?,* кому вы дали деньги? *With whom were you speaking?,* с кем вы говорили?

whomever *pron., objective case of* **whoever.** *Invite whomever you like,* пригласите кого вам угодно.

whoop *v.i.* выкрикивать; гикать. —*n.* выкрик; возглас.
whooping cough коклюш.
whooping crane американский журавль.
whopping *adj., colloq.* огромный. *A whopping 100 rubles,* целых сто рублей.
whore *n.* проститутка. —**whorehouse,** *n.* публичный дом.
whorl *n.* **1,** (curve) виток; завиток. **2,** *bot.* мутовка.
whortleberry *n.* черника.
whose *pron.* **1,** *interr.* чей?: *whose hat is this?,* чья эта шляпа? *Whose side are you on?,* вы на чьей стороне? **2,** *rel.* которого; которой: *the girl whose book I borrowed,* девушка, книгу которой я занял.
whosever *pron.* чей бы ни.
whosoever *pron.* кто бы ни.
why *adv.* почему: *why didn't you answer my letter?,* почему вы не ответили на моё письмо? *I don't understand why he objects,* не понимаю, почему он возражает. *The reason why he came,* причина, по которой он пришёл. *I see no reason why you can't go,* я не знаю, почему бы тебе не пойти. —*interj.* ведь: *why everyone knows that!,* ведь это известно всем! *Why it's Nina!,* да ведь это Нина! —**that's why,** вот почему; потому и. *That's why I asked,* потому я и спросил(а). —**which is why,** потому. —**why not?,** почему нет? *Why not ask him?,* почему бы не спросить его? —**why so?,** почему же?
wick *n.* фитиль.
wicked *adj.* **1,** (evil) злой; дурной. *Wicked man,* дурной человек. *Wicked deed,* злой *or* дурной поступок. *Wicked thoughts,* дурные мысли. **2,** (harmful; grievous) жестокий: *a wicked blow,* жестокий удар. —**wickedness,** *n.* зло.
wicker *n.* плетение. —*adj.* плетёный: *wicker basket,* плетёная корзина.
wickerwork *n.* плетение; плетёные изделия.
wicket *n.* **1,** (small door or gate) калитка. **2,** *croquet* ворота. **3,** *cricket* калитка.
wide *adj.* **1,** (broad; extensive) широкий: *wide street,* широкая улица; *wide assortment,* широкий ассортимент. **2,** (having a specified width) шириной в: *three feet wide,* шириной в три фута. **3,** (astray) мимо цели. *Be wide of the mark,* бить *or* попадать мимо цели; *fig.* попасть пальцем в небо. —*adv.* **1,** (to the full extent of opening) широко; настежь: *the windows were wide open,* окна были широко открыты; окна были настежь. **2,** (over a large area) широко. *Far and wide,* вдоль и поперёк. **3,** (astray) в сторону; мимо цели.
wide-angle *adj.* широкоугольный.
wide-eyed *adj.* с широко раскрытыми глазами. *Stare wide-eyed at,* смотреть на (+ *acc.*) большими глазами.
widely *adv.* широко. *Widely scattered,* широко разбросанный. *Vary widely,* широко расходиться. *Travel widely,* много путешествовать.
widen *v.t.* расширять. —*v.i.* расширяться.
widespread *adj.* распространённый.
widgeon *n.* свиязь.
widow *n.* вдова. —**widowed,** *adj.* вдовый; овдовевший. *Be/become widowed,* овдоветь.
widower *n.* вдовец.
widowhood *n.* вдовство.
width *n.* **1,** (breadth) ширина. **2,** (piece of material of a certain width) полотнище.
wield *v.t.* **1,** (brandish) махать; размахивать. **2,** (handle) работать; орудовать (*both with instr.*). **3,** (exercise, as power, influence, etc.) обладать; пользоваться.
wife *n.* жена. *Take (someone) for a wife,* взять кого-нибудь) в жёны.
wig *n.* парик.
wiggle *v.t.* шевелить: *wiggle one's toes,* шевелить пальцами ног. —*v.i.* ёрзать.
wigwam *n.* вигвам.
wild *adj.* **1,** (uncivilized; uncultivated; undomesticated) дикий: *wild duck/rose/region,* дикая утка/роза/местность. **2,** (boisterous; unruly) дикий; буйный. **3,** (fantastically impractical) дикий; сумасбродный; бредовой. **4,** (random; erratic) наугад: *make a wild guess,* сказать наугад; *fire a wild shot,* стрелять наугад. **5,** *colloq., fol. by* **about** (mad about) без ума (от). —*adv.* дико: *grow wild,* расти дико. —*n., often pl.* глушь; дебри. *Call of the wild,* зов природы. —**run wild,** буйствовать; буянить.
wild boar кабан.
wildcat *n.* дикая кошка.
wilderness *n.* пустыня; глушь. —**voice in the wilderness,** глас вопиющего в пустыне.
wildfire *n., in* **spread like wildfire,** распространяться с молниеносной быстротой *or* со скоростью лесного пожара.
wildflower *n.* дикорастущее растение; *pl.* полевые цветы.
wildlife *n.* дикие животные.
wildly *adv.* дико.
wile *n., usu. pl.* хитрости; уловки.
wilful *adj.* = **willful.**
will *n.* **1,** (in most meanings) воля: *the will of the people,* воля народа. *God's will,* божья *or* божия воля. *Good will,* добрая воля. *Ill will,* недоброжелательство. *The will to win/live,* воля к победе/жизни. *At will,* по желанию. *Of one's own free will,* по доброй воле. *Against one's will,* не по своей воле; против воли; поневоле. *Where there's a will there's a way,* при желании можно всего добиться. **2,** (testament) завещание. —*v.t.* **1,** (wish) хотеть: *do what you will,* делай, что хочешь. **2,** (decree; ordain) судить: *fate willed otherwise,* судьба сулила иначе. *God has willed that...,* божья воля (*or* богу угодно), что... **3,** (bequeath) завещать. —*v. aux.* **1,** *used to form the future tense: you will be sorry,* вы будете сожалеть об этом. *The window won't open,* окно не открывается. *Accidents will happen,* всегда бывают несчастные случаи. **2,** *in requests: will you have a cup of tea?,* можно вам предложить чашку чаю? *Won't you sit down?,* садитесь, пожалуйста! *Will you please be quiet!,* да замолчите же! **3,** *expressing probability: that will be Vera,* это, наверно, Вера. —**if you will,** если хотите.
willful *also,* **wilful** *adj.* **1,** (deliberate) преднамеренный; умышленный. **2,** (headstrong) своевольный; своевольный.
willing *adj.* **1,** (ready; disposed) готовый: *I'm willing to help,* я готов(а) помочь. **2,** (acting or performing gladly) услужливый; старательный. **3,** (readily given) добровольный. —**willingly,** *adv.* охотно. —**willingness,** *n.* готовность.
will-o'-the-wisp *n.* блуждающий огонёк.
willow *n.* ива. —*adj.* ивовый.
willowy *adj.* стройный.

will power сила воли.
willy-nilly *adv.* волей-неволей.
wilt *v.i.* **1,** (wither) вянуть; чахнуть. **2,** (lose strength or vigor) изнемогать: *wilt from the heat,* изнемогать от жары. —*v.t.* губить: *the heat wilted the flowers,* жара погубила цветы.
wily *adj.* хитрый; лукавый.
win *v.i.* выигрывать; побеждать: *who won?,* кто выиграл/победил? —*v.t.* **1,** (gain victory in) выигрывать: *win a game/bet/war,* выиграть игру/пари/войну. **2,** (gain in competition) завоёвывать: *win first place/a gold medal/,* завоевать первое место/золотую медаль/. *Win a prize,* взять *or* получить приз. **3,** (gain; earn) завоёвывать: *win one's freedom,* завоевать свободу. *Win recognition,* завоевать *or* снискать признание. *Win applause,* срывать аплодисменты. *Win someone's heart,* покорить чьё-нибудь сердце. —*n.* победа: *six wins and two losses,* шесть побед и два поражения. —**win back,** отыгрывать. —**win over, 1,** (charm) располагать к себе; привязывать к себе. **2,** (prevail upon) склонять в свою пользу. *Win over to one's side,* склонять *or* привлекать на свою сторону.
wince *v.i.* вздрагивать; морщиться (от боли).
winch *n.* лебёдка; ворот.
wind[1] (wind) *n.* **1,** (air in motion) ветер. **2,** (breath) дыхание: *second wind,* второе дыхание. *Get one's wind,* отдышаться. —**get wind of,** пронюхивать. —**see which way the wind blows,** узнать куда ветер дует. —**something is in the wind,** что-то затевается. *See also* **winded.**
wind[2] (waind) *v.t.* **1,** (turn) вертеть: *wind a crank,* вертеть рукоятку. **2,** (set going) заводить: *wind a watch/toy,* заводить часы/игрушку. **3,** (coil onto or around something) мотать. *Wind thread onto a spool,* намотать нитки на катушку. *Wind a scarf around one's head,* обмотать/обернуть/обвить шарф вокруг головы. —*v.i.* **1,** (move in a curving or twisting path) виться; извиваться. *The road winds through the mountains,* дорога вьётся по горам. **2,** *fol. by* **around** (twine around) обвиваться; обматываться (вокруг). —*n.* оборот; поворот. —**wind up, 1,** (wind onto a spool) сматывать. **2,** (tighten the spring of) заводить. **3,** (finish; conclude) заканчивать. **4,** (end up; find oneself) очутиться. **5,** *usu. passive* (make tense) взвинчивать. *All wound up,* взвинченный.
windbag *n., slang* пустозвон; пустослов; пустомеля; краснобай.
winded *adj.* запыхавшийся.
windfall *n.* золотой дождь; непредвиденный доход. *Windfall profits,* непредвиденная прибыль; сверхприбыль.
winding *adj.* **1,** (serving to wind) заводной; мотальный: *winding mechanism,* заводной/мотальный механизм. **2,** (twisting, as of a road) извилистый. *Winding staircase,* витая лестница.
wind instrument духовой инструмент.
windlass *n.* лебёдка; ворот; *naut.* брашпиль.
windless *adj.* безветренный.
windmill *n.* ветряная мельница. —**tilt at windmills,** сражаться с ветряными мельницами.
window *n.* **1,** (opening to let in light) окно. **2,** (display window of a store) витрина. —*adj.* оконный: *window curtain,* оконная занавеска.
window dressing мишура; декорации; показуха.
windowpane *n.* оконное стекло.
window shade штора.
window-shop *v.i.* рассматривать витрины.
window sill подоконник.
windpipe *n.* дыхательное горло.
windshield *n.* переднее стекло; ветровое стекло. —**windshield wiper,** стеклоочиститель; дворник.
windstorm *n.* буря.
wind tunnel аэродинамическая труба.
windward *adj.* наветренный.
windy *adj.* ветреный. *It is windy,* ветрено.
wine *n.* вино. —*adj.* винный: *wine bottle,* винная бутылка. —**wine cellar,** винный погреб.
wineglass *n.* бокал.
winegrower *n.* винодел. —**winegrowing,** *n.* виноделие.
wine list карта (*or* карточка) вин.
wine press давильный пресс.
wineskin *n.* бурдюк; мех для вина.
wing *n.* **1,** (of a bird; of a plane) крыло. **2,** (of fowl, when eaten) крылышко. **3,** (extension of a building) флигель; крыло. **4,** (side of a stage) кулиса: *in the wings,* за кулисами. **5,** (political faction) крыло. **6,** *Brit.* (fender) крыло. —*v.t.* **1,** (shoot; wound) подстреливать. **2,** *in* **wing one's way,** пролетать. —**on the wing,** на лету. —**take under one's wing,** брать под своё крылышко *or* покровительство; брать под защиту. —**take wing,** вспорхнуть.
winged *adj.* крылатый.
wingless *adj.* бескрылый.
wingspan *n.* размах крыльев. *Also,* **wingspread.**
wink *v.i.* мигать; моргать. —*n.* мигание. *Not sleep a wink,* совсем не спать; не смыкать глаз. —**wink at, 1,** (signal with a wink) мигать (+ *dat.*); моргать (+ *dat.*); подмигивать (+ *dat.*). **2,** (pretend not to notice) смотреть сквозь пальцы на.
winner *n.* победитель.
winning *adj.* **1,** (victorious) победивший. *Winning streak,* победное шествие. **2,** (leading to victory) выигрышный: *winning ticket/move,* выигрышный билет/ход. **3,** (captivating) подкупающий; обезоруживающий. —*n.* **1,** (victory) победа. **2,** *pl.* (money won) выигрыш.
winnow *v.t.* **1,** (blow the chaff from) веять. **2,** *fol. by* **out** (sift or separate out) отсеивать.
winnowing *n.* веяние. *Winnowing machine,* веялка.
winsome *adj.* привлекательный; располагающий.
winter *n.* зима. *In winter,* зимой. —*adj.* зимний: *winter clothes,* зимняя одежда. *Winter crops,* озимые культуры. —*v.i.* зимовать.
winterize *v.t.* утеплять; отеплять.
wintertime *n.* зима; зимнее время.
wintry *adj.* зимний.
wipe *v.t.* вытирать: *wipe the sweat from one's brow,* вытирать пот со лба; *wipe one's feet on the mat,* вытирать ноги о половик. *Wipe one's eyes,* осушать слёзы. *Wipe one's nose,* утереть (себе) нос. *Wipe from the face of the earth,* стирать с лица земли. —**wipe away,** вытирать; утирать: *wipe away the tears,* вытирать/утирать слёзы. —**wipe off,** стирать. —**wipe out,** уничтожать. —**wipe up,** подтирать.
wire *n.* **1,** (metal strand) проволока: *barbed wire,* колючая проволока. **2,** (electric, telegraph, etc.) провод. **3,** (telegram) телеграмма. —*adj.* проволочный:

wire netting, про́волочная сеть. —*v.t.* **1,** (fasten with wire) скрепля́ть про́волокой. **2,** (install wiring in) прокла́дывать провода́ в. **3,** (send a telegram to) телеграфи́ровать.

wire cutter куса́чки.

wireless *n., Brit.* = **radio.** —*adj.* беспро́волочный.

wire service телегра́фное аге́нство.

wiretap *v.t.* перехва́тывать. —**wiretapping,** *n.* перехва́т телефо́нных сообще́ний.

wiring *n.* прово́дка.

wiry *adj.* жи́листый.

wisdom *n.* му́дрость. —**wisdom tooth,** зуб му́дрости.

wise *adj.* **1,** (sagacious) му́дрый. **2,** (prudent) у́мный; благоразу́мный. **3,** *fol. by* **to** (aware of) в ку́рсе: *wise to what is going on,* в ку́рсе де́ла. **4,** *slang* (impudent; fresh) наха́льный. —**put wise,** *slang* вводи́ть в курс де́ла. —**wise up,** *slang* образу́миться.

wisecrack *n.* остро́та.

wisely *adv.* благоразу́мно.

wish *v.t.* **1,** (want; desire) хоте́ть; жела́ть: *I do not wish to see him,* не хочу́/жела́ю его́ ви́деть. *I wish I could stay longer,* я хоте́л бы до́льше оста́ться. *I wish you would stop bothering me!,* нельзя́ ли не беспоко́ить меня́? **2,** (bid) жела́ть: *I wish you luck,* жела́ю вам сча́стья. **3,** *fol. by* **on** (impose) навя́зывать: *who wished this job on us?,* кто навяза́л нам э́ту рабо́ту? —*n.* **1,** (desire) жела́ние; охо́та. *Act against someone's wishes,* поступи́ть вопреки́ чьи́м-нибудь жела́ниям. *She got her wish,* она́ добила́сь чего́ хоте́ла. **2,** *pl.* (expressed desire for someone's well-being) пожела́ние: *best wishes,* наилу́чшие пожела́ния.

wishful *adj. A wishful expression on one's face,* выраже́ние жела́ния на лице́. *Indulge in wishful thinking,* принима́ть жела́емое за действи́тельное.

wishy-washy *adj.* бесхара́ктерный; слабово́льный.

wisp *n.* **1,** (of hay, straw, etc.) пучо́к; клок. **2,** (of smoke, vapor, etc.) стру́йка.

wisteria *n.* глици́ния.

wistful *adj.* **1,** (melancholy) тосkли́вый. **2,** (pensive) заду́мчивый.

wit *n.* **1,** (wittiness) остроу́мие. *Man of great wit,* остроу́мный челове́к. **2,** (witty person) остря́к. **3,** *pl.* (innate intelligence) ум; мозги́. *Battle of wits,* игра́ ума́. *Use one's wits,* шевели́ть мозга́ми. *Live by one's wits,* жить хи́тростью. **4,** *pl.* (sanity) рассу́док: *lose one's wits,* теря́ть рассу́док. —**be at one's wits' end,** дойти́ до то́чки. *I am at my wits' end,* у меня́ ум за ра́зум захо́дит. —**frighten out of one's wits,** напуга́ть до́ смерти. —**keep one's wits about one,** не теря́ть головы́. —**to wit,** а и́менно.

witch *n.* ве́дьма.

witchcraft *n.* колдовство́.

witch doctor зна́харь.

witch hunt охо́та за ве́дьмами.

with *prep.* **1,** (in most meanings) с (+ *instr.): come with me,* иди́те со мно́й; *a house with a fireplace,* дом сками́ном; *read with difficulty,* чита́ть с трудо́м; *I agree with you,* я согла́сен с ва́ми. *Play/argue/cope/part with,* игра́ть/спо́рить/справля́ться/расстава́ться с. **2,** (by means of; using) *rendered by the instr. case: write with a pencil,* писа́ть карандашо́м; *work with one's hands,* рабо́тать рука́ми; *cut the meat with a knife,* ре́зать мя́со ножо́м. **3,** (at the home of) у: *stay with friends,* жить *or* гости́ть у друзе́й. **4,** (in the possession or care of) у: *leave the keys with the watchman,* оставля́ть ключи́ у сто́рожа. **5,** (in regard to): *satisfied with something,* дово́лен че́м-нибудь; *angry with someone,* серди́т на кого́-нибудь. **6,** (involving a material or substance) *rendered by the instr. case: covered with dust,* покры́т пы́лью; *be filled with smoke,* напо́лниться ды́мом. *Line a coat with silk,* подбива́ть пальто́ шёлком. **7,** (from) от: *tremble with fear,* дрожа́ть от хо́лода; *be green with envy,* ло́паться от за́висти. **8,** (beginning with) с (+ *gen.*): *let's start with you,* начнём с вас. *In German all nouns are written with a capital letter,* в неме́цком языке́ все существи́тельные пи́шутся с большо́й бу́квы. **9,** (having received) с (+ *gen.*): *with your permission,* с ва́шего разреше́ния.

withdraw *v.t.* **1,** (draw back; remove) отнима́ть; отдёргивать. **2,** (remove; evacuate, as troops) выводи́ть. **3,** (retract) снима́ть: *withdraw one's offer/motion,* снима́ть своё предложе́ние. **4,** (retire) изыма́ть: *withdraw from circulation,* изыма́ть из обраще́ния. **5,** (take out, as money from a bank) снима́ть со счёта. —*v.i.* **1,** (leave; retire) удаля́ться. **2,** (drop out) выходи́ть; выбыва́ть. **3,** *mil.* (retreat) отходи́ть; отступа́ть. **4,** *in* **withdraw into oneself,** уходи́ть в себя́; замыка́ться в себе́.

withdrawal *n.* **1,** (retreat) отхо́д. **2,** (dropping out) вы́ход. **3,** (removal, as of troops) вы́вод. **4,** (removal, as from circulation) изъя́тие. **5,** (retraction of a motion) сня́тие. **6,** (removal, as of funds) сня́тие со счёта. *Make a withdrawal,* снима́ть де́ньги со счёта. **7,** *med.* воздержа́ние от нарко́тиков.

withdrawn *adj.* (retiring; reticent) сде́ржанный; за́мкнутый.

wither *v.i.* **1,** (shrivel) вя́нуть; увяда́ть; со́хнуть; блёкнуть. **2,** *fol. by* **away** (gradually cease to exist) отмира́ть: *"The state will wither away",* госуда́рство отмира́ет. —*v.t.* иссуша́ть. —**withered,** *adj.* вя́лый; увя́дший; вы́сохший; блёклый. —**withering,** *adj.* уничтожа́ющий: *withering glance/crossfire,* уничтожа́ющий взгляд/перекрёстный ого́нь/.

withers *n. pl.* хо́лка; загри́вок.

withhold *v.t.* **1,** (hold back, as money) уде́рживать; заде́рживать. *Withhold payment,* заде́рживать вы́плату. **2,** (refrain from giving) возде́рживаться от: *withhold comment,* возде́рживаться от коммента́риев. **3,** (refuse to grant) не дава́ть: *withhold permission,* не дава́ть разреше́ния. **4,** (not divulge) ута́ивать: *withhold information,* ута́ивать све́дения.

within *prep.* **1,** (inside) в; внутри́. **2,** (not beyond) в; в преде́лах (+ *gen.*). *Within a radius of,* в ра́диусе (+ *gen.*); *within the framework of,* в ра́мках (+ *gen.*). *Within ten paces of,* в десяти́ шага́х от. *Within the city limits,* в преде́лах го́рода. *Within reach/earshot,* в преде́лах досяга́емости/слы́шимости. ♦*Also rendered by various other combinations: within my recollection,* на мое́й па́мяти. *Live within one's means,* жить по свои́м сре́дствам. *Is it within walking distance?,* туда́ мо́жно дойти́ пешко́м? *Guess someone's age within a year,* угада́ть че́й-нибудь во́зраст с то́чностью до го́да. **3,** (not later than) в; в тече́ние (+ *gen.*): *within a year,* в тече́ние го́да; *within 24 hours,* в два́дцать четы́ре часа́. —*adv.* внутри́. *From within,* изнутри́.

without *prep.* **1,** (lacking; free from) без: *without* *exception,* без исключе́ния. **2,** (failing to) без того́, что́бы (+ *inf.*); не (+ *verbal adverb*). *Without saying a word,* не говоря́ (*or* сказа́в) ни сло́ва. *Without saying goodbye to anyone,* ни с кем не простя́сь. **3,** (outside of) вне. —*adv.* снару́жи. *From without,* извне́. —**do (*or* go) without,** обходи́ться без.

withstand *v.t.* выде́рживать; устоя́ть про́тив; противостоя́ть. *Withstand the test of time,* выде́рживать прове́рку вре́менем.

witless *adj.* безмо́зглый.

witness *n.* свиде́тель. *Eyewitness,* очеви́дец. —*v.t.* **1,** (be present at; see) быть свиде́телем/очеви́дцем (+ *gen.*). **2,** (certify, as a signature) заверя́ть; удостоверя́ть. —**bear witness to,** свиде́тельствовать о. —**in witness whereof,** в удостовере́ние чего́.

witticism *n.* остро́та.

wittiness *n.* остроу́мие.

wittingly *adv.* созна́тельно; заве́домо.

witty *adj.* остроу́мный.

wizard *n.* **1,** (sorcerer) колду́н; чароде́й. **2,** *colloq.* (whiz) ге́ний.

wizardry *n.* колдовство́.

wizened *adj.* вы́сохший: *wizened old man,* вы́сохший стари́к.

wobble *v.i.* шата́ться; поша́тываться. —*n.* шата́ние. —**wobbly,** *adj.* ша́ткий.

woe *n.* го́ре. *Tale of woe,* печа́льный расска́з. *Woe (be it) to him who...,* го́ре тому́, кто... —**woe is me!,** го́ре мне!, бе́дная моя́ голо́вушка!

woebegone *adj.* удручённый; го́рестный.

woeful *adj.* **1,** (sad) го́рестный. **2,** (wretched) жа́лкий. —**knight of the woeful countenance,** ры́царь печа́льного о́браза.

wolf *n.* волк. —*adj.* [*also,* **wolf's**] во́лчий. —**wolf in sheep's clothing,** волк в ове́чьей шку́ре.

wolfhound *n.* (Irish) волкода́в; (Russian) борза́я.

wolverine *n.* росома́ха.

woman *n.* же́нщина. *Old woman,* стару́ха. —*adj.* **1,** (being a woman) же́нщина-: *woman doctor,* же́нщина-врач. **2,** [*usu.* **woman's** *or* **women's**] (of women) же́нский: *women's rights,* же́нские права́.

woman-hater *n.* женоненави́стник.

womanhood *n.* **1,** (maturity) зре́лость. **2,** (women collectively) же́нщины.

womanizer *n., colloq.* ба́бник; женолю́б.

womankind *n.* же́нщины; же́нский пол.

womanly *adj.* же́нственный.

womb *n.* ма́тка.

wonder *v.t.* хоте́ть знать. *I wonder what he wants/where she went/,* интере́сно, что он хо́чет/куда́ она́ пошла́/. *I wonder what's wrong with my watch,* не понима́ю, что с мои́ми часа́ми. —*v.i.* **1,** *fol. by* **at** (marvel) удивля́ться (+ *dat.*). **2,** (have doubts) сомнева́ться: *I wonder,* я в э́том сомнева́юсь; я не уве́рен(а). *I wonder about his sincerity,* я сомнева́юсь в его́ и́скренности. *I wonder if she'll ever get married,* задаю́ себе́ вопро́с, вы́йдет ли она́ за́муж? —*n.* **1,** (awe) удивле́ние; изумле́ние: *watch in/with wonder,* смотре́ть с удивле́нием/изумле́нием. **2,** (a marvel; miracle) чу́до: *work wonders,* твори́ть чудеса́. *It's a wonder that...,* удиви́тельно, что... —**no wonder,** не удиви́тельно; не ди́во; не мудрено́: *no wonder he's angry!,* не удиви́тельно/ди́во/мудрено́, что он рассерди́лся. *And no wonder!,* и не удиви́тельно!; и немудрено́!

wonderful *adj.* чуде́сный; чу́дный; замеча́тельный. —**wonderfully,** *adv.* чуде́сно; чу́дно; замеча́тельно.

wonderland *n.* страна́ чуде́с.

wonderment *n.* удивле́ние; изумле́ние.

wonder-working *adj.* чудоде́йственный; чудотво́рный.

wondrous *adj.* чу́дный; ди́вный.

wont *adj., used predicatively: be wont to,* име́ть привы́чку (+ *inf.*). —*n.* привы́чка; обыкнове́ние: *as was his wont,* по свое́й привы́чке; по своему́ обыкнове́нию.

woo *v.t.* уха́живать за.

wood *n.* **1,** (material) де́рево; древеси́на. **2,** (firewood) дрова́: *chop wood,* руби́ть/коло́ть дрова́. **3,** *usu. pl.* (forest) лес: *in the woods,* в лесу́. —*adj.* деревя́нный. —**out of the woods,** вне опа́сности.

wood alcohol древе́сный спирт.

wood block лубо́к.

woodchuck *n.* суро́к.

woodcock *n.* ва́льдшнеп.

woodcut *n.* гравю́ра на де́реве; лубо́к.

woodcutter *n.* лесору́б; дровосе́к.

wooded *adj.* леси́стый.

wooden *adj.* деревя́нный. *Wooden leg,* деревя́шка.

woodland *n.* леси́стая ме́стность.

wood louse мокри́ца.

woodman *n.* = **woodsman.**

woodpecker *n.* дя́тел.

wood pulp древе́сная ма́сса.

woods *see* **wood.**

woodshed *n.* дровяно́й сара́й.

woodsman *n.* лесору́б; лесни́к.

wood sorrel кисли́ца.

wood tar древе́сный дёготь.

woodwinds *n.pl.* деревя́нные духовы́е инструме́нты.

woodwork *n.* деревя́нные ча́сти (до́ма). —**woodworker,** *n.* деревообде́лочник. —**woodworking,** *adj.* деревообде́лочный.

woody *adj.* древе́сный; деревяни́стый.

woof *n., textiles* уто́к.

wool *n.* шерсть. —*adj.* шерстяно́й. —**pull the wool over someone's eyes,** втира́ть очки́ (+ *dat.*).

woolen *also,* **woollen** *adj.* шерстяно́й. —**woolens,** *n. pl.* шерстяны́е ве́щи.

woolly *adj.* шерсти́стый.

woozy *adj., slang* одуре́лый.

word *n.* **1,** (unit of speech) сло́во: *a rare word,* ре́дкое сло́во. *Harsh words,* ре́зкие слова́. *Just say the word!,* скажи́те то́лько сло́во! *Set words to music,* класть слова́ на му́зыку. **2,** (promise) сло́во: *give one's word,* дава́ть (че́стное) сло́во; *keep one's word,* сдержа́ть (своё) сло́во. **3,** (news; information) весть; изве́стие. *There hasn't been a word from him,* о нём (*or* от него́) ни слу́ху ни ду́ху. —*v.t.* выража́ть слова́ми; формули́ровать. —**by word of mouth,** у́стно; из уст в уста́. —**have a word with,** поговори́ть с. *May I have a word with you?,* мо́жно вас на полсло́ва? —**have words with,** име́ть кру́пный разгово́р с. —**in a word,** одни́м сло́вом. —**in other words,** други́ми слова́ми; ина́че говоря́. —**in so many words,** недвусмы́сленно. *I told her in so many words that...,* я так и сказа́л(а) ей, что... —**leave word,** оставля́ть запи́ску. —**man of his word,** челове́к сло́ва; хозя́ин своего́ сло́ва. —**of few words,**

немногосло́вный. —**take at one's word,** лови́ть на сло́ве. —**take one's word for it,** ве́рить (+ *dat.*) на́ слово. —**word for word,** сло́во в сло́во; досло́вно. —**word of honor,** че́стное сло́во.

wording *n.* формулиро́вка; реда́кция.

wordy *adj.* многосло́вный.

work *n.* **1,** (labor) рабо́та: *hard work,* тяжёлая рабо́та. **2,** (employment) рабо́та; слу́жба. *Out of work,* без рабо́ты; безрабо́тный. *What sort of work do you do?,* кем вы рабо́таете? **3,** (something done or produced) рабо́та: *stucco work,* лепна́я рабо́та. *Public works,* обще́ственные рабо́ты. *That's his work,* э́то его́ рабо́та; э́то его́ рук де́ло. *The blast was the work of terrorists,* взрыв – де́ло рук террори́стов. **4,** (literary or artistic creation) произведе́ние; сочине́ние; вещь. *Work of art,* произведе́ние иску́сства. *The complete works of Chekhov,* по́лное собра́ние сочине́ний Че́хова. *Two works by Glinka,* две ве́щи Гли́нки. **5,** *pl.* (factory) заво́д: *glassworks,* стеко́льный заво́д. **6,** *pl., mil.* сооруже́ния: *defensive works,* оборони́тельные сооруже́ния. **7,** [*usu.* **the works**] *slang* (everything) всё: *shoot the works,* идти́ на всё; идти́ ва-ба́нк. —*v.i.* **1,** (do work) рабо́тать: *work as a draftsman,* рабо́тать чертёжником. **2,** (function) рабо́тать: *the radio doesn't work,* радиоприёмник не рабо́тает. **3,** (prove effective, as of medicine) де́йствовать; возыме́ть де́йствие. **4,** (accomplish its purpose) удава́ться: *his idea didn't work,* его́ за́мысел не уда́лся. —*v.t.* **1,** (perform; accomplish) твори́ть: *work miracles,* твори́ть чудеса́. **2,** (operate) обраща́ться с: *know how to work a lathe,* уме́ть обраща́ться с тока́рным станко́м. **3,** (till, as the soil; treat, as metal) обраба́тывать. *Work a mine,* разраба́тывать рудни́к. **4,** (make work, as subordinates) заставля́ть рабо́тать. **5,** *in* **work one's way,** прокла́дывать себе́ доро́гу. *Work one's way out of debt,* вы́биться из долго́в. —**do its work,** сде́лать своё де́ло. —**go to work, 1,** (leave for work) идти́ на рабо́ту. **2,** (set to work) бра́ться за рабо́ту. —**work loose,** выпу́тываться; вывёртываться. —**work off, 1,** (pay off by working) отраба́тывать. **2,** (shed, as excess weight) сгоня́ть. —**work on, 1,** (do work on) рабо́тать над. **2,** (try to persuade) угова́ривать; склоня́ть. —**work out, 1,** (develop, as a plan) разраба́тывать; выраба́тывать. **2,** (solve) разга́дывать. **3,** (turn out) оберну́ться. **4,** (end successfully) устро́иться; обойти́сь. **5,** *sports* тренирова́ться; размина́ться. —**work up, 1,** (develop) разраба́тывать. **2,** (arouse) возбужда́ть. *Work up an appetite,* нагуля́ть себе́ аппети́т.

workable *adj.* выполни́мый; осуществи́мый.

workaday *adj.* бу́дничный; повседне́вный.

workbench *n.* верста́к.

workbook *n.* тетра́дь.

workday *n.* **1,** (day on which one works) бу́дний день. **2,** (time normally worked in one day) рабо́чий день.

worker *n.* **1,** (one who works) рабо́тник: *conscientious worker,* добросо́вестный рабо́тник. **2,** (member of the working class) рабо́чий; трудя́щийся.

workhouse *n.* **1,** (prison) исправи́тельный дом. **2,** *Brit.* (poorhouse) рабо́тный дом.

working *adj.* рабо́чий: *working class,* рабо́чий класс; *working clothes,* рабо́чая оде́жда. *Working conditions,* усло́вия труда́. *Working mothers,* рабо́тающие ма́тери. *In working order,* испра́вный; в испра́вности. *Working capital,* оборо́тный капита́л.

workingman *n.* рабо́чий.

workload *n.* нагру́зка.

workman *n.* рабо́тник.

workmanlike *adj.* иску́сный.

workmanship *n.* рабо́та; мастерство́; вы́делка; вы́работка. *Of marvelous workmanship,* великоле́пной рабо́ты.

workout *n.* трениро́вка.

workroom *n.* рабо́чая ко́мната.

workshop *n.* мастерска́я.

workweek *n.* рабо́чая неде́ля.

world *n.* мир; свет. *The ancient world,* дре́вний мир. *The Old/New World,* Ста́рый/Но́вый свет. *The next world,* тот свет. —*adj.* мирово́й: *a world record,* мирово́й реко́рд. —**be dead to the world,** спать мёртвым сном. —**bring/come into the world,** произвести́/появи́ться на свет. —**do someone a world of good,** о́чень идти́ на по́льзу (+ *dat.*). —**for all the world,** точь-в-точь. —**in the world, 1,** *literally* в ми́ре; на све́те. **2,** *used for emphasis: where in the world have you been?,* Куда́ же э́то вы пропа́ли? *Where in the world did you find it?,* где то́лько вы э́то нашли́? —**not for all the world,** ни за что на све́те. —**not long for this world,** не жиле́ц на э́том све́те. —**on top of the world,** на седьмо́м не́бе; на верху́ блаже́нства. —**out of this world,** из ря́да вон выходя́щий. —**think the world of,** быть о́чень высо́кого мне́ния о.

worldly *adj.* **1,** (earthly; mundane) мирско́й; жите́йский. **2,** (worldly-wise) быва́лый.

worldly-wise *adj.* вида́вший ви́ды; быва́лый.

world's fair всеми́рная вы́ставка.

world war мирова́я война́. *World War II,* втора́я мирова́я война́.

worldwide *adj.* мирово́й; всеми́рный.

worm *n.* червь; червя́к. *Intestinal worm,* глист. —*v.t.* **1,** *often fol. by* **out** (elicit, as a secret) вы́ведывать. **2,** *in* **worm one's way into,** вкра́дываться в; втира́ться в. —*v.i.* [*usu.* **worm out of**] вывёртываться (из); выпу́тываться (из).

worm-eaten *adj.* черви́вый.

worm gear червя́чная шестерня́.

wormhole *n.* червото́чина.

worm wheel червя́чное колесо́.

wormwood *n.* полы́нь.

wormy *adj.* черви́вый.

worn *adj.* **1,** (showing the effects of wear) поно́шенный. **2,** (haggard) изму́ченный; заму́ченный.

worn-out *also,* **worn out** *adj.* **1,** (no longer fit for wear) изно́шенный. **2,** (exhausted) изнурённый. *I am worn out,* я смерте́льно уста́л; я соверше́нно изму́чился.

worried *adj.* **1,** (experiencing worry) обеспоко́енный: *I am very worried,* я о́чень обеспоко́ен(а). **2,** (showing worry) беспоко́йный: *a worried look,* беспоко́йный вид.

worrisome *adj.* беспоко́йный.

worry *v.t.* беспоко́ить. —*v.i.* беспоко́иться. —*n.* **1,** (anxiety) беспоко́йство. **2,** (cause of anxiety) забо́та. *That's the least of my worries,* э́то меня́ ме́ньше всего́ беспоко́ит. *See also* **worried.**

worse *adj.* **1,** *modifier* ху́дший: *in worse shape,* в ху́дшем состоя́нии. **2,** *predicate* ху́же: *worse than I expected,* ху́же чем я ожида́л. *It could have been worse,* могло́ бы быть и ху́же. *Make worse,* ухудша́ть. *Get/grow worse,* стать ху́же; ухудша́ться. —*adv.* ху́же. —*n.* ху́дшее: *change for the worse,* переме́на к ху́дшему. *Take a turn for the worse,* принима́ть дурно́й оборо́т. —**be none the worse for,** ничу́ть не страда́ть от. —**for better or worse,** что бы ни случи́лось. —**go from bad to worse,** станови́ться всё ху́же и ху́же. —**so much the worse,** тем ху́же. —**what is worse; to make matters worse,** (и) что ещё ху́же. —**worse off,** в ху́дшем состоя́нии.

worsen *v.t.* ухудша́ть. —*v.i.* ухудша́ться.

worship *v.t.* **1,** (venerate, as a deity) поклоня́ться: *worship God,* поклоня́ться бо́гу. **2,** (idolize) обожа́ть; боготвори́ть. —*v.i.* моли́ться. —*n.* поклоне́ние. *Freedom of worship,* свобо́да вероисповеда́ния. *House of worship,* храм.

worshiper *also,* **worshipper** *n.* **1,** (person at prayer) моля́щийся. **2,** (fervent admirer) покло́нник.

worst *adj.* са́мый плохо́й; са́мый ху́дший; наиху́дший. *One's worst enemy,* зле́йший враг. *My worst mistake,* са́мая больша́я моя́ оши́бка. —*adv.* ху́же всего́; ху́же всех. —*n.* (са́мое) ху́дшее: *prepare for the worst,* гото́виться к ху́дшему. *Assume the worst,* предполага́ть са́мое ху́дшее. —**at worst,** в ху́дшем слу́чае. —**get the worst of it, 1,** (lose) быть в про́игрыше. **2,** (suffer most) страда́ть бо́льше всех. —**if worst comes to worst,** в кра́йнем слу́чае; на худо́й коне́ц. —**in the worst way,** *colloq.* о́чень; си́льно; стра́стно. —**the worst of it is that...,** ху́же всего́ то, что...

worsted *n.* камво́льная пря́жа; га́рус. —*adj.* камво́льный; га́русный.

worth *n.* **1,** (value) цена́; це́нность. *Know one's worth,* знать себе́ це́ну. *Show one's worth,* показа́ть себя́; прояви́ть себя́. **2,** *fol. by* **of** (amount to be had for a given sum) *rendered by* на: *a dollar's worth of stamps,* на до́ллар ма́рок. —*adj., used predicatively: rendered by the verb* сто́ить: *this painting is worth a thousand dollars,* э́та карти́на сто́ит ты́сячу до́лларов. *It is not worth the trouble,* не сто́ит труда́. *The play is worth seeing,* пье́су сто́ит посмотре́ть. *He is worth 100,000 dollars,* он име́ет капита́л в сто ты́сяч до́лларов. —**for all one is worth,** изо всех сил; что есть сил.

worthiness *n.* досто́инство.

worthless *adj.* **1,** (valueless) ничего́ не сто́ящий. *Be worthless,* ничего́ не сто́ить. **2,** (useless; good-for-nothing) него́дный; никчёмный. —**worthlessness,** *n.* него́дность.

worthwhile *adj.* сто́ящий. *Be worthwhile,* сто́ить; име́ть смысл.

worthy *adj.* досто́йный: *a worthy adversary,* досто́йный проти́вник. *Worthy of attention,* досто́йный внима́ния. *He is not worthy of her,* он не сто́ит её; он недосто́ин её.

would *v. aux.* **1,** *used to express futurity: he said he would be here by six,* он сказа́л, что придёт к шести́ часа́м. **2,** *used to form the conditional mood* бы: *I would go if I could,* я пошёл бы, е́сли б мог. **3,** *used to express a polite request or desire* бы: *I would like a glass of milk,* я бы хоте́л(а) стака́н молока́. *I would rather stay home,* я бы предпочёл оста́ться до́ма. *Would you like to see it?,* хоти́те посмотре́ть? *Would you be so kind,* бу́дьте добры́. **4,** *used to express customary action: he would often drop in to say hello,* он ча́сто заходи́л, что́бы поздоро́ваться с на́ми. *She would sit for hours in front of the fireplace,* она́, быва́ло, сиде́ла це́лыми часа́ми пе́редками́ном. **5,** *used to express a strong wish: would that he were here!,* о, е́сли бы он был здесь!

would-be *adj.* претенду́ющий на; с прете́нзией на.

wound *n.* ра́на; ране́ние. —*v.t.* ра́нить. *He was wounded in the chest,* он был ра́нен в грудь. *Wounded in action,* ра́нен в бою́.

wounded *adj.* ра́неный. *The wounded,* ра́неные.

woven *adj.* тка́ный.

wrack *v.t.* = **rack.** —**go to wrack and ruin,** пойти́ пра́хом.

wraith *n.* привиде́ние; при́зрак.

wrangle *v.i.* препира́ться. —*n.* препира́ния; перебра́нка.

wrap *v.t.* **1,** [*often* **wrap up**] (make a package of) завёртывать: *wrap a gift,* заверну́ть пода́рок. *Wrap something in paper,* заверну́ть *or* оберну́ть что́-нибудь в бума́гу. **2,** (enclose snugly) заку́тывать; уку́тывать; завёртывать: *wrap a child in a blanket,* заку́тывать/уку́тывать/завёртывать ребёнка одея́лом (*or* в одея́ло). **3,** *fol. by* **around** (wind around) обма́тывать; обёртывать: *wrap a towel around one's head,* обма́тывать/обёртывать полоте́нце вокру́г головы́. **4,** *fol. by* **up,** *colloq.* (finish; conclude) зака́нчивать; заключа́ть. —*v.i.* [*usu.* **wrap around**] обвива́ться (вокру́г). —*n.* шаль; наки́дка. —**under wraps,** под спу́дом. —**wrapped up in,** поглощён (+ *instr.*); погружён в; углублён в.

wrapper *n.* обёртка.

wrapping *n.* обёртка. —**wrapping paper,** обёрточная бума́га.

wrath *n.* гнев. —**wrathful,** *adj.* гне́вный.

wreak *v.t.* наноси́ть. *Wreak havoc on,* разоря́ть; опустоша́ть.

wreath *n.* **1,** (garland; crown) вено́к. **2,** (puff, as of smoke) кольцо́.

wreathe *v.t.* свива́ть. *His face was wreathed in smiles,* его́ лицо́ расплыло́сь в улы́бке.

wreck *v.t.* разбива́ть: *wreck a car,* разби́ть маши́ну. *Wreck someone's hopes,* разби́ть чьи́-нибудь наде́жды. —*n.* **1,** (crash) круше́ние: *train wreck,* круше́ние по́езда. **2,** (anything badly damaged; person in bad shape) разва́лина.

wreckage *n.* обло́мки.

wrecker *n.* **1,** (one who wrecks) разруши́тель. **2,** (truck) авари́йная маши́на.

wren *n.* крапи́вник.

wrench *n.* **1,** (tool) (га́ечный) ключ. *Monkey wrench,* францу́зский ключ. **2,** (sudden pull; yank) рыво́к. **3,** (sprain) вы́вих. **4,** (emotional shock) потрясе́ние. —*v.t.* **1,** (twist; sprain) вы́вихнуть; вы́вернуть. **2,** (wrest) вырыва́ть.

wrest *v.t.* вырыва́ть: *wrest a gun from one's assailant,* вырыва́ть пистоле́т у налётчика.

wrestle *v.i.* **1,** *sports* боро́ться. **2,** *fol. by* **with** (struggle with, as a problem) би́ться (над). —**wrestler,** *n.* боре́ц.

wrestling *n.* борьба́. *Wrestling match,* встре́ча по борьбе́.

wretch *n.* **1,** (unfortunate person) несча́стный. **2,** (despicable person) негодя́й.

wretched *adj.* **1,** (miserable) жа́лкий: *wretched existence,* жа́лкое существова́ние. **2,** (squalid) убо́гий; жа́лкий: *wretched hovel,* убо́гая/жа́лкая лачу́га. **3,** (awful) отврати́тельный: *wretched performance,* отврати́тельное исполне́ние.

wriggle *v.i.* **1,** (squirm) извива́ться. **2,** *fol. by* **out** (extricate oneself) выпу́тываться; вывёртываться: *wriggle out of a predicament,* выпу́тываться/вывёртываться из затрудни́тельного положе́ния. *Wriggle out of a commitment,* увíливать от обяза́тельства.

wring *v.t.* **1,** (twist) скру́чивать. *Wring one's hands,* лома́ть себе́ ру́ки. *Wring someone's neck,* сверну́ть ше́ю (+ *dat.*). **2,** *fol. by* **out** (squeeze the water from) выжима́ть; отжима́ть. **3,** (obtain by pressure or coercion) вырыва́ть; исторга́ть. —**wringing wet,** мо́крый, хоть вы́жми.

wringer *n.* пресс.

wrinkle *n.* морщи́на. —*v.t.* **1,** (crease) мять. **2,** (draw up; pucker) мо́рщить. —*v.i.* мя́ться; мо́рщиться.

wrinkled *adj.* **1,** (of one's face) морщи́нистый; смо́рщенный. *Become wrinkled,* мо́рщиться. **2,** (of fabric) мя́тый; измя́тый. *Become wrinkled,* мя́ться.

wrist *n.* запя́стье.

wristband *n.* напу́льсник.

wrist watch ручны́е *or* нару́чные часы́.

writ *n.* прика́з *or* распоряже́ние суда́; исполни́тельный лист. —**Holy Writ,** свяще́нное писа́ние.

write *v.t. & i.* писа́ть: *write a letter,* писа́ть письмо́. *Write a check,* вы́писать чек. *Know how to write,* уме́ть писа́ть. *This pen writes well,* э́та ру́чка хорошо́ пи́шет. —**write down,** запи́сывать. —**write in,** впи́сывать. —**write off, 1,** *bookkeeping* спи́сывать. **2,** *fig.* (acknowledge as a failure) махну́ть руко́й на. —**write out,** выпи́сывать. —**write up,** опи́сывать; писа́ть отчёт о. *See also* **written.**

writer *n.* писа́тель.

writhe *v.i.* ко́рчиться: *writhe in pain,* ко́рчиться от бо́ли.

writing *n.* **1,** (act of writing; ability to write) писа́ние; письмо́. *Reading, writing, arithmetic,* чте́ние, письмо́, арифме́тика. *He is good at writing,* он хорошо́ пи́шет. *Take up writing,* стать писа́телем. **2,** (something written on a surface): *read the writing on the blackboard,* чита́ть то, что напи́сано на доске́. **3,** *pl.* (written works) произведе́ния; сочине́ния: *the writings of Plato,* произведе́ния/сочине́ния Плато́на. **4,** (characters of a language) письмо́: *hieroglyphic writing,* иероглифи́ческое письмо́. *The language was only recently reduced to writing,* язы́к то́лько неда́вно стал пи́сьменным. —*adj.* пи́счий; пи́сьменный: *writing paper,* пи́счая бума́га; *writing table,* пи́сьменный стол. —**in writing,** пи́сьменно; в пи́сьменной фо́рме; в пи́сьменном ви́де.

written *adj.* **1,** (having been written) напи́санный: *well written,* хорошо́ напи́санный. **2,** (in writing) пи́сьменный: *written exam,* пи́сьменный экза́мен. *In written form,* в пи́сьменном ви́де; в пи́сьменной фо́рме.

wrong *adj.* **1,** (incorrect) непра́вильный; неве́рный: *wrong answer,* непра́вильный/неве́рный отве́т. *You are wrong,* вы непра́вы; вы ошиба́етесь. *My watch is wrong,* мои́ часы́ иду́т неве́рно. *Be on the wrong track,* быть на ло́жном пути́. **2,** *preceded by* **the** (not the one intended) не тот: *I took the wrong train,* я сел не на тот по́езд. *You have the wrong number,* вы не туда́ попа́ли. *You've come to the wrong place,* вы попа́ли не по а́дресу. **3,** (inappropriate) неподходя́щий: *at the wrong time,* в неподходя́щее вре́мя. *That was the wrong thing to say,* э́то не на́до бы́ло говори́ть. *Did I say something wrong?,* я что́-то не так сказа́л? **4,** (amiss) нела́дный: *something is wrong,* что́-то нела́дно. *Something is wrong with the phone,* что́-то случи́лось с телефо́ном. *What's wrong with you?,* что с ва́ми? *What's wrong with it?,* чем э́то пло́хо? **5,** (immoral) дурно́й; гре́шный. *It is wrong to kill,* грешно́ убива́ть. **6,** (not intended to be seen) ле́вый: *the wrong side,* ле́вая сторона́; изна́нка. *Wrong side out,* наизна́нку. —*adv.* **1,** (incorrectly) непра́вильно; неве́рно. **2,** (inside out) наизна́нку: *you've got your shirt on wrong,* у вас руба́шка наде́та наизна́нку. —*n.* зло: *right a wrong,* испра́вить зло. *Two wrongs don't make a right,* злом зла не попра́вишь. —*v.t.* обижа́ть: *wrong a friend,* обижа́ть дру́га. —**do wrong,** греши́ть. —**get (something) wrong,** пу́тать; перепу́тывать. —**go wrong, 1,** (go astray) заблуди́ться. **2,** (go awry) не вы́йти; не получи́ться. **3,** (degenerate) опуска́ться. —**in the wrong,** винова́тый.

wrongdoer *n.* правонаруши́тель. —**wrongdoing,** *n.* правонаруше́ние.

wrongful *adj.* **1,** (improper; illegal) незако́нный. **2,** (unjust) несправедли́вый; ло́жный. —**wrongfully,** *adv.* несправедли́во; ло́жно.

wrongly *adv.* **1,** (incorrectly; improperly) непра́вильно. **2,** (unjustly) несправедли́во; ло́жно.

wrought *adj.* отде́ланный: *finely wrought,* то́нко отде́ланный. —**wrought iron,** сва́рочное желе́зо.

wrought-up *adj.* взви́нченный.

wry *adj.* **1,** (twisted) криво́й. *Make a wry face,* криви́ться; мо́рщиться. **2,** (ironic; perverse) то́нкий: *wry humor,* то́нкий ю́мор.

X, x два́дцать четвёртая бу́ква англи́йского алфави́та; икс. —*n.* **1,** *math.* икс: *let x equal y,* пусть икс ра́вен и́греку. **2,** (mark in lieu of a signature) крест.

xenon *n.* ксено́н.

X-ray *n.* **1,** (picture) рентге́н; рентгеногра́мма; рентге́новский сни́мок. *Have X-rays taken,* идти́ на рентге́н. **2,** *pl.* (rays) рентге́новы лучи́; рентге́н. —*adj.* рентге́новский. —*v.t.* просве́чивать.

xylophone *n.* ксилофо́н.

Y

Y, y двáдцать пя́тая бу́ква англи́йского алфави́та; и́грек.

yacht *n.* я́хта. —**yachtsman**, *n.* яхтсмéн.

yak *n.* як.

yam *n.* **1,** (tropical plant) ямс. **2,** (sweet potato) батáт.

yammer *v.i., colloq.* **1,** (whine; complain) ныть. **2,** (talk loudly) орáть.

yank *v.t., colloq.* дёргать. *Yank the covers off someone,* стащи́ть одея́ла с когó-нибудь. —*n.* рывóк.

Yankee *n.* я́нки.

yap *v.i.* **1,** (bark) тя́вкать. **2,** *slang* (jabber) тараторить.

yard *n.* **1,** (unit of length) ярд. **2,** (area surrounded by buildings) двор. *Barnyard,* пти́чий двор. *Lumber yard,* леснóй склад. **3,** *R.R.* парк. *Freight yard,* товáрная стáнция.

yardstick *n.* **1,** (measuring stick) мéрка. **2,** *fig.* (standard) мéрка; мери́ло.

yarn *n.* **1,** (spun fiber) пря́жа. **2,** *colloq.* (story) рóссказни.

yawl *n.* ял.

yawn *v.i.* **1,** (open the mouth, when sleepy) зевáть. **2,** (gape, as of an opening) зия́ть: *yawning abyss,* зия́ющая прóпасть. —*n.* зевóк.

yaws *n.* фрамбéзия.

ye *pers. pron., archaic* вы. —*def. art., archaic* = **the.**

yea *adv., archaic* да. —*n.* за: *ten yeas, two nays,* дéсять за, два прóтив.

year *n.* год. *Three years,* три гóда. *Five years,* пять лет. *Year after year,* из гóда в год.

yearbook *n.* ежегóдник.

yearling *n.* годовáлое живóтное.

yearly *adj.* ежегóдный; годовóй. —*adv.* ежегóдно; раз в год.

yearn *v.i.* [*usu.* **yearn for**] **1,** (crave) жáждать. **2,** (long to see) тосковáть по. —**yearning,** *n.* тоскá: *yearning for one's homeland,* тоскá по рóдине.

year-old *adj.* годовáлый.

yeast *n.* дрóжжи.

yell *v.i.* кричáть. —*n.* крик.

yellow *adj.* жёлтый. —*n.* жёлтый цвет. —*v.i.* желтéть. —**yellowed,** *adj.* пожелтéлый.

yellow fever жёлтая лихорáдка.

yellowhammer *n.* (обыкновéнная) овся́нка.

yellowish *adj.* желтовáтый.

yellowjacket *n.* осá.

yelp *v.i.* тя́вкать; визжáть; взви́згивать. —*n.* визг; взвизг.

yen *n.* **1,** (monetary unit) иéна. **2,** *colloq.* (longing) жáжда; страсть.

yes *adv.* да: *yes or no,* да и́ли нет. *Yes, sir!, mil.* так тóчно!; есть! —**yes man,** *colloq.* подпевáла; подголóсок.

yesterday *n. & adv.* вчерá: *yesterday was Tuesday,* вчерá был втóрник. *Since yesterday,* со вчерáшнего дня. —*adj.* [*usu.* **yesterday's**] вчерáшний: *yesterday's weather,* вчерáшняя погóда. —**the day before yesterday,** позавчерá. —**yesterday morning,** вчерá ýтром.

yet *adv.* ещё: *not yet,* нет ещё. *He hasn't come yet,* он ещё не пришёл. *I'll beat him yet!,* я егó ещё (когдá-нибýдь) побью́! *Don't take your coat off yet,* не снимáйте покá пальтó. *Yet another example,* ещё оди́н при́мер. ♦*In interr. sentences* ужé: *have you eaten yet?,* вы ужé поéли? *Has the mail come yet?,* пóчта ужé прибылá? —*conj.* но; одна́ко: *yet he keeps trying,* но он всё старáется. —**as yet,** покá что; покá ещё; до сих пор.

yew *n.* тис.

Yiddish *n.* и́диш: *speak Yiddish,* говори́ть на и́дише. —*adj.* на и́дише: *a Yiddish newspaper,* газéта на и́дише.

yield *v.t.* **1,** (bear; produce) приноси́ть: *yield fruit/a profit/,* приноси́ть плоды́/при́быль. **2,** (give up; surrender) сдавáть; уступáть. *Yield the right of way,* уступáть дорóгу. *Yield the floor to,* давáть *or* предоставля́ть слóво (+ *dat.*). —*v.i.* **1,** (surrender) сдавáться. **2,** *fol. by* **to** (give in; succumb) уступáть (+ *dat.*); поддавáться (+ *dat.*): *yield to pressure,* уступáть/поддавáться давлéнию. **3,** (give way) подавáться: *the door yielded,* дверь поддалáсь. —*n.* **1,** (amount yielded) урожáй; урожáйность. *Yield of milk,* удóй; надóй. **2,** (return, as on an investment) дохóд.

yoga *n.* йóга. —**yogi** *n.* йог.

yogurt *n.* кефи́р.

yoke *n.* **1,** (device for coupling draft animals) ярмó. **2,** (for carrying buckets) корóмысло. **3,** (of a dress) кокéтка. **4,** *fig.* (oppressive force) и́го; гнёт; ярмó. —*v.t.* впрягáть в ярмó. *Yoke to a plow,* впрягáть (*e.g.* волóв) в плуг.

yokel *n.* деревéнщина.

yolk *n.* желтóк.

yonder *adj.* вон тот. —*adv.* вон там.

yore *n., in* **in days of yore,** во врéмя óно; *since days of yore,* и́здавна.

you *pers. pron.* **1,** *sing. (familiar)* ты; *(polite)* вы. *You are right,* ты прав/правá; вы правы́. *You are very funny,* ты/вы óчень смешнóй/смешнáя. **2,** *pl.* вы: *the three of you,* вы втроём.

young *adj.* молодо́й. —*n.* **1,** *preceded by* **the** (young people) молодёжь. **2,** (offspring) детёныши. —**young and old alike,** от ма́ла до вели́ка; стар и млад.
youngster *n.* ма́льчик; ю́ноша.
your *poss. adj.* **1,** *sing. (familiar)* твой; *polite* ваш: *your sisters,* твои́/ва́ши сёстры. *Wash your hands!,* вы́мой ру́ки! **2,** *pl.* ваш: *where are your bicycles?,* где ва́ши велосипе́ды?
yours *poss. pron.* твой; ваш: *is this coat yours?,* э́то твоё/ва́ше пальто́? *A friend of yours,* оди́н ваш друг; оди́н из ва́ших друзе́й.
yourself *pers. pron.* **1,** *used for emphasis* (ты) сам (сама́); (вы) са́ми. **2,** *used reflexively* себя́. *Did you hurt youself?,* вы ушиблись? *You ought to be ashamed of yourself!,* как вам не сты́дно! —**by yourself,** оди́н (одна́).
youth *n.* **1,** (quality of being young; one's early years) мо́лодость; ю́ность. *In my youth,* в мо́лодости/ю́ности. **2,** (young man) ю́ноша. **3,** (young people collectively) молодёжь. *Youth festival,* фестива́ль молодёжи.
youthful *adj.* ю́ный; молодо́й. *Youthful appearance,* моложа́вый вид.
ytterbium *n.* итте́рбий.
yttrium *n.* и́ттрий.
yucca *n.* ю́кка.
Yugoslav *adj.* [*also,* **Yugoslavian**] югосла́вский. —*n.* югосла́в; югосла́вка.
Yule *n.* свя́тки. *Also,* **Yuletide.**

Z

Z, z два́дцать шеста́я бу́ква англи́йского алфави́та. —**from A to Z,** от А до Я.
zeal *n.* усе́рдие; рве́ние. —**zealot,** *n.* фана́тик. —**zealous,** *adj.* усе́рдный; рети́вый; рья́ный. —**zealously,** *adv.* усе́рдно; рети́во.
zebra *n.* зе́бра.
zebu *n.* зе́бу.
zenith *n.* зени́т.
zephyr *n.* зефи́р.
zeppelin *n.* цеппели́н.
zero *n.* нуль. —*adj.* нулево́й. —*v.t.* [*usu.* **zero in**] пристре́ливать. —*v.i.* [*usu.* **zero in on**] пристре́ливать; пристре́ливаться по.
zest *n.* **1,** (keen enjoyment) смак. *Zest for life,* жизнера́достность. **2,** (flavor) пика́нтность; изю́минка.
Zeus *n.* Зевс.
zigzag *n.* зигза́г. —*adj.* зигзагообра́зный. —*v.i.* де́лать зигза́ги; петля́ть.
zinc *n.* цинк. —*adj.* ци́нковый. —**zinc oxide,** о́кись ци́нка. —**zinc white,** ци́нковые бели́ла.
zinnia *n.* ци́нния.
Zionism *n.* сиони́зм. —**Zionist,** *n.* сиони́ст. —*adj.* сиони́стский.
zip *n.* **1,** (whizzing sound) свист. **2,** *colloq.* (vim; pep) прыть.—*v.t.* [*usu.* **zip up**] застёгивать (на мо́лнию). —*v.i.* **1,** *colloq.* (move rapidly) мча́ться. **2,** *slang* (make a quick errand) сбе́гать.
zipper *n.* мо́лния.
zircon *n.* цирко́н.
zirconium *n.* цирко́ний.
zither *n.* ци́тра.
zloty *n.* зло́тый.
zodiac *n.* зодиа́к.
zonal *adj.* зона́льный.
zone *n.* зо́на; по́яс; полоса́. —*v.t.* разделя́ть на зо́ны.
zoo *n.* зоопа́рк.
zoology *n.* зооло́гия. —**zoological,** *adj.* зоологи́ческий. —**zoologist,** *n.* зоо́лог.
zoom *v.i.* **1,** (fly suddenly upwards) взмыва́ть. **2,** *fig.* (rise rapidly) подска́кивать. **3,** (move rapidly) мча́ться.
Zulu *n.* зулу́с. —*adj.* зулу́сский.
zwieback *n.* суха́рь.
zygote *n.* зиго́та.

Russian-English Section

A

А, а *n.neut.* first letter of the Russian alphabet. —**от А до Я,** from A to Z.

а *conj.* **1,** and: хорошо́!, а вы?, fine!, and you? Сего́дня гу́сто, а за́втра пу́сто, feast today and fast tomorrow. **2,** but: я приду́, а он нет, I'll come but he won't. —*particle* and; so: а что случи́лось с Бори́сом?, and what ever happened to Boris? А что он сказа́л?, and/so what did he say? —*interj., expressing various emotions* oh!; ah!; a!, что я наде́лал!, oh!, what have I done! А, вот молоде́ц!, ah, that's a fine fellow!

абажу́р *n.* lampshade.

абба́т *n.* abbot. —**аббати́са,** *n.* abbess. —**абба́тство,** *n.* abbey.

аббревиату́ра *n.* abbreviation.

аберра́ция *n.* aberration.

абза́ц *n.* **1,** indentation; indention. **2,** paragraph.

абитурие́нт *n.* **1,** *obs.* person graduating secondary school. **2,** applicant/candidate for admission to a university.

абонеме́нт *n.* subscription *(to a series of concerts, lectures, etc.).*

абоне́нт *n.* **1,** user *(of a telephone).* **2,** member; cardholder *(of a library).* **3,** subscriber *(to a series of cultural events).*

аборда́ж *n., naval* boarding *(of an enemy vessel).* —**брать на аборда́ж,** to board (an enemy vessel).

абориге́н *n.* aborigine.

або́рт *n.* abortion. —**аборти́вный,** *adj., med.* abortive.

абрази́в *n.* abrasive. —**абрази́вный,** *adj.* abrasive.

абракада́бра *n.* abracadabra.

абрико́с *n.* **1,** apricot. **2,** apricot tree. —**абрико́совый,** *adj.* apricot.

абсе́нт (сэ) *n.* absinthe.

абсолю́т *n.* absolute.

абсолюти́зм *n.* absolutism. —**абсолюти́ст,** *n.* absolutist. —**абсолюти́стский,** *adj.* absolutist.

абсолю́тно *adv.* absolutely.

абсолю́тный *adj.* absolute. —**абсолю́тный нуль, 1,** absolute zero. **2,** an absolute nothing *(said of a person).* —**абсолю́тный слух,** absolute (*or* perfect) pitch.

абсорби́ровать *v. impfv. & pfv.* [*pres.* **-рую, -руешь**] to absorb.

абсо́рбция *n.* absorption.

абстраги́ровать *v. impfv. & pfv.* [*pres.* **-рую, -руешь**] to abstract.

абстра́ктный *adj.* abstract. —**абстра́ктно,** *adv.* in an abstract manner; in the abstract.

абстракциони́зм *n.* abstract art. —**абстракциони́ст,** *n.* abstract artist.

абстра́кция *n.* abstraction.

абсу́рд *n.* absurdity. —**доводи́ть до абсу́рда,** to carry to the point of absurdity.

абсу́рдный *adj.* absurd; preposterous. —**абсу́рдность,** *n.f.* absurdity.

абсце́сс *n.* abscess.

абсци́сса *n.* abscissa.

абха́з *n.m.* [*fem.* **абха́зка**] Abkhaz *(one of a people inhabiting the Caucasus).* —**абха́зский,** *adj.* Abkhazian.

аванга́рд *n.* **1,** *mil.* advance guard. **2,** *fig.* vanguard: в аванга́рде, in the vanguard; in the forefront.

авангарди́зм *n.* avant gardism. —**авангарди́ст,** *n.* member of the avant-garde. —**авангарди́стский,** *adj.* avant-garde.

аванза́л *n.* anteroom; antechamber.

аванпо́ст *n., mil.* outpost.

ава́нс *n.* **1,** advance *(of money).* **2,** *pl., obs.* advances; overtures.

аванси́ровать *v. impfv. & pfv.* [*pres.* **-рую, -руешь**] to advance money to (an enterprise, organization, etc.).

ава́нсом *adv.* in advance.

авансце́на *n.* proscenium.

авантю́ра *n.* adventure; (risky) venture.

авантюри́зм *n.* adventurism.

авантюри́ст *n.* **1,** *obs.* adventurer. **2,** adventurist. —**авантюристи́ческий,** *adj.* adventuristic.

авантю́рный *adj.* **1,** speculative; risky. **2,** shady. **3,** *(of a story, novel, etc.)* adventure *(attrib.).*

ава́рец [*gen.* **-рца**] *n.m.* [*fem.* **-рка**] Avar *(one of a people inhabiting the Caucasus).* —**ава́рский,** *adj.* Avar.

авари́йность *n.f.* accident rate.

авари́йный *adj.* **1,** salvage *(attrib.);* wrecking *(attrib.):* авари́йная маши́на, wrecker; tow truck. **2,** emergency *(attrib.):* авари́йная поса́дка, emergency landing; crash landing.

ава́рия *n.* **1,** accident; crash; wreck. **2,** breakdown. **3,** mishap.

ава́ры *n.pl.* [*sing.* **ава́р**] Avars *(powerful Turkic people of the 6th-9th centuries).*

а́вгиев *adj., in* **а́вгиевы коню́шни,** Augean stables.

авгу́р *n.* augur.

а́вгуст *n.* August. —**а́вгустовский,** *adj.* August *(attrib.).*

авеню́ *n.f. indecl.* avenue.

авиа- *prefix* air-: авиаба́за, air base.

авиакомпáния *n.* **1,** aircraft company. **2,** airline.
авиаконстрýктор *n.* aircraft designer.
авиакосмúческий *adj.* aerospace *(attrib.).*
авиамодéль (дэ) *n.f.* model airplane.
авианóсец [*gen.* **-сца**] *n.* aircraft carrier.
авиапóчта *n.* air mail.
авиáтор *n.* aviator.
авиатрáсса *n.* air route.
авиациóнный *adj.* **1,** aviation *(attrib.).* **2,** aeronautical. **3,** aircraft *(attrib.);* airplane *(attrib.).*
авиáция *n.* **1,** aviation. **2,** airplanes; aircraft.
авокáдо *n. indecl.* avocado.
авóсь *particle, colloq.* maybe; perhaps. —**на авóсь,** hit or miss; by guesswork.
авóська [*gen. pl.* **-сек**] *n., colloq.* string bag.
аврáл *n.* **1,** *naval* job involving all hands. **2,** *colloq.* rush job.
аврóра *n.* aurora.
австралúец [*gen.* **-úйца**] *n.m.* [*fem.* **-úйка**] Australian. —**австралúйский,** *adj.* Australian.
австрúец [*gen.* **-úйца**] *n.m.* [*fem.* **-úйка**] Austrian. —**австрúйский,** *adj.* Austrian.
авто- *prefix* **1,** self-; auto-: автопортрéт, self-portrait; автобиогрáфия, autobiography. **2,** automatic: автопилóт, automatic pilot. **3,** automobile: автозавóд, automobile factory.
автобáза *n.* motor transport depot.
автобиогрáфия *n.* autobiography. —**автобиографúческий; автобиографúчный,** *adj.* autobiographical.
автóбус *n.* bus. —**автóбусный,** *adj.* bus *(attrib.).*
автóграф *n.* **1,** autograph. **2,** original handwritten manuscript.
автодрóм *n.* speedway.
автожúр *n.* autogiro.
автозавóд *n.* automobile factory.
автозапрáвочный *adj., in* **автозапрáвочная стáнция,** gas station; service station.
автокáр *n.* self-propelled cart.
автокрáт *n.* autocrat. —**автокрáтия,** *n.* autocracy. —**автократúческий,** *adj.* autocratic.
автóл *n.* motor oil.
автомагистрáль *n.f.* superhighway; expressway; thruway.
автомáт *n.* **1,** any automatic device: телефóн-автомáт, pay telephone. **2,** vending machine. **3,** automaton; robot. **4,** submachine gun; Tommy gun.
автоматизáция *n.* automation: автоматизáция произвóдства, automation of production.
автоматизúровать *v. impfv. & pfv.* [*pres.* **-рую, -руешь**] to automate.
автомáтика *n.* automation: век автомáтики, the age of automation.
автоматúчески *adv.* automatically.
автоматúческий *adj.* **1,** automatic; automatically operated. **2,** automatic; mechanical; involuntary.
автомáтчик *n.* submachine gunner.
автомашúна *n.* motor vehicle.
автомобилúст *n.* motorist.
автомобúль *n.m.* automobile. —**автомобúльный,** *adj.* automobile *(attrib.);* vehicle *(attrib.);* automotive.
автонóмия *n.* autonomy.
автонóмный *adj.* **1,** autonomous. **2,** *mech.* self-contained.
автопилóт *n.* automatic pilot.
автопортрéт *n.* self-portrait.
áвтор *n.* author.
автореферáт *n.* abstract *(by the author).*
авторизовáть *v. impfv. & pfv.* [*pres.* **-зýю, -зýешь**] to authorize (the translation, reproduction, etc. of a literary work).
авторитáрный *adj.* authoritarian.
авторитéт *n.* **1,** authority; prestige. **2,** an authority. —**авторитéтный,** *adj.* authoritative.
áвторский *adj.* author's. —**áвторское прáво,** copyright.
áвторство *n.* authorship.
авторýчка [*gen. pl.* **-чек**] *n.* fountain pen.
автострáда *n.* superhighway; expressway; thruway.
автотрáнспорт *n.* motor transport.
агá *interj.* aha!
агáва *n.* agave.
агáт *n.* agate. —**агáтовый,** *adj.* agate.
агглютинатúвный *adj.* agglutinative. —**агглютинáция,** *n.* agglutination.
агéнт *n.* agent. —**агéнтство,** *n.* agency.
агентýра *n.* **1,** intelligence agency; secret service. **2,** secret agents. —**агентýрный,** *adj.* intelligence *(attrib.).*
агиогрáфия *n.* hagiography.
агитáтор *n.* political agitator.
агитáция *n.* political agitation; propaganda work. —**агитациóнный,** *adj.* agitation *(attrib.);* propaganda *(attrib.).*
агитúровать *v. impfv.* [*pres.* **-рую, -руешь**] **1,** to agitate *(politically);* carry on propaganda work. **2,** [*pfv.* **сагитúровать**] *colloq.* to try to win over; try to persuade.
агúтка *n., colloq.* piece of art propaganda; propaganda play, novel, etc.
агитпýнкт *n.* local agitation and propaganda headquarters.
áгнец [*gen.* **áгнца**] *n., obs.* lamb.
агностицúзм *n.* agnosticism. —**агнóстик,** *n.* agnostic. —**агностúческий,** *adj.* agnostic.
агóния *n.* agony; throes of death.
агрáрный *adj.* agrarian.
агрегáт *n.* unit: силовóй агрегáт, power unit.
агрéссия *n.* aggression. —**агрессúвный,** *adj.* aggressive. —**агрéссор,** *n.* aggressor.
агронóмия *n.* agronomy. —**агронóм,** *n.* agronomist. —**агрономúческий,** *adj.* agronomic.
ад [*2nd loc.* **адý**] *n.* hell.
адáжио *adv. & n. indecl.* adagio.
адáмов *adj.* Adam's. —**адáмово яблоко,** Adam's apple.
адаптáция *n., biol.* adaptation.
адáптер (тэ) *n., mech.* adapter.
адвокáт *n.* lawyer; attorney. —**адвокáтский,** *adj.* lawyer's; lawyers'; legal.
адвокатýра *n.* **1,** the practice of law. **2,** lawyers collectively; the bar.
адеквáтный (дэ) *adj.* **1,** identical. **2,** adequate.
аденóид (дэ) *n.* adenoid.
адéпт (дэ) *n.* adherent; follower.
администратúвный *adj.* administrative.
администрáтор *n.* administrator; manager.
администрáция *n.* administration; management; managing officials.
администрúровать *v. impfv.* [*pres.* **-рую, -руешь**] to administer; manage.

адмира́л *n.* admiral.
адмиралте́йство *n.* **1,** admiralty. **2,** the Admiralty (building).
адмира́льский *adj.* admiral's.
адренали́н *n.* adrenalin.
а́дрес [*pl.* **адреса́**] *n.* address. —**по а́дресу** (+ *gen.*); **по (чьему-нибудь) а́дресу,** about; regarding; concerning; directed at/toward/against: по моему́ а́дресу, about me; directed against me. —**не по а́дресу,** to the wrong quarter, place, or party.
адреса́т *n.* addressee.
а́дресный *adj.* address *(attrib.).* —**а́дресная кни́га,** directory. —**а́дресный стол; а́дресное бюро́,** address bureau.
адресова́ть *v.impfv. & pfv.* [*pres.* **-су́ю, -су́ешь**] to address (a letter, question, etc.). —**адресова́ться,** *refl.* **1,** to be addressed. **2,** *(with* **к***)* to address (someone); apply (to).
а́дский *adj.* **1,** of hell. **2,** hellish. **3,** fiendish; diabolical. **4,** *colloq.* colossal; stupendous.
адсорби́ровать *v. impfv. & pfv.* [*pres.* **-рую, -руешь**] to adsorb.
адсо́рбция *n.* adsorption.
адъюта́нт *n.* aide-de-camp; adjutant.
адыге́ец [*gen.* **-е́йца**] *n.m.* [*fem.* **-е́йка**] Adygei *(one of a people inhabiting the Caucasus).* —**адыге́йский,** *adj.* Adygei.
ажиота́ж *n.* **1,** price fixing. **2,** *fig.* hullabaloo.
ажу́р *n.* **1,** *obs.* openwork. **2,** *bookkeeping* current basis. —**в ажу́ре,** *colloq.* in perfect order; shipshape.
ажу́рный *adj.* **1,** openwork *(attrib.).* **2,** finely wrought; delicate. —**ажу́рная стро́чка,** hemstitch.
аз [*gen.* **аза́**] *n.* **1,** old name of the letter A. **2,** *pl.* letters. **3,** *pl., fig.* rudiments; elements; fundamentals. —**начина́ть с азо́в,** to start from the beginning. —**ни аза́ не знать,** not to know a thing.
аза́лия *n.* azalea.
аза́рт *n.* zeal; ardor; fervor. —**войти́ в аза́рт,** to get carried away.
аза́ртный *adj.* **1,** ardent, zealous, fervent. **2,** heated; impassioned. —**аза́ртная игра́,** game of chance.
а́збука *n.* **1,** alphabet. **2,** alphabet book; primer. **3,** rudiments; ABC's.
а́збучный *adj.* **1,** alphabet *(attrib.).* **2,** alphabetical. —**а́збучная и́стина,** truism; obvious truth.
азербайджа́нец [*gen.* **-нца**] *n.m.* [*fem.* **-нка**] Azerbaijani. —**азербайджа́нский,** *adj.* Azerbaijani.
азиа́т *n.m.* [*fem.* **-а́тка**] Asian; Asiatic. —**азиа́тский,** *adj.* Asian; Asiatic.
а́зимут *n.* azimuth.
азо́т *n.* nitrogen. —**азо́тистый,** *adj.* nitrous. —**азо́тный,** *adj.* nitric; nitrogen *(attrib.).*
а́ист *n.* stork.
ай *interj.* **1,** oh! **2,** ouch!
айва́ *n.* **1,** quince. **2,** quince tree. —**айво́вый,** *adj.* quince.
айда́ *interj., colloq.* go!; let's go!
а́йсберг (бэ) *n.* iceberg.
акаде́мия *n.* academy. —**акаде́мик,** *n.* academician. —**академи́ческий,** *adj.* academic.
ака́нт *also,* **ака́нф** *n.* acanthus.
а́канье *n.* pronunciation of unstressed **о** as **а** in standard Russian.
а́кать *v. impfv.* to pronounce unstressed **о** as **а** in standard Russian.
ака́ция *n.* acacia.
аквала́нг *n.* aqualung. —**аквалангист,** *n.* skin diver.
аквамари́н *n.* aquamarine. —**аквамари́новый,** *adj.* aquamarine.
акваре́ль *n.f.* watercolors; watercolor painting. —**акваре́льный,** *adj.* watercolor *(attrib.).* —**акварели́ст,** *n.* watercolorist.
аква́риум *n.* **1,** aquarium. **2,** fishbowl; fish tank.
аквати́нта *n.* aquatint.
аквато́рия *n.* area of water *(on the globe).*
акведу́к *n.* aqueduct.
акклиматиза́ция *n.* acclimatization; acclimation.
акклиматизи́ровать *v. impfv. & pfv.* [*pres.* **-рую, -руешь**] to acclimatize; acclimate. —**акклиматизи́роваться,** *refl.* to become acclimatized; become acclimated.
аккомпанеме́нт *n., music* accompaniment.
аккомпаниа́тор *n.* accompanist.
аккомпани́ровать *v. impfv.* [*pres.* **-рую, -руешь**] *(with dat.) music* to accompany.
акко́рд *n.* **1,** *music* chord. **2,** *obs.* agreement; accord.
аккордео́н *n.* accordion. —**аккордеони́ст,** *n.* accordionist.
акко́рдный *adj.* by the piece: акко́рдная рабо́та, piecework.
аккредити́в *n.* letter of credit.
аккредитова́ть *v. impfv. & pfv.* [*pres.* **-ту́ю, -ту́ешь**] *dipl.* to accredit.
аккумуля́тор *n.* battery. —**аккумуля́торный,** *adj.,* in аккумуля́торная батаре́я, storage battery.
аккура́тно *adv.* **1,** neatly. **2,** punctually. **3,** efficiently. **4,** *colloq.* regularly. **5,** *colloq.* cautiously.
аккура́тность *n.f.* **1,** meticulousness; care. **2,** tidiness; neatness. **3,** punctuality; promptness.
аккура́тный *adj.* **1,** neat; tidy. **2,** punctual; prompt. **3,** efficient; thorough.
акони́т *n.* aconite; monkshood.
акр *n.* acre.
акроба́т *n.* acrobat. —**акроба́тика,** *n.* acrobatics. —**акробати́ческий,** *adj.* acrobatic.
акро́поль *n.m.* acropolis.
акрости́х *n.* acrostic.
акселера́тор *n.* accelerator.
аксельба́нт *n.* aiguillette; aglet.
аксессуа́р *n.* **1,** accessory. **2,** *pl.* secondary features; background details *(of a painting, literary work, etc.).* **3,** *pl.* stage props.
аксио́ма *n.* axiom. —**аксиомати́ческий,** *adj.* axiomatic.
акт *n.* **1,** act: престу́пный акт, criminal act. **2,** document; deed. **3,** *law* act. **4,** *theat.* act. **5,** graduation exercise; commencement.
актёр *n.* actor. —**актёрский,** *adj.* actor's; actors'.
актёрство *n.* **1,** acting *(as a profession).* **2,** affected behavior; play-acting.
акти́в *n.* **1,** most active members of an organization. **2,** *finance* assets. **3,** *bookkeeping & fig.* credit side of the ledger.
активизи́ровать *v. impfv. & pfv.* [*pres.* **-рую, -руешь**] to step up.
активи́ст *n.* political or social activist.
акти́вно *adv.* actively.
акти́вность *n.f.* activity; participation; involvement.
акти́вный *adj.* **1,** active. **2,** *econ.* favorable.
акти́ний *n.* actinium.

акти́ния *n.* sea anemone.
а́ктовый *adj., in* **а́ктовый зал,** assembly hall.
актри́са *n.* actress.
актуа́льность *n.f.* **1,** timeliness; relevance. **2,** urgency.
актуа́льный *adj.* current; timely; relevant.
аку́ла *n.* shark.
акупункту́ра *n.* acupuncture.
аку́стика *n.* acoustics. —**акусти́ческий,** *adj.* acoustic; acoustical.
акушёр *n.* obstetrician. —**акуше́рка,** *n.* midwife. —**акуше́рский,** *adj.* obstetric.
акуше́рство *n.* **1,** obstetrics. **2,** midwifery.
акце́нт *n.* accent: говори́ть с акце́нтом, to speak with an accent. —**де́лать акце́нт на** (+ *prepl.*), to accentuate; emphasize; place the emphasis on.
акценти́ровать *v. impfv. & pfv.* [*pres.* **-рую, -руешь**] **1,** *phonet.* to accent; stress. **2,** *fig.* to accentuate.
акци́з *n.* excise; excise tax. —**акци́зный,** *adj.* excise *(attrib.).*
акционе́р *n.* stockholder; shareholder.
акционе́рный *adj.* stockholder'; joint-stock *(attrib.):* акционе́рное о́бщество, joint-stock company.
а́кция *n.* **1,** share of stock. **2,** *pl., fig.* stock: его́ а́кции повыша́ются, his stock is rising. **3,** action.
алба́нец [*gen.* **-нца**] *n.m.* [*fem.* **-нка**] Albanian. —**алба́нский,** *adj.* Albanian.
а́лгебра *n.* algebra. —**алгебраи́ческий,** *adj.* algebraic.
алгори́тм *n.* algorithm.
алеба́рда *n.* halberd.
алеба́стр *n.* alabaster. —**алеба́стровый,** *adj.* alabaster.
александри́т *n.* alexandrite.
але́ть *v. impfv.* [*pfv.* **заале́ть**] **1,** to turn red; turn scarlet; blush. **2,** *(of anything red)* to glow; gleam.
алжи́рец [*gen.* **-рца**] *n.m.* [*fem.* **-рка**] Algerian. —**алжи́рский,** *adj.* Algerian.
а́либи *n. neut. indecl., law* alibi.
алиме́нты [*gen.* **-тов**] *n. pl.* alimony. —**алиме́нтный,** *adj.* alimony *(attrib.).*
алкало́ид *n.* alkaloid.
алка́ть *v. impfv.* [*pres.* **а́лчу, а́лчешь**] *(with gen.) obs.* to crave; hunger (for).
алка́ш [*gen.* **-каша́**] *n., colloq.* drunkard.
алкоголи́зм *n.* alcoholism. —**алкого́лик,** *n.* alcoholic.
алкого́ль *n.m.* alcohol. —**алкого́льный,** *adj.* alcohol *(attrib.).*
алла́х *n.* Allah.
аллего́рия *n.* allegory. —**аллегори́ческий,** *adj.* allegorical.
аллегре́тто *adv. & n. indecl.* allegretto.
алле́гро *adv. & n. indecl.* allegro.
аллерги́я *n.* allergy. —**аллерги́ческий,** *adj.* allergic.
алле́я *n.* tree-lined walk.
аллига́тор *n.* alligator.
аллилу́йя *interj.* hallelujah!
аллитера́ция *n.* alliteration.
алло́ *interj., used when answering the telephone* hello!
аллопа́тия *n.* allopathy. —**аллопа́т,** *n.* allopath. —**аллопати́ческий,** *adj.* allopathic.
аллю́вий *n.* alluvium. —**аллювиа́льный,** *adj.* alluvial.
аллю́р *n.* gait *(of a horse).*
алма́з *n.* diamond. —**алма́зный,** *adj.* diamond.
ало́э *n. neut. indecl.* **1,** aloe *(plant).* **2,** aloes *(drug).*
алта́ец [*gen.* **-а́йца**] *n.m.* [*fem.* **-а́йка**] Altai *(one of a people inhabiting southern Siberia).*
алта́йский *adj.* **1,** Altai. **2,** Altaic.
алта́рь [*gen.* **-таря́**] *n.m.* altar.
алты́н [*gen. pl.* **-ты́н**] *n.* old Russian coin worth three kopecks; altyn.
алфави́т *n.* alphabet. —**алфави́тный,** *adj.* alphabetical.
алхи́мия *n.* alchemy. —**алхи́мик,** *n.* alchemist.
а́лчный *adj.* greedy. —**а́лчность,** *n.f.* greed.
а́лый *adj.* scarlet.
алыча́ *n.* a variety of plum.
альбатро́с *n.* albatross.
альбини́зм *n.* albinism. —**альбино́с,** *n.* albino.
альбо́м *n.* album.
альбуми́н *n.* albumin.
альвео́ла *n.* alveolus. —**альвеоля́рный,** *adj.* alveolar.
алько́в *n.* alcove.
альмана́х *n.* **1,** literary miscellany. **2,** *obs.* almanac.
альпака́ *n. neut. indecl.* alpaca.
альпи́йский *adj.* Alpine.
альпини́зм *n.* mountain climbing. —**альпини́ст,** *n.* mountain climber. —**альпини́стский,** *adj.* mountain-climbing *(attrib.).*
альт [*gen.* **альта́**] *n.* **1,** alto *(voice or part).* **2,** viola.
альтернати́ва (тэ) *n.* alternative. —**альтернати́вный,** *adj.* alternative; alternate.
альтерна́тор (тэ) *n.* alternator.
альтиме́тр *n.* altimeter.
альто́вый *adj.* alto.
альтруи́зм *n.* altruism. —**альтруи́ст,** *n.* altruist. —**альтруисти́ческий,** *adj.* altruistic.
а́льфа *n.* alpha. —**а́льфа-лучи́,** alpha rays. —**а́льфа-части́ца,** alpha particle.
алья́нс *n.* alliance.
алюми́ний *n.* aluminum. —**алюми́ниевый,** *adj.* aluminum.
аляпова́тый *adj.* **1,** crude; crudely made. **2,** ugly.
амазо́нка [*gen. pl.* **-нок**] *n.* **1,** *myth.* Amazon. **2,** horsewoman. **3,** *obs.* riding habit.
амальга́ма *n.* **1,** amalgam. **2,** *fig.* amalgamation; mixture; blend.
амальгама́ция *n., chem.* amalgamation.
амальгами́ровать *v. impfv. & pfv.* [*pres.* **-рую, -руешь**] **1,** to amalgamate; alloy with mercury. **2,** to coat with an amalgam.
амара́нт *n.* amaranth.
амари́ллис *n.* amaryllis.
амба́р *n.* **1,** barn; granary. **2,** storehouse; warehouse. —**амба́рный,** *adj.* barn *(attrib.).*
амбицио́зный *adj.* ambitious.
амби́ция *n.* **1,** pride; self-respect. **2,** arrogance; conceit. —**уда́риться в амби́цию,** to take umbrage; get into a huff.
а́мбра *n.* ambergris.
амбразу́ра *n.* embrasure; loophole.
амбро́зия *n.* **1,** ambrosia. **2,** ragweed.
амбулато́рия *n.* outpatient clinic; dispensary.
амбулато́рный *adj.* dispensary *(attrib.).* —**амбулато́рный больно́й,** outpatient.
амёба *n.* ameba.
америка́нец [*gen.* **-нца**] *n.m.* [*fem.* **-нка**] American.
америка́нский *adj.* American.
амери́ций *n.* americium.
амети́ст *n.* amethyst. —**амети́стовый,** *adj.* amethyst.

аминокислота́ [*pl.* **-ло́ты**] *n.* amino acid.
ами́нь *particle & interj.* amen!
аммиа́к *n.* ammonia.
аммиа́чный *adj.* ammonia *(attrib.)*; ammonium *(attrib.)*. —**аммиа́чная сели́тра,** ammonium nitrate.
аммо́ний *n.* ammonium. —**аммо́ниевый,** *adj.* ammonium *(attrib.)*.
амнисти́ровать *v. impfv. & pfv.* [*pres.* **-рую, -руешь**] to grant amnesty to.
амни́стия *n.* amnesty.
амора́льный *adj.* amoral; immoral. —**амора́льность,** *n.f.* amorality; immorality.
амортиза́тор *n.* shock absorber.
амортизацио́нный *adj.* **1,** shock-absorbing. **2,** *finance* amortization *(attrib.)*.
амортиза́ция *n.* **1,** amortization; depreciation. **2,** shock absorption.
амортизи́ровать *v. impfv. & pfv.* [*pres.* **-рую, -руешь**] to amortize.
амо́рфный *adj.* amorphous.
ампе́р [*gen. pl.* **ампе́р**] *n.* ampere. —**амперме́тр,** *n.* ammeter.
амплиту́да *n., physics* amplitude.
амплуа́ *n. neut. indecl., theat.* (one's) kind of role.
а́мпула *n.* ampule.
ампута́ция *n.* amputation.
ампути́ровать *v. impfv. & pfv.* [*pres.* **-рую, -руешь**] to amputate.
амуле́т *n.* amulet; charm.
аму́р *n.* **1,** Cupid. **2,** *pl., obs., colloq.* love affairs.
амфи́бия *n.* **1,** amphibian. **2,** amphibious plane or vehicle.
амфитеа́тр *n.* **1,** amphitheater. **2,** *theat.* raised back rows of the orchestra.
анабапти́зм *n.* Anabaptism. —**анабапти́ст,** *n.* Anabaptist.
анагра́мма *n.* anagram.
анако́нда *n.* anaconda.
ана́лиз *n.* **1,** analysis. **2,** *med.* test: ана́лиз кро́ви, blood test.
анализи́ровать *v. impfv. & pfv.* [*pfv. also* **проанализи́ровать;** *pres.* **-рую, -руешь**] to analyze.
анали́тик *n.* analyst. —**аналити́ческий,** *adj.* analytic; analytical.
аналоги́чный *adj.* analogous.
анало́гия *n.* analogy.
анало́й *n.* lectern *(in a church)*.
ана́льный *adj.* anal.
анана́с *n.* pineapple. —**анана́сный,** *adj.* pineapple.
ана́пест *n.* anapest.
анархи́зм *n.* anarchism. —**анархи́ст,** *n.* anarchist. —**анархи́стский,** *adj.* anarchist *(attrib.)*. —**анархи́ческий,** *adj.* anarchistic. —**анархи́чный,** *adj.* anarchic; chaotic.
ана́рхия *n.* **1,** anarchy. **2,** *colloq.* chaos.
ана́том *n.* anatomist.
анатоми́ровать *v. impfv. & pfv.* [*pres.* **-рую, -руешь**] to anatomize; dissect.
анато́мия *n.* anatomy. —**анатоми́ческий,** *adj.* anatomical.
ана́фема *n.* anathema.
анахрони́зм *n.* anachronism. —**анахрони́ческий,** *adj.* anachronistic.
анаэро́б *n.* anaerobe. —**анаэро́бный,** *adj.* anaerobic.
анга́р *n.* hangar.
а́нгел *n.* angel. —**а́нгельский,** *adj.* angelic.
анги́на *n.* angina.
англизи́ровать *v. impfv. & pfv.* [*pres.* **-рую, -руешь**] to Anglicize.
англи́йский *adj.* **1,** English. **2,** British. —**англи́йская була́вка,** safety pin. —**англи́йская ми́ля,** statute mile. —**англи́йская соль,** Epsom salt(s).
англика́нский *adj.* Anglican.
англици́зм *n.* Anglicism.
англича́нин [*pl.* **-ча́не, -ча́н**] *n.* **1,** Englishman. **2,** *pl.* the English; the British.
англича́нка [*gen. pl.* **-нок**] *n.* Englishwoman.
англосаксо́нский *adj.* Anglo-Saxon.
англофи́л *n.* Anglophile.
анда́нте (тэ) *adv. & n. neut. indecl.* andante.
анекдо́т *n.* **1,** anecdote; joke. **2,** amusing incident; funny thing.
анекдоти́ческий *adj.* **1,** anecdotal. **2,** [*also,* **анекдоти́чный**] improbable; incredible.
анеми́я *n.* anemia. —**анеми́чный,** *adj.* anemic.
анемо́метр *n.* anemometer.
анемо́н *n.* anemone. *Also,* **анемо́на.**
анеро́ид *n.* aneroid barometer.
анестезио́лог (нэстэ) *n.* anesthesiologist.
анестези́ровать (нэстэ) *v. impfv. & pfv.* [*pres.* **-рую, -руешь**] to anesthetize.
анестези́рующий (нэстэ) *adj.* anesthetic. —**анестези́рующее сре́дство,** anesthetic.
анестези́я (нэстэ) *n.* anesthesia.
анили́н *n.* aniline. —**анили́новый,** *adj.* aniline.
аними́зм *n.* animism. —**аними́ст,** *n.* animist. —**анимисти́ческий,** *adj.* animistic.
ани́с *n.* anise.
ани́совка *n.* anisette.
ани́совый *adj.* anise.
анке́та *n.* **1,** questionnaire; form; blank. **2,** survey.
анке́тный *adj.* questionnaire *(attrib.)*. —**анке́тные да́нные,** biographical data.
ankла́в *n.* enclave.
анна́лы [*gen.* **-лов**] *n. pl.* annals.
аннекси́ровать *v. impfv. & pfv.* [*pres.* **-рую, -руешь**] to annex.
анне́ксия *n.* annexation.
аннота́ция *n.* synopsis.
аннули́рование *n.* annulment; cancellation; abrogation.
аннули́ровать *v. impfv. & pfv.* [*pres.* **-рую, -руешь**] to annul; cancel; abrogate.
ано́д *n.* anode.
анома́лия *n.* anomaly. —**анома́льный,** *adj.* anomalous.
анони́м *n.* **1,** anonymous author. **2,** anonymous work; anonymous letter.
анони́мный *adj.* anonymous. —**анони́мно,** *adv.* anonymously. —**анони́мность,** *n.f.* anonymity.
ано́нс *n.* announcement; notice *(of a performance)*.
анонси́ровать *v. impfv. & pfv.* [*pres.* **-рую, -руешь**] to announce; advertise (a performance).
анорма́льный *adj.* abnormal.
ано́фелес *n.* anopheles.
анса́мбль *n.m.* ensemble.
антагони́зм *n.* antagonism. —**антагони́ст,** *n.* antagonist. —**антагонисти́ческий,** *adj.* antagonistic.
антаркти́ческий *adj.* antarctic.
анте́нна (тэ) *n.* aerial; antenna.

антиамерикани́зм *n.* anti-Americanism. —**антиамерика́нский,** *adj.* anti-American.
антибио́тик *n.* antibiotic.
антивещество́ *n.* antimatter.
антиво́енный *adj.* antiwar.
антиге́н *n.* antigen.
антидемократи́ческий *adj.* undemocratic.
антиква́р *n.* antique dealer; antiquary. —**антиква́рный,** *adj.* antique.
антикоммуни́зм *n.* anticommunism. —**антикоммуни́ст,** *n.* anticommunist. —**антикоммунисти́ческий,** *adj.* anticommunist.
антило́па *n.* antelope.
антиобще́ственный *adj.* antisocial; harmful to society.
антиларти́йный *adj.* anti-party.
антипати́чный *adj.* unpleasant; disagreeable; antipathetic.
антипа́тия *n.* antipathy; aversion.
антираке́та *n.* anti-missile missile; anti-ballistic missile.
антирелигио́зный *adj.* antireligious.
антисанита́рный *adj.* unsanitary.
антисемити́зм *n.* anti-Semitism. —**антисеми́т,** *n.* anti-Semite. —**антисеми́тский,** *adj.* anti-Semitic.
антисе́птика (сэ) *n.* **1,** antisepsis. **2,** antiseptics. —**антисепти́ческий,** *adj.* antiseptic.
антисове́тский *adj.* anti-Soviet.
антите́за (тэ) *n.* antithesis; opposite.
антите́зис (тэ) *n., logic* antithesis.
антите́ло [*pl.* **-тела́**] *n.* antibody.
антитети́ческий (тэ) *adj.* antithetical.
антитокси́н *n.* antitoxin. —**антитокси́ческий,** *adj.* antitoxic.
антифри́з *n.* antifreeze.
анти́христ *n.* Antichrist.
анти́чный *adj.* ancient. —**анти́чность,** *n.f.* antiquity.
антоло́гия *n.* anthology.
анто́ним *n.* antonym.
анто́новка *n.* a variety of apple.
антра́кт *n.* **1,** *theat.* intermission. **2,** musical interlude.
антраци́т *n.* anthracite. —**антраци́тный; антраци́товый,** *adj.* anthracite *(attrib.).*
антреко́т *n.* rib steak.
антрепренёр *n.* **1,** impresario. **2,** *obs.* entrepreneur.
антресо́ли [*gen.* **-лей**] *n. pl.* **1,** attic. **2,** mezzanine.
антропо́ид *n.* anthropoid.
антрополо́гия *n.* anthropology. —**антропо́лог,** *n.* anthropologist. —**антропологи́ческий,** *adj.* anthropological.
антропоморфи́зм *n.* anthropomorphism. —**антропоморфи́ческий,** *adj.* anthropomorphic.
анфа́с *adv.* full-face: сня́ться анфа́с, to be photographed full-face.
анфила́да *n.* suite of rooms.
анча́р *n.* upas *(tree).*
анчо́ус *n.* anchovy.
аншла́г *n., theat.* "sold out" sign. —**идти́** (*or* **проходи́ть) с аншла́гом,** to be sold out; play to packed houses.
аню́тин *adj., in* **аню́тины гла́зки,** pansy.
ао́рта *n.* aorta.
апарта́мент *also,* **апартаме́нт** *n., usu. pl.* luxurious living quarters.
апарте́йд (тэ) *n.* apartheid.
апати́чный *adj.* apathetic.
апа́тия *n.* apathy.
апелли́ровать *v. impfv. & pfv.* [*pres.* **-рую, -руешь**] **1,** *law* to appeal. **2,** *(with* **к***)* to appeal (to).
апелляцио́нный *adj., law* of appeal; appellate.
апелля́ция *n.* **1,** *law* appeal. **2,** *(with* **к***)* plea; appeal.
апельси́н *n.* **1,** orange. **2,** orange tree. —**апельси́нный; апельси́новый,** *adj.* orange *(attrib.).*
аперту́ра *n.* aperture.
апплоди́ровать *v. impfv.* [*pres.* **-рую, -руешь**] *(with dat.)* to applaud.
аплодисме́нты [*gen.* **-тов**] *n. pl.* applause.
апло́мб *n.* self-assurance; aplomb.
апоге́й *n.* **1,** *astron.* apogee. **2,** *fig.* high point; pinnacle; acme.
апока́липсис *n.* **1,** apocalypse. **2,** *cap.* (book of) Revelation. —**апокалипси́ческий,** *adj.* apocalyptic.
апо́крифы [*gen.* **-фов**] *n. pl.* Apocrypha. —**апокрифи́ческий,** *adj.* Apocryphal.
аполити́чный *adj.* apolitical. —**аполити́чность,** *n.f.* indifference to politics.
Аполло́н *n.* Apollo.
апологе́т *n.* apologist.
апологе́тика *n.* apologetics.
аполо́гия *n.* apologia.
апоплекси́ческий *adj.* apoplectic.
апопле́ксия *n.* apoplexy; apoplectic stroke.
апосте́ори (тэ) *adv.* a posteori. —**апостерио́рный,** *adj.* a posteriori.
апо́стол *n.* apostle. —**апо́стольский,** *adj.* apostolic.
апостро́ф *n.* apostrophe.
апофео́з *n.* apotheosis.
аппара́т *n.* **1,** apparatus; device. **2,** *physiol.* system: дыха́тельный аппара́т, respiratory system. **3,** administrative machinery: госуда́рственный аппара́т, machinery of government. —**фотографи́ческий аппара́т,** camera.
аппарату́ра *n.* apparatus; equipment.
аппара́тчик *n.* **1,** maintenance man. **2,** party functionary.
аппе́ндикс *n., anat.* appendix. —**аппендици́т,** *n.* appendicitis.
апперце́пция *n., psychol.* apperception.
аппети́т *n.* appetite. —**прия́тного аппети́та**!, hearty appetite!
аппети́тный *adj.* appetizing.
аппликату́ра *n., music* fingering.
аппликáция *n.* appliqué work.
апре́ль *n.m.* April. —**апре́льский,** *adj.* April *(attrib.).*
априо́ри *adv.* a priori. —**априо́рный,** *adj.* a priori.
апроба́ция *n.* approbation; approval.
апроби́ровать *v. impfv. & pfv.* [*pres.* **-рую, -руешь**] to approve.
апси́да *n., archit.* apse; apsis.
апте́ка *n.* drugstore; pharmacy. —**как в апте́ке,** *colloq.* exactly.
апте́карь *n.m., obs.* druggist. —**апте́карский,** *adj.* pharmaceutical.
апте́чка [*gen. pl.* **-чек**] *n.* **1,** medicine chest; medicine cabinet. **2,** first-aid kit.
апте́чный *adj.* of or for drugs. —**апте́чный шкаф,** medicine chest; medicine cabinet.
ар *n.* are *(100 sq. meters).*
а́ра *n.* macaw.
ара́б *n.m.* [*fem.* **ара́бка**] Arab.
арабе́ска [*gen. pl.* **-сок**] *n.* arabesque. *Also,* **арабе́ск.**

ара́бский *adj.* **1,** Arab. **2,** Arabic.
арави́йский *adj.* Arabian.
араме́йский *adj.* Aramaic.
аранжи́ровать *v. impfv. & pfv.* [*pres.* **-рую, -руешь**] *music* to arrange.
аранжиро́вка *n., music* arrangement.
ара́п *n.* **1,** *obs.* Negro. **2,** *colloq.* cheat; crook.
ара́пник *n.* hunting whip.
ара́ра *n.* macaw.
ара́хис *n.* **1,** peanut plant. **2,** peanuts. —**ара́хисовый,** *adj.* peanut *(attrib.).*
арба́ [*pl.* **а́рбы**] *n.* a kind of cart used in the Crimea and the Caucasus.
арби́тр *n.* arbitrator; arbiter.
арбитра́ж *n.* arbitration. —**арбитра́жный,** *adj.* of arbitration: арбитра́жный суд, court of arbitration.
арбу́з *n.* watermelon. —**арбу́зный,** *adj.* watermelon *(attrib.).*
аргенти́нец [*gen.* **-нца**] *n.m.* [*fem.* **-нка**] Argentinean. —**аргенти́нский,** *adj.* Argentinean; Argentine.
арго́ *n. indecl.* jargon; argo; cant.
арго́н *n.* argon.
аргуме́нт *n.* argument.
аргумента́ция *n.* argumentation; line of reasoning.
аргументи́ровать *v. impfv. & pfv.* [*pres.* **-рую, -руешь**] to argue; adduce arguments.
аре́на *n.* **1,** arena. **2,** *fig.* field; sphere; arena.
аре́нда *n.* **1,** rental. **2,** rent. —**брать в аре́нду,** to take a lease on; rent. —**сдава́ть в аре́нду,** to rent out.
аренда́тор *n.* renter; tenant; lessee; leaseholder.
аре́ндный *adj.* rent *(attrib.)*; rental *(attrib.)*: аре́ндная пла́та, rent. —**аре́ндный догово́р,** lease.
арендова́ть *v. impfv. & pfv.* [*pres.* **-ду́ю, -ду́ешь**] to rent; take a lease on.
аре́ст *n.* **1,** arrest; custody: брать под аре́ст, to place under arrest; take into custody. **2,** *law* attachment.
ареста́нт *n., obs.* person under arrest.
аресто́ванный *n., decl. as an adj.* person arrested; prisoner.
арестова́ть *v. impfv. & pfv.* [*pres.* **-ту́ю, -ту́ешь**] to arrest.
ари́ец [*gen.* **ари́йца**] *n.m.* [*fem.* **ари́йка**] Aryan. —**ари́йский,** *adj.* Aryan.
аристокра́т *n.* aristocrat. —**аристократи́ческий; аристократи́чный,** *adj.* aristocratic. —**аристокра́тия,** *n.* aristocracy.
арифме́тика *n.* arithmetic. —**арифмети́ческий,** *adj.* arithmetic; arithmetical.
арифмо́метр *n.* automatic calculating machine; calculator.
а́рия *n.* aria.
а́рка [*gen. pl.* **а́рок**] *n.* arch.
арка́да *n., archit.* arcade.
арка́н *n.* lasso.
арка́нить *v. impfv.* [*pfv.* **зааркáнить**] to lasso.
аркти́ческий *adj.* arctic.
арлеки́н *n.* harlequin.
арма́да *n.* armada.
армату́ра *n.* **1,** steel framework. **2,** fittings; fixtures. **3,** armature.
арме́ец [*gen.* **-е́йца**] *n.* army man; serviceman.
арме́йский *adj.* army *(attrib.).*
а́рмия *n.* army.
армяни́н [*pl.* **-мя́не, -мя́н**] *n.m.* [*fem.* **-мя́нка**] Armenian. —**армя́нский,** *adj.* Armenian.
арома́т *n.* aroma; fragrance. —**арома́тный; аромати́чный; ароматический,** *adj.* aromatic; fragrant.
а́рочный *adj.* arched: а́рочный мост, arched bridge.
арпе́джио *adv. & n. indecl.* arpeggio.
арсена́л *n.* arsenal; armory.
арта́читься *v.r. impfv.* to balk.
артезиа́нский *adj.* artesian: артезиа́нский коло́дец, artesian well.
арте́ль *n.f.* workers' cooperative; artel. —**арте́льный,** *adj.* artel *(attrib.).* —**арте́льщик,** *n.* member of an artel.
артериа́льный *adj.* arterial.
артериосклеро́з *n.* arteriosclerosis.
арте́рия *n.* **1,** *anat.* artery. **2,** main route; artery. —**во́дная арте́рия,** waterway.
арти́кль *n.m., gram.* article.
артикули́ровать *v. impfv.* [*pres.* **-рую, -руешь**] to articulate.
артикуля́ция *n.* articulation.
артилле́рия *n.* artillery. —**артиллери́йский,** *adj.* artillery *(attrib.)*; gunnery *(attrib.)*; ordnance *(attrib.).* —**артиллери́ст,** *n.* artilleryman; gunner.
арти́ст *n.m.* [*fem.* **-ти́стка**] performing artist; performer.
артисти́ческий *adj.* **1,** artist's; performer's. **2,** artistic; masterly; masterful.
артисти́чность *n.f.* artistic talent; artistry.
арти́стка [*gen. pl.* **-ток**] *n., fem. of* **арти́ст.**
артишо́к *n.* artichoke.
артри́т *n.* arthritis. —**артрити́ческий,** *adj.* arthritic.
а́рфа *n.* harp. —**арфи́ст; арфи́стка,** *n.* harpist.
архаи́зм *n.* archaism. —**архаи́ческий; архаи́чный,** *adj.* archaic.
арха́нгел *n.* archangel.
археоло́гия *n.* archeology. —**архео́лог,** *n.* archeologist. —**археологи́ческий,** *adj.* archeological.
архи́в *n.* archives. —**сдать в архи́в,** to put away for good; consign to oblivion.
архива́риус *n.* archivist.
архи́вный *adj.* archive *(attrib.).*
архидья́кон *n.* archdeacon.
архиепи́скоп *n.* archbishop.
архиере́й *n., Orth. Ch.* bishop; archbishop; metropolitan.
архимандри́т *n., Orth. Ch.* archimandrite.
архипела́г *n.* archipelago.
архите́ктор *n.* architect. —**архите́кторский,** *adj.* architect's.
архитекту́ра *n.* architecture. —**архитекту́рный,** *adj.* architectural.
арши́н *n.* **1,** [*gen. pl.* **арши́н**] old Russian unit of length equal to approx. 28 inches; arshin. **2,** [*gen. pl.* **арши́нов**] ruler measuring an arshin in length. —**как арши́н проглоти́л,** ramrod straight. —**ме́рить на свой арши́н,** to measure by one's own yardstick.
арши́нный *adj.* **1,** of the length of an arshin. **2,** *(of writing, headlines, etc.)* huge.
арьерга́рд *n.* rear guard. —**арьерга́рдный,** *adj.* rearguard *(attrib.).*
ас *n.* ace (pilot).
асбе́ст *n.* asbestos. —**асбе́стовый,** *adj.* asbestos.
асе́птика (сэ) *n.* asepsis. —**асепти́ческий,** *adj.* aseptic.
асимметри́я *n.* asymmetry. —**асимметри́ческий; асимметри́чный,** *adj.* asymmetric; asymmetrical.

аскéт *n.* ascetic. —**аскети́зм,** *n.* asceticism. —**аскети́ческий,** *adj.* ascetic.

аскорби́новый *adj., in* **аскорби́новая кислотá,** ascorbic acid.

аспéкт *n.* aspect; viewpoint; perspective.

áспид *n.* **1,** asp *(snake).* **2,** *obs.* slate.

áспидный *adj.* **1,** slate. **2,** slate-black. —**áспидный слáнец,** slate.

аспирáнт *n.* graduate student. —**аспирантýра,** *n.* postgraduate course.

аспири́н *n.* aspirin.

ассамблéя *n.* assembly.

ассенизáция *n.* sewage disposal.

ассигновáние *n.* **1,** allocation; appropriation. **2,** allocated sum; appropriation.

ассигновáть *v. impfv. & pfv.* [*pres.* **-нýю, -нýешь**] to allocate; appropriate (funds).

ассимили́ровать *v. impfv. & pfv.* [*pres.* **-рую, -руешь**] to assimilate. —**ассимили́роваться,** *refl.* to assimilate; become assimilated.

ассимиля́ция *n.* assimilation.

ассири́ец [*gen.* **-и́йца**] *n.m.* [*fem.* **-и́йка**] Assyrian. —**ассири́йский,** *adj.* Assyrian.

ассистéнт *n.* **1,** assistant. **2,** lecturer; assistant professor.

ассисти́ровать *v. impfv.* [*pres.* **-рую, -руешь**] *(with dat.)* to assist.

ассонáнс *n.* assonance.

ассортимéнт *n.* selection; assortment.

ассоциáция *n.* **1,** association; society. **2,** association *(in one's mind).*

ассоции́ровать *v. impfv. & pfv.* [*pres.* **-рую, -руешь**] to associate *(in one's mind);* make an association between.

астати́н *n.* astatine.

астерóид (тэ) *n.* asteroid.

астигмати́зм *n.* astigmatism. —**астигмати́ческий,** *adj.* astigmatic.

áстма *n.* asthma. —**асмáтик,** *n., colloq.* asthmatic. —**астмати́ческий,** *adj.* asthmatic.

áстра *n.* aster.

астролóгия *n.* astrology. —**астрóлог,** *n.* astrologer. —**астрологи́ческий,** *adj.* astrological.

астроля́бия *n.* astrolabe.

астронавигáция *n.* celestial navigation.

астронóмия *n.* astronomy. —**астронóм,** *n.* astronomer. —**астрономи́ческий,** *adj.* astronomic(al).

астрофи́зика *n.* astrophysics. —**астрофи́зик,** *n.* astrophysicist. —**астрофизи́ческий,** *adj.* astrophysical.

асфáльт *n.* asphalt.

асфальти́ровать *v. impfv. & pfv.* [*pres.* **-рую, -руешь**] to asphalt.

асфáльтовый *adj.* asphalt.

асфи́ксия *n.* asphyxia; asphyxiation.

атави́зм *n.* atavism. —**атависти́ческий,** *adj.* atavistic.

атáка *n.* attack.

атаковáть *v. impfv. & pfv.* [*pres.* **-кýю, -кýешь**] to attack.

атакси́я *n.* ataxia.

атамáн *n.* Cossack chieftain; ataman.

атеи́зм (тэ) *n.* atheism. —**атеи́ст,** *n.* atheist. —**атеисти́ческий,** *adj.* atheistic.

ательé (тэ) *n. neut. indecl.* **1,** studio. **2,** dress shop; tailor shop.

атипи́ческий *adj.* atypical.

атланти́ческий *adj.* Atlantic.

áтлас *n.* atlas.

атлáс *n.* satin. —**атлáсный,** *adj.* satin.

атлéт *n.* athlete.

атлéтика *n.* athletics. —**лёгкая атлéтика,** track and field. —**тяжёлая атлéтика,** weightlifting.

атлети́ческий *adj.* athletic.

атмосфéра *n.* atmosphere. —**атмосфéрный,** *adj.* atmospheric.

атóлл *n.* atoll.

áтом *n.* atom.

áтомный *adj.* atomic. —**áтомная бóмба,** atomic bomb.

атонáльный *adj.* atonal. —**атонáльность,** *n.f.* atonality.

атрибýт *n.* **1,** attribute; characteristic. **2,** *gram.* modifier; qualifier; attribute; attributive. —**атрибути́вный,** *adj.* attributive.

атропи́н *n.* atropine.

атрофи́роваться *v.r. impfv. & pfv.* [*pres.* **-руется**] to atrophy; become atrophied.

атрофи́я *n.* atrophy.

атташé *n.m. indecl.* attaché.

аттестáт *n.* certificate; diploma. —**аттестáт зрéлости,** secondary-school diploma.

аттестáция *n.* written recommendation; character reference.

аттестовáть *v. impfv. & pfv.* [*pres.* **-тýю, -тýешь**] **1,** to recommend. **2,** to promote.

аттракциóн *n.* **1,** number; act. **2,** *pl.* amusements; attractions *(in a park).*

атý *interj., used in hunting with hounds* tallyho!; halloo! —**атý его!,** sic 'im!

аý *interj., shouted to another from a distance* hello there!

аудиéнция *n.* audience; formal interview.

аудитóрия *n.* **1,** auditorium; lecture hall. **2,** audience.

аýкать *v. impfv.* [*pfv.* **аýкнуть**] *colloq.* to shout "**аý**!" —**аýкаться,** *refl.* to exchange shouts of "**аý**!"

аукциóн *n.* auction. —**аукциони́ст,** *n.* auctioneer. —**аукциóнный,** *adj.* auction *(attrib.).*

аýл *n.* village in the Caucasus or Central Asia; aul.

аутенти́чный (тэ) *adj.* authentic; genuine. —**аутенти́чность,** *n.f.* authenticity.

аутсáйдер (дэ) *n., sports* outsider; long shot.

афáзия *n.* aphasia.

афгáнец [*gen.* **-нца**] *n.m.* [*fem.* **-нка**] Afghan. —**афгáнский,** *adj.* Afghan; Afghanistani.

афéлий *n.* aphelion.

афéра *n.* swindle; fraud. —**афери́ст,** *n.* swindler; crook.

афи́нский *adj.* Athenian.

афи́ша *n.* poster; bill.

афиши́ровать *v. impfv. & pfv.* [*pres.* **-рую, -руешь**] to flaunt; parade; advertise.

афори́зм *n.* aphorism. —**афористи́ческий; афористи́чный,** *adj.* aphoristic.

африкáнец [*gen.* **-нца**] *n.m.* [*fem.* **-нка**] African. —**африкáнский,** *adj.* African.

афрóнт *n., obs.* affront; insult.

аффéкт *n.* fit; paroxysm *(of rage, terror, despair, etc.).*

аффектáция *n.* affectation.

аффекти́рованный *adj.* affected.

ах *interj.* ah!; oh!

áхать *v. impfv.* [*pfv.* **áхнуть**] to shout "**ах**!"

ахиллéсов *adj., in* **ахиллéсова пятá,** Achilles' heel.

ахинéя *n., colloq.* nonsense: нести́ ахинéю, to talk nonsense.
áхнуть *v., pfv. of* **áхать.**
ахтерштéвень (тэ) [*gen.* **-вня**] *n.m.* sternpost.
ахти́ *interj., obs.* oh! —**не ахти́ как,** *colloq.* not particularly. —**не ахти́ какóй,** *colloq.* no great shakes; nothing to rave about.
ацетилéн *n.* acetylene. —**ацетилéновый,** *adj.* acetylene.
ацетóн *n.* acetone.
аэрáрий *n.* terrace for sunbathing.
аэрáция *n.* aeration.
аэровокзáл *n.* air terminal.
аэродинáмика *n.* aerodynamics.
аэродинами́ческий *adj.* aerodynamic. —**аэродинами́ческая трубá** wind tunnel.
аэродрóм *n.* airdrome; airfield.
аэрозóль *n.m.* aerosol.
аэронáвт *n.* balloonist; aeronaut. —**аэронáвтика,** *n.* aeronautics.
аэроплáн *n., obs.* airplane. —**аэроплáнный,** *adj., obs.* airplane *(attrib.).*
аэропóрт [*2nd loc.* **аэропортý**] *n.* airport.
аэросни́мок [*gen.* **-мка**] *n.* aerial photograph.
аэростáт *n.* balloon; aerostat. —**аэростáтика,** *n.* aerostatics.
аэрофотоаппарáт *n.* aerial camera.
аэрофотосъёмка *n.* aerial photography.
аятóлла *n.m.* ayatollah.

Б

Б, б *n. neut.* second letter of the Russian alphabet.
б *particle* = **бы.**
ба *interj., colloq., expressing surprise* well!
бáба *n.* **1,** *colloq.* woman. **2,** *colloq.* milksop; sissy. **3,** *mech.* ram. **4,** tall round cake. —**рóмовая бáба,** baba au rhum. —**снéжная бáба,** snowman.
бáбий [*fem.* **-бья**] *adj., colloq.* woman's. —**бáбье лéто,** Indian summer. —**бáбьи скáзки,** old wives' tales. —**бáбье цáрство,** petticoat government.
бáбка [*gen. pl.* **-бок**] *n.* **1,** *colloq.* grandmother. **2,** *colloq.* old woman. **3,** [*often,* **повивáльная бáбка**] *obs.* midwife. **4,** *anat.* pastern.
бáбник *n., colloq.* ladies' man.
бáбочка [*gen. pl.* **-чек**] *n.* **1,** butterfly. **2,** moth. **3,** *colloq.* bow tie.
бáбушка [*gen. pl.* **-шек**] *n.* grandmother.
бавáрский *adj.* Bavarian.
багáж [*gen.* **-гажá**] *n.* baggage; luggage.
багáжник *n.* **1,** luggage rack. **2,** trunk *(of an automobile).*
багáжный *adj.* baggage *(attrib.).*
багóр [*gen.* **-грá**] *n.* hook; boat hook. —**рыболóвный багóр,** gaff.
багровéть *v. impfv.* [*pfv.* **побагровéть**] to turn crimson; flush.
багрóвый *adj.* crimson.
багрянец [*gen.* **-нца**] *n.* crimson.
бадминтóн *n.* badminton.
бадья́ *n.* bucket; pail.
бáза *n.* **1,** base. **2,** basis; foundation. **3,** depot. **4,** camp; lodge.
базáльт *n.* basalt. —**базáльтовый,** *adj.* basalt.
базáр *n.* **1,** market; marketplace; bazaar. **2,** sale; fair; bazaar. **3,** *colloq.* clamor; hullabaloo. —**пти́чий базáр,** seashore colony of birds.
базáрный *adj.* market *(attrib.);* of the marketplace.
базéдов (зэ) *adj., in* **базéдова болéзнь,** exophthalmic goiter.
базили́к *n.* basil.
базили́ка *n.* basilica.
бази́ровать *v. impfv.* [*pres.* **-рую, -руешь**] to base. —**бази́роваться,** *refl. (with* **на** + *prepl.)* to be based (on).
бáзис *n.* base; basis.
бáзисный *adj.* base: бáзисная ценá, base price.
бáзовый *adj.* base *(attrib.);* of a base.
бай-бáй *interj.* bye-bye.
байбáк [*gen.* **-бакá**] *n.* a species of marmot; bobac.
байдáрка [*gen. pl.* **-рок**] *n.* kayak; canoe.
бáйка *n.* baize; flannel. —**бáйковый,** *adj.* baize; flannel.
бак *n.* **1,** tank; cistern. **2,** forecastle.
бакалáвр *n.* bachelor *(holder of a bachelor's degree).* —**стéпень бакалáвра,** bachelor's degree; baccalaureate.
бакалéя *n.* groceries. —**бакалéйный,** *adj.* grocery *(attrib.).* —**бакалéйщик,** *n.* grocer.
бакели́т *n.* bakelite.
бáкен *n.* buoy.
бакенбáрды [*gen.* **-бáрд**] *n. pl.* whiskers.
бáки [*gen.* **бак**] *n.pl.* = **бакенбáрды.**
баккарá *n. neut. indecl.* baccarat.
баклáга *n.* flask; canteen.
баклажáн *n.* eggplant. —**баклажáнный,** *adj.* eggplant *(attrib.).*
баклáн *n.* cormorant *(bird).*
баклýши *n. pl., in* **бить баклýши,** to twiddle one's thumbs.
бактериáльный *adj.* bacterial; bacteria *(attrib.).*
бактериолóгия *n.* bacteriology. —**бактериóлог,** *n.* bacteriologist. —**бактериологи́ческий,** *adj.* bacteriological.
бактéрия *n.* bacterium.

бал [*2nd loc.* **балу́;** *pl.* **балы́**] *n.* ball; formal dance. —**ко́нчен бал,** it's all over.
балага́н *n., obs.* **1,** carnival booth. **2,** side show. **3,** *fig.* farce.
балага́нить *v. impfv., colloq.* to play the buffoon; clown (around).
балага́нный *adj.* farcical.
балагу́р *n., colloq.* joker; jester.
балагу́рить *v. impfv., colloq.* to jest; joke.
балагу́рство *n.* witty talk; joking.
балала́ечник *n.* balalaika player.
балала́йка [*gen. pl.* **-ла́ек**] *n.* balalaika.
бала́нс *n.* **1,** balance; equilibrium. **2,** *econ.; finance* balance: платёжный/торго́вый бала́нс, balance of payments/trade. —**подводи́ть бала́нс, 1,** to balance the books. **2,** *fig.* to strike a balance.
балансёр *n.* balancer; tightrope walker.
баланси́р *n.* **1,** balancing pole. **2,** *mech.* balance beam. **3,** balance wheel.
баланси́ровать *v. impfv.* [*pfv.* **сбаланси́ровать;** *pres.* **-рую, -руешь**] **1,** [*impfv. only*] to balance oneself; remain balanced. **2,** [*impfv. only*] *(with instr.)* to balance (something precariously). **3,** to balance; bring into balance. **4,** *bookkeeping* to balance.
бала́нсовый *adj.* balance *(attrib.):* бала́нсовый отчёт, balance sheet.
балбе́с *n., colloq.* booby; nitwit.
балда́ *n.m. & f., colloq.* blockhead.
балдахи́н *n.* canopy.
балери́на *n.* ballerina.
бале́т *n.* ballet.
балетме́йстер *n.* ballet master.
бале́тный *adj.* ballet *(attrib.).*
балетома́н *n.* ballet lover.
ба́лка [*gen. pl.* **-лок**] *n.* **1,** beam; girder. **2,** ravine; gully.
балка́нский *adj.* Balkan.
балка́р [*gen. pl.* **-ка́р**] *n.m.* [*fem.* **-ка́рка**] Balkar *(one of a people inhabiting the Caucasus). Also,* **балка́рец** [*gen.* **-рца**].
балка́рский *adj.* Balkar.
балко́н *n.* balcony.
балл *n.* **1,** unit of measure of the intensity of winds, earthquakes, etc. **2,** mark *(in school).* **3,** *sports* point.
балла́да *n.* **1,** ballad. **2,** *music* ballade.
балла́ст *n.* ballast.
балли́стика *n.* ballistics. —**баллисти́ческий,** *adj.* ballistic.
балло́н *n.* **1,** cylinder; bottle. **2,** rubber tire.
баллоти́ровать *v. impfv.* [*pres.* **-рую, -руешь**] to vote on; vote for. —**баллоти́роваться,** *refl. (with* **в** *or* **на** + *acc.)* to run (for); be a candidate (for).
баллотиро́вка *n.* voting; balloting.
бало́ванный *adj., colloq.* spoiled; pampered.
балова́ть *v. impfv.* [*pfv.* **избалова́ть;** *pres.* **-лу́ю, -лу́ешь**] to spoil; pamper. —**балова́ться,** *refl.* [*impfv. only*] *colloq.* **1,** to be naughty; be mischievous. **2,** *(with* **с** + *instr.)* to play with (something dangerous). **3,** *(with instr.)* to dabble (in); indulge (in).
ба́ловень [*gen.* **-вня**] *n.m.* **1,** pet; favorite. **2,** mischievous child. —**ба́ловень судьбы́,** child of fortune; lucky person.
баловни́к [*gen.* **-ника́**] *n., colloq.* naughty child; mischievous child.
баловство́ *n., colloq.* **1,** spoiling. **2,** mischief.
балти́йский *adj.* Baltic.
бальза́м *n.* **1,** balsam. **2,** *fig.* balm.
бальзами́ровать *v. impfv.* [*pfv.* **набальзами́ровать;** *pres.* **-рую, -руешь**] to embalm.
бальзамиро́вщик *n.* embalmer.
ба́льный *adj.* of or for a ball; ball *(attrib.).*
балюстра́да *n.* balustrade.
баля́сина *n.* baluster.
баля́сы *n. pl., in* **баля́сы точи́ть,** *colloq.* to joke; jest; talk nonsense.
бамбу́к *n.* bamboo. —**бамбу́ковый,** *adj.* bamboo.
ба́мия *n.* okra; gumbo.
ба́мпер *n.* bumper.
бана́льность *n.f.* **1,** banality. **2,** platitude.
бана́льный *adj.* trite; banal.
бана́н *n.* banana. —**бана́новый,** *adj.* banana *(attrib.).*
ба́нда *n.* gang; band.
банда́ж [*gen.* **-дажа́**] *n.* **1,** abdominal support: грыжево́й банда́ж, truss. **2,** *mech.* tire; rim.
бандеро́ль *n.f.* **1,** wrapping for mailing printed matter. **2,** printed matter sent through the mail: отправля́ть бандеро́лью, to send as printed matter.
ба́нджо *n. indecl.* banjo.
банди́т *n.* bandit; thug. —**бандити́зм,** *n.* banditry. —**банди́тский,** *adj.* bandit *(attrib.).*
банк *n.* **1,** bank. **2,** faro *(card game).*
ба́нка [*gen. pl.* **-нок**] *n.* **1,** jar; can. **2,** *usu. pl.* cupping glass. **3,** shoal; sandbank. —**у́стричная ба́нка,** oyster bed.
банке́т *n.* banquet. —**банке́тный,** *adj.* banquet *(attrib.).*
банки́р *n.* banker.—**банки́рский,** *adj.* banking *(attrib.).*
банкно́т *n.* bank note.
ба́нковский *adj.* bank *(attrib.):* ба́нковская кни́жка, bankbook.
ба́нковый *adj.* bank *(attrib.);* banking *(attrib.).*
банкомёт *n.* banker *(in a game).*
банкро́т *n.* one who is bankrupt. —**банкро́тство,** *n.* bankruptcy.
ба́нный *adj.* bath *(attrib.):* ба́нное полоте́нце, bath towel.
бант *n.* bow: завяза́ть ба́нтом, to tie in a bow. —**ба́нтик,** *n.* small bow.
ба́нщик *n.* bathhouse attendant.
ба́ня *n.* **1,** public bath. **2,** *colloq.* steam bath. **3,** *colloq.* tongue-lashing; dressing-down. —**крова́вая ба́ня,** blood bath.
баоба́б *n.* baobab.
бапти́ст *n.* Baptist. —**бапти́стский,** *adj.* Baptist.
баптисте́рий *n.* baptistery.
бар *n.* **1,** bar; barroom. **2,** bar *(unit of pressure).*
бараба́н *n.* **1,** drum. **2,** cylinder *(of a revolver).*
бараба́нить *v. impfv.* **1,** to drum: бараба́нить па́льцами по́ столу, to drum on the table. **2,** *(of rain)* to patter.
бараба́нный *adj.* drum *(attrib.);* of drums. —**бараба́нная перепо́нка,** eardrum.
бараба́нщик *n.* drummer.
барабу́лька [*gen. pl.* **-лек**] *n.* red mullet.
бара́к *n.* hut.
бара́н *n.* **1,** ram. **2,** (wild) sheep. —**сне́жный бара́н,** bighorn sheep.
бара́ний [*fem.* **-нья**] *adj.* **1,** sheep's; sheep *(attrib.);*

ram's; ram *(attrib.)*. **2,** sheepskin. **3,** mutton *(attrib.)*. —**в бара́ний рог согну́ть,** to bend to one's will.
бара́нина *n.* **1,** mutton. **2,** lamb.
бара́нка [*gen. pl.* **-нок**] *n.* **1,** bagel. **2,** *colloq.* steering wheel.
барахло́ *n., colloq.* **1,** old things; old clothes. **2,** junk; trash.
бара́хтаться *v.r. impfv.* to flounder; thrash around.
бара́чный *adj.* like barracks.
бара́шек [*gen.* **-шка**] *n.* **1,** lamb. **2,** lambskin. **3,** *mech.* thumbscrew. **4,** *pl.* fleecy clouds. **5,** whitecaps *(on the sea)*.
бара́шковый *adj.* lamb *(attrib.)*; lambskin *(attrib.)*.
барбари́с *n.* **1,** barberries. **2,** a (single) barberry.
барбитура́т *n.* barbiturate.
барбо́с *n.* watchdog.
барви́нок [*gen.* **-нка**] *n.* periwinkle.
бард *n.* bard.
барелье́ф *n.* bas-relief. —**барелье́фный,** *adj.* bas-relief *(attrib.)*.
ба́ржа *also,* **баржа́** *n.* barge.
ба́рий *n.* barium.
ба́рин *n., pre-rev.* gentleman; nobleman; aristocrat. —**жить ба́рином,** to live like a king.
бари́т *n.* barite; heavy spar.
барито́н *n.* baritone.
баритона́льный *adj.* baritone. **баритона́льный бас,** bass baritone.
барито́нный *adj.* baritone.
барк *n.* bark *(sailing vessel)*.
ба́рка [*gen. pl.* **-рок**] *n.* barge.
баркаро́ла *n.* barcarole.
барка́с *n.* **1,** large rowboat. **2,** harbor vessel; launch.
баро́кко *n. indecl.* baroque.
баро́метр *n.* barometer. —**барометри́ческий,** *adj.* barometric.
баро́н *n.* baron.
барonéсса *n.* baroness.
бароне́т *n.* baronet.
баро́нство *n.* barony. —**баро́нский,** *adj.* baron's; baronial.
баро́чный *adj.* baroque.
ба́ррель *n.m.* barrel *(measure)*.
баррика́да *n.* barricade.
баррикади́ровать *v. impfv.* [*pfv.* **забаррикади́ровать;** *pres.* **-рую, -руешь**] to barricade.
барс *n.* snow leopard.
ба́рский *adj.* **1,** gentleman's; master's. **2,** haughty; supercilious.
ба́рственный *adj.* lordly.
ба́рство *n., pre-rev.* **1,** gentry; nobility. **2,** haughtiness. **3,** idle luxury.
барсу́к [*gen.* **-сука́**] *n.* badger.
барха́н *n.* sand dune.
ба́рхат *n.* velvet.
бархати́стый *adj.* velvety.
ба́рхатка [*gen. pl.* **-ток**] *n.* velvet ribbon.
ба́рхатный *adj.* velvet. —**ба́рхатный сезо́н,** warm months of early autumn in the south of Russia.
ба́рхатцы [*gen.* **-цев**] *n. pl.* (French *or* African) marigold.
ба́рыня *n., pre-rev.* wife of a **ба́рин.**
бары́ш [*gen.* **-рыша́**] *n., usu. pl.* profit.
бары́шник *n., obs.* **1,** horsetrader. **2,** profiteer. —**бары́шничество,** *n.* profiteering.
ба́рышня [*gen. pl.* **-шень**] *n., pre-rev.* **1,** unmarried daughter of a nobleman. **2,** young lady; miss.
барье́р *n.* **1,** barrier; bar. **2,** *sports* hurdle. —**барье́рный,** *adj.* hurdle *(attrib.)*: барье́рный бег, hurdle race; hurdles.
бас [*pl.* **басы́**] *n., music* bass.
баси́стый *adj., colloq.* deep; low *(in sound)*; bass.
баси́ть *v. impfv.* [*pres.* **башу́, баси́шь**] *colloq.* to speak (*or* sing) in a bass voice.
баск *n.m.* [*fem.* **-ко́нка**] Basque.
баскетбо́л *n.* basketball. —**баскетболи́ст,** *n.* basketball player. —**баскетбо́льный,** *adj.* basketball *(attrib.)*.
ба́скский *adj.* Basque.
баснопи́сец [*gen.* **-сца**] *n.* fabulist.
басносло́вный *adj.* **1,** fabled; legendary. **2,** fabulous; fantastic.
ба́сня [*gen. pl.* **ба́сен**] *n.* fable.
басо́вый *adj., music* bass.
бассе́йн *n.* **1,** pool: бассе́йн для пла́вания, swimming pool. **2,** *geol.* basin: бассе́йн реки́, river basin; у́гольный бассе́йн, coal basin.
ба́ста *interj., colloq.* enough!; that'll do!
бастио́н *n.* bastion.
бастова́ть *v. impfv.* [*pres.* **-сту́ю, -сту́ешь**] to strike; be on strike; go on strike.
батали́ст *n.* painter of battle scenes.
бата́лия *n.* **1,** *obs.* battle; fray. **2,** *colloq.* row; ruckus.
батальо́н *n.* battalion. —**батальо́нный,** *adj.* battalion.
батаре́йка [*gen. pl.* **-ре́ек**] *n.* small battery.
батаре́йный *adj.* **1,** battery *(attrib.)*; battery operated. **2,** *mil.* battery *(attrib.)*.
батаре́я *n.* **1,** *mil.* battery. **2,** *electricity* battery. —**батаре́я отопле́ния,** radiator.
бата́т *n.* sweet potato; yam.
ба́тенька *n.m., obs. familiar form of address* my friend; old boy.
бати́ст *n.* cambric; batiste. —**бати́стовый,** *adj.* made of this fabric.
бато́н *n.* **1,** long loaf of bread. **2,** stick of candy.
батра́к [*gen.* **-трака́**] *n.* farm worker; farm hand. —**батра́цкий,** *adj.* farm worker's.
батра́чество *n.* **1,** farm work. **2,** farm laborers; farmhands.
батра́чить *v. impfv.* to work as a farm laborer.
бату́т *n.* trampoline.
ба́тюшка *n.m.* **1,** *obs.* father. **2,** *(used in addresing a priest)* father. **3,** *obs., colloq.* old boy!; my dear fellow! **4,** *colloq.* father's name; patronymic. —**ба́тюшки (мои́)**!, good gracious!; dear me!
ба́ул *n.* steamer trunk.
бах *interj.* bang!
бахва́л *n., colloq.* braggart.
бахва́литься *v.r. impfv., colloq.* to brag.
бахва́льство *n., colloq.* bragging; boasting.
бахрома́ *n.* fringe. —**бахро́мчатый,** *adj.* fringed.
бахча́ *n.* melon field.
бац *interj.* bang!; smack!; crack!
баци́лла *n.* bacillus.
ба́шенка [*gen. pl.* **-нок**] *n.* small tower; turret.
ба́шенный *adj.* tower *(attrib.)*.
башка́ *n., colloq.* head; noggin.
башки́р [*gen. pl.* **-ки́р**] *n.m.* [*fem.* **-ки́рка**] Bashkir *(one of a people inhabiting central European Russia)*. —**башки́рский,** *adj.* Bashkir.
башкови́тый *adj., colloq.* brainy.

башма́к [*gen.* **-мака́**] *n.* shoe. —**под башмако́м у,** under the thumb of.
башма́чник *n., obs.* shoemaker; cobbler.
башма́чный *adj.* shoe *(attrib.).*
ба́шня [*gen. pl.* **ба́шен**] *n.* tower. —**ору́дийная ба́шня,** turret *(for a gun).*
баю́кать *v. impfv.* [*pfv.* **убаю́кать**] to lull/sing/rock to sleep.
бая́н *n.* accordion.
бде́ние *n., obs.* vigil; watch.
бди́тельный *adj.* vigilant. —**бди́тельность,** *n.f.* vigilance.
бег *n.* **1,** run; running. **2,** race. —**бег на ме́сте,** *sports* running in place. —**в бега́х,** on the run. —**на бегу́,** on the double.
бега́ [*gen.* **бего́в**] *n. pl.* harness racing; harness races.
бе́гать *v. impfv.* **1,** *indeterm. of* **бежа́ть. 2,** to move rapidly; flit; dart. **3,** *(with* **от***) colloq.* to avoid; get away from. **4,** *(with* **за** + *instr.) colloq.* to chase (after).
бегемо́т *n.* **1,** hippopotamus. **2,** *Bib.* behemoth.
бегле́ц [*gen.* **-леца́**] *n.m.* [*fem.* **-ля́нка**] fugitive; escaped convict.
бе́гло *adv.* **1,** fluently. **2,** with facility. **3,** in a cursory manner.
бе́глость *n.f.* **1,** fluency. **2,** facility.
бе́глый *adj.* **1,** fluent. **2,** facile. **3,** cursory. **4,** *phonet. (of a vowel)* fleeting. **5,** *in* бе́глый ого́нь, rapid fire. **6,** *obs.* fugitive; runaway. —*n.* fugitive.
бегля́нка [*gen. pl.* **-нок**] *n., fem. of* **бегле́ц.**
бегово́й *adj.* running *(attrib.);* racing *(attrib.);* race *(attrib.).* —**бегова́я доро́жка,** running track. —**бегова́я ло́шадь,** racehorse.
бего́м *adv.* running; on the double.
бего́ния *n.* begonia.
беготня́ *n., colloq.* running about; scurrying about.
бе́гство *n.* **1,** flight: обраща́ть в бе́гство, to put to flight. **2,** escape.
бегу́н [*gen.* **-гуна́**] *n.m.* [*fem.* **-гу́нья**] *sports* runner.
беда́ [*pl.* **бе́ды**] *n.* trouble; misfortune. —**беда́ в том, что...,** the trouble is... —**беда́ как,** *colloq.* very much. —**в то́м-то и беда́,** that's just the trouble.—**как на беду́,** as luck would have it. —**на беду́,** unfortunately. —**на свою́ беду́,** to one's cost. —**не беда́,** it doesn't matter; no harm done. —**что за беда́**!, what does it matter?
бедла́м *n.* bedlam; chaos.
бедне́ть *v. impfv.* [*pfv.* **обедне́ть**] to become poor.
бе́дно *adv.* **1,** in poor circumstances: они́ живу́т ужа́сно бе́дно, they live in utter poverty. **2,** shabbily: бе́дно оде́тый, shabbily dressed.
бе́дность *n.f.* poverty.
беднота́ *n.* **1,** the poor. **2,** *colloq.* poverty.
бе́дный *adj.* [*short form* **бе́ден, бедна́, бе́дно**] **1,** poor. **2,** meager.
бедня́га *n.m. & f., colloq.* poor fellow; poor devil. *Also,* **бедня́жка.**
бедня́к [*gen.* **-няка́**] *n.* poor person; pauper.
бедо́вый *adj., colloq.* **1,** daring. **2,** mischievous.
бедоку́р *n.m.* [*fem.* **-ку́рка**] *colloq.* mischief-maker.
бедоку́рить *v. impfv.* [*pfv.* **набедоку́рить**] *colloq.* to make mischief.
бе́дренный *adj.* hip *(attrib.);* thigh *(attrib.).* —**бе́дренная кость,** thighbone; femur.
бедро́ [*pl.* **бёдра, бёдер**] *n.* hip; thigh.
бе́дственный *adj.* calamitous; disastrous.
бе́дствие *n.* calamity; disaster. —**сигна́л бе́дствия,** distress signal.
бе́дствовать *v. impfv.* [*pres.* **-ствую, -ствуешь**] to live in poverty.
бедуи́н *n.* Bedouin.
беж *adj. indecl.* beige: пла́тье цве́та беж, beige dress.
бежа́ть *v. impfv.* [*pfv.* **побежа́ть;** *pres.* **бегу́, бежи́шь, ...бегу́т**] **1,** to run. **2,** to race. **3,** *fig.* to fly; flow; fleet. —*v. impfv. & pfv.* to escape; flee: бежа́ть из тюрьмы́, to escape from prison. *See also* **бе́гать.**
бе́жевый *adj., colloq.* beige.
бе́женец [*gen.* **-нца**] *n.m.* [*fem.* **-нка**] refugee.
без *also, before* **весь** *and* **вся́кий, безо** *prep., with gen.* **1,** without: идти́ без шля́пы, to go without a hat. **2,** *used to express minutes before the hour* to; before; of: без десяти́ семь, ten minutes to seven; без че́тверти три, a quarter to three. —**и без того́,** already: и без того́ сло́жное положе́ние, an already complicated situation.
без- *also,* **бес-, безъ-** *prefix* not; without; lacking; *often equivalent to English* **un-; in-; ir-; im-; il-; -less:** безалкого́льный, nonalcoholic; бесце́льный, aimless.
безала́берный *adj.* disorderly; slipshod.
безалкого́льный *adj.* nonalcoholic.
безапелляцио́нный *adj.* **1,** *law* not subject to appeal. **2,** categorical; peremptory.
беза́томный *adj.* atom-free.
безбе́дный *adj.* materially secure; comfortable. —**безбе́дно,** *adv.* comfortably: жить безбе́дно, to live comfortably.
безбиле́тный *adj.* having no ticket.
безбо́жие *n.* atheism. —**безбо́жник,** *n.* atheist.
безбо́жный *adj.* **1,** *obs.* godless. **2,** *colloq.* shameless; outrageous. —**безбо́жно,** *adv., colloq.* outrageously; something awful.
безболе́зненный *adj.* painless. —**безболе́зненно,** *adv.* painlessly.
безборо́дый *adj.* beardless.
безбоя́зненный *adj.* fearless; dauntless.
безбра́чие *n.* celibacy. —**безбра́чный,** *adj.* celibate.
безбре́жный *adj.* boundless; limitless.
безве́стный *adj.* unknown; obscure. —**безве́стность,** *n.f.* obscurity.
безве́тренный *adj.* **1,** windless. **2,** still; calm.
безве́трие *n.* absence of wind; calm.
безви́нный *adj.* innocent; guiltless.
безвку́сие *n.* poor taste; lack of taste; tastelessness. *Also, colloq.* **безвку́сица.**
безвку́сный *adj.* **1,** tasteless. **2,** in poor taste. **3,** lacking good taste. —**безвку́сно,** *adv.* without taste.
безвла́стие *n.* anarchy.
безво́дный *adj.* arid; waterless. —**безво́дье,** *n.* lack (*or* shortage) of water.
безвозвра́тный *adj.* **1,** irretrievable. **2,** not requiring repayment: безвозвра́тная ссу́да, outright grant. —**безвозвра́тно,** *adv.* for good; forever.
безвозду́шный *adj., in* **безвозду́шное простра́нство,** vacuum.
безвозме́здный *adj.* free (of charge). —**безвозме́здно,** *adv.* free of charge; gratis.
безво́лие *n.* lack of will.
безволо́сый *adj.* having no hair.
безво́льный *adj.* weak-willed.
безвре́дный *adj.* harmless; innocuous.
безвре́менный *adj. (of someone's death)* untimely.

безвы́ездно *adv.* **1,** without a break. **2,** all one's life.
безвы́ездный *adj. (of a stay or residence)* permanent.
безвы́ходный *adj.* hopeless; untenable.
безгла́зый *adj.* **1,** having no eyes. **2,** one-eyed.
безгла́сный *adj., obs.* **1,** mute. **2,** timid; reticent.
безголо́вый *adj.* **1,** headless. **2,** *colloq.* brainless; scatterbrained.
безголо́сый *adj.* **1,** voiceless; without a voice. **2,** having a poor voice.
безгра́мотный *adj.* **1,** illiterate. **2,** ungrammatical; full of mistakes. —**безгра́мотно,** *adv.* like an illiterate person. —**безгра́мотность,** *n.f.* illiteracy.
безграни́чный *adj.* boundless; limitless; infinite.
безда́рность *n.f.* **1,** lack of talent. **2,** *fig.* person without talent.
безда́рный *adj.* **1,** lacking (*or* without) talent. **2,** incompetent; inept. **3,** without merit; without a redeeming feature.
безде́йственный *adj.* inactive; idle.
безде́йствие *n.* inaction; inactivity; idleness.
безде́йствовать *v. impfv.* [*pres.* **-ствую, -ствуешь**] **1,** to do nothing; take no action. **2,** to be idle; be inoperative.
безде́лица *n., colloq.* trifle.
безделу́шка [*gen. pl.* **-шек**] *n.* trinket; knickknack.
безде́лье *n.* idleness.
безде́льник *n., colloq.* idler; loafer.
безде́льничать *v. impfv.* to idle; loaf; do nothing.
безде́нежный *adj.* **1,** not involving cash. **2,** *colloq.* penniless.
безде́нежье *n.* lack of money.
безде́тный *adj.* childless. —**безде́тность,** *n.f.* childlessness.
безде́ятельный *adj.* inactive; lethargic. —**безде́ятельность,** *n.f.* inactivity; lethargy.
бе́здна *n.* **1,** chasm; abyss. **2,** *colloq.* huge amount; endless number.
бездоказа́тельный *adj.* unsubstantiated; unsupported.
бездо́мный *adj.* homeless; stray.
бездо́нный *adj.* bottomless: бездо́нная про́пасть, bottomless pit.
бездоро́жье *n.* **1,** absence of passable roads; bad roads. **2,** time of year when roads are impassable.
безду́мный *adj.* thoughtless; unthinking.
безду́мье *n.* inability to think clearly; daze.
безду́шие *n.* heartlessness; callousness.
безду́шный *adj.* **1,** *obs.* dead; lifeless. **2,** *fig.* heartless; without a soul. **3,** *fig. (of a performance)* uninspired.
бездыха́нный *adj.* lifeless.
безжа́лостный *adj.* ruthless; merciless; pitiless. —**безжа́лостно,** *adv.* ruthlessly; mercilessly. —**безжа́лостность,** *n.f.* ruthlessness.
безжи́зненный *adj.* **1,** dead; lifeless. **2,** *fig.* without expression; blank.
беззабо́тный *adj.* carefree; happy-go-lucky. —**беззабо́тно,** *adv.* in a carefree manner; without a care. —**беззабо́тность,** *n.f.* unconcern.
беззаве́тный *adj.* selfless.
беззако́ние *n.* **1,** lawlessness. **2,** unlawful act.
беззако́нный *adj.* lawless; unlawful.
беззасте́нчивый *adj.* shameless; brazen.
беззащи́тный *adj.* defenseless; unprotected.
беззвёздный *adj.* starless.
беззву́чный *adj.* soundless; silent.
безземе́лье *n.* lack of land. —**безземе́льный,** *adj.* landless.
беззло́бие *n.* good nature. —**беззло́бный,** *adj.* good-natured.
беззубцо́вый *adj. (of postage stamps)* imperforate.
беззу́бый *adj.* toothless.
безле́сный *adj.* treeless.
безле́сье *n.* lack of forests.
безли́кий *adj.* faceless.
безли́чный *adj.* **1,** faceless. **2,** impersonal.
безлю́дный *adj.* **1,** uninhabited; sparsely populated. **2,** *(of streets, public places, etc.)* empty; deserted.
безлю́дье *n.* absence of people.
безме́н *n.* steelyard.
безме́рный *adj.* boundless; immeasurable. —**безме́рно,** *adv.* beyond measure; extraordinarily.
безмо́зглый *adj., colloq.* brainless; witless.
безмо́лвие *n.* silence.
безмо́лвный *adj.* silent; hushed; mute; speechless.
безмо́лвствовать *v. impfv.* [*pres.* **-ствую, -ствуешь**] to be silent; keep silent.
безмяте́жный *adj.* serene; tranquil. —**безмяте́жность,** *n.f.* serenity; tranquillity.
безнадёжный *adj.* hopeless. —**безнадёжность,** *n.f.* hopelessness.
безнадзо́рный *adj.* unsupervised, neglected.
безнака́занный *adj.* unpunished. —**безнака́занно,** *adv.* with impunity. —**безнака́занность,** *n.f.* impunity.
безнали́чный *adj.* not involving cash.
безнача́лие *n.* anarchy.
безно́гий *adj.* **1,** legless. **2,** having only one leg.
безнра́вственный *adj.* immoral. —**безнра́вственность,** *n.f.* immorality.
безо *prep., var. of* **без,** *used before* **весь** *and* **вся́кий.**
безоби́дный *adj.* inoffensive; innocuous; harmless.
безо́блачный *adj.* **1,** cloudless. **2,** *fig.* serene.
безобра́зие *n.* **1,** ugliness. **2,** outrage; scandal; disgrace.
безобра́зить *v. impfv.* [*pres.* **-жу, -зишь**] to mar the appearance of.
безобра́зник *n., colloq.* **1,** hooligan; rowdy. **2,** naughty child.
безобра́зничать *v. impfv., colloq.* to carry on; behave disgracefully.
безо́бразный *adj.* **1,** formless; shapeless. **2,** (*of writing*) lacking imagery.
безобра́зный *adj.* **1,** ugly; hideous; deformed. **2,** outrageous; scandalous; disgraceful.
безогля́дный *adj.* headlong.
безогово́рочный *adj.* unconditional; unreserved; unqualified.
безопа́сно *adv.* safely. —*adj., used predicatively* safe: здесь безопа́сно, it is safe here.
безопа́сность *n.f.* safety; security. —**Сове́т Безопа́сности,** Security Council. —**те́хника безопа́сности,** accident prevention; safety procedures.
безопа́сный *adj.* **1,** safe; secure. **2,** safety *(attrib.)*; security *(attrib.)*: безопа́сная бри́тва, safety razor.
безору́жный *adj.* **1,** unarmed. **2,** *fig.* defenseless.
безоснова́тельный *adj.* groundless; baseless.
безостано́вочный *adj.* **1,** ceaseless; uninterrupted. **2,** nonstop. —**безостано́вочно,** *adv.* nonstop.
безотве́тный *adj.* **1,** unrequited. **2,** silent. **3,** meek.

безотве́тственный *adj.* irresponsible. —**безотве́тственность,** *n.f.* irresponsibility.
безотка́зный *adj., colloq.* smooth; steady. —**безотка́зно,** *adv.* smoothly; perfectly.
безотка́тный *adj.* recoilless.
безотлага́тельный *adj.* urgent. —**безотлага́тельно,** *adv.* urgently.
безотлу́чный *adj.* **1,** ever-present. **2,** continual.
безотноси́тельно *adv. (with* **к***)* irrespective of; regardless of; without regard to.
безотра́дный *adj.* bleak; dismal; cheerless.
безотчётный *adj.* **1,** instinctive; unconscious. **2,** not accountable; not subject to control.
безоши́бочный *adj.* **1,** without error; perfect. **2,** unerring; infallible.
безрабо́тица *n.* unemployment.
безрабо́тный *adj.* unemployed. —*n.* unemployed person.
безра́достный *adj.* joyless; cheerless.
безразде́льный *adj.* undivided; absolute; complete.
безразли́чие *n.* indifference.
безразли́чно *adv.* with indifference. —*adj., used predicatively* immaterial: мне э́то безразли́чно, it's immaterial to me.
безразли́чный *adj.* **1,** indifferent. **2,** inconsequential; immaterial.
безразме́рный *adj. (of socks, stockings, etc.)* stretch.
безрассу́дный *adj.* rash; reckless; foolhardy. —**безрассу́дно,** *adv.* rashly; recklessly.
безрассу́дство *n.* **1,** recklessness; foolhardiness. **2,** rash act; reckless act.
безрезульта́тный *adj.* futile; unsuccessful. —**безрезульта́тно,** *adv.* without results; in vain.
безро́гий *adj.* hornless.
безро́дный *adj.* having no relatives; without kith or kin.
безро́потный *adj.* uncomplaining; mild-mannered. —**безро́потно,** *adv.* without complaining; without a murmur.
безрука́вка [*gen. pl.* **-вок**] *n.* sleeveless jacket. —**безрука́вный,** *adj.* sleeveless.
безру́кий *adj.* **1,** lacking one or both arms; lacking one or both hands. **2,** *colloq.* unhandy; clumsy.
безуда́рный *adj., phonet.* unaccented; unstressed.
безу́держный *adj.* unrestrained; unchecked; uncontrollable. —**безу́держная инфля́ция,** rampant (*or* runaway) inflation.
безукори́зненно *adv.* flawlessly; perfectly. —**безукори́зненно чи́стый,** spotlessly clean.
безукори́зненный *adj.* irreproachable; unimpeachable; flawless; impeccable.
безу́мец [*gen.* **-мца**] *n.* madman; lunatic.
безу́мие *n.* **1,** *obs.* madness; insanity. **2,** madness; folly. —**до безу́мия,** to distraction.
безу́мно *adv.* **1,** madly. **2,** *colloq.* terribly: безу́мно уста́л, terribly tired.
безу́мный *adj.* **1,** *obs.* mad; insane. **2,** *colloq.* crazy. **3,** *colloq.* extreme.
безумо́лчный *adj. (of noise)* incessant.
безу́мство *n.* madness; folly.
безу́мствовать *v. impfv.* [*pres.* **-ствую, -ствуешь**] to rant; rave; behave like a madman.
безупре́чный *adj.* irreproachable; unimpeachable; flawless; impeccable. —**безупре́чно,** *adv.* flawlessly; perfectly.
безусло́вно *adv.* certainly; absolutely; positively.
безусло́вный *adj.* absolute; unconditional.
безуспе́шный *adj.* unsuccessful; unavailing. —**безуспе́шно,** *adv.* without success; unsuccessfully.
безуста́нный *adj., obs.* **1,** tireless; untiring. **2,** ceaseless; endless.
безу́сый *adj.* **1,** having no mustache. **2,** *fig.* callow; beardless.
безуте́шный *adj.* inconsolable.
безуча́стие *n.* indifference; apathy.
безуча́стный *adj.* indifferent; apathetic. —**безуча́стность,** *n.f.* indifference; apathy.
безъя́дерный *adj.* nuclear-free.
безыде́йный *adj.* lacking proper ideological orientation. —**безыде́йность,** *n.f.* lack of proper ideological orientation.
безызве́стный *adj.* obscure; unknown. —**безызве́стность,** *n.f.* obscurity.
безымя́нный *adj.* nameless; anonymous. —**безымя́нный па́лец,** ring finger; fourth finger.
безынициати́вный *adj.* lacking initiative; unenterprising.
безыску́сственный *adj.* artless; ingenuous.
безысхо́дный *adj.* **1,** hopeless. **2,** endless.
бейсбо́л *n.* baseball. —**бейсбо́льный,** *adj.* baseball *(attrib.).*
бека́р *n., music* natural sign; natural.
бека́с *n.* snipe.
беко́н *n.* bacon.
белена́ *n.* henbane.
беле́ние *n.* bleaching.
белёный *adj.* bleached.
белёсый *adj.* whitish; off-white.
беле́ть *v. impfv.* [*pfv.* **побеле́ть**] **1,** to turn white. **2,** [*impfv. only*] *(of anything white)* to be visible; appear; shine; gleam.
белиберда́ *n., colloq.* nonsense; rubbish.
белизна́ *n.* whiteness.
бели́ла [*gen.* **-ли́л**] *n. pl.* **1,** whiting. **2,** ceruse *(cosmetic).* —**свинцо́вые бели́ла,** white lead; ceruse. —**ци́нковые бели́ла,** zinc white.
бели́льный *adj.* bleaching *(attrib.).*
бели́ть *v. impfv.* [*pres.* **белю́, бе́лишь** *or* **бели́шь**] **1,** [*pfv.* **побели́ть**] to whitewash; whiten. **2,** [*pfv.* **набели́ть**] to whiten (one's face) with ceruse. **3,** [*pfv.* **вы́белить**] to bleach. —**бели́ться,** *refl.* [*pfv.* **набели́ться**] to put on white makeup; whiten one's face with ceruse.
бе́личий [*fem.* **-чья**] *adj.* squirrel *(attrib.);* squirrel's.
бе́лка [*gen. pl.* **-лок**] *n.* squirrel. —**верте́ться как бе́лка в колесе́,** to be on a treadmill; go around in circles.
белко́вый *adj.* protein *(attrib.).*
белладо́нна *n.* belladonna.
беллетри́стика *n.* fiction. —**беллетри́ст,** *n.* fiction writer. —**беллетристи́ческий,** *adj.* fictional.
белобры́сый *adj., colloq.* towheaded.
белова́тый *adj.* whitish; off-white.
белови́к [*gen.* **-вика́**] *n.* clean copy.
белово́й *adj. (of a copy, manuscript, etc.)* clean; in final form.
белогварде́ец [*gen.* **-е́йца**] *n.* White Guard; counterrevolutionary. —**белогварде́йский,** *adj.* White-Guard *(attrib.).*
белоголо́вый *adj.* **1,** white-haired. **2,** fair-haired.

белóк [*gen.* -лкá] *n.* **1,** white of an egg; albumen. **2,** protein. **3,** white of the eye.
белокрóвие *n.* leukemia.
белокýрый *adj.* blond; fair-haired.
белолúцый *adj.* white-faced.
белорýс *n.m.* [*fem.* **-рýска**] Byelorussian. —**белорýсский,** *adj.* Byelorussian.
белорýчка *n.m & f., colloq.* one who disdains manual labor; one not wishing to dirty his hands.
белоснéжный *adj.* snow-white.
белошвéйка [*gen. pl.* **-éек**] *n.* seamstress.
белоэмигрáнт *n.* early emigrant from the Soviet Union.
белýга *n.* white sturgeon; beluga. —**ревéть белýгой,** to howl like a stuck pig.
белýха *n.* white whale; beluga.
бéлый *adj.* white. —*n.* **1,** white man; white. **2,** *neut.* white (clothes): одéт(а) в бéлое, dressed in white. **3,** *pl.* whites *(in the Russian Civil War).* **4,** *pl., chess* white: игрáть бéлыми, to be white; play the white pieces. —**бéлая ворóна,** rara avis. —**бéлый медвéдь,** polar bear. —**бéлые пятнá,** unexplored areas; blank spaces. —**бéлая совá,** snowy owl. —**бéлые стихú,** blank verse.
бельгúец [*gen.* **-úйца**] *n.m.* [*fem.* **-úйка**] Belgian. —**бельгúйский,** *adj.* Belgian.
бельё *n.* **1,** linen: столóвое бельё, table linen. **2,** laundry; wash. —**нúжнее бельё,** underwear.
бельевóй *adj* linen *(attrib.).*
бельмéс *n., colloq., in* **не знать** (*or* **не понимáть**) **ни бельмéса о,** not to know the first thing about.
бельмó *n.* walleye. —**бельмó на глазý,** thorn in one's side.
бельэтáж *n.* **1,** second floor. **2,** *theat.* mezzanine.
белЯк [*gen.* **-Якá**] *n.* **1,** white hare. **2,** *pl.* whitecaps.
бемóль *n.m., music* flat sign; flat.
бенгáлец [*gen.* **-льца**] *n.m.* [*fem.* **-лка**] Bengali. —**бенгáльский,** *adj.* Bengali.
бенефúс *n., theat.* benefit performance.
бензúн *n.* **1,** benzine. **2,** gasoline. —**бензúновый,** *adj.* gasoline *(attrib.).*
бензинoмéр *n.* gasoline gauge; fuel gauge.
бензобáк *n.* gas tank.
бензозаправочный *adj., in* **бензозапрáвочная колóнка,** gasoline pump; **бензозапрáвочная стáнция,** gas station; service station.
бензóин *n.* benzoin.
бензоколóнка [*gen. pl.* **-нок**] *n.* gas (*or* gasoline) pump.
бензóл *n.* benzene; benzol.
бенуáр *n., theat.* boxes *(at orchestra level).*
бéрег [*2nd loc.* **берегý;** *pl.* **берегá**] *n.* **1,** coast: плыть вдоль бéрега, to sail along the coast. **2,** bank *(of a river):* вы́ступить из берегóв, to overflow its banks. **3,** shore: достигáть бéрега, to reach the shore. Сойтú на бéрег, to go ashore. —**бéрег мóря,** seashore.
береговóй *adj.* coastal; shore *(attrib.).* —**береговáя лúния,** coastline. —**береговáя охрáна,** coast guard.
бередúть *v. impfv.* [*pfv.* **разбередúть;** *pres.* **-жý, -дúшь**] to irritate; aggravate (a wound). —**бередúть стáрые рáны,** to reopen old wounds.
бережлúвость *n.f.* **1,** thrift. **2,** *obs.* care.
бережлúвый *adj.* **1,** thrifty; economical. **2,** = **бéрежный.**
бéрежный *adj.* **1,** careful; gentle. **2,** solicitous; considerate. —**бéрежно,** *adv.* carefully; gently. —**бéрежность,** *n.f.* care.
берёза *n.* birch.
березнЯк [*gen.* **-нЯкá**] *n.* birch forest.
берёзовый *adj.* birch *(attrib.).*
берéйтор *n.* riding master.
берéменеть *v. impfv.* [*pfv.* **заберéменеть**] to become pregnant.
берéменная *adj.* pregnant. —*n.* pregnant woman.
берéменность *n.f.* pregnancy.
берёста *n.* birch bark.
берестянóй *adj.* birch-bark *(attrib.). Also,* **берёстовый.**
берéт *n.* beret.
берéчь *v. impfv.* [*pres.* **берегý, бережёшь, ...берегýт;** *past* **берёг, береглá, береглó**] **1,** to save; keep. **2,** to save; conserve. **3,** to guard; protect. —**берéчься,** *refl. (with gen.)* to watch out (for); beware (of).
бéри-бéри *n.f. indecl.* beriberi.
берúлл *n.* beryl.
берúллий *n.* beryllium.
беркéлий *n.* berkelium.
бéркут *n.* golden eagle.
берлóга *n.* den; lair *(of a bear).*
берцóвый *adj., in* **большáя берцóвая кость,** shinbone; tibia; **мáлая берцóвая кость,** fibula.
бес *n.* demon; evil spirit. —**рассыпáться мéлким бéсом пéред,** *colloq.* to curry favor with; play up to.
бес- *prefix, var. of* **без-** *(used before voiceless consonants).*
бесéда *n.* **1,** conversation; talk; chat. **2,** discussion. **3,** interview.
бесéдка [*gen. pl.* **-док**] *n.* summerhouse.
бесéдовать *v. impfv.* [*pres.* **-дую, -дуешь**] to talk; chat; converse.
бесёнок [*gen.* **-нка;** *pl.* **бесенЯта, -нЯт**] *n., colloq.* imp; little devil.
бесúть *v. impfv.* [*pfv.* **взбесúть;** *pres.* **бешý, бéсишь**] to enrage; infuriate. —**бесúться,** *refl.* **1,** to become enraged. **2,** *(of animals)* to become rabid.
бескáмерный *adj. (of a tire)* tubeless.
бесклáссовый *adj.* classless.
бескозы́рка [*gen. pl.* **-рок**] *n.* peakless cap.
бескомпромúссный *adj.* uncompromising.
бесконéчно *adv.* infinitely; endlessly. —**бесконéчно мáлый,** infinitesimal.
бесконéчность *n.f.* infinity. —**до бесконéчности,** endlessly; ad infinitum.
бесконéчный *adj.* **1,** endless; interminable. **2,** infinite.
бесконтрóльный *adj.* uncontrolled; unsupervised. —**бесконтрóльно,** *adv.* uncontrolled; without control.
бескоры́стие *n.* unselfishness. —**бескоры́стный,** *adj.* unselfish; disinterested.
бескрáйний *adj.* endless; boundless.
бескрúзисный *adj.* crisis-free.
бескрóвный *adj.* **1,** pallid; anemic. **2,** bloodless; without bloodshed. **3,** *obs.* homeless.
бескры́лый *adj.* **1,** wingless. **2,** *fig.* uninspired.
бескультýрье *n., colloq.* lack of culture.
бесновáтый *adj., obs.* mad; deranged.
бесновáться *v.r. impfv.* [*pres.* **-нýюсь, -нýешься**] to rant; rage.
бесóвский *adj.* diabolical; devilish.
беспáлый *adj.* **1,** having no fingers. **2,** having no toes.

беспа́мятный *adj., colloq.* forgetful.
беспа́мятство *n.* unconsciousness.
беспардо́нный *adj., colloq.* shameless; brazen.
беспарти́йный *adj.* non-party. —*n.* person not a member of the party.
бесперебо́йный *adj.* uninterrupted; regular; smooth. —**бесперебо́йно,** *adv.* without interruption; without a hitch.
беспереса́дочный *adj.* through; without transfer to another vehicle: беспереса́дочное сообще́ние, through connection.
бесперспекти́вный *adj.* having no prospects; hopeless.
беспе́чный *adj.* carefree; happy-go-lucky. —**беспе́чно,** *adv.* in a carefree manner; without a care. —**беспе́чность,** *n.f.* unconcern.
беспило́тный *adj.* not piloted; *(of a spacecraft)* unmanned.
беспи́сьменный *adj.* **1,** having no written language. **2,** *(of a language)* unwritten.
беспла́новый *adj.* unplanned.
беспла́тный *adj.* free (of charge): беспла́тное обуче́ние, free education. —**беспла́тно,** *adv.* free of charge; gratis.
бесплацка́ртный *adj.* **1,** *(of a car on a train)* unreserved; with unreserved seats. **2,** *(of a passenger)* having no reserved seat.
бесплодие *n.* **1,** sterility; infertility. **2,** barrenness; infertility *(of soil).*
беспло́дность *n.f.* **1,** barrenness; infertility *(of soil).* **2,** futility.
беспло́дный *adj.* **1,** barren; sterile. **2,** futile; fruitless.
беспло́тный *adj.* incorporeal.
бесповоро́тный *adj.* irrevocable.
бесподо́бный *adj., colloq.* incomparable; matchless; peerless.
беспозвоно́чный *adj.* invertebrate. —**беспозвоно́чные,** *n. pl.* invertebrates.
беспоко́ить *v. impfv.* to worry; trouble; bother; disturb. —**беспоко́иться,** *refl.* **1,** to worry. **2,** to trouble oneself; bother.
беспоко́йный *adj.* **1,** worried; troubled; anxious; uneasy. **2,** worrisome; disturbing. **3,** restless; uneasy.
беспоко́йство *n.* **1,** worry; anxiety; uneasiness; concern. **2,** trouble; disturbance; bother.
бесполе́зно *adv.* uselessly. —*adj., used predicatively* useless: спо́рить с ним бесполе́зно, it's useless to argue with him.
бесполе́зность *n.f.* uselessness.
бесполе́зный *adj.* **1,** useless. **2,** futile.
беспо́лый *adj.* sexless; asexual.
беспо́мощный *adj.* **1,** helpless. **2,** utterly without merit; hopeless. —**беспо́мощность,** *n.f.* helplessness.
беспоро́чный *adj.* faultless; irreproachable.
беспоря́док [*gen.* **-дка**] *n.* **1,** disorder; disarray; confusion. **2,** *pl.* disorders; disturbances; riots.
беспоря́дочный *adj.* **1,** disorderly; untidy. **2,** unsystematic; disorganized. —**беспоря́дочно,** *adv.* in disorder; haphazardly.
беспоса́дочный *adj. (of a flight)* nonstop.
беспо́чвенный *adj.* groundless; unfounded.
беспо́шлинный *adj.* duty-free.
беспоща́дный *adj.* merciless. —**беспоща́дно,** *adv.* mercilessly.
беспра́вие *n.* absence of rights.
беспра́вный *adj.* without rights.
беспреде́льный *adj.* boundless; limitless; infinite.
беспредме́тный *adj.* pointless; aimless.
беспрекосло́вный *adj.* unquestioning; absolute; implicit. —**беспрекосло́вно,** *adv.* without question; blindly; implicitly.
беспрепя́тственный *adj.* unhampered; unimpeded. —**беспрепя́тственно,** *adv.* without hindrance; unimpeded.
беспреры́вный *adj.* continuous; uninterrupted. —**беспреры́вно,** *adv.* continuously.
беспреста́нный *adj.* continual; incessant. —**беспреста́нно,** *adv.* continually; incessantly.
беспрецеде́нтный *adj.* unprecedented.
беспри́быльный *adj.* unprofitable; unremunerative.
бесприда́нница *n., obs.* girl without a dowry.
беспризо́рник *n.* street urchin; waif.
беспризо́рничать *v. impfv., colloq.* to live on the streets; be a waif.
беспризо́рный *adj.* **1,** neglected; uncared-for. **2,** homeless; stray. —*n.* = **беспризо́рник.**
бесприме́рный *adj.* unexampled; unparalleled.
беспринци́пный *adj.* unprincipled; unscrupulous.
беспристра́стие *n.* impartiality. —**беспристра́стный,** *adj.* impartial; unbiased.
беспричи́нный *adj.* lacking any visible cause; groundless. —**беспричи́нно,** *adv.* for no (apparent) reason.
бесприю́тный *adj.* homeless; lacking a roof over one's head.
беспробу́дный *adj.* **1,** *(of sleep)* deep. **2,** *colloq. (of drinking)* unrestrained.
беспро́волочный *adj.* wireless: беспро́волочный телегра́ф, wireless.
беспро́игрышный *adj.* risk-free; safe.
беспросве́тный *adj.* **1,** pitch black; pitch dark. **2,** *(of darkness)* absolute. **3,** *fig.* hopeless; unrelieved.
беспроце́нтный *adj.* interest-free.
беспу́тный *adj.* dissolute. —**беспу́тство,** *n.* dissoluteness.
бессвя́зный *adj.* rambling; disconnected; incoherent; disjointed. —**бессвя́зность,** *n.f.* incoherence.
бессеме́йный *adj.* having no family.
бессемя́нный *adj.* seedless.
бессерде́чие *n.* heartlessness; callousness. *Also,* **бессерде́чность,** *n.f.*
бессерде́чный *adj.* heartless; callous.
бесси́лие *n.* **1,** weakness; debility. **2,** helplessness; impotence. —**полово́е бесси́лие,** *med.* impotence.
бесси́льный *adj.* **1,** week; feeble. **2,** powerless; helpless; impotent.
бессисте́мный *adj.* unsystematic.
бессла́вие *n.* ignominy. —**бессла́вный,** *adj.* inglorious; ignominious.
бессле́дный *adj.* without a trace. —**бессле́дно,** *adv.* without a trace; completely.
бесслове́сный *adj.* **1,** mute; dumb. **2,** quiet; meek. —**бесслове́сная роль,** non-speaking part.
бессме́нный *adj.* **1,** permanent. **2,** continuous.
бессме́ртие *n.* immortality.
бессме́ртный *adj.* immortal.
бессмы́сленно *adv.* senselessly. —*adj., used predicatively* making no sense: сде́лать э́то – соверше́нно бессмы́сленно, it makes no sense whatever to do that.
бессмы́сленность *n.f.* senselessness.

бессмы́сленный *adj.* **1,** meaningless. **2,** senseless; irrational; wanton. **3,** inane. **4,** blank; vacant.
бессмы́слица *n., colloq.* foolishness; nonsense.
бессо́вестный *adj.* unscrupulous; unconscionable.
бессодержа́тельный *adj.* empty; shallow; insipid; dull.
бессозна́тельный *adj.* **1,** unconscious. **2,** involuntary; instinctive.
бессо́нница *n.* insomnia.
бессо́нный *adj.* sleepless.
бесспо́рный *adj.* indisputable; incontrovertible. —**бесспо́рно,** *adv.* unquestionably; without question.
бессро́чный *adj.* for an indefinite period; for an unlimited time.
бесстра́стие *n.* impassivity. —**бесстра́стный,** *adj.* impassive.
бесстра́шие *n.* fearlessness. —**бесстра́шный,** *adj.* fearless; intrepid.
бессты́дник *n.m.* [*fem.* **-ница**] *colloq.* shameless person.
бессты́дный *adj.* shameless; brazen. —**бессты́дство,** *n.* shamelessness.
бессчётный *adj.* countless; innumerable.
беста́ктность *n.f.* **1,** tactlessness. **2,** indiscretion: соверши́ть беста́ктность, to commit an indiscretion.
беста́ктный *adj.* tactless.
бесталáнный *adj.* **1,** lacking talent; untalented. **2,** luckless; ill-starred.
бестеле́сный *adj.* incorporeal.
бо́стил *n.* rogue; knave.
бестолко́вый *adj.* **1,** obtuse; stupid. **2,** incoherent; confused.
бестсе́ллер (сэ) *n.* best seller.
бесфо́рменный *adj.* formless; shapeless; amorphous.
бесхара́ктерный *adj.* lacking in character; weak-willed.
бесхи́тростный *adj.* artless; ingenuous.
бесхо́зный *adj., colloq.* = **бесхозя́йный.**
бесхозя́йный *adj.* without an owner; ownerless.
бесхозя́йственный *adj.* **1,** incompetent; inefficient. **2,** uneconomical; wasteful. —**бесхозя́йственность,** *n.f.* mismanagement.
бесхребе́тный *adj.* spineless; weak-willed.
бесцве́тный *adj.* **1,** colorless. **2,** *fig.* colorless; insipid; dull; drab. —**бесцве́тность,** *n.f.* dullness; drabness; monotony.
бесце́льный *adj.* **1,** aimless. **2,** pointless. —**бесце́льно,** *adv.* aimlessly.
бесце́нный *adj.* priceless; invaluable.
бесце́нок *n., in* **за бесце́нок,** for next to nothing; for a song.
бесцеремо́нный *adj.* unceremonious; familiar. —**бесцеремо́нно,** *adv.* unceremoniously. —**бесцеремо́нность,** *n.f.* familiarity.
бесчелове́чный *adj.* inhuman. —**бесчелове́чность,** *n.f.* inhumanity.
бесче́стить *v. impfv.* [*pfv.* **обесче́стить;** *pres.* **-щу, -стишь**] to disgrace; dishonor.
бесче́стный *adj.* dishonorable. —**бесче́стье,** *n.* disgrace; dishonor.
бесчи́нство *n.* outrage.
бесчи́нствовать *v. impfv.* [*pres.* **-ствую, -ствуешь**] to commit outrages.
бесчи́сленный *adj.* countless; innumerable.
бесчу́вственный *adj.* **1,** insensible; unconscious. **2,** insensitive; unfeeling.
бесчу́вствие *n.* **1,** insensibility; unconsciousness. **2,** insensitivity; indifference.
бесшаба́шный *adj., colloq.* reckless; devil-may-care.
бесшо́вный *adj.* *(of pipes)* seamless.
бесшу́мный *adj.* noiseless.
бе́та (бэ) *n.* beta. —**бе́та-лучи́,** beta rays. —**бе́та-части́ца,** beta particle.
бе́тель *n.m.* betel.
бето́н *n.* concrete.
бетони́ровать *v. impfv.* [*pfv.* **забетони́ровать;** *pres* **-рую, -руешь**] to pave with concrete.
бето́нный *adj.* concrete.
беф-стро́ганов *n.* beef stroganoff.
бечева́ *n.* towline; towrope.
бечёвка [*gen. pl.* **-вок**] *n.* string; twine.
бечевни́к [*gen.* **-ника́**] *n.* towpath. *Also,* **бечёвник.**
бечево́й *adj.* towing *(attrib.)*; tow *(attrib.)*.
бе́шенство *n.* **1,** rabies; hydrophobia. **2,** rage; fury.
бе́шеный *adj.* **1,** *(of an animal)* rabid; mad. **2,** violent furious. —**бе́шеные де́ньги, 1,** *obs.* quick (*or* easy) money. **2,** exorbitant price: плати́ть бе́шеные де́ньги, to pay through the nose.
библе́йский *adj.* Biblical.
библиогра́фия *n.* bibliography. —**библио́граф,** *n* bibliographer. —**библиографи́ческий,** *adj.* bibliographic.
библиоте́ка *n.* library.
библиоте́карь *n.m.* [*fem.* **-арша**] librarian.
библиотекове́дение *n.* library science.
библиоте́чный *adj.* library *(attrib.)*. —**библиоте́чное де́ло,** librarianship.
библиофи́л *n.* bibliophile.
би́блия *n.* the Bible; bible.
бива́к *also,* **бивуа́к** *n.* bivouac. —**жить (как) на бива́ках,** to camp out.
би́вень [*gen.* **-вня**] *n.m.* tusk.
бивуа́к *n.* = **бива́к.**
бигуди́ *n. pl. indecl.* (hair) curlers.
бидо́н *n.* large can: бидо́н для молока́, milk can.
бие́ние *n.* beating *(of the heart or pulse)*.
биза́нь *n.f.* mizzen *(sail)*.
би́знес (нэ) *n.* business. —**бизнесме́н,** *n.* businessman.
бизо́н *n.* bison.
биле́т *n.* **1,** ticket. **2,** membership card; identity card. **3,** bill; note: биле́т в пять до́лларов, five-dollar bill. —**креди́тный биле́т,** bank note. —**экзаменацио́нный биле́т,** question selected at random during an oral examination.
билетёр *n.m.* [*fem.* **-тёрша**] ticket collector; usher.
биле́тный *adj.* ticket *(attrib.)*.
биллио́н *n.* billion.
билль *n.m.* bill *(draft of a proposed law)*. —**билль о права́х,** Bill of Rights.
би́ло *n.* striking part *(of various mechanisms)*.
билья́рд *n.* **1,** billiards. **2,** billiard table; pool table. —**билья́рдная,** *n.* billiard room. —**билья́рдный,** *adj* billiard.
биметалли́зм *n.* bimetallism. —**биметалли́ческий,** *adj.* bimetallic.
бина́рный *adj.* binary.
бино́кль *n.m.* binoculars. —**полево́й бино́кль,** field glasses. —**театра́льный бино́кль,** opera glasses.

бинóм *n., math.* binomial.
бинт [*gen.* **бинтá**] *n.* bandage.
бинтовáть *v. impfv.* [*pfv.* **забинтовáть;** *pres.* **-тýю, -тýешь**] to bandage.
биогрáфия *n.* biography. —**биóграф,** *n.* biographer. —**биографи́ческий,** *adj.* biographical.
биолóгия *n.* biology. —**биóлог,** *n.* biologist. —**биологи́ческий,** *adj.* biological.
биóника *n.* bionics.
биопси́я *n.* biopsy.
биофи́зика *n.* biophysics.
биохи́мия *n.* biochemistry. —**биохи́мик,** *n.* biochemist. —**биохими́ческий,** *adj.* biochemical.
биплáн *n.* biplane.
би́ржа *n.* exchange; market: фóндовая би́ржа, stock exchange; stock market. —**би́ржа трудá, 1,** state employment agency. **2,** labor exchange.
биржеви́к [*gen.* **-викá**] *n.* trader in stocks.
биржевóй *adj.* stock *(attrib.);* stock market *(attrib.).*
би́рка [*gen. pl.* **-рок**] *n.* **1,** tally *(notched stick).* **2,** tag; marker; label.
бирмáнец [*gen.* **-нца**] *n.m.* [*fem.* **-нка**] Burmese: он бирмáнец, he is Burmese. —**бирмáнский,** *adj.* Burmese.
бирюзá *n.* turquoise. —**бирюзóвый,** *adj.* turquoise.
бирю́к [*gen.* **-юкá**] *n.* lone wolf *(lit. & fig.).* —**бирюкóм смотрéть,** to look sullen; scowl.
бирю́льки [*gen.* **-лек**] *n. pl.* jackstraws. —**игрáть в бирю́льки, 1,** to play jackstraws. **2,** *fig.* to trifle away one's time.
бис *interj.* encore! —**испóлнить (чтó-нибудь) на бис,** to perform (something) as an encore.
би́сер *n.* beads. —**метáть би́сер пéред сви́ньями,** to cast pearls before swine.
би́серина *n.* bead. *Also,* **би́серинка.**
би́серный *adj.* **1,** bead *(attrib.);* beaded. **2,** *(of handwriting)* tiny; minute.
биси́ровать *v. impfv.& pfv.* [*pres.* **-рую, -руешь**] to give an encore.
бискви́т *n.* sponge cake.
битá *n.* bat *(used in various games).*
би́тва *n.* battle.
биткóм *adv., in* **биткóм наби́ть,** to pack; jam; fill to capacity.
битóк [*gen.* **-ткá**] *n.* meatball.
битýм *n.* bitumen. —**битуминóзный; битýмный,** *adj.* bituminous.
би́тый *adj.* **1,** beaten. **2,** broken. —**би́тый час,** a whole (*or* good) hour.
бить *v. impfv.* [*pres.* **бью, бьёшь**] **1,** to beat; strike; hit. **2,** [*pfv.* **поби́ть**] to give a beating to; thrash. **3,** [*pfv.* **поби́ть**] to defeat; conquer; subdue. **4,** [*pfv.* **разби́ть**] to break; shatter; smash. **5,** [*pfv.* **проби́ть**] *(of clocks)* to strike; chime; *(of drums)* beat. **6,** [*pfv.* **проби́ть**] to sound (an alarm, retreat, etc.). **7,** [*pfv.* **проби́ть**] *(with* **в** + *acc.)* to beat (a drum); strike (a bell); clap (one's hands). **8,** to kill; shoot (game). **9,** to shoot; *(with* **из***)* fire (a weapon). **10,** to gush; spurt. —**бить в глазá,** to be striking; catch the eye. —**бить в цель,** to hit the mark. —**бить ми́мо цéли,** to be wide of the mark.
битьё *n.* **1,** *colloq.* beating; thrashing. **2,** breaking; smashing.
би́ться *v.r. impfv.* [*pres.* **бьюсь, бьёшься**] **1,** to fight; struggle. **2,** *(with* **над***)* *fig.* to struggle with; struggle over. **3,** *(with* **о** + *acc.)* to beat (against); strike (against); batter. **4,** *(of the heart, pulse, etc.)* to beat; pulsate. **5,** to writhe; toss about. **6,** to be fragile; be breakable. —**би́ться об заклáд,** to bet; wager. —**би́ться как ры́ба об лёд,** to struggle to keep body and soul together.
битю́г [*gen.* **-тюгá**] *n.* a type of dray horse.
бифштéкс (тэ) *n.* steak; beefsteak.
бихевиори́зм *n.* behaviorism.
би́цепс *n.* biceps.
бич [*gen.* **бичá**] *n.* **1,** whip; lash. **2,** *fig. (with gen.)* scourge (of).
бичевáние *n.* flagellation.
бичевáть *v. impfv.* [*pres.* **-чýю, -чýешь**] **1,** to whip; flog. **2,** *fig.* to castigate; excoriate.
бишь *particle, colloq., used when one has forgotten something:* о чём бишь мы говори́ли?, what is it we were talking about? —**то бишь,** *colloq.* or rather.
блáго[1] *n.* **1,** good: на блáго человéчества, for the good of mankind. **2,** *pl.* benefits; blessings. —**всех благ,** best wishes; all the best! —**ни за каки́е блáга,** not for anything in the world.
блáго[2] *conj., colloq.* since; inasmuch as.
блáговест *n.* ringing of church bells; call to prayer.
блáговестить *v. impfv.* [*pres.* **-щу, -стишь**] *obs.* to ring church bells.
благовéщение *n., relig.* Annunciation. —**благовéщенский,** *adj.* Annunciation *(attrib.):* Благовéщенский собóр, Cathedral of the Annunciation *(in the Kremlin).*
благови́дный *adj.* **1,** *obs.* attractive; good-looking. **2,** proper; suitable. **3,** *(of an excuse)* plausible; specious.
благоволéние *n., obs.* favor; good graces.
благоволи́ть *v. impfv.* **1,** *(with* **к***)* to like; regard with favor; be favorably disposed (toward). **2,** *(with inf.) obs.* to be so kind as to: благоволи́те отвéтить, kindly favor us with a reply.
благовоспи́танный *adj.* well-mannered; well-bred.
благоговéйный *adj.* reverent.
благоговéние *n. (with* **пéред***)* reverence (for); veneration (of).
благоговéть *v. impfv. (with* **пéред***)* to revere; venerate.
благодарéние *n., obs.* expression of gratitude; thanksgiving.
благодари́ть *v. impfv.* [*pfv.* **поблагодари́ть**] to thank. —**благодарю́ вас!,** thank you!
благодáрность *n.f.* **1,** gratitude. **2,** (expression of) thanks. —**не стóит благодáрности,** don't mention it!
благодáрный *adj.* [*short form* **-рен, -рна**] **1,** grateful; thankful; appreciative. **2,** worthy; worthwhile.
благодáрственный *adj., obs.* of thanks; of gratitude.
благодаря́ *prep., with dat.* thanks to; owing to. —**благодаря́ томý, что...,** owing to (*or* due to) the fact that...
благодáтный *adj.* **1,** bringing joy or happiness; blessed. **2,** fertile; abundant.
благодáть *n.f.* **1,** *obs.* blessing; divine gift. **2,** abundance; plenty. **3,** *colloq.* a delight.
благодéнствие *n., obs.* prosperity.
благодéнствовать *v. impfv.* [*pres.* **-ствую, -ствуешь**] to prosper; thrive.
благодéтель *n.m., obs.* benefactor.

благодéтельный *adj.* **1,** beneficial. **2,** *obs.* benevolent.

благодеяние *n.* **1,** good deed. **2,** blessing; boon.

благодýшие *n.* good nature. —**благодýшный,** *adj.* good-natured.

благожелáтельный *adj.* **1,** good-natured; kindly. **2,** favorable. —**благожелáтельность,** *n.f.* good will; benevolence.

благозвýчие *n.* harmony; euphony. *Also,* **благозвýчность,** *n.f.*

благозвýчный *adj.* euphonious; harmonious; melodious.

благóй *adj., obs.* good. —**кричáть благи́м мáтом,** *colloq.* to yell one's head off.

благонадёжный *adj.* reliable; trustworthy. —**благонадёжность,** *n.f.* reliability; trustworthiness.

благонамéренный *adj., obs.* well-intentioned; well-meaning.

благообрáзный *adj.* good-looking; handsome.

благополýчие *n.* welfare; well-being.

благополýчный *adj.* successful; happy; satisfactory. —**благополýчно,** *adv.* all right; safely; without mishap.

благопристóйный *adj., obs.* decorous; seemly.

благоприя́тный *adj.* favorable; propitious.

благоприя́тствовать *v. impfv.* [*pres.* **-ствую, -ствуешь**] *(with dat.)* to favor; work to the advantage of.

благоразýмие *n.* prudence; discretion; good sense.

благоразýмный *adj.* **1,** reasonable; prudent; judicious; discreet. **2,** *(of advice)* sensible. —**благоразýмно,** *adv.* prudently; judiciously; wisely.

благорóдный *adj.* noble. —**благорóдные метáллы,** precious metals. —**благорóдный олéнь,** red deer.

благорóдство *n.* nobility.

благосклóнный *adj.* favorable; kindly. —**благосклóнно,** *adv.* with favor; favorably. —**благосклóнность,** *n.f.* favor; good graces.

благословéние *n.* blessing.

благословéнный *adj., poetic* blessed.

благословля́ть *v. impfv.* [*pfv.* **благослови́ть**] to bless.

благосостоя́ние *n.* welfare; well-being.

блáгостный *adj.* **1,** lovely. **2,** serene.

благотвори́тель *n.m.* philanthropist. —**благотвори́тельность,** *n.f.* charity; philanthropy. —**благотвори́тельный,** *adj.* charitable; philanthropic.

благотвóрный *adj.* beneficial; wholesome; salutary.

благоустрóенный *adj.* well-designed; well-equipped; with all the modern conveniences.

благоустрóйство *n.* providing of public services and amenities.

благоухáние *n.* fragrance; sweet smell; redolence. —**благоухáнный,** *adj.* fragrant; sweet-smelling; redolent.

благоухáть *v. impfv.* to smell sweet; be fragrant.

благочести́вый *adj.* pious; devout. —**благочéстие,** *n.* piety.

блажéнный *adj.* **1,** blissful. **2,** blessed. **3,** *colloq.* wacky. —**блажéнной пáмяти,** of blessed memory. —**в блажéнном невéдении,** in blissful ignorance.

блажéнство *n.* bliss.

блажéнствовать *v. impfv.* [*pres.* **-ствую, -ствуешь**] **1,** to be blissfully happy; be in a state of bliss. **2,** to enjoy oneself.

блажь *n.f., colloq.* whim; fancy.

бланк *n.* form; blank.

блат *n.* **1,** thieves' jargon. **2,** *colloq.* pull; connections; influence: по блáту, by pulling strings.

блатнóй *adj.* thieves': блатнóй язы́к, thieves' jargon.

бледнéть *v. impfv.* [*pfv.* **побледнéть**] **1,** to turn pale; turn white. **2,** [*impfv. only*] *(with* **пéред***) fig.* to pale (before); suffer in comparison (with).

бледно- *prefix, used with colors* pale: бледно-зелёный, pale green.

блéдность *n.f.* pallor.

блéдный *adj.* [*short form* **-ден, -днá, -дно**] **1,** pale. **2,** *fig.* dull; colorless; insipid.

блёклый *adj.* faded; withered.

блёкнуть *v. impfv.* [*pfv.* **поблёкнуть;** *past* **блёк, -ла**] **1,** to fade. **2,** to wither.

блеск *n.* **1,** brilliance; luster. **2,** *fig.* magnificence; splendor: во всём блéске, in all its splendor. **3,** *(with gen.)* brilliance (*of wit, talent, etc.*). —**с блéском,** with flying colors.

блеснá [*pl.* **блёсны, блёсен**] *n.* spoon bait.

блеснýть *v. pfv.* **1,** *pfv. of* **блестéть. 2,** to flash across one's mind: у меня́ блеснýла мысль, the thought flashed across my mind.

блестéть *v. impfv.* [*pfv.* **блеснýть;** *pres.* **блещý, блести́шь** *or* **блéщешь**] **1,** to shine; sparkle; glitter; gleam. **2,** *fig. (with instr.)* to be blessed with: он не блéщет умóм, he is not the smartest person in the world.

блёстки *n. pl.* [*sing.* **блёстка**] **1,** spangles; sequins. **2,** *fig. (with gen.)* flashes *(of wit, talent, etc.)*.

блестя́щий *adj.* brilliant. —**блестя́ще,** *adv.* brilliantly.

блеф *n.* bluff.

блефовáть *v. impfv.* [*pres.* **-фýю, -фýешь**] *colloq.* to bluff.

блéяние *n.* bleat; bleating.

блéять *v. impfv.* [*pres.* **блéет**] to bleat.

ближáйший *adj.* **1,** nearest. **2,** next: в ближáйшие дни, in the next few days. **3,** immediate: ближáйший начáльник, immediate superior. **4,** *in* ближáйший рóдственник, nearest relative; next of kin. —**в ближáйшем бýдущем; в ближáйшее врéмя,** in the near future.

бли́же *adj., comp. of* **бли́зкий.**

ближневосточный *adj.* Middle East *(attrib.);* Middle Eastern.

бли́жний *adj.* near; nearby. —*n., obs.* neighbor; fellow human being. —**бли́жний бой,** close combat. —**Бли́жний Востóк,** Middle East.

близ *prep., with gen.* near; close to.

бли́зиться *v.r. impfv.* to approach; draw near.

бли́зкий *adj.* [*short form* **-зок, -зкá, -зко;** *comp.* **бли́же**] **1,** near; close *(in space or time).* **2,** close; intimate. —**бли́зкие,** *n.pl.* one's relatives.

бли́зко *adv.* near; close; nearby. —*adj., used predicatively* nearby; close to here: пóчта совсéм бли́зко, the post office is right nearby. —**бли́зко от,** near; close to.

близлежáщий *adj.* nearby; neighboring.

близнéц [*gen.* **-нецá**] *n.* **1,** twin. **2,** *pl., cap.* Gemini.

близорýкий *adj.* **1,** nearsighted; myopic. **2,** *fig.* shortsighted.

близорýкость *n.f.* **1,** nearsightedness; myopia. **2,** *fig.* shortsightedness.

бли́зость *n.f.* nearness; closeness; proximity.

блик *n.* patch of light.

блин [*gen.* **блинá**] *n.* pancake.

блинда́ж [*gen.* **-дажа́**] *n., mil.* dugout; bunker.
бли́нчатый *adj.* pancake *(attrib.).*
бли́нчик *n.* small pancake.
блиста́тельный *adj.* brilliant; glittering; resplendent.
блиста́ть *v. impfv.* to shine; sparkle; glitter. —**блиста́ть свои́м отсу́тствием,** to be conspicuous by one's absence.
блиц *n.* flash bulb.
блок *n.* **1,** bloc. **2,** block *(pulley).* **3,** *mech.* block: блок цили́ндров, cylinder block. **4,** (cement) block. **5,** *philately* block; souvenir sheet.
блока́да *n.* blockade.
блокга́уз *n., mil.* blockhouse.
блоки́ровать *v. impfv. & pfv.* [*pres.* **-рую, -руешь**] **1,** to blockade. **2,** *sports* to block. —**блоки́роваться,** *refl. (with* **с** + *instr.)* to form an alliance (with).
блокно́т *n.* writing pad; note pad; tablet.
блонди́н *n.* blond (man). —**блонди́нка,** *n.* blonde.
блоха́ [*pl.* **бло́хи, блох, блоха́м**] *n.* flea. —**блоши́ный,** *adj.* flea *(attrib.).*
бло́шки [*gen. pl.* **-шек**] *n. pl.* tiddlywinks.
блуд *n., obs.* lechery; debauchery.
блуди́ть *v. impfv.* [*pres.* **блужу́, блу́дишь**] *colloq.* to wander.
блу́дный *adj., in* **блу́дный сын,** prodigal son.
блужда́ть *v. impfv.* to roam; wander. —**блужда́ть в потёмках,** to feel one's way.
блужда́ющий *adj.* roaming; wandering. —**блужда́ющий огонёк,** will-o'-the wisp.
блу́за *n.* **1,** smock. **2,** *obs.* blouse.
блу́зка [*gen. pl.* **-зок**] *n.* (lady's) blouse.
блю́дечко [*gen. pl.* **-чек**] *n.* saucer.
блю́до *n.* **1,** platter. **2,** dish; food: моё люби́мое блю́до, my favorite dish/food. **3,** course: обе́д из трёх блюд, three-course dinner.
блю́дце [*gen. pl.* **-дец**] *n.* saucer.
блюз *n., music* blues.
блюсти́ *v. impfv.* [*pfv.* **соблюсти́;** *pres.* **блюду́, блюдёшь;** *past* **блюл, блюла́, блюло́**] **1,** to guard; watch over. **2,** to maintain; keep. **3,** to observe; abide by.
блюсти́тель *n.m., obs.* keeper; guardian. —**блюсти́тель поря́дка,** keeper of order; guardian of the law.
бля́ха *n.* name plate; badge. *Also,* **бля́шка.**
боа́ *n.m. indecl.* boa constrictor. —*n. neut. indecl., obs.* boa *(lady's scarf).*
боб [*gen.* **боба́**] *n.* bean. —**оста́ться на боба́х,** *colloq.* to be left with nothing.
бобёр [*gen.* **-бра́**] *n.* beaver fur.
бобо́вый *adj.* **1,** bean *(attrib.).* **2,** leguminous.
бобр [*gen.* **бобра́**] *n.* beaver.
бо́брик *n.* castor *(cloth).*
бобро́вый *adj.* beaver *(attrib.).*
бо́бслей *n.* bobsled.
бобы́ль [*gen.* **-быля́**] *n.m.* **1,** *obs.* poor landless peasant. **2,** *colloq.* lonely unmarried man.
бог *n., often cap.* God; god. —**бог его́ зна́ет**!, God knows! —**бог с** (+ *instr.*), to hell with...; forget about... —**дай бог**!, God grant. —**ей бо́гу**!, really!; truly! —**не дай бог**!, God forbid!; heaven forbid! —**ра́ди бо́га**!, for God's sake!; for goodness' sake!; for heaven's sake! —**сла́ва бо́гу**!, thank God!; thank goodness!; thank heaven!
богаде́льня [*gen. pl.* **-лен**] *n.* poorhouse; almshouse.
богате́ть *v. impfv.* [*pfv.* **разбогате́ть**] to get rich.
бога́то *adv.* richly.
бога́тство *n.* **1,** wealth; riches. **2,** richness. **3,** *pl.* (natural) resources. **4,** *(with gen.) fig.* wealth (of); profusion (of).
бога́тый *adj.* [*comp.* **бога́че**] **1,** rich; wealthy. **2,** abundant. **3,** *(of a collection)* large; *(of experience)* broad; *(of one's imagination)* fertile. **4,** luxurious; sumptuous. —*n.* rich man. —**чем бога́ты, тем и ра́ды,** you are welcome to what we have.
богаты́рь [*gen.* **-тыря́**] *n.m.* **1,** Russian epic hero. **2,** *fig.* big strapping man. —**богаты́рский,** *adj.* of a **богаты́рь.**
бога́ч [*gen.* **-гача́**] *n.* rich man.
бога́че *adj., comp. of* **бога́тый.**
боге́ма *n.* **1,** Bohemians. **2,** *colloq.* Bohemian way of life. —**боге́мный,** *adj., colloq.* Bohemian.
боге́мский *adj.* Bohemian; of or from Bohemia.
боги́ня *n.* goddess.
богобоя́зненный *adj.* god-fearing.
богома́терь *n.f., usu. cap.* Mother of God *(the Virgin Mary).*
богомо́л *n.* **1,** pilgrim. **2,** *zool.* (praying) mantis.
богомо́лец [*gen.* **-льца**] *n.m.* [*fem.* **-лка**] **1,** devout person. **2,** pilgrim. —**богомо́лье,** *n.* pilgrimage. —**богомо́льный,** *adj.* devout.
богоро́дица *n., usu. cap.* the Virgin Mary.
богосло́вие *n.* theology. —**богосло́в,** *n.* theologian. —**богосло́вский,** *adj.* theological.
богослуже́ние *n.* religious service.
боготвори́ть *v. impfv.* to idolize; worship.
богоху́льство *n.* blasphemy. —**богоху́льный,** *adj.* blasphemous.
богоху́льствовать *v. impfv.* [*pres.* **-ствую, -ствуешь**] to blaspheme; engage in blasphemy.
богоявле́ние *n., usu. cap.* Epiphany.
бода́ть *v. impfv.* to butt. —**бода́ться,** *refl.* **1,** to butt *(generally).* **2,** to butt each other.
бодли́вый *adj. (of an animal)* that butts a lot.
бодри́ть *v. impfv.* to invigorate. —**бодри́ться,** *refl.* to try to keep one's spirits up.
бо́дрость *n.f.* **1,** vigor. **2,** cheerfulness; good spirits.
бо́дрствовать *v. impfv.* [*pres.* **-ствую, -ствуешь**] to stay awake; keep vigil.
бо́дрый *adj.* **1,** cheerful; buoyant; jaunty. **2,** vigorous; hale and hearty.
бодря́щий *adj.* invigorating; bracing.
боеви́к [*gen.* **-вика́**] *n.* **1,** *hist.* worker taking part in the 1905 Revolution. **2,** *colloq.* hit *(movie).*
боеви́тость *n.f.* fighting spirit; enthusiasm. —**боеви́тый,** *adj.* active; energetic; lively; enthusiastic.
боево́й *adj.* **1,** fighting; battle *(attrib.);* combat *(attrib.).* **2,** *mil.* live: боевы́е патро́ны, live ammunition. **3,** militant; belligerent. **4,** urgent. —**боева́я часть; боева́я голо́вка,** warhead.
боеголо́вка [*gen. pl.* **-вок**] *n.* warhead.
боегото́вность *n.f.* combat readiness.
боеприпа́сы [*gen.* **-сов**] *n. pl.* ammunition.
боеспосо́бность *n.f., mil.* fighting efficiency; combat effectiveness. —**боеспосо́бный,** *adj.* battleworthy.
бое́ц [*gen.* **бойца́**] *n.* soldier; fighting man.
бо́же *n., vocative case of* **бог.** —*interj.* God! —**бо́же мой**!, God!; my God!
боже́ственный *adj.* **1,** divine. **2,** *colloq.* divine; idyllic; sublime. —**боже́ственность,** *n.f.* divinity.
божество́ *n.* deity.
бо́жий [*fem.* **-жья**] *adj.* God's. —**бо́жья коро́вка,**

ladybug; ladybird. —**ка́ждый бо́жий день,** every blessed day. —**ясно как бо́жий день,** as clear as day.

божи́ться *v.r. impfv.* [*pfv.* **побожи́ться**] to swear.

божо́к [*gen.* **-жка́**] *n.* **1,** figurine or statuette of a god. **2,** idol; one who is idolized.

бой [*2nd loc.* **бою́**; *pl.* **бои́, боёв**] *n.* **1,** combat; battle: пасть в бою́, to fall/be killed/in combat/battle/action. **2,** fight: кула́чный бой, fistfight; бой быко́в, bullfight. Без бо́я, without a fight. **3,** *pl.* fighting: тяжёлые бои́, heavy fighting. **4,** breaking; breakage. **5,** striking *(of a clock);* beating *(of drums).* **6,** killing; slaughter *(of fish, whales, etc.).* —**взять с бо́ю,** to take by force.

бо́йкий *adj.* [*short form* **бо́ек, бойка́, бо́йко**; *comp.* **бо́йче**] **1,** sharp; clever. **2,** lively; brisk. **3,** glib; facile.

бойко́т *n.* boycott.

бойкоти́ровать *v. impfv.* [*pres.* **-рую, -руешь**] to boycott.

бойни́ца *n.* loophole; embrasure.

бо́йня [*gen. pl.* **бо́ен**] *n.* **1,** slaughterhouse. **2,** massacre; slaughter; carnage.

бок [*2nd loc.* **боку́**; *pl.* **бока́**] *n.* side. —**бок о́ бок,** side by side. —**по́д боком,** nearby; close at hand. —**с бо́ку на́ бок,** from side to side. *See also* **бо́ком.**

бока́л *n.* wineglass; goblet.

боково́й *adj.* side *(attrib.);* lateral. —**отпра́виться на боковую,** *colloq.* to turn in; hit the hay.

бо́ком *adv.* sideways.

бокс *n.* boxing.

боксёр *n.* boxer. —**боксёрский,** *adj.* boxing *(attrib.).*

боксировать *v. impfv.* [*pres.* **-рую, -руешь**] *sports* to box.

бокси́т *n.* bauxite. —**бокси́товый,** *adj.* bauxite *(attrib.).*

болва́н *n.* **1,** *colloq.* dolt; blockhead. **2,** block *(for shaping hats).* **3,** *cards* dummy.

болга́рин [*pl.* **-га́ры, -га́р**] *n.m.* [*fem.* **-га́рка**] Bulgarian. —**болга́рский,** *adj.* Bulgarian.

бо́лее *adv.* **1,** more: я бо́лее чем дово́лен, I am more than satisfied. Бо́лее полуго́да тому́ наза́д, more than half a year ago. **2,** *used in forming compound comparatives* more: бо́лее интере́сный, more interesting. —**бо́лее или ме́нее,** more or less. —**бо́лее того́,** what is more. —**всё бо́лее** (+ *adj.*), more and more. —**тем бо́лее,** all the more; the more so. —**тем бо́лее, что...,** especially since; all the more so because...

болéзненно *adv.* **1,** painfully. **2,** with difficulty; hard.

болéзненность *n.f.* **1,** sickliness. **2,** morbidity.

болéзненный *adj.* **1,** sickly. **2,** painful; causing pain. **3,** of pain: болéзненный крик, a cry of pain. **4,** abnormal; morbid: болéзненное любопы́тство, morbid curiosity.

болéзнь *n.f.* illness; disease. —**болéзни ро́ста,** growing pains. —**морска́я болéзнь,** seasickness. —**о́тпуск по болéзни,** sick leave.

болéльщик *n., colloq., sports* fan.

бо́лен *see* **больно́й.**

болéть[1] *v. impfv.* [*pres.* **болéю, болéешь**] **1,** to be ill. **2,** *(with* **за** + *acc. or* **о***) colloq.* to agonize (over). **3,** *(with* **за** + *acc.) colloq.* to be a fan (of); root (for). —**болéть душо́й** *(with* **за** + *acc. or* **о***),* to feel for; take to heart.

болéть[2] *v. impfv.* [*pres.* **боли́т, боля́т**] to ache; hurt: у меня́ боли́т голова́, I have a headache. —**у меня́ душа́ боли́т за** (+ *acc.*), my heart aches for...

болеутоля́ющий *adj.* pain-relieving; analgesic. —**болеутоля́ющее сре́дство,** analgesic.

болиголо́в *n.* (poison) hemlock.

боли́д *n.* fireball *(meteor).*

боло́нка [*gen. pl.* **-нок**] *n.* small white poodle.

боло́то *n.* swamp; marsh. —**боло́тистый,** *adj.* swampy; marshy. —**боло́тный,** *adj.* marsh *(attrib.).*

болт [*gen.* **болта́**] *n., mech.* bolt.

болта́нка *n., aero., colloq.* bumpiness; turbulence.

болта́ть *v. impfv.* **1,** *colloq.* to talk; chatter. **2,** [*pfv.* **взболта́ть**] to shake; stir (a liquid). **3,** *(with instr.)* to dangle; swing. **4,** *in* **болта́ть языко́м,** *colloq.* to babble; prattle. —**болта́ться,** *refl.* **1,** to dangle. **2,** *colloq.* to hang around; loiter.

болтли́вый *adj.* talkative; loquacious; garrulous. —**болтли́вость,** *n.f.* loquaciousness.

болтовня́ *n., colloq.* chatter.

болту́н [*gen.* **-туна́**] *n.m.* [*fem.* **-ту́нья**] chatterbox.

болту́нья *n.* **1,** *fem. of* **болту́н.** **2,** *in* **я́ичница-болту́нья,** scrambled eggs.

боль *n.f.* pain; ache. —**с бо́лью в душé** *or* **в сéрдце,** with a heavy heart.

больни́ца *n.* hospital.

больни́чный *adj.* hospital *(attrib.).* —**больни́чный лист** *or* **листо́к,** medical/doctor's certificate *(certifying inability to work).*

бо́льно *adv.* **1,** badly: бо́льно ушиби́ться, to hurt oneself badly. **2,** *colloq.* terribly; a bit too. —*adj., used predicatively (with dat.)* painful: мне бо́льно, it is painful; it hurts. Мне бо́льно ви́деть..., it pains me to see... —**сдéлать бо́льно** (+ *dat.*), to hurt.

больно́й *adj.* [*short form* **бо́лен, больна́**] **1,** sick, ill. **2,** sore: больно́й зуб, a sore tooth. **3,** bad: больно́е сéрдце, a bad heart. —*n.* patient; sick person. —**больно́й вопро́с,** sore subject. —**больно́е мéсто,** sore spot; tender spot.

бо́льше *adj., comp. of* **большо́й,** bigger; larger; greater. —*adv., comp. of* **мно́го,** more. —**бо́льше всего́,** most of all. —**бо́льше не,** no more; anymore; any longer. —**бо́льше нигдé,** nowhere else. —**бо́льше никогда́,** never again. —**бо́льше никого́,** no one else. —**бо́льше ничего́,** nothing else. —**бо́льше того́,** what is more.

большеви́к [*gen.* **-вика́**] *n.* Bolshevik. —**большеви́стский,** *adj.* Bolshevik *(attrib.).*

бо́льший *adj., used only as a modifier, comp. of* **большо́й** *and* **вели́кий,** larger; greater. —**бо́льшая часть** (+ *gen.*), most (of). —**бо́льшей ча́стью; по бо́льшей ча́сти,** for the most part; mostly. —**са́мое бо́льшее, 1,** at (the) most. **2,** *(fol. by* **что***)* the most (that).

большинство́ *n.* **1,** majority. **2,** *(with gen. or* **из***)* most: в большинствé слу́чаев, in most cases; большинство́ из нас, most of us. —**в большинствé; в большинствé своём,** for the most part; mainly.

большо́й *adj.* [*comp.* **бо́льше** *and* **бо́льший**] **1,** big; large. **2,** great. **3,** *colloq.* grownup. —*n., usu. pl., colloq.* grownup. —**больша́я бу́ква,** capital letter. —**большо́й па́лец,** thumb. —**большо́е (вам) спаси́бо!,** thank you very much! *See also* **бо́льше** *and* **бо́льший.**

большу́щий *adj., colloq.* huge; tremendous.

боля́чка [*gen. pl.* **-чек**] *n., colloq.* sore.

бо́мба *n.* bomb.

бомбарди́р *n.* bombardier.

бомбардирова́ть *v. impfv.* [*pres.* **-ру́ю, -ру́ешь**] to bombard; bomb.

бомбардиро́вка *n.* bombardment; bombing. —**бомбардиро́вочный,** *adj.* bombing *(attrib.).*
бомбардиро́вщик *n.* bomber.
бомбёжка *n., colloq.* bombing.
бомби́ть *v. impfv.* [*pres.* **-блю́, -би́шь**] *colloq.* to bomb.
бо́мбовый *adj.* bomb *(attrib.).*
бомбодержа́тель *n.m.* bomb rack.
бомбомета́ние *n.* bombing.
бомбоубе́жище *n.* bomb shelter; air-raid shelter.
бо́ндарь *n.m.* cooper. *Also,* **бонда́рь** [*gen.* **-даря́**].
бо́нза *n.m., colloq.* bigwig; member of the elite.
бор[1] [*2nd loc.* **бору́;** *pl.* **боры́**] *n.* pine forest.
бор[2] *n.* boron.
бордо́ *n. indecl.* claret *(wine).* —*adj. indecl.* wine-colored; claret; maroon. —**бордо́вый,** *adj.* = **бордо́.**
бордю́р *n.* border; trimming.
боре́ц [*gen.* **-рца́**] *n.* **1,** *(often with* **за** + *acc.)* fighter (for). **2,** wrestler.
борза́я *n., decl. as an adj.* **1,** borzoi; Russian wolfhound. **2,** greyhound; whippet.
бо́рзый *adj., archaic (of a horse)* fleet; swift.
бормаши́на *n.* (dentist's) drill.
бормота́нье *n.* muttering; mumbling.
бормота́ть *v. impfv.* [*pfv.* **пробормота́ть;** *pres.* **-мочу́, -мо́чешь**] to mutter; mumble.
бо́рный *adj.* boric: бо́рная кислота́, boric acid.
бо́ров *n.* **1,** [*pl.* **бо́ровы, -во́в**] gelded hog. **2,** [*pl.* **борова́, -во́в**] chimney flue.
борода́ [*acc.* **бо́роду;** *pl.* **бо́роды, боро́д, -да́м**] *n.* **1,** beard. **2,** wattle *(of a bird).*
борода́вка [*gen. pl.* **-вок**] *n.* wart.
борода́вочник *n.* wart hog.
борода́вчатый *adj.* covered with warts.
борода́тый *adj.* bearded.
борода́ч [*gen.* **-дача́**] *n.* **1,** *colloq.* man with a beard. **2,** bearded vulture.
боро́дка [*gen. pl.* **-док**] *n.* small beard. —**козли́ная боро́дка,** goatee.
борозда́ [*pl.* **бо́розды, боро́зд, -да́м**] *n.* furrow.
борозди́ть *v. impfv.* [*pfv.* **изборозди́ть;** *pres.* **-зжу́, -зди́шь**] **1,** to furrow. **2,** *in* борозди́ть моря́ *or* океа́ны, to ply the seas.
борона́ [*acc.* **бо́рону;** *pl.* **бо́роны, боро́н, -на́м**] *n.* harrow.
борони́ть *v. impfv.* [*pfv.* **взборони́ть**] to harrow. *Also,* **бороно**ва́ть [*pres.* **-ну́ю, -ну́ешь**].
боро́ться *v.r. impfv.* [*pres.* **борю́сь, бо́решься**] **1,** to fight. **2,** *(with* **с** + *instr.)* to combat; fight; battle. **3,** to wrestle.
борт [*2nd loc.* **борту́;** *pl.* **борта́**] *n.* **1,** side *(of a ship).* **2,** breast *(of a coat).* **3,** cushion *(of a billiard table).* —**за́ борт; за бо́ртом,** overboard. —**на́ борт; на борту́,** aboard; on board. —**оста́вить/оста́ться за бо́ртом,** to leave/be left/out in the cold. —**челове́к за бо́ртом**!, man overboard!
бортмеха́ник *n.* flight engineer.
бортово́й *adj.* **1,** on-board. **2,** side *(attrib.).* —**бортова́я ка́чка,** rolling *(of a ship).*
бортпроводни́к [*gen.* **-ника́**] *n.* steward. —**бортпроводни́ца,** *n.* stewardess.
борщ [*gen.* **борща́**] *n.* borsch.
борьба́ *n.* **1,** struggle; fight. **2,** wrestling. —**япо́нская борьба́,** jujitsu.
босико́м *adv., colloq.* barefoot; in one's bare feet.
босо́й *adj.* **1,** barefoot. **2,** *(of feet)* bare. —**(надева́ть ту́фли) на босу́ но́гу,** (to put on one's shoes) without socks.
босоно́гий *adj.* barefoot.
босоно́жка [*gen. pl.* **-жек**] *n.* **1,** barefoot girl or woman. **2,** *usu. pl.* sandals.
босс *n.* (political) boss.
craft
бося́к [*gen.* **-сяка́**] *n.* vagabond; tramp.
бот *n.* **1,** boat. **2,** boot.
бота́ника *n.* botany. —**бота́ник,** *n.* botanist. —**ботани́ческий,** *adj.* botanical.
ботва́ *n.* vegetable tops.
ботви́нья *n.* cold soup made of kvass, cooked vegetables, and fish.
бо́тик *n.* **1,** small boat. **2,** lady's boot.
боти́нок [*gen.* **-нка;** *gen. pl.* **-нок**] *n.* shoe.
бо́цман *n.* boatswain.
боча́р [*gen.* **-чара́**] *n.* cooper.
бо́чка [*gen. pl.* **-чек**] *n.* barrel; keg. —**де́ньги на бо́чку,** cash on the barrel.
бочко́м *adv.* sideways.
бочо́нок [*gen.* **-нка**] *n.* small barrel; keg.
боязли́вый *adj.* timid; timorous. —**боязли́вость,** *n.f.* timidity.
боя́зно *adj., used predicatively (with dat.) colloq.* afraid.
боя́знь *n.f.* fear; dread.
боя́рин [*pl.* **боя́ре, боя́р**] *n., hist.* boyar. —**боя́рский,** *adj.* boyar *(attrib.);* boyars'. —**боя́рство,** *n.* the boyars.
боя́рышник *n.* hawthorn.
боя́ться *v.r. impfv.* [*pres.* **бою́сь, бои́шься**] **1,** *(with gen.)* to be afraid of; fear. **2,** *(with a dependent clause)* to be afraid; fear: бою́сь, что..., I'm afraid/I fear/ that... **3,** *(with gen.)* to be sensitive to. —**бою́сь сказа́ть,** I cannot say for sure.
бра *n. neut. indecl.* candlestick or lamp bracket mounted on a wall.
брава́да *n.* bravado.
брави́ровать *v. impfv.* [*pres.* **-рую, -руешь**] *(with instr.)* **1,** to flaunt; parade. **2,** to brave; defy.
брави́ссимо *interj.* bravissimo!
бра́во *interj.* bravo!
браву́рный *adj. (of music)* stirring. —**браву́рная му́зыка,** bravura.
бра́вый *adj.* dashing.
бра́га *n.* home-brewed beer.
бразды́ *n. pl., obs.* bridle; bit. —**бразды́ правле́ния,** the reins of government.
брази́лец [*gen.* **-льца**] *n.m.* [*fem.* **-лья́нка**] Brazilian. —**брази́льский,** *adj.* Brazilian.
брак *n.* **1,** marriage. **2,** defect; flaw. **3,** defective merchandise.
брако́ванный *adj. (of merchandise)* defective.
бракова́ть *v. impfv.* [*pfv.* **забракова́ть;** *pres.* **-ку́ю, -ку́ешь**] to reject as defective.
брако́вщик *n.* quality control inspector.
бракоде́л *n.* slipshod worker.
браконье́р *n.* poacher. —**браконье́рство,** *n.* poaching.
бракоразво́дный *adj.* divorce *(attrib.).*
бракосочета́ние *n.* wedding ceremony. —**дворе́ц бракосочета́ния,** wedding palace.
брами́н *n.* = **брахма́н.**
бра́мсель *n.m.* topgallant sail.
брам-сте́ньга *n.* topgallant mast.

брандспо́йт *n.* **1,** nozzle *(of a fire hose).* **2,** portable pump.
брани́ть *v. impfv.* to scold; berate. —**брани́ться,** *refl.* **1,** to quarrel. **2,** to swear; curse.
бра́нный *adj.* **1,** abusive: бра́нное сло́во, swearword. **2,** *archaic* martial.
брань *n.f.* **1,** swearing; profanity. **2,** *archaic* battle.
брасле́т *n.* bracelet.
брасс *n., swimming* breast stroke.
брат [*pl.* **бра́тья, бра́тьев**] *n.* brother.
брата́ние *n.* fraternization.
брата́ться *v.r. impfv.* [*pfv.* **побрата́ться**] to fraternize.
бра́тец [*gen.* **-тца**] *n.* **1,** *dim., endearing form of* **брат. 2,** *in direct address* old man; old chap.
брати́шка [*gen. pl.* **-шек**] *n.m., dim. of* **брат.**
бра́тия *n.* fraternity: литерату́рная бра́тия, literary fraternity.
братоуби́йство *n.* fratricide. —**братоуби́йственный,** *adj.* fratricidal.
бра́тский *adj.* brotherly; fraternal. —**бра́тская моги́ла,** common grave.
бра́тство *n.* brotherhood; fraternity.
брать *v. impfv.* [*pfv.* **взять;** *pres.* **беру́, берёшь;** *past fem.* **брала́**] **1,** to take. **2,** to seize. **3,** to buy; get. **4,** to levy; exact. **5,** to charge (a certain price). **6,** to clear (a hurdle, height, etc.). **7,** *(with instr.)* to succeed (by means of). **8,** *colloq.* to work; be effective: нож не берёт, the knife doesn't cut. —**брать верх,** *see* **верх.** —**брать за́ се́рдце** (*or* **за́ душу**), to touch someone's heart. —**брать курс на,** to make for; head for. —**брать на себя́,** to take upon oneself; assume. —**брать но́ту,** to strike *or* hit a note. —**брать приме́р с** (+ *gen.*), to follow someone's example. —**брать своё,** *see* **свой.** —**брать себя́ в ру́ки,** to pull oneself together. —**брать сло́во с** (+ *gen.*), to make someone promise. *See also* **взять.**
бра́ться *v.r. impfv.* [*pfv.* **взя́ться;** *pres.* **беру́сь, берёшься;** *past* **бра́лся, брала́сь, брало́сь**] **1,** *(with* **за** *+ acc.)* to take hold of; grasp. **2,** *(with* **за** *+ acc.)* to begin; take up; undertake. **3,** *(with inf.)* to take it upon oneself (to); dare (to); presume (to). **4,** to come (from): отку́да же они́ беру́тся?, where on earth do they come from? —**бра́ться за́ руки,** to join hands. —**бра́ться за ору́жие,** to take up arms. —**бра́ться за ум,** *colloq.* to come to one's senses. *See also* **взя́ться.**
брахма́н *also,* **брами́н** *n.* Brahman. —**брахмани́зм; брамани́зм,** *n.* Brahmanism.
бра́чный *adj.* marriage *(attrib.);* marital; matrimonial; conjugal; nuptial. —**бра́чный пери́од,** mating period; mating season.
бра́шпиль *n.m.* windlass.
бреве́нчатый *adj.* log *(attrib.);* made of logs.
бревно́ [*pl.* **брёвна, брёвен**] *n.* log.
бред [*2nd loc.* **бреду́**] *n.* **1,** delirium: быть в бреду́, to be delirious. **2,** ravings.
бре́день [*gen.* **-дня**] *n.m.* dragnet.
бре́дить *v. impfv.* [*pres.* **бре́жу, бре́дишь**] **1,** to be delirious; rave. **2,** *(with instr.) colloq.* to be crazy (about); be mad (about).
бре́дни [*gen.* **-ней**] *n. pl.* ravings; wild fantasy.
бредово́й *adj.* **1,** delirious. **2,** *fig.* nonsensical.
бре́згать *v. impfv.* [*pfv.* **побре́згать**] *(with instr. or inf.)* **1,** to be squeamish about; have an aversion to. **2,** to disdain; shrink from: не бре́згать никаки́ми сре́дствами, to stop at nothing.
брезгли́вый *adj.* squeamish. —**брезгли́вость,** *n.f.* squeamishness.
брезе́нт *n.* tarpaulin. —**брезе́нтовый,** *adj.* tarpaulin.
бре́зжить *v. impfv.* **1,** to glimmer; gleam faintly. **2,** *impers.* to dawn; get light. *Also,* **бре́зжиться,** *refl.*
брело́к *n.* charm *(on a chain or bracelet).*
бре́мя [*gen., dat., & prepl.* **бре́мени;** *instr.* **бре́менем**] *n. neut.* burden.
бре́нный *adj., obs.* perishable. —**бре́нные оста́нки,** mortal remains.
бренча́ть *v. impfv.* [*pres.* **-чу́, -чи́шь**] **1,** *v.i. (of inanimate objects)* to jingle; clink. **2,** *v.t. (with instr.)* to jingle; clink (something). **3,** *(with* **на** *+ prepl.) colloq.* to strum.
брести́ *v. impfv.* [*pres.* **бреду́, бредёшь;** *past* **брёл, брела́, брело́**] to trudge along; drag oneself along.
брете́лька (тэ) [*gen. pl.* **-лек**] *n.* strap *(of an undergarment).*
бреха́ть *v. impfv.* [*pfv.* **брехну́ть;** *pres.* **брешу́, бре́шешь**] *colloq.* **1,** to bark. **2,** to tell lies.
бреху́н [*gen.* **-хуна́**] *n.m.* [*fem.* **-ху́нья**] *colloq.* liar.
брешь *n.f.* breach; gap.
бре́ющий *pres. active part. of* **брить.** —*adj., in* **бре́ющий полёт,** low-altitude flight.
бриг *n.* brig *(ship).*
брига́да *n.* **1,** *mil.* brigade. **2,** team; crew; brigade *(of workers).* —**бригади́р,** *n.* foreman.
бридж *n., cards* bridge.
бри́джи [*gen.* **-жей**] *n. pl.* breeches.
бриз *n.* sea breeze.
брике́т *n.* briquette.
бриллиа́нт *also,* **брилья́нт** *n.* (cut) diamond. —**бриллиа́нтовый; брилья́нтовый,** *adj.* diamond.
брита́нский *adj.* British.
бри́тва *n.* razor.
бри́твенный *adj.* shaving *(attrib.):* бри́твенные принадле́жности, shaving equipment.
бри́тый *adj.* clean-shaven.
брить *v. impfv.* [*pfv.* **побри́ть;** *pres.* **бре́ю, бре́ешь**] to shave.
бритьё *n.* shaving; shave.
бри́ться *v.r.impfv.* [*pfv.* **побри́ться;** *pres.* **бре́юсь, бре́ешься**] to shave (oneself); get a shave.
бри́чка [*gen. pl.* **-чек**] *n.* light cart or carriage.
бровь [*pl.* **бро́ви, -ве́й, -вя́м**] *n.f.* eyebrow. —**попа́сть не в бровь, а в глаз,** to hit the nail on the head.
брод *n.* ford.
броди́льный *adj.* fermenting *(attrib.).*
броди́ть *v. impfv.* [*pres.* **брожу́, бро́дишь**] **1,** to wander; roam. **2,** to ferment.
бродя́га *n.m.* tramp; vagrant; vagabond; hobo.
бродя́жничать *v. impfv., colloq.* **1,** to lead the life of a tramp. **2,** to wander; roam. *Also,* **бродя́жить.**
бродя́жничество *n.* **1,** vagrancy. **2,** wandering.
бродя́чий *adj.* **1,** wandering; itinerant. **2,** *(of a dog or cat)* stray. **3,** nomadic.
броже́ние *n.* **1,** fermentation. **2,** *fig.* ferment.
бро́кколи *n.f. indecl.* broccoli.
бром *n.* **1,** bromine. **2,** *med.* bromide. —**броми́д,** *n., chem.* bromide. —**бро́мистый,** *adj.* bromide: бро́мистый ка́лий, potassium bromide.
бронеавтомоби́ль *n.m.* armored car.
бронебо́йный *adj.* armor-piercing.
броневи́к [*gen.* **-вика́**] *n.* = **бронеавтомоби́ль.**
бронево́й *adj.* armored. —**бронева́я плита́; бронево́й лист,** armor plate; armor plating.

бронемаши́на *n.* armored car.
броненóсец [*gen.* **-сца**] *n.* **1,** *hist.* battleship. **2,** armadillo.
броненóсный *adj.* armored: броненóсный крéйсер, armored cruiser.
бронепóезд *n.* armored train.
бронетáнковый *adj.* armored: бронетáнковые войскá, armored troops.
бронетранспортёр *n.* armored personnel carrier.
брóнза *n.* bronze.
бронзировáть *v. impfv. & pfv.* [*pres.* **-рýю, -рýешь**] to bronze.
брóнзовый *adj.* **1,** bronze; made of bronze. **2,** bronze *(in color).*
бронирóванный *adj.* armored. —**бронирóванный кулáк,** mailed fist.
брони́ровать *v. impfv. & pfv.* [*pfv. also* **заброни́ровать;** *pres.* **-рую, -руешь**] to reserve; book.
бронировáть *v. impfv. & pfv.* [*pfv. also* **забронировáть;** *pres.* **-рýю, -рýешь**] to armor; cover with armor.
бронтозáвр *n.* brontosaurus.
брóнхи *n. pl.* [*sing.* **бронх**] bronchi; bronchial tubes. —**бронхиáльный,** *adj.* bronchial.
бронхи́т *n.* bronchitis.
брóня *n.* reservation *(advance order).*
броня́ *n.* armor.
бросáть *v. impfv.* [*pfv.* **брóсить**] **1,** to throw; toss. **2,** to cast (a shadow, glance, etc.). **3,** to throw away. **4,** to abandon; forsake; desert. **5,** to give up; quit: брóсить кури́ть, to give up/quit smoking. **6,** *impers.* to careen: маши́ну бросáло из стороны́ в стóрону, the car careened from side to side. **7,** *impers.* to break into: егó брóсило в пот, he broke into a sweat. —**бросáть дéньги на вéтер,** to throw money away. —**бросáть жрéбий,** to cast lots; decide something by chance. —**бросáть орýжие,** to throw down one's weapons. —**бросáть я́корь,** to cast *or* drop anchor. —**брось!; брóсьте!,** stop!; stop it!
бросáться *v.r. impfv.* [*pfv.* **брóситься**] **1,** to rush; dash; fall; jump. **2,** *(with inf.)* to hasten (to). **3,** [*impfv. only*] *(with instr.)* to throw (something) at each other. —**бросáться в глазá,** to be striking; catch the eye. —**бросáться деньгáми,** to toss money around. —**бросáться словáми,** to make irresponsible statements; make idle promises.
брóсить [*infl.* **брóшу, брóсишь**] *v., pfv. of* **бросáть.** —**брóситься,** *refl., pfv. of* **бросáться.**
брóский *adj., colloq.* **1,** garish; loud. **2,** striking.
брóсовый *adj., colloq.* **1,** cheap; trashy; worthless. **2,** throwaway; disposable. —**брóсовые цéны,** prices below cost; giveaway prices.
бросóк [*gen.* **-скá**] *n.* **1,** throw. **2,** *sports* shot. **3,** spurt; burst of speed.
брошь *n.f.* brooch. *Also,* **брóшка.**
брошю́ра (шу) *n.* pamphlet; brochure.
брус [*pl.* **брýсья, брýсьев**] *n.* **1,** beam. **2,** *pl., sports* bars: параллéльные брýсья, parallel bars.
брусни́ка *n.* **1,** cowberries. **2,** a (single) cowberry.
брусóк [*gen.* **-скá**] *n.* **1,** bar. **2,** whetstone.
брýствер *n.* breastwork; parapet.
брусчáтка *n.* **1,** paving stones; paving blocks. **2,** *colloq.* paved road.
брусчáтый *adj.* made of paving blocks.
брýтто *adj. & adv. indecl.* gross: вес брýтто, gross weight; ценá брýтто, gross price.
бры́жи [*gen.* **-жей**] *n. pl., obs.* frilled collar; ruff.
бры́згать *v. impfv.* [*pfv.* **бры́знуть;** *pres.* **бры́зжу, бры́зжешь** *or* **бры́згаю, бры́згаешь**] **1,** *(with instr.)* to sprinkle; splash (a liquid). **2,** to sprinkle (something with a liquid). **3,** to spurt; gush; shoot forth; shoot out. —**бры́згаться,** *refl.* [*impfv. only*] **1,** *(with instr.)* to sprinkle; splash (a liquid); spray oneself (with a liquid). **2,** to splash each other.
бры́зги [*gen.* **брызг**] *n. pl.* spray.
брызгови́к [*gen.* **-викá**] *n.* mudguard.
бры́знуть *v., pfv. of* **бры́згать.**
брыкáть *v. impfv.* [*pfv.* **брыкнýть**] to kick. *Also,* **брыкáться,** *refl.*
бры́нза *n.* cheese made from sheep's milk.
брюзгá *n.m. & f.* grouch.
брюзгли́вый *adj.* grouchy; grumpy.
брюзжáть *v. impfv.* [*pres.* **-зжý, -зжи́шь**] to grumble; grouch.
брю́ква *n.* rutabaga.
брю́ки [*gen.* **брюк**] *n. pl.* trousers; pants.
брюнéт *n.m.* [*fem.* **-нéтка**] brunette.
брюссéльский (сэ) *adj., in* **брюссéльская капýста,** Brussels sprouts.
брю́хо *n.* **1,** belly *(of an animal).* **2,** *colloq.* paunch.
брюши́на *n.* peritoneum. —**воспалéние брюши́ны,** peritonitis.
брюшкó [*pl.* **-ки́, -кóв**] *n.* paunch; potbelly.
брюшнóй *adj.* abdominal. —**брюшнóй тиф,** typhoid.
бря́кать *v. impfv.* [*pfv.* **бря́кнуть**] *colloq.* **1,** *v.i.* to rattle; clang; clatter; jingle. **2,** *v.t. (with instr.)* to rattle; jingle. **3,** to slam down. **4,** to blurt out. —**бря́каться,** *refl., colloq.* to fall heavily; come crashing down.
бряцáние *n.* clank; jingling; jangling. —**бряцáние орýжием,** saber rattling.
бряцáть *v. impfv.* **1,** *v.i.* to clank; jingle; jangle. **2,** *v.i. (with* **на** *+ prepl.)* to strum. **3,** *v.t. (with instr.)* to jingle; jangle. —**бряцáть орýжием,** to brandish weapons; indulge in saber rattling.
бýбен [*gen.* **-бна**] *n.* tambourine.
бубенцы́ *n. pl.* [*sing.* **бубенéц**] small bells; sleigh bells.
бубéнчики *n. pl.* [*sing.* **бубéнчик**] = **бубенцы́.**
бýблик *n.* thick bagel.
бубни́ть *v. impfv.* [*pfv.* **пробубни́ть**] *colloq.* **1,** to mumble; mutter. **2,** [*impfv. only*] to drone (on and on).
бубнóвый *adj., cards* of diamonds: бубнóвый корóль, king of diamonds.
бýбны [*gen.* **бубён;** *dat.* **бубнáм**] *n. pl., cards* diamonds.
бубóн *n.* bubo.
бубóнный *adj.* bubonic. —**бубóнная чумá,** bubonic plague.
бугóр [*gen.* **-грá**] *n.* **1,** mound; knoll. **2,** bump; lump.
бугорóк [*gen.* **-ркá**] *n.* **1,** *dim. of* **бугóр. 2,** protuberance. **3,** *med.* tubercle.
бугóрчатый *adj.* **1,** covered with lumps. **2,** tuberous.
бугри́стый *adj.* **1,** hilly; uneven. **2,** bumpy.
будди́зм *n.* Buddhism. —**будди́йский,** *adj.* Buddhist.
будди́ст *n.m.* [*fem.* **-ди́стка**] Buddhist.
бýдет *v., 3rd person sing. of* **быть.** —*interj., colloq.* enough!; that'll do! —**что бýдет, то бýдет,** what will be will be.
буди́льник *n.* alarm clock.
буди́ть *v. impfv.* [*pres.* **бужý, бýдишь**] **1,** [*pfv.* **раз-**

буди́ть] to waken; awaken. **2,** [*pfv.* **пробуди́ть**] *fig.* to arouse; evoke.

бу́дка [*gen. pl.* **-док**] *n.* booth. —**карау́льная бу́дка,** sentry box. —**телефо́нная бу́дка,** telephone booth.

бу́дни [*gen.* **-ней**] *n. pl.* **1,** weekdays. **2,** *fig.* humdrum existence.

бу́дний *adj., in* **бу́дний день,** weekday.

бу́дничный *also,* **бу́днишний** *adj.* **1,** = **бу́дний. 2,** everyday; ordinary. **3,** *fig.* humdrum; routine.

будора́жить *v. impfv.* [*pfv.* **взбудора́жить**] *colloq.* to stir up; rouse; excite.

бу́дто *conj.* **1,** that *(implying doubt as to the truth of a statement):* говоря́т, бу́дто она́ за́мужем, they say she's married. **2,** [*also,* **как бу́дто**] as if: как бу́дто по волшебству́, as if by magic. У вас тако́й вид, бу́дто вы не по́няли, you look as if you did not understand. —*particle, colloq.* **1,** [*also,* **как бу́дто**] apparently: дождь как бу́дто ко́нчился, the rain appears to have stopped. **2,** really?: уж бу́дто ты так спеши́шь домо́й?, are you really in such a hurry to get home?

будуа́р *n.* boudoir.

бу́дучи *verbal adv. of* **быть,** being: бу́дучи в Ми́нске, being in Minsk; while in Minsk.

бу́дущее *n., decl. as an adj.* the future.

бу́дущий *adj.* **1,** future. **2,** next: в бу́дущем году́, next year.

бу́дущность *n.f.* future.

будь *v., imperative of* **быть.** ♦*Also, in contrary-to-fact constructions,* were: будь он сейча́с жив, were he alive today; будь я на её ме́сте, if I were in her place. —**будь то...,** be it... —**будь, что бу́дет,** come what may. —**не будь** (+ *gen.*), were it not for...

бу́ер [*pl.* **буера́**] *n.* iceboat.

бужени́на *n.* boiled pork.

бузина́ *n.* elder *(shrub).*

буй [*pl.* **буи́, буёв**] *n.* buoy.

бу́йвол *n.* buffalo. —**бу́йволовый,** *adj.* buffalo *(attrib.).*

бу́йный *adj.* **1,** wild; boisterous; unruly; rambunctious. **2,** *(of natural phenomena)* violent; stormy. **3,** *(of vegetation)* lush; luxuriant.

бу́йство *n.* unruly behavior.

бу́йствовать *v. impfv.* [*pres.* **-ствую, -ствуешь**] to run wild; run riot; go on a rampage; run amuck.

бук *n.* beech (tree).

бу́ка *n.m. & f., colloq.* **1,** bogeyman. **2,** surly, unfriendly person. —**смотре́ть бу́кой,** to look surly.

бука́шка [*gen. pl.* **-шек**] *n.* insect; bug.

бу́ква *n.* **1,** letter *(of the alphabet).* **2,** *fig. (with gen.)* the letter (of): бу́ква зако́на, the letter of the law. —**бу́ква в бу́кву,** word for word; literally.

буква́льный *adj.* literal. —**буква́льно,** *adv.* literally.

буква́рь [*gen.* **-варя́**] *n.m.* primer; book of ABC's.

бу́квенный *adj.* letter *(attrib.).*

буквое́д *n.* pedant.

буке́т *n.* bouquet. —**буке́тик,** *n.* small bouquet.

букини́ст *n.* secondhand book dealer. —**букинисти́ческий,** *adj.* secondhand-book *(attrib.).*

букле́т *n.* booklet.

букме́кер *n.* bookmaker.

бу́ковый *adj.* **1,** beech *(attrib.).* **2,** beechwood *(attrib.).*

букси́р *n.* **1,** tugboat. **2,** towline; towrope. —**брать на букси́р,** to take in tow *(lit. & fig.).*

букси́ровать *v. impfv.* [*pres.* **-рую, -руешь**] to tow.

буксиро́вка *n.* towing.

буксова́ть *v. impfv.* [*pres.* **-су́ет**] *(of wheels)* to spin around *(without gaining traction).*

булава́ *n.* mace *(weapon).*

була́вка [*gen. pl.* **-вок**] *n.* pin. —**англи́йская була́вка,** safety pin. —**де́ньги на була́вки,** pin money.

була́вочный *adj.* pin *(attrib.).*

бу́лка [*gen. pl.* **-лок**] *n.* roll; bun.

бу́лла *n.* (papal) bull.

бу́лочка [*gen. pl.* **-чек**] *n.* small roll; bun.

бу́лочная *n., decl. as an adj.* bakery.

бу́лочник *n.* baker.

булты́х *interj., colloq.* plop!; splash!

бултыха́ться *v.r. impfv.* [*pfv.* **булты́хнуться** *or* **бултыхну́ться**] *colloq.* **1,** to plunge; flop; plop *(into water).* **2,** [*impfv. only*] to flop about; thrash about.

булы́жник *n.* cobblestone. —**булы́жный,** *adj.* cobbled; cobblestone *(attrib.).*

бульва́р *n.* public walk; promenade; mall.

бульва́рный *adj.* **1,** of a **бульва́р. 2,** *fig. (of literature, a newspaper, etc.)* trashy.

бульдо́г *n.* bulldog.

бульдо́зер *n.* bulldozer.

бу́льканье *n.* gurgling; gurgle.

бу́лькать *v. impfv.* to gurgle.

бульо́н *n.* clear soup; broth; consommé; bouillon.

бум *n.* **1,** *econ.* boom. **2,** (media) sensation. —*interj.* boom!

бума́га *n.* **1,** paper. **2,** *pl.* papers; documents. **3,** *archaic* cotton. —**це́нные бума́ги,** securities.

бума́жка [*gen. pl.* **-жек**] *n.* **1,** piece of paper. **2,** *colloq.* bill; bank note: бума́жка в пять до́лларов, five-dollar bill.

бума́жник *n.* wallet; billfold.

бума́жный *adj.* **1,** paper. **2,** cotton.

бумера́нг *n.* boomerang.

бу́нкер [*pl.* **бункера́**] *n.* bunker; storage bin.

бунт *n.* **1,** [*gen.* **бу́нта;** *pl.* **бу́нты**] riot; uprising; rebellion; mutiny. **2,** [*gen.* **бунта́;** *pl.* **бунты́**] bundle; bale.

бунта́рский *adj.* rebellious; mutinous. —**бунта́рство,** *n.* rebelliousness.

бунта́рь [*gen.* **-таря́**] *n.m., obs.* rioter; rebel.

бунтова́ть *v. impfv.* [*pres.* **-ту́ю, -ту́ешь**] **1,** [*pfv.* **взбунтова́ться**] to rebel; revolt; mutiny. **2,** [*pfv.* **взбунтова́ть**] *archaic* to incite to rebellion.

бунтовщи́к [*gen.* **-щика́**] *n.* rioter; rebel.

бур *n.* **1,** drill; auger. **2,** Boer.

бура́ *n.* borax.

бура́в [*gen.* **-рава́**] *n.* auger; gimlet.

бура́вить *v. impfv.* [*pfv.* **пробура́вить;** *pres.* **-влю, -вишь**] to bore; drill.

бура́вчик *n.* auger; gimlet.

бура́к [*gen.* **-рака́**] *n., colloq.* beet.

бура́н *n.* blizzard.

бургоми́стр *n.* burgomaster.

бурда́ *n., colloq.* slop.

бурдю́к [*gen.* **-дюка́**] *n.* wineskin.

буреве́стник *n.* petrel *(bird).*

бурело́м *n.* fallen trees.

буре́ние *n.* boring; drilling.

буре́ть *v. impfv.* [*pfv.* **побуре́ть**] to become brown; turn brown.

буржуа́ *n.m. indecl.* bourgeois.

буржуази́я *n.* bourgeoisie. —**буржуа́зный,** *adj.* bourgeois.

working

бури́льный *adj.* boring *(attrib.);* drilling *(attrib.).*

бури́ть *v. impfv.* [*pfv.* **пробури́ть**] to bore; drill.
бу́рка [*gen. pl.* **-рок**] *n.* **1,** felt cloak *(worn in the Caucasus).* **2,** *usu. pl.* felt boot with a leather sole.
бу́ркать *v. impfv.* [*pfv.* **бу́ркнуть**] *colloq.* to mutter; growl.
бурла́к [*gen.* **-лака́**] *n.* bargeman.
бурле́ск *n.* burlesque.
бурли́вый *adj.* turbulent.
бурли́ть *v. impfv.* to seethe.
бу́рный *adj.* **1,** stormy. **2,** violent; wild. **3,** hectic; frantic. **4,** rapid.
буровой *adj.* boring *(attrib.);* drilling *(attrib.).* —**бурова́я вы́шка,** oil derrick.
бу́рский *adj.* Boer.
буру́н [*gen.* **-руна́**] *n.* breaker *(wave).*
бурунду́к [*gen.* **-дука́**] *n.* chipmunk.
бурча́ть *v. impfv.* [*pfv.* **пробурча́ть;** *pres.* **-чу́, -чи́шь**] *colloq.* **1,** to mumble; mutter. **2,** *(of one's stomach)* to rumble.
бу́рый *adj.* brown.
бурья́н *n.* (tall) weeds.
бу́ря *n.* storm. —**бу́ря в стака́не воды́,** tempest in a teapot.
буря́т [*gen. pl.* **буря́т**] *n.m.* [*fem.* **-ря́тка**] Buryat *(one of a people inhabiting southern Siberia).* —**буря́тский,** *adj.* Buryat.
бу́сина *n.* bead. *Also,* **бу́синка.**
буссо́ль *n.f.* surveyor's compass.
бу́сы [*gen.* **бус**] *n. pl.* beads.
бута́н *n.* butane.
бутафо́рия *n., theat.* properties; stage props. —**бутафо́р,** *n.* property man. —**бутафо́рский,** *adj.* of or for stage props.
бутербро́д (тэ) *n.* sandwich.
бути́л *n.* butyl.
бутиле́н *n.* butylene.
буто́н *n.* bud.
бутонье́рка [*gen. pl.* **-рок**] *n.* boutonniere.
буту́з *n., colloq.* roly-poly child.
буты́лка [*gen. pl.* **-лок**] *n.* bottle. —**буты́лочка,** *n.* small bottle.
буты́лочный *adj.* **1,** bottle *(attrib.).* **2,** bottled. —**буты́лочный цвет,** bottle green.
буты́ль *n.f.* large bottle.
бу́фер [*pl.* **буфера́**] *n.* **1,** bumper. **2,** *fig.* buffer. —**бу́ферный,** *adj.* buffer *(attrib.).*
буфе́т *n.* **1,** buffet; sideboard. **2,** snack bar.
буфе́тная *n., decl. as an adj.* pantry.
буфе́тчик *n.m.* [*fem.* **-чица**] **1,** person who works behind a counter. **2,** bartender; *fem.* barmaid.
буффо́н *n.* buffoon. —**буффона́да,** *n.* buffoonery.
буха́нка [*gen. pl.* **-нок**] *n.* loaf of bread.
бу́хать *v. impfv.* [*pfv.* **бу́хнуть**] *colloq.* **1,** to bang: бу́хнуть кулако́м в *or* по, to bang one's fist on. **2,** to drop (something) with a thud. **3,** *(of a door)* to slam; *(of a shot)* be heard. —**бу́хаться,** *refl., colloq.* to throw oneself; plop.
бухга́лтер *n.* bookkeeper; accountant.
бухгалте́рия *n.* **1,** bookkeeping; accounting. **2,** bookkeeping department; accounting department. —**бухга́лтерский,** *adj.* bookkeeping *(attrib.);* accounting *(attrib.).*
бу́хнуть[1] *v. impfv.* [*pfv.* **разбу́хнуть;** *past* **бух, -ла**] to swell; swell up.
бу́хнуть[2] [*past* **бу́хнул**] *v., pfv. of* **бу́хать.** —**бу́хнуться,** *refl., pfv. of* **бу́хаться.**
бу́хта *n.* small bay.
бу́хточка [*gen. pl.* **-чек**] *n.* cove; inlet.
бу́ча *n., colloq.* row; fuss.
бушева́ть *v. impfv.* [*pres.* **-шу́ю, -шу́ешь**] *(of a fire, storm, etc.)* to rage.
бу́шель *n.m.* bushel.
бушла́т *n.* pea jacket.
бушпри́т *n.* bowsprit.
буя́н *n.* rowdy; ruffian; roughneck.
буя́нить *v. impfv.* to run wild; run riot; go on a rampage; run amuck.
бы *also,* **б** *particle, used only with the inf. or past tense of a verb* **1,** would; should: я бы хоте́л(а) спроси́ть..., I would/should like to ask... Я бы сказа́л(а) вам е́сли бы вы спроси́ли, I would have told you if you had asked. **2,** *used to express a polite suggestion:* ты бы бро́сил кури́ть, you should give up smoking. Вам лу́чше бы пойти́ самому́, you had better go yourself. **3,** *used to express a profound wish:* был бы он здесь!, if only he were here!
быва́ло *particle, colloq.* would (often): он, быва́ло, ча́сто заходи́л к нам, he would often come to see us.
быва́лый *adj.* **1,** *obs.* former; olden; bygone. **2,** *colloq.* experienced; worldly-wise. —**э́то де́ло быва́лое,** it's nothing new; it has happened before.
быва́ть *v. impfv.* **1,** to be *(regularly or customarily):* он быва́ет в магази́не ка́ждый день, he is in the store every day. Он ча́сто быва́ет у нас, he is often over at our house. **2,** to happen: как э́то ча́сто быва́ет, as often happens. **3,** to take place; be held: заседа́ния быва́ют раз в ме́сяц, meetings are held once a month. —**как ни в чём не быва́ло,** as if nothing happened.
бы́вший *adj.* former; ex-.
бык [*gen.* **быка́**] *n.* **1,** bull. **2,** pier *(of a bridge).* —**бой быко́в,** bullfight; bullfighting. —**взять быка́ за рога́,** to take the bull by the horns.
были́на *n.* Russian epic poem.
были́нка [*gen. pl.* **-нок**] *n.* blade of grass.
было *particle (without stress)* just about to; on the point of: он встал было из-за стола́, когда́..., he was about to get up from the table when...
было́й *adj.* former; bygone. —**было́е,** *n.* the past.
быль *n.f.* **1,** *archaic* fact; event. **2,** true story.
быльё *n., obs.* weeds. —**быльём поросло́,** lost in oblivion.
быстрина́ [*pl.* **-три́ны**] *n.* rapids.
бы́стро *adv.* fast; quickly; rapidly.
быстроно́гий *adj.* fleet-footed.
быстрораствори́мый *adj.* dissolving quickly. —**быстрораствори́мый ко́фе,** instant coffee.
быстота́ *n.* speed; rapidity.
быстрохо́дный *adj.* fast-moving; high-speed.
бы́стрый *adj.* fast; quick; rapid; swift.
быт [*2nd loc.* **быту́**] *n.* **1,** way of life; life. **2,** daily life.
бытие́ *n.* **1,** being; existence. **2,** *cap., Bib.* Genesis: Кни́га Бытия́, the book of Genesis.
бы́тность *n.f., in* **в бы́тность (мою́, его́,** *etc.***),** during one's stay (in); *(with instr.)* when one was (in a certain capacity).
бытова́ть *v. impfv.* [*pres.* **-ту́ет**] to exist.
бытово́й *adj.* pert. to daily life; everyday.
быть *v., used only in the future* [**бу́ду, бу́дешь**] *and the past* [**был, была́, бы́ло, бы́ли;** *neg.* **не́ был, не была́, не́ было, не́ были**] to be. —**не́ было** *(with gen.),*

expressing the absence of something in the past: там никого́ не́ было, there was no one there. —**была́ не была́!,** come what may; whatever the risk. —**как бы то ни́ было,** be that as it may. —**как быть?,** what are we to do?; what is to be done? —**так и быть,** so be it. *See also* **бу́дет, будь, было.**

бытьё *n., archaic* life; existence.

быча́чий [*fem.* **-чья**] *adj.* ox *(attrib.);* bovine. *Also,* **бы́чий** [*fem.* **-чья**].

бычо́к [*gen.* **-чка́**] *n.* **1,** young bull; young ox. **2,** goby *(fish).* **3,** *colloq.* cigarette butt.

бюва́р *n.* letter case with leaves of blotting paper.

бюдже́т *n.* budget. —**бюдже́тный,** *adj.* budget *(attrib.);* budgetary.

бюллете́нь *n.m.* **1,** bulletin. **2,** ballot. **3,** *colloq.* doctor's certificate *(stating that one is ill).*

бю́ргер *n.* burgher.

бюро́ *n. indecl.* **1,** office; bureau. **2,** writing desk. —**бюро́ нахо́док,** lost and found department. —**спра́вочное бюро́,** information office.

бюрокра́т *n.* bureaucrat.

бюрократи́зм *n.* **1,** bureaucracy. **2,** red tape.

бюрокра́тия *n.* bureaucracy. —**бюрократи́ческий,** *adj.* bureaucratic.

бюст *n.* **1,** *sculpture* bust. **2,** bosom; bust.

бюстга́льтер (тэ) *n.* brassiere.

бязь *n.f.* heavy cloth; sheeting.

В

В, в *n. neut.* third letter of the Russian alphabet.

в *also,* **во** *prep.* A. *with acc.* **1,** to: ходи́ть в шко́лу, to go to school. **2,** into: попа́сть в лову́шку, to fall into a trap; вложи́ть письмо́ в конве́рт, to put the letter into an envelope. **3,** for *(a destination):* уйти́ в шко́лу, to leave for school. **4,** in *(a certain amount of time):* оде́ться в одну́ мину́ту, to get dressed in one minute. **5,** *(with the time of day)* at: в три часа́, at three o'clock. **6,** *(with days of the week)* on: в сре́ду, on Wednesday. **7,** a; per: два ра́за в неде́лю, twice a week. **8,** *in numerical comparisons:* в два ра́за бо́льше, twice as much. B. *with prepl.* **1,** in; at: в шко́ле, in/at school. **2,** *(with months, years, centuries)* in: в апре́ле, in April; в 1941-ом году́, in 1941; в 17-ом ве́ке, in the 17th century. **3,** at a distance of: в двух киломе́трах от гости́ницы, two kilometers from the hotel.

в- *also,* **во-, въ-** *prefix, indicating motion into:* входи́ть, to enter; вкла́дывать, to insert.

ва-ба́нк *adv., in* **идти́ ва-ба́нк,** to go for broke; shoot the works.

вавило́нский *adj.* Babylonian. —**вавило́нская ба́шня,** Tower of Babel.

ва́га *n.* **1,** weighing machine. **2,** lever; crowbar.

ваго́н *n.* (railroad) car; (trolley) car. —**ваго́н-рестора́н,** dining car; diner.

вагоне́тка [*gen. pl.* **-ток**] *n.* trolley; truck; car. —**подвесна́я вагоне́тка,** cable car.

ваго́нный *adj.* car *(attrib.);* wagon *(attrib.).*

вагоновожа́тый *n., decl. as an adj.* motorman *(on a streetcar).*

важне́йший *adj.* most important; paramount.

важне́цкий *adj., colloq.* excellent; first-rate.

ва́жничать *v. impfv., colloq.* to put on airs; give oneself airs.

ва́жно *adv.* proudly; with an air of importance. —*adj., used predicatively* important: э́то не ва́жно, it's not important; мне ва́жно знать, it is important for me to know.

ва́жность *n.f.* **1,** importance. **2,** self importance, pomposity.

ва́жный *adj.* [*short form* **ва́жен, важна́, ва́жно**] **1,** important. **2,** self-important; pompous.

ва́за *n.* vase; bowl.

вазели́н *n.* vaseline.

вазо́н *n.* flowerpot.

вака́нсия *n.* vacancy; opening. —**вака́нтный,** *adj.* vacant; unfilled.

ва́кса *n.* black shoe polish.

ва́ксить *v. impfv.* [*pfv.* **нава́ксить;** *pres.* **ва́кшу, ва́ксишь**] *colloq.* to shine; polish (shoes).

вакуо́ля [*gen. pl.* **-лей**] *n.* vacuole.

ва́куум *n.* vacuum. —**ва́куум-насо́с,** vacuum pump.

вакци́на *n.* vaccine. —**вакцина́ция,** *n.* vaccination.

вакцини́ровать *v. impfv. & pfv.* [*pres.* **-рую, -руешь**] to vaccinate.

вал [*pl.* **валы́**] *n.* **1,** earthen wall; bank; embankment. **2,** large wave; billow. **3,** shaft: коле́нчатый вал, crankshaft. —**крепостно́й вал,** rampart.

вале́жник *n.* windfallen branches.

валёк [*gen.* **-лька́**] *n.* **1,** roller. **2,** swingletree.

ва́ленок [*gen.* **-нка;** *gen. pl.* **-нок**] *n.* felt boot.

вале́нтность *n.f.* valence.

валерья́на *also,* **валериа́на** *n.* valerian. —**валерья́нка,** *n., colloq.* valerian drops. —**валерья́новый,** *adj.* valerian.

вале́т *n., cards* jack.

ва́лик *n.* **1,** roller. **2,** platen *(on a typewriter).* **3,** bolster *(pillow).*

вали́ть[1] *v. impfv.* [*pfv.* **свали́ть;** *pres.* **валю́, ва́лишь**] **1,** [*pfv. also* **повали́ть**] to knock down; fell; overturn; topple. **2,** *(with* **в** *+ acc.)* to throw (into); toss (into); dump (into): вали́ть в ку́чу, to toss into a pile. **3,** *(with* **на** *+ acc.) colloq.* to blame: вали́ть (вину́) на кого́-нибудь, to put the blame on someone. —**вали́ть с**

больно́й головы́ на здоро́вую, to lay the blame at someone else's doorstep.

вали́ть[2] *v. impfv.* [*pres.* **вали́т**] **1,** *(of people)* to flock; throng. **2,** *(of snow)* to fall heavily; *(of smoke)* to pour out.

вали́ться *v. r. impfv.* [*pfv.* **повали́ться** *or* **свали́ться;** *pres.* **валю́сь, ва́лишься**] to fall. —**вали́ться с ног,** to be exhausted; be falling off one's feet.

ва́лка *n.* chopping down; felling *(of trees)*.

ва́лкий *adj.* [*short form* **ва́лок, валка́, ва́лко**] unsteady; shaky; wobbly. —**ни ша́тко ни ва́лко,** fair to middling; so-so.

валли́ец [*gen.* **-и́йца**] *n.* Welshman. —**валли́йский,** *adj.* Welsh.

валово́й *adj., econ.* gross: валово́й дохо́д, gross income.

вало́м *adv., colloq., in* **вало́м вали́ть,** to flock; throng.

валто́рна *n.* French horn.

валу́н [*gen.* **-луна́**] *n.* boulder.

ва́льдшнеп (нэ) *n.* woodcock.

вальс *n.* waltz.

вальси́ровать *v. impfv.* [*pres.* **-рую, -руешь**] to waltz.

вальцева́ть *v. impfv.* [*pres.* **-цу́ю, -цу́ешь**] to roll; mill (metal).

вальцо́вка *n.* rolling; milling. —**вальцо́вый,** *adj.* rolling: вальцо́вая ме́льница, rolling mill.

валю́та *n.* currency.

валю́тный *adj.* currency *(attrib.)*. —**валю́тный курс,** rate of exchange.

валя́льщик *n.* fuller *(of cloth)*.

ва́ляный *adj. (of boots)* made of felt.

валя́ть *v. impfv.* **1,** [*pfv.* **повваля́ть**] *cooking* to roll (*e.g.* in bread crumbs). **2,** *(with* **по**) to drag (along). **3,** [*pfv.* **сваля́ть**] to full (cloth). **4,** *in* **валя́ть дурака́,** to play the fool. —**валя́ться,** *refl.* [*pfv.* **поваля́ться**] **1,** to roll; wallow. **2,** [*impfv. only*] to lie (scattered) about. **3,** to lie around; lounge; loll.

вам *pron., dat. of* **вы.**

ва́ми *pron., instr. of* **вы.**

вампи́р *n.* **1,** vampire. **2,** vampire bat.

вана́дий *n.* vanadium.

вани́ль *n.f.* vanilla. —**вани́льный,** *adj.* vanilla.

ва́нна *n.* **1,** bath. **2,** bathtub.

ва́нная *n., decl. as an adj.* bathroom.

ва́нночка [*gen. pl.* **-чек**] *n., dim. of* **ва́нна** (bath). —**глазна́я ва́нночка,** eyecup.

ва́нный *adj.* bath *(attrib.)*: ва́нная ко́мната, bathroom.

ва́нька-вста́нька *n.m.* self-righting toy doll.

вар *n.* pitch. —**сапо́жный вар,** cobbler's wax.

вара́н *n.* monitor lizard.

ва́рвар *n.* barbarian. —**варвари́зм,** *n.* (literary) barbarism. —**ва́рварский,** *adj.* barbarian; barbarous; barbaric. —**ва́рварство,** *n.* barbarity.

ва́режка [*gen. pl.* **-жек**] *n.* mitten.

варене́ц [*gen.* **-нца́**] *n.* fermented boiled milk.

варе́ние *n.* boiling.

варе́ник *n.* dumpling filled with cheese or fruit.

варёный *adj.* boiled.

варе́нье *n.* jam.

вариа́нт *n.* **1,** version. **2,** possibility; alternative.

вариа́ция *n.* variation.

варико́зный *adj.* varicose.

вари́ть *v. impfv.* [*pfv.* **свари́ть;** *pres.* **варю́, ва́ришь**] **1,** to boil; cook. **2,** to brew (beer); make (soap); weld (metals). —**вари́ться,** *refl.* to boil; be boiling; cook; be cooking.

ва́рка *n.* boiling.

варьете́ (тэ) *n. neut. indecl.* variety show; floor show.

варьи́ровать *v. impfv.* [*pres.* **-рую, -руешь**] to vary; modify. —**варьи́роваться,** *refl.* to vary.

варя́г *n.* Varangian. —**варя́жский,** *adj.* Varangian.

вас *pron., gen., acc., & prepl. of* **вы.**

василёк [*gen.* **-лька́**] *n.* cornflower.

васса́л *n.* vassal. —**васса́льный,** *adj.* vassal *(attrib.)*.

ва́та *n.* **1,** absorbent cotton. **2,** wadding; padding; stuffing.

вата́га *n., colloq.* crowd; throng; gang.

ватерли́ния (тэ) *n.* waterline.

ватерпа́с (тэ) *n.* spirit level.

ватерпо́ло (тэ) *n. indecl.* water polo.

Ватика́н *n.* Vatican.

вати́н *n.* batting *(sewn into a garment for extra warmth)*.

ва́тник *n., colloq.* quilted jacket.

ва́тный *adj.* wadded; quilted.

ватру́шка [*gen. pl.* **-шек**] *n.* pastry containing cheese or jam.

ватт [*gen. pl.* **ватт**] *n.* watt.

ва́фля [*gen. pl.* **-фель**] *n.* waffle. —**ва́фельница,** *n.* waffle iron.

ва́хта *n., naut.* watch: стоя́ть на ва́хте, to stand watch.

ва́хтенный *adj., naut.* watch *(attrib.)*. —**ва́хтенный журна́л,** (ship's) log.

вахтёр *n.* janitor; porter.

ваш [*fem.* **ва́ша;** *neut.* **ва́ше;** *pl.* **ва́ши**] *poss. adj. & pron.* your; yours.

вая́ние *n., obs.* sculpture. —**вая́тель,** *n.m., obs.* sculptor.

вая́ть *v. impfv.* [*pfv.* **извая́ть**] *obs.* to sculpture; chisel; carve; model.

вбега́ть *v. impfv.* [*pfv.* **вбежа́ть**] **1,** to run in. **2,** *(with* **в** + *acc.)* to run into. **3,** *(with* **на** + *acc.)*. to run up (a hill, stairs, etc.).

вбежа́ть [*infl. like* **бежа́ть**] *v., pfv. of* **вбега́ть.**

вбива́ть *v. impfv.* [*pfv.* **вбить**] to hammer in; drive in. —**вбива́ть в го́лову** (+ *dat.),* to get it through someone's head. —**вбива́ть себе́ в го́лову,** to get it into one's head.

вбира́ть *v. impfv.* [*pfv.* **вобра́ть**] to absorb; take in; draw in.

вбить [*infl.* **вобью́, вобьёшь**] *v., pfv. of* **вбива́ть.**

вблизи́ *adv.* **1,** near; nearby; close by. **2,** up close. —*prep., with gen.* near. —**вблизи́ от,** not far from.

вбо́к *adv.* to the side; to one side.

вброд *adv.* by wading: переходи́ть вброд, to wade across; ford.

вва́ливать *v. impfv.* [*pfv.* **ввали́ть**] *(with* **в** + *acc.) colloq.* to throw (into); toss (into). —**вва́ливаться,** *refl.* **1,** *(of one's cheeks)* to become sunken; become hollow. **2,** *(with* **в** + *acc.) colloq.* to fall into; plunge into. **3,** *(with* **в** + *acc.) colloq.* to burst into.

ввали́ть [*inf.* **ввалю́, вва́лишь**] *v., pfv. of* **вва́ливать.** —**ввали́ться,** *refl., pfv. of* **вва́ливаться.**

введе́ние *n.* introduction.

ввезти́ [*infl. like* **везти́**] *v., pfv. of* **ввози́ть.**

ввек *adv., colloq.* never.

вверга́ть *v. impfv.* [*pfv.* **вве́ргнуть**] **1,** *obs.* to hurl; toss. **2,** *fig.* to plunge; throw (into despair, confusion, etc.).

вве́ргнуть [*past* **вверг, -ла**] *v., pfv. of* **ввергáть.**

ввéрить *v., pfv. of* **вверя́ть.** —**ввéриться,** *refl., pfv. of* **вверя́ться.**

ввёртывать *v. impfv.* [*pfv.* **вверну́ть**] **1,** to screw in. **2,** *colloq.* to interject; interpose; put in (a word, remark, etc.).

вверх *adv., expressing motion or direction* up; upward(s). —**вверх дном; вверх ногáми,** upside down; topsy-turvy. —**вверх по,** up: вверх по течéнию, upstream.

вверху́ *adv., expressing location* **1,** above; overhead. **2,** at the top. —*prep., with gen.* at the top of.

вверя́ть *v. impfv.* [*pfv.* **ввéрить**] to entrust; confide. —**вверя́ться,** *refl. (with dat.)* to entrust oneself to; place oneself in the hands of.

ввести́ [*infl. like* **вести́**] *v., pfv. of* **вводи́ть.**

вви́ду *prep., with gen.* in view of.

вви́нчивать *v. impfv.* [*pfv.* **ввинти́ть**] to screw in. —**вви́нчиваться,** *refl.* to screw in.

ввод *n.* **1,** *mech.* lead-in. **2,** bringing in(to). **3,** putting into: ввод в дéйствие, putting into operation. **4,** input.

вводи́ть *v. impfv.* [*pfv.* **ввести́;** *pres.* **ввожу́, вво́дишь**] **1,** to bring in; bring into. **2,** to lead in; lead into. *Also fig.:* вводи́ть в соблáзн, to lead into temptation. **3,** to introduce; institute; initiate. **4,** to include; incorporate. **5,** *med.* to inject. —**вводи́ть в бой,** to commit to battle. —**вводи́ть в дéйствие, 1,** to put into effect. **2,** to put into operation. —**вводи́ть в курс дéла,** to brief; bring up to date. —**вводи́ть в расхо́д,** to put to expense. —**вводи́ть в строй,** to put into service; put into operation.

вво́дный *adj.* introductory. —**вво́дное сло́во,** *gram.* parenthetic word; introductory particle.

ввоз *n.* **1,** importing; importation. **2,** total imports.

ввози́ть *v. impfv.* [*pfv.* **ввезти́;** *pres.* **ввожу́, вво́зишь**] **1,** to import. **2,** *(with* **в** *+ acc.)* to convey into; transport into. **3,** *(with* **на** *+ acc.)* to convey up; convey to the top of.

ввозно́й *adj.* **1,** import *(attrib.).* **2,** imported.

вво́лю *adv., colloq.* = **вдо́воль.**

ввысь *adv.* upward; high into the air.

ввязáть [*infl.* **ввяжу́, ввя́жешь**] *v., pfv. of* **ввя́зывать.** —**ввязáться,** *refl., pfv. of* **ввя́зываться.**

ввя́зывать *v. impfv.* [*pfv.* **ввязáть**] *(with* **в** *+ acc.)* **1,** to knit in. **2,** *colloq.* to involve in; get (someone) mixed up in. —**ввя́зываться,** *refl. (with* **в** *+ acc.) colloq.* to meddle (in); get mixed up (in); become involved (in).

вгибáть *v. impfv.* [*pfv.* **вогну́ть**] to bend inwards; curve inwards.

вглубь *adv.* deep inside; deep into the interior. —*prep., with gen.* deep into; far into.

вглядéться [*infl.* **-жу́сь, -ди́шься**] *v.r., pfv. of* **вгля́дываться.**

вгля́дываться *v.r. impfv.* [*pfv.* **вглядéться**] **1,** to look closely; take a good look. **2,** *(with* **в** *+ acc.)* to peer into.

вгоня́ть *v. impfv.* [*pfv.* **вогнáть**] *(with* **в** *+ acc.)* **1,** to drive into; herd into. **2,** *colloq.* to hammer in; drive in. —**вгоня́ть в крáску,** to make (someone) blush. —**вгоня́ть в пот,** to make (someone) sweat *(from hard work).*

вдавáться *v.r. impfv.* [*pfv.* **вдáться;** *pres.* **вдаю́сь, вдаёшься**] *(with* **в** *+ acc.)* **1,** to protrude into; jut out into. **2,** *fig.* to sink into; lapse into. **3,** *fig.* to go into; delve into. —**вдавáться в кра́йности,** to go to extremes. —**вдавáться в подро́бности,** to go into detail.

вдави́ть [*infl.* **вдавлю́, вдáвишь**] *v., pfv. of* **вдáвливать.**

вдáвливать *v. impfv.* [*pfv.* **вдави́ть**] **1,** to press in; force in. **2,** to batter in; dent.

вдáлбливать *v. impfv.* [*pfv.* **вдолби́ть**] *colloq.* to drum in; drill in: вдолби́ть что́-нибудь в го́лову (+ *dat.*), to drum/drill something into someone's head.

вдалекé *adv.* in the distance. —**вдалекé от,** far from; a long way from.

вдали́ *adv.* in the distance. —**вдали́ от,** far from; a long way from.

вдаль *adv.* into the distance.

вдáться [*infl. like* **дáться**] *v.r., pfv. of* **вдавáться.**

вдвигáть *v. impfv.* [*pfv.* **вдви́нуть**] *(with* **в** *+ acc.)* to push into; thrust into.

вдво́е *adv.* **1,** twice as; double the: вдво́е бо́льше, twice as much; double the amount. **2,** (in) half: вдво́е мéньше, half as much; вдво́е сократи́ть, to reduce in half; halve. —**сложи́ть вдво́е,** to fold in half *or* in two.

вдвоём *adv.* **1,** two together: они́ вдвоём, the two of them together. **2,** together with one another.

вдвойнé *adv.* **1,** double; twice as much. **2,** *(with adjectives)* doubly.

вдевáть *v. impfv.* [*pfv.* **вдеть**] *(with* **в** *+ acc.)* to put in; put into. —**вдеть ни́тку в иго́лку,** to thread a needle.

вдéлывать *v. impfv.* [*pfv.* **вдéлать**] *(with* **в** *+ acc.)* **1,** to set (a gem, stone, etc.) into. **2,** to embed (in).

вдёргивать *v. impfv.* [*pfv.* **вдёрнуть**] to draw through; thread.

вдéсятеро *adv.* ten times; tenfold.

вдесятеро́м *adv.* ten together: они́ вдесятеро́м, the ten of them.

вдеть [*infl.* **вдéну, вдéнешь**] *v., pfv. of* **вдевáть.**

вдобáвок *adv., colloq.* besides; in addition; to boot.

вдовá [*pl.* **вдо́вы**] *n.* widow.

вдовéть *v. impfv.* to be a widow *or* widower.

вдовéц [*gen.* **-вцá**] *n.* widower.

вдо́воль *adv., colloq.* **1,** in abundance; as much as one could wish for. **2,** to one's heart's content: наéсться вдо́воль, to eat one's fill.

вдовствó *n.* widowhood.

вдо́вый *adj.* widowed.

вдого́нку *adv., colloq.* after; right behind; in pursuit of: бро́ситься вдого́нку за (+ *instr.*), to take off after. Кри́кнуть вдого́нку (+ *dat.*), to call after (someone).

вдолби́ть [*infl.* **-блю́, -би́шь**] *v., pfv. of* **вдáлбливать.**

вдоль *prep., with gen.* along: идти́ вдоль доро́ги, to walk along (the side of) the road. —*adv.* lengthwise. —**вдоль и поперёк, 1,** far and wide. **2,** *colloq.* thoroughly; inside out; backwards and forwards.

вдо́сталь *adv., colloq.* **1,** in abundance; as much as one could wish for. **2,** to one's heart's content.

вдох *n.* (a single) breath.

вдохновéние *n.* inspiration. —**вдохновéнно,** *adv.* with inspiration; in an inspired manner. —**вдохновéнный,** *adj.* inspired.

вдохнови́тель *n.m.* moving spirit; inspiration.

вдохновля́ть *v. impfv.* [*pfv.* **вдохнови́ть**] to inspire.

вдохну́ть *v. pfv.* **1,** *pfv.* of **вдыхáть. 2,** *(with* **в** *+ acc.)* to breathe (into): вдохну́ть жизнь в кого́-нибудь, to breathe new life into someone.

вдрéбезги *adv.* **1,** to pieces; to smithereens. **2,** *colloq.* completely; utterly: вдрéбезги пьян, dead drunk.

вдруг *adv.* **1,** suddenly; all of a sudden. **2,** *colloq.*

together; at once: не говори́те все вдруг, don't talk all at once. **3,** *colloq.* suppose...?; what if...?

вдува́ть *v. impfv.* [*pfv.* **вдуть**] *(with* **в** + *acc.)* to blow (*e.g.* air) into (something).

вду́маться *v.r., pfv. of* **вду́мываться.**

вду́мчивый *adj.* thoughtful; pensive.

вду́мываться *v.r. impfv.* [*pfv.* **вду́маться**] **1,** to reflect; ponder. **2,** *(with* **в** + *acc.)* to consider; go into.

вдуть [*infl.* **вду́ю, вду́ешь**] *v., pfv. of* **вдува́ть.**

вдыха́ние *n.* inhalation.

вдыха́тельный *adj.* **1,** respiratory. **2,** intake *(attrib.)*: вдыха́тельный кла́пан, intake valve.

вдыха́ть *v. impfv.* [*pfv.* **вдохну́ть**] to inhale; breathe in. *See also* **вдохну́ть.**

вегетариа́нец [*gen.* **-нца**] *n.* vegetarian. —**вегетариа́нский,** *adj.* vegetarian.

вегета́ция *n.* (process of) vegetation.

ве́дать *v. impfv.* **1,** *(with instr.)* to manage; be in charge of. **2,** *obs.* to know.

ве́дение *n.* authority; jurisdiction.

веде́ние *n.* *(with gen.)* keeping (of); conduct (of); handling (of); management (of).

ве́домо *n., in* **с/без ве́дома** (+ *gen.*), with/without the knowledge of.

ве́домость [*pl.* **ве́домости, -стей**] *n.f.* **1,** register; roll. **2,** *pl.* official bulletin. —**платёжная ве́домость,** payroll.

ве́домственный *adj.* departmental.

ве́домство *n.* (government) department.

ведо́мый *pres. passive part. of* **вести́.** —**ведо́мый самолёт,** supporting aircraft.

ведро́ [*pl.* **вёдра, вёдер**] *n.* bucket; pail. —**дождь льёт как из ведра́,** it is raining cats and dogs.

веду́щий *adj.* **1,** leading: веду́щий самолёт, lead aircraft. **2,** *fig.* leading; chief. **3,** *mech.* drive *(attrib.)*; transmission *(attrib.)*.

ведь *particle* **1,** why; after all; you know: ведь э́то всем изве́стно, why everyone knows that! Он ведь ребёнок, after all, he is only a child. **2,** isn't that so?: ведь он до́ма?, he is home, isn't he?

ве́дьма *n.* witch; hag.

ве́ер [*pl.* **веера́**] *n.* fan.

веерообра́зный *adj.* fan-shaped.

ве́жливый *adj.* polite; courteous. —**ве́жливо,** *adv.* politely; courteously. —**ве́жливость,** *n.f.* politeness; courtesy.

везде́ *adv.* everywhere. —**ведзе́, где...,** everywhere; wherever. —**везде́ и всю́ду,** absolutely everywhere.

вездесу́щий *adj.* omnipresent; ubiquitous.

вездехо́д *n.* cross-country vehicle; land rover. —**вездехо́дный,** *adj.* cross-country.

везе́ние *n., colloq.* luck.

везти́ *v. impfv.* [*pfv.* **повезти́;** *pres.* **везу́, везёшь;** *past* **вёз, везла́, везло́**] **1,** to carry; convey *(in a vehicle)*. **2,** *(with dat.) impers., colloq.* to be lucky; have luck: ему́ всегда́ везёт, he is always lucky. Вам повезло́, что..., you are lucky that...

век [*pl.* **века́**] *n.* **1,** century. **2,** age: ка́менный век, the Stone Age; сре́дние века́, the Middle Ages. **3,** *colloq.* life; lifetime: я мно́го повида́л на своём веку́, I have seen a lot in my life/lifetime. —**во ве́ки веко́в,** *archaic* for all time; for all eternity. —**в кои ве́ки; в ко́и-то ве́ки,** once in a blue moon. —**на ве́ки ве́чные,** forever. —**от ве́ка (веко́в); испоко́н веко́в,** since time immemorial.

ве́ко [*pl.* **ве́ки, век**] *n.* eyelid.

вeково́й *adj.* age-old.

ве́ксель [*pl.* **векселя́**] *n.m.* promissory note; bill of exchange.

ве́ктор *n.* vector. —**ве́кторный,** *adj.* vector *(attrib.)*.

веле́невый *adj.* *(of paper)* vellum.

веле́ние *n.* command; prescription; dictates.

веле́ть *v. impfv. & pfv.* [*pres.* **велю́, вели́шь**] *(with dat.)* **1,** to order; tell. **2,** *used negatively* not to allow; forbid.

велика́н *n.* giant.

вели́кий *adj.* **1,** great. **2,** [*short form only*] *(of clothes)* too big; too large: боти́нки мне велики́, the shoes are too big for me. —**от ма́ла до вели́ка,** young and old alike.

великоду́шие *n.* magnanimity. —**великоду́шный,** *adj.* magnanimous.

великоле́пие *n.* splendor; magnificence.

великоле́пно *adv.* **1,** magnificently. **2,** marvelously. **3,** *as an interj.* splendid!

великоле́пный *adj.* **1,** magnificent; splendid. **2,** *colloq.* wonderful; marvelous.

великопо́стный *adj.* Lenten.

велича́вый *adj.* stately; majestic.

велича́йший *adj., superl. of* **вели́кий,** greatest; utmost: де́ло велича́йшей ва́жности, a matter of the greatest/utmost importance.

велича́ть *v. impfv., obs.* **1,** to call *(by a certain name)*. **2,** to extol; sing the praises of.

вели́чественный *adj.* majestic; stately.

вели́чество *n.* Majesty: его́ вели́чество, His Majesty.

вели́чие *n.* greatness; grandeur. —**ма́ния вели́чия,** megalomania; delusions of grandeur.

величина́ [*pl.* **-чи́ны**] *n.* **1,** size. **2,** *math.* value; quantity. **3,** magnitude *(of a star)*. **4,** *fig.* eminent figure.

велого́нка [*gen. pl.* **-нок**] *n.* bicycle race. —**велого́нщик,** *n.* bicycle racer.

велодро́м *n.* velodrome.

велосипе́д *n.* bicycle. —**велосипеди́ст,** *n.* cyclist. —**велосипе́дный,** *adj.* bicycle *(attrib.)*.

вельве́т *n.* velveteen. —**вельве́товый,** *adj.* velveteen.

вельмо́жа *n.m.* **1,** *archaic* aristocrat. **2,** *ironic* bigwig.

велю́р *n.* velour. —**велю́ровый,** *adj.* velour.

веля́рный *adj.* velar.

ве́на *n.* vein.

венге́рка [*gen. pl.* **-рок**] *n.* **1,** Hungarian woman. **2,** Hungarian dance. **3,** Hungarian-style jacket.

венге́рский *adj.* Hungarian.

венгр *n.m.* [*fem.* **-ге́рка**] Hungarian.

Вене́ра *n.* Venus.

венери́ческий *adj.* venereal.

венесуэ́льский *adj.* Venezuelan.

вене́ц [*gen.* **-нца́**] *n.* **1,** crown. **2,** *poetic* wreath. **3,** *astron.* corona. **4,** *(with gen.)* crowning achievement (of). **5,** row of crossbeams. —**идти́ под вене́ц,** *obs.* to wed.

венециа́нский *adj.* Venetian.

вене́чный *adj.* coronary.

ве́нзель [*pl.* **вензеля́**] *n.m.* monogram.

ве́ник *n.* broom made of twigs.

вено́зный *adj.* venous.

вено́к [*gen.* **-нка́**] *n.* wreath.

ве́нский *adj.* of Vienna; Viennese.

вентили́ровать *v. impfv.* [*pfv.* **провентили́ровать;** *pres.* **-рую, -руешь**] to ventilate.

ве́нтиль *n.m.* valve.
вентиля́тор *n.* fan; blower.
вентиля́ция *n.* ventilation.
венча́льный *adj.* wedding *(attrib.).*
венча́ние *n.* **1,** (religious) wedding ceremony. **2,** coronation.
венча́ть *v. impfv.* **1,** [*pfv.* **увенча́ть**] to crown. **2,** [*pfv.* **повенча́ть** *or* **обвенча́ть**] to marry. —**венча́ться,** *refl.* **1,** to be crowned. **2,** to be married.
ве́нчик *n.* **1,** *dim. of* **вене́ц. 2,** corolla.
вепрь *n.m.* wild boar.
ве́ра *n.* faith; belief. —**дава́ть ве́ру** (+ *dat.*), to give credence to. —**принима́ть на ве́ру,** to take on faith. —**служи́ть ве́рой и пра́вдой,** to serve faithfully.
вера́нда *n.* veranda.
ве́рба *n.* pussy willow.
вербе́на *n.* verbena.
верблю́д *n.* camel.
верблю́жий [*fem.* **-жья**] *adj.* **1,** camel *(attrib.).* **2,** camel's-hair.
ве́рбный *adj.* pussy-willow *(attrib.).* —**ве́рбное воскресе́нье,** Palm Sunday.
вербова́ть *v. impfv.* [*pfv.* **завербова́ть;** *pres.* **-бу́ю, -бу́ешь**] to recruit.
вербо́вка *n.* recruitment. —**вербо́вщик,** *n.* recruiter.
ве́рбовый *adj.* pussy-willow *(attrib.).*
верди́кт *n.* verdict.
верёвка [*gen. pl.* **-вок**] *n.* rope; cord; string; line: верёвка для белья́, clothesline. —**вить верёвки из,** to twist around one's little finger.
верёвочный *adj.* rope *(attrib.);* string *(attrib.).*
верени́ца *n.* file; row; line.
ве́реск *n.* heather.
веретено́ [*pl.* **-тёна, -тён**] *n.* spindle.
верещáть *v. impfv.* [*pres.* **-щу́, -щи́шь**] to chirp.
верзи́ла *n.m. & f., colloq.* tall, ungainly person.
вери́ги *n.pl.* [*sing.* **вери́га**] chains worn by religious ascetics.
вери́тельный *adj., in* **вери́тельные гра́моты,** credentials *(of a diplomat).*
ве́рить *v. impfv.* [*pfv.* **пове́рить**] **1,** *(with dat.)* to believe. **2,** *(with* **в** + *acc.)* to believe in. **3,** [*impfv. only*] to believe (in God). **4,** *in* **ве́рить** (+ *dat.*) **на́ сло́во,** to take at one's word; take one's word for it. —**ве́риться,** *refl.* [*impfv. only*] *impers. (with dat.)* to believe: мне не ве́рится, I can't believe it.
вермише́ль *n.f.* vermicelli.
ве́рмут *n.* vermouth.
верне́е *adj., comp. of* **ве́рный.** —*particle* or rather; or to be more precise.
вернисáж *n.* **1,** opening day *(of an art exhibit).* **2,** preview; advance showing *(of an art exhibit).*
ве́рно *adv.* **1,** faithfully. **2,** correctly. —*adj., used predicatively* **1,** true: э́то не ве́рно, that is not true. **2,** correct; right: соверше́нно ве́рно, absolutely right. —*particle, colloq.* probably; most likely.
ве́рность *n.f.* **1,** fidelity; faithfulness; loyalty. **2,** correctness; accuracy.
верну́ть *v., pfv. of* **возвраща́ть.** —**верну́ться,** *refl., pfv. of* **возвраща́ться.**
ве́рный *adj.* [*short form* **ве́рен, верна́, ве́рно**] **1,** faithful; loyal; true. **2,** correct; right; true. **3,** reliable; sure; safe. **4,** sure; certain; inevitable.
ве́рование *n.* **1,** belief; conviction. **2,** *pl.* religious beliefs.
ве́ровать *v. impfv.* [*pres.* **-рую, -руешь**] **1,** *(with* **в** + *acc.)* to believe (in). **2,** to believe in God.
вероисповéдание *n.* faith; religion; creed; denomination.
вероло́мный *adj.* perfidious. —**вероло́мство,** *n.* perfidy.
вероуче́ние *n., relig.* teachings; dogma.
вероя́тно *adv.* probably.
вероя́тность *n.f.* probability; likelihood. —**по всей вероя́тности,** in all probability.
вероя́тный *adj.* probable; likely.
ве́рсия *n.* version.
верста́ [*pl.* **вёрсты**] *n.* old Russian unit of length equal to approx. one kilometer; verst. —**за́ версту,** from far off.
верста́к [*gen.* **-стака́**] *n.* carpenter's bench.
верста́ть *v. impfv.* [*pfv.* **сверста́ть**] *printing* to make up; make into pages.
вёрстка *n., printing* **1,** page make-up. **2,** page proofs.
верстово́й *adj., in* **верстово́й столб,** milepost; milestone.
ве́ртел [*pl.* **вертела́**] *n.* spit; skewer.
верте́п *n.* den *(of criminals, vice, etc.).*
верте́ть *v. impfv.* [*pres.* **верчу́, ве́ртишь**] **1,** to turn. **2,** to twirl. **3,** *(with instr.) colloq.* to boss about; twist around one's little finger. —**как ни верти́,** no matter what you do; like it or not.
верте́ться *v.r. impfv.* [*pres.* **верчу́сь, ве́ртишься**] **1,** to turn; spin; revolve; rotate. **2,** to fidget. **3,** *colloq.* to hang around. **4,** *colloq.* to beat around the bush. —**верте́ться на языке́** *or* **на ко́нчике языка́,** to be on the tip of one's tongue. —**верте́ться пе́ред глаза́ми** *(with* **у**), to pester. —**верте́ться под нога́ми** *(with* **у**), to be (*or* keep getting) in someone's way. —**как ни верти́сь = как ни верти́.**
вертика́ль *n.f.* **1,** vertical line. **2,** *chess* file.
вертика́льный *adj.* vertical. —**вертика́льно,** *adv.* vertically.
вёрткий *adj., colloq.* agile; nimble; spry.
вертлю́г [*gen.* **-люга́**] *n.* swivel.
вертля́вый *adj., colloq.* fidgety; frisky.
вертолёт *n.* helicopter.
верту́шка [*gen. pl.* **-шек**] *n., colloq.* **1,** any of a number of revolving devices; revolving door; revolving bookcase. **2,** flighty woman.
ве́рующий *n., decl. as an adj.* believer.
верфь *n.f.* shipyard.
верх [*2nd loc.* **верху́;** *pl.* **верхи́**] *n.* **1,** top. **2,** folding top *(of a carriage, automobile, etc.).* **3,** right side *(of material);* outer side *(of a garment).* **4,** *pl., colloq.* the leadership; the upper strata. **5,** *(with gen.)* the height (of); the acme (of). **6,** *pl., music* upper register; high notes. **7,** *pl.* superficial aspects: скользи́ть по верха́м, to skim the surface. —**брать** *or* **одержа́ть верх, 1,** to prevail; gain the upper hand; come out on top. **2,** *(with* **над***)* to prevail over; get the better (*or* best) of. —**совеща́ние в** *(or* **на***)* **верха́х,** summit conference. *See also* **ве́рхом** *and* **верхо́м.**
ве́рхний *adj.* upper; top. —**ве́рхняя оде́жда; ве́рхнее пла́тье,** outer clothing; outdoor clothes.
верхо́вный *adj.* supreme.
верхово́д *n., colloq.* boss.
верхово́дить *v. impfv.* [*pres.* **-жу, -дишь**] *colloq.* to be the boss; *(with instr.)* boss around.
верхово́й *adj.* **1,** horseback: верхова́я езда́, horse-

back riding. **2,** up-river: верховы́е сёла, towns located up-river. —*n.* horseman; rider.

верхо́вье *n.* upper reaches *(of a river);* headwaters.

верхола́з *n.* steeplejack.

ве́рхом *adv.* **1,** along the top; taking the high ground. **2,** to the brim; to overflowing.

верхо́м *adv.* (on) horseback: е́здить верхо́м, to ride horseback; ride a horse; ката́ться верхо́м, to go (horseback) riding. —**верхо́м на** (+ *prepl.),* astride.

верху́шка [*gen. pl.* **-шек**] *n.* **1,** peak; top. **2,** *colloq.* the leaders; the elite.

ве́рша *n.* creel.

верши́на *n.* **1,** top; peak; summit. **2,** *math.* apex *(of a triangle);* vertex *(of an angle).* **3,** *fig. (with gen.)* the acme (of); the pinnacle (of).

верши́ть *v. impfv.* **1,** to decide. **2,** *(with instr.)* to direct; control.

вершо́к [*gen.* **-шка́**] *n.* old Russian unit of length equal to approx. 1 3/4 inches.

вес *n.* weight. —**держа́ть(ся) на весу́,** to hold/remain suspended in midair. —**на вес зо́лота,** worth its weight in gold. See also **весы́.**

веселе́ть *v. impfv.* [*pfv.* **повеселе́ть**] to cheer up; become cheerful.

весели́ть *v. impfv.* **1,** to gladden; cheer. **2,** to amuse. —**весели́ться,** *refl.* to enjoy oneself; make merry; have fun.

ве́село *adv.* gaily; merrily. —*adj., used predicatively* gay; merry: на вечери́нке бы́ло о́чень ве́село, it was a very gay party.

весёлость *n.f.* gaiety; cheerfulness.

весёлый *adj.* [*short form* **ве́сел, весела́, ве́село**] gay; merry; cheerful.

весе́лье *n.* gaiety; merriment.

весельча́к [*gen.* **-чака́**] *n., colloq.* jolly fellow.

веселя́щий *adj., in* **веселя́щий газ,** laughing gas.

весе́нний *adj.* spring *(attrib.).* —**весе́ннее равноде́нствие,** vernal equinox.

ве́сить *v. impfv.* [*pres.* **ве́шу, ве́сишь**] to weigh (so many pounds).

ве́ский *adj.* weighty.

весло́ [*pl.* **вёсла, вёсел**] *n.* oar; paddle.

весна́ [*pl.* **вёсны, вёсен**] *n.* spring *(season).*

весно́й *also,* **весно́ю** *adv.* in (the) spring.

весну́шка [*gen. pl.* **-шек**] *n.* freckle. —**весну́шчатый,** *adj.* freckled; freckle-faced.

весо́мый *adj.* **1,** having weight; not weightless. **2,** *fig.* weighty.

вест *n., naut.* **1,** west. **2,** west wind.

вести́ *v. impfv.* [*pres.* **веду́, ведёшь;** *past* **вёл, вела́, вело́**] **1,** [*pfv.* **повести́**] to lead. **2,** *(of a road, path, etc.)* to lead (somewhere). **3,** to drive; steer; pilot. **4,** to conduct (a meeting, seminar, etc.). **5,** to carry on (a conversation, correspondence, etc.). **6,** to keep (a diary, the books, etc.). **7,** to wage (war, a struggle, etc.). **8,** to lead (a certain kind of life). **9,** [*pfv.* **повести́**] *(with* **к***)* to lead (to a certain result). **10,** *(with instr. and* **по***)* to pass; run (something over something). —**вести́ себя́,** to behave. *See also* **води́ть.**

вестибю́ль *n.m.* lobby; foyer.

вести́сь *v.r. impfv.* [*pres.* **ведётся**] **1,** to be conducted; be carried out. **2,** *impers., colloq.* to be the custom: так у нас не ведётся, that is not the way we do things.

ве́стник *n.* **1,** messenger; herald. **2,** bulletin *(title of a publication).*

вестово́й *n., decl. as an adj., obs.* orderly.

ве́сточка [*gen. pl.* **-чек**] *n., dim. of* **весть.** —**пришли́те мне ве́сточку,** drop me a line.

весть[1] [*pl.* **ве́сти, -сте́й, -стя́м**] *n.f.* (piece of) news. —**пропа́сть бе́з вести,** to be missing; disappear without a trace.

весть[2] *v., obs. 3rd person sing. of* **ве́дать.** —**бог весть,** God knows! —**не бог весть,** not particularly: не бог весть как далеко́, not particularly far; не бог весть кака́я кру́пная фигу́ра, not a particularly prominent figure.

весы́ [*gen.* **весо́в**] *n. pl.* **1,** scale(s). **2,** *cap.* Libra.

весь [*fem.* **вся;** *neut.* **всё;** *pl.* **все;** *gen.* **всего́, всей, всех;** *acc. fem.* **всю;** *dat.* **всему́, всей, всем;** *instr.* **всем, всей, все́ми;** *prepl.* **всём, всей, всех**] *adj.* all; the whole: весь день, all day; весь мир, the whole world; всё вре́мя, all the time; все стра́ны, all nations. —**весь в** (+ *acc.*), the image of: он весь в отца́, he is the image of his father. *See also* **всё, все, всего́.**

весьма́ *adv.* highly; extremely.

ветви́стый *adj.* having many branches.

ветвь [*pl.* **ве́тви, -ве́й, -вя́м**] *n.f.* branch; limb.

ве́тер [*gen.* **-тра**] *n.* wind. —**броса́ть де́ньги на ве́тер,** to toss money to the winds. —**броса́ть слова́ на ве́тер,** to waste words. —**держа́ть нос по ве́тру,** to follow the prevailing winds. —**ищи́ ве́тра в по́ле,** you'll never find it (him, her, *etc.*). —**куда́** *or* **отку́да ве́тер ду́ет,** which way the wind blows. —**у него́ ве́тер в голове́,** he hasn't got a brain in his head.

ветера́н *n.* veteran.

ветерина́р *n.* veterinarian. —**ветерина́рия,** *n.* veterinary medicine. —**ветерина́рный,** *adj.* veterinary.

ветеро́к [*gen.* **-рка́**] *n.* breeze.

ве́тка [*gen. pl.* **-ток**] *n.* branch; twig.

ветла́ [*pl.* **вётлы, вётел**] *n.* white willow.

ве́то *n. indecl.* veto.

ве́точка [*gen. pl.* **-чек**] *n.* twig; sprig.

ве́тошь *n.f.* tattered clothes; rags.

ве́треник *n., colloq.* frivolous person; flighty person; scatterbrain.

ве́треница *n.* **1,** *fem. of* **ве́треник. 2,** anemone.

ве́трено *adv.* frivolously. —*adj., used predicatively* windy: сего́дня ве́трено, it is windy today.

ве́треный *adj.* **1,** windy. **2,** *colloq.* frivolous.

ветрово́й *adj.* wind *(attrib.).* —**ветрово́е стекло́,** windshield.

ветроме́р *n.* anemometer.

ветря́нка *n., colloq.* chicken pox.

ветряно́й *adj.* wind *(attrib.).* —**ветряна́я ме́льница,** windmill.

ве́тряный *adj., in* **ве́тряная о́спа,** chicken pox.

ве́тхий *adj.* ramshackle; dilapidated. —**Ве́тхий заве́т,** the Old Testament.

ветхозаве́тный *adj.* Old Testament *(attrib.).*

ве́тхость *n.f.* disrepair; decay: приходи́ть в ве́тхость, to fall into disrepair.

ветчина́ *n.* ham.

ветша́ть *v. impfv.* [*pfv.* **обветша́ть**] to deteriorate; become dilapidated; fall into decay.

ве́ха *n.* **1,** signpost. **2,** *usu. pl., fig.* landmark; milestone.

ве́че *n., hist.* popular assembly in old Russia; veche.

ве́чер [*pl.* **вечера́**] *n.* **1,** evening. **2,** (evening) party; soirée. *See also* **ве́чером.**

вечере́ть *v. impfv., impers.* to grow dark: вечере́ет, dusk is falling; evening is coming on.

вечери́нка [*gen. pl.* **-нок**] *n.* (evening) party.
вече́рний *adj.* evening *(attrib.).* —**вече́рняя шко́ла,** night school.
вече́рня *n.* vespers.
ве́чером *adv.* in the evening. —**вчера́ ве́чером,** last evening; last night. —**за́втра ве́чером,** tomorrow evening; tomorrow night. —**сего́дня ве́чером,** this evening; tonight.
ве́черя *n., in* **та́йная ве́черя,** the Last Supper.
ве́чно *adv.* **1,** eternally; forever. **2,** *colloq.* constantly; always; forever.
вечнозелёный *adj.* evergreen.
ве́чность *n.f.* **1,** eternity. **2,** *in* це́лая ве́чность, ages: не ви́дел(а) вас це́лую ве́чность, I haven't seen you for ages. —**ка́нуть в ве́чность,** to sink into oblivion. —**отойти́ в ве́чность,** to pass into eternity.
ве́чный *adj.* **1,** eternal; everlasting; perpetual. **2,** *colloq.* endless; constant; continual. —**ве́чная па́мять** (+ *dat.*), may (someone's) memory live forever. —**ве́чное перо́,** *obs.* fountain pen. —**на ве́ки ве́чные,** forever. —**на ве́чные времена́,** for all time. —**засну́ть ве́чным сном,** to go to one's eternal rest.
ве́шалка [*gen. pl.* **-лок**] *n.* **1,** rack. **2,** hanger. **3,** *colloq.* cloakroom.
ве́шать *v. impfv.* **1,** [*pfv.* **пове́сить**] to hang; hang up. **2,** *in* **ве́шать нос** *or* **го́лову,** to be/become discouraged; lose heart. **3,** [*pfv.* **све́шать**] to weigh. —**ве́шаться,** *refl.* [*pfv.* **пове́ситься**] to hang oneself.
веща́ние *n.* **1,** broadcasting. **2,** prophesying. **3,** prophecy.
веща́ть *v. impfv.* **1,** *obs.* to prophesy. **2,** *colloq.* to preach; expound. **3,** to broadcast.
вещево́й *adj.* clothing *(attrib.).* —**вещево́й мешо́к,** knapsack. —**вещево́й склад,** warehouse.
веще́ственный *adj.* material. —**веще́ственные доказа́тельства,** material evidence.
вещество́ *n.* matter; substance. —**обме́н веще́ств,** metabolism.
ве́щий *adj., obs.* **1,** wise. **2,** prophetic.
вещи́ца *n.* **1,** *dim. of* **вещь. 2,** knickknack.
вещь [*pl.* **ве́щи, веще́й, веща́м**] *n.f.* **1,** thing. **2,** *pl.* things; belongings; clothes. **3,** work; piece *(of art, literature, music, etc.):* три ве́щи Проко́фьева, three works by Prokofiev.
ве́ялка [*gen. pl.* **-лок**] *n.* winnowing machine.
ве́яние *n.* **1,** winnowing. **2,** blowing *(of the wind).* **3,** sign; portent. **4,** trend; tendency.
ве́ять *v. impfv.* [*pres.* **ве́ю, ве́ешь**] **1,** to blow gently. **2,** *(with instr.) fig.* to be in the air: ве́ет весно́й, spring is in the air. **3,** to wave; flutter. **4,** *v.t.* [*pfv.* **прове́ять**] to winnow.
вжива́ться *v.r. impfv.* [*pfv.* **вжи́ться**] (with **в** + *acc.)* to get used to. —**вжива́ться в свою́ роль,** to get the feel of one's part.
вживля́ть *v. impfv.* [*pfv.* **вживи́ть**] *med.* to implant.
вжи́ться [*infl. like* **жить**] *v.r., pfv. of* **вжива́ться.**
взад *adv., colloq.* back. —**взад и вперёд,** back and forth; to and fro; up and down.
взаи́мный *adj.* mutual; reciprocal. —**взаи́мно,** *adv.* mutually. —**взаи́мность,** *n.f.* mutuality; reciprocity.
взаимовы́годный *adj.* mutually beneficial/advantageous.
взаимоде́йствие *n.* **1,** interaction; interplay. **2,** *mil.* cooperation; coordination.
взаимоде́йствовать *v. impfv.* [*pres.* **-ствую, -ствуешь**] **1,** to interact. **2,** *mil.* to cooperate.
взаимозави́симый *adj.* interdependent. —**взаимозави́симость,** *n.f.* interdependence.
взаимозаменя́емый *adj.* interchangeable.
взаимоотноше́ние *n.* relation; interrelation.
взаимопо́мощь *n.f.* mutual aid/assistance.
взаимопонима́ние *n.* mutual understanding.
взаимосвя́занный *adj.* interconnected; interrelated.
взаймы́ *adv.* on loan. —**дава́ть взаймы́,** to lend; loan. —**брать** *or* **получа́ть взаймы́,** to borrow.
взаме́н *adv.* **1,** instead. **2,** in return; in exchange. —*prep., with gen.* **1,** in return for; in exchange for. **2,** in place of.
взаперти́ *adv.* **1,** locked up; under lock and key. **2,** *fig.* in seclusion.
вза́пуски *adv., colloq.* racing (with) one another: бе́гать вза́пуски, to race each other.
взахлёб *adv., colloq.* avidly; with gusto.
взба́лмошный *adj., colloq.* eccentric; erratic; unbalanced.
взба́лтывать *v. impfv.* [*pfv.* **взболта́ть**] to shake (up).
взбега́ть *v. impfv.* [*pfv.* **взбежа́ть**] *(with* **на** + *acc. or* **по***)* to run up.
взбежа́ть [*infl. like* **бежа́ть**] *v., pfv. of* **взбега́ть.**
взбелени́ться *v.r. pfv., colloq.* to fly into a rage.
взбеси́ть *v., pfv. of* **беси́ть.** —**взбеси́ться,** *refl., pfv. of* **беси́ться.**
взбива́ть *v. impfv.* [*pfv.* **взбить**] **1,** to fluff (up). **2,** to whip (cream); beat (egg whites); churn up (water).
взбира́ться *v.r. impfv.* [*pfv.* **взобра́ться**] *(with* **на** + *acc. or* **по***)* to climb, climb up.
взби́тый *adj.* beaten; whipped: взби́тые сли́вки, whipped cream.
взбить [*infl.* **взобью́, взобьёшь**] *v., pfv. of* **взбива́ть.**
взбодри́ть *v. pfv., colloq.* to cheer up; hearten.
взболта́ть *v., pfv. of* **болта́ть** *(in sense #2) and* **взба́лтывать.**
взборони́ть *v., pfv. of* **борони́ть.**
взбреда́ть *v. impfv.* [*pfv.* **взбрести́**] *(with* **на** + *acc.) colloq.* to mount with difficulty. —**взбрести́ в го́лову** *or* **на ум** (+ *dat.*), to come into one's head.
взбрести́ [*infl. like* **брести́**] *v., pfv. of* **взбреда́ть.**
взбудора́жить *v., pfv. of* **будора́жить.**
взбунтова́ть *v., pfv. of* **бунтова́ть** *(in sense #2).* —**взбунтова́ться,** *refl., pfv. of* **бунтова́ть** *(in sense #1).*
взбуха́ть *v. impfv.* [*pfv.* **взбу́хнуть**] to swell out; bulge.
взбу́хнуть [*past* **взбух, -ла**] *v., pfv. of* **взбуха́ть.**
взбу́чка *n., colloq.* **1,** beating; thrashing. **2,** scolding; dressing-down.
вва́ливать *v. impfv.* [*pfv.* **взвали́ть**] *(with* **на** + *acc.)* **1,** to load (onto). **2,** *fig.* to load (work on someone). **3,** *fig.* to lay; place (blame).
взвали́ть [*infl.* **взвалю́, взва́лишь**] *v., pfv. of* **взва́ливать.**
взве́сить [*infl.* **-шу, -сишь**] *v., pfv. of* **взве́шивать.** —**взве́ситься,** *refl., pfv. of* **взве́шиваться.**
взвести́ [*infl. like* **вести́**] *v., pfv. of* **взводи́ть.**
взве́шивать *v. impfv.* [*pfv.* **взве́сить**] **1,** to weigh. **2,** *fig.* to weigh; ponder. —**взве́шиваться,** *refl.* to weigh oneself.
взвива́ть *v. impfv.* [*pfv.* **взвить**] to blow up; swirl.

—взвива́ться, *refl.* **1,** to fly up; soar. **2,** *(of a flag, curtain, etc.)* to go up.

взвизг *n., colloq.* screech; yelp.

взви́згивать *v. impfv.* [*pfv.* **взви́згнуть**] to screech; yelp.

взви́нчивать *v. impfv.* [*pfv.* **взвинти́ть**] *colloq.* **1,** to excite; arouse. **2,** to jack up (prices).

взви́ть [*infl.* **взовью́, взовьёшь**] *v., pfv. of* **взвива́ть.** —**взви́ться,** *refl., pfv. of* **взвива́ться.**

взвод *n.* **1,** platoon. **2,** cocking recess *(of a firearm):* на боево́м взво́де, cocked; ready to fire; на предохрани́тельном взво́де, at half cock. —**на взво́де,** *colloq.* tipsy.

взводи́ть *v. impfv.* [*pfv.* **взвести́;** *pres.* **-вожу́, -во́дишь**] **1,** to lead up. **2,** to level (an accusation). **3,** *in* взводи́ть куро́к, to cock a gun.

взво́дный *adj.* platoon *(attrib.).* —*n.* platoon leader.

взволно́ванный *adj.* agitated; anxious; uneasy.

взволнова́ть *v., pfv. of* **волнова́ть.** —**взволнова́ться,** *refl., pfv. of* **волнова́ться.**

взвыть *v. pfv.* [*infl.* **взво́ю, взво́ешь**] to howl.

взгляд *n.* **1,** look; glance. **2,** opinion; view: на мой взгляд, in my opinion. —**на пе́рвый взгляд,** at first glance; on the face of it. —**с пе́рвого взгля́да,** **1,** at first glance. **2,** at a glance; from the first.

взгля́дывать *v. impfv.* [*pfv.* **взгляну́ть**] *(with* **на** + *acc.)* to glance (at); take a look (at).

взго́рье *n., colloq.* hill.

взгроможда́ть *v. impfv.* [*pfv.* **взгромозди́ть**] *(with* **на** + *acc.) colloq.* to pile (onto); load (onto); hoist (onto). —**взгроможда́ться,** *refl. (with* **на** + *acc.) colloq.* to clamber up (on).

вздёргивать *v. impfv.* [*pfv.* **вздёрнуть**] *colloq.* **1,** to raise; hoist up; jerk up. **2,** to execute by hanging; string up.

вздёрнутый *adj., in* **вздёрнутый нос,** snub nose.

вздёрнуть *v., pfv. of* **вздёргивать.**

вздор *n.* nonsense.

вздо́рить *v. impfv.* [*pfv.* **повздо́рить**] *colloq.* to argue; squabble; bicker.

вздо́рный *adj., colloq.* **1,** absurd; preposterous. **2,** quarrelsome; cantankerous.

вздорожа́ть *v., pfv. of* **дорожа́ть.**

вздох *n.* deep breath; sigh.

вздохну́ть *v. pfv.* **1,** *pfv. of* **вздыха́ть. 2,** *colloq.* to take a short rest; take a breath.

вздра́гивать *v. impfv.* [*pfv.* **вздро́гнуть**] to give a start; jump; wince.

вздремну́ть *v. pfv., colloq.* to take a nap.

вздро́гнуть *v., pfv. of* **вздра́гивать.**

вздува́ть *v. impfv.* [*pfv.* **вздуть**] **1,** to blow up *(into the air).* **2,** to bloat. **3,** *fig., colloq.* to inflate (prices). —**вздува́ться,** *refl.* to swell up; puff up.

взду́мать *v. pfv., colloq.* to take a notion (to); take it into one's head (to). —**взду́маться,** *refl., impers., colloq.* = **взду́мать:** мне взду́малось, I took it into my head (to).

взду́тие *n.* swelling.

взду́тый *adj.* **1,** swollen. **2,** *fig.* inflated.

взду́ть [*infl.* **вздую́, вздуе́шь**] *v., pfv. of* **вздува́ть.** —**взду́ться,** *refl., pfv. of* **вздува́ться.**

взды́бливаться *v.r. impfv.* [*pfv.* **взды́биться**] *(of a horse)* to rear.

вздыма́ть *v. impfv.* to raise. —**вздыма́ться,** *refl.* **1,** to rise. **2,** *(of the chest)* to heave.

вздыха́ть *v. impfv.* [*pfv.* **вздохну́ть**] **1,** to sigh. **2,** [*impfv. only*] *(with* **по** + *prepl.)* to yearn (for); pine (for).

взима́ть *v. impfv.* to levy; collect. Взима́ть пла́ту, to charge a fee.

взира́ть *v. impfv., obs.* to look; gaze.

взла́мывать *v. impfv.* [*pfv.* **взлома́ть**] to break open; force open.

взлеза́ть *v. impfv.* [*pfv.* **взлезть**] *colloq.* to climb up.

взлезть [*infl. like* **лезть**] *v., pfv. of* **взлеза́ть.**

взлёт *n.* **1,** upward flight. **2,** *aero.* takeoff. **3,** *fig. (with gen.)* upsurge (of).

взлета́ть *v. impfv.* [*pfv.* **взлете́ть**] to fly up; soar; *(of an airplane)* take off. —**взлете́ть на во́здух,** to go up in smoke.

взлете́ть [*infl.* **-чу́, -ти́шь**] *v., pfv. of* **взлета́ть.**

взлётный *adj.* take-off *(attrib.).* —**взлётно-поса́дочная полоса́,** runway.

взло́м *n.* breaking in. —**кра́жа со взло́мом,** burglary.

взлома́ть *v., pfv. of* **взла́мывать.**

взло́мщик *n.* burglar.

взлохма́тить [*infl.* **-чу, -тишь**] *v., pfv. of* **взлохма́чивать.**

взлохма́ченный *adj.* disheveled.

взлохма́чивать *v. impfv.* [*pfv.* **взлохма́тить**] to muss; tousle.

взмах *n.* wave; sweep *(of the hand);* stroke *(of an oar);* flap *(of wings).*

взма́хивать *v. impfv.* [*pfv.* **взмахну́ть**] *(with instr.)* to flap; wave.

взметну́ть *v. pfv.* **1,** to throw up into the air; send flying. **2,** *(with instr.)* to flap (one's wings); throw up (one's hands). —**взметну́ться,** *refl.* to shoot up; fly up into the air.

взмоли́ться *v.r. pfv.* [*infl.* **-молю́сь, -мо́лишься**] to implore; *(with* **о***)* beg (for).

взмо́рье *n.* seashore.

взмыва́ть *v. impfv.* [*pfv.* **взмыть**] to soar.

взмы́ленный *adj. (of a horse)* foaming.

взмыть [*infl.* **взмо́ю, взмо́ешь**] *v., pfv. of* **взмыва́ть.**

взнос *n.* **1,** deposit; payment. **2,** fee; dues.

взну́здывать *v. impfv.* [*pfv.* **взнузда́ть**] to bridle (a horse).

взобра́ться [*infl. like* **брать**] *v.r., pfv. of* **взбира́ться.**

взойти́ [*infl.* **взойду́, взойдёшь;** *past* **взошёл, взошла́**] *v., pfv. of* **всходи́ть** *and* **восходи́ть.**

взор *n.* look; glance; gaze.

взорва́ть [*infl. like* **рвать**] *v., pfv. of* **взрыва́ть**[1]. —**взорва́ться,** *refl., pfv. of* **взрыва́ться.**

взрасти́ть [*infl.* **-щу́, -сти́шь**] *v., pfv. of* **взра́щивать.**

взра́щивать *v. impfv.* [*pfv.* **взрасти́ть**] **1,** to grow; cultivate. **2,** to raise; rear; bring up.

взреве́ть *v. pfv.* [*infl.* **-ву́, -вёшь**] to roar; let out a roar.

взро́слый *adj.* adult; grown. —*n.* adult; grownup.

взрыв *n.* **1,** explosion; blast. **2,** *fig. (with gen.)* burst: взрыв аплодисме́нтов, burst of applause.

взрыва́тель *n.m.* fuse.

взрыва́ть[1] *v. impfv.* [*pfv.* **взорва́ть**] **1,** to blow up (a bridge, building, etc.); set off (a charge). **2,** *fig., colloq.* to infuriate; send into a rage. —**взрыва́ться,** *refl.* **1,** to explode; burst; blow up; *(of a charge, grenade, etc.)* go off. **2,** *fig., colloq.* to blow up; become infuriated.

взрыва́ть[2] *v. impfv.* [*pfv.* **взрыть**] to dig up.

взрывно́й *adj.* blasting *(attrib.):* взрывны́е рабо́ты, blasting operations.

взрывча́тка *n., colloq.* explosives.
взры́вчатый *adj.* explosive.
взрыть [*infl.* **взро́ю, взро́ешь**] *v., pfv. of* **взрыва́ть**[2].
взрыхли́ть *v., pfv. of* **рыхли́ть** *and* **взрыхля́ть.**
взрыхля́ть *v. impfv.* [*pfv.* **взрыхли́ть**] to loosen; turn up (soil, dirt, etc.).
взъеда́ться *v.r. impfv.* [*pfv.* **взъе́сться**] *colloq.* **1,** to rant and rave. **2,** *(with* **на** + *acc.)* to lace into.
взъезжа́ть *v. impfv.* [*pfv.* **взъе́хать**] *(with* **на** + *acc.)* to drive up; ascend.
взъеро́шенный *adj.* disheveled.
взъеро́шить *v., pfv. of* **еро́шить.**
взъе́сться [*infl. like* **есть**] *v.r., pfv. of* **взъеда́ться.**
взъе́хать [*infl. like* **е́хать**] *v., pfv. of* **взъезжа́ть.**
взыва́ть *v. impfv.* [*pfv.* **воззва́ть**] to appeal.
взыгра́ть *v. pfv.* **1,** to become playful; act up. **2,** *(of the sea)* to become choppy. —**се́рдце во мне взыгра́ло,** my heart leaped for joy.
взыска́ние *n.* penalty.
взыска́тельный *adj.* exacting; demanding.
взыска́ть [*infl.* **взыщу́, взы́щешь**] *v., pfv. of* **взы́скивать.**
взы́скивать *v. impfv.* [*pfv.* **взыска́ть**] **1,** to exact; force payment of. **2,** *(with* **с** + *gen.)* to call to account; make answer.
взя́тие *n.* taking; capture; seizure.
взя́тка [*gen. pl.* **-ток**] *n.* **1,** bribe. **2,** *cards* trick.
взя́точник *n.* bribe taker. —**взя́точничество,** *n.* bribery.
взять *v. pfv.* [*infl.* **возьму́, возьмёшь;** *past fem.* **взяла́**] **1,** *pfv. of* **брать. 2,** to seize; arrest. **3,** *(with* **и, да** *or* **да и)** *denoting an unexpected action:* он взял и ушёл, he up and left. —**с чего́ вы взя́ли, что...?,** what made you think that...?; where did you get the idea that...?
взя́ться [*infl.* **возьму́сь, возьмёшься;** *past* **взя́лся, -ла́сь, -ло́сь, -ли́сь**] *v.r., pfv. of* **бра́ться.** —**отку́да ни возьми́сь,** from out of nowhere; from out of the blue.
виаду́к *n.* viaduct.
вибра́тор *n.* vibrator.
вибра́ция *n.* **1,** vibration. **2,** *music* tremolo.
вибри́ровать *v. impfv.* [*pres.* **-рует**] to vibrate.
виве́рра *n.* civet.
вивисе́кция *n.* vivisection.
вигва́м *n.* wigwam.
виго́нь *n.f.* vicuna. —**виго́невый,** *adj.* vicuna.
вид *n.* **1,** look; appearance. **2,** [*with* **в** + *an adj.)* state; condition: в пья́ном ви́де, drunk; in a drunken state. **3,** view: вид на мо́ре, view of the sea. **4,** sight: при ви́де (+ *gen.)*, at the sight of. **5,** *pl.* prospects. **6,** kind; sort. **7,** species. **8,** *gram.* aspect. **9,** *mil.* branch (of the armed forces). —**в ви́де** (+ *gen.*), in the form of. —**для ви́да,** for the sake of appearance. —**из ви́да; и́з виду,** from view. —**на вид; по ви́ду; с ви́ду,** in appearance. —**на виду́,** in the public eye. —**ни под каки́м ви́дом,** under no circumstances. —**под ви́дом** (+ *gen.)*, under the guise of. —**у всех на виду́,** on view; in full view of everyone. —**де́лать вид,** to pretend. —**име́ть в виду́, 1,** to have in mind. **2,** to bear in mind; keep in mind. —**име́ть ви́ды на** (+ *acc.*), **1,** to have an eye on; have designs on. **2,** to count on. —**поста́вить на вид** (+ *dat.*), to reprimand (someone).
ви́данный *adj., in* ви́данное ли э́то де́ло?, *colloq.* did you ever see such a thing?
вида́ть[1] *v. impfv.* [*pfv.* **повида́ть**] *colloq.* **1,** to see. **2,** *in* вида́ть ви́ды, to have seen a lot; have been through a lot. —**вида́ться,** *refl. (with* **с** + *instr.)* to see; visit.
вида́ть[2] *particle, colloq.* apparently; it seems.
ви́дение *n.* sight; vision.
виде́ние *n.* apparition; vision.
видеоза́пись *n.f.* video tape.
ви́деть *v. impfv.* [*pfv.* **уви́деть;** *pres.* **ви́жу, ви́дишь**] to see. —**ви́деться,** *refl.* **1,** [*impfv. only*] to be visible. **2,** *(with* **с** + *instr.)* to see; meet with. **3,** to see each other.
ви́димо *adv.* apparently; evidently.
ви́димость *n.f.* **1,** visibility. **2,** semblance; appearance. —**по всей ви́димости,** from all appearances.
ви́димый *adj.* **1,** visible. **2,** apparent; evident. **3,** *colloq.* seeming; apparent.
видне́ться *v.r. impfv.* to be seen; be visible.
ви́дно *adj., used predicatively* **1,** visible: моста́ ещё не ви́дно, the bridge cannot be seen as yet. **2,** clear; obvious: ви́дно, что он не придёт, it is clear/obvious that he is not coming. —*adv., colloq.* apparently; evidently.
ви́дный *adj.* [*short form* **ви́ден, видна́, ви́дно, ви́дны** *or* **видны́**] **1,** visible; in sight. **2,** noticeable; conspicuous. **3,** *(of a person)* prominent.
видово́й *adj.* **1,** *biol.* pert. to a species. **2,** *gram.* aspectual. —**видово́й фильм,** travel film.
видоизмене́ние *n.* **1,** modification; alteration. **2,** type; variety.
видоизменя́ть *v. impfv.* [*pfv.* **видоизмени́ть**] to modify; alter.
видоиска́тель *n.m., photog.* view finder.
ви́за *n.* visa.
визави́ *adv.* face to face. —*n.m. & f.indecl.* person opposite; person facing.
византи́йский *adj.* Byzantine.
визг *n.* squeal; screech; yelp.
визгли́вый *adj.* **1,** shrill. **2,** squealing; screeching.
визжа́ть *v. impfv.* [*pfv.* **ви́згнуть;** *pres.* **визжу́, визжи́шь**] to squeal; screech; yelp.
визи́р *n.* **1,** sight *(sighting device)*. **2,** *photog.* view finder.
визи́ровать *v. impfv. & pfv.* [*pres.* **-рую, -руешь**] **1,** to enter a visa in (a passport). **2,** to sight; aim.
визи́рь *n.m.* vizier.
визи́т *n.* visit; call. —**визитёр,** *n., obs.* visitor; caller.
визи́тка [*gen. pl.* **-ток**] *n.* morning coat.
визи́тный *adj.* of or for visiting. —**визи́тная ка́рточка,** business card; calling card.
ви́ка *n.* vetch.
вика́рий *n.* vicar.
ви́кинг *n.* Viking.
вико́нт *n.* viscount.
виктори́на *n.* quiz.
ви́лка [*gen. pl.* **-лок**] *n.* **1,** fork. **2,** plug *(for a socket)*.
ви́лла *n.* villa.
ви́ллис *n.* jeep.
вило́к [*gen.* **-лка́**] *n., colloq.* head of cabbage.
ви́лы [*gen.* **вил**] *n. pl.* pitchfork.
виля́ть *v. impfv.* [*pfv.* **вильну́ть**] **1,** *(with instr.)* to wag (one's tail). **2,** *(of one's tail)* to wag. **3,** to weave; zigzag. **4,** *colloq.* to equivocate; hedge.
вина́ *n.* **1,** fault; blame. **2,** guilt. **3,** misdeed; transgression: загла́живать вину́, to redress a wrong. —**всему́ вино́й** (+ *nom.)*, it's all because of; it's all due to.

—**не по мое́й вине́,** through no fault of mine. —**по вине́** (+ *gen.),* because of; on account of.
винегре́т *n.* **1,** Russian salad. **2,** *fig., colloq.* hodgepodge; potpourri.
вини́л *n.* vinyl.
вини́тельный *adj., in* **вини́тельный паде́ж,** accusative case.
вини́ть *v. impfv.* to blame.
виннока́менный *adj.* tartaric.
ви́нный *adj.* wine *(attrib.).* —**ви́нный ка́мень,** tartar; cream of tartar. —**ви́нный спирт,** ethyl alcohol. —**ви́нная я́года,** fig.
вино́ [*pl.* **ви́на**] *n.* wine.
винова́тый *adj.* **1,** guilty; at fault; to blame: я винова́т, it's my fault. **2,** *(of a look or expression)* guilty; apologetic. —**винова́т**!, I'm sorry!; I beg your pardon!
вино́вник *n.* **1,** culprit; guilty party. **2,** *(with gen.)* perpetrator (of); cause (of). —**вино́вник торжества́,** guest of honor; hero of the occasion.
вино́вность *n.f.* guilt; culpability.
вино́вный *adj.* guilty. —*n.* guilty person; guilty party.
виногра́д *n.* grapes. —**виногра́дарство,** *n.* viniculture; viticulture. —**виногра́дина,** *n.* a (single) grape. —**виногра́дник,** *n.* vineyard.
виногра́дный *adj.* grape *(attrib.).* —**виногра́дный са́хар,** grape sugar.
виноде́л *n.* winegrower. —**виноде́лие,** *n.* winegrowing. —**виноде́льческий,** *adj.* wine-growing *(attrib.).*
виноку́р *n.* distiller. —**винокуре́ние,** *n.* distilling. —**виноку́ренный,** *adj.* distilling *(attrib.).*
винт [*gen.* **винта́**] *n.* **1,** screw. **2,** propeller.
ви́нтик *n., dim. of* **винт.** —**у него́ ви́нтика не хвата́ет,** *colloq.* he has a screw loose.
винто́вка [*gen. pl.* **-вок**] *n.* rifle.
винтово́й *adj.* **1,** spiral: винтова́я ле́стница, spiral staircase. **2,** propeller-driven.
винто́вочный *adj.* rifle *(attrib.).*
винтообра́зный *adj.* spiral.
виньéтка [*gen. pl.* **-ток**] *n.* vignette.
вио́ла *n.* **1,** viol. **2,** viola.
виолончели́ст *n.* cellist.
виолонче́ль *n.f.* cello.
вира́ж *n.* **1,** [*gen.* **-ража́**] turn. **2,** [*gen.* **-ра́жа**] *photog.* toning agent.
виртуо́з *n.* virtuoso.
виртуо́зный *adj.* masterful; masterly. —**виртуо́зно,** *adv.* masterfully. —**виртуо́зность,** *n.f.* virtuosity.
вируле́нтный *adj.* virulent; deadly. —**вируле́нтность,** *n.f.* virulence.
ви́рус *n.* virus. —**ви́русный,** *adj.* viral.
ви́рши [*gen.* **-шей**] *n.pl.* poetry; doggerel.
ви́селица *n.* gallows.
висе́ть *v. impfv.* [*pres.* **виси́т, вися́т**] to hang. —**висе́ть в во́здухе,** to be up in the air; be undecided.
ви́ски *n. neut. indecl.* whiskey.
виско́за *n.* **1,** viscose. **2,** rayon. —**виско́зный,** *adj.* viscose.
вислоу́хий *adj.* lop-eared.
ви́смут *n.* bismuth.
ви́снуть *v. impfv.* [*past* **вис** *or* **ви́снул**] *colloq.* **1,** to hang. **2,** to droop.
висо́к [*gen.* **-ска́**] *n., anat.* temple.
високо́сный *adj., in* **високо́сный год,** leap year.
вист *n.* whist.
висю́лька [*gen. pl.* **-лек**] *n., colloq.* pendant.
вися́чий *adj.* hanging; suspended. —**вися́чий замо́к,** padlock. —**вися́чий мост,** suspension bridge.
витами́н *n.* vitamin. —**витами́нный,** *adj.* vitamin *(attrib.).* —**витамино́зный,** *adj.* rich in vitamins.
вита́ть *v. impfv.* **1,** *obs.* to be; live. **2,** *(with* **над***)* to hang (over); hover (over). —**вита́ть в облака́х,** to be up in the clouds.
витиева́тый *adj.* flowery; ornate.
вито́й *adj.* **1,** twisted: витая бу́лка, twist *(of bread).* **2,** winding; spiral.
вито́к [*gen.* **-тка́**] *n.* **1,** turn; loop; coil. **2,** strand. **3,** circuit *(of a planet by a space vehicle).*
витра́ж [*gen.* **-ража́**] *n.* stained-glass window.
витри́на *n.* **1,** store window. **2,** showcase.
вить *v. impfv.* [*pfv.* **свить;** *pres.* **вью, вьёшь;** *past fem.* **вила́**] **1,** to make *(by twisting).* **2,** *in* **вить/свить гнездо́,** to build a nest. —**ви́ться,** *refl.* [*past* **ви́лся, вила́сь, вило́сь, вили́сь**] [*impfv. only*] **1,** *(of hair)* to curl; *(of vines)* to twine. **2,** *(of a road)* to wind; *(of a snake)* to twist. **3,** *(of a bird)* to hover; *(of dust)* to swirl.
ви́тязь *n.m., obs., folk poetry* warrior; hero.
вихо́р [*gen.* **-хра́**] *n.* tuft *(of hair).*
вихрь *n.m.* **1,** whirlwind; vortex. **2,** swirl *(of dust);* eddy *(of snow).*
ви́це- *prefix* vice-: ви́це-президе́нт, vice-president; ви́це-адмира́л, vice-admiral. —**ви́це-коро́ль,** viceroy.
вишнёвка *n.* cherry brandy.
вишнёвый *adj.* **1,** cherry *(attrib.).* **2,** cherry-colored; cerise.
ви́шня [*gen. pl.* **-шен**] *n.* **1,** cherries. **2,** a (single) cherry. **3,** cherry tree.
вка́лывать *v. impfv.* [*pfv.* **вколо́ть**] *(with* **в** + *acc.)* to stick in; stick into.
вка́пывать *v. impfv.* [*pfv.* **вкопа́ть**] *(with* **в** + *acc.)* to implant; set (in the ground).
вкати́ть [*infl.* **вкачу́, вка́тишь**] *v., pfv. of* **вка́тывать.** —**вкати́ться,** *refl., pfv. of* **вка́тываться.**
вка́тывать *v. impfv.* [*pfv.* **вкати́ть**] **1,** *(with* **в** + *acc.)* to roll into; wheel into. **2,** *colloq.* to give; administer. —**вка́тываться,** *refl. (with* **в** + *acc.)* to roll into.
вклад *n.* **1,** deposit. **2,** *fig.* contribution.
вкла́дка [*gen. pl.* **-док**] *n.* supplement; insert *(in a publication).*
вкладно́й *adj.* **1,** deposit *(attrib.).* **2,** deposited. **3,** *in* **вкладно́й лист,** page insert.
вкла́дчик *n.* depositor.
вкла́дывание *n.* inserting; insertion.
вкла́дывать *v. impfv.* [*pfv.* **вложи́ть**] *(with* **в** + *acc.)* **1,** to put into; insert. **2,** to invest (money) in.
вкле́ивать *v. impfv.* [*pfv.* **вкле́ить**] *(with* **в** + *acc.)* to paste in.
вкле́йка [*gen. pl.* **-е́ек**] *n.* **1,** pasting in. **2,** inset.
вкли́нивать *v. impfv.* [*pfv.* **вкли́нить** *or* **вклини́ть**] *(with* **в** + *acc.)* to wedge (into). —**вкли́ниваться,** *refl.* **1,** to be wedged in. **2,** *(with* **в** + *acc.)* to drive a wedge (into).
включа́ть *v. impfv.* [*pfv.* **включи́ть**] **1,** to include. **2,** to turn on; switch on. —**включа́ться,** *refl. (with* **в** + *acc.)* to join in.
включа́я *prep., with acc.* including.
включе́ние *n.* **1,** inclusion. **2,** turning on; switching on.
включи́тельно *adv.* inclusive.
включи́ть *v., pfv. of* **включа́ть.** —**включи́ться,** *refl., pfv. of* **включа́ться.**
вкола́чивать *v. impfv.* [*pfv.* **вколоти́ть**] *colloq.* to hammer in; drive in.
вколоти́ть [*infl.* **-лочу́, -ло́тишь**] *v., pfv. of* **вкола́чивать.**

вколóть [*infl.* **вколю́, вкóлешь**] *v., pfv. of* **вка́лывать.**

вконéц *adv., colloq.* completely; entirely; utterly.

вкопа́ть *v., pfv. of* **вка́пывать.** —**как вкóпанный,** dead in one's tracks.

вкореня́ть *v. impfv.* [*pfv.* **вкорени́ть**] to implant; inculcate. —**вкореня́ться,** *refl.* to take root.

вкось *adv.* at an angle; diagonally; catty-corner.

вкра́дчивый *adj.* ingratiating.

вкра́дываться *v.r. impfv.* [*pfv.* **вкра́сться**] *(with* **в** + *acc.)* **1,** to creep in(to); steal in(to). **2,** *(of errors, misprints, etc.)* to creep in. —**вкра́дываться в довéрие к,** to worm one's way into the confidence of.

вкра́пить *v. pfv.* [*infl.* **-плю, -пишь**] to sprinkle *(usu. fig.)*: в доклáд бы́ли вкрáплены анекдóты, the report was sprinkled with (*or* contained numerous) anecdotes.

вкра́сться [*infl. like* **красть**] *v.r., pfv. of* **вкра́дываться.**

вкра́тце *adv.* in brief; briefly.

вкривь *adv., colloq.* aslant. —**вкривь и вкось, 1,** in all directions. **2,** without direction; aimlessly.

вкругову́ю *adv., colloq.* around; in a circle.

вкруту́ю *adv., in* **яйцó вкруту́ю,** hard-boiled egg.

вку́пе *adv., obs.* together.

вкус *n.* taste. —**быть по вку́су** (+ *dat.*); **быть в (чьём-нибудь) вку́се,** to be to someone's taste.

вкуси́ть [*infl.* **вкушу́, вку́сишь**] *v., pfv. of* **вкуша́ть.**

вку́сно *adv.* (*with verbs of eating, cooking, etc.*) well: вку́сно есть, eat well; вку́сно готóвить, be a good cook. —*adj., used predicatively* tasty; delicious: óчень вку́сно!, delicious!

вку́сный *adj.* tasty; delicious; good.

вкусовóй *adj.* taste (*attrib.*); gustatory.

вкуша́ть *v. impfv.* [*pfv.* **вкуси́ть**] to taste; savor.

вла́га *n.* moisture.

влага́лище *n.* vagina. —**влага́лищный,** *adj.* vaginal.

владéлец [*gen.* **-льца**] *n.m.* [*fem.* **-лица**] owner.

владéние *n.* **1,** ownership; possession. **2,** *obs.* property. **3,** *pl.* territories; possessions.

владéть *v. impfv.* (*with. instr.*) **1,** to own. **2,** to control (a territory). **3,** to hold (an audience, someone's attention, etc.). **4,** to know how to use; use with skill: владéть перóм, to be a talented writer; владéть инострáнным языкóм, to speak a foreign language. **5,** (*usu. neg.*) (not) to have the use of (a part of one's body). —**владéть собóй,** to control oneself; keep one's temper.

влады́ка *n.m., obs.* ruler; sovereign. —**влады́чество,** *n., obs.* dominion; sway.

вла́жность *n.f.* **1,** humidity. **2,** moisture; dampness.

вла́жный *adj.* **1,** humid. **2,** moist; damp.

вла́мываться *v.r. impfv.* [*pfv.* **вломи́ться**] (*with* **в** + *acc.*) **1,** to burst into. **2,** to break into.

вла́ствовать *v. impfv.* [*pres.* **-ствую, -ствуешь**] (*with* **над**) to rule; wield power (over).

властели́н *n.* **1,** absolute ruler. **2,** *fig.* (*with gen.*) master (of).

власти́тель *n.m., obs.* ruler. —**власти́тель дум,** major figure; major influence.

вла́стный *adj.* **1,** [*short form only; masc.* **вла́стен**] having power; (*with inf.*) having the power to. **2,** overpowering. **3,** overbearing; domineering. **4,** (*of one's tone of voice*) peremptory.

властолюби́вый *adj.* power-seeking; power-hungry. —**властолю́бие,** *n.* love of power.

власть *n.f.* **1,** power. **2,** rule: совéтская власть, Soviet rule; the Soviet regime. **3,** *pl.* [*gen.* **власте́й;** *dat.* **-стя́м**] the authorities. —**ва́ша власть,** *colloq.* as you wish; please yourself. —**во вла́сти** (+ *gen.*), at the mercy of.

власяни́ца *n.* hair shirt.

влачи́ть *v. impfv.* **1,** *obs.* to drag. **2,** *fig.* to lead; live: влачи́ть жáлкое существовáние, to lead a miserable existence.

влéво *adv.* to the left.

влеза́ть *v. impfv.* [*pfv.* **влезть**] **1,** (*with* **на** + *acc.*) to climb (a tree, wall, etc.); climb onto. **2,** (*with* **в** + *acc.*) to climb into; get into (a car, bathtub, etc.). **3,** (*with* **в** + *acc.*) *colloq.* to fit (into). —**влезть в довéрие к,** to gain the confidence of. —**влезть в долги́,** to get into debt. —**влезть в ду́шу** (*with gen., dat., or* **к**), **1,** to win over; gain the confidence of. **2,** to intrude into the personal life of.

влезть [*infl. like* **лезть**] *v., pfv. of* **влеза́ть.**

влепи́ть [*infl.* **влеплю́, влéпишь**] *v., pfv. of* **влепля́ть.**

влепля́ть *v. impfv.* [*pfv.* **влепи́ть**] **1,** to inlay. **2,** *colloq.* to give; let one have: влепи́ть пощёчину (+ *dat.*), to give someone a slap in the face.

влета́ть *v. impfv.* [*pfv.* **влетéть**] (*with* **в** + *acc.*) **1,** to fly into. **2,** *colloq.* to burst into; dash into. **3,** *impers.* (*with dat.*) *colloq.* to get into trouble: емý опя́ть влетéло, he is in trouble again.

влетéть [*infl.* **-чу́, -ти́шь**] *v., pfv. of* **влета́ть.**

влечéние *n.* (*with* **к**) **1,** bent (for); penchant (for). **2,** desire (for); lust (for): половóе влечéние, sexual desire/drive/appetite.

влечь *v. impfv.* [*pfv.* **повлéчь;** *pres.* **влеку́, влечёшь, ...влеку́т;** *past* **влёк, влекла́, влекло́**] **1,** to draw. **2,** to attract. —**влечь за собóй, 1,** to involve; entail. **2,** to lead to; bring in its wake.

влива́ние *n.* injection; infusion.

влива́ть *v. impfv.* [*pfv.* **влить**] (*with* **в** + *acc.*) **1,** to pour in; pour into. **2,** *fig.* to infuse; instill. —**влива́ться,** *refl.* (*with* **в** + *acc.*) **1,** to flow into. **2,** to be added to; join.

влипа́ть *v. impfv.* [*pfv.* **вли́пнуть**] (*with* **в** + *acc.*) **1,** to stick (to); get stuck (to); get stuck (in). **2,** *colloq.* to get into (trouble, a mess, etc.).

вли́пнуть [*past* **влип, -ла**] *v., pfv. of* **влипа́ть.**

влить [*infl.* **волью́, вольёшь;** *past fem.* **влила́**] *v., pfv. of* **влива́ть.** —**вли́ться,** *refl., pfv. of* **влива́ться.**

влия́ние *n.* influence.

влия́тельный *adj.* influential.

влия́ть *v. impfv.* [*pfv.* **повлия́ть**] (*with* **на** + *acc.*) to influence; affect; have an effect upon.

вложéние *n.* **1,** enclosure. **2,** investment.

вложи́ть [*infl.* **вложу́, влóжишь**] *v., pfv. of* **вкла́дывать.**

вломи́ться [*infl.* **вломлю́сь, влóмишься**] *v.r., pfv. of* **вла́мываться.**

влюби́ть [*infl.* **влюблю́, влю́бишь**] *v., pfv. of* **влюбля́ть.** —**влюби́ться,** *refl., pfv. of* **влюбля́ться.**

влюблённый *adj.* **1,** (*with* **в** + *acc.*) in love (with). **2,** loving; amorous. —*n., usu. pl.* lover(s).

влюбля́ть *v. impfv.* [*pfv.* **влюби́ть**] (*with* **в** + *acc.*) to make (someone) fall in love (with). —**влюбля́ться,** *refl.* (*with* **в** + *acc.*) to fall in love (with).

влю́бчивый *adj.* amorous. —**влю́бчивость,** *n.f.* amorousness.

вмени́ть [*infl.* **вменю́, вмени́шь**] *v., pfv. of* **вменя́ть.**

вменя́емый *adj., law* of sound mind. —**вменя́емость,** *n.f.* responsibility.

вменя́ть *v. impfv.* [*pfv.* **вмени́ть**] (*with* **в** + *acc.*) to regard; consider: вменя́ть что́-нибудь в недоста́ток (+ *gen.*), to regard something as a shortcoming of. —**вменя́ть (что́-нибудь) в вину́** (+ *dat.*), to impute something to someone; accuse of. —**вменя́ть себе́ в обя́занность** (+ *inf.*), to take upon oneself the job of.
вме́сте *adv.* together. —**вме́сте с,** together with; along with. —**вме́сте с тем,** at the same time.
вмести́лище *n.* container; receptacle.
вмести́мость *n.f.* capacity.
вмести́тельный *adj.* spacious; roomy. —**вмести́тельность,** *n.f.* spaciousness; roominess.
вмести́ть [*infl.* **-щу́, -сти́шь**] *v., pfv. of* **вмеща́ть.** —**вмести́ться,** *refl., pfv. of* **вмеща́ться.**
вме́сто *prep., with gen.* instead of; in place of: вме́сто меня́, instead of me; in my place. Вме́сто того́, что́бы оста́ться здесь, instead of remaining here.
вмеша́тельство *n.* (with **в** + *acc.*) interference (in); intervention (in); meddling (in).
вме́шиваться *v.r. impfv.* [*pfv.* **вмеша́ться**] (*with* **в** + *acc.*) to interfere (in); intervene (in); meddle (in).
вмеща́ть *v. impfv.* [*pfv.* **вмести́ть**] **1,** to hold; seat; accommodate; have a capacity of. **2,** (*with* **в** + *acc.*) to fit (into); get (into). —**вмеща́ться,** *refl.* (*with* **в** + *acc.*) to fit (into); go (into).
вмиг *adv.* in an instant; in a flash.
вмина́ть *v. impfv.* [*pfv.* **вмять**] **1,** to press in. **2,** to dent.
вмя́тина *n.* dent.
вмять [*infl.* **вомну́, вомнёшь**] *v., pfv. of* **вмина́ть.**
внаём *also,* **внаймы́** *adv., in* **брать внаём,** to rent; hire; **сдава́ть** *or* **отдава́ть внаём,** to rent (out).
внаки́дку *adv.* over one's shoulders: носи́ть пальто́ внаки́дку, to wear a coat over one's shoulders.
внакла́де *adv., colloq., in* **оста́ться внакла́де,** to be the loser; end up losing.
внакла́дку *adv., in* **пить чай внакла́дку,** to drink tea with sugar.
внача́ле *adv.* at first; in the beginning.
вне *prep., with gen.* **1,** outside: вне го́рода, outside the city. **2,** out of: вне о́череди, out of turn. **3,** *in* вне сомне́ния, beyond doubt; вне подозре́ний, above suspicion. —**вне себя́ (от),** beside oneself (with joy, grief, etc.). —**челове́к вне зако́на,** outlaw.
внебра́чный *adj.* **1,** extramarital. **2,** (*of a child*) illegitimate.
вневре́менный *adj.* timeless.
внедре́ние *n.* introduction; incorporation; adoption.
внедря́ть *v. impfv.* [*pfv.* **внедри́ть**] **1,** (*with* **в** + *acc.*) to instill (in); inculcate (in). **2,** to introduce: внедря́ть но́вую те́хнику, to introduce new equipment.
внеза́пно *adv.* suddenly.
внеза́пность *n.f.* **1,** suddenness. **2,** *mil.* (element of) surprise.
внеза́пный *adj.* **1,** sudden. **2,** *mil.* surprise: внеза́пное нападе́ние, surprise attack.
внекла́ссный *adj.* extracurricular.
внеочередно́й *adj.* **1,** out of turn; out of order. **2,** (*of a meeting, session, etc.*) extraordinary; special.
внесе́ние *n.* **1,** bringing in; carrying in. **2,** entering; insertion. **3,** putting forward; submission.
внести́ [*infl. like* **нести́**] *v., pfv. of* **вноси́ть.**
вне́шне *adv.* outwardly; on the surface.
вне́шний *adj.* **1,** outward; outer; outside; external. **2,** foreign: вне́шняя поли́тика, foreign policy.
вне́шность *n.f.* appearance; exterior.
внешта́тный *adj.* not on the permanent staff.
вниз *adv., expressing motion or direction* **1,** down; downward. **2,** downstairs. —**вниз по,** down: вниз по тече́нию, downstream.
внизу́ *adv., expressing location* **1,** below. **2,** downstairs. —*prep., with gen.* at the bottom of.
вника́ть *v. impfv.* [*pfv.* **вни́кнуть**] (*with* **в** + *acc.*) to go deeply into; delve into; probe.
вни́кнуть [*past* **вник** *or* **вни́кнул, вни́кла**] *v., pfv. of* **вника́ть.**
внима́ние *n.* **1,** attention: обраща́ть внима́ние на, to pay attention to. **2,** kindness; consideration. —**принима́ть во внима́ние,** to consider; take into account; take account of.
внима́тельно *adv.* **1,** attentively; closely. **2,** with consideration.
внима́тельность *n.f.* **1,** attentiveness. **2,** kindness; consideration.
внима́тельный *adj.* **1,** attentive. **2,** considerate; thoughtful.
внима́ть *v. impfv.* [*pfv.* **внять**] (*with dat.*) *poetic* to hearken (to); heed.
вничью́ *adv., sports; games* in a draw; in a tie: зако́нчиться вничью́, to end in a draw/tie. Сыгра́ть вничью́, to play to a draw/tie.
вновь *adv.* **1,** once again; once more. **2,** newly.
вноси́ть *v. impfv.* [*pfv.* **внести́;** *pres.* **вношу́, вно́сишь**] **1,** to bring in; carry in. **2,** to introduce; bring about. **3,** to cause; create: вноси́ть разла́д в семью́, to cause dissension in the family. **4,** to enter; insert. **5,** to put forward; submit. **6,** to contribute (one's share). Вноси́ть свой вклад (*with* **в** + *acc.*), to make one's contribution (to).
внук *n.* grandson; grandchild.
вну́тренний *adj.* **1,** internal; inner; interior; inside. **2,** domestic (*as opposed to foreign*). —**вну́тренне,** *adv.* inwardly.
вну́тренность *n.f.* **1,** interior; inside. **2,** *pl.* internal organs; innards.
внутри́ *adv.* inside. —*prep., with gen.* inside; within.
внутриве́нный *adj.* intravenous.
внутрь *adv., expressing direction* inside. —*prep., with gen.* into; inside.
внуча́та [*gen.* **-ча́т**] *n. pl., colloq.* grandchildren.
внуча́тый *adj., in* **внуча́тый племя́нник,** grandnephew; **внуча́тая племя́нница,** grandniece. *Also,* **внуча́тный.**
вну́чка [*gen. pl.* **-чек**] *n.* granddaughter.
внуша́ть *v. impfv.* [*pfv.* **внуши́ть**] **1,** to instill (respect, confidence, etc.); arouse (fear, envy, etc.): внуша́ть кому́-нибудь страх, to arouse fear in someone. **2,** to suggest (a thought, idea, etc.). **3,** (*with a dependent clause*) to convince; bring home to: он нам внуши́л, что..., he convinced us (of the fact) that...
внуше́ние *n.* **1,** *psychol.* suggestion. **2,** hypnosis. **3,** reprimand.
внуши́тельный *adj.* imposing; impressive.
внуши́ть *v., pfv. of* **внуша́ть.**
вня́тный *adj.* **1,** distinct; clear. **2,** intelligible.
внять *v.pfv., used only in the past* [*fem.* **вняла́**] *pfv. of* **внима́ть.**
во *prep.* = **в.**
вобра́ть [*infl.* **вберу́, вберёшь;** *past fem.* **вобрала́**] *v., pfv. of* **вбира́ть.**

вове́к *also,* **вове́ки** *adv.* **1,** forever. **2,** *with a neg. verb* never.

вовлека́ть *v. impfv.* [*pfv.* **вовле́чь**] (*with* **в** + *acc.*) to draw (into); involve (in).

вовлече́ние *n.* involvement.

вовле́чь [*infl. like* **влечь**] *v., pfv. of* **вовлека́ть.**

вовне́ *adv.* outside; without.

во́время *adv.* in time; on time. —**не во́время,** at the wrong time.

во́все *adv., colloq.* **1,** completely. **2,** (*with* **не**) not at all. —**во́все нет!,** not at all!

вовсю́ *adv., colloq.* with all one's might; as fast (*or* hard) as one can.

во-вторы́х secondly; in the second place.

вогна́ть [*infl.* **вгоню́, вго́нишь;** *past fem.* **вогнала́**] *v., pfv. of* **вгоня́ть.**

во́гнутый *adj.* concave. —**во́гнутость,** *n.f.* concavity.

вогну́ть *v., pfv. of* **вгиба́ть.**

вода́ [*acc.* **во́ду;** *pl.* **во́ды**] *n.* water.

водворе́ние *n.* **1,** settlement. **2,** establishment.

водворя́ть *v. impfv.* [*pfv.* **водвори́ть**] **1,** to settle; install (people somewhere). **2,** to put back (in its former place). **3,** *fig.* to establish; restore. —**водворя́ться,** *refl.* **1,** to settle. **2,** *fig.* to be established; set in.

водеви́ль *n.m.* vaudeville.

води́тель *n.m.* driver (*of a vehicle*).

води́тельский *adj.* driver (*attrib.*), driver's. —**води́тельские права́,** driver's license.

води́тельство *n., obs.* leadership.

води́ть *v. impfv.* [*pres.* **вожу́, во́дишь**] **1,** *indeterm. of* **вести́. 2,** *colloq.* to keep (animals, birds, etc.). —**води́ть дру́жбу с,** to keep up a friendship with. —**води́ть компа́нию с,** to keep company with.

води́ться *v.r. impfv.* [*pres.* **вожу́сь, во́дишься**] **1,** (*of animals, birds, etc.*) to be found (*in a certain area*). **2,** (*with* **с** + *instr.*) *colloq.* to associate (with); consort (with). **3,** (*with* **за** + *instr.*) (*of traits of character*) to be noticed; be observed: за ним никаки́х стра́нностей не води́лось, no peculiarities were observed in his behavior. —**как во́дится,** as usual.

во́дка *n.* vodka.

водноло́жный *adj., in* **водноло́жный спорт,** water-skiing.

во́дный *adj.* water (*attrib.*).

водобоя́знь *n.f.* rabies; hydrophobia.

водово́з *n.* water carrier.

водоворо́т *n.* **1,** whirlpool; eddy. **2,** *fig.* vortex; maelstrom.

водоём *n.* reservoir.

водоизмеще́ние *n., naut.* displacement; tonnage.

водока́чка [*gen. pl.* **-чек**] *n.* pumping station.

водола́з *n.* **1,** diver. **2,** Newfoundland dog. —**водола́зный,** *adj.* diving (*attrib.*).

Водоле́й *n.* Aquarius.

водоме́р *n.* water meter.

водонапо́рный *adj., in* **водонапо́рная ба́шня,** water tower.

водонепроница́емый *adj.* waterproof; watertight.

водоно́с *n.* water carrier.

водоотво́д *n.* drainage system. —**водоотво́дный,** *adj.* drain (*attrib.*); drainage (*attrib.*).

водопа́д *n.* waterfall.

водопла́вающий *adj., in* **водопла́вающая пти́ца,** water bird; waterfowl.

водопо́й *n.* **1,** watering place. **2,** watering (*of livestock*).

водопрово́д *n.* indoor plumbing; running water.

водопрово́дный *adj.* pert. to the carrying or supplying of water: водопрово́дная магистра́ль, water main. —**водопрово́дная вода́,** tap water.

водопрово́дчик *n.* plumber.

водоразбо́рный *adj., in* **водоразбо́рная коло́нка** *and* **водоразбо́рный кран,** hydrant.

водоразде́л *n.* watershed.

водоро́д *n.* hydrogen.

водоро́дный *adj.* hydrogen. —**водоро́дная бо́мба,** hydrogen bomb.

во́доросль *n.f.* algae; seaweed. *Often,* **морска́я во́доросль.**

водосви́нка [*gen. pl.* **-нок**] *n.* capybara.

водосли́в *n.* spillway.

водосто́к *n.* drain; gutter.

водосто́чный *adj., in* **водосто́чный жёлоб** *and* **водосто́чная кана́ва,** gutter; **водосто́чная труба́,** drainpipe.

водохрани́лище *n.* reservoir.

во́дочный *adj.* vodka (*attrib.*).

водружа́ть *v. impfv.* [*pfv.* **водрузи́ть**] to place firmly, plant; implant.

водяни́стый *adj.* **1,** watery. **2,** *fig.* colorless; insipid.

водя́нка *n.* dropsy.

водяно́й *adj.* water (*attrib.*); aquatic. —*n.* water sprite. —**водяно́й знак,** watermark. —**водяно́е колесо́,** water wheel. —**водяна́я ли́лия,** water lily.

воева́ть *v. impfv.* [*pres.* **вою́ю, вою́ешь**] **1,** (*with* **с** + *instr. or* **про́тив**) to be at war (with); fight (against). **2,** (*of a soldier*) to fight; see action.

воево́да *n.m., hist.* military governor in Old Russia (*from the 16th to the end of the 18th century*).

воеди́но *adv.* into one; together.

военача́льник *n.* commander (*of a large military or naval unit*).

вое́нно-возду́шный *adj., in* **вое́нно-возду́шные си́лы,** air force.

вое́нно-морско́й *adj., in* **вое́нно-морско́й флот,** navy.

военнообя́занный *n., decl. as an adj.* person subject to call-up; person subject to the draft.

военнопле́нный *n., decl. as an adj.* prisoner of war.

военнослу́жащий *n., decl. as an adj.* soldier; serviceman.

вое́нный *adj.* **1,** war (*attrib.*): вое́нное вре́мя, wartime. **2,** military. **3,** martial. —*n.* military man; serviceman. —**вое́нные де́йствия,** military operations; hostilities. —**вое́нный заво́д,** munitions factory. —**вое́нное положе́ние,** martial law. —**вое́нная промы́шленность,** the armaments industry. —**вое́нный суд,** court-martial.

вое́нщина *n.* the military; militarists.

вожа́к [*gen.* **-жака́**] *n.* **1,** leader. **2,** guide.

вожа́тый *n., decl. as an adj.* **1,** *obs.* guide. **2,** young pioneer leader. **3,** streetcar driver.

вожделе́ние *n.* **1,** longing; craving. **2,** desire; lust.

вожде́ние *n.* driving; steering; piloting.

вождь [*gen.* **вождя́**] *n.m.* leader.

во́жжи [*gen.* **вожже́й**] *n. pl.* [*sing.* **вожжа́**] reins.

воз [*2nd loc.* **возу́;** *pl.* **возы́**] *n.* **1,** cart. **2,** cartload. —**а воз и ны́не там,** things are right where they started. —**что с вóзу упáло, то пропáло,** there's no use crying over spilt milk.

воз- *also,* **вос-** *prefix,* **1,** *indicating upward direction:* возводи́ть, to erect; elevate; raise. **2,** *indicating repetition of an action:* воссоединя́ть, to reunite; воспроизводи́ть, to reproduce.

возбраня́ть *v. impfv.* [*pfv.* **возбрани́ть**] *obs.* to forbid. —**возбраня́ться,** *refl.* [*impfv. only*] *obs.* to be forbidden.

возбуди́мый *adj.* excitable. —**возбуди́мость,** *n.f.* excitability.

возбуди́тель *n.m.* agent; cause; stimulus.

возбуди́ть [*infl.* **-жу́, -ди́шь**] *v., pfv. of* **возбужда́ть.**

возбужда́ть *v. impfv.* [*pfv.* **возбуди́ть**] **1,** to arouse; rouse; excite. **2,** to stir up; incite. **3,** to raise (a question); bring (a lawsuit).

возбужда́ющий *adj.* rousing; stirring. —**возбужда́ющее сре́дство,** stimulant.

возбужде́ние *n.* **1,** excitation; stimulation. **2,** excitement.

возбуждённый *adj.* excited.

возведе́ние *n.* **1,** erection. **2,** leveling (*of an accusation*). **3,** *math.* raising (*to a certain power*).

возвели́чивать *v. impfv.* [*pfv.* **возвели́чить**] *obs.* to extol; exalt.

возвести́ [*infl. like* **вести́**] *v., pfv. of* **возводи́ть.**

возвеща́ть *v. impfv.* [*pfv.* **возвести́ть**] **1,** to announce. **2,** to herald; usher in.

возводи́ть *v. impfv.* [*pfv.* **возвести́;** *pres.* **-вожу́, -во́дишь**] **1,** to erect. **2,** to elevate (to a certain rank): возводи́ть на престо́л, to raise to the throne. **3,** to level (an accusation). **4,** to trace back (*in time*). **5,** *math.* to raise (to a certain power).

возвра́т *n.* **1,** return. **2,** recurrence. **3,** repayment.

возврати́ть [*infl.* **-щу́, -ти́шь**] *v., pfv. of* **возвраща́ть.** —**возврати́ться,** *refl., pfv. of* **возвраща́ться.**

возвра́тный *adj.* **1,** *obs.* return (*attrib.*): на возвра́тном пути́, on the way back. **2,** *gram.* reflexive: возвра́тный глаго́л, reflexive verb. —**возвра́тный тиф,** relapsing fever.

возвраща́ть *v. impfv.* [*pfv.* **верну́ть** *and* **возврати́ть**] **1,** to return; give back. **2,** to pay (a debt); repay (a loan). **3,** to restore. **4,** to recover; regain; get back. —**возвраща́ться,** *refl.* to return; come back; go back.

возвраще́ние *n.* **1,** return: по возвраще́нии домо́й, on returning home. **2,** return; giving back. **3,** repayment.

возвыша́ть *v. impfv.* [*pfv.* **возвы́сить**] **1,** to raise. **2,** [*impfv. only*] to uplift; ennoble. —**возвыша́ться,** *refl.* **1,** to rise. **2,** [*impfv. only*] (with **над**) to tower (over *or* above).

возвыше́ние *n.* **1,** rise; rising. **2,** platform; dais. **3,** elevation; hill.

возвы́шенность *n.f.* **1,** height; hill. **2,** loftiness.

возвы́шенный *adj.* **1,** high; elevated. **2,** *fig.* lofty.

возглавля́ть *v. impfv.* [*pfv.* **возгла́вить**] to head; be the head of.

во́зглас *n.* shout; cry; exclamation.

возглаша́ть *v. impfv.* [*pfv.* **возгласи́ть**] to proclaim.

возго́нка *n., chem.* sublimation.

возгоня́ть *v. impfv., chem.* to sublimate.

возгора́ться *v.r. impfv.* [*pfv.* **возгоре́ться**] **1,** to flare up. **2,** *fig.* (*with instr.*) to be stirred (with); be inflamed (*with*).

возгорди́ться *v.r. pfv.* [*infl.* **-жу́сь, -ди́шься**] (*with instr.*) to get a swelled head (over).

возгоре́ться *v.r., pfv. of* **возгора́ться.**

воздава́ть *v. impfv.* [*pfv.* **возда́ть;** *pres.* **-даю́, -даёшь**] **1,** to render. **2,** (*with instr.*) to repay (with). —**воздава́ть до́лжное,** *see* **до́лжное.**

возда́ть [*infl. like* **дать;** *past* **возда́л, -ла́, -да́ло**] *v., pfv. of* **воздава́ть.**

воздвига́ть *v. impfv.* [*pfv.* **воздви́гнуть**] to erect.

воздви́гнуть [*past* **-дви́г** *or* **-дви́гнул, -дви́гла**] *v., pfv. of* **воздвига́ть.**

возде́йствие *n.* influence; effect.

возде́йствовать *v. impfv. & pfv.* [*pres.* **-ствую, -ствуешь**] (*with* **на** + *acc.*) to influence; bring pressure to bear (on).

возде́лать *v., pfv. of* **возде́лывать.**

возде́лывать *v. impfv.* [*pfv.* **возде́лать**] to till; cultivate.

воздержа́вшийся *n., decl. as an adj.* abstention: при двух воздержа́вшихся, with two abstentions.

воздержа́ние *n.* **1,** (*with* **от**) abstention; abstinence. **2,** (*with* **в** + *prepl.*) moderation; temperance.

возде́ржанность *n.f.* moderation; temperance. —**возде́ржанный,** *adj.* observing moderation.

воздержа́ться [*infl.* **-держу́сь, -де́ржишься**] *v.r., pfv. of* **возде́рживаться.**

возде́рживаться *v.r. impfv.* [*pfv.* **воздержа́ться**] (*with* **от**) **1,** to refrain (from). **2,** to abstain (from).

возде́ть *v. pfv.* [*infl.* **-де́ну, -де́нешь**], *in* **возде́ть ру́ки,** *obs.* to lift up (*or* raise) one's hands.

во́здух *n.* air. —**на во́здух** *(with verbs of motion),* outdoors. —**на (откры́том) во́здухе,** outdoors; out of doors.

воздухоплáвание *n.* aeronautics. —**воздухоплáватель,** *n.m.* aeronaut. —**воздухоплáвательный,** *adj.* aeronautic; aeronautical.

воздушнодеса́нтный *adj., mil.* airborne: воздушнодеса́нтные войска́, airborne troops.

возду́шный *adj.* **1,** air (*attrib.*); aerial. **2,** airy. —**возду́шный шар,** balloon.

воззва́ние *n.* appeal.

воззва́ть [*infl. like* **звать**] *v., pfv. of* **взыва́ть.**

воззре́ние *n.* outlook; view.

вози́ть *v. impfv.* [*pres.* **вожу́, во́зишь**] *indeterm. of* **везти́.** —**вози́ться,** *refl.* **1,** to play; romp; frolic. **2,** *colloq.* to putter (about). **3,** (*with* **с** + *instr.*) *colloq.* to fiddle (with); tinker (with).

возлага́ть *v. impfv.* [*pfv.* **возложи́ть**] (*with* **на** + *acc.*) **1,** to place (on); lay (on): возложи́ть вено́к на моги́лу, to place/lay a wreath on a grave. **2,** to give; assign; turn over (work, a task, etc.) to. **3,** to place; pin (hopes, blame, responsibility, etc.) on.

во́зле *prep., with gen.* **1,** by; near. **2,** beside; alongside; next to. —*adv.* nearby.

возлия́ние *n.* libation.

возложи́ть [*infl.* **-ложу́, -ло́жишь**] *v., pfv. of* **возлага́ть.**

возлю́бленный *n., decl. as an adj.* loved one; sweetheart.

возме́здие *n.* retribution; requital.

возмеща́ть *v. impfv.* [*pfv.* **возмести́ть**] **1,** to refund (expenses); make up; recover (losses); make up for (lost time). **2,** (*with dat.*) to compensate; reimburse: возмеща́ть кому́-нибудь расхо́ды, to reimburse someone for his expenses.

возмеще́ние *n.* compensation; reimbursement.
возмо́жно *adv.* **1,** possibly. **2,** (*with comp. adjectives & adverbs*) as ... as possible: возмо́жно скоре́е, as soon as possible. —*adj., used predicatively* possible: э́то вполне́ возмо́жно, it/that is entirely possible.
возмо́жность *n.f.* **1,** possibility. **2,** opportunity; chance. **3,** *pl.* means; resources. **4,** *pl., mil.* capabilities. —**до после́дней возмо́жности,** to the utmost. —**по (ме́ре) возмо́жности,** as far as possible.
возмо́жный *adj.* possible. —**де́лать всё возмо́жное,** to do everything possible; do everything in one's power; do one's utmost.
возмужа́лый *adj.* mature; virile. —**возмужа́лость,** *n.f.* maturity; virility.
возмужа́ть *v. pfv.* (*of a young boy or girl*) to mature; develop.
возмути́тельно *adv.* outrageously. —*adj., used predicatively* outrageous: э́то возмути́тельно!, it's outrageous!; it's an outrage!
возмути́тельный *adj.* outrageous; disgraceful.
возмуща́ть *v. impfv.* [*pfv.* **возмути́ть**] to rouse the indignation of; outrage. —**возмуща́ться,** *refl.* to be indignant; be outraged.
возмуще́ние *n.* indignation; outrage.
возмущённый *adj.* indignant; outraged.
вознагражда́ть *v. impfv.* [*pfv.* **вознагради́ть**] to reward; compensate; remunerate; recompense.
вознагражде́ние *n.* reward; compensation; remuneration; recompense.
вознаме́риться *v.r. pfv.* (*with inf.*) *obs.* to decide (to); make up one's mind (to).
возненави́деть *v. pfv.* [*infl.* **-жу, -дишь**] to develop a hatred for.
вознесе́ние *n., relig.* **1,** the Ascension. **2,** Ascension Day.
вознести́ [*infl. like* **нести́**] *v., pfv. of* **возноси́ть.** —**вознести́сь,** *refl., pfv. of* **возноси́ться.**
возника́ть *v. impfv.* [*pfv.* **возни́кнуть**] to arise; spring up; crop up.
возникнове́ние *n.* origin; rise; beginning.
возни́кнуть [*past* **-ни́к, -ла**] *v., pfv. of* **возника́ть.**
возни́ца *n.m.* coachman.
возноси́ть *v. impfv.* [*pfv.* **вознести́;** *pres.* **-ношу́, -но́сишь**] **1,** to raise; lift up. **2,** to offer up (a prayer). —**возноси́ться,** *refl.* to loom up.
возня́ *n., colloq.* **1,** bustle; scurrying. **2,** trouble; bother. —**мыши́ная возня́,** petty cares.
возоблада́ть *v. pfv., obs.* to prevail.
возобнови́ть [*infl.* **-влю́, -ви́шь**] *v., pfv. of* **возобновля́ть.**
возобновле́ние *n.* renewal; resumption.
возобновля́ть *v. impfv.* [*pfv.* **возобнови́ть**] to renew; resume. —**возобновля́ться,** *refl.* to start again; resume.
возомни́ть *v. pfv.* [*usu. with* **себя́** *and instr.*] *colloq.* to to imagine oneself to be. —**возомни́ть о себе́,** to get a swelled head.
возража́ть *v. impfv.* [*pfv.* **возрази́ть**] to object; have an objection.
возраже́ние *n.* objection.
возрази́ть [*infl.* **-жу́, -зи́шь**] *v., pfv. of* **возража́ть.**
во́зраст *n.* age.
возраста́ние *n.* growth; increase.
возраста́ть *v. impfv.* [*pfv.* **возрасти́**] **1,** *obs.* to grow. **2,** to increase.
возрасти́ [*infl. like* **расти́**] *v., pfv. of* **возраста́ть.**
возрастно́й *adj.* age (*attrib.*).
возрожда́ть *v. impfv.* [*pfv.* **возроди́ть**] to revive; restore. —**возрожда́ться,** *refl.* **1,** to be revived. **2,** to be reborn.
возрожде́ние *n.* **1,** revival; rebirth; renaissance. **2,** *cap.* the Renaissance.
во́зчик *n.* carter.
возыме́ть *v. pfv.* **1,** *obs.* to acquire; achieve. **2,** to develop (a feeling, liking, etc.). —**возыме́ть де́йствие,** to have an effect; achieve the desired effect. —**возыме́ть обра́тное де́йствие,** to have the reverse effect. —**возыме́ть си́лу,** to go into effect; come into force.
во́ин *n.* warrior; soldier.
во́инский *adj.* military. —**во́инский эшело́н,** troop train.
вои́нственный *adj.* militant; warlike; belligerent; bellicose. —**вои́нственность,** *n.f.* militancy; belligerence; bellicosity.
вои́нствующий *adj.* militant.
вои́стину *adv., archaic* truly; verily.
вой *n.* howl; howling; wail; wailing.
во́йлок *n.* felt. —**во́йлочный,** *adj.* felt.
война́ [*pl.* **во́йны**] *n.* war.
войска́ [*gen.* **войск**] *n., pl. of* **во́йско,** troops.
во́йско *n.* army.
войсково́й *adj.* troop (*attrib.*).
войти́ [*infl.* **войду́, войдёшь;** *past* **вошёл, вошла́, вошло́**] *v., pfv. of* **входи́ть.**
вокали́ст *n.* voice teacher.
вока́льный *adj.* vocal.
вокза́л *n.* (railroad) station. —**вокза́льный,** *adj.* station (*attrib.*).
вокру́г *prep., with gen.* around. —*adv.* around; about. —**ходи́ть вокру́г да о́коло,** to beat around the bush.
вол [*gen.* **вола́**] *n.* ox.
вола́н *n.* **1,** flounce *(on a dress)*. **2,** shuttlecock.
волды́рь [*gen.* **-дыря́**] *n.m.* blister.
волево́й *adj.* **1,** volitional. **2,** strong-willed.
волейбо́л *n.* volleyball. —**волейболи́ст,** *n.* volleyball player. —**волейбо́льный,** *adj.* volleyball *(attrib.)*.
во́лей-нево́лей *adv.* having no other choice; perforce; willy-nilly.
волк [*pl.* **во́лки, волко́в, волка́м**] *n.* wolf. —**волк в ове́чьей шку́ре,** wolf in sheep's clothing. —**во́лком смотре́ть,** to scowl; glower. —**морско́й волк,** *colloq.* old sailor; sea dog.
волкода́в *n.* wolfhound.
волна́ [*pl.* **во́лны, волн, волна́м** *or* **во́лнам**] *n.* wave.
волне́ние *n.* **1,** rough seas; choppy seas. **2,** agitation; nervousness. **3,** *pl.* unrest; disturbances (*civil, political, etc.*).
волни́стый *adj.* **1,** wavy. **2,** rolling; undulating.
волнова́ть *v. impfv.* [*pfv.* **взволнова́ть;** *pres.* **-ну́ю, -ну́ешь**] **1,** to agitate; ruffle; stir. **2,** to excite; disturb; upset. —**волнова́ться,** *refl.* **1,** (*of the sea*) to be agitated; be choppy. **2,** to be excited; be disturbed; be nervous; be upset.
волноло́м *n.* breakwater.
волнообра́зный *adj.* undulating.
волноре́з *n.* breakwater.
волну́ющий *adj.* **1,** stirring; exciting; thrilling. **2,** disturbing; troubling; upsetting.
воло́вий [*fem.* **-вья**] *adj.* ox (*attrib.*).
во́лок *n.* (place of) portage.

волоки́та *n.f.* red tape. —*n.m., obs.* ladies' man.

волокни́стый *adj.* fibrous; stringy.

волокно́ [*pl.* **-о́кна, -о́кон**] *n.* fiber; filament.

волонтёр *n., obs.* volunteer.

во́лос [*pl.* **во́лосы, воло́с, -са́м**] *n.* **1,** a single hair. **2,** *pl.* hair. —**ни на́ волос,** not in the least; not a bit.

волоса́тый *adj.* hairy.

волосо́к [*gen.* **-ска́**] *n.* **1,** *dim. of* **во́лос. 2,** filament (*of a bulb*); hairspring (*of a watch*). —**висе́ть на волоске́,** to hang by a thread. —**на волосо́к (волоске́) от,** within a hairbreadth of.

во́лость *n.f., obs.* small administrative district.

волосяно́й *adj.* hair (*attrib.*).

волочи́ть *v. impfv.* [*pres.* **-лочу́, -ло́чишь**] to drag. —**волочи́ться,** *refl.* **1,** to drag; trail. **2,** to drag oneself along; shuffle along.

воло́чь *v. impfv.* [*pres.* **-локу́, -лочёшь, ...-локу́т;** *past* **воло́к, -локла́, -локло́**] *colloq.* = **волочи́ть.** —**воло́чься,** *refl.* = **волочи́ться.**

волхв [*gen.* **волхва́**] *n.* **1,** sorcerer. **2,** *pl.* the Magi.

волча́нка *n.* lupus (*skin disease*).

во́лчий [*fem.* **-чья**] *adj.* wolf (*attrib.*); wolf's. —**во́лчий аппети́т,** voracious appetite. —**во́лчья пасть,** cleft palate.

волчо́к [*gen.* **-чка́**] *n.* top (*toy*).

волчо́нок [*gen.* **-нка;** *pl.* **-ча́та, -ча́т**] *n.* wolf cub.

волше́бник *n.* magician; wizard; sorcerer.

волше́бный *adj.* **1,** magic; magical. **2,** *fig.* enchanting; captivating. —**волше́бная ска́зка,** fairy tale.

волшебство́ *n.* magic.

волы́нка *n.* **1,** bagpipe; bagpipes. **2,** *colloq.* delay; dawdling; procrastination. —**волы́нщик,** *n.* piper.

вольго́тный *adj., colloq.* free; free and easy.

волье́р *also,* **волье́ра** *n.* enclosure (*for animals or birds*).

во́льничать *v. impfv., colloq.* to take liberties.

во́льно *adv.* **1,** freely; voluntarily. **2,** loosely. **3,** *mil.* at ease. —*interj., mil.* at ease!; as you were!

вольноду́мец [*gen.* **-мца**] *n., obs.* freethinker. —**вольноду́мный,** *adj., obs.* freethinking. —**вольноду́мство,** *n., obs.* free thought.

вольнолюби́вый *adj.* freedom-loving.

вольнонаёмный *adj.* civilian.

вольнослу́шатель *n.m., obs.* non-matriculated student.

во́льность *n.f.* **1,** freedom; liberty; license. **2,** undue familiarity; liberties. —**поэти́ческая во́льность,** poetic license.

во́льный *adj.* **1,** free. **2,** unrestricted. **3,** unduly familiar. **4,** [*short form only* — **во́лен, вольна́**] (*with inf.*) free (to); at liberty (to).

вольт [*gen. pl.* **вольт**] *n.* volt.

вольта́ж [*gen.* **-тажа́**] *n.* voltage.

вольтме́тр *n.* voltmeter.

вольфра́м *n.* tungsten. —**вольфра́мовый,** *adj.* tungsten.

во́ля *n.* **1,** will. **2,** freedom. **3,** *hist.* emancipation. —**во́ля ва́ша,** as you please. —**дава́ть во́лю** (+ *dat.*), to give free rein to. —**до́брая во́ля,** good will. —**отпуска́ть на во́лю,** to set free. —**по до́брой во́ле,** of one's own free will. —**после́дняя во́ля,** last will and testament. —**си́ла во́ли,** will power.

вон *adv., colloq.* out; away: он вы́шел вон, he went out; пошёл вон!, away with you! У меня́ э́то из ума́ вон, it completely slipped my mind. —*particle* there; over there: вон там, over there. Вон он идёт, there he goes. —*interj.* be off!; get out!

вонза́ть *v. impfv.* [*pfv.* **вонзи́ть**] (*with* **в** + *acc.*) to thrust (into); plunge (into). —**вонза́ться,** *refl.* (*with* **в** + *acc.*) to pierce; enter.

вонзи́ть [*infl.* **вонжу́, вонзи́шь**] *v., pfv. of* **вонза́ть.** —**вонзи́ться,** *refl., pfv. of* **вонза́ться.**

вонь *n.f., colloq.* stink; stench.

воню́чий *adj., colloq.* stinking.

воню́чка [*gen. pl.* **-чек**] *n.* skunk.

воня́ть *v. impfv., colloq.* **1,** to stink. **2,** (*with* **от**) to reek (of).

вообража́емый *adj.* imaginary.

вообража́ть *v. impfv.* [*pfv.* **вообрази́ть**] to imagine.

воображе́ние *n.* imagination.

вообрази́мый *adj.* imaginable.

вообрази́ть [*infl.* **-жу́, -зи́шь**] *v., pfv. of* **вообража́ть.**

вообще́ *adv.* **1,** in general. **2,** always. **3,** *fol. by* **не** (not) at all. —**вообще́ говоря́,** generally speaking.

воодушеви́ть [*infl.* **-влю́, -ви́шь**] *v., pfv. of* **воодушевля́ть.**

воодушевле́ние *n.* enthusiasm; animation.

воодушевля́ть *v. impfv.* [*pfv.* **воодушеви́ть**] to inspire; fill with enthusiasm.

вооружа́ть *v. impfv.* [*pfv.* **вооружи́ть**] **1,** to arm. **2,** to equip; supply. **3,** (*with* **про́тив**) to set against. —**вооружа́ться,** *refl.* to arm (oneself).

вооруже́ние *n.* **1,** arming; armament. **2,** *often pl.* armaments; arms: го́нка вооруже́ний, arms race. —**брать** *or* **принима́ть (что́-нибудь) на вооруже́ние,** to add to one's arsenal; place in service.

вооружённый *adj.* armed. —**вооружённые си́лы,** armed forces.

вооружи́ть *v., pfv. of* **вооружа́ть.** —**вооружи́ться,** *refl., pfv. of* **вооружа́ться.**

воо́чию *adv.* **1,** with one's own eyes: воо́чию убеди́ться, to see for oneself. **2,** clearly; graphically.

во-пе́рвых in the first place; to begin with.

вопи́ть *v. impfv.* [*pres.* **воплю́, вопи́шь**] *colloq.* to cry out.

вопию́щий *adj.* **1,** outrageous; appalling. **2,** glaring; flagrant. —**глас вопию́щего в пусты́не,** voice in the wilderness.

воплоща́ть *v. impfv.* [*pfv.* **воплоти́ть**] to embody; personify. —**воплоща́ть в жизнь,** to make a reality of.

воплоще́ние *n.* embodiment.

вопль *n.m.* cry; howl; wail.

вопреки́ *prep., with dat.* contrary to; in defiance of.

вопро́с *n.* **1,** question. **2,** problem; matter. —**под вопро́сом,** open to question; undecided. —**ста́вить под вопро́с,** to question; call into question.

вопроси́тельный *adj.* **1,** questioning; inquiring. **2,** *gram.* interrogative. —**вопроси́тельный знак,** question mark.

вопро́сник *n.* questionnaire.

вор [*pl.* **во́ры, воро́в, вора́м**] *n.* thief. —**карма́нный вор,** pickpocket. —**магази́нный вор,** shoplifter.

во́рвань *n.f.* blubber.

ворва́ться [*infl. like* **рвать**] *v.r., pfv. of* **врыва́ться.**

вори́шка [*gen. pl.* **-шек**] *n.m.* petty thief.

воркова́ть *v. impfv.* [*pres.* **-ку́ю, -ку́ешь**] **1,** to coo. **2,** *fig.* to bill and coo.

воркотня́ *n., colloq.* grumbling; griping.

воробе́й [*gen.* **-бья́**] *n.* sparrow. —**стре́ляный воробе́й,** *colloq.* old hand.

воробьи́ный *adj.* sparrow's.
воро́ванный *adj.* stolen.
ворова́тый *adj.* **1,** thievish. **2,** furtive.
ворова́ть *v. impfv.* [*pres.* **-ру́ю, -ру́ешь**] to steal.
воро́вка [*gen. pl.* **-вок**] *n., fem. of* **вор.**
воровски́ *adv., colloq.* **1,** dishonestly. **2,** furtively.
воровско́й *adj.* thieves'.
воровство́ *n.* stealing; theft; larceny.
ворожба́ *n.* fortunetelling. —**ворожея́,** *n.* fortuneteller.
ворожи́ть *v. impfv.* [*pfv.* **поворожи́ть**] to tell fortunes.
во́рон *n.* raven.
воро́на *n.* crow.
воро́ний [*fem.* **-нья**] *adj.* **1,** crow's. **2,** of crows: воро́нья ста́я, flock of crows.
ворони́ть *v. impfv.* to burnish.
воро́нка [*gen. pl.* **-нок**] *n.* **1,** funnel. **2,** bomb crater.
вороно́й *adj.* (*of a horse*) black. —*n.* black horse.
во́рот *n.* **1,** collar. **2,** winch.
воро́та [*gen.* **воро́т**] *n. pl.* **1,** gate. **2,** *sports* goal; net.
вороти́ла *n.m., colloq.* bigwig.
вороти́ть *v. impfv.* [*pres.* **-рочу́, -ро́тишь**] *colloq.* to bring back. —**вороти́ться,** *refl., colloq.* to return; come back.
воротни́к [*gen.* **-ника́**] *n.* collar.
воротничо́к [*gen.* **-чка́**] *n., dim. of* **воротни́к.**
во́рох [*pl.* **вороха́**] *n.* pile; heap.
воро́чать *v. impfv.* **1,** to move; shift; roll; turn. **2,** (*with instr.*) *colloq.* to boss; manage; manipulate. —**воро́чаться,** *refl., colloq.* to turn from side to side; toss and turn.
вороши́ть *v. impfv.* **1,** to stir. **2,** to pitch (hay). —**вороши́ться,** *refl.* to stir; move about.
ворс *n.* nap; pile (*on cloth*).
ворси́нка [*gen. pl.* **-нок**] *n.* hair; fiber.
ворча́ние *n.* **1,** growling. **2,** *colloq.* grumbling; griping.
ворча́ть *v. impfv.* [*pres.* **-чу́, -чи́шь**] **1,** (*with* **на** + *acc.*) to growl (at). **2,** *colloq.* to grumble; gripe.
ворчли́вый *adj.* grumbling; grouchy; grumpy; surly.
ворчу́н [*gen.* **-чуна́**] *n.m.* [*fem.* **-чу́нья**] grumbler; griper.
вос- *prefix, var. of* **воз-** (*used before voiceless consonants*).
восвоя́си *adv., colloq.* home: пойти́ восвоя́си, to go home.
восемна́дцать *numeral* eighteen. —**восемна́дцатый,** *ordinal numeral* eighteenth.
во́семь [*gen., dat., & prepl.* **восьми́;** *instr.* **восьмью́** *or* **восемью́**] *numeral* eight.
во́семьдесят [*gen., dat., & prepl.* **восьми́десяти;** *instr.* **восьмью́десятью** *or* **восемью́десятью**] *numeral* eighty.
восемьсо́т [*gen.* **восьмисо́т;** *dat.* **восьмиста́м;** *instr.* **восьмьюста́ми** *or* **восемьюста́ми;** *prepl.* **восьмиста́х**] *numeral* eight hundred.
во́семью *adv.* eight times: во́семью де́сять – во́семьдесят, eight times ten is eighty.
воск *n.* wax.
воскли́кнуть *v., pfv. of* **восклица́ть.**
восклица́ние *n.* exclamation.
восклица́тельный *adj.* exclamatory; exclamation (*attrib.*). —**восклица́тельный знак,** exclamation point.
восклица́ть *v. impfv.* [*pfv.* **воскли́кнуть**] to exclaim.
восково́й *adj.* **1,** wax (*attrib.*). **2,** waxy; waxen.
воскреса́ть *v. impfv.* [*pfv.* **воскре́снуть**] **1,** to rise from the dead; come back to life. **2,** to regain one's strength; revive. **3,** to come back to mind.
воскресе́ние *n.* **1,** resurrection. **2,** *fig.* revival.
воскресе́нье *n.* Sunday.
воскреси́ть [*infl.* **-шу́, -си́шь**] *v., pfv. of* **воскреша́ть.**
воскре́снуть [*past* **-кре́с, -ла**] *v., pfv. of* **воскреса́ть.**
воскре́сный *adj.* Sunday (*attrib.*).
воскреша́ть *v. impfv.* [*pfv.* **воскреси́ть**] **1,** to resurrect; raise from the dead; bring back to life. **2,** to revive; resurrect (a custom, hopes, etc.). **3,** to revitalize. **4,** *in* воскреша́ть в па́мяти, to (re)call to mind.
воскреше́ние *n.* resurrection; revival.
воспале́ние *n.* inflammation. —**воспале́ние лёгких,** pneumonia. —**воспале́ние не́рвов,** neuritis.
воспалённый *adj.* inflamed.
воспали́тельный *adj.* inflammatory; inflammation (*attrib.*).
воспаля́ть *v. impfv.* [*pfv.* **воспали́ть**] *obs.* to inflame. —**воспаля́ться,** *refl.* to become inflamed.
воспева́ть *v. impfv.* [*pfv.* **воспе́ть**] to praise; extol (*in verse or song*).
воспе́ть [*infl.* **-пою́, -поёшь**] *v., pfv. of* **воспева́ть.**
воспита́ние *n.* **1,** raising; rearing; bringing up. **2,** upbringing. **3,** education. **4,** (good) breeding. **5,** fostering; cultivating.
воспи́танник *n.* **1,** pupil. **2,** adopted child; ward. **3,** (*with gen.*) graduate (of); alumnus (of).
воспи́танность *n.f.* (good) breeding.
воспи́танный *adj.* well-bred; well-mannered.
воспита́тель *n.m.* educator; teacher; mentor. —**воспита́тельница,** *n.* teacher; governess.
воспита́тельный *adj.* educational. —**воспита́тельный дом,** *pre-rev.* foundling home.
воспи́тывать *v. impfv.* [*pfv.* **воспита́ть**] **1,** to raise; bring up; rear. **2,** to educate; train. **3,** to foster; cultivate.
воспламене́ние *n.* **1,** combustion. **2,** ignition.
воспламени́ть *v., pfv. of* **воспламеня́ть.** —**воспламени́ться,** *refl., pfv. of* **воспламеня́ться.**
воспламеня́емость *n.f.* inflammability.
воспламеня́ть *v. impfv.* [*pfv.* **воспламени́ть**] **1,** to ignite; kindle. **2,** *fig.* to rouse; fire (up). —**воспламеня́ться,** *refl.* **1,** to flare up; burst into flames. **2,** *fig.* (*with instr.*) to become fired (with).
восполня́ть *v. impfv.* [*pfv.* **воспо́лнить**] to fill (a gap); make up for (a deficiency).
воспо́льзоваться *v.r., pfv. of* **по́льзоваться.**
воспомина́ние *n.* **1,** memory; recollection. **2,** *pl.* memoirs; reminiscences.
воспрепя́тствовать *v., pfv. of* **препя́тствовать.**
воспрети́ть [*infl.* **-щу́, -ти́шь**] *v., pfv. of* **воспреща́ть.**
воспреща́ть *v. impfv.* [*pfv.* **воспрети́ть**] **1,** to prohibit; forbid. **2,** *mil.* to interdict. —**воспреща́ться,** *refl.* [*impfv. only*] to be prohibited; be forbidden.
воспреще́ние *n.* **1,** prohibition. **2,** *mil.* interdiction.
восприи́мчивость *n.f.* **1,** receptivity. **2,** susceptibility.
восприи́мчивый *adj.* **1,** keen; receptive. **2,** (*with* **к**) susceptible (to).
воспринима́ть *v. impfv.* [*pfv.* **восприня́ть**] **1,** to perceive. **2,** to take in; assimilate; absorb (*mentally*). **3,** (*with* **как**) to take (as).
восприня́ть [*infl. like* **приня́ть**] *v., pfv. of* **воспринима́ть.**

восприя́тие *n.* perception.
воспроизведе́ние *n.* reproduction.
воспроизвести́ [*infl. like* **вести́**] *v., pfv. of* **воспроизводи́ть.**
воспроизводи́тельный *adj.* reproductive.
воспроизводи́ть *v. impfv.* [*pfv.* **воспроизвести́;** *pres.* **-вожу́, -во́дишь**] to reproduce.
воспроти́виться *v.r., pfv. of* **проти́виться.**
воспря́нуть *v. pfv., obs.* to leap up. —**воспря́нуть ду́хом,** to cheer up; perk up; take heart.
воспыла́ть *v. pfv.* **1,** *obs.* to flare up; burst into flame. **2,** *fig.* (*with instr.*) to become fired (with).
воссоедине́ние *n.* reunification.
воссоединя́ть *v. impfv.* [*pfv.* **воссоедини́ть**] to reunite. —**воссоединя́ться,** *refl.* to be reunited.
воссоздава́ть *v. impfv.* [*pfv.* **воссозда́ть;** *pres.* **-даю́, -даёшь**] **1,** to re-create. **2,** to (mentally) reconstruct.
воссозда́ть [*infl. like* **дать;** *past* **-да́л, -ла́, -да́ло**] *v., pfv. of* **воссоздава́ть.**
восстава́ть *v. impfv.* [*pfv.* **восста́ть;** *pres.* **-стаю́, -стаёшь**] to revolt; rebel.
восстана́вливать *v. impfv.* [*pfv.* **восстанови́ть**] **1,** to restore; re-establish. **2,** to recover; regain (one's health, strength, etc.). **3,** (*with* **про́тив**) to set against. —**восстана́вливать про́тив себя́,** to antagonize.
восста́ние *n.* revolt; rebellion; uprising; insurrection.
восстанови́ть [*infl.* **-новлю́, -но́вишь**] *v., pfv. of* **восстана́вливать.**
восстановле́ние *n.* **1,** restoration. **2,** recovery (*of one's health*).
восста́ть [*infl.* **-ста́ну, -ста́нешь**] *v., pfv. of* **восстава́ть.**
восто́к *n.* **1,** east. **2,** *cap.* the East.
востокове́д *n.* Orientalist. —**востокове́дение,** *n.* Oriental studies.
восто́рг *n.* ecstasy: быть в восто́рге от, to be in ecstasy over; be ecstatic about.
восторга́ть *v. impfv.* to delight; enchant; enrapture. —**восторга́ться,** *refl.* (*with instr.*) to be in ecstasy (over); be enchanted (with).
восто́рженность *n.f.* ecstasy; delight.
восто́рженный *adj.* ecstatic; rapturous.
восторжествова́ть *v., pfv. of* **торжествова́ть.**
восто́чный *adj.* **1,** eastern; East; easterly. **2,** oriental.
востре́бование *n.* claiming. —**до востре́бования,** general delivery.
востре́бовать *v. pfv.* [*infl.* **-бую, -буешь**] to claim.
востро́ *adv., in* **держа́ть у́хо востро́,** *colloq.* to be on one's guard.
восхвале́ние *n.* **1,** extolling. **2,** acclaim.
восхвали́ть [*infl.* **-хвалю́, -хва́лишь**] *v., pfv. of* **восхваля́ть.**
восхваля́ть *v. impfv.* [*pfv.* **восхвали́ть**] to laud; extol; eulogize.
восхити́тельный *adj.* captivating; enchanting.
восхити́ть [*infl.* **-щу́, -ти́шь**] *v., pfv. of* **восхища́ть.** —**восхити́ться,** *refl., pfv. of* **восхища́ться.**
восхища́ть *v. impfv.* [*pfv.* **восхити́ть**] to captivate; enchant. —**восхища́ться,** *refl.* (*with instr.*) to be captivated (by); be enchanted (with).
восхище́ние *n.* delight; enchantment; admiration.
восхо́д *n.* rise. —**восхо́д со́лнца,** sunrise.
восходи́ть *v. impfv.* [*pfv.* **взойти́;** *pres.* **-хожу́, -хо́дишь**] **1,** = **всходи́ть. 2,** [*impfv. only*] (*with* **к**) to go back to; date back to.
восходя́щий *adj.* rising. —**восходя́щая звезда́,** *fig.* rising star.
восхожде́ние *n.* ascent.
восше́ствие *n., obs.* ascent. —**восше́ствие на престо́л,** accession to the throne.
восьма́я *n., decl. as an adj.* eighth: одна́ восьма́я, one-eighth.
восьмёрка *n.* **1,** the numeral 8. **2,** *colloq.* anything numbered 8. **3,** figure eight (*in skating, flying, etc.*). **4,** *cards* eight.
во́сьмеро *collective numeral* eight.
восьмигра́нник *n.* octahedron. —**восьмигра́нный,** *adj.* octahedral.
восьмидеся́тый *ordinal numeral* eightieth.
восьмиле́тний *adj.* **1,** eight-year (*attrib.*). **2,** eight-year-old.
восьмино́г *n.* octopus.
восьмисо́тый *ordinal numeral* eight-hundredth.
восьмиуго́льник *n.* octagon. —**восьмиуго́льный,** *adj.* octagonal.
восьмичасово́й *adj.* eight-hour (*attrib.*).
восьмо́й *ordinal numeral* eighth.
восьму́шка [*gen. pl.* **-шек**] *n.* **1,** eighth of a pound. **2,** octavo.
вот *particle* **1,** here (is): вот ва́ша кни́га, here is your book; вот он идёт, here he comes. **2,** (*with* **где, как, что**) this is; that is: вот где я живу́, this is where I live. **3,** *used for emphasis:* вот э́то на́до посмотре́ть!, you really must see it! —**вот как!; вот что!,** really!; you don't say! —**вот так так!,** well, I never!; well, I'll be! —**вот тебе́ и...,** so much for... —**вот э́то да!,** now that's something like it!
вот-во́т *adv., colloq., used with future tense of verbs* (just) about to: он вот-во́т уйдёт, he is (just) about to leave.
воткну́ть *v., pfv. of* **втыка́ть.**
во́тум *n.* vote. —**во́тум (не)дове́рия,** vote of (no) confidence.
во́тчина *n., hist.* ancestral lands; estate; patrimony.
воцаря́ться *v.r. impfv.* [*pfv.* **воцари́ться**] **1,** *obs.* to ascend the throne. **2,** *fig.* to set in; be established: воцари́лась тишина́, silence reigned.
вошь [*gen., dat., & prepl.* **вши;** *instr.* **во́шью**] *n.f.* louse.
воща́нка *n.* wax paper.
вощёный *adj.* waxed.
вощи́ть *v. impfv.* [*pfv.* **навощи́ть**] to wax.
вою́ющий *adj.* warring; belligerent.
voя́ка *n.m., colloq., ironic* warrior.
впада́ть *v. impfv.* [*pfv.* **впасть**] **1,** [*impfv. only*] (*with* **в** + *acc.*) to flow (into); empty (into). **2,** to become hollow; become sunken. **3,** *fig.* (*with* **в** + *acc.*) to fall (into); sink (into); lapse (into).
впаде́ние *n.* **1,** emptying (*of a river into a larger body of water*). **2,** confluence: при впаде́нии (*or* у впаде́ния) реки́ Оки́ в Во́лгу, at the confluence of the Oka and Volga; where the Oka flows into the Volga.
впа́дина *n.* **1,** hollow; depression; cavity. **2,** *anat.* socket: глазна́я впа́дина, eye socket.
впа́лый *adj.* hollow; sunken.
впасть [*infl. like* **пасть**] *v., pfv. of* **впада́ть.**
впервы́е *adv.* first; for the first time.

вперева́лку *adv., colloq., in* **ходи́ть вперева́лку,** to waddle.

вперёд *adv.* **1,** forward; ahead. **2,** *colloq.* henceforth; from now on. **3,** *colloq.* ahead of time; beforehand; in advance.

впереди́ *adv.* **1,** in front; ahead. **2,** ahead; yet to occur: что нас ждёт впереди́?, what lies ahead for us? Развя́зка ещё впереди́, the climax is yet to come. —*prep., with gen.* in front of; ahead of.

впереме́жку *adv., colloq.* alternately.

впереме́шку *adv., colloq.* pell-mell; every which way.

впечатле́ние *n.* impression.

впечатли́тельный *adj.* impressionable.

впечатля́ющий *adj.* impressive.

впива́ть *v. impfv.* [*pfv.* **впить**] to absorb; imbibe. —**впива́ться,** *refl.* (*with* **в** + *acc.*) **1,** (*of something sharp*) to stick (in). **2,** (*with instr.*) to sink (one's teeth, claws, etc.) into. **3,** *fig.* (*with instr.*) to fix (one's eyes, gaze, etc.) on.

вписа́ть [*infl.* **впишу́, впи́шешь**] *v., pfv. of* **впи́сывать.** —**вписа́ться,** *refl., pfv. of* **впи́сываться.**

впи́сывать *v. impfv.* [*pfv.* **вписа́ть**] (*with* **в** + *acc.*) **1,** to write in; enter; insert. **2,** *math.* to inscribe. —**впи́сываться,** *refl.* (*with* **в** + *acc.*) **1,** *colloq.* to enroll (in); join. **2,** to blend in (with).

впи́тывать *v. impfv.* [*pfv.* **впита́ть**] to absorb; soak up.

впить [*infl.* **вопью́, вопьёшь;** *past fem.* **впила́**] *v., pfv. of* **впива́ть.** —**впи́ться,** *refl., pfv. of* **впива́ться.**

впи́хивать *v. impfv.* [*pfv.* **впихну́ть**] *colloq.* **1,** to stuff in; cram in; force in. **2,** to push in; shove in.

вплавь *adv.* by swimming.

вплести́ [*infl. like* **плести́**] *v., pfv. of* **вплета́ть.**

вплета́ть *v. impfv.* [*pfv.* **вплести́**] to entwine; intertwine.

вплотну́ю *adv.* **1,** closely; tightly. **2,** (*with* **к**) right up to; right up against. **3,** *fig., colloq.* in earnest.

вплоть *adv., usu. in* **вплоть до** (+ *gen.*), **1,** right up to. **2,** down to.

вплыва́ть *v. impfv.* [*pfv.* **вплыть**] **1,** to swim in. **2,** to sail in.

вплыть [*infl. like* **плыть**] *v., pfv. of* **вплыва́ть.**

впова́лку *adv., colloq.* side by side: лежа́ть/спать впова́лку, to lie/sleep side by side.

вполго́лоса *adv.* in a low voice; under one's breath; in an undertone.

вполза́ть *v. impfv.* [*pfv.* **вползти́**] (*with* **в** + *acc.*) **1,** to crawl into; creep into. **2,** to crawl up; creep up.

вползти́ [*infl. like* **ползти́**] *v., pfv. of* **вполза́ть.**

вполне́ *adv.* fully; entirely; completely; quite.

вполоборо́та *adv.* (*with* **к**) half-turned (toward).

впопа́д *adv., colloq.* to the point.

впопыха́х *adv.* **1,** hastily; hurriedly. **2,** in one's haste.

впо́ру *adv., colloq.* of the right size: пла́тье вам впо́ру, the dress is the right size for you.

впорхну́ть *v. pfv.* to fly in; flit in.

впосле́дствии *adv.* afterwards; subsequently; later on.

впотьма́х *adv.* in the dark.

впра́вду *adv., colloq.* really.

впра́ве *adv.* having a right: она́ впра́ве горди́ться, she has a right to be proud.

впра́вить [*infl.* **-влю, -вишь**] *v., pfv. of* **вправля́ть.**

вправля́ть *v. impfv.* [*pfv.* **впра́вить**] **1,** to set (a bone, joint, etc.). **2,** (*with* **в** + *acc.*) *colloq.* to tuck into.

впра́во *adv.* to the right.

впредь *adv.* hereafter; henceforth; from now on. —**впредь до,** until; pending.

вприку́ску *adv., in* **пить чай вприку́ску,** to drink tea holding a lump of sugar in one's mouth.

вприпры́жку *adv., in* **бежа́ть вприпры́жку,** to skip along.

вприся́дку *adv.* in a squatting position (*while dancing*).

впри́тык *adv.* (*with* **к**) *colloq.* flush (against).

впро́голодь *adv.* hungry: жить/пита́ться впро́голодь, to go hungry.

впрок *adv.* **1,** in store; for future use: заготовля́ть впрок, to store up; stock up on. **2,** (*usu. with* **идти́**) to one's advantage: э́то вам не пойдёт впрок, it won't do you any good. Ему́ всё (идёт) впрок, everything goes right for him.

впроса́к *adv., in* **попа́сть впроса́к,** *colloq.* to commit a gaffe; put one's foot in it.

впросо́нках *adv., colloq.* while half-asleep.

впро́чем *conj.* **1,** however; but; though. **2,** but then; but then again.

впры́гивать *v. impfv.* [*pfv.* **впры́гнуть**] **1,** (*with* **в** + *acc.*) to jump into. **2,** (*with* **на** + *acc.*) to jump onto.

впры́скивание *n.* injection.

впры́скивать *v. impfv.* [*pfv.* **впры́снуть**] to inject.

впряга́ть *v. impfv.* [*pfv.* **впрячь**] (*with* **в** + *acc.*) to harness (to); hitch (to).

впряму́ю *adv., colloq.* directly.

впрямь *adv., colloq.* really; indeed.

впрячь [*infl.* **впрягу́, впряжёшь, ...впрягу́т;** *past* **впряг, -ла́, -ло́**] *v., pfv. of* **впряга́ть.**

впуск *n.* **1,** admission; admittance. **2,** intake.

впуска́ть *v. impfv.* [*pfv.* **впусти́ть**] to admit; let in.

впусти́ть [*infl.* **впущу́, впу́стишь**] *v., pfv. of* **впуска́ть.**

впусту́ю *adv., colloq.* in vain; for nothing.

впу́тать *v., pfv. of* **пу́тать** (*in sense #6*) *and* **впу́тывать.** —**впу́таться,** *refl., pfv. of* **пу́таться** (*in sense #3*) *and* **впу́тываться.**

впу́тывать *v. impfv.* [*pfv.* **впу́тать**] (*with* **в** + *acc.*) *colloq.* to involve (in); embroil (in). —**впу́тываться,** *refl.* (*with* **в** + *acc.*) *colloq.* to get mixed up (in).

впя́теро *adv.* five times: впя́теро бо́льше, five times as much.

впятеро́м *adv.* five together: они́ впятеро́м, the five of them.

враг [*gen.* **врага́**] *n.* enemy.

вражда́ *n.* hostility; animosity; enmity.

вражде́бный *adj.* hostile. —**вражде́бно,** *adv.* with hostility; with animosity. —**вражде́бность,** *n.f.* hostility; animosity.

враждова́ть *v. impfv.* [*pres.* **-ду́ю, -ду́ешь**] (*with* **с** + *instr.*) to feud (with); be at odds (with).

вра́жеский *adj.* enemy (*attrib.*); hostile.

вразби́вку *adv., colloq.* at random; in no particular order.

вразбро́д *adv., colloq.* **1,** separately; not together. **2,** without coordination.

вразбро́с *adv., colloq.* scattered about; every which way.

вразва́лку *adv., colloq., in* **ходи́ть вразва́лку,** to waddle.

вразно́с *adv., colloq., in* **торгова́ть вразно́с,** to peddle.

вразре́з *adv., in* **идти́ вразре́з с** (+ *instr.*), to run counter to; go against.

вразумúтельный *adj.* clear; intelligible; understandable.
вразумля́ть *v. impfv.* [*pfv.* **вразумúть**] to make (someone) understand; bring to reason.
врáки [*gen.* **врак**] *n. pl., colloq.* **1,** nonsense. **2,** lies.
враль [*gen.* **враля́**] *n.m., colloq.* **1,** liar. **2,** chatterbox.
враньё *n., colloq.* **1,** lying. **2,** lies.
врасплóх *adv., in* **застáть** *or* **застúгнуть врасплóх,** to take by surprise; catch unawares.
врассыпнýю *adv.* in all directions; helter-skelter; every which way.
врастáть *v. impfv.* [*pfv.* **врастú**] (*with* **в** + *acc.*) **1,** to grow into. **2,** to become embedded (in).
врастú [*infl. like* **растú**] *v., pfv. of* **врастáть.**
врастя́жку *adv., colloq.* **1,** flat; stretched out. **2,** in a drawl.
вратáрь [*gen.* **-таря́**] *n.m.* **1,** *obs.* gatekeeper. **2,** *sports* goalkeeper; goalie.
врать *v. impfv.* [*pfv.* **совráть;** *pres.* **вру, врёшь;** *past fem.* **вралá**] *colloq.* to lie; tell lies.
врач [*gen.* **врачá**] *n.* doctor; physician. —**зубнóй врач,** dentist.
врачéбный *adj.* medical.
вращáтельный *adj.* rotary.
вращáть *v. impfv.* to rotate; turn (*trans. verb*). —**вращáться,** *refl.* **1,** to revolve; rotate; turn (*intrans.*). **2,** (*with* **в** + *prepl.*) *fig.* to move (*in certain circles*).
вращéние *n.* rotation.
вред [*gen.* **вредá**] *n.* harm; injury; damage. —**во вред** (+ *dat.*), to the detriment of.
вредúтель *n.m.* **1,** pest; *pl.* vermin. **2,** economic saboteur. —**вредúтельство,** *n.* economic sabotage.
вредúть *v. impfv.* [*pfv.* **повредúть;** *pres.* **врежý, вредúшь**] (*with dat.*) to harm; damage; be injurious to.
врéдно *adv.* in a harmful manner: врéдно дéйствовать на, to have a harmful effect on. —*adj., used predicatively* harmful; bad: врéдно для зрéния, bad for one's eyesight.
врéдный *adj.* harmful; damaging; detrimental; injurious.
вредонóсный *adj.* harmful.
врéзать [*infl.* **врéжу, врéжешь**] *v., pfv. of* **врезáть** *and* **врéзывать.** —**врéзаться,** *refl., pfv. of* **врезáться** *and* **врéзываться.**
врезáть *v. impfv.* [*pfv.* **врéзать**] (*with* **в** + *acc.*) **1,** to cut into; fit into. **2,** *fig.* to embed (in one's memory). —**врезáться,** *refl.* (*with* **в** + *acc.*) **1,** to cut into. **2,** (*of a vehicle, airplane, etc.*) to crash (into); slam (into); plunge (into). **3,** *fig.* to become ingrained (in one's memory).
врéзывать *v. impfv.* = **врезáть.** —**врéзываться,** *refl.* = **врезáться.**
врéменно *adv.* temporarily.
временнóй *adj.* time (*attrib.*); temporal.
врéменный *adj.* **1,** temporary. **2,** provisional.
врéмя [*gen., dat., & prepl.* **врéмени;** *instr.* **врéменем;** *pl.* **временá, времён, временáм**] *n. neut.* **1,** time. **2,** *gram.* tense. **3,** *in* врéмя гóда, season. —**во врéмя** (+ *gen.*), during. —**во временá** (+ *gen.*), in (someone's) time. —**во все временá,** at all times. —**в** (*or* **за**) **послéднее врéмя,** recently; of late. —**временáми,** at times; now and then. —**врéмя от врéмени,** from time to time. —**в своё врéмя, 1,** in one's time. **2,** in due time; in due course. —**всё врéмя,** all the time. —**в скóром врéмени,** before long; shortly. —**в то врéмя как,** while; whereas. —**в то же врéмя,** at the same time. —**на врéмя,** for a while; for a time. —**на врéмя** (+ *gen.*), for the duration of. —**однó врéмя,** at one time. —**пéрвое врéмя,** at first. —**по временáм,** from time to time. —**скóлько врéмени?, 1,** how long? **2,** what time?: скóлько врéмени сейчáс/у вас?/, what time is it/have you got? —**со врéменем,** in time. —**со врéмени** (+ *gen.*), since. —**тем врéменем,** meanwhile.
время́нка [*gen. pl.* **-нок**] *n., colloq.* temporary structure.
времяпрепровождéние *n.* way of spending time; pastime. *Also,* **времяпровождéние.**
врóвень *adv.* (*with* **с** + *instr.*) on a level (with); even (with); flush (with).
врóде *prep., with gen.* **1,** like; not unlike. **2,** a sort of. —*particle, colloq.* **1,** (*with nouns*) such as; like. **2,** (*with verbs*) seems to (have).
врождённый *adj.* innate; inborn; inherent; congenital.
врозь *adv.* apart: жить врозь, to live apart.
врубáть *v. impfv.* [*pfv.* **врубúть**] (*with* **в** + *acc.*) to place; set (in an opening that has been cut out). —**врубáться,** *refl.* (*with* **в** + *acc.*) to cut one's way (into *or* through).
врубúть [*infl.* **врублю́, врýбишь**] *v., pfv. of* **врубáть.** —**врубúться,** *refl., pfv. of* **врубáться.**
врукопáшную *adv.* in hand-to-hand combat: бúться врукопáшную, to engage in hand-to-hand combat.
врун [*gen.* **врунá**] *n.m.* [*fem.* **врýнья**] *colloq.* liar.
вручáть *v. impfv.* [*pfv.* **вручúть**] **1,** to hand over; deliver; present. **2,** *fig.* to entrust.
вручéние *n.* delivery; presentation.
вручúть *v., pfv. of* **вручáть.**
вручнýю *adv.* by hand; manually.
врывáть *v. impfv.* [*pfv.* **врыть**] (*with* **в** + *acc.*) to implant; set (in the ground).
врывáться *v.r. impfv.* [*pfv.* **ворвáться**] (*with* **в** + *acc.*) **1,** to burst into. **2,** to break into.
врыть [*infl.* **врóю, врóешь**] *v., pfv. of* **врывáть.**
вряд ли *particle* hardly; it is unlikely; I doubt whether...: вряд ли он придёт, I doubt whether he is coming.
всадúть [*infl.* **всажý, всáдишь**] *v., pfv. of* **всáживать.**
всáдник *n.* rider; horseman.
всáживать *v. impfv.* [*pfv.* **всадúть**] (*with* **в** + *acc.*) **1,** to plunge (a knife) into; put (a bullet) in. **2,** *colloq.* to sink (money) into.
всáсывание *n.* **1,** suction. **2,** absorption.
всáсывать *v. impfv.* [*pfv.* **всосáть**] to suck in; absorb. —**всáсываться,** *refl.* (*with* **в** + *acc.*) **1,** to be absorbed in. **2,** to be sucked into (a swamp, morass, etc.).
все *adj., pl. of* **весь.** —*indef. pron.* everybody; everyone. —**все и вся,** *colloq.* [*acc.* **всех и вся**] everybody and everything. *See also* **весь.**
всё *adj., neut. of* **весь:** всё врéмя, all the time. —*indef. pron.* everything; all: э́то всё, that's all; всё в поря́дке, everything is all right. —*adv., colloq.* **1,** constantly; all the time: телефóн всё звонúт, the phone keeps ringing (all the time). **2,** still. **3,** (*with comp. adjectives and some verbs*) more and more; -er and -er: всё лýчше и лýчше, better and better; все бóлее интерéсный, more and more interesting. Он всё слабéет, he keeps getting weaker and weaker. —**всё ещё; всё же,** still; all the same. —**всё равнó,** *see* **равнó.** —**при всём том,** for all that. *See also* **весь.**
всевéдение *n.* omniscience.

всеве́дущий *adj.* omniscient.
всевозмо́жный *adj.* all sorts of; all kinds of; every possible.
всегда́ *adv.* always. —**как всегда́,** as always; as usual.
всегда́шний *adj., colloq.* regular; usual; customary.
всего́ *adj., gen. of* **весь.** —*adv.* **1,** in all. **2,** only. —*interj.* so long! —**всего́ хоро́шего**!; **всего́ до́брого**!, all the best! —**всего́-на́всего,** only; nothing but.
всезна́йка *n.m. & f., colloq.* know-it-all.
вселе́ние *n.* moving in: вселе́ние в но́вый дом, moving into a new house.
вселе́нная *n., decl. as an adj.* universe.
вселе́нский *adj.* ecumenical.
вселя́ть *v. impfv.* [*pfv.* **всели́ть**] (*with* **в** + *acc.*) **1,** to move; settle (people) into. **2,** *fig.* to instill (hope, confidence, etc.) into; strike (fear) into. —**вселя́ться,** *refl.* (*with* **в** + *acc.*) **1,** to move into; settle in. **2,** *fig.* (*of an emotion*) to fill; seize.
всеме́рный *adj.* all possible: всеме́рная подде́ржка, all possible support. —**всеме́рно,** *adv.* in every (possible) way.
всеми́рный *adj.* world (*attrib.*); worldwide; universal. —**всеми́рная вы́ставка,** world's fair.
всемогу́щество *n.* omnipotence. —**всемогу́щий,** *adj.* all-powerful; almighty; omnipotent.
всенаро́дный *adj.* nationwide; national.
все́нощная *n., decl. as an adj.* vespers.
всео́бщий *adj.* universal; general.
всеобъе́млющий *adj.* all-embracing; comprehensive.
всеору́жие *n., in* **во всеору́жии,** fully armed. —**во всеору́жии зна́ний,** fully versed in one's subject.
всепобежда́ющий *adj.* all-conquering.
всепоглоща́ющий *adj.* all-consuming.
всеросси́йский *adj.* All-Russian.
всерьёз *adv.* seriously; in earnest. —**принима́ть всерьёз,** to take seriously.
всеси́льный *adj.* all-powerful; omnipotent.
всесою́зный *adj.* All-Union.
всесторо́нний *adj.* all-round; thorough; comprehensive.
всё-таки *conj.* still, all the same.
всеуслы́шание *n., in* **во всеуслы́шание,** publicly; for everyone to hear.
всеце́ло *adv.* completely.
всея́дный *adj.* omnivorous.
вска́кивать *v. impfv.* [*pfv.* **вскочи́ть**] **1,** (*with* **в** + *acc.*) to jump into; leap into. **2,** to jump up; (*with* **на** + *acc.*) jump onto. Вскочи́ть на́ ноги, to leap (*or* spring) to one's feet. **3,** *colloq.* (*of a bruise, pimple, etc.*) to appear.
вска́пывать *v. impfv.* [*pfv.* **вскопа́ть**] to dig; dig up.
вскара́бкиваться *v.r. impfv.* [*pfv.* **вскара́бкаться**] (*with* **на** + *acc.*) *colloq.* to climb (onto); scramble (up); clamber (up).
вска́рмливать *v. impfv.* [*pfv.* **вскорми́ть**] to raise (animals, birds, etc.). —**вскорми́ть и вспои́ть,** to raise; nurture (a child).
вскачь *adv.* at a gallop.
вски́дывать *v. impfv.* [*pfv.* **вски́нуть**] **1,** to throw up; toss up. **2,** (*with* **на** + *acc.*) to toss (onto). —**вски́нуть глаза́,** to look up suddenly. —**вски́нуть го́лову,** to toss one's head.
вскипа́ть *v. impfv.* [*pfv.* **вскипе́ть**] **1,** to boil up; come to a boil. **2,** (*of emotions*) to well up; flare up. **3,** [*also,* **вскипе́ть гне́вом**] to fly into a rage.
вскипе́ть [*infl.* **-плю́, -пи́шь**] *v., pfv. of* **вскипа́ть.**
вскипяти́ть *v., pfv. of* **кипяти́ть.** —**вскипяти́ться,** *refl., pfv. of* **кипяти́ться.**
всклоко́ченный *adj., colloq.* disheveled.
всколыхну́ть *v. pfv.* **1,** to stir. **2,** *fig.* to stir up; agitate.
вскользь *adv.* casually; in passing: упомяну́ть вскользь, to mention in passing.
вскопа́ть *v., pfv. of* **вска́пывать.**
вско́ре *adv.* soon; shortly; presently.
вскорми́ть [*infl.* **вскормлю́, вско́рмишь**] *v., pfv. of* **вска́рмливать.**
вскочи́ть [*infl.* **вскочу́, вско́чишь**] *v., pfv. of* **вска́кивать.**
вскри́кивать *v. impfv.* [*pfv.* **вскри́кнуть**] to cry out; scream; shriek.
вскрича́ть *v. pfv.* [*infl.* **-чу́, -чи́шь**] to exclaim; cry.
вскружи́ть *v. pfv., in* **вскружи́ть го́лову** (+ *dat.*), to turn someone's head; go to one's head.
вскрыва́ть *v. impfv.* [*pfv.* **вскрыть**] **1,** to open up; unseal. **2,** to expose; uncover; reveal. **3,** *med.* to lance. **4,** *med.* to dissect; perform an autopsy on. —**вскрыва́ться,** *refl.* **1,** to be revealed; come to light. **2,** (*of a river*) to become free of ice.
вскры́тие *n.* **1,** opening; unsealing. **2,** revelation; disclosure. **3,** thawing; breaking up (*of a frozen river*). **4,** *med.* autopsy; dissection. **5,** *med.* lancing.
вскрыть [*infl.* **вскро́ю, вскро́ешь**] *v., pfv. of* **вскрыва́ть.** —**вскры́ться,** *refl., pfv. of* **вскрыва́ться.**
всласть *adv., colloq.* to one's heart's content.
вслед *adv.* after; behind: идти́ вслед, to follow after, walk behind. —*prep., with dat.* after; following. Смотре́ть вслед (+ *dat.*), to follow with one's eyes. —**вслед за** (+ *instr.*), **1,** after; in pursuit of. **2,** right after; on the heels of. —**вслед за тем,** after that.
вспе́дствие *prep., with gen.* as a result of; on account of; owing to.
вслепу́ю *adv., colloq.* blind; blindly; blindfolded.
вслух *adv.* aloud; out loud.
вслу́шиваться *v.r. impfv.* [*pfv.* **вслу́шаться**] (*with* **в** + *acc.*) to listen carefully (to); strain one's ears to hear.
всма́триваться *v.r. impfv.* [*pfv.* **всмотре́ться**] (*with* **в** + *acc.*) to peer into; take a good look at.
всмотре́ться [*infl.* **всмотрю́сь, всмо́тришься**] *v.r., pfv. of* **всма́триваться.**
всмя́тку *adv., in* **яйцо́ всмя́тку,** soft-boiled egg.
всо́вывать *v. impfv.* [*pfv.* **всу́нуть**] (*with* **в** + *acc.*) to stick (into); slip (into); thrust (into).
всоса́ть [*infl.* **-су́, -сёшь**] *v., pfv. of* **вса́сывать.** —**всоса́ться,** *refl., pfv. of* **вса́сываться.**
вспа́ивать *v. impfv.* [*pfv.* **вспои́ть**] *colloq.* to raise; rear; bring up.
вспа́рывать *v. impfv.* [*pfv.* **вспоро́ть**] *colloq.* to cut open; rip open.
вспаха́ть [*infl.* **вспашу́, вспа́шешь**] *v., pfv. of* **паха́ть** *and* **вспа́хивать.**
вспа́хивать *v. impfv.* [*pfv.* **вспаха́ть**] to plow.
вспа́шка *n.* plowing.
вспе́нить *v., pfv. of* **пе́нить.** —**вспе́ниться,** *refl., pfv. of* **пе́ниться.**
всплакну́ть *v. pfv., colloq.* to have a little cry; shed a few tears.
всплеск *n.* splash; splashing.
всплёскивать *v. impfv.* [*pfv.* **всплесну́ть**] to splash.

—**всплесну́ть рука́ми,** to clasp one's hands (*in astonishment, dismay, etc.*).
всплыва́ть *v. impfv.* [*pfv.* **всплыть**] **1,** to float to the surface; (*of a submarine*) to surface. **2,** *fig.* to come to light.
всплыть [*infl. like* **плыть**] *v., pfv. of* **всплыва́ть.**
вспои́ть [*infl.* **вспою́, вспои́шь** *or* **вспо́ишь**] *v., pfv. of* **вспа́ивать.**
всполоши́ть *v. pfv., colloq.* to startle; alarm. —**всполоши́ться,** *refl., colloq.* to be startled; be alarmed.
вспомина́ть *v. impfv.* [*pfv.* **вспо́мнить**] **1,** to remember; recall; recollect. **2,** [*impfv. only*] to try to remember. **3,** [*impfv. only*] to recall; reminisce about. —**вспомина́ться,** *refl.* (*with dat.*) to come back to (someone); come back to (one's) mind.
вспомога́тельный *adj.* **1,** auxiliary; subsidiary. **2,** *gram.* auxiliary: вспомога́тельный глаго́л, auxiliary verb.
вспоро́ть [*infl.* **вспорю́, вспо́решь**] *v., pfv. of* **вспа́рывать.**
вспорхну́ть *v. pfv.* to take wing.
вспоте́ть *v. pfv.* **1,** *pfv. of* **поте́ть. 2,** to become fogged; fog up.
вспры́гивать *v. impfv.* [*pfv.* **вспры́гнуть**] (*with* **на** + *acc.*) to jump onto; jump up on.
вспры́скивание *n.* sprinkling.
вспры́скивать *v. impfv.* [*pfv.* **вспры́снуть**] to sprinkle.
вспу́гивать *v. impfv.* [*pfv.* **вспугну́ть**] to frighten away; scare away.
вспуха́ть *v. impfv.* [*pfv.* **вспу́хнуть**] to swell up.
вспу́хнуть [*past* **вспух, -ла**] *v., pfv. of* **вспуха́ть.**
вспыли́ть *v. pfv., colloq.* to flare up; fly into a rage.
вспы́льчивый *adj.* hot-tempered; quick-tempered; irascible.
вспы́хивать *v. impfv.* [*pfv.* **вспы́хнуть**] **1,** to blaze up; suddenly catch fire. Вспы́хнуть пла́менем, to burst into flames. **2,** (*of fire, war, panic, etc.*) to break out. **3,** to blush; flush. **4,** to flare up (*in anger*).
вспы́шка [*gen. pl.* **шек**] *n.* **1,** flash. **2,** *fig.* (*with gen.*) burst (of); outburst (of); outbreak (of). **3,** (angry) outburst. **4,** *photog.* flash gun.
вспять *adv.* back; in the opposite direction.
встава́ние *n.* standing up; rising.
встава́ть *v. impfv.* [*pfv.* **встать;** *pres.* **встаю́, встаёшь**] **1,** to stand up; get up; rise. **2,** (*of the sun*) to rise. **3,** *fig.* (*of a question, difficulty, etc.*) to arise; come up. **4,** to stand (*in a certain place*). **5,** *colloq.* (*of a machine or device*) to stop (working). —**встать на сто́рону** (+ *gen.*), to side with; take the side of.
вста́вить [*infl.* **-влю, -вишь**] *v., pfv. of* **вставля́ть.**
вста́вка [*gen. pl.* **-вок**] *n.* **1,** mounting; setting. **2,** an insertion. **3,** inset; front (*of a dress*).
вставля́ть *v. impfv.* [*pfv.* **вста́вить**] **1,** to put in; insert. **2,** to interject; interpose; put in (a word, remark, etc.).
вставно́й *adj.* that can be inserted and later removed. —**вставны́е зу́бы,** false teeth. —**вставны́е ра́мы,** storm windows.
встарь *adv.* in the old days; in olden times.
встать [*infl.* **вста́ну, вста́нешь**] *v., pfv. of* **встава́ть.**
встрево́женный *adj.* alarmed.
встрево́жить *v., pfv. of* **трево́жить.** —**встрево́житься,** *refl., pfv. of* **трево́житься.**
встрёпанный *adj., colloq.* disheveled.
встрепену́ться *v.r. pfv.* **1,** (*of a bird*) to ruffle its feathers. **2,** to give a start (and be aroused). **3,** (*of the heart*) to palpitate; begin to beat faster.
встре́тить [*infl.* **встре́чу, встре́тишь**] *v., pfv. of* **встреча́ть.** —**встре́титься,** *refl., pfv. of* **встреча́ться.**
встре́ча *n.* **1,** meeting; encounter. **2,** welcome; reception. **3,** *sports* match; contest. **4,** *in* встре́ча Но́вого го́да, New Year's Eve party. —**до (ско́рой) встре́чи!**, see you soon! До встре́чи в два часа́!, see you at two o'clock!
встреча́ть *v. impfv.* [*pfv.* **встре́тить**] **1,** to meet. **2,** to encounter; meet with; be met with. **3,** to greet; welcome; receive. **4,** to celebrate (a holiday, esp. New Year's Eve). —**встреча́ться,** *refl.* **1,** to meet (each other). **2,** to get together; see each other. **3,** (*with* **с** + *instr.*) to meet; encounter; come across. **4,** to be found; occur.
встре́чный *adj.* **1,** oncoming; approaching. **2,** counter-: встре́чный уда́р, counterblow. —*n.* passer-by. —**встре́чный ве́тер,** head wind. —**ка́ждый встре́чный и попере́чный,** *adj.* any (*or* every) Tom, Dick, or Harry. —**пе́рвый встре́чный,** the first person to come along; anyone.
встря́ска *n., colloq.* **1,** shaking. **2,** shock. **3,** dressing-down.
встря́хивать *v. impfv.* [*pfv.* **встряхну́ть**] to shake; shake out; shake up. —**встря́хиваться,** *refl.* **1,** to shake oneself off. **2,** *fig., colloq.* to cheer up; pull oneself together.
вступа́ть *v. impfv.* [*pfv.* **вступи́ть**] (*with* **в** + *acc.*) **1,** to enter; enter into: вступи́ть в но́вую э́ру, to enter a new era; вступи́ть в перепи́ску, to enter into correspondence. **2,** to join: вступи́ть в па́ртию, to join the party. —**вступи́ть в брак,** to marry; get married. —**вступи́ть в де́йствие** *or* **в строй,** to go into operation. —**вступи́ть в до́лжность,** to assume office. —**вступи́ть в свои́ права́,** to come into one's own. —**вступи́ть в си́лу,** to go into effect. —**вступи́ть на престо́л,** to assume *or* ascend the throne.
вступа́ться *v.r. impfv.* [*pfv.* **вступи́ться**] (*with* **за** + *acc.*) to come to the defense of; stand up for; stick up for.
вступи́тельный *adj.* **1,** introductory; opening. **2,** entrance (*attrib.*): вступи́тельный экза́мен, entrance examination.
вступи́ть [*infl.* **вступлю́, всту́пишь**] *v., pfv. of* **вступа́ть.** —**вступи́ться,** *refl., pfv. of* **вступа́ться.**
вступле́ние *n.* **1,** (*with* **в** + *acc.*) entry (*into a place*); joining (*an organization*); assumption (*of office*). **2,** introduction (*to a book, musical work, etc.*).
всу́е *adv., obs.* in vain.
всу́нуть *v., pfv. of* **всо́вывать.**
всухомя́тку *adv., colloq., in* **есть всухомя́тку,** to eat food dry (*without an accompanying beverage*).
всуху́ю *adv., colloq.* **1,** without grease. **2,** without having anything to drink. **3,** *sports* being shut out: проигра́ть всуху́ю, to be shut out.
всу́чивать *v. impfv.* [*pfv.* **всучи́ть**] (*with dat.*) *colloq.* to foist (on); palm off (on). *Also,* **всу́чивать.**
всучи́ть [*infl.* **всучу́, всу́чишь**] *v., pfv. of* **всуча́ть** *and* **всу́чивать.**
всхли́пывать *v. impfv.* [*pfv.* **всхли́пнуть**] to sniffle (*when crying*).
всходи́ть *v. impfv.* [*pfv.* **взойти́;** *pres.* **всхожу́, всхо́дишь**] **1,** (*with* **на** + *acc.*) to go up; mount; ascend; climb. **2,** (*of the sun, moon, etc.*) to rise. **3,** (*of plants, crops, etc.*) to sprout; come up.

всхо́ды [*gen.* **-дов**] *n. pl.* shoots; sprouts.
всхра́пывать *v. impfv.* to snore.
всы́пать [*infl.* **всы́плю, всы́плешь**] *v., pfv. of* **всыпа́ть.**
всыпа́ть *v. impfv.* [*pfv.* **всы́пать**] **1,** (*with* **в** + *acc.*) to pour into. **2,** (*with dat.*) *colloq.* to give (someone) a good licking.
всю́ду *adv.* everywhere.
вся *adj., fem. of* **весь.**
вся́кий *adj.* **1,** any. **2,** all sorts of; all kinds of. —*n.* anyone; anybody. —**во вся́ком слу́чае,** in any case; at any rate. —**на вся́кий слу́чай,** just in case.
вся́кое *n., decl. as an adj.* anything: вся́кое мо́жет случи́ться, anything can happen.
вся́чески *adv., colloq.* in every way.
вся́ческий *adj., colloq.* of every kind; of all kinds.
вся́чина *n., colloq., in* **вся́кая вся́чина,** all sorts of things.
вта́йне *adv.* secretly; in secret.
вта́лкивать *v. impfv.* [*pfv.* **втолкну́ть**] (*with* **в** + *acc.*) to push in; shove in; force in.
вта́птывать *v. impfv.* [*pfv.* **втопта́ть**] (*with* **в** + *acc.*) to trample into. —**втопта́ть в грязь,** to drag through the mud; vilify.
вта́скивать *v. impfv.* [*pfv.* **втащи́ть**] **1,** (*with* **в** + *acc.*) to drag in. **2,** (*with* **на** + *acc.*) to drag up.
втащи́ть [*infl.* **втащу́, вта́щишь**] *v., pfv. of* **вта́скивать.**
втека́ть *v. impfv.* [*pfv.* **втечь**] (*with* **в** + *acc.*) to flow into.
втере́ть [*infl.* **вотру́, вотрёшь;** *past* **втёр, -ла**] *v., pfv. of* **втира́ть.** —**втере́ться,** *refl., pfv. of* **втира́ться.**
втира́ние *n.* **1,** rubbing in. **2,** liniment.
втира́ть *v. impfv.* [*pfv.* **втере́ть**] **1,** (*with* **в** + *acc.*) to rub in. **2,** *in* **втира́ть очки́** (+ *dat.*), to pull the wool over someone's eyes. —**втира́ться,** *refl.* **1,** to be absorbed through rubbing. **2,** (*with* **в** + *acc.*) *colloq.* to make one's way (through); force one's way (into). **3,** (*with* **в** + *acc.*) *fig.* to worm one's way (into): втира́ться в дове́рие к, to worm one's way into the confidence of.
вти́скивать *v. impfv.* [*pfv.* **вти́снуть**] (*with* **в** + *acc.*) to squeeze (into); stuff (into); cram (into). —**вти́скиваться,** *refl.* (*with* **в** + *acc.*) *colloq.* to squeeze (into); crowd (into); jam (into).
втихомо́лку *adv., colloq.* secretly; stealthily; on the sly.
втолкну́ть *v., pfv. of* **вта́лкивать.**
втолкова́ть [*infl.* **-ку́ю, -ку́ешь**] *v., pfv. of* **втолко́вывать.**
втолко́вывать *v. impfv.* [*pfv.* **втолкова́ть**] (*with dat.*) *colloq.* to make (someone) understand; drive home the point (to).
втопта́ть [*infl.* **втопчу́, вто́пчешь**] *v., pfv. of* **вта́птывать.**
вторга́ться *v.r. impfv.* [*pfv.* **вто́ргнуться**] (*with* **в** + *acc.*) **1,** to invade. **2,** *fig.* to intrude (into). **3,** *fig.* to encroach (upon); infringe (upon).
вто́ргнуться [*past* **вто́ргся** *or* **вто́ргнулся, вто́рглась**] *v.r., pfv. of* **вторга́ться.**
вторже́ние *n.* invasion.
вто́рить *v. impfv.* (*with dat.*) **1,** *music* to sing second part (to). **2,** to echo; repeat.
втори́чно *adv.* a second time; for the second time.
втори́чный *adj.* **1,** second. **2,** secondary.
вто́рник *n.* Tuesday.
второго́дник *n.* pupil left back in school.
второ́е *n., decl. as an adj.* **1,** (*with dates*) second: сего́дня – второ́е апре́ля, today is April 2nd. **2,** main course; entrée.
Второзако́ние *n.* Deuteronomy.
второ́й *ordinal numeral & adj.* second. —**из вторы́х рук,** second hand; through an intermediary. *See also* **второ́е.**
второкла́ссник *n.* second-grade pupil.
второку́рсник *n.* second-year student; sophomore.
второпя́х *adv.* **1,** hastily; hurriedly. **2,** in one's haste.
второразря́дный *adj.* second-rate.
второсо́ртный *adj.* second-rate.
второстепе́нный *adj.* **1,** secondary. **2,** minor.
в-тре́тьих thirdly; in the third place.
втри́дорога *adv., colloq.* triple the price; three times as much. —**плати́ть втри́дорога,** to pay through the nose.
втро́е *adv.* **1,** three times; triple: втро́е бо́льше, three times as much. **2,** in three: сложи́ть втро́е, to fold in three.
втроём *adv.* three together: они́ втроём, the three of them.
втройне́ *adv.* triple; three times as much.
вту́лка [*gen. pl.* **-лок**] *n.* **1,** *mech.* bushing. **2,** plug; stopper.
вту́не *adv., obs.* for nothing; in vain.
втыка́ть *v. impfv.* [*pfv.* **воткну́ть**] (*with* **в** + *acc.*) to drive in; drive into; stick in; stick into.
втя́гивать *v. impfv.* [*pfv.* **втяну́ть**] **1,** to draw in; pull in. **2,** to breathe in; absorb. **3,** *colloq.* to draw into; involve. —**втя́гиваться,** *refl.* (*with* **в** + *acc.*) *colloq.* **1,** to make one's way into. **2,** (*of one's cheeks*) to become drawn. **3,** to become involved in; be drawn into. **4,** to get used to; come to enjoy.
втяну́ть [*infl.* **втяну́, втя́нешь**] *v., pfv. of* **втя́гивать.** —**втяну́ться,** *refl., pfv. of* **втя́гиваться.**
вуаль *n.f.* veil.
вуз *n., abbr. of* **вы́сшее уче́бное заведе́ние,** institution of higher learning.
ву́зовец [*gen.* **-вца**] *n.m.* [*fem.* **-вка**] *colloq.* student in a **вуз.**
вулка́н *n.* volcano.
вулканиза́ция *n.* vulcanization.
вулканизи́ровать *v. impfv. & pfv.* [*pres.* **-рую, -руешь**] to vulcanize.
вулкани́ческий *adj.* volcanic; volcano (*attrib.*).
вульгаризи́ровать *v. impfv. & pfv.* [*pres.* **-рую, -руешь**] to vulgarize.
вульгари́зм *n.* vulgarism.
вульга́рный *adj.* vulgar. —**вульга́рность,** *n.f.* vulgarity.
вундерки́нд (дэ) *n.* child prodigy.
вурдала́к *n., folklore* vampire.
вход *n.* **1,** entry. **2,** admission; admittance. **3,** entrance.
входи́ть *v. impfv.* [*pfv.* **войти́;** *pres.* **вхожу́, вхо́дишь**] (*with* **в** + *acc.*) **1,** to enter; come in; go in; walk in. **2,** to go into; be a part of. **3,** to fit into. **4,** to join. —**входи́ть во вкус** (+ *gen.*), to begin to enjoy. —**входи́ть в дове́рие к,** to gain the confidence of. —**входи́ть в исто́рию,** to go down in history. —**входи́ть в привы́чку,** to become a habit. —**входи́ть в роль,** to grow into a role. —**входи́ть в до́лю/мо́ду/обихо́д/посло́вицу/соста́в,** *see entry under noun.*

входно́й *adj.* entrance (*attrib.*); admission (*attrib.*): входна́я пла́та, admission/entrance fee.
входя́щий *adj.* incoming.
вхожде́ние *n.* (*with* **в** + *acc.*) entering; joining.
вхо́жий *adj., colloq.* having entrée: он вхож в лу́чшие дома́, he has entrée into the best homes.
вхолосту́ю *adv., in* **рабо́тать вхолосту́ю,** (*of a motor*) to idle.
вцепи́ться [*infl.* **вцеплю́сь, вце́пишься**] *v.r., pfv. of* **вцепля́ться.**
вцепля́ться *v.r. impfv.* [*pfv.* **вцепи́ться**] (*with* **в** + *acc.*) to seize; grab hold of.
вчера́ *adv.* yesterday.
вчера́шний *adj.* yesterday's; of yesterday. —**вчера́шний день,** yesterday.
вчерне́ *adv.* in the rough: докла́д напи́сан вчерне́, the report is written in the rough.
вче́тверо *adv.* **1,** four times; quadruple: вче́тверо бо́льше, four times as much. **2,** in four parts; in quarters.
вчетверо́м *adv.* four together: они́ вчетверо́м, the four of them.
в-четвёртых in the fourth place.
вчи́тываться *v.r. impfv.* [*pfv.* **вчита́ться**] (*with* **в** + *acc.*) *colloq.* **1,** to read carefully. **2,** to be thoroughly familiar with (*by reading*).
вшива́ть *v. impfv.* [*pfv.* **вшить**] (*with* **в** + *acc.*) to sew in; sew into.
вшивно́й *adj.* sown in.
вши́вый *adj.* infested with lice.
вширь *adv.* **1,** in breadth. **2,** over a great distance.
вшить [*infl.* **вошью́, вошьёшь**] *v., pfv. of* **вшива́ть.**
въеда́ться *v.r. impfv.* [*pfv.* **въе́сться**] (*with* **в** + *acc.*) **1,** to eat into. **2,** (*of something sharp*) to sink into.
въе́дливый *adj., colloq.* **1,** corrosive. **2,** meticulous.
въезд *n.* **1,** entry. **2,** entrance. —**въездно́й,** *adj.* entry (*attrib.*); entrance (*attrib.*).
въезжа́ть *v. impfv.* [*pfv.* **въе́хать**] (*with* **в** + *acc.*) **1,** to enter (*in a conveyance*); drive into. **2,** to move in; move into (a house, apartment, etc.). **3,** (*with* **на** + *acc.*) to ride up; drive up.
въе́сться [*infl. like* **есть**] *v.r., pfv. of* **въеда́ться.**
въе́хать [*infl.* **въе́ду, въе́дешь**] *v., pfv. of* **въезжа́ть.**
вы [*gen., acc., & prepl.* **вас;** *dat.* **вам;** *instr.* **ва́ми**] *pers. pron., 2nd person pl. and polite 2nd person sing.* you. —**быть с** (+ *instr.*) **на вы,** to address each other as "вы" (*as opposed to* "ты").
вы- *prefix* **1,** *indicating motion to the outside:* вы́бежать, to run out. **2,** *indicating thoroughness of an action or process:* вы́мокнуть, to get soaked. **3,** *indicating attainment of a goal:* вы́требовать, to demand and obtain. **4,** (*with* **-ся**) *indicating indulgence to the point of complete satisfaction:* вы́спаться, to have a good sleep; вы́плакаться, have a good cry.
выба́лтывать *v. impfv.* [*pfv.* **вы́болтать**] *colloq.* to blab; let out: вы́болтать секре́т, to let the cat out of the bag.
выбега́ть *v. impfv.* [*pfv.* **вы́бежать**] to run out.
вы́бежать [*infl. like* **бежа́ть**] *v., pfv. of* **выбега́ть.**
вы́белить *v., pfv. of* **бели́ть** (*in sense #3*).
выбива́ть *v. impfv.* [*pfv.* **вы́бить**] **1,** to knock out. **2,** to dislodge (an enemy). **3,** to beat down. **4,** to beat (a carpet). **5,** to strike (a medal); hammer out (metals). —**выбива́ться,** *refl.* **1,** *colloq.* to get out; work one's way out. **2,** to come out; appear. **3,** *in* **вы́биться из сил,** to be exhausted.
выбира́ть *v. impfv.* [*pfv.* **вы́брать**] **1,** to choose; select. **2,** to elect. **3,** to take out; remove (all of something). **4,** to haul in (a net); pull up (an anchor). **5,** *colloq.* to find (time, a spare moment, etc.). —**выбира́ться,** *refl.* **1,** to be chosen. **2,** (*with* **из**) to get out (of); find one's way out (of). **3,** *colloq.* to move (*change one's residence*). **4,** (*with* **в** + *acc.*) *colloq.* to find time to go to.
вы́бить [*infl.* **вы́бью, вы́бьешь**] *v., pfv. of* **выбива́ть.** —**вы́биться,** *refl., pfv. of* **выбива́ться.**
вы́боина *n.* **1,** dent; hole. **2,** pothole.
вы́болтать *v., pfv. of* **выба́лтывать.**
вы́бор *n.* **1,** choice. **2,** assortment. —**без вы́бора,** indiscriminately. —**на вы́бор** (*with* **предлага́ть**), one's choice; of one's choice *See also* **вы́боры.**
вы́борка *n.* **1,** choice; selection. **2,** sample; sampling: случа́йная вы́борка, random sample/sampling. **3,** *pl.* excerpts. —**произво́льная вы́борка,** random access.
вы́борность *n.f.* election; electing.
вы́борный *adj.* **1,** election (*attrib.*). **2,** elective; electoral. **3,** elected. —*n.* elected representative.
вы́борочный *adj.* selective. —**вы́борочная прове́рка,** spot check.
вы́борщик *n.* elector.
вы́боры [*gen.* **-ров**] *n. pl.* election; elections.
вы́бранить *v. pfv., colloq.* to chew out; give (someone) the devil.
выбра́сывание *n.* throwing out; ejection.
выбра́сывать *v. impfv.* [*pfv.* **вы́бросить**] **1,** to throw out: вы́бросить что́-нибудь в окно́, to throw something out the window. **2,** to throw away; throw out; discard. **3,** to hoist (a flag). **4,** *colloq.* to delete. **5,** *colloq.* to proclaim (a slogan). —**выбра́сывать из головы́,** to put out of one's head; dismiss from one's mind. —**выбра́сывать на у́лицу,** to put out (*or* turn out) on the street.
выбра́сываться *v.r. impfv.* [*pfv.* **вы́броситься**] to jump out.
вы́брать [*infl.* **-беру, -берешь**] *v., pfv. of* **выбира́ть.** —**вы́браться,** *refl.* **1,** *pfv. of* **выбира́ться. 2,** *colloq.* (*of time*) to become available.
выбрива́ть *v. impfv.* [*pfv.* **вы́брить**] to shave off; shave clean. —**выбрива́ться,** *refl.* to shave (oneself).
вы́брить [*infl.* **-брею, -бреешь**] *v., pfv. of* **выбрива́ть.** —**вы́бриться,** *refl., pfv. of* **выбрива́ться.**
вы́бросить [*infl.* **-шу, -сишь**] *v., pfv. of* **выбра́сывать.** —**вы́броситься,** *refl., pfv. of* **выбра́сываться.**
выбыва́ть *v. impfv.* [*pfv.* **вы́быть**] **1,** to leave; depart. **2,** (*with* **из**) to quit; drop out (of). **3,** *sports* to be eliminated. —**выбыва́ть из стро́я, 1,** to quit the ranks. **2,** to be put out of action.
вы́быть [*infl.* **-буду, -будешь**] *v., pfv. of* **выбыва́ть.**
выва́ливать *v. impfv.* [*pfv.* **вы́валить**] *colloq.* to throw out; dump out. —**выва́ливаться,** *refl., colloq.* to fall out.
выва́ривать *v. impfv.* [*pfv.* **вы́варить**] **1,** to remove by boiling. **2,** to overcook.
выве́дывать *v. impfv.* [*pfv.* **вы́ведать**] *colloq.* to worm (out); wangle; ferret out (a secret, information, etc.).
вы́везти [*infl. like* **везти́**] *v., pfv. of* **вывози́ть.**
вы́верить *v., pfv. of* **выверя́ть.**
вы́верка *n.* adjustment.
вы́вернуть *v., pfv. of* **вывёртывать.** —**вы́вернуться,** *refl., pfv. of* **вывёртываться.**
вы́верт *n., colloq.* **1,** turn; twist. **2,** quirk; eccentricity; idiosyncrasy.

вывёртывать *v. impfv.* [*pfv.* **вы́вернуть**] **1,** to unscrew. **2,** to turn inside out. **3,** *colloq.* to twist; wrench. —**вывёртываться,** *refl.* **1,** *colloq.* to come unscrewed. **2,** to be turned inside out. **3,** to wriggle out; slip away.

выверя́ть *v. impfv.* [*pfv.* **вы́верить**] **1,** to adjust. **2,** to check.

вы́весить [*infl.* **-шу, -сишь**] *v., pfv. of* **выве́шивать.**

вы́веска [*gen. pl.* **-сок**] *n.* sign; signboard.

вы́вести [*infl. like* **вести́**] *v., pfv. of* **выводи́ть.** —**вы́вестись,** *refl., pfv. of* **выводи́ться.**

выве́тривание *n.* **1,** ventilating; ventilation. **2,** erosion; decay.

выве́тривать *v. impfv.* [*pfv.* **вы́ветрить**] **1,** to get rid of (an odor) by ventilation. **2,** to erode; wear away. —**выве́триваться,** *refl.* **1,** (*of something in the air*) to disappear; be blown away. **2,** to erode; become eroded.

выве́шивать *v. impfv.* [*pfv.* **вы́весить**] **1,** to hang out. **2,** to put up; post. **3,** to weigh.

выви́нчивать *v. impfv.* [*pfv.* **вы́винтить**] to unscrew. —**выви́нчиваться,** *refl.* to come unscrewed.

вы́вих *n., med.* dislocation.

вы́вихнуть *v. pfv., med.* to dislocate.

вы́вод *n.* **1,** conclusion. **2,** derivation. **3,** withdrawal.

выводи́ть *v. impfv.* [*pfv.* **вы́вести;** *pres.* **-вожу́, -во́дишь**] **1,** to bring out; take out; lead out. **2,** to remove; withdraw. **3,** to remove; expel. **4,** to conclude; deduce; infer. **5,** to derive (a formula); draw (a conclusion). **6,** to grow; raise. **7,** to hatch. **8,** to construct; put up. **9,** to write carefully; trace. **10,** to give (a grade). **11,** to remove; take out (a stain). **12,** to exterminate (insects). —**выводи́ть из равнове́сия,** to disconcert; rattle. —**выводи́ть из себя́,** to drive (someone) crazy. —**выводи́ть из стро́я,** to put out of operation (*or* commission). —**выводи́ть из терпе́ния,** to make (someone) lose patience. —**выводи́ть на чи́стую во́ду,** to bring out into the open.

выводи́ться *v.r. impfv.* [*pfv.* **вы́вестись;** *pres.* **-вожу́сь, -во́дишься**] **1,** to disappear; become extinct. **2,** (*of a stain*) to come out. **3,** to hatch; be hatched; be born.

выводно́й *adj.* **1,** discharge (*attrib.*). **2,** *anat.* excretory.

вы́водок [*gen.* **-дка**] *n.* brood; litter.

вы́воз *n.* **1,** removal. **2,** exporting. **3,** exports.

вывози́ть *v. impfv.* [*pfv.* **вы́везти;** *pres.* **-вожу́, -во́зишь**] **1,** to take out; take away; cart out; cart away. **2,** to take; bring; deliver. **3,** to bring back (a souvenir). **4,** to export. **5,** *colloq.* to save; rescue.

вы́возка *n.* carting out; removal.

вывозно́й *adj.* export (*attrib.*).

выволáкивать *v. impfv.* [*pfv.* **вы́волочь**] *colloq.* to drag out.

вы́волочь [*infl.* **-локу, -лочешь, ...-локут;** *past* **-лок, -локла**] *v., pfv. of* **вывола́кивать.**

вывора́чивать *v. impfv.* [*pfv.* **вы́воротить**] *colloq.* **1,** to pull out; extract. **2,** to wrench; twist. **3,** to turn inside out.

вы́воротить [*infl.* **-чу, -тишь**] *v., pfv. of* **вывора́чивать.**

выга́дывать *v. impfv.* [*pfv.* **вы́гадать**] **1,** to gain. **2,** to save (time, money, etc.).

вы́гиб *n.* bend; curve.

выгиба́ть *v. impfv.* [*pfv.* **вы́гнуть**] to bend; arch. —**выгиба́ться,** *refl.* to bend; curve.

вы́гладить *v., pfv. of* **гла́дить** (*in sense #1*).

вы́глядеть *v. impfv.* [*pres.* **-жу, -дишь**] (*with an adv. or instr. case*) to look: она́ хорошо́ вы́глядит, she looks well. Он вы́глядит здоро́вым/старико́м, he looks healthy/like an old man/.

выгля́дывать *v. impfv.* [*pfv.* **вы́глянуть**] **1,** to look out. **2,** to appear; come into view.

вы́гнать [*infl.* **-гоню, -гонишь**] *v., pfv. of* **выгоня́ть.**

вы́гнутый *adj.* curved; bent.

вы́гнуть *v., pfv. of* **выгиба́ть.** —**вы́гнуться,** *refl., pfv. of* **выгиба́ться.**

выгова́ривать *v. impfv.* [*pfv.* **вы́говорить**] **1,** to pronounce; enunciate; articulate. **2,** (*with* **себе́**) *colloq.* to reserve for oneself. **3,** [*impfv. only*] (*with dat.*) to scold; berate.

вы́говор *n.* **1,** pronunciation. **2,** reprimand; rebuke.

вы́говорить *v., pfv. of* **выгова́ривать.** —**вы́говориться,** *refl., colloq.* to speak one's mind; sound off.

вы́года *n.* **1,** profit; gain. **2,** benefit; advantage.

вы́годно *adv.* **1,** to advantage; favorably. **2,** at a profit. —*adj., used predicatively* advantageous; profitable: кому́ э́то вы́годно?, whom is this good for?; who stands to gain from this?

вы́годный *adj.* **1,** profitable. **2,** favorable; advantageous.

вы́гон *n.* pasture.

выгоня́ть *v. impfv.* [*pfv.* **вы́гнать**] **1,** to drive out; chase out. **2,** *colloq.* to expel. **3,** *in* выгоня́ть с рабо́ты, *colloq.* to fire; give (someone) the sack. **4,** to force (plants).

выгора́живать *v. impfv.* [*pfv.* **вы́городить**] **1,** to fence off. **2,** *colloq.* to shield (from blame, responsibility, etc.).

выгора́ть *v. impfv.* [*pfv.* **вы́гореть**] **1,** to burn down. **2,** (*of colors*) to fade. **3,** *colloq.* to work out; pan out.

вы́городить [*infl.* **-жу, -дишь**] *v., pfv. of* **выгора́живать.**

вы́гравировать *v., pfv. of* **гравирова́ть.**

выгреба́ть *v. impfv.* [*pfv.* **вы́грести**] **1,** *v.t.* to rake out; scoop out; shovel out. **2,** *v.i.* to row: выгреба́ть к бе́регу, to row toward shore.

выгребно́й *adj., in* **выгребна́я я́ма,** cesspool.

вы́грести [*infl. like* **грести́**] *v., pfv. of* **выгреба́ть.**

выгружа́ть *v. impfv.* [*pfv.* **вы́грузить**] to unload (cargo). —**выгружа́ться,** *refl.* to disembark.

вы́грузка *n.* unloading.

выгрыза́ть *v. impfv.* [*pfv.* **вы́грызть**] to gnaw (a hole).

вы́грызть [*infl. like* **грызть**] *v., pfv. of* **выгрыза́ть.**

выдава́ть *v. impfv.* [*pfv.* **вы́дать;** *pres.* **-даю́, -даёшь**] **1,** to give out; issue. **2,** to deliver up; extradite. **3,** to give away; betray. **4,** (*with* **за** *+ acc.*) to pass (someone) off as; (*with* **себя́** *and* **за** *+ acc.*) pose as. —**выдава́ться,** *refl.* **1,** to stick out; jut out; protrude. **2,** to stand out; be distinguished. **3,** *colloq.* to turn out to be: вы́дался хоро́ший денёк, it turned out to be a nice day.

вы́давить [*infl.* **-влю, -вишь**] *v., pfv. of* **выда́вливать.**

выда́вливать *v. impfv.* [*pfv.* **вы́давить**] **1,** to press out; squeeze out. **2,** to break; knock out (*e.g.* a pane of glass). **3,** *fig.* to force (a smile, laugh, etc.).

выда́лбливать *v. impfv.* [*pfv.* **вы́долбить**] to hollow out.

вы́дать [*infl. like* **дать**] *v., pfv. of* **выдава́ть.** —**вы́даться,** *refl., pfv. of* **выдава́ться.**

вы́дача *n.* **1,** giving out; issuing; distribution. **2,** extradition.

выдаю́щийся *adj.* outstanding; distinguished; eminent; illustrious.

выдвига́ть *v. impfv.* [*pfv.* **вы́двинуть**] **1,** to pull out; draw out; move out. **2,** to advance; put forward (an idea, proposal, etc.). **3,** to nominate. **4,** to promote (*in rank*). —**выдвига́ться,** *refl.* **1,** to advance; move forward. **2,** to rise (*in rank*); work one's way up. **3,** [*impfv. only*] (*of a drawer*) to slide.

выдвиже́нец [*gen.* **-нца**] *n.m.* [*fem.* **-нка**] worker promoted to a position of responsibility.

выдвиже́ние *n.* **1,** moving forward. **2,** nomination. **3,** promotion.

выдвижно́й *adj.* sliding.

вы́двинуть *v., pfv. of* **выдвига́ть.** —**вы́двинуться,** *refl., pfv. of* **выдвига́ться.**

выдворя́ть *v. impfv.* [*pfv.* **вы́дворить**] **1,** to expel (from a country). **2,** *colloq.* to throw out; kick out.

вы́делать *v., pfv. of* **выде́лывать.**

выделе́ние *n.* **1,** allocation; allotment; apportionment. **2,** excretion; secretion; discharge. **3,** *pl.* (bodily) secretions.

выдели́тельный *adj.* secretory; excretory.

вы́делить *v., pfv. of* **выделя́ть.** —**вы́делиться,** *refl., pfv. of* **выделя́ться.**

вы́делка *n.* **1,** manufacturing. **2,** workmanship.

выде́лывать *v. impfv.* [*pfv.* **вы́делать**] **1,** to manufacture; make; fashion. **2,** to curry; dress (leather, hides, etc.). **3,** *colloq.* to do; perform.

выделя́ть *v. impfv.* [*pfv.* **вы́делить**] **1,** to single out. **2,** to set apart. **3,** to allot; allocate; apportion; earmark. **4,** to give off; excrete; secrete. **5,** *in* выделя́ть курси́вом, to italicize; set off in italics. —**выделя́ться,** *refl.* **1,** to stand out. **2,** to ooze; exude. **3,** to take one's inheritance and separate from the family.

выдёргивать *v. impfv.* [*pfv.* **вы́дернуть**] to pull out.

вы́держанность *n.f.* **1,** consistency. **2,** steadfastness. **3,** self-control.

вы́держанный *adj.* **1,** consistent. **2,** self-controlled; self-possessed. **3,** (*of wine, cheese, etc.*) aged; mellowed.

вы́держать [*infl.* **-держу, -держишь**] *v., pfv. of* **выде́рживать.**

выде́рживать *v. impfv.* [*pfv.* **вы́держать**] **1,** to bear; support. **2,** to endure; withstand. **3,** *v.i.* to control oneself; contain oneself. **4,** to maintain; keep up. **5,** to pass (an examination). **6,** to age (wine, cheese, etc.). —**выде́рживать хара́ктер,** to stand firm. —**не выде́рживать кри́тики,** not stand up (to criticism); not hold water.

вы́держка *n.* **1,** endurance; self-control. **2,** extract; excerpt. **3,** *photog.* exposure. —**на вы́держку,** picked at random.

вы́дернуть *v., pfv. of* **выдёргивать.**

выдира́ть *v. impfv.* [*pfv.* **вы́драть**] *colloq.* to tear out.

вы́долбить [*infl.* **-блю, -бишь**] *v., pfv. of* **выда́лбливать.**

вы́дох *n.* an outward breath; exhalation.

вы́дохнуть [*past* **-нул, -нула**] *v., pfv. of* **выдыха́ть.** —**вы́дохнуться,** *refl.* [*past* **-дохся, -дохлась**] *pfv. of* **выдыха́ться.**

вы́дра *n.* otter.

вы́драть [*infl.* **-деру -дерешь**] *v., pfv. of* **драть** (*in sense #3*) *and* **выдира́ть.**

вы́дрессировать *v., pfv. of* **дрессирова́ть.**

вы́дубить *v., pfv. of* **дуби́ть.**

выдува́ть *v. impfv.* [*pfv.* **вы́дуть**] to blow out.

вы́думанный *adj.* fictitious; made-up.

вы́думать *v., pfv. of* **выду́мывать.**

вы́думка *n.* **1,** *colloq.* inventiveness; imagination. **2,** invention. **3,** fabrication; fib.

вы́думщик *n., colloq.* **1,** one who thinks up anything. **2,** liar.

выду́мывать *v. impfv.* [*pfv.* **вы́думать**] **1,** to think up; invent. **2,** to make up; concoct.

вы́дуть [*infl.* **-дую, -дуешь**] *v., pfv. of* **выдува́ть.**

выдыха́ние *n.* exhalation.

выдыха́ть *v. impfv.* [*pfv.* **вы́дохнуть**] to exhale; breathe out. —**выдыха́ться,** *refl.* **1,** to lose its fragrance/taste/zest. **2,** *fig., colloq.* to fizzle; bog down; peter out.

выеда́ть *v. impfv.* [*pfv.* **вы́есть**] to eat away; corrode. —**вы́еденного яйца́ не сто́ит,** not worth a hill of beans.

вы́езд *n.* **1,** departure. **2,** exit; road leading out. **3,** horse and carriage. —**на вы́езде,** *sports* on the road.

вы́ездить [*infl.* **-езжу, -ездишь**] *v., pfv. of* **выезжа́ть** (*in sense #4*).

выездно́й *adj.* **1,** exit (*attrib.*). **2,** *(of a horse)* for riding.

выезжа́ть *v. impfv.* [*pfv.* **вы́ехать**] **1,** to drive out; depart; leave (*by conveyance*). **2,** to move out. **3,** (*with* **на** + *prepl.*) *colloq.* to exploit; make capital of. **4,** [*pfv.* **вы́ездить**] to break in (a horse).

вы́емка *n.* **1,** taking out; removing. **2,** hollow; depression. —**вы́емка пи́сем,** collection (*of mail*).

вы́есть [*infl. like* **есть**] *v., pfv. of* **выеда́ть.**

вы́ехать [*infl.* **-еду, -едешь**] *v., pfv. of* **выезжа́ть.**

вы́жать [*infl.* **-жму, -жмешь**] *v., pfv. of* **выжима́ть.**

вы́ждать [*infl.* **вы́жду, вы́ждешь**] *v., pfv. of* **выжида́ть.**

вы́жечь [*infl. like* **жечь**] *v., pfv. of* **выжига́ть.**

вы́жженный *past passive part. of* **вы́жечь.** —**страте́гия вы́жженной земли́,** scorched-earth policy.

выжива́ние *n.* survival. —**выжива́ние наибо́лее приспосо́бленных,** survival of the fittest.

выжива́ть *v. impfv.* [*pfv.* **вы́жить**] **1,** *v.i.* to survive; live; pull through. **2,** *v.t., colloq.* to drive out (by making life impossible). —**вы́жить из ума́,** to lose possession of one's faculties.

выжига́ние *n.* **1,** burning out. **2,** pyrography. **3,** cauterization.

выжига́ть *v. impfv.* [*pfv.* **вы́жечь**] **1,** to burn down; burn out. **2,** to burn in; trace by burning. **3,** to cauterize.

выжида́ние *n.* **1,** waiting. **2,** expectancy.

выжида́тельный *adj.* waiting; temporizing.

выжида́ть *v. impfv.* [*pfv.* **вы́ждать**] **1,** to wait for (the right moment): выжида́ть удо́бный слу́чай, to wait for an opportunity. **2,** to wait out; wait till the end of. **3,** to bide one's time; sit tight.

выжима́ть *v. impfv.* [*pfv.* **вы́жать**] to squeeze out; wring out. —**мо́крый, хоть вы́жми,** wringing/soaking/sopping wet.

вы́жить [*infl.* **-живу, -живешь**] *v., pfv. of* **выжива́ть.**

вы́звать [*infl.* **-зову, -зовешь**] *v., pfv. of* **вызыва́ть.** —**вы́званься,** *refl., pfv. of* **вызыва́ться.**

вызволя́ть *v. impfv.* [*pfv.* **вы́зволить**] *colloq.* to help out (of trouble).

выздора́вливать *v. impfv.* [*pfv.* **вы́здороветь**] to get well; recover; recuperate.

вы́здороветь [*infl.* **-ею, -еешь**] *v., pfv. of* **выздора́вливать.**

выздоровле́ние *n.* recovery.

вы́зов *n.* **1,** call: вы́зов по телефо́ну, telephone call. **2,** summons. **3,** challenge. **4,** invitation; affidavit (*from someone abroad to emigrate from the USSR*). —**бро́сить вы́зов** (+ *dat.*), to challenge.

вы́золотить *v., pfv. of* **золоти́ть.**

вы́золоченный *adj.* gilded; gilt.

вызрева́ть *v. impfv.* [*pfv.* **вы́зреть**] to ripen.

вызу́бривать *v. impfv.* [*pfv.* **вы́зубрить**] **1,** to notch; make notches in. **2,** *colloq.* to learn by rote.

вызыва́ть *v. impfv.* [*pfv.* **вы́звать**] **1,** to call. **2,** to summon. **3,** to challenge. **4,** to cause. **5,** to arouse; evoke. **6,** *in* **вызыва́ть к жи́зни,** to give rise to. —**вызыва́ться,** *refl.* to volunteer.

вызыва́ющий *adj.* defiant.

выи́грывать *v. impfv.* [*pfv.* **вы́играть**] **1,** to win. **2,** (*with* **у**) to defeat; beat. **3,** to gain.

вы́игрыш *n.* **1,** winnings. **2,** win; winning: игра́ть на вы́игрыш, to play to win; play for a win. **3,** gain; advantage. —**быть в вы́игрыше,** to be winning; be ahead of the game.

вы́игрышный *adj.* **1,** winning. **2,** advantageous.

вы́искать *v. pfv.* [*infl.* **-ищу, -ищешь**] *colloq.* to find; locate; turn up. —**вы́искаться,** *refl., colloq.* to turn up; appear.

выи́скивать *v. impfv., colloq.* to seek; try to find.

вы́йти [*infl.* **вы́йду, вы́йдешь;** *past* **вы́шел, вы́шла**] *v., pfv. of* **выходи́ть.**

вы́казать [*infl.* **-кажу, -кажешь**] *v., pfv. of* **выка́зывать.**

выка́зывать *v. impfv.* [*pfv.* **вы́казать**] *colloq.* to show; display; evince.

выка́лывать *v. impfv.* [*pfv.* **вы́колоть**] to put out; gouge out (someone's eye). —**темно́, хоть глаз вы́коли,** so dark you can't see your hand in front of your face.

выка́пывать *v. impfv.* [*pfv.* **вы́копать**] **1,** to dig (a hole, well, etc.). **2,** to dig up; dig out. **3,** to exhume, disinter. **4,** *fig.* to unearth.

выкара́бкиваться *v.r. impfv.* [*pfv.* **вы́карабкаться**] *colloq.* **1,** to scramble out; extricate oneself. **2,** *fig.* to pull through (an illness).

выка́рмливать *v. impfv.* [*pfv.* **вы́кормить**] to bring up; rear.

вы́катать *v., pfv. of* **ката́ть** (*in sense #4*).

вы́катить [*infl.* **-чу, -тишь**] *v., pfv. of* **выка́тывать.** —**вы́катиться,** *refl., pfv. of* **выка́тываться.**

выка́тывать *v. impfv.* [*pfv.* **вы́катить**] to roll out; wheel out. —**выка́тываться,** *refl.* to roll out.

выка́чивать *v. impfv.* [*pfv.* **вы́качать**] to pump; pump out.

выка́шливать *v. impfv.* [*pfv.* **вы́кашлять**] *colloq.* to cough up. —**выка́шливаться,** *refl., colloq.* to clear one's throat.

выки́дывать *v. impfv.* [*pfv.* **вы́кинуть**] **1,** to throw out. **2,** to delete. **3,** to raise; hoist (a flag). **4,** *v.i.* to have a miscarriage. **5,** *colloq.* to play (a trick).

вы́кидыш *n.* **1,** miscarriage; abortion. **2,** stillborn fetus.

вы́кинуть *v., pfv. of* **выки́дывать.**

выкипа́ть *v. impfv.* [*pfv.* **вы́кипеть**] to boil away.

вы́кладка *n.* **1,** *colloq.* laying out; spreading out. **2,** *usu. pl.* calculations. **3,** *mil.* kit: с по́лной вы́кладкой, with full kit.

выкла́дывать *v. impfv.* [*pfv.* **вы́ложить**] **1,** to lay out; spread out. **2,** *fig., colloq.* to tell; reveal; lay bare. **3,** (*with instr.*) to face (with); line (with); pave (with). —**выкла́дываться,** *refl., colloq.* to go all out. Он осо́бенно не выкла́дывался, he did not try especially hard.

вы́клевать [*infl.* **-клюю, -клюешь**] *v., pfv. of* **выклёвывать.**

выклёвывать *v. impfv.* [*pfv.* **вы́клевать**] to peck out.

выклика́ть *v. impfv.* [*pfv.* **вы́кликнуть**] to call out by name.

выключа́тель *n.m.* switch (*for turning something on or off*).

выключа́ть *v. impfv.* [*pfv.* **вы́ключить**] to turn off; switch off; shut off (a device); turn out (the light).

выкля́нчивать *v. impfv.* [*pfv.* **вы́клянчить**] *colloq.* to coax out of.

вы́ковать [*infl.* **-кую, -куешь**] *v., pfv. of* **выко́вывать.**

выко́вывать *v. impfv.* [*pfv.* **вы́ковать**] to forge.

выкола́чивать *v. impfv.* [*pfv.* **вы́колотить**] **1,** to knock out; beat out; hammer out. **2,** to beat (*in order to clean*).

вы́колоть [*infl.* **-колю, -колешь**] *v., pfv. of* **выка́лывать.**

вы́копать *v., pfv. of* **копа́ть** (*in sense #2*) *and* **выка́пывать.**

вы́кормить [*infl.* **-млю, -мишь**] *v., pfv. of* **выка́рмливать.**

вы́корчевать [*infl.* **-чую, -чуешь**] *v., pfv. of* **выкорчёвывать.**

выкорчёвывать *v. impfv.* [*pfv.* **вы́корчевать**] **1,** to uproot. **2,** to root out; eradicate.

выкра́дывать *v. impfv.* [*pfv.* **вы́красть**] to steal.

выкра́ивать *v. impfv.* [*pfv.* **вы́кроить**] **1,** to cut out the material for: вы́кроить пла́тье, to cut out (the material for) a dress. **2,** *fig., colloq.* to scrape up (money); find (time).

вы́красить [*infl.* **-шу, -сишь**] *v., pfv. of* **выкра́шивать.**

вы́красть [*infl. like* **красть**] *v., pfv. of* **выкра́дывать.**

выкра́шивать *v. impfv.* [*pfv.* **вы́красить**] to paint; dye.

вы́крик *n.* shout; cry; yell.

выкри́кивать *v. impfv.* [*pfv.* **вы́крикнуть**] to cry out; shout; yell.

вы́кроить *v., pfv. of* **выкра́ивать.**

вы́кройка [*gen. pl.* **-кроек**] *n.* pattern (*for sewing*).

выкрута́сы [*gen.* **-сов**] *n. pl., colloq.* **1,** twists and turns. **2,** *fig.* flourishes.

вы́крутить [*infl.* **-чу, -тишь**] *v., pfv. of* **выкру́чивать.** —**вы́крутиться,** *refl., pfv. of* **выкру́чиваться.**

выкру́чивать *v. impfv.* [*pfv.* **вы́крутить**] **1,** to twist; make by twisting. **2,** *colloq.* to twist: вы́крутить кому́-нибудь ру́ку, to twist someone's arm. **3,** *colloq.* to unscrew. —**выкру́чиваться,** *refl., colloq.* **1,** to come unscrewed. **2,** *fig.* to wiggle out (of a situation).

вы́куп *n.* **1,** redeeming; redemption. **2,** ransom.

вы́купать *v., pfv. of* **купа́ть.** —**вы́купаться,** *refl., pfv. of* **купа́ться.**

выкупа́ть *v. impfv.* [*pfv.* **вы́купить**] **1,** to redeem. **2,** to ransom.

выку́ривать *v. impfv.* [*pfv.* **вы́курить**] **1,** to finish smoking; smoke completely. **2,** to smoke out; flush out.

выла́вливать *v. impfv.* [*pfv.* **вы́ловить**] to fish out.

вы́лазка [*gen. pl.* **-зок**] *n.* **1,** *mil.* sortie; sally. **2,** excursion; outing.

вы́лакать *v., pfv. of* **лака́ть.**

выла́мывать *v. impfv.* [*pfv.* **вы́ломать**] to break open; break down (a door).

вы́лежать *v. pfv.* [*infl.* **-лежу, -лежишь**] *colloq. (of a sick person)* to remain in bed (for a certain length of time). —**вы́лежаться,** *refl.* **1,** *colloq.* to have a complete rest. **2,** to ripen; mature.

вылеза́ть *v. impfv.* [*pfv.* **вы́лезть** *or* **вы́лезти**] **1,** to crawl out; climb out. **2,** (*of hair*) to fall out.

вы́лезть *also,* **вы́лезти** [*infl. like* **лезть**] *v., pfv. of* **вылеза́ть.**

вы́лепить *v., pfv. of* **лепи́ть** (*in sense #1*).

вы́лет *n.* **1,** flight. **2,** takeoff. **3,** *mil.* mission.

вылета́ть *v. impfv.* [*pfv.* **вы́лететь**] **1,** to fly out. **2,** to leave; depart (*by plane*). **3,** (*of a plane*) to leave; take off. **4,** *fig.* to dash out; rush out. **5,** *colloq.* to be fired (from a job); be eliminated (from a tournament). —**вы́лететь из головы́,** to slip one's mind; go right out of one's mind.

вы́лететь [*infl.* **-чу, -тишь**] *v., pfv. of* **вылета́ть.**

выле́чивать *v. impfv.* [*pfv.* **вы́лечить**] (*with* **от**) to cure (of). —**выле́чиваться,** *refl.* (*with* **от**) to be cured (of).

вылива́ть *v. impfv.* [*pfv.* **вы́лить**] **1,** to pour out. **2,** *fig.* to vent (feelings). **3,** to cast; mold. —**вылива́ться,** *refl.* **1,** to run out; flow out. **2,** (*with* **в** + *acc.*) to take the form of; develop into; end up being.

вы́лизать [*infl.* **-лижу, -лижешь**] *v., pfv. of* **вылизывать.**

вылизывать *v. impfv.* [*pfv.* **вы́лизать**] to lick clean.

вы́линять *v., pfv. of* **линя́ть** (*in sense #2*).

вы́литый *adj., colloq., in* **вы́литый оте́ц** *and* **вы́литая мать,** the very image of one's father *or* mother.

вы́лить [*infl.* **вы́лью, вы́льешь**] *v., pfv. of* **вылива́ть.** —**вы́литься,** *refl., pfv. of* **вылива́ться.**

вы́ловить [*infl.* **-влю, -вишь**] *v., pfv. of* **выла́вливать.**

вы́ложить *v., pfv. of* **выкла́дывать.** —**вы́ложиться,** *refl., pfv. of* **выкла́дываться.**

вы́ломать *v., pfv. of* **выла́мывать.**

вы́лощить *v. pfv.* to polish.

вылупля́ться *v.r. impfv.* [*pfv.* **вы́лупиться**] to hatch.

вы́мазать [*infl.* **-мажу, -мажешь**] *v., pfv. of* **ма́зать** (*in senses #2 & #4*) *and* **выма́зывать.** —**вы́мазаться,** *refl., pfv. of* **ма́заться** (*in sense #2*).

выма́зывать *v. impfv.* [*pfv.* **вы́мазать**] (*with instr.*) to coat (with); cover (with).

выма́ливать *v. impfv.* [*pfv.* **вы́молить**] **1,** [*impfv. only*] to beg for; plead for. **2,** to get by begging or pleading.

выма́нивать *v. impfv.* [*pfv.* **вы́манить**] *colloq.* **1,** (*with* **из**) to lure out of. **2,** (*with* **у**) to coax out of. **3,** (*with* **у**) to cheat out of.

вы́марать *v., pfv. of* **мара́ть** (*in sense #3*) *and* **выма́рывать.**

выма́рывать *v. impfv.* [*pfv.* **вы́марать**] *colloq.* **1,** to soil; dirty. **2,** to cross out.

выма́тывать *v. impfv.* [*pfv.* **вы́мотать**] *colloq.* to exhaust; drain; use up.

выма́чивать *v. impfv.* [*pfv.* **вы́мочить**] **1,** (*of rain*) to soak; drench. **2,** to soak; steep.

выма́щивать *v. impfv.* [*pfv.* **вы́мостить**] to pave.

выме́нивать *v. impfv.* [*pfv.* **вы́менять**] to exchange; swap.

вы́мереть [*infl.* **вы́мрет;** *past* **вы́мер, -ла**] *v., pfv. of* **вымира́ть.**

вымерза́ть *v. impfv.* [*pfv.* **вы́мерзнуть**] **1,** to freeze; be destroyed by frost. **2,** to freeze solid.

вы́мерзнуть [*past* **вы́мерз, -ла**] *v., pfv. of* **вымерза́ть.**

вы́мерить *v., pfv. of* **вымеря́ть** *and* **выме́ривать.**

вы́мерший *adj.* extinct.

вымеря́ть *v. impfv.* [*pfv.* **вы́мерить**] to measure. *Also,* **выме́ривать.**

вы́мести [*infl. like* **мести́**] *v., pfv. of* **вымета́ть.**

вы́местить [*infl.* **-щу, -стишь**] *v., pfv. of* **вымеща́ть.**

вы́метать *v. pfv.* **1,** [*infl.* **-мечу, -мечешь**] *pfv. of* **вымётывать** (*in senses #1 & #2*). **2,** [*infl.* **-таю, -таешь**] *pfv. of* **вымётывать** (*in sense #3*).

вымета́ть *v. impfv.* [*pfv.* **вы́мести**] **1,** to sweep up; sweep out (refuse). **2,** to sweep (a surface).

вымётывать *v. impfv.* [*pfv.* **вы́метать**] **1,** to throw out. **2,** *in* **вымётывать икру́,** to spawn. **3,** to make (buttonholes).

вымеща́ть *v. impfv.* [*pfv.* **вы́местить**] **1,** to avenge. **2,** to vent (one's feelings): вымеща́ть свою́ доса́ду на ко́м-нибудь, to take out one's anger on someone.

вымира́ние *n.* dying out; extinction.

вымира́ть *v. impfv.* [*pfv.* **вы́мереть**] **1,** to die out; become extinct. **2,** to become depopulated; become desolate.

вымога́тель *n.m.* extortionist. —**вымога́тельство,** *n.* extortion.

вымога́ть *v. impfv.* to extort.

вы́мокнуть *v. pfv.* [*past* **вы́мок, -ла**] to get drenched; get soaked.

вы́молвить *v. pfv.* [*infl.* **-влю, -вишь**] *colloq.* to utter.

вы́молить *v., pfv. of* **выма́ливать.**

вымора́живать *v. impfv.* [*pfv.* **вы́морозить**] **1,** to air out. **2,** to kill by freezing.

вы́морить *v., pfv. of* **мори́ть** (*in sense #1*).

вы́морозить [*infl.* **-жу, -зишь**] *v., pfv. of* **вымора́живать.**

вы́мостить [*infl.* **-щу, -стишь**] *v., pfv. of* **мости́ть** *and* **выма́щивать.**

вы́мотать *v., pfv. of* **выма́тывать.**

вы́мочить *v., pfv. of* **выма́чивать.**

вы́мпел *n.* pennant.

вы́мученный *adj., colloq.* labored; forced; unnatural.

выму́чивать *v. impfv.* [*pfv.* **вы́мучить**] *colloq.* **1,** to force; wrest; wring. **2,** to force; produce only with great effort.

вы́муштровать *v., pfv. of* **муштрова́ть.**

вымыва́ть *v. impfv.* [*pfv.* **вы́мыть**] to wash. —**вымыва́ться,** *refl.* to wash; get washed.

вы́мысел [*gen.* **-сла**] *n.* **1,** fantasy; figment of the imagination. **2,** untruth; fiction; falsehood.

вы́мыть [*infl.* **-мою, -моешь**] *v., pfv. of* **мыть** *and* **вымыва́ть.** —**вы́мыться,** *refl., pfv. of* **мы́ться** *and* **вымыва́ться.**

вы́мышленный *adj.* fictitious; imaginary.

вы́мя [*gen., dat., & prepl.* **вы́мени;** *instr.* **вы́менем**] *n. neut.* udder.

вына́шивать *v. impfv.* [*pfv.* **вы́носить**] **1,** to carry; be pregnant with. **2,** to nurture (an idea); hatch (plans). **3,** *colloq.* to wear out.

вы́нести [*infl. like* **нести́**] *v., pfv. of* **выноси́ть.** —**вы́нестись,** *refl., pfv. of* **выноси́ться.**

вынима́ть *v. impfv.* [*pfv.* **вы́нуть**] to take out. —**вынь да поло́жь,** *colloq.* here and now; on the spot.

вы́нос *n.* **1,** carrying out. На вы́нос, (*of food*) to take out; "to go". **2,** funeral procession.
вы́носить [*infl.* **-ношу, -носишь**] *v., pfv. of* **вына́шивать.**
выноси́ть *v. impfv.* [*pfv.* **вы́нести;** *pres.* **-ношу́, -но́сишь**] **1,** to carry out; take out; bring out. **2,** to carry away. **3,** to get; come away with. **4,** to pass; render; pronounce; hand down (a decision, verdict, etc.). **5,** *in* вы́нести благода́рность (+ *dat.*), to thank. **6,** to stand; bear; endure: я его́ не выношу́, I can't stand him. —**выноси́ться,** *refl.* to dash out; dart out.
выно́сливый *adj.* sturdy; hardy; possessing great powers of endurance. —**выно́сливость,** *n.f.* endurance; staying power.
вынужда́ть *v. impfv.* [*pfv.* **вы́нудить**] **1,** to force; compel. **2,** to extract (a promise, confession, etc.).
вы́нужденный *adj.* forced: вы́нужденная поса́дка, forced landing; emergency landing.
вы́нуть *v., pfv. of* **вынима́ть.**
вы́нырнуть *v. pfv.* **1,** to come to the surface. **2,** *fig., colloq.* to emerge.
выня́нчивать *v. impfv.* [*pfv.* **вы́нянчить**] *colloq.* to bring up; raise; nurse.
вы́пад *n.* **1,** *sports* lunge; thrust. **2,** (verbal) attack.
выпада́ть *v. impfv.* [*pfv.* **вы́пасть**] **1,** to fall out. **2,** (*of rain, snow, etc.*) to fall. **3,** (*with dat.*) to fall to; befall. Выпада́ть на до́лю (+ *dat.*), to fall to someone's lot. **4,** to turn out to be: день вы́пал хоро́ший, it turned out to be a nice day.
выпаде́ние *n.* **1,** falling out (*of hair, teeth, etc.*). **2,** falling (*of rain, snow, etc.*). **3,** *med.* prolapse.
выпа́ливать *v. impfv.* [*pfv.* **вы́палить**] *colloq* **1,** to fire; shoot. **2,** *fig.* to blurt out.
вы́палить *v., pfv. of* **пали́ть** (*in sense #4*) *and* **выпа́ливать.**
выпа́ривать *v. impfv.* [*pfv.* **вы́парить**] to steam; steam-clean.
выпа́рывать *v. impfv.* [*pfv.* **вы́пороть**] to rip out.
вы́пасть [*infl. like* **пасть**] *v., pfv. of* **выпада́ть.**
вы́пачкать *v. pfv., colloq.* to soil; get (something) dirty. —**вы́пачкаться,** *refl., colloq.* to get (oneself) dirty.
выпека́ть *v. impfv.* [*pfv.* **вы́печь**] to bake.
вы́переть [*infl.* **-пру, -прешь;** *past* **вы́пер, -ла**] *v., pfv. of* **выпира́ть.**
вы́пестовать *v., pfv. of* **пе́стовать.**
вы́печка *n.* **1,** baking. **2,** batch (*of baked goods*).
вы́печь [*infl. like* **печь**] *v., pfv. of* **выпека́ть.**
выпива́ть *v. impfv., colloq.* to drink; like to drink; hit the bottle.
вы́пивка *n., colloq.* **1,** drinking spree; binge. **2,** drinks.
выпи́ливать *v. impfv.* [*pfv.* **вы́пилить**] to cut; cut out (*with a saw*).
выпира́ть *v. impfv.* [*pfv.* **вы́переть**] *colloq.* **1,** to push out; shove out; force out. **2,** [*impfv. only*] to stick out; jut out; protrude.
вы́писать [*infl.* **-пишу, -пишешь**] *v., pfv. of* **выпи́сывать.** —**вы́писаться,** *refl., pfv. of* **выпи́сываться.**
вы́писка *n.* **1,** writing out; copying out. **2,** (*with gen.*) subscription (to). **3,** discharge; release. **4,** excerpt.
выпи́сывать *v. impfv.* [*pfv.* **вы́писать**] **1,** to write out; make out. **2,** to copy out. **3,** to order (*by mail*). **4,** to subscribe to. **5,** to send for (*in writing*); summon; call home. **6,** to discharge. —**выпи́сываться,** *refl.* to be discharged (from a hospital).
вы́пить [*infl.* **вы́пью, вы́пьешь**] *v., pfv. of* **пить.**
выпи́хивать *v. impfv.* [*pfv.* **вы́пихнуть**] *colloq.* to push out; shove out.
вы́плавить [*infl.* **-влю, -вишь**] *v., pfv. of* **выплавля́ть.**
вы́плавка *n.* **1,** smelting. **2,** smelted metal; output of smelted metal.
выплавля́ть *v. impfv.* [*pfv.* **вы́плавить**] to smelt.
вы́плакать *v. pfv.* [*infl.* **-плачу, -плачешь**] **1,** to cry out; alleviate (sorrow, disappointment, etc.) by crying. **2,** *colloq.* to obtain by crying. **3,** *in* **вы́плакать все глаза́,** to cry one's eyes out. —**вы́плакаться,** *refl.* to have a good cry.
вы́плата *n.* payment.
вы́платить [*infl.* **-чу, -тишь**] *v., pfv. of* **выпла́чивать.**
выпла́чивать *v. impfv.* [*pfv.* **вы́платить**] **1,** to pay out; disburse. **2,** to pay; pay off; pay in full.
выплёвывать *v. impfv.* [*pfv.* **вы́плюнуть**] to spit out.
выплёскивать *v. impfv.* [*pfv.* **вы́плеснуть**] to splash out.
выплыва́ть *v. impfv.* [*pfv.* **вы́плыть**] **1,** to swim out. **2,** to sail out. **3,** to come to the surface. **4,** *fig.* to emerge; come up; come to light.
вы́плыть [*infl.* **-плыву, -плывешь**] *v., pfv. of* **выплыва́ть.**
вы́плюнуть *v., pfv. of* **выплёвывать.**
выпола́скивать *v. impfv.* [*pfv.* **вы́полоскать**] to rinse; rinse out.
выполза́ть *v. impfv.* [*pfv.* **вы́ползти**] to crawl out; creep out.
вы́ползти [*infl. like* **ползти́**] *v., pfv. of* **выполза́ть.**
выполне́ние *n.* **1,** fulfillment; execution. **2,** discharge; performance (*of one's duties*).
выполни́мый *adj.* feasible.
выполня́ть *v. impfv.* [*pfv.* **вы́полнить**] **1,** to fulfill; carry out; execute. **2,** to discharge; perform (one's duties).
вы́полоскать [*infl.* **-лощу, -лощешь**] *v., pfv. of* **полоска́ть** *and* **выпола́скивать.**
вы́полоть [*infl.* **-полю, -полешь**] *v., pfv. of* **поло́ть.**
вы́пороть [*infl.* **-порю, -порешь**] *v., pfv. of* **поро́ть** (*in sense #1*) *and* **выпа́рывать.**
вы́порхнуть *v. pfv.* **1,** to fly out; flit out. **2,** *colloq.* to dash out; dart out.
вы́потрошить *v., pfv. of* **потроши́ть.**
вы́править [*infl.* **-влю, -вишь**] *v., pfv. of* **выправля́ть.** —**вы́правиться,** *refl., pfv. of* **выправля́ться.**
вы́правка *n.* bearing; carriage.
выправля́ть *v. impfv.* [*pfv.* **вы́править**] **1,** to straighten. **2,** *fig.* to rectify; straighten out. **3,** to correct; make corrections in (a manuscript, proofs, etc.). —**выправля́ться,** *refl.* to get straightened out; straighten oneself out.
выпра́шивать *v. impfv.* [*pfv.* **вы́просить**] **1,** to obtain by persistent asking; coax out of; wheedle. **2,** [*impfv. only*] to try hard to get; keep asking for.
выпрова́живать *v. impfv.* [*pfv.* **вы́проводить**] *colloq.* to send on one's way; send packing.
вы́просить [*infl.* **-шу, -сишь**] *v., pfv. of* **выпра́шивать.**
выпры́гивать *v. impfv.* [*pfv.* **вы́прыгнуть**] to jump out; leap out.
выпряга́ть *v. impfv.* [*pfv.* **вы́прячь**] to unharness.
выпрямля́ть *v. impfv.* [*pfv.* **вы́прямить**] to straighten. —**выпрямля́ться,** *refl.* to stand erect; stand up straight.

вы́прячь [*infl.* **вы́прягу, вы́пряжешь, ...вы́прягут;** *past* **вы́пряг, -ла**] *v., pfv. of* **выпряга́ть.**

вы́пуклость *n.f.* **1,** convexity. **2,** bulge; protuberance.

вы́пуклый *adj.* **1,** convex. **2,** prominent; bulging.

вы́пуск *n.* **1,** issue; issuance. **2,** output. **3,** an issue; number; installment; edition. **4,** graduates; graduating class.

выпуска́ть *v. impfv.* [*pfv.* **вы́пустить**] **1,** to let out. **2,** to release; set free. **3,** to produce; turn out. **4,** to publish; put out. **5,** to issue (stamps, money, etc.). **6,** to graduate; turn out. **7,** to delete. **8,** to put out; let stick out. **9,** to let out (clothing). **10,** to fire (a bullet, shell, etc.). —**выпуска́ть в свет,** to bring out; publish. —**выпуска́ть из рук, 1,** to let go of. **2,** *fig.* to let slip; miss.

выпускни́к [*gen.* **-ника́**] *n.* **1,** senior. **2,** graduate.

выпускно́й *adj.* **1,** *mech.* exhaust (*attrib.*). **2,** graduation (*attrib.*); final.

вы́пустить [*infl.* **-щу, -стишь**] *v., pfv. of* **выпуска́ть.**

выпу́тывать *v. impfv.* [*pfv.* **вы́путать**] to extricate; disentangle. —**выпу́тываться,** *refl.* to extricate oneself; disentangle oneself.

вы́пучить *v. pfv., in* **вы́пучить глаза́,** to stare wide-eyed.

вы́пушка [*gen. pl.* **-шек**] *n.* edging; piping.

выпы́тывать *v. impfv.* [*pfv.* **вы́пытать**] *colloq.* to elicit; find out (information, a secret, etc.).

выпь *n.f.* bittern.

выпя́чивать *v. impfv.* [*pfv.* **вы́пятить**] *colloq.* **1,** to stick out; throw out (one's stomach, chest, etc.). **2,** *fig.* to emphasize; play up. —**выпя́чиваться,** *refl., colloq.* to stick out; jut out; protrude.

выраба́тывать *v. impfv.* [*pfv.* **вы́работать**] **1,** to make; produce; manufacture. **2,** to work out; draw up. **3,** to develop; cultivate. **4,** *colloq.* to earn. —**выраба́тываться,** *refl.* to develop. У него́ вы́работалась привы́чка (+ *inf.*), he has developed the habit of...

вы́работка *n.* **1,** making; manufacture. **2,** working out; drawing up. **3,** production; output. **4,** *colloq.* workmanship.

выра́внивание *n.* **1,** smoothing; leveling. **2,** alignment.

выра́внивать *v. impfv.* [*pfv.* **вы́ровнять**] **1,** to even; level; smooth out. **2,** to align; dress (a file, column, etc.). **3,** to straighten out (an airplane). **4,** *in* вы́ровнять шаг, to get in step; regain one's stride. —**выра́вниваться,** *refl.* **1,** to even out. **2,** to line up; dress. **3,** to develop (*physically*). **4,** to improve; get better.

выража́ть *v. impfv.* [*pfv.* **вы́разить**] to express. *See also* **вы́раженный.**

выража́ться *v.r. impfv.* [*pfv.* **вы́разиться**] **1,** to be expressed. **2,** to express oneself. Е́сли мо́жно так вы́разиться, if I (one) may say so. **3,** (*with* **в** + *prepl.*) to manifest itself (in). **4,** *in* выража́ться в су́мме (+ *gen.*), to amount to; come to. —**мя́гко выража́ясь,** to put it mildly.

выраже́ние *n.* **1,** expression; act of expressing. **2,** expression (*on one's face*). **3,** expression; feeling: чита́ть с выраже́нием, to read with expression. **4,** expression; phrase: идиомати́ческое выраже́ние, idiomatic expression.

вы́раженный *adj., usu. preceded by an adverb,* pronounced; marked. —**я́рко вы́раженная фо́рма боле́зни,** acute form of a disease.

вырази́тельный *adj.* expressive. —**вырази́тельность,** *n.f.* expressiveness.

вы́разить [*infl.* **-жу, -зишь**] *v., pfv. of* **выража́ть.** —**вы́разиться,** *refl., pfv. of* **выража́ться.**

выраста́ть *v. impfv.* [*pfv.* **вы́расти**] **1,** to grow; grow up. **2,** (*with* **из**) *colloq.* to outgrow; grow out of. **3,** (*with* **в** + *acc.*) to grow into; develop into. **4,** to appear; loom up. —**вы́расти в (чьи́х-нибудь) глаза́х,** to go up in someone's estimation.

вы́расти [*infl. like* **расти́**] *v., pfv. of* **расти́** *and* **выраста́ть.**

вы́растить [*infl.* **-щу, -стишь**] *v., pfv. of* **расти́ть** *and* **выра́щивать.**

выра́щивать *v. impfv.* [*pfv.* **вы́растить**] **1,** to raise; grow; cultivate (plants). **2,** to raise; breed (animals).

вы́рвать *v. pfv.* [*infl.* **вы́рву, вы́рвешь**] **1,** *pfv. of* **вырыва́ть. 2,** *pfv. of* **рвать** (*in sense #8*). —**вы́рваться,** *refl., pfv. of* **вырыва́ться.**

вы́рез *n.* cut; cut-out section: пла́тье с ни́зким/больши́м/глубо́ким вы́резом, low-cut dress; low-necked dress. —**треуго́льный вы́рез,** V-neck.

вы́резать [*infl.* **-режу, -режешь**] *v., pfv. of* **выреза́ть** *and* **выре́зывать.**

выреза́ть *v. impfv.* [*pfv.* **вы́резать**] **1,** to cut out; excise. **2,** to carve; engrave. **3,** to massacre; slaughter. *Also,* **выре́зывать.**

вы́резка [*gen. pl.* **-зок**] *n.* **1,** cutting out. **2,** clipping (*from a newspaper, magazine, etc.*). **3,** fillet; tenderloin (*of beef*).

вырезно́й *adj.* **1,** carved. **2,** to be cut out: вырезны́е карти́нки, pictures to be cut out.

выре́зывать *v. impfv.* = **выреза́ть.**

вы́рисовать [*infl.* **-сую, -суешь**] *v., pfv. of* **вырисо́вывать.** —**вы́рисоваться,** *refl., pfv. of* **вырисо́вываться.**

вырисо́вывать *v. impfv.* [*pfv.* **вы́рисовать**] to draw carefully; draw in great detail. —**вырисо́вываться,** *refl.* to loom; appear; be etched (*against a background*).

вы́ровнять *v., pfv. of* **выра́внивать.** —**вы́ровняться,** *refl., pfv. of* **выра́вниваться.**

вы́родиться *v.r., pfv. of* **вырожда́ться.**

вы́родок [*gen.* **-дка**] *n., colloq.* outcast.

вырожда́ться *v.r. impfv.* [*pfv.* **вы́родиться**] to degenerate.

вырожде́нец [*gen.* **-нца**] *n.* degenerate. —**вырожде́ние,** *n.* degeneration; degeneracy. —**вырожде́нческий,** *adj.* degenerative.

вы́ронить *v. pfv.* to drop.

выруба́ть *v. impfv.* [*pfv.* **вы́рубить**] **1,** to chop down; cut down. **2,** to cut out; hack out. **3,** to carve; carve out.

вы́рубка *n.* **1,** chopping down; cutting down. **2,** clearing; glade.

вы́ругать *v., pfv. of* **руга́ть.** —**вы́ругаться,** *refl., colloq.* to swear; curse.

выруча́ть *v. impfv.* [*pfv.* **вы́ручить**] **1,** to rescue; help out; come to the aid of. **2,** to make (money, a profit, etc.).

вы́ручка *n.* **1,** *colloq.* rescue: прийти́ на вы́ручку (+ *dat.*), to come to the rescue of. **2,** receipts; proceeds; takings.

вырыва́ть *v. impfv.* [*pfv.* **вы́рвать**] **1,** to tear out. **2,** to pull up (*from the ground*). **3,** to pull; extract (a tooth). **4,** to grab; snatch; wrest (something from someone). **5,** *fig.* to wring (a confession, concession, etc.); wrest (the initiative). **6,** *in* вырыва́ть из конте́кста, to take (*or* lift) out of context. **7,** [*pfv.* **вы́рыть**] to dig; dig up; exhume; unearth. —**вырыва́ться,** *refl.* [*pfv.* **вы́рвать-**

ся] **1,** to break away; break out; break loose. **2,** (*of pages*) to come out; come loose. **3,** to shoot forward; shoot ahead. **4,** (*of fire*) to shoot up; shoot out. **5,** (*of a sigh, groan, etc.*) to escape.

вы́рыть [*infl.* **-рою, -роешь**] *v., pfv. of* **рыть** *and* **вырыва́ть** (*in sense #7*).

выряжа́ть *v. impfv.* [*pfv.* **вы́рядить**] *colloq.* to dress up. —**выряжа́ться,** *refl., colloq.* to get dressed up.

вы́садить [*infl.* **-жу, -дишь**] *v., pfv. of* **выса́живать.** —**вы́садиться,** *refl., pfv. of* **выса́живаться.**

вы́садка *n.* **1,** debarkation; disembarkation. **2,** *mil.* landing. **3,** transplanting.

выса́живать *v. impfv.* [*pfv.* **вы́садить**] **1,** to drop off; let off; discharge (a passenger). **2,** to help out; help off (of or from a vehicle). **3,** to make (a passenger) get off; put off. **4,** *mil.* to land (troops); put ashore. **5,** to transplant. —**выса́живаться,** *refl.* to get off; disembark.

выса́сывать *v. impfv.* [*pfv.* **вы́сосать**] to suck out. —**вы́сосать из па́льца,** to fabricate; concoct.

высве́рливать *v. impfv.* [*pfv.* **вы́сверлить**] to drill; bore.

высвобожда́ть *v. impfv.* [*pfv.* **вы́свободить**] to free; release.

высева́ть *v. impfv.* [*pfv.* **вы́сеять**] to sow.

высека́ть *v. impfv.* [*pfv.* **вы́сечь**] to carve; carve out; hew.

выселе́ние *n.* **1,** eviction. **2,** resettlement.

выселя́ть *v. impfv.* [*pfv.* **вы́селить**] **1,** to evict. **2,** to resettle. —**выселя́ться,** *refl.* to move.

вы́сечь [*infl.* **-секу, -сечешь;** *past* **-сек, -ла**] *v., pfv. of* **сечь** (*in sense #2*) *and* **высека́ть.**

вы́сеять [*infl.* **-сею, -сеешь**] *v., pfv. of* **высева́ть.**

выси́живать *v. impfv.* [*pfv.* **вы́сидеть**] **1,** *colloq.* to sit; stay (for a certain length of time). **2,** *in* вы́сидеть до конца́ (+ *gen.*), to sit (something) out to the end. **3,** to hatch.

вы́ситься *v.r. impfv.* to tower; rise; loom.

выска́бливать *v. impfv.* [*pfv.* **вы́скоблить**] **1,** to scrape off; scrape clean. **2,** to scrape out; erase.

вы́сказать [*infl.* **-скажу, -скажешь**] *v., pfv. of* **выска́зывать.** —**вы́сказаться,** *refl., pfv. of* **выска́зываться.**

выска́зывание *n.* **1,** expression; utterance. **2,** statement; pronouncement. **3,** *logic* proposition.

выска́зывать *v. impfv.* [*pfv.* **вы́сказать**] to express. —**выска́зываться,** *refl.* **1,** to state one's opinion; have one's say. **2,** (*with* **за** *or* **про́тив**) to come out (in favor of *or* against).

выска́кивать *v. impfv.* [*pfv.* **вы́скочить**] **1,** to jump out. **2,** *colloq.* to dart out. **3,** *colloq.* (*of a sore, boil, etc.*) to appear. **4,** *colloq.* to fall out; slip out. —**вы́скочить из головы́,** to slip one's mind; go right out of one's mind.

выска́льзывать *v. impfv.* [*pfv.* **вы́скользнуть**] **1,** to slip out. **2,** to sneak out.

вы́скоблить *v., pfv. of* **выска́бливать.**

вы́скользнуть *v., pfv. of* **выска́льзывать.**

вы́скочить *v., pfv. of* **выска́кивать.**

вы́скочка *n.m. & f., colloq.* upstart.

вы́слать [*infl.* **вы́шлю, вы́шлешь**] *v., pfv. of* **высыла́ть.**

вы́следить *v. pfv.* [*infl.* **-жу, -дишь**] **1,** *pfv. of* **высле́живать. 2,** to track down; hunt down.

высле́живать *v. impfv.* [*pfv.* **вы́следить**] to follow; trail; track; shadow.

вы́слуга *n., in* **за вы́слугу лет,** by virtue of long service.

выслу́живать *v. impfv.* [*pfv.* **вы́служить**] **1,** to qualify for; receive (*through service*). **2,** *colloq.* to serve; serve out (a designated period). —**выслу́живаться,** *refl.* (*with* **пе́ред**) *colloq.* to curry favor (with).

вы́слушать *v., pfv. of* **выслу́шивать.**

выслу́шивание *n.* auscultation.

выслу́шивать *v. impfv.* [*pfv.* **вы́слушать**] **1,** to listen (to); hear out. **2,** *med.* to listen to; examine.

высма́тривать *v. impfv.* [*pfv.* **вы́смотреть**] **1,** to spot; spy; detect. **2,** (*with* **все** *or* **всё**) to look over; examine. **3,** [*impfv. only*] to look out.

высме́ивать *v. impfv.* [*pfv.* **вы́смеять**] to mock; deride; ridicule; make fun of.

вы́смеять [*infl.* **-смею, -смеешь**] *v., pfv. of* **высме́ивать.**

вы́смолить *v., pfv. of* **смоли́ть.**

вы́сморкать *v., pfv. of* **сморка́ть.** —**вы́сморкаться,** *refl., pfv. of* **сморка́ться.**

вы́смотреть [*infl.* **-трю, -тришь**] *v., pfv. of* **высма́тривать.**

высо́вывать *v. impfv.* [*pfv.* **вы́сунуть**] to stick out. —**высо́вываться,** *refl.* **1,** to stick out; jut out. **2,** to lean out.

высо́кий *adj.* [*short form* **высо́к, высока́, высоко́** *or* **высо́ко, высоки́** *or* **высо́ки;** *comp.* **вы́ше**] **1,** high. **2,** tall. **3,** *fig.* lofty; elevated. **4,** high; high-pitched.

высоко́ *also,* **высо́ко** *adv.* high: держа́ть го́лову высоко́, to hold one's head high. —*adj., used predicatively* **1,** high: о́кна бы́ли высоко́ от земли́, the windows were high off the ground. **2,** too high: э́то мне высоко́, it is too high for me.

высокока́чественный *adj.* high-quality; quality (*attrib.*).

высокоме́рие *n.* haughtiness; arrogance.

высокоме́рный *adj.* haughty; arrogant; supercilious.

высокоопла́чиваемый *adj.* high-paid.

высокопа́рный *adj.* high-flown; bombastic; grandiloquent. —**высокопа́рность,** *n.f.* grandiloquence; bombast.

высокопоста́вленный *adj.* high ranking: высокопоста́вленное лицо́, V.I.P.

высокора́звитый *adj.* highly developed.

вы́сосать *v., pfv. of* **выса́сывать.**

высота́ [*pl.* **высо́ты**] *n.* **1,** height. **2,** altitude. **3,** height(s): кома́ндные высо́ты, commanding heights. **4,** *music* pitch. —**быть на высоте́ (положе́ния),** to be equal to (*or* rise to) the occasion. —**на до́лжной высоте́,** up to the mark; up to par.

высо́тный *adj.* **1,** (*of a flight*) high-altitude. **2,** (*of a building*) very tall.

высотоме́р *n.* altimeter.

вы́сохнуть [*past* **вы́сох, -ла**] *v., pfv. of* **со́хнуть** *and* **высыха́ть.**

высоча́йший *adj.* **1,** *superl. of* **высо́кий. 2,** *pre-rev.* royal; imperial.

высоче́нный *adj., colloq.* very high; very tall.

высо́чество *n.* Highness (*title*).

вы́спаться [*infl.* **-сплюсь, -спишься**] *v.r., pfv. of* **высыпа́ться** (*in sense #2*).

выспра́шивать *v. impfv.* [*pfv.* **вы́спросить**] *colloq.* **1,** (*with acc. or* **у**) to ply with questions; pump. **2,** to find out (*by asking a lot of questions*).

выставить [*infl.* **-влю, -вишь**] *v., pfv. of* **выставлять.** —**выставиться,** *refl., pfv. of* **выставляться.**

выставка [*gen. pl.* **-вок**] *n.* **1,** exhibition; show. **2,** display. —**всемирная выставка,** world's fair.

выставлять *v. impfv.* [*pfv.* **выставить**] **1,** to put out; move out. **2,** to stick out. **3,** to exhibit; display. **4,** *colloq.* to send out; order out. **5,** to post (a guard). **6,** to put forth (demands, arguments, etc.). **7,** *colloq.* to present (in a certain light). **8,** to put down; enter (grades, a date, etc.). —**выставлять на свет,** to expose to the light. —**выставлять себя** (*instr.*), *colloq.* to make oneself out to be.

выставляться *v.r. impfv.* [*pfv.* **выставиться**] *colloq.* **1,** to stick out; lean out. **2,** *fig.* to show off.

выставочный *adj.* exhibition (*attrib.*).

выстаивать *v. impfv.* [*pfv.* **выстоять**] **1,** to stand; remain standing. **2,** *fig.* to hold out. —**выстаиваться,** *refl.* (*of wine*) to mature.

выстегать *v., pfv. of* **стегать** (*in sense #1*).

выстилать *v. impfv.* [*pfv.* **выстлать**] **1,** to cover. **2,** to pave.

выстирать *v., pfv. of* **стирать** (*in sense #4*).

выстлать [*infl.* **-стелю, -стелешь**] *v., pfv. of* **выстилать.**

выстоять [*infl.* **-стою, -стоишь**] *v., pfv. of* **выстаивать.** —**выстояться,** *refl., pfv. of* **выстаиваться.**

выстрадать *v. pfv.* **1,** to suffer; endure; have been (*or* gone) through. **2,** to achieve through suffering.

выстраивать *v. impfv.* [*pfv.* **выстроить**] *mil.* to form up. —**выстраиваться,** *refl.* **1,** *mil.* to form; line up. **2,** (*of a line*) to form.

выстрел *n.* shot: произвести выстрел, to fire a shot. —**без выстрела,** without firing a shot. —**на выстрел,** within gunshot.

выстрелить *v. pfv.* **1,** *pfv. of* **стрелять. 2,** (*of a gun*) to go off.

выстригать *v. impfv.* [*pfv.* **выстричь**] **1,** to cut off. **2,** to cut (one's hair in a certain style).

выстричь [*infl. like* **стричь**] *v., pfv. of* **выстригать.**

выстрогать *v., pfv. of* **строгать.**

выстроить *v. pfv.* **1,** *pfv. of* **выстраивать. 2,** to build. —**выстроиться,** *refl.* **1,** *pfv. of* **выстраиваться. 2,** to be built; go up.

выстукивать *v. impfv.* [*pfv.* **выстукать**] *colloq.* to tap out.

выступ *n.* **1,** projection. **2,** ledge.

выступать *v. impfv.* [*pfv.* **выступить**] **1,** to come forward; step forward. **2,** to appear (publicly): выступать на сцене, to appear on stage; выступать по телевидению, to appear on television; выступать на собрании, to address a meeting; выступать на соревнованиях, to appear (*or* take part) in a competition; выступать с речью, to give *or* deliver a speech. **3,** (*with* **за** + *acc.*) to come out in favor of; favor; advocate. **4,** (*with* **против**) to come out against; oppose. **5,** to appear (*on one's face or body*). **6,** (*of a river*) to overflow. **7,** [*impfv. only*] to jut out. **8,** [*impfv. only*] to strut; swagger.

выступить [*infl.* **-плю, -пишь**] *v., pfv. of* **выступать.**

выступление *n.* **1,** performance; appearance. **2,** speech; address.

высунуть *v., pfv. of* **высовывать.** —**высунуться,** *refl., pfv. of* **высовываться.**

высушивать *v. impfv.* [*pfv.* **высушить**] to dry; dry out. —**высушиваться,** *refl.* to dry out; become dry.

высушить *v., pfv. of* **сушить** *and* **высушивать.** —**высушиться,** *refl., pfv. of* **сушиться** *and* **высушиваться.**

высчитывать *v. impfv.* [*pfv.* **высчитать**] to calculate; compute.

высший *adj., used only as a modifier* **1,** highest: высшего качества, of the highest quality. **2,** higher: высшее учебное заведение, institution of higher learning. **3,** *with certain nouns* high: высшее командование, high command; высшая точка, the high point; climax. —**в высшей степени** (+ *adj.*), extraordinarily; most. —**высшая мера наказания,** the supreme penalty.

высылать *v. impfv.* [*pfv.* **выслать**] **1,** to send (out); mail (out). **2,** to send out; order out. **3,** to banish; exile; deport.

высылка *n.* **1,** sending; dispatch. **2,** banishment; deportation.

высыпать [*infl.* **-сыплю, -сыплешь**] *v., pfv. of* **высыпать.** —**высыпаться,** *refl., pfv. of* **высыпаться** (*in sense #1*).

высыпать *v. impfv.* [*pfv.* **высыпать**] **1,** to pour; empty (out of, into, onto). **2,** *colloq.* (*of many people*) to pour out; throng. **3,** *impers.* to break out (*in a rash*): у него высыпало на лице, his face is broken out.

высыпаться *v.r. impfv.* **1,** [*pfv.* **высыпаться**] to pour out; spill out. **2,** [*pfv.* **выспаться**] to have a good (night's) sleep.

высыхать *v. impfv.* [*pfv.* **высохнуть**] **1,** to dry out; dry up. **2,** to wither. **3,** to waste away.

высь *n.f.* **1,** height. **2,** *pl.* mountain tops.

выталкивать *v. impfv.* [*pfv.* **вытолкнуть**] to push out; throw out.

вытапливать *v. impfv.* [*pfv.* **вытопить**] **1,** to heat. **2,** to melt.

вытаптывать *v. impfv.* [*pfv.* **вытоптать**] to trample down.

вытаращить *v., pfv. of* **таращить.**

вытаскивать *v. impfv.* [*pfv.* **вытащить**] **1,** to pull out; drag out. **2,** to pull out; extract. **3,** to haul in (a fish). **4,** *colloq.* to drag (someone) somewhere against his will.

вытачать *v., pfv. of* **тачать.**

вытачивать *v. impfv.* [*pfv.* **выточить**] to make; fashion (*in a lathe*).

вытачка [*gen. pl.* **-чек**] *n.* tuck (*on a garment*).

вытащить *v., pfv. of* **тащить** (*in senses #3, 4, 5*) *and* **вытаскивать.**

вытвердить *v., pfv. of* **твердить** (*in sense #2*).

вытворять *v. impfv., colloq.* to do (something odd or foolish).

вытекать *v. impfv.* [*pfv.* **вытечь**] **1,** to flow out; run out; leak out. **2,** [*impfv. only*] to follow; result; ensue.

вытереть [*infl.* **вытру, вытрешь;** *past* **вытер, -ла**] *v., pfv. of* **вытирать.** —**вытереться,** *refl., pfv. of* **вытираться.**

вытерпеть *v. pfv.* [*infl.* **-плю, -пишь**] **1,** to endure. **2,** (*usu. neg.*) to stand it: наконец он не вытерпел, finally he could stand it no longer.

вытертый *adj., colloq.* threadbare.

вытесать [*infl.* **-тешу, -тешешь**] *v., pfv. of* **вытёсывать.**

вытеснение *n.* ouster; exclusion.

вытеснять *v. impfv.* [*pfv.* **вытеснить**] **1,** to crowd out; force out; oust. **2,** to replace; displace; supplant.

вытёсывать *v. impfv.* [*pfv.* **вытесать**] to hew.

вытечь [*infl. like* **течь**] *v., pfv. of* **вытекать.**

вытира́ть *v. impfv.* [*pfv.* **вы́тереть**] to wipe. —**вытира́ться,** *refl.* **1,** to dry oneself. **2,** *colloq.* to wear thin.
вытисня́ть *v. impfv.* [*pfv.* **вы́тиснить**] to imprint.
вы́ткать *v. pfv.* [*infl.* **вы́тку, вы́ткешь**] to weave.
вы́толкнуть *v., pfv. of* **выта́лкивать.**
вы́топить [*infl.* **-плю, -пишь**] *v., pfv. of* **выта́пливать.**
вы́топтать [*infl.* **-топчу, -топчешь**] *v., pfv. of* **выта́птывать.**
вы́торговать [*infl.* **-гую, -гуешь**] *v., pfv. of* **выторго́вывать.**
выторго́вывать *v. impfv.* [*pfv.* **вы́торговать**] *colloq.* **1,** to make; earn; clear; net. **2,** to get (a reduction in price) by bargaining.
вы́точить *v., pfv. of* **точи́ть** (*in sense #2*) *and* **выта́чивать.**
вы́травить [*infl.* **-влю, -вишь**] *v., pfv. of* **трави́ть** (*in senses #1,4, & 5*) *and* **вытравля́ть.**
вытравля́ть *v. impfv.* [*pfv.* **вы́травить**] **1,** to remove (a spot, mark, etc.). **2,** to exterminate. **3,** (*of cattle*) to trample down.
вы́требовать *v. pfv.* [*infl.* **-бую, -буешь**] **1,** to demand and obtain. **2,** to summon; send for.
вытрезви́тель *n.m.* sobering-up station.
вытрезвля́ть *v. impfv.* [*pfv.* **вы́трезвить**] to sober; sober up. —**вытрезвля́ться,** *refl.* to sober up; become sober.
вытряса́ть *v. impfv.* [*pfv.* **вы́трясти**] to shake out.
вы́трясти [*infl. like* **трясти́**] *v., pfv. of* **вытряса́ть.**
вытря́хивать *v. impfv.* [*pfv.* **вы́тряхнуть**] to shake out.
выть *v. impfv.* [*pres.* **во́ю, во́ешь**] to howl; wail.
вытьё *n., colloq.* howling; wailing.
вытя́гивать *v. impfv.* [*pfv.* **вы́тянуть**] **1,** to stretch. **2,** to draw out (air, smoke, etc.). **3,** *colloq.* to extract. **4,** *v.i., colloq.* to hold out; last.—**вытя́гиваться,** *refl.* **1,** to stretch; expand. **2,** to stretch; extend. **3,** to stretch out. **4,** *colloq.* to straighten up; stand up straight. **5,** *colloq.* to grow; shoot up. **6,** (*of one's face*) to fall.
вытяже́ние *n.* **1,** stretching. **2,** *med.* traction.
вы́тяжка *n.* **1,** drawing out. **2,** stretching. **3,** *chem.* extract.
вытяжно́й *adj.* exhaust (*attrib.*): вытяжно́й вентиля́тор, exhaust fan. —**вытяжно́й трос,** ripcord.
вы́тянутый *adj.* outstretched. —**вы́тянутое лицо́,** long face.
вы́тянуть *v., pfv. of* **вытя́гивать.** —**вы́тянуться,** *refl., pfv. of* **вытя́гиваться.**
выу́живать *v. impfv.* [*pfv.* **вы́удить**] **1,** to hook; catch (a fish). **2,** *fig., colloq.* to coax out; worm out.
вы́утюжить *v., pfv. of* **утю́жить.**
выу́чивать *v. impfv.* [*pfv.* **вы́учить**] **1,** to learn. **2,** to teach. —**выу́чиваться,** *refl.* (*with dat.*) to learn.
вы́учить [*infl.* **-учу, -учишь**] *v., pfv. of* **учи́ть** *and* **выу́чивать.** —**вы́учиться,** *refl., pfv. of* **учи́ться** (*in sense #2*) *and* **выу́чиваться.**
вы́учка *n.* **1,** training. **2,** level of training; skill.
выха́живать *v. impfv.* [*pfv.* **вы́ходить**] *colloq.* **1,** to nurse back to health. **2,** to bring up; raise.
выхва́тывать *v. impfv.* [*pfv.* **вы́хватить**] **1,** to grab; snatch. **2,** to pull out; whip out. **3,** to pick out (*at random*).
вы́хлоп *n., mech.* exhaust. —**выхлопно́й,** *adj.* exhaust (*attrib.*).
вы́хлопотать *v. pfv.* [*infl.* **-почу, -почешь**] to manage to obtain (*after much effort*).
вы́ход *n.* **1,** going out; coming out. **2,** *theat.* entrance (*onstage*). **3,** exit. **4,** *in* вы́ход к мо́рю, outlet to the sea. **5,** *fig.* way out. **6,** appearance; publication. **7,** output; yield. —**дать вы́ход** (+ *dat.*), to give vent to.
вы́ходец [*gen.* **-дца**] *n.* (*with* **из**) **1,** person originally from; émigré (from). **2,** person originally of a different social class. —**вы́ходец с того́ све́та,** apparition.
вы́ходить *v. pfv.* [*infl.* **-хожу, -ходишь**] *colloq.* **1,** *pfv. of* **выха́живать. 2,** to walk all over *or* around.
выходи́ть *v. impfv.* [*pfv.* **вы́йти;** *pres.* **-хожу́, -хо́дишь**] **1,** to go out; come out; walk out; get out. **2,** to leave. **3,** to run out; be used up. **4,** [*often* **выходи́ть в свет**] to appear; come out; be published. **5,** (*of a photograph or subject*) to come out. **6,** (*with instr.*) to come out; emerge: вы́йти победи́телем, to emerge the victor. **7,** (*of something unfortunate*) to occur. **8,** to work out; come off. **9,** to turn out: вы́шло, что..., it turned out that... **10,** (*with* **из**) to come of: из э́того ничего́ не вы́йдет, nothing will come of it. **11,** (*with* **из**) to make: из него́ вы́йдет хоро́ший врач, he will make a good doctor. **12,** [*impfv. only*] (*with* **в** *or* **на** + *acc.*) (*of a window*) to look out on; face. —**выходи́ть в мо́ре,** to put out to sea. —**выходи́ть из себя́,** to lose one's temper.
вы́ходка [*gen. pl.* **-док**] *n.* trick; prank; escapade.
выходно́й *adj.* **1,** serving as an exit. **2,** worn on social occasions: выходно́е пла́тье, party dress; cocktail dress. —*n., colloq.* day off. —**выходно́й день,** day off. —**выходно́е посо́бие,** severance pay. —**выходна́я роль,** bit part.
выхола́щивать *v. impfv.* [*pfv.* **вы́холостить**] **1,** to castrate. **2,** *fig.* to emasculate.
вы́холенный *adj.* well-groomed; trim; dapper.
вы́холостить [*infl.* **-щу, -стишь**] *v., pfv. of* **холости́ть** *and* **выхола́щивать.**
вы́хухоль *n.m.* desman.
выцара́пывать *v. impfv.* [*pfv.* **вы́царапать**] **1,** to scratch out. **2,** *colloq.* to get; obtain; wangle.
вы́цвести [*infl. like* **цвести́**] *v., pfv. of* **выцвета́ть.**
выцвета́ть *v. impfv.* [*pfv.* **вы́цвести**] to fade.
вы́цветший *adj.* faded.
вычека́нивать *v. impfv.* [*pfv.* **вы́чеканить**] to mint.
вычёркивание *n.* deleting; deletion.
вычёркивать *v. impfv.* [*pfv.* **вы́черкнуть**] to cross out; cross off; delete. —**вы́черкнуть из па́мяти,** to erase from one's memory. —**вы́черкнуть из свое́й жи́зни,** to put out of one's life.
вычё́рпывать *v. impfv.* [*pfv.* **вы́черпать**] to scoop out; bail out.
вычё́рчивать *v. impfv.* [*pfv.* **вы́чертить**] to draw; trace.
вы́чесать [*infl.* **-чешу, -чешешь**] *v., pfv. of* **вычёсывать.**
вы́честь [*infl.* **вы́чту, вы́чтешь;** *past* **вы́чел, вы́чла**] *v., pfv. of* **вычита́ть.**
вычёсывать *v. impfv.* [*pfv.* **вы́чесать**] to comb out.
вы́чет *n.* deduction. —**за вы́четом** (+ *gen.*), less; minus; after deducting.
вычисле́ние *n.* calculation; computation.
вычисли́тель *n.m.* **1,** calculator. **2,** computer. **3,** computer specialist.
вычисли́тельный *adj.* **1,** computing. **2,** computer (*attrib.*). —**вычисли́тельная маши́на,** computer.
вычисля́ть *v. impfv.* [*pfv.* **вы́числить**] to calculate; compute.

вы́чистить [*infl.* **-щу, -стишь**] *v., pfv. of* **чи́стить** *and* **вычища́ть.**

вычита́емое *n., decl. as an adj.* subtrahend.

вычита́ние *n.* subtraction.

вы́читать *v., pfv. of* **вычи́тывать.**

вычита́ть *v. impfv.* [*pfv.* **вы́честь**] **1,** to subtract. **2,** to deduct.

вычи́тывать *v. impfv.* [*pfv.* **вы́читать**] **1,** *colloq.* to learn; find out (*by reading*). **2,** to read; proofread.

вычища́ть *v. impfv.* [*pfv.* **вы́чистить**] to clean; clean out.

вы́чурный *adj.* fancy; elaborate.

вышвы́ривать *v. impfv.* [*pfv.* **вы́швырнуть**] *colloq.* to hurl out; toss out.

вы́ше *adj., comp. of* **высо́кий.** —*adv.* **1,** *comp. of* **высоко́. 2,** above. —*prep., with gen.* **1,** above; over. **2,** beyond: вы́ше моего́ понима́ния, beyond my comprehension.

вышеприведённый *adj.* cited above.

вышеска́занный *adj.* aforesaid.

вышестоя́щий *adj.* higher: вышестоя́щий о́рган, higher body.

вышеука́занный *adj.* foregoing.

вышеупомя́нутый *adj.* above-mentioned; aforementioned. —**вышеупомя́нутое,** *n.* the above.

вышиба́ла *n.m., colloq.* bouncer.

вышиба́ть *v. impfv.* [*pfv.* **вы́шибить**] *colloq.* **1,** to knock out; dislodge. **2,** to throw out; kick out.

вы́шибить [*infl.* **-бу, -бешь;** *past* **вы́шиб, -ла**] *v., pfv. of* **вышиба́ть.**

вышива́ние *n.* embroidery.

вышива́ть *v. impfv.* [*pfv.* **вы́шить**] to embroider.

вы́шивка *n.* embroidery.

вышина́ *n.* height. —**в вышине́, 1,** on high. **2,** in the sky.

вы́шитый *adj.* embroidered.

вы́шить [*infl.* **вы́шью, вы́шьешь**] *v., pfv. of* **вышива́ть.**

вы́шка [*gen. pl.* **-шек**] *n.* tower. —**бурова́я вы́шка,** oil derrick.

вы́школить *v., pfv. of* **шко́лить.**

выштукату́ривать *v. impfv.* [*pfv.* **вы́штукатурить**] to plaster; stucco.

вы́щипать [*infl.* **-плю, -плешь**] *v., pfv. of* **выщи́пывать.**

выщи́пывать *v. impfv.* [*pfv.* **вы́щипать**] to pull out; pluck.

вы́явить [*infl.* **-влю, -вишь**] *v., pfv. of* **выявля́ть.**

выявле́ние *n.* **1,** revelation. **2,** discovery.

выявля́ть *v. impfv.* [*pfv.* **вы́явить**] **1,** to reveal; display. **2,** to discover; bring to light.

выясне́ние *n.* clarification.

выясня́ть *v. impfv.* [*pfv.* **вы́яснить**] **1,** to clarify; clear up. **2,** to find out; ascertain. —**выясня́ться,** *refl.* **1,** to be discovered; become clear. **2,** to turn out: вы́яснилось, что..., it turned out that...

вьетна́мец [*gen.* **-мца**] *n.m.* [*fem.* **-мка**] Vietnamese. —**вьетна́мский,** *adj.* Vietnamese.

вью́га *n.* snowstorm; blizzard.

вьюк *n.* pack; load.

вьюно́к [*gen.* **-нка́**] *n.* bindweed.

вьюро́к [*gen.* **-рка́**] *n.* **1,** brambling. **2,** (*in combinations*) finch: го́рный вьюро́к, rosy finch.

вью́чить *v. impfv.* [*pfv.* **навью́чить**] to load (an animal).

вью́чный *adj.* pack (*attrib.*): вью́чное живо́тное, pack animal; beast of burden. —**вью́чное седло́,** packsaddle. —**вью́чная тропа́,** bridle path.

вью́шка [*gen. pl.* **-шек**] *n.* damper.

вью́щийся *adj.* **1,** (*of hair*) curly. **2,** (*of a plant*) climbing.

вя́жущий *adj.* astringent.

вяз *n.* elm.

вяза́льный *adj.* knitting (*attrib.*): вяза́льная спи́ца, knitting needle.

вяза́ние *n.* **1,** binding; tying. **2,** knitting; crocheting.

вяза́нка [*gen. pl.* **-нок**] *n.* bundle.

вя́заный *adj.* knitted.

вяза́ть *v. impfv.* [*pfv.* **связа́ть;** *pres.* **вяжу́, вя́жешь**] **1,** to bind; tie up. **2,** to knit; crochet. **3,** [*impfv. only*] *impers.* to be astringent: у меня́ вя́жет во рту, my mouth feels drawn. —**вяза́ться,** *refl.* [*impfv. only*] **1,** (*with* **с** + *instr.*) to accord (with); tally (with); square (with). **2,** (*usu. neg.*) (not) work out well: де́ло не вя́жется, things are not working out well.

вя́зка *n.* **1,** binding; tying. **2,** knitting; crocheting. **3,** *colloq.* bunch.

вя́зкий *adj.* [*short form* **-зок, -зка́, -зко;** *comp.* **вя́зче**] **1,** sticky; viscous. **2,** muddy; swampy. —**вя́зкость,** *n.f.* viscosity.

вя́знуть *v. impfv.* [*pfv.* **завя́знуть** *or* **увя́знуть;** *past* **вяз** *or* **вя́знул, вя́зла**] to get stuck.

вя́леный *adj.* dried; cured by drying.

вя́лить *v. impfv.* [*pfv.* **провя́лить**] to cure (meat) by drying.

вя́лый *adj.* **1,** faded; withered. **2,** flabby; limp. **3,** sluggish; listless. —**вя́ло,** *adv.* sluggishly; listlessly. —**вя́лость,** *n.f.* sluggishness; languor; lethargy.

вя́нуть *v. impfv.* [*pfv.* **завя́нуть** *or* **увя́нуть;** *past* **вял** *or* **вя́нул, вя́ла**] **1,** to wilt; wither. **2,** (*of a person*) to fade; decline. —**у́ши вя́нут,** one gets sick of hearing it.

вя́щий *adj., obs.* greater: для вя́щей убеди́тельности, in order to be more convincing.

Г

Г, г *n. neut.* fourth letter of the Russian alphabet.

габарди́н *n.* gabardine. —**габарди́новый,** *adj.* gabardine.

габари́т *n.* size; dimensions.

га́вань *n.f.* harbor.

га́га *n.* eider.

гага́ра *n.* loon (*bird*).

гага́рка [*gen. pl.* **-рок**] *n.* auk.

гага́т *n.* jet (*mineral*).

гаго́чий [*fem.* **-чья**] *adj.* eider (*attrib.*). —**гаго́чий пух,** eiderdown.

гад *n.* **1,** reptile. **2,** *colloq.* skunk; rat; louse.

гада́лка [*gen. pl.* **-лок**] *n.* fortuneteller.

гада́ние *n.* **1,** fortunetelling. **2,** guessing; guesswork; conjecture.

гада́тельный *adj.* doubtful; problematic; hypothetical; conjectural.

гада́ть *v. impfv.* **1,** to guess; speculate; conjecture. **2,** to tell fortunes.

га́дина *n., colloq.* = **гад.**

га́дкий *adj.* [*comp.* **га́же**] nasty; foul; vile. —**га́дкий утёнок,** ugly duckling.

гадли́вый *adj.* of disgust; of revulsion: гадли́вое чу́вство, feeling of disgust/revulsion. —**гадли́вость,** *n.f.* disgust; revulsion.

гадоли́ний *n.* gadolinium.

га́дость *n.f.* **1,** filth; muck. **2,** dirty trick; foul deed. **3,** *pl.* ugly/nasty remarks.

гадю́ка *n.* adder; viper.

га́ечный *adj., in* **га́ечный ключ,** wrench.

газ *n.* **1,** gas. **2,** *pl.* gas (*in one's stomach*). **3,** sheer silk; voile. —**дать газ,** *colloq.* to step on the gas. —**сба́вить газ,** *colloq.* to slow down.

газе́ль *n.f.* gazelle.

газе́та *n.* newspaper.

газе́тный *adj.* newspaper (*attrib.*). —**газе́тная бума́га,** newsprint. —**газе́тный киоск,** newsstand.

газе́тчик *n.* **1,** news vendor; newsboy. **2,** *colloq.* newsman; journalist.

газиро́ванный *adj.* carbonated.

гази́ровать *v. impfv.* [*pres.* **-рую, -руешь**] to carbonate.

га́зовый *adj.* **1,** gas (*attrib.*): га́зовый рожо́к, gas burner. **2,** made of sheer silk.

газоли́н *n.* gasoline.

газоме́р *n.* gas meter.

газо́н *n.* lawn. —**газонокоси́лка,** *n.* lawn mower.

газообра́зный *adj.* gaseous.

газопрово́д *n.* gas pipeline.

гаитя́нин [*pl.* **-тя́не, -тя́н**] *n.m.* [*fem.* **-тя́нка**] Haitian. —**гаитя́нский,** *adj.* Haitian.

га́ичка [*gen. pl.* **-чек**] *n.* chickadee.

га́йка [*gen. pl.* **га́ек**] *n.* nut (*for a bolt*).

гала́ктика *n.* galaxy. —**галакти́ческий,** *adj.* galactic.

галантере́я *n.* dry goods; haberdashery. —**галантере́йный,** *adj.* haberdashery (*attrib.*); haberdasher's. —**галантере́йщик,** *n.* haberdasher.

гала́нтный *adj.* gallant (*toward women*); chivalrous. —**гала́нтность,** *n.f.* gallantry; chivalry.

галдёж [*gen.* **-дежа́**] *n., colloq.* uproar; hubbub.

галде́ть *v. impfv.* [*pres.* **-ди́шь;** *1st person sing. not used*] *colloq.* to make a racket.

галени́т *n.* galena.

гале́ра *n.* galley (*ship*).

галере́я *n.* gallery.

галёрка [*gen. pl.* **-рок**] *n., colloq.* gallery (*in a theater*).

гале́та *n.* cracker; biscuit.

галиматья́ *n., colloq.* nonsense; rubbish.

галифе́ (фэ) *n. pl. or neut. indecl.* riding breeches.

га́лка [*gen. pl.* **-лок**] *n.* jackdaw. —**счита́ть га́лок, 1,** to gape. **2,** to loaf.

галл *n., bot.* gall.

га́ллий *n.* gallium.

галлици́зм *n.* Gallicism.

галло́н *n.* gallon.

га́лльский *adj.* Gallic.

галлюцина́ция *n.* hallucination.

галоге́н *n.* halogen.

гало́п *n.* gallop. —**гало́пом,** at a gallop.

галопи́ровать *v. impfv.* [*pres.* **-рую, руешь**] to gallop.

га́лочка [*gen. pl.* **-чек**] *n., colloq.* mark; check; tick.

гало́ши *n. pl.* [*sing.* **гало́ша**] rubbers; overshoes; galoshes.

галс *n., naut.* tack.

га́лстук *n.* tie; necktie.

галу́н [*gen.* **-луна́**] *n.* galloon.

галу́шки *n. pl.* [*sing.* **галу́шка**] dumplings.

гальванизи́ровать *v. impfv. & pfv.* [*pres.* **-рую, -руешь**] to galvanize.

гальвани́ческий *adj.* galvanic.

га́лька [*gen. pl.* **-лек**] *n.* **1,** pebble. **2,** pebbles.

гам *n., colloq.* racket; din; hubbub.

гама́к [*gen.* **-мака́**] *n.* hammock.

гама́ши [*gen.* **-ма́ш**] *n. pl.* leggings.

гамби́т *n.* gambit.

гаме́та *n.* gamete.

га́мма *n.* **1,** *music* scale. **2,** *fig.* gamut. —**га́мма-**

глобули́н, *n.* gamma globulin. —**га́мма-лучи́,** *n. pl.* gamma rays.
га́нглий *n.* ganglion.
гангре́на *n.* gangrene. —**гангрено́зный,** *adj.* gangrenous.
га́нгстер *n.* gangster.
гандбо́л *n.* team handball.
гандика́п *n., sports* handicap.
ганте́ль (тэ) *n.f., often pl.* dumbbell.
гара́ж [*gen.* **-ража́**] *n.* garage.
гаранти́ровать *v. impfv. & pfv.* [*pres.* **-рую, -руешь**] to guarantee.
гара́нтия *n.* guarantee.
гарде́ния *n.* gardenia.
гардеро́б *n.* **1,** cloakroom. **2,** wardrobe.
гардеро́бщик *n.m.* [*fem.* **-щица**] cloakroom attendant.
гарди́на *n.* window curtain.
гарево́й *also,* **га́ревый** *adj.* cinder (*attrib.*): гарева́я доро́жка, cinder path/track.
гаре́м *n.* harem.
га́ркать *v. impfv.* [*pfv.* **га́ркнуть**] *colloq.* to shout; bark.
гармонизи́ровать *v. impfv. & pfv.* [*pres.* **-рую, -руешь**] *music* to harmonize. *Also,* **гармонизова́ть** [*pres.* **-зу́ю, -зу́ешь**].
гармо́ника *n.* accordion. —**губна́я гармо́ника,** harmonica.
гармони́ровать *v. impfv.* [*pres.* **-рую, -руешь**] (*with* **с** + *instr.*) to harmonize (with); go well (with).
гармони́ст *n.* accordionist.
гармони́ческий *adj.* **1,** harmonic. **2,** harmonious.
гармони́чный *adj.* harmonious.
гармо́ния *n.* harmony.
гармо́нь *n.f., colloq.* = **гармо́ника.** *Also,* **гармо́шка.**
гарнизо́н *n.* garrison.
гарни́р *n.* garnish; trimmings.
гарни́ровать *v. impfv. & pfv.* [*pres.* **-рую, -руешь**] to garnish.
гарниту́р *n.* **1,** complete set. **2,** suite (*of furniture*).
гарпу́н [*gen.* **-пуна́**] *n.* harpoon.
гарпу́нить *v. impfv.* to harpoon.
га́рус *n.* worsted. —**га́русный,** *adj.* worsted.
гарцева́ть *v. impfv.* [*pres.* **-цу́ю, -цу́ешь**] to prance (*on a horse*).
га́ршнеп (нэ) *n.* jacksnipe.
гарь *n.f.* **1,** something burning: па́хнет га́рью, there is a smell of something burning. **2,** cinders.
гаси́ть *v. impfv.* [*pfv.* **погаси́ть;** *pres.* **гашу́, га́сишь**] **1,** to extinguish; put out. **2,** cancel (a stamp); liquidate (a debt). **3,** *fig.* to suppress; stifle. **4,** to slake (lime).
га́снуть *v. impfv.* [*pfv.* **пога́снуть** *or* **уга́снуть;** *past* **гас** *or* **га́снул, га́сла**] **1,** (*of a light, fire, etc.*) to go out. **2,** (*of emotions*) to fade; wane. **3,** (*of a person*) to be failing; sink.
гастри́т *n.* gastritis.
гастролёр *n.* guest performer.
гастроли́ровать *v. impfv.* [*pres.* **-рую, -руешь**] (*of a performer*) to tour; be on tour.
гастро́ль *n.f., usu. pl.* tour: выезжа́ть на гастро́ли, to go on tour. —**гастро́льный,** *adj.* touring; on tour.
гастроно́м *n.* **1,** gourmet. **2,** grocery store; delicatessen. —**гастрономи́ческий,** *adj.* gastronomic.
гастроно́мия *n.* **1,** gastronomy. **2,** groceries.
гать *n.f.* road of logs laid across a marshy area.
га́убица *n.* howitzer.
гауптва́хта *n., mil.* guardhouse; stockade.
га́фний *n.* hafnium.
гаше́ние *n.* **1,** extinguishing; extinction. **2,** cancellation (*on a postage stamp*).
гашёный *adj.* **1,** (*of a postage stamp*) used; canceled. **2,** *in* гашёная и́звесть, slaked lime.
гаше́тка [*gen. pl.* **-ток**] *n.* trigger.
гаши́ш *n.* hashish.
гвалт *n., colloq.* racket; hubbub.
гварде́ец [*gen.* **-де́йца**] *n.* guardsman. —**гварде́йский,** *adj.* guards (*attrib.*); of guards.
гва́рдия *n.* Guards: Кра́сная гва́рдия, Red Guards. —**ста́рая гва́рдия,** the old guard.
гво́здик *n.* small nail; tack.
гвозди́ка *n.* **1,** pink (*flower*); carnation. **2,** cloves. —**туре́цкая** *or* **борода́тая гвозди́ка,** sweet william.
гвозди́чный *adj.* clove (*attrib.*). —**гвозди́чный пе́рец,** allspice; pimento.
гвоздь [*gen.* **-здя́;** *pl.* **гво́зди, -зде́й, -здя́м**] *n.m.* **1,** nail. **2,** *colloq.* highlight; hit.
где *adv.* **1,** *interr.* where?: где вы рабо́таете?, where do you work? **2,** *rel.* where: я не зна́ю, где она́ живёт, I don't know where she lives. —**где бы ни,** wherever; no matter where.
где́-либо *adv.* = **где́-нибудь.**
где́-нибудь *adv.* somewhere; anywhere.
где́-то *adv.* somewhere; someplace.
гегемо́ния *n.* hegemony.
гедони́зм *n.* hedonism. —**гедони́ст,** *n.* hedonist. —**гедонисти́ческий,** *adj.* hedonistic.
гей *interj., colloq.* **1,** hey! **2,** gidd(y)ap!
ге́йзер *n.* geyser.
ге́йша *n.* geisha.
гекта́р *n.* hectare.
ге́лий *n.* helium.
гелио́граф *n.* heliograph.
гелиотро́п *n.* heliotrope.
гемоглоби́н *n.* hemoglobin.
геморро́й *n.* hemorrhoids; piles.
гемофили́я *n.* hemophilia.
ген *n.* gene.
генеало́гия *n.* genealogy. —**генеалоги́ческий,** *adj.* genealogical.
ге́незис (нэ) *n.* genesis; origin.
генера́л *n.* general. —**генера́л-майо́р,** major general (*equivalent to U.S. brigadier general*). —**генера́л-лейтена́нт,** lieutenant general (*equvalent to U.S. major general*). —**генера́л-полко́вник,** colonel general (*equivalent to U.S. lieutenant general*). —**генера́л а́рмии,** general of the army (*equivalent to U.S. full general*).
генерали́ссимус *n.* generalissimo.
генералите́т *n.* the generals.
генера́льный *adj.* general. —**Генера́льная Ассамбле́я,** General Assembly. —**генера́льный прокуро́р,** prosecutor general (*of the USSR*). —**генера́льная репети́ция,** dress rehearsal. —**генера́льный секрета́рь, 1,** secretary-general (*e.g. of the United Nations*). **2,** general secretary (*of a communist party*). —**генера́льное сраже́ние,** decisive battle; pitched battle. —**генера́льный штаб,** general staff.
генера́льский *adj.* of or for a general; general's.
генера́тор *n.* generator; oscillator.

гене́тика (нэ) *n.* genetics. —**гене́тик,** *n.* geneticist. —**генети́ческий,** *adj.* genetic.
гениа́льный *adj.* of genius. —**гениа́льность,** *n.f.* genius.
ге́ний *n.* genius.
геноци́д *n.* genocide.
геогра́фия *n.* geography. —**гео́граф,** *n.* geographer. —**географи́ческий,** *adj.* geographic.
геоде́зия (дэ) *n.* geodesy. —**геодези́ческий,** *adj.* geodetic.
геоло́гия *n.* geology. —**гео́лог,** *n.* geologist. —**геологи́ческий,** *adj.* geologic.
геоме́трия *n.* geometry. —**геометри́ческий,** *adj.* geometric; geometrical.
геополи́тика *n.* geopolitics.
георги́н *n.* dahlia. *Also,* **георги́на.**
геотерма́льный *adj.* geothermal. *Also,* **геотерми́ческий.**
геофи́зика *n.* geophysics. —**геофизи́ческий,** *adj.* geophysical.
геоцентри́ческий *adj.* geocentric.
гепа́рд *n.* cheetah.
гепати́т *n.* hepatitis.
гера́льдика *n.* heraldry. —**геральди́ческий,** *adj.* heraldic.
гера́нь *n.f.* geranium.
герб [*gen.* **герба́**] *n.* coat of arms.
герба́рий *n.* herbarium.
гербици́д *n.* herbicide; weed-killer.
ге́рбовый *adj.* bearing the coat of arms.
гериатри́я *n.* geriatrics. —**гериатри́ческий,** *adj.* geriatric.
Геркуле́с *n.* **1,** hercules. **2,** *l.c.* oatmeal.
герма́нец [*gen.* **-нца**] *n.m.* [*fem.* **-нка**] German.
герма́ний *n.* germanium.
герма́нский *adj.* **1,** German. **2,** Germanic.
гермафроди́т *n.* hermaphrodite.
гермети́чески *adv.* hermetically. —**гермети́ческий,** *adj.* airtight; pressurized.
герои́зм *n.* heroism. —**геро́ика,** *n.* heroic spirit.
герои́н *n.* heroin.
герои́ня *n.* heroine.
герои́ческий *adj.* heroic. —**герои́чески,** *adv.* heroically.
геро́й *n.* hero.
геро́йский *adj.* heroic. —**геро́йски,** *adv.* heroically.
геро́йство *n.* heroism.
геро́льд *n., hist.* herald.
геронтоло́гия *n.* gerontology.
геру́ндий *n.* gerund.
герц [*gen. pl.* **герц**] *n., electricity* cycle per second.
ге́рцог *n.* duke. —**герцоги́ня,** *n.* duchess. —**ге́рцогский,** *adj.* ducal.
ге́рцогство *n.* **1,** dukedom. **2,** duchy.
ге́тман *n., hist.* Ukrainian Cossack leader in the 17th and 18th centuries; hetman.
ге́тры *n. pl.* [*sing.* **ге́тра**] gaiters; spats.
ге́тто *n. indecl.* ghetto.
гиаци́нт *n.* hyacinth.
гиббо́н *n.* gibbon.
ги́бель *n.f.* **1,** destruction; death. **2,** wreck; crash. **3,** ruin; ruination. —**ги́бельный,** *adj.* disastrous; ruinous; fatal.
гиби́скус *n.* hibiscus.
ги́бкий *adj.* [*comp.* **ги́бче**] **1,** flexible. **2,** supple. —**ги́бкость,** *n.f.* flexibility.
ги́блый *adj., colloq.* hopeless; worthless. —**ги́блое де́ло,** hopeless case; lost cause.
ги́бнуть *v. impfv.* [*pfv.* **поги́бнуть;** *past* **гиб** *or* **ги́бнул, ги́бла**] to be killed; perish.
гибри́д *n.* hybrid. —**гибри́дный,** *adj.* hybrid.
гига́нт *n.* giant. —**гига́нтский,** *adj.* giant; gigantic.
гигие́на *n.* hygiene. —**гигиени́ческий,** *adj.* of or pert. to hygiene; hygienic. —**гигиени́чный,** *adj.* hygienic; clean; sanitary.
гид *n.* **1,** guide (*person*). **2,** *obs.* guidebook.
ги́дра *n.* hydra.
гидра́влика *n.* hydraulics. —**гидравли́ческий,** *adj.* hydraulic.
гидра́нт *n.* (fire) hydrant.
гидра́т *n.* hydrate.
гидродина́мика *n.* hydrodynamics.
гидро́лиз *n.* hydrolysis.
гидроло́гия *n.* hydrology.
гидролока́тор *n.* sonar (*device*). —**гидролока́ция,** *n.* sonar (*method*).
гидро́метр *n.* hydrometer.
гидроо́кись *n.f.* hydroxide.
гидропла́н *n.* seaplane.
гидросамолёт *n.* seaplane.
гидроста́тика *n.* hydrostatics.
гидроэлектри́ческий *adj.* hydroelectric.
гидроэлектроста́нция *n.* hydroelectric station.
гие́на *n.* hyena.
ги́кать *v. impfv.* [*pfv.* **ги́кнуть**] *colloq.* to shout; whoop.
гико́ри *n.m. indecl.* hickory.
ги́льдия *n., hist.* guild.
ги́льза *n.* **1,** shell; cartridge case. **2,** cigarette wrapper.
гильоти́на *n.* guillotine.
гильотини́ровать *v. impfv. & pfv.* [*pres.* **-рую, -руешь**] to guillotine.
гимн *n.* hymn. —**госуда́рственный гимн,** national anthem.
гимна́зия *n., pre-rev.* high school. —**гимнази́ст,** *n., pre-rev.* high school student.
гимна́ст *n.* gymnast.
гимнастерка [*gen. pl.* **-рок**] *n.* soldier's blouse.
гимна́стика *n.* gymnastics.
гимнасти́ческий *adj.* gymnastic. —**гимнасти́ческий зал,** gymnasium.
гинеколо́гия *n.* gynecology. —**гинеко́лог,** *n.* gynecologist. —**гинекологи́ческий,** *adj.* gynecological.
гине́я *n.* guinea.
гипе́рбола *n.* **1,** hyperbola. **2,** hyperbole. —**гиперболи́ческий,** *adj.* hyperbolic.
гипертони́я *n.* hypertension; high blood pressure.
гипно́з *n.* hypnosis. —**гипнотизёр,** *n.* hypnotist.
гипнотизи́ровать *v. impfv.* [*pfv.* **загипнотизи́ровать;** *pres.* **-рую, -руешь**] to hypnotize.
гипноти́зм *n.* hypnotism. —**гипноти́ческий,** *adj.* hypnotic.
гипо́теза *n.* hypothesis.
гипотену́за *n.* hypotenuse.
гипотети́ческий *also,* **гипотети́чный** *adj.* hypothetical.
гипо́физ *also,* **гипофи́з** *n.* pituitary gland.
гиппопота́м *n.* hippopotamus.
гипс *n.* **1,** gypsum. **2,** plaster of Paris. **3,** cast. —**ги́псовый,** *adj.* gypsum (*attrib.*); plaster.

гиреви́к [*gen.* **-вика́**] *n.* weightlifter.
гирля́нда *n.* garland.
гироко́мпас *n.* gyrocompass.
гироско́п *n.* gyroscope.
ги́ря *n.* **1,** weight. **2,** *sports* weight; dumbbell.
гистоло́гия *n.* histology.
гита́ра *n.* guitar. —**гитари́ст,** *n.* guitarist.
ги́чка [*gen. pl.* **-чек**] *n.* gig (*boat*).
глава́ [*pl.* **гла́вы**] *n.* **1,** *m. or f.* (*with gen.*) head (of): глава́ семьи́, head of the family. **2,** chapter. **3,** cupola; dome. **4,** *poetic* = **голова́.** —**во главе́** (+ *gen.*), at the head of. —**во главе́ с** (+ *instr.*), headed by; led by. —**ста́вить во главу́ угла́,** to put at the head of the list.
глава́рь [*gen.* **-варя́**] *n.m.* leader; ringleader.
главе́нство *n.* supremacy.
главе́нствовать *v. impfv.* [*pres.* **-ствую, -ствуешь**] **1,** to be dominant. **2,** (*with* **над**) to dominate; hold sway over.
главнокома́ндующий *n., decl. as an adj.* commander in chief.
гла́вный *adj.* **1,** main; chief; principal. **2,** head; chief. —**гла́вное,** *n.* the main thing. —**гла́вным о́бразом,** mainly; chiefly; for the most part.
глаго́л *n.* verb.
глаго́лица *n., hist.* one of the two original Slavonic alphabets; Glagolitic alphabet.
глаго́льный *adj.* verbal.
гладиа́тор *n.* gladiator.
глади́льный *adj.* ironing (*attrib.*): глади́льная доска́, ironing board.
гладио́лус *n.* gladiolus.
гла́дить *v. impfv.* [*pres.* **гла́жу, гла́дишь**] **1,** [*pfv.* **вы́гладить**] to iron; press. **2,** [*pfv.* **погла́дить**] to stroke; pet. —**гла́дить по голо́вке,** to give (someone) a pat on the back.
гла́дкий *adj.* [*short form* **-док, -дка́, -дко;** *comp.* **гла́же**] **1,** smooth. **2,** (*of material*) plain. —**гла́дко,** *adv.* smoothly.
гладкоство́льный *adj.* smoothbore.
гла́дкость *n.f.* smoothness.
гладь *n.f.* **1,** smooth surface. **2,** satin stitch.
гла́же *adj., comp. of* **гла́дкий.**
гла́женье *n.* ironing; pressing.
глаз [*2nd loc.* **глазу́;** *pl.* **глаза́, глаз**] *n.* eye. —**в глаза́ не ви́деть,** to have never seen (someone or something). —**в глаза́х** (+ *gen.*), in the eyes of. —**за глаза́, 1,** behind one's back. **2,** sight unseen. **3,** quite enough; more than enough. —**на глаза́х** (+ *gen. or* **у**), in plain view of; before the very eyes of. —**с гла́зу на глаз,** alone with one another; in private. —**с глаз доло́й, из се́рдца вон,** out of sight, out of mind.
глаза́стый *adj., colloq.* **1,** big-eyed. **2,** sharp-eyed.
глазе́ть *v. impfv., colloq.* to stare; gawk; gape.
глазиро́ванный *adj.* **1,** glazed. **2,** with icing. **3,** (*of paper*) glossy.
глазирова́ть *v. impfv. & pfv.* [*pres.* **-ру́ю, -ру́ешь**] **1,** to glaze (pottery). **2,** to put icing on. **3,** to give a glossy finish to.
глазни́к [*gen.* **-ника́**] *n., colloq.* eye doctor.
глазни́ца *n.* eye socket.
глазно́й *adj.* eye (*attrib.*).
глазо́к [*gen.* **-зка́**] *n.* **1,** [*pl.* **гла́зки**] *dim. of* **глаз. 2,** [*pl.* **глазки́**] *colloq.* peephole. —**де́лать** *or* **стро́ить гла́зки** (+ *dat.*), to make eyes (at). —**одни́м глазко́м,** with half an eye.
глазоме́р *n.* **1,** measurment with the naked eye. **2,** ability to so measure.
глазу́нья *n.* fried eggs. *Also,* **я́ичница-глазу́нья.**
глазу́рь *n.f.* **1,** glaze (*on pottery*). **2,** icing.
гла́нды *n. pl.* [*sing.* **гла́нда**] **1,** tonsils. **2,** *colloq.* swollen glands.
глас *n., archaic* voice. —**глас вопию́щего в пусты́не,** voice in the wilderness.
гласи́ть *v. impfv.* (*of a text, saying, etc.*) to read; say; go: как гласи́т погово́рка, as the saying goes.
гла́сность *n.f.* publicity. —**предава́ть (что́-нибудь) гла́сности,** to make public; publicize.
гла́сный *adj.* **1,** vowel (*attrib.*). **2,** open; public. —*n.* vowel.
глауко́ма *n.* glaucoma.
глаша́тай *n.* **1,** town crier. **2,** messenger; herald.
гле́тчер *n.* glacier.
гликоге́н *n.* glycogen.
гли́на *n.* clay.
гли́нистый *adj.* clay (*attrib.*); clayey. —**гли́нистый сла́нец,** shale.
глиноби́тный *adj.* clay (*attrib.*); mud (*attrib.*); adobe (*attrib.*).
гли́няный *adj.* **1,** clay (*attrib.*). **2,** earthenware (*attrib.*).
гли́ссер *n.* hydroplane (*boat*).
глист [*gen.* **глиста́**] *n.* (intestinal) worm.
глицери́н *n.* glycerine. —**глицери́новый,** *adj.* glycerine.
глици́ния *n.* wisteria.
глоба́льный *adj.* global.
гло́бус *n.* globe.
глода́ть *v. impfv.* [*pres.* **гложу́, гло́жешь**] to gnaw.
глокси́ния *n.* gloxinia.
гло́сса *n.* gloss (*commentary*).
глосса́рий *n.* glossary.
глота́ние *n.* swallowing.
глота́ть *v. impfv.* [*pfv.* **глотну́ть**] to swallow.
гло́тка [*gen. pl.* **-ток**] *n.* **1,** gullet. **2,** *colloq.* throat. —**во всю гло́тку,** at the top of one's lungs.
глотну́ть *v., pfv. of* **глота́ть.**
глото́к [*gen.* **-тка́**] *n.* **1,** swallow; gulp. **2,** mouthful.
гло́хнуть *v. impfv.* [*past* **глох** *or* **гло́хнул, гло́хла**] **1,** [*pfv.* **огло́хнуть**] to become deaf. **2,** [*pfv.* **загло́хнуть**] to die down; (*of an engine*) stall. **3,** [*pfv.* **загло́хнуть**] to become overgrown with weeds.
глу́бже *adj., comp. of* **глубо́кий.**
глубина́ [*pl.* **-би́ны**] *n.* **1,** depth. **2,** *pl.* depths: морски́е глуби́ны, ocean depths. —**в глубине́ души́,** in one's heart; deep down.
глуби́нный *adj.* **1,** deep; deep-water (*attrib.*). **2,** remote; out-of-the-way. —**глуби́нная бо́мба,** depth charge.
глубо́кий *adj.* [*short form* **-бо́к, -бока́, -боко́** *or* **-бо́ко, -боки́** *or* **-бо́ки;** *comp.* **глу́бже**] **1,** deep. **2,** profound. **3,** in-depth; thorough. —**глубо́кой но́чью,** in the dead of night. —**глубо́кая о́сень,** late autumn. —**глубо́кая ста́рость,** extreme old age.
глубоко́ *adv.* deeply; profoundly. —*adj., used predicatively* deep: здесь глубоко́, it is deep here.
глубоково́дный *adj.* deep-water; deep-sea.
глубокомы́сленный *adj.* profound. —**глубокомы́слие,** *n.* depth of thought; profundity.
глубокоуважа́емый *adj., used in salutations* honored; dear.

глубь *n.f.* depth; depths. —**в глубь** (+ *gen.*), deep into; far into.

глуми́ться *v.r. impfv.* [*pres.* **-млю́сь, -ми́шься**] (*with* **над**) to mock; deride.

глумле́ние *n.* mocking; derision.

глумли́вый *adj.* mocking; derisive.

глупе́ть *v. impfv.* [*pfv.* **поглупе́ть**] to become foolish; become stupid.

глупе́ц [*gen.* **-пца́**] *n.* dolt; oaf; dunce.

глупи́ть *v. impfv.* [*pres.* **-плю́, -пи́шь**] *colloq.* to be foolish; behave foolishly.

глу́по *adv.* foolishly; stupidly. —*adj., used predicatively* foolish; silly: глу́по волнова́ться из-за э́того, it is silly to get upset over that.

глупова́тый *adj.* dull; not very bright.

глу́пость *n.f.* **1,** foolishness; stupidity. **2,** foolish action; foolish thing. **3,** *usu. pl., colloq.* nonsense.

глу́пый *adj.* foolish; dumb; silly; stupid.

глупы́ш [*gen.* **-пыша́**] *n.* **1,** fulmar (*bird*). **2,** *colloq.* silly person.

глуха́рь [*gen.* **-харя́**] *n.m.* **1,** wood grouse. **2,** *colloq.* deaf person.

глу́хо *adv.* **1,** softly. **2,** vaguely. **3,** thickly. **4,** *colloq.* tight(ly). —*adj., used predicatively* quiet: в лесу́ было глу́хо, it was quiet in the woods.

глухо́й *adj.* **1,** deaf. **2,** (*of a sound*) muted; muffled; hollow. **3,** *phonet.* voiceless. **4,** closed up; having no openings. Глуха́я стена́, blank wall. **5,** latent; suppressed. **6,** (*of a forest*) dense. **7,** remote; desolate. Глуха́я у́лица, lonely street. **8,** *in* глуха́я о́сень, late autumn; глуха́я ночь, the dead of night. —*n.* deaf person.

глухома́нь *n.f.* remote corner; out-of-the-way place.

глухонемо́й *adj.* deaf-and-dumb. —*n.* deaf-mute.

глухота́ *n.* deafness.

глуши́тель *n.m.* muffler; silencer.

глуши́ть *v. impfv.* [*pfv.* **заглуши́ть**] **1,** to muffle; drown out. **2,** to deaden (pain). **3,** (*of weeds*) to choke. **4,** to turn off (the motor). **5,** to jam (a radio broadcast). **6,** *fig.* to stifle; suppress. **7,** *colloq.* [*pfv.* **оглуши́ть**] to stun (*with a blow*).

глушь [*gen., dat., & prepl.* **глуши́**; *instr.* **глу́шью**] *n.f.* **1,** wilderness; wilds. **2,** out-of-the-way place.

глы́ба *n.* **1,** block (*of ice, granite, etc.*). **2,** clod (*of earth*).

глюко́за *n.* glucose.

гляде́ть *v. impfv.* [*pfv.* **погляде́ть**; *pres.* **гляжу́, гляди́шь**] **1,** to look. **2,** (*with* **на** + *acc.*) to look at. **3,** (*with* **за** + *instr.*) *colloq.* to look after; keep an eye on. **4,** [*impfv. only*] (with **на** + *acc.*) to look out on. **5,** [*impfv. only*] *colloq.* (*with an adv.*) to look; appear; (*with instr.*) look like. —**гля́дя по** (+ *dat.*), depending on. —**идти́ куда́ глаза́ глядя́т**, to wander aimlessly; follow one's nose. —**того́ и гляди́**, one would expect (at any moment).

гляде́ться *v.r. impfv.* [*pfv.* **погляде́ться**; *pres.* **-жу́сь, -ди́шься**] to look at oneself: гляде́ться в зе́ркало, to look at oneself in the mirror.

гля́нец [*gen.* **-нца**] *n.* luster; gloss.

гля́нуть *v. pfv.* (*with* **на** + *acc.*) to glance (at).

гля́нцевый *adj.* glossy; lustrous. *Also,* **глянцеви́тый**.

гм *interj.* ahem!, hm!

гнать *v. impfv.* [*pres.* **гоню́, го́нишь**; *past fem.* **гнала́**] **1,** to drive (cattle). **2,** to urge on; ride *or* drive hard. **3,** *v.i.* to race; tear along. **4,** to hunt; chase (an animal). **5,** (*of the wind*) to blow (leaves, snow, etc.). **6,** to drive out. **7,** *colloq.* to drive (a car, truck, etc.). **8,** to distill. —**гна́ться**, *refl.* (*with* **за** + *instr.*) to chase; pursue.

гнев *n.* anger. —**гне́вный**, *adj.* angry; irate.

гнедо́й *adj.* (*of a horse*) bay.

гнезди́ться *v.r. impfv.* **1,** to nest. **2,** *fig.* to be lodged.

гнездо́ [*pl.* **гнёзда**] *n.* **1,** nest. **2,** socket. **3,** mortise.

гнёздышко [*pl.* **-шки, -шек**] *n., dim. of* **гнездо́**.

гнейс *n.* gneiss.

гнести́ *v. impfv.* [*pres.* **гнету́, гнетёшь**] to weigh on; oppress.

гнёт *n.* **1,** burden; weight; yoke. **2,** oppression.

гнету́щий *adj.* oppressive.

гни́да *n.* nit.

гние́ние *n.* rotting; decay.

гнило́й *adj.* **1,** rotten; decayed. **2,** (*of weather*) damp; muggy.

гни́лостный *adj.* putrid.

гни́лость *n.f.* rottenness.

гниль *n.f.* **1,** something rotten or decayed. **2,** mold. **3,** rot (*plant disease*).

гнить *v. impfv.* [*pfv.* **сгнить**; *pres.* **гнию́, гниёшь**; *past fem.* **гнила́**] to rot; decay.

гное́ние *n.* festering.

гнои́ть *v. impfv.* [*pfv.* **сгнои́ть**] **1,** to let rot; leave to rot. **2,** to cause to rot. —**гнои́ться**, *refl.* [*impfv. only*] to fester.

гной *n.* pus.

гнойни́к [*gen.* **-ника́**] *n.* abscess.

гнойничо́к [*gen.* **-чка́**] *n.* pustule.

гно́йный *adj.* festering.

гном *n.* gnome.

гну *n.m. indecl.* gnu.

гнус *n.* bloodsucking insects (*mosquitoes, gnats, etc.*).

гнуса́вить *v. impfv.* [*pres.* **-влю, -вишь**] to speak with a nasal twang.

гнуса́вый *adj.* **1,** (*of one's voice*) nasal. **2,** (*of a person*) speaking with a nasal twang.

гну́сность *n.f.* **1,** heinousness; infamy. **2,** heinous act; rotten thing.

гну́сный *adj.* vile; heinous; odious; infamous.

гнуть *v. impfv.* [*pfv.* **согну́ть**] **1,** to bend. **2,** [*impfv. only*] *colloq.* to drive at: куда́ ты гнёшь?, what are you driving at? —**гнуть спи́ну**, **1,** to break one's back (*i.e.* work hard). **2,** (*with* **пе́ред**) to kowtow (to).

гну́ться *v.r. impfv.* [*pfv.* **согну́ться**] to bend.

гнуша́ться *v.r. impfv.* [*pfv.* **погнуша́ться**] **1,** (*with gen. or instr.*) to disdain; have an aversion to. **2,** (*with inf.*) to disdain (to); be averse (to).

гобеле́н *n.* tapestry.

гобо́й *n.* oboe. —**гобои́ст**, *n.* oboist.

гове́ть *v. impfv.* to prepare for Communion (*by worship and fasting*).

го́вор *n.* **1,** sound of voices. **2,** manner of speaking; accent. **3,** dialect.

говори́ть *v. impfv.* [*pfv.* **сказа́ть**] **1,** [*impfv. only*] to speak; talk. **2,** to say; tell. **3,** to make; deliver (a speech, sermon, etc.). **4,** [*impfv. only*] (with **о**) to indicate; suggest: говори́ть о мно́гом, to say a lot; speak volumes. —**говори́ть само́ за себя́**, to speak for itself. —**да что вы говори́те!**, you don't say! —**и не говори́те!**, you can say that again! —**как говоря́т**, as they say. —**не говоря́ уже́ о**, not to mention; to say nothing of. —**не́чего и говори́ть**, it goes without saying. —**об э́том и говори́ть не́чего**, it is not even worth talking about; forget it. —**что и говори́ть**, to be sure; it cannot be denied. *See also* **сказа́ть**.

говори́ться *v.r. impfv.* to be said; be stated. —**как говори́тся,** as the saying goes; as they say.
говорли́вый *adj.* talkative; loquacious. —**говорли́вость,** *n.f.* loquaciousness.
говору́н [*gen.* **-руна́**] *n.m.* [*fem.* **-ру́нья**] *colloq.* habitual talker; chatterbox.
говя́дина *n.* beef.
говя́жий [*fem.* **-жья**] *adj.* beef (*attrib.*).
го́голь *n.m.* goldeneye (*duck*). —**ходи́ть го́голем,** to strut.
го́гот *n.* cackle (*of a goose*).
гогота́нье *n.* cackling (*of geese*).
гогота́ть *v. impfv.* [*pres.* **-гочу́, -го́чешь**] (*of geese*) to cackle.
год [*2nd loc.* **году́;** *nom. pl.* **го́ды** *and sometimes* **года́;** *gen. pl.* **лет** *and sometimes* **годо́в;** *other plural forms* **года́м, года́ми, года́х**] *n.* year. —**бе́з году неде́ля,** *colloq.* a very short time; only a few days. —**быть в года́х,** to be getting on in years. —**в мои́ го́ды,** at my age. —**год о́т году; год от го́да,** with each passing year. —**из го́да в год,** year after year; year in and year out. —**не по года́м,** beyond one's years: у́мный не по года́м, smart beyond one's years. —**с года́ми,** over the years. —**с Но́вым го́дом!,** Happy New Year! *See also* **лета́.**
годи́ться *v.r. impfv.* [*pres.* **-жу́сь, -ди́шься**] **1,** to do; be all right; fill the bill. **2,** (*with* **на** + *acc.*) to be good (for); do (for). **3,** (*with* **в** + *nom. pl.*) to be fit to be; be qualified to be: он не годи́тся в учителя́, he is not qualified to be a teacher. **4,** (*with* **в** + *nom. pl.*) to be old enough to be: я вам в отцы́ гожу́сь, I'm old enough to be your father. —**никуда́ не годи́ться,** to be of no use; be no good at all.
годи́чный *adj.* **1,** a year's; lasting a year. **2,** annual; yearly.
го́дность *n.f.* fitness; suitability.
го́дный *adj.* [*short form* **го́ден, годна́, го́дно, го́дны** *or* **годны́**] (*with* **к** *or* **для**) fit (for *or* to); suitable (for).
годова́лый *adj.* year-old.
годово́й *adj.* annual; yearly.
годовщи́на *n.* anniversary.
гол [*pl.* **голы́**] *n., sports* goal.
Голго́фа *n.* Calvary.
голени́ще *n.* boot top.
го́лень *n.f.* shin.
голла́ндец [*gen.* **-дца**] *n.m.* [*fem.* **-дка**] Dutchman.
голла́ндский *adj.* Dutch. —**голла́ндская печь,** tiled stove.
голова́ [*acc.* **го́лову;** *pl.* **го́ловы, голо́в, -ва́м**] *n.* head. —**в пе́рвую го́лову,** *colloq.* first of all. —**голова́ в го́лову,** neck and neck. —**на́ голову вы́ше** (+ *gen.*), head and shoulders above. —**над голово́й,** overhead. —**на све́жую го́лову,** with a fresh mind. —**на свою́ го́лову,** to one's detriment; to one's cost. —**с голово́й,** **1,** smart; bright; clever. **2,** *in* окуну́ться *or* уйти́ с голово́й в (+ *acc.*), to plunge into; become completely absorbed in. —**с головы́,** a/per head. —**с головы́ до ног,** from head to toe. —**че́рез го́лову** (+ *gen.*), over the head of; without letting someone know.
голова́стик *n.* tadpole.
голове́шка [*gen. pl.* **-шек**] *n.* smoldering piece of wood.
голо́вка [*gen. pl.* **-вок**] *n.* **1,** *dim. of* **голова́. 2,** head (*of a pin, match, etc.*). **3,** *colloq.* the people on top; the brass. —**боева́я голо́вка,** warhead.
головно́й *adj.* **1,** head (*attrib.*). **2,** *mil.* leading; advance.
головня́ [*gen. pl.* **-не́й**] *n.* **1,** charred log. **2,** smut (*plant disease*).
головокруже́ние *n.* dizziness. —**головокружи́тельный,** *adj.* dizzying; causing one's head to spin.
головоло́мка [*gen. pl.* **-мок**] *n.* puzzle; brain-twister. —**головоло́мный,** *adj.* baffling.
головомо́йка *n., colloq.* scolding; dressing-down.
головоре́з *n., colloq.* **1,** daredevil. **2,** bandit; cutthroat; desperado.
голо́вушка [*gen. pl.* **-шек**] *n., colloq. dim. of* **голова́.** —**бе́дная моя́ голо́вушка!,** woe is me!
голография *n.* holography.
го́лод *n.* **1,** hunger. **2,** starvation. **3,** famine. **4,** *fig.* dearth.
голода́ние *n.* starvation.
голода́ть *v. impfv.* to starve; go hungry.
голода́ющий *adj.* starving; hungry. —*n.* starving person; hungry person.
голо́дный *adj.* [*short form* **го́лоден, -дна́, го́лодны**] **1,** hungry. **2,** hunger (*attrib.*): голо́дные бо́ли, hunger pangs. **3,** *colloq.* (*of a meal*) meager. —*n.* hungry person. —**умира́ть голо́дной сме́ртью,** to die of hunger/starvation; starve to death.
голодо́вка *n.* **1,** *colloq.* starvation. **2,** hunger strike.
гололе́дица *n.* **1,** icy surface. **2,** icy conditions.
го́лос [*pl.* **голоса́**] *n.* **1,** voice. **2,** vote. —**во весь го́лос,** at the top of one's lungs. —**в оди́н го́лос,** with one voice.
голоси́стый *adj.* having a loud voice.
голоси́ть *v. impfv.* [*pres.* **-лошу́, -лоси́шь**] *colloq.* to wail.
голосло́вно *adv.* without (furnishing) any evidence.
голосло́вный *adj.* groundless; unfounded; unsubstantiated. —**что́бы не быть голосло́вным,** by way of evidence; to back up my statement.
голосова́ние *n.* voting; vote. —**ста́вить** (*e.g.* **вопро́с**) **на голосова́ние,** to put to the vote.
голосова́ть *v. impfv.* [*pfv.* **проголосова́ть;** *pres.* **-су́ю, -су́ешь**] **1,** (*with* **за** *or* **про́тив**) to vote (for *or* against). **2,** (*with a dir. obj.*) to vote on. **3,** *colloq.* to hitchhike; thumb a ride.
голосово́й *adj.* vocal.
голубе́ть *v. impfv.* [*pfv.* **поголубе́ть**] **1,** to turn blue; become blue. **2,** [*impfv. only*] (*of anything blue*) to shine; gleam.
голубизна́ *n.* bright blue color.
голуби́ный *adj.* pigeon (*attrib.*).
голу́бка [*gen. pl.* **-бок**] *n.* **1,** female pigeon. **2,** (*in direct address*) darling; sweetheart.
голубова́тый *adj.* bluish.
голубо́й *adj.* light blue; sky-blue.
голубо́к [*gen.* **-бка́**] *n., dim. of* **го́лубь.**
голубцы́ *n. pl.* [*sing.* **голубе́ц**] stuffed cabbage.
голу́бчик *n., used in direct address,* my dear fellow; my friend.
го́лубь [*pl.* **го́луби, -бе́й, -бя́м**] *n.m.* pigeon; dove.
голубя́тник *n.* pigeon lover.
голубя́тня [*gen. pl.* **-тен**] *n.* dovecote; pigeon house.
го́лый *adj.* naked; bare.
голы́ш [*gen.* **-ша́**] *n.* **1,** *colloq.* naked child. **2,** *obs.* pauper. **3,** pebble.
голышо́м *adv., colloq.* stark naked; in the nude.
голь *n.f., obs.* **1,** the poor. **2,** wasteland.
го́льмий *n.* holmium.

гольф *n.* golf.
гольян *n.* minnow.
гомеопа́тия *n.* homeopathy. —**гомеопа́т,** *n.* homeopath. —**гомеопати́ческий,** *adj.* homeopathic.
гомогенизи́ровать *v. impfv. & pfv.* [*pres.* **-рую, -руешь**] to homogenize.
гомоге́нный *adj.* homogenous.
го́мон *n., colloq.* hum (*of voices*); hubbub.
гомосексуали́зм *n.* homosexuality. —**гомосексуали́ст,** *n.* homosexual. —**гомосексуа́льный,** *adj.* homosexual.
гонг *n.* gong.
гондо́ла *n.* gondola. —**гондолье́р,** *n.* gondolier.
гоне́ние *n.* persecution.
гоне́ц [*gen.* **-нца́**] *n.* messenger.
гони́тель *n.m.* persecutor.
го́нка [*gen. pl.* **-нок**] *n.* **1,** *usu. pl.* race: автомоби́льные го́нки, automobile race. **2,** *colloq.* rush; hurry. **3,** *obs.* dressing-down. —**го́нка вооруже́ний,** arms race.
гоноко́кк *n.* gonococcus.
го́нор *n.* arrogance; conceit.
гонора́р *n.* fee; royalty; honorarium.
гоноре́я *n.* gonorrhea.
го́ночный *adj.* racing (*attrib.*).
гонт *n.* shingles (*for roofing*).
гонча́р [*gen.* **-чара́**] *n.* potter. —**гонча́рный,** *adj.* pottery (*attrib.*); potter's.
го́нчая *n., decl. as an adj.* hound; beagle.
го́нщик *n.* racing driver.
гоня́ть *v. impfv., indeterm. of* **гнать.** —**гоня́ться,** *refl., indeterm. of* **гна́ться.**
гопа́к [*gen.* **-пака́**] *n.* gopak (*Ukrainian dance*).
гора́ [*acc.* **го́ру;** *pl.* **го́ры, гор, гора́м**] *n.* mountain. —**в го́ру,** uphill. —**гора́ с плеч,** a load off one's shoulders. —**идти́ в го́ру,** to come up in the world. —**наде́яться на кого́-нибудь как на ка́менную го́ру,** to rely fully on; put implicit faith in. —**не за гора́ми,** not far off. —**по́д гору,** downhill. —**стоя́ть за кого́-нибудь горо́й,** to stand behind (someone) completely.
гора́зд *adj.* (*with* **на** + *acc. or* **в** + *prepl.*) *colloq.* good (at). —**кто во что гора́зд,** each in his own way.
гора́здо *adv., used only with comparative adjectives* much; far.
горб [*gen.* **горба́;** *2nd loc.* **горбу́**] *n.* hump.
горба́тый *adj.* **1,** hunchbacked; humpbacked. **2,** (*of one's nose*) hooked. —*n.* hunchback; humpback.
горби́на *n.* bump; rise.
горби́нка *n., in* **нос с горби́нкой,** hooked nose.
го́рбить *v. impfv.* [*pfv.* **сго́рбить;** *pres.* **-блю, -бишь**] to hunch. —**го́рбиться,** *refl.* to hunch one's back; be hunched over.
горбу́н [*gen.* **-буна́**] *n.m.* [*fem.* **-бу́нья**] hunchback; humpback.
горбу́шка [*gen. pl.* **-шек**] *n.* end crust.
горде́ливый *adj.* proud; haughty.
горде́ц [*gen.* **-деца́**] *n.* proud man; haughty man.
го́рдиев *adj., in* **го́рдиев у́зел,** Gordian knot.
горди́ться *v.r. impfv.* [*pres.* **-жу́сь, -ди́шься**] (*with instr.*) to be proud (of).
го́рдо *adv.* proudly.
го́рдость *n.f.* pride.
го́рдый *adj.* proud.
го́ре *n.* **1,** grief. Уби́тый го́рем, grief-stricken. **2,** misfortune. —**го́ре мне!,** woe is me! —**на своё го́ре,** to one's grief; to one's sorrow.
горева́ть *v. impfv.* [*pres.* **-рю́ю, -рю́ешь**] to mourn; grieve.
горе́лка [*gen. pl.* **-лок**] *n.* **1,** burner: га́зовая горе́лка, gas burner. **2,** torch: сва́рочная горе́лка, welding torch.
горе́лки [*gen.* **-лок**] *n. pl.* children's game similar to tag.
горе́лый *adj.* burnt.
горемы́ка *n.m. & f., colloq.* hapless creature; unlucky soul.
горе́ние *n.* **1,** burning; combustion. **2,** *fig.* ardor; enthusiasm.
го́рестный *adj.* sorrowful; mournful.
го́ресть *n.f.* **1,** sorrow; grief. **2,** *pl.* misfortunes; sorrows.
горе́ть *v. impfv.* [*pres.* **-рю́, -ри́шь**] **1,** to burn; be on fire. **2,** to be on; be burning. **3,** to shine; sparkle. **4,** *fig.* (*with instr.*) to burn; seethe (with an emotion).
го́рец [*gen.* **-рца**] *n.* mountaineer; highlander.
гореча́вка *n.* gentian.
го́речь *n.f.* **1,** bitter taste. **2,** something bitter. **3,** *fig.* bitterness.
горже́т *n.* fur neckpiece. *Also,* **горже́тка.**
горизо́нт *n.* horizon.
горизонта́ль *n.f.* **1,** horizontal line; horizontal. **2,** contour line.
горизонта́льный *adj.* horizontal. —**горизонта́льно,** *adv.* horizontally.
гори́лла *n.* gorilla.
гори́стый *adj.* mountainous.
горихво́стка [*gen. pl.* **-ток**] *n.* redstart.
го́рка [*gen. pl.* **-рок**] *n.* **1,** hill; hillock. **2,** (glass) cabinet. **3,** *aero.* vertical climb. **4,** sliding board.
го́ркнуть *v. impfv.* [*pfv.* **прого́ркнуть;** *past* **го́ркнул** *or* **горк, го́ркла**] to turn rancid.
горла́нить *v. impfv., colloq.* to bellow.
го́рлица *n.* turtledove. *Also,* **го́рлинка.**
го́рло *n.* **1,** throat. **2,** neck (*of a bottle*). —**во всё го́рло,** at the top of one's lungs.
горлово́й *adj.* **1,** throat (*attrib.*). **2,** guttural.
го́рлышко [*pl.* **-шки, -шек**] *n., dim. of* **го́рло.**
горля́нка *n.* calabash; gourd.
гормо́н *n.* hormone.
горн *n.* **1,** furnace; forge. **2,** bugle.
горни́ло *n.* crucible.
горни́ст *n.* bugler.
го́рничная *n., decl. as an adj.* maid; housemaid; chambermaid.
горнопромы́шленный *adj.* mining (*attrib.*).
горнорабо́чий *n., decl. as an adj.* miner.
горноста́й *n.* ermine. —**горноста́евый,** *adj.* ermine.
го́рный *adj.* **1,** mountain (*attrib.*). **2,** mountainous. **3,** mining (*attrib.*). **4,** mineral (*attrib.*). —**го́рное де́ло,** mining. —**го́рная поро́да,** *geol.* rock. —**го́рное со́лнце,** artificial sunlight. —**го́рный хруста́ль,** rock crystal.
горня́к [*gen.* **-няка́**] *n.* **1,** miner. **2,** mining engineer. **3,** mining student.
го́род [*pl.* **города́**] *n.* city; town. —**за́ город,** to the country; out of town. —**за́ городом,** in the country; out of town.
городи́ть *v. impfv.* [*pres.* **-рожу́, -ро́дишь** *or* **-роди́шь**] *colloq.* to talk (nonsense).

городки́ [*gen.* **-ко́в**] *n. pl.* game similar to skittles.
городо́к [*gen.* **-дка́**] *n.* **1,** small town. **2,** premises of an institution: медици́нский городо́к, medical center; вое́нный городо́к, military post; университе́тский городо́к, campus.
городско́й *adj.* city (*attrib.*); town (*attrib.*); municipal; urban.
горожа́нин [*pl.* **-жа́не, -жа́н**] *n.* city dweller; townsman.
гороско́п *n.* horoscope.
горо́х *n.* peas. —**как об сте́нку горо́х,** like talking to a stone wall.
горо́ховый *adj.* pea (*attrib.*).
горо́шек [*gen.* **-шка**] *n.* **1,** *dim. of* **горо́х. 2,** polka dots. —**души́стый горо́шек,** sweet peas.
горо́шина *n.* pea.
горсове́т *n.* municipal council (*contr. of* **городско́й сове́т**).
го́рсточка [*gen. pl.* **-чек**] *n.* handful.
го́рсть [*gen.* **го́рсти, -сте́й, -стя́м**] *n.f.* **1,** hollow of the hand. **2,** (*with gen.*) handful (of).
горта́нный *adj.* **1,** laryngeal. **2,** guttural.
горта́нь *n.f.* larynx.
горте́нзия (тэ) *n.* hydrangea.
горчи́ть *v. impfv.* to taste bitter; have a bitter taste.
горчи́ца *n.* mustard. —**горчи́чник,** *n.* mustard plaster. —**горчи́чница,** *n.* mustard pot. —**горчи́чный,** *adj.* mustard (*attrib.*).
горше́чник *n.* master potter.
горше́чный *adj.* **1,** pottery (*attrib.*); potter's. **2,** (*of plants*) potted.
горшо́к [*gen.* **-шка́**] *n.* (earthenware) pot. —**ночно́й горшо́к,** chamber pot.
го́рькая *n., decl. as an adj.* **1,** vodka. **2,** bitters.
го́рький *adj.* [*short form* **го́рек, горька́, го́рько;** *comp.* **го́рче**] bitter. —**го́рький пья́ница,** heavy drinker. —**пить го́рькую,** to drink hard; hit the bottle.
го́рько *adv.* bitterly. —*adj., used predicatively* **1,** bitter: у меня́ го́рько во рту, I have a bitter taste in my mouth. **2,** (*with inf.*) distressing: мне го́рько слы́шать таки́е слова́, it distresses me to hear such words.
горю́чее *n., decl. as an adj.* (motor) fuel. —**горю́честь,** *n.f.* combustibility. —**горю́чий,** *adj.* combustible; inflammable.
горя́чий *adj.* [*short form* **горя́ч, -ча́, -чо́**] **1,** hot. **2,** ardent; passionate. **3,** heated; intense. **4,** warm; hearty. **5,** hot-tempered. **6,** busy; hectic. —**по горя́чим следа́м, 1,** hot on the trail. **2,** without delay.
горячи́ть *v. impfv.* [*pfv.* **разгорячи́ть**] **1,** to heat; make hot. **2,** to excite; arouse. —**горячи́ться,** *refl.* to become excited; get hot under the collar.
горя́чка *n., colloq.* **1,** fever. **2,** fever; panic: биржева́я горя́чка, speculative fever. **3,** bustle; rush. **4,** *m. & f.* hothead.
горя́чность *n.f.* **1,** ardor; fervor. **2,** hot temper.
горячо́ *adv.* **1,** hotly; heatedly. **2,** ardently; fervently. —*adj., used predicatively* hot: куй желе́зо, пока́ горячо́, strike while the iron is hot.
госба́нк *n.* State Bank (*contr. of* **Госуда́рственный банк**).
госпитализа́ция *n.* hospitalization.
госпитализи́ровать *v. impfv. & pfv.* [*pres.* **-рую, -руешь**] to hospitalize.
го́спиталь *n.m.* (military) hospital. —**госпита́льный,** *adj.* hospital (*attrib.*).
госпо́день [*fem.* **-дня**] *adj.* the Lord's. —**гроб госпо́день,** the Holy Sepulcher. —**ле́та госпо́дня,** (*with dates*) of the year of our Lord. —**моли́тва госпо́дня,** the Lord's Prayer.
го́споди *interj.* good Lord!; good heavens! —**го́споди поми́луй!,** Lord have mercy!
господи́н [*pl.* **господа́, -по́д, -пода́м**] *n.* **1,** master. **2,** gentleman. **3,** (*in direct address to foreigners*) Mister; Mr.
госпо́дство *n.* **1,** domination; dominion. **2,** dominance; supremacy.
госпо́дствовать *v. impfv.* [*pres.* **-ствую, -ствуешь**] **1,** (*with* **над, в** *or* **на**) to dominate. **2,** to predominate. **3,** (*with* **над**) to dominate; tower over.
госпо́дствующий *adj.* **1,** ruling; dominant. **2,** prevailing.
госпо́дь *n.m., often cap.* Lord; God. *See also* **го́споди.**
госпожа́ *n., fem. of* **господи́н,** Mrs.; madam.
гostеприи́мный *adj.* hospitable. —**гостеприи́мство,** *n.* hospitality.
гости́ная *n., decl. as an adj.* living room; drawing room; sitting room; parlor.
гости́ница *n.* hotel.
гости́ный *adj., in* **гости́ный двор,** *pre-rev.* arcade.
гости́ть *v. impfv.* [*pres.* **гощу́, гости́шь**] (*with* **у**) to be a guest (of); stay (with).
гость [*pl.* **го́сти, -сте́й, -стя́м**] *n.m.* [*fem.* **го́стья**] guest. —**быть в гостя́х** (*with* **у**), to be a guest (of); be visiting. —**идти́ в го́сти,** to go visiting.
госуда́рственный *adj.* **1,** state (*attrib.*); government (*attrib.*). **2,** national: госуда́рственный гимн, national anthem. —**госуда́рственные дела́,** affairs of state. —**госуда́рственный де́ятель,** statesman. —**госуда́рственная изме́на,** high treason. —**госуда́рственный переворо́т,** coup d'état. —**госуда́рственное пра́во,** constitutional law. —**госуда́рственный слу́жащий,** civil servant. —**госуда́рственная слу́жба,** government service; civil service. —**госуда́рственный язы́к,** official language.
госуда́рство *n.* **1,** state. **2,** the State.
госуда́рь *n.m.* **1,** sovereign. **2,** (*in direct address*) Your Majesty; Sire.
гот *n.* Goth. —**го́тика,** *n.* Gothic architecture. —**готи́ческий,** *adj.* Gothic.
гото́вить *v. impfv.* [*pfv.* **пригото́вить;** *pres.* **-влю, -вишь**] **1,** to prepare. **2,** to cook. **3,** [*impfv. only*] to train. —**гото́виться,** *refl.* **1,** (*with* **к**) to prepare (for); get ready (for). **2,** [*impfv. only*] to be in the offing.
гото́вность *n.f.* **1,** readiness; preparedness. **2,** readiness; willingness.
гото́вый *adj.* **1,** ready. **2,** prepared. **3,** willing. **4,** (*of goods*) finished; (*of clothes*) ready-made; ready-to-wear; (*of a dish*) ready to serve.
го́тский *adj.* Gothic: го́тский язы́к, Gothic.
го́фер *n.* gopher.
гофрирова́ть *v. impfv. & pfv.* [*pres.* **-ру́ю, -ру́ешь**] **1,** to corrugate. **2,** to emboss.
граб *n.* hornbeam.
грабёж [*gen.* **-бежа́**] *n.* **1,** robbery. **2,** pillage. —**грабёж на большо́й доро́ге,** highway robbery.
граби́тель *n.m.* robber.
граби́тельский *adj.* **1,** predatory. **2,** (*of prices*) exorbitant; prohibitive.
гра́бить *v. impfv.* [*pfv.* **огра́бить;** *pres.* **-блю, -бишь**] **1,** to rob. **2,** to sack; plunder; pillage.

гра́бли [*gen.* **-бель** *or* **-блей**] *n. pl.* rake.

гравёр *n.* engraver; etcher.

гра́вий *n.* gravel.

гравирова́льный *adj.* engraving (*attrib.*).

гравирова́ние *n.* engraving.

гравирова́ть *v. impfv.* [*pfv.* **вы́гравировать;** *pres.* **-ру́ю, -ру́ешь**] to engrave; etch.

гравиро́вка *n.* engraving.

гравита́ция *n.* gravitation.

гравю́ра *n.* engraving; etching; print. —**гравю́ра на де́реве,** woodcut.

град *n.* **1,** hail: град идёт, it is hailing. **2,** *fig.* hail; flurry; shower; volley: град пуль, hail of bullets. **3,** *archaic* city.

града́ция *n.* gradation.

градие́нт *n., physics* gradient.

гра́дина *n., colloq.* hailstone.

гради́рня [*gen. pl.* **-рен**] *n.* **1,** salt pan. **2,** cooling tower.

гра́дом *adv.* thick and fast.

градострои́тельство *n.* town planning; urban planning; urban development.

градуи́ровать *v. impfv. & pfv.* [*pres.* **-рую, -руешь**] to calibrate. —**градуи́рованная шкала́,** graduated scale.

гра́дус *n.* degree: со́рок гра́дусов, 40°.

гра́дусник *n., colloq.* thermometer.

граждани́н [*pl.* **гра́ждане, -дан**] *n.m.* [*fem.* **-да́нка**] **1,** citizen. **2,** man.

гражда́нский *adj.* **1,** civil: гражда́нская война́, civil war. **2,** civilian: гражда́нское пла́тье, civilian clothes. **3,** civic: гражда́нский долг, civic duty.

гражда́нство *n.* citizenship.

грамза́пись *n.f.* recording.

грамм *n.* gram.

грамма́тика *n.* grammar. —**граммати́ст,** *n.* grammarian. —**граммати́ческий,** *adj.* grammatical.

граммофо́н *n.* phonograph. —**граммофо́нный,** *adj.* phonograph (*attrib.*).

гра́мота *n.* **1,** ability to read and write. **2,** document; deed. —**вери́тельные гра́моты,** credentials. —**ратификацио́нные гра́моты,** instruments of ratification.

гра́мотно *adv.* **1,** grammatically. **2,** competently.

гра́мотность *n.f.* **1,** literacy. **2,** grammatical correctness. **3,** knowledgeability.

гра́мотный *adj.* **1,** literate; educated. **2,** grammatically correct. **3,** knowledgeable; competent.

грампласти́нка [*gen. pl.* **-нок**] *n.* phonograph record (*contr. of* **граммофо́нная пласти́нка**).

гран [*gen. pl.* **гран**] *n.* grain (*unit of weight*).

грана́т *n.* **1,** pomegranate. **2,** garnet.

грана́та *n.* grenade. —**грана́тный,** *adj.* grenade (*attrib.*).

грана́товый *adj.* **1,** pomegranate (*attrib.*). **2,** garnet (*attrib.*).

гранатомёт *n.* grenade launcher.

грандио́зный *adj.* grandiose; vast; huge; tremendous. —**грандио́зность,** *n.f.* grandeur; immensity.

гранёный *adj.* (*of glass, gems, etc.*) cut.

грани́льный *adj.* lapidary. —**грани́льщик,** *n.* lapidary; diamond cutter.

грани́т *n.* granite. —**грани́тный,** *adj.* granite.

грани́ть *v. impfv.* to cut (glass, gems, etc.).

грани́ца *n.* **1,** border; boundary; frontier. **2,** *usu. pl.* limits; bounds: не знать грани́ц, to know no bounds. —**за грани́цей,** abroad (*location*). —**за грани́цу,** abroad (*direction*). —**из-за грани́цы,** from abroad.

грани́чить *v. impfv.* (*with* **с** + *instr.*) **1,** to border (on). **2,** *fig.* to border (on); verge (on).

гра́нка [*gen. pl.* **-нок**] *n.* (galley) proof.

гранули́ровать *v. impfv. & pfv.* [*pres.* **-рую, -руешь**] to granulate.

грануля́ция *n.* granulation.

грань *n.f.* **1,** boundary. **2,** verge; brink: на гра́ни вымира́ния, on the verge of extinction. **3,** side; surface (*of a geometric figure*). **4,** line (*i.e.* distinction); провести́ грань ме́жду, to draw a line/distinction between. **5,** facet (*of a gem*).

граф *n.* count; earl.

графа́ *n.* column (*of a page*).

гра́фик *n.* **1,** graph; chart. **2,** schedule; timetable. **3,** graphic artist.

гра́фика *n.* graphic arts.

графи́н *n.* carafe; decanter.

графи́ня *n.* countess.

графи́т *n.* **1,** graphite. **2,** lead (*for a pencil*). —**графи́товый,** *adj.* graphite (*attrib.*).

графи́ть *v. impfv.* [*pfv.* **разграфи́ть;** *pres.* **-флю́, -фи́шь**] to rule (paper).

графи́ческий *adj.* graphic.

графлёный *adj.* (*of paper*) ruled.

гра́фство *n.* county; shire.

грацио́зный *adj.* graceful. —**грацио́зно,** *adv.* gracefully.

гра́ция *n.* grace.

грач [*gen.* **грача́**] *n.* rook (*bird*).

гребёнка [*gen. pl.* **-нок**] *n.* comb. —**стричь кого́-нибудь под гребёнку,** to crop someone's hair. —**стричь под одну́ гребёнку,** to lump together.

гре́бень [*gen.* **-бня**] *n.m.* **1,** comb. **2,** comb (*of fowl*); crest (*of a bird*). **3,** crest (*of a wave, mountain, etc.*). **4,** ridge (*of a roof*). **5,** ridge (*of plowed land*).

гребе́ц [*gen.* **-бца́**] *n.* rower; oarsman.

гребешо́к [*gen.* **-шка́**] *n.* **1,** *dim. of* **гре́бень. 2,** scallop.

гре́бля *n.* rowing.

гребно́й *adj.* rowing (*attrib.*). —**гребно́й винт,** screw propeller. —**гребно́е колесо́,** paddle wheel. —**гребна́я ло́дка/шлю́пка,** rowboat.

гребо́к [*gen.* **-бка́**] *n.* **1,** stroke (*of an oar*). **2,** paddle.

грёза *n.* dream; vision. —**мир грёз; ца́рство грёз,** dreamworld; dreamland.

гре́зить *v. impfv.* [*pres.* **гре́жу, гре́зишь**] to dream; daydream. —**гре́зиться,** *refl.* [*pfv.* **пригре́зиться**] (*with dat.*) to appear in one's dreams: она́ ему́ ча́сто гре́зилась, he often dreamt about her.

гре́йдер (дэ) *n.* **1,** *mech.* grader. **2,** *colloq.* graded road.

гре́йпфрут *n.* grapefruit.

грек *n.m.* [*fem.* **греча́нка**] Greek.

гре́лка [*gen. pl.* **-лок**] *n.* hot-water bottle. —**электри́ческая гре́лка,** heating pad.

греме́ть *v. impfv.* [*pres.* **-млю́, -ми́шь**] **1,** to thunder; rumble. **2,** to ring out; resound. **3,** to clank; rattle; jingle. **4,** (*with instr.*) to rattle; jingle. **5,** *fig.* to be famous.

грему́чий *adj.* **1,** thundering. **2,** rattling. —**грему́чая змея́,** rattlesnake. —**грему́чая ртуть,** fulminate of mercury.

гренаде́р [*gen. pl.* **-де́р**] *n.* grenadier.

гренки́ *n. pl.* [*sing.* **грено́к**] croutons.

грести́ *v. impfv.* [*pres.* **гребу́, гребёшь;** *past* **грёб, гребла́, гребло́**] **1,** to row; paddle. **2,** to rake.

греть *v. impfv.* **1,** to warm. **2,** to provide warmth: со́лнце гре́ет, the sun is warm; шу́ба гре́ет, the coat keeps one warm. **3,** to heat; heat up. —**гре́ться,** *refl.* **1,** to warm oneself. **2,** to warm up; get warm. **3,** to bask (in the sun).

грех [*gen.* **греха́**] *n.* sin. —**как на грех,** as luck would have it. —**не́чего греха́ таи́ть,** we might as well admit it. —**от греха́ пода́льше,** out of harm's way. —**с грехо́м попола́м,** barely; by the skin of one's teeth.

гре́цкий *adj., in* **гре́цкий оре́х,** walnut.

греча́нка [*gen. pl.* **-нок**] *n.* Greek woman.

гре́ческий *adj.* Greek.

гречи́ха *n.* buckwheat.

гре́чневый *adj.* buckwheat (*attrib.*).

греши́ть *v. impfv.* **1,** [*pfv.* **согреши́ть**] to sin. **2,** [*pfv.* **погреши́ть**] (*with* **про́тив**) to go against: греши́ть про́тив ло́гики, to go against logic.

гре́шник *n.* sinner.

грешно́ *adv., used predicatively with inf.* it's a sin (to); it is wrong (to).

гре́шный *adj.* **1,** sinful. **2,** [*short form only* — **гре́шен, грешна́**] *colloq.* guilty. —**гре́шным де́лом,** I must admit; sad to say.

грешо́к [*gen.* **-шка́**] *n.* sin; peccadillo.

гриб [*gen.* **гриба́**] *n.* mushroom.

грибко́вый *adj.* fungous; fungus (*attrib.*).

грибно́й *adj.* mushroom (*attrib.*). —**грибно́й дождь,** rain that falls while the sun is shining.

грибо́к [*gen.* **-бка́**] *n.* **1,** *dim. of* **гриб. 2,** fungus.

гри́ва *n.* mane.

гри́венник *n., colloq.* ten-kopeck piece.

григориа́нский *adj.* Gregorian. —**григориа́нский календа́рь,** Gregorian calendar.

гри́зли *n.m. indecl.* grizzly bear.

грим *n.* make-up; grease paint.

грима́са *n.* grimace.

грима́сничать *v. impfv.* to make faces; grimace.

гримёр *n.* make-up artist.

гримирова́ть *v. impfv.* [*pres.* **-ру́ю, -ру́ешь**] *theat.* **1,** [*pfv.* **нагримирова́ть**] to make up; put make-up on. **2,** [*pfv.* **загримирова́ть**] (*with instr. or* **под** + *acc.*) to make (someone) up to look like. —**гримирова́ться,** *refl.* **1,** [*pfv.* **нагримирова́ться**] to put on one's make-up. **2,** [*pfv.* **загримирова́ться**] (*with instr. or* **под** + *acc.*) to make oneself up (as).

грипп *n.* grippe; influenza.

гриф *n.* **1,** vulture. **2,** *myth.* griffin. **3,** *music* finger board. **4,** rubber stamp. **5,** security classification (*stamped on a document*).

гри́фель *n.m.* slate pencil.

гри́фельный *adj.* slate (*attrib.*). —**гри́фельная доска́,** writing slate.

грифо́н *n.* **1,** *myth.* griffin. **2,** griffon (*dog*).

гроб [*2nd loc.* **гробу́;** *pl.* **гробы́**] *n.* coffin; casket. —**до гро́ба; по гроб жи́зни,** till the end of one's days; to one's dying day.

гробни́ца *n.* tomb.

гробово́й *adj.* **1,** coffin (*attrib.*). **2,** deathly; funereal: гробово́е молча́ние, deathly silence. —**до гробово́й доски́,** to the end of one's days.

гробовщи́к [*gen.* **-щика́**] *n.* coffin maker.

грог *n.* grog.

гроза́ [*pl.* **гро́зы**] *n.* storm; thunderstorm.

гроздь [*pl.* **гро́зди, -де́й, -дя́м** *or* **гро́здья, -дьев, -дьям**] *n.f.* cluster; bunch.

грози́ть *v. impfv.* [*pres.* **грожу́, -зи́шь**] (*with dat.*) to threaten.

гро́зный *adj.* **1,** threatening; menacing. **2,** fearsome; awesome; dread. —**Ива́н Гро́зный,** Ivan the Terrible.

грозово́й *adj.* storm (*attrib.*). —**грозова́я ту́ча,** storm cloud; thundercloud.

гром *n.* thunder. —**гром среди́ я́сного не́ба,** bolt from the blue.

грома́да *n.* huge mass; hulk: грома́да горы́, the great hulk of a mountain.

грома́дный *adj.* huge; enormous; tremendous; immense.

громи́ла *n.m., colloq.* **1,** burglar. **2,** thug.

громи́ть *v. impfv.* [*pfv.* **разгроми́ть;** *pres.* **-млю́, -ми́шь**] **1,** to smash; wreck. **2,** to rout; crush. **3,** *colloq.* to assail; fulminate against.

гро́мкий *adj.* [*short form* **-мок, -мка́, -мко;** *comp.* **гро́мче**] **1,** loud. **2,** famous; notorious. **3,** high-sounding; fine-sounding. —**гро́мко,** *adv.* loud; loudly.

громкоговори́тель *n.m.* loudspeaker.

гро́мкость *n.f.* loudness; volume.

громово́й *adj.* **1,** thunder (*attrib.*). **2,** thunderous. **3,** devastating; crushing.

громогла́сный *adj.* **1,** loud. **2,** loud-voiced.

громозди́ть *v. impfv.* [*pfv.* **нагромозди́ть;** *pres.* **-зжу́, -зди́шь**] to pile up. —**громозди́ться,** *refl.* [*impfv. only*] **1,** to tower; rise. **2,** (*with* **на** + *acc.*) *colloq.* to climb up on.

громо́здкий *adj.* bulky; cumbersome; unwieldy.

громоотво́д *n.* lightning rod.

громоподо́бный *adj.* thunderous.

гро́мче *adj., comp. of* **гро́мкий.**

громыха́ние *n., colloq.* rumble; rumbling.

громыха́ть *v. impfv., colloq.* to rumble; clatter.

гросс *n.* gross (*12 dozen*).

гроссбу́х *n.* ledger.

гроссме́йстер *n., chess* grandmaster.

грот *n.* **1,** grotto. **2,** mainsail.

гроте́ск (тэ) *n., art* grotesque style. —**гроте́скный,** *adj., art* grotesque.

грот-ма́чта *n.* mainmast.

гро́хать *v. impfv.* [*pfv.* **гро́хнуть**] *colloq.* **1,** to come crashing down. **2,** to bang down; slam down.

гро́хнуть *v., pfv. of* **гро́хать.** —**гро́хнуться,** *refl., colloq.* to fall with a bang; come crashing down.

гро́хот *n.* **1,** crash; din. **2,** screen; sieve.

грохота́ть *v. impfv.* [*pres.* **-хочу́, -хо́чешь**] **1,** to rumble. **2,** *colloq.* to howl (*with laughter*).

грош [*gen.* **гроша́**] *n.* **1,** *pre-rev.* half a kopeck. **2,** *colloq.* red cent; plug nickel. —**грош цена́** (+ *dat.*); **ни гроша́ не сто́ит; гроша́ ме́дного** (*or* **ло́маного**) **не сто́ит,** worthless; not worth two cents. —**ни в грош не ста́вить,** not give two cents for. —**ни за грош,** for nothing; completely in vain. —**ни на грош** (+ *gen.*), not a bit (*or* drop) of (*some admirable quality*).

грошо́вый *adj., colloq.* **1,** cheap (*in quality*). **2,** petty; paltry; insignificant.

грубе́ть *v. impfv.* [*pfv.* **огрубе́ть**] to become rough; become coarse.

груби́ть *v. impfv.* [*pfv.* **нагруби́ть;** *pres.* **-блю́, -би́шь**] (*with dat.*) **1,** to make rude or offensive remarks (to); be insulting (to). **2,** to talk back (to); answer back. *Also,* **грубия́нить** [*pfv.* **нагрубия́нить**].

грубия́н *n., colloq.* rude person; boor.

гру́бо *adv.* **1,** roughly. **2,** crudely. **3,** rudely. **4,** *in* гру́бо ошиби́ться, to make a gross mistake. —**гру́бо говоря́, 1,** roughly speaking. **2,** to put it rather crudely.

гру́бость *n.f.* **1,** rudeness. **2,** coarseness; crudity. **3,** rude remark; coarse remark.

гру́бый *adj.* **1,** rough. **2,** coarse; crude; rude. **3,** gross; flagrant.

гру́да *n.* heap; pile.

груди́на *n.* breastbone; sternum.

груди́нка *n.* brisket. —**копчёная груди́нка,** bacon.

грудни́ца *n.* mastitis.

грудно́й *adj.* **1,** chest (*attrib.*); thoracic; pectoral. **2,** (*of an infant*) suckling. —**грудна́я жа́ба,** angina pectoris. —**грудна́я железа́,** mammary gland. —**грудна́я кле́тка,** thorax.

грудобрю́шный *adj., in* **грудобрю́шная прегра́да,** *anat.* diaphragm.

грудь [*gen.* **гру́ди** *or* **груди́**; *2nd loc.* **груди́**; *pl.* **гру́ди, -де́й, -дя́м**] *n.f.* **1,** chest. **2,** breast. —**отнима́ть от груди́,** to wean. —**стоя́ть** *or* **встать гру́дью за** (+ *acc.*), to stand firmly behind.

гружёный *adj.* loaded.

груз *n.* **1,** load. **2,** freight; cargo.

груздь [*gen.* **-здя́**; *pl.* **гру́зди, -зде́й, -здя́м**] *n.m.* a variety of mushroom.

грузи́ло *n., fishing* sinker.

грузи́н [*gen. pl.* **-зи́н**] *n.m.* [*fem.* **-зи́нка**] Georgian. —**грузи́нский,** *adj.* Georgian.

грузи́ть *v. impfv.* [*pres.* **гружу́, гру́зишь** *or* **грузи́шь**] **1,** [*pfv.* **нагрузи́ть** *or* **загрузи́ть**] to load (a vehicle, vessel, etc.). **2,** [*pfv.* **погрузи́ть**] to load (cargo). —**грузи́ться,** *refl.* [*pfv.* **погрузи́ться**] **1,** to take on cargo. **2,** to get on board; (*with* **в** *or* **на** + *acc.*) to board.

гру́зный *adj.* **1,** heavy; weighty. **2,** stout; corpulent.

грузови́к [*gen.* **-вика́**] *n.* truck.

грузово́й *adj.* freight (*attrib.*); cargo (*attrib.*).

грузоотправи́тель *n.m.* shipper.

грузоподъёмный *adj., in* **грузоподъёмный кран,** (loading) crane.

гру́зчик *n.* longshoreman; stevedore.

грунт *n.* **1,** soil; ground. **2,** *painting* ground; priming.

грунтово́й *adj., in* **грунтова́я доро́га,** dirt road; **грунтовы́е во́ды,** ground water.

гру́ппа *n.* group. —**гру́ппа кро́ви,** blood type.

группирова́ть *v. impfv.* [*pfv.* **сгруппирова́ть**; *pres.* **-ру́ю, -ру́ешь**] to group; classify. —**группирова́ться,** *refl.* to group; form groups.

группиро́вка [*gen. pl.* **-вок**] *n.* **1,** grouping; classification. **2,** group; grouping.

группово́й *adj.* group (*attrib.*).

грусти́ть *v. impfv.* [*pres.* **грущу́, -сти́шь**] **1,** to be melancholy. **2,** (*with* **по** *or* **о**) to yearn for; mourn the loss of.

гру́стно *adv.* sadly. —*adj., used predicatively with dat.* sad: почему́ вам так гру́стно?, why are you so sad?

гру́стный *adj.* sad; melancholy.

грусть *n.f.* melancholy; sadness.

гру́ша *n.* **1,** pear. **2,** pear tree. —**земляна́я гру́ша,** Jerusalem artichoke.

гру́шевый *also,* **грушо́вый** *adj.* pear (*attrib.*).

гры́жа *n.* hernia; rupture.

грыжево́й *also,* **гры́жевый** *adj.* of or for a hernia; hernial. —**грыжево́й мешо́к,** hernial sac. —**грыжево́й банда́ж,** truss.

грызня́ *n., colloq.* **1,** fight (*between animals*). **2,** *fig.* squabble.

грызть *v. impfv.* [*pres.* **грызу́, грызёшь**; *past* **грыз, -ла**] **1,** to gnaw. **2,** to nibble (at). **3,** *colloq.* to nag; badger. **4,** to torment; beset. —**гры́зться,** *refl.* **1,** (*of animals*) to fight. **2,** *colloq.* to squabble; bicker.

грызу́н [*gen.* **-зуна́**] *n.* rodent.

гряда́ [*pl.* **гря́ды, гряд, гряда́м**] *n.* **1,** ridge (*of mountains*). **2,** bed (*for flowers or vegetables*). **3,** row; series. **4,** bank (*of clouds*).

гря́дка [*gen. pl.* **-док**] *n.* bed (*for flowers, vegetables, etc.*).

гряду́щий *adj.* coming; future. —**на сон гряду́щий,** *colloq.* at bedtime.

грязево́й *adj.* mud (*attrib.*).

грязни́ть *v. impfv.* [*pfv.* **загрязни́ть**] **1,** to soil; dirty. **2,** [*impfv. only*] to sully; besmirch. —**грязни́ться,** *refl.* to get dirty.

гря́зно *adv.* sloppily. —*adj., used predicatively* **1,** dirty; messy: здесь гря́зно, it is dirty/messy in here. **2,** muddy.

грязну́ля *n.m. & f., colloq.* slob. *Also,* **грязну́ха.**

гря́зный *adj.* [*short form* **-зен, -зна́, -зно**] dirty; filthy; muddy.

грязь [*2nd loc.* **грязи́**] *n.f.* **1,** mud. **2,** dirt; filth. **3,** *pl.* mud; mud baths. —**броса́ть** *or* **забра́сывать гря́зью** (+ *acc.*), to throw mud at.

гря́нуть *v. pfv.* **1,** to sound; ring out. **2,** to break out; erupt.

гуа́но *n. indecl.* guano.

гуа́шь *n.f.* gouache.

губа́ [*pl.* **гу́бы, губ, губа́м**] *n.* **1,** lip. **2,** inlet; bay (*in Northern Russia*).

губа́стый *adj., colloq.* thick-lipped.

губерна́тор *n.* governor. —**губерна́торский,** *adj.* governor's; gubernatorial. —**губерна́торство,** *n.* governorship.

губе́рния *n., pre-rev.* province.

губи́тельный *adj.* disastrous; devastating; pernicious; ruinous.

губи́ть *v. impfv.* [*pfv.* **погуби́ть**; *pres.* **гублю́, гу́бишь**] to ruin; destroy; kill.

гу́бка [*gen. pl.* **-бок**] *n.* **1,** *dim. of* **губа́. 2,** sponge.

губно́й *adj.* **1,** lip (*attrib.*). **2,** *phonet.* labial. —**губна́я пома́да,** lipstick.

гу́бчатый *adj.* spongy. —**гу́бчатая рези́на,** foam rubber.

гуверна́нтка [*gen. pl.* **-ток**] *n.* governess.

гувернёр *n.* tutor.

гугено́т *n.m.* [*fem.* **-но́тка**] Huguenot.

гугу́ *adv., in* **ни гугу́,** silent; mum. —**ни гугу́!,** mum's the word!

гуде́ние *n.* **1,** buzzing; droning; hum. **2,** honking (*of horns*).

гуде́ть *v. impfv.* [*pres.* **гужу́, гуди́шь**] **1,** to buzz; hum; drone. **2,** (*of a horn or factory whistle*) to sound; blow. **3,** *colloq.* to blow the horn (*of a car*).

гудо́к [*gen.* **-дка́**] *n.* **1,** (car) horn; (factory) whistle. **2,** hoot; toot; honk.

гудро́н *n.* petroleum tar.

гул *n.* hum; rumble; drone; din.

гу́лкий *adj.* **1,** resounding; booming. **2,** resonant.

гу́льден (дэ) *n.* guilder (*monetary unit of the Netherlands*).

гуля́ка *n.m. & f., colloq.* playboy; reveler.

гуля́нье *n.* **1,** walking; strolling. **2,** outdoor party. **3,** festival; celebration.
гуля́ть *v. impfv.* **1,** to walk; stroll. **2,** *colloq.* to make merry; live it up. **3,** *colloq.* to be off from work; have the day off. **4,** (*with* **с** + *instr.*) *colloq.* to run around (with); take up (with). —**води́ть гуля́ть,** to take for a walk. —**идти́ гуля́ть,** to go for a walk.
гуля́ш [*gen.* **-яша́**] *n.* goulash.
ГУМ *n., abbr. of* **Госуда́рственный универса́льный магази́н,** State Department Store (*on Red Square, Moscow*).
гумани́зм *n.* humanism. —**гумани́ст,** *n.* humanist. —**гуманисти́ческий,** *adj.* humanistic.
гуманита́рный *adj.* humanitarian. —**гуманита́рные нау́ки,** liberal arts; the humanities.
гума́нный *adj.* humane; humanitarian. —**гума́нно,** *adv.* humanely. —**гума́нность,** *n.f.* humaneness; humanity.
гу́мми *n. neut. indecl.* gum.
гуммиара́бик *n.* gum arabic.
гумно́ [*pl.* **гу́мна, гу́мен** *or* **гумён**] *n.* threshing floor.
гу́мус *n.* humus.
гунн *n., hist.* Hun.
гурма́н *n.* gourmet.
гурт [*gen.* **гурта́**] *n.* herd; flock.
гуртовщи́к [*gen.* **-щика́**] *n.* herdsman; drover.
гурто́м *adv., colloq.* **1,** wholesale; in bulk. **2,** in a group; as one group.
гурьба́ *n., colloq.* crowd; throng.
гуса́к [*gen.* **-сака́**] *n.* gander.
гуса́р [*gen. pl.* **гуса́р**] *n.* hussar.
гу́сеница *n.* **1,** caterpillar. **2,** *mech.* caterpillar track.
гу́сеничный *adj.* **1,** caterpillar (*attrib.*). **2,** *(of a vehicle)* tracked.
гусёнок [*gen.* **-нка;** *pl.* **-ся́та, -ся́т**] *n.* gosling.
гуси́ный *adj.* goose (*attrib.*). —**гуси́ная ко́жа,** goose flesh; goose pimples. —**гуси́ный шаг,** goose step.
гу́сли [*gen.* **-лей**] *n. pl.* old Russian stringed instrument; gusli.
густе́ть *v. impfv.* [*pfv.* **загусте́ть** *or* **погусте́ть**] to thicken.
гу́сто *adv.* **1,** densely. **2,** *colloq.* in abundance. —**то гу́сто, то пу́сто,** it's feast or famine.
густо́й *adj.* [*comp.* **гу́ще**] **1,** thick; dense. **2,** (*of a sound, voice, etc.*) deep; rich.
густонаселённый *adj.* densely populated.
густота́ *n.* **1,** thickness; density. **2,** richness (*of color, voice, etc.*).
гусы́ня *n.* female goose.
гусь [*pl.* **гу́си, гусе́й, гуся́м**] *n.m.* goose. —**как с гу́ся вода́,** like water off a duck's back.
гусько́м *adv.* (in) single file.
гуся́тина *n.* goose (*prepared as food*).
гуся́тник *n.* goose pen.
гутали́н *n.* shoe polish.
гуттапе́рча *n.* gutta-percha.
гу́ща *n.* **1,** dregs; grounds; lees. **2,** (*with gen.*) the thick of: в гу́ще ле́са, in the thick of the forest. —**гада́ть на кофе́йной гу́ще,** to guess in the dark.
гэ́льский *adj.* Gaelic.

Д

Д, д *n. neut.* fifth letter of the Russian alphabet.
да *particle* **1,** yes. **2,** right?; isn't that so? **3,** really?; indeed? **4,** *used for emphasis:* да замолчи́те же!, do be quiet! **5,** let; may: да бу́дет изве́стно, что..., let it be known that... Да испо́лнится ва́ше жела́ние!, may your wish be fulfilled! —*conj.* **1,** and: хлеб да вода́, bread and water. **2,** but: я и пошёл бы, да не могу́, I would like to go, but I can't. —**да и,** and; and besides. —**да ещё,** and besides; and what is more. —**да и то,** and even; at that: то́лько одна́ руба́шка, да и то потрёпанная, only one shirt and a tattered one at that. —**да и то́лько,** and nothing else: он смея́лся, да и то́лько, all he did was laugh; he just laughed and laughed.
дабы́ *conj., archaic* in order to; in order that.
дава́й *also,* **дава́йте** *verbal particle* **1,** *fol. by inf. or 1st person pl.* let's: дава́й чита́ть вме́сте, let's read together; дава́й ся́дем на авто́бус, let's take the bus. **2,** start!; go ahead!: ну, дава́йте!, O.K., go ahead!
дава́ть *v. impfv.* [*pfv.* **дать;** *pres.* **даю́, даёшь**] **1,** to give. **2,** to let: дай ему́ говори́ть, let him speak. **3,** *with certain nouns* to make: дава́ть обеща́ние/рекоменда́цию, to make a promise/recommendation. **4,** to yield; produce; provide. **5,** *in* дать звоно́к, to ring the bell; дать свисто́к, to blow a whistle. **6,** *in* дать течь, to spring a leak; дать тре́щину, to crack; дать осе́чку, misfire. **7,** *in* дать телегра́мму, to send a telegram. **8,** (*with dat.*) *colloq.* to hit; strike; clip: дать кому́-нибудь в зу́бы, to give someone a smack in the teeth. —**дать знать** (+ *dat.*), to let (someone) know. —**дать поня́ть,** to give to understand. —**дать себя́ знать** *or* **чу́вствовать,** to make itself felt. —**ни дать ни взять,** exactly alike.
дава́ться *v.r. impfv.* [*pfv.* **да́ться;** *pres.* **даю́сь, даёшься**] *colloq.* **1,** (*with* **в** + *acc.*) to allow oneself (to be): не дава́ться в оби́ду, not to allow oneself to be pushed around. **2,** (*usually with* **легко́** *and dat.*) to come easy (to): языки́ ему́ легко́ даю́тся, languages come easy to him.
дави́льный *adj.* for pressing: дави́льный пресс, wine press.

дави́льня [*gen. pl.* **-лен**] *n.* wine press.
дави́ть *v. impfv.* [*pres.* **давлю́, да́вишь**] **1,** to press down on; weigh heavily on. **2,** to squeeze. **3,** to pinch; be tight. **4,** [*pfv.* **раздави́ть**] to crush. **5,** [*pfv.* **раздави́ть** *or* **задави́ть**] to run over; kill. **6,** [*pfv.* **задави́ть**] *fig.* to suppress; stifle. —**дави́ться,** *refl.* [*pfv.* **подави́ться**] to choke.
да́вка *n.* crowding together; crush; jam.
давле́ние *n.* pressure.
да́вний *adj.* **1,** old; olden; ancient. **2,** long-standing; of long standing. —**с да́вних пор,** for a long time; for ages.
давни́шний *adj., colloq.* = **да́вний.**
давно́ *adv.* **1,** long ago; a long time ago: э́то случи́лось давно́, it happened long ago. **2,** a long time (*up to and including the present moment*): вы давно́ ждёте?, have you been waiting long? —**давны́м-давно́,** *colloq.* long long ago; ages ago.
давнопроше́дший *adj.* of long ago; that happened long ago. —**давнопроше́дшее вре́мя,** *gram.* pluperfect tense.
да́вность *n.f.* **1,** distance back in time: собы́тия сорокалётней да́вности, events which took place forty years ago. **2,** long history; long standing. **3,** *law* prescription. —**срок да́вности,** statute of limitations.
да́же *particle* even.
да́ктиль *n.m.* dactyl. —**дактили́ческий,** *adj.* dactylic.
да́лее *adv.* farther; further. —**и так да́лее,** and so on; and so forth; et cetera.
далёкий *adj.* [*short form* **далёк, далека́, далеко́** *or* **далёко, далеки́** *or* **далёки;** *comp.* **да́льше**] **1,** far; far away; faraway; distant. **2,** (*of a distance, journey, etc.*) long. **3,** [*short form only*] (*with* **от**) *fig.* far from: он не далёк от и́стины, he is not far wrong.
далеко́ *adv.* far: оста́вить далеко́ позади́, to leave far behind. Он пойдёт далеко́, he will go far. —*adj., used predicatively* far; far away: Москва́ далеко́, Moscow is far away. Туда́ ещё далеко́, it is still a long way to there. —**далеко́ до,** far beneath; not in the same class as: ему́ далеко́ до неё, he can't compare to her. —**далеко́ за** (+ *acc.*), well past: далеко́ за́ полночь, well past midnight. —**далеко́ иду́щий,** far-reaching. —**далеко́ не,** far from, by no means: далеко́ не уве́рен, far from/by no means/certain.
даль [*2nd loc.* **дали́**] *n.f.* **1,** distance: в таку́ю даль, such a great distance. **2,** expanse: бесконе́чная даль, endless expanse.
дальневосто́чный *adj.* Far Eastern.
дальне́йший *adj.* further. —**в дальне́йшем, 1,** in the future; hereafter. **2,** hereinafter.
да́льний *adj.* **1,** far-off; distant. **2,** (*of a trip, distance, etc.*) long. **3,** *in* да́льний ро́дственник, distant relative. —**без да́льних слов,** without wasting words; wasting no time on talk. —**Да́льний Восто́к,** Far East. —**да́льнего де́йствия,** *mil.* long-range.
дальнобо́йный *adj., mil.* long-range.
дальнови́дный *adj.* farsighted; having or showing foresight. —**дальнови́дность,** *n.f.* foresight.
дальнозо́ркий *adj., med.* farsighted. —**дальнозо́ркость,** *n.f., med.* farsightedness.
дальноме́р *n.* range finder.
да́льность *n.f.* **1,** distance. **2,** range. —**за да́льностью расстоя́ния,** because of the great distance.
дальтони́зм *n.* color blindness. —**дальто́ник,** *n., colloq.* color-blind person.
да́льше *adj., comp. of* **далёкий** *and* **далеко́.** —*adv.* **1,** *comp. of* **далеко́. 2,** then; next. **3,** further; on: чита́йте да́льше!, read on! **4,** continue!; go on! **5,** any longer: молча́ть да́льше бы́ло нельзя́, it was impossible to remain silent any longer. —*prep., with gen.* beyond: его́ не́ бы́ло слы́шно да́льше тре́тьего ря́да, he could not be heard beyond the third row.
да́ма *n.* **1,** lady. **2,** *cards* queen. **3,** partner (*in dancing*).
дама́н *n.* hyrax.
да́мба *n.* dike; levee.
да́мка [*gen. pl.* **-мок**] *n., checkers* king.
дамо́клов *adj., in* **дамо́клов меч,** sword of Damocles.
да́мский *adj.* lady's; ladies'.
да́нник *n.* one forced to pay tribute.
да́нные *n. pl., decl. as an adj.* **1,** data; facts. **2,** gifts; talent; ability.
да́нный *adj.* this; the given; the present. —**в да́нный моме́нт,** at the present moment. —**в да́нном слу́чае,** in the present case.
данти́ст *n., obs.* dentist.
дань *n.f.* **1,** *hist.* tribute (*exacted from the population*). **2,** *fig.* tribute; due: плати́ть *or* отдава́ть дань (+ *dat.*), to give someone (*or* something) his/its due.
дар [*pl.* **дары́**] *n.* **1,** gift. **2,** gift; talent: дар красноре́чия, the gift of eloquence.
дарёный *adj., colloq.* received as a gift. —**дарёному коню́ в зу́бы не смо́трят,** don't look a gift horse in the mouth.
дари́ть *v. impfv.* [*pfv.* **подари́ть;** *pres.* **дарю́, да́ришь**] to give (*as a gift*).
дармое́д *n., colloq.* sponger; parasite.
дарова́ние *n.* gift; talent.
дарова́ть *v. impfv. & pfv.* [*pres.* **-ру́ю, -ру́ешь**] *obs.* to grant; bestow.
дарови́тый *adj.* gifted.
даровой *adj., colloq.* free; given away free.
да́ром *adv.* **1,** gratis; free of charge. **2,** *colloq.* for next to nothing; for a song. **3,** in vain; for nothing; to no purpose. —**пропада́ть да́ром,** to go to waste; go for naught. —**не пройти́ да́ром, 1,** (*with dat.*) to have serious consequences for: э́то ему́ да́ром не пройдёт, he won't get away with that. **2,** (*with* **для**) (*of a lesson*) not to be lost upon.
да́та *n.* date.
да́тельный *adj., in* **да́тельный паде́ж,** dative case.
дати́ровать *v. impfv. & pfv.* [*pres.* **-рую, руешь**] to date.
да́тский *adj.* Danish.
датча́нин [*pl.* **-ча́не, -ча́н**] *n.m.* [*fem.* **-ча́нка**] Dane.
да́тчик *n.* sensor: теплово́й да́тчик, heat sensor.
дать [*infl.* **дам, дашь, даст, дади́м, дади́те, даду́т;** *past fem.* **дала́**] *v., pfv. of* **дава́ть.** —**да́ться,** *refl.* [*past* **да́лся, дала́сь, -ло́сь, -ли́сь**] *pfv. of* **дава́ться.**
да́ча *n.* **1,** country house; summer cottage; dacha. **2,** the country: жить на да́че, to live in the country. **3,** giving: да́ча ло́жных показа́ний, giving false evidence.
да́чник *n.* person spending the summer in the country.
да́чный *adj.* **1,** of or pert. to a dacha. **2,** suburban. **3,** *in* да́чный сезо́н, summer season.
два [*fem.* **две;** *gen. & prepl.* **двух;** *dat.* **двум;** *instr.* **двумя́**] *numeral* two. —**два-три** [*fem.* **две-три**], a couple; two or three.
двадцатиле́тие *n.* **1,** twentieth anniversary; twentieth birthday. **2,** twenty-year period.

двадцатиле́тний *adj.* **1,** twenty-year (*attrib.*). **2,** twenty-year-old.

двадцатипятиле́тие *n.* **1,** twenty-fifth anniversary; twenty-fifth birthday. **2,** twenty-five-year period.

двадцатипятиле́тний *adj.* **1,** twenty-five-year (*attrib.*). **2,** twenty-five-year-old.

двадца́тый *ordinal numeral* twentieth.

два́дцать [*gen., dat., & prepl.* **-цати́;** *instr.* **-цатью́**] *numeral* twenty.

два́жды *adv.* twice; two times. —**как два́жды два четы́ре,** as plain as day.

две *numeral, fem. of* **два.**

двенадцатипе́рстный *adj., in* **двенадцатипе́рстная кишка́,** duodenum.

двена́дцатый *ordinal numeral* twelfth.

двена́дцать [*gen., dat., & prepl.* **-цати;** *instr.* **-цатью**] *numeral* twelve.

две́рка [*gen. pl.* **-рок**] *n., dim. of* **дверь.**

дверно́й *adj.* door (*attrib.*).

две́рца [*gen. pl.* **-рец**] *n.* door.

дверь [*2nd loc.* **двери́;** *pl.* **две́ри, -ре́й, -ря́м, дверя́ми** *or* **дверьми́, -ря́х**] *n.f.* door. —**в дверя́х,** in the doorway. —**при закры́тых дверя́х,** behind closed doors.

две́сти [*gen.* **двухсо́т;** *dat.* **двумста́м;** *instr.* **двумяста́ми;** *prepl.* **двухста́х**] *numeral* two hundred.

дви́гатель *n.m.* motor; engine.

дви́гательный *adj.* motive. —**дви́гательный нерв,** motor nerve.

дви́гать *v. impfv.* [*pfv.* **дви́нуть;** *pres.* **-гаю, -гаешь** *or* **дви́жу, дви́жешь**] **1,** to move. **2,** (*with instr.*) to move (a part of one's body). **3,** [*impfv. only*] to drive: мото́р дви́гает колесо́, a motor drives the wheel. **4,** *fig.* to promote; further; advance. —**дви́гаться,** *refl.* **1,** to move. **2,** to stir; budge. **3,** *colloq.* to start out.

движе́ние *n.* **1,** motion; movement. **2,** traffic. **3,** *fig.* movement: освободи́тельное движе́ние, liberation movement.

дви́жимость *n.f., law* movable property; personal property.

дви́жимый *adj.* movable. —**дви́жимое иму́щество,** = **дви́жимость.**

дви́жущий *adj.* **1,** *in* **дви́жущая си́ла,** motive force. **2,** *in* **дви́жущие си́лы** (+ *gen.*), *fig.* the driving force (of); the forces which drive.

дви́нуть *v., pfv. of* **дви́гать.** —**дви́нуться,** *refl., pfv. of* **дви́гаться.**

дво́е [*gen. & prepl.* **двои́х;** *dat.* **двои́м;** *instr.* **двои́ми**] *collective numeral* two.

двоебра́чие *n.* bigamy.

двоевла́стие *n.* diarchy.

двоеже́нец [*gen.* **-нца**] *n.* bigamist. —**двоежёнство,** *n.* bigamy.

двоето́чие *n.* colon (*punctuation mark*).

двои́ться *v.r. impfv.* **1,** to divide in two. **2,** *impers.* to see double: у меня́ двои́тся в глаза́х, I am seeing double.

дво́йка *n.* **1,** the numeral 2. **2,** *colloq.* anything numbered 2. **3,** a grade of "two", signifying "poor". **4,** *cards* two; deuce.

двойни́к [*gen.* **-ника́**] *n.* **1,** (a person's) double. **2,** *colloq.* twin.

двойно́й *adj.* double; dual.

дво́йня [*gen. pl.* **дво́ен**] *n.* (set of) twins.

дво́йственность *n.f.* **1,** duality. **2,** ambivalence. **3,** duplicity.

дво́йственный *adj.* **1,** dual. **2,** bipartite. **3,** ambivalent. **4,** two-faced.

двор [*gen.* **двора́**] *n.* **1,** court (*of a sovereign*). **2,** yard; courtyard. **3,** peasant homestead. —**на дворе́,** out of doors; outdoors. —**не ко двору́,** not right; ill-suited.

дворе́ц [*gen.* **-рца́**] *n.* palace. —**дворе́ц съе́здов,** the Palace of Congresses (*in the Kremlin*).

дворе́цкий *n., decl. as an adj.* butler.

дво́рник *n.* **1,** caretaker. **2,** *colloq.* windshield wiper.

дво́рницкая *n., decl. as an adj., obs.* caretaker's house or quarters.

дворня́га *n., colloq.* mongrel. *Also,* **дворня́жка.**

дворо́вый *adj.* yard (*attrib.*). —**дворо́вая соба́ка,** watchdog.

дворцо́вый *adj.* palace (*attrib.*).

дворяни́н [*pl.* **-я́не, -я́н**] *n.m.* [*fem.* **-я́нка**] nobleman; noble. —**дворя́нский,** *adj.* nobleman's. —**дворя́нство,** *n.* the nobility; the gentry.

двою́родный *adj., denoting relationships of cousins:* двою́родный брат; двою́родная сестра́, first cousin. Двою́родный дя́дя; двою́родная тётка, cousin of one's father or mother. Двою́родный племя́нник; двою́родная племя́нница, child of one's first cousin. ♦*Also denoting other relationships:* двою́родная ба́бушка, great-aunt; двою́родный де́душка, great-uncle. Двою́родный внук, grandnephew; двою́родная вну́чка, grandniece.

двоя́кий *adj.* double; dual.

двоя́ко *adv.* in two ways.

двубо́ртный *adj.* double-breasted.

двугла́вый *adj.* two-headed. —**двугла́вая мы́шца,** biceps.

двугла́сный *adj., in* **двугла́сный звук,** diphthong. —*n.* diphthong.

двугра́нный *adj.* dihedral.

двугри́венный *n., decl. as an adj., colloq.* twenty-kopeck piece.

двудо́льный *adj.* dicotyledonous.

двузна́чный *adj.* two-digit.

двуко́лка [*gen. pl.* **-лок**] *n.* two-wheeled cart.

двукра́тный *adj.* **1,** twofold; double. **2,** second. **3,** two-time (*attrib.*).

двули́кий *adj.* **1,** having a dual nature. **2,** two-faced; double-dealing.

двули́чие *n.* duplicity. *Also,* **двули́чность,** *n.f.*

двули́чный *adj.* two-faced; double-dealing.

двуно́гий *adj.* two-legged.

двуо́кись *n.f.* dioxide.

двупо́лый *adj.* bisexual.

двуру́шник *n.* double-dealer. —**двуру́шнический,** *adj.* double-dealing. —**двуру́шничество,** *n.* double-dealing.

двуска́тный *adj., in* **двуска́тная кры́ша,** gable roof.

двусло́жный *adj.* two-syllable. *Also,* **двухсло́жный.**

двусмы́сленность *n.f.* **1,** ambiguity. **2,** double entendre.

двусмы́сленный *adj.* **1,** ambiguous. **2,** suggestive.

двуспа́льный *adj.* (*of a bed*) double. *Also,* **двухспа́льный.**

двуство́лка *also,* **двухство́лка** [*gen. pl.* **-лок**] *n., colloq.* double-barreled gun. —**двуство́льный,** *adj.* double-barreled.

двуство́рчатый *adj.* **1,** bivalve. **2,** (*of doors*) folding. *Also,* **двухство́рчатый.**

двусторо́нний *adj.* **1,** two-sided. **2,** bilateral; bipartite. **3,** two-way. **4,** (*of a garment*) reversible.

двууглеки́слый *adj., chem.* bicarbonate (of): двууглеки́слый на́трий, sodium bicarbonate; двууглеки́слая со́да, bicarbonate of soda.

двухвале́нтный *adj.* bivalent.

двухгоди́чный *adj.* two-year (*attrib.*).

двухдне́вный *adj.* two-day (*attrib.*).

двухколёсный *adj.* two-wheel(ed).

двухко́мнатный *adj.* two-room.

двухле́тний *adj.* **1,** two-year (*attrib.*). **2,** two-year-old. **3,** *bot.* biennial.

двухме́стный *adj.* accommodating two persons; for two.

двухме́сячник *n.* bimonthly (*publication*).

двухме́сячный *adj.* **1,** two-month (*attrib.*). **2,** two-month-old. **3,** bimonthly.

двухмото́рный *adj.* twin-engine.

двухнеде́льник *n.* biweekly (*publication*).

двухнеде́льный *adj.* **1,** two-week (*attrib.*). **2,** two-week-old. **3,** (*of a publication*) biweekly; fortnightly.

двухпала́тный *adj.* bicameral.

двухпарти́йный *adj.* **1,** two-party (*attrib.*). **2,** bipartisan.

двухсоле́тие *n.* bicentennial; bicentenary. —**двухсотле́тний,** *adj.* bicentennial.

двухсо́тый *ordinal numeral* two-hundredth.

двухфо́кусный *adj.* bifocal.

двухчасово́й *adj.* **1,** two hour (*attrib.*). **2,** *colloq.* two-o'clock (*attrib.*).

двухэта́жный *adj.* two-story.

двучле́н *n.* binomial. —**двучле́нный,** *adj.* binomial.

двуязы́чие *n.* bilingualism. —**двуязы́чный,** *adj.* bilingual.

двуяйцево́й *adj., in* **двуяйцевы́е близнецы́,** fraternal twins.

дебаркаде́р (дэ, дэ) *n.* pier; wharf; landing stage.

дебати́ровать *v. impfv.* [*pres.* **-рую, -руешь**] to debate.

деба́ты [*gen.* **-тов**] *n.pl.* debate; discussion.

дебе́лый *adj., colloq.* plump; buxom.

де́бет *n.* debit.

дебетова́ть *v. impfv. & pfv.* [*pres.* **-ту́ю, -ту́ешь**] to debit.

дебо́ш *n.* row; fracas; brawl.

дебоши́рить *v. impfv.* to carry on; run wild; kick up a row.

де́бри [*gen.* **-рей**] *n. pl.* **1,** jungle; wilderness; wilds. **2,** backwoods; sticks. **3,** maze; labyrinth.

дебю́т *n.* **1,** debut. **2,** *chess* opening.

дебюта́нт *n.m.* [*fem.* **-та́нтка**] person making his or her debut.

дебюти́ровать *v. impfv. & pfv.* [*pres.* **-рую, -руешь**] to make one's debut.

де́ва *n.* **1,** *archaic* maid; maiden. **2,** *relig.* the virgin. **3,** *cap.* Virgo. —**ста́рая де́ва,** old maid.

девальва́ция (дэ) *n.* devaluation.

девальви́ровать (дэ) *v. impfv. & pfv.* [*pres.* **-рую, -руешь**] to devalue.

дева́ть *v. impfv.* [*pfv.* **деть**] *colloq.* to put; do with: куда́ я дел мои́ очки́?, where did I put my glasses?; what did I do with my glasses? —**дева́ться,** *refl., colloq.* **1,** (*usu. with* **куда́**) to get (to); disappear (to): куда́ де́лась моя́ шля́па?, where has my hat gotten/disappeared to? **2,** (*with* **куда́** *or* **не́куда**) to go; hide: мне не́куда дева́ться, I have no place to go/hide.

де́верь [*pl.* **-рья́, -ре́й**] *n.m.* brother-in-law (*husband's brother*).

деви́з *n.* motto.

деви́ца *also,* **де́вица** *n., obs., poetic* maiden; damsel.

деви́ческий *adj.* = **де́вичий.** —**деви́чество,** *n.* girlhood; maidenhood.

де́вичий *also,* **деви́чий** [*fem.* **-чья**] *adj.* girlish; maidenly. —**де́вичья фами́лия,** maiden name.

де́вка [*gen. pl.* **-вок**] *n., colloq.* girl; wench.

де́вочка [*gen. pl.* **-чек**] *n.* (little) girl.

де́вственник *n.m.* [*fem.* **-ица**] virgin.

де́вственный *adj.* **1,** virgin; virginal. **2,** (*of a forest*) virgin; primeval. —**де́вственность,** *n.f.* virginity.

де́вушка [*gen. pl.* **-шек**] *n.* (teenage) girl; young lady.

девчо́нка [*gen. pl.* **-нок**] *n., colloq.* girl.

дявяно́сто [*gen., dat., instr., & prepl.* **девяно́ста**] *numeral* ninety. —**девяно́стый,** *ordinal numeral* ninetieth.

девя́тая *n., decl. as an adj.* ninth: одна́ девя́тая, one-ninth.

де́вятеро *collective numeral* nine.

девятиле́тний *adj.* **1,** nine-year (*attrib.*). **2,** nine-year-old.

девятисо́тый *ordinal numeral* nine-hundredth.

девя́тка *n.* **1,** the numeral 9. **2,** *colloq.* anything numbered 9. **3,** *cards* nine.

девятна́дцатый *ordinal numeral* nineteenth.

девятна́дцать *numeral* nineteen.

девя́тый *ordinal numeral* ninth.

де́вять [*gen., dat., & prepl.* **девяти́;** *instr.* **девятью́**] *numeral* nine.

девятьсо́т [*gen.* **девятисо́т;** *dat.* **девятиста́м;** *instr.* **девятьюста́ми;** *prepl.* **девятиста́х**] *numeral* nine hundred.

де́вятью *adv.* nine times: де́вятью де́сять — девяно́сто, nine times ten is ninety.

дегаза́ция (дэ) *n.* decontamination.

дегази́ровать (дэ) *v. impfv. & pfv.* [*pres.* **-рую, -руешь**] to decontaminate.

дегенера́т *n.* degenerate.

дегенера́ция *n.* degeneration.

дёготь [*gen.* **дёгтя**] *n.m.* tar. —**ло́жка дёгтя в бо́чке мёда,** fly in the ointment.

деграда́ция (дэ) *n.* degeneration.

деградИ́ровать (дэ) *v. impfv. & pfv.* [*pres.* **-рую, -руешь**] to degenerate.

дегтя́рный *adj.* tar (*attrib.*).

дегуста́тор (дэ) *n.* taster. —**дегуста́ция,** *n.* tasting: дегуста́ция вина́, wine-tasting.

дед *n.* grandfather. —**дед-моро́з,** Santa Claus; Grandfather Frost.

де́дов *adj.* belonging to one's grandfather; grandfather's.

де́довский *adj.* **1,** grandfather's. **2,** old-fashioned.

деду́кция *n., logic* deduction. —**дедукти́вный,** *adj., logic* deductive.

де́душка [*gen. pl.* **-шек**] *n.* grandfather.

дееприча́стие *n.* verbal adverb.

дееспосо́бность *n.f.* **1,** efficiency; energy; vitality. **2,** *law* competence.

дееспосо́бный *adj.* **1,** able to function. **2,** effective. **3,** *law* competent.

дежу́рить *v. impfv.* **1,** to be on duty. **2,** to keep vigil.

дежу́рный *adj.* **1,** on duty. **2,** (*of a store*) open extra hours. **3,** *fig.* everyday; ordinary. —*n.* person on duty. —**дежу́рное блю́до,** plat du jour.

дежу́рство *n.* duty: расписа́ние дежу́рств, duty roster.

дезерти́р *n.* deserter.

дезерти́ровать *v. impfv. & pfv.* [*pres.* **-рую, -руешь**] *mil.* to desert.

дезерти́рство *n., mil.* desertion.

дезинфе́кция *n.* disinfection.

дезинфици́ровать *v. impfv. & pfv.* [*pres.* **-рую, -руешь**] to disinfect.

дезинформа́ция (дэ) *n.* disinformation.

дезинформи́ровать (дэ) *v. impfv. & pfv.* [*pres.* **-рую, -руешь**] to misinform.

дезодора́тор (дэ) *n.* deodorant.

дезорганиза́ция *n.* disorganization; disruption.

дезорганизова́ть *v. impfv. & pfv.* [*pres.* **-зу́ю, -зу́ешь**] to disorganize; disrupt.

дезориента́ция *n.* disorientation.

дезориенти́ровать *v. impfv. & pfv.* [*pres.* **-рую, руешь**] to disorient.

деи́зм (дэ) *n.* deism. —**деи́ст,** *n.* deist. —**деисти́ческий,** *adj.* deistic.

де́йственный *adj.* effective; efficacious. —**де́йственность,** *n.f.* effectiveness; efficacy.

де́йствие *n.* **1,** action. **2,** *pl.* acts: незако́нные де́йствия, illegal acts. **3,** operation: вводи́ть в де́йствие, to put into operation. Приводи́ть в де́йствие, to start (*e.g.* a machine) going. **4,** effect: оказа́ть де́йствие на, to have an effect on. **5,** (legal) force; effect: вводи́ть зако́н в де́йствие, to put a law into effect; invoke a law. Продли́ть де́йствие догово́ра, to extend a treaty. **6,** act (*of a play*). —**вое́нные де́йствия,** military operations; hostilities. —**свобо́да де́йствий,** freedom of action.

действи́тельно *adv.* really; actually; truly; indeed.

действи́тельность *n.f.* **1,** reality: в действи́тельности, in reality. **2,** validity.

действи́тельный *adj.* **1,** real; actual; true. **2,** valid. **3,** effective. **4,** *mil.* active: действи́тельная слу́жба, active duty. —**действи́тельный зало́г,** *gram.* active voice. —**действи́тельное число́,** real number. —**действи́тельный член,** full member.

де́йствовать *v. impfv.* [*pres.* **-ствую, -ствуешь**] **1,** to act. **2,** to operate; function; work. **3,** (*with instr.*) *colloq.* to use; employ; operate; handle. **4,** [*pfv.* **поде́йствовать**] to take effect; work; (*with* **на** + *acc.*) have an effect (on). —**де́йствовать на не́рвы** (+ *dat.*), to get on someone's nerves.

де́йствующий *adj.* active; operating; functioning. —**де́йствующая а́рмия,** army in the field; front-line army. —**де́йствующее лицо́,** character (*in a play or story*).

дейте́рий (дэ,тэ) *n.* deuterium.

де́ка (дэ) *n., music* sounding board.

декабри́ст *n., hist.* Decembrist. —**декабри́стский,** *adj.* Decembrist.

дека́брь [*gen.* **-бря́**] *n.m.* December. —**дека́брьский,** *adj.* December (*attrib.*).

дека́да *n.* ten days; ten-day period.

декаде́нт *n.* decadent. —**декаде́нтский,** *adj.* decadent. —**декаде́нтство,** *n.* decadence.

дека́дный *adj.* ten-day (*attrib.*).

дека́н *n.* dean (*at a university*). —**декана́т,** *n.* dean's office.

деклама́тор *n.* reciter.

деклама́ция *n.* declamation; recitation. —**декламацио́нный,** *adj.* declamatory.

деклами́ровать *v. impfv.* [*pfv.* **продеклами́ровать;** *pres.* **-рую, -руешь**] to recite; declaim.

декларати́вный *adj.* **1,** declarative. **2,** solemn.

деклара́ция *n.* (solemn) declaration.

деклари́ровать *v. impfv. & pfv.* [*pres.* **-рую, -руешь**] to declare; proclaim.

декольте́ (дэ, тэ) *n. neut. indecl.* décolletage. —*adj. indecl.* low-necked; décolleté. —**декольти́рованный,** *adj.* = **декольте́.**

декорати́вный *adj.* **1,** decorative; ornamental. **2,** picturesque.

декора́тор *n.* **1,** stage designer. **2,** interior decorator.

декора́ция *n., usu. pl.* **1,** *theat.* scenery. **2,** *fig.* trappings; window dressing. —**переме́на декора́ций, 1,** *theat.* change of scenery. **2,** *fig.* change in the situation.

декори́ровать *v. impfv. & pfv.* [*pres.* **-рую, -руешь**] to decorate.

деко́рум (дэ) *n.* decorum.

декре́т *n.* decree.

декре́тный *adj.* established by decree. —**декре́тный о́тпуск,** maternity leave.

декстро́за (дэ) *n.* dextrose.

де́ланный *adj.* affected; unnatural. —**де́ланность,** *n.f.* affectation.

де́лать *v. impfv.* [*pfv.* **сде́лать**] **1,** to do. **2,** to make. **3,** *rendered by various English verbs depending on the noun:* де́лать опера́цию, to perform an operation; де́лать шаг, to take a step; де́лать комплиме́нт, to pay a compliment; де́лать пода́рок, to give a present; де́лать вы́вод, to draw a conclusion; де́лать уко́л, to give an injection; де́лать упо́р, to lay *or* place (the) emphasis. —**де́латься,** *refl.* **1,** [*impfv. only*] to be done (*in a certain way*). **2,** [*impfv. only*] (*with* **из**) to be made (of *or* from). **3,** (*with instr.*) to become. **4,** to happen; take place; be going on.

делега́т *n.* delegate. —**делега́ция,** *n.* delegation.

делеги́ровать *v. impfv. & pfv.* [*pres.* **-рую, -руешь**] to send as a delegate.

делёж [*gen.* **-лежа́**] *n., colloq.* dividing up; parceling out. *Also,* **делёжка.**

деле́ние *n.* **1,** division. **2,** fission. **3,** *math.* division. **4,** unit; point; notch (*on a scale, thermometer, etc.*).

деле́ц [*gen.* **-льца́**] *n.* shrewd businessman; smart operator.

деликате́с *n.* delicacy (*choice item of food*).

делика́тничать *v. impfv., colloq.* to be overly delicate; (*with* **с** + *instr.*) treat with kid gloves.

делика́тный *adj.* **1,** delicate; tactful. **2,** *colloq.* delicate; ticklish. **3,** *colloq.* delicate; frail. —**делика́тность,** *n.f.* delicacy; tact.

дели́мое *n., decl. as an adj., math.* dividend.

дели́мый *adj.* divisible. —**дели́мость,** *n.f.* divisibility.

дели́тель *n.m., math.* divisor.

дели́ть *v. impfv.* [*pfv.* **раздели́ть** *or* **подели́ть;** *pres.* **делю́, де́лишь**] **1,** to divide. **2,** to share. —**дели́ться,** *refl.* **1,** [*pfv.* **раздели́ться**] to divide; be divided. **2,** [*pfv.* **подели́ться**] (*with instr.*) to share: дели́ться с ке́м-нибудь куско́м хле́ба, to share a piece of bread with someone. **3,** [*pfv.* **подели́ться**] (*with* **с** + *instr.*)

to confide in. **4,** [*impfv. only*] (*with* **на** + *acc.*) *math.* to be divisible (by).

дели́шко *n., colloq., dim. of* **де́ло:** как ва́ши дели́шки?, how are you getting along?

де́ло [*pl.* **дела́, дел, дела́м**] *n.* **1,** matter; affair; business. **2,** deed; act. **3,** cause: де́ло ми́ра, the cause of peace. **4,** *law* case. **5,** file. **6,** *pl., colloq.* things; matters: как дела?, how are things? **7,** *in* го́рное де́ло, mining; печа́тное де́ло, printing; переплётное де́ло, bookbinding, etc. —**в са́мом де́ле,** really; truly; indeed. —**в то́м-то и де́ло,** that's just the point. —**в чём де́ло?,** what's the matter? —**говори́ть де́ло,** to talk sense. —**де́ло в том, что...,** the point is... —**де́ло рук** (+ *gen.*), one's doing; the work of; one's handiwork. —**име́ть де́ло с,** to deal with. —**ме́жду де́лом,** at odd moments; in between times. —**на де́ле,** in practice. —**на са́мом де́ле,** actually; in point of fact. —**не в э́том де́ло,** that is not the point. —**нет де́ла** (+ *dat.*) **до,** not to care about. —**пе́рвым де́лом,** *colloq.* first of all. —**сде́лать своё де́ло,** to do its work; have its effect. —**то и де́ло,** continually; constantly.

делови́тый *adj.* businesslike. —**делови́тость,** *n.f.* businesslike manner; efficiency.

делово́й *adj.* **1,** business (*attrib.*). **2,** businesslike. —**деловы́е ка́чества,** professional qualities.

делопроизво́дство *n.* office work; paper work.

де́льный *adj.* **1,** able; efficient. **2,** (*of advice, an idea, etc.*) practical; sensible; sound.

де́льта (дэ) *n.* delta.

дельтови́дный (дэ) *adj.* deltoid.

дельфи́н *n.* dolphin.

демаго́г *n.* demagogue. —**демагоги́ческий,** *adj.* demagogic. —**демаго́гия,** *n.* demagoguery; demagogy.

демаркацио́нный *adj., in* **демаркацио́нная ли́ния,** line of demarcation.

демарка́ция *n.* demarcation.

дема́рш (дэ) *n.* démarche.

демилитариза́ция (дэ) *n.* demilitarization.

демилитаризова́ть (дэ) *v. impfv. & pfv.* [*pres.* **-зу́ю, -зу́ешь**] to demilitarize.

демисезо́нный *adj.* (*of a coat*) worn in the spring or fall.

демобилиза́ция *n.* demobilization.

демобилизова́ть *v. impfv. & pfv.* [*pres.* **-зу́ю, -зу́ешь**] *mil.* **1,** to demobilize. **2,** to discharge. —**демобилизова́ться,** *refl.* to be discharged; receive one's discharge.

демогра́фия (дэ) *n.* demography. —**демо́граф,** *n.* demographer. —**демографи́ческий,** *adj.* demographic.

демокра́т *n.* democrat.

демократиза́ция *n.* democratization.

демократизи́ровать *v. impfv. & pfv.* [*pres.* **-рую, -руешь**] to democratize.

демокра́тия *n.* democracy. —**демократи́ческий,** *adj.* democratic.

де́мон *n.* demon. —**демони́ческий,** *adj.* demonic; demoniac.

демонстра́нт *n.* demonstrator (*one who takes part in a demonstration*).

демонстрати́вно *adv.* in a pointed or emphatic manner: демонстрати́вно поки́нуть собра́ние, to stalk out of the meeting.

демонстрати́вный *adj.* **1,** pointed; emphatic. **2,** employing visual aids. **3,** *mil.* diversionary.

демонстра́тор *n.* demonstrator (*one who demonstrates something*).

демонстрацио́нный *adj.* used for demonstrations.

демонстра́ция *n.* **1,** demonstration; march. **2,** demonstration; show. **3,** *mil.* diversionary action.

демонстри́ровать *v. impfv. & pfv.* [*pres.* **-рую, -руешь**] **1,** to demonstrate; participate in a demonstration. **2,** to demonstrate; show.

демонта́ж (дэ) *n.* dismantling.

демонти́ровать (дэ) *v. impfv. & pfv.* [*pres.* **-рую, -руешь**] to dismantle.

деморализа́ция (дэ) *n.* demoralization.

деморализова́ть (дэ) *v. impfv. & pfv.* [*pres.* **-зу́ю, -зу́ешь**] to demoralize.

де́мпинг (дэ) *n., econ.* dumping.

денатура́т *n.* denatured alcohol.

денатури́ровать *v. impfv. & pfv.* [*pres.* **-рую, -руешь**] to denature (alcohol).

дендра́рий (дэ) *n.* arboretum.

дендри́т (дэ) *n.* dendrite.

де́нежный *adj.* **1,** monetary; money (*attrib.*). **2,** *colloq.* affluent; well-to-do.

денёк [*gen.* **-нька́**] *n., dim. of* **день.** Вы́дался хоро́ший денёк, it turned out to be a nice day.

де́нно *adv., colloq., in* **де́нно и но́щно,** day and night.

денонси́ровать (дэ) *v. impfv. & pfv.* [*pres.* **-рую, -руешь**] to repudiate; renounce (a treaty, agreement, etc.).

денти́н (дэ) *n.* dentine.

день [*gen.* **дня**] *n.m.* day. —**день деньско́й,** all day long. —**день ото дня,** day by day; with each passing day. —**изо дня в день,** day after day; day in and day out. —**на днях, 1,** the other day. **2,** one of these days; some day soon. —**по сей день,** to this day. —**со дня на́ день, 1,** any day (now). **2,** from one day to the next. —**средь бе́ла дня,** in broad daylight.

де́ньги [*gen.* **де́нег;** *dat.* **деньга́м**] *n. pl.* money. —**быть при деньга́х,** to be in the chips. —**быть не при деньга́х,** to be short of cash.

департа́мент *n.* (governmental) department.

депе́ша *n.* **1,** dispatch. **2,** *obs.* telegram.

депо́ *n. indecl., R.R.* repair shop. —**пожа́рное депо́,** firehouse; fire station.

депре́ссия (дэ) *n.* **1,** depression; dejection. **2,** *econ.* depression.

депута́т *n.* deputy (*in a legislative body*). —**пала́та депута́тов,** Chamber of Deputies.

депута́ция *n.* deputation.

де́рби (дэ) *n. neut. indecl., horse racing* derby.

де́рбник *n.* merlin (*bird*).

де́рвиш *n.* dervish.

дёргать *v. impfv.* [*pfv.* **дёрнуть**] **1,** to pull; jerk; yank; tug at. **2,** (*with instr.*) to jerk (a part of one's body). **3,** [*impfv. only*] *impers.* to twitch: его́ всего́ дёргает, he is twitching all over. **4,** [*impfv. only*] *colloq.* to pull out; extract. **5,** [*impfv. only*] *colloq.* to harass. —**дёргаться,** *refl.* **1,** to quiver. **2,** to twitch. *See also* **дёрнуть** *and* **дёрнуться.**

дерга́ч [*gen.* **-гача́**] *n.* corn crake (*bird*).

деревене́ть *v. impfv.* [*pfv.* **одеревене́ть**] to become stiff; become numb.

дереве́нский *adj.* **1,** village (*attrib.*). **2,** country (*attrib.*); rural.

деревéнщина *n.m. & f., colloq.* country bumpkin; hick; yokel.

дерéвня [*pl.* **дерéвни, -вéнь, -вня́м**] *n.* **1,** village. **2,** the country (*as opposed to the city*).

дéрево *n.* **1,** [*pl.* **дерéвья, -вьев**] tree. **2,** wood. —**за дерéвьями лéса не ви́дно,** (one) cannot see the forest for the trees.

деревообдéлочник *n.* woodworker. —**деревообдéлочный,** *adj.* woodworking.

деревýшка [*gen. pl.* **-шек**] *n.* small village; hamlet.

дéревце *also,* **деревцó,** [*pl.* **-вцá, -вéц, -вцáм**] *n.* sapling.

деревяни́стый *adj.* woody.

деревя́нный *adj.* **1,** wooden; wood. **2,** *fig.* wooden; dull.

деревя́шка [*gen. pl.* **-шек**] *n.* **1,** piece of wood. **2,** *colloq.* wooden leg; peg leg.

держáва *n.* power: мировáя держáва, a world power.

держáтель *n.m.* holder.

держáть *v. impfv.* [*pres.* **держý, дéржишь**] **1,** to hold. **2,** to keep. **3,** to support; hold up. —**держáть курс** *or* **путь на** (+ *acc.*), to head for. —**держáть пари́,** to bet. —**держáть речь,** to make a speech. —**держáть себя́,** to behave. —**держáть чью-нибудь стóрону,** to take someone's side. —**держáть экзáмен,** to take an examination. —**держи́те вóра!,** stop thief!

держáться *v.r. impfv.* [*pres.* **держýсь, дéржишься**] **1,** (*with* **за** + *acc.*) to hold on to. **2,** (*with* **на** + *prepl.*) to be held up (by); be supported (by). **3,** to stay; remain: держáться на водé, to remain afloat. **4,** (*with gen.*) to keep to: держáться прáвой стороны́, to keep to the right. **5,** (*with gen.*) to adhere to. **6,** to hold together; remain in one piece. **7,** to hold out; stand firm. **8,** to behave. **9,** to last; persist. —**держáться бéрега,** to hug the shore. —**держáться вмéсте,** to stick together. —**держáться пря́мо,** to stand up straight.

дерзáние *n.* **1,** daring. **2,** *pl.* bold initiatives.

дерзáть *v. impfv.* [*pfv.* **дерзнýть**] **1,** [*impfv. only*] to be daring. **2,** to dare.

дерзи́ть *v. impfv.* [*pfv.* **надерзи́ть**] (*with dat.*) *colloq.* to be rude (to); be insolent (to).

дéрзкий *adj.* [*short form* **-зок, -зкá, -зко**] **1,** impudent; impertinent; insolent. **2,** daring; bold; audacious.

дерзнýть *v., pfv. of* **дерзáть** (*in sense* #2).

дéрзость *n.f.* **1,** impudence; impertinence; insolence. **2,** daring; audacity.

дери́ват (дэ) *n., chem.* derivative.

дерматолóгия (дэ) *n.* dermatology. —**дерматóлог,** *n.* dermatologist.

дёрн *n.* turf; sod.

дёрнуть *v. pfv.* **1,** *pfv. of* **дёргать. 2,** to lurch forward. —**дёрнуться,** *refl.* **1,** *pfv. of* **дёргаться. 2,** to lurch forward. **3,** to lunge.

дéррик (дэ) *n.* derrick. *Also,* **дéррик-кран.**

дерю́га *n.* sackcloth; burlap. —**дерю́жный,** *adj.* burlap.

десáнт *n., mil.* **1,** landing (*of troops*). **2,** landing party. —**десáнтник,** *n.* member of a landing party; commando. —**десáнтный,** *adj.* landing (*attrib.*).

десегрегáция (дэ) *n.* desegregation.

десегреги́ровать (дэ) *v. impfv. & pfv.* [*pres.* **-рую, -руешь**] to desegregate.

десéрт *n.* dessert. —**десéртный,** *adj.* dessert (*attrib.*).

дéскать *particle, colloq.* they say; he/she says.

деснá [*pl.* **дёсны, дёсен**] *n.* gum (*in the mouth*).

десни́ца *n., poetic* right hand

дéспот *n.* despot. —**деспоти́зм,** *n.* depotism. —**деспоти́ческий; деспоти́чный,** *adj.* despotic.

десть [*pl.* **дéсти, дестéй, дестя́м**] *n.f.* unit of quantity for sheets of paper: рýсская десть, quire; метри́ческая десть, fifty sheets.

деся́тая *n., decl. as an adj.* tenth: однá деся́тая, one-tenth.

дéсятеро *collective numeral* ten.

десятибóрье *n., sports* decathlon.

десятигрáнник *n.* decahedron. —**десятигрáнный,** *adj.* decahedral.

десятиднéвный *adj.* ten-day (*attrib.*).

десятикрáтный *adj.* tenfold.

десятилéтие *n.* **1,** tenth anniversary; tenth birthday. **2,** decade.

десятилéтка [*gen. pl.* **-ток**] *n.* ten-year secondary school.

десятилéтний *adj.* **1,** ten-year (*attrib.*). **2,** ten-year-old.

десяти́на *n.* **1,** *hist.* tithe. **2,** old Russian measure equal to approx 2.7 acres.

десятирублёвка [*gen. pl.* **-вок**] *n., colloq.* ten-ruble note.

десятиугóльник *n.* decagon.

десяти́чный *adj.* decimal (*attrib.*).

деся́тка *n.* **1,** the numeral 10. **2,** *colloq.* anything numbered 10. **3,** *colloq.* group of ten. **4,** *cards* ten. **5,** *colloq.* ten-ruble note.

деся́ток [*gen.* **-тка**] *n.* (*with gen. pl.*) **1,** ten: деся́ток я́блок, ten apples. **2,** decade (*of one's life*): емý идёт шестóй деся́ток, he is in his sixties. **3,** *pl.* tens of; dozens of: деся́тки раз, dozens of times; деся́тки ты́сяч рублéй, tens of thousands of rubles.

деся́тый *ordinal numeral* tenth.

дéсять [*gen., dat., & prepl.* **десяти́;** *instr.* **десятью́**] *numeral* ten.

дéсятью *adv.* ten times: дéсятью дéсять – сто, ten times ten is a hundred.

детализáция *n.* working out in detail.

детализи́ровать *v. impfv. & pfv.* [*pres.* **-рую, -руешь**] to work out in detail.

детáль *n.f.* **1,** detail. **2,** part; component.

детáльный *adj.* detailed. —**детáльно,** *adv.* in detail.

детворá *n., colloq.* children; kids.

детдóм *n.* children's home (*contr. of* **дéтский дом**).

детекти́в (дэ, тэ) *n.* **1,** detective. **2,** detective story. —**детекти́вный,** *adj.* detective (*attrib.*).

детéктор (дэ, тэ) *n.* detector. —**детéктор лжи,** lie detector.

детёныш *n.* young animal; cub; calf.

детермини́зм (дэ, тэ) *n.* determinism.

дéти [*gen.* **детéй;** *dat.* **дéтям;** *instr.* **детьми́;** *prepl.* **дéтях**] *n.pl.* children.

дети́шки [*gen.* **-шек**] *n. pl., colloq.* children; kids.

дéтище *n.* **1,** *obs.* child; offspring. **2,** *fig.* brainchild.

детонáтор *n.* detonator.

детонáция *n.* detonation.

детони́ровать *v. impfv.* [*pres.* **-рую, -руешь**] **1,** to detonate; go off. **2,** to be out of tune; be off key.

деторóдный *adj.* genital.

деторождéние *n.* **1,** childbearing. **2,** procreation.

детоуби́йство *n.* infanticide.

детса́д *n.* kindergarten; nursery school (*contr. of* **де́тский сад**).

де́тская *n., decl. as an adj.* nursery; room for children.

де́тский *adj.* **1,** children's; child's. **2,** childish; childlike. —**де́тское ме́сто,** afterbirth; placenta. —**де́тский сад,** kindergarten. —**де́тская сме́ртность,** infant mortality. —**де́тский труд,** child labor.

де́тство *n.* childhood. —**впада́ть в де́тство,** to be in one's second childhood; be in one's dotage.

деть [*infl.* **де́ну, де́нешь**] *v., pfv. of* **дева́ть.** —**де́ться,** *refl., pfv. of* **дева́ться.**

де-фа́кто (дэ) *adv.* de facto.

дефе́кт *n.* defect. —**дефекти́вный,** *adj.* handicapped. —**дефе́ктный,** *adj.* defective.

дефи́с *n.* hyphen.

дефици́т *n.* **1,** deficit. **2,** shortage: дефици́т в то́пливе, fuel shortage.

дефици́тный *adj.* **1,** operating at a loss; unprofitable. **2,** (*of goods*) scarce; in short supply.

дефля́ция (дэ) *n., econ.* deflation.

деформа́ция (дэ) *n.* deformation.

деформи́ровать (дэ) *v. impfv. & pfv.* [*pres.* **-рую, -руешь**] to change the shape of.

децентрализа́ция (дэ) *n.* decentralization.

децентрализова́ть (дэ) *v. impfv. & pfv.* [*pres.* **-зу́ю, -зу́ешь**] to decentralize.

децибе́л (дэ) *n.* decibel.

децигра́мм (дэ) *n.* decigram.

децили́тр (дэ) *n.* deciliter.

дециме́тр (дэ) *n.* decimeter.

дешеве́ть *v. impfv.* [*pfv.* **подешеве́ть**] to go down in price; become cheaper.

дешиви́зна *n.* (*with gen.*) low price level (of); low prices (for).

дешёвка *n., colloq.* **1,** low price. **2,** something low in price. —**по дешёвке,** dirt-cheap.

деше́вле *adj., comp. of* **дешёвый.**

дёшево *adv.* cheap; cheaply. —**дёшево и серди́то,** good and inexpensive. —**дёшево отде́латься,** to get off cheap.

дешёвый *adj.* [*short form* **дёшев, дешева́, дёшево;** *comp.* **деше́вле**] **1,** inexpensive; cheap. **2,** (*of a price*) low. **3,** *fig.* cheap; worthless; vulgar.

дешифри́ровать (дэ) *v. impfv. & pfv.* [*pres.* **-рую, -руешь**] to decipher. *Also,* **дешифрова́ть** [*pres.* **-ру́ю, -ру́ешь**].

дешифро́вка (дэ) *n.* decipherment; deciphering.

де-ю́ре (дэ) *adv.* de jure.

дея́ние *n.* deed; act.

де́ятель *n.m.* figure: обще́ственный де́ятель, public figure. —**госуда́рственный де́ятель,** statesman.

де́ятельность *n.f.* **1,** activity; activities. **2,** functioning; action.

де́ятельный *adj.* active.

джаз *n.* jazz. —**джа́зовый,** *adj.* jazz.

джем *n.* jam.

дже́мпер *n.* pullover; jersey.

джентльме́н *n.* gentleman.

джентльме́нский *adj.* gentlemanly. —**джентльме́нское соглаше́ние,** gentlemen's agreement.

джи́га *n.* jig (*dance*).

джиги́т *n.* skillful horseman.

джин *n.* **1,** gin. **2,** [*also,* **джинн**] genie.

джи́нсы [*gen.* **-ов**] *n. pl.* jeans.

джип *n.* jeep.

джи́у-джи́тсу *n. neut. indecl.* jujitsu.

джо́кер *n., cards* joker.

джо́нка [*gen. pl.* **-нок**] *n.* junk (*boat*).

джо́уль *n.m.* joule.

джу́нгли [*gen.* **-лей**] *n. pl.* jungle.

джут *n.* jute. —**джу́товый,** *adj.* jute.

дзюдо́ *n. indecl.* judo.

диабе́т *n.* diabetes. —**диабе́тик,** *n.* diabetic. —**диабети́ческий,** *adj.* diabetic.

диа́гноз *n.* diagnosis.

диагно́ст *n.* diagnostician. —**диагности́ческий,** *adj.* diagnostic.

диагона́ль *n.f.* diagonal. —**диагона́льный,** *adj.* diagonal.

диагра́мма *n.* diagram; chart; graph.

диаде́ма (дэ) *n.* diadem.

диакрити́ческий *adj.* diacritical.

диале́кт *n.* dialect.

диале́ктика *n.* dialectics. —**диалекти́ческий,** *adj.* dialectical.

диале́ктный *adj.* dialectal.

диало́г *n.* dialogue.

диа́метр *n.* diameter.

диаметра́льно *adv.* diametrically: диаметра́льно противополо́жный, diametrically opposite. —**диаметра́льный,** *adj.* diametrical.

диапазо́н *n.* **1,** *music* range. **2,** *radio* band. **3,** *fig.* range; scope.

диапозити́в *n., photog.* slide; transparency.

диатерми́я (тэ) *n.* diathermy.

диатони́ческий *adj.* diatonic.

диафра́гма *n., anat.; optics; photog.* diaphragm.

дива́н *n.* sofa; couch. —**дива́нный,** *adj.* sofa (*attrib.*); couch (*attrib.*).

диверса́нт *n.* saboteur.

диверсио́нный *adj.* **1,** *mil.* diversionary. **2,** of sabotage.

диверсифика́ция *n.* diversification.

диве́рсия *n.* **1,** *mil.* diversion. **2,** sabotage.

divиде́нд *n.* dividend.

дивизио́н *n.* (artillery) battalion.

дивизио́нный *adj., mil.* division (*attrib.*); divisional.

диви́зия *n., mil.* division.

диви́ть *v. impfv.* [*pres.* **дивлю́, диви́шь**] *colloq.* to surprise; startle. —**диви́ться,** *refl.* [*pfv.* **подиви́ться**] (*with dat.*) *colloq.* to wonder (at); marvel (at).

ди́вный *adj.* **1,** wonderful; marvelous. **2,** *obs.* amazing; remarkable.

ди́во *n.* wonder: ди́во, что..., it's a wonder that... —**ди́ву дава́ться,** to wonder; marvel. —**на ди́во,** wonderfully; marvelously.

дида́ктика *n.* didactics. —**дидакти́ческий,** *adj.* didactic.

дие́з *n., music* sharp: ля дие́з, A sharp.

дие́та *n.* diet.

диетвра́ч [*gen.* **-ча́**] *n.* dietitian.

диете́тика (тэ) *n.* dietetics; nutrition. —**диетети́ческий,** *adj.* dietetic.

диети́ческий *adj.* dietary.

диза́йн *n.* (industrial) design.

ди́зель *n.m.* diesel engine. —**ди́зельный,** *adj.* diesel.

дизентери́я *n.* dysentery.

дика́рь [*gen.* **-каря́**] *n.m.* [*fem.* **-ка́рка**] **1,** savage. **2,** *colloq.* unsociable person; loner.

ди́кий *adj.* **1,** wild. **2,** absurd; preposterous. **3,** shy;

retiring. —**ди́кое мя́со,** proud flesh. —**ди́кое я́блоко,** crab apple.

ди́ко *adv.* **1,** wild: расти́ ди́ко, to grow wild. **2,** wildly. —*adj., used predicatively* **1,** desolate: вокру́г бы́ло ди́ко, it was desolate all around. **2,** absurd: ди́ко да́же ду́мать об э́том, it is absurd even to think about it.

дикобра́з *n.* porcupine.

дико́вина *also,* **дико́винка** *n., colloq.* strange thing; wonder; novelty. —**быть в дико́вин(к)у** (+ *dat.*), to be amazing to.

дико́винный *adj., colloq.* odd; strange; bizarre.

дикорасту́щий *adj.* wild; growing wild.

ди́кость *n.f.* **1,** wild state; uncivilized state. **2,** savagery. **3,** lack of sociability. **4,** *colloq.* folly.

дикта́нт *n.* dictation (*classroom exercise*).

дикта́т *n.* imposed settlement. —**поли́тика дикта́та,** policy of dictating to others.

дикта́тор *n.* dictator. —**дикта́торский,** *adj.* dictatorial.

диктату́ра *n.* dictatorship.

диктова́ть *v. impfv.* [*pfv.* **продиктова́ть;** *pres.* **-ту́ю, -ту́ешь**] **1,** to dictate. **2,** *usu. passive* to prompt: реше́ние диктова́лось (*or* бы́ло продикто́вано) двумя́ фа́кторами, the decision was prompted by two factors.

дикто́вка *n.* dictation: писа́ть под дикто́вку, to take dictation. —**под дикто́вку** (+ *gen.*), at the urging of; at the behest of.

ди́ктор *n.* (radio) announcer.

диктофо́н *n.* dictaphone.

ди́кция *n.* diction; enunciation.

диле́мма *n.* dilemma.

дилета́нт *n.* amateur; dilettante. —**дилетанти́зм; дилета́нтство,** *n.* dilettantism. —**дилета́нтский,** *adj.* amateurish.

дилижа́нс *n.* stagecoach.

диминуэ́ндо *adv.* diminuendo.

ди́на *n.* dyne.

динами́зм *n.* dynamism.

дина́мика *n.* dynamics.

динами́т *n.* dynamite. —**динами́тный,** *adj.* dynamite (*attrib.*).

динами́ческий *adj.* **1,** of dynamics. **2,** dynamic.

динами́чный *adj.* dynamic. —**динами́чность,** *n.f.* dynamic quality.

дина́мо *n. indecl.* dynamo.

динамо́метр *n.* dynamometer.

дина́стия *n.* dynasty. —**династи́ческий,** *adj.* dynastic.

динoза́вр *n.* dinosaur.

дио́д *n.* diode.

дипло́м *n.* diploma; degree.

диплома́т *n.* diplomat.

дипломати́ческий *adj.* **1,** diplomatic. **2,** *fig.* diplomatic; tactful.

дипломати́чный *adj.* diplomatic; tactful. —**дипломати́чность,** *n.f.* diplomacy; tact.

диплома́тия *n.* diplomacy.

дипломи́рованный *adj.* having a degree: дипломи́рованный инжене́р, person with a degree in engineering.

дипло́мный *adj.* done toward a degree: дипло́мный прое́кт, project for one's degree.

директи́ва *n.* directive. —**директи́вный,** *adj.* containing instructions.

дире́ктор [*pl.* **директора́**] *n.* **1,** director; manager. **2,** *theat.* producer.

директора́т *n.* board of directors; directorate.

дире́кторский *adj.* director's; directorial.

дире́кция *n.* **1,** (top) management. **2,** director's office.

дирижа́бль *n.m.* dirigible.

дирижёр *n., music* conductor. —**дирижёрский,** *adj.* conductor's.

дирижи́ровать *v. impfv.* [*pres.* **-рую, -руешь**] *music (with instr.)* to conduct.

дисгармони́ровать *v. impfv.* [*pres.* **-рую, -руешь**] (*with* **с**) to clash (with).

дисгармо́ния *n.* disharmony.

диск *n.* **1,** disk. **2,** dial (*of a telephone*). **3,** turntable (*of a phonograph*). **4,** *sports* discus.

ди́скант *n., music* treble. —**дисканто́вый,** *adj.* treble.

дисквалифика́ция *n.* disqualification.

дисквалифици́ровать *v. impfv. & pfv.* [*pres.* **-рую, -руешь**] to disqualify.

ди́сковый *adj.* disk-shaped. —**ди́сковая борона́,** disk harrow. —**ди́сковый то́рмоз,** disk brake.

дискредити́ровать *v. impfv. & pfv.* [*pres.* **-рую, -руешь**] to discredit.

дискрецио́нный *adj.* discretionary.

дискримина́ция *n.* discrimination. —**дискриминацио́нный,** *adj.* discriminatory.

дискримини́ровать *v. impfv. & pfv.* [*pres.* **-рую, -руешь**] to discriminate (against).

дискуссио́нный *adj.* **1,** discussion (*attrib.*): в дискуссио́нном поря́дке, as a basis for discussion. **2,** debatable; controversial.

диску́ссия *n.* discussion; debate.

дискути́ровать *v. impfv.* [*pres.* **-рую, -руешь**] to discuss; debate.

дислока́ция *n., mil.* disposition (*of troops*).

дислоци́ровать *v. impfv. & pfv.* [*pres.* **-рую, -руешь**] *mil.* to deploy (troops).

диспансе́р (сэ) *n.* sanitarium; health center.

диспепси́я *n.* dyspepsia.

диспе́рсия *n., physics* dispersion.

диспе́тчер *n.* **1,** traffic manager. **2,** air traffic controller.

диспе́тчерская *n., decl. as an adj.* control tower. Also, **диспе́тчерская вы́шка.**

диспро́зий *n.* dysprosium.

диспропо́рция *n.* disproportion.

ди́спут *n.* (public) debate.

диссерта́ция *n.* dissertation; thesis.

диссона́нс *n.* **1,** *music* dissonance; discord. **2,** *fig.* disharmony; incongruity.

дистанцио́нный *adj.* controlled from a distance. —**дистанцио́нное управле́ние,** remote control.

диста́нция *n.* distance. —**сойти́ с диста́нции,** to drop out of a race; fail to go the distance.

дистилли́ровать *v. impfv. & pfv.* [*pres.* **-рую, -руешь**] to distill.

дистилля́ция *n.* distillation.

дистрофи́я *n.* dystrophy.

дисципли́на *n.* **1,** discipline. **2,** discipline (*branch of knowledge*).

дисциплина́рный *adj.* disciplinary. —**дисциплина́рное взыска́ние,** summary punishment.

дисциплини́ровать *v. impfv. & pfv.* [*pres.* **-рую, -руешь**] to discipline.

дитя́ *n. neut.* [*other cases rarely used*] child.

дифира́мб *n., in* **петь дифира́мбы** (+ *dat.*), to sing the praises of.

дифтери́я *also,* **дифтери́т** *n.* diphtheria. —**дифтери́йный,** *adj.* diphtheria (*attrib.*); diphtherial.

дифто́нг *n.* diphthong.

диффама́ция *n.* defamation.

дифференциа́л *n., math.; mech.* differential. —**дифференциа́льный,** *adj.* differential.

дифференциа́ция *n.* differentiation.

дифференци́ровать *v. impfv. & pfv.* [*pres.* **-рую, -руешь**] to differentiate.

диффу́зия *n., physics* diffusion.

despair

дича́ть *v. impfv.* [*pfv.* **одича́ть**] **1,** to become wild. **2,** to become shy; become unsociable.

дичи́ться *v.r. impfv., colloq.* **1,** to be shy; avoid people. **2,** (*with gen.*) to avoid.

дичь *n.f.* **1,** game (*animals, birds, etc.*): кру́пная дичь, big game. **2,** *colloq.* wilderness. **3,** *colloq.* nonsense.

длина́ *n.* length. —**в длину́,** lengthwise. —**длина́ волны́,** wavelength.

длинново́лновый *adj.* long-wave.

длинноволо́сый *adj.* long-haired.

длинноно́гий *adj.* long-legged.

длиннота́ [*pl.* **длинно́ты**] *n.* **1,** *obs.* (great) length. **2,** *pl.* long drawn-out passages.

дли́нный *adj.* [*short form* **дли́нен, длинна́, дли́нно**] long.

дли́тельный *adj.* long; lengthy; protracted; prolonged. —**дли́тельность,** *n.f.* length; duration.

дли́ться *v.r. impfv.* [*pfv.* **продли́ться**] to last.

для *prep., with gen.* for: кни́га для дете́й, a book for children. Корзи́на для бума́ги, a wastebasket. Хорошо́ вы́глядеть для своего́ во́зраста, to look well for one's age. —**для того́, что́бы,** *see* **что́бы.**

днева́льный *n., decl. as an adj., mil.* man on duty.

днева́ть *v. impfv.* [*pres.* **дню́ю, дню́ешь**] to spend the day (*in a certain place*). —**днева́ть и ночева́ть,** to spend all one's time; "live" (*in a certain place*).

дневни́к [*gen.* **-ника́**] *n.* diary.

дневно́й *adj.* **1,** day (*attrib.*). **2,** daytime (*attrib.*). **3,** a day's; one day's.

днём *adv.* during the day; in the daytime.

дни́ще *n.* bottom (*of a vessel or barrel*).

дно *n.* bottom. Морско́е дно, ocean floor; seabed. —**вверх дном,** upside down; topsy-turvy. —**идти́ ко дну,** (*of a ship*) to sink; go down. —**пить до дна,** to empty one's glass. —**пуска́ть ко дну,** to sink; send to the bottom.

до[1] *prep., with gen.* **1,** to; up to; as far as: дойти́ до ста́нции, to walk as far as the station. От Балти́йского до Чёрного мо́ря, from the Baltic to the Black Sea. **2,** before: до войны́, before the war. **3,** until: рабо́тать до двух часо́в но́чи, to work until two o'clock in the morning. **4,** to the point of: рабо́тать до изнеможе́ния, to work to the point of exhaustion. **5,** up to; as many as: зал вмеща́ет до ты́сячи челове́к, the hall accommodates up to a thousand people. —**до сих/тех пор; до тех пор пока́ (не),** *see* **пора́.** —**до того́,** so: до того́ уста́л, что..., so tired that... —**до того́, что,** until. —**не до,** not in the mood for: ему́ не до шу́ток, he is not in the mood for jokes. —**что до,** as for.

до[2] *n. neut., music* do; C.

до- *prefix* **1,** *indicating action or motion up to a point:* дойти́ до моста́, to walk as far as the bridge. **2,** *indicating completion of an action:* договори́ть, to finish speaking. **3,** *indicating something additional:* дополучи́ть, to receive in addition. **4,** (*with* **-ся**) *indicating attainment after persistent effort:* дозвони́ться, to ring until someone answers. **5,** (*with* **-ся**) *indicating an action to some extreme:* докрича́ться до хрипоты́, to shout oneself hoarse. **6,** *with adjectives* pre-: дошко́льный, preschool. **7,** *with adverbs* completely: до́суха, completely dry.

доба́вить [*infl.* **-влю, -вишь**] *v., pfv. of* **добавля́ть.**

доба́вка *n., colloq.* **1,** addition. **2,** second helping (*of food*).

добавле́ние *n.* **1,** addition (*act of adding*). **2,** an addition: примеча́ния и добавле́ния, notes and additions. —**в добавле́ние к,** in addition to.

добавля́ть *v. impfv.* [*pfv.* **доба́вить**] to add.

доба́вочный *adj.* **1,** additional; extra. **2,** (*with telephone numbers*) extension: доба́вочный со́рок два, extension 42. —**доба́вочный нало́г,** surtax.

добега́ть *v. impfv.* [*pfv.* **добежа́ть**] (*with* **до**) to run to; run up to; run as far as.

добежа́ть [*infl. like* **бежа́ть**] *v., pfv. of* **добега́ть.**

добела́ *adv.* **1,** until something is spotlessly clean. **2,** *in* **раскаля́ть добела́,** to make white-hot; **раскалённый добела́,** white-hot.

добива́ть *v. impfv.* [*pfv.* **доби́ть**] **1,** to kill; finish off; deal the finishing blow to. **2,** to crush; rout; smite. **3,** (*with* **до**) to beat to a certain point or state.

добива́ться *v. impfv.* [*pfv.* **доби́ться**] (*with gen.*) **1,** to achieve; obtain; get. **2,** [*impfv. only*] to seek; strive for. —**доби́ться своего́,** to gain one's objective; get one's way.

добира́ться *v.r. impfv.* [*pfv.* **добра́ться**] (*with* **до**) *colloq.* **1,** to reach; get to. **2,** to get one's hands on (someone).

доби́ть [*infl.* **-бью́, -бьёшь**] *v., pfv. of* **добива́ть.** —**доби́ться,** *refl., pfv. of* **добива́ться.**

до́блестный *adj.* valiant; valorous.

до́блесть *n.f.* valor.

добра́сывать *v. impfv.* [*pfv.* **добро́сить**] (*with* **до**) to throw as far as.

добра́ться [*infl. like* **брать**] *v.r., pfv. of* **добира́ться.**

добра́чный *adj.* before one is/was married; premarital.

добрести́ *v.pfv.* [*infl. like* **брести́**] (*with* **до**) to manage to reach; finally make it to.

добре́ть *v. impfv.* **1,** [*pfv.* **подобре́ть**] to become kind; become kinder. **2,** [*pfv.* **раздобре́ть**] *colloq.* to get fat; put on weight.

добро́ *n.* **1,** good: добро́ и зло, good and evil. Жела́ть кому́-нибудь добра́, to wish someone well. **2,** *colloq.* goods; property. —*adv., colloq.* good; all right. —**дать добро́ на** (+ *acc.*), *colloq.* to give the go-ahead for. —**добро́ бы,** *colloq.* it would be all right if; it would be one thing if. —**добро́ пожа́ловать!,** welcome! —**э́то не к добру́,** it's a bad omen.

доброво́лец [*gen.* **-льца**] *n.* volunteer.

доброво́льный *adj.* voluntary. —**доброво́льно,** *adv.* voluntarily.

доброво́льческий *adj.* volunteer (*attrib.*).

доброде́тель *n.f.* virtue. —**доброде́тельный,** *adj.* virtuous.

доброду́шие *n.* good nature. —**доброду́шный,** *adj.* good-natured.

доброжела́тель *n.m.* well-wisher. —**доброжела́тельный,** *adj.* good-natured; friendly. —**доброжела́тельство,** *n.* good will.

доброка́чественный *adj.* **1,** of good quality. **2,** *med.* benign; non-malignant.

добро́м *adv., colloq.* of one's own free will.

добросерде́чие *n.* kindheartedness. —**добросерде́чный,** *adj.* kindhearted; good-hearted.

добро́сить [*infl.* **-шу, -сишь**] *v., pfv. of* **добра́сывать.**

добросо́вестный *adj.* conscientious. —**добросо́вестность,** *n.f.* conscientiousness.

добрососе́дский *adj.* neighborly; good-neighbor.

доброта́ *n.* kindness.

добро́тный *adj.* of high quality; sound; durable.

до́брый *adj.* [*short form* **добр, добра́, до́бро**] **1,** kind. **2,** good: до́брое де́ло, good deed; до́брая во́ля, good will. **3,** *in greetings* good: до́брое у́тро!, good morning!; до́брый ве́чер!, good evening! **4,** *colloq.* a good; at least: до́брый час, a good hour. —**бу́дьте добры́** (+*imperative*), be so kind as to... —**в до́брый час!,** the best of luck (in your new venture)! —**всего́ до́брого!,** all the best! —**чего́ до́брого,** for all one knows.

добря́к [*gen.* **-бряка́**] *n., colloq.* good-natured person; good soul.

добуди́ться *v.r. pfv.* [*infl.* **-бужу́сь, -бу́дишься**] (*with gen.*) *colloq.* to succeed in waking.

добыва́ть *v. impfv.* [*pfv.* **добы́ть**] **1,** to obtain. **2,** to extract; mine.

добы́ть [*infl. like* **быть;** *past* **до́был** *or* **добы́л, добыла́, до́было** *or* **добы́ло**] *v., pfv. of* **добыва́ть.**

добы́ча *n.* **1,** extraction; mining. **2,** anything mined from the earth. **3,** booty; loot; plunder; spoils. **4,** prey.

дова́ривать *v. impfv.* [*pfv.* **довари́ть**] to finish cooking; finish making.

довари́ть [*infl.* **-варю́, -ва́ришь**] *v., pfv. of* **дова́ривать.**

довезти́ [*infl. like* **везти́**] *v., pfv. of* **довози́ть.**

дове́ренность *n.f.* power of attorney. —**по дове́ренности,** by proxy.

дове́ренный *adj.* authorized. —*n.* proxy; agent.

дове́рие *n.* confidence; trust.

довери́тельный *adj.* **1,** trusting. **2,** *obs.* secret; classified.

дове́рить *v., pfv. of* **доверя́ть.** —**дове́риться,** *refl., pfv. of* **доверя́ться.**

до́верху *adv.* to the top; to the brim. —**сни́зу до́верху,** from top to bottom.

дове́рчивый *adj.* trusting. —**дове́рчивость,** *n.f.* trusting nature.

доверша́ть *v. impfv.* [*pfv.* **доверши́ть**] to complete.

доверше́ние *n.* completion. —**в доверше́ние всего́,** to top it off.

доверши́ть *v., pfv. of* **доверша́ть.**

доверя́ть *v. impfv.* [*pfv.* **дове́рить**] **1,** [*impfv. only*] (*with dat.*) to trust. **2,** to entrust; confide. —**доверя́ться,** *refl.* (*with dat.*) to trust (in).

дове́сок [*gen.* **-ска**] *n.* makeweight.

довести́ [*infl. like* **вести́**] *v., pfv. of* **доводи́ть.** —**довести́сь,** *refl., pfv. of* **доводи́ться.**

довле́ть *v. impfv.* **1,** *obs.* to suffice. **2,** (*with* **над**) to hold sway over (*a usage generally considered incorrect*).

до́вод *n.* argument: до́воды за и про́тив, the arguments for and against; the pros and cons.

доводи́ть *v. impfv.* [*pfv.* **довести́;** *pres.* **-вожу́, -во́дишь**] (*with* **до**) **1,** to take to; bring to; accompany to. **2,** to drive; carry; reduce (*to a certain point or state*): доводи́ть до отча́яния/кра́йности/нищеты́, to drive to despair/carry to an extreme/reduce to poverty/. **3,** to convey (news, information, etc.). —**доводи́ть до конца́,** to see through to the end. —**доводи́ть до (чьего́-нибудь) све́дения,** *see* **све́дение.**

доводи́ться *v.r impfv.* [*pfv.* **довести́сь;** *pres.* **-вожу́сь, -во́дишься**] **1,** *impers.* (*with dat. and inf.*) *colloq.* to happen (to); have occasion (to): нам не довело́сь встре́титься, we did not have occasion to meet. **2,** [*impfv. only*] (*with dat. and instr.*) *colloq.* to be related in a certain way: он дово́дится мне дя́дей, he is my uncle.

довое́нный *adj.* prewar.

довози́ть *v. impfv.* [*pfv.* **довезти́;** *pres.* **-вожу́, -во́зишь**] (*with* **до**) to take to; bring to.

дово́льно *adv.* **1,** rather; fairly; pretty: дово́льно ча́сто, fairly often. **2,** enough: дово́льно крича́ть!, enough shouting! С меня́ дово́льно, I've had enough. **3,** contentedly.

дово́льный *adj.* **1,** [*short form* **-лен, -льна, -льно**] (*with instr.*) pleased (with); satisfied (with); contented (with). **2,** contented: дово́льный вид, contented look.

дово́льствие *n., mil.* allowance.

дово́льство *n.* **1,** satisfaction; contentment. **2,** *colloq.* comfortable circumstances.

дово́льствоваться *v.r. impfv.* [*pfv.* **удово́льствоваться;** *pres.* **-ствуюсь, -ствуешься**] (*with instr.*) to be content (with); be satistied (with).

дог *n.* mastiff. —**да́тский дог,** Great Dane.

догада́ться *v.r., pfv. of* **дога́дываться.**

дога́дка [*gen. pl.* **-док**] *n.* **1,** guess; conjecture. **2,** *pl.* guesswork. —**стро́ить дога́дки,** to conjecture; speculate. —**теря́ться в дога́дках,** to be at a loss.

дога́дливый *adj.* bright; clever; quick-witted.

дога́дываться *v.r. impfv.* [*pfv.* **догада́ться**] **1,** to guess. **2,** to figure out. **3,** to have the good sense to.

до́гма *n.* dogma. —**догмати́зм,** *n.* dogmatism. —**догма́тик,** *n.* dogmatist. —**догмати́ческий,** *adj.* dogmatic.

догна́ть [*infl. like* **гнать**] *v., pfv. of* **догоня́ть.**

догова́ривать *v. impfv.* [*pfv.* **договори́ть**] to finish speaking; have one's say. —**догова́риваться,** *refl.* **1,** to make arrangements: договори́лись!, it's all arranged/settled. **2,** (*with inf.*) to agree (to); arrange (to). **3,** (*with* **до**) to talk to some extreme: договори́ться до хрипоты́, to talk oneself hoarse. Догова́риваться до того́, что..., to go so far as to say.

догово́р *also,* **до́говор** *n.* **1,** treaty. **2,** contract. —**аре́ндный догово́р,** lease.

договорённость *n.f.* agreement; understanding.

договори́ть *v., pfv. of* **догова́ривать.** —**договори́ться,** *refl., pfv. of* **догова́риваться.**

догово́рный *adj.* **1,** treaty (*attrib.*). **2,** contractual.

догола́ *adv.* (*with verbs of undressing*) naked; to the skin.

догоня́ть *v. impfv.* [*pfv.* **догна́ть**] to overtake; catch up with.

догора́ть *v. impfv.* [*pfv.* **догоре́ть**] to burn down; burn out.

додава́ть *v. impfv.* [*pfv.* **дода́ть;** *pres.* **-даю́, -даёшь**] to pay the remainder: он додáст вам дéсять рублéй, he will pay you the remaining ten rubles.

додáть [*infl. like* **дать;** *past* **дóдал, додалá, дóдало**] *v., pfv. of* **додавáть.**

додéлывать *v. impfv.* [*pfv.* **додéлать**] to finish; complete.

додýмываться *v.r. impfv.* [*pfv.* **додýматься**] (*with* **до**) to think of; hit upon; come up with (an idea, solution, etc.).

доедáть *v. impfv.* [*pfv.* **доéсть**] to finish eating; eat up.

доезжáть *v. impfv.* [*pfv.* **доéхать**] (with **до**) **1,** to reach; arrive at. **2,** to go/drive/ride as far as.

доéние *n.* milking.

доéсть [*infl. like* **есть**] *v., pfv. of* **доедáть.**

доéхать [*infl.* **-éду, -éдешь**] *v., pfv. of* **доезжáть.**

дож *n.* doge.

дождáться *v.r. pfv.* [*infl. like* **ждать**] **1,** to wait (*as long as necessary*): я не могý дождáться, I can't wait. **2,** (*with gen.*) to wait (*until someone comes or something happens*): дождáться врачá, to wait till the doctor comes. Я éле дождáлся вас, I almost didn't wait for you. Он не дождáлся нас, he did not wait for us; he left before we came. —**ждать не дождáться,** *colloq.* to anxiously await.

дождевáльный *adj.* sprinkling (*attrib.*); sprinkler (*attrib.*): дождевáльная установка, sprinkler system.

дождевáние *n.* sprinkling (*of a lawn, crops, etc.*).

дождевúк [*gen.* **-викá**] *n., colloq.* raincoat.

дождевóй *adj.* rain (*attrib.*): дождевáя водá, rain water.

дóждик *n.* light rain; shower.

дождлúвый *adj.* rainy.

дождь [*gen.* **дождя́**] *n.m.* rain. —**дождь идёт; идёт дождь,** it is raining.

доживáть *v. impfv.* [*pfv.* **дожúть**] **1,** (*with* **до**) to live to; live to see. **2,** [*impfv. only*] to live out: доживáть послéдние дни, to be living out one's last days; be nearing the end of one's life. **3,** *colloq.* to spend the rest of: дожúть лéто на дáче, to spend the rest of the summer in the country.

дожúть [*infl.* **-живý, -живёшь;** *past* **дóжил, дожилá, дóжило**] *v., pfv. of* **доживáть.**

дóза *n.* dose.

дозапрáвить [*infl.* **-влю, -вишь**] *v., pfv. of* **дозаправля́ть.** —**дозапрáвиться,** *refl., pfv. of* **дозаправля́ться.**

дозапрáвка *n.* refueling.

дозаправля́ть *v. impfv.* [*pfv.* **дозапрáвить**] to refuel. —**дозаправля́ться,** *refl.* (*of a plane*) to refuel.

дозвáться *v.r. pfv.* [*infl. like* **звать**] (*with gen.*) *colloq.* (*usu. neg.*) to reach on the telephone: егó никáк не дозовёшься, you can't reach/get him on the phone.

дозвóленный *adj.* permitted; permissible.

дозволя́ть *v. impfv.* [*pfv.* **дозвóлить**] *obs.* to permit; allow.

дозвонúться *v.r. pfv.* (*with* **к**) *colloq.* to ring until one receives an answer; reach (*by telephone*).

дозвуковóй *adj.* subsonic.

дозирóвка *n.* dosage.

дознавáться *v.r. impfv.* [*pfv.* **дознáться;** *pres.* **-знаю́сь, -знаёшься**] *colloq.* **1,** to find out. **2,** [*impfv. only*] to inquire.

дознáние *n., law* inquest; inquiry.

дознáться *v.r., pfv. of* **дознавáться.**

дозóр *n.* patrol. —**дозóрный,** *adj.* patrol (*attrib.*).

дозревáть *v. impfv.* [*pfv.* **дозрéть**] to become fully ripe.

доигрывать *v. impfv.* [*pfv.* **доигрáть**] to finish playing; play to the end.

доúльный *adj.* used for milking: доúльная машúна, milking machine.

доискáться [*infl.* **-ищýсь, -úщешься**] *v.r., pfv. of* **доúскиваться.**

доúскиваться *v.r. impfv.* [*pfv.* **доискáться**] (*with gen.*) *colloq.* **1,** to try to find; search for (something) until it is found. **2,** to inquire into; try to find out; seek.

доисторúческий *adj.* prehistoric.

доúть *v. impfv.* [*pfv.* **подоúть;** *pres.* **дою́, дóишь** *or* **доúшь**] to milk. —**доúться,** *refl.* [*impfv. only*] to give milk.

дóйка *n.* milking.

дóйный *adj.* milch.

дойтú [*infl.* **дойдý, дойдёшь;** *past* **дошёл, дошлá, дошлó**] *v., pfv. of* **доходúть.**

док *n.* dock.

доказáтельный *adj.* demonstrative; conclusive.

доказáтельство *n.* proof; evidence.

доказáть [*infl.* **-кажý, -кáжешь**] *v., pfv. of* **докáзывать.**

доказýемый *adj.* demonstrable.

докáзывать *v. impfv.* [*pfv.* **доказáть**] **1,** to prove. **2,** [*impfv. only*] to try to prove; argue.

докáнчивать *v. impfv.* [*pfv.* **докóнчить**] **1,** to finish. **2,** *colloq.* to finish off (*i.e.* eating or drinking).

докáпывать *v. impfv.* [*pfv.* **докопáть**] to finish digging. —**докáпываться,** *refl.* (*with* **до**) **1,** to dig as far as. **2,** *fig., colloq.* to get to: докопáться до úстины, to get to the truth.

докатúться [*infl.* **-качýсь, -кáтишься**] *v.r., pfv. of* **докáтываться.**

докáтываться *v.r. impfv.* [*pfv.* **докатúться**] **1,** (*with* **до**) to roll to; roll as far as. **2,** *colloq.* (*of loud noises*) to thunder; resound. **3,** (*with* **до**) *fig., colloq.* to sink to.

дóкер *n.* dock worker; longshoreman.

доклáд *n.* **1,** report. **2,** lecture; paper. **3,** announcement (*of a visitor*): входúть без доклáда, to walk in unannounced.

докладнóй *adj., in* **докладнáя запúска,** report; memorandum.

доклáдчик *n.* person delivering a report; speaker.

доклáдывать *v. impfv.* [*pfv.* **доложúть**] **1,** to report. **2,** (*with* **о**) to announce (a visitor). **3,** *colloq.* to add.

докóле *adv., obs.* **1,** how long? **2,** as long as.

доконáть *v. pfv., colloq.* to finish; be the end of.

докóнчить *v., pfv. of* **докáнчивать.**

докопáть *v., pfv. of* **докáпывать.** —**докопáться,** *refl., pfv. of* **докáпываться.**

докраснá *also,* **дóкрасна** *adv.* **1,** until something is red. **2,** *in* **раскаля́ть докраснá,** to make red-hot; **раскалённый докраснá,** red-hot.

докричáться *v.r. pfv.* [*infl.* **-чýсь, -чúшься**] **1,** *colloq.* to shout until one is heard. **2,** (*with* **до**) to shout to some extreme: докричáться до хрипотý, to shout oneself hoarse.

дóктор [*pl.* **докторá**] *n.* **1,** doctor (*holder of a doctoral degree*): дóктор наýк, Doctor of Science; Ph.D. **2,** *colloq.* doctor; physician. —**дóкторский,** *adj.* doctor's; doctoral.

доктри́на *n.* doctrine. —**доктринёрский,** *adj.* doctrinaire.

докуме́нт *n.* document. —**документа́льный,** *adj.* documentary. —**документа́ция,** *n.* documentation.

документи́ровать *v. impfv. & pfv.* [*pres.* **-рую, -руешь**] to document.

докупа́ть *v. impfv.* [*pfv.* **докупи́ть**] to buy in addition.

докупи́ть [*infl.* **-куплю́, -ку́пишь**] *v., pfv. of* **докупа́ть.**

доку́ривать *v. impfv.* [*pfv.* **докури́ть**] to finish smoking.

докури́ть [*infl.* **-курю́, -ку́ришь**] *v., pfv. of* **доку́ривать.**

докуча́ть *v. impfv.* (*with dat.*) *colloq.* to bother; annoy; pester.

доку́чливый *adj., colloq.* annoying; bothersome.

дол *n., poetic* valley; vale; dale.

долби́ть *v. impfv.* [*pres.* **-блю́, -би́шь**] **1,** [*pfv.* **продолби́ть**] to gouge; hollow out. **2,** *colloq.* to bang (*repeatedly*). **3,** *colloq.* to memorize; learn by rote.

долг *n.* **1,** duty. **2,** [*2nd loc.* **долгу́;** *pl.* **долги́**] debt. —**в долгу́ пе́ред** *or* **у,** indebted to; in someone's debt. —**брать в долг,** to borrow. —**дава́ть в долг,** to lend. —**долг платежо́м кра́сен,** one good turn deserves another. —**не остава́ться в долгу́,** to reply in kind; (one was) not to be outdone. —**отда́ть после́дний долг** (+ *dat.*), to pay one's last respects to. —**по до́лгу слу́жбы,** in one's official capacity.

до́лгий *adj.* [*comp.* **до́льше** *and* **до́лее**] long (*in time*). —**до́лгие го́ды,** many long years.

до́лго *adv.* long; (for) a long time. —**как до́лго?,** how long?

долгове́чный *adj.* long-lasting; long-lived. —**долгове́чность,** *n.f.* longevity.

долгово́й *adj.* of or for a debt. —**долгово́е обяза́тельство,** promissory note. —**долгова́я тюрьма́; долгова́я я́ма,** debtor's prison.

долговре́менный *adj.* of long duration; lasting a long time.

долговя́зый *adj., colloq.* lanky; gangling.

долгожда́нный *adj.* long-awaited.

долгоигра́ющий *adj., in* **долгоигра́ющая пласти́нка,** long-playing record.

долголе́тие *n.* longevity. —**долголе́тний,** *adj.* of many years.

долгоно́жка [*gen. pl.* **-жек**] *n.* crane fly.

долгоно́сик *n.* weevil. —**хло́пковый долгоно́сик,** boll weevil.

долгосро́чный *adj.* long-term.

долгота́ *n.* **1,** length: долгота́ дня, the length of a day. **2,** [*pl.* **-го́ты**] longitude.

до́лее *adj., comp. of* **до́лгий.** —*adv., comp. of* **до́лго.**

долеза́ть *v. impfv.* [*pfv.* **доле́зть**] (*with* **до**) **1,** to climb as far as. **2,** to reach by climbing.

доле́зть [*infl. like* **лезть**] *v., pfv. of* **долеза́ть.**

долета́ть *v. impfv.* [*pfv.* **долете́ть**] (*with* **до**) **1,** to fly as far as. **2,** to reach by flying. **3,** (*of sounds, news, etc.*) to reach.

долете́ть [*infl.* **-чу́, -ти́шь**] *v., pfv. of* **долета́ть.**

до́лжен *adj., used predicatively* [*fem.* **-жна́;** *neut.* **-жно́;** *pl.* **-жны́**] **1,** must; have to: я до́лжен (должна́) идти́, I must go. **2,** should; ought to: она́ должна́ ско́ро прийти́, she should be here soon. **3,** due to; supposed to; scheduled to: по́езд до́лжен прибы́ть в семь часо́в, the train is due/scheduled to arrive at seven o'clock. **4,** to owe: он мне до́лжен два рубля́, he owes me two rubles. —**должно́ быть,** probably; must: он, должно́ быть, уже́ ушёл, he must have left already.

должни́к [*gen.* **-ника́**] *n.* debtor.

до́лжное *n., decl. as an adj.* one's due. —**отдава́ть/воздава́ть до́лжное** (+ *dat.*), to give someone his/her due; give someone credit. —**принима́ть как до́лжное,** to take as a matter of course; take for granted.

должностно́й *adj.* official. —**должностно́е лицо́,** official; officeholder. —**должностно́е преступле́ние,** malfeasance in office.

до́лжность [*pl.* **до́лжности, -сте́й, -стя́м**] *n.f.* post; position; office.

до́лжный *adj.* due; proper. —**до́лжным о́бразом,** properly. *See also* **до́лжное.**

долива́ть *v. impfv.* [*pfv.* **доли́ть**] **1,** to fill (*by pouring*). **2,** (*with gen.*) to pour more (of).

доли́на *n.* valley.

доли́ть [*infl.* **долью́, дольёшь;** *past* **до́лил** *or* **доли́л, долила́, до́лило** *or* **доли́ло**] *v., pfv. of* **долива́ть.**

до́ллар *n.* dollar.

доложи́ть [*infl.* **-ложу́, -ло́жишь**] *v., pfv. of* **докла́дывать.**

доло́й *adv.* **1,** (*with acc.*) down with...! **2,** off: ша́пки доло́й!, hats off! —**с глаз мои́х доло́й!,** out of my sight! —**с плеч доло́й,** (a load) off one's shoulders.

доломи́т *n.* dolomite.

долото́ [*pl.* **доло́та**] *n.* chisel.

до́лька [*gen. pl.* **-лек**] *n.* **1,** lobule. **2,** section (*of a citrus fruit*).

до́льше *adj., comp. of* **до́лгий.** —*adv., comp. of* **до́лго.**

до́ля [*pl.* **до́ли, доле́й, доля́м**] *n.* **1,** share; portion. **2,** lot: вы́пасть на до́лю (+ *dat.*), to fall to someone's lot. **3,** *anat.* lobe. **4,** *in* до́ля и́стины, grain of truth. —**войти́ в до́лю с** (+ *instr.*), to go shares with.

дом [*pl.* **дома́**] *n.* **1,** house; home. **2,** building. —**из до́ма,** from home. —**и́з дому,** out of the house. —**на́ дом,** to one's home. —**на дому́,** at home (*as opposed to one's place of work*). *See also* **до́ма** *and* **домо́й.**

до́ма *adv.* at home. —**бу́дьте как до́ма,** make yourself at home. —**у него́ не все до́ма,** he is not all there.

дома́шние *n.pl., decl. as an adj.* members of one's family.

дома́шний *adj.* **1,** home (*attrib.*); house (*attrib.*); household (*attrib.*). **2,** domestic. **3,** homemade; (*of a meal*) home-cooked. —**дома́шнее зада́ние,** homework. —**дома́шняя пти́ца,** poultry. —**дома́шняя хозя́йка,** housewife. —**дома́шнее хозя́йство,** housekeeping.

до́менный *adj., in* **до́менная печь,** blast furnace.

до́мик *n.* small house; cottage.

доминио́н *n.* dominion.

домини́ровать *v. impfv.* [*pres.* **-рую, -руешь**] **1,** (*of a thought, idea, etc.*) to be (pre)dominant. **2,** (*with* **над**) to dominate; tower over.

домини́рующий *adj.* dominant.

домино́ *n. indecl.* **1,** domino (*costume*). **2,** dominoes (*game*).

доми́шко [*pl.* **-шки, -шек**] *n.m.* **1,** tiny house. **2,** shack; hovel.

домкра́т *n.* jack (*for lifting*).

до́мна [*gen. pl.* **-мен**] *n.* blast furnace.

домови́тый *adj.* **1,** thrifty; economical. **2,** capable; efficient.
домовладе́лец [*gen.* **-льца**] *n.* homeowner.
домово́дство *n.* **1,** housekeeping. **2,** home economics.
домово́й *n., decl. as an adj.* elf; goblin.
домо́вый *adj.* house (*attrib.*). —**домо́вая кни́га,** register of tenants.
домога́тельство *n.* solicitation; *pl.* overtures.
домога́ться *v.r. impfv.* (*with gen.*) to seek; strive to obtain.
домо́й *adv.* home: идти́ домо́й, to go home.
доморо́щенный *adj.* **1,** homebred. **2,** *fig.* homespun; half-baked.
домосе́д *n.* stay-at-home; homebody.
домотка́ный *adj.* homespun.
домоуправле́ние *n.* **1,** building management. **2,** *colloq.* building manager's office.
домохозя́йка [*gen. pl.* **-я́ек**] *n.* housewife.
домоча́дцы [*gen.* **-цев**] *n. pl., obs.* household.
до́мра *n.* old Russian musical instrument resembling a mandolin.
домрабо́тница *n.* maid; housemaid.
домча́ть *v. pfv.* [*infl.* **-чу́, -чи́шь**] *colloq.* to deliver in a hurry; rush; whisk. —**домча́ться,** *refl.* (*with* **до**) *colloq.* to race to; rush to; dash to.
до́мысел [*gen.* **-сла**] *n.* conjecture; supposition.
донага́ *adv., colloq.* (*with verbs of undressing*) naked; to the skin.
дона́шивать *v. impfv.* [*pfv.* **доноси́ть**] **1,** to wear out. **2,** to carry (a baby) to full term.
доне́льзя *adv., colloq.* completely; utterly: доне́льзя уста́л, utterly exhausted.
донесе́ние *n.* message; dispatch.
донести́ [*infl. like* **нести́**] *v., pfv. of* **доноси́ть**[1]. —**донести́сь,** *refl., pfv. of* **доноси́ться.**
до́низу *adv.* to the bottom. —**све́рху до́низу,** from top to bottom.
донима́ть *v. impfv.* [*pfv.* **доня́ть**] *colloq.* to exasperate.
донкихо́тский *adj.* quixotic.
до́нор *n.* blood donor.
доно́с *n.* denunciation, accusation; report to the authorities.
доноси́ть[1] *v. impfv.* [*pfv.* **донести́;** *pres.* **-ношу́, -но́сишь**] **1,** (*with* **до**) to carry to; deliver to. **2,** to report. **3,** (*with* **на** + *acc.*) to report; inform against; squeal on. —**доноси́ться,** *refl.* **1,** to be heard; be sensed. **2,** (*with* **до**) to reach.
доноси́ть[2] [*infl.* **-ношу́, -но́сишь**] *v., pfv. of* **дона́шивать.**
доно́счик *n.* informer; stool pigeon.
донско́й *adj.* of the Don River. —**донско́й каза́к,** Don Cossack.
доны́не *adv., poetic* to this day.
доня́ть [*infl. like* **поня́ть**] *v., pfv. of* **донима́ть.**
допека́ть *v. impfv.* [*pfv.* **допе́чь**] **1,** to finish baking. **2,** *colloq.* to plague.
допе́чь [*infl. like* **печь**] *v., pfv. of* **допека́ть.**
допива́ть *v. impfv.* [*pfv.* **допи́ть**] to drink (up); finish drinking. —**допива́ться,** *refl.* (*with* **до**) *colloq.* to drink oneself into a state of.
дописа́ть [*infl.* **-пишу́, -пи́шешь**] *v., pfv. of* **допи́сывать.**
допи́сывать *v. impfv.* [*pfv.* **дописа́ть**] **1,** to finish writing. **2,** (*with* **до**) to write as far as. **3,** to write additionally; add (*by writing*).
допи́ть [*infl.* **-пью́, -пьёшь;** *past* **до́пил** *or* **допи́л, допила́, до́пило** *or* **допи́ло**] *v., pfv. of* **допива́ть.** —**допи́ться,** *refl.* [*past* **допи́лся** *or* **допился́, допила́сь, допи́лось** *or* **допило́сь**] *pfv. of* **допива́ться.**
допла́та *n.* additional charge; surcharge.
доплати́ть [*infl.* **-плачу́, -пла́тишь**] *v., pfv. of* **допла́чивать.**
допла́чивать *v. impfv.* [*pfv.* **доплати́ть**] **1,** to pay in addition; pay the remainder: доплати́ть два рубля́, to pay an additional (*or* the remaining) two rubles. **2,** to pay in full.
доплести́сь [*infl. like* **плести́**] *v.r., pfv. of* **доплета́ться.**
доплета́ться *v.r. impfv.* [*pfv.* **доплести́сь**] (*with* **до**) *colloq.* to drag oneself (to).
доплыва́ть *v. impfv.* [*pfv.* **доплы́ть**] (*with* **до**) to swim as far as.
доплы́ть [*infl. like* **плыть**] *v., pfv. of* **доплыва́ть.**
допо́длинный *adj., colloq.* true; authentic. —**допо́длинно,** *adv., colloq.* for certain.
допоздна́ *adv., colloq.* till late at night.
дополза́ть *v. impfv.* [*pfv.* **доползти́**] (*with* **до**) to crawl up to; crawl as far as.
доползти́ [*infl. like* **ползти́**] *v., pfv. of* **доползать.**
дополна́ *adv., colloq.* to the brim.
дополне́ние *n.* **1,** addition. **2,** supplement. **3,** *gram.* object. —**в дополне́ние к,** in addition to.
дополни́тельно *adv.* in addition.
дополни́тельный *adj.* **1,** additional; supplementary. **2,** (*of colors*) complementary. —**дополни́тельное вре́мя,** *sports* overtime.
дополня́ть *v. impfv.* [*pfv.* **допо́лнить**] to enlarge; expand; supplement; amplify; add to. —**дополня́ть друг дру́га,** to complement each other.
дополуча́ть *v. impfv.* [*pfv.* **дополучи́ть**] to receive in addition; receive the remainder.
дополучи́ть [*infl.* **-лучу́, -лу́чишь**] *v., pfv. of* **дополуча́ть.**
допото́пный *adj.* antediluvian.
допра́шивать *v. impfv.* [*pfv.* **допроси́ть**] to interrogate; question.
допро́с *n.* interrogation; questioning.
допроси́ть [*infl.* **-прошу́, -про́сишь**] *v., pfv. of* **допра́шивать.**
до́пуск *n.* **1,** admission; admittance. **2,** *mech.* tolerance.
допуска́ть *v. impfv.* [*pfv.* **допусти́ть**] **1,** to admit; let in. **2,** to allow; permit; tolerate. **3,** to commit (an error, indiscretion, etc.). **4,** to assume. **5,** to grant; concede.
допусти́мый *adj.* **1,** permissible. **2,** conceivable; possible.
допусти́ть [*infl.* **-пущу́, -пу́стишь**] *v., pfv. of* **допуска́ть.** —**допу́стим,** let us assume.
допуще́ние *n.* **1,** admission. **2,** assumption.
допы́тываться *v.r. impfv.* [*pfv.* **допыта́ться**] *colloq.* **1,** to find out. **2,** [*impfv. only*] to try to find out.
допьяна́ *also,* **до́пьяна** *adv., colloq.* till one is completely drunk.
дораба́тывать *v. impfv.* [*pfv.* **дорабо́тать**] **1,** *v.t.* to finish; put the finishing touches on. **2,** *v.i.* (*with* **до**) to work until. —**дораба́тываться,** *refl.* (*with* **до**) *colloq.* to work to some extreme: дорабо́таться до изнеможе́ния, to work to the point of exhaustion.

дорастáть *v. impfv.* [*pfv.* **дорасти́**] (*with* **до**) **1,** to grow to (a certain height). **2,** to reach the age of. **3,** (*with* **не**) not be old enough: он ещё не дорóс, чтóбы (+ *inf.*), he is not old enough to...

дорасти́ [*infl. like* **расти́**] *v., pfv. of* **дорастáть.**

дореволюциóнный *adj.* prerevolutionary.

дорóга *n.* **1,** road. **2,** way. **3,** trip: устáть с дорóги, to be tired from the trip. —**по** (*or* **в**) **дорóге,** on the way; en route. —**дать дорóгу** (+ *dat.*), to make way for. —**идти́ своéй дорóгой,** to go one's own way. —**стать поперёк дорóги** (+ *dat.*), to stand in someone's way. —**тудá емý и дорóга,** it serves him right.

дóрого *adv.* **1,** a lot (of money): заплати́ть/брать дóрого, to pay/charge a lot of money. **2,** dearly: э́то емý дóрого обошлóсь, it cost him dearly. —*adj., used predicatively* **1,** expensive: э́то не дóрого, that's not expensive. **2,** dear; precious: врéмя бы́ло дóрого, time was precious.

дороговизна *n.* **1,** high prices. **2,** (*with gen.*) the high cost of.

дорогóй *adj.* [*short form* **дóрог, дорогá, дóрого;** *comp.* **дорóже**] **1,** dear: дорогóй друг, a dear friend. **2,** expensive. **3,** (*of a price*) high. **4,** precious. —*n.* dear; my dear.

дорогостóящий *adj.* high-priced; expensive; costly.

дорóдный *adj.* stout; corpulent. —**дорóдность; дорóдство,** *n.* corpulence.

дорожáть *v. impfv.* [*pfv.* **вздорожáть** *or* **подорожáть**] to go up in price.

дорóже *adj., comp. of* **дорогóй.**

дорожи́ть *v. impfv.* (*with instr.*) to value; prize; treasure.

дорóжка [*gen. pl.* **-жек**] *n.* **1,** path; walk. **2,** track: беговáя дорóжка, running track. **3,** lane (*on a running track*). **4,** strip of carpet. —**звуковáя дорóжка,** sound track. —**лётная дорóжка,** runway.

дорóжный *adj.* **1,** road (*attrib.*): дорóжный знак, road sign. **2,** travel (*attrib.*); traveling (*attrib.*).

дортуáр *n., obs.* dormitory.

досáда *n.* annoyance; vexation. —**какáя досáда!,** how annoying!

досади́ть [*infl.* **-жý, -ди́шь**] *v., pfv. of* **досаждáть.**

досáдливый *adj.* expressing annoyance; of annoyance.

досáдный *adj.* **1,** annoying. **2,** regrettable. —**досáдно,** *adj., used predicatively* annoying: как досáдно!, how annoying!

досáдовать *v. impfv.* [*pres.* **-дую, -дуешь**] (*with* **на** + *acc.*) to be annoyed (with).

досаждáть *v. impfv.* [*pfv.* **досади́ть**] to annoy; vex.

досéле *adv., obs.* up to now.

досидéть [*infl.* **-жý, -ди́шь**] *v., pfv. of* **доси́живать.**

доси́живать *v. impfv.* [*pfv.* **досидéть**] (*with* **до**) to sit (until); stay (until).

доскá [*acc.* **дóску;** *pl.* **дóски, досóк, доскáм**] *n.* **1,** board. **2,** blackboard. **3,** plaque. —**от доски́ до доски́,** from cover to cover. —**стáвить на однý дóску,** to equate; place on a par.

досказáть *v. pfv.* [*infl.* **-скажý, -скáжешь**] **1,** to finish telling. **2,** (*with* **до**) to tell as far as.

досконáльный *adj.* thorough. —**досконáльно,** *adv.* thoroughly. —**досконáльность,** *n.f.* thoroughness.

дослóвный *adj.* literal; verbatim. —**дослóвно,** *adv.* literally; verbatim; word for word.

дослýживать *v. impfv.* [*pfv.* **дослужи́ть**] (with **до**) to serve (until). —**дослýживаться,** *refl.* (*with* **до**) to serve (until one reaches a certain rank): дослужи́ться до майóра, to rise to the rank of major.

дослужи́ть [*infl.* **-служý, -слýжишь**] *v., pfv. of* **дослýживать.** —**дослужи́ться,** *refl., pfv. of* **дослýживаться.**

дослýшать *v. pfv.* to listen (to something) till the end.

досмáтривать *v. impfv.* [*pfv.* **досмотрéть**] **1,** to watch to the end. **2,** to watch (until): досмотрéть пьéсу до трéтьего дéйствия, to watch a play till the third act.

досмóтр *n.* examination; inspection: тамóженный досмóтр, customs inspection.

досмотрéть [*infl.* **-смотрю́, -смóтришь**] *v., pfv. of* **досмáтривать.**

досмóтрщик *n.* customs inspector.

доспáть [*infl. like* **спать**] *v., pfv. of* **досыпáть.**

доспевáть *v. impfv.* [*pfv.* **доспéть**] to become fully ripe.

доспéхи [*gen.* **-хов**] *n. pl.* armor.

досрóчно *adv.* ahead of schedule. —**досрóчный,** *adj.* ahead of schedule; early.

доставáть *v. impfv.* [*pfv.* **достáть;** *pres.* **-стаю́, -стаёшь**] **1,** (*with* **до**) to reach; be able to touch. **2,** to take (*from a certain place*): достáть кни́гу с пóлки, to take a book from the shelf. **3,** to obtain; get. **4,** *impers.* (*with gen.*) *colloq.* to suffice: дéнег у нас достáнет, we have enough money. —**доставáться,** *refl., impers.* (*with dat.*) **1,** to pass into the possession of. **2,** to fall one's lot. **3,** *colloq.* to get it; catch it; catch hell.

достáвить [*infl.* **-влю, -вишь**] *v., pfv. of* **доставля́ть.**

достáвка *n.* delivery.

доставля́ть *v. impfv.* [*pfv.* **достáвить**] **1,** to deliver. **2,** to give; provide; afford (pleasure, an opportunity, etc.). **3,** to give; cause (trouble, anxiety, etc.).

достáток [*gen.* **-тка**] *n.* **1,** circumstances; means: лю́ди срéднего достáтка, people of moderate means. **2,** comfortable circumstances. **3,** *colloq.* sufficiency; plenty. **4,** *pl., colloq.* income.

достáточно *adv.* enough; sufficiently: достáточно широ́кий, wide enough. —*adj.* **1,** (*with gen.*) enough; sufficient: достáточно сил, enough strength. **2,** (*with inf.*) it is sufficient to: достáточно сказáть, suffice it to say. —*interj.* enough!

достáточность *n.f.* sufficiency.

достáточный *adj.* sufficient; ample.

достáть [*infl.* **-стáну, -стáнешь**] *v., pfv. of* **доставáть.** —**достáться,** *refl., pfv. of* **доставáться.**

достигáть *v. impfv.* [*pfv.* **дости́гнуть** *or* **дости́чь**] (*with gen.*) **1,** to reach. **2,** to achieve; attain.

дости́гнуть [*past* **-сти́г, -ла**] *v., pfv. of* **достигáть.**

достижéние *n.* achievement.

достижи́мый *adj.* attainable.

дости́чь [*infl. like* **дости́гнуть**] *v., pfv. of* **достигáть.**

достовéрно *adv.* for certain; for sure.

достовéрность *n.f.* **1,** reliability. **2,** authenticity.

достовéрный *adj.* (*of information or a source*) reliable.

достóинство *n.* **1,** dignity. **2,** merit; virtue; advantage. **3,** value; denomination (*of a bill or coin*). —**оцени́ть по достóинству,** *see* **оцéнивать.**

достóйно *adv.* **1,** in a worthy *or* fitting manner. **2,** *obs.* with dignity.

достóйный *adj.* [*short form* **-стóин, -стóйна**] **1,** (*with* *gen.*) worthy (of); deserving (of). **2,** deserved; well-deserved. **3,** fitting; worthy.

достопримеча́тельность *n.f.* sight; point of interest.

достопримеча́тельный *adj.* noteworthy.

достоя́ние *n.* **1,** property. **2,** *fig.* common property: стать достоя́нием наро́да, to become the common property of the people.

достра́ивать *v. impfv.* [*pfv.* **достро́ить**] to finish building.

до́ступ *n.* access.

досту́пность *n.f.* **1,** accessibility. **2,** availability.

досту́пный *adj.* **1,** accessible. **2,** (*of a person*) approachable. **3,** available. **4,** easily understood; understandable. **5,** (*of prices*) moderate; reasonable.

достуча́ться *v.r. pfv.* [*infl.* **-чу́сь, -чи́шься**] *colloq.* to knock until someone answers.

досу́г *n.* leisure. —**на досу́ге,** in one's spare time.

досу́жий *adj., colloq.* **1,** (*of time*) leisure. **2,** idle.

до́суха *adv.* dry; until thoroughly dry.

досыпа́ть *v. impfv.* [*pfv.* **доспа́ть**] *colloq.* **1,** to get enough sleep. **2,** (*with* **до**) to sleep until. **3,** to sleep through.

до́сыта *also,* **досы́та** *adv.* **1,** one's fill: нае́сться до́сыта, to eat one's fill. **2,** to one's heart's content.

досье́ *n. neut. indecl.* dossier.

досю́да *adv., colloq.* up to here; up to this point.

досяга́емость *n.f.* range; reach: вне досяга́емости, out of range.

дот *n.* pillbox (*abbr. of* **долговре́менная огнева́я то́чка**).

дота́скивать *v. impfv.* [*pfv.* **дотащи́ть**] (*with* **до**) to drag to; drag as far as. —**дота́скиваться,** *refl.* (*with* **до**) *colloq.* to drag oneself to.

дота́ция *n.* subsidy; grant.

дотащи́ть [*infl.* **-тащу́, -та́щишь**] *v., pfv. of* **дота́скивать.** —**дотащи́ться,** *refl., pfv. of* **дота́скиваться.**

дотемна́ *adv.* until dark; until nightfall.

дотла́ *adv.* to the ground: сгоре́ть дотла́, to burn to the ground.

дото́ле *adv., obs.* hitherto.

дото́шный *adj., colloq.* meticulous.

дотра́гиваться *v.r. impfv.* [*pfv.* **дотро́нуться**] (*with* **до**) to touch.

дотя́гивать *v. impfv.* [*pfv.* **дотяну́ть**] (*with* **до**) **1,** to drag as far as. **2,** to stretch as far as. **3,** *colloq.* to bring in (a disabled ship, aircraft, etc.). **4,** *colloq.* to make it to (a place). **5,** *colloq.* to live until; hold out until. —**дотя́гиваться,** *refl.* (*with* **до**) **1,** to reach; be able to touch. **2,** *colloq.* to stretch; extend (as far as). **3,** *colloq.* to make it (to a place).

дотяну́ть [*infl.* **-тяну́, -тя́нешь**] *v., pfv. of* **дотя́гивать.** —**дотяну́ться,** *refl., pfv. of* **дотя́гиваться.**

доу́чивать *v. impfv.* [*pfv.* **доучи́ть**] **1,** to finish teaching; (with **до**) teach up to. **2,** to finish learning; (with **до**) learn up to. —**доу́чиваться,** *refl.* **1,** to finish one's studies. **2,** (*with* **до**) to study up to a certain point: доучи́ться до восьмо́го кла́сса, to go through the eighth grade.

доучи́ть [*infl.* **-учу́, -у́чишь**] *v., pfv. of* **доу́чивать.** —**доучи́ться,** *refl., pfv. of* **доу́чиваться.**

дофи́н *n.* dauphin.

доха́ [*pl.* **до́хи**] *n.* heavy fur coat (*with fur both outside and inside*).

до́хлый *adj.* **1,** (*of animals, insects, fish, etc.*) dead. **2,** *colloq.* sickly.

дохля́тина *n., colloq.* carrion.

до́хнуть *v. impfv.* [*pfv.* **подо́хнуть;** *past* **дох** *or* **до́хнул, до́хла**] (*of animals*) to die.

дохну́ть *v. pfv.* to breathe; take a breath.

дохо́д *n.* income; revenue.

доходи́ть *v. impfv.* [*pfv.* **дойти́;** *pres.* **-хожу́, -хо́дишь**] (with **до**) **1,** to walk as far as. **2,** to reach. **3,** *colloq.* (*of a speech, play, etc.*) to come across (to). **4,** to reach the point of: дойти́ до отча́яния, to be on the point of despair; become desperate. Де́ло дошло́ до того́, что..., things got to the point where... —**дойти́ свои́м умо́м,** to figure it out by oneself. —**ру́ки не дохо́дят,** there is no time.

дохо́дный *adj.* lucrative; profitable; remunerative.

дохо́дчивый *adj.* lucid; easy to understand.

доце́нт *n.* associate professor.

доче́рний *adj.* **1,** one's daughter's. **2,** filial.

до́чиста *adv.* clean; till something is spotless. —**всё до́чиста,** absolutely everything; so that nothing is left.

дочи́тывать *v. impfv.* [*pfv.* **дочита́ть**] **1,** to finish reading. **2,** (*with* **до**) to read as far as.

до́чка [*gen. pl.* **-чек**] *n., dim. of* **дочь.**

дочь [*gen., dat., & prepl.* **до́чери;** *instr.* **до́черью;** *pl.* **до́чери, -ре́й, -ря́м, -рьми́, -ря́х**] *n.f.* daughter.

дошко́льник *n.* child of preschool age. —**дошко́льный,** *adj.* preschool.

до́шлый *adj., colloq.* clever; shrewd.

доща́тый *adj.* made of boards or planks.

доще́чка [*gen. pl.* **-чек**] *n.* **1,** small board. **2,** nameplate, plaque.

доя́рка [*gen. pl.* **-рок**] *n.* milkmaid.

дра́га *n.* dredge.

драгоце́нность *n.f.* **1,** jewel; gem. **2,** *pl.* jewelry. **3,** *pl.* valuables.

драгоце́нный *adj.* precious. —**драгоце́нный ка́мень, 1,** precious stone; gemstone. **2,** jewel; gem.

драгу́н [*gen. pl.* **-гу́н**] *n.* dragoon.

драже́ *n. neut. indecl.* drops (*candy*).

дразни́ть *v. impfv.* [*pres.* **дразню́, дра́знишь**] **1,** to tease. **2,** to whet; arouse (one's appetite, curiosity, etc.).

дра́ить *v. impfv.* to scrub; swab.

дра́ка *n.* fight: зате́ять дра́ку, to start a fight. —**дойти́ до дра́ки,** to come to blows.

драко́н *n.* dragon.

драко́новский *adj.* draconian: драко́новские ме́ры, draconian measures.

дра́ма *n.* **1,** drama. **2,** *fig.* tragedy; calamity.

драматизи́ровать *v. impfv. & pfv.* [*pres.* **-рую, -руешь**] to dramatize.

драмати́зм *n.* dramatic effect; drama.

драмати́ческий *adj.* dramatic.

драмату́рг *n.* playwright.

драматурги́я *n.* **1,** dramaturgy. **2,** plays; works.

драмкружо́к [*gen.* **-жка́**] *n.* dramatic circle (*contr. of* **драмати́ческий кружо́к**).

драндуле́т *n., colloq.* jalopy.

дра́нка [*gen. pl.* **-нок**] *n.* **1,** lath. **2,** shingle.

дра́ный *adj., colloq.* ragged; tattered.

драп *n.* heavy woolen cloth.

драпирова́ть *v. impfv.* [*pfv.* **задрапирова́ть;** *pres.* **-ру́ю, -ру́ешь**] to drape.

драпиро́вка [*gen. pl.* **-вок**] *n.* drapery.

драпиро́вщик *n.* upholsterer.
дра́повый *adj.* made of heavy woolen cloth.
драть *v. impfv.* [*pres.* **деру́, дерёшь;** *past fem.* **драла́**] **1,** *colloq.* to tear to pieces. **2,** to strip off. **3,** [*pfv.* **вы́драть**] to whip; thrash; flog. **4,** [*pfv.* **содра́ть**] *colloq.* to charge (an exorbitant price): драть вдво́е доро́же, чем..., to charge twice as much as. —**дра́ться,** *refl.* to fight.
дра́хма *n.* drachma (*monetary unit of Greece*).
драчли́вый *adj.* pugnacious; combative. —**драчли́вость,** *n.f.* pugnacity.
драчу́н [*gen.* **-чуна́**] *n., colloq.* scrapper; brawler.
дребеде́нь *n.f., colloq.* **1,** nonsense. **2,** junk.
дребезжа́ние *n.* rattling; rattle.
дребезжа́ть *v. impfv.* [*pres.* **-жи́т**] **1,** to rattle. **2,** to jingle.
древеси́на *n.* **1,** wood. **2,** timber.
древе́сница *n.* tree frog.
древе́сный *adj.* **1,** arboreal. **2,** wood (*attrib.*). —**древе́сная ма́сса,** wood pulp. —**древе́сный спирт,** wood alcohol. —**древе́сный у́голь,** charcoal.
дре́вко [*pl.* **-вки, -вков**] *n.* **1,** pole; staff (*for a flag or banner*). **2,** shaft (*of a spear*).
древнеангли́йский *adj.* Old English.
древнегре́ческий *adj.* ancient Greek.
древнеевре́йский *adj.* Hebrew.
древнеру́сский *adj.* Old Russian.
дре́вний *adj.* ancient. —**дре́вние,** *n. pl.* the ancients.
дре́вность *n.f.* **1,** antiquity; ancient times. **2,** *pl.* antiquities.
дре́во [*pl.* **древеса́, -ве́с, -веса́м**] *n., archaic & poetic* tree.
дредно́ут *n.* dreadnought.
дрези́на *n., R.R.* handcar.
дрейф *n., naut.* drift.
дрейфова́ть *v. impfv.* [*pres.* **-фу́ет**] *naut.* to drift.
дрель *n.f.* drill (*tool*).
дрема́ть *v. impfv.* [*pres.* **дремлю́, дре́млешь**] to doze; slumber.
дремо́та *n.* drowsiness.
дремо́тный *adj.* drowsy.
дрему́чий *adj.* (*of a forest*) thick; dense.
дрена́ж *n.* drainage. —**дрена́жный,** *adj.* drainage (*attrib.*); drain (*attrib.*).
дрени́ровать *v. impfv. & pfv.* [*pres.* **-рую, -руешь**] to drain.
дрессиро́ванный *adj.* (*of an animal*) trained.
дрессирова́ть *v. impfv.* [*pfv.* **вы́дрессировать;** *pres.* **-ру́ю, -ру́ешь**] to train (animals).
дрессиро́вка *n.* training (*of animals*). —**дрессиро́вщик,** *n.* animal trainer.
дроби́лка [*gen. pl.* **-лок**] *n.* crusher; crushing machine.
дроби́льный *adj.* crushing (*attrib.*). —**дроби́льная маши́на,** = **дроби́лка.**
дроби́на *n.* pellet. *Also,* **дроби́нка.**
дроби́ть *v. impfv.* [*pfv.* **раздроби́ть;** *pres.* **-блю́, -би́шь**] **1,** to crush; shatter; splinter. **2,** to divide up; split up; fragment. —**дроби́ться,** *refl.* **1,** to break into pieces; splinter. **2,** to split up.
дробле́ние *n.* **1,** crushing; grinding. **2,** splitting up; fragmentation.
дроблёный *adj.* crushed.
дро́бный *adj.* **1,** separate; fragmented. **2,** (*of sounds*) rhythmic; steady. **3,** *math.* fractional.
дробови́к [*gen.* **-вика́**] *n.* shotgun.
дробь *n.f.* **1,** shot: кру́пная дробь, buckshot. **2,** steady sound; beating; patter. **3,** [*pl.* **дро́би, -бе́й**] *math.* fraction. **4,** oblique stroke; slash.
дрова́ [*gen.* **дров**] *n. pl.* firewood.
дро́вни [*gen.* **-ней**] *n. pl.* sledge.
дровосе́к *n., obs.* woodcutter.
дровяно́й *adj.* wood (*attrib.*): дровяно́й сара́й, woodshed.
дро́ги [*gen.* **дрог**] *n. pl.* wagon; cart. —**похоро́нные дро́ги,** hearse.
дро́гнуть[1] *v. impfv.* [*past* **дрог, -ла**] to freeze; be chilled to the bone.
дро́гнуть[2] *v. pfv.* [*past* **дро́гнул**] **1,** to shake; tremble; quiver. **2,** to waver; falter; flinch.
дрожа́ние *n.* trembling; shivering; shaking.
дрожа́ть *v. impfv.* [*pres.* **-жу́, -жи́шь**] to tremble; shiver; shake.
дро́жжи [*gen.* **-е́й**] *n. pl.* yeast.
дро́жки [*gen.* **-жек**] *n. pl.* open carriage; droshky.
дрожь *n.f.* tremor; trembling.
дрозд [*gen.* **-зда́**] *n.* thrush. —**чёрный дрозд,** blackbird.
дрок *n.* furze.
дромаде́р (дэ) *n.* dromedary.
дро́ссель *n.m.* throttle; choke.
дро́тик *n.* javelin.
дрофа́ [*pl.* **дро́фы**] *n.* bustard.
друг [*pl.* **друзья́, -зе́й, -зья́м**] *n.* friend. —**друг дру́га,** each other; one another. —**друг за дру́гом,** one after another; one after the other. —**друг с дру́гом,** with each other.
друго́й *adj.* **1,** other; another: друго́е де́ло, another matter; други́е стра́ны, other countries. **2,** else: кто́-то друго́й, someone else; что́-то друго́е, something else. —*n.* **1,** the other (one). **2,** another person. **3,** *neut.* another thing; something else. **4,** *pl.* others. —**на друго́й день,** the next day. —**тот и́ли друго́й,** one...or another. —**и тот и друго́й,** both. —**ни тот ни друго́й,** neither (one).
дру́жба *n.* friendship.
дружелю́бие *n.* friendliness. —**дружелю́бный,** *adj.* friendly; amicable.
дру́жеский *adj.* friendly; amicable.
дру́жественный *adj.* friendly; amicable.
дружи́на *n.* **1,** *hist.* military retinue of a medieval Russian prince. **2,** *pre-rev.* militia unit; detachment. **3,** squad; brigade.
дружи́ть *v. impfv.* [*pres.* **дружу́, дру́жишь** *or* **дружи́шь**] (*with* **с** + *instr.*) to be friends (with). —**дружи́ться,** *refl.* [*pfv.* **подружи́ться**] (*with* **с** + *instr.*) to become friends (with); become friendly (with).
дру́жно *adv.* **1,** amicably. **2,** (all) together; in concert.
дру́жный *adj.* [*short form* **дру́жен, дружна́, дру́жны**] **1,** friendly; amicable; harmonious. **2,** [*short form only*] friendly; friends: он дру́жен с мои́м сы́ном, he is friendly with my son; he and my son are friends. **3,** on the part of everyone; concerted.
дружо́к [*gen.* **-жка́**] *n., colloq.* friend; pal.
дры́гать *v. impfv.* (*with instr.*) *colloq.* to kick (one's feet).
дря́блый *adj.* flabby; flaccid. —**дря́блость,** *n.f.* flabbiness.
дря́зги [*gen.* **дрязг**] *n. pl., colloq.* petty quarrels; squabbles.

дрянно́й *adj., colloq.* miserable; rotten; lousy.
дрянь *n.f., colloq.* **1,** rubbish; trash. **2,** nonsense. **3,** good-for-nothing. **4,** something that is no good: де́ло дрянь, things are lousy.
дряхле́ть *v. impfv.* [*pfv.* **одряхле́ть**] to become decrepit; become enfeebled.
дря́хлый *adj.* decrepit; enfeebled. —**дря́хлость,** *n.f.* decrepitude.
дуали́зм *n.* dualism. —**дуалисти́ческий,** *adj.* dualistic.
дуб [*pl.* **дубы́**] *n.* oak (*tree & wood*).
дуба́сить *v. impfv.* [*pres.* **-шу, -сишь**] *colloq.* **1,** to beat; thrash. **2,** (*with* **по** *or* **в**) to bang on.
дуби́льный *adj.* tanning (*attrib.*). —**дуби́льная кислота́,** tannic acid.
дуби́льня [*gen. pl.* **-лен**] *n.* tannery.
дуби́льщик *n.* tanner.
дуби́на *n.* club; cudgel; bludgeon; truncheon. *Also,* **дуби́нка.**
дуби́ть *v. impfv.* [*pfv.* **вы́дубить;** *pres.* **-блю́, -би́шь**] to tan (leather).
дубле́ние *n.* tanning.
дублёнка [*gen. pl.* **-нок**] *n., colloq.* sheepskin coat.
дублёный *adj.* tanned. —**дублёный полушу́бок,** sheepskin coat.
дублёр *n.* **1,** *theat.* understudy. **2,** *motion pictures* one who dubs in a part.
дубле́т *n.* duplicate.
дублика́т *n.* duplicate. —**дублика́тный,** *adj.* duplicate.
дубли́рование *n.* **1,** duplication. **2,** understudying. **3,** dubbing.
дубли́ровать *v. impfv.* [*pres.* **-рую, -руешь**] **1,** to duplicate. **2,** to understudy. **3,** to dub.
дубня́к [*gen.* **-няка́**] *n.* oak forest.
дубова́тый *adj., colloq.* clumsy; coarse.
дубо́вый *adj.* oak (*attrib.*).
дубо́к [*gen.* **-бка́**] *n.* young oak.
дубоно́с *n.* grosbeak.
дубра́ва *n.* oak forest.
дуга́ [*pl.* **ду́ги**] *n.* **1,** arc. **2,** shaft bow (*of a harness*).
дугообра́зный *adj.* arched.
дуде́ть *v. impfv., colloq.* **1,** *in* дуде́ть в ду́дку, to play a fife. **2,** to drone (on and on). —**дуде́ть в одну́ ду́дку,** to sing the same song.
ду́дка [*gen. pl.* **-док**] *n.* fife. —**пляса́ть под чью-нибудь ду́дку,** to dance to someone's tune.
ду́дник *n.* angelica.
ду́жка [*gen. pl.* **-жек**] *n.* **1,** hoop. **2,** handle.
дука́т *n.* ducat.
ду́ло *n.* muzzle (*of a gun*). —**под ду́лом пистоле́та,** at gunpoint.
ду́ма *n.* **1,** thought. **2,** *hist.* Duma.
ду́мать *v. impfv.* [*pfv.* **поду́мать**] to think. —**ду́маю, что нет,** I don't think so. —**мно́го ду́мать о себе́,** to have an exalted opinion of oneself. —**не ду́маю!,** I hardly think so; I doubt it. —**я ду́маю!,** I should think so! —**я так и ду́мал!,** I thought so!
ду́маться *v.r. impfv., impers.* (*with dat.*) to seem: мне ду́мается, it seems to me; I think.
ду́мка [*gen. pl.* **-мок**] *n., colloq.* small pillow.
дунове́ние *n.* puff; breath (*of wind, air, etc.*).
ду́нуть *v. pfv.* to blow.
ду́пель [*pl.* **дупеля́**] *n.m.* double snipe (*bird*).
дупле́т *n., billiards* bank shot.
дупли́стый *adj.* (*of a tree*) hollow.
дупло́ [*pl.* **ду́пла, ду́пел**] *n.* **1,** hollow (*in a tree*). **2,** cavity (*in a tooth*).
дура́к [*gen.* **-рака́**] *n.m.* [*fem.* **ду́ра**] fool. —**остава́ться в дурака́х,** to make a fool of oneself; look like a fool.
дурале́й *n., colloq.* fool; jerk; dope.
дура́цкий *adj., colloq.* **1,** fool's. **2,** ridiculous; idiotic.
дура́чество *n., colloq.* **1,** prank. **2,** *pl.* horseplay; tomfoolery.
дура́чить *v. impfv.* [*pfv.* **одура́чить**] to fool; make a fool of. —**дура́читься,** *refl.* [*impfv. only*] to fool around.
дурачо́к [*gen.* **-чка́**] *n., colloq.* **1,** little fool. **2,** idiot.
дура́шливый *adj., colloq.* **1,** silly. **2,** mischievous.
ду́рень [*gen.* **-рня**] *n.m., colloq.* dope; dolt.
дуре́ть *v. impfv.* [*pfv.* **одуре́ть**] *colloq.* to go crazy; lose one's wits.
дури́ть *v. impfv., colloq.* to play around; horse around.
дурма́н *n.* **1,** thorn apple; jimsonweed. **2,** narcotic; drug.
дурма́нить *v. impfv.* [*pfv.* **одурма́нить**] to dull one's mind; cloud one's mind.
дурне́ть *v. impfv.* [*pfv.* **подурне́ть**] to lose one's beauty; become less attractive.
ду́рно *adv.* badly. —*adj., used predicatively* faint; ill: мне ду́рно, I feel faint.
дурно́й *adj.* **1,** bad. **2,** evil; wicked. —**ду́рен (дурна́) собо́й,** homely; unattractive.
дурнота́ *n.* (feeling of) faintness: чу́вствовать дурноту́, to feel faint.
дурну́шка [*gen. pl.* **-шек**] *n., colloq.* plain girl; homely girl.
дуршла́г *n.* colander.
дурь *n.f., colloq.* foolishness; nonsense.
ду́тый *adj.* **1,** hollow. **2,** *fig.* inflated; exaggerated.
дуть *v. impfv.* [*pfv.* **поду́ть;** *pres.* **ду́ю, ду́ешь**] to blow.
дутьё *n.* **1,** blowing. **2,** blast.
ду́ться *v.r. impfv.* [*pres.* **ду́юсь, ду́ешься**] *colloq.* to pout; sulk.
дух *n.* spirit. —**быть в ду́хе,** to be in good spirits. —**быть не в ду́хе,** to be out of sorts. —**во весь дух,** full tilt. —**в том же ду́хе,** in the same vein; along the same lines. —**одни́м ду́хом, 1,** in one breath. **2,** all at once. —**что есть ду́ху, 1,** full tilt. **2,** at the top of one's lungs. —**что́-то в э́том ду́хе,** something of the sort.
духи́ [*gen.* **духо́в**] *n. pl.* perfume.
ду́хов *adj., in* **ду́хов день,** Whitmonday.
духове́нство *n.* clergy.
духо́вка [*gen. pl.* **-вок**] *n.* oven.
духовни́к [*gen.* **-ника́**] *n.* confessor.
духо́вный *adj.* **1,** spiritual. **2,** ecclesiastical. **3,** (*of a seminary, academy, etc.*) theological. —**духо́вное завеща́ние,** last will and testament. —**духо́вное о́ко,** mind's eye.
духово́й *adj.* **1,** *music,* духово́й инструме́нт, wind instrument; духово́й орке́стр, brass band. **2,** operated by heat: духова́я печь, oven. —**духово́е ружьё, 1,** air gun. **2,** blowgun.
духота́ *n.* **1,** stuffiness; closeness. **2,** sweltering heat.
душ *n.* **1,** shower. **2,** douche.
душа́ [*acc.* **ду́шу;** *pl.* **ду́ши**] *n.* soul. —**в душе́, 1,** inwardly; in one's heart. **2,** at heart. —**всей душо́й,**

with all one's heart. —**для души́,** for one's own pleasure. —**душá в ду́шу,** in perfect harmony. —**душá óбщества,** the life of the party. —**душóй и тéлом,** heart and soul. —**за душóй,** to one's name. —**на ду́шу населéния,** per capita. —**ни души́,** not a soul. —**от всей души́,** from the bottom of one's heart. —**по душé** (+ *dat.*), to one's liking. —**разговóр по душáм,** heart-to-heart talk. —**с бóлью на душé,** with a heavy heart. —**с душóй,** with feeling. —**скóлько душé угóдно,** to one's heart's content. —**стоя́ть над чьéй-либо душóй,** to stand over; breathe down someone's neck.

душевáя *n., decl. as an adj.* shower room.

душевнобольнóй *adj.* mentally ill. —*n.* mental patient; mental case.

душéвный *adj.* **1,** mental; emotional: душéвное состоя́ние, state of mind; душéвная болéзнь, mental illness. **2,** sincere; heartfelt.

душевóй *adj.* **1,** per capita. **2,** shower (*attrib.*).

душегу́б *n., obs., colloq.* killer; murderer.

душегу́бка [*gen. pl.* **-бок**] *n.* **1,** canoe. **2,** mobile gas chamber.

ду́шенька *n.f.* (*used in direct address*) dear; darling; sweetheart.

душеприкáзчик *n., obs.* executor (*of a will*).

душераздирáющий *adj.* heart-rending; harrowing; bloodcurdling.

ду́шечка *n.* = ду́шенька.

души́стый *adj.* fragrant; aromatic; sweet-smelling. —**души́стый горóшек,** sweet peas. —**души́стый пéрец,** allspice; pimento.

души́ть *v. impfv.* [*pfv.* **задуши́ть;** *pres.* **душу́, ду́шишь**] **1,** to strangle. **2,** *fig.* to stifle. **3,** [*impfv. only*] to choke: егó ду́шит кáшель, he is choking from a cough. **4,** [*pfv.* **надуши́ть**] to perfume. —**души́ться,** *refl.* [*pfv.* **надуши́ться**] to use perfume; put on perfume.

ду́шка [*gen. pl.* **-шек**] *n.m. & f., colloq.* **1,** dear person; lovely person. **2,** dear; darling.

ду́шно *adj., used predicatively* stuffy: здесь ду́шно, it is stuffy in here; мне ду́шно, I am suffocating.

ду́шный *adj.* stuffy; close.

душóк [*gen.* **-шкá**] *n., colloq.* **1,** smell of something beginning to decay. **2,** *fig.* taint; tinge.

дуэ́ль *n.f.* duel. —**дуэли́ст; дуэля́нт,** *n.* duelist.

дуэ́нья *n., obs.* chaperon.

дуэ́т *n.* duet.

ды́ба *n.* rack (*instrument of torture*).

ды́бом *adv., in* **станови́ться/стать ды́бом,** (*of hair*) to stand on end.

дыбы́ *adv., in* **станови́ться на дыбы́, 1,** (*of a horse*) to rear. **2,** to stand straight up in the air. **3,** *colloq.* to raise objections.

ды́лда *n.m. & f., colloq.* tall, ungainly person.

дым [*2nd loc.* **дыму́**] *n.* smoke.

дыми́ть *v. impfv.* [*pfv.* **надыми́ть**] **1,** to smoke; give off smoke. **2,** [*impfv. only*] (*with instr.*) to smoke (a cigarette, cigar, etc.). —**дыми́ться,** *refl.* [*impfv. only*] to give off smoke.

ды́мка *n.* haze.

ды́мный *adj.* smoky.

дымовóй *adj.* smoke (*attrib.*). —**дымовáя завéса,** smoke screen. —**дымовáя трубá,** chimney; smokestack.

дымóк [*gen.* **-мкá**] *n.* thin column of smoke.

дымохóд *n.* flue; stovepipe.

ды́мчатый *adj.* smoky; smoke-colored.

ды́нный *adj.* melon (*attrib.*). —**ды́нное дéрево,** papaya.

ды́ня *n.* melon.

дырá [*pl.* **ды́ры**] *n.* **1,** hole. **2,** *colloq.* out-of-the-way place.

ды́рка [*gen. pl.* **-рок**] *n.* (small) hole.

дырокóл *n., colloq.* punch; hole punch.

дыря́вый *adj.* having a hole; full of holes. —**дыря́вая пáмять,** memory like a sieve.

дыхáние *n.* breath; breathing; respiration. —**вторóе дыхáние,** second wind.

дыхáтельный *adj.* respiratory. —**дыхáтельное гóрло,** windpipe.

дышáть *v. impfv.* [*pres.* **дышу́, ды́шишь**] to breathe.

ды́шло *n.* pole; beam; shaft (*on a carriage*).

дья́вол *n.* devil. —**дья́вольский,** *adj.* devilish; diabolical.

дья́кон [*pl.* **дьяконá**] *n.* deacon.

дю́жий *adj., colloq.* hefty; robust; strapping.

дю́жина *n.* dozen.

дю́жинный *adj.* ordinary; run-of-the-mill.

дюйм *n.* inch. —**дюймóвый,** *adj.* one-inch; inch-long.

дю́на *n.* dune.

дюралюми́ний *n.* duralumin.

дя́гиль *n.m.* angelica.

дя́денька *n.m., colloq.* uncle. *Also,* **дя́дюшка.**

дя́дя [*gen. pl.* **дя́дей**] *n.m.* uncle.

дя́тел [*gen.* **-тла**] *n.* woodpecker.

E

Е, е *n. neut.* sixth letter of the Russian alphabet.

Ё, ё *n. neut.* not considered a separate letter of the Russian alphabet. Usually written E and e except in dictionaries and textbooks.

ева́нгелие *n.* gospel. —**евангели́ст,** *n., Bib.* Evangelist. —**евангели́ческий,** *adj.* evangelical. —**ева́нгельский,** *adj.* in *or* of the gospel.

евге́ника *n.* eugenics. —**евгени́ческий,** *adj.* eugenic.

е́внух *n.* eunuch.

еврази́йский *adj.* Eurasian.

евре́й *n.m.* [*fem.* **-ре́йка**] Jew. —**евре́йский,** *adj.* Jewish; Hebrew. —**евре́йство,** *n.* Jewry.

европе́ец [*gen.* **-е́йца**] *n.m.* [*fem.* **-е́йка**] European. —**европе́йский,** *adj.* European.

европео́ид *n.* Caucasoid; Caucasian. —**европео́идный,** *adj.* Caucasoid; Caucasian.

евро́пий *n.* europium.

евста́хиев *adj., in* **евста́хиева труба́,** Eustachian tube.

евхари́стия *n.* Eucharist.

е́герь [*pl.* **егеря́**] *n.m.* professional hunter.

еги́петский *adj.* Egyptian.

египтоло́гия *n.* Egyptology. —**египто́лог,** *n.* Egyptologist.

египтя́нин [*pl.* **-тя́не, -тя́н**] *n.m.* [*fem.* **-тя́нка**] Egyptian.

его́ (vo) *pron., gen. & acc. of* **он** *and* **оно́.** —*poss. adj. & pron.* his; its.

егоза́ *n.m. & f., colloq.* fidgety person; fidget.

егози́ть *v. impfv.* [*pres.* **-жу́, -зи́шь**] *colloq.* **1,** to fidget. **2,** (*with* **пе́ред**) to fawn (upon).

егозли́вый *adj., colloq.* fidgety.

еда́ *n.* **1,** meal. **2,** food.

едва́ *adv.* **1,** hardly; scarcely. **2,** just; barely. —**едва́..., как...,** hardly/scarcely..., when...: он едва́ ко́нчил говори́ть, как..., he had hardly finished speaking, when...—**едва́ ли,** hardly; it is unlikely (that). —**едва́ ли не,** nearly; almost; practically: едва́ ли не ка́ждый день, nearly every day. —**едва́ не,** almost; nearly: он едва́ не утону́л, he nearly drowned.

едине́ние *n.* unity.

едини́ца *n.* **1,** the numeral 1. **2,** a grade of "one", signifying "very poor". **3,** unit. **4,** *pl.* (only) a few individuals.

едини́чный *adj.* individual; isolated; unique.

едино- *prefix* **1,** one; single: единобо́жие, monotheism. **2,** same; of the same: единове́рный, of the same religion.

единобо́жие *n.* monotheism.

единобо́рство *n.* single combat.

единобра́чие *n.* monogamy. —**единобра́чный,** *adj.* monogamous.

единове́рец [*gen.* **-рца**] *n.* coreligionist.

единове́рный *adj.* of the same religion; of the same faith.

единовла́стие *n.* autocracy; absolute rule. —**единовла́стный,** *adj.* autocratic; having absolute power.

единовре́менный *adj.* one-time; given only once. —**единовре́менно,** *adv.* all at once; in a lump sum.

единогла́сие *n.* unanimity.

единогла́сный *adj.* unanimous. —**единогла́сно,** *adv.* unanimously.

единоду́шие *n.* unanimity.

единоду́шный *adj.* unanimous. —**единоду́шно,** *adv.* unanimously.

единокро́вный *adj., obs.* **1,** having the same father. **2,** kindred; consanguineous.

единоли́чный *adj.* individual. —**единоли́чно,** *adv.* alone; on one's own; singlehandedly.

единомы́слие *n.* harmony of views; agreement.

единомы́шленник *n.* **1,** person holding similar views. **2,** confederate; accomplice.

единообра́зие *n.* uniformity. —**единообра́зный,** *adj.* uniform.

единоро́г *n.* unicorn.

единоутро́бный *adj., obs.* having the same mother.

еди́нственно *adv.* only; solely. —**еди́нственно, что...,** the only thing that...: еди́нственно, что я могу́ сказа́ть, the only thing I can say is...; all I can say is...

еди́нственный *adj.* only; sole. —*n., fol. by* **кто,** the only one (who); the only person (who). —**еди́нственный в своём ро́де,** unique; the only one of its kind. —**еди́нственное число́,** *gram.* the singular.

еди́нство *n.* unity.

еди́ный *adj.* **1,** (*with* **ни** *or* **без**) (not) a single. **2,** united; unified. **3,** common; single. —**все до еди́ного,** everyone without exception; one and all.

е́дкий *adj.* **1,** caustic; corrosive. **2,** acrid; pungent. **3,** *fig.* cutting; sarcastic.

е́дкость *n.f.* **1,** corrosiveness; causticity. **2,** *fig.* cutting remark.

едо́к [*gen.* **едока́**] *n.* **1,** mouth to feed: пять едоко́в в семье́, five mouths to feed. **2,** *colloq.* eater: хоро́ший едо́к, good eater.

её *pron., gen. & acc. of* **она́.** —*poss. adj. & pron.* her; hers; its.

ёж [*gen.* **ежа́**] *n.* hedgehog. —**морско́й ёж,** sea urchin.

еже- *prefix* -ly; once a: ежеме́сячный, monthly; ежеме́сячно, once a month.
ежеви́ка *n.* **1,** blackberries. **2,** a (single) blackberry. **3,** blackberry bush.
ежего́дник *n.* yearbook; annual.
ежего́дный *adj.* yearly; annual. —**ежего́дно,** *adv.* annually.
ежедне́вный *adj.* daily. —**ежедне́вно,** *adv.* daily.
е́жели *conj., obs., colloq.* = **е́сли.**
ежеме́сячник *n.* monthly publication; monthly.
ежеме́сячный *adj.* monthly. —**ежеме́сячно,** *adv.* monthly; once a month.
ежеми́нутный *adj.* **1,** occurring once a minute. **2,** constant; incessant.
еженеде́льник *n.* weekly publication; weekly.
еженеде́льный *adj.* weekly. —**еженеде́льно,** *adv.* weekly; once a week.
ежено́щный *adj.* nightly. —**ежено́щно,** *adv.* nightly.
ежеча́сный *adj.* hourly.
ёжик *n., dim. of* **ёж.** —**ёжиком,** *adv.* in a crew cut: постри́чься ёжиком, to get a crew cut.
ёжиться *v.r. impfv.* [*pfv.* **съёжиться**] **1,** to huddle up (*from the cold*). **2,** *fig., colloq.* to hesitate; waver.
ежо́вый *adj.* hedgehog (*attrib.*). —**держа́ть в ежо́вых рукави́цах,** to rule with an iron hand.
езда́ *n.* ride; riding; drive; driving: два часа́ езды́, a two-hour ride/drive.
е́здить *v. impfv.* [*pres.* **е́зжу, е́здишь**] **1,** *indeterm. of* **е́хать. 2,** to ride: е́здить на велосипе́де, to ride a bicycle. Е́здить верхо́м, to ride a horse; ride horseback.
ездово́й *adj.* **1,** for riding. **2,** *in* **ездова́я соба́ка,** draft dog; harness dog. —*n., mil.* driver (*of a team of horses*).
ездо́к [*gen.* **-дока́**] *n.* rider; horseman. —**туда́ я бо́льше не ездо́к,** you won't catch me going there again.
е́зженый *adj., colloq.* (*of a road*) well-worn; well-trodden.
ей *pron., dat. & instr. of* **она́.**
ей-бо́гу *interj., colloq.* really; really and truly.
ёкать *v. impfv.* [*pfv.* **ёкнуть**] (*of one's heart*) to skip a beat: у меня́ се́рдце ёкнуло, my heart skipped a beat.
е́ле *adv.* **1,** hardly; scarcely. **2,** just; barely. *Also,* **е́ле-е́ле.**
еле́й *n.* **1,** holy oil; unction. **2,** *fig.* balm; solace.
еле́йный *adj.* unctuous.
ёлка [*gen. pl.* **ёлок**] *n.* **1,** spruce. **2,** Christmas tree. **3,** children's New Year's party.
ело́вый *adj.* spruce (*attrib.*).
ёлочка *n., dim. of* **ёлка.** —**ёлочкой; в ёлочку,** herringbone style.
ёлочный *adj.* of or for a Christmas tree.
ель *n.f.* spruce.
е́льник *n.* spruce grove.
ёмкий *adj.* capacious. —**ёмкость,** *n.f.* capacity; cubic content.
ему́ *pron., dat. of* **он** *and* **оно́.**
ено́т *n.* raccoon. —**ено́товый,** *adj.* raccoon (*attrib.*).
епа́рхия *n.* diocese.
епи́скоп *n.* bishop. —**епископа́льный,** *adj.* Episcopalian. —**епи́скопский,** *adj.* Episcopal.
ерала́ш *n., colloq.* muddle; jumble; confusion.
е́ресь *n.f.* heresy.
ерети́к [*gen.* **-тика́**] *n.m.* [*fem.* **-ти́чка**] heretic. —**ерети́ческий,** *adj.* heretical.
ёрзать *v. impfv., colloq.* to fidget.
ермо́лка [*gen. pl.* **-лок**] *n.* skullcap.
еро́шить *v. impfv.* [*pfv.* **взъеро́шить**] *colloq.* to muss; tousle.
ерунда́ *n., colloq.* **1,** nonsense. **2,** trifling amount: пять рубле́й – ерунда́, five rubles is nothing. **3,** a cinch; a snap; child's play.
ерундо́вый *adj., colloq.* **1,** nonsensical. **2,** trifling; petty.
ёрш [*gen.* **ерша́**] *n.* **1,** ruff (*fish*). **2,** brush; lamp brush.
ерши́ться *v.r. impfv., colloq.* **1,** (*of one's hair*) to bristle. **2,** *fig.* to flare up; get excited.
еса́ул *n., pre-rev.* Cossack captain.
е́сли *conj.* **1,** if: е́сли он прав, if he is right. **2,** when (*considering that*): заче́м убежда́ть его́, е́сли он и слу́шать не хо́чет?, why try to persuade him when he won't even listen? **3,** whereas: е́сли в 1970..., то сего́дня..., whereas in 1970..., today...—**е́сли бы не,** if it were not for; were it not for. —**е́сли бы то́лько,** if only. —**е́сли не...,** **1,** if not... **2,** unless. —**е́сли то́лько,** only if; provided; on condition that.
есте́ственник *n.* natural scientist; naturalist.
есте́ственно *adv.* **1,** naturally. **2,** naturally; of course. —*adj., used predicatively* natural: есте́ственно полага́ть, что..., it is natural to suppose that...
есте́ственный *adj.* natural.
естество́ *n.* essence.
естествове́д *n., obs.* natural scientist; naturalist.
естествове́дение *n., obs.* = **естествозна́ние.**
естествозна́ние *n.* natural sciences.
естествоиспыта́тель *n.m.* naturalist.
есть[1] *v. impfv.* [*pres.* **ем, ешь, ест, еди́м, еди́те, едя́т**] **1,** [*pfv.* **съесть**] to eat. **2,** [*pfv.* **пое́сть**] to eat; have something to eat.
есть[2] *v., 3rd person sing. pres. of* **быть. 1,** (he, she, it) is: зако́н есть зако́н, the law is the law. Ра́зница ма́ленькая, но всё-таки есть, it is a small difference but it exists nevertheless. **2,** there is; there are: есть таки́е лю́ди, there are such people. **3,** (*with* **у**) *indicating possession:* у вас есть спи́чка?, do you have a match? —*interj., mil.; naval* yes, sir!; aye aye, sir! —**есть когда́!,** *colloq.* there is still time. —**есть тако́е де́ло!,** *colloq.* agreed! —**ни на есть, 1,** any at all: кто ни на есть, anyone at all. **2,** (*with superl. adjectives*) the most: са́мый ни на есть обыкнове́нный челове́к, the most ordinary kind of person. —**так и есть,** and so it is.
ефре́йтор *n., mil.* private first class.
е́хать *v. impfv.* [*pfv.* **пое́хать;** *pres.* **е́ду, е́дешь**] to go (*by riding*); ride; drive. *See also* **е́здить.**
ехи́дна *n.* **1,** spiny anteater; echidna. **2,** *colloq.* vicious person; viper.
ехи́дный *adj.* malicious.
ехи́дство *n.* malice; spite.
ещё *adv.* **1,** still: он ещё ма́льчик, he is still a boy. **2,** yet: я ещё не ел, I haven't eaten yet. **3,** else: куда́ вы ещё е́здили?, where else did you go? **4,** more: хоти́те ещё хле́ба?, would you like some more bread? **5,** another: хоти́те ещё ча́шку ча́ю?, would you like another cup of tea? **6,** (*before comp. adjectives*) still; even: ещё бо́льше, still more; even greater. **7,** as long

ago as; as far back as: Москва́ была́ осно́вана ещё в 12-ом ве́ке, Moscow was founded as far back as the 12th century. **8,** as recently as: ещё в 1960-ом году́, as recently as 1960. —**всё ещё,** still; all the same. —**ещё бы!,** and how!; you can say that again! —**ещё раз,** again; once again. —**нет ещё,** not yet. —**никогда́ ещё,** never before.

е́ю *pron., instr. of* она́.

Ж, ж *n. neut.* seventh letter of the Russian alphabet.

ж *conj. & particle* = **же.**

жа́ба *n.* **1,** toad. **2,** *obs.* angina. —**грудна́я жа́ба,** angina pectoris.

жа́бры *n. pl.* [*sing.* **жа́бра**] gills.

жа́воронок [*gen.* **-нка**] *n.* lark.

жа́дничать *v. impfv., colloq.* to be greedy; be stingy.

жа́дно *adv.* **1,** greedily. **2,** avidly; eagerly.

жа́дность *n.f.* **1,** greed; avarice. **2,** stinginess. —**с жа́дностью,** eagerly; avidly.

жа́дный *adj.* [*short form* **жа́ден, жадна́, жа́дно**] **1,** greedy. **2,** (*with* **на, до, к**) hungry (for). **3,** (*of desire, curiosity, etc.*) avid. **4,** stingy.

жа́жда *n.* **1,** thirst. **2,** (*with gen.*) thirst (for); craving (for).

жа́ждать *v. impfv.* [*pres.* **-ду, -дешь**] **1,** (*with gen.*) to thirst for; crave. **2,** (*with inf.*) to long (to); be dying (to).

жаке́т *n.* woman's jacket. *Also,* **жаке́тка.**

жале́ть *v. impfv.* [*pfv.* **пожале́ть**] **1,** to feel sorry for; pity. **2,** to regret. **3,** to spare. **4,** to begrudge.

жа́лить *v. impfv.* [*pfv.* **ужа́лить**] to sting.

жа́лкий *adj.* [*short form* **жа́лок, жалка́, жа́лко**] **1,** pitiful; pathetic. **2,** wretched; miserable.

жа́лко *adv.* pitifully; pathetically. —*adj., used predicatively* = **жаль.**

жа́ло *n.* stinger.

жа́лоба *n.* complaint. —**кассацио́нная** *or* **апелляцио́нная жа́лоба,** *law* appeal.

жа́лобный *adj.* plaintive; mournful. —**жа́лобная кни́га,** complaints book.

жа́лобщик *n.* person registering a complaint.

жа́лованье *n.* wage(s); salary.

жа́ловать *v. impfv.* [*pfv.* **пожа́ловать;** *pres.* **-лую, -луешь**] **1,** *obs.* to grant; confer; award; bestow. **2,** [*impfv. only*] *colloq.* to like; favor. **3,** (*with* **к**) *obs.* to visit. **4,** *in* **добро́ пожа́ловать!,** welcome! —**жа́ловаться,** *refl.* (*with* **на** + *acc.*) to complain (about).

жа́лостливый *adj., colloq.* **1,** sympathetic; compassionate. **2,** sad; mournful.

жа́лостный *adj., colloq.* **1,** plaintive. **2,** sympathetic.

жа́лость *n.f.* pity.

жаль *predicate* **1,** it is a pity; it is a shame: жаль!, it's a shame! Жаль сиде́ть до́ма сего́дня, it's a shame/pity to have to sit home today. **2,** (*with dat.*) sorry for: мне жаль его́, I feel sorry for him. **3,** (*with dat.*) sorry about: мне жаль вас беспоко́ить, I am sorry to bother you. **4,** (*with dat.*) to hate to: мне жаль тра́тить де́ньги на э́то, I hate to spend money for that.

жалюзи́ *n. pl. indecl.* jalousie. —**подъёмные жалюзи́,** Venetian blinds.

жанда́рм *n.* gendarme. —**жандарме́рия,** *n.* gendarmerie.

жанр *n.* **1,** genre. **2,** genre painting. —**жа́нровый,** *adj.* genre (*attrib.*): жа́нровая жи́вопись, genre painting.

жар *n.* **1,** heat. **2,** fever; high temperature. **3,** *fig.* ardor; fervor. **4,** *colloq.* embers. —**в жару́,** running a high temperature. —**зада́ть жа́ру** (+ *dat.*), to rake over the coals.

жара́ *n.* heat.

жарго́н *n.* jargon; slang. —**жарго́нный,** *adj.* slang.

жа́реный *adj.* fried; roast; broiled.

жа́рить *v. impfv.* [*pfv.* **зажа́рить** *or* **изжа́рить**] **1,** to fry; roast; broil. **2,** [*impfv. only*] *colloq.* (*of the sun*) to beat down (on). —**жа́риться,** *refl.* **1,** (*of meat, coffee, etc.*) to fry; roast. **2,** [*impfv. only*] *colloq.* to bake (in the sun).

жа́ркий *adj.* [*comp.* **жа́рче**] **1,** hot. **2,** *fig.* heated; passionate; intense.

жа́рко *adj., used predicatively* hot: сего́дня жа́рко, it is hot today; мне жа́рко, I am hot.

жарко́е *n., decl. as an adj.* roast meat.

жаро́вня [*gen. pl.* **-вен**] *n.* roasting pan; brazier.

жар-пти́ца *n.* firebird.

жа́рче *adj., comp. of* **жа́ркий** *and* **жа́рко.**

жасми́н *n.* jasmine. —**жасми́нный; жасми́новый,** *adj.* jasmine.

жа́тва *n.* **1,** harvesting; reaping. **2,** harvest. **3,** harvest time.

жа́твенный *adj.* harvesting (*attrib.*). —**жа́твенная маши́на,** harvester; reaper.

жа́тка [*gen. pl.* **-ток**] *n.* harvester; reaper.

жать[1] *v. impfv.* [*pres.* **жму, жмёшь**] **1,** to squeeze; press. **2,** [*pfv.* **пожа́ть**] (*with* **ру́ку** + *dat.*) to shake (someone's hand). **3,** (*of clothes, shoes, etc.*) to pinch; be tight.

жать[2] *v. impfv.* [*pfv.* **сжать;** *pres.* **жну́, жнёшь**] to reap.

жа́ться *v.r. impfv.* [*pres.* **жмусь, жмёшься**] **1,** to huddle up. **2,** (*with* **к**) to press close against. **3,** to crowd together; squeeze together. **4,** *colloq.* to hesitate; waver. **5,** *colloq.* to economize; watch one's pocketbook.

жбан *n.* jug.
жва́чка *n.* cud.
жва́чный *adj. & n.* ruminant.
жгут [*gen.* **жгута́**] *n.* **1,** twisted strand; braid. **2,** tourniquet.
жгу́чий *adj.* burning.
ждать *v. impfv.* [*pfv.* **подожда́ть;** *pres.* **жду, ждёшь;** *past fem.* **ждала́**] **1,** to wait; wait for; await. **2,** [*impfv. only*] to expect. —**того́ и жди,** at any moment.
же *also,* **ж** *conj., expressing contrast:* я уезжа́ю, он же остаётся, I am leaving but he is staying. —*particle* **1,** *used for emphasis:* говори́те же!, speak up! Отку́да же я зна́ю?, how should I know? Вам лу́чше слу́шаться его́, он же ваш оте́ц, you had better obey him — after all, he is your father. **2,** *expressing sameness or identity:* тот же; тако́й же, the same; так же, in the same way; тогда́ же, at the same time; там же, in the same place.
жева́ние *n.* chewing; mastication.
жёваный *adj.* **1,** chewed. **2,** *colloq.* crumpled.
жева́тельный *adj.* chewing (*attrib.*): жева́тельный таба́к, chewing tobacco. —**жева́тельная рези́нка,** chewing gum.
жева́ть *v. impfv.* [*pres.* **жую́, жуёшь**] to chew.
жезл [*gen.* **жезла́**] *n.* rod; staff (*carried as a symbol of authority*).
жела́ние *n.* wish; desire. —**при всём моём жела́нии,** much as I would like to.
жела́нный *adj.* **1,** desired. **2,** welcome. **3,** *obs.* dearest.
жела́тельно *adj., used predicatively* desirable: жела́тельно, что́бы..., it is desirable that...
жела́тельный *adj.* **1,** desirable. **2,** desired. —**жела́тельность,** *n.f.* desirability.
желати́н *n.* gelatin. —**желати́новый,** *adj.* gelatinous; gelatin (*attrib.*).
жела́ть *v. impfv.* [*pfv.* **пожела́ть**] **1,** (*with gen.*) to wish for; desire. **2,** (*with inf.*) to wish (to); (*with* **что́бы**) wish (that). **3,** (*with dat. and gen.*) to wish (someone something): жела́ю вам всего́ хоро́шего, I wish you the best of everything. —**оставля́ть жела́ть лу́чшего,** to leave something to be desired.
жела́ющие *n. pl., decl. as an adj.* those wishing; those who wish.
желва́к [*gen.* **-вака́**] *n.* lump; swelling; tumor.
желе́ *n. neut. indecl.* jelly.
железа́ [*pl.* **же́лезы, желёз, железа́м**] *n.* gland.
желе́зистый *adj.* **1,** glandular. **2,** containing iron; ferrous.
желе́зка [*gen. pl.* **-зок**] *n.* **1,** *colloq.* piece of iron; iron bar. **2,** *obs., colloq.* railroad.
желёзка [*gen. pl.* **-зок**] *n.* glandule.
железнодоро́жник *n.* railway worker.
железнодоро́жный *adj.* railroad (*attrib.*); railway (*attrib.*).
желе́зный *adj.* iron. —**желе́зный блеск,** hematite. —**желе́зная доро́га,** railroad.
железня́к [*gen.* **-няка́**] *n.* iron ore. —**бу́рый железня́к,** limonite. —**кра́сный железня́к,** hematite. —**хро́мистый железня́к,** chromite.
желе́зо *n.* iron.
железобето́н *n.* reinforced concrete. —**железобето́нный,** *adj.* of reinforced concrete.
жёлоб [*pl.* **желоба́**] *n.* chute. —**водосто́чный жёлоб,** gutter.
желобо́к [*gen.* **-бка́**] *n.* groove.
желте́ть *v. impfv.* [*pfv.* **пожелте́ть**] **1,** to become yellow; turn yellow. **2,** (*of leaves*) to turn. **3,** [*impfv. only*] (*of anything yellow*) to appear; gleam.
желтизна́ *n.* yellow color; yellow hue.
желтова́тый *adj.* **1,** yellowish. **2,** sallow.
желто́к [*gen.* **-тка́**] *n.* yolk.
желторо́тый *adj.* **1,** yellow-beaked. **2,** *colloq.* immature; inexperienced; green.
желтофио́ль *n.f.* wallflower.
желту́ха *n.* (yellow) jaundice.
жёлтый *adj.* yellow.
желудёвый *adj.* acorn (*attrib.*).
желу́док [*gen.* **-дка**] *n.* stomach.
желу́дочек [*gen.* **-чка**] *n.* ventricle.
желу́дочный *adj.* stomach (*attrib.*); gastric.
жёлудь [*pl.* **жёлуди, -де́й, -дя́м**] *n.m.* acorn.
жёлчный *adj.* **1,** bilious. **2,** *fig.* ill-tempered; peevish. —**жёлчные ка́мни,** gallstones. —**жёлчный прото́к,** bile duct. —**жёлчный пузы́рь,** gall bladder.
жёлчь *n.f.* **1,** bile. **2,** *fig.* bitterness; rancor.
жема́ниться *v.r. impfv., colloq.* to put on airs.
жема́нный *adj.* unnatural; affected. —**жема́нство,** *n.* affectation.
же́мчуг [*pl.* **жемчуга́**] *n.* pearl; pearls.
жемчу́жина *n.* a (single) pearl. —**жемчу́жница,** *n.* pearl oyster. —**жемчу́жный,** *adj.* pearl (*attrib.*); pearly.
жена́ [*pl.* **жёны**] *n.* wife.
жена́тый *adj.* (*with* **на** + *prepl.*) (*of a man*) married (to): он жена́т на англича́нке, he is married to an Englishwoman.
жени́ть *v. impfv. & pfv.* [*pres.* **женю́, же́нишь**] to marry off (a son). —**жени́ться,** *refl.* (*with* **на** + *prepl.*) (*of a man*) to marry; get married (to).
жени́тьба *n.* marriage (*of a man*).
жени́х [*gen.* **-ниха́**] *n.* **1,** fiancé. **2,** groom; bridegroom. **3,** eligible bachelor.
женолю́б *n.* ladies' man; womanizer. —**женолюби́вый,** *adj.* having a fondness for women. —**женолю́бие,** *n.* fondness for women.
женоненави́стник *n.* woman-hater; misogynist. —**женоненави́стничество,** *n.* misogyny.
женоподо́бный *adj.* effeminate.
же́нский *adj.* **1,** feminine; female. **2,** woman's; women's.
же́нственный *adj.* feminine; womanly. —**же́нственность** *n.f.* femininity.
же́нщина *n.* woman.
женьше́нь *n.m.* ginseng.
жердь [*pl.* **же́рди, -де́й, -дя́м**] *n.f.* pole; long stick.
жеребёнок [*gen.* **-нка;** *pl.* **-бя́та, -бя́т**] *n.* **1,** colt. **2,** foal.
жеребе́ц [*gen.* **-бца́**] *n.* stallion.
жереби́ться *v.r. impfv.* [*pfv.* **ожереби́ться**] to foal.
жеребьёвка *n.* casting of lots.
жерло́ [*pl.* **жёрла**] *n.* **1,** mouth (*of a volcano*). **2,** muzzle (*of a gun*).
жёрнов [*pl.* **жернова́**] *n.* millstone.
же́ртва *n.* **1,** victim: пасть же́ртвой (+ *gen.*), to fall victim to. Жертв не́ было, there were no casualties. **2,** sacrifice: идти́ на же́ртвы, to make sacrifices. Принести́ (что́-нибудь) в же́ртву, to sacrifice (something).
же́ртвенник *n.* altar.
же́ртвенный *adj.* **1,** sacrificial. **2,** selfless.
же́ртвователь *n.m.* contributor; donor.
же́ртвовать *v. impfv.* [*pfv.* **поже́ртвовать;** *pres.*

-твую, -твуешь] **1,** (*with instr.*) to sacrifice. **2,** to contribute; donate.
жертвоприноше́ние *n.* sacrifice; (burnt) offering.
жест *n.* gesture.
жестикули́ровать *v. impfv.* [*pres.* **-рую, -руешь**] to gesticulate.
жестикуля́ция *n.* gesticulation.
жёсткий *adj.* [*short form* **жёсток, жестка́, жёстко;** *comp.* **жёстче**] **1,** hard. **2,** stiff; rigid. **3,** harsh. **4,** *fig.* rigid; strict. —**жёсткий ваго́н,** coach with hard (unupholstered) seats.
жёстко *adv.* **1,** harshly. **2,** abruptly. **3,** decisively. —*adj., used predicatively* hard: мне жёстко сиде́ть, this seat is too hard for me.
жёсткость *n.f.* **1,** hardness; toughness. **2,** stiffness; rigidity.
жесто́кий *adj.* [*short form* **жесто́к, -тока́, -то́ко**] **1,** cruel; brutal. **2,** bitter; fierce. **3,** severe; harsh.
жесто́ко *adv.* **1,** cruelly. **2,** severely; harshly.
жестокосе́рдие *n.* hardheartedness. —**жестокосе́рдный,** *adj.* hardhearted.
жесто́кость *n.f.* **1,** cruelty. **2,** atrocity. **3,** severity.
жёстче *adj., comp. of* **жёсткий.**
жесть *n.f.* tin.
жестя́нка [*gen. pl.* **-нок**] *n.* tin can.
жестяно́й *adj.* tin.
жестя́нщик *n.* tinsmith.
жето́н *n.* **1,** token; counter. **2,** badge; medal.
жечь *v. impfv.* [*pfv.* **сжечь;** *pres.* **жгу, жжёшь,... жгут;** *past* **жёг, жгла, жгло**] **1,** to burn. **2,** [*impfv. only*] to burn; sting. —**жечь свои́ корабли́** (*or* **мосты́**), to burn one's bridges.
жéчься *v.r. impfv.* [*pres.* **жгусь, жжёшься, ...жгу́тся**] *colloq.* **1,** (*of an object*) to get very hot; burn. **2,** to sting. **3,** to burn oneself.
жже́ние *n.* burning sensation.
жжёнка *n.* hot beverage made of rum or brandy with burnt sugar and spices.
жжёный *adj.* burnt.
живе́й *interj.* hurry!; speed it up!
живе́ц [*gen.* **-вца́**] *n.* small fish used for bait.
живи́тельный *adj.* **1,** life-giving. **2,** invigorating; bracing.
жи́вность *n.f., colloq.* **1,** living things. **2,** poultry; livestock.
жи́во *adv.* **1,** vividly. **2,** keenly. **3,** with great animation. **4,** *colloq.* quickly.
живодёр *n., colloq.* hustler.
живо́й *adj.* [*short form* **жив, жива́, жи́во**] **1,** living; alive; live. **2,** lively; active. **3,** vivacious; animated. **4,** real. **5,** vivid; expressive. **6,** (*of flowers*) real; natural. **7,** (*of a wound*) raw. —**жива́я си́ла, 1,** manpower. **2,** kinetic energy. —**задева́ть за живо́е,** to cut to the quick. —**на живу́ю ру́ку,** hastily; on the run. —**остава́ться в живы́х,** to survive; remain alive.
жи́вокость *n.f.* delphinium; larkspur.
живопи́сец [*gen.* **-сца**] *n.* painter.
живопи́сный *adj.* picturesque.
жи́вопись *n.f.* **1,** painting (*as an art*). **2,** paintings.
живородя́щий *adj.* viviparous.
жи́вость *n.f.* **1,** agility. **2,** liveliness; vivacity. **3,** vividness; intensity. **4,** clarity.
живо́т [*gen.* **-вота́**] *n.* **1,** stomach; belly; abdomen. **2,** *obs.* life. —**надрыва́ть животы́ (со́ смеху),** to laugh oneself silly; be in stitches.
животво́рный *adj.* life-giving. *Also,* **животворя́щий.**
живо́тик *n., colloq.* tummy.
животново́дство *n.* livestock breeding; cattle raising; animal husbandry.
живо́тное *n., decl. as an adj.* animal.
живо́тный *adj.* **1,** animal (*attrib.*). **2,** *fig.* bestial.
животрепе́щущий *adj.* timely; vital.
живу́честь *n.f.* ability to survive; hardiness.
живу́чий *adj.* **1,** hardy. **2,** *fig.* hard to change: предрассу́дки живу́чи, prejudices die hard.
жи́вчик *n., colloq.* **1,** lively person. **2,** noticeable pulsation of an artery in one's temple.
живьём *adv., colloq.* alive: брать кого́-нибудь живьём, to take someone alive.
жид [*gen.* **жида́**] *n.* Jew (*derogatory term*).
жи́дкий *adj.* [*comp.* **жи́же**] **1,** liquid; fluid. **2,** thin; watery; weak. **3,** (*of hair, a beard, etc.*) thin; scanty. **4,** (*of metal, lava, etc.*) molten. **5,** *colloq.* puny.
жи́дкость *n.f.* liquid; fluid.
жи́жа *n.* liquid; wash; swill. *Also,* **жи́жица.**
жи́же *adj., comp. of* **жи́дкий.**
жи́зненно *adv.* **1,** true to life. **2,** vitally.
жи́зненность *n.f.* **1,** vitality. **2,** closeness to life. **3,** lifelike quality.
жи́зненный *adj.* **1,** of life. **2,** lifelike. **3,** vital. —**жи́зненный у́ровень,** standard of living.
жизнеописа́ние *n.* biography.
жизнера́достный *adj.* buoyant; bubbling with life. —**жизнера́достность,** *n.f.* zest for life.
жизнеспосо́бный *adj.* viable. —**жизнеспосо́бность,** *n.f.* viability.
жизнь *n.f.* life. —**в жи́зни не** (+ *verb*), never in one's life. —**как жизнь?,** *colloq.* how are you?; how are things?; how is life (treating you)? —**на всю жизнь,** for life. —**не на жизнь, а на смерть,** to the death. —**никогда́ в жи́зни,** never. —**при жи́зни,** in/during one's lifetime.
жиклёр *n.* jet; nozzle.
жи́ла *n.* **1,** *anat.* vein. **2,** tendon; sinew. **3,** *mining* lode; vein.
жиле́т *n.* vest.
жиле́тка [*gen. pl.* **-ток**] *n., colloq.* vest.
жиле́тный *adj.* vest (*attrib.*).
жиле́ц [*gen.* **-льца́**] *n.m.* [*fem.* **-ли́ца**] tenant; lodger.—**не жиле́ц (на э́том све́те),** not long for this world.
жи́листый *adj.* **1,** sinewy; wiry. **2,** (*of meat*) stringy.
жили́ще *n.* dwelling; abode; living quarters. —**жили́щный,** *adj.* housing (*attrib.*).
жи́лка [*gen. pl.* **-лок**] *n.* **1,** vein. **2,** *fig.* bent: артисти́ческая жи́лка, artistic bent.
жило́й *adj.* **1,** living (*attrib.*); dwelling (*attrib.*): жило́е помеще́ние, living quarters; жила́я пло́щадь, floorspace. **2,** residential: жилы́е кварта́лы, residential districts; жило́й дом, apartment house. **3,** *in* жило́й вид, lived-in look.
жилпло́щадь *n.f.* floorspace (*contr. of* **жила́я пло́щадь**).
жильё *n.* **1,** habitation. **2,** *colloq.* living quarters; place to live.
жим *n., weightlifting* press.
жи́молость *n.f.* honeysuckle.
жир [*2nd loc.* **жиру́;** *pl.* **жиры́**] *n.* fat; grease. —**ры́бий жир,** cod-liver oil.
жира́ф *n.* giraffe. *Also,* **жира́фа.**

жире́ть *v. impfv.* [*pfv.* **ожире́ть** *or* **разжире́ть**] to get fat.
жи́рно *adv.* **1,** with a lot of butter or fat. Есть жи́рно, to eat a lot of rich (*or* fatty) food. **2,** *colloq.* too much.
жи́рный *adj.* **1,** fatty. **2,** (*of foods*) fattening; rich. **3,** greasy; oily. **4,** fat; plump. **5,** (*of a line*) thick; (*of type*) boldface; bold-faced. —**жи́рное пятно́,** grease spot.
жи́ро *n. indecl.* endorsement (*on a check*).
жирови́к [*gen.* **-вика́**] *n.* fatty tumor.
жирово́й *adj.* fatty.
жите́йский *adj.* worldly; mundane.
жи́тель *n.m.* inhabitant; resident.
жи́тельство *n.* residence. —**вид на жи́тельство,** residence permit.
жи́тница *n.* **1,** *obs.* granary. **2,** grain-producing region; granary; breadbasket.
жи́то *n., regional* grain; rye; barley.
жить *v. impfv.* [*pres.* **живу́, живёшь;** *past fem.* **жила́**] to live. —**как живёшь?; как живёте?,** how are you?; how are things?; how are you getting along?
житьё *n., colloq.* **1,** life; existence. **2,** habitation; occupancy.
жи́ться *v.r. impfv.* [*pres.* **живётся**] *colloq., used impersonally with the dat. case,* to live: им неплóхо живётся, they don't live badly.
жму́рить *v. impfv.* [*pfv.* **зажму́рить**] *in* **жму́рить глаза́** to squint. —**жму́риться,** *refl.* to squint.
жму́рки [*gen.* **-рок**] *n. pl.* blindman's bluff.
жне́йка [*gen. pl.* **жне́ек**] *n.* harvester; reaper.
жнец [*gen.* **жнеца́**] *n.m.* [*fem.* **жни́ца**] harvest hand.
жнивьё *n.* stubs of cut grain; stubble.
жоке́й *n.* jockey.
жонглёр *n.* juggler. —**жонглёрство,** *n.* juggling (*lit. & fig.*).
жонгли́ровать *v. impfv.* [*pres.* **-рую, -руешь**] (*with instr.*) to juggle (*lit. & fig.*).
жонки́ль *n.m. or f.* jonquil.
жрать *v. impfv.* [*pfv.* **сожра́ть;** *pres.* **жру, жрёшь;** *past fem.* **жрала́**] *vulg.* to eat; gobble up.
жре́бий *n.* **1,** lot: по жре́бию, by lot. **2,** lots: броса́ть/тяну́ть жре́бий, to cast/draw lots. —**жре́бий бро́шен,** the die is cast.
жрец [*gen.* **жреца́**] *n.* pagan priest.
жужжа́ние *n.* hum; buzz.
жужжа́ть *v. impfv.* [*pres.* **-жжу́, -жжи́шь**] to hum; buzz; drone.
жуи́р *n.* playboy.
жук [*gen.* **жука́**] *n.* beetle. —**ма́йский жук,** cockchafer.
жу́лик *n.* crook; swindler; cheat. —**жулико́ватый,** *adj.* roguish.
жу́льничать *v. impfv., colloq.* to cheat.
жу́льнический *adj., colloq.* crooked; underhand. —**жу́льничество,** *n., colloq.* cheating; trickery.
жу́пел *n.* bugaboo; bugbear.
жура́вль [*gen.* **-вля́**] *n.m.* **1,** crane (*bird*). **2,** well sweep.
жури́ть *v. impfv.* [*pfv.* **пожури́ть**] *colloq.* to chide.
журна́л *n.* **1,** magazine; journal. **2,** log: ва́хтенный журна́л, ship's log.
журнали́ст *n.* journalist; newspaperman.
журнали́стика *n.* **1,** journalism. **2,** periodic literature.
журнали́стский *adj.* journalist's; journalistic.
журна́льный *adj.* magazine (*attrib.*).
журча́ние *n.* babble; babbling (*of a stream, brook, etc.*).
журча́ть *v. impfv.* [*pres.* **-чи́т**] **1,** (*of water*) to rumble; (*of a brook*) to babble. **2,** (*of a speech, conversation, etc.*) to drone on.
жу́ткий *adj.* frightful; ghastly; gruesome; grim.
жу́тко *adv.* **1,** frighteningly. **2,** *colloq.* terribly. —*adj., used predicatively* **1,** terrified: мне бы́ло жу́тко, I was terrified. **2,** frightening: но́чью в лесу́ бы́ло жу́тко, it was frightening in the woods at night.
жуть *n.f., colloq.* horror.
жу́хлый *adj.* **1,** withered; dried up. **2,** (*of colors*) faded.
жу́хнуть *v. impfv.* [*past* **жух** *or* **жу́хнул, жу́хла**] **1,** to wither; dry up. **2,** (*of colors*) to fade.
жучо́к [*gen.* **-чка́**] *n., dim. of* **жук.**
жюри́ (жу) *n. neut. indecl.* **1,** judges; jury (*in a contest*). **2,** *law* jury: большо́е жюри́, grand jury.

З

З, з *n. neut.* eighth letter of the Russian alphabet.
за *prep.* A, *with acc.* **1,** behind (*with verbs of motion*): со́лнце зашло́ за ту́чи, the sun went behind the clouds. **2,** beyond (*with verbs of motion*): вы́йти за преде́лы (+ *gen.*), to go beyond the bounds of... **3,** (*with ages*) past; over: ему́ за со́рок, he is past/over forty. **4,** for; in exchange for: купи́ть за три рубля́, to buy for three rubles. **5,** for; in place of: расписа́ться за председа́теля, to sign for the chairman. **6,** for; in favor of: голосова́ть за кандида́та, to vote for a candidate. **7,** during: за э́то вре́мя, during that time. **8,** in (*a certain amount of time*): покры́ть расстоя́ние за три дня, to cover the distance in three days. **9,** (*with* **до**) before: за час до его́ отъе́зда, an hour before his departure. **10,** (*with verbs of sitting*) at; to: сесть за стол, to sit down at the table. **11,** (*with verbs of taking, grasping, holding*) by; on to: взять за́ руку, to take by the hand. **12,** (*with verbs

and nouns expressing fear, joy, struggle, death, forgiveness, gratitude, punishment, reward, and many others) for: боя́ться за свою́ жизнь, to fear for one's life; умере́ть за ро́дину, to die for one's country. В, *with instr.* **1,** behind: за мое́й спино́й, behind my back. **2,** beyond: за преде́лами го́рода, beyond the city limits. **3,** (following) after: оди́н за други́м, one after the other; one by one. **4,** for; to fetch: идти́ за папиро́сами, to go for some cigarettes; заходи́ть за това́рищем, to call for one's friend. **5,** after; in pursuit of: бежа́ть за ке́м-нибудь, to run after someone. **6,** at; occupied with; doing something: обсужда́ть вопро́с за обе́дом, to discuss a question at (*or* over) dinner; проводи́ть вре́мя за чте́нием, to spend time reading. **7,** (*with verbs of sitting*) at: сиде́ть за столо́м, to be sitting at the table. **8,** (*with verbs of watching, caring, etc.*) for; after: присма́тривать за детьми́, to look after the children. **9,** owing to; for: за неиме́нием ули́к, for lack of evidence. **10,** *indicating someone's turn:* сло́во за ва́ми, you have the floor; де́ло за ва́ми, it's up to you.

за- *prefix* **1,** *indicating the beginning of an action:* засмея́ться, to (begin to) laugh. **2,** *indicating motion behind or beyond:* заходи́ть, to go behind. **3,** *indicating action taken en route:* заходи́ть к кому́-нибудь, to drop in on someone. **4,** (*with* **-ся**) *indicating absorption to the point of forgetfulness:* засмотре́ться, to be lost in contemplation. **5,** (*with nouns and adjectives*) outside of: за́городный, out of town. **6,** (*with proper nouns and adjectives*) Trans-: Закавка́зье, Transcaucasia.

заале́ть *v., pfv. of* **але́ть.**

заарка́нить *v., pfv. of* **арка́нить.**

заатланти́ческий *adj.* transatlantic; located across the Atlantic.

заба́ва *n.* **1,** amusement; fun. **2,** pastime.

забавля́ть *v. impfv.* to amuse; entertain. —**забавля́ться,** *refl.* to amuse oneself.

заба́вник *n., colloq.* funny person; amusing fellow.

заба́вно *adv.* in an amusing way. —*adj., used predicatively* funny: заба́вно!, that's funny! Мне заба́вно, что..., I find it funny that...

заба́вный *adj.* funny; amusing.

забаллоти́ровать *v. pfv.* [*infl.* **-рую, -руешь**] to fail to elect; reject; blackball.

забаррикади́ровать *v., pfv. of* **баррикади́ровать.**

забастова́ть *v. pfv.* [*infl.* **-сту́ю, -сту́ешь**] to strike; go on strike.

забасто́вка [*gen. pl.* **-вок**] *n.* strike. —**забасто́вочный,** *adj.* strike (*attrib.*).

забасто́вщик *n.* striker.

забве́ние *n.* **1,** oblivion: предава́ть забве́нию, to consign to oblivion. **2,** (*with gen.*) neglect (of); disregard (of).

забе́г *n., sports* heat; race.

забега́ловка *n., colloq.* eating house.

забе́гать *v. pfv.* to start running. —**забе́гаться,** *refl., colloq.* to run oneself ragged.

забега́ть *v. impfv.* [*pfv.* **забежа́ть**] **1,** (*with* **в** *or* **на** + *acc.*) to run into. **2,** (*with* **к**) *colloq.* to drop in on. **3,** to run (far) away. —**забега́ть вперёд, 1,** to run ahead. **2,** to anticipate events; act in advance.

забежа́ть [*infl. like* **бежа́ть**] *v., pfv. of* **забега́ть.**

забели́ть *v. pfv.* [*infl.* **-белю́, -бе́лишь** *or* **-бели́шь**] **1,** to whiten; paint white. **2,** *colloq.* to add milk or sour cream to.

забере́менеть *v., pfv. of* **бере́менеть.**

забеспоко́иться *v.r. pfv.* to become anxious; become uneasy; begin to worry.

забетони́ровать *v., pfv. of* **бетони́ровать.**

забива́ть *v. impfv.* [*pfv.* **заби́ть**] **1,** to drive in; hammer in. **2,** to seal up; board up. **3,** to block up; clog. **4,** to beat to death; beat into submission. **5,** *colloq.* to outdo; surpass. **6,** *sports* to drive in (a ball); score (a goal). **7,** *in* **забива́ть чью́-нибудь го́лову** (+ *instr.*), to fill *or* stuff someone's head (with). **8,** *in* **забива́ть себе́ в го́лову,** to get it into one's head; develop a fixed idea. —**забива́ться,** *refl.* **1,** *colloq.* to hide; huddle. **2,** to become blocked; become clogged.

забинтова́ть *v., pfv. of* **бинтова́ть.**

забира́ть *v. impfv.* [*pfv.* **забра́ть**] **1,** to take. **2,** to take away. **3,** to arrest. **4,** to take in; shorten. **5,** *colloq. (of a feeling)* to come over (someone). **6,** to seal up; close up. **7,** to bear: забра́ть впра́во, to bear (to the) right. **8,** *in* **забира́ть в ру́ки,** to take over. **9,** *in* **забира́ть себе́ в го́лову,** to get it into one's head; develop a fixed idea. —**забира́ться,** *refl.* **1,** (*with* **на, в** *or* **под** + *acc.*) to climb. **2,** (*with* **в** + *acc.*) to get into; steal into. **3,** to get to: куда́ он забра́лся?, where has he gotten to? **4,** to hide.

заби́тый *adj.* downtrodden; cowed.

заби́ть *v. pfv.* [*infl.* **-бью́, -бьёшь**] **1,** *pfv. of* **забива́ть. 2,** to begin to strike. **3,** to sound (an alarm, retreat, etc.). —**заби́ться,** *refl.* **1,** *pfv. of* **забива́ться. 2,** to begin to beat.

забия́ка *n.m. & f., colloq.* roughneck; bully.

заблаговре́менно *adv.* beforehand; in advance; ahead of time.

заблагорассу́диться *v.r. pfv., impers.* (*with dat.*) to see fit: я сде́лаю, что мне заблагорассу́дится, I shall do as I see fit.

заблесте́ть *v. pfv.* [*infl. like* **блесте́ть**] to begin to shine; begin to sparkle.

заблуди́ться *v.r. pfv.* [*infl.* **-блужу́сь, -блу́дишься**] to lose one's way; get lost. —**заблуди́ться в трёх со́снах,** to be confounded by the simplest problem.

заблу́дший *adj.* **1,** lost; stray. **2,** *fig.* wayward; gone astray. —**заблу́дшая овца́,** lost sheep.

заблужда́ться *v.r. impfv.* to be mistaken.

заблужде́ние *n.* error; delusion; misconception. —**вводи́ть в заблужде́ние,** to mislead; delude; lead astray.

забода́ть *v. pfv.* to gore.

заболева́емость *n.f.* incidence; prevalence; rate; number of cases (*of a disease*).

заболева́ние *n.* illness; disease.

заболева́ть *v. impfv.* [*pfv.* **заболе́ть**] to become ill; fall ill; be taken ill.

заболе́ть *v. pfv.* **1,** [*infl.* **-е́ю, -е́ешь**] *pfv. of* **заболева́ть. 2,** [*infl.* **-и́т**] to begin to hurt; begin to ache.

за́болонь *n.f.* alburnum; sapwood.

заболта́ться *v.r. pfv., colloq.* to become engrossed in conversation.

забо́р *n.* fence.

забо́ристый *adj., colloq.* **1,** strong; pungent. **2,** racy; risqué.

забо́рный *adj.* **1,** fence (*attrib.*). **2,** coarse; vulgar.

забо́та *n.* **1,** care; concern: забо́та о челове́ке, concern for people. **2,** care; worry: без забо́т, without a care.

забо́титься *v.r. impfv.* [*pfv.* **позабо́титься;** *pres.* **-чусь, -тишься**] (*with* **о**) **1,** to take care of; care for; look after. **2,** to care about; be concerned about.

забо́тливый *adj.* thoughtful; solicitous; considerate. —**забо́тливость,** *n.f.* thoughtfulness; solicitude.

забракова́ть *v., pfv. of* **браковáть.**

забра́ло *n.* visor (*of a helmet*). —**с откры́тым забра́лом,** openly; frankly; boldly.

забра́сывать[1] *v. impfv.* [*pfv.* **заброса́ть**] (*with instr.*) **1,** to fill (with). **2,** to pelt (with): заброса́ть кого́-нибудь камня́ми, to throw stones at. **3,** *fig.* to shower (with); bombard (with): заброса́ть кого́-нибудь вопро́сами, to shower/bombard with questions.

забра́сывать[2] *v. impfv.* [*pfv.* **забро́сить**] **1,** to throw (*with force or over a distance*). **2,** to throw; toss (a part of one's body): забро́сить го́лову наза́д, to toss one's head back. **3,** to give up; drop; abandon. **4,** *colloq.* to deliver; drop off.

забра́ть [*infl. like* **брать**] *v., pfv. of* **забира́ть.** —**забра́ться,** *refl., pfv. of* **забира́ться.**

забрести́ *v. pfv.* [*infl. like* **брести́**] *colloq.* **1,** (*with* **в** + *acc.*) to wander into. **2,** to wander off.

заброни́ровать *v., pfv. of* **брони́ровать.**

забронирова́ть *v., pfv. of* **бронирова́ть.**

забро́с *n., colloq.* neglect: быть в забро́се, to be in a state of neglect.

заброса́ть *v., pfv. of* **забра́сывать**[1].

забро́сить [*infl.* **-шу, -сишь**] *v., pfv. of* **забра́сывать**[2].

забро́шенный *adj.* **1,** neglected. **2,** deserted; desolate.

забры́згивать *v. impfv.* [*pfv.* **забры́згать**] (*with instr.*) to splash (with); spatter (with); splatter (with).

забыва́ть *v. impfv.* [*pfv.* **забы́ть**] **1,** to forget: не забу́дьте!, don't forget! **2,** to leave (*accidentally*): забы́ть зо́нтик на рабо́те, to leave one's umbrella at work. —**забыва́ться,** *refl.* **1,** to doze off. **2,** to be lost in thought. **3,** to forget oneself. **4,** to be forgotten.

забы́вчивый *adj.* forgetful. —**забы́вчивость,** *n.f.* forgetfulness.

забы́тый *adj.* forgotten.

забы́ть [*infl.* **-бу́ду, -бу́дешь**] *v., pfv. of* **забыва́ть.** —**забы́ться,** *refl., pfv. of* **забыва́ться.**

забытьё [*prepl.* **в забытьи́**] *n.* **1,** drowsiness. **2,** semiconsciousness. **3,** (state of) distraction.

зава́л *n.* **1,** pile; accumulation: сне́жный зава́л, snowdrift. **2,** obstruction; barrier.

зава́ливать *v. impfv.* [*pfv.* **завали́ть**] **1,** to block up. **2,** (*with instr.*) *colloq.* to pile high (with); *fig.* overload (with); flood (with); swamp (with). —**зава́ливаться,** *refl.* **1,** to fall. **2,** *colloq.* to fall down; come tumbling down; collapse. **3,** *colloq.* to tilt to one side. **4,** *colloq.* to lie down; flop down.

завали́ть [*infl.* **-валю́, -ва́лишь**] *v., pfv. of* **зава́ливать.** —**завали́ться,** *refl., pfv. of* **зава́ливаться.**

за́валь *n.f., colloq.* unsold or unsalable merchandise; junk.

заваля́ться *v.r. pfv., colloq.* to lie unused; lie unsold; lie unattended to.

зава́ривать *v. impfv.* [*pfv.* **завари́ть**] to make; brew (coffee, tea, etc.). —**завари́ть ка́шу,** to stir up trouble.

завари́ть [*infl.* **-варю́, -ва́ришь**] *v., pfv. of* **зава́ривать.**

заварно́й *adj.* boiled. —**заварно́й крем,** custard. —**заварно́е пиро́жное,** pastry filled with custard.

заведе́ние *n.* institution; establishment. —**вы́сшее уче́бное заведе́ние,** institution of higher learning.

заве́дование *n.* management; supervision.

заве́довать *v. impfv.* [*pres.* **-дую, -дуешь**] (*with instr.*) to manage.

заве́домо *adv.* **1,** obviously; known to be. **2,** knowingly; wittingly.

заве́домый *adj.* **1,** notorious. **2,** obvious.

заве́дующий *n., decl. as an adj.* manager.

завезти́ [*infl. like* **везти́**] *v., pfv. of* **завози́ть.**

завербова́ть *v., pfv. of* **вербова́ть.**

завере́ние *n.* assurance.

заве́рить *v., pfv. of* **заверя́ть.**

заверну́ть *v., pfv. of* **завёртывать.** —**заверну́ться,** *refl., pfv. of* **завёртываться.**

заверте́ть *v. pfv.* [*infl.* **-верчу́, -ве́ртишь**] **1,** (*with instr.*) to begin to twirl. **2,** *fig., colloq.* to carry away. —**заверте́ться,** *refl.* **1,** to begin to spin; begin to whirl. **2,** *fig., colloq.* to be in a whirl.

завёртывать *v. impfv.* [*pfv.* **заверну́ть**] **1,** to wrap; wrap up; (*with* **в** + *acc.*) wrap in. **2,** to turn: заверну́ть за́ угол, to turn the corner. **3,** to turn up; roll up; tuck up. **4,** to screw tight; tighten. **5,** *colloq.* to turn off. **6,** (*with* **к**) *colloq.* to drop in (on). —**завёртываться,** *refl.* **1,** (*with* **в** + *acc.*) to wrap oneself (in). **2,** to be turned up; be folded *or* rolled back.

заверша́ть *v. impfv.* [*pfv.* **заверши́ть**] to complete. —**заверша́ться,** *refl.* **1,** to be completed. **2,** (*with instr.*) to be concluded (with *or* by).

заверша́ющий *adj.* concluding; closing. —**заверша́ющий уда́р,** crowning blow.

заверше́ние *n.* completion; conclusion; consummation.

заверши́ть *v., pfv. of* **заверша́ть.** —**заверши́ться,** *refl., pfv. of* **заверша́ться.**

заверя́ть *v. impfv.* [*pfv.* **заве́рить**] **1,** to assure. **2,** to witness; certify.

заве́са *n.* **1,** curtain. **2,** *fig.* veil; screen. —**дымова́я заве́са,** smoke screen.

заве́сить [*infl.* **-шу, -сишь**] *v., pfv. of* **заве́шивать** (*in sense #1*).

завести́ [*infl. like* **вести́**] *v., pfv. of* **заводи́ть.** —**завести́сь,** *refl., pfv. of* **заводи́ться.**

заве́т *n.* **1,** precept. **2,** *relig.* covenant. **3,** *obs.* vow. —**Ве́тхий заве́т,** Old Testament. —**Но́вый заве́т,** New Testament.

заве́тный *adj.* **1,** (*of a dream, desire, etc.*) fondest; lifelong. **2,** secret; hidden.

заве́шивать *v. impfv.* **1,** [*pfv.* **заве́сить**] to cover; curtain off. **2,** [*pfv.* **заве́шать**] to hang with: сте́ны бы́ли заве́шаны карти́нами, the walls were hung with paintings.

завеща́ние *n.* will. —**духо́вное завеща́ние,** last will and testament.

завеща́тель *n.m.* testator. —**завеща́тельница,** *n.* testatrix.

завеща́ть *v. impfv. & pfv.* to bequeath; will; leave.

завзя́тый *adj., colloq.* **1,** inveterate. **2,** avid; ardent.

завива́ть *v. impfv.* [*pfv.* **зави́ть**] to curl; wave. —**завива́ться,** *refl.* **1,** (*of hair*) to curl; become curly. **2,** to have one's hair curled.

зави́вка [*gen. pl.* **вок**] *n.* wave. —**шестиме́сячная зави́вка,** permanent wave.

зави́деть *v. pfv.* [*infl.* **-жу, -дишь**] *colloq.* to catch sight of (*from afar*).

зави́дно *adj., used predicatively* (*with dat.*) envious: ему́ зави́дно смотре́ть на неё, he is envious when he looks at her.

зави́дный *adj.* enviable.

зави́довать *v. impfv.* [*pfv.* **позави́довать;** *pres.* **-дую, -дуешь**] (*with dat.*) to envy; be jealous of.

завиду́щий *adj., colloq.* envious; covetous.

зави́нчивать *v. impfv.* [*pfv.* **завинти́ть**] to tighten (a screw, nut, etc.).

завира́ться *v.r. impfv.* [*pfv.* **завра́ться**] *colloq.* to become tangled in lies.

зави́сеть *v. impfv.* [*pres.* **-шу, -сишь**] (*with* **от**) to depend (on).

зави́симость *n.f.* dependence. —**в зави́симости от,** depending on. —**вне зави́симости от,** regardless of.

зави́симый *adj.* dependent.

зави́стливый *adj.* envious.

зави́стник *n.* envious person.

за́висть *n.f.* envy.

завито́й *adj.* (*of hair*) curled; waved.

завито́к [*gen.* **-тка́**] *n.* **1,** lock; ringlet. **2,** flourish (*in handwriting or oratory*).

завиту́шка [*gen. pl.* **-шек**] *n., colloq.* = **завито́к.**

зави́ть [*infl. like* **вить**] *v., pfv. of* **завива́ть.** —**зави́ться,** *refl., pfv. of* **завива́ться.**

завко́м *n.* factory committee (*contr. of* **заводско́й комите́т**).

завладева́ть *v. impfv.* [*pfv.* **завладе́ть**] (*with instr.*) **1,** to seize; take possession of; capture. **2,** *fig.* to grip: завладе́ть чьим-нибудь внима́нием, to grip someone's attention. **3,** *fig.* to captivate.

завлека́тельный *adj.* enticing; alluring.

завлека́ть *v. impfv.* [*pfv.* **завле́чь**] **1,** to entice; lure. **2,** to captivate; enthrall.

завле́чь [*infl. like* **влечь**] *v., pfv. of* **завлека́ть.**

заво́д *n.* **1,** factory; plant; mill; works. ♦*Used with various adjectives:* ко́нный заво́д, stud farm; пивова́ренный заво́д, brewery; са́харный заво́д, sugar refinery. **2,** winding mechanism.

заводи́ть *v. impfv.* [*pfv.* **завести́;** *pres.* **-вожу́, -во́дишь**] **1,** to take to; bring to. **2,** (*with* **в** +*acc.*) to bring into; lead into. **3,** to take out of one's way; take far away: куда́ ты нас завёл?, where have you taken us? **4,** to start; launch. **5,** to introduce; institute. **6,** to strike up (a conversation, acquaintance, etc.). **7,** to get; acquire. **8,** to wind (a watch); start (a car or motor). —**заводи́ться,** *refl.* **1,** to appear; turn up. **2,** to be established; start up. **3,** (*of an engine*) to start.

заводно́й *adj.* **1,** operated by winding; mechanical. **2,** serving to wind; winding: заводна́я рукоя́тка, hand crank.

заво́дский *also,* **заводско́й** *adj.* **1,** factory (*attrib.*). **2,** *in* заво́дская ло́шадь, stud horse.

заво́дчик *n.* factory owner.

за́водь *n.f.* inlet; creek.

завоева́ние *n.* **1,** conquest. **2,** *pl.* conquests. **3,** *pl.* achievements. —**завоева́тель,** *n.m.* conqueror.

завоева́ть [*infl.* **-вою́ю, -вою́ешь**] *v., pfv. of* **завоёвывать.**

завоёвывать *v. impfv.* [*pfv.* **завоева́ть**] **1,** to conquer. **2,** to gain; win.

заво́з *n.* delivery.

завози́ть *v. impfv.* [*pfv.* **завезти́;** *pres.* **-вожу́, -во́зишь**] **1,** to deliver; drop off. **2,** to take far away; take out of one's way. **3,** to bring into (a country).

завола́кивать *v. impfv.* [*pfv.* **заволо́чь**] to cloud; obscure: ту́чи заволокли́ со́лнце, clouds obscured the sun. *Also impers.:* её глаза́ заволокло́ слеза́ми, her eyes were clouded with tears.

заволнова́ться *v.r. pfv.* [*infl.* **-ну́юсь, -ну́ешься**] to become agitated.

заволо́чь [*infl. like* **воло́чь**] *v., pfv. of* **завола́кивать.**

завора́живать *v. impfv.* [*pfv.* **заворожи́ть**] **1,** to bewitch; cast a spell over. **2,** *fig.* to bewitch; captivate.

завора́чивать *v. impfv.* [*pfv.* **завороти́ть**] *colloq.* **1,** *v.i.* to turn; make a turn. **2,** *v.t.* to turn around; turn back. **3,** to turn up (an edge, sleeve, etc.). **4,** to drop in. **5,** [*impfv. only*] (*with instr.*) to be in charge of.

заворожённый *adj.* spellbound; bewitched.

заворожи́ть *v., pfv. of* **завора́живать.**

заворо́т *n., colloq.* **1,** sharp turn. **2,** bend (*in a road, river, etc.*).

завороти́ть [*infl.* **-рочу́, -ро́тишь**] *v., pfv. of* **завора́чивать.**

завра́ться [*infl. like* **врать**] *v.r., pfv. of* **завира́ться.**

завсегда́тай *n.* habitué.

за́втра *adv.* tomorrow.

за́втрак *n.* **1,** breakfast. **2,** lunch. **3,** luncheon.

за́втракать *v. impfv.* [*pfv.* **поза́втракать**] to have breakfast; have lunch.

за́втрашний *adj.* tomorrow's. —**за́втрашний день, 1,** tomorrow. **2,** the future.

завуали́ровать *v. pfv.* [*infl.* **-рую, -руешь**] to veil; conceal.

за́вуч *n., colloq.* director of studies (*contr. of* **заве́дующий уче́бной ча́стью**).

завхо́з *n., colloq.* steward; household manager (*contr. of* **заве́дующий хозя́йством**).

завыва́ть *v. impfv.* to howl; wail.

завыша́ть *v. impfv.* [*pfv.* **завы́сить**] to set (goals, norms, etc.) too high; give too high (a grade).

завяза́ть[1] [*infl.* **-вяжу́, -вя́жешь**] *v., pfv. of* **завя́зывать.** —**завяза́ться,** *refl., pfv. of* **завя́зываться.**

завяза́ть[2] *v. impfv.* [*pfv.* **завя́знуть;** *pres.* **-за́ю, -за́ешь**] **1,** to get stuck. **2,** *fig., colloq.* to become mired.

завя́зка [*gen. pl.* **-зок**] *n.* **1,** string; lace; band. **2,** beginning; starting point.

завя́знуть [*past* **-вя́з, -ла**] *v., pfv. of* **вя́знуть** *and* **завяза́ть**[2].

завя́зывать *v. impfv.* [*pfv.* **завяза́ть**] **1,** to tie; tie up. **2,** to bind; bind up. **3,** *in* завяза́ть глаза́ (+*dat.*), to blindfold. **4,** to start; strike up (a conversation, acquaintance, etc.). —**завя́зываться,** *refl.* **1,** to be tied; tie. **2,** to begin; develop; spring up.

за́вязь *n.f., bot.* ovary.

завя́нуть [*past* **-вя́л, -вя́ла**] *v., pfv. of* **вя́нуть.**

загада́ть *v., pfv. of* **зага́дывать.**

зага́дить [*infl.* **-жу, -дишь**] *v., pfv. of* **зага́живать.**

зага́дка [*gen. pl.* **-док**] *n.* **1,** riddle; puzzle. **2,** mystery; enigma.

зага́дочный *adj.* enigmatic; mysterious.

зага́дывать *v. impfv.* [*pfv.* **загада́ть**] **1,** to pose (a riddle). **2,** to think of; pick (*as part of a riddle*). **3,** to think ahead; look ahead.

зага́живать *v. impfv.* [*pfv.* **зага́дить**] *colloq.* to foul; dirty; pollute.

зага́р *n.* sunburn; sun tan.

загаси́ть *v. pfv.* [*infl.* **-гашу́, -га́сишь**] *colloq.* to put out; extinguish.

загво́здка [*gen. pl.* **-док**] *n., colloq.* hitch; catch; snag; rub.

заги́б *n.* **1,** bend. **2,** crease (*in a page*). **3,** *fig.* deviation.

загиба́ть *v. impfv.* [*pfv.* **загну́ть**] **1,** to turn up; turn down; fold down; fold over. **2,** *v.i., colloq.* to turn: загну́ть за́ угол, to turn the corner. **3,** *colloq.* to utter; come out with. —**загиба́ться,** *refl.* **1,** to turn up. **2,** to bend.

загипнотизи́ровать *v., pfv. of* **гипнотизи́ровать.**

загла́вие *n.* title.

загла́вный *adj.* title (*attrib.*). —**загла́вная бу́ква,** capital letter. —**загла́вный лист,** title page. —**загла́вная роль,** title role.

загла́дить [*infl.* **-жу, -дишь**] *v., pfv. of* **загла́живать.**

загла́живать *v. impfv.* [*pfv.* **загла́дить**] **1,** to smooth out; iron out. **2,** to redress; make amends for.

загла́зно *adv., colloq.* **1,** behind one's back. **2,** sight unseen.

загла́зный *adj., colloq.* said or done behind one's back.

загло́хнуть [*past* **-гло́х, -ла**] *v., pfv. of* **гло́хнуть** (*in senses #2 and #3*).

заглуша́ть *v. impfv.* [*pfv.* **заглуши́ть**] **1,** to muffle; drown out (sound); jam (radio broadcasts). **2,** to deaden (pain). **3,** (*of weeds*) to choke. **4,** *fig.* to stifle.

заглуши́ть *v., pfv. of* **глуши́ть** *and* **заглуша́ть.**

загляде́нье *n., colloq.* lovely sight; sight for sore eyes.

загляде́ться [*infl.* **-жу́сь, -ди́шься**] *v.r., pfv. of* **загля́дываться.**

загля́дывать *v. impfv.* [*pfv.* **загляну́ть**] **1,** (*with* **в** + *acc.*) to look (into); peep (into); (*with* **под** + *acc.*) look under. **2,** *colloq.* to drop in; drop by; (*with* **к**) drop in on; look in on. **3,** *in* загля́дывать вперёд, to look ahead. —**загля́дываться,** *refl.* [*pfv.* **загляде́ться**] to stare at (longingly); eye.

загляну́ть [*infl.* **-гляну́, -гля́нешь**] *v., pfv. of* **загля́дывать.**

загна́ивать *v. impfv.* [*pfv.* **загнои́ть**] *colloq.* to allow to fester; allow to rot. —**загна́иваться,** *refl.* to fester.

за́гнанный *adj.* **1,** (*of an animal*) exhausted (*from being chased*). **2,** *fig.* downtrodden; persecuted.

загна́ть [*infl. like* **гнать**] *v., pfv. of* **загоня́ть.**

загнива́ние *n.* **1,** rotting. **2,** *fig.* decay.

загнива́ть *v. impfv.* [*pfv.* **загни́ть**] to rot; decay.

загни́ть [*infl. like* **гнить**] *v., pfv. of* **загнива́ть.**

загнои́ть *v., pfv. of* **загна́ивать.** —**загнои́ться,** *refl., pfv. of* **загна́иваться.**

загну́ть *v., pfv. of* **загиба́ть.** —**загну́ться,** *refl., pfv. of* **загиба́ться.**

загова́ривать *v. impfv.* [*pfv.* **заговори́ть**] **1,** [*impfv. only*] (*with* **с** + *instr.*) to start a conversation (with). **2,** *colloq.* to talk (someone's) head off. **3,** to cast a spell over. **4,** *in* **загова́ривать зу́бы** (+ *dat.*), *colloq.* to fool (someone) with fine words. —**загова́риваться,** *refl.* **1,** [*impfv. only*] to ramble (*when speaking*). **2,** to become engrossed in conversation.

за́говор *n.* **1,** plot; conspiracy. **2,** incantation.

заговори́ть *v. pfv.* **1,** *pfv. of* **загова́ривать. 2,** to learn to speak. **3,** to begin to speak. —**заговори́ться,** *refl., pfv. of* **загова́риваться** (*in sense #2*).

загово́рщик *n.* conspirator; plotter. —**загово́рщический,** *adj.* conspiratorial.

за́годя *adv., colloq.* ahead of time; in advance.

заголо́вок [*gen.* **-вка**] *n.* **1,** headline. **2,** heading.

заго́н *n.* **1,** pen (*for cattle*). **2,** herding; rounding up. **3,** strip of land. —**быть в заго́не,** to be neglected; be in a state of neglect.

загоня́ть *v. impfv.* [*pfv.* **загна́ть**] **1,** (*with* **в** + *acc.*) to herd into; drive into. **2,** *colloq.* to drive in; hammer in. **3,** to drive away. **4,** to drive to exhaustion. **5,** to bring (an animal) to bay.

загора́живать *v. impfv.* [*pfv.* **загороди́ть**] **1,** to enclose; fence in. **2,** to bar; block; obstruct.

загора́ть *v. impfv.* [*pfv.* **загоре́ть**] **1,** to become (*or* get) sunburned. **2,** [*impfv. only*] to sun-bathe. —**загора́ться,** *refl.* **1,** to catch fire. **2,** (*of one's eyes*) to light up; (*of one's face*) be flushed. **3,** (*of an argument, fight, etc.*) to break out. **4,** (*with instr.*) to be consumed with (an emotion, idea, etc.). **5,** *impers.* (*with dat.*) *colloq.* to have a burning desire.

загоре́лый *adj.* sunburned; suntanned.

загоре́ть [*infl.* **-горю́, -гори́шь**] *v., pfv. of* **загора́ть.** —**загоре́ться,** *refl., pfv. of* **загора́ться.**

загороди́ть [*infl.* **-рожу́, -ро́дишь** *or* **-роди́шь**] *v., pfv. of* **загора́живать.**

загоро́дка [*gen. pl.* **-док**] *n., colloq.* **1,** fence. **2,** partition. **3,** enclosure.

за́городный *adj.* out-of-town; country (*attrib.*).

загости́ться *v.r. pfv.* [*infl.* **-гощу́сь, -сти́шься**] *colloq.* to overstay one's welcome.

загота́вливать *v. impfv.* = **заготовля́ть.**

загото́вить [*infl.* **-влю, -вишь**] *v., pfv. of* **загота́вливать** *and* **заготовля́ть.**

загото́вка *n.* **1,** storing up; stocking up. **2,** *often pl.* purchase(s) (*by the state*).

заготовля́ть *v. impfv.* [*pfv.* **загото́вить**] **1,** to prepare in advance. **2,** (*often fol. by* **впрок**) to store up; stock up on.

загради́тель *n.m.* minelayer. *Also,* **ми́нный загради́тель.**

загради́тельный *adj., mil.* protecting; covering. —**загради́тельный ого́нь,** covering fire; barrage.

загради́ть [*infl.* **-жу́, -ди́шь**] *v., pfv. of* **загражда́ть.**

загражда́ть *v. impfv.* [*pfv.* **загради́ть**] to bar; block; obstruct.

загражде́ние *n.* obstacle; barrier; obstruction.

грани́ца *n., colloq.* foreign countries. —**по заграни́цам,** abroad.

заграни́чный *adj.* foreign.

загреба́ть *v. impfv.* [*pfv.* **загрести́**] **1,** to rake together; rake up. **2,** *in* загреба́ть жар, to bank the fire (*in a furnace*). **3,** *colloq.* to rake in (money). —**чужи́ми рука́ми жар загреба́ть,** to make someone else do one's dirty work.

загреме́ть *v. pfv.* [*infl.* **-млю́, -ми́шь**] **1,** to begin to sound, clank, thunder, etc.; resound. **2,** (*with instr.*) to rattle. **3,** *colloq.* to come crashing down.

загрести́ [*infl. like* **грести́**] *v., pfv. of* **загреба́ть.**

загри́вок [*gen.* **-вка**] *n.* **1,** withers. **2,** *colloq.* nape of the neck.

загримирова́ть *v., pfv. of* **гримирова́ть** (*in sense #2*). —**загримирова́ться,** *refl., pfv. of* **гримирова́ться** (*in sense #2*).

загро́бный *adj.* occurring after death: загро́бный мир, the next world; загро́бная жизнь, life after death; afterlife.

загромождáть *v. impfv.* [*pfv.* **загромоздúть**] to clutter (up); jam.

загромоздúть [*infl.* **-зжý, -здúшь**] *v., pfv. of* **загромождáть.**

загрубéлый *adj.* calloused.

загрубéть *v. pfv.* **1,** to become calloused. **2,** *fig.* to become callous.

загружáть *v. impfv.* [*pfv.* **загрузúть**] **1,** to load (a vehicle, vessel, etc.). **2,** *fig.* to assign a full load of work to (someone); fill out (a period of time) with work. —**загружáться,** *refl.* to load up.

загрузúть [*infl.* **-гружý, -грýзишь** *or* **-грузúшь**] *v., pfv. of* **грузúть** (*in sense #1*) *and* **загружáть.** —**загрузúться,** *refl., pfv. of* **загружáться.**

загрýзка *n.* **1,** loading. **2,** *colloq.* workload; capacity.

загрустúть *v. pfv.* [*infl.* **-щý, -стúшь**] to become sad.

загрызáть *v. impfv.* [*pfv.* **загры́зть**] **1,** to kill; bite to death; tear to pieces. **2,** *colloq.* to nag; hound; badger.

загры́зть [*infl. like* **гры́зть**] *v., pfv. of* **загрызáть.**

загрязнéние *n.* **1,** soiling. **2,** pollution; contamination.

загрязнúть *v., pfv. of* **грязнúть** *and* **загрязнять.** —**загрязнúться,** *refl., pfv. of* **грязнúться** *and* **загрязня́ться.**

загрязня́ть *v. impfv.* [*pfv.* **загрязнúть**] **1,** to soil; dirty. **2,** to pollute; contaminate. —**загрязня́ться,** *refl.* to get dirty.

загс *n.* civilian registry office (*abbr. of* **зáпись áктов граждáнского состоя́ния**).

загубúть *v. pfv.* [*infl.* **-гублю́, -гýбишь**] *colloq.* **1,** to ruin. **2,** to squander.

загуля́ть *v. pfv., colloq.* to go on a spree. —**загуля́ться,** *refl., colloq.* **1,** to walk for too long a time. **2,** to carouse till one forgets the time.

загустéть *v., pfv. of* **густéть.**

зад [*2nd loc.* **задý;** *pl.* **зады́**] *n.* **1,** back; rear. **2,** behind; backside. **3,** rump; buttocks. **4,** *pl., colloq.* old stuff: повторя́ть зады́, to repeat old stuff; say what has been said many times before. *See also* **зáдом.**

задáбривать *v. impfv.* [*pfv.* **задóбрить**] **1,** to bring around; win over. **2,** to cajole; coax.

задавáть *v. impfv.* [*pfv.* **задáть;** *pres.* **-даю́, -даёшь**] **1,** to ask (a question); pose (a problem). **2,** to assign (a lesson, task, etc.). **3,** to set (the tone, fashion, etc.). **4,** *colloq.* to give; throw (a party, banquet, etc.). **5,** *colloq.* to give; administer (a scolding, punishment, etc.). —**задавáться,** *refl.* **1,** *in* задавáться цéлью (+ *inf.*), to set as one's goal. **2,** *in* задáться вопрóсом, to ask oneself a question. **3,** *colloq.* (*usu. neg.*) (not) turn out well. **4,** [*impfv. only*] *colloq.* to put on airs.

задавúть *v., pfv. of* **давúть** (*in senses #5 & #6*).

задáние *n.* task; assignment. —**домáшнее задáние,** homework.

задáривать *v. impfv.* [*pfv.* **задарúть**] **1,** to lavish gifts upon. **2,** *obs.* to bribe; "buy off".

задарúть [*infl.* **-дарю́, -дáришь**] *v., pfv. of* **задáривать.**

задáром *adv., colloq.* = **дáром.**

задáток [*gen.* **-тка**] *n.* **1,** deposit; down payment. **2,** *pl.* makings: задáтки хорóшего писáтеля, the makings of a good writer.

задáть [*infl. like* **дать;** *past* **зáдал, задалá, зáдало**] *v., pfv. of* **задавáть.** —**задáться,** *refl.* [*past* **задáлся, задалáсь, задалóсь**] *pfv. of* **задавáться.**

задáча *n.* **1,** task. **2,** (arithmetical) problem.

задáчник *n.* book of arithmetical problems.

задвигáть *v. impfv.* [*pfv.* **задвúнуть**] **1,** to push; slide (in, under, *or* behind). **2,** to close; slide shut. **3,** to close off. **4,** to draw (a curtain). **5,** to bolt (a door). —**задвигáться,** *refl.* **1,** to slide into place. **2,** [*impfv. only*] to be movable; slide.

задвúжка [*gen. pl.* **-жек**] *n.* bolt; catch (*for a door, gate, etc.*).

задвижнóй *adj.* sliding.

задвúнуть *v., pfv. of* **задвигáть.** —**задвúнуться,** *refl., pfv. of* **задвигáться.**

задвóрки [*gen.* **-рок**] *n. pl.* area behind a house. —**на задвóрках,** in the background.

задевáть *v. impfv.* [*pfv.* **задéть**] **1,** to brush against; graze. **2,** *v.i.* (*with* **за** + *acc.*) catch (on); snag (on). **3,** to affect. **4,** to touch; affect (*emotionally*). **5,** to arouse; whet (one's curiosity); hurt; wound (one's pride). **6,** *colloq.* to hurt; offend. —**задевáть за живóе,** to cut to the quick.

задéл *n., colloq.* **1,** beginning; start. **2,** reserve; margin.

задéлывать *v. impfv.* [*pfv.* **задéлать**] to close; seal up (a hole, crack, breach, etc.).

задёргать *v. pfv.* **1,** (*with instr.*) to tug at; give a tug. **2,** *colloq.* to wear out (a horse) by continually tugging at the reins. **3,** *colloq.* to harass.

задёргивать *v. impfv.* [*pfv.* **задёрнуть**] **1,** to draw (a curtain). **2,** to cover with a curtain.

задеревенéлый *adj., colloq.* stiff; numb.

задеревенéть *v. pfv., colloq.* to become numb; become stiff.

задержáние *n.* **1,** detention; arrest. **2,** retention (*of moisture, urine, etc.*).

задержáть [*infl.* **-держý, -дéржишь**] *v., pfv. of* **задéрживать.** —**задержáться,** *refl., pfv. of* **задéрживаться.**

задéрживать *v. impfv.* [*pfv.* **задержáть**] **1,** to delay; detain; hold up. **2,** to withhold; hold back. **3,** to arrest; detain. **4,** to retain (moisture). —**задéрживаться,** *refl.* **1,** to be delayed. **2,** to linger.

задéржка [*gen. pl.* **-жек**] *n.* delay. —**без задéржек,** without interruption.

задёрнуть *v., pfv. of* **задёргивать.**

задéть [*infl.* **-дéну, -дéнешь**] *v., pfv. of* **задевáть.**

задúра *n.m. & f., colloq.* roughneck; bully.

задирáть *v. impfv.* [*pfv.* **задрáть**] *colloq.* **1,** to lift up; stick up. **2,** [*impfv. only*] to tease; pick on. **3,** *in* **задирáть нос,** to turn up one's nose; put on airs. —**задирáться,** *refl.* [*impfv. only*] *colloq.* to pick a fight. *See also* **задрáть.**

задненёбный *adj.* velar.

заднепрохóдный *adj.* anal.

зáдний *adj.* rear; back; hind. —**зáдняя мысль,** ulterior motive. —**зáдний план,** background. —**зáдний прохóд,** anus. —**зáдним умóм крéпок,** wise after the event. —**зáдний ход,** reverse motion: дать зáдний ход, to go into reverse; back up; *fig.* reverse oneself. —**зáдним числóм,** later; afterwards; after the fact. —**помéтить зáдним числóм,** to backdate.

зáдник *n.* **1,** back (*of a shoe*). **2,** *theat.* backdrop.

задóбрить *v., pfv. of* **задáбривать.**

задóк [*gen.* **-дкá**] *n.* back (*of a vehicle, piece of furniture, or shoe*).

задóлго *adv.* [*usu.* **задóлго до**] long before.

задолжáть *v. pfv., colloq.* **1,** to borrow. **2,** to owe.

задóлженность *n.f.* indebtedness; debts.

за́дом *adv.* **1,** backward; backwards. **2,** (*with* **к**) with one's back to. —**за́дом напере́д,** *see* **напере́д.**
задо́р *n.* ardor; zeal; fervor.
задо́ринка *n., in* **ни/без сучка́, ни/без задо́ринки,** without a hitch.
задо́рный *adj.* **1,** ardent; passionate. **2,** lively; sprightly.
задохну́ться *v.r., pfv. of* **задыха́ться.**
задра́ивать *v. impfv.* [*pfv.* **задра́ить**] to batten down.
задрапирова́ть *v., pfv. of* **драпирова́ть.**
задра́ть *v. pfv.* [*infl. like* **драть**] **1,** *pfv. of* **задира́ть. 2,** to tear (the skin); break (a nail). **3,** to tear to pieces; kill. **4,** to whip; flog.
задрема́ть *v. pfv.* [*infl.* **-дремлю́, -дре́млешь**] to doze off.
задрожа́ть *v. pfv.* [*infl.* **-жу́, -жи́шь**] to begin to tremble; begin to shiver.
задува́ть *v. impfv.* [*pfv.* **заду́ть**] **1,** (*of the wind*) to begin to blow. **2,** [*impfv. only*] (*of the wind*) (*with a prep.*) A, *v.i.* to blow (into, through, etc.). B, *v.t.* to blow (something somewhere). **3,** to blow out (a candle).
заду́мать *v., pfv. of* **заду́мывать.** —**заду́маться,** *refl., pfv. of* **заду́мываться.**
заду́мчивый *adj.* thoughtful; pensive. —**заду́мчивость,** *n.f.* pensiveness; deep thought.
заду́мывать *v. impfv.* [*pfv.* **заду́мать**] **1,** to plan; conceive. **2,** to decide on; (*with inf.*) decide to. **3,** to think of; choose (*e.g.* a number in a game). —**заду́мываться,** *refl.* **1,** (*with* **над** *or* **о**) to ponder; meditate (over). **2,** to be lost in thought. **3,** to hesitate.
заду́ть [*infl.* **-ду́ю, -ду́ешь**] *v., pfv. of* **задува́ть.**
задуше́вный *adj.* **1,** sincere; heartfelt. **2,** intimate; innermost.
задуши́ть *v., pfv. of* **души́ть.**
задыми́ть *v. pfv.* [*infl.* **-млю́, -ми́шь**] **1,** to begin to emit smoke. **2,** to blacken with smoke.
задымлённый *adj.* smoky.
задыха́ться *v.r. impfv.* [*pfv.* **задохну́ться**] **1,** to gasp for breath; pant. **2,** to choke (*with anger, tears, etc.*). **3,** to suffocate.
заеда́ть *v. impfv.* [*pfv.* **зае́сть**] **1,** to chew to death; nibble to death. **2,** to take away the taste of (something) by eating something else: зае́сть лека́рство са́харом, to take sugar with the medicine. **3,** *fig.* to torment; harass. **4,** *fig.* to corrupt. **5,** *impers.* to stick; jam: ключ в замке́ зае́ло, the key stuck in the lock.
зае́зд *n.* **1,** visit; call. **2,** horse race.
зае́здить *v. pfv.* [*infl.* **-е́зжу, -е́здишь**] *colloq.* to overwork; wear out.
заезжа́ть *v. impfv.* [*pfv.* **зае́хать**] **1,** (*with* **в** + *acc. or* **к**) to stop in at; drop in on. **2,** (*with* **за** + *instr.*) to pick up; call for. **3,** (*with* **в** + *acc.*) to drive into (*accidentally*). **4,** to approach (from a certain direction).
зае́зженный *adj., colloq.* **1,** (*of a horse*) worn out. **2,** *fig.* hackneyed; trite.
зае́зжий *adj.* visiting; touring. —*n.* person passing through.
заём [*gen.* **за́йма**] *n.* loan. —**заёмщик,** *n.* borrower.
зае́сть [*infl. like* **есть**] *v., pfv. of* **заеда́ть.**
зае́хать [*infl.* **-е́ду, -е́дешь**] *v., pfv. of* **заезжа́ть.**
зажа́рить *v., pfv. of* **жа́рить.** —**зажа́риться,** *refl., pfv. of* **жа́риться.**
зажа́ть [*infl.* **-жму́, -жмёшь**] *v., pfv. of* **зажима́ть.**
зажда́ться *v.r. pfv.* [*infl. like* **ждать**] (*with gen.*) *colloq.* to get tired of waiting (for).
заже́чь [*infl. like* **жечь**] *v., pfv. of* **зажига́ть.** —**заже́чься,** *refl., pfv. of* **зажига́ться.**
зажива́ть *v. impfv.* [*pfv.* **зажи́ть**] to heal. —**зажива́ться,** *refl., colloq.* to live too long.
заживля́ть *v. impfv.* [*pfv.* **заживи́ть**] *colloq.* to heal (a wound).
за́живо *adv., used only with verbs of burying,* alive: хорони́ть за́живо, to bury alive.
зажига́лка [*gen. pl.* **-лок**] *n.* cigarette lighter.
зажига́ние *n.* **1,** lighting; act of lighting. **2,** *mech.* ignition.
зажига́тельный *adj.* **1,** incendiary. **2,** *fig.* fiery; inflammatory; incendiary.
зажига́ть *v. impfv.* [*pfv.* **заже́чь**] **1,** to light (a lamp *or* match); turn on (a light). **2,** *fig.* to fire up. **3,** *fig.* to kindle; spark; ignite (emotions). —**зажига́ться,** *refl.* **1,** (*of a match*) to light; (*of lights*) go to; (*of stars*) come out. **2,** (*with instr.*) (*of one's eyes*) to light up; blaze (with an emotion). **3,** (*of emotions*) to be aroused.
зажи́м *n.* **1,** clamp. **2,** *electricity* terminal.
зажима́ть *v. impfv.* [*pfv.* **зажа́ть**] **1,** to squeeze; clutch; grip. **2,** to stop up; block up; plug up. **3,** to hold (one's nose). **4,** *fig., colloq.* to stifle; suppress.
зажи́точный *adj.* prosperous; affluent; well-to-do. —**зажи́точность,** *n.f.* prosperity; affluence.
зажи́ть *v. pfv.* [*infl.* **-живу́, -живёшь;** *past* **за́жил, зажила́, за́жило**] **1,** *pfv. of* **зажива́ть. 2,** to begin to live: зажи́ть споко́йной жи́знью, to begin to live a quiet life. —**зажи́ться,** *refl.* [*past* **зажи́лся, -ла́сь, -ло́сь**] *pfv. of* **зажива́ться.**
зажму́рить *v., pfv. of* **жму́рить.** —**зажму́риться,** *refl., pfv. of* **жму́риться.**
зазва́ть [*infl. like* **звать**] *v., pfv. of* **зазыва́ть.**
зазвони́ть *v. pfv.* to begin to ring.
заздра́вный *adj., in* **заздра́вный тост,** toast to someone's health.
зазева́ться *v.r. pfv.* (*with* **на** + *acc.*) *colloq.* to stare (at); gape (at).
зазелене́ть *v. pfv.* to turn green.
заземле́ние *n., electricity* ground connection.
заземля́ть *v. impfv.* [*pfv.* **заземли́ть**] *electricity* to ground.
зазимова́ть *v. pfv.* [*infl.* **-му́ю, -му́ешь**] to winter; spend the winter.
зазнава́ться *v.r. impfv.* [*pfv.* **зазна́ться;** *pres.* **-зна́юсь, -знаёшься**] *colloq.* to get a swelled head.
зазна́йство *n., colloq.* conceit.
зазна́ться *v.r., pfv. of* **зазнава́ться.**
зазно́ба *n., colloq.* ladylove.
зазо́р *n., mech.* clearance.
зазо́рный *adj., colloq.* shameful.
зазре́ние *n., in* **без зазре́ния со́вести,** without any pangs of conscience; without compunction.
зазу́бренный *adj.* **1,** jagged; notched. **2,** *bot.* serrate(d). **3,** *colloq.* memorized; rote.
зазу́бривать *v. impfv.* [*pfv.* **зазубри́ть**] **1,** to notch; make notches in. **2,** *colloq.* to learn by rote.
зазу́брина *n.* notch.
зазубри́ть *v., pfv. of* **зубри́ть** *and* **зазу́бривать.**
зазыва́ть *v. impfv.* [*pfv.* **зазва́ть**] *colloq.* to invite repeatedly; urge to come.
заигра́ть *v. pfv.* **1,** *pfv. of* **заи́грывать. 2,** to begin to play.

заигрывание *n.* flirting; *pl.* advances.
заигрывать *v. impfv.* [*pfv.* **заиграть**] **1,** to wear out (cards, records, etc.) by playing. **2,** to make trite by repetition; play to death. **3,** [*impfv. only*] (*with* **с** + *instr.*) *colloq.* to flirt (with); play up to. —**заигрываться,** *refl.* to become absorbed in playing.
заика *n.m. & f.* stutterer.
заикание *n.* stutter; stuttering.
заикаться *v.r. impfv.* [*pfv.* **заикнуться**] **1,** [*impfv. only*] to stammer; stutter. **2,** (*with* **о**) *colloq.* to mention; breathe a word of.
заимодавец [*gen.* **-вца**] *n., obs.* moneylender.
заимствование *n.* borrowing.
заимствовать *v. impfv. & pfv.* [*pfv. also* **позаимствовать;** *pres.* **-ствую, -ствуешь**] to borrow; adopt; incorporate.
заиндеветь *v., pfv. of* **индеветь.**
заинтересованность *n.f.* interest.
заинтересованный *adj.* **1,** (*with* **в** + *prepl.*) interested (in). **2,** interested; concerned: заинтересованные стороны, the interested parties; the parties concerned.
заинтересовать *v. pfv.* [*infl.* **-сую, -суешь**] to interest; arouse the interest of. —**заинтересоваться,** *refl.* (*with instr.*) to become interested (in).
заинтриговать *v., pfv. of* **интриговать.**
заискивать *v. impfv.* (with **перед**) to try to ingratiate oneself (with); curry favor (with).
зайти [*infl.* **зайду, зайдёшь;** *past* **зашёл, зашла, зашло**] *v., pfv. of* **заходить.**
зайчик *n.* **1,** *dim. of* **заяц. 2,** *colloq.* spot of reflected light.
закабалять *v. impfv.* [*pfv.* **закабалить**] to enslave.
закавказский *adj.* Transcaucasian.
закадычный *adj., in* **закадычный друг,** *colloq.* bosom friend.
заказ *n.* order. —**на заказ,** (made) to order.
заказать [*infl.* **-кажу, -кажешь**] *v., pfv. of* **заказывать.**
заказной *adj., in* **заказное письмо,** registered letter.
заказчик *n.* customer.
заказывать *v. impfv.* [*pfv.* **заказать**] to order; place an order for.
закал *n.* **1,** tempering; hardening. **2,** toughness. **3,** *fig.* cast; stamp; breed: человек старого закала, man of the old school.
закалённый *adj.* tempered; hardened. —**закалённый в боях,** battle-hardened.
закалить *v., pfv. of* **закалять.** —**закалиться,** *refl., pfv. of* **закаляться.**
закалка *n.* **1,** hardening; tempering. **2,** *fig.* toughness.
закалывать *v. impfv.* [*pfv.* **заколоть**] **1,** to stab to death. **2,** to slaughter (an animal). **3,** to fasten with a pin.
закалять *v. impfv.* [*pfv.* **закалить**] **1,** to temper; harden. **2,** *fig.* to steel; inure. —**закаляться,** *refl.* **1,** to harden; become hard. **2,** *fig.* to become strong; become inured.
заканчивать *v. impfv.* [*pfv.* **закончить**] to finish. —**заканчиваться,** *refl.* to end; be over.
закапать *v. pfv.* **1,** to spot; stain. **2,** to begin to drip.
закапывать *v. impfv.* [*pfv.* **закопать**] **1,** to bury. **2,** to fill in (a hole).
закармливать *v. impfv.* [*pfv.* **закормить**] to overfeed; stuff.
закат *n.* **1,** sunset. **2,** *fig.* decline. —**на закате дней,** in one's declining years; in the twilight of one's life.
закатать *v., pfv. of* **закатывать**[1].
закатить [*infl.* **-качу, -катишь**] *v., pfv. of* **закатывать**[2]. —**закатиться,** *refl., pfv. of* **закатываться.**
закатывать[1] *v. impfv.* [*pfv.* **закатать**] **1,** (*with* **в** + *acc.*) to roll (in); roll up (in). **2,** *colloq.* to roll up (one's sleeves).
закатывать[2] *v. impfv.* [*pfv.* **закатить**] **1,** to roll; wheel (into, under, behind, etc.). **2,** *colloq.* to cause; create (a scandal); make (a scene). —**закатить глаза,** to roll up one's eyes. —**закатить истерику,** *colloq.* to go into hysterics.
закатываться *v.r. impfv.* [*pfv.* **закатиться**] **1,** to roll (into, under, behind, etc.). **2,** (*of the sun*) to set; go down.
закачать *v. pfv.* **1,** to rock to sleep. **2,** *impers.* to feel sick; feel nauseous (*from rocking or swaying*); меня закачало, I feel sick. **3,** to begin to shake.
закашлять *v. pfv.* to begin to cough. —**закашляться,** *refl.* to have a fit of coughing.
закаяться, *v.r. pfv.* [*infl.* **-каюсь, -каешься**] (*with inf.*) *colloq.* to swear off; swear never to do again.
заквасить [*infl.* **-шу, -сишь**] *v., pfv. of* **заквашивать.**
закваска *n.* **1,** leaven; ferment. **2,** *fig.* mold: одной закваски, of the same mold. **3,** *fig.* stuff: у него хорошая закваска, he is made of good stuff.
заквашивать *v. impfv.* [*pfv.* **заквасить**] to leaven; ferment.
закидывать[1] *v. impfv.* [*pfv.* **закидать**] = **забрасывать.**[1] —**шапками закидаем,** *colloq.* we'll win easily; we've got it won.
закидывать[2] *v. impfv.* [*pfv.* **закинуть**] = **забрасывать**[2]. —**закинуть словечко за** (+ *acc.*), to put in a word for. —**закинуть удочку,** to drop a hint; put out a feeler.
закипать *v. impfv.* [*pfv.* **закипеть**] **1,** to begin to boil; simmer. **2,** *fig.* (*with instr.*) to be seething (with). **3,** *fig.* to become agitated; become wrought up. **4,** *fig.* to get rolling; move into high gear.
закисать *v. impfv.* [*pfv.* **закиснуть**] **1,** to turn sour. **2,** *fig., colloq.* to become apathetic; become listless.
закиснуть [*past* **-кис, -ла**] *v., pfv. of* **закисать.**
закись *n.f.* protoxide. ♦*In compounds* —ous oxide: закись железа, ferrous oxide.
заклад *n., obs.* **1,** pawning: в закладе, in hock. **2,** bet; wager. —**биться об заклад,** to bet; wager.
закладка [*gen. pl.* **-док**] *n.* **1,** laying. **2,** bookmark.
закладная *n., decl. as an adj.* mortgage.
закладчик *n., obs.* **1,** mortgagor. **2,** one who has pawned something. **3,** pawnbroker.
закладывать *v. impfv.* [*pfv.* **заложить**] **1,** to put; place (*usually deep into something*). **2,** (*with* **за** + *acc.*) to put behind; place behind. **3,** to lay (mines, a foundation, etc.). **4,** to mark (a place in a book). **5,** to pawn; mortgage. **6,** to harness. **7,** (*with instr.*) to load (with); pile (with). **8,** to stop up; block. *See also* **заложить.**
заклевать [*infl.* **-клюю, -клюёшь**] *v., pfv. of* **заклёвывать.**
заклёвывать *v. impfv.* [*pfv.* **заклевать**] **1,** to peck to death. **2,** *fig., colloq.* to nag; harass.
заклеивать *v. impfv.* [*pfv.* **заклеить**] **1,** to seal up. **2,** to seal (an envelope). —**заклеиваться,** *refl.* to stick: конверт не заклеивается, the envelope doesn't stick.
заклеймить *v., pfv. of* **клеймить.**
заклепать *v., pfv. of* **заклёпывать.**

заклёпка [*gen. pl.* **-пок**] *n.* rivet.
заклёпывать *v. impfv.* [*pfv.* **заклепа́ть**] to rivet.
заклина́ние *n.* **1,** incantation. **2,** entreaty.
заклина́тель *n.m.* conjurer. —**заклина́тель змей,** snake charmer.
заклина́ть *v. impfv.* **1,** to bewitch; cast a spell over. **2,** to entreat; implore.
закли́нивать *v. impfv.* [*pfv.* **заклини́ть**] **1,** to wedge. **2,** to jam (a device, machine, etc.). **3,** *impers.* to jam; become jammed: дверь заклини́ло, the door jammed. —**закли́ниваться,** *refl.* **1,** to become wedged. **2,** to jam; become jammed.
заключа́ть *v. impfv.* [*pfv.* **заключи́ть**] **1,** to conclude; close; end. **2,** to conclude (a deal, peace, etc.); sign (a treaty, agreement, etc.); form (an alliance). **3,** to enclose: заключи́ть в ско́бки, to enclose in brackets. **4,** [*impfv. only*] (*often with* **в себе́**) to contain. **5,** to conclude; infer; gather. **6,** to imprison; confine; incarcerate. —**заключа́ться,** *refl.* [*impfv. only*] **1,** to conclude; close; end. **2,** (*of an agreement*) to be concluded; be signed. **3,** to be enclosed. **4,** (*with* **в** + *prepl.*) to be; consist of; lie in.
заключе́ние *n.* **1,** conclusion: прийти́ к заключе́нию, to come to/arrive at/ a conclusion. **2,** conclusion; end. **3,** signing (*of a treaty, agreement, etc.*). **4,** imprisonment; confinement. —**в заключе́ние,** in conclusion; in closing.
заключённый *n., decl. as an adj.* prisoner.
заключи́тельный *adj.* concluding; closing; final.
заключи́ть *v., pfv. of* **заключа́ть.**
закля́тие *n., obs.* **1,** incantation. **2,** oath; pledge.
закля́тый *adj.* (*of an enemy*) sworn: закля́тый враг, sworn enemy; archenemy.
закова́ть [*infl.* **-кую́, -куёшь**] *v., pfv. of* **зако́вывать.**
зако́вывать *v. impfv.* [*pfv.* **закова́ть**] to chain; shackle.
закола́чивать *v. impfv.* [*pfv.* **заколоти́ть**] *colloq.* **1,** to board up; seal up. **2,** to hammer in; drive in. **3,** to beat up; beat the life out of.
заколдо́ванный *adj.* charmed; bewitched; enchanted. —**заколдо́ванный круг,** vicious circle.
заколдова́ть [*infl.* **-ду́ю, -ду́ешь**] *v., pfv. of* **заколдо́вывать.**
заколдо́вывать *v. impfv.* [*pfv.* **заколдова́ть**] **1,** to cast a spell over. **2,** *fig.* to bewitch; charm.
зако́лка [*gen. pl.* **-лок**] *n., colloq.* **1,** bobby pin. **2,** tiepin.
заколоти́ть *v. pfv.* [*infl.* **-лочу́, -ло́тишь**] **1,** *pfv. of* **закола́чивать. 2,** to begin to knock.
заколо́ть [*infl.* **-колю́, -ко́лешь**] *v., pfv. of* **коло́ть** (*in sense #5*) *and* **зака́лывать.**
зако́н *n.* law. —**объяви́ть вне зако́на,** to outlaw.
зако́нник *n., colloq.* **1,** expert in law. **2,** one who strictly observes the law.
законнорождённый *adj.* (*of a child*) legitimate.
зако́нность *n.f.* legality; legitimacy.
зако́нный *adj.* **1,** legal; lawful; legitimate. **2,** legitimate; justifiable.
законове́д *n.* specialist in law; jurist. —**законове́дение,** *n.* jurisprudence.
законода́тель *n.m.* **1,** legislator; lawmaker. **2,** arbiter: законода́тель мод, arbiter of fashions.
законода́тельный *adj.* legislative. —**законода́тельство,** *n.* legislation.
закономе́рный *adj.* natural; regular; in accordance with the laws of nature. —**закономе́рность,** *n.f.* regularity; pattern; rule.
законопа́тить *v., pfv. of* **конопа́тить.**
законоположе́ние *n.* statute.
законопослу́шный *adj.* law-abiding.
законопрое́кт *n.* (legislative) bill.
законсерви́ровать *v., pfv. of* **консерви́ровать.**
законтрактова́ть *v., pfv. of* **контрактова́ть.**
зако́нченность *n.f.* completeness.
зако́нченный *adj.* **1,** complete; finished. **2,** (*of an artist, musician, etc.*) finished; accomplished; consummate.
зако́нчить *v., pfv. of* **зака́нчивать.** —**зако́нчиться,** *refl., pfv. of* **зака́нчиваться.**
закопа́ть *v., pfv. of* **зака́пывать.**
закопте́лый *adj.* sooty.
закопте́ть *v. pfv., colloq.* to become covered with soot.
закопти́ть *v., pfv. of* **копти́ть** (*in sense #1*). —**закопти́ться,** *refl.* to become covered with soot.
закорене́лый *adj.* **1,** chronic; ingrained; deep-rooted. **2,** inveterate; hardened; confirmed.
закорене́ть *v. pfv.* **1,** to become ingrained. **2,** (*with* **в** + *prepl.*) to become steeped in (prejudice, sin, etc.).
зако́рки *n. pl., colloq., in* **на зако́рки; на зако́рках,** on one's back; on one's shoulders; piggyback.
закорми́ть [*infl.* **-кормлю́, -ко́рмишь**] *v., pfv. of* **зака́рмливать.**
закорю́чка [*gen. pl.* **-чек**] *n., colloq.* **1,** hook; squiggle. **2,** trick; ploy. **3,** hitch; snag.
закосне́лый *adj.* **1,** inveterate; confirmed. **2,** ingrained; deep-seated.
закостене́лый *adj.* numb; stiff.
закостене́ть *v. pfv.* to become numb; become stiff.
закоу́лок [*gen.* **-у́лка**] *n.* **1,** back street. **2,** nook: все закоу́лки, every nook and cranny.
закочене́лый *adj.* frozen stiff; numb.
закочене́ть *v., pfv. of* **кочене́ть.**
закра́дываться *v.r. impfv.* [*pfv.* **закра́сться**] (*of feelings, doubts, etc.*) to creep in.
закра́сить [*infl.* **-шу, -сишь**] *v., pfv. of* **закра́шивать.**
закра́сться [*infl. like* **красть**] *v.r., pfv. of* **закра́дываться.**
закра́шивать *v. impfv.* [*pfv.* **закра́сить**] to paint over; cover over.
закрепи́тель *n.m., photog.* fixing agent.
закрепи́ть [*infl.* **-плю́, -пи́шь**] *v., pfv. of* **закрепля́ть.**
закрепле́ние *n.* **1,** fastening; securing. **2,** consolidation. **3,** *photog.* fixing.
закрепля́ть *v. impfv.* [*pfv.* **закрепи́ть**] **1,** to fasten; secure. **2,** to consolidate. **3,** (*with* **за** + *instr.*) to assign (to); set aside (for). Закрепи́ть за собо́й (+ *acc.*), to get; obtain; secure for oneself. **4,** *photog.* to fix.
закрепоща́ть *v. impfv.* [*pfv.* **закрепости́ть**] to enslave.
закрепоще́ние *n.* enslavement.
закрича́ть *v. pfv.* [*infl.* **-чу́, -чи́шь**] to cry out; shout; scream; yell.
закро́йщик *n.* cutter (*of cloth*).
за́кром [*pl.* **закрома́**] *n.* (grain) bin.
закругле́ние *n.* **1,** rounding; curving. **2,** curve.
закругля́ть *v. impfv.* [*pfv.* **закругли́ть**] to round off.
закружи́ть *v. pfv.* [*infl.* **-кружу́, -кру́жишь** *or* **-кружи́шь**] **1,** to begin to twirl/swirl/whirl; set spinning. **2,** to make dizzy. —**закружи́ться,** *refl.* **1,** to begin to whirl/swirl. **2,** to be dizzy; be in a whirl.

закрути́ть [*infl.* **-кручу́, -кру́тишь**] *v., pfv. of* **крути́ть** (*in sense #1*) *and* **закру́чивать.** —**закрути́ться,** *refl., pfv. of* **закру́чиваться.**

закру́чивать *v. impfv.* [*pfv.* **закрути́ть**] **1,** to twist. **2,** to twirl (one's mustache). **3,** (*with* **на** + *acc.*) to wind (around *or* onto). —**закру́чиваться,** *refl.* to become twisted.

закрыва́ть *v. impfv.* [*pfv.* **закры́ть**] **1,** to close; shut. **2,** to lock. **3,** to turn off; shut off (water, gas, etc.). **4,** to close down. **5,** to adjourn (a meeting). **6,** to cover. —**закрыва́ться,** *refl.* **1,** to close; shut; be closed; be shut. **2,** to lock: чемода́н закрыва́ется на ключ, the suitcase locks with a key. **3,** to cover oneself. **4,** (*of a meeting*) to adjourn.

закры́лок [*gen.* **-лка**] *n.* flap (*of an aircraft wing*).

закры́тие *n.* **1,** closing; shutting. **2,** close; end.

закры́тый *adj.* closed. —**закры́тый бассе́йн,** indoor pool. —**закры́тое голосова́ние,** secret ballot. —**закры́тое мо́ре,** inland sea. —**закры́тое пла́тье,** high-necked dress.

закры́ть [*infl.* **-кро́ю, -кро́ешь**] *v., pfv. of* **закрыва́ть.** —**закры́ться,** *refl., pfv. of* **закрыва́ться.**

закули́сный *adj.* occurring behind the scenes; backstage; offstage.

закупа́ть *v. impfv.* [*pfv.* **закупи́ть**] to buy up.

закупи́ть [*infl.* **-куплю́, -ку́пишь**] *v., pfv. of* **закупа́ть.**

заку́пка *n.* purchase.

заку́поривать *v. impfv.* [*pfv.* **заку́порить**] to plug up; stop up; cork.

заку́порка *n.* **1,** plugging up; stopping up. **2,** *med.* embolism; thrombosis; occlusion.

заку́почный *adj.* purchase (*attrib.*); purchasing.

заку́пщик *n.* (wholesale) buyer.

заку́ривать *v. impfv.* [*pfv.* **закури́ть**] **1,** *v.t.* to light (a cigarette, cigar, etc.). **2,** *v.i.* to light up; light a cigarette.

закури́ть *v. pfv.* [*infl.* **-курю́, -ку́ришь**] **1,** *pfv. of* **заку́ривать. 2,** to begin to smoke; take up smoking.

закуси́ть [*infl.* **-кушу́, -ку́сишь**] *v., pfv. of* **заку́сывать.**

заку́ска [*gen. pl.* **-сок**] *n.* **1,** snack; bite. **2,** hors d'oeuvre; appetizer.

заку́сочная *n., decl. as an adj.* snack bar.

заку́сывать *v. impfv.* [*pfv.* **закуси́ть**] **1,** to have a snack; have a bite to eat. **2,** (*with instr.*) to have (with); eat *or* drink (with): закуси́ть во́дку селёдкой, to have some vodka with one's herring. **3,** to bite. —**закуси́ть губу́** *or* **гу́бы,** to bite one's lip. —**закуси́ть язы́к,** to hold one's tongue. —**закуси́ть удила́,** to take the bit in one's teeth.

заку́тать *v., pfv. of* **ку́тать** *and* **заку́тывать.** —**заку́таться,** *refl., pfv. of* **ку́таться** *and* **заку́тываться.**

заку́тывать *v. impfv.* [*pfv.* **заку́тать**] (*with instr. or* **в** + *acc.*) to wrap (in); bundle (in). —**заку́тываться,** *refl.* (*with instr. or* **в** + *acc.*) to wrap/bundle oneself (in).

зал *n.* hall. —**а́ктовый зал,** assembly hall. —**гимнасти́ческий зал,** gymnasium. —**зал ожида́ния,** waiting room. —**зри́тельный зал,** auditorium. —**по́лный зал,** full house; packed house. —**чита́льный зал,** reading room.

за́ла *n., obs.* = **зал.**

зала́дить *v. pfv.* [*infl.* **-жу, -дишь**] *colloq.* **1,** to keep repeating. **2,** (*with inf.*) to take to (doing something). —**зала́дить одно́ и то же,** to harp on the same string.

зала́мывать *v. impfv.* [*pfv.* **заломи́ть**] **1,** to break (*by bending*). **2,** *colloq.* to charge (an exorbitant price). —**зала́мывать ру́ки,** to bend one's arms; twist one's arms. —**зала́мывать ша́пку,** to cock one's hat.

залата́ть *v., pfv. of* **лата́ть.**

зала́ять *v. pfv.* [*infl.* **-ла́ю, -ла́ешь**] to begin to bark.

залега́ть *v. impfv.* [*pfv.* **зале́чь**] **1,** to lie down (*for a long rest*). **2,** to lie low. **3,** to lie; be located (*in a low place*). **4,** *fig.* to become ingrained.

заледене́лый *adj.* **1,** covered with ice; icy. **2,** frozen; icy.

заледене́ть *v., pfv. of* **ледене́ть.**

залежа́лый *adj., colloq.* **1,** lying unused *or* unsold. **2,** stale.

залёживаться *v.r. impfv.* [*pfv.* **залежа́ться**] **1,** to lie around (unused *or* unsold). **2,** to become stale.

за́лежный *adj.* (*of land*) long fallow.

за́лежь *n.f.* **1,** (mineral) deposit. **2,** *pl.* accumulation. **3,** fallow land. **4,** *colloq.* unsold or unsalable merchandise.

залеза́ть *v. impfv.* [*pfv.* **зале́зть**] **1,** (*with* **на** + *acc.*) to climb; climb onto. **2,** (*with* **в** + *acc.*) to climb in; climb into. **3,** (*with* **под** + *acc.*) to climb under. **4,** (*with* **в** + *acc.*) *colloq.* to get into. —**зале́зть в долги́,** to get into debt. —**зале́зть в ду́шу,** *see* **влезть в ду́шу.** —**зале́зть в карма́н** (+ *dat.*), to pick the pocket of; rob.

зале́зть [*infl. like* **лезть**] *v., pfv. of* **залеза́ть.**

залени́ться *v.r. pfv.* [*infl.* **-леню́сь, -ле́нишься**] *colloq.* to become lazy.

залепи́ть [*infl.* **-леплю́, -ле́пишь**] *v., pfv. of* **залепля́ть.**

залепля́ть *v. impfv.* [*pfv.* **залепи́ть**] **1,** to seal up. **2,** to cover; plaster.

залета́ть *v. impfv.* [*pfv.* **залете́ть**] **1,** (*with* **в** + *acc.*) to fly into. **2,** (*with* **в** + *acc.*) to stop briefly (in); land briefly (in). **3,** (*with* **за** + *acc.*) to fly over; fly beyond.

залете́ть [*infl.* **-чу́, -ти́шь**] *v., pfv. of* **залета́ть.**

залётный *adj.* stray: залётная пу́ля, stray bullet. —**залётная пти́ца,** migratory bird.

зале́чивать *v. impfv.* [*pfv.* **залечи́ть**] **1,** to heal (a wound, sore, etc.). **2,** *colloq.* to doctor (someone) to death. —**зале́чиваться,** *refl. (of a wound)* to heal.

залечи́ть [*infl.* **-лечу́, -ле́чишь**] *v., pfv. of* **зале́чивать.** —**залечи́ться,** *refl., pfv. of* **зале́чиваться.**

зале́чь [*infl. like* **лечь**] *v., pfv. of* **залега́ть.**

зали́в *n.* bay; gulf.

залива́ть *v. impfv.* [*pfv.* **зали́ть**] **1,** (*of water, a river, etc.*) to flood. **2,** to stain (*by spilling something*): зали́ть ска́терть вино́м, to spill wine on the tablecloth. **3,** to douse (a fire). **4,** (*with instr.*) to cover (with); pave (with). **5,** *colloq.* to pour in; put in (gas, oil, etc.). **6,** *fig.* (*with instr.*) to suffuse (in); bathe (in): зали́тый со́лнцем, bathed in sunlight. —**залива́ться,** *refl.* **1,** (*with instr.*) to be filled; be covered (with a liquid). **2,** *fig.* (*with instr.*) to burst into; break into (tears, laughter, song, etc.). **3,** (*with* **в** + *acc.*) (*of liquids*) to run into; get into.

заливно́е *n., decl. as an adj.* aspic.

заливно́й *adj.* **1,** flood (*attrib.*): заливны́е по́ймы, flood plains; заливно́й луг, water meadow. **2,** jellied: заливна́я осетри́на, jellied sturgeon.

зализа́ть [*infl.* **-лижу́, -ли́жешь**] *v., pfv. of* **зали́зывать.**

зали́зывать *v. impfv.* [*pfv.* **зализа́ть**] **1,** to lick (a wound). **2,** *colloq.* to slick down (one's hair).

зали́ть [*infl. like* **лить;** *past* **за́лил** *or* **зали́л, залила́, за́лило** *or* **зали́ло**] *v., pfv. of* **залива́ть.** —**зали́ться,**

refl. [*past* зали́лся, залила́сь, залило́сь *or* зали́лось] *pfv. of* залива́ться.

залихва́тский *adj., colloq.* rollicking; devil-may-care.

зало́г *n.* **1,** pawning: отдава́ть в зало́г, to pawn. **2,** deposit; security. **3,** (*with gen.*) pledge (of): token (of). **4,** (*with gen.*) guarantee (of); key (to). **5,** *gram.* voice.

зало́говый *adj.* pawn (*attrib.*); mortgage (*attrib.*): зало́говая квита́нция, pawn ticket.

залогода́тель *n.m.* one who pawns or mortgages something.

залогодержа́тель *n.m.* pawnbroker.

заложи́ть *v. pfv.* [*infl.* -ложу́, -ло́жишь] **1,** *pfv. of* закла́дывать. **2,** *colloq.* to mislay. **3,** *impers.* (*with dat.*) *colloq., indicating a stuffy or heavy feeling:* мне заложи́ло нос/грудь, my nose is stuffed up; I feel a heaviness in my chest.

зало́жник *n.* hostage.

заломи́ть [*infl.* -ломлю́, -ло́мишь] *v., pfv. of* зала́мывать.

залп *n.* volley; salvo.

за́лпом *adv.* **1,** in one volley. **2,** *colloq.* without stopping; without pausing for breath; (*with verbs of drinking*) in one gulp; (*with verbs of reading*) in one stretch.

залуча́ть *v. impfv.* [*pfv.* залучи́ть] *colloq.* to entice; lure.

залюбова́ться *v.r. pfv.* [*infl.* -бу́юсь, -бу́ешься] (*with instr.*) to gaze with admiration (at); be lost in contemplation (of).

зама́зать [*infl.* -ма́жу, -ма́жешь] *v., pfv. of* зама́зывать.

зама́зка *n.* putty.

зама́зывать *v. impfv.* [*pfv.* зама́зать] **1,** to paint over. **2,** *fig., colloq.* to cover up; conceal. **3,** to seal up; putty. **4,** to smear; soil; dirty.

зама́лчивать *v. impfv.* [*pfv.* замолча́ть] *colloq.* to keep (something) quiet; keep quiet about; hush up.

зама́нивание *n.* enticing; enticement.

зама́нивать *v. impfv.* [*pfv.* замани́ть] to entice; lure; decoy.

замани́ть [*infl.* -маню́, -ма́нишь] *v., pfv. of* зама́нивать.

зама́нчивый *adj.* tempting; enticing; alluring.

замара́ть *v., pfv. of* мара́ть (*in sense #1*). —**замара́ться,** *refl., pfv. of* мара́ться.

замара́шка [*gen. pl.* -шек] *n., colloq.* slob.

замарино́вать *v., pfv. of* марино́вать.

замаскиро́ванный *adj.* **1,** masked. **2,** disguised; camouflaged.

замаскирова́ть *v., pfv. of* маскирова́ть. —**замаскирова́ться,** *refl., pfv. of* маскирова́ться.

зама́сливать *v. impfv.* [*pfv.* зама́слить] **1,** to spill oil or grease on. **2,** to treat with oil. **3,** *fig., colloq.* to butter up. —**зама́сливаться,** *refl.* to become soiled with oil or grease.

зама́тывать *v. impfv.* [*pfv.* замота́ть] *colloq.* **1,** to wind around *or* onto. **2,** (*with instr.*) to wrap (in *or* with). **3,** to wear out; tire out. —**зама́тываться,** *refl., colloq.* **1,** (*with* вокру́г) to be wound around. **2,** (*with instr.*) to wrap oneself (in). **3,** to be worn out.

зама́хиваться *v.r. impfv.* [*pfv.* замахну́ться] (*with instr. and* на + *acc.*) to threaten (with); brandish; wave: замахну́ться ножо́м на кого́-нибудь, to threaten someone with a knife.

зама́чивать *v. impfv.* [*pfv.* замочи́ть] **1,** to get (something) wet. **2,** to soak.

зама́шки *n. pl.* [*sing.* -ма́шка] *colloq.* ways; manner.

зама́щивать *v. impfv.* [*pfv.* замости́ть] to pave.

замедле́ние *n.* **1,** slowing down; deceleration. **2,** *obs.* delay.

заме́дленный *adj.* slow; slowed; slowed-down. —**заме́дленного де́йствия,** delayed-action (*attrib.*): бо́мба заме́дленного де́йствия, time bomb.

замедля́ть *v. impfv.* [*pfv.* заме́длить] **1,** to slow down. **2,** to delay. **3,** (*with inf. or* с + *instr.*) to be slow (in); be long (in). —**замедля́ться,** *refl.* to slow down; become slower.

заме́на *n.* **1,** substitution; replacement. **2,** substitute.

замени́мый *adj.* replaceable.

замени́тель *n.m.* substitute: замени́тель ко́жи, leather substitute.

замени́ть [*infl.* -меню́, -ме́нишь] *v., pfv. of* заменя́ть.

заменя́ть *v. impfv.* [*pfv.* замени́ть] **1,** (*with instr.*) to replace (with). **2,** to replace; take the place of; substitute for.

замере́ть [*infl.* -мру́, -мрёшь; *past* за́мер, замерла́, за́мерло] *v., pfv. of* замира́ть.

замерза́ние *n.* freezing.

замерза́ть *v. impfv.* [*pfv.* замёрзнуть] **1,** to freeze; become frozen. **2,** (*of a person*) to be freezing (cold); be frozen. **3,** to freeze to death; perish from the frost.

замёрзнуть [*past* -мёрз, -ла] *v., pfv. of* мёрзнуть *and* замерза́ть.

за́мертво *adv.* unconscious; in a dead faint.

замеси́ть [*infl.* -мешу́, -ме́сишь] *v., pfv. of* заме́шивать (*in sense #2*).

замести́ [*infl. like* мести́] *v., pfv. of* замета́ть[1].

замести́тель *n.m.* **1,** substitute; replacement. **2,** deputy: замести́тель дире́ктора, deputy director.

замести́ть [*infl.* -щу́, -сти́шь] *v., pfv. of* замеща́ть.

замета́ть[1] *v. impfv.* [*pfv.* замести́] **1,** (*with* в + *acc.*) to sweep; sweep into. **2,** (*of snow*) to cover. *Also impers.:* доро́гу замело́ сне́гом, the road is covered/blocked with snow. —**замета́ть следы́,** to cover up one's tracks; cover up the traces.

замета́ть[2] *v., pfv. of* замётывать.

замета́ться *v.r. pfv.* [*infl.* -мечу́сь, -ме́чешься] **1,** to begin rushing about. **2,** to begin tossing about (*in bed*). **3,** to become confused; become flustered.

заме́тить [*infl.* -чу, -тишь] *v., pfv. of* замеча́ть.

заме́тка [*gen. pl.* -ток] *n.* **1,** mark. **2,** note: путевы́е заме́тки, travel notes. **3,** notice; item (*in a newspaper*). —**брать на заме́тку,** to take/make note of.

заме́тно *adv.* noticeably; visibly: он заме́тно постаре́л, he has aged visibly. —*adj., used predicatively* noticeable: э́то едва́ заме́тно, it is hardly noticeable.

заме́тный *adj.* noticeable; visible; appreciable; marked.

замётывать *v. impfv.* [*pfv.* замета́ть] to baste.

замеча́ние *n.* **1,** remark; observation; comment. **2,** reprimand; rebuke.

замеча́тельно *adv.* **1,** remarkably. **2,** marvelously. —*adj., used predicatively* wonderful; marvelous: э́то замеча́тельно, that's wonderful.

замеча́тельный *adj.* remarkable; wonderful; marvelous.

замеча́ть *v. impfv.* [*pfv.* заме́тить] **1,** to notice. **2,** to note; make note of. **3,** to remark; comment; observe.

замечта́ться *v.r. pfv.* to fall to thinking; lapse into daydreaming.

замеша́тельство *n.* confusion; embarrassment.

замеша́ть *v., pfv. of* **заме́шивать** (*in sense #1*). —**замеша́ться,** *refl., pfv. of* **заме́шиваться.**

заме́шивать *v. impfv.* **1,** [*pfv.* **замеша́ть**] (*with* **в** + *acc.*) to mix up (in); implicate (in). **2,** [*pfv.* **замеси́ть**] to knead. —**заме́шиваться,** *refl.* [*pfv.* **замеша́ться**] **1,** to get lost: замеша́ться в толпе́/толпу́, to get lost in the crowd. **2,** (*with* **в** + *acc.*) to get mixed up (in); become implicated (in).

заме́шкаться *v.r. pfv., colloq.* to tarry; linger.

замеща́ть *v. impfv.* [*pfv.* **замести́ть**] **1,** to replace. **2,** to fill (a position). **3,** [*impfv. only*] to substitute for; fill in for.

замеще́ние *n.* **1,** substitution; replacement. **2,** filling (*of a position*).

замини́ровать *v., pfv. of* **мини́ровать.**

зами́нка [*gen. pl.* **-нок**] *n., colloq.* **1,** hitch; delay. **2,** hesitation (*in speech*).

замира́ние *n.* dying down. —**с замира́нием се́рдца,** with a sinking heart; with one's heart in one's mouth.

замира́ть *v. impfv.* [*pfv.* **замере́ть**] **1,** to freeze; stand motionless. **2,** *fig.* to come to a standstill. **3,** (*of a sound*) to die down. **4,** (*of one's heart*) to sink. **5,** [*impfv. only*] (*of one's voice*) to falter.

за́мкнутый *adj.* **1,** withdrawn; tight-lipped; close-mouthed. **2,** exclusive. **3,** secluded.

замкну́ть *v., pfv. of* **замыка́ть.** —**замкну́ться,** *refl., pfv. of* **замыка́ться.**

замоги́льный *adj.* **1,** *obs.* occurring after death. **2,** *colloq.* (*of a voice*) sepulchral.

за́мок [*gen.* **за́мка**] *n.* castle.

замо́к [*gen.* **-мка́**] *n.* lock. —**за семью́ замка́ми, 1,** guarded day and night. **2,** a deep dark secret. —**под замко́м,** under lock and key.

замо́лвить *v. pfv.* [*infl.* **-влю, -вишь**] *colloq., in* **замо́лвить сло́во** (*or* **слове́чко**) **за** (+ *acc.*), to put in a word for.

замолка́ть *v. impfv.* [*pfv.* **замо́лкнуть**] **1,** to fall silent. **2,** (*of noise, sounds, conversation, etc.*) to die away; stop; cease.

замо́лкнуть [*past* **-мо́лк, -ла**] *v., pfv. of* **замолка́ть.**

замолча́ть *v. pfv.* [*infl.* **-чу́, -чи́шь**] **1,** to stop talking; fall silent. **2,** *pfv. of* **зама́лчивать.**

замора́живание *n.* freezing.

замора́живать *v. impfv.* [*pfv.* **заморо́зить**] to freeze.

замори́ть *v. pfv., colloq.* **1,** *pfv. of* **мори́ть** (*in sense #2*). **2,** to starve. **3,** to assuage (one's hunger, appetite, etc.). —**замори́ть червяка́,** *colloq.* to have a bite to eat.

заморо́женный *adj.* **1,** frozen. **2,** icy; iced-up. **3,** *fig.* (*of a person, one's face, etc.*) cold; icy.

заморо́зить [*infl.* **-жу, -зишь**] *v., pfv. of* **замора́живать.**

за́морозки [*gen.* **-ков**] *n.pl.* light frost (*in spring or autumn*).

замо́рский *adj., obs.* foreign; from overseas.

замо́рыш *n., colloq.* puny creature; starveling.

замости́ть [*infl.* **-щу́, -сти́шь**] *v., pfv. of* **зама́щивать.**

замота́ть *v., pfv. of* **зама́тывать.** —**замота́ться,** *refl., pfv. of* **зама́тываться.**

замочи́ть [*infl.* **-мочу́, -мо́чишь**] *v., pfv. of* **мочи́ть** *and* **зама́чивать.**

замо́чный *adj.* of a lock. —**замо́чная сква́жина,** keyhole.

замполи́т *n.* deputy chief for political indoctrination.

за́муж *adv.* **1,** *in* **выходи́ть за́муж за** (+ *acc.*), (*of a woman*) to marry; get married (to). **2,** *in* **выдава́ть** (+ *acc.*) **за́муж за** (+ *acc.*), to marry off (a daughter) to.

за́мужем *adv.* (*with* **за** + *instr.*) (*of a woman*) married (to).

заму́жество *n.* marriage (*of a woman*).

заму́жняя *adj.* (*of a woman*) married.

замурова́ть [*infl.* **-ру́ю, -ру́ешь**] *v., pfv. of* **замуро́вывать.**

замуро́вывать *v. impfv.* [*pfv.* **замурова́ть**] to wall up.

замусо́ливать *v. impfv.* [*pfv.* **замусо́лить**] *colloq.* to soil.

замути́ть *v., pfv. of* **мути́ть** (*in sense #1*). —**замути́ться,** *refl., pfv. of* **мути́ться.**

заму́чить *v. pfv.* **1,** to torture to death. **2,** to torment; rack; wear out. —**заму́читься,** *refl.* to be exhausted.

за́мша *n.* suede; chamois. —**за́мшевый,** *adj.* suede.

замше́лый *adj.* moss-grown.

замыва́ть *v. impfv.* [*pfv.* **замы́ть**] to wash off; wash out.

замыка́ние *n.* locking; closing. —**коро́ткое замыка́ние,** short circuit.

замыка́ть *v. impfv.* [*pfv.* **замкну́ть**] **1,** *obs.* to lock. **2,** to close. **3,** to ring; surround. **4,** [*impfv. only*] *in* **замыка́ть ше́ствие,** to bring up the rear. —**замыка́ться,** *refl.* **1,** *obs.* to lock; be locked; lock oneself in. **2,** to close. **3,** *fig.* (*with* **в** + *acc. or prepl.*) to withdraw (into): замыка́ться в себе́, to withdraw into oneself.

за́мысел [*gen.* **-сла**] *n.* **1,** design; intention. **2,** idea; conception.

замы́слить *v., pfv. of* **замышля́ть.**

замыслова́тый *adj.* **1,** intricate; ingenious. **2,** abstruse; recondite. **3,** elaborate; fancy.

замы́ть [*infl.* **-мо́ю, -мо́ешь**] *v., pfv. of* **замыва́ть.**

замышля́ть *v. impfv.* [*pfv.* **замы́слить**] to plan; contemplate.

замя́ть *v. pfv.* [*infl.* **-мну́, -мнёшь**] *colloq.* to hush up; suppress. —**замя́ться,** *refl., colloq.* **1,** to become flustered. **2,** to stumble (*in speech*).

за́навес *n.* curtain.

занаве́сить [*infl.* **-шу, -сишь**] *v., pfv. of* **занаве́шивать.**

занаве́ска [*gen. pl.* **-сок**] *n.* (window) curtain.

занаве́шивать *v. impfv.* [*pfv.* **занаве́сить**] to curtain.

зана́шивать *v. impfv.* [*pfv.* **занosи́ть**] to wear out.

занемо́чь *v. pfv.* [*infl. like* **мочь**] *obs.* to be taken ill.

занесе́ние *n.* entering; recording.

занести́ [*infl. like* **нести́**] *v., pfv. of* **заноси́ть**[1]. —**занести́сь,** *refl., pfv. of* **заноси́ться.**

занижа́ть *v. impfv.* [*pfv.* **зани́зить**] to set (goals, norms, etc.) too low.

занима́тельный *adj.* entertaining; diverting.

занима́ть *v. impfv.* [*pfv.* **заня́ть**] **1,** to occupy. **2,** to take; take up (time, space, etc.). **3,** to entertain; keep amused. **4,** to borrow. —**занима́ться,** *refl.* **1,** (*with instr.*) to be occupied (with); be engaged (in). **2,** (*with instr.*) to go in for; take up. **3,** [*impfv. only*] to study: он меша́ет мне занима́ться, he is preventing me from studying. **4,** [*impfv. only*] (*with instr.*) to study (a certain subject). **5,** [*impfv. only*] (*with* **с** + *instr.*) to give special instruction to. **6,** to catch fire.

за́ново *adv.* all over again; anew.

зано́за *n.* splinter.
зано́зистый *adj., colloq.* **1,** rough; jagged. **2,** *fig.* abrasive.
занози́ть *v. pfv.* [*infl.* **-жу́, -зи́шь**] (*usu. with* **себе́**) to get a splinter in: занози́ть себе́ па́лец, to get a splinter in one's finger.
зано́с *n.* drift: сне́жный зано́с, snowdrift.
заноси́ть[1] *v. impfv.* [*pfv.* **занести́**; *pres.* **-ношу́, -но́сишь**] **1,** to bring; carry. **2,** to drop off; deliver (*on one's way*). **3,** (*with* **в** + *acc.*) to enter (on a list, in the minutes, etc.). **4,** to raise (*in order to strike with or put somewhere*). **5,** *impers.* to become covered with: доро́гу занесло́ сне́гом, the road is covered with snow. **6,** *impers.* to skid: маши́ну занесло́, the car skidded. —**заноси́ться,** *refl., colloq.* **1,** to get carried away. **2,** to get a swelled head.
заноси́ть[2] [*infl.* **-ношу́, -но́сишь**] *v., pfv. of* **зана́шивать.**
зано́счивый *adj.* arrogant. —**зано́счивость,** *n.f.* arrogance.
зано́шенный *adj.* worn; threadbare.
занумерова́ть *v., pfv. of* **нумерова́ть.**
заня́тие *n.* **1,** occupation (*act of occupying*). **2,** occupation; work. **3,** *pl.* studies; lessons. **4,** pastime.
заня́тный *adj., colloq.* amusing; entertaining.
занято́й *adj.* busy.
за́нятость *n.f.* **1,** being busy; pressure of work. **2,** *econ.* employment: по́лная за́нятость, full employment.
за́нятый *adj.* [*short form* **за́нят, занята́, за́нято**] **1,** busy. **2,** occupied.
заня́ть [*infl.* **займу́, займёшь;** *past* **за́нял, заняла́, за́няло**] *v., pfv. of* **занима́ть.** —**заня́ться,** *refl.* [*past* **занялся́, -ла́сь, -ло́сь**] *pfv. of* **занима́ться.**
заодно́ *adv.* **1,** jointly; together; in concert. **2,** *colloq.* at the same time. —**быть заодно́ с,** to be in agreement with; be at one with.
заокеа́нский *adj.* located across the ocean; transoceanic.
заострённый *adj.* sharp; pointed.
заостря́ть *v. impfv.* [*pfv.* **заостри́ть**] **1,** to sharpen. **2,** *fig.* to emphasize; point up. **3,** *fig.* to make more pointed. **4,** *in* заостря́ть внима́ние, to focus attention. —**заостря́ться,** *refl.* **1,** to taper off. **2,** *fig.* to become more acute.
зао́чник *n.* student taking correspondence courses.
зао́чно *adv.* **1,** in absentia: суди́ться зао́чно, to be tried in absentia. **2,** by correspondence.
зао́чный *adj.* **1,** in absentia. **2,** by correspondence: зао́чные ку́рсы, correspondence courses.
за́пад *n.* **1,** west. **2,** *cap.* the West.
запада́ть *v. impfv.* [*pfv.* **запа́сть**] **1,** to become hollow; become sunken. **2,** (*of piano keys*) to stick. **3,** (*with* **в** + *acc.*) *colloq.* to fall into. **4,** (*with* **в** + *acc.*) *fig.* to become ingrained in (one's memory, heart, etc.).
за́падный *adj.* western; West; westerly.
западня́ [*gen. pl.* **-не́й**] *n.* trap.
запа́здывание *n.* **1,** tardiness; lateness. **2,** time lag.
запа́здывать *v. impfv.* [*pfv.* **запозда́ть**] to be late.
запа́ивать *v. impfv.* [*pfv.* **запая́ть**] to solder.
запа́йка *n.* soldering.
запакова́ть [*infl.* **-ку́ю, -ку́ешь**] *v., pfv. of* **запако́вывать.**
запако́вывать *v. impfv.* [*pfv.* **запакова́ть**] to pack; pack up.
запа́л *n.* **1,** primer; fuse. **2,** *colloq.* ardor. **3,** heaves (*disease of horses*).
запали́ть *v. pfv., colloq.* to set fire to.
запа́льный *adj., in* **запа́льная свеча́,** spark plug.
запа́льчивый *adj.* hot-tempered; quick-tempered; explosive. —**запа́льчивость,** *n.f.* quick temper.
запанибра́та *adv., colloq.* as equals; on equal terms.
запа́ривать *v. impfv.* [*pfv.* **запа́рить**] to steam.
запарши́веть *v., pfv. of* **парши́веть.**
запа́рывать *v. impfv.* [*pfv.* **запоро́ть**] to whip to death; flog to death.
запа́с *n.* **1,** supply; stock; reserve. Запа́с зна́ний, fund of knowledge. Запа́с слов, stock of words; vocabulary. Запа́с про́чности, margin of safety. **2,** *mil.* reserve. **3,** *colloq.* hem. —**про запа́с,** as a reserve; in case of need. Держа́ть *or* оставля́ть про запа́с, to hold/keep in reserve.
запаса́ть *v. impfv.* [*pfv.* **запасти́**] to store up. —**запаса́ться,** *refl.* (*with instr.*) **1,** to stock up on. **2,** *in* запаса́ться терпе́нием, to steel oneself.
запа́сливый *adj.* provident.
запа́сник *n., mil., colloq.* reservist.
запасно́й *adj.* spare; reserve. —*n., mil.* reservist.
запа́сный *adj.* = **запасно́й.** —**запа́сный вы́ход,** emergency exit. —**запа́сный путь,** sidetrack; siding.
запасти́ [*infl. like* **пасти́**] *v., pfv. of* **запаса́ть.** —**запасти́сь,** *refl., pfv. of* **запаса́ться.**
запа́сть [*infl. like* **пасть**] *v., pfv. of* **запада́ть.**
за́пах *n.* smell; odor.
запаха́ть [*infl.* **-пашу́, -па́шешь**] *v., pfv. of* **запа́хивать** *(in sense #1).*
запа́хивать *v. impfv.* **1,** [*pfv.* **запаха́ть**] to plow. **2,** [*pfv.* **запахну́ть**] to wrap around oneself.
запа́хнуть *v. pfv.* [*past* **-па́х, -ла**] to begin to smell.
запахну́ть *v., pfv. of* **запа́хивать** (*in sense #2*).
запа́чкать *v., pfv. of* **па́чкать.** —**запа́чкаться,** *refl., pfv. of* **па́чкаться.**
запая́ть *v., pfv. of* **запа́ивать.**
запева́ла *n.m. & f.* **1,** leading singer in a choir. **2,** *fig.* guiding spirit.
запева́ть *v. impfv.* to be the first to sing; lead the singing.
запека́нка *n.* **1,** baked pudding. **2,** spiced brandy.
запека́ть *v. impfv.* [*pfv.* **запе́чь**] to bake. —**запека́ться,** *refl.* **1,** to bake; be baked. **2,** to clot; coagulate. **3,** (*of lips*) to become parched.
запелена́ть *v., pfv. of* **пелена́ть.**
запе́ниться *v.r. pfv.* to begin to foam.
запере́ть [*infl.* **-пру́, -прёшь;** *past* **за́пер, заперла́, за́перло**] *v., pfv. of* **запира́ть.** —**запере́ться,** *refl.* [*past* **заперся́** *or* **за́перся, заперла́сь, заперло́сь** *or* **за́перлось**] *pfv. of* **запира́ться.**
запе́ть *v. pfv.* [*infl.* **-пою́, -поёшь**] to begin to sing; break (*or* burst) into song. —**запе́ть друго́е; запе́ть на друго́й лад,** to change one's tune; sing a different tune.
запеча́тать *v., pfv. of* **запеча́тывать.**
запечатлева́ть *v. impfv.* [*pfv.* **запечатле́ть**] **1,** to set down; record; capture (*in writing, painting, on film, etc.*). **2,** to ingrain (in one's memory). **3,** to mark; commemorate. —**запечатлева́ться,** *refl.* to be stamped; be ingrained.
запеча́тывать *v. impfv.* [*pfv.* **запеча́тать**] to seal.
запе́чь [*infl. like* **печь**] *v., pfv. of* **запека́ть.** —**запе́чься,** *refl., pfv. of* **запека́ться.**

запивáть *v. impfv.* [*pfv.* **запи́ть**] **1,** [*past pfv.* **запи́л**] (*with instr.*) to wash down (with). **2,** [*past pfv.* **зáпил**] *colloq.* to take to drink.

запинáться *v.r. impfv.* [*pfv.* **запнýться**] **1,** (*with* **за** *or* **о** + *acc.*) to stumble (on). **2,** to stumble (*in speech*).

запи́нка *n.* stumbling (*in speech*). —**без запи́нки,** without stumbling once.

запирáтельство *n.* refusal to confess one's guilt.

запирáть *v. impfv.* [*pfv.* **заперéть**] **1,** to lock (a door, room, etc.). **2,** to lock; lock up; lock in (someone or something). **3,** to block. —**запирáться,** *refl.* **1,** to lock oneself in. **2,** (*of a door, lock, etc.*) to lock. **3,** [*impfv. only*] *colloq.* to refuse to admit one's guilt.

записáть [*infl.* **-пишý, -пи́шешь**] *v., pfv. of* **запи́сывать.** —**записáться,** *refl., pfv. of* **запи́сываться.**

запи́ска [*gen. pl.* **-сок**] *n.* **1,** note; short letter: оставля́ть запи́ску, to leave a note. **2,** memorandum. **3,** *pl.* notes.

записнóй *adj.* **1,** intended for notes: записнáя кни́жка, notebook. **2,** *colloq.* a true; real; out-and-out.

запи́сывание *n.* writing down; recording.

запи́сывать *v. impfv.* [*pfv.* **записáть**] **1,** to write down; record. **2,** to take notes of. **3,** (*with* **в** + *acc.*) to enter (in); enroll (in). **4,** (*with* **на** + *acc.*) to record (on film, tape, a phonograph record, etc.). —**запи́сываться,** *refl.* **1,** (*with* **в** *or* **на** + *acc.*) to sign up for; enroll in; join. **2,** (*with* **к**) to make an appointment (with).

зáпись *n.f.* **1,** writing down; recording. **2,** entry; notation. **3,** recording (*on a record, tape, etc.*). **4,** *pl.* notes.

запи́ть [*infl. like* **пить**] *v., pfv. of* **запивáть.**

запи́хивать *v. impfv.* [*pfv.* **запихáть** *or* **запихнýть**] (*with* **в** + *acc.*) *colloq.* to stuff (into); cram (into).

заплáканный *adj.* full of tears; tear-stained.

заплáкать *v. pfv.* [*infl.* **-плáчу, -плáчешь**] to begin to cry.

запланúровать *v., pfv. of* **планúровать** (*in sense #1*).

заплáта *n.* patch.

заплати́ть *v., pfv. of* **плати́ть.**

заплевáть [*infl.* **-плюю́, -плюёшь**] *v., pfv. of* **заплёвывать.**

заплёвывать *v. impfv.* [*pfv.* **заплевáть**] to spit on.

заплéсневелый *adj.* moldy; mildewed.

заплéсневеть *v., pfv. of* **плéсневеть.**

заплести́ [*infl. like* **плести́**] *v., pfv. of* **заплетáть.**

заплетáть *v. impfv.* [*pfv.* **заплести́**] to braid; plait. —**заплетáться,** *refl.* [*impfv. only*] **1,** (*of one's legs*) to wobble. **2,** (*with* **язы́к**): у негó язы́к заплетáется, his speech is slurred.

запломбировáть *v., pfv. of* **пломбировáть.**

заплутáться *v.r. pfv., colloq.* to lose one's way.

заплы́в *n., swimming* heat; lap.

заплывáть *v. impfv.* [*pfv.* **заплы́ть**] **1,** to swim (*to a distant point*). **2,** to be swollen; be bloated.

заплы́ть [*infl. like* **плыть**] *v., pfv. of* **заплывáть.**

запнýться *v.r., pfv. of* **запинáться.**

заповéдник *n.* reserve; preserve.

заповéдный *adj.* **1,** closed; off-limits. **2,** secret. **3,** cherished.

зáповедь *n.f.* **1,** *relig.* commandment. **2,** precept.

заподóзрить *v. pfv.* (*with* **в** + *prepl.*) to (begin to) suspect (of).

запóем *adv., colloq.* avidly; nonstop: читáть запóем, to read avidly; пить запóем, to drink like a fish; кури́ть запóем, to chain-smoke.

запоздáлый *adj.* belated; tardy.

запоздáние *n.* lateness; tardiness.

запоздáть *v., pfv. of* **запáздывать.**

запóй *n.* **1,** addiction to alcohol. **2,** drinking bout.

заползáть *v. impfv.* [*pfv.* **заползти́**] **1,** (*with* **в** + *acc.*) to crawl into. **2,** (*with* **под** + *acc.*) to crawl under.

заползти́ [*infl. like* **ползти́**] *v., pfv. of* **заползáть.**

заполня́ть *v. impfv.* [*pfv.* **запóлнить**] **1,** to fill. **2,** to fill out (a form).

запоминáть *v. impfv.* [*pfv.* **запóмнить**] **1,** to remember; make it a point to remember. **2,** to memorize. —**запоминáться,** *refl., impers.* (*with dat.*) to remain in one's memory.

зáпонка [*gen. pl.* **-нок**] *n.* cuff link; stud.

запóр *n.* **1,** bolt; lock. **2,** constipation.

запорóть [*infl.* **-порю́, -пóрешь**] *v., pfv. of* **запáрывать.**

запороши́ть *v. pfv.* (*of snow, dust, etc.*) to cover lightly.

запотевáть *v. impfv.* [*pfv.* **запотéть**] to become misty; steam up.

запотéлый *adj.* steamed up; misted up.

запотéть *v., pfv. of* **потéть** (*in sense #2*) *and* **запотевáть.**

заправи́ла *n.m., colloq.* **1,** boss; bigwig. **2,** ringleader; instigator.

заправить [*infl.* **-влю, -вишь**] *v., pfv. of* **заправля́ть.** —**заправиться,** *refl., pfv. of* **заправля́ться.**

заправка *n.* **1,** seasoning. **2,** refuelling.

заправля́ть *v. impfv.* [*pfv.* **заправить**] **1,** to tuck in; tuck under. **2,** (*with instr.*) to season (with). **3,** to put fuel in, put gas in. **4,** [*impfv. only*] (*with instr.*) *colloq.* to boss; run. —**заправля́ться,** *refl., colloq.* to take on fuel; refuel.

заправочный *adj.* (re)fueling (*attrib.*): заправочная стáнция, filling station.

заправский *adj., colloq.* real; true; regular.

запрáшивать *v. impfv.* [*pfv.* **запроси́ть**] **1,** (*with* **о**) to inquire (about). **2,** to question (someone). **3,** to charge (a high price).

запрéт *n.* prohibition; ban.

запрети́тельный *adj.* prohibitive.

запрети́ть [*infl.* **-щý, -ти́шь**] *v., pfv. of* **запрещáть.**

запрéтный *adj.* forbidden. —**запрéтная зóна,** forbidden zone; restricted area.

запрещáть *v. impfv.* [*pfv.* **запрети́ть**] **1,** (*with dat.*) to forbid (someone to do something). **2,** to forbid; prohibit; ban; outlaw. **3,** to suppress (a publication). —**запрещáться,** *refl.* [*impfv. only*] to be forbidden; be prohibited.

запрещéние *n.* prohibition; ban.

заприхóдовать *v., pfv. of* **прихóдовать.**

запрограмми́ровать *v., pfv. of* **программи́ровать.**

запроки́дывать *v. impfv.* [*pfv.* **запроки́нуть**] *colloq.* to throw back (one's head).

запрóс *n.* **1,** inquiry. **2,** demand. **3,** *pl.* needs; requirements. **4,** *pl.* aspirations; pretensions. **5,** *colloq.* overcharging.

запроси́ть [*infl.* **-прошý, -прóсишь**] *v., pfv. of* **запрáшивать.**

зáпросто *adv., colloq.* without ceremony; on an informal basis.

запрýда *n.* **1,** weir; dam. **2,** pond; reservoir (*formed by dammed-up water*).

запруди́ть [*infl.* **-пружу́, -пру́дишь** *or* **-пруди́шь**] *v., pfv. of* **пруди́ть** *and* **запру́живать.**
запру́живать *v. impfv.* [*pfv.* **запруди́ть**] **1,** to dam up. **2,** to jam; pack; throng.
запряга́ть *v. impfv.* [*pfv.* **запря́чь**] to harness; hitch up. —**запряга́ться,** *refl.* (*with* **в** + *acc.*) *colloq.* to buckle down to.
запря́жка *n.* **1,** harnessing. **2,** team of horses in harness.
запря́тать [*infl.* **-пря́чу, -пря́чешь**] *v., pfv. of* **запря́тывать.**
запря́тывать *v. impfv.* [*pfv.* **запря́тать**] *colloq.* to hide away; secrete.
запря́чь [*infl.* **-прягу́, -пряжёшь, ...-прягу́т;** *past* **-пря́г, -прягла́, -прягло́**] *v., pfv. of* **запряга́ть.** —**запря́чься,** *refl., pfv. of* **запряга́ться.**
запу́гивание *n.* intimidation.
запу́гивать *v. impfv.* [*pfv.* **запуга́ть**] to intimidate; cow; browbeat.
за́пуск *n.* **1,** starting. **2,** launching.
запуска́ть *v. impfv.* [*pfv.* **запусти́ть**] **1,** to launch; send up; fly (a rocket, balloon, kite, etc.). **2,** (*usu. with instr.*) *colloq.* to throw; hurl: запусти́ть ка́мнем в кого́-нибудь, to throw a stone at someone. **3,** to start; start up (a machine, motor, etc.). **4,** (*with* **в** + *acc.*) *colloq.* to thrust (into); plunge (into). **5,** to neglect.
запусте́лый *adj., obs.* neglected; deserted; abandoned.
запусте́ние *n.* **1,** desolation. **2,** (state of) neglect.
запусти́ть [*infl.* **-пущу́, -пу́стишь**] *v., pfv. of* **запуска́ть.**
запу́танный *adj.* **1,** tangled. **2,** *fig.* intricate; involved: запу́танный вопро́с, knotty problem. —**запу́танность,** *n.f.* confusion.
запу́тать *v., pfv. of* **пу́тать** *and* **запу́тывать.** —**запу́таться,** *refl., pfv. of* **пу́таться** (*in sense #1*) *and* **запу́тываться.**
запу́тывать *v. impfv.* [*pfv.* **запу́тать**] **1,** to tangle. **2,** to muddle; complicate. **3,** *colloq.* to confuse; mix up. **4,** (*with* **в** + *acc.*) *colloq.* to involve (in); embroil (in). —**запу́тываться,** *refl.* **1,** to become (en)tangled. **2,** *fig., colloq.* to become confused; get mixed up.
запуши́ть *v. pfv.* (*of snow, frost, etc.*) to cover lightly.
запу́щенный *adj.* neglected. —**запу́щенность,** *n.f.* neglect.
запыла́ть *v. pfv.* to flare up; burst into flame.
запыли́ть *v., pfv. of* **пыли́ть** (*in sense #2*). —**запыли́ться,** *refl., pfv. of* **пыли́ться.**
запыха́ться *v.r. impfv. & pfv., colloq.* to be out of breath; pant.
запя́стье *n.* **1,** wrist. **2,** *obs.* bracelet.
запята́я *n., decl. as an adj.* comma. —**то́чка с запято́й,** semicolon.
запятна́ть *v., pfv. of* **пятна́ть.**
зараба́тывать *v. impfv.* [*pfv.* **зарабо́тать**] to earn. Хорошо́ зараба́тывать, to earn good money. Зараба́тывать на жизнь, to earn a living; earn one's livelihood. —**зараба́тываться,** *refl., colloq.* to overwork.
зарабо́тать *v. pfv.* **1,** *pfv. of* **зараба́тывать. 2,** to start working. —**зарабо́таться,** *refl., pfv. of* **зараба́тываться.**
за́работный *adj., in* **за́работная пла́та,** wages; pay; salary.
за́работок [*gen.* **-тка**] *n.* earnings; wages; pay.
зара́внивать *v. impfv.* [*pfv.* **заровня́ть**] to fill; even up (a hole).
заража́ть *v. impfv.* [*pfv.* **зарази́ть**] **1,** to infect. **2,** to contaminate; pollute. **3,** *fig.* (*with instr.*) to infect (with); inspire (with). —**заража́ться,** *refl.* (*with instr.*) to become infected (with); catch.
зараже́ние *n.* infection. —**зараже́ние кро́ви,** blood poisoning.
зара́з *adv., colloq.* all at once; at one sitting; in one fell swoop.
зара́за *n.* infection.
зарази́тельный *adj.* infectious; contagious.
зарази́ть [*infl.* **-жу́, -зи́шь**] *v., pfv. of* **заража́ть.** —**зарази́ться,** *refl., pfv. of* **заража́ться.**
зара́зный *adj.* infectious; contagious; communicable.
зара́нее *adv.* beforehand; in advance.
зарапортова́ться *v.r. pfv.* [*infl.* **-ту́юсь, -ту́ешься**] *colloq.* to talk too much; run off at the mouth.
зараста́ть *v. impfv.* [*pfv.* **зарасти́**] **1,** (*with instr.*) to be overgrown (with). **2,** *colloq.* (*of a wound*) to heal.
зарасти́ [*infl. like* **расти́**] *v., pfv. of* **зараста́ть.**
зарва́ться [*infl. like* **рвать**] *v.r., pfv. of* **зарыва́ться** (*in sense #2*).
зарде́ться *v.r. pfv.* to flush with color; blush.
за́рево *n.* glow.
зарегистри́ровать *v., pfv. of* **регистри́ровать.** —**зарегистри́роваться,** *refl., pfv. of* **регистри́роваться.**
заре́з *n., in* **до заре́зу,** urgently; desperately.
заре́зать *v., pfv. of* **ре́зать** (*in sense #5*). —**заре́заться,** *refl., colloq.* to cut one's throat.
зарека́ться *v.r. impfv.* [*pfv.* **заре́чься**] (*with inf.*) *colloq.* to swear off.
зарекомендова́ть *v. pfv.* [*infl.* **-ду́ю, -ду́ешь**] (*with* **себя́** *and instr.*) to prove to be. —**хорошо́ зарекомендова́ть себя́,** to make a good showing; give a good account of oneself.
заре́чный *adj.* located on the other side of the river.
заре́чье *n.* area on the other side of a river.
заре́чься [*infl. like* **отре́чься**] *v.r., pfv. of* **зарека́ться.**
заржа́веть *v., pfv. of* **ржа́веть.**
заржа́вленный *adj.* rusty.
зарисова́ть [*infl.* **-су́ю, -су́ешь**] *v., pfv. of* **зарисо́вывать.**
зарисо́вка [*gen. pl.* **-вок**] *n.* **1,** sketching. **2,** sketch.
зарисо́вывать *v. impfv.* [*pfv.* **зарисова́ть**] to sketch.
за́риться *v.r. impfv.* [*pfv.* **поза́риться**] (*with* **на** + *acc.*) *colloq.* to covet.
зарни́ца *n.* summer lightning; heat lightning.
заровня́ть *v., pfv. of* **зара́внивать.**
зароди́ть [*infl.* **-жу́ -ди́шь**] *v., pfv. of* **зарожда́ть.** —**зароди́ться,** *refl., pfv. of* **зарожда́ться.**
заро́дыш *n.* embryo; fetus. —**подавля́ть в заро́дыше,** to nip in the bud.
заро́дышевый *adj.* embryonic.
зарожда́ть *v. impfv.* [*pfv.* **зароди́ть**] to generate; engender. —**зарожда́ться,** *refl.* to arise; originate; come into being.
зарожде́ние *n.* **1,** generation; engendering. **2,** *fig.* origin.
заро́к *n.* pledge; vow; resolution.
зарони́ть *v. pfv.* [*infl.* **-роню́, -ро́нишь**] **1,** *colloq.* to drop. **2,** *fig.* to arouse; inspire (feelings, thoughts, etc.).
за́росль *n.f., usu. pl.* undergrowth; brushwood.

зарпла́та *n.* wages; pay; salary (*contr. of* **за́работная пла́та**).

заруба́ть *v. impfv.* [*pfv.* **заруби́ть**] **1,** to slash to death; hack to death. **2,** to notch; make a notch in. —**заруби́те себе́ на носу́,** remember for the next time; don't you dare forget.

зарубе́жный *adj.* foreign.

заруби́ть [*infl.* **-рублю́, -ру́бишь**] *v., pfv. of* **заруба́ть.**

зару́бка [*gen. pl.* **-бок**] *n.* notch.

зарубцева́ться *v.r., pfv. of* **рубцева́ться.**

зарумя́нить *v., pfv. of* **румя́нить** (*in sense #2*). —**зарумя́ниться,** *refl., pfv. of* **румя́ниться** (*in sense #2*).

заручи́ться *v.r. pfv.* (*with instr.*) to enlist; secure; obtain (one's support, services, etc.).

зару́чка *n., colloq.* influence; pull.

зарыва́ть *v. impfv.* [*pfv.* **зары́ть**] to bury. —**зарыва́ться,** *refl.* **1,** [*pfv.* **зары́ться**] to bury oneself. **2,** [*pfv.* **зарва́ться**] *colloq.* to go too far; go to extremes; overdo things.

зары́ть [*infl.* **-ро́ю, -ро́ешь**] *v., pfv. of* **зарыва́ть.** —**зары́ться,** *refl., pfv. of* **зарыва́ться.**

заря́ *n.* **1,** glow on the horizon before sunrise or after sunset. **2,** (*often with* **у́тренняя**) dawn; daybreak: на заре́, at dawn. **3,** (*often with* **вече́рняя**) dusk; nightfall. **4,** *fig.* dawn; beginning. **5,** [*acc.* **зо́рю**] *mil.* reveille; taps. —**ни свет ни заря́,** before dawn; at the crack of dawn. —**от зари́ до зари́, 1,** from dawn to dusk. **2,** from night to morn.

заря́д *n.* **1,** (powder) charge. **2,** *electricity* charge. **3,** cartridge. **4,** warhead. **5,** *fig.* (*with gen.*) fund; supply; store.

заряди́ть *v. pfv.* [*infl.* **-ряжу́, -ряди́шь**] **1,** *pfv. of* **заряжа́ть. 2,** *colloq.* to keep repeating. **3,** *colloq.* (*of rain*) to keep coming down.

заря́дка *n.* **1,** loading (*of a gun*); charging (*of a battery*). **2,** exercise(s); calisthenics.

заря́дный *adj.* charging (*attrib.*): заря́дный агрега́т, battery charger. —**заря́дный я́щик,** caisson; ammunition wagon.

заряжа́ние *n.* loading (*of a gun or camera*); charging (*of a battery*).

заряжа́ть *v. impfv.* [*pfv.* **заряди́ть**] to load (a gun, camera, etc.); charge (a battery).

заря́нка [*gen. pl.* **-нок**] *n.* robin.

заса́да *n.* ambush.

засади́ть [*infl.* **-сажу́, -са́дишь**] *v., pfv. of* **заса́живать.**

заса́живать *v. impfv.* [*pfv.* **засади́ть**] **1,** to plant: заса́живать сад цвета́ми, to plant a garden with flowers. **2,** *colloq.* to confine; keep confined (at home, in/to prison, etc.). **3,** (*with* **за** + *acc.*) *colloq.* to sit down (to): заса́живать кого́-нибудь за кни́гу, to sit someone down to a book. **4,** (*with* **в** + *acc.*) *colloq.* to stick; thrust; plunge (something into something).

заса́ливать *v. impfv.* **1,** [*pfv.* **заса́лить**] to soil; get grease on. **2,** [*pfv.* **засоли́ть**] to salt; pickle.

заса́сывать *v. impfv.* [*pfv.* **засоса́ть**] to suck in; swallow up.

заса́харенный *adj.* candied.

засвети́ть *v. pfv.* [*infl.* **-свечу́, -све́тишь**] **1,** to light (a candle, lamp, etc.). **2,** *photog.* to spoil (a roll of film) by exposing it to light. —**засвети́ться,** *refl.* **1,** to (begin to) shine; sparkle. **2,** (*of one's eyes*) to light up. **3,** (*of film*) to be spoiled.

за́светло *adv.* before dark.

засвиде́тельствовать *v. pfv.* [*infl.* **-ствую, -ствуешь**] **1,** to attest (to). **2,** to certify; notarize. —**засвиде́тельствовать почте́ние** (+ *dat.*), *obs.* to pay one's respects to.

засе́в *n.* **1,** sowing. **2,** sown area.

засева́ть *v. impfv.* [*pfv.* **засе́ять**] to sow.

заседа́ние *n.* session; meeting.

заседа́тель *n.m.* (people's) representative.

заседа́ть *v. impfv.* to be in session; meet.

засе́ивать *v. impfv.* = **засева́ть.**

засе́ка *n.* barricade of felled trees.

засека́ть *v. impfv.* [*pfv.* **засе́чь**] **1,** [*past pfv.* **-се́к, -секла́, -секло́**] to notch. **2,** [**-се́к, -секла́, -секло́**] to locate; plot (*on a map*). **3,** [**-се́к, -се́кла, -се́кло**] to whip brutally; flog to death. —**засе́чь вре́мя** [*past fem.* **-секла́**], to note the time.

засекре́ченный *adj.* **1,** secret. **2,** (*of documents*) classified.

засекре́чивать *v. impfv.* [*pfv.* **засекре́тить**] **1,** to classify (as secret). **2,** *colloq.* to give (someone) access to classified documents; clear.

заселе́ние *n.* **1,** settlement (*of an area*). **2,** occupancy (*of a building*).

заселя́ть *v. impfv.* [*pfv.* **засели́ть**] **1,** to populate; settle. **2,** to settle (in); occupy.

засе́сть *v. pfv.* [*infl. like* **сесть**] *colloq.* **1,** (*with* **за** + *acc.*) to sit down (to); settle down to: засе́сть за рабо́ту, to sit down to work. **2,** to ensconce oneself. **3,** (*with* **в** + *prepl.*) (*of a bullet*) to lodge (in).

засе́чка [*gen. pl.* **-чек**] *n.* notch.

засе́чь [*infl. like* **сечь**] *v., pfv. of* **засека́ть.**

засе́ять [*infl.* **-се́ю, -се́ешь**] *v., pfv. of* **засева́ть** *and* **засе́ивать.**

засиде́ться [*infl.* **-жу́сь, -ди́шься**] *v.r., pfv. of* **заси́живаться.**

заси́живаться *v.r. impfv.* [*pfv.* **засиде́ться**] *colloq.* **1,** to sit a long time; sit up late. **2,** *fig.* to remain for a long time.

заси́лье *n.* domination; dominance.

засия́ть *v. pfv.* **1,** to begin to shine. **2,** (*of something bright*) to appear.

заско́к *n., colloq.* quirk; idiosyncrasy.

заскору́злый *adj.* **1,** hardened; calloused. **2,** *fig.* callous.

засла́ть [*infl.* **-шлю́, -шлёшь**] *v., pfv. of* **засыла́ть.**

засло́н *n.* **1,** barrier; screen. **2,** *mil.* covering force.

заслони́ть *v., pfv. of* **заслоня́ть.**

засло́нка [*gen. pl.* **-нок**] *n.* **1,** oven door. **2,** damper.

заслоня́ть *v. impfv.* [*pfv.* **заслони́ть**] **1,** to shield. **2,** *fig.* to overshadow. —**заслоня́ть свет** (+ *dat.*), to stand in someone's light.

заслу́га *n.* **1,** *usu. pl.* services; contribution; accomplishments; achievements. **2,** merit; virtue. —**по заслу́гам,** according to one's deserts; as one deserves. —**получи́ть по заслу́гам,** to get what one deserves; get one's just deserts/reward. —**ста́вить что́-нибудь в заслу́гу** (+ *dat.*), to give (someone) credit for something.

заслу́женно *adv.* deservedly.

заслу́женный *adj.* **1,** deserved; well-earned. **2,** distinguished. **3,** (*in titles*) Honored.

заслу́живать *v. impfv.* (*with gen.*) to deserve; merit; be worthy of.

заслужи́ть *v. pfv.* [*infl.* **-служу́, -слу́жишь**] to deserve; earn; win; gain.

заслу́шивать *v. impfv.* [*pfv.* **заслу́шать**] to listen to; hear (a report, speech, etc.). —**заслу́шиваться,** *refl.* (*with gen.*) to listen (to) with rapt attention.
заслы́шать *v. pfv.* [*infl.* **-шу, -шишь**] to hear; catch the sound of.
засма́тривать *v. impfv.* (*with* **в** + *acc.*) *colloq.* to peep into; peer into.
засма́триваться *v.r. impfv.* [*pfv.* **засмотре́ться**] (*with* **на** + *acc.*) **1,** to be lost in contemplation of. **2,** [*impfv. only*] *colloq.* to stare at; eye.
засмея́ться *v.r. pfv.* [*infl.* **-смею́сь, -смеёшься**] to laugh; begin to laugh.
засмотре́ться [*infl.* **-смотрю́сь, -смо́тришься**] *v.r., pfv. of* **засма́триваться.**
засне́женный *also,* **заснежённый** *adj.* snow-clad; snow-covered.
засну́ть *v., pfv. of* **засыпа́ть**[1].
засня́ть *v. pfv.* [*infl. like* **снять**] to photograph; film; shoot.
засо́в *n.* bolt; bar.
засо́вывать *v. impfv.* [*pfv.* **засу́нуть**] **1,** to stick; thrust. **2,** *colloq.* to put (somewhere and be unable to find).
засо́л *n.* salting; pickling.
засоли́ть [*infl.* **-солю́, -со́лишь** *or* **-соли́шь**] *v., pfv. of* **заса́ливать** (*in sense #2*).
засоре́ние *n.* clogging up. —**засоре́ние желу́дка,** constipation.
засоря́ть *v. impfv.* [*pfv.* **засори́ть**] **1,** to litter. **2,** to clog (up). **3,** to choke (with weeds). **4,** to clutter up. —**засоря́ться,** *refl.* to become clogged.
засоса́ть [*infl.* **-сосу́, -сосёшь**] *v., pfv. of* **заса́сывать.**
засо́хнуть [*past* **-со́х, -ла**] *v., pfv. of* **засыха́ть.**
за́спанный *adj.* sleepy; sleepy-eyed.
заспа́ться *v.r. impfv.* [*infl. like* **спать**] *colloq.* to oversleep.
заста́ва *n.* **1,** gate; gates (*to a city*). **2,** *mil.* security detachment. Пограни́чная заста́ва, frontier post.
застава́ть *v. impfv.* [*pfv.* **заста́ть;** *pres.* **-стаю́, -стаёшь**] to find; catch (*at a certain moment*): заста́ть кого́-нибудь до́ма, to find someone at home. Заста́ть кого́-нибудь врасплóх, to catch someone unawares.
заста́вить [*infl.* **-влю, -вишь**] *v., pfv. of* **заставля́ть.**
заставля́ть *v. impfv.* [*pfv.* **заста́вить**] **1,** to make; force; compel. **2,** to cram; jam; clutter. **3,** to block off; close off.
заста́иваться *v.r. impfv.* [*pfv.* **застоя́ться**] **1,** to stand too long. **2,** to become stale; become stagnant.
застаре́лый *adj.* chronic; inveterate.
заста́ть [*infl.* **-ста́ну, -ста́нешь**] *v., pfv. of* **застава́ть.**
застёгивать *v. impfv.* [*pfv.* **застегну́ть**] to button (up); fasten; hook. —**застёгиваться,** *refl.* **1,** to button; hook. **2,** to button oneself up.
застёжка [*gen. pl.* **-жек**] *n.* clasp; fastener. —**застёжка-мо́лния,** zipper.
застекля́ть *v. impfv.* [*pfv.* **застекли́ть**] to glaze; fit with glass.
засте́нок [*gen.* **-нка**] *n.* torture chamber.
засте́нчивый *adj.* shy; timid; bashful; diffident. —**засте́нчивость,** *n.f.* shyness; timidity; bashfulness; diffidence.
застига́ть *v. impfv.* [*pfv.* **засти́гнуть** *or* **засти́чь**] to catch (unawares); take by surprise.
засти́гнуть [*past* **-сти́г, -ла**] *v., pfv. of* **застига́ть.**
застила́ть *v. impfv.* [*pfv.* **застла́ть**] **1,** to cover. **2,** to cloud; obscure.
засти́рывать *v. impfv.* [*pfv.* **застира́ть**] *colloq.* **1,** to wash out (a spot, stain, etc.). **2,** to ruin in the wash.
засти́чь [*infl. like* **засти́гнуть**] *v., pfv. of* **застига́ть.**
застла́ть [*infl.* **-стелю́, -сте́лешь**] *v., pfv. of* **застила́ть.**
засто́й *n.* **1,** standing still; immobility. **2,** *fig.* stagnation. **3,** *in* засто́й кро́ви, *med.* congestion. —**засто́йный,** *adj.* stagnant.
засто́лье *n., colloq.* meal; repast.
засто́льный *adj.* occurring at the table: засто́льная бесе́да, table talk.
засто́порить *v., pfv. of* **сто́порить.** —**засто́пориться,** *refl., pfv. of* **сто́пориться.**
застоя́ться *v.r., pfv. of* **заста́иваться.**
застра́ивать *v. impfv.* [*pfv.* **застро́ить**] to build up (an area).
застрахова́ть [*infl.* **-ху́ю, -ху́ешь**] *v., pfv. of* **страхова́ть** *and* **застрахо́вывать.** —**застрахова́ться,** *refl., pfv. of* **страхова́ться** *and* **застрахо́вываться.**
застрахо́вывать *v. impfv.* [*pfv.* **застрахова́ть**] to insure. —**застрахо́вываться,** *refl.* to insure oneself; take out insurance.
застра́чивать *v. impfv.* [*pfv.* **застрочи́ть**] to sew up; stitch up.
застра́щивать *v. impfv.* [*pfv.* **застраща́ть**] *colloq.* to intimidate; frighten.
застрева́ть *v. impfv.* [*pfv.* **застря́ть**] to stick; get stuck.
застрели́ть *v. pfv.* [*infl.* **-стрелю́, -стре́лишь**] to shoot; kill. —**застрели́ться,** *refl.* to shoot oneself; kill oneself.
застре́льщик *n.* leader; initiator; pioneer.
застро́ить *v., pfv. of* **застра́ивать.**
застро́йка *n.* building up; development. —**застро́йщик,** *n.* builder; developer.
застрочи́ть *v. pfv.* [*infl.* **-строчу́, -строчи́шь** *or* **-стро́чишь**] **1,** *pfv. of* **застра́чивать. 2,** (*of a machine gun*) to blaze away.
застря́ть [*infl.* **-стря́ну, -стря́нешь**] *v., pfv. of* **застрева́ть.**
застуди́ться *v.r. pfv.* [*infl.* **-стужу́сь, -сту́дишься**] *colloq.* to catch cold.
за́ступ *n.* spade.
заступа́ться *v.r. impfv.* [*pfv.* **заступи́ться**] (*with* **за** + *acc.*) to come to the defense of; stand up for; stick up for.
заступи́ться [*infl.* **-ступлю́сь, -сту́пишься**] *v.r., pfv. of* **заступа́ться.**
засту́пник *n.* defender; intercessor. —**засту́пничество,** *n.* intercession.
застыва́ть *v. impfv.* [*pfv.* **засты́ть**] **1,** to thicken; harden; congeal. **2,** *colloq.* to freeze; be frozen. **3,** *fig.* to freeze: засты́ть от у́жаса, to freeze in horror.
застыди́ть *v. pfv.* [*infl.* **-жу́, -ди́шь**] *colloq.* to shame. —**застыди́ться,** *refl.* to become embarrassed.
засты́ть [*infl.* **-сты́ну, -сты́нешь**] *v., pfv. of* **застыва́ть.**
засу́нуть *v., pfv. of* **засо́вывать.**
за́суха *n.* drought.
засу́чивать *v. impfv.* [*pfv.* **засучи́ть**] to roll up (one's sleeves).
засучи́ть [*infl.* **-сучу́, -су́чишь**] *v., pfv. of* **засу́чивать.**

засу́шивать *v. impfv.* [*pfv.* **засуши́ть**] to dry; press (flowers).
засуши́ть [*infl.* **-сушу́, -су́шишь**] *v., pfv. of* **засу́шивать.**
засу́шливый *adj.* drought-afflicted; arid.
засчи́тывать *v. impfv.* [*pfv.* **засчита́ть**] (*with* **в** + *acc.*) to count (toward); apply (toward). —**засчи́тываться,** *refl.* [*impfv. only*] (*with* **в** + *acc.*) to count (toward); be counted (toward).
засыла́ть *v. impfv.* [*pfv.* **засла́ть**] *colloq.* **1,** to send out (*on a secret mission*). **2,** to send (*far away or to the wrong place*).
засы́пать [*infl.* **-сы́плю, -сы́плешь**] *v., pfv. of* **засыпа́ть.**[2] —**засы́паться,** *refl., pfv. of* **засыпа́ться.**
засыпа́ть[1] *v. impfv.* [*pfv.* **засну́ть**] to fall asleep.
засыпа́ть[2] *v. impfv.* [*pfv.* **засы́пать**] (*with instr.*) **1,** to fill up (with dirt, sand, etc.). **2,** to cover; strew (with dust, papers, etc.). **3,** *fig.* to shower; deluge; bombard (with questions, gifts, etc.).—**засыпа́ться,** *refl.* **1,** (*with* **в** + *acc.*) (*of sand, snow, etc.*) to get into. **2,** (*with instr.*) to be covered (with).
засыха́ть *v. impfv.* [*pfv.* **засо́хнуть**] **1,** to dry up. **2,** to wither.
зата́ивать *v. impfv.* [*pfv.* **затаи́ть**] **1,** *colloq.* to hide; conceal. **2,** to bear; harbor; nurse (a grudge). **3,** to hold (one's breath): затаи́в дыха́ние; с затаённым дыха́нием, with bated breath.
зата́лкивать *v. impfv.* [*pfv.* **затолкну́ть**] *colloq.* to push; shove (into, under, etc.).
зата́пливать *v. impfv.* [*pfv.* **затопи́ть**] to light (a stove).
зата́птывать *v. impfv.* [*pfv.* **затопта́ть**] **1,** to trample down; trample upon. **2,** (*with* **в** + *acc.*) to press into (the ground). **3,** to stamp out (a fire, cigarette, etc.). **4,** *colloq.* to leave footmarks on; track up. —**зата́птывать в грязь,** to drag through the mud.
зата́сканный *adj., colloq.* **1,** worn; worn out; threadbare. **2,** *fig.* trite; hackneyed.
зата́скивать *v. impfv.* **1,** [*pfv.* **затащи́ть**] to drag away; drag off. **2,** [*pfv.* **затаска́ть**] *colloq.* to wear out; *fig.* make trite.
зата́чивать *v. impfv.* [*pfv.* **заточи́ть**] to sharpen.
затащи́ть [*infl.* **-тащу́, -та́щишь**] *v., pfv. of* **зата́скивать** (*in sense #1*).
затвердева́ть *v. impfv.* [*pfv.* **затверде́ть**] to harden; become hard.
затверде́лый *adj.* hardened.
затверде́ние *n.* **1,** hardening. **2,** hard lump.
затверде́ть *v., pfv. of* **тверде́ть** *and* **затвердева́ть.**
затверди́ть *v., pfv. of* **тверди́ть** (*in sense #2*).
затво́р *n.* **1,** *colloq.* bolt (*of a door*). **2,** bolt (*of a gun*); shutter (*of a camera*).
затвори́ть [*infl.* **-творю́, -тво́ришь**] *v., pfv. of* **затворя́ть.** —**затвори́ться,** *refl., pfv. of* **затворя́ться.**
затво́рник *n.* hermit; recluse. —**затво́рнический,** *adj.* of a hermit; solitary. —**затво́рничество,** *n.* solitary life.
затворя́ть *v. impfv.* [*pfv.* **затвори́ть**] to close; shut. —**затворя́ться,** *refl.* **1,** to close; be closed. **2,** to shut oneself in.
затева́ть *v. impfv.* [*pfv.* **зате́ять**] *colloq.* **1,** to start; undertake; launch. **2,** (*with inf.*) to decide (to); make up one's mind (to). **3,** *in* затева́ть недо́брое, to be up to something; be up to no good. —**затева́ться,** *refl., colloq.* **1,** to start. **2,** [*impfv. only*] to be afoot.
зате́йливый *adj.* **1,** elaborate; fancy. **2,** intricate. **3,** clever; ingenious.
зате́йник *n.* **1,** amusing fellow; jokester. **2,** organizer of social activities; social director.
затека́ть *v. impfv.* [*pfv.* **зате́чь**] (*with* **в** + *acc.*) **1,** to leak (into); get (into). **2,** to swell; swell up. **3,** to become numb.
зате́м *adv.* **1,** then; next. **2,** that is why. —**зате́м, что́бы,** to; in order to.
затемне́ние *n.* **1,** darkening. **2,** blackout. **3,** *fig.* obscuring.
затемни́ть *v., pfv. of* **затемня́ть.**
за́темно *adv., colloq.* before dawn; before daybreak; before daylight.
затемня́ть *v. impfv.* [*pfv.* **затемни́ть**] **1,** to darken; black out. **2,** *fig.* to obscure; cloud; blur.
затеня́ть *v. impfv.* [*pfv.* **затени́ть**] to shade; shield.
затере́ть [*infl. like* **тере́ть**] *v., pfv. of* **затира́ть.**
зате́рянный *adj.* lost; forgotten.
затеря́ть *v. pfv., colloq.* to lose; mislay. —**затеря́ться,** *refl., colloq.* **1,** to be lost. **2,** to disappear.
затеса́ться *v.r. pfv.* [*infl.* **-тешу́сь, -те́шешься**] (*with* **в** *or* **на** + *acc.*) *colloq.* to get into; worm one's way into.
зате́чь [*infl. like* **течь**] *v., pfv. of* **затека́ть.**
зате́я *n.* **1,** undertaking; venture. **2,** game; amusement. —**без зате́й** [*often,* **по́просту, без зате́й**], simply; without fanfare.
зате́ять [*infl.* **-те́ю, -те́ешь**] *v., pfv. of* **затева́ть.** —**зате́яться,** *refl., pfv. of* **затева́ться.**
затира́ть *v. impfv.* [*pfv.* **затере́ть**] **1,** to rub out; efface. **2,** to hem in; trap; hold fast. —**затёртый льда́ми,** icebound.
зати́скивать *v. impfv.* [*pfv.* **зати́снуть**] *colloq.* to squeeze in.
затиха́ть *v. impfv.* [*pfv.* **зати́хнуть**] to subside; abate; die down.
зати́хнуть [*past* **-ти́х, -ла**] *v., pfv. of* **затиха́ть.**
зати́шье *n.* calm; lull. —**зати́шье пе́ред грозо́й,** the calm before the storm.
заткну́ть *v., pfv. of* **затыка́ть.** —**заткну́ться,** *refl., colloq.* to shut up: заткни́сь!, shut up!
затмева́ть *v. impfv.* [*pfv.* **затми́ть**] **1,** to obscure. **2,** *fig.* to outshine; overshadow.
затме́ние *n.* eclipse.
затми́ть *v., pfv. of* **затмева́ть.**
зато́ *conj.* but; but then; but on the other hand.
затолка́ть *v. pfv.* **1,** to push; shove. **2,** to jostle; elbow.
затолкну́ть *v., pfv. of* **зата́лкивать.**
зато́н *n.* inlet; creek.
затону́ть *v. pfv.* [*infl.* **-тону́, -то́нешь**] to sink.
затопи́ть [*infl.* **-топлю́, -то́пишь**] *v., pfv. of* **зата́пливать** *and* **затопля́ть.**
затопле́ние *n.* **1,** sinking. **2,** flooding.
затопля́ть *v. impfv.* [*pfv.* **затопи́ть**] **1,** to flood; inundate. **2,** to sink.
затопта́ть [*infl.* **-топчу́, -то́пчешь**] *v., pfv. of* **зата́птывать.**
зато́р *n.* jam (*of people, traffic, etc.*).
затормози́ть *v., pfv. of* **тормози́ть.**
заточа́ть *v. impfv.* [*pfv.* **заточи́ть**] *obs.* to imprison; incarcerate.
заточе́ние *n., obs.* imprisonment; incarceration.
заточи́ть *v. pfv.* **1,** [*infl.* **-точу́, -то́чишь**] *pfv. of* **зата́чивать.** **2,** [*infl.* **-точу́, -точи́шь**] *pfv. of* **заточа́ть.**

затрави́ть *v., pfv. of* **трави́ть** (*in sense #3*).
затра́гивать *v. impfv.* [*pfv.* **затро́нуть**] **1,** (*of a bullet*) to touch; graze. **2,** to affect. **3,** *fig.* to wound (someone's pride). **4,** to touch upon; broach.
затра́та *n.* **1,** expenditure. **2,** *usu. pl.* expenses.
затра́тить [*infl.* **-чу, -тишь**] *v., pfv. of* **затра́чивать.**
затра́чивать *v. impfv.* [*pfv.* **затра́тить**] to spend; expend.
затре́бовать *v. pfv.* [*infl.* **-бую, -буешь**] to request; demand; require; order.
затрепа́ть *v. pfv.* [*infl.* **-треплю́, -тре́плешь**] *colloq.* to wear out.
затре́щина *n., colloq.* box on the ears.
затро́нуть *v., pfv. of* **затра́гивать.**
затрудне́ние *n.* **1,** difficulty. **2,** predicament.
затруднённый *adj.* difficult; labored.
затрудни́тельный *adj.* difficult; awkward; embarrassing.
затрудня́ть *v. impfv.* [*pfv.* **затрудни́ть**] **1,** to bother; trouble; inconvenience. **2,** to hamper; make difficult. —**затрудня́ться,** *refl.* to have difficulty; find it difficult.
затума́нивать *v. impfv.* [*pfv.* **затума́нить**] to cloud; obscure. —**затума́ниваться,** *refl.* **1,** to cloud up; become clouded. **2,** (*of the senses*) to become muddled.
затума́нить *v., pfv. of* **тума́нить** *and* **затума́нивать.** —**затума́ниться,** *refl., pfv. of* **тума́ниться** *and* **затума́ниваться.**
затупи́ть *v., pfv. of* **тупи́ть.** —**затупи́ться,** *refl., pfv. of* **тупи́ться.**
затуха́ть *v. impfv.* [*pfv.* **зату́хнуть**] *colloq.* (*of something burning*) to go out.
зату́хнуть [*past* **-ту́х, -ла**] *v., pfv. of* **затуха́ть.**
затушева́ть [*infl.* **-шу́ю, -шу́ешь**] *v., pfv. of* **тушева́ть** *and* **затушёвывать.**
затушёвывать *v. impfv.* [*pfv.* **затушева́ть**] **1,** to shade; add shading to. **2,** *fig.* to veil; obscure.
затуши́ть *v. pfv.* [*infl.* **-тушу́, -ту́шишь**] *colloq.* **1,** to put out; extinguish. **2,** to suppress.
за́тхлый *adj.* musty.
затыка́ть *v. impfv.* [*pfv.* **заткну́ть**] **1,** to stop up; plug up; cork up. **2,** to stick; thrust. —**заткну́ть за́ пояс,** *colloq.* to outdo; outshine; put to shame.
заты́лок [*gen.* **-лка**] *n.* back of the head. —**в заты́лок,** single file; one behind the other.
заты́лочный *adj.* cervical.
заты́чка [*gen. pl.* **-чек**] *n., colloq.* stopper; plug.
затя́гивать *v. impfv.* [*pfv.* **затяну́ть**] **1,** to tighten; pull tight; draw tight. **2,** (*with instr.*) to cover (with); clothe (in). **3,** to delay; drag out. **4,** to suck in. **5,** (*with* **в** + *acc.*) to draw (into); involve (in). **6,** *colloq.* to strike up (a song). —**затя́гиваться,** *refl.* **1,** to tighten something around oneself: затяну́ться по́ясом, to tighten one's belt. **2,** (*of a wound*) to heal over. **3,** (*of the sky*) to become obscured. **4,** to drag out; last a long time. **5,** to inhale (*when smoking*).
затя́жка [*gen. pl.* **-жек**] *n.* **1,** tightening; drawing. **2,** delay; dragging out. **3,** puff; drag (*on a cigarette*).
затяжно́й *adj.* lengthy; protracted.
затяну́ть [*infl.* **-тяну́, -тя́нешь**] *v., pfv. of* **затя́гивать.** —**затяну́ться,** *refl., pfv. of* **затя́гиваться.**
зау́мный *adj.* abstruse; esoteric; arcane.
зауны́вный *adj.* mournful; plaintive.
заупоко́йный *adj.* for the repose of the dead. Заупоко́йная слу́жба, funeral service.
заупря́миться *v.r., pfv. of* **упря́миться.**
зауря́дный *adj.* ordinary; mediocre.
заусе́ница *n.* **1,** hangnail. **2,** burr (*on metal*).
зау́треня *n.* matins; Morning Prayer.
зау́ченный *adj.* **1,** studied; affected. **2,** mechanical; automatic.
зау́чивать *v. impfv.* [*pfv.* **заучи́ть**] to memorize; learn by heart. —**зау́чиваться,** *refl., colloq.* to study too hard; study too much.
заучи́ть [*infl.* **-учу́, -у́чишь**] *v., pfv. of* **зау́чивать.** —**заучи́ться,** *refl., pfv. of* **зау́чиваться.**
заушá́тельский *adj.* vicious; abusive. —**заушá́тельство,** *n.* vicious criticism; abuse.
зафикси́ровать *v., pfv. of* **фикси́ровать.**
зафрахтова́ть *v., pfv. of* **фрахтова́ть.**
заха́живать *v. impfv., colloq.* to drop in; stop in.
захва́ливать *v. impfv.* [*pfv.* **захвали́ть**] *colloq.* to praise excessively.
захвали́ть [*infl.* **-хвалю́, -хва́лишь**] *v., pfv. of* **захва́ливать.**
захва́т *n.* seizure; capture.
захва́танный *adj., colloq.* soiled by fingering; full of finger marks.
захвата́ть *v., pfv. of* **захва́тывать** (*in sense #6*).
захвати́ть [*infl.* **-хвачу́, -хва́тишь**] *v., pfv. of* **захва́тывать.**
захва́тнический *adj.* (*of a policy*) expansionist; (*of wars*) of conquest.
захва́тчик *n.* invader.
захва́тывать *v. impfv.* [*pfv.* **захвати́ть**] **1,** to seize; capture. **2,** to take (along). **3,** to carry away; thrill; engross. **4,** *colloq.* to catch; take by surprise. **5,** *colloq.* to stop; check (in time). **6,** [*pfv.* **захвата́ть**] *colloq.* to soil (*by fingering*). —**от э́того дух захва́тывает,** it takes one's breath away.
захва́тывающий *adj.* exciting; thrilling; gripping; engrossing; absorbing.
захвора́ть *v. pfv., colloq.* **1,** to be taken ill. **2,** (*with instr.*) to come down with.
захире́ть *v., pfv. of* **хире́ть.**
захлёбываться *v.r. impfv.* [*pfv.* **захлебну́ться**] **1,** to choke. **2,** *fig.* (*with* **от**) to be breathless (with an emotion). **3,** to bog down; peter out. **4,** (*of an engine*) to stall.
захлёстывать *v. impfv.* [*pfv.* **захлестну́ть**] **1,** (*with* **за** + *acc.*) to wind around. **2,** (*with instr.*) to secure (with a rope, lasso, etc.). **3,** (*of water*) to sweep over.
захло́пывать *v. impfv.* [*pfv.* **захло́пнуть**] to slam; slam shut. —**захло́пываться,** *refl.* (*of a door*) to slam shut; close with a bang.
захо́д *n.* stop; call. —**захо́д со́лнца,** sunset.
заходи́ть[1] *v. impfv.* [*pfv.* **зайти́;** *pres.* **-хожу́, -хо́дишь**] **1,** (*with* **в** + *acc.*) to stop (in) at; (*with* **к**) to call on; drop in on. **2,** (*with* **за** + *instr.*) to call for. **3,** (*with* **за** + *acc.*) to go behind. **4,** to go (far). **5,** (*of the sun*) to set. **6,** (*with* **о**) (*of an argument*) to arise (over); (*of a conversation*) to turn (to).
заходи́ть[2] *v. pfv.* [*infl.* **-хожу́, -хо́дишь**] **1,** to begin to walk. **2,** to circulate. **3,** (*of an object*) to begin to shake.
захолу́стный *adj.* **1,** remote; out-of-the-way. **2,** provincial.
захолу́стье *n.* out-of-the-way place.
захорони́ть *v. pfv.* [*infl.* **-роню́, -ро́нишь**] to bury.
захоте́ть *v. pfv.* [*infl. like* **хоте́ть**] to want. —**захоте́ться,** *refl., impers.* (*with dat.*) to want.

захуда́лый *adj.* **1,** impoverished. **2,** insignificant. **3,** *colloq.* (*of a child*) frail; (*of a horse*) run-down.
зацвести́ *v. pfv.* [*infl. like* **цвести́**] to begin to bloom.
зацелова́ть *v. pfv.* [*infl.* **-лу́ю, -лу́ешь**] *colloq.* to smother with kisses.
зацепи́ть [*infl.* **-цеплю́, -це́пишь**] *v., pfv. of* **зацепля́ть.** —**зацепи́ться,** *refl., pfv. of* **зацепля́ться.**
заце́пка [*gen. pl.* **-пок**] *n., colloq.* **1,** hook; peg. **2,** pull; influence; connections. **3,** hitch; catch; snag.
зацепля́ть *v. impfv.* [*pfv.* **зацепи́ть**] **1,** to hook. **2,** (*with* **за** + *acc.*) to catch (on); snag (on). —**зацепля́ться,** *refl.* (*with* **за** + *acc.*) to get caught (on); get snagged (on).
зачаро́ванный *adj.* **1,** enchanted. **2,** bewitched. **3,** spellbound.
зачарова́ть [*infl.* **-ру́ю, -ру́ешь**] *v., pfv. of* **зачаро́вывать.**
зачаро́вывать *v. impfv.* [*pfv.* **зачарова́ть**] to bewitch; charm; enchant; captivate.
зачасти́ть *v. pfv.* [*infl.* **-щу́, -сти́шь**] *colloq.* **1,** to increase in intensity. **2,** to begin to speak rapidly. **3,** (*with* **к**) to begin to visit frequently.
зачасту́ю *adv., colloq.* often; frequently.
зача́тие *n., physiol.* conception.
зача́ток [*gen.* **-тка**] *n.* **1,** embryo. **2,** *usu. pl.* beginning; early stages.
зача́точный *adj.* rudimentary.
зача́ть *v. pfv.* [*infl.* **-чну́, -чнёшь;** *past fem.* **зачала́**] to conceive (a child).
зача́хнуть *v., pfv. of* **ча́хнуть.**
заче́м *adv.* **1,** why?; what for? **2,** why; what ...for: он забы́л, заче́м пришёл, he forgot what he came for. —**вот заче́м,** that's why.
заче́м-то *adv.* for some reason or other.
зачёркивать *v. impfv.* [*pfv.* **зачеркну́ть**] to cross out.
заче́рпывать *v. impfv.* [*pfv.* **зачерпну́ть**] to scoop up; ladle.
зачерстве́лый *adj.* **1,** stale; hard. **2,** *fig.* callous.
зачерстве́ть *v., pfv. of* **черстве́ть** (*in sense #1*).
зачеса́ть *v. pfv.* [*infl.* **-чешу́, -че́шешь**] **1,** *pfv. of* **зачёсывать. 2,** *colloq.* to scratch; begin to scratch (an itch). —**зачеса́ться,** *refl.* to itch; begin to itch.
заче́сть [*infl.* **-чту́, -чтёшь;** *past* **-чёл, -чла́**] *v., pfv. of* **зачи́тывать**[2]. —**заче́сться,** *refl., pfv. of* **зачи́тываться.**
зачёсывать *v. impfv.* [*pfv.* **зачеса́ть**] to comb.
зачёт *n.* test (*in school*).
зачётный *adj.* **1,** test (*attrib.*). **2,** record (*attrib.*): зачётная кни́жка, (student's) record book.
зачина́тель *n.m.* founder; initiator; pioneer.
зачи́нивать *v. impfv.* [*pfv.* **зачини́ть**] *colloq.* **1,** to mend; repair. **2,** to sharpen (a pencil).
зачини́ть [*infl.* **-чиню́, -чи́нишь**] *v., pfv. of* **зачи́нивать.**
зачи́нщик *n.* instigator; ringleader.
зачисле́ние *n.* enrollment.
зачисля́ть *v. impfv.* [*pfv.* **зачи́слить**] **1,** to enroll; take in (a student); hire; take on (an employee). **2,** to enter; record. —**зачисля́ться,** *refl.* to enroll; join.
зачи́тывать[1] *v. impfv.* [*pfv.* **зачита́ть**] **1,** to read out. **2,** *colloq.* to read (a book) until it is tattered. **3,** *colloq.* to fail to return (a borrowed book). —**зачи́тываться,** *refl.* (*with instr.*) *colloq.* to become engrossed in reading (a book, novel, etc.).
зачи́тывать[2] *v. impfv.* [*pfv.* **заче́сть**] **1,** (*with* **в** + *acc.*) to apply (toward). **2,** to accept; pass (academic work). —**зачи́тываться,** *refl.* to count; be counted.
зашага́ть *v. pfv.* to set out on foot.
зашевели́ть *v. pfv.* (*with acc. or instr.*) to (begin to) stir. —**зашевели́ться,** *refl.* **1,** to move slightly; begin to stir. **2,** *colloq.* to begin to take action; begin to move.
зашива́ть *v. impfv.* [*pfv.* **заши́ть**] to sew up; mend.
заши́ть [*infl.* **-шью́, -шьёшь**] *v., pfv. of* **зашива́ть.**
зашифрова́ть *v., pfv. of* **шифрова́ть.**
зашнурова́ть *v., pfv. of* **шнурова́ть.**
зашпаклева́ть *v., pfv. of* **шпаклева́ть.**
зашпи́ливать *v. impfv.* [*pfv.* **зашпи́лить**] to pin; fasten with a pin.
заштемпелева́ть *v., pfv. of* **штемпелева́ть.**
зашто́пать *v., pfv. of* **што́пать.**
заштрихова́ть *v., pfv. of* **штрихова́ть.**
защёлка [*gen. pl.* **-лок**] *n.* latch; catch.
защёлкивать *v. impfv.* [*pfv.* **защёлкнуть**] to snap; snap shut. —**защёлкиваться,** *refl.* to snap shut.
защеми́ть *v. pfv.* [*infl.* **-млю́, -ми́шь**] **1,** *pfv. of* **защемля́ть. 2,** (*of one's heart*) to ache.
защемля́ть *v. impfv.* [*pfv.* **защеми́ть**] **1,** to squeeze; crush. **2,** *colloq.* to catch; jam.
защи́та *n.* defense; protection. —**брать (кого́-нибудь) под защи́ту,** to take under one's wing.
защити́тельный *adj., in* **защити́тельная речь,** speech for the defense.
защити́ть [*infl.* **-щу́, -ти́шь**] *v., pfv. of* **защища́ть.** —**защити́ться,** *refl., pfv. of* **защища́ться.**
защи́тник *n.* **1,** defender; protector. **2,** defense attorney. **3,** *sports* defenseman; back.
защи́тный *adj.* protective. —**защи́тная окра́ска,** protective coloration. —**защи́тный цвет,** khaki.
защища́ть *v. impfv.* [*pfv.* **защити́ть**] **1,** to defend. **2,** to protect. —**защища́ться,** *refl.* to defend oneself; protect oneself.
заяви́ть [*infl.* **-явлю́, -я́вишь**] *v., pfv. of* **заявля́ть.**
зая́вка [*gen. pl.* **-вок**] *n.* **1,** claim. **2,** order; application; requisition.
заявле́ние *n.* **1,** announcement; statement. **2,** application.
заявля́ть *v. impfv.* [*pfv.* **заяви́ть**] **1,** (*with* **о**) to announce: заяви́ть о своём реше́нии, to announce one's decision. **2,** (*with a dependent clause*) to state (that)...; declare (that)... **3,** to file; lodge (a protest, complaint, etc.). **4,** to report: заяви́ть о происше́ствии в мили́цию, to report an incident to the police.
зая́длый *adj., colloq.* inveterate; avid.
за́яц [*gen.* **за́йца**] *n.* **1,** hare. **2,** *colloq.* stowaway: е́хать за́йцем, to stow away.
за́ячий [*fem.* **-чья**] *adj.* hare (*attrib.*); hare's. —**за́ячья губа́,** harelip.
зва́ние *n.* **1,** rank: во́инское зва́ние, military rank. **2,** title: зва́ние чемпио́на, championship title.
зва́ный *adj.* **1,** invited: зва́ный гость, invited guest. **2,** with invited guests: зва́ный обе́д, dinner party.
зва́тельный *adj., in* **зва́тельный паде́ж,** vocative case.
звать *v. impfv.* [*pfv.* **позва́ть;** *pres.* **зову́, зовёшь;** *past fem.* **звала́**] **1,** to call. **2,** to invite. **3,** [*impfv. only*] to name; call: как вас зову́т?, what is your name? Меня́ зову́т Ири́на, my name is Irina. —**зва́ться,** *refl.* [*impfv. only*] to be called.
звезда́ [*pl.* **звёзды**] *n.* star. —**морска́я звезда́,** starfish. —**но́вая звезда́,** nova.

звёздный *adj.* **1,** star (*attrib.*); stellar. **2,** starry.
звездочёт *n., obs.* astrologer.
звёздочка [*gen. pl.* **-чек**] *n.* **1,** little star. **2,** asterisk.
звене́ть *v. impfv.* [*pres.* **-ню́, -ни́шь**] **1,** *v.i.* to ring; jingle: колоко́льчики звеня́т, sleighbells are ringing. **2,** *v.t.* (*with instr.*) to jingle: звене́ть моне́тами, to jingle coins.
звено́ [*pl.* **зве́нья, зве́ньев**] *n.* **1,** link. **2,** unit; section (*of a device or structure*). **3,** team; group; unit. **4,** flight (*of aircraft*). **5,** *mil.* level; echelon.
зверёк [*gen.* **-рька́**] *n.* small animal.
зверёныш *n., colloq.* cub.
звере́ть *v. impfv.* [*pfv.* **озвере́ть**] to become like an animal.
зверинец [*gen.* **-нца**] *n., obs., colloq.* menagerie.
звери́ный *adj.* **1,** animal (*attrib.*). **2,** brutal; savage.
зверобо́й *n.* **1,** hunter (*of aquatic mammals*). **2,** St.-John's-wort.
зверолóв *n.* trapper.
зве́рский *adj.* **1,** brutal; savage. **2,** *colloq.* beastly; frightful. —**зве́рски,** *adv.* brutally.
зве́рство *n.* **1,** brutality; bestiality. **2,** *usu. pl.* atrocities.
зверь [*pl.* **зве́ри, звере́й, зверя́м**] *n.m.* (wild) animal; beast. —**смотре́ть зве́рем,** to glare; glower.
зверьё *n., colloq.* wild animals.
звон *n.* **1,** ringing; pealing; tolling. **2,** jingling; tinkling.
звона́рь [*gen.* **-наря́**] *n.m.* bell ringer.
звони́ть *v. impfv.* [*pfv.* **позвони́ть**] **1,** (*of a bell, phone, alarm clock, etc.*) to ring. **2,** (*with* **в** + *acc.*) to ring: звони́ть в ко́локол, to ring a bell. **3,** (*with dat.*) to call; phone: я вам позвоню́, I'll call/phone you. Звони́ть на вокза́л, to call/phone the station.
зво́нкий *adj.* **1,** clear; ringing; resounding. **2,** *phonet.* voiced. —**зво́нкая моне́та,** specie; coin. —**зво́нкая фра́за,** high-sounding phrase.
зво́нница *n.* bell tower; belfry.
звоно́к [*gen.* **-нка́**] *n.* **1,** bell. **2,** ring. **3,** *colloq.* phone call.
звук *n.* sound.
звуково́й *adj.* sound (*attrib.*). —**звуково́й фильм,** talking film.
звукоза́пись *n.f.* sound recording.
звуконепроница́емый *adj.* soundproof.
звукоопера́тор *n.* sound technician.
звукоподража́ние *n.* onomatopoeia.
звукоусиле́ние *n.* amplification. —**систе́ма звукоусиле́ния,** amplification system; public-address system.
звуча́ние *n.* **1,** sound. **2,** *fig.* significance: пьеса огро́много звуча́ния, play of enormous significance.
звуча́ть *v. impfv.* [*pfv.* **прозвуча́ть;** *pres.* **-чу́, -чи́шь**] to sound; be heard.
зву́чный *adj.* **1,** ringing; resounding. **2,** resonant.
звя́канье *n.* tinkling; jingling; jangling.
звя́кать *v. impfv.* [*pfv.* **звя́кнуть**] to tinkle; jingle; jangle.
зги *n., in* **ни зги не ви́дно,** it is pitch dark.
зда́ние *n.* building.
здесь *adv.* here.
зде́шний *adj., colloq.* of this place; local.
здоро́ваться *v.r. impfv.* [*pfv.* **поздоро́ваться**] (*with* **с** + *instr.*) to say hello (to); greet.
здорове́нный *adj., colloq.* robust; healthy.
здорове́ть *v. impfv.* [*pfv.* **поздорове́ть**] *colloq.* to grow healthy.
здо́рово *adv., colloq.* **1,** very; awfully; terribly. **2,** marvelously; splendidly. —*adj., used predicatively* nice; wonderful: как здо́рово бы́ло бы (+ *inf.*), how nice/wonderful it would be to...
здоро́во *adv. & adj.* healthy: вы́глядеть здоро́во, to look healthy. —**(за) здоро́во живёшь,** *colloq.* just like that.
здоро́вый *adj.* healthy. —**бу́дьте здоро́вы!, 1,** stay well! **2,** (*after a sneeze*) bless you! —**жив и здоро́в,** alive and well; safe and sound.
здоро́вье *n.* health. —**за ва́ше здоро́вье!,** to your health!; to good health! —**как ва́ше здоро́вье?,** how are you? —**на здоро́вье,** help yourself; take as much as you like.
здоровя́к [*gen.* **-яка́**] *n., colloq.* healthy person; robust person.
здра́вица *n.* toast to one's health.
здра́вница *n.* health resort.
здра́во *adv.* **1,** soundly. **2,** sensibly.
здравомы́слящий *adj.* sensible; of sound judgment.
здравоохране́ние *n.* public health.
здра́вствовать *v. impfv.* [*pres.* **-ствую, -ствуешь**] to be well; be healthy; thrive. —**здра́вствуйте!,** *interj.* hello! —**да здра́вствует...!,** long live...!
здра́вый *adj.* sensible; sound. —**в здра́вом уме́,** of sound mind; sane. —**здра́вый смысл,** common sense.
зе́бра *n.* zebra.
зе́бу *n.m. indecl.* zebu.
зев *n.* pharynx. —**льви́ный зев,** snapdragon.
зева́ка *n.m. & f., colloq.* idle onlooker.
зева́ть *v. impfv.* **1,** [*pfv.* **зевну́ть**] to yawn. **2,** [*impfv. only*] *colloq.* to gape. **3,** [*pfv.* **прозева́ть**] *colloq.* to let an opportunity slip by.
зево́к [*gen.* **-вка́**] *n.* yawn.
зево́та *n.* yawning.
Зевс *n.* Zeus.
зелене́ть *v. impfv.* [*pfv.* **позелене́ть**] **1,** to become green; turn green. **2,** [*impfv. only*] (*of anything green*) to loom; appear.
зеленщи́к [*gen.* **-щика́**] *n.* greengrocer.
зелёный *adj.* green. —**зелёная ску́ка** *or* **тоска́,** utter boredom. —**зелёная у́лица,** the green light.
зе́лень *n.f.* **1,** greenery; verdure. **2,** greens; vegetables.
зе́лье *n., obs.* **1,** poison. **2,** potion: любо́вное зе́лье, love potion.
земе́льный *adj.* land (*attrib.*).
землеве́дение *n.* physical geography.
землевладе́лец [*gen.* **-льца**] *n.* landowner. —**землевладе́льческий,** *adj.* landowner's. —**землевладе́ние,** *n.* ownership of land.
земледе́лец [*gen.* **-льца**] *n.* farmer.
земледе́лие *n.* farming. —**земледе́льческий,** *adj.* farming (*attrib.*).
землеко́п *n.* digger.
землеме́р *n., obs.* surveyor. —**землеме́рный,** *adj.* surveying (*attrib.*).
землеро́йка [*gen. pl.* **-ро́ек**] *n.* shrew.
землеро́йный *adj.* excavation (*attrib.*). —**землеро́йная маши́на,** steam shovel.
землетрясе́ние *n.* earthquake.
земли́стый *adj.* **1,** earthy. **2,** (*of one's complexion*) sallow.
земля́ [*acc.* **зе́млю;** *pl.* **зе́мли, земе́ль, зе́млям**] *n.* **1,** land; ground; earth. **2,** *cap.* the earth.

земля́к [*gen.* **-ляка́**] *n.m.* [*fem.* **-ля́чка**] compatriot; fellow countryman.

земляни́ка *n.* **1,** (wild) strawberries. **2,** a (single) strawberry. —**земляни́чный,** *adj.* strawberry (*attrib.*).

земля́нка [*gen. pl.* **-нок**] *n.* dugout; mud hut.

земляно́й *adj.* earthen. —**земляно́й оре́х,** peanut. —**земляно́й червь,** earthworm.

земново́дный *adj.* amphibious. —**земново́дные,** *n. pl.* amphibia; amphibians.

земно́й *adj.* **1,** of the earth; the earth's; terrestrial. **2,** earthly; mundane.

зе́мский *adj.* **1,** *hist.* national; people's: зе́мский собо́р, zemski sobor (*legislative assembly in old Russia*). **2,** of or pert. to the zemstvos.

зе́мство *n., hist.* zemstvo (*local assembly in 19th-cent. Russia*).

зени́т *n.* zenith.

зени́тка [*gen. pl.* **-ток**] *n., colloq.* antiaircraft gun.

зени́тный *adj.* **1,** *astron.* zenith (*attrib.*). **2,** *mil.* antiaircraft.

зени́ца *n., obs.* pupil of the eye. —**бере́чь как зени́цу о́ка,** to guard like the apple of one's eye.

зе́ркало [*pl.* **-кала́, -ка́л**] *n.* mirror.

зерка́льный *adj.* **1,** mirror (*attrib.*). **2,** having a mirror. **3,** mirror-like. **4,** (*of a telescope*) reflecting; (*of a camera*) reflex. —**зерка́льное стекло́,** plate glass.

зе́ркальце [*gen. pl.* **-лец**] *n.* small mirror.

зерни́стый *adj.* **1,** grainy. **2,** granular. —**зерни́стая икра́,** soft caviar.

зерно́ [*pl.* **зёрна, зёрен**] *n.* **1,** grain: произво́дства зерна́, grain production. **2,** *fig.* grain; particle: зерно́ и́стины, grain of truth. —**жемчу́жное зерно́,** a pearl. —**кофе́йные зёрна,** coffee beans.

зерново́й *adj.* grain (*attrib.*); cereal (*attrib.*).

зернохрани́лище *n.* granary.

зёрнышко [*gen. pl.* **-шек**] *n.* grain; granule.

зефи́р *n.* **1,** *obs.* zephyr (*gentle breeze*). **2,** zephyr (*lightweight cloth*). **3,** a kind of candy; marshmallow.

зигза́г *n.* zigzag. —**зигзагообра́зный,** *adj.* zigzag.

зиго́та *n.* zygote.

зи́ждиться *v.r. impfv.* [*pres.* **-ждется**] (*with* **на** + *prepl.*) to be based (upon).

зима́ [*acc.* **зи́му;** *pl.* **зи́мы**] *n.* winter.

зи́мний *adj.* **1,** winter (*attrib.*). **2,** wintry.

зимова́ть *v. impfv.* [*pfv.* **прозимова́ть;** *pres.* **-му́ю, -му́ешь**] to spend the winter.

зимо́вка *n.* **1,** wintering; spending the winter. **2,** winter camp; winter quarters.

зимо́вье *n.* winter camp; winter quarters.

зимо́й *adv.* in (the) winter. *Also,* **зимо́ю.**

зиморо́док [*gen.* **-дка**] *n.* halcyon; kingfisher.

зимосто́йкий *adj.* winter (*attrib.*); winter-hardy.

зипу́н [*gen.* **-пуна́**] *n.* homespun peasant's coat worn in old Russia.

зия́ние *n., ling.* hiatus.

зия́ть *v. impfv.* (*of a wound, abyss, etc.*) to gape; yawn.

зла́ки *n. pl.* [*sing.* **злак**] cereals. —**зла́ковый,** *adj.* cereal (*attrib.*).

зла́то *n., poetic* gold.

зле́йший *adj.* worst; bitterest.

злить *v. impfv.* [*pfv.* **обозли́ть** *or* **разозли́ть**] to anger. —**зли́ться,** *refl.* to become angry.

зло[1] [*gen. pl.* **зол**] *n.* **1,** evil. **2,** wrong. **3,** harm. **4,** *colloq.* spite: со зла, out of spite. —**из двух зол выбира́ть ме́ньшее,** to choose the lesser of two evils.

зло[2] *adv.* maliciously. Зло подшути́ть (над), to play a mean trick (on).

зло́ба *n.* **1,** spite; malice. **2,** grudge: таи́ть зло́бу, to bear a grudge. —**зло́ба дня,** topic of the day.

зло́бный *adj.* malicious; spiteful. —**зло́бно,** *adv.* maliciously.

злободне́вный *adj.* (*of a question, issue, etc.*) timely; vital.

зло́бствовать *v. impfv.* [*pres.* **-ствую, -ствуешь**] (*with* **на** + *acc.*) to bear malice (towards).

злове́щий *adj.* ominous; sinister.

злово́ние *n.* stench. —**злово́нный,** *adj.* stinking; fetid.

зловре́дный *adj.* harmful; pernicious.

злоде́й *n.* evildoer; villain; scoundrel.

злоде́йский *adj.* **1,** vicious; heinous. **2,** insidious.

злоде́йство *n.* **1,** villainy. **2,** evil deed.

злодея́ние *n.* evil deed; crime; outrage.

злой *adj.* [*short form* **зол, зла, зло**] **1,** wicked; evil. **2,** cross; ill-tempered. **3,** [*short form only*] (*with* **на** + *acc.*) angry (at); cross (with). **4,** mean; malicious. **5,** (*of animals*) mean; ferocious. **6,** biting; acerbic. **7,** *colloq.* severe.

злока́чественный *adj., med.* malignant. —**злока́чественное малокро́вие,** pernicious anemia.

злоключе́ние *n.* misadventure; mishap.

злонаме́ренный *adj.* malicious.

злопа́мятный *adj.* bearing a grudge; rancorous.

злополу́чный *adj.* ill-fated; ill-starred; hapless.

злопыха́тель *n.m.* malicious critic; mudslinger. —**злопыха́тельский,** *adj.* malicious. —**злопыха́тельство,** *n.* maliciousness.

злора́дный *adj.* gloating.

злора́дство *n.* malicious pleasure.

злора́дствовать *v. impfv.* [*pres.* **-ствую, -ствуешь**] to gloat.

злосло́вие *n.* malicious gossip.

злосло́вить *v. impfv.* [*pres.* **-влю, -вишь**] to utter malicious gossip.

зло́стный *adj.* **1,** malicious. **2,** (*of an offender, defaulter, etc.*) persistent; habitual.

злость *n.f.* **1,** malice. **2,** rage; fury.

зло́тый *n., decl. as an adj.* zloty (*monetary unit of Poland*).

злоупотреби́ть [*infl.* **-блю́, -би́шь**] *v., pfv. of* **злоупотребля́ть.**

злоупотребле́ние *n.* **1,** (*with instr.*) misuse (of); abuse (of): злоупотребле́ние вла́стью, abuse of power. **2,** abuse; instance of wrongdoing.

злоупотребля́ть *v. impfv.* [*pfv.* **злоупотреби́ть**] (*with instr.*) to misuse; abuse.

злю́ка *n.m. & f., colloq.* ill-tempered person; grouch.

змееви́дный *adj.* like a serpent; serpentine.

змеи́ный *adj.* snake (*attrib.*); snake's.

змеи́ться *v.r. impfv.* to wind; snake.

змей [*gen. & acc.* **змея́**] *n.* **1,** dragon. **2,** kite.

змея́ [*pl.* **зме́и, змей, зме́ям**] *n.* snake.

знава́ть *v. impfv., colloq., used only in the past tense* to have known: он знава́л лу́чшие времена́, he has known better times.

знак *n.* **1,** sign. **2,** signal. **3,** mark; point: зна́ки препина́ния, punctuation marks; восклица́тельный знак, exclamation point. —**в знак** (+ *gen.*), as a sign, token, or gesture of. —**под зна́ком** (+ *gen.*), under the banner (of).

знако́мить *v. impfv.* [*pfv.* **познако́мить;** *pres.* **-млю,**

-мишь] (*with* с + *instr.*) **1,** to introduce (to). **2,** to acquaint (with); familiarize (with). —**знако́миться,** *refl.* (*with* с + *instr.*) **1,** to make the acquaintance (of); become acquainted (with). **2,** to familiarize oneself (with); become familiar (with).

знако́мство *n.* **1,** acquaintance. **2,** (circle of) acquaintances. **3,** familiarity; knowledge.

знако́мый *adj.* **1,** acquainted: вы знако́мы?, are you acquainted?; do you know each other? **2,** familiar: знако́мый звук, a familiar sound. Я знако́м с э́тим вопро́сом, I am familiar with the matter. —*n.* acquaintance.

знамена́тель *n.m.* denominator. —**приводи́ть к одному́** (or **к о́бщему**) **знамена́телю,** to reduce to a common denominator.

знамена́тельный *adj.* **1,** momentous; memorable. **2,** significant; revealing.

зна́мение *n., obs.* sign. —**зна́мение вре́мени,** sign of the times. —**кре́стное зна́мение,** sign of the cross.

знамени́тость *n.f.* **1,** fame; eminence; celebrity. **2,** a celebrity.

знамени́тый *adj.* famous; celebrated.

знаменова́ть *v. impfv.* [*pfv.* **ознаменова́ть;** *pres.* **-ну́ю, -ну́ешь**] (*often with* **собо́й**) to mark; signify; represent.

знамено́сец [*gen.* **-сца**] *n.* standard-bearer.

зна́мя [*gen., dat. & prepl.* **зна́мени;** *instr.* **зна́менем;** *pl.* **знамёна, знамён**] *n. neut.* banner.

зна́ние *n., often pl.* knowledge. —**со зна́нием де́ла, 1,** knowledgeably. **2,** with great skill.

зна́тный *adj.* **1,** from among the nobility *or* elite. **2,** prominent; noted: зна́тные лю́ди, notables. **3,** *colloq.* sizable. **4,** *colloq.* splendid.

знато́к [*gen.* **-тока́**] *n.* expert; connoisseur.

знать[1] *v. impfv.* to know. —**как зна́ешь,** as you wish. —**как знать?,** how is one to know? —**кто его́ зна́ет?,** who knows? —**то и знай,** *colloq.* continually.

знать[2] *n.f.* aristocracy; nobility.

зна́ться *v.r. impfv.* (*with* с + *instr.*) *colloq.* to associate (with); have to do with.

зна́харь *n.m.* [*fem.* **зна́харка**] medicine man; witch doctor; quack. —**зна́харство,** *n.* quackery.

зна́чащий *adj.* meaningful; significant.

значе́ние *n.* **1,** meaning; sense: двойно́е значе́ние, dual meaning. **2,** significance; importance: не име́ть значе́ния, to be of no significance. Име́ть большо́е значе́ние для, to be of great importance to. **3,** value: коне́чное значе́ние, finite value.

зна́чимый *adj.* significant. —**зна́чимость,** *n.f.* significance.

зна́чит *particle, colloq.* so; then.

значи́тельно *adv.* considerably; significantly; substantially.

значи́тельность *n.f.* significance; importance.

значи́тельный *adj.* **1,** considerable. **2,** significant.

зна́чить *v. impfv.* to mean; signify. —**зна́читься,** *refl.* to be listed.

значо́к [*gen.* **-чка́**] *n.* **1,** badge. **2,** mark.

зна́ющий *adj.* knowledgeable.

знobи́ть *v. impfv., impers.* to have a chill; be chilled: меня́ зноби́т, I have a chill.

зной *n.* intense heat.

зно́йный *adj.* burning hot; sultry.

зоб *n.* **1,** craw; crop (*of a bird*). **2,** *med.* goiter.

зо́бный *adj., in* **зо́бная железа́,** thymus.

зов *n.* **1,** call. **2,** *colloq.* invitation.

зодиа́к *n.* zodiac.

зо́дчество *n.* architecture. —**зо́дческий,** *adj.* architectural.

зо́дчий *n., decl. as an adj.* architect.

зол *adj., short form of* **злой.** —*n., gen. pl. of* **зло.**

зола́ *n.* **1,** ashes. **2,** ash: вулкани́ческая зола́, volcanic ash.

золо́вка [*gen. pl.* **-вок**] *n.* sister-in-law *(husband's sister).*

золота́рник *n.* goldenrod.

золоти́стый *adj.* golden.

золоти́ть *v. impfv.* [*pfv.* **позолоти́ть** *or* **вы́золотить;** *pres.* **-чу́, -ти́шь**] to gild. —**золоти́ть пилю́лю,** to sweeten the pill.

золотни́к [*gen.* **-ника́**] *n.* old Russian measure of weight equal to about 1/6 of an ounce. —**мал золотни́к, да до́рог,** good things come in small packages.

зо́лото *n.* gold. —**на вес зо́лота,** worth its weight in gold.

золотоиска́тель *n.m.* prospector (*for gold*).

золото́й *adj.* gold; golden. —**золоты́х дел ма́стер,** goldsmith. —**золото́е дно,** gold mine (*fig.*). —**золото́й дождь,** windfall. —**золото́й мешо́к,** rich man; moneybags.

золотоно́сный *adj.* containing gold.

золоту́ха *n., obs.* scrofula.

золоче́ние *n.* gilding.

золочёный *adj.* gilded; gilt.

Зо́лушка *n.* Cinderella.

зо́на *n.* zone. —**зона́льный,** *adj.* zone (*attrib.*); zonal.

зонд *n.* **1,** *med.* probing device: желу́дочный зонд, stomach pump. **2,** weather balloon.

зонди́ровать *v. impfv.* [*pres.* **-рую, -руешь**] **1,** to probe; sound. **2,** *fig.* to sound out. —**зонди́ровать по́чву,** to get the lay of the land.

зонт [*gen.* **зонта́**] *n.* **1,** umbrella. **2,** awning.

зо́нтик *n.* umbrella.

зооло́гия *n.* zoology. —**зоо́лог,** *n.* zoologist. —**зоологи́ческий,** *adj.* zoological.

зоопа́рк *n.* zoo.

зо́ркий *adj.* **1,** sharp-eyed. **2,** perceptive. —**зо́рко,** *adv.* with a watchful eye. —**зо́ркость,** *n.f.* keen vision.

зра́зы [*gen.* **зраз**] *n.pl.* meat patties stuffed with rice, kasha, etc.

зрачо́к [*gen.* **-чка́**] *n.* pupil (*of the eye*).

зре́лище *n.* **1,** sight; spectacle. **2,** show.

зре́лость *n.f.* **1,** ripeness. **2,** maturity. —**полова́я зре́лость,** puberty.

зре́лый *adj.* **1,** ripe. **2,** mature.

зре́ние *n.* sight; eyesight; vision. —**по́ле зре́ния,** field of vision. —**то́чка зре́ния,** point of view; viewpoint. —**у́гол зре́ния,** viewpoint; standpoint.

зреть[1] *v. impfv.* [*pfv.* **созре́ть;** *pres.* **зре́ю, зре́ешь**] to ripen; mature.

зреть[2] *v. impfv.* [*pfv.* **узре́ть;** *pres.* **зрю, зришь**] *archaic* to behold.

зри́тель *n.m.* **1,** spectator. **2,** *pl.* audience.

зри́тельный *adj.* **1,** visual. **2,** optic. —**зри́тельный зал,** auditorium.

зря *adv., colloq.* in vain; for nothing; to no purpose.

зря́чий *adj.* able to see; sighted. —*n.* sighted person.

зуб *n.* **1,** [*pl.* **зу́бы, зубо́в, зуба́м**] tooth. **2,** [*pl.* **зу́бья, зу́бьев**] tooth (*of a saw, gear, etc.*). —**име́ть зуб на** *or* **про́тив,** to have a grudge against. —**класть зу́бы на по́лку,** to go hungry; suffer hard times. —**не**

по зуба́м (+ *dat.*), *colloq.* too much for; beyond one.
зуба́стый *adj., colloq.* **1,** having large teeth; toothy. **2,** *fig.* sharp-tongued.
зубе́ц [*gen.* **-бца́**] *n.* tooth; cog; prong.
зуби́ло *n.* cutting tool; chisel.
зубно́й *adj.* tooth (*attrib.*); dental. —**зубно́й врач,** dentist. —**зубна́я па́ста,** toothpaste. —**зубна́я щётка,** toothbrush.
зубовраче́бный *adj.* of or pert. to dentistry; dental.
зубо́к [*gen.* **-бка́**] *n., colloq., dim. of* **зуб.** —**на зубо́к,** *colloq.* **1,** as a present for a new-born child. **2,** (*with verbs of knowing or learning*) thoroughly; inside out. —**попа́сть на зубо́к** (+ *dat.*), to be subjected to (someone's) criticism or ridicule; be the target of someone's tongue.
зубоска́л *n., colloq.* joker; kidder. —**зубоска́льство,** *n., colloq.* scoffing; kidding.
зубочи́стка [*gen. pl.* **-ток**] *n.* toothpick.
зубр *n.* European bison.
зубрёжка *n., colloq.* cramming.
зубри́ла *n.m. & f., colloq.* crammer; grind. *Also,* **зубри́лка.**
зубри́ть *v. impfv.* [*pfv.* **зазубри́ть;** *pres.* **зубрю́, зубри́шь** *or* **зу́бришь**] **1,** to notch; make notches in. **2,** *colloq.* to cram (*study hard*). **3,** *colloq.* to learn by rote.
зубцо́вка *n.* perforation (*on stamps*). —**зубцо́вый,** *adj.* perforate; perforated.
зубча́тый *adj.* **1,** toothed. **2,** jagged. **3,** (*of a wall of a fortress*) crenelated. —**зубча́тое колесо́,** cogwheel.
зуд *n.* itch.
зуде́ть *v. impfv.* [*pres.* **-ди́т**] *colloq.* to itch.
зуёк [*gen.* **зуйка́**] *n.* plover.
зулу́с *n.m.* [*fem.* **-ка**] Zulu. —**зулу́сский,** *adj.* Zulu.
зу́ммер *n.* buzzer.
зы́бкий *adj.* **1,** unsteady; unstable. **2,** shifting; rippling. **3,** *fig.* vacillating.
зыбу́чий *adj.* shifting: зыбу́чий песо́к, shifting sands.
зыбь *n.f.* rippling; undulating (*of water*). —**лёгкая зыбь,** ripples. —**мёртвая зыбь,** groundswell.
зы́чный *adj.* loud; resounding.
зюйд *n., naut.* **1,** south. **2,** south wind.
зя́бкий *adj., colloq.* sensitive to cold.
зя́блик *n.* chaffinch.
зя́бнуть *v. impfv.* [*past* **зяб, -ла**] to be frozen; be chilled to the bone.
зябь *n.f.* **1,** autumn plowing. **2,** land plowed in autumn for spring sowing.
зять [*pl.* **зятья́, зятьёв**] *n.m.* **1,** son-in-law. **2,** brother-in-law (*sister's husband or husband's sister's husband*).

И

И, и *n. neut.* ninth letter of the Russian alphabet.
и *conj.* **1,** and: причи́на и сле́дствие, cause and effect. **2,** *used for emphasis:* вы себе́ и предста́вить не мо́жете!, you just can't imagine! **3,** also; as well: он опозда́л и на второ́й по́езд, he missed the second train as well. **4,** (*with negatives*) either: э́то не легко́ и для меня́, it is not easy for me either. **5,** even: он и спаси́бо не сказа́л, he didn't even say thank you. —**и ... и,** both: и мужчи́ны и же́нщины, both men and women.
и́бис *n.* ibis.
и́бо *conj.* for; as.
и́ва *n.* willow. —**плаку́чая и́ва,** weeping willow.
ива́новский *adj., in* **во всю ива́новскую,** at the top of one's lungs.
ивня́к [*gen.* **-няка́**] *n.* **1,** willow bed. **2,** willow branches.
и́вовый *adj.* willow (*attrib.*).
и́волга *n.* European oriole.
иври́т *n.* (modern) Hebrew.
игла́ [*pl.* **и́глы, игл**] *n.* **1,** needle. **2,** quill (*of an animal*).
игли́стый *adj.* covered with needles or quills.
иглова́тый *adj.* **1,** needle-like. **2,** *colloq.* prickly.
иглови́дный *adj.* needle-shaped. *Also,* **иглообра́зный.**
иглотерапи́я *n.* acupuncture. *Also,* **иглоука́лывание.**
и́глу *n. neut. indecl.* igloo.
игнори́ровать *v. impfv. & pfv.* [*pres.* **-рую, -руешь**] to ignore; disregard.
и́го *n.* yoke (*of oppression*).
иго́лка [*gen. pl.* **-лок**] *n.* needle. —**быть** *or* **сиде́ть как на иго́лках,** to be on pins and needles; be on tenterhooks.
иго́лочка [*gen. pl.* **-чек**] *n., dim. of* **игла́** *and* **иго́лка.** —**с иго́лочки,** brand-new. —**одет с иго́лочки,** impeccably dressed.
иго́лочный *adj.* needle (*attrib.*).
иго́льник *n.* needle cushion; needle case.
иго́льный *adj.* of a needle; needle (*attrib.*): иго́льное ушко́, eye of a needle.
иго́льчатый *adj.* needle-shaped.
иго́рный *adj.* gambling (*attrib.*); gaming (*attrib.*).
игра́ [*pl.* **и́гры, игр**] *n.* **1,** game. **2,** play; playing: игра́ на роя́ле, playing (of) the piano. **3,** performance; acting. —**игра́ воображе́ния,** figment of the imagination. —**игра́ приро́ды, 1,** extraordinary natural phenomenon. **2,** freak of nature. —**игра́ слов,** play on words. —**игра́ судьбы́** *or* **слу́чая,** quirk of fate. —**игра́ ума́,** battle of wits.
игра́льный *adj.* playing (*attrib.*). —**игра́льные ко́сти,** dice.
игра́ть *v. impfv.* [*pfv.* **сыгра́ть**] **1,** to play. **2,** (*with* **в** + *acc.*) to play (a game). **3,** (*with* **на** + *prepl.*) to play (an

instrument). **4,** to act; perform. **5,** [*impfv. only*] (*with instr.*) to play (with); toy (with); trifle (with). **6,** [*impfv. only*] (*with instr.*) to play (with); fiddle (with); twiddle. **7,** [*impfv. only*] (*of beverages*) to sparkle. **8,** (*with instr.*) *chess* to move (a pawn or piece). —**игра́ть в зага́дки,** to talk in riddles. —**игра́ть глаза́ми,** to ogle. —**игра́ть на́ руку** (+ *dat.*), to play into the hands of. —**игра́ть слова́ми,** to make plays on words; pun. —**игра́ть с огнём,** to play with fire.

игра́ючи *adv., colloq.* effortlessly; as if it were child's play.

и́грек *n.* the letter y.

игри́вый *adj.* playful. —**игри́вость,** *n.f.* playfulness.

игри́стый *adj.* (*of wine, champagne, etc.*) sparkling.

игрово́й *adj.* **1,** playing (*attrib.*). **2,** acting (*attrib.*). **3,** (*of a film, play, etc.*) full of action.

игро́к [*gen.* **игрока́**] *n.* **1,** player. **2,** gambler.

игру́шечный *adj.* **1,** toy (*attrib.*). **2,** miniature.

игру́шка [*gen. pl.* **шек**] *n.* **1,** toy. **2,** *fig.* plaything.

игуа́на *n.* iguana.

игу́мен *n.* abbot; father superior (*of a Russian Orthodox monastery*). —**игу́менья,** *n.* abbess; mother superior (*of a Russian Orthodox convent*).

идеа́л *n.* ideal.

идеализи́ровать *v. impfv. & pfv.* [*pres.* **-рую, -руешь**] to idealize.

идеали́зм *n.* idealism. —**идеали́ст,** *n.* idealist. —**идеалисти́ческий,** *adj.* idealistic.

идеа́льный *adj.* **1,** ideal; sublime. **2,** ideal; perfect.

иде́йность *n.f.* **1,** ideological content. **2,** progressive character. **3,** high-mindedness.

иде́йный *adj.* **1,** ideological. **2,** progressive; high-minded. **3,** *in* иде́йный за́мысел, the basic idea; the point (*of a novel, play, etc.*).

иденти́чный (дэ) *adj.* identical. —**иденти́чность,** *n.f.* identity.

идеогра́мма *n.* ideogram; ideograph.

идеоло́гия *n.* ideology. —**идео́лог,** *n.* ideologist. —**идеологи́ческий,** *adj.* ideological.

иде́я *n.* idea.

иди́ллия *n.* idyll. —**идилли́ческий,** *adj.* idyllic.

идио́ма *n.* idiom. —**идиомати́ческий,** *adj.* idiomatic.

идио́т *n.* idiot; imbecile. —**идиоти́зм,** *n.* idiocy; imbecility. —**идио́тский,** *adj.* idiotic; imbecilic. —**идио́тство,** *n., colloq.* idiocy; nonsense.

и́диш *n.* Yiddish.

и́дол *n.* idol. —**(сиде́ть** *or* **стоя́ть) и́долом,** motionless; like a statue.

идолопокло́нник *n.* idolater. —**идолопокло́ннический,** *adj.* idolatrous. —**идолопокло́нство,** *n.* idolatry.

идти́ *v. impfv.* [*pfv.* **пойти́;** *pres.* **иду́, идёшь;** *past* **шёл, шла, шло**] **1,** to go. **2,** to come: вот они́ иду́т, here they come. **3,** to come out: дым идёт из трубы́, smoke is coming out of the chimney. **4,** to go; proceed; progress: рабо́та идёт хорошо́, the work is going well. **5,** to be in progress: иду́т экза́мены, exams are in progress. **6,** (*of time*) to pass; go by: вре́мя бы́стро идёт, time passes quickly. **7,** (*of mail*) to take a certain amout of time to reach: пи́сьма сюда́ иду́т о́чень до́лго, the mail takes a long time to get here. **8,** (*of rain, snow, etc.*): идёт дождь, it is raining. **9,** (*of a road, mountain range, etc.*) to run; extend. **10,** (*of a device*) to work: мои́ часы́ не иду́т, my watch is not working. **11,** (*of a film or play*) to be playing. **12,** (*with* **на** + *acc.*) to be used for; go into the making of: де́рево идёт на изготовле́ние бума́ги, wood is used in making paper. **13,** (*with dat.*) to become: шля́па вам идёт, the hat is becoming to you. **14,** (*with* **на** + *acc.*) to make (*with certain nouns*): идти́ на усту́пки/же́ртвы, to make concessions/sacrifices. **15,** *cards* to play; lead: идти́ с туза́, to play/lead an ace; идти́ ко́зырем, to play/lead a trump. **16,** (*with instr.*) *chess* to move: идти́ пе́шкой, to move a pawn. **17,** *colloq.* to sell: това́р хорошо́ идёт, the merchandise is selling well. **18,** (*with* **в** *or* **на** + *acc.*) *colloq.* to go into; go onto: гвоздь не идёт в сте́ну, the nail will not go into the wall; боти́нок не идёт на́ ногу, the shoe will not go onto my foot. *See also* **ходи́ть** *and* **пойти́.**

и́ды [*gen.* **ид**] *n. pl.* ides: и́ды ма́рта, the ides of March.

иезу́ит *n.* Jesuit. —**иезу́итский,** *adj.* Jesuit.

ие́на *n.* yen (*monetary unit of Japan*).

иера́рхия *n.* hierarchy. —**иерархи́ческий,** *adj.* hierarchical.

иеро́глифы *n. pl.* [*sing.* **иеро́глиф**] (Egyptian) hieroglyph(ic)s; (Chinese) characters. —**иероглифи́ческий,** *adj.* hieroglyphic.

иждиве́нец [*gen.* **-нца**] *n.m.* [*fem.* **-нка**] dependent.

иждиве́ние *n.* maintenance; support. —**на иждиве́нии кого́-нибудь,** dependent on someone for support.

из *also,* **изо** *prep., with gen.* **1,** from: прие́хать из Пари́жа, to arrive from Paris. Из достове́рных исто́чников, from reliable sources. **2,** out of: вы́йти из ко́мнаты, to go out of the room. **3,** of; made of: стол из де́рева, a table made of wood. **4,** of; consisting of: буке́т из роз, a bouquet of roses. **5,** of (*a group*): оди́н из них, one of them. **6,** (*with emotions*) out of: из жа́лости, out of pity.

из- *also,* **ис-, изо-, изъ-** *prefix* **1,** out of; ex-: извлека́ть, to extract; исключа́ть, to exclude. **2,** covering a surface: исписа́ть лист бума́ги, to fill up a sheet of paper with writing. **3,** entirely; all over: изъе́здить всю страну́, to travel all over the country. **4,** thoroughly; severely: измока́ть, to get soaked; исцара́пывать, to scratch severely. **5,** (*with* **-ся**) to the point of exhaustion: избе́гаться, to run oneself ragged.

изба́ [*pl.* **и́збы**] *n.* peasant's hut; log cabin.

избави́тель *n.m.* deliverer; savior; redeemer.

изба́вить [*infl.* **-влю, -вишь**] *v., pfv. of* **избавля́ть.** —**изба́виться,** *refl., pfv. of* **избавля́ться.**

избавле́ние *n.* deliverance.

избавля́ть *v. impfv.* [*pfv.* **изба́вить**] (*with* **от**) to save (from); rescue (from); deliver (from); spare. —**избавля́ться,** *refl.* (*with* **от**) **1,** to get rid of; rid oneself of. **2,** to avoid; escape.

избало́ванный *adj.* spoiled.

избалова́ть [*infl.* **-лу́ю, -лу́ешь**] *v., pfv. of* **балова́ть** *and* **избало́вывать.** —**избалова́ться,** *refl., pfv. of* **избало́вываться.**

избало́вывать *v. impfv.* [*pfv.* **избалова́ть**] to spoil; pamper. —**избало́вываться,** *refl.* to become spoiled.

избе́гать *v. pfv., colloq.* to run all over (a place).

избега́ть *v. impfv.* [*pfv.* **избежа́ть** *or* **избе́гнуть**] (*with gen.*) to avoid; evade.

избе́гаться *v.r. pfv., colloq.* to run oneself ragged.

избе́гнуть [*past* **-бе́г** *or* **-бе́гнул, -бе́гла**] *v., pfv. of* **избега́ть.**

избежа́ние *n., in* **во избежа́ние** (+ *gen.*), in order to avoid.

избежа́ть [*infl. like* **бежа́ть**] *v., pfv. of* **избега́ть.**

избива́ть *v. impfv.* [*pfv.* **изби́ть**] **1,** to beat up. **2,** *obs.* to slaughter; massacre.

избие́ние *n.* **1,** beating. **2,** slaughter; massacre. **3,** *law* assault and battery.

избира́тель *n.m.* voter.

избира́тельный *adj.* electoral; election (*attrib.*). —**избира́тельный бюллете́нь,** ballot. —**избира́тельное пра́во,** suffrage. —**избира́тельная у́рна,** ballot box. —**избира́тельный уча́сток, 1,** voting district. **2,** polling place.

избира́ть *v. impfv.* [*pfv.* **избра́ть**] **1,** to select. **2,** to elect.

изби́тый *adj.* **1,** beaten up. **2,** *fig.* (*of a road, path, etc.*) familiar; well-trodden. **3,** trite; hackneyed. —**изби́тая и́стина,** truism.

изби́ть [*infl.* **изобью́, изобьёшь**] *v., pfv. of* **избива́ть.**

избородди́ть *v., pfv. of* **борозди́ть.**

избра́ние *n.* election.

избра́нник *n.* chosen one.

и́збранные *n. pl., decl. as an adj.* select people.

и́збранный *adj.* **1,** elected. **2,** select. —**и́збранные сочине́ния,** selected works.

избра́ть [*infl. like* **брать**] *v., pfv. of* **избира́ть.**

избу́шка [*gen. pl.* **-шек**] *n.* hut; log cabin.

избы́ток [*gen.* **-тка**] *n.* **1,** surplus; excess. **2,** abundance. —**в избы́тке; с избы́тком,** in abundance.

избы́точный *adj.* surplus; excess.

изваа́ние *n.* piece of sculpture; sculptured figure.

изваа́ть *v., pfv. of* **ваа́ть.**

изве́дывать *v. impfv.* [*pfv.* **изве́дать**] to experience.

и́зверг *n.* fiend; monster.

изверга́ть *v. impfv.* [*pfv.* **изве́ргнуть**] to spew forth. —**изверга́ться,** *refl.* **1,** (*of a volcano*) to erupt. **2,** (*of lava*) to spew forth.

изве́ргнуть [*past* **-ве́рг** *or* **-ве́ргнул, -ве́ргла**] *v., pfv. of* **изверга́ть.** —**изве́ргнуться,** *refl., pfv. of* **изверга́ться.**

изверже́ние *n.* **1,** eruption. **2,** ejection; expulsion. **3,** *fig.* outpouring; torrent (*of words, abuse, etc.*).

изве́рженный *adj., geol.* igneous.

изве́риться *v.r. pfv.* (*with* **в** + *prepl. or acc.*) *colloq.* to lose faith (in); lose confidence (in).

извернУ́ться *v.r., pfv. of* **изворА́чиваться.**

извести́ [*infl. like* **вести́**] *v., pfv. of* **изводи́ть.** —**извести́сь,** *refl., pfv. of* **изводи́ться.**

изве́стие *n.* **1,** piece of news. **2,** *pl.* news.

извести́ть [*infl.* **-щу́, -сти́шь**] *v., pfv. of* **извеща́ть.**

извёстка *n., colloq.* = **и́звесть.**

известко́вый *adj.* lime. —**известко́вая вода́,** limewater.

изве́стно *adj., used predicatively* known: как изве́стно, as is known. Изве́стно, что..., it is known that... Наско́лько мне изве́стно, as far as I know. —**одному́ бо́гу изве́стно,** God alone knows.

изве́стность *n.f.* **1,** fame; notoriety; renown. **2,** *colloq.* a celebrity. —**поста́вить в изве́стность,** to inform; notify.

изве́стный *adj.* [*short form* **-стен, -стна**] **1,** known. **2,** well-known. **3,** notorious. **4,** a certain: до изве́стной сте́пени, to a certain degree. —**изве́стное де́ло,** naturally; of course.

известня́к [*gen.* **-няка́**] *n.* limestone. —**известняко́вый,** *adj.* limestone.

и́звесть *n.f.* lime. —**хло́рная и́звесть,** bleaching powder.

изве́чный *adj.* primeval; age-old; ancient.

извеща́ть *v. impfv.* [*pfv.* **извести́ть**] to inform; notify.

извеще́ние *n.* notice; notification.

изви́в *n.* bend (*in a river*); curve (*in a road*).

извива́ться *v.r. impfv.* **1,** to wriggle; squirm. **2,** (*of a river, road, etc.*) to wind; meander.

изви́лина *n.* bend (*in a river*); curve (*in a road*).

изви́листый *adj.* winding.

извине́ние *n.* **1,** apology. **2,** pardon: проси́ть извине́ния у, to beg someone's pardon. **3,** excuse: э́то не мо́жет служи́ть извине́нием, that's no excuse.

извини́тельный *adj.* **1,** pardonable; excusable. **2,** apologetic.

извиня́ть *v. impfv.* [*pfv.* **извини́ть**] to excuse; pardon: извини́те!, excuse me!; pardon me! —**извиня́ться,** *refl.* (*with* **перед**) to apologize (to).

извиня́ющийся *adj.* apologetic.

извлека́ть *v. impfv.* [*pfv.* **извле́чь**] **1,** to extract. **2,** to derive.

извлече́ние *n.* **1,** extraction. **2,** excerpt; extract.

извле́чь [*infl. like* **влечь**] *v., pfv. of* **извлека́ть.**

извне́ *adv.* from without; from the outside.

изводи́ть *v. impfv.* [*pfv.* **извести́;** *pres.* **-вожу́, -во́дишь**] *colloq.* **1,** to use up; waste; exhaust. **2,** to destroy; exterminate. **3,** to torment; exasperate. —**изводи́ться,** *refl., colloq.* **1,** to tire oneself out. **2,** to eat one's heart out. **3,** to waste away. **4,** to be used up.

изво́зчик *n.* **1,** driver; coachman (*of a hired carriage*). **2,** carriage for hire.

изво́лить *v. impfv., obs.* to wish; desire. —**изво́льте,** (*with inf.*) please; be so kind as to...

изворА́чиваться *v.r. impfv.* [*pfv.* **извернУ́ться**] **1,** to twist and turn. **2,** *fig., colloq.* to use cunning; resort to trickery.

изворо́т *n.* **1,** *obs.* bend. **2,** *usu. pl.* twist. **3,** *fig.* trick.

изворо́тливый *adj.* **1,** (*of a person*) shifty; clever; resourceful. **2,** (*of an animal*) elusive; slippery.

извраща́ть *v. impfv.* [*pfv.* **изврати́ть**] **1,** to distort; misrepresent. **2,** to corrupt; pervert.

извраще́ние *n.* **1,** distortion; misrepresentation. **2,** corruption; perversion. —**извращённость,** *n.f.* perversity.

изги́б *n.* bend; curve.

изгиба́ть *v. impfv.* [*pfv.* **изогну́ть**] to bend; curve; arch. —**изгиба́ться,** *refl.* **1,** to bend; become bent. **2,** (*of a path, river, etc.*) to curve; wind.

изгла́живать *v. impfv.* [*pfv.* **изгла́дить**] to efface; blot out; obliterate.

изгна́ние *n.* **1,** banishment; expulsion; ostracism. **2,** exile: жить в изгна́нии, to live in exile. —**изгна́нник,** *n.* exile; outcast.

изгна́ть [*infl. like* **гнать**] *v., pfv. of* **изгоня́ть.**

изго́й *n.* outcast.

изголо́вье *n.* head of a bed.

изголода́ться *v.r. pfv.* **1,** to starve; be starving. **2,** (*with* **по** + *dat.*) to yearn (for).

изгоня́ть *v. impfv.* [*pfv.* **изгна́ть**] to drive out; banish; exile; ostracize.

и́згородь *n.f.* fence. —**жива́я и́згородь,** hedge.

изгота́вливать *v.* = **изготовля́ть.**

изгото́вить [*infl.* **-влю, -вишь**] *v., pfv. of* **изготовля́ть** *and* **изгота́вливать.**

изгото́вка *n., in* **на изгото́вку,** (*of a gun*) at the ready.

изготовле́ние *n.* manufacture.

изготовля́ть *v. impfv.* [*pfv.* **изгото́вить**] to make; manufacture.

издава́ть *v. impfv.* [*pfv.* **изда́ть;** *pres.* **-даю́, -даёшь**] **1,** to publish. **2,** to issue; promulgate. **3,** to emit; utter. **4,** to emit; give off (an odor).

и́здавна *adv.* **1,** since olden times; since days of yore. **2,** for a very long time; for as long as one can remember.

издалека́ *also,* **издалёка** *adv.* from a distance; from afar.

и́здали *adv.* from a distance; from afar.

изда́ние *n.* **1,** issuance; promulgation. **2,** publication. **3,** a publication. **4,** edition.

изда́тель *n.m.* publisher. —**изда́тельский,** *adj.* publishing (*attrib.*). —**изда́тельство,** *n.* publishing house.

изда́ть [*infl. like* **дать;** *past* **изда́л, издала́, изда́ло**] *v., pfv. of* **издава́ть.**

издева́тельский *adj.* mocking; derisive.

издева́тельство *n.* (*usu. with* **над**) **1,** mockery; derision. **2,** harassment; persecution; violation of one's dignity. **3,** *usu. pl.* malicious insults.

издева́ться *v.r. impfv.* (*with* **над**) to mock; taunt.

издёвка [*gen. pl.* **-вок**] *n., colloq.* **1,** gibe. **2,** mockery. Говори́ть с издёвкой, to speak in a mocking tone.

изде́лие *n.* **1,** make; manufacture. **2,** manufactured article. **3,** *pl.* goods: ко́жаные изде́лия, leather goods.

издёргать *v. pfv., colloq.* to harry; harass; unnerve. —**издёргаться,** *refl., colloq.* to be unnerved.

издержа́ть [*infl.* **-держу́, -де́ржишь**] *v., pfv. of* **изде́рживать.** —**издержа́ться,** *refl., pfv. of* **изде́рживаться.**

изде́рживать *v. impfv.* [*pfv.* **издержа́ть**] to spend; expend. —**изде́рживаться,** *refl., colloq.* to spend all one's money.

изде́ржки [*gen.* **-жек**] *n. pl.* expenses; costs.

издо́льщик *n.* sharecropper. *Also,* **издо́льник.**

издо́хнуть [*past* **-до́х, -ла**] *v., pfv. of* **издыха́ть.**

издре́вле *adv.* from time immemorial.

издыха́ние *n.* last breath; dying gasp. —**до после́днего издыха́ния,** to one's last breath; to the death. —**при после́днем издыха́нии,** breathing one's last; near death.

издыха́ть *v. impfv.* [*pfv.* **издо́хнуть**] (*of animals*) to die.

изжа́рить *v., pfv. of* **жа́рить.** —**изжа́риться,** *refl., pfv. of* **жа́риться.**

изжива́ть *v. impfv.* [*pfv.* **изжи́ть**] to rid oneself of; eliminate. —**изжи́ть себя́,** to become obsolete.

изжи́ть [*infl. like* **жить**] *v., pfv. of* **изжива́ть.**

изжо́га *n.* heartburn.

из-за *prep., with gen.* **1,** from behind. **2,** because of; on account of.

иззя́бнуть *v. pfv.* [*past* **-зя́б, -ла**] *colloq.* to be chilled to the bone.

излага́ть *v. impfv.* [*pfv.* **изложи́ть**] to state; set forth; expound.

изла́мывать *v. impfv.* [*pfv.* **излома́ть**] **1,** to smash; shatter. **2,** *colloq.* to warp; pervert. —**изла́мываться,** *refl.* to be broken; be smashed.

излени́ться *v.r. pfv.* [*infl.* **-леню́сь, -ле́нишься**] *colloq.* to become incorrigibly lazy.

излёт *n., in* **на излёте,** (*of a bullet*) spent.

излече́ние *n.* **1,** medical treatment. **2,** recovery.

изле́чивать *v. impfv.* [*pfv.* **излечи́ть**] to cure. —**изле́чиваться,** *refl.* (*with* **от**) to be cured (of).

излечи́мый *adj.* curable.

излечи́ть [*infl.* **-лечу́, -ле́чишь**] *v., pfv. of* **изле́чивать.** —**излечи́ться,** *refl., pfv. of* **изле́чиваться.**

излива́ть *v. impfv.* [*pfv.* **изли́ть**] **1,** *obs.* to pour out. **2,** *fig.* to pour out; give vent to. **3,** *in* **излива́ть ду́шу,** to pour out one's heart/soul. —**излива́ться,** *refl.* to give vent to one's feelings.

изли́ть [*infl.* **изолью́, изольёшь;** *past* **изли́л, излила́, изли́ло**] *v., pfv. of* **излива́ть.** —**изли́ться,** *refl., pfv. of* **излива́ться.**

изли́шек [*gen.* **-шка**] *n.* **1,** surplus. **2,** excess. —**с изли́шком,** with something to spare.

изли́шество *n.* **1,** *obs.* excess; overabundance. **2,** excess; immoderation; *pl.* excesses. —**до изли́шества,** to excess.

изли́шне *adv.* excessively. —*adj., used predicatively* superfluous; unnecessary: изли́шне сказа́ть, что..., it is superfluous/unnecessary to say that...

изли́шний *adj.* **1,** excessive. **2,** superfluous; unnecessary.

излия́ние *n., usu. pl.* outpouring (*of emotion*).

излови́ть *v. pfv.* [*infl.* **-ловлю́, -ло́вишь**] *colloq.* to catch.

изловчи́ться *v.r. pfv., colloq.* to manage; contrive.

изложе́ние *n.* exposition; presentation.

изложи́ть [*infl.* **-ложу́, -ло́жишь**] *v., pfv. of* **излага́ть.**

изло́м *n.* **1,** break; fracture. **2,** sharp turn; sharp curve.

изло́манный *adj.* **1,** broken; fractured. **2,** crooked; winding. **3,** *fig.* warped; perverted.

излома́ть *v., pfv. of* **изла́мывать.** —**излома́ться,** *refl., pfv. of* **изла́мываться.**

излуча́ть *v. impfv.* to radiate. —**излуча́ться,** *refl.* to radiate; emanate.

излуче́ние *n.* radiation.

излу́чина *n.* bend; curve.

излю́бленный *adj.* favorite; pet.

изма́зать [*infl.* **-ма́жу, -ма́жешь**] *v., pfv. of* **изма́зывать.** —**изма́заться,** *refl., pfv. of* **изма́зываться.**

изма́зывать *v. impfv.* [*pfv.* **изма́зать**] *colloq.* to smear; get dirty. —**изма́зываться,** *refl.* (*with instr.*) *colloq.* to get (dirt, paint, ink, etc.) all over oneself.

изма́тывать *v. impfv.* [*pfv.* **измота́ть**] *colloq.* to exhaust; wear out. —**изма́тываться,** *refl., colloq.* to be exhausted; be worn out.

изма́яться *v.r. pfv., colloq.* to be exhausted.

измельча́ть[1] *v., pfv. of* **мельча́ть.**

измельча́ть[2] *v. impfv.* [*pfv.* **измельчи́ть**] to grind down; reduce to fine particles.

изме́на *n.* **1,** treason. **2,** betrayal. **3,** infidelity.

измене́ние *n.* change; alteration.

измени́ть [*infl.* **-меню́, -ме́нишь**] *v., pfv. of* **изменя́ть.** —**измени́ться,** *refl., pfv. of* **изменя́ться.**

изме́нник *n.* traitor. —**изме́ннический,** *adj.* traitorous; treasonable.

изме́нчивый *adj.* changeable; fickle. —**изме́нчивость,** *n.f.* changeability.

изменя́ть *v. impfv.* [*pfv.* **измени́ть**] **1,** to change; alter. **2,** (*with dat.*) to betray; be unfaithful to. **3,** (*with dat.*) to fail: си́лы ему́ измени́ли, his strength failed him.

изменя́ться *v.r. impfv.* [*pfv.* **измени́ться**] to change: времена́ измени́лись, times have changed. —**измени́ться в лице́,** to change the expression on one's face.

измере́ние *n.* **1,** measurement; measuring. **2,** taking (*of temperature*). **3,** dimension.

измери́мый *adj.* measurable.

измери́тель *n.m.* **1,** measuring device; gauge. **2,** indicator; index. —**измери́тельный,** *adj.* (for) measuring.

измеря́ть *v. impfv.* [*pfv.* **изме́рить**] to measure. —**измеря́ть температу́ру** (+ *dat.*), to take someone's temperature.

изможде́нный *adj.* haggard; gaunt; emaciated.

измока́ть *v. impfv.* [*pfv.* **измо́кнуть**] *colloq.* to get drenched; get soaked.

измо́кнуть [*past* **-мо́к, -ла**] *v., pfv. of* **измока́ть.**

измо́р *n., in* **взять измо́ром, 1,** to starve into submission. **2,** *fig.* to wear down; wear down the resistance of.

измори́ть *v.t., colloq.* to wear out; exhaust.

и́зморозь *n.f.* frost; hoarfrost.

и́зморось *n.f.* drizzle.

измота́ть *v., pfv. of* **изма́тывать.** —**измота́ться,** *refl., pfv. of* **изма́тываться.**

изму́ченный *adj.* worn out; exhausted.

изму́чить *v. pfv.* **1,** to wear out; exhaust. **2,** to torment; rack. —**изму́читься,** *refl.* to be worn out; be exhausted.

измыва́ться *v.r. impfv.* (*with* **над**) *colloq.* to make fun of; poke fun at.

измы́слить *v., pfv. of* **измышля́ть.**

измышле́ние *n.* fabrication; falsehood; invention.

измышля́ть *v. impfv.* [*pfv.* **измы́слить**] **1,** to invent; fabricate. **2,** to think up; devise.

измя́тый *adj.* **1,** crumpled; creased. **2,** battered. **3,** haggard.

измя́ть *v. pfv.* [*infl.* **изомну́, изомнёшь**] **1,** *pfv. of* **мять** (*in sense #2*). **2,** to batter. —**измя́ться,** *refl., pfv. of* **мя́ться** (*in sense #1*).

изна́нка *n.* **1,** wrong side; reverse side. **2,** *fig.* seamy side.

изнаси́лование *n.* rape.

изнаси́ловать *v., pfv. of* **наси́ловать.**

изнача́льный *adj.* primordial.

изна́шивание *n.* wearing out.

изна́шивать *v. impfv.* [*pfv.* **износи́ть**] to wear out (clothing, machinery, etc.). —**изна́шиваться,** *refl.* to wear out; be worn out.

изне́женный *adj.* soft; spoiled.

изне́живать *v. impfv.* [*pfv.* **изне́жить**] to spoil; pamper.

изнемога́ть *v. impfv.* [*pfv.* **изнемо́чь**] to be exhausted; be worn out.

изнеможе́ние *n.* utter exhaustion.

изнеможённый *adj.* utterly exhausted.

изнемо́чь [*infl. like* **мочь**] *v., pfv. of* **изнемога́ть.**

изне́рвничаться *v.r. pfv., colloq.* to be a nervous wreck.

изно́с *n.* wear; wear and tear. —**нет изно́су** (+ *dat.*), immune to wear: э́тим боти́нкам нет изно́су, these shoes will never wear out.

износи́ть [*infl.* **-ношу́, -но́сишь**] *v., pfv. of* **изна́шивать.** —**износи́ться,** *refl., pfv. of* **изна́шиваться.**

изно́шенный *adj.* worn out; threadbare.

изнуре́ние *n.* exhaustion.

изнури́тельный *adj.* **1,** exhausting; grueling. **2,** enervating; debilitating.

изнуря́ть *v. impfv.* [*pfv.* **изнури́ть**] to exhaust.

изнутри́ *adv.* **1,** from inside; from within. **2,** on the inside.

изныва́ть *v. impfv.* [*pfv.* **изны́ть**] to languish.

изны́ть [*infl.* **-но́ю, -но́ешь**] *v., pfv. of* **изныва́ть.**

изо *prep.* = **из.**

изоба́ра *n.* isobar.

изоби́лие *n.* abundance; plenty. —**рог изоби́лия,** horn of plenty; cornucopia.

изоби́ловать *v. impfv.* [*pfv.* **-лует**] (*with instr.*) to abound (in).

изоби́льный *adj.* abundant.

изоблича́ть *v. impfv.* [*pfv.* **изобличи́ть**] **1,** to expose; convict. **2,** [*impfv. only*] to reveal; give away: акце́нт изобличи́л в нём иностра́нца, his accent gave him away as a foreigner.

изобличе́ние *n.* exposure.

изобличи́тель *n.m.* exposer. —**изобличи́тельный,** *adj.* incriminating.

изобличи́ть *v., pfv. of* **изобличáть.**

изобража́ть *v. impfv.* [*pfv.* **изобрази́ть**] to depict; portray; represent. —**изобража́ть из себя́** (+ *acc.*), *colloq.* to make oneself out to be.

изображе́ние *n.* **1,** portrayal; representation. **2,** image; picture.

изобрази́тельный *adj.* graphic. —**изобрази́тельные иску́сства,** fine arts.

изобрази́ть [*infl.* **-жу́, -зи́шь**] *v., pfv. of* **изобража́ть.**

изобрести́ [*infl.* **-брету́, -бретёшь;** *past* **-брёл, -брела́, -брело́**] *v., pfv. of* **изобрета́ть.**

изобрета́тель *n.m.* inventor. —**изобрета́тельность,** *n.f.* inventiveness. **изобрета́тельный,** *adj.* inventive.

изобрета́ть *v. impfv.* [*pfv.* **изобрести́**] to invent.

изобрете́ние *n.* invention.

изо́гнутый *adj.* bent, curved.

изогну́ть *v., pfv. of* **изгиба́ть.** —**изогну́ться,** *refl., pfv. of* **изгиба́ться.**

изодра́ть *v. pfv.* [*infl.* **издеру́, издерёшь;** *past fem.* **изодрала́**] *colloq.* to tear up; tear to shreds.

изойти́ [*infl.* **изойду́, изойдёшь;** *past* **изошёл, изошла́**] *v., pfv. of* **исходи́ть**[1] (*in sense #4*).

изолга́ться *v.r. pfv.* [*infl. like* **лгать**] to become a habitual liar.

изоли́ровать *v. impfv. & pfv.* [*pres.* **-рую, -руешь**] **1,** to isolate. **2,** to quarantine. **3,** to insulate.

изоля́тор *n.* **1,** insulator. **2,** isolation ward.

изоляциони́зм *n.* isolationism. —**изоляциони́ст,** *n.* isolationist. —**изоляциони́стский,** *adj.* isolationist.

изоляцио́нный *adj.* **1,** isolation (*attrib.*). **2,** quarantine (*attrib.*). **3,** insulation (*attrib.*).

изоля́ция *n.* **1,** isolation. **2,** quarantine. **3,** insulation.

изоме́р *n.* isomer.

изо́рванный *adj.* torn; tattered.

изорва́ть *v. pfv.* [*infl. like* **рвать**] to tear up; tear to shreds. —**изорва́ться,** *refl.* **1,** to be torn to shreds. **2,** *colloq.* to be in shreds; become full of holes.

изото́п *n.* isotope.

изощре́ние *n.* refinement; perfection.

изощрённый *adj.* acute; keen.

изощря́ть *v. impfv.* [*pfv.* **изощри́ть**] to sharpen (one's hearing, mind, etc.); refine; cultivate (one's taste); perfect (one's skills). —**изощря́ться,** *refl.* **1,** to become refined. **2,** (*with* **в** + *prepl.*) to excel (in); be a master of.

из-под *prep., with gen.* **1,** from under: из-под стола́, from under the table. Вода́ из-под кра́на, water from the tap; tap water. **2,** from somewhere near. **3,** (*of a container*) for holding: буты́лка из-под вина́, a wine bottle.

изразе́ц [*gen.* **-зца́**] *n.* (glazed) tile. —**изразцо́вый,** *adj.* tile (*attrib.*); tiled.
изра́ильский *adj.* Israeli.
израильтя́нин [*pl.* **-тя́не, -тя́н**] *n.m.* [*fem.* **-тя́нка**] **1,** *hist.* Israelite. **2,** Israeli.
изра́нить *v. pfv.* to wound severely; wound in many places.
израсхо́довать *v., pfv. of* **расхо́довать.** —**израсхо́довать,** *refl.* to be used up; be consumed.
и́зредка *adv.* now and then; from time to time.
изре́занный *adj.* **1,** cut up; sliced up. **2,** (*of a coastline*) irregular; indented; jagged. **3,** (*of a region*) rugged.
изре́зать [*infl.* **-ре́жу, -ре́жешь**] *v., pfv. of* **изре́зывать.**
изре́зывать *v. impfv.* [*pfv.* **изре́зать**] **1,** to cut up; cut to pieces. **2,** to gash; slash. **3,** to cut across; crisscross.
изрека́ть *v. impfv.* [*pfv.* **изре́чь**] *obs.* to utter; state.
изрече́ние *n.* saying; maxim; adage; dictum.
изре́чь [*infl.* **-реку́, -речёшь, ...-реку́т;** *past* **-рёк, -рекла́, рекло́**] *v., pfv. of* **изрека́ть.**
изреше́чивать *v. impfv.* [*pfv.* **изрешети́ть**] to riddle (with bullets, shrapnel, etc.).
изрисова́ть *v. pfv.* [*inf.* **-су́ю, -су́ешь**] to cover with drawings.
изруби́ть *v. pfv.* [*infl.* **-рублю́, -ру́бишь**] **1,** to chop up; hack to pieces. **2,** to massacre (*by sword*).
изруга́ть *v. pfv., colloq.* to curse (someone) roundly; heap abuse on.
изрыва́ть *v. impfv.* [*pfv.* **изры́ть**] to dig up; tear up; churn up.
изрыга́ть *v. impfv.* [*pfv.* **изрыгну́ть**] **1,** to belch up; regurgitate. **2,** to belch forth (flames, smoke, etc.). **3,** *fig.* to utter (profanities).
изры́тый *adj.* **1,** dug up. **2,** rough; bumpy; uneven. —**изры́тый о́спой,** pockmarked.
изры́ть [*infl.* **-ро́ю, -ро́ешь**] *v., pfv. of* **изрыва́ть.**
изря́дно *adv., colloq.* **1,** (*with adjectives*) rather; pretty. **2,** (*with verbs*) quite a lot.
изря́дный *adj., colloq.* quite a; a pretty fair; a handsome; a goodly.
изуве́р *n.* **1,** fanatic. **2,** *fig.* monster; fiend.
изуве́рский *adj.* **1,** fanatical. **2,** *fig.* savage; barbaric.
изуве́рство *n.* **1,** fanaticism. **2,** *fig.* barbarity.
изуве́чивать *v. impfv.* [*pfv.* **изуве́чить**] to maim.
изукра́шивать *v. impfv.* [*pfv.* **изукра́сить**] to decorate lavishly; bedeck.
изуми́тельно *adv.* **1,** amazingly. **2,** marvelously.
изуми́тельный *adj.* **1,** amazing; astonishing. **2,** wonderful; marvelous.
изуми́ть [*infl.* **-млю́, -ми́шь**] *v., pfv. of* **изумля́ть.** —**изуми́ться,** *refl., pfv. of* **изумля́ться.**
изумле́ние *n.* amazement; astonishment.
изумля́ть *v. impfv.* [*pfv.* **изуми́ть**] to amaze; astonish. —**изумля́ться,** *refl.* (*with dat.*) to be amazed (at); be astonished (at).
изумру́д *n.* emerald. —**изумру́дный,** *adj.* emerald.
изуро́дованный *adj.* disfigured.
изуро́довать *v., pfv. of* **уро́довать.**
изуча́ть *v. impfv.* [*pfv.* **изучи́ть**] to study.
изуче́ние *n.* study; studying.
изучи́ть *v. pfv.* [*infl.* **-учу́, -у́чишь**] **1,** *pfv. of* **изуча́ть.** **2,** to learn. **3,** to get to know.
изъеда́ть *v. impfv.* [*pfv.* **изъе́сть**] **1,** to eat away. **2,** to eat into.
изъе́здить *v. pfv.* [*infl.* **-е́зжу, -е́здишь**] *colloq.* to travel all over (an area).
изъе́сть [*infl. like* **есть**] *v., pfv. of* **изъеда́ть.**
изъяви́тельный *adj., in* **изъяви́тельное наклоне́ние,** *gram.* indicative mood.
изъяви́ть [*infl.* **-явлю́, -я́вишь**] *v., pfv. of* **изъявля́ть.**
изъявле́ние *n.* expression; declaration.
изъявля́ть *v. impfv.* [*pfv.* **изъяви́ть**] to express.
изъязвля́ть *v. impfv.* [*pfv.* **изъязви́ть**] to ulcerate. —**изъязвля́ться,** *refl.* to ulcerate; become ulcerated.
изъя́н *n.* defect; flaw (*in merchandise*).
изъясня́ться *v.r. impfv.* [*pfv.* **изъясни́ться**] **1,** *obs.* to express oneself. **2,** [*impfv. only*] to speak.
изъя́тие *n.* **1,** withdrawal; removal. **2,** exception.
изъя́ть [*infl.* **изыму́, изы́мешь**] *v., pfv. of* **изыма́ть.**
изыма́ть *v. impfv.* [*pfv.* **изъя́ть**] **1,** to withdraw; remove. **2,** to seize; confiscate.
изыска́ние *n.* **1,** seeking. **2,** *usu. pl.* research. **3,** *usu. pl.* surveying; prospecting.
изы́сканный *adj.* refined; exquisite. —**изы́сканность,** *n.f.* refinement.
изыска́тель *n.m.* prospector.
изыска́ть [*infl.* **изыщу́, изы́щешь**] *v., pfv. of* **изы́скивать.**
изы́скивать *v. impfv.* [*pfv.* **изыска́ть**] **1,** to find; obtain. **2,** [*impfv. only*] to seek; look for.
изю́бр *also,* **изю́брь** *n.m.* a variety of red deer; Altai wapiti.
изю́м *n.* raisins. —**не фунт изю́му,** nothing to be sneezed at.
изю́мина *n.* a (single) raisin.
изю́минка [*gen. pl.* **-нок**] *n.* **1,** a (single) raisin. **2,** *fig.* spark; sparkle (*in a person*).
изя́щество *n.* elegance; grace.
изя́щно *adv.* elegantly.
изя́щный *adj.* elegant; graceful. —**изя́щные иску́сства,** fine arts.
Иису́с *n.* Jesus.
ика́ть *v. impfv.* [*pfv.* **икну́ть**] to hiccup.
ико́на *n.* icon. —**ико́нный,** *adj.* icon (*attrib.*).
иконобо́рец [*gen.* **-рца**] *n.* iconoclast. —**иконобо́р(че)ство,** *n.* iconoclasm. —**иконобо́рческий,** *adj.* iconoclastic.
иконопи́сец [*gen.* **-сца**] *n.* icon painter. —**и́конопись,** *n.f.* icon painting.
иконоста́с *n.* iconostasis.
ико́та *n.* hiccups.
икра́ *n.* **1,** fish eggs; roe. **2,** caviar. **3,** [*pl.* **и́кры**] calf (*of the leg*).
икромета́ние *n.* spawning.
икс *n.* the letter x.
ил *n.* silt.
и́ли *conj.* or. —**и́ли..., и́ли...,** either..., or...
и́листый *adj.* silty; slimy; muddy.
иллюзиони́ст *n.* magician.
иллю́зия *n.* illusion.
иллюзо́рный *adj.* illusory.
иллюмина́тор *n.* porthole.
иллюмина́ция *n.* illumination; decorative lighting.
иллюминова́ть *v. impfv. & pfv.* [*pres.* **-ну́ю, -ну́ешь**] to decorate with lights. *Also,* **иллюмини́ровать** [*pres.* **-рую, -руешь**].
иллюстра́ция *n.* illustration. —**иллюстрати́вный,** *adj.* illustrative. —**иллюстра́тор,** *n.* illustrator.

иллюстри́ровать *v. impfv. & pfv.* [*pfv. also* **проиллюстри́ровать;** *pres.* **-рую, -руешь**] to illustrate.
и́лька [*gen. pl.* **и́лек**] *n.* fisher (*animal*).
ильм *n.* elm.
им *pron.* **1,** *instr. of* **он** *and* **оно́. 2,** *dat. of* **они́.**
имби́рь [*gen.* **-ря́**] *n.m.* ginger. —**имби́рный,** *adj.* ginger.
име́ние *n.* estate.
имени́ны [*gen.* **-ни́н**] *n. pl.* name day; one's saint's day. —**имени́нник,** *n.* person celebrating his name day. —**имени́нный,** *adj.* of or pert. to one's name day.
имени́тельный *adj., in* **имени́тельный паде́ж,** nominative case.
имени́тый *adj.* prominent; distinguished; eminent.
и́менно *particle* **1,** just; exactly; precisely. Вот и́менно!, exactly!; precisely! **2,** [*often* **а и́менно**] namely; to wit.
именно́й *adj.* inscribed with the owner's name. —**именно́й спи́сок,** roll; list of names.
имено́ванный *adj., in* **имено́ванное число́,** *math.* concrete number.
именова́ть *v. impfv.* [*pfv.* **наименова́ть;** *pres.* **-ну́ю, -ну́ешь**] to name. —**именова́ться,** *refl.* [*impfv. only*] to be called.
име́ть *v. impfv.* **1,** to have: име́ть возмо́жность (+ *inf.*), to have the opportunity to. **2,** *rendered by various English verbs according to the noun:* име́ть вес, to carry weight; име́ть успе́х, to be successful; име́ть схо́дство с, to bear a resemblance to; не име́ть смы́сла, to make no sense; не име́ть значе́ния, to be of no significance. —**ничего́ не име́ть про́тив,** to have no objection.
име́ться *v.r. impfv.* to be; exist; be available. В го́роде име́ется мно́го кни́жных магази́нов, there are many bookstores in town. Возраже́ний не име́ется, there are no objections.
име́ющийся *adj.* available; on hand.
и́ми *pron., instr. of* **они́.**
имита́тор *n.* imitator; mimic.
имита́ция *n.* **1,** imitation; mimicry. **2,** imitation; fake.
имити́ровать *v. impfv.* [*pres.* **-рую, -руешь**] to imitate.
иммигра́нт *n.m.* [*fem.* **-ка**] immigrant.
иммигра́ция *n.* immigration. —**иммиграцио́нный,** *adj.* immigration (*attrib.*).
иммигри́ровать *v. impfv. & pfv.* [*pres.* **-рую, -руешь**] to immigrate.
иммуниза́ция *n.* immunization.
иммунизи́ровать *v. impfv. & pfv.* [*pres.* **-рую, -руешь**] to immunize.
иммуните́т *n.* immunity.
императи́вный *adj.* **1,** imperative; obligatory. **2,** imperious; peremptory.
импера́тор *n.* emperor. —**импера́торский,** *adj.* emperor's; imperial.
императри́ца *n.* empress.
империали́зм *n.* imperialism. —**империали́ст,** *n.* imperialist. —**империалисти́ческий,** *adj.* imperialist; imperialistic.
импе́рия *n.* empire. —**импе́рский,** *adj.* imperial.
импи́чмент *n.* impeachment.
импоза́нтный *adj.* imposing; impressive.
импони́ровать *v. impfv.* [*pres.* **-рую, -руешь**] (*with dat.*) to impress; make an impression on.
и́мпорт *n.* **1,** import; importation. **2,** imports. —**импортёр,** *n.* importer.
импорти́ровать *v. impfv. & pfv.* [*pres.* **-рую, -руешь**] to import.
и́мпортный *adj.* **1,** import (*attrib.*). **2,** imported.
импоте́нтный *adj., med.* impotent. —**импоте́нция,** *n., med.* impotence.
импреса́рио *n.m. indecl.* impresario.
импрессиони́зм *n.* impressionism. —**импрессиони́ст,** *n.* impressionist. —**импрессионисти́ческий; импрессиони́стский,** *adj.* impressionist(ic).
импровиза́ция *n.* improvisation. —**импровиза́тор,** *n.* improviser.
импровизи́рованный *adj.* improvised; extemporaneous; impromptu.
импровизи́ровать *v. impfv. & pfv.* [*pres.* **-рую, -руешь**] to improvise.
и́мпульс *n.* impulse; impetus. —**импульси́вный,** *adj.* impulsive.
иму́щественный *adj.* property (*attrib.*).
иму́щество *n.* **1,** property. **2,** *mil.* equipment. **3,** *colloq.* belongings. —**недви́жимое иму́щество,** real estate.
иму́щий *adj.* propertied. —**власть иму́щие,** those in power; the powers that be.
и́мя [*gen., dat., & prepl.* **и́мени;** *instr.* **и́менем;** *pl.* **имена́, имён, имена́м**] *n. neut.* **1,** name; first name. **2,** name; reputation: сде́лать себе́ и́мя, to make a name for oneself. **3,** noun: и́мя со́бственное, proper noun. **4,** *in* **и́мя существи́тельное,** noun; **и́мя прилага́тельное,** adjective; **и́мя числи́тельное,** numeral. —**во и́мя** (+ *gen.*), in the name of; for the sake of. —**на и́мя** (+ *gen.*), addressed to. —**от и́мени** (+ *gen.*), on behalf of. —**по и́мени, 1,** by name. **2,** (*fol. by a name*) by the name of. —**и́менем** (+ *gen.*), in the name of: и́менем зако́на, in the name of the law. —**и́мени** (+ *gen.*), named in honor of: институ́т и́мени Па́влова, the Pavlov Institute.
инакомы́слие *n.* dissent; dissidence. —**инакомы́слящий,** *adj. & n.* dissident.
инаугура́ция *n.* inauguration.
ина́че *also,* **и́наче** *adv.* differently; otherwise. Сде́лать что́-нибудь ина́че, to do something differently. Вы́шло ина́че, it turned out otherwise. —*conj., colloq.* or; or else; otherwise. Спеши́те, ина́че вы опозда́ете, hurry, or you'll be late. —**ина́че говоря́,** in other words. —**так и́ли ина́че,** somehow or other; one way or another.
инвали́д *n.* invalid. —**инвали́дность,** *n.f.* disability.
инвали́дный *adj.* invalid (*attrib.*); invalid's. —**инвали́дное кре́сло,** wheelchair.
инвентариза́ция *n.* (taking of) inventory.
инвентаризи́ровать *v. impfv. & pfv.* [*pres.* **-рую, -руешь**] to take inventory of. *Also,* **инвентаризова́ть** [*pres.* **-зу́ю, -зу́ешь**].
инвента́рный *adj.* inventory (*attrib.*).
инвента́рь [*gen.* **-ря́**] *n.m.* inventory. —**живо́й инвента́рь,** livestock. —**мёртвый инвента́рь,** farm tools and equipment.
инве́рсия *n., gram.; chem.; meteorol.* inversion.
инвеститу́ра *n.* investiture.
ингаля́тор *n., med.* inhaler.
ингредие́нт *n.* ingredient.
ингу́ш [*gen.* **-ша́**] *n.m.* [*fem.* **-гу́шка**] Ingush (*one of a*

people inhabiting the Caucasus). —**ингу́шский,** *adj.* Ingush.

и́ндеветь *v. impfv.* [*pfv.* **заи́ндеветь**] to become covered with frost.

инде́ец [*gen.* **-де́йца**] *n.m.* [*fem.* **-диа́нка**] American Indian.

инде́йка [*gen. pl.* **-де́ек**] *n.* turkey.

инде́йский *adj.* (American) Indian.

и́ндекс (дэ) *n.* index: и́ндекс цен, price index.

индиа́нка [*gen. pl.* **-нок**] *n.* **1,** Indian woman; woman of India. **2,** American Indian woman; squaw.

индиви́д *n.* individual.

индивидуали́зм *n.* individualism. —**индивидуали́ст,** *n.* individualist.

индивидуа́льный *adj.* individual. —**индивидуа́льность,** *n.f.* individuality.

индиви́дуум *n.* individual.

инди́го *n. indecl.* indigo.

инди́ец [*gen.* **-ди́йца**] *n.m.* [*fem.* **-диа́нка**] Indian; native of India.

и́ндий *n.* indium.

инди́йский *adj.* Indian; of India.

индика́тор *n.* indicator.

индиффере́нтный *adj.* indifferent. —**индиффере́нтность,** *n.f.* indifference.

индоевропе́йский *adj.* Indo-European.

индонези́ец [*gen.* **-и́йца**] *n.m.* [*fem.* **-и́йка**] Indonesian. —**индонези́йский,** *adj.* Indonesian.

индоссаме́нт *n., comm.* endorsement.

индосси́ровать *v. impfv. & pfv.* [*pres.* **-рую, -руешь**] *comm.* to endorse.

индуи́зм *n.* Hinduism.

индукти́вный *adj.* inductive.

инду́ктор *n.* inductor.

индукцио́нный *adj.* induction (*attrib.*): индукцио́нная кату́шка, induction coil.

инду́кция *n., logic; electricity* induction.

инду́с *n.m.* [*fem.* **-ду́ска**] Hindu. —**инду́сский,** *adj.* Hindu.

индустриализа́ция *n.* industrialization.

индустриализи́ровать *v. impfv. & pfv.* [*pres.* **-рую, -руешь**] to industrialize.

индустриа́льный *adj.* industrial.

инду́стрия *also,* **индустри́я** *n.* industry.

индю́к [*gen.* **-дюка́**] *n.* turkey cock.

индю́шка [*gen. pl.* **-шек**] *n., colloq.* turkey.

и́ней *n.* frost; hoarfrost.

ине́ртный *adj.* **1,** *chem.* inert. **2,** inert; sluggish. —**ине́ртность,** *n.f.* inertia; sluggishness.

ине́рция *n.* **1,** inertia. **2,** momentum. **3,** *fig.* inertia; sluggishness.

инжене́р *n.* engineer. —**инжене́р-меха́ник,** mechanical engineer. —**инжене́р-строи́тель,** civil engineer. —**инжене́р-хи́мик,** chemical engineer. —**инжене́р-эле́ктрик,** electrical engineer.

инжене́рный *adj.* **1,** engineering (*attrib.*). **2,** *mil.* engineer (*attrib.*): инжене́рные войска́, engineer troops.

инжи́р *n.* **1,** fig. **2,** fig tree.

инициа́лы [*gen.* **-лов**] *n. pl.* initials.

инициати́ва *n.* initiative. —**инициати́вный,** *adj.* with initiative; possessing intiative.

инициа́тор *n.* initiator.

инквизи́ция *n.* inquisition. —**инквизи́тор,** *n.* inquisitor.

инко́гнито *adv.* incognito.

инкорпора́ция *n.* incorporation.

инкорпори́ровать *v. impfv. & pfv.* [*pres.* **-рую, -руешь**] to incorporate.

инкримини́ровать *v. impfv. & pfv.* [*pres.* **-рую, -руешь**] (*with dat.*) to charge; accuse.

инкруста́ция *n.* inlaid work; inlay.

инкрусти́ровать *v. impfv. & pfv.* [*pres.* **-рую, -руешь**] to inlay; encrust.

инкуба́тор *n.* incubator.

инкуба́ция *n.* incubation. —**инкубацио́нный,** *adj.* incubation (*attrib.*).

иногда́ *adv.* sometimes.

иногоро́дный *adj.* from another city; out-of-town.

инозе́мец [*gen.* **-мца**] *n.m.* [*fem.* **-мка**] *obs.* foreigner. —**инозе́мный,** *adj.* foreign.

ино́й *adj.* **1,** other; another. **2,** else: никто́ ино́й, no one else. **3,** some; certain. —**ино́й раз,** sometimes. —**не кто ино́й, как,** none other than. —**не что ино́е, как,** nothing but; nothing less than. —**тот и́ли ино́й,** some ... or other; one ... or another.

и́нок *n., obs.* monk.

иноро́дный *adj.* foreign: иноро́дное те́ло, foreign body.

иносказа́ние *n.* allegory. —**иносказа́тельный,** *adj.* allegorical.

инostра́нец [*gen.* **-нца**] *n.m.* [*fem.* **-нка**] foreigner.

иностра́нный *adj.* foreign.

инохо́дец [*gen.* **-дца**] *n.* pacer (*horse*).

и́ноходь *n.f.* amble; pace: идти́ и́ноходью, to amble; pace.

иноязы́чный *adj.* **1,** speaking another language. **2,** belonging to another language; foreign.

инсектици́д *n.* insecticide.

инсинуа́ция *n.* insinuation; innuendo.

инспекти́ровать *v. impfv.* [*pres.* **-рую, -руешь**] to inspect.

инспе́ктор [*pl.* **инспектора́**] *n.* inspector. —**инспе́кторский,** *adj.* inspector's.

инспе́кция *n.* **1,** inspection. **2,** inspectors. —**инспекцио́нный,** *adj.* inspection (*attrib.*).

инспири́ровать *v. impfv. & pfv.* [*pres.* **-рую, -руешь**] **1,** to influence. **2,** to inspire; instigate.

инста́нция *n.* **1,** level of authority; echelon. **2,** *law* instance: суд пе́рвой инста́нции, court of first instance. —**кома́ндные инста́нции,** *mil.* chain of command.

инсти́нкт *n.* instinct.

инстинкти́вный *adj.* instinctive. —**инстинкти́вно,** *adv.* instinctively.

институ́т *n.* **1,** institute. **2,** institution: институ́т бра́ка, the institution of marriage.

инструкта́ж *n., colloq.* **1,** instructing. **2,** instructions; *mil.* briefing.

инструкти́вный *adj.* instructional.

инструкти́рование *n.* instructing; instruction.

инструкти́ровать *v. impfv. & pfv.* [*pres.* **-рую, -руешь**] **1,** to instruct. **2,** to brief.

инстру́ктор *n.* instructor.

инстру́кция *n.* instructions; directions.

инструме́нт *n.* **1,** tool; instrument. **2,** *music* instrument.

инструментали́ст *n.* instrumentalist.

инструмента́льный *adj.* **1,** tool (*attrib.*); used in making tools. **2,** *music* instrumental.

инструмента́льщик *n.* toolmaker.

инструмента́рий *n.* tools; instruments.

инструментова́ть *v. impfv. & pfv.* [*pres.* **-ту́ю, -ту́ешь**] to orchestrate.
инструменто́вка *n.* orchestration.
инсули́н *n.* insulin.
инсу́льт *n., med.* stroke.
инсцени́ровать *v. impfv. & pfv.* [*pres.* **-рую, -руешь**] **1,** to stage; adapt for the stage. **2,** *fig.* to feign.
инсцениро́вка *n.* staging.
интегра́л (тэ) *n., math.* integral.
интегра́льный (тэ) *adj.* **1,** *math.* integral. **2,** *electronics* integrated: интегра́льная схе́ма, integrated circuit.
интегра́ция (тэ) *n.* integration. *Also,* **интегри́рование.**
интегри́ровать (тэ) *v. impfv. & pfv.* [*pres.* **-рую, -руешь**] to integrate.
интелле́кт *n.* intellect.
интеллектуа́л *n.* intellectual. —**интеллектуа́льный,** *adj.* intellectual.
интеллиге́нт *n.* intellectual.
интеллиге́нтный *adj.* cultured; educated.
интеллиге́нция *n.* intelligentsia.
интенда́нт *n., mil.* quartermaster. —**интенда́нтство,** *n.* quartermaster corps; commissariat.
интенси́вный (тэ) *adj.* intensive. —**интенси́вность,** *n.f.* intensity.
интерва́л *n.* interval; space. —**че́рез два интерва́ла,** double-spaced.
интерве́нция *n.* intervention.
интервью́ (тэ) *n. neut. indecl.* interview. —**интервьюе́р,** *n.* interviewer.
интервьюи́ровать (тэ) *v. impfv. & pfv.* [*pres.* **-рую, -руешь**] to interview.
интере́с *n.* interest. —**в интере́сах** (+ *gen.*), in the interest of; for the sake of.
интере́сно *adv.* in an interesting manner. —*adj., used predicatively* **1,** interesting: интере́сно знать, кто э́то сказа́л, it would be interesting to know who said that. **2,** (*with dat.*) interested: е́сли вам интере́сно знать, in case you're interested; if it is of any interest to you. **3,** I wonder: интере́сно, куда́ он пошёл, I wonder where he went.
интере́сный *adj.* [*short form* **-сен, -сна**] **1,** interesting. **2,** *colloq.* attractive; good-looking; cute. —**в интере́сном положе́нии,** in the family way.
интересова́ть *v. impfv.* [*pres.* **-су́ю, -су́ешь**] to interest. —**интересова́ться,** *refl.* (*with instr.*) to be interested (in).
интерлю́дия (тэ) *n., music* interlude.
интерме́ццо (тэ) *n. indecl.* intermezzo.
инте́рн (тэ) *n.* intern.
интерна́т (тэ) *n.* dormitory. —**шко́ла-интерна́т,** boarding school.
Интернациона́л (тэ) *n.* **1,** International (*socialist organization*). **2,** the Internationale (*revolutionary hymn*).
интернационали́зм (тэ) *n.* internationalism.
интернациона́льный (тэ) *adj.* international.
интерни́рование (тэ) *n.* internment.
интерни́ровать (тэ) *v. impfv. & pfv.* [*pres.* **-рую, -руешь**] to intern.
интерполи́ровать (тэ) *v. impfv. & pfv.* [*pres.* **-рую, -руешь**] to interpolate.
интерполя́ция (тэ) *n.* interpolation.
интерпрета́тор (тэ) *n.* interpreter.
интерпрета́ция (тэ) *n.* interpretation.
интерпрети́ровать (тэ) *v. impfv. & pfv.* [*pres.* **-рую, -руешь**] to interpret.
интерье́р (тэ) *n.* interior (*of a building*).
инти́мный *adj.* intimate. —**инти́мно,** *adv.* intimately. —**инти́мность,** *n.f.* intimacy.
интона́ция *n.* intonation.
интри́га *n.* **1,** intrigue. **2,** plot (*of a novel*). **3,** *obs.* love affair.
интрига́н *n.* schemer.
интригова́ть *v. impfv.* [*pfv.* **заинтригова́ть;** *pres.* **-гу́ю, -гу́ешь**] **1,** to intrigue; fascinate. **2,** [*impfv. only*] to engage in intrigue; scheme.
интроду́кция *n., music* introduction.
интроспе́кция *n.* introspection. —**интроспекти́вный,** *adj.* introspective.
интуити́вный *adj.* intuitive. —**интуити́вно,** *adv.* intuitively.
интуи́ция *n.* intuition.
инфа́ркт *n.* heart attack.
инфе́кция *n.* infection. —**инфекцио́нный,** *adj.* infectious.
инфинити́в *n.* infinitive.
инфля́ция *n.* inflation. —**инфляцио́нный,** *adj.* inflation (*attrib.*); inflationary.
информа́тор *n.* informant.
информа́ция *n.* information. —**информацио́нный,** *adj.* information (*attrib.*).
информи́ровать *v. impfv. & pfv.* [*pfv. also* **проинформи́ровать;** *pres.* **-рую, -руешь**] to inform.
инфракра́сный *adj.* infrared.
инциде́нт *n.* incident.
инъе́кция *n.* injection.
ио́н *n.* ion.
иониза́ция *n.* ionization.
ионизи́ровать *v. impfv. & pfv.* [*pres.* **-рую, -руешь**] to ionize. *Also,* **ионизова́ть** [*pres.* **-зу́ю, -зу́ешь**].
ио́нный *adj.* ionic; ion (*attrib.*).
ионосфе́ра *n.* ionosphere.
иорда́нский *adj.* Jordanian.
ипоме́я *n.* morning-glory.
ипоте́ка *n.* mortgage.
ипохо́ндрия *n.* hypochondria. —**ипохо́ндрик,** *n.* hypochondriac.
ипподро́м *n.* racetrack.
ипри́т *n.* mustard gas.
ира́кский *adj.* Iraqi.
ира́нец [*gen.* **-нца**] *n.m.* [*fem.* **-нка**] Iranian. —**ира́нский,** *adj.* Iranian.
ири́дий *n.* iridium.
и́рис *n.* iris (*flower*).
ири́с *n.* taffy.
ирла́ндец [*gen.* **-дца**] *n.m.* [*fem.* **-дка**] Irishman. —**ирла́ндский,** *adj.* Irish.
иронизи́ровать *v. impfv.* [*pres.* **-рую, -руешь**] to speak ironically; be ironic.
ирони́ческий *adj.* ironic; ironical. —**ирони́чески,** *adv.* ironically.
иро́ния *n.* irony. —**по иро́нии судьбы́,** by an irony of fate; ironically.
иррадиа́ция *n.* irradiation.
иррациона́льный *adj., math.* irrational.
ирига́ция *n.* irrigation. —**ирригацио́нный,** *adj.* irrigation (*attrib.*).
ис- *prefix, var. of* **из-** (*used before voiceless consonants*).
иск *n.* suit; lawsuit.
искажа́ть *v. impfv.* [*pfv.* **искази́ть**] **1,** to distort; contort. **2,** to distort; misrepresent.

искажéние *n.* distortion.
исказить [*infl.* **-жу́, -зи́шь**] *v., pfv. of* **искажáть.**
искалéчить *v., pfv. of* **калéчить.**
искáлывать *v. impfv.* [*pfv.* **исколóть**] to prick all over.
искáние *n., often pl.* search; quest.
искáпывать *v. impfv.* [*pfv.* **ископáть**] to dig up.
искáтель *n.m.* seeker. —**искáтель приключéний,** adventure-seeker; adventurer.
искáть *v. impfv.* [*pres.* **ищу́, и́щешь**] **1,** (*with acc.*) to look for; search for. **2,** (*with gen. or acc.*) to seek; try to obtain.
исключáть *v. impfv.* [*pfv.* **исключи́ть**] **1,** to expel; dismiss; remove. **2,** to eliminate. **3,** to exclude; preclude; rule out: э́то исключенó, that is out of the question. **4,** to delete; drop; strike off *or* from.
исключáя *prep., with acc.* except; excepting; excluding; barring.
исключéние *n.* **1,** exception: за исключéнием (+ *gen.*), with the exception of. **2,** elimination; exclusion. **3,** expulsion.
исключи́тельно *adv.* **1,** exceptionally. **2,** exclusively; only; solely.
исключи́тельность *n.f.* **1,** exceptional nature. **2,** superiority: рáсовая исключи́тельность, racial superiority.
исключи́тельный *adj.* **1,** exceptional. **2,** exclusive.
исключи́ть *v., pfv. of* **исключáть.**
исковéркать *v., pfv. of* **ковéркать.**
исколеси́ть *v. pfv.* [*infl.* **-шу́, -си́шь**] *colloq.* to travel all over (an area).
исколоти́ть *v. pfv.* [*infl.* **-лочу́, -лóтишь**] *colloq.* to beat up.
исколóть [*infl.* **-колю́, -кóлешь**] *v., pfv. of* **искáлывать.**
искóмый *adj.* **1,** sought after. **2,** *math.* sought; to be found. —**искóмое,** *n., math.* unknown.
искони́ *adv., obs.* from time immemorial.
искóнный *adj.* **1,** age-old; long-standing. **2,** native.
ископáемое *n., decl. as an adj.* fossil. —**полéзные ископáемые,** minerals.
ископáемый *adj.* **1,** extracted from the earth. **2,** fossil (*attrib.*); fossilized.
ископáть *v., pfv. of* **искáпывать.**
искоренéние *n.* eradication; rooting out.
искореня́ть *v. impfv.* [*pfv.* **искорени́ть**] to eradicate; stamp out; root out.
и́скорка [*gen. pl.* **-рок**] *n., dim. of* **и́скра.**
и́скоса *adv.* askance; out of the corner of one's eye.
и́скра *n.* **1,** spark. **2,** *fig.* (*with gen.*) ray; glimmer (*of hope*); seed (*of doubt, suspicion, etc.*). —**у негó и́скры из глаз посы́пались,** he saw stars.
и́скренний *adj.* sincere. —**и́скренне; и́скренно,** *adv.* sincerely. —**и́скренность,** *n.f.* sincerity.
искриви́ть [*infl.* **-влю́, -ви́шь**] *v., pfv. of* **искривля́ть.**
искривлéние *n.* curvature.
искривля́ть *v. impfv.* [*pfv.* **искриви́ть**] **1,** to bend out of shape. **2,** to distort; contort.
искри́стый *adj.* sparkling.
и́скриться *also,* **искри́ться** *v.r. impfv.* to sparkle.
искромётный *adj.* sparkling; flashing; dazzling.
искромсáть *v., pfv. of* **кромсáть.**
искроши́ть *v., pfv. of* **кроши́ть.** —**искроши́ться,** *refl., pfv. of* **кроши́ться.**
искупáть *v. impfv.* [*pfv.* **искупи́ть**] **1,** to atone for; expiate. **2,** to make up for; make amends for.
искупи́тельный *adj.* expiatory.
искупи́ть [*infl.* **-куплю́, -ку́пишь**] *v., pfv. of* **искупáть.**
искуплéние *n.* (*with gen.*) expiation (of); atonement (for).
иску́с *n.* **1,** ordeal. **2,** test.
искусáть *v. pfv.* to sting; bite (*in many places*).
искуси́тель *n.m.* tempter.
искуси́ть [*infl.* **-кушу́, -куси́шь**] *v., pfv. of* **искушáть.** —**искуси́ться,** *refl.* (*with* **в** + *prepl.*) *obs.* to become experienced in; become an expert at.
иску́сник *n., colloq.* master craftsman; past master.
иску́сный *adj.* skillful. —**иску́сно,** *adv.* skillfully.
иску́сственный *adj.* **1,** artificial; imitation. **2,** artificial; unnatural. —**иску́сственно,** *adv.* artificially. —**иску́сственность,** *n.f.* artificiality.
иску́сство *n.* **1,** art: изя́щные иску́сства, fine arts; произведéние иску́сства, work of art; иску́сство шитья́, the art of sewing. **2,** skill: с больши́м иску́сством, with great skill.
искусствовéд *n.* art critic. —**искусствовéдение,** *n.* art criticism; study of art.
искушáть *v. impfv.* [*pfv.* **искуси́ть**] to tempt. —**искушáть судьбу́,** to tempt fate; press *or* stretch one's luck.
искушéние *n.* temptation.
искушённый *adj.* experienced; knowledgeable.
ислáм *n.* Islam.
ислáндец [*gen.* **-дца**] *n.m.* [*fem.* **-дка**] Icelander. —**ислáндский,** *adj.* Icelandic.
испáнец [*gen.* **-нца**] *n.m.* [*fem.* **-нка**] Spaniard.
испáнка [*gen. pl.* **-нок**] *n.* **1,** Spanish woman. **2,** *colloq.* influenza; flu.
испáнский *adj.* Spanish.
испарéние *n.* **1,** evaporation. **2,** *pl.* vapor; fumes.
испáрина *n.* perspiration.
испари́тель *n.m.* vaporizer.
испаря́ть *v. impfv.* [*pfv.* **испари́ть**] to evaporate; convert to vapor. —**испаря́ться,** *refl.* **1,** to evaporate; turn into vapor. **2,** *colloq.* to vanish; evaporate.
испáчкать *v., pfv. of* **пáчкать.** —**испáчкаться,** *refl., pfv. of* **пáчкаться.**
испепеля́ть *v. impfv.* [*pfv.* **испепели́ть**] to incinerate; reduce to ashes.
испестря́ть *v. impfv.* [*pfv.* **испестри́ть**] to color; make colorful.
испéчь *v., pfv. of* **печь.** —**испéчься,** *refl., pfv. of* **пéчься** (*in sense #1*).
испещря́ть *v. impfv.* [*pfv.* **испещри́ть**] **1,** to dot with color. **2,** to mark up.
исписáть [*infl.* **-пишу́, -пи́шешь**] *v., pfv. of* **испи́сывать.** —**исписáться,** *refl., pfv. of* **испи́сываться.**
испи́сывать *v. impfv.* [*pfv.* **исписáть**] **1,** to cover with writing. **2,** to use up (paper, a pencil, etc.). —**испи́сываться,** *refl.* **1,** (*of a pencil*) to be used up; be worn to a stump. **2,** *colloq.* (*of a writer*) to lose one's creativity; become stale.
испитóй *adj., colloq.* haggard; gaunt; drawn.
исповедáльня [*gen. pl.* **-лен**] *n.* confessional.
исповéдание *n.* **1,** profession (*of a certain faith*). **2,** *obs.* faith; creed.
исповéдник *n.* confessor.
исповéдовать *v. impfv. & pfv.* [*pres.* **-дую, -дуешь**] *relig.* **1,** to hear the confession of. **2,** to profess (a religion). —**исповéдоваться,** *refl.* to confess; confess one's sins.
и́споведь *n.f.* confession.

исподволь *adv., colloq.* gradually; slowly; little by little.
исподлóбья *adv., in* **смотрéть исподлóбья (на),** to glower (at).
исподтишкá *adv., colloq.* secretly; stealthily; on the sly.
испокóн *adv., in* **испокóн векóв** (*or* **вéку),** since time immemorial.
исполи́н *n.* giant. —**исполи́нский,** *adj.* giant; gigantic.
исполкóм *n.* executive committee (*contr. of* **исполни́тельный комитéт).**
исполнéние *n.* **1,** execution; fulfillment; performance. **2,** performance; rendition. —**приводи́ть в исполнéние,** to carry out.
испóлненный *adj.* (*with gen.*) full (of).
исполни́мый *adj.* feasible.
исполни́тель *n.m.* **1,** executor. **2,** performer. —**состáв исполни́телей,** cast. —**судéбный исполни́тель,** bailiff.
исполни́тельный *adj.* **1,** executive. **2,** efficient; industrious. —**исполни́тельный комитéт,** executive committee. —**исполни́тельный лист,** writ.
исполня́ть *v. impfv.* [*pfv.* **испóлнить**] **1,** to fulfill; execute; carry out. **2,** to perform (a song, dance, role, etc.). —**исполня́ться,** *refl.* **1,** to be fulfilled. **2,** (*of an anniversary*) to occur; be. **3,** *impers.* (*with dat.*) *indicating attainment of a certain age:* зáвтра мне испóлнится двáдцать оди́н год, tomorrow I will be twenty-one.
испóльзование *n.* utilization; use.
испóльзовать *v. impfv. & pfv.* [*pres.* **-зую, -зуешь**] to use; utilize; make use of; exploit.
испóльщик *n.* sharecropper.
испóртить *v., pfv. of* **пóртить.** —**испóртиться,** *refl., pfv. of* **пóртиться.**
испóрченный *adj.* **1,** spoiled; rotten; tainted. **2,** damaged. **3,** depraved; perverted.
исправи́мый *adj.* **1,** reparable; rectifiable; remediable. **2,** repairable.
исправи́тельный *adj.* corrective; remedial. —**исправи́тельный дом,** reformatory; reform school; house of correction.
испрáвить [*infl.* **-влю, -вишь**] *v., pfv. of* **исправля́ть.** —**испрáвиться,** *refl., pfv. of* **исправля́ться.**
исправлéние *n.* **1,** repairing; correcting. **2,** correction.
исправля́ть *v. impfv.* [*pfv.* **испрáвить**] **1,** to correct. **2,** to repair. **3,** to reform. —**исправля́ться,** *refl.* to reform; mend one's ways.
испрáвность *n.f.* good condition; good working order.
испрáвный *adj.* **1,** in good condition; in good working order. **2,** conscientious; industrious.
испражнéние *n.* **1,** defecation. **2,** *pl.* excrement; feces.
испражня́ться *v.r. impfv.* [*pfv.* **испражни́ться**] to defecate.
испрáшивать *v. impfv.* [*pfv.* **испроси́ть**] *obs.* to solicit; formally request.
испрóбовать *v. pfv.* [*infl.* **-бую, -буешь**] **1,** to test; try out. **2,** to experience.
испроси́ть *v. pfv.* [*infl.* **-прошу́, -прóсишь**] **1,** *pfv. of* **испрáшивать. 2,** to obtain; receive (*by asking*).
испу́г *n.* fright.
испу́ганный *adj.* frightened; scared.
испугáть *v., pfv. of* **пугáть.** —**испугáться,** *refl., pfv. of* **пугáться.**
испускáние *n.* emission.
испускáть *v. impfv.* [*pfv.* **испусти́ть**] **1,** to emit; give off. **2,** to emit; utter. —**испусти́ть дух** *or* **послéдний вздох,** to breathe one's last.
испусти́ть [*infl.* **-пущу́, -пу́стишь**] *v., pfv. of* **испускáть.**
испытáние *n.* **1,** test; trial. **2,** examination. **3,** trial; ordeal.
испы́танный *adj.* tried; tested; proven.
испытáтель *n.m.* tester. —**лётчик-испытáтель,** test pilot.
испытáтельный *adj.* test (*attrib.*); trial (*attrib.*).
испытáть *v., pfv. of* **испы́тывать.**
испыту́ющий *adj.* searching; penetrating.
испы́тывать *v. impfv.* [*pfv.* **испытáть**] **1,** to test; try out. **2,** to experience; feel. **3,** to try; tax (someone's patience). **4,** *in* испы́тывать судьбу́, to tempt fate; press one's luck.
иссекáть *v. impfv.* [*pfv.* **иссéчь**] **1,** to carve. **2,** *med.* to excise. **3,** to slash in many places. **4,** *obs.* to flog.
иссечéние *n., med.* excision.
иссéчь *v. pfv.* [*infl. like* **сечь**] **1,** [*past* **-сéк, -секлá, секлó**] *pfv. of* **иссекáть** (*in senses #1 & #2*). **2,** [*past* **-сéк, -сéкла, сéкло**] *pfv. of* **иссекáть** (*in senses #3 & #4*).
исслéдование *n.* **1,** research. **2,** a study (*piece of research*). **3,** exploration.
исслéдователь *n.m.* **1,** researcher. **2,** explorer.
исслéдовательский *adj.* research (*attrib.*).
исслéдовать *v. impfv. & pfv.* [*pres.* **-дую, -дуешь**] **1,** to explore. **2,** to examine. **3,** to study; do research in.
иссóп *n.* hyssop.
иссóхнуть [*past* **-сóх, -ла**] *v., pfv. of* **иссыхáть.**
и́сстари *adv.* since ancient times.
исстрадáться *v.r. pfv.* to be worn out with suffering.
исступлéние *n.* frenzy.
исступлённый *adj.* frenzied.
иссушáть *v. impfv.* [*pfv.* **иссуши́ть**] **1,** to dry thoroughly; dry completely. **2,** *fig.* to drain; exhaust (someone).
иссуши́ть [*infl.* **-сушу́, -су́шишь**] *v., pfv. of* **иссушáть.**
иссыхáть *v. impfv.* [*pfv.* **иссóхнуть**] **1,** to dry up. **2,** *fig.* to shrink away to nothing.
иссякáть *v. impfv.* [*pfv.* **иссякнуть**] **1,** to dry up; run dry. **2,** to give out; run out; be used up; be exhausted.
исся́кнуть [*past* **-ся́к, -ла**] *v., pfv. of* **иссякáть.**
истáпливать *v. impfv.* [*pfv.* **истопи́ть**] **1,** to heat; heat up (a stove). **2,** *colloq.* to use; consume (firewood). **3,** *colloq.* to melt completely; melt all of.
истáптывать *v. impfv.* [*pfv.* **истоптáть**] **1,** to trample. **2,** *colloq.* to track up (a clean floor). **3,** *colloq.* to wear out (shoes).
истáскивать *v. impfv.* [*pfv.* **истаскáть**] *colloq.* to wear out.
истáчивать *v. impfv.* [*pfv.* **источи́ть**] **1,** to wear down (*by repeated rubbing*). **2,** to eat away.
истекáть *v. impfv.* [*pfv.* **истéчь**] **1,** *obs.* to flow out. **2,** *in* истекáть крóвью, to bleed profusely. **3,** (*of time*) to elapse; expire; run out; be up. **4,** [*impfv. only*] (*with* **от** *or* **из**) to emanate (from); stem (from).
истéкший *adj.* past: за истéкший год, during the past year.
истерéть [*infl.* **изотру́, изотрёшь** *past* **истёр, -ла**] *v., pfv. of* **истирáть.**
истéрзанный *adj.* **1,** slashed to bits. **2,** bedraggled. **3,** tormented.

истерзáть *v. pfv.* **1,** to tear to pieces. **2,** *fig.* to beset; torment; wrack.
истéрик *n., colloq.* person often going into fits of hysteria.
истéрика *n.* hysterics.
истери́ческий *adj.* hysterical.
истери́чка [*gen. pl.* **-чек**] *n., colloq.* hysterical woman.
истери́чный *adj.* hysterical.
истери́я *n.* hysteria.
истёртый *adj.* **1,** worn out; worn down. **2,** *fig.* trite; overused.
истéц [*gen.* **истцá**] *n.* plaintiff.
истечéние *n.* **1,** outflow. **2,** expiration.
истéчь [*infl. like* **течь**] *v., pfv. of* **истекáть.**
и́стина *n.* truth.
и́стинный *adj.* true; veritable. —**и́стинно,** *adv.* truly.
истирáние *n.* abrasion; wear.
истирáть *v. impfv.* [*pfv.* **истерéть**] **1,** to grate; shred. **2,** to wear away (a surface); wear out (clothes or furniture); wear down (an eraser).
истлевáть *v. impfv.* [*pfv.* **истлéть**] **1,** to rot; decay. **2,** to burn to ashes.
и́стовый *adj., obs.* **1,** real; true. **2,** energetic; vigorous. **3,** proper; sedate.
истóк *n.* **1,** source (*of a river*); *pl.* headwaters. **2,** *usu. pl.* source; origin.
истолковáние *n.* interpretation.
истолковáтель *n.m.* interpreter; commentator.
истолковáть [*infl.* **-кýю, -кýешь**] *v., pfv. of* **истолкóвывать.**
истолкóвывать *v. impfv.* [*pfv.* **истолковáть**] to interpret; construe.
истолóчь *v., pfv. of* **толóчь.**
истóма *n.* languor; lassitude.
истоми́ть [*infl.* **-млю́, -ми́шь**] *v., pfv. of* **томи́ть** *and* **истомля́ть.**
истомля́ть *v. impfv.* [*pfv.* **истоми́ть**] to tire; weary; fatigue; exhaust.
истопи́ть [*infl.* **-топлю́, -тóпишь**] *v., pfv. of* **истáпливать.**
истопни́к [*gen.* **-никá**] *n.* boilerman; stoker.
истоптáть [*infl.* **-топчý, -тóпчешь**] *v., pfv. of* **истáптывать.**
исторгáть *v. impfv.* [*pfv.* **истóргнуть**] *obs.* **1,** to banish. **2,** to wrest; grab. **3,** to rescue; deliver. **4,** to elicit; evoke. **5,** to extract; extort.
истóргнуть [*past* **-тóрг** *or* **-тóргнул, -тóргла**] *v., pfv. of* **исторгáть.**
истори́зм *n.* historical method.
истóрик *n.* historian.
историогрáфия *n.* historiography. —**истóриóграф,** *n.* historiographer.
истори́ческий *adj.* **1,** historical. **2,** historic. —**истори́чески,** *adv.* historically.
истóрия *n.* **1,** history. **2,** story. **3,** *colloq.* incident; untoward event: попáсть *or* вли́пнуть в истóрию, to get into an unpleasant situation. —**истóрия болéзни,** case history.
истосковáться *v.r. pfv.* [*infl.* **-кýюсь, -кýешься**] (*with* **по** + *dat.*) *colloq.* to miss greatly; yearn for.
источáть *v. impfv.* **1,** *obs.* to shed (tears). **2,** to give off; emit.
источи́ть [*infl.* **-точý, -тóчишь**] *v., pfv. of* **истáчивать.**
истóчник *n.* **1,** spring. **2,** *fig.* source.
истóшный *adj., colloq.* heart-rending; blood-curdling.
истощáть *v. impfv.* [*pfv.* **истощи́ть**] **1,** to exhaust; tire out. **2,** to exhaust; deplete; use up. —**истощáться,** *refl.* **1,** to be exhausted (*physically*). **2,** to be exhausted; be used up; run out.
истощéние *n.* **1,** exhaustion: нéрвное истощéние, nervous exhaustion. **2,** exhaustion; depletion. —**войнá на истощéние,** war of attrition.
истощённый *adj.* **1,** exhausted. **2,** emaciated.
истощи́ть *v., pfv. of* **истощáть.** —**истощи́ться,** *refl., pfv. of* **истощáться.**
истрáтить *v., pfv. of* **трáтить.** —**истрáтиться,** *refl., pfv. of* **трáтиться.**
истреби́тель *n.m.* **1,** (*with gen.*) destroyer (of). **2,** fighter (*aircraft*).
истреби́тельный *adj.* **1,** destructive. Истреби́тельная войнá, war of annihilation. **2,** *aero.* fighter (*attrib.*).
истреби́ть [*infl.* **-блю́, би́шь**] *v., pfv. of* **истребля́ть.**
истреблéние *n.* destruction; extermination.
истребля́ть *v. impfv.* [*pfv.* **истреби́ть**] to destroy; annihilate; exterminate; wipe out.
истрепáть [*infl.* **-треплю́, -трéплешь**] *v., pfv. of* **трепáть** (*in sense #4*) *and* **истрёпывать.** —**истрепáться,** *refl., pfv. of* **трепáться** (*in sense #2*) *and* **истрёпываться.**
истрёпывать *v. impfv.* [*pfv.* **истрепáть**] *colloq.* to wear out. —**истрёпываться,** *refl., colloq.* to be worn out.
истукáн *n.* idol. —**(сидéть** *or* **стоя́ть) истукáном,** motionless; like a statue.
иступи́ть *v., pfv. of* **тупи́ть.** —**иступи́ться,** *refl., pfv. of* **тупи́ться.**
и́стый *adj.* true; real.
истязáние *n.* torture. —**истязáтель,** *n.m.* torturer.
истязáть *v. impfv.* to torture.
исхóд *n.* **1,** end; close. **2,** outcome. **3,** way out (*of a situation*). **4,** outlet (*for one's emotions*). **5,** *Bib.* exodus; *cap.* (book of) Exodus. —**на исхóде, 1,** drawing to a close. **2,** (*with gen.*) at the end (of). **3,** running low; running out.
исходи́ть[1] *v. impfv.* [*pres.* **-хожý, -хóдишь**] **1,** (*with* **из** *or* **от**) (*of smoke, an odor, etc.*) to come (from); issue (from). **2,** (*with* **из** *or* **от**) to originate (from); emanate (from). **3,** (*with* **из**) to proceed on (an assumption, premise, etc.). **4,** [*pfv.* **изойти́**] (*with instr.*) *colloq.* to be drained of (tears, blood, etc.).
исходи́ть[2] *v. pfv.* [*infl.* **-хожý, -хóдишь**] *colloq.* to walk all over (a place).
исхóдный *adj.* initial; starting.
исходя́щий *adj.* (*of mail, documents, etc.*) outgoing.
исхудáлый *adj.* emaciated; haggard; gaunt.
исхудáть *v. pfv.* to become emaciated.
исцарáпывать *v. impfv.* [*pfv.* **исцарáпать**] to scratch severely; scratch in many places.
исцелéние *n.* **1,** cure; healing. **2,** recovery. —**исцели́тель,** *n.m.* healer.
исцеля́ть *v. impfv.* [*pfv.* **исцели́ть**] to cure; heal.
исчáдие *n., obs.* child; offspring. —**исчáдие áда,** the devil incarnate.
исчáхнуть *v. pfv.* [*past* **-чáх, -ла**] to waste away.
исчезáть *v. impfv.* [*pfv.* **исчéзнуть**] to disappear; vanish.
исчезновéние *n.* disappearance.
исчéзнуть [*past* **-чéз, -ла**] *v., pfv. of* **исчезáть.**
исчéрпывать *v. impfv.* [*pfv.* **исчéрпать**] **1,** to exhaust. **2,** to settle; close (a matter).

исчéрпывающий *adj.* exhaustive.
исчерти́ть [*infl.* **-черчу́, -чéртишь**] *v., pfv. of* **исчéрчивать.**
исчéрчивать *v. impfv.* [*pfv.* **исчерти́ть**] to cover with lines.
исчислéние *n.* **1,** calculation. **2,** calculus.
исчисля́ть *v. impfv.* [*pfv.* **исчи́слить**] to calculate; estimate. —**исчисля́ться,** *refl.* [*impfv. only*] (*with instr. or* **в** + *acc.*) to number in; amount to.
ита́к *conj.* so; and so; thus.
италья́нец [*gen.* **-нца**] *n.m.* [*fem.* **-нка**] Italian.
италья́нский *adj.* Italian. —**италья́нская забастóвка,** sit-down strike.
и т.д. *abbr. of* **и так да́лее,** and so forth; et cetera.
итóг *n.* **1,** sum; total. **2,** result. —**в итóге,** as a result. —**в конéчном итóге,** in the final analysis. —**подводи́ть итóг** *or* **итóги** (+ *dat.*), to total; add up; *fig.* sum up.
итогó *adv.* **1,** in all; altogether. **2,** (*at the bottom of a column of figures*) total.
итóговый *adj.* **1,** total. **2,** final.
иттéрбий *n.* ytterbium.
и́ттрий *n.* yttrium.
Иу́да *n.* Judas.
иудаи́зм *n.* Judaism.
иудéй *n.* Jew. —**иудéйский,** *adj.* Judaic. —**иудéйство,** *n.* Judaism.
их *pron., gen. & acc. of* **они́.** —*poss. adj. & pron.* their; theirs.
ихневмóн *n.* ichneumon.
и́хний *adj., colloq.* their; theirs.
ихтиолóгия *n.* ichthyology.
иша́к [*gen.* **ишака́**] *n.* donkey.
и́шиас *n.* sciatica.
ишь *particle, colloq.* see!; look!; oh! —**ишь ты, 1,** = **ишь. 2,** oh come on!; what are you talking about!
ищéйка [*gen. pl.* **ищéек**] *n.* **1,** bloodhound. **2,** *colloq.* sleuth.
ию́ль *n.m.* July. —**ию́льский,** *adj.* July (*attrib.*).
ию́нь *n.m.* June. —**ию́ньский,** *adj.* June (*attrib.*).

Й

Й, й *n. neut., called* **и кра́ткое,** tenth letter of the Russian alphabet.
йог *n.* yogi. —**йóга,** *n.* yoga.
йод *n.* iodine.
йóдистый *adj.* **1,** containing iodine. **2,** iodide (of): йóдистый ка́лий, potassium iodide.
йóдный *adj.* iodine (*attrib.*).
йóта *n.* iota. —**ни на йóту,** not a bit; not one iota.

К

К, к *n. neut.* eleventh letter of the Russian alphabet.
к *also,* **ко** *prep., with dat.* **1,** to; toward; in the direction of: идти́ к доскé, to go to the blackboard; подходи́ть к концу́, to draw to a close. **2,** to; to the home or place of business of: идти́ к врачу́, to go to the doctor. Он ча́сто приходи́л к нам, he often came to visit us. **3,** *with emotions* of; for; toward: любóвь к рóдине, love of one's country; мои́ чу́вства к ней, my feelings toward her. **4,** *in introductory expressions* to: к моему́ удивлéнию, to my surprise. К сча́стью, fortunately; к сожалéнию, unfortunately. **5,** *with expressions of time* by: к тому́ врéмени, by that time; by then. —**к тому́ же,** moreover; besides.
-ка *particle, colloq., used to lessen the force of a suggestion, request, command, etc.:* ну́-ка, well?; встава́й-ка!, get up, now!; закрóй-ка окнó!, close the window, will you?
каба́к [*gen.* **-бака́**] *n.* **1,** *pre-rev.* tavern. **2,** *colloq.* mess.
кабала́ *n.* servitude; bondage.
каба́льный *adj.* **1,** serving to enslave. **2,** (*of a treaty, provisions, etc.*) one-sided.
каба́н [*gen.* **-бана́**] *n.* **1,** wild boar. **2,** male hog.
кабарга́ [*gen. pl.* **-рóг**] *n.* musk deer.
кабарди́нец [*gen.* **-нца**] *n.m.* [*fem.* **-нка**] Kabardian (*one of a people inhabiting the Caucasus*). —**кабарди́нский,** *adj.* Kabardian.

кабаре́ (рэ) *n. neut. indecl.* cabaret.
кабачо́к [*gen.* **-чка́**] *n.* **1,** cheap restaurant. **2,** squash (*vegetable*).
ка́бель *n.m.* cable. —**ка́бельный,** *adj.* cable (*attrib.*).
кабеста́н *n.* capstan.
каби́на *n.* **1,** booth; cubicle. **2,** cab (*of a truck*). **3,** *aero.* cabin; cockpit.
кабине́т *n.* **1,** private office; study. **2,** (specially equipped) room: рентге́новский кабине́т, X-ray room. **3,** set of office furniture. **4,** private room in a restaurant. **5,** *polit.* cabinet.
кабине́тный *adj.* office (*attrib.*). —**кабине́тный роя́ль,** baby grand piano. —**кабине́тный страте́г,** armchair strategist.
каби́нка [*gen. pl.* **-нок**] *n., dim. of* **каби́на.**
каблогра́мма *n.* cablegram.
каблу́к [*gen.* **-блука́**] *n.* heel (*of a shoe*). —**под каблуко́м у,** under the thumb of.
каблучо́к [*gen.* **-чка́**] *n., dim. of* **каблу́к.**
кабриоле́т *n.* cabriolet; gig.
кабы́ *conj., colloq.* **1,** if. **2,** if only.—**е́сли бы да кабы́, (то во рту росли́ б грибы́),** if wishes were horses (beggars would ride).
кавале́р *n.* **1,** escort; dancing partner. **2,** holder (*of an order or award*). **3,** *colloq.* admirer.
кавале́рия *n.* cavalry. —**кавалери́йский,** *adj.* cavalry (*attrib.*). —**кавалери́ст,** *n.* cavalryman.
кавалька́да *n.* cavalcade.
каварда́к [*gen.* **-дака́**] *n., colloq.* confusion; disorder; mess.
ка́верза *n., colloq.* **1,** intrigue; chicanery. **2,** mean trick.
ка́верзный *adj., colloq.* **1,** scheming. **2,** tricky; intricate.
каве́рна *n., med.* cavity.
кавака́зец [*gen.* **-зца**] *n.m.* [*fem.* **-зка**] native of the Caucasus. —**кавка́зский,** *adj.* Caucasian; Caucasus (*attrib.*).
кавы́чки [*gen.* **-чек**] *n. pl.* quotation marks.
каде́нция (дэ) *n., music* **1,** cadence. **2,** cadenza.
каде́т *n.* **1,** *pre-rev.* (military) cadet. **2,** *hist.* member of the Constitutional Democrat party; Cadet.
каде́тский *adj.* **1,** *pre-rev.* cadet (*attrib.*). **2,** *hist.* of or pert. to the Constitutional Democrats.
кади́ло *n.* censer.
кади́ть *v. impfv.* [*pres.* **кажу́, кади́шь**] to gently wave a container of burning incense.
ка́дка [*gen. pl.* **-док**] *n.* tub.
ка́дмий *n.* cadmium.
кадр *n., motion pictures* **1,** frame. **2,** shot; scene.
кадри́ль *n.f.* quadrille.
ка́дровый *adj.* **1,** (*of a worker*) trained; skilled. **2,** *mil.* regular.
ка́дры [*gen.* **-ров**] *n. pl.* **1,** personnel. **2,** cadres.
кады́к [*gen.* **-дыка́**] *n.* Adam's apple.
каёмка [*gen. pl.* **-мок**] *n.* border; edging.
каждодне́вный *adj.* daily; everyday.
ка́ждый *adj.* every; each: ка́ждый день, every day. —*indef. pron.* **1,** each one. **2,** everyone; everybody. **3,** anyone; anybody. —**ка́ждому своё,** to each his own.
ка́жущийся *adj.* apparent; seeming; imaginary.
каза́к [*gen.* **-зака́**] *n.* Cossack.
каза́рка [*gen. pl.* **-рок**] *n.* brant goose. —**белощёкая каза́рка,** barnacle goose. —**кана́дская каза́рка,** Canada goose.
каза́рма *n.* **1,** *usu. pl.* barracks. **2,** *colloq.* ugly building. —**каза́рменный,** *adj.* barracks (*attrib.*).
каза́ться *v.r. impfv.* [*pfv.* **показа́ться;** *pres.* **кажу́сь, ка́жешься**] (*with instr.*) to seem: каза́ться стра́нным, to seem strange. *Also impers.:* ка́жется, it seems. Мне ка́жется, что..., it seems to me that... —**каза́лось бы, 1,** it would seem. **2,** seemingly.
каза́х *n.m.* [*fem.* **-за́шка**] Kazakh (*one of a people living mainly in the Kazakh S.S.R.*). —**каза́хский,** *adj.* Kazakh.
каза́цкий *adj.* Cossack (*attrib.*).
каза́чество *n.* the Cossacks.
каза́чий [*fem.* **-чья**] *adj.* Cossack (*attrib.*).
казачо́к [*gen.* **-чка́**] *n.* **1,** a lively Ukrainian dance. **2,** *obs.* boy servant; page.
казеи́н *n.* casein.
казема́т *n.* **1,** casemate. **2,** cell for solitary confinement.
казённый *adj.* **1,** public; belonging to, issued by, or paid for by the government. **2,** *fig.* bureaucratic; formal. —**казённая часть,** breech (*of a firearm*).
казино́ *n. indecl.* casino.
казна́ *n., obs.* **1,** treasury. **2,** the State. **3,** money.
казначе́й *n.* **1,** treasurer. **2,** purser; paymaster. —**казначе́йский,** *adj.* treasury (*attrib.*): казначе́йский биле́т, treasury note. —**казначе́йство,** *n., pre-rev.* treasury.
казни́ть *v. impfv. & pfv.* to execute; put to death. —**казни́ться,** *refl.* to suffer acute remorse; blame oneself bitterly.
казнокра́д *n.* embezzler of public funds.
казнь *n.f.* execution. —**сме́ртная казнь,** the death penalty; capital punishment.
казуи́стика *n.* casuistry. —**казуи́ст,** *n.* casuist. —**казуисти́ческий,** *adj.* casuistic.
ка́зус *n.* **1,** complex legal case. **2,** *colloq.* incident.
ка́зусный *adj.* involved; complex.
ка́йзер (зэ) *n.* Kaiser.
кайло́ [*pl.* **ка́йла**] *n.* pick; hack. *Also,* **кайла́.**
кайма́ [*gen. pl.* **каём**] *n.* border; edging.
ка́йра *n.* murre (*bird*).
как *adv.* **1,** how: как дела́?, how are things?; как краси́во!, how beautiful! Я забы́л, как туда́ пройти́, I forgot how to get there. **2,** *in certain expressions* what?: как ва́ше и́мя?, what is your name?; как э́то называ́ется?, what is this called? —*conj.* **1,** as; like: как обы́чно, as usual; бе́лый как снег, white as snow; рабо́тать как вол, to work like a horse. **2,** *following verbs of perceiving:* я ви́дел, как он ушёл, I saw him leave. **3,** (*with* **не**) but; besides: кто мо́жет э́то сде́лать, как не вы?, who can do it but/besides you? **4,** *when preceded and followed by the same word* like any other: го́род как го́род, a city like any other city. —**как бы, 1,** as if. **2,** seeming to. **3,** a sort of. —**как бы не,** that (*something might happen*). —**как бы то ни́ было,** *see* **быть.** —**как быть?,** *see* **быть.** —**как же!,** why, of course! —**как ни,** however; no matter how: как он ни стара́лся, no matter how he tried. —**как раз,** *see* **раз.** —**как..., так и,** both..., and. —**как то́лько,** as soon as.
какаду́ *n.m. indecl.* cockatoo.
кака́о *n. indecl.* **1,** cacao. **2,** cocoa.
ка́к-либо *adv.* somehow.
ка́к-нибудь *adv.* **1,** somehow. **2,** *colloq.* haphazardly; any which way. **3,** *colloq.* sometime; someday.

как-никáк *adv., colloq.* **1,** despite all; still and all. **2,** after all; in the end.

какóв [*fem.* **каковá;** *pl.* **каковы́**] *pron.* **1,** *interr.* what is?; what are?: каковы́ фáкты?, what are the facts? **2,** *interr.* what is... like?; what kind of... is...?: какóв он?, what is he like?; какóв он собóй?, what does he look like? **3,** *rel.* what kind of; the sort of: я тебé расскажý, каковы́ э́ти лю́ди, I'll tell you what kind of people they are. **4,** *rel.* such as: какóв он есть, such as he is. —**какóв..., такóв и...,** like..., like...: какóв отéц, такóв и сын, like father, like son.

каковó *pron., neut. of* **какóв.** —*interr. & rel. adv., colloq.* how: каковó ей живётся?, how is she getting along?

каковóй *rel. pron., obs.* which.

какóй *adj.* **1,** which?; what?: в какýю стóрону он пошёл?, which way did he go? До какóй стéпени?, to what extent? **2,** what is...?: какóй счёт?, what's the score? Какóе сегóдня числó?, what is today's date? **3,** what sort of; what kind of: какáя сегóдня погóда?, what sort of weather is it today?; what is the weather like today? **4,** *in exclamations* what...!: какóе чýдное мéсто!, what a delightful place! —*rel. pron.* such as; the kind of: он не такóй знатóк, какóй ты дýмал, he is not the expert you thought he was. —**какóй (бы) ни,** whatever; whichever. —**какóй бы то ни́ было,** any whatsoever. —**ни** (+ *prep.*) **какóй,** not any; no: ни под каки́м ви́дом, under no circumstances. Он не отвечáл ни на какúе вопрóсы, he did not answer any questions.

какóй-либо *adj.* = **какóй-нибудь.**

какóй-нибудь *adj.* **1,** some; a: дáйте мне какóй-нибудь примéр, give me an example. **2,** (*with numerals*) *colloq.* about; some.

какóй-то *adj.* **1,** some: вас спрáшивает какóй-то человéк, some man is asking for you. **2,** a kind of; a sort of.

какофóния *n.* cacophony. **какофони́ческий,** *adj.* cacophonous.

кáк-то *adv.* **1,** somehow. **2,** *colloq.* once; one day. **3,** *colloq.* I wonder how. **4,** *colloq.* namely. —**кáк-то раз,** once.

кáктус *n.* cactus.

кал *n.* excrement.

каламбýр *n.* pun. —**каламбури́ст,** *n.* punster.

каламбýрить *v. impfv.* to pun; make puns.

калáн *n.* sea otter.

калáндр *n.* calender.

каланчá *n.* **1,** watch tower (*of a fire station*). **2,** *colloq.* beanpole (*tall person*).

калáч [*gen.* **-лачá**] *n.* a kind of roll with a distinctive shape. —**тёртый калáч,** old hand; person who has been around.

калáчик *n., dim. of* **калáч.** —**свернýться калáчиком,** to curl up into a ball.

калейдоскóп *n.* kaleidoscope. —**калейдоскопи́ческий,** *adj.* kaleidoscopic.

калéка *n.m. & f.* cripple.

календáрь [*gen.* **-дaря́**] *n.m.* calendar. —**календáрный,** *adj.* calendar (*attrib.*).

калéние *n.* incandescence. —**бéлое калéние,** white heat.

калёный *adj.* **1,** red-hot. **2,** (*of nuts*) roasted.

калéчить *v. impfv.* [*pfv.* **искалéчить**] **1,** to maim; cripple. **2,** *fig.* to pervert; warp.

кали́бр *n.* **1,** caliber (*of a gun or bullet*). **2,** gauge.

калибровáние *n.* calibration.

калибровáть *v. impfv.* [*pres.* **-рýю, -рýешь**] to calibrate.

кáлий *n.* potassium. —**кáлиевый; кали́йный,** *adj.* potassium (*attrib.*).

кали́льный *adj.* used for heating or smelting metals. —**кали́льная сéтка,** (incandescent) mantle.

кали́на *n.* viburnum.

кали́тка [*gen. pl.* **-ток**] *n.* gate in a fence.

кали́ть *v. impfv.* **1,** to make red-hot. **2,** to roast.

кали́ф *n.* caliph.

калифóрний *n.* californium.

каллигрáфия *n.* calligraphy. —**каллиграфи́ческий,** *adj.* calligraphic.

калмы́к *n.m.* [*fem.* **-мы́чка**] Kalmyk; Kalmuck (*one of a Mongol people inhabiting the Volga delta*). —**калмы́цкий,** *adj.* Kalmyk; Kalmuck.

калóрия *n.* calorie. —**калори́йность,** *n.f.* caloric content. —**калори́метр,** *n.* calorimeter.

калóши *n. pl.* [*sing.* **калóша**] rubbers. —**сесть в калóшу,** *colloq.* to make a fool of oneself; put one's foot in it. *Also,* **галóши.**

калýжница *n.* marsh marigold.

кáлька [*gen. pl.* **-лек**] *n.* **1,** [*usu.* **бумáжная кáлька**] tracing paper. **2,** a tracing. **3,** *ling.* loan translation; calque.

кальки́ровать *v. impfv.* [*pfv.* **скальки́ровать;** *pres.* **-рую, -руешь**] to trace.

калькули́ровать *v. impfv.* [*pfv.* **скалькули́ровать;** *pres.* **-рую, -руешь**] to calculate.

калькуля́тор *n.* calculator.

кальмáр *n.* squid.

кальсóны [*gen.* **-сóн**] *n. pl.* men's drawers; long underpants.

кáльций *n.* calcium. —**кáльциевый,** *adj.* calcium (*attrib.*).

каля́кать *v. impfv., colloq.* to chatter.

камáринская *n., decl. as an adj.* Russian folk dance.

кáмбала *n.* flounder; plaice; sole.

кáмбий *n.* cambium.

кáмбуз *n.* **1,** ship's galley. **2,** ship's boiler.

камвóльный *adj.* worsted.

камéдь *n.f.* gum.

камелёк [*gen.* **-лькá**] *n.* small fireplace.

камéлия *n.* camellia.

каменéть *v. impfv.* [*pfv.* **окаменéть**] **1,** to turn to stone; become petrified; petrify. **2,** to stiffen; freeze. **3,** *fig.* to harden; become callous.

камени́стый *adj.* stony; rocky.

каменноугóльный *also,* **каменноýгольный** *adj.* coal (*attrib.*).

кáменный *adj.* **1,** stone. **2,** *fig.* stony. —**кáменный век,** the Stone Age. —**кáменная соль,** rock salt. —**кáменный ýголь,** (anthracite or bituminous) coal.

каменолóмня [*gen. pl.* **-мен**] *n.* quarry.

каменотёс *n.* stonemason.

кáменщик *n.* mason; bricklayer.

кáмень [*gen.* **-мня;** *pl.* **кáмни, -нéй, -ня́м**] *n.m.* stone; rock. —**кáмня на кáмне не остáвить,** not to leave a stone standing.

кáмера *n.* **1,** chamber. **2,** cell (*of a prison*). **3,** inner tube. **4,** camera. —**кáмера хранéния (багажá),** baggage room.

камергéр *n.* chamberlain.

камерди́нер *n.* valet.
камери́стка [*gen. pl.* **-ток**] *n.* lady's maid.
ка́мерный *adj.* **1,** *mech.* having chambers. **2,** *music* chamber (*attrib.*): ка́мерная му́зыка, chamber music.
камерто́н *n.* tuning fork.
ка́мешек [*gen.* **-шка**] *n.* small stone; pebble. —**броса́ть ка́мешки в чей-нибудь огоро́д,** to make snide remarks about someone.
каме́я *n.* cameo.
ками́н *n.* fireplace. —**электри́ческий ками́н,** electric heater.
ками́нный *adj.* fireplace (*attrib.*). —**ками́нная по́лка,** mantel; mantelpiece. —**ками́нная решётка,** fire screen. —**ками́нные щипцы́,** fire irons.
камнедроби́лка *n.* stone crusher; rock crusher.
камнело́мка *n.* saxifrage.
камнере́з *n.* stonecutter.
камо́рка [*gen. pl.* **-рок**] *n.* tiny room; closet.
кампа́ния *n.* campaign.
камуфли́ровать *v. impfv. & pfv.* [*pres.* **-рую, -руешь**] to camouflage.
камуфля́ж *n.* camouflage.
ка́мушек [*gen.* **-шка**] *n.* = **ка́мешек.**
камфара́ *also,* **ка́мфора** *n.* camphor. —**камфа́рный; ка́мфорный,** *adj.* camphor.
камы́ш [*gen.* **-мыша́**] *n.* reed; rush; cane. —**камышо́вый,** *adj.* made of reed/rush/cane.
кана́ва *n.* ditch. —**сто́чная** *or* **водосто́чная кана́ва,** gutter.
кана́дец [*gen.* **-дца**] *n.m.* [*fem.* **-дка**] Canadian. —**кана́дский,** *adj.* Canadian.
кана́л *n.* **1,** canal. **2,** *anat.* duct. **3,** bore (*of a firearm*). **4,** *television* channel. **5,** *fig.* channel: дипломати́ческие кана́лы, diplomatic channels.
канализа́ция *n.* sewage system. —**канализацио́нный,** *adj.* sewage (*attrib.*).
канаре́ечный *adj.* **1,** canary (*attrib.*). **2,** canary-yellow.
канаре́йка [*gen. pl.* **-ре́ек**] *n.* canary.
кана́т *n.* **1,** rope. **2,** cable. —**кана́тный,** *adj.* rope (*attrib.*); cable (*attrib.*).
канатохо́дец [*gen.* **-дца**] *n.* tightrope walker.
канва́ *n.* **1,** canvas (*for needlework*). **2,** *fig.* background.
кандалы́ [*gen.* **-ло́в**] *n. pl.* shackles; fetters.
канделя́бр *n.* candelabrum.
кандида́т *n.* **1,** candidate. **2,** holder of an academic degree roughly equivalent to a master's degree; candidate: кандида́т нау́к, candidate of science. —**кандида́т в чле́ны** (+ *gen.*), candidate (*or* alternate) member (of).
кандида́тский *adj.* candidate's.
кандидату́ра *n.* candidacy. —**выдвига́ть** *or* **выставля́ть чью-нибудь кандидату́ру,** to nominate someone. —**выдвига́ть** *or* **выставля́ть свою́ кандидату́ру,** to announce one's candidacy; run.
кани́кулы [*gen.* **-кул**] *n. pl.* vacation (*from school*). —**каникуля́рный,** *adj.* vacation (*attrib.*).
кани́телиться *v.r. impfv.* [*pfv.* **прокани́телиться**] *colloq.* to dawdle.
кани́тель *n.f.* **1,** gold or silver thread. **2,** *colloq.* long drawn-out affair; waste of time. —**кани́тельный,** *adj., colloq.* long drawn-out.
канифо́ль *n.f.* rosin.
канка́н *n.* cancan.
каннниба́л *n.* cannibal. —**каннибали́зм,** *n.* cannibalism. —**каннииба́льский,** *adj.* cannibalistic. —**каннииба́льство,** *n.* cannibalism.
канои́ст *n.* canoeist.
кано́н *n.* canon.
канона́да *n.* cannonade.
канонe\u0301рка [*gen. pl.* **-рок**] *n.* gunboat. —**канонe\u0301рский,** *adj., in* **канонe\u0301рская ло́дка,** gunboat.
канонизи́ровать *v. impfv. & pfv.* [*pres.* **-рую, -руешь**] to canonize.
кано́ник *n.* canon (*clergyman*).
канони́ческий *adj.* canonical. —**канони́ческое пра́во,** canon law.
кано́э *n. neut. indecl.* canoe.
кант *n.* edging; piping. *Also,* **ка́нтик.**
канталу́па *n.* cantaloupe.
канта́та *n.* cantata.
кантова́ть *v. impfv.* [*pfv.* **окантова́ть;** *pres.* **-ту́ю, -ту́ешь**] **1,** to mount (a picture). **2,** [*impfv. only*] to invert; turn over: "не кантова́ть", "do not invert".
канто́н *n.* canton. —**кантона́льный,** *adj.* cantonal.
ка́нтор *n.* cantor.
кану́н *n.* eve. —**в кану́н** (+ *gen.*), on the eve of.
ка́нуть *v. pfv.* **1,** *obs.* to drip; drop. **2,** *obs.* to sink. **3,** to disappear; fade from memory. —**как в во́ду ка́нуть,** to vanish into thin air. —**ка́нуть в ве́чность,** to sink into oblivion.
канцеляри́ст *n.* **1,** *obs.* clerk. **2,** *fig.* bureaucrat.
канцеля́рия *n.* **1,** office. **2,** chancellery.
канцеля́рский *adj.* **1,** office (*attrib.*). **2,** *fig.* (*of language*) bureaucratic.
канцеля́рщина *n.* **1,** routine office work. **2,** bureaucracy; red tape.
канцероге́н *n.* carcinogen. —**канцероге́нный,** *adj.* carcinogenic.
ка́нцлер *n.* chancellor.
каньо́н *n.* canyon.
каню́к [*gen.* **-нюка́**] *n.* buzzard.
каоли́н *n.* kaolin.
ка́панье *n.* dripping; drip.
ка́пать *v. impfv.* [*pfv.* **ка́пнуть**] **1,** to drip; fall in drops. **2,** to pour a drop at a time. **3,** to drip; spill: ка́пать себе́ на га́лстук, to spill something on one's tie; ка́пать вино́м на ска́терть, to drip wine on the tablecloth. —**над на́ми не ка́плет** (*old conjugation*), there's no rush.
капе́лла *n.* **1,** choir. **2,** chapel.
капелла́н *n.* chaplain.
ка́пелька [*gen. pl.* **-лек**] *n.* **1,** *dim. of* **ка́пля. 2,** *fig.* drop; grain; ounce; particle; modicum. —**до ка́пельки, 1,** to the last drop. **2,** completely; absolutely. —**ни ка́пельки,** not a bit.
ка́пельку *adv., colloq.* a little; just a bit.
капельме́йстер *n.* conductor; bandmaster.
ка́пельница *n.* dropper; eye dropper; medicine dropper.
ка́персы [*gen.* **-сов**] *n. pl.* capers (*condiment*).
капилля́р *n.* capillary. —**капилля́рный,** *adj.* capillary.
капита́л *n.* capital.
капитализа́ция *n.* capitalization.
капитализи́ровать *v. impfv. & pfv.* [*pres.* **-рую, -руешь**] to capitalize; convert into capital.
капитали́зм *n.* capitalism. —**капитали́ст,** *n.* capitalist. —**капиталисти́ческий,** *adj.* capitalist.
капиталовложе́ния *n. pl.* [*sing.* **-ние**] capital investment.

капита́льный *adj.* **1,** *econ.* capital (*attrib.*). **2,** major: капита́льный ремо́нт, major repairs.
капита́н *n.* captain. —**капита́н пе́рвого ра́нга,** *naval* captain. —**капита́н второ́го ра́нга,** *naval* commander. —**капита́н тре́тьего ра́нга,** *naval* lieutenant commander.
капита́нский *adj.* captain's.
капито́лий *n.* capitol.
капитули́ровать *v. impfv.* & *pfv.* [*pres.* **-рую, -руешь**] to capitulate.
капитуля́ция *n.* surrender; capitulation.
ка́пище *n.* pagan temple.
капка́н *n.* trap; snare.
каплу́н [*gen.* **-луна́**] *n.* capon.
ка́пля [*gen. pl.* **-пель**] *n.* **1,** drop: ка́пля воды́, a drop of water. Ка́пли по́та, beads of perspiration. **2,** *pl.* drops: глазны́е ка́пли, eye drops. —**ка́пля в мо́ре,** a drop in the bucket. —**ка́пля за ка́плей; ка́пля по ка́пле,** bit by bit. —**ни ка́пли,** not a bit. —**по ка́пле,** a drop at a time. —**после́дняя ка́пля,** the last straw. —**похо́жи как две ка́пли воды́,** like two peas in a pod.
ка́пнуть *v., pfv. of* **ка́пать.**
капо́к [*gen.* **-пка́**] *n.* kapok.
ка́пор *n.* bonnet.
капо́т *n.* **1,** *obs.* housecoat. **2,** *mech.* hood.
капра́л *n.* corporal.
капри́з *n.* whim; caprice.
капри́зничать *v. impfv.* to be capricious.
капри́зный *adj.* capricious.
капро́н *n.* kapron (*a kind of nylon*). —**капро́новый,** *adj.* kapron.
ка́псула *n.* **1,** capsule. **2,** space capsule.
ка́псюль *n.m.* percussion cap; primer.
капу́ста *n.* cabbage. —**брюссе́льская капу́ста,** Brussels sprouts. —**ки́слая капу́ста,** sauerkraut. —**морска́я капу́ста,** sea kale. —**спа́ржевая капу́ста,** broccoli. —**цветна́я капу́ста,** cauliflower.
капу́стница *n.* cabbage butterfly.
капу́стный *adj.* cabbage (*attrib.*).
капу́т *adv.* (*with dat.*) *colloq.* done for: ему́ капу́т, he's done for.
капуци́н *n.* **1,** Capuchin (*monk*). **2,** capuchin (*monkey*).
капюшо́н *n.* hood.
ка́ра *n.* punishment; retribution.
караби́н *n.* carbine.
кара́бкаться *v.r. impfv.* to clamber; scramble.
карава́й *n.* round loaf of bread.
карава́н *n.* **1,** caravan. **2,** convoy (*of ships*).
карavéлла *n.* caravel.
карака́тица *n.* cuttlefish.
кара́ковый *adj.* (*of a horse*) dark bay.
кара́куль *n.m.* Persian lamb; astrakhan; caracul. —**кара́кулевый,** *adj.* Persian lamb (*attrib.*).
кaraку́льский *adj., in* **караку́льская овца́,** caracul sheep.
каракульча́ *n.* broadtail.
кара́куля *n., usu. pl.* scrawl; scribble.
карамбо́ль *n.m., billiards* carom (shot).
караме́ль *n.f.* **1,** caramels. **2,** a (single) caramel.
караме́лька [*gen. pl.* **-лек**] *n., colloq.* a (single) caramel.
караме́льный *adj.* caramel.
каранда́ш [*gen.* **-даша́**] *n.* pencil. —**каранда́шный,** *adj.* pencil (*attrib.*).
каранти́н *n.* quarantine.
кара́сь [*gen.* **-ся́**] *n.m.* European carp.
кара́т *n.* carat.
кара́тельный *adj.* punitive.
кара́ть *v. impfv.* [*pfv.* **покара́ть**] to punish. —**кара́ться,** *refl.* [*impfv. only*] (*with instr.*) to be punishable (by).
карау́л *n.* **1,** guard: почётный карау́л, honor guard. **2,** guard duty; sentry duty. —**брать (взять) на карау́л,** to present arms.
карау́лить *v. impfv.* **1,** to guard; watch over. **2,** *colloq.* to watch for; lie in wait for.
карау́льный *adj.* guard (*attrib.*); sentry (*attrib.*). —*n.* sentry. —**карау́льная,** *n.f.* guardhouse.
карау́льня [*gen. pl.* **-лен**] *n.* guardhouse.
карау́льщик *n., colloq.* watchman.
кара́чки *n. pl., colloq., in* **на кара́чки** *and* **на кара́чках,** on one's hands and knees; on all fours.
карби́д *n.* carbide.
карбо́лка *n., colloq.* carbolic acid.
карбо́ловый *adj.* carbolic.
карбона́т *n.* carbonate.
карбору́нд *n.* carborundum.
карбу́нкул *n.* carbuncle.
карбюра́тор *n.* carburetor.
карга́ *n., colloq.* hag.
кардина́л *n.* **1,** cardinal (*prelate*). **2,** cardinal (*bird*).
кардина́льный *adj.* cardinal; fundamental.
кардиогра́мма *n.* cardiogram.
кардио́граф *n.* cardiograph.
кардиоло́гия *n.* cardiology. —**кардио́лог,** *n.* cardiologist.
каре́та *n.* coach; carriage. —**каре́та ско́рой по́мощи,** *obs.* ambulance.
каре́тка [*gen. pl.* **-ток**] *n.* **1,** *dim. of* **каре́та. 2,** carriage (*of a typewriter*).
каре́тный *adj.* of or for a coach. —**каре́тный сара́й,** coach house.
кариати́да *n.* caryatid.
ка́риес *n.* caries. —**ка́риес зубо́в,** tooth decay.
ка́рий *adj.* (*of one's eyes*) brown.
карикату́ра *n.* **1,** cartoon. **2,** caricature. —**карикатури́ст,** *n.* cartoonist.
карикату́рный *adj.* **1,** of or like a cartoon. **2,** *fig.* grotesque; ludicrous.
карильо́н *n.* carillon.
карио́з *n.* = **ка́риес.** —**карио́зный,** *adj.* carious.
ка́рканье *n.* caw; cawing.
карка́с *n.* frame; framework. —**карка́сный,** *adj.* frame (*attrib.*): карка́сный дом, frame house.
ка́ркать *v. impfv.* [*pfv.* **ка́ркнуть**] (*of a bird*) to caw.
ка́рлик *n.m.* [*fem.* **ка́рлица**] midget; dwarf. —**ка́рликовый,** *adj.* midget; tiny.
карма́н *n.* pocket. —**бить** *or* **ударя́ть по карма́ну,** to put a hole in one's pocketbook. —**э́то мне не по карма́ну,** I can't afford it.
карма́нный *adj.* pocket (*attrib.*). —**карма́нный вор,** pickpocket.
карми́н *n.* carmine. —**карми́нный; карми́новый,** *adj.* carmine.
карнава́л *n.* carnival.
карни́з *n.* cornice.
карп *n.* carp.
ка́рта *n.* **1,** map. **2,** playing card. —**(с)пу́тать чьи́-нибудь ка́рты,** to upset someone's plans. —**(с)пу́тать все ка́рты,** to upset the applecart. —**ста́вить (что́-нибудь) на ка́рту,** to stake.

картáвить *v. impfv.* [*pres.* **-влю, -вишь**] to have difficulty pronouncing the sounds "R" and "L".
картáвость *n.f.* improper pronunciation of the letters "L" and "R"; burr.
картёжник *n., colloq.* inveterate cardplayer.
картёжный *adj., colloq.* of or pert. to card playing.
картéль (тэ) *n.m.* cartel.
кáртер *n.* crankcase.
картéчь *n.f.* **1,** canister shot. **2,** buckshot.
картúна *n.* **1,** picture. **2,** painting. **3,** *theat.* scene (*part of an act of a play*). **4,** *colloq.* movie.
картúнка [*gen. pl.* **-нок**] *n., dim. of* **картúна.** —**мóдная картúнка,** fashion plate. —**составнáя картúнка,** jigsaw puzzle.
картúнный *adj.* **1,** picture (*attrib.*). **2,** picturesque.
картóграф *n.* cartographer.
картографúровать *v. impfv.* [*pres.* **-рую, -руешь**] to map; draw a map of.
картогрáфия *n.* cartography. —**картографúческий,** *adj.* cartographic.
картóн *n.* cardboard.
картонáж *n.* article made of cardboard. —**картонáжный,** *adj.* cardboard.
картóнка [*gen. pl.* **-нок**] *n.* cardboard box; carton. —**картóнка для шля́пы,** hatbox; bandbox.
картóнный *adj.* cardboard.
картотéка *n.* card index; card file. —**картотéчный,** *adj.* of or for a card file.
картóфелина *n., colloq.* a (single) potato.
картóфель *n.m.* potatoes.
картóфельный *adj.* potato (*attrib.*). —**картóфельный жук,** potato beetle (*or* bug). —**картóфельное пюрé,** mashed potatoes.
кáрточка [*gen. pl.* **-чек**] *n.* **1,** card. **2,** small photograph.
кáрточный *adj.* card (*attrib.*). —**кáрточный дóмик,** house of cards. —**кáрточная систéма,** rationing.
картóшка [*gen. pl.* **-шек**] *n., colloq.* **1,** potatoes. **2,** a (single) potato.
картýз [*gen.* **-тузá**] *n.* peaked cap.
карусéль *n.f.* merry-go-round; carousel.
кáрцер *n.* prison cell (usu. dark and cold) used for special punishment.
канцерогéн *n.* carcinogen.
карьéр *n.* **1,** full gallop. **2,** quarry. —**с мéста в карьéр,** right away; at once.
карьéра *n.* career. —**бы́стро сдéлать карьéру,** to rise (very) rapidly.
карьерúст *n.* careerist.
касáние *n.* touch; contact.
касáтельная *n., decl. as an adj., geom.* tangent.
касáтельно *prep., with gen.* regarding; concerning.
касáтельство *n.* relation; connection.
касáтик *n.* iris (*flower*).
касáтка [*gen. pl.* **-ток**] *n.* barn swallow.
касáться *v.r. impfv.* [*pfv.* **коснýться**] (*with gen.*) **1,** to touch. **2,** to touch upon. **3,** to concern; have to do with. —**что касáется** (+ *gen.*), as to; as for; as far as... is concerned.
касáющийся *prep., with gen.* regarding; concerning.
кáска [*gen. pl.* **-сок**] *n.* helmet.
каскáд *n.* cascade.
кáсса *n.* **1,** cashier's office; cashier's desk: платúть в кáссу, to pay the cashier. **2,** box office; ticket office. **3,** cash register. **4,** cash box; till. **5,** ticket machine (*on a bus or trolley*). **6,** cash. **7,** *typography* case. —**несгорáемая кáсса,** safe; strongbox. —**сберегáтельная кáсса,** savings bank.
кассáция *n., law* appeal. —**кассациóнный,** *adj.* appeal (*attrib.*); of appeal.
кассéта *n.* cassette.
кассúр *n.m.* [*fem.* **-úрша**] *n.* **1,** cashier. **2,** (bank) teller. **3,** ticket seller.
кассúровать *v. impfv. & pfv.* [*pres.* **-рую, -руешь**] *law* to annul; set aside.
кáссовый *adj.* cash (*attrib.*): кáссовая кнúга, cashbook.
кáста *n.* caste.
кастаньéты *n. pl.* [*sing.* **-ньéта**] castanets.
кастеля́нша *n.* woman in charge of linen (*in a hotel, hospital, etc.*).
кастéт *n.* brass knuckles.
кáстовый *adj.* caste (*attrib.*).
кастóр *n.* castor (*heavy woolen cloth*).
кастóрка *n., colloq.* castor oil.
кастóровый *adj.* **1,** made of castor or beaver fur. **2,** *in* **кастóровое мáсло,** castor oil.
кастрáт *n.* castrated man or boy. —**кастрáция,** *n.* castration.
кастрúровать *v. impfv. & pfv.* [*pres.* **-рую, -руешь**] to castrate.
кастрю́ля *n.* pot; saucepan. *Also,* **кастрю́лька.**
катаклúзм *n.* cataclysm.
катакóмбы *n. pl.* [*sing.* **-кóмба**] catacombs.
каталáнский *adj.* = **каталóнский.**
каталéпсия *n.* catalepsy. —**каталептúческий; каталепсúческий,** *adj.* cataleptic.
катáлиз *n.* catalysis.
катализáтор *n.* catalyst. —**каталитúческий,** *adj.* catalytic.
каталóг *n.* catalogue.
каталогизáтор *n.* cataloguer.
каталогизúровать *v. impfv. & pfv.* [*pres.* **-рую, -руешь**] to catalogue.
каталóжный *adj.* catalogue (*attrib.*). —**каталóжная,** *n.* catalogue room (*in a library*).
каталóнский *adj.* Catalan. *Also,* **каталáнский.**
катáние *n.* **1,** rolling. **2,** riding; driving. —**катáние на велосипéде/конькáх/лóдке,** bicycling/skating/boating.
катáнье *n.* = **катáние.** —**не мытьём, так кáтаньем** (*with different stress*), by hook or by crook.
катапýльта *n.* **1,** catapult. **2,** *aero.* ejection seat.
катáр *n.* catarrh.
катарáкт *n.* cataract (*waterfall*).
катарáкта *n.* cataract (*of the eye*).
катастрóфа *n.* **1,** catastrophe; disaster; calamity. **2,** accident; crash. —**катастрофúческий,** *adj.* catastrophic; disastrous.
катáть *v. impfv.* **1,** *indeterm. of* **катúть. 2,** [*pfv.* **покатáть**] to take for a ride *or* drive. **3,** to roll (dough); make (little balls). **4,** [*pfv.* **вы́катать**] to mangle; press in a mangle.
катáться *v.r. impfv.* **1,** *indeterm. of* **катúться. 2,** [*pfv.* **покатáться**] to ride; go riding: катáться на машúне, to go for a drive; катáться верхóм, to go horseback riding; катáться на велосипéде, to go bicycle riding. Катáться на конькáх, to go skating. Катáться на лóдке, to go boating. —**катáться как сыр в мáсле,**

to be in clover. —**ката́ться со́ смеху,** to roar with laughter.

катафа́лк *n.* **1,** hearse. **2,** bier; catafalque.

категори́ческий *adj.* categorical. —**категори́чески,** *adv.* categorically.

катего́рия *n.* category.

ка́тер [*pl.* **катера́**] *n.* cutter; launch. ♦*In combinations* boat: сторожево́й ка́тер, patrol boat; торпе́дный ка́тер, PT boat.

кате́тер (тэтэ) *n.* catheter.

катехи́зис *n.* catechism.

кати́ть *v. impfv.* [*pfv.* **покати́ть;** *pres.* **качу́, ка́тишь**] **1,** to roll; wheel. **2,** *v.i., colloq.* (*of a vehicle*) to roll along. **3,** to stir; cause to move slightly. —**кати́ться,** *refl.* **1,** to roll. **2,** (*of a vehicle*) to roll along. **3,** to slide down. **4,** to flow; stream. **5,** (*of a sound*) to roll; resound. *See also* **ката́ть** *and* **ката́ться.**

като́д *n.* cathode. —**като́дный,** *adj.* cathode (*attrib.*): като́дные лучи́, cathode rays.

като́к [*gen.* **-тка́**] *n.* **1,** skating rink. **2,** roller: парово́й като́к, steamroller. **3,** mangle; rolling press.

като́лик *n.m.* [*fem.* **-ли́чка**] Catholic. —**католици́зм,** *n.* Catholicism. —**католи́ческий,** *adj.* Catholic. —**католи́чество,** *n.* Catholicism.

ка́торга *n.* penal servitude; hard labor.

ка́торжник *n.* convict.

ка́торжный *adj.* **1,** of or pert. to penal servitude. **2,** *fig.* backbreaking. —**ка́торжные рабо́ты,** penal servitude; hard labor.

кату́шка [*gen. pl.* **-шек**] *n.* **1,** spool; reel; bobbin. **2,** roll (*of film*). **3,** *electricity* coil.

катю́ша *n.* rocket launcher mounted on a vehicle; Katyusha.

каусти́ческий *adj.* caustic.

каучу́к *n.* rubber. —**каучу́ковый,** *adj.* rubber. —**каучуконо́с,** *n.* rubber plant.

кафе́ *n. neut. indecl.* café.

ка́федра *n.* **1,** pulpit; rostrum. **2,** department (*of a university*). **3,** chair; professorship.

кафедра́льный *adj., in* **кафедра́льный собо́р,** cathedral.

ка́фель *n.m.* (glazed) tile. —**ка́фельный,** *adj.* tiled; tile (*attrib.*).

кафете́рий (тэ) *n.* cafeteria.

кафта́н *n.* caftan.

кача́лка [*gen. pl.* **-лок**] *n.* rocking chair.

кача́ние *n.* **1,** rocking; swinging. **2,** pumping.

кача́ть *v. impfv.* [*pfv.* **качну́ть**] **1,** to rock; swing. **2,** *impers.* (*of a boat*) to toss; pitch; roll: ло́дку кача́ет, the boat is tossing. **3,** to pump. **4,** *in* кача́ть голово́й, to shake one's head; nod one's head. —**кача́ться,** *refl.* **1,** to swing; rock. **2,** to reel; stagger.

каче́ли [*gen.* **-лей**] *n. pl.* (child's) swing.

ка́чественный *adj.* **1,** qualitative. **2,** high-quality; high-grade.

ка́чество *n.* quality. —**в ка́честве** (+ *gen.*), as; by way of; in the capacity of.

ка́чка *n.* tossing; pitching; rolling (*of a ship*).

качну́ть *v., pfv. of* **кача́ть.** —**качну́ться,** *refl., pfv. of* **кача́ться.**

качу́рка [*gen. pl.* **-рок**] *n.* petrel (*bird*).

ка́ша *n.* cooked cereal; porridge; kasha. —**овся́ная ка́ша,** oatmeal.

кашало́т *n.* sperm whale.

кашева́р *n., mil.* cook.

ка́шель [*gen.* **-шля**] *n.m.* cough.

кашеми́р *n.* cashmere. —**кашеми́ровый,** *adj.* cashmere.

каши́ца *also,* **ка́шица** *n.* gruel.

ка́шка *n.* pap.

ка́шлять *v. impfv.* [*pfv.* **ка́шлянуть**] to cough.

кашне́ (нэ) *n. neut. indecl.* muffler; scarf.

кашта́н *n.* **1,** chestnut. **2,** chestnut tree.

кашта́новый *adj.* **1,** (of) chestnut. **2,** chestnut-colored; brown.

каю́та *n.* cabin; stateroom.

ка́ющийся *adj.* repentant; penitent.

кая́к *n.* kayak.

ка́яться *v.r. impfv.* [*pfv.* **пока́яться;** *pres.* **ка́юсь, ка́ешься**] **1,** to repent; be sorry. **2,** to confess. Публи́чно ка́яться, to publicly recant.

квадра́нт *n.* quadrant.

квадра́т *n.* **1,** square (*figure*). **2,** *math.* square (*second power*): возводи́ть в квадра́т, to square.

квадра́тный *adj.* square. —**квадра́тный ко́рень,** square root. —**квадра́тные ско́бки,** brackets. —**квадра́тное уравне́ние,** quadratic equation.

квадрату́ра *n.* squaring. —**квадрату́ра кру́га,** squaring the circle.

квадрильо́н *also,* **квадриллио́н** *n.* quadrillion.

кваза́р *n.* quasar.

ква́канье *n.* croaking.

ква́кать *v. impfv.* [*pfv.* **ква́кнуть**] to croak.

ква́кер *n.* Quaker. —**ква́керский,** *adj.* Quaker.

ква́кша *n.* tree frog.

квалифика́ция *n.* qualification; skill.

квалифици́рованный *adj.* skilled.

квалифици́ровать *v. impfv. & pfv.* [*pres.* **-рую, -руешь**] to characterize; categorize.

квант *n., physics* quantum. —**ква́нтовый,** *adj.* quantum (*attrib.*).

ква́рта *n.* **1,** quart. **2,** *music* fourth.

кварта́л *n.* **1,** quarter; section (*of a city*). **2,** block (*in a city*). **3,** quarter (*of a year*). —**кварта́льный,** *adj.* quarterly.

кварте́т *n., music* quartet.

кварти́ра *n.* **1,** apartment. **2,** *pl., mil.* quarters; billets. —**квартира́нт,** *n., colloq.* lodger; tenant.

квартирме́йстер *n.* quartermaster.

кварти́рный *adj.* housing (*attrib.*); billeting (*attrib.*). —**кварти́рная пла́та,** rent.

квартирова́ть *v. impfv.* [*pres.* **-ру́ю, -ру́ешь**] **1,** *colloq.* to lodge; live. **2,** *mil.* to be quartered; be billeted.

квартпла́та *n., colloq.* rent (*contr. of* **кварти́рная пла́та**).

кварц *n.* quartz. —**ква́рцевый,** *adj.* quartz.

кварци́т *n.* quartzite.

квас *n.* kvass (*fermented drink*).

ква́сить *v. impfv.* [*pres.* **-шу, -сишь**] to pickle; make sour.

квасно́й *adj.* kvass (*attrib.*).

квасцы́ [*gen.* **-цо́в**] *n. pl.* alum.

ква́шеный *adj.* pickled; sour.

квашня́ [*gen. pl.* **-не́й**] *n.* kneading trough.

кве́рху *adv.* up; upward(s). —**лицо́м кве́рху,** face up; right side up.

квинте́т *n.* quintet.

квинтэссе́нция *n.* quintessence.

квит *also,* **квиты** *adj., colloq.* all even: мы (с ва́ми) квиты, we are all even.

квита́нция *n.* **1,** receipt. **2,** sales slip.
кво́рум *n.* quorum.
кво́та *n.* quota.
КГБ *abbr. of* **Комитéт госуда́рственной безопа́сности,** Committee of State Security; the KGB.
кегельба́н *n.* bowling alley.
ке́гля [*gen. pl.* **-лей**] *n.* **1,** bowling pin. **2,** *pl.* bowling (*game*).
кедр *n.* cedar. —**кедро́вый,** *adj.* cedar.
ке́ды [*gen.* **-дов**] *n. pl.* sneakers.
кекс *n.* fruit cake.
келе́йный *adj.* **1,** like that in a monastic cell. **2,** *fig.* secret; private.
ке́льнер *n.* waiter, esp. in Germany. —**ке́льнерша,** *n.* waitress.
кельт *n.* Celt. —**ке́льтский,** *adj.* Celtic.
ке́лья *n.* monastic cell.
кем *pron., instr. of* **кто.**
ке́мпинг (кэ) *n.* campsite.
кенгуру́ *n.m. indecl.* kangaroo.
кента́вр *n.* centaur.
ке́пка [*gen. pl.* **-пок**] *n.* cap.
кера́мика *n.* ceramics. —**керами́ческий,** *adj.* ceramic.
keрога́з *n.* kerosene stove.
кероси́н *n.* kerosene.
кероси́нка [*gen. pl.* **-нок**] *n.* kerosene stove.
кероси́новый *adj.* kerosene (*attrib.*).
ке́сарев *adj., in* **ке́сарево сече́ние,** Caesarean section.
кессо́н *n.* caisson.
кессо́нный *adj.* caisson (*attrib.*). —**кессо́нная боле́знь,** the bends.
ке́та *n.* Siberian salmon.
кетгу́т *n.* catgut.
ке́товый *adj., in* **ке́товая икра́,** red caviar.
кефа́ль *n.f.* (gray) mullet.
кефи́р *n.* yogurt.
киберне́тика (нэ) *n.* cybernetics.
киби́тка [*gen. pl.* **-ток**] *n.* **1,** covered wagon. **2,** nomad's tent. **3,** mud house (*found in Central Asia*).
кива́ть *v. impfv.* [*pfv.* **кивну́ть**] **1,** (*with instr.*) to nod (one's head). **2,** (*with* **на** + *acc.*) to nod (to). **3,** (*with* **на** + *acc.*) *colloq.* to try to put the blame on.
ки́ви-ки́ви *n.f. or neut. indecl.* kiwi.
кивну́ть *v., pfv. of* **кива́ть.**
киво́к [*gen.* **-вка́**] *n.* nod.
кида́ть *v. impfv.* [*pfv.* **ки́нуть**] **1,** to throw; toss; cast. **2,** *in* **куда́ не кинь,** wherever you look. —**кида́ться,** *refl.* **1,** to throw oneself; rush; dash. **2,** [*impfv. only*] (*with instr.*) to throw (something) at each other.
кизи́л *n.* dogwood. *Also,* **кизи́ль,** *n.m.* [*gen.* **кизиля́**].
кий [*gen.* **кия́** *or* **ки́я**; *pl.* **кии́**; **киёв**] *n.* billiard cue.
кики́мора *n., folklore* female hobgoblin.
кило́ *n. indecl.* = **килогра́мм.**
килова́тт [*gen. pl.* **-ва́тт**] *n.* kilowatt. —**килова́тт-ча́с,** *n.* kilowatt-hour.
килоге́рц [*gen. pl.* **-ге́рц**] *n.* kilocycle.
килогра́мм *n.* kilogram.
киломе́тр *n.* kilometer.
килото́нна *n.* kiloton.
киль *n.m.* keel.
кильва́тер (тэ) *n., naut.* wake.
ки́лька [*gen. pl.* **-лек**] *n.* sprat.
кимоно́ *n. indecl.* kimono.
кинемато́граф *n.* **1,** motion-picture camera; movie camera. **2,** *obs.* movie theater.
кинематогра́фия *n.* cinematography.
кинеско́п *n.* kinescope; picture tube.
кине́тика (нэ) *n.* kinetics. —**кинети́ческий,** *adj.* kinetic.
кинжа́л *n.* dagger.
кино́ *n. indecl.* **1,** motion pictures; films; movies; the cinema. Немо́е кино́, silent pictures/films. Ходи́ть в кино́, to go to the movies. **2,** movie theater.
киноактёр *n.* movie actor. —**киноактри́са,** *n.* movie actress.
киноаппара́т *n.* motion-picture camera; movie camera.
киноарти́ст *n.* movie actor. —**киноарти́стка,** *n.* movie actress.
ки́новарь *n.f.* cinnabar; vermilion.
киножурна́л *n.* short subject.
кинозвезда́ [*pl.* **-звёзды**] *n., colloq.* movie star.
кинока́мера *n.* movie camera.
кинокарти́на *n., colloq.* film; picture; movie.
кинокри́тик *n.* film critic.
кинопле́нта *n.* film.
киномеха́ник *n.* projectionist.
киноопера́тор *n.* cameraman.
киноплёнка *n.* movie film.
кинорежиссёр *n.* film director.
киносту́дия *n.* movie studio.
кинотеа́тр *n.* movie theater.
киноустано́вка [*gen. pl.* **-вок**] *n.* movie projector.
кинофестива́ль *n.m.* film festival.
кинофи́льм *n.* film; picture; movie.
кинохро́ника *n.* newsreel.
ки́нуть *v., pfv. of* **кида́ть.** —**ки́нуться,** *refl., pfv. of* **кида́ться.**
кио́ск *n.* kiosk; booth; stand.
кио́т *n.* icon case.
ки́па *n.* **1,** pile; stack. **2,** bale (*measure*).
кипари́с *n.* cypress. —**кипари́сный; кипари́совый,** *adj.* cypress (*attrib.*).
кипе́ние *n.* boiling. —**то́чка кипе́ния,** boiling point.
кипе́ть *v. impfv.* [*pres.* **-плю́, -пи́шь**] **1,** to boil. **2,** to seethe. **3,** (*of emotions*) to boil; rage. **4,** (*of activity*) to be in full swing. **5,** (*with instr.*) to boil; seethe; burn (with anger, indignation, etc.).
кипу́чий *adj.* **1,** seething. **2,** ebullient. **3,** frenetic.
кипяти́ть *v. impfv.* [*pfv.* **вскипяти́ть**; *pres.* **-чу́, -ти́шь**] to boil. —**кипяти́ться,** *refl.* **1,** to boil. **2,** *colloq.* to get excited; flare up.
кипято́к [*gen.* **-тка́**] *n.* **1,** boiling water. **2,** *colloq.* hothead.
кипяче́ние *n.* boiling.
кипячёный *adj.* boiled.
кира́са *n.* cuirass.
кирги́з *n.m.* [*fem.* **-ка**] Kirghiz (*one of a people living mainly in the Kirghiz S.S.R.*). —**кирги́зский,** *adj.* Kirghiz.
кири́ллица *n.* the Cyrillic alphabet.
ки́рка [*gen. pl.* **-рок**] *n.* Protestant church. *Also,* **ки́рха.**
кирка́ [*pl.* **ки́рки, ки́рок**] *n.* pick (*tool*).
кирпи́ч [*gen.* **-пича́**] *n.* brick.
кирпи́чный *adj.* **1,** brick (*attrib.*). **2,** brick-red.
ки́са *n., colloq.* pussy cat.
кисе́йный *adj.* muslin.

кисе́ль [*gen.* **-селя́**] *n.m.* dessert made of fruit, berries and potato- (or corn-) starch and served with milk.
кисе́т *n.* tobacco pouch.
кисея́ *n.* muslin.
ки́ска [*gen. pl.* **-сок**] *n.* pussy cat.
кисли́ца *n.* wood sorrel.
кислоро́д *n.* oxygen. —**кислоро́дный,** *adj.* oxygen (*attrib.*).
ки́сло-сла́дкий *adj.* sweet-and-sour.
кислота́ *n.* **1,** [*pl.* **кисло́ты**] acid. **2,** acidity.
кисло́тный *adj.* acid (*attrib.*). —**кисло́тность,** *n.f.* acidity.
ки́слый *adj.* [*short form* **ки́сел, кисла́, ки́сло**] sour.
ки́снуть *v. impfv.* [*pfv.* **проки́снуть;** *past* **кис** *or* **ки́снул, ки́сла**] **1,** to turn sour. **2,** *fig., colloq.* (*of a person*) A, to stagnate; vegetate. B, to mope.
киста́ *n.* cyst.
кисте́нь [*gen.* **-теня́**] *n.m.* slung shot.
ки́сточка [*gen. pl.* **-чек**] *n., dim. of* **кисть.** —**ки́сточка для бритья́,** shaving brush.
кисть [*pl.* **ки́сти, -сте́й, -стя́м**] *n.f.* **1,** hand. **2,** cluster; bunch. **3,** *bot.* raceme. **4,** tassel. **5,** paintbrush. **6,** painting; brushwork.
кит [*gen.* **кита́**] *n.* whale.
кита́ец [*gen.* **-а́йца**] *n.m.* [*fem.* **-a я́нка**] Chinese (man): он кита́ец, he is Chinese. —**кита́йский,** *adj.* Chinese.
ки́тель [*pl.* **кителя́**] *n.m.* tunic.
китобо́ец [*gen.* **-бо́йца**] *n.* whaling ship.
китобо́й *n.* **1,** whaler (*person*). **2,** whaling ship. —**китобо́йный,** *adj.* whaling (*attrib.*).
кито́вый *adj.* whale (*attrib.*). —**кито́вый жир,** whale oil. —**кито́вый ус,** whalebone.
кичи́ться *v.r. impfv.* **1,** to boast; sing one's own praises. **2,** (*with instr.*) to brag about; trumpet.
кичли́вый *adj.* conceited; arrogant. —**кичли́вость,** *n.f.* conceit.
кише́ть *v. impfv.* [*pres.* **киши́т**] **1,** to swarm. **2,** (*with instr.*) to swarm (with); teem (with).
кише́чник *n.* bowels; intestines.
кише́чный *adj.* intestinal.
кишка́ [*gen. pl.* **-шо́к**] *n.* **1,** intestine. **2,** hose. —**пряма́я кишка́,** rectum. —**слепа́я кишка́,** cecum.
кишмя́ *adv., in* **кишмя́ кише́ть,** to swarm.
клавеси́н *n.* harpsichord.
клавиату́ра *n.* keyboard.
клавико́рды [*gen.* **-дов**] *n. pl.* clavichord.
кла́виша *n.* key (*of a piano, organ, typewriter, etc.*).
клад *n.* **1,** buried treasure. **2,** *colloq.* treasure.
кла́дбище *n.* cemetery; graveyard. —**кладби́щенский,** *adj.* cemetery (*attrib.*).
кла́дезь *n.m., archaic* = **коло́дец.** —**кла́дезь прему́дрости,** fountain of information.
кла́дка *n.* laying (*of stone or brick*). —**ка́менная кла́дка,** masonry. —**кирпи́чная кла́дка,** brickwork.
кладова́я *n., decl. as an adj.* pantry; larder; storeroom.
кладо́вка [*gen. pl.* **-вок**] *n., colloq.* small pantry.
кладовщи́к [*gen.* **-щика́**] *n.* storekeeper; keeper of supplies.
кладь *n.f.* load. —**ручна́я кладь,** hand luggage.
кла́ка *n.* claque. —**клакёр,** *n.* claqueur.
клан *n.* clan.
кла́няться *v.r. impfv.* [*pfv.* **поклони́ться**] **1,** to bow. **2,** (*with dat.*) to give one's regards (to).
кла́пан *n.* **1,** valve. **2,** flap (*of a pocket*).
кларне́т *n.* clarinet. —**кларнети́ст,** *n.* clarinetist.
класс *n.* **1,** (social) class: рабо́чий класс, the working class. **2,** class (*category*): е́хать пе́рвым кла́ссом, to travel first class. **3,** class; classroom: идти́/войти́ в класс, to go to/enter the/class. Класс оживи́лся, the class came alive. **4,** grade: быть в тре́тьем кла́ссе, to be in the third grade.
кла́ссик *n.* **1,** classical writer. **2,** classicist.
кла́ссика *n.* the classics.
классифика́ция *n.* classification.
классифици́ровать *v. impfv. & pfv.* [*pres.* **-рую, -руешь**] to classify.
классици́зм *n.* classicism.
класси́ческий *adj.* **1,** classical. **2,** classic: класси́ческий приме́р, classic example.
кла́ссный *adj.* **1,** class (*attrib.*); classroom (*attrib.*). **2,** *sports* first-class; top-level. —**кла́ссный ваго́н,** railway passenger car. —**кла́ссная доска́,** blackboard.
кла́ссовый *adj.* class (*attrib.*): кла́ссовая борьба́, class struggle.
кла́ссы [*gen.* **-сов**] *n. pl.* hopscotch.
класть *v. impfv.* [*pfv.* **положи́ть;** *pres.* **кладу́, кладёшь;** *past* **клал, кла́ла**] **1,** to lay; put; place. **2,** to apply (*to a surface*). **3,** [*impfv. only*] to build; erect. **4,** [*impfv. only*] to lay (eggs). **5,** to put (work, effort, etc.) into. **6,** *colloq.* to set aside; lay aside; put aside. —**класть не на ме́сто,** to put in the wrong place; misplace. —**класть но́гу на́ ногу,** to cross one's legs. *See also* **положи́ть.**
клаустрофо́бия *n.* claustrophobia.
клева́ть *v. impfv.* [*pfv.* **клю́нуть;** *pres.* **клюю́, клюёшь**] **1,** to peck. **2,** to bite; take the bait. —**клева́ть но́сом,** to nod; be drowsy. —**у него́ де́нег ку́ры не клюю́т,** he has money to burn.
кле́вер *n.* clover. —**кле́верный,** *adj.* of clover.
клевета́ *n.* slander; libel.
клевета́ть *v. impfv.* [*pfv.* **наклевета́ть;** *pres.* **-вещу́, -ве́щешь**] (*with* **на** + *acc.*) to slander.
клеветни́к [*gen.* **-ника́**] *n.* slanderer.
клеветни́ческий *adj.* slanderous; libelous.
клево́к [*gen.* **-вка́**] *n.* peck.
клевре́т *n.* follower; supporter; minion.
клеёнка *n.* oilcloth. —**клеёнчатый,** *adj.* oilcloth (*attrib.*).
кле́ить *v. impfv.* [*pfv.* **скле́ить**] **1,** to glue; paste. **2,** to hang (wallpaper). **3,** to make (*by gluing or pasting something together*). —**кле́иться,** *refl.* **1,** *colloq.* to get sticky. **2,** to stick. **3,** *colloq.* (*usu. neg.*) to go well: де́ло не кле́ится, things are not going well.
клей [*2nd loc.* **на клею́**] *n.* glue. —**пти́чий клей,** birdlime. —**ры́бий клей,** isinglass.
кле́йкий *adj.* sticky; gummy. —**кле́йкость,** *n.f.* stickiness.
клейми́ть *v. impfv.* [*pfv.* **заклейми́ть;** *pres.* **-млю́, -ми́шь**] **1,** to stamp; mark. **2,** to brand (cattle). **3,** *fig.* to brand; stigmatize.
клеймо́ [*pl.* **кле́йма, клейм**] *n.* **1,** mark; stamp. **2,** brand (*on cattle*). **3,** branding iron. —**клеймо́ позо́ра,** stigma.
кле́йстер *n.* paste.
клёкот *n.* screech.
клекота́ть *v. impfv.* [*pres.* **-ко́чет**] to screech.
клён *n.* maple (tree). —**клено́вый,** *adj.* maple.
клепа́льщик *n.* riveter.
клепа́ть *v. impfv.* to rivet.
клёпка [*gen. pl.* **-пок**] *n.* **1,** riveting. **2,** barrel stave.

клептома́н *n.* kleptomaniac. —**клептома́ния,** *n.* kleptomania.

клерк *n.* clerk.

клёст [*gen.* **клеста́**] *n.* crossbill.

кле́тка [*gen. pl.* **-ток**] *n.* **1,** cage. **2,** check; square. **3,** *biol.* cell. —**грудна́я кле́тка,** thorax. —**ле́стничная кле́тка,** stairwell.

кле́точка *n., dim. of* **кле́тка.**

кле́точный *adj.* cellular.

клету́шка [*gen. pl.* **-шек**] *n., colloq.* tiny room; cubicle.

клетча́тка *n.* cellulose.

кле́тчатый *adj.* checked.

клёцки [*gen.* **-цек**] *n. pl.* [*sing.* **клёцка**] dumplings.

клёш *n.* flare (*in a skirt or trousers*): ю́бка клёш, flared skirt; брю́ки клёш, bell-bottom trousers.

клешня́ [*gen. pl.* **-не́й**] *n.* claw; nipper.

клещ [*gen.* **клеща́**] *n.* tick; mite.

кле́щи [*gen.* **-ще́й**] *n. pl.* pincers; tongs.

клещи́ [*gen.* **-ще́й**] *n. pl.* **1,** = **кле́щи. 2,** *mil.* pincers movement.

кли́вер [*pl.* **кливера́**] *n., naut.* jib.

клие́нт *n.* client; customer.

клиенту́ра *n.* clientele.

кли́зма *n.* enema.

клик *n.* **1,** call. **2,** honk (*of geese*).

кли́ка *n.* clique.

кли́кать *v. impfv.* [*pfv.* **кли́кнуть;** *pres.* **кли́чу, кли́чешь**] **1,** *colloq.* to call. **2,** (*of swans and geese*) to honk.

климакте́рий *n.* menopause.

кли́мат *n.* climate. —**климати́ческий,** *adj.* climatic.

клин [*pl.* **кли́нья, кли́ньев**] *n.* **1,** wedge. **2,** gore; gusset.

кли́ника *n.* clinic. —**клини́ческий,** *adj.* clinical.

клинови́дный *adj.* wedge-shaped.

клино́к [*gen.* **-нка́**] *n.* blade (*of a sword, knife, etc.*).

клинообра́зный *adj.* wedge-shped.

кли́нопись *n.f.* cuneiform.

кли́пер [*pl.* **клипера́**] *n., naut.* clipper.

клипс *n.* earring (*for an unpierced ear*).

кли́ринг *n., comm.* clearing.

кли́рос *n.* choir (*part of a church*).

кли́тор *n.* clitoris.

клич *n.* call; appeal. —**боево́й клич,** war cry; battle cry.

кли́чка [*gen. pl.* **-чек**] *n.* **1,** name of a household pet. **2,** nickname.

клише́ *n. neut. indecl.* cliché.

клоа́ка *n.* **1,** sewer; cesspool. **2,** *fig.* foul place; sewer.

клок [*gen.* **клока́;** *pl.* **кло́чья, кло́чьев** *or* **клоки́, клоко́в**] *n.* **1,** shred. **2,** tuft (*of hair*); wisp (*of hay*).

клокота́ть *v. impfv.* [*pres.* **-кочу́, -ко́чешь**] **1,** (*of liquids*) to bubble. **2,** *fig.* (*of emotions*) to bubble; seethe.

клони́ть *v. impfv.* [*pres.* **клоню́, кло́нишь**] **1,** to bend; incline. *Also impers.:* ло́дку клони́ло на́ бок, the boat was listing. **2,** (*of sleep*) to overcome. *Also impers.:* его́ кло́нит ко сну, he is drowsy. **3,** (*with* **к**) *fig.* to incline (toward); predispose (toward). **4,** *fig.* to guide; steer (a conversation, affair, etc.). **5,** (*with* **к**) *colloq.* to get at; drive at: к чему́ ты кло́нишь?, what are you getting/driving at? —**клони́ться,** *refl.* **1,** to bow; bend. **2,** (*with* **к**) to be nearing. **3,** (*with* **к**) *fig.* to be leading to: к чему́ всё э́то кло́нится?, what is all this leading to?

клоп [*gen.* **клопа́**] *n.* bedbug.

кло́ун *n.* clown.

кло́унский *adj.* **1,** clown (*attrib.*); clown's. **2,** clownish.

клохта́нье *n.* cluck; clucking.

клохта́ть *v. impfv.* [*pres.* **клохчу́, кло́хчешь**] to cluck.

клочо́к [*gen.* **-чка́**] *n.* **1,** scrap (*of paper*). **2,** shred. **3,** wisp (*of hay*). **4,** small plot; patch. **5,** patch (*of fog, blue sky, etc.*).

клуб *n.* **1,** [*pl.* **клу́бы**] club. **2,** [*pl.* **клубы́**] puff (*of smoke*); cloud (*of dust*).

клу́бень [*gen.* **-бня**] *n.m.* tuber.

клуби́ть *v. impfv.* to swirl; blow into the air. —**клуби́ться,** *refl.* **1,** to swirl (*in the wind*). **2,** (*of smoke*) to curl.

клубнево́й *adj.* tuberous.

клубни́ка *n.* **1,** strawberries. **2,** a (single) strawberry. —**клубни́чный,** *adj.* strawberry (*attrib.*).

клу́бный *adj.* club (*attrib.*).

клубо́к [*gen.* **бка́**] *n.* **1,** ball (*of thread or yarn*). **2,** *fig.* (*with gen.*) tangle (of); maze (of). —**клубо́к в го́рле,** lump in one's throat.

клу́мба *n.* flower bed.

клык [*gen.* **клыка́**] *n.* **1,** fang. **2,** tusk. **3,** canine tooth.

клюв *n.* beak; bill.

клюка́ *n.* cane; walking stick.

клю́ква *n.* **1,** cranberries. **2,** a (single) cranberry. **3,** cranberry bush. —**клю́квенный,** *adj.* cranberry (*attrib.*).

клю́нуть *v., pfv. of* **клева́ть.**

ключ [*gen.* **ключа́**] *n.* **1,** key. **2,** [*also,* **га́ечный ключ**] wrench: францу́зский ключ, monkey wrench. **3,** *music* clef; key. **4,** spring: го́рные ключи́, mountain springs. —**бить ключо́м, 1,** to spurt; spout. **2,** *fig.* to throb; be bursting (with life, energy, etc.).

ключево́й *adj.* **1,** key (*attrib.*). **2,** *fig.* key; vital. **3,** coming from underground: ключева́я вода́, spring water.

клю́чик *n., dim. of* **ключ.**

ключи́ца *n.* collarbone; clavicle.

клю́шка [*gen. pl.* **-шек**] *n.* **1,** hockey stick. **2,** golf club.

кля́кса *n.* inkblot.

кля́нчить *v. impfv., colloq.* to beg; pester.

кляп *n.* gag.

клясть *v. impfv.* [*pres.* **кляну́, клянёшь;** *past* **клял, кляла́, кля́ло**] to curse. —**кля́сться,** *refl.* [*pfv.* **покля́сться**] to swear; vow.

кля́тва *n.* oath; vow. —**дава́ть кля́тву,** to take an oath; swear.

кля́твенный *adj.* (*of a promise, oath, etc.*) solemn; sworn.

клятвопреступле́ние *n.* perjury. —**клятвопресту́пник,** *n.* perjurer.

кля́уза *n.* **1,** petty lie; petty complaint. **2,** *obs.* petty lawsuit.

кля́узничать *v. impfv., colloq.* to tell petty lies; spread malicious gossip.

кля́ча *n.* old horse; nag; jade.

кни́га *n.* book.

книголю́б *n.* bibliophile.

кни́жка [*gen. pl.* **-жек**] *n., dim. of* **кни́га.** —**сберега́тельная кни́жка,** bankbook; passbook. —**трудова́я кни́жка,** work-record book. —**че́ковая кни́жка,** checkbook.

кни́жник *n.* **1,** lover of books; bibliophile. **2,** one who has only book knowledge. **3,** *colloq.* bookseller. **4,** *Bib.* scribe.

книжный *adj.* **1,** book (*attrib.*). **2,** *fig.* bookish.

книзу *adv.* down; downward(s).

книксен (сэ) *n.* curtsy.

кнопка [*gen. pl.* **-пок**] *n.* **1,** button; push button. **2,** thumbtack. **3,** snap; snap fastener.

кнут [*gen.* **кнута**] *n.* whip; knout.

кнутовище *n.* whip handle.

княгиня *n.* princess (*wife of a prince*).

княжеский *adj.* **1,** prince's. **2,** princely.

княжество *n.* principality. —**великое княжество,** grand duchy.

княжить *v. impfv.* to reign (*as prince*).

княжна [*gen. pl.* **-жон**] *n.* princess (*daughter of a prince*).

князь [*pl.* **князья, -зей, -зьям**] *n.m., pre-rev.* prince. —**великий князь,** grand duke.

ко *prep.* = **к.**

коагулянт *n.* coagulant. —**коагуляция,** *n.* coagulation.

коаксиальный *adj., in* **коаксиальный кабель,** coaxial cable.

коалиция *n.* coalition. —**коалиционный,** *adj.* coalition (*attrib.*).

кобальт *n.* cobalt. —**кобальтовый,** *adj.* cobalt.

кобель [*gen.* **-беля**] *n.m.* male dog.

кобра *n.* cobra.

кобура *n.* holster.

кобыла *n.* **1,** mare. **2,** *gymnastics* horse.

кобылка [*gen. pl.* **-лок**] *n.* **1,** filly. **2,** bridge (*of a stringed instrument*).

кованый *adj.* **1,** forged; hammered. **2,** *fig.* terse; concise.

коварный *adj.* insidious; treacherous. —**коварство,** *n.* treachery.

ковать *v. impfv.* [*pres.* **кую, куёшь**] **1,** to forge. **2,** to shoe (a horse). **3,** *fig.* to forge; carve out (a victory). —**куй железо, пока горячо,** strike while the iron is hot; make hay while the sun shines.

ковбой *n.* cowboy.

ковбойка [*gen. pl.* **-боек**] *n., colloq.* man's checked shirt.

ковбойский *adj.* cowboy (*attrib.*); cowboy's.

ковёр [*gen.* **-вра**] *n.* carpet; rug.

коверкать *v. impfv.* [*pfv.* **исковеркать**] **1,** to break; damage; wreck; mangle. **2,** to warp; distort. **3,** to mispronounce (a word, name, etc.); murder; butcher (a language).

ковка *n.* **1,** forging. **2,** shoeing.

ковкий *adj.* [*short form* **-вок, -вка, -вко**] malleable; ductile. —**ковкость,** *n.f.* malleability.

коврига *n.* large round loaf of bread.

коврижка [*gen. pl.* **-жек**] *n.* **1,** *dim. of* **коврига. 2,** honey cake; gingerbread. —**ни за какие коврижки,** *colloq.* not for the world.

коврик *n.* **1,** small rug. **2,** mat.

ковровый *adj.* carpet (*attrib.*); rug (*attrib.*).

ковчег *n.* ark: Ноев ковчег, Noah's ark. —**ковчег завета,** ark of the covenant.

ковш [*gen.* **ковша**] *n.* scoop; dipper.

ковыль [*gen.* **-выля**] *n.m.* feather grass.

ковылять *v. impfv.* **1,** to hobble. **2,** (*of a child*) to toddle.

ковырять *v. impfv., colloq.* **1,** to dig up (earth, soil, etc.). **2,** (*with* **в** + *prepl.*) to pick (one's teeth, nose, etc.). —**ковыряться,** *refl.* (*with* **в** + *prepl.*) *colloq.* to rummage (in).

когда *adv.* **1,** *interr.* when?: когда он придёт?, when is he coming? **2,** *rel.* when: бывали дни, когда..., there were days when... —*conj.* **1,** when: когда я был (была) в Москве, when I was in Moscow. **2,** while; as: когда мы обедали, while/as we were having dinner. —**вот когда...,** that was when... —**есть когда!,** *colloq.* there is no time. —**когда бы ни,** whenever; no matter when. —**когда как; как когда,** *colloq.* it depends. —**теперь, когда...,** now that... —**тогда, когда...,** when...

когда-либо *adv.* **1,** sometime. **2,** ever: больше чем когда-либо раньше, more than ever before.

когда-нибудь *adv.* **1,** sometime. **2,** (*in interr. sentences*) ever: вы когда-нибудь бывали там?, have you ever been there?

когда-то *adv.* **1,** at one time; once. **2,** someday; sometime.

кого (vo) *pron., gen. & acc. of* **кто.**

коготь [*gen.* **-гтя;** *pl.* **-гти, -гтей, -гтям**] *n.m.* claw. —**в когтях смерти,** in the jaws of death. —**показывать когти,** to show one's teeth. —**попасть в когти** (*with* **к**), to fall into the clutches of.

когтистый *adj.* having sharp claws.

когтить *v. impfv.* to claw.

код *n.* code.

кодеин *n.* codeine.

кодекс (дэ) *n.* code (*of law, principles, etc.*).

кодировать *v. impfv. & pfv.* [*pres.* **-рую, -руешь**] to encode.

кодификация *n.* codification.

кодифицировать *v. impfv. & pfv.* [*pres.* **-рую, -руешь**] to codify.

кодовый *adj.* code (*attrib.*).

кое-где *adv.* in some places; here and there.

кое-как *adv.* **1,** carelessly; any which way. **2,** somehow; with great difficulty.

кое-какой *adj.* some.

кое-когда *adv.* now and then.

кое-кто *indef. pron.* someone; some people.

кое-куда *adv.* somewhere.

кое-что *indef. pron.* something.

кожа *n.* **1,** skin. **2,** leather. —**гусиная кожа,** goose flesh; goose pimples.

кожаный *adj.* leather.

кожевенный *adj.* leather (*attrib.*). —**кожевенный завод,** tannery.

кожевник *n.* currier.

кожимит *n.* imitation leather.

кожица *n.* **1,** *dim. of* **кожа. 2,** thin skin (*e.g. of a sausage*). **3,** skin; peel; rind.

кожный *adj.* skin (*attrib.*).

кожура *n.* rind; skin; peel.

кожух [*gen.* **-жуха**] *n.* **1,** sheepskin coat. **2,** housing; casing.

коза [*pl.* **козы**] *n.* (nanny) goat.

козёл [*gen.* **-зла**] *n.* goat; billy goat. —**козёл отпущения,** scapegoat.

козерог *n.* **1,** ibex. **2,** *cap.* Capricorn: тропик Козерога, Tropic of Capricorn.

козий [*fem.* **-зья**] *adj.* goat (*attrib.*); goat's.

козлёнок [*gen.* **-нка;** *pl.* **-лята, -лят**] *n.* young goat; kid.

ко́злик *n., dim. of* **козёл.**
козли́ный *adj.* **1,** goat (*attrib.*); goat's. **2,** goatskin (*attrib.*). —**козли́ная боро́дка,** goatee.
козло́вый *adj.* goatskin (*attrib.*).
ко́злы [*gen.* **-зел**] *n. pl.* **1,** coachman's seat. **2,** trestle. **3,** sawhorse.
козля́тина *n.* goat meat.
ко́зни [*gen.* **-ней**] *n. pl.* intrigues; machinations.
козодо́й *n.* goatsucker (*bird*).
ко́зочка [*gen. pl.* **-чек**] *n., dim. of* **коза́.**
козырёк [*gen.* **-рька́**] *n.* peak; visor. —**взять** *or* **сде́лать под козырёк,** to salute.
козырно́й *also,* **козы́рный** *adj.* trump (*attrib.*); of trump: козырно́й/козы́рный туз, ace of trump.
козырну́ть *v., pfv. of* **козыря́ть.**
ко́зырь [*pl.* **ко́зыри, -ре́й, -ря́м**] *n.m.* **1,** trump. **2,** *fig.* trump card. —**пусти́ть в ход после́дний ко́зырь,** to play one's trump card.
козыря́ть *v. impfv.* [*pfv.* **козырну́ть**] *colloq.* **1,** to play a trump. **2,** (*with instr.*) to flaunt. **3,** to salute.
козя́вка [*gen. pl.* **-вок**] *n., colloq.* insect; bug.
кой *adj., archaic* = **како́й** *and* **кото́рый.** —**в ко́и ве́ки,** once in a blue moon. —**ни в ко́ем слу́чае,** under no circumstances.
ко́йка [*gen. pl.* **ко́ек**] *n.* **1,** berth; bunk. **2,** hospital bed. —**подвесна́я ко́йка,** hammock.
койо́т *n.* coyote.
кок *n.* cook (*on board a ship*).
ко́ка *n.* coca.
кокаи́н *n.* cocaine.
кока́рда *n.* cockade.
коке́тка [*gen. pl.* **-ток**] *n.* **1,** coquette; flirt. **2,** yoke (*of a dress*).
коке́тливый *adj.* **1,** coquettish; flirtatious. **2,** attractive; fetching.
коке́тничать *v. impfv.* **1,** to flirt. **2,** (*with instr.*) to flaunt.
коке́тство *n.* coquetry; flirting.
кокк *n.* coccus.
коклю́ш *n.* whooping cough.
ко́кон *n.* cocoon.
коко́с *n.* **1,** coconut. **2,** coconut palm; coconut tree. —**коко́совый,** *adj.* coconut (*attrib.*).
коко́тка [*gen. pl.* **-ток**] *n.* kept woman.
коко́шник *n.* woman's headdress worn in old Russia.
кокс *n.* coke. —**ко́ксовый; коксова́льный,** *adj.* coke (*attrib.*). —**коксу́ющийся,** *adj., in* **коксу́ющийся у́голь,** coking coal.
кокте́йль (тэ) *n.m.* cocktail. —**моло́чный кокте́йль,** milk shake.
кол [*gen.* **кола́**] *n.* **1,** [*pl.* **ко́лья, ко́льев**] stake; picket. Посади́ть на́ кол, to impale on a stake. **2,** [*pl.* **колы́, коло́в**] *colloq.* one (*lowest grade in school*).
ко́лба *n.* flask; retort.
колбаса́ [*pl.* **-ба́сы**] *n.* sausage.
колба́сник *n.* sausage maker.
колба́сный *adj.* sausage (*attrib.*).
колго́тки [*gen.* **-ток**] *n. pl.* panty hose.
колдо́бина *n., colloq.* rut; pothole.
колдова́ть *v. impfv.* [*pres.* **-ду́ю, -ду́ешь**] to practice witchcraft.
колдовство́ *n.* sorcery; witchcraft.
колду́н [*gen.* **-дуна́**] *n.* sorcerer.
колду́нья *n.* sorceress.
колеба́ние *n.* **1,** swaying. **2,** oscillation; vibration. **3,** fluctuation; variation. **4,** *often pl.* hesitation; hesitancy; vacillation: без колеба́ний, without hesitation.
колеба́ть *v. impfv.* [*pfv.* **поколеба́ть;** *pres.* **-ле́блю, -ле́блешь**] to shake. —**колеба́ться,** *refl.* **1,** to sway; swing to and fro. **2,** to oscillate. **3,** to fluctuate; vary. **4,** to hesitate; waver; vacillate.
коле́нка [*gen. pl.* **-нок**] *n., colloq.* knee.
коленко́р *n.* buckram. —**э́то совсе́м друго́й коленко́р,** that's a horse of a different color.
коле́нный *adj.* knee (*attrib.*). —**коле́нная ча́шка** *or* **ча́шечка,** kneecap.
коле́но *n.* **1,** [*pl.* **коле́ни, -ней** *or* **-ле́н**] knee; *pl.* lap. **2,** [*pl.* **коле́нья, -ьев**] bend (*in a pipe, river, road, etc.*). **3,** [*pl.* **-ья, -ьев**] section (*of a pipe, river, road, etc.*). **4,** [*pl.* **коле́на, -ле́н**] *colloq., music* part; *dance* figure. **5,** [*pl.* **-на, -ле́н**] generation. Брат (сестра́) во второ́м коле́не, cousin twice removed. **6,** [*pl.* **-на, -ле́н**] *Bib.* tribe: коле́на Изра́илевы, the tribes of Israel. —**ему́ мо́ре по коле́но,** *colloq.* he doesn't care about anything.
коле́нчатый *adj.* consisting of several branches. —**коле́нчатый вал,** crankshaft.
колёсико *n.* **1,** *dim. of* **колесо́. 2,** caster.
колеси́ть *v. impfv.* [*pres.* **-шу́, -си́шь**] *colloq.* **1,** to travel in a roundabout way; zigzag. **2,** to travel about (a place); travel all over.
колесни́ца *n.* chariot. —**погреба́льная колесни́ца,** hearse.
колёсный *adj.* **1,** wheel (*attrib.*). **2,** wheeled.
колесо́ [*pl.* **колёса**] *n.* wheel. —**вставля́ть па́лки в колёса, 1,** to throw a monkey wrench into the works. **2,** (*with dat.*) to put a spoke in someone's wheel.
колесова́ть *v. impfv. & pfv.* [*pres.* **-су́ю, -су́ешь**] to break on the wheel.
коле́чко [*gen. pl.* **-чек**] *n., dim. of* **кольцо́.**
колея́ *n.* **1,** rut. **2,** *R.R.* track; gauge. **3,** *fig.* normal routine. —**войти́ в колею́,** to settle into one's normal routine. —**вы́бить из колеи́,** to unsettle; upset someone's routine.
ко́ли *also,* **коли́** *and* **коль** *conj., obs.* if.
коли́бри *n.m. or f. indecl.* hummingbird.
колизе́й *n.* coliseum.
ко́лики [*gen.* **-лик**] *n. pl.* colic.
коли́т *n.* colitis.
коли́чественный *adj.* quantitative. —**коли́чественное числи́тельное,** cardinal number.
коли́чество *n.* quantity; number; amount.
ко́лкий *adj.* **1,** prickly. **2,** *fig.* biting; mordant; caustic.
ко́лкость *n.f.* **1,** causticity; mordancy. **2,** caustic remark.
коллаборациони́ст *n.* collaborator.
колле́га *n.m. & f.* colleague.
коллегиа́льный *adj.* collective; joint.
колле́гия *n.* **1,** board: редакцио́нная колле́гия, editorial board. **2,** collegium; college. **3,** *in* суде́йская колле́гия, panel of judges.
колле́дж *n.* college.
коллекти́в *n.* collective; body; group.
коллективиза́ция *n.* collectivization.
коллективизи́ровать *v. impfv. & pfv.* [*pres.* **-рую, -руешь**] to collectivize.
коллективи́зм *n.* collectivism.
коллекти́вный *adj.* collective. —**коллекти́вное хозя́йство,** collective farm(ing).
коллекционе́р *n.* collector.

коллекциони́ровать *v. impfv.* [*pres.* **-рую, -руешь**] to collect.
колле́кция *n.* collection.
ко́лли *n.m. indecl.* collie.
колло́дий *n.* collodion. *Also,* **колло́диум.**
колло́ид *n.* colloid. —**колло́идный,** *adj.* colloidal.
колло́квиум *n.* oral examination.
колобро́дить *v. impfv.* [*pres.* **-жу, -дишь**] *colloq.* **1,** to wander; drift; loiter. **2,** to carouse; live it up.
коловоро́т *n.* drill brace.
коло́да *n.* **1,** log. **2,** chopping block. **3,** deck (*of cards*). —**че́рез пень коло́ду,** in a slipshod manner.
коло́дезный *adj.* well (*attrib.*): коло́дезная вода́, well water.
коло́дец [*gen.* **-дца**] *n.* well.
коло́дка [*gen. pl.* **-док**] *n.* **1,** shoetree. **2,** last (*for a shoe*). **3,** shoe (*of a brake*). **4,** *pl.* stocks (*instrument of punishment*).
коло́к [*gen.* **-лка́**] *n.* peg (*of a musical instrument*).
ко́локол [*pl.* **колокола́**] *n.* bell.
колоко́льный *adj.* of bells: колоко́льный звон, ringing/tolling of bells.
колоко́льня [*gen. pl.* **-лен**] *n.* bell tower. —**смотре́ть (на что́-нибудь) со свое́й колоко́льни,** to look at (solely) from one's own point of view.
колоко́льчик *n.* **1,** small bell. **2,** bluebell; bellflower; campanula.
колониали́зм *n.* colonialism.
колониа́льный *adj.* colonial.
колониза́тор *n.* **1,** colonialist; colonizer. **2,** colonist. —**колониза́ция,** *n.* colonization.
колонизи́ровать *v. impfv. & pfv.* [*pres.* **-рую, -руешь**] to colonize. *Also,* **колонизова́ть** [*pres.* **-зу́ю, -зу́ешь**].
колони́ст *n.* colonist; settler.
коло́ния *n.* colony.
коло́нка [*gen. pl.* **-нок**] *n.* **1,** *dim. of* **коло́нна. 2,** column (*of print, figures, etc.*). **3,** any of a number of devices dispensing liquid: бензи́новая коло́нка, gasoline pump. **4,** hot-water heater. —**рулева́я коло́нка,** steering column.
коло́нна *n.* **1,** column; pillar. **2,** column; file: коло́нна демонстра́нтов, column of demonstrators/marchers. **3,** column (*of print, figures, etc.*).
колонна́да *n.* colonnade.
коло́нный *adj.* columned.
колоно́к [*gen.* **-нка́**] *n.* kolinsky (*Russian mink*).
колонти́тул *n.* running head.
колорату́ра *n.* coloratura. —**колорату́рный,** *adj.* coloratura.
колори́т *n.* coloring; color. —**ме́стный колори́т,** local color.
колори́тный *adj.* colorful.
ко́лос [*pl.* **коло́сья, коло́сьев**] *n.* ear (*of a cereal plant*).
колосовы́е *n. pl., decl. as an adj.* cereals.
коло́сс *n.* colossus.
колосса́льный *adj.* colossal; huge; tremendous.
колоти́ть *v. impfv.* [*pres.* **-лочу́, -ло́тишь**] **1,** (*with* **в** + *acc. or* **по**) to strike; bang; thump. **2,** *colloq.* to beat; whip; thrash. **3,** *colloq.* to break; smash. —**колоти́ться,** *refl., colloq.* **1,** (*with* **о** + *acc.*) to beat (against); strike (against). **2,** (*of the heart*) to thump; pound.
колоту́шка [*gen. pl.* **-шек**] *n.* **1,** wooden hammer; mallet. **2,** watchman's stick.
коло́ть *v. impfv.* [*pfv.* **кольну́ть;** *pres.* **колю́, ко́лешь**] **1,** to prick. **2,** to stab. **3,** *impers.* to have a sharp pain: у меня́ ко́лет в боку́, I have a sharp pain in my side. **4,** [*pfv.* **расколо́ть**] to crack (nuts); chop (wood). **5,** [*pfv.* **заколо́ть**] to slaughter (an animal). **6,** to taunt. —**коло́ться,** *refl.* [*impfv. only*] **1,** to be prickly. **2,** to split. **3,** to slash each other.
колпа́к [*gen.* **-пака́**] *n.* **1,** tall pointed cap. **2,** cone-shaped cover. **3,** hubcap. **4,** cowl.
колпачо́к [*gen.* **-чка́**] *n.* **1,** *dim. of* **колпа́к. 2,** cap: буты́лочный колпачо́к, bottle cap.
ко́лпица *n.* spoonbill.
колумби́йский *adj.* **1,** Colombian. **2,** Columbia (*attrib.*): колумби́йский университе́т, Columbia University.
колу́н [*gen.* **-луна́**] *n.* heavy ax.
колхо́з *n.* collective farm (*contr. of* **коллекти́вное хозя́йство**). —**колхо́зник,** *n.* collective farmer; member of a collective farm. —**колхо́зный,** *adj.* of or pert. to a collective farm.
колча́н *n.* quiver.
колчеда́н *n.* pyrites.
колчено́гий *adj., colloq.* having one leg shorter than the other.
колыбе́ль *n.f.* cradle.
колыбе́льный *adj.* cradle (*attrib.*). —**колыбе́льная пе́сня,** lullaby.
колыма́га *n.* **1,** old-fashioned coach. **2,** *colloq.* rattletrap; jalopy.
колыха́ние *n.* swaying.
колыха́ть *v. impfv.* [*pfv.* **колыхну́ть;** *pres.* **-лы́шу, -лы́шешь**] to sway. —**колыха́ться,** *refl.* to sway; wave; flutter.
ко́лышек [*gen.* **-шка**] *n.* peg.
коль *conj.* = **ко́ли.** —**коль ско́ро, 1,** if. **2,** as soon as.
кольдкре́м *n.* cold cream.
колье́ *n. neut. indecl.* necklace.
кольну́ть *v., pfv. of* **коло́ть.**
кольра́би *n.f. indecl.* kohlrabi.
кольцево́й *adj.* circular.
кольцо́ [*pl.* **ко́льца, коле́ц, ко́льцам**] *n.* ring.
ко́льчатый *adj.* **1,** made of rings. **2,** ring-shaped.
кольчу́га *n.* mail; chain mail.
колю́чий *adj.* **1,** prickly. **2,** itchy. **3,** *fig.* biting; cutting; sarcastic. —**колю́чая про́волока,** barbed wire.
колю́чка [*gen. pl.* **-чек**] *n.* thorn; barb.
ко́люшка [*gen. pl.* **-шек**] *n.* stickleback.
ко́лющий *adj.* stabbing: ко́лющая боль, stabbing pain.
коля́дка [*gen. pl.* **-док**] *n.* Christmas carol.
коля́ска [*gen. pl.* **-сок**] *n.* carriage. —**де́тская коля́ска,** baby carriage.
ком[1] [*pl.* **ко́мья, ко́мьев**] *n.* lump; clod. Сне́жный ком, snowball. —**ком в го́рле,** lump in one's throat.
ком[2] *pron., prepl. of* **кто.**
ко́ма *n.* coma.
кома́нда *n.* **1,** command; order. **2,** command: под кома́ндой (+ *gen.*), under the command of. **3,** crew (*of a ship*). **4,** *sports* team. **5,** *mil.* party; team. —**пожа́рная кома́нда,** fire brigade. —**спаса́тельная кома́нда,** rescue party.
команди́р *n.* **1,** commander. **2,** (ship's) captain.

командирова́ть *v. impfv. & pfv.* [*pres.* **-ру́ю, -ру́ешь**] to send on an assignment; dispatch.
командиро́вка [*gen. pl.* **-вок**] *n.* assignment; business trip.
командиро́вочный *adj.* connected with an assignment or business trip. —*n.* **1,** person on an assignment or business trip. **2,** *pl., colloq.* travel allowance.
кома́ндный *adj.* **1,** command (*attrib.*). **2,** team (*attrib.*). **3,** *fig.* commanding: кома́ндная высота́, commanding heights.
кома́ндование *n.* **1,** command: принима́ть кома́ндование, to assume command. **2,** command; commanding officers: верхо́вное кома́ндование, high command.
кома́ндовать *v. impfv.* [*pres.* **-дую, -дуешь**] **1,** to command; give orders. **2,** (*with instr.*) to command; be in command of. **3,** (*with* **над**) *colloq.* to order about.
кома́ндующий *n., decl. as an adj.* commander.
кома́р [*gen.* **-мара́**] *n.* mosquito. —**комари́ный,** *adj.* mosquito (*attrib.*).
комато́зный *adj.* comatose.
комба́йн *n.* combine (*harvesting machine*).
комбина́т *n.* **1,** (industrial) combine. **2,** center: комбина́т бытово́го обслу́живания, service center. —**уче́бный комбина́т,** training center.
комбина́ция *n.* **1,** combination. **2,** *sports* maneuver. **3,** *fig.* scheme. **4,** (lady's) slip.
комбинезо́н *n.* overalls.
комбини́ровать *v. impfv.* [*pfv.* **скомбини́ровать;** *pres.* **-рую, -руешь**] to combine.
комеди́йный *adj.* comedy (*attrib.*).
коме́дия *n.* comedy. —**разы́грывать** *or* **лома́ть коме́дию,** to put on an act.
ко́мель [*gen.* **-мля**] *n.m.* thick end; stump; base.
коменда́нт *n.* **1,** commandant. **2,** superintendent.
коменда́нтский *adj., in* **коменда́нтский час,** curfew.
комендату́ра *n.* commandant's headquarters.
коме́та *n.* comet.
коми́зм *n.* comedy; humor.
ко́мик *n.* comedian; comic actor.
ко́микс *n., usu. pl.* comics.
Коминте́рн (тэ) *n.* the Comintern (*contr. of* **Коммунисти́ческий Интернациона́л**).
комисса́р *n.* **1,** commissar. **2,** commissioner. —**комиссариа́т,** *n.* commissariat.
комиссионе́р *n.* broker; agent.
комиссио́нный *adj.* commission (*attrib.*). —**комиссио́нные,** *n. pl.* commission; fee.
коми́ссия *n.* **1,** commission; committee; board. **2,** commission: брать ве́щи на коми́ссию, to accept items for sale on a commission basis.
комите́т *n.* committee.
коми́ческий *adj.* **1,** comic. **2,** comical.
коми́чный *adj.* comical; funny.
ко́мкать *v. impfv.* [*pfv.* **ско́мкать**] **1,** to crumple. **2,** *colloq.* to rush through; cut short.
комкова́тый *adj.* bumpy; uneven.
коммента́рий *n.* **1,** commentary. **2,** *pl.* comment: никаки́х коммента́риев, no comment.
коммента́тор *n.* commentator.
комменти́ровать *v. impfv. & pfv.* [*pres.* **-рую, -руешь**] **1,** to annotate. **2,** to comment on; interpret.
коммерса́нт *n.* merchant.
комме́рция *n.* commerce. —**комме́рческий,** *adj.* commercial.
коммивояжёр *n.* traveling salesman.
комму́на *n.* commune.
коммуна́льный *adj.* **1,** public; municipal. **2,** (*of an apartment*) communal.
коммуни́зм *n.* communism.
коммуника́бельный *adj.* communicative; approachable; easy to talk to.
коммуника́ция *n., mil., often pl.* communications. —**коммуникацио́нный,** *adj.* of communication.
коммуни́ст *n.* communist. —**коммунисти́ческий,** *adj.* communist.
коммута́тор *n.* switchboard.
коммюнике́ *n. neut. indecl.* communiqué.
ко́мната *n.* room.
ко́мнатный *adj.* **1,** room (*attrib.*). **2,** indoor: ко́мнатные расте́ния, indoor plants. —**ко́мнатные и́гры,** indoor games; parlor games. —**ко́мнатная соба́чка,** lap dog.
комо́д *n.* bureau; dresser.
комо́к [*gen.* **-мка́**] *n.* lump. —**комо́к в го́рле,** lump in one's throat. —**комо́к не́рвов,** bundle of nerves.
комо́лый *adj.* hornless.
компа́ктный *adj.* compact; solid.
компане́йский *adj., colloq.* sociable; companionable; outgoing.
компа́ния *n.* **1,** company: води́ть компа́нию с, to keep company with. Он тебе́ не компа́ния, he is not the proper company for you. **2,** group: отдели́ться от компа́нии, to become separated from the group. Пойти́ всей компа́нией, to go in a group. **3,** *comm.* company: нефтяна́я компа́ния, oil company.
компаньо́н *n.* **1,** (male) companion. **2,** partner. —**компаньо́нка,** *n.* (female) companion.
компа́ртия *n.* Communist Party (*contr. of* **коммунисти́ческая па́ртия**).
ко́мпас *n.* compass. —**ко́мпасный,** *adj.* compass (*attrib.*).
компе́ндиум *also,* **компе́ндий** *n.* compendium; digest.
компенса́ция *n.* compensation. —**компенсацио́нный,** *adj.* compensatory.
компенси́ровать *v. impfv. & pfv.* [*pres.* **-рую, -руешь**] **1,** to compensate. **2,** to compensate for; make up for; offset.
компете́нтный *adj.* **1,** competent; qualified. **2,** competent; having jurisdiction. —**компете́нтность,** *n.f.* competence.
компете́нция *n.* jurisdiction.
компили́ровать *v. impfv.* [*pfv.* **скомпили́ровать;** *pres.* **-рую, -руешь**] to compile.
компиля́ция *n.* compilation. —**компиля́тор,** *n.* compiler.
ко́мплекс *n.* **1,** complex. **2,** series. **3,** system. **4,** *psychoanalysis* complex: ко́мплекс неполноце́нности, inferiority complex.
ко́мплексный *adj.* **1,** complex; composite; multiple. **2,** integrated. **3,** all-round; comprehensive.
компле́кт *n.* **1,** (complete) set. **2,** complement (*of personnel*). —**компле́ктный,** *adj.* (*of a set*) complete.
комплектова́ть *v. impfv.* [*pfv.* **укомплектова́ть;** *pres.* **-ту́ю, -ту́ешь**] **1,** to complete (a set); acquire a complete set of. **2,** to bring up to full strength.
компле́кция *n.* build; figure; frame.

комплимéнт *n.* compliment.
композúтор *n.* composer.
композúция *n.* composition.
компонéнт *n.* component.
компоновáть *v. impfv.* [*pfv.* **скомпоновáть;** *pres.* **-нýю, -нýешь**] to arrange; put together.
компонóвка *n.* arrangement; layout.
компóст *n.* compost.
компóстер *n.* punch (*for punching tickets*).
компостúровать *v. impfv.* [*pfv.* **прокомпостúровать;** *pres.* **-рую, -руешь**] to punch (a ticket).
компóт *n.* fruit compote; stewed fruit.
компрéсс *n.* compress.
компрéссор *n.* compressor.
компрометáция *n.* compromising (*of someone or something*).
компрометúровать *v. impfv.* [*pfv.* **скомпрометúровать;** *pres.* **-рую, -руешь**] to compromise; place in a compromising position.
компромúсс *n.* compromise. —**компромúссный,** *adj.* compromise (*attrib.*).
компьютер *n.* computer.
комсомóл *n.* Komsomol; Communist Youth League (*contr. of* **Коммунистúческий Союз Молодёжи**).
комсомóлец [*gen.* **-льца**] *n.m.* [*fem.* **-лка**] member of the Komsomol.
комсомóльский *adj.* Komsomol (*attrib.*).
комý *pron., dat. of* **кто.**
комфóрт *n.* comfort.
комфортáбельный *adj.* comfortable.
конвéйер *n.* conveyer. —**сбóрочный конвéйер,** assembly line.
конвéйерный *adj.* conveyer (*attrib.*): конвéйерная лéнта, conveyer belt.
конвéнт *n., hist.* convention.
конвéнция *n.* convention; compact.
конвéрт *n.* envelope.
конвéртер (тэ) *n.* converter. *Also,* **конвéртор.**
конвертúровать *v. impfv. & pfv.* [*pres.* **-рую, -руешь**] *finance* to convert.
конвоúр *n.* **1,** armed guard; escort. **2,** escort (*for ships*).
конвоúровать *v. impfv.* [*pres.* **-рую, -руешь**] *mil.* to escort.
конвóй *n.* (armed) escort: под конвóем, under escort; under guard.
конвóйный *adj.* escort (*attrib.*). —*n.* armed guard; escort.
конвýльсия *n.* convulsion. —**конвульсúвный,** *adj.* convulsive.
конгломерáт *n.* **1,** conglomeration. **2,** conglomerate.
конгрéсс *n.* **1,** congress: Вéнский конгрéсс, Congress of Vienna. **2,** Congress (*of the U.S.*). —**конгрессмéн,** *n.* (U.S.) congressman.
конгруэ́нтный *adj., math.* congruent. —**конгруэ́нция,** *n., math.* congruence.
конденсáтор (дэ) *n.* **1,** *chem.* condenser. **2,** *electricity* capacitator; condenser.
конденсáция (дэ) *n., physics* condensation. —**конденсациóнный,** *adj.* obtained by condensation.
конденсúровать (дэ) *v. impfv. & pfv.* [*pres.* **-рую, -руешь**] *physics* to condense.
кондúтер *n.* pastry cook; pastry chef; confectioner.
кондúтерская *n., decl. as an adj.* pastry shop; confectionery. —**кондúтерский,** *adj.* pastry (*attrib.*); confectionery (*attrib.*).
кондиционéр *n.* air conditioner.
кондиционúрование *n.* conditioning. —**кондиционúрование вóздуха,** air conditioning.
кондиционúровать *v. impfv. & pfv.* [*pres.* **-рую, -руешь**] to air-condition.
кондомúниум *n.* condominium.
кóндор *n.* condor.
кондотьéр *n.* soldier of fortune.
кондýктор [*pl.* **кондукторá**] *n.* conductor (*on a train, bus, etc.*). —**кондýкторский,** *adj.* conductor's.
коневóдство *n.* horse breeding. —**коневóд,** *n.* horse breeder. —**коневóдческий,** *adj.* of or pert. to breeding horses: коневóдческая фéрма, stud farm.
конёк [*gen.* **-нькá**] *n.* **1,** *dim. of* **конь. 2,** *pl.* skates (*esp.* ice skates). **3,** *fig.* one's chief interest; one's favorite topic of conversation. **4,** ridge (*of a roof*). **5,** carved horse's head used as a decoration for a roof. —**морскóй конёк,** sea horse.
конéц [*gen.* **-нцá**] *n.* end. —**без концá,** endlessly. —**в концé концóв,** in the end; after all; when all is said and done. —**в одúн конéц,** (*of a trip*) one-way. —**до концá, 1,** to the end. **2,** completely; totally. —**и дéло с концóм,** *colloq.* and that will be the end of it. —**и концы́ в вóду,** and no one will know the difference; and none will be the wiser. —**на худóй конéц,** *colloq.* if worst comes to worst. —**со всех концóв** (+ *gen.*), from every corner of.
конéчно *adv.* of course; certainly.
конéчность *n.f.* extremity (*of the body*).
конéчный *adj.* **1,** final; last. **2,** ultimate; eventual. **3,** finite. —**в конéчном итóге** *or* **счёте,** ultimately; in the final analysis.
конúна *n.* horsemeat.
конúческий *adj.* conic; conical.
кóнка [*gen. pl.* **-нок**] *n.* horsecar.
конклáв *n., relig.* conclave.
конкордáт *n.* concordat.
конкретизúровать *v. impfv. & pfv.* [*pres.* **-рую, -руешь**] to make specific; spell out.
конкрéтный *adj.* concrete; specific.
конкурéнт *n.* (business) competitor. —**конкурентоспосóбный,** *adj.* able to compete; competitive. —**конкурéнция,** *n.* (business) competition.
конкурúровать *v. impfv.* [*pres.* **-рую, -руешь**] to compete.
кóнкурс *n.* competition; contest. —**кóнкурсный,** *adj.* competitive.
кóнник *n.* cavalryman.
кóнница *n.* cavalry.
коннозавóдство *n.* horse breeding.
кóнный *adj.* **1,** horse (*attrib.*). **2,** horse-drawn. **3,** mounted. **4,** (*of a statue*) equestrian. —**кóнный двор,** stable. —**кóнный завóд,** stud farm.
коновáл *n.* horse doctor.
кóновязь *n.f.* hitching post.
конокрáд *n.* horse thief. —**конокрáдство,** *n.* horse stealing.
конопáтить *v. impfv.* [*pfv.* **законопáтить;** *pres.* **-чу, -тишь**] to caulk.
коноплá *n.* hemp.
коноплянка [*gen. pl.* **-нок**] *n.* linnet.
конопляный *adj.* hemp (*attrib.*).
коносамéнт *n.* bill of lading.

консерва́нт *n.* preservative.
консервати́вный *adj.* conservative. —**консерва-ти́зм,** *n.* conservatism. —**консерва́тор,** *n.* conservative.
консервато́рия *n.* conservatory (*of music*).
консерва́ция *n.* **1,** preservation. **2,** temporary closing.
консерви́ровать *v. impfv. & pfv.* [*pfv. also* **закон-серви́ровать;** *pres.* **-рую, -руешь**] **1,** to can; preserve. **2,** to close down temporarily.
консе́рвный *adj.* canning (*attrib.*). —**консе́рвная ба́нка,** tin can. —**консе́рвный нож,** can opener. —**консе́рвная фа́брика,** cannery.
консе́рвы [*gen.* **-вов**] *n.pl.* canned food; canned goods: мясны́е консе́рвы, canned meat; овощны́е консе́рвы, canned vegetables.
конси́лиум *n.* consultation (*between doctors*).
консисте́нция *n.* consistency (*firmness*).
ко́нский *adj.* horse (*attrib.*). —**ко́нский во́лос,** horsehair.
консолида́ция *n.* consolidation.
консо́ль *n.f.* **1,** console (*bracket*). **2,** pedestal; stand. —**консо́льный,** *adj.* cantilever (*attrib.*): консо́льный мост, cantilever bridge.
консона́нс *n.* consonance.
консо́рциум *n.* consortium.
конспе́кт *n.* synopsis; outline; abstract.
конспекти́вный *adj.* concise; brief.
конспекти́ровать *v. impfv.* [*pfv.* **проконспекти́ро-вать;** *pres.* **-рую, -руешь**] to abstract; make an abstract of.
конспирати́вный *adj.* secret. —**конспира́тор,** *n.* conspirator. —**конспира́ция,** *n.* secrecy.
конста́нта *n., physics; math.* constant.
констата́ция *n.* establishment; certification.
констати́ровать *v. impfv. & pfv.* [*pres.* **-рую, -ру-ешь**] to establish; certify.
консте́бль *n.m.* constable.
конститу́ция *n.* constitution. —**конституцио́нный,** *adj.* constitutional.
конструи́ровать *v. impfv.* [*pfv.* **сконструи́ровать;** *pres.* **-рую, -руешь**] **1,** to construct; design. **2,** to organize.
конструкти́вный *adj.* **1,** structural. **2,** *fig.* constructive.
констру́ктор *n.* designer.
констру́кторский *adj.* design (*attrib.*). —**констру́к-торское бюро́,** design office (*in a factory*).
констру́кция *n.* **1,** construction; design. **2,** a structure. **3,** *gram.* construction.
ко́нсул *n.* consul. —**ко́нсульский,** *adj.* consular. —**ко́нсульство,** *n.* consulate.
консульта́нт *n.* **1,** consultant. **2,** consulting physician.
консультати́вный *adj.* consultative; advisory.
консульта́ция *n.* **1,** consultation. **2,** expert advice; expert opinion. **3,** guidance center; clinic.
консульти́ровать *v. impfv.* [*pfv.* **проконсульти́ро-вать;** *pres.* **-рую, -руешь**] **1,** to advise; give advice to. **2,** [*impfv. only*] (*with* **с** + *instr.*) to consult. —**кон-сульти́роваться,** *refl.* (*with* **с** + *instr.*) to consult.
конта́кт *n.* contact.
конта́ктный *adj.* contact (*attrib.*). —**конта́ктные ли́нзы,** contact lenses.
контéйнер (тэ) *n.* container (*for shipping goods*). —**конте́йнерный,** *adj.* container (*attrib.*).
конте́кст *n.* context: вырыва́ть из конте́кста, to take out of context.
континге́нт *n.* **1,** contingent. **2,** quota.
контине́нт *n.* continent. —**континента́льный,** *adj.* continental.
конто́ра *n.* office.
конто́рка [*gen. pl.* **-рок**] *n.* **1,** small office. **2,** high old-fashioned writing desk.
конто́рский *adj.* office (*attrib.*).
ко́нтра *n., colloq.* **1,** rebel; counterrevolutionary. **2,** *pl.* quarrel; falling-out. —**быть в ко́нтрах с** (+ *instr.*), to be on the outs with.
контраба́нда *n.* **1,** smuggling. **2,** contraband goods. —**контрабанди́ст,** *n.* smuggler. —**контраба́ндный,** *adj.* contraband.
контраба́с *n.* bass viol; double bass; contrabass.
контраге́нт *n.* contractor.
контр-адмира́л *n.* rear admiral.
контра́кт *n.* contract.
контрактова́ть *v. impfv.* [*pfv.* **законтрактова́ть;** *pres.* **-ту́ю, ту́ешь**] to contract (for).
контра́льто *n. neut. indecl.* contralto (*voice*). —*n. fem. indecl.* contralto (*singer*). —**контра́льтовый,** *adj.* contralto.
контрама́рка [*gen. pl.* **-рок**] *n.* free pass; complimentary ticket.
контрапу́нкт *n., music* counterpoint. —**контрапунк-ти́ческий,** *adj.* contrapuntal.
контра́ст *n.* contrast.
контрасти́ровать *v. impfv.* [*pres.* **-рую, -руешь**] to contrast; form a contrast.
контра́стный *adj.* contrasting.
контрата́ка *n.* counterattack.
контратакова́ть *v. impfv. & pfv.* [*pres.* **-ку́ю, -ку́ешь**] to counterattack.
контрафаго́т *n.* double bassoon; contrabassoon.
контрибу́ция *n.* levy; tribute.
контрме́ра *n.* countermeasure.
контрнаступле́ние *n.* counteroffensive.
контролёр *n.* **1,** controller. **2,** inspector; examiner. **3,** ticket collector. —**фина́нсовый контролёр,** auditor.
контроли́ровать *v. impfv.* [*pfv.* **проконтроли́ро-вать;** *pres.* **-рую, -руешь**] **1,** to check. **2,** [*impfv. only*] to control.
контро́ль *n.m.* **1,** control. **2,** inspection; supervision; monitoring.
контро́льный *adj.* **1,** control (*attrib.*). **2,** check (*attrib.*): контро́льный пункт, checkpoint. **3,** monitoring: контро́льный аппара́т/прибо́р, monitoring device. —**контро́льный о́пыт,** control experiment. —**конт-ро́льная рабо́та,** test (*in school*). —**контро́льные ци́фры,** control figures (*in a planned economy*).
контрпредложе́ние *n.* counteroffer; counterproposal.
контрразве́дка *n.* counterintelligence; counterespionage. —**контрразве́дчик,** *n.* counterintelligence agent.
контрреволю́ция *n.* counterrevolution. —**контр-революционе́р,** *n.* counterrevolutionary. —**контр-революцио́нный,** *adj.* counterrevolutionary.
контруда́р *n.* counterblow.
контрфо́рс *n.* buttress.
конту́зить *v. impfv.* [*pres.* **-жу, -зишь**] to contuse.
конту́зия *n.* contusion.
ко́нтур *n.* **1,** contour. **2,** *electricity* circuit. —**ко́нтур-ный,** *adj.* contour (*attrib.*).

конура́ *n.* **1,** kennel; doghouse. **2,** *colloq.* hovel; dump.

ко́нус *n., geom.* cone.

конусообра́зный *adj.* cone-shaped.

конфедера́ция (дэ) *n.* confederation; confederacy. —**конфедерати́вный,** *adj.* confederate.

конферансье́ *n.m. indecl.* master of ceremonies.

конфере́нц-за́л *n.* conference hall.

конфере́нция *n.* conference.

конфе́та *also,* **конфе́тка** *n.* **1,** piece of candy. **2,** *pl.* candy. —**конфе́тный,** *adj.* candy (*attrib.*).

конфетти́ *n. neut. indecl.* confetti.

конфигура́ция *n.* configuration.

конфиденциа́льный *adj.* confidential. —**конфиденциа́льно,** *adv.* confidentially.

конфирма́ция *n., relig.* confirmation.

конфирмова́ть *v. impfv. & pfv.* [*pres.* **-му́ю, -му́ешь**] *relig.* to confirm.

конфиска́ция *n.* confiscation.

конфискова́ть *v. impfv. & pfv.* [*pres.* **-ку́ю, -ку́ешь**] to confiscate.

конфли́кт *n.* conflict.

конфо́рка [*gen. pl.* **-рок**] *n.* burner (*on a stove*).

конформи́зм *n.* conformism.

конфронта́ция *n.* confrontation.

конфу́з *n.* embarrassment.

конфу́зить *v. impfv.* [*pfv.* **сконфу́зить;** *pres.* **-жу, -зишь**] to embarrass. —**конфу́зиться,** *refl.* **1,** to be embarrassed. **2,** (*with gen.*) to be shy (in the presence of).

конфу́зливый *adj.* bashful; shy.

конфу́зный *adj., colloq.* embarrassing; awkward.

концентра́т *n.* concentrate.

концентрацио́нный *adj., in* **концентрацио́нный ла́герь,** concentration camp.

концентра́ция *n.* concentration.

концентри́ровать *v. impfv.* [*pfv.* **сконцентри́ровать;** *pres.* **-рую, -руешь**] to concentrate. —**концентри́роваться,** *refl.* **1,** to concentrate; mass. **2,** [*impfv. only*] (*with* **на** + *prepl.*) to concentrate (on).

концентри́ческий *adj.* concentric.

конце́пция *n.* conception.

конце́рн *n.* (business) concern.

конце́рт *n.* **1,** concert; recital. **2,** concerto.

концерта́нт *n.m.* [*fem.* **-та́нтка**] concert performer.

концерти́но *n. indecl.* concertina.

концерти́ровать *v. impfv.* [*pres.* **-рую, -руешь**] to give concerts.

концертме́йстер *n.* concertmaster.

конце́ртный *adj.* concert (*attrib.*).

конце́ссия *n., comm.* concession. —**концессионе́р,** *n.* concessionaire.

концла́герь [*pl.* **-лагеря́**] *n.m.* concentration camp (*contr. of* **концентрацио́нный ла́герь**).

конча́ть *v. impfv.* [*pfv.* **ко́нчить**] **1,** to finish. **2,** to close; conclude. **3,** to stop. **4,** to graduate from. **5,** *in* **пло́хо ко́нчить,** to end up badly; come to a bad end. —**конча́ться,** *refl.* **1,** to end; come to an end; be over. **2,** to be used up; run out.

ко́нченый *adj., colloq.* hopeless. —**ко́нченый челове́к,** failure; has-been.

ко́нчик *n.* tip; point.

кончи́на *n.* death; passing; demise.

ко́нчить *v., pfv. of* **конча́ть.** —**ко́нчиться,** *refl., pfv. of* **конча́ться.**

конъюнктиви́т *n.* conjunctivitis.

конъюнкту́ра *n.* situation; state of affairs.

конъюнкту́рный *adj.* temporary; of the moment: конъюнкту́рные соображе́ния, considerations of the moment.

конь [*gen.* **коня́;** *pl.* **ко́ни, коне́й, коня́м**] *n.m.* **1,** horse. **2,** *chess* knight. **3,** *gymnastics* horse. —**ко́нь-кача́лка,** hobbyhorse.

коньки́ *n. pl. See* **конёк.**

конькобе́жец [*gen.* **-жца**] *n.* skater. —**конькобе́жный,** *adj.* skating.

конья́к [*gen.* **-яка́**] *n.* cognac; brandy.

ко́нюх *n.* stable hand; groom.

коню́шня [*gen. pl.* **-шен**] *n.* stable.

кооперати́в *n.* **1,** cooperative. **2,** *colloq.* cooperative store. —**кооперати́вный,** *adj.* cooperative.

коопера́ция *n.* **1,** *econ.* cooperation. **2,** cooperative.

координа́та *n.* **1,** *math.* coordinate. **2,** *pl., colloq.* whereabouts.

координа́ция *n.* coordination.

координи́ровать *v. impfv. & pfv.* [*pres.* **-рую, -руешь**] to coordinate.

копа́л *n.* copal.

копа́ние *n.* digging.

копа́тель *n.m., obs.* digger.

копа́ть *v. impfv.* **1,** [*pfv.* **копну́ть**] to dig. **2,** [*pfv.* **вы́копать**] to dig; dig up; dig out. —**копа́ться,** *refl.* [*impfv. only*] (*with* **в** + *prepl.*) **1,** to dig in (the sand, dirt, etc.). **2,** to rummage through. **3,** to delve (into); probe. **4,** (*with* **с** + *instr.*) *colloq.* to dawdle (over).

копе́ечка [*gen. pl.* **-чек**] *n., dim. of* **копе́йка.** —**обойти́сь** (*or* **влете́ть**) **в копе́ечку,** to cost a fortune.

копе́ечный *adj.* **1,** worth one kopeck; one-kopeck (*attrib.*). **2,** (*of expenses*) minor; trifling. **3,** *fig.* petty.

копе́йка [*gen. pl.* **-пе́ек**] *n.* **1,** kopeck. **2,** *in idiomatic expressions* penny: копе́йка в копе́йку, penny for penny; до после́дней копе́йки, to the last penny. —**без копе́йки,** penniless.

копёр [*gen.* **-пра́**] *n.* pile driver.

ко́пи [*gen.* **ко́пей**] *n. pl.* mines.

копи́лка [*gen. pl.* **-лок**] *n.* money box; piggy bank.

копи́рка *n., colloq.* carbon paper.

копирова́льный *adj.* copying (*attrib.*). —**копирова́льная бума́га,** carbon paper.

копи́рование *n.* copying.

копи́ровать *v. impfv.* [*pfv.* **скопи́ровать;** *pres.* **-рую, -руешь**] **1,** to copy; make a copy of. **2,** to copy; imitate.

копиро́вка *n., colloq.* copying. —**копиро́вщик,** *n.* copier; copyist.

копи́ть *v. impfv.* [*pfv.* **накопи́ть;** *pres.* **коплю́, ко́пишь**] to accumulate; amass. —**копи́ться,** *refl.* to accumulate; pile up.

ко́пия *n.* **1,** copy. **2,** (*with gen.*) *colloq.* the image of: то́чная (*or* жива́я) ко́пия своего́ отца́, the living image of his father.

копна́ [*pl.* **ко́пны, копён, копна́м**] *n.* **1,** haycock. **2,** shock (*of hair*).

копну́ть *v., pfv. of* **копа́ть.**

ко́поть *n.f.* soot.

копоши́ться *v.r. impfv.* **1,** (*of insects*) to swarm about; (*of fish*) to swim about. **2,** *colloq.* (*of a person*) to putter about.

ко́пра *n.* copra.

копте́ть *v. impfv.* [*pres.* **-пчу́, -пти́шь**] **1,** to smoke; emit smoke. **2,** *colloq.* to vegetate; stagnate. **3,** (*with* **над**) *colloq.* to pore over.

копти́лка [*gen. pl.* **-лок**] *n.* wick lamp.
копти́льня [*gen. pl.* **-лен**] *n.* smokehouse.
копти́ть *v. impfv.* [*pres.* **-пчу́, -пти́шь**] **1,** [*pfv.* **закопти́ть**] to smoke (ham, fish, glass, etc.). **2,** [*pfv.* **накопти́ть**] (*of a lamp, candle, etc.*) to smoke; emit smoke. —**не́бо копти́ть,** to sit around doing nothing.
ко́птский *adj.* Coptic.
копче́ние *n.* smoking (*of meat*).
копчёности *n. pl.* [*sing.* **-ность**] smoked products.
копчёный *adj.* smoked.
ко́пчик *n.* coccyx.
копы́тный *adj.* **1,** hoof (*attrib.*). **2,** hoofed; ungulate.
копы́то *n.* hoof.
копьё [*pl.* **ко́пья, ко́пий**] *n.* spear.
кора́ *n.* **1,** bark. **2,** *bot.* cortex. **3,** crust: земна́я кора́, the earth's crust. —**кора́ головно́го мо́зга,** *anat.* cortex.
корабе́льный *adj.* ship (*attrib.*); ship's.
кораблевожде́ние *n.* navigation.
кораблекруше́ние *n.* shipwreck.
кораблестрое́ние *n.* shipbuilding. —**кораблестро́итель,** *n.m.* shipbuilder.
кора́блик *n.* **1,** *dim. of* **кора́бль. 2,** nautilus.
кора́бль [*gen.* **-бля́**] *n.m.* **1,** ship. **2,** *archit.* nave. —**косми́ческий кора́бль,** spaceship.
кора́лл *n.* coral. —**кора́лловый,** *adj.* coral.
кора́н *n.* the Koran.
корве́т *n.* corvette.
кордебале́т (дэ) *n.* corps de ballet.
кордо́н *n.* **1,** cordon. **2,** post; station.
коре́ец [*gen.* **-е́йца**] *n.m.* [*fem.* **-ея́нка**] Korean. —**коре́йский,** *adj.* Korean.
коре́йка *n.* brisket (*of pork or veal*).
корена́стый *adj.* stocky; thickset; heavyset.
корени́ться *v.r. impfv.* (*with* **в** + *prepl.*) to be rooted (in).
коренни́к [*gen.* **-ника́**] *n.* wheel horse.
коренно́й *adj.* **1,** native; indigenous. **2,** fundamental; radical. —**коренно́й зуб,** molar. —**коренна́я ло́шадь** = **коренни́к.** —**коренны́м о́бразом,** radically.
ко́рень [*gen.* **ко́рня;** *pl.* **ко́рни, -не́й, -ня́м**] *n.m.* root. —**в ко́рне,** radically. —**вырыва́ть с ко́рнем,** to uproot. —**знак ко́рня,** *math.* radical sign. —**ко́рень зла,** the root of all evil.—**на корню́,** (*of timber, crops, etc.*) standing; not (yet) cut down. —**пресека́ть в ко́рне,** to nip in the bud. —**пуска́ть ко́рни, 1,** to develop roots; put down roots. **2,** to take root. —**смотре́ть в ко́рень** (+ *gen.*), to get to the root (*or* heart) of.
коре́нья [*gen.* **-ньев**] *n. pl., cooking* roots.
корешо́к [*gen.* **-шка́**] *n.* **1,** *dim. of* **ко́рень. 2,** spine (*of a book*). **3,** counterfoil; stub.
ко́ржик *n.* cookie.
корзи́на *n.* basket. —**корзи́на для бума́ги,** wastebasket.
корзи́нка [*gen. pl.* **-нок**] *n.* small basket.
кориа́ндр *n.* coriander. —**кориа́ндровый,** *adj.* coriander (*attrib.*).
коридо́р *n.* corridor; hall.
коридо́рный *adj.* corridor (*attrib.*); hall (*attrib.*). —*n.* bellboy.
кори́нка *n.* currants (*seedless raisins*).
кори́нфский *adj.* Corinthian.
кори́ть *v. impfv., colloq.* to scold; rebuke; upbraid.
корифе́й *n.* leading light; luminary.
кори́ца *n.* cinnamon.
кори́чневый *adj.* brown.
ко́рка *n.* **1,** crust. **2,** rind; peel. —**от ко́рки до ко́рки,** from cover to cover.
корм [*pl.* **корма́**] *n.* **1,** forage; feed; fodder. **2,** feeding. —**пти́чий корм,** birdseed.
корма́ *n., naut.* stern.
кормёжка *n., colloq.* feeding.
корми́лец [*gen.* **-льца**] *n.* breadwinner.
корми́лица *n.* **1,** wet nurse. **2,** (female) breadwinner.
корми́ло *n., archaic* helm. —**стоя́ть у корми́ла вла́сти** (*or* **правле́ния**), to be at the helm of state.
корми́ть *v. impfv.* [*pfv.* **накорми́ть** *or* **покорми́ть;** *pres.* **кормлю́, ко́рмишь**] **1,** to feed. **2,** to suckle; nurse. —**корми́ться,** *refl.* [*impfv. only*] (*with instr.*). to eat; live on; live by.
кормле́ние *n.* **1,** feeding. **2,** suckling; nursing.
кормово́й *adj.* **1,** *naut.* stern (*attrib.*). **2,** fodder (*attrib.*); forage (*attrib.*).
корму́шка [*gen. pl.* **-шек**] *n.* feeding trough.
ко́рмчий *n., decl. as an adj.* helmsman.
корневи́ще *n.* rhizome.
корнево́й *adj.* root (*attrib.*).
корне́т *n.* cornet.
корнишо́н *n.* gherkin.
ко́роб [*pl.* **короба́**] *n.* basket. —**це́лый ко́роб новосте́й,** all sorts of news; loads of news.
коробе́йник *n.* peddler.
коро́бить *v. impfv.* [*pfv.* **покоро́бить**] **1,** to warp: жар коро́бил де́рево, the heat warped the wood. *Also impers. & intrans.* до́ски покоро́било, the boards have warped. **2,** *fig., colloq.* to irk; grate on: его́ э́то покоро́било (*or impers.* его́ покоро́било от э́того), it irked/grated on/him. —**коро́биться,** *refl.* to warp; buckle.
коро́бка [*gen. pl.* **-бок**] *n.* **1,** box. **2,** frame (*of a building, door, etc.*). —**коро́бка переда́ч/скоросте́й,** gearbox. —**черепна́я коро́бка,** cranium.
коро́бление *n.* warping.
коробо́к [*gen.* **-бка́**] *n.* small box.
коро́бочка [*gen. pl.* **-чек**] *n.* **1,** small box. **2,** *bot.* boll.
коро́ва *n.* cow. Ста́до коро́в, herd of cattle. —**морска́я коро́ва,** sea cow.
коро́вий [*fem.* **-вья**] *adj.* cow (*attrib.*); cow's. —**коро́вья о́спа,** cowpox.
коро́вка [*gen. pl.* **-вок**] *n., dim. of* **коро́ва.** —**бо́жья коро́вка,** ladybug; ladybird.
коро́вник *n.* cowshed.
короле́ва *n.* queen.
короле́вский *adj.* **1,** king's; queen's. **2,** royal. **3,** *chess* king's.
короле́вство *n.* kingdom.
королёк [*gen.* **-лька́**] *n.* **1,** kinglet (*bird*). **2,** blood orange.
коро́ль [*gen.* **-ля́**] *n.m.* **1,** king. **2,** *cards; chess* king.
коромы́сло [*gen. pl.* **-сел**] *n.* yoke (*for carrying buckets*).
коро́на *n.* **1,** crown. **2,** *astron.* corona.
корона́ция *n.* coronation.
коро́нка [*gen. pl.* **-нок**] *n.* **1,** *dim. of* **коро́на. 2,** crown (*of or for a tooth*).
коро́нный *adj.* crown (*attrib.*). —**коро́нный но́мер, 1,** best-known number (*of a performer*). **2,** *colloq.* one's usual trick: э́то его́ коро́нный но́мер, that's his usual trick; he's always doing that. —**коро́нная роль,** best-known role (*of an actor*).

короновáть *v. impfv. & pfv.* [*pres.* **-нýю, -нýешь**] to crown.

корóста *n.* sores; pustules.

коростéль [*gen.* **-стеля́**] *n.m.* corn crake (*bird*).

коротáть *v. impfv.* [*pfv.* **скоротáть**] *colloq.* to while away (the time).

корóтенький *adj., colloq.* short.

корóткий *adj.* [*short form* **кóрóток, -ткá, кóрóткó, кóрóтки́**; *comp.* **корóче**] short.

кóротко *adv.* **1,** short. **2,** briefly. **3,** intimately.

коротковóлновый *adj.* short-wave.

короткометрáжный *adj., in* **короткометрáжный фильм,** short.

корóткость *n.f.* **1,** shortness. **2,** intimacy; familiarity.

короты́ш [*gen.* **-тыша́**] *n., colloq.* shrimp; runt. *Also,* **короты́шка.**

корóче *adj., comp. of* **корóткий.** —**корóче говоря́,** in short.

корпéть *v. impfv.* [*pres.* **-плю́, -пи́шь**] (*with* **над**) *colloq.* to pore over.

кóрпия *n.* lint (*for surgical dressings*).

корпорáция *n.* corporation. —**корпорати́вный,** *adj.* corporate; corporative.

кóрпус *n.* **1,** [*pl.* **-ы**] body; trunk; torso. **2,** [*pl.* **-á**] body; casing; frame. **3,** [*pl.* **-á**] hull (*of a ship*). **4,** [*pl.* **-á**] building (*one of several in a complex*). **5,** [*no pl.*] corps: дипломати́ческий кóрпус, diplomatic corps. **6,** [*pl.* **-á**] *mil.* corps. **7,** [*pl.* **-ы**] *horse racing* length. —**кóрпусный; корпуснóй,** *adj.* corps (*attrib.*).

корректи́в *n.* correction; modification; change.

корректи́вный *adj.* remedial: корректи́вное чтéние, remedial reading.

корректи́ровать *v. impfv.* [*pfv.* **прокорректи́ровать;** *pres.* **-рую, -руешь**] **1,** to correct; adjust. **2,** to proofread.

корректирóвщик *n., mil.* **1,** spotter. **2,** spotter plane.

коррéктный *adj.* correct; proper. —**коррéктность,** *n.f.* proper behavior.

коррéктор *n.* proofreader.

корректýра *n.* **1,** proofreading. **2,** proofs. —**держáть** *or* **прáвить корректýру,** to read proofs; proofread.

корреспондéнт *n.* correspondent. —**корреспондéнтский,** *adj.* correspondent's; press (*attrib.*).

корреспондéнция *n.* **1,** correspondence; mail. **2,** report; dispatch.

коррóзия *n.* corrosion.

коррýпция *n.* corruption.

корсáж *n.* bodice.

корсáр *n.* corsair.

корсéт *n.* corset.

корт *n.* tennis court.

кортéж (тэ) *n.* **1,** cortege; procession. **2,** motorcade.

кортизóн *n.* cortisone.

кóртик *n.* dagger.

кóрточки *n. pl., in* **сидéть на кóрточках; сесть** (*or* **присéсть**) **на кóрточки,** to squat.

корýнд *n.* corundum.

корчевáть *v. impfv.* [*pres.* **-чýю, -чýешь**] to uproot; tear up by the roots.

кóрчи [*gen.* **-чей**] *n. pl.* [*sing.* **кóрча**] *colloq.* cramps; convulsions.

кóрчить *v. impfv.* [*pfv.* **скóрчить**] **1,** *impers.* to writhe: егó кóрчит от бóли, he is writhing in pain. **2,** [*impfv. only*] (*with* **из себя́** + *acc.*) *colloq.* to pose (as): кóрчить из себя́ знатокá мýзыки, to pose as an expert on music. **3,** *in* **кóрчить рóжи** *or* **гримáсы,** to make faces. —**кóрчиться,** *refl.* to writhe.

корчмá [*gen. pl.* **-чéм**] *n., pre-rev.* tavern; inn.

кóршун *n.* kite (*bird*).

коры́стный *adj.* mercenary; selfish.

корыстолюби́вый *adj.* mercenary. —**корыстолю́бие,** *n.* self-interest.

коры́сть *n.f.* **1,** profit; advantage; gain. **2,** self-interest.

коры́то *n.* washtub; trough. —**остáться** (*or* **оказáться**) **у разби́того коры́та,** to be left with nothing.

корь *n.f.* measles.

кóрюшка [*gen. pl.* **-шек**] *n.* smelt (*fish*).

коря́вый *adj.* **1,** twisted; gnarled. **2,** *colloq.* clumsy; maladroit. **3,** *colloq.* pockmarked.

коря́га *n.* snag (*tree or branch lying in the water*).

косá [*acc.* **кóсу;** *pl.* **кóсы**] *n.* **1,** scythe. **2,** braid; plait. **3,** spit (*of land*). —**нашлá косá на кáмень,** stone cutting stone; a clash of wills.

косáрь [*gen.* **-ря́**] *n.m.* **1,** one who mows grass, cuts hay, etc. **2,** chopping knife.

косáтка [*gen. pl.* **-ток**] *n.* killer whale.

кóсвенно *adv.* indirectly; obliquely.

кóсвенный *adj.* indirect; oblique. —**кóсвенные ули́ки,** circumstantial evidence.

косéканс (сэ) *n.* cosecant.

косéц [*gen.* **-цá**] *n.* one who mows grass, cuts hay, etc.

коси́лка [*gen. pl.* **-лок**] *n.* mower.

кóсинус *n.* cosine.

коси́ть[1] *v. impfv.* [*pfv.* **скоси́ть;** *pres.* **кошý, кóсишь**] **1,** to mow; cut. **2,** *fig.* to mow down; wipe out; decimate.

коси́ть[2] *v. impfv.* [*pfv.* **скоси́ть;** *pres.* **кошý, коси́шь**] **1,** to twist; contort. **2,** (*with acc. or instr.*) to cock (one's eye). **3,** *v.i.* [*impfv. only*] to be crosseyed; (*of one's eyes*) be crossed. —**коси́ться,** *refl.* [*pfv.* **покоси́ться**] **1,** to slant. **2,** to look sideways. **3,** [*impfv. only*] *fig.* to look askance.

коси́чка [*gen. pl.* **-чек**] *n.* pigtail.

космáтый *adj.* shaggy.

космéтика *n.* **1,** make-up; cosmetics. **2,** cosmetology.

космети́ческий *adj.* cosmetic. —**космети́ческий кабинéт,** beauty parlor.

космети́чка [*gen. pl.* **-чек**] *n., colloq.* beautician.

косми́ческий *adj.* **1,** space (*attrib.*): косми́ческий корáбль, spaceship. **2,** cosmic.

космогóния *n.* cosmogony.

космодрóм *n.* space center.

космолóгия *n.* cosmology.

космонáвт *n.* cosmonaut; astronaut; spaceman.

космополи́т *n.* cosmopolite; cosmopolitan. —**космополити́зм,** *n.* cosmopolitanism. —**космополити́ческий,** *adj.* cosmopolitan.

кóсмос *n.* (outer) space; the cosmos.

кóсмы [*gen.* **косм**] *n. pl., colloq.* long disheveled locks of hair.

коснéть *v. impfv.* **1,** to stagnate. **2,** *fig.* (*with* **в** + *prepl.*) to wallow (in). **3,** (*of the tongue*) to become stiff.

кóсность *n.f.* lethargy; indolence; resistance to change.

косноязы́чие *n.* tongue-tie. —**косноязы́чный,** *adj.* tongue-tied.

коснýться *v.r., pfv. of* **касáться.**

кóсный *adj.* negative; unreceptive to new ideas.

кóсо *adv.* obliquely; aslant; askew. —**смотрéть кóсо,** to look askance.

кособóкий *adj.* lopsided; crooked.

косоворо́тка [*gen. pl.* **-ток**] *n.* man's blouse (*with the collar fastening at the side*).
косогла́зие *n.* strabismus; cross-eye. —**косогла́зый,** *adj.* cross-eyed.
косого́р *n.* **1,** hillside. **2,** slope.
косо́й *adj.* **1,** slanting; oblique. **2,** (*of a person*) cross-eyed; (*of eyes*) slanting. **3,** crooked. —**косо́й взгляд, 1,** glance to one side. **2,** suspicious look. —**косо́й па́рус,** fore-and-aft sail.
косола́пый *adj.* **1,** pigeon-toed. **2,** *colloq.* clumsy; awkward.
костёл *n.* Roman Catholic church, esp. in Poland.
костене́ть *v. impfv.* [*pfv.* **окостене́ть**] **1,** to become numb (*from the cold*). **2,** (*of a corpse*) to become stiff; ossify.
костёр [*gen.* **-стра́**] *n.* fire; campfire; bonfire.
кости́стый *adj.* bony (*full of bones*).
костля́вый *adj.* bony (*skinny*).
ко́стный *adj.* bone (*attrib.*). —**ко́стный мозг,** marrow.
костое́да *n.* bone decay; caries.
ко́сточка [*gen. pl.* **-чек**] *n.* **1,** *dim. of* **кость. 2,** pit; stone (*of fruit*). **3,** stay (*for a corset, collar, etc.*).
косты́ль [*gen.* **-ля́**] *n.m.* **1,** crutch. **2,** large nail; spike.
кость [*pl.* **ко́сти, -сте́й, -стя́м**] *n.f.* **1,** bone. **2,** *pl.* dice. **3,** *in* **слоно́вая кость,** ivory. —**до мо́зга косте́й,** to the marrow of one's bones; through and through. —**лечь костьми́,** to be killed (*in battle*). —**продро́гнуть до мо́зга косте́й,** to be chilled to the bone. —**промо́кнуть до косте́й,** to be soaked to the skin. —**язы́к без косте́й,** loose tongue.
костю́м *n.* **1,** suit. **2,** outfit; attire. **3,** costume.
костюме́р *n.m.* [*fem.* **-ме́рша**] costume designer.
костюми́рованный *adj.* costumed. —**костюми́рованный бал,** costume party; masquerade.
костю́мный *adj.* of or for a suit.
костя́к [*gen.* **-яка́**] *n.* **1,** skeleton. **2,** *fig.* backbone.
костяно́й *adj.* made of bone; bone (*attrib.*). —**костяна́я мука́,** bone meal.
костя́шка [*gen. pl.* **-шек**] *n., colloq.* **1,** knuckle. **2,** ball; bead; button.
косу́ля *n.* roe deer.
косы́нка [*gen. pl.* **-нок**] *n.* triangular kerchief or scarf.
косьба́ *n.* mowing.
кося́к [*gen.* **-сяка́**] *n.* **1,** doorpost; jamb. **2,** school (*of fish*); flock (*of birds*); herd (*of horses*).
кот [*gen.* **кота́**] *n.* **1,** male cat; tomcat. **2,** *in* **морско́й кот,** stingray. —**кот напла́кал,** *colloq.* practically none: де́нег у меня́ кот напла́кал, I have practically no money. —**купи́ть кота́ в мешке́,** to buy a pig in a poke.
кота́нгенс *n.* contangent.
котёл [*gen.* **-тла́**] *n.* **1,** caldron. **2,** boiler.
котело́к [*gen.* **-лка́**] *n.* **1,** pot. **2,** mess tin. **3,** bowler (*hat*); derby.
коте́льная *n., decl. as an adj.* boiler room.
коте́льный *adj.* boiler (*attrib.*).
котёнок [*gen.* **-нка;** *pl.* **-тя́та, -тя́т**] *n.* kitten.
ко́тик *n.* **1,** *dim. of* **кот. 2,** [*also,* **морско́й ко́тик**] fur seal. **3,** sealskin. —**ко́тиковый,** *adj.* sealskin.
котильо́н *n.* cotillion.
коти́ровать *v. impfv. & pfv.* [*pres.* **-рую, -руешь**] *finance to* quote.
котиро́вка *n., finance* quotation.
коти́ться *v.r. impfv.* [*pfv.* **окоти́ться**] to have kittens.
котле́та *n.* chop; cutlet: свина́я котле́та, pork chop; теля́чья котле́та, veal cutlet. —**отбивна́я котле́та,** chop; cutlet. —**ру́бленая котле́та,** hamburger.
котлова́н *n.* foundation pit.
котлови́на *n.* hollow; depression.
кото́мка [*gen. pl.* **-мок**] *n.* knapsack; shoulder pack.
кото́рый *pron.* **1,** *interr.* what?; which?: в кото́ром часу́?, at what time? Кото́рый из них ста́рше?, which (one) of them is older? **2,** *rel.* who; that; which: челове́к, кото́рый то́лько что ушёл, the man who just left. Кни́га, кото́рую вы мне одолжи́ли, the book that/which you lent me.—**в кото́рый раз,** once again; for the umpteenth time. —**кото́рый раз?,** how many times?: кото́рый раз я тебе́ говорю́?, how many times have I told you?
котте́дж (тэ) *n.* cottage.
ко́фе *n.m. indecl.* coffee.
кофеи́н *n.* caffeine.
кофе́йник *n.* coffeepot.
кофе́йница *n.* coffee mill.
кофе́йный *adj.* **1,** coffee (*attrib.*). **2,** coffee-colored.
ко́фта *n.* woman's jacket.
ко́фточка [*gen. pl.* **-чек**] *n.* blouse.
коча́н [*gen.* **-чана́**] *n.* head of cabbage.
кочева́ть *v. impfv.* [*pres.* **-чу́ю, -чу́ешь**] **1,** to lead a nomadic life; be a nomad. **2,** (*of animals, birds, etc.*) to migrate.
коче́вник *n.* nomad.
кочево́й *adj.* nomadic; nomad's.
коче́вье *n.* **1,** migration. **2,** nomads' encampment. **3,** territory where nomads roam.
кочега́р *n.* stoker; fireman (*on a locomotive*).
кочене́ть *v. impfv.* [*pfv.* **окочене́ть** *or* **закочене́ть**] to become numb (*from the cold*).
кочерга́ [*gen. pl.* **-рёг**] *n.* poker (*for a fire*).
кочеры́жка [*gen. pl.* **-жек**] *n.* cabbage stump.
ко́чка [*gen. pl.* **-чек**] *n.* hummock.
коша́чий [*fem.* **-чья**] *adj.* cat (*attrib.*); cat's; feline.
кошелёк [*gen.* **-лька́**] *n.* purse.
кошёлка [*gen. pl.* **-лок**] *n., colloq.* basket.
кошени́ль *n.f.* cochineal.
коше́рный *adj.* kosher.
ко́шечка [*gen. pl.* **-чек**] *n.* pussy cat.
ко́шка [*gen. pl.* **-шек**] *n.* **1,** cat. **2,** *pl.* cat-o'-nine-tails. **3,** grapnel; grappling iron. **4,** *pl.* climbing irons. —**жить как ко́шка с соба́кой,** to be at each other's throat. —**ме́жду ни́ми пробежа́ла чёрная ко́шка,** they have had a falling-out; something has come between them.
кошма́р *n.* nightmare. —**кошма́рный,** *adj.* nightmarish.
Коще́й *n., folklore* a bony old man who knows the secret of eternal life.
кощу́нство *n.* sacrilege; blasphemy. —**кощу́нственный,** *adj.* sacrilegious; blasphemous.
кощу́нствовать *v. impfv.* [*pres.* **-ствую, -ствуешь**] to blaspheme; commit a sacrilege.
коэффицие́нт *n.* coefficient; factor; ratio. —**коэффицие́нт поле́зного де́йствия,** efficiency (*of a machine in transmitting energy*).
краб *n.* crab. —**кра́бовый,** *adj.* crab (*attrib.*).
кра́ги [*gen.* **краг**] *n. pl.* leggings; puttees.
кра́деное *n., decl. as an adj.* stolen goods; loot.
кра́деный *adj.* stolen.
кра́дучись *adv.* stealthily.
кра́дущийся *adj.* stealthy; furtive.

краеве́дение *n.* the study of a particular region. —**краеве́дческий,** *adj., in* **краеве́дческий музе́й,** regional museum.

краево́й *adj.* of or pert. to a **край;** regional.

краеуго́льный *adj., in* **краеуго́льный ка́мень,** cornerstone.

кра́ешек [*gen.* **-шка**] *n., colloq.* edge.

кра́жа *n.* theft; larceny. —**кра́жа со взло́мом,** burglary.

край [*2nd loc.* **краю́;** *pl.* **края́, краёв**] *n.* **1,** edge; rim; brim; brink. **2,** land; country; *pl.* places; parts: в э́тих края́х, in these places/parts. **3,** large administrative division of the USSR; krai. —**кра́ем у́ха, 1,** (*with* **слу́шать**) to listen with half an ear. **2,** (*with* **слы́шать**) to happen to hear. —**на край све́та** (*or* **земли́**), to the ends of the earth. —**по́лный до краёв,** filled to the brim.—**че́рез край, 1,** over the edge: ли́ться че́рез край, to overflow. **2,** *fig.* in abundance. **3,** *in* хвати́ть че́рез край, *see* **хвати́ть. 4,** *in* хлебну́ть че́рез край, *colloq.* to have had a bit too much to drink.

кра́йне *adv.* extremely.

кра́йний *adj.* **1,** extreme. **2,** last: кра́йняя ко́мната спра́ва, the last room on the right. **3,** *fig.* (*of surprise, exhaustion, etc.*) complete; utter. **4,** *fig.* dire. **5,** *in* кра́йний срок, deadline. **6,** *in* кра́йний Се́вер, the Far North. **7,** *in* кра́йняя цена́, lowest price; rock-bottom price. —**в кра́йнем слу́чае,** if worst comes to worst; as a last resort. —**по кра́йней ме́ре,** at least.

кра́йность *n.f.* **1,** extreme. **2,** extreme situation. —**до кра́йности,** to an extreme.

крамо́ла *n., obs.* uprising; revolt. —**крамо́льный,** *adj., obs.* seditious; rebellious.

кран *n.* **1,** faucet; spigot; tap. **2,** [*also,* **подъёмный кран**] crane. —**водоразбо́рный кран,** hydrant. —**пожа́рный кран,** fire hydrant.

крап *n.* spots; specks.

кра́пать *v. impfv.* [*pres.* **кра́плет** *or* **кра́пает**] (*of rain*) to drizzle; fall in drops.

крапи́ва *n.* nettle.

крапи́вник *n.* wren.

крапи́вница *n.* hives.

кра́пинка [*gen. pl.* **-нок**] *n.* dot; spot; speckle. —**в кра́пинку,** dotted; speckled. —**в кра́сную кра́пинку,** with red dots. *Also,* **кра́пина.**

краплёный *adj.* (*of cards*) marked.

кра́пчатый *adj.* spotted; speckled.

краса́ *n.* **1,** *archaic* beauty. **2,** (*with gen.*) the pride (of).

краса́вец [*gen.* **-вца**] *n.* **1,** very handsome man. **2,** a beauty.

краса́вица *n.* **1,** beautiful woman. **2,** a beauty.

краси́вый *adj.* beautiful; handsome; good-looking. —**краси́во,** *adv.* beautifully.

краси́льный *adj.* dye (*attrib.*); dyeing (*attrib.*).

краси́льня [*gen. pl.* **-лен**] *n.* dye works. —**краси́льщик,** *n.* dyer.

краси́тель *n.m.* dye.

кра́сить *v. impfv.* [*pfv.* **покра́сить;** *pres.* **кра́шу, кра́сишь**] **1,** to paint; dye. **2,** [*impfv. only*] to become; make (someone) look pretty. —**кра́ситься,** *refl.* [*pfv.* **накра́ситься**] *colloq.* to put on make-up.

кра́ска [*gen. pl.* **-сок**] *n.* **1,** paint. **2,** dye. **3,** *pl.* colors. **4,** flush (*of anger, embarrassment, etc.*). —**ма́сляная кра́ска,** oil color. —**типогра́фская кра́ска,** printer's ink.

краскопу́льт *n.* spray gun.

красне́ть *v. impfv.* [*pfv.* **покрасне́ть**] **1,** to turn red; redden; flush. **2,** to blush. **3,** [*impfv. only*] (*of anything red*) to appear prominently; shine; gleam.

краснобა́й *n.* windbag; big talker.

краснова́тый *adj.* reddish.

красногварде́ец [*gen.* **-де́йца**] *n.* Red Guard. —**красногварде́йский,** *adj.* Red Guard (*attrib.*).

красноко́жий *adj.* red-skinned. —*n.* redskin; American Indian.

красноле́сье *n.* pine forest.

красноли́цый *adj.* ruddy-faced.

красноречи́вый *adj.* eloquent.

красноре́чие *n.* eloquence.

краснота́ *n.* redness.

краснота́л *n.* red willow.

красну́ха *n.* German measles.

кра́сный *adj.* **1,** red. **2,** *obs., poetic* beautiful. —*n.* **1,** the red one. **2,** *pl.* reds (*communists*). —**кра́сное де́рево,** mahogany. —**кра́сная доска́,** roll of honor. —**кра́сная строка́,** new paragraph. —**кра́сный уголо́к,** recreation and reading room.

красова́ться *v.r. impfv.* [*pres.* **-су́юсь, -су́ешься**] **1,** to stand out (in all its splendor). **2,** to show off.

красота́ *n.* **1,** beauty. **2,** [*pl.* **-со́ты**] beauty: красо́ты приро́ды, the beauties of nature.

красо́тка [*gen. pl.* **-ток**] *n., colloq.* pretty girl.

кра́сочный *adj.* **1,** paint (*attrib.*); dye (*attrib.*). **2,** colorful.

красть *v. impfv.* [*pfv.* **укра́сть;** *pres.* **краду́, крадёшь;** *past* **крал, кра́ла**] to steal. —**кра́сться,** *refl.* [*impfv. only*] to sneak; creep; steal.

кра́сящий *adj.* dye (*attrib.*); dyeing (*attrib.*). —**кра́сящее вещество́,** dyestuff.

крат *n., in* **во́ сто крат,** a hundredfold.

кра́тер *n.* crater.

кра́ткий *adj.* [*short form* **-ток, -тка́, -тко**] short; brief; concise. —**в кра́тких слова́х,** briefly; in a few words.

кра́тко *adv.* briefly.

кратковре́менный *adj.* brief; of short duration.

краткосро́чный *adj.* short-term.

кра́ткость *n.f.* brevity. —**для кра́ткости,** for short.

кра́тный *adj.* (*of a number*) divisible by another number. —**кра́тное,** *n.* multiple.

кратча́йший *adj., superl. of* **кра́ткий.**

крах *n.* **1,** (financial) crash. Крах ба́нка, bank failure. **2,** *fig.* collapse.

крахма́л *n.* starch. —**крахма́листый,** *adj.* starchy.

крахма́лить *v. impfv.* [*pfv.* **накрахма́лить**] to starch.

крахма́льный *adj.* starched.

кра́чка [*gen. pl.* **-чек**] *n.* tern.

кра́ше *adj., colloq.* more beautiful.

кра́шение *n.* dyeing.

кра́шеный *adj.* **1,** painted. **2,** dyed. **3,** wearing make-up; made up.

краю́ха *n., colloq.* hunk (*of bread*).

креве́тка [*gen. pl.* **-ток**] *n.* shrimp.

кре́дит *n., bookkeeping* credit.

креди́т *n.* credit: в креди́т, on credit. —**креди́тный,** *adj.* credit (*attrib.*).

кредитова́ть *v. impfv. & pfv.* [*pres.* **-ту́ю, -ту́ешь**] **1,** to extend credit (to). **2,** to extend credit for; finance.

кредито́р *n.* creditor.

кре́до *n. indecl.* credo.

кре́йсер *n.* cruiser.

кре́йсерский *adj.* cruiser (*attrib.*). —**кре́йсерская ско́рость,** cruising speed.

крейси́ровать *v. impfv.* [*pres.* **-рую, -руешь**] to cruise.

крем *n.* **1,** cream; lotion. **2,** cream (*used in desserts*). **3,** *in* сапо́жный крем, shoe polish.

кремато́рий *n.* crematorium.

крема́ция *n.* cremation.

креме́нь [*gen.* **-мня́**] *n.m.* flint.

креми́ровать *v. impfv. & pfv.* [*pres.* **-рую, -руешь**] to cremate.

кремлёвский *adj.* of the Kremlin; Kremlin (*attrib.*).

Кремль [*gen.* **-мля́**] *n.m.* **1,** the Kremlin (*in Moscow*). **2,** *l.c.* fortress or citadel in old Russian towns; kremlin.

кремнёвый *adj.* made of flint; flint (*attrib.*).

кремнезём *n.* silica.

кре́мниевый *adj.* silicic: кре́мниевая кислота́, silicic acid.

кре́мний *n.* silicon.

кремни́стый *adj.* **1,** siliceous. **2,** stony.

кре́мовый *adj.* **1,** cream (*attrib.*). **2,** cream-colored.

крен *n.* **1,** *naut.* list. **2,** *aero.* bank.

кре́ндель [*pl.* **кре́ндели, -ле́й, -ля́м**] *n.m.* pretzel.

крени́ть *v. impfv.* [*pfv.* **накрени́ть**] to tip; tilt. —**крени́ться,** *refl.* to tilt; list.

креозо́т *n.* creosote.

крео́л *n.* Creole. —**крео́льский,** *adj.* Creole.

креп *n.* crepe.

крепи́тельный *adj.* **1,** *obs.* invigorating; refreshing. **2,** *med.* binding.

крепи́ть *v. impfv.* [*pres.* **-плю́, -пи́шь**] **1,** to fasten. **2,** to strengthen. **3,** to constipate. *Also impers.:* его́ крепи́т, he is constipated. —**крепи́ться,** *refl.* to hold out; stand firm; bear up.

кре́пкий *adj.* [*short form* **-пок, -пка́, -пко;** *comp.* **кре́пче**] **1,** strong; durable. **2,** strong; sturdy; robust. **3,** (*of tea, wine, etc.*) strong. **4,** (*of frost*) hard. **5,** (*of sleep*) sound.

кре́пко *adv.* **1,** firmly. **2,** sturdily: кре́пко сложённый, sturdily built. **3,** tight(ly): держа́ться кре́пко, to hold tight. —**кре́пко спать,** to be sound/fast asleep.

крепколо́бый *adj., colloq.* stubborn; pigheaded.

крепле́ние *n.* **1,** strengthening; fastening. **2,** mount; mounting. —**у́зел крепле́ния дви́гателя,** engine mount.

кре́пнуть *v. impfv.* [*pfv.* **окре́пнуть;** *past* **креп** *or* **кре́пнул, кре́пла**] to grow stronger; regain one's strength.

крепостни́чество *n.* serfdom.

крепостно́й *adj.* **1,** serf (*attrib.*). **2,** of a fortress. —*n.* serf. —**крепостно́е пра́во,** serfdom.

кре́пость *n.f.* **1,** strength. **2,** [*pl.* **кре́пости, -сте́й, -стя́м**] fortress.

крепча́ть *v. impfv.* **1,** to increase in intensity; (*of the wind*) blow harder. **2,** *colloq.* (*of a person*) to grow stronger; gain strength.

кре́пче *adj., comp. of* **кре́пкий.**

крепы́ш [*gen.* **-пыша́**] *n., colloq.* robust man; sturdy youngster.

кре́сло [*gen. pl.* **-сел**] *n.* armchair; easy chair. —**инвали́дное кре́сло,** wheelchair.

кресс *n.* cress. —**водяно́й кресс,** watercress. —**кресс-сала́т,** garden cress.

крест [*gen.* **креста́**] *n.* **1,** cross. **2,** the sign of the cross. —**ста́вить крест на** (+ *prepl.*), to give up on; give up as hopeless.

кресте́ц [*gen.* **-тца́**] *n.* **1,** *anat.* sacrum. **2,** rump (*of an animal*).

кре́стик *n.* **1,** *dim. of* **крест. 2,** *printing* dagger (†).

крести́льный *adj.* baptismal.

крести́ны [*gen.* **-ти́н**] *n. pl.* christening.

крести́ть *v. impfv.* [*pres.* **крещу́, кре́стишь**] **1,** [*pfv.* **окрести́ть**] to baptize; christen. **2,** [*impfv. only*] to be a godfather *or* godmother to. **3,** [*pfv.* **перекрести́ть**] to make the sign of the cross over. —**крести́ться,** *refl.* **1,** [*pfv.* **окрести́ться**] to be baptized. **2,** [*pfv.* **перекрести́ться**] to cross oneself.

крест-на́крест *adv.* crosswise; crisscross.

крёстная *n., decl. as an adj., colloq.* godmother.

кре́стник *n.* godson; godchild. —**кре́стница,** *n.* goddaughter; godchild.

кре́стный *adj., in* **1, кре́стное зна́мение,** the sign of the cross. **2, кре́стный ход** religious procession.

крёстный *adj., in* **крёстный оте́ц,** godfather; **крёстная мать,** godmother; **крёстный сын,** godson; **крёстная дочь,** goddaughter. —*n.* godfather.

крестови́на *n.* crosspiece.

кресто́вый *adj., in* **кресто́вый похо́д,** *hist.* crusade.

кресто́носец [*gen.* **-сца**] *n., hist.* crusader.

крестообра́зный *adj.* in the shape of a cross; cruciform. —**крестообра́зно,** *adv.* crosswise.

крестья́нин [*pl.* **-я́не, -я́н**] *n.m.* [*fem.* **-я́нка**] peasant. —**крестья́нский,** *adj.* peasant (*attrib.*). —**крестья́нство,** *n.* peasantry.

крети́н *n.* cretin. —**кретини́зм,** *n.* cretinism.

крето́н *n.* cretonne. —**крето́нный; крето́новый.** *adj.* cretonne.

кре́чет *n.* gyrfalcon.

креще́ндо *adv. & n. indecl.* crescendo.

креще́ние *n.* **1,** baptism; christening. **2,** Epiphany.

крещёный *adj.* baptized.

крива́я *n., decl. as an adj., math.* curve.

кривизна́ *n.* **1,** curvature. **2,** crookedness.

криви́ть *v. impfv.* [*pfv.* **покриви́ть** *or* **скриви́ть;** *pres.* **-влю́, -ви́шь**] **1,** to twist; contort. **2,** *in* **(по)криви́ть душо́й,** to play the hypocrite. —**криви́ться,** *refl.* **1,** to become bent; get out of shape. **2,** *colloq.* to make a face; grimace.

кривля́ка *n.m. & f., colloq.* affected person.

кривля́нье *n.* affectation; artificiality.

кривля́ться *v.r. impfv.* **1,** to make faces. **2,** to put on airs.

кри́во *adv.* **1,** in a crooked line. **2,** askew; awry.

кривобо́кий *adj.* lopsided.

криво́й *adj.* **1,** crooked. **2,** *colloq.* one-eyed; blind in one eye. —**криво́е зе́ркало,** distorting mirror. —**кривы́е пути́,** crooked ways. —**крива́я улы́бка,** wry smile.

криволине́йный *adj.* curvilinear.

кривоно́гий *adj.* bowlegged; bandy-legged; knock-kneed.

кривото́лки [*gen.* **-ков**] *n. pl.* false rumors; idle gossip; loose talk.

кривоши́п *n., mech.* crank.

кри́зис *n.* crisis. —**кри́зисный,** *adj.* crisis (*attrib.*); critical.

крик *n.* cry; shout; scream; yell. —**после́дний крик мо́ды,** the latest thing in fashion.

кри́кет *n., sports* cricket.

крикли́вый *adj.* **1,** loud; noisy. **2,** *fig.* loud; flashy; garish.
кри́кнуть *v., pfv. of* **крича́ть.**
крику́н [*gen.* **-куна́**] *n.m.* [*fem.* **-ку́нья**] *colloq.* noisy person; loudmouth.
кримина́л *n., colloq.* a crime.
криминали́ст *n.* criminal lawyer. —**криминали́стика,** *n.* criminal law. —**криминалисти́ческий,** *adj.* of or pert. to criminal law.
кримина́льный *adj.* criminal.
криминоло́гия *n.* criminology. —**кримино́лог,** *n.* criminologist.
кри́нка [*gen. pl.* **-нок**] *n.* = **кры́нка.**
кринoли́н *n.* hoop skirt.
криптогра́мма *n.* cryptogram.
криптогра́фия *n.* cryptography. —**криптографи́ческий,** *adj.* cryptographic.
крипто́н *n.* krypton.
криста́лл *n.* crystal.
кристаллиза́ция *n.* crystallization.
кристаллизова́ть *v. impfv. & pfv.* [*pres.* **-зу́ю, -зу́ешь**] to crystallize. —**кристаллизова́ться,** *refl.* to crystallize; take shape.
кристалли́ческий *adj.* crystalline.
криста́льный *adj.* **1,** crystal-clear. **2,** pure; perfect.
крите́рий *n.* criterion.
кри́тик *n.* critic.
кри́тика *n.* criticism.
критика́н *n.* faultfinder. —**критика́нство,** *n.* carping; faultfinding.
критикова́ть *v. impfv.* [*pres.* **-ку́ю, -ку́ешь**] to criticize.
крити́ческий *adj.* **1,** critical; containing criticism. **2,** critical; crucial.
крича́ть *v. impfv.* [*pfv.* **кри́кнуть;** *pres.* **-чу́, -чи́шь**] to shout; yell; scream.
крича́щий *adj.* loud; flashy; garish.
кров *n.* shelter. —**оста́ться без кро́ва,** to be left without a roof over one's head.
крова́вый *adj.* **1,** bloody. **2,** blood-red. **3,** (*of meat*) rare; underdone. —**крова́вая ба́ня,** blood bath. —**крова́вое пятно́,** bloodstain.
крова́тка [*gen. pl.* **-ток**] *n.* small bed; child's bed.
крова́ть *n.f.* bed. —**де́тская крова́ть,** crib.
кро́вельный *adj.* roofing (*attrib.*).
кро́вельщик *n.* roofer.
кровено́сный *adj.* of the circulatory system. —**кровено́сная систе́ма,** circulatory system. —**кровено́сный сосу́д,** blood vessel.
крови́нка [*gen. pl.* **-нок**] *n., colloq.* drop of blood. —**ни крови́нки в лице́,** white as a sheet.
кро́вля [*gen. pl.* **-вель**] *n.* **1,** roof. **2,** roofing.
кро́вно *adv.* **1,** by blood: кро́вно свя́занный, bound by ties of blood. **2,** vitally: кро́вно заинтересо́ванный, vitally interested. **3,** grievously: кро́вно оби́деть кого́-нибудь, to grievously offend someone.
кро́вный *adj.* **1,** blood (*attrib.*); related by blood. **2,** thoroughbred. **3,** *fig.* vital. —**кро́вный враг,** mortal enemy. —**кро́вные де́ньги,** hard-earned money. —**кро́вная месть,** vendetta. —**кро́вная оби́да,** grievous insult.
кровожа́дный *adj.* bloodthirsty.
кровоизлия́ние *n.* hemorrhage.
кровообраще́ние *n.* circulation (*of the blood*).
кровоостана́вливающий *adj.* styptic. —**кровоостана́вливающее сре́дство,** styptic agent.
кровопи́йца *n.m. & f.* bloodsucker.
кровоподтёк *n.* bruise.
кровопроли́тие *n.* bloodshed.
кровопуска́ние *n.* bloodletting; phlebotomy.
кровосмеше́ние *n.* incest. —**кровосмеси́тельный,** *adj.* incestuous.
кровосо́с *n.* vampire bat.
кровотече́ние *n.* bleeding; hemorrhaging.
кровоточи́вость *n.f.* **1,** bleeding: кровоточи́вость дёсен, bleeding gums. **2,** hemophilia.
кровоточи́ть *v. impfv.* to bleed.
кровь [*2nd loc.* **крови́**] *n.f.* blood. —**в кровь** (*with verbs of beating*), till one bleeds. —**в крови́,** bloody; covered with blood. —**э́то у него́ в крови́,** it's in his blood.
кровяно́й *adj.* blood (*attrib.*). —**кровяно́е давле́ние,** blood pressure. —**кровяны́е ша́рики,** corpuscles.
крои́ть *v. impfv.* [*pfv.* **скрои́ть**] to cut; cut out (material or a garment).
кро́йка *n.* cutting.
кроке́т *n.* croquet.
крокоди́л *n.* crocodile. —**крокоди́лов,** *adj., in* **крокоди́ловы слёзы,** crocodile tears. —**крокоди́ловый,** *adj.* made of crocodile skin; crocodile (*attrib.*).
кро́кус *n.* crocus.
кро́лик *n.* rabbit. —**кро́личий,** *adj.* [*fem.* **-чья**] rabbit (*attrib.*).
кроль *n.m., swimming* crawl.
кро́ме *prep., with gen.* **1,** except (for); but. **2,** besides; in addition to. —**кро́ме как,** except. —**кро́ме того́,** besides; moreover; furthermore; in addition.
кроме́шный *adj., in* **ад кроме́шный,** sheer hell; **тьма кроме́шная,** absolute darkness.
кро́мка [*gen. pl.* **-мок**] *n.* **1,** selvage. **2,** edge.
кромса́ть *v. impfv.* [*pfv.* **искромса́ть**] *colloq.* to cut up, hack.
кро́на *n.* **1,** crown (*of a tree*). **2,** crown (*monetary unit*).
кронци́ркуль *n.m.* calipers.
кро́ншнеп (нэ) *n.* curlew (*bird*).
кронште́йн (тэ) *n.* bracket; holder.
кропи́ть *v. impfv.* [*pres.* **-плю́, -пи́шь**] **1,** to sprinkle. **2,** (*of rain*) to fall lightly.
кропотли́вый *adj.* laborious; painstaking.
кросс *n.* cross-country race.
кроссво́рд *n.* crossword puzzle.
крот [*gen.* **крота́**] *n.* **1,** mole. **2,** moleskin.
кро́ткий *adj.* [*short form* **-ток, -тка́, -тко**] meek.
кρото́вый *adj.* **1,** mole (*attrib.*); mole's. **2,** moleskin.
кро́тость *n.f.* meekness.
кроха́ [*acc.* **кро́ху;** *pl.* **кро́хи, крох, -ха́м**] *n.* **1,** *obs.* crumb. **2,** *pl.* crumbs: кро́хи зна́ний, crumbs of knowledge.
кроха́ль [*gen.* **-каля́**] *n.m.* merganser.
кро́хотный *adj., colloq.* tiny. *Also,* **кро́шечный.**
кроши́ть *v. impfv.* [*pfv.* **искроши́ть;** *pres.* **крошу́, кро́шишь**] **1,** to chop up. **2,** to crumble. **3,** [*impfv. only*] to spill crumbs. —**кроши́ться,** *refl.* to crumble; disintegrate.
кро́шка [*gen. pl.* **-шек**] *n.* crumb. —**ни кро́шки,** not a bit.
круг [*2nd loc.* **кру́ге** *or* **кругу́;** *pl.* **круги́**] *n.* **1,** circle. **2,** *fig.* (*with gen.*) circle (*of people*); sphere; range (*of activities*). **3,** detour: сде́лать круг, to make a de-

tour. **4,** *sports* lap. —**гонча́рный круг,** potter's wheel. —**поворо́тный круг,** turntable. —**спаса́тельный круг,** life buoy.

кру́гленький *adj.* **1,** round. **2,** chubby; plump. —**кру́гленькая су́мма,** a tidy sum.

кругле́ть *v. impfv.* to become round.

круглоли́цый *adj.* round-faced.

круглосу́точный *adj.* twenty-four-hour (*attrib.*); round-the-clock.

кру́глый *adj.* **1,** round. **2,** (*with periods of time*) all: кру́глые су́тки, day and night; round the clock. **3,** *colloq.* utter. —**кру́глый** (*or* **кру́глая**) **сирота́,** child who has lost both parents. —**кру́глая су́мма,** a tidy sum. —**кру́глым счётом,** in round figures.

кругово́й *adj.* circular. —**кругова́я доро́га,** roundabout route. —**кругова́я систе́ма,** *sports* round robin. —**кругова́я ча́ша,** loving cup.

круговоро́т *n.* **1,** rotation. **2,** *fig.* constant flow (*of events, life, etc.*).

кругозо́р *n.* **1,** range of vision. **2,** *fig.* outlook; range of interests.

круго́м *adv.* **1,** (all) around. **2,** *colloq.* entirely. —*prep., with gen., colloq.* around. —*interj., mil.* about face!

кругообра́зный *adj.* circular.

кругосве́тный *adj.* round-the-world.

кружевно́й *adj.* lace (*attrib.*).

кру́жево [*often pl.* **-жева́, кру́жев, -жева́м**] *n.* lace.

круже́ние *n.* whirling; swirling.

кружи́ть *v. impfv.* [*pres.* **кружу́, кру́жишь** *or* **кружи́шь**] **1,** *v.t.* to twirl; whirl; swirl. **2,** *v.i.* to spin; circle; swirl. **3,** *colloq.* to wander. —**кружи́ть го́лову** (+ *dat.*), **1,** to make (someone) dizzy. **2,** [*pfv.* **вскружи́ть**] to turn someone's head; go to one's head.

кружи́ться *v.r. impfv.* [*pres.* **кружу́сь, кру́жишься** *or* **кружи́шься**] **1,** to spin; whirl; go round: у меня́ кру́жится голова́, my head is spinning. **2,** (*of a bird, plane, etc.*) to circle. **3,** (*of dust, snow, etc.*) to swirl. **4,** *colloq.* to wander.

кру́жка [*gen. pl.* **-жек**] *n.* **1,** mug; tankard. **2,** poorbox.

кру́жный *adj., colloq.* roundabout; circuitous.

кружо́к [*gen.* **-жка́**] *n.* **1,** *dim. of* **круг. 2,** circle; group; club.

круи́з *n.* cruise.

круп *n.* **1,** *med.* croup. **2,** croup (*of a horse*).

крупа́ *n.* **1,** groats. **2,** sleet. —**гре́чневая крупа́,** buckwheat. —**ма́нная крупа́,** farina. —**овся́ная крупа́,** oatmeal. —**перло́вая крупа́,** pearl barley.

крупи́нка [*gen. pl.* **-нок**] *n.* grain.

крупи́ца *n.* **1,** grain. **2,** *fig.* grain; ounce; particle.

кру́пно *adv.* **1,** into large pieces. **2,** with large strides or strokes. **3,** using strong language: кру́пно поговори́ть с, to use strong language with.

крупномасшта́бный *adj.* (*of a map*) large-scale.

кру́пный *adj.* **1,** large. **2,** major; prominent; important. **3,** (*of sand*) coarse. —**кру́пный план,** close-up. —**кру́пный разгово́р,** sharp words; sharp exchange.

крупча́тый *adj.* grainy; coarse.

крупье́ *n.m. indecl.* croupier.

крупяно́й *adj.* groats (*attrib.*).

крутизна́ *n.* **1,** steepness. **2,** steep slope.

крути́ть *v. impfv.* [*pres.* **кручу́, кру́тишь**] **1,** [*pfv.* **закрути́ть**] to turn; twist; twirl. **2,** [*pfv.* **скрути́ть**] to twist (cloth, rope, etc.); roll (a cigarette). **3,** [*impfv. only*] to whirl; swirl (dust, snow, etc.). **4,** *v.i.* [*impfv. only*] (*of a snowstorm*) to swirl. —**крути́ться,** *refl.* [*impfv. only*] **1,** to turn; spin; gyrate; whirl. **2,** *fig., colloq.* to hang around.

кру́то *adv.* **1,** steeply. **2,** abruptly; sharply. **3,** tightly. **4,** harshly.

круто́й *adj.* [*comp.* **кру́че**] **1,** steep. **2,** sharp; abrupt. **3,** drastic. **4,** stern. **5,** (*of foods*) thick. —**круто́е яйцо́,** hard-boiled egg.

кру́тость *n.f.* **1,** steepness; slope. **2,** sternness.

кру́ча *n.* steep slope.

кру́че *adj., comp. of* **круто́й.**

круче́ние *n.* **1,** twisting. **2,** torsion.

кручи́на *n., poetic* sorrow; grief.

круше́ние *n.* **1,** crash; wreck. **2,** *fig.* downfall; collapse.

круши́на *n.* buckthorn.

круши́ть *v. impfv.* to destroy; shatter; smite.

крыжо́вник *n.* **1,** gooseberries. **2,** a (single) gooseberry. **3,** gooseberry shrub.

крыла́тый *adj.* winged. —**крыла́тая ракéта,** cruise missile. —**крыла́тые слова́,** pithy saying; popular expression.

крыле́чко [*gen. pl.* **-чек**] *n., dim. of* **крыльцо́.**

крыло́ [*pl.* **кры́лья, -льев, -льям**] *n.* **1,** wing. **2,** fender. **3,** blade; vane.

кры́лышко [*gen. pl.* **-шек**] *n., dim. of* **крыло́.** —**взять под своё кры́лышко,** to take under one's wing.

крыльцо́ [*pl.* **кры́льца, -ле́ц, -льца́м**] *n.* porch.

кры́мский *adj.* Crimean.

кры́нка [*gen. pl.* **-нок**] *n.* milk jug.

кры́са *n.* rat. —**крыси́ный,** *adj.* rat (*attrib.*).

крысоло́вка [*gen. pl.* **-вок**] *n.* rattrap.

кры́тый *adj.* covered; sheltered.

крыть *v. impfv.* [*pfv.* **покры́ть;** *pres.* **кро́ю, кро́ешь**] to cover. —**кры́ться,** *refl.* [*impfv. only*] to lie (beneath the surface): что за э́тим кро́ется?, what's behind it all?

кры́ша *n.* roof. —**застеклённая кры́ша,** skylight.

кры́шка [*gen. pl.* **-шек**] *n.* lid; cover.

крюк [*gen.* **крюка́;** *pl.* **крю́чья, -чьев** *or* **крюки́, -ко́в**] *n.* **1,** hook. **2,** *colloq.* detour.

крючкова́тый *adj.* hooked.

крючкотво́рство *n., obs.* pettifoggery; chicanery.

крючо́к [*gen.* **-чка́**] *n.* **1,** hook. **2,** curlicue. —**рыболо́вный крючо́к,** fishhook. —**спусково́й крючо́к,** trigger.

крюшо́н *n.* punch made of white wine, liqueur, and fruit.

кря́ду *adv., colloq.* in a row; running.

кряж *n.* **1,** ridge (*of mountains*). **2,** block; stump (*of wood*).

кря́жистый *adj.* **1,** (*of a tree*) sturdy. **2,** *fig.* stocky; thickset.

кря́канье *n.* **1,** quacking. **2,** grunting.

кря́кать *v. impfv.* [*pfv.* **кря́кнуть**] **1,** to quack. **2,** *colloq.* to grunt.

кря́ква *n.* wild duck; mallard.

кря́кнуть *v., pfv. of* **кря́кать.**

кряхте́ть *v. impfv.* [*pres.* **-хчу́, -хти́шь**] *colloq.* to groan.

ксено́н *n.* xenon.

ксилогра́фия *n.* wood engraving.

ксилофо́н *n.* xylophone.

кста́ти *adv.* **1,** incidentally; by the way. **2,** timely; apropos; to the point. **3,** at the same time; while you're at it. —**приходи́ться кста́ти,** to come in handy.

кто [*gen. & acc.* **кого́;** *dat.* **кому́;** *instr.* **кем;** *prepl.*

ком] *pron.* **1,** *interr.* who?; whom?: кто знáет?, who knows? **2,** *rel.* who; whom: те, кто хóчет идти́..., those wishing to go... Он тот, когó никтó не лю́бит, he is the one (whom) no one likes. **3,** *indef., colloq.* anyone; someone: éсли кто спрóсит, if anyone asks. —**кто (бы) ни,** whoever. —**кто бы то ни́ был,** whoever it may be. —**кто где,** in various places. —**кто как,** in various ways. —**кто кудá,** in various directions.

ктó-либо *indef. pron.* = **ктó-нибудь.**

ктó-нибудь *indef. pron.* someone; somebody; anyone; anybody.

ктó-то *indef. pron.* someone; somebody.

куб [*pl.* **кубы́**] *n.* **1,** cube (*figure*). **2,** *math.* cube (*third power*). **3,** *colloq.* cubic meter. **4,** boiler. —**перегóнный куб,** still (*for distilling liquids*).

кýбарем *adv., colloq., in* **кати́ться кýбарем,** to roll head over heels.

кубáрь [*gen.* **-баря́**] *n.m.* peg top.

кубатýра *n.* cubic capacity.

куби́зм *n., art* cubism.

кýбик *n.* **1,** *dim. of* **куб. 2,** *pl.* (children's) blocks. **3,** *colloq.* cubic centimeter.

куби́нец [*gen.* **-нца**] *n.m.* [*fem.* **-нка**] Cuban. —**куби́нский,** *adj.* Cuban.

куби́ческий *adj.* cubic. —**куби́ческий кóрень,** cube root.

кýбовый *adj.* deep blue.

кýбок [*gen.* **-бка**] *n.* **1,** goblet. **2,** *sports* trophy; cup.

кубомéтр *n.* cubic meter.

кýбрик *n., naut.* crew's quarters.

кубы́шка [*gen. pl.* **-шек**] *n.* **1,** money box. **2,** *colloq.* plump woman.

кувáлда *n.* sledgehammer.

кувши́н *n.* pitcher; jug.

кувши́нка [*gen. pl.* **-нок**] *n.* water lily.

кувыркáться *v.r. impfv.* [*pfv.* **кувыркнýться** *or* **кувырнýться**] to somersault; turn somersaults; tumble.

кувыркóм *adv., colloq.* head over heels.

кугуáр *n.* cougar.

кудá *adv.* **1,** *interr.* (*with verbs of motion*) where?; which way?: кудá ты идёшь?, where are you going? Кудá мне э́то положи́ть?, where should I put it? **2,** *rel.* (*with verbs of motion*) where; to which: я не знáю, кудá мы идём, I don't know where we're going. Гóрод, кудá егó сослáли, the city to which he was exiled. **3,** *colloq.* what for?: кудá вам стóлько дéнег?, what do you need all that money for? **4,** *colloq.* much; much more: кудá лýчше, much better. —**кудá (бы) ни,** wherever. —**кудá ни шло,** all right; very well.

кудá-либо *adv.* = **кудá-нибудь.**

кудá-нибудь *adv.* somewhere; anywhere.

кудá-то *adv.* somewhere; to some place.

кудáхтанье *n.* cackle.

кудáхтать *v. impfv.* [*pres.* **-хчу, -хчешь**] to cackle.

кудéль *n.f.* tow (*fiber*).

кудéсник *n.* sorcerer.

кудлáтый *adj., colloq.* shaggy.

кýдри [*gen.* **-дрéй**] *n. pl.* curls.

кудря́вый *adj.* **1,** (*of hair*) curly. **2,** curly-headed. **3,** leafy; lush. **4,** *fig.* flowery.

кудря́шки *n. pl.* [*sing.* **-шка**] ringlets (*of hair*).

кузéн (зэ) *n.* (male) cousin.

кузи́на *n.* (female) cousin.

кузнéц [*gen.* **-нецá**] *n.* blacksmith.

кузнéчик *n.* grasshopper.

кузнéчный *adj.* blacksmith's.

кýзница *n.* blacksmith's shop; smithy; forge.

кýзов [*pl.* **кузовá**] *n.* **1,** basket. **2,** body (*of a car or carriage*).

кукарéканье *n.* crowing; crow (*of a rooster*).

кукарéкать *v. impfv.* (*of a rooster*) to crow.

кýкиш *n., colloq.* fig (*insulting gesture*).

кýкла [*gen. pl.* **-кол**] *n.* **1,** doll. **2,** puppet.

куковáть *v. impfv.* [*pres.* **-кýет**] to cuckoo; cry "cuckoo".

кýколка [*gen. pl.* **-лок**] *n.* **1,** *dim. of* **кýкла. 2,** *zool.* chrysalis; pupa.

кýколь *n.m.* cockle (*weed*).

кýкольный *adj.* **1,** doll (*attrib.*). **2,** puppet (*attrib.*).

кýкситься *v.r. impfv.* [*pres.* **-шусь, -сишься**] *colloq.* to sulk; mope.

кукурýза *n.* corn. —**кукурýзный,** *adj.* corn (*attrib.*).

кукýшка [*gen. pl.* **-шек**] *n.* cuckoo.

кулáк [*gen.* **-лакá**] *n.* **1,** fist. **2,** kulak. **3,** *mech.* cam. —**держáть в кулакé,** to keep under one's thumb. —**смея́ться в кулáк,** to laugh up one's sleeve.

кулáцкий *adj.* of the kulaks; kulak (*attrib.*).

кулáчество *n.* the kulaks.

кулáчки *n. pl., in* **би́ться** *or* **дрáться на кулáчках,** to engage in fisticuffs; spar.

кулачкóвый *adj., in* **кулачкóвый вал,** camshaft.

кулáчный *adj.* with fists: кулáчный бой, fisticuffs.

кулачóк [*gen.* **-чкá**] *n.* **1,** *dim. of* **кулáк. 2,** *mech.* cam.

кулебя́ка *n.* pie with meat, fish, or cabbage filling.

кулёк [*gen.* **-лькá**] *n.* small bag.

кýли *n.m. indecl.* coolie.

кули́к [*gen.* **-ликá**] *n.* snipe.

кулинáрия *n.* **1,** (the art of) cooking; cookery. **2,** delicatessen: отдéл кулинáрии, delicatessen department. —**кулинáрный,** *adj.* culinary.

кули́сы *n. pl.* [*sing.* **кули́са**] *theat.* wings. —**за кули́сами,** backstage; behind the scenes.

кули́ч [*gen.* **-личá**] *n.* Easter cake.

кули́чки *n. pl., in* **у чёрта на кули́чках,** in the middle of nowhere; at the ends of the earth.

кулóн *n.* **1,** pendant. **2,** coulomb (*unit of electricity*).

кулуáры [*gen. pl.* **-ров**] *n. pl.* corridors. —**кулуáрный,** *adj.* in the corridors: кулуáрные разговóры, talk in the corridors.

куль [*gen.* **куля́**] *n.m.* sack.

кульминáция *n.* culmination. —**кульминациóнный,** *adj.* climactic: кульминациóнный пункт, climax; culmination.

культ *n.* cult.

культиви́ровать *v. impfv.* [*pres.* **-рую, -руешь**] to cultivate.

культýра *n.* **1,** culture. **2,** (*with gen.*) standard (of); level (of). **3,** (*with gen.*) *agric.* cultivation (of). **4,** crop: кормовы́е культýры, forage crops. **5,** *bacteriology* culture.

культýрность *n.f.* level of culture; high degree of culture.

культýрный *adj.* **1,** cultural. **2,** cultured. **3,** refined; gracious.

культя́ *n.* stump (*of an amputated limb*).

кум [*pl.* **кумовья́, -вьёв**] *n.* **1,** godfather of one's child. **2,** father of one's godchild. **3,** (*with respect to a godmother*) co-sponsor; godparent in common.

кумá *n.* **1,** godmother of one's child. **2,** mother of one's

godchild. **3,** (*with respect to a godfather*) co-sponsor; godparent in common.
кума́ника *n.* bramble (*shrub*).
кума́ч [*gen.* **-мача́**] *n.* bright red cotton cloth. —**кума́чный,** *adj.* made of this material.
куми́р *n.* idol.
кумовство́ *n., colloq.* nepotism.
кумуляти́вный *adj.* cumulative.
ку́мушка [*gen. pl.* **-шек**] *n.* **1,** *dim. of* **кума́. 2,** gossipmonger.
кумы́к *n.m.* [*fem.* **-мы́чка**] Kumyk (*one of a people inhabiting the Caucasus*). —**кумы́кский,** *adj.* Kumyk.
кумы́с *n.* fermented mare's milk; kumiss.
кунжу́т *n.* sesame. —**кунжу́тный,** *adj.* sesame (*attrib.*).
куни́ца *n.* marten.
ку́па *n.* clump (*of trees, bushes, etc.*).
купа́льник *n., colloq.* bathing suit.
купа́льный *adj.* bathing (*attrib.*): купа́льный костю́м, bathing suit.
купа́льня [*gen. pl.* **-лен**] *n.* bathhouse.
купа́льщик *n.* bather.
купа́ние *n.* bathing.
купа́ть *v. impfv.* [*pfv.* **вы́купать**] to bathe; give a bath to. —**купа́ться,** *refl.* **1,** to bathe; take a bath. **2,** to go bathing; go swimming.
купе́ (пэ) *n. neut. indecl.* compartment (*on a train*).
купе́ль *n.f., eccles.* font; baptistery.
купе́ц [*gen.* **-пца́**] *n.* merchant. —**купе́ческий,** *adj.* merchants'. —**купе́чество,** *n.* the merchants (*as an economic class*).
Купидо́н *n.* Cupid.
купи́ть [*infl.* **куплю́, ку́пишь**] *v., pfv. of* **покупа́ть.**
купле́т *n.* **1,** verse; stanza. **2,** *pl.* satiric songs.
ку́пля *n.* purchase.
ку́пол [*pl.* **купола́**] *n.* dome; cupola.
купо́н *n.* coupon.
купоро́с *n.* vitriol. —**желе́зный купоро́с,** green vitriol; ferrous sulfate. —**ме́дный купоро́с,** blue vitriol; copper sulfate. —**ци́нковый купоро́с,** white vitriol; zinc sulfate.
купчи́ха *n.* **1,** woman merchant. **2,** merchant's wife.
купю́ра *n.* **1,** cut; deletion. **2,** *finance* denomination.
курага́ *n.* dried apricots.
кура́житься *v.r. impfv., colloq.* **1,** to swagger; boast. **2,** (*with* **над**) to lord it over. **3,** to act coy.
кура́нты [*gen.* **-тов**] *n. pl.* chimes.
курга́н *n.* burial mound.
курд *n.m.* [*fem.* **-дя́нка**] Kurd. —**ку́рдский,** *adj.* Kurdish.
ку́рево *n., colloq.* something to smoke.
куре́ние *n.* **1,** smoking. **2,** incense.
кури́льница *n.* censer.
кури́льня [*gen. pl.* **-лен**] *n.* place where narcotics are smoked: кури́льня о́пиума, opium den.
кури́льщик *n.* smoker; one who smokes.
кури́ный *adj.* chicken (*attrib.*); chicken's; hen's. —**кури́ная слепота́,** night blindness.
кури́тельный *adj.* smoking (*attrib.*).
кури́ть *v. impfv.* [*pres.* **курю́, ку́ришь**] to smoke. —**кури́ться,** *refl.* to smoke; give off smoke.
ку́рица [*pl.* **ку́ры, кур**] *n.* hen; chicken. —**мо́края ку́рица,** milksop.
ку́рия *n.* curia.
курку́ма *n.* turmeric.
курно́сый *adj.* **1,** *in* **курно́сый нос,** pug nose. **2,** pug-nosed; snub-nosed.
курово́дство *n.* poultry breeding.
куро́к [*gen.* **-рка́**] *n.* cock; hammer (*of a firearm*). —**спуска́ть куро́к,** to pull the trigger.
куропа́тка [*gen. pl.* **ток**] *n.* partridge. —**бе́лая куропа́тка,** ptarmigan.
куро́рт *n.* resort. —**куро́ртник,** *n., colloq.* person staying at a resort. —**куро́ртный,** *adj.* resort (*attrib.*).
курослéп *n.* buttercup.
ку́рочка [*gen. pl.* **-чек**] *n.* **1,** pullet. **2,** crake. —**водяна́я ку́рочка,** gallinule.
курс *n.* **1,** course: измени́ть курс, to change course. **2,** policy: ми́рный курс, peaceful policy. **3,** course (*of instruction*): (про)слу́шать курс, to take a course. **4,** year (*in school*). **5,** rate: курс валю́ты, rate of exchange. **6,** *in* курс лече́ния, course of treatment. —**быть в ку́рсе** (+ *gen.*), to be up on. —**в ку́рсе де́ла,** up on things; aware of what is going on. —**вводи́ть (кого́-нибудь) в курс (де́ла),** to bring someone up to date. —**держа́ть (кого́-нибудь) в ку́рсе,** to keep someone informed.
курса́нт *n.* **1,** student. **2,** cadet.
курси́в *n.* italics. —**курси́вный,** *adj.* italic.
курси́ровать *v. impfv.* [*pres.* **-рую, -руешь**] to ply; travel back and forth.
курсо́вка *n.* document entitling the bearer to treatment and meals (but not accommodations) at a sanitarium.
курсово́й *adj.* course (*attrib.*). —**курсова́я рабо́та,** term paper. —**курсово́й экза́мен,** final examination.
куртиза́нка [*gen. pl.* **-нок**] *n.* courtesan.
ку́ртка [*gen. pl.* **-ток**] *n.* (man's) jacket.
курча́вый *adj.* **1,** (*of hair*) curly. **2,** curly-headed.
ку́ры *n., pl. of* **ку́рица.**
курьёз *n.* funny thing; queer thing. —**курьёзный,** *adj.* strange; odd; queer; curious.
курье́р *n.* **1,** courier. **2,** messenger; errand boy.
курье́рский *adj.* courier's. —**курье́рский по́езд,** express train.
куря́тина *n., colloq.* chicken (*as food*).
куря́тник *n.* henhouse; chicken coop.
куря́щий *n., decl. as an adj.* smoker. —**ваго́н для куря́щих,** smoking car.
куса́ть *v. impfv.* [*pfv.* **укуси́ть**] to bite. —**куса́ться,** *refl.* [*impfv. only*] **1,** to bite; have a tendency to bite. **2,** to bite each other.
куса́чки [*gen.* **-чек**] *n. pl.* cutting pliers; wire cutter.
кусково́й *adj.* lump (*attrib.*): кусково́й са́хар, lump sugar.
кусо́к [*gen.* **-ска́**] *n.* **1,** piece; bit. **2,** slice (*of bread*); lump (*of sugar*); bar (*of soap*).
кусо́чек [*gen.* **-чка**] *n., dim. of* **кусо́к.**
куст [*gen.* **куста́**] *n.* bush; shrub.
куста́рник *n.* bushes; shrubs; shrubbery.
куста́рный *adj.* **1,** handicraft (*attrib.*). **2,** *fig.* crude; primitive.
куста́рь [*gen.* **-таря́**] *n.m.* handicraftsman.
ку́тать *v. impfv.* [*pfv.* **заку́тать**] to wrap; bundle. —**ку́таться,** *refl.* (*with* **в** + *acc.*) to wrap/bundle oneself in.
кутёж [*gen.* **-тежа́**] *n.* drinking spree; binge.
кутерьма́ *n., colloq.* commotion.
кути́ла *n.m., colloq.* reveler; carouser.
кути́ть *v. impfv.* [*pres.* **кучу́, ку́тишь**] to carouse.
куту́зка [*gen. pl.* **-зок**] *n., obs., colloq.* jail; hoosegow.
куха́рка [*gen. pl.* **-рок**] *n.* cook.

ку́хня [*gen. pl.* **-хонь**] *n.* **1,** kitchen. **2,** cooking; cuisine; cookery. —**ку́хонный,** *adj.* kitchen (*attrib.*).
ку́цый *adj.* **1,** (*of a tail*) short. **2,** short-tailed. **3,** (*of clothes*) skimpy. **4,** *fig.* limited; reduced; incomplete.
ку́ча *n.* **1,** pile; heap. **2,** (*with gen.*) *colloq.* heaps (of); lots (of). —**вали́ть в одну́ ку́чу,** to lump together.
кучево́й *adj.* (*of clouds*) cumulous.
ку́чер [*pl.* **кучера́**] *n.* coachman.
ку́чка [*gen. pl.* **-чек**] *n.* **1,** *dim. of* **ку́ча. 2,** small circle (*of people*).
куш *n.* **1,** bet (*in a card game*). **2,** *colloq.* large sum of money. —**сорва́ть куш,** to clean up; make a killing.
куша́к [*gen.* **-шака́**] *n.* sash.
ку́шанье *n.* food.
ку́шать *v. impfv.* [*pfv.* **поку́шать**] to eat.
куше́тка [*gen. pl.* **-ток**] *n.* couch.
кш *interj.* shoo! *Also,* **кыш.**
кюве́т *n.* ditch (*along the side of a road*).
кю́рий *n.* curium.

Л

Л, л *n. neut.* twelfth letter of the Russian alphabet.
лабири́нт *n.* labyrinth; maze.
лабора́нт *n.* laboratory assistant.
лаборато́рия *n.* laboratory. —**лаборато́рный,** *adj.* laboratory (*attrib.*).
ла́ва *n.* lava.
лава́нда *n.* lavender. —**лава́ндовый,** *adj.* lavender (*attrib.*).
лави́на *n.* avalanche.
лави́ровать *v. impfv.* [*pres.* **-рую, -руешь**] **1,** *naut.* to tack with the wind. **2,** *fig.* to maneuver.
ла́вка [*gen. pl.* **-вок**] *n.* **1,** bench. **2,** shop; store.
ла́вочка [*gen. pl.* **-чек**] *n.* **1,** small bench. **2,** small shop; small store. —**закры́ть ла́вочку,** to close up shop.
ла́вочник *n., obs.* shopkeeper.
лавр *n.* **1,** laurel. **2,** laurel wreath. **3,** *pl., fig.* laurels: почива́ть на ла́врах, to rest on one's laurels.
ла́вра *n.* large monastery: Пече́рская ла́вра, Monastery of the Caves (*in Kiev*).
лавро́вый *also,* **ла́вровый** *adj.* laurel (*attrib.*). —**лавро́вый лист,** bay leaf.
лавса́н *n.* a polyester fiber similar to dacron; lavsan.
ла́герный *adj.* camp (*attrib.*).
ла́герь *n.m.* **1,** [*pl.* **лагеря́**] camp. **2,** [*pl.* **ла́гери**] *fig.* camp; side; faction.
лагу́на *n.* lagoon.
лад [*2nd loc.* **ладу́;** *pl.* **лады́**] *n.* **1,** *colloq.* harmony (*between people*). **2,** way: на друго́й лад, a different way. **3,** *music* key; tone. **4,** *usu. pl.* fret (*of a stringed instrument*); key (*of an accordion*). —**в лад, 1,** in harmony; in tune. **2,** (*with dat.*) in time to. —**в ладу́; в лада́х,** on good terms. —**на все лады́,** thoroughly; from all angles. —**не в ладу́; не в лада́х,** on the outs. —**де́ло идёт на лад,** *colloq.* things are going well. —**запе́ть на друго́й лад,** to change one's tune; sing a different tune. —**перестро́ить на вое́нный лад,** to place on a war footing.
ла́дан *n.* **1,** incense. **2,** *in* **ро́сный ла́дан,** benzoin. —**дыша́ть на ла́дан,** to be near death; have one foot in the grave. —**как черт от ла́дана,** (*with verbs of shunning, fearing, etc.*) like the plague.
ла́данка [*gen. pl.* **-нок**] *n.* amulet.
ла́дить *v. impfv.* [*pres.* **ла́жу, ла́дишь**] (*with* **с** + *instr.*) to get along (with); be on good terms (with). —**ла́диться,** *refl.* to get on well; proceed satisfactorily: де́ло не ла́дится, things are not working out well.
ла́дно *particle, colloq.* all right; O.K. —*adv., colloq.* **1,** harmoniously. **2,** well.
ла́дный *adj., colloq.* **1,** graceful. **2,** harmonious. **3,** well-built; well-made.
ладо́нь *n.f.* palm of the hand. —**ви́дно как на ладо́ни,** clearly visible.
ладо́ши *n. pl., in* **хло́пать** *or* **бить в ладо́ши,** to clap one's hands.
ладья́ *n., chess* rook; castle.
лаз *n.* manhole.
ла́занье *n.* climbing.
лазаре́т *n.* **1,** field hospital. **2,** infirmary.
лазе́йка [*gen. pl.* **-зе́ек**] *n.* **1,** small opening. **2,** *fig.* loophole: оста́вить себе́ лазе́йку, to leave oneself a loophole.
ла́зер *n.* laser. —**ла́зерный,** *adj.* laser (*attrib.*).
ла́зить *v. impfv.* [*pres.* **ла́жу, ла́зишь**] *indeterm. of* **лезть.**
лазу́рный *adj.* light-blue; azure.
лазу́рь *n.f.* light blue; azure. —**берли́нская лазу́рь,** Prussian blue.
лазу́тчик *n., obs.* **1,** scout. **2,** spy.
лай *n.* bark; barking.
ла́йка [*gen. pl.* **ла́ек**] *n.* **1,** husky (*dog*). **2,** kidskin. —**ла́йковый,** *adj.* kid (*attrib.*); kidskin (*attrib.*): ла́йковые перча́тки, kid gloves.
лайм *n.* lime (*fruit & tree*).
ла́йнер *n.* ocean liner. —**возду́шный ла́йнер,** airliner.
лак *n.* lacquer; varnish; polish. —**лак для ногте́й,** nail polish.
лака́ть *v. impfv.* [*pfv.* **вылакать**] to lap; lap up.
лаке́й *n.* **1,** footman. **2,** *fig.* lackey.
лаке́йский *adj.* **1,** of a footman. **2,** *fig.* servile.
лакиро́ванный *adj.* **1,** lacquered. Лакиро́ванные

изде́лия, lacquerware. **2,** gleaming; lustrous. —**лаки-ро́ванная ко́жа,** patent leather. —**лакиро́ванные ту́фли,** patent-leather shoes.
лакирова́ть *v. impfv.* [*pfv.* **отлакирова́ть;** *pres.* **-ру́ю, -ру́ешь**] **1,** to lacquer; varnish. **2,** [*impfv. only*] *fig.* to varnish; embellish.
лакиро́вка *n.* lacquering; varnishing.
ла́кмус *n.* litmus. —**ла́кмусовый,** *adj.* litmus (*attrib.*): ла́кмусовая бума́га, litmus paper.
ла́ковый *adj.* **1,** lacquer (*attrib.*). **2,** lacquered.
ла́комиться *v.r. impfv.* [*pfv.* **пола́комиться;** *pres.* **-млюсь, -мишься**] (*with instr.*) to feast on.
ла́комка [*gen. pl.* **-мок**] *n.m. & f., colloq.* person with a sweet tooth.
ла́комство *n.* **1,** *usu. pl.* sweets. **2,** delicacy.
ла́комый *adj.* **1,** tasty; luscious. **2,** [*short form only*] (*with* **до**) *colloq.* fond (of); having a weakness (for). —**ла́комый кусо́чек,** tempting morsel; prize catch.
лакони́зм *n.* terseness; brevity.
лакони́ческий *adj.* laconic.
лакони́чный *adj.* laconic. —**лакони́чность,** *n.f.* terseness; brevity.
лакри́ца *n.* licorice. —**лакри́чный,** *adj.* licorice.
лакта́ция *n.* lactation.
лакто́за *n.* lactose.
лакфио́ль *n.f.* wallflower.
ла́ма[1] *n.* llama.
ла́ма[2] *n.* lama. —**ламаи́зм,** *n.* Lamaism. —**ламаи́ст-ский,** *adj.* of or pert. to Lamaism.
ламанти́н *n.* manatee.
ла́мпа *n.* **1,** lamp. **2,** *radio* tube: электро́нная ла́мпа, vacuum tube. —**ла́мпа дневно́го све́та,** daylight lamp.
лампа́да *n.* icon lamp.
лампа́с *n.* stripe (*on the side of uniform trousers*).
ла́мповый *adj.* lamp (*attrib.*).
ла́мпочка [*gen. pl.* **-чек**] *n.* **1,** *dim. of* **ла́мпа. 2,** (electric light) bulb.
ланге́т *n.* sliced steak.
лангу́ст *also,* **лангу́ста** *n.* spiny lobster.
ландша́фт *n.* landscape.
ла́ндыш *n.* lily of the valley.
ланоли́н *n.* lanolin.
ланта́н *n.* lanthanum.
ланце́т *n.* lancet.
лань *n.f.* fallow deer.
ла́па *n.* **1,** paw. **2,** claw (*of a hammer*); fluke (*of an anchor*). —**попа́сть в ла́пы** (+ *dat. or with* **к**), to fall into the clutches of.
ла́пка [*gen. pl.* **-пок**] *n.* **1,** paw. **2,** *in* **гуси́ные ла́пки,** crow's-feet (*near the eye*). —**ходи́ть на за́дних ла́пках пе́ред,** to kowtow to; bow and scrape to.
ла́поть [*gen.* **-птя;** *pl.* **ла́пти, -пте́й, -птя́м**] *n.m.* sandal made of bark.
лапта́ *n.* **1,** Russian game, somewhat like baseball. **2,** wooden bat used in this game.
лапша́ *n.* **1,** noodles. **2,** noodle soup.
лапше́вник *n.* noodle pudding.
ла́рго *n. neut. & adv., music* largo.
ларёк [*gen.* **-рька́**] *n.* stall; booth.
ларе́ц [*gen.* **-рца́**] *n.* small box or case (*for valuables*).
ларинги́т *n.* laryngitis.
ла́рчик *n.* small box. —**а ла́рчик про́сто открыва́лся,** the explanation was quite simple.
ларь [*gen.* **ларя́**] *n.m.* bin.
ла́ска *n.* **1,** [*gen. pl.* **ласк**] caress. **2,** [*sing. only*] kindness. **3,** [*gen. pl.* **ла́сок**] weasel.
ласка́тельный *adj.* **1,** tender. **2,** *gram.* of endearment: ласка́тельное и́мя, endearing form of a name.
ласка́ть *v. impfv.* **1,** to caress; fondle; pet. **2,** *fig.* to please; delight (the senses). —**ласка́ться,** *refl.* (*with* **к**) **1,** to snuggle up (to). **2,** *obs.* to play up to.
ла́сковый *adj.* **1,** affectionate; tender. **2,** *fig.* (*of a breeze, sound, etc.*) gentle.
лассо́ *n. indecl.* lasso; lariat.
ласт *n.* flipper (*of a seal, walrus, etc.*).
ла́стик *n.* **1,** lasting. **2,** *colloq.* eraser.
ла́сточка [*gen. pl.* **-чек**] *n.* swallow (*bird*). —**пе́рвая ла́сточка,** first sign. —**прыжо́к в во́ду ла́сточкой,** swan dive.
ла́сточкин *adj.* of a swallow; swallows': ла́сточкино гнездо́, swallows' nest. —**ла́сточкин хвост,** dovetail.
лата́ть *v. impfv.* [*pfv.* **залата́ть**] *colloq.* to patch; patch up.
латви́йский *adj.* Latvian.
ла́текс *n.* latex.
лате́нтный *adj.* latent.
лати́нский *adj.* **1,** Latin. **2,** (*of the alphabet, characters, etc.*) Roman.
ла́тный *adj.* armor (*attrib.*). —**ла́тные доспе́хи,** suit of armor.
лату́к *n.* lettuce.
лату́нь *n.f.* brass. —**лату́нный,** *adj.* brass.
ла́ты [*gen.* **лат**] *n. pl.* armor.
латы́нь *n.f., colloq.* Latin.
латы́ш [*gen.* **-тыша́**] *n.m.* [*fem.* **-ты́шка**] Latvian; Lett. —**латы́шский,** *adj.* Latvian; Lettish.
лауреа́т *n.* laureate.
лафе́т *n.* gun carriage.
ла́цкан *n.* lapel.
лачу́га *n.* shanty; hovel.
ла́ять *v. impfv.* [*pres.* **ла́ю, ла́ешь**] to bark.
лганьё *n.* **1,** lying. **2,** lies.
лгать *v. impfv.* [*pfv.* **солга́ть;** *pres.* **лгу, лжёшь, ... лгут;** *past fem.* **лгала́**] to lie; tell lies.
лгун [*gen.* **лгуна́**] *n.m.* [*fem.* **лгу́нья**] liar.
лебеди́ный *adj.* **1,** swan (*attrib.*); swan's; of swans. **2,** like that of a swan; graceful. —**лебеди́ная пе́сня,** swan song.
лебёдка [*gen. pl.* **-док**] *n.* **1,** female swan. **2,** *mech.* winch.
ле́бедь [*pl.* **ле́беди, -де́й, -дя́м**] *n.m.* swan.
лебези́ть *v. impfv.* [*pres.* **-жу́, -зи́шь**] (*with* **пе́ред**) *colloq.* to be obsequious (to); kowtow (to).
лебя́жий [*fem.* **-жья**] *adj.* swan (*attrib.*); swan's.
лев [*gen.* **льва**] *n.* **1,** lion. **2,** *cap.* Leo. —**морско́й лев,** sea lion.
леве́ть *v. impfv.* [*pfv.* **полеве́ть**] to move to the left (*politically*).
левиафа́н *n.* leviathan.
Леви́т *n.* Leviticus.
левко́й *n.* gillyflower.
левре́тка [*gen. pl.* **-ток**] *n.* Italian greyhound.
левша́ *n.m. & f.* left-handed person.
ле́вый *adj.* **1,** left; lefthand. **2,** *polit.* left; left-wing. **3,** (*of a side of material*) wrong. **4,** *naut.* port. —*n.* left-winger; leftist. —**встать с ле́вой ноги́,** to get up on the wrong side of the bed.
лега́вый *adj., in* **лега́вая соба́ка,** pointer; setter.
легализа́ция *n.* legalization.

легализи́ровать *v. impfv. & pfv.* [*pres.* **-рую, -руешь**] to legalize. *Also,* **легализова́ть** [*pres.* **-зу́ю, -зу́ешь**].

лега́льный *adj.* legal. —**лега́льность,** *n.f.* legality.

лега́то *n. neut. & adv., music* legato.

леге́нда *n.* legend. —**легенда́рный,** *adj.* legendary.

легио́н *n.* legion. —**легионе́р,** *n.* legionnaire.

лёгкий *adj.* [*short form* **лёгок, легка́, легко́;** *comp.* **ле́гче**] **1,** light (*in weight*). **2,** easy. **3,** not severe; light; slight; mild. **4,** graceful; light. **5,** (*of a breeze, nudge, etc.*) slight; gentle. **6,** (*of foods*) light; soft; bland; (*of a meal*) light. **7,** (*of music, reading, etc.*) light. **8,** easygoing. **9,** (*of behavior*) lax; loose. **10,** (*of industry, artillery, etc.*) light. —**лёгкая атле́тика,** track and field. —**лёгкая фигу́ра,** *chess* minor piece. —**лёгок на подъём,** always ready and willing. —**лёгок на поми́не!,** talk of the devil! —**с лёгкой руки́** (+ *gen.*), thanks to; at the initiative of. —**у него́ лёгкая рука́,** he brings luck; he has a magic touch. *See also* **ле́гче.**

легко́ *adv.* **1,** easily. **2,** lightly. **3,** *in* легко́ ра́неный, slightly wounded. —*adj., used predicatively* easy: легко́ ошиба́ться, it is easy to make a mistake.

легкоатле́т *n.* (track and field) athlete; one taking part in any track or field event. —**легкоатлети́ческий,** *adj.* track-and-field.

легкове́рие *n.* credulity; gullibility. —**легкове́рный,** *adj.* credulous; gullible.

легкове́с *n., sports* lightweight.

легкове́сный *adj.* **1,** lightweight. **2,** *fig.* frivolous.

легково́й *adj., in* **легково́й автомоби́ль,** passenger car.

лёгкое *n., decl. as an adj.* lung.

легкомы́сленный *adj.* frivolous; flighty. —**легкомы́слие,** *n.* frivolity.

лёгкость *n.f.* **1,** lightness. **2,** ease; facility.

лёгочный *adj.* lung (*attrib.*); pulmonary.

легча́ть *v. impfv.* [*pfv.* **полегча́ть**] *colloq.* **1,** to abate; moderate. **2,** *impers.* (*with dat.*) to feel better.

ле́гче *adj., comp. of* **лёгкий.** —**ле́гче на поворо́тах!,** *colloq.* take it easy!; watch what you're saying! —**ста́ло ле́гче** (*with dat.*), one is feeling somewhat better. —**час о́т часу не ле́гче!,** things are getting worse by the minute.

лёд [*gen.* **льда;** *2nd loc.* **льду**] *n.* ice.

ледене́ть *v. impfv.* [*pfv.* **заледене́ть** *or* **оледене́ть**] to freeze; become numb.

ледене́ц [*gen.* **-нца́**] *n.* piece of hard candy.

ледени́ть *v. impfv.* [*pfv.* **оледени́ть**] to freeze; cause to freeze.

ле́ди *n.f. indecl.* lady.

ле́дник *n.* **1,** ice house; ice cellar. **2,** icebox; refrigerator.

ледни́к [*gen.* **-ника́**] *n.* glacier. —**леднико́вый,** *adj.* glacial.

ледо́вый *adj.* **1,** ice (*attrib.*). **2,** (*of a voyage*) made through icy regions.

ледоко́л *n.* icebreaker (*ship*).

ледоста́в *n.* freeze-up (*of a river*).

ледохо́д *n.* drifting of ice.

леды́шка [*gen. pl.* **-шек**] *n., colloq.* piece of ice.

ледяно́й *adj.* **1,** of ice; ice (*attrib.*). **2,** icy; ice-cold. **3,** *fig.* icy: ледяно́й взгляд, icy look.

лёжа *adv.* in a reclining position; lying down.

лежа́лый *adj.* stale; old.

лежа́нка [*gen. pl.* **-нок**] *n.* sleeping ledge over a Russian chimney stove.

лежа́ть *v. impfv.* [*pres.* **лежу́, лежи́шь**] **1,** to lie. **2,** to be; be situated; lie. **3,** (*of responsibility, duties, etc.*) to lie; rest. —**лежа́ть на боку́,** *colloq.* to loaf. —**всё, что пло́хо лежи́т,** everything in sight; everything that is not tied down. —**у него́ душа́ не лежи́т к э́тому,** his heart isn't in it; he has no appetite for it.

лежа́чий *adj.* **1,** lying; recumbent. **2,** *colloq.* confined to bed. —*n., in* **бить лежа́чего,** to hit a man when he is down.

ле́жбище *n.* breeding ground (*of seals, walruses, etc.*).

лежебо́ка *n.m. & f., colloq.* loafer; lazybones.

лежмя́ *adv., colloq., in* **лежмя́ лежа́ть,** to lie prostrate.

ле́звие *n.* blade (*of a knife, axe, etc.*). —**ле́звие бри́твы,** razor blade.

лезги́н [*gen. pl.* **-ги́н**] *n.m.* [*fem.* **-ги́нка**] Lezgin (*one of a people inhabiting the Caucasus*). —**лезги́нский,** *adj.* Lezgin.

лезть *v. impfv.* [*pfv.* **поле́зть;** *pres.* **ле́зу, ле́зешь;** *past* **лез, ле́зла**] **1,** to climb. **2,** (*with* **в** + *acc.*) to sneak (into). **3,** (*with* **в** + *acc.*) *colloq.* to reach (into). **4,** [*impfv. only*] *usu. neg.* to fit: ша́пка тебе́ не ле́зет, the hat doesn't fit you. **5,** (*of hair, fur, etc.*) to fall out. **6,** to stick out. —**лезть в буты́лку,** *colloq.* to fly off the handle. —**лезть в го́лову,** (*of thoughts*) to pop into one's head. —**лезть в дра́ку,** to be spoiling for a fight. —**лезть в ду́шу** (+ *dat.*), to worm one's way into someone's confidence. —**лезть в карма́н** (+ *dat.*), to pick someone's pocket. —**лезть в пе́тлю,** to risk one's neck. —**лезть из ко́жи вон,** to try in every way. —**лезть на глаза́** (+ *dat.*), *colloq.* to (try to) catch one's eye. —**лезть (поле́зть) на лоб,** (*of one's eyes*) to pop out of one's head. —**лезть на́ стену,** *colloq.* to fly off the handle; hit the ceiling. —**не лезть в карма́н за сло́вом,** never to be at a loss for words.

лейбори́ст *n.* Labourite. —**лейбори́стский,** *adj.* Labour (*attrib.*).

ле́йка [*gen. pl.* **ле́ек**] *n.* **1,** watering can; sprinkling can. **2,** *colloq.* funnel.

лейкеми́я *n.* leukemia.

лейкоци́т *n.* leukocyte.

лейтена́нт *n.* lieutenant.

лейтмоти́в *n.* leitmotiv.

лека́ло *n.* French curve.

лека́рственный *adj.* medicinal.

лека́рство *n.* medicine.

ле́карь [*pl.* **ле́кари, -ре́й, -ря́м**] *n.m., obs.* doctor.

ле́ксика *n.* vocabulary; lexicon.

лексикогра́фия *n.* lexicography. —**лексико́граф,** *n.* lexicographer. —**лексикографи́ческий,** *adj.* lexicographic.

лексико́н *n.* lexicon.

лекси́ческий *adj.* lexical.

ле́ктор *n.* lecturer.

ле́кция *n.* lecture. —**лекцио́нный,** *adj.* lecture (*attrib.*).

леле́ять *v. impfv.* [*pres.* **леле́ю, леле́ешь**] **1,** to care for lovingly. **2,** *fig.* to cherish; nurture (a dream, hope, etc.).

ле́мех *also,* **леме́х** [*pl.* **лемеха́**] *n.* plowshare.

ле́мминг *n.* lemming.

лему́р *n.* lemur.

лён [*gen.* **льна**] *n.* flax.

лени́вец [*gen.* **-вца**] *n.* **1,** lazy person. **2,** *zool.* sloth.

лени́вый *adj.* **1,** lazy. **2,** sluggish.

ле́нинец [*gen.* **-нца**] *n.* Leninist. —**ленини́зм,** *n.* Leninism. —**ле́нинский,** *adj.* Leninist.
лени́ться *v.r. impfv.* [*pres.* **леню́сь, ле́нишься**] **1,** to be lazy. **2,** (*with inf.*) to be too lazy (to).
ле́ность *n.f.* laziness.
ле́нта *n.* **1,** ribbon. **2,** tape. **3,** band. **4,** film. —**конве́йерная ле́нта,** conveyer belt. —**патро́нная ле́нта,** cartridge belt.
ле́нто *n. neut. & adv., music* lento.
ле́нточный *adj.* tape (*attrib.*); band (*attrib.*). —**ле́нточная пила́,** band saw. —**ле́нточный транспортёр,** conveyer belt. —**ле́нточный червь,** tapeworm.
лентя́й *n.m.* [*fem.* **-тя́йка**] *colloq.* lazy person; lazybones.
лентя́йничать *v. impfv., colloq.* to loaf; idle.
ленца́ *n., colloq.* lazy streak: челове́к с ленцо́й, person with a lazy streak.
ленч *n.* lunch.
лень *n.f.* laziness. —*predicate* (*with dat.*) *colloq.* too lazy: мне лень идти́, I am too lazy to go.
леопа́рд *n.* leopard. —**леопа́рдовый,** *adj.* leopard (*attrib.*); leopard's.
лепесто́к [*gen.* **-стка́**] *n.* petal.
ле́пет *n.* babble; prattle.
лепета́ние *n.* babbling; prattling.
лепета́ть *v. impfv.* [*pres.* **-печу́, -пе́чешь**] to babble; prattle.
лепёшка [*gen. pl.* **-шек**] *n.* **1,** small cake; crumpet. **2,** tablet; lozenge. **3,** (*with gen.*) clod (*of dirt*).
лепи́ть *v. impfv.* [*pres.* **леплю́, ле́пишь**] **1,** [*pfv.* **вы́лепить**] to model; fashion; sculpture. **2,** [*pfv.* **слепи́ть**] to make; build (a nest, hive, etc.). —**лепи́ться,** *refl.* [*impfv. only*] to nestle.
ле́пка *n.* modeling.
лепно́й *adj.* sculptured. —**лепно́е украше́ние,** molding.
ле́пта *n.* small contribution; mite: вноси́ть свою́ ле́пту, to contribute one's (small) share; do one's bit.
лес [*2nd loc.* **лесу́;** *pl.* **леса́**] *n.* **1,** forest; woods. **2,** timber; lumber. —**быть как в лесу́,** to be all at sea.
леса́[1] *also,* **ле́са** [*pl.* **лёсы**] *n.* fishing line.
леса́[2] [*gen.* **лесо́в**] *n. pl.* scaffolding.
лесбия́нка [*gen. pl.* **-нок**] *n.* lesbian. —**лесби́йский,** *adj.* lesbian.
ле́сенка [*gen. pl.* **-нок**] *n.* **1,** small ladder. **2,** short flight of stairs.
леси́стый *adj.* wooded.
ле́ска [*gen. pl.* **-сок**] *n.* fishing line.
лесни́к [*gen.* **-ника́**] *n.* forest ranger.
лесни́чество *n.* forest district.
лесни́чий *n., decl. as an adj.* forester.
лесно́й *adj.* **1,** forest (*attrib.*). **2,** timber (*attrib.*); lumber (*attrib.*). **3,** of forestry. —**лесна́я земляни́ка,** wild strawberries. —**лесно́й оре́х,** hazelnut.
лесово́д *n.* specialist in forestry. —**лесово́дство,** *n.* forestry.
лесозаво́д *n.* lumber mill.
лесоматериа́л *n., usu. pl.* timber; lumber.
лесопи́лка [*gen. pl.* **-лок**] *n., colloq.* sawmill.
лесопи́льный *adj.* sawing; saw (*attrib.*). —**лесопи́льный заво́д,** sawmill.
лесору́б *n.* woodcutter; lumberjack.
ле́стница *n.* **1,** stairs; staircase; stairway. **2,** ladder. —**пожа́рная ле́стница,** fire escape.
ле́стничный *adj.* stair (*attrib.*).
ле́стно *adv.* in flattering terms. —*adj., used predicatively* flattering: мне бы́ло ле́стно, что..., it was flattering to me that...; I was flattered that...
ле́стный *adj.* flattering; complimentary.
лесть *n.f.* flattery.
лёт *n.* flight; flying. —**на лету́,** in midair; on the fly; on the wing. —**лови́ть на лету́,** *fig.* to be quick to grasp.
лета́ [*gen.* **лет**] *n. pl.* years: пять лет, five years. Мне два́дцать лет, I am twenty years old. —**быть в лета́х,** to be getting on in years. —**мно́гая ле́та** (*with different stress*), here's to long life! —**одни́х лет,** the same age. —**с де́тских** (*or* **с ма́лых**) **лет,** since childhood. —**ско́лько вам лет?,** how old are you? —**сре́дних лет,** middle-aged.
летарги́я *n.* lethargy. —**летарги́ческий,** *adj.* lethargic.
лета́тельный *adj.* flying (*attrib.*).
лета́ть *v. impfv., indeterm. of* **лете́ть.**
лете́ть *v. impfv.* [*pfv.* **полете́ть;** *pres.* **лечу́, лети́шь**] to fly. —**лете́ть вверх,** *colloq.* to soar. —**лете́ть вниз,** *colloq.* to plummet.
ле́тний *adj.* summer (*attrib.*).
лётный *adj.* flying (*attrib.*). —**лётная доро́жка,** runway. —**лётное по́ле,** airfield. —**лётный соста́в,** flight personnel.
ле́то *n.* summer. —**ле́том,** *adv.* in (the) summer.
летоисчисле́ние *n.* method of numbering the years.
летопи́сец [*gen.* **-сца**] *n.* chronicler.
ле́топись *n.f.* chronicle.
летосчисле́ние *n.* = **летоисчисле́ние.**
летýн [*gen.* **-туна́**] *n., colloq.* **1,** flier. **2,** person continually changing jobs.
лету́честь *n.f.* volatility.
лету́чий *adj.* **1,** flying. **2,** fleeting; momentary. **3,** *chem.* volatile. —**лету́чая мышь,** *zool.* bat. —**лету́чая ры́ба,** flying fish.
лету́чка [*gen. pl.* **-чек**] *n., colloq.* **1,** leaflet. **2,** quick meeting. **3,** mobile unit.
лётчик *n.* pilot. —**лётчик-испыта́тель,** test pilot. —**лётчик-истреби́тель,** fighter-pilot.
летя́га *n.* flying squirrel.
лече́бница *n.* hospital; nursing home.
лече́бный *adj.* **1,** medical. **2,** medicinal; curative.
лече́ние *n.* (medical) treatment.
лечи́ть *v. impfv.* [*pres.* **лечу́, ле́чишь**] to treat (*medically*). —**лечи́ться,** *refl.* **1,** to undergo (medical) treatment. **2,** to treat oneself.
лечь [*infl.* **ля́гу, ля́жешь, ...ля́гут;** *past* **лёг, легла́, легло́**] *v., pfv. of* **ложи́ться.**
ле́ший *n., decl. as an adj.* wood goblin.
лещ [*gen.* **леща́**] *n.* bream (*fish*).
лещи́на *n.* hazel (*tree*).
лженау́ка *n.* pseudoscience. —**лженау́чный,** *adj.* pseudoscientific.
лжесвиде́тель *n.m.* false witness; perjurer. —**лжесвиде́тельство,** *n.* false evidence; perjury.
лжесвиде́тельствовать *v. impfv.* [*pres.* **-ствую, -ствуешь**] to give false evidence; commit perjury; perjure oneself.
лжец [*gen.* **лжеца́**] *n.* liar.
лжи́вый *adj.* lying; untruthful; false. —**лжи́вость,** *n.f.* falsity.
ли *conj.* if; whether: я не зна́ю, смогу́ ли я пойти́, I don't know if I'll be able to go. Он попро́бовал,

хорошо́ ли вино́, he tasted the wine to see if it was good. —*interr. particle:* есть ли у вас спи́чка?, do you have a match?; have you a match? Нра́вится ли вам э́то?, do you like it?

либера́л *n.* liberal. —**либерали́зм,** *n.* liberalism.

либера́льничать *v. impfv., colloq.* to be overly tolerant.

либера́льный *adj.* liberal.

ли́бо *conj.* or. —**ли́бо..., ли́бо...,** either..., or...

либре́тто *n. indecl.* libretto. —**либретти́ст,** *n.* librettist.

лива́нский *adj.* Lebanese.

ли́вень [*gen.* **ли́вня**] *n.m.* rainstorm; downpour; cloudburst; thundershower.

ли́вер *n.* giblets.

ли́верный *adj., in* **ли́верная колбаса́,** liverwurst.

ливи́йский *adj.* Libyan.

ливмя́ *adv., colloq., in* **ливмя́ лить,** (*of rain*) to come down in torrents.

ливре́я *n.* livery. —**ливре́йный,** *adj.* livery (*attrib.*); liveried; in livery.

ли́га *n.* **1,** league: Ли́га на́ций, League of Nations. **2,** *music* slur.

лигату́ра *n.* ligature.

лигни́т *n.* lignite.

лигрои́н *n.* naphtha.

ли́дер *n.* leader.

ли́дерство *n.* **1,** leadership. **2,** *sports* lead (*in a race, contest, etc.*).

лиди́ровать *v. impfv. & pfv.* [*pres.* **-рую, -руешь**] *sports* to lead; be in the lead.

лиза́ние *n.* licking.

лиза́ть *v. impfv.* [*pfv.* **лизну́ть;** *pres.* **лижу́, ли́жешь**] to lick.

лизоблю́д *n., colloq.* bootlicker.

лик *n.* **1,** *archaic* face; countenance. **2,** face (*of the moon, sun, etc.*). **3,** *eccles.* assembly. —**причи́слить к ли́ку святы́х,** to canonize.

ликвида́ция *n.* liquidation.

ликвиди́ровать *v. impfv. & pfv.* [*pres.* **-рую, -руешь**] **1,** to liquidate. **2,** to eliminate.

ликви́дный *adj., finance* liquid: ликви́дные сре́дства, liquid assets. —**ликви́дность,** *n.f.* liquidity.

ликёр *n.* liqueur; cordial.

ликова́ние *n.* rejoicing; jubilation; exultation.

ликова́ть *v. impfv.* [*pres.* **-ку́ю, -ку́ешь**] to rejoice; exult.

лику́ющий *adj.* jubilant; exultant.

ли́лия *n.* lily. —**водяна́я ли́лия,** water lily.

лилове́ть *v. impfv.* to turn purple.

лило́вый *adj.* purple.

лима́н *n.* estuary.

лими́т *n.* limit; quota.

лимити́ровать *v. impfv. & pfv.* [*pres.* **-рую, -руешь**] to limit.

лимо́н *n.* **1,** lemon. **2,** lemon tree.

лимона́д *n.* **1,** lemonade. **2,** carbonated fruit drink; squash.

лимо́нный *adj.* lemon. —**лимо́нная кислота́,** citric acid.

лимузи́н *n.* limousine.

ли́мфа *n.* lymph. —**лимфати́ческий,** *adj.* lymph (*attrib.*); lymphatic.

лингви́ст *n.* linguist. —**лингви́стика,** *n.* linguistics. —**лингвисти́ческий,** *adj.* linguistic.

лине́йка [*gen. pl.* **-не́ек**] *n.* **1,** ruled line (*on paper*). В лине́йку, (*of paper*) lined; ruled. **2,** ruler; straight edge. **3,** line; file: вы́строиться в лине́йку, to form a line. **4,** line-up; assembly (*in a camp*). —**логарифми́ческая лине́йка,** slide rule.

лине́йный *adj.* linear. —**лине́йный кора́бль,** battleship.

ли́нза *n.* lens.

ли́ния *n.* line. —**по ли́нии** (+ *gen.*), through; under the auspices of.

линко́р *n.* battleship (*contr. of* **лине́йный кора́бль**).

лино́ванный *adj.* lined; ruled.

линова́ть *v. impfv.* [*pfv.* **налинова́ть;** *pres.* **-ну́ю, -ну́ешь**] to rule; draw lines on.

лино́леум *n.* linoleum.

линоти́п *n.* linotype.

линчева́ние *n.* lynching.

линчева́ть *v. impfv. & pfv.* [*pres.* **-чу́ю, -чу́ешь**] to lynch.

ли́нька *n.* molting.

линю́чий *adj., colloq.* (*of material*) that fades easily.

линя́лый *adj., colloq.* faded; discolored.

линя́ть *v. impfv.* **1,** [*pfv.* **полиня́ть**] (*of material*) to fade; (*of colors*) to run. **2,** [*pfv.* **вы́линять**] (*of animals*) to shed hair; (*of birds*) to molt.

ли́па *n.* linden tree; lime tree.

ли́пкий *adj.* sticky; adhesive. —**ли́пкий пла́стырь,** sticking plaster.

ли́пнуть *v. impfv.* [*past* **лип** *or* **ли́пнул, ли́пла**] (*with* **к**) to stick (to).

ли́повый *adj.* **1,** linden (*attrib.*); lime (*attrib.*). **2,** *colloq.* false; fake; phony.

липу́чий *adj., colloq.* sticky.

липу́чка *n., colloq.* **1,** sticky paper: липу́чка от мух, flypaper. **2,** sticking plaster.

ли́ра *n.* **1,** lyre. **2,** lira (*monetary unit of Italy and Turkey*).

лири́зм *n.* lyricism.

ли́рик *n.* lyric poet.

ли́рика *n.* **1,** lyric poetry. **2,** lyric poem. —**лири́ческий,** *adj.* lyric; lyrical.

лиса́ [*pl.* **ли́сы**] *n.* fox.

ли́сий [*fem.* **-сья**] *adj.* **1,** fox (*attrib.*). **2,** *fig.* foxy.

лиси́ца *n.* fox. —**морска́я лиси́ца,** thresher shark.

лиси́чка [*gen. pl.* **-чек**] *n.* a kind of edible mushroom; chanterelle.

лист [*gen.* **листа́**] *n.* **1,** [*pl.* **ли́стья, ли́стьев**] leaf. **2,** [*pl.* **листы́, листо́в**] sheet (*of paper, metal, etc.*). **3,** [*pl.* **листы́, листо́в**] any of various official documents: опро́сный лист, questionnaire; исполни́тельный лист, writ. —**с листа́,** from sight: чита́ть с листа́, to sight-read.

листа́ть *v. impfv., colloq.* to leaf through.

листва́ *n.* foliage.

ли́ственница *n.* larch (*tree*).

ли́ственный *adj.* leafy; leaf-bearing.

листо́вка [*gen. pl.* **-вок**] *n.* leaflet.

листово́й *adj.* **1,** sheet (*attrib.*): листово́й мета́лл, sheet metal. **2,** leaf (*attrib.*).

листо́к [*gen.* **-стка́**] *n.* **1,** leaf. **2,** sheet (*of paper*).

листопа́д *n.* falling of leaves. —**листопа́дный,** *adj.* deciduous.

лита́вры *n. pl.* [*sing.* **лита́вра**] kettledrums.

лита́ния *n.* litany.

литéйный *adj.* founding; casting. —**литéйный завóд,** foundry.

литéйщик *n.* founder; caster.

литерáтор *n.* man of letters.

литератýра *n.* literature. —**литератýрный,** *adj.* literary.

лúтерный *adj.* **1,** designated by a letter. **2,** (*of a seat*) reserved.

лúтий *n.* lithium.

литóвец [*gen.* **-вца**] *n.m.* [*fem.* **-вка**] Lithuanian. —**литóвский,** *adj.* Lithuanian.

литóграф *n.* lithographer.

литографúровать *v. impfv. & pfv.* [*pres.* **-рую, -руешь**] to lithograph.

литогрáфия *n.* **1,** lithography. **2,** lithograph. —**литогрáфский,** *adj.* lithographic.

литóй *adj.* (*of metals*) cast.

литорúна *n.* periwinkle (*mollusk*).

литосфéра *n.* lithosphere.

литр *n.* liter. —**литрóвый,** *adj.* with a capacity of one liter.

литургúя *n.* liturgy. —**литургúческий,** *adj.* liturgical.

лить *v. impfv.* [*pres.* **лью, льёшь;** *past fem.* **лилá**] **1,** to pour. **2,** to emit (sound, light, etc.). **3,** to shed (tears, blood, etc.). **4,** to cast; form; make. **5,** *v.i., colloq.* (*of liquids*) to flow; stream; run; (*of rain*) to come down.

литьё *n.* **1,** casting (*process*). **2,** castings.

лúться *v.r. impfv.* [*pres.* **льётся;** *past* **лúлся, лилáсь, лúлось** *or* **лилóсь, лúлись** *or* **лилúсь**] to flow; stream; pour.

лиф *n.* bodice.

лифт *n.* elevator.

лифтёр *n.* elevator operator. —**лифтёрша,** *n., colloq.* (female) elevator operator.

лúфчик *n.* underbodice.

лихáч [*gen.* **-хачá**] *n.* **1,** daredevil. **2,** reckless driver. **3,** *obs.* coachman (*equipped with a good horse and carriage*).

лихáчество *n.* recklessness; foolhardiness.

лихвá *n., obs.* interest (*on a loan*). —**с лихвóй,** with something to spare: окупáться с лихвóй, to more than pay for itself.

лúхо *n., colloq.* evil; misfortune. —*adv., colloq.* **1,** dashingly; jauntily. **2,** *colloq.* at a brisk pace. —**не поминáйте лúхом,** don't think badly of me. —**почём фунт лúха,** what misfortune is all about.

лихóй *adj.* **1,** *obs.* evil; hard. **2,** *colloq.* daring; dashing; jaunty. **3,** *colloq.* rapid; fast; brisk. **4,** *colloq.* deft.

лихорáдить *v. impfv., impers.* to have a fever: егó лихорáдит, he has a fever; he is feverish.

лихорáдка *n.* fever. —**лихорáдочный,** *adj.* feverish.

лúхость *n.f.* daring; audacity; bravado.

лúхтер *n., naut.* lighter.

лицевóй *adj.* **1,** facial. **2,** *in* лицевáя сторонá, the right side (*of material, a coin, etc.*). —**лицевáя рýкопись,** illuminated manuscript. —**лицевóй счёт,** personal account.

лицезрéть *v. impfv., obs.* to behold.

лицéй *n.* lycée.

лицемéр *n.* hypocrite. —**лицемéрие,** *n.* hypocrisy.

лицемéрить *v. impfv.* to be hypocritical; play the hypocrite.

лицемéрный *adj.* hypocritical.

лицéнзия *n.* (commercial) license.

лицó [*pl.* **лúца**] *n.* **1,** face. **2,** person; individual; personage. **3,** face; right side (*of an object, fabric, etc.*). **4,** *gram.* person. —**в лицé** (+ *gen.*), in the person of. —**в лицó** (+ *dat.*), to one's face. —**знать в лицó,** to know (someone) by sight. —**к лицý** (+ *dat.*), becoming: плáтье вам к лицý, the dress is becoming to you. —**лицóм к,** facing. —**лицóм квéрху,** face up; right side up. —**лицóм к лицý,** face to face. —**на нём (ней) нет лицá,** he (she) looks awful. —**на однó лицó,** all alike; exactly alike. —**от лицá** (+ *gen.*), on behalf of. —**пéред лицóм** (+ *gen.*), in the face of. —**показáть своё настоящее лицó,** to show one's true colors. —**показáть товáр лицóм,** to show something in its best light; put one's best foot forward. —**с лицá землú,** from the face of the earth. —**смотрéть** (+ *dat.*) **в лицó,** to face (squarely): смотрéть фáктам в лицó, to face facts.

лúчико *n., dim. of* **лицó.**

личúна *n.* mask.

личúнка *n.* **1,** larva. **2,** maggot. —**личúночный,** *adj.* larval.

лúчно *adv.* **1,** personally. **2,** in person.

личнóй *adj.* face (*attrib.*).

лúчность *n.f.* **1,** person; figure; individual; character. **2,** personality. **3,** identity. —**переходúть на лúчности,** to get personal.

лúчный *adj.* **1,** personal. **2,** private. —**лúчный состáв,** personnel; staff.

лишáй [*gen.* **-шая́**] *n.* **1,** [*also,* **лишáйник**] lichen. **2,** *med.* herpes. —**опоясывающий лишáй,** shingles. —**стригýщий лишáй,** ringworm.

лишáть *v. impfv.* [*pfv.* **лишúть**] (*with gen.*) to deprive (of); rob (of). —**лишáться,** *refl.* (*with gen.*) to be deprived (of); lose.

лишéние *n.* **1,** deprivation. **2,** *pl.* privations; hardships.

лишённый *adj.* (*with gen.*) devoid (of); void (of); lacking; without.

лишúть *v., pfv. of* **лишáть.** —**лишúться,** *refl., pfv. of* **лишáться.**

лúшнее *n., decl. as an adj.* too much: брать лúшнее, to overcharge. —**с лúшним,** *colloq.* a little over: три дóллара с лúшним, three dollars and change.

лúшний *adj.* **1,** superfluous; excess. **2,** spare; extra. —**лúшний раз,** once again; once more. —**не лúшнее,** worthwhile; not a bad idea.

лишь *adv.* only. —**лишь бы, 1,** if only. **2,** as long as. —**лишь тóлько,** as soon as.

лоб [*gen.* **лба;** *2nd loc.* **лбу**] *n.* forehead; brow. —**в лоб,** frontally; head-on. —**пустúть себé пýлю в лоб,** to blow one's brains out. —**что в лоб, что пó лбу,** it's as broad as it is long.

лóбби *n. neut. indecl., polit.* lobby. —**лоббúзм,** *n.* lobbying. —**лоббúст,** *n.* lobbyist.

лобзáть *v. impfv., archaic* to kiss.

лóбзик *n.* fret saw.

лóбный *adj., anat.* frontal. —**лóбное мéсто,** *hist.* place of execution (*in a public square*).

лобовóй *adj.* **1,** *mil.* frontal. **2,** front.

лоботрýс *n., colloq.* lazybones; loafer.

лобызáть *v. impfv.* =**лобзáть.**

лов *n.* catch (*of fish*).

ловелáс *n.* ladies' man.

ловéц [*gen.* **-вцá**] *n.* **1,** fisherman. **2,** hunter.

ловúть *v. impfv.* [*pfv.* **поймáть;** *pres.* **ловлю́, лó-**

вишь] **1,** to (try to) catch. **2,** *colloq.* to pick up (a radio signal). —**ловúть кáждое слóво,** to devour (*or* hang on) every word. —**ловúть на слóве,** to take at one's word. —**ловúть момéнт** *or* **слýчай,** to seize the opportunity. —**ловúть рыбу в мýтной водé,** to fish in troubled waters. —**ловúть себя на** (+ *prepl.*), to catch oneself doing something. —**ловúть чéй-нибудь взгляд,** to catch someone's eye.

ловкáч [*gen.* **-качá**] *n., colloq.* clever fellow.

лóвкий *adj.* [*short form* **лóвок, ловкá, лóвко;** *comp.* **лóвче**] **1,** adroit; deft. **2,** *colloq.* clever; shrewd.

лóвко *adv.* **1,** adroitly. **2,** *colloq.* well: лóвко сдéлано!, well done!

лóвкость *n.f.* **1,** adroitness; dexterity. **2,** *colloq.* ingenuity. —**лóвкость рук,** sleight of hand; legerdemain.

лóвля *n.* catching (*of fish*); trapping (*of animals*). —**рыбная лóвля,** fishing.

ловýшка [*gen. pl.* **-шек**] *n.* trap.

лóвчий *adj.* hunting (*attrib.*).

лог [*2nd loc.* **лóге** *or* **логý;** *pl.* **логá**] *n.* ravine.

логарúфм *n.* logarithm. —**логарифмúческий,** *adj.* logarithmic.

лóгик *n.* logician.

лóгика *n.* logic.

логúческий *adj.* logical. —**логúчески,** *adv.* logically.

логúчный *adj.* logical. —**логúчно,** *adv.* logically. —**логúчность,** *n.f.* logic.

лóговище *n.* lair; den. *Also,* **лóгово.**

логопéдия *n.* speech therapy. —**логопéд,** *n.* speech therapist.

лóдка [*gen. pl.* **-док**] *n.* boat. —**подвóдная лóдка,** submarine.

лóдочка [*gen. pl.* **-чек**] *n.* **1,** small boat. **2,** pump (*shoe*).

лóдочник *n.* boatman.

лóдочный *adj.* boat (*attrib.*); boating (*attrib.*).

лодыжка [*gen. pl.* **-жек**] *n.* ankle.

лóдырничать *v. impfv., colloq.* to loaf.

лóдырь *n.m., colloq.* loafer; idler.

лóжа *n.* **1,** *theat.* box. **2,** *obs.* (masonic) lodge. **3,** rifle stock.

ложбúна *n.* dale; glen.

лóже *n.* **1,** *archaic; poetic* bed. **2,** river bed.

лóжечка [*gen. pl.* **-чек**] *n., dim. of* **лóжка.** —**под лóжечкой,** in the pit of one's stomach.

ложúться *v.r. impfv.* [*pfv.* **лечь**] **1,** to lie down. **2,** (*of shadows, light, etc.*) to fall. **3,** (*with* **в** + *acc.*) to go into; enter (a hospital, clinic, etc.). **4,** *fig.* (*of responsibility, suspicion, etc.*) to lie; fall. —**лечь в могúлу** *or* **в гроб,** to die. —**лечь на курс,** (*of an aircraft or ship*) to embark (*or* set off) on a certain course. —**лечь/ложúться спать,** to go to sleep; go to bed.

лóжка [*gen. pl.* **-жек**] *n.* **1,** spoon. **2,** spoonful. **3,** ladle: разливáтельная лóжка, soup ladle. —**чéрез час по чáйной лóжке,** in dribs and drabs.

лóжно *adv.* **1,** falsely; wrongfully. **2,** incorrectly; wrongly.

лóжный *adj.* **1,** false. **2,** erroneous; fallacious. —**лóжность,** *n.f.* falsity.

ложь [*gen., dat., & prepl.* **лжи;** *instr.* **лóжью**] *n.f.* **1,** lie; falsehood. **2,** lying; lies.

лозá [*pl.* **лóзы**] *n.* **1,** vine: виногрáдная лозá, grapevine. **2,** twig: ѝвовая лозá, willow twig.

лозня́к [*gen.* **-някá**] *n.* willow shrub.

лóзунг *n.* slogan.

локализáция *n.* localization.

локализовáть *v. impfv. & pfv.* [*pres.* **-зýю, -зýешь**] to localize. —**локализовáться,** *refl.* to become localized.

локáльный *adj.* local.

локáтор *n.* locator; detector; radar.

локáут *n.* lockout.

локомотúв *n.* locomotive.

лóкон *n.* lock; curl.

лóкоть [*gen.* **лóктя;** *pl.* **лóкти, локтéй, локтя́м**] *n.m.* **1,** elbow. Толкнýть лóктем, to nudge. **2,** elbow (*of a garment*): потёртый на локтя́х, worn at the elbows. **3,** cubit (*ancient measure*). —**блúзок лóкоть, да не укýсишь,** so near and yet so far. —**чýвство лóктя,** feeling of comradeship.

локтевóй *adj.* elbow (*attrib.*). —**локтевáя кость,** funny bone.

лом *n.* **1,** [*pl.* **лóмы, ломóв, ломáм**] crowbar. **2,** scrap: желéзный лом, scrap iron.

ломáка *n.m. & f., colloq.* affected person.

лóманый *adj.* broken.

ломáть *v. impfv.* [*pfv.* **сломáть**] **1,** to break. **2,** to tear down. **3,** [*impfv. only*] to quarry. **4,** to break down (old beliefs or customs). **5,** [*pfv.* **поломáть**] to alter; transform. **6,** to ruin; wreck. —**ломáть себé гóлову,** to rack one's brains. —**ломáть себé рýки,** to wring one's hands.

ломáться *v.r. impfv.* [*pfv.* **сломáться**] **1,** to break. **2,** [*impfv. only*] to be breakable. **3,** [*impfv. only*] (*of one's voice*) to break; crack; (*of a young man's voice*) to change. **4,** (*of something well-established*) to break down; collapse; crumble. **5,** [*pfv.* **поломáться**] to be coy; put on airs.

ломбáрд *n.* pawnshop; hockshop. —**ломбáрдный,** *adj.* of or pert. to a pawnshop: ломбáрдная квитáнция, pawn ticket.

лóмберный *adj., in* **лóмберный стол,** card table.

ломúть *v. impfv.* [*pres.* **ломлю́, лóмишь**] **1,** *colloq.* to break. **2,** *impers.* to ache: у меня́ лóмит спúну, my back aches; I have a pain in my back. —**ломúться,** *refl.* **1,** to break; snap. **2,** (*with* **от**) to be loaded (with); be weighed down (with). **3,** (*with* **в** + *acc.*) *colloq.* to break through; force one's way into. **4,** *in* **ломúться в открытую дверь,** to belabor the obvious.

лóмка *n.* breaking; breakup.

лóмкий *adj.* fragile; brittle. —**лóмкость,** *n.f.* fragility.

ломовúк [*gen.* **-викá**] *n., colloq.* carter.

ломовóй *adj.* dray (*attrib.*): ломовáя лóшадь, dray horse. —*n.* [*also,* **ломовóй извóзчик**] carter.

ломонóс *n.* clematis.

ломóта *n.* dull ache (*in the joints, muscles, etc.*).

ломóть [*gen.* **-мтя́**] *n.m.* hunk; chunk (*of bread, meat, etc.*).

лóмтик *n.* slice.

лонжерóн *n., aero.* spar.

лóно *n., poetic* **1,** bosom. **2,** lap: на лóне прирóды, in the lap of nature.

лóпасть [*pl.* **лóпасти, -стéй, -стя́м**] *n.f.* blade (*of an oar, propeller, etc.*).

лопáта *n.* shovel.

лопáтка [*gen. pl.* **-ток**] *n.* **1,** small shovel; trowel. **2,** blade. **3,** shoulder blade. **4,** chuck (*cut of beef*). —**бежáть во все лопáтки,** *colloq.* to run for all one is worth. —**положúть на óбе лопáтки, 1,** *wrestling* to pin down. **2,** *fig.* to beat; get the best (*or* better) of.

ло́пать *v. impfv.* [*pfv.* **сло́пать**] *colloq.* to eat; gobble.
ло́паться *v.r. impfv.* [*pfv.* **ло́пнуть**] **1,** to burst; break; snap. **2,** (*of one's patience*) to be at an end. **3,** *colloq.* to fail; go broke.
лопота́ть *v. impfv.* [*pres.* **-почу́, -по́чешь**] *colloq.* to mumble; mutter.
лопоу́хий *adj., colloq.* lop-eared.
лопу́х [*gen.* **-пуха́**] *n.* burdock.
лорд *n.* lord.
лорне́т *n.* lorgnette.
лоси́на *n.* **1,** elk skin. **2,** elk meat. **3,** *pl.* buckskin breeches.
лоси́ный *adj.* **1,** elk (*attrib.*); elk's. **2,** made of elk skin.
лоск *n.* luster; gloss; sheen.
лоску́т [*gen.* **-кута́**; *pl.* **-куты́, -куто́в** *or* **-ку́тья, -ку́тьев**] *n.* shred; scrap of cloth.
лоску́тный *adj.* made of patches; patchwork (*attrib.*): лоску́тное одея́ло, patchwork quilt.
лосни́ться *v.r. impfv.* to be glossy; shine.
лососёвый *adj.* salmon (*attrib.*).
лососи́на *n.* salmon (*prepared as food*).
лосо́сь *also,* **ло́сось** *n.m.* salmon.
лось [*pl.* **ло́си, -се́й, -ся́м**] *n.m.* elk; moose.
лосьо́н *n.* face lotion.
лот *n.* **1,** *naut.* plumb line. **2,** old Russian unit of weight equal to 12.8 grams.
лотере́я *n.* lottery; raffle. —**лотере́йный,** *adj.* lottery (*attrib.*).
лото́ *n. indecl.* lotto; bingo.
лото́к [*gen.* **-тка́**] *n.* **1,** tray (*of a street peddler*). **2,** chute: ме́льничный лото́к, millrace.
ло́тос *n.* lotus.
лото́чник *n.* street vendor.
лоха́нь *n.f.* washtub. *Also,* **лоха́нка.**
лохма́тый *adj.* **1,** shaggy. **2,** disheveled.
лохмо́тья [*gen.* **-тьев**] *n. pl.* tatters.
ло́ция *n.* book of navigational information for a certain body of water.
ло́цман *n.* **1,** harbor pilot. **2,** pilot fish.
лошади́ный *adj.* horse (*attrib.*). —**лошади́ная си́ла,** horsepower.
лоша́дка [*gen. pl.* **-док**] *n., dim. of* **ло́шадь.**
ло́шадь [*pl.* **ло́шади, -де́й, -дя́м, -дьми́, -дя́х**] *n.f.* horse.
лоша́к [*gen.* **-шака́**] *n.* hinny.
лощёный *adj.* **1,** glossy. **2,** *fig.* polished.
лощи́на *n.* dale; glen.
лощи́ть *v. impfv.* [*pfv.* **налощи́ть**] to buff; polish.
лоя́льный *adj.* loyal. —**лоя́льность,** *n.f.* loyalty.
луб *n.* bast.
лубо́к [*gen.* **-бка́**] *n.* **1,** strip of bast. **2,** splint. **3,** wood block; woodcut.
лубяно́й *adj.* bast (*attrib.*).
луг [*2nd loc.* **лугу́**; *pl.* **луга́**] *n.* meadow.
лугови́на *n., colloq.* small meadow.
лугово́й *adj.* meadow (*attrib.*).
луди́льщик *n.* tinsmith.
луди́ть *v. impfv.* [*pfv.* **полуди́ть**; *pres.* **лужу́, лу́дишь** *or* **луди́шь**] to tin; tin-plate.
лу́жа *n.* puddle. —**сесть в лу́жу,** *colloq.* to make a fool of oneself; put one's foot in it.
лужа́йка [*gen. pl.* **-а́ек**] *n.* **1,** clearing (*in a forest*). **2,** lawn.
лужёный *adj.* tin-plated. —**лужёный желу́док,** cast-iron stomach.
лу́жица *n., dim. of* **лу́жа.**
лужо́к [*gen.* **-жка́**] *n., dim. of* **луг.**
лу́за *n.* pocket (*of a billiard table*). —**лу́зный,** *adj., in* **лу́зный бильярд,** pocket billiards.
луизиа́нский мох Spanish moss.
лук *n.* **1,** onions. **2,** bow (*for shooting arrows*). —**лук-поре́й,** leek.
лука́ [*pl.* **лу́ки**] *n.* **1,** bend (*in a road or river*). **2,** pommel (*of a saddle*).
лука́вить *v. impfv.* [*pres.* **-влю, -вишь**] to be cunning.
лука́вство *n.* cunning.
лука́вый *adj.* cunning; sly; crafty.
лу́ковица *n.* **1,** an onion. **2,** *bot.* bulb. **3,** onion dome (*of a Russian church*). —**лу́ковичный,** *adj.* bulbous.
лу́ковый *adj.* onion (*attrib.*).
луна́ [*pl.* **лу́ны**] *n.* moon.
лу́на-па́рк *n.* amusement park.
луна́-ры́ба [*pl.* **луны́-ры́бы**] *n.* sunfish.
лунати́зм *n.* sleepwalking; somnambulism. —**луна́тик,** *n.* sleepwalker; somnambulist.
лу́нка [*gen. pl.* **-нок**] *n.* **1,** small hole. **2,** alveolus.
лу́нный *adj.* **1,** moon (*attrib.*); lunar. **2,** moonlit.
лунь [*gen.* **луня́**] *n.m.* harrier (*bird*).
лу́па *n.* magnifying glass.
лупи́ть *v. impfv.* [*pres.* **луплю́, лу́пишь**] *colloq.* **1,** [*pfv.* **облупи́ть** *or* **слупи́ть**] to peel off. **2,** [*pfv.* **слупи́ть**] to charge (an exorbitant price). **3,** [*pfv.* **отлупи́ть**] to beat; thrash. —**лупи́ться,** *refl.* [*pfv.* **облупи́ться**] *colloq.* **1,** to peel off; come off. **2,** (*of one's face*) to peel.
луфа́рь [*gen.* **-фаря́**] *n.m.* bluefish.
луч [*gen.* **луча́**] *n.* ray; beam.
лучево́й *adj.* radial. —**лучева́я боле́знь,** radiation sickness.
лучеза́рный *adj.* radiant; effulgent.
лучеиспуска́ние *n.* radiation.
лучи́на *n.* thin stick; sliver (*of kindling wood*).
лучи́стый *adj.* radiant.
лучи́ться *v.r. impfv.* **1,** to shine; sparkle. **2,** *fig.* (*with instr.*) to radiate.
лучко́вый *adj., in* **лучко́вая пила́,** whipsaw.
лу́чше *adj. & adv., comp. of* **хоро́ший** *and* **хорошо́,** better. —**лу́чше всего́,** best of all. —**тем лу́чше,** so much the better.
лу́чшее *n., decl. as an adj.* something better: я ожида́л лу́чшего, I expected something better. —**жела́ю вам всего́ (са́мого) лу́чшего,** I wish you all the best. —**оставля́ть жела́ть мно́го лу́чшего,** to leave much to be desired. —**переме́на к лу́чшему,** change for the better.
лу́чший *adj., used only as a modifier, comp. and superl. of* **хоро́ший** **1,** (a) better. **2,** (the) best. —**в лу́чшем слу́чае,** at best. —**измени́ться в лу́чшую сто́рону,** to change for the better.
лущи́ть *v. impfv.* [*pfv.* **облущи́ть**] to shell; husk; hull.
лы́жа *n.* ski. —**лы́жник,** *n.* skier. —**лы́жный,** *adj.* ski (*attrib.*); skiing (*attrib.*).
лыжня́ [*gen. pl.* **-не́й**] *n.* track left by skis.
лы́ко *n.* bast. —**не лы́ком шит,** *colloq.* no slouch.
лы́ковый *adj.* made of bast.
лысе́ть *v. impfv.* [*pfv.* **облысе́ть** *or* **полысе́ть**] to become bald.
лы́сина *n.* bald spot.
лысу́ха *n.* coot.
лы́сый *adj.* bald.

ль *conj.* = **ли.**
львёнок [*gen.* **-нка;** *pl.* **львя́та, львят**] *n.* lion cub.
льви́ный *adj.* lion's. —**льви́ная до́ля,** the lion's share. —**льви́ный зев; льви́ная пасть,** snapdragon.
льви́ца *n.* lioness.
льго́та *n.* privilege; benefit.
льго́тный *adj.* **1,** favorable; preferential: на льго́тных усло́виях, on favorable terms. **2,** (*of a price, fare, etc.*) reduced; (*of a ticket*) cut-rate. —**льго́тный срок,** grace period. Три́дцать льго́тных дней, 30-day grace period.
льди́на *n.* block of ice. —**плаву́чая льди́на,** ice field.
льнуть *v. impfv.* [*pfv.* **прильну́ть**] (*with* **к**) **1,** to cling (to). **2,** [*impfv. only*] *fig.* to feel drawn toward.
льняно́й *adj.* **1,** flax (*attrib.*). **2,** linen (*attrib.*). **3,** (*of hair*) flaxen. —**льняно́е ма́сло,** linseed oil.
льстец [*gen.* **льстеца́**] *n.* flatterer.
льсти́вый *adj.* flattering; ingratiating.
льстить *v. impfv.* [*pfv.* **польсти́ть;** *pres.* **льщу, льстишь**] (*with dat.*) to flatter.
любвеоби́льный *adj.* loving; full of love.
любе́зничать *v. impfv.* (*with* **с** + *instr.*) *colloq.* to exchange pleasantries with; say nice things to.
любе́зно *adv.* kindly; graciously. —*adj., used predicatively* kind; gracious: о́чень любе́зно с ва́шей стороны́, very kind/gracious of you.
любе́зность *n.f.* **1,** courtesy; graciousness. **2,** *pl.* kind words; compliments. **3,** favor; kindness; good turn.
любе́зный *adj.* [*short form* **-зен, -зна**] kind; gracious. —**бу́дьте любе́зны** (+ *imperative*), be so kind as to...
люби́мец [*gen.* **-мца**] *n.m.* [*fem.* **-мица**] favorite; pet.
люби́мчик *n., colloq.* favorite; pet.
люби́мый *adj.* **1,** loved. **2,** favorite; pet.
люби́тель *n.m.* **1,** lover: люби́тель му́зыки, music lover. **2,** amateur; dilettante. —**люби́тельский,** *adj.* amateur.
люби́ть *v. impfv.* [*pres.* **люблю́, лю́бишь**] **1,** to love. **2,** to like; be fond of.
лю́бо *predicate, used with inf., colloq.* it is a pleasure (to).
любова́ться *v.r. impfv.* [*pfv.* **полюбова́ться;** *pres.* **-бу́юсь, -бу́ешься**] (*with instr. or* **на** + *acc.*) to admire; watch with pleasure.
любо́вник *n.* lover; paramour.
любо́вница *n.* lover; mistress.
любо́вный *adj.* **1,** love (*attrib.*). **2,** loving; tender. **3,** amorous. —**любо́вно,** *adv.* lovingly.
любо́вь [*gen., dat., & prepl.* **любви́;** *instr.* **любо́вью**] *n.f.* love.
любозна́тельный *adj.* curious; inquisitive; thirsty for knowledge. —**любозна́тельность,** *n.f.* (intellectual) curiosity; inquisitiveness.
любо́й *adj.* **1,** any. **2,** either. —*n.* **1,** anyone; anybody. **2,** either one. —**в любо́м слу́чае,** in either case; either way.
любопы́тно *adv.* curiously; with curiosity. —*adj., used predicatively* curious: мне любопы́тно знать, куда́ они́ пое́хали, I am curious to know where they went.
любопы́тный *adj.* curious. —**любопы́тство,** *n.* curiosity.
любопы́тствовать *v. impfv.* [*pfv.* **полюбопы́тствовать;** *pres.* **-ствую, -ствуешь**] to be curious.
лю́бящий *adj.* loving.
люд *n., colloq.* people.
лю́ди [*gen.* **люде́й;** *dat.* **лю́дям;** *instr.* **людьми́;** *prepl.* **лю́дях**] *n. pl.* people. —**вы́вести в лю́ди,** to put (someone) on his feet. —**вы́йти** *or* **вы́биться в лю́ди,** to make one's way in the world. —**на лю́дях,** in public.
лю́дный *adj.* **1,** populous. **2,** crowded.
людое́д *n.* cannibal. —**людое́дский,** *adj.* cannibalistic. —**людое́дство,** *n.* cannibalism.
людска́я *n., decl. as an adj.* servants' quarters.
людско́й *adj.* human.
люк *n.* hatch; manhole; trap door. —**светово́й люк,** skylight.
люкс *adj. indecl.* de luxe: гости́ница-люкс, de luxe hotel.
лю́лька [*gen. pl.* **-лек**] *n.* cradle.
люмба́го *n. indecl.* lumbago.
люмина́л *n.* phenobarbital.
люминесце́нтный *adj.* luminescent. —**люминесце́нтная ла́мпа,** fluorescent lamp.
люминесце́нция *n.* luminescence.
лю́стра *n.* chandelier.
лютера́нин [*pl.* **-ра́не, -ра́н**] *n.m.* [*fem.* **-ра́нка**] Lutheran. —**лютера́нский,** *adj.* Lutheran. —**лютера́нство,** *n.* Lutheranism.
люте́ций (тэ) *n.* lutetium.
лю́тик *n.* buttercup.
лю́тня [*gen. pl.* **-тен**] *n.* lute.
лю́тый *adj.* **1,** fierce; ferocious. **2,** (*of cold, hatred, etc.*) bitter. **3,** (*of pain*) excruciating. —**лю́тость,** *n.f.* ferocity.
люце́рна *n.* alfalfa.
ля *n. neut., music* la; A.
ляга́ть *v. impfv.* [*pfv.* **лягну́ть**] (*of a horse*) to kick. *Also,* **ляга́ться** [*impfv. only*].
лягу́шечий *also,* **лягуша́чий** [*fem.* **-чья**] *adj.* frog's; frogs'.
лягу́шка [*gen. pl.* **-шек**] *n.* frog.
ля́жка [*gen. pl.* **-жек**] *n., colloq.* thigh; haunch.
лязг *n.* clang; clank.
ля́згать *v. impfv.* [*pfv.* **ля́згнуть**] **1,** to clang; clank; make a clanking sound. **2,** (*with instr.*) to rattle; clank.
лякро́сс *n.* lacrosse.
ля́мка [*gen. pl.* **-мок**] *n.* shoulder strap. —**тяну́ть ля́мку,** *colloq.* to slave; toil.
ля́пис *n.* silver nitrate.
ля́пис-лазу́рь *n.f.* lapis-lazuli.
ля́пнуть *v. pfv., colloq.* to blurt out.
ля́псус *n.* blunder.

M

М, м *n. neut.* thirteenth letter of the Russian alphabet.
мавзоле́й *n.* mausoleum.
мавр *n.* Moor. —**маврита́нский,** *adj.* Moorish.
маг *n.* magician; wizard.
магази́н *n.* **1,** store; shop. **2,** magazine (*of a firearm, camera, etc.*).
магази́нный *adj.* **1,** store (*attrib.*); shop (*attrib.*). **2,** *mil.* magazine (*attrib.*). —**магази́нная винто́вка,** repeating rifle. —**магази́нный вор,** shoplifter.
магара́джа *n.m.* maharajah.
маги́стр *n.* **1,** holder of a master's degree. **2,** master's degree. **3,** grandmaster (*of a monastic or knightly order*).
магистра́ль *n.f.* **1,** highway; thoroughfare. **2,** *R.R.* main line. **3,** main: га́зовая магистра́ль, gas main. —**магистра́льный,** *adj.* main; arterial.
магистра́т *n.* city council. —**магистрату́ра,** *n.* magistracy.
маги́ческий *adj.* magic; magical.
ма́гия *n.* magic.
магна́т *n.* magnate; tycoon.
магне́зия *n.* magnesia.
магнети́зм *n.* **1,** magnetism. **2,** magnetics.
магнети́т *n.* magnetite.
магнети́ческий *adj.* magnetic.
магне́то *n. indecl.* magneto.
магнетро́н *n.* magnetron.
ма́гниевый *adj.* magnesium (*attrib.*).
ма́гний *n.* magnesium.
магни́т *n.* magnet. —**магни́тный,** *adj.* magnetic.
магнитофо́н *n.* tape recorder. —**магнитофо́нный,** *adj.* of a tape recorder: магнитофо́нная за́пись, tape recording.
магно́лия *n.* magnolia.
магомета́нин [*pl.* **-та́не, -та́н**] *n.m.* [*fem.* **-та́нка**] Mohammedan. —**магомета́нский,** *adj.* Mohammedan. —**магомета́нство,** *n.* Mohammedanism.
мада́м *n.f. indecl.* madam.
мадемуазе́ль (дмуазэ) *n.f. indecl.* mademoiselle.
маде́ра *n.* Madeira wine.
мадо́нна *n.* madonna.
мадрига́л *n.* madrigal.
мадья́р *n.m.* [*fem.* **-ка**] Magyar. —**мадья́рский,** *adj.* Magyar.
маёвка [*gen. pl.* **-вок**] *n.* **1,** illegal May-day meeting (*in pre-rev. Russia*). **2,** spring outing; picnic.
мажо́р *n.* **1,** *music* major key: тона́льность до мажо́р, key of C major. **2,** *colloq.* good/high spirits.
мажордо́м *n.* majordomo.
мажо́рный *adj.* **1,** *music* major. **2,** *fig.* buoyant; exuberant.
ма́занка [*gen. pl.* **-нок**] *n.* clay-walled hut.
ма́зать *v. impfv.* [*pres.* **ма́жу, ма́жешь**] **1,** [*pfv.* **нама́зать** *or* **пома́зать**] (*with instr.*) to smear (with): ма́зать хлеб ма́слом, to smear butter on bread; butter one's bread. **2,** [*pfv.* **вы́мазать**] (*with instr.*) to coat (with): ма́зать сте́ны кра́ской, to paint the walls. **3,** [*pfv.* **нама́зать**] *colloq.* to paint (one's lips); put make-up on (one's face). **4,** [*pfv.* **вы́мазать**] *colloq.* to soil. **5,** [*pfv.* **нама́зать**] *colloq.* to paint poorly; daub. **6,** [*pfv.* **прома́зать**] *colloq.* to miss (*in shooting or games*). —**ма́заться,** *refl.* **1,** [*pfv.* **нама́заться**] to put on make-up; (*with instr.*) put on (salve, make-up, etc.). **2,** [*pfv.* **вы́мазаться**] *colloq.* to soil; get dirty.
мазня́ *n., colloq.* poor painting.
мазо́к [*gen.* **-зка́**] *n.* **1,** dab; stroke (*with a paintbrush*). **2,** *med.* smear.
мазохи́зм *n.* masochism. —**мазохи́ст,** *n.* masochist. —**мазохи́стский,** *adj.* masochistic.
мазу́рка *n.* mazurka.
мазу́т *n.* fuel oil.
мазь *n.f.* **1,** ointment. **2,** grease. **3,** *in* сапо́жная мазь, shoe polish. —**де́ло на мази́,** *colloq.* things are moving right along.
маис *n.* maize.
май *n.* May.
ма́йка [*gen. pl.* **ма́ек**] *n.* T-shirt.
майоне́з *n.* mayonnaise.
майо́р *n.* major.
майора́н *n.* marjoram.
майо́рский *adj.* major's.
ма́йский *adj.* May (*attrib.*).
мак *n.* **1,** poppy. **2,** poppy seeds.
мака́ка *n.* macaque.
макаро́ны [*gen.* **-ро́н**] *n. pl.* macaroni.
мака́ть *v. impfv.* [*pfv.* **макну́ть**] to dip; dunk.
македо́нский *adj.* Macedonian.
маке́т *n.* **1,** model; mock-up. **2,** *printing* dummy.
макиаве́ллевский *adj.* Machiavellian.
макинто́ш *n.* mackintosh.
ма́клер *n.* stockbroker. —**ма́клерский,** *adj.* of a broker; brokerage (*attrib.*). —**ма́клерство,** *n.* brokerage.
макну́ть *v., pfv. of* **мака́ть.**
ма́ковка [*gen. pl.* **-вок**] *n.* **1,** poppy head. **2,** dome; cupola (*of a church*). **3,** *colloq.* top.
ма́ковый *adj.* poppy (*attrib.*).
макре́ль *n.f.* mackerel.

макрокосм *n.* macrocosm.
максимальный *adj.* maximum. —**максимально,** *adv.* to the maximum.
максимум *n.* maximum. —*adv.* a maximum of; at (the) most.
макулатура *n.* **1,** pages spoiled in printing. **2,** literary trash.
макушка [*gen. pl.* **-шек**] *n.* **1,** top. **2,** crown of the head.
малага *n.* Malaga wine.
малаец [*gen.* **-айца**] *n.m.* [*fem.* **-айка**] Malay. —**малайский,** *adj.* Malay.
малахит *n.* malachite. —**малахитовый,** *adj.* malachite.
малевать *v. impfv.* [*pfv.* **намалевать;** *pres.* **малюю, малюешь**] *colloq.* to paint.
малейший *adj., superl. of* **малый,** the least; the slightest; the faintest. —**ни в малейшей степени,** not in the least.
малёк [*gen.* **-лька**] *n.* young fish; newly-hatched fish.
маленький *adj.* [*comp.* **меньше**] little; small. —*n.* the little one; the baby. *See also* **меньше.**
маленько *adv., colloq.* a little; a bit; somewhat.
малина *n.* **1,** raspberries. **2,** a (single) raspberry.
малиновка [*gen. pl.* **-вок**] *n.* robin (redbreast).
малиновый *adj.* **1,** raspberry (*attrib.*). **2,** crimson.
мало *adv.* **1,** little; not much: мало сделать, to do little; not do much; мало времени, little time; not much time. **2,** few; not many: мало народу, few people; not many people. **3,** hardly: мало кто, hardly anyone; мало что, hardly anything. **4,** (*with* **ли**) many; lots of; all kinds of: мало ли что, all kinds of things; anything. —**мало (ли) что** (+ *past tense verb*), what of it!; what if I (you, *etc.*) did...? —**мало того,** moreover. —**мало того, что...,** not only...; it is not enough that...
маловажный *adj.* of little importance; of little significance.
маловато *adv., colloq.* not quite enough.
маловер *n.* skeptic.
маловероятный *adj.* not likely; unlikely; improbable. —**маловероятность,** *n.f.* unlikelihood.
маловодный *adj.* **1,** shallow. **2,** arid.
маловодье *n.* **1,** shortage of water. **2,** low level of water (*in a river, lake, etc.*).
малогабаритный *adj.* small-size; compact.
малограмотный *adj.* semiliterate.
малодоступный *adj.* **1,** inaccessible. **2,** *fig.* esoteric.
малодушие *n.* faintheartedness; cowardice. —**малодушный,** *adj.* fainthearted; craven; cowardly.
малозаметный *adj.* **1,** hardly noticeable. **2,** ordinary; undistinguished.
малознакомый *adj.* unfamiliar.
малоизвестный *adj.* little-known.
малоинтересный *adj.* of little interest; uninteresting.
малокровие *n.* anemia. —**малокровный,** *adj.* anemic.
малолетний *adj.* underage. —*n.* juvenile. —**малолетство,** *n., colloq.* childhood.
малолитражный *adj.* fuel-efficient.
малолюдный *adj.* **1,** sparsely populated. **2,** with few people to be seen. **3,** (*of a meeting*) poorly attended.
мало-мальски *adv., colloq.* the least bit; the slightest bit: каждый, кто мало-мальски знаком с..., anyone who is the least acquainted with...
маломощный *adj.* not powerful; low-powered.
малонадёжный *adj.* not very reliable.
малонаселённый *adj.* sparsely populated.
мало-помалу *adv., colloq.* little by little; bit by bit.
малопонятный *adj.* difficult to understand.
малоприбыльный *adj.* showing little profit.
малоразвитый *adj.* **1,** undeveloped; underdeveloped. **2,** limited (*in intellect*).
малорослый *adj.* undersized.
малосведущий *adj.* poorly informed.
малосемейный *adj.* having a small family.
малосильный *adj.* **1,** weak. **2,** low-powered.
малосодержательный *adj.* containing little of interest; lacking substance.
малосольный *adj.* lightly salted.
малость *n.f.* **1,** *obs.* small size. **2,** tiny bit. **3,** *colloq.* trifle. —*adv., colloq.* a little; a bit.
малотиражный *adj.* **1,** having a small circulation. **2,** (*of an edition*) limited.
малоупотребительный *adj.* little used; rarely used.
малоценный *adj.* of little value.
малочисленный *adj.* small in number; not numerous. —**малочисленность,** *n.f.* small number.
малый *adj.* **1,** small. **2,** [*short form only* — **мал, мала, мало, малы**] (too) small: ботинки мне малы, the shoes are too small for me. —*n.* **1,** *colloq.* fellow; chap; guy: добрый малый, a decent fellow. **2,** *neut.* little: довольствоваться малым, to be satisfied with little. **3,** *pl.* little ones; children. —**без мала; без малого,** *colloq.* almost, nearly. —**за малым дело стало,** only one small matter is holding things up. —**от мала до велика,** young and old alike. —**самое малое, 1,** the least. **2,** at (the) least. —**с малых лет,** since childhood.
малыш [*gen.* **-лыша**] *n.* small child; tot.
мальва *n.* mallow.
мальтоза *n.* maltose.
мальчик *n.* boy.
мальчишеский *adj.* **1,** boy's. **2,** childish. —**мальчишество,** *n.* childish behavior.
мальчишка [*gen. pl.* **-шек**] *n.m., colloq.* (little) boy.
мальчуган *n., colloq.* little boy; little fellow.
малюсенький *adj., colloq.* tiny; wee; minuscule.
малютка [*gen. pl.* **-ток**] *n.m. & f.* little one.
маляр [*gen.* **-яра**] *n.* house painter.
малярийный *adj.* malarial.
малярия *n.* malaria.
малярный *adj.* painting (*attrib.*); paint (*attrib.*). —**малярная кисть,** paintbrush. —**малярный цех,** paint shop (*in a factory*).
мама *n.* mama; mommy.
мамалыга *n.* hominy.
мамаша *n., colloq.* = **мама.**
маменька *n., obs.* = **мама.**
маменькин *adj., colloq.* mother's. —**маменькин сынок,** mother's boy; mama's boy.
мамин *adj.* mother's.
мамонт *n.* mammoth.
мамочка *n.* mother dear.
манатки [*gen.* **-ток**] *n. pl., colloq.* (one's) things; belongings.
манганит *n.* manganite.
манго *n. indecl.* **1,** mango. **2,** mango tree.
мангуста *n.* mongoose.
мандарин *n.* **1,** tangerine; mandarin. **2,** mandarin (*Chinese official*). —**мандаринный; мандариновый,**

adj. tangerine (*attrib.*). —**мандари́нский,** *adj.* Mandarin: мандари́нский язы́к, Mandarin.
мандáт *n.* **1,** mandate. **2,** warrant.
мандáтный *adj.* mandate (*attrib.*); mandated. —**мандáтная коми́ссия,** credentials committee.
мандоли́на *n.* mandolin.
мандрагóра *n.* mandrake.
мандри́л *n.* mandrill.
манёвр *n.* maneuver.
манёвренный *adj.* **1,** *mil.* mobile: манёвренная войнá, mobile warfare. **2,** maneuverable. —**манёвренность,** *n.f.* mobility; maneuverability.
маневри́ровать *v. impfv.* [*pres.* **-рую, -руешь**] **1,** to maneuver. **2,** *fig.* (*with instr.*) to manipulate.
манéж *n.* **1,** riding academy; riding school. **2,** circus arena; ring. **3,** playpen.
манекéн *n.* mannequin; dummy.
манекéнщик *n.m.* [*fem.* **-щица**] model.
манéр *n., colloq.* manner; way. —**на манéр** (+ *gen.*), in the manner of. На рýсский манéр, in the Russian manner; Russian-style.
манéра *n.* **1,** manner. **2,** *pl.* manners.
манéрный *adj.* affected; mannered. —**манéрность,** *n.f.* affectation.
манжéта *n.* cuff.
маниакáльный *adj.* maniacal; manic. —**маниакáльно-депресси́вный,** *adj.* manic-depressive.
маникю́р *n.* manicure. —**маникю́рный,** *adj.* manicure (*attrib.*). —**маникю́рша,** *n.* manicurist.
маниóка *n.* manioc; cassava.
манипули́ровать *v. impfv.* [*pres.* **-рую, -руешь**] (*with instr.*) to manipulate.
манипуля́тор *n.* manipulator.
манипуля́ция *n.* manipulation.
мани́ть *v. impfv.* [*pfv.* **помани́ть;** *pres.* **маню́, мáнишь**] **1,** to beckon. **2,** *fig.* to draw; attract: егó мáнит мóре, he feels drawn to the sea.
манифéст *n.* manifesto.
манифестáция *n.* demonstration; march.
мани́шка [*gen. pl.* **-шек**] *n.* shirt front; dickey.
мáния *n.* mania. —**мáния вели́чия,** delusions of grandeur; megalomania. —**мáния преслéдования,** persecution complex.
манки́ровать *v. impfv. & pfv.* [*pres.* **-рую, -руешь**] **1,** (*with instr.*) to neglect. **2,** *obs.* to be absent.
мáнна *n.* manna.
мáнный *adj.* **1,** *in* **мáнная крупá,** farina. **2,** *in* **мáнная кáша,** cereal made from farina.
мановéние *n., obs.* wave (*of the hand*); nod (*of the head*). —**как по мановéнию волшéбного жезлá,** instantly; as if by magic.
манóметр *n.* pressure gauge; manometer. —**манометри́ческий,** *adj.* manometric.
мансáрда *n.* garret.
мансáрдный *adj.* of a garret; garret (*attrib.*). —**мансáрдная кры́ша,** mansard roof.
манти́лья *n.* mantilla.
мáнтия *n.* mantle; cloak; robe; gown.
мантó *n. indecl.* (woman's) fur coat.
мануфактýра *n.* **1,** *hist.* manufacturing. **2,** *obs.* textile mill. **3,** textiles; soft goods.
мануфактýрный *adj.* **1,** manufacturing (*attrib.*). **2,** textile (*attrib.*); soft-goods (*attrib.*).
маньчжýр *n.* Manchu. —**маньчжýрский,** *adj.* Manchu.
манья́к *n.* maniac.
маня́щий *adj.* alluring.
марабý *n.m. indecl.* marabou.
марáзм *n.* marasmus.
марáл *n.* a variety of red deer; maral.
марáнье *n., colloq.* **1,** soiling. **2,** scribble; scrawl.
мараски́н *n.* maraschino.
марáть *v. impfv., colloq.* **1,** [*pfv.* **замарáть**] to soil; dirty. **2,** [*pfv.* **намарáть**] to scribble. **3,** [*pfv.* **вымарать**] to cross out. —**марáться,** *refl.* [*pfv.* **замарáться**] *colloq.* to get oneself dirty.
марафóнский *adj., in* **марафóнский бег,** marathon (race).
мáрганец [*gen.* **-нца**] *n.* manganese. —**мáрганцевый,** *adj.* manganese (*attrib.*).
маргари́н *n.* margarine.
маргари́тка [*gen. pl.* **-ток**] *n.* daisy; English daisy.
маргинáлии *n. pl.* [*sing.* **маргинáлия**] marginalia.
мáрево *n.* **1,** mirage. **2,** haze.
марéна *n.* madder (*plant*).
мари́ец [*gen.* **-и́йца**] *n.m.* [*fem.* **-и́йка**] *n.* Mari (*one of a people inhabiting central European Russia*). —**мари́йский,** *adj.* Mari.
мари́на *n.* seascape.
маринáд *n.* marinade.
марини́ст *n.* painter of seascapes.
маринóванный *adj.* pickled; marinated.
мариновáть *v. impfv.* [*pfv.* **замариновáть;** *pres.* **-нýю, -нýешь**] **1,** to pickle; marinate. **2,** *colloq.* to delay; shelve; put off.
марионéтка [*gen. pl.* **-ток**] *n.* **1,** puppet; marionette. **2,** *fig.* puppet. —**марионéточный,** *adj., fig.* puppet (*attrib.*): марионéточное прави́тельство, puppet government.
марихуáна *n.* marijuana.
мáрка [*gen. pl.* **-рок**] *n.* **1,** (postage) stamp. **2,** make; model; brand. **3,** mark: фабри́чная мáрка, trademark. **4,** counter; token (*used as payment*). **5,** chip (*used in games*). **6,** mark (*German monetary unit*). **7,** *fig.* reputation: держáть мáрку, to uphold one's reputation. —**всех мáрок,** of every stamp. —**вы́сшей мáрки, 1,** of the highest quality. **2,** (*of a type of person*) of the worst type. —**под мáркой** (+ *gen.*), under the guise of.
марки́з *n.* marquis.
марки́за *n.* **1,** marquise; marchioness. **2,** sun blind.
мáркий *adj.* [*short form* **мáрок, -рка, -рко**] that soils easily.
маркировáть *v. impfv. & pfv.* [*pres.* **-рýю, -рýешь**] to mark.
маркси́зм *n.* Marxism. —**маркси́ст,** *n.* Marxist. —**маркси́стский,** *adj.* Marxist; Marxian.
мáрля *n.* gauze. —**мáрлевый,** *adj.* gauze (*attrib.*).
мармелáд *n.* fruit jellies (*candy*).
мародёр *n.* **1,** marauder. **2,** *colloq.* profiteer. —**мародёрский,** *adj.* marauding. —**мародёрство,** *n.* marauding.
мародёрствовать *v. impfv.* [*pres.* **-ствую, -ствуешь**] to maraud.
мáрочный *adj., in* **мáрочные ви́на,** fine wines; vintage wines.
Марс *n.* Mars.
марсалá *n.* Marsala wine.
мáрсель *n.m.* topsail.
Марсельéза *n.* Marseillaise.

марсиа́нин [*pl.* **-а́не, -а́н**] *n.* Martian. —**марсиа́нский,** *adj.* Martian.
март *n.* March (*month*).
марте́н (тэ) *n.* open-hearth furnace. —**марте́новский,** *adj.* open-hearth (*attrib.*): марте́новская печь, open-hearth furnace.
ма́ртовский *adj.* March (*attrib.*).
марты́шка [*gen. pl.* **-шек**] *n.* marmoset.
марципа́н *n.* marchpane; marzipan.
марш *n.* **1,** march. **2,** (*as a military command*) forward, march! **3,** flight of stairs.
ма́ршал *n.* marshal. —**ма́ршальский,** *adj.* marshal's.
марширова́ть *v. impfv.* [*pres.* **-ру́ю, -ру́ешь**] to march.
марширо́вка *n.* marching. —**марширо́вочный,** *adj.* marching (*attrib.*).
маршру́т *n.* route; itinerary.
ма́ска [*gen. pl.* **-сок**] *n.* **1,** mask. **2,** *fig.* mask; guise.
маскара́д *n.* masquerade. —**маскара́дный,** *adj.* masquerade (*attrib.*).
маскирова́ть *v. impfv.* [*pfv.* **замаскирова́ть;** *pres.* **-ру́ю, -ру́ешь**] **1,** to disguise. **2,** *fig.* to mask; conceal. **3,** to camouflage. —**маскирова́ться,** *refl.* **1,** (*with instr.*) to dress up (as); come disguised (as). **2,** to camouflage oneself.
маскиро́вка *n.* **1,** masking; disguising; concealment. **2,** *mil.* camouflage.
маскиро́вочный *adj.* camouflage (*attrib.*).
ма́сленица *n.* Shrovetide; Mardi gras.
маслёнка [*gen. pl.* **-нок**] *n.* **1,** butter dish. **2,** lubricator; oilcan.
маслёнок [*gen.* **-нка**] *n.* a variety of edible mushroom.
ма́сленый *adj.* **1,** buttered. **2,** oily. **3,** *fig.* unctuous.
масли́на *n.* **1,** olive. **2,** olive tree.
ма́слить *v. impfv.* [*pfv.* **нама́слить**] *colloq.* **1,** to butter. **2,** to oil; grease.
ма́сличный *adj.* yielding edible oil; oil-bearing. —**ма́сличное се́мя,** oilseed.
масли́чный *adj.* olive (*attrib.*).
ма́сло *n.* **1,** butter. **2,** oil. **3,** *art* oil; oils: писа́ть ма́слом, to paint in oils. —**всё идёт как по ма́слу,** everything is hunky-dory. —**подлива́ть ма́сла в ого́нь,** to add fuel to the fire.
маслобо́йка [*gen. pl.* **-бо́ек**] *n.* churn.
маслобо́йня [*gen. pl.* **-бо́ен**] *n.* creamery.
маслоде́лие *n.* butter making. —**маслоде́льный,** *adj.* butter-making.
маслозаво́д *n.* creamery.
масляни́стый *adj.* oily.
ма́сляный *adj.* oil (*attrib.*); grease (*attrib.*).
масо́н *n.* Mason; Freemason. —**масо́нский,** *adj.* Masonic; Mason's; Freemason's. —**масо́нство,** *n.* Masonry; Freemasonry.
ма́сса *n.* **1,** mass. **2,** *pl.* the masses. **3,** pulp: древе́сная ма́сса, wood pulp. **4,** (*with gen.*) *colloq.* a lot (of); heaps (of). —**в (о́бщей) ма́ссе,** on the whole; for the most part. —**основна́я ма́сса** (+ *gen.*), the bulk (of).
масса́ж *n.* massage. —**массажи́ст,** *n.* masseur. —**массажи́стка,** *n.* masseuse.
масси́в *n.* **1,** mountain range. **2,** tract of land.
масси́вный *adj.* massive.
масси́ровать *v. impfv. & pfv.* [*pres.* **-рую, -руешь**] **1,** to massage. **2,** *mil.* to mass. —**масси́роваться,** *refl., mil.* to mass.
массо́вка *n., colloq.* **1,** secret meeting. **2,** group excursion. **3,** *theat.; motion pictures* crowd scene.
ма́ссовый *adj.* **1,** mass (*attrib.*). **2,** for the masses; popular. —**ма́ссовое произво́дство,** mass production.
ма́стер [*pl.* **мастера́**] *n.* **1,** skilled craftsman. Сапо́жный ма́стер, shoemaker. Ма́стер по ремо́нту (+ *gen.*), repairman (*TV, washing machine, etc.*). **2,** master: ма́стер расска́за, master storyteller. **3,** foreman. —**ма́стер на все ру́ки,** jack-of-all-trades.
мастери́ть *v. impfv.* [*pfv.* **смастери́ть**] *colloq.* to make; fashion; build.
мастерска́я *n., decl. as an adj.* **1,** shop; repair shop; workshop: поши́вочная мастерска́я, tailor's/dressmaker's shop; обувна́я мастерска́я, shoe repair shop; железнодоро́жные мастерски́е, railroad workshops. **2,** shop (*in a factory*). **3,** (artist's) studio.
мастерски́ *adv.* in a masterful fashion; like an expert.
мастерско́й *adj.* masterly; masterful.
мастерство́ *n.* **1,** skill. **2,** handicraft; trade.
масти́ка *n.* **1,** mastic. **2,** floor polish. —**масти́ковый,** *adj.* mastic.
масти́т *n.* mastitis.
масти́тый *adj.* venerable.
мастодо́нт *n.* mastodon.
масть [*pl.* **ма́сти, -сте́й, -стя́м**] *n.f.* **1,** color (*of an animal*). **2,** *cards* suit. —**всех масте́й,** of every stripe. —**ходи́ть в масть,** to follow suit.
масшта́б *n.* **1,** scale (*of a map*). **2,** *fig.* scale: в большо́м масшта́бе, on a large scale.
мат *n.* **1,** *chess* mate; checkmate. **2,** floor mat. **3,** *obs.* mat (*dull surface*). **4,** obscene language. —**крича́ть благи́м ма́том,** *colloq.* to yell one's head off.
матема́тика *n.* mathematics. —**матема́тик,** *n.* mathematician. —**математи́ческий,** *adj.* mathematical.
матереуби́йство *n.* matricide.
материа́л *n.* **1,** material: строи́тельные материа́лы, building materials; материа́л для докла́да, material for a report. **2,** material; fabric.
материали́зм *n.* materialism.
материализова́ть *v. impfv. & pfv.* [*pres.* **-зу́ю, -зу́ешь**] to give material form to. —**материализова́ться,** *refl.* to assume material form.
материали́ст *n.* materialist. —**материалисти́ческий,** *adj.* materialistic.
материа́льно *adv.* materially.
материа́льный *adj.* **1,** material. **2,** financial: материа́льные затрудне́ния, financial difficulties. —**материа́льная часть,** matériel.
матери́к [*gen.* **-рика́**] *n.* **1,** continent; mainland. **2,** subsoil.
материко́вый *adj.* continental. —**материко́вая поро́да,** bedrock.
матери́нский *adj.* maternal.
матери́нство *n.* motherhood; maternity.
мате́рия *n.* **1,** matter. **2,** material; fabric. **3,** *colloq.* subject; topic.
ма́терный *adj., colloq.* obscene.
матёрчатый *adj.* cloth (*attrib.*); made of cloth.
матёрый *adj.* **1,** (*of an animal*) full-grown. **2,** *colloq.* experienced; veteran. **3,** inveterate.
ма́тка [*gen. pl.* **-ток**] *n.* **1,** uterus; womb. **2,** female (*of animals*). **3,** queen bee.
ма́товый *adj.* mat; dull. —**ма́товое стекло́,** frosted glass.

ма́точный *adj.* uterine.
матра́с *also,* **матра́ц** *n.* mattress. —**матра́сный,** *adj.* mattress (*attrib.*).
матрёшка [*gen. pl.* **-шек**] *n.* set of nesting dolls.
матриарха́льный *adj.* matriarchal. —**матриарха́т,** *n.* matriarchy.
матримониа́льный *adj., obs.* matrimonial.
ма́трица *n.* matrix.
матро́на *n.* matron.
матро́с *n.* sailor; seaman.
матро́ска [*gen. pl.* **-сок**] *n.* sailor's jacket.
матро́сский *adj.* sailor's; sailor (*attrib.*).
ма́тушка *n., archaic* mother.
матч *n., sports* match.
мать [*gen., dat., & prepl.* **ма́тери;** *instr.* **ма́терью;** *pl.* **ма́тери, -ре́й, -ря́м**] *n.f.* mother.
ма́узер (зэ) *n.* Mauser.
мах *n., colloq.* stroke. —**дать ма́ху,** to commit a blunder. —**одни́м ма́хом, 1,** with one stroke. **2,** at a single bound. —**с ма́ху, 1,** with all one's might. **2,** rashly; without thinking.
махао́н *n.* swallowtail (*butterfly*).
маха́ть *v. impfv.* [*pfv.* **махну́ть;** *pres.* **машу́, ма́шешь**] (*with instr.*) **1,** to wave: маха́ть руко́й (+ *dat.*), to wave to someone. **2,** to wag (one's tail); flap (one's wings). —**махну́ть руко́й на** (+ *acc.*), to give up on; give up as hopeless.
махи́на *n., colloq.* large cumbersome object.
махина́ция *n.* machination.
махну́ть *v., pfv. of* **маха́ть.**
махови́к [*gen.* **-вика́**] *n.* flywheel.
махово́й *adj., in* **махово́е колесо́,** flywheel.
махо́рка *n.* **1,** a kind of low-grade tobacco. **2,** the plant from which it comes.
махро́вый *adj.* **1,** made of terry cloth: махро́вая ткань, terry cloth. **2,** *bot.* double: махро́вая ро́за, double rose. **3,** *fig.* blatant; out-and-out. **4,** *fig.* rabid; fanatical.
маца́ *n.* matzo.
ма́чеха *n.* stepmother.
ма́чта *n.* mast (*of a ship*).
маши́на *n.* **1,** machine: стира́льная маши́на, washing machine. **2,** car. **3,** vehicle: боева́я маши́на, combat vehicle. **4,** engine: парова́я маши́на, steam engine.
машина́льный *adj.* mechanical; automatic; subconscious.
машиниза́ция *n.* mechanization.
машинизи́ровать *v. impfv. & pfv.* [*pres.* **-рую, -руешь**] to mechanize.
машини́ст *n.* **1,** machinist. **2,** engineer; motorman.
машини́стка [*gen. pl.* **-ток**] *n.* (female) typist.
маши́нка [*gen. pl.* **-нок**] *n.* **1,** machine. **2,** device. —**пи́шущая маши́нка,** typewriter.
маши́нный *adj.* machine (*attrib.*).
машинопи́сный *adj.* typewritten.
маши́нопись *n.f.* typing.
машинострое́ние *n.* machine building. —**машинострои́тельный,** *adj.* machine-building.
маэ́стро *n.m. indecl.* maestro.
мая́к [*gen.* **маяка́**] *n.* lighthouse.
ма́ятник *n.* **1,** pendulum. **2,** balance wheel.
ма́яться *v.r. impfv., colloq.* **1,** to toil; slave. **2,** to suffer.
ма́ячить *v. impfv., colloq.* to loom up; appear in the distance.
мгла *n.* **1,** haze. **2,** gloom; darkness. —**мгли́стый,** *adj.* hazy.
мгнове́ние *n.* instant; moment. —**в мгнове́ние о́ка,** in the twinkling of an eye.
мгнове́нный *adj.* **1,** instantaneous. **2,** momentary. —**мгнове́нно,** *adv.* instantly.
ме́бель *n.f.* furniture. —**ме́бельный,** *adj.* furniture (*attrib.*). —**ме́бельщик,** *n.* furniture maker.
меблиро́ванный *adj.* furnished.
меблирова́ть *v. impfv. & pfv.* [*pres.* **-ру́ю, -ру́ешь**] to furnish.
меблиро́вка *n.* **1,** furnishing. **2,** furniture; furnishings.
мегаге́рц [*gen. pl.* **-ге́рц**] *n.* megacycle.
мегато́нна *n.* megaton.
мегафо́н *n.* megaphone.
меге́ра *n.* shrew; termagant; virago.
мёд [*2nd loc.* **меду́**] *n.* **1,** honey. **2,** mead.
медали́ст *n.m.* [*fem.* **-ли́стка**] medal winner; medalist.
меда́ль *n.f.* medal. —**оборо́тная сторона́ меда́ли,** the other side of the coin.
медальо́н *n.* medallion; locket.
медве́дица *n.* female bear. —**Больша́я Медве́дица,** Big Dipper; Ursa Major. —**Ма́лая Медве́дица,** Little Dipper; Ursa Minor.
медве́дь *n.m.* bear. —**бе́лый** *or* **поля́рный медве́дь,** polar bear.
медве́жий [*fem.* **-жья**] *adj.* **1,** bear (*attrib.*); bear's. **2,** bearskin. —**медве́жий у́гол,** godforsaken place. —**медве́жья услу́га,** a well-meaning gesture that backfires.
медвежо́нок [*gen.* **-нка;** *pl.* **-жа́та, -жа́т**] *n.* bear cub.
медвя́ный *adj.* smelling of honey. —**медвя́ная роса́,** honeydew.
медиа́на *n.* median.
ме́дик *n.* **1,** *obs.* physician; doctor. **2,** *colloq.* medical student.
медикаме́нты [*gen.* **-тов**] *n. pl.* medicines.
ме́диум *n.* medium; spiritualist.
медици́на *n.* medicine (*the science*).
медици́нский *adj.* medical. —**медици́нский осмо́тр,** physical examination. —**медици́нская сестра́,** (hospital) nurse.
ме́дленный *adj.* slow. —**ме́дленно,** *adv.* slowly. —**ме́дленность,** *n.f.* slowness.
медли́тельный *adj.* slow; slow-moving; sluggish. —**медли́тельность,** *n.f.* slowness; sluggishness.
ме́длить *v. impfv.* to be slow; delay; tarry.
ме́дник *n.* coppersmith.
ме́дный *adj.* copper. —**ме́дный лоб,** *colloq.* blockhead.
медо́вый *adj.* **1,** honey (*attrib.*). **2,** sweet-smelling. **3,** *fig.* honeyed; sugary. —**медо́вый ме́сяц,** honeymoon.
медоно́сный *adj.* yielding or producing honey. —**медоно́сная пчела́,** honeybee.
медосмо́тр *n.* physical examination (*contr. of* **медици́нский осмо́тр**).
медпу́нкт *n.* first-aid station (*contr. of* **медици́нский пункт**).
медсестра́ *n.* (hospital) nurse (*contr. of* **медици́нская сестра́**).
меду́за *n.* jellyfish; medusa.
медь *n.f.* copper.
медя́к [*gen.* **-дяка́**] *n., colloq.* copper coin.
медя́нка *n.* **1,** a species of non-poisonous snake. **2,** verdigris.

меж *prep.* = **мéжду.**

межá [*pl.* **мéжи, меж, межáм**] *n.* boundary (*between property*).

междомéтие *n., gram.* interjection.

междоусóбие *also,* **междоусóбица** *n.* civil strife. —**междоусóбный,** *adj.* internecine.

мéжду *prep., with instr.* **1,** between: мéжду окнóм и двéрью, between the window and the door; мéжду пятью́ и шестью́ часáми, between five and six o'clock. **2,** among: мéжду собóй, among oneselves. ♦ *Also with gen. in certain set expressions:* читáть мéжду строк, to read between the lines. —**мéжду нáми,** between you and me; confidentially. —**мéжду прóчим,** by the way. —**мéжду тем,** meanwhile; in the meantime. —**мéжду тем как,** while; whereas.

междугорóдный *adj.* **1,** intercity; interurban. **2,** (*of a phone call*) long-distance.

междунарóдный *adj.* international.

междуцáрствие *n.* interregnum.

межевáние *n.* surveying.

межевáть *v. impfv.* [*pres.* **-жу́ю -жу́ешь**] to survey; set boundaries to.

межевóй *adj.* **1,** boundary (*attrib.*): межевóй знáк, boundary marker. **2,** surveying (*attrib.*).

межéнь *n.f.* lowest water level (*of a river or lake*).

межзвёздный *adj.* interstellar.

межконтинентáльный *adj.* intercontinental.

межпланéтный *adj.* interplanetary

межсезóнье *n.* off-season

мезозóйский *adj.* Mesozoic.

мезóн *n.* meson.

мезони́н *n.* attic.

мексикáнец [*gen.* **-нца**] *n.m.* [*fem.* **-нка**] Mexican. —**мексикáнский,** *adj.* Mexican.

мел *n.* chalk.

меланхóлия *n.* **1,** melancholy. **2,** *med.* melancholia. —**меланхóлик,** *n.* melancholic person. —**меланхоли́ческий; меланхоли́чный,** *adj.* melancholic; melancholy.

мелéть *v. impfv.* [*pfv.* **обмелéть**] to become shallow.

мелиорáция *n.* land reclamation.

мéлкий *adj.* [*short form* **мéлок, мелкá, мéлко;** *comp.* **мéльче;** *superl.* **мельчáйший**] **1,** small; minute. **2,** (*of rain, sand, etc.*) fine. **3,** shallow. **4,** minor: мéлкий чинóвник/ремóнт, minor official/repairs. **5,** petty: мéлкие забóты, petty cares. **6,** *fig.* petty; small-minded. —**мéлкая буржуази́я,** petty bourgeoisie. —**мéлкие дéньги,** small change. —**мéлкая крáжа,** petty larceny. —**мéлкая тарéлка,** (flat) plate; dinner plate.

мéлко *adv.* fine; into small particles.

мелкобуржуáзный *adj.* petty-bourgeois.

мелковóдный *adj.* shallow.

мелковóдье *n.* shallow water.

мелкотá *n., colloq.* **1,** small size. **2,** small fry.

меловóй *adj.* **1,** chalk (*attrib.*); chalky. **2,** *geol.* cretaceous.

мелóдика *n.* melodics.

мелоди́ческий *adj.* **1,** melodic. **2,** melodious.

мелоди́чный *adj.* melodious. —**мелоди́чность,** *n.f.* melodiousness.

мелóдия *n.* melody; tune.

мелодрáма *n.* melodrama. —**мелодрамати́ческий,** *adj.* melodramatic.

мелóк [*gen.* **-лкá**] *n.* piece of chalk. —**игрáть на мелóк,** *cards* to play on credit.

меломáн *n.* music lover.

мéлочный *also,* **мелочнóй** *adj.* petty; picayune. —**мéлочность,** *n.f.* pettiness.

мéлочь [*pl.* **мéлочи, -чéй, -чáм**] *n.f.* **1,** small things; small items. **2,** (small) change. **3,** trifle.

мель [*2nd loc.* **мели́**] *n.f.* **1,** shoal. **2,** *in* **песчáная мель,** sandbank. —**на мели́, 1,** aground. **2,** *fig.* high and dry; on the rocks. —**сесть на мель,** to run aground.

мелькáть *v. impfv.* [*pfv.* **мелькну́ть**] **1,** to flash; flash by: у меня́ мелькну́ла мысль, the thought flashed across my mind. **2,** (*of stars*) to glimmer.

мéльком *adv.* **1,** for a moment; briefly; quickly: ви́деть мéльком, to catch a glimpse of; слы́шать мéльком, chance to hear. **2,** cursorily; perfunctorily.

мéльник *n.* miller.

мéльница *n.* mill. —**лить вóду на чью́-нибудь мéльницу,** to be grist for (*or* bring grist to) someone's mill.

мельхиóр *n.* nickel silver.

мельчáть *v. impfv.* [*pfv.* **измельчáть**] **1,** to become smaller. **2,** to become shallow. **3,** *fig.* to deteriorate; degenerate.

мéльче *adj., comp. of* **мéлкий.**

мельчи́ть *v. impfv.* to crush; grind.

мелюзгá *n., colloq.* small fry.

мембрáна *n.* diaphragm (*in an earphone, microphone, etc.*).

меморáндум *n.* memorandum.

мемориáльный *adj.* memorial.

мемуáры [*gen.* **-ров**] *n. pl.* memoirs.

менделéвий *n.* mendelevium.

мéнее *adv., used in forming compound comparatives* less: мéнее интерéсный, less interesting. —**бóлее или мéнее,** more or less. —**тем не мéнее,** nevertheless.

менестрéль *n.m.* minstrel; troubadour.

мензу́рка [*gen. pl.* **-рок**] *n.* measuring glass.

менинги́т *n.* meningitis.

меновóй *adj.* of exchange: меновáя едини́ца, unit of exchange. —**меновáя торгóвля,** barter.

менструáция *n.* menstruation. —**менструáльный,** *adj.* menstrual.

менструи́ровать *v. impfv.* [*pres.* **-рую, -руешь**] to menstruate.

ментóл *n.* menthol. —**ментóловый,** *adj.* menthol (*attrib.*); mentholated.

мéнтор *n., obs.* mentor.

менуэ́т *n.* minuet.

мéньше *adj., comp. of* **мáлый** *and* **мáленький,** smaller. —*adv., comp. of* **мáло,** less. —**мéньше всегó,** least of all.

меньшеви́к [*gen.* **-викá**] *n.* Menshevik. —**меньшеви́стский,** *adj.* Menshevik (*attrib.*).

мéньший *adj., used only as a modifier, comp. of* **мáлый** *and* **мáленький,** smaller; lesser. —**по мéньшей мéре, 1,** at least. **2,** to say the least. —**сáмое мéньшее, 1,** the least. **2,** at the least.

меньшинствó *n.* minority.

меню́ *n. neut. indecl.* menu.

меня́ *pron., gen. & acc. of* **я.**

меня́ла *n.m.* moneychanger.

меня́ть *v. impfv.* [*pfv.* **поменя́ть**] **1,** to change. **2,** to exchange. —**меня́ться,** *refl.* **1,** [*impfv. only*] to change. **2,** (*with instr.*) to exchange; trade: меня́ться роля́ми, to exchange roles; меня́ться места́ми, to trade places.

ме́ра *n.* **1,** measure: ме́ра жи́дкости, liquid measure. **2,** extent; degree; measure: в большо́й ме́ре, to a great extent/degree; in large measure. **3,** measure (*action*): круты́е ме́ры, drastic measures. —**в ме́ру, 1,** sufficiently; in the right amount. **2,** (*with gen.*) to the extent of. —**в по́лной ме́ре,** fully; in full measure. —**знать ме́ру,** to know one's limits; know when to stop. —**не в ме́ру,** excessively. —**по кра́йней ме́ре,** at least. —**по ме́ньшей ме́ре, 1,** at least. **2,** to say the least. —**по ме́ре** (+ *gen.*), in proportion to; to the extent of: по ме́ре возмо́жности, to the fullest extent possible. —**по ме́ре того́, как,** as. —**сверх ме́ры; че́рез ме́ру,** excessively. —**чу́вство ме́ры,** sense of proportion.

ме́ргель *n.m., geol.* marl.

мере́жка *n.* openwork.

мере́нга *n.* meringue.

мере́ть *v. impfv.* [*pres.* **мрёт, мрут;** *past* **мёр, -ла**] *colloq.* to die (*in large numbers*).

мере́щиться *v.r. impfv.* [*pfv.* **помере́щиться**] (*with dat.*) *colloq.* to seem (to).

мерза́вец [*gen.* **-вца**] *n.* scoundrel.

ме́рзкий *adj.* [*short form* **-зок, -зка́, -зко**] **1,** loathsome; vile. **2,** *colloq.* rotten; foul.

мерзлота́ *n.* frozen earth. —**ве́чная мерзлота́,** permafrost.

мёрзлый *adj.* frozen.

мёрзнуть *v. impfv.* [*pfv.* **замёрзнуть;** *past* **мёрз, -ла**] **1,** to freeze; become frozen. **2,** (*of a person*) to be freezing (cold); be frozen. **3,** to freeze to death; perish from the frost.

ме́рзость *n.f.* vile thing; abomination.

меридиа́н *n.* meridian.

мери́ло *n.* standard; criterion; yardstick; gauge.

ме́рин *n.* gelding. —**врать как си́вый ме́рин,** to be a habitual liar.

мерино́с *n.* **1,** merino sheep. **2,** merino wool. —**мерино́совый,** *adj.* merino.

ме́рить *v.impfv.* **1,** to measure. **2,** to try on. —**ме́риться,** *refl.* [*pfv.* **поме́риться**] (*with instr.*) to measure: ме́риться си́лами с, to measure one's strength against.

ме́рка [*gen. pl.* **-рок**] *n.* **1,** measurements. **2,** measuring rod; yardstick. **3,** *fig.* yardstick; criterion. —**по ме́рке,** to measure.

меркантили́зм *n.* mercantilism. —**меркantíльный,** *adj.* mercantile.

ме́ркнуть *v. impfv.* [*pfv.* **поме́ркнуть;** *past* **мерк, -ла**] **1,** to grow dim. **2,** *fig.* to fade; wane.

Мерку́рий *n.* Mercury (*the planet*).

мерлу́шка *n.* lambskin (*attrib.*). —**мерлу́шковый,** *adj.* lambskin (*attrib.*).

ме́рный *adj.* measured; rhythmical.

мероприя́тие *n.* measure; step.

ме́ртвенный *adj.* **1,** lifeless; dead. **2,** *fig.* deathly.

мертве́ть *v. impfv.* [*pfv.* **омертве́ть** *or* **помертве́ть**] **1,** to become numb. **2,** *fig.* to be paralyzed (*with fear, terror, etc.*).

мертве́ц [*gen. & acc.* **-веца́**] *n.* dead person.

мертве́цкая *n., decl. as an adj., colloq.* mortuary; morgue.

мертве́цки *adv., colloq., in* **мертве́цки пьян,** dead drunk; **спать мертве́цки,** be dead to the world.

мертвечи́на *n.* carrion.

мертви́ть *v. impfv.* [*pres.* **-влю́, -ви́шь**] **1,** to kill; destroy. **2,** *fig.* to deaden.

мертворождённый *adj.* stillborn.

мёртвый *adj.* dead. —*n.* **1,** dead person. **2,** *pl.* the dead. —**мёртвая бу́ква,** dead letter. —**мёртвый груз,** dead weight. —**мёртвая то́чка,** dead center: сдви́нуть(ся) с мёртвой то́чки, to move off dead center. —**на мёртвой то́чке,** deadlocked; at a standstill. —**ни жив ни мёртв,** in a state of shock. —**спать мёртвым сном,** to be dead to the world.

мерца́ние *n.* glimmer; twinkling; flickering.

мерца́ть *v. impfv.* to twinkle; flicker; glimmer; shimmer.

ме́сиво *n., colloq.* **1,** liquid refuse; slop. **2,** mud; mire. **3,** swill; mash (*fed to livestock*).

меси́ть *v. impfv.* [*pres.* **мешу́, ме́сишь**] to knead. —**меси́ть грязь,** to slosh through the mud.

ме́сса *n., relig.* Mass.

месси́я *n.* Messiah. —**мессиа́нский,** *adj.* Messianic.

месте́чко [*pl.* **-чки, -чек**] *n.* **1,** *dim. of* **ме́сто. 2,** small town. —**тёплое месте́чко,** soft job.

мести́ *v. impfv.* [*pres.* **мету́, метёшь;** *past* **мёл, мела́, мело́**] **1,** to sweep. **2,** to scatter; swirl. **3,** (*of a snowstorm*) to be raging. **4,** *impers.* to be snowing: сего́дня си́льно метёт, it is snowing hard today.

ме́стность *n.f.* **1,** area; region; district: се́льская/боло́тистая ме́стность, rural/marshy area. **2,** country; terrain: холми́стая ме́стность, hilly country; пересечённая ме́стность, rugged terrain.

ме́стный *adj.* local. —**ме́стный паде́ж,** locative case.

ме́сто [*pl.* **места́**] *n.* **1,** place. **2,** (*with gen.*) site (of); scene (of). **3,** space; room. **4,** seat; place. **5,** (*with gen.*) part; place (*of/in a book, story, etc.*). **6,** berth. **7,** job; position. **8,** piece (*of luggage*). **9,** *pl.* provinces; outlying areas. —**знать своё ме́сто,** to know one's place. —**име́ть ме́сто, 1,** to take place. **2,** to exist; be found. —**класть не на ме́сто,** to misplace. —**места́ми,** in places; in spots; here and there. —**на ва́шем ме́сте,** in your place; if I were you. —**на ме́сте, 1,** in place: стоя́ть на ме́сте, to stand in place; stand still. **2,** on the spot: уби́ть кого́-нибудь на ме́сте, to kill someone on the spot. —**на своём ме́сте,** in one's proper place; doing what one should be doing. —**не к ме́сту; не у ме́ста,** inappropriate; out of place. —**не ме́сто, 1,** (*with dat.*) not to belong: здесь вам не ме́сто, you don't belong here. **2,** not the place to: здесь не ме́сто говори́ть об э́том, this is not the place to talk about it. —**ни с ме́ста, 1,** (*as a command*) don't move!; stay put! **2,** making no progress; getting nowhere. —**поста́вить кого́-нибудь на (своё) ме́сто,** to put someone in his place.

местожи́тельство *n.* (place of) residence.

местоиме́ние *n.* pronoun. —**местоиме́нный,** *adj.* pronominal.

местонахожде́ние *n.* location; whereabouts.

местоположе́ние *n.* location; site.

местопребыва́ние *n.* residence; abode. —**местопребыва́ние прави́тельства,** the seat of government.

месторожде́ние *n.* **1,** deposit; field: месторожде́ние не́фти, oil field. **2,** *obs.* place of birth.

месть *n.f.* revenge; vengeance. —**кро́вная месть,** vendetta.

ме́сяц *n.* **1,** month. **2,** moon. —**медо́вый ме́сяц,** honeymoon.

ме́сячник *n.* month (*devoted to a special cause*): ме́сячник де́тской кни́ги, children's book month.
ме́сячный *adj.* **1,** lasting a month; a month's. **2,** monthly.
ме́та *n.* **1,** mark. **2,** *obs.* target.
мета́лл *n.* metal. —**металли́ст,** *n.* metalworker. —**металли́ческий,** *adj.* metal (*attrib.*); metallic.
металло́ид *n.* metalloid.
металлоло́м *n.* scrap metal.
металлоно́сный *adj.* metalliferous.
металлоплави́льный *adj.* smelting (*attrib.*).
металлу́ргия *also,* **металлурги́я** *n.* metallurgy. —**металлу́рг,** *n.* metallurgist. —**металлурги́ческий,** *adj.* metallurgic.
метаморфо́з *n., biol.* metamorphosis. —**метаморфо́за,** *n., fig.* metamorphosis; complete transformation.
мета́н *n.* methane.
мета́ние *n.* **1,** throwing: мета́ние ди́ска, discus throw. **2,** *in* **мета́ние икры́,** spawning.
метаста́з *n.* metastasis.
мета́тель *n.m., sports* thrower: мета́тель ди́ска, discus thrower.
мета́тельный *adj.* to be thrown or launched: мета́тельный снаря́д, missile; projectile.
мета́ть[1] *v. impfv.* [*pfv.* **метну́ть;** *pres.* **мечу́, ме́чешь**] to throw; hurl; fling; cast. —**мета́ть банк,** *cards* to keep the bank. —**мета́ть гро́мы и мо́лнии,** to fulminate; rant and rave. —**мета́ть икру́,** to spawn. —**мета́ть се́но,** to stack hay.
мета́ть[2] *v. impfv.* [*pfv.* **смета́ть;** *pres.* **-та́ю, -та́ешь**] to baste. —**мета́ть пе́тли, 1,** to make buttonholes. **2,** to foul the trail. **3,** to confuse the issue.
мета́ться *v.r. impfv.* [*pres.* **мечу́сь, ме́чешься**] **1,** to rush about. **2,** to toss about (*in bed*); toss (*in one's sleep*).
метафи́зика *n.* metaphysics. —**метафи́зик,** *n.* metaphysician; metaphysicist. —**метафизи́ческий,** *adj.* metaphysical.
мета́фора *n.* metaphor. —**метафори́ческий,** *adj.* metaphorical.
мете́лица *n.* = **мете́ль.**
метёлка [*gen. pl.* **-лок**] *n.* **1,** whisk broom. **2,** *bot.* panicle.
мете́ль *n.f.* snowstorm; blizzard.
метео́р *n.* meteor.
метеори́зм *n., med.* flatulence.
метеори́т *n.* meteorite.
метео́рный *adj.* meteor (*attrib.*); meteoric.
метеороло́гия *n.* meteorology. —**метеоро́лог,** *n.* meteorologist. —**метеорологи́ческий,** *adj.* meteorological.
метеоспу́тник *n.* weather satellite.
метиза́ция *n.* crossbreeding.
мети́л *n.* methyl.
метиле́н *n.* methylene.
мети́ловый *adj.* methyl (*attrib.*).
мети́с *n.* **1,** mongrel. **2,** mestizo.
ме́тить *v. impfv.* [*pres.* **ме́чу, ме́тишь**] **1,** [*pfv.* **наме́тить** *or* **поме́тить**] to mark. **2,** (*with* **в** + *acc.*) to aim (at). **3,** (*with* **в** + *nom. pl.*) *colloq.* to aim (to become); aspire (to).
ме́тка [*gen. pl.* **-ток**] *n.* **1,** marking. **2,** mark. **3,** name tape containing one's initials.
ме́ткий *adj.* [*short form* **-ток, -тка́, -тко**] **1,** (*of a marksman, weapon, etc.*) accurate. **2,** (*of a blow, bullet, etc.*) well-aimed. **3,** (*of one's eye*) keen. **4,** *fig.* (*of a comment, remark, etc.*) pointed; apt.
ме́ткость *n.f.* **1,** accuracy; marksmanship. **2,** keenness (*of eyesight*).
метла́ [*pl.* **мётлы, мётел**] *n.* broom.
метну́ть *v., pfv. of* **мета́ть**[1].
ме́тод *n.* method.
методи́зм *n.* Methodism.
мето́дика *n.* methods.
методи́ст *n.* **1,** Methodist. **2,** specialist in the methodology of teaching. —**методи́стский,** *adj.* Methodist.
методи́ческий *adj.* **1,** [*also,* **методи́чный**] methodical; systematic. **2,** pert. to the methodology of teaching.
методоло́гия *n.* methodology. —**методологи́ческий,** *adj.* methodological.
метр *n.* **1,** meter (*unit of length*). **2,** measuring rod *or* tape (*one meter in length*). **3,** *pros.* meter.
метра́ж [*gen.* **-жа́**] *n.* **1,** length (*in meters*). **2,** *motion pictures* footage. **3,** area (*in square meters*).
метрдоте́ль (тэ) *n.m.* maître d'hotel; headwaiter.
ме́трика *n.* **1,** birth certificate. **2,** *pros.* metrics.
метри́ческий *adj.* **1,** metric. **2,** pert. to the registration of births, marriages, and deaths: метри́ческое свиде́тельство, birth certificate.
метро́ *n. indecl.* subway.
метроно́м *n.* metronome.
метрополите́н (тэ) *n.* subway.
метропо́лия *n.* parent state, home country (*of an empire*).
ме́тчик *n.* marker; one who marks.
мех *n.* **1,** [*pl.* **меха́**] fur. **2,** [*pl.* **мехи́**] skin (*vessel*); wineskin. —**на меху́,** fur-lined. *See also* **мехи́.**
механиза́тор *n.* **1,** specialist in mechanization. **2,** machine operator; machine servicer (*in agriculture*).
механиза́ция *n.* mechanization.
механизи́ровать *v. impfv. & pfv.* [*pres.* **-рую, -руешь**] to mechanize.
механи́зм *n.* mechanism.
меха́ник *n.* **1,** mechanical engineer. **2,** mechanic.
меха́ника *n.* mechanics.
механи́ческий *adj.* **1,** mechanical. **2,** power-driven; power (*attrib.*). **3,** *fig.* mechanical; automatic. —**механи́ческий цех; механи́ческая мастерска́я,** machine shop.
мехи́ [*gen.* **мехо́в**] *n. pl.* bellows.
мехово́й *adj.* fur.
меховщи́к [*gen.* **-щика́**] *n.* furrier.
мецена́т *n.* patron of the arts.
ме́ццо-сопра́но *n. neut. indecl.* mezzo-soprano (*voice*). —*n.f. indecl.* mezzo-soprano (*singer*).
меч [*gen.* **меча́**] *n.* sword.
мечено́сец [*gen.* **-сца**] *n.* **1,** sword-bearer. **2,** *hist.* Teutonic knight.
ме́ченый *adj.* marked.
мече́ть *n.f.* mosque.
меч-ры́ба *n.* swordfish.
мечта́ *n.* **1,** dream: заве́тная мечта́, lifelong dream. **2,** daydreaming: предава́ться мечта́м, to give way to daydreaming.
мечта́ние *n.* daydreaming; reverie.
мечта́тель *n.m.* dreamer; visionary.
мечта́тельный *adj.* **1,** given to dreaming. **2,** dreamy. **3,** visionary. —**мечта́тельность,** *n.f.* reverie.
мечта́ть *v. impfv.* **1,** to dream. **2,** to daydream.

мешáлка [*gen. pl.* **-лок**] *n.* mixer.
мешанѝна *n., colloq.* mishmash; hodgepodge.
мешáть *v. impfv.* [*pfv.* **помешáть**] **1,** (*with dat.*) to bother; disturb; hinder; impede; prevent. **2,** to stir. **3,** [*pfv.* **смешáть**] to mix; blend. —**мешáться,** *refl.* [*pfv.* **смешáться**] **1,** to mix; blend; mingle. **2,** to become confused. **3,** [*impfv. only*] (*with* **в** + *acc.*) *colloq.* to interfere (in). **4,** [*impfv. only*] *colloq.* to be a hindrance; get in the way.
мéшкать *v. impfv., colloq.* to tarry; dally; dawdle.
мешковáтый *adj.* **1,** (*of clothing*) baggy. **2,** clumsy; awkward.
мешковѝна *n.* sacking; sackcloth.
мéшкотный *adj., colloq.* **1,** sluggish. **2,** laborious.
мешóк [*gen.* **-шкá**] *n.* bag; sack. —**дéнежный мешóк,** moneybags; rich man. —**мешкѝ под глазáми,** bags under one's eyes. —**сидéть мешкóм,** (*of a garment*) to be too big; be baggy.
мешóчек [*gen.* **-чка**] *n.* **1,** *dim. of* **мешóк. 2,** sac. —**яйцó в мешóчек,** medium-boiled egg.
мещанѝн [*pl.* **-щáне, -щáн**] *n.m.* [*fem.* **-щáнка**] **1,** petty bourgeois. **2,** *fig.* person of narrow or petty interests.
мещáнский *adj.* **1,** petty-bourgeois. **2,** *fig.* narrow-minded.
мещáнство *n.* **1,** lower middle class; petty bourgeoisie. **2,** *fig.* narrow-mindedness.
мзда *n., obs.* **1,** payment. **2,** bribe.
ми *n. neut., music* mi; E.
миáзмы *n. pl.* [*sing.* **миáзма**] miasma.
миг *n.* moment; instant. —**в одѝн миг,** in a flash; in a jiffy.
мигáлка [*gen. pl.* **-лок**] *n., colloq.* **1,** wick lamp. **2,** blinking light; blinker; flasher.
мигáние *n.* **1,** wink (*of the eye*). **2,** blinking (*of a light*).
мигáть *v. impfv.* [*pfv.* **мигнýть**] **1,** to blink. **2,** (*with instr.*) to blink (one's eyes). **3,** (*with dat.*) to wink (at). **4,** to twinkle; flicker.
мѝгом *adv., colloq.* in a flash; in a jiffy.
мигрáция *n.* migration.
мигрéнь *n.f.* migraine.
мигрѝровать *v. impfv.* [*pres.* **-рую, -руешь**] to migrate.
мѝдия *n.* mussel.
мизансцéна *n., theat.* staging.
мизантрóпия *n.* misanthropy. —**мизантрóп,** *n.* misanthrope. —**мизантропѝческий,** *adj.* misanthropic.
мизéрный *adj.* **1,** wretched. **2,** paltry; meager; measly.
мизѝнец [*gen.* **-нца**] *n.* **1,** little finger. **2,** little toe.
микрóб *n.* microbe; germ.
микробиолóгия *n.* microbiology. —**микробиóлог,** *n.* microbiologist.
микрокóсм *n.* microcosm.
микрóметр *n.* micrometer.
микрóн [*gen. pl.* **-крóн**] *n.* micron.
микроорганѝзм *n.* microorganism.
микроскóп *n.* microscope. —**микроскопѝческий,** *adj.* microscopic.
микросхéма *n.* microcircuit.
микрофѝльм *n.* microfilm.
микрофóн *n.* microphone.
микстýра *n.* mixture; medicine.
мѝлая *n., decl. as an adj.* sweetheart; darling.
мѝленький *adj., colloq.* **1,** pretty; cute. **2,** dear; sweet. **3,** (*in direct address*) darling.
милитаризáция *n.* militarization.
милитаризѝровать *v. impfv. & pfv.* [*pres.* **-рую, -руешь**] to militarize. *Also,* **милитаризовáть** [*pres.* **-зýю, -зýешь**].
милитарѝзм *n.* militarism. —**милитарѝст,** *n.* militarist. —**милитаристѝческий,** *adj.* militaristic.
милицéйский *adj.* **1,** militia (*attrib.*). **2,** police (*attrib.*).
милиционéр *n.* **1,** policeman. **2,** militiaman.
милѝция *n.* **1,** the police. **2,** militia.
миллиáрд *n.* (*U.S.*) billion; (*Brit.*) milliard. —**миллиардéр,** (дэ) *n.* multimillionaire.
миллиáрдный *ordinal numeral* billionth. —*adj.* **1,** containing or consisting of billions. **2,** worth billions.
миллигрáмм *n.* milligram.
миллимéтр *n.* millimeter.
миллиóн *n.* million. —**миллионéр,** *n.* millionaire.
миллиóнный *ordinal numeral* millionth. —*adj.* **1,** containing or consisting of millions. **2,** worth millions.
мѝло *adv.* **1,** nicely. **2,** prettily. —*adj., used predicatively* nice; kind: как мѝло, что вы пришлѝ, how nice/kind of you to come!
мѝловать *v. impfv.* [*pres.* **-лую, -луешь**] *obs.* to show mercy to; pardon.
миловѝдный *adj.* pretty; good-looking.
милосéрдие *n.* **1,** mercy. **2,** clemency. —**милосéрдный,** *adj.* merciful; charitable.
мѝлостивый *adj., obs.* kind; gracious.
мѝлостыня *n.* alms.
мѝлость *n.f.* **1,** favor; good graces: быть в мѝлости у, to be in the good graces of. **2,** favor; good turn: сдéлать мѝлость (+ *dat.*), to do (someone) a favor. **3,** mercy. —**мѝлости прóсим!,** you are always welcome! —**по мѝлости** (+ *gen.*), **1,** thanks to. **2,** through the fault of. —**сдавáться на мѝлость** (+ *gen.*), to surrender unconditionally to. —**скажѝ(те) на мѝлость, 1,** would you please tell (*or* mind telling) me. **2,** you don't say!
мѝлый *adj.* **1,** nice; sweet. **2,** dear: мѝлый друг, dear friend. —*n.* darling; sweetheart.
мѝля *n.* mile. —**англѝйская мѝля,** statute mile.
мим *n.* mime (*farce performed in ancient times*).
мѝмика *n.* **1,** facial expressions. **2,** mimicry.
мимикрѝя *n., biol.* mimicry.
мимѝст *n.* mimic. —**мимѝческий,** *adj.* mimic.
мѝмо *prep., with gen.* past; by: проходѝть мѝмо дóма, to walk past/by the house. —*adv.* past; by: солдáты прошлѝ мѝмо, the soldiers walked past (*or* passed by). —**мѝмо цéли,** wide of the mark.
мимóза *n.* mimosa.
мимолётный *adj.* passing; fleeting.
мимохóдом *adv.* **1,** while passing by; on the way. **2,** *colloq.* in passing: упомянýть мимохóдом, to mention in passing.
мѝна *n.* **1,** *mil.* mine. **2,** mortar shell. **3,** facial expression; countenance. —**дéлать хорóшую (весёлую) мѝну при плохóй игрé,** to put up a bold front. —**подклáдывать (*or* подводѝть) мѝну** (+ *dat. or with* **под** + *acc.*), to play a dirty trick on.
минарéт *n.* minaret.
миндалевѝдный *adj.* almond-shaped. —**миндалевѝдная железá,** tonsil.
миндáлина *n.* tonsil.
миндáль [*gen.* **-далѝ**] *n.m.* **1,** almonds. **2,** almond tree. —**миндáльный,** *adj.* almond (*attrib.*).
минёр *n.* specialist in mine-laying.

минера́л *n.* mineral.
минерало́гия *n.* mineralogy. —**минерало́г,** *n.* mineralogist. —**минералоги́ческий,** *adj.* mineralogical.
минера́льный *adj.* mineral.
миниатю́ра *n.* miniature.
миниатю́рный *adj.* **1,** miniature. **2,** tiny.
минима́льный *adj.* minimum; minimal.
ми́нимум *n.* minimum. —*adv.* a minimum of; at least.
мини́ровать *v. impfv. & pfv.* [*pfv. also* **замини́ровать;** *pres.* **-рую, -руешь**] *mil.* to mine.
министе́рский *adj.* ministerial.
министе́рство *n.* ministry.
мини́стр *n.* minister. —**мини́стр иностра́нных дел,** foreign minister. —**мини́стр фина́нсов,** finance minister; (*U.S.*) Secretary of the Treasury. —**мини́стр юсти́ции,** Minister of Justice; (*U.S.*) Attorney General.
ми́нный *adj., mil.* mine (*attrib.*). —**ми́нное по́ле,** minefield. —**ми́нный по́рох,** blasting powder.
минова́ть *v. pfv.* [*infl.* **-ну́ю, -ну́ешь**] **1,** [*also impfv.*] *v.t.* to pass; pass by. **2,** *v.i.* to pass; be over. **3,** (*usu. neg.*) to avoid; escape. —**мину́я подро́бности,** omitting details.
мино́га *n.* lamprey.
миноиска́тель *n.m.* mine detector.
миномёт *n., mil.* mortar. —**миномётный,** *adj.* mortar (*attrib.*).
миноно́сец [*gen.* **-сца**] *n.* torpedo boat. —**эска́дренный миноно́сец,** destroyer.
мино́р *n.* **1,** *music* minor key: сона́та си мино́р, sonata in B minor. **2,** *colloq.* melancholy; the blues; the dumps: быть в мино́ре, to be in the dumps.
мино́рный *adj.* **1,** *music* minor. **2,** *colloq.* melancholy; gloomy.
мину́вший *adj.* past; bygone.
ми́нус *n.* **1,** *math.* minus. **2,** minus sign. **3,** *fig., colloq.* minus; drawback. —*adv.* minus: пять ми́нус два равно́ трём, five minus two equals three; ми́нус де́сять гра́дусов, ten degrees below freezing.
мину́та *n.* **1,** minute. **2,** moment: незабыва́емая мину́та, unforgettable moment. —**мину́та в мину́ту,** on the dot. —**с мину́ты на мину́ту,** any minute.
мину́тка [*gen. pl.* **-ток**] *n., dim. of* **мину́та.**
мину́тный *adj.* **1,** minute (*attrib.*): мину́тная стре́лка, minute hand. **2,** lasting a moment; momentary.
мину́точка [*gen. pl.* **-чек**] *n., colloq., dim. of* **мину́тка.**
мину́ть *v. pfv.* [*infl.* **ми́нет**] **1,** [*past* **мину́л**] to pass. **2,** [*past* **ми́нуло**] *impers.* (*with dat.*) *indicating attainment of a certain age:* ему́ ми́нуло со́рок лет, he has turned forty.
мир [*pl.* **миры́**] *n.* **1,** world. **2,** peace: мир во всём ми́ре, peace throughout the world. **3,** *hist.* village community; mir. —**не от ми́ра сего́,** (*of a person*) from (*or* living in) a different world. —**пусти́ть по́ миру,** to bankrupt; make a beggar out of (someone). —**ходи́ть по́ миру,** to live by begging.
мира́ж *n.* mirage.
мириа́ды [*gen.* **-а́д**] *n. pl.* myriads.
мири́ть *v. impfv.* [*pfv.* **помири́ть** *or* **примири́ть**] to reconcile. —**мири́ться,** *refl.* **1,** to become reconciled (*after a quarrel*); make up. **2,** (*with* **с** + *instr.*) to reconcile oneself (to); resign oneself (to); (learn to) accept.
ми́рный *adj.* **1,** peace (*attrib.*). **2,** peaceful. —**ми́рно,** *adv.* peacefully.
мирова́я *n., decl. as an adj., colloq.* amicable agreement: пойти́ на мирову́ю, to reach an amicable agreement.
мировоззре́ние *n.* world outlook; world view.
миров́ой *adj.* **1,** world (*attrib.*). Втора́я мирова́я война́, World War II. **2,** *law* of arbitration: миров́ой суд, court of arbitration. Миров́ой судья́, justice of the peace.
мироздáние *n.* the universe.
миролюби́вый *adj.* peace-loving; peaceful. —**миролю́бие,** *n.* peaceful nature.
миропома́зание *n.* anointing; unction.
миротво́рец [*gen.* **-рца**] *n.* peacemaker.
ми́рра *n.* myrrh.
мирско́й *adj.* **1,** worldly; mundane. **2,** secular; lay. **3,** *hist.* pert. to a **мир.**
мирт *n.* myrtle. —**ми́ртовый,** *adj.* myrtle.
миря́нин [*pl.* **-я́не, -я́н**] *n.* **1,** *obs.* layman. **2,** *hist.* member of a **мир.**
ми́ска [*gen. pl.* **-сок**] *n.* bowl; tureen.
мисс *n.f. indecl.* miss; Miss.
миссионе́р *n.* missionary. —**миссионе́рский,** *adj.* missionary. —**миссионе́рство,** *n.* missionary work.
ми́ссис *n.f. indecl.* Mrs.
ми́ссия *n.* **1,** mission (*assignment*). **2,** delegation; mission. **3,** legation; diplomatic mission. **4,** *relig.* mission.
ми́стер *n.* mister; Mr.
ми́стик *n.* mystic.
ми́стика *n.* mysticism.
мистифика́ция *n.* hoax; practical joke.
мистици́зм *n.* mysticism.
мисти́ческий *adj.* mystical.
ми́тинг *n.* mass meeting; rally.
митка́ль [*gen.* **-каля́**] *n.m.* calico (*plain unfinished cloth*). —**миткалёвый; митка́левый,** *adj.* calico.
мито́з *n.* mitosis.
ми́тра *n.* miter (*worn by a bishop*).
митрополи́т *n., Orth. Ch.* metropolitan.
миф *n.* myth. —**мифи́ческий,** *adj.* mythical.
мифоло́гия *n.* mythology. —**мифологи́ческий,** *adj.* mythological.
ми́чман *n., naval* warrant officer.
мише́нь *n.f.* target. —**я́блоко мише́ни,** bull's-eye.
ми́шка [*gen. pl.* **-шек**] *n.* teddy bear.
мишура́ *n.* **1,** tinsel. **2,** *fig.* ostentation.
мишу́рный *adj.* **1,** tinsel (*attrib.*). **2,** *fig.* showy; tawdry; ostentatious.
младе́нец [*gen.* **-нца**] *n.* infant; baby. —**младе́нческий,** *adj.* infantile. —**младе́нчество,** *n.* infancy.
младо́й *adj., archaic* young. —**стар и млад,** young and old (alike).
мла́дший *adj., used only as a modifier* **1,** younger. **2,** youngest. **3,** junior. —**мла́дший лейтена́нт,** second lieutenant.
млекопита́ющее *n., decl. as an adj.* mammal.
млеть *v. impfv.* **1,** (with **от**) to be overcome (*with an emotion*). **2,** to languish. **3,** *colloq.* to become numb.
мле́чный *adj., archaic* = **моло́чный.** —**Мле́чный Путь,** the Milky Way.
мне *pron., dat. & prepl. of* **я.**
мнемо́ника *n.* mnemonics. —**мнемони́ческий,** *adj.* mnemonics.
мне́ние *n.* opinion. —**быть высо́кого мне́ния о,** to have a high opinion of. —**быть одного́ мне́ния,** to be of one mind. —**по моему́ мне́нию,** in my opinion. —**я того́ мне́ния, что...,** I am of the opinion that...

мни́мый *adj.* **1,** imaginary. **2,** false; feigned.
мни́тельный *adj.* **1,** forever worrying about one's health. **2,** suspicious; distrustful.
мни́ть *v. impfv., obs.* to imagine. —**мнить себя́** (+ *instr.*), to imagine oneself to be; see oneself as; like to think of oneself as. —**мно́го** (*or* **высоко́**) **мнить о себе́,** to have a high opinion of oneself.
мно́гие *adj.* many: мно́гие дома́, many houses; со мно́гими друзья́ми, with many friends. —*indef. pron.* many; many people: мно́гие счита́ют, что..., many people believe that...
мно́го *adv.* much; a lot; a great deal: я мно́го о вас слы́шал(а), I've heard a lot about you. Ви́деть и слы́шать мно́го, to see and hear a great deal. —*adj.* (*with gen.*) many; much; a lot of; a great deal of: мно́го рабо́ты, a lot of work; мно́го друзе́й, many friends. —**ни мно́го ни ма́ло,** as much as; no less than. *See also* **мно́гое.**
многобо́жие *n.* polytheism.
многобра́чие *n.* polygamy. —**многобра́чный,** *adj.* polygamous.
многова́то *adv., colloq.* a bit too much.
многогра́нник *n.* polyhedron. —**многогра́нный,** *adj.* polyhedral; many-sided.
мно́гое [*gen.* **мно́гого;** *dat.* **мно́гому;** *instr.* **мно́гим;** *prepl.* **мно́гом**] *n., decl. as an adj.* much; a great deal: о́пыт нас у́чит мно́гому, experience teaches us a great deal. Я мно́гим ему́ обя́зан, I am much indebted to him. —**во мно́гом,** in many respects; largely; in large part.
многоже́нец [*gen.* **-нца**] *n.* polygamist. —**многожёнство,** *n.* polygamy.
многозначи́тельный *adj.* **1,** significant. **2,** (*of a look, smile, etc.*) knowing.
многокра́сочный *adj.* multicolored; polychromatic.
многокра́тный *adj.* **1,** repeated; frequent. **2,** *gram.* frequentative: многокра́тный вид, frequentative aspect. —**многокра́тно,** *adv.* repeatedly.
многоле́тний *adj.* **1,** of many years. **2,** long-lived. **3,** *bot.* perennial.
многолю́дный *adj.* **1,** populous. **2,** crowded.
многомиллио́нный *adj.* consisting of many millions.
многонациона́льный *adj.* multinational.
многоно́жка [*gen. pl.* **-жек**] *n.* myriapod; centipede; millipede.
многообеща́ющий *adj.* promising; up-and-coming.
многообра́зие *n.* variety; diversity.
многообра́зный *adj.* varied; diverse.
многоречи́вый *adj.* loquacious; verbose; long-winded.
многосеме́йный *adj.* having a large family.
многосло́вие *n.* verbosity. —**многосло́вный,** *adj.* long-winded; verbose.
многосло́жный *adj.* polysyllabic.
многосторо́нний *adj.* **1,** multilateral. **2,** *fig.* versatile. —**многосторо́нность,** *n.f.* versatility.
многострада́льный *adj.* long-suffering.
многоступе́нчатый *adj.* multistage.
многотира́жка [*gen. pl.* **-жек**] *n., colloq.* company newspaper; house organ.
многотира́жный *adj.* (*of a publication*) having a large circulation.
многото́мный *adj.* multivolume.
многото́чие *n.* suspension points (......).
многоуважа́емый *adj.* (*in salutations of letters*) dear: многоуважа́емый Ива́н Петро́вич, Dear Ivan Petrovich.
многоуго́льник *n.* polygon. —**многоуго́льный,** *adj.* polygonal.
многоцве́тный *adj.* multicolored; polychromatic.
многочи́сленность *n.f.* **1,** great number. **2,** large size (*of a family, army, etc.*).
многочи́сленный *adj.* **1,** numerous. **2,** consisting of many people; large.
многочле́н *n.* polynomial. —**многочле́нный,** *adj.* polynomial.
многоэта́жный *adj.* multistoried.
многоязы́чный *adj.* multilingual; polyglot.
мно́жественность *n.f.* multiplicity.
мно́жественный *adj.* plural. —**мно́жественное число́,** *gram.* the plural.
мно́жество *n.* **1,** (*with gen.*) a great number (of); a multitude (of). **2,** *math. set:* тео́рия мно́жеств, theory of sets. —**во мно́жестве,** in great numbers.
мно́жимое *n., decl. as an adj., math.* multiplicand.
мно́житель *n.m., math.* **1,** multiplier. **2,** factor.
мно́жить *v. impfv.* [*pfv.* **помно́жить** *or* **умно́жить**] **1,** *math.* to multiply. **2,** *fig.* to increase; augment. —**мно́житься,** *refl.* [*pfv.* **умно́житься**] to multiply; increase in number.
мной *also,* **мно́ю** *pron., instr. of* **я.**
мобилиза́ция *n.* mobilization. —**мобилизацио́нный,** *adj.* mobilization (*attrib.*).
мобилизова́ть *v. impfv. & pfv.* [*pres.* **-зу́ю, -зу́ешь**] **1,** to mobilize. **2,** *fig.* to mobilize; muster; rally. —**мобилизова́ться,** *refl.* **1,** to mobilize; be mobilized. **2,** *fig.* to brace oneself; buckle down.
моби́льный *adj.* mobile. —**моби́льность,** *n.f.* mobility.
моги́ла *n.* grave. —**своди́ть в моги́лу,** to be the death of. —**стоя́ть одно́й ного́й в моги́ле,** to have one foot in the grave.
моги́льный *adj.* **1,** grave (*attrib.*); burial (*attrib.*). **2,** deathly; sepulchral. —**моги́льная плита́,** gravestone.
моги́льщик *n.* gravedigger.
896го́л *n.* Mogul.
могу́чий *adj.* powerful; mighty.
могу́щественный *adj.* powerful; mighty.
могу́щество *n.* power; might.
мо́да *n.* fashion; style; vogue: быть в мо́де, to be in style. —**войти́ в мо́ду,** to come into fashion. —**вы́йти из мо́ды,** to go out of style.
мода́льный *adj.* modal.
модели́ровать (дэ) *v. impfv. & pfv.* [*pres.* **-рую, -руешь**] to design (clothes).
моде́ль (дэ) *n.f.* model.
моделье́р (дэ) *n.* designer (*of clothes*).
моде́льный (дэ) *adj.* **1,** model (*attrib.*); pattern (*attrib.*): моде́льный цех, pattern shop. **2,** fashionable.
моде́льщик (дэ) *n.* modeler.
моде́рн (дэ) *n.* modernist style. —*adj. indecl.* modern: та́нец моде́рн, modern dance.
модерниза́ция (дэ) *n.* modernization.
модернизи́ровать (дэ) *v. impfv. & pfv.* [*pres.* **-рую, -руешь**] to modernize.
модерни́зм (дэ) *n.* modernism. —**модерни́ст,** *n.* modernist. —**модерни́стский,** *adj.* modernistic.
моди́стка [*gen. pl.* **-сток**] *n.* milliner.
модифика́ция *n.* modification.

модифици́ровать *v. impfv. & pfv.* [*pres.* **-рую, -руешь**] to modify.
мо́дник *n.m.* [*fem.* **-ница**] *colloq.* fashion plate.
мо́дничать *v. impfv., colloq.* to dress fashionably; dress in the latest fashions.
мо́дно *adv.* stylishly; fashionably. —*adj., used predicatively* fashionable: стать мо́дно, to become fashionable.
мо́дный *adj.* **1,** fashionable; stylish. **2,** fashion (*attrib.*): мо́дный журна́л, fashion magazine.
модули́ровать *v. impfv.* [*pres.* **-рую, -руешь**] to modulate.
мо́дуль *n.m.* module; modulus.
модуля́тор *n.* modulator.
модуля́ция *n.* modulation. —**частóтная модуля́ция,** frequency modulation.
моёвка [*gen. pl.* **-вок**] *n.* kittiwake.
можжеве́льник *n.* juniper. —**можжевёловый,** *adj.* juniper (*attrib.*).
мо́жно *predicate* may; can; it is permitted: мо́жно войти́?, may I come in? Здесь мо́жно кури́ть, you may smoke here; you are allowed to smoke here. —**как мо́жно** (+ *comp.*), as ... as possible: как мо́жно бо́льше, as much as possible; как мо́жно скоре́е, as soon as possible.
моза́ика *n.* mosaic; inlay. —**моза́ичный,** *adj.* mosaic; inlaid.
мозг [*2nd loc.* **мозгу́**; *pl.* **мозги́**] *n.* **1,** brain. **2,** *pl.* brains (*food*). —**головно́й мозг,** cerebrum. —**ко́стный мозг,** marrow. —**продолгова́тый мозг,** medulla oblongata. —**спинно́й мозг,** spinal cord.
мозгови́тый *adj., colloq.* brainy.
мозгово́й *adj.* brain (*attrib.*); cerebral.
мозжечо́к [*gen.* **-чка́**] *n.* cerebellum.
мозо́листый *adj.* calloused.
мозо́ль *n.f.* callus; corn. —**мозо́льный,** *adj.* for removing corns: мозо́льный пла́стырь, corn plaster.
мой [*fem.* **моя́**; *neut.* **моё**; *pl.* **мои́**; *gen.* **моего́, мое́й, мои́х**; *acc. fem.* **мою́**; *dat.* **моему́, мое́й, мои́м**; *instr.* **мои́м, мое́й, мои́ми**; *prepl.* **моём, мое́й, мои́х**] *poss. adj. & pron.* my; mine.
мо́йка *n.* **1,** *colloq.* washing. **2,** washer (*machine*).
мо́йщик *n.* washer (*one who washes*).
мокаси́н [*gen. pl.* **-си́н**] *n.* moccasin.
мокаси́новый *adj., in* **мокаси́новая змея́,** moccasin (*snake*).
мо́кко *n.indecl.* mocha.
мо́кнуть *v. impfv.* [*past* **мок, -ла**] **1,** to become wet; get wet. **2,** to soak.
мокри́ца *n.* wood louse.
мокрова́тый *adj.* moist; damp.
мокро́та *n.* phlegm.
мокрота́ *n., colloq.* **1,** dampness; humidity. **2,** light rain; wet snow.
мо́крый *adj.* wet. —**у неё глаза́ на мо́кром ме́сте,** she is easily moved to tears.
мол[1] *n.* breakwater; jetty.
мол[2] *particle, colloq.* he says; they say.
молва́ *n.* rumors; talk.
мо́лвить *v. impfv. & pfv.* [*pres.* **-влю, -вишь**] *obs., poetic* to say.
молдава́нин [*pl.* **-ва́не, -за́н**] *n.m.* [*fem.* **-ва́нка**] Moldavian. —**молда́вский,** *adj.* Moldavian.
моле́бен [*gen.* **-бна**] *n.* short church service.
моле́кула *n.* molecule. —**молекуля́рный,** *adj.* molecular.
моле́льня [*gen. pl.* **-лен**] *n.* prayer house; meeting house.
моле́ние *n.* **1,** prayer service: соверши́ть моле́ние, to hold a prayer service. **2,** entreaty; supplication.
молески́н *n.* moleskin (*cloth*). —**молески́новый,** *adj.* moleskin.
молибде́н (дэ) *n.* molybdenum. —**молибде́новый,** *adj.* molybdic.
моли́тва *n.* prayer. —**моли́твенник,** *n.* prayer book. —**моли́твенный,** *adj.* of prayer.
моли́ть *v. impfv.* [*pres.* **молю́, мо́лишь**] (*with* **о**) to beg (for); plead (for). —**моли́ться,** *refl.* **1,** [*pfv.* **помоли́ться**] to pray. **2,** (*with* **на** + *acc.*) *colloq.* to idolize.
моллю́ск *n.* mollusk.
молниено́сный *adj.* quick as lightning; lightning-fast. —**молниено́сная война́,** blitzkrieg.
молниеотво́д *n.* lightning rod.
мо́лния *n.* **1,** lightning. **2,** [*also,* **застёжка-мо́лния**] zipper. **3,** express telegram. **4,** special edition (*of a newspaper*).
молодёжный *adj.* youth (*attrib.*).
молодёжь *n.f.* youth; young people.
моло́денький *adj., colloq.* young; very young.
молоде́ть *v. impfv.* [*pfv.* **помолоде́ть**] to get younger; become young again.
молоде́ц [*gen.* **-дца́**] *n.* good boy; fine fellow. —*interj.* well done!
молоде́цкий *adj.* bold; dashing.
молоде́чество *n.* daring; bravado.
молоди́ть *v. impfv.* [*pres.* **-ложу́, -лоди́шь**] to make (someone) look younger; give a youthful appearance (to).
молодня́к [*gen.* **-няка́**] *n.* **1,** saplings. **2,** young animals. **3,** *colloq.* youth; the younger generation.
молодожёны [*gen.* **-жёнов**] *n. pl.* newlyweds.
молодо́й *adj.* [*short form* **мо́лод, молода́, мо́лодо**; *comp.* **моло́же**] **1,** young. **2,** (*of qualities or emotions*) youthful: молодо́й задо́р, youthful enthusiasm. **3,** (*of potatoes, wine, etc.*) new. —**молоды́е,** *n. pl.* **1,** young people. **2,** young couple; newlyweds. **3,** (*of animals*) newly-born; (their) young.
мо́лодость *n.f.* youth. —**втора́я мо́лодость,** new lease on life. —**не пе́рвой мо́лодости,** getting on in years; no spring chicken. —**по мо́лодости лет,** through inexperience.
молодцева́тый *adj.* dashing.
моло́дчик *n., colloq.* punk; thug.
молодчи́на *n.m., colloq.* = **молоде́ц.**
моложа́вый *adj.* young-looking; youthful.
моло́же *adj., comp. of* **молодо́й.**
моло́ки [*gen.* **-ло́к**] *n. pl.* milt; soft roe.
молоко́ *n.* milk. —**кровь с молоко́м,** the picture of health.
молокосо́с *n., colloq.* greenhorn; neophyte.
мо́лот *n.* (large) hammer; sledgehammer.
молоти́лка [*gen. pl.* **-лок**] *n.* thresher; threshing machine.
молоти́льщик *n.* thresher (*one who threshes*).
молоти́ть *v. impfv.* [*pres.* **-лочу́, -ло́тишь**] **1,** to thresh. **2,** *colloq.* to thrash.
молото́к [*gen.* **-тка́**] *n.* hammer. —**продава́ть с молотка́,** to auction (off).
мо́лот-ры́ба *n.* hammerhead (*fish*).

мо́лотый *adj.* ground.
моло́ть *v. impfv.* [*pfv.* **смоло́ть;** *pres.* **мелю́, ме́лешь**] **1,** to grind. **2,** [*impfv. only*] *colloq.* to talk (nonsense).
молотьба́ *n.* **1,** threshing. **2,** threshing season.
моло́чная *n., decl. as an adj.* dairy.
моло́чник *n.* **1,** milk pitcher. **2,** milkman; dairyman.
моло́чница *n.* **1,** dairymaid. **2,** thrush (*disease*).
моло́чный *adj.* **1,** milk (*attrib.*). **2,** dairy (*attrib.*). **3,** milky. **4,** suckling. **5,** lactic. —**моло́чные же́лезы,** mammary glands. —**моло́чный зуб,** baby tooth. —**моло́чная коро́ва,** milch cow. —**моло́чный са́хар,** milk sugar; lactose. —**моло́чный скот,** dairy cattle.
мо́лча *adv.* silently; in silence.
молчали́вый *adj.* **1,** taciturn; reticent. **2,** tacit. —**молчали́вость,** *n.f.* taciturnity; reticence.
молча́ние *n.* silence. —**обойти́ (что́-нибудь) молча́нием,** to pass over in silence. —**храни́ть молча́ние,** to maintain silence; keep/remain silent.
молча́ть *v. impfv.* [*pres.* **-чу́, -чи́шь**] to be quiet; keep quiet; be silent.
моль *n.f.* moth; clothes moth.
мольба́ *n.* entreaty; supplication.
мольбе́рт *n.* easel.
моля́щийся *n., decl. as an adj.* worshiper.
моме́нт *n.* **1,** moment; instant: в да́нный моме́нт, at the present moment. **2,** feature; element; factor; aspect.
момента́льно *adv.* instantly; instantaneously; immediately. —**момента́льный,** *adj.* instantaneous.
мона́рх *n.* monarch. —**монархи́зм,** *n.* monarchism. —**монархи́ст,** *n.* monarchist. —**монархи́ческий,** *adj.* monarchist; monarchical. —**мона́рхия,** *n.* monarchy.
монасты́рь [*gen.* **-ря́**] *n.m.* monastery; convent; cloister. —**монасты́рский,** *adj.* of a monastery; monasterial.
мона́х *n.* monk. —**постри́чься в мона́хи,** to take the monastic vows.
мона́хиня *n.* nun. —**постри́чься в мона́хини,** to take the veil.
мона́шенка [*gen. pl.* **-нок**] *n., colloq.* nun.
мона́шеский *adj.* monastic.
мона́шество *n.* **1,** monasticism; monkhood. **2,** monks.
монго́л *n.m.* [*fem.* **-го́лка**] Mongol. —**монго́льский,** *adj.* Mongol; Mongolian.
моне́та *n.* coin. Ме́лкая *or* разме́нная моне́та, small change. —**плати́ть той же моне́той,** to repay in kind. —**принима́ть за чи́стую моне́ту,** to take in good faith; take at face value.
моне́тный *adj.* monetary. —**моне́тный двор,** mint.
мони́зм *n.* monism. —**монисти́ческий,** *adj.* monistic.
мони́сто *n.* necklace (*of beads or coins*).
монога́мия *n.* monogamy. —**монога́мный,** *adj.* monogamous.
моногра́мма *n.* monogram.
моногра́фия *n.* monograph. —**монографи́ческий,** *adj.* monographic.
моно́кль *n.m.* monocle.
моноли́т *n.* monolith.
моноли́тный *adj.* monolithic. —**моноли́тность,** *n.f.* monolithic nature.
моноло́г *n.* monologue.
мононуклео́з *n.* mononucleosis.
монопла́н *n.* monoplane.
монополиза́ция *n.* monopolization.
монополизи́ровать *v. impfv. & pfv.* [*pres.* **-рую, -руешь**] to monopolize.
монополи́ст *n.* monopolist. —**монополисти́ческий,** *adj.* monopolistic.
монопо́лия *n.* monopoly.
монопо́льный *adj.* **1,** monopoly (*attrib.*). **2,** exclusive.
монотеи́зм (тэ) *n.* monotheism. —**монотеисти́ческий,** *adj.* monotheistic.
моноти́п *n.* monotype.
моното́нный *adj.* **1,** monotone. **2,** monotonous. —**моното́нность,** *n.f.* monotony.
монохромати́ческий *adj.* monochromatic.
монсеньёр *n.* Monsignor.
монта́ж [*gen.* **-жа́**] *n.* **1,** assembling; installing (*of machinery*). **2,** editing (*of a film or literary work*); arrangement (*of a musical composition*). **3,** montage.
монтёр *n.* **1,** fitter. **2,** electrician.
монти́ровать *v. impfv.* [*pfv.* **смонти́ровать;** *pres.* **-рую, -руешь**] **1,** to assemble. **2,** to edit (a film).
монуме́нт *n.* monument. —**монумента́льный,** *adj.* monumental.
мопе́д *n.* motorbike; moped.
мопс *n.* pug (*dog*).
морализи́ровать *v. impfv.* [*pres.* **-рую, -руешь**] to moralize.
морали́ст *n.* moralist.
мора́ль *n.f.* **1,** morals; morality. **2,** moral; moral lesson. **3,** *colloq.* moralizing. —**чита́ть мора́ль** (+ *dat.*), to lecture; preach (to).
мора́льно *adv.* morally.
мора́льный *adj.* moral. —**мора́льное состоя́ние,** morale. —**мора́льный изно́с,** obsolescence.
морато́рий *n.* moratorium.
морг *n.* morgue; mortuary.
морганати́ческий *adj.* morganatic.
морга́ть *v. impfv.* [*pfv.* **моргну́ть**] **1,** to blink. **2,** (*with instr.*) to blink (one's eyes). **3,** (*with dat.*) to wink (at). **4,** to twinkle; flicker. —**гла́зом не моргну́в,** without batting an eye.
мо́рда *n.* **1,** snout; muzzle. **2,** *colloq.* face; mug.
мордви́н *n.m.* [*fem.* **-ви́нка**] Mordvin (*one of a people inhabiting central European Russia*). —**мордо́вский,** *adj.* Mordvinian; Mordovian.
мо́ре [*pl.* **моря́, море́й**] *n.* sea. —**вы́йти в мо́ре,** to put (out) to sea.
море́на *n.* moraine.
морёный *adj.* stained: морёный дуб, stained oak.
морепла́вание *n.* navigation. —**морепла́ватель,** *n.m.* navigator.
морехо́д *n.* = **морепла́ватель.**
морехо́дный *adj.* **1,** nautical; navigational. **2,** seaworthy.
морж [*gen.* **моржа́**] *n.* walrus.
Мо́рзе (зэ) *n. indecl., in* **а́збука Мо́рзе,** Morse code.
мори́лка *n.* stain (*for wood*).
мори́ть *v. impfv.* **1,** [*pfv.* **вы́морить**] to exterminate; poison (insects, rodents, etc.). **2,** [*pfv.* **замори́ть**] *colloq.* to wear out; exhaust. **3,** [*impfv. only*] to stain (wood). —**мори́ть го́лодом,** to starve.
морко́вь *n.f.* **1,** carrots. **2,** a (single) carrot. —**морко́вный,** *adj.* carrot (*attrib.*).
мормо́н *n.* Mormon. —**мормо́нский,** *adj.* Mormon.
моро́женое *n., decl. as an adj.* ice cream.
моро́женщик *n.* ice-cream vendor.

моро́женый *adj.* frozen.
моро́з *n.* **1,** frost: де́сять гра́дусов моро́за, ten degrees of frost. **2,** freezing weather.
моро́зец [*gen.* **-зца**] *n., colloq.* slight frost.
моро́зилка *also,* **морози́лка** [*gen. pl.* **-лок**] *n.* freezing compartment; freezer.
моро́зить *v. impfv.* [*pres.* **-жу, -зишь**] **1,** to freeze. **2,** *impers.* to be freezing: на дворе́ моро́зит, it is freezing outside.
моро́зный *adj.* frosty; freezing.
морозосто́йкий *adj.* frost-resistant; hardy.
мороси́ть *v. impfv.* to drizzle.
моро́чить *v. impfv.* [*pfv.* **обморо́чить**] *colloq.* to trick; fool. —**моро́чить го́лову** (+ *dat.*), to mislead; deceive.
моро́шка *n.* **1,** cloudberries. **2,** a (single) cloudberry.
морс *n.* fruit drink.
морско́й *adj.* sea (*attrib.*); maritime; marine; naval; nautical. —**морска́я боле́знь,** seasickness. —**морска́я пехо́та,** the marines. —**морско́й флот,** navy.
морти́ра *n., mil.* mortar.
морфе́ма *n.* morpheme.
мо́рфий *n.* morphine.
морфини́ст *n.* morphine addict.
морфоло́гия *n.* morphology. —**морфологи́ческий,** *adj.* morphological.
морщи́на *n.* wrinkle. —**морщи́нистый,** *adj.* wrinkled.
мо́рщить *v. impfv.* [*pfv.* **намо́рщить** *or* **смо́рщить**] to wrinkle; pucker. —**мо́рщиться,** *refl.* **1,** [*pfv.* **намо́рщиться**] (*of one's skin, eyebrows, etc.*) to become wrinkled; contract; pucker. **2,** [*pfv.* **смо́рщиться** *or* **помо́рщиться**] to make a face; wince. **3,** [*pfv.* **смо́рщиться**] *colloq.* (*of material*) to crease; become creased.
морщи́ть *v. impfv., colloq.* (*of material*) to become creased; pucker.
моря́к [*gen.* **-яка́**] *n.* sailor; seaman.
москате́ль *n.f.* paint supplies. —**москате́льный,** *adj.* pert. to paint supplies: москате́льный магази́н, store selling paint supplies.
москви́ч [*gen.* **-вича́**] *n.* Muscovite; native of Moscow.
моски́т *n.* sand fly.
моско́вский *adj.* Moscow (*attrib.*).
мост [*gen.* **мо́ста** *or* **моста́**; *2nd loc.* **мосту́**; *pl.* **мосты́**] *n.* bridge.
мо́стик *n.* **1,** small bridge; footbridge. **2,** bridge (*of a ship*).
мости́ть *v. impfv.* [*pfv.* **вы́мостить**; *pres.* **мощу́, мости́шь**] to pave.
мостки́ [*gen.* **-ко́в**] *n. pl.* **1,** planked walkway; footbridge. **2,** wooden platform (*extending out over water*).
мостова́я *n., decl. as an adj.* roadway.
мостово́й *adj.* bridge (*attrib.*).
мосье́ *n.m. indecl.* monsieur.
мо́ська *n., colloq.* pug (*dog*).
мот *n., colloq.* spendthrift.
мота́льный *adj., mech.* winding.
мота́ть *v. impfv.* [*pfv.* **намота́ть**] **1,** to wind. **2,** [*impfv. only*] (*with instr.*) *colloq.* to shake (one's head). —**мота́ть себе́ на ус,** *colloq.* to make a mental note of.
мота́ться *v.r. impfv., colloq.* to dangle; bob.
моте́ль (тэ) *n.m.* motel.
моти́в *n.* **1,** motive; reason. **2,** motif; theme. **3,** tune; melody.
мотиви́ровать *v. impfv. & pfv.* [*pres.* **-рую, -руешь**] to explain; justify; give reasons for; show just cause for.
мотиviро́вка *n.* reasons; justification.
мотобо́л *n.* football (soccer) played on motorcycles.
мотовство́ *n.* extravagance; prodigality.
мотого́нки [*gen.* **-нок**] *n. pl.* motorcycle races/racing.
мото́к [*gen.* **-тка́**] *n.* skein; hank (*of thread*).
мотопехо́та *n.* motorized infantry.
мотопила́ *n.* power saw.
мото́р *n.* motor; engine.
моторизо́ванный *adj.* motorized.
мото́рный *adj.* motor (*attrib.*).
моторо́ллер *n.* motor scooter.
мотоци́кл *also,* **мотоцикле́т** *n.* motorcycle. —**мотоцикли́ст,** *n.* motorcyclist.
моты́га *n.* hoe.
моты́жить *v. impfv.* to hoe.
мотылёк [*gen.* **-лька́**] *n.* moth.
мох [*gen.* **мха** *or* **мо́ха**] *n.* moss.
мохе́р *n.* mohair. —**мохе́ровый,** *adj.* mohair.
мохна́тый *adj.* shaggy; hairy. —**мохна́тое полоте́нце,** Turkish towel.
моцио́н *n.* exercise.
моча́ *n.* urine.
моча́лка [*gen. pl.* **-лок**] *n.* piece of bast used as a bath sponge.
моча́ло *n.* bast.
мочеви́на *n.* urea.
мочево́й *adj.* **1,** urinary. **2,** uric. —**мочева́я кислота́,** uric acid. —**мочево́й песо́к,** *med.* gravel.
мочего́нный *adj.* diuretic. —**мочего́нное сре́дство,** diuretic.
мочеиспуска́ние *n.* urination.
мочеиспуска́тельный *adj.* urinary. —**мочеиспуска́тельный кана́л,** urethra.
мочёный *adj.* (*of foods*) soaked.
мочи́ть *v. impfv.* [*pfv.* **намочи́ть** *or* **замочи́ть**; *pres.* **мочу́, мо́чишь**] **1,** to wet. **2,** to get (something) wet. **3,** to soak. —**мочи́ться,** *refl.* [*pfv.* **помочи́ться**] to urinate.
мо́чка [*gen. pl.* **-чек**] *n.* **1,** wetting; soaking. **2,** ear lobe.
мочь[1] *v. impfv.* [*pfv.* **смочь**; *pres.* **могу́, мо́жешь, ...мо́гут**; *past* **мог, могла́, могло́**] to be able. —**мо́жет быть,** perhaps; maybe. —**не мо́жет быть!,** impossible!; it can't be! —**не мочь не** (+ *inf.*), one can't help: я не могу́ не ду́мать об э́том, I can't help thinking about it.
мочь[2] *n.f., colloq.* power; might. —**во всю мочь,** with all one's might.
моше́нник *n.* swindler.
моше́нничать *v. impfv.* [*pfv.* **смоше́нничать**] to practice fraud.
моше́ннический *adj.* fraudulent. —**моше́нничество,** *n.* swindle; swindling; fraud.
мо́шка [*gen. pl.* **-шек**] *n.* gnat; midge. —**мошкара́,** *n.* gnats.
мошо́нка *n.* scrotum.
моще́ние *n.* paving.
мощёный *adj.* paved.
мо́щи [*gen.* **моще́й**] *n. pl.* earthly remains (*of a saint*).
мо́щность *n.f.* **1,** power. **2,** output; capacity: рабо́тать на по́лную мо́щность, to operate at full capacity.
мо́щный *adj.* powerful.
мощь *n.f.* power; might.
мо́ющий *adj., in* **мо́ющее сре́дство,** cleanser; detergent.

мрак *n.* darkness; gloom.
мракобе́с *n.* obscurantist. —**мракобе́сие,** *n.* obscurantism.
мра́мор *n.* marble. —**мра́морный,** *adj.* marble.
мрачне́ть *v. impfv.* [*pfv.* **помрачне́ть**] to grow dark; become gloomy.
мра́чный *adj.* **1,** gloomy; dismal; dreary. **2,** somber; morose; glum. —**мра́чность,** *n.f.* gloominess; dreariness; moroseness.
мсти́тель *n.m.* avenger.
мсти́тельный *adj.* vindictive. —**мсти́тельность,** *n.f.* vindictiveness.
мстить *v. impfv.* [*pfv.* **отомсти́ть;** *pres.* **мщу, мстишь**] **1,** (*with dat.*) to take revenge on. **2,** (*with* **за** + *acc.*) to avenge.
муа́р *n.* moire. —**муа́ровый,** *adj.* moiré.
мудрено́ *adj., used predicatively* difficult; next to impossible: мудрено́ поня́ть его́, there is no making him out. —**не мудрено́,** it is no wonder.
мудрёный *adj., colloq.* **1,** difficult; hard to understand; esoteric. **2,** (*of a task*) difficult; formidable. **3,** intricate; fancy. **4,** odd; queer.
мудре́ц [*gen.* **-реца́**] *n.* wise man; sage.
мудри́ть *v. impfv., colloq.* to (try to) be clever.
му́дрость *n.f.* wisdom.
му́дрствовать *v. impfv.* [*pres.* **-ствую, -ствуешь**] *colloq.* to philosophize. —**не му́дрствуя лука́во,** without equivocation; without beating around the bush.
му́дрый *adj.* wise.
муж [*pl.* **мужья́, муже́й, мужья́м**] *n.* husband.
мужа́ть *v. impfv.* to mature; become a man. —**мужа́ться,** *refl.* (*usu. imperative*) to be brave.
мужеподо́бный *adj.* mannish.
му́жественно *adv.* bravely; courageously.
му́жественность *n.f.* **1,** courageousness. **2,** manliness; masculinity.
му́жественный *adj.* **1,** brave; courageous. **2,** manly.
му́жество *n.* courage.
мужи́к [*gen.* **-ика́**] *n., pre-rev.* Russian peasant; muzhik.
мужско́й *adj.* **1,** masculine; male. **2,** man's; men's.
мужчи́на *n.m.* man.
му́за *n.* muse.
музе́й *n.* museum.
музе́йный *adj.* museum (*attrib.*). —**музе́йная ре́дкость,** museum piece.
му́зыка *n.* music. —**испо́ртить всю му́зыку,** *colloq.* to upset the applecart.
музыка́льный *adj.* **1,** music (*attrib.*). **2,** musical. —**музыка́льный ве́чер,** musicale. —**музыка́льный слух,** ear for music. —**музыка́льная шкату́лка; музыка́льный я́щик,** music box.
музыка́нт *n.* musician.
музыкове́д *n.* musicologist. —**музыкове́дение,** *n.* musicology.
му́ка *n.* **1,** torment; torture. **2,** *pl.* pangs; throes.
мука́ *n.* **1,** flour. **2,** meal.
мукомо́льный *adj.* flour-milling (*attrib.*).
мул *n.* mule.
мула́т *n.m.* [*fem.* **-ка**] mulatto.
мулла́ *n.m.* mullah.
мультимиллионе́р *n.* multimillionaire.
мультипликацио́нный *adj., in* **мультипликацио́нный фильм,** animated cartoon.
мультиплика́ция *n.* **1,** making of animated cartoons. **2,** cartoon.
му́льча *n.* mulch.
му́мия *n.* mummy.
мунди́р *n.* uniform dress coat. —**карто́фель в мунди́ре,** potatoes boiled in their skins.
мундшту́к [*gen.* **-штука́**] *n.* **1,** mouthpiece. **2,** cigarette holder; cigar holder.
муниципалите́т *n.* municipality.
муниципа́льный *adj.* municipal.
мура́ *n., colloq.* rubbish; nonsense.
мураве́й [*gen.* **-вья́**] *n.* ant.
мураве́йник *n.* anthill.
муравье́д *n.* anteater.
муравьи́ный *adj.* **1,** ant (*attrib.*); ants'. **2,** *chem.* formic.
мура́шки *n. pl, colloq., in* **мура́шки бе́гают (забе́гали, поползли́) по спине́** (*with* **у**), to get the creeps; get chills up and down one's spine.
муре́на *n.* moray (eel).
мурлы́канье *n.* purr; purring.
мурлы́кать *v. impfv.* [*pres.* **-лы́чу, -лы́чешь**] **1,** to purr. **2,** *colloq.* to hum.
муска́т *n.* **1,** nutmeg. **2,** muscat (*grape*). **3,** muscatel (*wine*). —**муска́тник,** *n.* nutmeg (*tree*).
муска́тный *adj.* nutmeg. —**муска́тное вино́,** muscatel wine. —**муска́тный оре́х,** nutmeg. —**муска́тный цвет,** mace (*spice*).
му́скул *n.* muscle. —**мускулату́ра,** *n.* muscles; musculature. —**му́скулистый,** *adj.* muscular; brawny. —**му́скульный,** *adj.* muscle (*attrib.*); muscular.
му́скус *n.* musk. —**му́скусный,** *adj.* musk (*attrib.*).
мусли́н *n.* muslin. —**мусли́новый,** *adj.* muslin.
му́сор *n.* garbage; rubbish; refuse; trash.
му́сорный *adj.* garbage (*attrib.*); rubbish (*attrib.*); refuse (*attrib.*); trash (*attrib.*). —**му́сорный я́щик,** garbage can; trash can.
мусоропрово́д *n.* garbage chute; refuse chute.
мусоросжига́тельный *adj., in* **мусоросжига́тельная печь,** incinerator.
му́сорщик *n.* garbage collector.
мусс *n.* mousse.
мусси́ровать *v. impfv.* [*pres.* **-рую, -руешь**] to spread; fan (rumors, fears, etc.).
муссо́н *n.* monsoon.
муста́нг *n.* mustang.
мусульма́нин [*pl.* **-ма́не, -ма́н**] *n.m.* [*fem.* **-ма́нка**] Moslem. —**мусульма́нский,** *adj.* Moslem. —**мусульма́нство,** *n.* Mohammedanism; Islam.
мута́ция *n.* mutation.
мути́ть *v. impfv.* [*pres.* **мучу́, мути́шь** *or* **му́тишь**] **1,** [*pfv.* **замути́ть**] to make turbid; muddy (water). **2,** [*pfv.* **помути́ть**] to dull; cloud (the senses). **3,** *in* **мути́ть во́ду,** *fig.* to muddy the waters. **4,** *impers., colloq.* to feel nauseous: его́ мути́т, he feels nauseous. —**мути́ться,** *refl.* [*pfv.* **замути́ться** *or* **помути́ться**] **1,** to become cloudy. **2,** to be dulled.
мутне́ть *v. impfv.* [*pfv.* **помутне́ть**] to become cloudy; become muddy.
му́тный *adj.* **1,** turbid; murky. **2,** clouded; misty. **3,** dull; dim. —**му́тность,** *n.f.* turbidity.
муто́вка [*gen. pl.* **-вок**] *n.* **1,** *bot.* whorl. **2,** stick for churning or whipping.
муть *n.f.* **1,** dregs; lees. **2,** haze; mist.
му́фта *n.* **1,** muff. **2,** *mech.* coupling; clutch.
му́фтий *n.* mufti (*interpreter of Moslem law*).
му́ха *n.* fly (*insect*). —**де́лать из му́хи слона́,** to make a mountain out of a molehill. —**кака́я му́ха его́ укуси́ла?,** what's eating him? —**он и му́хи не оби́дит,** he wouldn't hurt a fly. —**слы́шно, как му́ха пролети́т,** you could have heard a pin drop.
мухоло́вка [*gen. pl.* **-вок**] *n.* **1,** flytrap; flycatcher. **2,** flycatcher (*bird*). **3,** flytrap (*plant*).

мухомо́р *n.* a variety of poisonous mushroom; fly agaric.
муче́ние *n.* torment; torture.
му́ченик *n.* martyr. —**му́ченический,** *adj.* martyr's. —**му́ченичество,** *n.* martyrdom.
мучи́тель *n.m.* tormentor.
мучи́тельно *adv.* **1,** painfully. **2,** terribly. —*adj., used predicatively* agonizing: мучи́тельно смотре́ть на них, it is an agony/ordeal to look at them.
мучи́тельный *adj.* **1,** painful; agonizing; excruciating. **2,** of anguish; anguished.
му́чить *v. impfv.* [*pfv.* **му́чу, му́чишь** *or* **му́чаю, му́чаешь**] to torment; harass; plague. —**му́читься,** *refl.* **1,** to suffer. **2,** (*with instr.*) to be plagued (with). **3,** (*with* **с** *or* **над**) to slave (over).
мучни́стый *adj.* farinaceous. —**мучни́стая роса́,** mildew.
мучно́й *adj.* flour (*attrib.*).
му́шка [*gen. pl.* **-шек**] *n.* **1,** *dim. of* **му́ха. 2,** beauty spot. **3,** front sight (*on a firearm*). —**взять на му́шку,** to draw a bead on.
мушке́т *n.* musket. —**мушкетёр,** *n.* musketeer.
мушмула́ *n.* medlar.
муштра́ *n.* **1,** drill; drilling. **2,** strict discipline; regimentation.
муштрова́ть *v. impfv.* [*pfv.* **вымуштровать;** *pres.* **-тру́ю, -тру́ешь**] to drill.
муштро́вка *n.* drilling.
муэдзи́н *n.* muezzin.
мчать *v. impfv.* [*pfv.* **помча́ть;** *pres.* **мчу, мчишь**] to rush; whisk. —**мча́ться,** *refl.* to race; speed along; tear along.
мши́стый *adj.* mossy.
мще́ние *n.* revenge; vengeance.
мы [*gen., acc., & prepl.* **нас;** *dat.* **нам;** *instr.* **на́ми**] *pers. pron., 1st person pl.* **1,** we. **2,** (*with* **с** + *instr.*) and I: мы с ва́ми, you and I.
мы́лить *v. impfv.* [*pfv.* **намы́лить**] to soap; lather. —**мы́литься,** *refl.* to soap oneself.
мы́лкий *adj.* (*of soap*) soft; easily lathering.
мы́ло *n.* soap.
мыловаре́ние *n.* soap making.
мылова́ренный *adj., in* **мылова́ренный заво́д,** soap works.
мы́льница *n.* soap dish.
мы́льный *adj.* **1,** soap (*attrib.*). **2,** soapy.
мыльня́нка *n.* soapwort.
мыс *n., geog.* cape.
мы́сленный *adj.* mental. —**мы́сленно,** *adv.* mentally; in one's mind.
мы́слимый *adj.* conceivable.
мысли́тель *n.m.* thinker.
мы́слить *v. impfv.* to think; reason.
мысль *n.f.* **1,** thought. **2,** idea. —**за́дняя мысль,** ulterior motive. —**о́браз мы́слей,** way of thinking. —**ход мы́слей,** train of thought.
мы́слящий *adj.* thinking; capable of thinking.
мыта́рить *v. impfv., colloq.* to torment. —**мыта́риться,** *refl., colloq.* to suffer; have a hard time of it; go through hell.
мыта́рство *n., usu. pl.* ordeal; tribulation.
мыть *v. impfv.* [*pfv.* **помы́ть** *or* **вы́мыть;** *pres.* **мо́ю, мо́ешь**] to wash.
мытьё *n.* washing.
мы́ться *v.r. impfv.* [*pfv.* **помы́ться** *or* **вы́мыться;** *pres.* **мо́юсь, мо́ешься**] to wash; wash oneself.
мыча́ние *n.* **1,** moo; mooing. **2,** *colloq.* mumbling.
мыча́ть *v. impfv.* [*pres.* **-чу́, -чи́шь**] **1,** to moo; bellow. **2,** *colloq.* to mumble.
мышело́вка [*gen. pl.* **-вок**] *n.* mousetrap.
мы́шечный *adj.* muscle (*attrib.*); muscular.
мыши́ный *adj.* **1,** mouse (*attrib.*). **2,** like that of a mouse. —**мыши́ная возня́,** fuss over nothing.
мы́шка [*gen. pl.* **-шек**] *n.* **1,** *dim. of* **мышь. 2,** *in* **под мы́шкой** *and* **под мы́шку,** under one's arm: нести́ под мы́шкой, to carry under one's arm. —**игра́ в ко́шки-мы́шки,** cat-and-mouse game.
мышле́ние *also,* **мы́шление** *n.* thinking; thought.
мышо́нок [*gen.* **-нка;** *pl.* **-ша́та, -ша́т**] *n.* baby mouse.
мы́шца *n.* muscle.
мышь [*pl.* **мы́ши, мыше́й, мыша́м**] *n.f.* mouse. —**лету́чая мышь,** bat.
мышья́к [*gen.* **-яка́**] *n.* arsenic. —**мышьяко́вый,** *adj.* arsenic (*attrib.*).
мэр *n.* mayor.
мэ́рия *n.* **1,** city administration. **2,** city hall.
мю́зикл *n.* musical.
мю́зик-хо́лл *n.* music hall.
мя́гкий *adj.* [*short form* **мя́гок, мягка́, мя́гко;** *comp.* **мя́гче**] **1,** soft. **2,** mild. **3,** gentle. **4,** (*of punishment, a sentence, etc.*) light. —**мя́гкий ваго́н,** coach with soft (upholstered) seats. —**мя́гкий знак,** soft sign (ь).
мя́гко *adv.* **1,** softly. **2,** mildly. —**мя́гко выража́ясь,** to put it mildly.
мягкосерде́чие *n.* softheartedness; tenderheartedness. *Also,* **мягкосерде́чность,** *n.f.*
мягкосерде́чный *adj.* softhearted; tenderhearted.
мя́гкость *n.f.* softness; mildness; gentleness.
мягкоте́лый *adj.* **1,** flabby; soft. **2,** *fig.* spineless.
мя́гче *adj., comp. of* **мя́гкий.**
мягчи́ть *v. impfv.* to soften (*the skin*).
мяки́на *n.* chaff.
мя́киш *n.* the soft part of bread.
мя́кнуть *v. impfv.* [*pfv.* **размя́кнуть;** *past* **мяк, -ла**] to become soft; become flabby.
мя́коть *n.f.* **1,** flesh. **2,** pulp (*of fruit*).
мя́млить *v. impfv.* [*pfv.* **промя́млить**] *colloq.* **1,** to mumble. **2,** [*impfv. only*] to procrastinate. —**тяну́ть и мя́млить,** to hem and haw.
мя́мля *n.m. & f., colloq.* wishy-washy person.
мяси́стый *adj.* meaty; fleshy.
мясна́я *n., decl. as an adj., colloq.* butcher shop.
мясни́к [*gen.* **-ника́**] *n.* butcher.
мясно́й *adj.* meat (*attrib.*); beef (*attrib.*). —**мясна́я ла́вка,** butcher shop.
мя́со *n.* **1,** meat. **2,** flesh. —**сла́дкое мя́со,** sweetbread.
мясокомбина́т *n.* meat-packing plant.
мясору́бка [*gen. pl.* **-бок**] *n.* meat grinder.
мя́та *n., bot.* mint.
мяте́ж [*gen.* **-тежа́**] *n.* mutiny; revolt; rebellion. —**мяте́жник,** *n.* mutineer; rebel; insurgent.
мяте́жный *adj.* **1,** mutinous; rebellious. **2,** stormy; restless.
мя́тный *adj.* **1,** mint (*attrib.*). **2,** mint-flavored; peppermint.
мя́тый *adj.* crushed; crumpled; creased.
мять *v. impfv.* [*pres.* **мну, мнёшь**] **1,** [*pfv.* **размя́ть**] to knead. **2,** [*pfvs.* **измя́ть, помя́ть, смять**] to rumple; crease; wrinkle; crush. **3,** [*pfv.* **смять**] to crush; crumble. **4,** [*pfv.* **помя́ть**] *colloq.* to press; squeeze. —**мя́ться,** *refl.* **1,** [*pfv.* **из-, по-, с-**] to become rumpled; become creased. **2,** [*pfv.* **по-**] *colloq.* to hesitate; waver.
мяу́канье *n.* meow; meowing.
мяу́кать *v. impfv.* to meow.
мяч [*gen.* **мяча́**] *n.* ball.
мя́чик *n., dim. of* **мяч.**

Н

Н, н *n. neut.* fourteenth letter of the Russian alphabet.

на[1] *prep.* A, *with acc.* **1,** on; onto: положи́ть кни́гу на стол, to put the book on the table. **2,** to (*used in place of* **в** *with certain nouns denoting a large building, an open place, an event, or direction*): идти́ на по́чту, на вокза́л, на фа́брику, на пло́щадь, на рабо́ту, на собра́ние, to go to the post office, station, factory, square, work, meeting. **3,** for: уро́к на за́втра, the lesson for tomorrow; обе́д на двои́х, dinner for two. Он прие́хал на три дня, he has come to stay for three days. **4,** *expressing the degree of difference, as in comparisons:* он на три го́да ста́рше меня́, he is three years older than I. Населе́ние увели́чилось на три миллио́на, the population has increased by three million. **5,** by: продава́ть на фунт, to sell by the pound; шесть ме́тров на три, six meters by three; помно́жить семь на пять, to multiply seven by five. **6,** (*with dates*) as of: на пе́рвое ию́ля 1980, as of July 1, 1980. **7,** worth of: на рубль ма́рок, a ruble's worth of stamps. B, *with prepl.* **1,** on: кни́га лежи́т на столе́, the book is (lying) on the table. **2,** in; at (*used in place of* **в** *as above*): на пло́щади, in the square; на конце́рте, at the concert. **3,** by (*with modes of travel*): е́хать на по́езде, to go by train.

на[2] *particle, colloq.* here!: на, возьми́те!, here, take it! Да́йте мне, пожа́луйста, кни́гу! На!, Give me the book, please! Here! —**вот тебе́ и на**!, look what happened!; see what happened!

на- *prefix* **1,** on; onto: наплева́ть, to spit on. **2,** *indicating accidental meeting or collision:* нае́хать, to run over; run down. **3,** (*with pfv. verbs only*) a quantity of: накупи́ть, to buy a quantity of. **4,** (*with* **-ся**) to one's heart's content: наигра́ться, to play to one's heart's content.

наба́вить [*infl.* **-влю, -вишь**] *v., pfv. of* **набавля́ть.**

набавля́ть *v. impfv.* [*pfv.* **наба́вить**] **1,** to add on (a certain amount to the price of something). **2,** to raise (a price).

набалда́шник *n.* handle; knob (*of a walking stick*).

набальзами́ровать *v., pfv. of* **бальзами́ровать.**

наба́т *n.* alarm: бить (в) наба́т, to sound the alarm.

наба́тный *adj.* alarm (*attrib.*): наба́тный ко́локол, alarm bell.

набе́г *n.* raid; foray; incursion.

набега́ть *v. impfv.* [*pfv.* **набежа́ть**] **1,** (*with* **на** + *acc.*) to run into; smash into; dash against. **2,** to appear suddenly; gather suddenly.

набе́гаться *v.r. pfv., colloq.* **1,** to run to one's heart's content. **2,** to tire oneself out by running.

набедоку́рить *v., pfv. of* **бедоку́рить.**

набе́дренный *adj., in* **набе́дренная повя́зка,** loincloth.

набежа́ть [*infl. like* **бежа́ть**] *v., pfv. of* **набега́ть.**

набекре́нь *adv., colloq.* cocked; at an angle; on one side.

набели́ть *v., pfv. of* **бели́ть** (*in sense #2*). —**набели́ться,** *refl., pfv. of* **бели́ться.**

на́бело *adv.* (*of something written*) in final form; without corrections or erasures.

на́бережная *n., decl. as an adj.* embankment.

набива́ть *v. impfv.* [*pfv.* **наби́ть**] **1,** to stuff; fill; cram; pack. **2,** to nail; attach. **3,** *textiles* to print. —**наби́ть ру́ку на** (+ *prepl.*), *colloq.* to become experienced at. —**наби́ть це́ну,** to jack up the price. —**наби́ть себе́ це́ну,** to build oneself up.

набива́ться *v.r. impfv.* [*pfv.* **наби́ться**] **1,** (*with* **в** + *acc.*) to crowd into. **2,** (*with instr.*) to be crammed (with); be jammed (with). **3,** *colloq.* to force; impose (oneself): набива́ться в друзья́, to force one's friendship on someone; набива́ться в го́сти, invite oneself somewhere.

наби́вка *n.* **1,** (act of) stuffing. **2,** stuffing; filling; packing; padding. **3,** *textiles* printing. —**наби́вка чу́чел,** taxidermy.

набивно́й *adj.* (*of fabric*) printed.

наби́вщик *n.* one who stuffs anything. —**наби́вщик чу́чел,** taxidermist.

набира́ть *v. impfv.* [*pfv.* **набра́ть**] **1,** (*with gen. or acc.*) to gather; collect (a quantity of something). **2,** to gain (strength, experience, altitude, etc.). **3,** to recruit; enlist. **4,** to form; make up (a group, team, etc.). **5,** *printing* to compose; set in type. **6,** to dial (a telephone number). **7,** *sports* to score (points). —**набира́ться,** *refl.* **1,** to collect; gather; accumulate. **2,** to amount to; add up to. **3,** (*with gen.*) *colloq.* to summon up; muster (courage, strength, etc.). **4,** (*with gen.*) *colloq.* to pick up; acquire. **5,** *in* **набра́ться ума́,** to get smart. **6,** *colloq.* to get drunk.

наби́тый *adj.* stuffed; tightly packed; crammed. —**наби́тый дура́к,** *colloq.* utter fool.

наби́ть [*infl.* **-бью́, -бьёшь**] *v., pfv. of* **набива́ть.** —**наби́ться,** *refl., pfv. of* **набива́ться.**

наблюда́тель *n.m.* observer.

наблюда́тельный *adj.* **1,** observant. **2,** observation (*attrib.*). —**наблюда́тельность,** *n.f.* keenness of observation; powers of observation.

наблюда́ть *v. impfv.* **1,** (*with acc. or* **за** + *instr.*) to observe; watch. **2,** (*with* **за** + *instr.*) to look after;

keep an eye on. **3,** (*with* **за** + *instr.*) to see that (order, cleanliness, etc.) is maintained. —**наблюда́ться,** *refl.* to exist; be seen: наблюда́ются определённые тру́дности, certain difficulties exist (*or* are to be seen).

наблюде́ние *n.* **1,** observation. **2,** supervision. **3,** surveillance. —**вести́ наблюде́ние,** to keep a lookout.

на́божный *adj.* pious; devout. —**на́божность,** *n.f.* piety.

набо́йка [*gen. pl.* **-бо́ек**] *n.* **1,** printed fabric. **2,** lift; tap (*on a heel*).

на́бок *adv.* to one side.

наболе́вший *adj.* painful; sore. —**наболе́вший вопро́с,** sore subject; sore point.

наболе́ть *v. pfv.* [*infl.* **-е́ет** *or* **-и́т**] to become painful.

наболта́ть *v. pfv., colloq.* to talk (a lot of).

набо́р *n.* **1,** recruitment; enrollment. **2,** set; collection. **3,** *printing* composition. —**набо́р высоты́,** *aero.* climb. —**набо́р слов,** gibberish.

набо́рный *adj.* typesetting (*attrib.*); composition (*attrib.*).

набо́рщик *n.* typesetter; compositor.

набра́сывать[1] *v. impfv.* [*pfv.* **наброса́ть**] **1,** to toss (a quantity of something). **2,** to sketch; outline. **3,** to jot down; dash off.

набра́сывать[2] *v. impfv.* [*pfv.* **набро́сить**] to throw on; throw over: набро́сить что́-нибудь на́ пол/на пле́чи/, to throw something on the floor/over one's shoulders/. —**набра́сываться,** *refl.* (*with* **на** + *acc.*) **1,** to attack; pounce on. **2,** *colloq.* to jump on; jump down someone's throat.

набра́ть [*infl. like* **брать**] *v., pfv. of* **набира́ть.** —**набра́ться,** *refl., pfv. of* **набира́ться.**

набрести́ *v. pfv.* [*infl. like* **брести́**] **1,** (*with* **на** + *acc.*) to come upon; wander upon; *fig.* hit upon (an idea). **2,** (*neut. past tense only*) to gather: набрело́ мно́го наро́ду, a large crowd gathered.

наброса́ть *v., pfv. of* **набра́сывать**[1].

набро́сить [*infl.* **-шу, -сишь**] *v., pfv. of* **набра́сывать**[2]. —**набро́ситься,** *refl., pfv. of* **набра́сываться.**

набро́сок [*gen.* **-ска**] *n.* sketch; draft; outline.

набры́згать *v. pfv.* (*with instr. or gen.*) to spill; splash.

набрю́шник *n.* abdominal band.

набуха́ть *v. impfv.* [*pfv.* **набу́хнуть**] to swell.

набу́хнуть [*past* **-бу́х, -ла**] *v., pfv. of* **набуха́ть.**

нава́га *n.* a variety of codfish found in northern waters.

наважде́ние *n.* delusion; hallucination.

нава́ксить *v., pfv. of* **ва́ксить.**

нава́ливать *v. impfv.* [*pfv.* **навали́ть**] **1,** (*with* **на** + *acc.*) to load on; pile on. **2,** *colloq.* to toss into a pile; pile up. **3,** *impers.* (*of snow*) to pile up. —**нава́ливаться,** *refl.* (*with* **на** + *acc.*) **1,** to lean heavily on; put all one's weight on. **2,** *colloq.* to attack; pounce on; tear into.

навали́ть [*infl.* **-валю́, -ва́лишь**] *v., pfv. of* **нава́ливать.** —**навали́ться,** *refl., pfv. of* **нава́ливаться.**

нава́лом *adv., colloq.* **1,** in a pile; in a heap. **2,** (*with gen.*) piles of; tons of: рабо́ты у меня́ нава́лом, I have piles/tons of work.

нава́р *n.* fat (*forming on the surface of soup*).

нава́ривать *v. impfv.* [*pfv.* **навари́ть**] to weld on.

нава́ристый *adj.* (*of soup*) rich; concentrated.

навари́ть [*infl.* **-варю́, -ва́ришь**] **1,** *pfv. of* **нава́ривать.** **2,** to cook (a quantity of something).

наварно́й *adj.* welded.

навева́ть *v. impfv.* [*pfv.* **наве́ять**] **1,** (*of the wind*) to bring on; waft. **2,** *fig.* to bring on; induce.

наве́даться *v.r., pfv. of* **наве́дываться.**

наведе́ние *n.* **1,** aiming (*of a gun*). **2,** applying; application (*of a polish*). **3,** *aerospace* guidance. **4,** *in* наведе́ние спра́вок, making of inquiries.

наве́дываться *v.r. impfv.* [*pfv.* **наве́даться**] (*with* **к**) *colloq.* to drop in on; call on.

навезти́ *v. pfv.* [*infl. like* **везти́**] to bring (a quantity of something).

наве́к *also,* **наве́ки** *adv.* forever.

навербова́ть *v. pfv.* [*infl.* **-бу́ю, -бу́ешь**] to recruit (a quantity of people).

наве́рно *adv.* **1,** probably; most likely. **2,** *obs.* certainly; for sure. *Also,* **наве́рное.**

наверну́ть *v., pfv. of* **навёртывать.** —**наверну́ться,** *refl., pfv. of* **навёртываться.**

наверняка́ *adv., colloq.* **1,** for sure. **2,** when one is sure of success.

навёрстывать *v. impfv.* [*pfv.* **наверста́ть**] to make up for: наверста́ть потёрянное вре́мя, to make up for lost time.

наверте́ть *v. pfv.* [*infl.* **-верчу́, -ве́ртишь**] **1,** *pfv. of* **навёртывать** (*in sense #1*). **2,** (*with gen.*) to make (*by spinning or drilling*).

навёртывать *v. impfv.* [*pfv.* **наверну́ть**] (*with* **в** + *acc.*) **1,** [*pfv. also* **наверте́ть**] to wind onto; wind around. **2,** to screw onto. —**навёртываться,** *refl.* [*pfv.* **наверну́ться**] (*of tears*) to well up: у неё наверну́лись слёзы, tears came to her eyes.

наве́рх *adv., expressing motion or direction* **1,** up; upward(s). **2,** upstairs.

наверху́ *adv., expressing location* **1,** above. **2,** upstairs.

наве́с *n.* **1,** awning. **2,** *fig.* cover: под наве́сом (+ *gen.*), under a cover of.

навеселе́ *adv., colloq.* tipsy; high.

наве́сить [*infl.* **-шу, -сишь**] *v., pfv. of* **наве́шивать.**

навесно́й *adj.* hanging.

навести́ [*infl. like* **вести́**] *v., pfv. of* **наводи́ть.**

навести́ть [*infl.* **-щу́, -сти́шь**] *v., pfv. of* **навеща́ть.**

наве́т *n., obs.* slander; calumny.

наве́тренный *adj.* windward.

наве́чно *adv.* forever; for all time.

наве́шать *v. pfv.* **1,** to hang up; hang out (a quantity of something). **2,** to weigh; weigh out (a quantity of something).

наве́шивать *v. impfv.* [*pfv.* **наве́сить**] to hang; install by hanging.

навеща́ть *v. impfv.* [*pfv.* **навести́ть**] to visit.

наве́ять *v. pfv.* [*infl.* **-ве́ю, -ве́ешь**] **1,** *pfv. of* **навева́ть.** **2,** to winnow (a quantity of something).

на́взничь *adv.* flat on one's back: упа́сть на́взничь, to fall flat on one's back.

навзры́д *adv., in* **пла́кать навзры́д,** to sob uncontrollably.

навига́тор *n.* navigator.

навига́ция *n.* navigation. —**навигацио́нный,** *adj.* navigation (*attrib.*); navigational.

навида́ться *v.r. pfv.* (*with gen.*) *colloq.* to have seen a lot (*or* enough) of.

нави́нчивать *v. impfv.* [*pfv.* **навинти́ть**] to screw on. —**нави́нчиваться,** *refl.* (*of an object*) to screw on.

нависа́ть *v. impfv.* [*pfv.* **нави́снуть**] **1,** (*with* **на** + *acc. or* **над**) to hang over; overhang. **2,** (*with* **над**) *fig.* (*of danger, a threat, etc.*) to hang over.

нави́снуть [*past* **-ви́с, -ла**] *v., pfv. of* **нависа́ть.**
нави́сший *adj.* overhanging. —**с нави́сшими бровя́ми,** beetle-browed.
навлека́ть *v. impfv.* [*pfv.* **навле́чь**] (*with* **на себя́**) to incur.
навле́чь [*infl. like* **влечь**] *v., pfv. of* **навлека́ть.**
наводи́ть *v. impfv.* [*pfv.* **навести́;** *pres.* **-вожу́, -во́дишь**] **1,** (*with* **на** + *acc.*) to lead (to); guide (to). **2,** to aim; point; train; direct. **3,** (*with* **на** + *acc.*) to suggest (a thought); give rise to (doubts). **4,** to cause; arouse; inspire (sadness, fear, etc.). **5,** to apply; apply a coat of. —**наводи́ть блеск** *or* **лоск на** (+ *acc.*), to give a luster/sheen to. —**наводи́ть (на себя́) красоту́,** to make oneself beautiful. —**наводи́ть кри́тику на** (+ *acc.*), to level criticism at. —**наводи́ть мост,** to throw up a bridge. —**наводи́ть (кого́-нибудь) на ум,** to bring to one's senses; bring to reason. —**наводи́ть поря́док в** (+ *prepl.*), to put in order. —**наводи́ть спра́вки,** to make inquiries. —**наводи́ть чистоту́ в** (+ *prepl.*), to bring an air of cleanliness to.
наво́дка *n.* **1,** aiming (*of a weapon*). **2,** application (*of a coat or layer of something*). **3,** throwing up (*of a bridge*).
наводне́ние *n.* flood.
наводня́ть *v. impfv.* [*pfv.* **наводни́ть**] **1,** *obs.* to flood; inundate. **2,** *fig.* to flood: наводня́ть ры́нок, to flood the market.
наво́дчик *n., mil.* one who aims a gun.
наводя́щий *adj., in* наводя́щий вопро́с, leading question.
наво́з *n.* manure; dung.
наво́зить *v. impfv.* [*pfv.* **унаво́зить;** *pres.* **-во́жу, -во́зишь**] to treat with manure.
навози́ть *v. pfv.* [*infl.* **-вожу́, -во́зишь**] to bring in (a supply of something).
наво́зник *n.* dung beetle.
наво́зный *adj.* manure (*attrib.*); dung (*attrib.*). —**наво́зный жук,** dung beetle.
на́волочка [*gen. pl.* **-чек**] *n.* pillowcase.
навора́чивать *v. impfv.* [*pfv.* **наворoти́ть**] *colloq.* **1,** to pile up. **2,** [*impfv. only*] (*with* **на** + *acc.*) to wind onto.
наворова́ть *v. pfv.* [*infl.* **-ру́ю, -ру́ешь**] to steal (a quantity of something).
навороти́ть [*infl.* **-рочу́, -ро́тишь**] *v., pfv. of* **навора́чивать.**
навостри́ть *v. pfv., colloq.* to sharpen. —**навостри́ть лы́жи,** *colloq.* to take to one's heels. —**навостри́ть у́ши,** *colloq.* to prick up one's ears.
навощи́ть *v., pfv. of* **вощи́ть.**
навра́ть *v. pfv.* [*infl. like* **врать**] *colloq.* **1,** to tell lies. **2,** (*with* **на** + *acc.*) to tell lies about. **3,** (*with* **в** + *prepl.*) to make a mistake (in).
навреди́ть *v. pfv.* [*infl.* **-жу́, -ди́шь**] (*with dat.*) *colloq.* to harm; do a great deal of harm to.
навря́д ли *particle, colloq.* = **вряд ли.**
навсегда́ *adv.* forever; for good. —**раз (и) навсегда́,** once and for all.
навстре́чу *adv.* in someone's direction. —*prep., with dat.* toward; to meet: вы́йти навстре́чу гостя́м, to go out to meet the guests. —**идти́ навстре́чу** (+ *dat.*), to meet halfway; cooperate with; accommodate.
навы́ворот *adv., colloq.* **1,** inside out. **2,** *fig.* upside down; backwards: всё получи́лось навы́ворот, everything turned out backwards.
на́вык *n.* skill; ability: на́выки чте́ния/письма́, reading/writing skills.
навы́кат *also,* **навы́кате** *adv., in* **глаза́ навы́кат(е),** bulging eyes.
навы́лет *adv.* (*of a bullet, wound, etc.*) going right through (one's body).
навы́нос *adv., colloq.* for comsumption off the premises.
навы́пуск *adv., in* брю́ки навы́пуск, trousers worn over one's boots.
навы́рез *adv., in* **купи́ть арбу́з навы́рез,** to buy watermelon with the right to sample a piece.
навы́тяжку *adv., in* **стоя́ть навы́тяжку,** to stand at attention.
навью́чить *v., pfv. of* **вью́чить.**
навяза́ть[1] *v. impfv.* [*pfv.* **навя́знуть;** *pres.* **-за́ю, -за́ешь**] to stick; get stuck. —**навя́знуть у** (+ *gen.*) **в зуба́х,** *colloq.* to bore to death; make sick and tired.
навяза́ть[2] *v. pfv.* [*infl.* **-вяжу́, -вя́жешь**] **1,** *pfv. of* **навя́зывать. 2,** to knit (a quantity of something). —**навяза́ться,** *refl., pfv. of* **навя́зываться.**
навя́знуть [*past* **-вя́з, -ла**] *v., pfv. of* **навяза́ть**[1].
навя́зчивый *adj.* **1,** obtrusive; irksome; pesky. **2,** (*of an idea, thought, etc.*) fixed; obsessive. **3,** (*of a melody*) haunting.
навя́зывать *v. impfv.* [*pfv.* **навяза́ть**] **1,** (*with* **на** + *acc.*) to tie (to); attach (to); fasten (to). **2,** (*with dat.*) to impose (upon); force (upon); foist (upon): навяза́ть свою́ во́лю кому́-нибудь, to impose one's will on someone. —**навя́зываться,** *refl.* to intrude; obtrude.
нага́йка [*gen. pl.* **-га́ек**] *n.* whip.
нага́н *n.* revolver.
нага́р *n.* snuff (*of a candle*).
нагиба́ть *v. impfv.* [*pfv.* **нагну́ть**] to bend. —**нагиба́ться,** *refl.* to bend over; bend down; stoop.
нагишо́м *adv., colloq.* stark naked.
нагла́живать *v. impfv.* [*pfv.* **нагла́дить**] *colloq.* **1,** to iron. **2,** to smooth out.
нагла́зник *n.* **1,** eyeshade. **2,** blinker; blinder.
нагле́ть *v. impfv.* [*pfv.* **обнагле́ть**] to become insolent.
нагле́ц [*gen.* **-леца́**] *n.* insolent person; impudent person.
на́глость *n.f.* **1,** insolence; impudence; impertinence. **2,** effrontery; gall.
наглота́ться *v.r. pfv.* (*with gen.*) to swallow (a quantity of something).
на́глухо *adv.* (*with verbs of closing*) tightly; tight.
на́глый *adj.* insolent; impudent; impertinent.
нагляде́ться *v.r. pfv.* [*infl.* **-жу́сь, -ди́шься**] (*with* **на** + *acc.*) to see a lot (of); see enough (of).
нагля́дно *adv.* graphically.
нагля́дность *n.f.* **1,** clarity. Для нагля́дности, for clarity; for visual effect; to demonstrate one's point. **2,** use of visual aids.
нагля́дный *adj.* **1,** graphic: нагля́дный приме́р, graphic example. **2,** employing visual aids: нагля́дное обуче́ние, instruction using visual aids. —**нагля́дные посо́бия,** visual aids. —**нагля́дный уро́к,** object lesson.
нагна́ть [*infl. like* **гнать**] *v., pfv. of* **нагоня́ть.**
нагнести́ [*infl. like* **гнести́**] *v., pfv. of* **нагнета́ть.**
нагнета́тель *n.m.* supercharger.
нагнета́ть *v. impfv.* [*pfv.* **нагнести́**] to force; pump (liquid, air, etc.).
нагное́ние *n.* festering; suppuration.
нагнои́ться *v.r. pfv.* to fester.
нагну́ть *v., pfv. of* **нагиба́ть.** —**нагну́ться,** *refl., pfv. of* **нагиба́ться.**
нагова́ривать *v. impfv.* [*pfv.* **наговори́ть**] **1,** (*with* **на** + *acc.*) *colloq.* to slander. **2,** *in* нагова́ривать плас-

ти́нку, to record one's voice. —**нагова́риваться,** *refl.* to have a long talk; say all one wishes to say.

нагово́р *n., colloq.* slander; calumny.

наговори́ть *v. pfv.* **1,** *pfv. of* **нагова́ривать. 2,** to say; utter (a lot of things). —**наговори́ться,** *refl., pfv. of* **нагова́риваться.**

наго́й *adj.* naked; nude; bare.

на́голо *adv., in* **стричь на́голо,** to cut off all of someone's hair; shave someone's head.

наголо́ *adv.* (*of a sword, saber, etc.*) drawn.

на́голову *adv., in* **разби́ть на́голову,** to rout; defeat utterly.

наголода́ться *v.r. pfv., colloq.* to go hungry; be half-starved.

нагоня́й *n., colloq.* scolding; bawling out; dressing-down; tongue-lashing.

нагоня́ть *v. impfv.* [*pfv.* **нагна́ть**] **1,** to overtake; catch up to. **2,** to make up for. **3,** to drive together; gather together. **4,** *colloq.* to cause; arouse; evoke (fear; boredom, etc.).

нагора́ть *v. impfv.* [*pfv.* **нагоре́ть**] **1,** (*of a candle*) to be covered with snuff. **2,** *impers., colloq.* (*of fuel or electricity*) to be consumed. **3,** *impers., colloq.* to get it; catch it; catch hell.

наго́рный *adj.* **1,** situated in the mountains; mountain (*attrib.*). **2,** (*of a river bank*) high. —**Наго́рная про́поведь,** the Sermon on the Mount.

нагороди́ть *v. pfv.* [*infl.* **-рожу́, -ро́дишь** *or* **-роди́шь**] **1,** to erect; put up. **2,** *colloq.* to heap up. **3,** *colloq.* to talk (nonsense).

наго́рье *n.* upland.

нагота́ *n.* nakedness, nudity.

наготове *adv.* in readiness.

нагото́вить *v. pfv.* [*infl.* **-влю, -вишь**] *colloq.* **1,** to lay in (a supply of something). **2,** to cook (a large quantity of something).

награ́бить *v. pfv.* [*infl.* **-блю, -бишь**] to rob (a quantity of something), amass by robbing.

награ́да *n.* **1,** reward. **2,** award; decoration.

награди́ть [*infl.* **-жу́, -ди́шь**] *v., pfv. of* **награжда́ть.**

наградно́й *adj.* reward (*attrib.*). —**наградны́е,** *n. pl.* bonus.

награжда́ть *v. impfv.* [*pfv.* **награди́ть**] **1,** to reward. **2,** to award. **3,** *fig.* to endow.

награжде́ние *n.* **1,** rewarding; awarding. **2,** *obs.* reward; award.

награждённый *n., decl. as an adj.* recipient of an award.

нагре́в *n.* heat; heating.

нагрева́ние *n.* heating.

нагрева́тель *n.m.* heater. —**нагрева́тельный,** *adj.* heating (*attrib.*).

нагрева́ть *v. impfv.* [*pfv.* **нагре́ть**] **1,** to warm; heat. **2,** *in* **нагре́ть ру́ки,** to line one's pocket; feather one's nest. —**нагрева́ться,** *refl.* to become warm; get warm.

нагримирова́ть *v., pfv. of* **гримирова́ть** (*in sense #1*). —**нагримирова́ться,** *refl., pfv. of* **гримирова́ться** (*in sense #1*).

нагроможда́ть *v. impfv.* [*pfv.* **нагромозди́ть**] to pile up. —**нагроможда́ться,** *refl.* to pile up; accumulate.

нагроможде́ние *n.* **1,** piling up. **2,** disorderly pile.

нагромозди́ть [*infl.* **-зжу́, -зди́шь**] *v., pfv. of* **громозди́ть** *and* **нагроможда́ть.** —**нагромозди́ться,** *refl., pfv. of* **нагроможда́ться.**

нагруби́ть *v., pfv. of* **груби́ть.**

нагрубия́нить *v., pfv. of* **грубия́нить.**

нагру́дник *n.* **1,** bib. **2,** breastplate.

нагру́дный *adj.* breast (*attrib.*); worn over the breast.

нагружа́ть *v. impfv.* [*pfv.* **нагрузи́ть**] **1,** to load (a vehicle, vessel, etc.). **2,** *fig., colloq.* to burden. —**нагружа́ться,** *refl.* (*with instr.*) to load up (with); take on.

нагрузи́ть [*infl.* **-гружу́, -гру́зишь** *or* **-грузи́шь**] *v., pfv. of* **грузи́ть** (*in sense #1*) *and* **нагружа́ть.** —**нагрузи́ться,** *refl., pfv. of* **нагружа́ться.**

нагру́зка *n.* **1,** loading. **2,** load. **3,** workload. —**поле́зная нагру́зка,** payload.

нагря́нуть *v. pfv.* **1,** to arrive unexpectedly. **2,** (*with* **к**) to descend on.

нагу́ливать *v. impfv.* [*pfv.* **нагуля́ть**] *colloq.* to develop; work up (*as the result of walking*): нагуля́ть аппети́т, to work up an appetite.

нагуля́ть *v., pfv. of* **нагу́ливать.** —**нагуля́ться,** *refl.* to have had a long walk; have walked enough.

над *also,* **надо** *prep., with instr.* **1,** over: кры́ша над голово́й, a roof over one's head; побе́да над враго́м, victory over the enemy. **2,** above: над у́ровнем мо́ря, above sea level. **3,** *used with certain verbs and nouns:* рабо́тать над, to work on; смея́ться над, to laugh at. Суд над ке́м-нибудь, the trial of someone.

над- *also,* **надо-** *prefix* **1,** adding on: надстра́ивать, to build on; надставля́ть, to lengthen. **2,** supervision: надзира́ть; надсма́тривать, to supervise. **3,** *indicating partial or superficial action:* надрыва́ть, to tear slightly; надкуси́ть, to take a bite of.

надава́ть *v. pfv.* [*infl.* **-даю́, -даёшь**] *colloq.* to give (a quantity of something).

надави́ть [*infl.* **-давлю́, -да́вишь**] *v., pfv. of* **нада́вливать.**

нада́вливать *v. impfv.* [*pfv.* **надави́ть**] (*with acc. or* **на** + *acc.*) to press (on).

надари́ть *v. pfv.* [*infl.* **-дарю́, -да́ришь**] *colloq.* to give (a quantity of gifts).

надба́вить [*infl.* **-влю, -вишь**] *v., pfv. of* **надбавля́ть.**

надба́вка *n.* **1,** increase. **2,** raise (*in pay*).

надбавля́ть *v. impfv.* = **набавля́ть.**

надбива́ть *v. impfv.* [*pfv.* **надби́ть**] *colloq.* to chip (a glass, cup, etc.).

надби́ть [*infl.* **-добью́, -добьёшь**] *v., pfv. of* **надбива́ть.**

надвига́ть *v. impfv.* [*pfv.* **надви́нуть**] (*with* **на** + *acc.*) to pull; pull down (over one's ears, forehead, etc.). —**надвига́ться,** *refl.* **1,** to approach; come on. **2,** to be impending; be imminent.

надвига́ющийся *adj.* imminent; impending.

надви́нуть *v., pfv. of* **надвига́ть.** —**надви́нуться,** *refl., pfv. of* **надвига́ться.**

надво́дный *adj.* surface (*attrib.*): надво́дный кора́бль, surface vessel. —**надво́дная часть,** topsides.

на́двое *adv.* in two; in half. —**ба́бушка на́двое сказа́ла,** it (*or* that) remains to be seen.

надво́рный *adj.* situated outside: надво́рная постро́йка, outbuilding.

надгорта́нник *n.* epiglottis.

надгро́бие *n.* **1,** tombstone. **2,** *obs.* epitaph.

надгро́бный *adj.* **1,** grave (*attrib.*); tomb (*attrib.*): надгро́бный ка́мень; надгро́бная плита́, gravestone; tombstone. Надгро́бная на́дпись, epitaph. **2,** funeral (*attrib.*): надгро́бная речь, funeral oration.

надгрыза́ть *v. impfv.* [*pfv.* **надгры́зть**] to nibble at; nibble on.

надгры́зть [*infl. like* **грызть**] *v., pfv. of* **надгрыза́ть.**
надева́ние *n.* putting on; donning.
надева́ть *v. impfv.* [*pfv.* **наде́ть**] **1,** to put on. **2,** to wear: что мне наде́ть?, what should I wear?
наде́жда *n.* hope.
надёжный *adj.* **1,** reliable; dependable; trustworthy. **2,** safe: в надёжных рука́х, in safe hands. **3,** firm; steady. —**надёжность,** *n.f.* reliability; dependability.
наде́л *n., hist.* parcel of land (*given to a peasant*).
наде́лать *v. pfv.* **1,** to make (a quantity of something). **2,** (*with gen.*) to do (damage); make (mistakes); cause (trouble). —**что ты наде́лал?,** what have you done?
наделе́ние *n.* allotment.
наделя́ть *v. impfv.* [*pfv.* **надели́ть**] (*with instr.*) **1,** to allot; provide with. **2,** *fig.* to endow (with).
надерзи́ть *v., pfv. of* **дерзи́ть.**
наде́ть [*infl.* **-де́ну, -де́нешь**] *v., pfv. of* **надева́ть.**
наде́яться *v.r. impfv.* [*pres.* **наде́юсь, наде́ешься**] **1,** to hope; (*with* **на** + *acc.*) hope for. **2,** (*with* **на** + *acc.*) to rely on; count on.
надзе́мный *adj.* above-ground; overhead; elevated.
надзира́тель *n.m.* **1,** supervisor; overseer. **2,** (prison) guard. —**надзира́тельский,** *adj.* supervisory.
надзира́ть *v. impfv.* (*with* **за** + *instr.*) **1,** to supervise; oversee. **2,** to look after; keep an eye on. **3,** to see that (something) is maintained.
надзо́р *n.* **1,** supervision. **2,** surveillance.
надиви́ться *v.r. pfv., colloq., in* **не мочь надиви́ться,** to not but wonder; not get over; never cease to be amazed.
нади́р *n., astron.* nadir.
надка́лывать *v. impfv.* [*pfv.* **надколо́ть**] to split (slightly).
надколо́ть [*infl.* **-колю́, -ко́лешь**] *v., pfv. of* **надка́лывать.**
надкуси́ть [*infl.* **-кушу́, -ку́сишь**] *v., pfv. of* **надку́сывать.**
надку́сывать *v. impfv.* [*pfv.* **надкуси́ть**] to bite into; take a bite (out) of.
надла́мывать *v. impfv.* [*pfv.* **надломи́ть**] **1,** to break partly; fracture; crack. **2,** *fig.* to overtax; undermine. —**надла́мываться,** *refl.* **1,** to crack. **2,** to break down.
надлежа́ть *v. impfv.* [*pres.* **-жи́т**] *impers.* to be required: э́то надлежи́т сде́лать в ука́занный срок, this must (*or* is to) be done within the period indicated. Вам надлежи́т яви́ться в де́вять часо́в, you are to appear at nine o'clock.
надлежа́щий *adj.* proper; appropriate. —**надлежа́щим о́бразом,** properly.
надло́м *n.* **1,** break; crack. **2,** *fig.* breakdown.
надломи́ть [*infl.* **-ломлю́, -ло́мишь**] *v., pfv. of* **надла́мывать.** —**надломи́ться,** *refl., pfv. of* **надла́мываться.**
надло́мленный *adj.* **1,** broken; cracked. **2,** *fig.* shattered; broken (*in spirit*).
надме́нный *adj.* haughty; arrogant; supercilious. —**надме́нность,** *n.f.* haughtiness; arrogance.
надо *prep.* = **над** (*used mainly in the combination* **надо мной**).
на́до *adv.* (one) must; (one) has to: на́до соблюда́ть пра́вила, one must observe the rules; мне на́до идти́, I have to go. —**не на́до, 1,** (one) must not: не на́до так говори́ть, you must not talk like that. **2,** (one) does not have to; (one) need not: не на́до боя́ться, you need not be afraid. —**так ему́ и на́до,** it serves him right.
на́добно *adv., obs.* = **на́до.**
на́добность *n.f.* necessity; need.
на́добный *adj., obs.* necessary; needed.
надое́да *n.m. & f., colloq.* pest; nuisance. *Also,* **надоеда́ла.**
надоеда́ть *v. impfv.* [*pfv.* **надое́сть**] (*with dat.*) **1,** to pester; bother; bore. **2,** *impers.* to be tired of; be sick of: мне надое́ло безде́льничать, I am tired of doing nothing.
надое́дливый *adj.* **1,** annoying; irksome. **2,** tiresome; boring.
надое́сть [*infl. like* **есть**] *v., pfv. of* **надоеда́ть.**
надои́ть *v. pfv.* [*infl.* **-дою́, -до́ишь** *or* **-дои́шь**] to draw (a quantity of milk).
надо́й *n.* yield (*of milk*).
надо́лго *adv.* for a long time (*subsequent to the action expressed in the verb*): он уе́хал надо́лго, he went away (*or* has gone away) for a long time.
надо́мник *n.* person who works at home.
надорва́ть [*infl. like* **рвать**] *v., pfv. of* **надрыва́ть.** —**надорва́ться,** *refl.* **1,** *pfv. of* **надрыва́ться. 2,** *colloq.* to strain oneself. **3,** *fig.* to break down; crack up.
надоу́мить *v. pfv.* [*infl.* **-млю, -мишь**] *colloq.* to suggest; give someone the idea (to *or* that).
надпа́рывать *v. impfv.* [*pfv.* **надпоро́ть**] to rip partly open; remove a few stitches from.
надпи́ливать *v. impfv.* [*pfv.* **надпили́ть**] to saw a little; saw partially.
надпили́ть [*infl.* **-пилю́, -пи́лишь**] *v., pfv. of* **надпи́ливать.**
надписа́ть [*infl.* **-пишу́, -пи́шешь**] *v., pfv. of* **надпи́сывать.**
надпи́сывать *v. impfv.* [*pfv.* **надписа́ть**] **1,** to inscribe; autograph. **2,** *obs.* to address (a letter).
на́дпись *n.f.* inscription.
надпоро́ть [*infl.* **-порю́, -по́решь**] *v., pfv. of* **надпа́рывать.**
надпо́чечник *n.* adrenal gland.
надпо́чечный *adj.* adrenal.
надра́ть *v. pfv.* [*infl. like* **драть**] to tear off (a quantity of something). —**надра́ть у́ши** (+ *dat.*), *colloq.* to pull someone's ears.
надре́з *n.* cut; incision.
надре́зать [*infl.* **-ре́жу, -ре́жешь**] *v., pfv. of* **надреза́ть** *and* **надре́зывать.**
надреза́ть *v. impfv.* [*pfv.* **надре́зать**] to cut slightly; make an incision in. *Also,* **надре́зывать.**
надруга́тельство *n.* an outrage.
надруга́ться *v.r. pfv.* (*with* **над**) to commit an outrage (against).
надры́в *n.* **1,** (slight) tear. **2,** *fig.* great effort. **3,** *fig.* breakdown. **4,** *fig.* emotional outburst.
надрыва́ть *v. impfv.* [*pfv.* **надорва́ть**] **1,** to tear slightly. **2,** to strain; overtax. —**надрыва́ться,** *refl.* **1,** to have a slight tear; be slightly torn. **2,** [*impfv. only*] to overexert oneself. **3,** [*impfv. only*] to yell at the top of one's lungs. **4,** [*impfv. only*] (*with* **от**) to suffer grievously. **5,** *in* се́рдце надрыва́ется, one's heart aches.
надры́вный *adj.* heart-rending; (*of laughter*) hysterical.
надсма́тривать *v. impfv.* (*with* **над** *or* **за** + *instr.*) to supervise; oversee; watch over.
надсмо́тр *n.* supervision.
надсмо́трщик *n.* overseer; supervisor.
надста́вить [*infl.* **-влю, -вишь**] *v., pfv. of* **надставля́ть.**

надста́вка [*gen. pl.* **-вок**] *n.* **1,** lengthening. **2,** extra piece.

надставля́ть *v. impfv.* [*pfv.* **надста́вить**] to lengthen (a garment).

надстра́ивать *v. impfv.* [*pfv.* **надстро́ить**] **1,** to build on (*at the top*). **2,** to increase the height of; make taller.

надстро́йка [*gen. pl.* **-стро́ек**] *n.* **1,** building on(to). **2,** superstructure.

надстро́чный *adj.* written above the line. —**надстро́чный знак,** superscript.

надтре́снутый *adj.* cracked.

надува́ла *n.m. & f., colloq.* swindler; cheat.

надува́ние *n.* inflation; blowing up.

надува́тельство *n., colloq.* cheating; trickery; deceit. —**надува́тельский,** *adj., colloq.* deceitful; underhand.

надува́ть *v. impfv.* [*pfv.* **наду́ть**] **1,** to inflate; blow up. **2,** *in* **надува́ть гу́бы,** to pout; show displeasure. **3,** *colloq.* to swindle; cheat; dupe. —**надува́ться,** *refl.* **1,** to become filled with air. **2,** to puff up one's cheeks. **3,** *colloq.* to swell; become swollen. **4,** *fig., colloq.* to get a swelled head. **5,** *fig., colloq.* to pout; sulk.

надувно́й *adj.* inflatable.

наду́манный *adj.* farfetched, artificial; forced.

наду́мать *v. pfv., colloq.* **1,** to decide. **2,** to think up; devise.

наду́тый *adj.* **1,** inflated. **2,** swollen. **3,** *colloq.* haughty; puffed up. **4,** (*of a style of writing*) pompous. **5,** *colloq.* peeved.

наду́ть *v. pfv.* [*infl.* **-ду́ю, -ду́ешь**] **1,** *pfv. of* **надува́ть. 2,** *impers., colloq.* to be affected (*by sitting in a draft*): мне наду́ло (в) шéю, I have a stiff neck. —**наду́ться,** *refl., pfv. of* **надува́ться.**

надуши́ть *v., pfv. of* **души́ть** (*in sense #4*). —**надуши́ться,** *refl., pfv. of* **души́ться.**

надшива́ть *v. impfv.* [*pfv.* **надши́ть**] **1,** to lengthen (*by sewing*). **2,** (*with* **к** *or* **на**) to sew onto.

надши́ть [*infl.* **надошью́, надошьёшь**] *v., pfv. of* **надшива́ть.**

надыми́ть *v., pfv. of* **дыми́ть.**

наеда́ться *v.r. impfv.* [*pfv.* **нае́сться**] to eat one's fill.

наедине́ *adv.* **1,** in private; privately. **2,** (*with* **с** + *instr.*) alone (with).

нае́зд *n.* quick visit: он быва́ет там то́лько нае́здом (*or* нае́здами), he goes there only on quick visits.

нае́здить *v. pfv.* [*infl.* **-е́зжу, -е́здишь**] **1,** *pfv. of* **наезжа́ть** (*in sense #3*) *and* **нае́зживать. 2,** to travel (a certain distance *or* amount of time).

нае́здник *n.* horseman; rider. —**нае́здничество,** *n.* horsemanship.

наезжа́ть *v. impfv.* **1,** [*pfv.* **нае́хать**] (*with* **на** + *acc.*) to run into; strike: на него́ нае́хала маши́на, he was struck by a car. **2,** [*pfv.* **нае́хать**] *colloq.* to arrive in large numbers. **3,** [*pfv.* **нае́здить**] to smooth down (a road). **4,** [*impfv. only*] (*with* **в** + *acc.*) *colloq.* to make periodic visits (to).

нае́зженный *adj.* (*of a road*) worn; well-trodden.

нае́зживать *v. impfv.* [*pfv.* **нае́здить**] to smooth down (a road).

наём [*gen.* **на́йма**] *n.* **1,** hiring. **2,** renting. —**рабо́тать по на́йму,** to work as a hired hand.

наёмник *n.* **1,** hireling. **2,** mercenary (*soldier*).

наёмный *adj.* **1,** hired. **2,** mercenary.

нае́сться [*infl. like* **есть**] *v.r., pfv. of* **наеда́ться.**

нае́хать [*infl.* **-е́ду, -е́дешь**] *v., pfv. of* **наезжа́ть.**

нажа́рить *v. pfv.* to roast; fry (a quantity of something).

нажа́ть[1] *v.pfv.* [*infl.* **-жму́, -жмёшь**] **1,** *pfv. of* **нажима́ть. 2,** to squeeze (a quantity of something).

нажа́ть[2] *v.pfv.* [*infl.* **-жну́, -жнёшь**] to harvest (a quantity of something).

нажда́к [*gen.* **-дака́**] *n.* emery.

нажда́чный *adj.* emery (*attrib.*). —**нажда́чная бума́га,** sandpaper.

наже́чь *v. pfv.* [*infl. like* **жечь**] to burn (a quantity of something).

нажи́ва *n.* **1,** making money. **2,** bait.

нажива́ть *v. impfv.* [*pfv.* **нажи́ть**] **1,** to make; amass (a fortune). **2,** to contract (a disease). **3,** (*with gen.*) to make (trouble, enemies, etc.) for oneself. —**нажива́ться,** *refl.* (*with* **на** + *prepl.*) to get rich (on).

наживи́ть [*infl.* **-влю́, -ви́шь**] *v., pfv. of* **наживля́ть.**

нажи́вка *n.* bait.

наживля́ть *v. impfv.* [*pfv.* **наживи́ть**] to bait.

нажи́м *n.* pressure.

нажима́ть *v. impfv.* [*pfv.* **нажа́ть**] **1,** (*with acc. or* **на** + *acc.*) to press (on). **2,** (*with* **на** + *acc.*) *colloq.* to put pressure on.

нажи́ть [*infl.* **-живу́, -живёшь;** *past* **на́жил, нажила́, на́жило**] *v., pfv. of* **нажива́ть.** —**нажи́ться,** *refl.* [*past* **нажи́лся, -ла́сь, -ло́сь**] *pfv. of* **нажива́ться.**

наза́втра *adv., colloq.* the next day.

наза́д *adv.* back; backwards. —*interj.* stand back! —**тому́ наза́д,** ago.

назва́ние *n.* **1,** name; appellation. **2,** title (*of a book, film, etc.*).

назва́ть [*infl. like* **звать**] *v., pfv. of* **называ́ть.** —**назва́ться,** *refl., pfv. of* **называ́ться.**

назе́мный *adj.* ground (*attrib.*); surface (*attrib.*); overland.

на́земь *adv., colloq.* to the ground.

назида́ние *n.* edification. —**в назида́ние** (+ *dat.*), for the edification of.

назида́тельный *adj.* **1,** edifying; instructive. **2,** didactic: назида́тельный тон, didactic tone.

назло́ *also,* **на́зло** *adv.* for spite; out of spite. —*prep., with dat.* to spite (someone). —**как назло́,** as luck would have it.

назнача́ть *v. impfv.* [*pfv.* **назна́чить**] **1,** to set; schedule. **2,** to appoint; name. **3,** to assign. **4,** to designate; earmark. **5,** to award; grant. **6,** *colloq.* to prescribe.

назначе́ние *n.* **1,** setting (of a date); awarding (of a pension or scholarship); prescribing (of medicine). **2,** assignment; appointment. **3,** function; purpose. —**ме́сто назначе́ния,** destination.

назна́чить *v., pfv. of* **назнача́ть.**

назо́йливый *adj.* obtrusive; officious.

назрева́ть *v. impfv.* [*pfv.* **назре́ть**] **1,** to ripen; mature. **2,** *fig.* to come to a head.

назре́вший *adj.* (*of a problem or question*) urgent.

назубо́к *adv., colloq.* (*with verbs of knowing, learning, etc.*) thoroughly; by heart.

называ́емый *adj., in* **так называ́емый,** the so-called.

называ́ть *v. impfv.* [*pfv.* **назва́ть**] **1,** to call; name. **2,** *in* наз(ы)ва́ть себя́, to identify oneself; give one's name. —**называ́ть ве́щи свои́ми имена́ми,** to call a spade a spade.

называ́ться *v.r. impfv.* [*pfv.* **назва́ться**] **1,** to call oneself. **2,** [*impfv. only*] to be called. **3,** to identify oneself; give one's name. **4,** *colloq.* to invite oneself. —**что называ́ется,** as they say.

наибо́лее *adv., used in forming compound superla-*

tives the most: наибо́лее уда́чный спо́соб, the most successful method.
наибо́льший *adj.* the greatest; the largest.
наи́вный *adj.* naïve. —**наи́вность,** *n.f.* naïveté.
наивы́сший *adj.* the highest; the greatest.
наи́гранный *adj.* affected; pretended.
наигра́ть *v., pfv. of* **наи́грывать.** —**наигра́ться,** *refl.* to play to one's heart's content; play as much as one wishes.
наи́грывать *v. impfv.* [*pfv.* **наигра́ть**] **1,** *colloq.* to win (money) in a game. **2,** to make (a record); record. **3,** [*impfv. only*] to play softly.
наизна́нку *adv.* inside out.
наизу́сть *adv.* by heart.
наилу́чший *adj.* the best: наилу́чшим о́бразом, in the best possible manner. —**наилу́чшие пожела́ния,** best wishes.
наиме́нее *adv., used in forming compound superlatives* the least: наиме́нее вероя́тный слу́чай, the least probable case.
наименова́ние *n.* name; appellation.
наименова́ть *v., pfv. of* **именова́ть.**
наиме́ньший *adj.* the least; the least amount.
наискосо́к *adv., colloq.* = **на́искось.**
на́искось *adv.* at an angle; diagonally; catty-corner.
наи́тие *n.* inspiration. —**по наи́тию,** instinctively; intuitively.
наиху́дший *adj.* the worst.
найдёныш *n.* foundling.
найми́т *n.* hireling.
найти́ [*infl.* **найду́, найдёшь;** *past* **нашёл, нашла́, нашло́**] *v., pfv. of* **находи́ть.** —**найти́сь,** *refl., pfv. of* **находи́ться.**
нака́з *n.* **1,** *obs.* order; instructions. **2,** mandate (*from the voters*). **3,** *hist.* set of instructions issued by Catherine II.
наказа́ние *n.* punishment.
наказа́ть [*infl.* **-кажу́, -ка́жешь**] *v., pfv. of* **нака́зывать.**
наказу́емый *adj., law* punishable.
нака́зывать *v. impfv.* [*pfv.* **наказа́ть**] to punish.
нака́л *n.* **1,** incandescence. **2,** *fig.* fever pitch. —**бе́лый/кра́сный нака́л,** white/red heat.
накалённый *adj.* **1,** burning hot; incandescent. **2,** *fig.* tense; charged; explosive.
нака́ливание *n., in* **ла́мпа нака́ливания,** incandescent lamp.
нака́ливать *v. impfv.* [*pfv.* **накали́ть**] **1,** to make red hot. **2,** *fig.* to inflame. —**нака́ливаться,** *refl.* **1,** to become red hot. **2,** *fig.* to heat up.
накали́ть *v., pfv. of* **нака́ливать** *and* **накаля́ть.** —**накали́ться,** *refl., pfv. of* **нака́ливаться** *and* **накаля́ться.**
нака́лывать *v. impfv.* [*pfv.* **наколо́ть**] **1,** to prick. **2,** (*with* **на** + *acc.*) to pin on. —**нака́лываться,** *refl.* to prick oneself.
накаля́ть *v. impfv.* = **нака́ливать.** —**накаля́ться,** *refl.* = **нака́ливаться.**
накану́не *adv.* the day before. —*prep., with gen.* on the eve of.
нака́пливать *v. impfv.* = **накопля́ть.** —**нака́пливаться,** *refl.* = **накопля́ться.**
наката́ть *v. pfv.* **1,** *pfv. of* **нака́тывать** (*in sense #1*). **2,** to roll (a quantity of something).
накати́ть [*infl.* **-качу́, -ка́тишь**] *v., pfv. of* **нака́тывать** (*in sense #2*).
нака́тывать *v. impfv.* **1,** [*pfv.* **наката́ть**] to wear down; smooth down (a road). **2,** [*pfv.* **накати́ть**] (*with* **на** + *acc.*) to roll onto.
нака́чивать *v. impfv.* [*pfv.* **накача́ть**] **1,** to pump. **2,** to pump up; inflate.
наки́дка [*gen. pl.* **-док**] *n.* **1,** cape. **2,** pillow cover. **3,** *colloq.* extra charge.
наки́дывать *v. impfv.* [*pfv.* **наки́нуть**] **1,** to throw on; throw over. **2,** *colloq.* to add on (a certain amount). —**наки́дываться,** *refl.* (*with* **на** + *acc.*) to attack; pounce (on).
накипа́ть *v. impfv.* [*pfv.* **накипе́ть**] **1,** (*of scum*) to form. **2,** *fig.* (*of passions*) to smolder.
на́кипь *n.f.* scum.
накла́д *n., in* **в накла́де,** *see* **внакла́де.**
накла́дка [*gen. pl.* **-док**] *n.* **1,** hairpiece; wig. **2,** protective plate, pad, or strap. —**тормозна́я накла́дка,** brake lining.
накладна́я *n., decl. as an adj.* invoice; bill of lading.
накладно́й *adj.* **1,** superimposed. **2,** (*of hair, a beard, etc.*) false. —**накладно́й карма́н,** patch pocket. —**накладны́е расхо́ды,** overhead (costs).
накла́дывать *v. impfv.* [*pfv.* **наложи́ть**] **1,** to lay on; lay over; superimpose. **2,** to apply (a bandage, makeup, etc.). **3,** to load (with); pack (with). **4,** to load; pack; pile (a quantity of something). —**накла́дывать на себя́ ру́ки,** to kill oneself; commit suicide. —**накла́дывать свой отпеча́ток на** (+ *acc.*), to leave its mark upon. —**накла́дывать себе́ на таре́лку** (+ *gen.*), to help oneself to.
наклевета́ть *v., pfv. of* **клевета́ть.**
накле́ивать *v. impfv.* [*pfv* **накле́ить**] **1,** to glue on; paste on; affix. **2,** to paste up; post (a notice).
накле́йка [*gen. pl.* **-е́ек**] *n.* **1,** pasting on; gluing on. **2,** sticker; label. **3,** hinge (*for a postage stamp*).
накли́кать [*infl.* **-кли́чу, -кли́чешь**] *v., pfv. of* **наклика́ть.**
наклика́ть *v. impfv.* [*pfv.* **накли́кать**] to invite; court; bring on (trouble, disaster, etc.).
накло́н *n.* **1,** inclination. **2,** slope; incline.
наклоне́ние *n.* **1,** inclination. **2,** *gram.* mood.
наклони́ть [*infl.* **-клоню́, -кло́нишь**] *v., pfv. of* **наклоня́ть.** —**наклони́ться,** *refl., pfv. of* **наклоня́ться.**
накло́нность *n.f.* inclination; tendency; leaning; propensity.
накло́нный *adj.* inclined; sloping; slanting.
наклоня́ть *v. impfv.* [*pfv.* **наклони́ть**] to incline; lean; tilt; bow. —**наклоня́ться,** *refl.* to bend over; lean over.
накова́льня [*gen. pl.* **-лен**] *n.* anvil. —**ме́жду мо́лотом и накова́льней,** between the devil and the deep blue sea.
нако́жный *adj.* appearing on the skin: нако́жная сыпь, skin rash.
наколе́нник *n.* kneepad.
наколо́ть *v. pfv.* [*infl.* **-колю́, -ко́лешь**] **1,** *pfv. of* **нака́лывать. 2,** to chop; split (a quantity of wood). **3,** to slaughter; kill (a quantity of animals, fish, etc.). —**наколо́ться,** *refl., pfv. of* **нака́лываться.**
наконе́ц *adv.* at last; finally.
наконе́чник *n.* tip.
накопа́ть *v. pfv.* **1,** to dig. **2,** to dig (a quantity of something).
накопи́ть [*infl.* **-коплю́, -ко́пишь**] *v., pfv. of* **копи́ть, накопля́ть,** *and* **нака́пливать.** —**накопи́ться,** *refl., pfv. of* **копи́ться, накопля́ться,** *and* **нака́пливаться.**

накопле́ние *n.* accumulation.
накопля́ть *v. impfv.* [*pfv.* **накопи́ть**] to accumulate; amass. —**накопля́ться,** *refl.* to accumulate; pile up; build up.
накопти́ть *v. pfv.* [*infl.* **-пчу́, -пти́шь**] **1,** *pfv. of* **копти́ть** (*in sense #2*). **2,** to smoke (a quantity of ham, fish, glass, etc.).
накорми́ть *v., pfv. of* **корми́ть.**
накоротке́ *adv., colloq.* **1,** from close up; at close range. **2,** for a short time; for a moment. **3,** (*with* **с** + *instr.*) on friendly terms (with).
накра́пывать *v. impfv.* (*of rain*) to fall lightly. *Also impers.:* ста́ло накра́пывать, it began to drizzle.
накра́сить *v. pfv.* [*infl.* **-шу, -сишь**] **1,** *pfv. of* **накра́шивать. 2,** to paint (a quantity of something). —**накра́ситься,** *refl., pfv. of* **кра́ситься** *and* **накра́шиваться.**
накра́сть *v. pfv.* [*infl. like* **красть**] to steal (a quantity of something).
накрахма́лить *v., pfv. of* **крахма́лить.**
накра́шивать *v. impfv.* [*pfv.* **накра́сить**] to paint (one's lips, face, etc.). —**накра́шиваться,** *refl., colloq.* to put on make-up.
накрени́ть *v., pfv. of* **крени́ть** *and* **накреня́ть.** —**накрени́ться,** *refl., pfv. of* **крени́ться** *and* **накреня́ться.**
накреня́ть *v. impfv.* [*pfv.* **накрени́ть**] **1,** *v.t.* to tip; tilt. **2,** *v.i., impers.* to tilt to one side: дом/ло́дку накрени́ло, the house/boat tilted to one side. —**накреня́ться,** *refl.* to tip over; list; tilt to one side.
на́крепко *adv.* **1,** firmly; fast. **2,** *colloq.* strictly. —**кре́пко-на́крепко,** *intensive form of* **кре́пко:** кре́пко-на́крепко засну́ть, to fall fast asleep.
на́крест *adv.* crosswise. *Also,* **кре́ст-на́крест.**
накрича́ть *v. pfv.* [*infl.* **-чу́, -чи́шь**] to shout; (*with* **на** + *acc.*) shout at.
накрои́ть *v. pfv.* to cut out (a quantity of something).
накроши́ть *v. pfv.* [*infl.* **-крошу́, -кро́шишь**] to crumble; chop up (a quantity of something).
накрути́ть [*infl.* **-кручу́, -кру́тишь**] *v., pfv. of* **накру́чивать.**
накру́чивать *v. impfv.* [*pfv.* **накрути́ть**] (*with* **на** + *acc.*) to wind (onto); wind (around).
накрыва́ть *v. impfv.* [*pfv.* **накры́ть**] **1,** to cover. **2,** *mil.* to hit; strike. **3,** *colloq.* to catch in the act. **4,** *in* накрыва́ть (на) стол, to set the table. **5,** *in* накрыва́ть за́втрак/обе́д/у́жин, to set the table for breakfast/dinner/supper. —**накрыва́ться,** *refl.* (*with instr.*) to cover oneself (with).
накры́ть [*infl.* **-кро́ю, -кро́ешь**] *v., pfv. of* **накрыва́ть.** —**накры́ться,** *refl., pfv. of* **накрыва́ться.**
накупи́ть *v. pfv.* [*infl.* **-куплю́, -ку́пишь**] to buy (a quantity of something).
накури́ть *v. pfv.* [*infl.* **-курю́, -ку́ришь**] to fill (a room) with smoke. —**накури́ться,** *refl.* to smoke to one's heart's content.
налага́ть *v. impfv.* [*pfv.* **наложи́ть**] to impose (a fine, penalty, duty, etc.). —**налага́ть аре́ст на иму́щество,** to seize (someone's) property. —**налага́ть запре́т на** (+ *acc.*), to place a ban on.
нала́дить [*infl.* **-жу, -дишь**] *v., pfv. of* **нала́живать.** —**нала́диться,** *refl., pfv. of* **нала́живаться.**
нала́дчик *n.* adjuster.
нала́живание *n.* adjustment; setting right.
нала́живать *v. impfv.* [*pfv.* **нала́дить**] to adjust; repair; put right. —**нала́живаться,** *refl.* to settle down; take shape; work out.
налакирова́ть *v. pfv.* [*infl.* **-ру́ю, -ру́ешь**] to varnish; lacquer.
налга́ть *v. pfv.* [*infl. like* **лгать**] **1,** to lie; tell lies. **2,** (*with* **на** + *acc.*) to tell lies about; slander.
нале́во *adv.* to the left; on the left.
налега́ть *v. impfv.* [*pfv.* **нале́чь**] (*with* **на** + *acc.*) **1,** to lean (on); put one's weight on. **2,** to wield (*vigorously*); ply (*with energy*). **3,** *colloq.* to apply oneself (to).
налегке́ *adv.* **1,** with little or no baggage or cargo: путеше́ствовать налегке́, to travel light. **2,** lightly dressed.
налеза́ть *v. impfv.* [*pfv.* **нале́зть**] *colloq.* **1,** to come swarming in. **2,** (*of clothes*) to fit.
нале́зть [*infl. like* **лезть**] *v., pfv. of* **налеза́ть.**
налепи́ть *v. pfv.* [*infl.* **-леплю́, -ле́пишь**] **1,** *pfv. of* **налепля́ть. 2,** to make (a quantity of something by modeling).
налепля́ть *v. impfv.* [*pfv.* **налепи́ть**] *colloq.* to stick on; paste on.
налёт *n.* **1,** raid. **2,** holdup. **3,** thin layer; thin coating. **4,** *fig.* touch; tinge. —**с налёта, 1,** on the run; at full speed. **2,** in a flash; with only a moment's thought.
налета́ть[1] *v. impfv.* [*pfv.* **налете́ть**] **1,** (*with* **на** + *acc.*) to fly into; fly onto; swoop down on; pounce on. **2,** (*with* **на** + *acc.*) to run into; smash into. **3,** (*of a storm*) to blow up.
налета́ть[2] *v. pfv.* to fly (a certain distance *or* amount of time).
налете́ть *v. pfv.* [*infl.* **-чу́, -ти́шь**] **1,** *pfv. of* **налета́ть**[1]. **2,** to fly in (*in large numbers*).
налётчик *n.* robber; assailant.
нале́чь [*infl. like* **лечь**] *v., pfv. of* **налега́ть.**
налива́ть *v. impfv.* [*pfv.* **нали́ть**] **1,** to pour. **2,** (*with instr.*) to fill (with a liquid). **3,** (*with gen. or acc.*) to spill. —**налива́ться,** *refl.* **1,** (*with* **в** + *acc.*) (*of liquids*) to flow into; get into. **2,** (*with instr.*) to become filled with. **3,** (*of fruits*) to ripen. **4,** *in* **нали́ться кро́вью,** to become bloodshot.
нали́вка *n.* fruit liqueur.
наливно́й *adj.* **1,** liquid: наливно́й груз, liquid cargo. **2,** designed to carry liquids: наливно́е су́дно, tanker. **3,** fully ripe.
нали́м *n.* burbot (*fish*).
налинова́ть *v., pfv. of* **линова́ть.**
налипа́ть *v. impfv.* [*pfv.* **нали́пнуть**] (*with* **на** + *acc.*) (*of dirt, leaves, etc.*) to stick (to); collect (on).
нали́пнуть [*past* **-ли́п, -ла**] *v., pfv. of* **налипа́ть.**
нали́ть [*infl.* **налью́, нальёшь;** *past* **на́лил** *or* **нали́л, налила́, на́лило** *or* **нали́ло**] *v., pfv. of* **налива́ть.** —**нали́ться,** *refl., pfv. of* **налива́ться.**
налицо́ *adv.* present; on hand.
нали́чие *n.* presence; existence. —**быть в нали́чии,** to be available; be on hand.
нали́чность *n.f.* **1,** cash on hand. **2,** = **нали́чие.**
нали́чный *adj.* (*of money*) available; on hand. —**нали́чные,** *n. pl.* [*also,* **нали́чные де́ньги**] cash.
налови́ть *v. pfv.* [*infl.* **-ловлю́, -ло́вишь**] to catch (a quantity of something).
наловчи́ться *v.r. pfv.* (*with inf. or* **в** + *prepl.*) *colloq.* to become proficient (at); get the hang (of).
нало́г *n.* tax. —**нало́говый,** *adj.* tax (*attrib.*).
налогообложе́ние *n.* taxation.

налогоплате́льщик *n.* taxpayer.
наложе́ние *n.* **1,** application (*of a bandage, make-up, etc.*). **2,** imposition (*of a fine, tax, etc.*).
нало́женный *adj., in* **нало́женным платежо́м,** C.O.D.
наложи́ть [*infl.* **-ложу́, -ло́жишь**] *v., pfv. of* **накла́дывать** *and* **налага́ть.**
нало́жница *n., obs.* concubine.
налома́ть *v. pfv.* to break (a quantity of something).
налощи́ть *v., pfv. of* **лощи́ть.**
налущи́ть *v. pfv.* to shell; husk (a quantity of something).
налюбова́ться *v.r. pfv.* [*infl.* **-бу́юсь, -бу́ешься**] (*with* **на** + *acc.*) to gaze at to one's heart's content: не могу́ налюбова́ться на э́ту карти́ну, I never get tired of looking at that picture.
нам *pron., dat. of* **мы.**
намагни́чивать *v. impfv.* [*pfv.* **намагни́тить**] to magnetize.
нама́зать *v., pfv. of* **ма́зать.** —**нама́заться,** *refl., pfv. of* **ма́заться** (*in sense #1*).
намалева́ть *v., pfv. of* **малева́ть.**
намара́ть *v., pfv. of* **мара́ть** (*in sense #2*).
нама́слить *v., pfv. of* **ма́слить.**
нама́тывать *v. impfv.* [*pfv.* **намота́ть**] to wind onto; wind around. —**намота́ть себе́ на ус,** *colloq.* to make a mental note of.
нама́чивать *v. impfv.* [*pfv.* **намочи́ть**] **1,** to wet; moisten. **2,** to soak. **3,** (*with* **на** + *prepl.*) *colloq.* to make a puddle (on).
намёк *n.* hint.
намека́ть *v. impfv.* [*pfv.* **намекну́ть**] **1,** (*with* **на** + *acc.*) to hint (at); allude (to). **2,** to suggest; infer; intimate (that).
наменя́ть *v. pfv.* **1,** to obtain (a quantity of something) by exchanging. **2,** to change (a quantity of money).
намерева́ться *v.r. impfv.* to intend.
наме́рен *adj., used predicatively* intending: что вы наме́рены сде́лать?, what do you intend to do?
наме́рение *n.* intention.
наме́ренный *adj.* intentional; deliberate. —**наме́ренно,** *adv.* intentionally; deliberately.
намерза́ть *v. impfv.* [*pfv.* **намёрзнуть**] (*with* **на** + *prepl.*) (*of a layer of ice*) to form (on).
намёрзнуть [*past* **-мёрз, -ла**] *v., pfv. of* **намерза́ть.**
на́мертво *adv., colloq.* firmly; fast.
намести́ [*infl. like* **мести́**] *v., pfv. of* **намета́ть**[1].
наме́стник *n., obs.* **1,** deputy. **2,** provincial governor.
намета́ть[1] *v. impfv.* [*pfv.* **намести́**] **1,** to sweep together (a quantity of something). **2,** (*of a storm, the wind, etc.*) to form (snowdrifts); drift (the snow). **3,** *impers.* to drift; pile up: намело́ мно́го сне́гу, large snowdrifts had formed.
намета́ть[2] *v., pfv. of* **намётывать.**
наме́тить [*infl.* **-чу, -тишь**] *v., pfv. of* **ме́тить** (*in sense #1*) *and* **намеча́ть.** —**наме́титься,** *refl., pfv. of* **намеча́ться.**
намётка [*gen. pl.* **-ток**] *n.* **1,** basting. **2,** basting thread. **3,** rough draft; outline.
намётывать *v. impfv.* [*pfv.* **намета́ть**] **1,** to pile up (a quantity of something). **2,** *colloq.* (*with* **глаз** *or* **ру́ку**) to train: намётанный глаз, trained eye. Намета́ть ру́ку на (+ *prepl.*), to become proficient at. **3,** to baste.
намеча́ть *v. impfv.* [*pfv.* **наме́тить**] **1,** to mark. **2,** to plan; map out; outline. **3,** to set; schedule. **4,** to nominate. —**намеча́ться,** *refl.* **1,** to appear; be visible. **2,** *fig.* to emerge; take shape. **3,** [*impfv. only*] to be planned; be scheduled.
на́ми *pron., instr. of* **мы.**
намно́го *adv.* **1,** (*with comp. adjectives*) much; far. **2,** (*with verbs*) greatly; considerably.
намока́ть *v. impfv.* [*pfv.* **намо́кнуть**] to get wet; get soaked.
намо́кнуть [*past* **-мо́к, -ла**] *v., pfv. of* **намока́ть.**
намоло́ть *v. pfv.* [*infl.* **-мелю́, -ме́лешь**] to grind (a quantity of something).
намо́рдник *n.* muzzle.
намо́рщить *v., pfv. of* **мо́рщить.** —**намо́рщиться,** *refl., pfv. of* **мо́рщиться** (*in sense #1*).
намота́ть *v. pfv.* **1,** *pfv. of* **мота́ть** *and* **нама́тывать.** **2,** to wind (a quantity of something).
намочи́ть [*infl.* **-мочу́, -мо́чишь**] *v., pfv. of* **мочи́ть** *and* **нама́чивать.**
наму́читься *v.r. pfv., colloq.* **1,** to suffer; go through hell. **2,** (*with* **с** + *instr.*) to have a hell of a time with.
намы́ливать *v. impfv.* [*pfv.* **намы́лить**] **1,** to soap; lather. **2,** *in* **намы́лить го́лову** (+ *dat.*), *colloq.* to chew someone out. —**намы́ливаться,** *refl.* to soap oneself.
намы́лить *v., pfv. of* **мы́лить** *and* **намы́ливать.** —**намы́литься,** *refl., pfv. of* **мы́литься** *and* **намы́ливаться.**
намя́ть *v. pfv.* [*infl.* **-мну́, -мнёшь**] *colloq.* **1,** to trample down; flatten. **2,** to irritate; chafe. —**намя́ть бока́** *or* **ше́ю** (+ *dat.*), *colloq.* to administer a beating to; beat up.
нанесе́ние *n.* **1,** inflicting; causing. **2,** tracing; plotting. **3,** applying; laying.
нанести́ [*infl. like* **нести́**] *v., pfv. of* **наноси́ть.**
наниза́ть [*infl.* **-нижу́, -ни́жешь**] *v., pfv. of* **низа́ть** *and* **нани́зывать.**
нани́зывать *v. impfv.* [*pfv.* **наниза́ть**] to string; thread.
нанима́тель *n.m.* **1,** tenant. **2,** employer.
нанима́ть *v. impfv.* [*pfv.* **наня́ть**] **1,** to hire; employ. **2,** to hire; rent. —**нанима́ться,** *refl.* to get a job.
на́ново *adv., colloq.* anew; over again.
нано́с *n.* alluvium.
наноси́ть *v. impfv.* [*pfv.* **нанести́;** *pres.* **-ношу́, -но́сишь**] **1,** to inflict: нанести́ кому́-нибудь уда́р/пораже́ние, to inflict a blow/defeat on someone. **2,** to drift; pile up (snow, sand, etc.); (*of water*) wash up. **3,** to trace; plot (*on a map*). **4,** to apply a layer of. **5,** *impers.* to strike; run into: ло́дку нанесло́ на ка́мень, the boat struck a rock. **6,** *in* наноси́ть визи́т (+ *dat.*), to pay a visit on.
нано́сный *adj.* **1,** alluvial. **2,** *fig.* alien; external.
наня́ть [*infl. like* **поня́ть**] *v., pfv. of* **нанима́ть.** —**наня́ться,** *refl.* [*past* **наня́лся́, -ла́сь**] *pfv. of* **нанима́ться.**
наоборо́т *adv.* **1,** backwards. **2,** the other way round. **3,** (*with* **и** *or* **или**) vice versa. **4,** on the contrary.
наобу́м *adv., colloq.* **1,** without thinking. **2,** at random.
нао́тмашь *adv.* **1,** (*with verbs of striking, throwing, etc.*) with a full sweep of one's arm. **2,** (*of one's arms*) stretched out; fully extended.
наотре́з *adv.* flatly; pointblank.
напа́дать *v. pfv.* to fall (*in large quantities*).
напада́ть *v. impfv.* [*pfv.* **напа́сть**] (*with* **на** + *acc.*) **1,** to attack. **2,** to run across; come across; come upon. **3,** to come up with; hit upon (an idea). **4,** *colloq.*

to attack; assail; jump on. **5,** (*of a feeling*) to come over.

нападáющий *n., decl. as an adj., sports* forward (*offensive player*).

нападéние *n.* attack.

напáдки [*gen.* **-док**] *n. pl.* (verbal) attacks.

напáивать *v. impfv.* [*pfv.* **напои́ть**] **1,** to give to drink. **2,** to make drunk. **3,** [*pfv.* **напая́ть**] to solder on.

напáлм *n.* napalm. —**напáлмовый,** *adj.* napalm.

напáрник *n., colloq.* partner; buddy; mate.

напáрывать *v. impfv.* [*pfv.* **напорóть**] *colloq.* to cut: напорóть нóгу на гвоздь, to cut one's foot on a nail. —**напáрываться,** *refl.* (*with* **на** + *acc.*) *colloq.* **1,** to cut oneself (on). **2,** to run into; encounter.

напáсть[1] *v. pfv.* [*infl. like* **пасть**] **1,** *pfv. of* **нападáть. 2,** to fall (*in large quantities*).

напáсть[2] *n.f., colloq.* misfortune.

напая́ть *v., pfv. of* **напáивать** (*in sense #3*).

напéв *n.* tune; melody; air.

напевáть *v. impfv.* [*pfv.* **напéть**] **1,** to sing. **2,** to record; make (a record). **3,** [*impfv. only*] to hum.

напéвный *adj.* melodious.

наперебóй *adv., colloq.* **1,** interrupting one another. **2,** vying with one another; trying to outdo one another.

напереве́с *adv.* (*of a weapon*) pointed forward.

наперегонки́ *also,* **наперегóнки** *adv., colloq.* racing one another: бежáть наперегонки́, to race each other.

напере́д *adv., colloq.* **1,** forward. **2,** in advance. —**зáдом напере́д,** backwards: надéть шля́пу зáдом напере́д, to put one's hat on backwards.

наперекóр *prep., with dat.* contrary to; in defiance of.

наперере́з *prep., with dat.* so as to cut across the path of; so as to intercept; so as to head off.

напереры́в *adv., colloq.* = **наперебóй.**

напере́чёт *adv., colloq.* **1,** (*with verbs of knowing*) inside out; like a book; (*with* **все**) every single one. **2,** few and far between.

напéрсник *n., obs.* confidant.

напéрсный *adj., in* **напéрсный крест,** pectoral cross.

напёрсток [*gen.* **-стка**] *n.* thimble.

наперстя́нка *n.* foxglove; digitalis.

напéть [*infl.* **-пою́, -поёшь**] *v., pfv. of* **напевáть.**

напечáтать *v., pfv. of* **печáтать.** —**напечáтаться,** *refl., pfv. of* **печáтаться.**

напéчь *v. pfv.* [*infl. like* **печь**] to bake (a quantity of something).

напивáться *v.r. impfv.* [*pfv.* **напи́ться**] **1,** to drink one's fill. **2,** (*with gen.*) to have a drink of. **3,** to get drunk.

напили́ть *v. pfv.* [*infl.* **-пилю́, -пи́лишь**] to saw (a quantity of something).

напи́лок [*gen.* **-лка**] *n., colloq.* = **напи́льник.**

напи́льник *n.* file (*tool*).

напирáть *v. impfv.* (*with* **на** + *acc.*) *colloq.* **1,** to press; put pressure on. **2,** to stress; emphasize.

написáние *n.* **1,** writing. **2,** spelling.

написáть *v., pfv. of* **писáть.**

напитáть *v. pfv.* **1,** *pfv. of* **напи́тывать. 2,** *colloq.* to feed.

напи́ток [*gen.* **-тка**] *n.* drink; beverage.

напи́тывать *v. impfv.* [*pfv.* **напитáть**] to saturate.

напи́ться [*infl. like* **пить**] *v.r., pfv. of* **напивáться.**

напи́хивать *v. impfv.* [*pfv.* **напихáть**] *colloq.* to stuff; cram.

напи́чкать *v., pfv. of* **пи́чкать.**

наплавнóй *adj., in* **наплавнóй мост,** floating bridge.

наплáкать *v. pfv.* [*infl.* **-плáчу, -плáчешь**], *in* наплáкать себé глазá, to have red eyes from crying. —**наплáкаться,** *refl.* **1,** to have a good cry. **2,** (*with* **с** + *instr.*) *colloq.* to have trouble (with).

напластовáние *n., geol.* bedding; stratification.

наплевáтельский *adj., colloq.* couldn't-care-less: наплевáтельское отношéние, couldn't-care-less attitude.

наплевáть *v. pfv.* [*infl.* **-плюю́, -плюёшь**] (*with* **на** + *acc.*) **1,** to spit on. **2,** *colloq.* not to give a damn: емý наплевáть на э́то, he doesn't give a damn about it.

наплести́ *v. pfv.* [*infl. like* **плести́**] **1,** to weave (a quantity of something). **2,** *colloq.* to talk a lot of (nonsense).

наплы́в *n.* **1,** influx. **2,** excrescence (*on trees*).

наповáл *adv., in* **уби́ть наповáл,** to kill outright; kill on the spot.

наподóбие *prep., with gen.* like; resembling.

напои́ть [*infl.* **-пою́, -пóишь** *or* **-пои́шь**] *v., pfv. of* **пои́ть** *and* **напáивать.**

напокáз *adv.* **1,** on display. **2,** for show.

наползáть *v. impfv.* [*pfv.* **наползти́**] *colloq.* **1,** (*with* **на** + *acc.*) to crawl onto. **2,** to crawl in (*in large numbers*).

наползти́ [*infl. like* **ползти́**] *v., pfv. of* **наползáть.**

наполнéние *n.* (act of) filling.

наполни́тель *n.m.* filler.

наполня́ть *v. impfv.* [*pfv.* **напóлнить**] to fill. —**наполня́ться,** *refl.* to be filled; become filled.

наполови́ну *adv.* **1,** half: наполови́ну пуст, half-empty. **2,** in half; by half: уменьши́ть наполови́ну, to reduce in/by half.

напомáдить *v., pfv. of* **помáдить.** —**напомáдиться,** *refl., pfv. of* **помáдиться.**

напоминáние *n.* **1,** reminder. **2,** mention: при напоминáнии о..., at the mention of...

напоминáть *v. impfv.* [*pfv.* **напóмнить**] **1,** (*with dat.*) to remind: напоминáть комý-нибудь о встрéче, to remind someone about an appointment. Вы напоминáете мне моегó мýжа, you remind me of my husband. **2,** [*impfv. only*] to resemble: фóрма кýпола напоминáет лýковицу, the shape of the dome resembles an onion.

напóр *n.* pressure.

напóристый *adj.* assertive; aggressive.

напóрный *adj.* pressure (*attrib.*).

напорóть *v. pfv.* [*infl.* **-порю́, -пóрешь**] **1,** *pfv. of* **напáрывать. 2,** (*with gen. or acc.*) to talk a lot of (nonsense). —**напорóться,** *refl., pfv. of* **напáрываться.**

напóртить *v. pfv.* [*infl.* **-чу, -тишь**] *colloq.* **1,** to damage (a quantity of something). **2,** (*with dat.*) to harm.

напослéдок *adv., colloq.* **1,** finally; at last; in the end. **2,** in conclusion.

напрáвить [*infl.* **-влю, -вишь**] *v., pfv. of* **направля́ть.** —**напрáвиться,** *refl., pfv. of* **направля́ться.**

направлéние *n.* **1,** direction. **2,** trend. **3,** assignment. **4,** order; permit. **5,** *mil.* axis.

напрáвленность *n.f.* direction; orientation.

напрáвленный *adj.* **1,** purposeful. **2,** *radio* directional.

направля́ть *v. impfv.* [*pfv.* **напрáвить**] **1,** to direct. **2,** to aim (a blow); point (a weapon). **3,** to send. **4,** to sharpen. —**направля́ться,** *refl.* (*with* **в, на,** *or* **к**) to head for; make for.

напра́во *adv.* to the right; on the right.
напрактикова́ться *v.r. pfv.* [*infl.* **-ку́юсь, -ку́ешься**] (*with* **в** + *prepl.*) *colloq.* to become proficient (at); get the knack (of).
напра́слина *n., colloq.* false charge; false allegation.
напра́сно *adv.* in vain; for nothing. Вы напра́сно ждёте её, you're wasting your time waiting for her. Вы напра́сно обвиня́ете его́, you have no reason to accuse him.
напра́сный *adj.* **1,** vain; futile. **2,** (*of fears, anxiety, etc.*) needless; groundless.
напра́шиваться *v.r. impfv.* [*pfv.* **напроси́ться**] *colloq.* **1,** (*with* **на** + *acc.*) to invite oneself (to); (try to) get invited (to). Напра́шиваться в го́сти, to (try to) wangle an invitation. **2,** (*with* **на** + *acc.*) to ask for; look for; invite (trouble); fish for (a compliment). **3,** [*impfv. only*] to come to mind; suggest itself.
наприме́р *adv.* for example; for instance.
напрока́зить *v., pfv. of* **прока́зить.**
напрока́зничать *v., pfv. of* **прока́зничать.**
напрока́т *adv.* on a rental basis. —**брать напрока́т,** to rent; hire. —**дава́ть** *or* **отдава́ть напрока́т,** to rent; rent out. —**сдава́ться напрока́т,** to be for hire.
напролёт *adv., colloq.* through; long; straight: всю ночь напролёт, the whole night through/long; весь день напролёт, all day long; два дня напролёт, two days straight.
напроло́м *adv., colloq.* straight ahead (*regardless of obstacles*).
напропалу́ю *adv., colloq.* headlong; for all one is worth.
напроро́чить *v., pfv. of* **проро́чить.**
напроси́ться [*infl.* **-прошу́сь, -про́сишься**] *v.r., pfv. of* **напра́шиваться.**
напро́тив *adv.* **1,** opposite. **2,** across the street. **3,** on the contrary. —*prep., with gen.* opposite; facing.
на́прочь *adv., colloq.* completely.
напру́живать *v. impfv.* [*pfv.* **напру́жить**] *colloq.* to strain; make taut.
напряга́ть *v. impfv.* [*pfv.* **напря́чь**] to strain; exert. —**напряга́ться,** *refl.* **1,** to become taut. **2,** to strain oneself; exert oneself.
напряже́ние *n.* **1,** straining; exertion. **2,** tension; strain; stress. **3,** *electricity* tension; voltage.
напряжённость *n.f.* tension: междунаро́дная напряжённость, international tension.
напряжённый *adj.* **1,** tense; strained. **2,** intense; strenuous. **3,** (*of attention*) rapt.
напрями́к *adv., colloq.* **1,** straight; in a straight line. **2,** *fig.* to the point; pointblank.
напря́чь [*infl.* **-прягу́, -пряжёшь, ...-прягу́т;** *past* **-пря́г, -прягла́, -прягло́**] *v., pfv. of* **напряга́ть.** —**напря́чься,** *refl., pfv. of* **напряга́ться.**
напуга́ть *v. pfv.* to frighten; scare. —**напуга́ться,** *refl.* to become frightened; become scared.
напу́дрить *v., pfv. of* **пу́дрить.** —**напу́дриться,** *refl., pfv. of* **пу́дриться.**
напу́льсник *n.* wristband.
напуска́ть *v. impfv.* [*pfv.* **напусти́ть**] **1,** to let in. **2,** (*with* **на** + *acc.*) *colloq.* to sic (an animal) on. **3,** (*with* **на** + *acc.*) *colloq.* to strike (fear, terror, etc.) into. **4,** (*with* **на себя́**) *colloq.* to affect; assume an air of. **5,** *in* **напуска́ть тума́ну,** to confuse the issue. —**напуска́ться,** *refl.* (*with* **на** + *acc.*) *colloq.* to attack; pounce on.
напускно́й *adj.* affected; assumed.
напусти́ть [*infl.* **-пущу́, -пу́стишь**] *v., pfv. of* **напуска́ть.** —**напусти́ться,** *refl., pfv. of* **напуска́ться.**
напу́тать *v. pfv., colloq.* **1,** to make a mess of; botch. **2,** (*with* **в** + *prepl.*) to get (something) wrong; get (something) mixed up.
напу́тственный *adj.* parting; farewell.
напу́тствие *n.* parting words.
напу́тствовать *v. impfv. & pfv.* [*pres.* **-ствую, -ствуешь**] (*with instr.*) to say (*when parting*).
напуха́ть *v. impfv.* [*pfv.* **напу́хнуть**] *colloq.* to swell up.
напу́хнуть [*past* **-пу́х, -ла**] *v., pfv. of* **напуха́ть.**
напы́житься *v.r., pfv. of* **пы́житься.**
напыли́ть *v., pfv. of* **пыли́ть** (*in sense #1*).
напы́щенность *n.f.* **1,** pomposity. **2,** bombast.
напы́щенный *adj.* **1,** pompous. **2,** bombastic; high-flown.
напя́ливать *v. impfv.* [*pfv.* **напя́лить**] **1,** to stretch (material) on a frame. **2,** *colloq.* to pull on (an item of clothing that is too small).
нарабо́тать *v. pfv., colloq.* **1,** to produce (a quantity of something). **2,** to earn (a sum of money). —**нарабо́таться,** *refl., colloq.* to do a lot of work; do enough work.
наравне́ *adv.* (*with* **с** + *instr.*) **1,** even (with); on a level (with). **2,** equally (with); on a par (with); on an equal footing (with).
нараспа́шку *adv., colloq.* unbuttoned; unfastened. —**душа́ нараспа́шку,** open-hearted; not one to hold back.
нараспе́в *adv.* in a singsong voice.
нараста́ние *n.* growth; expansion.
нараста́ть *v. impfv.* [*pfv.* **нарасти́**] **1,** (*with* **на** + *prepl.*) to grow (on); form (on). **2,** to grow; expand. **3,** to increase; build up; mount. **4,** (*of debts*) to pile up; (*of interest*) to accrue.
нарасти́ [*infl. like* **расти́**] *v., pfv. of* **нараста́ть.**
нарасти́ть [*infl.* **-щу́, -сти́шь**] *v., pfv. of* **нара́щивать.**
нарасхва́т *adv., colloq.* **1,** in great demand. **2,** *in* **продава́ться нарасхва́т,** to sell like hot cakes.
нара́щивание *n.* increase; build-up.
нара́щивать *v. impfv.* [*pfv.* **нарасти́ть**] **1,** [*impfv. only*] to increase; augment; step up; build up. **2,** to grow; develop (muscles, corns, etc.). **3,** to lengthen; extend.
нарва́л *n.* narwhal.
нарва́ть *v. pfv.* [*infl. like* **рвать**] **1,** *pfv. of* **нарыва́ть. 2,** to pick (a quantity of something). **3,** to tear (a quantity of something). —**нарва́ться,** *refl., pfv. of* **нарыва́ться.**
нард *n.* nard; spikenard.
наре́зать [*infl.* **-ре́жу, -ре́жешь**] *v., pfv. of* **нареза́ть.**
нареза́ть *v. impfv.* [*pfv.* **наре́зать**] **1,** to cut; slice. **2,** to thread (a screw); rifle (a gun barrel).
наре́зка *n.* **1,** cutting; slicing. **2,** thread (*of a screw*).
нарека́ние *n.* censure; reprimand.
нарека́ть *v. impfv.* [*pfv.* **наре́чь**] *obs.* to name.
наре́чие *n.* **1,** adverb. **2,** dialect. —**наре́чный,** *adj.* adverbial.
наре́чь [*infl.* **-реку́, -речёшь, ...-реку́т;** *past* **-рёк, -рекла́, -рекло́**] *v., pfv. of* **нарека́ть.**
нарза́н *n.* a kind of mineral water; narzan.
нарисова́ть *v., pfv. of* **рисова́ть.**
нарица́тельный *adj., in* **и́мя нарица́тельное,** common noun.

наркóз *n.* **1,** anesthesia. **2,** *colloq.* anesthetic.
наркомáн *n.* drug addict. —**наркомáния,** *n.* drug addiction.
наркотизи́ровать *v. impfv. & pfv.* [*pres.* **-рую, -руешь**] to anesthetize; drug.
наркóтик *n.* **1,** narcotic; drug. **2,** *colloq.* drug addict.
наркоти́ческий *adj.* narcotic. —**наркоти́ческие срéдства,** narcotics; drugs.
нарóд *n.* **1,** a people: совéтский нарóд, the Soviet people. **2,** the (common) people: человéк из нарóда, a man of the people. **3,** people: мнóго нарóду, a lot of people; a big crowd.
народи́ть *v. pfv.* [*infl.* **-жý, -ди́шь**] *colloq.* to give birth to (a number of children). —**народи́ться,** *refl., pfv. of* **нарождáться.**
нарóдник *n., hist.* Populist. —**нарóднический,** *adj.* Populist. —**нарóдничество,** *n.* Populism.
нарóдность *n.f.* **1,** nationality; people. **2,** national character; national roots.
нарóдный *adj.* **1,** people's. **2,** national. **3,** folk-: нарóдная пéсня, folk song.
народонаселéние *n.* population.
нарождáться *v.r. impfv.* [*pfv.* **народи́ться**] **1,** *colloq.* to be born. **2,** *fig.* to arise; come into being.
нарóст *n.* growth; tumor.
нарочи́тый *adj.* deliberate; intentional. —**нарочи́то,** *adv.* deliberately; intentionally.
нарóчно *adv.* **1,** deliberately; on purpose. **2,** (*with* **для**) specifically (for); expressly (for). **3,** for spite; just to be contrary. **4,** *colloq.* for fun. —**как нарóчно,** as luck would have it.
нáрочный *n., decl. as an adj.* special messenger; courier.
нáрты [*gen.* **нарт**] *n. pl.* dog sled; reindeer sled.
наруби́ть *v. pfv.* [*infl.* **-рублю́, -рýбишь**] to chop (a quantity of something).
нарýжно *adv., colloq.* outwardly.
нарýжное *n., decl. as an adj.* medicine to be taken externally.
нарýжность *n.f.* **1,** appearance; looks. **2,** exterior.
нарýжный *adj.* **1,** external; outward. **2,** (*of a wall*) outside. **3,** outward: нарýжное спокóйствие, outward calm.
нарýжу *adv.* ouside; outward(s); out. —**весь нарýжу,** (*of a person*) completely open about everything. —**вы́вести нарýжу,** to bring out into the open; bring to light. —**вы́йти нарýжу,** to come to the surface; come to light.
нарукáвник *n.* sleeve cover; sleeve protector.
нарукáвный *adj.* worn on the sleeve: нарукáвная повя́зка, armband.
нарумя́нить *v., pfv. of* **румя́нить.** —**нарумя́ниться,** *refl., pfv. of* **румя́ниться** (*in sense #1*).
нарýчники *n. pl.* [*sing.* **нарýчник**] handcuffs; manacles.
нарýчный *adj.* worn on the arm. —**нарýчные часы́,** wrist watch.
нарушáть *v. impfv.* [*pfv.* **нарýшить**] **1,** to violate; break. **2,** to disturb; disrupt.
нарушéние *n.* **1,** violation; breach; infringement. **2,** disturbance; disruption.
наруши́тель *n.m.* violator.
нарýшить *v., pfv. of* **нарушáть.**
нарци́сс *n.* narcissus; daffodil.
нáры [*gen.* **нар**] *n. pl.* plank bed.
нары́в *n.* abscess; boil.
нарывáть *v. impfv.* [*pfv.* **нарвáть**] to become infected and swollen. —**нарывáться,** *refl.* (*with* **на** + *acc.*) *colloq.* to run into; bump into.
нары́ть *v. pfv.* [*infl.* **-рóю, -рóешь**] to dig (a quantity of something).
наря́д *n.* **1,** dress; attire; apparel. **2,** order; warrant. **3,** *mil.* detail. **4,** *mil.* duty.
наряди́ть [*infl.* **-ряжý, -ряди́шь** *or* **-ря́дишь**] *v., pfv. of* **наряжáть.** —**наряди́ться,** *refl., pfv. of* **наряжáться.**
наря́дный *adj.* **1,** well-dressed. **2,** (*of an item of clothing*) good-looking; smart.
нарядý *adv.* (*with* **с** + *instr.*) **1,** along (with); side by side (with). **2,** on a level (with); on a par (with). —**нарядý с э́тим,** at the same time.
наряжáть *v. impfv.* [*pfv.* **наряди́ть**] **1,** to dress; dress up. **2,** to order; assign; detail. —**наряжáться,** *refl.* to dress up.
нас *pron., gen. & prepl. of* **мы.**
насади́ть *v. pfv.* [*infl.* **-сажý, -сáдишь**] **1,** *pfv. of* **насáживать** *and* **насаждáть. 2,** to plant (a quantity of something). **3,** (*with* **в** + *acc.*) *colloq.* to stuff (people or animals) into.
насáдка [*gen. pl.* **-док**] *n.* **1,** putting on. **2,** attachment (*for a camera or other device*). **3,** bait.
насажáть *v. pfv.* = **насади́ть** (*in senses #2 & #3*).
насаждáть *v. impfv.* [*pfv.* **насади́ть**] to implant; instill.
насаждéние *n.* **1,** planting. **2,** *fig.* implanting. **3,** *usu. pl.* plantings (*trees, plants, etc.*).
насáживать *v. impfv.* [*pfv.* **насади́ть**] **1,** to plant. **2,** (*with* **на** + *acc.*) to put; fix; stick; fasten (onto a hook, spit, etc.).
насáливать *v. impfv.* [*pfv.* **насоли́ть**] **1,** to salt; pickle. **2,** (*with dat.*) *colloq.* to hurt; injure; spite.
насáхаривать *v. impfv.* [*pfv.* **насáхарить**] *colloq.* to sugar; put sugar into.
насви́стывать *v. impfv.* to whistle.
наседáть *v. impfv.* [*pfv.* **насéсть**] **1,** (*of dust*) to settle; collect. **2,** (*with* **на** + *acc.*) *colloq.* to pounce on; *fig.* press; put pressure on (someone).
насéдка [*gen. pl.* **-док**] *n.* brood hen.
насекáть *v. impfv.* [*pfv.* **насéчь**] **1,** to carve (*on a surface*). **2,** to carve up; slice.
насекóмое *n., decl. as an adj.* insect.
населéние *n.* population.
населённость *n.f.* population density.
населённый *adj.* populated.
населя́ть *v. impfv.* [*pfv.* **насели́ть**] **1,** to populate; settle. **2,** [*impfv. only*] to inhabit.
насéст *n.* roost; perch.
насéсть *v. pfv.* [*infl. like* **сесть**] **1,** *pfv. of* **наседáть. 2,** (*of many people*) to sit down.
насéчка [*gen. pl.* **-чек**] *n.* **1,** notch; groove. **2,** inlay.
насéчь [*infl. like* **сечь;** *past* **-сéк, -секлá, -секлó**] *v., pfv. of* **насекáть.**
насéять *v. pfv.* to sow (a quantity of something).
насидéть [*infl.* **-жý, -ди́шь**] *v., pfv. of* **наси́живать.** —**насидéться,** *refl., colloq.* to sit a long time; sit long enough.
наси́женный *adj., in* **наси́женное мéсто,** place where one has always lived; one's home of many years.
наси́живать *v. impfv.* [*pfv.* **насидéть**] to hatch (an egg).

наси́лие *n.* violence.
наси́ловать *v. impfv.* [*pfv.* **изнаси́ловать;** *pres.* **-лую, -луешь**] **1,** to force; coerce. **2,** to rape.
наси́лу *adv., colloq.* barely; with great difficulty.
наси́льник *n.* **1,** tyrant; oppressor. **2,** rapist.
наси́льно *adv.* by force; forcibly.
наси́льственный *adj.* forcible; violent.
наска́кивать *v. impfv.* [*pfv.* **наскочи́ть**] (*with* **на** + *acc.*) **1,** to run into; collide (with). **2,** to pounce on. **3,** *fig., colloq.* to jump on; assail.
наскandáлить *v., pfv. of* **сканда́лить.**
наскво́зь *adv.* **1,** through; right through. **2,** *fig.* through and through; to the core. —**видеть насквозь,** to see through (someone).
наско́к *n., colloq.* **1,** lunge. **2,** attack. —**с наско́ку, 1,** with a swoop; by swooping down. **2,** on impulse; on the spur of the moment.
наско́лько *adv.* **1,** (*with adjectives and adverbs*) how: наско́лько э́то ве́рно?, how true is this? **2,** as far as: наско́лько я зна́ю, as far as I know.
на́скоро *adv., colloq.* hastily; hurriedly.
наскочи́ть [*infl.* **-скочу́, -ско́чишь**] *v., pfv. of* **наска́кивать.**
наскрести́ *v. pfv.* [*infl. like* **скрести́**] to scrape up; scrape together (*lit. & fig.*).
наску́чить *v. pfv.* (*with dat.*) *colloq.* to bore.
наслажда́ться *v.r. impfv.* [*pfv.* **наслади́ться**] (*with instr.*) to enjoy; take pleasure in.
наслажде́ние *n.* delight; pleasure; enjoyment.
насла́иваться *v.r. impfv.* [*pfv.* **наслои́ться**] to accumulate; pile up.
насла́ть *v. pfv.* [*infl.* **-шлю́, -шлёшь**] **1,** *pfv. of* **насыла́ть. 2,** to send (a quantity of something).
насле́дие *n.* legacy; heritage.
наследи́ть *v., pfv. of* **следи́ть** (*in sense #6*).
насле́дник *n.* heir. —**насле́дница,** *n.* heiress.
насле́дный *adj., in* **насле́дный принц/князь,** crown prince.
насле́дование *n.* inheritance. —**пра́во насле́дования,** succession.
насле́довать *v. impfv. & pfv.* [*pfv. also* **унасле́довать;** *pres.* **-дую, -дуешь**] **1,** to inherit. **2,** (*with dat.*) to succeed (someone) to the throne.
насле́дственность *n.f.* heredity.
насле́дственный *adj.* hereditary; inherited.
насле́дство *n.* inheritance. —**получи́ть (что́-нибудь) в насле́дство,** to inherit.
наслое́ние *n.* **1,** stratification. **2,** layer.
наслои́ться *v.r., pfv. of* **насла́иваться.**
наслу́шаться *v.r. pfv.* (*with gen.*) **1,** to hear a lot of. **2,** to hear enough of.
наслы́шаться *v.r. pfv.* [*infl.* **-шусь, -шишься**] (*with* **о**) *colloq.* to hear enough (about).
насма́рку *adv., colloq., in* **идти́/пойти́ насма́рку,** to go awry; go down the drain.
на́смерть *adv.* **1,** to death; mortally. Разби́ться на́смерть, to be killed (*in a crash, fall, etc.*). **2,** to the death: сража́ться на́смерть, to fight to the death. **3,** *fig., colloq.* to an extreme degree: испуга́ть на́смерть, to frighten to death; ненави́деть на́смерть, to hate with a passion.
насмеха́ться *v.r. impfv.* **1,** to sneer; scoff. **2,** (*with* **над**) to mock; ridicule; deride.
насмеши́ть *v., pfv. of* **смеши́ть.**
насме́шка [*gen. pl.* **-шек**] *n.* mockery; ridicule; derision.
насме́шливый *adj.* **1,** (*of a person*) sarcastic. **2,** mocking; derisive.
насме́шник *n., colloq.* mocker.
насме́шничать *v. impfv., colloq.* to scoff; sneer; (*with* **над**) scoff at; deride.
насмея́ться *v.r. pfv.* [*infl.* **-смею́сь, -смеёшься**] **1,** *colloq.* to have a lot of laughs. **2,** (*with* **над**) to laugh at; make fun of; deride.
на́сморк *n.* (head) cold.
насмотре́ться *v.r. pfv.* [*infl.* **-смотрю́сь, -смо́тришься**] **1,** (*with gen.*) to see a lot of. **2,** (*with* **на** + *acc.*) to see enough of: не могу́ насмотре́ться на..., I can't see enough of...
насоли́ть [*infl. like* **соли́ть**] *v., pfv. of* **наса́ливать.**
насори́ть *v., pfv. of* **сори́ть.**
насо́с *n.* pump.
насо́сный *adj.* pump (*attrib.*); pumping.
на́спех *adv.* hastily; hurriedly; in a hurry.
наспле́тничать *v., pfv. of* **спле́тничать.**
наст *n.* frozen crust on snow.
настава́ть *v. impfv.* [*pfv.* **наста́ть;** *pres.* **-стаёт**] (*of time, a season, etc.*) to come.
настави́тельный *adj.* didactic.
наста́вить *v. pfv.* [*infl.* **-влю, -вишь**] **1,** *pfv. of* **наставля́ть. 2,** to place (a quantity of something).
наставле́ние *n.* **1,** instructions. **2,** admonition. **3,** *mil.* manual.
наставля́ть *v. impfv.* [*pfv.* **наста́вить**] **1,** to lengthen. **2,** to aim; point. **3,** to teach; enlighten. —**наставля́ть нос** (+ *dat.*), to fool; dupe.
наста́вник *n.* teacher; tutor; mentor.
наста́ивать *v. impfv.* [*pfv.* **настоя́ть**] (*with* **на** + *prepl.*) to insist (on). —**наста́ивать на своём,** to insist on having one's own way. —**настоя́ть на своём,** to have one's way.
наста́ть [*infl.* **-ста́нет**] *v., pfv. of* **настава́ть.**
на́стежь *adv.* **1,** (*with verbs of opening*) wide. **2,** wide open.
насте́нный *adj.* wall (*attrib.*).
настига́ть *v. impfv.* [*pfv.* **насти́гнуть** *or* **насти́чь**] to overtake; catch up to.
насти́гнуть [*past* **-сти́г, -ла**] *v., pfv. of* **настига́ть.**
насти́л *n.* flooring.
настила́ть *v. impfv.* [*pfv.* **настла́ть**] to lay (a floor, carpet, etc.).
насти́лка *n., colloq.* flooring.
насти́чь [*infl. like* **насти́гнуть**] *v., pfv. of* **настига́ть.**
настла́ть [*infl.* **-стелю́, -сте́лешь**] *v., pfv. of* **настила́ть.**
насто́й *n.* extract.
насто́йка *n.* **1,** (fruit) brandy: вишнёвая насто́йка, cherry brandy. **2,** tincture: насто́йка йо́да, tincture of iodine.
насто́йчивый *adj.* persistent; insistent. —**насто́йчивость,** *n.f.* persistence; perseverance.
насто́лько *adv.* **1,** (*with adjectives*) so: э́то бы́ло насто́лько невероя́тно, что..., it was so unbelievable that... **2,** (*with verbs*) so much: он насто́лько вы́рос, что..., he has grown so much that... —**насто́лько..., наско́лько,** as..., as: она́ насто́лько умна́, наско́лько краси́ва, she is as intelligent as she is beautiful.
насто́льный *adj.* **1,** table (*attrib.*); desk (*attrib.*). **2,** *fig.* continually referred to: насто́льная кни́га, book

of ready reference; one's "bible". —**насто́льный те́ннис,** table tennis.
настора́живать *v. impfv.* [*pfv.* **насторожи́ть**] **1,** to put on one's guard. **2,** *in* насторожи́ть у́ши, to prick up one's ears. —**настора́живаться,** *refl.* to prick up one's ears; become alert.
настороже́ *adv.* on the alert; on the lookout; on one's guard.
насторо́женный *also,* **насторожённый** *adj.* **1,** watchful. **2,** guarded.
насторожи́ть *v., pfv. of* **настора́живать.** —**насторожи́ться,** *refl., pfv. of* **настора́живаться.**
настоя́ние *n.* insistence.
настоя́тель *n.m.* **1,** abbot. **2,** dean (*of a cathedral*). —**настоя́тельница,** *n.* mother superior.
настоя́тельный *adj.* **1,** insistent; persistent. **2,** vital; urgent. —**настоя́тельно,** *adv.* urgently. —**настоя́тельность,** *n.f.* persistence.
настоя́ть [*infl.* **-стою́, -стои́шь**] *v., pfv. of* **наста́ивать.**
настоя́щее *n., decl. as an adj.* the present.
настоя́щий *adj.* **1,** present: в настоя́щее вре́мя, at the present time. **2,** the present; this. **3,** real; true; genuine. —**настоя́щее вре́мя,** *gram.* present tense.
настрада́ться *v.r.pfv.* to suffer much.
настра́ивать *v. impfv.* [*pfv.* **настро́ить**] **1,** to tune (a musical instrument); tune in (a radio). **2,** to adjust (a device). **3,** to put (someone) in a certain mood: настро́ить кого́-нибудь на весёлый лад, to put someone in a happy frame of mind. ♦*Often passive.* Он пло́хо настро́ен, he is in a bad mood. Я настро́ен(а) пойти́ в кино́, I am in the mood to go to the movies. **4,** to influence; dispose: настро́ить кого́-нибудь в по́льзу (*or* про́тив) чего́-нибудь, to influence someone in favor of (*or* against) something. Настро́ить (кого́-нибудь) в свою́ по́льзу, to win over. Настро́ить сы́на про́тив отца́, to turn a son against his father. Он настро́ен про́тив меня́, he has something against me. —**настра́иваться,** *refl.* **1,** (*with* **на** + *acc.*) to tune in (a program, station, etc.). **2,** (*with* **к** *or* **про́тив**) to feel disposed (in a certain way toward or against). **3,** (*with inf.*) to make up one's mind to; (*with* **на** + *acc.*) decide upon.
настреля́ть *v. pfv.* to shoot (a quantity of something).
на́строго *adv., colloq.* strictly.
настрое́ние *n.* mood; frame of mind. —**у меня́ нет настрое́ния** (+ *inf.*), I am not in the mood for...
настро́енность *n.f.* mood; attitude.
настро́ить *v. pfv.* **1,** *pfv. of* **настра́ивать. 2,** to build (a quantity of something). —**настро́иться,** *refl., pfv. of* **настра́иваться.**
настро́йка *n.* tuning.
настро́йщик *n.* tuner.
настрочи́ть *v., pfv. of* **строчи́ть** (*in sense #2*).
настря́пать *v. pfv.* to cook; whip up (a quantity of something).
наступа́тельный *adj., mil.* offensive.
наступа́ть *v. impfv.* [*pfv.* **наступи́ть**] **1,** (*with* **на** + *acc.*) to step on; tread on. **2,** [*impfv. only*] to attack; assume the offensive; (*with* **на** + *acc.*) attack; advance on *or* against. **3,** [*impfv. only*] (*with* **на** + *acc.*) to harass; nag. **4,** [*impfv. only*] (*of natural phenomena*) to advance. **5,** (*of time, a season, etc.*) to come.
наступи́ть [*infl.* **-ступлю́, -сту́пишь**] *v., pfv. of* **наступа́ть.**
наступле́ние *n.* **1,** *mil.* offensive. **2,** coming (*of a season, time, etc.*). До наступле́ния темноты́, before nightfall.
насту́рция *n.* nasturtium.
насу́пить *v. pfv.* [*infl.* **-су́плю, -су́пишь**], *in* **насу́пить бро́ви,** to frown. —**насу́питься,** *refl.* to scowl; frown.
на́сухо *adv.* dry: вы́тереть на́сухо, to wipe dry.
насуши́ть *v. pfv.* [*infl.* **-сушу́, -су́шишь**] to dry (a quantity of something).
насу́щный *adj.* vital. —**насу́щный хлеб,** daily bread.
насчёт *prep., with gen.* about; regarding; concerning. —**как насчёт** (+ *gen.*), how about...?; what about...?
насчи́тывать *v. impfv.* [*pfv.* **насчита́ть**] **1,** to count. **2,** [*impfv. only*] to number; consist of: а́рмия насчи́тывала де́сять ты́сяч солда́т, the army numbered/consisted of/10,000 soldiers. —**насчи́тываться,** *refl.* [*impfv. only*] *impers.* to number: в го́роде насчи́тывается сто ты́сяч жи́телей, the city's inhabitants number 100,000; the city has a population of 100,000.
насыла́ть *v. impfv.* [*pfv.* **насла́ть**] (*of divine powers*) to send down; inflict (destruction, a calamity, etc.).
насы́пать [*infl.* **-сы́плю, -сы́плешь**] *v., pfv. of* **насыпа́ть.**
насыпа́ть *v. impfv.* [*pfv.* **насы́пать**] **1,** to sprinkle; spread. **2,** to pour: насыпа́ть муки́ в мешо́к, to pour flour into a sack. **3,** to fill: насыпа́ть мешо́к муко́й, to fill a sack with flour. **4,** to build (*out of dirt, sand, etc.*).
на́сыпь *n.f.* embankment.
насы́тить [*infl.* **-сы́щу, -сы́тишь**] *v., pfv. of* **насыща́ть.** —**насы́титься,** *refl., pfv. of* **насыща́ться.**
насыща́ть *v. impfv.* [*pfv.* **насы́тить**] **1,** to satiate; sate. **2,** to saturate. —**насыща́ться,** *refl.* **1,** to be full; be sated. **2,** to be saturated.
насыще́ние *n.* **1,** satiation. **2,** saturation.
ната́лкивать *v. impfv.* [*pfv.* **натолкну́ть**] **1,** *colloq.* to push into/against/onto: натолкну́ть кого́-нибудь на стол, to push someone into/against the table. **2,** *fig.* to lead (to): ната́лкивать кого́-нибудь на мысль, to lead someone to think; give someone an idea. —**ната́лкиваться,** *refl.* (*with* **на** + *acc.*) **1,** to run into; bump into; strike. **2,** *fig.* to run into; encounter. **3,** *fig.* to run across; come across.
ната́птывать *v. impfv.* [*pfv.* **натопта́ть**] (*with* **на** + *prepl.*) *colloq.* to track up.
натаска́ть *v. pfv.* **1,** *pfv. of* **ната́скивать. 2,** to bring, drag, store, or steal (a quantity of something). **3,** *colloq.* to cull; drag up (from various sources).
ната́скивать *v. impfv.* [*pfv.* **натаска́ть**] **1,** to train (a dog). **2,** *colloq.* to coach; teach (*quickly or superficially*). **3,** [*pfv.* **натащи́ть**] *colloq.* to pull on (an item of clothing); pull over.
натащи́ть *v. pfv.* [*infl.* **-тащу́, -та́щишь**] **1,** *pfv. of* **ната́скивать** (*in sense #3*). **2,** = **натаска́ть** (*in sense #2*).
натвори́ть *v. pfv., colloq.* to do (something harmful): что ты натвори́л?, what have you done?
на́те *particle, colloq.* here is; here you are.
натека́ть *v. impfv.* [*pfv.* **нате́чь**] (*of water*) to accumulate.
нате́льный *adj.* worn next to the skin: нате́льное бельё, underwear.
натере́ть *v. pfv.* [*infl. like* **тере́ть**] **1,** *pfv. of* **натира́ть. 2,** to grate (a quantity of something). —**натере́ться,** *refl., pfv. of* **натира́ться.**

натерпе́ться *v.r. pfv.* [*infl.* **-терплю́сь, -те́рпишься**] *colloq.* **1,** to suffer greatly. **2,** (*with gen.*) to suffer (a great deal of). —**натерпе́ться стра́ху,** to have a terrible fright.

нате́чь [*infl. like* **течь**] *v., pfv. of* **натека́ть.**

нате́шиться *v.r. pfv., colloq.* **1,** to enjoy oneself to the full. **2,** (*with* **над**) to have a good laugh (over).

натира́ть *v. impfv.* [*pfv.* **натере́ть**] **1,** to rub. **2,** to rub; irritate. Натере́ть себе́ мозо́ль, to get a corn. **3,** to polish. —**натира́ться,** *refl.* (*with instr.*) to rub oneself (with).

на́тиск *n.* onslaught; charge.

натка́ть *v. pfv.* [*infl. like* **ткать**] to weave (a quantity of something).

наткну́ться *v.r., pfv. of* **натыка́ться.**

натолкну́ть *v., pfv. of* **ната́лкивать.** —**натолкну́ться,** *refl., pfv. of* **ната́лкиваться.**

натоло́чь *v. pfv.* [*infl. like* **толо́чь**] to pound; crush (a quantity of something).

натопи́ть *v. pfv.* [*infl.* **-топлю́, -то́пишь**] **1,** to heat well. **2,** to melt (a quantity of something).

натопта́ть [*infl.* **-топчу́, -то́пчешь**] *v., pfv. of* **ната́птывать.**

наточи́ть *v., pfv. of* **точи́ть** (*in sense #1*).

натоща́к *adv.* on an empty stomach.

натр *n., in* **е́дкий натр,** caustic soda; sodium hydroxide.

натрави́ть [*infl.* **-травлю́, -тра́вишь**] *v., pfv. of* **натра́вливать.**

натра́вливать *v. impfv.* [*pfv.* **натрави́ть**] (*with* **на** + *acc.*) **1,** to sic (an animal on). **2,** *colloq.* to set (people against each other).

натренирова́ть *v., pfv. of* **тренирова́ть.** —**натренирова́ться,** *refl., pfv. of* **тренирова́ться.**

на́триевый *adj.* sodium (*attrib.*). —**на́триевая ла́мпа,** sodium-vapor lamp. —**на́триевая сели́тра,** sodium nitrate.

на́трий *n.* sodium.

на́трое *adv.* in three; into three parts.

натруди́ть *v. pfv.* [*infl.* **-тружу́, -тру́дишь** *or* **-труди́шь**] *colloq.* to overexert; wear out (a part of one's body).

нату́га *n., colloq.* strain; exertion.

на́туго *adv., colloq.* very tightly.

нату́живать *v. impfv.* [*pfv.* **нату́жить**] *colloq.* to strain; stretch; exert. —**нату́живаться,** *refl., colloq.* to make a supreme effort; bear down.

нату́жный *adj., colloq.* **1,** strenuous. **2,** strained. —**нату́жно,** *adv., colloq.* with great effort.

нату́ра *n.* **1,** nature; temperament; disposition. **2,** *art* real life: писа́ть с нату́ры, to paint from real life. **3,** model (*one who poses*). **4,** *motion pictures* location: на нату́ре, on location. —**нату́рой,** in kind: получа́ть жа́лованье нату́рой, to receive one's wages in kind.

натуриза́ция *n.* naturalization.

натурали́зм *n.* naturalism.

натурализова́ть *v. impfv. & pfv.* [*pres.* **-зу́ю, -зу́ешь**] to naturalize (*confer citizenship upon*). —**натурализова́ться,** *refl.* to become naturalized.

натурали́ст *n.* naturalist. —**натуралисти́ческий,** *adj.* naturalist (*attrib.*); naturalistic.

натура́льный *adj.* **1,** natural (*in various meanings*). **2,** (*of a product, material, etc.*) natural; real. **3,** (*of a person, gesture, etc.*) natural; genuine. —**в натура́льную величину́,** life-size.

нату́рщик *n.m.* [*fem.* **-щица**] model (*one who poses*).

натыка́ть *v. pfv., colloq.* to stick in (a quantity of something).

натыка́ться *v.r. impfv.* [*pfv.* **наткну́ться**] (*with* **на** + *acc.*) **1,** to run into; run against (a sharp object). **2,** *fig.* to run into; encounter. **3,** *colloq.* to run across; come across; stumble upon.

натюрмо́рт *n.* still life.

натя́гивать *v. impfv.* [*pfv.* **натяну́ть**] **1,** to draw (a bow, reins, etc.). **2,** to draw tight; tighten. **3,** to pull on; slip on. **4,** to pull over: натяну́ть ша́пку на́ уши, to pull one's cap over one's ears. —**натя́гиваться,** *refl.* to become taut.

натяже́ние *n.* pull; tension.

натя́жка *n.* **1,** stretching. **2,** *fig.* stretching of a point: с натя́жкой, by stretching a point.

натя́нутость *n.f.* tension; strain.

натя́нутый *adj.* **1,** strained. **2,** unnatural; forced.

натяну́ть [*infl.* **-тяну́, -тя́нешь**] *v., pfv. of* **натя́гивать.** —**натяну́ться,** *refl., pfv. of* **натя́гиваться.**

наугá́д *adv.* **1,** at random. **2,** by guesswork.

наугó́льник *n.* bevel; bevel square.

наудá́чу *adv.* at random.

науди́ть *v. pfv.* [*infl.* **-ужу́, -у́дишь**] to catch (a quantity of fish).

нау́ка *n.* **1,** science. **2,** *colloq.* lesson: э́то тебе́ нау́ка!, let that be a lesson to you!

нау́ськивать *v. impfv.* [*pfv.* **нау́ськать**] *colloq.* **1,** to sic (a dog). **2,** to egg on; incite.

наутёк *adv., colloq., in* **пусти́ться** *or* **бро́ситься наутёк,** to take to one's heels.

наутофо́н *n.* foghorn.

нау́тро *adv.* the next morning.

научи́ть *v., pfv. of* **учи́ть** (*in sense #1*). —**научи́ться,** *refl., pfv. of* **учи́ться** (*in sense #2*).

нау́чный *adj.* scientific. —**нау́чно,** *adv.* scientifically.

нау́шник *n.* **1,** earlap; earmuff. **2,** earphone; headphone. **3,** *colloq.* informer; tattletale.

нау́шничать *v. impfv., colloq.* to spread malicious gossip.

нау́шничество *n., colloq.* malicious gossip.

наще́ние *n., obs.* urging; instigation.

нафтали́н *n.* naphthalene.

нафто́л *n.* naphthol.

наха́л *n.m.* [*fem.* **-ка**] insolent person.

наха́льничать *v. impfv., colloq.* to be insolent; behave insolently.

наха́льный *adj.* impudent; insolent; impertinent.

наха́льство *n.* **1,** insolence; impudence; impertinence. **2,** effrontery; gall.

нахва́ливать *v. impfv.* [*pfv.* **нахвали́ть**] *colloq.* to extol.

нахвали́ть [*infl.* **-хвалю́, -хва́лишь**] *v., pfv. of* **нахва́ливать.** —**нахвали́ться,** *refl.* (*with instr.*) to praise sufficiently: не могу́ им нахвали́ться, I cannot praise him too highly.

нахвата́ть *v. pfv., colloq.* to acquire; pick up (a quantity of something). —**нахвата́ться,** *refl.* (*with gen.*) *colloq.* to pick up (bits of knowledge, a few words of a language, etc.).

нахле́бник *n.* **1,** *obs.* boarder. **2,** parasite; hanger-on.

нахлеста́ть [*infl.* **-хлещу́, -хле́щешь**] *v., pfv. of* **нахлёстывать.**

нахлёстывать *v. impfv.* [*pfv.* **нахлеста́ть**] *colloq.* to whip.

нахлобу́чивать *v. impfv.* [*pfv.* **нахлобу́чить**] *colloq.* to pull down (a hat) over one's eyes, ears, etc.
нахлобу́чка [*gen. pl.* **-чек**] *n., colloq.* scolding; bawling out; dressing-down.
нахлы́нуть *v. pfv.* **1,** (*of liquids*) to stream; flow; gush. **2,** (*of people*) to rush; throng; surge. **3,** *fig.* (*of thoughts*) to spring to mind.
нахму́ренный *adj.* **1,** frowning. **2,** gloomy.
нахму́рить *v., pfv. of* **хму́рить.** —**нахму́риться,** *refl., pfv. of* **хму́риться.**
находи́ть *v. impfv.* [*pfv.* **найти́;** *pres.* **-хожу́, -хо́дишь**] **1,** to find: найти́ свой портфе́ль, to find one's briefcase. Находи́ть до́вод убеди́тельным, to find an argument convincing. **2,** (*with* **на** + *acc.*) to strike; run into. **3,** (*with* **на** + *acc.*) to come upon. **4,** (*with* **на** + *acc.*) (*of emotions*) to come over. **5,** (*of clouds, twilight, etc.*) to gather. **6,** (*with* **на** + *acc.*) (*of clouds*) to cover; obscure. **7,** *impers.* (*of a crowd*) to gather: нашло́ мно́го наро́ду, a large crowd gathered. **8,** *in* найти́ свою́ смерть, to meet one's death/end. —**находи́ться,** *refl.* **1,** [*impfv. only*] to be; be found; be located. **2,** to be found; turn up. **3,** to come up with a quick answer; shoot back. Я не нашёлся, что отве́тить, I was at a loss as to how to answer.
нахо́дка [*gen. pl.* **-док**] *n.* a find.
нахо́дчивый *adj.* resourceful. —**нахо́дчивость,** *n.f.* resourcefulness.
нахожде́ние *n.* **1,** finding. **2,** being (somewhere).
нахо́хлиться *v.r., pfv. of* **хо́хлиться.**
нахохота́ться *v.r. pfv.* [*infl.* **-хочу́сь, -хо́чешься**] *colloq.* to have a good laugh.
нацара́пать *v., pfv. of* **цара́пать** (*in sense #2*).
нацеди́ть *v. pfv.* [*infl.* **-цежу́, -це́дишь**] to strain (a quantity of something).
наце́ливать *v. impfv.* [*pfv.* **наце́лить**] to aim (a weapon). —**наце́ливаться,** *refl.* **1,** to take aim. **2,** (*with inf.*) to get ready (to).
наце́нивать *v. impfv.* [*pfv.* **нацени́ть**] to mark up; raise the price of.
нацени́ть [*infl.* **-ценю́, -це́нишь**] *v., pfv. of* **наце́нивать.**
наце́нка *n.* markup; increase in price.
нацепи́ть [*infl.* **-цеплю́, -це́пишь**] *v., pfv. of* **нацепля́ть.**
нацепля́ть *v. impfv.* [*pfv.* **нацепи́ть**] (*with* **на** + *acc.*) to fasten to; hook onto; pin to.
наци́зм *n.* Nazism.
национализа́ция *n.* nationalization.
национализи́ровать *v. impfv. & pfv.* [*pres.* **-рую, -руешь**] to nationalize.
национали́зм *n.* nationalism. —**национали́ст,** *n.* nationalist. —**националисти́ческий,** *adj.* nationalist (*attrib.*); nationalistic.
национа́льность *n.f.* nationality.
национа́льный *adj.* national.
наци́ст *n.* Nazi. —**наци́стский,** *adj.* Nazi.
на́ция *n.* nation.
начади́ть *v., pfv. of* **чади́ть.**
нача́ло *n.* **1,** beginning: с са́мого нача́ла, from the very beginning; from the outset. **2,** origin; source. **3,** *pl.* basis: на доброво́льных нача́лах, on a voluntary basis. **4,** *pl.* principles: нача́ла хи́мии, principles of chemistry. —**брать нача́ло,** to originate; (*of a river*) rise. —**вести́ своё нача́ло от,** to have its origin in. —**дать нача́ло** (+ *dat.*), to give rise to. —**для нача́ла,** to start with; for a start. —**под нача́лом** (+ *gen. or* **у**), under the direction of. —**положи́ть нача́ло** (+*dat.*), **1,** to begin; initiate. **2,** to mark the beginning of. —**по нача́лу,** at first.
нача́льник *n.* chief; head; boss; superior. —**нача́льник ста́нции,** stationmaster —**нача́льник шта́ба,** chief of staff.
нача́льный *adj.* **1,** first; initial. **2,** (*of education, a school, etc.*) elementary; primary.
нача́льственный *adj.* overbearing; domineering.
нача́льство *n.* **1,** the authorities. **2,** command; direction. **3,** *colloq.* boss; chief.
нача́льствование *n.* command.
нача́льствовать *v. impfv.* [*pres.* **-ствую, -ствуешь**] (*with* **над**) *obs.* to command.
нача́тки *n. pl.* [*sing.* **нача́ток**] rudiments.
нача́ть [*infl.* **начну́, начнёшь;** *past* **на́чал, начала́, на́чало**] *v., pfv. of* **начина́ть.** —**нача́ться,** *refl.* [*past* **начался́, начала́сь, начало́сь**] *pfv. of* **начина́ться.**
начеку́ *adv.* on one's guard; on the alert.
начерни́ть *v., pfv. of* **черни́ть** (*in sense #1*).
на́черно *adv.* in the rough: писа́ть (что́-нибудь) на́черно, to make a rough draft of.
начерта́ние *n.* **1,** tracing. **2,** outline.
начерта́тельный *adj., in* **начерта́тельная геоме́трия,** descriptive geometry.
начерта́ть *v. pfv.* **1,** *obs.* to trace; inscribe. **2,** *fig.* to set forth; outline.
начерти́ть *v., pfv. of* **черти́ть.**
начёс *n.* nap (*of cloth*).
начётчик *n.* pedant.
начина́ние *n.* project; undertaking.
начина́тельный *adj., gram.* inceptive: начина́тельный глаго́л, inceptive verb (*e.g.* забе́гать, to begin to run).
начина́ть *v. impfv.* [*pfv.* **нача́ть**] **1,** to begin; start (something). **2,** (*with inf.*) to begin (to); start (to). —**начина́ться,** *refl.* (*of something*) to begin; start.
начина́ющий *adj.* beginning. —*n.* beginner.
начина́я *prep.* (*with* **с** + *gen.*) beginning (with).
начини́ть *v. pfv.* **1,** [*infl.* **-чиню́, -чини́шь**] *pfv. of* **начиня́ть. 2,** [*infl.* **-чиню́, -чи́нишь**] to mend (a quantity of something); sharpen (a quantity of pencils).
начи́нка *n.* stuffing; filling.
начиня́ть *v. impfv.* [*pfv.* **начини́ть**] to stuff.
начи́стить *v. pfv.* [*infl.* **-щу, -стишь**] **1,** *pfv. of* **начища́ть. 2,** to peel (a quantity of something).
на́чисто *adv.* **1,** clean: на́чисто вы́бритый, clean-shaven. Переписа́ть (что́-нибудь) на́чисто, to make a clean copy of. **2,** *colloq.* completely; utterly. **3,** *colloq.* openly; candidly.
начистоту́ *adv.* frankly; without equivocation; straight from the shoulder.
начи́танный *adj.* well-read. —**начи́танность,** *n.f.* erudition.
начита́ть *v. pfv., colloq.* to read (a quantity of something). —**начита́ться,** *refl.* (*with gen.*) to read a great deal of.
начища́ть *v. impfv.* [*pfv.* **начи́стить**] *colloq.* to polish; shine.
наш [*fem.* **на́ша;** *neut.* **на́ше;** *pl.* **на́ши**] *poss. adj. & pron.* our; ours.
нашали́ть *v. pfv.* to be naughty; act up.
нашаты́рный *adj., in* **нашаты́рный спирт,** liquid ammonia.

нашатырь [*gen.* **-тыря́**] *n.m.* ammonium chloride.
нашепта́ть *v. pfv.* [*infl.* **-шепчу́, -ше́пчешь**] **1,** to whisper. **2,** (*with dat.*) to whisper in someone's ear.
наше́ствие *n.* invasion.
нашива́ть *v. impfv.* [*pfv.* **наши́ть**] to sew on.
наши́вка [*gen. pl.* **-вок**] *n., mil.* stripe; chevron.
нашивно́й *adj.* sewn-on.
наши́ть *v. pfv.* [*infl.* **-шью́, -шьёшь**] **1,** *pfv. of* **нашива́ть. 2,** to sew (a quantity of something).
нашпигова́ть *v., pfv. of* **шпигова́ть.**
нашпи́ливать *v. impfv.* [*pfv.* **нашпи́лить**] **1,** to place (*or* stick) on a pin. **2,** to pin on.
нашуме́вший *adj.* sensational; much talked about; having caused quite a stir.
нашуме́ть *v. pfv.* [*infl.* **-млю́, -ми́шь**] **1,** to make a lot of noise. **2,** *fig.* to cause a sensation.
нащипа́ть *v. pfv.* [*infl.* **-щиплю́, -щи́плешь**] **1,** to pluck; pick (a quantity of something). **2,** *colloq.* to pinch.
нащу́пывать *v. impfv.* [*pfv.* **нащу́пать**] **1,** [*impfv. only*] to grope for; fumble for; feel about for. **2,** to feel (someone's pulse). **3,** to find; come upon (*after groping*). **4,** *fig.* to find; discover; detect. —**нащу́пывать по́чву,** to get the lay of the land; sound out the possibilities.
наэлектризова́ть *v., pfv. of* **электризова́ть.**
ная́бедничать *v., pfv. of* **я́бедничать.**
наяву́ *adv.* while awake; not in one's dreams.
ная́да *n.* naiad.
не *neg. particle* **1,** not: э́то не ве́рно, that is not true; лифт не рабо́тает, the elevator is not working. **2,** *inserted between such words as* ничего́, никто́, никогда́, *etc. and a verb following:* никто́ не зна́ет, no one knows. Мы почти́ никогда́ не ви́дим её, we almost never see her. **3,** (*with imperatives*) don't: не забу́дьте!, don't forget! **4,** *occurring as a separate word when* не́чего, не́кого, *and their oblique case forms are separated to permit the insertion of a preposition in between:* ему́ не́ с кем игра́ть, he has no one to play with. **5,** (*with past tense verbal adverbs*) without: гла́зом не моргну́в, without batting an eye. **6,** (*with inf.*) will never; would never: его́ не узна́ть, you would never recognize him. —**не́ за что!**, not at all!; don't mention it! —**не то что** *or* **что́бы...,** it is not that...
неаккура́тность *n.f.* **1,** lack of punctuality. **2,** carelessness. **3,** sloppiness.
неаккура́тный *adj.* **1,** not punctual. **2,** careless; sloppy; inefficient. **3,** untidy.
неандерта́лец [*gen.* **-льца**] *n.* Neanderthal man. —**неандерта́льский,** *adj.* Neanderthal.
неаппети́тный *adj.* unappetizing.
небезопа́сный *adj.* somewhat dangerous; unsafe.
небезоснова́тельный *adj.* not without foundation.
небезразли́чный *adj.* **1,** not indifferent; interested. **2,** (*with dat. or* **для**) of interest (to).
небезызве́стный *adj.* not unknown; rather well-known.
небезынтере́сный *adj.* rather interesting.
небелёный *adj.* unbleached.
небе́сный *adj.* heavenly; celestial. —**небе́сный свод,** firmament.
неблагови́дный *adj.* unseemly; improper.
неблагода́рный *adj.* **1,** ungrateful. **2,** thankless. —**неблагода́рность,** *n.f.* ingratitude.
неблагожела́тельный *adj.* unfriendly; hostile. —**неблагожела́тельность,** *n.f.* ill will.
неблагозву́чие *n.* dissonance; disharmony. —**неблагозву́чный,** *adj.* dissonant; discordant.
неблагонадёжный *adj.* (politically) unreliable.
неблагополу́чие *n.* trouble; troubles.
неблагополу́чный *adj.* unhappy; unfortunate. —**неблагополу́чно,** *adv.* badly; in an unhappy way.
неблагопристо́йный *adj.* improper; indecent.
неблагоприя́тный *adj.* unfavorable.
неблагоразу́мие *n.* imprudence. —**неблагоразу́мный,** *adj.* imprudent; unwise; ill-advised.
неблагоро́дный *adj.* ignoble. —**неблагоро́дные мета́ллы,** base metals.
неблагоскло́нный *adj.* ill-disposed; unfavorably disposed. —**неблагоскло́нность,** *n.f.* unfavorable attitude.
неблагоустро́енный *adj.* (*of premises*) lacking amenities or conveniences.
неблестя́щий *adj.* not outstanding; mediocre.
нёбный *adj.* palatal. —**нёбная занаве́ска,** *anat.* uvula.
не́бо [*pl.* **небеса́, небе́с, небеса́м**] *n.* sky; heaven. —**ме́жду не́бом и землёй,** without a roof over one's head. —**на седьмо́м не́бе,** in seventh heaven. —**под откры́тым не́бом,** in the open air. —**попа́сть па́льцем в не́бо,** to be wide of the mark. —**превозноси́ть до небе́с,** to praise to the skies.
нёбо *n.* palate; roof of the mouth.
небога́тый *adj.* **1,** not rich; of modest means. **2,** modest; unpretentious. **3,** meager; scanty.
небоеспосо́бный *adj.* unfit for (military) action; disabled.
небольшо́й *adj.* **1,** small; not large; not great. **2,** (*of time, distance, etc.*) short. —**с небольши́м,** a little over; a little past: в три с небольши́м, a little after three.
небосво́д *n.* firmament.
небоскло́н *n.* lower part of the sky near the horizon.
небоскрёб *n.* skyscraper.
небо́сь *particle, colloq.* in all probability; most likely.
небре́жный *adj.* **1,** careless; negligent. **2,** sloppy; slipshod. **3,** casual. —**небре́жно,** *adv.* carelessly. —**небре́жность,** *n.f.* carelessness; negligence.
небри́тый *adj.* unshaven.
небыва́лый *adj.* **1,** unprecedented; unheard-of. **2,** fantastic; unreal.
небыли́ца *n.* tall story; cock-and-bull story.
небытие́ *n.* nonexistence.
небью́щийся *adj.* unbreakable; nonbreakable; shatterproof.
нева́жно *adv.* **1,** not well; poorly. **2,** *as an exclamation* never mind!; it doesn't matter!
нева́жный *adj.* **1,** unimportant. **2,** *colloq.* poor; not so good.
невдалеке́ *adv.* not far away; not far off.
невдомёк *adv., with dat., colloq.* having no idea: мне невдомёк, I had no idea; it never occurred to me.
неве́дение *n.* ignorance. —**держа́ть в неве́дении,** to keep in the dark.
неве́домо *adv., colloq.* there is no telling; there is no way of knowing.
неве́домый *adj.* **1,** unknown. **2,** mysterious.
неве́жа *n.m. & f.* boor; lout.
неве́жда *n.m. & f.* ignoramus.
неве́жество *n.* ignorance. —**неве́жественный,** *adj.* ignorant.

невéжливый *adj.* impolite; rude. —**невéжливость,** *n.f.* impoliteness; rudeness.
невезéние *n., colloq.* bad luck.
невезýчий *adj., colloq.* unlucky.
невели́кий *adj., usu. used in short form* [*fem.* **ликá;** *neut.* **-ли́ко** *or* **-ликó**] **1,** small; not large. Невели́к рóстом, short (*in height*). **2,** not great; slight; insignificant.
невéрие *n.* **1,** disbelief. **2,** lack of faith.
невéрно *adv.* **1,** incorrectly. **2,** with an uncertain gait.
невéрность *n.f.* **1,** error; fallacy. **2,** infidelity.
невéрный *adj.* **1,** incorrect; wrong; erroneous. **2,** unfaithful; untrue. **3,** unsteady; faltering. **4,** *in* невéрная нóта, false note. —*n.* infidel.
невероя́тно *adv.* incredibly; unbelievably.
невероя́тность *n.f.* **1,** improbability. **2,** unbelievability. **3,** *pl.* unbelievable stories. —**до невероя́тности,** unbelievably; incredibly; to an incredible degree.
невероя́тный *adj.* incredible; unbelievable.
невéрующий *adj.* nonbelieving; irreligious. —*n.* nonbeliever.
невесёлый *adj.* melancholy; sad; blue.
невесóмый *adj.* weightless. —**невесóмость,** *n.f.* weightlessness.
невéста *n.* **1,** fiancée. **2,** bride.
невéстка [*gen. pl.* **-ток**] *n.* **1,** daughter-in-law. **2,** sister-in-law (*brother's wife* or *spouse's brother's wife*).
невéсть *adv., colloq.* heaven knows; God knows.
невещéственный *adj.* immaterial.
невзви́деть *v. pfv., in* **свéта невзви́деть,** *colloq.* **1,** (*from shock or surprise*) to be stupefied. **2,** (*from pain*) to see stars.
невзгóда *n.* adversity; misfortune.
невзирáя на (*with acc.*) in spite of; regardless of.
невзлюби́ть *v. pfv.* [*infl.* **-люблю́, -лю́бишь**] to dislike; take a disliking to.
невзначáй *adv., colloq.* by chance; accidentally.
невзнóс *n.* nonpayment of dues.
невзрáчный *adj.* ugly; homely; unattractive.
невзыскáтельный *adj.* undemanding.
нéвидаль *n.f., colloq.* wonder; something to marvel at. —**вот** (*or* **э́ка**) **нéвидаль!,** what's all the fuss?
неви́данный *adj.* extraordinary; unprecedented.
невиди́мка [*gen. pl.* **-мок**] *n.m. & f.* invisible man or creature. —*n.f.* invisible hairpin.
неви́димый *adj.* invisible.
неви́дный *adj.* **1,** invisible. **2,** *colloq.* insignificant. **3,** *colloq.* unattractive.
неви́дящий *adj.* **1,** unseeing; sightless; blind. **2,** (*of a look*) blank; absent; vacant.
неви́нность *n.f.* **1,** innocence. **2,** virginity.
неви́нный *adj.* **1,** innocent; guiltless. **2,** innocent; naïve; ingenuous. **3,** innocent; innocuous; harmless. **4,** innocent; virginal.
невинóвный *adj.* innocent; not guilty. —**невинóвность,** *n.f.* innocence.
невкýсный *adj.* tasteless; unpalatable.
невменя́емый *adj., law* not responsible for one's actions.
невмешáтельство *n.* noninterference; nonintervention.
невмоготý *adv., colloq.* too much; more than one can bear.
невнимáние *n.* **1,** inattention. **2,** lack of consideration.
невнимáтельность *n.f.* **1,** carelessness. **2,** lack of consideration.
невнимáтельный *adj.* **1,** inattentive. **2,** inconsiderate.
невнуши́тельный *adj.* unimpressive.
невня́тный *adj.* indistinct; scarcely audible.
нéвод [*pl.* **неводá**] *n.* large fishing net.
невозврáтный *adj.* **1,** irretrievable. **2,** (*of a loss*) irreparable.
невозвращéнец [*gen.* **-нца**] *n.* defector.
невоздéланный *adj.* untilled, uncultivated.
невоздержáние *n.* intemperance; immoderation.
невоздéржанный *also,* **невоздéржный** *adj.* intemperate; immoderate. —**невоздéржанность; невоздéржность,** *n.f.* intemperance, immoderation.
невозмóжно *adj., used predicatively* impossible: э́то практи́чески невозмóжно, it is practically impossible.
невозмóжное *n., decl. as an adj.* the impossible.
невозмóжность *n.f.* impossibility. —**до невозмóжности,** to the extreme.
невозмóжный *adj.* impossible.
невозмути́мый *adj.* **1,** imperturbable; unflappable. **2,** (*of calm, quiet, etc.*) perfect; undisturbed. —**невозмути́мость,** *n.f.* imperturbability; coolness.
невознагради́мый *adj.* **1,** irreparable. **2,** that can never be repaid.
невóлить *v. impfv., colloq.* to force; compel.
невóльник *n.* slave. —**невóльничество,** *n.* slavery. —**невóльничий,** *adj.* [*fem.* **-чья**] slave (*attrib.*).
невóльно *adv.* **1,** unintentionally. **2,** instinctively. **3,** against one's will.
невóльный *adj.* **1,** unintentional; involuntary. **2,** involuntary; forced.
невóля *n.* **1,** slavery. **2,** captivity: размножáться в невóле, to breed in captivity. **3,** *colloq.* necessity.
невообрази́мый *adj.* inconceivable; unimaginable.
невооружённый *adj.* unarmed. —**невооружённым глáзом,** with the naked (*or* unaided) eye.
невоспéтый *adj.* unsung.
невоспи́танный *adj.* ill-bred; ill-mannered. —**невоспи́танность,** *n.f.* lack of upbringing.
невоспламеня́емый *adj.* incombustible; nonflammable.
невосполни́мый *adj.* irreparable.
невосприи́мчивый *adj.* **1,** slow to absorb or learn. **2,** (*with* к) immune (to). —**невосприи́мчивость,** *n.f.* immunity.
невострéбованный *adj.* unclaimed.
невою́ющий *adj.* nonbelligerent.
невпопáд *adv., colloq.* not to the point: он отвечáл невпопáд, his answers were not to the point.
невразуми́тельный *adj.* unintelligible.
невралги́я *n.* neuralgia. —**невралги́ческий,** *adj.* neuralgic.
неврастени́я *n.* nervous breakdown; nervous exhaustion; neurasthenia.
невреди́мый *adj.* unharmed; safe. —**цел и невреди́м,** safe and sound.
неврéдный *adj.* harmless.
неври́т *n.* neuritis.
неврóз *n.* neurosis.
невролóгия *n.* neurology. —**неврóлог,** *n.* neurologist. —**неврологи́ческий,** *adj.* neurological.
невропатóлог *n.* neurologist.
невроти́ческий *adj.* neurotic.

невы́года *n.* **1,** disadvantage. **2,** loss.
невы́годно *adv.* **1,** not to one's advantage. **2,** at a loss. *—adj., used predicatively* disadvantageous; not a good idea.
невы́годный *adj.* **1,** unprofitable. **2,** unfavorable; disadvantageous. **3,** unattractive.
невы́держанный *adj.* **1,** lacking self-control. **2,** uneven. **3,** (*of wine, cheese, etc.*) not aged; new. —**невы́держанность,** *n.f.* lack of self-control.
невыла́зный *adj., colloq.* **1,** impassable. **2,** offering no way out.
невыноси́мый *adj.* unbearable; unendurable; insufferable. —**невыноси́мо,** *adv.* unbearably.
невыполне́ние *n.* nonfulfillment; failure to carry out.
невы́полненный *adj.* unfulfilled.
невыполни́мый *adj.* impracticable; unfeasible. —**невыполни́мость,** *n.f.* impracticability.
невырази́мый *adj.* inexpressible. —**невырази́мые,** *n. pl., jocular* unmentionables.
невырази́тельный *adj.* inexpressive; unexpressive. —**невырази́тельность,** *n.f.* lack of expression.
невы́сказанный *adj.* unexpressed; unspoken.
невысо́кий *adj.* low. —**невысо́кого ка́чества,** low-grade; of poor quality.
невы́ход *n.* failure to appear.
не́га *n.* **1,** comfort; contentment; ease. **2,** bliss.
негати́в *n., photog.* negative.
негати́вный *adj.* negative.
негашёный *adj.* **1,** (*of stamps*) uncanceled; unused. **2,** *in* негашёная и́звесть, quicklime.
не́где *adv., used with inf.* nowhere; no place: мне не́где сесть, I have no place to sit.
неги́бкий *adj.* stiff; rigid; inflexible. —**неги́бкость,** *n.f.* stiffness.
негла́сный *adj.* secret.
неглиже́ *n. neut. indecl.* negligee.
неглубо́кий *adj.* **1,** shallow. **2,** *fig.* shallow; superficial.
неглу́пый *adj.* **1,** quite intelligent. **2,** (*of advice*) sound; sensible.
негну́щийся *adj.* stiff.
него́ (vo) *pron., var. of* **его́,** *used after prepositions.*
него́дник *n., colloq.* **1,** good-for-nothing. **2,** brat.
него́дность *n.f.* **1,** lack of fitness. **2,** uselessness. —**приходи́ть в него́дность, 1,** to fall into disrepair. **2,** to become unusable.
него́дный *adj.* **1,** unfit. **2,** *colloq.* worthless; good-for-nothing.
негодова́ние *n.* indignation.
негодова́ть *v. impfv.* [*pres.* **-ду́ю, -ду́ешь**] to be indignant.
негоду́ющий *adj.* indignant.
негодя́й *n.* scoundrel.
негостеприимный *adj.* inhospitable.
негото́вый *adj.* unready.
негр *n.* Negro; black.
негра́мотный *adj.* **1,** illiterate. **2,** full of errors (*in grammar, spelling, etc.*). —**негра́мотность,** *n.f.* illiteracy.
негритёнок [*gen.* **-нка;** *pl.* **-тя́та, -тя́т**] *n.* Negro child; black child.
негритя́нка [*gen. pl.* **-нок**] *n.* Negro woman; black woman.
негритя́нский *adj.* Negro; black.
негро́идный *adj.* Negroid.
негро́мкий *adj.* low; not loud. —**негро́мко,** *adv.* in a low voice.
неда́вний *adj.* recent. —**до неда́внего вре́мени,** until recently.
неда́вно *adv.* recently; not long ago.
недалёкий *adj.* **1,** nearby; not far off. **2,** near (*in time*). В недалёком про́шлом, in the recent past. **3,** not very bright.
недалеко́ *also,* **недалёко** *adv.* not far. *—adj. used predicatively* not far: по́чта недалеко́ от вокза́ла, the post office is not far from the station.
недальнови́дный *adj.* shortsighted. —**недальнови́дность,** *n.f.* shortsightedness.
неда́ром *adv.* for a reason; not for nothing; (it is) no wonder.
недви́жимость *n.f.* real estate.
недви́жимый *also,* **недвижи́мый** *adj.* immovable. —**недви́жимое иму́щество,** real estate.
недвусмы́сленный *adj.* unequivocal; unambiguous. —**недвусмы́сленно,** *adv.* unequivocally.
недееспосо́бный *adj.* **1,** unable to function. **2,** *law* incompetent. —**недееспосо́бность,** *n.f., law* incompetence.
недействи́тельный *adj.* **1,** *obs.* ineffective; ineffectual. **2,** invalid; null and void.
неделика́тный *adj.* indelicate; tactless. —**неделика́тность,** *n.f.* indelicacy; tactlessness.
недели́мый *adj.* **1,** indivisible. **2,** (*of numbers*) prime. —**недели́мость,** *n.f.* indivisibility.
неде́льный *adj.* a week's.
неде́ля *n.* week.
недержа́ние *n., med.* incontinence.
недёшево *adv., colloq.* not cheap: сто́ить недёшево, to cost a pretty penny.
недисциплини́рованный *adj.* undisciplined.
недобо́р *n.* shortage; shortfall.
недоброжела́тельный *adj.* unfriendly; hostile. —**недоброжела́тельность,** *n.f.;* **недоброжела́тельство,** *n.neut.* ill will.
недоброка́чественный *adj.* poor-quality; low-grade; inferior; shoddy. —**недоброка́чественность,** *n.f.* poor quality.
недобросо́вестность *n.f.* **1,** lack of conscientiousness; negligence. **2,** lack of integrity; bad faith.
недобросо́вестный *adj.* **1,** unconscientious. **2,** unscrupulous.
недо́брый *adj.* **1,** unkind; mean; malicious. **2,** evil; bad. —**недо́брое,** *n.* trouble: чу́ять недо́брое, to sense trouble; smell a rat.
недова́ривать *v. impfv.* [*pfv.* **недовари́ть**] to undercook.
недовари́ть [*infl.* **-варю́, -ва́ришь**] *v., pfv. of* **недова́ривать.**
недове́рие *n.* **1,** distrust; mistrust. **2,** incredulity.
недове́рчивый *adj.* **1,** distrustful; mistrustful. **2,** incredulous. —**недове́рчивость,** *n.f.* distrust; mistrust.
недово́льный *adj.* [*short form* **-лен, -льна**] dissatisfied; discontented; displeased. —*n.* malcontent.
недово́льство *n.* dissatisfaction; discontent; displeasure.
недовыполне́ние *n.* failure to fulfill completely; underfulfillment.
недовыполня́ть *v. impfv.* [*pfv.* **недовы́полнить**] to fail to fulfill completely.
недога́дливый *adj.* slow to grasp things; dull; dense.
недогляде́ть *v. pfv.* [*infl.* **-жу́, -ди́шь**] *colloq.* **1,** to overlook. **2,** (*with* **за** + *instr.*) to fail to look after.

недогова́ривать *v. impfv.* [*pfv.* **недоговори́ть**] to hold back; leave unsaid: вы что-то недогова́риваете, you're holding something back.

недоговорённость *n.f.* **1,** lack of agreement; lack of coordination. **2,** failure to tell all.

недоговори́ть *v., pfv. of* **недогова́ривать.**

недодава́ть *v. impfv.* [*pfv.* **недода́ть;** *pres.* **-даю́, -даёшь**] to give less than the required amount: он мне недо́дал три рубля́, he gave me three rubles less than he was supposed to.

недода́ть [*infl. like* **дать;** *past* **недо́дал, -дала́, недо́дало**] *v., pfv. of* **недодава́ть.**

недоде́ланный *adj.* unfinished.

недоде́лать *v. pfv.* to fail to do; fail to finish.

недоде́лка [*gen. pl.* **-лок**] *n., colloq.* defect; imperfection.

недодержа́ть [*infl.* **-держу́, -де́ржишь**] *v., pfv. of* **недоде́рживать.**

недоде́рживать *v. impfv.* [*pfv.* **недодержа́ть**] *photog.* to underexpose.

недоде́ржка *n., photog.* underexposure.

недоеда́ние *n.* malnutrition.

недоеда́ть *v. impfv.* to be underfed; be undernourished.

недожа́ривать *v. impfv.* [*pfv.* **недожа́рить**] to undercook.

недозво́ленный *adj.* unauthorized; unlawful; illicit.

недозре́лый *adj.* **1,** not fully ripe. **2,** *fig.* immature.

недои́мка [*gen. pl.* **-мок**] *n.* arrears; back rent; back taxes. —**недои́мщик,** *n.* person in arrears.

недока́занный *adj.* unproved; unproven.

недоказу́емый *adj.* that cannot be proved.

недолга́ *adv., in* **(вот) и вся недолга́,** *colloq.* and that's (all there is to) it!

недо́лгий *adj.* short; brief.

недо́лго *adv.* not long. —**недо́лго ду́мая,** without pausing to think. —**недо́лго и** (+ *inf.*), *colloq.* easily: недо́лго и утону́ть, one could easily drown.

недолгове́чный *adj.* short-lived.

недолю́бливать *v. impfv.* to have little liking for; not particularly like.

недомога́ние *n.* indisposition.

недомога́ть *v. impfv.* to be unwell; be ailing; be indisposed.

недомо́лвка [*gen. pl.* **-вок**] *n.* allusion; innuendo.

недомы́слие *n.* thoughtlessness; foolishness.

недонесе́ние *n.* failure to report a crime.

недоно́сок [*gen.* **-ска**] *n.* prematurely born baby.

недоно́шенный *adj.* born prematurely.

недооце́нивать *v. impfv.* [*pfv.* **недооцени́ть**] to underestimate.

недооцени́ть [*infl.* **-ценю́, -це́нишь**] *v., pfv. of* **недооце́нивать.**

недооце́нка *n.* underestimation.

недопечённый *adj.* half-baked.

недоплати́ть [*infl.* **-плачу́, -пла́тишь**] *v., pfv. of* **недопла́чивать.**

недопла́чивать *v. impfv.* [*pfv.* **недоплати́ть**] to underpay: недоплати́ть пять рубле́й, to underpay by five rubles.

недополуча́ть *v. impfv.* [*pfv.* **недополучи́ть**] to receive less than one should: недополучи́ть де́сять рубле́й, to receive ten rubles less than one was supposed to.

недополучи́ть [*infl.* **-лучу́, -лу́чишь**] *v., pfv. of* **недополуча́ть.**

недопроизво́дство *n.* underproduction.

недопусти́мый *adj.* impermissible; intolerable.

недораба́тывать *v. impfv.* [*pfv.* **недорабо́тать**] **1,** *v.i.* to work less than the required time. **2,** *v.t.* to fail to complete.

недора́звитый *adj.* underdeveloped.

недоразуме́ние *n.* misunderstanding.

недо́рого *adv.* inexpensively; for a reasonable price.

недорого́й *adj.* inexpensive.

недоро́д *n.* poor harvest; crop failure.

не́доросль *n.m.* ignorant young man.

недоро́сток [*gen.* **-стка**] *n., colloq.* shrimp; runt.

недослы́шать *v. impfv. & pfv.* [*infl.* **-шу, -шишь**] **1,** [*v. pfv.*] to fail to hear entirely. **2,** [*v. impfv.*] *colloq.* to be somewhat hard of hearing.

недосмо́тр *n.* oversight.

недосмотре́ть *v. pfv.* [*infl.* **-смотрю́ -смо́тришь**] *colloq.* **1,** to overlook. **2,** (*with* за + *instr.*) to fail to look after.

недоспа́ть [*infl. like* **спать**] *v., pfv. of* **недосыпа́ть.**

недоспе́лый *adj.* not fully ripe.

недостава́ть *v. impfv.* [*pfv.* **недоста́ть;** *pres.* **-стаёт**] *impers.* (*with gen.*) **1,** to be insufficient; be lacking: чего́ вам недостаёт?, what are you lacking? Нам недостаёт де́нег, we are short of money. **2,** [*impfv. only*] to be missing: недостаёт двух страни́ц, two pages are missing. **3,** [*impfv. only*] to be missed: нам вас недостава́ло, we missed you.

недоста́ток [*gen.* **-тка**] *n.* **1,** shortage; scarcity; lack. **2,** defect; shortcoming; deficiency.

недоста́точно *adv.* not...enough; insufficiently. —*adj., used predicatively* not enough; insufficient: пять рубле́й недоста́точно, five rubles is not enough.

недоста́точный *adj.* insufficient; inadequate. —**недоста́точность,** *n.f.* insufficiency; inadequacy.

недоста́ть [*infl.* **-ста́нет**] *v., pfv. of* **недостава́ть.**

недоста́ча *n., colloq.* shortage.

недостаю́щий *adj.* missing: недостаю́щее звено́, missing link.

недостижи́мый *adj.* unattainable.

недостове́рный *adj.* of doubtful authenticity; unreliable.

недосто́йно *adv.* badly; improperly. —*adj., used predicatively* (*with gen.*) unworthy of; beneath: э́то его́ недосто́йно, it is unworthy of him; it is beneath him.

недосто́йный *adj.* [*short form* **-сто́ин, -сто́йна**] **1,** unworthy: он её недосто́ин, he is unworthy of her. **2,** undignified. **3,** dishonorable.

недостро́енный *adj.* (*of something being built*) unfinished.

недосту́пный *adj.* **1,** inaccessible. **2,** unattainable. **3,** distant; unapproachable. **4,** beyond one's comprehension. **5,** beyond one's means; more than one can afford. —**недосту́пность,** *n.f.* inaccessibility.

недосу́г *n., colloq., used impersonally with dat.* lack of (leisure) time: мне недосу́г, I am too busy.

недосчи́тываться *v.r. impfv.* [*pfv.* **недосчита́ться**] (*with subject in gen.*) to be short; be missing.

недосыпа́ние *n.* lack of sleep.

недосыпа́ть *v. impfv.* [*pfv.* **недоспа́ть**] not to get enough sleep.

недосяга́емый *adj.* **1,** unattainable. **2,** inaccessible.

недотёпа *n.m. & f., colloq.* maladroit person; clod.

недотро́га *n.* touch-me-not (*flower*). —*n.m. & f., colloq.* touchy person.

недоу́здок [*gen.* **-дка**] *n.* halter (*for a horse*).
недоумева́ть *v. impfv.* to be puzzled; be perplexed; be bewildered.
недоумева́ющий *adj.* puzzled; perplexed; bewildered.
недоуме́ние *n.* bewilderment; perplexity.
недоуме́нный *adj.* **1,** puzzling; perplexing; baffling. **2,** puzzled; perplexed.
недоу́чка [*gen. pl.* **-чек**] *n.m. & f., colloq.* person with little education.
недочёт *n.* **1,** shortage; deficit. **2,** defect; shortcoming.
не́дра [*gen.* **недр**] *n.pl.* **1,** bowels of the earth. **2,** *fig.* innermost depths.
недре́млющий *adj.* vigilant; watchful.
не́друг *n.* enemy; foe.
недружелю́бие *n.* unfriendliness. —**недружелю́бный,** *adj.* unfriendly.
неду́г *n.* ailment.
недурно́й *adj.* **1,** not bad. **2,** (*with* **собо́й**) not bad-looking. —**неду́рно,** *adv.* rather well.
недю́жинный *adj.* unusual; uncommon; outstanding; exceptional.
неё *pron., var. of* **её,** *used after prepositions.*
нестéственный *adj.* unnatural.
нежда́нный *adj., colloq.* unexpected.
нежела́ние *n.* unwillingness; reluctance; disinclination.
нежела́тельный *adj.* undesirable.
не́жели *conj., archaic* than.
нежена́тый *adj.* (*of a man*) unmarried; single.
не́женка [*gen. pl.* **-нок**] *n.m. & f., colloq.* sissy.
неживо́й *adj.* **1,** lifeless; dead. **2,** inorganic. **3,** listless; apathetic. **4,** (*of light*) faint.
нежи́зненный *adj.* **1,** unrealistic; impractical. **2,** unreal; weird.
нежило́й *adj.* **1,** unoccupied; vacant; unlived-in. **2,** unfit for occupation.
не́жить *v. impfv.* to pamper; coddle. —**не́житься,** *refl.* **1,** to lounge around; loll. **2,** to luxuriate; bask (in the sun).
не́жничать *v. impfv., colloq.* to be overly gentle.
не́жно *adv.* **1,** tenderly. **2,** gently.
не́жность *n.f.* **1,** tenderness; gentleness. **2,** *pl., colloq.* tender words.
не́жный *adj.* tender; gentle; delicate.
незабве́нный *adj.* unforgettable.
незаброни́рованный *adj.* unreserved: заброни́рованное ме́сто, unreserved seat.
незабу́дка [*gen. pl.* **-док**] *n.* forget-me-not.
незабыва́емый *adj.* unforgettable.
незавершённый *adj.* uncompleted; unfinished.
незави́дный *adj.* unenviable.
незави́симо *adv.* independently. —**незави́симо от,** regardless of; irrespective of.
незави́симость *n.f.* independence.
незави́симый *adj.* independent.
незави́сящий *adj., in* **по незави́сящим от** (+ *gen.*) **обстоя́тельствам,** due to circumstances beyond (one's) control.
незада́ча *n., colloq.* bad luck.
незада́чливый *adj., colloq.* unlucky; luckless.
незадо́лго *adv.* (*with* **до**) shortly (before); not long (before).
незаинтересо́ванный *adj.* disinterested.
незако́нно *adv.* unlawfully; illegally.
незаконнорождённый *adj.* (*of a child*) illegitimate.
незако́нный *adj.* unlawful; illegal; illegitimate. —**незако́нность,** *n.f.* illegality.
незако́нченный *adj.* unfinished.
незамедли́тельный *adj.* immediate.
незамени́мый *adj.* **1,** irreplaceable; indispensable. **2,** irreparable.
незаме́тно *adv.* **1,** without being seen. **2,** *fig.* imperceptibly; unnoticed: пройти́ незаме́тно, to pass unnoticed. —*adj., used predicatively* **1,** not noticeable: незаме́тно, что́бы..., it is not noticeable that...; you could not tell that... **2,** (*with* **для**) unnoticed (by); without (someone) noticing it. Незаме́тно для себя́, without realizing it.
незаме́тный *adj.* **1,** imperceptible. **2,** inconspicuous. **3,** insignificant.
незаме́ченный *adj.* unnoticed.
незаму́жняя *adj.* (*of a woman*) unmarried.
незамыслова́тый *adj., colloq.* simple; unimaginative.
неза́нятый *adj.* unoccupied.
незапа́мятный *adj.* immemorial. —**с незапа́мятных времён,** since time immemorial.
неза́пертый *adj.* unlocked.
незапя́тнанный *adj.* unblemished; unsullied.
незара́зный *adj.* noncontagious.
незаря́женный *also,* **незаряжённый** *adj.* **1,** (*of a rifle, pistol, etc.*) unloaded. **2,** (*of a battery*) not charged.
незаселённый *adj.* unsettled.
незаслу́женный *adj.* undeserved.
незате́йливый *adj.* simple; unpretentious.
незауря́дный *adj.* outstanding.
не́зачем *adv.* (*with inf.*) *colloq.* there is no need (to); there is no point (in).
незащищённый *adj.* unprotected; undefended.
незва́ный *adj.* uninvited.
незде́шний *adj.* **1,** *colloq.* not of this place: я незде́шний, I am not from around here. **2,** *obs.* unearthly; supernatural.
нездоро́виться *v.r. impfv., impers.* (*with dat.*) to feel ill: мне нездоро́вится, I feel ill; I am not feeling well.
нездоро́вый *adj.* **1,** unwell. **2,** unhealthy; unwholesome.
нездоро́вье *n.* **1,** ill health. **2,** ailment.
неземно́й *adj.* unearthly.
незло́й *adj.* kind; good-natured.
незлопа́мятный *adj.* forgiving; not one to bear a grudge.
незнако́мец [*gen.* **-мца**] *n.m.* [*fem.* **-мка**] stranger.
незнако́мство *n.* lack of familiarity; unfamiliarity.
незнако́мый *adj.* **1,** unfamiliar; unknown. **2,** (*with* **с** + *instr.*) unacquainted (with). —*n., colloq.* stranger.
незна́ние *n.* ignorance.
незна́чащий *adj.* insignificant.
незначи́тельный *adj.* **1,** insignificant; very slight; negligible. **2,** insignificant; minor; trivial. —**незначи́тельность,** *n.f.* insignificance.
незре́лый *adj.* **1,** unripe; green. **2,** *fig.* immature. —**незре́лость,** *n.f.* immaturity.
незри́мый *adj.* invisible.
незря́чий *adj.* unseeing; sightless; blind.
незы́блемый *adj.* **1,** firm; solid. **2,** *fig.* steadfast; unwavering; unshakable.
неизбе́жный *adj.* inevitable; unavoidable. —**неизбе́жно,** *adv.* inevitably. —**неизбе́жность,** *n.f.* inevitability.

неизве́данный *adj.* **1,** unexplored. **2,** never before experienced.
неизве́стно *adj., used predicatively* unknown; not known: кто он тако́й – неизве́стно, who he is is not known.
неизве́стное *n., decl. as an adj., math.* unknown.
неизве́стность *n.f.* **1,** lack of information; uncertainty. Быть в неизве́стности (о), to be unaware (of); have no knowledge (of). **2,** obscurity: жить в неизве́стности, to live in obscurity.
неизве́стный *adj.* unknown. —*n.* unknown person; stranger.
неизглади́мый *adj.* indelible.
нeíзданный *adj.* unpublished.
неизлечи́мый *adj.* incurable.
неизме́нный *adj.* **1,** invariable; unchanging. **2,** unfailing; devoted. —**неизме́нно,** *adv.* invariably.
неизменя́емый *adj.* unalterable; unchanging; fixed.
неизмери́мый *adj.* immeasurable; unfathomable. —**неизмери́мо,** *adv.* immeasurably; infinitely.
неизъясни́мый *adj.* **1,** unexplainable. **2,** inexpressible.
неиме́ние *n., in* **за неиме́нием** (+ *gen.*), owing to the lack of; for want of. За неиме́нием лу́чшего, for want of anything better.
неимове́рный *adj.* incredible; fantastic.
неиму́щий *adj.* poor; indigent; needy.
неинтеллиге́нтный *adj.* not cultured; unsophisticated.
неинтере́сный *adj.* uninteresting.
неискорени́мый *adj.* ineradicable; ingrained.
нeи́скренний *adj.* insincere. —**нeи́скренность,** *n.f.* insincerity.
неискушённый *adj.* unsophisticated; inexperienced.
неисповеди́мый *adj.* inscrutable.
неисполне́ние *n.* nonperformance; failure to carry out; failure to obey.
неисполни́мый *adj.* **1,** impossible to carry out; impracticable. **2,** impossible to perform. **3,** unrealizable. Неисполни́мая мечта́, impossible dream. —**неисполни́мость,** *n.f.* impracticability.
неиспо́льзованный *adj.* unused.
неиспо́рченный *adj.* **1,** unspoiled. **2,** innocent; pure.
неисправи́мый *adj.* **1,** incorrigible. **2,** irreparable.
неиспра́вность *n.f.* **1,** disrepair. **2,** failure; malfunction(ing). **3,** carelessness.
неиспра́вный *adj.* **1,** defective; faulty; out of order. **2,** careless.
неиспы́танный *adj.* **1,** untried; untested. **2,** never before experienced.
неиссле́дованный *adj.* unexplored.
неиссяка́емый *adj.* inexhaustible.
неи́стовство *n.* **1,** fury; rage. **2,** atrocity.
неи́стовствовать *v. impfv.* [*pres.* **-ствую, -ствуешь**] **1,** to rage; rave. **2,** to run wild; go on a rampage. **3,** (*of a storm, the sea, etc.*) to rage.
неи́стовый *adj.* furious; violent.
неистощи́мый *adj.* inexhaustible.
неисцели́мый *adj.* incurable.
неисчерпа́емый *adj.* inexhaustible.
неисчисли́мый *adj.* countless; incalculable; innumerable.
ней *pers. pron., variant of* **ей,** *used after prepositions.*
нейло́н *n.* nylon. —**нейло́новый,** *adj.* nylon.
нейро́н *n.* neuron.
нейрохирурги́я *n.* neurosurgery. —**нейрохиру́рг,** *n.* neurosurgeon.
нейтрализа́ция *n.* neutralization.
нейтрализова́ть *v. impfv. & pfv.* [*pres.* **-зу́ю, -зу́ешь**] to neutralize.
нейтралите́т *n.* neutrality.
нейтра́льный *adj.* neutral.
нейтро́н *n.* neutron. —**нейтро́нный,** *adj.* neutron (*attrib.*): нейтро́нная бо́мба, neutron bomb.
неказ́истый *adj., colloq.* ugly; homely; unattractive.
неквалифици́рованный *adj.* unskilled.
не́кий *indef. pron.* a certain; someone named: вас спра́шивал не́кий Ива́нов, someone named Ivanov was asking for you.
не́когда *adv.* **1,** no time: мне не́когда, I have no time. **2,** once; formerly; at one time.
не́кого *indef. pron., gen. & acc.* [*dat.* **не́кому;** *instr.* **не́кем;** *prepl.* **не́** (+ *prep.*) **ком**] *used with inf.* there is no one; there is nobody: не́кого посла́ть, there is no one to send; мне не́кого спроси́ть, there is no one I can ask. *See also* **не́кому.**
неколеби́мый *adj.* = **непоколеби́мый.**
некомпете́нтный *adj.* incompetent; unqualified.
не́кому *indef. pron.* **1,** *dat. of* **не́кого. 2,** there is no one: не́кому его́ замени́ть, there is no one to replace him.
неконституцио́нный *adj.* unconstitutional.
некороно́ванный *adj.* uncrowned.
некорре́ктный *adj.* improper; indecorous.
не́которые *indef. pron.* some; some people; certain people. —**не́которые из,** some of.
не́который *adj.* **1,** *pl.* some; certain: не́которые лю́ди, some/certain people. **2,** some; a certain amount of: не́которое сомне́ние, some doubt. —**не́которое вре́мя,** for some time; (for) a while. —**с не́которых пор,** for some time (now).
некраси́вый *adj.* **1,** ugly; unattractive. **2,** *colloq.* improper; not nice: э́то некраси́во, that's not nice.
некра́шеный *adj.* unpainted.
некре́пкий *adj.* **1,** not strong; not firm; flimsy. **2,** not robust. **3,** weak; diluted.
некрити́ческий *adj.* uncritical.
некро́з *n.* necrosis.
некроло́г *n.* obituary.
некста́ти *adv.* **1,** at the wrong time; at an inopportune moment. **2,** out of place; inappropriate.
некта́р *n.* nectar.
не́кто *indef. pron.* **1,** someone; somebody. **2,** a certain; someone named: вас спра́шивал не́кто Ива́нов, someone named Ivanov was asking for you.
не́куда *adv., used with inf.* nowhere; no place: мне е́хать не́куда, I have nowhere to go.
некульту́рный *adj.* **1,** uncivilized; uncultured. **2,** (*of plants*) uncultivated. —**некульту́рность,** *n.f.* lack of culture; lack of refinement.
некуря́щий *adj.* nonsmoking. —*n.* nonsmoker.
нела́дно *adv.* badly. —*adj., used predicatively* wrong: что́-то с ним нела́дно, something is wrong with him.
нела́дный *adj., colloq.* **1,** wrong: что́-то нела́дное происхо́дит, something wrong is going on. **2,** ungainly. —**нела́дное,** *n.* something wrong: чу́вствовать нела́дное, to sense that something is wrong.
нелады́ [*gen.* **-до́в**] *n. pl., colloq.* disagreements; friction; failure to get along: у них нелады́, they are not getting along.

нелакиро́ванный *adj.* not lacquered; unvarnished.
нела́сковый *adj.* cold; unfriendly.
нелега́льный *adj.* illegal. —**нелега́льно,** *adv.* illegally. —**нелега́льность,** *n.f.* illegality.
нелёгкий *adj.* **1,** not easy; hard; difficult. **2,** heavy; not light.
нелегко́ *adv.* not easily: языки́ даю́тся ему́ нелегко́, languages do not come easy to him.
неле́пость *n.f.* **1,** absurdity (*of something*). **2,** nonsense.
неле́пый *adj.* ridiculous; absurd.
неле́стный *adj.* unflattering; uncomplimentary.
нелётный *adj.* non-flying; unsuitable for flying.
нели́шний *adj.* useful; necessary. —**нели́шне,** *adj., used predicatively* useful; worthwhile: нели́шне отме́тить, что..., it is worth noting that...
нело́вкий *adj.* **1,** awkward; clumsy. **2,** awkward; uncomfortable; embarrassing: нело́вкое молча́ние, awkward silence.
нело́вко *adv.* awkwardly. —*adj., used predicatively* awkward; ill at ease: чу́вствовать себя́ нело́вко, to feel awkward/ill at ease/.
нело́вкость *n.f.* **1,** awkwardness. **2,** (an) indiscretion. **3,** (sense of) awkwardness; embarrassment.
нелоги́чный *adj.* illogical.
нелоя́льный *adj.* disloyal. —**нелоя́льность,** *n.f.* disloyalty.
нельзя́ *adv.* **1,** it is impossible; one cannot: нельзя́ сказа́ть, it is impossible to say; one cannot say. **2,** it is forbidden; one may not: нельзя́ кури́ть, smoking is forbidden. —**как нельзя́ лу́чше,** perfectly. —**нельзя́ ли...,** can't you...?; couldn't you...?: нельзя́ ли поти́ше?, can't/couldn't you be a little more quiet?
нелюбе́зный *adj.* ungracious.
нелюби́мый *adj.* unloved.
нелюбо́вь [*infl. like* **любо́вь**] *n.f.* dislike.
нелюди́м *n.m.* [*fem.* **-ка**] unsociable person.
нелюди́мый *adj.* unsociable. —**нелюди́мость,** *n.f.* unsociability.
нём *pron., prepl. of* **он** *and* **оно́.**
нема́ло *adv.* **1,** (*with gen.*) quite a bit of; considerable. **2,** (*with verbs*) quite; quite a bit; quite a lot.
немалова́жный *adj.* of no small importance; not unimportant.
нема́лый *adj.* rather large; considerable.
немеблиро́ванный *adj.* unfurnished.
неме́дленный *adj.* immediate. —**неме́дленно,** *adv.* immediately; at once.
неме́для *adv.* immediately; at once.
Немези́да *n.* **1,** Nemesis (*Greek goddess*). **2,** (one's) nemesis.
неме́ркнущий *adj.* **1,** never fading. **2,** *fig.* undying.
неме́ть *v. impfv.* [*pfv.* **онеме́ть**] **1,** to be speechless; be dumfounded. **2,** to become numb.
не́мец [*gen.* **-мца**] *n.m.* [*fem.* **-мка**] German. —**не́мецкий,** *adj.* German.
неми́лостивый *adj., obs.* **1,** ungracious. **2,** unmerciful.
неми́лость *n.f.* disfavor; disgrace.
немину́емый *adj.* inevitable; unavoidable. —**немину́емо,** *adv.* inevitably; unavoidably.
не́мка [*gen. pl.* **-мок**] *n.* German woman.
немно́гие *adj.* a few: в немно́гих слова́х, in a few words. —*indef. pron.* **1,** few people; not many people. **2,** the few: немно́гие, кто..., the few who... —**немно́гим,** *adv., used with comp. adjectives* a little.
немно́го *adv.* **1,** a little; a bit of. **2,** little; not much. **3,** a little; rather; somewhat.
немно́гое *n., in* **то немно́гое, что...,** the little that...; what little...
немногосло́вный *adj.* of few words; laconic.
немногочи́сленный *adj.* **1,** small (*in number of people, members, etc.*). **2,** *pl.* the few: немногочи́сленные доброво́льцы, the few volunteers.
немно́жко *adv., colloq.* = **немно́го.**
немну́щийся *adj.* (*of fabric*) crease-resistant.
немо́й *adj.* **1,** dumb; mute. **2,** (*of a film*) silent. —*n.* mute.
немолодо́й *adj.* not young.
немота́ *n.* inability to speak.
не́мочь *n.f., colloq.* sickness; illness.
немощёный *adj.* unpaved.
не́мощный *adj.* feeble.
не́мощь *n.f.* debility.
нему́ *pron., variant of* **ему́,** *used after prepositions.*
немудрено́ *adv.* no wonder: немудрено́, что он не отве́тил, no wonder he didn't answer.
немудрёный *adj., colloq.* simple; plain.
нему́дрый *adj.* **1,** not very bright. **2,** *colloq.* = **немудрёный.**
немы́слимый *adj.* unthinkable.
ненаблюда́тельный *adj.* unobservant.
ненави́деть *v. impfv.* [*pres.* **-ви́жу, -ви́дишь**] to hate; detest.
ненави́стник *n.* person who hates. —**ненави́стничество,** *n.* hostile attitude.
ненави́стный *adj.* hated; hateful; abhorrent.
не́нависть *n.f.* hatred; hate.
ненагля́дный *adj.* beloved.
ненадёжный *adj.* unreliable. —**ненадёжность,** *n.f.* unreliability.
нена́добность *n.f.* lack of need (for). —**за нена́добностью,** for lack of use. —**за нена́добностью** (+ *gen.*), there being no need (for).
ненадо́лго *adv.* for a short time; for a short while (*subsequent to the action expressed by the verb*): я уезжа́ю ненадо́лго, I am going away for a short time/while.
нена́званный *adj.* unnamed.
ненаказу́емый *adj.* not punishable by law.
ненаме́ренный *adj.* unintentional. —**ненаме́ренно,** *adv.* unintentionally.
ненападе́ние *n.* nonaggression.
ненаро́ком *adv., colloq.* by chance: он ненаро́ком зашёл, he just happened to drop in.
нена́стный *adj.* inclement.
нена́стье *n.* inclement weather.
ненасы́тный *adj.* insatiable.
ненасы́щенный *adj.* unsaturated.
ненатура́льный *adj.* **1,** artificial. **2,** unnatural.
ненау́чный *adj.* unscientific.
не́нец [*gen.* **-нца**] *n.m.* [*fem.* **-нка**] Nenets (*one of a people inhabiting northernmost Russia*). —**не́нецкий,** *adj.* Nenets.
ненорма́льный *adj.* abnormal. —**ненорма́льно,** *adv.* abnormally. —**ненорма́льность,** *n.f.* abnormality.
нену́жность *n.f.* **1,** uselessness. **2,** *usu. pl.* useless things.
нену́жный *adj.* unneeded; needless; unnecessary.
необду́манный *adj.* not thought out; rash.

необескура́женный *adj.* not discouraged; undismayed.
необеспе́ченный *adj.* without means; unprovided for.
необеспоко́енный *adj.* unworried; undisturbed.
необита́емый *adj.* uninhabited.
необозри́мый *adj.* boundless; vast. —**необозри́мость,** *n.f.* vastness.
необосно́ванный *adj.* **1,** groundless; unfounded. **2,** unsound.
необрабо́танный *adj.* **1,** uncultivated; untilled. **2,** crude; rough; unfinished.
необразо́ванный *adj.* uneducated. —**необразо́ванность,** *n.f.* lack of education.
необрати́мый *adj.* irreversible.
необу́зданный *adj.* unrestrained; unbridled.
необу́ченный *adj.* untrained.
необходи́мо *adj., used predicatively* necessary; essential: необходи́мо де́йствовать без промедле́ния, it is essential to act without delay. Необходи́мо приня́ть сро́чные ме́ры, urgent measures must be taken.
необходи́мое *n., decl. as an adj.* necessities; essentials: всё необходи́мое, all the necessities; everything one needs.
необходи́мость *n.f.* necessity; need. —**по необходи́мости,** out of necessity. —**при необходи́мости,** when necessary. —**предме́ты пе́рвой необходи́мости,** the barest necessities.
необходи́мый *adj.* necessary; essential.
необщи́тельный *adj.* unsociable; antisocial. —**необщи́тельность,** *n.f.* unsociability.
необъекти́вный *adj.* not objective; biased. —**необъекти́вность,** *n.f.* lack of objectivity.
необъя́вленный *adj.* (*of a war*) undeclared.
необъясни́мый *adj.* inexplicable; unexplainable; unaccountable.
необъя́тный *adj.* boundless; vast.
необыкнове́нный *adj.* unusual; uncommon; extraordinary. —**необыкнове́нно,** *adv.* unusually; uncommonly.
необыча́йность *n.f.* **1,** (*with gen.*) extraordinary nature (of). **2,** extraordinary event.
необыча́йный *adj.* extraordinary; exceptional.
необы́чный *adj.* unusual.
необяза́тельный *adj.* **1,** optional; not obligatory. **2,** (*of a person*) not obliging.
неограни́ченный *adj.* unlimited.
неодина́ковый *adj.* different; dissimilar.
неоднокра́тно *adv.* repeatedly; more than once. —**неоднокра́тный,** *adj.* repeated.
неоднoро́дный *adj.* **1,** heterogeneous. **2,** dissimilar. —**неоднoро́дность,** *n.f.* heterogeneity.
неодобре́ние *n.* disapproval.
неодобри́тельный *adj.* disapproving. —**неодобри́тельно,** *adv.* in disapproval.
неодоли́мый *adj.* **1,** (*of a force, urge, etc.*) irresistible. **2,** invincible.
неодушевлённый *adj.* inanimate.
неожи́данно *adv.* unexpectedly.
неожи́данность *n.f.* **1,** suddenness. **2,** unexpected development; surprise: кака́я прия́тная неожи́данность!, what a pleasant surprise!
неожи́данный *adj.* unexpected.
неоклассици́зм *n.* neoclassicism. —**неоклассі́ческий,** *adj.* neoclassical.
неоконча́тельный *adj.* not final.
неоко́нченный *adj.* unfinished.
неолити́ческий *adj.* neolithic.
неологи́зм *n.* neologism.
нео́н *n.* neon. —**нео́новый,** *adj.* neon.
неопа́сный *adj.* not dangerous.
неопера́бельный *adj., med.* inoperable.
неопери́вшийся *adj.* **1,** unfledged. **2,** *fig., colloq.* callow.
неопису́емый *adj.* indescribable.
неопла́тный *adj.* **1,** that cannot be repaid. **2,** unable to pay one's debts.
неопла́ченный *adj.* unpaid.
неопо́знанный *adj.* unidentified.
неопра́вданный *adj.* **1,** unjustified; unwarranted. **2,** unfounded.
неопределённо *adv.* vaguely.
неопределённость *n.f.* **1,** vagueness. **2,** uncertainty.
неопределённый *adj.* **1,** indefinite; uncertain; indeterminate. **2,** vague; unclear. —**неопределённая фо́рма глаго́ла,** infinitive.
неопредели́мый *adj.* indefinable.
неопровержи́мый *adj.* irrefutable; incontrovertible; conclusive. —**неопровержи́мо,** *adv.* conclusively.
неопря́тный *adj.* untidy. —**неопря́тность,** *n.f.* untidiness.
неопублико́ванный *adj.* unpublished.
нео́пытный *adj.* inexperienced. —**нео́пытность,** *n.f.* inexperience; lack of experience.
неорганизо́ванный *adj.* unorganized; disorganized. —**неорганизо́ванность,** *n.f.* lack of organization; disorganization.
неоргани́ческий *adj.* inorganic.
неосведомлённый *adj.* uninformed. —**неосведомлённость,** *n.f.* lack of information; ignorance.
неосвещённый *adj.* unlighted; unlit.
неосла́бный *adj.* unflagging; unremitting. С неосла́бным внима́нием, with rapt attention. *Also,* **неослабева́ющий.**
неосмотри́тельный *adj.* imprudent; indiscreet. —**неосмотри́тельность,** *n.f.* imprudence; indiscretion.
неоснова́тельный *adj.* **1,** groundless; unfounded. **2,** *colloq.* frivolous; superficial; shallow.
неоспори́мый *adj.* indisputable; incontestable; undeniable.
неосторо́жно *adv.* carelessly.
неосторо́жность *n.f.* carelessness: по неосторо́жности, through carelessness.
неосторо́жный *adj.* careless; incautious.
неосуществи́мый *adj.* impracticable; infeasible. —**неосуществи́мость,** *n.f.* impracticability.
неосяза́емый *adj.* intangible.
неотврати́мый *adj.* inevitable. —**неотврати́мость,** *n.f.* inevitability.
неотвя́зный *adj., colloq.* **1,** (*of a thought, question, etc.*) nagging. **2,** (*of a person*) bothersome; annoying. *Also,* **неотвя́зчивый.**
неотдели́мый *adj.* inseparable. —**неотдели́мость,** *n.f.* inseparability.
неотёсанный *adj., colloq.* crude; uncouth.
неотзы́вчивый *adj.* unresponsive.

нéоткуда *adv., used with inf.* there is no place (from): мне нéоткуда э́то достáть, there is no place I can get it from.
неотлóжка *n., colloq.* ambulance (service): вы́звать неотлóжку, to call an ambulance.
неотлóжный *adj.* urgent. —**неотлóжность,** *n.f.* urgency.
неотлу́чный *adj.* always present; ever-present. —**неотлу́чно,** *adv.* constantly.
неотполирóванный *adj.* unpolished.
неотрази́мый *adj.* irresistible. —**неотрази́мость,** *n.f.* irresistibility.
неотсту́пный *adj.* persistent; relentless. —**неотсту́пность,** *n.f.* persistence; relentlessness.
неотчётливый *adj.* indistinct. —**неотчётливость,** *n.f.* indistinctness.
неотшлифóванный *adj.* unpolished.
неотъéмлемый *adj.* inalienable. —**неотъéмлемая часть,** integral part.
неофи́т *n.* neophyte.
неофициáльный *adj.* unofficial.
неохóта *n.* reluctance; unwillingness. —**мне неохóта** (+ *inf.*), I don't feel like...; I don't care to...
неохóтно *adv.* reluctantly. —**неохóтный,** *adj.* reluctant.
неоцени́мый *adj.* inestimable; invaluable.
неочи́щенный *adj.* unrefined; crude.
неощути́мый *adj.* imperceptible. *Also,* **неощути́тельный.**
непáрный *adj.* odd (*one of an incomplete pair*).
непарти́йный *adj.* **1,** non-party; not belonging to the party. **2,** non-partylike; not befitting a member of the party.
непереводи́мый *adj.* untranslatable.
непередавáемый *adj.* indescribable; inexpressible.
непереноси́мый *adj.* unbearable.
неперехóдный *adj.* (*of a verb*) intransitive.
неперспекти́вный *adj.* having poor prospects; unpromising.
непечáтный *adj., colloq.* unprintable (*i.e. obscene*).
непи́саный *adj.* unwritten.
неплатёж [*gen.* **-тежá**] *n.* nonpayment.
неплатёжеспосóбный *adj.* insolvent. —**неплатёжеспосóбность,** *n.f.* insolvency.
неплатéльщик *n.* person who has not paid; defaulter.
неплодорóдный *adj.* barren; infertile. —**неплодорóдность,** *n.f.* barrenness; infertility.
неплóтно *adv.* not tightly: неплóтно закры́тый, not closed tightly. —**неплóтный,** *adj.* not dense; thin.
неплóхо *adv.* quite well; rather well. —*adj., used predicatively* not bad: э́то неплóхо, that's not bad.
неплохóй *adj.* not (a) bad.
непобеди́мый *adj.* invincible; unconquerable. —**непобеди́мость,** *n.f.* invincibility.
непови́нный *adj.* innocent.
неповиновéние *n.* disobedience; insubordination.
неповорóтливый *adj.* clumsy. —**неповорóтливость,** *n.f.* clumsiness.
неповтори́мый *adj.* inimitable; unique.
непогóда *n.* bad weather.
непогóжий *adj., colloq.* overcast; dreary.
непогреши́мый *adj.* infallible. —**непогреши́мость,** *n.f.* infallibility.
неподалёку *adv.* **1,** not far away; not far off. **2,** (*with* **от**) not far (from).
неподáтливый *adj.* unyielding; intractable.
неподви́жный *adj.* **1,** motionless; stationary; immobile. **2,** (*of a look, stare, etc.*) fixed. —**неподви́жно,** *adv.* motionless. —**неподви́жность,** *n.f.* immobility.
неподготóвленный *adj.* **1,** unprepared. **2,** untrained.
неподдéльный *adj.* **1,** genuine; authentic. **2,** genuine; unfeigned; sincere.
неподку́пный *adj.* incorruptible. —**неподку́пность,** *n.f.* incorruptibility.
неподобáющий *adj.* improper; unseemly.
неподражáемый *adj.* inimitable.
неподтверждённый *adj.* unconfirmed.
неподходя́щий *adj.* unsuitable; inappropriate.
неподчинéние *n.* insubordination. —**неподчинéние судéбному постановлéнию,** contempt of court.
непозволи́тельный *adj.* impermissible.
непоколеби́мый *adj.* unshakable; unwavering; steadfast. —**непоколеби́мость,** *n.f.* steadfastness.
непокóрный *adj.* rebellious; recalcitrant; unruly. —**непокóрность,** *n.f.* rebelliousness; recalcitrance.
непокры́тый *adj.* uncovered.
неполáдки *n. pl.* [*sing.* **-дка**] *colloq.* **1,** defects; bugs. **2,** arguments; squabbles.
неполнопрáвный *adj.* not enjoying full rights.
неполнотá *n.* incompleteness.
неполноцéнный *adj.* inferior. —**неполноцéнность,** *n.f.* inferiority.
непóлный *adj.* **1,** (*of a container*) partially filled; not completely full. **2,** incomplete. —**рабóтать непóлный день,** to work part-time.
непомéрный *adj.* excessive; inordinate; exorbitant.
непонимáние *n.* lack of understanding; failure to understand; incomprehension.
непоня́тливый *adj.* slow to grasp things; dull; dense.
непоня́тно *adv.* incomprehensibly. —*adj., used predicatively* incomprehensible; impossible to understand: мне непоня́тно, как э́то случи́лось, I cannot understand how it happened.
непоня́тный *adj.* incomprehensible; unintelligible. —**непоня́тность,** *n.f.* incomprehensibility; unintelligibility.
непопадáние *n.* miss (*in shooting*).
непоправи́мый *adj.* irreparable; irretrievable.
непопуля́рный *adj.* unpopular. —**непопуля́рность,** *n.f.* unpopularity.
непорóчность *n.f.* innocence; purity; chastity.
непорóчный *adj.* innocent; pure; chaste. —**непорóчное зачáтие,** the Immaculate Conception.
непóртящийся *adj.* nonperishable.
непоря́док [*gen.* **-дка**] *n.* disorder.
непоря́дочный *adj.* dishonorable.
непосвящённый *adj.* uninitiated.
непосéда *n.m. & f., colloq.* fidgety person; fidget.
непосéдливый *adj.* restless; fidgety. —**непосéдливость,** *n.f.* restlessness.
непосещéние *n.* (*with gen.*) failure to attend.
непоси́льный *adj.* exhausting; backbreaking.
непослéдовательный *adj.* inconsistent. —**непослéдовательность,** *n.f.* inconsistency.
непослушáние *n.* disobedience.
непослу́шный *adj.* disobedient.
непосрéдственный *adj.* **1,** immediate; direct. **2,** natural; spontaneous. —**непосрéдственно,** *adv.* im-

mediately; directly. —**непосре́дственность,** *n.f.* spontaneity.

непостижи́мый *adj.* incomprehensible. —**непостижи́мость,** *n.f.* incomprehensibility.

непостоя́нный *adj.* inconstant; changeable; fickle. —**непостоя́нство,** *n.* inconstancy.

непоти́зм *n.* nepotism.

непотопля́емый *adj.* unsinkable.

непотре́бный *adj., obs.* indecent; obscene.

непохо́жий *adj.* (*with* **на** + *acc.*) unlike; different (from).

непоча́тый *adj.* untouched; unopened; unused. —**непоча́тый край** (+ *gen.*), no end (of); tons (of).

непочте́ние *n.* disrespect.

непочти́тельный *adj.* disrespectful. —**непочти́тельность,** *n.f.* disrespect.

непра́вда *n.* **1,** untruth; falsehood; lie. **2,** deception; trickery. —*interj.* not so! —**все́ми пра́вдами и непра́вдами,** by hook or by crook.

неправдоподо́бие *n.* improbability; unlikelihood.

неправдоподо́бный *adj.* **1,** improbable; unlikely. **2,** implausible.

непра́ведный *adj., obs.* unjust; unfair.

непра́вильно *adv.* incorrectly. —*adj., used predicatively* incorrect: бы́ло бы непра́вильно (+ *inf.*), it would be incorrect to...

непра́вильность *n.f.* **1,** error; fallacy. **2,** irregularity.

непра́вильный *adj.* **1,** wrong; incorrect. **2,** irregular. **3,** (*of a fraction*) improper.

неправомо́чный *adj.* not legally qualified; incompetent. —**неправомо́чность,** *n.f., law* incompetence.

неправота́ *n.* error.

непра́вый *adj., usu. used predicatively* wrong: она́ была́ неправа́, she was wrong.

непракти́чный *adj.* impractical. —**непракти́чность,** *n.f.* impracticality.

непревзойдённый *adj.* unsurpassed; unexcelled.

непредви́денный *adj.* unforeseen.

непреднаме́ренный *adj.* unintentional; unpremeditated.

непредприи́мчивый *adj.* unenterprising.

непредсказу́емый *adj.* unpredictable.

непредубеждённый *adj.* unbiased; unprejudiced.

непредуму́шленный *adj.* unpremeditated. —**непредуму́шленное уби́йство,** manslaughter.

непредусмотри́тельный *adj.* lacking foresight; improvident. —**непредусмотри́тельность,** *n.f.* lack of foresight; improvidence.

непреклóнный *adj.* inflexible; intransigent; adamant. —**непреклóнность,** *n.f.* inflexibility; intransigence.

непрело́жный *adj.* immutable.

непреме́нно *adv.* **1,** absolutely; definitely; without fail. **2,** sure; bound: он непреме́нно опозда́ет, he is sure/bound to be late. —**непреме́нный,** *adj.* necessary; essential.

непреобори́мый *adj.* irresistible.

непреодоли́мый *adj.* **1,** insurmountable; insuperable. **2,** irresistible.

непререка́емый *adj.* unquestionable; indisputable.

непреры́вный *adj.* continuous; uninterrupted. —**непреры́вно,** *adv.* continuously. —**непреры́вность,** *n.f.* continuity.

непреста́нный *adj.* incessant; continual. —**непреста́нно,** *adv.* incessantly; continually.

неприве́тливый *adj.* **1,** unfriendly; ungracious. **2,** uninviting; forbidding. —**неприве́тливость,** *n.f.* unfriendliness; ungraciousness.

непривлека́тельный *adj.* unattractive.

непривы́чка *n.* not being used to something: с непривы́чки (+ **к** *or inf.*), not being used to...

непривы́чно *adv.* unusually. —*adj., used predicatively* (*with dat.*) unaccustomed; not used to: (мне) непривы́чно по́здно ложи́ться, I am not used to going to bed late.

непривы́чный *adj.* **1,** strange; unfamiliar. **2,** (*with* **к**) unaccustomed (to). **3,** inexperienced; untrained.

непригля́дный *adj.* unattractive; unsightly.

неприго́дный *adj.* unfit; unusable; useless. —**неприго́дность,** *n.f.* uselessness.

неприе́млемый *adj.* unacceptable. —**неприе́млемость,** *n.f.* unacceptability.

непризна́ние *n.* nonrecognition.

непри́знанный *adj.* unrecognized.

неприкаса́емые *n. pl., decl. as an adj.* untouchables (*in India*).

неприка́яннный *adj., colloq.* aimless; not knowing what to do with oneself.

неприкоснове́нность *n.f.* inviolability. —**дипломати́ческая неприкоснове́нность,** diplomatic immunity.

неприкоснове́нный *adj.* **1,** saved for an emergency: неприкоснове́нный запа́с, emergency reserve. **2,** *fig.* inviolable.

неприкра́шенный *adj.* plain; unadorned; unvarnished: неприкра́шенная пра́вда, the unvarnished truth.

неприкреплённый *adj.* unattached.

неприкры́тый *adj.* **1,** slightly open; ajar. **2,** uncovered; unprotected; undefended. **3,** *fig.* naked; barefaced; undisguised.

неприли́чие *n.* impropriety; indecency.

неприли́чный *adj.* improper; indecent. —**неприли́чно,** *adv.* improperly; indecently.

неприме́ни́мый *adj.* inapplicable.

неприме́тный *adj.* **1,** imperceptible. **2,** not noteworthy; ordinary.

непримеча́тельный *adj.* ordinary; undistinguished.

непримири́мый *adj.* irreconcilable. —**непримири́мость,** *n.f.* irreconcilability.

непринуждённый *adj.* natural; casual; relaxed; nonchalant. —**непринуждённость,** *n.f.* ease; abandon; nonchalance.

неприсоедине́ние *n.* nonalignment. —**неприсоедини́вшийся,** *adj.* nonaligned.

неприспосо́бленный *adj.* unable to adjust easily; maladjusted. —**неприспосо́бленность,** *n.f.* inability to adjust; maladjustment.

непристо́йность *n.f.* **1,** obscenity. **2,** *often pl.* an obscenity. —**непристо́йный,** *adj.* obscene.

непристу́пный *adj.* **1,** impregnable; unassailable. **2,** *fig.* (*of a person*) unapproachable.

непритво́рный *adj.* unfeigned; genuine.

непритяза́тельный *adj.* unpretentious; unassuming.

неприхотли́вый *adj.* unpretentious; simple; plain.

неприча́стность *n.f.* noninvolvement.

неприча́стный *adj.* [*short form* **-стен, -стна**] (*with* **к**) not implicated (in); not involved (in).

неприя́зненный *adj.* hostile; unfriendly.

неприя́знь *n.f.* hostility; enmity.

неприятель *n.m.* enemy. —**неприятельский,** *adj.* enemy (*attrib.*).

неприятно *adj., used predicatively* unpleasant: мне неприятно слышать это, it is unpleasant to hear it; I am distressed to hear it.

неприятность *n.f.* **1,** unpleasantness. **2,** *pl.* trouble.

неприятный *adj.* unpleasant; disagreeable.

непробиваемый *adj.* impenetrable.

непробудный *adj.* **1,** (*of sleep*) deep. **2,** *colloq.* (*of drinking*) unrestrained; (*of a drinker*) chronic.

непроверенный *adj.* unverified.

непроводник [*gen.* **-ника**] *n., physics* nonconductor.

непроглядный *adj.* **1,** pitch-dark. **2,** (*of darkness, fog, etc.*) impenetrable.

непродолжительный *adj.* short; of short duration. —**непродолжительность,** *n.f.* shortness; short duration.

непродуктивный *adj.* unproductive. —**непродуктивность,** *n.f.* unproductiveness.

непродуманный *adj.* not thought through; hasty; rash.

непроезжий *adj.* impassable.

непрозрачный *adj.* opaque. —**непрозрачность,** *n.f.* opacity; opaqueness.

непроизводительный *adj.* **1,** unproductive. **2,** nonproductive. —**непроизводительность,** *n.f.* unproductiveness.

непроизвольный *adj.* involuntary.

непроизносимый *adj.* unpronounceable.

непролазный *adj., colloq.* impassable.

непромокаемый *adj.* waterproof. —**непромокаемый плащ,** raincoat.

непроницаемый *adj.* impenetrable. —**непроницаемость,** *n.f.* impenetrability.

непропорциональный *adj.* disproportionate. —**непропорционально,** *adv.* disproportionately. —**непропорциональность,** *n.f.* disproportion.

непросвещённый *adj.* unenlightened.

непростительный *adj.* unforgivable; inexcusable; unpardonable.

непроходимость *n.f.* **1,** impassability; impenetrability. **2,** *med.* obstruction; blockage.

непроходимый *adj.* **1,** impassable; impenetrable. **2,** *colloq.* utter.

непрочный *adj.* **1,** not durable; flimsy. **2,** *fig.* tenuous. —**непрочность,** *n.f.* flimsiness.

непрошеный *adj.* **1,** uninvited. **2,** unsought; unsolicited.

непрямой *adj.* **1,** indirect. **2,** devious; evasive.

Нептун *n.* Neptune.

нептуний *n.* neptunium.

непутёвый *adj., colloq.* shiftless; good-for-nothing.

непьющий *adj.* not drinking; who does not drink. —*n.* nondrinker.

неработоспособный *adj.* disabled; incapacitated.

нерабочий *adj.* **1,** nonworking. **2,** off: нерабочий день, day off; нерабочее время, time off. **3,** *colloq.* not conducive to work.

неравенство *n.* inequality.

неравнодушный *adj.* [*short form* **-шен, -шна**] (*with* **к**) not indifferent (to).

неравномерный *adj.* uneven. —**неравномерно,** *adv.* unevenly. —**неравномерность,** *n.f.* unevenness.

неравноправие *n.* lack of equal rights; inequality. —**неравноправный,** *adj.* not enjoying equal rights; unequal.

неравный *adj.* unequal.

нерадение *n., obs.* = **нерадивость.**

нерадивый *adj.* lackadaisical. —**нерадивость,** *n.f.* lackadaisical attitude.

неразбериха *n., colloq.* confusion; chaos; disorder.

неразборчивость *n.f.* **1,** illegibility. **2,** lack of discrimination.

неразборчивый *adj.* **1,** illegible. **2,** not particular; undiscriminating. —**неразборчивый в средствах,** unscrupulous.

неразведанный *adj.* unexplored; untapped.

неразвитый *also,* **неразвитой** *adj.* **1,** undeveloped. **2,** backward; retarded. —**неразвитость,** *n.f.* backwardness; retardation.

неразгаданный *adj.* unsolved.

неразговорчивый *adj.* taciturn; uncommunicative. —**неразговорчивость,** *n.f.* taciturnity.

неразделимый *adj.* indivisible.

нераздельный *adj.* **1,** (*of property*) commonly held. **2,** indivisible; inseparable.

неразличимый *adj.* **1,** indistinguishable. **2,** indiscernible.

неразлучный *adj.* inseparable. —**неразлучность,** *n.f.* inseparability.

неразрезанный *adj.* uncut.

неразрешённый *adj.* **1,** unsolved; unresolved. **2,** forbidden; prohibited.

неразрешимый *adj.* insoluble.

неразрушимый *adj.* indestructible.

неразрывный *adj.* indissoluble.

неразумный *adj.* **1,** unreasonable; irrational. **2,** unwise; injudicious. —**неразумность,** *n.f.* unreasonableness; irrationality.

нераскаянный *adj., obs.* impenitent; unrepentant.

нерасположение *n.* (*with* **к**) dislike (of/for).

нераспорядительный *adj.* lacking administrative ability.

нераспространение *n.* nonproliferation.

нерассказанный *adj.* untold.

нерассудительный *adj.* irrational; lacking common sense. —**нерассудительность,** *n.f.* irrationality; lack of common sense.

нерастворимый *adj.* insoluble; indissoluble.

нерасторжимый *adj.* indissoluble.

нерасторопный *adj.* sluggish; inert.

нерастроганный *adj.* unmoved.

нерасчётливость *n.f.* **1,** extravagance. **2,** lack of foresight; improvidence.

нерасчётливый *adj.* **1,** extravagant; wasteful. **2,** shortsighted; improvident.

нерациональный *adj.* inefficient.

нерв *n.* nerve.

нервировать *v. impfv.* [*pres.* **-рую, -руешь**] to make nervous; unnerve.

нервический *adj., obs.* nervous.

нервничать *v. impfv.* to be nervous; become fidgety.

нервнобольной *adj.* suffering from a nervous disorder. —*n.* person suffering from a nervous disorder.

нервность *n.f.* nervousness.

нервный *adj.* **1,** nerve (*attrib.*): нервные клетки, nerve cells. **2,** nervous. **3,** irritable; high-strung. **4,** trying (on one's nerves). —**нервная система,** nervous system.

нервозный *adj.* nervous; high-strung. —**нервозность,** *n.f.* nervousness.

нереа́льный *adj.* **1,** unreal. **2,** unrealistic; impractical.
нерегуля́рный *adj.* irregular. —**нерегуля́рность,** *n.f.* irregularity.
нере́дкий *adj.* not infrequent; not uncommon.
нере́дко *adv.* quite often.
нерента́бельный *adj.* unprofitable.
не́рест *n.* spawning. —**нерести́лище,** *n.* spawning ground.
нерешённый *adj.* unresolved; unsolved.
нереши́мость *n.f.* indecision. —**быть в нереши́мости,** to be undecided.
нереши́тельность *n.f.* **1,** indecisiveness. **2,** indecision: быть в нереши́тельности, to be undecided. —**нереши́тельный,** *adj.* irresolute; indecisive.
нержаве́ющий *adj.* rust-resistant. —**нержаве́ющая сталь,** stainless steel.
неритми́чный *adj.* irregular; uneven.
неро́бкий *adj.* not timid; brave.
неро́вный *adj.* [*short form* **-вен, -вна́, -вно**] **1,** uneven. **2,** crooked. **3,** (*of one's pulse, breathing, etc.*) irregular. **4,** *fig.* erratic. —**неро́вно,** *adv.* unevenly. —**неро́вность,** *n.f.* unevenness.
неро́вня *also,* **неровня́** *n.m. & f., colloq.* person not the equal of another.
не́рпа *n.* ringed seal.
нерукотво́рный *adj.* not created by human hands.
неру́сский *adj.* non-Russian.
неруши́мый *adj.* inviolable; indissoluble. —**неруши́мость,** *n.f.* inviolability.
неря́ха *n.m. & f.* slovenly person; slob.
неря́шливый *adj.* **1,** sloppy; slovenly. **2,** slipshod. —**неря́шливость,** *n.f.;* **неря́шество,** *n. neut.* sloppiness; slovenliness.
несбы́точный *adj.* unrealizable; vain.
несваре́ние *n., in* **несваре́ние желу́дка,** indigestion.
несве́дущий *adj.* **1,** ignorant; uninformed. **2,** (*with* в + *prepl.*) unfamiliar (with); unconversant (with); unversed (in); ungrounded (in).
несве́жий *adj.* **1,** not fresh; stale; spoiled. **2,** worn; dirty; soiled. **3,** worn; tired; drawn.
несвоевре́менно *adv.* **1,** at an inopportune time. **2,** too late.
несвоевре́менный *adj.* **1,** ill-timed; untimely. **2,** tardy; belated.
несвя́зный *adj.* rambling; disconnected; incoherent; disjointed. —**несвя́зность,** *n.f.* incoherence.
несгиба́емый *adj.* unbending; inflexible.
несгово́рчивый *adj.* uncooperative; intractable.
несгора́емый *adj.* fireproof; incombustible; noninflammable. —**несгора́емый шкаф,** safe. —**несгора́емый я́щик,** strongbox.
несде́ржанный *adj.* **1,** broken; unkept. **2,** unrestrained; violent.
несдоброва́ть *v. pfv., used in inf. only with dat. case:* ему́ несдоброва́ть; he is in for trouble.
несекре́тный *adj.* **1,** not secret. **2,** unclassified.
несе́ние *n.* performance; execution; carrying out.
несерьёзный *adj.* **1,** not serious. **2,** casual; lackadaisical. **3,** trivial; unimportant.
несессе́р (нэ-сэ-сэр) *n.* traveling case; toilet case.
несимметри́чный *adj.* asymmetrical. —**несимметри́чность,** *n.f.* asymmetry.
несказа́нный *adj.* indescribable; unspeakable.
нескла́дица *n., colloq.* incoherent talk; nonsense; prattle.
нескла́дный *adj.* **1,** awkward; ungainly. **2,** incoherent. **3,** discordant. **4,** absurd.
несклоня́емый *adj., gram.* indeclinable.
не́сколько *adj.* a few; some; several: не́сколько люде́й, a few people; в не́скольких слова́х, in a few words. —*adv.* somewhat: не́сколько удивлён, somewhat surprised.
несконча́емый *adj.* endless; unending; interminable.
нескро́мность *n.f.* **1,** immodesty. **2,** indiscretion.
нескро́мный *adj.* **1,** immodest. **2,** indiscreet. **3,** indecent.
нескрыва́емый *adj.* unconcealed; undisguised.
несла́женный *adj.* uncoordinated; disorganized.
несло́жный *adj.* uncomplicated; simple.
неслы́ханный *adj.* unheard-of.
неслы́шный *adj.* inaudible.
несме́лый *adj.* timid; diffident.
несменя́емый *adj.* **1,** ever-present; never removed. **2,** (*of a position*) permanent; (*of a person*) having tenure. —**несменя́емость,** *n.f.* irremovability from office; tenure.
несме́тный *adj.* countless; incalculable.
несмолка́емый *adj.* (*of a noise or sound*) incessant.
несмотря́ на (*with acc.*) despite; in spite of. —**несмотря́ ни на что,** despite all; in spite of everything.
несмыва́емый *adj.* indelible.
несмышлёный *adj., colloq.* slow to grasp things; dull; dense.
несно́сный *adj.* unbearable; unendurable.
несоблюде́ние *n.* failure to observe.
несовершенноле́тие *n.* minority (*being under legal age*).
несовершенноле́тний *adj.* under legal age. —*n.* minor.
несоверше́нный *adj.* **1,** imperfect. **2,** *gram.* imperfective: несоверше́нный вид, imperfective aspect.
несоверше́нство *n.* **1,** lack of perfection. **2,** *usu. pl.* imperfection.
несовмести́мый *adj.* incompatible. —**несовмести́мость,** *n.f.* incompatibility.
несогла́сие *n.* **1,** disagreement; difference of opinion. **2,** disagreement; discord. **3,** refusal; rejection.
несогла́сный *adj.* **1,** in disagreement. **2,** (*with* с + *instr.*) inconsistent (with). **3,** uncoordinated. **4,** discordant.
несогласо́ванный *adj.* uncoordinated. —**несогласо́ванность,** *n.f.* lack of coordination.
несозна́тельный *adj.* **1,** thoughtless; irresponsible. **2,** lacking political consciousness.
несоизмери́мый *adj.* incommensurable. —**несоизмери́мость,** *n.f.* incommensurability.
несокращённый *adj.* unabridged.
несокруши́мый *adj.* indestructible; unshakable.
несо́лоно *adv., in* **несо́лоно хлеба́вши,** having accomplished nothing.
несомне́нно *adv.* undoubtedly; doubtlessly; indubitably; unquestionably. —*adj., used predicatively* certain: одно́ несомне́нно, one thing is certain.
несомне́нный *adj.* undoubted; indubitable; unquestioned.
несообрази́тельный *adj.* slow to grasp things; dull; dense.
несообра́зный *adj.* **1,** incongruous. **2,** absurd. —**несообра́зность,** *n.f.* incongruity; absurdity.
несоотве́тствие *n.* discrepancy; disparity.

несоразме́рно *adv.* disproportionately. —**несоразме́рно с** (+ *instr.*), out of proportion to.
несоразме́рный *adj.* disproportionate; incommensurate. —**несоразме́рность,** *n.f.* disproportion.
несостоя́тельность *n.f.* **1,** insolvency; bankruptcy. **2,** fallacy.
несостоя́тельный *adj.* **1,** of modest means. **2,** insolvent; bankrupt. **3,** powerless; helpless. **4,** unsound; untenable.
несочу́вствующий *adj.* unsympathetic.
неспе́лый *adj.* unripe.
неспе́шный *adj.* unhurried.
неспоко́йно *adv.* anxiously. —*adj., used predicatively* uneasy: на душе́ у него́ неспоко́йно, he feels uneasy.
неспоко́йный *adj.* **1,** restless. **2,** anxious; uneasy.
неспорти́вный *adj.* unsportsmanlike.
неспосо́бность *n.f.* inability.
неспосо́бный *adj.* [*short form* **-бен, -бна**] **1,** not bright. **2,** (*with* **к**) having no aptitude (for). **3,** (with **к** *or* **на**) incapable (of).
несправедли́во *adv.* **1,** unjustly; unfairly. **2,** incorrectly; erroneously.
несправедли́вость *n.f.* injustice; unfairness.
несправедли́вый *adj.* **1,** unjust; unfair. **2,** incorrect.
неспровоци́рованный *adj.* unprovoked.
неспроста́ *adv., colloq.* for a definite reason; not by chance.
несравне́нно *adv.* **1,** incomparably. **2,** (*with comparisons*) far; infinitely. —**несравне́нный,** *adj.* incomparable; matchless; peerless.
несравни́мый *adj.* incomparable.
нестерпи́мый *adj.* unbearable; unendurable.
нестеснённый *adj.* uninhibited.
нести́ *v. impfv.* [*pfv.* **понести́;** *pres.* **несу́, несёшь;** *past* **нёс, несла́, несло́**] **1,** to carry. **2,** to carry swiftly; whisk. **3,** to suffer; sustain; incur. **4,** [*impfv. only*] to bear (responsibility). **5,** [*impfv. only*] to perform (duties). Нести́ слу́жбу, *mil.* to serve; see service. **6,** [*impfv. only*] to bring (death, freedom, ruin, etc.). **7,** *impers.* (*with instr.*) *colloq.* to blow: от окна́ несёт хо́лодом, there is a draft from the window. **8,** *impers.* (*with instr.*) to reek (of): от него́ несёт во́дкой, he reeks of vodka. **9,** *colloq.* to talk (nonsense.). **10,** [*pfv.* **снести́**] to lay (eggs). —**нести́сь,** *refl.* **1,** to race; tear along. **2,** *colloq.* to rush; dash. **3,** to float; drift (*on water or through the air*). **4,** to be heard. **5,** [*pfv.* **снести́сь**] to lay eggs. *See also* **носи́ть** *and* **носи́ться.**
несто́йкий *adj.* **1,** unstable. **2,** (*of an odor*) slight; (*of perfume*) weak.
несто́ящий *adj., colloq.* worthless; good-for-nothing.
нестроево́й *adj.* **1,** unfit for building purposes. **2,** *mil.* noncombatant. —*n., mil.* noncombatant.
нестро́йный *adj.* **1,** ungraceful; ungainly. **2,** irregular; disorderly. **3,** discordant.
несть *predicate, obs.* there is no... —**несть конца́** *or* **числа́** (+ *dat.*), there is no end of...
несудохо́дный *adj.* unnavigable.
несура́зный *adj.* **1,** ridiculous; absurd. **2,** awkward; ungainly.
несусве́тный *adj., colloq.* **1,** utter; absolute; unmitigated. **2,** not of this world; not to be believed.
несу́шка [*gen. pl.* **-шек**] *n.* hen that lays eggs; layer.
несуще́ственный *adj.* minor; unimportant; inconsequential.
несуществу́ющий *adj.* nonexistent.
несхо́дный *adj.* different; dissimilar; disparate. —**несхо́дство,** *n.* difference; dissimilarity; disparity.
несчастли́вец [*gen.* **-вца**] *n.m.* [*fem.* **-вица**] *colloq.* unlucky person.
несчастли́вый *adj.* **1,** unhappy. **2,** unlucky; unfortunate.
несча́стный *adj.* **1,** unhappy. **2,** unfortunate. —**несча́стный слу́чай,** accident.
несча́стье *n.* misfortune. —**к несча́стью,** unfortunately.
несчётный *adj.* countless; innumerable.
несъедо́бный *adj.* inedible; uneatable.
нет *neg. particle* **1,** no. **2,** not: нет ещё, not yet; почему́ нет?, why not? Вы идёте или нет?, are you going or not? Я иду́, а он нет, I am going but he isn't. **3,** (*with gen.*) *indicating the absence of something:* нет вре́мени, there is no time. Его́ нет, he is not here. Там никого́ нет, there is no one there. У меня́ нет спи́чек, I don't have any matches. —**нет и нет** (*with gen.*), not a sign of (someone). —**нет-нет да и,** once in a while. —**своди́ть на нет,** to negate; nullify. —**своди́ться** *or* **сходи́ть на нет,** to come to naught.
нетакти́чный *adj.* tactless. —**нетакти́чность,** *n.f.* tactlessness.
немала́нтливый *adj.* untalented; lacking talent.
нетвёрдо *adv.* not firmly: нетвёрдо держа́ться на нога́х, to be unsteady on one's feet.
нетвёрдый *adj.* **1,** not hard; soft. **2,** unsteady; shaky. **3,** irresolute; uncertain.
нетерпели́вый *adj.* impatient. —**нетерпели́во,** *adv.* impatiently. —**нетерпели́вость,** *n.f.* impatience.
нетерпе́ние *n.* impatience. —**ждать с нетерпе́нием, 1,** to await impatiently; await anxiously. **2,** to look forward to.
нетерпи́мость *n.f.* intolerance.
нетерпи́мый *adj.* **1,** intolerable. **2,** intolerant.
нетипи́чный *adj.* not typical.
нетле́нный *adj.* **1,** *obs.* imperishable. **2,** *fig.* eternal; immortal.
нетопы́рь [*gen.* **-пыря́**] *n.m.* pipistrelle (*bat*).
неторопли́вый *adj.* leisurely; unhurried. —**неторопли́во,** *adv.* leisurely.
нето́чность *n.f.* **1,** inaccuracy. **2,** *usu. pl.* inaccuracies.
нето́чный *adj.* inaccurate; inexact; imprecise.
нетре́бовательный *adj.* not demanding; undemanding.
нетре́звый *adj.* not sober; drunk: в нетре́звом ви́де, in a drunken state.
нетро́нутый *adj.* **1,** untouched; untapped. **2,** *fig.* pure; unsullied; virginal. **3,** unmoved.
нетру́дный *adj.* not difficult.
нетрудово́й *adj.* **1,** nonworking. **2,** unearned.
нетрудоспосо́бный *adj.* disabled; incapacitated. —**нетрудоспосо́бность,** *n.f.* disability; incapacity.
не́тто (нэ) *adj. & adv., indecl.* net: вес не́тто, net weight; цена́ не́тто, net price.
не́ту *particle, colloq.* = **нет.**
неубеди́тельный *adj.* unconvincing.
неу́бранный *adj.* **1,** (*of a room*) not straightened up; (*of a bed*) not made; (*of dishes*) not taken away. **2,** (of crops) not gathered; not harvested.
неуваже́ние *n.* disrespect; lack of respect.
неуважи́тельный *adj.* **1,** (*of a reason or excuse*) invalid. **2,** *colloq.* disrespectful.

неуве́ренность *n.f.* uncertainty; lack of confidence. —**неуве́ренный,** *adj.* uncertain.

неувяда́емый *adj.* **1,** *obs.* never fading. **2,** *fig.* undying. *Also,* **неувяда́ющий.**

неувя́зка [*gen. pl.* **-зок**] *n., colloq.* mix-up; slip-up; hitch.

неугаси́мый *adj.* **1,** unquenchable. **2,** *fig.* undying.

неуго́дный *adj.* disagreeable; objectionable.

неугомо́нный *adj., colloq.* **1,** indefatigable; always on the go. **2,** (*of a sound or noise*) incessant.

неуда́ча *n.* failure; reverse.

неуда́чливый *adj.* unlucky.

неуда́чник *n.* unlucky person; failure.

неуда́чно *adv.* **1,** unsuccessfully. **2,** poorly; badly.

неуда́чный *adj.* **1,** unsuccessful. **2,** unfortunate; having turned out badly.

неудержи́мый *adj.* irrepressible; uncontrollable.

неудиви́тельный *adj.* not surprising. —**неудиви́тельно,** *adj., used predicatively* not surprising: неудиви́тельно, что..., it is not surprising that...

неудо́бно *adv.* uncomfortably. —*adj., used predicatively* **1,** uncomfortable: мне неудо́бно так лежа́ть, I am uncomfortable lying that way. **2,** inconvenient. **3,** awkward.

неудо́бный *adj.* **1,** uncomfortable. **2,** inconvenient. **3,** awkward.

неудобовари́мый *adj.* indigestible.

неудобопроизноси́мый *adj.* difficult to pronounce; unpronounceable.

неудобочита́емый *adj.* difficult to read.

неудо́бство *n.* **1,** inconvenience; discomfort. **2,** awkwardness; embarrassment.

неудовлетворе́ние *n.* dissatisfaction.

неудовлетворённый *adj.* dissatisfied. —**неудовлетворённость,** *n.f.* dissatisfaction.

неудовлетвори́тельно *adv.* **1,** unsatisfactorily. **2,** (*as a school grade*) "unsatisfactory". —**неудовлетвори́тельный,** *adj.* unsatisfactory.

неудово́льствие *n.* displeasure.

неуёмный *adj., colloq.* **1,** irrepressible; indefatigable. **2,** (*of an emotion*) uncontrollable.

неуже́ли *interr. particle* really?; is it possible?

неужи́вчивый *adj.* hard to get along with.

неузнава́емость *n.f., in* **до неузнава́емости,** beyond recognition.

неузнава́емый *adj.* unrecognizable.

неука́занный *adj.* **1,** not indicated; unspecified. **2,** *obs.* not permitted.

неукло́нный *adj.* **1,** steady: неукло́нный рост, steady growth. **2,** steadfast; unwavering.

неуклю́жий *adj.* awkward; clumsy. —**неуклю́же,** *adv.* awkwardly; clumsily. —**неуклю́жесть,** *n.f.* awkwardness; clumsiness.

неукосни́тельный *adj.* absolute; total. —**неукосни́тельно,** *adv.* unfailingly.

неукроти́мый *adj.* **1,** untamable. **2,** uncontrollable. **3,** indomitable.

неулови́мый *adj.* **1,** elusive. **2,** barely audible or visible. —**неулови́мость,** *n.f.* elusiveness.

неуме́лый *adj.* clumsy; inept.

неуме́ние *n.* inability; lack of ability.

неуме́ренный *adj.* **1,** immoderate. **2,** intemperate. —**неуме́ренность,** *n.f.* immoderation.

неуме́стность *n.f.* **1,** impropriety. **2,** irrelevance.

неуме́стный *adj.* **1,** inappropriate; out of place; uncalled-for. **2,** irrelevant.

неу́мный *adj.* **1,** unintelligent. **2,** unwise.

неумоли́мый *adj.* **1,** implacable. **2,** inexorable.

неумолка́емый *adj.* (*of a sound or noise*) incessant.

неумо́лчный *adj.* = **неумолка́емый.**

неумы́шленный *adj.* unintentional.

неупла́та *n.* failure to pay; nonpayment.

неупла́ченный *adj.* unpaid; outstanding.

неупотреби́тельный *adj.* not in use.

неуравнове́шенный *adj.* unbalanced; unstable. —**неуравнове́шенность,** *n.f.* (mental) instability.

неурегули́рованный *adj.* (*of questions, issues, etc.*) unsettled; outstanding.

неурожа́й *n.* crop failure; poor harvest. —**неурожа́йный,** *adj., in* **неурожа́йный год,** year of poor harvest.

неуро́чный *adj.* untimely; inopportune.

неуря́дица *n., colloq.* **1,** confusion; disorder. **2,** squabbling; squabbles.

неуси́дчивый *adj.* **1,** restless. **2,** not diligent; not persevering.

неуспева́емость *n.f.* poor progress (*among pupils*); pupils' failure.

неуспева́ющий *adj.* (*of a student*) poor; not making satisfactory progress.

неуспе́х *n.* failure.

неуспе́шный *adj.* unsuccessful.

неуста́нный *adj.* **1,** untiring; tireless. **2,** unceasing; ceaseless.

неусто́йка *n.* **1,** *law* forfeit. **2,** *colloq.* failure.

неусто́йчивость *n.f.* instability.

неусто́йчивый *adj.* **1,** shaky; unstable; unsteady. **2,** fluctuating; variable; changeable.

неустрани́мый *adj.* **1,** irremovable. **2,** insurmountable. **3,** inevitable.

неустраши́мый *adj.* fearless; intrepid. —**неустраши́мость,** *n.f.* fearlessness; intrepidity.

неустро́енный *adj.* **1,** unsettled. **2,** poorly organized. **3,** not provided for. —**неустро́енность,** *n.f.* unsettled state.

неустро́йство *n.* disorder.

неусту́пчивый *adj.* unyielding; uncompromising. —**неусту́пчивость,** *n.f.* obstinacy; unwillingness to compromise.

неусы́пный *adj.* **1,** untiring; tireless. **2,** unflagging; constant.

неутеши́тельный *adj.* unencouraging; inauspicious.

неуте́шный *adj.* inconsolable; disconsolate.

неутоли́мый *adj.* unquenchable.

неутоми́мый *adj.* indefatigable; tireless. —**неутоми́мость,** *n.f.* indefatigability.

не́уч *n., colloq.* ignoramus.

неучти́вый *adj.* impolite; discourteous. —**неучти́вость,** *n.f.* impoliteness; discourtesy.

неую́тный *adj.* lacking in comforts. —**неую́тно,** *adj., used predicatively* uncomfortable: чу́вствовать себя́ неую́тно, to feel uncomfortable.

неуязви́мый *adj.* invulnerable. —**неуязви́мость,** *n.f.* invulnerability.

нефри́т *n.* **1,** nephritis. **2,** nephrite; jade.

нефтеналивно́й *adj.* carrying oil: нефтеналивно́е су́дно, oil tanker.

нефтено́сный *adj.* containing oil; yielding oil: нефтено́сный сла́нец, oil shale.

нефтеперего́нный *adj., in* **нефтеперего́нный заво́д,** oil refinery.
нефтепрово́д *n.* oil pipeline.
нефтехими́ческий *adj.* petrochemical.
нефтехрани́лище *n.* oil storage tank.
нефть *n.f.* oil; petroleum.
нефтяно́й *adj.* oil (*attrib.*); petroleum (*attrib.*).
нехаракте́рный *adj.* not typical.
нехва́тка [*gen. pl.* **-ток**] *n., colloq.* shortage.
неху́трый *adj.* **1,** without guile; ingenuous. **2,** *colloq.* simple; unpretentious.
неходово́й *adj.* **1,** not in working order; out of commission. **2,** (*of merchandise*) not selling well; not in great demand.
нехоро́ший *adj.* bad. —**нехоро́ш собо́й,** ugly; unattractive.
нехорошо́ *adv.* badly. —*adj., used predicatively* **1,** not good; bad: нехорошо́, что..., it's not good that... **2,** ill: ему́ ста́ло нехорошо́, he began to feel ill.
не́хотя *adv.* **1,** unwillingly; reluctantly. **2,** accidentally; inadvertently.
нецелесообра́зный *adj.* **1,** inadvisable. **2,** pointless.
нецензу́рный *adj.* unprintable; obscene.
нецеремо́нный *adj.* unceremonious.
нецивилизо́ванный *adj.* uncivilized.
нечаянный *adj.* **1,** unexpected; chance. **2,** accidental; inadvertent. —**неча́янно,** *adv.* accidentally; inadvertently; by chance.
не́чего *indef. pron., gen. & acc.* [*dat.* **не́чему;** *instr.* **не́чем;** *prepl.* **не́** (+ *prep.*) **чем**] *used with inf.* there is nothing: не́чего чита́ть, there is nothing to read. Мне не́чего де́лать, I have nothing to do. —*adv., colloq. used with inf.* **1,** there is no need: не́чего беспоко́иться, there is no need to worry. **2,** there is no point; it is no use: не́чего жа́ловаться, there is no point (*or* it's no use) complaining. —**не́чего и говори́ть; и говори́ть не́чего,** *see* **говори́ть.** —**не́чего сказа́ть, 1,** of course; to be sure. **2,** I must say! —**от не́чего де́лать,** having nothing better to do.
нечелове́ческий *adj.* **1,** inhuman. **2,** superhuman.
нечёсаный *adj.* unkempt.
нечести́вый *adj., obs.* wicked; unholy.
нече́стный *adj.* dishonest. —**нече́стно,** *adv.* dishonestly. —**нече́стность,** *n.f.* dishonesty.
не́чет *n., colloq.* odd number.
нечёткий *adj.* **1,** unclear; illegible. **2,** careless; slipshod.
нечётный *adj.* (*of a number*) odd.
нечистокро́вный *adj.* half-blooded.
нечистопло́тный *adj.* **1,** dirty; sloppy. **2,** *fig.* unscrupulous; shady.
нечистота́ [*pl.* **-то́ты**] *n.* **1,** uncleanliness; impurity. **2,** *pl.* sewage. **3,** *pl.* impurities.
нечи́стый *adj.* **1,** unclean; dirty. **2,** impure; adulterated. **3,** (*of sounds or speech*) unclear. **4,** *fig.* dishonest; shady. —**на́ руку нечи́ст,** light-fingered.
не́чисть *n.f., colloq.* **1,** evil spirits. **2,** *fig.* scum.
нечленоразде́льный *adj.* inarticulate; unintelligible.
не́что *indef. pron.* something.
нечувстви́тельный *adj.* insensitive. —**нечувстви́тельность,** *n.f.* insensitivity.
нечу́ткий *adj.* **1,** insensitive; not keen; dull. **2,** insensitive; not caring; indifferent.
нешу́точный *adj., colloq.* not to be taken lightly: нешу́точное де́ло, no laughing matter.
неща́дный *adj.* merciless. —**неща́дно,** *adv.* mercilessly.
неэконо́мный *adj.* uneconomical.
неэкспони́рованный *adj.* (*of film*) unexposed.
неэтили́рованный *adj.* (*of gasoline*) unleaded.
неэти́чный *adj.* unethical.
неэффекти́вность *n.f.* **1,** inefficacy. **2,** inefficiency.
неэффекти́вный *adj.* **1,** ineffective. **2,** inefficient.
нея́вка *n.* failure to appear.
нея́ркий *adj.* **1,** dim; faint. **2,** pale; subdued.
нея́сно *adv.* dimly; faintly. —*adj., used predicatively* unclear: ещё нея́сно, что бу́дет, it is still unclear as to what will happen.
нея́сность *n.f.* **1,** lack of clarity; vagueness. **2,** unclear point; ambiguity.
нея́сный *adj.* [*short form* **-сен, -сна́, -сно**] **1,** unclear; indistinct. **2,** (*of sounds*) faint; indistinct. **3,** vague.
нея́сыть *n.f.* tawny owl.
ни *neg. particle* **1,** not a: на не́бе ни о́блачка, there is not a cloud in the sky. ♦*Often used with* оди́н: он не сказа́л ни одного́ сло́ва, he did not say a single word. **2,** *occurring as a separate word when* никто́, ничто́, никако́й, *and their oblique case forms are separated to permit the insertion of a preposition in between:* ни за что на све́те, not for anything in the world. Он не отвеча́л ни на каки́е вопро́сы, he did not answer any questions. Я ни с кем не встре́тился, I did not meet anyone. —*indef. particle, equivalent to English* -ever: что ни *or* что бы ни, whatever; где ни *or* где бы ни, wherever. Кто бы он ни́ был, whoever he is. Куда́ ни посмо́тришь, wherever you look. —**ни...ни,** neither ...nor: ни за ни про́тив, neither for nor against; ни тот ни друго́й, neither one.
ни́ва *n.* **1,** field of grain. **2,** *fig.* field (of endeavor): на ни́ве просвеще́ния, in the field of education.
нивели́р *n.* level (*instrument*).
нивели́ровать *v. impfv. & pfv.* [*pres.* **-рую, -руешь**] to level.
нивелиро́вка *n.* leveling.
нивя́ник *n.* (oxeye) daisy.
нигде́ *adv.* nowhere; no place.
нигили́зм *n.* nihilism. —**нигили́ст,** *n.* nihilist. —**нигилисти́ческий,** *adj.* nihilistic.
нидерла́ндец [*gen.* **-дца**] *n.m.* [*fem.* **-дка**] Dutchman. —**нидерла́ндский,** *adj.* Dutch; Netherlands (*attrib.*).
ни́же *adj., comp. of* **ни́зкий.** —*adv.* below. —*prep., with gen.* **1,** below: ни́же нуля́, below zero. **2,** beneath: ни́же его́ досто́инства, beneath his dignity.
нижеподписа́вшийся *n., decl. as an adj.* the undersigned.
нижесле́дующий *adj.* the following.
нижестоя́щий *adj.* (*of an organization, governmental body, etc.*) lower-level.
ни́жний *adj.* **1,** lower. **2,** bottom. —**ни́жнее бельё,** underwear. —**ни́жняя руба́шка,** undershirt. —**ни́жний эта́ж,** ground floor.
низ [*2nd loc.* **низу́;** *pl.* **низы́**] *n.* **1,** bottom. **2,** *pl., music* low notes. **3,** *pl., colloq.* lower classes; lower strata.
низа́ть *v. impfv.* [*pfv.* **наниза́ть;** *pres.* **нижу́, ни́жешь**] to string; thread.
низверга́ть *v. impfv.* [*pfv.* **низве́ргнуть**] **1,** to throw (down); plunge. **2,** *fig.* to overthrow; bring down. —**низверга́ться,** *refl.* (*of water*) to come rushing down; cascade down.

низве́ргнуть [*past* **-ве́рг, -ла**] *v., pfv. of* **низверга́ть.** —**низве́ргнуться,** *refl., pfv. of* **низверга́ться.**
низверже́ние *n.* overthrow.
низвести́ [*infl. like* **вести́**] *v., pfv. of* **низводи́ть.**
низводи́ть *v. impfv.* [*pfv.* **низвести́;** *pres.* **-вожу́, -во́дишь**] **1,** to bring down. **2,** *fig.* (*with* **до**) to reduce (to).
низи́на *n.* low-lying area. —**низи́нный,** *adj.* low-lying.
ни́зкий *adj.* [*short form* **ни́зок, низка́, ни́зко;** *comp.* **ни́же**] **1,** low. **2,** (*of quality*) poor. **3,** base; despicable. **4,** (*of a sound, voice, etc.*) deep. —**ни́зкого ро́ста,** short (*in height*).
ни́зко *adv.* **1,** low: поклони́ться ни́зко, to bow low. **2,** despicably.
низкоопла́чиваемый *adj.* low-paid.
низкопокло́нник *n.* sycophant.
низкопокло́нничать *v. impfv.* (*with* **пе́ред**) to grovel (before); bow and scrape (before).
низкопокло́нство *n.* servility.
низкопро́бный *adj.* **1,** (*of gold or silver*) base-alloy; low-grade. **2,** *fig.* low-grade; second-rate.
низкоро́слый *adj.* undersized.
низкосо́ртный *adj.* low-quality; low-grade.
низлага́ть *v. impfv.* [*pfv.* **низложи́ть**] to overthrow; depose; bring down.
низложе́ние *n.* overthrow.
низложи́ть [*infl.* **-ложу́, -ло́жишь**] *v., pfv. of* **низлага́ть.**
ни́зменность *n.f.* **1,** lowland. **2,** baseness; meanness.
ни́зменный *adj.* **1,** *geog.* low-lying. **2,** base; mean.
низово́й *adj.* **1,** low; close to the ground. **2,** located downstream. **3,** local; at the local level.
низо́вье *n.* lower reaches (*of a river*).
ни́зом *adv.* along the bottom; along the lower route.
ни́зость *n.f.* baseness; meanness.
ни́зший *adj., superl. of* **ни́зкий,** lowest. —**ни́зшее образова́ние,** elementary education.
ника́к *adv.* (in) no way: я ника́к не мог откры́ть дверь, there was no way I could open the door; I simply could not open the door. Ника́к не могу́ вспо́мнить, I simply (*or* just) can't remember. Это ника́к не помо́жет, that won't help at all. —**ника́к нельзя́,** absolutely impossible.
никако́й *adj.* not any; no: не мо́жет быть никако́го сомне́ния, there can be no doubt. Никаки́х извине́ний!, no apologies!
ни́келевый *adj.* nickel.
никелирова́ть *v. impfv. & pfv.* [*pres.* **-ру́ю, -ру́ешь**] to plate with nickel; nickel-plate.
никелиро́вка *n.* **1,** nickel-plating. **2,** nickle plate.
ни́кель *n.m.* nickel.
нике́м *pron., instr. of* **никто́.**
ни́кнуть *v. impfv.* [*pfv.* **пони́кнуть;** *past* **ник** *or* **ни́кнул, ни́кла**] to droop.
никогда́ *adv.* never. —**бо́льше никогда́,** never again. —**как никогда́,** more than ever; as never before. —**никогда́ ещё,** never before.
никого́ *pron., gen. & acc. of* **никто́.**
нико́й *adj., in* **нико́им о́бразом** *and* **ни в ко́ем слу́чае,** under no circumstances.
никому́ *pron., dat. of* **никто́.**
никоти́н *n.* nicotine. —**никоти́нный; никоти́новый,** *adj.* nicotine (*attrib.*).
никто́ *indef. pron.* [*gen. & acc.* **никого́;** *dat.* **никому́;** *instr.* **нике́м;** *prepl.* **ни** (+ *prep.*) **ком**] no one; nobody.
никуда́ *adv.* nowhere; no place. —**никуда́ не годи́ться,** to be no good at all.
никуды́шный *adj., colloq.* useless; worthless; good-for-nothing.
никчёмный *adj., colloq.* useless; worthless; good-for-nothing. —**никчёмность,** *n.f., colloq.* uselessness; worthlessness.
ним *pron., variant of* **им,** *used after prepositions.*
нима́ло *adv.* not at all; not in the least; not a bit.
нимб *n.* nimbus.
ни́ми *pron., variant of* **и́ми,** *used after prepositions.*
ни́мфа *n.* nymph.
нимфома́ния *n.* nymphomania. —**нимфома́нка,** *n.* nymphomaniac.
нио́бий *n.* niobium.
неоди́мий *n.* neodymium.
ниотку́да *adv.* from nowhere; not from anywhere.
нипочём *adv., colloq.* **1,** (*with dat.*) it is nothing (for someone): ему́ нипочём пройти́ два́дцать киломе́тров, it is nothing for him to walk twenty kilometers. **2,** dirt-cheap.
ни́ппель [*pl.* **ниппеля́**] *n.m.* nipple (*threaded pipe*).
нирва́на *n.* nirvana.
ниско́лько *adv.* not at all; not a bit; not in the least.
ниспада́ть *v. impfv.* to hand down.
ниспроверга́ть *v. impfv.* [*pfv.* **ниспрове́ргнуть**] to overthrow.
ниспрове́ргнуть [*past* **-ве́рг, -ла**] *v., pfv. of* **ниспроверга́ть.**
ниспроверже́ние *n.* overthrow.
нисходя́щий *adj.* descending.
ни́тка [*gen. pl.* **-ток**] *n.* **1,** thread. **2,** string (*of pearls, beads, etc.*). —**до ни́тки, 1,** (*with* **всё**) down to the last penny. **2,** (*with the verb* **промо́кнуть**) to the skin. —**на живу́ю ни́тку,** hastily; crudely. —**шит бе́лыми ни́тками,** transparent; poorly disguised.
ни́точка [*gen. pl.* **-чек**] *n., dim. of* **ни́тка.**
ни́точный *adj.* of or for thread.
нитра́т *n.* nitrate. —**нитра́тный,** *adj.* containing nitrate; nitrate (*attrib.*).
нитри́т *n.* nitrite.
нитроглицери́н *n.* nitroglycerin(e).
нить *n.f.* **1,** thread. **2,** filament. **3,** suture. —**потеря́ть нить разгово́ра,** to lose the thread of the conversation. —**проходи́ть кра́сной ни́тью** (*with* **в** + *prepl. or* **че́рез**) to be the dominant theme of; run through.
ни́тяный *adj.* made of thread.
них *pers. pron., var. of* **их,** *used after prepositions.*
ниц *adv.* with one's face touching the ground. —**пасть ниц,** to prostrate oneself.
ничего́ *pron., gen. of* **ничто́,** nothing: ничего́ осо́бенного, nothing special. —*adv. & adj., colloq.* [*also,* **ничего́ себе́**] not bad; pretty good; pretty well. —**ничего́!,** no matter!; it doesn't matter!; never mind!
ничегонеде́лание *n., colloq.* idleness.
ниче́й *indef. pron.* [*infl. like* **чей**] nobody's; no one's. —**ничья́ земля́,** no man's land.
ниче́йный *adj.* **1,** *sports; games* drawn; tied. **2,** *colloq.* no man's: ниче́йная земля́, no man's land.
ниче́м *pron., instr. of* **ничто́.**
ничему́ *pron., dat. of* **ничто́.**
ничко́м *adv.* prone; face down.
ничто́ *indef. pron.* [*gen. & acc.* **ничего́;** *dat.* **ничему́;** *instr.* **ниче́м;** *prepl.* **ни** (+ *prep.*) **чём**] nothing. *See also* **ничего́.**

ничто́жество *n.* nonentity; nobody.
ничто́жность *n.f.* **1,** insignificance. **2,** nonentity; nobody.
ничто́жный *adj.* **1,** (*of an amount*) insignificant; infinitesimal; paltry. **2,** insignificant; meaningless. **3,** (*of a person*) worthless; good-for-nothing.
ничу́ть *adv., colloq.* not at all; not the least; not a bit. —**ничу́ть не быва́ло,** *colloq.* **1,** not at all; not in the least. **2,** but it was not that way; but that was not the case.
ничья́ [*gen., dat., & instr.* **ничье́й;** *acc.* **ничью́**] *n., sports; games* tie; draw.
ни́ша *n.* niche; recess; alcove.
нища́ть *v. impfv.* [*pfv.* **обнища́ть**] to become impoverished.
ни́щенка [*gen. pl.* **-нок**] *n.* beggar (woman).
ни́щенский *adj.* **1,** beggarly. **2,** *fig.* paltry.
ни́щенство *n.* **1,** begging. **2,** poverty; destitution.
ни́щенствовать *v. impfv.* [*pres.* **-ствую, -ствуешь**] **1,** to beg; go begging. **2,** to live in poverty.
нищета́ *n.* poverty.
ни́щий *adj.* destitute; poverty-stricken. —*n.* beggar.
но *conj.* but.
Но́белевский *adj., in* **Но́белевская пре́мия,** Nobel Prize.
нобе́лий *n.* nobelium.
нова́тор *n.* innovator. —**нова́торский,** *adj.* innovative. —**нова́торство,** *n.* innovation.
нове́йший *adj., superl. of* **но́вый,** newest; latest.
нове́лла *n.* short story; novella.
новелли́ст *n.* short story writer.
но́венький *adj.* new. —*n., colloq.* **1,** newcomer. **2,** freshman. —**что но́венького?,** *colloq.* what's new?
новизна́ *n.* novelty; newness.
нови́нка [*gen. pl.* **-нок**] *n.* something new: кни́жные нови́нки, new books. —**э́то мне в нови́нку,** it is new to me; it is something I've never done before.
новичо́к [*gen.* **-чка́**] *n.* **1,** novice. **2,** new boy *or* girl (*in school*).
новобра́нец [*gen.* **-нца**] *n.* recruit.
новобра́чный *n., decl. as an adj.* newlywed.
нововведе́ние *n.* innovation.
новогóдний *adj.* New Year's.
новогре́ческий *adj.* modern Greek.
новозаве́тный *adj.* New Testament (*attrib.*).
новозела́ндец [*gen.* **-дца**] *n.m.* [*fem.* **-дка**] New Zealander. —**новозела́ндский,** *adj.* New Zealand (*attrib.*).
новоиспечённый *adj., colloq.* **1,** newly made. **2,** newly appointed.
новокаи́н *n.* novocaine. —**новокаи́новый,** *adj.* novocaine.
новолу́ние *n.* new moon.
новомо́дный *adj.* **1,** in the latest style. **2,** (*of words*) currently fashionable.
новообразова́ние *n.* **1,** new formation. **2,** neoplasm; new growth. **3,** newly coined word.
новообращённый *adj.* newly converted (*to another religion*). —*n.* neophyte; convert; proselyte.
новоприбы́вший *adj.* newly arrived; recently arrived. —*n.* newcomer.
новорождённый *adj.* newborn. —*n.* newborn baby.
новосёл *n.* **1,** new settler. **2,** new tenant.
новосе́лье *n.* **1,** new home. **2,** housewarming.
новостро́йка [*gen. pl.* **-о́ек**] *n.* **1,** new building. **2,** construction project.
но́вость [*pl.* **но́вости, -сте́й, -стя́м**] *n.f.* **1,** news. **2,** a novelty; something new. **3,** newness.
но́вшество *n.* innovation; novelty.
но́вый *adj.* [*short form* **нов, нова́, но́во**] **1,** new. **2,** (*of history, languages, etc.*) modern. —**Но́вый год,** the New Year. —**Но́вый свет,** the New World. —**но́вый стиль,** New Style (*of dates*). —**что но́вого?,** what's new?
новь *n.f.* virgin soil.
нога́ [*acc.* **но́гу;** *pl.* **но́ги, ног, нога́м**] *n.* **1,** leg. **2,** foot. —**быть без ног,** to be falling off one's feet. —**вверх нога́ми,** upside down; topsy-turvy. —**идти́ в но́гу,** to keep in step. —**идти́ в но́гу с,** to keep up with; keep pace with. —**идти́ нога́ за́ ногу,** to amble along. —**к ноге́!,** *mil.* order arms! —**на дру́жеской (***or* **на коро́ткой) ноге́ с,** on good terms with. —**на нога́х, 1,** on one's feet. **2,** awake; up. **3,** on the go. **4,** up and about. —**на ра́вной ноге́ с,** on an equal footing with. —**ни ного́й,** never going to: мы туда́ ни ного́й, we never set foot in there. —**одна́ нога́ здесь, друга́я там,** be quick about it! —**со всех ног,** as fast as one's legs would carry one. —**с головы́ до ног,** from head to toe.
нога́ец [*gen.* **-а́йца**] *n.m.* [*fem.* **-а́йка**] Nogai (*one of a people inhabiting the Caucasus*). —**нога́йский,** *adj.* Nogai.
ноготки́ [*pl.* **-ко́в**] *n. pl.* marigold.
но́готь [*gen.* **-гтя;** *pl.* **но́гти, -те́й, -тя́м**] *n.m.* nail; fingernail; toenail. —**до конца́ ногте́й,** to the tips of one's toes.
нож [*gen.* **ножа́**] *n.* knife. —**быть на ножа́х,** to be at swords' points.
ножево́й *also,* **ножо́вый** *adj.* knife (*attrib.*). —**ножево́й това́р; ножевы́е изде́лия,** cutlery.
но́жик *n.* small knife.
но́жка [*gen. pl.* **-жек**] *n.* **1,** *dim. of* **нога́. 2,** leg (*of a chair, table, etc.*). **3,** stem (*of a goblet*). **4,** stem (*of a mushroom*).
но́жницы [*gen.* **-ниц**] *n. pl.* **1,** scissors. **2,** shears.
ножно́й *adj.* foot (*attrib.*).
но́жны [*gen.* **но́жен**] *n. pl.* scabbard; sheath. *Also,* **ножны́** [*gen.* **ножо́н**].
ножо́вка [*gen. pl.* **-вок**] *n.* handsaw; hacksaw.
ноздрева́тый *adj.* porous.
ноздря́ [*pl.* **но́здри, -ре́й, -ря́м**] *n.* nostril.
нока́ут *n., boxing* knockout.
нокаути́ровать *v. impfv. & pfv.* [*pres.* **-рую, -руешь**] *boxing* to knock out.
нокда́ун *n., boxing* knockdown.
ноктю́рн *n.* nocturne.
нолево́й *adj.* = **нулево́й.**
ноль [*gen.* **ноля́**] *n.m.* = **нуль.**
номенклату́ра *n.* **1,** nomenclature. **2,** *USSR, colloq.* top-level governmental positions. —**номенклату́рный,** *adj.* (*of a post or the person holding it*) top-level.
но́мер [*pl.* **номера́**] *n.* **1,** number. **2,** issue (*of a newspaper*). **3,** size (*of an article of clothing*). **4,** hotel room. **5,** number; item (*on a program*). **6,** *colloq.* trick; ploy: но́мер не прошёл, the ploy didn't work.
номерно́й *adj.* containing a number: номерно́й знак, license plate. —*n.* room attendant (*in a hotel*).
номеро́к [*gen.* **-рка́**] *n.* **1,** small room (*in a hotel*). **2,** check; ticket.

номинáл *n., finance* par; face value.
номинáльный *adj.* nominal.
норá [*pl.* **нóры**] *n.* hole; burrow (*of an animal*).
норвéжец [*gen.* **-жца**] *n.m.* [*fem.* **-жка**] Norwegian. —**норвéжский,** *adj.* Norwegian.
норд *n., naut.* **1,** north. **2,** north wind.
норд-вéст *n., naut.* **1,** northwest. **2,** northwester (*wind*).
нóрдовый *adj., naut.* north.
норд-óст *n., naut.* **1,** northeast. **2,** northeaster (*wind*).
нóрка [*gen. pl.* **-рок**] *n.* **1,** *dim. of* **норá. 2,** mink. —**нóрковый,** *adj.* mink (*attrib.*).
нóрма *n.* **1,** norm; standard. **2,** quota. **3,** rate. —**войти́ в нóрму,** to return to normal.
нормализáция *n.* normalization.
нормализовáть *v. impfv. & pfv.* [*pres.* **-зýю, -зýешь**] **1,** to standardize. **2,** to normalize.
нормáль *n.f., math.* normal.
нормáльно *adv.* normally. —*adj., used predicatively, colloq.* all right; O.K.: всё нормáльно, everything is all right/O.K. —**нормáльность,** *n.f.* normality. —**нормáльный,** *adj.* normal.
нормáндский *adj.* Norman: Нормáндское завоевáние Áнглии, the Norman Conquest.—**Нормáндские островá,** Channel Islands.
нормáнн *n.* Norseman. —**нормáнский; нормáннский,** *adj.* Norse.
нормати́в *n.* norm. —**нормати́вный,** *adj.* normative.
нормировáние *n.* **1,** standardization; setting of norms. **2,** rationing.
нормировáть *v. impfv. & pfv.* [*pres.* **-рýю, -рýешь**] **1,** to standardize; set. **2,** to ration.
нóров *n., colloq.* character; temperament; disposition. —**с нóровом,** (*of a person*) stubborn; strong-willed; (*of a horse*) restive; balky.
норови́стый *adj., colloq.* (*of a horse*) restive; balky.
норови́ть *v. impfv.* [*pres.* **-влю́, -ви́шь**] *colloq.* to try (to).
нос [*2nd loc.* **носý;** *pl.* **носы́**] *n.* **1,** nose. **2,** *naut.* prow; bow. **3,** *geog.* point. —**води́ть зá нос,** to lead (someone) on; string (someone) along; take in. —**из-под сáмого нóса,** from under one's very nose. —**на носý,** near at hand; just around the corner: веснá на носý, spring is just around the corner. —**под сáмым нóсом; пóд носом,** under one's very nose. —**оставáить с нóсом,** *colloq.* to leave (someone) holding the bag. —**остáться с нóсом,** *colloq.* to be left holding the bag. —**с нóса; с нóсу,** *colloq.* apiece; a head.
носáтый *adj., colloq.* big-nosed.
нóсик *n.* **1,** *dim. of* **нос. 2,** spout (*on a teapot, watering can, etc.*).
носи́лки [*gen.* **-лок**] *n. pl.* stretcher; litter.
носи́льщик *n.* porter.
носи́тель *n.m.* **1,** transmitter (*e.g. of new ideas*). **2,** speaker (*of a certain language*). **3,** carrier (*of a disease*).
носи́ть *v. impfv.* [*pres.* **ношý, нóсишь**] **1,** *indeterm. of* **нести́.** Носи́ть орýжие, to bear arms. **2,** to wear. **3,** to bear (characteristics, traces, etc.). **4,** *in* **носи́ть на рукáх,** to dote on. —**носи́ться,** *refl.* **1,** *indeterm. of* **нести́сь. 2,** to rush about; dash about. **3,** (*of clothing*) to wear: э́то плáтье хорошó нóсится, this dress wears well. **4,** (*with* **с** + *instr.*) *colloq.* to fuss (over); make too much (of).
нóска *n.* **1,** carrying. **2,** wearing; wear: от дóлгой нóски, from long wear. **3,** laying (*of eggs*).
нóский *adj.* **1,** *colloq.* giving long wear; durable. **2,** producing eggs in large quantity: нóская кýрица, a good layer.
носовóй *adj.* nose (*attrib.*); nasal. —**носовóй кóнус,** nose cone. —**носовóй платóк,** handkerchief.
носóк [*gen.* **-скá**] *n.* **1,** sock. **2,** toe (*of a shoe*).
носорóг *n.* rhinoceros.
ностальги́я *n.* nostalgia. —**ностальги́ческий,** *adj.* nostalgic.
носýха *n.* coati.
нóта *n.* **1,** *music* note. **2,** *pl.* music: игрáть по нóтам, to play from music. **3,** *dipl.* note. —**разы́грывать (что́-нибудь) как по нóтам,** to carry out like clockwork.
нотáриус *n.* notary public. —**нотариáльный,** *adj.* notary (*attrib.*).
нотáция *n.* **1,** notation. **2,** admonition; talking-to: читáть нотáцию (+ *dat.*), to give someone a talking-to.
нóтка [*gen. pl.* **-ток**] *n.* faint note; trace; hint; suggestion.
нóтный *adj.* music (*attrib.*): нóтный пюпи́тр, music stand. —**нóтный стан,** *music* staff.
нотонóсец [*gen.* **-сца**] *n., music* staff.
ночевáть *v. impfv. & pfv.* [*pres.* **-чýю, -чýешь**] to spend the night.
ночёвка *n., colloq.* spending the night.
ночлéг *n.* **1,** place to spend the night. **2,** spending the night: останови́ться на ночлéг, to stop for the night; spend the night.
ночлéжка [*gen. pl.* **-жек**] *n., colloq.* = **ночлéжный дом.**
ночлéжный *adj., in* **ночлéжный дом,** flophouse.
ночни́к [*gen.* **-никá**] *n.* night light.
ночнóй *adj.* night (*attrib.*). —**ночнóй горшóк,** chamber pot. —**ночнóй стóлик,** night table.
ночь [*pl.* **нóчи, ночéй, ночáм**] *n.f.* night. —**нá ночь, 1,** for the night; overnight. **2,** before going to bed. —**по ночáм,** at night. —**спокóйной нóчи!,** good night!
нóчью *adv.* at night.
нóша *n.* **1,** load. **2,** *fig.* burden.
ношéние *n.* **1,** carrying; bearing. **2,** wearing.
нóщно *adv., in* **дéнно и нóщно,** *colloq.* day and night.
нóющий *adj.* (*of a pain*) gnawing; nagging.
ноя́брь [*gen.* **-бря́**] *n.m.* November. —**ноя́брьский,** *adj.* November (*attrib.*).
нрав *n.* disposition; temperament. —**быть** (*or* **приходи́ться) по нрáву** (+ *dat.*), to please: всё емý не по нрáву, nothing pleases him. *See also* **нрáвы.**
нрáвиться *v.r. impfv.* [*pfv.* **понрáвиться;** *pres.* **-влюсь, -вишься**] (*with dat.*) to please; be to the liking of: онá мне нрáвится, I like her; пьéса мне не понрáвилась, I did not like (*or* enjoy) the play.
нравоучéние *n.* moral admonition.
нравоучи́тельный *adj.* moralizing; moralistic.
нрáвственно *adv.* morally.
нрáвственность *n.f.* **1,** morality. **2,** morals.
нрáвственный *adj.* moral.
нрáвы [*gen.* **нрав**] *n. pl.* customs; ways; way of life.
ну *interj., colloq.* well; well then; why; now: ну, я пошёл, well, I'm off; ну, конéчно!, why of course! —**а ну** (+ *gen.*), to hell with...—**да ну?,** you don't say so! —**ну и...,** what...!: ну и погóда!, what weather! —**ну и что?,** well, what of it?
нугá *n.* nougat.
нýдный *adj., colloq.* **1,** boring; tiresome. **2,** inane.
нуждá [*pl.* **нýжды**] *n.* **1,** (dire) need; dire straits: жить

в нужде́, to live in dire straits. **2,** need; necessity: в слу́чае нужды́, in case of need; if need be. **3,** *pl.* needs: ну́жды населе́ния, the needs of the populace.
нужда́ться *v.r. impfv.* **1,** to be in need; be poor. **2,** (*with* **в** + *prepl.*) to need; be in need of.
ну́жно *adv.* **1,** (one) must; (one) has to; (one) needs to: э́то ну́жно сде́лать сейча́с, this must be done at once; мне ну́жно идти́, I have to go. **2,** needed: для чего́ э́то вам ну́жно?, what do you need that for?
ну́жный *adj.* [*short form* **ну́жен, нужна́, ну́жно, нужны́**] **1,** necessary: ну́жные да́нные, the necessary data. Находи́ть ну́жным (+ *inf.*), to find it necessary to. **2,** needed: я здесь ну́жен (нужна́), I am needed here. **3,** (*with dat.*) one needs: ему́ ну́жен о́тдых, he needs rest; мне нужны́ де́ньги, I need money.
ну́-ка *interj., colloq.* well?; well then?; how about it?
нулево́й *adj.* zero (*attrib.*).
нуль [*gen.* **нуля́**] *n.m.* **1,** zero; naught. **2,** *fig.* (*of a person*) a nothing; a nobody. —**своди́ть к нулю́,** to negate; nullify. —**своди́ться к нулю́,** to come to naught.
нумера́тор *n.* numbering machine.
нумера́ция *n.* numeration; numbering.
нумеро́ванный *adj.* numbered. —**нумеро́ванное ме́сто,** reserved seat.
нумерова́ть *v. impfv.* [*pfv.* **занумерова́ть** *or* **пронумерова́ть;** *pres.* **-ру́ю, -ру́ешь**] to number.
нумизма́тика *n.* numismatics. —**нумизма́т,** *n.* numismatist. —**нумизмати́ческий,** *adj.* numismatic.
ну́нций *n.* nuncio.
нут *n.* chickpea.
ну́трия *n.* coypu; nutria.
нутро́ *n., colloq.* **1,** insides; innards. **2,** interior. **3,** essence. **4,** instinct. —**не по нутру́** (+ *dat.*), not to one's liking.
ны́не *adv.* now.
ны́нешний *adj., colloq.* present.
ны́нче *adv., colloq.* now; nowadays. —**не ны́нче – за́втра,** any day now.
нырну́ть *v., pfv. of* **ныря́ть.**
нырóк [*gen.* **-рка́**] *n.* **1,** *colloq.* dive. **2,** pochard (*duck*).
ныря́льщик *n., colloq.* diver.
ныря́ть *v. impfv.* [*pfv.* **нырну́ть**] to dive.
ны́тик *n., colloq.* whiner.
ныть *v. impfv.* [*pres.* **но́ю, но́ешь**] **1,** to ache. **2,** *colloq.* to whine.
нытьё *n.* **1,** whining; complaining. **2,** dull pain.
нэп *n., abbrev. of* **но́вая экономи́ческая поли́тика,** N.E.P.; New Economic Policy (1921-27).
нюа́нс *n.* nuance.
ню́ни *n. pl., in* **распуска́ть ню́ни,** *colloq.* **1,** to start crying. **2,** to whine; start whining.
ню́ня *n.m. & f., colloq.* crybaby; whiner.
нюх *n., colloq.* **1,** sense of smell (*of an animal*). **2,** *fig.* (keen) sense: име́ть нюх на, to have a nose for.
ню́хательный *adj.* for smelling; to be smelled: ню́хательная соль, smelling salts. —**ню́хательный таба́к,** snuff.
ню́хать *v. impfv.* [*pfv.* **поню́хать**] to smell; sniff; take a whiff of.
ня́нчить *v. impfv.* to nurse; take care of. —**ня́нчиться,** *refl.* (*with* **с** + *instr.*) **1,** to nurse; take care of. **2,** *colloq.* to fuss with.
ня́нька [*gen. pl.* **-нек**] *n., colloq.* = **ня́ня.**
ня́ня *n.* **1,** nurse; nursemaid. **2,** *colloq.* nurse's aide.

О

О, о *n. neut.* fifteenth letter of the Russian alphabet.
о[1] *also,* **об** *and* **обо** *prep.* A, *with prepl.* about; of: говори́ть о поли́тике, to talk about politics; кни́га о Че́хове, a book about Chekhov. Он ду́мает то́лько о себе́, he thinks only of himself. B, *with acc.* **1,** against (*involving contact or collision*): опира́ться о сте́ну, to lean against the wall; во́лны бью́тся о бе́рег, the waves are beating against the shore. **2,** *in* бок о́ бок, side by side; рука́ о́б руку, hand in hand.
о[2] *interj.* oh!
о- *also,* **об-, обо-, объ-** *prefix* **1,** *indicating motion around:* обходи́ть, to walk around; оплыва́ть, to swim around. **2,** *indicating action affecting everyone present:* обноси́ть, to serve (everyone present). **3,** *indicating the gaining of an advantage:* обы́грывать, to beat; defeat; обсчи́тывать, to shortchange. **4,** (*with* **-ся**) *indicating a mistake or misstep:* ослы́шаться, to hear incorrectly; оступи́ться, to stumble. **5,** (*with* **-ся**) *indicating excess:* объеда́ться, to overeat.
оа́зис *n.* oasis.
об *prep.* = **о** (*used when the word following begins with a vowel*).
о́ба [*fem.* **о́бе;** *gen. & prepl.* **обо́их, обе́их;** *dat.* **обо́им, обе́им;** *instr.* **обо́ими, обе́ими**] *numeral, m. & neut.* (*nominative forms govern gen. sing.*) both: о́ба ма́льчика, both boys; обе́ими рука́ми, with both hands. —**смотре́ть** *or* **гляде́ть в о́ба, 1,** to be on one's guard. **2,** (*with* **в/на** + *acc. or* **за** + *instr.*) to keep a watchful eye on.
обагря́ть *v. impfv.* [*pfv.* **обагри́ть**] to give a reddish or purplish hue to. —**обагря́ть кро́вью,** to stain with blood.
обалде́лый *adj., colloq.* dazed; groggy.
обалде́ть *v. pfv., colloq.* to lose one's wits.
обанкро́титься *v.r. pfv.* [*infl.* **-чусь, -тишься**] to go bankrupt.
обая́ние *n.* charm; attraction.
обая́тельный *adj.* charming; enchanting.

обва́л *n.* **1,** collapse; cave-in. **2,** slide; landslide.

обва́ливать *v. impfv.* **1,** [*pfv.* **обвали́ть**] to cause to collapse; bring down. **2,** [*pfv.* **обваля́ть**] to roll (in flour, bread crumbs, etc.). —**обва́ливаться,** *refl.* [*pfv.* **обвали́ться**] to collapse; cave in; come tumbling down.

обвали́ть [*infl.* **-валю́, -ва́лишь**] *v., pfv. of* **обва́ливать** (*in sense #1*). —**обвали́ться,** *refl., pfv. of* **обва́ливаться.**

обваля́ть *v., pfv. of* **обва́ливать** (*in sense #2*).

обва́ривать *v. impfv.* [*pfv.* **обвари́ть**] **1,** to pour boiling water over. **2,** to scald. —**обва́риваться,** *refl.* to scald oneself.

обвари́ть [*infl.* **-варю́, -ва́ришь**] *v., pfv. of* **обва́ривать.** —**обвари́ться,** *refl., pfv. of* **обва́риваться.**

обвева́ть *v. impfv.* [*pfv.* **обве́ять**] (*of the wind*) to blow upon; fan.

обвенча́ть *v., pfv. of* **венча́ть** (*in sense #2*). —**обвенча́ться,** *refl., pfv. of* **венча́ться** (*in sense #2*).

обвёртывать *v. impfv.* [*pfv.* **обверну́ть**] to wrap; bundle.

обве́сить [*infl.* **-шу, -сишь**] *v., pfv. of* **обве́шивать** (*in sense #1*).

обвести́ [*infl. like* **вести́**] *v., pfv. of* **обводи́ть.**

обве́тренный *adj.* **1,** weather-beaten; weather-worn. **2,** (*of one's hands, lips, etc.*) chapped.

обве́трить *v. pfv., usu. in the past passive part.,* to chap. —**обве́триться,** *refl.* **1,** to become weather-beaten. **2,** to become chapped.

обветша́лый *adj.* ramshackle; dilapidated.

обветша́ть *v., pfv. of* **ветша́ть.**

обве́шивать *v. impfv.* **1,** [*pfv.* **обве́сить**] to cheat in weighing. **2,** [*pfv.* **обве́шать**] *colloq.* to hang (with); cover (with).

обве́ять [*infl.* **-ве́ю, -ве́ешь**] *v., pfv. of* **обвева́ть.**

обвива́ть *v. impfv.* [*pfv.* **обви́ть**] to wind around. —**обвива́ться,** *refl.* (*with* **вокру́г**) to wind (around); twine (around); coil (around).

обвине́ние *n.* **1,** accusation; charge. **2,** *law* the prosecution.

обвини́тель *n.m.* **1,** accuser. **2,** prosecutor.

обвини́тельный *adj.* of accusation; accusatory. —**обвини́тельный акт; обвини́тельное заключе́ние,** (bill of) indictment. —**обвини́тельный пригово́р,** verdict of "guilty".

обвини́ть *v., pfv. of* **обвиня́ть.**

обвиня́емый *n., decl. as an adj.* the accused; defendant.

обвиня́ть *v. impfv.* [*pfv.* **обвини́ть**] (*with* **в** + *prepl.*) to accuse (of); charge (with).

обвиса́ть *v. impfv.* [*pfv.* **обви́снуть**] to hang down; droop.

обви́слый *adj., colloq.* drooping.

обви́снуть [*past* **-ви́с, -ла**] *v., pfv. of* **обвиса́ть.**

обви́ть [*infl.* **обовью́, обовьёшь;** *past fem.* **обвила́**] *v., pfv. of* **обвива́ть.** —**обви́ться,** *refl., pfv. of* **обвива́ться.**

обводи́ть *v. impfv.* [*pfv.* **обвести́;** *pres.* **-вожу́, -во́дишь**] **1,** to lead around; walk around; take around. **2,** *sports* to sidestep; dodge. **3,** to enclose; surround; ring. **4,** to circle; outline; draw a line around. **5,** *in* обводи́ть (что́-нибудь) взгля́дом *or* глаза́ми, to look around at. —**обвести́ (кого́-нибудь) вокру́г па́льца,** to twist around one's little finger.

обвола́кивать *v. impfv.* [*pfv.* **обволо́чь**] (*of smoke, clouds, etc.*) to envelop.

обволо́чь [*infl. like* **воло́чь**] *v., pfv. of* **обвола́кивать.**

обвора́живать *v. impfv.* [*pfv.* **обворожи́ть**] to charm; captivate; enchant.

обворова́ть [*infl.* **-ру́ю, -ру́ешь**] *v., pfv. of* **обворо́вывать.**

обворо́вывать *v. impfv.* [*pfv.* **обворова́ть**] *colloq.* to rob.

обворожи́тельный *adj.* charming; enchanting; bewitching.

обворожи́ть *v., pfv. of* **обвора́живать.**

обвяза́ть [*infl.* **-вяжу́, -вя́жешь**] *v., pfv. of* **обвя́зывать.** —**обвяза́ться,** *refl., pfv. of* **обвя́зываться.**

обвя́зывать *v. impfv.* [*pfv.* **обвяза́ть**] to tie around: обвяза́ть го́лову платко́м, to tie a kerchief around one's head. —**обвя́зываться,** *refl.* (*with instr.*) to tie (something) around oneself.

обго́н *n.* passing: обго́н запрещён!, no passing!

обгоня́ть *v. impfv.* [*pfv.* **обогна́ть**] **1,** to pass (*on the road, in a race, etc.*). **2,** *fig.* to outstrip; surpass; excel.

обгора́ть *v. impfv.* [*pfv.* **обгоре́ть**] **1,** to be partially burned. **2,** *colloq.* to get a bad sunburn.

обгоре́лый *adj.* charred; burnt; scorched.

обгоре́ть *v., pfv. of* **обгора́ть.**

обгрыза́ть *v. impfv.* [*pfv.* **обгры́зть**] to nibble (at).

обгры́зть [*infl. like* **гры́зть**] *v., pfv. of* **обгрыза́ть.**

обдава́ть *v. impfv.* [*pfv.* **обда́ть;** *past* **-даю́, -даёшь**] **1,** to douse (with water); splash (with mud). **2,** *impers.* to be seized with; be filled with: меня́ о́бдало хо́лодом, I suddenly felt very cold.

обда́ть [*infl. like* **дать;** *past* **о́бдал, обдала́, о́бдало**] *v., pfv. of* **обдава́ть.**

обде́лать *v., pfv. of* **обде́лывать.**

обдели́ть [*infl.* **-делю́, -де́лишь**] *v., pfv. of* **обделя́ть.**

обде́лывать *v. impfv.* [*pfv.* **обде́лать**] **1,** to finish; dress. **2,** to set (a precious stone). **3,** *colloq.* to arrange; manage; handle.

обделя́ть *v. impfv.* [*pfv.* **обдели́ть**] to cheat (someone) out of his rightful share; give (someone) less than his due.

обдира́ть *v. impfv.* [*pfv.* **ободра́ть**] **1,** to skin; flay. **2,** *colloq.* to lacerate. **3,** *colloq.* to wear out. **4,** *colloq.* to rob; fleece.

обдува́ть *v. impfv.* [*pfv.* **обду́ть**] **1,** (*of the wind*) to blow on. **2,** to blow off (dust, ashes, etc.). **3,** *colloq.* to swindle; dupe.

обду́манный *adj.* **1,** considered; carefully thought out. **2,** deliberate.

обду́мывать *v. impfv.* [*pfv.* **обду́мать**] to think over; consider carefully.

обду́ть [*infl.* **-ду́ю, -ду́ешь**] *v., pfv. of* **обдува́ть.**

о́бе *numeral, fem. of* **о́ба.**

обе́гать *v., pfv. of* **обега́ть** (*in sense #2*).

обега́ть *v. impfv.* [*pfv.* **обежа́ть**] **1,** to run around. **2,** [*pfv. also* **обе́гать**] to run all over; make the rounds of.

обе́д *n.* midday meal; dinner; lunch.

обе́дать *v. impfv.* [*pfv.* **пообе́дать**] to have dinner; have lunch.

обе́денный *adj.* dinner (*attrib.*); lunch (*attrib.*).

обедне́вший *adj.* impoverished.

обедне́ние *n.* impoverishment.

обедне́ть *v., pfv. of* **бедне́ть.**

обедни́ть *v., pfv. of* **обедня́ть.**

обе́дня [*gen. pl.* **-ден**] *n., relig.* Mass.

обедня́ть *v. impfv.* [*pfv.* **обедни́ть**] to impoverish.

обежáть [*infl. like* **бежáть**] *v., pfv. of* **обегáть** (*in sense #1*).
обезбóливание *n.* anesthetization.
обезбóливать *v. impfv.* [*pfv.* **обезбóлить**] to anesthetize.
обезбóливающий *adj.* anesthetic. —**обезбóливающее срéдство,** anesthetic.
обезбóлить *v., pfv. of* **обезбóливать.**
обезвóдить [*infl.* **-жу, -дишь**] *v., pfv. of* **обезвóживать.**
обезвóживание *n.* dehydration.
обезвóживать *v. impfv.* [*pfv.* **обезвóдить**] to dehydrate.
обезврéживать *v. impfv.* [*pfv.* **обезврéдить**] to render harmless.
обезглáвить [*infl.* **-влю, -вишь**] *v., pfv. of* **обезглáвливать.**
обезглáвливание *n.* beheading; decapitation.
обезглáвливать *v. impfv.* [*pfv.* **обезглáвить**] to behead; decapitate.
обездéнежеть *v. pfv., colloq.* to run out of money.
обездóленный *adj.* indigent; destitute.
обездóливать *v. impfv.* [*pfv.* **обездóлить**] **1,** *obs.* to deprive of one's share. **2,** to leave destitute.
обезжи́ривать *v. impfv.* [*pfv.* **обезжи́рить**] to remove the fat from.
обеззарáживание *n.* disinfection; decontamination.
обеззарáживать *v. impfv.* [*pfv.* **обеззарáзить**] to disinfect; decontaminate.
обезземéливать [*pfv.* **обезземéлить**] to dispossess of one's land.
обезлéсение *n.* deforestation.
обезлéсить *v. pfv.* to deforest.
обезли́чивать *v. impfv.* [*pfv.* **обезли́чить**] to rob of one's individuality; depersonalize.
обезлю́деть *v. pfv.* to become depopulated.
обезлю́дить *v. pfv.* to depopulate.
обезобрáживание *n.* disfigurement.
обезобрáживать *v. impfv.* [*pfv.* **обезобрáзить**] to disfigure.
обезопáсить *v. pfv.* [*infl.* **-шу, -сишь**] to secure.
обезорýживать *v. impfv.* [*pfv.* **обезорýжить**] to disarm.
обезýметь *v. pfv.* to lose one's senses; lose one's head.
обезья́на *n.* monkey; ape.
обезья́ний [*fem.* **-нья**] *adj.* **1,** monkey (*attrib.*). **2,** ape-like.
обезья́нничать *v. impfv., colloq.* to ape; imitate.
обезьяноподóбный *adj.* ape-like.
обезьяночеловéк [*pl.* **обезьянолю́ди**] *n.* ape-man.
обели́ск *n.* obelisk.
обеля́ть *v. impfv.* [*pfv.* **обели́ть**] to vindicate; clear of a charge; prove the innocence of.
оберегáть *v. impfv.* [*pfv.* **оберéчь**] to guard; protect.
оберéчь [*infl. like* **берéчь**] *v., pfv. of* **оберегáть.**
обернýть *v., pfv. of* **обёртывать** *and* **оборáчивать.** —**обернýться,** *refl., pfv. of* **обёртываться** *and* **оборáчиваться.**
обёртка [*gen. pl.* **-ток**] *n.* **1,** wrapping; wrapper. **2,** cover (*for a book*).
обертóн *n., music* overtone.
обёрточный *adj.* wrapping: обёрточная бумáга, wrapping paper.
обёртывание *n., med.* pack.
обёртывать *v. impfv.* [*pfv.* **обернýть**] **1,** (*with* **вокрýг**) to wrap (around). **2,** (*with instr. or* **в** + *acc.*) to wrap (in). **3,** *in* **обернýть (когó-нибудь) вокрýг пáльца,** to twist around one's little finger. —**обёртываться,** *refl.* = **оборáчиваться.**
обескрóвливать *v. impfv.* [*pfv.* **обескрóвить**] **1,** to drain of blood; bleed white. **2,** *fig.* to rob of vitality.
обескурáженность *n.f., colloq.* discouragement.
обескурáживать *v. impfv.* [*pfv.* **обескурáжить**] to discourage; dishearten.
обеспáмятеть *v. pfv., colloq.* **1,** to lose one's memory. **2,** to lose consciousness. **3,** to lose one's senses.
обеспéчение *n.* **1,** (*with instr.*) providing (with); supplying (with). **2,** ensuring; securing. **3,** (financial) security. **4,** security; guarantee.
обеспéченность *n.f.* **1,** (*with instr.*) supply: обеспéченность учéбниками, supply of textbooks. **2,** (financial) security; material well-being.
обеспéченный *adj.* well-to-do.
обеспéчивать *v. impfv.* [*pfv.* **обеспéчить**] **1,** to ensure; secure. **2,** (*with instr.*) to provide (with); supply (with). **3,** to provide for; support. **4,** (*with* **от**) *obs.* to protect (from).
обеспокóить *v. pfv.* to worry; trouble; disturb. —**обеспокóиться,** *refl.* to be worried; be disturbed.
обесси́леть *v. pfv.* to lose one's strength; become weak.
обесси́ливать *v. impfv.* [*pfv.* **обесси́лить**] to weaken; debilitate; rob of one's strength.
обесслáвить *v. pfv.* [*infl.* **-влю, -вишь**] to disgrace.
обессмéртить *v. pfv.* [*infl.* **-рчу, -ртишь**] to immortalize.
обесцвéтить [*infl.* **-чу, -тишь**] *v., pfv. of* **обесцвéчивать.**
обесцвéчивание *n.* discoloration.
обесцвéчивать *v. impfv.* [*pfv.* **обесцвéтить**] to discolor.
обесцéнение *n.* depreciation.
обесцéнивать *v. impfv.* [*pfv.* **обесцéнить**] to cheapen; lessen the value of. —**обесцéниваться,** *refl.* to depreciate; decrease in value.
обесчéстить *v., pfv. of* **бесчéстить.**
обéт *n.* vow; pledge.
обетовáнный *adj., in* **обетовáнная земля́,** the Promised Land.
обещáние *n.* promise.
обещáть *v. impfv. & pfv.* **1,** (*with dat.*) to promise. **2,** *impers.* to promise: день обещáет быть хорóшим, the day promises to be nice; it promises to be a nice day.
обжáлование *n., law* appeal.
обжáловать *v. pfv.* [*infl.* **-лую, -луешь**] to appeal (a verdict, decision, etc.).
обжéчь [*infl.* **обожгý, обожжёшь, ...обожгýт;** *past* **обжёг, обожглá**] *v., pfv. of* **обжигáть.** —**обжéчься,** *refl., pfv. of* **обжигáться.**
обживáть *v. impfv.* [*pfv.* **обжи́ть**] *colloq.* to make habitable. —**обживáться,** *refl., colloq.* to make oneself at home; feel at home.
обжигáтельный *adj.* used for burning or baking. —**обжигáтельная печь,** kiln.
обжигáть *v. impfv.* [*pfv.* **обжéчь**] **1,** to burn. **2,** to bake (pottery, bricks, etc.). —**обжигáться,** *refl.* **1,** to burn oneself. **2,** *fig.* to get burned; burn one's fingers.
обжи́ть [*infl.* **-живý, -живёшь;** *past* **óбжил, обжилá, óбжило**] *v., pfv. of* **обживáть.** —**обжи́ться,** *refl.* [*past* **-жи́лся, -лáсь, -лóсь**] *pfv. of* **обживáться.**

обжо́ра *n.m. & f., colloq.* glutton. —**обжо́рливый,** *adj., colloq.* gluttonous. —**обжо́рство,** *n., colloq.* gluttony.

обжу́ливать *v. impfv.* [*pfv.* **обжу́лить**] *colloq.* to swindle; cheat; gyp.

обзавести́сь [*infl. like* **вести́**] *v.r., pfv. of* **обзаводи́ться.**

обзаводи́ться *v.r. impfv.* [*pfv.* **обзавести́сь;** *pres.* **-вожу́сь, -во́дишься**] (*with instr.*) *colloq.* **1,** to acquire; provide oneself with. **2,** to make (friends); start (a family). —**обзаводи́ться хозя́йством,** to set up house.

обзо́р *n.* **1,** observation. **2,** survey; roundup. **3,** field of vision.

обзыва́ть *v. impfv.* [*pfv.* **обозва́ть**] *colloq.* to call (someone something insulting): обозва́ть кого́-нибудь глупцо́м, to call someone a dunce.

обива́ть *v. impfv.* [*pfv.* **оби́ть**] **1,** to upholster; cover. **2,** to knock off; shake off. **3,** *colloq.* to wear out; wear thin. —**обива́ть (все) поро́ги,** to knock on every door.

оби́вка *n.* **1,** upholstering. **2,** upholstery.

оби́да *n.* **1,** offense; insult. **2,** offense; resentment. —**быть в оби́де на** (+ *acc.*), to be offended (*or* angry) with. —**не в оби́ду будь ска́зано,** no offense meant. —**не дать (кого́-нибудь) в оби́ду,** to allow no harm to come to. —**не дава́ться в оби́ду,** not to allow oneself to be pushed around.

оби́деть [*infl.* **оби́жу, оби́дишь**] *v., pfv. of* **обижа́ть.** —**оби́деться,** *refl., pfv. of* **обижа́ться.**

оби́дно *adj., used predicatively* unfortunate; distressing: оби́дно э́то слы́шать, I am sorry to hear it. Оби́дно, что вы опозда́ли, it's a pity that you were late.

оби́дный *adj.* **1,** insulting; offensive. **2,** *colloq.* annoying.

оби́дчивый *adj.* touchy; sensitive. —**оби́дчивость,** *n.f.* touchiness.

оби́дчик *n., colloq.* person who has offended someone.

обижа́ть *v. impfv.* [*pfv.* **оби́деть**] **1,** to offend; hurt the feelings of. **2,** *colloq.* to harm; wrong. —**обижа́ться,** *refl.* (*with* **на** + *acc.*) to take offense (at); be offended (by); resent.

оби́женный *adj.* **1,** offended. Вы оби́жены на меня́?, are you offended/angry/annoyed with me? **2,** resentful.

оби́лие *n.* abundance; plenty.

оби́льный *adj.* abundant; plentiful; bountiful. —**оби́льно,** *adv.* abundantly.

обиня́к [*gen.* **-няка́**] *n., in* **говори́ть обиняка́ми,** to beat around the bush; **говори́ть без обиняко́в,** to speak straight to the point.

обира́ть *v. impfv.* [*pfv.* **обобра́ть**] *colloq.* **1,** to gather; pick. **2,** to rob; fleece.

обита́емый *adj.* inhabited.

обита́тель *n.m.* inhabitant.

обита́ть *v. impfv.* (*with* **в** + *prepl.*) to dwell (in); inhabit.

оби́тель *n.f., obs.* monastery.

оби́тый *adj.* upholstered.

оби́ть [*infl.* **обобью́, обобьёшь**] *v., pfv. of* **обива́ть.**

обихо́д *n.* **1,** everyday life; day-to-day existence. **2,** use: входи́ть в обихо́д, to come into use. —**предме́ты дома́шнего обихо́да,** (everyday) household items.

обихо́дный *adj.* everyday.

обка́пывать *v. impfv., colloq.* **1,** [*pfv.* **обка́пать**] to stain (*by spilling drops of something on*). **2,** [*pfv.* **обкопа́ть**] to dig around.

обка́рмливать *v. impfv.* [*pfv.* **обкорми́ть**] to give (someone) too much to eat; stuff.

обка́тывать *v. impfv.* [*pfv.* **обката́ть**] **1,** to make round or smooth by rolling. **2,** to wear smooth. **3,** to break in (a car, motor, etc.).

обкла́дывать *v. impfv.* [*pfv.* **обложи́ть**] **1,** to surround (*by laying objects around*). **2,** to face (*with stone, marble, etc.*). **3,** (*of clouds*) to cover. *Also impers.*: не́бо обложи́ло ту́чами, the sky is overcast. **4,** to surround; lay siege to. **5,** *impers.* to become coated: у меня́ обложи́ло язы́к, my tongue is coated. —**обкла́дываться,** *refl.* (*with instr.*) to surround oneself (with).

обко́м *n.* regional committee (*contr. of* **областно́й комите́т**).

обкопа́ть *v., pfv. of* **обка́пывать** (*in sense #2*).

обкорми́ть [*infl.* **-кормлю́, -ко́рмишь**] *v., pfv. of* **обка́рмливать.**

обкра́дывать *v. impfv.* [*pfv.* **обокра́сть**] to rob.

обку́ривать *v. impfv.* [*pfv.* **обкури́ть**] **1,** to break in (a pipe). **2,** *colloq.* to stain by exposure to smoke.

обкури́ть [*infl.* **-курю́, -ку́ришь**] *v., pfv. of* **обку́ривать.**

обку́сывать *v. impfv.* [*pfv.* **обкуса́ть**] to bite around the edges of; nibble.

обла́ва *n.* **1,** hunt (*involving surrounding, driving out, and shooting animals*). **2,** (police) raid; roundup; dragnet.

облага́ть *v. impfv.* [*pfv.* **обложи́ть**] to assess; tax. Облага́ть кого́-нибудь нало́гом, to impose a tax on.

облагора́живать *v. impfv.* [*pfv.* **облагоро́дить**] to ennoble.

облада́ние *n.* possession. —**облада́тель,** *n.m.* possessor.

облада́ть *v. impfv.* (*with instr.*) to possess; have.

о́блако [*pl.* **облака́, облако́в**] *n.* cloud.

обла́мывать *v. impfv.* [*pfv.* **oблома́ть** *or* **обломи́ть**] to break off.

обла́пить *v. pfv.* [*infl.* **-плю, -пишь**] *colloq.* (*of an animal*) to grab in its paws.

обласка́ть *v. pfv.* to show kindness toward.

областно́й *adj.* of an oblast; regional; provincial.

о́бласть [*pl.* **о́бласти, -сте́й, -стя́м**] *n.f.* **1,** oblast: моско́вская о́бласть, Moscow oblast. **2,** area; region. **3,** *fig.* field; sphere; domain.

обла́тка [*gen. pl.* **-ток**] *n.* **1,** capsule; tablet. **2,** *relig.* wafer.

облача́ть *v. impfv.* [*pfv.* **облачи́ть**] **1,** to robe; clothe (a clergyman). **2,** *colloq.* to dress up; deck out.

облаче́ние *n.* **1,** *relig.* vestment(s). **2,** *obs.* clothes.

облачи́ть *v., pfv. of* **облача́ть.**

о́блачко [*pl.* **облачка́, -ко́в**] *n., dim. of* **о́блако.**

о́блачность *n.f.* cloudiness.

о́блачный *adj.* **1,** cloud (*attrib.*): о́блачный покро́в, cloud cover. **2,** cloudy.

обла́ять *v. pfv.* [*infl.* **-ла́ю, -ла́ешь**] *colloq.* to bark furiously at.

облега́ть *v. impfv.* [*pfv.* **обле́чь**] **1,** to envelop; shroud. **2,** [*impfv. only*] (*of clothes*) to fit snugly; cling to.

облегча́ть *v. impfv.* [*pfv.* **облегчи́ть**] **1,** to lighten. **2,** to ease; facilitate. **3,** to ease; relieve; alleviate. —**облегча́ться,** *refl.* **1,** to lighten; become lighter. **2,** to become easier. **3,** to be relieved.

облегче́ние *n.* **1,** lightening; facilitating. **2,** (feeling of) relief.

облегчённый *adj.* **1,** made lighter. **2,** of relief: облегчённый вздох, sigh of relief. —**облегчённо,** *adv.* with (a sense of) relief.

облегчи́ть *v., pfv. of* **облегча́ть.** —**облегчи́ться,** *refl., pfv. of* **облегча́ться.**

обледене́лый *adj.* ice-covered; ice-coated.

обледене́ние *n.* icing up; icing over.

обледене́ть *v. pfv.* to ice up; be coated with ice.

облеза́ть *v. impfv.* [*pfv.* **обле́зть**] *colloq.* **1,** to lose one's fur; become mangy. **2,** (*of something painted*) to peel. **3,** (*of paint, varnish, etc.*) to peel off.

обле́злый *adj., colloq.* **1,** (*of an animal*) mangy. **2,** with the paint having worn off; shabby.

обле́зть [*infl. like* **лезть**] *v., pfv. of* **облеза́ть.**

облека́ть *v. impfv.* [*pfv.* **обле́чь**] **1,** *obs.* to clothe. **2,** to envelop; shroud. **3,** to vest (with power, authority, etc.). **4,** (*with* **в** + *acc.*) to express; couch (in certain language).

обле́ниваться *v.r. impfv.* [*pfv.* **облени́ться**] to become lazy.

облени́ться [*infl.* **-леню́сь, -ле́нишься**] *v., pfv. of* **обле́ниваться.**

облепи́ть [*infl.* **-леплю́, -ле́пишь**] *v., pfv. of* **облепля́ть.**

облепля́ть *v. impfv.* [*pfv.* **облепи́ть**] **1,** to stick to; cling to. **2,** to cover; plaster. **3,** *fig., colloq.* to swarm around.

облета́ть[1] *v. impfv.* [*pfv.* **облете́ть**] **1,** to fly around. **2,** to fly all over. **3,** *fig.* to spread all over: весть облете́ла весь го́род, the news spread all over town. **4,** (*of leaves*) to fall.

облета́ть[2] *v. pfv.* **1,** to fly all over. **2,** to test-fly.

облете́ть [*infl.* **-чу́, -ти́шь**] *v., pfv. of* **облета́ть**[1].

обле́чь *v. pfv.* **1,** [*infl. like* **лечь**] *pfv. of* **облега́ть. 2,** [*infl. like* **течь**] *pfv. of* **облека́ть.**

облива́ние *n.* **1,** dousing (*with water*). **2,** douche.

облива́ть *v. impfv.* [*pfv.* **обли́ть**] **1,** to pour water over; douse. **2,** to cover (*with tears, sweat, etc.*). **3,** to soil; stain (*by spilling something on*): облива́ть ска́терть су́пом, to spill soup all over the tablecloth. —**облива́ть (кого́-нибудь) гря́зью** *or* **помо́ями,** to vilify; drag through the mud.

облига́ция *n., finance* bond.

облиза́ть [*infl.* **-лижу́, -ли́жешь**] *v., pfv. of* **обли́зывать.** —**облиза́ться,** *refl., pfv. of* **обли́зываться.**

обли́зывать *v. impfv.* [*pfv.* **облиза́ть**] **1,** to lick. **2,** *in* **па́льчики обли́жешь,** you'll love it! —**обли́зываться,** *refl.* **1,** to lick oneself. **2,** [*impfv. only*] to lick one's lips; *fig.* lick one's chops.

о́блик *n.* **1,** look; appearance. **2,** *fig.* character; make-up.

облиня́ть *v. pfv., colloq.* to fade.

обли́ть [*infl.* **оболью́, обольёшь;** *past* **о́блил** *or* **обли́л, облила́, о́блило** *or* **обли́ло**] *v., pfv. of* **облива́ть.**

облицева́ть [*infl.* **-цу́ю, -цу́ешь**] *v., pfv. of* **облицо́вывать.**

облицо́вка *n.* facing; revetment.

облицо́вывать *v. impfv.* [*pfv.* **облицева́ть**] to face (*with stone, marble, etc.*).

облича́ть *v. impfv.* [*pfv.* **обличи́ть**] **1,** to expose (wrongs, misdeeds, etc.). **2,** [*impfv. only*] to reveal; indicate. Всё облича́ет в нём вое́нного, everything points to his being a military man.

обличе́ние *n.* exposure.

обличи́тель *n.m.* exposer. —**обличи́тельный,** *adj.* serving to expose something.

обличи́ть *v., pfv. of* **облича́ть.**

обли́чье *n., colloq.* look; appearance.

облобыза́ть *v. pfv., obs.* to kiss.

обложе́ние *n.* **1,** levying: обложе́ние нало́гами, levying of taxes. **2,** *obs.* siege.

обложи́ть [*infl.* **-ложу́, -ло́жишь**] *v., pfv. of* **обкла́дывать** *and* **облага́ть.** —**обложи́ться,** *refl., pfv. of* **обкла́дываться.**

обло́жка [*gen. pl.* **-жек**] *n.* **1,** cover (*of a book or magazine*). **2,** folder (*for papers*); case (*for documents*).

обложно́й *adj., in* **обложно́й до́ждь,** *colloq.* steady downpour.

облока́чиваться *v.r. impfv.* [*pfv.* **облокоти́ться**] (*with* **на** *or* **о** + *acc.*) to lean one's elbows (on *or* against).

облокоти́ться [*infl.* **-кочу́сь, -ко́тишься** *or* **-коти́шься**] *v.r., pfv. of* **облока́чиваться.**

облома́ть *v., pfv. of* **обла́мывать.**

обломи́ть [*infl.* **-ломлю́, -ло́мишь**] *v., pfv. of* **обла́мывать.**

обло́мовщина *n.* lethargy; apathy; sluggishness (*after* **Обло́мов,** *hero of the novel of the same name by Goncharov*).

обло́мок [*gen.* **-мка**] *n.* **1,** fragment. **2,** *pl.* wreckage; debris.

облупи́ть [*infl.* **-луплю́, -лу́пишь**] *v., pfv. of* **лупи́ть** (*in sense #1*) *and* **облу́пливать.** —**облупи́ться,** *refl., pfv. of* **лупи́ться** *and* **облу́пливаться.**

облу́пливать *v. impfv.* [*pfv.* **облупи́ть**] *colloq.* **1,** to peel; shell. **2,** *fig.* to swindle; fleece. —**облу́пливаться,** *refl.* (*of paint, plaster, etc.*) to come off; peel off.

облуча́ть *v. impfv.* [*pfv.* **облучи́ть**] to treat with rays; expose to rays.

облуче́ние *n.* irradiation; exposure to radiation; radiation treatment.

облучи́ть *v., pfv. of* **облуча́ть.**

облучо́к [*gen.* **-чка́**] *n.* coachman's seat.

облущи́ть *v., pfv. of* **лущи́ть.**

облысе́лый *adj.* bald.

облысе́ть *v., pfv. of* **лысе́ть.**

облюбова́ть *v. pfv.* [*infl.* **-бу́ю, -бу́ешь**] to choose; select; settle on.

обма́зать [*infl.* **-ма́жу, -ма́жешь**] *v., pfv. of* **обма́зывать.**

обма́зывать *v. impfv.* [*pfv.* **обма́зать**] **1,** to coat (with). **2,** to smear (with).

обма́кивать *v. impfv.* [*pfv.* **обмакну́ть**] to dip.

обма́н *n.* **1,** deception; deceit; fraud. **2,** illusion; delusion. —**обма́н зре́ния; опти́ческий обма́н,** optical illusion.

обма́нка *n., in* **рогова́я обма́нка,** hornblende; **смоляна́я обма́нка,** pitchblende.

обма́нный *adj.* fraudulent; deceitful.

обману́ть [*infl.* **-ману́, -ма́нешь**] *v., pfv. of* **обма́нывать.** —**обману́ться,** *refl., pfv. of* **обма́нываться.**

обма́нчивый *adj.* **1,** deceptive. **2,** illusory.

обма́нщик *n.* one who deceives; faker; cheat.

обма́нывать *v. impfv.* [*pfv.* **обману́ть**] **1,** to deceive. **2,** to trick; cheat. **3,** to disappoint; let down. **4,** to betray (someone's trust); fail to live up to (hopes, expectations, etc.). **5,** to be unfaithful to (one's spouse). **6,** to seduce. —**обма́нываться,** *refl.* **1,** to be deceived. **2,** to be mistaken.

обма́тывать *v. impfv.* [*pfv.* **обмота́ть**] to wind around; wrap around. —**обма́тываться,** *refl.* **1,** (*with* *instr.*) to wrap oneself in. **2,** (*with* **вокру́г**) to wrap around; be wrapped around.

обма́хивать *v. impfv.* [*pfv.* **обмахну́ть**] **1,** to fan. **2,** to brush off. **3,** to brush away. —**обма́хиваться,** *refl.* to fan oneself.

обма́чивать *v. impfv.* [*pfv.* **обмочи́ть**] to wet; moisten.

обмеле́ть *v., pfv. of* **меле́ть.**

обме́н *n.* exchange. —**обме́н веще́ств,** metabolism.

обме́нивать *v. impfv.* [*pfv.* **обменя́ть**] to exchange; trade; swap (*one thing for another*). —**обме́ниваться,** *refl.* **1,** (*of two people*) to trade; swap; make a trade. **2,** (*with instr.*) to exchange (*similar things*): обме́ниваться места́ми, to exchange places. Обме́ниваться впечатле́ниями, to compare notes.

обмени́ть *v. pfv.* [*infl.* **-меню́, -ме́нишь**] *colloq.* to exchange.

обме́нный *adj.* exchange (*attrib.*).

обменя́ть *v., pfv. of* **обме́нивать.** —**обменя́ться,** *refl., pfv. of* **обме́ниваться.**

обме́р *n.* **1,** measurement. **2,** *colloq.* dishonesty in measuring.

обмере́ть [*infl.* **обомру́, обомрёшь;** *past* **о́бмер, обмерла́, о́бмерло**] *v., pfv. of* **обмира́ть.**

обме́ривать *v. impfv.* [*pfv.* **обме́рить**] **1,** to measure. **2,** to cheat in measuring.

обмести́ [*infl. like* **мести́**] *v., pfv. of* **обмета́ть**[1].

обмета́ть[1] *v. impfv.* [*pfv.* **обмести́**] to sweep off; dust off; brush off.

обмета́ть[2] [*infl.* **-мечу́, -ме́чешь**] *v., pfv. of* **обмётывать.**

обмётывать *v. impfv.* [*pfv.* **обмета́ть**] *sewing* to overcast.

обмина́ть *v. impfv.* [*pfv.* **обмя́ть**] to press down; trample down.

обмира́ть *v. impfv.* [*pfv.* **обмере́ть**] *colloq.* **1,** to faint. **2,** to go numb (*from fear, shock, etc.*). **3,** (*of one's heart*) to skip a beat.

обмозгова́ть [*infl.* **-гу́ю, -гу́ешь**] *v., pfv. of* **обмозго́вывать.**

обмозго́вывать *v. impfv.* [*pfv.* **обмозгова́ть**] *colloq.* to think over; mull over.

обмола́чивать *v. impfv.* [*pfv.* **обмолоти́ть**] to thresh.

обмо́лвиться *v.r. impfv.* [*infl.* **-влюсь, -вишься**] **1,** to make a slip of the tongue. **2,** (*with instr.*) to utter.

обмо́лвка [*gen. pl.* **-вок**] *n.* slip of the tongue.

обмолоти́ть [*infl.* **-лочу́, -ло́тишь**] *v., pfv. of* **обмола́чивать.**

обмора́живать *v. impfv.* [*pfv.* **обморо́зить**] to get (a part of one's body) frostbitten: я обморо́зил себе́ ру́ки, my hands are frostbitten. —**обмора́живаться,** *refl.* to suffer frostbite.

обморо́жение *also,* **обмороже́ние** *n.* frostbite.

обморо́женный *adj.* frostbitten.

обморо́зить [*infl.* **-жу, -зишь**] *v., pfv. of* **обмора́живать.** —**обморо́зиться,** *refl., pfv. of* **обмора́живаться.**

о́бморок *n.* fainting spell. —**упа́сть в о́бморок,** to faint.

обморо́чить *v., pfv. of* **моро́чить.**

обмота́ть *v., pfv. of* **обма́тывать.** —**обмота́ться,** *refl., pfv. of* **обма́тываться.**

обмо́тки [*gen.* **-ток**] *n. pl.* puttees.

обмочи́ть [*infl.* **-мочу́, -мо́чишь**] *v., pfv. of* **обма́чивать.**

обмундирова́ние *n.* **1,** fitting out (*with uniforms*). **2,** uniform.

обмундирова́ть *v. pfv.* [*infl.* **-ру́ю, -ру́ешь**] to fit out (*with uniforms*).

обмундиро́вка *n., colloq.* = **обмундирова́ние.**

обмыва́ть *v. impfv.* [*pfv.* **обмы́ть**] to wash; bathe. —**обмыва́ться,** *refl.* to bathe (oneself).

обмы́лок [*gen.* **-лка**] *n., colloq.* remaining piece of a bar of soap.

обмы́ть [*infl.* **-мо́ю, -мо́ешь**] *v., pfv. of* **обмыва́ть.** —**обмы́ться,** *refl., pfv. of* **обмыва́ться.**

обмяка́ть *v. impfv.* [*pfv.* **обмя́кнуть**] *colloq.* **1,** to become soft. **2,** *fig.* to become flabby.

обмя́кнуть [*past* **-мя́к, -ла**] *v., pfv. of* **обмяка́ть.**

обмя́ть [*infl.* **обомну́, обомнёшь**] *v., pfv. of* **обмина́ть.**

обнагле́ть *v., pfv. of* **нагле́ть.**

обнадёживать *v. impfv.* [*pfv.* **обнадёжить**] to reassure; give hope to; raise the hopes of.

обнажа́ть *v. impfv.* [*pfv.* **обнажи́ть**] **1,** to bare; expose; uncover. **2,** to denude. **3,** to draw; unsheathe (a sword). **4,** *fig.* to reveal; lay bare. **5,** *mil.* to expose. —**обнажа́ться,** *refl.* **1,** to take off all one's clothes. **2,** to be exposed. **3,** to be denuded.

обнажённый *adj.* bare; naked; nude.

обнажи́ть *v., pfv. of* **обнажа́ть.** —**обнажи́ться,** *refl., pfv. of* **обнажа́ться.**

обнаро́дование *n.* promulgation.

обнаро́довать *v. pfv.* [*infl.* **-дую, -дуешь**] to promulgate.

обнару́жение *also,* **обнаруже́ние** *n.* **1,** discovery; detection. **2,** revelation; disclosure.

обнару́живать *v. impfv.* [*pfv.* **обнару́жить**] **1,** to reveal; display; show. **2,** to discover.

обна́шивать *v. impfv.* [*pfv.* **обноси́ть**] *colloq.* **1,** to wear in; break in (new clothes). **2,** to wear out (clothes). —**обна́шиваться,** *refl., colloq.* **1,** (*of new clothes*) to become broken in. **2,** (*of clothes*) to wear out.

обнести́ [*infl. like* **нести́**] *v., pfv. of* **обноси́ть**[1].

обнима́ть *v. impfv.* [*pfv.* **обня́ть**] **1,** to embrace; hug. **2,** *fig.* to engulf; envelop. **3,** *fig.* to take in; embrace. —**обнима́ться,** *refl.* (*of two people*) to embrace; hug.

обни́мка *n., colloq., in* **в обни́мку,** in each other's embrace.

обнища́лый *adj.* impoverished; destitute.

обнища́ние *n.* impoverishment; destitution.

обнища́ть *v., pfv. of* **нища́ть.**

обно́ва *n., colloq.* = **обно́вка.**

обнови́ть [*infl.* **-влю́, -ви́шь**] *v., pfv. of* **обновля́ть.**

обно́вка [*gen. pl.* **-вок**] *n., colloq.* article of clothing just bought; new acquisition; new outfit.

обновле́ние *n.* **1,** renovation. **2,** renewal. **3,** replenishment.

обновля́ть *v. impfv.* [*pfv.* **обнови́ть**] **1,** to renovate; refurbish; revamp. **2,** to renew; revitalize. **3,** to replenish. **4,** *colloq.* to wear for the first time.

обноси́ть[1] *v. impfv.* [*pfv.* **обнести́;** *pres.* **-ношу́, -но́сишь**] **1,** to carry around. **2,** to enclose; fence in. **3,** to serve (everyone): обноси́ть госте́й шампа́нским, to serve champagne to all the guests. **4,** to pass by (*while serving*); not serve.

обноси́ть[2] [*infl.* **-ношу́, -но́сишь**] *v., pfv. of* **обна́-**

шивать. —**обноси́ться,** *refl.* **1,** *pfv. of* **обна́шиваться. 2,** to wear out all one's clothes.
обно́ски [*gen.* **-сков**] *n. pl., colloq.* old clothes.
обня́ть [*infl.* **-ниму́, -ни́мешь;** *past* **о́бнял, обняла́, о́бняло**] *v., pfv. of* **обнима́ть.** —**обня́ться,** *refl.* [*past* **обня́лся** *or* **обнялся́, -ла́сь, -ло́сь, -ли́сь**] *pfv. of* **обнима́ться.**
обо *prep.* = **о** (*used before* **мне, всем, всей,** *and* **всех.**
обобра́ть [*infl.* **оберу́, оберёшь;** *past fem.* **обобрала́**] *v., pfv. of* **обира́ть.**
обобща́ть *v. impfv.* [*pfv.* **обобщи́ть**] to summarize; synthesize.
обобще́ние *n.* **1,** summarizing; synthesizing. **2,** generalization.
обобществи́ть [*infl.* **-влю́, -ви́шь**] *v., pfv. of* **обобществля́ть.**
обобществле́ние *n.* socialization; collectivization.
обобществля́ть *v. impfv.* [*pfv.* **обобществи́ть**] to socialize; collectivize.
обобщи́ть *v., pfv. of* **обобща́ть.**
обогаща́ть *v. impfv.* [*pfv.* **обогати́ть**] to enrich. —**обогаща́ться,** *refl.* **1,** to get rich; enrich oneself. **2,** *fig.* to be enriched.
обогаще́ние *n.* enrichment.
обогна́ть [*infl.* **обгоню́, обго́нишь;** *past fem.* **обогнала́**] *v., pfv. of* **обгоня́ть.**
обогну́ть *v., pfv. of* **огиба́ть.**
обоготворе́ние *n.* deification.
обоготворя́ть *v. impfv.* [*pfv.* **обоготвори́ть**] to deify.
обогрева́ние *n.* heating.
обогрева́тель *n.m.* **1,** heater. **2,** defroster.
обогрева́ть *v. impfv.* [*pfv.* **обогре́ть**] to warm; heat. —**обогрева́ться,** *refl.* to warm up; get warm.
о́бод [*pl.* **обо́дья, обо́дьев**] *n.* rim (*of a wheel*).
ободо́к [*gen.* **-дка́**] *n.* **1,** thin rim; ring. **2,** band.
ободо́чный *adj., in* **ободо́чная кишка́,** *anat.* colon.
ободра́нец [*gen.* **-нца**] *n., colloq.* ragamuffin.
обо́дранный *adj., colloq.* ragged; torn; tattered.
ободра́ть [*infl.* **обдеру́, обдерёшь;** *past fem.* **ободрала́**] *v., pfv. of* **обдира́ть.**
ободре́ние *n.* encouragement; reassurance. —**ободри́тельный,** *adj.* encouraging; reassuring.
ободря́ть *v. impfv.* [*pfv.* **ободри́ть**] to cheer up; hearten; encourage; reassure. —**ободря́ться,** *refl.* to cheer up; take heart.
обо́его *numeral, obs.* of both. —**ли́ца обо́его по́ла,** people of both sexes.
обожа́ние *n.* adoration.
обожа́тель *n.m., colloq.* worshiper; admirer.
обожа́ть *v. impfv.* to adore; worship.
обожда́ть *v. pfv.* [*infl. like* **ждать**] *colloq.* to wait; wait a while.
обожестви́ть [*infl.* **-влю́, -ви́шь**] *v., pfv. of* **обожествля́ть.**
обожествле́ние *n.* deification.
обожествля́ть *v. impfv.* [*pfv.* **обожестви́ть**] to deify.
обо́з *n.* line; string; column (*of vehicles*).
обозва́ть [*infl.* **обзову́, обзовёшь;** *past fem.* **обозвала́**] *v., pfv. of* **обзыва́ть.**
обозли́ть *v., pfv. of* **злить.** —**обозли́ться,** *refl., pfv. of* **зли́ться.**
обозна́ться *v.r. pfv., colloq.* to mistake someone for someone else.
обознача́ть *v. impfv.* [*pfv.* **обозна́чить**] **1,** to mark; indicate; designate. **2,** [*impfv. only*] to mean; signify; denote. **3,** to highlight; accentuate (*visually*). —**обознача́ться,** *refl.* **1,** to appear; become visible. **2,** to be felt; be sensed. **3,** to become clear.
обозначе́ние *n.* **1,** indication. **2,** symbol; designation.
обозна́чить *v., pfv. of* **обознача́ть.** —**обозна́читься,** *refl., pfv. of* **обознача́ться.**
обозрева́тель *n.m.* commentator; columnist.
обозрева́ть *v. impfv.* [*pfv.* **обозре́ть**] **1,** to look around; survey; view. **2,** *fig.* to review; survey.
обозре́ние *n.* **1,** viewing. **2,** review; survey. **3,** review (*publication*). **4,** *theat.* revue.
обозре́ть [*infl.* **-зрю́, -зри́шь**] *v., pfv. of* **обозрева́ть.**
обозри́мый *adj.* visible. —**в обозри́мом бу́дущем,** in the foreseeable future.
обо́и [*gen.* **обо́ев**] *n. pl.* wallpaper.
обо́йма *n.* cartridge clip.
обо́йный *adj.* wallpaper (*attrib.*).
обойти́ [*infl.* **обойду́, обойдёшь;** *past* **обошёл, обошла́, обошло́**] *v., pfv. of* **обходи́ть.** —**обойти́сь,** *refl., pfv. of* **обходи́ться.**
обо́йщик *n.* **1,** upholsterer. **2,** paperhanger.
о́бок *adv., colloq.* alongside. —*prep., with gen., colloq.* alongside.
обокра́сть [*infl.* **обкраду́, обкрадёшь**] *v., pfv. of* **обкра́дывать.**
оболва́нить *v. pfv., colloq.* to dupe; make a fool of.
оболга́ть *v. pfv.* [*infl. like* **лгать**] to slander; calumniate.
оболо́чка [*gen. pl.* **-чек**] *n.* **1,** shell (*of a fruit or seed*). **2,** *anat.* membrane: сли́зистая оболо́чка, mucous membrane. **3,** *fig.* shell: вне́шняя оболо́чка, one's outer shell. —**ра́дужная оболо́чка,** iris. —**рогова́я оболо́чка,** cornea. —**се́тчатая оболо́чка,** retina.
обо́лтус *n., colloq.* blockhead; oaf.
обольсти́тель *n.m.* seducer. —**обольсти́тельный,** *adj.* seductive.
обольсти́ть [*infl.* **-льщу́, -льсти́шь**] *v., pfv. of* **обольща́ть.** —**обольсти́ться,** *refl., pfv. of* **обольща́ться.**
обольща́ть *v. impfv.* [*pfv.* **обольсти́ть**] **1,** to beguile. **2,** to seduce. —**обольща́ться,** *refl.* **1,** [*impfv. only*] to flatter oneself; delude oneself. **2,** (*with instr.*) to be carried away (by): обольща́ться успе́хами, to be carried away by one's own success; let success go to one's head.
обольще́ние *n.* **1,** seduction. **2,** lure; temptation. **3,** delusion.
обомле́ть *v. pfv., colloq.* to be stunned; freeze (*in shock, surprise, etc.*).
обомше́лый *adj.* moss-grown.
обоня́ние *n.* sense of smell. —**обоня́тельный,** *adj.* olfactory.
обоня́ть *v. impfv.* to smell (something).
обора́чивать *v. impfv.* [*pfv.* **оберну́ть**] to turn. —**обора́чиваться,** *refl.* **1,** to turn around; look around. **2,** *fig.* to turn out; work out. **3,** *colloq.* to go and return. **4,** *colloq.* to manage; get by.
оборва́нец [*gen.* **-нца**] *n., colloq.* vagabond; hobo.
обо́рванный *adj.* ragged; torn; tattered.
оборва́ть [*infl. like* **рвать**] *v., pfv. of* **обрыва́ть.** —**оборва́ться,** *refl., pfv. of* **обрыва́ться.**
обо́рвыш *n., colloq.* ragamuffin.
обо́рка [*gen. pl.* **-рок**] *n.* frill; flounce; ruffle.
оборо́на *n.* **1,** defense. **2,** defensive: быть в оборо́не, to be on the defensive. **3,** defenses.

оборони́тельный *adj.* defensive.

оборони́ть *v., pfv. of* **обороня́ть.** —**оборони́ться,** *refl., pfv. of* **обороня́ться.**

оборо́нный *adj.* defense (*attrib.*).

обороня́ть *v. impfv.* [*pfv.* **оборони́ть**] to defend. —**обороня́ться,** *refl.* to defend oneself.

оборо́т *n.* **1,** revolution: сто оборо́тов в мину́ту, 100 r.p.m. **2,** *fig.* turn: оборо́т ре́чи, turn of speech. Приня́ть дурно́й оборо́т, to take a bad turn; take a turn for the worse. **3,** use; circulation: пуска́ть в оборо́т, to put into circulation. **4,** back; reverse side: смотри́ на оборо́те, please turn over. **5,** *finance* turnover. —**брать в оборо́т, 1,** to take in hand. **2,** to take to task.

о́боротень [*gen.* **-тня**] *n.m.* werewolf.

оборо́тливый *adj., colloq.* clever; resourceful. *Also,* **оборо́тистый.**

оборо́тный *adj.* **1,** *finance* circulating; negotiable. Оборо́тный капита́л, working capital. **2,** (*of a side*) back; reverse.

обору́дование *n.* **1,** equipping. **2,** equipment.

обору́довать *v. impfv. & pfv.* [*pres.* **-дую, -дуешь**] to equip.

обоснова́ние *n.* **1,** substantiation. **2,** basis; grounds.

обосно́ванный *adj.* sound; well-founded. —**обосно́ванность,** *n.f.* validity.

обоснова́ть [*infl.* **-ную́, -нуёшь**] *v., pfv. of* **обосно́вывать.** —**обоснова́ться,** *refl., pfv. of* **обосно́вываться.**

обосно́вывать *v. impfv.* [*pfv.* **обоснова́ть**] to substantiate. —**обосно́вываться,** *refl.* **1,** to be substantiated. **2,** to settle (*in a certain place*).

обосо́бить [*infl.* **-блю, -бишь**] *v., pfv. of* **обособля́ть.** —**обосо́биться,** *refl., pfv. of* **обособля́ться.**

обособле́ние *n.* isolation.

обосо́бленный *adj.* **1,** isolated; separate. **2,** solitary.

обособля́ть *v. impfv.* [*pfv.* **обосо́бить**] to isolate. —**обособля́ться,** *refl.* to stand apart; remain aloof.

обостре́ние *n.* **1,** intensification. **2,** aggravation; exacerbation.

обострённый *adj.* **1,** (*of facial features*) prominent. **2,** (*of the senses*) unusually keen. **3,** (*of relations*) strained.

обостря́ть *v. impfv.* [*pfv.* **обостри́ть**] **1,** to intensify; increase; heighten. **2,** to aggravate; exacerbate; strain. —**обостря́ться,** *refl.* **1,** to become more acute. **2,** (*of the senses*) to become keener. **3,** (*of pain*) to become more intense. **4,** (*of relations*) to be strained; worsen.

обо́чина *n.* **1,** side of a road; shoulder. **2,** curb.

обою́дный *adj.* mutual; reciprocal. —**обою́дно,** *adv.* mutually. —**обою́дность,** *n.f.* mutuality; reciprocity.

обоюдоо́стрый *adj.* double-edged.

обраба́тывать *v. impfv.* [*pfv.* **обрабо́тать**] **1,** to work; treat; process. **2,** to till; cultivate. **3,** to cleanse (a wound). **4,** to work up; put in final form. **5,** to refine; perfect. **6,** *colloq.* to work on; work over (someone); indoctrinate.

обрабо́тка *n.* **1,** working; treatment; processing. **2,** tillage; cultivation. **3,** refinement. **4,** *colloq.* indoctrination. —**брать в обрабо́тку,** to work on (someone); twist someone's arm.

обра́довать *v., pfv. of* **ра́довать.** —**обра́доваться,** *refl., pfv. of* **ра́доваться.**

о́браз *n.* **1,** image. **2,** way; mode; manner: о́браз жи́зни, way of life; о́браз мы́слей, way of thinking. О́браз правле́ния, form of government. **3,** [*pl.* **образа́**] icon. **4,** *used in forming adverbial expressions:* до́лжным о́бразом, properly; коренны́м о́бразом, radically; суще́ственным о́бразом, substantially. —**гла́вным о́бразом,** chiefly; mainly; for the most part. —**каки́м о́бразом?,** how?; in what way? —**не́которым о́бразом,** of sorts; after a fashion. —**нико́им о́бразом,** under no circumstances. —**ра́вным о́бразом,** by the same token. —**таки́м о́бразом, 1,** this way; like this. **2,** thus.

обра́зе́ц [*gen.* **-зца́**] *n.* **1,** sample: образе́ц обо́ев, a wallpaper sample. **2,** model: образе́ц самоотве́рженности, a model of selflessness. **3,** pattern.

о́бразно *adv.* **1,** vividly. **2,** using imagery. —**о́бразно говоря́,** figuratively speaking.

о́бразность *n.f.* **1,** vividness. **2,** imagery.

о́бразный *adj.* **1,** vivid; colorful; graphic. **2,** using imagery.

образова́ние *n.* **1,** formation. **2,** education.

образо́ванный *adj.* educated; cultured; cultivated.

образова́тельный *adj.* educational.

образова́ть [*infl.* **-зу́ю, -зу́ешь**] *v., pfv. of* **образо́вывать.** —**образова́ться,** *refl., pfv. of* **образо́вываться.**

образо́вывать *v. impfv.* [*pfv.* **образова́ть**] to form. —**образо́вываться,** *refl.* **1,** to form; appear; come into being. **2,** *colloq.* to be all right: всё образу́ется, everything will be all right.

образу́мить *v. pfv.* [*infl.* **-млю, -мишь**] *colloq.* to bring to reason. —**образу́миться,** *refl., colloq.* to come to one's senses.

образцо́вый *adj.* model; exemplary.

обра́зчик *n.* **1,** sample. **2,** (*with gen.*) *fig., colloq.* sample (of); example (of).

обрамля́ть *v. impfv.* [*pfv.* **обра́мить**] to frame.

обраста́ть *v. impfv.* [*pfv.* **обрасти́**] (*with instr.*) **1,** to become overgrown (with). **2,** *colloq.* to be covered (with a layer of). **3,** *colloq.* to surround oneself (with).

обрасти́ [*infl. like* **расти́**] *v., pfv. of* **обраста́ть.**

обрати́мость *n.f.* **1,** reversibility. **2,** convertibility.

обрати́мый *adj.* **1,** reversible. **2,** convertible.

обрати́ть [*infl.* **-щу́, -ти́шь**] *v., pfv. of* **обраща́ть.** —**обрати́ться,** *refl., pfv. of* **обраща́ться.**

обра́тно *adv.* **1,** back. **2,** *colloq.* the other way round. **3,** *in* обра́тно пропорциона́льный (+ *dat.*), inversely proportional (to). —**биле́т туда́ и обра́тно,** round-trip ticket. —**пое́здка туда́ и обра́тно,** round trip.

обра́тное *n., decl. as an adj.* the opposite; the reverse.

обра́тный *adj.* **1,** reverse. **2,** opposite. **3,** return (*attrib.*): обра́тный а́дрес/биле́т/путь, return address/ticket/trip. С обра́тной по́чтой, by return mail. **4,** *math.* inverse.

обраща́ть *v. impfv.* [*pfv.* **обрати́ть**] **1,** to turn; direct. **2,** (*with* **в** + *acc.*) to turn (into); convert (to). —**обраща́ть внима́ние на** (+ *acc.*), to pay attention to. —**обраща́ть чьё-нибудь внима́ние на** (+ *acc.*), to draw *or* call someone's attention to. —**обрати́ть в бе́гство,** to put to flight. —**обрати́ть в прах,** to reduce to dust (*or* ashes).

обраща́ться *v.r. impfv.* [*pfv.* **обрати́ться**] **1,** (*with* **к**) to apply (to); appeal (to); address. **2,** (*with* **к**) to turn to (*for advice or information*); consult; go to; see. **3,** (*with* **в** + *acc.*) to turn into; become. **4,** [*impfv. only*] to circulate; be in circulation. **5,** [*impfv. only*] (*with* **с** + *instr.*) to treat; handle (someone) in a certain way. **6,** [*impfv. only*] (*with* **с** + *instr.*) to handle; operate. **7,**

(*with* **в** + *acc.*) to convert (to another faith). —**обраща́ться в бе́гство,** to take flight.
обраще́ние *n.* **1,** (*with* **к**) turning (toward). **2,** conversion. **3,** appeal. **4,** form of address: обраще́ние на "ты", familiar form of address. **5,** (*with* **с** + *instr.*) treatment (of); handling (of). **6,** circulation.
обре́з *n.* **1,** edge. **2,** sawed-off rifle. —**в обре́з,** *colloq.* barely enough: у меня́ вре́мени в обре́з, I barely have enough time; I am pressed for time.
обре́зание *n.* circumcision.
обреза́ние *n.* cutting; trimming.
обре́зать [*infl.* **-ре́жу, -ре́жешь**] *v., pfv. of* **обреза́ть** *and* **обре́зывать.** —**обре́заться,** *refl., pfv. of* **обреза́ться.**
обреза́ть *v. impfv.* [*pfv.* **обре́зать**] **1,** to trim; clip; prune. **2,** to cut (*accidentally*). **3,** *fig., colloq.* to cut short; interrupt. **4,** to circumcise. —**обреза́ться,** *refl., colloq.* to cut oneself.
обре́зок [*gen.* **-зка**] *n., usu. pl.* scrap (*of meat, paper, etc.*).
обре́зывать *v. impfv.* = **обреза́ть.**
обрека́ть *v. impfv.* [*pfv.* **обре́чь**] (*with* **на** + *acc.*) to doom (to).
обремени́тельный *adj.* burdensome; onerous.
обременя́ть *v. impfv.* [*pfv.* **обремени́ть**] to burden.
обрести́ [*infl.* **обрету́, обретёшь;** *past* **обрёл, обрела́, обрело́**] *v., pfv. of* **обрета́ть.**
обрета́ть *v. impfv.* [*pfv.* **обрести́**] to find.
обречённый *adj.* doomed. —**обречённость,** *n.f.* (impending) doom.
обре́чь [*infl.* **-реку́, -речёшь, ...-реку́т;** *past* **-рёк, -рекла́, -рекло́**] *v., pfv. of* **обрека́ть.**
обрисова́ть [*infl.* **-су́ю, -су́ешь**] *v., pfv. of* **обрисо́вывать.** —**обрисова́ться,** *refl., pfv. of* **обрисо́вываться.**
обрисо́вывать *v. impfv.* [*pfv.* **обрисова́ть**] **1,** to draw a line around. **2,** to highlight. **3,** *fig.* to describe; portray. —**обрисо́вываться,** *refl.* **1,** to appear (in outline). **2,** *fig.* to become clear.
обри́ть *v. pfv.* [*infl.* **обре́ю, обре́ешь**] to shave; shave off. —**обри́ться,** *refl.* to shave one's head; shave off one's beard, mustache, etc.
обро́к *n., hist.* tax paid by a peasant to the state for the use of land allotted to him; obrok.
oброни́ть *v. pfv.* [*infl.* **-роню́, -ро́нишь**] *colloq.* **1,** to drop. **2,** to let (a remark) drop.
обруба́ть *v. impfv.* [*pfv.* **обруби́ть**] **1,** to chop off; lop off. **2,** to chop the end off of.
обруби́ть [*infl.* **-рублю́, -ру́бишь**] *v., pfv. of* **обруба́ть.**
обру́бок [*gen.* **-бка**] *n.* stump.
обруга́ть *v. pfv.* **1,** to curse out; call names. **2,** *colloq.* to criticize; attack; pan.
обрусе́ть *v. pfv.* to become Russified.
о́бруч [*pl.* **о́бручи, обруче́й, -ча́м**] *n.* hoop.
обруча́льный *adj.* engagement (*attrib.*). —**обруча́льное кольцо́,** engagement ring; wedding ring.
обруча́ть *v. impfv.* [*pfv.* **обручи́ть**] to betroth; affiance. —**обруча́ться,** *refl.* (*with* **с** + *instr.*) to become engaged (to).
обруче́ние *n.* engagement; betrothal.
обручи́ть *v., pfv. of* **обруча́ть.** —**обручи́ться,** *refl., pfv. of* **обруча́ться.**
обру́шивать *v. impfv.* [*pfv.* **обру́шить**] **1,** to bring down; send crashing to the ground. **2,** (*with* **на** + *acc.*) to bring down (on); rain (blows, bombs, etc.) on; hurl (epithets) at. —**обру́шиваться,** *refl.* **1,** to collapse; cave in; come tumbling down. **2,** (*with* **на** + *acc.*) (*of the elements*) to pound; batter. **3,** (*with* **на** + *acc.*) to befall. **4,** (*with* **на** + *acc.*) to attack; pounce upon. **5,** (*with* **на** + *acc.*) to assail (*verbally*).
обру́шить *v., pfv. of* **обру́шивать.** —**обру́шиться,** *refl., pfv. of* **обру́шиваться.**
обры́в *n.* precipice.
обрыва́ть *v. impfv.* [*pfv.* **оборва́ть**] **1,** to tear off; pluck. **2,** to break; snap. **3,** *fig.* to cut short; interrupt. —**обрыва́ться,** *refl.* **1,** to break; snap. **2,** to slip; fall. **3,** *fig.* to stop suddenly; be suddenly cut short.
обры́вистый *adj.* steep; precipitous.
обры́вок [*gen.* **-вка**] *n.* **1,** scrap. **2,** *fig.* snatch (*of a song, conversation, etc.*). —**обры́вочный,** *adj.* (*of thoughts, phrases, etc.*) disjointed.
обры́згивать *v. impfv.* [*pfv.* **обры́згать**] **1,** to spatter; splash. **2,** to sprinkle.
обры́скать *v. pfv., colloq.* to roam: обры́скать свет, to roam the world.
обрю́зглый *adj.* flabby.
обрю́згнуть *v. pfv.* [*past* **обрю́зг, -ла**] to become flabby.
обрю́згший *adj.* flabby.
обря́д *n.* rite; ceremony. —**обря́довый,** *adj.* ritual; ceremonial.
обсади́ть [*infl.* **-сажу́, -са́дишь**] *v., pfv. of* **обса́живать.**
обса́живать *v. impfv.* [*pfv.* **обсади́ть**] to plant around; plant along: обса́живать доро́гу дере́вьями, to plant trees along a road.
обсервато́рия *n.* observatory.
обсе́сть *v. pfv.* [*infl. like* **сесть**] *colloq.* to sit around.
обскака́ть [*infl.* **-скачу́, -ска́чешь**] *v., pfv. of* **обска́кивать.**
обска́кивать *v. impfv.* [*pfv.* **обскака́ть**] **1,** to gallop around. **2,** (*of a horse*) to outrun.
обскура́нт *n.* obscurant. —**обскуранти́зм,** *n.* obscurantism.
обсле́дование *n.* **1,** inspection. **2,** *med.* checkup. —**обсле́дователь,** *n.m.* inspector.
обсле́довать *v. impfv. & pfv.* [*pres.* **-дую, -дуешь**] to inspect.
обслу́живание *n.* **1,** service. **2,** servicing; maintenance.
обслу́живать *v. impfv.* [*pfv.* **обслужи́ть**] **1,** to serve. **2,** to wait on. **3,** to service. **4,** [*impfv. only*] to operate (a machine).
обслужи́ть [*infl.* **-служу́, -слу́жишь**] *v., pfv. of* **обслу́живать.**
обсо́хнуть [*past* **-со́х, -ла**] *v., pfv. of* **обсыха́ть.**
обста́вить [*infl.* **-влю, -вишь**] *v., pfv. of* **обставля́ть.**
обставля́ть *v. impfv.* [*pfv.* **обста́вить**] **1,** to surround (with). **2,** to furnish (a home, room, etc.). **3,** *fig.* to arrange; organize.
обстано́вка *n.* **1,** situation: междунаро́дная обстано́вка, the international situation. **2,** *fig.* atmosphere; setting: в дру́жественной обстано́вке, in a friendly atmosphere. **3,** furniture. **4,** *theat.* set. —**переме́на обстано́вки,** change of scenery (*fig.*).
обсти́рывать *v. impfv.* [*pfv.* **обстира́ть**] *colloq.* to do all the washing for.
обстоя́тельный *adj.* **1,** thorough; detailed. **2,** *colloq.* steady; reliable.

обстоя́тельство *n.* circumstance.

обстоя́ть *v. impfv.* to be; stand: как обстои́т де́ло с (+ *instr.*), how do matters stand with...? Вот как обстои́т де́ло, this is the way things stand; this is the way it is.

обстра́ивать *v. impfv.* [*pfv.* **обстро́ить**] **1,** to surround (with buildings); line (with buildings). **2,** to build; build up. —**обстра́иваться,** *refl., colloq.* **1,** to build a house for oneself. **2,** to be built up.

обстре́л *n.* fire; firing; shelling: попа́сть под обстре́л, to come under fire. —**взять под обстре́л,** to rake over the coals.

обстре́ливать *v. impfv.* [*pfv.* **обстреля́ть**] to fire upon; shell.

обстре́лянный *adj.* battle-hardened.

обстреля́ть *v., pfv. of* **обстре́ливать.**

обстро́ить *v., pfv. of* **обстра́ивать.** —**обстро́иться,** *refl., pfv. of* **обстра́иваться.**

обструкциони́зм *n.* obstructionism. —**обструкциони́ст,** *n.* obstructionist. —**обструкцио́нный,** *adj.* obstructionist.

обстру́кция *n.* obstruction; delaying tactics.

обступа́ть *v. impfv.* [*pfv.* **обступи́ть**] to surround; crowd around; cluster around.

обступи́ть [*infl.* **-ступлю́, -сту́пишь**] *v., pfv. of* **обступа́ть.**

обсуди́ть [*infl.* **-сужу́, -су́дишь**] *v., pfv. of* **обсужда́ть.**

обсужда́ть *v. impfv.* [*pfv.* **обсуди́ть**] to discuss.

обсужде́ние *n.* discussion.

обсу́шивать *v. impfv.* [*pfv.* **обсуши́ть**] to dry; dry out. —**обсу́шиваться,** *refl.* to dry oneself off; get dry.

обсуши́ть [*infl.* **-сушу́, -су́шишь**] *v., pfv. of* **обсу́шивать.** —**обсуши́ться,** *refl., pfv. of* **обсу́шиваться.**

обсчи́тывать *v. impfv.* [*pfv.* **обсчита́ть**] to shortchange. —**обсчи́тываться,** *refl.* to make an error in counting; miscount.

обсы́пать [*infl.* **-сыплю, -сыплешь**] *v., pfv. of* **обсыпа́ть.**

обсыпа́ть *v. impfv.* [*pfv.* **обсы́пать**] to sprinkle (with).

обсыха́ть *v. impfv.* [*pfv.* **обсо́хнуть**] to dry; dry off. —**у него́ молоко́ на губа́х не обсо́хло,** he is still wet behind the ears.

обта́чивать *v. impfv.* [*pfv.* **обточи́ть**] to grind smooth.

обтека́емый *adj.* streamlined.

обтека́ть *v. impfv.* [*pfv.* **обте́чь**] **1,** to flow around. **2,** to bypass; skirt.

обтере́ть [*infl.* **оботру́, оботрёшь;** *past* **обтёр, -ла**] *v., pfv. of* **обтира́ть.** —**обтере́ться,** *refl., pfv. of* **обтира́ться.**

обтеса́ть [*infl.* **-тешу́, -те́шешь**] *v., pfv. of* **обтёсывать.**

обтёсывать *v. impfv.* [*pfv.* **обтеса́ть**] **1,** to trim; rough-hew. **2,** *fig., colloq.* to teach (someone) good manners.

обте́чь [*infl. like* **течь**] *v., pfv. of* **обтека́ть.**

обтира́ние *n.* rubdown.

обтира́ть *v. impfv.* [*pfv.* **обтере́ть**] **1,** to wipe. **2,** to wipe away. **3,** to rub (with). —**обтира́ться,** *refl.* **1,** to dry oneself. **2,** to sponge oneself down. **3,** *colloq.* to wear thin.

обточи́ть [*infl.* **-точу́, -то́чишь**] *v., pfv. of* **обта́чивать.**

обтрёпанный *adj.* **1,** frayed; tattered. **2,** shabbily dressed.

обтрепа́ть *v. pfv.* [*infl.* **-треплю́, -тре́плешь**] to fray. —**обтрепа́ться,** *refl.* to fray; become frayed.

обтя́гивать *v. impfv.* [*pfv.* **обтяну́ть**] **1,** to cover; upholster. **2,** (*of clothes*) to fit tightly; hug. —**обтя́гиваться,** *refl.* **1,** to become covered. **2,** (*of one's face*) to become drawn.

обтя́жка *n.* **1,** covering. **2,** cover. —**в обтя́жку,** close-fitting; tight-fitting.

обтяну́ть [*infl.* **-тяну́, -тя́нешь**] *v., pfv. of* **обтя́гивать.** —**обтяну́ться,** *refl., pfv. of* **обтя́гиваться.**

обува́ть *v. impfv.* [*pfv.* **обу́ть**] **1,** to put on (someone's) shoes. **2,** to put on (one's shoes). **3,** to provide with shoes. —**обува́ться,** *refl.* to put on one's shoes.

обувно́й *adj.* shoe (*attrib.*).

о́бувь *n.f.* shoes; footwear.

обу́гливать *v. impfv.* [*pfv.* **обу́глить**] to char.

обу́за *n.* **1,** burdensome chore. **2,** burden.

обузда́ние *n.* restraint.

обу́здывать *v. impfv.* [*pfv.* **обузда́ть**] **1,** to bridle (a horse). **2,** *fig.* to restrain; curb.

обурева́ть *v. impfv.* (*of fears, doubts, etc.*) to seize; grip.

обусло́вливать *v. impfv.* [*pfv.* **облусло́вить**] **1,** to condition; make conditional. **2,** to cause; occasion. —**обусло́вливаться,** *refl.* (*with instr.*) **1,** to be conditional (upon); be determined (by). **2,** to be the result (of); be due (to).

обу́ть [*infl.* **обу́ю, обу́ешь**] *v., pfv. of* **обува́ть.** —**обу́ться,** *refl., pfv. of* **обува́ться.**

о́бух *also,* **обу́х** *n.* butt; butt end. —**бить/ударя́ть кого́-нибудь как о́бухом (обухо́м) по голове́,** to hit someone like a thunderbolt.

обуча́ть *v. impfv.* [*pfv.* **обучи́ть**] to teach; instruct; train: обуча́ть кого́-нибудь ремеслу́, to teach someone a trade. —**обуча́ться,** *refl.* **1,** (*with dat.*) to learn: обуча́ться ремеслу́, to learn a trade. **2,** [*impfv. only*] to study (in a certain institution).

обуче́ние *n.* **1,** (*with gen.*) teaching; training (*of people*). Обуче́ние взро́слых, adult education. **2,** (*with dat.*) teaching (*of a subject*); instruction (in): обуче́ние ремеслу́, teaching of a trade. Беспла́тное обуче́ние, free tuition.

обучи́ть [*infl.* **-учу́, -у́чишь**] *v., pfv. of* **обуча́ть.** —**обучи́ться,** *refl., pfv. of* **обуча́ться.**

обуя́ть *v. pfv.* (*of a feeling or physical state*) to seize; come over.

обха́живать *v. impfv., colloq.* **1,** to walk all over. **2,** to care for. **3,** to play up to; cultivate.

обхва́т *n.* **1,** circumference; girth: метр в обхва́те, a meter in circumference. **2,** circumference equal to a span of the arm: дуб в три обхва́та, an oak tree three spans in circumference.

обхвати́ть [*infl.* **-хвачу́, -хва́тишь**] *v., pfv. of* **обхва́тывать.**

обхва́тывать *v. impfv.* [*pfv.* **обхвати́ть**] **1,** to put one's arms around. **2,** *fig.* to take in; embrace; encompass.

обхо́д *n.* **1,** going around. **2,** detour; bypass. **3,** rounds; beat: идти́ в обхо́д, to make one's rounds. **4,** *mil.* flanking movement. —**в обхо́д** (+ *gen.*), skirting; bypassing.

обходи́тельный *adj.* polite; courteous. —**обходи́тельность** *n.f.* politeness.

обходи́ть *v. impfv.* [*pfv.* **обойти́;** *pres.* **-хожу́, -хо́дишь**] **1,** to go around; walk around. **2,** *mil.* to outflank.

3, to walk around; bypass; avoid. **4,** to pass over; ignore. **5,** to circumvent; get around (a law, rule, etc.). **6,** to pass over; fail to promote. **7,** *colloq.* to pass; outpace. **8,** (*with* **весь**) to walk all over. **9,** (*with* **все**) to make the rounds of; go to every one of. **10,** to spread all over: но́вость обошла́ весь го́род, the news spread all over town. —**обходи́ться,** *refl.* **1,** (*with* **с** + *instr.*) to treat. **2,** *colloq.* to cost. **3,** *colloq.* to get along; manage. **4,** *colloq.* to turn out; work out.

обхо́дный *adj.* **1,** roundabout; circuitous: обхо́дным путём, by a roundabout way. **2,** *mil.* outflanking: обхо́дное движе́ние, outflanking movement.

обхо́дчик *n.* inspector. —**путево́й обхо́дчик,** *R.R.* trackwalker.

обхожде́ние *n.* **1,** behavior; manners; attitude. **2,** treatment.

обче́сться *v.r. pfv.* [*infl.* **обочту́сь, обочтёшься;** *past* **обчёлся, обочла́сь**] *colloq.* = **обсчита́ться.** —**раз, два и обчёлся,** you can count them on the fingers of one hand.

обчи́стить [*infl.* **-чи́щу, -чи́стишь**] *v., pfv. of* **обчища́ть.**

обчища́ть *v. impfv.* [*pfv.* **обчи́стить**] *colloq.* **1,** to clean. **2,** (*in gambling*) to clean out; take to the cleaners.

обша́ривать *v. impfv.* [*pfv.* **обша́рить**] *colloq.* to rummage; ransack.

обша́рпанный *adj., colloq.* dilapidated; run-down.

обшива́ть *v. impfv.* [*pfv.* **обши́ть**] **1,** (*with instr.*) to edge (with); border (with); trim (with). **2,** (*with instr.*) to plank (with boards). **3,** *colloq.* to sew all the clothes for.

обши́вка *n.* **1,** edging; bordering; trimming. **2,** plating; sheeting; planking.

обши́рный *adj.* vast; extensive. —**обши́рность,** *n.f.* extent; magnitude.

обши́ть [*infl.* **обошью́, обошьёшь**] *v., pfv. of* **обшива́ть.**

обшла́г [*gen. sing. & nom. pl.* **обшлага́**] *n.* cuff.

обща́ться *v.r. impfv.* (*with* **с** + *instr.*) to associate (with); consort (with); socialize (with).

общедосту́пный *adj.* **1,** available to all. **2,** understandable to all; popular. **3,** (*of prices*) moderate; reasonable.

общежи́тие *n.* **1,** dormitory. **2,** society; everyday life.

общеизве́стный *adj.* generally known; known to all. Общеизве́стно, что..., it is common knowledge that...

общенаро́дный *adj.* national; of all the people.

обще́ние *n.* association; contact; intercourse.

общеобразова́тельный *adj.* (*of a school, subject, etc.*) general; not specialized.

общепри́нятый *adj.* generally accepted; conventional.

обще́ственник *n.* person active in public life.

обще́ственность *n.f.* **1,** the public. **2,** public opinion. **3,** public-mindedness. **4,** socially active members.

обще́ственный *adj.* public; social.

о́бщество *n.* **1,** society. **2,** company: в о́бществе друзе́й, in the company of friends. **3,** society: литерату́рное о́бщество, literary society.

о́бщий *adj.* **1,** general; common. **2,** total; overall. —**в о́бщем,** in general; on the whole. —**в о́бщем и це́лом,** on the whole; all in all. —**о́бщее ме́сто,** platitude. —**о́бщая су́мма; о́бщий ито́г,** sum total; grand total. —**не име́ть ничего́ о́бщего с,** to have nothing in common with.

о́бщина *also,* **общи́на** *n.* **1,** community. **2,** commune.

общи́нный *adj.* communal.

общипа́ть [*infl.* **-щиплю́, -щи́плешь**] *v., pfv. of* **щипа́ть** (*in sense #3*) *and* **общи́пывать.**

общи́пывать *v. impfv.* [*pfv.* **общипа́ть**] to pluck.

общи́тельный *adj.* sociable; gregarious. —**общи́тельность,** *n.f.* sociability.

о́бщность *n.f.* commonality: о́бщность интере́сов, commonality of interests.

объего́ривать *v. impfv.* [*pfv.* **объего́рить**] *colloq.* to swindle; cheat; gyp.

объеда́ть *v. impfv.* [*pfv.* **объе́сть**] **1,** to eat around; nibble at. **2,** *colloq.* to eat out of house and home. —**объеда́ться,** *refl.* **1,** to overeat. **2,** (*with instr. or gen.*) to eat too much of.

объеде́ние *n.* **1,** overeating. **2,** *colloq.* something delicious; something out of this world.

объедине́ние *n.* **1,** unification. **2,** amalgamation; merger. **3,** union; association. **4,** *mil.* large formation (*front, army, etc.*).

объединённый *adj.* **1,** united: Объединённые На́ции, United Nations. **2,** joint: объединённый комите́т, joint committee.

объединя́ть *v. impfv.* [*pfv.* **объедини́ть**] **1,** to unite; unify. **2,** to combine (into one); amalgamate. **3,** to join; combine (forces, efforts, etc.). —**объединя́ться,** *refl.* to unite; combine; amalgamate.

объе́дки [*gen.* **-ков**] *n.pl., colloq.* leftovers; scraps.

объе́зд *n.* **1,** traveling around. **2,** detour.

объе́здить [*infl.* **-е́зжу, -е́здишь**] *v., pfv. of* **объезжа́ть.**

объе́здка *n.* breaking in (*of a horse*).

объе́здчик *n.* warden; ranger.

объезжа́ть *v. impfv.* **1,** [*pfv.* **объе́хать**] to go around; drive around; detour around. **2,** [*pfv.* **объе́хать** *or* **объе́здить**] to drive all over; travel throughout (a city, region, etc.). **3,** [*pfv.* **объе́здить**] to break in (a horse).

объе́кт *n.* **1,** object. **2,** establishment; installation. **3,** *mil.* objective.

объекти́в *n.* lens.

объекти́вный *adj.* objective. —**объекти́вно,** *adv.* objectively. —**объекти́вность,** *n.f.* objectivity.

объе́ктный *adj., in* **объе́ктный паде́ж,** objective case.

объём *n.* **1,** volume (*of a geometric figure, trade, etc.*). **2,** *fig.* scope; range.

объёмистый *adj., colloq.* large; bulky; voluminous.

объёмный *adj.* **1,** by volume. **2,** volumetric. **3,** (*of an image, film, etc.*) three-dimensional.

объе́сть [*infl. like* **есть**] *v., pfv. of* **объеда́ть.** —**объе́сться,** *refl., pfv. of* **объеда́ться.**

объе́хать [*infl.* **-е́ду, -е́дешь**] *v., pfv. of* **объезжа́ть.**

объяви́ть [*infl.* **-явлю́, -я́вишь**] *v., pfv. of* **объявля́ть.** —**объяви́ться,** *refl., pfv. of* **объявля́ться.**

объявле́ние *n.* **1,** declaration: объявле́ние войны́, declaration of war. **2,** announcement: объявле́ние о собра́нии, announcement of a meeting. **3,** advertisement. —**доска́ объявле́ний,** bulletin board.

объявля́ть *v. impfv.* [*pfv.* **объяви́ть**] **1,** to declare. **2,** (*with acc. or* **о** + *prepl.*) to announce. —**объявля́ться,** *refl.* **1,** *colloq.* to turn up; show up. **2,** (*with instr.*) to declare oneself to be.

объясне́ние *n.* **1,** explanation. **2,** face-to-face meeting (*to settle something*). **3,** *in* объясне́ние в любви́, declaration of love.

объясни́мый *adj.* explainable; explicable.

объясни́тельный *adj.* explanatory.

объясня́ть *v. impfv.* [*pfv.* **объясни́ть**] to explain. —**объясня́ться,** *refl.* **1,** (*with* **с** + *instr.*) to have a talk (with); have it out with. **2,** *obs.* to explain oneself; explain one's behavior. **3,** to become clear. **4,** [*impfv. only*] to express oneself; make oneself understood. **5,** [*impfv. only*] (*with instr.*) to be explained (by); be accounted for (by): чем э́то объясня́ется?, how do you account for this? Этим объясня́ется его́ поведе́ние, this accounts for his behavior. **6,** *in* **объясни́ться в любви́** (+ *dat.*), to make a declaration of love (to).

объя́тие *n., usu. pl.* embrace. —**с распростёртыми объя́тиями,** with open arms.

объя́ть *v. pfv.* [*infl.* **обойму́, обоймёшь;** *past* **объя́л, объя́ла**] **1,** to embrace. **2,** to engulf; envelop. **3,** (*of an emotion*) to fill; seize; come over.

обыва́тель *n.m.* **1,** *obs.* inhabitant; resident. **2,** person of narrow or petty interests. —**обыва́тельский,** *adj.* narrow; narrow-minded.

обы́грывать *v. impfv.* [*pfv.* **обыгра́ть**] to beat; defeat (*in a game*).

обы́денный *adj.* ordinary; everyday.

обыкнове́ние *n.* habit. —**по обыкнове́нию,** as usual; as is his/her custom *or* wont.

обыкнове́нно *adv.* usually.

обыкнове́нный *adj.* **1,** usual; customary. **2,** ordinary.

о́быск *n.* search (*of a person, premises, etc.*).

обыска́ть [*infl.* **обыщу́, обы́щешь**] *v., pfv. of* **обы́скивать.**

обы́скивать *v. impfv.* [*pfv.* **обыска́ть**] to search; conduct a search of.

обы́чай *n.* custom.

обы́чно *adv.* usually; generally; ordinarily. —**как обы́чно,** as usual.

обы́чный *adj.* **1,** usual; customary. Ра́ньше обы́чного, earlier than usual. **2,** ordinary. **3,** (*of weapons*) conventional. —**обы́чное пра́во,** common law.

обя́занность *n.f.* duty; responsibility.

обя́занный *adj.* **1,** (*with inf.*) obliged (to); required (to). **2,** (*with dat.*) obliged (to); indebted (to); obligated (to).

обяза́тельно *adv.* **1,** without fail. **2,** necessarily. **3,** *as an interj.* of course!; absolutely!

обяза́тельный *adj.* **1,** compulsory; obligatory; mandatory. **2,** obliging; accommodating.

обяза́тельство *n.* obligation; commitment. —**долгово́е обяза́тельство,** promissory note.

обяза́ть [*infl.* **обяжу́, обя́жешь**] *v., pfv. of* **обя́зывать.** —**обяза́ться,** *refl., pfv. of* **обя́зываться.**

обя́зывать *v. impfv.* [*pfv.* **обяза́ть;** *pres.* **-ваю, -ваешь** *or* **-зу́ю, -зу́ешь**] **1,** to oblige; obligate; bind; commit. **2,** to oblige; do (someone) a favor. —**обя́зываться,** *refl.* (*with inf.*) to pledge (to); undertake (to).

ова́л *n.* oval. —**ова́льный,** *adj.* oval.

ова́ция *n.* ovation: устро́ить ова́цию (+ *dat.*), to give an ovation (to).

овдове́ть *v. pfv.* (*of a woman*) to become widowed; (*of a man*) to become a widower.

овева́ть *v. impfv.* [*pfv.* **ове́ять**] **1,** (*of the wind*) to blow upon; fan. **2,** *fig.* to pervade; infuse.

ове́н [*gen.* **овна́;** *pl.* **о́вны**] *n.* **1,** *obs.* ram. **2,** *cap.* Aries.

овёс [*gen.* **овса́**] *n.* oats.

ове́чий [*fem.* **-чья**] *adj.* sheep (*attrib.*); sheep's. —**волк в ове́чьей шку́ре,** wolf in sheep's clothing.

ове́чка [*gen. pl.* **-чек**] *n., dim. of* **овца́.**

ове́ять [*infl.* **ове́ю, ове́ешь**] *v., pfv. of* **овева́ть.**

ОВИ́Р *abbr. of* **отде́л виз и регистра́ции,** visa and registration department; OVIR.

овладева́ть *v. impfv.* [*pfv.* **овладе́ть**] (*with instr.*) **1,** to seize; capture. **2,** to control; dominate. **3,** (*of emotions*) to seize; grip; come over. **4,** to master (a subject, theory, technique, etc.). —**овладе́ть собо́й,** to compose oneself; regain one's composure.

овладе́ние *n.* **1,** capture. **2,** mastery.

овладе́ть *v., pfv. of* **овладева́ть.**

о́вод [*pl.* **о́воды** *or* **овода́**] *n.* gadfly.

о́вощи [*gen.* **овоще́й**] *n.pl.* [*sing.* **о́вощ**] vegetables.

овощно́й *adj.* vegetable (*attrib.*).

овра́г *n.* ravine.

овся́нка [*gen. pl.* **-нок**] *n.* **1,** oatmeal. **2,** bunting (*bird*). Обыкнове́нная овся́нка, yellowhammer. Садо́вая овся́нка, ortolan.

овся́ный *also,* **овсяно́й** *adj.* oat (*attrib.*). —**овся́ная ка́ша; овся́ная крупа́,** oatmeal.

овуля́ция *n.* ovulation.

овца́ [*pl.* **о́вцы, ове́ц, о́вцам**] *n.* **1,** sheep. **2,** ewe.

овцебы́к *n.* musk ox.

овцево́д *n.* sheep farmer. —**овцево́дство,** *n.* sheep raising. —**овцево́дческий,** *adj.* pert. to the raising of sheep: овцево́дческая фе́рма, sheep farm.

овча́рка [*gen. pl.* **-рок**] *n.* sheep dog. —**неме́цкая овча́рка,** German shepherd.

овча́рня [*gen. pl.* **-рен**] *n.* sheepfold.

овчи́на *also,* **овчи́нка** *n.* sheepskin. —**овчи́нный,** *adj.* sheepskin.

ога́рок [*gen.* **-рка**] *n.* candle end.

огиба́ть *v. impfv.* [*pfv.* **обогну́ть**] **1,** to bend around; wind around. **2,** to round; go around; skirt.

оглавле́ние *n.* table of contents.

огласи́ть [*infl.* **-шу́, -си́шь**] *v., pfv. of* **оглаша́ть.**

огла́ска *n.* publicity.

оглаша́ть *v. impfv.* [*pfv.* **огласи́ть**] **1,** to announce; read out. **2,** *obs.* to divulge; make public. **3,** to fill (the air, a room, etc.) with a certain sound.

огло́бля [*gen. pl.* **-бель**] *n.* shaft (*for harnessing a horse to a carriage*).

огло́хнуть [*past* **огло́х, -ла**] *v., pfv. of* **гло́хнуть** (*in sense #1*).

оглуша́ть *v. impfv.* [*pfv.* **оглуши́ть**] **1,** to deafen. **2,** to stun.

оглуши́тельный *adj.* deafening.

оглуши́ть *v., pfv. of* **глуши́ть** (*in sense #7*) *and* **оглуша́ть.**

огляде́ть [*infl.* **-жу́, -ди́шь**] *v., pfv. of* **огля́дывать.** —**огляде́ться,** *refl.* **1,** *pfv. of* **огля́дываться** (*in sense #1*). **2,** *fig.* to get used to one's surroundings.

огля́дка *n., obs.* looking back. —**без огля́дки, 1,** (*with verbs of running*) without looking back; like a jack rabbit. **2,** without second thoughts; without looking back. —**с огля́дкой,** with caution; cautiously.

огля́дывать *v. impfv.* [*pfv.* **огляде́ть** *or* **огляну́ть**] to look over; examine. —**огля́дываться,** *refl.* **1,** [*pfv.* **огляде́ться**] to look around. **2,** [*pfv.* **огляну́ться**] to look back; turn around and look.

огляну́ть [*infl.* **огляну́, огля́нешь**] *v., pfv. of* **огля́дывать.** —**огляну́ться,** *refl., pfv. of* **огля́дываться** (*in sense #2*).

огнево́й *adj.* **1,** fire (*attrib.*): огнева́я мощь, firepower. **2,** fiery. **3,** fiery red. —**огнево́й вал,** covering fire; barrage. —**огнева́я то́чка,** gun emplacement.

огнемёт *n.* flame thrower.
о́гненный *adj.* **1,** fiery; ablaze. **2,** fiery red. **3,** *fig.* fiery; impassioned.
огнеопа́сный *adj.* flammable; inflammable.
огнесто́йкий *adj.* fireproof.
огнестре́льный *adj., in* **огнестре́льное ору́жие,** firearm; firearms; **огнестре́льная ра́на,** gunshot wound.
огнетуши́тель *n.m.* fire extinguisher.
огнеупо́рный *adj.* heat-resistant; refractory.
ого́ *interj.* oho!
огова́ривать *v. impfv.* [*pfv.* **оговори́ть**] **1,** to stipulate. **2,** to slander. —**огова́риваться,** *refl.* **1,** to point out in advance. **2,** to qualify one's statement. **3,** to make a slip of the tongue.
огово́р *n.* slander.
оговори́ть *v., pfv. of* **огова́ривать.** —**оговори́ться,** *refl., pfv. of* **огова́риваться.**
огово́рка [*gen. pl.* **-рок**] *n.* **1,** reservation; stipulation; proviso; qualification. **2,** slip of the tongue.
оголённый *adj.* bare; nude.
оголи́ть *v., pfv. of* **оголя́ть.** —**оголи́ться,** *refl., pfv. of* **оголя́ться.**
оголте́лый *adj., colloq.* mad; rabid; fanatical.
оголя́ть *v. impfv.* [*pfv.* **оголи́ть**] **1,** to bare; expose. **2,** to denude. **3,** to draw; unsheathe (a sword). **4,** *mil.* to expose. —**оголя́ться,** *refl.* to be exposed.
огонёк [*gen.* **-нька́**] *n.* **1,** light; dot of light: огоньки́ го́рода, the lights of a city. **2,** *fig.* zest; verve. —**зайти́ на огонёк** (*with* **к**), to drop in (on).
ого́нь [*gen.* **огня́**] *n.m.* **1,** fire. **2,** light: огни́ го́рода, the lights of a city. **3,** fire (*from a gun*): пулемётный ого́нь, machine-gun fire. Откры́ть ого́нь, to open fire. —**в огне́,** on fire; aflame; ablaze. —**днём с огнём (не найти́, не сыска́ть,** *etc.* **),** seldom seen anywhere; not to be found anywhere. —**игра́ть с огнём,** to play with fire. —**идти́/пойти́ в ого́нь и в во́ду за** (+ *acc. or instr.*), to be willing to do anything for. —**ме́жду двух огне́й,** between the devil and the deep blue sea. —**пройти́ ого́нь и во́ду,** to have been through the mill.
огора́живать *v. impfv.* [*pfv.* **огороди́ть**] to fence in; enclose.
огоро́д *n.* vegetable garden.
огороди́ть [*infl.* **-рожу́, -ро́дишь** *or* **-роди́шь**] *v., pfv. of* **огора́живать.**
огоро́дник *n.* truck farmer. —**огоро́дничество,** *n.* truck farming.
огоро́дный *adj.* garden (*attrib.*).
огоро́шить *v. pfv., colloq.* to take aback.
огорча́ть *v. impfv.* [*pfv.* **огорчи́ть**] to distress; grieve. —**огорча́ться,** *refl.* to be distressed.
огорче́ние *n.* distress; chagrin. —**огорчи́тельный,** *adj.* distressing.
огорчи́ть *v., pfv. of* **огорча́ть.** —**огорчи́ться,** *refl., pfv. of* **огорча́ться.**
огра́бить *v., pfv. of* **гра́бить.**
ограбле́ние *n.* robbery.
огра́да *n.* fence.
оградить [*infl.* **-жу́, -ди́шь**] *v., pfv. of* **огражда́ть.**
огражда́ть *v. impfv.* [*pfv.* **огради́ть**] **1,** *obs.* to fence in. **2,** to protect; shield.
огражде́ние *n.* **1,** fencing in. **2,** protection. **3,** fence; barrier.
ограниче́ние *n.* limitation; restriction.
ограни́ченный *adj.* **1,** limited. **2,** (*of a person*) of limited intellect.
ограни́чивать *v. impfv.* [*pfv.* **ограни́чить**] to limit; restrict; confine. —**ограни́чиваться,** *refl.* (*with instr.*) **1,** to limit/restrict/confine oneself (to). **2,** to be limited (to).
ограничи́тельный *adj.* **1,** restrictive. **2,** *fig.* narrow: ограничи́тельное толкова́ние, narrow interpretation.
ограни́чить *v., pfv. of* **ограни́чивать.** —**ограни́читься,** *refl., pfv. of* **ограни́чиваться.**
огре́ть *v.pfv., colloq.* to smack; whack.
огре́х *n., colloq.* fault; shortcoming; imperfection.
огро́мный *adj.* enormous; huge; tremendous; immense. —**огро́мность,** *n.f.* immensity.
огрубе́лый *adj.* rough; coarse; callous(ed).
огрубе́ть *v., pfv. of* **грубе́ть.**
огрыза́ть *v. impfv.* [*pfv.* **огры́зть**] *colloq.* to nibble at. —**огрыза́ться,** *refl.* [*pfv.* **огрызну́ться**] **1,** (*with* **на** + *acc.*) (*of a dog*) to snap (at). **2,** *colloq.* to snap; retort sharply.
огры́зок [*gen.* **-зка**] *n.* **1,** leftover bit (*of an apple, piece of meat, etc.*). **2,** stub (*of a pencil*).
огры́зть [*infl. like* **грызть**] *v., pfv. of* **огрыза́ть.**
огу́лом *adv., colloq.* **1,** indiscriminately; wholesale. **2,** in one lot; in a lump. **3,** all together; en masse.
огу́льно *adv.* **1,** without grounds; unfairly. **2,** indiscriminately; wholesale.
огу́льный *adj.* **1,** unfounded; groundless. **2,** *colloq.* indiscriminate; wholesale; sweeping.
огуре́ц [*gen.* **-рца́**] *n.* cucumber. —**огуре́чный,** *adj.* cucumber (*attrib.*).
о́да *n.* ode.
ода́лживать *v. impfv.* [*pfv.* **одолжи́ть**] to lend.
одарённость *n.f.* gifts; talents; endowments.
одарённый *adj.* gifted.
одаря́ть *v. impfv.* [*pfv.* **одари́ть**] (*with instr.*) **1,** *obs.* to give (as a gift). **2,** to endow (with).
одева́ть *v. impfv.* [*pfv.* **оде́ть**] to dress; clothe. —**одева́ться,** *refl.* to dress; get dressed.
оде́жда *n.* clothes; clothing.
одеколо́н *n.* eau de Cologne.
оделя́ть *v. impfv.* [*pfv.* **одели́ть**] (*with instr.*) to present (with): оделя́ть дете́й сластя́ми, to present sweets to the children.
одёр [*gen.* **одра́**] *n., colloq.* old horse; jade.
одёргивать *v. impfv.* [*pfv.* **одёрнуть**] **1,** to pull down; straighten (an article of clothing). **2,** *colloq.* to restrain; silence.
одеревене́лый *adj.* **1,** stiff; numb. **2,** *fig.* lifeless.
одеревене́ть *v. pfv.* **1,** *pfv.of* **деревене́ть. 2,** *fig.* to become indifferent; become apathetic.
одержа́ть *v. pfv.* [*infl.* **одержу́, оде́ржишь**] *in* **одержа́ть побе́ду,** to score a victory. —**одержа́ть верх,** *see* **верх.**
одержи́мость *n.f.* obsession; preoccupation.
одержи́мый *adj.* (*with instr.*) obsessed (by); possessed (by).
одёрнуть *v., pfv. of* **одёргивать.**
оде́ть [*infl.* **оде́ну, оде́нешь**] *v., pfv. of* **одева́ть.** —**оде́ться,** *refl., pfv. of* **одева́ться.**
одея́ло *n.* blanket; cover.
одея́ние *n., obs.* clothing; raiment.
оди́н [*fem.* **одна́**; *neut.* **одно́**; *pl.* **одни́**; *gen.* **одного́, одно́й, одни́х**; *acc. fem.* **одну́**; *dat.* **одному́, одно́й,**

одни́м; *instr.* одни́м, одно́й, одни́ми; *prepl.* одно́м, одно́й, одни́х] *numeral* one: оди́н биле́т, one ticket; одна́ ко́мната, one room; одни́ часы́, one watch. —*pron.* **1,** one: оди́н из са́мых лу́чших, one of the best. Оди́н друго́го удиви́тельнее, one more surprising than the next. **2,** *pl.* some; certain: одни́ бо́льше, чем други́е, some are larger than others. —*adj.* **1,** a; a certain. **2,** alone; by oneself: он живёт оди́н, he lives alone. **3,** only: в це́ркви бы́ли одни́ стару́шки, there were only old women in the church. **4,** the same: жить в одно́м до́ме, to live in the same house; они́ одни́х лет, they are the same age. —**все до одного́,** (everyone) to a man. —**все как оди́н,** one and all alike. —**ни оди́н,** not a single: он не сказа́л ни одного́ сло́ва, he did not say a single word. —**оди́н за други́м,** one by one; one after the other. —**оди́н и тот же,** the same. —**оди́н на оди́н,** face to face. —**оди́н то́лько,** alone: в одно́й то́лько Фра́нции, in France alone. —**по одному́,** one by one; one at a time. *See also* **одно́.**

одина́ково *adv.* **1,** identically. **2,** equally.

одина́ковый *adj.* identical. Они́ одина́кового ро́ста; они́ одина́ковы по ро́сту, they are of identical height; they are identical in height. —**в одина́ковой ме́ре,** in equal measure.

одина́рный *adj.* single.

оди́ннадцатый *ordinal numeral* eleventh.

оди́ннадцать [*gen., dat., & prepl.* **-цати;** *instr.* **-цатью**] *numeral* eleven.

одино́кий *adj.* **1,** lone; solitary. **2,** lonely; lonesome. **3,** single; unmarried. —*n.* single person; unmarried person.

одино́ко *adv.* **1,** alone. **2,** lonely: чу́вствовать себя́ одино́ко, to feel lonely.

одино́чество *n.* solitude; loneliness.

одино́чка [*gen. pl.* **-чек**] *n.m. & f.* lone person; person on his/her own. ♦*Often in compounds:* мать-одино́чка, unwed mother; single mother. —*n.f., colloq.* solitary (confinement) cell. —**в одино́чку,** alone; by oneself; on one's own. —**одино́чкой,** alone. —**по одино́чке,** one by one.

одино́чный *adj.* **1,** lone; solitary. **2,** for one person; single. —**одино́чный бой,** single combat. —**одино́чное заключе́ние,** solitary confinement.

одио́зный *adj.* odious; offensive.

одиссе́я *n.* odyssey.

одича́лый *adj.* (*of an animal, plant, etc.*) wild.

одича́ть *v., pfv. of* **дича́ть.**

одна́жды *adv.* **1,** once. **2,** once; one day; once upon a time.

одна́ко *conj.* however; but.

одно́ *numeral, neut. of* **оди́н.** —*pron.* one thing: одно́ несомне́нно, one thing is certain. —**одно́ и то же,** the same thing.

однобо́кий *adj.* **1,** lopsided. **2,** *fig.* one-sided.

однобо́ртный *adj.* single-breasted.

одновре́менно *also,* **одновреме́нно** *adv.* simultaneously; at the same time.

одновре́менность *also,* **одновреме́нность** *n.f.* simultaneity.

одновре́менный *also,* **одновреме́нный** *adj.* simultaneous.

одногла́зый *adj.* one-eyed.

одногоди́чный *adj.* one-year (*attrib.*).

одного́док [*gen.* **-дка**] *n.m.* [*fem.* **-дка**] *colloq.* = **одноле́ток.**

однодне́вный *adj.* one-day (*attrib.*).

однозна́чный *adj.* **1,** synonymous. **2,** having only one meaning. **3,** (*of a number*) one-digit.

одноимённый *adj.* of the same name.

однока́шник *n., colloq.* fellow student.

однокла́ссник *n.* classmate.

одноклéточный *adj.* one-celled.

одноколе́йный *adj.* single-track (*attrib.*).

одноко́лка *n.* gig.

одноко́мнатный *adj.* one-room (*attrib.*).

однокра́тный *adj., gram.* semelfactive: однокра́тный глаго́л, semelfactive verb (*e.g.* кри́кнуть).

одноку́рсник *n.* person enrolled in the same course; classmate.

одноле́тний *adj.* **1,** one-year (*attrib.*); one-year-old. **2,** *bot.* annual.

одноле́ток [*gen.* **-тка**] *n.m.* [*fem.* **-тка**] *colloq.* contemporary; person the same age.

одноме́стный *adj.* having one seat; having room for one; single-seat (*attrib.*).

одноно́гий *adj.* one-legged.

однообра́зие *n.* monotony. —**однообра́зный,** *adj.* monotonous.

однопала́тный *adj.* unicameral.

однопо́лый *adj.* unisexual.

однорéльсовый *adj.* single-rail (*attrib.*). —**однорéльсовая желе́зная доро́га,** monorail.

одноро́дный *adj.* **1,** homogeneous. **2,** similar; uniform. —**одноро́дность,** *n.f.* homogeneity.

однору́кий *adj.* one-armed.

односельча́нин [*pl.* **-ча́не, -ча́н**] *n.m.* [*fem.* **-ча́нка**] person from the same village.

односло́жный *adj.* **1,** one-syllable; monosyllabic. **2,** *fig.* one-syllable; terse.

односпа́льный *adj., in* **односпа́льная крова́ть,** single bed.

односторо́нний *adj.* **1,** one-sided. **2,** unilateral. **3,** (*of movement, traffic, etc.*) one-way.

одноти́пный *adj.* of the same type.

одното́мный *adj.* one-volume (*attrib.*).

одното́нный *adj.* **1,** monotone. **2,** single-colored. **3,** (*of a color*) solid.

однофами́лец [*gen.* **-льца**] *n.m.* [*fem.* **-лица**] person with the same (last) name.

одноцве́тный *adj.* one-color (*attrib.*); plain.

одноэта́жный *adj.* one-story.

одобре́ние *n.* approval.

одобри́тельный *adj.* approving. —**одобри́тельно,** *adv.* approvingly.

одобря́ть *v. impfv.* [*pfv.* **одо́брить**] to approve (of).

одолева́ть *v. impfv.* [*pfv.* **одоле́ть**] **1,** to overcome. **2,** *colloq.* to master.

одолжа́ть *v. impfv.* [*pfv.* **одолжи́ть**] **1,** to lend; loan. **2,** *obs.* to oblige; do (someone) a favor.

одолже́ние *n.* favor: сде́лать одолже́ние (+ *dat.*), to do someone a favor.

одолжи́ть *v., pfv. of* **одолжа́ть** *and* **ода́лживать.**

одома́шнивание *n.* domestication. *Also,* **одома́шнение.**

одома́шнивать *v. impfv.* [*pfv.* **одома́шнить**] to domesticate.

одо́метр *n.* odometer.

одонтоло́гия *n.* odontology.

одр [*gen.* **одра́**] *n., obs.* bed. —**на сме́ртном одре́,** on one's deathbed.
одряхле́вший *adj.* decrepit; enfeebled.
одряхле́ть *v., pfv. of* **дряхле́ть.**
одува́нчик *n.* dandelion.
оду́мываться *v.r. impfv.* [*pfv.* **оду́маться**] **1,** to change one's mind; think better of it. **2,** to collect oneself; come to one's senses.
одура́чить *v., pfv. of* **дура́чить.**
одуре́лый *adj., colloq.* dazed; groggy.
одуре́ние *n., colloq.* stupor: пить до одуре́ния, to drink oneself into a stupor.
одуре́ть *v., pfv. of* **дуре́ть.**
одурма́нить *v., pfv. of* **дурма́нить.**
о́дурь *n.f., colloq.* daze; trance; stupor.
одуря́ть *v. impfv., colloq.* to cloud; befuddle (the mind).
одутлова́тый *adj.* puffy.
одухотворя́ть *v. impfv.* [*pfv.* **одухотвори́ть**] **1,** to ascribe intelligent powers to. **2,** to animate; inspire.
одушеви́ть [*infl.* **-влю́, -ви́шь**] *v., pfv. of* **одушевля́ть.**
одушевле́ние *n.* enthusiasm; animation.
одушевлённый *adj.* **1,** animate. **2,** animated.
одушевля́ть *v. impfv.* [*pfv.* **одушеви́ть**] to animate.
оды́шка *n.* shortness of breath.
ожереби́ться *v.r., pfv. of* **жереби́ться.**
ожере́лье *n.* necklace.
ожесточа́ть *v. impfv.* [*pfv.* **ожесточи́ть**] **1,** to harden. **2,** to embitter.
ожесточе́ние *n.* **1,** bitterness. **2,** *fig.* great zeal; great force.
ожесточённый *adj.* bitter; fierce.
ожесточи́ть *v., pfv. of* **ожесточа́ть.**
ожива́ть *v. impfv.* [*pfv.* **ожи́ть**] **1,** to come back to life. **2,** *fig.* to perk up; come alive.
оживи́ть [*infl.* **-влю́, -ви́шь**] *v., pfv. of* **оживля́ть.** —**оживи́ться,** *refl., pfv. of* **оживля́ться.**
оживле́ние *n.* **1,** revival; resuscitation. **2,** animation.
оживлённый *adj.* **1,** animated; lively. **2,** (*of a street*) busy; (*of trade*) brisk. —**оживлённо,** *adv.* with great animation.
оживля́ть *v. impfv.* [*pfv.* **оживи́ть**] **1,** to bring back to life. **2,** to revive; resuscitate. **3,** *fig.* to liven up; enliven; brighten. —**оживля́ться,** *refl.* to perk up; come alive.
ожида́ние *n.* **1,** waiting; wait. **2,** expectation: сверх вся́кого ожида́ния, beyond all expectations. —**в ожида́нии** (+ *gen.*), while waiting; pending.
ожида́ть *v. impfv.* (*with gen.*) **1,** to expect. **2,** to wait for; await.
ожире́ние *n.* obesity.
ожире́ть *v., pfv. of* **жире́ть.**
ожи́ть [*infl.* **оживу́, оживёшь;** *past* **о́жил, ожила́, о́жило**] *v., pfv. of* **ожива́ть.**
ожо́г *n.* burn.
озабо́тить [*infl.* **-чу, -тишь**] *v., pfv. of* **озабо́чивать.** —**озабо́титься,** *refl., pfv. of* **озабо́чиваться.**
озабо́ченный *adj.* anxious; concerned; worried; apprehensive. —**озабо́ченность,** *n.f.* anxiety; concern.
озабо́чивать *v. impfv.* [*pfv.* **озабо́тить**] to cause (someone) anxiety. —**озабо́чиваться,** *refl.* (*with instr.*) to see to; attend to.
озагла́вливать *v. impfv.* [*pfv.* **озагла́вить**] to entitle.
озада́ченный *adj.* puzzled; perplexed; baffled. —**озада́ченность,** *n.f.* puzzlement; perplexity; bafflement.
озада́чивать *v. impfv.* [*pfv.* **озада́чить**] to perplex; baffle; confound; bewilder; take aback.
озаря́ть *v. impfv.* [*pfv.* **озари́ть**] **1,** to light up. **2,** *fig.* (*of a thought or idea*) to strike; dawn upon. —**озаря́ться,** *refl.* to light up.
озвере́лый *adj.* crazed.
озвере́ние *n.* brutality; ferocity.
озвере́ть *v., pfv. of* **звере́ть.**
оздорови́тельный *adj.* health (*attrib.*); sanitary (*attrib.*).
оздорови́ть [*infl.* **-влю́, -ви́шь**] *v., pfv. of* **оздоровля́ть.**
оздоровле́ние *n.* **1,** making healthier. **2,** *fig.* improvement.
оздоровля́ть *v. impfv.* [*pfv.* **оздорови́ть**] **1,** to make healthy; make healthier. **2,** *fig.* to improve.
озелене́ние *n.* planting of trees and shrubs.
озеленя́ть *v. impfv.* [*pfv.* **озелени́ть**] to plant trees and shrubs (in).
о́земь *adv., colloq.* to the ground.
озёрный *adj.* of a lake; lake (*attrib.*).
о́зеро [*pl.* **озёра, озёр**] *n.* lake.
ози́мый *adj.* (*of crops*) winter. —**ози́мые,** *n. pl.* winter crops.
о́зимь *n.f.* winter crop(s).
озира́ть *v. impfv.* to look over. —**озира́ться,** *refl.* to look around.
озло́бить [*infl.* **-блю, -бишь**] *v., pfv. of* **озлобля́ть.** —**озло́биться,** *refl., pfv. of* **озлобля́ться.**
озлобле́ние *n.* bitterness; animosity.
озлобля́ть *v. impfv.* [*pfv.* **озло́бить**] to embitter. —**озлобля́ться,** *refl.* to become embittered.
ознако́мить [*infl.* **-млю, -мишь**] *v., pfv. of* **ознакомля́ть.** —**ознако́миться,** *refl., pfv. of* **ознакомля́ться.**
ознакомле́ние *n.* **1,** acquainting; familiarizing. **2,** acquaintance; familiarization.
ознакомля́ть *v. impfv.* [*pfv.* **ознако́мить**] (*with* **с** + *instr.*) to acquaint (with); familiarize (with). —**ознакомля́ться,** *refl.* (*with* **с** + *instr.*) to familiarize oneself (with); become familiar (with).
ознаменова́ние *n., in* **в ознаменова́ние** (+ *gen.*), in honor of; to mark; in commemoration of.
ознаменова́ть *v. pfv.* [*infl.* **-ну́ю, -ну́ешь**] **1,** *pfv. of* **знаменова́ть. 2,** to celebrate; observe; commemorate.
означа́ть *v. impfv.* to mean; signify; denote.
озно́б *n.* shivering; chill.
озокери́т *n.* ozocerite.
озолоти́ть *v. pfv.* [*infl.* **-чу́, -ти́шь**] **1,** to give a golden color to. **2,** *colloq.* to shower with money, gifts, etc.
озо́н *n.* ozone. —**озо́новый,** *adj.* ozone (*attrib.*).
озорни́к [*gen.* **-ника́**] *n., colloq.* mischief-maker.
озорнича́ть *v. impfv., colloq.* to be naughty; make mischief.
озорно́й *adj.* mischievous.
озорство́ *n.* mischief.
озя́бнуть *v. pfv.* [*past* **озя́б, -ла**] *colloq.* to be cold; freeze.
ой *interj.* **1,** oh!; o! **2,** ouch!
оказа́ние *n.* rendering; providing; giving.
оказа́ть [*infl.* **окажу́, ока́жешь**] *v., pfv. of* **ока́зывать.** —**оказа́ться,** *refl., pfv. of* **ока́зываться.**
ока́зия *n.* **1,** *obs.* opportunity. **2,** *colloq.* unexpected event.

оказывать *v. impfv.* [*pfv.* **оказать**] **1,** to render; provide (assistance, support, etc.). **2,** to give (preference, a welcome, reception, etc.). **3,** to exert; put; apply; bring to bear (pressure). **4,** to exert; have (influence). **5,** to accord (respect); put (confidence); extend (hospitality). **6,** to offer (resistance). —**оказываться,** *refl.* **1,** to find oneself (in a certain place). **2,** (*with instr.*) to turn out to be: он оказался старым знакомым, he turned out to be an old acquaintance. **3,** *impers.* to turn out: оказалось, что..., it turned out that... **4,** to be: оказаться в большинстве, to be in the majority. **5,** (*with* **не**) *indicating the absence of something:* в холодильнике продуктов не оказалось, there was no food in the refrigerator.

окаймлять *v. impfv.* [*pfv.* **окаймить**] to border; edge.

окалина *n.* dross.

окаменелость *n.f.* fossil.

окаменелый *adj.* **1,** petrified. **2,** *fig.* stony; impassive.

окаменеть *v., pfv. of* **каменеть.**

окантовать *v., pfv. of* **кантовать.**

оканчивать *v. impfv.* [*pfv.* **окончить**] **1,** to finish; end; complete. **2,** to graduate (from). —**оканчиваться,** *refl.* **1,** to finish; end; be over. **2,** [*impfv. only*] (*with instr.*) to end (in); terminate (in).

оканье *n.* pronunciation of unstressed Russian **о** as **о** rather than **а.**

окапи *n.m. indecl.* okapi.

окапывать *v. impfv.* [*pfv.* **окопать**] **1,** to dig around. **2,** to dig a ditch around. —**окапываться,** *refl.* to dig in; entrench oneself.

окарина *n.* ocarina.

окатить [*infl.* **окачу, окатишь**] *v., pfv. of* **окачивать.**

окать *v. impfv.* to pronounce unstressed Russian **о** as **о** rather than **а.**

окачивать *v. impfv.* [*pfv.* **окатить**] (*with instr.*) to douse (with). —**окатить кого-нибудь холодной водой,** to dampen one's enthusiasm.

океан *n.* ocean.

океанография *n.* oceanography. —**океанограф,** *n.* oceanographer. —**океанографический,** *adj.* oceanographic.

океанский *adj.* ocean (*attrib.*); oceanic.

окидывать *v. impfv.* [*pfv.* **окинуть**] *in* **окидывать взглядом** (+*acc.*), to cast a glance (at).

окисел [*gen.* **-сла**] *n.* oxide.

окисление *n.* oxidation.

окислять *v. impfv.* [*pfv.* **окислить**] to oxidize. —**окисляться,** *refl.* to oxidize; become oxidized.

окись *n.f.* oxide: окись железа, ferric oxide.

оккультизм *n.* occultism. —**оккультный,** *adj.* occult.

оккупант *n.* invader.

оккупация *n.* (military) occupation. —**оккупационный,** *adj.* occupying; of occupation: оккупационная армия, army of occupation.

оккупировать *v. impfv. & pfv.* [*pres.* **-рую, -руешь**] *mil.* to occupy.

оклад *n.* salary; wages; rate of pay.

оклеветать *v. pfv.* [*infl.* **-вещу, -вещешь**] to slander; smear.

оклеивать *v. impfv.* [*pfv.* **оклеить**] to cover by pasting something on: оклеивать комнату обоями, to paper a room.

оклик *n.* **1,** call. **2,** challenge (*of a sentry*).

окликать *v. impfv.* [*pfv.* **окликнуть**] **1,** to call to; hail. **2,** (*of a sentry*) to challenge.

окно [*pl.* **окна, окон, окнам**] *n.* window.

око [*pl.* **очи, очей, очам**] *n., archaic* eye. —**око за око, зуб за зуб,** an eye for an eye, a tooth for a tooth.

оковать [*infl.* **окую, окуёшь**] *v., pfv. of* **оковывать.**

оковы [*gen.* **оков**] *n. pl.* shackles; fetters.

оковывать *v. impfv.* [*pfv.* **оковать**] **1,** to bind (with metal). **2,** *fig.* to shackle.

околачиваться *v.r. impfv., colloq.* to knock about; hang around.

околдовать [*infl.* **-дую, -дуешь**] *v., pfv. of* **околдовывать.**

околдовывать *v. impfv.* [*pfv.* **околдовать**] to bewitch; cast a spell over.

околевать *v. impfv.* [*pfv.* **околеть**] (*of animals*) to die.

околёсица *n., colloq.* nonsense.

околеть *v., pfv. of* **околевать.**

околица *n.* **1,** fence surrounding a village. **2,** outskirts of a village.

околичности *n. pl.* [*sing.* **околичность**] *obs.* circumlocution. —**без околичностей,** plainly; to the point.

около *prep., with gen.* **1,** near; close to. **2,** about; approximately. —*adv.* around; about: никого нет около, there is no one around/about. —**ходить вокруг да около,** to beat around the bush.

околоплодник *n.* pericarp.

околосердечный *adj., in* **околосердечная сумка,** pericardium.

околоток [*gen.* **-тка**] *n., obs.* neighborhood; district.

околощитовидный *adj., in* **околощитовидная железа,** parathyroid gland.

околпачивать *v. impfv.* [*pfv.* **околпачить**] *colloq.* to fool; dupe; make a fool of.

околыш *n.* hatband.

окольный *adj.* roundabout; circuitous: окольным путём, by a roundabout route.

оконечность *n.f.* extremity (*of an island or continent*).

оконный *adj.* window (*attrib.*).

окончание *n.* **1,** completion; termination. **2,** end. **3,** graduation. **4,** *gram.* ending. **5,** concluding installment: окончание в следующем номере, to be concluded in the next issue.

окончательно *adv.* **1,** finally; definitively. **2,** utterly; completely. **3,** for good.

окончательность *n.f.* finality.

окончательный *adj.* final; definitive.

окончить *v., pfv. of* **оканчивать.** —**окончиться,** *refl., pfv. of* **оканчиваться.**

окоп *n., mil.* trench.

окопать *v., pfv. of* **окапывать.** —**окопаться,** *refl., pfv. of* **окапываться.**

окопный *adj.* trench (*attrib.*). —**окопная война,** trench warfare.

окорок [*pl.* **окорока**] *n.* ham; leg of veal; leg of mutton.

окостенелый *adj.* **1,** ossified. **2,** numb; stiff.

окостенение *n.* ossification.

окостенеть *v., pfv. of* **костенеть.**

окотиться *v.r., pfv. of* **котиться.**

окоченелый *adj.* **1,** numb (*from the cold*). **2,** (*of a corpse*) stiff.

окоченение *n.* rigidity. —**трупное окоченение,** rigor mortis.

окоченеть *v., pfv. of* **коченеть.**

окошко [*pl.* **-шки, -шек**] *n., dim. of* **окно.**

окра́ина *n.* **1,** edge. **2,** outskirts (*of a city*). **3,** remote area (*of a country*).
окра́инный *adj.* outlying.
окра́сить [*infl.* **-шу, -сишь**] *v., pfv. of* **окра́шивать.**
окра́ска *n.* **1,** painting. **2,** color; coloring; coloration. **3,** *fig.* coloration; complexion. —**защи́тная** *or* **покрови́тельственная окра́ска,** protective coloration.
окра́шивать *v. impfv.* [*pfv.* **окра́сить**] to paint.
окре́пнуть [*past* **окре́п, -ла**] *v., pfv. of* **кре́пнуть.**
окрести́ть *v. pfv.* [*infl.* **окрещу́, окре́стишь**] **1,** *pfv. of* **крести́ть** (*in sense #1*). **2,** *colloq.* to nickname. —**окрести́ться,** *refl., pfv. of* **крести́ться** (*in sense* #1).
окре́стность *n.f., usu. pl.* environs; suburbs.
окре́стный *adj.* **1,** neighboring; adjacent. **2,** local; living nearby.
о́крик *n.* shout; cry.
окри́кнуть *v. pfv.* to shout to; call to.
окрова́вить *v. pfv.* [*infl.* **-влю, -вишь**] to stain with blood.
окрова́вленный *adj.* bloodstained.
окропля́ть *v. impfv.* [*pfv.* **окропи́ть**] to sprinkle; besprinkle.
окро́шка *n.* **1,** cold soup made from kvass with meat and vegetables. **2,** *colloq.* hodgepodge.
о́круг [*pl.* **округа́**] *n.* district.
окру́га *n., colloq.* neighborhood.
округли́ть *v., pfv. of* **округля́ть.** —**округли́ться,** *refl., pfv. of* **округля́ться.**
окру́глый *adj.* round; rounded.
округля́ть *v. impfv.* [*pfv.* **округли́ть**] **1,** to round; make round. **2,** to round off. **3,** *in* округля́ть глаза́, to stare wide-eyed. **4,** *colloq.* to enlarge (one's holdings). —**округля́ться,** *refl.* **1,** to become round. **2,** to fill out.
окружа́ть *v. impfv.* [*pfv.* **окружи́ть**] **1,** to surround; encircle. **2,** to gather round. **3,** to lavish: окружа́ть кого́-нибудь забо́той, to lavish care upon someone.
окружа́ющий *adj.* surrounding. —**окружа́ющее,** *n. neut.* one's surroundings: всё окружа́ющее, everything around one. —**окружа́ющие,** *n. pl.* those around one.
окруже́ние *n.* **1,** encirclement. **2,** surroundings; environment. **3,** entourage. —**в окруже́нии** (+ *gen.*), accompanied by; surrounded by; in the midst of.
окружи́ть *v., pfv. of* **окружа́ть.**
окружно́й *adj.* district (*attrib.*). —**окружна́я желе́зная доро́га,** suburban railway (*circling a city*). —**окружно́й суд,** circuit court.
окру́жность *n.f.* circumference.
окрути́ть [*inf.* **окручу́, окру́тишь**] *v., pfv. of* **окру́чивать.**
окру́чивать *v. impfv.* [*pfv.* **окрути́ть**] *colloq.* to wind around: окрути́ть про́волоку ле́нтой, to wind tape around a wire.
окрыля́ть *v. impfv.* [*pfv.* **окрыли́ть**] to inspire.
окры́ситься *v.r. pfv.* (*with* **на** + *acc.*) *colloq.* to snap (at).
окта́ва *n.* octave.
окта́н *n.* octane.
окте́т *n.* octet.
октя́брь [*gen.* **-бря́**] *n.m.* **1,** October. **2,** *cap.* the October Revolution (*of 1917*).
октя́брьский *adj.* **1,** October (*attrib.*). **2,** *cap.* of or pert. to the October Revolution.
окули́ст *n.* oculist.
окуля́р *n.* eyepiece.
окуна́ть *v. impfv.* [*pfv.* **окуну́ть**] (*with* **в** + *acc.*) to dip (something into a liquid). —**окуна́ться,** *refl.* (*with* **в** + *acc.*) **1,** to dip (into). **2,** *fig.* to be plunged into (darkness). **3,** *fig.* to be absorbed in; be engrossed in.
о́кунь [*pl.* **о́куни, окуне́й, окуня́м**] *n.m.* perch (*fish*).
окупа́ть *v. impfv.* [*pfv.* **окупи́ть**] to cover (a cost); cover the cost of. —**окупа́ться,** *refl.* **1,** to pay for itself. **2,** *fig.* to be justified; be worth it.
окупи́ть [*infl.* **окуплю́, оку́пишь**] *v., pfv. of* **окупа́ть.** —**окупи́ться,** *refl., pfv. of* **окупа́ться.**
оку́ривание *n.* fumigation.
оку́ривать *v. impfv.* [*pfv.* **окури́ть**] to fumigate.
окури́ть [*infl.* **окурю́, оку́ришь**] *v., pfv. of* **оку́ривать.**
оку́рок [*gen.* **-рка**] *n.* cigarette butt; cigar stub.
оку́тывать *v. impfv.* [*pfv.* **оку́тать**] **1,** to wrap. **2,** *fig.* to envelop; shroud.
ола́дья [*gen. pl.* **-дий**] *n.* pancake; fritter.
олеа́ндр *n.* oleander. —**олеа́ндровый,** *adj.* oleander (*attrib.*).
оледене́лый *adj.* frozen.
оледене́ть *v., pfv. of* **ледене́ть.**
оледени́ть *v., pfv. of* **ледени́ть.**
оленебы́к [*gen.* **-быка́**] *n.* eland (*antelope*).
оленево́д *n.* reindeer breeder. —**оленево́дство,** *n.* reindeer breeding. —**оленево́дческий,** *adj.* reindeer-breeding (*attrib.*).
оле́ний [*fem.* **-нья**] *adj.* **1,** deer (*attrib.*); deer's; reindeer (*attrib.*). **2,** deerskin. —**оле́ньи рога́,** antlers.
оле́нина *n.* venison.
олену́ха *n.* doe (*female deer*).
оле́нь *n.m.* deer. —**благоро́дный оле́нь,** red deer. —**се́верный оле́нь,** reindeer.
оли́ва *n.* **1,** olive. **2,** olive tree. *Also,* **оли́вка.**
оли́вковый *adj.* **1,** olive (*attrib.*). **2,** olive-green.
олига́рх *n.* oligarch. —**олигархи́ческий,** *adj.* oligarchic. —**олига́рхия,** *n.* oligarchy.
олимпиа́да *n.* **1,** Olympiad. **2,** Olympics.
олимпи́йский *adj.* Olympian; Olympic. —**Олимпи́йские и́гры,** Olympic Games.
оли́фа *n.* drying oil.
олицетворе́ние *n.* personification; embodiment.
олицетворя́ть *v. impfv.* [*pfv.* **олицетвори́ть**] to personify; embody.
о́лово *n.* tin. —**оловя́нный,** *adj.* tin.
о́лух *n., colloq.* oaf; dolt; blockhead.
о́луша *n.* gannet (*bird*).
ольха́ [*pl.* **о́льхи**] *n.* alder. —**ольхо́вый,** *adj.* alder (*attrib.*).
оля́пка [*gen. pl.* **-пок**] *n.* water ouzel; dipper.
ом *n.* ohm.
ома́р *n.* lobster.
оме́га *n.* omega.
оме́ла *n.* mistletoe.
омерзе́ние *n.* loathing.
омерзи́тельный *adj.* loathsome; disgusting; revolting.
омертве́лый *adj.* **1,** (*of tissues, cells, etc.*) dead. **2,** *fig.* stiff; numb. **3,** *fig.* deserted; lifeless.
омертве́ть *v., pfv. of* **мертве́ть.**
омёт *n.* stack of straw.
омле́т *n.* omelet.
о́мнибус *n., obs.* horse-drawn coach (*carrying paying passengers*).
омове́ние *n.* ablution.

омола́живать *v. impfv.* [*pfv.* **омолоди́ть**] to rejuvenate.
омоложе́ние *n.* rejuvenation.
омо́ним *n.* homonym.
омрача́ть *v. impfv.* [*pfv.* **омрачи́ть**] **1,** *obs.* to darken. **2,** to dull (the senses). **3,** to dampen; cast a pall over.
о́мут *n.* **1,** deep place in a river or lake. **2,** whirlpool. **3,** *fig.* maelstrom.
омыва́ть *v. impfv.* [*pfv.* **омы́ть**] **1,** to wash. **2,** [*impfv. only*] (*of waves, the sea, etc.*) to wash (the shore).
омы́ть [*infl.* **омо́ю, омо́ешь**] *v., pfv. of* **омыва́ть.**
он [*gen. & acc.* **его́**; *dat.* **ему́**; *instr.* **им**; *prepl.* **нём**] *pers. pron., 3rd person sing. masc.* he; (*of inanimate objects*) it.
она́ [*gen. & acc.* **её**; *dat.* **ей**; *instr.* **е́ю** *or* **ей**; *prepl.* **ней**] *pers. pron., 3rd person sing. fem.* she; (*of inanimate objects*) it.
она́гр *n.* onager.
онани́зм *n.* masturbation.
онани́ровать *v. impfv.* [*pres.* **-рую, -руешь**] to masturbate.
онда́тра *n.* muskrat.
онеме́лый *adj.* **1,** numb; stiff. **2,** *obs.* dumb; mute.
онеме́ние *n.* **1,** numbness. **2,** inability to speak.
онеме́ть *v., pfv. of* **неме́ть.**
онёры *n. pl.* [*sing.* **онёра**] *cards* honors.
они́ [*gen. & acc.* **их**; *dat.* **им**; *instr.* **и́ми**; *prepl.* **них**] *pers. pron., 3rd person pl.* they.
о́никс *n.* onyx. —**о́никсовй,** *adj.* onyx.
о́но *see* **о́ный.**
оно́ [*infl. like* **он**] *pers. pron., 3rd person sing. neut.* it.
онтоло́гия *n.* ontology. —**онтологи́ческий,** *adj.* ontological.
ону́ча [*gen. pl.* **ону́ч**] *n.* piece of cloth wrapped around the foot and worn instead of a stocking.
о́ный *adj., obs.* that. —**во вре́мя о́но,** long ago; way back when.
опада́ть *v. impfv.* [*pfv.* **опа́сть**] **1,** (*of leaves*) to fall; (*of fruit or petals*) to fall off. **2,** (*of wind*) to subside. **3,** (*of a swelling*) to go down. **4,** *colloq.* (*of one's face or cheeks*) to become sunken.
опа́здывать *v. impfv.* [*pfv.* **опозда́ть**] to be late: опозда́ть в шко́лу/на рабо́ту/к обе́ду/, to be late for school/work/dinner. Опозда́ть с отве́том, to be late in answering. Опозда́ть на полчаса́, to be half an hour late.
опа́ивать *v. impfv.* [*pfv.* **опои́ть**] **1,** to give (an animal) too much to drink. **2,** to make (someone) drunk. **3,** *obs.* to poison.
опа́л *n.* opal.
опа́ла *n.* disgrace: быть в опа́ле, to be in disgrace.
опа́ливать *v. impfv.* [*pfv.* **опали́ть**] **1,** to scorch; sear. **2,** to singe (feathers, a chicken, etc.).
опали́ть *v., pfv. of* **пали́ть** (*in sense # 1*), **опаля́ть,** *and* **опа́ливать.**
опа́ловый *adj.* opal; opaline.
опа́льный *adj.* disgraced; in disgrace; in disfavor.
опаля́ть *v. impfv.* = **опа́ливать.**
опа́ра *n.* leavened dough.
опарши́веть *v., pfv. of* **паршѝветь.**
опаса́ться *v.r. impfv.* **1,** (*with gen.*) to fear. **2,** (*with gen. or inf.*) to avoid; refrain from.
опасе́ние *n.* fear; apprehension.
опа́ска *n., colloq., in* **с опа́ской,** cautiously; **без опа́ски,** without fear.
опа́сливый *adj., colloq.* cautious; fearful.
опа́сно *adv.* dangerously. —*adj., used predicatively* dangerous: по э́той доро́ге опа́сно е́хать, it is dangerous to drive on this road.
опа́сность *n.f.* danger.
опа́сный *adj.* dangerous. —**опа́сная бри́тва,** straight razor.
опа́сть [*infl. like* **пасть**] *v., pfv. of* **опада́ть.**
опаха́ло *n.* large fan.
опе́ка *n.* guardianship; tutelage. —**Междунаро́дная опе́ка,** International Trusteeship. —**Сове́т по Опе́ке,** Trusteeship Council (*of the United Nations*).
опека́емый *n., decl. as an adj.* ward.
опека́ть *v. impfv.* **1,** to be the guardian of. **2,** *fig.* to watch over.
опеку́н [*gen.* **-куна́**] *n.* guardian. —**опеку́нский,** *adj.* of a guardian; guardian's; tutelary. —**опеку́нство,** *n.* guardianship
о́пера *n.* opera.
операти́вный *adj.* **1,** operative; surgical: операти́вное вмеша́тельство, surgical intervention. **2,** *mil.* operations (*attrib.*); operational. **3,** effective; efficient.
опера́тор *n.* **1,** operator. **2,** cameraman. **3,** *obs.* surgeon.
операцио́нный *adj.* **1,** *med.* operating. **2,** *mil.* operations (*attrib.*). —**операцио́нная,** *n.* operating room.
опера́ция *n., med., mil., finance, etc.* operation.
опережа́ть *v. impfv.* [*pfv.* **опереди́ть**] **1,** to pass; outdistance; leave behind. **2,** to do something ahead of (someone); beat (someone) to it. **3,** to surpass; excel.
опере́ние *n.* plumage.
оперённый *adj.* feathered.
опере́тта *n.* operetta; musical comedy. —**опере́точный,** *adj.* of operetta; musical-comedy (*attrib.*).
опере́ть [*infl.* **обопру́, обопрёшь**; *past* **опёр, оперла́, оперло́**] *v., pfv. of* **опира́ть.** —**опере́ться,** *refl.* [*past* **опёрся, оперла́сь, оперло́сь**] *pfv. of* **опира́ться.**
опери́ровать *v. impfv.* [*pres.* **-рую, -руешь**] **1,** to operate on. **2,** *mil.* to operate. **3,** (*with instr.*) to use.
опери́ться *v.r., pfv. of* **опери́ться.**
о́перный *adj.* opera (*attrib.*); operatic.
оперя́ться *v.r. impfv.* [*pfv.* **опери́ться**] **1,** (*of a bird*) to become fully fledged. **2,** *fig.* to become independent; stand on one's own feet.
опеча́ленный *adj.* sad; sorrowful.
опеча́лить *v., pfv. of* **печа́лить.** —**опеча́литься,** *refl., pfv. of* **печа́литься.**
опеча́тать *v., pfv. of* **опеча́тывать.**
опеча́тка [*gen. pl.* **-ток**] *n.* misprint.
опеча́тывать *v. impfv.* [*pfv.* **опеча́тать**] to seal up.
опе́шить *v. pfv., colloq.* to be taken aback.
опива́ться *v.r. impfv.* [*pfv.* **опи́ться**] *colloq.* to drink to excess; have too much to drink; (*with instr.*) drink too much (of); have too much (of something) to drink.
о́пий *n.* opium. —**о́пийный,** *adj.* opium (*attrib.*).
опи́ливать *v. impfv.* [*pfv.* **опили́ть**] to saw.
опили́ть [*infl.* **опилю́, опи́лишь**] *v., pfv. of* **опи́ливать.**
опи́лки [*gen.* **-лок**] *n. pl.* **1,** filings. **2,** sawdust.
опира́ть *v. impfv.* [*pfv.* **опере́ть**] (*with* **на** *or* **о** + *acc.*) to lean (something) on *or* against. —**опира́ться,** *refl.* (*with* **на** *or* **о** + *acc.*) **1,** to lean on; lean against. **2,** *fig.* to rely on; depend on.

описа́ние *n.* description. —**описа́тельный,** *adj.* descriptive.

описа́ть [*infl.* **опишу́, опи́шешь**] *v., pfv. of* **опи́сывать.** —**описа́ться,** *refl.* to make a slip of the pen.

опи́ска [*gen. pl.* **-сок**] *n.* slip of the pen.

опи́сывать *v. impfv.* [*pfv.* **описа́ть**] **1,** to describe. **2,** to take inventory of. **3,** *math.* to circumscribe. **4,** to make; move in; describe (a circle, arc, etc.).

о́пись *n.f.* inventory.

опи́ться [*infl.* **обопью́сь, обопьёшься;** *past* **опи́лся, опила́сь, опило́сь**] *v.r., pfv. of* **опива́ться.**

о́пиум *n.* opium. —**о́пиумный,** *adj.* opium (*attrib.*).

опла́кать [*infl.* **опла́чу, опла́чешь**] *v., pfv. of* **опла́кивать.**

опла́кивать *v. impfv.* [*pfv.* **опла́кать**] to mourn; mourn the loss of.

опла́та *n.* pay; payment.

оплати́ть [*infl.* **оплачу́, опла́тишь**] *v., pfv. of* **опла́чивать.**

опла́чиваемый *adj.* paid: опла́чиваемый о́тпуск, paid vacation.

опла́чивать *v. impfv.* [*pfv.* **оплати́ть**] to pay.

оплева́ть [*infl.* **оплюю́, оплюёшь**] *v., pfv. of* **оплёвывать.**

оплёвывать *v. impfv.* [*pfv.* **оплева́ть**] *colloq.* to spit on (*lit. & fig.*).

оплести́ [*infl. like* **плести́**] *v., pfv. of* **оплета́ть.**

оплета́ть *v. impfv.* [*pfv.* **оплести́**] to entwine; string: оплести́ и́згородь колю́чей про́волокой, to entwine/string a fence with barbed wire.

оплеу́ха *n., colloq.* slap in the face.

оплеши́веть *v., pfv. of* **плеши́веть.**

оплодотворе́ние *n.* fertilization; impregnation; insemination.

оплодотворя́ть *v. impfv.* [*pfv.* **оплодотвори́ть**] to fertilize; impregnate.

опло́т *n.* bulwark; bastion.

оплоша́ть *v. pfv., colloq.* to make a mistake; slip up.

опло́шность *n.f.* mistake; blunder.

оплыва́ть *v. impfv.* [*pfv.* **оплы́ть**] **1,** to swim around; sail around. **2,** to swell up; become swollen. **3,** (*of a candle*) to drip.

оплы́ть [*infl. like* **плыть**] *v., pfv. of* **оплыва́ть.**

оповеща́ть *v. impfv.* [*pfv.* **оповести́ть**] to notify; inform.

оповеще́ние *n.* notification.

опо́ек [*gen.* **опо́йка**] *n.* calfskin.

опозда́ние *n.* **1,** lateness; tardiness. Нача́ть собра́ние с опозда́нием, to start the meeting late. **2,** delay.

опозда́ть *v., pfv. of* **опа́здывать.**

опознава́тельный *adj.* identification (*attrib.*); identifying. —**опознава́тельный знак, 1,** identification mark. **2,** landmark.

опознава́ть *v. impfv.* [*pfv.* **опозна́ть;** *pres.* **-знаю́, знаёшь**] to identify.

опозна́ние *n.* identification.

опозна́ть *v., pfv. of* **опознава́ть.**

опозо́рить *v., pfv. of* **позо́рить.** —**опозо́риться,** *refl., pfv. of* **позо́риться.**

опои́ть [*infl.* **опою́, опо́ишь** *or* **опои́шь**] *v., pfv. of* **опа́ивать.**

опо́йковый *adj.* calfskin (*attrib.*).

опола́скивать *v. impfv.* [*pfv.* **ополосну́ть**] to rinse.

ополза́ть *v. impfv.* [*pfv.* **оползти́**] **1,** to crawl around. **2,** (*of the ground or a building*) to slip; sink.

о́ползень [*gen.* **-зня**] *n.m.* landslide; mudslide.

оползти́ [*infl. like* **ползти́**] *v., pfv. of* **ополза́ть.**

ополосну́ть *v., pfv. of* **опола́скивать.**

ополча́ться *v.r. impfv.* [*pfv.* **ополчи́ться**] (*with* **на** + *acc. or* **про́тив**) **1,** to take up arms (against). **2,** *fig.* to assail; sail into.

ополче́нец [*gen.* **-нца**] *n.* militiaman.

ополче́ние *n.* militia.

ополчи́ться *v.r., pfv. of* **ополча́ться.**

опо́мниться *v.r. pfv.* **1,** to regain consciousness. **2,** to come to one's senses.

опо́р *n., in* **во весь опо́р,** at top speed; full tilt.

опо́ра *n.* **1,** support. **2,** basis. —**то́чка опо́ры, 1,** fulcrum. **2,** foothold: найти́ то́чку опо́ры, to gain a foothold.

опора́жнивать *v. impfv.* [*pfv.* **опоро́жнить** *or* **опорожни́ть**] to empty. —**опора́жниваться,** *refl.* to empty; become empty.

опо́рки *n. pl.* [*sing.* **опо́рок**] worn-out shoes.

опо́рный *adj.* supporting: опо́рная коло́нна, supporting column. —**опо́рный пункт,** *mil.* strong point.

опоро́жнить *also,* **опорожни́ть** *v., pfv. of* **опора́жнивать** *and* **опорожня́ть.** —**опоро́жни́ться,** *refl., pfv. of* **опора́жниваться** *and* **опорожня́ться.**

опорожня́ть *v. impfv.* = **опора́жнивать.** —**опорожня́ться,** *refl.* = **опора́жниваться.**

опоро́с *n.* farrow.

опоро́чить *v., pfv. of* **поро́чить.**

опо́ссум *n.* opossum.

опосты́леть *v. pfv.* (*with dat.*) *colloq.* to become hateful (to).

опохмеля́ться *v.r. impfv.* [*pfv.* **опохмели́ться**] *colloq.* to take a drink in order to cure a hangover.

опочи́ть *v. pfv.* [*infl.* **-чи́ю, -чи́ешь**] *obs.* **1,** to go to sleep. **2,** to die.

опошля́ть *v. impfv.* [*pfv.* **опо́шлить**] **1,** to vulgarize; debase. **2,** to make trite by overuse.

опоя́сать [*infl.* **опоя́шу, опоя́шешь**] *v., pfv. of* **опоя́сывать.** —**опоя́саться,** *refl., pfv. of* **опоя́сываться.**

опоя́сывать *v. impfv.* [*pfv.* **опоя́сать**] **1,** to gird. **2,** to circle; girdle. —**опоя́сываться, 1,** [*also,* опоя́сываться ремнём] to put on one's belt. **2,** *fig.* (*with instr.*) to be circled (by); be surrounded (by).

оппози́ция *n., polit.* opposition. —**оппозицио́нный,** *adj.* opposition (*attrib.*).

оппоне́нт *n.* opponent (*in a debate or argument*).

оппони́ровать *v. impfv.* (*with dat.*) to oppose (*in a discussion, debate, etc.*).

оппортуни́зм *n.* opportunism. —**оппортуни́ст,** *n.* opportunist. —**оппортунисти́ческий,** *adj.* opportunistic.

опра́ва *n.* **1,** mount; setting. **2,** frame; rim (*for eyeglasses*).

оправда́ние *n.* **1,** justification. **2,** excuse. **3,** *law* acquittal.

оправда́тельный *adj., in* **оправда́тельный пригово́р,** verdict of "not guilty".

оправда́ть *v., pfv. of* **опра́вдывать.** —**оправда́ться,** *refl., pfv. of* **опра́вдываться.**

опра́вдывать *v. impfv.* [*pfv.* **оправда́ть**] **1,** to justify. **2,** to excuse. **3,** to acquit. **4,** to live up to. **5,** *in* **оправда́ть себя́,** to prove its worth; prove worthwhile. —**опра́вдываться,** *refl.* **1,** to justify oneself; justify one's actions. **2,** to justify itself; be justified. **3,** to (try to) prove one's innocence. **4,** to prove to be correct. **5,** to be realized; materialize; come true.

опра́вить [*infl.* **-влю, -вишь**] *v., pfv. of* **оправля́ть.** —**опра́виться,** *refl., pfv. of* **оправля́ться.**

опра́вка [*gen. pl.* **-вок**] *n.* mandrel.

оправля́ть *v. impfv.* [*pfv.* **опра́вить**] **1,** to straighten; adjust. **2,** to mount; set in a mount. —**оправля́ться,** *refl.* **1,** to straighten one's clothes; tidy oneself up. **2,** to recover; get well.

опра́шивать *v. impfv.* [*pfv.* **опроси́ть**] **1,** to poll; canvass. **2,** to question; examine.

определе́ние *n.* **1,** determination. **2,** definition. **3,** *law* decision; ruling. **4,** *gram.* attribute; modifier.

определённо *adv.* definitely.

определённый *adj.* **1,** definite. **2,** certain: при определённых усло́виях, under certain conditions.

определи́тель *n.m.* **1,** determining factor. **2,** *math.* determinant.

определя́ть *v. impfv.* [*pfv.* **определи́ть**] **1,** to determine. **2,** to define. **3,** to fix; set. **4,** to diagnose (an illness). —**определя́ться,** *refl.* **1,** to be determined. **2,** to be formed; take shape. **3,** to determine one's position.

опресне́ние *n.* desalinization; desalination.

опресня́ть *v. impfv.* [*pfv.* **опресни́ть**] to desalinate.

опри́чнина *n., hist.* oprichnina (*period of terror during the reign of Tsar Ivan IV; also those charged with carrying it out*).

опро́бовать *v. pfv.* [*infl.* **-бую, -буешь**] to test.

опроверга́ть *v. impfv.* [*pfv.* **опрове́ргнуть**] **1,** to refute; rebut; disprove. **2,** to deny.

опрове́ргнуть [*past* **-ве́рг, -ла**] *v., pfv. of* **опроверга́ть.**

опроверже́ние *n.* **1,** refutation. **2,** denial. **3,** disclaimer; retraction.

опроки́дывать *v. impfv.* [*pfv.* **опроки́нуть**] to overturn; upset; tip over; knock over; topple. —**опроки́дываться,** *refl.* **1,** to overturn; fall over; tip over; topple over. **2,** (*of a boat*) to capsize.

опроме́тчивый *adj.* rash; impetuous. —**опроме́тчиво,** *adv.* rashly; impetuously. —**опроме́тчивость,** *n.f.* rashness; impetuosity.

о́прометью *adv.* headlong.

опро́с *n.* **1,** questioning. **2,** poll; survey. **3,** quiz (*in school*).

опроси́ть [*infl.* **опрошу́, опро́сишь**] *v., pfv. of* **опра́шивать.**

опро́сный *adj., in* **опро́сный лист,** questionnaire.

опроста́ть *v. pfv., colloq.* to empty; empty the contents of.

опростоволо́ситься *v.r. pfv.* [*infl.* **-шусь, -сишься**] *colloq.* to make a fool of oneself.

опротестова́ть *v. pfv.* [*infl.* **-сту́ю, -сту́ешь**] *law* to appeal; protest; contest.

опроти́веть *v. pfv.* (*with dat.*) to become loathsome (to).

опры́скивать *v. impfv.* [*pfv.* **опры́скать**] **1,** to sprinkle. **2,** to spray.

опря́тный *adj.* neat; tidy. —**опря́тно,** *adv.* neatly. —**опря́тность,** *n.f.* neatness; tidiness.

о́птик *n.* optician; optometrist. —**о́птика,** *n.* optics.

оптима́льный *adj.* optimum.

оптими́зм *n.* optimism. —**оптими́ст,** *n.* optimist. —**оптимисти́ческий,** *adj.* optimistic.

о́птимум *n.* optimum.

опти́ческий *adj.* optical.

оптови́к [*gen.* **-вика́**] *n.* wholesaler. —**опто́вый,** *adj.* wholesale. —**о́птом,** *adv.* wholesale.

опубликова́ние *n.* **1,** publication. **2,** promulgation.

опубликова́ть *v. pfv.* [*infl.* **-ку́ю, -ку́ешь**] **1,** *pfv. of* **публикова́ть.** **2,** to promulgate.

опу́нция *n.* prickly pear.

о́пус *n.* opus.

опуска́ть *v. impfv.* [*pfv.* **опусти́ть**] **1,** to lower; let down. **2,** (*with* **в** + *acc.*) to put (into); drop; deposit: опуска́ть письмо́ в почто́вый я́щик, to mail a letter. **3,** to omit; leave out. —**как в во́ду опу́щенный,** dejected; crestfallen. —**опуска́ть ру́ки,** to become disheartened; lose heart.

опуска́ться *v.r. impfv.* [*pfv.* **опусти́ться**] **1,** to go down; descend; sink. **2,** *fig.* to go downhill; go to seed.

опусте́лый *adj.* deserted.

опусте́ть *v., pfv. of* **пусте́ть.**

опусти́ть [*infl.* **опущу́, опу́стишь**] *v., pfv. of* **опуска́ть.** —**опусти́ться,** *refl., pfv. of* **опуска́ться.**

опустоша́ть *v. impfv.* [*pfv.* **опустоши́ть**] to devastate; ravage; lay waste.

опустоше́ние *n.* devastation.

опустоши́тельный *adj.* devastating.

опустоши́ть *v., pfv. of* **опустоша́ть.**

опу́тывать *v. impfv.* [*pfv.* **опу́тать**] **1,** to wind around; tie around: опу́тать что́-нибудь веревкой, to tie/wind a string around something. **2,** *fig.* to entangle.

опуха́ть *v. impfv.* [*pfv.* **опу́хнуть**] to swell (up); become swollen.

опу́хлый *adj., colloq.* swollen.

опу́хнуть [*past* **опу́х, -ла**] *v., pfv. of* **опуха́ть.**

о́пухоль *n.f.* **1,** swelling. **2,** tumor.

опуша́ть *v. impfv.* [*pfv.* **опуши́ть**] **1,** to trim with fur. **2,** (*with instr.*) to cover with (fur, snow, frost, etc.).

опу́шка [*gen. pl.* **-шек**] *n.* **1,** edge of a forest. **2,** fur trimming.

опуще́ние *n.* **1,** lowering; coming down. **2,** omission. **3,** *med.* prolapse.

опыле́ние *n.* pollination.

опы́ливать *v. impfv.* [*pfv.* **опыли́ть**] to dust (crops).

опыли́ть *v., pfv. of* **опыля́ть** *and* **опы́ливать.**

опыля́ть *v. impfv.* [*pfv.* **опыли́ть**] to pollinate.

о́пыт *n.* **1,** experience. **2,** experiment.

о́пытный *adj.* **1,** experienced. **2,** experimental.

опьяне́лый *adj., colloq.* intoxicated.

опьяне́ние *n.* intoxication.

опьяне́ть *v., pfv. of* **пьяне́ть.**

опьяни́ть *v., pfv. of* **пьяни́ть** *and* **опьяня́ть.**

опьяня́ть *v. impfv.* [*pfv.* **опьяни́ть**] to intoxicate; make drunk.

опя́ть *adv.* again. —**опя́ть-таки,** **1,** again. **2,** and what is more.

ора́ва *n., colloq.* **1,** crowd; mob. **2,** throng; horde.

ора́кул *n.* oracle.

ора́ло *n., obs.* plow. —**перекова́ть мечи́ на ора́ла,** to beat swords into plowshares.

орангута́нг *n.* orangutan.

ора́нжевый *adj.* orange.

оранжере́я *n.* hothouse; greenhouse. —**оранжере́йный,** *adj.* hothouse (*attrib.*).

ора́тор *n.* speaker; orator

орато́рия *n.* oratorio.

ора́торский *adj.* oratorical. —**ора́торское иску́сство,** oratory; public speaking.

ора́торствовать *v. impfv.* [*pres.* **-ствую, -ствуешь**] *colloq.* to orate; perorate.

ора́ть *v. impfv.* [*pres.* **ору́, орёшь**] *colloq.* to yell; scream.

орби́та *n.* **1,** orbit. **2,** eye socket. —**орбита́льный,** *adj.* orbital.

орга́зм *n.* orgasm.

о́рган *n.* **1,** *physiol.* organ: о́рганы ре́чи, organs of speech. **2,** (governmental) organ; body: о́рганы вла́сти, organs of power; законода́тельный о́рган, legislative body. **3,** organ; publication.

орга́н *n.* organ (*musical instrument*).

организа́тор *n.* organizer. —**организа́торский,** *adj.* organizational.

организацио́нный *adj.* of organization; organizational.

организа́ция *n.* **1,** organization. **2,** an organization.

органи́зм *n.* organism.

организо́ванный *adj.* organized; well-organized. —**организо́ванно,** *adv.* in an organized manner. —**организо́ванность,** *n.f.* (good) organization.

организова́ть *v. impfv. & pfv.* [*pres.* **-зу́ю, -зу́ешь**] to organize. —**организова́ться,** *refl.* **1,** to be organized. **2,** to organize; get organized.

органи́ст *n.* organist.

органи́ческий *adj.* organic.

орга́нный *adj., music* organ (*attrib.*).

о́ргия *n.* orgy.

орда́ [*pl.* **о́рды**] *n.* horde. —**Золота́я орда́,** the Golden Horde.

о́рден *n.* **1,** [*pl.* **ордена́**] order (*medal*): о́рден Кра́сного Зна́мени, Order of the Red Banner. **2,** [*pl.* **о́рдены**] order (*society*): масо́нский о́рден, the Masonic Order.

орденоно́сец [*gen.* **-сца**] *n.* holder of an order.

о́рдер [*pl.* **ордера́**] *n.* **1,** order; warrant; writ. **2,** voucher.

ордина́рец [*gen.* **-рца**] *n., mil.* orderly.

ордина́рный *adj.* ordinary.

ордина́та *n., geom.* ordinate.

орёл [*gen.* **орла́**] *n.* eagle. —**орёл и́ли ре́шка?,** heads or tails?

орео́л *n.* **1,** halo. **2,** *fig.* aura.

оре́х *n.* **1,** nut. **2,** walnut (*tree & wood*). —**доста́ться на оре́хи** (+ *dat.*), *colloq.* to get it hot; get it good. —**разде́лывать под оре́х, 1,** to rake over the coals. **2,** to rout.

оре́ховый *adj.* **1,** nut (*attrib.*). **2,** walnut (*attrib.*).

оре́шек [*gen.* **-шка**] *n., dim. of* **оре́х.** —**бу́ковый оре́шек,** beechnut. —**черни́льный оре́шек,** gallnut.

оре́шник *n.* hazel (*tree*).

оригина́л *n.* **1,** original: чита́ть в оригина́ле, to read in the original. **2,** *colloq.* queer bird; queer duck; unique character.

оригина́льничать *v. impfv., colloq.* to try to be clever.

оригина́льный *adj.* original. —**оригина́льность,** *n.f.* originality.

ориента́льный *adj.* oriental.

ориента́ция *n.* orientation; getting one's bearings.

ориенти́р *n.* landmark; reference point.

ориенти́ровать *v. impfv. & pfv.* [*pres.* **-рую, -руешь**] to orient. —**ориенти́роваться,** *refl.* **1,** [*pfv. also* **сориенти́роваться**] to orient oneself; get one's bearings. **2,** (*with* **на** + *acc.*) to be oriented (toward); direct one's efforts (toward).

ориентиро́вка *n.* orientation; getting one's bearings. —**чу́вство ориентиро́вки,** sense of direction.

ориентиро́вочно *adv.* **1,** approximately. **2,** tentatively.

ориентиро́вочный *adj.* **1,** reference (*attrib.*): ориентиро́вочный пункт, reference point. **2,** preliminary; tentative. **3,** approximate.

орке́стр *n.* **1,** orchestra. **2,** orchestra pit.

оркестрова́ть *v. impfv. & pfv.* [*pres.* **-стру́ю, -стру́ешь**] to orchestrate.

оркестро́вка *n.* orchestration.

оркестро́вый *adj.* orchestral.

орла́н *n.* sea eagle; bald eagle.

орлёнок [*gen.* **-нка;** *pl.* **орля́та, -ля́т**] *n.* eaglet.

орли́ный *adj.* eagle (*attrib.*). —**орли́ный нос,** aquiline nose.

орна́мент *n.* ornamental design; decorative pattern.

орнитоло́гия *n.* ornithology. —**орнито́лог,** *n.* ornithologist. —**орнитологи́ческий,** *adj.* ornithological.

оробе́лый *adj.* frightened; timid.

оробе́ть *v. pfv.* to become shy; lose one's nerve.

ороси́тельный *adj.* irrigation (*attrib.*).

ороси́ть [*infl.* **-шу́, -си́шь**] *v., pfv. of* **ороша́ть.**

ороша́ть *v. impfv.* [*pfv.* **ороси́ть**] to irrigate.

ороше́ние *n.* irrigation.

ортодокса́льный *adj.* orthodox. —**ортодо́ксия,** *n.* orthodoxy.

ортодонти́я *n.* orthodontia.

ортопе́дия *n.* orthopedics. —**ортопе́д,** *n.* orthopedics. —**ортопеди́ческий,** *adj.* orthopedic.

ору́дие *n.* **1,** instrument; implement. Ору́дие пы́тки, instrument of torture. **2,** *fig.* instrument; tool: ору́дия произво́дства, instruments/tools of production. **3,** *fig.* tool: ору́дие в рука́х (+ *gen.*), a tool in the hands of. **4,** *mil.* gun.

оруди́йный *adj., mil.* gun (*attrib.*).

ору́довать *v. impfv.* [*pres.* **-дую, -дуешь**] *colloq.* **1,** (*with instr.*) to handle; wield (an instrument). **2,** (*with instr.*) to be in charge of; boss. **3,** to be active; operate.

оруже́йник *n.* gunsmith.

оруже́йный *adj.* gun (*attrib.*); arms (*attrib.*); weapons (*attrib.*). —**оруже́йный ма́стер,** gunsmith. —**Оруже́йная пала́та,** the Armory (*in the Kremlin*).

ору́жие *n.* **1,** weapon. **2,** weapons; arms. **3,** *in* **си́лой ору́жия,** by force of arms. **4,** *in* **това́рищ по ору́жию,** comrade in arms. —**бить (кого́-нибудь) его́ же ору́жием,** to turn the tables on; beat (someone) at his own game.

орфогра́фия *n.* orthography; spelling. —**орфографи́ческий,** *adj.* orthographic; spelling (*attrib.*).

орхиде́я (дэ) *n.* orchid.

оса́ [*pl.* **о́сы**] *n.* wasp.

оса́да *n.* siege. —**в оса́де,** under siege.

осади́ть [*infl.* **осажу́, оса́дишь**] *v., pfv. of* **осажда́ть** *and* **оса́живать.**

оса́дка *n.* **1,** sinking; settling. **2,** draft (*of a sailing vessel*).

оса́дный *adj.* siege (*attrib.*). —**оса́дное положе́ние,** state of siege.

оса́док [*gen.* **-дка**] *n.* **1,** sediment. **2,** *fig.* aftertaste. **3,** *pl.* precipitation. —**радиоакти́вные оса́дки,** (radioactive) fallout.

оса́дочный *adj.* sedimentary.

осажда́ть *v. impfv.* [*pfv.* **осади́ть**] **1,** to lay siege to;

besiege. **2,** *fig.* (*with instr.*) to besiege (with questions, requests, etc.).

оса́живать *v. impfv.* [*pfv.* **осади́ть**] **1,** to rein in (a horse). **2,** *v.i.* (*of an animal*) to stop short and retreat. **3,** to force back. **4,** *fig.* to silence; put in one's place.

оса́нистый *adj.* imposing; stately.

оса́нка *n.* carriage; bearing.

оса́нна *n.* hosanna.

осва́ивать *v. impfv.* [*pfv.* **осво́ить**] **1,** to master. **2,** to settle; open up; develop (new territory). —**осва́иваться,** *refl.* **1,** to (come to) feel at home. **2,** (*with* **с** + *instr.*) to get used to; adjust to. **3,** (*with* **с** + *instr.*) to familiarize oneself with.

осведоми́тель *n.m.* informer; informant. —**осведоми́тельный,** *adj.* pert. to information; information (*attrib.*).

осве́домить [*infl.* **-млю, -мишь**] *v., pfv. of* **осведомля́ть.**

осведомле́ние *n.* notification.

осведомлённый *adj.* well-informed; knowledgeable. —**осведомлённость,** *n.f.* knowledgeability.

осведомля́ть *v. impfv.* [*pfv.* **осве́домить**] to inform; notify. —**осведомля́ться,** *refl.* (*with* **о**) to inquire about.

освежа́ть *v. impfv.* [*pfv.* **освежи́ть**] to refresh; freshen (up); invigorate. —**освежа́ться,** *refl.* **1,** to be refreshed. **2,** to freshen up. **3,** to revive one's energies.

освежа́ющий *adj.* refreshing.

освежева́ть *v., pfv. of* **свежева́ть.**

освеже́ние *n.* refreshment.

освежи́тельный *adj.* refreshing.

освежи́ть *v., pfv. of* **освежа́ть.** —**освежи́ться,** *refl., pfv. of* **освежа́ться.**

освети́тельный *adj.* lighting (*attrib.*); illuminating.

освети́ть [*infl.* **-щу́, -ти́шь**] *v., pfv. of* **освеща́ть.** —**освети́ться,** *refl., pfv. of* **освеща́ться.**

освеща́ть *v. impfv.* [*pfv.* **освети́ть**] **1,** to light up; illuminate. **2,** *fig.* to elucidate; shed light on. —**освеща́ться,** *refl.* to light up.

освеще́ние *n.* **1,** lighting; illumination. **2,** *fig.* interpretation. **3,** *fig.* coverage (*in the press*).

освещённость *n.f.* luminosity.

освиде́тельствовать *v. pfv.* [*infl.* **-ствую, -ствуешь**] to examine.

освиста́ть [*infl.* **освищу́, осви́щешь**] *v., pfv. of* **осви́стывать.**

осви́стывать *v. impfv.* [*pfv.* **освиста́ть**] to hiss (a performer).

освободи́тель *n.m.* liberator; emancipator. —**освободи́тельный,** *adj.* liberation (*attrib.*); освободи́тельное движе́ние, liberation movement.

освободи́ть [*infl.* **-жу́, -ди́шь**] *v., pfv. of* **освобожда́ть.** —**освободи́ться,** *refl., pfv. of* **освобожда́ться.**

освобожда́ть *v. impfv.* [*pfv.* **освободи́ть**] **1,** to free; liberate. **2,** (*with* **из**) to release (from). **3,** (*with* **от**) to excuse (from); exempt (from). **4,** (*with* **от**) to relieve (of a position); remove (from office). **5,** to vacate. **6,** to clear; empty. —**освобожда́ться,** *refl.* **1,** to be freed; be released. **2,** to free oneself; get free. **3,** to be cleared; be vacated.

освобожде́ние *n.* **1,** liberation. **2,** release. **3,** evacuation. **4,** exemption.

освое́ние *n.* **1,** mastering; mastery. **2,** settling; developing (*of new territory*).

осво́ить *v., pfv. of* **осва́ивать.** —**осво́иться,** *refl., pfv. of* **осва́иваться.**

освяща́ть *v. impfv.* [*pfv.* **освяти́ть**] to sanctify; hallow; consecrate. —**освящённый века́ми,** time-honored.

освяще́ние *n.* sanctification; consecration.

осево́й *adj.* axial. —**осева́я ли́ния,** center line (*in a road*).

оседа́ть *v. impfv.* [*pfv.* **осе́сть**] **1,** to settle; sink. **2,** to settle; establish residence.

оседла́ть *v. pfv.* **1,** *pfv. of* **седла́ть. 2,** *colloq.* to sit astride; straddle. **3,** *fig.* to get control of; dominate.

осе́длость *n.f.* settled way of life. —**черта́ осе́длости,** the Pale of Settlement; the Jewish Pale.

осе́длый *adj.* settled: осе́длый о́браз жи́зни, settled way of life.

осека́ться *v.r. impfv.* [*pfv.* **осе́чься**] **1,** *obs.* (*of a gun*) to misfire. **2,** to stop short (*in speaking); (of one's voice*) to break off. **3,** *colloq.* to suffer a setback.

осёл [*gen.* **осла́**] *n.* donkey; ass.

осело́к [*gen.* **-лка́**] *n.* **1,** whetstone. **2,** *fig.* touchstone.

осемене́ние *n.* insemination.

осени́ть *v., pfv. of* **осеня́ть.**

осе́нний *adj.* autumn (*attrib.*); fall (*attrib.*).

о́сень *n.f.* autumn; fall.

о́сенью *adv.* in autumn; in (the) fall.

осеня́ть *v. impfv.* [*pfv.* **осени́ть**] **1,** to shade. **2,** (*of a thought*) to strike: меня́ осени́ла мысль, the thought struck me. —**осени́ть** (+ *acc.*) **кре́стным зна́мением,** to make the sign of the cross over.

осе́сть [*infl. like* **сесть**] *v., pfv. of* **оседа́ть.**

осети́н [*gen. pl.* **-ти́н**] *n.m.* [*fem.* **-ти́нка**] Ossetian (*one of a people inhabiting the Caucasus*). —**осети́нский,** *adj.* Ossetian.

осётр [*gen.* **осетра́**] *n.* sturgeon. —**осетри́на,** *n.* sturgeon (*used as food*). —**осетро́вый,** *adj.* sturgeon (*attrib.*).

осе́чка [*gen. pl.* **-чек**] *n.* misfire. —**дать осе́чку,** to misfire.

осе́чься [*infl. like* **сечь;** *past* **осе́кся, -лась**] *v.r., pfv. of* **осека́ться.**

оси́ливать *v. impfv.* [*pfv.* **оси́лить**] *colloq.* **1,** to overpower. **2,** *fig.* to overcome. **3,** to manage; handle. **4,** to master (a subject); get through (a book).

оси́на *n.* aspen. —**оси́нник,** *n.* aspen grove.

оси́новый *adj.* aspen (*attrib.*). —**дрожа́ть как оси́новый лист,** to shake like a leaf.

оси́ный *adj.* wasp's. —**оси́ное гнездо́,** hornets' nest.

оси́плый *adj.* hoarse; husky.

оси́пнуть *v. pfv.* [*past* **оси́п, -ла**] to become hoarse.

осироте́лый *adj.* orphan (*attrib.*); orphaned.

осироте́ть *v., pfv. of* **сироте́ть.**

оска́л *n., in* **оска́л зубо́в,** bared teeth.

оска́лить *v. pfv., in* **оска́лить зу́бы,** to bare one's teeth; show one's teeth. —**оска́литься,** *refl.* = **оска́лить зу́бы.**

оскверне́ние *n.* desecration.

оскверня́ть *v. impfv.* [*pfv.* **оскверни́ть**] to desecrate; profane; defile.

оскла́биться *v.r. pfv.* [*infl.* **-блюсь, -бишься**] *colloq.* to grin.

оско́лок [*gen.* **-лка**] *n.* splinter; fragment.

оско́лочный *adj., mil.* **1,** fragmentation (*attrib.*): оско́лочная бо́мба, fragmentation bomb. **2,** shrapnel (*attrib.*): оско́лочная ра́на, shrapnel wound.

оско́мина *n.* soreness of the mouth. —**набива́ть**

оско́мину (+ *dat.*), **1,** to make one's mouth sore. **2,** *fig.* to bore to death.
оскопля́ть *v. impfv.* [*pfv.* **оскопи́ть**] to castrate.
оскорби́тельный *adj.* insulting; abusive.
оскорби́ть [*infl.* **-блю́, -би́шь**] *v., pfv. of* **оскорбля́ть.** —**оскорби́ться,** *refl., pfv. of* **оскорбля́ться.**
оскорбле́ние *n.* insult; affront. —**оскорбле́ние де́йствием,** assault and battery.
оскорбля́ть *v. impfv.* [*pfv.* **оскорби́ть**] to insult; offend. —**оскорбля́ться,** *refl.* to be insulted.
оскуде́ть *v., pfv. of* **скуде́ть.**
ослабева́ть *v. impfv.* [*pfv.* **ослабе́ть**] **1,** to weaken; grow weak. **2,** to slacken. **3,** to loosen; come loose.
ослабе́лый *adj., colloq.* weakened; enfeebled.
ослабе́ть *v., pfv. of* **слабе́ть** *and* **ослабева́ть.**
осла́бить [*infl.* **-блю, -бишь**] *v., pfv. of* **ослабля́ть.**
ослабле́ние *n.* **1,** weakening. **2,** relaxation; slackening.
ослабля́ть *v. impfv.* [*pfv.* **осла́бить**] **1,** to weaken. **2,** to relax; slacken. **3,** to loosen.
осла́бнуть *v. pfv.* [*past* **осла́б, -ла**] *colloq.* = **ослабе́ть.**
осла́вить *v. pfv.* [*infl.* **-влю, -вишь**] *colloq.* to malign; defame. —**осла́виться,** *refl., colloq.* to get a bad reputation.
ослепи́тельный *adj.* blinding; dazzling.
ослепи́ть [*infl.* **-плю́, -пи́шь**] *v., pfv. of* **ослепля́ть.**
ослепле́ние *n.* **1,** (act of) blinding. **2,** *fig.* blindness.
ослепля́ть *v. impfv.* [*pfv.* **ослепи́ть**] **1,** to blind. **2,** to dazzle.
осле́пнуть [*past* **осле́п, -ла**] *v., pfv. of* **сле́пнуть.**
о́слик *n.* small donkey; burro.
осли́ный *adj.* donkey's.
осли́ца *n.* female donkey.
осложне́ние *n.* complication.
осложня́ть *v. impfv.* [*pfv.* **осложни́ть**] to complicate. —**осложня́ться,** *refl.* **1,** to become complicated. **2,** (*with instr.*) to be complicated (by).
ослуша́ние *n., obs.* disobedience.
ослу́шаться *v.r. pfv.* (*with gen.*) *colloq.* to disobey.
ослы́шаться *v.r. pfv.* [*infl.* **-шусь, -шишься**] to hear incorrectly.
ослы́шка *n., colloq.* something heard incorrectly.
осма́тривать *v. impfv.* [*pfv.* **осмотре́ть**] **1,** to examine; inspect. **2,** to see; visit (a museum, the sights, etc.). —**осма́триваться,** *refl.* to look around.
осме́ивать *v. impfv.* [*pfv.* **осмея́ть**] to ridicule; deride.
осмеле́ть *v., pfv. of* **смеле́ть.**
осме́ливаться *v.r. impfv.* [*pfv.* **осме́литься**] (*with inf.*) to dare; venture: осме́люсь сказа́ть, I dare say; I venture to say.
осмея́ние *n.* ridicule; derision; mockery.
осмея́ть [*infl.* **осмею́, осмеёшь**] *v., pfv. of* **осме́ивать.**
о́смий *n.* osmium.
о́смос *n.* osmosis.
осмо́тр *n.* examination; inspection; checkup.
осмотре́ть [*infl.* **осмотрю́, осмо́тришь**] *v., pfv. of* **осма́тривать.** —**осмотре́ться,** *refl., pfv. of* **осма́триваться.**
осмотри́тельный *adj.* wary; circumspect. —**осмотри́тельность,** *n.f.* circumspection.
осмо́трщик *n.* inspector.
осмысле́ние *n.* comprehension.
осмы́сленный *adj.* **1,** intelligent (*able to reason*). **2,** conscious.
осмы́сливать *v. impfv.* [*pfv.* **осмы́слить**] **1,** to comprehend; grasp. **2,** to interpret. *Also,* **осмысля́ть.**
оснасти́ть [*infl.* **-щу́, -сти́шь**] *v., pfv. of* **оснаща́ть.**
осна́стка *n.* **1,** fitting out. **2,** *naut.* rig; rigging.
оснаща́ть *v. impfv.* [*pfv.* **оснасти́ть**] to equip; fit out.
оснаще́ние *n.* **1,** equipping; fitting out. **2,** equipment.
осне́женный *also,* **оснежённый** *adj.* snow-covered.
осно́ва *n.* **1,** base. **2,** *fig.* basis. **3,** *pl.* fundamentals. **4,** *textiles* warp. **5,** *ling.* stem. —**класть (что́-нибудь) в осно́ву; брать** *or* **принима́ть (что́-нибудь) за осно́ву,** to take as a starting point. —**лежа́ть в осно́ве; лечь в осно́ву** (+ *gen.*), **1,** to form the basis of. **2,** to underlie. —**осно́ва осно́в** (+ *gen.*), the cornerstone (of).
основа́ние *n.* **1,** founding. **2,** foundation. **3,** *fig.* basis. **4,** reason; grounds: име́ть основа́ния ду́мать, что..., to have reasons to think that... На како́м основа́нии?, on what grounds? **5,** *chem.; math.* base. —**до основа́ния,** to the ground; to its foundations: разру́шить до основа́ния, to raze to the ground. —**на основа́нии** (+ *gen.*), on the basis of; on the strength of.
основа́тель *n.m.* founder.
основа́тельно *adv.* thoroughly; soundly.
основа́тельность *n.f.* **1,** soundness. **2,** thoroughness.
основа́тельный *adj.* **1,** sound; well-founded. **2,** sound; firm; stable. **3,** (*of a person*) solid; dependable. **4,** thorough. **5,** *colloq.* sizable.
основа́ть [*infl.* **-ну́ю, -нуёшь**] *v., pfv. of* **осно́вывать.** —**основа́ться,** *refl., pfv. of* **осно́вываться.**
основно́й *adj.* **1,** basic; fundamental; primary. **2,** main; principal; primary. —**в основно́м,** mainly; for the most part; in the main. —**основна́я ма́сса,** (+ *gen.*), the bulk (of).
основополага́ющий *adj.* fundamental.
основополо́жник *n.* founder (*of a school of thought*).
осно́вывать *v. impfv.* [*pfv.* **основа́ть**] **1,** to found. **2,** (*with* **на** + *prepl.*) to base (on). Это обвине́ние ни на чём не осно́вано, the charge is completely baseless. —**осно́вываться,** *refl.* **1,** [*impfv. only*] (*with* **на** + *prepl.*) to be based (on). **2,** to be formed. **3,** to settle (down).
осо́ба *n.f.* person.
осо́бенно *adv.* especially; particularly.
осо́бенность *n.f.* particular feature; distinctive feature. —**в осо́бенности,** in particular.
осо́бенный *adj.* special; particular; peculiar. —**ничего́ осо́бенного,** nothing special; nothing in particular.
особня́к [*gen.* **-няка́**] *n.* private house; mansion.
особняко́м *adv.* apart; by oneself. —**держа́ться особняко́м,** to remain aloof.
осо́бо *adv.* **1,** separately; apart. **2,** especially; particularly.
осо́бый *adj.* **1,** special; particular: осо́бый тип/ме́тод, special type/method. **2,** special; separate: осо́бая ко́мната, special/separate room.
о́собь *n.f.* **1,** individual. **2,** specimen.
осознава́ть *v. impfv.* [*pfv.* **осозна́ть;** *pres.* **-знаю́, -знаёшь**] to realize; become aware of.
осозна́ние *n.* realization; awareness.
осозна́ть [*infl.* **-зна́ю, -зна́ешь**] *v., pfv. of* **осознава́ть.**

осóка *n.* sedge.
осокóрь *n.m.* black poplar.
осолове́лый *adj., colloq.* bleary-eyed.
óспа *n.* **1,** pox. **2,** smallpox. **3,** *colloq.* pockmarks: изры́тый óспой, pockmarked. —**ве́тряная óспа,** chicken pox. —**корóвья óспа,** cowpox. —**чёрная óспа,** (black) smallpox.
оспа́ривать *v. impfv.* [*pfv.* **оспóрить**] **1,** to challenge; dispute; contest. **2,** [*impfv. only*] to contend for; contest (a championship, prize, etc.).
óспенный *adj.* smallpox (*attrib.*).
óспина *n.* pockmark.
оспопрививáние *n.* vaccination.
оспори́мый *adj.* questionable; debatable.
оспóрить *v., pfv. of* **оспа́ривать.**
осрами́ть *v., pfv. of* **срами́ть.**
ост *n., naut.* **1,** east. **2,** east wind.
оставáться *v.r. impfv.* [*pfv.* **остáться;** *pres.* **остаю́сь, остаёшься**] **1,** to remain; stay. **2,** to be left; remain: скóлько врéмени остáлось?, how much time is left?; how much time remains? Остáться сиротóй, to be left an orphan. Дверь остáлась незáпертой, the door was left unlocked. Остаётся тóлько добáвить, что..., it remains only to add that... **3,** *impers.* (*with dat.*) to have: емý остáлось недóлго жить, he hasn't long to live. Нам не остается ничегó другóго, как..., we have no choice but to... —**оставáться на вторóй год,** to be left back (*in school*).
остáвить [*infl.* **-влю, -вишь**] *v., pfv. of* **оставля́ть.**
оставля́ть *v. impfv.* [*pfv.* **остáвить**] **1,** to leave. **2,** to give up; abandon. **3,** to keep; retain. —**остáвьте!,** stop it! —**оставля́ть без внимáния,** to disregard; take no notice of. —**оставля́ть желáть мнóго лýчшего,** to leave much to be desired. —**оставля́ть за собóй,** to reserve: оставля́ть за собóй прáво, to reserve the right. —**оставля́ть на вторóй год,** to leave back (*in school*). —**оставля́ть пóсле урóков,** to keep in after school.
остальнóе *n., decl. as an adj.* the rest.
остальнóй *adj.* the other; the remaining; the rest of. —**в остальнóм,** in all other respects.
остальны́е *n. pl., decl. as an adj.* the others; the rest.
останáвливать *v. impfv.* [*pfv.* **останови́ть**] **1,** to stop; bring to a stop. **2,** *in* останáвливать взгляд на (+ *prepl.*), to rest one's gaze on. **3,** *in* останáвливать свой вы́бор на (+ *prepl.*), to choose; opt for. —**останáвливаться,** *refl.* **1,** to stop; come to a stop. **2,** to stay (at a hotel, with friends, etc.). **3,** (*with* **на** + *prepl.*) to dwell on (a subject, details, etc.). **4,** (*with* **на** + *prepl.*) to settle on; decide on. **5,** *in* ни пéред чем не останови́ться, to stop at nothing.
остáнки [*gen.* **-ков**] *n. pl.* remains (*of a human being*). —**брéнные остáнки,** mortal remains.
останови́ть [*infl.* **-новлю́, -нóвишь**] *v., pfv. of* **останáвливать.** —**останови́ться,** *refl., pfv. of* **останáвливаться.**
останóвка [*gen. pl.* **-вок**] *n.* **1,** stop; stopping. **2,** stop; stay. **3,** stop (*of or for a vehicle*): слéдующая останóвка, the next stop; автóбусная останóвка, bus stop.
остáток [*gen.* **-тка**] *n.* **1,** remainder; rest. **2,** *pl.* remains; vestiges. **3,** residue. **4,** *math.* remainder.
остáточный *adj.* **1,** remaining. **2,** vestigial. **3,** residual.
остáться [*infl.* **остáнусь, остáнешься**] *v.r., pfv. of* **оставáться.**
остеклени́ть *v., pfv. of* **стеклени́ть.**
остеолóгия (тэ) *n.* osteology. —**остеóлог,** *n.* osteologist.
остепени́ть *v. pfv.* to steady (someone) down. —**остепени́ться,** *refl.* to steady down; have sown one's wild oats.
остервенéлый *adj.* frenzied. —**остервенéние,** *n.* frenzy.
остервенéть *v. pfv.* to become enraged.
остервени́ть *v. pfv.* to enrage. —**остервени́ться,** *refl.* = **остервенéть.**
остерегáть *v. impfv.* [*pfv.* **остерéчь**] (*with* **от**) to warn (against); caution (against). —**остерегáться,** *refl.* **1,** to be careful. **2,** (*with gen.*) to beware (of); be wary (of). **3,** (*with gen. or inf.*) to avoid.
остерéчь [*infl. like* **стерéчь**] *v., pfv. of* **остерегáть.** —**остерéчься,** *refl., pfv. of* **остерегáться.**
óстов *n.* **1,** frame; framework. **2,** *anat.* skeleton.
остолбенéлый *adj., colloq.* stupefied; dumfounded. —**остолбенéние,** *n.* stupefaction; stupor.
остолбенéть *v., pfv. of* **столбенéть.**
остолóп *n., colloq.* blockhead; bonehead.
осторóжно *adv.* carefully; cautiously. —*interj.* careful!; be careful!; look out!; watch out!; watch it!
осторóжность *n.f.* care; caution.
осторóжный *adj.* [*short form* **-жен, -жна**] careful; cautious.
осточертéть *v. pfv.* (*with dat.*) *colloq.* to make sick and tired: э́то мне осточертéло, I am sick and tired of it; I am fed up with it.
остраки́зм *n.* ostracism.
острáстка *n., colloq.* warning: для острáстки, as a warning.
остригáть *v. impfv.* = **стричь.** —**остригáться,** *refl.* = **стри́чься.**
остриё *n.* **1,** (sharp) point. **2,** cutting edge. **3,** *fig.* (*with gen.*) cutting edge (*of a joke, criticism, etc.*).
остри́ть *v.impfv.* **1,** to sharpen. **2,** to make jokes; crack jokes.
остри́чь [*infl. like* **стричь**] *v., pfv. of* **стричь** *and* **остригáть.** —**остри́чься,** *refl., pfv. of* **стри́чься** *and* **остригáться.**
óстро *adv.* **1,** (*with verbs of sharpening*) to a fine point. **2,** *fig.* sharply: óстро критиковáть, to sharply criticize. Óстро пáхнуть, to have a sharp/strong smell. Óстро нуждáться в, to be in dire need of.
óстров [*pl.* **островá**] *n.* island.
островитя́нин [*pl.* **-тя́не**] *n.m.* [*fem.* **-тя́нка**] islander.
островнóй *adj.* island (*attrib.*); insular.
островóк [*gen.* **-вкá**] *n.* small island.
острóг *n., obs.* jail.
острогá *n.* spear; harpoon: бить ры́бу острогóй, to spear a fish.
остроглáзый *adj., colloq.* sharp-eyed.
острогýбцы [*gen. pl.* **-цев**] *n.pl.* cutting pliers.
остроконéчный *adj.* pointed; coming to a point.
остроли́ст *n.* holly.
острóта *n.* witticism; quip; wisecrack.
остротá *n.* sharpness; keenness; pungency.
остроýмие *n.* wit.
остроýмно *adv.* **1,** with great wit. **2,** cleverly.
остроýмный *adj.* **1,** witty. **2,** clever; ingenious.
óстрый *adj.* **1,** sharp. **2,** acute. **3,** keen. **4,** pungent. **5,** (*of a situation, moment, etc.*) critical.
остря́к [*gen.* **-ряка́**] *n.* witty person; wit.

остуди́ть [*infl.* **остужу́, осту́дишь**] *v., pfv. of* **студи́ть** *and* **остужа́ть.**

остужа́ть *v. impfv.* [*pfv.* **остуди́ть**] to cool; chill.

оступа́ться *v.r. impfv.* [*pfv.* **оступи́ться**] to stumble.

оступи́ться [*infl.* **оступлю́сь, осту́пишься**] *v.r., pfv. of* **оступа́ться.**

остыва́ть *v. impfv.* [*pfv.* **осты́ть**] **1,** to get cold. **2,** *fig.* to cool off; calm down. **3,** (*with* **к**) to grow cool towards. **4,** (*of strong emotions*) to cool.

осты́ть [*infl.* **осты́ну, осты́нешь**] *v., pfv. of* **остыва́ть.**

осуди́ть [*infl.* **осужу́, осу́дишь**] *v., pfv. of* **осужда́ть.**

осужда́ть *v. impfv.* [*pfv.* **осуди́ть**] **1,** to condemn; denounce. **2,** to convict. **3,** to condemn (*e.g.* to death); sentence.

осужде́ние *n.* **1,** condemnation; denunciation; censure. **2,** conviction.

осуждённый *n., decl. as an adj.* convict.

осу́нуться *v.r. pfv.* to become drawn in the face.

осуша́ть *v. impfv.* [*pfv.* **осуши́ть**] **1,** to dry. **2,** to drain (a swamp, glass of wine, etc.). —**осуша́ть (свои́) слёзы,** to stop crying. —**осуша́ть слёзы** (+ *dat.*), to console.

осуше́ние *n.* drainage. —**осуши́тельный,** *adj.* drainage (*attrib.*).

осуши́ть [*infl.* **осушу́, осу́шишь**] *v., pfv. of* **осуша́ть.**

осуществи́мый *adj.* feasible; practicable. —**осуществи́мость,** *n.f.* feasibility; practicability.

осуществи́ть [*infl.* **-влю́, -ви́шь**] *v., pfv. of* **осуществля́ть.** —**осуществи́ться,** *refl., pfv. of* **осуществля́ться.**

осуществле́ние *n.* realization; fulfillment; implementation.

осуществля́ть *v. impfv.* [*pfv.* **осуществи́ть**] **1,** to carry out; implement. **2,** to accomplish; realize. **3,** to exercise (a right, control, etc.). —**осуществля́ться,** *refl.* to be realized; come true.

осцилло́граф *n.* oscillograph.

осциллоско́п *n.* oscilloscope.

осцилля́тор *n.* oscillator.

осчастли́вить *v. pfv.* [*infl.* **-влю, -вишь**] to make happy.

осы́пать [*infl.* **осы́плю, осы́плешь**] *v., pfv. of* **осыпа́ть.** —**осы́паться,** *refl., pfv. of* **осыпа́ться.**

осыпа́ть *v. impfv.* [*pfv.* **осы́пать**] (*with instr.*) **1,** to sprinkle (with); strew (with). **2,** *fig.* to shower (with gifts); rain (blows); hurl (insults); heap (ridicule) upon. —**осыпа́ться,** *refl.* **1,** (*of plaster*) to peel off. **2,** to crumble. **3,** (*of leaves*) to fall. **4,** (*with instr.*) to be strewn with.

ось [*pl.* **о́си, осе́й, ося́м**] *n.f.* **1,** axis. **2,** axle.

осьмино́г *n.* octopus.

осяза́емый *adj.* tangible; palpable.

осяза́ние *n.* touch: чу́вство осяза́ния, sense of touch.

осяза́тельный *adj.* **1,** tactile. **2,** tangible.

осяза́ть *v. impfv.* to feel; perceive.

от *also,* **ото** *prep., with gen.* **1,** from: письмо́ от А́ни, a letter from Anya; от Москвы́ до Ленингра́да, from Moscow to Leningrad; счита́ть от одного́ до десяти́, to count from one to ten. Отходи́ть от стола́, to walk away from the table. **2,** *indicating cause:* дрожа́ть от стра́ха, to tremble from/with fear; умере́ть от ра́ка, to die of cancer. **3,** to; belonging to: ключ от ко́мнаты, the key to a room; пу́говица от пальто́, a button to a coat. **4,** for (*an illness*): что́-нибудь от ка́шля, something for a cough; лечи́ть больно́го от я́звы, to treat a patient for an ulcer. **5,** of (*a certain date*): ва́ше письмо́ от седьмо́го ма́рта, your letter of March 7.

от- *also,* **ото-, отъ-,** *prefix* **1,** *indicating motion away, aside or back:* отходи́ть, to walk away; step back; отта́лкивать, to push away; push aside. **2,** *indicating separation, detachment, etc.:* отделя́ть, to separate; отреза́ть, to cut off. **3,** *indicating unfastening, unhooking, etc.:* отстёгивать, to unfasten; отпряга́ть, to unharness; отку́поривать, to uncork. **4,** *indicating response, return, etc.:* отвеча́ть, to answer; отклика́ться, to respond; отдава́ть, to give back; отпла́чивать, to pay back. **5,** *indicating rejection, refusal, etc.:* отка́зываться, to refuse; отверга́ть, to reject; отрека́ться, to renounce. **6,** *indicating completion of an action:* отобе́дать, to be finished with dinner; отде́лывать, to put into final form.

ота́пливать *v. impfv.* [*pfv.* **отопи́ть**] to heat (a building).

ота́ра *n.* flock (*of sheep*).

отбавля́ть *v. impfv.* [*pfv.* **отба́вить**] (*with gen.*) to pour off (a certain amount of). —**хоть отбавля́й,** more than enough; enough and then some.

отбараба́нить *v. pfv., colloq.* **1,** to stop drumming. **2,** to bang out (*on a musical instrument*). **3,** to rattle off (a speech, answers, etc.).

отбега́ть *v. impfv.* [*pfv.* **отбежа́ть**] to run away; run back.

отбежа́ть [*infl. like* **бежа́ть**] *v., pfv. of* **отбега́ть.**

отбе́ливать *v. impfv.* [*pfv.* **отбели́ть**] to bleach.

отбели́ть [*infl.* **отбелю́, отбе́лишь** *or* **отбели́шь**] *v., pfv. of* **отбе́ливать.**

отбива́ть *v. impfv.* [*pfv.* **отби́ть**] **1,** to break off. **2,** to beat off; repel; repulse (an attack); beat back (an attacker); parry; deflect (a blow). **3,** to recapture; retake. **4,** *colloq.* to take away; remove (a taste, odor, desire, etc.). **5,** to hurt; injure. **6,** to sharpen; whet. **7,** to beat (time); sound (a call). **8,** *sports* to return (a ball). —**отбива́ться,** *refl.* **1,** to be broken off. **2,** (*with* **от**) to fight off. **3,** to fall behind; (with **от**) stray (from). **4,** (*with* **от**) *colloq.* to drift away from; get away from. **5,** *in* **отби́ться от рук,** to get out of hand.

отбивно́й *adj., in* отбивна́я котле́та, chop; cutlet. Бара́нья/свина́я отбивна́я, lamb/pork chop. Теля́чья отбивна́я, veal chop; veal cutlet.

отбира́ть *v. impfv.* [*pfv.* **отобра́ть**] **1,** to take away; take (from): отбира́ть конфе́ты у ребёнка, to take candy (away) from a child. **2,** to select.

отби́ть [*infl.* **отобью́, отобьёшь**] *v., pfv. of* **отбива́ть.** —**отби́ться,** *refl., pfv. of* **отбива́ться.**

отблагодари́ть *v. pfv.* **1,** to thank. **2,** to show one's appreciation to.

о́тблеск *n.* **1,** reflection. **2,** *fig.* (*with gen.*) spark (of); trace (of).

отбо́й *n.* **1,** *mil.* retreat: дава́ть *or* бить отбо́й, to sound retreat. **2,** the all-clear signal. —**бить отбо́й, 1,** to beat a retreat. **2,** *fig.* to back down. —**дать отбо́й,** to ring off; hang up (the receiver). —**отбо́ю нет от,** no end of: у меня́ нет отбо́ю от предложе́ний, I've had no end of offers.

отбо́йный *adj., in* **отбо́йный молото́к,** mechanical pick; **пневмати́ческий отбо́йный молото́к,** jackhammer.

отбо́р *n.* selection.

отбо́рный *adj.* **1,** select; choice. Отбо́рные войска́, crack troops. **2,** *colloq.* (*of swearwords*) choice; unprintable.

отбо́рочный *adj.* selection (*attrib.*). —**отбо́рочные соревнова́ния,** *sports* trials.

отбоя́риваться *v.r. impfv.* [*pfv.* **отбоя́риться**] (*with* **от**) *colloq.* to get out of; avoid.

отбра́сывать *v. impfv.* [*pfv.* **отбро́сить**] **1,** to throw aside; cast aside. **2,** *mil.* to throw back; hurl back. **3,** to cast (light, a shadow, etc.). **4,** *fig.* to cast aside (thoughts, doubts, etc.).

отбро́сить [*infl.* **-шу, -сишь**] *v., pfv. of* **отбра́сывать.**

отбро́сы [*gen.* **-сов**] *n.pl.* refuse; garbage.

отбыва́ть *v. impfv.* [*pfv.* **отбы́ть**] **1,** *v.i.* to leave; depart. **2,** *v.t.* to serve; serve out (time, a sentence, etc.).

отбы́тие *n.* **1,** departure. **2,** serving; completion (*of a sentence, term, etc.*).

отбы́ть [*infl.* **-бу́ду, -бу́дешь;** *past* **о́тбыл, отбыла́, о́тбыло**] *v., pfv. of* **отбыва́ть.**

отва́га *n.* courage; bravery.

отва́живать *v. impfv.* [*pfv.* **отва́дить**] (*with* **от**) *colloq.* **1,** to break (someone) of the habit (of). **2,** to drive off; scare off. —**отва́живаться,** *refl.* **1,** [*pfv.* **отва́диться**] (*with* **от**) *colloq.* to break the habit of; get out of the habit of. **2,** [*pfv.* **отва́житься**] to dare; venture.

отва́жный *adj.* courageous; brave. —**отва́жно,** *adv.* courageously; bravely.

отва́л *n.* **1,** casting off (*of a boat*). **2,** heap; dump: отва́л шла́ка, slag heap. —**до отва́ла,** to the bursting point.

отва́ливать *v. impfv.* [*pfv.* **отвали́ть**] **1,** to push aside. **2,** *v.i.* (*of a boat*) to cast off. **3,** *colloq.* to hand out (money). —**отва́ливаться,** *refl.* **1,** to fall off. **2,** *colloq.* to lean back.

отвали́ть [*infl.* **-валю́, -ва́лишь**] *v., pfv. of* **отва́ливать.** —**отвали́ться,** *refl., pfv. of* **отва́ливаться.**

отва́р *n.* decoction. —**мясно́й отва́р,** stock. —**ри́совый отва́р,** rice water.

отва́ривать *v. impfv.* [*pfv.* **отвари́ть**] to boil.

отвари́ть [*infl.* **-варю́, -ва́ришь**] *v., pfv. of* **отва́ривать.**

отварно́й *adj.* boiled.

отве́дывать *v. impfv.* [*pfv.* **отве́дать**] *colloq.* **1,** to try; taste. **2,** to taste; experience.

отвезти́ [*infl. like* **везти́**] *v., pfv. of* **отвози́ть.**

отверга́ть *v. impfv.* [*pfv.* **отве́ргнуть**] to reject; turn down.

отве́ргнуть [*past* **-ве́рг, -ла**] *v., pfv. of* **отверга́ть.**

отвердева́ть *v. impfv.* [*pfv.* **отверде́ть**] to harden; solidify.

отверде́лый *adj.* hard; hardened.

отверде́ть *v., pfv. of* **отвердева́ть.**

отве́рженный *adj. & n.* outcast.

отверну́ть *v., pfv. of* **отвёртывать** *and* **отвора́чивать.** —**отверну́ться,** *refl., pfv. of* **отвёртываться** *and* **отвора́чиваться.**

отве́рстие *n.* opening; hole.

отверте́ться [*infl.* **-верчу́сь, -ве́ртишься**] *v.r., pfv. of* **отвёртываться** (*in sense #3*).

отвёртка [*gen. pl.* **-ток**] *n.* screwdriver.

отвёртывать *v. impfv.* [*pfv.* **отверну́ть**] **1,** = **отвора́чивать. 2,** to turn on (a faucet). **3,** to unscrew; screw off. —**отвёртываться,** *refl.* **1,** = **отвора́чиваться. 2,** to come unscrewed. **3,** [*pfv.* **отверте́ться**] *colloq.* to get out of it; get off.

отве́с *n.* **1,** plumb. **2,** sheer cliff.

отве́сить [*infl.* **-шу, -сишь**] *v., pfv. of* **отве́шивать.**

отве́сный *adj.* sheer; vertical; perpendicular. —**отве́сная скала́,** cliff.

отвести́ [*infl. like* **вести́**] *v., pfv. of* **отводи́ть.**

отве́т *n.* answer; reply: в отве́т на (+ *acc.*), in answer/reply to. —**без отве́та,** unanswered: оста́вить/оста́ться без отве́та, to leave/remain unanswered. —**(быть) в отве́те за** (+ *acc.*), to be responsible for.

ответви́ться *v.r., pfv. of* **ответвля́ться.**

ответвле́ние *n.* branch; offshoot.

ответвля́ться *v.r. impfv.* [*pfv.* **ответви́ться**] to branch off.

отве́тить [*infl.* **-чу, -тишь**] *v., pfv. of* **отвеча́ть.**

отве́тный *adj.* **1,** return (*attrib.*): отве́тный визи́т, return visit. **2,** in reply: отве́тная речь, speech in reply. **3,** retaliatory.

отве́тственность *n.f.* responsibility: нести́ отве́тственность за (+ *acc.*), to bear the responsibility for.

отве́тственный *adj.* **1,** responsible: отве́тственный за рабо́ту, responsible for the work. **2,** crucial; (very) important. —**отве́тственный рабо́тник,** senior official. —**отве́тственный реда́ктор,** managing editor.

отве́тчик *n., law* defendant.

отвеча́ть *v. impfv.* [*pfv.* **отве́тить**] **1,** (*with dat.*) to answer; reply (to) (a person); (*with* **на** + *acc.*) (a question, letter, etc.). **2,** (*with* **на** + *acc.*) to respond to (a request, appeal, etc.). **3,** [*impfv. only*] (*with* **за** + *acc.*) to answer (for); be responsible (for). **4,** [*pfv. only*] (*with* **за** + *acc.*) to pay for: вы за э́то отве́тите!, you'll pay for this! **5,** [*impfv. only*] (*with dat.*) to meet; answer (needs, requirements, etc.). **6,** *in* отвеча́ть уро́к, to recite one's lesson.

отве́шивать *v. impfv.* [*pfv.* **отве́сить**] **1,** to weigh out. **2,** *colloq.* to deal; dish out (a blow). **3,** *in* отве́шивать покло́н, to make a bow.

отви́ливать *v. impfv.* [*pfv.* **отвильну́ть**] (*with* **от**) *colloq.* to avoid; dodge.

отви́нчивать *v. impfv.* [*pfv.* **отвинти́ть**] to unscrew; screw off.

отвиса́ть *v. impfv.* [*pfv.* **отви́снуть**] to hang down; sag; droop.

отви́слый *adj.* loose-hanging; drooping; flaccid.

отви́снуть [*past* **-ви́с, -ла**] *v., pfv. of* **отвиса́ть.**

отвлека́ть *v. impfv.* [*pfv.* **отвле́чь**] to distract; divert. —**отвлека́ться,** *refl.* **1,** to be distracted. **2,** (*with* **от**) to digress (from).

отвлече́ние *n.* **1,** distraction; diversion. **2,** *obs.* abstraction.

отвлечённый *adj.* abstract. —**отвлечённо,** *adv.* in an abstract manner; in the abstract.

отвле́чь [*infl. like* **влечь**] *v., pfv. of* **отвлека́ть.** —**отвле́чься,** *refl., pfv. of* **отвлека́ться.**

отво́д *n.* **1,** taking; delivering. **2,** draining off (*of water*). **3,** allocation (*of land*). **4,** diversion: для отво́да глаз, to divert attention. **5,** rejection (*of a candidate*); challenge (*to a witness*).

отводи́ть *v. impfv.* [*pfv.* **отвести́;** *pres.* **-вожу́, -во́дишь**] **1,** to take (someone on foot to a certain place). **2,** to lead away; take away. **3,** to deflect; ward off. **4,** to draw aside. **5,** to drain; drain off (water). **6,** to allot; set aside. **7,** to reject (someone's candidacy); challenge (a witness). —**отводи́ть глаза́,** to turn one's eyes away. —**отводи́ть глаза́** (+ *dat.*), to mislead; delude; lead astray. —**отводи́ть ду́шу,** to unburden oneself.

отвóдный *adj.* drainage (*attrib.*); drain (*attrib.*).
отвоевáть *v. pfv.* [*infl.* **-воюю, -воюешь**] **1,** *pfv. of* **отвоёвывать. 2,** *colloq.* to fight (*for a certain length of time*). **3,** *colloq.* to finish fighting.
отвоёвывать *v. impfv.* [*pfv.* **отвоевáть**] to win back (*in war*); retake.
отвози́ть *v. impfv.* [*pfv.* **отвезти́;** *pres.* **-вожу́, -вóзишь**] **1,** to take; drive (someone to a certain place). **2,** to take away; cart away.
отворáчивать *v. impfv.* [*pfv.* **отвернýть**] **1,** to turn away; turn aside. **2,** to turn down; fold down. **3,** *v.i., colloq.* to turn; make a turn. —**отворáчиваться,** *refl.* (*with* **от**) to turn away (from); turn one's back (on).
отвори́ть [*infl.* **-творю́, -твóришь**] *v., pfv. of* **отворя́ть.** —**отвори́ться,** *refl., pfv. of* **отворя́ться.**
отворóт *n.* **1,** lapel. **2,** cuff.
отворя́ть *v. impfv.* [*pfv.* **отвори́ть**] to open. —**отворя́ться,** *refl.* to open; come open.
отврати́тельный *adj.* **1,** disgusting. **2,** *colloq.* miserable; rotten.
отвращáть *v. impfv.* [*pfv.* **отврати́ть**] **1,** *obs.* to turn away. **2,** to avert; ward off.
отвращéние *n.* disgust; repugnance; loathing; aversion.
отвыкáть *v. impfv.* [*pfv.* **отвы́кнуть**] (*with* **от**) **1,** to become unaccustomed to. **2,** to get out of the habit of. **3,** to become estranged from.
отвы́кнуть [*past* **-вы́к, -ла**] *v., pfv. of* **отвыкáть.**
отвязáть [*infl.* **-вяжу́, -вя́жешь**] *v., pfv. of* **отвя́зывать.** —**отвязáться,** *refl., pfv. of* **отвя́зываться.**
отвя́зывать *v. impfv.* [*pfv.* **отвязáть**] to untie; unfasten. —**отвя́зываться,** *refl.* **1,** to come untied; come loose. **2,** to break loose. **3,** (*with* **от**) *colloq.* to get rid of; rid oneself of; shake off. **4,** (*with* **от**) *colloq.* to leave alone; leave in peace.
отгадáть *v., pfv. of* **отгáдывать.**
отгáдка [*gen. pl.* **-док**] *n.* answer; solution (*to a riddle*).
отгáдчик *n., colloq.* guesser.
отгáдывать *v. impfv.* [*pfv.* **отгадáть**] **1,** to guess (*correctly*). **2,** to solve (a riddle).
отгибáть *v. impfv.* [*pfv.* **отогнýть**] **1,** to unbend; straighten. **2,** to turn down; turn back.
отглагóльный *adj., gram.* verbal: отглагóльное существи́тельное, verbal noun.
отглáживать *v. impfv.* [*pfv.* **отглáдить**] to iron; press.
отговáривать *v. impfv.* [*pfv.* **отговори́ть**] (*with inf. or* **от**) **1,** to dissuade; talk out of. **2,** [*impfv. only*] to try to dissuade; try to talk out of. —**отговáриваться,** *refl.* **1,** to beg off (*by giving excuses*). **2,** (*with instr.*) to plead (illness, ignorance, etc.).
отговóрка [*gen. pl.* **-рок**] *n.* excuse.
отголóсок [*gen.* **-ска**] *n.* **1,** echo. **2,** faint sound. **3,** sympathetic response. **4,** *pl.* repercussions; aftereffects; aftermath.
отгоня́ть *v. impfv.* [*pfv.* **отогнáть**] to drive away; drive off.
отгорáживать *v. impfv.* [*pfv.* **отгороди́ть**] **1,** to fence off; partition off. **2,** *fig.* to shut off; isolate.
отгороди́ть [*infl.* **-рожу́, -рóдишь** *or* **-роди́шь**] *v., pfv. of* **отгорáживать.**
отгребáть *v. impfv.* [*pfv.* **отгрести́**] **1,** *v.t.* to rake away. **2,** *v.i.* to row away.
отгремéть *v. pfv.* to die down; fall silent.
отгрести́ [*infl. like* **грести́**] *v., pfv. of* **отгребáть.**
отгружáть *v. impfv.* [*pfv.* **отгрузи́ть**] to ship.
отгрузи́ть [*infl.* **-гружу́, -грýзишь** *or* **-грузи́шь**] *v., pfv. of* **отгружáть.**
отгрýзка *n.* shipment.
отгрызáть *v. impfv.* [*pfv.* **огры́зть**] to bite off; gnaw off.
отгры́зть [*infl. like* **гры́зть**] *v., pfv. of* **отгрызáть.**
отгýл *n.* compensatory leave.
отгýливать *v. impfv.* [*pfv.* **отгуля́ть**] *colloq.* to take (time) off; take compensatory leave: отгýливать два дня, to take two days off; take two days compensatory leave.
отгуля́ть *v. pfv., colloq.* **1,** *pfv. of* **отгýливать. 2,** to reach the end of (one's vacation). **3,** to celebrate (a holiday, wedding, etc.). **4,** to finish celebrating.
отдавáть *v. impfv.* [*pfv.* **отдáть;** *pres.* **-даю́, -даёшь**] **1,** to give back; return. **2,** to hand over; turn over. **3,** to devote: отдавáть жизнь теáтру, to devote one's life to the theater. **4,** (*with* **в** + *acc.*) to have (cleaned, repaired, etc.): отдáть (чтó-нибудь) в чи́стку/ремóнт, to have (something) cleaned/repaired. **5,** *v.i.* (*of a gun*) to recoil. **6,** *v.i.* [*impfv. only*] (*with instr.*) to taste of; smell of; smack of. —**отдавáть (когó-нибудь) в шкóлу,** to put *or* place (someone) in school. —**отдавáть долг,** to repay a debt. —**отдавáть дóлжное,** *see* **дóлжное.** —**отдавáть жизнь за** (+ *acc.*), to give one's life for. —**отдавáть (когó-нибудь) под суд,** to prosecute; bring to trial. —**отдавáть послéдний долг** (+ *dat.*), to pay one's last respects to. —**отдавáть предпочтéние** (+ *dat.*), to give preference (to). —**отдавáть прикáз,** to give an order. —**отдавáть свой гóлос** (+ *dat.*), to cast one's vote (for). —**отдавáть себé отчёт,** *see* **отчёт.** —**отдавáть честь** (+ *dat.*), *mil.* to salute.
отдавáться *v.r. impfv.* [*pfv.* **отдáться;** *pres.* **-даю́сь, -даёшься**] **1,** (*with dat.*) to give oneself up (to). **2,** (*with dat.*) (*of a woman*) to give in (to). **3,** (*with dat.*) to devote oneself (to). **4,** (*of a sound*) to resound. **5,** (*of a pain*) to be felt. В моём сéрдце отдавáлось бóлью, I felt sick at heart.
отдалéние *n.* **1,** removal. **2,** estrangement. **3,** distance. —**в отдалéнии,** in the distance. —**на отдалéнии,** at a distance.
отдалённый *adj.* remote; distant. —**отдалённость,** *n.f.* remoteness.
отдаля́ть *v. impfv.* [*pfv.* **отдали́ть**] **1,** to remove; move away. **2,** to postpone; put off. **3,** to estrange; alienate. —**отдаля́ться,** *refl.* (*with* **от**) **1,** to drift away (from). **2,** to digress (from).
отдáривать *v. impfv.* [*pfv.* **отдари́ть**] *colloq.* to give (a gift) in return.
отдáть [*infl. like* **дать;** *past* **óтдал, отдалá, óтдало**] *v., pfv. of* **отдавáть.** —**отдáться,** *refl.* [*past* **отдáлся, -лáсь, -лóсь**] *pfv. of* **отдавáться.**
отдáча *n.* **1,** return. **2,** recoil; kick (*of a gun*).
отдéл *n.* **1,** section. **2,** department: отдéл закáзов, order department.
отдéлать *v., pfv. of* **отдéлывать.** —**отдéлаться,** *refl., pfv. of* **отдéлываться.**
отделéние *n.* **1,** separation. **2,** department; section; division; branch. Почтóвое отделéние, local post office. **3,** compartment; section. **4,** part (*of a concert, performance, etc.*). **5,** *mil.* squad. —**котéльное отделéние,** boiler room. —**маши́нное отделéние,** engine room.

отделить [*infl.* **-делю, -делишь**] *v., pfv. of* **отделять.** —**отделиться,** *refl., pfv. of* **отделяться.**

отделка *n.* **1,** finishing; decorating. **2,** trimming; trim.

отделывать *v. impfv.* [*pfv.* **отделать**] **1,** to put into final form. **2,** to decorate; trim. **3,** to finish (a surface). **4,** *colloq.* to rebuke; bawl out. —**отделываться,** *refl., colloq.* **1,** (*with* **от**) to finish; be done with; get out of the way. **2,** (*with* **от**) to get rid of. **3,** (*with instr.*) to get off (with). **4,** (*with an adverb*) to get off (cheap, easily, etc.).

отдельно *adv.* **1,** separately; apart. **2,** individually.

отдельность *n.f., in* **в отдельности,** individually; separately.

отдельный *adj.* **1,** separate. **2,** individual.

отделять *v. impfv.* [*pfv.* **отделить**] **1,** to separate. **2,** [*impfv. only*] to divide; serve as the boundary between. —**отделяться,** *refl.* (*with* **от**) **1,** to become separated from. **2,** to come off. **3,** to move away from.

отдёргивать *v. impfv.* [*pfv.* **отдёрнуть**] **1,** to pull back; draw back. **2,** to pull aside; draw aside.

отдирать *v. impfv.* [*pfv.* **отодрать**] to tear off; rip off.

отдохнуть *v., pfv. of* **отдыхать.**

отдувать *v. impfv.* [*pfv.* **отдуть**] **1,** to blow away. **2,** to puff up (one's cheeks). —**отдуваться,** *refl.* **1,** to become puffed up. **2,** [*impfv. only*] to pant; puff. **3,** [*impfv. only*] (*with* **за** + *acc.*) *colloq.* to take the rap for.

отдумывать *v. impfv.* [*pfv.* **отдумать**] (*with inf.*) *colloq.* to change one's mind (about).

отдуть [*infl.* **-дую, -дуешь**] *v., pfv. of* **отдувать.** —**отдуться,** *refl., pfv. of* **отдуваться.**

отдушина *n.* **1,** vent; air-vent. **2,** *fig.* outlet (*for one's emotions*).

отдых *n.* rest. —**дом отдыха,** rest home.

отдыхать *v. impfv.* [*pfv.* **отдохнуть**] **1,** to rest. **2,** to be on vacation; take a vacation.

отдышаться *v.r. pfv.* [*infl.* **-дышусь, -дышишься**] to catch one's breath.

отёк *n., med.* edema.

отекать *v. impfv.* [*pfv.* **отечь**] **1,** to swell up, become swollen. **2,** to become numb. **3,** (*of a candle*) to drip.

отелится *v.r., pfv. of* **телиться.**

отель (тэ) *n.m.* hotel.

отеплять *v. impfv.* [*pfv.* **отеплить**] to winterize.

отец [*gen.* **отца**] *n.* father. —**отеческий,** *adj.* fatherly; paternal.

отечественный *adj.* **1,** native. **2,** domestically produced. —**Великая Отечественная война,** the Great Patriotic War (*World War II*).

отечество *n.* native land; homeland; fatherland.

отечь [*infl. like* **течь**] *v., pfv. of* **отекать.**

отжать [*infl.* **отожму, отожмёшь**] *v., pfv. of* **отжимать.**

отжечь [*infl.* **отожгу, отожжёшь, ...отожгут;** *past* **отжёг, отожгла**] *v., pfv. of* **отжигать.**

отживать *v. impfv.* [*pfv.* **отжить**] to die out; become a thing of the past. *See also* **отжить.**

отживший *adj.* **1,** having lived out one's life. **2,** out-of-date; obsolete.

отжигать *v. impfv.* [*pfv.* **отжечь**] to anneal.

отжимать *v. impfv.* [*pfv.* **отжать**] **1,** to wring out. **2,** to squeeze out (liquid). **3,** *colloq.* to push back; force back.

отжить *v. pfv.* [*infl.* **-живу, -живёшь;** *past* **отжил, отжила, отжило**] **1,** *pfv. of* **отживать. 2,** to have lived one's life. —**отжить свой век,** to become a thing of the past; have had one's day.

отзвонить *v. pfv.* **1,** (*of a clock*) to strike (a certain hour). **2,** to stop ringing.

отзвук *n.* **1,** echo. **2,** faint sound. **3,** *fig.* sympathetic response. **4,** *fig.* reverberations.

отзыв *n.* **1,** review; comment: получить благоприятные отзывы, to receive favorable reviews/comment. **2,** (character) reference. **3,** *fig.* responsive chord. **4,** reply (*to a password*).

отзыв *n.* recall (*of an ambassador, representative, etc.*).

отзывать *v. impfv.* [*pfv.* **отозвать**] **1,** to take aside. **2,** to recall (an ambassador.). **3,** *v.i.* [*impfv. only*] (*with instr.*) *colloq.* to have the taste of; smell faintly of. —**отзываться,** *refl.* **1,** to answer. **2,** (*with* **на** + *acc.*) to respond to (an appeal, request, etc.). **3,** (*with* **на** + *prepl.*) to affect; have an effect on. **4,** (*with* **о**) to speak (well, badly, etc.) of.

отзывчивый *adj.* responsive; kindhearted; sympathetic. —**отзывчивость,** *n.f.* sympathy; kindheartedness; empathy.

отказ *n.* **1,** refusal. **2,** repudiation; renunciation; disavowal. **3,** failure; breakdown: действовать *or* работать без отказа, to work perfectly. —**набитый до отказа,** chock-full; filled to the brim.

отказать [*infl.* **-кажу, -кажешь**] *v., pfv. of* **отказывать.** —**отказаться,** *refl., pfv. of* **отказываться.**

отказывать *v. impfv.* [*pfv.* **отказать**] **1,** to say no: он не умеет отказывать, he doesn't kow how to say no. **2,** (*with dat.*) to turn (someone) down: ему отказали, they turned him down; he was turned down. **3,** (*with dat. and* **в** + *prepl.*) to refuse; deny: отказывать кому-нибудь в помощи, to refuse help to someone; отказывать себе в самом необходимом, to deny oneself (even) the barest necessities. Ему нельзя отказать в остроумии, you can't say he is not clever. **4,** *colloq.* (*of a machine*) to break down; fail to operate. **5,** *obs.* to leave; bequeath. —**отказываться,** *refl.* **1,** (*with inf.*) to refuse. **2,** (*with* **от**) to turn down; decline. **3,** (*with* **от**) to abandon; give up; relinquish. **4,** (*with* **от**) to renounce; repudiate; disavow; disown.

откалывать *v. impfv.* [*pfv.* **отколоть**] **1,** to chop off; break off. **2,** to unpin. —**откалываться,** *refl.* **1,** to break off; break away. **2,** *fig.* to break away; cut oneself off. **3,** to come unpinned.

откапывать *v. impfv.* [*pfv.* **откопать**] **1,** to dig up; disinter; exhume. **2,** *fig., colloq.* to dig up; unearth.

откармливать *v. impfv.* [*pfv.* **откормить**] to fatten up.

откат *n.* recoil (*of a field gun*).

откатить [*infl.* **-качу, -катишь**] *v., pfv. of* **откатывать.** —**откатиться,** *refl., pfv. of* **откатываться.**

откатывать *v. impfv.* [*pfv.* **откатить**] to roll (away, aside, *or* back). —**откатываться,** *refl.* **1,** to roll away; roll back. **2,** (*of troops*) to retreat; fall back. **3,** (*of a field gun*) to recoil.

откачивать *v. impfv.* [*pfv.* **откачать**] **1,** to pump out. **2,** to give artificial respiration to.

откачнуться *v.r. pfv.* **1,** to swing to one side. **2,** to reel back; slump back.

откашливаться *v.r. impfv.* [*pfv.* **откашляться**] to clear one's throat.

откидной *adj.* folding; collapsible.

откидывать *v. impfv.* [*pfv.* **откинуть**] **1,** to cast aside; throw aside; toss aside. **2,** (*with* **назад**) to throw back. **3,** to fold back; fold aside; raise; open. —**откидываться,** *refl.* to lean back; settle back.

откла́дывать *v. impfv.* [*pfv.* **отложи́ть**] **1,** to lay aside; put aside; set aside. **2,** to postpone; put off; defer. **3,** *chess* to adjourn (a game). **4,** to unhitch; unharness.

откла́ниваться *v.r. impfv.* [*pfv.* **откла́няться**] *obs.* to depart; take one's leave.

откле́ивать *v. impfv.* [*pfv.* **откле́ить**] to peel off (something stuck). —**откле́иваться,** *refl.* to come unstuck; come off.

о́тклик *n.* **1,** response. **2,** echo. **3,** *pl.* reaction; comments. **4,** *fig.* responsive chord.

отклика́ться *v.r. impfv.* [*pfv.* **откли́кнуться**] **1,** to answer; reply. **2,** (*with* **на** + *acc.*) to respond (to).

отклоне́ние *n.* **1,** rejection; denial. **2,** deviation; departure; digression. **3,** deflection.

отклони́ть [*infl.* **-клоню́, -кло́нишь**] *v., pfv. of* **отклоня́ть.** —**отклони́ться,** *refl., pfv. of* **отклоня́ться.**

отклоня́ть *v. impfv.* [*pfv.* **отклони́ть**] **1,** to deflect. **2,** to reject; turn down; decline. **3,** to deter; talk out of. —**отклоня́ться,** *refl.* (*with* **от**) to deviate (from); digress (from); stray (from).

отключа́ть *v. impfv.* [*pfv.* **отключи́ть**] to cut off; shut off; disconnect. —**отключа́ться,** *refl.* to become disconnected.

откозыря́ть *v.pfv.* (*with dat.*) *colloq.* to salute.

отколоти́ть *v. pfv.* [*infl.* **-лочу́, -ло́тишь**] *colloq.* **1,** to knock off; hammer off. **2,** to beat up.

отколо́ть [*infl.* **-колю́, -ко́лешь**] *v., pfv. of* **отка́лывать.** —**отколо́ться,** *refl., pfv. of* **отка́лываться.**

откомандирова́ть [*infl.* **-ру́ю, -ру́ешь**] *v., pfv. of* **откомандиро́вывать.**

откомандиро́вывать *v. impfv.* [*pfv.* **откомандирова́ть**] **1,** to send (*on an assignment*). **2,** to assign; transfer.

откопа́ть *v., pfv. of* **отка́пывать.**

откорми́ть [*infl.* **-кормлю́, -ко́рмишь**] *v., pfv. of* **отка́рмливать.**

отко́с *n.* slope; side (*of a hill, embankment, etc.*): свали́ться под отко́с, to go/tumble over the embankment. Пусти́ть по́езд под отко́с, to derail a train. —**пойти́ под отко́с,** to fall apart; go to pieces.

открепля́ть *v. impfv.* [*pfv.* **открепи́ть**] **1,** to unfasten. **2,** to strike off the list.

откре́щиваться *v.r. impfv.* (*with* **от**) *colloq.* **1,** to try to avoid; shun. **2,** to disavow; disown.

открове́ние *n.* revelation.

открове́нничать *v. impfv.* (*with* **с** + *instr.*) *colloq.* to be frank (with); open up (to).

открове́нно *adv.* frankly. —**открове́нно говоря́,** frankly speaking; to be perfectly frank.

открове́нность *n.f.* frankness; candor.

открове́нный *adj.* **1,** frank; candid; outspoken. **2,** undisguised; unconcealed.

открути́ть [*infl.* **-кручу́, -кру́тишь**] *v., pfv. of* **откру́чивать.**

откру́чивать *v. impfv.* [*pfv.* **открути́ть**] to untwist; unscrew.

открыва́тель *n.m.* discoverer.

открыва́ть *v. impfv.* [*pfv.* **откры́ть**] **1,** to open. **2,** to uncover; reveal. **3,** to unveil (a monument). **4,** to discover. **5,** to reveal (a secret). **6,** to begin; launch. **7,** *colloq.* to turn on (water, gas, etc.). **8,** *in* откры́ть счёт, to score first; be the first to score. —**открыва́ться,** *refl.* **1,** to open; be opened. **2,** (*with* **пе́ред**) to open up before one's eyes. **3,** *fig.* to be revealed; come to light. **4,** (*with dat.*) to open up to; confide in.

откры́тие *n.* **1,** opening. **2,** discovery.

откры́тка [*gen. pl.* **-ток**] *n.* postcard.

откры́то *adv.* openly.

откры́тый *adj.* **1,** open. **2,** (*of a dress*) low-cut. —**в откры́тую,** openly.

откры́ть [*infl.* **-кро́ю, -кро́ешь**] *v., pfv. of* **открыва́ть.** —**откры́ться,** *refl., pfv. of* **открыва́ться.**

отку́да *adv.* **1,** from where: отку́да вы?, where are you from? Он верну́лся туда́, отку́да он пришёл, he returned to the place from which he came. **2,** from what source?; how?: отку́да вы э́то зна́ете?, how do you (happen to) know that? Отку́да же я зна́ю?, how should I know? —**отку́да ни возьми́сь,** from out of nowhere; from out of the blue.

отку́да-либо *adv.* = **отку́да-нибудь.**

отку́да-нибудь *adv.* from somewhere or other.

отку́да-то *adv.* from somewhere.

о́ткуп *n.* tax farming. —**брать на о́ткуп,** to acquire exclusive rights to. —**отдава́ть на о́ткуп,** to farm out.

отку́поривать *v. impfv.* [*pfv.* **отку́порить**] to uncork; open.

откуси́ть [*infl.* **-кушу́, -ку́сишь**] *v., pfv. of* **отку́сывать.**

отку́сывать *v. impfv.* [*pfv.* **откуси́ть**] to bite off.

отлага́тельство *n.* delay. —**не терпе́ть отлага́тельства,** to brook no delay.

отлакирова́ть *v., pfv. of* **лакирова́ть.**

отла́мывать *v. impfv.* [*pfv.* **отлома́ть** *or* **отломи́ть**] to break off. —**отла́мываться,** *refl.* to break off; fall off; come off.

отлега́ть *v. impfv.* [*pfv.* **отле́чь**] (*of a pain, feeling, etc.*) to pass. —**у меня́ отлегло́ от се́рдца,** I felt relieved.

отлежа́ть [*infl.* **-лежу́, -лежи́шь**] *v., pfv. of* **отлёживать.** —**отлежа́ться,** *refl., pfv. of* **отлёживаться.**

отлёживать *v. impfv.* [*pfv.* **отлежа́ть**] to cause to become numb: я отлежа́л(а) но́гу, my foot has gone to sleep. —**отлёживаться,** *refl., colloq.* **1,** to recover (*after spending time in bed*). **2,** [*impfv. only*] to lie low.

отлёт *n.* departure (*by flying*). —**на отлёте, 1,** off at a distance. **2,** away from everything. **3,** about to leave. —**держа́ть (что́-нибудь) на отлёте,** to hold at arm's length.

отлета́ть *v. impfv.* [*pfv.* **отлете́ть**] **1,** to fly away; fly off. **2,** to be thrown (*from a blow or jolt*). **3,** to rebound; ricochet. **4,** *colloq.* to come off; come loose.

отлете́ть [*infl.* **-чу́, -ти́шь**] *v., pfv. of* **отлета́ть.**

отле́чь [*infl. like* **лечь**] *v., pfv. of* **отлега́ть.**

отли́в *n.* **1,** ebb; ebb tide. **2,** *fig.* ebb; decline; falling off. **3,** tint; fleck (*of color*). —**прили́в и отли́в,** ebb and flow of the tides. —**прили́вы и отли́вы,** tide; tides.

отлива́ть *v. impfv.* [*pfv.* **отли́ть**] **1,** to pour off. **2,** to pump out. **3,** to cast; found. **4,** *v.i.* (*of a liquid*) to flow; rush: кровь отлила́ от его́ лица́, the blood rushed from his face (*i.e.* he turned pale). **5,** *colloq.* to revive (*by throwing water on*). **6,** *v.i.* [*impfv. only*] (*with instr.*) to be streaked with (a certain color).

отли́вка *n.* founding; casting.

отлипа́ть *v. impfv.* [*pfv.* **отли́пнуть**] *colloq.* to come unstuck; come off.

отли́пнуть [*past* **-ли́п, -ла**] *v., pfv. of* **отлипа́ть.**

отли́ть [*infl.* **отолью́, отольёшь;** *past* **о́тлил** *or* **отли́л, отлила́, о́тлило** *or* **отли́ло**] *v., pfv. of* **отлива́ть.**

отличáть *v. impfv.* [*pfv.* **отличи́ть**] **1,** to distinguish. **2,** to reward; honor. **3,** [*impfv. only*] to distinguish; set apart. **4,** [*impfv. only*] to single out. —**отличáться,** *refl.* **1,** to stand out. **2,** to distinguish oneself. **3,** [*impfv. only*] (*with* **от**) to differ (from). **4,** [*impfv. only*] (*with instr.*) to be remarkable (for); be notable (for). Он не отличáется умóм, he is not particularly bright.

отли́чие *n.* **1,** difference; distinction. **2,** distinguished service. **3,** honors; distinction: окóнчить шкóлу с отли́чием, to graduate with honors. **4,** *in* знак отли́чия, *mil.* decoration; *pl.* insignia. —**в отли́чие от,** unlike; as opposed to; in contrast to; as distinct from.

отличи́тельный *adj.* distinguishing; distinctive.

отличи́ть *v., pfv. of* **отличáть.** —**отличи́ться,** *refl., pfv. of* **отличáться.**

отли́чник *n.* **1,** A-student. **2,** outstanding worker.

отли́чно *adv.* excellently; very well. —*adj., used predicatively* excellent. —*n.indecl.* a grade of A (*in school*): сдать экзáмен на отли́чно, to get an A on an examination.

отли́чный *adj.* **1,** excellent. **2,** (*with* **от**) different (from).

отлóгий *adj.* not steep; gently sloping.

отложéние *n.* **1,** *geol.* sediment. **2,** deposit: жировы́е отложéния, fatty deposits.

отложи́ть [*infl.* **-ложу́, -лóжишь**] *v., pfv. of* **откладывать.**

отложнóй *adj.* (*of a collar*) turndown.

отломáть *v., pfv. of* **отлáмывать.** —**отломáться,** *refl., pfv. of* **отлáмываться.**

отломи́ть [*infl.* **-ломлю́, -лóмишь**] *v., pfv. of* **отлáмывать.** —**отломи́ться,** *refl., pfv. of* **отлáмываться.**

отлупи́ть *v., pfv. of* **лупи́ть** (*in sense #3*).

отлучáть *v. impfv.* [*pfv.* **отлучи́ть**] **1,** *obs.* to remove; separate. **2,** *in* **отлучáть от цéркви,** to excommunicate. —**отлучáться,** *refl.* to go away; leave; absent oneself.

отлучéние *n.* **1,** *obs.* separation. **2,** *in* отлучéние от цéркви, excommunication.

отлучи́ть *v., pfv. of* **отлучáть.** —**отлучи́ться,** *refl., pfv. of* **отлучáться.**

отлу́чка *n.* absence: быть в отлу́чке, to be absent; be away. —**самовóльная отлу́чка,** absence without leave.

отлы́нивать *v. impfv.* (*with* **от**) *colloq.* to shirk.

отмáлчиваться *v.r. impfv.* [*pfv.* **отмолчáться**] *colloq.* to keep silent; say nothing.

отмáтывать *v. impfv.* [*pfv.* **отмотáть**] to wind off.

отмахáть [*infl.* **-махáю, -махáешь**] *v., pfv. of* **отмáхивать** (*in sense #2*).

отмáхивать *v. impfv.* **1,** [*pfv.* **отмахну́ть**] to brush away; chase away. **2,** [*pfv.* **отмахáть**] *colloq.* to cover (a certain distance). —**отмáхиваться,** *refl.* [*pfv.* **отмахну́ться**] **1,** to wave one's hand (*in disagreement or to object*). **2,** (*with* **от**) to brush away; chase away. **3,** (*with* **от**) *fig.* to brush aside; dismiss.

отмáчивать *v. impfv.* [*pfv.* **отмочи́ть**] to soak off.

отмежевáть [*infl.* **-жу́ю, -жу́ешь**] *v., pfv. of* **отмежёвывать.** —**отмежевáться,** *refl., pfv. of* **отмежёвываться.**

отмежёвывать *v. impfv.* [*pfv.* **отмежевáть**] to mark off; delimit. —**отмежёвываться,** *refl.* (*with* **от**) to dissociate oneself (from).

óтмель *n.f.* bank; shoal. —**песчáная óтмель,** sandbank; sand bar.

отмéна *n.* **1,** abolition. **2,** cancellation. **3,** repeal.

отмени́ть [*infl.* **-меню́, -мéнишь**] *v., pfv. of* **отменя́ть.**

отмéнный *adj.* excellent; splendid.

отменя́ть *v. impfv.* [*pfv.* **отмени́ть**] **1,** to abolish. **2,** to cancel. **3,** to repeal; rescind.

отмерéть [*infl.* **отомрёт;** *past* **óтмер, отмерлá, óтмерло**] *v., pfv. of* **отмирáть.**

отмерзáть *v. impfv.* [*pfv.* **отмёрзнуть**] **1,** to perish from the frost. **2,** *colloq.* (*of one's hands, ears, etc.*) to be frozen.

отмёрзнуть [*past* **-мёрз, -ла**] *v., pfv. of* **отмерзáть.**

отмéривать *v. impfv.* [*pfv.* **отмéрить**] to measure off. *Also,* **отмеря́ть.**

отмести́ [*infl. like* **мести́**] *v., pfv. of* **отметáть.**

отмéстка *n., colloq.* revenge. —**в отмéстку,** in revenge; in retaliation.

отметáть *v. impfv.* [*pfv.* **отмести́**] **1,** to sweep away; sweep off. **2,** *fig.* to reject; sweep aside.

отмéтина *n.* **1,** mark. **2,** spot of color (*on an animal or bird*).

отмéтить [*infl.* **-чу, -тишь**] *v., pfv. of* **отмечáть.** —**отмéтиться,** *refl., pfv. of* **отмечáться.**

отмéтка [*gen. pl.* **-ток**] *n.* **1,** mark; note. **2,** grade; mark (*in school*).

отмечáть *v. impfv.* [*pfv.* **отмéтить**] **1,** to mark. **2,** to note; take note of. **3,** to mark; celebrate; commemorate. —**отмечáться,** *refl.* **1,** to register. **2,** to be noticed. **3,** to be noted.

отмирáть *v. impfv.* [*pfv.* **отмерéть**] **1,** to die; die off. **2,** *fig.* to die out; disappear.

отмокáть *v. impfv.* [*pfv.* **отмóкнуть**] **1,** to get wet. **2,** to come off (*as a result of being wet*).

отмóкнуть [*past* **-мóк, -ла**] *v., pfv. of* **отмокáть.**

отмолчáться [*infl.* **-чу́сь, -чи́шься**] *v., pfv. of* **отмáлчиваться.**

отморáживать *v. impfv.* [*pfv.* **отморóзить**] (*with* **себé**) to get (a part of one's body) frostbitten: он отморóзил себé нос, his nose was frostbitten.

отморóжение *n.* frostbite.

отморóзить [*infl.* **-жу, -зишь**] *v., pfv. of* **отморáживать.**

отмотáть *v., pfv. of* **отмáтывать.**

отмочи́ть [*infl.* **-мочу́, -мóчишь**] *v., pfv. of* **отмáчивать.**

отмывáть *v. impfv.* [*pfv.* **отмы́ть**] **1,** to wash off. **2,** to wash; wash clean. —**отмывáться,** *refl.* **1,** to wash oneself off. **2,** to come clean. **3,** to come off; come out (*when something is washed*).

отмыкáть *v. impfv.* [*pfv.* **отомкну́ть**] to unlock.

отмы́ть [*infl.* **-мóю, -мóешь**] *v., pfv. of* **отмывáть.** —**отмы́ться,** *refl., pfv. of* **отмывáться.**

отмы́чка [*gen. pl.* **-чек**] *n.* **1,** master key; skeleton key. **2,** jimmy.

отнéкиваться *v.r. impfv., colloq.* to decline (by making excuses).

отнести́ [*infl. like* **нести́**] *v., pfv. of* **относи́ть.** —**отнести́сь,** *refl., pfv. of* **относи́ться.**

отнимáть *v. impfv.* [*pfv.* **отня́ть**] **1,** to take away. **2,** to withdraw; remove (one's hand). **3,** to rob of (hope, faith, etc.). **4,** to take (a certain amount of time, effort, etc.). **5,** *colloq.* to amputate. **6,** *colloq.* to subtract; take away. —**отнимáться,** *refl.* (*of a part of the body*) to become paralyzed.

относи́тельно *adv.* relatively. —*prep., with gen.* regarding; concerning.

относи́тельность *n.f.* relativity. —**тео́рия относи́тельности,** theory of relativity.

относи́тельный *adj.* relative. —**относи́тельное местоиме́ние,** relative pronoun.

относи́ть *v. impfv.* [*pfv.* **отнести́;** *pres.* **-ношу́, -но́сишь**] **1,** to take; carry; deliver (to a certain place). **2,** (*of the wind, current, etc.*) to carry away; sweep away. **3,** (*with* **к**) to attribute (to); ascribe (to); consider (among); place (among). Относи́ть на счёт (+ *gen.*), to attribute to; put down to. —**относи́ться,** *refl.* (*with* **к**) **1,** to behave (toward); act (toward); treat. **2,** to react (toward); have a certain attitude (toward). **3,** [*impfv. only*] to belong to; be among. **4,** [*impfv. only*] to apply to; pertain to. Это не отно́сится к де́лу, that is beside the point; that is irrelevant. **5,** [*impfv. only*] to date (from).

отноше́ние *n.* **1,** (*with* **к**) attitude (toward). **2,** (*with* **к**) relation; relationship; connection: не име́ть никако́го отноше́ния к, bear no relation(ship) to; have no connection with; have nothing to do with. **3,** *pl.* relations: междунаро́дные отноше́ния, international relations. Быть в хоро́ших отноше́ниях с, to be on good terms with. **4,** respect; regard; connection: в э́том отноше́нии, in this connection; во мно́гих отноше́ниях, in many respects. **5,** ratio. **6,** memorandum. —**в отноше́нии** (+ *gen.*); **по отноше́нию к,** with respect to; with regard to.

отны́не *adv.* hereafter; henceforth; from now on.

отню́дь *adv.* [*usu.* **отню́дь не**] by no means; in no way.

отня́тие *n.* **1,** taking away; seizure. **2,** amputation.

отня́ть [*infl.* **отниму́, отни́мешь;** *past* **о́тнял, отняла́, о́тняло**] *v., pfv. of* **отнима́ть.** —**отня́ться,** *refl.* [*past* **отня́лся, -ла́сь, -ло́сь**] *pfv. of* **отнима́ться.**

ото *prep.* = **от** (*used before words beginning with a double consonant*).

отобе́дать *v. pfv.* to have finished dinner.

отобража́ть *v. impfv.* [*pfv.* **отобрази́ть**] to reflect; depict; represent.

отображе́ние *n.* reflection; representation.

отобрази́ть [*infl.* **-жу́, -зи́шь**] *v., pfv. of* **отобража́ть.**

отобра́ть [*infl.* **отберу́, отберёшь;** *past fem.* **отобрала́**] *v., pfv. of* **отбира́ть.**

отовсю́ду *adv.* from everywhere.

отогна́ть [*infl.* **отгоню́, отго́нишь;** *past fem.* **отогнала́**] *v., pfv. of* **отгоня́ть.**

отогну́ть *v., pfv. of* **отгиба́ть.**

отогрева́ть *v. impfv.* [*pfv.* **отогре́ть**] to warm. —**отогрева́ться,** *refl.* to warm oneself; warm up; get warm.

отодвига́ть *v. impfv.* [*pfv.* **отодви́нуть**] **1,** to move aside; move away. **2,** *colloq.* to put off; postpone. **3,** *in* отодвига́ть на за́дний план, to relegate to the background. —**отодвига́ться,** *refl.* **1,** to move aside; step aside. **2,** to move back; draw back. **3,** *colloq.* to be put off; be postponed.

отодра́ть [*infl.* **отдеру́, отдерёшь;** *past fem.* **отодрала́**] *v., pfv. of* **отдира́ть.**

отождествля́ть *also,* **отожествля́ть** *v. impfv.* [*pfv.* **отождестви́ть** *or* **отожестви́ть**] to equate.

отозва́ть [*infl.* **отзову́, отзовёшь;** *past fem.* **отозвала́**] *v., pfv. of* **отзыва́ть.** —**отозва́ться,** *refl., pfv. of* **отзыва́ться.**

отойти́ [*infl.* **отойду́, отойдёшь;** *past* **отошёл, отошла́, отошло́**] *v., pfv. of* **отходи́ть.**

отомкну́ть *v., pfv. of* **отмыка́ть.**

отомсти́ть *v., pfv. of* **мстить.**

отопи́тельный *adj.* heating (*attrib.*). Отопи́тельный сезо́н, season when heat is required.

отопи́ть [*infl.* **отоплю́, ото́пишь**] *v., pfv. of* **ота́пливать.**

отопле́ние *n.* heating.

ото́рванность *n.f.* isolation; being cut off.

оторва́ть [*infl. like* **рвать**] *v., pfv. of* **отрыва́ть.** —**оторва́ться,** *refl., pfv. of* **отрыва́ться.**

оторопе́лый *adj., colloq.* dazed; dumfounded.

оторопе́ть *v. pfv., colloq.* to be struck dumb; be dumfounded.

о́торопь *n.f., colloq.* confusion; panic; fright.

оторо́чка *n.* edging; trimming.

отосла́ть [*infl.* **отошлю́, отошлёшь**] *v., pfv. of* **отсыла́ть.**

отоспа́ться [*infl.* **-сплю́сь, -спи́шься**] *v.r., pfv. of* **отсыпа́ться.**

отоща́лый *adj., colloq.* emaciated.

отоща́ть *v., pfv. of* **тоща́ть.**

отпада́ть *v. impfv.* [*pfv.* **отпа́сть**] **1,** to fall off; come off; peel off. **2,** (*with* **от**) to drop out of (an organization). **3,** to cease to have significance; be no longer relevant. **4,** (*of a feeling*) to pass.

отпари́ровать *v. pfv.* [*infl.* **-рую, -руешь**] **1,** to parry (a blow). **2,** *fig.* to rebut (attacks, an argument, etc.). **3,** to retort.

отпа́рывать *v. impfv.* [*pfv.* **отпоро́ть**] to snip off; slit off. —**отпа́рываться,** *refl.* to come off; tear off.

отпа́сть [*infl. like* **пасть**] *v., pfv. of* **отпада́ть.**

отпева́ние *n.* (religious) funeral service.

отпева́ть *v. impfv.* [*pfv.* **отпе́ть**] to hold a funeral service in honor of. *See also* **отпе́ть.**

отпере́ть [*infl.* **отопру́, отопрёшь;** *past* **о́тпер, отперла́, о́тперло**] *v., pfv. of* **отпира́ть.** —**отпере́ться,** *refl.* [*past* **отпёрся** *or* **отперся́, отперла́сь, отперло́сь**] *pfv. of* **отпира́ться.**

отпе́тый *adj., colloq.* incorrigible.

отпе́ть *v. pfv.* [*infl.* **-пою́, -поёшь**] **1,** *pfv. of* **отпева́ть.** **2,** to sing; chant (a song, prayer, etc.). **3,** to stop singing; finish singing.

отпеча́тать *v., pfv. of* **отпеча́тывать.** —**отпеча́таться,** *refl., pfv. of* **отпеча́тываться.**

отпеча́ток [*gen.* **-тка**] *n.* **1,** print; imprint: отпеча́ток па́льца, fingerprint. **2,** *fig.* imprint; mark: накла́дывать свой отпеча́ток на (+ *acc.*), to leave its mark upon.

отпеча́тывать *v. impfv.* [*pfv.* **отпеча́тать**] **1,** to print; run off. **2,** to type (something) on a typewriter. **3,** to make (fingerprints or footprints): отпеча́тать следы́ на песке́, to make footprints in the sand.

отпива́ть *v. impfv.* [*pfv.* **отпи́ть**] to take a sip of.

отпи́ливать *v. impfv.* [*pfv.* **отпили́ть**] to saw off.

отпили́ть [*infl.* **-пилю́, -пи́лишь**] *v., pfv. of* **отпи́ливать.**

отпира́тельство *n.* persistent denial; refusal to confess.

отпира́ть *v. impfv.* [*pfv.* **отпере́ть**] to unlock. —**отпира́ться,** *refl.* **1,** to unlock; come unlocked. **2,** *colloq.* to deny; (*with* **от**) disavow.

отписа́ть [*infl.* **-пишу́, -пи́шешь**] *v., pfv. of* **отпи́сывать.** —**отписа́ться,** *refl., pfv. of* **отпи́сываться.**

отпи́ска [*gen. pl.* **-сок**] *n.* noncommittal answer; answer that is not really an answer.

отпи́сывать *v. impfv.* [*pfv.* **отписа́ть**] *obs.* **1,** to confiscate. **2,** to bequeath. —**отпи́сываться,** *refl., colloq.* to write a purely formal reply.

отпи́ть *v. pfv.* [*infl.* **отопью́, отопьёшь;** *past* **о́тпил, отпила́, о́тпило**] **1,** *pfv. of* **отпива́ть. 2,** *colloq.* to finish drinking.

отпи́хивать *v. impfv.* [*pfv.* **отпихну́ть**] *colloq.* to push away; push aside; shove aside.

отпла́та *n.* repayment. —**в отпла́ту за,** in repayment for; in return for.

отплати́ть [*infl.* **-плачу́, -пла́тишь**] *v., pfv. of* **отпла́чивать.**

отпла́чивать *v. impfv.* [*pfv.* **отплати́ть**] (*with dat.*) to pay back; repay (someone).

отплёвывать *v. impfv.* [*pfv.* **отплю́нуть**] *colloq.* **1,** *v.t.* to spit out. **2,** *v.i.* to spit (a certain distance). —**отплёвываться,** *refl.* [*impfv. only*] to spit (*in disgust*).

отплыва́ть *v. impfv.* [*pfv.* **отплы́ть**] **1,** to swim away. **2,** (*of a ship*) to sail; depart.

отплы́тие *n.* sailing; departure.

отплы́ть [*infl. like* **плыть**] *v., pfv. of* **отплыва́ть.**

отплю́нуть *v., pfv. of* **отплёвывать.**

о́тповедь *n.f.* rebuke; reproof.

отполза́ть *v. impfv.* [*pfv.* **отползти́**] to crawl away.

отползти́ [*infl. like* **ползти́**] *v., pfv. of* **отполза́ть.**

отполирова́ть *v., pfv. of* **полирова́ть.**

отпо́р *n.* rebuff.

отпоро́ть [*infl.* **-порю́, -по́решь**] *v., pfv. of* **отпа́рывать.** —**отпоро́ться,** *refl., pfv. of* **отпа́рываться.**

отправи́тель *n.m.* sender.

отпра́вить [*infl.* **-влю, -вишь**] *v., pfv. of* **отправля́ть.** —**отпра́виться,** *refl., pfv. of* **отправля́ться.**

отпра́вка *n., colloq.* dispatch; shipment.

отправле́ние *n.* **1,** sending; dispatch. **2,** departure. **3,** item of mail. **4,** exercise; performance; discharge. **5,** *pl.* functions (*of an organism*). —**то́чка отправле́ния,** point of departure.

отправля́ть *v. impfv.* [*pfv.* **отпра́вить**] **1,** to send; dispatch. **2,** [*impfv. only*] to discharge; perform. Отправля́ть правосу́дие, to administer justice. —**отправля́ться,** *refl.* **1,** to leave; start out; set out. **2,** [*impfv. only*] (*with* **от**) to proceed from (*in one's thinking*).

отправно́й *adj.* **1,** dispatch (*attrib.*); shipping (*attrib.*). **2,** initial. —**отправно́й пункт; отправна́я то́чка,** starting point.

отпра́здновать *v., pfv. of* **пра́здновать.**

отпра́шиваться *v.r. impfv.* [*pfv.* **отпроси́ться**] **1,** [*usu. impfv.*] to request permission to be absent. **2,** [*usu. pfv.*] to obtain permission to be absent: отпроси́ться на одну́ неде́лю, to get a week off.

отпроси́ться [*infl.* **-прошу́сь, -про́сишься**] *v.r., pfv. of* **отпра́шиваться.**

отпры́гивать *v. impfv.* [*pfv.* **отпры́гнуть**] to jump back; jump aside.

о́тпрыск *n.* **1,** *bot.* shoot. **2,** *fig., obs.* offspring.

отпряга́ть *v. impfv.* [*pfv.* **отпря́чь**] to unharness.

отпря́нуть *v. pfv.* to jump back; recoil.

отпря́чь [*infl.* **-прягу́, -пряжёшь, ...-прягу́т;** *past* **-пря́г, -прягла́, -прягло́**] *v., pfv. of* **отпряга́ть.**

отпу́гивать *v. impfv.* [*pfv.* **отпугну́ть**] to frighten away; frighten off.

о́тпуск [*pl.* **отпуска́**] *n.* **1,** vacation: в о́тпуске (*or colloquially* в отпуску́), on vacation. **2,** leave: о́тпуск по боле́зни, sick leave.

отпуска́ть *v. impfv.* [*pfv.* **отпусти́ть**] **1,** to let go of. **2,** to let go; release. **3,** to loosen; slacken. **4,** *v.i., colloq.* (*of pain*) to lessen; ease. **5,** to grow (a beard, mustache, etc.). **6,** to allot; allow. **7,** to sell. **8,** to remit (a sin). **9,** *colloq.* to utter (a remark); crack (a joke).

отпускни́к [*gen.* **-ника́**] *n.* person on vacation; person on leave.

отпускно́й *adj.* vacation (*attrib.*).

отпусти́ть [*infl.* **-пущу́, -пу́стишь**] *v., pfv. of* **отпуска́ть.**

отпуще́ние *n.* **1,** remission (*of sins*). **2,** *in* отпуще́ние на во́лю, emancipation. —**козёл отпуще́ния,** scapegoat.

отраба́тывать *v. impfv.* [*pfv.* **отрабо́тать**] **1,** to work off (a debt). **2,** to perfect; polish.

отрабо́тать *v. pfv.* **1,** *pfv. of* **отраба́тывать. 2,** to work (*for a certain length of time*). **3,** *colloq.* to finish working; stop working.

отра́ва *n.* poison.

отрави́ть [*infl.* **отравлю́, отра́вишь**] *v., pfv. of* **отравля́ть.** —**отрави́ться,** *refl., pfv. of* **отравля́ться.**

отравле́ние *n.* poisoning. —**отравле́ние свинцо́м,** lead poisoning.

отравля́ть *v. impfv.* [*pfv.* **отрави́ть**] **1,** to poison. **2,** *fig.* to spoil; mar. —**отравля́ться,** *refl.* **1,** to poison oneself; take poison. **2,** to be poisoned; suffer poisoning.

отра́да *n.* joy; delight.

отра́дный *adj.* pleasing; gratifying. Отра́дно, что..., it is gratifying that...,

отража́тель *n.m.* reflector.

отража́ть *v. impfv.* [*pfv.* **отрази́ть**] **1,** to reflect. **2,** to repulse; repel; parry; ward off. —**отража́ться,** *refl.* **1,** to be reflected. **2,** (*with* **на** + *prepl.*) to affect; have an effect upon.

отраже́ние *n.* **1,** reflection. **2,** repulsing; repelling.

отрази́ть [*infl.* **-жу́, -зи́шь**] *v., pfv. of* **отража́ть.** —**отрази́ться,** *refl., pfv. of* **отража́ться.**

отрапортова́ть *v.pfv.* [*infl.* **-ту́ю, -ту́ешь**] to report.

отраслево́й *adj.* of a particular branch or field. —**отраслева́я библиогра́фия,** bibliography by subject.

о́трасль *n.f.* branch; field.

отраста́ть *v. impfv.* [*pfv.* **отрасти́**] (*of hair, nails, etc.*) to grow.

отрасти́ [*infl. like* **расти́**] *v., pfv. of* **отраста́ть.**

отрасти́ть [*infl.* **-щу́, -сти́шь**] *v., pfv. of* **отра́щивать.**

отра́щивать *v. impfv.* [*pfv.* **отрасти́ть**] **1,** to let (one's hair, nails, etc.) grow. **2,** to grow (a beard, paunch, etc.).

отреаги́ровать *v. pfv.* [*infl.* **-рую, -руешь**] to react.

отре́бье *n.* rabble. —**отре́бье о́бщества,** the dregs of society.

отрегули́ровать *v., pfv. of* **регули́ровать** (*in sense #2*).

отредакти́ровать *v., pfv. of* **редакти́ровать.**

отре́з *n.* **1,** cut. **2,** length (*of material*). **3,** perforated line (*for tearing off something*).

отре́зать [*infl.* **-ре́жу, -ре́жешь**] *v., pfv. of* **отреза́ть** *and* **отре́зывать.**

отреза́ть *v. impfv.* [*pfv.* **отре́зать**] **1,** to cut off. **2,** *colloq.* to snap back (*when answering*). *Also,* **отре́зывать.**

отрезве́ть *v., pfv. of* **трезве́ть.**

отрезви́ть [*infl.* **-влю́, -ви́шь**] *v., pfv. of* **отрезвля́ть.** —**отрезви́ться,** *refl., pfv. of* **отрезвля́ться.**

отрезвля́ть *v. impfv.* [*pfv.* **отрезви́ть**] to sober; sober up. —**отрезвля́ться,** *refl.* to sober up; become sober.

отрезно́й *adj.* **1,** to be torn off. **2,** detachable.

отре́зок [*gen.* **-зка**] *n.* **1,** piece; length (*of material*). **2,** segment; section; part. Отре́зок вре́мени, segment/stretch/span of time.

отре́зывать *v.impfv.* = **отреза́ть.**

отрека́ться *v.r. impfv.* [*pfv.* **отре́чься**] (*with* **от**) **1,** to renounce; disavow; repudiate. **2,** *in* отрека́ться от престо́ла, to abdicate.

отрекомендова́ть *v.pfv.* [*infl.* **-ду́ю, -ду́ешь**] **1,** to recommend. **2,** *obs.* to introduce. —**отрекомендова́ться,** *refl.* to introduce oneself.

отремонти́ровать *v., pfv. of* **ремонти́ровать.**

отре́пье *n., often pl., colloq.* rags; tatters.

отрече́ние *n.* (*with* **от**) **1,** renunciation; disavowal; repudiation. **2,** *in* отрече́ние от престо́ла, abdication.

отре́чься [*infl.* **-реку́сь, -речёшься, ...-реку́тся;** *past* **-рёкся, -рекла́сь, -рекло́сь**] *v.r., pfv. of* **отрека́ться.**

отреша́ть *v. impfv.* [*pfv.* **отреши́ть**] *obs.* to remove; dismiss; suspend. —**отреша́ться,** *refl.* (*with* **от**) **1,** to rid oneself of; get away from. **2,** to renounce.

отрешённый *adj.* **1,** aloof; isolated. **2,** (*of a look*) blank; distracted. —**отрешённость,** *n.f.* aloofness; isolation.

отреши́ть *v., pfv. of* **отреша́ть.** —**отреши́ться,** *refl., pfv. of* **отреша́ться.**

отрица́ние *n.* **1,** denial. **2,** negation. **3,** *gram.* negative.

отрица́тельно *adv.* **1,** negatively. **2,** in the negative. **3,** adversely.

отрица́тельный *adj.* negative.

отрица́ть *v. impfv.* to deny.

отро́г *n.* spur (*of a mountain range*).

о́троду *adv.* (*with* **не**) *colloq.* never in one's life; never in all one's born days.

отро́сток [*gen.* **-стка**] *n.* **1,** shoot; sprout. **2,** *anat.* outgrowth.

о́троческий *adj.* adolescent. —**о́трочество,** *n.* adolescence.

отруба́ть *v. impfv.* [*pfv.* **отруби́ть**] to chop off.

о́труби [*gen.* **-бе́й**] *n.pl.* bran.

отруби́ть *v. pfv.* [*infl.* **-рублю́, -ру́бишь**] **1,** *pfv. of* **отруба́ть. 2,** *colloq.* to snap back (*in answering*).

отру́гиваться *v.r. impfv., colloq.* to answer back; answer curses with curses.

отры́в *n.* **1,** tearing off. **2,** break; hiatus. **3,** alienation; isolation. —**в отры́ве от,** isolated from; cut off from. —**отры́в от земли́, 1,** takeoff. **2,** liftoff.

отрыва́ть *v. impfv.* [*pfv.* **оторва́ть**] **1,** to tear off. **2,** (*with* **от**) to tear away (from): я не мог оторва́ть мы́слей от э́того, I couldn't stop thinking about it. Я не могла́ оторва́ть глаз от э́того, I couldn't take my eyes off it. **3,** [*pfv.* **отры́ть**] to dig up; unearth.

отрыва́ться *v.r. impfv.* [*pfv.* **оторва́ться**] **1,** to come off; be torn off. **2,** (*with* **от**) to break away (from); give (someone) the slip. **3,** *in* оторва́ться от земли́, (*of a plane*) to take off. **4,** (*with* **от**) to lose touch (with); lose contact (with). **5,** (*with* **от**) to tear oneself away (from work, a book, etc.). —**не отрыва́ясь,** without a break; nonstop.

отры́вистый *adj.* **1,** (*of sounds*) staccato. **2,** (*of speech*) uneven; disjointed.

отрывно́й *adj.* **1,** that can be torn off. **2,** with sheets that can be torn off.

отры́вок [*gen.* **-вка**] *n.* **1,** passage; excerpt. **2,** fragment; snatch: отры́вки разгово́ра, snatches of a conversation.

отры́вочный *adj.* **1,** fragmentary. **2,** disjointed.

отры́гивать *v. impfv.* [*pfv.* **отрыгну́ть**] to belch up.

отры́жка *n.* **1,** belch. **2,** *fig., colloq.* vestige.

отры́ть [*infl.* **-ро́ю, -ро́ешь**] *v., pfv. of* **отрыва́ть** (*in sense #3*).

отря́д *n.* **1,** *mil.* detachment. **2,** group: пионе́рский отря́д, (young) pioneer group. **3,** *zool.* order.

отряжа́ть *v. impfv.* [*pfv.* **отряди́ть**] **1,** to dispatch; send (*on a certain assignment*). **2,** *mil.* to assign; detail.

отряса́ть *v. impfv.* [*pfv.* **отрясти́**] to shake off. —**отрясти́ прах от свои́х ног,** to shake the dust from one's feet.

отрясти́ [*infl. like* **трясти́**] *v., pfv. of* **отряса́ть.**

отря́хивать *v. impfv.* [*pfv.* **отряхну́ть**] to shake off.

отсади́ть [*infl.* **-сажу́, -са́дишь**] *v., pfv. of* **отса́живать.**

отса́живать *v. impfv.* [*pfv.* **отсади́ть**] **1,** to seat apart. **2,** to separate (animals, birds, etc.). **3,** to transplant.

отса́сывать *v. impfv.* [*pfv.* **отсоса́ть**] to draw off; draw out; suck out.

отсве́т *also,* **о́тсвет** *n.* reflection.

отсве́чивать *v. impfv.* to shine; gleam (*by reflecting light*).

отсебя́тина *n., colloq.* words of one's own.

отсе́в *n.* **1,** sifting out (*lit. & fig.*). **2,** *fig.* dropping out: проце́нт отсе́ва, dropout rate.

отсе́ивать *v. impfv.* [*pfv.* **отсе́ять**] **1,** to sift out. **2,** *fig.* to weed out; winnow out. —**отсе́иваться,** *refl.* to drop out.

отсе́к *n.* **1,** compartment. **2,** (space) module. —**бо́мбовый отсе́к,** bomb bay.

отсека́ть *v. impfv.* [*pfv.* **отсе́чь**] to chop off.

отсече́ние *n.* chopping off. —**дать го́лову** (*or* **ру́ку**) **на отсече́ние,** to stake one's life on it.

отсе́чь [*infl. like* **сечь;** *past* **-се́к, -секла́, -секло́**] *v., pfv. of* **отсека́ть.**

отсе́ять [*infl.* **-се́ю, -се́ешь**] *v., pfv. of* **отсе́ивать.**

отсиде́ть [*infl.* **-жу́, -ди́шь**] *v., pfv. of* **отси́живать.** —**отсиде́ться,** *refl., pfv. of* **отси́живаться.**

отси́живать *v. impfv.* [*pfv.* **отсиде́ть**] **1,** to make numb (*by sitting*): я отсиде́л себе́ но́гу, my foot is asleep. **2,** *colloq.* to sit through: отсиде́ть весь спекта́кль, to sit through the entire performance. **3,** to serve out; finish serving (a prison term). —**отси́живаться,** *refl., colloq.* to take cover.

отска́бливать *v. impfv.* [*pfv.* **отскобли́ть**] to scrape off.

отска́кивать *v. impfv.* [*pfv.* **отскочи́ть**] **1,** to jump back; jump aside. **2,** to rebound; (*with* **от**) bounce off. **3,** *colloq.* to come off; fly off.

отскобли́ть [*infl.* **-скоблю́, -ско́блишь** *or* **-скобли́шь**] *v., pfv. of* **отска́бливать.**

отскочи́ть [*infl.* **-скочу́, -ско́чишь**] *v., pfv. of* **отска́кивать.**

отсла́ивать *v. impfv.* [*pfv.* **отслои́ть**] to remove layer by layer. —**отсла́иваться,** *refl.* to come off in layers.

отсло́йка *n., in* **отсло́йка сетча́тки; отсло́йка се́тчатой оболо́чки,** detached retina.

отслужи́ть *v. pfv.* [*infl.* **-служу́, -слу́жишь**] **1,** to serve out; finish serving. **2,** to be worn out (*from use*).

отсове́товать *v. pfv.* [*infl.* **-тую, -туешь**] (*with dat. & inf.*) to dissuade (from); talk out of.

отсоса́ть [*infl.* **-сосу́, -сосёшь**] *v., pfv. of* **отса́сывать.**

отсо́хнуть [*past* **-со́х, -ла**] *v., pfv. of* **отсыха́ть.**

отсро́чивать *v. impfv.* [*pfv.* **отсро́чить**] **1,** to postpone; defer. **2,** to extend (a passport, license, etc.).

отсро́чка [*gen. pl.* **-чек**] *n.* postponement; deferment; delay.

отстава́ние *n.* lag; lagging behind.

отстава́ть *v. impfv.* [*pfv.* **отста́ть;** *pres.* **-стаю́, -стаёшь**] **1,** (*with* **от**) to lag behind; be behind; fall behind. **2,** (*of a clock or watch*) to be slow. **3,** to come off; peel off. **4,** (*with* **от**) *colloq.* to lose touch (with). **5,** (*with* **от**) *colloq.* to leave alone; leave in peace. —**отстава́ть от жи́зни/вре́мени,** to be behind the times. —**отстава́ть от по́езда,** to fail to get back on a train in time.

отста́вить [*infl.* **-влю, -вишь**] *v., pfv. of* **отставля́ть.**

отста́вка *n.* **1,** resignation. **2,** retirement. —**в отста́вке,** retired. —**вы́йти** *or* **уйти́ в отста́вку. 1,** to resign. **2,** to retire.

отставля́ть *v. impfv.* [*pfv.* **отста́вить**] **1,** to move aside. **2,** *obs.* to discharge; dismiss. —**отста́вить!,** *mil.* as you were!

отставно́й *adj.* retired.

отста́ивать *v. impfv.* [*pfv.* **отстоя́ть**] **1,** to defend. **2,** *fig.* to uphold (a principle); assert (one's rights). —**отста́иваться,** *refl.* (*of a liquid*) to settle. *See also* **отстоя́ть.**

отста́лый *adj.* **1,** backward. **2,** retarded. —**отста́лость,** *n.f.* backwardness.

отста́ть [*infl.* **-ста́ну, -ста́нешь**] *v., pfv. of* **отстава́ть.**

отстега́ть *v., pfv. of* **стега́ть** (*in sense #2*).

отстёгивать *v. impfv.* [*pfv.* **отстегну́ть**] to unfasten; undo. —**отстёгиваться,** *refl.* to come unfastened; come undone.

отсти́рывать *v. impfv.* [*pfv.* **отстира́ть**] to wash off; wash out. —**отсти́рываться,** *refl.* to come out in the wash.

отстоя́ть[1] *v. pfv.* [*infl.* **-стою́, -стои́шь**] **1,** *pfv. of* **отста́ивать. 2,** to stand through: отстоя́ть весь конце́рт, to stand through the entire concert. —**отстоя́ться,** *refl., pfv. of* **отста́иваться.**

отстоя́ть[2] *v. impfv.* [*pres.* **-стою́, -стои́шь**] (*with* **от**) to be; be located (a certain distance from).

отстра́ивать *v. impfv.* [*pfv.* **отстро́ить**] **1,** to build; finish building. **2,** to rebuild (*after a disaster*).

отстране́ние *n.* removal; dismissal.

отстраня́ть *v. impfv.* [*pfv.* **отстрани́ть**] **1,** to push aside. **2,** to remove; dismiss; suspend. —**отстраня́ться,** *refl.* **1,** to step aside. **2,** (*with* **от**) to avoid; dodge. **3,** (*with* **от**) to keep away (from); remain aloof (from).

отстре́ливать *v. impfv.* [*pfv.* **отстрели́ть**] to shoot off. —**отстре́ливаться,** *refl.* [*pfv.* **отстреля́ться**] to shoot back; fire back; (*with* **от**) fire back upon.

отстрели́ть [*infl.* **-стрелю́, -стре́лишь**] *v., pfv. of* **отстре́ливать.**

отстреля́ться *v.r., pfv. of* **отстре́ливаться.**

отстрига́ть *v. impfv.* [*pfv.* **отстри́чь**] to cut off (someone's hair).

отстри́чь [*infl. like* **стричь**] *v., pfv. of* **отстрига́ть.**

отстро́ить *v., pfv. of* **отстра́ивать.**

о́тступ *n.* indention; indentation (*in writing or printing*).

отступа́ть *v. impfv.* [*pfv.* **отступи́ть**] **1,** to step back. **2,** to recede. **3,** to retreat. **4,** to back down. **5,** (*with* **от**) to give up; abandon. **6,** (*with* **от**) to deviate (from); depart (from); digress (from). **7,** to indent. —**отступа́ться,** *refl.* (*with* **от**) to give up on; abandon; retreat from; turn one's back on.

отступи́ть [*infl.* **-ступлю́, -сту́пишь**] *v., pfv. of* **отступа́ть.** —**отступи́ться,** *refl., pfv. of* **отступа́ться.**

отступле́ние *n.* **1,** retreat. **2,** deviation; departure. **3,** digression.

отсту́пник *n.* apostate. —**отсту́пнический,** *adj.* apostate. —**отсту́пничество,** *n.* apostasy.

отступно́е *n., decl. as an adj.* indemnity; compensation.

отступя́ *adv.* away; off: немно́го отступя́, a short distance away.

отсу́тствие *n.* **1,** absence: в моё отсу́тствие, in my absence. **2,** lack.

отсу́тствовать *v. impfv.* [*pres.* **-ствую, -ствуешь**] **1,** to be absent: отсу́тствовать на собра́нии, to be absent from a meeting. **2,** to be lacking: ули́ки отсу́тствуют, evidence is lacking.

отсу́тствующий *adj.* **1,** absent. **2,** (*of a look*) absent; blank; vacant. —*n.* absentee.

отсчёт *n.* **1,** counting out; marking off. **2,** reading (*on an instrument*). —**обра́тный отсчёт вре́мени,** countdown. —**то́чка отсчёта,** reference point.

отсчи́тывать *v. impfv.* [*pfv.* **отсчита́ть**] **1,** to count out: отсчита́ть сто рубле́й, to count out 100 rubles. **2,** to mark off; count off: отсчита́ть де́сять шаго́в, to mark off ten paces.

отсыла́ть *v. impfv.* [*pfv.* **отосла́ть**] **1,** to send off. **2,** to send away; dismiss. **3,** (*with* **к**) to refer (someone) to.

отсы́лка *n.* **1,** sending; dispatch. **2,** reference.

отсы́пать [*infl.* **-сы́плю, -сы́плешь**] *v., pfv. of* **отсыпа́ть.**

отсыпа́ть *v. impfv.* [*pfv.* **отсы́пать**] (*usu. with gen.*) to pour out (a quantity or portion of something).

отсыпа́ться *v.r. impfv.* [*pfv.* **отоспа́ться**] to catch up on one's sleep.

отсыре́лый *adj.* damp; soggy.

отсыре́ть *v., pfv. of* **сыре́ть.**

отсыха́ть *v. impfv.* [*pfv.* **отсо́хнуть**] to wither.

отсю́да *adv.* **1,** from here. **2,** hence. Отсю́да сле́дует, что..., from this it follows that...

otта́ивать *v. impfv.* [*pfv.* **отта́ять**] *v.t. & i.* to thaw; thaw out. —**отта́ивать чьё-нибудь се́рдце,** to melt someone's heart.

отта́лкивать *v. impfv.* [*pfv.* **оттолкну́ть**] **1,** to push back; push away; push aside. **2,** to repel; antagonize; alienate. —**отта́лкиваться,** *refl.* (*with* **от**) to push off (from shore, land, etc.).

отта́лкивающий *adj.* repulsive; repellent.

отта́скивать *v. impfv.* [*pfv.* **оттащи́ть**] **1,** to pull aside; drag aside. **2,** to pull away.

отта́чивать *v. impfv.* [*pfv.* **отточи́ть**] **1,** to sharpen; hone. **2,** *fig.* to polish; perfect.

оттащи́ть [*infl.* **-тащу́, -та́щишь**] *v., pfv. of* **отта́скивать.**

отта́ять [*infl.* **-та́ю, -та́ешь**] *v., pfv. of* **отта́ивать.**

оттени́ть *v., pfv. of* **оттеня́ть.**

отте́нок [*gen.* **-нка**] *n.* **1,** tint; hue. **2,** shade; nuance. **3,** (*with gen.*) trace (of); tinge (of).

оттеня́ть *v. impfv.* [*pfv.* **оттени́ть**] **1,** to shade; shade in. **2,** *fig.* to set off.

о́ттепель *n.f.* thaw.

оттере́ть [*infl.* **ототру́, ототрёшь;** *past* **оттёр, -ла**] *v., pfv. of* **оттира́ть.**

оттеснять *v. impfv.* [*pfv.* **оттеснить**] **1,** to drive back; force back. **2,** *fig.* to force out; crowd out.
оттирать *v. impfv.* [*pfv.* **оттереть**] **1,** to rub off; rub out. **2,** to rub (one's hands, ears, etc.) until the feeling returns. **3,** *colloq.* to push aside; force aside.
оттиск *n.* **1,** imprint; print; impression. **2,** print; proof. **3,** reprint.
оттискивать *v. impfv.* [*pfv.* **оттиснуть**] **1,** *colloq.* to push back. **2,** to imprint.
оттого *adv.* (*often* **оттого и**) that is why; which is why. —**оттого что,** because.
оттолкнуть *v., pfv. of* **отталкивать.** —**оттолкнуться,** *refl., pfv. of* **отталкиваться.**
оттоманка [*gen. pl.* **-нок**] *n.* ottoman.
оттопыренный *adj.* protruding; prominent.
оттопыривать *v. impfv.* [*pfv.* **оттопырить**] *colloq.* to stick out. —**оттопыриваться,** *refl., colloq.* to stick out; bulge; protrude.
отторгать *v. impfv.* [*pfv.* **отторгнуть**] to tear away; forcibly detach or separate.
отторгнуть [*past* **-торг** *or* **-торгнул, -торгла**] *v., pfv. of* **отторгать.**
отточить [*infl.* **-точу, -точишь**] *v., pfv. of* **оттачивать.**
оттуда *adv.* from there.
оттузить *v., pfv. of* **тузить.**
оттягивать *v. impfv.* [*pfv.* **оттянуть**] **1,** to draw aside; pull aside. **2,** *mil.* to draw off. **3,** to weigh down. **4,** to delay; put off. —**оттягивать время,** to play for time; stall for time.
оттяжка [*gen. pl.* **-жек**] *n., colloq.* (deliberate) delay.
оттянуть [*infl.* **-тяну, -тянешь**] *v., pfv. of* **оттягивать.**
отуманивать *v. impfv.* [*pfv.* **отуманить**] **1,** to blur; dim; obscure. **2,** to dull; cloud (the senses).
отупелый *adj., colloq.* dazed.
отупение *n.* daze; stupor; torpor.
отупеть *v. pfv.* to become dazed.
отутюживать *v. impfv.* [*pfv.* **отутюжить**] to iron; press.
отучать *v. impfv.* [*pfv.* **отучить**] (*with* **от** *or inf.*) to break (someone) of the habit of; train not to; wean away from. —**отучаться,** *refl.* (*with* **от** *or inf.*) to break oneself (of a habit); break the habit of.
отучить [*infl.* **-учу, -учишь**] *v., pfv. of* **отучать.** —**отучиться,** *refl., pfv. of* **отучаться.**
отхаживать *v. impfv.* [*pfv.* **отходить**] *colloq.* to nurse back to health.
отхаркивать *v. impfv.* [*pfv.* **отхаркнуть**] to cough up. —**отхаркиваться,** *refl.* to clear one's throat.
отхватить [*infl.* **-хвачу, -хватишь**] *v., pfv. of* **отхватывать.**
отхватывать *v. impfv.* [*pfv.* **отхватить**] *colloq.* to cut off; slice off; snip off.
отхлёбывать *v. impfv.* [*pfv.* **отхлебнуть**] *colloq.* **1,** to take a sip of. **2,** (*with* **из**) to sip (from).
отхлестать *v. pfv.* [*infl.* **-хлещу, -хлещешь**] *colloq.* to give (someone) a lashing; horsewhip.
отхлынуть *v. pfv.* to surge back.
отход *n.* **1,** departure. **2,** *mil.* withdrawal. **3,** *fig.* departure; deviation; retreat. **4,** *pl.* waste; waste matter.
отходить[1] *v. impfv.* [*pfv.* **отойти;** *pres.* **-хожу, -ходишь**] **1,** (*with* **от**) to walk away (from); step back (from). **2,** (*of a train*) to leave; depart. **3,** *mil.* to withdraw; fall back. **4,** (*with* **от**) to deviate (from); depart (from); digress (from). **5,** (*with* **от**) to drift away (from). **6,** to come off; peel off; (*of a stain*) come out. **7,** to recover; come round. **8,** to calm down. **9,** (*with* **к**) (*of property*) to pass (to). **10,** *obs.* to pass; come to an end. —**отойти в прошлое** *or* **в историю,** to pass into history; become a thing of the past.
отходить[2] [*infl.* **-хожу, -ходишь**] *v., pfv. of* **отхаживать.**
отходная *n., decl. as an adj.* prayer said for a dying person.
отходчивый *adj.* disposed quickly to forgive; not such as to harbor a grudge.
отхожий *adj., in* **отхожее место,** outhouse; latrine.
отцвести [*infl. like* **цвести**] *v., pfv. of* **отцветать.**
отцветать *v. impfv.* [*pfv.* **отцвести**] **1,** to cease to bloom. **2,** *fig.* to lose its bloom; fade.
отцепить [*infl.* **-цеплю, -цепишь**] *v., pfv. of* **отцеплять.** —**отцепиться,** *refl., pfv. of* **отцепляться.**
отцеплять *v. impfv.* [*pfv.* **отцепить**] to unhook; uncouple. —**отцепляться,** *refl.* to come unhooked; come uncoupled.
отцеубийство *n.* patricide.
отцовский *adj.* **1,** one's father's. **2,** paternal. —**отцовство,** *n.* paternity; fatherhood.
отчаиваться *v.r. impfv.* [*pfv.* **отчаяться**] (*with inf. or* **в** + *prepl.*) to despair (of).
отчаливать *v. impfv.* [*pfv.* **отчалить**] (*of a boat*) to cast off.
отчасти *adv.* partly; in part.
отчаяние *n.* despair.
отчаянно *adv.* **1,** desperately. **2,** *colloq.* frightfully.
отчаянный *adj.* **1,** desperate. **2,** *colloq.* reckless. **3,** *colloq.* frightful; awful.
отчаяться *v.r., pfv. of* **отчаиваться.**
отчего *adv.* why. —*conj.* and as a result; and because of that.
отчего-нибудь *adv.* for some reason or other. *Also,* **отчего-либо.**
отчего-то *adv.* for some unknown reason.
отчеканить *v., pfv. of* **чеканить.**
отчёркивать *v. impfv.* [*pfv.* **отчеркнуть**] to mark; mark off.
отчество *n.* patronymic (name).
отчёт *n.* account; report. —**отдавать себе отчёт в** (+ *prepl.*), to realize; be aware of.
отчётливый *adj.* distinct; clear. —**отчётливо,** *adv.* distinctly; clearly.
отчётность *n.f.* **1,** accounting; bookkeeping. **2,** accounts; records. —**проверка отчётности,** audit; auditing.
отчётный *adj.* **1,** of or pert. to a report. Отчётный доклад, report. **2,** covered in a report: отчётный период, the period covered.
отчизна *n., archaic* native land; fatherland.
отчий *adj., obs.* one's father's.
отчим *n.* stepfather.
отчисление *n.* **1,** deduction. **2,** *pl.* money deducted; deductions. **3,** dismissal.
отчислять *v. impfv.* [*pfv.* **отчислить**] **1,** to deduct. **2,** to dismiss.
отчистить [*infl.* **-щу, -стишь**] *v., pfv. of* **отчищать.**
отчитывать *v. impfv.* [*pfv.* **отчитать**] *colloq.* to tell off; give (someone) a talking-to. —**отчитываться,** *refl.* **1,** to report; give a report. **2,** (*with* **в** + *prepl.*) to account for.
отчищать *v. impfv.* [*pfv.* **отчистить**] **1,** to clean; scour. **2,** to remove (a stain, rust, etc.).

отчуждáть *v. impfv.* [*pfv.* **отчудить**] to alienate; estrange.
отчуждéние *n.* alienation; estrangement.
отчуждённость *n.f.* estrangement; aloofness; distance.
отшагáть *v. pfv., colloq.* to walk (a certain distance).
отшагнýть *v. pfv., colloq.* to step aside; step back.
отшáтываться *v.r. impfv.* [*pfv.* **отшатнýться**] **1,** to jump back; recoil. **2,** (*with* **от**) *fig.* to turn one's back on.
отшвы́ривать *v. impfv.* [*pfv.* **отшвырнýть**] *colloq.* to throw away; fling away.
отшéльник *n.* hermit; recluse. —**отшéльнический,** *adj.* (like that) of a hermit; solitary. —**отшéльничество,** *n.* solitary life.
отши́б *n., in* **на отши́бе, 1,** at a distance. **2,** alone; by oneself. **3,** (*with* **от**) apart (from); aloof (from).
отшибáть *v. impfv.* [*pfv.* **отшиби́ть**] *colloq.* **1,** to hurt: отшиби́ть себé нóгу, to hurt one's leg. **2,** *impers.* to lose (one's memory, appetite, etc.): у негó отши́бло аппети́т, he lost his appetite.
отшиби́ть [*infl.* **-бý, -бёшь;** *past* **отши́б, -ла**] *v., pfv. of* **отшибáть.**
отшлёпать *v. pfv., colloq.* to spank.
отшлифовáть *v., pfv. of* **шлифовáть.**
отшути́ться [*infl.* **-шучýсь, -шýтишься**] *v.r., pfv. of* **отшýчиваться.**
отшýчиваться *v.r. impfv.* [*pfv.* **отшути́ться**] *colloq.* to reply with a joke; come back with a joke.
отщепéнец [*gen.* **-нца**] *n.* renegade.
отщепля́ть *v. impfv.* [*pfv.* **отщепи́ть**] to chip off. —**отщепля́ться,** *refl.* to chip off; be chipped off.
отщи́пывать *v. impfv.* [*pfv.* **отщипнýть**] to pinch off (*usu.* a piece of bread).
отъедáть *v. impfv.* [*pfv.* **отъéсть**] to bite off. —**отъедáться,** *refl.* to put on weight from good food.
отъéзд *n.* departure. —**быть в отъéзде,** to be away; be out of town.
отъезжáть *v. impfv.* [*pfv.* **отъéхать**] to drive away; drive off; ride away; ride off.
отъéсть [*infl. like* **есть**] *v., pfv. of* **отъедáть.** —**отъéсться,** *refl., pfv. of* **отъедáться.**
отъéхать [*infl.* **-éду, -éдешь**] *v., pfv. of* **отъезжáть.**
отъя́вленный *adj.* arrant; unmitigated; out-and-out.
оты́грывать *v. impfv.* [*pfv.* **отыгрáть**] to win back. —**оты́грываться,** *refl.* **1,** to recoup one's losses. **2,** *colloq.* to wiggle out of a situation.
отыскáть [*infl.* **отыщý, оты́щешь**] *v., pfv. of* **оты́скивать.** —**отыскáться,** *refl., pfv. of* **оты́скиваться.**
оты́скивать *v. impfv.* [*pfv.* **отыскáть**] **1,** to find. **2,** [*impfv. only*] to look for; search for; try to find. —**оты́скиваться,** *refl.* to be found; turn up.
отягощáть *v. impfv.* [*pfv.* **отяготи́ть**] to weigh down; burden.
отягчáть *v. impfv.* [*pfv.* **отягчи́ть**] **1,** to weigh down; burden. **2,** to aggravate: отягчáющие винý обстоя́тельства, aggravating circumstances.
отяжелéть *v. pfv.* to grow heavy; become heavy.
отяжеля́ть *v. impfv.* [*pfv.* **отяжели́ть**] **1,** to make heavy. **2,** to weigh down.
офицéр *n.* officer. —**офицéрский,** *adj.* officer (*attrib.*); officer's; officers'.
офицéрство *n.* **1,** the officers. **2,** officer's rank; commission.
официáльный *adj.* **1,** official. **2,** *fig.* formal. —**официáльно,** *adv.* officially.
официáнт *n.* waiter.
официáнтка [*gen. pl.* **-ток**] *n.* waitress.
официóз *n.* semi-official publication.
официóзный *adj.* semi-official.
оформи́тель *n.m.* **1,** designer. **2,** stage designer.
офóрмить [*infl.* **-млю, -мишь**] *v., pfv. of* **оформля́ть.**
оформлéние *n.* **1,** design. **2,** legalization. **3,** processing (*of documents*). **4,** taking on; hiring.
оформля́ть *v. impfv.* [*pfv.* **офóрмить**] **1,** to design; arrange; lay out. **2,** to legalize; formalize; make official. **3,** to process; validate (documents). **4,** to take on; hire. —**оформля́ться,** *refl.* **1,** to take shape. **2,** to go through the formalities; complete the paperwork.
офóрт *n.* etching.
офсéт *n.* offset. —**офсéтный,** *adj.* offset (*attrib.*): офсéтная печáть, offset printing.
офтальмолóгия *n.* ophthalmology. —**офтальмóлог,** *n.* ophthalmologist.
ох *interj.* oh!; ah!
охáивать *v. impfv.* [*pfv.* **охáять**] *colloq.* to find fault with; run down.
óханье *n.* moaning; groaning.
охáпка [*gen. pl.* **-пок**] *n.* armful. —**в охáпку; в охáпке,** in one's arms.
охарактеризовáть *v. pfv.* [*infl.* **-зýю, -зýешь**] to characterize; describe.
óхать *v. impfv.* [*pfv.* **óхнуть**] to moan; groan.
охáять [*infl.* **охáю, охáешь**] *v., pfv. of* **охáивать.**
охвáт *n.* **1,** encompassing. **2,** scope; range. **3,** *mil.* envelopment.
охвати́ть [*infl.* **охвачý, охвáтишь**] *v., pfv. of* **охвáтывать.**
охвáтывать *v. impfv.* [*pfv.* **охвати́ть**] **1,** (*usu. with* **рукáми**) to put one's arms around; embrace. **2,** to engulf; envelop: плáмя охвати́ло здáние, flames engulfed the building. **3,** (*of emotions, feelings, etc.*) to seize; grip. **4,** *fig.* to take in; include; embrace; encompass. —**охвати́ть (чтó-нибудь) взгля́дом,** to take in; survey. —**охвати́ть (чтó-нибудь) умóм,** to grasp; encompass in one's mind.
охладевáть *v. impfv.* [*pfv.* **охладéть**] **1,** (*with* **к**) to grow cold (toward). **2,** (*of feelings*) to die down.
охлаждáть *v. impfv.* [*pfv.* **охлади́ть**] **1,** to cool; chill. **2,** *fig.* to calm down. **3,** *fig.* to dampen (one's ardor, enthusiasm, etc.). —**охлаждáться,** *refl.* to cool; cool off; cool down.
охлаждéние *n.* **1,** cooling. **2,** *fig.* coolness (*toward someone*).
охмелéть *v.pfv., colloq.* to become intoxicated.
óхнуть *v., pfv. of* **óхать.**
охóта *n.* **1,** hunt; hunting: идти́ на охóту, to go hunting. **2,** wish; desire. Мне (не) охóта (+ *inf.*), I (don't) feel like (reading, walking, etc.). —**что за охóта; охóта вам** (+ *inf.*), *colloq.* why do you want to...?; why bother...?; what's the use of...?
охóтиться *v.r. impfv.* [*pres.* **-чусь, -тишься**] (*with* **на** + *acc. or* **за** + *instr.*) to hunt; go hunting (for).
охóтник *n.* **1,** hunter. **2,** volunteer. **3,** (*with* **до**) enthusiast: быть охóтником до шáхмат, to be a chess enthusiast.
охóтничий [*fem.* **-чья**] *adj.* hunting (*attrib.*). —**охóтничий дóмик,** hunting lodge. —**охóтничий расскáз,** fish story. —**охóтничья собáка,** hunting dog; hound.
охóтно *adv.* gladly; willingly.

óxpa *n.* ocher.
охрáна *n.* **1,** guarding; protection. Быть под охрáной, to be under guard. **2,** guard; guards.
охранéние *n.* safeguarding; protection.
охранúть *v., pfv. of* **охранять.**
охрáнка *n., colloq.* secret police in tsarist Russia; Okhranka.
охрáнный *adj.* safe-conduct: охрáнная грáмота; охрáнный лист, safe-conduct pass.
охранять *v. impfv.* [*pfv.* **охранúть**] **1,** to guard. **2,** *fig.* to safeguard.
охрúплый *adj., colloq.* hoarse. *Also,* **охрúпший.**
охрúпнуть *v. pfv.* [*past* **охрúп, -ла**] to become hoarse.
оцарáпать *v. pfv.* to scratch.
оцелóт *n.* ocelot.
оцéнивать *v. impfv.* [*pfv.* **оценúть**] **1,** to appraise; assess; evaluate. **2,** to estimate. —**оценúть по достóинству, 1,** to assess properly. **2,** to appreciate; recognize the value of.
оценúть [*infl.* **оценю́, оцéнишь**] *v., pfv. of* **оцéнивать.**
оцéнка [*gen. pl.* **-нок**] *n.* **1,** (monetary) appraisal. **2,** assessment; appraisal; evaluation. **3,** grade; mark.
оцéнщик *n.* appraiser.
оцепенéлый *adj.* dazed; stunned.
оцепенéние *n.* stupor; torpor.
оцепенéть *v., pfv. of* **цепенéть.**
оцеплять *v. impfv.* [*pfv.* **оцепúть**] to surround; seal off; cordon off.
очáг [*gen.* **очагá**] *n.* **1,** hearth; fireside. **2,** *fig.* center; hotbed; breeding ground.
очаровáние *n.* charm; fascination; enchantment.
очарóванный *adj.* **1,** charmed. **2,** spellbound.
очаровáтельный *adj.* charming.
очаровáть [*infl.* **-ру́ю, -ру́ешь**] *v., pfv. of* **очарóвывать.**
очарóвывать *v. impfv.* [*pfv.* **очаровáть**] to charm; captivate.
очевúдец [*gen.* **-дца**] *n.* eyewitness.
очевúдно *adv.* **1,** obviously. **2,** evidently. —*adj., used predicatively* obvious: бы́ло очевúдно, что..., it was obvious that...
очевúдный *adj.* [*short form* **-ден, -дна**] obvious.
очеловéчивать *v. impfv.* [*pfv.* **очеловéчить**] to humanize.
óчень *adv.* **1,** very. **2,** (*before verbs*) very much.
очервúветь *v., pfv. of* **червúветь.**
очереднóй *adj.* **1,** next; immediate; at hand. **2,** regular; regularly scheduled. **3,** ordinary; routine; just another.
очерёдность *n.f.* (prescribed) order; sequence.
óчередь [*pl.* **óчереди, -дéй, -дям**] *n.f.* **1,** turn: ждать своéй óчереди, to wait one's turn. **2,** line: стоять в óчереди, to stand in line. **3,** order; sequence. **4,** burst of fire: пулемётная óчередь, burst of machine-gun fire. —**в пéрвую óчередь,** first of all. —**в свою́ óчередь,** for one's part: я, в свою́ óчередь, for my part. —**на óчереди,** next (in turn). —**по óчереди, 1,** in turn. **2,** alternately.
óчерк *n.* essay. —**очеркúст,** *n.* essayist.
очернúть *v., pfv. of* **чернúть** (*in sense #2*).
очерствéлый *adj.* callous.
очерствéть *v., pfv. of* **черствéть** (*in sense #2*).
очерствлять *v. impfv.* [*pfv.* **очерствúть**] to harden (someone's heart).
очертáние *n., usu. pl.* outline; contour.
очертúть [*infl.* **очерчу́, очéртишь**] *v., pfv. of* **очéрчивать.**
очéрчивать *v. impfv.* [*pfv.* **очертúть**] **1,** to draw a line around. **2,** *fig.* to describe; outline; sketch. —**очертя гóлову,** headlong; rashly.
очёски [*gen.* **-ков**] *n. pl.* combings.
очинúть [*infl.* **очиню́, очúнишь**] *v., pfv. of* **чинúть** (*in sense #2*).
очистúтельный *adj.* cleansing. —**очистúтельный завóд,** refinery.
очúстить [*infl.* **-щу, -стишь**] *v., pfv. of* **чúстить** (*in sense #4*) *and* **очищáть.** —**очúститься,** *refl., pfv. of* **очищáться.**
очúстка *n.* **1,** cleaning. **2,** clearing. **3,** purification. —**для очúстки сóвести,** to clear one's conscience.
очúстки [*gen.* **-ков**] *n. pl.* peelings: картóфельные очúстки, potato peelings.
очищáть *v. impfv.* [*pfv.* **очúстить**] **1,** to clean. **2,** to purify; refine. **3,** to cleanse; purge. **4,** to clear; clear up; clear out. **5,** *colloq.* to rob; clean out. —**очищáться,** *refl.* **1,** to clear; clear up. **2,** (*with* **от**) to become clear (of).
очищéние *n.* **1,** clearing. **2,** cleansing. **3,** purification.
очкú [*gen.* **очкóв**] *n. pl.* glasses; eyeglasses.
очкó [*pl.* **очкú, очкóв**] *n.* **1,** point (*scored in a game*). **2,** pip (*on a playing card, die, domino, etc.*). **3,** small opening; mesh.
очковтирáтельство *n., colloq.* fakery.
очкóвый *adj., sports* based on points scored. —**очкóвая змея,** cobra.
очну́ться *v.r. pfv.* **1,** to awaken. **2,** to regain consciousness.
óчный *adj.* **1,** *in* **óчное обучéние,** classroom instruction (*as opposed to correspondence courses*). **2,** *in* **óчная стáвка,** simultaneous questioning of witnesses or defendants (*in order to resolve contradictions*). **3,** *in* **óчный цвет,** pimpernel.
очумéть *v.pfv., colloq.* to lose one's head.
очутúться *v.r.pfv.* [*infl.* **очу́тишься;** *1st person sing. not used*] to find oneself; wind up; end up (in a certain place).
очу́хаться *v.r. pfv., colloq.* to come to; regain one's senses.
ошалéть *v., pfv. of* **шалéть.**
ошарáшивать *v. impfv.* [*pfv.* **ошарáшить**] *colloq.* to dumfound; flabbergast.
ошéйник *n.* collar (*for a dog*).
ошеломúтельный *adj.* stunning; staggering.
ошеломлять *v. impfv.* [*pfv.* **ошеломúть**] to stun; stagger.
ошельмовáть *v., pfv. of* **шельмовáть.**
ошибáться *v.r. impfv.* [*pfv.* **ошибúться**] **1,** to make a mistake. **2,** to be mistaken; be wrong.
ошибúться [*infl.* **-бу́сь, -бёшься;** *past* **ошúбся, ошúблась**] *v.r., pfv. of* **ошибáться.**
ошúбка [*gen. pl.* **-бок**] *n.* mistake; error.
ошúбочно *adv.* **1,** erroneously; mistakenly. **2,** by mistake.
ошúбочный *adj.* erroneous; mistaken; fallacious. —**ошúбочность,** *n.f.* fallaciousness.
ошúкать *v. pfv., colloq.* to hiss; boo (a performer, play, etc.).
ошпáривать *v. impfv.* [*pfv.* **ошпáрить**] *colloq.* to scald. —**ошпáриваться,** *refl., colloq.* to scald oneself.

оштрафова́ть *v., pfv. of* **штрафова́ть.**
оштукату́рить *v., pfv. of* **штукату́рить.**
ощени́ться *v.r., pfv. of* **щени́ться.**
ощети́ниться *v.r., pfv. of* **щети́ниться.**
ощипа́ть [*infl.* **ощиплю́, ощи́плешь**] *v., pfv. of* **щипа́ть** (*in sense #3*) *and* **ощи́пывать.**
ощи́пывать *v. impfv.* [*pfv.* **ощипа́ть**] **1,** to pluck. **2,** to pick (clean).
ощу́пывать *v. impfv.* [*pfv.* **ощу́пать**] to feel (*with one's fingers*).
о́щупь *n.f., in* **на о́щупь, 1,** to the touch. **2,** by touch.
о́щупью *adv.* by groping one's way: идти́ о́щупью, to grope one's way; иска́ть о́щупью, to grope for.
ощути́мый *adj.* **1,** perceptible; tangible; palpable. **2,** noticeable; marked; appreciable. *Also,* **ощути́тельный.**
ощуща́ть *v. impfv.* [*pfv.* **ощути́ть**] to feel; sense. —**ощуща́ться,** *refl.* [*impfv. only*] to be felt; be sensed.
ощуще́ние *n.* sensation; feeling.
оягни́ться *v.r., pfv. of* **ягни́ться.**

П

П, п *n. neut.* sixteenth letter of the Russian alphabet.
па *n. neut. indecl.* step (*in dancing*).
па́ва *n.* peahen.
павиа́н *n.* baboon.
павильо́н *n.* **1,** pavilion. **2,** film studio.
павли́н *n.* peacock. —**павли́ний,** *adj.* [*fem.* **-нья**] peacock (*attrib.*).
па́водок [*gen.* **-дка**] *n.* high water; flood.
па́вший *adj.* fallen.
пагина́ция *n.* pagination.
па́года *n.* pagoda.
па́губа *n., obs.* ruin; downfall.
па́губный *adj.* ruinous; pernicious; disastrous.
па́даль *n.f.* carrion.
па́дать *v. impfv.* [*pfv.* **упа́сть** *or* **пасть**] **1,** to fall: упа́сть на зе́млю, to fall to the ground. Пасть в бою́, to fall in battle. **2,** to decline; go down; fall: це́ны па́дают, prices are going down. —**па́дать ду́хом,** to lose heart. —**па́дать в о́бморок,** to faint.
па́дающий *adj.* falling. —**па́дающая звезда́,** shooting star. —**па́дающий мо́лот,** triphammer.
паде́ж [*gen.* **-дежа́**] *n., gram.* case.
падёж [*gen.* **-дежа́**] *n.* murrain.
паде́жный *adj., gram.* case (*attrib.*).
паде́ние *n.* **1,** fall. **2,** drop; decline. **3,** downfall. **4,** *physics* incidence.
па́дкий *adj.* [*short form* **па́док, па́дка**] (*with* **на** + *acc. or* **до**) having a weakness (for); susceptible (to): па́дкий на лесть, susceptible to flattery.
па́дуб *n.* holly.
паду́чий *adj., obs.* falling. —**паду́чая боле́знь,** *obs.* epilepsy.
па́дчерица *n.* stepdaughter.
па́дший *adj.* fallen. —**па́дшая же́нщина,** fallen woman.
паёк [*gen.* **пайка́**] *n.* ration.
паж [*gen.* **пажа́**] *n.* page; attendant.
паз [*2nd loc.* **пазу́;** *pl.* **пазы́**] *n.* **1,** crack; crevice. **2,** slot; groove; mortise.
па́зуха *n.* **1,** bosom. **2,** *anat.* sinus. **3,** *bot.* axil. —**держа́ть ка́мень за па́зухой,** to bear a grudge.
па́инька [*gen. pl.* **-нек**] *n.m. & f., colloq.* good child.
пай [*pl.* **пай**] *n.* share.
па́йка *n.* soldering.
па́йщик *n.* shareholder.
пакга́уз *n.* warehouse.
паке́т *n.* **1,** package. **2,** packet. **3,** paper bag.
пакетбо́т *n.* packet (*steamship*).
пакиста́нец [*gen.* **-нца**] *n.m.* [*fem.* **-нка**] Pakistani. —**пакиста́нский,** *adj.* Pakistani.
па́кля *n.* oakum; tow.
пакова́ть *v. impfv.* [*pfv.* **упакова́ть;** *pres.* **-ку́ю, -ку́ешь**] to pack (things).
па́костить *v. impfv.* [*pres.* **-щу, -стишь**] *colloq.* **1,** to soil; dirty. **2,** to spoil. **3,** (*with dat.*) to play dirty tricks on; do nasty things to.
па́костный *adj., colloq.* nasty; foul; vile.
па́кость *n.f., colloq.* **1,** dirty trick; mean trick. **2,** dirty word; obscenity.
пакт *n.* pact: пакт о ненападе́нии, nonaggression pact.
паланти́н *n.* (fur) stole.
пала́та *n.* **1,** house (*of a legislature*): пала́та представи́телей/о́бщин/ло́рдов, House of Representatives/Commons/Lords. **2,** bureau; chamber: торго́вая пала́та, chamber of commerce; пала́та мер и весо́в, Bureau of Weights and Measures. —**у него́ ума́ пала́та,** he is as smart as they come.
палатализа́ция *n.* palatalization.
палатализова́ть *v. impfv. & pfv.* [*pres.* **-зу́ю, -зу́ешь**] *phonet.* to palatalize.
палата́льный *adj., phonet.* palatal.
пала́тка [*gen. pl.* **-ток**] *n.* **1,** tent. **2,** stall; booth.
пала́точный *adj.* tent (*attrib.*).
пала́ч [*gen.* **-лача́**] *n.* executioner; hangman; *fig.* butcher.
пала́ш [*gen.* **-лаша́**] *n.* broadsword.
па́левый *adj.* pale yellow; straw-colored.
палёный *adj.* singed; scorched.
палеоазиа́тский *adj.* Paleo-Asiatic.
палеогра́фия *n.* paleography. —**палео́граф,** *n.* paleographer. —**палеографи́ческий,** *adj.* paleographic.

палеозо́йский *adj.* Paleozoic.

палеолити́ческий *adj.* paleolithic.

палеонтоло́гия *n.* paleontology. —**палеонто́лог,** *n.* paleontologist. —**палеонтологи́ческий,** *adj.* paleontological.

палести́нец [*gen.* **-нца**] *n.m.* [*fem.* **-нка**] Palestinian. —**палести́нский,** *adj.* Palestinian.

па́лец [*gen.* **-льца**] *n.* **1,** finger. Большо́й па́лец, thumb. **2,** *in* **па́лец ноги́; па́лец на ноге́,** toe. —**знать (что́-нибудь) как свой пять па́льцев,** to know like the back of one's hand. —**па́льца в рот не клади́** (+ *dat.*), *colloq.* watch out for...!; be on your guard against...! —**па́лец о па́лец не уда́рить,** not to lift a finger. —**пока́зывать** *or* **ука́зывать па́льцем на** (+ *acc.*), to point one's finger at. —**попа́сть па́льцем в не́бо,** to be wide of the mark. —**смотре́ть сквозь па́льцы на** (+ *acc.*), to wink at; deliberately overlook; turn a blind eye to.

палиса́д *n.* palisade.

палиса́дник *n.* small garden.

палиса́ндр *n.* rosewood. —**палиса́ндровый,** *adj.* rosewood (*attrib.*).

пали́тра *n.* palette.

пали́ть *v. impfv.* **1,** [*pfv.* **опали́ть**] to singe (an animal). **2,** [*pfv.* **спали́ть**] to singe; scorch (*accidentally*). **3,** [*impfv. only*] (*of the sun*) to beat down. **4,** [*pfv.* **вы́палить**] *colloq.* to fire; shoot.

па́лка [*gen. pl.* **-лок**] *n.* **1,** stick. **2,** cane; walking stick. —**из-под па́лки,** under compulsion. —**па́лка о двух конца́х,** double-edged sword.

палла́дий *n.* palladium.

паллиати́в *n.* palliative. —**паллиати́вный,** *adj.* palliative.

пало́мник *n.* pilgrim.

пало́мничать *v. impfv.* to go on a pilgrimage.

пало́мничество *n.* pilgrimage. —**пало́мнический,** *adj.* pilgrim (*attrib.*); pilgrims'.

па́лочка [*gen. pl.* **-чек**] *n.* **1,** small stick: бараба́нная па́лочка, drumstick. **2,** baton; wand. **3,** bacillus.

па́лочный *adj.* with or using a stick. —**па́лочная дисципли́на,** discipline enforced with the rod.

па́лтус *n.* halibut.

па́луба *n.* deck (*of a ship*). —**па́лубный,** *adj.* deck (*attrib.*).

пальба́ *n., colloq.* firing: откры́ть пальбу́, to open fire.

па́льма *n.* palm (tree). —**па́льма пе́рвенства,** the crown; the chief laurels.

па́льмовый *adj.* palm (*attrib.*).

пальто́ *n. indecl.* overcoat.

па́льчик *n., dim. of* **па́лец**. —**ма́льчик с па́льчик,** Tom Thumb.

паля́щий *adj.* burning; scorching; searing.

пампа́сы [*gen.* **-сов**] *n. pl.* pampas.

памфле́т *n.* (political) pamphlet. —**памфлети́ст,** *n.* pamphleteer.

па́мятка [*gen. pl.* **-ток**] *n.* **1,** reminder. **2,** book of instructions.

па́мятливый *adj., colloq.* having a retentive memory. —**па́мятливость,** *n.f., colloq.* retentive memory.

па́мятник *n.* monument; memorial. —**надгро́бный па́мятник,** monument; (large) tombstone.

па́мятный *adj.* **1,** memorable. **2,** serving as a reminder: па́мятная кни́жка, memorandum book; notebook. **3,** memorial; commemorative: па́мятная доска́, memorial plaque; па́мятная ма́рка, commemorative stamp. —**па́мятная запи́ска,** memorandum; aide-mémoire. —**па́мятный пода́рок,** memento.

па́мятовать *v. impfv., in* **па́мятуя о,** remembering; recalling.

па́мять *n.f.* memory. —**без па́мяти, 1,** unconscious. **2,** (*with verbs of running or racing*) madly; for all one is worth. **3,** (*with* **от**) madly in love with. **4,** (*with* **люби́ть**) to distraction. —**в па́мять** (+ *gen.*), in memory of. —**на чьей-нибудь па́мяти,** in (*or* within) someone's memory. —**на па́мять, 1,** by heart. **2,** from memory. **3,** as a keepsake. —**по па́мяти,** from memory. —**по ста́рой па́мяти, 1,** by force of habit. **2,** (in) the old (*or* traditional) way. —**приходи́ть на па́мять** (+ *dat.*), to come to mind.

пана́ма *n.* Panama hat.

панаце́я *n.* panacea.

па́нда *n.* panda.

пандеми́я (дэ) *n.* pandemic.

панеги́рик *n.* panegyric; eulogy. —**панегири́ст,** *n.* panegyrist.

пане́ль *n.f.* **1,** pavement; sidewalk. **2,** paneling; wainscot.

панибра́тский *adj., colloq.* overly familiar. —**панибра́тство,** *n., colloq.* undue familiarity.

па́ника *n.* panic.

паникёр *n.* alarmist.

панихи́да *n.* funeral service; requiem.

пани́ческий *adj.* panicky; panic-stricken.

пано́птикум *n.* wax museum.

панора́ма *n.* panorama; panoramic view. —**панора́мный,** *adj.* panoramic.

пансио́н *n.* **1,** boarding house. **2,** room and board: жить на пансио́не, to receive room and board. **3,** *pre-rev.* boarding school.

пансиона́т *n.* (resort) hotel.

пансионе́р *n.* **1,** *pre-rev.* boarding-school student. **2,** boarder; roomer.

пантало́ны [*gen.* **-ло́н**] *n. pl.* **1,** *obs.* pants. **2,** (women's) drawers.

пантал́ык *n., colloq., in* **сбить с пантал́ыку,** to confuse; **сби́ться с пантал́ыку,** to become confused.

пантеи́зм (тэ) *n.* pantheism. —**пантеи́ст,** *n.* pantheist. —**пантеисти́ческий,** *adj.* pantheistic.

пантео́н (тэ) *n.* pantheon.

панте́ра *n.* panther; leopard.

пантоми́ма *n.* pantomime. —**пантоми́мный; пантомими́ческий,** *adj.* pantomime.

панхромати́ческий *adj.* panchromatic.

па́нцирь *n.m.* **1,** armor; coat of mail. **2,** shell (*of a turtle*); armor (*of an armadillo*).

па́па *n.m.* **1,** papa; daddy. **2,** Pope.

папа́ха *n.* tall fur hat.

папа́ша *n.m., colloq.* daddy.

па́перть *n.f.* portico of a church.

папильо́тка [*gen. pl.* **-ток**] *n.* (hair) curler.

папиро́са *n.* cigarette.

папиро́сница *n.* cigarette case.

папиро́сный *adj.* cigarette (*attrib.*). —**папиро́сная бума́га,** tissue paper.

папи́рус *n.* papyrus.

па́пка [*gen. pl.* **-пок**] *n.* (cardboard) folder.

па́поротник *n.* fern.

па́прика *n.* paprika.

па́пский *adj.* papal. —**па́пство,** *n.* papacy.

па́пула *n.* papule.

папье́-маше́ *n. neut. indecl.* papier-mâché.
пар [*2nd loc.* **пару́**; *pl.* **пары́**] *n.* **1,** steam. **2,** vapor. **3,** fallow land: лежа́ть под па́ром, to lie fallow. —**на всех пара́х, 1,** under a full head of steam. **2,** *fig.* at top speed.
па́ра *n.* **1,** pair: па́ра чуло́к, pair of stockings. **2,** (married) couple: счастли́вая па́ра, happy couple. **3,** (*with gen. or* **к**) mate (*other of a pair*): э́та перча́тка – па́ра (к) утёрянной, this glove is the mate to the one that was lost. **4,** (*with dat.*) *colloq.* suitable mate (for); good match (for): он ей не па́ра, he is not a good match for her. **5,** (*with gen. pl.*) *colloq.* a few: мо́жно попроси́ть вас на па́ру слов?, may I have a few words (*or* a word) with you? **6,** man's suit. —**стать** *or* **встать в па́ры,** to line up in pairs. —**ходи́ть** *or* **гуля́ть па́рами,** to walk in pairs.
пара́бола *n.* parabola. —**параболи́ческий,** *adj.* parabolic.
пара́граф *n.* paragraph.
пара́д *n.* parade.
паради́гма *n.* paradigm.
пара́дный *adj.* **1,** parade (*attrib.*). **2,** (*of clothes*) formal; dress. **3,** gala; festive. **4,** (*of an entrance, staircase, etc.*) main; front. —**пара́дное,** *n.* front door.
парадо́кс *n.* paradox. —**парадокса́льный,** *adj.* paradoxical.
парази́т *n.* **1,** *biol.* parasite. **2,** *fig.* parasite; sponger. —**паразити́зм,** *n.* parasitism. —**паразити́ческий; парази́тный,** *adj.* parasitic.
парализова́ть *v. impfv. & pfv.* [*pres.* **-зу́ю, -зу́ешь**] to paralyze.
парали́тик *n.* paralytic. —**паралити́ческий,** *adj.* paralytic.
парали́ч [*gen.* **-лича́**] *n.* paralysis. —**парали́чный,** *adj.* paralytic.
паралла́кс *n.* parallax.
параллелепи́пед *n.* parallelepiped.
параллели́зм *n.* parallelism.
параллелогра́мм *n.* parallelogram.
паралле́ль *n.f.* parallel.
паралле́льно *adv.* **1,** (*with dat.*) parallel to: паралле́льно доро́ге, parallel to the road. **2,** (*with* **с** + *instr.*) *fig.* parallel to: паралле́льно с э́тим, parallel to this.
паралле́льный *adj.* parallel.
пара́метр *n.* parameter.
параме́ция *n.* paramecium.
парано́ик *n., colloq.* paranoiac. —**параноический,** *adj.* paranoid.
парано́йя *n.* paranoia.
парапе́т *n.* parapet.
параплеги́я *n.* paraplegia.
парати́ф *n.* paratyphoid (fever).
парафи́н *n.* paraffin. —**парафи́новый,** *adj.* paraffin.
парафи́ровать *v. impfv. & pfv.* [*pres.* **-рую, -руешь**] to initial (a treaty, document, etc.).
парафра́за *n.* periphrasis.
парашю́т (шу) *n.* parachute. —**парашюти́зм,** *n.* parachute jumping (*as a sport*). —**парашюти́ст,** *n.* parachutist; parachute jumper; paratrooper. —**парашю́тный,** *adj.* parachute (*attrib.*).
паращитови́дный *adj., in* **паращитови́дная железа́,** parathyroid gland.
паре́з (рэ) *n.* paresis.
па́реный *adj.* steamed. —**дешёвле па́реной ре́пы,** *colloq.* dirt-cheap.
па́рень [*gen.* **-рня;** *pl.* **па́рни, -ней́, -ня́м**] *n.m., colloq.* fellow; lad; chap; guy.
пари́ *n. neut. indecl.* bet; wager.
парижа́нин [*pl.* **-жа́не, -жа́н**] *n.m.* [*fem.* **-жа́нка**] Parisian.
пари́жский *adj.* of Paris; Parisian.
пари́к [*gen.* **-рика́**] *n.* wig.
парикма́хер *n.* barber; hairdresser. —**парикма́херская,** *n., decl. as an adj.* barbershop.
пари́льня [*gen. pl.* **-лен**] *n.* steam room.
пари́ровать *v. impfv. & pfv.* [*pres.* **-рую, -руешь**] **1,** to parry; ward off. **2,** *fig.* to parry; counter.
парите́т *n.* parity. —**парите́тный,** *adj.* equal.
па́рить *v. impfv.* **1,** to steam. **2,** to stew. **3,** *impers.* to be sultry: сего́дня па́рит, it is sultry today. —**па́риться,** *refl.* **1,** to steam; sweat (*in a bath*). **2,** (*of food*) to stew.
пари́ть *v. impfv.* to soar; glide.
па́рия *n.* pariah; outcast.
парк *n.* **1,** park. **2,** depot; yard. **3,** fleet; stock: автомоби́льный парк США, the total number of cars in the USA.
па́рка [*gen. pl.* **-рок**] *n.* parka.
парке́т *n.* parquetry; parquet. —**парке́тный,** *adj.* parquet.
парла́мент *n.* parliament. —**парламентари́зм,** *n.* parliamentarianism. —**парламента́рий,** *n.* member of parliament. —**парламента́рный,** *adj.* parliamentary.
парламентёр *n.* bearer of a flag of truce.
парла́ментский *adj.* parliamentary.
парни́к [*gen.* **-ника́**] *n.* hotbed.
парнико́вый *adj.* hotbed (*attrib.*); hothouse (*attrib.*): парнико́вые расте́ния, hothouse plants.
парни́шка [*gen. pl.* **-шек**] *n.m., colloq.* lad; boy.
парно́й *adj.* **1,** (*of milk*) fresh from the cow; (*of meat*) freshly killed. **2,** *colloq.* stuffy; sultry.
па́рный *adj.* **1,** being one (or the other) of a pair. **2,** arranged or done in pairs. —**па́рная игра́,** doubles (*in tennis*).
парово́з *n.* locomotive.
парово́зный *adj.* locomotive (*attrib.*). —**парово́зное депо́,** roundhouse.
парово́й *adj.* **1,** steam (*attrib.*); steam-driven: парова́я маши́на, steam engine. **2,** (*of food*) steamed. **3,** (*of land*) fallow.
пароди́ровать *v. impfv. & pfv.* [*pres.* **-рую, -руешь**] to parody.
паро́дия *n.* parody; travesty. —**пароди́ст,** *n.* parodist.
пароксي́зм *n.* paroxysm.
паро́ль *n.m.* password.
паро́м *n.* ferry. —**паро́мный,** *adj.* ferry (*attrib.*). —**паро́мщик,** *n.* ferryman.
парообра́зный *adj.* vaporous.
парообразова́ние *n.* vaporization; generation of steam.
парохо́д *n.* ship; steamship. —**парохо́дный,** *adj.* steamship (*attrib.*). —**парохо́дство,** *n.* steamship line.
па́рочка [*gen. pl.* **-чек**] *n., colloq.* **1,** pair. **2,** couple.
па́рта *n.* school desk.
партбиле́т *n.* Party (membership) card (*contr. of* **парти́йный биле́т**).
партеногене́з (тэ, нэ) *n.* parthenogenesis.
парте́р (тэ) *n., theat.* orchestra.
парти́ец [*gen.* **-йица**] *n., colloq.* member of the (communist) party.

партиза́н [*gen. pl.* **-за́н**] *n.* partisan; guerrilla. —**партиза́нский,** *adj.* guerrilla (*attrib.*). —**партиза́нство,** *n.* guerrilla activity.
парти́йность *n.f.* **1,** party membership. **2,** party spirit. **3,** reflection of party principles (*in literature, art, etc.*).
парти́йный *adj.* party (*attrib.*); Party (*attrib.*).
партиту́ра *n., music* score.
па́ртия *n.* **1,** (political) party. **2,** party; team; group. **3,** batch; lot; consignment. **4,** game. **5,** *music* part. **6,** *obs.* match; suitable mate.
партнёр *n.m.* [*fem.* **-нёрша**] **1,** partner. **2,** player. **3,** (one's) opponent (*in a game*).
парто́рг *n.* party organizer (*contr. of* **парти́йный организа́тор**).
па́рус [*pl.* **паруса́**] *n.* sail. —**на всех паруса́х,** (at) full speed.
паруси́на *n.* canvas. —**паруси́новый,** *adj.* canvas.
па́русник *n.* **1,** sailing vessel. **2,** sailfish. **3,** swallowtail (*butterfly*).
па́русный *adj.* sail (*attrib.*): па́русная ло́дка, sailboat.
Парфено́н *n.* Parthenon.
парфюме́рия *n.* perfumes. —**парфюме́р,** *n.* perfumer. —**парфюме́рный,** *adj.* perfume (*attrib.*).
парча́ *n.* brocade. —**парчо́вый,** *adj.* brocade; brocaded.
парша́ *n.* mange.
парши́веть *v. impfv.* [*pfv.* **запарши́веть** *or* **опарши́веть**] *colloq.* to become mangy.
парши́вый *adj.* **1,** mangy. **2,** *colloq.* rotten; lousy.
пас *n., cards; sports* pass. —*predicate, colloq.* over one's head: в э́том де́ле я пас, this is way over my head; this is beyond me.
па́сека *n.* apiary; bee garden. —**па́сечник,** *n.* beekeeper.
па́сквиль *n.m.* scurrilous piece of writing; libel; slander; hatchet job.
паску́дный *adj., colloq.* foul; vile.
паслён *n.* nightshade.
па́смурный *adj.* **1,** overcast; dreary; dismal. **2,** gloomy; sullen; morose.
пасова́ть *v. impfv.* [*pfv.* **спасова́ть;** *pres.* **-су́ю, -су́ешь**] **1,** *cards* to pass. **2,** *fig.* (*with* **пе́ред**) to shrink (from); retreat in the face of. **3,** [*impfv. only*] *sports* to pass (a ball, puck, etc.).
па́спорт [*pl.* **паспорта́**] *n.* passport. —**па́спортный,** *adj.* passport (*attrib.*).
пасса́ж *n.* **1,** arcade. **2,** *music* passage.
пассажи́р *n.* passenger. —**пассажи́рский,** *adj.* passenger (*attrib.*).
пасса́т *n.* trade wind.
пасси́в *n.* **1,** *comm.* liabilities. **2,** *gram.* passive voice.
пасси́вный *adj.* **1,** passive. **2,** *econ.* unfavorable. —**пасси́вность,** *n.f.* passivity.
па́ссия *n., obs.* passion; flame.
па́ста *n.* paste. —**зубна́я па́ста,** toothpaste.
па́стбище *n.* pasture. —**па́стбищный,** *adj.* pasture (*attrib.*); grazing (*attrib.*).
па́ства *n.* flock; congregation; parishioners.
пасте́ль (тэ) *n.f.* pastel. —**пасте́льный,** *adj.* pastel.
пастериза́ция (тэ) *n.* pasteurization.
пастеризова́ть (тэ) *v. impfv. & pfv.* [*pres.* **-зу́ю, -зу́ешь**] to pasteurize.
пастерна́к *n.* parsnip.
пасти́ *v. impfv.* [*pres.* **пасу́, пасёшь;** *past* **пас, пасла́, пасло́**] to tend; graze; herd. —**пасти́сь,** *refl.* to graze.
пастила́ [*pl.* **-сти́лы**] *n.* a confection made of fruit, sugar, and egg whites.
па́стор *n.* pastor; minister.
пастора́ль *n.f.* **1,** pastoral. **2,** pastorale. —**пастора́льный,** *adj.* pastoral.
пасту́х [*gen.* **-стуха́**] *n.* shepherd.
пасту́шеский *adj.* **1,** shepherd's. **2,** *obs.* pastoral.
пасту́ший [*fem.* **-шья**] *adj.* shepherd's.
пастушо́к [*gen.* **-шка́**] *n.* **1,** young shepherd. **2,** swain. **3,** rail (*bird*).
па́стырь *n.m.* **1,** *poetic* shepherd. **2,** pastor.
пасть[1] [*infl.* **паду́, падёшь;** *past* **пал, па́ла**] *v., pfv. of* **па́дать.**
пасть[2] *n.f.* mouth (*of an animal*). —**во́лчья пасть,** cleft palate.
пастьба́ *n.* pasturage.
па́сха *n.* **1,** Easter. **2,** Passover. **3,** traditional Easter dish make of cottage cheese and other ingredients. —**пасха́льный,** *adj.* Easter (*attrib.*); Passover (*attrib.*); paschal.
па́сынок [*gen.* **-нка**] *n.* stepchild; stepson.
пасья́нс *n., cards* solitaire.
пат *n., chess* stalemate.
пате́нт *n.* patent. —**пате́нтный,** *adj.* patent (*attrib.*).
патенто́ванный *adj.* patent; patented.
патентова́ть *v. impfv. & pfv.* [*pres.* **-ту́ю, -ту́ешь**] to patent; take out a patent on.
патети́ческий (тэ) *adj.* passionate; impassioned.
патефо́н *n.* small portable phonograph. —**патефо́нный,** *adj.* phonograph (*attrib.*).
па́тио *n. indecl.* patio.
па́тлы [*gen.* **патл**] *n. pl., colloq.* long disheveled locks of hair.
па́тока *n.* molasses; treacle.
патоло́гия *n.* pathology. —**пато́лог,** *n.* pathologist. —**патологи́ческий,** *adj.* pathological.
па́точный *adj.* **1,** made of molasses. **2,** *fig.* sugary; saccharine.
патриа́рх *n.* patriarch. —**патриарха́льный,** *adj.* patriarchal. —**патриарха́т,** *n.* patriarchy. —**патриа́ршество,** *n.* patriarchate.
патрио́т *n.* **1,** patriot. **2,** *fig.* supporter; booster. —**патриоти́зм,** *n.* patriotism. —**патриоти́ческий,** *adj.* patriotic.
патри́ций *n.* patrician.
патро́н *n.* **1,** *obs.* patron. **2,** cartridge. **3,** *mech.* chuck. **4,** socket (*for a bulb*).
патро́нник *n.* chamber (*of a gun*).
патро́нный *adj.* cartridge (*attrib.*).
патронта́ш *n.* ammunition belt.
патрули́ровать *v. impfv.* [*pres.* **-рую, -руешь**] to patrol.
патру́ль [*gen.* **-труля́**] *n.m.* patrol.
патру́льный *adj.* patrol (*attrib.*). —*n.* man on patrol.
па́уза *n.* **1,** pause. **2,** *music* rest.
пау́к [*gen.* **паука́**] *n.* spider.
паути́на *n.* spider web; cobweb.
па́фос *n.* fervor; zeal.
пах [*2nd loc.* **паху́**] *n.* groin.
па́харь *n.m.* plowman.
паха́ть *v. impfv.* [*pfv.* **вспаха́ть;** *pres.* **пашу́, па́шешь**] to plow.
па́хнуть *v. impfv.* [*past* **пах** *or* **па́хнул, па́хла**] **1,** (*with an adv.*) to smell (good, bad, nice, etc.). **2,** (*with instr.*) to smell (of).

пахну́ть *v. pfv., usu. impers.* (*of air, a fragrance, etc.*) to blow in: со двора́ пахну́ло хо́лодом, a gust of cold air blew in from the yard.
па́хота *n.* **1,** plowing. **2,** plowed land.
па́хотный *adj.* arable.
па́хта *n.* buttermilk.
па́хтать *v. impfv.* to churn.
паху́чий *adj.* strong-smelling. —**паху́честь,** *n.f.* strong smell; strong odor.
пацие́нт *n.m.* [*fem.* **-ка**] patient.
пацифи́зм *n.* pacifism. —**пацифи́ст,** *n.* pacifist. —**пацифи́стский,** *adj.* pacifist.
па́че *n., obs.* more. —**па́че того́; тем па́че,** the more so; all the more. —**па́че ча́яния,** contrary to (*or* beyond one's) expectations.
па́чка [*gen. pl.* **-чек**] *n.* **1,** pack; bundle; batch. **2,** tutu.
па́чкать *v. impfv.* [*pfv.* **запа́чкать** *or* **испа́чкать**] **1,** to soil; dirty; stain. **2,** [*impfv. only*] *colloq.* to daub. —**па́чкаться,** *refl.* to become dirty; become soiled.
пачкотня́ *n., colloq.* poorly painted picture; daub.
пачку́н [*gen.* **-куна́**] *n., colloq.* **1,** slovenly person. **2,** poor painter.
паша́ [*gen. pl.* **-ше́й**] *n.m.* pasha.
па́шня [*gen. pl.* **-шен**] *n.* plowed land; land under cultivation.
паште́т *n.* pâté.
па́юсный *adj., in* **па́юсная икра́,** pressed caviar.
пая́льник *n.* soldering iron.
пая́льный *adj.* soldering (*attrib.*). —**пая́льная ла́мпа,** blowtorch. —**пая́льная тру́бка,** blowpipe.
пая́льщик *n.* solderer.
пая́ние *n.* soldering.
пая́сничать *v. impfv., colloq.* to clown around.
пая́ть *v. impfv.* to solder.
пая́ц *n.* clown; buffoon.
певе́ц [*gen.* **-вца́**] *n.* singer.
певи́ца *n.* (female) singer.
певу́н [*gen.* **-вуна́**] *n.m.* [*fem.* **-ву́нья**] *colloq.* person who likes to sing.
певу́чий *adj.* melodious. —**певу́честь,** *n.f.* melodiousness.
пе́вчий *adj., in* **пе́вчая пти́ца,** songbird. —*n.* chorister; choirboy.
пега́нка [*gen. pl.* **-нок**] *n.* sheldrake.
пе́гий *adj.* piebald.
педаго́г *n.* teacher; pedagogue. —**педаго́гика,** *n.* pedagogy. —**педагоги́ческий,** *adj.* pedagogical.
педа́ль *n.f.* pedal.
педа́нт *n.* pedant. —**педанти́зм,** *n.* pedantry. —**педанти́чный,** *adj.* pedantic.
педера́стия *n.* sodomy.
педиатри́я *n.* pediatrics. —**педиа́тр,** *n.* pediatrician. —**педиатри́ческий,** *adj.* pediatric.
педикю́р *n.* pedicure; chiropody. —**педикю́рша,** *n.* (woman) chiropodist.
педо́метр *n.* pedometer.
пезе́та *n.* = **песе́та.**
пе́зо *n.* = **пе́со.**
пейза́ж *n.* **1,** landscape. **2,** landscape painting. —**пейзажи́ст,** *n.* landscape painter. —**пейза́жный,** *adj.* landscape (*attrib.*).
пека́н *n.* pecan.
пе́кари *n.m. indecl.* peccary.
peка́рный *adj.* baking (*attrib.*).
пека́рня [*gen. pl.* **-рен**] *n.* bakery.
пе́карь [*pl.* **пекаря́** *or* **пе́кари**] *n.m.* baker. —**пе́карский,** *adj.* baker's.
пеклева́нный *adj.* (*of flour*) fine; finely ground. —**пеклева́нный хлеб,** fine rye bread.
пе́кло *n., colloq.* **1,** intense heat. **2,** hell. **3,** *fig.* (*with gen.*) the heat (of); the thick (of).
пелена́ [*gen. pl.* **-лён**] *n.* cover; veil; shroud (*of clouds, fog, snow, smoke, etc.*).
пелена́ть *v. impfv.* [*pfv.* **спелена́ть** *or* **запелена́ть**] to diaper; swaddle.
пе́ленг *n., navigation* bearing.
пеленга́тор *n.* direction finder.
пеленгова́ть *v. impfv. & pfv.* [*pres.* **-гу́ю, -гу́ешь**] to take a bearing on.
пелёнка [*gen. pl.* **-нок**] *n.* diaper. —**с пелёнок,** from the cradle.
пелери́на *n.* cape.
пелика́н *n.* pelican.
пелла́гра *n.* pellagra.
пельме́ни *n. pl.* [*sing.* **пельме́нь,** *m.*] meat dumplings.
пе́мза *n.* pumice; pumice stone.
пе́на *n.* **1,** foam. **2,** lather; suds: мы́льная пе́на, soapsuds. **3,** scum.
пена́л *n.* pencil case.
пенёк [*gen.* **-нька́**] *n.* stump (*of a tree*).
пе́ние *n.* singing.
пе́нистый *adj.* foamy.
пе́нить *v. impfv.* [*pfv.* **вспе́нить**] to froth; cause to foam. —**пе́ниться,** *refl.* to froth; foam.
пеницилли́н *n.* penicillin.
пе́нка *n.* **1,** skin (*forming on milk*). **2,** [*also,* **морска́я пе́нка**] meerschaum. —**пе́нковый,** *adj.* meerschaum.
пе́нни *n. neut. indecl.* penny (*in Great Britain*).
пе́нный *adj.* foamy. —**пе́нный огнетуши́тель,** foam fire extinguisher.
пенопла́ст *n.* foam plastic; expanded plastic.
пенс *n.* penny (*in Great Britain*); *pl.* pence.
пе́нсия *n.* pension. Вы́йти *or* уйти́ на пе́нсию, to retire (*on a pension*). —**пенсионе́р,** *n.* pensioner. —**пенсио́нный,** *adj.* pension (*attrib.*).
пенсне́ (нэ) *n. neut. indecl.* pince-nez.
Пентаго́н *n.* the Pentagon.
пента́метр *n.* pentameter.
пень [*gen.* **пня**] *n.m.* stump (*of a tree*). —**стоя́ть как пень,** to stand (there) like a dummy.
пенька́ *n.* hemp. —**пенько́вый,** *adj.* hemp (*attrib.*).
пеньюа́р *n.* peignoir.
пе́ня *n.* fine; penalty.
пеня́ть *v. impfv.* [*pfv.* **попеня́ть**] *colloq.* to reproach; blame.
пео́н *n.* peon. —**пеона́ж,** *n.* peonage.
пе́пел [*gen.* **пе́пла**] *n.* **1,** ashes. **2,** (volcanic) ash.
пепели́ще *n.* site of a fire.
пе́пельница *n.* ashtray.
пе́пельный *adj.* ash-colored.
пепси́н *n.* pepsin.
пепто́н *n.* peptone.
перве́йший *adj., colloq.* **1,** primary. **2,** the very best.
пе́рвенец [*gen.* **-нца**] *n.* first-born.
пе́рвенство *n.* **1,** championship. **2,** primacy.
пе́рвенствовать *v. impfv.* [*pres.* **-ствую, -ствуешь**] **1,** to come in first; finish first. **2,** (*with* **над**) to take precedence (over). **3,** (*with* **ме́жду** *or* **среди́**) to stand out (among); dominate.
перви́чный *adj.* primary; initial.

первобы́тный *adj.* **1,** primitive. **2,** primeval; pristine.

пе́рвое *n., decl. as an adj.* **1,** the first thing: пе́рвое, что на́до сде́лать, the first thing to be done. **2,** (*with dates*) first: сего́дня – пе́рвое ма́рта, today is March 1st. **3,** first course.

первозда́нный *adj.* primordial; primeval.

первоисто́чник *n.* original source; primary source.

первокла́ссный *adj.* first-class; first-rate.

первоку́рсник *n.* freshman.

первома́йский *adj.* May-Day (*attrib.*).

первонача́льный *adj.* **1,** original. **2,** initial; primary. **3,** elementary. —**первонача́льно,** *adv.* originally.

первоо́браз *n.* prototype.

первоочередно́й *adj.* primary; immediate.

первоQразря́дный *adj.* first-rate; first-class.

перворо́дный *adj.* **1,** *obs.* first-born. **2,** *fig.* pristine. —**перворо́дный грех,** original sin.

перворо́дство *n.* primogeniture.

первосвяще́нник *n.* high priest.

первосо́ртный *adj.* **1,** of the highest quality. **2,** *colloq.* first-rate; first-class.

первостепе́нный *adj.* paramount.

первоцве́т *n.* primrose.

пе́рвый *ordinal numeral & adj.* first: пе́рвая страни́ца, the first page. —*n.* **1,** the first. **2,** the former. —**в пе́рвую о́чередь,** first of all. —**из пе́рвых рук,** first-hand. —**пе́рвое вре́мя; на пе́рвых пора́х,** at first; in the beginning. —**пе́рвым де́лом; пе́рвым до́лгом,** *colloq.* first thing; first of all. *See also* **пе́рвое.**

перга́мент *n.* parchment. —**перга́ментный,** *adj.* parchment.

пере- *prefix* **1,** *indicating motion over or across:* перейти́ че́рез у́лицу, to cross the street; перелете́ть че́рез забо́р, to fly over the fence. **2,** *indicating motion to another place:* переле́чь на друго́й дива́н, to lie on another couch; переве́сить карти́ну на другу́ю сте́ну, to hang the picture on another wall. **3,** *indicating repetition of an action:* перечита́ть, to reread; перепрода́ть, to resell. **4,** *indicating excess:* перее́сть, to overeat; переплати́ть, to overpay. **5,** (*with pfv. verbs only*) *colloq., indicating thoroughness or completeness of an action:* переиска́ть, to search everywhere; перемо́кнуть, to get completely drenched. **6,** (*with pfv. verbs only*) *colloq., indicating outdoing someone:* перепи́ть, to outdrink; перехитри́ть, to outwit. **7,** (*with pfv. verbs only*) *colloq., used when the subject is all or many:* все цветы́ перемёрзли, all the flowers perished from the frost. **8,** (*with pfv. verbs only*) *colloq., used when the object is all or many:* перекупа́ть всех дете́й, to bathe all the children; переме́рить мно́го шляп, to try on many hats. **9,** (*with* **-ся**) *indicating reciprocity or exchange:* перепи́сываться, to correspond; перемигиваться, to wink at each other.

переадресова́ть [*infl.* **-су́ю, -су́ешь**] *v., pfv. of* **переадресо́вывать.**

переадресо́вывать *v. impfv.* [*pfv.* **переадресова́ть**] to readdress; forward.

перебази́ровать *v. pfv.* [*infl.* **-рую, -руешь**] to shift; transfer; relocate.

переба́рщивать *v. impfv.* [*pfv.* **переборщи́ть**] *colloq.* to overdo it; go too far.

перебега́ть *v. impfv.* [*pfv.* **перебежа́ть**] **1,** to run across. **2,** to run from one place to another. **3,** to defect. —**перебега́ть доро́гу** (+ *dat.*), to stand in someone's way.

перебежа́ть [*infl. like* **бежа́ть**] *v., pfv. of* **перебега́ть.**

перебе́жка [*gen. pl.* **-жек**] *n.* **1,** run; rush; dash. **2,** defection. **3,** *sports* rerunning (*of a race*).

перебе́жчик *n.* defector; turncoat.

перебе́ливать *v. impfv.* [*pfv.* **перебели́ть**] **1,** to repaint; give a fresh coat of white paint. **2,** to make a clean copy of; put in final form.

перебели́ть [*infl.* **-белю́, -бе́лишь** *or* **-бели́шь**] *v., pfv. of* **перебе́ливать.**

перебеси́ться *v.r. pfv.* [*infl.* **-бешу́сь, -бе́сишься**] **1,** (*of dogs*) to become rabid. **2,** *colloq.* to settle down (*after leading a wild life*).

перебива́ть *v. impfv.* [*pfv.* **переби́ть**] **1,** to interrupt. **2,** to drown out. **3,** to reupholster. **4,** *colloq.* to snatch up (*ahead of someone else*). —**перебива́ться,** *refl.* **1,** to be smashed; be shattered. **2,** *colloq.* to manage; get along; make ends meet.

перебинтова́ть *v. pfv.* [*infl.* **-ту́ю, -ту́ешь**] **1,** to rebandage; change the bandage on. **2,** to bandage all of; bandage entirely.

перебира́ть *v. impfv.* [*pfv.* **перебра́ть**] **1,** to sort out. **2,** to go through; run through. **3,** to run one's fingers over. **4,** [*often,* **перебира́ть в па́мяти**] to turn (*or* run) over in one's mind. **5,** *printing* to reset. —**перебира́ться,** *refl., colloq.* **1,** to cross; get across. **2,** to move (*change residence*).

переби́ть *v. pfv.* [*infl.* **-бью́, -бьёшь**] **1,** *pfv. of* **перебива́ть. 2,** to slaughter; massacre. **3,** to break; fracture. **4,** to break (all of something). —**переби́ться,** *refl., pfv. of* **перебива́ться.**

перебо́й *n.* interruption; irregularity: пульс с перебо́ями, irregular pulse.

переболе́ть[1] *v. pfv.* [*infl.* **-ле́ю, -ле́ешь**] (*with instr.*) **1,** to have had (a certain illness). **2,** (*of many people*) to come down with (a certain illness).

переболе́ть[2] *v. pfv.* [*infl.* **-ли́т**] *fig.* (*of one's heart*) to ache: се́рдце переболе́ло (*or* душа́ переболе́ла) за тебя́, my heart ached for you.

перебо́рка [*gen. pl.* **-рок**] *n.* **1,** sorting out. **2,** partition. **3,** *naut.* bulkhead.

переборо́ть *v. pfv.* [*infl.* **-борю́, -бо́решь**] to overcome. —**переборо́ть себя́,** to keep control of oneself.

переборщи́ть *v., pfv. of* **переба́рщивать.**

перебра́ниваться *v.r. impfv., colloq.* to exchange angry words.

перебра́нка *n., colloq.* squabble; hassle.

перебра́сывать *v. impfv.* [*pfv.* **перебро́сить**] **1,** to throw over. **2,** to throw across. **3,** to transport; transfer. —**перебра́сываться,** *refl.* **1,** to jump over. **2,** to spread. **3,** (*with instr.*) to exchange.

перебра́ть [*infl. like* **брать**] *v., pfv. of* **перебира́ть.** —**перебра́ться,** *refl., pfv. of* **перебира́ться.**

переброди́ть *v. pfv.* [*infl.* **-брожу́, -бро́дишь**] **1,** to ferment. **2,** *fig., colloq.* to mellow.

перебро́сить [*infl.* **-шу, -сишь**] *v., pfv. of* **перебра́сывать.** —**перебро́ситься,** *refl., pfv. of* **перебра́сываться.**

перебро́ска *n.* transfer.

перебыва́ть *v. pfv., used mainly in the past tense* **1,** to have been (in all or many places). **2,** (*with* **у**) to visit; go see (all or many people). **3,** (*of all or many people*) to have been (somewhere).

перева́л *n.* **1,** crossing. **2,** mountain pass.

перева́ливать *v. impfv.* [*pfv.* **перевали́ть**] **1,** to turn over on one's/its other side. **2,** to cross; traverse. **3,**

(*with* за + *acc.*) *colloq.* to exceed; (*of a person*) be past a certain age: ему́ перевали́ло за со́рок, he is past forty. —**перева́ливаться**, *refl.* **1,** to roll over. **2,** [*impfv. only*] to waddle.

перевали́ть [*infl.* **-валю́, -ва́лишь**] *v., pfv. of* **перева́ливать.** —**перевали́ться**, *refl., pfv. of* **перева́ливаться.**

перева́лка *n.* **1,** transfer of cargo; transshipment. **2,** transshipment point. **3,** *colloq.* waddle. —**перева́лочный**, *adj.* transfer (*attrib.*); transshipment (*attrib.*).

перева́ривать *v. impfv.* [*pfv.* **перевари́ть**] **1,** to recook. **2,** to overcook. **3,** to digest. **4,** *colloq.* to put up with; stomach.

перевари́ть [*infl.* **-варю́, -ва́ришь**] *v., pfv. of* **перева́ривать.**

перевезти́ [*infl. like* **везти́**] *v., pfv. of* **перевози́ть.**

переверну́ть *v., pfv. of* **перевёртывать** *and* **перевора́чивать.** —**переверну́ться**, *refl., pfv. of* **перевёртываться** *and* **перевора́чиваться.**

перeверте́ть [*infl.* **-верчу́, -ве́ртишь**] *v., pfv. of* **перевёртывать** (*in sense #5*).

перевёртывание *n.* inversion.

перевёртывать *v. impfv.* [*pfv.* **переверну́ть**] **1,** to turn over; invert. **2,** *colloq.* to overturn; upset. **3,** to turn (a page). **4,** *colloq.* to change completely; transform. **5,** [*pfv.* **переверте́ть**] to turn too far; overwind (a watch). —**перевёртываться**, *refl.* **1,** to turn over. **2,** to capsize.

переве́с *n.* **1,** superiority; preponderance. **2,** advantage; edge. **3,** *colloq.* excess weight.

переве́сить [*infl.* **-шу, -сишь**] *v., pfv. of* **переве́шивать.** —**переве́ситься**, *refl., pfv. of* **переве́шиваться.**

перевести́ [*infl. like* **вести́**] *v., pfv. of* **переводи́ть.** —**перевести́сь**, *refl., pfv. of* **переводи́ться.**

переве́шивать *v. impfv.* [*pfv.* **переве́сить**] **1,** to move by hanging elsewhere. **2,** to weigh again. **3,** *fig.* to outweigh. **4,** *v.i.* to prevail. —**переве́шиваться**, *refl.* (*with* **в, на,** *or* **че́рез**) to hang over; lean over.

перевива́ть *v. impfv.* [*pfv.* **переви́ть**] to interweave; intertwine.

перевира́ть *v. impfv.* [*pfv.* **перевра́ть**] *colloq.* to garble; misquote.

переви́ть [*infl. like* **вить**] *v., pfv. of* **перевива́ть.**

перево́д *n.* **1,** transfer. **2,** translation. **3,** remittance: де́нежный перево́д, money order. **4,** conversion (*to a different unit of measurement*). **5,** (*with gen.*) *colloq.* waste (of).

переводи́ть *v. impfv.* [*pfv.* **перевести́**; *pres.* **-вожу́, -во́дишь**] **1,** to lead across; take across. **2,** to transfer. **3,** to shift. **4,** to translate. **5,** to convert (to a different unit of measurement). **6,** to remit (money). **7,** *colloq.* to exterminate. **8,** *colloq.* to waste. **9,** *in* **перевести́ дух** *or* **дыха́ние**, to catch one's breath. —**переводи́ться**, *refl.* **1,** to switch; shift. **2,** *colloq.* to disappear; cease to exist. **3,** *colloq.* to be in short supply; be spent: у него́ де́ньги никогда́ не перево́дятся, he is never lacking for money.

переводно́й *adj.* **1,** of or for a money order. **2,** *in* переводна́я бума́га, carbon paper; переводна́я карти́нка, decal.

перево́дческий *adj.* of translating; of a translator.

перево́дчик *n.* translator; interpreter.

перево́з *n.* **1,** transporation. **2,** ferrying station.

перевози́ть *v. impfv.* [*pfv.* **перевезти́**; *pres.* **-вожу́, -во́зишь**] **1,** to transport; move; convey. **2,** to take across; transport across; ferry across.

перево́зка *n.* transportation.

перево́зочный *adj., in* **перево́зочные сре́дства**, means of conveyance.

перево́зчик *n.* **1,** ferryman. **2,** *colloq.* mover. **3,** sandpiper.

перевооружа́ть *v. impfv.* [*pfv.* **перевооружи́ть**] to rearm (*supply with new arms*). —**перевооружа́ться**, *refl.* to rearm (*acquire new arms*).

перевооруже́ние *n.* rearmament.

перевооружи́ть *v., pfv. of* **перевооружа́ть.** —**перевооружи́ться**, *refl., pfv. of* **перевооружа́ться.**

перевоплоща́ть *v. impfv.* [*pfv.* **перевоплоти́ть**] to reincarnate.

перевоплоще́ние *n.* reincarnation.

перевора́чивать *v. impfv.* = **перевёртывать.** —**перевора́чиваться**, *refl.* = **перевёртываться.**

переворо́т *n.* revolution; upheaval; coup. —**госуда́рственный переворо́т**, coup d'état.

перевороши́ть *v. pfv., colloq.* **1,** to toss (hay). **2,** to mess up; disarrange. **3,** to turn over in one's mind. **4,** *fig.* to turn upside down.

перевоспита́ние *n.* re-education.

перевоспи́тывать *v. impfv.* [*pfv.* **перевоспита́ть**] to re-educate.

перевра́ть [*infl. like* **врать**] *v., pfv. of* **перевира́ть.**

перевы́боры [*gen.* **-ров**] *n. pl.* **1,** election. **2,** new election.

перевыполне́ние *n.* overfulfillment.

перевыполня́ть *v. impfv.* [*pfv.* **перевы́полнить**] to exceed; overfulfill.

перевяза́ть [*infl.* **-вяжу́, -вя́жешь**] *v., pfv. of* **перевя́зывать.** —**перевяза́ться**, *refl., pfv. of* **перевя́зываться.**

перевя́зка *n.* **1,** tying up. **2,** bandaging; dressing. **3,** *colloq.* bandage.

перевя́зочный *adj.* for the dressing of wounds: перевя́зочный пункт, place where wounds are dressed.

перевя́зывать *v. impfv.* [*pfv.* **перевяза́ть**] **1,** to tie; tie up. **2,** to bandage. **3,** to retie. **4,** to rebandage. **5,** to knit again. —**перевя́зываться**, *refl.* to bandage oneself.

пе́ревязь *n.f.* **1,** *mil.* shoulder belt. **2,** *med.* sling.

переги́б *n.* **1,** bend. **2,** *fig.* excess; extreme.

перегиба́ть *v. impfv.* [*pfv.* **перегну́ть**] **1,** to bend. **2,** *in* **перегну́ть па́лку**, to go too far; go overboard. —**перегиба́ться**, *refl.* to bend over; lean over.

перегласо́вка *n., phonet.* mutation.

перегля́дываться *v.r. impfv.* [*pfv.* **перегляну́ться**] to exchange glances.

перегляну́ться [*infl.* **-гляну́сь, -гля́нешься**] *v.r., pfv. of* **перегля́дываться.**

перегна́ть [*infl. like* **гнать**] *v., pfv. of* **перегоня́ть.**

перегнива́ть *v. impfv.* [*pfv.* **перегни́ть**] to rot through.

перегни́ть [*infl. like* **гнить**] *v., pfv. of* **перегнива́ть.**

перегно́й *n.* humus.

перегну́ть *v., pfv. of* **перегиба́ть.** —**перегну́ться**, *refl., pfv. of* **перегиба́ться.**

перегова́риваться *v.r. impfv.* **1,** to be engaged in conversation. **2,** (*with* **с** + *instr.*) to converse (with).

переговори́ть *v. pfv.* **1,** to talk; have a talk. **2,** *colloq.* to outtalk; talk down.

перегово́ры [*gen.* **-ров**] *n. pl.* **1,** negotiations. **2,** talks.

перегóн *n.* **1,** driving (*of cattle*). **2,** space between two stations. **3,** stage; leg (*of a journey*).

перегóнка *n.* distillation.

перегóнный *adj.* of or for distilling. —**перегóнный завóд,** distillery. —**перегóнный куб,** still.

перегоня́ть *v. impfv.* [*pfv.* **перегна́ть**] **1,** to outdistance; outrun. **2,** *fig.* to outstrip; surpass; leave behind. **3,** to drive (to another place). **4,** *colloq.* to move; ship; transport. **5,** to distill.

перегора́живать *v. impfv.* [*pfv.* **перегороди́ть**] to partition (off).

перегора́ть *v. impfv.* [*pfv.* **перегорéть**] **1,** (*of a bulb, fuse, etc.*) to burn out. **2,** to be burned down to nothing. **3,** (*of a fire*) to burn itself out. **4,** *fig.* (*of emotions*) to die down.

перегороди́ть [*infl.* **-рожу́, -рóдишь** *or* **-роди́шь**] *v., pfv. of* **перегора́живать.**

перегорóдка [*gen. pl.* **-док**] *n.* **1,** partition. **2,** *fig.* barrier.

перегрéв *n.* overheating. *Also,* **перегревáние.**

перегрева́ть *v. impfv.* [*pfv.* **перегрéть**] to overheat. —**перегрева́ться,** *refl.* **1,** to overheat; become overheated. **2,** to get too much sun.

перегружа́ть *v. impfv.* [*pfv.* **перегрузи́ть**] **1,** to load from one place to another. **2,** to overload; overburden. —**перегружа́ться,** *refl.* to be overloaded.

перегрузи́ть [*infl.* **-гружу́, -гру́зишь** *or* **-грузи́шь**] *v., pfv. of* **перегружа́ть.** —**перегрузи́ться,** *refl., pfv. of* **перегружа́ться.**

перегру́зка *n.* **1,** transfer of cargo; transshipment. **2,** overloading. —**перегру́зочный,** *adj.* transfer (*attrib.*); transshipment (*attrib.*).

перегруппирова́ть [*infl.* **-ру́ю, -ру́ешь**] *v., pfv. of* **перегруппирóвывать.** —**перегруппирова́ться,** *refl., pfv. of* **перегруппирóвываться.**

перегруппирóвка *n.* regrouping.

перегруппирóвывать *v. impfv.* [*pfv.* **перегруппирова́ть**] to regroup. —**перегруппирóвываться,** *refl.* to regroup.

перегрыза́ть *v. impfv.* [*pfv.* **перегры́зть**] to gnaw through. —**перегрыза́ться,** *refl., colloq.* **1,** (*of animals*) to fight; scrap. **2,** *fig.* (*of people*) to squabble.

перегры́зть [*infl. like* **грызть**] *v., pfv. of* **перегрыза́ть.** —**перегры́зться,** *refl., pfv. of* **перегрыза́ться.**

пéред *prep., with instr.* **1,** in front of; before: сидéть пéред зéркалом, to sit in front of the mirror; предстáть пéред судóм, to appear before the court. **2,** before (*in time*): пéред обéдом, before dinner. **3,** compared to: э́то ничтó пéред..., that's nothing compared to... —**пéред тем, как,** before: пéред тем, как вы́йти и́з дому, before leaving the house; пéред тем, как он вы́шел и́з дому, before he left the house.

перёд [*gen.* **пéреда;** *pl.* **переда́**] *n.* front.

передава́ть *v. impfv.* [*pfv.* **переда́ть;** *pres.* **-даю́, -даёшь**] **1,** to hand over; (*at the table*) to pass. **2,** to transmit; convey. Передáйте емý (от меня́) привéт, give him my regards. Передáйте ей, что..., tell her that... **3,** to refer; turn over (a matter). **4,** to turn over; transfer (property). **5,** to transmit: передавáть по рáдио, to broadcast; передавáть по телеви́дению, to televise. **6,** *colloq.* to overpay.

переда́точный *adj.* transmission (*attrib.*); gear (*attrib.*): передáточный ремéнь, transmission belt; передáточное числó, gear ratio.

переда́тчик *n.* **1,** transmitter. **2,** messenger.

переда́ть [*infl. like* **дать;** *past* **пéредал, -дала́, пéредало**] *v., pfv. of* **передава́ть.**

переда́ча *n.* **1,** transmission. **2,** transfer. **3,** broadcast. **4,** *mech.* transmission; gear; drive. **5,** parcel (*for a hospital patient, prisoner, etc.*). **6,** *sports* pass.

передвига́ть *v. impfv.* [*pfv.* **передви́нуть**] to move; shift (*from one place to another*). —**передвига́ться,** *refl.* **1,** to move. **2,** [*impfv. only*] to walk.

передвижéние *n.* **1,** movement; transportation. **2,** movement; locomotion. —**срéдства передвижéния,** means of conveyance.

передви́жка *n., colloq.* movement. —**библиотéка-передви́жка,** mobile library; bookmobile.

передвижнóй *adj.* **1,** movable. **2,** traveling; mobile.

передви́нуть *v., pfv. of* **передвига́ть.** —**передви́нуться,** *refl., pfv. of* **передвига́ться.**

передéл *n.* redistribution.

передéлать *v. pfv.* **1,** *pfv. of* **передéлывать.** **2,** *colloq.* to do (all or everything).

передели́ть [*infl.* **-делю́, -дéлишь**] *v., pfv. of* **переделя́ть.**

передéлка *n.* **1,** alteration; doing over. **2,** adaptation (*of a book, play, etc.*). **3,** fix; mess; jam: попáсть в передéлку, to get into a mess.

передéлывать *v. impfv.* [*pfv.* **передéлать**] **1,** to alter (a garment). **2,** to redo; do over. **3,** to remake; make into something else.

переделя́ть *v. impfv.* [*pfv.* **передели́ть**] to redistribute.

передёргивать *v. impfv.* [*pfv.* **передёрнуть**] **1,** to pull; tug on; jerk. **2,** *impers.* to wince: егó передёрнуло от э́тих слов, he winced on hearing those words. **3,** *colloq.* to cheat (at cards); juggle (facts).

передержа́ть [*infl.* **-держу́, -дéржишь**] *v., pfv. of* **передéрживать.**

передéрживать *v. impfv.* [*pfv.* **передержа́ть**] **1,** to keep in too long. **2,** *photog.* to overexpose. **3,** to retake (an examination).

передéржка *n.* **1,** *photog.* overexposure. **2,** *colloq.* misstatement; distortion of the facts.

передёрнуть *v., pfv. of* **передёргивать.**

перéдний *adj.* front. —**перéдний план,** foreground.

перéдник *n.* apron.

перéдняя *n., decl. as an adj.* vestibule; hall.

передо *prep.* = **пéред** (*used mainly in the combination* **передо мной**).

передова́я *n., decl. as an adj.* **1,** lead article. **2,** *mil.* front line.

передоверя́ть *v. impfv.* [*pfv.* **передовéрить**] to transfer (legal title, power of attorney, etc.).

передови́к [*gen.* **-вика́**] *n.* outstanding worker.

передови́ца *n., colloq.* = **передова́я статья́.**

передовóй *adj.* **1,** forward. Передовóй отря́д, advance guard. **2,** advanced; progressive. —**передова́я статья́,** lead article.

передóк [*gen.* **-дка́**] *n.* **1,** front (*of a vehicle*). **2,** vamp (*of a shoe*).

передóхнуть *v. pfv.* [*past* **-дóх, -ла**] *colloq.* (*of many animals*) to die.

передохну́ть *v. pfv.* **1,** to take a breath. **2,** *colloq.* to pause for breath; take a short rest.

передра́знивать *v. impfv.* [*pfv.* **передразни́ть**] to mimic; imitate.

передразни́ть [*infl.* **-дразню́, -дра́знишь**] *v., pfv. of* **передра́знивать.**

передра́ться *v.r. pfv.* [*infl. like* **драть**] (*of many people*) to fight; scrap.

передря́га *n., colloq.* scrape; row: попа́сть в передря́гу, to get into a scrape.

переду́мывать *v. impfv.* [*pfv.* **переду́мать**] **1,** to change one's mind. **2,** (*with acc. or* **о**) *colloq.* to think over carefully.

передышка [*gen. pl.* **-шек**] *n.* breathing space; respite.

переда́ть *v. impfv.* [*pfv.* **перее́сть**] **1,** to overeat. **2,** to corrode; eat away.

перее́зд *n.* **1,** (act of) crossing. **2,** crossing (*place to cross*). **3,** move; moving (*to another residence*).

переезжа́ть *v. impfv.* [*pfv.* **перее́хать**] **1,** to cross. **2,** to move (to another residence). **3,** *colloq.* to run over.

перее́сть [*infl. like* **есть**] *v., pfv. of* **переда́ть.**

перее́хать [*infl. like* **е́хать**] *v., pfv. of* **переезжа́ть.**

пережа́ривать *v. impfv.* [*pfv.* **пережа́рить**] to overcook; overdo.

пережда́ть [*infl. like* **ждать**] *v., pfv. of* **пережида́ть.**

пережева́ть [*infl.* **-жую́, -жуёшь**] *v., pfv. of* **пережёвывать.**

пережёвывать *v. impfv.* [*pfv.* **пережева́ть**] **1,** to chew. **2,** [*impfv. only*] *fig.* to keep repeating.

пережени́ть *v. pfv.* [*infl.* **-женю́, -же́нишь**] *colloq.* to marry off (many or all one's sons). —**пережени́ться,** *refl.* (*of many men*) to get married.

пережéчь *v. pfv.* [*infl. like* **жечь**] **1,** *pfv. of* **пережига́ть. 2,** to burn (all or much of something).

пережива́ние *n., usu. pl.* **1,** (emotional) experiences. **2,** sufferings; tribulations.

пережива́ть *v. impfv.* [*pfv.* **пережи́ть**] **1,** to go through; experience. **2,** to survive. **3,** to outlive. **4,** *v.i.* [*impfv. only*] *colloq.* to be upset.

пережига́ть *v. impfv.* [*pfv.* **пережéчь**] **1,** to heat to excess. **2,** to burn out (a bulb, fuse, etc.). **3,** *colloq.* to burn too much (fuel, electricity, etc.).

пережида́ть *v. impfv.* [*pfv.* **пережда́ть**] to wait out; wait until (something) is over.

пережито́е *n., decl. as an adj.* past experiences; what one has experienced or gone through.

пережи́ток [*gen.* **-тка**] *n.* vestige; remnant; survival.

пережи́ть [*infl. like* **жить;** *past* **пе́режил** *or* **пережи́л, -жила́, пе́режило** *or* **пережи́ло**] *v., pfv. of* **пережива́ть.**

перезабы́ть *v. pfv.* [*infl.* **-бу́ду, -бу́дешь**] *colloq.* to forget (much or everything).

перезаключа́ть *v. impfv.* [*pfv.* **перезаключи́ть**] to renew (a contract).

перезаряди́ть [*infl.* **-ряжу́, -ря́дишь** *or* **-ряди́шь**] *v., pfv. of* **перезаряжа́ть.**

перезаряжа́ть *v. impfv.* [*pfv.* **перезаряди́ть**] **1,** to recharge. **2,** to overcharge. **3,** to reload.

перезво́н *n.* ringing of bells.

перезимова́ть *v. pfv.* [*infl.* **-му́ю, -му́ешь**] to winter; spend the winter.

перезрева́ть *v. impfv.* [*pfv.* **перезре́ть**] to become overripe.

перезре́лый *adj.* overripe.

перезре́ть *v., pfv. of* **перезрева́ть.**

переигра́ть *v. pfv.* **1,** *pfv. of* **переи́грывать. 2,** to play; perform (all or many of something).

переи́грывать *v. impfv.* [*pfv.* **переигра́ть**] **1,** to replay. **2,** *colloq.* to outplay. **3,** *theat., colloq.* to overplay (a part); overact.

переизбира́ть *v. impfv.* [*pfv.* **переизбра́ть**] to re-elect.

переизбра́ние *n.* re-election.

переизбра́ть [*infl. like* **брать**] *v., pfv. of* **переизбира́ть.**

переиздава́ть *v. impfv.* [*pfv.* **переизда́ть;** *pres.* **-даю́, -даёшь**] to republish; reissue.

переизда́ние *n.* **1,** republication. **2,** new edition.

переизда́ть [*infl. like* **дать**] *v., pfv. of* **переиздава́ть.**

переименова́ть *v. pfv.* [*infl.* **-ну́ю, -ну́ешь**] to rename.

переи́мчивый *adj., colloq.* imitative.

переина́чивать *v. impfv.* [*pfv.* **переина́чить**] *colloq.* to modify; alter.

перейти́ [*infl.* **перейду́, перейдёшь;** *past* **перешёл, перешла́**] *v., pfv. of* **переходи́ть.**

перека́лывать *v. impfv.* [*pfv.* **переколо́ть**] to pin (somewhere else). *See also* **переколо́ть.**

перека́пывать *v. impfv.* [*pfv.* **перекопа́ть**] **1,** to dig (all of something). **2,** to dig again. **3,** to dig across.

перека́рмливать *v. impfv.* [*pfv.* **перекорми́ть**] to overfeed.

перека́т *n.* **1,** *usu. pl.* sharp sound; crack (*of shots being fired*); clap (*of thunder*). **2,** sandbank; shoal.

перекати́-по́ле *n.* tumbleweed.

перекати́ть [*infl.* **-качу́, -ка́тишь**] *v., pfv. of* **перека́тывать.** —**перекати́ться,** *refl., pfv. of* **перека́тываться.**

перека́тывать *v. impfv.* [*pfv.* **перекати́ть**] to roll (from one place to another). —**перека́тываться,** *refl.* to roll (over, across, etc.).

перека́шивать *v. impfv.* [*pfv.* **перекоси́ть**] *usu. impers.* to distort; warp; twist: (лицо́) его́ перекоси́ло, his face became distorted. —**перека́шиваться,** *refl.* to become distorted; become warped.

переквалифика́ция *n.* retraining.

переквалифици́ровать *v. impfv. & pfv.* [*pres.* **-рую, -руешь**] to retrain. —**переквалифици́роваться,** *refl.* to be retrained; learn a new trade.

переки́дывать *v. impfv.* [*pfv.* **переки́нуть**] = **перебра́сывать.** —**переки́дываться,** *refl.* = **перебра́сываться.**

перекипа́ть *v. impfv.* [*pfv.* **перекипе́ть**] **1,** to boil too long. **2,** *fig., colloq.* to calm down.

пе́рекись *n.f.* peroxide: пе́рекись водоро́да, hydrogen peroxide.

перекла́дина *n.* **1,** crossbeam; crossbar; transom. **2,** *sports* horizontal bar.

перекла́дывать *v. impfv.* [*pfv.* **переложи́ть**] **1,** to move (from one place to another). **2,** *fig.* to shift (a job, responsibility, etc.). **3,** (*with instr.*) to pack (with); interlay (with). **4,** to pile up again. **5,** *music; lit.* to rearrange; (*with* **в** *or* **на** + *acc.*) set (to music); put (into verse). **6,** *colloq.* to put too much (salt, sugar, etc.).

перекле́ивать *v. impfv.* [*pfv.* **перекле́ить**] **1,** to glue again; paste again. **2,** to glue; paste (somewhere else).

переклика́ть *v. impfv., colloq.* to call the roll. —**перекли́каться,** *refl.* **1,** to call; shout (to one another). **2,** (*with* **с** + *instr.*) *fig.* to have certain things in common (with).

перекли́чка *n.* roll call: де́лать перекли́чку, to call the roll.

переключа́тель *n.m.* switch: переключа́тель све́та, light switch.

переключа́ть *v. impfv.* [*pfv.* **переключи́ть**] to switch; shift. —**переключа́ться,** *refl.* (*with* **на** + *acc.*) to switch (to); shift (to).

переключе́ние *n.* switch; switching over; changeover.

переключи́ть *v., pfv. of* **переключа́ть.** —**переключи́ться,** *refl., pfv. of* **переключа́ться.**

перекова́ть [*infl.* **-кую́, -куёшь**] *v., pfv. of* **перeко́вывать.**

перeко́вывать *v. impfv.* [*pfv.* **перекова́ть**] **1,** to reforge. **2,** *fig.* to remold. **3,** to make a new shoe for (a horse).

переколо́ть *v. pfv.* [*infl.* **-колю́, -ко́лешь**] **1,** *pfv. of* **перека́лывать. 2,** to prick in many places. **3,** to slaughter; massacre. **4,** to chop (all or much of something).

переконструи́ровать *v. impfv. & pfv.* [*pres.* **-рую, руешь**] to redesign.

перекопа́ть *v., pfv. of* **перека́пывать.**

перекорми́ть [*infl.* **-кормлю́, -ко́рмишь**] *v., pfv. of* **перека́рмливать.**

переко́ры [*gen.* **-ров**] *n.pl., colloq.* squabble.

перекоси́ть [*infl.* **-кошу́, -коси́шь**] *v., pfv. of* **перека́шивать.** —**перекоси́ться,** *refl., pfv. of* **перека́шиваться.**

перекочева́ть [*infl.* **-чу́ю, -чу́ешь**] *v., pfv. of* **перекочёвывать.**

перекочёвывать *v. impfv.* [*pfv.* **перекочева́ть**] to wander; migrate (from one place to another).

переко́шенный *adj.* **1,** twisted out of shape. **2,** (*of one's face*) twisted; contorted.

перекра́ивать *v. impfv.* [*pfv.* **перекрои́ть**] **1,** to cut again. **2,** to refashion; revamp. **3,** *in* перекра́ивать ка́рту ми́ра, to recarve the map of the world.

перекра́сить *v. pfv.* [*infl.* **-шу, -сишь**] **1,** *pfv. of* **перекра́шивать. 2,** to paint (all or many things). —**перекра́ситься,** *refl., pfv. of* **перекра́шиваться.**

перекра́шивать *v. impfv.* [*pfv.* **перекра́сить**] to paint (something) a different color; repaint. —**перекра́шиваться,** *refl.* **1,** to change color. **2,** *fig., colloq.* to hide one's true colors.

перекрести́ть [*infl.* **-крещу́, -кре́стишь**] *v., pfv. of* **крести́ть** (*in sense #3*) *and* **перекре́щивать.** —**перекрести́ться,** *refl., pfv. of* **крести́ться** (*in sense #2*) *and* **перекре́щиваться.**

перекрёстный *adj.* cross. —**перекрёстный допро́с,** cross-examination. —**перекрёстный ого́нь,** crossfire. —**перекрёстная ссы́лка,** cross-reference.

перекрёсток [*gen.* **-стка**] *n.* intersection; crossing. —**крича́ть на всех перекрёстках,** to shout from the rooftops.

перекре́щивать *v. impfv.* [*pfv.* **перекрести́ть**] **1,** to make the sign of the cross over. **2,** *colloq.* to rename; rechristen. **3,** *colloq.* to lie across; crisscross. —**перекре́щиваться,** *refl.* to intersect; crisscross.

перекрича́ть *v. pfv.* [*infl.* **-чу́, -чи́шь**] to shout down.

перекрои́ть *v., pfv. of* **перекра́ивать.**

перекрути́ть [*infl.* **-кручу́, -кру́тишь**] *v., pfv. of* **перекру́чивать.**

перекру́чивать *v. impfv.* [*pfv.* **перекрути́ть**] *colloq.* **1,** to twist. **2,** to twist too far; turn too far.

перекрыва́ть *v. impfv.* [*pfv.* **перекры́ть**] **1,** to cover again; recover. **2,** *colloq.* to exceed. **3,** to block; bar. **4,** to dam (a river).

перекры́ть [*infl.* **-кро́ю, -кро́ешь**] *v., pfv. of* **перекрыва́ть.**

перекувырну́ть *v. pfv., colloq.* to upset; overturn. —**перекувырну́ться,** *refl., colloq.* **1,** to tip over; topple over. **2,** to turn a somersault (*in the air*).

перекупа́ть[1] *v. impfv.* [*pfv.* **перекупи́ть**] *colloq.* **1,** to buy by outbidding someone else. **2,** to buy back.

перекупа́ть[2] *v. pfv., colloq.* **1,** to bathe too long. **2,** to bathe (all or many people). —**перекупа́ться,** *refl., colloq.* to bathe too long; stay in the water too long.

перекупи́ть [*infl.* **-куплю́, -ку́пишь**] *v., pfv. of* **перекупа́ть**[1].

переку́пщик *n.* one who buys for resale; dealer.

переку́р *n., colloq.* smoke break.

перекуси́ть *v. pfv.* [*infl.* **-кушу́, -ку́сишь**] **1,** to bite in half. **2,** to bite through. **3,** *colloq.* to have a bite to eat.

перела́мывать *v. impfv.* [*pfv.* **переломи́ть**] **1,** to break in two; fracture. **2,** to alter; transform. **3,** *colloq.* to overcome; conquer (a feeling). —**перела́мываться,** *refl.* to be broken in two; be fractured.

перелеза́ть *v. impfv.* [*pfv.* **переле́зть**] to climb over.

переле́зть [*infl. like* **лезть**] *v., pfv. of* **перелеза́ть.**

переле́ска *n.* hepatica.

переле́сок [*gen.* **-ска**] *n.* coppice; copse.

перелёт *n.* **1,** (long) flight. **2,** migration (*of birds*). **3,** overshooting (*of a target*).

перелета́ть *v. impfv.* [*pfv.* **перелете́ть**] **1,** to fly over; fly across. **2,** to fly (from one place to another).

перелете́ть [*infl.* **-чу́, -ти́шь**] *v., pfv. of* **перелета́ть.**

перелётный *adj.* (*of a bird*) migratory.

переле́чь *v. pfv.* [*infl. like* **лечь**] to lie down (somewhere else).

перели́в *n.* **1,** flowing. **2,** *usu. pl.* play (*of colors*). **3,** *usu. pl.* modulation.

перелива́ние *n.* **1,** pouring (*from one container to another*). **2,** transfusion: перелива́ние кро́ви, blood transfusion.

перелива́ть *v. impfv.* [*pfv.* **перели́ть**] **1,** to pour (from one vessel to another). **2,** *in* перелива́ть кровь (+ *dat.*), to give a blood transfusion (to). **3,** to recast. **4,** [*impfv. only*] to gleam; glisten. —**перелива́ться,** *refl.* **1,** to flow (from one place to another). **2,** to overflow. **3,** [*impfv. only*] to gleam; glisten. **4,** [*impfv. only*] (*of sounds*) to modulate.

перели́вчатый *adj.* **1,** (*of colors*) iridescent. **2,** (*of a voice*) lilting.

перели́стывать *v. impfv.* [*pfv.* **перелиста́ть**] to leaf through.

перели́ть [*infl. like* **лить**] *v., pfv. of* **перелива́ть.** —**перели́ться,** *refl., pfv. of* **перелива́ться.**

перелицева́ть [*infl.* **-цу́ю, -цу́ешь**] *v., pfv. of* **перелицо́вывать.**

перелицо́вывать *v. impfv.* [*pfv.* **перелицева́ть**] **1,** to alter by turning inside out. **2,** *fig., colloq.* to give a new face to.

переловить *v. pfv.* [*infl.* **-ловлю́, -ло́вишь**] to catch (all or many of something).

переложе́ние *n.* **1,** (with **в** *or* **на** + *acc.*) setting (to); turning into (verse, music, etc.). **2,** *music* arrangement; transposition.

переложи́ть [*infl.* **-ложу́, -ло́жишь**] *v., pfv. of* **перекла́дывать.**

перело́м *n.* **1,** break; fracture. **2,** *fig.* critical period; turning point. **3,** *fig.* sudden change.

перелома́ть *v. pfv.* to break (all or many things). —**перелома́ться,** *refl.* (*of many things*) to be broken.

перелом́ить [*infl.* **-ломлю́, -ло́мишь**] *v., pfv. of* **перела́мывать.** —**перелом́иться,** *refl., pfv. of* **перела́мываться.**

перело́мный *adj.* critical; crucial.

перема́зать *v. pfv.* [*infl.* **-ма́жу, -ма́жешь**] *colloq.* to smear; make dirty. —**перема́заться,** *refl., colloq.* to get all dirty.

перема́нивать *v. impfv.* [*pfv.* **переман́ить**] to entice; win over.

переман́ить [*infl.* **-маню́, -ма́нишь**] *v., pfv. of* **перема́нивать.**

перема́тывать *v. impfv.* [*pfv.* **перемота́ть**] **1,** to wind (onto something else). **2,** to rewind.

перема́хивать *v. impfv.* [*pfv.* **перемахну́ть**] *colloq.* to jump over.

перемежа́ть *v. impfv.* **1,** to alternate: перемежа́ть рабо́ту (с) о́тдыхом, to alternate work and rest. **2,** to intersperse: перемежа́ть расска́з анекдо́тами, to intersperse a story with anecdotes. —**перемежа́ться,** *refl.* to alternate.

перемежа́ющийся *adj.* intermittent.

переме́на *n.* **1,** change. **2,** recess; break (*between classes*).

перемен́ить *v. pfv.* [*infl.* **-меню́, -ме́нишь**] to change. —**перемен́иться,** *refl.* **1,** to change. **2,** (with **к**) to change one's attitude (toward); act differently (toward). **3,** (*with instr.*) to change; exchange; trade.

переме́нный *adj.* variable. —**переме́нная величина́,** *math.* variable. —**переме́нный ток,** alternating current. —**с переме́нным успе́хом,** with varying (degrees of) success.

переме́нчивый *adj., colloq.* changeable.

перемерза́ть *v. impfv.* [*pfv.* **перемёрзнуть**] **1,** to freeze up; freeze solid. **2,** *colloq.* to freeze; be frozen.

перемёрзнуть *v. pfv.* [*past* **-мёрз, -ла**] **1,** *pfv. of* **перемерза́ть. 2,** (*of all of something, usu. plants*) to perish from the frost.

переме́ривать *v. impfv.* [*pfv.* **переме́рить**] **1,** to remeasure. **2,** to try on again.

переме́рить *v. pfv.* **1,** *pfv. of* **переме́ривать. 2,** to measure (all or many things). **3,** to try on (all or many things).

переместить [*infl.* **-щу́, -сти́шь**] *v., pfv. of* **перемеща́ть.** —**переместиться,** *refl., pfv. of* **перемеща́ться.**

переме́тить *v. pfv.* [*infl.* **-чу, -тишь**] **1,** *pfv. of* **перемеча́ть. 2,** to mark (all or many of something).

переметну́ться *v.r. pfv., colloq.* **1,** to jump across; dart across. **2,** to defect (to the enemy).

перемётный *adj., in* **перемётная сума́,** saddlebag.

перемеча́ть *v. impfv.* [*pfv.* **переме́тить**] to mark again.

переме́шивать *v. impfv.* [*pfv.* **перемеша́ть**] **1,** to mix. **2,** to stir. **3,** to mix up; disarrange. **4,** *colloq.* to mix up; confuse. —**переме́шиваться,** *refl.* **1,** (with **с** + *instr.*) to mix (with); blend (with). **2,** to get mixed up.

перемеща́ть *v. impfv.* [*pfv.* **перемести́ть**] to move; shift; transfer. —**перемеща́ться,** *refl.* to move.

перемеще́ние *n.* **1,** shift; movement. **2,** displacement. **3,** transfer.

перемещённый *adj., in* **перемещённые ли́ца,** displaced persons.

перемиѓиваться *v.r. impfv.* [*pfv.* **перемигну́ться**] to wink to each other.

перемина́ться *v.r. impfv., colloq.* (*often with* **с ноги́ на́ ногу**) to shift from foot to foot (*in anxiety*).

переми́рие *n.* truce; armistice.

перемога́ть *v. impfv., colloq.* to fight off (drowsiness, an illness, etc.). —**перемога́ться,** *refl., colloq.* to try to fight off an illness.

перемо́лвить *v. pfv.* [*infl.* **-влю, -вишь**] *colloq., in* перемо́лвить сло́во с (+ *instr.*), to have a word with.

перемота́ть *v., pfv. of* **перема́тывать.**

перемыва́ть *v. impfv.* [*pfv.* **перемы́ть**] to wash again. —**перемыва́ть ко́сточки** (+ *dat.*), to say malicious things about.

перемы́ть *v. pfv.* [*infl.* **-мо́ю, -мо́ешь**] **1,** *pfv. of* **перемыва́ть. 2,** to wash (all or many of something).

перемы́чка [*gen. pl.* **-чек**] *n.* **1,** crosspiece. **2,** lintel. **3,** bulkhead.

перенапряга́ть *v. impfv.* [*pfv.* **перенапря́чь**] to overexert.

перенапряже́ние *n.* overexertion.

перенапря́чь [*infl. like* **напря́чь**] *v., pfv. of* **перенапряга́ть.**

перенаселе́ние *n.* overpopulation.

перенаселённый *adj.* overpopulated. —**перенаселённость,** *n.f.* overpopulation.

перенаселя́ть *v. impfv.* [*pfv.* **перенаселить**] to overpopulate.

перенесе́ние *n.* **1,** moving, shifting; transferring. **2,** postponement; putting off. **3,** enduring.

перенести́ [*infl. like* **нести́**] *v., pfv. of* **переноси́ть.** —**перенести́сь,** *refl., pfv. of* **переноси́ться.**

перенима́ть *v. impfv.* [*pfv.* **переня́ть**] *colloq.* to adopt; copy; imitate.

перено́с *n.* **1,** moving; shifting; transferring. **2,** *in* перено́с сло́ва, dividing a word at the end of a line; word division. **3,** hyphen (*at the end of a line*).

переноси́ть *v. impfv.* [*pfv.* **перенести́**; *pres.* **-ношу́, -но́сишь**] **1,** to carry across; carry somewhere else. **2,** to move; shift; transfer. **3,** to postpone; put off. **4,** to endure; bear; stand: переноси́ть жару́, to endure the heat. Я не переношу́ его́, I can't stand him. **5,** to come through (an illness, operation, etc.). **6,** *in* переноси́ть сло́во, to carry over part of a word to the next line. —**переноси́ться,** *refl.* **1,** *colloq.* to dash from one place to another; (*with* **че́рез**) dash across. **2,** (*of thoughts, attention, etc.*) to shift. **3,** to shift one's thoughts; turn one's thoughts.

перено́сица *n.* bridge of the nose.

перено́сный *adj.* **1,** portable. **2,** figurative: в перено́сном смы́сле, in the figurative sense.

перено́счик *n.* **1,** carrier. **2,** carrier (*of a disease*). **3,** *obs.* spreader of gossip.

переночева́ть *v. pfv.* [*infl.* **-чу́ю, -чу́ешь**] to spend the night.

перенумерова́ть *v.pfv.* [*infl.* **-ру́ю, -ру́ешь**] **1,** to renumber. **2,** to number (all or many of something).

переня́ть [*infl.* **переймý, переймёшь;** *past* **пе́ренял, -няла́, пе́реняло**] *v., pfv. of* **перенима́ть.**

переобору́дование *n.* re-equipping.

переобору́довать *v. impfv. & pfv.* [*pres.* **-дую, -дуешь**] to re-equip.

переобременя́ть *v. impfv.* [*pfv.* **переобремени́ть**] to overburden.

переобува́ть *v. impfv.* [*pfv.* **переобу́ть**] to change someone's shoes: переобу́ть ребёнка, to change a child's shoes. Переобу́ть боти́нки, to change (one's) shoes. —**переобува́ться**, *refl.* **1,** to change (one's) shoes. **2,** (with **в** + *acc.*) to change into (different shoes). **3,** to put one's shoes back on.

переобу́ть [*infl.* **-бу́ю, -бу́ешь**] *v., pfv. of* **переобува́ть.** —**переобу́ться**, *refl., pfv. of* **переобува́ться.**

переодева́ть *v. impfv.* [*pfv.* **переоде́ть**] **1,** to change (someone's) clothes. **2,** *colloq.* to change (an article of clothing). **3,** (*with instr. or* **в** + *acc.*) to dress (as); disguise (as). —**переодева́ться**, *refl.* **1,** to change clothes. **2,** (*with* **в** + *acc.*) to change (into). **3,** (*with instr. or* **в** + *acc.*) to dress up (as); disguise oneself (as).

переоде́ть [*infl.* **-де́ну, -де́нешь**] *v., pfv. of* **переодева́ть.** —**переоде́ться**, *refl., pfv. of* **переодева́ться.**

переоце́нивать *v. impfv.* [*pfv.* **переоцени́ть**] **1,** to reappraise; reassess. **2,** to overestimate; overrate.

переоцени́ть [*infl.* **-ценю́, -це́нишь**] *v., pfv. of* **переоце́нивать.**

переоце́нка *n.* **1,** reappraisal; reassessment. **2,** overestimation.

перепада́ть *v. impfv.* [*pfv.* **перепа́сть**] **1,** (*of rain, snow, etc.*) to fall intermittently. **2,** (*with dat.*) *colloq.* to come one's way.

перепа́ивать *v. impfv.* [*pfv.* **перепои́ть**] **1,** to give (an animal) too much to drink. **2,** *colloq.* to make (a person) drunk.

перепа́лка [*gen. pl.* **-лок**] *n., colloq.* **1,** exchange of gunfire. **2,** squabble; wrangle.

перепа́сть [*infl. like* **пасть**] *v., pfv. of* **перепада́ть.**

перепа́чкать *v. impfv.* to get (something) all dirty. —**перепа́чкаться**, *refl.* to get all dirty.

перепе́в *n.* **1,** hum. **2,** *fig.* repetition; rehash.

пе́репел [*pl.* **перепела́**] *n.* quail.

перепелена́ть *v. pfv.* to change (a baby).

перепёлка [*gen. pl.* **-лок**] *n.* female quail.

перепеля́тник *n.* sparrow hawk.

перепе́рчивать *v. impfv.* [*pfv.* **перепе́рчить**] to put too much pepper in.

перепеча́тать *v., pfv. of* **перепеча́тывать.**

перепеча́тка [*gen. pl.* **-ток**] *n.* **1,** (act of) reprinting. **2,** reprint.

перепеча́тывать *v. impfv.* [*pfv.* **перепеча́тать**] **1,** to reprint. **2,** to retype.

перепива́ть *v. impfv.* [*pfv.* **перепи́ть**] *colloq.* **1,** to have too much to drink. **2,** to outdrink. —**перепива́ться**, *refl., colloq.* to get completely drunk.

перепи́ливать *v. impfv.* [*pfv.* **перепили́ть**] to saw in two.

перепили́ть *v. pfv.* [*infl.* **-пилю́, -пи́лишь**] **1,** *pfv. of* **перепи́ливать. 2,** to saw (all of something).

переписа́ть [*infl.* **-пишу́, -пи́шешь**] *v., pfv. of* **перепи́сывать.**

перепи́ска *n.* **1,** copying. **2,** correspondence. Быть в перепи́ске с, to correspond with.

перепи́счик *n.* copier; copyist.

перепи́сывать *v. impfv.* [*pfv.* **переписа́ть**] **1,** to rewrite. **2,** to copy over. **3,** to make a list of. —**перепи́сываться**, *refl.* [*impfv. only*] to correspond (*by mail*).

пе́репись *n.f.* census.

перепи́ть [*infl. like* **пить**] *v., pfv. of* **перепива́ть.** —**перепи́ться**, *refl., pfv. of* **перепива́ться.**

переплавля́ть *v. impfv.* [*pfv.* **перепла́вить**] **1,** (*with* **в** *or* **на** + *acc.*) to melt down (into something else). **2,** to float; transport by floating downstream.

перепла́та *n., colloq.* overpayment.

переплати́ть [*infl.* **-плачу́, -пла́тишь**] *v., pfv. of* **перепла́чивать.**

перепла́чивать *v. impfv.* [*pfv.* **переплати́ть**] to overpay.

переплести́ [*infl. like* **плести́**] *v., pfv. of* **переплета́ть.** —**переплести́сь**, *refl., pfv. of* **переплета́ться.**

переплёт *n.* **1,** cover; binding (*of a book*). **2,** sash: око́нный переплёт, window sash. **3,** *colloq.* fix; mess; jam: попа́сть в переплёт, to get into a mess.

переплета́ть *v. impfv.* [*pfv.* **переплести́**] **1,** to bind (a book). **2,** to interlace; interweave; intertwine. **3,** to lock together; interlock (one's fingers, arms, etc.). **4,** to braid again. —**переплета́ться**, *refl.* **1,** to become intertwined. **2,** *fig.* to be intertwined; be interwoven.

переплете́ние *n.* **1,** interlacing; interweaving. **2,** *textiles* weave; texture.

переплётная *n., decl. as an adj.* bindery.

переплётный *adj.* bookbinding (*attrib.*). —**переплётное де́ло**, bookbinding.

переплётчик *n.* bookbinder.

переплыва́ть *v. impfv.* [*pfv.* **переплы́ть**] **1,** to swim across. **2,** to sail across.

переплы́ть [*infl. like* **плыть**] *v., pfv. of* **переплыва́ть.**

переподгота́вливать *v. impfv.* [*pfv.* **переподгото́вить**] to provide with additional training; give (someone) a refresher course.

переподгото́вка *n.* additional training; refresher course.

перепои́ть *v. pfv.* [*infl.* **-пою́, -по́ишь** *or* **-пои́шь**] **1,** *pfv. of* **перепа́ивать. 2,** to give (everyone or many people) something to drink.

переполза́ть *v. impfv.* [*pfv.* **переползти́**] to crawl across; creep across.

переползти́ [*infl. like* **ползти́**] *v., pfv. of* **переполза́ть.**

переполне́ние *n.* **1,** overfilling. **2,** overcrowding.

перепо́лненный *adj.* crowded; jammed; packed.

переполня́ть *v. impfv.* [*pfv.* **перепо́лнить**] **1,** to overfill. **2,** to overcrowd. **3,** *fig.* to overwhelm (with emotion). —**переполня́ться**, *refl.* to be filled to overflowing; be crowded/packed/jammed.

переполо́х *n.* **1,** alarm; panic. **2,** turmoil; commotion.

переполоши́ть *v. pfv., colloq.* to throw into a panic. —**переполоши́ться**, *refl., colloq.* to be thrown into a panic.

перепо́нка [*gen. pl.* **-нок**] *n.* **1,** membrane. **2,** *zool.* web. —**бараба́нная перепо́нка**, eardrum.

перепо́нчатый *adj., zool.* webbed: перепо́нчатые ла́пы, webbed feet.

перепоруча́ть *v. impfv.* [*pfv.* **перепоручи́ть**] to turn over; hand over; entrust.

перепоручи́ть [*infl.* **-ручу́, -ру́чишь**] *v., pfv. of* **перепоруча́ть.**

перепра́ва *n.* **1,** crossing (*of a river*). **2,** place to cross (a river).

переправля́ть *v. impfv.* [*pfv.* **перепра́вить**] **1,** to carry across; ferry across. **2,** to forward. **3,** *colloq.* to correct. —**переправля́ться**, *refl.* to cross; make one's way across.

перепрева́ть *v. impfv.* [*pfv.* **перепре́ть**] **1,** to rot. **2,** (*of food*) to be overcooked.

перепре́лый *adj.* rotten.

перепре́ть *v., pfv. of* **перепрева́ть.**

перепро́бовать *v. pfv.* [*infl.* **-бую, -буешь**] to try; taste (all or many of something).

перепродава́ть *v. impfv.* [*pfv.* **перепрода́ть**; *pres.* **-даю́, -даёшь**] to resell.

перепрода́жа *n.* resale.

перепрода́ть [*infl. like* **прода́ть**] *v., pfv. of* **перепродава́ть.**

перепроизво́дство *n.* overproduction.

перепры́гивать *v. impfv.* [*pfv.* **перепры́гнуть**] **1,** to jump over; jump across. **2,** to jump from place to place; jump from one thing to another.

перепу́г *n., colloq.* fright.

перепуга́ть *v. pfv.* to frighten; scare. —**перепуга́ться,** *refl.* to be frightened; be terrified.

перепу́тать *v., pfv. of* **пу́тать** *and* **перепу́тывать.** —**перепу́таться,** *refl., pfv. of* **пу́таться** *and* **перепу́тываться.**

перепу́тывать *v. impfv.* [*pfv.* **перепу́тать**] **1,** to tangle. **2,** to mix up; disarrange. **3,** to confuse; get (two or more things) mixed up. —**перепу́тываться,** *refl.* **1,** to become (en)tangled. **2,** to get mixed up. **3,** to get confused.

перепу́тье *n.* crossroads. —**на перепу́тье,** at the crossroads.

перераба́тывать *v. impfv.* [*pfv.* **перерабо́тать**] **1,** to process; refine. **2,** (*with* **в** *or* **на** + *acc.*) to make (into); convert (into). **3,** to rework; revise. **4,** to work overtime. **5,** *colloq.* to overwork; tire oneself out.

перерабо́тка *n.* **1,** processing; refining. **2,** reworking; revision. **3,** *colloq.* overtime work.

перераспределе́ние *n.* redistribution.

перераспределя́ть *v. impfv.* [*pfv.* **перераспредели́ть**] to redistribute.

перераста́ние *n.* **1,** outgrowing. **2,** (*with* **в** + *acc.*) development (into); *mil.* escalation (into).

перераста́ть *v. impfv.* [*pfv.* **перерасти́**] **1,** to outgrow. **2,** (*with* **в** + *acc.*) to develop (into); evolve (into).

перерасти́ [*infl. like* **расти́**] *v., pfv. of* **перераста́ть.**

перерасхо́д *n.* overexpenditure.

перерасхо́довать *v. impfv. & pfv.* [*pres.* **-дую, -дуешь**] to use too much (of).

перерва́ть [*infl. like* **рвать**] *v., pfv. of* **перерыва́ть** (*in sense #1*).

пере́резать *v. pfv.* [*infl.* **-ре́жу, -ре́жешь**] **1,** *pfv. of* **перереза́ть. 2,** *colloq.* to kill (all or many of something).

перереза́ть *v. impfv.* [*pfv.* **пере́резать**] **1,** to cut (*usu. in two*). **2,** to cut off (a road, army, etc.).

перереша́ть *v. impfv.* [*pfv.* **перереши́ть**] *colloq.* **1,** to change one's mind. **2,** to solve in a different manner.

перерисова́ть [*infl.* **-су́ю, -су́ешь**] *v., pfv. of* **перерисо́вывать.**

перерисо́вывать *v. impfv.* [*pfv.* **перерисова́ть**] to draw again; make a copy of.

перерожда́ть *v. impfv.* [*pfv.* **перероди́ть**] to regenerate; make a new man of. —**перерожда́ться,** *refl.* **1,** *colloq.* to be reborn. **2,** to be (completely) regenerated; become a new person. **3,** to degenerate.

перерожде́ние *n.* **1,** regeneration. **2,** degeneration.

переро́сток [*gen.* **-стка**] *n.* youngster who is slow to develop (*and therefore older than his classmates*).

перерուба́ть *v. impfv.* [*pfv.* **перерубить**] to cut in two; chop in two.

переруби́ть *v. pfv.* [*infl.* **-рублю́, -ру́бишь**] **1,** *pfv. of* **перерубать. 2,** to cut down (all or many of something).

переруга́ть *v. pfv., colloq.* to swear at (everyone). —**переруга́ться,** *refl., colloq.* to swear at each other; cuss each other out.

перeру́гиваться *v.r. impfv., colloq.* to swear at each other; swear back and forth.

переры́в *n.* recess; break. —**с переры́вами,** intermittently; off and on.

перерыва́ть *v. impfv.* **1,** [*pfv.* **перерва́ть**] to break; snap. **2,** [*pfv.* **переры́ть**] to dig up; *fig.* rummage through.

переры́ть [*infl.* **-ро́ю, -ро́ешь**] *v., pfv. of* **перерыва́ть** (*in sense #2*).

переряди́ть [*infl.* **-ряжу́, -ря́дишь**] *v., pfv. of* **переряжа́ть.** —**переряди́ться,** *refl., pfv. of* **переряжа́ться.**

переряжа́ть *v. impfv.* [*pfv.* **переряди́ть**] (*with instr. or* **в** + *acc.*) *colloq.* to dress up (as); disguise (as). —**переряжа́ться,** *refl., colloq.* **1,** to disguise oneself. **2,** (*with instr. or* **в** + *acc.*) to dress up (as); disguise oneself (as).

пересади́ть [*infl.* **-сажу́, -са́дишь**] *v., pfv. of* **переса́живать.**

переса́дка [*gen. pl.* **-док**] *n.* **1,** change (*of trains, planes, etc.*). **2,** transplant; transplantation.

переса́живать *v. impfv.* [*pfv.* **пересади́ть**] **1,** to seat somewhere else; move; transfer. **2,** to transplant; graft. —**переса́живаться,** *refl.* [*pfv.* **пересе́сть**] **1,** to change one's seat. **2,** to change trains; change planes.

переса́ливать *v. impfv.* [*pfv.* **пересоли́ть**] **1,** to put too much salt in. **2,** *fig., colloq.* to go too far; overdo it.

пересдава́ть *v. impfv.* [*pfv.* **пересда́ть**; *pres.* **-сдаю́, -сдаёшь**] **1,** to rent again; sublet. **2,** *cards* to deal again. **3,** *colloq.* to retake (an examination).

пересда́ть [*infl. like* **дать**] *v., pfv. of* **пересдава́ть.**

пересека́ть *v. impfv.* [*pfv.* **пересе́чь**] **1,** to cross; traverse. **2,** to cross; intersect. **3,** *in* пересека́ть путь *or* доро́гу (+ *dat.*), to bar the way (to). —**пересека́ться,** *refl.* to cross (each other); intersect (each other).

переселе́нец [*gen.* **-нца**] *n.* **1,** migrant. **2,** settler.

переселе́ние *n.* **1,** migration; transmigration. **2,** moving; resettlement. —**переселе́ние душ,** *relig.* transmigration.

переселя́ть *v. impfv.* [*pfv.* **пересели́ть**] to move; resettle. —**переселя́ться,** *refl.* **1,** to migrate. **2,** to move; relocate.

пересе́сть [*infl. like* **сесть**] *v., pfv. of* **переса́живаться.**

пересече́ние *n.* **1,** crossing. **2,** intersection.

пересечённый *adj.* (*of terrain*) rough; broken; rugged.

пересе́чь [*infl. like* **сечь**; *past* **-се́к, -секла́, -секло́**] *v., pfv. of* **пересека́ть.** —**пересе́чься,** *refl., pfv. of* **пересека́ться.**

переси́живать *v. impfv.* [*pfv.* **пересиде́ть**] *colloq.* **1,** to sit longer than; stay longer than. **2,** to sit too long; stay too long. **3,** to sit out; wait out.

пересиливать *v. impfv.* [*pfv.* **переси́лить**] **1,** to overpower. **2,** *fig.* to overcome; master.

переска́з *n.* **1,** retelling. **2,** exposition.

пересказа́ть *v. pfv.* [*infl.* **-скажу́, -ска́жешь**] **1,** *pfv. of* **переска́зывать. 2,** to tell (all or many of something).

переска́зывать *v. impfv.* [*pfv.* **пересказа́ть**] to retell.

переска́кивать *v. impfv.* [*pfv.* **перескочи́ть**] **1,** to jump over; jump across. **2,** to jump from place to place;

jump from one thing to another. **3,** *fig., colloq.* to skip over (*when reading or telling something*).

перескочи́ть [*infl.* **-скочу́, -ско́чишь**] *v., pfv. of* **переска́кивать.**

пересла́ть [*infl.* **-шлю́, -шлёшь**] *v., pfv. of* **пересыла́ть.**

пересма́тривать *v. impfv.* [*pfv.* **пересмотре́ть**] **1,** to look over; go over again. **2,** to re-examine; reconsider; review. **3,** to revise.

пересме́иваться *v.r. impfv., colloq.* to look at each other and giggle.

пересме́шник *n.* **1,** mockingbird. **2,** *colloq.* one who likes to tease.

пересмо́тр *n.* **1,** reconsideration; review. **2,** revision.

пересмотре́ть [*infl.* **-смотрю́, -смо́тришь**] *v., pfv. of* **пересма́тривать.**

переснима́ть *v. impfv.* [*pfv.* **пересня́ть**] **1,** to make a copy of (a photograph). **2,** to reshoot (a film, scene, etc.).

пересня́ть [*infl. like* **снять**] *v., pfv. of* **переснима́ть.**

пересоздава́ть *v. impfv.* [*pfv.* **пересозда́ть;** *pres.* **-даю́, -даёшь**] to re-create.

пересозда́ть [*infl. like* **дать**] *v., pfv. of* **пересоздава́ть.**

пересо́л *n.* excess of salt.

пересоли́ть [*infl.* **-солю́, -со́лишь** *or* **-соли́шь**] *v., pfv. of* **переса́ливать.**

пересо́хнуть [*past* **-со́х, -ла**] *v., pfv. of* **пересыха́ть.**

переспа́ть *v. pfv.* [*infl. like* **спать**] *colloq.* **1,** to oversleep. **2,** to spend the night (somewhere).

переспева́ть *v. impfv.* [*pfv.* **переспе́ть**] to become overripe.

переспе́лый *adj.* overripe.

переспе́ть *v., pfv. of* **переспева́ть.**

переспо́рить *v. pfv.* to win an argument from; get the best of in an argument.

переспра́шивать *v. impfv.* [*pfv.* **переспроси́ть**] to ask again.

переспроси́ть *v. pfv.* [*infl.* **-спрошу́, -спро́сишь**] **1,** *pfv. of* **переспра́шивать. 2,** *colloq.* to ask (many people or everyone).

перессо́рить *v. pfv., colloq.* to cause a quarrel between. —**перессо́риться,** *refl.* (*of many people*) to quarrel.

переставáть *v. impfv.* [*pfv.* **переста́ть;** *pres.* **-стаю́, -стаёшь**] to stop; cease.

переставля́ть *v. impfv.* [*pfv.* **переста́вить**] **1,** to move (from one place to another). **2,** to rearrange; transpose. —**переставля́ть но́ги,** to plod along. —**е́ле переставля́ть но́ги,** to be scarcely able to walk.

переста́ивать *v. impfv.* [*pfv.* **перестоя́ть**] **1,** to be left standing too long (and turn sour). **2,** *colloq.* to wait out; wait till something passes.

перестано́вка [*gen. pl.* **-вок**] *n.* **1,** rearrangement; transposition. **2,** *math.* permutation.

перестара́ться *v.r. pfv., colloq.* to try too hard; overdo it.

переста́ть [*infl.* **-ста́ну, -ста́нешь**] *v., pfv. of* **перестава́ть.**

перестила́ть *v. impfv.* [*pfv.* **перестла́ть**] **1,** to remake (a bed). **2,** to re-lay (a floor).

перестира́ть *v. pfv.* **1,** *pfv. of* **перести́рывать. 2,** to wash; launder (all of something).

перести́рывать *v. impfv.* [*pfv.* **перестира́ть**] to wash again; launder again.

перестла́ть [*infl.* **-стелю́, -сте́лешь**] *v., pfv. of* **перестила́ть.**

перестоя́ть [*infl.* **-стою́, -стои́шь**] *v., pfv. of* **переста́ивать.**

перестрада́ть *v. pfv.* **1,** to suffer a great deal. **2,** to suffer through; go through.

перестра́ивать *v. impfv.* [*pfv.* **перестро́ить**] **1,** to rebuild; reconstruct. **2,** to reorganize. **3,** *mil.* to re-form. **4,** to tune. —**перестра́иваться,** *refl.* **1,** to change one's methods of work. **2,** *mil.* to re-form.

перестрахова́ть [*infl.* **-ху́ю, -ху́ешь**] *v., pfv. of* **перестрахо́вывать.** —**перестрахова́ться,** *refl., pfv. of* **перестрахо́вываться.**

перестрахо́вка *n.* **1,** reinsurance. **2,** *colloq.* excessive caution. —**для перестрахо́вки,** to be on the safe side.

перестрахо́вщик *n., colloq.* person who never takes any chances.

перестрахо́вывать *v. impfv.* [*pfv.* **перестрахова́ть**] to reinsure. —**перестрахо́вываться,** *refl.* **1,** to reinsure oneself. **2,** *fig., colloq.* to play safe; make extra sure.

перестре́ливаться *v.r. impfv.* to exchange shots; exchange gunfire.

перестре́лка [*gen. pl.* **-лок**] *n.* exchange of gunfire.

перестреля́ть *v. pfv.* **1,** to shoot (all or many of something). **2,** *colloq.* to use up (*in shooting*).

перестро́ить *v., pfv. of* **перестра́ивать.** —**перестро́иться,** *refl., pfv. of* **перестра́иваться.**

перестро́йка *n.* **1,** rebuilding; reconstruction. **2,** reorganization. **3,** retuning.

пересту́киваться *v.r. impfv.* (*of prisoners*) to communicate with each other by tapping.

переступа́ть *v. impfv.* [*pfv.* **переступи́ть**] **1,** to step across; step over. **2,** [*impfv. only*] to walk; step; move. **3,** *fig.* to overstep; transgress. —**переступа́ть с ноги́ на́ ногу,** to shift from foot to foot.

переступи́ть [*infl.* **-ступлю́, -сту́пишь**] *v., pfv. of* **переступа́ть.**

пересу́ды [*gen.* **-дов**] *n. pl., colloq.* gossip.

пересу́шивать *v. impfv.* [*pfv.* **пересуши́ть**] **1,** to dry again. **2,** to dry too much.

пересуши́ть *v. pfv.* [*infl.* **-сушу́, -су́шишь**] **1,** *pfv. of* **пересу́шивать. 2,** to dry (all of something).

пересчёт *n.* recount; recounting.

пересчи́тывать *v. impfv.* [*pfv.* **пересчита́ть**] **1,** to count. **2,** to recount.

пересыла́ть *v. impfv.* [*pfv.* **пересла́ть**] to send; remit; forward by mail.

пересы́лка *n.* **1,** sending; forwarding. **2,** remittance (*of money*). **3,** postage: плати́ть за пересы́лку, to pay the postage.

пересы́пать [*infl.* **-сыплю, -сыплешь**] *v., pfv. of* **пересыпа́ть.**

пересыпа́ть *v. impfv.* [*pfv.* **пересы́пать**] **1,** to pour (into another container). **2,** (*with instr.*) to sprinkle (with). **3,** *colloq.* to pour too much.

пересыха́ть *v. impfv.* [*pfv.* **пересо́хнуть**] **1,** to dry up; become dry. **2,** *impers.* to become parched: у меня́ в го́рле пересо́хло, my throat is parched.

перета́пливать *v. impfv.* [*pfv.* **перетопи́ть**] **1,** to light (a stove) again. **2,** to melt; melt down.

перетаска́ть *v. pfv., colloq.* **1,** to carry; haul (from one place to another). **2,** to carry off; steal.

перета́скивать *v. impfv.* [*pfv.* **перетащи́ть**] **1,** to drag over; drag across. **2,** to drag (from one place to another); move (something heavy).

перетасова́ть [*infl.* **-су́ю, -су́ешь**] *v., pfv. of* **перетасо́вывать.**

перетасо́вка *n.* shuffling; reshuffle.

перетасо́вывать *v. impfv.* [*pfv.* **перетасова́ть**] **1,** to shuffle (cards). **2,** *fig., colloq.* to shuffle; reshuffle; move around.

перетащи́ть [*infl.* **-тащу́, -та́щишь**] *v., pfv. of* **перета́скивать.**

перетере́ть *v. pfv.* [*infl. like* **тере́ть**] **1,** *pfv. of* **перетира́ть. 2,** to wipe (all of something). —**перетере́ться,** *refl., pfv. of* **перетира́ться.**

перетерпе́ть *v. pfv.* [*infl.* **-терплю́, -те́рпишь**] *colloq.* to endure; suffer.

перетира́ть *v. impfv.* [*pfv.* **перетере́ть**] **1,** to break; wear through (a rope). **2,** to grind; grate. —**перетира́ться,** *refl.* (*of a rope*) to wear through.

перето́лки [*gen.* **-ков**] *n.pl., colloq.* gossip.

перетолкова́ть *v. pfv.* [*infl.* **-ку́ю, -ку́ешь**] **1,** *pfv. of* **перетолко́вывать. 2,** *colloq.* to talk (with many people); talk over (many things).

перетолко́вывать *v. impfv.* [*pfv.* **перетолкова́ть**] to misinterpret; misconstrue.

перетопи́ть [*infl.* **-топлю́, -то́пишь**] *v., pfv. of* **перета́пливать.**

перетряса́ть *v. impfv.* [*pfv.* **перетрясти́**] **1,** to shake out. **2,** to rummage through.

перетрясти́ [*infl. like* **трясти́**] *v., pfv. of* **перетряса́ть.**

перетря́хивать *v. impfv.* [*pfv.* **перетряхну́ть**] to shake out.

пере́ть *v. impfv.* [*pres.* **пру, прёшь;** *past* **пёр, -ла**] *colloq.* **1,** to go; make one's way. **2,** to force one's way. **3,** to haul. **4,** to come out; stream out.

перетя́гивать *v. impfv.* [*pfv.* **перетяну́ть**] **1,** to pull (from one place to another). **2,** *v.i., colloq.* to make it (to a certain place). **3,** *fig., colloq.* to win over (to one's side). **4,** (*with instr.*) to tie tightly (with). **5,** to retighten. **6,** *v.i.* to weigh more. —**перетя́гиваться,** *refl.* (*with instr.*) to tie (something) tightly around one's waist.

перетяну́ть [*infl.* **-тяну́, -тя́нешь**] *v., pfv. of* **перетя́гивать.** —**перетяну́ться,** *refl., pfv. of* **перетя́гиваться.**

переубежда́ть *v. impfv.* [*pfv.* **переубеди́ть**] to change (someone's mind); make (someone) change his mind. —**переубежда́ться,** *refl.* to change one's mind.

переу́лок [*gen.* **-лка**] *n.* side street.

переустра́ивать *v. impfv.* [*pfv.* **переустро́ить**] **1,** to reconstruct. **2,** to reorganize.

переустро́йство *n.* **1,** reconstruction. **2,** reorganization.

переутоми́ть [*infl.* **-млю́, -ми́шь**] *v., pfv. of* **переутомля́ть.** —**переутоми́ться,** *refl., pfv. of* **переутомля́ться.**

переутомле́ние *n.* exhaustion; fatigue; overwork.

переутомля́ть *v. impfv.* [*pfv.* **переутоми́ть**] to tire out; wear out. —**переутомля́ться,** *refl.* to tire oneself out; wear oneself out.

переуче́сть [*infl. like* **уче́сть**] *v., pfv. of* **переучи́тывать.**

переучёт *n.* stock-taking; inventory.

переу́чивать *v. impfv.* [*pfv.* **переучи́ть**] **1,** to teach again; retrain. **2,** to study again; study a second time. —**переу́чиваться,** *refl.* **1,** to be retrained; undergo retraining. **2,** (*with dat.*) to relearn.

переучи́тывать *v. impfv.* [*pfv.* **переуче́сть**] to take stock of; take inventory of.

переучи́ть [*infl.* **-учу́, -у́чишь**] *v., pfv. of* **переу́чивать.** —**переучи́ться,** *refl., pfv. of* **переу́чиваться.**

перефрази́ровать *v. impfv. & pfv.* [*pres.* **-рую, -руешь**] to reword; rephrase; paraphrase.

перефразиро́вка *n.* paraphrase.

перехва́ливать *v. impfv.* [*pfv.* **перехвали́ть**] to praise excessively; give undue praise to.

перехвали́ть [*infl.* **-хвалю́, -хва́лишь**] *v., pfv. of* **перехва́ливать.**

перехва́т *n., colloq.* interception. —**перехва́т телефо́нных сообще́ний,** wiretapping.

перехвати́ть [*infl.* **-хвачу́, -хва́тишь**] *v., pfv. of* **перехва́тывать.**

перехва́тчик *n.* one who intercepts something. —**истреби́тель-перехва́тчик,** *aero.* interceptor.

перехва́тывать *v. impfv.* [*pfv.* **перехвати́ть**] **1,** to intercept. **2,** to grab. **3,** to tie around: перехвати́ть но́гу жгуто́м, to tie a tourniquet around one's leg. **4,** *fig.* to traverse. **5,** to stop; cut off (one's breathing, voice, etc.). **6,** *colloq.* to borrow for a short time. **7,** *v.i., colloq.* to have a quick bite to eat. **8,** *v.i., colloq.* to go too far; overdo it.

перехитри́ть *v. pfv.* to outwit; outsmart; outfox.

перехо́д *n.* **1,** (act of) crossing. **2,** crossing (*place to cross*). **3,** passage; passageway. **4,** *mil.* day's march. **5,** shift; switch. **6,** transition. **7,** conversion (*to another religion*).

переходи́ть *v. impfv.* [*pfv.* **перейти́;** *pres.* **-хожу́, -хо́дишь**] **1,** to cross. **2,** to go; walk; pass (from one place to another). **3,** to shift; switch. **4,** to pass (into the hands of). **5,** (*with* **в** + *acc.*) to turn into. **6,** (*with* **в** + *acc.*) to adopt; be converted to (another religion).

перехо́дный *adj.* **1,** connecting. **2,** transitional. **3,** (*of a grade*) passing. **4,** (*of a verb*) transitive.

переходя́щий *adj.* **1,** transitory. **2,** *finance* carried over to the following year. —**переходя́щие дожди́,** intermittent showers. —**переходя́щий ку́бок,** challenge cup.

пе́рец [*gen.* **-рца**] *n.* pepper.

перецара́пать *v. pfv.* to scratch severely. —**перецара́паться,** *refl.* **1,** to scratch each other. **2,** *colloq.* to scratch oneself.

пе́речень [*gen.* **-чня**] *n.m.* list; enumeration; inventory.

перечёркивать *v. impfv.* [*pfv.* **перечеркну́ть**] to cross out.

перечерти́ть [*infl.* **-черчу́, -че́ртишь**] *v., pfv. of* **перече́рчивать.**

перече́рчивать *v. impfv.* [*pfv.* **перечерти́ть**] **1,** to draw again. **2,** to copy.

перече́сть *v. pfv.* [*infl.* **-чту́, -чтёшь;** *past* **-чёл, -чла́**] *colloq.* = **перечита́ть** *and* **пересчита́ть.**

перечини́ть *v. pfv.* [*infl.* **-чиню́, -чи́нишь**] **1,** to repair; mend (all or many of something). **2,** to repair again; mend again.

перечисле́ние *n.* **1,** enumeration. **2,** transfer.

перечисля́ть *v. impfv.* [*pfv.* **перечи́слить**] **1,** to enumerate. **2,** to transfer.

перечита́ть *v. pfv.* **1,** *pfv. of* **перечи́тывать. 2,** to read (all or many of something).

перечи́тывать *v. impfv.* [*pfv.* **перечита́ть** *or* **перече́сть**] to reread.
пере́чить *v. impfv.* (*with dat.*) *colloq.* to contradict.
пе́речница *n.* pepper shaker.
пе́речный *adj.* pepper (*attrib.*).
перечу́вствовать *v. pfv.* [*infl.* **-ствую, -ствуешь**] to experience; live through; go through (a great deal).
переша́гивать *v. impfv.* [*pfv.* **перешагну́ть**] **1,** to step over. **2,** *fig.* to overcome. **3,** (*with* **за** + *acc.*) to be past (a certain age).
перешее́к [*gen.* **-ше́йка**] *n.* isthmus; neck of land.
перешёптываться *v.r. impfv.* to whisper to each other.
перешиба́ть *v. impfv.* [*pfv.* **перешиби́ть**] *colloq.* to break; fracture.
перешиби́ть [*infl.* **-бу́, -бёшь;** *past* **-ши́б, -ла**] *v., pfv. of* **перешиба́ть.**
перешива́ть *v. impfv.* [*pfv.* **переши́ть**] to alter (*by sewing*).
переши́ть [*infl.* **-шью́, -шьёшь**] *v., pfv. of* **перешива́ть.**
перещеголя́ть *v. pfv., colloq.* to outdo; surpass.
переэкзаменова́ть *v. pfv.* [*infl.* **-ну́ю, -ну́ешь**] to give (someone) a second examination. —**переэкзаменова́ться,** *refl.* to take an examination for a second time.
переэкзамено́вка *n.* repeat examination (*for one who has failed the first time*).
периге́й *n.* perigee.
периге́лий *n.* perihelion.
пери́ла [*gen.* **-ри́л**] *n.pl.* banister; railing.
пери́метр *n.* perimeter.
пери́на *n.* feather bed.
пери́од *n.* **1,** period (*of time*). **2,** (historical) period.
перио́дика *n.* periodicals.
периоди́ческий *adj.* **1,** [*also,* **периоди́чный**] periodic. **2,** (*of a publication*) periodical. **3,** (*of a decimal*) repeating. —**периоди́чески,** *adv.* periodically.
перипети́я *n., usu. pl.* vicissitudes; ups and downs.
перisко́п *n.* periscope.
периста́льтика *n.* peristalsis. —**перистальти́ческий,** *adj.* peristaltic.
перисти́ль *n.m.* peristyle.
пе́ристый *adj.* **1,** feathered. **2,** *bot.* pinnate. **3,** (*of clouds*) fleecy.
перитони́т *n.* peritonitis.
перифери́я *n.* **1,** periphery. **2,** outlying districts; the provinces. —**перифери́йный,** *adj.* provincial. —**перифери́ческий,** *adj.* peripheral.
перифра́за *n.* periphrasis.
пёрка [*gen. pl.* **-рок**] *n.* drill bit.
перка́ль *n.m. or f.* percale. —**перка́левый,** *adj.* percale.
перл *n., obs.* pearl.
перламу́тр *n.* mother-of-pearl. —**перламу́тровый,** *adj.* mother-of-pearl (*attrib.*).
пе́рлинь *also,* **перли́нь** *n.m.* hawser.
пе́рловый *adj., obs.* made of pearls; pearl (*attrib.*).
перло́вый *adj.* **1,** *in* **перло́вая крупа́,** pearl barley. **2,** made of pearl barley.
перлюстра́ция *n.* secret opening of mail.
перманéнт *n.* permanent wave.
перманéнтный *adj.* permanent.
перна́тый *adj.* feathered. —**перна́тые,** *n.pl.* birds.
перо́ [*pl.* **пе́рья, пе́рьев**] *n.* **1,** feather. **2,** pen. —**взя́ться за перо́,** to take pen in hand. —**вы́йти из-под пера́** (+ *gen.*), to emerge from the pen of.
перочи́нный *adj., in* **перочи́нный нож (но́жик),** penknife.
перпендикуля́р *n.* perpendicular. —**перпендикуля́рный,** *adj.* perpendicular.
перро́н *n.* platform (*in a railroad station*).
перс *n.m.* [*fem.* **персия́нка**] Persian. —**перси́дский,** *adj.* Persian.
пе́рсик *n.* **1,** peach. **2,** peach tree. —**пе́рсиковый,** *adj.* peach (*attrib.*).
персо́на *n.* person. —**со́бственной персо́ной,** in person.
персона́ж *n.* character; personage.
персона́л *n.* personnel. —**персона́льный,** *adj.* personal.
перспекти́ва *n.* **1,** perspective. **2,** vista; view. **3,** prospect: в перспекти́ве, in prospect. **4,** *pl.* prospects; outlook.
перспекти́вный *adj.* **1,** perspective. **2,** long-term; long-range. **3,** having good prospects; promising.
перст [*gen.* **перста́**] *n., obs.* finger. —**оди́н как перст,** all alone in the world.
пе́рстень [*gen.* **-стня**] *n.m.* ring set with a stone.
пертурба́ция *n., astron. & fig.* perturbation.
перуа́нский *adj.* Peruvian.
перфе́кт (пэ, фэ) *n., gram.* perfect; the perfect tense.
перфока́рта *n.* punch card.
перфора́тор *n.* **1,** perforator; punch. **2,** drill. —**перфора́ция,** *n.* perforation.
перфори́ровать *v. impfv. & pfv.* [*pres.* **-рую, -руешь**] to perforate.
перхо́та *n., colloq.* tickling sensation in one's throat.
пе́рхоть *n.f.* dandruff.
перцо́вка *n.* pepper brandy.
перцо́вый *adj.* pepper (*attrib.*).
перча́тка [*gen. pl.* **-ток**] *n.* glove. —**бро́сить перча́тку,** to throw down the gauntlet.
пе́рчить *v. impfv.* to put pepper in *or* on.
перши́ть *v impfv., impers., colloq.* to have a tickling sensation in one's throat: у меня́ перши́т в го́рле, I have a tickling sensation in my throat; my throat tickles.
пёрышко [*gen. pl.* **-шек**] *n.* small feather.
пёс [*gen.* **пса**] *n.* dog.
пе́сенка [*gen. pl.* **-нок**] *n., dim. of* **пе́сня.** —**его́ пе́сенка спе́та,** he is done for; he has had it.
пе́сенник *n.* **1,** member of a chorus. **2,** songwriter. **3,** songbook.
песе́та *n.* peseta (*monetary unit of Spain*).
песе́ц [*gen.* **-сца́**] *n.* polar fox.
пеਸка́рь [*gen.* **-каря́**] *n.m.* gudgeon (*fish*).
песнопе́ние *n.* **1,** religious song; hymn; chant. **2,** *obs.* poem; poetry.
песнь *n.f.* **1,** *obs.* song. **2,** canto. —**Песнь Пе́сней,** Song of Songs.
пе́сня [*gen. pl.* **-сен**] *n.* song. —**до́лгая пе́сня,** a long story. —**ста́рая пе́сня,** the same old story. —**тяну́ть всё ту же пе́сню,** to harp on the same string.
пе́со *n. indecl.* peso (*monetary unit of a number of Latin American countries*).
песо́к [*gen.* **-ска́**] *n.* sand. —**золото́й песо́к,** gold dust. —**са́харный песо́к,** granulated sugar.
песо́чник *n.* sandpiper.
песо́чница *n.* sandbox.

песо́чный *adj.* **1,** sand (*attrib.*). **2,** *colloq.* sand-colored; sandy. **3,** (*of pastry*) short: песо́чный торт, shortcake. —**песо́чные часы́,** hourglass.

пессими́зм *n.* pessimism. —**пессими́ст,** *n.* pessimist. —**пессимисти́ческий,** *adj.* pessimistic.

пест [*gen.* **песта́**] *n.* pestle.

пе́стик *n.* **1,** *dim. of* **пест. 2,** *bot.* pistil.

пе́стовать *v. impfv.* [*pfv.* **вы́пестовать;** *pres.* **-тую, -туешь**] **1,** *obs.* to nurse. **2,** *fig.* to nurture.

пестре́ть[1] *v. impfv.* [*pres.* **-ре́ет**] **1,** (*of something brightly colored or multicolored*) to appear; strike the eye. **2,** (*with instr.*) to be bright (with); be gay (with).

пестре́ть[2] *v. impfv.* [*pres.* **-ри́т**] **1,** to be everywhere; be all over. **2,** to turn up continually.

пестри́ть *v. impfv.* **1,** to make colorful. **2,** (*with instr.*) to sprinkle (with); intersperse (with). **3,** (*with instr.*) to abound (in); be filled (with); be replete (with). **4,** *impers.* to be dazzled: у меня́ пестри́ло в глаза́х, I was dazzled.

пестрота́ *n.* **1,** diversity of colors. **2,** *fig.* diversity; diverse nature.

пёстрый *adj.* **1,** multicolored; motley. **2,** *fig.* mixed; diverse; motley; heterogeneous.

песча́ник *n.* sandstone.

песча́нка [*gen. pl.* **-нок**] *n.* **1,** gerbil. **2,** sanderling.

песча́ный *adj.* **1,** sand (*attrib.*): песча́ная о́тмель, sandbank. **2,** sandy.

песчи́нка [*gen. pl.* **-нок**] *n.* grain of sand.

петá́рда *n.* **1,** petard. **2,** firecracker.

пе́телька [*gen. pl.* **-лек**] *n.* **1,** *dim. of* **пе́тля. 2,** eyelet.

пети́ция *n.* petition.

петли́ца *n.* **1,** buttonhole (*in a lapel*). **2,** colored patch or stripe (*on a uniform*).

пе́тля [*gen.pl.* **-тель**] *n.* **1,** loop. **2,** noose. **3,** buttonhole. **4,** stitch: спусти́ть пе́тлю, to drop a stitch. **5,** hinge (*of a door*). **6,** *aero.* [*often* **мёртвая пе́тля**] loop: де́лать (мёртвую) пе́тлю, to loop the loop. —**лезть в пе́тлю,** to risk one's neck.

петля́ть *v. impfv., colloq.* **1,** to weave; zigzag. **2,** *fig.* to equivocate; prevaricate.

петру́шка *n.f.* parsley. —*n.m.* **1,** puppet show. **2,** chief character in this show.

пету́ния *also,* **пету́нья** *n.* petunia.

пету́х [*gen.* **-туха́**] *n.* rooster; cock. —**встава́ть с петуха́ми,** to get up at the crack of dawn. —**пусти́ть кра́сного петуха́,** to start a fire.

пету́ший [*fem.* **-шья**] *adj.* rooster's; cock's. —**пету́ший гребешо́к,** cockscomb (*plant*).

петуши́ный *adj.* rooster (*attrib.*); cock (*attrib.*). —**петуши́ный бой,** cockfight; cockfighting. —**петуши́ный гре́бень,** cockscomb.

петуши́ться *v.r. impfv., colloq.* to get on one's high horse.

петушо́к [*gen.* **-шка́**] *n.* cockerel.

петь *v. impfv.* [*pfv.* **спеть** *or* **пропе́ть;** *pres.* **пою́, поёшь**] to sing.

пехо́та *n.* infantry. —**морска́я пехо́та,** the marines.

пехоти́нец [*gen.* **-нца**] *n.* infantryman; foot soldier. —**морско́й пехоти́нец,** marine.

пехо́тный *adj.* infantry (*attrib.*).

печа́лить *v. impfv.* [*pfv.* **опеча́лить**] to sadden. —**печа́литься,** *refl.* to be sad; be saddened; grieve.

печа́ль *n.f.* sorrow; sadness.

печа́льный *adj.* [*short form* **-лен, -льна**] sad. —**печа́льно,** *adv.* sadly.

печа́тание *n.* printing.

печа́тать *v. impfv.* [*pfv.* **напеча́тать**] **1,** to print. **2,** *in* печа́тать на маши́нке, to type. **3,** to publish. **4,** to have (something) published. —**печа́таться,** *refl.* to have something published.

печа́тка [*gen. pl.* **-ток**] *n.* signet.

печа́тник *n.* printer.

печа́тный *adj.* **1,** printing (*attrib.*): печа́тный стано́к, printing press. **2,** printed. **3,** published. —**печа́тные бу́квы,** block letters. —**печа́тный лист,** signature (*of 16 pages*). —**печа́тное сло́во,** the printed word.

печа́ть *n.f.* **1,** seal; stamp. **2,** printing: кни́га сейча́с в печа́ти, the book is being printed right now. **3,** type; print. **4,** the press: освеща́ться в печа́ти, to be covered in the press. —**выходи́ть из печа́ти,** to come off the press; come out.

пече́ние *n.* baking.

печёнка *n.* liver (*meat*).

печёночник *n.* liverwort.

печёночница *n.* hepatica.

печёночный *adj.* liver (*attrib.*); hepatic.

печёный *adj.* baked.

пе́чень *n.f., anat.* liver.

пече́нье *n.* pastry; cookies.

пе́чка [*gen. pl.* **-чек**] *n.* stove.

печно́й *adj.* stove (*attrib.*).

печу́рка [*gen. pl.* **-рок**] *n.* small portable stove.

печь[1] *v. impfv.* [*pfv.* **испе́чь;** *pres.* **пеку́, печёшь, ...пеку́т;** *past* **пёк, пекла́, пекло́**] **1,** to bake. **2,** [*impfv. only*] (*of the sun*) to beat down on; (*intrans.*) to be burning hot. —**пе́чься,** *refl.* **1,** to bake; be baked. **2,** [*impfv. only*] (*with* **о**) to care (about).

печь[2] [*2nd loc.* **печи́;** *pl.* **пе́чи, пече́й, печа́м**] *n.f.* **1,** stove; oven. **2,** furnace: до́менная печь, blast furnace. —**обжига́тельная печь,** kiln.

пешехо́д *n.* pedestrian. —**пешехо́дный,** *adj.* pedestrian (*attrib.*).

пе́ший *adj.* traveling on foot.

пе́шка [*gen. pl.* **-шек**] *n., chess & fig.* pawn.

пешко́м *adv.* on foot.

пеще́ра *n.* cave; cavern.

пеще́рный *adj.* cave (*attrib.*): пеще́рный челове́к, cave man.

пиани́но *n. indecl.* upright piano.

пиани́ссимо *adv. & n. indecl.* pianissimo.

пиани́ст *n.m.* [*fem.* **-ни́стка**] pianist.

пиа́но *adv., music* piano; soft.

пиано́ла *n.* player piano.

пиа́стр *n.* piaster (*monetary unit of several Middle Eastern countries*).

пивна́я *n., decl. as an adj.* tavern; saloon; pub.

пивно́й *adj.* beer (*attrib.*).

пи́во *n.* beer.

пивова́р *n.* brewer. —**пивоваре́ние,** *n.* brewing. —**пивова́ренный,** *adj.* brewing (*attrib.*): пивова́ренный заво́д, brewery.

пи́галица *n.* lapwing; pewit.

пигме́й *n.* pygmy.

пигме́нт *n.* pigment. —**пигмента́ция,** *n.* pigmentation.

пиджа́к [*gen.* **-жака́**] *n.* (man's) suit jacket; coat.

пижа́ма *n.* pajamas.

пижо́н *n., colloq.* fop; dandy.

пик *n.* **1,** mountain peak. **2,** peak (*of work, traffic, etc.*). —**часы́ пик,** rush hours.

пи́ка *n.* lance; pike. —**в пи́ку** (+ *dat.*), in order to spite someone.
пика́нтный *adj.* **1,** piquant; pungent. **2,** *fig.* spicy. —**пика́нтность,** *n.f.* piquancy.
пика́п *n.* pickup truck.
пике́ *n. neut. indecl.* **1,** piqué. **2,** *aero.* dive. —**пике́йный,** *adj.* piqué.
пике́т *n.* **1,** picket line. **2,** *mil.* picket. **3,** bench mark. **4,** piquet (*card game*).
пикети́ровать *v. impfv.* [*pres.* **-рую, -руешь**] to picket.
пике́тчик *n.* picket (*one who pickets*).
пи́ки [*gen.* **пик**] *n. pl., cards* spades.
пики́рование *n., aero.* dive; diving.
пики́ровать *v. impfv. & pfv.* [*pres.* **-рую, -руешь**] *aero.* to dive; go into a dive.
пики́роваться *v.r. impfv.* [*pres.* **-руюсь, -руешься**] to squabble; bicker; trade insults.
пикиро́вка *n.* squabbling; bickering.
пикиро́вщик *n.* dive bomber.
пики́рующий *adj., in* **пики́рующий бомбардиро́вщик,** dive bomber.
пи́кколо *n. indecl.* piccolo.
пикни́к [*gen.* **-ника́**] *n.* picnic.
пи́кнуть *v. pfv., colloq., usu. used negatively,* to object: он и пи́кнул не успе́л, before he had a chance to say "no".
пи́ковый *adj.* **1,** *cards* of spades: пи́ковая да́ма, queen of spades. **2,** *colloq.* awkward; sticky: пи́ковое положе́ние, awkward situation. —**остава́ться при пи́ковом интере́се,** to be left holding the bag.
пиктогра́мма *n.* pictograph. —**пиктогра́фия,** *n.* pictography. —**пиктографи́ческий,** *adj.* pictographic.
пи́кули [*gen.* **-лей**] *n.pl.* pickles.
пи́кша *n.* haddock.
пила́ [*pl.* **пи́лы**] *n.* saw.
пила́в *n.* pilaf.
пила́-ры́ба *n.* sawfish.
пилёный *adj.* sawed. —**пилёный са́хар,** lump sugar.
пилигри́м *n., obs.* pilgrim.
пили́кать *v. impfv., colloq.* to scrape (on a musical instrument).
пили́ть *v. impfv.* [*pres.* **пилю́, пи́лишь**] **1,** to saw. **2,** *fig.* to nag.
пи́лка [*gen. pl.* **-лок**] *n.* **1,** sawing. **2,** small handsaw. **3,** nail file.
пи́ллерс *n., naut.* stanchion.
пило́н *n.* pylon.
пило́т *n.* pilot. —**пилота́ж,** *n.* piloting; flying.
пилоти́ровать *v. impfv.* [*pres.* **-рую, -руешь**] to pilot.
пило́тка [*gen. pl.* **-ток**] *n., mil.* overseas cap.
пи́льщик *n.* sawyer; woodcutter.
пилю́ля *n.* pill.
пиля́стра *n.* pilaster.
пина́ть *v. impfv.* [*pfv.* **пнуть**] *colloq.* to kick.
пингви́н *n.* penguin.
пинг-по́нг *n.* ping-pong.
пи́ния *n.* stone pine.
пино́к [*gen.* **-нка́**] *n., colloq.* kick.
пи́нта *n.* pint.
пинце́т *n.* tweezers.
пио́н *n.* peony.
пионе́р *n.* pioneer. —**пионе́рский,** *adj.* pioneer (*attrib.*).
пиоре́я *n.* pyorrhea.
пипе́тка [*gen. pl.* **-ток**] *n.* eye dropper; medicine dropper.
пир [*2nd loc.* **пиру́**; *pl.* **пиры́**] *n.* feast; banquet. —**пир горо́й; пир на весь мир,** lavish banquet; sumptuous feast.
пирами́да *n.* pyramid. —**пирамида́льный,** *adj.* pyramidal.
пира́т *n.* pirate. —**пира́тский,** *adj.* pirate (*attrib.*); piratical. —**пира́тство,** *n.* piracy.
пири́т *n.* pyrite.
пирова́ть *v. impfv.* [*pres.* **-ру́ю, -ру́ешь**] to feast; have a feast.
пиро́г [*gen.* **-рога́**] *n.* pie.
пиро́жное *n., decl. as an adj.* pastry.
пирожо́к [*gen.* **-жка́**] *n.* small pie; patty.
пирома́ния *n.* pyromania.
пироте́хника *n.* pyrotechnics.
пи́рров *adj., in* **пи́ррова побе́да,** Pyrrhic victory.
пирс *n.* pier.
пиру́шка [*gen. pl.* **-шек**] *n., colloq.* lively party.
пируэ́т *n.* pirouette.
пи́ршество *n., obs.* sumptuous feast.
писа́ка *n.m. & f., colloq.* poor writer; hack writer; scribbler.
писа́ние *n.* writing. —**свяще́нное писа́ние,** Holy Scripture; Holy Writ.
пи́саный *adj.* handwritten. —**пи́саная краса́вица,** picture of beauty.
пи́сарь [*pl.* **писаря́**] *n.m., usu. mil.* clerk.
писа́тель *n.m.* [*fem.* **-ница**] writer. —**писа́тельский,** *adj.* writer; writer's. —**писа́тельство,** *n., colloq.* writing; being a writer.
писа́ть *v. impfv.* [*pfv.* **написа́ть**; *pres.* **пишу́, пи́шешь**] **1,** to write. **2,** to paint. **3,** *in* писа́ть на маши́нке, to type. —**писа́ться,** *refl.* [*impfv. only*] **1,** to be spelled: как пи́шется э́то сло́во?, how is this word spelled? **2,** *impers.* (*with dat.*) to feel like writing: мне сего́дня не пи́шется, I don't feel like writing today; I can't get myself to do any writing today.
писе́ц [*gen.* **-сца́**] *n.* scribe.
писк *n.* peep; cheep.
пискли́вый *adj.* squeaky.
пи́скнуть *v., pfv. of* **пища́ть.**
писсуа́р *n.* urinal.
пистоле́т *n.* pistol; gun. —**пистоле́т-пулемёт,** submachine gun.
пистоле́тный *adj.* pistol (*attrib.*).
писто́н *n.* **1,** percussion cap. **2,** *music* piston.
пису́лька [*gen. pl.* **-лек**] *n., colloq.* short letter; note.
писчебума́жный *adj.* stationery (*attrib.*).
пи́счий *adj.* writing (*attrib.*): пи́счая бума́га, writing paper.
письмена́ [*gen.* **-мён**] *n. pl.* characters; letters.
пи́сьменно *adv.* in writing.
пи́сьменность *n.f.* **1,** written language; system of writing. **2,** literature; literary texts (*of an ancient people*).
пи́сьменный *adj.* **1,** writing (*attrib.*): пи́сьменный стол, desk. **2,** written: пи́сьменная про́сьба, written request.
письмо́ [*pl.* **пи́сьма, пи́сем**] *n.* **1,** letter: писа́ть письмо́, to write a letter. **2,** writing: чте́ние и письмо́, reading and writing. **3,** script: ара́бское письмо́, the Arabic script.
письмоно́сец [*gen.* **-сца**] *n.* mailman.

пита́ние *n.* **1,** feeding. **2,** food; diet; nourishment; nutrition. **3,** power supply.

пита́тельный *adj.* **1,** nourishing; nutritious. **2,** feeding (*attrib.*). —**пита́тельная среда́,** culture medium.

пита́ть *v. impfv.* **1,** to feed; nourish. **2,** to supply (with energy). **3,** *fig.* to harbor (a feeling); have a feeling of. —**пита́ться,** *refl.* **1,** to eat; take one's meals. **2,** (*with instr.*) to feed (on).

пито́мец [*gen.* **-мца**] *n.m.* [*fem.* **-мица**] **1,** charge; ward. **2,** pupil. **3,** graduate; alumnus.

пито́мник *n.* **1,** nursery (*for plants*). **2,** farm (*for breeding and raising animals*).

пито́н *n.* python.

пить *v. impfv.* [*pfv.* **вы́пить;** *pres.* **пью, пьёшь;** *past fem.* **пила́**] to drink. Я хочу́ пить, I am thirsty. —**как пить дать,** *colloq.* for sure.

питьё *n.* **1,** drinking: го́дный для питья́, fit to drink. **2,** drink; beverage.

питьево́й *adj.* drinking (*attrib.*): питьева́я вода́, drinking water. —**питьева́я со́да,** baking soda; bicarbonate of soda.

пифаго́ров *adj., in* **пифаго́рова теоре́ма,** Pythagorean theorem.

пиха́ть *v. impfv.* [*pfv.* **пихну́ть**] *colloq.* **1,** to push; shove. **2,** (*with* **в** + *acc.*) to stuff (into); cram (into).

пи́хта *n.* fir. —**пи́хтовый,** *adj.* fir (*attrib.*).

пиццика́то *adv. & n. indecl.* pizzicato.

пи́чкать *v. impfv.* [*pfv.* **напи́чкать**] (*with instr.*) *colloq.* to stuff (with food, drink, medicine, etc.).

пичу́га *n., colloq.* small bird. *Also,* **пичу́жка.**

пиччика́то *adv. & n. indecl.* pizzicato.

пи́шущий *adj., in* **пи́шущая маши́нка,** typewriter.

пи́ща *n.* food. —**пи́ща для ума́/размышле́ния,** food for thought.

пища́ль *n.f.* arquebus; harquebus.

пища́ть *v. impfv.* [*pfv.* **пи́скнуть;** *pres.* **пищу́, пищи́шь**] to peep; cheep.

пищеваре́ние *n.* digestion. —**расстро́йство пищеваре́ния,** indigestion.

пищевари́тельный *adj.* digestive. —**пищевари́тельный кана́л,** alimentary canal.

пищево́д *n.* gullet; esophagus.

пищево́й *adj.* food (*attrib.*).

пищу́ха *n.* **1,** pika (*animal*). **2,** creeper (*bird*).

пия́вка [*gen. pl.* **-вок**] *n.* leech.

плав *n., in* **на плаву́,** afloat.

пла́вание *n.* **1,** swimming. **2,** voyage.

пла́вательный *adj.* swimming (*attrib.*).

пла́вать *v. impfv.* **1,** *indeterm. of* **плыть. 2,** to float (*not sink*). **3,** *colloq.* to flounder; be at sea.

пла́вающий *adj.* **1,** swimming. **2,** floating. **3,** (*of a vehicle*) amphibious.

пла́вень [*gen.* **-вня**] *n.m., metall.* flux.

плавико́вый *adj., in* **плавико́вая кислота́,** hydrofluoric acid; **плавико́вый шпат,** fluorspar; fluorite.

плави́льный *adj.* melting (*attrib.*); smelting (*attrib.*). —**плави́льный котёл,** melting pot.

плави́льня [*gen. pl.* **-лен**] *n.* smelting plant. —**плави́льщик,** *n.* smelter.

пла́вить *v. impfv.* [*pres.* **-влю, -вишь**] to melt; smelt. —**пла́виться,** *refl.* to melt.

пла́вка *n.* melting; smelting.

пла́вки [*gen.* **-вок**] *n. pl.* swimming trunks.

пла́вкий *adj.* capable of being melted.

плавле́ние *n.* melting. —**то́чка плавле́ния,** melting point.

плавни́к [*gen.* **-ника́**] *n.* **1,** fin (*of a fish*). **2,** driftwood.

пла́вный *adj.* **1,** (*of movements*) smooth; graceful. **2,** (*of sounds or speech*) smooth; fluent. —**пла́вность,** *n.f.* smoothness.

плаву́нчик *n.* phalarope.

плаву́честь *n.f.* buoyancy.

плаву́чий *adj.* **1,** floating. **2,** buoyant. —**плаву́чая ба́за,** *naut.* tender. —**плаву́чая льди́на,** ice field.

плагиа́т *n.* plagiarism. —**плагиа́тор,** *n.* plagiarist.

пла́зма *n.* plasma.

плака́т *n.* poster; placard.

пла́кать *v. impfv.* [*pres.* **пла́чу, пла́чешь**] to cry; weep. —**пла́каться,** *refl.* (*with* **на** + *acc.*) *colloq.* to cry (about); bemoan.

пла́кса *n.m. & f., colloq.* crybaby.

плакси́вый *adj., colloq.* whining.

плаку́чий *adj.* **1,** *obs.* whining. **2,** (*of trees*) weeping: плаку́чая и́ва, weeping willow.

пламене́ть *v. impfv.* to blaze; flame.

пла́менный *adj.* **1,** flaming; fiery. **2,** *fig.* fiery; ardent.

пла́мя [*gen., dat., & prepl.* **пла́мени;** *instr.* **пла́менем**] *n. neut.* flame; blaze.

план *n.* **1,** plan. **2,** diagram: план кварти́ры, floor plan of an apartment; план го́рода, city map. **3,** *fig.* aspect; context. —**за́дний план,** background. —**кру́пный план,** close-up. —**пере́дний план,** foreground. —**учё́бный план,** curriculum.

планёр *n., aero.* glider. —**планери́зм,** *n.* gliding. —**планери́ст,** *n.* glider pilot. —**планёрный,** *adj.* gliding (*attrib.*).

плане́та *n.* planet.

планета́рий *n.* planetarium.

плане́тный *adj.* planetary.

планиме́трия *n.* plane geometry.

плани́рование *n.* **1,** planning. **2,** *aero.* gliding; glide.

плани́ровать *v. impfv.* [*pfv.* **сплани́ровать;** *pres.* **-рую, -руешь**] **1,** [*pfv. also* **заплани́ровать**] to plan. **2,** *aero.* to glide; glide down.

планирова́ть *v. impfv.* [*pfv.* **распланирова́ть;** *pres.* **-ру́ю, -ру́ешь**] to lay out.

планиро́вка *n.* **1,** planning. **2,** laying out. **3,** layout; design.

планиро́вщик *n.* planner; one who lays out a city, town, etc.

пла́нка [*gen. pl.* **-нок**] *n.* **1,** plank; strip. **2,** bar; crossbar (*used in high jumping*).

планкто́н *n.* plankton.

планови́к [*gen.* **-вика́**] *n.* (economic) planner.

пла́новый *adj.* **1,** planned: пла́новое хозя́йство, planned economy. **2,** planning (*attrib.*): пла́новый отде́л, planning department.

планоме́рный *adj.* planned; systematic.

планта́тор *n.* plantation owner; planter. —**планта́ция,** *n.* plantation.

планшё́т *n.* map case.

планши́р *n.* gunwale.

пласт [*gen.* **-ста́**] *n.* **1,** layer. **2,** *geol.* stratum. —**лежа́ть пласто́м,** (*of a sick person*) to be flat on one's back.

пла́стик *n.* plastic.

пла́стика *n.* **1,** plastic arts. **2,** grace of movement.

пла́стиковый *adj.* plastic. —**пла́стиковая бо́мба,** plastic bomb.

пласти́нка [*gen. pl.* **-нок**] *n.* **1,** metal plate. **2,** phonograph record. **3,** photographic plate. **4,** blade (*of a leaf*). —**кровяны́е пласти́нки,** platelets.

пласти́ческий *adj.* **1,** plastic. **2,** (*of movements of the body*) rhythmical; graceful.

пласти́чный *adj.* **1,** plastic. **2,** supple; pliant; plastic. **3,** rhythmical; graceful.

пластма́сса *n.* plastic. —**пластма́ссовый,** *adj.* plastic.

пла́стырь *n.m.* plaster (*applied to a sore or wound*).

пла́та *n.* **1,** pay; payment. **2,** fee; charge: входна́я пла́та, admission charge. —**за́работная пла́та,** pay; wages; salary. —**кварти́рная пла́та,** rent.

плата́н *n.* plane tree.

платёж [*gen.* **-тежа́**] *n.* payment. —**нало́женным платежо́м,** C.O.D.

платёжеспосо́бный *adj.* solvent. —**платёжеспосо́бность,** *n.f.* solvency.

платёжный *adj.* pay (*attrib.*); payment (*attrib.*). —**платёжный бала́нс,** balance of payments. —**платёжная ве́домость,** payroll.

плате́льщик *n.* payer.

пла́тина *n.* platinum. —**пла́тиновый,** *adj.* platinum.

плати́ть *v. impfv.* [*pfv.* **заплати́ть;** *pres.* **плачу́, пла́тишь**] to pay: плати́ть кому́-нибудь за (+ *acc.*), to pay someone for (something). —**плати́ться,** *refl.* [*pfv.* **поплати́ться**] to pay; pay the penalty: поплати́ться жи́знью за (+ *acc.*), to pay for (something) with one's life.

пла́тный *adj.* **1,** requiring payment. **2,** paying. **3,** paid.

плато́ *n. indecl.* plateau.

плато́к [*gen.* **-тка́**] *n.* kerchief. —**носово́й плато́к,** handkerchief. —**ше́йный плато́к,** neckerchief.

платони́ческий *adj.* platonic.

платфо́рма *n.* **1,** platform. **2,** flatcar. **3,** (political) platform.

пла́тье *n.* **1,** [*gen. pl.* **-тьев**] dress; gown. **2,** clothes; clothing.

платяно́й *adj.* clothes (*attrib.*). —**платяно́й шкаф,** wardrobe.

плафо́н *n.* **1,** decorated ceiling. **2,** shade (*for a lamp suspended from a ceiling*).

пла́ха *n.* **1,** block; log. **2,** execution block.

плац [*2nd loc.* **плацу́**] *n.* parade ground.

плацда́рм *n.* **1,** bridgehead; beachhead. **2,** springboard; jumping-off place; staging area.

плаце́нта *n.* placenta.

плацка́рта *n.* reserved seat coupon (*for a train*). —**плацка́ртный,** *adj.* reserved.

плач *n.* weeping; crying.

плаче́вный *adj.* **1,** mournful; sad. **2,** lamentable; deplorable; sorry.

плашмя́ *adv.* flat: лежа́ть плашмя́, to lie flat.

плащ [*gen.* **плаща́**] *n.* **1,** cloak. **2,** raincoat.

плебе́й *n.* plebeian. —**плебе́йский,** *adj.* plebeian.

плебисци́т *n.* plebiscite.

плебс *n.* the common people; hoi polloi.

плева́ *n.* membrane. —**де́вственная плева́,** hymen.

плева́тельница *n.* spittoon; cuspidor.

плева́ть *v. impfv.* [*pfv.* **плю́нуть;** *pres.* **плюю́, плюёшь**] **1,** to spit. **2,** (*with* **на** + *acc.*) *colloq.* to ignore; shrug off; brush off. **3,** (*with inf.*) *colloq.* not to give a damn: ему́ плева́ть на э́то, he doesn't give a damn about it. —**плева́ться,** *refl.* [*impfv. only*] *colloq.* = **плева́ть.**

пле́вел *n.* **1,** darnel. **2,** *fig.* weed.

плево́к [*gen.* **-вка́**] *n.* spit; spittle; sputum.

пле́вра *n.* pleura. —**плевра́льный,** *adj.* pleural.

плеври́т *n.* pleurisy.

плёвый *adj., colloq.* **1,** miserable; rotten. **2,** trifling; insignificant.

плед *n.* laprobe; steamer rug.

плексигла́с *n.* plexiglass.

плектр *n.* plectrum.

племенно́й *adj.* **1,** tribal. **2,** pedigreed. **3,** breeding (*attrib.*); stud (*attrib.*).

пле́мя [*gen., dat., & prepl.* **пле́мени;** *instr.* **пле́менем;** *pl.* **племена́, -мён, -мена́м**] *n. neut.* tribe.

племя́нник *n.* nephew.

племя́нница *n.* niece.

плен [*2nd loc.* **плену́**] *n.* captivity. —**брать/взять в плен,** to take (someone) prisoner. —**попа́сть в плен,** to be taken prisoner.

плена́рный *adj.* plenary.

плене́ние *n., obs.* **1,** taking prisoner; capture. **2,** captivity.

плени́тельный *adj.* captivating; enchanting.

плени́ть *v. pfv.* **1,** *pfv. of* **пленя́ть. 2,** *obs.* to take prisoner. —**плени́ться,** *refl., pfv. of* **пленя́ться.**

плёнка [*gen. pl.* **-нок**] *n.* **1,** thin layer (*of ice, dust, fat, etc.*). **2,** *photog.* film. **3,** tape: записа́ть на плёнку, to tape; tape-record. **4,** pellicle.

пле́нник *n.* prisoner; captive.

пле́нный *adj.* captive. —*n.* prisoner; captive.

плёночный *adj.* film (*attrib.*). —**плёночный фотоаппара́т,** roll-film camera.

пле́нум *n.* plenum; plenary session.

пленя́ть *v. impfv.* [*pfv.* **плени́ть**] to captivate; enchant. —**пленя́ться,** *refl.* (*with instr.*) to be captivated (by); be fascinated (with).

плёс *n.* stretch; section (*of a river*).

пле́сень *n.f.* mold.

плеск *n.* **1,** splash; splashing. **2,** lapping (*of waves*).

плеска́ть *v. impfv.* [*pfv.* **плесну́ть;** *pres.* **плещу́, пле́щешь**] **1,** *v.i.* (*of water or other liquids*) to splash. **2,** *v.t.* to splash: плеска́ть во́ду (*or* водо́й) на́ пол, to splash water on the floor. **3,** *v.i.* (*of waves*) to lap (against something). —**плеска́ться,** *refl.* [*impfv. only*] **1,** to splash. **2,** to spill.

пле́сневеть *v. impfv.* [*pfv.* **запле́сневеть**] to grow moldy.

плесну́ть *v., pfv. of* **плеска́ть.**

плести́ *v. impfv.* [*pfv.* **сплести́;** *pres.* **плету́, плетёшь;** *past* **плёл, плела́, плело́**] **1,** to weave; braid; plait. **2,** *colloq.* to weave (intrigues); spin (a tale); utter (nonsense). —**плести́ть,** *refl.* [*impfv. only*] *colloq.* to plod along; trudge along.

плете́ние *n.* **1,** weaving. **2,** wickerwork.

плетёнка [*gen. pl.* **-нок**] *n., colloq.* **1,** wicker basket. **2,** wicker enclosure. **3,** twist (*of bread*).

плетёный *adj.* wicker (*attrib.*); wattled.

плете́нь [*gen.* **-тня́**] *n.m.* wattle fence. —**навести́ тень на плете́нь,** to confuse the issue.

плётка [*gen. pl.* **-ток**] *n.* lash.

плеть [*pl.* **пле́ти, -те́й, -тя́м**] *n.f.* lash.

плечево́й *adj.* shoulder (*attrib.*).

пле́чико [*pl.* **-ки, -ков**] *n.* **1,** *dim. of* **плечо́. 2,** shoulder strap. **3,** *pl.* clothes hanger; coat hanger.

плечи́стый *adj.* broad-shouldered.

плечо́ [*pl.* **пле́чи, плеч, плеча́м**] *n.* shoulder. —**вы-**

носи́ть на свои́х плеча́х, to carry on one's shoulders; bear the full burden of. —**за плеча́ми, 1,** behind one. **2,** close at hand. —**име́ть го́лову на плеча́х,** to have a good head on one's shoulders. —**не по плечу́** (+ *dat.*), *colloq.* too much for; beyond one. —**плечо́м к плечу́,** shoulder to shoulder —**с плеч доло́й,** off one's back; over and done with.

плеши́веть *v. impfv.* [*pfv.* **оплеши́веть**] to grow bald.

плеши́вый *adj.* bald. —**плеши́вость,** *n.f.* baldness.

плешь *n.f.* bald spot.

плея́да *n.* brilliant assemblage; galaxy. —**Плея́ды,** *n. pl., astron.* Pleiades.

пли́нтус *n.* plinth.

плиссе́ (сэ) *n. neut. indecl.* accordion pleats. —*adj., indecl.* with accordion pleats.

плиссирова́ть *v. impfv.* [*pres.* **-ру́ю, -ру́ешь**] to pleat; make pleats in.

плита́ [*pl.* **пли́ты**] *n.* **1,** slab. **2,** flagstone. **3,** (electric) stove; range. —**моги́льная плита́,** gravestone.

пли́тка [*gen. pl.* **-ток**] *n.* **1,** thin slab; tile. **2,** bar (*of chocolate*). **3,** small stove.

плитня́к [*gen.* **-няка́**] *n.* flagstone. —**плитняко́вый,** *adj.* flagstone.

пли́точный *adj.* tiled: пли́точный пол, tiled floor.

пловéц [*gen.* **-вца́**] *n.m.* [*fem.* **пловчи́ха**] swimmer.

плод [*gen.* **плода́**] *n.* **1,** fruit. **2,** fetus. **3,** *fig.* fruit: плоды́ на́ших трудо́в, the fruits of our labor. —**плод воображе́ния,** product (*or* figment) of the imagination.

плоди́ть *v. impfv.* [*pres.* **пложу́, плоди́шь**] **1,** to produce. **2,** *fig.* to generate; engender. —**плоди́ться,** *refl.* to propagate; multiply; breed.

пло́дный *adj.* **1,** of a fruit. **2,** producing fruit. **3,** fertilized. **4,** fetal.

плодови́тый *adj.* **1,** (*of animals*) prolific; fertile; fecund. **2,** (*of a writer, composer, etc.*) prolific. —**плодови́тость,** *n.f.* fertility.

плодово́дство *n.* fruit growing.

плодо́вый *adj.* **1,** fruit (*attrib.*). **2,** fruit-bearing.

плодоноси́ть *v. impfv.* [*pres.* **-но́сит**] to bear fruit.

плодоно́сный *adj.* fruit-bearing.

плодоро́дие *n.* fertility.

плодоро́дный *adj.* fertile.

плодотво́рный *adj.* fruitful; productive.

пло́мба *n.* **1,** seal (*for a door or package*). **2,** filling (*for a tooth*).

пломби́р *n.* ice cream topped with fruit.

пломбирова́ть *v. impfv.* [*pfv.* **запломбирова́ть;** *pres.* **-ру́ю, -ру́ешь**] **1,** to seal. **2,** to fill (a tooth).

пло́ский *adj.* [*short form* **-сок, -ска́, -ско;** *comp.* **пло́ще**] **1,** flat. **2,** *fig.* flat; vapid; banal. —**пло́ская стопа́,** flatfoot. —**пло́ский червь,** flatworm.

плоского́рье *n.* plateau; tableland.

плоскогру́дый *adj.* flat-chested.

плоского́бцы [*gen.* **-цев**] *n. pl.* pliers.

плоскодо́нка [*gen. pl.* **-нок**] *n., colloq.* flat-bottomed boat.

плоскодо́нный *adj.* flat-bottomed.

плоскосто́пие *n.* flatfoot; fallen arches.

пло́скость [*pl.* **пло́скости, -сте́й, -стя́м**] *n.f.* **1,** flatness. **2,** plane. **3,** *fig.* plane; level; sphere. **4,** *fig.* platitude; banality.

плот [*gen.* **плота́;** *2nd loc.* **плоту́**] *n.* raft.

плотва́ *n.* roach (*fish*).

плоти́на *n.* dam.

пло́тник *n.* carpenter.

пло́тничать *v. impfv.* to work as a carpenter.

пло́тничество *n.* carpentry.

пло́тничий [*fem.* **-чья**] *adj.* carpenter's (*attrib.*). *Also,* **пло́тничный.**

пло́тно *adv.* **1,** tightly. **2,** densely. **3,** *in* пое́сть пло́тно, to eat heartily.

пло́тность *n.f.* **1,** density. **2,** solidity.

пло́тный *adj.* [*short form* **-тен, -тна́, -тно**] **1,** dense; compact. **2,** (*of material*) closely woven. **3,** *colloq.* stocky; solidly built. **4,** *colloq.* (*of a meal*) hearty.

плотоя́дный *adj.* carnivorous. —**плотоя́дное живо́тное,** carnivore.

пло́тский *adj., obs.* carnal.

плоть *n.f.* flesh. —**во плоти́,** in the flesh. —**плоть и кровь моя́,** my own flesh and blood. —**плоть от пло́ти мое́й,** flesh of my flesh. —**кра́йняя плоть,** *anat.* foreskin.

пло́хо *adv.* badly; poorly. Пло́хо па́хнуть, to smell bad. —*adj., used predicatively* **1,** bad: э́то пло́хо, that's bad. **2,** (*with dat.*) ill; not well: ему́ пло́хо, he is not well. **3,** (*with dat.*) in a bad way: ей пло́хо, she is in a bad way.

плохо́й *adj.* [*short form* **плох, плоха́, пло́хо, пло́хи** *or* **плохи́;** *comp.* **ху́же**] bad; poor.

плоша́ть *v. impfv.* (*usu. used negatively*) *colloq.* to make a mistake.

площа́дка [*gen. pl.* **-док**] *n.* **1,** ground; site; area: площа́дка для игр, playground; строи́тельная площа́дка, building site. **2,** *sports* court: те́ннисная/баскетбо́льная площа́дка, tennis/basketball court. **3,** landing (*of a staircase*). **4,** platform (*of a railway car or streetcar*). —**пускова́я** *or* **ста́ртовая площа́дка,** launching pad.

площадно́й *adj.* coarse; crude; vulgar; of the gutter.

пло́щадь [*pl.* **пло́щади, -де́й, -дя́м**] *n.f.* **1,** area. **2,** space: жила́я пло́щадь, living space. **3,** square: Кра́сная пло́щадь, Red Square.

плуг [*pl.* **плуги́**] *n.* plow.

плу́нжер *n.* plunger.

плут [*gen.* **плута́**] *n.* cheat; swindler.

плута́ть *v. impfv., colloq.* to stray; wander.

плути́шка [*gen. pl.* **-шек**] *n.m.* imp; rascal.

плу́тни [*gen.* **-ней**] *n. pl., colloq.* tricks.

плутова́тый *adj.* crafty; cunning.

плутова́ть *v. impfv.* [*pfv.* **сплутова́ть;** *pres.* **-ту́ю, -ту́ешь**] *colloq.* to cheat.

плутовско́й *adj.* **1,** crooked; underhanded. **2,** (*of one's face, eyes, etc.*) roguish. **3,** *lit.* picaresque.

плутовство́ *n.* **1,** cheating. **2,** trickery.

плутокра́т *n.* plutocrat. —**плутократи́ческий,** *adj.* plutocratic. —**плутокра́тия,** *n.* plutocracy.

Плуто́н *n.* Pluto (*the planet*).

плуто́ний *n.* plutonium.

плыть *v. impfv.* [*pfv.* **поплы́ть;** *pres.* **плыву́, плывёшь;** *past fem.* **плыла́**] **1,** to swim. **2,** to sail. **3,** to float. —**плыть сто́я,** to tread water. *See also* **пла́вать.**

плюга́вый *adj., colloq.* **1,** ugly; miserable-looking. **2,** *fig.* trivial; piddling.

плюма́ж *n.* plume (*on a hat.*).

плю́нуть *v., pfv. of* **плева́ть.**

плюс *n.* **1,** plus sign. **2,** *fig., colloq.* plus; advantage. —*adv.* plus: два плюс три равно́ пяти́, two plus three equals five. Плюс пять гра́дусов, five degrees above freezing.

плюсна́ [*pl.* **плю́сны, -сен**] *n.* metatarsus. —**плюснево́й,** *adj.* metatarsal.

плю́хаться *v.r. impfv.* [*pfv.* **плю́хнуться**] (*with* **в** *or* **на** + *acc.*) *colloq.* to flop into/onto.

плюш *n.* plush (*fabric*). —**плю́шевый,** *adj.* plush.

плю́шка [*gen. pl.* **-шек**] *n.* sweet roll; bun.

плющ [*gen.* **плюща́**] *n.* ivy. —**плющево́й,** *adj.* ivy (*attrib.*).

пляж *n.* beach. —**пля́жный,** *adj.* beach (*attrib.*).

пляс *n., colloq.* dance.

пляса́ть *v. impfv.* [*pfv.* **спляса́ть;** *pres.* **пляшу́, пля́шешь**] to dance.

пля́ска [*gen. pl.* **-сок**] *n.* dance. —**пля́ска свято́го Ви́тта; ви́ттова пля́ска,** Saint Vitus' dance.

плясово́й *adj.* dance (*attrib.*); dancing. —**плясова́я,** *n.* dance tune.

плясу́н [*gen.* **-суна́**] *n.m.* [*fem.* **-су́нья**] *colloq.* dancer.

пневмати́ческий *adj.* pneumatic.

пнуть *v., pfv. of* **пина́ть.**

по *prep.* A, *with dat.* **1,** along: идти́ по у́лице, to walk along the street. **2,** about; around; through: ходи́ть по ко́мнате, to pace about the room; е́здить по стране́, to travel around/through a country. **3,** in *or* to various places: ходи́ть по магази́нам, to go shopping; размести́ть това́ры по по́лкам, to arrange the merchandise on the shelves. **4,** in the direction of: по ве́тру, with the wind; по тече́нию, downstream. **5,** by: по оши́бке, by mistake; по желе́зной доро́ге, by rail; по профе́ссии, by profession. **6,** through; due to; on account of: не по мое́й вине́, through no fault of mine; отсу́тствовать по боле́зни, to be absent on account of illness. **7,** according to: по пра́вилам, according to the rules; по мои́м часа́м, according to my watch. **8,** in the field of: кни́га по иску́сству, art book; чемпио́н по бо́ксу, boxing champion. **9,** to; for the purpose of: кампа́ния по привлече́нию тури́стов, campaign to attract tourists; опера́ция по удале́нию пу́ли, operation to remove a bullet. **10,** *with verbs of striking:* уда́рить кулако́м по́ столу, to bang one's fist on the table. **11,** *with expressions of time* each; every; on: по вечера́м, each evening; по среда́м, on Wednesdays. B, *with acc.* **1,** *with expressions of time* through: с ию́ля по сентя́брь, from July through September. По сей день, to this day. **2,** up to; down to (*on one's body*): ко́сы по по́яс, braids down to one's waist; грязь была́ по коле́но, the mud was knee-deep. **3,** on (*a side or direction*): по ту сто́рону, on the other side; по ле́вую ру́ку, on the left. **4,** *obs.* for; to fetch: идти́ по́ воду, to go for water. C, *with prepl.* on; upon; after: по сме́рти отца́, on the death of his father; по оконча́нии университе́та, upon graduation from the university. D, *with dat. or acc.* **1,** each; apiece: де́ти получи́ли по я́блоку, each child received an apple. Чле́ны получи́ли по два биле́та, each member received two tickets. Я купи́л четы́ре кни́ги по рублю́, I bought four books at one ruble each. **2,** by; in: по одному́, one by one; по́ двое, two by two; по́ два, in twos. —**по мне,** as far as I am concerned.

по- *prefix* **1,** *used to form the perfective aspect:* побледне́ть, *pfv. of* бледне́ть. **2,** *indicating the beginning of an action:* побежа́ть, to begin to run. **3,** *indicating action of short duration:* почита́ть, to read for a while. **4,** (*with* **-ива** *or* **-ыва** *verbs*) *indicating action performed intermittently:* пописывать, to write from time to time. **5,** (*with comp. adjectives*) a little: погро́мче, a little louder. **6,** *in various combinations:* по-мо́ему, in my opinion; по-ра́зному, in different ways; говори́ть по-ру́сски, to speak Russian.

побагрове́ть *v., pfv. of* **багрове́ть.**

поба́иваться *v.r. impfv.* (*with gen. or inf.*) *colloq.* to be somewhat afraid.

поба́ливать *v. impfv., colloq.* to ache a little; ache on and off; ache now and then.

побе́г *n.* **1,** escape. **2,** *bot.* sprout; shoot.

побе́гать *v. pfv.* to do a little running.

побегу́шки *n. pl., in* **быть на побегу́шках,** *colloq.* **1,** to run errands. **2,** (*with* **у**) to be at someone's beck and call.

побе́да *n.* victory.

победи́тель *n.m.* victor; winner.

победи́ть [*infl.* **-ди́шь, -ди́т;** *1st person sing. not used*] *v., pfv. of* **побежда́ть.**

побе́дный *adj.* **1,** victory (*attrib.*); of victory. **2,** victorious; triumphant.

победоно́сный *adj.* victorious; triumphant.

побежа́ть *v. pfv.* [*infl. like* **бежа́ть**] **1,** *pfv. of* **бежа́ть. 2,** to begin to run.

побежда́ть *v. impfv.* [*pfv.* **победи́ть**] **1,** to defeat; vanquish; conquer. **2,** *v.i.* to triumph; win. **3,** *fig.* to conquer; overcome.

побеле́ть *v., pfv. of* **беле́ть.**

побели́ть *v., pfv. of* **бели́ть** (*in sense #1*).

побе́лка *n.* whitewashing.

побере́жье *n.* coast; seacoast.

побере́чь *v. pfv.* [*infl. like* **бере́чь**] **1,** to save; preserve. **2,** to take care of. **3,** to watch; look after. —**побере́чься,** *refl.* to take care of oneself.

побесе́довать *v. pfv.* [*infl.* **-дую, -дуешь**] to have a chat.

побеспоко́ить *v. pfv.* to trouble; disturb. —**побеспоко́иться,** *refl.* **1,** to trouble oneself. **2,** to be concerned.

побира́ться *v.r. impfv., colloq.* to beg; live by begging.

поби́ть *v. pfv.* [*infl.* **-бью́, -бьёшь**] **1,** *pfv. of* **бить** (*in senses #2 & #3*). **2,** to beat up. **3,** to kill; slaughter; destroy. **4,** (*of rain, hail, etc.*) to beat down; flatten; (*of frost*) to nip. **5,** *sports* to break (a record). —**поби́ться,** *refl.* **1,** to break; be broken. **2,** (*of fruit*) to be bruised; be damaged.

поблагодари́ть *v., pfv. of* **благодари́ть.**

побла́жка *n., colloq.* indulgence. —**дава́ть побла́жку** (+ *dat.*), to be lenient with.

побледне́ть *v., pfv. of* **бледне́ть.**

поблёклый *adj.* faded.

поблёкнуть *v., pfv. of* **блёкнуть.**

побли́зости *adv.* nearby. —**побли́зости от,** near.

побожи́ться *v.r., pfv. of* **божи́ться.**

побо́и [*gen.* **-бо́ев**] *n. pl.* beating.

побо́ище *n.* **1,** *obs.* bloody battle. **2,** brawl. —**ледо́вое побо́ище,** Battle on the Ice (*famous battle fought on the ice of Lake Peipus in 1242*).

поболта́ть *v. pfv.* **1,** *colloq.* to have a chat. **2,** *colloq.* to shake; agitate. **3,** (*with instr.*) to dangle.

побо́льше *adj.* a little larger. —*adv.* a little more.

побо́рник *n.* champion; defender.

поборо́ть *v. pfv.* [*infl.* **-борю́, -бо́решь**] **1,** to defeat; conquer. **2,** *fig.* to overcome (a feeling). —**поборо́ть себя́,** to control oneself.

побо́ры [*gen.* **-ров**] *n. pl.* **1,** bribery. **2,** extortion.

побо́чный *adj.* **1,** occurring or done on the side; secondary; incidental: побо́чный проду́кт, by-product; побо́чные эффе́кты, side effects; побо́чная рабо́та, sideline. **2,** *obs.* illegitimate.

побоя́ться *v.r. pfv.* (*with gen. or inf.*) to be afraid.

побрани́ть *v. pfv.* to scold slightly; chide. —**побрани́ться,** *refl.* to have a quarrel.

побрата́таться *v.r., pfv. of* **брата́ться.**

побра́ть *v. pfv.* [*infl. like* **брать**] *colloq.* to take (all or many of something). —**чёрт побери́!**, what the hell!

побре́згать *v., pfv. of* **бре́згать.**

побрести́ *v. pfv.* [*infl. like* **брести́**] to trudge.

побри́ть *v., pfv. of* **брить.** —**побри́ться,** *refl., pfv. of* **бри́ться.**

поброди́ть *v. pfv.* [*infl.* **-брожу́, -бро́дишь**] *colloq.* to wander (*for a while*).

поброса́ть *v. pfv.* **1,** to throw; toss. **2,** to forsake; desert.

побряку́шка [*gen. pl.* **-шек**] *n., colloq.* **1,** trinket. **2,** (child's) rattle.

побуди́тельный *adj.* serving to cause or induce. —**побуди́тельная причи́на,** motive; incentive.

побуди́ть [*infl.* **-жу́, -ди́шь**] *v., pfv. of* **побужда́ть.**

побу́дка *n.* reveille.

побужда́ть *v. impfv.* [*pfv.* **побуди́ть**] to impel; induce; prompt; motivate.

побужде́ние *n.* **1,** urge: внеза́пное побужде́ние, a sudden urge. **2,** motive; reason: из коры́стных побужде́ний, for selfish motives/reasons. **3,** initiative: по со́бственному побужде́нию, on one's own initiative; on one's own.

побуре́ть *v., pfv. of* **буре́ть.**

побыва́ть *v. pfv.* **1,** (*with* **в** *or* **на** + *prepl.*) to visit; have been (to a place or to many places). **2,** (*with* **у**) to visit; go see (a person).

побы́вка *n., colloq.* **1,** short visit; stay. **2,** *mil.* furlough; leave.

побы́ть *v. pfv.* [*infl.* **-бу́ду, -бу́дешь;** *past* **по́был, побыла́, по́было**] to stay (somewhere).

пова́дить *v. pfv.* [*infl.* **-ва́жу, -ва́дишь**] *colloq.* to train. —**пова́диться,** *refl., colloq.* **1,** (*with inf.*) to get into the habit of. **2,** (*with a prep.*) to go to all the time; drop in on constantly.

пова́дка [*gen. pl.* **-док**] *n., colloq.* **1,** habit; mannerism. **2,** *pl.* manner; ways.

пова́дно *adv., colloq., in* **что́бы не́ было** (+ *dat.*) **пова́дно** (+ *inf.*), so as to be certain that one will not do it again.

повали́ть[1] [*infl.* **-валю́, -ва́лишь**] *v., pfv. of* **вали́ть**[1] (*in sense #1*). —**повали́ться,** *refl., pfv. of* **вали́ться.**

повали́ть[2] *v. pfv.* [*infl.* **-ва́лит**] *colloq.* **1,** to flock; throng. **2,** (*of snow*) to begin to fall heavily; (*of smoke*) begin to pour out.

пова́льный *adj.* general; mass.

поваля́ть *v., pfv. of* **валя́ть** (*in sense #1*). —**поваля́ться,** *refl., pfv. of* **валя́ться.**

по́вар [*pl.* **повара́**] *n.* cook.

пова́ренный *adj.* culinary. —**пова́ренная кни́га,** cookbook. —**пова́ренная соль,** common salt; table salt.

по-ва́шему *adv.* **1,** in your opinion. **2,** as you wish: пусть бу́дет по-ва́шему, have it your way.

пове́дать *v. pfv.* to announce; reveal; disclose.

поведе́ние *n.* behavior; conduct.

повезти́ *v., pfv. of* **везти́.**

повелева́ть *v. impfv.* [*pfv.* **повеле́ть**] **1,** (*with dat.*) to order; command. **2,** [*impfv. only*] (*with instr.*) to rule; rule over.

повеле́ние *n.* command.

повеле́ть [*infl.* **-велю́, -вели́шь**] *v., pfv. of* **повелева́ть.**

повели́тель *n.m.* **1,** sovereign; ruler. **2,** *colloq.* lord and master.

повели́тельный *adj.* imperious; peremptory. —**повели́тельное наклоне́ние,** *gram.* imperative mood.

повенча́ть *v., pfv. of* **венча́ть** (*in sense #2*). —**повенча́ться,** *refl., pfv. of* **венча́ться** (*in sense #2*).

поверга́ть *v. impfv.* [*pfv.* **пове́ргнуть**] **1,** *obs.* to knock down; topple. **2,** *obs.* to defeat. **3,** (*with* **в** + *acc.*) to plunge into (a state, mood, etc.).

пове́ргнуть [*past* **-ве́рг, -ла**] *v., pfv. of* **поверга́ть.**

пове́ренный *n., decl. as an adj.* **1,** attorney. **2,** confidant. —**пове́ренный в дела́х,** chargé d'affaires.

пове́рить *v., pfv. of* **ве́рить** *and* **поверя́ть.**

пове́рка *n.* **1,** check. **2,** roll call. —**на пове́рку,** in actual fact; in reality.

поверну́ть *v., pfv. of* **повёртывать** *and* **повора́чивать.** —**поверну́ться,** *refl., pfv. of* **повёртываться** *and* **повора́чиваться.**

поверте́ть *v. pfv.* [*infl.* **-верчу́, -ве́ртишь**] **1,** to turn slightly. **2,** to turn this way and that. —**поверте́ться,** *refl.* to turn; turn this way and that.

повёртывать *v. impfv.* = **повора́чивать.** —**повёртываться,** *refl.* = **повора́чиваться.**

пове́рх *prep., with gen.* over. —*adv.* above; overhead.

пове́рхностный *adj.* **1,** surface (*attrib.*). **2,** superficial. —**пове́рхностно,** *adv.* superficially. —**пове́рхностность,** *n.f.* superficiality.

пове́рхность *n.f.* surface.

по́верху *adv., colloq.* on top; on the surface.

пове́рье *n.* popular belief; superstition.

поверя́ть *v. impfv.* [*pfv.* **пове́рить**] **1,** to confide; entrust. **2,** *obs.* to check; verify.

пове́са *n.m.* playboy.

повеселе́ть *v., pfv. of* **веселе́ть.**

повесели́ть *v. pfv.* to amuse; entertain. —**повесели́ться,** *refl.* to have fun.

пове́сить [*infl.* **-шу, -сишь**] *v., pfv. of* **ве́шать.** —**пове́ситься,** *refl., pfv. of* **ве́шаться.**

повествова́ние *n.* narration; narrative.

повествова́тельный *adj.* **1,** narrative. **2,** *gram.* declarative.

повествова́ть *v. impfv.* [*pres.* **-ству́ю, -ству́ешь**] to tell; relate; narrate.

повести́ *v. pfv.* [*infl. like* **вести́**] **1,** *pfv. of* **вести́** *and* **поводи́ть**[1]. **2,** to begin; start; launch. **3,** to manage; handle.

повести́сь *v.r. pfv.* [*infl. like* **вести́**] **1,** *impers.* to be the custom: и́сстари повело́сь (+ *inf.*), since ancient times it has been the custom to... **2,** (*with* **с** + *instr.*) *colloq.* to take up with (someone).

пове́стка [*gen. pl.* **-ток**] *n.* notice; notification. —**пове́стка в суд,** summons; subpoena. —**пове́стка дня,** agenda.

по́весть [*pl.* **по́вести, -сте́й, -стя́м**] *n.f.* story; tale.

пове́трие *n.* **1,** *obs.* epidemic. **2,** *colloq.* rage; craze; fad.

пове́шение *n.* hanging (*method of execution*).

пове́ять *v. pfv.* **1,** to begin to blow. **2,** *impers.* (*with instr.*) to be in the air: пове́яло весно́й, spring was in the air; пове́яло прохла́дой, there was a coolness in the air.

повздо́рить *v., pfv. of* **вздо́рить.**

повзросле́ть *v. pfv.* to grow up; become an adult.

повива́льный *adj., in* **повива́льная ба́бка,** *obs.* midwife.

повида́ть *v., pfv. of* **вида́ть.** —**повида́ться,** *refl., pfv. of* **вида́ться.**

по-ви́димому *adv.* apparently; evidently.

пови́дло *n.* jam.

пови́нная *n., decl. as an adj.* admission; confession (*of guilt*). —**принести́ пови́нную,** to confess one's guilt. —**яви́ться** *or* **прийти́ с пови́нной,** to give oneself up.

пови́нность *n.f.* obligation; duty. —**во́инская пови́нность,** military conscription; the draft.

пови́нный *adj.* [*short form* **пови́нен, -нна**] (*with* **в** + *prepl.*) guilty (of). *See also* **пови́нная.**

повинова́ться *v.r. impfv. & pfv.* [*pres.* **-ну́юсь, -ну́ешься**] (*with dat.*) to obey.

повинове́ние *n.* obedience.

повиса́ть *v. impfv.* [*pfv.* **пови́снуть**] **1,** to hang; remain suspended. **2,** (*with* **на** + *prepl.*) to hang onto; cling to. **3,** to hang down; droop. —**повиса́ть в во́здухе, 1,** to remain poised in midair. **2,** *fig.* to be up in the air.

пови́снуть [*past* **-ви́с, -ла**] *v., pfv. of* **повиса́ть.**

повиту́ха *n., obs., colloq.* midwife.

повле́чь *v., pfv. of* **влечь.**

повлия́ть *v., pfv. of* **влия́ть.**

по́вод[1] *n.* grounds; cause; reason. —**по по́воду** (+ *gen.*), regarding; with regard to. —**по э́тому по́воду,** in this connection.

по́вод[2] [*2nd loc.* **поводу́;** *pl.* **пово́дья, пово́дьев**] *n.* rein. —**быть на поводу́ у,** to be under the thumb of. —**вести́ на поводу́,** to lead by the nose. —**идти́/пойти́ на поводу́ у,** to knuckle under to.

поводи́ть[1] *v. impfv.* [*pfv.* **повести́;** *pres.* **-вожу́, -во́дишь**] (*with instr.*) **1,** to move; wiggle. Он и бро́вью не повёл, he didn't bat an eye. **2,** to run along the surface of something: поводи́ть па́льцами по мате́рии, to run one's fingers over the material.

поводи́ть[2] *v. pfv.* [*infl.* **-вожу́, -во́дишь**] to lead (a person); walk (a horse).

поводо́к [*gen.* **-дка́**] *n.* leash.

поводы́рь [*gen.* **-дыря́**] *n.m.* **1,** one who leads a blind person. **2,** *colloq.* guide.

пово́зка [*gen. pl.* **-зок**] *n.* wagon.

пово́йник *n.* kerchief worn around the head by married peasant women in old Russia.

поволо́ка *n., in* **глаза́ с поволо́кой,** languishing eyes.

повора́чивать *v. impfv.* [*pfv.* **поверну́ть**] **1,** *v.t.* to turn: поверну́ть кран, to turn the faucet. **2,** *v.i.* to turn: поверну́ть напра́во, to turn right. —**куда́** (*or* **как**) **ни поверни́,** any way you look at it.

повора́чиваться *v.r. impfv.* [*pfv.* **поверну́ться**] **1,** to turn: ключ не повора́чивается, the key won't turn. **2,** [*often with* **круго́м**] to turn around. **3,** *fig.* to turn out. —**поверну́ться спино́й к,** to turn one's back on (*figuratively*). —**у меня́ язы́к не поверну́лся,** I couldn't bring myself (to tell him, say it, etc.).

поворожи́ть *v., pfv. of* **ворожи́ть.**

поворо́т *n.* **1,** turn: круто́й поворо́т, sharp turn. **2,** *fig.* turn; change; turning point.

поворо́тливость *n.f.* **1,** agility. **2,** maneuverability.

поворо́тливый *adj.* **1,** nimble, agile. **2,** (*of a vehicle*) maneuverable.

поворо́тный *adj.* **1,** rotary; turning; swivel (*attrib.*): поворо́тный круг, turntable; поворо́тное сиде́нье, swivel seat. **2,** *fig.* turning; decisive: поворо́тный пункт, turning point.

повреди́ть [*infl.* **-жу́, -ди́шь**] *v., pfv. of* **вреди́ть** *and* **поврежда́ть.**

поврежда́ть *v. impfv.* [*pfv.* **повреди́ть**] to hurt; injure; damage.

поврежде́ние *n.* **1,** damage. **2,** injury.

повремени́ть *v. pfv., colloq.* **1,** (*with* **с** + *instr.*) to delay; hold off (doing something). **2,** to wait.

повреме́нный *adj.* **1,** periodic. **2,** (*of work, pay, etc.*) by the hour, day, week, etc.

повседне́вный *adj.* daily; day-to-day; everyday.

повсеме́стный *adj.* general; to be found everywhere. —**повсеме́стно,** *adv.* everywhere.

повста́нец [*gen.* **-нца**] *n.* rebel; insurgent. —**повста́нческий,** *adj.* rebel (*attrib.*); insurgent.

повстреча́ть *v. pfv., colloq.* to run into; meet. —**повстреча́ться,** *refl.* (*with* **с** + *instr.*) *colloq.* to run into; meet.

повсю́ду *adv.* everywhere.

повторе́ние *n.* **1,** repetition. **2,** recurrence. **3,** review.

повтори́тельный *adj.* repeat (*attrib.*). —**повтори́тельный курс,** refresher course.

повтори́ть *v., pfv. of* **повторя́ть.** —**повтори́ться,** *refl., pfv. of* **повторя́ться.**

повто́рный *adj.* a second; repeat (*attrib.*). —**повто́рно,** *adv.* for the second time; once again.

повторя́ть *v. impfv.* [*pfv.* **повтори́ть**] **1,** to repeat. **2,** to review; go over. **3,** to equal; tie (a record). —**повторя́ться,** *refl.* **1,** to happen again. **2,** to sound again; be heard again. **3,** to repeat itself. **4,** [*impfv. only*] to repeat oneself.

повыша́ть *v. impfv.* [*pfv.* **повы́сить**] **1,** to raise. **2,** to increase; heighten. **3,** to improve; enhance. **4,** to promote; give a promotion to. —**повыша́ться,** *refl.* **1,** to rise. **2,** to increase. **3,** to be promoted.

повыше́ние *n.* **1,** rise; increase. Повыше́ние зарпла́ты, pay raise. **2,** *in* повыше́ние по слу́жбе, promotion.

повы́шенный *adj.* increased; heightened. Повы́шенная температу́ра, a (slight) temperature.

повяза́ть [*infl.* **-вяжу́, -вя́жешь**] *v., pfv. of* **повя́зывать.** —**повяза́ться,** *refl., pfv. of* **повя́зываться.**

повя́зка [*gen. pl.* **-зок**] *n.* **1,** band. **2,** bandage.

повя́зывать *v. impfv.* [*pfv.* **повяза́ть**] to tie. —**повя́зываться,** *refl.* (*with instr.*) to tie (something) around oneself.

пога́нить *v. impfv., colloq.* **1,** to soil; get dirty. **2,** *fig.* to defile.

пога́нка [*gen. pl.* **-нок**] *n.* **1,** toadstool. **2,** grebe (*bird*).

пога́ный *adj.* **1,** (*of food*) inedible; impure. **2,** *colloq.* foul; vile. —**пога́ное ведро́,** garbage pail.

погаса́ть *v. impfv.* [*pfv.* **пога́снуть**] **1,** (*of lights, a fire, etc.*) to go out. **2,** *fig.* to dim; fade.

погаси́ть [*infl.* **-гашу́, -га́сишь**] *v., pfv. of* **гаси́ть** *and* **погаша́ть.**

пога́снуть [*past* **пога́с, -ла**] *v., pfv. of* **га́снуть** *and* **погаса́ть.**

погаша́ть *v. impfv.* [*pfv.* **погаси́ть**] **1,** to cancel (a stamp). **2,** to pay off (a debt, loan, etc.).

погаше́ние *n.* **1,** cancellation (*of a stamp*). **2,** paying off.

погиба́ть *v. impfv.* [*pfv.* **поги́бнуть**] **1,** to be killed; perish. **2,** (*of a ship or plane*) to go down.

поги́бнуть [*past* **-ги́б, -ла**] *v., pfv. of* **ги́бнуть** *and* **погиба́ть.**

погла́дить *v., pfv. of* **гла́дить** (*in sense #2*).

погла́живать *v. impfv.* to stroke from time to time.

поглоща́ть *v. impfv.* [*pfv.* **поглоти́ть**] **1,** to absorb; take in; soak up. **2,** to consume; use up. **3,** to engulf. **4,** *fig.* to absorb; engross. **5,** *fig.* to devour (books, stories, etc.).

поглоще́ние *n.* absorption.

поглупе́ть *v., pfv. of* **глупе́ть.**

погляде́ть *v., pfv. of* **гляде́ть.** —**погляде́ться,** *refl., pfv. of* **гляде́ться.**

погля́дывать *v. impfv.* **1,** to glance from time to time. **2,** (*with* **за** + *instr.*) *colloq.* to keep an eye on.

погна́ть *v. pfv.* [*infl. like* **гнать**] to drive. —**погна́ться,** *refl.* (*with* **за** + *instr.*) to chase after; take off after.

погну́ть *v. pfv.* to bend. —**погну́ться,** *refl.* to bend; become bent.

погнуша́ться *v.r., pfv. of* **гнуша́ться.**

погова́ривать *v. impfv., colloq.* to talk: погова́ривают, что..., there is talk that...; it is rumored that...

поговори́ть *v. pfv.* to have a talk.

погово́рка [*gen. pl.* **-рок**] *n.* saying.

пого́да *n.* weather. —**де́лать пого́ду,** to make the difference. —**ждать у мо́ря пого́ды,** to wait for a miracle to happen.

погоди́ть *v. pfv.* [*infl.* **-гожу́, -годи́шь**] *colloq.* to wait a while. —**немно́го погодя́,** a little while later.

пого́дный *adj.* **1,** yearly. **2,** weather (*attrib.*).

пого́док [*gen.* **-дка**] *n.* one of a pair of siblings a year apart in age: Ива́н и О́льга пого́дки, Ivan and Olga are a year apart in age.

пого́жий *adj.* (*of the weather*) fine: пого́жий день, a fine day.

поголо́вный *adj.* general; total; all-inclusive. —**поголо́вно,** *adv.* to a man: все поголо́вно, everyone to the last man.

поголо́вье *n.* total amount of livestock.

поголубе́ть *v., pfv. of* **голубе́ть.**

пого́н *n., mil.* shoulder strap.

пого́нщик *n.* driver; drover.

пого́ня *n.* **1,** pursuit; chase. **2,** pursuers. **3,** *fig.* pursuit: пого́ня за сча́стьем, pursuit of happiness.

погоня́ть *v. impfv.* **1,** to drive; urge on (animals). **2,** *colloq.* to hurry; rush (someone).

погоре́лец [*gen.* **-льца**] *n.* person made homeless by a fire.

погоре́ть *v. pfv.* **1,** *colloq.* to lose everything in a fire. **2,** *colloq.* to burn down. **3,** *colloq.* (*of many things*) to be burned. **4,** to burn for a while.

пого́ст *n.* village cemetery.

погости́ть *v. pfv.* [*infl.* **-щу́, -сти́шь**] (*with* **у**) to stay for a while (at the home of).

пограни́чник *n.* border guard.

пограни́чный *adj.* border (*attrib.*); boundary (*attrib.*); frontier (*attrib.*).

по́греб [*pl.* **погреба́**] *n.* cellar. —**порохово́й по́греб, 1,** powder magazine. **2,** *fig.* powder keg.

погреба́льный *adj.* funeral (*attrib.*).

погреба́ть *v. impfv.* [*pfv.* **погрести́**] to bury; inter.

погребе́ние *n.* burial.

погрему́шка [*gen. pl.* **-шек**] *n.* (child's) rattle.

погрести́ *v. pfv.* [*infl. like* **грести́**] **1,** *pfv. of* **погреба́ть. 2,** to row (*for a while*).

погре́ть *v. pfv.* to warm (*for a while*). —**погре́ться,** *refl.* to warm oneself (*for a while*); warm up a little.

погреши́ть *v., pfv. of* **греши́ть** (*in sense #2*).

погре́шность *n.f.* error.

погрози́ть *v. pfv.* [*infl.* **-жу́, -зи́шь**] to make a threatening gesture: погрози́ть па́льцем (+ *dat.*), to shake one's finger at.

погро́м *n.* **1,** massacre. **2,** pogrom. —**погро́мный,** *adj.* (*of a speech*) rabble-rousing. —**погро́мщик,** *n.* one taking part in a pogrom; thug.

погружа́ть *v. impfv.* [*pfv.* **погрузи́ть**] **1,** to dip; immerse. **2,** *fig.* to plunge: го́род был погружён в темноту́, to city was plunged into darkness. **3,** *fig.* to absorb; engross: весь погружён в рабо́ту, completely absorbed in one's work; погружён в размышле́ния, lost in thought. —**погружа́ться,** *refl.* (*with* **в** + *acc.*) **1,** to sink (into); be submerged (in). **2,** *fig.* to be plunged into (darkness); become absorbed in (one's work); be lost in (thought).

погруже́ние *n.* immersion; submersion.

погрузи́ть [*infl.* **-гружу́, -гру́зишь** *or* **-грузи́шь**] *v., pfv. of* **грузи́ть** (*in sense #2*) *and* **погружа́ть.** —**погрузи́ться,** *refl., pfv. of* **грузи́ться** *and* **погружа́ться.**

погру́зка *n.* loading. —**погру́зочный,** *adj.* loading (*attrib.*).

погряза́ть *v. impfv.* [*pfv.* **погря́знуть**] (*with* **в** + *prepl.*) to become mired in; get bogged down in.

погря́знуть *v. pfv.* [*past* **-гря́з, -ла**] **1,** *pfv. of* **погряза́ть. 2,** *fig.* (*with* **в** + *prepl.*) to wallow (in).

погуби́ть *v., pfv. of* **губи́ть.**

погу́дка [*gen. pl.* **-док**] *n., colloq.* **1,** tune; melody. **2,** story; tale. —**ста́рая погу́дка на но́вый лад,** the same old story with a new twist.

погу́ливать *v. impfv., colloq.* **1,** to stroll; walk up and down. **2,** to carouse (*from time to time*).

погуля́ть *v. pfv.* to go for a walk; take a walk.

погусте́ть *v., pfv. of* **густе́ть.**

под *also,* **подо** *prep.* A, *with instr.* **1,** under (*with verbs of location*): быть под водо́й, to be under water; сиде́ть под де́ревом, to be sitting under a tree. **2,** (*in various figurative senses*) under: под прися́гой, under oath; под чужи́м и́менем, under an assumed name. **3,** in the environs of (a city): жить под Москво́й, to live in the environs of Moscow. B, *with acc.* **1,** under (*with verbs of motion*): мяч закати́лся под дива́н, the ball rolled under the couch; поста́вьте чемода́н под крова́ть, put the suitcase under the bed. **2,** (*with numbers denoting age*) under; not yet: ему́ под со́рок, he is under/not yet/forty. **3,** (*with certain nouns*) toward: под ве́чер, toward evening. **4,** to the sound of: танцева́ть под му́зыку, to dance to the music. **5,** in imitation: ме́бель под кра́сное де́рево, furniture in imitation mahogany. C, *with acc. or instr.* (*of a container*) used to hold: ба́нка под варе́нье (*or* под варе́ньем), jelly jar.

под- *also,* **подо-, подъ-** *prefix* **1,** *indicating motion upward or from under:* подбра́сывать, to toss up; подпира́ть, to prop up. **2,** *indicating motion under:* подле́зть под дива́н, to crawl under the couch. **3,** *indicating motion toward:* подходи́ть, to approach. **4,** *indicating action to a slight degree:* поджа́рить, to fry lightly; подмёрзнуть, to be slightly frozen. **5,** *indicating the adding of something:* подлива́ть сли́вок в ко́фе, to add some cream to the coffee. **6,** *indicating stealth:* подслу́шивать, to eavesdrop. **7,** joining in; going along: подпева́ть, to join in singing. **8,** (*with nouns*) under; sub-: подпо́лье, underground; подразделе́ние, subdivision. **9,** (*with adjectives*) on the outskirts of: подмоско́вный, on the outskirts of Moscow.

подава́льщик *n.* waiter; server. —**подава́льщица,** *n.* waitress.

подава́ть *v. impfv.* [*pfv.* **пода́ть;** *pres.* **-даю́, -даёшь**] **1,** (*with certain nouns*) to give: пода́ть сове́т/сигна́л/кома́нду, to give advice/a signal/a command/. **2,** to serve (food, a meal, etc.). **3,** *v.i.* to give alms. **4,** to bring; deliver (a vehicle). **5,** to hand in; submit; file; lodge; register. **6,** to help on with: подава́ть кому́-нибудь пальто́, to help someone on with his (her) coat. **7,** *tennis* to serve. —**подава́ть в отста́вку,** to submit (*or* tender) one's resignation. —**подава́ть в суд, 1,** to sue; go to court. **2,** (*with* **на** + *acc.*) to bring (*or* file) suit against. —**подава́ть го́лос, 1,** to announce one's presence. **2,** to cast one's vote. —**подава́ть наде́жду, 1,** to offer hope. **2,** to give (*or show*) promise. —**подава́ть приме́р,** to set an example. —**подава́ть при́знаки жи́зни,** to show signs of life. —**подава́ть ру́ку,** to offer (*or* extend) one's hand. —**не подава́ть ви́ду,** not to show; not let on. —**руко́й пода́ть,** a stone's throw (from).

подава́ться *v.r. impfv.* [*pfv.* **пода́ться;** *pres.* **-даю́сь, -даёшься**] **1,** to be served. **2,** to move. **3,** *colloq.* to yield; give way. **4,** (*with* **в** *or* **на** + *acc.*) to leave (for); set out (for).

подави́ть [*infl.* **-давлю́, -да́вишь**] *v., pfv. of* **подавля́ть.** —**подави́ться,** *refl., pfv. of* **дави́ться.**

подавле́ние *n.* suppression.

пода́вленный *adj.* **1,** (*of a sound*) muffled. **2,** (*of a feeling*) suppressed. **3,** depressed; despondent. —**пода́вленность.** *n.f.* depression; despondency.

подавля́ть *v. impfv.* [*pfv.* **подави́ть**] **1,** to press down; weigh down. **2,** to suppress; put down; crush. **3,** to suppress; repress (a feeling, laugh, etc.). **4,** to depress; dispirit. **5,** to overwhelm.

подавля́ющий *adj.* **1,** overwhelming: подавля́ющее большинство́, overwhelming majority. **2,** depressing.

пода́вно *adv.* [*usu.* **и пода́вно**] *colloq.* even more (so): весно́й там жа́рко, а ле́том и пода́вно, it's hot there in spring and even more so in summer.

пода́гра *n.* gout.

пода́льше *adv., colloq.* a little farther.

подари́ть *v., pfv. of* **дари́ть.**

пода́рок [*gen.* **-рка**] *n.* gift; present. Получи́ть что́-нибудь в пода́рок, to receive something as a gift.

пода́тель *n.m.* bearer.

пода́тливый *adj.* **1,** pliable; malleable. **2,** *fig.* pliable; amenable.

по́дать *n.f., pre-rev.* tax. —**податно́й,** *adj.* tax (*attrib.*).

пода́ть [*infl. like* **дать;** *past* **по́дал, подала́, по́дало**] *v., pfv. of* **подава́ть.** —**пода́ться,** *refl.* [*past* **пода́лся, -ла́сь, -ло́сь**] *pfv. of* **подава́ться.**

пода́ча *n.* **1,** giving; presenting; handing in. **2,** supply; delivery. **3,** *tennis* serve; service.

пода́чка [*gen. pl.* **-чек**] *n., colloq.* handout.

подая́ние *n., obs.* alms.

подбавля́ть *v. impfv.* [*pfv.* **подба́вить**] (*with gen.*) to add a little (of something).

подбега́ть *v. impfv.* [*pfv.* **подбежа́ть**] (*with* **к**) to come running (up to).

подбежа́ть [*infl. like* **бежа́ть**] *v., pfv. of* **подбега́ть.**

подбива́ть *v. impfv.* [*pfv.* **подби́ть**] **1,** to nail on. **2,** to line (a garment). **3,** *mil.* to cripple; knock out. **4,** *colloq.* to incite; put up to. —**подби́ть глаз** (+ *dat.*), to give (someone) a black eye.

подбира́ть *v. impfv.* [*pfv.* **подобра́ть**] **1,** to pick up. **2,** to tuck up. **3,** to draw up (the edge of a garment); put up (one's hair). **4,** to draw in (reins, one's stomach, etc.). **5,** to purse (one's lips). **6,** to select; choose. —**подбира́ться,** *refl.* **1,** to be selected; be chosen. **2,** (*with* **к**) to sneak up to *or* on. **3,** (*with* **под** + *acc.*) *colloq.* to crawl under. **4,** *colloq.* to draw oneself up; straighten up. **5,** *colloq.* to draw oneself in; huddle up.

подби́ть [*infl.* **подобью́, подобьёшь**] *v., pfv. of* **подбива́ть.**

подбодря́ть *v. impfv.* [*pfv.* **подбодри́ть**] to cheer up; hearten. —**подбодря́ться,** *refl.* to cheer up; take heart.

подбо́р *n.* **1,** selection; selecting. **2,** selection; assortment. —**как на подбо́р,** choice: я́блоки как на подбо́р, choice apples.

подбо́рка *n.* **1,** selection. **2,** group of related articles under a single heading in a newspaper.

подборо́док [*gen.* **-дка**] *n.* chin.

подбоче́ниться *v.r. pfv., colloq.* to stand with arms akimbo.

подбра́сывать *v. impfv.* [*pfv.* **подбро́сить**] **1,** to throw up; toss up. **2,** (*with* **под** + *acc.*) to throw under; toss under. **3,** to throw in; throw on (more of something). **4,** to slip; place surreptitiously. **5,** to abandon (a child). **6,** to shake; toss up and down. *Also impers.:* маши́ну/пассажи́ров си́льно подбра́сывало, the car/passengers was/were tossed all around (*or* kept bouncing up and down).

подбро́сить [*infl.* **-шу, -сишь**] *v., pfv. of* **подбра́сывать.**

подва́л *n.* **1,** basement. **2,** special article (*in a newspaper*).

подва́льный *adj.* basement (*attrib.*).

подвезти́ [*infl. like* **везти́**] *v., pfv. of* **подвози́ть.**

подвене́чный *adj.* wedding (*attrib.*); bridal.

подверга́ть *v. impfv.* [*pfv.* **подве́ргнуть**] (*with dat.*) to subject (to); expose (to). —**подверга́ться,** *refl.* (*with dat.*) to be subjected (to); be exposed (to); undergo.

подве́ргнуть [*past* **-ве́рг, -ла**] *v., pfv. of* **подверга́ть.** —**подве́ргнуться,** *refl., pfv. of* **подверга́ться.**

подве́рженный *adj.* (*with dat.*) subject (to); liable (to); prone (to); susceptible (to). —**подве́рженность,** *n.f.* susceptibility.

подвёртывать *v. impfv.* [*pfv.* **подверну́ть**] **1,** to turn up; fold up. **2,** to tuck under; fold under. **3,** to sprain; twist: подверну́ть себе́ но́гу, to sprain/twist/turn one's ankle. **4,** to tighten; screw tight. —**подвёртываться,** *refl.* **1,** to be turned inward. **2,** *colloq.* to turn up; show up; appear.

подве́сить [*infl.* **-шу, -сишь**] *v., pfv. of* **подве́шивать.**

подве́ска [*gen. pl.* **-сок**] *n.* **1,** hanging up. **2,** *mech.* suspension. **3,** pendant.

подвесно́й *adj.* hanging; suspended. —**подвесна́я доро́га,** aerial railway. —**подвесно́й мост,** suspension bridge. —**подвесно́й мото́р,** outboard motor.

подвести́ [*infl. like* **вести́**] *v., pfv. of* **подводи́ть.**

подве́тренный *adj.* leeward.

подве́шивать *v. impfv.* [*pfv.* **подве́сить**] to hang; suspend.

подвива́ть *v. impfv.* [*pfv.* **подви́ть**] to curl slightly.

по́двиг *n.* feat; exploit.

подви́гать *v. pfv.* (*with instr.*) to move (a part of one's body) slightly; wiggle. —**подви́гаться,** *refl.* to move a little.

подвига́ть *v. impfv.* [*pfv.* **подви́нуть**] **1,** to move. **2,** *fig., colloq.* to give a push to; get (something) moving. —**подвига́ться,** *refl.* **1,** to move. **2,** to move over. **3,** to edge (toward, forward, etc.). **4,** *fig.* to make progress.

подви́д *n.* subspecies.

подви́жник *n.* **1,** religious ascetic. **2,** (*with gen.*) champion (of).

подвижно́й *adj.* mobile. —**подвижно́й соста́в,** rolling stock.

подви́жность *n.f.* **1,** mobility. **2,** liveliness.

подви́жный *adj.* lively; active; quick.

подвиза́ться *v.r. impfv.* to work (in a certain field): подвиза́ться на своём по́прище, to ply one's trade.

подвинти́ть [*infl.* **-чу́, -ти́шь**] *v., pfv. of* **подви́нчивать.**

подви́нуть *v., pfv. of* **подвига́ть.** —**подви́нуться,** *refl., pfv. of* **подвига́ться.**

подви́нчивать *v. impfv.* [*pfv.* **подвинти́ть**] to tighten; screw tight.

подви́ть [*infl.* **подовью́, подовьёшь;** *past fem.* **подвила́**] *v., pfv. of* **подвива́ть.**

подвла́стный *adj.* (*with dat.*) subject (to); under the control (of).

подво́да *n.* cart; wagon.

подводи́ть *v. impfv.* [*pfv.* **подвести́;** *pres.* **-вожу́, -во́дишь**] **1,** (*with* **к**) to lead up to; bring to. **2,** *mil.* to bring up (reserves). **3,** to extend: подводи́ть доро́гу к реке́, to extend a road as far as the river. **4,** (*with* **под** + *acc.*) to place under; place beneath (*for support*); lay (a foundation, mine, etc.). **5,** (*with* **под** + *acc.*) to place; subsume (in a certain category). **6,** to adjust (a clock). **7,** to touch up (*with make-up*): подвести́ бро́ви, to pencil one's eyebrows. **8,** *colloq.* to let down; disappoint. —**подводи́ть бала́нс,** to strike a balance. —**подводи́ть итог** *or* **ито́ги** (+ *dat.*), to add up; total; *fig.* sum up. —**подводи́ть к концу́,** to complete; finish. —**у меня́ живо́т подвело́,** I have an empty feeling in my stomach.

подво́дный *adj.* **1,** underwater. **2,** submarine (*attrib.*). —**подво́дный ка́мень, 1,** reef. **2,** *fig.* pitfall. —**подво́дное крыло́,** hydrofoil. —**подво́дная ло́дка,** submarine. —**подво́дная скала́,** reef. —**подво́дное тече́ние,** undercurrent; undertow.

подво́з *n.* supply; delivery; transport.

подвози́ть *v. impfv.* [*pfv.* **подвезти́;** *pres.* **-вожу́, -во́зишь**] **1,** to transport; bring; deliver. **2,** to pick up along the way; give (someone) a lift.

подворо́тня [*gen. pl.* **-тен**] *n.* **1,** space beneath a gate. **2,** board covering this space.

подво́х *n., colloq.* (dirty or sneaky) trick.

подвы́пивший *adj., colloq.* tipsy; high; tight.

подвяза́ть [*infl.* **-вяжу́, -вя́жешь**] *v., pfv. of* **подвя́зывать.** —**подвяза́ться,** *refl., pfv. of* **подвя́зываться.**

подвя́зка [*gen. pl.* **-зок**] *n.* garter.

подвя́зывать *v. impfv.* [*pfv.* **подвяза́ть**] **1,** to tie up (*so as not to fall*). **2,** to tie around oneself. —**подвя́зываться,** *refl.* (*with instr.*) to tie (something) around oneself.

подгиба́ть *v. impfv.* [*pfv.* **подогну́ть**] **1,** to fold over; tuck in. **2,** to bend (one's knees). **3,** *in* подгиба́ть но́ги под себя́, to tuck one's legs under one. —**подгиба́ться,** *refl.* **1,** to be turned up; be folded up. **2,** (*of one's legs or knees*) to bend; sag.

подгляде́ть *v. pfv.* [*infl.* **-гляжу́, -гляди́шь**] **1,** *pfv. of* **подгля́дывать. 2,** to catch sight of; spot; detect.

подгля́дывать *v. impfv.* [*pfv.* **подгляде́ть**] **1,** to watch secretly. **2,** (*with* **в** + *acc.*) to peep through. **3,** (*with* **за** + *instr.*) to peep at.

подгнива́ть *v. impfv.* [*pfv.* **подгни́ть**] **1,** to rot from under; rot on the bottom. **2,** to rot slightly.

подгни́ть [*infl. like* **гнить**] *v., pfv. of* **подгнива́ть.**

подгова́ривать *v. impfv.* [*pfv.* **подговори́ть**] (*with inf. or* **на** + *acc.*) to incite (to); put up to.

подголо́сок [*gen.* **-ска**] *n.* **1,** *music* second part; supporting voice. **2,** *fig., colloq.* yes man.

подгоня́ть *v. impfv.* [*pfv.* **подогна́ть**] **1,** to drive; steer (to a certain place). **2,** to drive on; urge on. **3,** to adjust; fit. **4,** *colloq.* to time; schedule.

подгора́ть *v. impfv.* [*pfv.* **подгоре́ть**] (*of food*) to be slightly burnt.

подгоре́лый *adj.* slightly burnt.

подгоре́ть *v., pfv. of* **подгора́ть.**

подгота́вливать *v. impfv.* [*pfv.* **подгото́вить**] **1,** to prepare. **2,** to train. —**подгота́вливаться,** *refl.* (*with* **к**) to prepare (for); get ready (for).

подготови́тельный *adj.* preparatory.

подгото́вить [*infl.* **-влю, -вишь**] *v., pfv. of* **подгота́вливать** *and* **подготовля́ть.** —**подгото́виться,** *refl., pfv. of* **подгота́вливаться** *and* **подготовля́ться.**

подгото́вка *n.* **1,** preparation. **2,** training. **3,** grounding; background.

подгото́вленность *n.f.* preparedness.

подготовля́ть *v. impfv.* = **подгота́вливать.** —**подготовля́ться,** *refl.* = **подгота́вливаться.**

подгру́док [*gen.* **-дка**] *n.* dewlap; jowl.

подгру́ппа *n.* subgroup.

подгу́зник *n.* diaper.

поддава́ть *v. impfv.* [*pfv.* **подда́ть;** *pres.* **поддаю́, поддаёшь**] **1,** to strike; kick. **2,** (*with gen.*) *colloq.* to increase; step up. **3,** *colloq.* (*in certain games*) to give away (a card, piece, etc.). —**поддава́ться,** *refl.* (*with dat.*) **1,** to give in (to); yield (to); succumb (to). **2,** [*impfv. only*] to respond (to treatment); lend itself (to translation); (*with* **не**) defy (description).

поддавки́ [*gen.* **-ко́в**] *n. pl.* giveaway checkers.

подда́кивать *v. impfv.* [*pfv.* **подда́кнуть**] (*with dat.*) *colloq.* to say yes (to); agree (with); nod assent (to).

по́дданный *n., decl. as an adj.* subject; citizen: англи́йский по́дданный, British subject; америка́нский по́дданный, American citizen.

по́дданство *n.* citizenship.

подда́ть [*infl. like* **дать;** *past* **по́ддал, -дала́, по́ддало**] *v., pfv. of* **поддава́ть.** —**подда́ться,** *refl.* [*past* **подда́лся, -ла́сь, -ло́сь**] *pfv. of* **поддава́ться.**

поддева́ть *v. impfv.* [*pfv.* **подде́ть**] **1,** to raise slightly (*from underneath*). **2,** to hook; snag. **3,** (*with* **под** + *acc.*) *colloq.* to put on; wear (underneath). **4,** *fig., colloq.* to needle (someone).

поддёвка [*gen. pl.* **-вок**] *n.* man's long coat with a fitted waist.

подде́лать *v., pfv. of* **подде́лывать.** —**подде́латься,** *refl., pfv. of* **подде́лываться.**

подде́лка [*gen. pl.* **-лок**] *n.* forgery.

подде́лыватель *n.m.* forger; counterfeiter.

подде́лывать *v. impfv.* [*pfv.* **подде́лать**] to forge;

counterfeit. —**подде́лываться**, *refl.* **1,** (*with* **под** + *acc.*) to imitate; pose (as). **2,** (*with* **к**) *colloq.* to ingratiate oneself (with); play up to.

подде́льный *adj.* **1,** forged; counterfeit. **2,** artificial; imitation (*attrib.*).

поддержа́ние *n.* maintenance.

поддержа́ть [*infl.* **поддержу́, подде́ржишь**] *v., pfv. of* **подде́рживать.**

подде́рживать *v. impfv.* [*pfv.* **поддержа́ть**] **1,** to support; hold up. **2,** to support: подде́рживать кандида́та, to support a candidate. Подде́рживать предложе́ние, to support a proposal; second a motion. **3,** to maintain; keep up (order, a correspondence, etc.).

подде́ржка *n.* support.

подде́ть [*infl.* **подде́ну, подде́нешь**] *v., pfv. of* **поддева́ть.**

поддра́знивать *v. impfv.* [*pfv.* **поддразни́ть**] to tease.

поддразни́ть [*infl.* **-дразню́, -дра́знишь**] *v., pfv. of* **поддра́знивать.**

поддува́ло *n.* ash pit (*of a furnace*).

поддува́ть *v. impfv., impers.* to blow slightly: от окна́ поддува́ет, there is a slight draft from the window.

поде́йствовать *v., pfv. of* **де́йствовать** (*in sense #4*).

поде́лать *v. pfv., colloq.* to do. —**ничего́ не поде́лаешь,** there is nothing you can do about it.

подели́ть *v., pfv. of* **дели́ть.** —**подели́ться**, *refl., pfv. of* **дели́ться** (*in senses #2 & #3*).

поде́лка [*gen. pl.* **-лок**] *n.* **1,** *usu. pl.* odd jobs. **2,** homemade article.

подело́м *adv., colloq.* deservedly; properly. —**ему́/ей подело́м,** it serves him/her right.

поде́лывать *v. impfv., colloq., in* **что (вы) поде́лываете?,** how are you doing?; how are you getting along?

подёнка [*gen. pl.* **-нок**] *n.* mayfly.

подённый *adj.* by the day. —*n.* dayworker; day laborer. —**подённая**, *n., colloq.* daywork.

подёнщик *n.m.* [*fem.* **-щица**] dayworker; day laborer. —**подёнщина**, *n.* daywork.

подёргать *v. pfv.* (*with acc. or* **за** + *acc.*) to pull at (*a number of times*).

подёргивание *n.* (nervous) twitch.

подёргивать *v. impfv.* **1,** (*with acc. or* **за** + *acc.*) to pull (at). **2,** (*with instr.*) to twitch. *Also impers.:* его́ подёргивало, he was twitching. —**подёргиваться**, *refl.* to twitch.

подёржанный *adj.* secondhand; used.

подержа́ть *v. pfv.* [*infl.* **-держу́, -де́ржишь**] **1,** to hold (*for a while*). **2,** to keep (*for a while*). —**подержа́ться**, *refl.* **1,** (*with* **за** + *acc.*) to hold onto (*for a while*). **2,** to hold out (*for a while*).

подёрнуть *v. pfv.* **1,** to cover (with a thin layer of something). **2,** to shroud; envelop.

подешеве́ть *v., pfv. of* **дешеве́ть.**

поджа́ривать *v. impfv.* [*pfv.* **поджа́рить**] **1,** to roast; broil; fry (*lightly*). **2,** to toast (bread).

поджа́ристый *adj.* brown; nice and brown.

поджа́рить *v., pfv. of* **поджа́ривать.**

поджа́рый *adj., colloq.* lean; wiry.

поджа́ть [*infl.* **подожму́, подожмёшь**] *v., pfv. of* **поджима́ть.**

поджелу́дочный *adj.* pancreatic. —**поджелу́дочная железа́,** pancreas.

подже́чь [*infl.* **подожгу́, подожжёшь, ...подожгу́т;** *past* **поджёг, подожгла́**] *v., pfv. of* **поджига́ть.**

поджига́тель *n.m.* **1,** arsonist. **2,** *fig.* instigator. —**поджига́тель войны́,** warmonger.

поджига́ть *v. impfv.* [*pfv.* **подже́чь**] **1,** to set fire to; set on fire. **2,** *colloq.* to burn (food) slightly.

поджида́ть *v. impfv.* (*with gen.*) to wait for; await.

поджи́лки [*gen.* **-лок**] *n. pl., colloq.* tendons of the knee. —**у меня́ поджи́лки затрясли́сь,** my knees were shaking; I was quaking in my boots.

поджима́ть *v. impfv.* [*pfv.* **поджа́ть**] to draw up (one's legs); purse (one's lips); put (one's tail) between one's legs.

поджо́г *n.* arson.

подзаголо́вок [*gen.* **-вка**] *n.* subtitle; subheading.

подзадо́ривать *v. impfv.* [*pfv.* **подзадо́рить**] *colloq.* to goad; egg on.

подзаты́льник *n., colloq.* blow on the back of the head.

подзащи́тный *n., decl. as an adj., law* client.

подземе́лье *n.* underground cave, cell, or vault.

подзе́мный *adj.* underground; subterranean. —**подзе́мный толчо́к,** earth tremor.

подзерка́льник *n.* pier table.

подзо́л *n.* podzol.

подзо́рный *adj., in* **подзо́рная труба́,** spyglass.

подзыва́ть *v. impfv.* [*pfv.* **подозва́ть**] to call to; beckon.

поди́ *v., imperative of* **пойти́,** *colloq.:* поди́ прочь!, go away! Поди́ поспо́рь с ним!, go argue with him!; just try arguing with him! —*particle, colloq.* probably; I dare say.

подиви́ться *v.r., pfv. of* **диви́ться.**

подира́ть *v. impfv., usu. in* **подира́ть по ко́же,** to go up and down one's spine. —**моро́з по ко́же подира́ет** (*with* **у**), to get the creeps (*or* shivers); get chills up and down one's spine.

подка́лывать *v. impfv.* [*pfv.* **подколо́ть**] **1,** to pin up. **2,** (*with* **к**) to append (to). **3,** *colloq.* to needle; twit. **4,** (*with gen.*) to chop up some more of.

подка́пывать *v. impfv.* [*pfv.* **подкопа́ть**] **1,** to undermine. **2,** to tunnel under. —**подка́пываться**, *refl.* **1,** (*with* **под** + *acc.*) to dig under. **2,** to tunnel under. **3,** *fig., colloq.* to undercut (someone).

подкарау́ливать *v. impfv.* [*pfv.* **подкарау́лить**] *colloq.* to watch for; be on the lookout for.

подка́рмливать *v. impfv.* [*pfv.* **подкорми́ть**] *colloq.* **1,** to feed. **2,** to fatten up.

подкати́ть [*infl.* **-качу́, -ка́тишь**] *v., pfv. of* **подка́тывать.** —**подкати́ться**, *refl., pfv. of* **подка́тываться.**

подка́тывать *v. impfv.* [*pfv.* **подкати́ть**] (*with* **к**) **1,** *v.t.* to roll (a ball, barrel, etc.) up to; drive (a vehicle) up to. **2,** *v.i., colloq.* to roll up to; pull up to. **3,** *v.i., colloq.* to press against: у меня́ ком подкати́л к го́рлу (*or impers.* у меня́ подкати́ло к го́рлу), I felt a lump in my throat. —**подка́тываться**, *refl.* **1,** (*with* **к**) to roll over to. **2,** (*with* **под** + *acc.*) to roll under. **3,** (*with* **к**) *colloq.* to roll up to; pull up to.

подка́шивать *v. impfv.* [*pfv.* **подкоси́ть**] **1,** to cut; trim (grass). **2,** to knock off one's feet; (*of a bullet*) cut down. **3,** *fig.* to demoralize. —**подка́шиваться**, *refl.* (*of one's legs*) to give way.

подки́дывать *v. impfv.* [*pfv.* **подки́нуть**] **1,** to throw up; toss up. **2,** to slip; place surreptitiously. **3,** to abandon (a child).

подки́дыш *n.* abandoned child; foundling.

подки́нуть *v., pfv. of* **подки́дывать.**

подкла́дка [*gen. pl.* **-док**] *n.* lining.

подкладно́й *adj.* placed underneath. —**подкладно́е су́дно,** bedpan.

подкла́дывать *v. impfv.* [*pfv.* **подложи́ть**] **1,** (*with* **под** + *acc.*) to place under; lay under. **2,** (*with* **к**) to apply (to); append (to). **3,** (*with gen.*) to add; put some more. **4,** to put furtively; slip; stick; plant. **5,** (*with* **под** + *acc.*) *colloq.* to line: подкла́дывать шёлк под пальто́, to line a coat with silk.

подкла́сс *n.* subclass.

подкле́ивать *v. impfv.* [*pfv.* **подкле́ить**] **1,** to glue under; paste under. **2,** to glue up; paste up.

подключа́ть *v. impfv.* [*pfv.* **подключи́ть**] to connect; hook up. —**подключа́ться,** *refl.* **1,** to be connected. **2,** (*with* **к**) *colloq.* to join.

подко́ва *n.* horseshoe.

подкова́ть [*infl.* **-кую́, -куёшь**] *v., pfv. of* **подко́вывать.**

подко́вывать *v. impfv.* [*pfv.* **подкова́ть**] **1,** to shoe (a horse). **2,** *fig., colloq.* to train; ground: хорошо́ подко́ван в фи́зике, well-grounded in physics.

подко́жный *adj.* hypodermic.

подколо́дный *adj., in* **змея́ подколо́дная,** *colloq.* snake in the grass.

подколо́ть [*infl.* **-колю́, -ко́лешь**] *v., pfv. of* **подка́лывать.**

подкоми́ссия *n.* subcommittee.

подкомите́т *n.* subcommittee.

подко́п *n.* **1,** undermining. **2,** underground passage; tunnel. **3,** *pl., colloq.* schemes; machinations.

подкопа́ть *v., pfv. of* **подка́пывать.** —**подкопа́ться,** *refl., pfv. of* **подка́пываться.**

подкорми́ть [*infl.* **-кормлю́, -ко́рмишь**] *v., pfv. of* **подка́рмливать.**

подко́с *n.* strut; cross brace.

подкоси́ть [*infl.* **-кошу́, -ко́сишь**] *v., pfv. of* **подка́шивать.** —**подкоси́ться,** *refl., pfv. of* **подка́шиваться.**

подкра́дываться *v.r. impfv.* [*pfv.* **подкра́сться**] (*with* **к**) to sneak up to *or* on; steal up to.

подкра́сить [*infl.* **-шу, -сишь**] *v., pfv. of* **подкра́шивать.** —**подкра́ситься,** *refl., pfv. of* **подкра́шиваться.**

подкра́сться [*infl. like* **красть**] *v.r., pfv. of* **подкра́дываться.**

подкра́шивать *v. impfv.* [*pfv.* **подкра́сить**] to touch up. —**подкра́шиваться,** *refl., colloq.* to put on some make-up.

подкрепи́ть [*infl.* **-плю́, -пи́шь**] *v., pfv. of* **подкрепля́ть.**

подкрепле́ние *n.* **1,** reinforcement. **2,** *pl., mil.* reinforcements. **3,** *colloq.* sustenance. —**в подкрепле́ние** (+ *gen.*), to support (an argument, assertion, etc.).

подкрепля́ть *v. impfv.* [*pfv.* **подкрепи́ть**] **1,** to reinforce. **2,** to fortify (with food, drink, etc.). **3,** *fig.* to support; bolster. —**подкрепля́ться,** *refl.* to fortify oneself (*with food or drink*).

по́дкуп *n.* **1,** bribery. **2,** graft.

подкупа́ть *v. impfv.* [*pfv.* **подкупи́ть**] **1,** to bribe. **2,** *fig.* to win over. **3,** (*with gen.*) *colloq.* to buy an additional quantity of.

подкупа́ющий *adj.* winning; appealing; engaging.

подкупи́ть [*infl.* **-куплю́, -ку́пишь**] *v., pfv. of* **подкупа́ть.**

подла́живаться *v.r. impfv.* [*pfv.* **подла́диться**] *colloq.* **1,** (*with* **под** + *acc. or* **к**) to adapt (to); adjust (to). **2,** (*with* **к**) to try to please; play up to.

подла́мывать *v. impfv.* [*pfv.* **подломи́ть**] to break. —**подла́мываться,** *refl.* **1,** to give way; cave in; collapse. **2,** (*of one's legs, knees, etc.*) to buckle.

по́дле *prep., with gen.* beside; alongside of; near. —*adv.* alongside; nearby.

подлежа́ть *v. impfv.* [*pres.* **-жу́, -жи́шь**] (*with dat.*) to be subject to; be liable to.

подлежа́щее *n., decl. as an adj., gram.* subject.

подлежа́щий *adj.* (*with dat.*) subject (to); liable (to).

подлеза́ть *v. impfv.* [*pfv.* **подле́зть**] (*with* **под** + *acc.*) to crawl under.

подле́зть [*infl. like* **лезть**] *v., pfv. of* **подлеза́ть.**

подле́сок [*gen.* **-ска**] *n.* underbrush; undergrowth.

подлета́ть *v. impfv.* [*pfv.* **подлете́ть**] (*with* **к**) **1,** to fly up to. **2,** *colloq.* to rush up to.

подлете́ть [*infl.* **-чу́, -ти́шь**] *v., pfv. of* **подлета́ть.**

подле́ц [*gen.* **-леца́**] *n.* scoundrel.

подлива́ть *v. impfv.* [*pfv.* **подли́ть**] (*with gen.*) to add a little more (*by pouring*). —**подлива́ть ма́сла в ого́нь,** to add fuel to the fire; pour oil on the flames.

подли́вка *n.* sauce; gravy.

подли́за *n.m. & f., colloq.* bootlicker.

подли́зываться *v.r. impfv.* [*pfv.* **подлиза́ться**] (*with* **к**) *colloq.* to lick (someone's) boots.

по́длинник *n.* original: чита́ть в по́длиннике, to read in the original.

по́длинный *adj.* **1,** original. **2,** genuine; authentic. **3,** true; real. —**по́длинно,** *adv.* truly; really. —**по́длинность,** *n.f.* authenticity.

подли́ть [*infl.* **подолью́, подольёшь;** *past fem.* **подлила́**] *v., pfv. of* **подлива́ть.**

по́дличать *v. impfv.* **1,** to be mean; do mean things. **2,** to be servile; (*with* **пе́ред**) cater to; play up to.

по́дло *adv.* despicably.

подло́г *n.* forgery.

подло́дка [*gen. pl.* **-док**] *n., colloq.* submarine (*contr. of* **подво́дная ло́дка**).

подложи́ть [*infl.* **-ложу́, -ло́жишь**] *v., pfv. of* **подкла́дывать.**

подло́жный *adj.* forged; counterfeit.

подлоко́тник *n.* armrest.

подломи́ть [*infl.* **-ломлю́, -ло́мишь**] *v., pfv. of* **подла́мывать.** —**подломи́ться,** *refl., pfv. of* **подла́мываться.**

по́длость *n.f.* **1,** meanness; baseness. **2,** mean trick; dirty trick.

по́длый *adj.* mean; base; miserable; despicable.

подма́зать [*infl.* **-ма́жу, -ма́жешь**] *v., pfv. of* **подма́зывать.** —**подма́заться,** *refl., pfv. of* **подма́зываться.**

подма́зывать *v. impfv.* [*pfv.* **подма́зать**] **1,** to grease. **2,** *colloq.* to grease the palm of. —**подма́зываться,** *refl., colloq.* **1,** to put on some make-up. **2,** (*with* **к**) to play up to; curry favor with.

подманда́тный *adj., in* **подманда́тная террито́рия,** mandated territory.

подмасте́рье [*gen. pl.* **-рьев**] *n.m.* apprentice.

подма́хивать *v. impfv.* [*pfv.* **подмахну́ть**] *colloq.* to sign hurriedly; sign without reading.

подма́чивать *v. impfv.* [*pfv.* **подмочи́ть**] **1,** to wet slightly. **2,** *colloq.* to damage (one's reputation).

подме́на *also,* **подме́н** *n.* (improper or illegal) substitution.

подменить [*infl.* **-меню, -ме́нишь**] *v., pfv. of* **подменя́ть.**

подменя́ть *v. impfv.* [*pfv.* **подмени́ть**] **1,** to remove (stealthily) and replace with something else: подменя́ть че́й-нибудь экзаменацио́нный биле́т свои́м, to replace someone's exam paper with one's own; substitute one's own exam paper for someone else's. Кто́-то подмени́л мне шля́пу, someone took my hat (and left his own instead). **2,** to replace; take the place of (*for a short time*).

подмерза́ть *v. impfv.* [*pfv.* **подмёрзнуть**] to freeze slightly; become slightly frozen.

подмёрзнуть [*past* **-мёрз, -ла**] *v., pfv. of* **подмерза́ть.**

подмести́ [*infl. like* **мести́**] *v., pfv. of* **подмета́ть.**

подмета́льщик *n.m.* [*fem.* **-щица**] sweeper.

подмета́ть *v. impfv.* [*pfv.* **подмести́**] to sweep.

подме́тить [*infl.* **-чу, -тишь**] *v., pfv. of* **подмеча́ть.**

подмётка [*gen. pl.* **-ток**] *n.* sole (*of a shoe*). —**в подмётки не годи́ться** (+ *dat.*), to be unable to hold a candle to.

подмеча́ть *v. impfv.* [*pfv.* **подме́тить**] to notice; spot; detect.

подме́шивать *v. impfv.* [*pfv.* **подмеша́ть**] (*with gen.*) to add a little (*by mixing*).

подми́гивать *v. impfv.* [*pfv.* **подмигну́ть**] (*with dat.*) to wink (at).

подмина́ть *v. impfv.* [*pfv.* **подмя́ть**] (*often with* **под себя́**) **1,** to pin down. **2,** *fig.* to crush.

подмо́га *n., colloq.* help.

подмока́ть *v. impfv.* [*pfv.* **подмо́кнуть**] to get slightly wet.

подмо́кнуть [*past* **-мо́к, -ла**] *v., pfv. of* **подмока́ть.**

подмора́живать *v. impfv.* [*pfv.* **подморо́зить**] **1,** to freeze slightly; put in the refrigerator for a while. **2,** *impers.* to freeze up: но́чью подморо́зило, there was some frost during the night.

подмоско́вный *adj.* located near (*or* on the outskirts of) Moscow.

подмо́стки [*gen.* **-ков**] *n. pl.* **1,** scaffold. **2,** the stage: на подмо́стках, on the stage; before the footlights.

подмо́ченный *adj.* **1,** slightly wet. **2,** *colloq.* (*of one's reputation*) damaged.

подмочи́ть [*infl.* **-мочу́, -мо́чишь**] *v., pfv. of* **подма́чивать.**

подмыва́ть *v. impfv.* [*pfv.* **подмы́ть**] **1,** to wash (*from underneath*). **2,** to wash away. **3,** [*impfv. only*] *impers., colloq.* to be dying to: меня́ так и подмыва́ет сказа́ть ей, I am dying to tell her.

подмы́ть [*infl.* **-мо́ю, -мо́ешь**] *v., pfv. of* **подмыва́ть.**

подмы́шка [*gen. pl.* **-шек**] *n.* armpit.

подмы́шник *n.* (perspiration) shield (*sewn to the armhole of a dress*).

подмя́ть [*infl.* **подомну́, подомнёшь**] *v., pfv. of* **подмина́ть.**

поднадзо́рный *adj.* under surveillance. —*n.* person under surveillance.

поднебе́сье *n.* the heavens; the skies.

поднево́льный *adj.* **1,** dependent. **2,** (*of labor*) forced.

поднесе́ние *n.* **1,** giving (*of a gift*). **2,** *obs.* gift.

поднести́ [*infl. like* **нести́**] *v., pfv. of* **подноси́ть.**

поднима́ть *v. impfv.* [*pfv.* **подня́ть**] **1,** to raise; lift. **2,** to pick up. **3,** to take up; carry up. **4,** *fig.* to rouse: поднима́ть на борьбу́, to rouse to action. **5,** *fig.* to raise (a fuss); start (a revolt). **6,** to plow up: поднима́ть целину́, to plow up (*or* turn up) virgin soil. —**поднима́ть на во́здух,** to blow up; blow sky-high. —**поднима́ть на́ смех,** to hold up to ridicule. —**поднима́ть ру́ку на** (+ *acc.*), to lift a hand against.

поднима́ться *v.r. impfv.* [*pfv.* **подня́ться**] **1,** to go up; rise. **2,** (*with* **на** + *acc.*) to mount; ascend. **3,** *fig.* to arise; break out; develop. —**рука́ не поднима́ется** (*with* **у** *and inf.*), one cannot bring oneself (to).

подновля́ть *v. impfv.* [*pfv.* **поднови́ть**] to freshen up; touch up.

подного́тная *n., decl. as an adj., colloq., in* **вся подного́тная,** inside information; all there is to know.

подно́жие *n.* **1,** foot (*of a mountain*). **2,** pedestal.

подно́жка [*gen. pl.* **-жек**] *n.* **1,** running board. **2,** *in* **дава́ть подно́жку** (+ *dat.*), *colloq.* to trip (someone) up.

подно́жный *adj.* situated or placed under one's feet. —**подно́жный корм,** pasturage.

подно́с *n.* tray.

подноси́ть *v. impfv.* [*pfv.* **поднести́;** *pres.* **-ношу́, -но́сишь**] **1,** (*with* **к**) to bring (to); carry (to). **2,** (*with* **к**) to hold up (to); lift up (to). **3,** to give; present (a gift).

подно́счик *n.* **1,** *mil.* carrier; handler. **2,** server of drinks (*in a tavern*).

подноше́ние *n.* **1,** giving; presenting. **2,** gift; present.

подны́ривать *v. impfv.* [*pfv.* **поднырну́ть**] (*with* **под** + *acc.*) to dive under.

подня́тие *n.* raising; lifting.

подня́ть [*infl.* **-ниму́, -ни́мешь;** *past* **по́днял, подняла́, по́дняло**] *v., pfv. of* **поднима́ть.** —**подня́ться,** *refl.* [*past* **подня́лся** *or* **поднялся́, -ла́сь, -ло́сь**] *pfv. of* **поднима́ться.**

подо *prep.* = **под.**

подоба́ть *v. impfv.* (*with dat.*) to befit; become.

подоба́ющий *adj.* proper; befitting; becoming.

подо́бие *n.* (*with gen.*) something resembling; semblance (of); likeness (of).

подо́бно *prep., with dat.* like: подо́бно отцу́, он..., like his father, he... —**подо́бно тому́ как,** just as.

подо́бный *adj.* [*short form* **подо́бен, -бна**] **1,** (*with dat.*) similar (to); like. **2,** such. **3,** *geom.* (*of figures*) similar. —**и тому́ подо́бное,** and so on; and so forth; and the like; et cetera. —**ничего́ подо́бного,** nothing of the sort; nothing of the kind.

подобостра́стие *n.* obsequiousness; servility. —**подобостра́стный,** *adj.* obsequious; servile.

подобра́ть [*infl.* **подберу́, подберёшь;** *past fem.* **подобрала́**] *v., pfv. of* **подбира́ть.** —**подобра́ться,** *refl., pfv. of* **подбира́ться.**

подобре́ть *v., pfv. of* **добре́ть** (*in sense #1*).

подобру́-поздоро́ву *adv., colloq.* (*with verbs of leaving*) while the going (*or* getting) is good.

подогна́ть [*infl.* **подгоню́, подго́нишь;** *past fem.* **подогнала́**] *v., pfv. of* **подгоня́ть.**

подогну́ть *v., pfv. of* **подгиба́ть.** —**подогну́ться,** *refl., pfv. of* **подгиба́ться.**

подогрева́ть *v. impfv.* [*pfv.* **подогре́ть**] **1,** to warm up. **2,** to reheat; warm over.

пододвига́ть *v. impfv.* [*pfv.* **пододви́нуть**] (*with* **к**) to move up (to); move closer (to). —**пододвига́ться,** *refl.* (*with* **к**) to move over (to); move closer (to).

пододея́льник *n.* blanket cover.

подожда́ть *v., pfv. of* **ждать.**

подозва́ть [*infl.* **подзову́, подзовёшь;** *past fem.* **подозвала́**] *v., pfv. of* **подзыва́ть.**

подозрева́емый *adj.* suspect(ed); under suspicion. —*n.* suspect.

подозрева́ть *v. impfv.* (*with* **в** + *prepl.*) to suspect (of).

подозре́ние *n.* suspicion.

подозри́тельный *adj.* suspicious. —**подозри́тельно,** *adv.* suspiciously.

подои́ть *v., pfv. of* **дои́ть.**

подо́йник *n.* milk pail.

подойти́ [*infl.* **подойду́, подойдёшь;** *past* **подошёл, подошла́, подошло́**] *v., pfv. of* **подходи́ть.**

подоко́нник *n.* window sill.

подо́л *n.* lap (*of a skirt*).

подо́лгу *adv.* for a long time; for hours on end.

подольща́ться *v.r. impfv.* [*pfv.* **подольсти́ться**] (*with* **к**) to ingratiate oneself (with).

подо́нки [*gen.* **-ков**] *n. pl.* dregs; residue. —**подо́нки о́бщества,** dregs of society.

подопе́чный *adj.* under the care of a guardian. —*n.* ward; charge. —**подопе́чная террито́рия,** trust territory.

подоплёка *n.* underlying cause; underlying basis.

подо́пытный *adj.* experimental; used for experimental purposes. —**подо́пытный кро́лик,** guinea pig.

подорва́ть [*infl. like* **рвать**] *v., pfv. of* **подрыва́ть.**

подорожа́ть *v., pfv. of* **дорожа́ть.**

подоро́жник *n.* plantain.

подоро́жный *adj.* situated along a road.

подосла́ть [*infl.* **-шлю́, -шлёшь**] *v., pfv. of* **подсыла́ть.**

подосно́ва *n.* true cause; underlying cause.

подоспе́ть *v. pfv., colloq.* **1,** (*of time*) to come. **2,** to arrive in time; come at the right time.

подостла́ть [*infl.* **подстелю́, -сте́лешь**] *v., pfv. of* **подстила́ть.**

подоткну́ть *v., pfv. of* **подтыка́ть.**

подотчётный *adj.* **1,** (*of money*) on account. **2,** (*with dat.*) accountable (to). —**подотчётность,** *n.f.* accountability.

подо́хнуть [*past* **-до́х, -ла**] *v., pfv. of* **до́хнуть.**

подохо́дный *adj., in* **подохо́дный нало́г,** income tax.

подо́шва *n.* **1,** sole (*of a shoe*). **2,** *colloq.* sole (*of the foot*). **3,** foot (*of a mountain*).

подпада́ть *v. impfv.* [*pfv.* **подпа́сть**] (*with* **под** + *acc.*) to fall under; come under (the power, influence, etc. of someone).

подпа́ивать *v. impfv.* [*pfv.* **подпои́ть**] *colloq.* to give (someone) too much to drink; intentionally make (someone) drunk.

подпа́ливать *v. impfv.* [*pfv.* **подпали́ть**] *colloq.* **1,** to singe; scorch. **2,** to set fire to; set on fire.

подпа́лина *n.* **1,** *colloq.* burn mark. **2,** spot; dapple.

подпали́ть *v., pfv. of* **подпа́ливать.**

подпа́сок [*gen.* **-ска**] *n.* shepherd boy.

подпа́сть [*infl. like* **пасть**] *v., pfv. of* **подпада́ть.**

подпева́ла *n.m. & f., colloq.* lackey; yes man.

подпева́ть *v. impfv.* **1,** to sing along; join in singing. **2,** (*with dat.*) to sing along with. **3,** (*with dat.*) *fig., colloq.* to echo; parrot.

подпере́ть [*infl.* **подопру́, -прёшь;** *past* **подпёр, -ла**] *v., pfv. of* **подпира́ть.** —**подпере́ться,** *refl., pfv. of* **подпира́ться.**

подпи́ливать *v. impfv.* [*pfv.* **подпили́ть**] **1,** to saw at the base of. **2,** to shorten (*by sawing*).

подпили́ть [*infl.* **-пилю́, -пи́лишь**] *v., pfv. of* **подпи́ливать.**

подпира́ть *v. impfv.* [*pfv.* **подопре́ть**] to prop up. —**подпира́ться,** *refl., colloq.* to prop oneself up.

подписа́ние *n.* signing.

подписа́ть [*infl.* **-пишу́, -пи́шешь**] *v., pfv. of* **подпи́сывать.** —**подписа́ться,** *refl., pfv. of* **подпи́сываться.**

подпи́ска [*gen. pl.* **-сок**] *n.* **1,** subscription. **2,** signed statement; written pledge.

подписно́й *adj.* subscription (*attrib.*).

подпи́счик *n.* subscriber.

подпи́сывать *v. impfv.* [*pfv.* **подписа́ть**] **1,** to sign. **2,** to write at the bottom; add at the end. **3,** (*with* **на** + *acc.*) to take out a subscription for (someone) to (a publication). —**подпи́сываться,** *refl.* **1,** to sign one's name. **2,** (*with* **на** + *acc.*) to subscribe (to).

по́дпись *n.f.* **1,** signature. **2,** caption.

подплыва́ть *v. impfv.* [*pfv.* **подплы́ть**] (*with* **к**) **1,** to swim up to. **2,** to sail up to.

подплы́ть [*infl. like* **плыть**] *v., pfv. of* **подплыва́ть.**

подпои́ть [*infl.* **-пою́, -по́ишь** *or* **-пои́шь**] *v., pfv. of* **подпа́ивать.**

подполза́ть *v. impfv.* [*pfv.* **подползти́**] **1,** (*with* **к**) to crawl up to; creep up to. **2,** (*with* **под** + *acc.*) to crawl under; creep under.

подползти́ [*infl. like* **ползти́**] *v., pfv. of* **подполза́ть.**

подполко́вник *n.* lieutenant colonel.

подпо́лье *n.* **1,** cellar. **2,** *fig.* underground: уйти́ в подпо́лье, to go underground. —**подпо́льный,** *adj.* underground (*attrib.*). —**подпо́льщик,** *n.* member of the underground.

подпо́ра *n.* prop; support. *Also* **подпо́рка.**

подпо́рный *adj.* supporting. —**подпо́рная сте́нка,** retaining wall.

подпору́чик *n., pre-rev.* second lieutenant.

подпо́чва *n.* subsoil.

подпоя́сать [*infl.* **-поя́шу, -поя́шешь**] *v., pfv. of* **подпоя́сывать.** —**подпоя́саться,** *refl., pfv. of* **подпоя́сываться.**

подпоя́сывать *v. impfv.* [*pfv.* **подпоя́сать**] to put a belt on; tie a belt around. —**подпоя́сываться,** *refl.* to put one's belt on.

подпра́вить [*infl.* **-влю, -вишь**] *v., pfv. of* **подправля́ть.**

подправля́ть *v. impfv.* [*pfv.* **подпра́вить**] to fix up; straighten; put right.

подпру́га *n.* bellyband; surcingle.

подпры́гивать *v. impfv.* [*pfv.* **подпры́гнуть**] **1,** to jump up and down. **2,** to bounce up and down; bob up and down.

подпуска́ть *v. impfv.* [*pfv.* **подпусти́ть**] **1,** to allow to approach; allow to come near. **2,** *colloq.* to add. **3,** *colloq.* to utter; get in.

подпусти́ть [*infl.* **-пущу́, -пу́стишь**] *v., pfv. of* **подпуска́ть.**

подраба́тывать *v. impfv.* [*pfv.* **подрабо́тать**] *colloq.* **1,** to work up; work out. **2,** to earn on the side.

подра́внивать *v. impfv.* [*pfv.* **подровня́ть**] **1,** to level; make even. **2,** to trim (one's hair, beard, etc.).

подра́гивать *v. impfv., colloq.* **1,** to quiver. **2,** (*with instr.*) to shake (a part of one's body).

подража́ние *n.* imitation. —**подража́тель,** *n.m.* imitator. —**подража́тельный,** *adj.* imitative.

подража́ть *v. impfv.* (*with dat.*) to imitate.

подразделéние *n.* **1,** subdivision. **2,** *mil.* subunit.
подразделя́ть *v. impfv.* [*pfv.* **подраздели́ть**] to subdivide. —**подразделя́ться,** *refl.* to subdivide; be subdivided.
подразумевáть *v. impfv.* to mean; have in mind. —**подразумевáться,** *refl.* to be meant; be understood.
подрастáть *v. impfv.* [*pfv.* **подрасти́**] to grow; grow up.
подрасти́ [*infl. like* **расти́**] *v., pfv. of* **подрастáть.**
подрáться *v.r. pfv.* [*infl. like* **драть**] to fight; get into a fight.
подрéзать [*infl.* **-рéжу, -рéжешь**] *v., pfv. of* **подрезáть.**
подрезáть *v. impfv.* [*pfv.* **подрéзать**] to cut; trim; clip; prune.
подрисовáть [*infl.* **-сýю, -сýешь**] *v., pfv. of* **подрисóвывать.**
подрисóвывать *v. impfv.* [*pfv.* **подрисовáть**] **1,** to touch up. **2,** to paint in.
подрóбно *adv.* in detail.
подрóбность *n.f.* detail.
подрóбный *adj.* detailed.
подровня́ть *v., pfv. of* **подрáвнивать.**
подрóсток [*gen.* **-стка**] *n.* adolescent; teenager.
подрубáть *v. impfv.* [*pfv.* **подруби́ть**] **1,** to chop (*at the base*). **2,** to hem.
подруби́ть [*infl.* **-рублю́, -рýбишь**] *v., pfv. of* **подрубáть.**
подрýга *n.* (female) friend.
подружи́ться *v.r., pfv. of* **дружи́ться.**
подрýливать *v. impfv.* [*pfv.* **подрули́ть**] *aero.* (*with* **к**) to taxi up to.
подрумя́нивать *v. impfv.* [*pfv.* **подрумя́нить**] **1,** to redden; flush. **2,** to put some rouge on. **3,** to brown; toast. —**подрумя́ниваться,** *refl.* **1,** to flush; become flushed. **2,** to put on some rouge. **3,** (*of food*) to become nice and brown.
подрýчный *adj.* **1,** on hand; handy. **2,** improvised; makeshift. **3,** assistant. —*n.* assistant.
подры́в *n.* **1,** blowing up. **2,** *fig.* undermining.
подрывáть *v. impfv.* [*pfv.* **подорвáть**] **1,** to blow up. **2,** *fig.* to undermine. **3,** [*pfv.* **подры́ть**] to dig under; dig the ground from under.
подрывни́к [*gen.* **-никá**] *n.* demolition expert.
подрывнóй *adj.* **1,** demolition (*attrib.*); blasting (*attrib.*). **2,** *fig.* subversive.
подры́ть [*infl.* **-рóю, -рóешь**] *v., pfv. of* **подрывáть** (*in sense #3*).
подря́д *n.* contract. —*adv.* in a row; in succession.
подряди́ть [*infl.* **-жý, -ди́шь**] *v., pfv. of* **подряжáть.**
подря́дный *adj.* contract (*attrib.*); done on contract.
подря́дчик *n.* contractor.
подряжáть *v. impfv.* [*pfv.* **подряди́ть**] to hire.
подсади́ть [*infl.* **-сажý, -сáдишь**] *v., pfv. of* **подсáживать.**
подсáживать *v. impfv.* [*pfv.* **подсади́ть**] (*with* **в** *or* **на** + *acc.*) **1,** to help (someone) into *or* onto. **2,** (*with* **к**) to seat next to. **3,** (*with gen.*) to plant (an additional quantity of something). —**подсáживаться,** *refl.* [*pfv.* **подсéсть**] (*with* **к**) to sit down near; take a seat near.
подсáливать *v. impfv.* [*pfv.* **подсоли́ть**] to salt lightly; add a little salt to.
подсвéчник *n.* candlestick.
подсевáть *v. impfv.* [*pfv.* **подсéять**] (*with gen.*) to sow (an additional quantity of something).
подсекáть *v. impfv.* [*pfv.* **подсéчь**] to chop off; chop down (*at the base*).
подсéсть [*infl. like* **сесть**] *v., pfv. of* **подсáживаться.**
подсéчь [*infl. like* **сечь;** *past* **-сéк, -лá, -лó**] *v., pfv. of* **подсекáть.**
подсéять [*infl.* **-сéю, -сéешь**] *v., pfv. of* **подсевáть.**
подси́живать *v. impfv.* [*pfv.* **подсидéть**] *colloq.* **1,** to lie in wait for. **2,** to plot against; scheme against.
подси́нивать *v. impfv.* [*pfv.* **подсини́ть**] **1,** to color blue. **2,** to rinse in bluing; blue.
подсини́ть *v., pfv. of* **сини́ть** *and* **подси́нивать.**
подскáбливать *v. impfv.* [*pfv.* **подскобли́ть**] to scrape off.
подсказáть [*infl.* **-скажý, -скáжешь**] *v., pfv. of* **подскáзывать.**
подскáзывать *v. impfv.* [*pfv.* **подсказáть**] **1,** (*with dat.*) to prompt: не подскáзывать!, no prompting! **2,** to suggest (an idea, solution, etc.).
подскакáть [*infl.* **-скачý, -скáчешь**] *v., pfv. of* **подскáкивать** (*in sense #4*).
подскáкивать *v. impfv.* [*pfv.* **подскочи́ть**] **1,** to jump up. **2,** *colloq.* (*of prices, temperature, etc.*) to shoot up; soar; skyrocket. **3,** (*with* **к**) to run up to; come running up to. **4,** [*pfv.* **подскакáть**] (*with* **к**) to come galloping up to.
подскобли́ть [*infl.* **-скоблю́, -скóблишь** *or* **-скобли́шь**] *v., pfv. of* **подскáбливать.**
подскочи́ть [*infl.* **-скочý, -скóчишь**] *v., pfv. of* **подскáкивать.**
подслáщивать *v. impfv.* [*pfv.* **подсласти́ть**] to sweeten.
подслéдственный *adj.* under investigation.
подслеповáтый *adj.* having poor vision.
подслýживаться *v.r. impfv.* [*pfv.* **подслужи́ться**] (*with* **к**) *colloq.* to curry favor (with); play up to.
подслужи́ться [*infl.* **-служýсь, -слýжишься**] *v.r., pfv. of* **подслýживаться.**
подслýшать *v., pfv. of* **подслýшивать.**
подслýшивание *n.* eavesdropping. —**пункт/пост подслýшивания,** listening post.
подслýшивать *v. impfv.* [*pfv.* **подслýшать**] **1,** to overhear. **2,** [*impfv. only*] to eavesdrop.
подсмáтривать *v. impfv.* [*pfv.* **подсмотрéть**] **1,** to watch secretly. **2,** (*with* **в** + *acc.*) to peep through. **3,** (*with* **за** + *instr.*) to spy on.
подсмéиваться *v.r. impfv.* (*with* **над**) to make fun of.
подсмотрéть *v. pfv.* [*infl.* **-смотрю́, -смóтришь**] **1,** *pfv. of* **подсмáтривать. 2,** to catch sight of; spot; detect.
подснéжник *n.* snowdrop.
подсóбный *adj.* auxiliary; subsidiary; accessory; additional.
подсóвывать *v. impfv.* [*pfv.* **подсýнуть**] **1,** (*with* **под** + *acc.*) to put under; shove under. **2,** *colloq.* to slip; put furtively. **3,** *colloq.* to palm off.
подсознáние *n.* the subconscious. —**подсознáтельный,** *adj.* subconscious.
подсоли́ть [*infl.* **-солю́, -сóлишь** *or* **-соли́шь**] *v., pfv. of* **подсáливать.**
подсóлнечник *n.* sunflower. —**подсóлнечный,** *adj.* sunflower (*attrib.*).
подсóлнух *n., colloq.* **1,** sunflower. **2,** *usu. pl.* sunflower seeds.
подсóхнуть [*past* **-сóх, -ла**] *v., pfv. of* **подсыхáть.**
подспóрье *n., colloq.* help; support.

подспу́дный *adj.* hidden; secret; latent. —**подспу́дно,** *adv.* secretly.
подста́вить [*infl.* **-влю, -вишь**] *v., pfv. of* **подставля́ть.**
подста́вка [*gen. pl.* **-вок**] *n.* stand; support.
подставля́ть *v. impfv.* [*pfv.* **подста́вить**] **1,** (*with* **под** + *acc.*) to place under. **2,** (*with* **к**) to place near (to). Подста́вить стул (+ *dat.*), to bring up a chair for. **3,** (*with dat.*) to turn toward: подставля́ть лицо́ со́лнцу, to turn one's face toward the sun. **4,** to expose; leave vulnerable. **5,** to substitute. —**подставля́ть другу́ю щёку,** to turn the other cheek. —**подставля́ть но́жку** (+ *dat.*), to trip (someone) up.
подставно́й *adj.* **1,** placed near or under. **2,** false. —**подставно́е лицо́,** dummy; front.
подстака́нник *n.* glass holder (*for use when drinking*).
подстано́вка *n., math.* substitution.
подста́нция *n.* substation.
подстёгивать *v. impfv.* [*pfv.* **подстегну́ть**] **1,** *colloq.* to fasten (on). **2,** to urge on; whip (a horse). **3,** *fig., colloq.* to stir up; spur on.
подстерега́ть *v. impfv.* [*pfv.* **подстере́чь**] to lie in wait for.
подстере́чь [*infl. like* **стере́чь**] *v., pfv. of* **подстерега́ть.**
подстила́ть *v. impfv.* [*pfv.* **подостла́ть**] (*with* **под** + *acc.*) to lay under; spread under.
подсти́лка [*gen. pl.* **-лок**] *n.* bedding.
подстра́ивать *v. impfv.* [*pfv.* **подостро́ить**] **1,** (*with* **к**) to build on to. **2,** *colloq.* to cook up. **3,** *in* подстро́ить шу́тку/по́длость/па́кость (+ *dat.*), to play a dirty trick on.
подстрека́тель *n.m.* instigator. —**подстрека́тельство,** *n.* instigation.
подстрека́ть *v. impfv.* [*pfv.* **подстрекну́ть**] **1,** to incite; goad; egg on; put up to. **2,** to arouse (a feeling).
подстре́ливать *v. impfv.* [*pfv.* **подстрели́ть**] to wound (an animal); wing (a bird).
подстрели́ть [*infl.* **-стрелю́, -стре́лишь**] *v., pfv. of* **подстре́ливать.**
подстрига́ть *v. impfv.* [*pfv.* **подстри́чь**] to clip; trim; crop. —**подстрига́ться,** *refl.* to get a haircut; get a trim.
подстри́чь [*infl. like* **стричь**] *v., pfv. of* **подстрига́ть.**
подстро́ить *v., pfv. of* **подстра́ивать.**
подстро́чник *n.* word-for-word translation.
подстро́чный *adj.* **1,** (*of a translation*) word-for-word. **2,** placed under a line or at the bottom of a page: подстро́чное примеча́ние, footnote.
по́дступ *n.* approach.
подступа́ть *v. impfv.* [*pfv.* **подступи́ть**] **1,** (*with* **к**) to approach. **2,** [*often with* **к го́рлу** *or* **к се́рдцу**] (*of emotions, tears, etc.*) to come; come over; (*of a lump*) to form. —**подступа́ться,** *refl.* (*with* **к**) to approach.
подступи́ть [*infl.* **-ступлю́, -сту́пишь**] *v., pfv. of* **подступа́ть.** —**подступи́ться,** *refl., pfv. of* **подступа́ться.**
подсуди́мый *n., decl. as an adj.* defendant.
подсу́дный *adj.* (*with dat.*) within the jurisdiction (of). —**подсу́дность,** *n.f.* jurisdiction.
подсу́мок [*gen.* **-мка**] *n.* cartridge pouch.
подсу́нуть *v., pfv. of* **подсо́вывать.**
подсу́шивать *v. impfv.* [*pfv.* **подсуши́ть**] to dry (something) a little.
подсуши́ть [*infl.* **-сушу́, -су́шишь**] *v., pfv. of* **подсу́шивать.**
подсчёт *n.* **1,** count(ing). **2,** *pl.* calculations.
подсчи́тывать *v. impfv.* [*pfv.* **подсчита́ть**] to count up; calculate; compute.
подсыла́ть *v. impfv.* [*pfv.* **подосла́ть**] to send on a secret mission.
подсы́пать [*infl.* **-сы́плю, -сы́плешь**] *v., pfv. of* **подсыпа́ть.**
подсыпа́ть *v. impfv.* [*pfv.* **подсы́пать**] (*with gen. or acc.*) to add a little (of something) by sprinkling.
подсыха́ть *v. impfv.* [*pfv.* **подсо́хнуть**] to dry out a little.
подта́ивать *v. impfv.* [*pfv.* **подта́ять**] to melt a little; melt slightly.
подта́лкивать *v. impfv.* [*pfv.* **подтолкну́ть**] **1,** to push slightly; shove slightly; nudge. **2,** *fig.* to prompt; encourage; spur on.
подта́пливать *v. impfv.* [*pfv.* **подтопи́ть**] to heat slightly; warm slightly.
подта́скивать *v. impfv.* [*pfv.* **подтащи́ть**] (*with* **к**) to pull up to; drag up to.
подтасова́ть [*infl.* **-су́ю, -су́ешь**] *v., pfv. of* **подтасо́вывать.**
подтасо́вка *n.* **1,** dishonest shuffling (*of cards*). **2,** *fig.* juggling (*of facts*).
подтасо́вывать *v. impfv.* [*pfv.* **подтасова́ть**] **1,** to shuffle (cards) dishonestly. **2,** *fig.* to juggle (facts).
подта́чивать *v. impfv.* [*pfv.* **подточи́ть**] **1,** to sharpen. **2,** to eat away; corrode. **3,** *fig.* to undermine; sap.
подтащи́ть [*infl.* **-тащу́, -та́щишь**] *v., pfv. of* **подта́скивать.**
подта́ять [*infl.* **-та́ет**] *v., pfv. of* **подта́ивать.**
подтверди́ть [*infl.* **-жу́, -ди́шь**] *v., pfv. of* **подтвержда́ть.**
подтвержда́ть *v. impfv.* [*pfv.* **подтверди́ть**] to confirm; corroborate. Подвержда́ть получе́ние (+ *gen.*), to acknowledge receipt of.
подтвержде́ние *n.* confirmation; corroboration.
подтёк *n.* **1,** streak. **2,** bruise.
подтека́ть *v. impfv.* [*pfv.* **подте́чь**] **1,** (*with* **под** + *acc.*) to flow under; run under. **2,** *colloq.* (*of a container*) to leak.
подте́кст *n.* underlying theme.
подтере́ть [*infl.* **подотру́, -трёшь;** *past* **подтёр, -ла**] *v., pfv. of* **подтира́ть.**
подте́чь [*infl. like* **течь**] *v., pfv. of* **подтека́ть.**
подтира́ть *v. impfv.* [*pfv.* **подтере́ть**] to wipe up.
подтолкну́ть *v., pfv. of* **подта́лкивать.**
подтопи́ть [*infl.* **-топлю́, -то́пишь**] *v., pfv. of* **подта́пливать.**
подточи́ть [*infl.* **-точу́, -то́чишь**] *v., pfv. of* **подта́чивать.**
подтру́нивать *v. impfv.* [*pfv.* **подтруни́ть**] (*with* **над**) to poke fun at.
подтыка́ть *v. impfv.* [*pfv.* **подоткну́ть**] to tuck in; tuck under.
подтя́гивать *v. impfv.* [*pfv.* **подтяну́ть**] **1,** to tighten; pull tight. **2,** (*with* **к**) to pull up to; drag up to. **3,** (*with* **под** + *acc.*) to pull under; drag under. **4,** *mil.* to bring up (troops). **5,** to get after; clamp down on. **6,** *v.i.* to join in singing. —**подтя́гиваться,** *refl.* **1,** to tighten one's belt. **2,** to pull oneself up. **3,** (*of troops*) to move up. **4,** *fig., colloq.* to catch up with the rest.
подтя́жка [*gen. pl.* **-жек**] *n.* suspender.

подтя́нутый *adj.* smart; neat; fresh.
подтяну́ть [*infl.* **-тяну́, -тя́нешь**] *v., pfv. of* **подтя́гивать. —подтяну́ться,** *refl., pfv. of* **подтя́гиваться.**
поду́мать *v. pfv.* **1,** *pfv. of* **ду́мать. 2,** to think for a moment. **—и не поду́маю!,** I wouldn't dream of it! **—поду́мать то́лько!,** just think!; just imagine!
поду́мывать *v. impfv.* (*with inf. or* **о**) *colloq.* to be thinking of; be considering (a possibility).
подурне́ть *v., pfv. of* **дурне́ть.**
поду́ть *v. pfv.* **1,** *pfv. of* **дуть. 2,** to begin to blow.
поду́чивать *v. impfv.* [*pfv.* **подучи́ть**] *colloq.* **1,** to teach. **2,** to learn. **3,** to egg on; put up to. **—поду́чиваться,** *refl.* (*with dat. or inf.*) *colloq.* to learn.
подучи́ть [*infl.* **-учу́, -у́чишь**] *v., pfv. of* **поду́чивать. —подучи́ться,** *refl., pfv. of* **поду́чиваться.**
поду́шечка [*gen. pl.* **-чек**] *n., dim. of* **поду́шка. —поду́шечка для була́вок,** pincushion.
подуши́ть *v. pfv.* [*infl.* **-душу́, -ду́шишь**] to perfume; put some perfume on. **—подуши́ться,** *refl.* to put on some perfume.
поду́шка [*gen. pl.* **-шек**] *n.* pillow; cushion. **—поду́шка для штемпеле́й,** stamp pad; ink pad.
поду́шный *adj., in* **поду́шный нало́г; поду́шная по́дать,** poll tax; tax per head.
подфа́рник *n.* parking light.
подхали́м *n.* toady; sycophant.
подхали́мничать *v. impfv., colloq.* **1,** to be servile; bow and scrape. **2,** (*with* **пе́ред**) to curry favor with; play up to.
подхали́мство *n.* toadyism.
подхвати́ть [*infl.* **-хвачу́, -хва́тишь**] *v., pfv. of* **подхва́тывать.**
подхва́тывать *v. impfv.* [*pfv.* **подхвати́ть**] **1,** to catch; grasp; snatch. **2,** *colloq.* to catch; pick up (an illness). **3,** to pick up (information, an expression, etc.). **4,** to join in (singing, a conversation, etc.).
подхлёстывать *v. impfv.* [*pfv.* **подхлестну́ть**] **1,** to whip; urge on (a horse). **2,** *fig., colloq.* to spur on.
подхо́д *n.* approach.
подходи́ть *v. impfv.* [*pfv.* **подойти́**; *pres.* **-хожу́, -хо́дишь**] **1,** (*with* **к**) to approach; come up to; walk up to. **2,** to approach; come near. **3,** to do; be suitable. **4,** (*with dat.*) to suit; fit; be right for.
подходя́щий *adj.* suitable; proper; appropriate; right.
подцепи́ть [*infl.* **-цеплю́, -це́пишь**] *v., pfv. of* **подцепля́ть.**
подцепля́ть *v. impfv.* [*pfv.* **подцепи́ть**] **1,** to hook on; couple. **2,** *fig., colloq.* to get; acquire; catch.
подча́с *adv.* sometimes; at times.
подчёркивать *v. impfv.* [*pfv.* **подчеркну́ть**] **1,** to underline. **2,** to emphasize; stress.
подчине́ние *n.* **1,** subordination. Быть в подчине́нии у, to be subordinate to. **2,** submission. **3,** subjugation.
подчинённый *adj. & n.* subordinate. **—подчинённость,** *n.f.* subordination.
подчиня́ть *v. impfv.* [*pfv.* **подчини́ть**] **1,** to subjugate; subdue. **2,** (*with dat.*) to subordinate (to); subject (to). **3,** (*with dat.*) to place under the command or jurisdiction of. **—подчиня́ться,** *refl.* (*with dat.*) to submit (to); yield (to); obey.
подчи́стить [*infl.* **-щу, -стишь**] *v., pfv. of* **подчища́ть.**
подчи́стка *n.* **1,** cleaning up. **2,** *colloq.* erasure.
подчи́тчик *n.* [*usu.* **корре́ктор-подчи́тчик**] copyholder.
подчища́ть *v. impfv.* [*pfv.* **подчи́стить**] **1,** to clean up. **2,** to erase; rub out.
подшива́ть *v. impfv.* [*pfv.* **подши́ть**] **1,** to sew in; sew on. **2,** to sew a hem in. **3,** to sole (a shoe). **4,** to file (newspapers, documents, etc.).
подши́вка [*gen. pl.* **-вок**] *n.* **1,** hemming. **2,** soling (*of shoes*). **3,** filing. **4,** *colloq.* file: газе́тная подши́вка, newspaper file.
подши́пник *n., mech.* bearing: ша́риковый подши́пник, ball bearing.
подши́ть [*infl.* **подошью́, -шьёшь**] *v., pfv. of* **подшива́ть.**
подшта́нники [*gen.* **-ков**] *n. pl., colloq.* men's drawers.
подшути́ть [*infl.* **-шучу́, -шу́тишь**] *v., pfv. of* **подшу́чивать.**
подшу́чивать *v. impfv.* [*pfv.* **подшути́ть**] (*with* **над**) **1,** to make fun of. **2,** to play a trick on.
подъе́зд *n.* **1,** approach. **2,** entrance; doorway.
подъездно́й *adj.* of approach. **—подъездна́я доро́га,** access road.
подъезжа́ть *v. impfv.* [*pfv.* **подъе́хать**] (*with* **к**) to drive up to; ride up to; draw up to; pull up to.
подъём *n.* **1,** raising; lifting. **2,** ascent; upgrade. **3,** *fig.* rise; upsurge. **4,** enthusiasm. **5,** instep. **6,** reveille. **—лёгок на подъём,** always ready to get up and go. **—тяжёл на подъём,** hard to get moving.
подъёмник *n.* lift; hoist.
подъёмный *adj.* lifting (*attrib.*). **—подъёмный кран,** crane. **—подъёмный мост,** drawbridge. **—подъёмная си́ла, 1,** lifting capacity. **2,** *aero.* lift.
подъе́хать [*infl. like* **е́хать**] *v., pfv. of* **подъезжа́ть.**
поды́грывать *v. impfv.* [*pfv.* **подыгра́ть**] (*with dat.*) *colloq.* to accompany (*on a musical instrument*). **—поды́грываться,** *refl.* (*with* **к**) *colloq.* to play up to.
подыма́ть *v. impfv.* = **поднима́ть.**
подыска́ть [*infl.* **подыщу́, поды́щешь**] *v., pfv. of* **поды́скивать.**
поды́скивать *v. impfv.* [*pfv.* **подыска́ть**] **1,** to find. **2,** [*impfv. only*] to look for; seek; try to find.
подыто́живать *v. impfv.* [*pfv.* **подыто́жить**] **1,** to add up; total. **2,** to sum up.
подыша́ть *v. pfv.* [*infl.* **-дышу́, -ды́шишь**] (*with instr.*) to breathe; take a breath of.
поеда́ть *v. impfv.* [*pfv.* **пое́сть**] **1,** to eat up. **2,** (*of insects, rodents, etc.*) to eat; devour.
поеди́нок [*gen.* **-нка**] *n.* duel.
поедо́м *also,* **по́едом** *adv., colloq. in* **есть (кого́-нибудь) поедо́м,** to make someone's life miserable (*by nagging*).
по́езд [*pl.* **поезда́**] *n.* train.
пое́здить *v. pfv.* [*infl.* **-е́зжу, -е́здишь**] to travel about; travel widely.
пое́здка [*gen.pl.* **-док**] *n.* trip.
поездно́й *adj.* train (*attrib.*).
пое́сть [*infl. like* **есть**] *v., pfv. of* **есть** (*in sense #2*) *and* **поеда́ть.**
пое́хать *v. pfv.* [*infl.* **пое́ду, пое́дешь**] **1,** *pfv. of* **е́хать. 2,** (*of a vehicle*) to start moving. **—пое́хали!,** let's go!; let's get started!; let's be off!
пожале́ть *v., pfv. of* **жале́ть.**
пожа́ловать *v., pfv. of* **жа́ловать. —пожа́ловаться,** *refl., pfv. of* **жа́ловаться.**
пожа́луй *particle* **1,** possibly; probably: пожа́луй, вы пра́вы, you may be right; you are probably right. **2,** well, all right! (*indicating reluctant consent*).

пожа́луйста *particle* **1,** please! **2,** you're welcome!; don't mention it! **3,** certainly!; by all means!
пожа́р *n.* a fire: лесно́й пожа́р, forest fire.
пожа́рище *n.* scene of a fire; burned-out area.
пожа́рник *n.* fireman.
пожа́рный *adj.* fire (*attrib.*). —*n.* fireman. —**пожа́рная ле́стница,** fire escape. —**пожа́рная маши́на,** fire engine.
пожа́тие *n.* handshake.
пожа́ть *v. pfv.* **1,** [*infl.* **-жму́, -жмёшь**] *pfv. of* **жать**[1] (*in sense #2*) *and* **пожима́ть. 2,** [*infl.* **-жну́, -жнёшь**] *pfv. of* **пожина́ть.**
пожева́ть *v. pfv.* [*infl.* **-жую́, -жуёшь**] to chew.
пожела́ние *n.* wish: наилу́чшие пожела́ния, best wishes.
пожела́ть *v., pfv. of* **жела́ть.**
пожелте́лый *adj.* yellowed.
пожелте́ть *v., pfv. of* **желте́ть.**
пожени́ться *v.r. pfv.* [*infl.* **-же́нится**] (*of two people*) to get married.
поже́ртвование *n.* contribution; donation.
поже́ртвовать *v., pfv. of* **же́ртвовать.**
пожи́ва *n., colloq.* easy money.
пожива́ть *v. impfv., in* **как вы пожива́ете?,** how are you?; how are you getting along?
поживи́ться *v.r. pfv.* [*infl.* **-влю́сь, -ви́шься**] *colloq.* **1,** (*with instr.*) to make money (off of *or* out of). **2,** (*with* **за счёт**) to profit (at the expense of).
пожи́зненный *adj.* life (*attrib.*); for life; lifetime (*attrib.*): пожи́зненное заключе́ние, life imprisonment. —**пожи́зненно,** *adv.* for life: назнача́ться пожи́зненно, to be appointed for life.
пожило́й *adj.* getting on in years.
пожима́ние *n.* shaking (of hands); shrug (of the shoulder).
пожима́ть *v. impfv.* [*pfv.* **пожа́ть**] **1,** to shake: пожима́ть ру́ку (+ *dat.*), to shake someone's hand. **2,** *in* пожима́ть плеча́ми, to shrug one's shoulders.
пожина́ть *v. impfv.* [*pfv.* **пожа́ть**] **1,** *obs.* to reap. **2,** *fig.* to reap; gain: пожина́ть ла́вры, to reap the laurels.
пожира́ть *v. impfv.* [*pfv.* **пожра́ть**] **1,** to devour; consume. **2,** *colloq.* to eat; gobble.
пожи́тки [*pl.* **-ков**] *n. pl., colloq.* belongings.
пожи́ть *v. pfv.* [*infl.* **-живу́, -живёшь;** *past* **по́жил, пожила́, по́жило**] **1,** to live for a while. **2,** *colloq.* to live it up. —**поживём – уви́дим,** we'll see what happens.
пожра́ть [*infl. like* **жрать**] *v., pfv. of* **пожира́ть.**
пожури́ть *v., pfv. of* **жури́ть.**
по́за *n.* **1,** pose; position. **2,** *fig.* affectation; pretense.
позаба́вить *v. pfv.* [*infl.* **-влю, -вишь**] to amuse; entertain. —**позаба́виться,** *refl., colloq.* to have a little fun.
позабо́титься *v.r., pfv. of* **забо́титься.**
позабыва́ть *v. impfv.* [*pfv.* **позабы́ть**] *colloq.* to forget all about; completely forget.
позабы́ть [*infl.* **-бу́ду, -бу́дешь**] *v., pfv. of* **позабыва́ть.**
позави́довать *v., pfv. of* **зави́довать.**
поза́втракать *v., pfv. of* **за́втракать.**
позавчера́ *adv.* the day before yesterday.
позади́ *adv.* behind. —*prep., with gen.* behind.
позаимствовать *v., pfv. of* **заимствовать.**
позапро́шлый *adj.* before last: позапро́шлый год, the year before last.
поза́риться *v.r., pfv. of* **за́риться.**
позва́ть *v., pfv. of* **звать.**
позволе́ние *n.* permission. —**с позволе́ния сказа́ть, 1,** if I may say so. **2,** if you could call it that.
позволи́тельный *adj.* permissible.
позволя́ть *v. impfv.* [*pfv.* **позво́лить**] (*with dat.*) **1,** to allow; permit. **2,** to enable; make it possible for. —**позво́льте, 1,** (*with inf.*) allow me to... **2,** excuse me!; I beg your pardon! —**позво́лить себе́, 1,** (*with inf.*) to venture (to); take the liberty of. **2,** to allow oneself; be able to afford: не могу́ себе́ э́того позво́лить, I can't afford it.
позвони́ть *v., pfv. of* **звони́ть.**
позвоно́к [*gen.* **-нка́**] *n.* vertebra.
позвоно́чник *n.* spine; backbone.
позвоно́чный *adj.* vertebrate; vertebral. Позвоно́чный столб, spinal column. —**позвоно́чные,** *n. pl.* vertebrates.
по́здний *adj.* late. —**до по́здней но́чи,** till late at night.
по́здно *adv.* late. —*adj., used predicatively* late: уже́ по́здно, it is already late.
поздоро́ваться *v.r., pfv. of* **здоро́ваться.**
поздорове́ть *v., pfv. of* **здорове́ть.**
поздоро́виться *v.r. pfv., colloq., impers., used negatively with dat.* to be bad for: ему́ не поздоро́вится от э́того, it will be bad for him; he will come out the worse for it.
поздрави́тельный *adj.* congratulatory.
поздра́вить [*infl.* **-влю, -вишь**] *v., pfv. of* **поздравля́ть.**
поздравле́ние *n.* congratulation. Приими́те мои́ поздравле́ния, (please) accept my congratulations.
поздравля́ть *v. impfv.* [*pfv.* **поздра́вить**] **1,** to congratulate. **2,** (*on holidays, birthdays, etc.*) to wish a happy...: поздра́вить кого́-нибудь с Но́вым го́дом, to wish someone a happy New Year.
позелене́ть *v., pfv. of* **зелене́ть.**
позёр *n.* play-actor. —**позёрство,** *n.* play-acting.
по́зже *adv., comp. of* **по́здно,** later.
пози́ровать *v. impfv.* [*pres.* **-рую, -руешь**] to pose.
позити́в *n., photog.* positive.
позитиви́зм *n.* positivism.
позити́вный *adj.* positive.
позитро́н *n.* positron.
позицио́нный *adj.* positional.
пози́ция *n.* **1,** position. **2,** *fig.* position; viewpoint: изложи́ть свою́ пози́цию, to state one's position.
познава́тельный *adj.* cognitive.
познава́ть *v. impfv.* [*pfv.* **позна́ть;** *pres.* **-знаю́, -знаёшь**] **1,** to get to know. **2,** to experience. —**познава́ться,** *refl.* [*impfv. only*] to become known; become recognized (*for what one is*).
познако́мить *v., pfv. of* **знако́мить.** —**познако́миться,** *refl., pfv. of* **знако́миться.**
позна́ние *n.* **1,** cognition. **2,** *pl.* knowledge. —**тео́рия позна́ния,** epistemology.
позна́ть [*infl.* **-зна́ю, -зна́ешь**] *v., pfv. of* **познава́ть.**
позоло́та *n.* gilding; gilt.
позолоти́ть *v., pfv. of* **золоти́ть.**
позоло́ченний *adj.* gilded; gilt.
позо́р *n.* shame; disgrace.
позо́рить *v. impfv.* [*pfv.* **опозо́рить**] to disgrace. —**позо́риться,** *refl.* to disgrace oneself.
позо́рище *n., colloq.* shameful event; disgrace; scandal.

позóрный *adj.* disgraceful; shameful. —**позóрный столб,** pillory.
позумéнт *n.* galloon; braid.
позы́в *n.* urge; desire.
позывнóй *adj., in* **позывнóй сигнáл,** call sign. —**позывны́е,** *n. pl.* call sign.
поигрáть *v. pfv.* to play (*for a while*).
поимённо *adv.* by name.
поимённый *adj.* of names: поимённый спи́сок, list of names. —**поимённое голосовáние,** roll-call vote.
поименовáть *v. pfv.* [*infl.* **-ну́ю, -ну́ешь**] **1,** to call; name. **2,** to mention; list.
пои́мка *n.* catching; capture.
поинтересовáться *v.r. pfv.* [*infl.* **-су́юсь, -су́ешься**] (*with instr.*) **1,** to show an interest (in). **2,** to look into; check into.
пóиск *n., often pl.* **1,** search; quest. **2,** retrieval (*of information*). **3,** *mil.* reconnaissance raid. —**в пóисках** (+ *gen.*), in search of. —**пойти́** *or* **отпрáвиться на пóиски** (+ *gen.*), to set out in search of.
поискáть *v. pfv.* [*infl.* **-ищу́, -и́щешь**] to look for.
поискóвый *also,* **пóисковый** *adj.* **1,** search (*attrib.*): поискóвая грýппа, search party. **2,** exploring; prospecting.
пои́стине *adv.* truly; indeed.
пои́ть *v. impfv.* [*pfv.* **напои́ть;** *pres.* **пою́, пóишь** *or* **пои́шь**] **1,** to give (someone) something to drink. **2,** to water (cattle).
пóйло *n.* mash; swill.
пóйма *n.* flood plain.
поймáть *v., pfv. of* **лови́ть.**
пóйнтер [*pl.* **пойнтерá**] *n.* pointer (*dog*).
пойти́ *v. pfv.* [*infl.* **пойду́, пойдёшь;** *past* **пошёл, пошлá, пошлó**] **1,** *pfv. of* **идти́. 2,** to begin to walk; set out. **3,** (*of a vehicle*) to start moving. **4,** (*of rain, snow, etc.*) to begin to fall: пошёл дождь, it began to rain. **5,** (*of a liquid*) to begin to flow. **6,** (*with* **на** + *acc.*) to do; take the step of: он не пойдёт на э́то, he won't do (something like) that. **7,** (*with inf.*) *colloq.* to begin (to). **8,** *past tense only, giving imperative meaning,* go!; leave!; go away! Пошёл вон!, away with you!; be off. —**я пошёл,** *colloq.* I'm leaving; I'm off. —**éсли (уж) на то пошлó,** for that matter; if it comes to that.
покá *adv.* for the time being; for the present; for the moment; for now. —*conj.* **1,** while: покá я ждал, while I was waiting. **2,** as long as: покá я бу́ду жив, as long as I live. **3,** (*with* **не**) until: покá онá не придёт, until she comes. **4,** (*with* **не**) before: покá не пóздно, before it is too late. —*interj.* [*also,* **ну, покá**] *colloq.* so long! —**покá ещё; покá что, 1,** for the time being; for the present. **2,** so far; thus far; as yet.
покáз *n.* showing; demonstration.
показáние *n.* **1,** evidence; testimony. **2,** affidavit; deposition. **3,** reading (*on an instrument*).
показáтель *n.m.* **1,** index; indicator. **2,** *pl.* figures. **3,** *math.* exponent.
показáтельный *adj.* **1,** indicative; significant; revealing. **2,** model (*attrib.*); demonstration (*attrib.*). —**показáтельный суд,** show trial.
показáть [*infl.* **-кажу́, -кáжешь**] *v., pfv. of* **покáзывать.** —**показáться,** *refl.* **1,** *pfv. of* **казáться. 2,** *pfv. of* **покáзываться.**
показнóй *adj.* **1,** for show; done for effect. **2,** ostentatious.
показу́ха *n., colloq.* show; window dressing.
покáзывать *v. impfv.* [*pfv.* **показáть**] **1,** to show. **2,** (*with* **на** + *acc.*) to point at; point to. **3,** to register; read. **4,** to show; display (a quality, emotion, etc.). **5,** *sports* to achieve (a certain result). **6,** to stick out (one's tongue); turn (one's back); thumb (one's nose). **7,** to perform (a trick, play, etc.). **8,** to testify; (*with* **на** + *acc.*) testify against. **9,** (*with dat.*) *colloq.* to show; teach (someone) a lesson. —**не покáзывать ви́ду,** not to show; not let on. —**показáть (кому́-нибудь) на дверь,** to show (someone) the door (*i.e.* order out). —**показáть примéр** (+ *dat.*), to serve as an example to. —**показáть себя́, 1,** to prove oneself; show one's worth. **2,** (*with instr.*) to prove to be; show oneself to be.
покáзываться *v.r. impfv.* [*pfv.* **показáться**] **1,** to appear; come into view. **2,** to show up; turn up. Показáться врачу́, to see a doctor. —**покáзываться на глазáх у,** (*of tears*) to come to one's eyes. —**покáзываться на глазá** (+ *dat.*), to show one's face to; allow oneself to be seen by.
покáлывать *v. impfv., colloq.* **1,** to prick. **2,** *impers.* to have an intermittent pain: у меня́ покáлывает в бокý, I have an intermittent pain in my side.
покáмест *adv. & conj., colloq.* = **покá.**
покарáть *v., pfv. of* **карáть.**
покатáть *v., pfv. of* **катáть** (*in sense #2*). —**покатáться,** *refl., pfv. of* **катáться** (*in sense #2*).
покати́ть *v., pfv. of* **кати́ть.** —**покати́ться,** *refl.* **1,** *pfv. of* **кати́ться. 2,** *in* **покати́ться có смеху,** *colloq.* to roar with laughter.
покáтость *n.f.* slope; incline.
покáтываться *v.r. impfv., colloq., in* **покáтываться có смеху,** *colloq.* to roar with laughter.
покáтый *adj.* **1,** slanting; sloping. **2,** *in* покáтый лоб, receding forehead.
покачáть *v. pfv.* **1,** to rock; swing. **2,** *in* покачáть головóй, to shake one's head. —**покачáться,** *refl.* **1,** to rock. **2,** to swing back and forth. **3,** *in* покачáться на качéлях, to ride a swing.
покáчивать *v. impfv.* to rock slightly. —**покáчиваться,** *refl.* to rock, toss, or waver slightly.
покачну́ть *v. pfv.* **1,** to shake. **2,** to tip; tilt. —**покачну́ться,** *refl.* **1,** to sway. **2,** to lurch. **3,** to tilt. **4,** *fig., colloq.* to take a turn for the worse.
покáшливать *v. impfv.* to have a slight cough; cough intermittently.
покáшлять *v. pfv.* to cough (*momentarily*).
покая́ние *n.* **1,** (religious) confession. **2,** repentance; penitence.
покая́нный *adj.* of repentance; repentant; penitent.
покáяться *v.r., pfv. of* **кáяться.**
поквартáльный *adj.* quarterly. —**поквартáльно,** *adv.* quarterly.
поквитáться *v.r. pfv.* (*with* **с** + *instr.*) *colloq.* to get even (with); settle scores (with).
пóкер *n.* poker (*card game*).
покидáть *v. impfv.* [*pfv.* **поки́нуть**] to leave; desert; abandon; forsake.
покладáя *verbal adv., in* **рабóтать не покладáя рук,** to work untiringly.
поклáдистый *adj.* amenable; agreeable.
поклáжа *n.* **1,** load. **2,** baggage; luggage.
поклёп *n., colloq.* slander; calumny.
поклóн *n.* **1,** bow. **2,** regards; greetings; best wishes. —**идти́ на поклóн к,** to go begging to.
поклонéние *n.* (*with dat.*) worship (of): поклонéние и́долам, worship of idols.

поклони́ться [*infl.* **-клоню́сь, -кло́нишься**] *v.r., pfv. of* **кла́няться.**

покло́нник *n.* **1,** admirer. **2,** devotee. **3,** suitor. **4,** *relig.* worshiper.

поклоня́ться *v.r. impfv.* (*with dat.*) to worship.

покля́сться *v.r., pfv. of* **кля́сться.**

поко́иться *v.r. impfv.* **1,** (*with* **на** + *prepl.*) to rest (on). **2,** to repose; lie: здесь поко́ится..., here lies...

поко́й *n.* **1,** peace (of mind): оставля́ть в поко́е, to leave in peace. **2,** quiet. **3,** rest: в состоя́нии поко́я, in a state of rest. **4,** *obs.* room; apartment. —**ве́чный поко́й,** eternal rest. —**приёмный поко́й,** reception office (*in a hospital*). —**уходи́ть на поко́й,** to retire.

поко́йник *n.m.* [*fem.* **-ница**] the deceased.

поко́йницкая *n., decl. as an adj.* morgue; mortuary.

поко́йный *adj.* **1,** calm; tranquil; serene. **2,** (*of a deceased person*) the late. —*n.* the deceased.

поколеба́ть *v., pfv. of* **колеба́ть.** —**поколеба́ться,** *refl., pfv. of* **колеба́ться.**

поколе́ние *n.* generation.

поколоти́ть *v. pfv.* [*infl.* **-лочу́, -ло́тишь**] *colloq.* **1,** to beat; whip; thrash. **2,** (*with* **в** + *acc. or* **по**) to bang (on).

поколо́ть *v. pfv.* [*infl.* **-колю́, -ко́лешь**] **1,** to prick. **2,** to slaughter. **3,** to chop (all or a quantity of something).

поко́нчить *v. pfv.* (*with* **с** + *instr.*) **1,** to finish. **2,** to put an end to. —**поко́нчить жизнь самоуби́йством; поко́нчить с собо́й,** to commit suicide. —**поко́нчить счёты с** (+ *instr.*), to break off with.

покоре́ние *n.* conquest.

покори́тель *n.m.* conqueror. —**покори́тель серде́ц,** lady-killer.

покори́ть *v., pfv. of* **покоря́ть.** —**покори́ться,** *refl., pfv. of* **покоря́ться.**

покорми́ть *v., pfv. of* **корми́ть.**

поко́рный *adj.* **1,** submissive; obedient. **2,** humble: поко́рная про́сьба, humble request. —**поко́рно,** *adv.* humbly. —**поко́рность,** *n.f.* submissiveness.

покоро́бить *v., pfv. of* **коро́бить.** —**покоро́биться,** *refl., pfv. of* **коро́биться.**

покоря́ть *v. impfv.* [*pfv.* **покори́ть**] **1,** to conquer; subdue. **2,** *fig.* to win the heart of. —**покоря́ться,** *refl.* (*with dat.*) **1,** to submit (to). **2,** to resign oneself (to).

поко́с *n.* **1,** mowing. **2,** meadow.

покоси́ть[1] *v. pfv.* [*infl.* **-кошу́, -ко́сишь**] *colloq.* to mow; cut.

покоси́ть[2] *v. pfv.* [*infl.* **-кошу́, -коси́шь**] **1,** to tilt. **2,** (*with acc. or instr.*) to cock (one's eye). —**покоси́ться,** *refl., pfv. of* **коси́ться.**

покра́сить *v., pfv. of* **кра́сить.**

покрасне́ть *v., pfv. of* **красне́ть.**

покриви́ть *v., pfv. of* **криви́ть.** —**покриви́ться,** *refl., pfv. of* **криви́ться.**

покри́кивать *v. impfv., colloq.* to shout.

покро́в *n.* **1,** cover; covering. **2,** *fig.* cover; cloak; mantle: под покро́вом но́чи, under cover of night. **3,** *obs.* coverlet. —**ко́жный покро́в,** skin. —**леднико́вый покро́в,** icecap. —**о́блачный покро́в,** cloud cover. —**по́чвенный покро́в,** topsoil. —**сне́жный покро́в,** blanket of snow.

покрови́тель *n.m.* patron; protector; sponsor.

покрови́тельственный *adj.* **1,** protective. **2,** patronizing. —**покрови́тельственная окра́ска,** protective coloration. —**покрови́тельственный тари́ф,** protective tariff.

покрови́тельство *n.* patronage; sponsorship. Под покрови́тельством (+ *gen.*), under the auspices of.

покрови́тельствовать *v. impfv.* [*pres.* **-ствую, -ствуешь**] (*with dat.*) to patronize; sponsor.

покро́й *n.* cut (*of a garment*). —**все на оди́н покро́й,** all alike.

покроши́ть *v. pfv.* [*infl.* **-крошу́, -кро́шишь**] **1,** to chop up. **2,** to crumble.

покружи́ть *v. pfv.* [*infl.* **-кружу́, -кру́жишь**] **1,** *v.t.* to spin around. **2,** *v.i.* to wander (*for a while*). **3,** *v.i.* (*of an aircraft*) to circle several times. —**покружи́ться,** *refl.* **1,** to spin around. **2,** to wander (*for a while*). **3,** (*of a bird*) to circle.

покрути́ть *v. pfv.* [*infl.* **-кручу́, -кру́тишь**] (*with acc. or instr.*) to twist.

покрыва́ло *n.* **1,** cloth cover. **2,** bedspread; counterpane. **3,** covering; layer: нефтяно́е покрыва́ло, oil slick.

покрыва́ть *v. impfv.* [*pfv.* **покры́ть**] **1,** to cover. **2,** to coat (with paint, lacquer, etc.). **3,** to hide; cover up; shield. **4,** to cover; defray (expenses, losses, etc.). **5,** to drown out.

покры́тие *n.* **1,** (act of) covering. **2,** covering; coating; surface. **3,** defrayal (*of expenses*); discharge (*of debts*). **4,** roofing.

покры́ть [*infl.* **-кро́ю, -кро́ешь**] *v., pfv. of* **крыть** *and* **покрыва́ть.**

покры́шка [*gen. pl.* **-шек**] *n.* **1,** tire. **2,** *colloq.* cover; lid.

поку́да *adv. & conj., colloq.* = **пока́.**

покупа́тель *n.m.* buyer; customer.

покупа́тельный *adj.* buying (*attrib.*); purchasing (*attrib.*): покупа́тельная спосо́бность, purchasing power.

покупа́ть *v. impfv.* [*pfv.* **купи́ть**] to buy; purchase.

поку́пка [*gen. pl.* **-пок**] *n.* **1,** purchase; (act of) purchasing. **2,** a purchase: де́лать поку́пки, to go shopping.

покупно́й *adj.* **1,** purchased; bought. **2,** *in* **покупна́я цена́,** purchase price.

покури́ть *v. pfv.* [*infl.* **-курю́, -ку́ришь**] to have a smoke.

покуса́ть *v. pfv.* to bite; sting.

покуси́ться [*infl.* **-шу́сь, -си́шься**] *v.r., pfv. of* **покуша́ться.**

поку́шать *v., pfv. of* **ку́шать.**

покуша́ться *v.r. impfv.* [*pfv.* **покуси́ться**] (*with* **на** + *acc.*) **1,** to make an attempt upon: покуси́ться на чью́-нибудь жизнь, to make an attempt on someone's life. **2,** to encroach (upon).

покуше́ние *n.* (*with* **на** + *acc.*) attempted assassination of; attempt on the life of.

пол *n.* **1,** [*2nd loc.* **полу́;** *pl.* **полы́, поло́в**] floor. **2,** [*pl.* **по́лы, поло́в**] sex.

пол- *prefix* **1,** half: полчаса́, half an hour. **2,** *colloq.* (*in telling time*) half (*before the next hour*): полшесто́го, half-past five.

пола́ [*pl.* **по́лы**] *n.* **1,** flap (*of a garment*). **2,** flap; fold (*of a tent*). —**из-под полы́,** (*of a purchase, sale, etc.*) under the table (*or* counter).

полага́ть *v. impfv.* to think; believe; suppose. На́до полага́ть, one may assume; it may be assumed. —**полага́ться,** *refl.* **1,** *impers.* to be proper; be in order; be expected. Как полага́ется, as it should be; as expected. Не полага́ется, not supposed to; not the thing to do. **2,** (*with dat.*) to be due to; be payable to. **3,** [*pfv.* **положи́ться**] (*with* **на** + *acc.*) to rely on.

пола́дить *v. pfv.* [*infl.* **-ла́жу, -ла́дишь**] *colloq.* **1,** to reach an agreement. **2,** to get along.

пола́комиться *v.r., pfv. of* **ла́комиться.**

полбеды́ *n.f., colloq., in* **э́то ещё полбеды́,** it's not so terrible; it's no calamity.

полве́ка [*gen.* **полуве́ка**] *n.m.* half a century. В тече́ние полуве́ка, for half a century.

полго́да [*gen.* **полуго́да**] *n.m.* half a year. Бо́льше полуго́да, more than half a year.

по́лдень [*gen.* **полу́дня**] *n.m.* noon. —**полдне́вный,** *adj.* noon (*attrib.*); midday (*attrib.*).

по́лдник *n.* mid-afternoon snack.

полдоро́ги *n.f.* halfway point: на полдоро́ге, halfway; at the halfway point.

полдю́жины *n.f.* half a dozen.

по́ле [*pl.* **поля́, поле́й**] *n.* **1,** field. **2,** *fig.* field (*of activity*). **3,** background (*of a painting*). **4,** *pl.* brim (*of a hat*). **5,** *pl.* margin. —**по́ле би́твы; по́ле бо́я; по́ле сраже́ния,** battlefield. —**по́ле зре́ния,** field of vision.

полеве́ть *v., pfv. of* **леве́ть.**

полёвка [*gen. pl.* **-вок**] *n.* vole.

полево́дство *n.* field crop farming.

полево́й *adj.* field (*attrib.*). —**полева́я мышь,** field mouse. —**полевы́е цветы́,** wildflowers.

полего́ньку *adv., colloq.* slowly; little by little.

полегча́ть *v., pfv. of* **легча́ть.**

полежа́ть *v. pfv.* [*infl.* **-лежу́, -лежи́шь**] to lie for a while; lie down for a while.

поле́зно *adj., used predicatively* **1,** useful. **2,** healthy; good: по́сле обе́да поле́зно отдохну́ть, it is good to rest after dinner.

поле́зность *n.f.* usefulness.

поле́зный *adj.* [*short form* **-зен, -зна**] **1,** useful; helpful. **2,** wholesome. **3,** good (for): поле́зный для здоро́вья, good for one's health. —**чем могу́ быть поле́зен (поле́зна)?,** what can I do for you?

поле́зть *v. pfv.* [*infl. like* **лезть**] **1,** *pfv. of* **лезть. 2,** to begin to climb.

полемизи́ровать *v. impfv.* [*pres.* **-рую, -руешь**] to engage in polemics.

поле́мика *n.* polemics. —**полеми́ст,** *n.* polemicist. —**полеми́ческий,** *adj.* polemic(al).

полени́ться *v.r. pfv.* [*infl.* **-леню́сь, -ле́нишься**] (*with inf.*) to be too lazy (to).

поле́нница *n.* stack of logs; stack of firewood.

поле́но [*pl.* **поле́нья, -ньев**] *n.* log (*for burning*).

поле́сье *n.* marshy woodlands.

полёт *n.* flight; flying. —**полёт фанта́зии,** flight of fantasy.

полета́ть *v. pfv.* to fly (*for a while*).

полете́ть *v. pfv.* [*infl.* **-чу́, -ти́шь**] **1,** *pfv. of* **лете́ть. 2,** to begin to fly; take off. **3,** *colloq.* to fall.

полётный *adj.* flight (*attrib.*); flying.

полечи́ть *v. pfv.* [*infl.* **-лечу́, -ле́чишь**] to treat (*for a while*). —**полечи́ться,** *refl.* to be treated; get some treatment.

поле́чь *v. pfv.* [*infl. like* **лечь**] (*of all or many people*) **1,** *colloq.* to lie down. **2,** to be killed (*in battle*).

по́лзать *v. impfv., indeterm. of* **ползти́.**

ползко́м *adv.* by crawling; on all fours.

ползти́ *v. impfv.* [*pfv.* **поползти́;** *pres.* **ползу́, ползёшь;** *past* **полз, ползла́, ползло́**] **1,** to crawl. **2,** to creep (along). **3,** to trickle. **4,** *colloq.* (*of fabric*) to come apart.

ползу́н [*gen.* **-зуна́**] *n., colloq.* baby still in the crawling stage.

ползуно́к [*gen.* **-нка́**] *n., colloq.* **1,** = **ползу́н. 2,** *pl.* crawlers (*baby's garment*).

ползу́чий *adj.* (*of a plant*) creeping: ползу́чее расте́ние, creeper.

полиа́ндрия *n.* polyandry.

полива́ть *v. impfv.* [*pfv.* **поли́ть**] to water (plants). —**полива́ться,** *refl.* (*with instr.*) to pour (water) on oneself.

поли́вка *n.* watering (*of plants*).

полига́мия *n.* polygamy. —**полигами́ческий; полига́мный,** *adj.* polygamous.

полигло́т *n.* polyglot.

полиго́н *n.* **1,** firing range. **2,** training ground. —**испыта́тельный полиго́н,** proving ground.

полиграфи́я *n.* printing. —**полиграфи́ческий,** *adj.* printing (*attrib.*).

поликли́ника *n.* polyclinic.

полиме́р *n.* polymer. —**полиме́рный,** *adj.* polymeric.

полинези́ец [*gen.* **-и́йца**] *n.m.* [*fem.* **-и́йка**] Polynesian. —**полинези́йский,** *adj.* Polynesian.

полиня́лый *adj.* faded.

полиня́ть *v., pfv. of* **линя́ть** (*in sense #1*).

полиомиели́т *n.* poliomyelitis.

поли́п *n.* polyp.

полирова́льный *adj.* polishing (*attrib.*). —**полирова́льная маши́на,** buffing machine.

полиро́ванный *adj.* polished.

полирова́ть *v. impfv.* [*pfv.* **отполирова́ть;** *pres.* **-ру́ю, -ру́ешь**] to polish.

полиро́вка *n.* **1,** polishing. **2,** polish; gloss; finish. —**полиро́вочный,** *adj.* polishing (*attrib.*). —**полиро́вщик,** *n.* polisher.

по́лис *n., in* **страхово́й по́лис,** insurance policy.

полисме́н *n.* policeman (*in the U.S. or Great Britain*).

полиста́ть *v. pfv.* to flip through.

полистиро́л *n.* polystyrene.

политбюро́ *n. indecl.* Politburo.

политеи́зм (тэ) *n.* polytheism. —**политеи́ст,** *n.* polytheist. —**политеисти́ческий,** *adj.* polytheistic.

полите́хникум *n.* polytechnic school.

политехни́ческий *adj.* polytechnic.

политзаключённый *n., decl. as an adj.* political prisoner.

поли́тик *n.* politician.

поли́тика *n.* **1,** policy. **2,** politics.

политика́н *n.* (unscrupulous) politician.

полити́ческий *adj.* political. —**полити́ческий де́ятель,** political figure; politician.

полити́чный *adj., colloq.* politic; diplomatic.

политру́к *n.* political instructor in the Soviet armed forces (*contr. of* **полити́ческий руководи́тель**).

политу́ра *n.* polish; varnish.

поли́ть *v. pfv.* [*infl.* **-лью́, -льёшь;** *past* **по́лил** *or* **поли́л, полила́, по́лило** *or* **поли́ло**] **1,** *pfv. of* **полива́ть. 2,** (*of rain*) to begin to come down. —**поли́ться,** *refl.* [*past* **поли́лся, полила́сь, полило́сь** *or* **поли́лось**] **1,** *pfv. of* **полива́ться. 2,** to begin to flow.

полице́йский *adj.* police (*attrib.*). —*n.* policeman.

поли́ция *n.* police.

поли́чное *n., decl. as an adj., in* **с поли́чным,** red-handed: пойма́ть/попа́сться с поли́чным, to catch/be caught/red-handed.

полиэтиле́н *n.* polyethylene. —**полиэтиле́новый,** *adj.* polyethylene.

полиэфи́р *n.* polyester. —**полиэфи́рный,** *adj.* polyester.

полк [*gen.* **полка́**; *2nd loc.* **полку́**] *n.* regiment. —**на́шего полку́ при́было,** our numbers have grown.
по́лка [*gen. pl.* **-лок**] *n.* **1,** shelf. **2,** berth.
полко́вник *n.* colonel.
полково́дец [*gen.* **-дца**] *n.* military leader.
полково́й *adj.* regimental.
полне́ть *v. impfv.* [*pfv.* **пополне́ть**] to put on weight; get fat.
полни́ть *v. impfv., colloq.* to make (someone) look fat.
по́лно *predicate, colloq.* **1,** enough!; stop! **2,** don't be silly!
полно́ *adv., colloq.* filled; packed: в за́ле бы́ло полно́ наро́да, the hall was packed with people.
полнове́сный *adj.* **1,** full-weight. **2,** heavy; weighty.
полновла́стие *n.* full power; absolute power. —**полновла́стный,** *adj.* having full or absolute power.
полново́дный *adj.* (*of a river or lake*) at a high level.
полново́дье *n.* high water.
полногру́дый *adj.* buxom.
полнокро́вие *n., med.* plethora.
полнокро́вный *adj.* full-blooded; red-blooded.
полнолу́ние *n.* full moon.
полнометра́жный *adj.* (*of a film*) feature-length.
полномо́чие *n.* authority; power. —**полномо́чный,** *adj.* plenipotentiary.
полнопра́вие *n.* full rights, equality. —**полнопра́вный,** *adj.* enjoying full rights: полнопра́вный член, full member.
по́лностью *adv.* **1,** in full. **2,** fully; completely.
полнота́ *n.* **1,** fullness; completeness. **2,** obesity; corpulence. —**для полноты́ карти́ны,** to complete the picture. —**от полноты́ се́рдца,** out of the fullness of one's heart. —**со всей полното́й; во всей полноте́,** in its entirety.
полноце́нный *adj.* **1,** worth its full value. **2,** *fig.* full-fledged.
по́лночь [*gen.* **полу́ночи** *or* **по́лночи**] *n.f.* midnight. —**полно́чный,** *adj.* midnight (*attrib.*).
по́лный *adj.* [*short form* **по́лон, полна́, по́лно** *or* **полно́**] **1,** full. **2,** complete; total. **3,** fat; stout. —**в по́лной ме́ре,** fully; in full measure.
по́ло *n. indecl.* polo. —**во́дное по́ло,** water polo.
полови́к [*gen.* **-вика́**] *n.* floor mat; doormat.
полови́на *n.* **1,** half. **2,** (*with ordinal numbers*) half-past: полови́на тре́тьего, half-past two. **3,** middle: в полови́не ме́сяца, in the middle of the month.
полови́нный *adj.* half; half a; a half: полови́нная до́ля, a half share. —**полови́нная но́та,** half note. —**в полови́нном соста́ве,** at half strength.
полови́нчатый *adj.* halfway; indecisive.
полови́ца *n.* floorboard.
поло́вник *n., colloq.* ladle.
полово́дье *n.* high water (*resulting from the melting of snow*).
полово́й *adj.* **1,** sexual; sex (*attrib.*). **2,** floor (*attrib.*).
по́лог *n.* **1,** canopy. **2,** *fig.* cover.
поло́гий *adj.* not steep; gently sloping.
положе́ние *n.* **1,** position: сидя́чее положе́ние, sitting position. **2,** situation: отча́янное положе́ние, desperate situation. **3,** status. **4,** tenet; thesis; proposition. **5,** regulations. **6,** provision. —**в (интере́сном) положе́нии,** pregnant. —**положе́ние веще́й/дел,** state of affairs. —**входи́ть в (чьё-нибудь) положе́ние,** to put oneself in someone's place; empathize with.
поло́женный *adj.* agreed-upon; prescribed.
поло́жено *short form neut. of past passive part. of* **положи́ть** (*with dat.*) *colloq.* (one) should; (one) is supposed to. —**как поло́жено,** as one should; as it should be.
положи́тельно *adv.* **1,** positively: положи́тельно заряже́нное ядро́, a positively charged nucleus. **2,** positively; favorably. **3,** positively; absolutely: положи́тельно некраси́в, positively ugly; положи́тельно ничего́, absolutely nothing.
положи́тельный *adj.* **1,** positive. **2,** affirmative. **3,** *colloq.* absolute; utter.
положи́ть [*infl.* **-ложу́, -ло́жишь**] *v., pfv. of* **класть.** —**поло́жим,** let us say; let us assume. —**положи́ть коне́ц** (+ *dat.*), to put an end to. —**положи́ть слова́ на му́зыку,** to set words to music.
положи́ться [*infl.* **-ложу́сь, -ло́жишься**] *v. r., pfv. of* **полага́ться** (*in sense #3*).
по́лоз [*pl.* **поло́зья, -зьев**] *n.* runner (*of a sleigh*).
полома́ть *v. pfv.* **1,** to break. **2,** *colloq.* to disrupt. **3,** *colloq., pfv. of* **лома́ть** (*in sense #5*). —**полома́ться,** *refl.* **1,** to break; break down. **2,** *pfv. of* **лома́ться** (*in sense #5*).
поло́мка [*gen. pl.* **-мок**] *n.* **1,** breakage. **2,** breakdown (*of a machine*). **3,** broken part.
поломо́йка [*gen. pl.* **-мо́ек**] *n., colloq.* woman who washes floors.
полоне́з *n.* polonaise.
поло́ний *n.* polonium.
полони́ть *v. pfv., archaic* to take prisoner.
полоса́ [*acc.* **полосу́** *or* **по́лосу**; *pl.* **по́лосы, поло́с, -са́м**] *n.* **1,** strip (*of metal, paper, etc.*). **2,** stripe (*in a design*). **3,** strip (*of land*); lane (*of a highway*). **4,** belt; region; zone. **5,** band (*of frequencies, the spectrum, etc.*). **6,** welt (*from a blow*). **7,** (*with gen.*) period (of); spell (of): полоса́ хоро́шей пого́ды, spell of good weather. **8,** page (*of a newspaper, book, etc.*).
полоса́тик *n.* rorqual (*whale*).
полоса́тый *adj.* striped.
поло́ска [*gen. pl.* **-сок**] *n., dim. of* **полоса́.** —**в поло́ску,** striped.
полоска́ние *n.* **1,** rinsing; gargling. **2,** mouthwash.
полоска́тельница *n.* slop basin.
полоска́ть *v. impfv.* [*pfv.* **вы́полоскать** *or* **прополоска́ть**; *pres.* **-лощу́, -ло́щешь**] **1,** to rinse. **2,** *in* полоска́ть го́рло, to gargle. —**полоска́ться,** *refl.* [*impfv. only*] **1,** to splash about (*in water*). **2,** (*of a flag, sail, etc.*) to flutter.
по́лость [*pl.* **по́лости, -сте́й, -стя́м**] *n.f.* **1,** cavity. **2,** lap robe.
полоте́нце [*gen. pl.* **-нец**] *n.* towel.
полотёр *n.* floor-polisher.
поло́тнище *n.* **1,** width (*of cloth*): простыня́ в два поло́тнища, a sheet of two widths. **2,** leaf (*of a door, gate, etc.*).
полотно́ [*pl.* **поло́тна, поло́тен**] *n.* **1,** linen. **2,** canvas; painting. **3,** roadbed. **4,** blade (*of a saw, axe, etc.*).
полотня́ный *adj.* linen.
поло́ть *v. impfv.* [*pfv.* **вы́полоть**; *pres.* **полю́, по́лешь**] **1,** to weed (a garden). **2,** to pull up (weeds).
полоу́мие *n., colloq.* madness. —**полоу́мный,** *adj., colloq.* mad; crazy.
полпути́ *n.m.* halfway point: на полпути́, halfway; at the halfway point.
полсло́ва [*gen.* **полсло́ва** *or* **полусло́ва**] *n. neut.* **1,**

a (brief) word: мо́жно вас на полсло́ва?, may I have a word with you? **2,** a word half uttered: останови́ться на полусло́ве, to stop short (*when speaking*); прерва́ть на полусло́ве, to cut (someone) short. —**ни полсло́ва,** not a single word. —**поня́ть с полусло́ва,** to get the point immediately.

полти́нник *n., colloq.* fifty kopecks; fifty-kopeck coin.

полтора́ [*fem.* **полторы́**; *gen., dat., instr., & prepl.* **полу́тора**] *numeral* one and a half.

полтора́ста [*gen., dat., instr., & prepl.* **полу́тораста**] *numeral* one hundred and fifty.

полуавтомати́ческий *adj.* semiautomatic.

полубессозна́тельный *adj.* semiconscious.

полубо́г *n.* demigod.

полуботи́нок [*gen.* **-нка;** *gen. pl.* **-нок**] *n.* shoe.

полувое́нный *adj.* paramilitary.

полуго́дие *n.* half a year; half of a calendar year. —**полугоди́чный; полугодово́й,** *adj.* half-year (*attrib.*); six-month (*attrib.*). —**полугодова́лый,** *adj.* six-month-old.

полуголо́дный *adj.* half-starved.

полугра́мотный *adj.* semiliterate.

полу́денный *adj.* noon (*attrib.*); midday (*attrib.*).

полуди́ть *v., pfv. of* **луди́ть.**

полуживо́й *adj.* more dead than alive.

полузабытьё [*2nd loc.* **-тьи́**] *n.* (state of) semi-consciousness.

полузащи́тник *n., sports* halfback.

полукро́вка [*gen. pl.* **-вок**] *n.* half-breed.

полукро́вный *adj.* half-blooded.

полукру́г *n.* semicircle. —**полукру́глый,** *adj.* semicircular.

полулежа́ть *v. impfv.* [*pres.* **-жу́, -жи́шь**] to recline.

полумёртвый *adj.* half-dead; more dead than alive.

полуме́сяц *n.* half-moon.

полуме́сячный *adj.* half a month's.

полумра́к *n.* semidarkness.

полуно́чник *n., colloq.* night owl.

полуно́чничать *v. impfv., colloq.* to stay up most of the night; burn the midnight oil.

полу́ночный *also,* **полуно́чный** *adj.* midnight (*attrib.*).

полуоборо́т *n.* half-turn.

полуо́стров [*pl.* **полуострова́**] *n.* peninsula. —**полуостровно́й,** *adj.* peninsular.

полуотво́ренный *adj.* half-open; ajar. *Also,* **полуоткры́тый.**

полуприце́п *n.* semitrailer.

полупроводни́к [*gen.* **-ника́**] *n.* semiconductor.

полупрозра́чный *adj.* translucent.

полуразру́шенный *adj.* tumble-down; ramshackle.

полураспа́д *n., in* **пери́од полураспа́да,** half-life.

полусве́т *n.* dim light.

полусме́рть *n.f., in* **до полусме́рти,** (half) to death: испуга́ть до полусме́рти, to frighten (half) to death. —**изби́ть до полусме́рти,** to beat within an inch of one's life.

полусозна́тельный *adj.* semiconscious.

полусо́н [*gen.* **-сна́**] *n.* state of being half asleep: в полусне́, half asleep. —**полусо́нный,** *adj.* half asleep.

полуста́нок [*gen.* **-нка**] *n.* small station; way station.

полуте́нь [*2nd loc.* **-тени́**] *n.f.* penumbra.

полуто́н *n.* **1,** *music* half tone. **2,** *art* halftone.

полутьма́ *n.* semidarkness.

полуфабрика́т *n.* **1,** semi-finished product. **2,** *pl.* partially prepared food.

полуфина́л *n.* semifinal; semifinals. —**полуфинали́ст,** *n.* semifinalist. —**полуфина́льный,** *adj.* semifinal.

получасово́й *adj.* half-hour (*attrib.*).

получа́тель *n.m.* recipient.

получа́ть *v. impfv.* [*pfv.* **получи́ть**] **1,** to receive; get. **2,** to obtain; get. **3,** to gain. **4,** *colloq.* to catch; get (a cold, illness, etc.). —**получа́ться,** *refl.* **1,** to be received; be obtained. **2,** to come about; result. **3,** to come out; turn out.

получе́ние *n.* **1,** receiving; receipt. **2,** obtaining.

получи́ть [*infl.* **-лучу́, -лу́чишь**] *v., pfv. of* **получа́ть.** —**получи́ться,** *refl., pfv. of* **получа́ться.**

полу́чка *n., colloq.* **1,** (act of) receiving; receipt. **2,** sum (*of money*). **3,** pay; paycheck.

полуша́рие *n.* hemisphere.

полу́шка [*gen. pl.* **-шек**] *n., pre-rev.* old coin worth 1/4 of a kopeck. —**ни полу́шки,** not a penny; not a plug nickel.

полушу́бок [*gen.* **-бка**] *n.* short sheepskin coat.

полушутя́ *adv.* half in jest.

полцены́ *n.f.* half-price: купи́ть за полцены́, to buy at half-price.

полчаса́ [*gen.* **получа́са**] *n.m.* half an hour. Ка́ждые полчаса́, every half hour.

по́лчище *n.* **1,** horde. **2,** *fig.* swarm.

по́лый *adj.* hollow. —**по́лая вода́,** floodwaters.

по́лымя *n. neut., in* **из огня́ да в по́лымя,** out of the frying pan into the fire.

полы́нный *adj.* wormwood (*attrib.*). —**полы́нная во́дка,** absinthe.

полы́нь *n.f.* wormwood; sagebrush.

полынья́ [*gen. pl.* **-не́й**] *n.* unfrozen patch of water in the ice; polynya.

полысе́ть *v., pfv. of* **лысе́ть.**

полыха́ть *v. impfv.* to blaze.

по́льза *n.* use; benefit; good. Кака́я от э́того по́льза?, what good will it do? —**в по́льзу** (+ *gen.*), **1,** in favor of. **2,** for; for the sake of; on behalf of. —**быть** *or* **идти́ на по́льзу** (+ *dat.*), to do (someone) good; be good for.

по́льзование *n.* **1,** use. **2,** (*with instr.*) enjoyment (of).

по́льзоваться *v.r. impfv.* [*pfv.* **воспо́льзоваться;** *pres.* **-зуюсь, -зуешься**] (*with instr.*) **1,** to use; make use of; take advantage of. **2,** [*impfv. only*] to enjoy (an advantage, good health, etc.).

по́лька [*gen. pl.* **-лек**] *n.* **1,** Polish woman. **2,** polka (*dance*).

по́льский *adj.* Polish.

польсти́ть *v., pfv. of* **льсти́ть.**

полюби́ть *v. pfv.* [*infl.* **-люблю́, -лю́бишь**] **1,** to come to love; fall in love with. **2,** to come to like; grow fond of. —**полюби́ться,** *refl.* (*with dat.*) *colloq.* to catch the fancy of.

полюбова́ться *v.r., pfv. of* **любова́ться.**

полюбо́вный *adj.* (*of an agreement, settlement, etc.*) amicable. —**полюбо́вно,** *adv.* amicably.

полюбопы́тствовать *v., pfv. of* **любопы́тствовать.**

по́люс *n.* pole: Се́верный по́люс, North Pole; Ю́жный по́люс, South Pole. Они́ – два по́люса, they are poles apart.

поля́к *n.* Pole.

поля́на *n.* clearing (*in the woods*); glade.

поляриза́ция *n.* polarization.
поляризова́ть *v. impfv. & pfv.* [*pres.* **-зу́ю, -зу́ешь**] to polarize.
поля́рность *n.f.* polarity.
поля́рный *adj.* polar. —**Поля́рная звезда́,** the North Star. —**Поля́рный круг,** the Arctic *or* Antarctic Circle.
пома́да *n.* pomade. —**губна́я пома́да,** lipstick.
пома́дить *v. impfv.* [*pfv.* **напома́дить;** *pres.* **-ма́жу, -ма́дишь**] **1,** to pomade (one's hair). **2,** to paint (one's lips). —**пома́диться,** *refl.* **1,** to pomade one's hair. **2,** to put on lipstick.
пома́дка *n.* fruit candy.
помáзание *n., relig.* anointment.
пома́зать [*infl.* **-ма́жу, -ма́жешь**] *v., pfv. of* **ма́зать** (*in sense #1*) *and* **пома́зывать.**
помазо́к [*gen.* **-зка́**] *n.* small brush; shaving brush.
пома́зывать *v. impfv.* [*pfv.* **пома́зать**] to anoint.
помале́ньку *adv., colloq.* **1,** at a leisurely pace; without hurrying. **2,** modestly: жить помале́ньку, to live modestly. **3,** tolerable; all right.
пома́лкивать *v. impfv., colloq.* to keep quiet; hold one's tongue.
помани́ть *v., pfv. of* **мани́ть.**
пома́рка [*gen. pl.* **-рок**] *n.* pencil mark; correction.
помаха́ть *v. pfv.* [*infl.* **-машу́, -ма́шешь**] **1,** (*with dat.*) to wave (to). **2,** (*with instr.*) to wave (something).
пома́хивать *v. impfv.* (*with instr.*) **1,** to wave (*back and forth*). **2,** to wag; swish (one's tail).
поме́длить *v. pfv.* (*with inf. or* **с** + *instr.*) to delay; be slow.
помело́ *n.* broom (*for cleaning out stoves and chimneys*).
поме́ньше *adj.* a little smaller. —*adv.* a little less.
поменя́ть *v., pfv. of* **меня́ть.** —**поменя́ться,** *refl., pfv. of* **меня́ться.**
помера́нец [*gen.* **-нца**] *n.* wild bitter orange. —**помера́нцевый,** *adj.* orange (*attrib.*).
помере́ть [*infl.* **помру́, помрёшь;** *past* **по́мер, померла́, по́мерло**] *v., pfv. of* **помира́ть.**
помере́щиться *v.r., pfv. of* **мере́щиться.**
помёрзнуть *v. pfv.* [*past* **-мёрз, -ла**] *colloq.* to perish from the frost.
поме́рить *v. pfv.* to try on. —**поме́риться,** *refl., pfv. of* **ме́риться.**
поме́ркнуть *v., pfv. of* **ме́ркнуть.**
помертве́лый *adj.* **1,** deathly pale. **2,** lifeless.
помертве́ть *v., pfv. of* **мертве́ть.**
помести́тельный *adj.* spacious; roomy. —**помести́тельность,** *n.f.* spaciousness; roominess.
помести́ть [*infl.* **-щу́, -сти́шь**] *v., pfv. of* **помеща́ть.** —**помести́ться,** *refl., pfv. of* **помеща́ться.**
поме́стный *adj.* **1,** estate (*attrib.*). **2,** landed: поме́стное дворя́нство, landed gentry.
поме́стье *n.* estate; manor.
по́месь *n.f.* **1,** hybrid; cross. **2,** *colloq.* mixture (*of two different elements*).
поме́сячный *adj.* monthly. —**поме́сячно,** *adv.* monthly; each month; by the month.
помёт *n.* **1,** dung; droppings. **2,** litter; brood.
поме́та *n.* mark; note.
поме́тить [*infl.* **-чу, -тишь**] *v., pfv. of* **ме́тить** (*in sense #1*) *and* **помеча́ть.**
поме́тка [*gen. pl.* **-ток**] *n.* mark; note.
поме́ха *n.* **1,** hindrance; obstacle. **2,** interruption. **3,** *pl.* static; interference.
помеча́ть *v. impfv.* [*pfv.* **поме́тить**] **1,** to mark. **2,** to date; write the date on.
поме́шанный *adj.* **1,** mad; crazy; insane. **2,** (*with* **на** + *prepl.*) *colloq.* addicted (to); hooked (on). —*n.* madman; lunatic.
помеша́тельство *n.* madness; insanity.
помеша́ть *v., pfv. of* **меша́ть.** —**помеша́ться,** *refl.* **1,** to go mad; go crazy. **2,** (*with* **на** + *prepl.*) *colloq.* to develop a passion (for); become a nut (about).
помеща́ть *v. impfv.* [*pfv.* **помести́ть**] **1,** to place; put. **2,** to house; lodge; accommodate. **3,** to invest. **4,** to publish (*in a newspaper, magazine, etc.*). —**помеща́ться,** *refl.* **1,** [*impfv. only*] to be; be placed; be situated. **2,** to be housed; be lodged. **3,** to fit: помеща́ться за столо́м, to fit around the table.
помеще́ние *n.* **1,** placing; placement. **2,** quarters; accommodations; housing. **3,** premises.
поме́щик *n.* landowner.
поме́щичий [*fem.* **-чья**] *adj.* **1,** of or pert. to a landowner. **2,** manorial. —**поме́щичий дом,** manor house.
помидо́р *n.* tomato. —**помидо́рный,** *adj.* tomato (*attrib.*).
поми́лование *n.* **1,** pardon; forgivenes. **2,** clemency; a pardon.
поми́ловать *v. pfv.* [*infl.* **-лую, -луешь**] to pardon. —**Го́споди, поми́луй!,** Lord have mercy!
поми́мо *prep., with gen.* **1,** besides; apart from; aside from. **2,** without the knowledge of. —**поми́мо всего́ про́чего,** in addition to/apart from/everything else; all else aside.
помин *n., obs.* mention. —**и в поми́не нет** (*preceded by gen.*), there is not a trace of; (something is) not to be found anywhere. —**и поми́ну нет** (*preceded by* **о** + *prepl.*), there is no trace/mention/question of; (something is) out of the question. —**лёгок на поми́не,** talk of the devil.
помина́ть *v. impfv.* [*pfv.* **помяну́ть**] **1,** to remember; recall. **2,** (*with* **о**) to mention. **3,** to pray for. **4,** to give (*or* attend) a funeral repast in memory of. —**помина́ть добро́м** (+ *acc.*), to speak well of. —**не помина́й (меня́) ли́хом,** don't think ill of me. —**помина́й как зва́ли,** he (she, it) disappeared without a trace.
поми́нки [*gen.* **-нок**] *n. pl.* funeral repast.
поминутный *adj.* **1,** by the minute. **2,** continual; constant. —**помину́тно,** *adv.* continually; constantly.
помира́ть *v. impfv.* [*pfv.* **помере́ть**] *colloq.* to die. —**помира́ть со́ смеху,** *colloq.* to die laughing.
помири́ть *v., pfv. of* **мири́ть.** —**помири́ться,** *refl., pfv. of* **мири́ться.**
по́мнить *v. impfv.* **1,** to remember. **2,** *in* **не по́мнить себя́,** to get carried away; lose control of oneself; (*with* **от**) be beside oneself (with). —**по́мниться,** *refl.* **1,** (*with dat.*) to remember: мне по́мнится, I remember; I seem to remember. **2,** *impers., colloq.* to remember (*said of oneself*): как по́мнится, as I recall.
помно́гу *adv., colloq.* **1,** a lot. **2,** (*with gen.*) many.
помножа́ть *v. impfv.* [*pfv.* **помно́жить**] **1,** *math.* to multiply. **2,** *fig.* to increase; augment.
помно́жить *v., pfv. of* **мно́жить** *and* **помножа́ть.**
помога́ть *v. impfv.* [*pfv.* **помо́чь**] (*with dat.*) to help.
по-мо́ему *adv.* in my opinion.
помо́и [*gen.* **-мо́ев**] *n. pl.* kitchen waste; dirty dishwater. —**облива́ть помо́ями,** to vilify; drag through the mud.
помо́йка [*gen. pl.* **-мо́ек**] *n., colloq.* garbage pit.

помо́йный *adj.* garbage (*attrib.*): помо́йное ведро́, garbage pail. —**помо́йная я́ма,** cesspool.

помо́л *n.* **1,** grinding. **2,** grind: ме́лкого помо́ла, finely ground; fine-ground.

помо́лвить *v. pfv.* [*infl.* **-влю, -вишь**] (*with* **с** + *instr.*) *obs.* to betroth (to).

помо́лвка *n.* engagement; betrothal.

помоли́ться *v.r., pfv. of* **моли́ться** (*in sense #1*).

помолоде́ть *v., pfv. of* **молоде́ть.**

помолча́ть *v. pfv.* [*infl.* **-чу́, -чи́шь**] to be silent (*for a while*).

помо́рщиться *v.r., pfv. of* **мо́рщиться** (*in sense #2*).

помо́рье *n.* coastal region.

помо́ст *n.* dais; podium.

по́мочи [*gen.* **-че́й**] *n. pl.* suspenders. —**быть** *or* **ходи́ть на помоча́х у** (+ *gen.*), to be tied to someone's apron strings. —**води́ть на помоча́х,** to keep on a leash (*fig.*).

помочи́ть *v.pfv.* [*infl.* **-мочу́, -мо́чишь**] to moisten slightly. —**помочи́ться,** *refl., pfv. of* **мочи́ться.**

помо́чь [*infl. like* **мочь**] *v., pfv. of* **помога́ть.**

помо́щник *n.m.* [*fem.* **-ница**] assistant; helper. Помо́щник дире́ктора, assistant director.

по́мощь *n.f.* help; aid; assistance. —**на по́мощь!**, help! —**при по́мощи; с по́мощью** (+ *gen.*), with the help of; by means of.

по́мпа *n.* **1,** pump. **2,** pomp.

помпе́зный *adj.* lavish; extravagant.

помпо́н *n.* pompon.

помрачне́ть *v., pfv. of* **мрачне́ть.**

помути́ть *v., pfv. of* **мути́ть** (*in sense #2*). —**помути́ться,** *refl., pfv. of* **мути́ться.**

помутне́ние *n.* clouding; dimming.

помутне́ть *v., pfv. of* **мутне́ть.**

пому́чить *v. pfv.* to tease; torment; make suffer. —**пому́читься,** *refl.* to suffer.

помча́ть *v., pfv. of* **мчать.** —**помча́ться,** *refl., pfv. of* **мча́ться.**

помыка́ть *v. impfv.* (*with instr.*) *colloq.* to order about.

по́мысел [*gen.* **-сла**] *n.* thought; idea; intention.

помы́слить *v., pfv. of* **помышля́ть.**

помы́ть *v., pfv. of* **мыть.** —**помы́ться,** *refl., pfv. of* **мы́ться.**

помышля́ть *v. impfv.* [*pfv.* **помы́слить**] (*with* **о**) to think (about); contemplate.

помяну́ть [*infl.* **-мяну́, -мя́нешь**] *v., pfv. of* **помина́ть.** —**помяни́те моё сло́во,** mark my words!

помя́тый *adj.* **1,** crumpled; creased. **2,** (*of one's face*) lined; wrinkled.

помя́ть *v., pfv. of* **мять** (*in senses #2 & #4*). —**помя́ться,** *refl., pfv. of* **мя́ться.**

понаде́яться *v. r. pfv.* (*with* **на** + *acc.*) to count on.

пона́добиться *v.r. pfv.* [*infl.* **-блюсь, -бишься**] (*with dat.*) **1,** to be needed: е́сли вам э́то когда́-нибудь пона́добится, if you ever have need of it. **2,** to be necessary.

понапра́сну *adv., colloq.* **1,** in vain. **2,** for no reason; for nothing.

понаслы́шке *adv., colloq.* through hearsay.

поbriefly

понача́лу *adv., colloq.* at first.

по-на́шему *adv.* in our opinion.

понево́ле *adv., colloq.* against one's will; willy-nilly.

понеде́льник *n.* Monday.

понеде́льный *adj.* weekly. —**понеде́льно,** *adv.* weekly; each week; by the week.

понемно́гу *adv.* **1,** a little at a time. **2,** little by little.

понести́ *v. pfv.* [*infl. like* **нести́**] **1,** *pfv. of* **нести́. 2,** (*of a horse*) to bolt. —**понести́сь,** *refl.* **1,** *pfv. of* **нести́сь. 2,** to dash off.

по́ни *n.m. indecl.* pony.

понижа́ть *v. impfv.* [*pfv.* **пони́зить**] **1,** to lower; reduce. **2,** to demote. —**понижа́ться,** *refl.* to go down; drop; decline.

пониже́ние *n.* **1,** lowering; reduction. **2,** drop; fall; decline. **3,** *in* пониже́ние в до́лжности (*or* по слу́жбе), demotion.

пони́зить [*infl.* **-жу, -зишь**] *v., pfv. of* **понижа́ть.** —**пони́зиться,** *refl., pfv. of* **понижа́ться.**

по́низу *adv.* low; close to the ground.

поника́ть *v. impfv.* [*pfv.* **пони́кнуть**] **1,** to droop. **2,** *in* поника́ть голово́й, to hang one's head.

пони́кнуть [*past* **-ни́к, -ла**] *v., pfv. of* **ни́кнуть** *and* **поника́ть.**

понима́ние *n.* **1,** understanding; comprehension. **2,** interpretation.

понима́ть *v. impfv.* [*pfv.* **поня́ть**] **1,** to understand: понима́ть по-ру́сски, to understand Russian. Поня́ть намёк, to take a hint. **2,** to realize: он сра́зу по́нял, что..., he immediately realized that... **3,** [*impfv. only*] (*with acc. or* **в** + *prepl.*) to have an understanding of; know something about: я ничего́ не понима́ю в спо́рте, I know nothing about sports.

поножо́вщина *n., colloq.* fight involving the use of knives.

понома́рь [*gen.* **-маря́**] *n.m.* sexton.

поно́с *n.* diarrhea.

поноси́ть[1] *v. impfv.* [*pres.* **-ношу́, -но́сишь**] to vilify; revile; defame.

поноси́ть[2] *v. pfv.* [*infl.* **-ношу́, -но́сишь**] to carry (*for a while*).

поноше́ние *n.* **1,** vilification; defamation. **2,** *usu. pl.* verbal abuse. **3,** disgrace.

поно́шенный *adj.* **1,** worn; shabby; threadbare. **2,** *colloq.* somewhat the worse for wear.

понра́виться *v.r., pfv. of* **нра́виться.**

понтифика́т *n.* pontificate.

понто́н *n.* pontoon. —**понто́нный,** *adj.* pontoon (*attrib.*): понто́нный мост, pontoon bridge.

понужда́ть *v. impfv.* [*pfv.* **пону́дить**] to force; compel.

понужде́ние *n.* compulsion.

понука́ть *v. impfv.* **1,** to urge on (an animal). **2,** *colloq.* to hurry; rush.

пону́рить *v. pfv.* to hang (one's head). —**пону́риться,** *refl.* to hang one's head; look despondent.

пону́рый *adj.* **1,** downcast; despondent. **2,** bowed; bent.

по́нчик *n.* doughnut.

по́нчо *n. indecl.* poncho.

поны́не *adv., archaic* until now.

поню́хать *v., pfv. of* **ню́хать.**

поню́шка [*gen. pl.* **-шек**] *n., colloq.* pinch of snuff.

поня́тие *n.* concept; notion; idea.

поня́тливый *adj.* bright; clever; sharp.

поня́тно *adv.* **1,** clearly; intelligibly. **2,** *colloq.* naturally; understandably. —*adj., used predicatively* **1,** understandable: э́то поня́тно, that is understandable. **2,** I understand. **3,** *interrogatively* do you understand?; is that understood? **4,** obvious: соверше́нно поня́тно, что..., it is quite obvious that...

поня́тность *n.f.* intelligibility.

поня́тный *adj.* **1,** understandable; comprehensible; intelligible. **2,** understandable; justified; justifiable. —**поня́тное де́ло,** *colloq.* naturally; understandably.

понято́й *n., decl. as an adj.* witness (*present during a search or when something is being counted.*).

поня́ть [*infl.* **пойму́, поймёшь;** *past* **по́нял, поняла́, по́няло**] *v., pfv. of* **понима́ть.**

пообе́дать *v., pfv. of* **обе́дать.**

пообеща́ть *v. pfv.* to promise.

поо́даль *adv.* at a distance: держа́ться поо́даль, to keep one's distance.

поодино́чке *adv.* one at a time; one by one.

поочерёдный *adj.* alternating; done in turn. —**поочерёдно,** *adv.* in turn.

поощре́ние *n.* encouragement.

поощри́тельный *adj.* serving to encourage: поощри́тельная улы́бка, a smile of encouragement. Поощри́тельная пре́мия, incentive bonus.

поощря́ть *v. impfv.* [*pfv.* **поощри́ть**] to encourage; stimulate.

поп [*gen.* **попа́**] *n., colloq.* priest.

попада́ние *n.* hit: прямо́е попада́ние, direct hit.

попада́ть *v. impfv.* [*pfv.* **попа́сть**] **1,** (*with* **в** *or* **на** + *acc.*) to get (to a place). **2,** (*with* **в** + *acc.*) to get into (a building, college, situation, trouble, etc.). **3,** (*with* **в** + *acc.*) to fall into (a trap, someone's hands, etc.). **4,** (*with* **в** + *acc.*) to end up (in); wind up (in). **5,** (*with* **на** + *acc.*) to catch; make; be on time for (a train, bus, etc.). **6,** (*with* **в** *or* **под** + *acc.*) to get caught in: попа́сть в мете́ль, to get caught in a snowstorm; попа́сть под дождь, to get caught in the rain. **7,** (*with* **под** + *acc.*) to be run over (by). **8,** (*with* **на** + *acc.*) to find; come upon: попа́сть на рабо́ту, to land a job. **9,** (*with* **в** + *acc.*) (*of a missile*) to hit; strike: попа́сть в цель, to hit the target. Пу́ля попа́ла ему́ в грудь, the bullet struck him in the chest. **10,** (*with instr. and* **в** + *acc.*) to get (something into a small opening): попа́сть ключо́м в замо́к, to get the key into the lock. **11,** (*with* **под** + *acc.*) to come under (suspicion, someone's influence, etc.). **12,** *impers.* (*with dat.*) *colloq.* to get a scolding; catch it: мне попадёт от отца́, I'll catch it from my father. —**попа́сть в плен,** to be taken prisoner. —**попа́сть в ру́ки** (+ *gen.*), to come/fall into the hands of. Мне попа́л(а) в ру́ки (+ *nom.*), I came across... —**попа́сть** (*or* **попа́сться) по́д руку** (+ *dat.*), to turn up (*by chance*): всё, что ему́ попада́ло по́д руку, anything (*or* whatever) he could get his hands on. —**попа́сть под суд,** to be brought to trial. —**где попа́ло; куда́ попа́ло,** anywhere; wherever one happens to be. —**как попа́ло,** helter-skelter; in a hit or miss fashion. —**кто попа́ло,** anyone; the first one who comes along. —**что попа́ло,** anything; anything that comes along.

попада́ться *v.r. impfv.* [*pfv.* **попа́сться**] **1,** to be caught: попа́сться на кра́же, to be caught stealing. **2,** (*with dat.*) *colloq.* to come across: мне попа́лась интере́сная кни́га, I came across an interesting book. —**попада́ться на глаза́** (+ *dat.*), to catch someone's eye. —**попа́сться на у́дочку,** to swallow the bait. —**пе́рвый попа́вшийся,** the first one to come along.

попадья́ *n., colloq.* priest's wife.

попа́рно *adv.* in pairs; two by two.

попа́сть [*infl. like* **пасть**] *v., pfv. of* **попада́ть.** —**попа́сться,** *refl., pfv. of* **попада́ться.**

попа́хивать *v. impfv.* (*with instr.*) *colloq.* to smell slightly (of).

попеня́ть *v., pfv. of* **пеня́ть.**

поперёк *adv.* across. —*prep., with gen.* across; athwart. —**знать вдоль и поперёк,** to know inside out. —**стать поперёк го́рла** (+ *dat.*), to stick in someone's throat. —**стоя́ть поперёк доро́ги** (+ *dat.*), to stand in someone's way.

попереме́нно *adv.* alternately; in turn.

попере́чина *n.* crossbeam; crossbar; crosspiece.

попере́чник *n.* diameter.

попере́чный *adj.* transverse; cross-: попере́чный разре́з; попере́чное сече́ние, cross section. Попере́чная пила́, cross-cut saw. —**ка́ждый встре́чный и попере́чный,** any (*or* every) Tom, Dick, or Harry.

поперхну́ться *v.r. pfv.* (*with instr.*) to choke (on).

попече́ние *n.* care; charge: быть на попече́нии (+ *gen.*), to be in the care/charge of; име́ть (+ *acc.*) на попече́нии, to have charge of.

попечи́тель *n.m.* guardian; trustee. —**попечи́тельство,** *n.* guardianship; trusteeship.

попива́ть *v. impfv., colloq.* **1,** *v.t.* to drink (something) slowly. **2,** *v.i.* to drink from time to time.

попира́ть *v. impfv.* [*pfv.* **попра́ть**] to trample upon; violate; flout.

пописа́ть *v. pfv.* [*infl.* **-пишу́, -пи́шешь**] to write (*for a while*).

popи́сывать *v. impfv., colloq.* to write occasionally; write from time to time.

попи́ть *v. pfv.* [*infl.* **-пью́, -пьёшь;** *past* **по́пил** *or* **попи́л, попила́, по́пило** *or* **попи́ло**] *colloq.* **1,** (*with gen.*) to have a drink of. **2,** to have something to drink.

popла́вать *v. pfv.* to go for a swim; have a swim.

поплаво́к [*gen.* **-вка́**] *n.* **1,** float (*marker*). **2,** fishing float; bob. **3,** *colloq.* floating restaurant.

попла́кать *v. pfv.* [*infl.* **-пла́чу, -пла́чешь**] to have a brief cry; shed a few tears.

поплати́ться *v.r., pfv. of* **плати́ться.**

поплести́сь *v.r. pfv.* [*infl. like* **плести́**] to trudge along.

попли́н *n.* poplin. —**попли́новый,** *adj.* poplin.

поплы́ть *v. pfv.* [*infl. like* **плыть**] **1,** *pfv. of* **плыть. 2,** to begin to swim. **3,** to begin to drift.

попляса́ть *v. pfv.* [*infl.* **-пляшу́, -пля́шешь**] *colloq.* to dance (*for a while*).

попо́вич *n., colloq.* priest's son.

попо́вна [*gen. pl.* **-вен**] *n., colloq.* priest's daughter.

попо́вник *n.* (oxeye) daisy.

попо́зже *adv.* a little later.

попо́йка [*gen. pl.* **-по́ек**] *n., colloq.* drinking bout.

попола́м *adv.* **1,** in half; in two. **2,** half and half: снег попола́м с дождём, half snow, half rain.

по́ползень [*gen.* **-зня**] *n.m.* nuthatch (*bird*).

поползнове́ние *n.* impulse; inclination.

поползти́ *v. pfv.* [*infl. like* **ползти́**] **1,** *pfv. of* **ползти́. 2,** to begin to crawl.

пополне́ние *n.* **1,** replenishment. **2,** *mil., often pl.* reinforcements; additional personnel.

пополне́ть *v., pfv. of* **полне́ть.**

пополня́ть *v. impfv.* [*pfv.* **попо́лнить**] **1,** to replenish (a supply of something). **2,** to supply with more of something. **3,** *fig.* to expand; broaden; enlarge. **4,** *mil.* to reinforce; beef up.

пополу́дни *adv.* in the afternoon; p.m.

попо́мнить *v. pfv., colloq.* to remember. —**попо́мните моё сло́во!,** mark my words!

попо́на *n.* horsecloth.
попо́ртить *v. pfv.* [*infl.* **-чу, -тишь**] *colloq.* to damage slightly.
попо́тчевать *v., pfv. of* **по́тчевать.**
поправе́ть *v., pfv. of* **праве́ть.**
поправи́мый *adj.* **1,** (*of an error*) rectifiable. **2,** (*of a situation*) not beyond repair; not hopeless.
попра́вить [*infl.* **-влю, -вишь**] *v., pfv. of* **поправля́ть.** —**попра́виться,** *refl., pfv. of* **поправля́ться.**
попра́вка [*gen. pl.* **-вок**] *n.* **1,** correction. **2,** amendment. **3,** repair. **4,** adjustment. **5,** recovery: у него́ де́ло идёт на попра́вку, he is on the road to recovery; he is on the mend.
поправле́ние *n.* **1,** correcting; correction. **2,** adjustment. **3,** straightening out; putting right.
поправля́ть *v. impfv.* [*pfv.* **попра́вить**] **1,** to correct. **2,** to repair; fix; mend. **3,** to straighten; adjust; set right; put right. **4,** to restore (one's health). —**поправля́ться,** *refl.* **1,** to correct oneself. **2,** to improve; get better. **3,** to get well; recover. **4,** to put on weight.
попра́ть *v., used in the past tense only, pfv. of* **попира́ть.**
по-пре́жнему *adv.* as before.
попрёк *n., colloq.* critical remark. Ве́чные попрёки, endless nagging.
попрека́ть *v. impfv.* [*pfv.* **попрекну́ть**] *colloq.* to reproach.
по́прище *n.* field (of endeavor): нау́чное по́прище, the scientific field.
попро́бовать *v., pfv. of* **про́бовать.**
попроси́ть *v., pfv. of* **проси́ть.** —**попроси́ться,** *refl., pfv. of* **проси́ться.**
по́просту *adv.* simply. —**по́просту говоря́,** to put it bluntly; in plain words.
попроша́йка [*gen. pl.* **-ша́ек**] *n.m. & f., colloq.* beggar.
попроша́йничать *v. impfv., colloq.* to beg.
попроша́йничество *n., colloq.* begging.
попроща́ться *v.r., pfv. of* **проща́ться.**
попры́гать *v. pfv.* **1,** to jump. **2,** to hop.
попры́гивать *v. impfv., colloq.* to hop about; hop around.
попрыгу́н *n.m.* [*fem.* **-гу́нья**] *colloq.* fidgety person; fidget.
попря́тать *v. pfv.* [*infl.* **-пря́чу, -пря́чешь**] *colloq.* to hide (all or many of something). —**попря́таться,** *refl., colloq.* (*of all or many of something*) to hide.
попуга́й *n.* parrot.
попуга́ть *v. pfv., colloq.* to frighten a little; scare.
попу́дрить *v. pfv.* to powder. —**попу́дриться,** *refl.* to powder one's nose.
популяриза́ция *n.* popularization.
популяризи́ровать *v. impfv. & pfv.* [*pres.* **-рую, -руешь**] to popularize. *Also,* **популяризова́ть** [*pres.* **-зу́ю, -зу́ешь**].
популя́рно *adv.* in understandable terms; in a way that is easy to understand.
популя́рность *n.f.* popularity.
популя́рный *adj.* [*short form* **-я́рен, -я́рна**] **1,** popular. **2,** written or set forth in understandable terms.
попурри́ *n. neut. indecl., music* medley.
попусти́тельство *n.* **1,** tolerance (of); permissive attitude (toward). **2,** connivance.
попусти́тельствовать *v. impfv.* [*pres.* **-ствую, -ствуешь**] (*with dat.*) to permit; tolerate; put up with; do nothing about.
по́пусту *adv., colloq.* to no purpose; for nothing. *Also,* **по-пусто́му.**
попу́тно *adv.* **1,** at the same time; while one is (*or* was) at it. **2,** in passing: попу́тно отме́тить, to mention in passing.
попу́тный *adj.* **1,** going the same way. **2,** situated along the way: попу́тная ста́нция, way station. **3,** *fig.* passing: попу́тное замеча́ние, a passing remark. —**попу́тный ве́тер,** favorable wind; tail wind.
попу́тчик *n.* **1,** traveling companion. **2,** *polit.* fellow traveler.
попыта́ть *v. pfv., colloq.* to try: попыта́ть сча́стья, to try one's luck. —**попыта́ться,** *refl., pfv. of* **пыта́ться.**
попы́тка [*gen. pl.* **-ток**] *n.* attempt; try.
попы́хивать *v. impfv., colloq.* **1,** to give off occasional puffs of smoke. **2,** (*with instr.*) to puff on (a cigar, pipe, etc.).
попя́титься *v.r., pfv. of* **пя́титься.**
попя́тный *adj., obs.* backward; reverse. —**идти́ на попя́тный** *or* **попя́тную,** *colloq.* to go back on one's word.
по́ра *n.* pore.
пора́ [*acc.* **по́ру**] *n.* **1,** time. **2,** *impers.* it is time: нам пора́ домо́й, it is time for us to be going home. —**в (са́мую) по́ру,** at (just) the right time. —**в ту по́ру,** then; at that time. —**в э́ту по́ру,** now; at this time. —**до каки́х пор?,** until when? —**до поры́ до вре́мени,** for the time being. —**до сих пор,** until now; up to now. —**до тех пор,** until then. —**до тех пор пока́,** as long as. —**до тех пор пока́ не,** until the time when. —**на пе́рвых пора́х,** at first. —**с да́вних пор,** for a long time. —**с каки́х пор?,** since when? —**с не́которых пор,** for some time now. —**с тех пор,** since then. —**с тех пор, как,** since.
порабо́тать *v. pfv.* to do some work.
поработи́тель *n.m.* enslaver; oppressor.
порабоща́ть *v. impfv.* [*pfv.* **поработи́ть**] to enslave.
порабоще́ние *n.* enslavement.
поравня́ть *v. pfv., colloq.* to make equal; place on an equal footing. —**поравня́ться,** *refl.* (*with* **с** + *instr.*) to pull alongside (of); draw even (with).
пора́довать *v. pfv.* [*infl.* **-дую, -дуешь**] to gladden; make happy. —**пора́доваться,** *refl.* to be glad; be happy.
поража́ть *v. impfv.* [*pfv.* **порази́ть**] **1,** to strike; smite. **2,** to hit (a target). **3,** to strike; astonish. **4,** (*of an illness*) to strike; affect. **5,** to defeat; rout.
пораже́нец [*gen.* **-нца**] *n.* defeatist.
пораже́ние *n.* **1,** defeat. **2,** damage; destruction.
пораже́нчество *n.* defeatism. —**пораже́нческий,** *adj.* defeatist.
порази́тельный *adj.* striking; astonishing. —**порази́тельно,** *adv.* strikingly.
порази́ть [*infl.* **-жу́, -зи́шь**] *v., pfv. of* **поража́ть.**
по-ра́зному *adv.* differently; in different ways.
пора́нить *v. pfv.* to wound; injure. —**пора́ниться,** *refl.* to injure oneself; hurt oneself.
пора́ньше *adv.* a little earlier.
пораски́нуть *v. pfv., colloq., in* **пораски́нуть умо́м,** to think it over.
пороста́ть *v. impfv.* [*pfv.* **порасти́**] (*with instr.*). to become overgrown (with).
порасти́ [*infl. like* **расти́**] *v., pfv. of* **пороста́ть.**
порва́ть *v. pfv.* [*infl. like* **рвать**] **1,** *pfv. of* **рвать** *and* **порыва́ть. 2,** to break; disrupt (communications). —**порва́ться,** *refl.* **1,** *pfv.* of **рва́ться** *and* **порыва́ться. 2,** to break; snap.
пореде́ть *v., pfv. of* **реде́ть.**

поре́з *n.* cut.
поре́зать *v. pfv.* [*infl.* **-ре́жу, -ре́жешь**] **1,** to cut (*accidentally*). **2,** to slice. —**поре́заться,** *refl.* to cut oneself.
поре́й *n.* leek.
порекомендова́ть *v., pfv. of* **рекомендова́ть.**
по́ристый *adj.* porous. —**по́ристость,** *n.f.* porosity.
порица́ние *n.* condemnation; censure.
порица́ть *v. impfv.* to condemn; censure.
по́рка *n.* **1,** unstitching. **2,** *colloq.* whipping; thrashing; flogging.
порногра́фия *n.* pornography. —**порнографи́ческий,** *adj.* pornographic.
по́ровну *adv.* equally; in equal parts.
поро́г *n.* **1,** threshold; doorstep. **2,** *usu. pl.* rapids (*of a river*). —**на поро́ге, 1,** at hand; just around the corner. **2,** (*with gen.*) on the brink of. —**обива́ть (все) поро́ги,** to knock on every door.
поро́да *n.* **1,** breed; strain. **2,** *fig.* breed; type (*of person*). —**го́рная поро́да,** *geol.* rock.
поро́дистый *adj.* thoroughbred; pedigreed.
породи́ть [*infl.* **-жу́, -ди́шь**] *v., pfv. of* **порожда́ть.**
породни́ть *v., pfv. of* **родни́ть.** —**породни́ться,** *refl., pfv. of* **родни́ться.**
порожда́ть *v. impfv.* [*pfv.* **породи́ть**] **1,** *obs.* to give birth to; beget. **2,** to give rise to; generate; engender.
порожде́ние *n.* product; result.
поро́жистый *adj.* (*of a river*) full of rapids.
поро́жний *adj., colloq.* empty. —**перелива́ть из пусто́го в поро́жнее,** to engage in idle chatter.
порожня́к [*gen.* **-няка́**] *n.* empty trains; empty cars. —**порожняко́м,** *adv., colloq.* empty; without cargo; without passengers.
по́рознь *adv.* separately; apart.
порозове́ть *v., pfv. of* **розове́ть.**
поро́й *adv.* at times; occasionally; now and then.
поро́к *n.* **1,** vice. **2,** defect.
поросёнок [*gen.* **-нка;** *pl.* **-ся́та, -ся́т**] *n.* piglet; suckling pig.
по́росль *n.f.* **1,** sprouts; shoots. **2,** thicket. **3,** *colloq.* growth of hair.
пороси́тина *n.* suckling pig (*served as food*).
поро́ть *v. impfv.* [*pres.* **порю́, по́решь**] **1,** [*pfv.* **вы́пороть**] *colloq.* to whip; flog. **2,** [*pfv.* **распоро́ть**] to unstitch. **3,** [*impfv. only*] *colloq.* to talk (nonsense).
по́рох *n.* powder; gunpowder. —**не ню́хать по́роху,** never to have been in combat. —**па́хнет по́рохом,** war is in the air. —**тра́тить по́рох да́ром,** to waste one's energies. —**у него́ по́роху не хвата́ет,** he hasn't got it in him; he is not up to it.
порохово́й *adj.* powder (*attrib.*); gunpowder (*attrib.*): порохова́я бо́чка, powder keg.
поро́чить *v. impfv.* [*pfv.* **опоро́чить**] **1,** to sully; besmirch (someone's reputation). **2,** to disparage; run down. **3,** to discredit.
поро́чность *n.f.* depravity.
поро́чный *adj.* **1,** vicious; depraved. **2,** faulty; unsound. —**поро́чный круг,** vicious circle.
поро́ша *n.* fresh snow; newly-fallen snow.
пороши́ть *v. impfv.* **1,** (*of snow*) to fall lightly. **2,** *impers.* to be snowing lightly.
порошкообра́зный *adj.* powdery.
порошо́к [*gen.* **-шка́**] *n.* **1,** powder. **2,** *in* моло́чный порошо́к, powdered milk; яи́чный порошо́к, powdered eggs. —**стере́ть в порошо́к,** to make mincemeat of.
порт [*2nd loc.* **порту́;** *pl.* **по́рты, -то́в, -та́м**] *n.* port.
порта́л *n.* portal.
портати́вный *adj.* portable.
портве́йн *n.* port (wine).
по́ртик *n.* portico.
по́ртить *v. impfv.* [*pfv.* **испо́ртить;** *pres.* **по́рчу, по́ртишь**] **1,** to spoil; damage; mar; impair. **2,** to corrupt. —**по́ртиться,** *refl.* **1,** to spoil; decay. **2,** to deteriorate. **3,** to stop working; break down. **4,** (*of the weather*) to turn bad.
портмоне́ (нэ) *n. neut. indecl., obs.* purse.
портни́ха *n.* dressmaker.
портно́вский *adj.* tailor's.
портно́й *n., decl. as an adj.* tailor.
портня́жничать *v. impfv., colloq.* to be a tailor; work as a tailor.
портня́жный *adj.* tailor's. —**портня́жное де́ло,** tailoring.
портови́к [*gen.* **-вика́**] *n.* dock worker.
портово́й *adj.* port (*attrib.*). —**порто́вый го́род,** seaport. —**порто́вый рабо́чий,** dock worker.
портре́т *n.* portrait. —**портрети́ст,** *n.* portrait painter. —**портре́тный,** *adj.* portrait (*attrib.*).
портсига́р *n.* cigarette case.
португа́лец [*gen.* **-льца**] *n.m.* [*fem.* **-лка**] Portuguese. —**португа́льский,** *adj.* Portuguese.
портула́к *n.* portulaca; purslane.
портупе́я *n.* sword belt.
портфе́ль *n.m.* **1,** briefcase; portfolio. **2,** portfolio; office: мини́стр без портфе́ля, minister without portfolio.
портше́з *n.* sedan chair.
портье́ *n.m. indecl.* desk clerk (*in a hotel*).
портье́ра *n.* heavy curtain (*for a door or window*).
портя́нка [*gen. pl.* **-нок**] *n.* foot wrapping (*worn in place of socks*).
поруби́ть *v. pfv.* [*infl.* **-рублю́, -ру́бишь**] **1,** to chop down. **2,** to chop.
пору́бка *n.* chopping down (*of trees*).
поруга́ние *n.* humiliation.
поруга́ть *v. pfv.* to tell off; curse out. —**поруга́ться,** *refl.* **1,** (*with* **с** + *instr.*) to quarrel (with); have words (with). **2,** to swear; curse.
пору́ка *n.* bail; surety; guarantee. Брать на пору́ки, to bail (someone) out. —**отпуска́ть на пору́ки,** to release on bail. —**кругова́я пору́ка, 1,** collective responsibility. **2,** covering up for each other.
поруча́ть *v. impfv.* [*pfv.* **поручи́ть**] (*with dat.*) **1,** to instruct; charge; commission. **2,** to entrust.
поруче́ние *n.* assignment; mission; errand.
пору́чик *n., pre-rev.* lieutenant.
поручи́тель *n.m.* person who vouches for another; sponsor.
поручи́тельство *n.* **1,** statement vouching for another person; reference. **2,** bail.
поручи́ть [*infl.* **-ручу́, -ру́чишь**] *v., pfv. of* **поруча́ть.** —**поручи́ться,** *refl., pfv. of* **руча́ться.**
по́ручни [*gen.* **-ней**] *n. pl.* handrail.
порфи́р *n.* porphyry.
порха́ть *v. impfv.* [*pfv.* **порхну́ть**] to flit.
порцио́нный *adj.* à la carte.
по́рция *n.* portion; helping.
по́рча *n.* **1,** damage; spoilage. **2,** *fig.* deterioration.
по́ршень [*gen.* **-шня**] *n.m.* piston.
поршнево́й *adj.* piston (*attrib.*).

поры́в *n.* **1,** gust (*of wind*). **2,** fit; burst (*of emotion*). **3,** impulse.

порыва́ть *v. impfv.* [*pfv.* **порва́ть**] **1,** *v.i.* (*with* **с** + *instr.*) to break (with). **2,** *v.t.* to break off; sever (ties, relations, etc.). —**порыва́ться,** *refl.* **1,** (*of ties, relations, etc.*) to be broken off. **2,** [*impfv. only*] to try to move; try to get up. **3,** [*impfv. only*] (*with inf.*) to try (to); strive (to).

поры́вистый *adj.* **1,** (*of the wind*) gusty. **2,** (*of movements*) jerky. **3,** (*of a person*) impetuous; impulsive.

порыже́ть *v., pfv. of* **рыже́ть.**

поры́ться *v.r., pfv. of* **ры́ться.**

поря́дковый *adj., in* **поря́дковое числи́тельное,** ordinal number; **поря́дковый но́мер,** serial number.

поря́дком *adv., colloq.* **1,** rather; pretty. **2,** properly.

поря́док [*gen.* **-дка**] *n.* **1,** order; sequence: по поря́дку, in order; in sequence; in succession. **2,** (proper) order: всё в поря́дке, everything is in order; everything is all right (*or* o.k.). **3,** procedure. **4,** order; regime: ста́рый поря́док, the old order. **5,** *mil.* order; formation. **6,** *in* в спе́шном поря́дке, in short order; в обяза́тельном поря́дке, without fail; в служе́бном поря́дке, in line of duty. —**в поря́дке** (+ *gen.*), as; by way of. —**в поря́дке веще́й,** in the nature of things. —**идти́ свои́м поря́дком,** to take its normal course. —**поря́дка** (+ *gen.*), on the order of; approximately.

поря́дочно *adv.* **1,** honestly. **2,** *colloq.* quite a bit; quite a while; quite a ways. **3,** *colloq.* fairly well.

поря́дочность *n.f.* honesty; decency.

поря́дочный *adj.* **1,** honest; decent. **2,** fairly good; decent. **3,** considerable; sizable. **4,** utter; out-and-out.

посади́ть [*infl.* **-сажу́, -са́дишь**] *v., pfv. of* **сажа́ть.**

поса́дка *n.* **1,** (act of) planting. **2,** *pl.* plantings. **3,** boarding; embarkation. **4,** landing (*of an aircraft*). **5,** manner of sitting (*when riding*).

поса́дочный *adj.* **1,** planting (*attrib.*). **2,** boarding (*attrib.*). **3,** landing (*attrib.*).

поса́пывать *v. impfv., colloq.* to breathe heavily; sniff; snort.

поса́сывать *v. impfv., colloq.* to suck (on *or* at).

посва́тать *v., pfv. of* **сва́тать.** —**посва́таться,** *refl., pfv. of* **сва́таться.**

посвеже́ть *v., pfv. of* **свеже́ть.**

посвети́ть *v. pfv.* [*infl.* **-свечу́, -све́тишь**] **1,** *pfv. of* **свети́ть** (*in sense #2*). **2,** to shine (*for a while*).

посветле́ть *v., pfv. of* **светле́ть.**

по́свист *n.* whistle; whistling.

посвиста́ть *v. pfv.* [*infl.* **-свищу́, -сви́щешь**] to whistle; give a whistle. *Also,* **посвисте́ть** [*infl.* **-свищу́, -свисти́шь**].

посви́стывание *n.* whistling.

посви́стывать *v. impfv.* to whistle (*softly or from time to time*).

по-своему *adv.* in one's own way.

по-сво́йски *adv., colloq.* **1,** in one's own way. **2,** as a friend.

посвяти́ть [*infl.* **-щу́, -ти́шь**] *v., pfv. of* **посвяща́ть.**

посвяща́ть *v. impfv.* [*pfv.* **посвяти́ть**] **1,** (*with dat.*) to devote (to); dedicate (to). **2,** (*with* **в** + *acc.*) to let in on: посвяти́ть кого́-нибудь в та́йну, to let someone in on a secret. **3,** (*with* **в** + *nom. pl.*) to ordain: посвяти́ть кого́-нибудь в свяще́нники, to ordain someone as priest.

посвяще́ние *n.* **1,** dedication. **2,** letting (someone) in on (a secret). **3,** consecration; ordination; initiation.

посе́в *n.* **1,** sowing. **2,** *usu. pl.* crops.

посевна́я *n., decl. as an adj., colloq.* sowing campaign.

посевно́й *adj.* sowing (*attrib.*). —**посевна́я пло́щадь,** area under cultivation.

поседе́лый *adj.* turned gray.

поседе́ть *v., pfv. of* **седе́ть.**

посейча́с *adv., colloq.* until now; up to now.

поселе́нец [*gen.* **-нца**] *n.* **1,** settler. **2,** *pre-rev.* exile (*person sent into exile*).

поселе́ние *n.* **1,** settling. **2,** settlement. **3,** *pre-rev.* exile.

посели́ть *v., pfv. of* **поселя́ть.** —**посели́ться,** *refl., pfv. of* **поселя́ться.**

поселко́вый *adj.* village (*attrib.*).

посёлок [*gen.* **-лка**] *n.* village; community; settlement.

поселя́ть *v. impfv.* [*pfv.* **посели́ть**] **1,** to settle. **2,** *fig.* to arouse; engender. —**поселя́ться,** *refl.* to settle; take up residence.

посему́ *adv., obs.* therefore.

посеребри́ть *v., pfv. of* **серебри́ть.** —**посеребри́ться,** *refl., pfv. of* **серебри́ться.**

посереди́не *adv.* in the middle. —*prep., with gen.* in the middle of.

посере́ть *v., pfv. of* **сере́ть.**

посети́тель *n.m.* visitor.

посети́ть [*infl.* **-щу́, -ти́шь**] *v., pfv. of* **посеща́ть.**

посе́товать *v., pfv. of* **се́товать.**

посеща́емость *n.f.* (regularity) of attendance.

посеща́ть *v. impfv.* [*pfv.* **посети́ть**] **1,** to visit. **2,** to attend.

посеще́ние *n.* **1,** visit. **2,** attendance.

посе́ять *v., pfv. of* **се́ять.**

посиде́ть *v. pfv.* [*infl.* **-жу́, -ди́шь**] to sit (*for a while*).

поси́льный *adj.* **1,** within one's power to do. **2,** (*of help, payment, etc.*) whatever one can give.

посине́ть *v., pfv. of* **сине́ть.**

поскака́ть *v. pfv.* [*infl.* **-скачу́, -ска́чешь**] **1,** to hop off (to another place). **2,** to gallop off.

поскользну́ться *v.r. pfv.* to slip (and fall).

поско́льку *conj.* **1,** since; inasmuch as; as long as. **2,** as far as; to the extent that.

по́сконь *n.f.* male hemp. —**поско́нный,** *adj.* hemp (*attrib.*).

поскупи́ться *v.r., pfv. of* **скупи́ться.**

послабле́ние *n., often pl.* relaxation of discipline; leniency.

посла́нец [*gen.* **-нца**] *n.* messenger; envoy.

посла́ние *n.* message.

посла́нник *n.* envoy; minister.

по́сланный *n., decl. as an adj.* messenger; envoy.

посла́ть [*infl.* **пошлю́, пошлёшь**] *v., pfv. of* **слать** *and* **посыла́ть.**

по́сле *prep., with gen.* **1,** after: по́сле обе́да, after dinner. **2,** since: по́сле его́ возвраще́ния, since his return. —*adv.* afterward. —**по́сле того́, как,** after: по́сле того́, как он ушёл, after he left. —**по́сле того́, что,** after; in view of. —**по́сле чего́,** whereupon.

послевое́нный *adj.* postwar.

после́д *n.* placenta.

последи́ть *v. pfv.* [*infl.* **-жу́, -ди́шь**] (*with* **за** + *instr.*) to watch; look after.

после́дний *adj.* **1,** last. **2,** past: за после́днюю неде́лю, during the past week. **3,** recent: в *or* за после́дние го́ды, in recent years. **4,** the latest: после́дние изве́стия, the latest news. **5,** the latter. **6,** the lowest; the worst. —**в** *or* **за после́днее вре́мя,** recently; lately; of late. —**до после́днего,** to the last; to the utmost; to the bitter end. —**после́дними слова́ми,** in the crudest possible language.

после́дователь *n.m.* follower.

после́довательно *adv.* **1,** consecutively; in succession. **2,** consistently.

после́довательность *n.f.* **1,** succession; sequence. **2,** consistency.

после́довательный *adj.* **1,** consecutive; successive. **2,** consistent.

после́довать *v., pfv. of* **сле́довать** (*in senses #1 & #2*).

после́дствие *n.* consequence. —**оставля́ть без после́дствий,** to fail to act on; take no action on.

после́дующий *adj.* subsequent.

после́дыш *n., colloq.* **1,** youngest child in a family. **2,** *fig.* last to propound a certain (reactionary) doctrine.

послеза́втра *adv.* the day after tomorrow.

послеобе́денный *adj.* after-dinner.

послеоперацио́нный *adj.* postoperative. —**послеоперацио́нная пала́та,** recovery room.

послереволюцио́нный *adj.* post-revolutionary.

послеродово́й *adj.* postnatal.

послесло́вие *n.* epilogue; postscript.

посло́вица *n.* proverb. —**войти́ в посло́вицу,** to become proverbial.

послужи́ть *v. pfv.* [*infl.* **-служу́, -слу́жишь**] **1,** *pfv. of* **служи́ть. 2,** to serve (*for a while*)

послужно́й *adj., in* **послужно́й спи́сок,** service record.

послуша́ние *n.* obedience.

послу́шать *v., pfv. of* **слу́шать** (*in sense #2*). —**послу́шаться,** *refl., pfv. of* **слу́шаться.**

по́слушник *n., eccles.* novice.

послу́шный *adj.* obedient.

послы́шаться *v.r., pfv. of* **слы́шаться.**

послюни́ть *v., pfv. of* **слюни́ть.**

посма́тривать *v. impfv.* to look from time to time.

посме́иваться *v.r. impfv.* **1,** to chuckle. **2,** (*with* **над**) to poke fun at.

посме́нный *adj.* shift (*attrib.*): посме́нная рабо́та, shift work. —**посме́нно,** *adv.* in shifts.

посме́ртно *adv.* posthumously.

посме́ртный *adj.* posthumous. —**посме́ртная ма́ска,** death mask.

посме́ть *v., pfv. of* **сметь.**

посме́шище *n.* laughingstock. —**выставля́ть (кого́-нибудь) на посме́шище,** to make a laughingstock of.

посмея́ться *v.r. pfv.* [*infl.* **-смею́сь, -смеёшься**] **1,** to laugh a little. **2,** (*with* **над**) to poke fun at.

посмотре́ть *v., pfv. of* **смотре́ть.** —**посмотре́ться,** *refl., pfv. of* **смотре́ться.**

посо́бие *n.* **1,** allowance; benefits: посо́бие по безрабо́тице, unemployment benefits. **2,** textbook. **3,** *pl.* study aids: нагля́дные посо́бия, visual aids.

посо́бник *n.* accomplice. —**посо́бничество,** *n.* complicity.

посо́веститься *v.r., pfv. of* **со́веститься.**

посове́товать *v., pfv. of* **сове́товать.** —**посове́товаться,** *refl., pfv. of* **сове́товаться.**

посо́л [*gen.* **-сла́**] *n.* ambassador.

посоли́ть *v., pfv. of* **соли́ть.**

посолове́лый *adj., colloq.* bleary-eyed.

посолове́ть *v. pfv., colloq.* to become bleary-eyed.

посо́льский *adj.* **1,** ambassadorial. **2,** embassy (*attrib.*).

посо́льство *n.* embassy.

по́сох *n.* **1,** staff; crook. **2,** crosier.

посо́хнуть *v. pfv.* [*past* **-со́х, -ла**] (*of all or many things*) to wither.

поспа́ть *v. pfv.* [*infl. like* **спать**] to sleep a bit; take a nap.

поспева́ть *v. impfv.* [*pfv.* **поспе́ть**] **1,** to ripen. **2,** *colloq.* to be on time. **3,** (*with* **за** + *instr.*) to keep up with; keep pace with.

поспе́ть *v., pfv. of* **спеть**[1] *and* **поспева́ть.**

поспеши́ть *v., pfv. of* **спеши́ть.** —**поспеши́шь – люде́й насмеши́шь,** haste makes waste.

поспе́шный *adj.* hasty; hurried. —**поспе́шно,** *adv.* hastily; hurriedly; in a hurry. —**поспе́шность,** *n.f.* haste.

поспо́рить *v., pfv. of* **спо́рить.**

посрами́ть [*infl.* **-млю́, -ми́шь**] *v., pfv. of* **посрамля́ть.**

посрамле́ние *n.* disgrace.

посрамля́ть *v. impfv.* [*pfv.* **посрами́ть**] to disgrace.

посреди́ *prep., with gen.* in the middle of. —*adv.* in the middle.

посреди́не *adv. & prep.* = **посереди́не.**

посре́дник *n.* **1,** middleman; intermediary. **2,** mediator; go-between.

посре́дничать *v. impfv.* to mediate; serve as a go-between.

посре́дничество *n.* mediation. —**посре́днический,** *adj.* mediation (*attrib.*); middleman (*attrib.*); intermediary.

посре́дственно *adv.* so-so; not particularly well. —*n. indecl.* "fair"; "mediocre" (*school grade*).

посре́дственность *n.f.* **1,** mediocrity. **2,** mediocre person; a mediocrity.

посре́дственный *adj.* mediocre.

посре́дство *n., in* **при посре́дстве** *and* **че́рез посре́дство** (+ *gen.*), **1,** through, by means of. **2,** through the intercession of; thanks to.

посре́дством *prep., with gen.* through; by means of.

поссо́рить *v., pfv. of* **ссо́рить.** —**поссо́риться,** *refl., pfv. of* **ссо́риться.**

пост [*gen.* **поста́;** *2nd loc.* **посту́**] *n.* **1,** post: наблюда́тельный пост, observation post. **2,** post; position: пост дире́ктора, the post/position of director. **3,** *relig.* fast. —**вели́кий пост,** Lent.

поста́вить [*infl.* **-влю, -вишь**] *v., pfv. of* **ста́вить** *and* **поставля́ть.**

поста́вка [*gen. pl.* **-вок**] *n.* delivery.

поставля́ть *v. impfv.* [*pfv.* **поста́вить**] to supply.

поставщи́к [*gen.* **-щика́**] *n.* supplier.

постаме́нт *n.* pedestal; base.

постанови́ть [*infl.* **-новлю́, -но́вишь**] *v., pfv. of* **постановля́ть.**

постано́вка *n.* **1,** *theat.* production. **2,** position; carriage (*of a part of the body*). **3,** organization. **4,** stating; posing: постано́вка вопро́са, the way a question is put. **5,** *in* постано́вка го́лоса, voice training.

постановле́ние *n.* **1,** decision; resolution. **2,** decree.

постановля́ть *v. impfv.* [*pfv.* **постанови́ть**] to decide; resolve; decree.

постано́вочный *adj., theat.* production (*attrib.*).

постано́вщик *n., theat.* director.

постара́ться *v.r., pfv. of* **стара́ться.**

постарéть *v., pfv. of* **старéть.**
постéль *n.f.* bed. —**постéльный,** *adj.* bed (*attrib.*).
постепéнный *adj.* gradual. —**постепéнно,** *adv.* gradually.
постесня́ться *v.r., pfv. of* **стесня́ться** (*in sense #2*).
постигáть *v. impfv.* [*pfv.* **пости́гнуть** *or* **пости́чь**] **1,** to comprehend; grasp. **2,** (*of misfortune*) to befall; overtake.
пости́гнуть [*past* **-сти́г, -ла**] *v., pfv. of* **постигáть.**
постижéние *n.* comprehension; grasp.
постижи́мый *adj.* comprehensible.
постилáть *v. impfv.* [*pfv.* **постлáть**] to lay (a rug, tablecloth, etc.); make (a bed).
постирáть *v. pfv., colloq.* to wash; launder.
пости́ться *v.r. impfv.* [*pres.* **пощу́сь, пости́шься**] to fast.
пости́чь [*infl. like* **пости́гнуть**] *v., pfv. of* **постигáть.**
постлáть [*infl. like* **стлать**] *v., pfv. of* **стлать** *and* **постилáть.**
пóстник *n.* person who fasts.
пóстничать *v. impfv., colloq.* to fast.
пóстный *adj.* **1,** fast (*attrib.*): пóстный день, fast day. **2,** containing no milk or meat. **3,** *colloq.* (*of meat*) lean. **4,** *fig.* dreary. **5,** *fig.* pious; sanctimonious.
постовóй *adj.* **1,** duty (*attrib.*); sentry (*attrib.*): постовáя бу́дка, sentry box. **2,** on duty: постовóй милиционéр, policeman on duty. —*n.* man on duty.
постóй *n.* quartering; billeting (*of troops*). —**стáвить на постóй,** to billet.
постóльку *conj., in* **постóльку, поскóльку,** insofar as; to the extent that.
посторони́ться *v.r., pfv. of* **сторони́ться.**
посторóнний *adj.* outside; foreign; extraneous. —*n.* stranger; outsider.
постоя́лец [*gen.* **-льца**] *n., obs.* lodger; guest (*at a hotel or inn*).
постоя́лый *adj., in* **постоя́лый двор,** *obs.* inn; hostelry.
постоя́нно *adv.* constantly; continually.
постоя́нный *adj.* **1,** constant. **2,** permanent. **3,** regular; steady. —**постоя́нная áрмия,** standing army. —**постоя́нный ток,** direct current.
постоя́нство *n.* constancy.
постоя́ть *v. pfv.* [*infl.* **-стою́, -стои́шь**] **1,** to stand (*for a while*). **2,** (*with* **за** + *acc.*) to stand up for. —**постóй!; постóйте!,** wait a minute!; stop!
пострадáвший *n., decl. as an adj.* victim (*of a disaster*).
пострадáть *v. pfv.* **1,** *pfv. of* **страдáть. 2,** to be injured; be damaged; suffer damage.
пострéл *n., colloq.* imp; rascal; brat.
пострéливать *v. impfv.* to fire an occasional shot.
пострeля́ть *v. pfv.* **1,** *v.i.* to fire a gun (*for a while*); do some shooting. **2,** *v.t., colloq.* to shoot (many of something); bag.
постригáть *v. impfv.* [*pfv.* **пострúчь**] **1,** to cut (one's hair, beard, etc.). **2,** to give (someone) a haircut. —**постригáться,** *refl.* **1,** to cut one's hair. **2,** to get a haircut.
пострúчь [*infl. like* **стричь**] *v., pfv. of* **постригáть.** —**пострúчься,** *refl., pfv. of* **постригáться.**
построéние *n.* **1,** building; construction. **2,** *mil.* formation.
пострóить *v., pfv. of* **стрóить.** —**пострóиться,** *refl., pfv. of* **стрóиться.**
пострóйка [*gen. pl.* **-óек**] *n.* **1,** building; edifice. **2,** building; construction.
пострóмка [*gen. pl.* **-мок**] *n.* trace (*of a harness*).
постскри́птум *n.* postscript; P.S.
посту́кивать *v. impfv.* to tap; rap; knock.
постулáт *n.* postulate.
постули́ровать *v. impfv. & pfv.* [*pres.* **-рую, -руешь**] to postulate.
поступáтельный *adj.* forward; progressive.
поступáть *v. impfv.* [*pfv.* **поступи́ть**] **1,** to act. **2,** (*with* **с** + *instr.*) to treat. **3,** (*with* **в** *or* **на** + *acc.*) to join; enter; enlist (in). Поступáть на рабóту, to take a job; go to work. Поступáть на ку́рсы, to enroll in courses. **4,** to arrive; be received; come in. **5,** *in* поступи́ть в продáжу, to go on sale; поступи́ть в произвóдство, to go into production. —**поступáться,** *refl.* (*with instr.*) to waive; forgo.
поступи́ть [*infl.* **-ступлю́, -сту́пишь**] *v., pfv. of* **поступáть.** —**поступи́ться,** *refl., pfv. of* **поступáться.**
поступлéние *n.* **1,** joining; entering. **2,** receipt. **3,** coming in; arrival. **4,** *pl.* receipts.
посту́пок [*gen.* **-пка**] *n.* act; deed.
пóступь *n.f.* walk; gait.
постучáть *v., pfv. of* **стучáть.** —**постучáться,** *refl., pfv. of* **стучáться.**
постыди́ться *v.r., pfv. of* **стыди́ться.**
посты́дный *adj.* shameful; disgraceful.
посты́лый *adj., colloq.* repellent; odious.
посу́да *n.* **1,** dishes: мыть посу́ду, to wash the dishes. **2,** ware: эмалирóванная посу́да, enamelware. **3,** utensils. **4,** *colloq.* vessel; utensil.
посу́дина *n., colloq.* **1,** vessel; container. **2,** boat; tub.
посуди́ть *v. pfv.* [*infl.* **-сужу́, -су́дишь**] to judge: посуди́те сáми, judge for yourself.
посу́дный *adj.* **1,** for dishes; dish (*attrib.*). **2,** china (*attrib.*): посу́дный шкаф, china closet.
посудомóечный *adj., in* **посудомóечная маши́на,** dishwasher.
посудомóйка [*gen. pl.* **-мóек**] *n., colloq.* dishwasher.
посу́л *n., colloq.* promise.
посули́ть *v., pfv. of* **сули́ть.**
пóсуху *adv., colloq.* over dry land.
посчастли́виться *v.r. pfv., impers.* (*with dat.*) to be lucky.
посчитáть *v. pfv.* **1,** to count. **2,** *colloq.* to consider. —**посчитáться,** *refl.* **1,** *pfv. of* **считáться** (*in sense #1*). **2,** (*with* **с** + *instr.*) to get even (with); settle scores (with).
посылáть *v. impfv.* [*pfv.* **послáть**] to send.
посы́лка [*gen. pl.* **-лок**] *n.* **1,** package; parcel. **2,** sending; mailing. **3,** premise. —**быть на посы́лках,** to run errands.
посы́лочный *adj.* **1,** for a package or packages. **2,** mail-order: посы́лочная торгóвля, mail-order business.
посы́льный *n., decl. as an adj.* messenger.
посы́пать [*infl.* **-сыплю, -сыплешь**] *v., pfv. of* **посыпáть.** —**посыпáться,** *refl.* **1,** to begin to fall. **2,** (*of questions, blows, etc.*) to rain down.
посыпáть *v. impfv.* [*pfv.* **посы́пать**] to sprinkle.
посягáтельство *n.* encroachment; infringement.
посягáть *v. impfv.* [*pfv.* **посягну́ть**] (*with* **на** + *acc.*) to infringe (upon); encroach (upon).
пот [*2nd loc.* **поту́**] *n.* perspiration; sweat: весь в поту́, all perspired. —**в пóте лицá,** by the sweat of

one's brow. —**по́том и кро́вью,** by one's own sweat and blood.

потайно́й *adj.* secret; hidden.

потака́ние *n.* (*with dat.*) *colloq.* indulgence (of); catering (to).

потака́ть *v. impfv.* (*with dat.*) *colloq.* to indulge; cater to.

потанцева́ть *v. pfv.* [*infl.* **-цу́ю, -цу́ешь**] to dance (*for a while*); have a dance: потанцу́ем?, shall we dance?

потаску́ха *n., colloq.* strumpet; tart.

потасо́вка [*gen. pl.* **-вок**] *n., colloq.* **1,** brawl; fight. **2,** whipping; beating.

пота́чка [*gen. pl.* **-чек**] *n., colloq.* favor; indulgence.

пота́ш [*gen.* **-таша́**] *n.* potash. —**пота́шный,** *adj.* potash (*attrib.*).

потащи́ть *v., pfv. of* **тащи́ть.** —**потащи́ться,** *refl., pfv. of* **тащи́ться.**

потво́рство *n.* (*with dat.*) leniency (toward); indulgence (of).

потво́рствовать *v. impfv.* [*pres.* **-ствую, -ствуешь**] (*with dat.*) to indulge; be lenient (toward); look the other way (at).

потёк *n.* streak.

потёмки [*gen.* **-мок**] *n. pl.* darkness.

потёмкинский *adj., in* **потёмкинская дере́вня,** Potemkin village.

потемне́ние *n.* darkening.

потемне́ть *v., pfv. of* **темне́ть** (*in sense #1*).

потенциа́л (тэ) *n.* potential. —**потенциа́льный,** *adj.* potential.

потепле́ние *n.* warming.

потепле́ть *v., pfv. of* **тепле́ть.**

потере́ть *v. pfv.* [*infl. like* **тере́ть**] to rub. —**потере́ться,** *refl., pfv. of* **тере́ться.**

потерпе́вший *adj., law* aggrieved: потерпе́вшая сторона́, the aggrieved party. —*n., law* victim: потерпе́вший от пожа́ра, victim of a fire.

потерпе́ть *v. pfv.* [*infl.* **-терплю́, -те́рпишь**] **1,** *pfv. of* **терпе́ть** (*in sense #3*). **2,** to be patient. **3,** (*usu. neg.*) to tolerate; put up with.

потёртость *n.f.* sore spot (*caused by rubbing or chafing*).

потёртый *adj.* shabby; threadbare.

поте́ря *n.* **1,** loss. **2,** waste (*of time, money, etc.*). **3,** *pl.* losses; casualties.

поте́рянный *adj.* **1,** lost. **2,** confused; bewildered. **3,** *colloq.* gone to the dogs. —**как поте́рянный,** like a lost soul.

потеря́ть *v., pfv. of* **теря́ть.** —**потеря́ться,** *refl., pfv. of* **теря́ться.**

потесни́ть *v., pfv. of* **тесни́ть** (*in sense #1*). —**потесни́ться,** *refl.* to crowd together; squeeze together (*so as to make room for someone else*).

поте́ть *v. impfv.* **1,** [*pfv.* **вспоте́ть**] to perspire; sweat. **2,** [*pfv.* **запоте́ть**] *colloq.* to become misty; steam up.

поте́ха *n.* **1,** fun; amusement. **2,** funny incident; funny thing.

поте́чь *v. pfv.* [*infl. like* **течь**] **1,** to begin to flow. **2,** to begin to leak.

потеша́ть *v. impfv., colloq.* to entertain; amuse. —**потеша́ться,** *refl.* **1,** *colloq.* to amuse oneself. **2,** (*with* **над**) to make fun of.

поте́шить *v., pfv. of* **те́шить.** —**поте́шиться,** *refl., pfv. of* **те́шиться.**

поте́шный *adj., colloq.* funny; amusing.

потира́ть *v. impfv.* to rub. —**потира́ть ру́ки,** to rub one's hands (*with glee, worry, etc.*).

потихо́ньку *adv., colloq.* **1,** quietly; silently. **2,** secretly; on the sly. **3,** slowly; gradually.

потни́к [*gen.* **-ника́**] *n.* saddlecloth.

потни́ца *n.* prickly heat; heat rash.

по́тный *adj.* **1,** sweaty; covered with perspiration. **2,** steamed up; misted up.

потово́й *adj.* sweat (*attrib.*): потовы́е же́лезы, sweat glands.

потого́нный *adj.* **1,** inducing perspiration. **2,** involving sweatshop conditions: потого́нная фа́брика, sweatshop. —**потого́нное,** *n.* something taken to induce perspiration.

пото́к *n.* stream; torrent; flood.

потолкова́ть *v. pfv.* [*infl.* **-ку́ю, -ку́ешь**] *colloq.* to talk (*for a while*); have a talk.

потоло́к [*gen.* **-лка́**] *n.* ceiling. —**взять с потолка́,** to take (*e.g.* facts) out of the air. —**плева́ть в потоло́к,** to sit around doing nothing.

потолсте́ть *v., pfv. of* **толсте́ть.**

пото́м *adv.* **1,** then; next. **2,** afterward(s); later (on).

пото́мок [*gen.* **-мка**] *n.* descendant; offspring.

пото́мственный *adj.* **1,** *obs.* hereditary; ancestral. **2,** by birth: пото́мственный дворяни́н, a nobleman by birth. Он пото́мственный актёр, he comes from a long line of actors.

пото́мство *n.* **1,** progeny. **2,** posterity.

потому́ *adv.* which is why. —**потому́...и,** that is why: потому́ я и спра́шиваю, that's why I ask. —**потому́ что,** because.

потону́ть *v., pfv. of* **тону́ть** (*in sense #1*).

пото́п *n.* **1,** *Bib.* flood. **2,** *colloq.* flood; deluge.

потопи́ть *v., pfv. of* **топи́ть** (*in sense #4*).

потопле́ние *n.* sinking.

потопта́ть *v. pfv.* [*infl.* **-топчу́, -то́пчешь**] to trample down.

потора́пливать *v. impfv., colloq.* to hurry; urge on. —**потора́пливаться,** *refl., colloq.* to hurry: потора́пливайтесь!, hurry up!; get a move on!

поторопи́ть *v., pfv. of* **торопи́ть.** —**поторопи́ться,** *refl., pfv. of* **торопи́ться.**

пото́чный *adj.* done on an assembly line: пото́чное произво́дство, assembly-line production.

потра́ва *n.* damage done to crops by cattle.

потрави́ть *v., pfv. of* **трави́ть** (*in sense #2*).

потра́тить *v., pfv. of* **тра́тить.** —**потра́титься,** *refl., pfv. of* **тра́титься.**

потрафля́ть *v. impfv.* [*pfv.* **потра́фить**] (*with dat.*) *colloq.* to please; satisfy.

потреби́тель *n.m.* consumer. —**потреби́тельский,** *adj.* consumer (*attrib.*); consumers'.

потреби́ть [*infl.* **-блю́, -би́шь**] *v., pfv. of* **потребля́ть.**

потребле́ние *n.* consumption. —**това́ры широ́кого потребле́ния,** consumer goods.

потребля́ть *v. impfv.* [*pfv.* **потреби́ть**] to consume.

потре́бность *n.f.* need; requirement.

потре́бный *adj.* necessary; required; requisite.

потре́бовать *v., pfv. of* **тре́бовать.** —**потре́боваться,** *refl., pfv. of* **тре́боваться.**

потрево́жить *v., pfv. of* **трево́жить** (*in sense #2*).

потрёпанный *adj.* tattered; shabby; threadbare.

потрепа́ть *v. pfv.* [*infl.* **-треплю́, -тре́плешь**] **1,** *pfv.*

of **трепа́ть. 2,** *mil.* to inflict heavy losses on. **3,** *fig.* to scar.

потре́скаться *v.r., pfv. of* **тре́скаться.**

потре́скивать *v. impfv.* to crackle.

потро́гать *v. pfv.* to touch; feel; finger.

потроха́ [*gen.* **-хо́в**] *n. pl.* giblets.

потроши́ть *v. impfv.* [*pfv.* **вы́потрошить**] to eviscerate; disembowel.

потруди́ться *v.r. pfv.* [*infl.* **-тружу́сь, -тру́дишься**] **1,** to work (*for a while*). **2,** (*with inf.*) to bother (to); take the trouble (to).

потряса́ть *v. impfv.* [*pfv.* **потрясти́**] **1,** to shake. **2,** (*with instr.*) to shake; brandish. **3,** *fig.* to shake; shock; stagger; stun.

потряса́ющий *adj.* **1,** staggering; stunning. **2,** tremendous; stupendous. **3,** *colloq.* marvelous; fabulous.

потрясе́ние *n.* **1,** shock. **2,** upheaval.

потрясти́ [*infl. like* **трясти́**] *v., pfv. of* **потряса́ть.**

потря́хивать *v. impfv.* (*with acc. or instr.*) *colloq.* to shake.

поту́ги [*gen.* **-ту́г**] *n. pl.* **1,** spasms. Родовы́е поту́ги, birth pains; labor pains. **2,** *fig.* vain attempts.

потупля́ть *v. impfv.* [*pfv.* **поту́пить**] to lower (one's eyes, head, etc.). —**потупля́ться,** *refl.* to lower one's eyes; lower one's head.

потускне́лый *adj.* dull; tarnished.

потускне́ть *v., pfv. of* **тускне́ть.**

потусторо́нний *adj., in* **потусторо́нний мир,** the next world.

потуха́ть *v. impfv.* [*pfv.* **поту́хнуть**] **1,** (*of something burning*) to go out. **2,** to die out; fade away.

поту́хнуть [*past* **-ту́х, -ла**] *v., pfv. of* **ту́хнуть** (*in sense #1*) *and* **потуха́ть.**

поту́хший *adj.* **1,** dull; lifeless. **2,** (*of a volcano*) extinct.

потучне́ть *v., pfv. of* **тучне́ть.**

потуши́ть *v., pfv. of* **туши́ть** (*in sense #1*).

по́тчевать *v. impfv.* [*pfv.* **попо́тчевать;** *pres.* **-чую, -чуешь**] (*with instr.*) *colloq.* to treat to (food, drink, etc.).

потяга́ться *v.r., pfv. of* **тяга́ться.**

потя́гивать *v. impfv.* **1,** to pull at; tug at. **2,** to draw on (a cigarette, pipe, etc.). **3,** to sip. —**потя́гиваться,** *refl.* [*pfv.* **потяну́ться**] to stretch; take a stretch.

потяну́ть *v., pfv. of* **тяну́ть.** —**потяну́ться,** *refl., pfv. of* **тяну́ться** (*in sense #3*) *and* **потя́гиваться.**

поу́жинать *v., pfv. of* **у́жинать.**

поумне́ть *v., pfv. of* **умне́ть.**

поуро́чный *adj.* **1,** of *or* for a lesson. **2,** (*of payment*) by the lesson.

поутру́ *adv., colloq.* in the morning.

поуча́ть *v. impfv.* **1,** to teach; instruct. **2,** to preach to; lecture.

поуче́ние *n.* **1,** edification: в поуче́ние (+ *dat.*), for the edification of. **2,** sermon; homily.

поучи́тельный *adj.* instructive.

поучи́ть *v. pfv.* [*infl.* **-учу́, -у́чишь**] to teach (*for a while*).

поха́бный *adj., colloq.* dirty; lewd; obscene.

поха́живать *v. impfv., colloq.* **1,** to walk back and forth; pace. **2,** (*with* **к**) to drop in on (*from time to time*).

похвала́ *n.* praise.

похвали́ть *v., pfv. of* **хвали́ть.** —**похвали́ться,** *refl., pfv. of* **хвали́ться.**

похвальба́ *n., colloq.* bragging; boasting.

похва́льный *adj.* laudable; commendable; admirable; praiseworthy. —**похва́льная гра́мота,** certificate of good work and conduct (*in school*).

похваля́ться *v.r. impfv.* (*with instr.*) *colloq.* to boast (about); brag (about).

похва́статься *v.r., pfv. of* **хва́статься.**

похити́тель *n.m.* **1,** thief. **2,** kidnaper; abductor. **3,** hijacker.

похища́ть *v. impfv.* [*pfv.* **похи́тить**] **1,** to steal. **2,** to kidnap; abduct. **3,** to hijack.

похище́ние *n.* **1,** theft. **2,** kidnaping; abduction. **3,** hijacking.

похлёбка *n.* pottage.

похло́пать *v., pfv. of* **хло́пать.**

похлопота́ть *v., pfv. of* **хлопота́ть.**

похло́пывать *v. impfv., colloq.* to clap; tap; pat.

похме́лье *n.* hangover.

похо́д *n.* **1,** excursion; outing; hike. Туристи́ческий похо́д, hiking expedition; walking tour. Лы́жный/ло́дочный похо́д, skiing/boat trip. **2,** march. **3,** *mil.* campaign. **4,** campaign; drive. —**кресто́вый похо́д,** *hist.* crusade.

походата́йствовать *v., pfv. of* **хода́тайствовать.**

походи́ть[1] *v. impfv.* [*pres.* **-хожу́, -хо́дишь**] (*with* **на** + *acc.*) to resemble; look like; be like.

походи́ть[2] *v. pfv.* [*infl.* **-хожу́, -хо́дишь**] to walk (*for a while*); take a walk.

похо́дка *n.* walk; gait.

похо́дный *adj., mil.* **1,** field (*attrib.*): похо́дная ку́хня, (mobile) field kitchen. **2,** march (*attrib.*); marching.

по́ходя *adv., colloq.* **1,** hastily; on the run. **2,** at the same time; while one is (was) at it. **3,** casually; without thinking twice about it.

похожде́ние *n.* adventure.

похо́жий *adj.* (*with* **на** + *acc.*) similar (to); like; alike. Это на него́ не похо́же, that's not like him. Похо́же, что бу́дет дождь, it looks like rain.

похолода́ние *n.* drop in temperature; cold snap.

похолода́ть *v. pfv., impers.* to get cold; turn cold.

похолоде́ть *v., pfv. of* **холоде́ть.**

похорони́ть *v., pfv. of* **хорони́ть.**

похоро́нный *adj.* funeral (*attrib.*).

по́хороны [*gen.* **-ро́н;** *dat.* **-рона́м**] *n. pl.* funeral.

похороше́ть *v., pfv. of* **хороше́ть.**

похотли́вый *adj.* lustful; lewd; lascivious. —**похотли́вость,** *n.f.* lewdness; lasciviousness.

похотни́к [*gen.* **-ника́**] *n.* clitoris.

по́хоть *n.f.* lust.

похуде́ть *v., pfv. of* **худе́ть.**

поцелова́ть *v., pfv. of* **целова́ть.** —**поцелова́ться,** *refl., pfv. of* **целова́ться.**

поцелу́й *n.* kiss.

почасово́й *adj.* by the hour; hourly.

поча́ток [*gen.* **-тка**] *n.* ear (*of corn*).

по́чва *n.* **1,** soil; ground. **2,** *fig.* basis; foundation: не име́ть (под собо́й) по́чвы, to be without foundation. —**на по́чве** (+ *gen.*), due to; owing to; on account of. —**выбива́ть по́чву из-под чьих-нибудь ног,** to cut the ground from under someone's feet. —**подгота́вливать по́чву для,** to prepare the ground for; pave the way for; set the stage for. —**теря́ть по́чву под нога́ми,** to feel the ground slipping from beneath one's feet.

по́чвенный *adj.* soil (*attrib.*).

почвове́д *n.* soil scientist. —**почвове́дение,** *n.* soil science.

почём *adv., colloq.* how much is?; how much are?; what is the price of? —**почём знать?,** who knows?; how is one to know? —**почём я зна́ю?,** how should I know?

почему́ *adv.* **1,** *interr.* why? **2,** *rel.* why: я не зна́ю, почему́ он э́то сказа́л, I don't know why he said that. —*conj.* which is why. —**вот почему́,** that is why. —**почему́ бы не** (+ *inf.*), why not...?: почему́ бы не спроси́ть её?, why not ask her? —**почему́ нет?,** why not?

почему́-ли́бо *adv.* for some reason; for any reason. *Also,* **почему́-нибудь.**

почему́-то *adv.* for some reason or other.

по́черк *n.* handwriting.

почерне́лый *adj.* darkened; blackened.

почерне́ть *v., pfv. of* **черне́ть.**

почерпа́ть *v. impfv.* [*pfv.* **почерпну́ть**] **1,** *colloq.* to draw (water). **2,** *fig.* to glean; cull.

почерстве́ть *v., pfv. of* **черстве́ть** (*in sense #1*).

почеса́ть *v., pfv. of* **чеса́ть.** —**почеса́ться,** *refl., pfv. of* **чеса́ться** (*in sense #2*).

по́чести [*gen.* **-стей**] *n.pl.* honor; homage: ока́зывать *or* воздава́ть по́чести (+ *dat.*), to pay homage to.

почёсывать *v. impfv., colloq.* to scratch occasionally. —**почёсываться,** *refl., colloq.* to scratch oneself occasionally.

почёт *n.* honor; respect; esteem.

почётный *adj.* **1,** honored; of honor: почётное ме́сто, place of honor. **2,** honorary. **3,** honorable. —**почётный карау́л,** guard of honor; honor guard.

по́чечный *adj.* kidney (*attrib.*); renal.

почива́ть *v. impfv.* [*pfv.* **почи́ть**] *obs.* **1,** to sleep. **2,** [*impfv. only*] to lie; repose (in one's grave). —**почива́ть (почи́ть) на ла́врах,** to rest on one's laurels.

почи́вший *n., decl. as an adj.* the deceased.

почи́н *n.* **1,** initiative. **2,** *colloq.* start; beginning.

почини́ть *v., pfv. of* **чини́ть** (*in sense #1*).

почи́нка *n.* mending; repair.

почи́стить *v., pfv. of* **чи́стить.**

почита́й *adv., colloq.* **1,** almost. **2,** probably.

почита́тель *n.m.* admirer.

почита́ть[1] *v. impfv.* **1,** to respect; honor; revere. **2,** *obs.* to consider.

почита́ть[2] *v. pfv.* **1,** to read (*for a while*). **2,** *colloq.* to read (a book, article, etc.).

почи́тывать *v. impfv., colloq.* to read from time to time.

почи́ть [*infl.* **-чи́ю, -чи́ешь**] *v., pfv. of* **почива́ть.**

по́чка [*gen. pl.* **-чек**] *n.* **1,** bud. **2,** kidney.

по́чта *n.* **1,** mail. **2,** post office. —**дипломати́ческая по́чта,** diplomatic pouch.

почтальо́н *n.* mailman; postman.

почта́мт *n.* main post office.

почте́ние *n.* **1,** respect; deference. **2,** reverence. —**с почте́нием,** (*at the close of a letter*) respectfully yours.

почте́нный *adj.* **1,** worthy. **2,** venerable. **3,** *colloq.* considerable.

почти́ *adv.* almost; nearly. —**почти́ что** = **почти́.**

почти́тельность *n.f.* respect; deference.

почти́тельный *adj.* respectful; reverent; deferential. —**держа́ться на почти́тельном расстоя́нии,** to keep at a distance; keep one's distance.

почти́ть *v. pfv.* [*infl. like* **чтить**] to honor.

почтме́йстер *n., obs.* postmaster.

почто́вый *adj.* postal; mail (*attrib.*). —**почто́вая бума́га,** stationery. —**почто́вый го́лубь,** carrier pigeon; homing pigeon. —**почто́вая ка́рточка,** postcard. —**почто́вая ма́рка,** postage stamp. —**почто́вые расхо́ды,** postage. —**почто́вый ште́мпель,** postmark. —**почто́вый я́щик,** mailbox.

почу́вствовать *v., pfv. of* **чу́вствовать.** —**почу́вствоваться,** *refl., pfv. of* **чу́вствоваться.**

почу́диться *v.r., pfv. of* **чу́диться.**

почу́ять *v., pfv. of* **чу́ять.**

пошаба́шить *v., pfv. of* **шаба́шить.**

поша́ливать *v. impfv., colloq.* to act up.

пошатну́ть *v. pfv.* to shake. —**пошатну́ться,** *refl.* **1,** to stagger. **2,** to be shaken. **3,** *fig.* (*of one's health*) to be impaired.

поша́тывать *v. impfv.* **1,** to shake. **2,** *impers.* to totter: его́ поша́тывает, he is unsteady on his feet. —**поша́тываться,** *refl.* **1,** to sway; totter; wobble. **2,** (*of a tooth*) to be loose.

пошевели́ть *v., pfv. of* **шевели́ть.** —**пошевели́ться,** *refl., pfv. of* **шевели́ться.**

поши́б *n., colloq.* manner; style. —**одного́ поши́ба,** two of a kind; from the same mold.

поши́вка *n.* sewing.

поши́вочный *adj., in* **поши́вочная мастерска́я,** tailor's shop; dressmaker's shop.

по́шлина *n.* duty; customs.

по́шлость *n.f.* **1,** pettiness. **2,** trite remark; banality.

по́шлый *adj.* **1,** common; petty; shallow. **2,** coarse; vulgar. **3,** banal; trite.

пошля́к [*gen.* **-ляка́**] *n., colloq.* common *or* shallow person.

пошту́чный *adj.* by the piece. —**пошту́чно,** *adv.* by the piece.

пошуме́ть *v. pfv.*[*infl.* **-млю́, -ми́шь**] to make (some) noise.

пошути́ть *v., pfv. of* **шути́ть.**

поща́да *n.* mercy.

пощади́ть *v., pfv. of* **щади́ть.**

пощекота́ть *v., pfv. of* **щекота́ть.**

пощёчина *n.* slap in the face.

пощи́пывать *v. impfv.* **1,** to pinch from time to time. **2,** *impers.* to prick; tingle: у меня́ щёки пощи́пывает, my cheeks are tingling.

пощу́пать *v., pfv. of* **щу́пать.**

поэ́зия *n.* poetry.

поэ́ма *n.* (long) poem.

поэ́т *n.* poet.

поэте́сса (тэ) *n.* poetess.

поэти́ческий *adj.* poetic.

поэ́тому *adv.* therefore.

появи́ться [*infl.* **-явлю́сь, -я́вишься**] *v.r., pfv. of* **появля́ться.**

появле́ние *n.* appearance.

появля́ться *v.r. impfv.* [*pfv.* **появи́ться**] to appear.

по́яс [*pl.* **пояса́**] *n.* **1,** belt. **2,** waist: кла́няться в по́яс, to bow from the waist. **3,** [*pl.* **по́ясы**] zone: часово́й по́яс, time zone. —**спаса́тельный по́яс,** life belt; life preserver.

поясне́ние *n.* explanation.

поясни́тельный *adj.* explanatory.

поясни́ть *v., pfv. of* **поясня́ть.**

поясни́ца *n.* small of the back. —**поясни́чный,** *adj.* lumbar.

поясно́й *adj.* **1,** belt (*attrib.*). **2,** to the waist; from the waist. **3,** zonal. —**поясно́й портре́т,** half-length portrait.

поясня́ть *v. impfv.* [*pfv.* **поясни́ть**] to explain; elucidate.

праба́бка [*gen. pl.* **-бок**] *n.* great-grandmother. *Also,* **праба́бушка.**

пра́вда *n.* truth. Это пра́вда, that is true; that's the truth. Пра́вда ли, что...?, is it true that...? —*adv.* **1,** really; indeed. **2,** true; admittedly; to be sure. **3,** *in questions,* isn't that so?; don't you think so? —**все́ми пра́вдами и непра́вдами,** by hook or by crook. —**по пра́вде говоря́; по пра́вде сказа́ть,** to tell the truth...

правди́вый *adj.* **1,** (*of a person*) truthful. **2,** (*of a story, answer, etc.*) true; truthful. —**правди́вость,** *n.f.* truthfulness; veracity.

правдоподо́бие *n.* plausibility; credibility; verisimilitude. —**правдоподо́бный,** *adj.* plausible; believable; credible.

пра́ведник *n.* righteous man.

пра́ведный *adj.* **1,** righteous. **2,** just. —**пра́ведность,** *n.f.* righteousness.

праве́ть *v. impfv.* [*pfv.* **поправе́ть**] to shift to the right; become more conservative.

пра́вило *n.* **1,** rule: пра́вило орфогра́фии, spelling rule. **2,** *pl.* rules; regulations: пра́вила безопа́сности, rules of safety; safety regulations. —**как пра́вило,** as a rule. —**взять себе́ за пра́вило** (+ *inf.*), to make it a rule (to).

пра́вильно *adv.* **1,** correctly. **2,** properly. **3,** regularly; evenly. —*adj., used predicatively* right; correct: соверше́нно пра́вильно, absolutely right.

пра́вильность *n.f.* **1,** rightness; correctness. **2,** regularity.

пра́вильный *adj.* **1,** right; correct. **2,** proper. **3,** regular: пра́вильный глаго́л, regular verb; пра́вильные черты́ лица́, regular features. —**пра́вильная дробь,** proper fraction.

прави́тель *n.m.* ruler.

прави́тельство *n.* government. —**прави́тельственный,** *adj.* governmental; government (*attrib.*).

пра́вить *v. impfv.* [*pres.* **-влю, -вишь**] **1,** (*with instr.*) to rule; govern. **2,** (*with instr.*) to drive; steer. **3,** (*with acc.*) to read; correct (something written). **4,** (*with acc.*) to sharpen; hone.

пра́вка *n.* reading; correcting: пра́вка корректу́ры, proofreading.

правле́ние *n.* **1,** government; rule. **2,** management; board of directors.

пра́внук *n.* great-grandson.

пра́внучка [*gen. pl.* **-чек**] *n.* great-granddaughter.

пра́во [*pl.* **права́**] *n.* **1,** right: пра́во на труд, the right to work; пра́во го́лоса, the right to vote. **2,** law: уголо́вное пра́во, criminal law. Изуча́ть пра́во, to study law. **3,** *pl., colloq.* (driver's) license. —*particle, colloq.* **1,** really. **2,** believe me! —**на права́х** (+ *gen.*), as; in the capacity of. —**по пра́ву,** rightfully; deservedly.

правове́рный *adj.* orthodox; faithful.

правово́й *adj.* legal; of (the) law.

правоме́рный *adj.* legitimate.

правомо́чный *adj., law* competent.

правонаруше́ние *n.* offense; violation of the law. —**правонаруши́тель,** *n.m.* offender; lawbreaker; wrongdoer.

правописа́ние *n.* orthography; spelling.

правосла́вие *n.* the Orthodox faith.

правосла́вный *adj.* orthodox. —*n.* member of the Orthodox Church.

правосу́дие *n.* justice.

правота́ *n.* rightness; correctness.

пра́вый *adj.* **1,** right; right-hand. **2,** *polit.* right; right-wing. **3,** *naut.* starboard. **4,** [*short form* **прав, права́, пра́во, пра́вы**] right; correct. **5,** (*of a cause*) just. —*n.* right-winger; rightist.

пра́вящий *adj.* ruling: пра́вящие круги́, ruling circles.

прагмати́зм *n.* pragmatism. —**прагмати́ст,** *n.* pragmatist. —**прагмати́ческий,** *adj.* pragmatic.

пра́дед *n.* **1,** great-grandfather. **2,** *pl.* ancestors; forefathers.

пра́зднество *n.* **1,** festival; celebration. **2,** *pl.* festivities.

пра́здник *n.* **1,** holiday: с пра́здником!, happy holiday! **2,** celebration. —**бу́дет и на на́шей у́лице пра́здник,** our day will come.

пра́здничный *adj.* **1,** holiday (*attrib.*). **2,** festive.

пра́здно *adv.* idly.

пра́зднование *n.* celebration.

пра́здновать *v. impfv.* [*pfv.* **отпра́здновать;** *pres.* **-ную, -нуешь**] to celebrate.

пра́здный *adj.* idle. —**пра́здность,** *n.f.* idleness.

празеоди́м *n.* praseodymium.

пра́ктик *n.* **1,** practical worker. **2,** practical person.

пра́ктика *n.* **1,** practice: на пра́ктике, in practice. **2,** practical experience. **3,** practical work. **4,** *obs.* practice (*of a physician or lawyer*).

практика́нт *n.* person undergoing practical training; trainee.

практикова́ть *v. impfv.* [*pres.* **-ку́ю, -ку́ешь**] **1,** *v.t.* to practice; try out. **2,** *v.i., obs.* (*of a physician, lawyer, etc.*) to practice. —**практикова́ться,** *refl.* **1,** (*with* **в** + *prepl.*) to practice. **2,** to be practiced; be done.

пра́ктикум *n.* practical work; practical training.

практи́чески *adv.* **1,** in a practical manner; practically. **2,** practically; virtually; for all practical purposes.

практи́ческий *adj.* practical: практи́ческий челове́к/курс/о́пыт, practical person/course/experience.

практи́чный *adj.* practical: практи́чный челове́к/костю́м/автомоби́ль, practical person/suit/car. —**практи́чность,** *n.f.* practicality.

пра́отец [*gen.* **-тца**] *n., obs.* forefather; ancestor.

пра́порщик *n., mil.* **1,** warrant officer. **2,** *pre-rev.* ensign; lieutenant.

прапраба́бка [*gen. pl.* **-бок**] *n.* great-great-grandmother. *Also,* **прапраба́бушка.**

прапра́внук *n.* great-great-grandson.

прапра́внучка [*gen. pl.* **-чек**] *n.* great-great-granddaughter.

прапра́дед *n.* great-great-grandfather.

прах *n.* **1,** *poetic* dust. **2,** (earthly) remains. —**мир пра́ху его́,** may he rest in peace. —**обрати́ть** *or* **преврати́ть в прах,** to reduce to dust (*or* ashes). —**пойти́ пра́хом,** to go to the dogs.

пра́чечная *n., decl. as an adj.* laundry.

пра́чка [*gen. pl.* **-чек**] *n.* laundress.

праща́ *n.* sling (*for hurling stones*).

пра́щур *n.* ancestor; forefather.

пре- *prefix* **1,** *indicating a high degree:* превозноси́ть, to extol; пресыща́ть, to satiate. **2,** *indicating excess:* преувели́чивать, to exaggerate. **3,** *indicating transfor-*

mation: превраща́ть, to turn into. **4,** *indicating the overcoming of something:* преодолева́ть/превозмога́ть, to overcome. **5,** (*with adjectives*) *indicating a high degree:* престаре́лый, very old.

преа́мбула *n.* preamble.

пребыва́ние *n.* **1,** (one's) stay: во вре́мя на́шего пребыва́ния в Пари́же, during our stay in Paris. **2,** tenure: пребыва́ние в до́лжности, tenure in office. —**ме́сто постоя́нного пребыва́ния,** permanent residence.

пребыва́ть *v. impfv.* to be.

превали́ровать *v. impfv.* [*pres.* **-рую, -руешь**] **1,** to predominate. **2,** (*with* **над**) to dominate; take precedence over.

превенти́вный *adj.* preventive.

превзойти́ [*infl.* **-взойду́, -взойдёшь;** *past* **-взошёл, -взошла́, -взошло́**] *v., pfv. of* **превосходи́ть.**

превозмога́ть *v. impfv.* [*pfv.* **превозмо́чь**] to overcome.

превозмо́чь [*infl. like* **мочь**] *v., pfv. of* **превозмога́ть.**

превознести́ [*infl. like* **нести́**] *v., pfv. of* **превозноси́ть.**

превозноси́ть *v. impfv.* [*pfv.* **превознести́;** *pres.* **-ношу́, -но́сишь**] to extol. —**превозноси́ть до небе́с,** to praise to the skies.

превосходи́тельство *n.* Excellency: ва́ше превосходи́тельство, Your Excellency.

превосходи́ть *v. impfv.* [*pfv.* **превзойти́;** *pres.* **-хожу́, -хо́дишь**] **1,** to excel. **2,** to exceed; surpass. —**превосходи́ть (самого́) себя́,** to outdo oneself.

превосхо́дный *adj.* **1,** excellent; superb. **2,** *gram.* superlative: превосхо́дная сте́пень, superlative degree.

превосхо́дство *n.* superiority.

преврати́ть [*infl.* **-щу́, -ти́шь**] *v., pfv. of* **превраща́ть.** —**преврати́ться,** *refl., pfv. of* **превраща́ться.**

превра́тно *adv.* incorrectly: превра́тно истолкова́ть, to misinterpret.

превра́тность *n.f.* **1,** error; fallacy. **2,** *pl.* vicissitudes: превра́тности судьбы́, the vicissitudes of life.

превра́тный *adj.* **1,** wrong; incorrect; erroneous. **2,** *obs.* (*of luck, fate, etc.*) fickle; capricious.

превраща́ть *v. impfv.* [*pfv.* **преврати́ть**] (*with* **в** + *acc.*) **1,** to turn into; convert into. **2,** to reduce to (rubble, ashes, etc.). —**превраща́ться,** *refl.* (*with* **в** + *acc.*) to turn to; turn into; become.

превраще́ние *n.* **1,** conversion. **2,** transformation.

превы́сить [*infl.* **-шу, -сишь**] *v., pfv. of* **превыша́ть.**

превыша́ть *v. impfv.* [*pfv.* **превы́сить**] to exceed.

превыше́ние *n.* **1,** exceeding. **2,** excess.

прегра́да *n.* obstacle; barrier.

прегради́ть [*infl.* **-жу́, -ди́шь**] *v., pfv. of* **преграждать.**

прегражда́ть *v. impfv.* [*pfv.* **прегради́ть**] to block; bar; obstruct.

прегражде́ние *n.* blocking; barring; obstructing.

прегреше́ние *n., obs.* sin; transgression; iniquity.

пред *prep.* = **пе́ред.**

пред- *prefix, indicating prior action:* предви́деть, to foresee; предвосхища́ть, to anticipate.

предава́ть *v. impfv.* [*pfv.* **преда́ть;** *pres.* **-даю́, -даёшь**] **1,** to betray. **2,** (*with dat.*) to commit (to): предава́ть (что́-нибудь) огню́, to commit to the flames. **3,** *in* предава́ть гла́сности, to make public; предава́ть сме́рти, to put to death; предава́ть суду́, to prosecute; put on trial. —**предава́ться,** *refl.* (*with dat.*) to give way to; indulge in.

преда́ние *n.* **1,** legend. **2,** (*with dat.*) committing (to); putting (to).

пре́данность *n.f.* devotion; dedication.

пре́данный *adj.* devoted; dedicated. —**пре́данный вам,** yours truly.

преда́тель *n.m.* traitor.

преда́тельский *adj.* **1,** traitorous; treasonable. **2,** treacherous.

преда́тельство *n.* **1,** betrayal. **2,** treachery. **3,** treason.

преда́ть [*infl. like* **дать;** *past* **пре́дал, предала́, пре́дало**] *v., pfv. of* **предава́ть.** —**преда́ться,** *refl.* [*past* **преда́лся, -ла́сь, -ло́сь**] *pfv. of* **предава́ться.**

предвари́тельно *adv.* beforehand; in advance; ahead of time.

предвари́тельный *adj.* **1,** preliminary. **2,** advance; prior.

предваря́ть *v. impfv.* [*pfv.* **предвари́ть**] **1,** to anticipate. **2,** *obs.* to forewarn.

предве́стие *n.* omen; augury; portent.

предве́стник *n.* harbinger; precursor; forerunner.

предвеща́ть *v. impfv.* to portend; presage; augur. Предвеща́ть хоро́шее, to augur well; bode well.

предвзя́тость *n.f.* prejudice; bias. —**предвзя́тый,** *adj.* preconceived.

предви́дение *n.* **1,** foresight. **2,** anticipation: в предви́дении (+ *gen.*), in anticipation of. **3,** prediction.

предви́деть *v. impfv.* [*pres.* **-ви́жу, -ви́дишь**] to foresee.

предвкуси́ть [*infl.* **-вкушу́, -вку́сишь**] *v., pfv. of* **предвкуша́ть.**

предвкуша́ть *v. impfv.* [*pfv.* **предвкуси́ть**] to anticipate with pleasure; look forward to.

предвкуше́ние *n.* **1,** foretaste. **2,** anticipation.

предводи́тель *n.m.* leader. —**предводи́тельство,** *n.* leadership.

предводи́тельствовать *v. impfv.* [*pres.* **-ствую, -ствуешь**] **1,** to be the leader; be in charge. **2,** (*with instr.*) to lead; command; be the leader of.

предвое́нный *adj.* prewar.

предвосхища́ть *v. impfv.* [*pfv.* **предвосхи́тить**] to anticipate.

предвосхище́ние *n.* anticipation.

предвы́борный *adj.* election (*attrib.*).

предго́рье *n.* foothill.

преддве́рие *n.* threshold: в преддве́рии (+ *gen.*), on the threshold (of).

преде́л *n.* **1,** limit. **2,** *pl.* bounds: вы́йти за преде́лы (+ *gen.*), to go beyond the bounds of. **3,** (*with gen.*) height (of); acme (of); pinnacle (of): преде́л жела́ний, the pinnacle of one's desires. —**в преде́лах** (+ *gen.*), within. —**за преде́лами** (+ *gen.*), outside; beyond.

преде́льно *adv.* utterly; to the extreme.

преде́льный *adj.* **1,** boundary (*attrib.*): преде́льная ли́ния, boundary line. **2,** maximum: преде́льный во́зраст, maximum age. Преде́льный срок, time limit. **3,** *fig.* utmost: с преде́льной быстрото́й, with the utmost speed.

предержа́щий *adj., in* **вла́сти предержа́щие,** *obs.* the powers that be; the authorities.

предзнаменова́ние *n.* omen; augury; portent.

предика́т *n., gram.* predicate. —**предикати́вный,** *adj., gram.* predicative.
предисло́вие *n.* preface; foreword.
предлага́ть *v. impfv.* [*pfv.* **предложи́ть**] **1,** to offer. **2,** to propose. **3,** to suggest. **4,** to pose (a question, riddle, etc.). **5,** to order (someone to do something).
предло́г *n.* **1,** pretext; excuse. **2,** preposition.
предложе́ние *n.* **1,** offer. **2,** proposal; proposition. **3,** suggestion. **4,** motion (*made at a meeting*). **5,** *gram.* sentence; clause. **6,** *econ.* supply: спрос и предложе́ние, supply and demand.
предложи́ть [*infl.* **-ложу́, -ло́жишь**] *v., pfv. of* **предлага́ть.**
предло́жный *adj., in* **предло́жный паде́ж,** prepositional case.
предме́стье *n.* suburb.
предме́т *n.* **1,** object: неодушевлённый предме́т, inanimate object. **2,** article; item: предме́т ро́скоши, luxury item. **3,** object; target: предме́т насме́шек, object of ridicule. **4,** subject; topic. **5,** subject (*in school*). —**на предме́т** (+ *gen.*), for; for the purpose of.
предме́тный *adj.* **1,** subject (*attrib.*): предме́тный катало́г, subject catalogue. **2,** material; physical. —**предме́тное стекло́,** slide (*for a microscope*). —**предме́тный указа́тель,** index. —**предме́тный уро́к,** object lesson.
предмо́стный *adj.* located at the foot of a bridge. —**предмо́стное укрепле́ние,** bridgehead.
предназнача́ть *v. impfv.* [*pfv.* **предназна́чить**] (*with* **на** + *acc. or* **для**) **1,** to mean; intend; design (for). **2,** to set aside; earmark (for).
предназначе́ние *n.* **1,** mission; calling. **2,** *obs.* fate; destiny.
предназна́чить *v., pfv. of* **предназнача́ть.**
преднаме́ренный *adj.* premeditated; intentional; deliberate. —**преднаме́ренно,** *adv.* intentionally; deliberately. —**преднаме́ренность,** *n.f.* premeditation.
предначерта́ние *n.* prescription; requirement.
предначерта́ть *v. pfv.* to destine; predetermine; foreordain.
предо *prep.* = **пред** *and* **пе́ред.**
пре́док [*gen.* **-дка**] *n.* ancestor; forefather.
предопределе́ние *n.* **1,** predetermination. **2,** *obs.* predestination.
предопределя́ть *v. impfv.* [*pfv.* **предопредели́ть**] to predetermine; predestine; foreordain.
предоста́вить [*infl.* **-влю, -вишь**] *v., pfv. of* **предоставля́ть.**
предоставле́ние *n.* granting; giving.
предоставля́ть *v. impfv.* [*pfv.* **предоста́вить**] **1,** to grant; give. **2,** to leave (*to do something*): нам предоста́вили э́то сде́лать, it was left for us to do. —**предоставля́ть самому́ себе́,** to leave on one's own; leave to one's own devices.
предостерега́ть *v. impfv.* [*pfv.* **предостере́чь**] (*with* **от**) to warn (against); caution (against).
предостереже́ние *n.* warning; caution.
предостере́чь [*infl. like* **стере́чь**] *v., pfv. of* **предостерега́ть.**
предосторо́жность *n.f.* **1,** caution; precaution. **2,** *usu. pl.* precautions. —**ме́ры предосторо́жности,** precautionary measures.
предосуди́тельный *adj.* reprehensible; blameworthy.
предотвраща́ть *v. impfv.* [*pfv.* **предотврати́ть**] to avert; prevent.
предотвраще́ние *n.* prevention; preventing; averting.
предохране́ние *n.* protection.
предохрани́тель *n.m.* safety device; safety catch; safety lock.
предохрани́тельный *adj.* **1,** precautionary; preventive. **2,** safety (*attrib.*): предохрани́тельный кла́пан, safety valve.
предохраня́ть *v. impfv.* [*pfv.* **предохрани́ть**] to protect.
предписа́ние *n.* order: предписа́ния врача́, doctor's orders.
предписа́ть [*infl.* **-пишу́, -пи́шешь**] *v., pfv. of* **предпи́сывать.**
предпи́сывать *v. impfv.* [*pfv.* **предписа́ть**] **1,** to order; direct. **2,** to prescribe.
предпле́чье *n.* forearm.
предплюсна́ [*pl.* **-плю́сны, -плю́сен**] *n., anat.* tarsus. —**предплюснево́й,** *adj.* tarsal.
предполага́емый *adj.* **1,** planned. **2,** supposed; presumed.
предполага́ть *v. impfv.* [*pfv.* **предположи́ть**] **1,** to suppose; assume; presume. **2,** [*impfv. only*] to intend; plan. **3,** [*impfv. only*] to presuppose. —**предполага́ться,** *refl.* [*impfv. only*] **1,** to be planned. **2,** *impers.* to be assumed: предполага́лось, что..., it was assumed that...
предположе́ние *n.* **1,** supposition; assumption. **2,** plan; project.
предположи́тельно *adv.* **1,** by making an assumption; hypothetically. **2,** supposedly; presumably; probably.
предположи́тельный *adj.* hypothetical; conjectural.
предположи́ть [*infl.* **-ложу́, -ло́жишь**] *v., pfv. of* **предполага́ть.**
предпосла́ть [*infl.* **-шлю́, -шлёшь**] *v., pfv. of* **предпосыла́ть.**
предпосле́дний *adj.* next to last.
предпосыла́ть *v. impfv.* [*pfv.* **предпосла́ть**] (*with dat.*) to preface: предпосыла́ть расска́зу анекдо́т, to preface one's story with an anecdote. Предпосыла́ть не́сколько слов к расска́зу, to preface one's story with a few words.
предпосы́лка [*gen. pl.* **-лок**] *n.* **1,** prerequisite; precondition. **2,** premise.
предпоче́сть [*infl.* **-чту́, -чтёшь;** *past* **-чёл, -чла́, -чло́**] *v., pfv. of* **предпочита́ть.**
предпочита́ть *v. impfv.* [*pfv.* **предпоче́сть**] to prefer.
предпочте́ние *n.* preference.
предпочти́тельный *adj.* **1,** preferable; preferred. Си́ний цвет предпочти́тельнее зелёного, blue is preferable to green. **2,** (*of a tariff*) preferential.
предприи́мчивый *adj.* enterprising. —**предприи́мчивость,** *n.f.* enterprise; initiative.
предпринима́тель *n.m.* entrepreneur; businessman.
предпринима́тельство *n.* enterprise: свобо́дное предпринима́тельство, free enterprise.
предпринима́ть *v. impfv.* [*pfv.* **предприня́ть**] **1,** to undertake. **2,** to make (an attempt, efforts, etc.). **3,**

to take (steps, measures, action, etc.). **4,** to mount (an attack, offensive, etc.).

предприня́ть [*infl. like* **приня́ть**] *v., pfv. of* **предпринима́ть.**

предприя́тие *n.* **1,** undertaking; venture. **2,** enterprise: промы́шленное предприя́тие, an industrial enterprise.

предрасполага́ть *v. impfv.* [*pfv.* **предрасположи́ть**] (*with* **к** *or* **в по́льзу**) to predispose (toward *or* in favor of).

предрасположе́ние *n.* (*with* **к**) predisposition (to *or* toward).

предрасполо́женный *adj.* (*with* **к**) predisposed (to).

предрасположи́ть [*infl.* **-ложу́, -ло́жишь**] *v., pfv. of* **предрасполага́ть.**

предрассу́док [*gen.* **-дка**] *n.* prejudice.

предрека́ть *v. impfv.* [*pfv.* **предре́чь**] **1,** to predict. **2,** to portend.

предре́чь [*infl. like* **печь**] *v., pfv. of* **предрека́ть.**

предреша́ть *v. impfv.* [*pfv.* **предреши́ть**] **1,** to decide beforehand. **2,** to predetermine.

предродово́й *adj.* prenatal.

председа́тель *n.m.* chairman. —**председа́тельский,** *adj.* chairman's. —**председа́тельство,** *n.* chairmanship.

председа́тельствовать *v. impfv.* [*pres.* **-ствую, -ствуешь**] to preside.

предсе́рдие *n.* auricle (*of the heart*).

предсказа́ние *n.* prediction.

предсказа́тель *n.m.* forecaster; prognosticator.

предсказа́ть [*infl.* **-скажу́, -ска́жешь**] *v., pfv. of* **предска́зывать.**

предсказу́емый *adj.* predictable.

предска́зывать *v. impfv.* [*pfv.* **предсказа́ть**] to predict.

предсме́ртный *adj.* **1,** occurring just before death; death (*attrib.*). **2,** (*of words, a wish, etc.*) dying.

представи́тель *n.m.* **1,** representative. **2,** spokesman.

представи́тельный *adj.* **1,** representative. **2,** impressive; imposing.

представи́тельство *n.* **1,** representation. **2,** representative office: вое́нное представи́тельство, military representative's office.

предста́вить [*infl.* **-влю, -вишь**] *v., pfv. of* **представля́ть.** —**предста́виться,** *refl., pfv. of* **представля́ться.**

представле́ние *n.* **1,** presentation; submission. **2,** idea; notion. **3,** picture (*in one's mind*). **4,** performance; show. **5,** representation (*formal statement*).

представля́ть *v. impfv.* [*pfv.* **предста́вить**] **1,** to present; submit. **2,** to introduce; present (a person). **3,** (*with* **себе́**) to imagine. **4,** [*impfv. only*] to represent. **5,** [*impfv. only*] (*often with* **собо́й**) to be; represent; constitute: представля́ть (собо́й) опа́сность (для), to represent a danger (to). Представля́ть угро́зу, to pose a threat. Представля́ть интере́с (для), to be of interest (to). Представля́ть тру́дности *or* затрудне́ния, to present difficulties. Что он собо́й представля́ет?, what sort of person is he?; what is he like? —**представля́ться,** *refl.* **1,** to introduce oneself. **2,** (*of an opportunity*) to arise; present itself. **3,** (*with dat.*) to appear (before). **4,** (*with dat.*) to seem (to). **5,** (*with instr.*) *colloq.* to pretend (to be).

предста́тельный *adj.*, *in* **предста́тельная железа́,** prostate gland.

предста́ть *v. pfv.* [*infl.* **-ста́ну, -ста́нешь**] (*with* **пе́ред**) to appear (before).

предстоя́ть *v. impfv.* [*pres.* **-стои́т**] **1,** to lie ahead; be in the offing. **2,** (*with dat.*) to be in store (for). Нам предстои́т холо́дная зима́, we are in for a cold winter. **3,** (*with dat. and inf.*) to have to: мне предстои́т пое́хать туда́, I shall have to go there.

предстоя́щий *adj.* forthcoming; impending.

предте́ча *n.m. & f., archaic* forerunner; precursor. —**Иоа́нн Предте́ча,** John the Baptist.

предубежда́ть *v. impfv.* [*pfv.* **предубеди́ть**] *obs.* to prejudice.

предубежде́ние *n.* prejudice; bias. —**предубежде́нный,** *adj.* prejudiced; biased.

предуга́дывать *v. impfv.* [*pfv.* **предугада́ть**] **1,** to guess; divine. **2,** to foresee; anticipate.

предупреди́тельный *adj.* **1,** precautionary; preventive. **2,** warning (*attrib.*): предупреди́тельный вы́стрел, warning shot. **3,** considerate; thoughtful; attentive.

предупреди́ть [*infl.* **-жу́, -ди́шь**] *v., pfv. of* **предупрежда́ть.**

предупрежда́ть *v. impfv.* [*pfv.* **предупреди́ть**] **1,** to warn. **2,** to notify. **3,** to prevent. **4,** to anticipate. **5,** to beat (someone) to it.

предупрежде́ние *n.* **1,** warning. **2,** notification; notice. **3,** prevention.

предусма́тривать *v. impfv.* [*pfv.* **предусмотре́ть**] **1,** to foresee; envisage; anticipate. **2,** [*impfv. only*] to provide for; stipulate.

предусмотре́ть [*infl.* **-смотрю́, -смо́тришь**] *v., pfv. of* **предусма́тривать.**

предусмотри́тельный *adj.* having foresight; farsighted. —**предусмотри́тельность,** *n.f.* foresight.

предчу́вствие *n.* presentiment; premonition; foreboding.

предчу́вствовать *v. impfv.* [*pres.* **-ствую, -ствуешь**] **1,** to have a premonition about. **2,** (*with* **что**) to have a feeling that...

предше́ственник *n.* **1,** predecessor. **2,** forerunner; precursor.

предше́ствовать *v. impfv.* [*pres.* **-ствую, -ствуешь**] (*with dat.*) to precede.

предше́ствующий *adj.* preceding; previous.

предъяви́тель *n.m.* bearer (*of a document*). —**предъяви́тель и́ска,** plaintiff.

предъяви́ть [*infl.* **-явлю́, -я́вишь**] *v., pfv. of* **предъявля́ть.**

предъявле́ние *n.* **1,** presentation (*of a document*). **2,** bringing (*of a suit, charges, etc.*).

предъявля́ть *v. impfv.* [*pfv.* **предъяви́ть**] **1,** to present; produce; show (a document). **2,** to bring (a lawsuit); press; prefer (charges). **3,** to make (demands); assert (one's rights).

предыду́щий *adj.* previous. —**предыду́щее,** *n.* the foregoing.

пре́мник *n.* successor.

пре́мственность *n.f.* **1,** succession. **2,** continuity.

пре́мственный *adj.* successive.

пре́мство *n.* succession.

пре́жде *adv.* **1,** before; formerly. **2,** first. —*prep., with gen.* before; ahead of. —**пре́жде всего́,** first of all; first and foremost. —**пре́жде чем,** before.

преждевре́менный *adj.* **1,** premature. **2,** untimely. —**преждевре́менно,** *adv.* prematurely.

пре́жний *adj.* **1,** former. **2,** previous. —**в пре́жнее вре́мя; в пре́жние времена́,** in former times.

презента́бельный *adj.* presentable; proper.

презервати́в *n.* contraceptive device; contraceptive.

президе́нт *n.* president. —**президе́нтский,** *adj.* presidential. —**президе́нтство,** *n.* presidency.

прези́диум *n.* presidium.

презира́ть *v. impfv.* [*pfv.* **презре́ть**] **1,** [*impfv. only*] to despise; scorn; hold in contempt. **2,** to disregard; scorn.

презре́ние *n.* (with **к**) **1,** contempt; scorn (for someone). **2,** disdain; disregard (of danger, death, etc.).

презре́нный *adj.* contemptible; despicable. —**презре́нный мета́лл,** filthy lucre.

презре́ть [*infl.* **-зрю́, -зри́шь**] *v., pfv. of* **презира́ть** (*in sense #2*).

презри́тельный *adj.* scornful; contemptuous; disdainful.

презу́мпция *n.* presumption.

преиму́щественно *adv.* mainly; chiefly; primarily.

преиму́щественный *adj.* **1,** primary; paramount. **2,** preferred.

преиму́щество *n.* advantage: преиму́щество пе́ред сопе́рником, advantage over one's rival. —**по преиму́ществу,** mainly; chiefly; primarily.

преиспо́дняя *n., decl. as an adj., obs.* hell; the nether world.

преиспо́лненный *adj.* (*with gen.*) filled (with); full (of).

преисполня́ть *v. impfv.* [*pfv.* **преиспо́лнить**] **1,** to fill. **2,** *fig.* to imbue.

прейскура́нт *n.* price list; catalogue. —**прейскура́нтный,** *adj.* of a price list: прейскура́нтная цена́, list price.

преклоне́ние *n.* (with **пе́ред**) worship (of); admiration (of); reverence (for).

преклони́ть [*infl.* **-клоню́, -клони́шь**] *v., pfv. of* **преклоня́ть.** —**преклони́ться,** *refl., pfv. of* **преклоня́ться.**

прекло́нный *adj.* (*of age*) old; advanced.

преклоня́ть *v. impfv.* [*pfv.* **преклони́ть**] **1,** to bend (one's knees); bow (one's head). **2,** *in* **преклоня́ть коле́на** (*or* **коле́ни**) **пе́ред,** to kneel before; bow down to. —**преклоня́ться,** *refl.* (*with* **пе́ред**) **1,** to kneel (before); bow down (to). **2,** to worship; revere. **3,** to admire; take off one's hat to.

прекосло́вить *v. impfv.* [*pres.* **-влю, -вишь**] (*with dat.*) to contradict.

прекра́сно *adv.* **1,** marvelously. Она́ прекра́сно вы́глядит, she looks marvelous/wonderful. **2,** perfectly well: я прекра́сно зна́ю, что..., I know perfectly well that... **3,** *as an interj.* wonderful!; fine!; perfect!

прекра́сное *n., decl. as an adj.* the beautiful; that which is beautiful.

прекра́сный *adj.* **1,** beautiful. **2,** excellent; wonderful. **3,** *in* **прекра́сный пол,** the fair sex. —**в оди́н прекра́сный день,** one fine day. —**ра́ди чьих-нибудь прекра́сных глаз,** for love.

прекрати́ть [*infl.* **-щу́, -ти́шь**] *v., pfv. of* **прекраща́ть.** —**прекрати́ться,** *refl., pfv. of* **прекраща́ться.**

прекраща́ть *v. impfv.* [*pfv.* **прекрати́ть**] to halt; cease; break off; terminate; suspend; discontinue. —**прекраща́ться,** *refl.* to end; stop; cease.

прекраще́ние *n.* halt; cessation; suspension. —**прекраще́ние огня́,** cease-fire. —**прекраще́ние пре́ний,** cloture.

прела́т *n.* prelate.

преле́стный *adj.* charming; delightful; lovely.

пре́лесть *n.f.* **1,** charm. **2,** a delight: пря́мо пре́лесть!, it's an absolute delight; it's simply delightful.

преломи́ть [*infl.* **-ломлю́, -ло́мишь**] *v., pfv. of* **преломля́ть.**

преломле́ние *n.* refraction.

преломля́ть *v. impfv.* [*pfv.* **преломи́ть**] to refract.

пре́лый *adj.* rotten.

прель *n.f.* rot; mold.

прельсти́ть [*infl.* **-льщу́, -льсти́шь**] *v., pfv. of* **прельща́ть.** —**прельсти́ться,** *refl., pfv. of* **прельща́ться.**

прельща́ть *v. impfv.* [*pfv.* **прельсти́ть**] **1,** to charm; captivate. **2,** to tempt; entice; lure. —**прельща́ться,** *refl.* (*with instr.*) to be enticed (by); fall for.

прелюбоде́й *n.* adulterer. —**прелюбоде́йка,** *n.* adulteress. —**прелюбоде́йный,** *adj.* adulterous.

прелюбоде́йствовать *v. impfv.* [*pres.* **-ствую, -ствуешь**] to commit adultery.

прелюбодея́ние *n.* adultery.

прелю́дия *n.* **1,** *music* prelude. **2,** *fig.* (*with* **к**) prelude (to).

премиа́льный *adj.* bonus (*attrib.*). —**премиа́льные,** *n. pl.* bonus.

преми́нуть *v. pfv., used negatively with inf.* not to fail (to).

премирова́ть *v. impfv. & pfv.* [*pres.* **-ру́ю, -ру́ешь**] to give a bonus to; award a prize to.

пре́мия *n.* **1,** prize. **2,** bonus. **3,** premium.

прему́дрость *n.f.* **1,** *obs.* wisdom. **2,** *usu. pl.* mysteries; intricacies. —**невелика́ прему́дрость,** it's not that difficult.

прему́дрый *adj.* **1,** *obs.* possessing great wisdom. **2,** abstruse; arcane.

премье́р *n.* **1,** premier. **2,** leading actor; star performer.

премье́ра *n.* première.

премье́р-мини́стр *n.* prime minister.

премье́рша *n., colloq., theat.* leading lady.

пренебрега́ть *v. impfv.* [*pfv.* **пренебре́чь**] (*with instr.*) **1,** to scorn; disdain; look down on. **2,** to disregard; ignore (rules, advice, etc.). **3,** to neglect (one's duties, health, etc.).

пренебреже́ние *n.* **1,** scorn; disdain. **2,** disregard. **3,** neglect.

пренебрежи́тельный *adj.* scornful; disdainful.

пренебре́чь [*infl.* **-брегу́, -брежёшь, ...-брегу́т;** *past* **-брёг, -брегла́, -брегло́**] *v., pfv. of* **пренебрега́ть.**

пре́ния [*gen.* **-ний**] *n.pl.* debate.

преоблада́ние *n.* **1,** predominance. **2,** preponderance.

преоблада́ть *v. impfv.* **1,** to predominate. **2,** (*with* **над**) to prevail over.

преоблада́ющий *adj.* predominant; prevailing.

преобража́ть *v. impfv.* [*pfv.* **преобрази́ть**] **1,** to transform. **2,** to transfigure.

преображе́ние *n.* **1,** transformation. **2,** *relig.* the Transfiguration.

преобрази́ть [*infl.* **-жу́, -зи́шь**] *v., pfv. of* **преобража́ть.**

преобразова́ние *n.* **1,** transformation. **2,** *pl.* reforms.

преобразова́тель *n.m.* **1,** reformer. **2,** *electricity* transformer.
преобразова́ть [*infl.* **-зу́ю, -зу́ешь**] *v., pfv. of* **преобразо́вывать.**
преобразо́вывать *v. impfv.* [*pfv.* **преобразова́ть**] **1,** to transform; reorganize; reform. **2,** *electricity; physics* to transform.
преодолева́ть *v. impfv.* [*pfv.* **преодоле́ть**] to overcome; surmount.
преодоле́ние *n.* overcoming; surmounting.
преодоле́ть *v., pfv. of* **преодолева́ть.**
преодоли́мый *adj.* surmountable.
препара́т *n.* **1,** laboratory specimen. **2,** preparation; compound.
препина́ние *n., in* **зна́ки препина́ния,** punctuation marks.
препира́тельство *n.* squabble; hassle.
препира́ться *v.r. impfv.* to squabble; wrangle.
преподава́ние *n.* teaching.
преподава́тель *n.m.* [*fem.* **-ница**] teacher. —**преподава́тельский,** *adj.* teaching (*attrib.*).
преподава́ть *v. impfv.* [*pres.* **-даю́, -даёшь**] to teach.
преподнести́ [*infl. like* **нести́**] *v., pfv. of* **преподноси́ть.**
преподноси́ть *v. impfv.* [*pfv.* **преподнести́**; *pres.* **-ношу́, -но́сишь**] **1,** to present (a gift, award, etc.). **2,** *colloq.* to give (a surprise, bad news, etc.). **3,** to present (facts, material, etc.).
преподо́бие *n.* Reverence (*title*). —**преподо́бный,** *adj.* Reverend.
препо́на *n., obs.* obstacle; impediment.
препроводи́ть [*infl.* **-вожу́, -води́шь** *or* **-во́дишь**] *v., pfv. of* **препровожда́ть.**
препровожда́ть *v. impfv.* [*pfv.* **препроводи́ть**] **1,** to send. **2,** to forward.
препровожде́ние *n.* **1,** sending; forwarding. **2,** passing (*of time*).
препя́тствие *n.* **1,** obstacle. **2,** *sports* obstacle; hurdle: бег/ска́чка с препя́тствиями, hurdle/steeplechase race.
препя́тствовать *v. impfv.* [*pfv.* **воспрепя́тствовать;** *pres.* **-ствую, -ствуешь**] (*with dat.*) to hinder; impede.
прерва́ть [*infl. like* **рвать**] *v., pfv. of* **прерыва́ть.** —**прерва́ться,** *refl., pfv. of* **прерыва́ться.**
пререка́ние *n., usu. pl.* squabble; argument.
пререка́ться *v.r. impfv.* to argue; squabble; bicker.
пре́рия *n.* prairie.
прерогати́ва *n.* prerogative.
прерыва́ние *n.* interruption.
прерыва́тель *n.m.* circuit breaker.
прерыва́ть *v. impfv.* [*pfv.* **прерва́ть**] **1,** to interrupt. **2,** to break; break off; sever. —**прерыва́ться,** *refl.* **1,** to be interrupted. **2,** (*of one's voice*) to break.
преры́вистый *adj.* irregular; intermittent.
пресви́тер *n.* presbyter.
пресвитериа́нин [*pl.* **-иа́не, -иа́н**] *n.* Presbyterian. *Also,* **пресвитериа́нец** [*gen.* **-нца;** *fem.* **-нка**].
пресвитериа́нский *adj.* Presbyterian.
пресека́ть *v. impfv.* [*pfv.* **пресе́чь**] **1,** to put a stop to. **2,** to head off; nip: пресека́ть в ко́рне, to nip in the bud. **3,** to cut short. —**пресека́ться,** *refl.* **1,** to stop. **2,** to end. **3,** (*of one's voice*) to break.
пресе́чь [*infl. like* **сечь;** *past* **-се́к, -секла́** *or* **-се́кла, -секло́** *or* **-се́кло**] *v., pfv. of* **пресека́ть.** —**пресе́чься,** *refl., pfv. of* **пресека́ться.**
пресле́дование *n.* **1,** pursuit. **2,** persecution. **3,** prosecution.
пресле́дователь *n.m.* **1,** persecutor. **2,** pursuer.
пресле́довать *v. impfv.* [*pres.* **-дую, -дуешь**] **1,** to pursue. **2,** to persecute. **3,** *fig.* (*of a thought, melody, etc.*) to haunt. **4,** to prosecute.
преслову́тый *adj.* notorious; famous.
пресмыка́ться *v.r. impfv.* (*with* **пе́ред**) to grovel (before).
пресмыка́ющееся *n., decl. as an adj.* reptile.
пресново́дный *adj.* fresh-water.
пре́сный *adj.* **1,** (*of water*) fresh. **2,** (*of bread or dough*) unleavened. **3,** (*of food*) tasteless. **4,** *fig.* insipid; vapid.
пресс *n.* press (*machine*).
пре́сса *n.* the press.
пресс-конфере́нция *n.* press conference; news conference.
прессова́ние *n.* pressing.
прессова́ть *v. impfv.* [*pfv.* **спрессова́ть;** *pres.* **-су́ю, -су́ешь**] to press.
прессо́вка *n.* pressing.
прессовщи́к [*gen.* **-щика́**] *n.* presser; pressman.
пресс-папье́ *n. neut. indecl.* **1,** paperweight. **2,** blotter.
преста́виться *v.r. pfv., obs.* to die; pass away.
престаре́лый *adj.* very old; aged. —**дом для престаре́лых,** old age home.
прести́ж *n.* prestige.
прести́жный *adj.* **1,** prestigious. **2,** of prestige: прести́жный вопро́с, matter of prestige.
пре́сто *n. indecl. & adj., music* presto.
престо́л *n.* throne. —**па́пский престо́л,** Holy/Apostolic See.
престолонасле́дие *n.* succession (to the throne).
престо́льный *adj.* throne (*attrib.*). —**престо́льный пра́здник,** patron saint's day.
преступа́ть *v. impfv.* [*pfv.* **преступи́ть**] *obs.* to break; overstep (the law).
преступи́ть [*infl.* **-ступлю́, -сту́пишь**] *v., pfv. of* **преступа́ть.**
преступле́ние *n.* crime.
престу́пник *n.* criminal.
престу́пность *n.f.* **1,** crime: рост престу́пности, the rise in crime. **2,** criminal nature; criminality. —**де́тская престу́пность,** juvenile delinquency.
престу́пный *adj.* criminal.
пресыща́ть *v. impfv.* [*pfv.* **пресы́тить**] to satiate; surfeit.
пресыще́ние *n.* satiation; satiety; surfeit.
претворя́ть *v. impfv.* [*pfv.* **претвори́ть**] *obs.* to change; transform. —**претворя́ть в жизнь,** to make a reality of; put into practice.
претенде́нт *n.* (*with* **на** + *acc.*) **1,** contender; aspirant. **2,** applicant; claimant. **3,** challenger. **4,** pretender (to the throne).
претендова́ть *v. impfv.* [*pres.* **-ду́ю, -ду́ешь**] (*with* **на** + *acc.*) **1,** to lay claim to. **2,** to seek; aspire to. **3,** to have pretensions of.
прете́нзия *n.* **1,** claim. **2,** complaint; grievance. **3,** pretension. —**быть в прете́нзии на** (+ *acc.*), to have something against; have it in for. —**с прете́нзиями,** pretentious.

претенцио́зный (тэ) *adj.* pretentious. —**претенцио́зность,** *n.f.* pretentiousness.

претерпева́ть *v. impfv.* [*pfv.* **претерпе́ть**] **1,** to suffer; endure. **2,** to undergo (changes).

претерпе́ть [*infl.* **-терплю́, -те́рпишь**] *v., pfv. of* **претерпева́ть.**

прети́ть *v. impfv.* (*with dat.*) to sicken; disgust. *Also impers.:* мне прети́т от э́того, I'm sick of it; it makes me sick.

преткнове́ние *n., in* **ка́мень преткнове́ния,** stumbling block.

пре́тор *n.* praetor.

пре́ть *v. impfv.* [*pfv.* **сопре́ть**] to rot.

преувеличе́ние *n.* exaggeration.

преувели́чивать *v. impfv.* [*pfv.* **преувели́чить**] to exaggerate.

преуменьша́ть *v. impfv.* [*pfv.* **преуменьши́ть** *or* **преуме́ньшить**] **1,** to underestimate; underrate. **2,** to understate; minimize; play down.

преуменьше́ние *n.* underestimation.

преуменьши́ть *also,* **преуме́ньшить** *v., pfv. of* **преуменьша́ть.**

преуспева́ть *v. impfv.* [*pfv.* **преуспе́ть**] **1,** to succeed; be successful. **2,** [*impfv. only*] to thrive; prosper.

префе́кт *n.* prefect. —**префекту́ра,** *n.* prefecture.

префера́нс *n.* preference (*card game*).

пре́фикс *n.* prefix. —**префикса́ция,** *n.* prefixion.

преходя́щий *adj.* transient; transitory; ephemeral; momentary.

прецеде́нт *n.* precedent.

при *prep., with prepl.* **1,** near; by; at: при впаде́нии реки́ Оки́ в Во́лгу, where the Oka River flows into the Volga. Би́тва при Бородине́, the Battle of Borodino. Быть при́ смерти, to be near death. **2,** attached to: я́сли при заво́де, nursery attached to a factory; указа́тель при кни́ге, index to a book. **3,** in the presence of: при мне, in my presence; при свиде́телях, in the presence of witnesses. **4,** during: при жи́зни (+ *gen.*), during the life of; при Ива́не Гро́зном, during the reign of Ivan the Terrible. **5,** under (*a ruler or regime*): при Ста́лине, under Stalin; жить при коммуни́зме, to live under communism. **6,** at; on; upon; when: при упомина́нии о, at the mention of; при перехо́де че́рез у́лицу, when crossing the street. **7,** on the person of: докуме́нты при себе́, documents on one's person. **8,** having; possessing: быть при деньга́х, to have plenty of money. **9,** under; in view of; given: при таки́х усло́виях, under such conditions. **10,** (*with* **всём** *or* **всей**) for all; despite: при всём том, for all that. При всём моём жела́нии, much as I would like to. —**ни при чём** (*often preceded by* **тут**), **1,** innocent. **2,** having nothing to do with it; irrelevant. **3,** *in* оста́ться ни при чём, to be left with nothing. —**при чём тут** (+ *nom.*), what has this to do with...? —**при э́том,** here; in the process; in so doing.

при- *prefix* **1,** *indicating arrival:* приходи́ть, to come; прилета́ть, to arrive (*by plane*). **2,** *indicating attachment:* привя́зывать, to tie to; пришива́ть, to sew on. **3,** *indicating addition:* прибавля́ть, to add; прикупа́ть, to buy some more. **4,** *indicating partial or slight action:* приотворя́ть, to open slightly; приспуска́ть, to lower slightly.

приба́вить [*infl.* **-влю, -вишь**] *v., pfv. of* **прибавля́ть.** —**приба́виться,** *refl., pfv. of* **прибавля́ться.**

приба́вка [*gen. pl.* **-вок**] *n.* **1,** adding; addition. **2,** something added; addition. **3,** increase; raise (*in pay*).

прибавле́ние *n.* **1,** adding; addition. **2,** something added; addition. **3,** increase (*in weight*); rise (*of water*).

прибавля́ть *v. impfv.* [*pfv.* **приба́вить**] **1,** to add: прибавля́ть соль (*or* со́ли) к су́пу, to add salt to the soup; прибавля́ть не́сколько слов, to add a few words. **2,** (*with acc. or gen.*) to increase. **3,** *in* прибавля́ть в ве́се, *colloq.* to put on weight. —**прибавля́ться,** *refl.* **1,** to be added. **2,** to increase; rise. **3,** (*of the day*) to grow longer. **4,** (*of the moon*) to wax.

приба́вочный *adj.* **1,** additional. **2,** *econ.* surplus: приба́вочная сто́имость, surplus value.

прибалти́йский *adj.* Baltic.

прибау́тка [*gen. pl.* **-ток**] *n.* humorous saying.

прибега́ть *v. impfv.* **1,** [*pfv.* **прибежа́ть**] to come running. **2,** [*pfv.* **прибе́гнуть**] (*with* **к**) to resort to.

прибе́гнуть [*past* **-бе́г** *or* **-бе́гнул, -бе́гла**] *v., pfv. of* **прибега́ть** (*in sense #2*).

прибедня́ться *v. impfv.* [*pfv.* **прибедни́ться**] *colloq.* **1,** to pretend to be poorer than one is. **2,** to play down one's achievements; be excessively modest.

прибежа́ть [*infl. like* **бежа́ть**] *v., pfv. of* **прибега́ть** (*in sense #1*).

прибе́жище *n.* refuge.

приберега́ть *v. impfv.* [*pfv.* **прибере́чь**] to put aside; hold aside.

прибере́чь [*infl. like* **бере́чь**] *v., pfv. of* **приберега́ть.**

прибива́ть *v. impfv.* [*pfv.* **приби́ть**] **1,** to nail; nail down. **2,** (*of wind, rain, etc.*) to beat down; flatten. —**приби́ть к бе́регу,** *usu. impers.* to wash ashore: ло́дку приби́ло к бе́регу, the boat was washed ashore.

прибира́ть *v. impfv.* [*pfv.* **прибра́ть**] *colloq.* **1,** to put in order; tidy up. **2,** to put away. —**прибра́ть к рука́м, 1,** to take (someone) in hand. **2,** to seize; expropriate.

приби́ть [*infl.* **-бью́, -бьёшь**] *v., pfv. of* **прибива́ть.**

приближа́ть *v. impfv.* [*pfv.* **прибли́зить**] to bring near; bring nearer. —**приближа́ться,** *refl.* **1,** to draw near. **2,** (*with* **к**) to approach; near. **3,** (*with* **к**) to approximate.

приближе́ние *n.* **1,** bringing near. **2,** approach.

приближённый *adj.* **1,** (*of people*) close; trusted. **2,** *math.* approximate; rough. —*n.* close associate (*of a ruler or high-ranking person*).

приблизи́тельно *adv.* approximately; roughly. —**приблизи́тельный,** *adj.* approximate.

прибли́зить [*infl.* **-жу, -зишь**] *v., pfv. of* **приближа́ть.** —**прибли́зиться,** *refl., pfv. of* **приближа́ться.**

прибо́й *n.* surf; breakers.

прибо́р *n.* **1,** instrument; device; apparatus; appliance. **2,** set: бри́твенный прибо́р, shaving set. Черни́льный прибо́р, inkstand. **3,** (place) setting. Накры́ть стол на шесть прибо́ров, to set the table for six.

прибо́рный *adj., in* **прибо́рная доска́,** instrument panel; dashboard.

прибра́ть [*infl. like* **брать**] *v., pfv. of* **прибира́ть.**

прибре́жный *adj.* **1,** offshore. **2,** coastal.

прибыва́ть *v. impfv.* [*pfv.* **прибы́ть**] **1,** to arrive. **2,** to increase in size or number; grow larger: толпа́ всё прибыва́ла, the crowd kept getting larger and larger. **3,** (*of water*) to rise; (*of the moon*) to wax.

при́быль *n.f.* **1,** profit. **2,** *colloq.* benefit; gain. **3,** increase; rise. —**при́быльный,** *adj.* profitable; lucrative.

прибы́тие *n.* arrival.

прибы́ть [*infl.* **-бу́ду, -бу́дешь;** *past* **при́был, прибыла́, при́было**] *v., pfv. of* **прибыва́ть.**

прива́л *n.* **1,** halt; rest. **2,** resting place.

прива́ливать *v. impfv.* [*pfv.* **привали́ть**] **1,** (*with* **к**) to lean (a heavy object) against. **2,** *colloq.* to arrive in great numbers. **3,** (*with dat.*) *colloq.* (*of luck*) to strike; descend on. —**прива́ливаться,** *refl.* (*with* **к**) *colloq.* to lean against.

привали́ть [*infl.* **-валю́, -ва́лишь**] *v., pfv. of* **прива́ливать.** —**привали́ться,** *refl., pfv. of* **прива́ливаться.**

прива́тный *adj., obs.* private.

приведе́ние *n.* **1,** bringing. **2,** citing; adducing. **3,** putting (in order, motion, etc.).

привезти́ [*infl. like* **везти́**] *v., pfv. of* **привози́ть.**

приверéдливый *adj., colloq.* choosy; finicky; fussy.

приве́рженец [*gen.* **-нца**] *n.* adherent; supporter.

приве́рженность *n.f.* **1,** adherence. **2,** devotion. —**приве́рженный,** *adj.* (*with dat.*) devoted (to); loyal (to).

привёртывать *v. impfv.* [*pfv.* **приверну́ть**] **1,** to tighten (a screw). **2,** (*with* **к**) to screw (onto). **3,** to turn down (a flame, lamp, etc.).

приве́сить [*infl.* **-шу, -сишь**] *v., pfv. of* **приве́шивать.**

привести́ [*infl. like* **вести́**] *v., pfv. of* **приводи́ть.** —**привести́сь,** *refl., pfv. of* **приводи́ться.**

приве́т *n.* regards; greetings. —*interj., colloq.* hello there!; hi!

приве́тливый *adj.* friendly; amiable; affable. —**приве́тливость,** *n.f.* friendliness, amiability; affability.

приве́тственный *adj.* of welcome; welcoming.

приве́тствие *n.* greeting.

приве́тствовать *v. impfv.* [*pres.* **-ствую, -ствуешь**] **1,** to greet; welcome. **2,** to welcome (a proposal, decision, etc.).

приве́шивать *v. impfv.* [*pfv.* **приве́сить**] to hang up.

привива́ть *v. impfv.* [*pfv.* **приви́ть**] **1,** to graft. **2,** (*with dat.*) to inoculate: привива́ть кому́-нибудь холе́ру, to inoculate someone for cholera. **3,** *fig.* to instill (in): привива́ть кому́-нибудь хоро́шие мане́ры, to instill good manners in someone. —**привива́ться,** *refl.* **1,** (*of a vaccine*) to take. **2,** *fig.* to take root; take hold; (*of a name, word, style, etc.*) catch on.

приви́вка *n.* inoculation: сде́лать приви́вку (+ *dat.*), to inoculate. —**приви́вка о́спы,** (smallpox) vaccination.

привиде́ние *n.* ghost; apparition.

приви́деться *v.r. pfv.* (*with dat.*) *colloq.* to appear in one's dreams: мне приви́делось, I dreamt.

привилегиро́ванный *adj.* privileged.

привиле́гия *n.* privilege.

приви́нчивать *v. impfv.* [*pfv.* **привинти́ть**] **1,** to screw on. **2,** (*with* **к**) to screw onto.

привира́ть *v. impfv.* [*pfv.* **привра́ть**] *colloq.* **1,** *v.i.* to lie. **2,** *v.t.* to make up; add (fictional details).

приви́ть [*infl. like* **вить**] *v., pfv. of* **привива́ть.** —**приви́ться,** *refl.* [*past* **-ви́лся, -ла́сь, -ло́сь**] *pfv. of* **привива́ться.**

при́вкус *n.* **1,** aftertaste. **2,** taste; flavor. **3,** *fig.* touch; trace; tinge.

привлека́тельный *adj.* attractive. —**привлека́тельность,** *n.f.* attractiveness.

привлека́ть *v. impfv.* [*pfv.* **привле́чь**] **1,** to attract. **2,** to bring in; call in. **3,** to win over: привлека́ть на свою́ сто́рону, to win over to one's side. —**привлека́ть к суду́,** to arraign; bring to trial. —**привлека́ть к отве́ту** *or* **к отве́тственности,** to bring to account.

привлече́ние *n.* **1,** attracting. **2,** bringing in; calling in. —**привлече́ние к отве́тственности,** bringing to account. —**привлече́ние к суду́,** arraignment.

привле́чь [*infl. like* **влечь**] *v., pfv. of* **привлека́ть.**

приво́д *n.* **1,** (forcible) arrest. **2,** *mech.* drive.

приводи́ть *v. impfv.* [*pfv.* **привести́;** *pres.* **-вожу́, -во́дишь**] **1,** to bring (*on foot*). **2,** (*of a road, tracks, etc.*) to lead (somewhere). **3,** (*with* **к**) to lead (to a certain result). **4,** (*with* **в** + *acc.*) to bring to a certain state or condition: приводи́ть в поря́док, to put in order; приводи́ть в движе́ние, to set in motion; приводи́ть в смяте́ние, to throw into confusion. **5,** to cite; adduce. —**приводи́ть в де́йствие,** to start (*e.g.* a machine) going. —**приводи́ть в исполне́ние,** to carry out. —**приводи́ть в себя́** (*or* **в чу́вство**), **1,** to revive; resuscitate; bring around. **2,** to bring back to reality (a person lost in thought). —**приводи́ть к о́бщему знамена́телю,** to reduce to a common denominator.

приводи́ться *v.r. impfv.* [*pfv.* **привести́сь;** *pres.* **-во́дится**] *impers.* (*with dat. & inf.*) *colloq.* to happen to; have occasion to: мне не привело́сь быть там, I have not had occasion to be there.

приводне́ние *n.* landing on water; splashdown.

приводни́ться *v.r., pfv. of* **приводня́ться.**

приводно́й *adj., mech.* drive (*attrib.*); transmission (*attrib.*): приводно́й вал, drive shaft; приводно́й реме́нь, transmission belt.

приводня́ться *v.r. impfv.* [*pfv.* **приводни́ться**] to land on water.

приво́з *n.* **1,** bringing in; delivery. **2,** *colloq.* a shipment.

привози́ть *v. impfv.* [*pfv.* **привезти́;** *pres.* **-вожу́, -во́зишь**] to bring (*by vehicle*).

привозно́й *adj.* imported. *Also,* **приво́зный.**

приво́лье *n.* **1,** wide open spaces. **2,** freedom to move about.

приво́льный *adj.* **1,** open; spacious. **2,** free.

привора́живать *v. impfv.* [*pfv.* **приворожи́ть**] to bewitch; charm.

привра́тник *n.* gatekeeper; doorkeeper.

привра́ть [*infl. like* **врать**] *v., pfv. of* **привира́ть.**

привска́кивать *v. impfv.* [*pfv.* **привскочи́ть**] to jump up.

привскочи́ть [*infl.* **-вскочу́, -вско́чишь**] *v., pfv. of* **привска́кивать.**

привстава́ть *v. impfv.* [*pfv.* **привста́ть;** *pres.* **-стаю́, -стаёшь**] to rise (*halfway*).

привста́ть [*infl.* **-вста́ну, -вста́нешь**] *v., pfv. of* **привстава́ть.**

привыка́ть *v. impfv.* [*pfv.* **привы́кнуть**] (*with* **к** *or inf.*) **1,** to be *or* get used to; grow accustomed to. **2,** to be *or* get into the habit of.

привы́кнуть [*past* **-вы́к, -ла**] *v., pfv. of* **привыка́ть.**

привы́чка [*gen. pl.* **-чек**] *n.* habit. Это вошло́ у меня́ в привы́чку, it has become a habit with me. Не в мои́х привы́чках по́здно ложи́ться, I don't usually go to bed late.

привы́чный *adj.* **1,** habitual; usual; customary. **2,** (*with* **к**) *colloq.* used to; accustomed (to). **3,** *colloq.* (*of a person*) of set habits; (*of an eye, hands, etc.*) practiced.

привя́занность *n.f.* (*with* **к**) (emotional) attachment (to). —**привя́занный,** *adj.* attached.

привяза́ть [*infl.* **-вяжу́, -вя́жешь**] *v., pfv. of* **привя́зывать.** —**привяза́ться,** *refl., pfv. of* **привя́зываться.**

привязно́й *adj.* fastened; secured. —**привязно́й ре-ме́нь,** seat belt.
привя́зчивый *adj., colloq.* **1,** easily forming attachments. **2,** annoying; bothersome.
привя́зывать *v. impfv.* [*pfv.* **привяза́ть**] **1,** (*with* **к**) to tie (to); bind (to); attach (to). **2,** (*with* **к себе́**) to win over. —**привя́зываться,** *refl.* (with **к**) **1,** to become attached (to). **2,** to attach oneself (to). **3,** *colloq.* to pester.
при́вязь *n.f.* **1,** leash. **2,** tether.
пригвожда́ть *v. impfv.* [*pfv.* **пригвозди́ть**] (*with* **к**) **1,** to nail (to). **2,** *fig.* to nail (to); rivet (to); chain (to): пригвождённый к ме́сту, nailed/riveted to the spot.
пригиба́ть *v. impfv.* [*pfv.* **пригну́ть**] to bend; bend down (a tree, branch, etc.). —**пригиба́ться,** *refl.* to bend down.
пригла́живать *v. impfv.* [*pfv.* **пригла́дить**] **1,** to smooth. **2,** to slick down (one's hair).
пригласи́тельный *adj.* conveying an invitation. —**пригласи́тельный биле́т,** ticket of admission (*to invited guests only*).
пригласи́ть [*infl.* **-шу́, -си́шь**] *v., pfv. of* **приглаша́ть.**
приглаша́ть *v. impfv.* [*pfv.* **пригласи́ть**] to invite.
приглаше́ние *n.* invitation.
приглашённый *adj.* invited. —*n.* person invited; invited guest. —**приглашённый дирижёр,** guest conductor.
приглуша́ть *v. impfv.* [*pfv.* **приглуши́ть**] to muffle; deaden; absorb (sound).
пригляде́ть [*infl.* **-жу́, -ди́шь**] *v., pfv. of* **пригля́дывать.** —**пригляде́ться,** *refl., pfv. of* **пригля́дываться.**
пригля́дывать *v. impfv.* [*pfv.* **пригляде́ть**] *colloq.* **1,** (*with* **за** + *instr.*) to look after; keep an eye on. **2,** to pick out. —**пригля́дываться,** *refl., colloq.* **1,** (*with* **к**) to stare (at); scrutinize. **2,** (*with* **к**) to get used to. **3,** (*with dat.*) to pall (on); become boring (to).
пригляну́ться *v.r. pfv.* [*infl.* **-гляну́сь, -гля́нешься**] (*with dat.*) *colloq.* to catch the fancy of.
пригна́ть [*infl. like* **гнать**] *v., pfv. of* **пригоня́ть.**
пригну́ть *v., pfv. of* **пригиба́ть.** —**пригну́ться,** *refl., pfv. of* **пригиба́ться.**
пригова́ривать *v. impfv.* [*pfv.* **приговори́ть**] **1,** (*with* **к**) to sentence (to); condemn (to). **2,** [*impfv. only*] *colloq.* to repeat; keep saying.
пригово́р *n.* **1,** verdict. **2,** sentence.
приговори́ть *v., pfv. of* **пригова́ривать.**
пригоди́ться *v.r. pfv.* [*infl.* **-жу́сь, -ди́шься**] (*with dat.*) to come in handy; be useful (to); stand in good stead.
приго́дный *adj.* (*with* **к** *or* **для**) fit (for); suitable (for). —**приго́дность,** *n.f.* fitness; suitability.
пригоня́ть *v. impfv.* [*pfv.* **пригна́ть**] **1,** to drive home; bring in (cattle). **2,** to fit; adjust.
пригора́ть *v. impfv.* [*pfv.* **пригоре́ть**] to be slightly burnt.
пригоре́лый *adj.* burnt.
пригоре́ть *v., pfv. of* **пригора́ть.**
при́город *n.* suburb. —**при́городный,** *adj.* suburban.
приго́рок [*gen.* **-рка**] *n.* hillock; knoll.
при́горшня *also,* **приго́ршня** [*gen. pl.* **-шней**] *n.* handful.
приготови́тельный *adj.* preparatory.
пригото́вить [*infl.* **-влю, -вишь**] *v., pfv. of* **гото́вить** *and* **приготовля́ть.** —**пригото́виться,** *refl., pfv. of* **гото́виться** *and* **приготовля́ться.**
приготовле́ние *n.* **1,** preparation. **2,** *pl.* preparations.
приготовля́ть *v. impfv.* [*pfv.* **пригото́вить**] **1,** to prepare. **2,** to cook. —**приготовля́ться,** *refl.* (*with* **к**) to prepare (for); get ready (for).
пригрева́ть *v. impfv.* [*pfv.* **пригре́ть**] **1,** to warm. **2,** *fig., colloq.* to give shelter to.
пригре́зиться *v.r., pfv. of* **гре́зиться.**
пригре́ть *v., pfv. of* **пригрева́ть.**
пригрози́ть *v. pfv.* [*infl.* **-жу́, -зи́шь**] (*with dat.*) to threaten.
приго́бить *v. pfv.* [*infl.* **-блю, -бишь**] to take a sip of; taste.
придава́ть *v. impfv.* [*pfv.* **прида́ть;** *pres.* **-даю́, -даёшь**] **1,** to give; impart. **2,** to attach (significance, importance, etc.). **3,** *mil.* to assign; attach (to a certain unit).
придави́ть [*infl.* **-давлю́, -да́вишь**] *v., pfv. of* **прида́вливать.**
прида́вливать *v. impfv.* [*pfv.* **придави́ть**] **1,** to press down upon; weigh down. **2,** (*with* **к**) to press (something) against (something).
прида́ние *n.* **1,** giving; imparting. **2,** *mil.* assigning; attaching.
прида́ное *n., decl. as an adj.* **1,** dowry. **2,** trousseau. **3,** layette.
прида́ток [*gen.* **-тка**] *n.* appendage; adjunct.
прида́точный *adj., in* **прида́точное предложе́ние,** dependent clause; subordinate clause.
прида́ть [*infl. like* **дать;** *past* **при́дал, придала́, при́дало**] *v., pfv. of* **придава́ть.**
прида́ча *n.* **1,** giving; imparting. **2,** *mil.* assigning; attaching. **3,** addition. —**в прида́чу,** besides; in addition; to boot; into the bargain.
придвига́ть *v. impfv.* [*pfv.* **придви́нуть**] (*with* **к**) to move (something) toward; move (something) closer to. —**придвига́ться,** *refl.* (*with* **к**) to move closer (to).
придво́рный *adj.* court (*attrib.*). —*n.* courtier.
приде́лывать *v. impfv.* [*pfv.* **приде́лать**] (*with* **к**) to attach (to); fasten (to).
придержа́ть [*infl.* **-держу́, -де́ржишь**] *v., pfv. of* **приде́рживать.**
приде́рживать *v. impfv.* [*pfv.* **придержа́ть**] **1,** to hold; hold still; hold in place. **2,** *colloq.* to hold back; withhold. **3,** *in* **придержа́ть язы́к,** to hold one's tongue. —**приде́рживаться,** *refl.* **1,** (*with* **за** + *acc.*) to hold onto. **2,** (*with gen.*) to keep to; stick to: приде́рживаться пра́вой стороны́, to keep/stick to the right. **3,** *fig.* (*with gen.*) to stick to; adhere to (a subject, opinion, agreement, etc.).
приди́ра *n.m. & f., colloq.* faultfinder; quibbler.
придира́ться *v.r. impfv.* [*pfv.* **придра́ться**] (*with* **к**) to find fault (with); carp (at); pick on.
приди́рка [*gen. pl.* **-рок**] *n.* cavil; quibble.
приди́рчивый *adj.* captious; carping; hypercritical.
придоро́жный *adj.* roadside; wayside.
придра́ться [*infl. like* **драть**] *v.r., pfv. of* **придира́ться.**
приду́мывать *v. impfv.* [*pfv.* **приду́мать**] to think of; think up; devise.
придуркова́тый *adj., colloq.* dumb; stupid.
при́дурь *n.f., colloq., in* **с при́дурью,** slightly touched in the head.
придуши́ть *v. pfv.* [*infl.* **-душу́, -ду́шишь**] *colloq.* to strangle; choke.

придыха́ние *n., phonet.* aspiration. —**придыха́тельный,** *adj.* aspirate.

приеда́ться *v.r. impfv.* [*pfv.* **прие́сться**] (*with dat.*) *colloq.* to pall (on); become boring (to).

прие́зд *n.* arrival. —**с прие́здом!**, welcome!

приезжа́ть *v. impfv.* [*pfv.* **прие́хать**] to come (*by vehicle*); arrive.

прие́зжий *adj.* **1,** newly arrived. **2,** visiting; touring. —*n.* newcomer.

приём *n.* **1,** receiving. **2,** admission. **3,** reception; welcome. **4,** reception (*social gathering*). **5,** dose. **6,** method; technique. **7,** trick; ploy. **8,** *radio; television* reception. —**в оди́н приём, 1,** in one gulp. **2,** in one sitting.

прие́млемый *adj.* acceptable.

приёмная *n., decl. as an adj.* waiting room.

приёмник *n.* (radio) receiver.

приёмный *adj.* **1,** receiving (*attrib.*); reception (*attrib.*). Приёмные часы́, office hours. **2,** admission (*attrib.*). Приёмная коми́ссия, selection committee. **3,** (*of a parent*) foster; adoptive; (*of a child*) adopted.

приёмыш *n., colloq.* adopted child.

прие́сться [*infl. like* **есть**] *v.r., pfv. of* **приеда́ться.**

прие́хать [*infl.* **-е́ду, -е́дешь**] *v., pfv. of* **приезжа́ть.**

прижа́ть [*infl.* **-жму́, -жмёшь**] *v., pfv. of* **прижима́ть.** —**прижа́ться,** *refl., pfv. of* **прижима́ться.**

приже́чь [*infl. like* **жечь**] *v., pfv. of* **прижига́ть.**

прижива́льщик *n.m.* [*fem.* **-ва́лка**] sponger; hanger-on.

прижива́ться *v.r. impfv.* [*pfv.* **прижи́ться**] to become acclimated.

прижига́ние *n.* cauterization.

прижига́ть *v. impfv.* [*pfv.* **приже́чь**] to cauterize.

прижи́зненный *adj.* occurring in one's lifetime; occurring before one's death.

прижима́ть *v. impfv.* [*pfv.* **прижа́ть**] **1,** (*with* **к**) to press (to *or* against). **2,** (*with* **к**) to pin (to): прижима́ть к земле́, to pin to the ground; pin down. Прижима́ть к стене́, to pin/drive against the wall; *fig.* drive into a corner. **3,** *fig., colloq.* to put pressure on. —**прижима́ться,** *refl.* (*with* **к**) to snuggle up to; cuddle up to; nestle close to.

прижи́мистый *adj., colloq.* tight-fisted.

прижи́ться [*infl. like* **жить**; *past* **-жи́лся, -ла́сь, -ло́сь**] *v.r., pfv. of* **прижива́ться.**

приз [*pl.* **призы́**] *n.* prize.

призаду́мываться *v.r. impfv.* [*pfv.* **призаду́маться**] to become thoughtful; become pensive.

призанима́ть *v. impfv.* [*pfv.* **призаня́ть**] *colloq.* to borrow.

призаня́ть [*infl. like* **заня́ть**] *v., pfv. of* **призанима́ть.**

призва́ние *n.* vocation; calling.

призва́ть [*infl. like* **звать**] *v., pfv. of* **призыва́ть.**

призе́мистый *adj.* stocky; thickset; heavyset; squat.

приземле́ние *n.* landing.

приземля́ть *v. impfv.* [*pfv.* **приземли́ть**] to land (a plane). —**приземля́ться,** *refl.* to land; touch down.

призёр *n.* prizewinner.

при́зма *n.* prism. —**призмати́ческий,** *adj.* prismatic.

признава́ть *v. impfv.* [*pfv.* **призна́ть**; *pres.* **-знаю́, -знаёшь**] **1,** to recognize. **2,** to admit; acknowledge. **3,** to declare; pronounce; find: его́ призна́ли душевнобольны́м, he was declared insane. —**признава́ться,** *refl.* **1,** to confess (that). **2,** (*with* **в** + *prepl.*) to confess (to): признава́ться в преступле́нии, to confess to a crime. **3,** *in* призна́ться в любви́, to make a declaration of love.

при́знак *n.* sign; indication; symptom.

призна́ние *n.* **1,** confession; admission; acknowledgment. **2,** recognition: получи́ть призна́ние, to receive recognition. **3,** *in* призна́ние в любви́, declaration of love.

при́знанный *adj.* recognized; acknowledged.

призна́тельный *adj.* grateful; appreciative. —**призна́тельность,** *n.f.* gratitude; appreciation.

призна́ть [*infl.* **-зна́ю, -зна́ешь**] *v., pfv. of* **признава́ть.** —**призна́ться,** *refl., pfv. of* **признава́ться.**

призово́й *adj.* prize (*attrib.*).

при́зрак *n.* specter; ghost; apparition.

при́зрачный *adj.* **1,** ghostly; eerie. **2,** unreal; illusory.

призы́в *n.* **1,** appeal; call. **2,** slogan. **3,** *mil.* call-up.

призыва́ть *v. impfv.* [*pfv.* **призва́ть**] **1,** (*with inf.*) to call upon (to); urge (to). **2,** (*with* **на** + *acc. or* **к**) to call (for); appeal (for). **3,** *mil.* to call up; draft. **4,** *past passive part. only,* A, to destine: он при́зван быть врачо́м, he is destined to be a doctor. B, to intend: рабо́та при́звана воспи́тывать люде́й, the work is intended to teach people. —**призыва́ть к отве́ту,** to call to account.

призывни́к [*gen.* **-ника́**] *n.* draftee; inductee; conscript.

призывно́й *adj.* of or pert. to the military draft: призывно́й во́зраст, draft age; призывна́я коми́ссия, selective service commission; призывно́й пункт, draft board; induction center.

при́иск *n., often pl.* mine: алма́зные при́иски, diamond mines.

прийти́ [*infl.* **приду́, придёшь**; *past* **пришёл, пришла́, пришло́**] *v., pfv. of* **приходи́ть.** —**прийти́сь,** *refl., pfv. of* **приходи́ться.**

прика́з *n.* order; command. —**по прика́зу** (+ *gen.*), by order of.

приказа́ние *n.* order; command.

приказа́ть [*infl.* **-кажу́, -ка́жешь**] *v., pfv. of* **прика́зывать.**

прика́зчик *n., obs.* **1,** salesman; clerk. **2,** steward (*on a large estate*).

прика́зывать *v. impfv.* [*pfv.* **приказа́ть**] (*with dat.*) to order; command. —**приказа́ть до́лго жить,** *colloq.* to die; depart this world.

прика́лывать *v. impfv.* [*pfv.* **приколо́ть**] **1,** (*with* **к**) to pin (to). **2,** *colloq.* to stab to death.

прика́нчивать *v. impfv.* [*pfv.* **прико́нчить**] *colloq.* **1,** to terminate; wind up. **2,** to finish off (a quantity of food or drink). **3,** to kill; finish off.

прикарма́нивать *v. impfv.* [*pfv.* **прикарма́нить**] *colloq.* to pocket.

прикаса́ться *v.r. impfv.* [*pfv.* **прикосну́ться**] (*with* **к**) to touch.

прикати́ть [*infl.* **-качу́, -ка́тишь**] *v., pfv. of* **прика́тывать.** —**прикати́ться,** *refl., pfv. of* **прика́тываться.**

прика́тывать *v. impfv.* [*pfv.* **прикати́ть**] **1,** *v.t.* to roll (something somewhere). **2,** *v.i., colloq.* to come rolling up; arrive. —**прика́тываться,** *refl.* (*with* **к**) to roll up to.

прики́дывать *v. impfv.* [*pfv.* **прики́нуть**] *colloq.* **1,** to add; throw in; toss in. **2,** to estimate; reckon. **3,** to try on. —**прики́дываться,** *refl.* (*with instr.*) *colloq.* to pretend (to be).

прикла́д *n.* **1,** rifle butt. **2,** *sewing* findings.

прикладно́й *adj.* applied: прикладны́е нау́ки, applied sciences.
прикла́дывать *v. impfv.* [*pfv.* **приложи́ть**] (*with* **к**) **1,** to put (against); place (against). **2,** to apply (to); affix (to). **3,** *in* **приложи́ть ру́ку к,** to have a hand in; put one's hand to. **4,** *in* **ума́ не приложу́,** I have no idea; I can't imagine; I am at a loss. —**прикла́дываться,** *refl.* **1,** (*with instr.* and **к**) to put (one's eye, ear, etc.) to. **2,** (*with* **к**) to kiss reverently. **3,** to take aim.
прикле́ивать *v. impfv.* [*pfv.* **прикле́ить**] (*with* **к**) to glue (to); paste (to). —**прикле́иваться,** *refl.* (*with* **к**) to stick (to).
приклёпывать *v. impfv.* [*pfv.* **приклепа́ть**] to rivet.
приклони́ть *v. pfv.* [*infl.* **-клоню́, -кло́нишь**] to lay (one's head): ему́ не́где го́лову приклони́ть, he has nowhere to lay his head.
приключа́ться *v.r. impfv.* [*pfv.* **приключи́ться**] *colloq.* to happen; occur.
приключе́ние *n.* **1,** adventure. **2,** incident. —**приключе́нческий,** *adj.* adventure (*attrib.*).
приключи́ться *v.r., pfv. of* **приключа́ться.**
прикова́ть [*infl.* **-кую́, -куёшь**] *v., pfv. of* **прико́вывать.**
прико́вывать *v. impfv.* [*pfv.* **прикова́ть**] **1,** (*with* **к**) to chain (to). **2,** (*with* **к**) *fig.* to tie down; nail; rivet (to a place): прикова́ть к ме́сту, to rivet to the spot. **3,** *fig.* to fix (one's gaze); rivet (one's attention). —**прико́ванный к посте́ли,** bedridden.
прико́л *n., naut., in* **на прико́ле, 1,** tied up; moored. **2,** idle; laid up.
прикола́чивать *v. impfv.* [*pfv.* **приколоти́ть**] to nail down; fasten with nails.
приколоти́ть [*infl.* **-лочу́, -ло́тишь**] *v., pfv. of* **прикола́чивать.**
приколо́ть [*infl.* **-колю́, -ко́лешь**] *v., pfv. of* **прика́лывать.**
прикомандирова́ть *v. pfv.* [*infl.* **-ру́ю, -ру́ешь**] (with **к**) to assign (to).
прико́нчить *v., pfv. of* **прика́нчивать.**
прикорну́ть *v. pfv., colloq.* to curl up; settle down (*for a nap*).
прикоснове́ние *n.* **1,** touch. **2,** *fig.* involvement.
прикосну́ться *v.r., pfv. of* **прикаса́ться.**
прикра́сить [*infl.* **-шу, -сишь**] *v., pfv. of* **прикра́шивать.**
прикра́сы *n. pl.* [*sing.* **прикра́са**] *colloq.* embellishments (*in telling or describing something*): без прикра́с, without embellishment.
прикра́шивать *v. impfv.* [*pfv.* **прикра́сить**] to embellish; embroider; exaggerate.
прикрепи́ть [*infl.* **-плю́, -пи́шь**] *v., pfv. of* **прикрепля́ть.** —**прикпепи́ться,** *refl., pfv. of* **прикрепля́ться.**
прикрепле́ние *n.* **1,** fastening; attaching. **2,** assigning. **3,** registration.
прикрепля́ть *v. impfv.* [*pfv.* **прикрепи́ть**] (*with* **к**) **1,** to fasten (to); attach (to). **2,** to assign (to); attach (to). —**прикрепля́ться,** *refl.* (*with* **к**) **1,** to fasten (onto). **2,** to register (at).
прикри́кивать *v. impfv.* [*pfv.* **прикри́кнуть**] (*with* **на** + *acc.*) to shout (at).
прикрыва́ть *v. impfv.* [*pfv.* **прикры́ть**] **1,** to close (*but not tightly*). **2,** to cover (*but not completely*). **3,** to cover up; conceal. **4,** to shield; protect. **5,** *colloq.* to close down; liquidate. —**прикрыва́ться,** *refl.* **1,** (*with instr.*) to cover *or* shield oneself (with). **2,** (*of a door, window, etc.*) to close. **3,** *fig.* (*with instr.*) to cover up one's actions (by); take refuge (in).
прикры́тие *n.* **1,** concealment. **2,** protection. **3,** cover; shelter. **4,** *mil.* cover.
прикры́ть [*infl.* **-кро́ю, -кро́ешь**] *v., pfv. of* **прикрыва́ть.** —**прикры́ться,** *refl., pfv. of* **прикрыва́ться.**
прикупа́ть *v. impfv.* [*pfv.* **прикупи́ть**] to buy some more of.
прикупи́ть [*infl.* **-куплю́, -ку́пишь**] *v., pfv. of* **прикупа́ть.**
прику́ривать *v. impfv.* [*pfv.* **прикури́ть**] **1,** to light up; light a cigarette. **2,** to get a light from another cigarette.
прикури́ть [*infl.* **-курю́, -ку́ришь**] *v., pfv. of* **прику́ривать.**
прику́с *n., dent.* bite.
прикуси́ть [*infl.* **-кушу́, -ку́сишь**] *v., pfv. of* **прику́сывать.**
прику́сывать *v. impfv.* [*pfv.* **прикуси́ть**] to bite (one's tongue, lip, etc.).
прила́вок [*gen.* **-вка**] *n.* counter.
прилага́тельный *adj., in* **и́мя прилага́тельное,** adjective. —**прилага́тельное,** *n., decl. as an adj.* adjective.
прилага́ть *v. impfv.* [*pfv.* **приложи́ть**] **1,** (*with* **к**) to attach (to); append (to); enclose (in). **2,** to apply; exert: прилага́ть все уси́лия, to make every effort.
прила́живать *v. impfv.* [*pfv.* **прила́дить**] to fit; adjust.
приласка́ть *v. pfv.* **1,** to caress; pet. **2,** to be nice to. —**приласка́ться,** *refl.* (*with* **к**) **1,** to snuggle up to. **2,** to make up to.
прилега́ть *v. impfv.* (*with* **к**) **1,** to adjoin; lie adjacent (to). **2,** (*of clothes*) to fit; fit snugly.
прилега́ющий *adj.* adjoining; adjacent; contiguous.
прилежа́ние *n.* diligence.
приле́жный *adj.* diligent. —**приле́жно,** *adv.* diligently. —**приле́жность,** *n.f.* diligence.
прилепи́ть [*infl.* **-леплю́, -ле́пишь**] *v., pfv. of* **прилепля́ть.** —**прилепи́ться,** *refl., pfv. of* **прилепля́ться.**
прилепля́ть *v. impfv.* [*pfv.* **прилепи́ть**] (*with* **к**) to stick (to); affix (to). —**прилепля́ться,** *refl.* (with **к**) to stick (to).
прилёт *n.* arrival (*of air passengers or birds*).
прилета́ть *v. impfv.* [*pfv.* **прилете́ть**] **1,** to come flying in; arrive by plane. **2,** (*of a plane*) to arrive.
прилете́ть [*infl.* **-чу́, -ти́шь**] *v., pfv. of* **прилета́ть.**
приле́чь *v. pfv.* [*infl. like* **лечь**] to lie down for a while.
прили́в *n.* **1,** rising tide. **2,** rush (*of blood*). **3,** *fig.* influx. **4,** *fig.* wave; surge; burst. —**прили́в и отли́в,** ebb and flow of the tides. —**прили́вы и отли́вы,** tide; tides.
прилива́ть *v. impfv.* [*pfv.* **прили́ть**] **1,** to flow. **2,** (*of blood*) to rush.
прили́вный *adj.* tidal.
прили́занный *adj., colloq.* sleek.
прилипа́ние *n.* adhesion.
прилипа́ть *v. impfv.* [*pfv.* **прили́пнуть**] (*with* **к**) to stick (to); adhere (to).
прили́пнуть [*past* **-ли́п, -ла**] *v., pfv. of* **прилипа́ть.**
прили́пчивый *adj.* **1,** sticky. **2,** *fig., colloq.* catching; contagious. **3,** *fig., colloq.* bothersome; pesky.
прили́ть [*infl. like* **лить**] *v., pfv. of* **прилива́ть.**
прили́чие *n.* **1,** propriety; decency; decorum. **2,** *pl.* the proprieties; rules of propriety.

прили́чно *adv.* **1,** decently; properly. **2,** *colloq.* quite well.

прили́чный *adj.* **1,** decent; proper. **2,** *colloq.* decent; passable.

приложе́ние *n.* **1,** application. **2,** enclosure. **3,** supplement; appendix. **4,** *gram.* apposition.

приложи́ть [*infl.* **-ложу́, -ло́жишь**] *v., pfv. of* **прилага́ть** *and* **прикла́дывать.** —**приложи́ться,** *refl., pfv. of* **прикла́дываться.**

прилуне́ние *n.* moon landing.

прилуни́ться *v.r. pfv.* to land on the moon.

прильну́ть *v., pfv. of* **льнуть.**

примадо́нна *n.* prima donna.

прима́нивать *v. impfv.* [*pfv.* **примани́ть**] to entice; lure; decoy.

примани́ть [*infl.* **-маню́, -ма́нишь**] *v., pfv. of* **прима́нивать.**

прима́нка *n.* **1,** bait; lure. **2,** *fig.* lure; attraction.

прима́с *n., eccles.* primate.

прима́т *n.* **1,** primacy. **2,** *pl., zool.* primates.

примелька́ться *v.r. pfv.* (*with dat.*) to become (overly) familiar to: го́род мне примелька́лся, I have seen (more than) enough of the city.

примене́ние *n.* application; use; employment. —**в примене́нии к,** as applied to.

примени́мый *adj.* applicable. —**примени́мость,** *n.f.* applicability.

примени́тельно *adv.* (*with* **к**) as it applies to; with reference to.

примени́ть [*infl.* **-меню́, -ме́нишь**] *v., pfv. of* **применя́ть.** —**примени́ться,** *refl., pfv. of* **применя́ться.**

применя́ть *v. impfv.* [*pfv.* **примени́ть**] to apply; employ; use. —**применя́ться,** *refl.* **1,** to be used. **2,** (*with* **к**) to adjust (to).

приме́р *n.* example. —**для приме́ра,** as an example. —**к приме́ру,** for example. —**не в приме́р, 1,** (*with dat.*) unlike; as distinct from. **2,** (*with comp. adjectives*) much more; far more. —**по приме́ру** (+ *gen.*), after/following the example of.

примерза́ть *v. impfv.* [*pfv.* **примёрзнуть**] (*with* **к**) to freeze (to).

примёрзнуть [*past* **-мёрз, -ла**] *v., pfv. of* **примерза́ть.**

приме́рить *v., pfv. of* **примеря́ть.**

приме́рка *n.* **1,** trying on. **2,** fitting: сде́лать приме́рку, to have a fitting.

приме́рно *adv.* **1,** in an exemplary manner. **2,** approximately. **3,** *colloq.* for example.

приме́рный *adj.* **1,** exemplary; model. **2,** approximate.

приме́рочная *n., decl. as an adj.* dressing room (*for trying on clothes*).

примеря́ть *v. impfv.* [*pfv.* **приме́рить**] to try on.

при́месь *n.f.* **1,** admixture. **2,** *fig., colloq.* touch; dash; trace.

приме́та *n.* **1,** mark; sign. **2,** omen. —**брать на приме́ту,** to take note of. —**име́ть на приме́те,** to have an eye on.

примета́ть *v., pfv. of* **примётывать.**

приме́тить [*infl.* **-чу, -тишь**] *v., pfv. of* **примеча́ть.**

приме́тливый *adj., colloq.* observant.

приме́тный *adj.* **1,** noticeable; perceptible. **2,** conspicuous.

примётывать *v. impfv.* [*pfv.* **примета́ть**] to stitch; baste.

примеча́ние *n.* note; footnote; explanatory note.

примеча́тельный *adj.* noteworthy; notable.

примеча́ть *v. impfv.* [*pfv.* **приме́тить**] *colloq.* **1,** to notice. **2,** to note; take note of; make a mental note of.

приме́шивать *v. impfv.* [*pfv.* **примеша́ть**] to add (something to something) by mixing.

примина́ть *v. impfv.* [*pfv.* **примя́ть**] to crush; flatten; trample down.

примире́ние *n.* reconciliation.

примири́тель *n.m.* conciliator. —**примири́тельный,** *adj.* conciliatory.

примири́ть *v., pfv. of* **мири́ть** *and* **примиря́ть.** —**примири́ться,** *refl., pfv. of* **мири́ться** *and* **примиря́ться.**

примиря́ть *v. impfv.* [*pfv.* **примири́ть**] to reconcile. —**примиря́ться,** *refl.* **1,** to become reconciled (*after a quarrel*). **2,** (*with* **с** + *instr.*) to become reconciled (to); reconcile oneself (to).

примити́вный *adj.* primitive.

примкну́ть *v., pfv. of* **примыка́ть.** —**при́мкнутые штыки́,** fixed bayonets.

примо́лкнуть *v. pfv.* [*past* **-мо́лк, -ла**] *colloq.* to fall silent.

примо́рский *adj.* **1,** seaside (*attrib.*). **2,** maritime.

примо́рье *n.* area near the seashore.

примости́ться *v.r. pfv.* [*infl.* **-щу́сь, -сти́шься**] *colloq.* to settle down, perch (*in an uncomfortable place*).

примо́чка [*gen. pl.* **-чек**] *n.* wash: примо́чка для глаз, eyewash.

при́мула *n.* primrose.

при́мус *n.* small kerosene stove.

примча́ться *v.r. pfv.* [*infl.* **-мчу́сь, -мчи́шься**] to arrive on the run; come tearing along

примыка́ть *v. impfv.* [*pfv.* **примкну́ть**] (*with* **к**) **1,** to join; side with. **2,** [*impfv. only*] to adjoin; abut. —**примыка́ть/примкну́ть штыки́,** to fix bayonets.

примя́ть [*infl.* **-мну́, -мнёшь**] *v., pfv. of* **примина́ть.**

принадлежа́ть *v. impfv.* [*pres.* **-лежу́, -лежи́шь**] **1,** (*with dat.*) to belong to. **2,** (*with* **к**) to belong to; be a member of. —**принадлежа́ть к числу́** (+ *gen.*), to be among; number among.

принадле́жность *n.f.* **1,** *pl.* accessories; articles; gear. **2,** (*with* **к**) belonging (to); affiliation (with). **3,** characteristic; attribute.

принале́чь *v. pfv.* [*infl. like* **лечь**] (*with* **на** + *acc.*) *colloq.* **1,** to lean (on). **2,** *fig.* to apply oneself (to).

принаряжа́ть *v. impfv.* [*pfv.* **принаряди́ть**] *colloq.* to dress up; deck out. —**принаряжа́ться,** *refl., colloq.* to get dressed up.

принево́ливать *v. impfv.* [*pfv.* **принево́лить**] *colloq.* to force; make; compel.

принесе́ние *n.* **1,** bringing. **2,** *in* принесе́ние прися́ги, taking of the oath. **3,** *in* принесе́ние поздравле́ний, offering of congratulations.

принести́ [*infl. like* **нести́**] *v., pfv. of* **приноси́ть.**

принижа́ть *v. impfv.* [*pfv.* **прини́зить**] **1,** to humiliate; humble. **2,** to disparage; belittle.

приниже́ние *n.* **1,** humiliation. **2,** disparagement.

прини́женный *adj.* **1,** humble. **2,** humiliating.

прини́зить [*infl.* **-жу, -зишь**] *v., pfv. of* **принижа́ть.**

принока́ть *v. impfv.* [*pfv.* **прини́кнуть**] (*with* **к**) to press against; nestle close to. Прини́кнуть губа́ми к (чему́-нибудь), to press one's lips against.

прини́кнуть [*past* **-ни́к, -ла**] *v., pfv. of* **приника́ть.**

принима́ть *v. impfv.* [*pfv.* **приня́ть**] **1,** to accept. **2,** to receive (a person *or* persons). **3,** to admit; allow to enter. **4,** to take (food, medicine, measures, a bath, etc.). **5,** to assume; take on. **6,** to take over. **7,** to adopt (a resolution, amendment, etc.); pass (a law). **8,** to adopt (a religion, citizenship, etc.). **9,** [*impfv. only*] to receive; pick up (a signal). **10,** (*with* **за** + *acc.*) to take for; mistake for. **11,** [*impfv. only*] to deliver (a baby). —**принимáть во внимáние** *or* **в расчёт** *or* **к свéдению,** to take account of; take into account; take into consideration. —**принимáть (блúзко) к сéрдцу,** to take to heart. —**принимáть на вéру,** to take on faith. —**принимáть на свой счёт,** to take personally. —**принимáть решéние,** to make a decision. —**принимáть стóрону** (+ *gen.*), to take someone's side. —**принимáть учáстие** (*with* **в** + *prepl.*), to take part (in); participate (in).

принимáться *v.r. impfv.* [*pfv.* **принúться**] **1,** (*with inf. or* **за** + *acc.*) to begin; set about. **2,** (*of a plant*) to take root; (*of a vaccine*) to take.

принорáвливать *v. impfv.* [*pfv.* **приноровúть**] (*with* **к**) *colloq.* **1,** to adapt (to). **2,** to time to coincide with. —**принорáвливаться,** *refl.* (*with* **к**) *colloq.* **1,** to adjust (to). **2,** to get the knack of.

приносúть *v. impfv.* [*pfv.* **принестú;** *pres.* **-ношý, -нóсишь**] **1,** to bring. **2,** to yield; bear. **3,** to offer (an apology, one's thanks, etc.). —**приносúть (чтó-нибудь) в жéртву,** to sacrifice. —**приносúть жéртву,** to make a sacrifice. —**приносúть пóльзу,** to be of use; be of benefit. —**приносúть присúгу,** to take the oath.

приношéние *n.* offering; gift.

принудúтельный *adj.* **1,** (*of labor*) forced. **2,** (*of measures*) coercive.

принýдить [*infl.* **-жу, -дишь**] *v., pfv. of* **принуждáть.**

принуждáть *v. impfv.* [*pfv.* **принýдить**] to force; compel.

принуждéние *n.* compulsion; coercion; duress: по принуждéнию, under duress.

принуждённый *adj.* forced; constrained; unnatural. —**принуждённость,** *n.f.* constraint.; stiffness; lack of spontaneity.

принц *n.* prince. —**принцéсса,** *n.* princess.

прúнцип *n.* principle. —**в прúнципе,** in principle. —**из прúнципа,** on principle.

принципиáльно *adv.* **1,** in principle. **2,** fundamentally.

принципиáльность *n.f.* adherence to principle.

принципиáльный *adj.* **1,** of principle: принципиáльный человéк, man of principle. **2,** fundamental: имéть принципиáльное значéние, to be of fundamental importance.

принюхиваться *v.r. impfv.* [*pfv.* **принюхаться**] (*with* **к**) *colloq.* **1,** to sniff. **2,** to get used to the smell of.

принятие *n.* **1,** acceptance. **2,** receiving. **3,** admission; admittance. **4,** taking (*of food, medicine, measures, an oath, etc.*). **5,** assumption; taking on. **6,** making (*a decision*).

прúнятый *past passive part. of* **принúть,** accepted. Это не прúнято, that is (just) not done. У нас не прúнято (+ *inf.*), it is not our custom (*or* practice) to...

принúть [*infl.* **примý, прúмешь;** *past* **прúнял, принялá, прúняло**] *v., pfv. of* **принимáть.** —**принúться,** *refl.* [*past* **принялсú, -лáсь, -лóсь**] *pfv. of* **принимáться.**

приободрúть *v. impfv.* [*pfv.* **приободрúть**] to cheer up; hearten. —**приободрúться,** *refl.* to cheer up; feel better.

приобрестú [*infl.* **-бретý, -бретёшь;** *past* **-брёл, -бреля́, -брелó**] *v., pfv. of* **приобретáть.**

приобретáть *v. impfv.* [*pfv.* **приобрестú**] to acquire; gain.

приобретéние *n.* acquisition.

приобщáть *v. impfv.* [*pfv.* **приобщúть**] **1,** (*with* **к**) to introduce (to); acquaint (with); initiate (into). **2,** (*with* **к**) to attach (to); append (to). **3,** to administer the sacrament to. —**приобщáться,** *refl.* (*with* **к**) to join; enter into; become a part of.

приодéть *v. pfv.* [*infl.* **-дéну, -дéнешь**] *colloq.* to dress (someone) up. —**приодéться,** *refl., colloq.* to get dressed up.

приóр *n., eccles.* prior.

приоритéт *n.* **1,** being first. Емý принадлежúт приоритéт открытия (+ *gen.*), to him belongs the distinction of having invented... **2,** priority.

приосáниваться *v.r. impfv.* [*pfv.* **приосáниться**] *colloq.* to assume a dignified air.

приостанáвливать *v. impfv.* [*pfv.* **приостановúть**] to halt; interrupt; suspend. —**приостанáвливаться,** *refl.* to stop for a moment; pause.

приостановúть [*infl.* **-новлю́, -нóвишь**] *v., pfv. of* **приостанáвливать.** —**приостановúться,** *refl., pfv. of* **приостанáвливаться.**

приостанóвка *n.* halt; suspension.

приостановлéние *n.* halt; suspension. —**приостановлéние исполнéния приговóра,** stay of execution.

приотворúть [*infl.* **-ворю́, -вóришь**] *v., pfv. of* **приотворя́ть.** —**приотворúться,** *refl., pfv. of* **приотворя́ться.**

приотворя́ть *v. impfv.* [*pfv.* **приотворúть**] *v.t.* to open slightly. —**приотворя́ться,** *refl.* (*of a door*) to open slightly.

приоткрывáть *v. impfv.* [*pfv.* **приоткры́ть**] *v.t.* to open slightly. —**приоткрывáться,** *refl.* (*of a door*) to open slightly.

приоткры́ть [*infl.* **-крóю, -крóешь**] *v., pfv. of* **приоткрывáть.**

приохóтить *v. pfv.* [*infl.* **-хóчу, -хóтишь**] to instill (in someone) an appreciation for: приохóтить когó-нибудь к чтéнию, to instill in someone a taste for reading. —**приохóтиться,** *refl.* (*with* **к**) *colloq.* to take to.

припадáть *v. impfv.* [*pfv.* **припáсть**] **1,** (with **к**) to press (oneself) close to. Припадáть ýхом к землé, to press one's ear to the ground. **2,** (*with* **на** + *acc.*) to drop (to): припáсть на однó колéно, to drop to one knee. **3,** [*impfv. only*] *colloq.* to be slightly lame; (*with* **на** + *acc.*) limp slightly (on).

припáдок [*gen.* **-дка**] *n.* fit; attack.

припáдочный *adj.* **1,** of an attack or fit. **2,** *colloq.* subject to attacks. —*n.* person subject to attacks.

припáивать *v. impfv.* [*pfv.* **припая́ть**] (*with* **к**) to solder (to).

припáйка *n.* soldering.

припáрка [*gen. pl.* **-рок**] *n., usu. pl.* poultice.

припасáть *v. impfv.* [*pfv.* **припастú**] *colloq.* to store (up); lay in a supply of.

припастú [*infl. like* **пастú**] *v., pfv. of* **припасáть.**

припáсть [*infl. like* **пасть**] *v., pfv. of* **припадáть.**

припáсы [*gen.* **-сов**] *n. pl.* supplies. —**боевы́е** *or*

огнестре́льные припа́сы, ammunition. —**съестны́е припа́сы,** provisions; rations.

припая́ть *v., pfv. of* **припа́ивать.**

припе́в *n.* refrain.

припева́ть *v. impfv., colloq.* to sing (*while doing something*).

припева́ючи *adv., colloq., in* **жить припева́ючи,** to live in clover.

припёк *n.* intense heat from the sun: на припёке, in the hot sun; right in the sun.

припека́ть *v. impfv.* (*of the sun*) to be very hot; beat down.

припере́ть [*infl. like* **пере́ть**] *v., pfv. of* **припира́ть.**

припира́ть *v. impfv.* [*pfv.* **припере́ть**] **1,** (*with* **к**) to place (something) firmly against (something). **2,** to secure: припира́ть дверь сту́лом, to secure a door by placing a chair against it. **3,** *colloq.* to set (a door or window) ajar. —**припере́ть к стене́,** to drive against the wall; drive into a corner.

приписа́ть [*infl.* **-пишу́, -пи́шешь**] *v., pfv. of* **припи́сывать.** —**приписа́ться,** *refl., pfv. of* **припи́сываться.**

припи́ска [*gen. pl.* **-сок**] *n.* **1,** postscript. **2,** codicil. **3,** registration.

припи́сывать *v. impfv.* [*pfv.* **приписа́ть**] **1,** to add (*to something written*). **2,** (*with* **к**) to register (at). **3,** (*with dat.*) to ascribe (to); attribute (to). —**припи́сываться,** *refl.* **1,** (*with dat.*) to be attributed (to). **2,** to register.

припла́та *n.* extra charge; surcharge.

приплати́ть [*infl.* **-плачу́, -пла́тишь**] *v., pfv. of* **припла́чивать.**

припла́чивать *v. impfv.* [*pfv.* **приплати́ть**] to pay (a certain amount) extra.

припло́д *n.* litter; offspring.

приплыва́ть *v. impfv.* [*pfv.* **приплы́ть**] (*with* **к**) to swim up to; reach by swimming.

приплы́ть [*infl. like* **плыть**] *v., pfv. of* **приплыва́ть.**

приплю́снутый *adj.* flat; flattened.

приплю́щивать *v. impfv.* [*pfv.* **приплю́снуть**] to flatten.

припля́сывать *v. impfv.* to dance up and down.

приподнима́ть *v. impfv.* [*pfv.* **приподня́ть**] to raise slightly. —**приподнима́ться,** *refl.* **1,** to raise oneself slightly. **2,** to sit up.

припо́днятый *adj.* **1,** (*of one's mood*) elated; exultant. **2,** (*of style, language, etc.*) elevated.

приподня́ть [*infl. like* **подня́ть**] *v., pfv. of* **приподнима́ть.** —**приподня́ться,** *refl., pfv. of* **приподнима́ться.**

припо́й *n.* solder.

приполза́ть *v. impfv.* [*pfv.* **приползти́**] (*with* **к**) to crawl to; reach by crawling.

приползти́ [*infl. like* **ползти́**] *v., pfv. of* **приполза́ть.**

припомина́ть *v. impfv.* [*pfv.* **припо́мнить**] to remember; recall; recollect.

припра́ва *n.* seasoning; flavoring; relish; dressing; condiment.

припра́вить [*infl.* **-влю, -вишь**] *v., pfv. of* **приправля́ть.**

приправля́ть *v. impfv.* [*pfv.* **припра́вить**] to season; flavor.

припря́тать [*infl.* **-пря́чу, -пря́чешь**] *v., pfv. of* **припря́тывать.**

припря́тывать *v. impfv.* [*pfv.* **припря́тать**] *colloq.* **1,** to put away; store. **2,** *fig.* to hide; conceal.

припу́гивать *v. impfv.* [*pfv.* **припугну́ть**] *colloq.* to frighten; scare; intimidate.

припу́дривать *v. impfv.* [*pfv.* **припу́дрить**] to powder. —**припу́дриваться,** *refl.* to powder oneself.

припуска́ть *v. impfv.* [*pfv.* **припусти́ть**] *colloq.* **1,** (*with* **к**) to allow to come near; let at. **2,** to urge on (a horse). **3,** to let out (a garment). **4,** *v.i.* to quicken one's pace. **5,** *v.i.* (*of rain*) to come down harder. —**припуска́ться,** *refl., colloq.* to quicken one's pace.

припусти́ть [*infl.* **-пущу́, -пу́стишь**] *v., pfv. of* **припуска́ть.** —**припусти́ться,** *refl., pfv. of* **припуска́ться.**

припуха́ть *v. impfv.* [*pfv.* **припу́хнуть**] to be slightly swollen.

припу́хлый *adj.* slightly swollen. —**припу́хлость,** *n.f.* slight swelling.

припу́хнуть [*past* **-пу́х, -ла**] *v., pfv. of* **припуха́ть.**

прираба́тывать *v. impfv.* [*pfv.* **прирабо́тать**] to earn (extra money).

при́работок [*gen.* **-тка**] *n.* extra money earned.

прира́внивать *v. impfv.* [*pfv.* **приравня́ть**] (*with* **к**) to equate (with).

прираста́ть *v. impfv.* [*pfv.* **прирасти́**] **1,** (*with* **к**) to grow on to. **2,** (*with* **к**) *fig.* to become rooted to; become frozen to. **3,** to increase; grow.

прирасти́ [*infl. like* **расти́**] *v., pfv. of* **прираста́ть.**

прираще́ние *n.* **1,** increase. **2,** increment.

приревнова́ть *v. pfv.* [*infl.* **-ну́ю, -ну́ешь**] to be jealous of.

прире́зать [*infl.* **-ре́жу, -ре́жешь**] *v., pfv. of* **прireза́ть** *and* **прире́зывать.**

прireза́ть *v. impfv.* [*pfv.* **прире́зать**] **1,** to cut (someone's) throat. **2,** to slaughter (animals). **3,** to add on (a piece of land). *Also,* **прире́зывать.**

приро́да *n.* **1,** nature: дары́ приро́ды, the gifts of nature; изуча́ть приро́ду, to study nature. **2,** climate; environment (*of a region*): суро́вая приро́да Сиби́ри, the harsh climate (*or* rugged environment) of Siberia. **3,** *colloq.* (a person's) nature. Челове́ческая приро́да, human nature. —**в приро́де веще́й,** in the nature of things. —**от приро́ды,** from birth. —**по приро́де,** by nature.

приро́дный *adj.* **1,** natural. **2,** innate; inborn; inherent.

прирождённый *adj.* **1,** innate; inborn. **2,** (*of a person*) born: прирождённый поэ́т, a born poet.

приро́ст *n.* increase; growth.

прируча́ть *v. impfv.* [*pfv.* **приручи́ть**] to tame; domesticate.

прируче́ние *n.* taming; domestication.

прирученный *adj.* tame.

приручи́ть *v., pfv. of* **прируча́ть.**

приса́дка *n.* additive.

приса́живаться *v.r. impfv.* [*pfv.* **присе́сть**] to sit down; have a seat; take a seat.

приса́ливать *v. impfv.* [*pfv.* **присоли́ть**] *colloq.* to add a touch of salt to.

приса́сываться *v.r. impfv.* [*pfv.* **присоса́ться**] (*with* **к**) **1,** to adhere to (*by suction*). **2,** *fig., colloq.* to worm one's way into.

присва́ивать *v. impfv.* [*pfv.* **присво́ить**] **1,** to appropriate; take for one's own. **2,** to pass off as one's own. **3,** (*with dat.*) to award (a degree to); confer (a title on); give (a name to).

при́свист *n.* whistle; whistling.

присви́стывать *v. impfv.* [*pfv.* **присви́стнуть**] to whistle.

присвое́ние *n.* **1,** appropriation. **2,** conferring.
присво́ить *v., pfv. of* **присва́ивать.**
приседа́ние *n.* **1,** squat. **2,** *obs.* curtsy.
приседа́ть *v. impfv.* [*pfv.* **присе́сть**] **1,** to squat; crouch. **2,** *obs.* to curtsy.
присе́ст *n., obs.* sitting. —**в** (*or* **за**) **оди́н присе́ст,** at one sitting; at a stretch.
присе́сть [*infl. like* **сесть**] *v., pfv. of* **приса́живаться** *and* **приседа́ть.**
при́сказка [*gen. pl.* **-зок**] *n.* **1,** introduction; prelude. **2,** saying.
прискака́ть *v. pfv.* [*infl.* **-скачу́, -ска́чешь**] to arrive at a gallop.
приско́рбие *n., obs.* sorrow; regret. —**к моему́ приско́рбию,** to my regret.
приско́рбный *adj.* **1,** sad; sorrowful. **2,** regrettable; deplorable.
прску́чить *v. pfv., colloq.* **1,** to become boring. **2,** (*with dat.*) to bore.
присла́ть [*infl.* **-шлю́, -шлёшь**] *v., pfv. of* **присыла́ть.**
прислоня́ть *v. impfv.* [*pfv.* **прислони́ть**] (*with* **к**) **1,** to lean; rest (something) against. **2,** to place; stand (something) against. —**прислоня́ться,** *refl.* (*with* **к**) to lean against; rest against.
прислу́га *n.* **1,** *obs.* servant; maid. **2,** *obs.* servants. **3,** *mil.* crew; team.
прислу́живать *v. impfv.* **1,** to be a servant. **2,** (*with dat.*) *colloq.* to wait on. —**прислу́живаться,** *refl.* (*with dat. or* **к**) to play up to.
прислу́жник *n.* **1,** *obs.* servant. **2,** *colloq.* lackey.
прислу́шиваться *v.r. impfv.* [*pfv.* **прислу́шаться**] (*with* **к**) **1,** to listen (to). **2,** to heed. **3,** *colloq.* to get used to the sound of.
присма́тривать *v. impfv.* [*pfv.* **присмотре́ть**] **1,** (*with* **за** + *instr.*) to look after; keep an eye on. **2,** [*impfv. only*] to look for. —**присма́триваться,** *refl.* (*with* **к**) **1,** to look closely (at). **2,** to grow accustomed to.
присмире́ть *v. pfv.* to calm down; grow quiet.
присмо́тр *n.* supervision.
присмотре́ть *v. pfv.* [*infl.* **-смотрю́, -смо́тришь**] **1,** *pfv. of* **присма́тривать. 2,** to find. —**присмотре́ться,** *refl., pfv. of* **присма́триваться.**
присни́ться *v.r., pfv. of* **сни́ться.**
присоедине́ние *n.* **1,** addition. **2,** joining. **3,** annexation.
присоединя́ть *v. impfv.* [*pfv.* **присоедини́ть**] (*with* **к**) **1,** to add (something) to. **2,** to join (something) to. **3,** to annex (to). —**присоединя́ться,** *refl.* (*with* **к**) **1,** to be added to. **2,** to join. **3,** to endorse; subscribe to.
присоли́ть [*infl.* **-солю́, -со́лишь** *or* **-соли́шь**] *v., pfv. of* **приса́ливать.**
присоса́ться *v.r., pfv. of* **приса́сываться.**
присосе́диться *v.r. pfv.* [*infl.* **-жусь, -дишься**] (*with* **к**) *colloq.* to sit down next to.
присо́сок [*gen.* **-ска**] *n., bot., zool.* sucker. *Also,* **присо́ска.**
присо́хнуть [*past* **-со́х, -ла**] *v., pfv. of* **присыха́ть.**
приспе́ть *v. pfv., colloq.* (*of time*) to be ripe.
приспе́шник *n.* henchman.
приспоса́бливать *v. impfv.* = **приспособля́ть.** —**приспоса́бливаться,** *refl.* = **приспособля́ться.**
приспосо́бить [*infl.* **-блю, -бишь**] *v., pfv. of* **приспособля́ть** *and* **приспоса́бливать.** —**приспосо́биться,** *refl., pfv. of* **приспособля́ться** *and* **приспоса́бливаться.**
приспособле́ние *n.* **1,** device. **2,** adaptation; adjustment.
приспособля́емость *n.f.* adaptability.
приспособля́ть *v. impfv.* [*pfv.* **приспосо́бить**] **1,** to adapt. **2,** (*with* **под** + *acc.*) to convert (into). —**приспособля́ться,** *refl.* (*with* **к**) to adjust (to); become adjusted (to); adapt (to).
приспуска́ть *v. impfv.* [*pfv.* **приспусти́ть**] **1,** to lower slightly. **2,** to lower (a flag) to half-mast.
приспусти́ть [*infl.* **-спущу́, -спу́стишь**] *v., pfv. of* **приспуска́ть.**
при́став [*pl.* **пристава́**] *n., pre-rev.* police officer. —**суде́бный при́став,** *pre-rev.* bailiff.
пристава́ние *n., usu. pl.* nagging; pestering.
пристава́ть *v. impfv.* [*pfv.* **приста́ть;** *pres.* **-стаю́, -стаёшь**] (*with* **к**) **1,** to stick (to); adhere (to). **2,** *colloq.* to nag; pester. **3,** *colloq.* to join. **4,** (*of a boat*) to put in (to); pull up (to). **5,** *colloq.* (*of a disease*) to be transmitted (to). *See also* **приста́ть.**
приста́вить [*infl.* **-влю, -вишь**] *v., pfv. of* **приставля́ть.**
приста́вка [*gen. pl.* **-вок**] *n.* **1,** prefix. **2,** attachment; accessory.
приставля́ть *v. impfv.* [*pfv.* **приста́вить**] **1,** (*with* **к**) to place (against); lean (against). **2,** to add on. **3,** *colloq.* to appoint to look after.
приставно́й *adj.* attached.
приста́вочный *adj.* **1,** prefixed. **2,** (*of a collar, cuffs, etc.*) detachable.
при́стальный *adj.* (*of a look*) intent; (*of attention*) rapt. —**при́стально,** *adv.* intently.
приста́нище *n.* refuge; shelter; haven.
при́стань [*pl.* **при́стани, -не́й, -ня́м**] *n.f.* dock; pier; wharf.
приста́ть *v. pfv.* [*infl.* **-ста́ну, -ста́нешь**] **1,** *pfv. of* **пристава́ть. 2,** *impers.* (*with dat.*) *colloq.* to befit; become.
пристёгивать *v. impfv.* [*pfv.* **пристегну́ть**] to fasten; button; hook; buckle; pin. —**пристёгиваться,** *refl.* to hook on.
присто́йный *adj.* proper; decorous.
пристра́ивать *v. impfv.* [*pfv.* **пристро́ить**] **1,** (*with* **к**) to build on (to); add on (to). **2,** *colloq.* to place; find a job for. —**пристра́иваться,** *refl., colloq.* **1,** to ensconce oneself; perch. **2,** to get a job. **3,** (*with* **к**) to get into formation (with).
пристра́стие *n.* (*with* **к**) **1,** predilection; bent. **2,** partiality; bias.
пристрасти́ть *v. pfv.* [*infl.* **-щу́, -сти́шь**] *colloq.* to develop (in someone) a love of: пристрасти́ть кого́-нибудь к кни́гам, to develop in someone a love of books. —**пристрасти́ться,** *refl.* (*with* **к**) to develop a passion (for).
пристра́стный *adj.* **1,** partial; biased. **2,** (*with* **к**) partial (to); drawn (to). —**пристра́стно,** *adv.* in a biased manner. —**пристра́стность,** *n.f.* partiality; bias.
пристра́чивать *v. impfv.* [*pfv.* **пристрочи́ть**] (*with* **к**) to sew on (to).
пристре́ливать *v. impfv.* **1,** [*pfv.* **пристрели́ть**] to shoot; kill. **2,** [*pfv.* **пристреля́ть**] to zero in (a weapon); zero in on (a target). —**пристре́ливаться,** *refl.* [*pfv.* **пристреля́ться**] to zero in.
пристрели́ть [*infl.* **-стрелю́, -стре́лишь**] *v., pfv. of* **пристре́ливать** (*in sense #1*).

пристре́лка *n.* zeroing in (*of a weapon*); zeroing in on (*a target*).
пристреля́ть *v., pfv. of* **пристре́ливать** (*in sense #2*). —**пристреля́ться,** *refl., pfv. of* **пристре́ливаться.**
пристро́ить *v., pfv. of* **пристра́ивать.** —**пристро́иться,** *refl., pfv. of* **пристра́иваться.**
пристро́йка [*gen. pl.* **-стро́ек**] *n.* annex; extension.
пристрочи́ть [*infl.* **-строчу́, -строчи́шь** *or* **-стро́чишь**] *v., pfv. of* **пристра́чивать.**
пристру́нивать *v. impfv.* [*pfv.* **пристру́нить**] *colloq.* to clamp down on; crack down on.
присту́кивать *v. impfv.* [*pfv.* **присту́кнуть**] (*with instr.*) **1,** to rap. **2,** to click (one's heels).
при́ступ *n.* **1,** fit; attack. **2,** *mil.* attack; assault.
приступа́ть *v. impfv.* [*pfv.* **приступи́ть**] (*with* **к**) to proceed (to); begin; set about. —**приступа́ться,** *refl.* (*with* **к**) *colloq.* to approach; come near (to).
приступи́ть [*infl.* **-ступлю́, -сту́пишь**] *v., pfv. of* **приступа́ть.** —**приступи́ться,** *refl., pfv. of* **приступа́ться.**
пристыди́ть *v., pfv. of* **стыди́ть.**
присуди́ть [*infl.* **-сужу́, -су́дишь**] *v., pfv. of* **присужда́ть.**
присужда́ть *v. impfv.* [*pfv.* **присуди́ть**] **1,** (*with* **к**) to sentence (to). **2,** to award; confer.
присужде́ние *n.* awarding; conferring.
прису́тствие *n.* presence: в моём прису́тствии, in my presence. —**прису́тствие ду́ха,** presence of mind.
прису́тствовать *v. impfv.* [*pres.* **-ствую, -ствуешь**] to be present: прису́тствовать на собра́нии/в за́ле/при разгово́ре/, to be present at a meeting/in the hall/during a conversation/.
прису́тствующий *n., decl. as an adj.* person present.
прису́щий *adj.* (*with dat.*) inherent (in): с прису́щим ему́ доброду́шием, with his inherent good nature.
присчи́тывать *v. impfv.* [*pfv.* **присчита́ть**] to add on.
присыла́ть *v. impfv.* [*pfv.* **присла́ть**] to send.
присы́пать [*infl.* **-сы́плю, -сы́плешь**] *v., pfv. of* **присыпа́ть.**
присыпа́ть *v. impfv.* [*pfv.* **присы́пать**] **1,** (*with gen.*) to pour some more (of). **2,** to sprinkle (a surface): присыпа́ть что́-нибудь песко́м, to sprinkle something with sand.
присы́пка *n.* **1,** sprinkling. **2,** powder: де́тская присы́пка, baby powder.
присыха́ть *v. impfv.* [*pfv.* **присо́хнуть**] (*with* **к**) to stick (to); adhere (*in drying*).
прися́га *n.* oath. —**дава́ть прися́гу,** to swear. —**приводи́ть (кого́-нибудь) к прися́ге,** to swear in; administer the oath to. —**приноси́ть** *or* **принима́ть прися́гу,** to take the oath.
присяга́ть *v. impfv.* [*pfv.* **присягну́ть**] to swear.
прися́жный *n., decl. as an adj.* **1,** juror. **2,** *pl.* jury.
притаи́ть *v. pfv., colloq.* **1,** to conceal. **2,** to harbor. —**притаи́ться,** *refl.* to hide.
прита́птывать *v. impfv.* [*pfv.* **притопта́ть**] to trample; trample down.
прита́скивать *v. impfv.* [*pfv.* **притащи́ть**] to bring in; drag in. —**прита́скиваться,** *refl., colloq.* to drag oneself along.
притащи́ть [*infl.* **-тащу́, -та́щишь**] *v., pfv. of* **прита́скивать.** —**притащи́ться,** *refl., pfv. of* **прита́скиваться.**
притвори́ть [*infl.* **-творю́, -тво́ришь**] *v., pfv. of* **притворя́ть.** —**притвори́ться,** *refl.* **1,** [*infl.* **-тво́рится**] *pfv. of* **притворя́ться** (*in sense #1*). **2,** [*infl.* **-творю́сь, -твори́шься**] *pfv. of* **притворя́ться** (*in sense #2*).
притво́рный *adj.* feigned; pretended. —**притво́рно,** *adv.* pretending to: притво́рно рассерди́ться, to pretend to be angry.
притво́рство *n.* sham; pretense. —**притво́рщик,** *n.* hypocrite.
притворя́ть *v. impfv.* [*pfv.* **притвори́ть**] to close; shut. —**притворя́ться,** *refl.* **1,** to be closed; be shut. **2,** (*with instr.*) to pretend (to be).
притека́ть *v. impfv.* [*pfv.* **прите́чь**] **1,** to leak in. **2,** *fig.* to filter in.
притерпе́ться *v.r. pfv.* [*infl.* **-терплю́сь, -те́рпишься**] (*with* **к**) *colloq.* to get used to; learn to live with.
притёртый *adj.* ground in; ground smooth. —**притёртое стекло́,** ground glass.
притесне́ние *n.* oppression.
притесни́тель *n.m.* oppressor.
притесня́ть *v. impfv.* [*pfv.* **притесни́ть**] to oppress; keep down.
прите́чь [*infl. like* **течь**] *v., pfv. of* **притека́ть.**
прити́скивать *v. impfv.* [*pfv.* **прити́снуть**] (*with* **к**) to press (something) against (something).
притиха́ть *v. impfv.* [*pfv.* **прити́хнуть**] **1,** to quiet down; (*of noise*) die down. **2,** to subside; abate.
прити́хнуть [*past* **-ти́х, -ла**] *v., pfv. of* **притиха́ть.**
приткну́ть *v. pfv., colloq.* to stick; put; lay. —**приткну́ться,** *refl., colloq.* to find room for oneself; find a place to stay.
прито́к *n.* **1,** inflow (*of water, air, etc.*). **2,** *fig.* influx. **3,** *fig.* surge (*of energy, an emotion, etc.*). **4,** tributary.
при́толока *n.* lintel.
прито́м *conj.* besides; moreover; furthermore.
прито́н *n.* den: иго́рный прито́н, gambling den.
прито́пнуть *v., pfv. of* **прито́пывать.**
притопта́ть [*infl.* **-топчу́, -то́пчешь**] *v., pfv. of* **прита́птывать.**
прито́пывать *v. impfv.* [*pfv.* **прито́пнуть**] (*with instr.*) **1,** to stamp (one's foot). **2,** to tap (one's foot in time to music).
притормози́ть *v. pfv.* [*infl.* **-жу́, -зи́шь**] to slow down (*trans. & intrans.*).
при́торный *adj.* sugary; saccharine.
притра́гиваться *v.r. impfv.* [*pfv.* **притро́нуться**] (*with* **к**) to touch.
притупи́ть [*infl.* **-туплю́, -ту́пишь**] *v., pfv. of* **притупля́ть.** —**притупи́ться,** *refl., pfv. of* **притупля́ться.**
притупля́ть *v. impfv.* [*pfv.* **притупи́ть**] **1,** to blunt. **2,** *fig.* to dull (the mind, senses, etc.). —**притупля́ться,** *refl.* **1,** to become dull. **2,** *fig.* to fade; wane.
притуши́ть *v. pfv.* [*infl.* **-тушу́, -ту́шишь**] *colloq.* **1,** to put out; extinguish. **2,** to dim (lights).
при́тча *n.* **1,** parable. **2,** *in exclamations, colloq.* strange thing: что за при́тча!, what a strange thing! —**при́тча во язы́цех,** the talk of the town.
притяга́тельный *adj.* attractive; magnetic.
притя́гивать *v. impfv.* [*pfv.* **притяну́ть**] **1,** to pull in (a boat). **2,** to attract; draw. **3,** *colloq.* to summon: притяну́ть к отве́ту, to call to account. —**притя́нутый за́ волосы,** farfetched.
притяжа́тельный *adj., gram.* possessive.
притяже́ние *n.* attraction; gravitation; gravity.
притяза́ние *n.* (*with* **на** + *acc.*) claim (to).
притяза́тельный *adj.* demanding; exacting.

притянýть [*infl.* **-тянý, -тя́нешь**] *v., pfv. of* **притя́гивать.**

приукрáшивать *v. impfv.* [*pfv.* **приукрáсить**] *colloq.* **1,** to decorate; spruce up; brighten up. **2,** to embellish (a story, an account, etc.). —**приукрáшиваться,** *refl., colloq.* to spruce up.

приурóчивать *v. impfv.* [*pfv.* **приурóчить**] (*with* **к**) to time (for); time to coincide (with).

приучáть *v. impfv.* [*pfv.* **приучи́ть**] (*with* **к** *or inf.*) **1,** to teach (to); train (to). **2,** to inure (to). —**приучáться,** *refl.* (*with* **к** *or inf.*) **1,** to train oneself (to). **2,** to get used to.

приучи́ть [*infl.* **-учý, -ýчишь**] *v., pfv. of* **приучáть.** —**приучи́ться,** *refl., pfv. of* **приучáться.**

прифронтовóй *adj., mil.* forward; front-line. —**прифронтовáя полосá,** forward area.

прихвáрывать *v. impfv.* [*pfv.* **прихворнýть**] *colloq.* to be ailing; be unwell.

прихвастнýть *v. pfv., colloq.* to brag a little; boast a little.

прихвати́ть [*infl.* **-хвачý, -хвáтишь**] *v., pfv. of* **прихвáтывать.**

прихвáтывать *v. impfv.* [*pfv.* **прихвати́ть**] *colloq.* **1,** to grab; grip. **2,** to take along. **3,** to tie up; fasten. **4,** (*of frost*) to nip; damage.

прихворнýть *v., pfv. of* **прихвáрывать.**

при́хвостень [*gen.* **-тня**] *n.m., colloq.* toady; sycophant.

прихлебáтель *n.m., colloq.* parasite; sponger.

прихлёбывать *v. impfv.* [*pfv.* **прихлебнýть**] *colloq.* to sip.

прихлóпывать *v. impfv.* [*pfv.* **прихлóпнуть**] **1,** to slap; bang. **2,** to slam (shut). **3,** *colloq.* to catch: прихлóпнуть пáлец двéрью, to catch one's finger in a door. **4,** [*impfv. only*] to clap (*in rhythm*).

прихлы́нуть *v. pfv.* to rush; surge.

прихóд *n.* **1,** coming; arrival. **2,** income; receipts. **3,** parish; congregation.

приходи́ть *v. impfv.* [*pfv.* **прийти́;** *pres.* **-хожý, -хóдишь**] **1,** to come; arrive. **2,** (*with* **к**) to come to; arrive at; reach (a decision, conclusion, agreement, etc.). **3,** (*with* **в** + *acc.*) to reach a certain state or condition: приходи́ть в ýжас, to be horrified; приходи́ть в вéтхость, to fall into disrepair. —**приходи́ть в гóлову** (+ *dat.*), to come to mind; occur to. —**приходи́ть в себя́,** to regain consciousness; come to.

приходи́ться *v.r. impfv.* [*pfv.* **прийти́сь;** *pres.* **-хожýсь, -хóдишься**] **1,** (*with* **по**) to fit: сапоги́ пришли́сь по ногé, the shoes fitted well. **2,** (*with* **по**) (*of a blow or flying object*) to land (on); fall (on). **3,** (*with* **на** + *acc.*) to fall (*on a certain date*). **4,** *impers.* (*with dat. and inf.*) to have to: емý придётся подождáть, he will have to wait. **5,** *impers.* (*with dat. and inf.*) to happen to; have occasion to: мне чáсто приходи́лось (+ *inf.*), I frequently had occasion to... Удивля́ться не прихóдится, one should not (*or* there is no reason to) be surprised. **6,** *impers.* (*with dat. and adverb*) to have a certain time of it: емý пришлóсь тяжелó *or* нелегкó, he has had a hard time of it. **7,** *impers.* (*with* **на** + *acc.*) to number; account for: на кáждую жéнщину приходи́лось по трóе мужчи́н, there were three men for every woman. Чéтверть всегó э́кспорта прихóдится на нефть, oil accounts for one-fourth of all exports. **8,** *impers.* to be due: на кáждого пришлóсь по рублю́, each person had to pay a ruble. С вас прихóдится пять рублéй, you owe five rubles. **9,** [*impfv. only*] to be related in a certain way: кем он вам прихóдится?, how is he related to you? **10,** *in* приходи́ться по вкýсу (+ *dat.*), to be to someone's taste; приходи́ться по душé (+ *dat.*), to suit; please; be to one's liking. —**где придётся,** wherever one can. —**как придётся,** in whatever way one can. —**чем придётся,** with whatever happens to be on hand.

прихóдный *adj.* receipts (*attrib.*): прихóдная кни́га, receipts book.

прихóдовать *v. impfv.* [*pfv.* **заприхóдовать;** *pres.* **-дую, -дуешь**] *bookkeeping* to credit (*enter on the credit side of the ledger*).

прихóдо-расхóдный *adj., in* **прихóдо-расхóдная кни́га,** receipts and disbursements book.

прихóдский *adj.* parish (*attrib.*). —**прихóдская шкóла,** parochial school.

прихожáнин [*pl.* **-жáне, -жáн**] *n.m.* [*fem.* **-жáнка**] parishioner.

прихóжая *n., decl. as an adj.* vestibule; hall.

прихорáшивать *v. impfv., colloq.* to spruce up; doll up. —**прихорáшиваться,** *refl., colloq.* to spruce up.

прихотли́вый *adj.* **1,** (*of a person*) whimsical; capricious. **2,** (*of a design*) quaint; intricate. **3,** (*of a dream*) fanciful.

при́хоть *n.f.* whim; whimsy; caprice.

прихрáмывать *v. impfv.* to limp slightly.

прицéл *n.* sight (*on a gun*). —**взять на прицéл,** to take aim at; draw a bead on.

прицéливание *n.* aiming (*of a weapon*).

прицéливаться *v.r. impfv.* [*pfv.* **прицéлиться**] **1,** to take aim. **2,** (*with* **в** + *acc.*) to aim (at).

прицéльный *adj.* **1,** aiming; sighting: прицéльное приспособлéние, sighting device. **2,** aimed: прицéльный огóнь, aimed fire.

прицéниваться *v.r. impfv.* [*pfv.* **прицени́ться**] (*with* **к**) *colloq.* to ask the price of.

прицени́ться [*infl.* **-ценю́сь, -цéнишься**] *v.r., pfv. of* **прицéниваться.**

прицéп *n.* trailer.

прицепи́ть [*infl.* **-цеплю́, -цéпишь**] *v., pfv. of* **прицепля́ть.** —**прицепи́ться,** *refl., pfv. of* **прицепля́ться.**

прицéпка [*gen. pl.* **-пок**] *n.* **1,** hitching; hooking. **2,** *colloq.* cavil; quibble.

прицепля́ть *v. impfv.* [*pfv.* **прицепи́ть**] (*with* **к**) **1,** to hitch (to); hook (to). **2,** *colloq.* to pin (to). —**прицепля́ться,** *refl.* (*with* **к**) **1,** to be hitched (to); hook (onto). **2,** to stick (to); cling (to). **3,** *fig., colloq.* to join. **4,** *fig., colloq.* to attach oneself to. **5,** *fig., colloq.* to pick on.

прицепнóй *adj.* towed; that needs to be towed.

причáл *n.* **1,** mooring; moorage. **2,** mooring line. **3,** berth (*at a pier*).

причáливать *v. impfv.* [*pfv.* **причáлить**] **1,** *v.t.* to moor. **2,** *v.i.* (*with* **к**) to tie up (at).

причáльный *adj.* mooring (*attrib.*): причáльный канáт, mooring line.

причáстие *n.* **1,** *gram.* participle. **2,** *relig.* communion; Eucharist.

причасти́ть [*infl.* **-щý, -сти́шь**] *v., pfv. of* **причащáть.** —**причасти́ться,** *refl., pfv. of* **причащáться.**

причáстный *adj.* **1,** (*with* **к**) involved (in); being a party to; connected (with); concerned (with). **2,** *gram.* participial. —**причáстность,** *n.f.* involvement.

причащáть *v. impfv.* [*pfv.* **причастúть**] to give communion to. —**причащáться**, *refl.* to receive communion.

причём *conj.* **1**, in which connection. **2**, at that. ♦*Often not translated:* супрýги развелúсь, причём сын остáлся у отцá, the couple was divorced, the son remaining with the father.

причесáть [*infl.* **-чешý, -чéшешь**] *v., pfv. of* **причёсывать.** —**причесáться**, *refl., pfv. of* **причёсываться.**

причёска [*gen. pl.* **-сок**] *n.* hairdo.

причёсывать *v. impfv.* [*pfv.* **причесáть**] to comb. —**причёсываться**, *refl.* **1**, to comb one's hair. **2**, to have one's hair done.

причúна *n.* **1**, cause. **2**, reason: по э́той причúне, for this reason. —**безо вся́кой причúны**, for no reason whatever.

причинúть *v., pfv. of* **причиня́ть.**

причúнный *adj.* causal; causative. —**причúнность**, *n.f.* causality.

причиня́ть *v. impfv.* [*pfv.* **причинúть**] to cause: причиня́ть вред (+ *dat.*), to cause damage to.

причисля́ть *v. impfv.* [*pfv.* **причúслить**] (*with* **к**) **1**, to add (to). **2**, to number (among). —**причисля́ться**, *refl.* (*with* **к**) to belong to.

причитáние *n.* lamentation.

причитáть *v. impfv.* to wail; moan (*in grief*). —**причитáться**, *refl.* **1**, (*with dat.*) to be owed (to); be due (to). **2**, (*with* **с** + *gen.*) to owe; be obliged to pay: с вас причитáется три рубля́, you owe three rubles.

причмóкивать *v. impfv.* [*pfv.* **причмóкнуть**] to smack one's lips. *Also,* **причмóкивать губáми.**

причýда *n.* whim; whimsy; caprice.

причýдливый *adj.* **1**, quaint; intricate. **2**, *colloq.* whimsical; capricious.

пришвартовáть *v., pfv. of* **швартовáть.** —**пришвартовáться**, *refl., pfv. of* **швартовáться.**

пришéлец [*gen.* **-льца**] *n.* newcomer.

пришёптывать *v. impfv.* to whisper.

пришéствие *n.* coming; appearance; advent. —**до вторóго пришéствия**, till doomsday.

пришúбленный *adj., colloq.* crushed; crestfallen.

пришивáть *v. impfv.* [*pfv.* **пришúть**] to sew on.

пришúть [*infl.* **-шью́, -шьёшь**] *v., pfv. of* **пришивáть.**

прúшлый *adj.* having come from somewhere else; newly arrived.

пришпúливать *v. impfv.* [*pfv.* **пришпúлить**] **1**, to pin on. **2**, (*with* **к**) to pin to.

пришпóривать *v. impfv.* [*pfv.* **пришпóрить**] **1**, to spur (a horse). **2**, *fig., colloq.* to spur on; urge on.

прищёлкивать *v. impfv.* [*pfv.* **прищёлкнуть**] (*with instr.*) to snap; crack.

прищемля́ть *v. impfv.* [*pfv.* **прищемúть**] to catch: прищемúть пáлец двéрью, to catch one's finger in a door.

прищéпка [*gen. pl.* **-пок**] *n.* clothespin.

прищýривать *v. impfv.* [*pfv.* **прищýрить**], *in* **прищýривать глазá**, to squint. —**прищýриваться**, *refl.* to squint.

прию́т *n.* **1**, shelter; refuge. **2**, *pre-rev.* orphanage; foundling home.

приютúть *v. pfv.* [*infl.* **-ючý, -ютúшь**] to shelter; give refuge to. —**приютúться**, *refl.* to take shelter.

прия́тель *n.m.* [*fem.* **-ница**] friend. —**прия́тельский**, *adj.* friendly.

прия́тно *adv.* pleasantly. —*adj., used predicatively* pleasant; nice: прия́тно э́то слы́шать, it is nice to hear it. Мне бýдет прия́тно (+ *inf.*), I will be happy to...; it will be a pleasure to...

прия́тный *adj.* [*short form* **-ятен, -ятна**] pleasant; pleasing; nice.

про *prep., with acc.* about: говорúть про дрýга, to talk about a friend. —**про запáс**, *see* **запáс.** —**про себя́**, to oneself: читáть про себя́, to read to oneself.

про- *prefix* **1**, *indicating motion through:* пробирáться сквозь толпý, to make one's way through a crowd. **2**, *indicating motion past:* проéхать мúмо стáнции, to ride past the station. **3**, *indicating thoroughness of an action:* просýшивать, to dry thoroughly. **4**, *indicating failure, error, etc.:* проигрáть, to lose; промахнýться, to miss; провалúться, to fail; просчитáться, to miscalculate. **5**, (*with pfv. verbs only*) *indicating action performed over or throughout a certain period of time:* прожúть три гóда за границéй, to live abroad for three years; проспáть всё ýтро, to sleep through the entire morning. **6**, (*with adjectives*) pro-: проамерикáнский, pro-American.

проанализúровать *v., pfv. of* **анализúровать.**

прóба *n.* **1**, test; trial. **2**, sample. **3**, a unit of fineness of precious metals based on 96 parts for pure metals: зóлото пятьдеся́т шестóй прóбы, 14-karat gold. **4**, hallmark (*of precious metals*). —**высóкой/вы́сшей прóбы**, of a high/the highest/ order. —**нúзкой** *or* **нúзшей прóбы**, of the worst type.

пробавля́ться *v.r. impfv.* (*with instr.*) *colloq.* to get along (on); subsist (on).

пробáлтывать *v. impfv.* [*pfv.* **проболтáть**] *colloq.* to blab; blurt out; let out. —**пробáлтываться**, *refl., colloq.* to shoot off one's mouth; let the cat out of the bag; spill the beans.

пробéг *n.* **1**, run. **2**, race. —**прóбный пробéг**, test run; road test.

пробéгать *v. pfv.* to run (*for a certain length of time*).

пробегáть *v. impfv.* [*pfv.* **пробежáть**] **1**, to run; (*with* **по**) run along; run down; (*with* **чéрез**) run through; (*with* **мúмо**) run past. **2**, (*with* **по**) to pass over; sweep over. **3**, (*with instr. and* **по**) to run (something over something): пробежáть пáльцами по клавиатýре, to run one's fingers over the keyboard. **4**, to glance over; run through; scan.

пробежáть [*infl. like* **бежáть**] *v., pfv. of* **пробегáть.** —**пробежáться**, *refl.* (*with* **по**) to run about; race about.

пробéжка [*gen. pl.* **-жек**] *n.* run.

пробéл *n.* **1**, blank space; blank. **2**, *fig.* gap: пробéлы в знáниях, gaps in one's knowledge.

пробивáть *v. impfv.* [*pfv.* **пробúть**] **1**, to make a hole in; pierce. **2**, to break through; breach. **3**, to make (a hole). **4**, *colloq.* to lay (a road); clear (a path). —**пробивáть себé дорóгу**, **1**, to force one's way through. **2**, *fig.* to make one's way in the world.

пробивáться *v.r. impfv.* [*pfv.* **пробúться**] **1**, (*with* **к, сквозь** *or* **чéрез**) to force one's way (to *or* through); break through (to). **2**, (*with* **в** + *acc. or* **сквозь**) to seep through; filter through. **3**, (*of plants, hair, etc.*) to push through; come out; appear.

пробивнóй *adj., colloq.* aggressive; pushy.

пробирáть *v. impfv.* [*pfv.* **пробрáть**] *colloq.* **1**, (*of cold*) to penetrate; (*of fear*) to seize. **2**, to bawl out.

—**пробира́ться,** *refl.* **1,** to make one's way. **2,** to sneak; steal (into *or* through).
проби́рка [*gen. pl.* **-рок**] *n.* test tube.
проби́рный *adj.* pert. to the analyzing of precious metals. —**проби́рный ка́мень,** touchstone.
проби́ть [*infl.* **-бью́, -бьёшь**] *v., pfv. of* **бить** *and* **пробива́ть.** —**проби́ться,** *refl., pfv. of* **пробива́ться.**
про́бка [*gen. pl.* **-бок**] *n.* **1,** cork. **2,** plug; stopper. **3,** *fig.* jam; congestion. **4,** fuse. —**глуп как про́бка,** dumb as they come.
про́бковый *adj.* cork (*attrib.*). —**про́бковый по́яс,** life belt.
пробле́ма *n.* problem.
проблема́тика *n.* problems. —**проблемати́ческий; проблемати́чный,** *adj.* problematic(al).
про́блеск *n.* **1,** flash; gleam. **2,** *fig.* glimmer (*of hope*).
проблужда́ть *v. pfv.* to wander (*for a certain length of time*).
про́бный *adj.* **1,** test (*attrib.*); trial (*attrib.*). **2,** sample (*attrib.*). —**про́бный ка́мень,** touchstone. —**про́бный шар,** trial balloon.
про́бовать *v. impfv.* [*pfv.* **попро́бовать;** *pres.* **-бую, -буешь**] **1,** to try. **2,** to test. **3,** to taste.
прободе́ние *n., med.* perforation. —**прободно́й,** *adj., med.* perforated: прободна́я я́зва, perforated ulcer.
пробо́ина *n.* hole; breach.
пробо́й *n.* hasp.
проболе́ть *v. pfv.* **1,** [*infl.* **-е́ю, -е́ешь**] to be ill (*for a certain length of time*). **2,** [*infl.* **-ли́т**] to hurt (*for a certain length of time*).
проболта́ть *v. pfv.* **1,** *pfv. of* **проба́лтывать. 2,** (*of two people*) to talk (*for a certain length of time*). —**проболта́ться,** *refl., pfv. of* **проба́лтываться.**
пробо́р *n.* part (*in one's hair*).
пробормота́ть *v., pfv. of* **бормота́ть.**
про́бочник *n., colloq.* corkscrew.
пробра́ть [*infl. like* **брать**] *v., pfv. of* **пробира́ть.** —**пробра́ться,** *refl., pfv. of* **пробира́ться.**
пробро́дить *v. pfv.* [*infl.* **-брожу́, -бро́дишь**] to wander (*for a certain length of time*).
пробубни́ть *v., pfv. of* **бубни́ть.**
пробуди́ть *v. pfv.* **1,** [*infl.* **-бужу́, -бу́дишь**] *pfv. of* **пробужда́ть** (*in sense #1*). **2,** [*infl.* **-бужу́, -буди́шь**] *pfv. of* **буди́ть** (*in sense #2*) *and* **пробужда́ть** (*in sense #2*). —**пробуди́ться,** *refl., pfv. of* **пробужда́ться.**
пробужда́ть *v. impfv.* [*pfv.* **пробуди́ть**] **1,** to wake up; awaken. **2,** *fig.* to rouse; arouse. —**пробужда́ться,** *refl.* **1,** to wake up. **2,** *fig.* to be aroused; be awakened.
пробужде́ние *n.* awakening.
пробура́вить *v., pfv. of* **бура́вить.**
пробури́ть *v., pfv. of* **бури́ть.**
пробурча́ть *v., pfv. of* **бурча́ть.**
пробы́ть *v. pfv.* [*infl.* **-бу́ду, -бу́дешь;** *past* **про́был, пробыла́, про́было**] to stay (*for a certain length of time*); spend (*a certain amount of time*).
прова́л *n.* **1,** collapse; cave-in. **2,** depression; hole. **3,** failure. **4,** exposure (*of illegal activity*). **5,** lapse: прова́л па́мяти, lapse of memory.
прова́ливать *v. impfv.* [*pfv.* **провали́ть**] **1,** to cause to collapse; cause to cave in. **2,** *fig., colloq.* to ruin; make a mess of. **3,** *fig., colloq.* to fail (a student). **4,** *fig., colloq.* to reject.—**прова́ливаться,** *refl.* **1,** (*with* **в** + *acc.*) to fall (into). **2,** to collapse; cave in; come tumbling down. **3,** to fail. **4,** *colloq.* to disappear. **5,** *in* **как сквозь зе́млю провали́ться,** to vanish into thin air.
провали́ть [*infl.* **-валю́, -ва́лишь**] *v., pfv. of* **прова́ливать.** —**провали́ться,** *refl., pfv. of* **прова́ливаться.**
прованса́ль *n.m.* mayonnaise. —**капу́ста прованса́ль,** pickled cabbage with a dressing added.
прова́нский *adj., in* **прова́нское ма́сло,** olive oil.
прова́ривать *v. impfv.* [*pfv.* **провари́ть**] to boil thoroughly; cook thoroughly.
провари́ть [*infl.* **-варю́, -ва́ришь**] *v., pfv. of* **прова́ривать.**
прове́дать *v., pfv. of* **прове́дывать.**
проведе́ние *n.* **1,** guiding; conducting. **2,** building; construction. **3,** installation. **4,** conducting; carrying out; holding.
прове́дывать *v. impfv.* [*pfv.* **прове́дать**] *colloq.* **1,** to call on; pay a visit on. **2,** to find out; learn.
провезти́ [*infl. like* **везти́**] *v., pfv. of* **провози́ть.**
провентили́ровать *v., pfv. of* **вентили́ровать.**
прове́ренный *adj.* tested; of proven ability.
прове́рить *v., pfv. of* **проверя́ть.**
прове́рка [*gen. pl.* **-рок**] *n.* **1,** check; checking. **2,** verification. **3,** testing.
провернуть *v., pfv. of* **провёртывать.**
прове́рочный *adj.* **1,** control (*attrib.*). **2,** test (*attrib.*): прове́рочная рабо́та, test paper (*in school*).
провёртывать *v. impfv.* [*pfv.* **проверну́ть**] *colloq.* **1,** to drill; bore (a hole). **2,** to drill a hole in.
проверя́ть *v. impfv.* [*pfv.* **прове́рить**] **1,** to check. **2,** to test.
провести́ *v. pfv.* [*infl. like* **вести́**] **1,** *pfv. of* **проводи́ть**². **2,** *colloq.* to trick; take in.
прове́тривание *n.* ventilation.
прове́тривать *v. impfv.* [*pfv.* **прове́трить**] to air out; ventilate. —**прове́триваться,** *refl.* **1,** to be aired out. **2,** *colloq.* to get some fresh air.
прове́ять *v., pfv. of* **ве́ять** (*in sense #4*).
прови́дение *n.* foresight; vision.
провиде́ние *n., relig.* Providence. —**провиденциа́льный,** *adj.* providential.
прови́деть *v. impfv.* [*pres.* **-ви́жу, -ви́дишь**] to foresee.
прови́дец [*gen.* **-дца**] *n.* prophet; seer.
прови́зия *n.* food; provisions.
прови́зор *n.* pharmacist.
провини́ться *v.r. pfv.* (*with* **в** + *prepl.*) to be guilty (of); do (something) wrong.
прови́нность *n.f., colloq.* **1,** fault. **2,** misdeed.
провинциа́л *n.* a provincial; hick. —**провинциали́зм,** *n.* provincialism. —**провинциа́льный,** *adj.* provincial.
прови́нция *n.* **1,** province. **2,** the provinces.
провиса́ть *v. impfv.* [*pfv.* **прови́снуть**] to be weighed down; sag.
прови́снуть [*past* **-ви́с, -ла**] *v., pfv. of* **провиса́ть.**
про́вод [*pl.* **провода́**] *n.* **1,** wire. **2,** (telephone) line: прямо́й про́вод, direct line. —**быть на про́воде,** to be calling; be on the line.
проводи́мость *n.f.* conductivity.
проводи́ть¹ [*infl.* **-вожу́, -во́дишь**] *v., pfv. of* **провожа́ть.**
проводи́ть² *v. impfv.* [*pfv.* **провести́;** *pres.* **-вожу́, -во́дишь**] **1,** to lead; guide; conduct; take; steer. **2,** (*with instr. and* **по**) to run (one's hand, fingers, etc.) over the surface of. **3,** to build; construct (a railroad,

canal, etc.). **4,** to install (a telephone, electricity, etc.). **5,** to conduct (a meeting, investigation, etc.); carry out (reforms); hold (elections). **6,** to spend (time). Хорошо́ провести́ вре́мя, to have a good time. **7,** to draw (a line, boundary, etc.). **8,** to draw; make (a distinction, comparison, etc.). **9,** to get (a proposal, bill, etc.) through. **10,** [*impfv. only*] to conduct (electricity, heat, etc.). —**провести́ в жизнь,** to put into practice; make a reality of. *See also* **провести́.**

прово́дка *n.* **1,** guiding; conducting. **2,** building; construction. **3,** installation. **4,** wiring.

проводни́к [*gen.* **-ника́**] *n.* **1,** guide. **2,** conductor (*on a train*). **3,** *physics* conductor.

про́воды [*gen.* **-дов**] *n. pl.* send-off.

провожа́тый *n., decl. as an adj.* guide; escort.

провожа́ть *v. impfv.* [*pfv.* **проводи́ть**] **1,** to accompany. **2,** (*with* **в** *or* **на** + *acc.*) to see (someone) off (at). **3,** (*with* **до**) to walk to; see to: проводи́ть (кого́-нибудь) до гости́ницы/две́ри, to walk (someone) to the hotel; see to the door. **4,** to send off (to the army, war, etc.). **5,** to follow (*with one's eyes*).

прово́з *n.* **1,** transport; delivery. **2,** smuggling in. —**пла́та за прово́з,** freight charges; carrying charges.

провозгласи́ть [*infl.* **-шу́, -си́шь**] *v., pfv. of* **провозглаша́ть.**

провозглаша́ть *v. impfv.* [*pfv.* **провозгласи́ть**] **1,** to proclaim. **2,** to propose (a toast).

провозглаше́ние *n.* proclamation.

провози́ть[1] *v. impfv.* [*pfv.* **провезти́**; *pres.* **-вожу́, -во́зишь**] **1,** to transport; convey. **2,** to smuggle (in).

провози́ть[2] *v. pfv.* [*infl.* **-вожу́, -во́зишь**] to convey; carry; deliver (*for a certain length of time*). —**провози́ться,** *refl.* (*with* **с** + *instr.*) to be busy with; concern oneself with (*for a certain length of time*).

провока́тор *n.* **1,** agent provocateur. **2,** instigator.

провока́ция *n.* provocation. —**провокацио́нный,** *adj.* provocative.

про́волока *n.* wire. —**колю́чая про́волока,** barbed wire.

про́волочка [*gen. pl.* **-чек**] *n.* **1,** short piece of wire. **2,** fine wire.

проволо́чка [*gen. pl.* **-чек**] *n., colloq.* delay.

про́волочный *adj.* wire (*attrib.*).

провоня́ть *v. pfv., colloq.* **1,** *v.i.* to smell; stink. **2,** *v.t.* to smell up; stink up.

прово́рный *adj.* **1,** agile; nimble; adroit; dexterous. **2,** quick; swift; brisk.

проворова́ться *v.r. pfv.* [*infl.* **-ру́юсь, -ру́ешься**] *colloq.* to be caught stealing.

прово́рство *n.* **1,** agility; dexterity. **2,** promptness.

проворча́ть *v. pfv.* [*infl.* **-чу́, -чи́шь**] to mumble; grumble.

провоци́ровать *v. impfv. & pfv.* [*pfv. also* **спровоци́ровать;** *pres.* **-рую, -руешь**] to provoke.

провы́ть *v. pfv.* [*infl.* **-во́ю, -во́ешь**] to howl; wail.

провя́лить *v., pfv. of* **вя́лить.**

прога́дывать *v. impfv.* [*pfv.* **прогада́ть**] *colloq.* to miscalculate.

прога́лина *n., colloq.* **1,** clearing; glade. **2,** space; gap.

проги́б *n.* sagging; sag.

прогиба́ть *v. impfv.* [*pfv.* **прогну́ть**] to bend; weigh down; cause to sag. —**прогиба́ться,** *refl.* to bend; sag.

прогла́дить *v. pfv.* [*infl.* **-жу, -дишь**] **1,** *pfv. of* **прогла́живать. 2,** to iron (*for a certain length of time*).

прогла́живать *v. impfv.* [*pfv.* **прогла́дить**] to iron.

прогла́тывать *v. impfv.* [*pfv.* **проглоти́ть**] to swallow. —**проглоти́ть язы́к,** to keep quiet; hold one's tongue. —**язы́к проглóтишь,** it will make your mouth water.

проглоти́ть [*infl.* **-глочу́, -гло́тишь**] *v., pfv. of* **прогла́тывать.**

прогляде́ть *v. pfv.* [*infl.* **-жу́, -ди́шь**] **1,** *pfv. of* **прогля́дывать** (*in sense #1*). **2,** to overlook. **3,** to gaze at; stare at (*for a certain length of time*).

прогля́дывать *v. impfv.* **1,** [*pfv.* **прогляде́ть**] *colloq.* to look over; skim; scan. **2,** [*pfv.* **прогляну́ть**] to appear; come partly into view; peep.

прогляну́ть [*infl.* **-гляну́, -гля́нешь**] *v., pfv. of* **прогля́дывать** (*in sense #2*).

прогна́ть [*infl. like* **гнать**] *v., pfv. of* **прогоня́ть.**

прогнива́ть *v. impfv.* [*pfv.* **прогни́ть**] to rot through.

прогни́ть [*infl. like* **гнить**] *v., pfv. of* **прогнива́ть.**

прогно́з *n.* prognosis; forecast.

прогну́ть *v., pfv. of* **прогиба́ть.** —**прогну́ться,** *refl., pfv. of* **прогиба́ться.**

прогова́ривать *v. impfv.* [*pfv.* **проговори́ть**] to say; utter. —**прогова́риваться,** *refl.* to let the cat out of the bag; spill the beans.

проговори́ть *v. pfv.* **1,** *pfv. of* **прогова́ривать. 2,** to talk; converse (*for a certain length of time*). —**проговори́ться,** *refl., pfv. of* **прогова́риваться.**

проголода́ться *v.r. pfv.* to be hungry; get hungry.

проголосова́ть *v., pfv. of* **голосова́ть.**

прого́н *n.* **1,** driving (*of animals*). **2,** girder. **3,** stairwell.

прогоня́ть *v. impfv.* [*pfv.* **прогна́ть**] **1,** to drive (animals). **2,** to drive away; chase away. **3,** *fig., colloq.* to dispel. **4,** *colloq.* to fire; dismiss.

прогора́ть *v. impfv.* [*pfv.* **прогоре́ть**] **1,** (*of wood*) to be burned completely. **2,** to be damaged (*by fire*). **3,** *fig., colloq.* to go bankrupt; go broke.

прого́рклый *adj.* rancid.

прого́ркнуть [*past* **-го́рк, -ла**] *v., pfv. of* **го́ркнуть.**

програ́мма *n.* **1,** program. **2,** syllabus.

программи́рование *n.* (computer) programming.

программи́ровать *v. impfv.* [*pfv.* **запрограмми́ровать;** *pres.* **-рую, -руешь**] to program.

программи́ст *n.* (computer) programmer.

програ́ммный *adj.* **1,** program (*attrib.*): програ́ммная му́зыка, program music. **2,** programmed.

прогрева́ть *v. impfv.* [*pfv.* **прогре́ть**] to warm up; make warm. —**прогрева́ться,** *refl.* to warm up; become warm.

прогреме́ть *v. pfv.* [*infl.* **-млю́, -ми́шь**] to thunder; ring out.

прогре́сс *n.* progress.

прогресси́вный *adj.* progressive.

прогресси́ровать *v. impfv.* [*pres.* **-рую, -руешь**] **1,** to progress; make progress. **2,** (*of an illness*) to grow progressively worse.

прогре́ссия *n., math.* progression.

прогре́ть *v., pfv. of* **прогрева́ть.** —**прогре́ться,** *refl., pfv. of* **прогрева́ться.**

прогрыза́ть *v. impfv.* [*pfv.* **прогры́зть**] to gnaw through.

прогры́зть [*infl. like* **грызть**] *v., pfv. of* **прогрыза́ть.**

прогуде́ть *v. pfv.* [*infl.* **-жу́, -ди́шь**] **1,** to buzz; hum; drone. **2,** (*of a horn or factory whistle*) to sound; blow.

прогу́л *n.* unexcused absence from work or school; truancy.

прогу́ливать *v. impfv.* [*pfv.* **прогуля́ть**] **1,** to miss;

fail to show up for: прогу́ливать уро́ки, to play hooky; play truant. **2,** [*impfv. only*] to walk; take for a walk. —**прогу́ливаться,** *refl.* to take a walk; go for a stroll.

прогу́лка [*gen. pl.* **-лок**] *n.* **1,** walk; stroll. **2,** outing; ride; drive.

прогу́лочный *adj.* excursion (*attrib.*); pleasure (*attrib.*). —**прогу́лочная па́луба,** promenade deck. —**прогу́лочный шаг,** leisurely pace.

прогу́льщик *n.* **1,** shirker. **2,** truant.

прогуля́ть *v. pfv.* **1,** *pfv. of* **прогу́ливать. 2,** to walk; stroll (*for a certain length of time*). —**прогуля́ться,** *refl., pfv. of* **прогу́ливаться.**

продава́ть *v. impfv.* [*pfv.* **прода́ть;** *pres.* **-даю́, -даёшь**] **1,** to sell. **2,** to sell out; betray. —**продава́ться,** *refl.* **1,** [*impfv. only*] to sell; be selling (*well, poorly, etc.*). **2,** [*impfv. only*] to be for sale. **3,** to sell oneself. **4,** to be a traitor; (*with dat.*) sell out to.

продаве́ц [*gen.* **-вца́**] *n.* seller; salesman; salesperson.

продави́ть [*infl.* **-давлю́, -да́вишь**] *v., pfv. of* **прода́вливать.**

прода́вливать *v. impfv.* [*pfv.* **продави́ть**] to bend in; cause to sag in the middle.

продавщи́ца *n.* saleslady; salesgirl.

прода́жа *n.* sale. —**в прода́же,** in stock; available. —**нет в прода́же,** out of stock; not on sale.

прода́жность *n.f.* corruption; venality.

прода́жный *adj.* **1,** sale (*attrib.*); selling (*attrib.*): прода́жная цена́, selling price. **2,** for sale. **3,** corrupt; venal. —**прода́жная же́нщина,** prostitute.

прода́ть [*infl. like* **дать;** *past* **про́дал, продала́, про́дало**] *v., pfv. of* **продава́ть.** —**прода́ться,** *refl.* [*past* **прода́лся, -ла́сь, -ло́сь**] *pfv. of* **продава́ться.**

продвига́ть *v. impfv.* [*pfv.* **продви́нуть**] **1,** to move (something) forward. **2,** (*with* **к**) to move toward; (*with* **че́рез**) move through. **3,** to promote; advance. **4,** *colloq.* to move along; expedite. —**продвига́ться,** *refl.* **1,** to move forward; move ahead; advance. **2,** *fig.* to advance; move up. **3,** *colloq.* to move along; make progress.

продвиже́ние *n.* **1,** movement. **2,** advancement; promotion.

продви́нутый *adj.* advanced.

продви́нуть *v., pfv. of* **продвига́ть.** —**продви́нуться,** *refl., pfv. of* **продвига́ться.**

продева́ть *v. impfv.* [*pfv.* **проде́ть**] to pass through: продева́ть ни́тку в иго́лку, to thread a needle.

продеклами́ровать *v., pfv. of* **деклами́ровать.**

проде́лать *v., pfv. of* **проде́лывать.**

проде́лка [*gen. pl.* **-лок**] *n.* prank; trick.

проде́лывать *v. impfv.* [*pfv.* **проде́лать**] **1,** to make (a hole). **2,** to do; perform. **3,** to play (a trick).

продемонстри́ровать *v. pfv.* [*infl.* **-рую, -руешь**] to demonstrate; display; show.

продёргивать *v. impfv.* [*pfv.* **продёрнуть**] *colloq.* to pass through: продёргивать ни́тку в иго́лку, to thread a needle.

продержа́ть *v. pfv.* [*infl.* **-держу́, -де́ржишь**] to hold; keep (*for a certain length of time*). —**продержа́ться,** *refl.* **1,** to remain (*in a certain position*). **2,** to last. **3,** to hold out.

продёрнуть *v., pfv. of* **продёргивать.**

проде́ть [*infl.* **-де́ну, -де́нешь**] *v., pfv. of* **продева́ть.**

продешеви́ть *v. pfv.* [*infl.* **-влю́, -ви́шь**] to sell (something) cheap.

продиктова́ть *v., pfv. of* **диктова́ть.**

продира́ть *v. impfv.* [*pfv.* **продра́ть**] *colloq.* to tear; wear through. —**продира́ться,** *refl., colloq.* **1,** to be torn; be worn through. **2,** to make one's way; force one's way.

продлева́ть *v. impfv.* [*pfv.* **продли́ть**] to prolong; extend.

продле́ние *n.* extension; prolongation.

продли́ть *v., pfv. of* **продлева́ть.** —**продли́ться,** *refl., pfv. of* **дли́ться.**

продово́льственный *adj.* food (*attrib.*). —**продово́льственный магази́н,** grocery store. —**продово́льственные това́ры,** foodstuffs.

продово́льствие *n.* food; provisions.

продолби́ть *v., pfv. of* **долби́ть** (*in sense #1*).

продолгова́тый *adj.* oblong.

продолжа́тель *n.m.* continuer.

продолжа́ть *v. impfv.* [*pfv.* **продо́лжить**] **1,** [*usu. impfv.*] to continue. **2,** [*usu. pfv.*] to extend; prolong. —**продолжа́ться,** *refl.* to last; continue; go on.

продолже́ние *n.* **1,** continuation. **2,** sequel. —**в продолже́ние** (+ *gen.*), during; in the course of. —**продолже́ние сле́дует,** to be continued.

продолжи́тельность *n.f.* length; duration. —**продолжи́тельность жи́зни,** life expectancy.

продолжи́тельный *adj.* prolonged; long.

продо́лжить *v., pfv. of* **продолжа́ть.** —**продо́лжиться,** *refl., pfv. of* **продолжа́ться.**

продо́льный *adj.* **1,** longitudinal. **2,** *naut.* fore-and-aft. —**продо́льная пила́,** ripsaw.

продохну́ть *v. pfv., colloq.* to take a deep breath. —**не** (*or* **нельзя́**) **продохну́ть,** it's impossible to breathe.

продра́ть [*infl. like* **драть**] *v., pfv. of* **продира́ть.** —**продра́ться,** *refl., pfv. of* **продира́ться.**

продро́гнуть *v. pfv.* [*past* **-дро́г, -ла**] to be chilled to the bone.

продува́ть *v. impfv.* [*pfv.* **проду́ть**] **1,** to blow out; clean out by blowing. **2,** [*impfv. only*] (*of a wind, draft, etc.*) *colloq.* to blow through. **3,** *impers.* to be chilled through (*by the wind*): меня́ проду́ло, I am chilled (from the wind).

продувно́й *adj., colloq.* sly; crafty.

проду́кт *n.* **1,** product. **2,** *pl.* food products; groceries: моло́чные проду́кты, dairy products; заморо́женные проду́кты, frozen food(s).

продукти́вный *adj.* productive. —**продукти́вность,** *n.f.* productivity.

продукто́вый *adj.* food (*attrib.*). —**продукто́вый магази́н,** grocery store.

проду́кция *n.* production; output.

проду́манный *adj.* considered; carefully thought out.

проду́мывать *v. impfv.* [*pfv.* **проду́мать**] to think out; think through.

проду́ть [*infl.* **-ду́ю, -ду́ешь**] *v., pfv. of* **продува́ть.**

продыря́вливать *v. impfv.* [*pfv.* **продыря́вить**] *colloq.* **1,** to make a hole in. **2,** to wear holes in. —**продыря́вливаться,** *refl., colloq.* to develop holes; become full of holes.

продю́сер (сэ) *n.* producer (*of a motion picture*).

проеда́ть *v. impfv.* [*pfv.* **прое́сть**] **1,** to eat away; corrode. **2,** *colloq.* to spend (one's money) on food.

прое́зд *n.* **1,** passage; getting across: туда́ нет прое́зда, you cannot get there; there is no way to get there. **2,** trip: де́ньги на прое́зд, money for the trip.

Плáта за проéзд, fare. Скóлько стóит проéзд в...?, what is the fare to...? **3,** passage; passageway. **4,** street; thoroughfare. —**проéздом,** *colloq.* passing through.

проéздить *v. pfv.* [*infl.* **-éзжу, -éздишь**] **1,** to travel (*for a certain length of time*). **2,** *colloq.* to spend (a certain amount of money) on a trip.

проезднóй *adj., in* **проезднáя плáта,** fare; **проезднóй билéт,** ticket.

проезжáть *v. impfv.* [*pfv.* **проéхать**] **1,** to ride; drive (along, through, past, etc.). **2,** (*with* **мúмо**) to pass (by). **3,** to go (right) past (*inadvertently*). **4,** to cover (a certain distance).

проéзжий *adj.* **1,** passing by; passing through. **2,** (*of a road*) fit for traffic; used for traffic. —*n.* person passing through.

проéкт *n.* **1,** project; plan; design. **2,** draft: проéкт резолюции, draft resolution.

проектúровать *v. impfv.* [*pfv.* **спроектúровать;** *pres.* **-рую, -руешь**] **1,** to design. **2,** [*impfv. only*] to plan. **3,** *math.* to project. **4,** to project (*onto a screen*).

проектирóвщик *n.* designer.

проéктный *adj.* **1,** planning (*attrib.*). **2,** planned; projected. —**проéктная мóщность, 1,** planned production capacity (*of a factory*). **2,** rated capacity (*of a machine*).

проéктор *n.* projector.

проекциóнный *adj., in* **проекциóнный фонáрь,** projector.

проéкция *n.* projection.

проём *n.* opening (*for a door, window, etc.*).

проéсть [*infl. like* **есть**] *v., pfv. of* **проедáть.**

проéхать [*infl. like* **éхать**] *v., pfv. of* **проезжáть.** —**проéхаться,** *refl., colloq.* to go for a ride; go for a drive.

прожáренный *adj.* (*of meat*) well-done.

прожáривать *v. impfv.* [*pfv.* **прожáрить**] to roast thoroughly; fry thoroughly.

прождáть *v. pfv.* [*infl. like* **ждать**] to wait (*for a certain length of time*).

прожевáть [*infl.* **-жую, -жуёшь**] *v., pfv. of* **прожёвывать.**

прожёвывать *v. impfv.* [*pfv.* **прожевáть**] to chew well; chew thoroughly.

прожектёр *n.* promoter of impractical schemes.

прожéктор *n.* searchlight; floodlight.

прожéчь [*infl. like* **жечь**] *v., pfv. of* **прожигáть.**

прожжённый *adj., colloq.* arch; arrant; out-and-out.

проживáние *n.* **1,** residing; residence. **2,** squandering.

проживáть *v. impfv.* [*pfv.* **прожúть**] **1,** [*impfv. only*] to live; reside. **2,** to spend; run through (a sum of money).

прожигáть *v. impfv.* [*pfv.* **прожéчь**] **1,** to burn: прожигáть дырý в (+ *prepl.*), to burn a hole in. **2,** to burn through. —**прожигáть жизнь,** to lead a dissolute life.

прожúлка [*gen. pl.* **-лок**] *n.* vein; streak.

прожúтие *n., in* **на прожúтие,** to live on: дéньги на прожúтие, money to live on.

прожúточный *adj., in* **прожúточный мúнимум,** living wage; subsistence wage.

прожúть *v. pfv.* [*infl.* **-живý, -живёшь;** *past* **прóжил, прожилá, прóжило**] **1,** *pfv. of* **проживáть** (*in sense #2*). **2,** to live (*for a certain length of time*).

прожóрливый *adj.* voracious; gluttonous.

прожужжáть *v. pfv.* [*infl.* **-жжý, -жжúшь**] to buzz. —**прожужжáть ýши** (+ *dat.*), to tell (someone) over and over.

прóза *n.* prose.

прозáик *n.* writer of prose.

прозаúческий *adj.* **1,** prose (*attrib.*). **2,** [*also,* **прозáичный**] prosaic. **3,** practical; businesslike.

прозвáние *n.* nickname.

прозвáть [*infl. like* **звать**] *v., pfv. of* **прозывáть.**

прозвенéть *v. pfv.* [*infl.* **-нúт, -нят**] to ring out; resound.

прóзвище *n.* nickname.

прозвонúть *v. pfv.* **1,** (*of a bell*) to ring. **2,** to announce by ringing a bell.

прозвучáть *v., pfv. of* **звучáть.**

прозевáть *v., pfv. of* **зевáть** (*in sense #3*).

прозелúт *n.* proselyte.

прозимовáть *v., pfv. of* **зимовáть.**

прозорлúвый *adj.* sagacious; perspicacious. —**прозорлúвость,** *n.f.* sagacity; perspicacity.

прозрáчный *adj.* **1,** transparent. **2,** (*of water, air, etc.*) clear. **3,** (*of material*) very thin; gauzy. —**прозрáчность,** *n.f.* transparency.

прозревáть *v. impfv.* [*pfv.* **прозрéть**] **1,** to regain one's sight. **2,** *fig.* to see things clearly; see the light.

прозрéние *n.* **1,** recovery of one's sight. **2,** *fig.* insight; discernment.

прозрéть [*infl.* **-зрю, -зрúшь**] *v., pfv. of* **прозревáть.**

прозывáть *v. impfv.* [*pfv.* **прозвáть**] to nickname.

прозябáть *v. impfv.* to vegetate (*lit. & fig.*).

прозябнуть *v. pfv.* [*past* **-зяб, -ла**] *colloq.* to be frozen; be chilled to the bone.

проигрáть *v. pfv.* **1,** *pfv. of* **проúгрывать. 2,** to play (*for a certain length of time*). —**проигрáться,** *refl., pfv. of* **проúгрываться.**

проúгрыватель *n.m.* record player.

проúгрывать *v. impfv.* [*pfv.* **проигрáть**] **1,** to lose. **2,** to gamble away. **3,** *colloq.* to play; perform. —**проúгрываться,** *refl.* to gamble away all one's money.

прóигрыш *n.* **1,** loss; defeat. **2,** losses (*in gambling*). —**быть в прóигрыше,** to be the loser; end up losing.

прóигрышный *adj.* losing.

произведéние *n.* **1,** making (*of something*). **2,** work (*of art or literature*). **3,** *math.* product.

произвестú [*infl. like* **вестú**] *v., pfv. of* **производúть.**

производúтель *n.m.* **1,** producer. **2,** sire. —**производúтель рабóт,** construction superintendent.

производúтельный *adj.* productive. —**производúтельность,** *n.f.* productivity.

производúть *v. impfv.* [*pfv.* **произвестú;** *pres.* **-вожý, -вóдишь**] **1,** [*usu. impfv.*] to produce; manufacture. **2,** to conduct; carry out. **3,** to produce; cause; create. **4,** to make (an impression, calculation, repairs, etc.). **5,** to produce; give birth to. Производúть на свет, to bring into the world. **6,** (*with* **в** + *nom. pl.*) to promote (to): егó произвелú в капитáны, he was promoted to captain.

произвóдный *adj.* derivative. —**произвóдная,** *n., math.* derivative. —**произвóдное,** *n., chem.* derivative.

произвóдственный *adj.* production (*attrib.*); industrial.

произвóдство *n.* **1,** production. **2,** manufacture. **3,** conducting; carrying out. **4,** promotion.

произвóл *n.* **1,** arbitrary rule; tyranny; despotism. **2,** arbitrariness. —**оставлять** *or* **бросáть на произвóл судьбы,** to leave to the mercy of fate.

произво́льный *adj.* **1,** arbitrary. **2,** *physiol.* voluntary. —**произво́льно,** *adv.* arbitrarily.

произнесе́ние *n.* **1,** pronouncing (*of a sentence*). **2,** giving (*of a speech*).

произнести́ [*infl. like* **нести́**] *v., pfv. of* **произноси́ть.**

произноси́ть *v. impfv.* [*pfv.* **произнести́;** *pres.* **-ношу́, -но́сишь**] **1,** to pronounce. **2,** to utter (a word); deliver (a speech, sermon, toast, etc.).

произноше́ние *n.* pronunciation.

произойти́ [*infl.* **-изойдёт;** *past* **-изошёл, -изошла́**] *v., pfv. of* **происходи́ть.**

произраста́ть *v. impfv.* [*pfv.* **произрасти́**] to sprout; spring up.

произрасти́ [*infl. like* **расти́**] *v., pfv. of* **произраста́ть.**

проиллюстри́ровать *v., pfv. of* **иллюстри́ровать.**

проинформи́ровать *v., pfv. of* **информи́ровать.**

про́иски [*gen.* **-сков**] *n. pl.* intrigues; schemes; machinations.

проистека́ть *v. impfv.* [*pfv.* **происте́чь**] (*with* **из** *or* **от**) to arise (out of); stem (from); spring (from); result (from).

происте́чь [*infl. like* **течь**] *v., pfv. of* **проистека́ть.**

происходи́ть *v. impfv.* [*pfv.* **произойти́;** *pres.* **-хожу́, -хо́дишь**] **1,** to happen; occur; take place. **2,** (*with* **от**) to result (from); be the result (of). **3,** (*with* **от**) to be descended (from).

происхожде́ние *n.* **1,** origin. **2,** parentage; descent; extraction; ancestry. Англича́нин по происхожде́нию, of English origin; English by birth.

происше́ствие *n.* incident.

пройдо́ха *n.m. & f., colloq.* sly person; rascal.

про́йма *n.* armhole.

пройти́ [*infl.* **пройду́, пройдёшь;** *past* **прошёл, прошла́, прошло́**] *v., pfv. of* **проходи́ть.** —**пройти́сь,** *refl., pfv. of* **проха́живаться.**

прок [*2nd gen.* **про́ку**] *n., colloq.* use; good: како́й прок в э́том?; что про́ку от э́того?, what's the good of it?

прокажённый *adj.* leprous. —*n.* leper.

прока́за *n.* **1,** leprosy. **2,** prank; trick.

прока́зить *v. impfv.* [*pfv.* **напрока́зить;** *pres.* **-жу, -зишь**] *colloq.* = **прока́зничать.**

прока́зливый *adj., colloq.* mischievous.

прока́зник *n.* mischief-maker; prankster.

прока́зничать *v. impfv.* [*pfv.* **напрока́зничать**] to play pranks; horse around.

прока́лывать *v. impfv.* [*pfv.* **проколо́ть**] to prick; pierce; puncture.

проканите́литься *v.r., pfv. of* **каните́литься.**

прока́пывать *v. impfv.* [*pfv.* **прокопа́ть**] **1,** to dig (a canal, ditch, etc.). **2,** to dig through.

прока́т *n.* **1,** rental. **2,** rolling (*of metal*). **3,** rolled metal.

проката́ть *v., pfv. of* **прока́тывать.**

прокати́ть *v. pfv.* [*infl.* **-качу́, -ка́тишь**] **1,** to roll. **2,** to take for a ride. **3,** *v.i.* to roll by; roll past. **4,** *colloq.* to fail to elect; reject at the polls. **5,** *colloq.* to berate; roundly condemn. —**прокати́ться,** *refl.* **1,** to roll; roll along. **2,** to go for a ride. **3,** (*with* **по**) to sweep across; sweep over.

прока́тка *n.* rolling (*of metal*).

прока́тный *adj.* **1,** for rent; rented; rental (*attrib.*). **2,** of or pert. to the rolling of metal: прока́тный стан, rolling mill. **3,** (*of metal*) rolled.

прока́тывать *v. impfv.* [*pfv.* **проката́ть**] **1,** to roll flat; press. **2,** to roll (metal).

прока́шливаться *v.r. impfv.* [*pfv.* **прока́шляться**] to clear one's throat.

прокипяти́ть *v. pfv.* [*infl.* **-чу́, -ти́шь**] to boil (thoroughly).

проки́снуть [*past* **-ки́с, -ла**] *v., pfv. of* **ки́снуть.**

прокла́дка *n.* **1,** laying (*of a road, pipe, etc.*). **2,** padding. **3,** washer; gasket.

прокла́дывать *v. impfv.* [*pfv.* **проложи́ть**] **1,** to lay; build (a road, pipeline, etc.). **2,** to make; form (a path, trail, etc.). **3,** (*with instr.*) to interlay (with); pack (with). —**прокла́дывать путь, 1,** to blaze a trail. **2,** (*with dat.*) to pave the way (for). —**прокла́дывать себе́ доро́гу,** to make one's way in the world.

проклама́ция *n.* leaflet.

проклами́ровать *v. impfv. & pfv.* [*pres.* **-рую, -руешь**] to proclaim.

прокле́ивать *v. impfv.* [*pfv.* **прокле́ить**] to smear; cover (*with paste or glue*).

проклина́ть *v. impfv.* [*pfv.* **прокля́сть**] to damn; curse.

прокля́сть [*infl.* **-кляну́, -клянёшь;** *past* **про́клял, -кляла́, про́кляло**] *v., pfv. of* **проклина́ть.**

прокля́тие *n.* **1,** curse: налага́ть прокля́тие на, to place a curse on. **2,** damnation; perdition. **3,** curse word; swearword. —*interj.* damn it!; damn it all!

про́клятый *past passive part. of* **прокля́сть:** будь я про́клят (про́клята), е́сли..., I'll be damned if...

прокля́тый *adj.* cursed; damned; accursed.

проко́л *n.* puncture.

проколо́ть [*infl.* **-колю́, -ко́лешь**] *v., pfv. of* **прока́лывать.**

прокомменти́ровать *v. pfv.* [*infl.* **-рую, -руешь**] to comment on; provide commentary on.

прокомпости́ровать *v., pfv. of* **компости́ровать.**

проконспекти́ровать *v., pfv. of* **конспекти́ровать.**

проко́нсул *n.* proconsul.

проконсульти́ровать *v., pfv. of* **консульти́ровать.** —**проконсульти́роваться,** *refl., pfv. of* **консульти́роваться.**

проконтроли́ровать *v., pfv. of* **контроли́ровать.**

прокопа́ть *v., pfv. of* **прока́пывать.**

прокопте́лый *adj., colloq.* sooty; covered with soot.

проко́рм *n.* nourishment; sustenance.

прокорми́ть *v. pfv.* [*infl.* **-кормлю́, -ко́рмишь**] to feed; provide sustenance for. —**прокорми́ться,** *refl., colloq.* **1,** to feed oneself; sustain oneself. **2,** (*with instr.*) to subsist (on).

прокорректи́ровать *v., pfv. of* **корректи́ровать.**

проко́с *n.* swath.

прокра́дываться *v.r. impfv.* [*pfv.* **прокра́сться**] to sneak; steal; creep (into, through, etc.).

прокра́сться [*infl. like* **красть**] *v.r., pfv. of* **прокра́дываться.**

прокрича́ть *v. pfv.* [*infl.* **-чу́, -чи́шь**] **1,** to shout. **2,** *fig.* to trumpet; crow.

прокурату́ра *n.* office of the public prosecutor.

прокуро́р *n.* public prosecutor. —**прокуро́рский,** *adj.* public prosecutor's.

прокуси́ть [*infl.* **-кушу́, -ку́сишь**] *v., pfv. of* **проку́сывать.**

проку́сывать *v. impfv.* [*pfv.* **прокуси́ть**] to bite through.

прокути́ть *v. pfv.* [*infl.* **-кучу́, -ку́тишь**] **1,** *v.t.* to squander; dissipate. **2,** *v.i.* to go on a binge.

прола́мывать *v. impfv.* [*pfv.* **проломи́ть**] **1,** to break through; make a hole in. **2,** to fracture (one's skull). —**прола́мываться,** *refl.* to break; give way.

пролега́ть *v. impfv.* (*of a road*) to lie; run; pass.

пролежа́ть *v. pfv.* [*infl.* **-лежу́, -лежи́шь**] to lie (*for a certain length of time*).

про́лежень [*gen.* **-жня**] *n.m.* bedsore.

пролеза́ть *v. impfv.* [*pfv.* **проле́зть**] **1,** (*with* **сквозь** *or* **че́рез**) to climb through. **2,** (*with* **в** + *acc.*) to fit through; get through; go through. **3,** (*with* **в** + *acc.*) *colloq.* to worm one's way into.

проле́зть [*infl. like* **лезть**] *v., pfv. of* **пролеза́ть.**

пролёт *n.* **1,** flight. **2,** open space. **3,** span (*of a bridge*). **4,** *archit.* bay. **5,** stairwell. **6,** *colloq.* distance between two railway stations.

пролетариа́т *n.* proletariat. —**пролета́рий,** *n.* proletarian; worker. —**пролета́рский,** *adj.* proletarian.

пролета́ть *v. impfv.* [*pfv.* **пролете́ть**] **1,** to fly; (*with* **над**) fly over; (*with* **че́рез**) fly across; (*with* **ми́мо**) fly past. **2,** to fly (a certain distance). **3,** *fig.* (*of time*) to fly by.

пролете́ть [*infl.* **-чу́, -ти́шь**] *v., pfv. of* **пролета́ть.**

пролётка [*gen. pl.* **-ток**] *n.* open carriage.

проли́в *n.* strait; channel.

пролива́ть *v. impfv.* [*pfv.* **проли́ть**] **1,** to spill. **2,** to shed (light, tears, blood, etc.). —**пролива́ться,** *refl.* (*of a liquid*) to spill.

проливно́й *adj.* (*of rain*) driving; torrential.

проли́ть [*infl.* **-лью́, -льёшь;** *past* **про́лил** *or* **проли́л, пролила́, про́лило** *or* **проли́ло**] *v., pfv. of* **пролива́ть.** —**проли́ться,** *refl., pfv. of* **пролива́ться.**

проло́г *n.* prologue.

проложи́ть [*infl.* **-ложу́, -ло́жишь**] *v., pfv. of* **прокла́дывать.**

проло́м *n.* break; breach.

проломи́ть [*infl.* **-ломлю́, -ло́мишь**] *v., pfv. of* **прола́мывать.** —**проломи́ться,** *refl., pfv. of* **прола́мываться.**

прома́зать [*infl.* **-ма́жу, -ма́жешь**] *v., pfv. of* **ма́зать** (*in sense #6*) *and* **прома́зывать.**

прома́зывать *v. impfv.* [*pfv.* **прома́зать**] **1,** to oil; grease. **2,** *colloq.* to miss (*in shooting or games*).

прома́сливать *v. impfv.* [*pfv.* **прома́слить**] to treat with oil.

прома́тывать *v. impfv.* [*pfv.* **промота́ть**] *colloq.* to squander; dissipate.

про́мах *n.* **1,** miss (*in shooting*). **2,** *fig.* blunder. —**ма́лый не про́мах,** nobody's fool.

промахну́ться *v.r. pfv.* **1,** to miss (*in striking, shooting, etc.*). **2,** *colloq.* to make a blunder.

прома́чивать *v. impfv.* [*pfv.* **промочи́ть**] to drench; soak.

промедле́ние *n.* delay.

проме́длить *v. pfv.* to delay; procrastinate.

проме́жность *n.f.* crotch.

промежу́ток [*gen.* **-тка**] *n.* **1,** space (*between two objects*). **2,** interval (*of time*).

промежу́точный *adj.* **1,** intermediate. **2,** intervening; interim. —**промежу́точные вы́боры,** off-year elections.

промелькну́ть *v. pfv.* **1,** to flash by; flash past. **2,** (*of a thought*) to flash across one's mind. **3,** *fig.* to appear momentarily; be faintly perceptible.

проме́нивать *v. impfv.* [*pfv.* **променя́ть**] to exchange; trade; barter.

промерза́ть *v. impfv.* [*pfv.* **промёрзнуть**] **1,** to be frozen solid. **2,** *colloq.* to be chilled through.

промёрзлый *adj.* frozen.

промёрзнуть [*past* **-мёрз, -ла**] *v., pfv. of* **промерза́ть.**

проме́ривать *v. impfv.* [*pfv.* **проме́рить**] to measure; survey.

промеря́ть *v. impfv.* = **проме́ривать.**

Промете́й *n.* Prometheus.

проме́тий *n.* promethium.

проме́шкать *v. pfv., colloq.* to linger; dawdle.

промо́зглый *adj.* dank; damp.

промока́тельный *adj., in* **промока́тельная бума́га,** blotting paper.

промока́ть *v. impfv.* [*pfv.* **промо́кнуть**] **1,** to get wet; get soaked; get drenched. **2,** [*impfv. only*] to be not waterproof: плащ промока́ет, the raincoat is not waterproof. **3,** *v.t.* [*pfv.* **промокну́ть**] to blot; dry (ink).

промока́шка [*gen. pl.* **-шек**] *n., colloq.* blotter.

промо́кнуть [*past* **-мо́к, -ла**] *v., pfv. of* **промока́ть.**

промокну́ть [*past* **-мокну́л**] *v., pfv. of* **промока́ть** (*in sense #3*).

промо́лвить *v. pfv.* [*infl.* **-влю, -вишь**] to utter; say.

промолча́ть *v. pfv.* [*infl.* **-чу́, -чи́шь**] to keep silent; say nothing.

проморга́ть *v. pfv., colloq.* **1,** to fail to notice. **2,** to miss; let slip by.

промота́ть *v., pfv. of* **прома́тывать.**

промочи́ть [*infl.* **-мочу́, -мо́чишь**] *v., pfv. of* **прома́чивать.**

промтова́рный *adj., in* **промтова́рный магази́н,** general store (*selling clothes, manufactured items, etc.*).

промтова́ры [*gen.* **-ров**] *n. pl.* manufactured goods (*contr. of* **промы́шленные това́ры**).

промча́ться *v.r. pfv.* [*infl.* **-чу́сь, -чи́шься**] to flash by; race by; speed by.

промыва́ть *v. impfv.* [*pfv.* **промы́ть**] **1,** to wash; cleanse; bathe. **2,** to pan (gold).

про́мысел [*gen.* **-сла**] *n.* **1,** trade: пушно́й про́мысел, fur trade. Куста́рный про́мысел, cottage industry. **2,** hunting; catching. Ры́бный про́мысел, fishing. **3,** *pl.* fields; mines: нефтяны́е про́мыслы, oil fields; соляны́е про́мыслы, salt mines.

про́мысл *n., relig.* Providence.

промысло́вый *adj.* **1,** commercial. **2,** sold commercially: промысло́вая пти́ца, game bird; промысло́вая ры́ба, food fish. **3,** producers': промысло́вая коопера́ция, producers' cooperative.

промы́ть [*infl.* **-мо́ю, -мо́ешь**] *v., pfv. of* **промыва́ть.**

промы́шленник *n.* manufacturer; industrialist.

промы́шленность *n.f.* industry. —**промы́шленный,** *adj.* industrial.

промышля́ть *v. impfv.* (*with instr.*) to earn one's living (by); make a living (from).

промя́млить *v., pfv. of* **мя́млить.**

прона́шивать *v. impfv.* [*pfv.* **проноси́ть**] to wear out (clothes). —**прона́шиваться,** *refl.* (*of clothes*) to wear out.

пронести́ [*infl. like* **нести́**] *v., pfv. of* **проноси́ть**[1]. —**пронести́сь,** *refl., pfv. of* **проноси́ться.**

пронза́ть *v. impfv.* [*pfv.* **пронзи́ть**] to pierce; impale.

пронзи́тельный *adj.* piercing.
пронзи́ть [*infl.* **-нжу́, -нзи́шь**] *v., pfv. of* **пронза́ть.**
пронизáть [*infl.* **-нижу́, -ни́жешь**] *v., pfv. of* **прони́зывать.**
прони́зывать *v. impfv.* [*pfv.* **пронизáть**] **1,** to pierce. **2,** *fig.* to penetrate; permeate.
проника́ть *v. impfv.* [*pfv.* **прони́кнуть**] (*with* **в** + *acc.*) **1,** to penetrate. **2,** to get to; reach. **3,** *fig.* to delve into; (try to) fathom. —**проника́ться,** *refl.* (*with instr.*) to be imbued (with); be filled (with).
проникнове́ние *n.* **1,** penetration. **2,** feeling; sincerity.
проникнове́нный *adj.* heartfelt; earnest. —**проникнове́нность,** *n.f.* feeling; sincerity.
прони́кнуть [*past* **-ни́к, -ла**] *v., pfv. of* **проника́ть.** —**прони́кнуться,** *refl., pfv. of* **проника́ться.**
пронима́ть *v. impfv.* [*pfv.* **проня́ть**] *colloq.* **1,** (*of cold, wind, etc.*) to penetrate. **2,** *fig.* to move; touch; affect.
проница́емый *adj.* permeable. —**проница́емость,** *n.f.* permeability.
проница́тельный *adj.* **1,** astute; shrewd; penetrating; perspicacious. **2,** (*of a look*) penetrating. —**проница́тельность,** *n.f.* astuteness; perspicacity; acumen; insight.
проноси́ть[1] *v. impfv.* [*pfv.* **пронести́;** *pres.* **-ношу́, -но́сишь**] **1,** to carry. **2,** (*with* **че́рез**) to carry through; (*with* **ми́мо**) carry past. **3,** to carry quickly; whisk. **4,** to smuggle (something) into, past, *or* out of. **5,** *impers.* to pass: грозу́ пронесло́, the storm passed. —**проноси́ться,** *refl.* **1,** to rush past; flash by; sweep over. **2,** (*of a rumor*) to spread; (*of time*) to fly by.
проноси́ть[2] *v. pfv.* [*infl.* **-ношу́, -но́сишь**] **1,** *pfv. of* **прона́шивать. 2,** to carry (*for a certain length of time*). **3,** to wear (*for a certain length of time*). —**проноси́ться,** *refl.* **1,** *pfv. of* **прона́шиваться. 2,** (*of clothes*) to last (*a certain length of time*).
пронумерова́ть *v., pfv. of* **нумерова́ть.**
проны́ра *n.m. & f., colloq.* one always able to gain access; wire-puller. —**проны́рливый,** *adj., colloq.* sneaky; slippery; able to worm one's way in.
проню́хивать *v. impfv.* [*pfv.* **пронюхать**] *colloq.* to hear about; get wind of.
проня́ть [*infl. like* **поня́ть**] *v., pfv. of* **пронима́ть.**
прообраз *n.* prototype.
пропага́нда *n.* **1,** propaganda. **2,** (*with gen.*) propagandizing (of).
пропаганди́ровать *v. impfv.* [*pres.* **-рую, -руешь**] to propagandize.
пропаганди́ст *n.* propagandist. —**пропаганди́стский,** *adj.* propagandistic; propaganda (*attrib.*).
пропада́ть *v. impfv.* [*pfv.* **пропа́сть**] **1,** to disappear; be missing: где вы пропада́ли?; куда́ вы пропа́ли?, where did you disappear to?; where have you been? У меня́ пропа́л зо́нтик, my umbrella has disappeared; I've lost my umbrella. **2,** to die; perish. **3,** to be lost; be done for. **4,** to be wasted. —**пиши́ пропа́ло,** it's hopeless. —**пропади́ про́падом**!, *colloq.* damn it all!
пропа́жа *n.* **1,** disappearance; loss. **2,** *colloq.* lost object; missing thing.
пропа́лывать *v. impfv.* [*pfv.* **прополо́ть**] to weed.
пропа́н *n.* propane.
про́пасть [*pl.* **про́пасти, -сте́й, -стя́м**] *n.f.* **1,** abyss; chasm. **2,** *fig.* gulf; chasm. **3,** (*with gen.*) *colloq.* lots of; tons of. —**на краю́ про́пасти,** on the brink of disaster.
пропа́сть [*infl. like* **пасть**] *v., pfv. of* **пропада́ть.**
пропа́хнуть *v. pfv.* [*past* **-па́х, -ла**] (*with instr.*) to become permeated with the smell of; reek (of).
пропа́щий *adj., colloq.* **1,** lost; gone for good. **2,** hopeless.
пропека́ть *v. impfv.* [*pfv.* **пропе́чь**] to bake (*thoroughly*). —**пропека́ться,** *refl.* to be baked thoroughly.
пропе́ллер *n.* propeller.
пропе́ть *v. pfv.* [*infl.* **-пою́, -поёшь**] **1,** *pfv. of* **петь. 2,** to sing (*for a certain length of time*).
пропе́чь [*infl. like* **печь**] *v., pfv. of* **пропека́ть.** —**пропе́чься,** *refl., pfv. of* **пропека́ться.**
пропива́ть *v. impfv.* [*pfv.* **пропи́ть**] to drink away; squander by drinking.
пропи́ливать *v. impfv.* [*pfv.* **пропили́ть**] to saw through.
пропили́ть [*infl.* **-пилю́, -пи́лишь**] *v., pfv. of* **пропи́ливать.**
прописа́ть [*infl.* **-пишу́, -пи́шешь**] *v., pfv. of* **пропи́сывать.** —**прописа́ться,** *refl., pfv. of* **пропи́сываться.**
пропи́ска [*gen. pl.* **-сок**] *n.* **1,** registration. **2,** residence permit.
прописно́й *adj.* **1,** *in* прописна́я бу́ква, capital letter. **2,** conventional: прописна́я мора́ль, conventional morality. —**прописна́я и́стина,** truism.
пропи́сывать *v. impfv.* [*pfv.* **прописа́ть**] **1,** to prescribe (medicine). **2,** to register. —**пропи́сываться,** *refl.* to register (*e.g.* in a hotel).
про́пись *n.f.* sample of writing. —**про́писью,** *adv.* written out: написа́ть число́ про́писью, to write out a number (*using letters*).
пропита́ние *n.* **1,** subsistence: сре́дства пропита́ния, means of subsistence. **2,** food; sustenance.
пропи́тывать *v. impfv.* [*pfv.* **пропита́ть**] to saturate; impregnate.
пропи́ть *v. pfv.* [*infl.* **-пью́, -пьёшь;** *past* **про́пил** *or* **пропи́л, пропила́, про́пило** *or* **пропи́ло**] **1,** *pfv. of* **пропива́ть. 2,** to drink (*for a certain length of time*).
пропла́вать *v. pfv.* to swim (*for a certain length of time*).
пропла́кать *v. pfv.* [*infl.* **-пла́чу, -пла́чешь**] to cry (*for a certain length of time*). —**пропла́кать глаза́,** *colloq.* to cry one's eyes out.
проплыва́ть *v. impfv.* [*pfv.* **проплы́ть**] **1,** to swim; sail; float; drift. **2,** (*with acc. or* **ми́мо**) to swim past; sail past. **3,** to swim; sail (a certain distance).
проплы́ть [*infl. like* **плыть**] *v., pfv. of* **проплыва́ть.**
пропове́дник *n.* **1,** preacher. **2,** *fig.* advocate; exponent; proponent.
пропове́довать *v. impfv.* [*pres.* **-дую, -дуешь**] **1,** to preach; propagate (a religion, idea, etc.). **2,** *v.i.* to preach (*deliver a sermon*).
про́поведь *n.f.* **1,** sermon. **2,** spreading; propagation.
пропо́йца *n.m. & f., colloq.* drunkard; drunk.
проползáть *v. impfv.* [*pfv.* **проползти́**] to crawl; creep.
проползти́ [*infl. like* **ползти́**] *v., pfv. of* **проползáть.**
прopо́лка *n.* weeding.
прополоска́ть *v., pfv. of* **полоска́ть.**
прополо́ть [*infl.* **-полю́, -по́лешь**] *v., pfv. of* **пропа́лывать.**
пропорциона́льно *adv.* **1,** proportionally; proportionately. **2,** (*with dat.*) proportionately with; in proportion to. —**пропорциона́льность,** *n.f.* proportion.

пропорциона́льный *adj.* **1,** proportional; proportionate. **2,** well-proportioned.

пропо́рция *n.* proportion.

пропоте́ть *v. pfv.* **1,** to perspire heavily. **2,** *colloq.* (*of an item of clothing*) to become drenched with perspiration.

про́пуск *n.* **1,** admission; admittance. **2,** passing through; letting through. **3,** omission. **4,** failure to attend; absence. **5,** blank; gap. **6,** [*pl.* **-ска́**] pass; permit. **7,** [*pl.* **-ска́**] password.

пропуска́ть *v. impfv.* [*pfv.* **пропусти́ть**] **1,** to admit; let in; let pass; let through. **2,** to serve; accommodate (a certain number of people). **3,** *sports* to allow (a goal, point to be scored, etc.). **4,** to let in (light, water, etc.). **5,** to pass through; run through; put through. **6,** to omit; leave out. **7,** to skip; pass over. **8,** to miss; fail to attend. **9,** to miss; let slip by.

пропускно́й *adj.* admission (*attrib.*). —**пропускна́я бума́га,** blotting paper. —**пропускна́я спосо́бность,** (carrying) capacity.

пропусти́ть [*infl.* **-пущу́, -пу́стишь**] *v., pfv. of* **пропуска́ть.**

проpа́б *n.* construction superintendent (*contr. of* **производи́тель рабо́т**).

прораба́тывать *v. impfv.* [*pfv.* **прорабо́тать**] *colloq.* **1,** to work over; study carefully. **2,** to give (someone) a going over.

прорабо́тать *v. pfv.* **1,** *pfv. of* **прораба́тывать. 2,** to work (*for a certain length of time*).

прораста́ние *n.* germination; sprouting.

прораста́ть *v. impfv.* [*pfv.* **прорасти́**] to germinate; sprout.

прорасти́ [*infl. like* **расти́**] *v., pfv. of* **прораста́ть.**

прорва́ть [*infl. like* **рвать**] *v., pfv. of* **прорыва́ть**[1]. —**прорва́ться,** *refl., pfv. of* **прорыва́ться.**

проре́з *n.* cut; slit; opening.

проре́зать [*infl.* **-ре́жу, -ре́жешь**] *v., pfv. of* **прореза́ть.** —**проре́заться,** *refl., pfv. of* **прореза́ться.**

прореза́ть *v. impfv.* [*pfv.* **проре́зать**] to cut; cut through. —**прореза́ться,** *refl.* (*of teeth*) to cut through: у ребёнка прореза́ются зу́бы, the child is teething.

прорези́нивать *v. impfv.* [*pfv.* **прорези́нить**] to rubberize.

про́резь *n.f.* cut; slit; opening.

прорепети́ровать *v., pfv. of* **репети́ровать.**

проре́ха *n.* **1,** tear. **2,** *colloq.* shortcoming; deficiency.

прорецензи́ровать *v., pfv. of* **рецензи́ровать.**

проржа́веть *v. pfv.* to rust through.

прорица́ние *n.* prophecy; prediction. —**прорица́тель,** *n.m.* prophet.

прорица́ть *v. impfv.* to prophesy.

проро́к *n.* prophet.

пророни́ть *v. pfv.* [*infl.* **-роню́, -ро́нишь**] **1,** to utter: не пророни́ть ни сло́ва, not to utter a word. **2,** to miss: он бо́йтся пророни́ть сло́во, he is afraid to miss a word. —**не пророни́ть (ни) слезы́** *or* **слези́нки,** not to shed a tear.

проро́ческий *adj.* prophetic. —**проро́чество,** *n.* prophecy.

проро́чить *v. impfv.* [*pfv.* **напроро́чить**] to prophesy.

проруба́ть *v. impfv.* [*pfv.* **проруби́ть**] to cut through; hack through.

проруби́ть [*infl.* **-рублю́, -ру́бишь**] *v., pfv. of* **проруба́ть.**

про́рубь *n.f.* hole in the ice.

проры́в *n.* **1,** bursting. **2,** breach. **3,** *mil.* breakthrough. **4,** *fig.* hitch; lag (*in production*).

прорыва́ть[1] *v. impfv.* [*pfv.* **прорва́ть**] **1,** to tear. **2,** to break through. **3,** *impers.* to burst: плоти́ну прорва́ло, the dam burst. —**прорыва́ться,** *refl.* **1,** to tear; break; burst. **2,** to break through; (*with* **из**) break out of.

прорыва́ть[2] *v. impfv.* [*pfv.* **проры́ть**] to dig (a hole, tunnel, canal, etc.).

проры́ть [*infl.* **-ро́ю, -ро́ешь**] *v., pfv. of* **прорыва́ть**[2].

проса́ливать *v. impfv.* **1,** [*pfv.* **проса́лить**] to grease. **2,** [*pfv.* **просоли́ть**] to salt.

проса́чивание *n.* **1,** seepage. **2,** penetration; infiltration.

проса́чиваться *v.r. impfv.* [*pfv.* **просочи́ться**] **1,** to seep. **2,** (*with* **в** + *acc.*) to penetrate; infiltrate. **3,** *fig.* (*of news, a rumor, etc.*) to leak out; (*with* **в** + *acc.*) filter (into).

просве́рливать *v. impfv.* [*pfv.* **просверли́ть**] **1,** to drill; bore (a hole). **2,** to drill through; drill a hole in.

просверли́ть *v., pfv. of* **сверли́ть** (*in sense #1*) *and* **просве́рливать.**

просве́т *n.* **1,** narrow shaft of light (*shining through an opening onto a surface*). **2,** *fig.* bright spot (*in a situation, one's life, etc.*). **3,** open space; empty space. **4,** opening; crack (*in a door or window*). **5,** *mil.* stripe (*on shoulder insignia*).

просвети́тельный *adj.* educational.

просвети́ть *v. pfv.* **1,** [*infl.* **-свечу́, -све́тишь**] *pfv. of* **просве́чивать. 2,** [*infl.* **-свещу́, -свети́шь**] *pfv. of* **просвеща́ть.**

просветле́ние *n.* **1,** brightening (*of the sky*). **2,** *fig.* lucid moment.

просветле́ть *v., pfv. of* **светле́ть.**

просве́чивание *n.* X-raying; X-ray examination.

просве́чивать *v. impfv.* [*pfv.* **просвети́ть**] **1,** (*of the sun*) to light up. **2,** to X-ray. **3,** [*impfv. only*] to be translucent. **4,** [*impfv. only*] (*with* **сквозь**) to appear through; shine through.

просвеща́ть *v. impfv.* [*pfv.* **просвети́ть**] to enlighten.

просвеще́ние *n.* **1,** enlightenment. **2,** education.

просвира́ *n., Orth. Ch.* communion bread.

просви́рник *n.* marsh mallow. *Also,* **просвирня́к** [*gen.* **-няка́**].

просвиста́ть [*infl.* **-свищу́, -сви́щешь**] *v., pfv. of* **просви́стывать.** *Also,* **просвисте́ть** [*infl.* **-свищу́, -свисти́шь**].

просви́стывать *v. impfv.* [*pfv.* **просвиста́ть** *or* **просвисте́ть**] to whistle.

про́седь *n.f.* streaks of gray.

просе́ивать *v. impfv.* [*pfv.* **просе́ять**] to sift.

про́сека *n.* cleared path in a forest.

просёлок [*gen.* **-лка**] *n.* country road; byroad.

просёлочный *adj., in* **просёлочная доро́га,** = **просёлок.**

просе́ять [*infl.* **-се́ю, -се́ешь**] *v., pfv. of* **просе́ивать.**

просиде́ть [*infl.* **-жу́, -ди́шь**] *v., pfv. of* **проси́живать.**

проси́живать *v. impfv.* [*pfv.* **просиде́ть**] **1,** to sit (*for a certain length of time*). **2,** to stay (*for a certain length of time*). **3,** to wear out the seat of; wear out by sitting on.

про́синь *n.f.* bluish tint.

проси́тель *n.m., obs.* applicant; suppliant.

проси́тельный *adj.* pleading; suppliant.

проси́ть *v. impfv.* [*pfv.* **попроси́ть**; *pres.* **прошу́, про́сишь**] **1,** to ask: попроси́те его́ войти́, ask him to come in. **2,** to ask for; request: проси́ть кни́гу, to ask for a book; проси́ть разреше́ния, to ask (for) permission; проси́ть (о) по́мощи, to ask for help. **3,** to beg: проси́ть проще́ния, to beg someone's pardon. Я вас о́чень прошу́!, please!; I beg of you! **4,** to invite; call; ask. **5,** [*impfv. only*] to ask; charge (a price). **6,** (*with* **за** + *acc.*) to plead for (someone). —**прошу́ вас**!, please go ahead!; (*when serving food*) please help yourself!; (*when offering a chair*) please have a seat!; (*when entering a doorway*) after you!

проси́ться *v.r. impfv.* [*pfv.* **попроси́ться**; *pres.* **прошу́сь, про́сишься**] **1,** (*with inf. or* **в/на** + *acc.*) to ask (for); apply (for); ask permission (to). **2,** [*impfv. only*] (*with* **на** + *acc.*): проси́ться на язы́к, to be on the tip of one's tongue; проси́ться на карти́ну, to cry out to be painted.

просия́ть *v. pfv.* **1,** (*of the sun*) to begin to shine. **2,** *fig.* (*with instr.*) to beam (with joy); light up (with a smile).

проскака́ть *v. pfv.* [*infl.* **-скачу́, -ска́чешь**] **1,** to gallop. **2,** (*with* **ми́мо**) to gallop past.

проска́кивать *v. impfv.* [*pfv.* **проскочи́ть**] **1,** *v.t.* to race through; race past. Проскочи́ть светофо́р, to go through a traffic light. **2,** (*with* **сквозь**) to get through; slip through. **3,** to slip (into a small opening). **4,** *colloq.* (*of time*) to slip by. **5,** *colloq.* (*of mistakes*) to creep in.

проска́льзывание *n.* slippage.

проска́льзывать *v. impfv.* [*pfv.* **проскользну́ть**] **1,** to slip (through a small opening). **2,** to slip; sneak (into, past, through, etc.).

просклоня́ть *v., pfv. of* **склоня́ть** (*in sense #5*).

проскользну́ть *v., pfv. of* **проска́льзывать.**

проскочи́ть [*infl.* **-скочу́, -ско́чишь**] *v., pfv. of* **проска́кивать.**

проскрипе́ть *v., pfv. of* **скрипе́ть.**

проскурня́к [*gen.* **-няка́**] *n.* marsh mallow.

проскуча́ть *v. pfv.* to be bored (*for a certain length of time*).

просла́вить [*infl.* **-влю, -вишь**] *v., pfv. of* **прославля́ть.** —**просла́виться,** *refl., pfv. of* **прославля́ться.**

прославле́ние *n.* glorification.

просла́вленный *adj.* celebrated; renowned.

прославля́ть *v. impfv.* [*pfv.* **просла́вить**] **1,** to make famous. **2,** to glorify; celebrate (*in song, poetry, etc.*). —**прославля́ться,** *refl.* (*with instr.*) to become famous (for).

проследи́ть [*infl.* **-жу́, -ди́шь**] *v., pfv. of* **просле́живать.**

просле́живать *v. impfv.* [*pfv.* **проследи́ть**] **1,** to follow; trail; shadow. **2,** *fig.* to trace; trace the development of. **3,** (*with* **за** + *instr.*) *colloq.* to monitor; keep tabs on.

прослези́ться *v.r. pfv.* [*infl.* **-жу́сь, -зи́шься**] to shed a few tears.

просло́йка [*gen. pl.* **-о́ек**] *n.* **1,** layer. **2,** *fig.* social stratum.

прослужи́ть *v. pfv.* [*infl.* **-служу́, -слу́жишь**] **1,** to serve (*for a certain length of time*). **2,** (*of a product*) to last (*for a certain length of time*).

прослу́шать *v. pfv.* **1,** *pfv. of* **слу́шать** (*in sense #4*). *and* **прослу́шивать. 2,** *colloq.* to fail to hear; fail to catch; miss.

прослу́шивать *v. impfv.* [*pfv.* **прослу́шать**] **1,** to listen to (*from beginning to end*). **2,** *med.* to examine (*by listening to*). **3,** to "bug" (a room); tap (a telephone).

прослы́ть *v., pfv. of* **слыть.**

прослы́шать *v. pfv.* [*infl.* **-шу, -шишь**] (*with* **о**) *colloq.* to hear (about).

просма́тривать *v. impfv.* [*pfv.* **просмотре́ть**] **1,** to look over; glance over; scan. **2,** to examine; view. **3,** to overlook; miss. —**просма́триваться,** *refl.* [*impfv. only*] to be visible.

просмо́тр *n.* **1,** examination. **2,** viewing: предвари́тельный просмо́тр, preview. **3,** oversight; error.

просмотре́ть [*infl.* **-смотрю́, -смо́тришь**] *v., pfv. of* **просма́тривать.**

просну́ться *v.r., pfv. of* **просыпа́ться.**

про́со *n.* millet.

просо́вывать *v. impfv.* [*pfv.* **просу́нуть**] to stick; thrust (into, through, etc.).

просо́дия *n.* prosody. —**просоди́ческий,** *adj.* prosodic.

просоли́ть [*infl.* **-солю́, -со́лишь** *or* **-соли́шь**] *v., pfv. of* **проса́ливать** (*in sense #2*).

просо́хнуть [*past* **-со́х, -ла**] *v., pfv. of* **просыха́ть.**

просочи́ться *v.r., pfv. of* **проса́чиваться.**

проспа́ть *v. pfv.* [*infl. like* **спать**] **1,** *pfv. of* **просыпа́ть**[2]. **2,** to sleep (*for a certain length of time*). —**проспа́ться,** *refl., colloq.* to sleep it off.

проспе́кт *n.* **1,** broad street; avenue: Не́вский проспе́кт, the Nevsky Prospekt (*main street of Leningrad*). **2,** outline; prospectus. **3,** advertisement: рекла́мные проспе́кты, advertisements; promotional material.

проспо́рить *v. pfv.* **1,** to lose (*in a bet*). **2,** to argue (*for a certain length of time*).

проспряга́ть *v., pfv. of* **спряга́ть.**

просро́ченный *adj.* **1,** overdue. **2,** expired.

просро́чивать *v. impfv.* [*pfv.* **просро́чить**] **1,** to be behind in. **2,** to exceed (a time limit). **3,** to allow to expire: мой па́спорт просро́чен, my passport has expired.

просро́чка *n.* **1,** delinquency (*in paying*). **2,** expiration.

проста́вить [*infl.* **-влю, -вишь**] *v., pfv. of* **проставля́ть.**

проставля́ть *v. impfv.* [*pfv.* **проста́вить**] to write in; fill in; enter.

проста́ивать *v. impfv.* [*pfv.* **простоя́ть**] **1,** to stand; stay (*for a certain length of time*). **2,** to stand idle; sit idle; lie idle. **3,** to stand; remain.

проста́к [*gen.* **-стака́**] *n.* simpleton.

простáта *n.* prostate (gland).

просте́йшие *n. pl., decl. as an adj.* protozoa.

просте́нок [*gen.* **-нка**] *n.* space between windows; pier.

простере́ть [*past* **-стёр, -ла**; *future rarely used*] *v., pfv. of* **простира́ть**[1]. —**простере́ться,** *refl., pfv. of* **простира́ться.**

простёртый *adj.* **1,** (*of one's hand or arm*) outstretched. **2,** stretched out on the floor or ground.

просте́цкий *adj., colloq.* simple; humble; unpretentious.

простира́ть[1] *v. impfv.* [*pfv.* **простере́ть**] to stretch out; hold out; extend. —**простира́ться,** *refl.* to extend; stretch.

простира́ть[2] *v., pfv. of* **прости́рывать.**

прости́рывать *v. impfv.* [*pfv.* **простира́ть**] *colloq.* to wash; launder.

процеди́ть [*infl.* **-цежу́, -це́дишь**] *v., pfv. of* **проце́живать.**

процеду́ра *n.* **1,** procedure. **2,** *usu. pl., med.* treatment (*baths, massages, etc.*). —**процеду́рный,** *adj.* procedural.

проце́живать *v. impfv.* [*pfv.* **процеди́ть**] **1,** to strain; filter. **2,** to mutter.

проце́нт *n.* **1,** percent: два́дцать проце́нтов, twenty percent. **2,** percentage. **3,** *pl.* interest.

проце́нтный *adj.* **1,** percentage (*attrib.*). **2,** interest-bearing.

проце́сс *n.* **1,** process. **2,** [*often* **суде́бный проце́сс**] A, trial. B, lawsuit. **3,** *med.* condition. Проце́сс в лёгких, tuberculosis of the lungs.

проце́ссия *n.* procession.

процити́ровать *v., pfv. of* **цити́ровать.**

прочерти́ть [*infl.* **-черчу́, -че́ртишь**] *v., pfv. of* **проче́рчивать.** —**прочерти́ться,** *refl., pfv. of* **проче́рчиваться.**

проче́рчивать *v. impfv.* [*pfv.* **прочерти́ть**] to draw (a line). —**проче́рчиваться,** *refl.* to stand out.

прочеса́ть [*infl.* **-чешу́, -че́шешь**] *v., pfv. of* **прочёсывать.**

проче́сть [*infl.* **-чту́, -чтёшь;** *past* **-чёл, -чла́, -чло́**] *v., pfv. of* **чита́ть.**

прочёсывать *v. impfv.* [*pfv.* **прочеса́ть**] **1,** to comb (flax, fiber, etc.). **2,** *fig., colloq.* to comb; search.

про́чий *adj.* other. —**про́чие,** *n. pl.* the others. —**и про́чее,** and so on; and so forth. —**ме́жду про́чим,** by the way. —**поми́мо всего́ про́чего,** *see* **поми́мо.** —**при про́чих ра́вных усло́виях,** other things being equal.

прочи́стить [*infl.* **-щу, -стишь**] *v., pfv. of* **прочища́ть.**

прочита́ть *v. pfv.* **1,** *pfv. of* **чита́ть. 2,** to read (*for a certain length of time*).

про́чить *v. impfv.* **1,** to intend; have in mind: про́чить кого́-нибудь в зятья́, to have someone in mind to be one's son-in-law. **2,** to predict: ему́ про́чат блестя́щее бу́дущее, a brilliant future is being predicted for him.

прочища́ть *v. impfv.* [*pfv.* **прочи́стить**] **1,** to clean out. **2,** to clear (a road, forest, etc.).

про́чно *adv.* firmly; solidly; securely.

про́чность *n.f.* **1,** strength; durability. **2,** soundness; solidity.

про́чный *adj.* **1,** firm; durable. **2,** *fig.* (*of peace, a friendship, etc.*) lasting.

прочте́ние *n.* **1,** reading. **2,** reciting. **3,** giving (*of lectures*).

прочу́вствовать *v. pfv.* [*infl.* **-ствую, -ствуешь**] **1,** to feel deeply. **2,** to experience; live through.

прочь *adv.* away; off: ру́ки прочь!, hands off! —*interj.* begone! Прочь отсю́да!, get away from here! Прочь с доро́ги!, get out of the way! —**быть не прочь** (+ *inf.*), not to mind; not be averse to.

проше́дшее *n., decl. as an adj.* the past.

проше́дший *adj.* last; past. —**проше́дшее вре́мя,** *gram.* the past tense.

проше́ние *n., obs.* application; petition; formal request.

прошепта́ть *v., pfv. of* **шепта́ть.**

проше́ствие *n., in* **по проше́ствии** (+ *gen.*), with the passage (of); upon the expiration (of).

прошива́ть *v. impfv.* [*pfv.* **проши́ть**] **1,** to sew; stitch. **2,** *colloq.* to riddle (with bullets); rack (with a bomb).

проши́вка *n.* lace trim.

проши́ть [*infl.* **-шью́, -шьёшь**] *v., pfv. of* **прошива́ть.**

прошлого́дний *adj.* last year's.

про́шлое *n., decl. as an adj.* the past. —**отойти́ в про́шлое,** to become a thing of the past.

про́шлый *adj.* **1,** last: в про́шлом году́, last year. **2,** past: про́шлые во́йны/оши́бки, past wars/mistakes.

прошмы́гивать *v. impfv.* [*pfv.* **прошмыгну́ть**] *colloq.* to sneak; slip (into, past, etc.).

проштуди́ровать *v., pfv. of* **штуди́ровать.**

проща́й *interj.* farewell!; adieu! *Also,* **проща́йте.**

проща́льный *adj.* parting; farewell (*attrib.*).

проща́ние *n.* parting; farewell. —**на проща́ние,** at parting.

проща́ть *v. impfv.* [*pfv.* **прости́ть**] to forgive; excuse; pardon. —**проща́ться,** *refl.* [*pfv.* **прости́ться** *or* **попроща́ться**] (*with* **с** + *instr.*) to say goodbye (to); bid farewell.

про́ще *adj., comp. of* **просто́й.**

проще́ние *n.* forgiveness; pardon: прошу́ проще́ния!, I beg your pardon!

прощу́пывать *v. impfv.* [*pfv.* **прощу́пать**] **1,** to feel. **2,** *fig.* to reconnoiter. **3,** *fig.* to size up. —**прощу́пывать по́чву,** to get the lay of the land; sound out the possibilities.

проэкзаменова́ть *v., pfv. of* **экзаменова́ть.** —**проэкзаменова́ться,** *refl., pfv. of* **экзаменова́ться.**

прояви́тель *n.m., photog.* developer.

прояви́ть [*infl.* **-явлю́, -я́вишь**] *v., pfv. of* **проявля́ть.** —**прояви́ться,** *refl., pfv. of* **проявля́ться.**

проявле́ние *n.* **1,** display; manifestation. **2,** *photog.* developing.

проявля́ть *v. impfv.* [*pfv.* **прояви́ть**] **1,** to show; display (a quality or emotion). **2,** *photog.* to develop. —**прояви́ть себя́, 1,** to show one's worth. **2,** (*with instr.*) to prove to be.

проявля́ться *v.r. impfv.* [*pfv.* **прояви́ться**] to reveal itself; manifest itself.

проя́снеть *v. pfv., colloq.* (*of the sky*) to clear up.

проясне́ть *v. pfv.* **1,** to become clear. **2,** to brighten up.

проясня́ть *v. impfv.* [*pfv.* **проясни́ть**] to make clear. —**проясня́ться,** *refl.* **1,** to clear up. **2,** *fig.* to become clear. **3,** to brighten up.

пруд [*gen.* **пруда́;** *2nd loc.* **пруду́**] *n.* pond.

пруди́ть *v. impfv.* [*pfv.* **запруди́ть;** *pres.* **пружу́, пру́дишь** *or* **пруди́шь**] to dam up. —**хоть пруд пруди́,** plenty; galore.

пружи́на *n.* **1,** spring. **2,** *in* гла́вная пружи́на, mainspring. —**нажа́ть на все пружи́ны,** to pull out all the stops.

пружи́нистый *adj.* springy; resilient.

пружи́нить *v. impfv.* to be springy; be resilient. —**пружи́ниться,** *refl., colloq.* = **пружи́нить.**

пружи́нный *adj.* spring (*attrib.*): пружи́нный матра́с, spring mattress.

руса́к [*gen.* **-сака́**] *n.* Croton bug; German cockroach.

прусса́к [*gen.* **-ссака́**] *n.* Prussian. —**пру́сский,** *adj.* Prussian.

прут [*gen.* **пру́та** *or* **прута́;** *pl.* **пру́тья, пру́тьев**] *n.* **1,** twig. **2,** rod.

прыга́ние *also,* **пры́ганье** *n.* jumping.

пры́гать *v. impfv.* [*pfv.* **пры́гнуть**] **1,** to jump; leap. **2,** to bounce. —**пры́гать на одно́й ноге́,** to hop.

прыгу́н [*gen.* **-гуна́**] *n.* jumper.

прости́тельный *adj.* pardonable; forgivable; excusable.

проститу́тка [*gen. pl.* **-ток**] *n.* prostitute. —**проститу́ция,** *n.* prostitution.

прости́ть [*infl.* **прощу́, прости́шь**] *v., pfv. of* **проща́ть.** —**прости́ться,** *refl., pfv. of* **проща́ться.**

про́сто *adv.* simply. —*adj., used predicatively* simple: Это не так про́сто, it's not so simple. Вам про́сто критикова́ть, it is easy for you to criticize. —**про́сто-на́просто,** simply (*used for emphasis*). —**про́сто так, 1,** as usual; in the usual manner. **2,** for no particular reason.

простова́тый *adj., colloq.* **1,** simple-minded. **2,** naïve; ingenuous.

простоволо́сый *adj., colloq.* bareheaded.

простоду́шие *n.* simple-heartedness.

простоду́шный *adj.* **1,** simple-hearted. **2,** artless; ingenuous.

просто́й[1] *adj.* [*short form* **прост, проста́, про́сто;** *comp.* **про́ще**] **1,** simple. **2,** plain: просто́й материа́л, plain material; проста́я пи́ща, plain food. **3,** mere: просто́й сме́ртный, mere mortal. —**просты́м гла́зом,** with the naked eye. —**просто́е число́,** prime number.

просто́й[2] *n.* idle time; downtime.

простоква́ша *n.* thick sour milk; clabber.

простонаро́дье *n., obs.* the common people. —**простонаро́дный,** *adj., obs.* of the common people.

простона́ть *v. pfv.* [*infl.* **-стону́, -сто́нешь**] to groan; moan.

просто́р *n.* **1,** space; expanse. **2,** range; scope; freedom.

просторе́чие *n.* vernacular; common speech. —**просторе́чный,** *adj.* vernacular.

просто́рный *adj.* spacious; roomy.

простосерде́чие *n.* simple-heartedness. —**простосерде́чный,** *adj.* simple-hearted.

простота́ *n.* simplicity.

простофи́ля *n.m. & f., colloq.* nincompoop.

простоя́ть [*infl.* **-стою́, -стои́шь**] *v., pfv. of* **проста́ивать.**

простра́нный *adj.* **1,** vast; extensive. **2,** (*of a speech, letter, etc.*) lengthy; wordy; long-winded.

простра́нство *n.* space. —**простра́нственный,** *adj.* spatial.

простра́ция *n.* prostration.

простра́чивать *v. impfv.* [*pfv.* **прострочи́ть**] to stitch.

простре́л *n.* lumbago.

простре́ливать *v. impfv.* [*pfv.* **прострели́ть**] **1,** to shoot through. **2,** [*impfv. only*] to rake with (machine-gun) fire.

прострели́ть [*infl.* **-стрелю́, -стре́лишь**] *v., pfv. of* **простре́ливать.**

прострочи́ть *v., pfv. of* **строчи́ть** (*in sense #1*) *and* **простра́чивать.**

просту́да *n.* a cold.

простуди́ть [*infl.* **-стужу́, -сту́дишь**] *v., pfv. of* **простужа́ть.** —**простуди́ться,** *refl., pfv. of* **простужа́ться.**

просту́дливый *adj., colloq.* susceptible to colds; easily catching cold.

просту́дный *adj.* of or from a cold.

простужа́ть *v. impfv.* [*pfv.* **простуди́ть**] to allow to catch cold. —**простужа́ться,** *refl.* to catch cold.

просту́женный *adj.* **1,** having a cold: я просту́жен(а), I have a cold. **2,** showing the effects of a cold.

просту́кивать *v. impfv.* [*pfv.* **просту́кать**] to tap.

проступа́ть *v. impfv.* [*pfv.* **проступи́ть**] **1,** to ooze. **2,** to appear; become faintly visible.

проступи́ть [*infl.* **-сту́пит**] *v., pfv. of* **проступа́ть.**

просту́пок [*gen.* **-пка**] *n.* **1,** misdeed; offense. **2,** *law* misdemeanor.

простуча́ть *v. pfv.* [*infl.* **-чу́, -чи́шь**] **1,** to tap out (a message). **2,** to come rolling by; come rattling by.

простыва́ть *v. impfv.* [*pfv.* **просты́ть**] *colloq.* to get cold. —**его́ и след просты́л,** he vanished without a trace.

просты́нный *adj.* of or for sheets: просты́нное полотно́, sheeting.

простыня́ [*pl.* **про́стыни, -сты́нь, -стыня́м**] *n.* sheet; bed sheet.

просты́ть [*infl.* **-сты́ну, -сты́нешь**] *v., pfv. of* **простыва́ть.**

просу́нуть *v., pfv. of* **просо́вывать.**

просу́шивать *v. impfv.* [*pfv.* **просуши́ть**] to dry (*thoroughly*). —**просу́шиваться,** *refl.* to dry out thoroughly.

просуши́ть [*infl.* **-сушу́, -су́шишь**] *v., pfv. of* **просу́шивать.**

просуществова́ть *v. pfv.* [*infl.* **-ству́ю, -ству́ешь**] **1,** to exist; subsist. **2,** to last; endure.

просце́ниум *n.* proscenium.

просчёт *n.* **1,** error (*in counting or calculation*). **2,** *fig.* miscalculation.

просчита́ть *v., pfv. of* **просчи́тывать.** —**просчита́ться,** *refl., pfv. of* **просчи́тываться.**

просчи́тывать *v. impfv.* [*pfv.* **просчита́ть**] **1,** to count. **2,** to miscount. —**просчи́тываться,** *refl.* **1,** to miscount. **2,** *fig.* to miscalculate.

про́сып *also,* **просы́п** *n., colloq., in* спать без про́сыпу/про́сыпа, to sleep on and on; sleep like a log.

просы́пать [*infl.* **-сыплю, -сыплешь**] *v., pfv. of* **просыпа́ть**[1].

просыпа́ть[1] *v. impfv.* [*pfv.* **просы́пать**] to spill.

просыпа́ть[2] *v. impfv.* [*pfv.* **проспа́ть**] **1,** to oversleep. **2,** *colloq.* to sleep through. —**просыпа́ться,** *refl.* [*pfv.* **просну́ться**] to wake up.

просыха́ть *v. impfv.* [*pfv.* **просо́хнуть**] to dry out.

про́сьба *n.* request. У меня́ к вам про́сьба, I have a favor to ask of you. Про́сьба не кури́ть!, you are requested not to smoke.

просяно́й *adj.* millet (*attrib.*).

prося́щий *adj.* pleading; supplicating.

протагони́ст *n.* protagonist.

протакти́ний *n.* protactinium.

прота́лина *n.* thawed patch; place where the snow has melted.

прота́лкивать *v. impfv.* [*pfv.* **протолкну́ть**] **1,** to push; press; force (into, through, forward, etc.). **2,** *colloq.* to expedite (a matter); give (something) a little push. —**прота́лкиваться,** *refl.* [*pfv.* **протолка́ться** *or* **протолкну́ться**] *colloq.* to force one's way; elbow one's way.

протанцева́ть *v. pfv.* [*infl.* **-цу́ю, -цу́ешь**] **1,** to dance. **2,** to dance (*for a certain length of time*).

прота́пливать *v. impfv.* [*pfv.* **протопи́ть**] **1,** to heat properly; heat sufficiently. **2,** [*impfv. only*] to heat slightly; warm slightly.

прота́птывать *v. impfv.* [*pfv.* **протопта́ть**] **1,** to beat (a path). **2,** *colloq.* to wear holes in (a carpet, pair of socks, etc.).

протара́нить *v., pfv. of* **тара́нить.**

протаскивать *v. impfv.* [*pfv.* **протащи́ть**] **1,** to drag. **2,** to drag through; pull through. **3,** *colloq.* to push through (a law, resolution, etc.). **4,** *colloq.* to give (someone) a going over (*in the press*).

прота́чивать *v. impfv.* [*pfv.* **проточи́ть**] to eat through; gnaw through.

протащи́ть [*infl.* **-тащу́, -та́щишь**] *v., pfv. of* **прота́скивать.**

прота́ять *v. pfv.* [*infl.* **-та́ет**] to melt.

протеже́ (тэ) *n.m. & f., indecl.* protégé.

проте́з (тэ) *n.* prosthetic device; artificial limb. —**зубно́й проте́з,** denture.

проте́зный (тэ) *adj.* prosthetic.

протеи́н (тэ) *n.* protein. —**протеи́новый,** *adj.* protein (*attrib.*).

протека́ть *v. impfv.* [*pfv.* **проте́чь**] **1,** to flow. **2,** to leak; seep. **3,** to leak; have a leak. **4,** (*of time, life, etc.*) to pass; go by. **5,** (*of an event, illness, etc.*) to proceed. Боле́знь протека́ет без осложне́ний, the illness is taking its normal course.

проте́ктор *n.* **1,** *obs.* protector; patron. **2,** tread (*on tires*).

протектора́т *n.* protectorate.

протекциони́зм *n.* protectionism.

проте́кция *n.* patronage; influence.

протере́ть [*infl. like* **тере́ть**] *v., pfv. of* **протира́ть.** —**протере́ться,** *refl., pfv. of* **протира́ться.**

проте́ст *n.* protest.

протеста́нт *n.* **1,** Protestant. **2,** protester. —**протеста́нти́зм; протеста́нство,** *n.* Protestantism. —**протеста́нтский,** *adj.* Protestant.

протестова́ть *v. impfv.* [*pres.* **-ту́ю, -ту́ешь**] (*with* **про́тив**) to protest.

проте́чь [*infl. like* **течь**] *v., pfv. of* **протека́ть.**

про́тив *prep., with gen.* **1,** against. **2,** opposite; facing. **3,** against; contrary to. **4,** against; compared to. —*predicate,* against: я не про́тив, I am not against it. —*n., colloq.* con: все за и про́тив, all the pros and cons. —**ничего́ не име́ть про́тив,** to have no objection (to).

про́тивень [*gen.* **-вня**] *n.m.* baking sheet; roasting pan.

противи́ться *v.r. impfv.* [*pfv.* **воспроти́виться;** *pres.* **-влюсь, -вишься**] (*with dat.*) to oppose; resist.

проти́вник *n.* **1,** enemy. **2,** opponent; adversary.

проти́вно *adv.* in a disgusting way. Проти́вно па́хнуть, have a disgusting odor. —*adj., used predicatively* disgusting; revolting: мне проти́вно (+ *inf.*), I find it disgusting/revolting to have to... —*prep., with dat., obs.* against; contrary to.

проти́вный *adj.* **1,** *obs.* opposite; facing. **2,** contrary. **3,** opposing. **4,** disgusting; repugnant. —**в проти́вном слу́чае,** otherwise; failing which.

противоа́томный *adj., in* **противоа́томная защи́та,** defense/protection against nuclear attack.

противове́с *n.* counterbalance; counterweight. —**в противове́с** (+ *dat.*), in contrast to; as distinct from. —**для противове́са,** for balance.

противовозду́шный *adj., in* **противовозду́шная оборо́на,** air defense.

противога́з *n.* gas mask.

противоде́йствие *n.* opposition; counteraction.

противоде́йствовать *v. impfv.* [*pres.* **-ствую, -ствуешь**] (*with dat.*) to oppose; counteract.

противоесте́ственный *adj.* unnatural; perverted.

противозако́нный *adj.* illegal; unlawful. —**противозако́нность,** *n.f.* illegality.

противозача́точный *adj.* contraceptive. —**противозача́точные сре́дства,** contraceptives.

противолежа́щий *adj.* **1,** opposite; facing. **2,** (*of an angle*) alternate.

противопехо́тный *adj., mil.* anti-personnel.

противопожа́рный *adj.* fire-prevention (*attrib.*).

противополо́жное *n., decl. as an adj.* the opposite.

противополо́жность *n.f.* **1,** opposition; contrast. **2,** opposite: пряма́я противополо́жность, exact opposite. —**в противополо́жность** (+ *dat.*), **1,** unlike; in contrast to. **2,** as opposed to; in contradistinction to.

противополо́жный *adj.* **1,** opposite: в противополо́жном направле́нии, in the opposite direction. **2,** opposite; contrary: противополо́жные взгля́ды, opposite views.

противопоста́вить [*infl.* **-влю, -вишь**] *v., pfv. of* **противопоставля́ть.**

противопоставле́ние *n.* **1,** contrasting. **2,** opposition.

противопоставля́ть *v. impfv.* [*pfv.* **противопоста́вить**] (*with dat.*) **1,** to compare (to); contrast (with). **2,** to oppose: противопоставля́ть си́ле си́лу, to oppose force with force.

противоречи́вый *adj.* contradictory; conflicting.

противоре́чие *n.* contradiction.

противоре́чить *v. impfv.* (*with dat.*) **1,** to contradict (someone). **2,** to contradict; be contrary to; be at variance with.

противостоя́ние *n., astron.* opposition.

противостоя́ть *v. impfv.* [*pres.* **-стою́, -стои́шь**] (*with dat.*) **1,** to resist; withstand. **2,** to oppose; be opposed to.

противота́нковый *adj.* antitank.

противоя́дие *n.* antidote.

протира́ть *v. impfv.* [*pfv.* **протере́ть**] **1,** to wear a hole in. **2,** to wipe; wipe clean. **3,** to strain; grate. —**протира́ться,** *refl.* to be worn through.

проти́скивать *v. impfv.* [*pfv.* **проти́снуть**] to force; press; squeeze (something) into *or* through. —**проти́скиваться,** *refl.* to squeeze into; squeeze through; squeeze between.

проткну́ть *v., pfv. of* **протыка́ть.**

протодья́кон *n., Orth. Ch.* archdeacon.

прото́к *n.* **1,** channel. **2,** *anat.* duct.

протоко́л *n.* **1,** minutes (*of a meeting*). **2,** report (*of an incident, interrogation, etc.*). **3,** protocol (*between states*).

протолка́ться *v.r., pfv. of* **прота́лкиваться.**

протолкну́ть *v., pfv. of* **прота́лкивать.** —**протолкну́ться,** *refl., pfv. of* **прота́лкиваться.**

прото́н *n.* proton.

протопи́ть [*infl.* **-топлю́, -то́пишь**] *v., pfv. of* **прота́пливать.**

протопла́зма *n.* protoplasm.

протопта́ть [*infl.* **-топчу́, -то́пчешь**] *v., pfv. of* **прота́птывать.**

проторённый *adj.* (*of a road or path*) beaten; well-trodden.

протора́ть *v. impfv.* [*pfv.* **протори́ть**], *usu. in* **протори́ть путь** *or* **доро́гу,** **1,** to beat a path. **2,** *fig.* to open the way.

прототи́п *n.* prototype.

проточи́ть [*infl.* **-точу́, -то́чишь**] *v., pfv. of* **прота́чивать.**

прото́чный *adj.* (*of water*) running; flowing; (*of a pond*) not stagnant; fed by springs.

протра́ва *n.* mordant.

протрезви́ть [*infl.* **-влю́, -ви́шь**] *v., pfv. of* **протрезвля́ть.** —**протрезви́ться,** *refl., pfv. of* **протрезвля́ться.**

протрезвля́ть *v. impfv.* [*pfv.* **протрезви́ть**] to sober up; make sober. —**протрезвля́ться,** *refl.* to sober up; become sober.

протрруби́ть *v., pfv. of* **труби́ть.**

протуха́ть *v. impfv.* [*pfv.* **проту́хнуть**] to spoil; rot.

проту́хнуть [*past* **-ту́х, -ла**] *v., pfv. of* **ту́хнуть** (*in sense #2*) *and* **протуха́ть.**

проту́хший *adj.* rotten.

протыка́ть *v. impfv.* [*pfv.* **проткну́ть**] to pierce.

протя́гивать *v. impfv.* [*pfv.* **протяну́ть**] **1,** to extend; stretch (a rope, wire, etc.). **2,** to stretch out; hold out; offer; extend. **3,** to sustain (a note, sound, etc.). —**протя́гиваться,** *refl.* **1,** to reach out. **2,** to stretch; extend. **3,** *colloq.* to stretch out. **4,** *colloq.* to last; go on. *See also* **протяну́ть.**

протяже́ние *n.* length; extent. —**на протяже́нии** (+ *gen.*), for; over a period of.

протяжённость *n.f.* length; extent.

протя́жный *adj.* (*of speech, a sound, etc.*) slow; prolonged.

протяну́ть *v. pfv.* [*infl.* **-тяну́, -тя́нешь**] **1,** *pfv. of* **протя́гивать. 2,** *colloq.* to delay; drag out. **3,** *v.i., colloq.* to hold out; live a while longer. **4,** *in* **протяну́ть но́ги,** *colloq.* to kick the bucket. —**протяну́ться,** *refl., pfv. of* **протя́гиваться.**

проучи́ть *v. pfv.* [*infl.* **-учу́, -у́чишь**] **1,** *colloq.* to teach (someone) a (good) lesson. **2,** to teach (*for a certain length of time*). —**проучи́ться,** *refl.* to study (*for a certain length of time*).

профа́н *n.* ignoramus.

профана́ция *n.* profanation.

профани́ровать *v. impfv. & pfv.* [*pres.* **-рую, -руешь**] to profane.

профессиона́л *n.* professional.

профессиона́льный *adj.* professional. —**профессиона́льная боле́знь,** occupational disease. —**профессиона́льное образова́ние,** vocational training.

профе́ссия *n.* profession. —**челове́к свобо́дной профе́ссии,** professional man (*in private practice*).

профе́ссор [*pl.* **профессора́**] *n.* professor. Профе́ссор исто́рии, professor of history; history professor. —**профе́ссорский,** *adj.* professorial. —**профе́ссорство,** *n.* professorship.

профессу́ра *n.* **1,** professorship. **2,** professors.

профила́ктика *n.* **1,** *med.* prophylaxis. **2,** preventive measures: пожа́рная профила́ктика, fire prevention. —**профилакти́ческий,** *adj.* prophylactic.

про́филь *n.m.* **1,** profile. **2,** *fig.* type: худо́жники разли́чного про́филя, painters of various types/styles/schools. Специали́ст широ́кого про́филя, broad specialist.

профо́рма *n., colloq.* formality. —**для профо́рмы,** as a matter of form.

профсою́з *n.* trade union (*contr. of* **профессиона́льный сою́з**). —**профсою́зный,** *adj.* trade-union (*attrib.*).

проха́живаться *v.r. impfv.* [*pfv.* **пройти́сь**] **1,** to walk; stroll. **2,** (*with* **насчёт** *or* **по а́дресу**) *colloq.* to make slighting remarks about; take a swipe at.

прохвати́ть [*infl.* **-хвачу́, -хва́тишь**] *v., pfv. of* **прохва́тывать.**

прохва́тывать *v.impfv.* [*pfv.* **прохвати́ть**] *colloq.* **1,** (*of cold, wind, etc.*) to penetrate. **2,** *impers.* to get a chill: меня́ прохвати́ло в откры́той маши́не, I got a chill in the open car.

прохво́ст *n., colloq.* scoundrel.

прохла́да *n.* cool; coolness: вече́рняя прохла́да, the cool of the evening.

прохла́дец *also,* **прохла́дца** *n., in* **с прохла́дцем; с прохла́дцей,** *colloq.* leisurely; without making much effort.

прохлади́тельный *adj.* cooling; refreshing.

прохлади́ться [*infl.* **-жу́сь, -ди́шься**] *v.r., pfv. of* **прохлажда́ться.**

прохла́дно *adv.* coolly. —*adj., used predicatively* **1,** cool: сего́дня прохла́дно, it is cool today. **2,** chilly: мне прохла́дно, I am chilly.

прохла́дный *adj.* cool.

прохла́дца *n. see* **прохла́дец.**

прохлажда́ться *v.r. impfv.* [*pfv.* **прохлади́ться**] *colloq.* **1,** to cool off. **2,** [*impfv. only*] to idle; loaf.

прохо́д *n.* **1,** passing. **2,** passage; passageway. **3,** aisle. **4,** *in* **за́дний прохо́д,** anus. **5,** *in* **пра́во прохо́да,** right of way. —**не дава́ть прохо́да** (+ *dat.*), to give someone no peace. —**прохо́да нет от,** there is no getting away from...

проходи́мец [*gen.* **-мца**] *n., colloq.* scoundrel; crook; rogue.

проходи́мость *n.f.* **1,** ability (of a surface) to carry traffic. **2,** ability (of a vehicle) to travel cross-country.

проходи́мый *adj.* passable.

проходи́ть[1] *v. impfv.* [*pfv.* **пройти́;** *pres.* **-хожу́, -хо́дишь**] **1,** to walk (along, through, past, into, etc.). **2,** (*with* **ми́мо**) to pass (by). **3,** to go (right) past (*inadvertently*). **4,** (*with* **че́рез**) to pass through. **5,** (*with* **в** + *acc.*) to fit into; fit through. **6,** to cover (a certain distance); traverse (a route or path); walk the length of (*e.g.* a street). **7,** (*of roads, a border, etc.*) to run; extend. **8,** to pass; elapse; go by. **9,** (*of pain, rain, etc.*) to pass; stop. **10,** to go: заседа́ние прошло́ уда́чно, the meeting went well. **11,** to undergo (treatment, training, etc.); complete (a course). **12,** *colloq.* to study.

проходи́ть[2] *v. pfv.* [*infl.* **-хожу́, -хо́дишь**] to walk (*for a certain length of time*).

проходна́я *n., decl. as an adj.* checkpoint (*at the entrance to a factory or other building*).

проходно́й *adj.* (*of a room, courtyard, etc.*) connecting; communicating. —**проходно́й балл,** lowest passing score (*on an entrance examination*). —**проходна́я бу́дка,** entrance gate; checkpoint. —**проходна́я пе́шка,** *chess* passed pawn.

прохожде́ние *n.* passing; passage.

прохо́жий *adj.* **1,** passing. **2,** passing through; in transit. —*n.* passer-by.

прохрипе́ть *v. pfv.* [*infl.* **-плю́, -пи́шь**] to utter in a hoarse voice.

прохуди́ться *v.r. pfv., colloq.* to wear out.

процвета́ние *n.* prosperity.

процвета́ть *v. impfv.* to prosper; flourish; thrive.

прыжóк [*gen.* **-жкá**] *n.* jump; leap. —**прыжки́ в вóду,** diving. —**прыжóк в вóду,** dive. —**прыжóк в высотý,** high jump. —**прыжóк в длинý,** broad jump. —**прыжóк с мéста,** standing broad jump. —**прыжóк с разбéга,** running broad jump. —**прыжóк с шестóм,** pole vault. —**тройнóй прыжóк,** hop, step, and jump.

прыскать *v. impfv.* [*pfv.* **пры́снуть**] (*with instr.*) *colloq.* to sprinkle.

пры́снуть *v. pfv., colloq.* **1,** *pfv. of* **пры́скать. 2,** (*of blood*) to gush. **3,** to dart; dash. **4,** to burst out laughing.

пры́ткий *adj.* [*comp.* **пры́тче**] *colloq.* quick; nimble; agile.

прыть *n.f., colloq.* **1,** speed. **2,** energy; vim; pep. —**во всю прыть,** at full speed.

прыщ [*gen.* **-щá**] *n.* pimple.

прыщáвый *adj., colloq.* pimply.

прядéние *n.* spinning.

пря́деный *adj.* spun.

пряди́льный *adj.* spinning (*attrib.*).

пряди́льщик *n.m.* [*fem.* **-щица**] *n.* spinner.

прядь *n.f.* strand (*of hair*).

пря́жа *n.* yarn.

пря́жка [*gen. pl.* **-жек**] *n.* buckle.

пря́лка [*gen. pl.* **-лок**] *n.* **1,** distaff. **2,** spinning wheel.

прямáя *n., decl. as an adj.* straight line. —**по прямóй,** as the crow flies.

прямизнá *n.* straightness.

прямикóм *adv., colloq.* **1,** straight; in a straight line. **2,** straight to the point.

пря́мо *adv.* **1,** straight. **2,** straight ahead. **3,** right; directly. **4,** openly; frankly. **5,** *colloq.* really; truly. **6,** *colloq.* simply; just: я пря́мо не знáю, I just don't know.

прямодýшие *n.* directness; straightforwardness. —**прямодýшный,** *adj.* direct; straightforward.

прямóй *adj.* **1,** straight. **2,** erect; upright. **3,** direct. **4,** straightforward. **5,** *in* **прямóй ýгол,** right angle. —**прямóй расчёт** *or* **смысл** (+ *inf.*), *colloq.* there is every reason to...; it makes a lot of sense to... *See also* **прямáя.**

прямолинéйный *adj.* **1,** rectilinear. **2,** *fig.* straightforward.

прямотá *n.* directness; straightforwardness.

прямоуróльник *n.* rectangle. —**прямоуróльный,** *adj.* rectangular.

пря́ник *n.* cake: медóвый пря́ник, honey cake. Имби́рный пря́ник, gingerbread. —**поли́тика кнутá и пря́ника,** the carrot and stick.

пря́ность *n.f.* spice. —**пря́ный,** *adj.* spicy.

прясть *v. impfv.* [*pfv.* **спрясть;** *pres.* **прядý, прядёшь;** *past* **прял, прялá** *or* **пря́ла, пря́ло**] to spin (cloth, yarn, etc.).

пря́тание *also,* **пря́танье** *n.* hiding.

пря́тать *v. impfv.* [*pfv.* **спря́тать;** *pres.* **пря́чу, пря́чешь**] to hide; conceal. —**пря́таться,** *refl.* to hide; be hiding.

пря́тки [*gen.* **-ток**] *n. pl.* hide-and-seek.

пря́ха *n.* (woman) spinner.

псалóм [*gen.* **-лмá**] *n.* psalm.

псалты́рь *n.m. or f.* [*gen.* **-ты́ри** *or* **-тыря́**] Psalter.

псáрня [*gen. pl.* **-рен**] *n.* kennel.

псевдони́м *n.* pseudonym; pen name.

пси́на *n., colloq.* **1,** dogmeat. **2,** smell of a dog.

псих *n., colloq.* madman; lunatic; nut.

психиатри́я *n.* psychiatry. —**психиáтр,** *n.* psychiatrist. —**психиатри́ческий,** *adj.* psychiatric.

пси́хика *n.* psyche. —**психи́ческий,** *adj.* psychic.

психоанáлиз *n.* psychoanalysis. —**психоаналити́ческий,** *adj.* psychoanalytic(al).

психóз *n.* psychosis.

психолóгия *n.* psychology. —**психóлог,** *n.* psychologist. —**психологи́ческий,** *adj.* psychological.

психопáт *n.* psychopath. —**психопати́ческий,** *adj.* psychopathic. —**психопáтия,** *n.* psychopathy.

психосомати́ческий *adj.* psychosomatic.

психотерапи́я *n.* psychotherapy. —**психотерапéвт,** *n.* psychotherapist.

психоти́ческий *adj.* psychotic.

псориáз *n.* psoriasis.

птáшка [*gen. pl.* **-шек**] *n., colloq.* little bird; birdie. —**рáнняя птáшка,** early bird.

птенéц [*gen.* **-нцá**] *n.* baby bird; nestling; fledgling.

птеродáктиль *n.m.* pterodactyl.

пти́ца *n.* bird. —**домáшняя пти́ца,** poultry.

птицевóд *n.* poultry farmer; poultry breeder. —**птицевóдство,** *n.* poultry farming, poultry breeding.

птицелóв *n.* fowler. —**птицелóвство,** *n.* fowling.

пти́чий [*fem.* **-чья**] *adj.* **1,** bird (*attrib.*); bird's. **2,** birdlike. **3,** *in* **пти́чий двор,** barnyard. —**вид с пти́чьего полёта,** bird's-eye view. —**жить на пти́чьих правáх,** to live from hand to mouth.

пти́чка [*gen. pl.* **-чек**] *n.* **1,** *dim. of* **пти́ца. 2,** check; check mark; tick [✓].

пти́чник *n.* poultry yard; hen house.

пýблика *n.* **1,** (the) public. **2,** audience. **3,** *colloq.* people.

публикáция *n.* **1,** publication. **2,** (published) announcement; notice.

публиковáть *v. impfv.* [*pfv.* **опубликовáть;** *pres.* **-кýю, -кýешь**] to publish.

публици́ст *n.* commentator; columnist; publicist.

публи́чно *adv.* publicly; in public.

публи́чный *adj.* public. —**публи́чный дом,** brothel.

пýгало *n.* **1,** scarecrow. **2,** *fig.* bugaboo; bugbear.

пýганый *adj.* frightened.

пугáть *v. impfv.* [*pfv.* **испугáть**] to frighten; scare. —**пугáться,** *refl.* (*with gen.*) to be frightened (of); be scared (of).

пугáч [*gen.* **-гачá**] *n.* toy pistol.

пугли́вый *adj.* easily frightened; fearful; timorous.

пýговица *n.* button.

пуд [*pl.* **пуды́**] *n.* old Russian unit of weight equal to approx. 36 pounds; pood.

пýдель *n.m.* poodle.

пýдинг *n.* pudding.

пýдра *n.* powder. —**сáхарная пýдра,** powdered sugar.

пýдреница *n.* (lady's) compact.

пýдрить *v. impfv.* [*pfv.* **напýдрить**] to powder. —**пýдриться,** *refl.* to powder one's face; powder one's nose.

пузáтый *adj., colloq.* potbellied.

пýзо *n., colloq.* belly; paunch.

пузырёк [*gen.* **-рькá**] *n.* **1,** small bottle; vial. **2,** bubble.

пузы́риться *v.r. impfv., colloq.* **1,** to bubble. **2,** (*of clothes*) to billow.

пузы́рь [*gen.* **-зыря́**] *n.m.* **1,** bubble. **2,** *colloq.* blister. **3,** bladder: жёлчный пузы́рь, gall bladder; мочевóй пузы́рь, urinary bladder. **4,** bag: пузы́рь со льдом, ice bag.

пук [*pl.* **пуки́**] *n.* bunch; bundle; tuft; wisp.

пулевóй *adj.* bullet (*attrib.*).

пулемёт *n.* machine gun. —**пулемётный,** *adj.* machine-gun (*attrib.*). —**пулемётчик,** *n.* machine gunner.
пулесто́йкий *adj.* bulletproof. *Also,* **пуленепробива́емый; пуленепроница́емый.**
пуло́вер *n.* pullover.
пульвериза́тор *n.* atomizer; sprayer.
пу́льпа *n.* pulp (*of a tooth*).
пульс *n.* pulse.
пульса́р *n.* pulsar.
пульса́ция *n.* pulsation.
пульси́ровать *v. impfv.* [*pres.* **-рует**] to pulsate.
пульт *n.* **1,** music stand: дирижёрский пульт, conductor's stand. **2,** console; control panel.
пу́ля *n.* bullet.
пуля́рка [*gen. pl.* **-рок**] *n.* fattened chicken.
пу́ма *n.* puma.
пункт *n.* **1,** point: поворо́тный пункт, turning point. Са́мый се́верный пункт страны́, the northernmost point in the country. **2,** station; post; center: медици́нский пункт, first-aid station; наблюда́тельный пункт, observation post; призывно́й пункт, induction center. **3,** point; paragraph; item (*in a document*). **4,** *in* пу́нкты обвине́ния, counts (*of an indictment*). —**по пу́нктам; пункт за пу́нктом,** point by point.
пункти́р *n.* dotted line. —**пункти́рный,** *adj., in* **пункти́рная ли́ния,** = **пункти́р.**
пунктуа́льный *adj.* punctual. —**пунктуа́льность,** *n.f.* punctuality.
пунктуа́ция *n.* punctuation.
пу́нкция *n., med.* puncture; tapping.
пу́ночка [*gen. pl.* **-чек**] *n.* snow bunting.
пунцо́вый *adj.* crimson.
пунш *n.* punch.
пуп [*gen.* **пупа́**] *n., colloq.* navel; bellybutton.
пупа́вка [*gen. pl.* **-вок**] *n.* camomile.
пупови́на *n.* umbilical cord.
пупо́к [*gen.* **-пка́**] *n.* navel.
пупо́чный *adj.* umbilical.
пупы́рышек [*gen.* **-шка**] *n., colloq.* pimple. —**пупы́рчатый,** *adj., colloq.* pimply.
пурга́ *n.* blizzard; snowstorm.
пури́зм *n.* purism. —**пури́ст,** *n.* purist.
пурита́нин [*pl.* **-та́не, -та́н**] *n.m.* [*fem.* **-та́нка**] **1,** *hist.* Puritan. **2,** puritan.
пурита́нский *adj.* **1,** Puritan. **2,** puritanical.
пурпу́рный *adj.* purple; crimson. *Also,* **пурпу́ровый.**
пуск *n.* **1,** starting; setting in motion. **2,** launching.
пуска́й *particle* = **пусть.**
пуска́ть *v. impfv.* [*pfv.* **пусти́ть**] **1,** to let go (of). **2,** to let (someone) go (somewhere). **3,** to let in; admit. **4,** to take in (lodgers). **5,** to start up; switch on; set in motion. **6,** to throw; toss. **7,** to fire; shoot. **8,** to blow (smoke, bubbles, etc.). **9,** (*with* **в** + *acc.*) to put (into production, into circulation, on sale, etc.). **10,** to sprout (buds, shoots, etc.). **11,** *colloq.* to start; set afloat (a rumor, gossip, etc.). —**пуска́ть в де́ло,** to put to use. —**пуска́ть в ход,** *see* **ход.** —**пуска́ть ко́рни,** *see* **ко́рень.** —**пуска́ть кровь** (+ *dat.*), to bleed (someone). —**пуска́ть себе́ пу́лю в лоб,** to blow one's brains out.
пуска́ться *v.r. impfv.* [*pfv.* **пусти́ться**] **1,** to set out; set off. **2,** to dash; race. **3,** (*with inf.*) to begin (to); start (to). **4,** (*with* **в** *or* **на** + *acc.*) to enter into; embark upon.
пусково́й *adj.* starting (*attrib.*); launching (*attrib.*). —**пускова́я устано́вка,** launcher.
пустельга́ *n.* kestrel.
пусте́ть *v. impfv.* [*pfv.* **опусте́ть**] to become empty; become deserted.
пусти́ть [*infl.* **пущу́, пу́стишь**] *v., pfv. of* **пуска́ть.** —**пусти́ться,** *refl., pfv. of* **пуска́ться.**
пу́сто *adj., used predicatively* empty; deserted: на у́лицах бы́ло пу́сто, the streets were empty/deserted.
пустова́ть *v. impfv.* [*pres.* **-сту́ет**] to be empty; stand empty.
пустоголо́вый *adj., colloq.* empty-headed.
пустозво́н *n., colloq.* windbag.
пусто́й *adj.* [*short form* **пуст, пуста́, пу́сто**] **1,** empty. **2,** *fig.* empty; vain; hollow. **3,** *fig.* lacking depth; shallow. —**пусто́е ме́сто, 1,** blank space. **2,** a nothing; nonentity; nobody. —**пуста́я тра́та** (+ *gen.*), a waste (of). —**с пусты́ми рука́ми,** empty-handed.
пустоме́ля *n.m. & f., colloq.* windbag.
пустопоро́жний *adj., colloq.* empty.
пустосло́в *n., colloq.* windbag. —**пустосло́вие,** *n., colloq.* idle talk; twaddle; hot air.
пустосло́вить *v. impfv.* [*pres.* **-влю, -вишь**] *colloq.* to babble; chatter.
пустота́ [*pl.* **пусто́ты**] *n.* **1,** emptiness. **2,** vacuum. **3,** *fig.* void.
пустоте́лый *adj.* hollow.
пустоцве́т *n.* **1,** sterile flower. **2,** *fig.* person who has amounted to nothing.
пу́стошь *n.f.* uncultivated plot of land.
пусты́нник *n.* hermit.
пусты́нный *adj.* **1,** desert (*attrib.*). **2,** uninhabited; deserted. **3,** bleak; desolate.
пусты́ня *n.* **1,** desert. **2,** wilderness; wasteland.
пусты́рь [*gen.* **-стыря́**] *n.m.* abandoned lot; neglected plot of land.
пусть *particle* let: пусть он говори́т, let him speak. Пусть икс ра́вен и́греку, let x equal y. —*conj.* **1,** though: зада́ча, пусть тру́дная, но выполни́ма, the task, though difficult, can be accomplished. **2,** granted; so what if...?: пусть он мне помо́г, ра́зве э́то даёт пра́во (+ *inf.*), so what if he helped me? Does that give him the right to...? —**пусть бу́дет по-ва́шему,** have it your way. —**пусть бу́дет так,** so be it.
пустя́к [*gen.* **-тяка́**] *n.* **1,** trifle. **2,** *pl.* nonsense. —**па́ра пустяко́в,** child's play. —**пустяки́!,** never mind!; it's nothing!
пустяко́вый *adj., colloq.* trifling; trivial.
пу́таник *n., colloq.* muddle-headed person.
пу́таница *n.* mess; muddle; jumble.
пу́таный *adj.* **1,** tangled. **2,** confused; rambling; incoherent. **3,** *colloq.* (*of a person*) confused; mixed up.
пу́тать *v. impfv.* **1,** [*pfv.* **спу́тать, запу́тать,** *or* **перепута́ть**] to tangle. **2,** [*pfv.* **перепу́тать**] to mix up (*objects previously in order*). **3,** [*pfv.* **спу́тать** *or* **запу́тать**] to confuse; mix (someone) up. **4,** [*pfv.* **спу́тать** *or* **перепу́тать**] to confuse; get (two or more things) mixed up. **5,** [*impfv. only*] to ramble (*in speech*). **6,** [*pfv.* **запу́тать** *or* **впу́тать**] (*with* **в** + *acc.*) *colloq.* to involve (in); embroil (in). **7,** [*pfv.* **спу́тать**] to hobble; fetter (a horse). —**пу́таться,** *refl.* **1,** [*pfv.* **с-, за-, пере-**] to become (en)tangled. **2,** [*pfv.* **с-, пере-**] *colloq.* to become confused. **3,** [*pfv.* **в-**] (*with* **в** + *acc.*) *colloq.* to interfere (in); meddle (in). **4,** [*pfv.* **с-**] (*with* **с** + *instr.*) *colloq.* to consort (with); keep company (with).
путёвка [*gen. pl.* **-вок**] *n.* **1,** pass; permit; authori-

zation. **2,** ticket for a group tour; place in a tourist group. —**путёвка в жизнь,** a start in life.

путеводи́тель *n.m.* guidebook.

путево́дный *adj.* guiding. —**путево́дная звезда́,** guiding star; lodestar. —**путево́дная нить,** clue.

путево́й *adj.* **1,** travel (*attrib.*): путевы́е заме́тки, travel notes. **2,** *R.R.* track (*attrib.*): путево́й обхо́дчик, trackman; lineman. —**путева́я ка́рта,** road map. —**путева́я ско́рость,** ground speed.

путе́ец [*gen.* **-те́йца**] *n.* railway engineer.

путём *prep., with gen.* by means of; by.

путепрово́д *n.* overpass.

путеше́ственник *n.* traveler.

путеше́ствие *n.* trip; journey; voyage.

путеше́ствовать *v. impfv.* [*pres.* **-ствую, -ствуешь**] to travel.

пу́тник *n.* traveler.

пу́тный *adj., colloq.* **1,** sensible. **2,** worthwhile. —**из него́ ничего́ пу́тного не вы́йдет,** he'll never amount to anything.

путч *n.* putsch.

пу́ты [*gen.* **пут**] *n. pl.* fetters; shackles (*lit. & fig.*).

путь [*gen., dat., & prepl.* **пути́;** *instr.* **путём;** *pl.* **пути́, путе́й, путя́м**] *n.m.* **1,** way; route: на обра́тном пути́, on the way back. Око́льным путём, by a roundabout way/route. **2,** journey; traveling: два дня пути́, a two-day journey; two days of traveling. Отпра́виться в путь, to start/set out on a journey. Счастли́вого пути́!, bon voyage! **3,** *fig.* path: и́збранный путь, one's chosen path. **4,** *fig.* track: на ло́жном пути́, on the wrong track. **5,** way; means; method: каки́м путём?, in what way?; by what means? **6,** *R.R.* track: запа́сный путь, sidetrack; siding. **7,** *pl., anat.* passage; tract: дыха́тельные пути́, respiratory tract. —**по пути́, 1,** [*also,* **в пути́**] on the way; along the way; en route. **2,** (*with dat.*) going one's way: мне с ва́ми по пути́, I am going your way. *See also* **путём.**

пуф *n.* padded stool; hassock.

пух *n.* down; fluff; fuzz. —**в пух и прах, 1,** thoroughly; utterly. **2,** (*with verbs of dressing*) in one's finest. —**ни пу́ха ни пера́!,** good luck!

пу́хлый *adj.* chubby; pudgy; plump.

пу́хнуть *v. impfv.* [*past* **пух, -ла**] to swell.

пухови́к [*gen.* **-вика́**] *n.* feather bed.

пухо́вка [*gen. pl.* **-вок**] *n.* powder puff.

пухо́вый *adj.* made of down; downy.

пучегла́зый *adj., colloq.* goggle-eyed.

пучи́на *n.* ocean depths.

пучо́к [*gen.* **-чка́**] *n.* **1,** bunch (*of flowers*); tuft (*of grass*). **2,** wisp (*of hay, straw, etc.*). **3,** beam: пучо́к све́та, beam of light. **4,** bun: носи́ть во́лосы пучко́м, to wear one's hair in a bun.

пу́шечный *adj.* gun (*attrib.*); cannon (*attrib.*). —**пу́шечное мя́со,** cannon fodder. —**пу́шечное ядро́,** cannon ball.

пуши́нка [*gen. pl.* **-нок**] *n.* **1,** bit of fluff. **2,** tiny flake (*of snow*).

пуши́стый *adj.* downy; fluffy; fuzzy.

пуши́ть *v. impfv.* [*pfv.* **распуши́ть**] to fluff (up).

пу́шка [*gen. pl.* **-шек**] *n.* **1,** gun. **2,** cannon. —**как из пу́шки,** punctually; right on time.

пушка́рь [*gen.* **-каря́**] *n.m., obs.* gunner; artilleryman.

пушни́на *n.* fur; furs.

пушно́й *adj.* **1,** fur (*attrib.*). **2,** fur-bearing.

пушо́к [*gen.* **-шка́**] *n.* fluff; fuzz.

пу́ща *n.* dense forest.

пу́ще *adv., colloq.* more.

пу́щий *adj., obs.* **1,** greatest. **2,** *preceded by* **для,** greater: для пу́щей ва́жности, for greater effect.

пуэрторика́нец [*gen.* **-нца**] *n.m.* [*fem.* **-нка**] Puerto Rican. —**пуэрторика́нский,** *adj.* Puerto Rican.

пчела́ [*pl.* **пчёлы**] *n.* bee.

пчели́ный *adj.* bee (*attrib.*). —**пчели́ный воск,** beeswax.

пчелово́д *n.* beekeeper. —**пчелово́дство,** *n.* beekeeping.

пче́льник *n.* apiary.

пшени́ца *n.* wheat. —**твёрдая пшени́ца,** durum wheat.

пшени́чный *adj.* wheat (*attrib.*).

пшено́ *n.* millet.

пыж [*gen.* **пыжа́**] *n.* wad (*used in loading a firearm*).

пы́жик *n.* baby reindeer.

пы́житься *v.r. impfv.* [*pfv.* **напы́житься**] *colloq.* **1,** to make every effort; strain every nerve. **2,** to act high and mighty.

пыл [*2nd loc.* **пылу́**] *n.* ardor. —**в пылу́** (+ *gen.*), in the heat of (battle, an argument, etc.); in a moment of (anger, passion, etc.). —**с пы́лу, с жа́ру,** piping hot.

пыла́ть *v. impfv.* **1,** to flame; blaze. **2,** (*of one's face*) to glow. **3,** (*with instr.*) to burn (with love, rage, etc.).

пылесо́с *n.* vacuum cleaner.

пыли́нка [*gen. pl.* **-нок**] *n.* speck of dust.

пыли́ть *v. impfv.* **1,** *v.i.* [*pfv.* **напыли́ть**] to raise (a cloud of) dust. **2,** *v.t.* [*pfv.* **запыли́ть**] to get dust on. —**пыли́ться,** *refl.* [*pfv.* **запыли́ться**] to get dusty; gather dust.

пы́лкий *adj.* ardent; fervent; fiery. —**пы́лкость,** *n.f.* ardor; fervor.

пыль [*2nd loc.* **пыли́**] *n.f.* dust. —**пуска́ть пыль в глаза́, 1,** to put on a false front. **2,** (*with dat.*) to throw dust in someone's eyes.

пы́льник *n.* **1,** *bot.* anther. **2,** smock to protect against dust; duster. **3,** light summer overcoat.

пы́льный *adj.* **1,** dust (*attrib.*). **2,** dusty.

пыльца́ *n.* pollen.

пыта́ть *v. impfv.* **1,** to torture. **2,** *fig.* to torment.

пыта́ться *v.r. impfv.* [*pfv.* **попыта́ться**] to attempt; try; endeavor.

пы́тка [*gen. pl.* **-ток**] *n.* **1,** torture. **2,** *fig.* torture; agony; sheer hell.

пытли́вый *adj.* inquisitive. —**пытли́вость,** *n.f.* inquisitiveness.

пы́хать *v. impfv.* [*pres.* **пы́шу, пы́шешь**] *colloq.* **1,** to blaze. **2,** (*with instr.*) to radiate: пы́хать сча́стьем, to radiate happiness. Он пы́шет здоро́вьем, he is the picture of health.

пыхте́ние *n.* panting; puffing.

пыхте́ть *v. impfv.* [*pres.* **пыхчу́, пыхти́шь**] to puff; pant.

пы́шка [*gen. pl.* **-шек**] *n.* **1,** bun. **2,** *colloq.* plump child.

пы́шный *adj.* **1,** sumptuous; magnificent. **2,** fluffy. **3,** (*of vegetation*) luxuriant; lush. **4,** pompous; high-flown. —**пы́шность,** *n.f.* sumptuousness; splendor; pomp

пьедеста́л *n.* pedestal.

пье́са *n.* (stage) play.

пью́щий *adj.* (*of a person*) who drinks. —*n.* drinker.

пьяне́ть *v. impfv.* [*pfv.* **опьяне́ть**] to get drunk.

пьяни́ть *v. impfv.* [*pfv.* **опьяни́ть**] to intoxicate; make drunk.

пья́ница *n.m. & f.* drunkard.
пья́нство *n.* drunkenness.
пья́нствовать *v. impfv.* [*pres.* **-ствую, -ствуешь**] to drink too much; be frequently drunk.
пья́ный *adj. & n.* drunk.
пэр *n.* peer. —**пэ́рство,** *n.* title of peer.
пюпи́тр *n.* stand: но́тный пюпи́тр, music stand.
пюре́ (рэ) *n. neut. indecl.* purée. —**я́блочное пюре́,** applesauce. —**карто́фельное пюре́,** mashed potatoes.
пядь [*pl.* **пя́ди, -де́й, -дя́м**] *n.f.* span (*distance from thumb to forefinger*). —**пядь земли́,** dot of land. —**не отда́ть** *or* **не уступи́ть ни пя́ди земли́,** not to yield an inch. —**будь он семи́ пяде́й во лбу,** even if he were a genius/the smartest man in the world/.
пя́лить *v. impfv., colloq., in* **пя́лить глаза́ на** (+ *acc.*), to stare at.
пя́льцы [*gen.* **-лец**] *n. pl.* tambour (*embroidery frame*).
пясть *n.f.* metacarpus.
пята́ [*pl.* **пя́ты, пят, пята́м**] *n.* **1,** *obs.* heel. **2,** abutment. —**до пят,** (*of a garment*) extending down to one's ankles. —**по пята́м,** on someone's heels. —**под пято́й** (+ *gen.*), under the heel of.
пята́к [*gen.* **-така́**] *n., colloq.* five-kopeck piece.
пятачо́к [*gen.* **-чка́**] *n., colloq.* **1,** = **пята́к. 2,** pig's snout.
пя́тая *n., decl. as an adj.* fifth: одна́ пя́тая, one-fifth.
пятёрка *n.* **1,** the numeral 5. **2,** *colloq.* anything numbered 5. **3,** a grade of "five", signifying "excellent". **4,** *cards* five. **5,** *colloq.* five-ruble note.
пятерня́ *n., colloq.* one's hand.
пя́теро *collective numeral* five.
пятибо́рье *n.* pentathlon.
пятигра́нник *n.* pentahedron.
пятидесятиле́тие *n.* **1,** fiftieth anniversary; fiftieth birthday. **2,** fifty-year period.
пятидесятиле́тний *adj.* **1,** fifty-year (*attrib.*). **2,** fifty-year-old.
пятидеся́тница *n.* Pentecost.
пятидеся́тый *ordinal number* fiftieth.
пятидне́вный *adj.* five-day (*attrib.*).
пятикни́жие *n.* the Pentateuch.
пятиконе́чный *adj.* (*of a star*) five-pointed.
пятикра́тный *adj.* fivefold.
пятиле́тие *n.* **1,** fifth anniversary; fifth birthday. **2,** five-year period.
пятиле́тка [*gen. pl.* **-ток**] *n.* five-year plan.
пятиле́тний *adj.* **1,** five-year (*attrib.*). **2,** five-year-old.
пятирублёвка [*gen. pl.* **-вок**] *n., colloq.* five-ruble note.
пятисо́тый *ordinal numeral* five-hundredth.
пятисто́пный *adj.* pentameter. —**пятисто́пный стих,** pentameter. —**пятисто́пный ямб,** iambic pentameter.
пя́титься *v.r. impfv.* [*pfv.* **попя́титься;** *pres.* **-чусь, -тишься**] **1,** to back up; move backwards. **2,** *colloq.* to back out; (*with* **от**) go back on.
пятиуго́льник *n.* pentagon. —**пятиуго́льный,** *adj.* pentagonal.
пя́тка [*gen. pl.* **-ток**] *n.* heel. —**лиза́ть пя́тки** (+ *dat.*), to lick someone's boots. —**наступа́ть на пя́тки** (+ *dat.*), to be close on the heels of. —**показа́ть пя́тки,** to take to one's heels. —**у меня́ душа́ ушла́ в пя́тки,** my heart sank.
пятна́дцатый *ordinal numeral* fifteenth.
пятна́дцать [*gen., dat., & prepl.* **-цати;** *instr.* **-цатью**] *numeral* fifteen.
пятна́ть *v. impfv.* [*pfv.* **запятна́ть**] **1,** to spot; stain. **2,** *fig.* to sully; tarnish.
пятна́шки [*gen.* **-шек**] *n. pl.* tag (*game*).
пятни́стый *adj.* spotted.
пя́тница *n.* Friday.
пятно́ [*pl.* **пя́тна, пя́тен**] *n.* spot; stain; blemish.
пя́тнышко [*pl.* **-шки, -шек**] *n., dim. of* **пятно́.**
пято́к [*gen.* **-тка́**] *n.* (*with gen. pl.*) *colloq.* five (*similar objects*).
пя́тый *ordinal numeral* fifth.
пять [*gen., dat., & prepl.* **пяти́;** *instr.* **пятью́**] *numeral* five.
пятьдеся́т [*gen., dat., & prepl.* **пяти́десяти;** *instr.* **пятью́десятью**] *numeral* fifty.
пятьсо́т [*gen.* **пятисо́т;** *dat.* **пятиста́м;** *instr.* **пятьюста́ми;** *prepl.* **пятиста́х**] *numeral* five hundred.
пя́тью *adv.* five times: пя́тью пять – два́дцать пять, five times five is 25.

Р

Р, р *n. neut.* seventeenth letter of the Russian alphabet.
раб [*gen.* **раба́**] *n.m.* [*fem.* **раба́**] slave.
рабовладе́лец [*gen.* **-льца**] *n.* slaveowner. —**рабовладе́льческий,** *adj.* slave-owning.
раболе́пный *adj.* servile. —**раболе́пие; раболе́пство,** *n.* servility.
раболе́пствовать *v. impfv.* [*pres.* **-ствую, -ствуешь**] (*with* **пе́ред**) to be servile (to); kowtow (to); grovel (before).
рабо́та *n.* **1,** work. **2,** job: меня́ть рабо́ту, to change jobs. **3,** *in* курсова́я рабо́та, term paper. **4,** *pl.* work; operations: стро́ительные рабо́ты, construction work; спаса́тельные рабо́ты, rescue operations. **5,** *pl.* works (*of an artist, writer, etc.*). **6,** workmanship: превосхо́дной рабо́ты, of superb workmanship.

—**брать в рабо́ту, 1,** to take in hand. **2,** to take to task.
рабо́тать *v. impfv.* **1,** to work. **2,** (*with instr.*) to use; handle; wield (a tool). **3,** (*of a device*) to work; function; operate. **4,** to be open (*to the public*). **5,** *in* **рабо́тать над собо́й,** to work to improve oneself. —**рабо́таться,** *refl., impers.* **1,** *indicating the progress of work:* сего́дня хорошо́ рабо́тается, the work is going well today. **2,** (*with dat.*) to feel like working: мне сего́дня не рабо́тается, I don't feel like working today; I can't get down to work today.
рабо́тник *n.* **1,** worker: отли́чный рабо́тник, excellent worker. Рабо́тник иску́сства, person who works in the arts. Нау́чный рабо́тник, person engaged in scientific research. **2,** employee; official: рабо́тник посо́льства, embassy employee/official. Руководя́щий рабо́тник, person in a supervisory position.
рабо́тница *n.* woman worker.
рабо́тный *adj., obs.* working (*attrib.*). —**рабо́тный дом,** workhouse.
работода́тель *n.m.* employer.
работорго́вец [*gen.* **-вца**] *n.* slave trader. —**работорго́вля,** *n.* slave trade.
работоспосо́бный *adj.* **1,** able-bodied. **2,** hard-working; industrious. —**работоспосо́бность,** *n.f.* ability to work; capacity for work.
работя́га *n.m. & f., colloq.* hard worker.
работя́щий *adj., colloq.* hard-working; industrious.
рабо́чий *adj.* work (*attrib.*); working; worker's. —*n.* worker; workman. —**рабо́чий день,** workday. —**рабо́чий класс,** the working class. —**рабо́чие ру́ки,** workmen; hands. —**рабо́чая си́ла,** manpower. —**рабо́чий скот,** draft animals. —**рабо́чий сце́ны,** stage hand. —**в рабо́чем поря́дке,** in the course of work; (while) on the job.
ра́бский *adj.* **1,** slave (*attrib.*). **2,** servile; slavish.
ра́бство *n.* slavery; servitude; bondage.
рабы́ня *n.* slave; bondwoman.
равви́н *n.* rabbi. —**равви́нский,** *adj.* rabbinical.
ра́венство *n.* equality.
равне́ние *n., mil.* alignment.
равни́на *n.* plain.
равни́нный *adj.* **1,** of the plains. **2,** (*of terrain*) flat.
равно́ *adv.* equally. —*adj., used predicatively* (*with dat.*) equal (to): два плюс три равно́ пяти́, two plus three equals five. —**всё равно́, 1,** it is all the same; it makes no difference. **2,** still; all the same; nevertheless. —**всё равно́, что,** just the same as. —**равно́ и; равно́ как,** as well as.
равнобе́дренный *adj., math.* isosceles.
равнове́сие *n.* balance; equilibrium. —**выводи́ть из равнове́сия,** to disconcert; rattle.
равноде́нствие *n.* equinox.
равноду́шие *n.* indifference.
равноду́шный *adj.* [*short form* **-шен, -шна**] (*with* **к**) indifferent (to). —**равноду́шно,** *adv.* with indifference.
равнозна́чный *adj.* equivalent.
равноме́рный *adj.* even; uniform.
равнопра́вие *n.* equal rights; equality.
равнопра́вный *adj.* **1,** equal; enjoying equal rights. **2,** equitable.
равноси́льный *adj.* **1,** of equal strength. **2,** (*with dat.*) equivalent (to); tantamount (to).
равносторо́нний *adj.* equilateral.
равноуго́льный *adj.* equiangular.
равноце́нный *adj.* **1,** equal in price. **2,** of equal value.
ра́вный *adj.* [*short form* **ра́вен, равна́, равно́, равны́**] equal. —*n.* equal: пе́рвый среди́ ра́вных, first among equals. —**на ра́вной ноге́ с,** on an equal footing with. —**при про́чих ра́вных усло́виях,** other things being equal. —**ра́вным о́бразом,** by the same token.
равня́ть *v. impfv.* [*pfv.* **сравня́ть**] **1,** to make equal; equalize. **2,** [*impfv. only*] (*with* **с** + *instr.*) to equate (with). —**равня́ться,** *refl.* [*impfv. only*] **1,** (*with dat.*) to equal. **2,** (*with dat.*) to amount to; be tantamount to. **3,** (*with* **с** + *instr.*) *colloq.* to compete (with); compare (with). **4,** (*with* **по**) to emulate. **5,** *mil.* to dress.
рагу́ *n. neut. indecl.* ragout; stew.
рад *adj., used predicatively* (*with inf., dat., or* **что**) glad; pleased: о́чень рад (ра́да) познако́миться с ва́ми!, pleased to meet you! Я рад слу́чаю (+ *inf.*), I am glad/pleased to have the opportunity to...
рада́р *n.* radar. —**рада́рный,** *adj.* radar (*attrib.*).
ра́джа *n.m.* rajah.
ра́ди *prep., with gen.* for; for the sake of. —**ра́ди бо́га!,** *see* **бог.**
радиа́льный *adj.* radial.
радиа́тор *n.* radiator.
радиа́ция *n.* radiation.
ра́дий *n.* radium. —**ра́диевый,** *adj.* radium.
радика́л *n.* **1,** *polit.* radical. **2,** *math.* radical sign. **3,** *chem.* radical. —**радикали́зм,** *n.* radicalism.
радика́льный *adj.* **1,** *polit.* radical. **2,** radical; drastic. —**радика́льно,** *adv.* radically.
ра́дио *n. indecl.* **1,** radio: по ра́дио, on/over the radio. **2,** = **радиоприёмник.**
радиоакти́вный *adj.* radioactive. —**радиоакти́вность,** *n.f.* radioactivity.
радиовеща́ние *n.* broadcasting. —**радиовеща́тельный,** *adj.* broadcasting.
радиогра́мма *n.* radio message; radiogram.
радио́ла *n.* radio-phonograph.
радиоло́гия *n.* radiology. —**радио́лог,** *n.* radiologist.
радиолока́тор *n.* radar (set). —**радиолока́ция,** *n.* radar; detection by radar. —**радиолокацио́нный,** *adj.* radar (*attrib.*).
радиолюби́тель *n.m.* amateur radio operator; ham.
радиомая́к [*gen.* **-маяка́**] *n.* (radio) beacon.
радиопеленга́тор *n.* (radio) direction finder.
радиопереда́тчик *n.* radio transmitter.
радиопереда́ча *n.* radio broadcast; radio transmission.
радиоприёмник *n.* radio: включи́ть радиоприёмник, to turn on the radio.
радиосвя́зь *n.f.* radio communication.
радиослу́шатель *n.m.* (radio) listener.
радиоста́нция *n.* radio station.
радиотелеграфи́я *n.* radiotelegraphy.
радиотелефо́н *n.* radiotelephone. —**радиотелефони́я,** *n.* radiotelephony.
радиотерапи́я *n.* radiotherapy.
радиоте́хник *n.* radio mechanic. —**радиоте́хника,** *n.* radio engineering.
ради́ровать *v. impfv. & pfv.* [*pres.* **-рую, -руешь**] to radio.
ради́ст *n.* radio operator.
ра́диус *n.* radius. —**ра́диус де́йствий,** range (*of an aircraft, missile, etc.*).
ра́довать *v. impfv.* [*pfv.* **обра́довать;** *pres.* **-дую,**

-дуешь] to gladden; make happy. —**ра́доваться,** *refl.* to be glad; be happy; rejoice. Ра́доваться изве́стию, to be happy about the news; rejoice over the news.

радо́н *n.* radon.

ра́достно *adv.* with joy. —*adj., used predicatively* (*with dat.*) delighted: мне бы́ло ра́достно, что..., I was delighted that...

ра́достный *adj.* joyful; joyous. Ра́достное изве́стие, joyful news; glad tidings.

ра́дость *n.f.* joy; gladness.

ра́дуга *n.* rainbow.

ра́дужность *n.f.* iridescence.

ра́дужный *adj.* **1,** iridescent; opalescent. **2,** *fig.* bright; rosy. **3,** (*of hopes, spirits, etc.*) high. —**ра́дужная оболо́чка,** *anat.* iris.

раду́шие *n.* cordiality; hospitality.

раду́шный *adj.* cordial. —**раду́шно,** *adv.* cordially.

раж *n., colloq.* passion; frenzy. —**войти́ в раж,** to become very emotional; get all worked up.

раз [*pl.* **разы́, раз**] *n.* **1,** time: два ра́за, two times. **2,** *in counting,* one: раз, два, три, one, two, three. —*adv.* once: раз по́здно ве́чером, once late at night. —*conj., colloq.* since; if: раз не зна́ешь, не говори́, if you don't know, don't talk. —**в са́мый раз, 1,** the right time. **2,** the right size. —**вся́кий раз, когда́,** every time; whenever. —**ещё раз,** again; once again. —**как раз,** just; exactly; precisely: как раз то, что мне ну́жно, just what I need. —**не раз,** more than once. —**ни ра́зу,** not a single time. —**раз за ра́зом,** time after time; time and again.

раз- *also,* **рас-, разо-, разъ-,** *prefix* **1,** *indicating breaking asunder:* разбива́ть, to smash. **2,** (*with* **-ся**) *indicating dispersal:* разъезжа́ться, to depart (*in various directions*). **3,** *indicating distribution:* раздава́ть, to hand out. **4,** *indicating undoing or unfastening:* развя́зывать, to untie. **5,** *indicating reversal of action:* разлюби́ть, to cease to love. **6,** (*with* **-ся**) [*with pfv. verbs only*] *indicating warming up to one's activity:* разговори́ться, to warm to one's subject.

разба́вить [*infl.* **-влю, -вишь**] *v., pfv. of* **разбавля́ть.**

разбавля́ть *v. impfv.* [*pfv.* **разба́вить**] to dilute.

разбаза́ривать *v. impfv.* [*pfv.* **разбаза́рить**] *colloq.* to squander.

разба́лтывать *v. impfv.* [*pfv.* **разболта́ть**] *colloq.* **1,** to shake up; stir. **2,** to work loose; knock loose. **3,** to give away (a secret). —**разба́лтываться,** *refl., colloq.* **1,** to come loose. **2,** to get carried away (*while speaking*). **3,** *fig.* to get out of hand.

разбе́г *n.* running approach (*before jumping, diving, taking off, etc.*). —**с разбе́га; с разбе́гу,** while running at full speed. —**прыжо́к с разбе́га/разбе́гу,** running broad jump.

разбега́ться *v.r. impfv.* [*pfv.* **разбежа́ться**] **1,** to scatter; disperse. **2,** to run at top speed. **3,** to make a running approach. —**у меня́ глаза́ разбежа́лись,** I didn't know where to look first.

разбежа́ться [*infl. like* **бежа́ть**] *v.r., pfv. of* **разбега́ться.**

разбереди́ть *v., pfv. of* **береди́ть.**

разбива́ть *v. impfv.* [*pfv.* **разби́ть**] **1,** to break; smash; shatter. **2,** to hurt badly; fracture. **3,** to defeat; crush. **4,** to demolish (an argument, theory, etc.). **5,** to divide; break up. **6,** to lay out (a garden, park, etc.). **7,** to pitch (a tent); set up (camp). —**разбива́ться,** *refl.* **1,** to break; be smashed. **2,** to break up; split up. **3,** (*of a plane*) to crash. **4,** to be badly hurt. **5,** *in* разби́ться на́смерть, to be killed (*in a crash, fall, etc.*).

разби́вка *n.* **1,** dividing up. **2,** laying out.

разбинтова́ть [*infl.* **-ту́ю, -ту́ешь**] *v., pfv. of* **разбинто́вывать.**

разбинто́вывать *v. impfv.* [*pfv.* **разбинтова́ть**] to unbandage.

разбира́тельство *n.* investigation. —**суде́бное разбира́тельство,** *law* hearing.

разбира́ть *v. impfv.* [*pfv.* **разобра́ть**] **1,** to take apart; dismantle. **2,** to analyze; examine; look into. **3,** to sort out. **4,** to buy up. **5,** to make out; discern. **6,** to make out; decipher (something written). **7,** *gram.* to parse. **8,** *colloq.* (*of an emotion*) to seize; come over. **9,** [*impfv. only*] *colloq.* to stop to choose; take time to choose. —**разбира́ться,** *refl.* (*with* **в** + *prepl.*) to understand; have an understanding of.

разбитно́й *adj., colloq.* **1,** capable; adept. **2,** sprightly; outgoing.

разби́тый *adj.* **1,** broken. **2,** defeated. **3,** ruined; shattered. **4,** worn out; jaded. —**разби́т параличо́м,** paralyzed.

разби́ть [*infl.* **разобью́, разобьёшь**] *v., pfv. of* **бить** (*in sense #4*) *and* **разбива́ть.** —**разби́ться,** *refl., pfv. of* **разбива́ться.**

разбогате́ть *v., pfv. of* **богате́ть.**

разбо́й *n.* robbery. —**разбо́йник,** *n.* robber.

разбо́йничать *v. impfv.* to commit robberies.

разбо́йничий [*fem.* **-чья**] *adj.* robbers'. *Also,* **разбо́йнический.**

разболе́ться *v.r. pfv., colloq.* **1,** [*infl.* **-е́юсь, -е́ешься**] to become seriously ill. **2,** [*infl.* **-и́тся**] to begin to hurt.

разболта́ть *v., pfv. of* **разба́лтывать.** —**разболта́ться,** *refl., pfv. of* **разба́лтываться.**

разбомби́ть *v. pfv.* [*infl.* **-блю́, -би́шь**] to destroy; wipe out (*by bombing*); bomb out.

разбо́р *n.* **1,** taking apart. **2,** analysis. **3,** investigation. **4,** sorting out. **5,** selectivity: без разбо́ра, indiscriminately. **6,** *gram.* parsing. **7,** *colloq.* quality; caliber.

разбо́рка *n.* **1,** taking apart; dismantling. **2,** sorting out.

разбо́рный *adj.* **1,** collapsible. **2,** (*of furniture*) sectional.

разбо́рчиво *adv.* legibly.

разбо́рчивость *n.f.* **1,** discrimination. **2,** legibility.

разбо́рчивый *adj.* **1,** discriminating. **2,** legible.

разбрани́ть *v. pfv., colloq.* to scold; bawl out; berate. —**разбрани́ться,** *refl.* (*with* **с** + *instr.*) *colloq.* to quarrel (with).

разбра́сывать *v. impfv.* [*pfv.* **разброса́ть**] to scatter. —**разбра́сываться,** *refl.* **1,** to stretch out. **2,** *fig.* to do too many things at once; spread oneself thin.

разбреда́ться *v.r. impfv.* [*pfv.* **разбрести́сь**] (*of many people*) to wander off (*in different directions*).

разбрести́сь [*infl. like* **брести́**] *v.r., pfv. of* **разбреда́ться.**

разбро́д *n.* **1,** confusion; disorder. **2,** discord; dissension.

разбро́санный *adj.* **1,** scattered; dispersed. **2,** *colloq.* disconnected; incoherent.

разброса́ть *v., pfv. of* **разбра́сывать.** —**разброса́ться,** *refl., pfv. of* **разбра́сываться.**

разбры́згивать *v. impfv.* [*pfv.* **разбры́згать**] to

splash; sprinkle; spray. —**разбры́згиваться,** *refl.* to splash; spatter.

разбуди́ть *v., pfv. of* **буди́ть** (*in sense #1*).

разбуха́ть *v. impfv.* [*pfv.* **разбу́хнуть**] to swell.

разбу́хнуть [*past* **-бу́х, -ла**] *v., pfv. of* **бу́хнуть**[1] *and* **разбуха́ть.**

разбушева́ться *v.r. impfv.* [*infl.* **-шу́юсь, -шу́ешься**] **1,** (*of a storm, the sea, etc.*) to rage. **2,** *colloq.* to become enraged; fly into a rage.

разва́л *n.* collapse; breakdown.

разва́ливать *v. impfv.* [*pfv.* **развали́ть**] **1,** to tear down. **2,** *fig.* to ruin; make a mess of. —**разва́ливаться,** *refl.* **1,** to collapse; come tumbling down. **2,** to fall apart; go to pieces. **3,** *colloq.* to sprawl out.

разва́лина *n.* **1,** *pl.* ruins. **2,** *colloq.* (physical) wreck.

развали́ть [*infl.* **-валю́, -ва́лишь**] *v., pfv. of* **разва́ливать.** —**развали́ться,** *refl., pfv. of* **разва́ливаться.**

разва́ривать *v. impfv.* [*pfv.* **разва́рить**] to boil until soft.

развари́ть [*infl.* **-варю́, -ва́ришь**] *v., pfv. of* **разва́ривать.**

ра́зве *particle* **1,** really? **2,** (*with inf.*) perhaps one should...; shouldn't one...? **3,** (*with* **не**) isn't it...?: ра́зве не я́сно, что..., isn't it clear that...? —*conj., obs.* unless. —**ра́зве то́лько; ра́зве что,** except: ра́зве то́лько на кра́йнем се́вере, except in the extreme north. Он почти́ не постаре́л, ра́зве что стал чу́точку седе́е, he has hardly aged at all except for becoming a bit grayer.

развева́ть *v. impfv.* to blow about; cause to wave. —**развева́ться,** *refl.* to flutter.

разве́дать *v., pfv. of* **разве́дывать.**

разведе́ние *n.* raising; breeding.

разведённый *adj.* divorced. —*n.* divorced man. —**разведённая,** *n.* divorcée.

разве́дка *n.* **1,** (gathering of) intelligence. **2,** intelligence service. **3,** reconnaissance. **4,** prospecting; exploration.

разве́дочный *adj.* **1,** exploratory. **2,** reconnaissance (*attrib.*); intelligence (*attrib.*).

разве́дчик *n.* **1,** *mil.* scout. **2,** intelligence agent. **3,** prospector. **4,** reconnaissance plane.

разве́дывательный *adj.* intelligence (*attrib.*); reconnaissance (*attrib.*).

разве́дывать *v. impfv.* [*pfv.* **разве́дать**] **1,** (*with* **о**) *colloq.* to find out (about). **2,** *mil.* to reconnoiter. **3,** to prospect; explore.

развезти́ [*infl. like* **везти́**] *v., pfv. of* **развози́ть.**

разве́ивать *v. impfv.* [*pfv.* **разве́ять**] **1,** (*of the wind*) to scatter; disperse. **2,** *fig.* to dispel.

разве́нчивать *v. impfv.* [*pfv.* **развенча́ть**] to discredit.

развёрнутый *adj.* **1,** *mil.* deployed; extended. **2,** all-out; full-scale. **3,** detailed; comprehensive.

разверну́ть *v., pfv. of* **развёртывать** *and* **развора́чивать** (*in sense #1*). —**разверну́ться,** *refl., pfv. of* **развёртываться** *and* **развора́чиваться.**

развёрстка *n.* **1,** apportionment; allotment. **2,** assessment (*of a tax*).

развёртка [*gen. pl.* **-ток**] *n.* reamer.

развёртывание *n.* **1,** unfolding; unwrapping; unrolling. **2,** *mil.* deployment. **3,** *fig.* development.

развёртывать *v. impfv.* [*pfv.* **разверну́ть**] **1,** to unfold; unwrap. **2,** to unroll; unfurl. **3,** *mil.* to deploy. **4,** to launch (a campaign, movement, etc.). **5,** to develop; expand. —**развёртываться,** *refl.* **1,** to come unfolded; come unrolled; come undone. **2,** *mil.* to deploy. **3,** *fig.* to develop.

развесели́ть *v. pfv.* to cheer up; gladden. —**развесели́ться,** *refl.* to cheer up; become cheerful.

развесёлый *adj., colloq.* gay; merry; jolly.

разве́систый *adj.* (*of a tree*) spreading.

разве́сить [*infl.* **-шу, -сишь**] *v., pfv. of* **разве́шивать.**

разве́ска *n.* weighing.

развесно́й *adj.* sold by weight.

развести́ [*infl. like* **вести́**] *v., pfv. of* **разводи́ть.** —**развести́сь,** *refl., pfv. of* **разводи́ться.**

разветви́ть [*infl.* **-влю́, -ви́шь**] *v., pfv. of* **разветвля́ть.** —**разветви́ться,** *refl., pfv. of* **разветвля́ться.**

разветвле́ние *n.* fork (*in a road*).

разветвля́ться *v.r. impfv.* [*pfv.* **разветви́ться**] **1,** (*of a tree or bush*) to form branches. **2,** (*of a road*) to fork; divide.

разве́шивать *v. impfv.* [*pfv.* **разве́сить**] **1,** to weigh out. **2,** [*pfv. also* **разве́шать**] to hang out (a number of objects). **3,** (*of a tree*) to spread (its branches).

разве́ять *v., pfv. of* **разве́ивать.**

развива́ть *v. impfv.* [*pfv.* **разви́ть**] **1,** to develop. **2,** to unwind; unravel. —**развива́ться,** *refl.* **1,** to develop. **2,** to come unwound.

разви́лина *n.* fork (*in a road or branches of a tree*).

разви́листый *adj.* forked.

разви́лка [*gen. pl.* **-лок**] *n.* fork (*in a road*).

развинти́ть [*infl.* **-чу́, -ти́шь**] *v., pfv. of* **разви́нчивать.** —**развинти́ться,** *refl., pfv. of* **разви́нчиваться.**

разви́нченный *adj.* **1,** unscrewed. **2,** (*of one's gait*) unsteady. **3,** *colloq.* unnerved.

разви́нчивать *v. impfv.* [*pfv.* **развинти́ть**] to unscrew. —**разви́нчиваться,** *refl.* **1,** to come unscrewed; come loose. **2,** *colloq.* to go to pieces. **3,** *colloq.* (*of one's nerves*) to be shot.

разви́тие *n.* development. —**разви́тие собы́тий,** course of events.

развито́й *adj.* [*short form* **ра́звит, развита́, ра́звито**] **1,** highly developed. **2,** mature.

разви́ть [*infl.* **разовью́, разовьёшь;** *past fem.* **развила́**] *v., pfv. of* **развива́ть.** —**разви́ться,** *refl., pfv. of* **развива́ться.**

развлека́тельный *adj.* done purely for pleasure or entertainment; entertainment (*attrib.*).

развлека́ть *v. impfv.* [*pfv.* **развле́чь**] to entertain; amuse. —**развлека́ться,** *refl.* to amuse oneself; seek diversion.

развлече́ние *n.* amusement; entertainment; diversion; recreation.

развле́чь [*infl. like* **влечь**] *v., pfv. of* **развлека́ть.** —**развле́чься,** *refl., pfv. of* **развлека́ться.**

разво́д *n.* **1,** divorce. В разво́де, divorced. **2,** posting (*of sentries*). **3,** breeding. *See also* **разво́ды.**

разводи́ть *v. impfv.* [*pfv.* **развести́;** *pres.* **-вожу́, -во́дишь**] **1,** to take; conduct (*each to his place*). **2,** *mil.* to post (sentries). **3,** to separate; pull apart. **4,** to dilute; dissolve. **5,** to raise; breed. **6,** to grow; cultivate (plants). **7,** to build; make (a fire). **8,** *in* **разводи́ть рука́ми,** to throw up one's hands. —**разводи́ться,** *refl.* **1,** (*with* **с** + *instr.*) to divorce; get a divorce from. **2,** to breed; multiply.

разво́дка *n., colloq.* separating. Разво́дка моста́, opening up of a drawbridge.

разводно́й *adj., in* **разводно́й мост,** drawbridge.

разво́ды [*gen.* **-дов**] *n. pl.* **1,** design; pattern. **2,** *colloq.* streaks; stains.
разво́з *n.* delivery; conveyance; transport.
развози́ть *v. impfv.* [*pfv.* **развезти́;** *pres.* **-вожу́, -во́зишь**] **1,** to deliver; convey; transport (*each to his or its destination*). **2,** *impers., colloq.* to become impassable: доро́гу развезло́, the road became impassable.
разво́зка *n., colloq.* delivery; conveyance; transport.
разволнова́ть *v. pfv.* [*infl.* **-ну́ю, -ну́ешь**] to upset; throw into a state. —**разволнова́ться,** *refl.* to become highly upset.
развора́чивать *v. impfv.* **1,** [*pfv.* **разверну́ть**] to turn (a vehicle) around. **2,** [*pfv.* **разворoти́ть**] *colloq.* to upset; throw into disorder. —**развора́чиваться,** *refl.* [*pfv.* **разверну́ться**] to turn around (*in a vehicle*).
разворова́ть [*infl.* **-ру́ю, -ру́ешь**] *v., pfv. of* **разворо́вывать.**
разворо́вывать *v. impfv.* [*pfv.* **разворова́ть**] *colloq.* to steal; make off with.
разворо́т *n.* **1,** U-turn. **2,** turn (*in a road*). **3,** (*with gen.*) *colloq.* development (of). **4,** inside (*of something that folds over*). **5,** double page; centerfold.
развороти́ть [*infl.* **-рочу́, -ро́тишь**] *v., pfv. of* **развора́чивать** (*in sense #2*).
развра́т *n.* debauchery; depravity.
разврати́ть [*infl.* **-щу́, -ти́шь**] *v., pfv. of* **развраща́ть.** —**разврати́ться,** *refl., pfv. of* **развраща́ться.**
развра́тник *n.* profligate; lecher; libertine; rake; roué.
развра́тничать *v. impfv.* to lead a dissolute life.
развра́тный *adj.* dissolute; licentious.
развраща́ть *v. impfv.* [*pfv.* **разврати́ть**] to corrupt; deprave; debauch. —**развраща́ться,** *refl.* **1,** to become corrupted. **2,** to give way to debauchery.
развраще́ние *n.* (*with gen.*) corruption (of).
развращённый *adj.* corrupt; depraved; dissolute. —**развращённость,** *n.f.* depravity.
развью́чивать *v. impfv.* [*pfv.* **развью́чить**] to unload (a pack animal).
развяза́ть [*infl.* **-вяжу́, -вя́жешь**] *v., pfv. of* **развя́зывать.** —**развяза́ться,** *refl., pfv. of* **развя́зываться.**
развя́зка [*gen. pl.* **-зок**] *n.* **1,** outcome; upshot. **2,** climax; dénouement.
развя́зный *adj.* overly familiar; forward.
развя́зывать *v. impfv.* [*pfv.* **развяза́ть**] **1,** to untie. **2,** *fig., colloq.* to free; release. —**развяза́ть войну́,** to unleash a war. —**развяза́ть язы́к, 1,** (*with dat.*) to loosen someone's tongue. **2,** to start talking.
развя́зываться *v.r. impfv.* [*pfv.* **развяза́ться**] **1,** to come untied; come loose; come undone. **2,** *fig.* (*with* **с** + *instr.*) *colloq.* to get rid of; finish with.
разгада́ть *v., pfv. of* **разга́дывать.**
разга́дка [*gen. pl.* **-док**] *n.* **1,** solving; unraveling. **2,** solution.
разга́дывать *v. impfv.* [*pfv.* **разгада́ть**] **1,** to solve; unravel. **2,** to figure out; divine.
разга́р *n.* high point; height: в разга́р сезо́на, at the height of the season. —**в (по́лном** *or* **са́мом) разга́ре,** at its height; in full swing.
разгиба́ть *v. impfv.* [*pfv.* **разогну́ть**] to unbend; straighten. —**рабо́тать, не разгиба́я спины́,** to work without letup.
разгиба́ться *v.r. impfv.* [*pfv.* **разогну́ться**] to straighten up.
разгильдя́й *n., colloq.* slob.
разглаго́льствовать *v. impfv.* [*pres.* **-ствую, -ствуешь**] *colloq.* to speak at length; hold forth.
разгла́живать *v. impfv.* [*pfv.* **разгла́дить**] **1,** to smooth out. **2,** to iron out.
разглаша́ть *v. impfv.* [*pfv.* **разгласи́ть**] to divulge; make known.
разглаше́ние *n.* divulging; divulgence.
разгляде́ть *v. pfv.* [*infl.* **-жу́, -ди́шь**] to discern; make out.
разгля́дывать *v. impfv.* to examine closely; look over.
разгне́ванный *adj.* furious; enraged; incensed.
разгне́вать *v. pfv.* to infuriate; enrage. —**разгне́ваться,** *refl.* to fly into a rage.
разгова́ривать *v. impfv.* to talk; speak; converse. Разгова́ривать по-ру́сски, to speak Russian. Они́ не разгова́ривают друг с дру́гом, they don't talk to each other; they are not on speaking terms.
разгове́ться *v.r. pfv.* to break the Lenten fast.
разгово́р *n.* **1,** conversation. **2,** talk: то́лько и разгово́ру, что об э́том, it's all people are talking about. **3,** subject: перемени́ть разгово́р, to change the subject. Это друго́й разгово́р, that's another matter; that's something else again. —**без разгово́ров!; и никаки́х разгово́ров!,** and no argument!; I want to hear nothing more about it!
разговори́ться *v.r. pfv., colloq.* **1,** to get into a conversation; get to talking. **2,** to warm to one's subject.
разгово́рник *n.* phrase book.
разгово́рный *adj.* **1,** conversational. **2,** colloquial. —**разгово́рная бу́дка,** telephone booth.
разгово́рчивый *adj.* talkative; loquacious. —**разгово́рчивость,** *n.f.* loquaciousness.
разго́н *n.* **1,** dispersal. **2,** momentum. —**в разго́не,** (*of a number of people*) away on an errand or assignment. —**с разго́на,** full speed; full tilt.
разгоня́ть *v. impfv.* [*pfv.* **разогна́ть**] **1,** to disperse; break up. **2,** *fig.* to dispel (a feeling). **3,** to drive at high speed; race. —**разгоня́ться,** *refl.* to gather momentum.
разгора́живать *v. impfv.* [*pfv.* **разгороди́ть**] to partition off; fence off.
разгора́ться *v.r. impfv.* [*pfv.* **разгоре́ться**] **1,** to begin to burn properly. **2,** (*of one's cheeks*) to become flushed. **3,** *fig.* (*of passions, an argument, etc.*) to flare.
разгороди́ть [*infl.* **-рожу́, -ро́дишь** *or* **-роди́шь**] *v., pfv. of* **разгора́живать.**
разгорячи́ть *v., pfv. of* **горячи́ть.** —**разгорячи́ться,** *refl., pfv. of* **горячи́ться.**
разгра́бить *v. pfv.* [*infl.* **-блю, -бишь**] to rob; loot; ransack.
разграбле́ние *n.* plundering; looting.
разграниче́ние *n.* **1,** delimitation. **2,** differentiation.
разграни́чивать *v. impfv.* [*pfv.* **разграни́чить**] **1,** to delimit; demarcate. **2,** to distinguish; differentiate.
разграфи́ть *v., pfv. of* **графи́ть.**
разгреба́ть *v. impfv.* [*pfv.* **разгрести́**] to rake aside; shovel aside.
разгрести́ [*infl. like* **грести́**] *v., pfv. of* **разгреба́ть.**
разгро́м *n.* **1,** crushing defeat; rout. **2,** destruction; devastation. **3,** *colloq.* havoc; chaos.
разгроми́ть *v., pfv. of* **громи́ть.**
разгружа́ть *v. impfv.* [*pfv.* **разгрузи́ть**] **1,** to unload (a vehicle, vessel, etc.). **2,** *fig., colloq.* to relieve (of part of one's work). —**разгружа́ться,** *refl.* to unload; discharge cargo.

разгрузи́ть [*infl.* **-гружу́, -гру́зишь** *or* **-грузи́шь**] *v., pfv. of* **разгружа́ть.** —**разгрузи́ться,** *refl., pfv. of* **разгружа́ться.**

разгру́зка *n.* unloading.

разгрыза́ть *v. impfv.* [*pfv.* **разгры́зть**] to bite in two; crack between one's teeth.

разгры́зть [*infl. like* **грызть**] *v., pfv. of* **разгрыза́ть.**

разгу́л *n.* **1,** carousing. **2,** *fig.* (*with gen.*) wave: разгу́л наси́лия, wave of violence.

разгу́ливать *v. impfv.* [*pfv.* **разгуля́ть**] *colloq.* **1,** [*impfv. only*] to take a stroll. **2,** to dispel (a feeling). **3,** to amuse so as to keep awake. —**разгу́ливаться,** *refl., colloq.* **1,** to live it up; let oneself go. **2,** to become wide-awake. **3,** (*of the weather*) to clear up.

разгу́лье *n., colloq.* revelry.

разгу́льный *adj., colloq.* wild; fast; loose.

разгуля́ть *v., pfv. of* **разгу́ливать.** —**разгуля́ться,** *refl., pfv. of* **разгу́ливаться.**

раздава́ть *v. impfv.* [*pfv.* **разда́ть**; *pres.* **-даю́, -даёшь**] to distribute; give out; hand out. —**раздава́ться,** *refl.* **1,** to be heard; resound; ring out. **2,** to move aside; make way. **3,** *colloq.* to become fatter; fill out.

раздави́ть *v. pfv.* [*infl.* **-давлю́, -да́вишь**] **1,** *pfv. of* **дави́ть** (*in senses #4 & #5*). **2,** to overwhelm; crush.

разда́ривать *v. impfv.* [*pfv.* **раздари́ть**] to give away (*as gifts*).

раздари́ть [*infl.* **-дарю́, -да́ришь**] *v., pfv. of* **разда́ривать.**

разда́точный *adj.* distributing; distribution (*attrib.*).

разда́ть [*infl. like* **дать**; *past* **ро́здал** *or* **разда́л, раздала́, ро́здало** *or* **разда́ло**] *v., pfv. of* **раздава́ть.** —**разда́ться,** *refl.* [*past* **разда́лся, -дала́сь, -дало́сь** *or* **-да́лось**] *pfv. of* **раздава́ться.**

разда́ча *n.* distribution.

раздва́ивать *v. impfv.* [*pfv.* **раздвои́ть**] to divide in half. —**раздва́иваться,** *refl.* to divide; be divided.

раздвига́ть *v. impfv.* [*pfv.* **раздви́нуть**] **1,** to draw apart; spread apart; pull apart. **2,** to draw aside; move aside. **3,** to push one's way through (a crowd). **4,** to extend (a table). —**раздвига́ться,** *refl.* **1,** (*of a curtain*) to part; (*of a crowd*) to step aside; make way. **2,** [*impfv. only*] (*of a table*) to expand; open up.

раздвижно́й *adj.* **1,** expandable; extensible: раздвижно́й стол, expandable table. **2,** sliding: раздвижна́я дверь, sliding door; раздвижно́й за́навес, draw curtain.

раздви́нуть *v., pfv. of* **раздвига́ть.** —**раздви́нуться,** *refl., pfv. of* **раздвига́ться.**

раздвое́ние *n.* split; division. —**раздвое́ние ли́чности,** split personality.

раздво́енный *adj.* divided; double. —**раздво́енное копы́то,** cloven hoof.

раздвои́ть *v., pfv. of* **раздва́ивать.** —**раздвои́ться,** *refl., pfv. of* **раздва́иваться.**

раздева́лка [*gen. pl.* **-лок**] *n., colloq.* cloakroom; checkroom.

раздева́льня [*gen. pl.* **-лен**] *n.* **1,** cloakroom; checkroom. **2,** dressing room; locker room.

раздева́ние *n.* undressing.

раздева́ть *v. impfv.* [*pfv.* **разде́ть**] to undress. —**раздева́ться,** *refl.* **1,** to get undressed. **2,** to take off one's coat.

разде́л *n.* **1,** division; dividing up. **2,** section; part (*of a book, article, etc.*).

разде́лать *v., pfv. of* **разде́лывать.** —**разде́латься,** *refl., pfv. of* **разде́лываться.**

разделе́ние *n.* division.

раздели́тельный *adj.* **1,** dividing. **2,** *gram.* partitive; disjunctive.

раздели́ть [*infl.* **-делю́, -де́лишь**] *v., pfv. of* **дели́ть** *and* **разделя́ть.** —**раздели́ться,** *refl., pfv. of* **дели́ться** *and* **разделя́ться.**

разде́лывать *v. impfv.* [*pfv.* **разде́лать**] **1,** to dress; prepare (*for cooking*). **2,** (*with* **под** + *acc.*) to finish (in imitation wood grain, marble, etc.). —**разде́лываться,** *refl.* (*with* **с** + *instr.*) *colloq.* **1,** to settle (debts); settle up with (someone). **2,** to get even with; settle scores with.

разде́льный *adj.* **1,** separate. **2,** (*of speech*) clear; distinct.

разделя́ть *v. impfv.* [*pfv.* **раздели́ть**] **1,** to divide. **2,** to share. **3,** to separate. —**разделя́ться,** *refl.* **1,** to divide; be divided. **2,** to break up; split up. **3,** [*impfv. only*] (*with* **на** + *acc.*) to fall into (different categories).

разде́ть [*infl.* **-де́ну, -де́нешь**] *v., pfv. of* **раздева́ть.** —**разде́ться,** *refl., pfv. of* **раздева́ться.**

раздира́ть *v. impfv.* [*pfv.* **разодра́ть**] **1,** to tear to pieces. **2,** [*impfv. only*] *fig.* to tear apart. —**раздира́ться,** *refl., colloq.* to tear; rip.

раздира́ющий *adj.* heart-rending; heartbreaking.

раздобре́ть *v., pfv. of* **добре́ть** (*in sense #2*).

раздобыва́ть *v. impfv.* [*pfv.* **раздобы́ть**] *colloq.* to obtain; wangle; get hold of.

раздобы́ть [*infl. like* **быть**; *past fem.* **-была́**] *v., pfv. of* **раздобыва́ть.**

раздо́лье *n.* **1,** open space; expanse. **2,** *fig.* freedom.

раздо́льный *adj., colloq.* **1,** vast; spacious; far-flung. **2,** *fig.* free; carefree.

раздо́р *n., often pl.* discord; dissension.

раздоса́довать *v. pfv.* [*infl.* **-дую, -дуешь**] *colloq.* to vex.

раздража́ть *v. impfv.* [*pfv.* **раздражи́ть**] **1,** to irritate; annoy. **2,** to irritate (the skin, eyes, etc.). —**раздража́ться,** *refl.* to become irritated.

раздраже́ние *n.* irritation.

раздражи́тель *n.m.* irritant.

раздражи́тельный *adj.* irritable. —**раздражи́тельность,** *n.f.* irritability.

раздражи́ть *v., pfv. of* **раздража́ть.** —**раздражи́ться,** *refl., pfv. of* **раздража́ться.**

раздразни́ть *v. pfv.* [*infl.* **-дразню́, -дра́знишь**] **1,** to tease; provoke. **2,** to whet (a desire, one's appetite, etc.).

раздроби́ть [*infl.* **-блю́, -би́шь**] *v., pfv. of* **дроби́ть** *and* **раздробля́ть.** —**раздроби́ться,** *refl., pfv. of* **дроби́ться** *and* **раздробля́ться.**

раздро́бленность *n.f.* disunity; division; fragmentation.

раздробля́ть *v. impfv.* [*pfv.* **раздроби́ть**] **1,** to smash; splinter. **2,** *fig.* to fragment; splinter. **3,** to reduce; convert (into smaller units). —**раздробля́ться,** *refl.* to splinter.

раздува́ть *v. impfv.* [*pfv.* **разду́ть**] **1,** to fan (a fire). **2,** to inflate. **3,** to stir up; whip up; foment. **4,** *colloq.* to exaggerate; blow up. **5,** *impers., colloq.* to be puffed up: у него́ разду́ло щёку, his cheek is puffed up. —**раздува́ться,** *refl.* **1,** to swell up; become swollen. **2,** to bulge.

раздумать *v. pfv.* to change one's mind. —**раздуматься,** *refl.* (*with* **о**) *colloq.* to begin to reflect (on).
раздумывать *v. impfv.* to ponder; think; deliberate. —**не раздумывая,** without a moment's hesitation.
раздумье *n.* **1,** thought; meditation. **2,** *usu. pl.* thoughts. **3,** second thoughts; doubts.
раздутый *adj., colloq.* **1,** swollen; puffed up. **2,** inflated; excessive. **3,** exaggerated; overblown.
раздуть [*infl.* **-дую, -дуешь**] *v., pfv. of* **раздувать.** —**раздуться,** *refl., pfv. of* **раздуваться.**
разевать *v. impfv.* [*pfv.* **разинуть**] *colloq.* to open (one's mouth) wide. —**разинув рот,** open-mouthed.
разжалобить *v. pfv.* [*infl.* **-блю, -бишь**] to move to pity; stir.
разжалование *n., obs.* demotion.
разжаловать *v. pfv.* [*infl.* **-лую, -луешь**] *obs.* to demote.
разжать [*infl.* **разожму, разожмёшь**] *v., pfv. of* **разжимать.** —**разжаться,** *refl., pfv. of* **разжиматься.**
разжевать [*infl.* **-жую, -жуёшь**] *v., pfv. of* **разжёвывать.**
разжёвывать *v. impfv.* [*pfv.* **разжевать**] to chew; masticate.
разжечь [*infl.* **разожгу, разожжёшь, ...разожгут;** *past* **разжёг, разожгла**] *v., pfv. of* **разжигать.** —**разжечься,** *refl., pfv. of* **разжигаться.**
разжигание *n.* **1,** kindling. **2,** *fig.* igniting (of conflicts); unleashing (of war).
разжигать *v. impfv.* [*pfv.* **разжечь**] **1,** to kindle; light. **2,** *fig.* to kindle; inflame. **3,** *fig.* to unleash (a war). —**разжигаться,** *refl.* to catch (fire); start burning.
разжижать *v. impfv.* [*pfv.* **разжидить**] *colloq.* to dilute.
разжижение *n.* dilution.
разжимать *v. impfv.* [*pfv.* **разжать**] to unclench; relax; release. —**разжиматься,** *refl.* to open; part; relax.
разжиреть *v., pfv. of* **жиреть.**
разжиться *v.r. pfv.* [*infl. like* **жить;** *past* **-жился, -жилась, -жилось**] *colloq.* to get rich.
разинуть *v., pfv. of* **разевать.**
разиня *n.m. & f., colloq.* scatterbrain.
разительный *adj.* striking.
разить *v. impfv.* [*pres.* **ражу, разишь**] **1,** to strike. **2,** to defeat; crush. **3,** *impers.* (*with instr.*) *colloq.* to reek (of): от него разит водкой, he reeks of vodka.
разлагать *v. impfv.* [*pfv.* **разложить**] **1,** to separate (*or* break down) into (its) constituent parts. **2,** *math.* to expand. **3,** *fig.* to corrupt. —**разлагаться,** *refl.* **1,** to decompose; decay. **2,** to degenerate. **3,** to disintegrate; collapse; go to pieces.
разлад *n.* **1,** lack of coordination; disorder. **2,** discord; dissension.
разлаживать *v. impfv.* [*pfv.* **разладить**] *colloq.* **1,** to put out of commission. **2,** to disrupt. —**разлаживаться,** *refl., colloq.* **1,** to go out of commission. **2,** *fig.* to go bad.
разламывать *v. impfv.* **1,** [*pfv.* **разломать**] to tear down. **2,** [*pfv.* **разломать** *or* **разломить**] to break (*into parts or pieces*). —**разламываться,** *refl.* to break apart.
разлениться *v.r. pfv.* [*infl.* **-ленюсь, -ленишься**] *colloq.* to become utterly lazy.
разлетаться *v.r. impfv.* [*pfv.* **разлететься**] **1,** to fly in all directions; scatter into the air. **2,** *fig.* (*of news*) to spread. **3,** to shatter. **4,** *fig.* (*of hopes, dreams, etc.*) to vanish; be shattered; be dashed. **5,** (*with* **в** + *acc. or* **к**) *colloq.* to rush; dash (into *or* up to).
разлечься *v.r. pfv.* [*infl. like* **лечь**] *colloq.* to stretch out.
разлив *n.* **1,** bottling. **2,** overflowing. **3,** high water; spring flood. —**в разлив,** for consumption on the premises.
разливание *n.* pouring.
разливательный *adj., in* **разливательная ложка,** ladle.
разливать *v. impfv.* [*pfv.* **разлить**] **1,** to spill. **2,** to pour (into many containers). **3,** *fig.* to spread; diffuse. **4,** *in* **(их) водой не разольёшь,** the two of them are inseparable. —**разливаться,** *refl.* **1,** to spill. **2,** (*of a river*) to overflow its banks. **3,** to spread. **4,** [*impfv. only*] *colloq.* to sing (melodiously); say (with feeling); sob (bitterly).
разливной *adj.* (*of beer*) on draft; on tap.
разлиновать *v. pfv.* [*infl.* **-ную, -нуешь**] to rule; line.
разлить [*infl.* **разолью, разольёшь;** *past fem.* **разлила**] *v., pfv. of* **разливать.** —**разлиться,** *refl., pfv. of* **разливаться.**
различать *v. impfv.* [*pfv.* **различить**] **1,** to distinguish; tell apart. **2,** to discern; make out. —**различаться,** *refl.* [*impfv. only*] to differ.
различие *n.* **1,** difference: различие во взглядах, difference of opinion. **2,** distinction: делать/проводить различие, to make/draw a distinction. —**знаки различия,** insignia.
различимый *adj.* **1,** distinguishable. **2,** discernible.
различительный *adj.* distinctive; distinguishing.
различить *v., pfv. of* **различать.**
различный *adj.* **1,** different; differing. **2,** various; diverse.
разложение *n.* **1,** decomposition. **2,** *fig.* decay; degeneration; disintegration.
разложить [*infl.* **-ложу, -ложишь**] *v., pfv. of* **раскладывать** *and* **разлагать.**
разлом *n.* **1,** breaking up. **2,** break.
разломать *v., pfv. of* **разламывать.** —**разломаться,** *refl., pfv. of* **разламываться.**
разломить [*infl.* **-ломлю, -ломишь**] *v., pfv. of* **разламывать** (*in sense #2*). —**разломиться,** *refl., pfv. of* **разламываться.**
разлука *n.* **1,** separation. Жить в разлуке, to be separated. **2,** parting.
разлучать *v. impfv.* [*pfv.* **разлучить**] to separate; part. —**разлучаться,** *refl.* to part company; separate.
разлюбить *v. pfv.* [*infl.* **-люблю, -любишь**] to cease to love; no longer love.
размагничивать *v. impfv.* [*pfv.* **размагнитить**] to demagnetize.
размазать [*infl.* **-мажу, -мажешь**] *v., pfv. of* **размазывать.** —**размазаться,** *refl., pfv. of* **размазываться.**
размазня *n., colloq.* **1,** gruel. **2,** wishy-washy person.
размазывать *v. impfv.* [*pfv.* **размазать**] **1,** to spread; smear. **2,** *colloq.* to pad (a story, report, etc.). —**размазываться,** *refl.* to smear.
размалывать *v. impfv.* [*pfv.* **размолоть**] to grind.
разматывать *v. impfv.* [*pfv.* **размотать**] to unwind unreel. —**разматываться,** *refl.* to unwind; become unwound.
размах *n.* **1,** swing; sweep (*of one's arm*). **2,** span:

размáх кры́льев, wingspan. **3,** *fig.* range; scope. —**со всего́ размáху,** with all one's might.

размáхивать *v. impfv.* [*pfv.* **размахну́ть**] (*with instr.*) **1,** [*impfv. only*] to wave; swing; brandish. **2,** to draw back (*in order to strike with*). —**размáхиваться,** *refl.* to draw back one's arm (*in order to strike someone or something*); haul off.

размахну́ть *v., pfv. of* **размáхивать.** —**размахну́ться,** *refl., pfv. of* **размáхиваться.**

размáчивать *v. impfv.* [*pfv.* **размочи́ть**] to soak; steep.

размáшистый *adj., colloq.* **1,** (*of a motion*) sweeping. **2,** (*of handwriting*) sprawling. **3,** (*of an expanse of land*) broad.

размежевáть [*infl.* **-жу́ю, -жу́ешь**] *v., pfv. of* **размежёвывать.**

размежёвывать *v. impfv.* [*pfv.* **размежевáть**] to delimit.

размельчáть *v. impfv.* [*pfv.* **размельчи́ть**] to crush; grind; reduce to small particles.

размéн *n.* exchange. —**размéн дéнег,** changing of money.

размéнивать *v. impfv.* [*pfv.* **разменя́ть**] to change (money). —**размéниваться,** *refl., colloq.* **1,** (*with instr.*) to exchange. **2,** to waste one's energies.

размéнный *adj.* change (*attrib.*): размéнная кáсса, change booth. —**размéнная монéта,** small change.

разменя́ть *v., pfv. of* **размéнивать.** —**разменя́ться,** *refl., pfv. of* **размéниваться.**

размéр *n.* **1,** size: размéр кóмнаты, the size of a room. Я ношу́ боти́нки деся́того размéра, I wear a size ten shoe. **2,** amount. В двойнóм размéре, twice as much. Ссу́да в размéре ты́сячи дóлларов, a $1000 loan. **3,** *often pl.* scale; extent; proportions. **4,** *pros.* meter. **5,** *music* measure.

размéренный *adj.* measured.

размеря́ть *v. impfv.* [*pfv.* **размéрить**] to measure.

размеси́ть [*infl.* **-мешу́, -мéсишь**] *v., pfv. of* **размéшивать** (*in sense #1*).

размести́ [*infl. like* **мести́**] *v., pfv. of* **разметáть**[1].

размести́ть [*infl.* **-щу́, -сти́шь**] *v., pfv. of* **размещáть.** —**размести́ться,** *refl., pfv. of* **размещáться.**

разметáть[1] *v. impfv.* [*pfv.* **размести́**] **1,** to sweep; sweep clean. **2,** to sweep away; sweep up.

разметáть[2] [*infl.* **-мечу́, -мéчешь**] *v., pfv. of* **размётывать.** —**разметáться,** *refl.* **1,** to lie with one's arms and legs outstretched. **2,** (*of one's hair*) to hang loosely.

размéтить [*infl.* **-чу, -тишь**] *v., pfv. of* **размечáть.**

размéтка [*gen. pl.* **-ток**] *n.* **1,** marking. **2,** mark.

размётывать *v. impfv.* [*pfv.* **разметáть**] **1,** to scatter; disperse. **2,** to destroy; demolish. **3,** to stretch out; spread apart.

размечáть *v. impfv.* [*pfv.* **размéтить**] to mark; mark up; mark out.

размéшивать *v. impfv.* **1,** [*pfv.* **размеси́ть**] to knead. **2,** [*pfv.* **размешáть**] to stir.

размещáть *v. impfv.* [*pfv.* **размести́ть**] **1,** to place; arrange; station (many people or items). **2,** to find lodging for; quarter (troops). **3,** to distribute; assign. **4,** to place (orders); float (a loan). —**размещáться,** *refl.* **1,** (*of many people*) to take their places; take seats. **2,** to be quartered.

размещéние *n.* **1,** placement; arrangement; stationing. **2,** distribution. **3,** quartering; billeting (*of troops*). **4,** placing (*of orders*); floating (*of a loan*).

разминáть *v. impfv.* [*pfv.* **размя́ть**] **1,** to mash; knead. **2,** *colloq.* to stretch (one's legs). —**разминáться,** *refl., colloq.* **1,** to stretch one's legs. **2,** to limber up.

размини́ровать *v. impfv. & pfv.* [*pres.* **-рую, -руешь**] to clear of mines.

рази́нка *n., colloq.* limbering up; warm-up.

размину́ться *v.r. pfv., colloq.* **1,** to miss one another; fail to meet. **2,** (*of letters*) to cross in the mail. **3,** to pass by each other (*in a narrow place*).

размножáть *v. impfv.* [*pfv.* **размнóжить**] **1,** to make copies of. **2,** to raise; breed. —**размножáться,** *refl.* to multiply; reproduce; breed; propagate.

размножéние *n.* **1,** copying; reproducion. **2,** reproduction; propagation.

размнóжить *v., pfv. of* размножáть. —**размнóжиться,** *refl., pfv. of* **размножáться.**

размозжи́ть *v. pfv.* to smash; shatter.

размокáть *v. impfv.* [*pfv.* **размнóкнуть**] to become soggy.

размóкнуть [*past* **-мóк, -ла**] *v., pfv. of* **размокáть.**

размóл *n.* **1,** grinding; milling. **2,** *in* кру́пного размóла, coarse; мéлкого размóла, finely ground.

размóлвка [*gen. pl.* **-вок**] *n.* spat; tiff.

размолóть [*infl.* **-мелю́, -мéлешь**] *v., pfv. of* **размáлывать.**

разморáживать *v. impfv.* [*pfv.* **разморóзить**] to defrost; unfreeze. —**размораживаться**, *refl.* to defrost; melt.

размотáть *v., pfv. of* **размáтывать.** —**размотáться,** *refl., pfv. of* **размáтываться.**

размочи́ть [*infl.* **-мочу́, -мóчишь**] *v., pfv. of* **размáчивать.**

размы́в *n.* washing away; erosion.

размывáть *v. impfv.* [*pfv.* **размы́ть**] **1,** to wash away; wash out: водá размы́ла дорóгу, the water/floodwaters washed out the road. **2,** to erode.

размыкáть *v. impfv.* [*pfv.* **разомкну́ть**] **1,** to open. **2,** to break (a circuit).

размы́ть [*infl.* **-мóю, -мóешь**] *v., pfv. of* **размывáть.**

размышлéние *n.* reflection; meditation; thought. —**по зрéлом размышлéнии,** on second thought.

размышля́ть *v. impfv.* to reflect; meditate; ponder.

размягчáть *v. impfv.* [*pfv.* **размягчи́ть**] to soften.

размягчéние *n.* softening.

размягчи́ть *v., pfv. of* **размягчáть.**

размя́кнуть [*past* **-мя́к, -ла**] *v., pfv. of* **мя́кнуть.**

размя́ть [*infl.* **разомну́, разомнёшь**] *v., pfv. of* **мять** (*in sense #1*) *and* **разминáть.** —**размя́ться,** *refl., pfv. of* **разминáться.**

разнаря́дка [*gen. pl.* **-док**] *n.* order; voucher.

разнáшивать *v. impfv.* [*pfv.* **разноси́ть**] to break in (shoes).

разнести́ [*infl. like* **нести́**] *v., pfv. of* **разноси́ть**[1] —**разнести́сь,** *refl., pfv. of* **разноси́ться.**

разнимáть *v. impfv.* [*pfv.* **разня́ть**] *colloq.* to separate; pull apart.

рáзниться *v.r. impfv.* to differ.

рáзница *n.* difference. —**большáя рáзница,** it makes a big difference. —**какáя рáзница?,** what difference does it make?

разнобóй *n.* lack of coordination; inconsistency.

разнови́дность *n.f.* a variety.

разновремéнный *adj.* occurring at different times.

разногла́сие *n.* **1,** disagreement. **2,** discrepancy.

разноголо́сица *n., colloq.* **1,** dissonance. **2,** disageement. **3,** discrepancy.

разноголо́сый *adj.* discordant.

ра́зное *n., decl. as an adj.* **1,** various things. **2,** (*as a heading*) miscellaneous.

разнообра́зие *n.* variety; diversity.

разнообра́зить *v. impfv.* [*pres.* **-жу, -зишь**] to vary; diversify.

разнообра́зный *adj.* diverse; varied.

разноречи́вый *adj.* conflicting; contradictory.

разноро́дный *adj.* heterogeneous. —**разноро́дность,** *n.f.* heterogeneity.

разно́с *n.* **1,** carrying; delivery. **2,** *colloq.* sharp rebuke; dressing-down.

разноси́ть[1] *v. impfv.* [*pfv.* **разнести́;** *pres.* **-ношу́, -но́сишь**] **1,** to carry; deliver (*each to its place*). **2,** to distribute; hand around. **3,** to enter; record. **4,** *colloq.* to scatter; disperse. **5,** *colloq.* to spread. **6,** *colloq.* to shatter; destroy. **7,** *colloq.* to berate; upbraid. **8,** *colloq.* to criticize; excoriate; pan. **9,** *impers., colloq.* to swell: у меня́ щёку разнесло́, my cheek is swollen. —**разноси́ться,** *refl.* **1,** to spread rapidly. **2,** to sound; resound.

разноси́ть[2] [*infl.* **-ношу́, -но́сишь**] *v., pfv. of* **разна́шивать.**

разно́ска *n., colloq.* distribution; handing out.

разно́сный *adj., colloq.* scathing; blistering.

разносторо́нний *adj.* **1,** *math.* scalene. **2,** multifaceted; versatile. **3,** (*of education*) all-round. —**разносторо́нность,** *n.f.* versatility.

ра́зность *n.f.* **1,** *obs.* difference. **2,** *math.* difference. —**ра́зные ра́зности,** various things; this and that.

разно́счик *n.* **1,** delivery man. **2,** peddler.

разноцве́тный *adj.* of different colors.

разношёрстный *adj.* **1,** (*of animals*) of different colors. **2,** *fig., colloq.* motley.

разну́зданный *adj.* **1,** (*of a horse*) unbridled. **2,** *fig.* rowdy; unruly.

разну́здывать *v. impfv.* [*pfv.* **разнузда́ть**] to unbridle.

ра́зный *adj.* **1,** different; differing: ра́зные вку́сы, different/differing tastes. **2,** different; not the same: говори́ть на ра́зных языка́х, to speak different languages; not speak the same language. **3,** various: ра́зные тео́рии, various theories. **4,** *colloq.* all sorts of: ра́зная ру́хлядь, all sorts of junk. *See also* **ра́зное.**

разню́хивать *v. impfv.* [*pfv.* **разню́хать**] *colloq.* **1,** to smell out. **2,** *fig.* to smell about; nose about.

разня́ть [*infl.* **-ниму́, -ни́мешь;** *past* **разня́л** *or* **ро́знял, разняла́, разня́ло** *or* **ро́зняло**] *v., pfv. of* **разнима́ть.**

разоблача́ть *v. impfv.* [*pfv.* **разоблачи́ть**] to expose; unmask.

разоблаче́ние *n.* exposure.

разоблачи́ть *v., pfv. of* **разоблача́ть.**

разобра́ть [*infl.* **разберу́, разберёшь;** *past fem.* **разобрала́**] *v., pfv. of* **разбира́ть.** —**разобра́ться,** *refl., pfv. of* **разбира́ться.**

разобща́ть *v. impfv.* [*pfv.* **разобщи́ть**] **1,** to cut off. **2,** to alienate.

ра́зовый *adj.* one-time; for one-time use only.

разогна́ть [*infl.* **разгоню́, разго́нишь;** *past fem.* **разогнала́**] *v., pfv. of* **разгоня́ть.** —**разогна́ться,** *refl., pfv. of* **разгоня́ться.**

разогну́ть *v., pfv. of* **разгиба́ть.** —**разогну́ться,** *refl., pfv. of* **разгиба́ться.**

разогрева́ть *v. impfv.* [*pfv.* **разогре́ть**] **1,** to heat up; warm up. **2,** to reheat; warm over: разогре́тый обе́д, warmed-over dinner. —**разогрева́ться,** *refl.* to get hot; get warm.

разоде́ть *v. pfv.* [*infl.* **-оде́ну, -оде́нешь**] *colloq.* to dress up. —**разоде́ться,** *refl., colloq.* to dress up; get dressed up.

разодра́ть [*infl.* **раздеру́, раздерёшь;** *past fem.* **разодрала́**] *v., pfv. of* **раздира́ть.** —**разодра́ться,** *refl.* **1,** *pfv. of* **раздира́ться. 2,** *colloq.* to have a fight.

разозли́ть *v., pfv. of* **злить.** —**разозли́ться,** *refl., pfv. of* **зли́ться.**

разойти́сь [*infl.* **разойду́сь, разойдёшься;** *past* **разошёлся, разошла́сь**] *v.r., pfv. of* **расходи́ться.**

ра́зом *adv., colloq.* **1,** at once; at the same time. **2,** at once; instantly. **3,** at once; in one gulp; with one stroke.

разомкну́ть *v., pfv. of* **размыка́ть.**

разорва́ть [*infl. like* **рвать**] *v., pfv. of* **разрыва́ть.** —**разорва́ться,** *refl., pfv. of* **разрыва́ться.**

разоре́ние *n.* **1,** destruction; devastation. **2,** bankruptcy; ruin.

разори́тельный *adj.* devastating; ruinous.

разори́ть *v., pfv. of* **разоря́ть.** —**разори́ться,** *refl., pfv. of* **разоря́ться.**

разоружа́ть *v. impfv.* [*pfv.* **разоружи́ть**] *v.t.* to disarm. —**разоружа́ться,** *refl.* to disarm.

разоруже́ние *n.* disarmament.

разоружи́ть *v., pfv. of* **разоружа́ть.** —**разоружи́ться,** *refl., pfv. of* **разоружа́ться.**

разоря́ть *v. impfv.* [*pfv.* **разори́ть**] **1,** to ravage; devastate. **2,** to ruin. —**разоря́ться,** *refl.* **1,** to be ruined. **2,** to lose everything; go broke.

разосла́ть [*infl.* **-шлю́, -шлёшь**] *v., pfv. of* **рассыла́ть.**

разоспа́ться *v.r. pfv.* [*infl. like* **спать**] *colloq.* to fall fast asleep.

разостла́ть [*infl.* **расстелю́, рассте́лешь**] *v., pfv. of* **расстила́ть.**

разочарова́ние *n.* disappointment; disillusionment; disenchantment.

разочаро́ванный *adj.* disappointed; disillusioned; disenchanted.

разочарова́ть [*infl.* **-ру́ю, -ру́ешь**] *v., pfv. of* **разочаро́вывать.** —**разочарова́ться,** *refl., pfv. of* **разочаро́вываться.**

разочаро́вывать *v. impfv.* [*pfv.* **разочарова́ть**] to disappoint; disillusion. —**разочаро́вываться,** *refl.* (*with* **в** + *prepl.*) to be disappointed (with); become disillusioned (with).

разраба́тывать *v. impfv.* [*pfv.* **разрабо́тать**] **1,** to work out; develop (a plan, theory, device, etc.). **2,** to cultivate (land). **3,** to work (a mine); mine (a certain mineral).

разрабо́тка *n.* **1,** development. **2,** cultivation (*of land*). **3,** mining; extraction.

разра́внивать *v. impfv.* [*pfv.* **разровня́ть**] to level.

разража́ться *v.r. impfv.* [*pfv.* **разрази́ться**] **1,** to break out. **2,** (*with instr.*) to burst into (tears, laughter, etc.).

разраста́ться *v.r. impfv.* [*pfv.* **разрасти́сь**] to grow, expand; increase in size.

разрасти́сь [*infl. like* **расти́**] *v.r., pfv. of* **разраста́ться.**

разрежа́ть *v. impfv.* [*pfv.* **разреди́ть**] **1,** to thin out. **2,** to rarefy (the air).

разре́з *n.* **1,** cut; split. **2,** *med.* incision. **3,** section: попере́чный разре́з, cross section. **4,** *fig.* sense; aspect: в друго́м разре́зе, in a different sense/way/ light. —**в разре́зе** (+ *gen.*), in the light of.

разре́зать [*infl.* **-ре́жу, -ре́жешь**] *v., pfv. of* **разреза́ть.**

разреза́ть *v. impfv.* [*pfv.* **разре́зать**] **1,** to cut; slit. **2,** to lance. **3,** to bisect; divide in half.

разреша́ть *v. impfv.* [*pfv.* **разреши́ть**] **1,** (*with dat.*) to permit; allow. **2,** to solve (a problem). **3,** to settle; resolve (a dispute, conflict, etc.). —**разреша́ться,** *refl.* **1,** [*impfv. only*] (*with dat.*) to be permitted; be allowed: ему́ не разреша́ется (+ *inf.*), he is not permitted/ allowed to... **2,** to be solved; be settled. **3,** *in* **разреши́ться от бре́мени** (+ *instr.*), to give birth to; be delivered of.

разреше́ние *n.* **1,** permission: с ва́шего разреше́ния, with your permission. **2,** solution; resolution; settlement. **3,** *colloq.* permit.

разреши́мый *adj.* solvable.

разреши́ть *v., pfv. of* **разреша́ть.** —**разреши́ться,** *refl., pfv. of* **разреша́ться.**

разрисова́ть *v. pfv.* [*infl.* **-су́ю, -су́ешь**] to draw all over: сте́ны бы́ли разрисо́ваны цвета́ми, the walls had flowers drawn all over them.

разровня́ть *v., pfv. of* **разра́внивать.**

разро́зненный *adj.* **1,** (*of a set*) incomplete; (*of one of such a set*) odd. **2,** uncoordinated.

разро́знивать *v. impfv.* [*pfv.* **разро́знить**] to break; break up (a set of something).

разруба́ть *v. impfv.* [*pfv.* **разруби́ть**] **1,** to chop up. **2,** to cut up.

разруби́ть [*infl.* **-рублю́, -ру́бишь**] *v., pfv. of* **разруба́ть.**

разруга́ть *v. pfv., colloq.* **1,** to berate; chastise. **2,** to tear apart; pan (a book, play, etc.). —**разруга́ться,** *refl., colloq.* to quarrel.

разру́ха *n.* (economic) ruin.

разруша́ть *v. impfv.* [*pfv.* **разру́шить**] **1,** to destroy; demolish. **2,** *fig.* to wreck (one's plans, hopes, etc.); ruin (one's health). —**разруша́ться,** *refl.* **1,** to be destroyed; collapse. **2,** *fig.* to be ruined.

разруше́ние *n.* **1,** destruction (*act of destroying*). **2,** *pl.* destruction (*heavy damage*).

разруши́тель *n.m.* destroyer; wrecker.

разруши́тельный *adj.* destructive.

разру́шить *v., pfv. of* **разруша́ть.** —**разру́шиться,** *refl., pfv. of* **разруша́ться.**

разры́в *n.* **1,** break; rupture. **2,** breaking (*of relations*); breakup. **3,** burst (*of a shell*). **4,** gap.

разрыва́ть *v. impfv.* [*pfv.* **разорва́ть**] **1,** to tear; tear open; tear up. **2,** to blow up. **3,** *impers.* to burst: котёл разорва́ло, the boiler burst. **4,** *fig.* to break off; sever (relations, ties, etc.). **5,** *v.i.* (*with* **с** + *instr.*) *colloq.* to break (with someone). **6,** [*pfv.* **разры́ть**] to dig; dig up. —**разрыва́ться,** *refl.* [*pfv.* **разорва́ться**] **1,** to tear; be torn. **2,** to break; snap. **3,** to burst; explode; go off. **4,** (*of relations*) to be broken off.

разрывно́й *adj.* explosive.

разрыда́ться *v.r. pfv.* to burst into tears; begin to sob.

разры́ть [*infl.* **-ро́ю, -ро́ешь**] *v., pfv. of* **разрыва́ть** (*in sense #6*).

разрыхля́ть *v. impfv.* [*pfv.* **разрыхли́ть**] to loosen (soil, dirt, etc.).

разря́д *n.* **1,** category. **2,** class; rank: спортсме́н пе́рвого разря́да, top-class athlete; сле́сарь тре́тьего разря́да, metalworker of the third rank. **3,** discharge (*of electricity, a weapon, etc.*).

разряди́ть [*infl.* **-ряжу́, -ря́дишь** *or* **-ряди́шь**] *v., pfv. of* **разряжа́ть.** —**разряди́ться,** *refl., pfv. of* **разряжа́ться.**

разря́дка *n.* **1,** unloading (*of a weapon*); using up (*of a battery*). **2,** *fig.* relaxation; lessening (*of tension*); détente.

разряжа́ть *v. impfv.* [*pfv.* **разряди́ть**] **1,** to unload (a weapon). **2,** to use up; run down (a battery). **3,** *fig.* to relax (tension); defuse (a situation). Разряди́ть атмосфе́ру, to clear the air. **4,** *colloq.* to dress up; deck out. —**разряжа́ться,** *refl.* **1,** (*of a battery*) to run down. **2,** *fig.* to become less tense. **3,** *colloq.* to get dressed up.

разубежда́ть *v. impfv.* [*pfv.* **разубеди́ть**] (*with* **в** + *prepl.*) to change someone's mind (about); convince to the contrary. —**разубежда́ться,** *refl.* (*with* **в** + *prepl.*) to change one's mind (about).

разува́ть *v. impfv.* [*pfv.* **разу́ть**] to take off (someone's) shoes. —**разува́ться,** *refl.* to take off one's shoes.

разуверя́ть *v. impfv.* [*pfv.* **разуве́рить**] (*with* **в** + *prepl.*) to disillusion (about); disabuse (of); change someone's mind (about). —**разуверя́ться,** *refl.* (*with* **в** + *prepl.*) to lose faith (in); lose hope (of).

разузнава́ть *v. impfv.* [*pfv.* **разузна́ть;** *pres.* **-знаю́, -знаёшь**] *colloq.* **1,** [*impfv. only*] to make inquiries; try to find out. **2,** to find out.

разукра́шивать *v. impfv.* [*pfv.* **разукра́сить**] *colloq.* to adorn; embellish.

разукрупня́ть *v. impfv.* [*pfv.* **разукрупни́ть**] to break up into smaller units.

ра́зум *n.* reason; intellect. —**у меня́ ум за ра́зум захо́дит,** I am at my wits' end.

разуме́ние *n., obs.* understanding.

разуме́ть *v. impfv.* **1,** to mean. **2,** *obs.* to understand.

разуме́ться *v.r. impfv.* to be understood; be taken to mean. —**разуме́ется,** naturally; of course. —**само́ собо́й разуме́ется,** it goes without saying.

разу́мно *adv.* sensibly; rationally. —*adj., used predicatively* reasonable: э́то вполне́ разу́мно, that is entirely reasonable.

разу́мный *adj.* **1,** intelligent; rational. **2,** clever. **3,** reasonable; sensible; logical.

разу́ть [*infl.* **-зу́ю, -зу́ешь**] *v., pfv. of* **разува́ть.** —**разу́ться,** *refl., pfv. of* **разува́ться.**

разу́чивать *v. impfv.* [*pfv.* **разучи́ть**] to learn. —**разу́чиваться,** *refl.* to forget; forget how (to); lose one's ability (to).

разучи́ть [*infl.* **-учу́, -у́чишь**] *v., pfv. of* **разу́чивать.** —**разучи́ться,** *refl., pfv. of* **разу́чиваться.**

разъеда́ть *v. impfv.* [*pfv.* **разъе́сть**] to eat away; corrode.

разъедине́ние *n.* **1,** separation. **2,** disconnecting. **3,** disengagement.

разъединя́ть *v. impfv.* [*pfv.* **разъедини́ть**] **1,** to separate. **2,** to disconnect. —**разъединя́ться,** *refl.* **1,** to come apart. **2,** to disengage.

разъе́зд *n.* **1,** departure (*of people in different directions*). **2,** *pl.* travels: в разъе́здах, traveling; on the move. **3,** *mil.* mounted patrol. **4,** *R.R.* short stretch of double track.
разъездно́й *adj.* **1,** traveling. **2,** for traveling.
разъезжа́ть *v. impfv.* to travel. —**разъезжа́ться,** *refl.* [*pfv.* **разъе́хаться**] **1,** to depart (*in various directions*). **2,** to pass by each other; miss each other; fail to meet. **3,** to be able to pass by each other (*on a narrow street, road, etc.*). **4,** (*of a married couple*) to separate; break up. **5,** *colloq.* to fall apart; come apart.
разъе́сть [*infl. like* **есть**] *v., pfv. of* **разъеда́ть.**
разъе́хаться [*infl.* **разъе́дусь, разъе́дешься**] *v.r., pfv. of* **разъезжа́ться.**
разъяря́ть *v. impfv.* [*pfv.* **разъяри́ть**] to enrage; infuriate.
разъясне́ние *n.* explanation; clarification.
разъясни́тельный *adj.* explanatory.
разъясня́ть *v. impfv.* [*pfv.* **разъясни́ть**] to explain; elucidate; clarify. —**разъясня́ться,** *refl.* to become clear; clear up.
разы́грывать *v. impfv.* [*pfv.* **разыгра́ть**] **1,** to perform; put on. **2,** to play (a certain card, chess opening, etc.). **3,** to raffle (off). **4,** to pose as; play the role of. **5,** *colloq.* to fool; make a fool of. —**разы́грываться,** *refl.* **1,** to play; frolic. **2,** *colloq.* (*of a performer*) to warm to one's part. **3,** *fig.* to increase in intensity; build up.
разыска́ть *v. pfv.* [*infl.* **разыщу́, разы́щешь**] **1,** *pfv. of* **разы́скивать. 2,** to find.
разы́скивать *v. impfv.* [*pfv.* **разыска́ть**] to search for; hunt for; seek.
рай [*2nd loc.* **раю́**] *n.* paradise.
райко́м *n.* district committee (*contr. of* **райо́нный комите́т**).
райо́н *n.* **1,** area; region. **2,** district (*of a city*). **3,** subdivision of an oblast; rayon. —**райо́нный,** *adj.* district (*attrib.*).
ра́йский *adj.* heavenly. —**ра́йская пти́ца,** bird of paradise.
рак *n.* **1,** crawfish. **2,** cancer (*disease*). **3,** *cap., astron.* Cancer: тро́пик Ра́ка, Tropic of Cancer.
ра́ка *n.* shrine (*of a saint*).
раке́та *n.* **1,** rocket. **2,** missile.
раке́тка [*gen. pl.* **-ток**] *n.* (tennis) racket.
раке́тный *adj.* rocket (*attrib.*); missile (*attrib.*).
ра́ковина *n.* **1,** shell. **2,** sink. **3,** bandstand. —**ушна́я ра́ковина,** auricle (*of the ear*).
ра́ковый *adj.* **1,** of (a) crawfish. **2,** cancer (*attrib.*); cancerous.
ракообра́зное *n., decl. as an adj.* crustacean.
раку́рс *also,* **ра́курс** *n.* **1,** *art* foreshortening. В ра́курсе, foreshortened. **2,** *fig.* perspective.
раку́шка [*gen. pl.* **-шек**] *n.* shell; sea shell.
ра́ма *n.* frame.
ра́мка [*gen. pl.* **-мок**] *n.* **1,** small frame. **2,** *pl.* limits; bounds. —**в ра́мках** (+ *gen.*), within the framework of.
ра́мочный *adj.* frame (*attrib.*).
ра́мпа *n., theat.* footlights.
ра́на *n.* wound.
ранг *n.* rank.
ранго́ут *n., naut.* masts and spars. —**рангоу́тный,** *adj., in* **рангоу́тное де́рево,** *naut.* spar.
ра́нее *adv.* earlier; sooner.
ране́ние *n.* **1,** wounding; injuring. **2,** wound; injury: получи́ть ране́ние, to be wounded; be injured.
ра́неный *adj.* wounded; injured. —*n.* wounded man; casualty. Ухо́д за ра́неными, care of the wounded.
ра́нец [*gen.* **-нца**] *n.* **1,** knapsack. **2,** satchel.
ранжи́р *n., in* **по ранжи́ру,** in size order.
ра́нить *v. impfv. & pfv.* to wound; injure. Он был ра́нен в но́гу, he was wounded in the leg.
ра́нний *adj.* early.
ра́но *adv.* early. —*adj., used predicatively* early: ещё ра́но, it is still early. —**ра́но и́ли по́здно,** sooner or later.
рант [*2nd loc.* **ранту́**] *n.* welt (*of a shoe*).
ра́нчо *n. indecl.* ranch.
рань *n.f., colloq.* early morning hours: в таку́ю рань, at such an ungodly hour.
ра́ньше *adv.* **1,** earlier; sooner. **2,** before. **3,** (*with gen.*) before; ahead of. **4,** before; formerly. —**ра́ньше вре́мени; ра́ньше сро́ка,** ahead of time; ahead of schedule.
рапи́ра *n.* rapier; foil.
ра́порт *n.* report.
рапортова́ть *v. impfv. & pfv.* [*pres.* **-ту́ю, -ту́ешь**] to report.
рапс *n.* rape (*plant*). —**ра́псовый,** *adj.* rape (*attrib.*): ра́псовое ма́сло, rape oil.
рапсо́дия *n.* rhapsody.
рас- *prefix, var. of* **раз-** (*used before voiceless consonants*).
ра́са *n.* race: жёлтая ра́са, the yellow race.
раси́зм *n.* racism. —**раси́ст,** *n.* racist. —**раси́стский,** *adj.* racist.
раска́иваться *v.r. impfv.* [*pfv.* **раска́яться**] to repent; be sorry.
раскалённый *adj.* scorching; burning; red-hot.
раскали́ть *v., pfv. of* **раскаля́ть.** —**раскали́ться,** *refl., pfv. of* **раскаля́ться.**
раска́лывать *v. impfv.* [*pfv.* **расколо́ть**] **1,** to split; cleave. **2,** *fig.* to split; divide. —**раска́лываться,** *refl.* to split; split up.
раскаля́ть *v. impfv.* [*pfv.* **раскали́ть**] to make red-hot. —**раскаля́ться,** *refl.* to become red-hot.
раска́пывать *v. impfv.* [*pfv.* **раскопа́ть**] **1,** to dig; dig up. **2,** to excavate. **3,** *fig., colloq.* to dig up; unearth.
раска́рмливать *v. impfv.* [*pfv.* **раскорми́ть**] to fatten (up).
раска́т *n.* peal; clap; burst (*of thunder, laughter, etc.*).
раската́ть *v., pfv. of* **раска́тывать**[1].
раска́тистый *adj.* rolling; resounding.
раскати́ть [*infl.* **-качу́, -ка́тишь**] *v., pfv. of* **раска́тывать**[2]. —**раскати́ться,** *refl., pfv. of* **раска́тываться.**
раска́тывать[1] *v. impfv.* [*pfv.* **раската́ть**] **1,** to unroll. **2,** to smooth out; level. **3,** to roll (dough).
раска́тывать[2] *v. impfv.* [*pfv.* **раскати́ть**] to set in motion by rolling. —**раска́тываться,** *refl.* **1,** to gather speed. **2,** to roll about. **3,** to resound.
раска́чивать *v. impfv.* [*pfv.* **раскача́ть**] **1,** to rock. **2,** [*impfv. only*] (*with instr.*) to swing. **3,** *fig., colloq.* to rouse to action. —**раска́чиваться,** *refl.* **1,** to swing back and forth. **2,** [*impfv. only*] *colloq.* to sway (*while walking*). **3,** *fig., colloq.* to bestir oneself; get (oneself) moving.
раска́шляться *v.r. pfv.* to have a fit of coughing.
раска́яние *n.* repentance; remorse.

раскáяться [*infl.* **-кáюсь, -кáешься**] *v.r., pfv. of* **раскáиваться.**

расквартировáние *n.* quartering; billeting.

расквартировáть *v. pfv.* [*infl.* **-рýю, -рýешь**] to quarter; billet.

расквáшивать *v. impfv.* [*pfv.* **расквáсить**] *colloq.* to smash in; bloody: расквáсить нос (+ *dat.*), to bloody someone's nose.

расквитáться *v.r. pfv.* (*with* **с** + *instr.*) *colloq.* **1,** to settle one's debts (with); square one's accounts (with). **2,** to get even (with).

раскидáть *v., pfv. of* **раскидывать** (*in sense #4*).

раскидистый *adj.* (*of a tree*) spreading.

раскидывать *v. impfv.* [*pfv.* **раскинуть**] **1,** to spread; spread out. **2,** to pitch (a tent); set up (camp). **3,** *in* **раскидывать умóм,** *colloq.* to ponder. **4,** [*pfv.* **раскидáть**] to scatter. —**раскидываться,** *refl.* [*pfv.* **раскинуться**] **1,** to stretch; extend (*over a wide area*). **2,** *colloq.* to stretch out; sprawl.

раскинуть *v., pfv. of* **раскидывать.** —**раскинуться,** *refl., pfv. of* **раскидываться.**

раскисáть *v. impfv.* [*pfv.* **раскиснуть**] *colloq.* **1,** to become soggy; become limp. **2,** *fig.* to become listless; become apathetic. **3,** *fig.* to become very emotional.

раскиснуть [*past* **-кис, -ла**] *v., pfv. of* **раскисáть.**

расклáдка *n.* **1,** laying out; spreading. **2,** making (*of a fire, bed, etc.*). **3,** apportionment.

раскладнóй *adj.* folding.

раскладýшка [*gen. pl.* **-шек**] *n., colloq.* cot.

расклáдывать *v. impfv.* [*pfv.* **разложить**] **1,** to put (*each in its place*); put away. **2,** to lay out; spread out. **3,** to distribute; apportion. **4,** to make; build (a fire). —**расклáдываться,** *refl., colloq.* to lay one's things out.

расклáниваться *v.r. impfv.* [*pfv.* **расклáняться**] **1,** to bow. **2,** (*of a performer*) to take a bow. **3,** (*with* **с** + *instr.*) *colloq.* to take leave of.

расклéивать *v. impfv.* [*pfv.* **расклéить**] **1,** to unglue; unseal. **2,** to post (a notice, placard, etc.) in many places. —**расклéиваться,** *refl.* **1,** to come unstuck; come apart. **2,** *fig., colloq.* to fall through. **3,** *fig., colloq.* to feel run-down.

расклéйка *n.* posting; hanging up.

раскóванный *adj.* uninhibited; unconstrained. Чýвствовать себя раскóванно, to feel uninhibited; feel free to do what one pleases.

расковáть [*infl.* **-кую, -куёшь**] *v., pfv. of* **раскóвывать.**

раскóвывать *v. impfv.* [*pfv.* **расковáть**] **1,** to unshoe (a horse). **2,** to unchain; unshackle.

раскóл *n.* split; schism; cleavage.

расколóть [*infl.* **-колю, -кóлешь**] *v., pfv. of* **колóть** (*in sense #4*) *and* **раскáлывать.** —**расколóться,** *refl., pfv. of* **раскáлываться.**

раскóльник *n.* **1,** religious dissenter. **2,** *fig.* person exerting a divisive influence; splitter.

раскóльнический *adj.* schismatic; divisive.

раскопáть *v., pfv. of* **раскáпывать.**

раскóпки [*gen.* **-пок**] *n.pl.* excavations.

раскормить [*infl.* **-кормлю, -кóрмишь**] *v., pfv. of* **раскáрмливать.**

раскоря́ка *n.m. & f., colloq.* bowlegged person.

раскóсый *adj.* (*of one's eyes*) slanting.

раскошéливаться *v.r. impfv.* [*pfv.* **раскошéлиться**] *colloq.* to pay up; loosen one's purse strings.

раскрáдывать *v. impfv.* [*pfv.* **раскрáсть**] to rob; steal.

раскрáивать *v. impfv.* [*pfv.* **раскроить**] to cut out.

раскрáсить [*infl.* **-шу, -сишь**] *v., pfv. of* **раскрáшивать.**

раскрáска *n.* **1,** coloring. **2,** coloration.

раскраснéться *v.r. pfv.* to blush; become flushed; turn red.

раскрáсть [*infl. like* **красть**] *v., pfv. of* **раскрáдывать.**

раскрáшивать *v. impfv.* [*pfv.* **раскрáсить**] to paint; color.

раскрепощáть *v. impfv.* [*pfv.* **раскрепостить**] to emancipate.

раскрепощéние *n.* emancipation.

раскритиковáть *v. pfv.* [*infl.* **-кýю, -кýешь**] to criticize severely.

раскричáться *v.r. pfv.* [*infl.* **-чýсь, -чишься**] *colloq.* **1,** to start shouting. **2,** (*with* **на** + *acc.*) to start swearing (at); call (someone) a lot of names.

раскроить *v., pfv. of* **раскрáивать.**

раскрошить *v. pfv.* [*infl.* **-крошý, -крóшишь**] to crumble.

раскрутить [*infl.* **-кручý, -крýтишь**] *v., pfv. of* **раскрýчивать.** —**раскрутиться,** *refl., pfv. of* **раскрýчиваться.**

раскрýчивать *v. impfv.* [*pfv.* **раскрутить**] to untwist. —**раскрýчиваться,** *refl.* to come untwisted.

раскрывáть *v. impfv.* [*pfv.* **раскрыть**] **1,** to open. **2,** to uncover; expose; bare. **3,** to reveal. **4,** to discover. **5,** *in* **раскрыть свои кáрты,** to reveal (*or* tip) one's hand. —**раскрывáться,** *refl.* **1,** to open. **2,** to uncover oneself; expose onself. **3,** to be uncovered; be exposed. **4,** to come out; come to light. **5,** to reveal one's secrets; tell one's story.

раскрытие *n.* **1,** opening. **2,** exposure. **3,** revelation; disclosure.

раскрыть [*infl.* **-крóю, -крóешь**] *v., pfv. of* **раскрывáть.** —**раскрыться,** *refl., pfv. of* **раскрывáться.**

раскупáть *v. impfv.* [*pfv.* **раскупить**] to buy up.

раскупить [*infl.* **-куплю, -кýпишь**] *v., pfv. of* **раскупáть.**

раскýпоривать *v. impfv.* [*pfv.* **раскýпорить**] to uncork.

раскýривать *v. impfv.* [*pfv.* **раскурить**] **1,** to get (a pipe, cigarette, etc.) lighted. **2,** [*impfv. only*] *colloq.* to pass the time smoking.

раскурить [*infl.* **-курю, -кýришь**] *v., pfv. of* **раскýривать.**

раскусить *v. pfv.* [*infl.* **-кушý, -кýсишь**] **1,** *pfv. of* **раскýсывать. 2,** *fig., colloq.* to see through (someone).

раскýсывать *v. impfv.* [*pfv.* **раскусить**] to bite; bite into pieces.

раскýтывать *v. impfv.* [*pfv.* **раскýтать**] to unwrap.

рáсовый *adj.* racial; race (*attrib.*).

распáд *n.* **1,** disintegration; breakup. **2,** *chem.; physics* decay.

распадáться *v.r. impfv.* [*pfv.* **распáсться**] **1,** to disintegrate; fall apart. **2,** *fig.* to break up.

распáивать *v. impfv.* [*pfv.* **распаять**] to unsolder.

распаковáть [*infl.* **-кýю, -кýешь**] *v., pfv. of* **распакóвывать.** —**распаковáться,** *refl., pfv. of* **распакóвываться.**

распакóвка *n.* unpacking.

распако́вывать *v. impfv.* [*pfv.* **распакова́ть**] to unpack. —**распако́вываться,** *refl., colloq.* to unpack; get unpacked.

распаля́ть *v. impfv.* [*pfv.* **распали́ть**] **1,** *colloq.* to make burning hot. **2,** *fig.* to fire up.

распа́ривать *v. impfv.* [*pfv.* **распа́рить**] **1,** to steam; stew. **2,** *colloq.* to cause to sweat.

распа́рывать *v. impfv.* [*pfv.* **распоро́ть**] **1,** to unstitch. **2,** to rip open. —**распа́рываться,** *refl.* to rip; split.

распа́сться [*infl. like* **пасть**] *v.r., pfv. of* **распада́ться.**

распаха́ть [*infl.* **-пашу́, -па́шешь**] *v., pfv. of* **распа́хивать** (*in sense #1*).

распа́хивать *v. impfv.* **1,** [*pfv.* **распаха́ть**] to plow; plow up. **2,** [*pfv.* **распахну́ть**] to throw open; fling open. —**распа́хиваться,** *refl.* [*pfv.* **распахну́ться**] to swing open; fly open.

распахну́ть *v., pfv. of* **распа́хивать** (*in sense #2*). —**распахну́ться,** *refl., pfv. of* **распа́хиваться.**

распашо́нка [*gen. pl.* **-нок**] *n.* baby's short-sleeved undershirt that opens down the back.

распая́ть *v., pfv. of* **распа́ивать.**

распева́ть *v. impfv., colloq.* to sing (*loudly or gaily*).

распека́ть *v. impfv.* [*pfv.* **распе́чь**] *colloq.* to tell off; upbraid.

распе́ться *v.r. pfv.* [*infl.* **-пою́сь, -поёшься**] *colloq.* **1,** (*of a singer*) to warm up. **2,** to sing away.

распеча́тывать *v. impfv.* [*pfv.* **распеча́тать**] to unseal; break the seal of.

распе́чь [*infl. like* **печь**] *v., pfv. of* **распека́ть.**

распива́ть *v. impfv.* [*pfv.* **распи́ть**] *colloq.* **1,** to drink up (together with someone else). **2,** [*impfv. only*] to drink slowly; linger over.

распи́ливать *v. impfv.* [*pfv.* **распили́ть**] to saw up.

распили́ть [*infl.* **-пилю́, -пи́лишь**] *v., pfv. of* **распи́ливать.**

распина́ть *v. impfv.* [*pfv.* **распя́ть**] to crucify. —**распина́ться,** *refl.* [*impfv. only*] *colloq.* **1,** (*with* **за** + *acc.*) to go to bat for. **2,** (*with* **о**) to crow (about).

расписа́ние *n.* schedule; timetable.

расписа́ть [*infl.* **-пишу́, -пи́шешь**] *v., pfv. of* **распи́сывать.** —**расписа́ться,** *refl., pfv. of* **распи́сываться.**

распи́ска [*gen. pl.* **-сок**] *n.* (written) receipt.

расписно́й *adj., colloq.* painted (*with designs*).

распи́сывать *v. impfv.* [*pfv.* **расписа́ть**] **1,** to write down; note down; copy down; enter (a number of items). **2,** to schedule; assign. **3,** to paint; decorate. **4,** *fig., colloq.* to describe in glowing terms. —**распи́сываться,** *refl.* **1,** to sign one's name. **2,** *colloq.* to register one's marriage. **3,** (*with* **в** + *prepl.*) *colloq.* to openly admit; openly advertise.

распи́ть [*infl.* **разопью́, разопьёшь;** *past* **распи́л** *or* **ро́спил, распила́, распи́ло** *or* **ро́спило**] *v., pfv. of* **распива́ть.**

распи́хивать *v. impfv.* [*pfv.* **распиха́ть**] *colloq.* **1,** to push aside; force one's way through. **2,** to shove; stuff.

распла́вить [*infl.* **-влю, -вишь**] *v., pfv. of* **расплавля́ть.**

распла́вленный *adj.* molten.

расплавля́ть *v. impfv.* [*pfv.* **распла́вить**] to melt; melt down.

распла́каться *v.r. pfv.* [*infl.* **-пла́чусь, -пла́чешься**] to burst into tears.

распла́нировать *v. pfv.* [*infl.* **-рую, -руешь**] to plan out (one's day, work, etc.).

распланирова́ть [*infl.* **-ру́ю, -ру́ешь**] *v., pfv. of* **планирова́ть.**

распла́стывать *v. impfv.* [*pfv.* **распласта́ть**] **1,** to slice into layers. **2,** to spread; spread out; spread flat. —**распла́стываться,** *refl.* to lie flat.

распла́та *n.* **1,** payment. **2,** *fig.* retribution. —**день** (*or* **час**) **распла́ты,** day of reckoning.

расплати́ться [*infl.* **-плачу́сь, -пла́тишься**] *v.r., pfv. of* **распла́чиваться.**

распла́чиваться *v.r. impfv.* [*pfv.* **расплати́ться**] **1,** (*with* **с** + *instr.*) to pay off; settle accounts (with). **2,** (*with* **с** + *instr.*) to get even (with). **3,** (*with* **за** + *acc.*) to pay (for); take the punishment (for).

расплеска́ть [*infl.* **-плещу́, -пле́щешь**] *v., pfv. of* **расплёскивать.** —**расплеска́ться,** *refl., pfv. of* **расплёскиваться.**

расплёскивать *v. impfv.* [*pfv.* **расплеска́ть**] to spill. —**расплёскиваться,** *refl.* (*of a liquid*) to spill.

расплести́ [*infl. like* **плести́**] *v., pfv. of* **расплета́ть.**

расплета́ть *v. impfv.* [*pfv.* **расплести́**] to untwist; unbraid.

расплоди́ть *v. pfv.* [*infl.* **-жу́, -ди́шь**] to breed. —**расплоди́ться,** *refl.* to breed; multiply.

расплыва́ться *v.r. impfv.* [*pfv.* **расплы́ться**] **1,** (*of a liquid*) to run; (*of something in the air*) to spread. **2,** *fig.* to become blurred. **3,** *fig., colloq.* to grow fat. **4,** *fig.* (*of a smile, look of satisfaction, etc.*) to spread across one's face. —**расплыва́ться в улы́бке,** (*of one's face*) to break into a smile.

расплы́вчатый *adj.* **1,** indistinct. **2,** *fig.* vague.

расплы́ться [*infl. like* **плыть**] *v.r., pfv. of* **расплыва́ться.**

расплю́щивать *v. impfv.* [*pfv.* **расплю́щить**] to flatten; crush; squash.

распознава́ть *v. impfv.* [*pfv.* **распозна́ть;** *pres.* **-знаю́, -знаёшь**] **1,** to recognize; identify. **2,** to diagnose (an illness). **3,** to discern; make out.

распозна́ть [*infl.* **-зна́ю, -зна́ешь**] *v., pfv. of* **распознава́ть.**

располага́ть *v. impfv.* **1,** (*with instr.*) to have; have at one's disposal. **2,** (*with instr.*) to dispose of; do with. **3,** (*with* **к**) to be conducive to. **4,** *obs.* to intend; plan. **5,** [*pfv.* **расположи́ть**] to arrange; station; post. **6,** [*pfv.* **расположи́ть**] (*often with* **к себе́**) to win over. —**располага́ться,** *refl.* [*pfv.* **расположи́ться**] **1,** to settle down; sit down. **2,** *in* располага́ться ла́герем, to camp; encamp; set up camp. **3,** [*impfv. only*] *obs.* to intend; plan.

располага́ющий *adj.* pleasing; attractive.

располза́ться *v.r. impfv.* [*pfv.* **расползти́сь**] **1,** to crawl; crawl away (*in different directions*). **2,** *colloq.* to come apart at the seams.

расползти́сь [*infl. like* **ползти́**] *v.r., pfv. of* **располза́ться.**

расположе́ние *n.* **1,** arrangement; layout; disposition. **2,** location; position. **3,** favor; sympathies; liking. **4,** (*with* **к**) inclination (toward); tendency (toward). **5,** *colloq.* mood; desire: у меня́ нет расположе́ния (+ *inf.*), I am not in the mood to... —**расположе́ние ду́ха,** mood; frame of mind.

располо́женный *adj.* **1,** located; situated. **2,** (*with* **к**) fond (of). **3,** (*with* **к**) inclined (to); disposed (toward). **4,** (*with inf.*) of a mood (to); in the mood (for).

расположи́ть [*infl.* **-ложу́, -ло́жишь**] *v., pfv. of* **располага́ть** (*in senses #5 & #6*). —**расположи́ться,** *refl.* **1,** *pfv. of* **располага́ться. 2,** (*with inf.*) *obs.* to decide (to); make up one's mind (to).

распоро́ть [*infl.* **-порю́, -по́решь**] *v., pfv. of* **поро́ть** (*in sense #2*) *and* **распа́рывать.**—**распоро́ться,** *refl., pfv. of* **распа́рываться.**

распоряди́тель *n.m.* manager; superintendent; person in charge.

распоряди́тельный *adj.* efficient; businesslike.

распоряди́ться [*infl.* **-жу́сь, -ди́шься**] *v.r., pfv. of* **распоряжа́ться.**

распоря́док [*gen.* **-дка**] *n.* order; routine.

распоряжа́ться *v.r. impfv.* [*pfv.* **распоряди́ться**] **1,** (*with inf. or* **о**) to order (*that something be done*). **2,** [*impfv. only*] to be in charge; give orders; (*with instr.*) be in charge of; direct; manage. **3,** (*with instr.*) to handle; dispose of (money, property, etc.).

распоряже́ние *n.* **1,** (*with instr.*) disposition (of). **2,** order; command. **3,** disposal: име́ть в своём распоряже́нии, to have at one's disposal; предоста́вить в распоряже́ние (+ *gen.*), to place at the disposal of.

распоя́сать [*infl.* **-поя́шу, -поя́шешь**] *v., pfv. of* **распоя́сывать.** —**распоя́саться,** *refl., pfv. of* **распоя́сываться.**

распоя́сывать *v. impfv.* [*pfv.* **распоя́сать**] to ungird. —**распоя́сываться,** *refl.* **1,** to take off one's belt. **2,** *fig., colloq.* to cast off all restraint; let oneself go.

распра́ва *n.* (with **с** + *instr.*) harsh treatment (of); savage punishment (of); reprisals (against).

распра́вить [*infl.* **-влю, -вишь**] *v., pfv. of* **расправля́ть.** —**распра́виться,** *refl., pfv. of* **расправля́ться.**

расправля́ть *v. impfv.* [*pfv.* **распра́вить**] **1,** to smooth out. **2,** to straighten. **3,** *in* **расправля́ть кры́лья,** to spread one's wings (*lit. & fig.*). —**расправля́ться,** *refl.* **1,** to get smoothed out. **2,** (*with* **с** + *instr.*) to deal with (*severely or cruelly*). **3,** (*with* **с** + *instr.*) *colloq.* to dispose of; finish off. **4,** *in* **расправля́ться без суда́,** to take the law into one's own hands.

распределе́ние *n.* distribution; allocation.

распредели́тель *n.m.* **1,** distributor (*person*). **2,** distribution center. **3,** *mech.* distributor.

распредели́тельный *adj.* distribution (*attrib.*); distributing; distributive. —**распредели́тельный вал,** camshaft. —**распредели́тельный щит,** switchboard.

распределя́ть *v. impfv.* [*pfv.* **распредели́ть**] to distribute; allocate.

распродава́ть *v. impfv.* [*pfv.* **распрода́ть;** *pres.* **-даю́, -даёшь**] to sell out; sell completely.

распрода́жа *n.* sale; clearance sale.

распрода́ть [*infl. like* **прода́ть**] *v., pfv. of* **распродава́ть.**

распростере́ть [*past* **-стёр, -ла,** *not used in future*] *v., pfv. of* **распростира́ть.** —**распростере́ться,** *refl., pfv. of* **распростира́ться.**

распростёртый *adj.* **1,** outstretched. **2,** prostrate. —**с распростёртыми объя́тиями,** with open arms.

распростира́ть *v. impfv.* [*pfv.* **распростере́ть**] to stretch out; spread; extend. —**распростира́ться,** *refl.* **1,** to lie with arms outstretched. **2,** *fig.* to stretch; extend.

распрости́ться *v.r. pfv.* [*infl.* **-щу́сь, -сти́шься**] (*with* **с** + *instr.*) *colloq.* to say goodbye (to); bid farewell (to); take leave (of).

распростране́ние *n.* **1,** spreading. **2,** dissemination. **3,** expansion; extension. **4,** prevalence; distribution: име́ть большо́е распростране́ние, to be widespread. О́бласть распростране́ния живо́тного, area over which an animal is to be found.

распространённый *adj.* widespread; prevalent.

распространя́ть *v. impfv.* [*pfv.* **распространи́ть**] **1,** to spread. **2,** to disseminate. **3,** to expand. **4,** to extend. **5,** to give off. —**распространя́ться,** *refl.* **1,** to spread. **2,** to extend. **3,** (*with* **о**) *colloq.* to dwell at great length (upon). **4,** *in* распространя́ться на те́му, to dwell/enlarge/expand on a subject.

ра́спря *n., usu. pl.* discord; contention; strife.

распряга́ть *v. impfv.* [*pfv.* **распря́чь**] to unharness.

распрямля́ть *v. impfv.* [*pfv.* **распрями́ть**] to straighten; unbend. —**распрямля́ться,** *refl.* to straighten up.

распря́чь [*infl.* **-прягу́, -пряжёшь, ...-прягу́т;** *past* **-пря́г, -прягла́, -прягло́**] *v., pfv. of* **распряга́ть.**

распу́гивать *v. impfv.* [*pfv.* **распуга́ть**] *colloq.* to frighten away; scare away.

распуска́ть *v. impfv.* [*pfv.* **распусти́ть**] **1,** to dismiss; disband; dissolve. **2,** to loosen; let out (reins); let down (one's hair). **3,** to open; spread; unfurl. **4,** *colloq.* to be too lenient with; let get out of hand. **5,** *colloq.* to spread (rumors, gossip, etc.). **6,** *colloq.* to dissolve; melt. **7,** *in* **распуска́ть язы́к,** *colloq.* to speak too freely. **8,** *in* **распуска́ть со́пли, слю́ни, ню́ни,** *see* **со́пли, слю́ни, ню́ни.** —**распуска́ться,** *refl.* **1,** (*of buds*) to open. **2,** *colloq.* to come undone. **3,** *colloq.* to become flabby. **4,** *colloq.* to let oneself go. **5,** *colloq.* to get out of hand.

распусти́ть [*infl.* **-пущу́, -пу́стишь**] *v., pfv. of* **распуска́ть.** —**распусти́ться,** *refl., pfv. of* **распуска́ться.**

распу́тать *v., pfv. of* **распу́тывать.** —**распу́таться,** *refl., pfv. of* **распу́тываться.**

распу́тица *n.* time of year when roads are impassable.

распу́тник *n.* profligate; lecher; libertine.

распу́тничать *v. impfv.* to lead a dissolute life.

распу́тный *adj.* dissolute; licentious.

распу́тство *n.* profligacy; licentiousness; dissoluteness.

распу́тывать *v. impfv.* [*pfv.* **распу́тать**] **1,** to untangle; disentangle; unravel. **2,** *fig.* to unravel. —**распу́тываться,** *refl.* **1,** to come untangled. **2,** *fig., colloq.* to be cleared up; be settled. **3,** *fig., colloq.* to disentangle oneself (*from a situation*). **4,** *in* распу́таться с долга́ми, to free oneself of debt.

распу́тье *n.* crossroads. —**на распу́тье,** at the crossroads.

распуха́ть *v. impfv.* [*pfv.* **распу́хнуть**] **1,** to swell; swell up. **2,** to bulge.

распу́хнуть [*past* **-пу́х, -ла**] *v., pfv. of* **распуха́ть.**

распуши́ть *v., pfv. of* **пуши́ть.**

распу́щенность *n.f.* **1,** lack of discipline; laxity. **2,** dissoluteness; dissipation.

распу́щенный *adj.* **1,** (*of one's hair*) loose; hanging down. **2,** *colloq.* undisciplined. **3,** dissolute.

распыли́тель *n.m.* sprayer; atomizer.

распыля́ть *v. impfv.* [*pfv.* **распыли́ть**] **1,** to pulverize. **2,** to spray. **3,** to disperse; scatter.

распя́тие *n.* **1,** crucifixion. **2,** crucifix.

распя́ть [*infl.* **-пну́, -пнёшь**] *v., pfv. of* **распина́ть.**

расса́да *n.* seedlings.

рассади́ть [*infl.* **-сажу́, -са́дишь**] *v., pfv. of* **расса́живать.**
расса́дник *n.* **1,** nursery (*for plants*). **2,** *fig.* center (*of learning*); breeding ground (*of crime, infection, etc.*).
расса́живать *v. impfv.* [*pfv.* **рассади́ть**] **1,** to seat (*each in his place*). **2,** to separate; seat apart. **3,** to plant farther apart. —**расса́живаться,** *refl.* [*pfv.* **рассе́сться**] (*of many people*) to take their (respective) seats.
расса́сываться *v.r. impfv.* [*pfv.* **рассоса́ться**] **1,** (*of a tumor*) to dissolve. **2,** *colloq.* (*of a crowd*) to melt away.
рассвести́ [*infl.* **-светёт;** *past* **-свело́**] *v., pfv. of* **рассвета́ть.**
рассве́т *n.* dawn; daybreak.
рассвета́ть *v. impfv.* [*pfv.* **рассвести́**] *impers.* to dawn: рассвета́ет, day is dawning; day is breaking.
рассвирепе́ть *v., pfv. of* **свирепе́ть.**
расседа́ться *v.r. impfv.* [*pfv.* **рассе́сться**] to crack.
рассёдлывать *v. impfv.* [*pfv.* **расседла́ть**] to unsaddle.
рассе́ивание *n.* scattering; dispersion; dispersal.
рассе́ивать *v. impfv.* [*pfv.* **рассе́ять**] **1,** to disperse. **2,** to diffuse (light). **3,** *fig.* to dispel (doubts, fears, etc.). **4,** *fig.* to take someone's mind off things. —**рассе́иваться,** *refl.* **1,** to scatter; disperse. **2,** (*of fog*) to lift; (*of clouds*) to disappear. **3,** to get one's mind off things.
рассека́ть *v. impfv.* [*pfv.* **рассе́чь**] **1,** to cleave; split. **2,** to slash; gash. **3,** to cut in two.
рассекре́чивать *v. impfv.* [*pfv.* **рассекре́тить**] to declassify.
рассе́лина *n.* cleft; fissure.
расселя́ть *v. impfv.* [*pfv.* **рассели́ть**] **1,** to settle (many people). **2,** to separate; settle separately. —**расселя́ться,** *refl.* to settle in different places.
рассерди́ть *v., pfv. of* **серди́ть.** —**рассерди́ться,** *refl., pfv. of* **серди́ться.**
рассе́сться [*infl. like* **сесть**] *v.r., pfv. of* **расса́живаться** *and* **расседа́ться.**
рассе́чь [*infl. like* **сечь;** *past* **-се́к, -секла́, -секло́**] *v., pfv. of* **рассека́ть.**
рассе́яние *n.* **1,** dispersion. **2,** diffusion (*of light*). **3,** dispelling (*of doubts, rumors, etc.*).
рассе́янный *adj.* **1,** scattered; dispersed. **2,** (*of light*) diffused. **3,** absent-minded. —**рассе́янно,** *adv.* absent-mindedly; absently. —**рассе́янность,** *n.f.* absent-mindedness.
рассе́ять [*infl.* **-се́ю, -се́ешь**] *v., pfv. of* **рассе́ивать.** —**рассе́яться,** *refl., pfv. of* **рассе́иваться.**
расска́з *n.* **1,** story; tale. **2,** account.
рассказа́ть [*infl.* **-скажу́, -ска́жешь**] *v., pfv. of* **расска́зывать.**
расска́зчик *n.* narrator; storyteller.
расска́зывание *n.* telling; narration.
расска́зывать *v. impfv.* [*pfv.* **рассказа́ть**] to tell; relate; recount.
рассла́бить [*infl.* **-блю, -бишь**] *v., pfv. of* **расслабля́ть.**
расслабле́ние *n.* weakness; debility. *Also,* **рассла́бленность,** *n.f.*
рассла́бленный *adj.* **1,** weak; debilitated. **2,** (*of a gait*) unsure; unsteady.
расслабля́ть *v. impfv.* [*pfv.* **рассла́бить**] **1,** to weaken; debilitate. **2,** to relax (muscles).
рассла́ивать *v. impfv.* [*pfv.* **расслои́ть**] to stratify.
рассле́дование *n.* investigation; inquiry.
рассле́довать *v. impfv. & pfv.* [*pres.* **-дую, -дуешь**] to investigate; inquire into.
расслое́ние *n.* stratification: расслое́ние о́бщества, stratification of society.
расслои́ть *v., pfv. of* **рассла́ивать.**
рассль́ішать *v. pfv.* [*infl.* **-шу, -шишь**] to hear; catch.
рассма́тривать *v. impfv.* [*pfv.* **рассмотре́ть**] **1,** to examine; scrutinize. **2,** to consider; take up; examine. **3,** [*impfv. only*] (*with* **как**) to regard (as); consider (to be). *See also* **рассмотре́ть.**
рассмеши́ть *v., pfv. of* **смеши́ть.**
рассмея́ться *v.r. pfv.* [*infl.* **-смею́сь, -смеёшься**] to burst out laughing.
рассмотре́ние *n.* examination; consideration.
рассмотре́ть *v. pfv.* [*infl.* **-смотрю́, -смо́тришь**] **1,** *pfv. of* **рассма́тривать. 2,** to discern; make out; spot.
рассо́л *n.* brine.
рассо́льник *n.* soup with pickled cucumbers.
рассо́рить *v. pfv.* to set to quarreling; cause a quarrel between. —**рассо́риться,** *refl.* (*with* **с** + *instr.*) to have a falling-out (with).
рассортирова́ть *v., pfv. of* **сортирова́ть.**
рассортиро́вка *n.* sorting out.
рассоса́ться [*infl. like* **соса́ть**] *v.r., pfv. of* **расса́сываться.**
рассо́хнуться [*past* **-со́хся, -со́хлась**] *v.r., pfv. of* **рассыха́ться.**
расспра́шивать *v. impfv.* [*pfv.* **расспроси́ть**] to question.
расспроси́ть [*infl.* **-спрошу́, -спро́сишь**] *v., pfv. of* **расспра́шивать.**
расспро́сы [*gen.* **-сов**] *n. pl.* questions; questioning.
рассро́чивать *v. impfv.* [*pfv.* **рассро́чить**] to spread (payments) over a period of time.
рассро́чка *n., usu. in* **в рассро́чку,** on the installment plan; on time.
расстава́ние *n.* parting; taking leave.
расстава́ться *v.r. impfv.* [*pfv.* **расста́ться;** *pres.* **-стаю́сь, -стаёшься**] (*with* **с** + *instr.*) **1,** to part (with). **2,** to leave (a place). **3,** *fig.* to give up (an idea, dream, etc.).
расста́вить [*infl.* **-влю, -вишь**] *v., pfv. of* **расставля́ть.**
расставля́ть *v. impfv.* [*pfv.* **расста́вить**] **1,** to place; arrange. **2,** to assign (personnel); post (sentries). **3,** to spread; move apart.
расстано́вка *n.* **1,** placement; arrangement. **2,** intermittent pauses. —**говори́ть с расстано́вкой,** to speak in measured tones.
расста́ться [*infl.* **-ста́нусь, -ста́нешься**] *v.r., pfv. of* **расстава́ться.**
расстёгивать *v. impfv.* [*pfv.* **расстегну́ть**] to unfasten; unbutton; unhook; undo. —**расстёгиваться,** *refl.* **1,** to come undone. **2,** to unbutton one's coat.
расстила́ть *v. impfv.* [*pfv.* **разостла́ть**] to spread out. —**расстила́ться,** *refl.* **1,** to be spread out. **2,** to stretch; extend.
расстоя́ние *n.* distance.
расстра́ивать *v. impfv.* [*pfv.* **расстро́ить**] **1,** to throw into disorder; break up. **2,** to impair; damage; ruin; shatter. **3,** to disrupt; upset. **4,** to frustrate; thwart; foil. **5,** to upset (*emotionally*); disturb. **6,** to throw out of tune. **7,** *in* расстра́ивать желу́док, to upset one's stomach; cause indigestion. **8,** *in* расстро́ить сва́дьбу,

to break off one's engagement. —**расстра́иваться,** *refl.* **1,** to be thrown into disorder. **2,** to collapse; break down. **3,** to fall through. **4,** to become upset. **5,** to get out of tune.

расстре́л *n.* execution by a firing squad.

расстре́ливать *v. impfv.* [*pfv.* **расстреля́ть**] **1,** to execute by a firing squad. **2,** to shoot up; rake with fire. **3,** to use up; exhaust (one's ammunition).

расстри́га *n.m.* unfrocked monk; unfrocked priest.

расстрига́ть *v. impfv.* [*pfv.* **расстри́чь**] to unfrock; defrock.

расстри́чь [*infl. like* **стричь**] *v., pfv. of* **расстрига́ть.**

расстро́енный *adj.* **1,** disorganized; thrown into disorder. **2,** upset (*emotionally*). **3,** (*of one's health*) impaired. **4,** out of tune.

расстро́ить *v., pfv. of* **расстра́ивать.** —**расстро́иться,** *refl., pfv. of* **расстра́иваться.**

расстро́йство *n.* **1,** upsetting; disruption. **2,** disorder; disarray. **3,** *med.* disorder. **4,** *colloq.* discomfiture; distress. —**расстро́йство желу́дка,** upset stomach. —**расстро́йство пищеваре́ния,** indigestion.

расступа́ться *v.r. impfv.* [*pfv.* **расступи́ться**] **1,** to step aside; make way. **2,** to part; open.

расступи́ться [*infl.* **-ступлю́сь, -сту́пишься**] *v.r., pfv. of* **расступа́ться.**

рассуди́тельный *adj.* reasonable; sensible; judicious; prudent. —**рассуди́тельность,** *n.f.* prudence; discretion; good sense.

рассуди́ть *v. pfv.* [*infl.* **-сужу́, -су́дишь**] **1,** to settle a dispute between. **2,** (*with* **что**) to decide (that); come to the conclusion (that). **3,** to think; reflect.

рассу́док [*gen.* **-дка**] *n.* **1,** reason. **2,** sanity. **3,** common sense. —**в по́лном рассу́дке,** in full possession of one's faculties.

рассу́дочный *adj.* rational.

рассужда́ть *v. impfv.* **1,** to reason. **2,** (*with* **о**) to discuss. **3,** (*with* **о**) to discourse (on); expound (on).

рассужде́ние *n.* **1,** reasoning. **2,** *pl.* discussion; comments; remarks. **3,** *pl.* objections; arguments: без (вся́ких) рассужде́ний, without any arguments.

рассу́чивать *v. impfv.* [*pfv.* **рассучи́ть**] **1,** to untwist. **2,** to roll down (one's sleeves).

рассучи́ть [*infl.* **-сучу́, -су́чишь**] *v., pfv. of* **рассу́чивать.**

рассчи́танный *adj.* **1,** calculated; intentional. **2,** (*with* **на** + *acc.*) intended (for); designed (for); meant (for).

рассчи́тывать *v. impfv.* [*pfv.* **рассчита́ть**] **1,** to calculate. **2,** to figure; plan. **3,** to dismiss; discharge; fire. **4,** [*impfv. only*] to intend; expect. **5,** [*impfv. only*] (*with* **на** + *acc.*) to count on. —**рассчи́тываться,** *refl.* **1,** (*with* **с** + *instr.*) to settle up with (someone); pay off (one's debts). **2,** (*with* **с** + *instr.*) to settle scores (with); get even (with). **3,** *colloq.* to lose one's job. **4,** [*impfv. only*] (*with* **за** + *acc.*) to answer for; pay for.

рассыла́ть *v. impfv.* [*pfv.* **разосла́ть**] to send out; mail out; circulate.

рассы́лка *n.* sending out; mailing out.

рассы́льный *n., decl. as an adj.* errand boy.

рассы́пать [*infl.* **-сы́плю, -сы́плешь**] *v., pfv. of* **рассыпа́ть.** —**рассы́паться,** *refl., pfv. of* **рассыпа́ться.**

рассыпа́ть *v. impfv.* [*pfv.* **рассы́пать**] to spill; scatter; strew. —**рассыпа́ться,** *refl.* **1,** to spill; be strewn. **2,** to crumble; fall to pieces. **3,** to scatter; disperse. **4,** (*of one's hair*) to hang loosely. **5,** (*with* **в** + *prepl.*) *colloq.* to shower (with praises, compliments, etc.): рассыпа́ться кому́-нибудь в комплиме́нтах, to shower someone with compliments. Рассыпа́ться в извине́ниях, to apologize profusely.

рассы́пчатый *adj.* friable; crumbly.

рассыха́ться *v.r. impfv.* [*pfv.* **рассо́хнуться**] to crack (*as a result of drying up*).

раста́лкивать *v. impfv.* [*pfv.* **растолка́ть**] *colloq.* **1,** to push (everyone) aside. **2,** to awaken; arouse (*by shaking*).

раста́пливать *v. impfv.* [*pfv.* **растопи́ть**] **1,** to light (a stove). **2,** to melt. —**раста́пливаться,** *refl.* **1,** (*of a stove*) to light. **2,** to melt.

раста́птывать *v. impfv.* [*pfv.* **растопта́ть**] to trample; crush.

растаска́ть *v., pfv. of* **раста́скивать** (*in senses #1 & #2*).

раста́скивать *v. impfv.* [*pfv.* **растащи́ть**] **1,** [*pfv. also* **растаска́ть**] to carry away; remove (*one at a time, bit by bit*). **2,** [*pfv. also* **растаска́ть**] to steal; make off with. **3,** *colloq.* to pull apart; separate.

раста́чивать *v. impfv.* [*pfv.* **расточи́ть**] to chisel out.

растащи́ть [*infl.* **-тащу́, -та́щишь**] *v., pfv. of* **раста́скивать.**

раста́ять *v., pfv. of* **та́ять.**

раство́р *n.* solution: щелочно́й раство́р, alkaline solution. —**строи́тельный раство́р,** mortar.

растворе́ние *n.* dissolution; solution.

раствори́мый *adj.* soluble. —**раствори́мость,** *n.f.* solubility.

раствори́тель *n.m.* solvent.

раствори́ть *v. pfv.* **1,** [*infl.* **-творю́, -тво́ришь**] *pfv. of* **растворя́ть** (*in sense #1*). **2,** [*infl.* **-творю́, -твори́шь**] *pfv. of* **растворя́ть** (*in sense #2*). —**раствори́ться,** *refl.* [*same distinction in stress*] *pfv. of* **растворя́ться.**

растворя́ть *v. impfv.* [*pfv.* **раствори́ть**] **1,** to open. **2,** to dissolve. —**растворя́ться,** *refl.* **1,** (*of a door, window, etc.*) to open; swing open. **2,** (*of a substance*) to dissolve.

растворя́ющий *adj.* solvent.

растека́ться *v.r. impfv.* [*pfv.* **расте́чься**] **1,** (*of liquids*) to run; spread. **2,** (*of a crowd*) to set out (*in various directions*). **3,** (*with* **по**) (*of a smile, feeling, etc.*) to come over (one's face, body, etc.). **4,** [*impfv. only*] *colloq.* to go into unnecessary detail.

расте́ние *n.* plant.

растениево́дство *n.* plant growing; plant cultivation.

растере́ть [*infl.* **разотру́, разотрёшь;** *past* **растёр, -ла**] *v., pfv. of* **растира́ть.**

расте́рзанный *adj.* **1,** torn to shreds. **2,** disheveled.

растерза́ть *v. pfv.* **1,** to tear to pieces. **2,** to torment. Растерза́ть чьё-нибудь се́рдце, to tear at one's heart; tear one's heart out.

расте́рянный *adj.* confused; bewildered. —**расте́рянно,** *adv.* in bewilderment. —**расте́рянность,** *n.f.* confusion; bewilderment.

растеря́ть *v. pfv.* to lose (many things). —**растеря́ться,** *refl.* **1,** (*of many things*) to be lost. **2,** to become confused; be bewildered; become flustered.

расте́чься [*infl. like* **течь**] *v.r., pfv. of* **растека́ться.**

расти́ *v. impfv.* [*pfv.* **вы́расти;** *pres.* **расту́, растёшь;** *past* **рос, росла́, росло́**] **1,** to grow. **2,** to grow up. **3,** to grow; increase; rise; go up.

растира́ние *n.* **1,** grinding. **2,** rubbing; massaging.

растира́ть *v. impfv.* [*pfv.* **растере́ть**] **1,** to grind (into

small particles). **2,** to rub (onto the surface of something). **3,** to rub; massage.
расти́тельность *n.f.* **1,** vegetation. **2,** *colloq.* hair (*on one's face or body*).
расти́тельный *adj.* plant (*attrib.*); vegetable (*attrib.*). —**расти́тельное ма́сло,** vegetable oil.
расти́ть *v. impfv.* [*pfv.* **вы́растить;** *pres.* **ращу́, расти́шь**] **1,** to raise; bring up (children). **2,** to train (personnel). **3,** to raise; grow; cultivate (plants).
растлева́ть *v. impfv.* [*pfv.* **растли́ть**] **1,** to violate; ravish (a minor). **2,** *fig.* to corrupt.
растле́ние *n.* **1,** violation; rape (*of a minor*). **2,** decay; decadence.
растле́нный *adj.* corrupt; decadent.
растли́ть *v., pfv. of* **растлева́ть.**
растолка́ть *v., pfv. of* **раста́лкивать.**
растолкова́ть [*infl.* **-ку́ю, -ку́ешь**] *v., pfv. of* **растолко́вывать.**
растолко́вывать *v. impfv.* [*pfv.* **растолкова́ть**] to explain.
растоло́чь *v., pfv. of* **толо́чь.**
растолсте́ть *v. pfv.* to grow fat; put on a lot of weight.
растопи́ть [*infl.* **-топлю́, -то́пишь**] *v., pfv. of* **топи́ть** (*in sense #3*) *and* **раста́пливать.** —**растопи́ться,** *refl., pfv. of* **раста́пливаться.**
расто́пка *n.* **1,** lighting (*of a stove*). **2,** *colloq.* kindling wood.
растопта́ть [*infl.* **-топчу́, -то́пчешь**] *v., pfv. of* **раста́птывать.**
растопы́ривать *v. impfv.* [*pfv.* **растопы́рить**] *colloq.* to spread apart.
расторга́ть *v. impfv.* [*pfv.* **расто́ргнуть**] to annul; abrogate.
расто́ргнуть [*past* **-то́рг** *or* **-то́ргнул, -то́ргла**] *v., pfv. of* **расторга́ть.**
расторже́ние *n.* annulment; abrogation.
расторо́пный *adj.* capable; competent; efficient. —**расторо́пность,** *n.f.* capability; competence; efficiency.
расточа́ть *v. impfv.* [*pfv.* **расточи́ть**] **1,** to squander; dissipate. **2,** to lavish; shower: расточа́ть похвалы́ (+ *dat.*), to lavish praise upon.
расточе́ние *n.* squandering; dissipation.
расточи́тель *n.m.* squanderer; spendthrift.
расточи́тельный *adj.* extravagant; wasteful. —**расточи́тельность,** *n.f.* extravagance; wastefulness.
расточи́ть *v. pfv.* **1,** [*infl.* **-точу́, -точи́шь**] *pfv. of* **расточа́ть. 2,** [*infl.* **-точу́, -то́чишь**] *pfv. of* **раста́чивать.**
растрави́ть [*infl.* **-травлю́, -тра́вишь**] *v., pfv. of* **растравля́ть.**
растравля́ть *v. impfv.* [*pfv.* **растрави́ть**] **1,** to irritate; *fig.* rub salt on (a wound). **2,** *colloq.* to revive; reopen (something unpleasant).
растранжи́рить *v., pfv. of* **транжи́рить.**
растра́та *n.* **1,** squandering; waste. **2,** embezzlement.
растра́тить [*infl.* **-чу, -тишь**] *v., pfv. of* **растра́чивать.**
растра́тчик *n.* embezzler.
растра́чивать *v. impfv.* [*pfv.* **растра́тить**] **1,** to squander; dissipate. **2,** to embezzle.
растрево́жить *v. pfv.* **1,** to alarm; upset. **2,** to stir up; disturb.
растрёпа *n.m. & f., colloq.* slovenly person; slob.
растрёпанный *adj.* **1,** disheveled. **2,** tattered.
растрепа́ть *v. pfv.* [*infl.* **-треплю́, -тре́плешь**] **1,** to mess up; muss. **2,** to wear out; tatter.
растре́скаться *v.r. pfv.* to crack all over.
растро́ганный *adj.* deeply touched; deeply moved.
растро́гать *v. pfv.* to move; touch; affect deeply. —**растро́гаться,** *refl.* to be (deeply) touched; be (deeply) moved.
растру́б *n.* **1,** flare (*of a garment, bell, etc.*). **2,** bell (*of a musical instrument*).
растряса́ть *v. impfv.* [*pfv.* **растрясти́**] **1,** to strew; scatter. **2,** *fig., colloq.* to waste; spend needlessly. **3,** *impers.* to be shaken up (*while riding*): его́ растрясло́, he was shaken up.
растрясти́ [*infl. like* **трясти́**] *v., pfv. of* **растряса́ть.**
растя́гивать *v. impfv.* [*pfv.* **растяну́ть**] **1,** to stretch. **2,** to strain; sprain. **3,** to spread out. **4,** to prolong; drag out. **5,** *in* растя́гивать слова́, to drawl. —**растя́гиваться,** *refl.* **1,** to stretch; become stretched. **2,** to extend; be stretched out. **3,** *colloq.* to stretch out. **4,** *colloq.* to tumble headlong. **5,** to be stretched out; be dragged out (*over a period of time*).
растяже́ние *n.* strain; sprain.
растяжи́мость *n.f.* **1,** stretchability. **2,** tensile strength.
растяжи́мый *adj.* **1,** stretchable. **2,** *fig.* loose; imprecise.
растя́жка *n.* stretching: отда́ть ту́фли на растя́жку, to have one's shoes stretched.
растя́нутый *adj.* **1,** stretched out; extended. **2,** *fig.* long-winded; verbose.
растяну́ть [*infl.* **-тяну́, -тя́нешь**] *v., pfv. of* **растя́гивать.** —**растяну́ться,** *refl., pfv. of* **растя́гиваться.**
растя́па *n.m. & f., colloq.* dolt; dope; dullard.
расфасова́ть *v., pfv. of* **фасова́ть.**
расфасо́вка *n.* packaging.
расформирова́ть [*infl.* **-ру́ю, -ру́ешь**] *v., pfv. of* **расформиро́вывать.**
расформиро́вывать *v. impfv.* [*pfv.* **расформирова́ть**] to disband.
расха́живать *v. impfv.* to pace back and forth.
расхва́ливать *v. impfv.* [*pfv.* **расхвали́ть**] to extol; rave about; praise to the skies.
расхвали́ть [*infl.* **-хвалю́, -хва́лишь**] *v., pfv. of* **расхва́ливать.**
расхва́рываться *v.r. impfv.* [*pfv.* **расхвора́ться**] *colloq.* to become ill.
расхва́статься *v.r. pfv., colloq.* to brag endlessly.
расхва́тывать *v. impfv.* [*pfv.* **расхвата́ть**] *colloq.* to buy up; snap up; snatch up.
расхвора́ться *v.r., pfv. of* **расхва́рываться.**
расхити́тель *n.m.* embezzler (*of public property*).
расхища́ть *v. impfv.* [*pfv.* **расхи́тить**] to steal; embezzle; misappropriate.
расхище́ние *n.* theft; embezzlement; misappropriation.
расхля́банный *adj., colloq.* **1,** rickety; wobbly. **2,** *fig.* lax; slack. —**расхля́банность,** *n.f., colloq.* laxity.
расхо́д *n.* **1,** *usu. pl.* expenses. **2,** (*with gen.*) expenditure (of); consumption (of); outlay (of). —**в расхо́де,** *colloq.* in use (*and therefore unavailable*). —**вы́вести** *or* **пусти́ть в расхо́д,** *colloq.* to shoot; execute.
расходи́ться *v.r. impfv.* [*pfv.* **разойти́сь;** *pres.* **-хожу́сь, -хо́дишься**] **1,** to depart (*in different directions*); disperse. **2,** to pass by each other; miss each other; fail to meet. **3,** to be able to pass by each other

(*in a narrow place*). **4,** to part company; (*of a married couple*) separate; break up. **5,** to come apart. **6,** to divide; diverge. **7,** to differ; be at variance. Расходи́ться во мнéниях, to be of different opinions. **8,** (*of an item*) to sell; be sold out; (*of money*) to be spent. **9,** to gather speed. **10,** *fig.* to get worked up.

расхóдный *adj.* expense (*attrib.*).

расхóдование *n.* **1,** spending. **2,** expenditure.

расхóдовать *v. impfv.* [*pfv.* **израсхóдовать;** *pres.* **-дую, -дуешь**] **1,** to spend; expend. **2,** *colloq.* to use (up); consume (fuel).

расхождéние *n.* **1,** divergence. **2,** discrepancy. **3,** difference: расхождéние во мнéниях, difference of opinion.

расхóжий *adj., colloq.* **1,** everyday; for everyday use or wear. **2,** in great demand; in great vogue.

расхолáживать *v. impfv.* [*pfv.* **расхолоди́ть**] to dim the enthusiasm of; dampen the ardor of.

расхотéть *v. pfv.* [*infl. like* **хотéть**] *colloq.* to want no longer; lose all desire (to *or* for). —**расхотéться,** *refl., impers.* (*with dat.*) *colloq.* = **расхотéть.**

расхохотáться *v.r. pfv.* [*infl.* **-хохочýсь, -хохóчешься**] to burst out laughing; roar with laughter.

расцарáпывать *v. impfv.* [*pfv.* **расцарáпать**] to scratch (severely).

расцвести́ [*infl. like* **цвести́**] *v., pfv. of* **расцветáть.**

расцвéт *n.* **1,** flowering; blooming; blossoming. **2,** *fig.* flowering; golden age. **3,** *fig.* peak; prime: в расцвéте сил *or* своегó талáнта, at the peak of one's powers; в расцвéте лет, in the prime of life.

расцветáть *v. impfv.* [*pfv.* **расцвести́**] **1,** to flower; blossom; bloom. **2,** *fig.* (*of a person*) to blossom. **3,** *fig.* (*of one's face*) to light up. **4,** *fig.* to flourish.

расцвети́ть [*infl.* **-цвечý, -цвети́шь**] *v., pfv. of* **расцвéчивать.**

расцвéтка *n.* color scheme; color combination.

расцвéчивать *v. impfv.* [*pfv.* **расцвети́ть**] *colloq.* to deck; adorn (*with something colorful*).

расцеловáть *v. pfv.* [*infl.* **-лýю, -лýешь**] to kiss fervently; shower with kisses.

расцéнивать *v. impfv.* [*pfv.* **расцени́ть**] **1,** to price; set a price on. **2,** to assess; estimate; rate. **3,** (*with* **как**) to regard (as); consider (to be).

расцени́ть [*infl.* **-ценю́, -цéнишь**] *v., pfv. of* **расцéнивать.**

расцéнка *n.* **1,** appraisal; valuation. **2,** price; rate. **3,** *usu. pl.* wage rate.

расцепи́ть [*infl.* **-цеплю́, -цéпишь**] *v., pfv. of* **расцепля́ть.** —**расцепи́ться,** *refl., pfv. of* **расцепля́ться.**

расцепля́ть *v. impfv.* [*pfv.* **расцепи́ть**] to unhook; unhitch; uncouple. —**расцепля́ться,** *refl.* to come unhitched.

расчесáть [*infl.* **-чешý, -чéшешь**] *v., pfv. of* **расчёсывать.** —**расчесáться,** *refl., pfv. of* **расчёсываться.**

расчёска [*gen. pl.* **-сок**] *n., colloq.* comb.

расчéсть *v. pfv.* [*infl.* **разочтý, разочтёшь;** *past* **расчёл, разочлá, разочлó**] *colloq.* = **рассчитáть.** —**расчéсться,** *refl., colloq.* = **рассчитáться.**

расчёсывать *v. impfv.* [*pfv.* **расчесáть**] **1,** to comb. **2,** to scratch (and thus further irritate). —**расчёсываться,** *refl., colloq.* to comb one's hair.

расчёт *n.* **1,** calculation; reckoning: по моемý расчёту, by my calculations. Это не входи́ло в мои́ расчёты, that did not enter into my calculations; I had not allowed for that. **2,** payment; settlement. Быть в расчёте с, to be all even with. **3,** discharge; dismissal: дать расчёт (+ *dat.*), to dismiss; fire. **4,** *fig.* retribution: с ним бýдет корóткий расчёт, retribution will be swift. **5,** assumption; expectation: в расчёте на (+ *acc.*), on the expectation of. С таки́м расчётом, что..., on the assumption that...; with the idea that... **6,** selfish consideration: брак по расчёту, marriage for money; marriage of convenience. **7,** *colloq.* benefit; advantage: нет расчёта (+ *inf.*), there is no point in... **8,** *mil.* crew. —**принимáть в расчёт,** *see* **принимáть.**

расчётливость *n.f.* **1,** thrift. **2,** prudence.

расчётливый *adj.* **1,** thrifty. **2,** prudent.

расчётный *adj.* **1,** calculation (*attrib.*). **2,** of payments; pay (*attrib.*). —**расчётная палáта,** clearing house.

расчи́стить [*infl.* **-щу, -стишь**] *v., pfv. of* **расчищáть.**

расчи́стка *n.* clearing (*of land, roads, etc.*).

расчихáться *v.r. pfv., colloq.* to have a fit of sneezing.

расчищáть *v. impfv.* [*pfv.* **расчи́стить**] to clear; rid of obstacles.

расчленéние *n.* **1,** division. **2,** dismemberment.

расчленя́ть *v. impfv.* [*pfv.* **расчлени́ть**] **1,** to divide. **2,** to dismember. **3,** to break down (*into component parts*).

расчýвствоваться *v.r. pfv.* [*infl.* **-ствуюсь, -ствуешься**] *colloq.* to be deeply touched.

расшáркиваться *v.r. impfv.* [*pfv.* **расшáркаться**] **1,** to bow, scraping one's feet. **2,** (*with* **пéред**) *colloq.* to bow and scrape (before).

расшáтанный *adj.* **1,** wobbly; rickety. **2,** (*of one's health*) seriously impaired; (*of one's nerves*) shattered.

расшáтывать *v. impfv.* [*pfv.* **расшатáть**] **1,** to shake loose; knock loose. **2,** to make unsteady; make wobbly. **3,** *fig.* to undermine; impair. —**расшáтываться,** *refl.* **1,** to come loose. **2,** to be (*or* become) rickety. **3,** *fig* to break down; collapse; go to pieces. **4,** *fig.* (*of one's nerves*) to be shattered; (*of one's health*) to give way.

расшвы́ривать *v. impfv.* [*pfv.* **расшвыря́ть**] *colloq.* to toss in all directions.

расшевели́ть *v. pfv., colloq.* to stir; rouse.

расшибáть *v. impfv.* [*pfv.* **расшиби́ть**] *colloq.* to hurt; bruise; stub. —**расшибáться,** *refl., colloq.* to hurt oneself.

расшиби́ть [*infl.* **-бý, -бёшь;** *past* **-ши́б, -ла**] *v., pfv. of* **расшибáть.** —**расшиби́ться,** *refl., pfv. of* **расшибáться.**

расшивáть *v. impfv.* [*pfv.* **расши́ть**] **1,** to rip open. **2,** to embroider.

расширéние *n.* **1,** widening; broadening. **2,** expansion. **3,** *med.* dilation. —**расширéние вен,** varicose veins.

расширя́ть *v. impfv.* [*pfv.* **расши́рить**] **1,** to widen; broaden. **2,** to enlarge. **3,** *fig.* to broaden; expand. —**расширя́ться,** *refl.* to widen; broaden; expand.

расши́ть [*infl.* **разошью́, разошьёшь**] *v., pfv. of* **расшивáть.**

расшифровáть [*infl.* **-рýю, -рýешь**] *v., pfv. of* **расшифрóвывать.**

расшифрóвка *n.* decipherment.

расшифрóвывать *v. impfv.* [*pfv.* **расшифровáть**] to decipher; decode.

расшнуровáть [*infl.* **-рýю, -рýешь**] *v., pfv. of* **расшнурóвывать.**

расшнурóвывать *v. impfv.* [*pfv.* **расшнуровáть**] to unlace; untie.

расшуме́ться *v.r. pfv.* [*infl.* **-млю́сь, -ми́шься**] *colloq.* to become noisy; raise a rumpus.
расще́лина *n.* cleft; crevice; fissure.
расщепи́ть [*infl.* **-плю́, -пи́шь**] *v., pfv. of* **расщепля́ть.** —**расщепи́ться,** *refl., pfv. of* **расщепля́ться.**
расщепле́ние *n.* **1,** splitting: расщепле́ние а́тома, splitting of the atom. **2,** fission: расщепле́ние ядра́, nuclear fission.
расщепля́ть *v. impfv.* [*pfv.* **расщепи́ть**] to split. —**расщепля́ться,** *refl.* to split; be split.
ратификацио́нный *adj.* ratification (*attrib.*): ратификацио́нные гра́моты, instruments of ratification.
ратифика́ция *n.* ratification.
ратифици́ровать *v. impfv. & pfv.* [*pres.* **-рую, -руешь**] to ratify.
ра́тник *n., obs.* warrior; soldier.
ра́тный *adj., obs.* military.
ра́товать *v. impfv.* [*pres.* **-тую, -туешь**] **1,** *obs.* to fight in battle. **2,** (*with* **за** + *acc.*) to fight for; advocate; (*with* **про́тив**) inveigh (against).
ра́туша *n.* town hall; city hall.
рать *n.f., archaic* **1,** army. **2,** battle.
ра́унд *n., boxing* round.
рафина́д *n.* lump sugar.
рафини́ровать *v. impfv. & pfv.* [*pres.* **-рую, -руешь**] to refine.
раха́т-луку́м *n.* Turkish delight.
рахи́т *n.* rickets.
рацио́н *n.* ration.
рационализа́ция *n.* application of modern means of efficiency; streamlining.
рационализи́ровать *v. impfv. & pfv.* [*pres.* **-рую, -руешь**] to apply modern methods of efficiency to; streamline.
рационали́зм *n.* rationalism.
рационали́ст *n.* **1,** rationalist. **2,** rational person. —**рационалисти́ческий,** *adj.* rationalistic.
рациона́льный *adj.* **1,** rational. **2,** efficient. **3,** *math.* rational. —**рациона́льность,** *n.f.* rationality.
ра́ция *n.* portable two-way radio; walkie-talkie.
ра́чий [*fem.* **-чья**] *adj.* of (a) crawfish. —**ра́чьи глаза́,** bulging eyes.
рачи́тельный *adj., obs.* zealous; diligent.
ра́шпер *n.* gridiron; grill.
ра́шпиль *n.m.* rasp.
рвану́ть *v. pfv.* **1,** to tug; jerk. **2,** *colloq.* to dart; dash. **3,** *colloq.* to start with a jerk; lurch forward. —**рвану́ться,** *refl., colloq.* = **рвану́ть** (*in senses #2 & #3*).
рва́ный *adj.* **1,** torn; full of holes. **2,** uneven; jagged. **3,** *in* **рва́ная ра́на,** laceration.
рвань *n.f., colloq.* **1,** tatters; rags. **2,** riffraff.
рвать *v. impfv.* [*pres.* **рву, рвёшь;** *past fem.* **рвала́**] **1,** [*pfv.* **порва́ть**] to tear; tear up. **2,** [*pfv.* **порва́ть**] to break; snap. **3,** to pull out; tear out; snatch. **4,** to pull off; yank off. **5,** to pick; pluck (flowers). **6,** [*pfv.* **порва́ть**] to break off; sever (ties, relations, etc.). **7,** to blow up. **8,** [*pfv.* **вы́рвать**] *impers., colloq.* to vomit; throw up: его́ рвёт, he is throwing up. —**рвать и мета́ть,** to be in a rage; rant and rave. —**рвать на себе́ во́лосы,** to tear one's hair. —**рвать на ча́сти,** to harass; harry; beset.
рва́ться *v.r. impfv.* [*pfv.* **порва́ться;** *pres.* **рвусь; рвёшься;** *past* **рва́лся, рвала́сь, рвало́сь** *or* **рва́лось, рвали́сь** *or* **рва́лись**] **1,** to tear; become torn. **2,** (*of a rope, thread, etc.*) to break; snap. **3,** [*impfv. only*] to burst; explode. **4,** (*of ties, relations, etc.*) to be broken off. **5,** [*impfv. only*] (*with various prepositions*) to thirst for; be dying for.
рвач [*gen.* **рвача́**] *n., colloq.* crook; chiseler.
рве́ние *n.* zeal; ardor.
рво́та *n.* vomiting.
рво́тный *adj.* **1,** pert. to vomiting: рво́тная ма́сса, vomit. **2,** inducing vomiting; emetic: рво́тное сре́дство, an emetic. —**рво́тное,** *n.* emetic.
рдест *n.* pondweed.
рдеть *v. impfv.* (*of anything red*) to glow.
ре *n. neut., music* re; D.
реабилита́ция *n.* rehabilitation.
реабилити́ровать *v. impfv. & pfv.* [*pres.* **-рую, -руешь**] to rehabilitate.
реаге́нт *n.* reagent.
реаги́ровать *v. impfv.* [*pres.* **-рую, -руешь**] (*with* **на** + *acc.*) to react (to).
реакти́в *n.* reagent.
реакти́вный *adj.* **1,** reactive. **2,** jet; jet-propelled. **3,** rocket (*attrib.*): реакти́вная устано́вка, rocket launcher. Реакти́вный снаря́д, missile.
реа́ктор *n.* reactor.
реакционе́р *n.* reactionary.
реакцио́нный *adj.* reactionary.
реа́кция *n.* **1,** reaction (*in various senses*). **2,** *polit.* reaction; extreme conservatism.
реализа́ция *n.* **1,** realization; achievement. **2,** selling; converting to cash.
реали́зм *n.* realism.
реализова́ть *v. impfv. & pfv.* [*pres.* **-зу́ю, -зу́ешь**] **1,** to realize; bring about; see fulfilled. **2,** to sell; convert into cash. —**реализова́ться,** *refl.* to be realized; materialize.
реали́ст *n.* realist. —**реалисти́ческий,** *adj.* realistic.
реа́льность *n.f.* reality.
реа́льный *adj.* [*short form* **реа́лен, реа́льна**] **1,** real. **2,** realistic; practical. —**реа́льное учи́лище,** *pre-rev.* secondary school stressing scientific subjects (*as opposed to the classics*).
реанима́ция *n.* reanimation; resuscitation.
ребёнок [*gen.* **-нка;** *pl.* **ребя́та, ребя́т**] *n.* child; baby.
рёберный *adj.* rib (*attrib.*).
ребо́рда *n.* flange (*of a wheel*).
ребри́стый *adj.* **1,** having prominent ribs. **2,** ribbed.
ребро́ [*pl.* **рёбра, рёбер**] *n.* **1,** rib. **2,** edge. —**поста́вить вопро́с ребро́м,** to put a question pointblank.
ре́бус *n.* **1,** rebus. **2,** *fig.* enigma.
ребя́та [*gen.* **ребя́т**] *n. pl.* **1,** *pl. of* **ребёнок. 2,** *colloq.* lads; boys.
ребяти́шки [*gen.* **-шек**] *n. pl., colloq.* children; kids.
ребя́ческий *adj.* **1,** child's; of a child. **2,** childish.
ребя́чество *n.* **1,** *obs.* childhood. **2,** childishness.
ребя́чий [*fem.* **-чья**] *adj., colloq.* **1,** child's; children's. **2,** childish.
ребя́читься *v.r. impfv., colloq.* to behave childishly.
рёв *n.* **1,** roar. **2,** *colloq.* howl (*of a child*).
рева́нш *n.* **1,** revenge (*after a defeat*): взять рева́нш, to gain revenge. **2,** return match. —**реванши́зм,** *n.* revanchism. —**реванши́ст,** *n.* revanchist.
реве́нь [*gen.* **ревеня́**] *n.m.* rhubarb. —**реве́нный,** *adj.* rhubarb.
ревера́нс *n.* curtsy.
реверберáция *n.* reverberation.
реве́ть *v. impfv.* [*pres.* **реву́, ревёшь**] **1,** to roar. **2,**

fig. (*of a storm, the sea, etc.*) to rage. **3,** *colloq.* to howl; bawl.

ревизиони́зм *n.* revisionism. —**ревизиони́ст,** *n.* revisionist. —**ревизиони́стский,** *adj.* revisionist (*attrib.*).

реви́зия *n.* **1,** inspection. **2,** audit; auditing. **3,** revision. —**ревизио́нный,** *adj.* inspection (*attrib.*); auditing.

ревизова́ть *v. impfv. & pfv.* [*pres.* **-зу́ю, -зу́ешь**] **1,** to inspect. **2,** to audit. **3,** to revise.

ревизо́р *n.* inspector.

ревмати́зм *n.* rheumatism. —**ревма́тик,** *n., colloq.* rheumatic. —**ревмати́ческий,** *adj.* rheumatic.

ревмя́ *adv., in* **ревмя́ реве́ть,** *colloq.* to howl.

ревни́вец [*gen.* **-вца**] *n., colloq.* jealous person.

ревни́вый *adj.* jealous. —**ревни́во,** *adv.* jealously.

ревни́тель *n.m., obs.* ardent supporter.

ревнова́ть *v. impfv.* [*pres.* **-ну́ю, -ну́ешь**] to be jealous of: он ревну́ет жену́ к Са́ше, he is jealous of Sasha because his wife likes him; he is jealous over the fact that his wife likes Sasha.

ре́вностный *adj.* ardent; zealous.

ре́вность *n.f.* **1,** jealousy. **2,** *obs.* zeal; ardor.

револьве́р *n.* revolver.

револьве́рный *adj.* revolver (*attrib.*). —**револьве́рный стано́к,** turret lathe.

революционе́р *n.* revolutionary; revolutionist.

революционизи́ровать *v. impfv. & pfv.* [*pres.* **-рую, -руешь**] to revolutionize.

револю́ция *n.* revolution. —**революцио́нный,** *adj.* revolutionary.

реву́н [*gen.* **-вуна́**] *n.* **1,** *colloq.* child who is always crying or yelling. **2,** howling monkey.

ревю́ *n. neut. indecl.* revue.

рега́лии *n. pl.* [*sing.* **рега́лия**] regalia.

рега́та *n.* regatta.

ре́гби (рэ) *n. neut. indecl.* rugby.

регенера́ция *n.* regeneration. —**регенерати́вный,** *adj.* regenerative.

ре́гент *n.* **1,** regent. **2,** director of a church choir. —**ре́гентство,** *n.* regency.

регио́н *n.* region. —**региона́льный,** *adj.* regional.

реги́стр *n.* **1,** register; list. **2,** *music* register. **3,** *music* stop (*of an organ, reed instrument, etc.*).

регистра́тор *n.* registering clerk; registrar. —**регистрату́ра,** *n.* registration office; registry.

регистра́ция *n.* registration. —**регистрацио́нный,** *adj.* registration (*attrib.*).

регистри́ровать *v. impfv.* [*pfv.* **зарегистри́ровать;** *pres.* **-рую, -руешь**] to register; record. —**регистри́роваться,** *refl.* **1,** to register. **2,** to register one's marriage.

регла́мент *n.* **1,** *obs.* regulations; rules. **2,** order of business; agenda. **3,** *colloq.* speaker's allotted time.

регламента́ция *n.* regulation.

регламенти́ровать *v. impfv. & pfv.* [*pres.* **-рую, -руешь**] to regulate.

регла́н *n.* raglan.

регре́сс *n.* regression; retrogression. —**регресси́вный,** *adj.* regressive; retrogressive.

регресси́ровать *v. impfv.* [*pres.* **-рую, -руешь**] to regress; retrogress.

регули́рование *n.* regulation; adjustment.

регули́ровать *v. impfv.* [*pres.* **-рую, -руешь**] **1,** to regulate. **2,** [*pfv.* **отрегули́ровать**] to adjust.

регулиро́вка *n.* **1,** regulation. **2,** adjustment.

регуля́рный *adj.* regular. —**регуля́рно,** *adv.* regularly. —**регуля́рность,** *n.f.* regularity.

регуля́тор *n., mech.* regulator; governor.

редакти́рование *n.* editing.

редакти́ровать *v. impfv.* [*pfv.* **отредакти́ровать;** *pres.* **-рую, -руешь**] to edit.

реда́ктор *n.* editor. —**реда́кторский,** *adj.* editorial; editor's.

редакцио́нный *adj.* editorial; editing (*attrib.*). —**редакцио́нная колле́гия,** editorial board. —**редакцио́нная статья́,** editorial.

реда́кция *n.* **1,** editing. Под реда́кцией (+ *gen.*), edited by... **2,** wording. **3,** version; edition: первонача́льная реда́кция, original version/edition. **4,** editorial staff. **5,** editorial office: письмо́ в реда́кцию, letter to the editor.

реде́ть *v. impfv.* [*pfv.* **пореде́ть**] to thin out.

реди́с *n.* **1,** radish (*plant*). **2,** radishes.

реди́ска [*gen. pl.* **-сок**] *n.* radish.

ре́дкий *adj.* [*comp.* **ре́же**] **1,** rare. **2,** (*of trains, visits, etc.*) infrequent. **3,** (*of a forest, vegetation, etc.*) sparse. **4,** (*of hair*) thin; (*of teeth*) widely spaced.

ре́дко *adv.* rarely; seldom. —**ре́дко когда́,** very rarely; very seldom.

редколле́гия *n.* = **редакцио́нная колле́гия.**

ре́дкостный *adj.* rare.

ре́дкость *n.f.* **1,** rarity. **2,** a rarity. **3,** thinness; sparseness. —**на ре́дкость,** exceptionally: зима́ была́ на ре́дкость холо́дной, the winter was exceptionally cold.

реду́кция *n.* reduction (*in various technical senses*).

реду́т *n.* redoubt.

ре́дька *n.* radish.

редюи́т *n.* redoubt.

рее́стр *n.* register; list; log.

ре́же *adj., comp. of* **ре́дкий.** —*adv., comp. of* **ре́дко.**

режи́м *n.* **1,** regime. **2,** regimen: больни́чный режи́м, hospital regimen. **3,** procedures: режи́м безопа́сности, safety procedures. **4,** conditions: температу́рный режи́м, temperature conditions.

режиссёр *n., theat.* director.

режисси́ровать *v. impfv.* [*pres.* **-рую, -руешь**] *theat.* to direct.

режиссу́ра *n.* **1,** direction (*of a play or film*). **2,** directors.

ре́жущий *adj.* **1,** cutting. **2,** (*of a pain*) sharp.

реза́к [*gen.* **-зака́**] *n.* large knife; cutter.

ре́зальщик *n.* cutter (*person*).

ре́зание *n.* cutting.

ре́заный *adj.* **1,** cut. **2,** sliced.

ре́зать *v. impfv.* [*pres.* **ре́жу, ре́жешь**] **1,** to cut. **2,** to slice. **3,** *colloq.* to cut open (*surgically*). **4,** to carve; engrave. **5,** [*pfv.* **заре́зать**] to kill; slaughter. **6,** [*pfv.* **сре́зать**] *sports* to slice (a ball). —**ре́зать глаз** *or* **глаза́,** to offend the eye. —**ре́зать у́хо** *or* **слух,** to grate on one's ears.

ре́заться *v.r. impfv.* [*pres.* **ре́жусь, ре́жешься**] **1,** to cut; be cut; be able to be cut. **2,** *colloq.* to fight (*with swords*). **3,** *colloq.* (*of teeth*) to cut through: у ребёнка ре́жутся зу́бы, the child is teething.

резви́ться *v.r. impfv.* [*pres.* **-влю́сь, -ви́шься**] to romp; frolic; rollick.

ре́звость *n.f.* **1,** playfulness. **2,** speed (*of a horse*).

ре́звый *adj.* **1,** playful; frisky. **2,** (*of a horse*) fast; fast-running.

резеда́ *n.* mignonette.

резе́кция *n., med.* resection.

резе́рв *n.* **1,** reserve: резе́рвы зерна́, reserves of grain. Име́ть в резе́рве, to have in reserve. **2,** *mil.* reserve; reserves.
резерва́ция *n.* (Indian) reservation.
резерви́ровать *v. impfv. & pfv.* [*pres.* **-рую, -руешь**] to keep in reserve.
резерви́ст *n.* reservist.
резе́рвный *adj.* reserve (*attrib.*).
резервуа́р *n.* reservoir.
резе́ц [*gen.* **-зца́**] *n.* **1,** cutting tool; cutter. **2,** incisor (*tooth*).
резиде́нт *n.* **1,** resident governor. **2,** resident alien. **3,** chief of a country's intelligence operations in another country.
резиде́нция *n.* residence.
рези́на *n.* rubber.
рези́нка [*gen. pl.* **-нок**] *n.* **1,** eraser. **2,** elastic band. **3,** rubber band. **4,** garter. —**жева́тельная рези́нка,** chewing gum.
рези́новый *adj.* rubber.
ре́зка *n.* cutting.
ре́зкий *adj.* [*short form* **ре́зок, резка́, ре́зко;** *comp.* **ре́зче**] **1,** (*of a voice*) shrill. **2,** (*of an odor*) pungent. **3,** (*of light*) glaring. **4,** (*of cold, wind, etc.*) biting. **5,** (*of features*) sharp. **6,** (*of movements*) jerky. **7,** (*of words, criticism, etc.*) harsh. **8,** (*of a change*) abrupt; drastic. **9,** (*of a person, manners, etc.*) abrupt; brusque.
ре́зко *adv.* **1,** sharply. **2,** harshly. **3,** abruptly.
ре́зкость *n.f.* **1,** harshness; sharpness; abruptness. **2,** sharpness; clarity; definition. **3,** *pl.* harsh words.
резно́й *adj.* carved.
резня́ *n.* slaughter; massacre; butchery; carnage.
резолю́ция *n.* resolution.
резо́н *n., colloq.* reason.
резона́нс *n.* **1,** resonance. **2,** *fig.* reaction; response.
резона́тор *n.* resonator.
резонёр *n.* sermonizer; preacher.
резони́ровать *v. impfv.* [*pres.* **-рую, -руешь**] to resound.
резо́нный *adj., colloq.* reasonable.
результа́т *n.* **1,** result. **2,** *sports* (one's) score; showing: показа́ть лу́чший результа́т, to achieve the best score. —**в результа́те, 1,** as a result. **2,** (*with gen.*) as a result of.
результати́вный *adj.* effective; successful.
ре́зче *adj., comp. of* **ре́зкий.**
ре́зчик *n.* carver; engraver.
резь *n.f.* sharp pain.
резьба́ *n.* **1,** carving. **2,** thread (*of a screw*).
резюме́ (мэ) *n. neut. indecl.* résumé.
резюми́ровать *v. impfv. & pfv.* [*pres.* **-рую, -руешь**] to summarize; sum up.
рейд *n.* **1,** *naut.* roadstead. **2,** *mil.* raid. **3,** unannounced investigation.
ре́йка [*gen. pl.* **ре́ек**] *n.* **1,** strip of wood. **2,** measuring rod. —**зубча́тая ре́йка,** rack (*for a pinion*).
рейс *n.* **1,** trip; voyage: пе́рвый рейс, maiden voyage. **2,** flight: рейс сто во́семь, flight 108.
рейсши́на *n.* T square.
рейту́зы [*gen.* **-ту́з**] *n. pl.* **1,** riding breeches. **2,** long knit pants.
река́ [*acc.* **реку́** *or* **ре́ку;** *pl.* **ре́ки, рек, река́м** *or* **ре́кам**] *n.* river.
ре́квием *n.* requiem.
реквизи́ровать *v. impfv. & pfv.* [*pres.* **-рую, -руешь**] to requisition; commandeer.
реквизи́т *n., theat.* properties; stage props.
реквизи́ция *n.* requisitioning.
рекла́ма *n.* **1,** advertising; publicity. **2,** advertisement; commercial. **3,** sign: нео́новая рекла́ма, neon sign.
реклами́ровать *v. impfv. & pfv.* [*pres.* **-рую, -руешь**] to advertise; publicize.
рекла́мный *adj.* advertising (*attrib.*); publicity (*attrib.*); promotional. —**рекла́мный щит,** billboard.
рекогносци́ровать *v. impfv. & pfv.* [*pres.* **-рую, -руешь**] to reconnoiter.
рекогносциро́вка *n.* reconnaissance. —**рекогносциро́вочный,** *adj.* reconnaissance (*attrib.*).
рекоменда́тельный *adj.* of recommendation: рекоменда́тельное письмо́, letter of recommendation.
рекоменда́ция *n.* recommendation: дать рекоменда́цию, to make a recommendation.
рекомендова́ть *v. impfv. & pfv.* [*pfv. also* **порекомендова́ть;** *pres.* **-ду́ю, -ду́ешь**] to recommend. —**рекомендова́ться,** *refl.* **1,** [*impfv. only*] to be recommended. **2,** [*pfv. also* **отрекомендова́ться**] to introduce oneself.
реконструи́ровать *v. impfv. & pfv.* [*pres.* **-рую, -руешь**] to reconstruct.
реконстру́кция *n.* reconstruction. —**реконструкти́вный,** *adj.* reconstruction (*attrib.*).
реко́рд *n.* record: поста́вить реко́рд, to set a record.
рекорди́ст *n.* **1,** record holder. **2,** (*of an animal*) prizewinner.
реко́рдный *adj.* record (*attrib.*); record-breaking.
рекордсме́н *n.* record holder.
ре́крут *n., pre-rev.* recruit.
ре́ктор *n.* rector (*of a university*).
реле́ (рэ) *n. neut. indecl., electricity* relay.
религио́зный *adj.* religious.
рели́гия *n.* religion.
рели́квия *n.* relic.
рели́кт *n.* relic; ancient artifact.
релье́ф *n., art; topog.* relief.
релье́фно *adv.* in relief.
релье́фный *adj.* **1,** carved in relief. **2,** (*of a surface, design, etc.*) raised. **3,** *fig.* vivid; graphic. —**релье́фная ка́рта,** relief map.
рельс *n., R.R.* rail; track. —**ре́льсовый,** *adj.* rail (*attrib.*).
рема́рка [*gen. pl.* **-рок**] *n.* **1,** note. **2,** *theat.* stage direction.
ремённый *adj.* **1,** of, from, or for a belt. **2,** *mech.* belt (*attrib.*): ремённый приво́д; ремённая переда́ча, belt drive.
реме́нь [*gen.* **ремня́**] *n.m.* **1,** strap. **2,** belt. —**привязно́й реме́нь,** seat belt. —**реме́нь вентиля́тора,** fan belt.
реме́сленник *n.* craftsman; artisan.
реме́сленный *adj.* **1,** craft (*attrib.*). **2,** *fig.* pedestrian; unimaginative. —**реме́сленное учи́лище,** vocational school.
ремесло́ [*pl.* **реме́сла, -сел**] *n.* trade; craft.
ремешо́к [*gen.* **-шка́**] *n.* small strap.
реми́ссия *n., med.* remission.
ремо́нт *n.* repair; repairs. Быть в ремо́нте, to be under (*or* undergoing) repair.
ремонти́ровать *v. impfv. & pfv.* [*pfv. also* **отремон-**

ти́ровать; *pres.* **-ру́ю, -ру́ешь**] to repair; renovate; refurbish; overhaul; recondition.

ремо́нтный *adj.* repair (*attrib.*).

ренега́т *n.* renegade; turncoat. —**ренега́тство,** *n.* desertion; apostasy.

ре́ний *n.* rhenium.

рено́нс *n., cards* revoke.

ре́нта *n., econ.* rent. —**ежего́дная ре́нта,** annuity.

рента́бельный *adj.* profitable; paying. Рента́бельное предприя́тие, going concern.

рентге́н *n., colloq.* **1,** X-rays. **2,** X-ray machine.

рентге́нов *adj., in* **рентге́новы лучи́,** X-rays.

рентге́новский *adj.* X-ray (*attrib.*).

рентгеногра́мма *n.* X-ray; X-ray photograph.

рентгеноло́гия *n.* radiology. —**рентгено́лог,** *n.* radiologist.

рентгеноскопи́я *n.* X-raying; X-ray examination.

рентгенотерапи́я *n.* X-ray therapy.

реорганиза́ция *n.* reorganization.

реорганизова́ть *v. impfv. & pfv.* [*pres.* **-зу́ю, -зу́ешь**] to reorganize.

реоста́т *n.* rheostat.

ре́па *n.* turnip.

репара́ции *n. pl.* [*sing.* **-ция**] reparations. —**репарацио́нный,** *adj.* reparations (*attrib.*).

репатриа́нт *n.* repatriate. —**репатриа́ция,** *n.* repatriation.

репатрии́ровать *v. impfv. & pfv.* [*pres.* **-ру́ю, -ру́ешь**] to repatriate.

репе́йник *n.* **1,** burdock. **2,** bur.

репе́р *n.* bench mark.

репертуа́р *n.* repertoire. —**репертуа́рный,** *adj.* repertory (*attrib.*).

репети́ровать *v. impfv.* [*pfv.* **прорепети́ровать;** *pres.* **-ру́ю, -ру́ешь**] **1,** to rehearse. **2,** [*impfv. only*] to coach; tutor.

репети́тор *n.* tutor; coach. —**репети́торский,** *adj.* tutoring (*attrib.*); tutorial. —**репети́торство,** *n.* tutoring.

репети́ция *n.* rehearsal. —**репетицио́нный,** *adj.* rehearsal (*attrib.*).

ре́плика *n.* **1,** retort; rejoinder. **2,** *theat.* cue.

реполо́в *n.* linnet.

репорта́ж *n.* **1,** report (*in the news media*). **2,** reporting.

репортёр *n.* reporter.

репресси́вный *adj.* repressive.

репресси́ровать *v. impfv. & pfv.* [*pres.* **-ру́ю, -ру́ешь**] to subject to repression.

репре́ссия *n.* repression.

репри́за *n.* reprise.

репроду́ктор *n.* loudspeaker.

репроду́кция *n.* reproduction; copy.

репута́ция *n.* reputation.

ре́пчатый *adj., in* **ре́пчатый лук,** onion.

ресни́ца *n.* eyelash.

респекта́бельный *adj.* respectable. —**респекта́бельность,** *n.f.* respectability.

респира́тор *n.* respirator.

респу́блика *n.* republic.

республика́нец [*gen.* **-нца**] *n.* republican.

республика́нский *adj.* **1,** republican. **2,** of a republic of the USSR.

рессо́ра *n.* spring (*on a vehicle*). —**рессо́рный,** *adj.* on springs; having springs.

реставра́тор *n.* restorer (*of works of art*).

реставра́ция *n.* restoration.

реставри́ровать *v. impfv. & pfv.* [*pres.* **-ру́ю, -ру́ешь**] to restore.

рестора́н *n.* restaurant. —**рестора́нный,** *adj.* restaurant (*attrib.*).

ресу́рс *n.* **1,** *pl.* resources: приро́дные ресу́рсы, natural resources. **2,** resort; recourse: после́дний ресу́рс, last resort.

рети́вый *adj.* zealous. —**рети́во,** *adv.* zealously. —**рети́вость,** *n.f.* zeal.

рети́на *n.* retina.

ретирова́ться *v. impfv. & pfv.* [*pres.* **-ру́юсь, -ру́ешься**] to retire; withdraw.

рето́рта *n.* retort (*vessel*).

ретроспекти́вный *adj.* retrospective. —**ретроспе́кция,** *n.* retrospection.

ретушёр *n.* retoucher.

ретуши́ровать *v. impfv. & pfv.* [*pres.* **-ру́ю, -ру́ешь**] *photog.* to retouch.

ре́тушь *n.f.* retouching.

рефера́т *n.* **1,** synopsis; abstract. **2,** paper; essay.

рефере́ндум *n.* referendum.

рефере́нт *n.* **1,** reader; reviewer. **2,** adviser; consultant.

рефери́ровать *v. impfv. & pfv.* [*pres.* **-ру́ю, -ру́ешь**] to abstract; make a synopsis of.

рефле́кс *n.* reflex.

рефлекти́вный *adj.* = **рефлекто́рный.**

рефле́ктор *n.* **1,** reflector. **2,** reflecting telescope.

рефлекто́рный *adj.* reflex: рефлекто́рная реа́кция, reflex reaction.

рефо́рма *n.* reform. —**реформа́тор,** *n.* reformer.

реформа́тский *adj., in* **реформа́тская це́рковь,** Reformed Church.

реформа́ция *n., hist.* the Reformation.

реформи́ровать *v. impfv. & pfv.* [*pres.* **-ру́ю, -ру́ешь**] to reform.

рефра́ктор *n.* refracting telescope; refractor.

рефра́кция *n.* refraction.

рефре́н *n.* refrain.

рефрижера́тор *n.* refrigerator.

рехну́ться *v.r. pfv., colloq.* to go mad; go crazy.

реценз́ент *n.* reviewer; critic.

рецензи́ровать *v. impfv.* [*pfv.* **прорецензи́ровать;** *pres.* **-ру́ю, -ру́ешь**] to review.

реце́нзия *n.* review: реце́нзия на кни́гу (*or* о кни́ге), book review.

реце́пт *n.* **1,** prescription. **2,** recipe.

рецесси́вный *adj., biol.* recessive.

рециди́в *n.* **1,** recurrence. **2,** *med.* relapse. **3,** *law* second offense.

рецидиви́зм *n.* recidivism. —**рецидиви́ст,** *n.* recidivist.

речево́й *adj.* speech (*attrib.*).

рече́ние *n.* expression; locution.

речи́стый *adj., colloq.* **1,** eloquent. **2,** talkative.

речитати́в *n., music* recitative. —**говори́ть** *or* **чита́ть речитати́вом,** to intone.

ре́чка [*gen. pl.* **-чек**] *n.* small river.

речно́й *adj.* river (*attrib.*).

речь [*pl.* **ре́чи, рече́й, реча́м**] *n.f.* **1,** speech: о́рганы ре́чи, organs of speech. **2,** a speech: произноси́ть речь, to make a speech. —**речь идёт о,** the question is one of; it is a question of. —**об э́том не мóжет быть и рéчи,** that is out of the question.

решáть *v. impfv.* [*pfv.* **решúть**] **1,** (*with inf.*) to decide (to). **2,** to decide (an issue, the outcome of something, etc.). **3,** to solve. —**решáться,** *refl.* **1,** (*with inf.*) to make up one's mind (to); (*with* **на** + *acc.*) decide on. **2,** (*with inf.*) to dare (to); bring oneself (to). **3,** to be decided.

решáющий *adj.* deciding; decisive. —**с решáющим гóлосом,** voting: член с решáющим гóлосом, voting member.

решéние *n.* **1,** decision. **2,** solution.

решётка [*gen. pl.* **-ток**] *n.* grating; grate; lattice; grille. Камúнная решётка, fire screen. —**посадúть за решётку,** to put behind bars; imprison. —**сидéть за решёткой,** to be behind bars.

решетó [*pl.* **решёта**] *n.* strainer; sieve.

решётчатый *adj.* lattice (*attrib.*); latticed.

решúмость *n.f.* determination; resoluteness; resolve.

решúтельно *adv.* **1,** decisively. **2,** strongly; emphatically; categorically. **3,** absolutely.

решúтельность *n.f.* **1,** decisiveness. **2,** determination.

решúтельный *adj.* **1,** (*of a person, action, result, moment, etc.*) decisive. **2,** (*of an answer*) definite. **3,** (*of a refusal, protest, gesture, etc.*) emphatic.

решúть *v., pfv. of* **решáть.** —**решúться,** *refl., pfv. of* **решáться.**

рéшка *n., in* **орёл úли рéшка?,** heads or tails?

рéять *v. impfv.* [*pres.* **рéю, рéешь**] **1,** to soar; glide. **2,** to hover. **3,** to flutter.

ржáветь *v. impfv.* [*pfv.* **заржáветь**] to rust.

ржáвчина *n.* rust.

ржáвый *adj.* **1,** rusty. **2,** rust-colored.

ржáние *n.* neighing.

ржáнка [*gen. pl.* **-нок**] *n.* plover.

ржанóй *adj.* rye (*attrib.*): ржанóй хлеб, rye bread.

ржать *v. impfv.* [*pres.* **ржёт**] to neigh.

рúга *n.* threshing barn.

рúза *n.* **1,** chasuble. **2,** metal plating on an icon.

рúзница *n.* sacristy; vestry.

рикошéт *n.* ricochet; rebound. —**рикошéтом,** on the rebound.

рикошетúровать *v. impfv. & pfv.* [*pres.* **-рует**] to ricochet.

рúкша [*gen. pl.* **рикш**] *n.* **1,** *n.f.* rickshaw. **2,** *n.m.* rickshaw driver.

рúмлянин [*pl.* **рúмляне, рúмлян**] *n.m.* [*fem.* **рúмлянка**] Roman.

рúмский *adj.* Roman.

ринг *n.* boxing ring.

рúнуться *v.r. pfv.* **1,** to dash; rush: рúнуться к выходý, to dash/rush for the exit. Рúнуться помóчь (+ *dat.*), to rush to help (someone). **2,** *fig.* (*with* **в** + *acc.*) to plunge into (a task, battle, etc.).

рис *n.* rice.

риск *n.* risk. Идтú на риск, to take a risk; take a chance. —**на свой страх и риск,** at one's own risk.

рискнýть *v. pfv.* **1,** *pfv. of* **рисковáть. 2,** (*with inf.*) to dare (to); venture (to).

рискóванный *adj.* **1,** risky. **2,** risqué.

рисковáть *v. impfv.* [*pfv.* **рискнýть;** *pres.* **-кýю, -кýешь**] **1,** to take a chance; take chances. **2,** (*with instr.*) to risk. **3,** (*with inf.*) to risk; run the risk of.

рисовáльный *adj.* drawing (*attrib.*).

рисовáльщик *n.* (graphic) artist.

рисовáние *n.* drawing.

рисовáть *v. impfv.* [*pfv.* **нарисовáть;** *pres.* **-сýю, -сýешь**] **1,** to draw. **2,** *fig.* to paint; portray. —**рисовáться,** *refl.* [*impfv. only*] **1,** to appear; loom; be silhouetted. **2,** *fig.* (*with dat.*) to appear (to); seem (to). **3,** to show off.

рисóвка *n.* **1,** *obs.* drawing. **2,** showing off; pretentiousness.

рúсовый *adj.* rice (*attrib.*).

рисýнок [*gen.* **-нка**] *n.* **1,** a drawing. **2,** design; pattern. **3,** (*when accompanying a scientific article*) figure.

ритм *n.* rhythm.

рúтмика *n.* **1,** rhythm. **2,** rhythmics.

ритмúческий *adj.* rhythmic; rhythmical.

ритмúчный *adj.* rhythmic; rhythmical. —**ритмúчность,** *n.f.* rhythm.

ритóрика *n.* rhetoric. —**риторúческий,** *adj.* rhetorical.

ритуáл *n.* ritual. —**ритуáльный,** *adj.* ritual.

риф *n.* reef.

рифлёный *adj.* corrugated; fluted.

рúфма *n.* rhyme.

рифмáч [*gen.* **-мачá**] *n., colloq.* rhymer; rhymester.

рифмовáть *v. impfv.* [*pres.* **-мýю, -мýешь**] to rhyme; make (something) rhyme. —**рифмовáться,** *refl.* (*of words, sounds, etc.*) to rhyme.

рифмоплёт *n., colloq.* rhymer; rhymester.

рóба *n.* overalls.

рóббер *n., cards* rubber.

робéть *v. impfv.* to be timid; be shy.

рóбкий *adj.* [*short form* **рóбок, робкá, рóбко;** *comp.* **рóбче**] timid; shy. —**не из рóбкого десятка,** not the timid type.

рóбко *adv.* timidly.

рóбость *n.f.* timidity; shyness.

рóбот *n.* robot.

ров [*gen.* **рва;** *2nd loc.* **рву**] *n.* ditch. —**крепостнóй ров,** moat.

ровéсник *n.* person one's own age; contemporary.

рóвно *adv.* **1,** evenly. **2,** exactly; precisely: рóвно в дéсять часóв, at ten o'clock sharp. **3,** *colloq.* absolutely: рóвно ничегó, absolutely nothing.

рóвность *n.f.* **1,** evenness. **2,** *fig.* equanimity.

рóвный *adj.* [*short form* **рóвен, ровнá, рóвно**] **1,** even; level. **2,** straight. **3,** even; steady; equable. **4,** *fig.* even-tempered. —**для рóвного счёта,** to make it come out even. —**рóвным счётом, 1,** exactly. **2,** only. —**рóвным счётом ничегó,** absolutely nothing.

рóвня *also,* **ровня́** *n.m. & f., colloq.* (one's) equal.

ровня́ть *v. impfv.* [*pfv.* **сровня́ть**] to even; level.

рог [*pl.* **рогá**] *n.* **1,** horn; antler. **2,** horn: трубúть в рог, to blow a horn. —**брать быкá за рогá,** to take the bull by the horns. —**наставля́ть рогá** (+ *dat.*), *colloq.* to cuckold.

рогáстый *adj., colloq.* having large horns or antlers.

рогáтка [*gen. pl.* **-ток**] *n.* **1,** bar; barrier. **2,** *fig.* obstacle. **3,** slingshot.

рогáтый *adj.* horned. —**крýпный/мéлкий рогáтый скот,** *see* **скот.**

рогáч [*gen.* **-гачá**] *n.* **1,** stag; hart. **2,** stag beetle.

роговúца *n.* cornea.

роговóй *adj.* **1,** made of horn. **2,** (*of glasses*) horn-rimmed. **3,** horny. **4,** *music* for (the) horn. —**роговáя обмáнка,** hornblende. —**роговáя оболóчка,** cornea.

рого́жа *n.* matting.
рого́з *n.* cattail.
рогоно́сец [*gen.* **-сца**] *n., colloq.* cuckold.
род *n.* **1,** family. **2,** birth; origin; stock. **3,** sort; kind. **4,** gender. **5,** genus. **6,** *in* челове́ческий род, the human race. **7,** *in* род заня́тий *or* де́ятельности, line of work; occupation; profession. **8,** *in* род войск, *mil.* arm of service. —**вести́ свой род от...,** to trace one's ancestry back to... —**в не́котором ро́де,** to a certain extent; in a certain sense; in a way. —**в своём ро́де,** in his way; in its way. —**вся́кого ро́да** (+ *nom.*), all sorts of. —**из ро́да в род,** from generation to generation. —**о́т ро́ду,** of age: ему́ два́дцать лет о́т роду, he is twenty years of age. —**своего́ ро́да,** a kind of. —**тако́го ро́да** (+ *nom.*), such. —**что́-то в э́том ро́де,** something like that. *See also* **ро́дом** *and* **ро́ды.**
ро́дий *n.* rhodium.
роди́льница *n.* woman who has just given birth.
роди́льный *adj.* **1,** maternity (*attrib.*): роди́льное отделе́ние, maternity ward; delivery room. **2,** puerperal: роди́льная горя́чка, puerperal fever.
роди́мый *adj., colloq.* **1,** native. **2,** one's own. —**роди́мое пятно́,** birthmark.
ро́дина *n.* native land; homeland; motherland.
ро́динка [*gen. pl.* **-нок**] *n.* mole; birthmark.
роди́тели [*gen.* **-лей**] *n. pl.* parents.
роди́тельный *adj., in* **роди́тельный паде́ж,** genitive case.
роди́тельский *adj.* parental; parents'.
роди́ть *v. pfv.* [*infl.* **рожу́, роди́шь;** *past fem.* **родила́**] **1,** *pfv. of* **рожа́ть** *and* **рожда́ть. 2,** to sire; father; beget. —**роди́ться,** *refl., pfv. of* **рожда́ться.**
родни́к [*gen.* **-ника́**] *n.* spring (*of water*). —**роднико́вый,** *adj.* spring (*attrib.*).
родни́ть *v. impfv.* [*pfv.* **сродни́ть** *or* **породни́ть**] to unite; bring together. —**родни́ться,** *refl.* [*pfv.* **породни́ться**] (*with* **с** + *instr.*) to become related to.
родно́й *adj.* **1,** related by blood. Родно́й брат, brother (*as opposed to* двою́родный брат – cousin). **2,** native: родна́я дере́вня, one's native village. Родно́й го́род, home town. **3,** *in direct address,* my dear. —**родны́е,** *n. pl.* relatives.
родня́ *n.* **1,** relatives. **2,** *colloq.* relative.
родови́тый *adj.* of noble birth. —**родови́тость,** *n.f.* noble birth.
родово́й *adj.* **1,** family (*attrib.*). **2,** ancestral. **3,** tribal. **4,** *biol.* generic. **5,** *gram.* gender (*attrib.*). **6,** birth (*attrib.*): родовы́е поту́ги, birth pains; labor pains.
рододе́ндрон (дэ) *n.* rhododendron.
ро́дом *adv.* by birth: он ро́дом из Фра́нции, he is a native of France; he is a Frenchman by birth.
родонача́льник *n.* **1,** progenitor. **2,** *fig.* father; founder.
родосло́вие *n.* genealogy; pedigree; lineage. *Also,* **родосло́вная.**
родосло́вный *adj.* genealogical. —**родосло́вное де́рево,** family tree.
ро́дственник *n.* relative; relation.
ро́дственный *adj.* **1,** family (*attrib.*): ро́дственные свя́зи, family ties; ties of kinship. **2,** (*of languages, peoples, sciences, etc.*) related. **3,** *fig.* warm; cordial.
родство́ *n.* **1,** relationship; kinship: быть в родстве́ с, to be related to. **2,** *colloq.* relatives. **3,** affinity.
ро́ды [*gen.* **ро́дов**] *n. pl.* birth; childbirth.
ро́жа *n.* **1,** erysipelas (*skin disease*). **2,** *colloq.* ugly face; ugly mug; ugly puss.
рожа́ть *v. impfv.* [*pfv.* **роди́ть**] **1,** *v.i.* to give birth; have a baby. **2,** *v.t.* to give birth to; bear.
рожда́емость *n.f.* birth rate.
рожда́ть *v. impfv.* [*pfv.* **роди́ть**] **1,** = **рожа́ть. 2,** *fig.* to give rise to; engender. —**рожда́ться,** *refl.* to be born.
рожде́ние *n.* birth. —**день рожде́ния,** birthday.
рождённый *past passive part. of* **роди́ть,** born: рождённый для сце́ны, born for the stage.
рожде́ственский *adj.* Christmas (*attrib.*).
рождество́ *n.* Christmas.
роже́ница *also,* **рожени́ца** *n.* woman giving birth.
рожо́к [*gen.* **-жка́;** *pl.* **ро́жки, ро́жек** *in sense #1;* **рожки́, рожко́в** *in other senses*] *n.* **1,** small horn. **2,** *music* horn. **3,** shoehorn. **4,** nursing bottle. —**англи́йский рожо́к,** English horn. —**га́зовый рожо́к,** gas burner. —**слухово́й рожо́к,** ear trumpet.
рожь [*gen., dat., & prepl.* **ржи;** *instr.* **ро́жью**] *n.f.* rye.
ро́за *n.* **1,** rose. **2,** rosebush.
ро́зан *n., colloq.* rose.
ро́звальни [*gen.* **-ней**] *n. pl.* low wide sled.
ро́зга [*gen. pl.* **ро́зог**] *n.* rod (*for whipping*).
ро́зговенье *n.* first day following a period of fasting.
розе́тка [*gen. pl.* **-ток**] *n.* **1,** rosette. **2,** small jam dish. **3,** electric outlet.
розмари́н *n.* rosemary.
ро́зница *n., in* **в ро́зницу,** retail. —**ро́зничный,** *adj.* retail.
ро́зно *adv., obs.* apart; separately.
рознь *n.f.* **1,** dissension; discord. **2,** (*with dat.*) *indicating diversity of similar things:* челове́к челове́ку – рознь, there are all kinds of people; there are people, and then there are people.
розове́ть *v. impfv.* [*pfv.* **порозове́ть**] **1,** to turn pink. **2,** [*impfv. only*] (*of anything rose or pink*) to appear; be seen.
розовощёкий *adj.* rosy-cheeked.
ро́зовый *adj.* **1,** rose (*attrib.*). **2,** rose-colored; pink. **3,** *fig.* rosy. —**сквозь ро́зовые очки́,** through rose-colored glasses.
ро́зыгрыш *n.* **1,** drawing (*in a lottery*). **2,** *sports* play; competition. **3,** draw; tie; drawn game.
ро́зыск *n.* **1,** search. **2,** investigation. —**уголо́вный ро́зыск,** department of criminal investigation.
рои́ться *v.r. impfv.* to swarm.
рой [*pl.* **рои́**] *n.* swarm.
рок *n.* fate.
рокирова́ть *v. impfv. & pfv.* [*pres.* **-ру́ю, -ру́ешь**] *chess* to castle. *Also,* **рокирова́ться.**
рокиро́вка *n., chess* castling: де́лать рокиро́вку, to castle.
роково́й *adj.* fatal.
рококо́ *n. indecl.* rococo.
ро́кот *n.* **1,** roar; rumble. **2,** murmur.
рокота́ть *v. impfv.* [*pres.* **-кочу́, -ко́чешь**] to rumble; resound.
ро́лик *n.* **1,** roller; caster. **2,** *pl.* roller skates. **3,** reel (*for movie film*).
ро́ликовый *adj.* roller (*attrib.*). —**ро́ликовые коньки́,** roller skates. —**ро́ликовый подши́пник,** roller bearing.
роль [*pl.* **ро́ли, роле́й, роля́м**] *n.f.* role; part. —**игра́ть роль,** to play a role/part.

ром *n.* rum.

рома́н *n.* **1,** novel. **2,** *colloq.* romance; love affair.

романи́ст *n.* **1,** novelist. **2,** specialist in Romance philology.

рома́нс *n., music* romance.

рома́нский *adj.* **1,** Romance: рома́нские языки́, Romance languages. **2,** Romanesque.

романтизи́ровать *v. impfv. & pfv.* [*pres.* **-рую, -руешь**] to romanticize.

романти́зм *n.* romanticism.

рома́нтик *n.* romanticist.

рома́нтика *n.* **1,** romanticism. **2,** romance; romantic appeal.

романти́ческий *adj.* romantic. *Also,* **романти́чный.**

рома́шка [*gen. pl.* **-шек**] *n.* camomile.

ромб *n.* rhombus. —**ромби́ческий,** *adj.* rhombic.

ромбо́ид *n.* rhomboid.

ро́мовый *adj.* rum (*attrib.*).

ромште́кс (тэ) *n.* rump steak.

ро́ндо *n. indecl.* rondo.

роня́ть *v. impfv.* [*pfv.* **урони́ть**] **1,** to drop. **2,** [*impfv. only*] to shed (leaves, tears, etc.). **3,** *fig.* to demean: роня́ть/урони́ть себя́, to demean oneself.

ро́пот *n.* **1,** murmur (*of disapproval*); grumbling. **2,** murmuring; rustling; rippling.

ропта́ть *v. impfv.* [*pres.* **ропщу́, ро́пщешь**] to grumble; murmur.

роса́ *n.* dew.

роси́нка [*gen. pl.* **-нок**] *n.* dewdrop.

роси́стый *adj.* dewy.

роско́шествовать *v. impfv.* [*pres.* **-ствую, -ствуешь**] to live in luxury; live sumptuously. *Also,* **роско́шничать.**

роско́шный *adj.* luxurious; sumptuous.

ро́скошь *n.f.* luxury.

ро́слый *adj.* strapping; husky; burly.

ро́сный *adj., in* **ро́сный ла́дан,** benzoin.

росома́ха *n.* wolverine.

ро́спись *n.f.* painting; mural.

ро́спуск *n.* dismissal; dissolution.

росси́йский *adj.* Russian.

ро́ссказни [*gen.* **-ней**] *n. pl., colloq.* tale; yarn; cock-and-bull story.

ро́ссыпь *n.f.* (mineral) deposit.

рост *n.* **1,** growth. **2,** height. Высо́кого ро́ста, tall. Ни́зкого ро́ста, short. Он ро́стом шесть фу́тов, he is six feet tall. Существо́ в рост челове́ка, a creature the height of a man. **3,** rise; increase. **4,** length (*of a garment*): брю́ки сорокового́ разме́ра пе́рвого ро́ста, trousers size forty short. —**во весь рост, 1,** to one's full height. **2,** (*of a portrait*) full-length. **3,** *fig.* in all its magnitude. —**не по ро́сту,** (*of a garment*) not the right size. —**по ро́сту,** according to size; in size order.

ро́стбиф *n.* roast beef.

ростовщи́к [*gen.* **-щика́**] *n.* **1,** moneylender. **2,** usurer. —**ростовщи́ческий,** *adj.* usurious. —**ростовщи́чество,** *n.* usury.

росто́к [*gen.* **-тка́**] *n.* sprout; shoot.

ро́счерк *n.* flourish. —**одни́м ро́счерком пера́,** with a stroke of the pen.

рося́нка *n.* sundew.

росяно́й *adj.* dew (*attrib.*).

рот [*gen.* **рта;** *2nd loc.* **рту**] *n.* mouth. Во рту, in one's mouth. Изо рта, from one's mouth. —**во весь рот, 1,** at the top of one's lungs. **2,** from ear to ear. —**набра́ть воды́ в рот,** to keep silent; keep mum. —**не брать в рот** (+ *gen.*), not to touch (a certain food or drink). —**смотре́ть в рот** (+ *dat.*), to listen spellbound (to someone).

ро́та *n., mil.* company.

рота́нг *n.* rattan. —**рота́нговый,** *adj.* rattan.

рота́тор *n.* mimeograph.

ротацио́нный *adj.* rotary. —**ротацио́нная (печа́тная) маши́на,** rotary press.

ро́тный *adj., mil.* company (*attrib.*). —*n.* company commander.

ротово́й *adj.* of the mouth; oral.

ротозе́й *n., colloq.* **1,** onlooker; bystander. **2,** dimwit; dullard.

ротозе́йство *n., colloq.* extreme absent-mindedness.

рото́нда *n.* rotunda.

ро́тор *n.* rotor.

ро́ща *n.* grove.

рояли́зм *n.* royalism. —**рояли́ст,** *n.* royalist. —**рояли́стский,** *adj.* royalist.

роя́ль *n.m.* piano.

ртуть *n.f.* mercury. —**рту́тный,** *adj.* mercury (*attrib.*).

руба́нок [*gen.* **-нка**] *n.* plane (*tool*).

руба́ха *n.* shirt.

руба́шка [*gen. pl.* **-шек**] *n.* **1,** shirt. **2,** casing. **3,** back (*of a playing card*). —**ночна́я руба́шка, 1,** nightshirt. **2,** nightgown. —**роди́ться в руба́шке,** to be born with a silver spoon in one's mouth.

рубе́ж [*gen.* **-бежа́**] *n.* **1,** border; boundary. **2,** *mil.* line: огнево́й рубе́ж, firing line. —**за рубежо́м,** abroad.

рубе́ц [*gen.* **-бца́**] *n.* **1,** scar; welt. **2,** hem. **3,** rumen; paunch (*of an animal*). **4,** tripe.

руби́дий *n.* rubidium.

Рубико́н *n., in* **перейти́ Рубико́н,** to cross the Rubicon.

руби́н *n.* ruby. —**руби́новый,** *adj.* ruby (*attrib.*).

руби́ть *v. impfv.* [*pres.* **рублю́, ру́бишь**] **1,** to chop. **2,** to chop down; cut down; fell. **3,** to slash. **4,** to build (*out of logs*). —**руби́ться,** *refl.* to fight with swords.

ру́бище *n.* rags; tatters.

ру́бка [*gen. pl.* **-бок**] *n.* **1,** chopping; felling. **2,** *naut.* deckhouse. —**боева́я ру́бка,** conning tower. —**рулева́я ру́бка,** pilothouse.

рублёвка [*gen. pl.* **-вок**] *n., colloq.* one-ruble note. —**рублёвый,** *adj.* ruble (*attrib.*); one-ruble (*attrib.*).

ру́бленый *adj.* **1,** chopped. **2,** made of logs.

рубль [*gen.* **рубля́**] *n.m.* ruble.

ру́брика *n.* heading.

рубцева́ться *v.r. impfv.* [*pfv.* **зарубцева́ться;** *pres.* **-цу́ется**] (*of a wound*) to form a scar.

ру́бчатый *adj.* (*of material*) ribbed.

ру́бчик *n.* **1,** *dim. of* **рубе́ц. 2,** rib; ridge (*on material*).

ру́гань *n.f.* swearing; profanity.

руга́тельный *adj.* abusive. —**руга́тельство,** *n.* swearword; expletive.

руга́ть *v. impfv.* [*pfv.* **вы́ругать**] to curse out; swear at. —**руга́ться,** *refl.* [*impfv. only*] **1,** to swear; curse. **2,** to swear at one another.

руда́ [*pl.* **ру́ды**] *n.* ore.

рудиме́нт *n.* rudimentary organ. —**рудимента́рный,** *adj.* rudimentary.

рудни́к [*gen.* **-ника́**] *n.* mine. —**руднико́вый; рудни́чный,** *adj.* mine (*attrib.*).

ру́дный *adj.* ore (*attrib.*); of ore.

рудоко́п *n., obs.* miner.

руже́йник *n.* gunsmith.

руже́йный *adj.* gun (*attrib.*); rifle (*attrib.*).

ружьё [*pl.* **ру́жья, ру́жей, ру́жьям**] *n.* **1,** gun. **2,** *in various set expressions,* arms: быть под ружьём, to be under arms; призыва́ть под ружьё, to call to arms.

руи́ны *n. pl.* [*sing.* **руи́на**] ruins.

рука́ [*acc.* **ру́ку;** *pl.* **ру́ки, рук, рука́м**] *n.* **1,** hand. **2,** arm. —**в рука́х,** in one's hands. —**из пе́рвых рук,** (*of information*) firsthand. —**из рук вон (пло́хо),** atrociously; miserably. —**из рук в ру́ки,** from hand to hand. —**на рука́х, 1,** in one's arms. **2,** *fig.* on one's hands. —**на́ руку** (+ *dat.*), to one's liking. —**не с руки́** (+ *dat.*), inconvenient (for); inappropriate (for). —**от рук** (+ *gen.*), at the hands of. —**от руки́,** in longhand. —**по рука́м!,** it's a deal! —**по руке́,** the right size. —**под руко́й,** on hand; at hand. —**по́д руку, 1,** arm in arm. **2,** *in* говори́ть кому́-нибудь по́д руку, to speak to someone when he (she) is busy. —**рука́ в ру́ку; рука́ о́б руку,** hand in hand. —**ру́ки вверх!,** hands up! —**ру́ки прочь!,** hands off! —**руко́й пода́ть,** a stone's throw.

рука́в [*gen. sing. & nom. pl.* **рукава́**] *n.* **1,** sleeve. **2,** branch (*of a river*). **3,** hose. —**спустя́ рукава́,** carelessly; in a slipshod manner.

рукави́ца *n.* mitten.

руководи́тель *n.m.* **1,** leader. **2,** supervisor; head.

руководи́ть *v. impfv.* [*pres.* **-вожу́, -води́шь**] (*with instr.*) **1,** to direct; manage; run. **2,** to lead; head. **3,** to guide; supervise. —**руководи́ться,** *refl.* (*with instr.*) to be guided (by).

руково́дство *n.* **1,** leadership. **2,** guidance; supervision. **3,** guide: руково́дство к де́йствию, guide to action. **4,** manual; handbook. **5,** leaders.

руково́дствоваться *v.r. impfv.* [*pres.* **-ствуюсь, -ствуешься**] (*with instr.*) to be guided (by).

руководя́щий *adj.* **1,** leading; guiding. **2,** senior; supervisory. —**руководя́щий комите́т,** steering committee.

рукоде́лие *n.* needlework. —**рукоде́льница,** *n.* needleworker.

рукомо́йник *n.* washstand.

рукопа́шный *adj., in* **рукопа́шный бой,** hand-to-hand fighting/combat.

рукопи́сный *adj.* **1,** manuscript (*attrib.*). **2,** handwritten. **3,** cursive.

ру́копись *n.f.* manuscript.

рукоплеска́ние *n., usu. pl.* applause.

рукоплеска́ть *v. impfv.* [*pres.* **-плещу́, -пле́щешь**] to applaud.

рукопожа́тие *n.* handshake.

рукоположе́ние *n., Orth. Ch.* ordination.

рукоя́тка [*gen. pl.* **-ток**] *n.* handle. *Also,* **рукоя́ть,** *n.f.*

рула́да *n., music* roulade.

рулево́й *adj.* rudder (*attrib.*); steering (*attrib.*). —*n.* helmsman.

руле́т *n.* meat (*or* potato) loaf.

руле́тка [*gen. pl.* **-ток**] *n.* **1,** tape measure. **2,** roulette; roulette wheel.

рули́ть *v. impfv., aero.* to taxi.

руло́н *n.* roll; bolt (*of cloth*).

руль [*gen.* **руля́**] *n.m.* **1,** rudder; helm. **2,** steering wheel. **3,** handlebar(s). —**за рулём,** at (*or* behind) the wheel. —**стать за руль,** to take the helm. —**стоя́ть у руля́,** to be at the helm.

ру́мба *n.* rumba.

румы́н [*gen. pl.* **румы́н**] *n.m.* [*fem.* **-мы́нка**] Romanian. —**румы́нский,** *adj.* Romanian.

румя́на [*gen.* **-мя́н**] *n.pl.* rouge.

румя́нец [*gen.* **-нца**] *n.* color in one's face; redness in one's cheeks.

румя́нить *v. impfv.* [*pfv.* **нарумя́нить**] **1,** to rouge; apply rouge to. **2,** [*pfv. also* **зарумя́нить**] to redden; put color in; give a reddish glow to. —**румя́ниться,** *refl.* **1,** [*pfv.* **нарумя́ниться**] to put on rouge. **2,** [*pfv.* **зарумя́ниться**] to turn red; flush.

румя́ный *adj.* ruddy; rosy.

руно́ [*pl.* **ру́на**] *n.* fleece. —**золото́е руно́,** the Golden Fleece.

ру́ны *n. pl.* [*sing.* **ру́на**] runes. —**руни́ческий,** *adj.* runic.

ру́пия *n.* rupee.

ру́пор *n.* **1,** megaphone. **2,** *fig.* mouthpiece.

руса́к [*gen.* **-сака́**] *n.* **1,** European hare. **2,** *colloq.* Russian.

руса́лка [*gen. pl.* **-лок**] *n.* mermaid.

руси́ст *n.* specialist in the Russian language.

русифика́ция *n.* Russification.

русифици́ровать *v. impfv. & pfv.* [*pres.* **-рую, -руешь**] to Russify.

ру́сло *n.* **1,** river bed; channel. **2,** *fig.* course; direction.

русофи́л *n.* Russophile.

русофо́б *n.* Russophobe. —**русофо́бство,** *n.* Russophobia.

ру́сский *adj.* Russian: ру́сский язы́к, the Russian language. —*n.* Russian (*person*).

русскоязы́чный *adj.* Russian-language (*attrib.*).

ру́сый *adj.* **1,** (*of hair*) light brown. **2,** (*of a person*) with light brown hair.

руте́ний *n.* ruthenium.

рути́на *n.* resistance to change; conservatism. —**рутинёр,** *n.* conservative; traditionalist. —**рути́нный,** *adj.* staid; conservative; traditional.

ру́хлядь *n.f., colloq.* junk.

ру́хнуть *v. pfv.* **1,** to collapse; come tumbling down. **2,** *fig.* (*of hopes, plans, etc.*) to collapse; fall through; come to naught.

руча́тельство *n.* guarantee.

руча́ться *v.r. impfv.* [*pfv.* **поручи́ться**] (*with* **за** + *acc.*) to vouch for; guarantee.

ручеёк [*gen.* **-чейка́**] *n., dim. of* **ручей.**

руче́й [*gen.* **-чья́**] *n.* brook; stream.

ру́чка [*gen. pl.* **-чек**] *n.* **1,** *dim. of* **рука́. 2,** handle; knob. **3,** arm (*of a chair, sofa, etc.*). **4,** penholder. **5,** pen. —**автомати́ческая ру́чка,** fountain pen.

ручно́й *adj.* **1,** hand (*attrib.*). **2,** manual. **3,** tame; domesticated. —**ручны́е часы́,** wrist watch.

ру́шить *v. impfv.* to tear down. —**ру́шиться,** *refl.* **1,** to collapse; come tumbling down. **2,** *fig.* to collapse; fall through.

ры́ба *n.* **1,** fish. **2,** *pl., cap.* Pisces. —**ни ры́ба ни мя́со,** neither fish nor fowl.

рыба́к [*gen.* **-бака́**] *n.* (commercial) fisherman.

рыба́лка *n., colloq.* fishing: идти́ на рыба́лку, to go fishing.

рыба́цкий *adj.* fishing (*attrib.*); fisherman's. *Also,* **ры-ба́чий** [*fem.* **-чья**].
рыба́чить *v. impfv.* to fish.
рыбёшка [*gen. pl.* **-шек**] *n., colloq.* small fish.
ры́бий [*fem.* **-бья**] *adj.* fish (*attrib.*). —**ры́бий жир,** cod-liver oil. —**ры́бий клей,** isinglass.
ры́бка [*gen. pl.* **-бок**] *n., dim. of* **ры́ба.** —**золота́я ры́бка,** goldfish.
ры́бный *adj.* fish (*attrib.*). —**ры́бная ло́вля,** fishing.
рыболо́в *n.* fisherman; angler. —**рыболо́вный,** *adj.* fishing (*attrib.*). —**рыболо́вство,** *n.* fishing (*as an economic activity*).
рыво́к [*gen.* **-вка́**] *n.* **1,** jerk. **2,** spurt. **3,** *weightlifting* snatch.
рыга́ть *v. impfv.* [*pfv.* **рыгну́ть**] to belch.
рыда́ние *n.* sobbing.
рыда́ть *v. impfv.* to sob.
рыжеволо́сый *adj.* redheaded.
рыже́ть *v. impfv.* [*pfv.* **порыже́ть**] to become red; turn red.
ры́жий *adj.* **1,** red. **2,** redheaded. **3,** (*of a horse*) chestnut. —*n., colloq.* circus clown.
ры́жик *n.* a variety of edible mushroom.
рык *n.* roar.
рыка́ть *v. impfv.* to roar.
ры́ло *n.* **1,** snout. **2,** *colloq.* mug; puss; kisser.
ры́льце [*gen. pl.* **-лец**] *n.* **1,** *dim. of* **ры́ло. 2,** *bot.* stigma.
ры́нда *n.* ship's bell.
ры́нок [*gen.* **-нка**] *n.* market. —**ры́ночный,** *adj.* market (*attrib.*).
рыса́к [*gen.* **-сака́**] *n.* trotter (*horse*).
ры́сий [*fem.* **-сья**] *adj.* **1,** lynx (*attrib.*). **2,** (*of one's eyes*) piercing.
рыси́стый *adj., in* **рыси́стые бега́,** trotting races; **рыси́стая ло́шадь,** trotter.
рыси́ть *v. impfv.* (*of a horse*) to trot.
ры́скать *v. impfv.* [*pres.* **ры́щу, ры́щешь**] **1,** to prowl; be on the prowl. **2,** *colloq.* to wander about; roam.
рысца́ *n.* slow trot; jog trot.
рысь *n.f.* **1,** lynx; bobcat. **2,** trot: ры́сью (*or* на рыся́х), at a trot.
ры́твина *n.* rut; pothole.
рыть *v. impfv.* [*pfv.* **вы́рыть;** *pres.* **ро́ю, ро́ешь**] **1,** to dig. **2,** to dig up.
рытьё *n.* digging.
ры́ться *v.r. impfv.* [*pfv.* **поры́ться;** *pres.* **ро́юсь, ро́ешься**] (*with* **в** + *prepl.*) **1,** [*impfv. only*] to dig (in the dirt, sand, etc.). **2,** to search; rummage; ransack. —**ры́ться/поры́ться в па́мяти,** to rack one's brains; try hard to remember.
рыхле́ть *v. impfv.* to become soft; lose its firmness.
рыхли́ть *v. impfv.* [*pfv.* **взрыхли́ть**] to loosen; turn up (soil, dirt, etc.).
ры́хлый *adj.* loose; crumbly; friable.
ры́царский *adj.* **1,** knight's; knights'. **2,** chivalrous.
ры́царство *n.* **1,** knights. **2,** knighthood. **3,** chivalry.
ры́царь *n.m.* knight.
ры́чаг [*gen.* **-чага́**] *n.* lever.
рыча́ние *n.* growling; snarling.
рыча́ть *v. impfv.* [*pres.* **-чи́т**] to growl; snarl.
рья́ный *adj.* zealous. —**рья́но,** *adv.* zealously. —**рья́ность,** *n.f.* zeal.
рэ́кет *n.* racket. —**рэкети́р,** *n.* racketeer.
рюкза́к [*gen.* **-зака́**] *n.* knapsack.
рю́мка [*gen. pl.* **-мок**] *n.* small liquor glass.
рю́мочка [*gen. pl.* **-чек**] *n., dim. of* **рю́мка.**
ряби́на *n.* **1,** mountain ash; rowan tree. **2,** rowanberries. **3,** pockmark.
ряби́ть *v. impfv.* **1,** to ripple (*trans. & intrans.*). **2,** (*usu. with* **в глаза́х**) to dance before one's eyes. *Also impers.:* у меня́ в глаза́х ряби́т, things are dancing (*or* flashing) before my eyes.
рябо́й *adj.* **1,** pockmarked. **2,** spotted.
ря́бчик *n.* hazel grouse; hazel hen.
рябь *n.f.* ripples.
ря́вкать *v. impfv.* [*pfv.* **ря́вкнуть**] *colloq.* to roar; bellow.
ряд [*gen.* **ря́да,** *but after 2, 3, & 4* **ряда́;** *2nd loc.* **ряду́;** *pl.* **ряды́**] *n.* **1,** row. **2,** *mil.* file. **3,** *pl., mil.* ranks. **4,** row of stalls (*in a market*). **5,** [*prepl.* **в ря́де**] series; number: це́лый ряд (+ *gen.*), a whole series of; в ря́де слу́чаев, in a number of cases. —**в ряд/ряду́,** abreast. —**в ряду́** (+ *gen.*), among. —**из ря́да вон выходя́щий,** exceptional; out of the ordinary. —**стоя́ть в одно́м ряду́ с,** to be/rank on a par with.
рядово́й *adj.* **1,** common; ordinary; average. **2,** *mil.* of the rank and file: рядово́й соста́в, the rank and file; enlisted personnel. —*n., mil.* private.
ря́дом *adv.* **1,** alongside. **2,** next to each other. **3,** nearby. **4,** next door. —**ря́дом с** (+ *instr.*), **1,** next to; beside; alongside. **2,** next door to.
ря́са *n.* monk's habit; cassock; frock.
ря́ска *n.* duckweed.

С

С, с *n. neut.* eighteenth letter of the Russian alphabet.

с *also,* **со** *prep.* A, *with instr.* **1,** with: я пойду́ с ва́ми, I'll go with you; чита́ть с трудо́м, to read with difficulty. **2,** and: мы с тобо́й, you and I; три с полови́ной, three and a half; хлеб с ма́слом, bread and butter. **3,** on (*a specified train, plane etc.*): уе́хать с ра́нним по́ездом, to leave on the early-morning train. **4,** *used in greetings:* с пра́здником!, happy holiday!; с Но́вым го́дом!, Happy New Year! B, *with gen.* **1,** off; down from; down: сойти́ с ре́льсов, to go off the tracks; упа́сть с ле́стницы, to fall down the stairs; доста́ть кни́гу с по́лки, to take a book from the shelf. **2,** from: с вокза́ла, from the station; с рабо́ты, from work. С са́мого нача́ла, from the very beginning. С головы́ до ног, from head to toe. С ру́сского на англи́йский, from Russian to English. **3,** *indicating cause:* ката́ться со́ смеху, to roar with laughter; умира́ть с го́лоду, to die of hunger. **4,** with: с ва́шего разреше́ния, with your permission. **5,** since: с де́тства, since childhood; с тех пор, since then. C, *with acc.* about; approximately: с ме́сяц, about a month; величино́й с дом, about the size of a house. —**с тем, что́бы,** *see* **что́бы.**

с- *also,* **со-, съ-,** *prefix* **1,** *indicating motion off or down:* сойти́ с ле́стницы, to go down the stairs; соскользну́ть со стола́, to slip off the table. **2,** *indicating removal from a surface:* соска́бливать, to scrape off. **3,** *indicating bringing or gathering together:* собира́ть, to gather; соединя́ть, to unite. **4,** (*with* **-ся**) *indicating coming together from various places:* съезжа́ться, to gather; assemble (*from various places*). **5,** *indicating joining or fastening together:* свя́зывать, to tie together. **6,** (*with pfv. verbs only*) *indicating motion to a place and back:* сбе́гать, to run (*to a place and return*). **7,** (*with* **-ся**) *indicating harmony in doing something:* спева́ться, to sing in harmony; сраба́тываться, to achieve harmony in work.

саа́м *n.m.* [*fem.* **саа́мка**] Lapp; Laplander. —**саа́мский,** *adj.* Lapp; Lappish.

са́бля [*gen. pl.* **-бель**] *n.* saber. —**са́бельный,** *adj.* saber (*attrib.*).

сабота́ж *n.* sabotage. —**сабота́жник,** *n.* saboteur.

сабота́жничать *v. impfv., colloq.* = **саботи́ровать.**

саботи́ровать *v. impfv. & pfv.* [*pres.* **-рую, -руешь**] to sabotage.

са́ван *n.* **1,** shroud. **2,** *fig.* cover; blanket; mantle (*of snow, ice, fog, etc.*).

сава́нна *n.* savanna; savannah.

савра́сый *adj.* (*of a horse*) light brown with a black mane and tail.

са́га *n.* saga.

сагити́ровать *v., pfv. of* **агити́ровать** (*in sense #2*).

сад [*2nd loc.* **саду́;** *pl.* **сады́**] *n.* garden. —**ботани́ческий сад,** botanical gardens. —**де́тский сад,** kindergarten. —**фрукто́вый сад,** orchard. —**я́блоневый сад,** apple orchard.

сади́зм *n.* sadism.

са́дик *n., dim. of* **сад.**

сади́ст *n.* sadist. —**сади́стский,** *adj.* sadistic.

сади́ть *v. impfv.* [*pres.* **сажу́, са́дишь**] *colloq.* = **сажа́ть.**

сади́ться *v.r. impfv.* [*pfv.* **сесть;** *pres.* **сажу́сь, сади́шься**] **1,** to sit; sit down; take a seat. Сади́тесь!, sit down!; have a seat! Сесть за стол/рабо́ту, to sit down at a table; sit (*or* get) down to work. Сесть в посте́ли, to sit up in bed. **2,** (*with* **в** *or* **на** + *acc.*) to take; board; get on (a train, bus, etc.); get into (a car); get on(to); mount (a horse). **3,** (*of a bird, insect, etc.*) to alight; perch. **4,** (*of dust, fog, etc.*) to settle. **5,** (*of an airplane*) to land. **6,** (*of the sun, stars, etc.*) to set. **7,** (*of a building, foundation, etc.*) to sink. **8,** (*of material*) to shrink.

са́днить *v. impfv.* **1,** to scratch; abrade. **2,** to smart; sting; burn. В го́рле са́днит, my throat feels scratchy.

садо́вник *n.* gardener.

садово́д *n.* horticulturist; gardener. —**садово́дство,** *n.* horticulture; gardening. —**садово́дческий,** *adj.* horticultural.

садо́вый *adj.* **1,** garden (*attrib.*). **2,** cultivated. —**садо́во-па́рковое иску́сство,** landscape architecture.

садо́к [*gen.* **-дка́**] *n.* **1,** fish tank. **2,** pen; coop; warren.

са́жа *n.* soot. —**в са́же,** sooty.

сажа́лка [*gen. pl.* **-лок**] *n.* planter (*machine*).

сажа́ть *v. impfv.* [*pfv.* **посади́ть**] **1,** to plant. **2,** to seat; sit (someone) down. **3,** to place; put. **4,** to set down; land (an aircraft). **5,** to put in prison. **6,** *colloq.* to make (a stain, blot, etc.). —**сажа́ть/посади́ть в кле́тку,** to cage. —**сажа́ть/посади́ть на́ кол,** to impale on a stake. —**сажа́ть/посади́ть на цепь,** to chain; chain up. —**сажа́ть/посади́ть под аре́ст,** to place under arrest.

са́женец [*gen.* **-нца**] *n.* seedling.

саже́нь *also,* **са́жень** *n.f.* old Russian unit of length equal to approx. 7 feet. —**морска́я са́жень,** fathom.

саза́н *n.* carp (*fish*).

сайга́ *also,* **сайга́к** *n.* a variety of antelope; saiga.
са́йка [*gen. pl.* **са́ек**] *n.* roll (*of bread*).
саквоя́ж *n.* traveling bag.
сакрамента́льный *adj.* **1,** ritual (*attrib.*). **2,** sacred. **3,** traditional.
сакс *n., hist.* Saxon.
саксау́л *n.* tree native to Central Asia; saxaul.
саксо́нский *adj.* Saxon.
саксофо́н *n.* saxophone.
сала́зки [*gen.* **-зок**] *n. pl.* small sled; toboggan.
салама́ндра *n.* salamander.
сала́т *n.* **1,** lettuce. **2,** salad. —**сала́тник,** *n.* salad bowl.
сала́тный *adj.* **1,** lettuce (*attrib.*); salad (*attrib.*). **2,** light green.
са́лить *v. impfv.* to grease.
са́лки [*gen.* **-лок**] *n. pl.* tag (*game*).
са́ло *n.* **1,** fat; lard. **2,** grease. **3,** tallow. **4,** thin ice.
сало́н *n.* **1,** salon. **2,** lounge (*in a hotel, on a train, ship, etc.*). **3,** passenger section (*on an airplane*). **4,** showroom. —**сало́н-ваго́н,** parlor car.
сало́нный *adj.* light; trivial: сало́нный разгово́р, small talk.
салфе́тка [*gen. pl.* **-ток**] *n.* napkin.
са́льдо *n. indecl., bookkeeping* balance. —**акти́вное/отрица́тельное са́льдо торго́вого бала́нса,** trade surplus/deficit.
са́льность *n.f.* profanity; obscenity.
са́льный *adj.* **1,** tallow (*attrib.*). **2,** greasy. **3,** salacious. —**са́льные же́лезы,** sebaceous glands.
са́льто *n. indecl.* somersault. *Also,* **са́льто-морта́ле.**
салю́т *n.* salute.
салютова́ть *v. impfv. & pfv.* [*pres.* **-ту́ю, -ту́ешь**] (*with dat.*) to salute.
саля́ми *n.f. indecl.* salami.
сам *emphatic pron.* [*fem.* **сама́**; *neut.* **само́**; *pl.* **са́ми**; *gen.* **самого́, само́й, сами́х**; *dat.* **самому́, само́й, сами́м**; *acc. fem.* **саму́** *or* **самоё**; *instr.* **сами́м, само́й, сами́ми**; *prepl.* **само́м, само́й, сами́х**] oneself; myself; yourself; himself; herself; ourselves, etc.: я сам э́то сде́лаю, I'll do it myself. Письмо́ от самого́ президе́нта, a letter from the President himself. —**быть сами́м собо́й,** to be oneself. Будь сам (сама́) собо́й!, be yourself! —**сам не свой (сама́ не своя́),** not oneself; out of sorts. —**сам по себе́, 1,** oneself; in and of itself; per se. **2,** independently; on one's own. —**сам собо́й,** by itself; of itself.
сама́н *n.* adobe. —**сама́нный,** *adj.* adobe.
сама́рий *n.* samarium.
саме́ц [*gen.* **-мца́**] *n.* male (*of animals*): саме́ц оле́ня, male deer; buck.
самизда́т *n.* underground publication of manuscripts (*in the USSR*).
са́мка [*gen. pl.* **-мок**] *n.* female (*of animals*): са́мка оле́ня, female deer; doe.
само- *prefix* self-.
самоана́лиз *n.* self-analysis; introspection.
самобы́тный *adj.* original; distinctive.
самова́р *n.* samovar.
самовла́стие *n.* **1,** *obs.* one-man rule. **2,** *fig.* despotism. —**самовла́стный,** *adj.* despotic.
самовлюблённый *adj.* conceited.
самовнуше́ние *n.* autosuggestion.
самовозгора́ние *n.* spontaneous combustion.
самово́лие *n.* arbitrariness; high-handedness.
самово́льный *adj.* **1,** self-willed. **2,** arbitrary; high-handed. **3,** unauthorized: самово́льная отлу́чка, absence without leave. —**самово́льно,** *adv.* without permission.
самовоспламене́ние *n.* spontaneous combustion.
самого́н *n.* homemade whiskey.
самодви́жущийся *adj.* self-propelled.
самоде́льный *adj.* homemade.
самодержа́вие *n.* autocracy. —**самодержа́вный,** *adj.* autocratic.
самоде́ржец [*gen.* **-жца**] *n.* autocrat.
самоде́ятельность *n.f.* **1,** individual initiative. **2,** amateur activities; amateur production.
самоде́ятельный *adj.* **1,** independent. **2,** amateur.
самоди́йский *adj.* Samoyed.
самодисципли́на *n.* self-discipline.
самодовле́ющий *adj.* self-contained; independent.
самодово́льный *adj.* self-satisfied; self-complacent; smug. —**самодово́льство,** *n.* self-satisfaction; self-complacency; smugness.
самоду́р *n.* high-handed person. —**самоду́рство,** *n.* high-handedness.
самозарожде́ние *n.* spontaneous generation.
самозащи́та *n.* self-defense.
самозва́нец [*gen.* **-нца**] *n.m.* [*fem.* **-нка**] impostor; pretender.
самозва́нный *also,* **самозва́ный** *adj.* pseudo-; false; self-styled.
самока́т *n.* scooter.
самокри́тика *n.* self-criticism. —**самокрити́ческий,** *adj.* self-critical.
самолёт *n.* plane; airplane; aircraft.
самоли́чно *adv., colloq.* oneself; personally.
самолюби́вый *adj.* proud. —**самолю́бие,** *n.* pride; self-respect.
самомне́ние *n.* conceit.
самонаблюде́ние *n.* introspection.
самонаде́янный *adj.* self-assured; presumptuous. —**самонаде́янность,** *n.f.* self-assurance; presumption.
самоназва́ние *n.* self-designation.
самооблада́ние *n.* self-control; equanimity; composure.
самообма́н *n.* self-deception.
самооборо́на *n.* self-defense.
самообслу́живание *n.* self-service.
самоопределе́ние *n.* self-determination.
самоотверже́ние *n.* = **самоотве́рженность.**
самоотве́рженный *adj.* selfless. —**самоотве́рженность,** *n.f.* selflessness.
самоотрече́ние *n.* self-denial.
самоочеви́дный *adj.* self-evident.
самопи́сец [*gen.* **-сца**] *n.* recorder: бортово́й самопи́сец, flight recorder.
самопи́ска [*gen. pl.* **-сок**] *n., colloq.* fountain pen.
самопоже́ртвование *n.* self-sacrifice.
самопроизво́льный *adj.* spontaneous. —**самопроизво́льность,** *n.f.* spontaneity.
самопу́ск *n.* self-starter.
самоpо́док [*gen.* **-дка**] *n.* **1,** nugget. **2,** *fig.* person with exceptional natural talent.
самоса́д *n., colloq.* home-grown tobacco.
самосва́л *n.* dump truck.
самосожже́ние *n.* self-immolation.
самосозна́ние *n.* consciousness.
самосохране́ние *n.* self-preservation.

самостоя́тельный *adj.* independent. —**самостоя́тельно,** *adv.* independently. —**самостоя́тельность,** *n.f.* independence.

самостре́л *n.* **1,** crossbow. **2,** self-inflicted wound (*made to evade military service*). **3,** *colloq.* soldier with a self-inflicted wound.

самосу́д *n.* mob law; lynching.

самотёк *n.* aimless unplanned progression; drift: пусти́ть де́ло на самотёк, to let matters take their course.

самотёком *adv.* **1,** (*of the movement of liquids*) by gravity. **2,** *fig.* spontaneously; on its own momentum.

самоуби́йство *n.* suicide: поко́нчить жизнь самоуби́йством, to commit suicide. —**самоуби́йственный,** *adj.* suicidal.

самоуби́йца *n.m. & f.* person who has committed suicide.

самоуваже́ние *n.* self-respect; self-esteem.

самоуве́ренный *adj.* self-confident; self-assured. —**самоуве́ренность,** *n.f.* self-confidence; self-assurance.

самоуничтоже́ние *n.* self-destruction.

самоуправле́ние *n.* self-government. —**самоуправля́ющийся,** *adj.* self-governing.

самоупра́вный *adj.* arbitrary. —**самоупра́вство,** *n.* arbitrariness.

самоучи́тель *n.m.* manual of self-instruction.

самоу́чка [*gen. pl.* **-чек**] *n.m. & f., colloq.* self-taught person; self-educated person.

самохва́льство *n., colloq.* boasting; self-congratulation.

самохо́дка [*gen. pl.* **-док**] *n., colloq.* self-propelled gun.

самохо́дный *adj.* self-propelled.

самоцве́т *n.* semiprecious stone. —**самоцве́тный,** *adj.* semiprecious.

самоце́ль *n.f.* end in itself.

самочи́нный *adj.* **1,** arbitrary. **2,** done on one's own initiative.

самочу́вствие *n.* general physical and mental state. Как ва́ше самочу́вствие?, how do you feel (in general)?

самура́й *n.* samurai.

самши́т *n.* box tree.

са́мый *adj.* **1,** the very: до са́мого конца́, to the very end. **2,** *in* **тот са́мый** *or* **тот же са́мый,** the same: тот са́мый челове́к, the same person. **3,** *used in forming superlatives:* са́мый ва́жный вопро́с, the most important question. **4,** *in* са́мое бо́льшее, the most; at (the) most; са́мое по́зднее, at the latest.

сан *n.* rank; title. —**посвяща́ть в духо́вный сан,** to ordain (*as a clergyman*).

санато́рий *n.* sanitarium; sanatorium.

сангвини́ческий *adj.* excitable; mercurial.

санда́л *n.* sandalwood.

санда́лия *n.* sandal.

санда́ловый *adj.* sandalwood.

са́ни [*gen.* **сане́й;** *dat.* **саня́м**] *n. pl.* sleigh; sled.

санита́р *n.* **1,** (medical) orderly. **2,** [*also,* **санита́р-носи́льщик**] stretcher-bearer.

санитари́я *n.* sanitation.

санита́рный *adj.* **1,** sanitary: санита́рное состоя́ние, sanitary conditions. **2,** *mil.* medical: санита́рный батальо́н, medical battalion. —**санита́рное су́дно,** hospital ship. —**санита́рная су́мка,** first-aid kit.

са́нки [*gen.* **-нок**] *n. pl., colloq.* sled; sleigh.

санкциони́ровать *v. impfv. & pfv.* [*pres.* **-рую, -руешь**] to sanction.

са́нкция *n.* **1,** sanction; approval. **2,** *pl.* sanctions.

са́нный *adj.* sled (*attrib.*); sleigh (*attrib.*).

сanови́тый *adj.* = **сано́вный.**

сано́вник *n.* dignitary; high official.

сано́вный *adj.* **1,** high-ranking; distinguished. **2,** stately; dignified.

санскри́т *n.* Sanskrit. —**санскри́тский,** *adj.* Sanskrit.

сантигра́мм *n.* centigram.

санти́м *n.* centime.

сантиме́тр *n.* **1,** centimeter. **2,** tape measure.

сап *n.* glanders.

са́па *n., mil.* trench; sap. —**ти́хой са́пой,** on the sly.

сапёр *n., mil.* sapper.

сапо́г [*gen.* **-пога́;** *gen. pl.* **-по́г**] *n.* boot.

сапо́жник *n.* shoemaker.

сапо́жный *adj.* shoe (*attrib.*).

сапса́н *n.* peregrine falcon.

сапфи́р *n.* sapphire. —**сапфи́рный; сапфи́ровый,** *adj.* sapphire.

сара́й *n.* shed. —**дровяно́й сара́й,** woodshed. —**каре́тный сара́й,** coach house. —**ло́дочный сара́й,** boathouse.

саранча́ *n.* **1,** locusts. **2,** a (single) locust.

сарафа́н *n., pre-rev.* peasant woman's dress.

сарде́лька [*gen. pl.* **-лек**] *n.* small sausage.

сарди́на *n.* sardine. *Also,* **сарди́нка.**

сардони́ческий *adj.* sardonic.

са́ржа *n.* serge. —**са́ржевый,** *adj.* serge.

сарка́зм *n.* sarcasm.

саркасти́ческий *adj.* sarcastic. —**саркасти́чески,** *adv.* sarcastically.

саркофа́г *n.* sarcophagus.

сары́ч [*gen.* **-рыча́**] *n.* buzzard.

сатана́ *n.* Satan. —**сатани́нский,** *adj.* satanic.

сателли́т *n.* satellite.

сати́н *n.* sateen. —**сати́новый,** *adj.* sateen.

сати́р *n.* satyr.

сати́ра *n.* satire. —**сати́рик,** *n.* satirist. —**сатири́ческий,** *adj.* satirical.

сатра́п *n.* satrap. —**сатра́пия,** *n.* satrapy.

Сату́рн *n.* Saturn.

сафло́р *n.* safflower.

сафья́н *n.* morocco; morocco leather. —**сафья́нный; сафья́новый,** *adj.* morocco.

са́хар *n.* sugar.

сахари́н *n.* saccharin.

са́харистый *adj.* containing sugar; rich in sugar.

са́харница *n.* sugar bowl.

са́харный *adj.* **1,** sugar (*attrib.*). **2,** *fig.* sugary; honeyed. —**са́харная боле́знь,** diabetes. —**са́харная голова́,** sugar loaf. —**са́харный заво́д,** sugar refinery. —**са́харный песо́к,** granulated sugar. —**са́харная пу́дра,** powdered sugar. —**са́харная свёкла,** sugar beet. —**са́харный тростни́к,** sugar cane.

сахаро́за *n.* sucrose.

сачо́к [*gen.* **-чка́**] *n.* net with a hoop on a long handle.

сба́вить [*infl.* **-влю, -вишь**] *v., pfv. of* **сбавля́ть.**

сба́вка *n., colloq.* reduction.

сбавля́ть *v. impfv.* [*pfv.* **сба́вить**] **1,** to take off (from a price). **2,** to reduce (a price, speed, etc.). —**сбавля́ть вес** *or* **в ве́се,** to lose weight.

сбаланси́рованный *adj.* balanced.

сбаланси́ровать *v. pfv.* [*infl.* **-рую, -руешь**] **1,** *pfv. of* **баланси́ровать. 2,** to regain one's balance.
сбе́гать *v. pfv., colloq.* **1,** to run (*somewhere and return*). **2,** (*with* **за** + *instr.*) to run and fetch.
сбега́ть *v. impfv.* [*pfv.* **сбежа́ть**] **1,** to run down. **2,** to run away; escape. **3,** to disappear; fade (*from one's face*). —**сбега́ться,** *refl.* (*of many people*) to come running.
сбежа́ть [*infl. like* **бежа́ть**] *v., pfv. of* **сбега́ть.** —**сбежа́ться,** *refl., pfv. of* **сбега́ться.**
сберега́тельный *adj.* savings (*attrib.*). —**сберега́тельная ка́сса,** savings bank. —**сберега́тельная кни́жка,** bankbook; passbook.
сберега́ть *v. impfv.* [*pfv.* **сбере́чь**] **1,** to guard; protect. **2,** to save; conserve. **3,** to put aside (*for future use*).
сбереже́ние *n.* **1,** (*with gen.*) conservation (of). **2,** *pl.* savings.
сбере́чь [*infl. like* **бере́чь**] *v., pfv. of* **сберега́ть.**
сберка́сса *n.* savings bank (*contr. of* **сберега́тельная ка́сса**).
сберкни́жка [*gen. pl.* **-жек**] *n.* bankbook; passbook (*contr. of* **сберега́тельная кни́жка**).
сбива́ть *v. impfv.* [*pfv.* **сбить**] **1,** to knock off: сбить (кого́-нибудь) с ног, to knock off one's feet. **2,** to shoot down. **3,** to throw off; disconcert. **4,** to knock together. **5,** to wear down (shoes, heels, etc.). **6,** to reduce; bring down. **7,** to churn (butter); whip (cream, eggs, etc.). —**сбива́ть с пути́,** to lead astray. —**сбива́ть с то́лку,** to confuse.
сбива́ться *v.r. impfv.* [*pfv.* **сби́ться**] **1,** to slip off; slip out of position. **2,** to become confused; be disconcerted. **3,** to be off; be wrong. **4,** (*of footwear*) to become worn down. **5,** to crowd together; huddle together. —**сбива́ться с ног,** to be exhausted; be falling off one's feet. —**сбива́ться с ноги́,** to break step. —**сбива́ться с пути́,** to go astray; lose one's way. —**сбива́ться с то́лку,** to become confused.
сби́вчивый *adj.* **1,** confusing; muddled. **2,** inconsistent; contradictory.
сбить [*infl.* **собью́, собьёшь**] *v., pfv. of* **сбива́ть.** —**сби́ться,** *refl., pfv. of* **сбива́ться.**
сближа́ть *v. impfv.* [*pfv.* **сбли́зить**] to draw together; bring closer together. —**сближа́ться,** *refl.* **1,** to draw nearer; come closer together. **2,** (*with* **с** + *instr.*) to become close friends (with).
сближе́ние *n.* **1,** coming together; drawing together. **2,** rapprochement. **3,** *mil.* approach; closing in. **4,** *obs.* resemblance.
сбли́зить [*infl.* **-жу, -зишь**] *v., pfv. of* **сближа́ть.** —**сбли́зиться,** *refl., pfv. of* **сближа́ться.**
сбо́ку *adv.* **1,** from the side; from one side. **2,** on the side; on one side. —*prep., with gen.* beside; alongside.
сболтну́ть *v. pfv., colloq.* to blurt out.
сбор *n.* **1,** collection. **2,** gathering. **3,** *theat.* receipts. Де́лать по́лные сбо́ры, to play to packed houses. **4,** duty; toll; levy. **5,** meeting; gathering; assembly. **6,** *mil.* muster. **7,** short course of instruction. **8,** *pl.* preparations (*for a trip*). —**в сбо́ре,** present; on hand.
сбо́рище *n., colloq.* gathering; crowd.
сбо́рка [*gen. pl.* **-рок**] *n.* **1,** assembly; putting together. **2,** gather (*in clothing*).
сбо́рная *n., decl. as an adj.* = **сбо́рная кома́нда.**
сбо́рник *n.* collection; anthology.
сбо́рный *adj.* **1,** gathering (*attrib.*); meeting (*attrib.*); assembly (*attrib.*). **2,** mixed; combined; of various kinds. **3,** prefabricated. —**сбо́рная кома́нда,** combined team; all-star team.
сбо́рочный *adj.* assembly (*attrib.*).
сбо́рщик *n.* **1,** collector (*of taxes, signatures, etc.*). **2,** picker (*of cotton*). **3,** assembler.
сбра́сывать *v. impfv.* [*pfv.* **сбро́сить**] **1,** to throw off; throw down. **2,** to drop (bombs). **3,** *fig.* to overthrow. **4,** to shed. **5,** *fig.* to shake off (apathy, an illness, etc.). **6,** (*with* **в** + *acc.*) *colloq.* to toss (into). **7,** *cards* to discard. **8,** *finance* to dump. —**сбра́сывать со счето́в,** to rule out; count out.
сбрива́ть *v. impfv.* [*pfv.* **сбрить**] to shave off.
сбрить [*infl.* **сбре́ю, сбре́ешь**] *v., pfv. of* **сбрива́ть.**
сброд *n., colloq.* rabble; riffraff.
сбро́сить [*infl.* **-шу, -сишь**] *v., pfv. of* **сбра́сывать.**
сбру́я *n.* harness.
сбыва́ть *v. impfv.* [*pfv.* **сбыть**] **1,** to sell; market. **2,** to get rid of. Сбыва́ть с рук, to get off one's hands. **3,** *v.i.* (*of rising waters*) to recede. —**сбыва́ться,** *refl.* to come true; be realized.
сбыт *n.* sale.
сбыть [*infl. like* **быть**] *v., pfv. of* **сбыва́ть.** —**сбы́ться,** *refl.* [*past* **сбы́лся, сбыла́сь, сбыло́сь**] *pfv. of* **сбыва́ться.**
сва́дебный *adj.* wedding (*attrib.*).
сва́дьба [*gen. pl.* **-деб**] *n.* wedding.
сва́йный *adj.* built on piles.
сва́ливать *v. impfv.* [*pfv.* **свали́ть**] **1,** to knock down. **2,** to throw down. **3,** to toss together; toss into a pile. **4,** *colloq.* to overthrow. **5,** *fig.* to throw off; cast off. **6,** (*with* **на** + *acc.*) *colloq.* to shift; dump (work, blame, etc.) on(to) someone else. **7,** *colloq.* (*of sleep*) to overcome; (*of an illness*) to strike. **8,** *v.i., colloq.* (*of a large crowd*) to depart. **9,** *v.i., colloq.* to abate. —**сва́ливаться,** *refl.* **1,** to fall. **2,** to collapse; come tumbling down. **3,** *colloq.* to lean; tilt. **4,** *colloq.* to appear from nowhere. **5,** *colloq.* to fall ill. **6,** *colloq.* (*of cattle*) to die.
свали́ть [*infl.* **свалю́, сва́лишь**] *v., pfv. of* **вали́ть**[1] *and* **сва́ливать.** —**свали́ться,** *refl., pfv. of* **вали́ться** *and* **сва́ливаться.**
сва́лка [*gen. pl.* **-лок**] *n.* **1,** dump; dumping ground. **2,** *colloq.* brawl; scuffle.
сваля́ть *v., pfv. of* **валя́ть** (*in sense #3*).
сва́ривать *v. impfv.* [*pfv.* **свари́ть**] to weld together.
свари́ть [*infl.* **сварю́, сва́ришь**] *v., pfv. of* **вари́ть** *and* **сва́ривать.**
сва́рка *n.* welding.
сварли́вый *adj.* quarrelsome; cantankerous.
сварно́й *adj.* welded.
сва́рочный *adj.* welding (*attrib.*). —**сва́рочное желе́зо,** wrought iron.
сва́рщик *n.* welder.
сва́стика *n.* swastika.
сват *n.* **1,** matchmaker. **2,** father of one's son-in-law or daughter-in-law.
сва́тать *v. impfv.* [*pfv.* **посва́тать** *or* **сосва́тать**] **1,** to match up; arrange a match for; (*with dat. or* **за** + *acc.*) match (someone) up with. **2,** to propose to; ask for one's hand; request permission to marry. —**сва́таться,** *refl.* [*pfv.* **посва́таться**] (*with* **за** + *acc. or* **к**) to propose to.
сватовство́ *n.* matchmaking.
сва́тья *n.* mother of one's son-in-law or daughter-in-law.

сва́ха *n.* matchmaker.
сва́я *n.* pile: мост на сва́ях, bridge on piles.
све́дение *n.* **1,** *usu. pl.* information. **2,** *pl.* knowledge. —**доводи́ть до (чьего́-нибудь) све́дения,** to inform; bring to the attention of: довожу́ до ва́шего све́дения, I beg to inform you. —**доходи́ть до (чьего́-нибудь) све́дения,** to come to the attention of. —**к ва́шему све́дению,** for your information. —**принима́ть к све́дению,** *see* **принима́ть.**
сведе́ние *n.* **1,** leading down; leading away. **2,** joining together; bringing together. **3,** removal (*of stains*). **4,** reduction; squaring; reconciling. **5,** cramp.
све́дущий *adj.* knowledgeable; well-versed.
свежева́ть *v. impfv.* [*pfv.* **освежева́ть;** *pres.* **-жу́ю, жу́ешь**] to skin; dress (an animal).
све́жесть *n.f.* **1,** freshness. **2,** cool air. —**не пе́рвой све́жести, 1,** not very fresh. **2,** (*of clothes*) not very clean.
свеже́ть *v. impfv.* [*pfv.* **посвеже́ть**] **1,** to become cool; become chilly; cool off. **2,** *naut.* (*of the wind*) to blow up. **3,** (*of a person*) to take on a healthy color.
све́жий *adj.* [*short form* **свеж, свежа́, свежо́, све́жи** *or* **свежи́**] **1,** fresh. **2,** cool; chilly. **3,** the latest: све́жий но́мер, the latest issue. —**на све́жую го́лову,** with a fresh mind. —**на све́жую па́мять,** while (something is) still fresh in one's memory. —**со све́жими си́лами,** with renewed strength *or* vigor.
свезти́ *v. pfv.* [*infl. like* **везти́**] **1,** *pfv. of* **свози́ть. 2,** to take; drive (to a certain place). **3,** to take; drive (to and back).
свёкла *n.* **1,** beets. **2,** a (single) beet.
свеклови́ца *n.* sugar beet. —**свеклови́чный,** *adj.* beet (*attrib.*); sugar-beet (*attrib.*); beet-sugar (*attrib.*).
свеклоса́харный *adj.* beet-sugar (*attrib.*).
свеко́льник *n.* **1,** beet soup. **2,** beet tops.
свеко́льный *adj.* **1,** beet (*attrib.*). **2,** beet-colored.
свёкор [*gen.* **-кра**] *n.* father-in-law (*husband's father*).
свекро́вь *n.f.* mother-in-law (*husband's mother*).
сверга́ть *v. impfv.* [*pfv.* **све́ргнуть**] **1,** *obs.* to throw down. **2,** to overthrow.
све́ргнуть [*past* **сверг, -ла**] *v., pfv. of* **сверга́ть.**
сверже́ние *n.* overthrow.
све́рить *v., pfv. of* **сверя́ть.**
сверка́ние *n.* **1,** sparkle. **2,** glare.
сверка́ть *v. impfv.* [*pfv.* **сверкну́ть**] **1,** to sparkle; glitter; shine. **2,** (*of lightning*) to flash.
сверли́льный *adj.* boring (*attrib.*); drilling (*attrib.*).
сверли́ть *v. impfv.* **1,** [*pfv.* **просверли́ть**] to drill; drill a hole in; bore through. **2,** *impers.* to cause a gnawing pain: у меня́ сверли́т в у́хе, I have a gnawing pain in my ear. **3,** (*of a thought*) to haunt; weigh on one's mind. **4,** *in* сверли́ть (кого́-нибудь) глаза́ми, to stare right through (someone).
сверло́ [*pl.* **свёрла**] *n.* drill (*tool*).
сверля́щий *adj.* **1,** (*of a pain*) gnawing. **2,** (*of a sound*) shrill; piercing.
сверну́ть *v., pfv. of* **свёртывать** *and* **свора́чивать.** —**сверну́ться,** *refl., pfv. of* **свёртываться.**
сверста́ть *v., pfv. of* **верста́ть.**
све́рстник *n.* person one's own age; contemporary; peer.
свёрток [*gen.* **-тка**] *n.* **1,** roll (*of paper, material, etc.*). **2,** package.
свёртывание *n.* **1,** rolling up. **2,** curtailment. **3,** coagulation.
свёртывать *v. impfv.* [*pfv.* **сверну́ть**] **1,** to roll up. **2,** to curtail; cut back. **3,** *in* **сверну́ть ше́ю** (+ *dat.*), to wring someone's neck; **сверну́ть себе́ ше́ю,** to break one's neck; get killed. —**свёртываться,** *refl.* **1,** to roll up; curl up. **2,** to congeal; curdle; coagulate.
сверх *prep., with gen.* **1,** over. **2,** in addition to; over and above; in excess of. **3,** *fig.* beyond: сверх сил, beyond one's strength; сверх вся́кого ожида́ния, beyond all expectations. —**сверх всего́,** on top of everything (else). —**сверх того́,** moreover; furthermore.
сверх- *prefix* super-.
сверхдержа́ва *n.* superpower.
сверхзвуково́й *adj.* supersonic.
сверхпла́новый *adj.* in excess of the plan; over and above the plan.
сверхпри́быль *n.f.* excess profits.
сверхсро́чный *adj.* **1,** additional; extra: сверхсро́чная слу́жба, additional time in service. **2,** *colloq.* extremely urgent.
све́рху *adv.* **1,** from above; from the top. **2,** on top. —**све́рху до́низу,** from top to bottom.
сверхуро́чный *adj.* overtime (*attrib.*). —**сверхуро́чно,** *adv.* overtime: рабо́тать сверхуро́чно, to work overtime. —**сверхуро́чные,** *n. pl.* overtime (pay).
сверхчелове́к *n.* superman. —**сверхчелове́ческий,** *adj.* superhuman.
сверхчувстви́тельный *adj.* supersensitive.
сверхшта́тный *adj.* supernumerary.
сверхъесте́ственный *adj.* supernatural.
сверчо́к [*gen.* **-чка́**] *n.* cricket (*insect*).
сверша́ть *v. impfv.* [*pfv.* **сверши́ть**] = **соверша́ть.**
сверя́ть *v. impfv.* [*pfv.* **све́рить**] to check; compare; collate.
све́сить *v. pfv.* [*infl.* **-шу, -сишь**] **1,** *pfv. of* **све́шивать. 2,** *colloq.* to weigh. —**све́ситься,** *refl., pfv. of* **све́шиваться.**
свести́ [*infl. like* **вести́**] *v., pfv. of* **своди́ть.** —**свести́сь,** *refl., pfv. of* **своди́ться.**
свет[1] [*2nd loc.* **на свету́**] *n.* light. —**в све́те** (+ *gen.*), in the light of. —**при све́те** (+ *gen.*), by the light of. —**чуть свет,** at the crack of dawn.
свет[2] *n.* **1,** world. **2,** society: вы́сший свет, high society. —**ни за что на све́те,** not for (anything in) the world. —**тот свет,** the next (*or* other) world. —**вы́йти в свет,** to come out; be published. —**появи́ться на свет,** to come into the world; be born. —**производи́ть на свет,** to bring into the world. —**уви́деть свет, 1,** to see the light of day; be published. **2,** = появи́ться на свет.
света́ть *v. impfv., impers.* to dawn: света́ет, day is dawning; day is breaking.
свети́ло *n.* **1,** heavenly body. **2,** *fig.* luminary.
свети́льник *n.* (oil) lamp.
свети́ть *v. impfv.* [*pres.* **свечу́, све́тишь**] **1,** (*of the sun, moon, etc.*) to shine. **2,** [*pfv.* **посвети́ть**] (*with instr.*) to shine (a light); (*with dat.*) shine a light on; hold up a light for. —**свети́ться,** *refl.* (*of lights, stars, one's eyes, etc.*) to shine.
светле́ть *v. impfv.* [*pfv.* **посветле́ть** *or* **просветле́ть**] to brighten (up); become bright.
светло́ *adj., used predicatively* light: уже́ светло́, it is light already.
светло- *prefix, used with colors,* light: светло-зелёный, light green.

светловоло́сый *adj.* light-haired; fair-haired.
све́тлость *n.f.* **1,** lightness; brightness. **2,** (*with* **ва́ша, его́, её,** *etc.*) lordship; grace: ва́ша све́тлость, your lordship; your grace.
све́тлый *adj.* **1,** light. **2,** bright. **3,** (*of liquids, glass, etc.*) clear. **4,** *fig.* lucid: све́тлый ум, lucid mind. **5,** *fig.* happy; radiant. —**све́тлая ли́чность,** fine person. —**све́тлая па́мять,** blessed memory.
светля́к [*gen.* **-ляка́**] *n.* firefly; lightning bug.
светлячо́к [*gen.* **-чка́**] *n.* = **светля́к.**
светово́й *adj.* **1,** light (*attrib.*). **2,** luminous. **3,** illuminated. —**светово́й год,** light year.
светомаскиро́вка *n.* blackout.
светонепроница́емый *adj.* lightproof.
светопреставле́ние *n.* the end of the world.
светофо́р *n.* traffic light.
све́точ *n.* **1,** *obs.* torch. **2,** *fig.* (*with gen.*) torch: све́точ и́стины, the torch of truth. **3,** *fig.* luminary; leading light.
светочувстви́тельный *adj., photog.* sensitive to light.
све́тский *adj.* **1,** fashionable. **2,** refined; polite. **3,** secular; lay.
светя́щийся *adj.* luminous; luminescent.
свеча́ [*pl.* **све́чи, свече́й, свеча́м**] *n.* **1,** candle. При све́те свечи́; при свеча́х, by candlelight. **2,** (unit of) candlepower. **3,** *in* **запа́льная свеча́,** spark plug. **4,** suppository. —**игра́ не сто́ит свеч,** the game is not worth the candle.
свече́ние *n.* **1,** luminescence. **2,** fluorescence. **3,** phosphorescence.
све́чка [*gen. pl.* **-чек**] *n.* **1,** candle. **2,** suppository.
свечно́й *adj.* candle (*attrib.*).
све́шать *v., pfv. of* **ве́шать** (*in sense #3*).
све́шивать *v. impfv.* [*pfv.* **све́сить**] **1,** (*with* **с** + *gen.*) to hang (something from something). **2,** to let down; lower (a rope); dangle (one's legs). —**све́шиваться,** *refl.* **1,** to hang down; dangle. **2,** *colloq.* (*with* **из**) to lean out of; (*with* **че́рез**) lean over.
свива́льник *n.* swaddling clothes.
свива́ть *v. impfv.* [*pfv.* **свить**] **1,** to twist. **2,** to weave. **3,** to roll; roll up. **4,** [*impfv. only*] to swaddle. —**свива́ться,** *refl.* to roll up.
свида́ние *n.* **1,** appointment; date; meeting; rendezvous. **2,** visit (*with a prisoner, patient, etc.*). —**до свида́ния!,** goodbye! —**до ско́рого свида́ния!,** see you soon!
свиде́тель *n.m.* witness.
свиде́тельство *n.* **1,** evidence. **2,** testimony. **3,** certificate; license: свиде́тельство о рожде́нии, birth certificate; бра́чное свиде́тельство, marriage license.
свиде́тельствовать *v. impfv.* [*pres.* **-ствую, -ствуешь**] **1,** to testify; give evidence. **2,** (*with* **о**) to attest to; bear witness to. —**свиде́тельствовать почте́ние** (+ *dat.*), *obs.* to pay one's respects to.
свина́рник *n.* pigpen; pigsty.
свине́ц [*gen.* **-нца́**] *n.* lead.
свини́на *n.* pork.
сви́нка [*gen. pl.* **-нок**] *n.* **1,** little pig. **2,** mumps. —**морска́я сви́нка,** guinea pig.
свино́й *adj.* **1,** pig (*attrib.*); hog (*attrib.*). **2,** pork (*attrib.*).
свинома́тка [*gen. pl.* **-ток**] *n.* sow (*pig*).
свинопа́с *n.* swineherd.
сви́нский *adj., colloq.* swinish.
сви́нство *n., colloq.* **1,** squalor; filth. **2,** despicable act. **3,** scandal; outrage.
свинти́ть [*infl.* **-чу́, -ти́шь**] *v., pfv. of* **сви́нчивать.**
свинцо́вый *adj.* **1,** lead (*attrib.*). **2,** leaden; dull gray. —**свинцо́вые бели́ла,** white lead; ceruse. —**свинцо́вый блеск,** galena.
сви́нчивать *v. impfv.* [*pfv.* **свинти́ть**] **1,** to screw together. **2,** *colloq.* to unscrew.
свинья́ [*pl.* **сви́ньи, свине́й, сви́ньям**] *n.* **1,** pig; hog; swine. **2,** *in* **морска́я свинья́,** porpoise. —**подложи́ть свинью́** (+ *dat.*), to play a dirty trick on.
свире́ль *n.f.* reed (*primitive musical instrument*).
свирепе́ть *v. impfv.* [*pfv.* **рассвирепе́ть**] to become violent; become enraged.
свире́пость *n.f.* ferocity.
свире́пствовать *v. impfv.* [*pres.* **-ствую, -ствуешь**] **1,** to go on a rampage; wreak havoc. **2,** (*of a storm, fire, etc.*) to rage.
свире́пый *adj.* fierce; ferocious.
свиристе́ль *n.m.* waxwing (*bird*).
свиса́ть *v. impfv.* [*pfv.* **сви́снуть**] to hang down; droop.
сви́снуть [*past* **свис, -ла**] *v., pfv. of* **свиса́ть.**
свист *n.* **1,** whistle; whistling. **2,** hiss; hissing.
свиста́ть *v. impfv.* [*pres.* **свищу́, сви́щешь**] = **свисте́ть.**
свисте́ть *v. impfv.* [*pfv.* **сви́стнуть;** *pres.* **свищу́, свисти́шь**] **1,** to whistle. **2,** to hiss.
свисто́к [*gen.* **-стка́**] *n.* whistle (*instrument or sound*).
свистопля́ска *n., colloq.* bedlam; chaos.
свисту́лька [*gen. pl.* **-лек**] *n., colloq.* whistle; tin whistle.
свисту́н [*gen.* **-туна́**] *n., colloq.* whistler (*one who whistles*).
свистя́щий *adj. & n.* sibilant.
сви́та *n.* suite; retinue.
сви́тер (тэ) *n.* sweater.
сви́ток [*gen.* **-тка**] *n.* **1,** roll. **2,** scroll.
свить [*infl.* **совью́, совьёшь;** *past fem.* **свила́**] *v., pfv. of* **вить** *and* **свива́ть.** —**сви́ться,** *refl., pfv. of* **свива́ться.**
свихну́ть *v. pfv., colloq.* to dislocate. —**свихну́ться,** *refl., colloq.* **1,** to go mad; go nuts. **2,** to go astray.
свищ [*gen.* **свища́**] *n.* **1,** knothole. **2,** *med.* fistula.
свия́зь *n.f.* widgeon (*duck*).
свобо́да *n.* freedom; liberty. —**на свобо́де, 1,** at large. **2,** in one's leisure time. —**выпуска́ть** *or* **отпуска́ть на свобо́ду,** to set free.
свобо́дно *adv.* **1,** freely. **2,** easily. **3,** loosely. **4,** fluently. **5,** in a relaxed manner. —*adj., used predicatively* unoccupied: здесь свобо́дно?, is this seat taken?
свобо́дный *adj.* [*short form* **-ден, -дна**] **1,** free. **2,** vacant; unoccupied. **3,** loose. **4,** (*of time*) spare; free. **5,** free and easy; relaxed.
свободолюби́вый *adj.* freedom-loving. —**свободолю́бие,** *n.* love of freedom.
свободомы́слие *n.* free thought.
свободомы́слящий *adj.* freethinking. —*n.* freethinker.
свод *n.* **1,** code: свод зако́нов, code of laws. **2,** *archit.* arch. —**небе́сный свод,** the firmament.
своди́ть[1] *v. impfv.* [*pfv.* **свести́;** *pres.* **свожу́, сво́дишь**] **1,** to lead down; take down; help (someone) down. **2,** to take (a person somewhere on foot). **3,** to lead away. **4,** to join; tie together. **5,** *fig.* to bring

together. **6,** to remove (a stain, wart, etc.). **7,** (*with* **на** + *acc. or* **к** *or* **до**) to reduce: своди́ть к ми́нимуму, to reduce to a minimum. **8,** (*with* **в** + *acc.*) to incorporate (into): своди́ть в табли́цу, to tabulate. **9,** to square; settle: своди́ть счёты с, to settle scores with. **10,** *fig.* to turn; switch (a conversation, one's thoughts, etc.). **11,** to cramp. *Also impers.:* у меня́ свело́ но́гу, I have a cramp in my leg. —**не своди́ть глаз с** (+ *gen.*), not take one's eyes off... —**своди́ть в моги́лу,** to be the death of. —**своди́ть дру́жбу с,** to make friends with. —**своди́ть концы́ с конца́ми,** to make ends meet. —**своди́ть на нет,** to negate; nullify. —**своди́ть с ума́,** to drive mad; drive out of one's mind.

своди́ть2 *v. pfv.* [*infl.* **свожу́, сво́дишь**] to take to and back; lead to and back.

своди́ться *v.r. impfv.* [*pfv.* **свести́сь;** *pres.* **сво́дится**] to come (down) to: своди́ться на нет *or* к нулю́, to come to naught. Всё де́ло сво́дится к э́тому, the whole thing comes (*or* boils) down to this.

сво́дка [*gen. pl.* **-док**] *n.* summary. Сво́дка пого́ды, weather report; weather forecast.

сво́дник *n.* procurer; pimp.

сво́дничать *v. impfv.* to pander.

сво́дничество *n.* procuring.

сво́дный *adj.* combined; consolidated; composite. —**сво́дный брат, 1,** stepbrother. **2,** half brother. —**сво́дная сестра́, 1,** stepsister. **2,** half sister.

сво́дчатый *adj.* arched; vaulted.

своево́лие *n.* arbitrariness; high-handedness; capriciousness.

своево́льный *adj.* strong-willed; headstrong.

своевре́менный *adj.* timely; opportune. —**своевре́менно,** *adv.* in time. —**своевре́менность,** *n.f.* timeliness.

своекоры́стие *n.* self-interest. —**своекоры́стный,** *adj.* self-seeking.

своенра́вие *n.* arbitrariness; capriciousness. —**своенра́вный,** *adj.* arbitrary; capricious.

своеобра́зие *n.* distinctive quality.

своеобра́зный *adj.* distinctive; singular; peculiar.

свози́ть1 *v. impfv.* [*pfv.* **свезти́;** *pres.* **свожу́, сво́зишь**] **1,** to gather together (*in one place*). **2,** to drive down. **3,** to take away; cart away. *See also* **свезти́.**

свози́ть2 *v. pfv.* [*infl.* **свожу́, сво́зишь**] to drive; take (someone) to and back.

свой [*infl. like* **мой**] *poss. adj. & pron., used when the possessor is the subject of the sentence.* **1,** one's; my; his; her; their: снять свою́ шля́пу, to take off one's hat. **2,** one's own: у них своя́ маши́на, they have their own car; they have a car of their own. —**свои́,** *n. pl.* one's own people. —**брать своё, 1,** to succeed; prevail. **2,** to take its toll. —**доби́ться своего́,** to gain one's objective; get one's way. —**наста́ивать на своём,** to insist on having one's own way. —**настоя́ть на своём,** to have one's own way. —**оста́ться при свои́х,** to break even (*in gambling*). —**получи́ть своё,** to get one's just reward. —**стоя́ть на своём,** to stand one's ground.

сво́йственник *n.* relative by marriage; in-law.

сво́йственный *adj.* (*with dat.*) characteristic: со сво́йственным ему́ ю́мором, with his characteristic humor. Челове́ку сво́йственно ошиба́ться, to err is human.

сво́йство *n.* property; attribute; characteristic.

свойство́ *n.* relationship by marriage.

свола́кивать *v. impfv.* [*pfv.* **своло́чь**] *colloq.* to drag; drag off; drag down.

сво́лочь *n.f., vulg.* **1,** riffraff; rabble. **2,** swine; scoundrel.

своло́чь [*infl.* **-локу́, -лочёшь, ...-локу́т;** *past* **-ло́к, -локла́, -локло́**] *v., pfv. of* **свола́кивать.**

сво́ра *n.* **1,** leash. **2,** pack (*of dogs, wolves, etc.*). **3,** gang.

свора́чивать *v. impfv.* [*pfv.* **сверну́ть**] **1,** *v.i.* to turn: свора́чивать с доро́ги/в переу́лок/, to turn off the road/down a side street/. **2,** *v.t., colloq.* to turn: свора́чивать маши́ну нале́во, to turn a car to the left.

своя́к [*gen.* **свояка́**] *n.* brother-in-law (*wife's sister's husband*).

своя́ченица *n.* sister-in-law (*wife's sister*).

свыка́ться *v.r. impfv.* [*pfv.* **свы́кнуться**] (*with* **с** + *instr.*) to get used to.

свы́кнуться [*past* **свы́кся, свы́клась**] *v.r., pfv. of* **свыка́ться.**

свысока́ *adv.* **1,** *obs.* from on high. **2,** with disdain: смотре́ть на (+ *acc.*) свысока́, to look down on.

свы́ше *adv.* from above; from on high. —*prep., with gen.* **1,** over; more than. **2,** beyond: свы́ше мои́х сил, beyond me; more than I can handle.

свя́занный *adj.* **1,** related; connected. **2,** (*of movements*) awkward; (*of speech*) halting. *See also* **свя́зывать** (*sense #5*).

связа́ть [*infl.* **свяжу́, свя́жешь**] *v., pfv. of* **вяза́ть** *and* **свя́зывать.** —**связа́ться,** *refl., pfv. of* **свя́зываться.**

связи́ст *n.* **1,** *mil.* signalman. **2,** telephone or telegraph worker.

свя́зка [*gen. pl.* **-зок**] *n.* **1,** bunch; bundle. **2,** ligament. —**глаго́л-свя́зка,** linking verb. —**голосовы́е свя́зки,** vocal cords.

связно́й *adj.* liaison (*attrib.*); communications (*attrib.*). —*n.* messenger.

свя́зный *adj.* coherent; connected. —**свя́зность,** *n.f.* coherence.

связу́ющий *adj.* connecting.

свя́зывать *v. impfv.* [*pfv.* **связа́ть**] **1,** to tie; bind; tie together. **2,** to connect; link; join. **3,** to put in touch with. **4,** *fig.* to bind: свя́зан обеща́нием, bound by a promise. Судьба́ их связа́ла, fate bound them together. **5,** *past passive part. only,* A, to connect; associate: всё, что свя́зано с э́тим, everything connected/associated/having to do/with it. B, to involve; entail: э́то свя́зано с ри́ском, it involves/entails risk. —**связа́ть свою́ судьбу́ с,** to cast one's lot with. —**связа́ть по рука́м и нога́м, 1,** to bind hand and foot. **2,** *fig.* to tie someone's hands.

свя́зываться *v.r. impfv.* [*pfv.* **связа́ться**] (*with* **с** + *instr.*) **1,** to contact; get in touch (with). **2,** *colloq.* to get involved (with).

связь *n.f.* **1,** connection. **2,** tie; link: торго́вые свя́зи, trade ties. **3,** contact; touch: потеря́ть связь с, to lose contact/touch with. **4,** (illicit) affair; liaison. **5,** communication(s). **6,** *pl.* (personal) contacts; connections. **7,** coupling; tie. **8,** *mil.* liaison. —**в свя́зи с** (+ *instr.*), **1,** in connection with. **2,** because of; owing to. —**в свя́зи с э́тим, 1,** in this connection. **2,** as a result. —**в э́той свя́зи,** in this connection.

святе́йшество *n.* Holiness: его́ святе́йшество, His Holiness.

святи́лище *n.* **1,** *obs.* temple; sanctuary. **2,** *fig.* revered place.
свя́тки [*gen.* **-ток**] *n. pl.* yuletide; the period from Christmas through January 6th.
свя́то *adv.* **1,** as if sacred: свя́то чтить что́-нибудь, to hold something sacred. **2,** scrupulously: свя́то соблюда́ть что́-нибудь, to observe something scrupulously.
свято́й *adj.* holy; sacred. —*n.* saint. —**свята́я и́стина,** gospel truth. —**свята́я святы́х,** holy of holies.
свя́тость *n.f.* holiness; sanctity.
святота́тство *n.* sacrilege. —**святота́тственный,** *adj.* sacrilegious.
святота́тствовать *v. impfv.* [*pres.* **-ствую, -ствуешь**] to commit sacrilege.
свя́точный *adj.* Christmas (*attrib.*).
свято́ша *n.m. & f.* pious hypocrite.
свя́тцы [*gen.* **-цев**] *n. pl.* church calendar.
святы́ня *n.* sacred object; holy place.
свяще́нник *n.* **1,** priest. **2,** clergyman.
свяще́ннический *adj.* **1,** priestly; sacerdotal. **2,** clergyman's; clergy's.
свяще́нный *adj.* sacred; holy.
свяще́нство *n.* priesthood.
сгиб *n.* **1,** bend. **2,** crook; joint.
сгиба́ть *v. impfv.* [*pfv.* **согну́ть**] to bend. —**сгиба́ться,** *refl.* **1,** (*of an object*) to bend. **2,** (*of a person*) to bend over.
сги́нуть *v. pfv., colloq.* to disappear; vanish.
сгла́дить [*infl.* **-жу, -дишь**] *v., pfv. of* **сгла́живать.**
сгла́живать *v. impfv.* [*pfv.* **сгла́дить**] **1,** to smooth; smooth out. **2,** *fig.* to smooth over.
сгла́зить *v. pfv.* [*infl.* **-жу, -зишь**] to jinx; put a hex on; give (someone) the evil eye.
сглупи́ть *v. pfv.* [*infl.* **-плю́, -пи́шь**] *colloq.* to do or say something foolish.
сгнить *v., pfv. of* **гнить.**
сгнои́ть *v., pfv. of* **гнои́ть.**
сгова́риваться *v.r. impfv.* [*pfv.* **сговори́ться**] **1,** to arrange (to do something). Та́йно сговори́ться (+ *inf.*), to secretly conspire to... **2,** to reach an agreement: с ним тру́дно сговори́ться, it is hard to reach an agreement with him; he is hard to deal with.
сго́вор *n.* **1,** conspiracy. **2,** collusion. **3,** *obs.* agreement; understanding. **4,** *obs.* betrothal.
сговори́ться *v.r., pfv. of* **сгова́риваться.**
сгово́рчивый *adj.* amenable.
сгоня́ть *v. impfv.* [*pfv.* **согна́ть**] **1,** to drive away; drive off; chase away; chase off. **2,** to drive together; round up. **3,** *colloq.* to take off (weight).
сгора́ние *n.* combustion. —**дви́гатель вну́треннего сгора́ния,** internal-combustion engine.
сгора́ть *v. impfv.* [*pfv.* **сгоре́ть**] **1,** to burn (up); be burned (up); burn down. **2,** (*of fuel, firewood, etc.*) to be consumed. **3,** (*of vegetation*) to wither; shrivel. **4,** *fig.* to burn oneself out. **5,** *fig.* (*with* **от** *or* **с** + *gen.*) to be dying (of shame, curiosity, etc.).
сго́рбить *v., pfv. of* **го́рбить.** —**сго́рбиться,** *refl., pfv. of* **го́рбиться.**
сго́рбленный *adj.* hunched; stooped.
сгоре́ть [*infl.* **-рю́, -ри́шь**] *v., pfv. of* **сгора́ть.**
сгоряча́ *adv.* in the heat of the moment; in a fit of temper.
сгреба́ть *v. impfv.* [*pfv.* **сгрести́**] **1,** to rake; sweep. **2,** *colloq.* to sweep off; brush off; shovel off.
сгрести́ [*infl. like* **грести́**] *v., pfv. of* **сгреба́ть.**
сгруди́ться *v.r. pfv., colloq.* to congregate; cluster.
сгружа́ть *v. impfv.* [*pfv.* **сгрузи́ть**] to unload.
сгрузи́ть [*infl.* **сгружу́, сгру́зишь** *or* **сгрузи́шь**] *v., pfv. of* **сгружа́ть.**
сгруппирова́ть *v., pfv. of* **группирова́ть.** —**сгруппирова́ться,** *refl., pfv. of* **группирова́ться.**
сгрыза́ть *v. impfv.* [*pfv.* **сгрызть**] to chew up.
сгрызть [*infl. like* **грызть**] *v., pfv. of* **сгрыза́ть.**
сгуби́ть *v. pfv.* [*infl.* **сгублю́, сгу́бишь**] *colloq.* to ruin.
сгусти́ть [*infl.* **-щу́, -сти́шь**] *v., pfv. of* **сгуща́ть.** —**сгусти́ться,** *refl., pfv. of* **сгуща́ться.**
сгу́сток [*gen.* **-тка**] *n.* **1,** clot: сгу́сток кро́ви, blood clot. **2,** *fig.* bundle: сгу́сток эне́ргии, bundle of energy.
сгуща́ть *v. impfv.* [*pfv.* **сгусти́ть**] **1,** to thicken; make thick. **2,** to condense. **3,** to clot; coagulate (blood). —**сгуща́ть кра́ски, 1,** to (grossly) exaggerate. **2,** to make things out to be worse than they are.
сгуща́ться *v.r. impfv.* [*pfv.* **сгусти́ться**] to thicken; condense; clot; coagulate.
сгуще́ние *n.* thickening; coagulation; clotting.
сгущённый *adj., in* **сгущённое молоко́,** condensed milk; evaporated milk.
сда́бривать *v. impfv.* [*pfv.* **сдо́брить**] to season; flavor; spice.
сдава́ть *v. impfv.* [*pfv.* **сдать;** *pres.* **сдаю́, сдаёшь**] **1,** to hand in; turn in. **2,** to hand over; turn over. **3,** to rent; lease; let. **4,** to surrender; give up. **5,** *cards* to deal. **6,** *v.i., colloq.* to decline (*in health*). **7,** *v.i., colloq.* to break down; give out. **8,** *in* сдава́ть экза́мен, to take an examination; сдать экза́мен, to pass an examination. —**сдава́ться,** *refl.* **1,** to surrender; give up. **2,** (*in a game, esp. chess*) to resign. **3,** [*impfv. only*] to be for rent. **4,** [*impfv. only*] (*with dat.*) *colloq.* to seem; appear.
сдави́ть [*infl.* **сдавлю́, сда́вишь**] *v., pfv. of* **сда́вливать.**
сда́вливать *v. impfv.* [*pfv.* **сдави́ть**] **1,** to squeeze. **2,** to constrict.
сда́точный *adj.* delivery (*attrib.*).
сдать [*infl. like* **дать**] *v., pfv. of* **сдава́ть.** —**сда́ться,** *refl.* [*past* **сда́лся, сдала́сь, сдало́сь**] *pfv. of* **сдава́ться.**
сда́ча *n.* **1,** handing over; handing in; turning in. **2,** returning; giving back. **3,** renting; leasing. **4,** surrender; giving up. **5,** taking (*of an examination*). **6,** *cards* deal; dealing. **7,** change (*money given back*). **8,** *fig., colloq.* riposte. —**дава́ть сда́чи** (*with dat.*), **1,** to hit back; strike back. **2,** to give (someone) tit for tat.
сдва́ивать *v. impfv.* [*pfv.* **сдвои́ть**] to double.
сдвиг *n.* **1,** shift; change. **2,** *fig.* progress; step forward; change for the better. **3,** *geol.* fault.
сдвига́ть *v. impfv.* [*pfv.* **сдви́нуть**] **1,** to move (*from a certain place*). **2,** to move together; draw together. **3,** *in* сдви́нуть бро́ви, to knit one's brows.
сдвига́ться *v.r. impfv.* [*pfv.* **сдви́нуться**] **1,** to move; budge. **2,** to move closer together. —**сдвига́ться с ме́ста, 1,** to move; budge. **2,** *fig.* to make headway.
сдвои́ть *v., pfv. of* **сдва́ивать.**
сде́лать *v., pfv. of* **де́лать.** —**сде́латься,** *refl., pfv. of* **де́латься** (*in senses #3 & #4*).
сде́лка [*gen. pl.* **-лок**] *n.* transaction; bargain; deal.
сде́льный *adj.* by the piece. —**сде́льная рабо́та,** piecework.
сде́льщик *n.* pieceworker.

сде́льщина *n.* piecework.
сдёргивать *v. impfv.* [*pfv.* **сдёрнуть**] to pull off.
сде́ржанный *adj.* restrained; reserved. —**сде́ржанность,** *n.f.* restraint; reserve.
сдержа́ть *v. pfv.* [*infl.* **сдержу́, сде́ржишь**] **1,** *pfv. of* **сде́рживать. 2,** to keep (one's word, a promise, etc.). —**сдержа́ться,** *refl., pfv. of* **сде́рживаться.**
сде́рживать *v. impfv.* [*pfv.* **сдержа́ть**] **1,** to restrain; hold back; hold in check. **2,** to hold back; suppress; repress (tears, laughter, a feeling, etc.). **3,** to withstand. —**сде́рживаться,** *refl.* to restrain oneself.
сдёрнуть *v., pfv. of* **сдёргивать.**
сдира́ть *v. impfv.* [*pfv.* **содра́ть**] **1,** to strip; tear off; remove. **2,** *colloq.* to cheat; "rip off".
сдо́ба *n.* **1,** shortening. **2,** sweet rolls; buns.
сдо́бный *adj.* (*of pastry*) rich. —**сдо́бная бу́лка,** bun.
сдо́брить *v., pfv. of* **сда́бривать.**
сдоброва́ть *v. pfv., in* ему́ (ей) не сдоброва́ть, it will not turn out well for him (her).
сдо́хнуть *v. pfv.* [*past* **сдох, -ла**] (*of animals*) to die.
сдружи́ть *v. pfv.* [*infl.* **сдружу́, сдружи́шь** *or* **сдру́жишь**] to bring together; make friends of. —**сдружи́ться,** *refl.* to become friends.
сдува́ть *v. impfv.* [*pfv.* **сдуть**] *v.t.* to blow away; blow off. *Also impers. and intrans.:* у него́ шля́пу сду́ло, his hat blew off. —**как ве́тром сду́ло,** disappeared completely.
сду́ру *adv., colloq.* foolishly; stupidly.
сдуть [*infl.* **сду́ю, сду́ешь**] *v., pfv. of* **одува́ть.**
сё *dem. pron.* [*gen.* **сего́**] *used only in certain idiomatic expressions.* —**то-сё; то и сё; то да сё,** this and that: поговори́ть о том, о сём, to talk about this and that. —**ни то ни сё,** ordinary; nondescript. —**ни с того́ ни с сего́,** for no apparent reason; without rhyme or reason.
сеа́нс *n.* **1,** performance; show. **2,** sitting (*for a portrait*). **3,** session. —**сеа́нс одновре́менной игры́,** simultaneous chess exhibition.
себе́ *pron., dat. & prepl. of* **себя́.** *See* **себя́.**
себесто́имость *n.f.* (prime) cost.
себя́ *refl. pron.* [*dat. & prepl.* **себе́;** *instr.* **собо́й**] oneself (myself, yourself, himself, etc.): недооцени́ть себя́, to underestimate oneself; владе́ть собо́й, control oneself; отвеча́ть за себя́, answer for oneself; ду́мать то́лько о себе́, think only of oneself. —**быть сами́м собо́й,** *see* **сам.** —**вне себя́,** beside oneself: вне себя́ от ра́дости, beside oneself with joy. —**к себе́, 1,** to one's home. **2,** (*sign on doors*) "pull". —**ме́жду собо́й,** among oneselves. —**не по себе́** (+ *dat.*), not to be feeling well. —**от себя́, 1,** for oneself; personally. **2,** (*sign on doors*) "push". —**про себя́,** to oneself: чита́ть про себя́, to read to oneself. —**сам по себе́,** *see* **сам.** —**сам собо́й,** by itself; of itself. —**так себе́,** so-so. —**у себя́,** at home.
себялю́бец [*gen.* **-бца**] *n.* self-centered person.
себялюби́вый *adj.* selfish; self-centered. —**себялю́бие,** *n.* selfishness; egoism.
сев *n.* sowing.
се́вер *n.* north.
се́верный *adj.* northern; North; northerly.
се́веро-восто́к *n.* northeast. —**се́веро-восто́чный,** *adj.* northeast; northeastern; northeasterly.
се́веро-за́пад *n.* northwest. —**се́веро-за́падный,** *adj.* northwest; northwestern; northwesterly.
северя́нин [*pl.* **-я́не, -я́н**] *n.m.* [*fem.* **-я́нка**] northerner.
севооборо́т *n.* crop rotation.
севрю́га *n.* a variety of sturgeon.
сегме́нт *n., math.* segment.
сего́дня (vo) *adv.* today. Сего́дня у́тром, this morning. Сего́дня ве́чером, this evening; tonight. —**не сего́дня-за́втра,** any day now.
сего́дняшний (vo) *adj.* today's. —**сего́дняшний день,** today.
сегрега́ция *n.* segregation.
седа́лище *n., obs.* seat; place to sit.
седа́лищный *adj.* sciatic: седа́лищный нерв, sciatic nerve.
седе́льник *n.* saddler.
седе́льный *adj.* saddle (*attrib.*).
седе́ть *v. impfv.* [*pfv.* **поседе́ть**] to turn gray.
седи́ль *n.m.* cedilla.
седина́ [*pl.* **седи́ны**] *n., often pl.* gray hair. —**дожи́ть до седи́н,** to live to be old and gray.
седла́ть *v. impfv.* [*pfv.* **оседла́ть**] to saddle.
седло́ [*pl.* **сёдла, сёдел**] *n.* saddle.
седлови́на *n.* depression; dip.
седоволо́сый *adj.* gray-haired; white-haired. *Also,* **седовла́сый.**
седо́й *adj.* **1,** (*of hair*) gray; white. **2,** gray-haired; white-haired. —**дожи́ть до седы́х воло́с,** to live to be old and gray.
седо́к [*gen.* **-дока́**] *n.* **1,** rider; horseman. **2,** rider; passenger (*in a carriage*).
седьма́я *n., decl. as an adj.* seventh: одна́ седьма́я, one-seventh.
седьмо́й *ordinal numeral* seventh.
сеза́м *n.* sesame. —**сеза́мовый,** *adj.* sesame.
сезо́н *n.* season. —**сезо́нный,** *adj.* season (*attrib.*); seasonal.
сей *dem. pron.* [*fem.* **сия́;** *neut.* **сие́;** *pl.* **сии́;** *gen.* **сего́, сей, сих;** *acc. fem.* **сию́;** *dat.* **сему́, сей, сим;** *instr.* **сим, сей, си́ми;** *prepl.* **сём, сей, сих**] *obs.* this. —**до сих пор,** until now. —**на сей раз,** this time. —**по сей день,** to this day. —**при сём,** hereto; herewith. —**сего́ го́да,** (*with dates — usu. abbr. to* с.г.) of this year. —**сим,** hereby. —**сию́ мину́ту,** this minute; this instant.
сейсми́ческий *adj.* seismic.
сейсмо́граф *n.* seismograph.
сейсмоло́гия *n.* seismology. —**сейсмо́лог,** *n.* seismologist. —**сейсмологи́ческий,** *adj.* seismological.
сейф *n.* safe.
сейча́с *adv.* **1,** now; right now; at present: он сейча́с за́нят, he is busy right now. **2,** right now; right away; at once; immediately: я сейча́с верну́сь, I'll be right back. **3,** just; just now: она́ сейча́с звони́ла, she just called. —**сейча́с же, 1,** right now; immediately; at once. **2,** right away; immediately (*in the past*).
се́канс *n., trig.* secant.
сека́ч [*gen.* **-кача́**] *n.* chopper (*tool*).
секве́стр *n.* sequestration.
секвестрова́ть *v. impfv. & pfv.* [*pres.* **-ру́ю, -ру́ешь**] to sequester.
секво́йя *n.* sequoia; redwood.
секи́ра *n.* poleax.
секре́т *n.* secret: большо́й секре́т, a big secret. Держа́ть (что́-нибудь) в секре́те, to keep (something) secret. —**по секре́ту,** confidentially; in confidence.

—**под больши́м** (*or* **по́лным**) **секре́том,** in strict confidence.
секретариа́т *n.* secretariat.
секрета́рский *adj.* secretarial.
секрета́рствовать *v. impfv.* [*pres.* **-ствую, -ствуешь**] to serve as secretary.
секрета́рь [*gen.* **-таря́**] *n.m.* [*fem.* **-та́рша**] secretary. —**генера́льный секрета́рь,** *see* **генера́льный.** —**госуда́рственный секрета́рь,** secretary of state.
секрете́р (тэ) *n.* desk; writing table.
секре́тничать *v. impfv., colloq.* **1,** to keep things secret. **2,** to talk confidentially.
секре́тно *adv.* secretly; in secret. —**соверше́нно секре́тно,** top secret.
секре́тность *n.f.* secrecy.
секре́тный *adj.* secret.
секре́ция *n.* secretion. —**железа́ вну́тренней секре́ции,** ductless gland; endocrine gland.
секс *n.* sex.
се́кста *n., music* sixth.
секста́нт *n.* sextant.
сексте́т *n.* sextet.
сексуа́льный *adj.* sexual. —**сексуа́льность,** *n.f.* sexuality.
се́кта *n.* sect.
секта́нт *n.* sectarian. —**секта́нтский,** *adj.* sectarian. —**секта́нтство,** *n.* sectarianism.
се́ктор *n.* sector.
секуляриза́ция *n.* secularization.
секуляризи́ровать *v. impfv. & pfv.* [*pres.* **-рую, -руешь**] to secularize.
секу́нда *n.* **1,** second (*of time or angular measurement*). **2,** *music* second.
секунда́нт *n.* second (*in a duel, chess match, etc.*).
секу́ндный *adj.* **1,** second (*attrib.*): секу́ндная стре́лка, second hand (*on a watch*). **2,** lasting only a second; momentary.
секундоме́р *n.* stopwatch.
секу́щая *n., decl. as an adj., geom.* secant.
секцио́нный *adj.* sectional.
се́кция *n.* section.
селёдка [*gen. pl.* **-док**] *n., colloq.* herring. —**селёдочный,** *adj.* herring (*attrib.*).
селезёнка *n.* spleen. —**селезёночный,** *adj.* splenetic.
се́лезень [*gen.* **-зня**] *n.m.* drake; male duck.
селе́кция *n.* breeding (*of plants and animals*).
селе́н *n.* selenium.
селе́ние *n.* village; settlement.
селени́т *n.* selenite.
сели́тра *n.* saltpeter; niter. —**аммиа́чная** *or* **аммо́ниевая сели́тра,** ammonium nitrate. —**ка́лиевая** *or* **кали́йная сели́тра,** potassium nitrate. —**на́триевая сели́тра,** sodium nitrate.
сели́тряный *adj.* saltpeter (*attrib.*); nitric.
сели́ть *v. impfv.* to settle. —**сели́ться,** *refl.* to settle; take up residence.
село́ [*pl.* **сёла**] *n.* village. —**ни к селу́ ни к го́роду,** apropos of nothing; for no apparent reason.
сельдере́й *n.* celery. —**сельдере́йный,** *adj.* celery (*attrib.*).
сельдь [*pl.* **се́льди, -де́й, -дя́м**] *n.f.* herring. —**как се́льди в бо́чке,** like sardines.
се́льский *adj.* **1,** rural. **2,** village (*attrib.*). —**се́льское хозя́йство,** agriculture.
сельскохозя́йственный *adj.* agricultural; farm (*attrib.*).
сельсове́т *n.* village soviet (*contr. of* **се́льский сове́т**).
се́льтерский *adj., in* **се́льтерская вода́,** seltzer water.
сема́нтика *n.* semantics. —**семанти́ческий,** *adj.* semantic.
семафо́р *n.* semaphore.
сёмга *n.* smoked salmon; lox.
семе́йный *adj.* family (*attrib.*).
семе́йственность *n.f.* **1,** attachment to family; family spirit. **2,** nepotism.
семе́йственный *adj.* attached to one's family; home-loving.
семе́йство *n.* **1,** = **семья́. 2,** *biol.* family.
семени́ть *v. impfv., colloq., in* **семени́ть нога́ми,** to trip (along); walk with mincing steps.
семенни́к [*gen.* **-ника́**] *n.* **1,** seed plant. **2,** testicle.
семенно́й *adj.* **1,** seed (*attrib.*). **2,** seminal.
семёрка *n.* **1,** the numeral 7. **2,** *colloq.* anything numbered 7. **3,** *cards* seven.
се́меро *collective numeral* seven.
семе́стр *n.* semester.
се́мечко [*gen. pl.* **-чек**] *n.* **1,** *dim. of* **се́мя. 2,** *pl.* sunflower seeds.
семидесятиле́тие *n.* **1,** seventieth anniversary; seventieth birthday. **2,** seventy-year period.
семидесятиле́тний *adj.* **1,** seventy-year (*attrib.*). **2,** seventy-year-old.
семидеся́тый *ordinal numeral* seventieth.
семидне́вный *adj.* seven-day (*attrib.*).
семикра́тный *adj.* sevenfold.
семиле́тие *n.* **1,** seventh anniversary; seventh birthday. **2,** seven-year period.
семиле́тка [*gen. pl.* **-ток**] *n.* **1,** seven-year school. **2,** Seven-Year Plan.
семиле́тний *adj.* **1,** seven-year (*attrib.*). **2,** seven-year-old.
семина́р *n.* seminar.
семина́рия *n.* seminary. —**семинари́ст,** *n.* seminary student; seminary graduate.
семисо́тый *ordinal numeral* seven-hundredth.
семи́тский *adj.* Semitic. *Also,* **семити́ческий.**
семиуго́льник *n.* heptagon. —**семиуго́льный,** *adj.* heptagonal.
семичасово́й *adj.* seven-hour: семичасово́й рабо́чий день, seven-hour working day.
семна́дцать *numeral* seventeen. —**семна́дцатый,** *ordinal numeral* seventeenth.
семь [*gen., dat., & prepl.* **семи́;** *instr.* **семью́**] *numeral* seven.
се́мьдесят [*gen., dat., & prepl.* **семи́десяти;** *instr.* **семью́десятью**] *numeral* seventy.
семьсо́т [*gen.* **семисо́т;** *dat.* **семиста́м;** *instr.* **семьюста́ми;** *prepl.* **семиста́х**] *numeral* seven hundred.
се́мью *adv.* seven times: се́мью пять – три́дцать пять, seven times five is 35.
семья́ [*pl.* **се́мьи, семе́й, се́мьям**] *n.* family.
семьяни́н *n.* family man.
се́мя [*gen., dat., & prepl.* **се́мени;** *instr.* **се́менем;** *pl.* **семена́, семя́н, семена́м**] *n. neut.* **1,** seed. **2,** semen. —**пойти́ в семена́,** (*of a plant*) to go to seed.
семядо́ля *n.* cotyledon.

семяизлия́ние *n.* ejaculation.

семяпо́чка [*gen. pl.* **-чек**] *n., bot.* ovule.

сена́т *n.* senate. —**сена́тор,** *n.* senator. —**сена́торский,** *adj.* senator's; senatorial. —**сена́тский,** *adj.* senate (*attrib.*).

сенберна́р (сэ) *n.* Saint Bernard (*dog*).

се́ни [*gen.* **сене́й**] *n. pl.* entrance hall; vestibule.

сенни́к [*gen.* **-ника́**] *n.* straw mattress.

сенно́й *adj.* hay (*attrib.*). —**сенна́я лихора́дка,** hay fever.

се́но *n.* hay. —**соба́ка на се́не,** dog in the manger.

сенова́л *n.* hayloft.

сеноко́с *n.* **1,** haymaking. **2,** hayfield.

сенокоси́лка [*gen. pl.* **-лок**] *n.* machine for mowing hay.

сенса́ция *n.* sensation. —**сенсацио́нный,** *adj.* sensational.

сенсо́рный (сэ) *adj.* sensory.

сентенцио́зный (сэ,тэ) *adj.* sententious.

сенте́нция (сэ, тэ) *n.* maxim; adage.

сентимента́льничать (сэ) *v. impfv.* **1,** to be sentimental. **2,** to be soft; be lenient.

сентимента́льный (сэ) *adj.* sentimental. —**сентимента́льность,** *n.f.* sentimentality.

сентя́брь [*gen.* **-бря́**] *n.m.* September. —**сентя́брьский,** *adj.* September (*attrib.*).

сень [*2nd loc.* **сени́**] *n.f., archaic* canopy. —**под се́нью** (+ *gen.*), under the protection of.

сепарати́зм *n.* separatism. —**сепарати́ст,** *n.* separatist. —**сепарати́стский,** *adj.* separatist.

сепара́тный *adj., polit.* separate: сепара́тный мир, separate peace.

сепара́тор *n.* separator.

се́пия (сэ) *n.* **1,** sepia. **2,** cuttlefish.

се́псис (сэ) *n.* sepsis.

се́птима (сэ) *n., music* seventh.

септи́ческий (сэ) *adj.* septic.

се́ра *n.* sulfur. —**ушна́я се́ра,** earwax.

сера́ль *n.m.* seraglio.

серафи́м *n.* seraph.

серб *n.m.* [*fem.* **се́рбка**] Serb.

сербохорва́тский *adj.* Serbo-Croatian.

се́рбский *adj.* Serbian.

сербскохорва́тский *adj.* Serbo-Croatian.

серва́нт *n.* sideboard.

серви́з *n.* set (*of dishes or silverware*): фарфо́ровый серви́з, set of china.

сервирова́ть *v. impfv. & pfv.* [*pres.* **-ру́ю, -ру́ешь**] **1,** to set (a table). **2,** to serve (a meal).

сервиро́вка *n.* [*often with* **стола́**] *n.* **1,** (act of) setting (*a table*). **2,** table arrangement.

серде́чник *n., colloq.* **1,** person with a heart ailment. **2,** heart specialist.

серде́чно *adv.* **1,** cordially; warmly. **2,** sincerely.

серде́чно-сосу́дистый *adj.* cardiovascular.

серде́чность *n.f.* warmth; cordiality.

серде́чный *adj.* **1,** heart (*attrib.*); cardiac. **2,** hearty; cordial. **3,** warmhearted; kind. **4,** heartfelt; sincere. **5,** of the heart; love (*attrib.*); romantic.

серди́тый *adj.* (*with* **на** + *acc.*) angry (at). —**серди́то,** *adv.* angrily.

серди́ть *v. impfv.* [*pfv.* **рассерди́ть;** *pres.* **сержу́, се́рдишь**] to anger; make angry. —**серди́ться,** *refl.* (*with* **на** + *acc.*) to be angry (at); become angry (with).

сердобо́лие *n., obs.* compassion. —**сердобо́льный,** *adj., colloq.* tenderhearted.

се́рдце [*pl.* **сердца́, серде́ц, сердца́м**] *n.* heart. —**всем се́рдцем,** with all one's heart. —**в сердца́х,** *colloq.* in a fit of anger. —**от всего́ се́рдца,** from the bottom of one's heart. —**от полноты́ се́рдца,** in the fullness of one's heart. —**от чи́стого се́рдца,** in all sincerity. —**по́ сердцу** (+ *dat.*), to one's liking. —**брать за́ сердце,** to move deeply. —**положа́ ру́ку на́ сердце,** in all honesty. —**принима́ть (бли́зко) к се́рдцу,** to take to heart.

сердцебие́ние *n.* **1,** heartbeat. **2,** palpitation of the heart.

сердцеви́дка [*gen. pl.* **-док**] *n.* cockle (*mollusk*).

сердцеви́дный *adj.* heart-shaped.

сердцеви́на *n.* **1,** core. **2,** *fig.* core; heart.

сердцее́д *n., colloq.* lady-killer.

серебри́стый *adj.* silvery.

серебри́ть *v. impfv.* [*pfv.* **посеребри́ть**] to silver; silver-plate. —**серебри́ться,** *refl.* to become silvery.

серебро́ *n.* silver.

сере́бряник *n.* silversmith.

сере́бряный *adj.* silver. —**сере́бряных дел ма́стер,** silversmith.

середи́на *n.* middle. —**золота́я середи́на,** the golden mean; happy medium.

середи́нный *adj.* **1,** middle. **2,** *fig.* halfway; compromise (*attrib.*).

серёдка [*gen. pl.* **-док**] *n., colloq.* middle; center.

середня́к [*gen.* **-няка́**] *n.* middle-class peasant.

серёжка [*gen. pl.* **-жек**] *n.* **1,** earring. **2,** catkin. **3,** *colloq.* wattle (*on fowl*).

серена́да *n.* serenade.

сере́ть *v. impfv.* [*pfv.* **посере́ть**] to turn gray.

сержа́нт *n.* sergeant. —**сержа́нтский,** *adj.* sergeant's.

сери́йный *adj.* **1,** (*of production*) mass. **2,** mass-produced.

се́рия *n.* **1,** series. **2,** set (*of postage stamps*). **3,** part (*of a film*): кинофи́льм в трех се́риях, three-part film.

сермя́га *n.* **1,** a coarse undyed cloth. **2,** robe made of this cloth.

се́рна *n.* chamois.

серни́стый *adj.* **1,** containing sulfur: серни́стые краси́тели, sulfur dyes. **2,** sulfurous; sulfide (of): серни́стая кислота́, sulfurous acid; серни́стый водоро́д, hydrogen sulfide.

сернобы́к [*gen.* **-быка́**] *n.* oryx.

серноки́слый *adj.* sulfate (of): серноки́слый аммо́ний/ба́рий/на́трий, ammonium/barium/sodium sulfate. —**серноки́слая соль,** sulfate.

се́рный *adj.* **1,** sulfur (*attrib.*). **2,** sulfuric.

сероводоро́д *n.* hydrogen sulfide.

серolо́гия *n.* serology.

серп [*gen.* **серпа́**] *n.* sickle. —**серп луны́,** crescent moon.

серпанти́н *n.* (paper) streamer.

сертифика́т *n.* certificate.

се́рый *adj.* **1,** gray. **2,** *fig.* dull; drab.

серьга́ [*pl.* **се́рьги, серёг, серьга́м**] *n.* earring.

серьёзно *adv.* **1,** seriously. Я говорю́ серьезно, I'm serious. **2,** (*in direct address*) seriously?; really?

серьёзность *n.f.* seriousness.

серьёзный *adj.* [*short form* **-зен, -зна**] serious.

се́ссия *n.* session.

сестрá [*pl.* **сёстры, сестёр, сёстрам**] *n.* sister. —**медицúнская сестрá,** (hospital) nurse.
сестрёнка [*gen. pl.* **-нок**] *n.* little sister.
сéстрин *adj.* one's sister's.
сестрúца *also,* **сестрúчка** *n., dim. of* **сестрá.**
сесть [*infl.* **сядy, сядешь;** *past* **сел, сéла**] *v., pfv. of* **садúться.**
сет (сэ) *n., tennis* set.
сéтка [*gen. pl.* **-ток**] *n.* **1,** net. **2,** netting. **3,** window screen. **4,** *colloq.* string bag. **5,** grid.
сéтование *n.* **1,** complaining. **2,** *usu. pl.* complaint.
сéтовать *v. impfv.* [*pfv.* **посéтовать;** *pres.* **-тую, туешь**] **1,** (*with* **на** + *acc. or a dependent clause*) to complain. **2,** (*with* **о** *or a dependent clause*) to lament; bewail; bemoan.
сéттер (сэ, тэ) *n.* setter.
сетчáтка *n.* retina.
сéтчатый *adj.* made of netting or gauze. —**сéтчатая оболóчка,** retina.
сеть [*2nd loc.* **сетú;** *pl.* **сéти, сетéй, сетям**] *n.f.* **1,** net. **2,** network.
сечéние *n.* section: конúческое сечéние, conic section; поперéчное сечéние, cross section.
сéчка [*gen. pl.* **-чек**] *n.* **1,** chopping knife. **2,** fine-cut straw; chaff.
сечь *v. impfv.* [*pres.* **секý, сечёшь, ...секýт**] **1,** [*impfv. only; past* **сек, секлá, секлó**] to cut to pieces; slash. **2,** [*pfv.* **вы́сечь;** *past* **сек, сéкла, сéкло**] to whip; flog. —**сéчься,** *refl.* [*impfv. only*] [*past* **сéкся, секлáсь, секлóсь**] **1,** (*of hair*) to be brittle; break. **2,** (*of fabric*) to tear; fray.
сéялка [*gen. pl.* **-лок**] *n.* seeding machine; seeder.
сéянец [*gen.* **-нца**] *n.* seedling.
сéятель *n.m.* sower.
сéять *v. impfv.* [*pfv.* **посéять;** *pres.* **сéю, сéешь**] to sow.
сжáлиться *v.r. pfv.* (*with* **над**) to take pity on.
сжáтие *n.* **1,** compression. **2,** constriction. **3,** grip; grasp.
сжáтость *n.f.* conciseness.
сжáтый *adj.* **1,** (*of air*) compressed. **2,** (*of fists*) clenched. **3,** concise. —**в сжáтые срóки,** in a short space of time.
сжать[1] [*infl.* **сожмý, сожмёшь**] *v., pfv. of* **сжимáть.** —**сжáться,** *refl., pfv. of* **сжимáться.**
сжать[2] [*infl.* **сожнý, сожнёшь**] *v., pfv. of* **жать**[2].
сжечь [*infl.* **сожгý, сожжёшь,...сожгýт;** *past* **сжёг, сожглá, сожглó**] *v., pfv. of* **жечь** *and* **сжигáть.**
сживáть *v. impfv.* [*pfv.* **сжить**] **1,** *colloq.* to make (someone) move out (*by making life unbearable*). **2,** *in* **сживáть со свéта** *or* **сó свету,** to be the death of. —**сживáться,** *refl.* (*with* **с** + *instr.*) *colloq.* **1,** to make friends with; become friendly with. **2,** to get used to.
сжигáть *v. impfv.* [*pfv.* **сжечь**] to burn.
сжижáть *v. impfv.* [*pfv.* **сжидúть**] to liquefy.
сжижéние *n.* liquefaction.
сжúженный *adj.* liquefied.
сжимáть *v. impfv.* [*pfv.* **сжать**] **1,** to squeeze. **2,** to clench (one's fist, teeth, etc.). **3,** to compress. **4,** to constrict (one's throat). **5,** *fig.* to reduce; condense. —**сжимáться,** *refl.* **1,** to be compressed; be clenched. **2,** to shrink; contract. **3,** to tighten; close. **4,** to shrink; huddle up (from cold, fear, etc.).
сжить [*infl. like* **жить**] *v., pfv. of* **сживáть.** —**сжúться,** *refl.* [*past* **сжúлся, -лáсь, -лóсь**] *pfv. of* **сживáться.**
сзáди *adv.* **1,** behind. **2,** from behind; from the rear. —*prep., with gen.* behind.
сзывáть *v. impfv.* = **созывáть.**
си *n. neut., music* si; ti; B.
сиáмский *adj.* Siamese.
сибарúт *n.* sybarite. —**сибарúтский,** *adj.* sybaritic.
сибúрский *adj.* Siberian. —**сибúрская кóшка,** Persian cat. —**сибúрская язва,** anthrax.
сибиряк [*gen.* **-якá**] *n.m.* [*fem.* **-ячка**] Siberian.
сúвка [*gen. pl.* **-вок**] *n.m. & f., colloq.* gray horse. —*n.f.* golden plover. —**сúвка глýпая,** dotterel.
сивýха *n.* raw vodka.
сúвый *adj.* **1,** (*of a horse*) gray. **2,** *colloq.* (*of hair*) gray.
сиг [*gen.* **сигá**] *n.* whitefish.
сигáра *n.* cigar.
сигарéта *n.* cigarette. —**сигарéтный,** *adj.* cigarette (*attrib.*).
сигáрный *adj.* cigar (*attrib.*).
сигнáл *n.* signal.
сигнализáтор *n.* signaling device.
сигнализáция *n.* **1,** signaling. **2,** alarm system. **3,** signaling system.
сигнализúровать *v. impfv. & pfv.* [*pres.* **-рую, -руешь**] **1,** to signal. **2,** *fig.* (*with acc. or* **о**) to warn (of).
сигнáльный *adj.* signal (*attrib.*). —**сигнáльный огóнь,** signal light; beacon.
сигнáльщик *n.* signalman; flagman.
сигнатýра *n.* label (*on a medicine bottle*).
сидéлка [*gen. pl.* **-лок**] *n.* nurse.
сидéние *n.* sitting.
сúдень [*gen.* **-дня**] *n.m., obs.* stay-at-home. —**сúднем сидéть,** to stay home all the time.
сидéнье *n.* seat.
сидéть *v. impfv.* [*pres.* **сижý, сидúшь**] **1,** to sit; be sitting: сидéть на полý, be sitting on the floor. Сидéть за урóками, to sit doing one's lessons. Сидéть без дéла, to sit around doing nothing. **2,** (*with certain nouns*) to be: сидéть на диéте, to be on a diet. **3,** (*of clothes*) to fit. **4,** to be in prison. —**сидéться,** *refl., used negatively with dat.* to be restless; be unable to sit for long (in a certain place): емý не сидúтся на мéсте, he can't sit still.
сидр *n.* cider. —**сúдровый,** *adj.* cider (*attrib.*).
сидячий *adj.* **1,** sitting. **2,** sedentary. —**сидячая забастóвка,** sit-down strike.
сиéна *n.* sienna.
сизáль *n.m.* sisal.
сúзый *adj.* blue-gray.
сикомóр *n.* sycamore.
сúла *n.* **1,** strength. **2,** force: сúла удáра, the force of a blow. Сúлой орýжия, by force of arms. **3,** power: лошадúная сúла, horsepower. Сúла печáтного слóва, the power of the printed word. **4,** effect; force: вступáть в сúлу, to go into effect/force. **5,** *pl., mil.* forces: вооружённые сúлы, armed forces. **6,** *pl.* forces; elements: реакциóнные сúлы, reactionary forces/elements. —**быть (не) в сúлах,** (not) to be able; (not) have the strength (*fig.*). —**в мéру сил; по мéре сил,** as far as one is able. —**всё, что в (чьих-нибудь) сúлах,** everything in one's power. —**всéми сúлами,** in every way. —**в сúлу** (+ *gen.*), on the strength of; by virtue of. —**изо всех сил,** with all one's might.

—**не под си́лу** (+ *dat.*), too much for; beyond one. —**от си́лы,** at the most. —**че́рез си́лу,** with the utmost difficulty; by forcing oneself. —**что есть сил,** for all one is worth.

сила́ч [*gen.* **-лача́**] *n.* strong man.

силикаге́ль *n.m.* silica gel.

силика́т *n.* silicate.

силико́н *n.* silicone.

си́литься *v.r. impfv., colloq.* to try; make an effort.

силлоги́зм *n.* syllogism. —**силлогисти́ческий; силлоги́ческий,** *adj.* syllogistic.

силово́й *adj.* power (*attrib.*): силова́я ста́нция, power station; power plant.

сило́к [*gen.* **-лка́**] *n.* snare.

силоме́р *n.* dynamometer.

си́лос *n.* **1,** silage. **2,** silo. —**си́лосный,** *adj.* silage (*attrib.*).

силу́эт *n.* silhouette.

си́льно *adv.* **1,** strongly; powerfully. **2,** very much; greatly.

си́льный *adj.* [*short form* **си́лен** *or* **силён, сильна́, си́льно, си́льны** *or* **сильны́**] **1,** strong; powerful. **2,** severe; intense; violent. **3,** (*of a student*) good.

сильф *n.* sylph. —**сильфи́да,** *n.* sylphid.

сим *see* **сей.**

симбио́з *n.* symbiosis.

си́мвол *n.* symbol.

символизи́ровать *v. impfv. & pfv.* [*pres.* **-рую, -руешь**] to symbolize; be symbolic of.

символи́зм *n.* symbolism.

симво́лика *n.* **1,** symbolism. **2,** symbols.

символи́ческий *adj.* symbolic. *Also,* **символи́чный.**

симметри́я *n.* symmetry. —**симметри́ческий; симметри́чный,** *adj.* symmetrical.

симпатизи́ровать *v. impfv.* [*pres.* **-рую, -руешь**] (*with dat.*) **1,** to like; be fond of. **2,** to be in sympathy with.

симпати́ческий *adj., anat.; physiol.* sympathetic: симпати́ческая не́рвная систе́ма, sympathetic nervous system. —**симпати́ческие черни́ла,** invisible ink.

симпати́чный *adj.* likable; nice.

симпа́тия *n.* **1,** (*with* **к**) liking (for). **2,** *pl.* sympathies: симпа́тии слу́шателей, the sympathies of the audience.

симпо́зиум *n.* symposium.

симпто́м *n.* symptom. —**симптомати́ческий,** *adj., med.* symptomatic.

симптомати́чный *adj.* **1,** symptomatic; significant; indicative of something. **2,** = **симптомати́ческий.**

симули́ровать *v. impfv. & pfv.* [*pres.* **-рую, -руешь**] to simulate; feign.

симуля́нт *n.* **1,** simulator. **2,** malingerer.

симуля́ция *n.* **1,** simulation. **2,** malingering.

симфони́ческий *adj.* **1,** symphony (*attrib.*). **2,** symphonic.

симфо́ния *n.* symphony.

синаго́га *n.* synagogue.

синдика́т *n.* syndicate.

синдро́м *n.* syndrome.

синева́ *n.* **1,** blue color. **2,** blue expanse. —**синева́ под глаза́ми,** blue circles under one's eyes.

синева́тый *adj.* bluish.

синегла́зый *adj.* blue-eyed.

синеку́ра *n.* sinecure.

сине́ль *n.f.* chenille.

сине́ть *v. impfv.* [*pfv.* **посине́ть**] **1,** to turn blue; become blue. **2,** [*impfv. only*] (*of anything blue*) to appear.

си́ний *adj.* (dark) blue.

сини́льный *adj., in* **сини́льная кислота́,** prussic acid.

сини́ть *v. impfv.* [*pfv.* **подсини́ть**] **1,** to dye blue. **2,** to rinse in bluing; blue.

сини́ца *n.* titmouse; tomtit.

синко́па *n.* **1,** *music* syncopation. **2,** *gram.* syncope.

синкопи́ровать *v. impfv. & pfv.* [*pres.* **-рую, -руешь**] *music* to syncopate.

сино́д *n.* synod. —**синода́льный,** *adj.* synodal.

сино́ним *n.* synonym. —**синоними́ческий; синоними́чный,** *adj.* synonymous.

сино́птика *n.* weather forecasting. —**сино́птик,** *n.* weather forecaster.

синопти́ческий *adj.* pert. to weather forecasting: синопти́ческая ка́рта, weather map.

си́нтаксис *n.* syntax. —**синтакси́ческий,** *adj.* syntactical.

си́нтез (тэ) *n.* **1,** synthesis. **2,** *physics* fusion.

синтези́ровать (тэ) *v. impfv. & pfv.* [*pres.* **-рую, руешь**] to synthesize.

синтети́ческий (тэ) *adj.* synthetic.

синтои́зм *n.* Shinto; Shintoism.

си́нус *n.* **1,** *math.* sine. **2,** *anat.* sinus. —**синуи́т; синуси́т,** *n.* sinusitis.

синхрониза́ция *n.* synchronization.

синхронизи́ровать *v. impfv. & pfv.* [*pres.* **-рую, руешь**] to synchronize.

синхрони́ческий *adj.* synchronic.

синхро́нный *adj.* synchronous. —**синхро́нный перево́д,** simultaneous translation.

синь *n.f.* blue color.

си́нька *n.* **1,** blueing. **2,** blueprint.

синю́ха *n.* cyanosis.

синю́шность *n.f.* = **синю́ха.**

синя́к [*gen.* **-яка́**] *n.* **1,** bruise; black-and-blue mark. **2,** *in* синяки́ под глаза́ми, dark patches under one's eyes. —**избива́ть до синяко́в,** to beat black-and-blue.

сиони́зм *n.* Zionism. —**сиони́ст,** *n.* Zionist. —**сиони́стский,** *adj.* Zionist.

сип *n.* griffon vulture.

сипе́ть *v. impfv.* [*pres.* **сиплю́, сипи́шь**] **1,** (*of something hot*) to hiss. **2,** to speak in a hoarse voice. **3,** *impers.* to be hoarse: у меня́ в го́рле сипи́т, my throat is hoarse.

си́плый *adj.* hoarse; husky.

си́пнуть *v. impfv.* [*past* **сип** *or* **си́пнул, си́пла**] to become hoarse.

сипу́ха *n.* barn owl.

сире́на *n.* siren.

сире́нь *n.f.* lilac. —**сире́невый,** *adj.* lilac.

си́речь *conj., archaic* that is to say.

сири́ец [*gen.* **-и́йца**] *n.m.* [*fem.* **-и́йка**] Syrian. —**сири́йский,** *adj.* Syrian.

сиро́кко *n.m. indecl.* sirocco.

сиро́п *n.* syrup.

сирота́ [*pl.* **сиро́ты**] *n.m. & f.* orphan. —**кру́глый** *or* **кру́глая сирота́,** child who has lost both parents.

сироте́ть *v. impfv.* [*pfv.* **осироте́ть**] to be orphaned.

сиротли́вый *adj.* lonely.

сиро́тский *adj.* orphan (*attrib.*); orphan's. —**сиро́тский дом** *or* **прию́т,** orphanage; orphan asylum.

сиро́тство *n.* orphanhood.

систе́ма *n.* system.
систематизи́ровать *v. impfv. & pfv.* [*pres.* **-рую, руешь**] to systematize.
системати́ческий *adj.* systematic. —**системати́чески,** *adv.* systematically.
си́стола *n.* systole. —**систоли́ческий,** *adj.* systolic.
си́тец [*gen.* **си́тца**] *n.* printed cotton fabric; chintz.
си́течко [*gen. pl.* **-чек**] *n.* filter; strainer.
си́тник *n.* **1,** rush (*plant*). **2,** *colloq.* bread made of sifted flour.
си́то *n.* sieve; strainer.
ситуа́ция *n.* situation.
си́тцевый *adj.* made of printed cotton; chintz (*attrib.*).
си́филис *n.* syphilis. —**сифили́тик,** *n., colloq.* syphilitic. —**сифилити́ческий,** *adj.* syphilitic.
сифо́н *n.* siphon.
сия́ние *n.* **1,** glow. **2,** halo. **3,** *fig.* radiance. —**се́верное сия́ние,** northern lights; aurora borealis.
сия́ть *v. impfv.* to shine; beam; glow.
скабрёзный *adj.* indecent; off-color; bawdy; dirty. —**скабрёзность,** *n.f.* dirty word; *pl.* indecent language.
сказ *n.* epic tale.
сказа́ние *n.* folk legend.
ска́занное *n., decl. as an adj.* what has been said.
сказа́ть [*infl.* **скажу́, ска́жешь**] *v., pfv. of* **говори́ть.** —**е́сли не сказа́ть** (+ *adj.*), if not... —**мо́жно сказа́ть,** you might say. —**не́чего сказа́ть,** *see* **не́чего.** —**сказа́ть своё сло́во,** to have one's say; make one's presence felt. —**так сказа́ть,** so to speak; as it were. —**хоте́ть сказа́ть,** to mean. —**что́бы не сказа́ть бо́льше,** to say the least.
сказа́ться [*infl.* **скажу́сь, ска́жешься**] *v.r., pfv. of* **ска́зываться.**
сказа́тель *n.m.* teller of folk tales.
ска́зка [*gen. pl.* **-зок**] *n.* tale.
ска́зочник *n.* storyteller.
ска́зочный *adj.* **1,** fairy-tale (*attrib.*). **2,** fabulous; fantastic.
сказу́емое *n., decl. as an adj., gram.* predicate.
ска́зываться *v.r. impfv.* [*pfv.* **сказа́ться**] **1,** *colloq.* to be told. **2,** (*with* **в** + *prepl.*) to be manifest (in); be seen (in). **3,** (*with* **на** + *prepl.*) to have an effect (upon); tell (on *or* upon). **4,** (*with instr.*) *colloq.* to pose as; pretend to be. **5,** *obs.* to give warning; give notice.
скака́лка [*gen. pl.* **-лок**] *n.* jump rope.
скака́ть *v. impfv.* [*pres.* **скачу́, ска́чешь**] **1,** to jump; skip. **2,** to gallop (*on horseback*). **3,** (*of a horse*) to race. —**скака́ть на одно́й ноге́,** to hop.
скаково́й *adj.* racing (*attrib.*). —**скакова́я ло́шадь,** racehorse.
скаку́н [*gen.* **-куна́**] *n.* fast horse; racer.
скала́ [*pl.* **ска́лы**] *n.* **1,** rock. **2,** [*often* **отве́сная скала́**] cliff. —**подво́дная скала́,** reef.
скали́стый *adj.* rocky.
ска́лить *v. impfv., in* **ска́лить зу́бы, 1,** to bare one's teeth. **2,** *colloq.* to laugh; smile; grin.
ска́лка [*gen. pl.* **-лок**] *n.* rolling pin.
ска́лывать *v. impfv.* [*pfv.* **сколо́ть**] **1,** to chop away; chip away. **2,** to pin together.
скальки́ровать *v., pfv. of* **кальки́ровать.**
скалькули́ровать *v., pfv. of* **калькули́ровать.**
скальп *n.* scalp (*taken from the head of an enemy*).
ска́льпель *n.m.* scalpel.
скальпи́ровать *v. impfv. & pfv.* [*pres.* **-рую, -руешь**] to scalp.
скаме́ечка [*gen. pl.* **-чек**] *n.* small bench.
скаме́йка [*gen. pl.* **-ме́ек**] *n.* bench. —**скаме́йка для ног,** footstool.
скамья́ [*pl.* **скамьи́** *or* **ска́мьи, скаме́й, скамья́м**] *n.* **1,** bench. **2,** *in* скамья́ подсуди́мых, the dock. —**со шко́льной скамьи́,** right out of school.
сканда́л *n.* **1,** scandal. **2,** row; brawl.
скандализи́ровать *v. impfv. & pfv.* [*pres.* **-рую, -руешь**] to scandalize.
скандали́ст *n.* trouble-maker; rowdy.
сканда́лить *v. impfv.* [*pfv.* **насканда́лить**] to make a fuss; kick up a row.
сканда́льный *adj.* **1,** scandalous. **2,** rowdy; boisterous. **3,** *colloq.* (*of a person*) always making a fuss.
ска́ндий *n.* scandium.
скандина́в *n.m.* [*fem.* **-на́вка**] Scandinavian. —**скандина́вский,** *adj.* Scandinavian.
сканди́ровать *v. impfv. & pfv.* [*pres.* **-рую, -руешь**] **1,** to scan (verse). **2,** to enunciate. **3,** (*of a crowd*) to chant.
ска́пливать *v. impfv.* [*pfv.* **скопи́ть**] to save up; amass. —**ска́пливаться,** *refl.* **1,** to pile up; accumulate. **2,** to gather; congregate.
скарабе́й *n.* scarab.
скарб *n., colloq.* household belongings.
ска́редный *adj., colloq.* miserly; stingy.
скарлати́на *n.* scarlet fever. —**скарлати́нный,** *adj., colloq.* of scarlet fever.
ска́рмливать *v. impfv.* [*pfv.* **скорми́ть**] to feed: ска́рмливать се́но лошадя́м, to feed hay to the horses.
скат *n.* **1,** slope; incline. **2,** ramp; slide. **3,** *zool.* ray; skate.
ската́ть *v., pfv. of* **ска́тывать** (*in sense #1*).
ска́терть [*pl.* **ска́терти, -те́й, -тя́м**] *n.f.* tablecloth. —**ска́тертью доро́га!,** good riddance!
скати́ть [*infl.* **скачу́, ска́тишь**] *v., pfv. of* **ска́тывать** (*in sense #2*). —**скати́ться,** *refl., pfv. of* **ска́тываться.**
ска́тывать *v. impfv.* **1,** [*pfv.* **ската́ть**] to roll up (*into a ball or bundle*). **2,** [*pfv.* **скати́ть**] to roll down (a slope). —**ска́тываться,** *refl.* [*pfv.* **скати́ться**] **1,** to roll down; slide down. **2,** *fig.* (*with* **в, на,** *or* **к**) to slide into; slip into.
ска́ут *n.* boy scout.
скафа́ндр *n.* **1,** diving suit. **2,** space suit.
ска́чка [*gen. pl.* **-чек**] *n.* **1,** horse race. **2,** *pl.* the races.
скачкообра́зный *adj.* uneven; spasmodic.
скачо́к [*gen.* **-чка́**] *n.* **1,** jump; leap. **2,** *fig.* sudden change. —**скачка́ми,** by leaps and bounds.
ска́шивать *v. impfv.* [*pfv.* **скоси́ть**] **1,** to mow; cut. **2,** *fig.* to strike down; cut down. **3,** to twist; tilt. **4,** to cock (one's eye). **5,** to bevel; miter.
сква́жина *n.* chink; slit. —**замо́чная сква́жина,** keyhole. —**нефтяна́я сква́жина,** oil well.
сквайр *n.* squire.
сквалы́га *n.m. & f., colloq.* cheapskate; skinflint. *Also,* **сквалы́жник,** *n.m.*
сква́ттер (тэ) *n.* squatter.
сквер *n.* public garden.
скве́рно *adv.* badly; bad.
скверносло́в *n.* foul-mouthed person. —**скверносло́вие,** *n.* foul language.

скверносло́вить *v. impfv.* [*pres.* **-влю, -вишь**] to swear; use foul language.

скве́рный *adj.* **1,** foul; nasty. **2,** vulgar; indecent. **3,** *colloq.* bad; awful; lousy.

сквита́ть *v. pfv., obs.* to repay. —**сквита́ться,** *refl.* (*with* **с** + *instr.*) *colloq.* **1,** to settle up (with). **2,** to settle scores (with).

сквози́ть *v. impfv.* **1,** *impers.* to be drafty: здесь сквози́т, there is a draft in here. **2,** (*with* **че́рез**) (*of wind*) to blow through; get through; (*of light*) pass through; filter through. **3,** to be transparent; admit light. **4,** (*with* **сквозь**) to be seen (through). **5,** *fig.* to creep in: в его́ отве́те сквози́ло раздраже́ние, a trace of irritation crept into his answer.

сквозно́й *adj.* **1,** (*of a hole or wound*) going all the way through. **2,** thin; sheer. —**сквозно́й ве́тер,** draft.

сквозня́к [*gen.* **-няка́**] *n.* draft: сиде́ть на сквозняке́, to be (*or* sit) in a draft.

сквозь *prep., with acc.* through: пробира́ться сквозь толпу́, to make one's way through a crowd.

скворе́ц [*gen.* **-рца́**] *n.* starling.

скворе́чник *n.* bird house (*for starlings*). *Also,* **скворе́чня** [*gen. pl.* **-чен**].

скеле́т *n.* skeleton. —**скеле́тный,** *adj.* skeletal.

ске́птик *n.* skeptic. —**скептици́зм,** *n.* skepticism. —**скепти́ческий,** *adj.* skeptical.

ске́рцо *n. indecl.* scherzo.

скетч *n.* sketch; skit.

ски́дка [*gen. pl.* **-док**] *n.* **1,** discount; reduction. **2,** *fig.* (*with* **на** + *acc.*) allowance (for).

ски́дывать *v. impfv.* [*pfv.* **ски́нуть**] **1,** to throw off; throw down. **2,** *fig., colloq.* to overthrow. **3,** *colloq.* to take off. **4,** *fig.* to shake off (laziness, a feeling, etc.). **5,** to take off; knock off (from a price). —**ски́дывать со счето́в,** to rule out; count out.

ски́ния *n., Bib.* tabernacle.

ски́нуть *v., pfv. of* **ски́дывать.**

ски́петр *n.* scepter.

скипида́р *n.* turpentine. —**скипида́рный,** *adj.* turpentine (*attrib.*).

скирд [*gen.* **скирда́**; *pl.* **скирды́, -до́в, -да́м**] *n.* haystack. *Also,* **скирда́** [*pl.* **ски́рды, скирд, -да́м**].

скиса́ть *v. impfv.* [*pfv.* **ски́снуть**] **1,** to turn sour. **2,** *fig., colloq.* to lose heart; lose interest.

ски́снуть [*past* **скис, -ла**] *v., pfv. of* **скиса́ть.**

скита́лец [*gen.* **-льца**] *n.* wanderer. —**скита́ние,** *n.* wandering.

скита́ться *v.r. impfv.* to wander; roam.

скиф *n.* **1,** Scythian. **2,** skiff. —**ски́фский,** *adj.* Scythian.

склад *n.* **1,** supply; stock; store. **2,** warehouse; storehouse; depot. **3,** way; mode; tenor: склад жи́зни, way of life. **4,** style (*of writing or speaking*). **5,** build; physique. **6,** *in* **склад ума́,** mentality; turn of mind. —**ни скла́ду ни ла́ду,** no sense whatever. *See also* **склады́.**

скла́дка [*gen. pl.* **-док**] *n.* **1,** fold; crease; pleat. **2,** wrinkle. —**в скла́дку,** pleated.

скла́дно *adv.* smoothly.

складно́й *adj.* folding; collapsible.

скла́дный *adj., colloq.* **1,** well-built; well-proportioned. **2,** (*of speech*) smooth; (*of something written*) well put together.

скла́дчатый *adj.* pleated.

скла́дчина *n.* pooling of resources. —**в скла́дчину,** jointly.

склады́ [*gen.* **-до́в**] *n. pl., obs.* syllables.—**чита́ть по склада́м,** to read a syllable at a time.

скла́дывать *v. impfv.* [*pfv.* **сложи́ть**] **1,** to lay together; pile (up). **2,** to pack. **3,** to fold. **4,** *math.* to add. **5,** to compose. **6,** to set down; lay down. —**сиде́ть сложа́ ру́ки,** to sit with one's hands folded (*i.e. doing nothing*). —**сложи́ть го́лову за** (+ *acc.*), to lay down one's life (for). —**сложи́ть ору́жие,** to lay down one's arms.

скла́дываться *v.r. impfv.* [*pfv.* **сложи́ться**] **1,** to form; take shape. **2,** to develop. **3,** to fold. **4,** *colloq.* to pool one's resources.

скле́ивать *v. impfv.* [*pfv.* **скле́ить**] to glue together; paste together. —**скле́иваться,** *refl.* to stick together.

скле́ить *v., pfv. of* **кле́ить** *and* **скле́ивать.** —**скле́иться,** *refl., pfv. of* **кле́иться** *and* **скле́иваться.**

склеп *n.* burial vault; crypt.

склёпывать *v. impfv.* [*pfv.* **склепа́ть**] to rivet.

склеро́з *n.* sclerosis. —**склероти́ческий,** *adj.* sclerotic.

скли́кать [*infl.* **скли́чу, скли́чешь**] *v., pfv. of* **скликáть.**

склика́ть *v. impfv.* [*pfv.* **скли́кать**] *colloq.* to call together; summon.

скло́ка *n.* squabble; row.

склон *n.* slope; incline. —**на скло́не лет,** in the twilight of one's life.

склоне́ние *n.* **1,** inclining; disposing. **2,** *gram.* declension. **3,** *astron.* declination.

склони́ть [*infl.* **склоню́, скло́нишь**] *v., pfv. of* **склоня́ть.** —**склони́ться,** *refl., pfv. of* **склоня́ться.**

скло́нность *n.f.* (*with* **к**) **1,** inclination (toward); tendency (toward); disposition (toward). **2,** aptitude (for); talent (for); bent (for).

скло́нный *adj.* [*short form* **-нен, -нна́, -нно**] (*with* **к** *or inf.*) inclined (to); given (to); prone (to).

склоня́емый *adj., gram.* declinable.

склоня́ть *v. impfv.* [*pfv.* **склони́ть**] **1,** to incline; bend; bow. **2,** *in* склоня́ть го́лову пе́ред, to bow to; yield to. **3,** *in* склоня́ть в свою́ по́льзу, to win over; склоня́ть на свою́ сто́рону, to win over to one's side. **4,** *fig.* to persuade. **5,** [*pfv.* **просклоня́ть**] *gram.* to decline. —**склоня́ться,** *refl.* **1,** to bend; bend over. **2,** (*with* **пе́ред**) to submit (to); yield (to). **3,** (*with* **на** + *acc. or* **к**) to lean (toward); be inclined (toward). **4,** (*with* **на** + *acc. or* **к**) *colloq.* to agree (to). **5,** [*impfv. only*] *gram.* to be declined.

скло́чный *adj., colloq.* argumentative; contentious.

скля́нка [*gen. pl.* **-нок**] *n.* **1,** small bottle; vial. **2,** *naut.* bell: во́семь скля́нок, eight bells.

скоба́ [*pl.* **ско́бы, скоб, скоба́м**] *n.* bracket; staple.

ско́бка [*gen. pl.* **-бок**] *n.* **1,** = **скоба́. 2,** *pl.* parentheses. **3,** [*also,* **квадра́тные ско́бки**] brackets. —**в ско́бках,** parenthetically.

скобли́ть *v. impfv.* [*pres.* **скоблю́, ско́блишь** *or* **скобли́шь**] to scrape.

скобяно́й *adj.* hardware (*attrib.*): скобяно́й това́р; скобяны́е изде́лия, hardware.

ско́ванность *n.f.* awkwardness; constraint.

ско́ванный *adj.* awkward; constrained. —**ско́ванный льда́ми,** (*of a river*) frozen over; icebound.

скова́ть [*infl.* **скую́, скуёшь**] *v., pfv. of* **ско́вывать.**

сковорода́ [*pl.* **ско́вороды, сковоро́д, -рода́м**] *n.* frying pan.

сковоро́дка [*gen. pl.* **-док**] *n., colloq.* frying pan.

ско́вывать *v. impfv.* [*pfv.* **скова́ть**] **1,** to make; forge. **2,** to forge together; *fig.* unite. **3,** to chain; shackle. **4,** to constrain. **5,** *mil.* to tie down. **6,** to freeze: лёд скова́л ре́ку, the river was frozen over.

скола́чивать *v. impfv.* [*pfv.* **сколоти́ть**] **1,** to nail together. **2,** to knock together (*i.e.* build). **3,** *fig., colloq.* to put together; form. **4,** *colloq.* to scrape together (money).

сколоти́ть [*infl.* **-лочу́, -ло́тишь**] *v., pfv. of* **скола́чивать.**

сколо́ть [*infl.* **сколю́, ско́лешь**] *v., pfv. of* **ска́лывать.**

сколь *adv., obs.* how.

скольже́ние *n.* sliding; slippage; skid(ding).

скользи́ть *v. impfv.* [*pfv.* **скользну́ть;** *pres.* **-льжу́, -льзи́шь**] **1,** to slide. **2,** to glide (*along a surface*). **3,** to slip. —**скользи́ть по верха́м** *or* **по пове́рхности,** to skim the surface.

ско́льзкий *adj.* [*short form* **-зок, -зка́, -зко**] **1,** slippery. **2,** *fig.* tricky; treacherous. **3,** *fig.* ticklish; delicate. —**ско́льзко,** *adj., used predicatively* slippery: на у́лицах ско́льзко, the streets are slippery.

скользну́ть *v. pfv.* **1,** *pfv. of* **скользи́ть. 2,** (*with* **по**) (*of a bullet*) to graze; glance off. **3,** to slip (into, by, past, under, etc.).

скользя́щий *adj.* sliding: скользя́щая шкала́, sliding scale. —**скользя́щий уда́р,** glancing blow. —**скользя́щий у́зел,** slipknot.

ско́лько *adv.* how much?; how many?: ско́лько миль?, how many miles? Ско́лько э́то сто́ит?, how much does it cost? —**во ско́лько?,** *colloq.* (at) what time? —**ско́лько вре́мени,** *see* **вре́мя.** —**ско́лько ни,** however much; as much as. —**ско́лько хоти́те; ско́лько уго́дно,** as much as you like.

ско́лько-нибудь *adv.* **1,** (*with gen.*) any...at all. **2,** (*with verbs and adjectives*) the least bit.

скома́ндовать *v. pfv.* [*infl.* **-дую, -дуешь**] to order; command.

скомбини́ровать *v., pfv. of* **комбини́ровать.**

ско́мкать *v., pfv. of* **ко́мкать.**

скоморо́х *n., colloq.* buffoon; clown. —**скоморо́шество,** *n., colloq.* buffoonery.

скомпили́ровать *v., pfv. of* **компили́ровать.**

скомпонова́ть *v., pfv. of* **компонова́ть.**

скомпромети́ровать *v., pfv. of* **компромети́ровать.**

сконструи́ровать *v., pfv. of* **конструи́ровать.**

сконфу́женный *adj.* confused; flustered; embarrassed; bewildered.

сконфу́зить *v., pfv. of* **конфу́зить.** —**сконфу́зиться,** *refl., pfv. of* **конфу́зиться.**

сконцентри́ровать *v., pfv. of* **концентри́ровать.** —**сконцентри́роваться,** *refl., pfv. of* **концентри́роваться.**

сконча́ться *v.r. pfv.* to die; pass away.

скопа́ *n.* osprey.

скопе́ц [*gen.* **-пца́**] *n.* **1,** castrated man or boy. **2,** *hist.* member of the *skoptsy,* a religious sect practicing castration.

скопидо́м *n., colloq.* cheapskate; skinflint. —**скопидо́мство,** *n., colloq.* miserliness.

скопи́ровать *v., pfv. of* **копи́ровать.**

скопи́ть [*infl.* **скоплю́, ско́пишь**] *v., pfv. of* **ска́пливать.** —**скопи́ться,** *refl., pfv. of* **ска́пливаться.**

ско́пище *n.* crowd; throng.

скопле́ние *n.* **1,** accumulating; accumulation. **2,** crowd; accumulation; concentration.

ско́пом *adv., colloq.* in a group; in a crowd; en masse.

скорбе́ть *v. impfv.* [*pres.* **-блю́, -би́шь**] to grieve; mourn.

ско́рбный *adj.* sorrowful; mournful. —**ско́рбно,** *adv.* sorrowfully; sadly.

скорбь *n.f.* grief; sorrow.

скоре́е *also,* **скоре́й** *adj., comp. of* **ско́рый.** —*adv.* **1,** *comp. of* **ско́ро. 2,** hurry up! Иди́ скоре́й!, come quickly! **3,** rather; sooner. **4,** more likely. **5,** more: скоре́е похо́ж на, more like. —**скоре́е всего́,** most probably; most likely.

скорлупа́ [*pl.* **-лу́пы**] *n.* shell (*of an egg, nut, etc.*). —**уйти́ в свою́ скорлупу́,** to withdraw into one's shell.

скорми́ть [*infl.* **скормлю́, ско́рмишь**] *v., pfv. of* **ска́рмливать.**

скорня́жный *adj.* fur (*attrib.*).

скорня́к [*gen.* **-няка́**] *n.* furrier.

ско́ро *adv.* **1,** fast; quickly. **2,** soon. —**не ско́ро,** not for some time; not for a long time.

скорогово́рка [*gen. pl.* **-рок**] *n.* **1,** rapid speech; patter. **2,** tongue twister.

скоро́мный *adj.* not to be eaten on fast days. —**скоро́мный день,** non-fast day.

скоропали́тельный *adj., colloq.* hasty; rash.

ско́ропись *n.f.* cursive writing.

скороподъёмность *n.f., aero.* rate of climb.

скоропо́ртящийся *adj.* perishable.

скоропости́жный *adj.* (*of death*) sudden.

скоро́спелый *adj.* **1,** early-ripening; fast-maturing. **2,** *fig., colloq.* hasty; premature.

скоростни́к [*gen.* **-ника́**] *n.* high-speed worker.

скоростно́й *adj.* **1,** of speed; speed (*attrib.*). **2,** high-speed. —**скоростно́й бег на конька́х,** speed skating.

скоростре́льный *adj.* (*of a gun*) rapid-firing.

ско́рость [*pl.* **ско́рости, -сте́й, -стя́м**] *n.f.* **1,** speed; velocity. **2,** gear: переключа́ться на пе́рвую ско́рость, to shift into first gear.

скоросшива́тель *n.m.* binder (*for papers*).

скорота́ть *v., pfv. of* **корота́ть.**

скороте́чный *adj.* transitory; short-lived.

скорохо́д *n.* **1,** *obs.* footman. **2,** *colloq.* fast runner.

скорпио́н *n.* **1,** scorpion. **2,** *cap.* Scorpio.

ско́рчить *v., pfv. of* **ко́рчить.** —**ско́рчиться,** *refl., pfv. of* **ко́рчиться.**

ско́рый *adj.* **1,** fast; quick; swift; speedy. **2,** impending; forthcoming. —**в ско́ром бу́дущем,** in the near future. —**в ско́ром вре́мени,** before long; shortly. —**на ско́рую ру́ку, 1,** in a slapdash manner. **2,** in a hurry; on the run. —**ско́рая по́мощь, 1,** first aid. **2,** *colloq.* ambulance.

скос *n.* **1,** slope; slant. **2,** bevel; miter.

скоси́ть *v. pfv.* **1,** [*infl.* **скошу́, ско́сишь**] *pfv. of* **коси́ть**[1] *and* **ска́шивать** (*in senses #1 & #2*). **2,** [*infl.* **скошу́, скоси́шь**] *pfv. of* **коси́ть**[2] *and* **ска́шивать** (*in senses #3, 4, 5*).

скот [*gen.* **скота́;** *acc.* **скот**] *n.* cattle; livestock. —**ме́лкий рога́тый скот,** sheep and goats. —**кру́пный рога́тый скот,** cattle (*cows, oxen, etc.*). —**рабо́чий скот,** draft animals.

скоти́на *n., colloq.* **1,** = **скот. 2,** animal.

скóтник *n.* **1,** person who tends cattle. **2,** *colloq.* cattle yard.
скóтный *adj.* cattle (*attrib.*). —**скóтный двор, 1,** stockyard. **2,** farmyard.
скотобóйня [*gen. pl.* **-бóен**] *n.* slaughterhouse.
скотовóд *n.* cattle breeder. —**скотовóдство,** *n.* cattle raising; cattle breeding. —**скотовóдческий,** *adj.* cattle-breeding (*attrib.*).
скотолóжство *n.* sodomy.
скотопригóнный *adj., in* **скотопригóнный двор,** stockyard.
скóтский *adj.* **1,** cattle (*attrib.*). **2,** *fig.* like that of an animal.
скóтство *n.* **1,** animal-like existence. **2,** *colloq.* crudity; barbarity.
скрáдывать *v. impfv.* to conceal.
скрáшивать *v. impfv.* [*pfv.* **скрáсить**] **1,** to make more attractive. **2,** *fig.* to soften the effect of; tone down; relieve. **3,** *fig.* to brighten up (one's life, existence, etc.).
скребнѝца *n.* currycomb.
скребóк [*gen.* **-бкá**] *n.* scraper.
скрéжет *n.* **1,** grinding; grating; clanking. **2,** grinding; gnashing (*of teeth*).
скрежетáть *v. impfv.* [*pres.* **скрежещý, скрежéщешь**] **1,** *v.i.* to grind; grate; clank. **2,** (*with instr.*) to grind; gnash (one's teeth).
скрéпа *n.* **1,** clamp; brace. **2,** *fig.* tie; bond. **3,** countersignature.
скрепить [*infl.* **-плю́, -пи́шь**] *v., pfv. of* **скреплять.**
скрéпка [*gen. pl.* **-пок**] *n.* paper clip.
скреплять *v. impfv.* [*pfv.* **скрепи́ть**] **1,** to fasten together; clamp together. **2,** *fig.* to cement (a friendship, ties, etc.). **3,** to countersign. —**скрепя́ сéрдце,** reluctantly; grudgingly.
скрести́ *v. impfv.* [*pres.* **скребý, скребёшь;** *past* **скрёб, скреблá, скребló**] to scrape. —**скрести́сь,** *refl.* (*of a cat, mouse, etc.*) to scratch; make a scratching noise.
скрести́ть [*infl.* **-щý, -сти́шь**] *v., pfv. of* **скрéщивать.**
скрещéние *n.* **1,** crossing: скрещéние шпаг, crossing of swords. **2,** crossing; intersection.
скрéщивание *n.* **1,** crossing. **2,** crossbreeding.
скрéщивать *v. impfv.* [*pfv.* **скрести́ть**] **1,** to cross; place crosswise. **2,** to cross; crossbreed. —**скрéщивать шпáги** *or* **мечи́,** to cross swords.
скриви́ть *v., pfv. of* **криви́ть.** —**скриви́ться,** *refl., pfv. of* **криви́ться.**
скрижáль *n.f.* **1,** tablet (*bearing a sacred text*). **2,** *pl.* (*with gen.*) annals (of).
скрип *n.* squeak; creak.
скрипáч [*gen.* **-пачá**] *n.m.* [*fem.* **-пáчка**] violinist.
скрипéть *v. impfv.* [*pfv.* **проскрипéть;** *pres.* **-плю́, -пи́шь**] to squeak; creak.
скрипи́чный *adj.* violin (*attrib.*). —**скрипи́чный ключ,** treble clef.
скри́пка [*gen. pl.* **-пок**] *n.* violin. —**игрáть пéрвую скри́пку,** to play the leading role; be top dog. —**игрáть вторýю скри́пку,** to play second fiddle.
скрипýчий *adj., colloq.* squeaky; creaky.
скрои́ть *v., pfv. of* **крои́ть.**
скрóмник *n.* modest person.
скрóмничать *v. impfv.* to be excessively modest.
скрóмный *adj.* modest. —**скрóмно,** *adv.* modestly. —**скрóмность,** *n.f.* modesty.
скрупулёзный *adj.* scrupulous; meticulous.
скрути́ть *v. pfv.* [*infl.* **скручý, скрýтишь**] **1,** *pfv. of* **крути́ть** (*in sense #2*) *and* **скрýчивать. 2,** *colloq.* to subdue; bend to one's will. **3,** *colloq.* (*of an illness*) to lay (someone) low.
скрýчивать *v. impfv.* [*pfv.* **скрути́ть**] **1,** to twist (cloth, rope, etc.). **2,** to roll (a cigarette). **3,** to tie up; bind securely. **4,** *in* скрути́ть рýки комý-нибудь за спинóй, to tie/twist someone's arms behind his back.
скрывáть *v. impfv.* [*pfv.* **скрыть**] to hide; conceal. —**скрывáться,** *refl.* **1,** to hide; be hiding. **2,** to disappear: скрывáться из виду, to disappear from view; pass out of sight. **3,** [*impfv. only*] to be concealed. **4,** *colloq.* to steal away; make off.
скры́тие *n.* hiding; concealment.
скры́тничать *v. impfv., colloq.* to be secretive.
скры́тность *n.f.* **1,** secretiveness. **2,** *colloq.* secrecy.
скры́тный *adj.* secretive.
скры́тый *adj.* **1,** hidden; concealed. **2,** latent.
скрыть [*infl.* **скрóю, скрóешь**] *v., pfv. of* **скрывáть.** —**скры́ться,** *refl., pfv. of* **скрывáться.**
скрю́чивать *v. impfv.* [*pfv.* **скрю́чить**] *colloq.* **1,** to bend. **2,** *impers.* to be bent: егó скрю́чило от бóли, he was doubled up in pain. —**скрю́чиваться,** *refl., colloq.* to be bent; be doubled up.
скря́га *n.m. & f.* miser; skinflint.
скря́жничать *v. impfv., colloq.* to be a miser.
скудéть *v. impfv.* [*pfv.* **оскудéть**] to become depleted.
скýдный *adj.* scanty; meager. —**скýдность; скýдость,** *n.f.* scarcity; paucity.
скýка *n.* boredom.
скулá [*pl.* **скýлы**] *n.* cheekbone.
скулáстый *adj.* having high cheekbones.
скули́ть *v. impfv.* to whine; whimper.
скýльптор *n.* sculptor.
скульптýра *n.* sculpture.
скульптýрный *adj.* **1,** sculptural; sculptor's. **2,** *fig.* statuesque.
скýмбрия *n.* mackerel.
скунс *n.* skunk. —**скýнсовый,** *adj.* skunk (*attrib.*).
скупáть *v. impfv.* [*pfv.* **скупи́ть**] to buy up.
скупердя́й *n., colloq.* cheapskate; skinflint; tightwad.
скупéц [*gen.* **-пцá**] *n.* miser.
скупи́ть [*infl.* **скуплю́, скýпишь**] *v., pfv. of* **скупáть.**
скупи́ться *v.r. impfv.* [*pfv.* **поскупи́ться;** *pres.* **скуплю́сь, скупи́шься**] **1,** to be stingy. **2,** to scrimp; skimp. **3,** (*with* **на** + *acc. pl.*) to stint; be sparing with.
скупóй *adj.* **1,** stingy. **2,** (*of light, soil, sun, etc.*) poor; weak; (*of rainfall, supplies, rations, etc.*) meager. **3,** (*with* **на** + *acc. pl.*) sparing (with). —**скýпо,** *adv.* stingily. —**скýпость,** *n.f.* stinginess.
скýпщик *n.* buyer (*of items for resale*).
скуфья́ [*gen. pl.* **-фéй**] *n.* skullcap. *Also,* **скуфéйка** [*gen. pl.* **-фéек**].
скучáть *v. impfv.* **1,** to be bored. **2,** (*with* **по** + *dat., but prepl. with pers. pronouns*) to miss; long for; yearn for.
скучáющий *adj.* bored.
скýченный *adj.* congested; overcrowded. —**скýченность,** *n.f.* congestion; overcrowding.
скýчиваться *v.r. impfv.* [*pfv.* **скýчиться**] *colloq.* to crowd together; cluster.
скýчно *adv.* in a boring manner. —*adj., used predicatively* **1,** bored: мне скýчно, I am bored. **2,** boring: скýчно сидéть одномý, it is boring to be alone.

скýчный *adj.* **1,** boring; tiresome; tedious. **2,** bored.

скýшать *v. pfv.* to eat; eat up.

слабéть *v. impfv.* [*pfv.* **ослабéть**] **1,** to weaken; become weak; grow weak. **2,** (*of one's health, eyesight, etc.*) to fail; get worse. **3,** to slacken; subside.

слабинá *n.* **1,** slack (*in a rope*). **2,** weak spot.

слаби́тельный *adj.* cathartic; purgative. —**слаби́тельное,** *n.* laxative.

слáбить *v. impfv., impers.* to have diarrhea: егó слáбит, he has diarrhea.

слáбо *adv.* **1,** weakly; faintly. **2,** poorly.

слабовóлие *n.* weakness of will. —**слабовóльный,** *adj.* weak-willed.

слаборáзвитый *adj.* (*of countries*) underdeveloped.

слабоси́лие *n.* weakness; lack of strength.

слабоси́льный *adj.* **1,** weak; feeble. **2,** low-powered.

слáбость *n.f.* weakness. Имéть слáбость к, to have a weakness for.

слабоýмие *n.* feeble-mindedness.

слабоýмный *adj.* feeble-minded. —*n.* feeble-minded person; imbecile; moron.

слáбый *adj.* **1,** weak. **2,** faint; slight. **3,** poor; weak; bad. **4,** loose; lax; slack.

слáва *n.* **1,** glory. **2,** fame. **3,** reputation. **4,** *colloq.* rumors; talk. —**во слáву** (+ *gen.*), to the glory of. —**на слáву,** marvelously; wonderfully well: удáться на слáву, to be a great success. —**слáва бóгу!**, *see* **бог.**

слави́ст *n.* Slavicist. —**слави́стика,** *n.* Slavic studies.

слáвить *v. impfv.* [*pres.* **-влю, -вишь**] **1,** to glorify. **2,** to sing the praises of. —**слáвиться,** *refl.* (*with instr. or* **как**) to be famous (for *or* as); be renowned (for).

слáвка [*gen. pl.* **-вок**] *n.* warbler.

слáвно *adv., colloq.* wonderfully. —*adj., used predicatively, colloq.* nice; wonderful: как слáвно!, how nice!; how wonderful!

слáвный *adj.* **1,** glorious. **2,** famous; renowned. **3,** *colloq.* nice.

славословие *n.* **1,** glorification. **2,** *pl.* paeans of praise.

славяни́н [*pl.* **-я́не, -я́н**] *n.m.* [*fem.* **-я́нка**] Slav.

славянофи́л *n.* Slavophile.

славя́нский *adj.* Slavic; Slavonic.

слагáемое *n., decl. as an adj.* element; component.

слагáть *v. impfv.* [*pfv.* **сложи́ть**] **1,** to compose. **2,** (*with* **с себя́**) to give up; relinquish; decline. —**слагáться,** *refl.* [*impfv. only*] (*with* **из**) to be composed of; consist of.

слад *n., colloq., in* **слáду нет с** (+ *instr.*), he (she) is impossible; there is no dealing with him (her).

слáдить [*infl.* **-жу, -дишь**] *v., pfv. of* **слáживать.**

слáдкий *adj.* [*short form* **-док, -дкá, -дко;** *comp.* **слáще**] sweet. —**слáдкое мя́со,** sweetbread.

слáдко *adv.* sweetly; sweet.

слáдкое *n., decl. as an adj.* **1,** sweets. **2,** dessert.

сладкоéжка [*gen. pl.* **-жек**] *n.m. & f., colloq.* person with a sweet tooth.

сладкозвýчный *adj.* sweet-sounding.

сладкоречи́вый *adj.* smooth-spoken.

слáдостный *adj.* sweet.

сладострáстие *n.* sensuality. —**сладострáстный,** *adj.* sensual.

слáдость *n.f.* **1,** sweetness. **2,** *pl.* sweets. **3,** *fig., colloq.* delight.

слáженный *adj.* harmonious; well-coordinated. —**слáженность,** *n.f.* harmony.

слáживать *v. impfv.* [*pfv.* **слáдить**] *colloq.* **1,** to arrange. **2,** (*with* **с** + *instr.*) to handle; cope (with).

слáзить *v. pfv.* [*infl.* **слáжу, слáзишь**] **1,** to climb up (to an attic, onto a roof, etc.). **2,** to go down (to a cellar, basement, etc.).

слáлом *n.* slalom.

слáнец [*gen.* **-нца**] *n.* slate; shale. —**слáнцевый,** *adj.* slate (*attrib.*); shale (*attrib.*).

сластёна *n.m. & f., colloq.* person with a sweet tooth.

слáсти [*gen.* **-стéй;** *dat.* **-стя́м**] *n. pl.* sweets.

сластолюби́вый *adj.* sensual.

слать *v. impfv.* [*pfv.* **послáть;** *pres.* **шлю, шлёшь**] to send.

слащáвый *adj.* sugary; honeyed.

слáще *adj., comp. of* **слáдкий.**

слéва *adv.* **1,** from the left. **2,** to (*or* on) the left.

слегкá *adv.* **1,** slightly; a little. **2,** lightly; gently.

след [*gen.* **следá** *or* **слéда;** *dat.* **слéду;** *2nd loc.* **следý;** *pl.* **следы́**] *n.* **1,** track: свéжие следы́, fresh tracks. **2,** trail: напáсть на след (+ *gen.*), to come upon the trail of... **3,** trace: от э́того не остáлось ни следá, not a trace of it remains. **4,** footprint; footstep. **5,** mark; scar: следы́ шин, tire marks; следы́ óспы, smallpox scars. *See also* **слéдом.**

следи́ть *v. impfv.* [*pres.* **слежý, следи́шь**] (*with* **за** + *instr.*) **1,** to follow (*with one's eye*). **2,** to watch; look after; keep an eye on. **3,** to see that (order, discipline, etc.) is maintained. **4,** *fig.* to follow; keep abreast of. **5,** to keep under surveillance. **6,** [*pfv.* **наследи́ть**] *colloq.* to leave footmarks: следи́ть сапогáми на полý, to track up the floor.

слéдование *n.* **1,** following. **2,** movement; travel. —**пóезд дáльнего слéдования,** long-distance train.

слéдователь *n.m.* investigator.

слéдовательно *adv.* consequently.

слéдовать *v. impfv.* [*pres.* **-дую, -дуешь**] **1,** [*pfv.* **послéдовать**] (*with* **за** + *instr.*) to follow; come *or* go after: слéдовать за проводникóм, to follow the guide. Лéто слéдует за веснóй, summer follows spring. **2,** [*pfv.* **послéдовать**] (*with dat.*) to follow (rules, advice, an example, etc.). **3,** *impers.* (*with* **из**) to follow (from): из э́того слéдует, что..., from this it follows that... **4,** (*with* **в** *or* **до**) (*of a train or ship*) to be bound for. **5,** *impers.* one should: слéдует отмéтить, что..., it should be noted that... Как и слéдовало ожидáть, as was to be expected. **6,** *impers.* (*with* **с** + *gen.*) to be owed; be due: скóлько с меня́ слéдует?, how much do I owe? —**как слéдует,** properly. —**комý слéдует,** to the proper person. —**кудá слéдует,** to the proper quarter.

слéдом *adv.* **1,** right behind; in someone's footsteps. **2,** immediately afterward. —**слéдом за** (+ *instr.*), right after; immediately after.

следопы́т *n.* **1,** hunter (who tracks down animals). **2,** *fig.* pioneer; trailblazer.

слéдственный *adj.* of inquiry; investigatory.

слéдствие *n.* **1,** consequence; result. **2,** investigation; inquiry. —**причи́на и слéдствие,** cause and effect.

слéдуемый *adj.* due: слéдуемая мне сýмма, the amount due me.

слéдующий *adj.* **1,** next: на слéдующий день, the next day. **2,** following: слéдующим óбразом, in the following manner. —**слéдующее,** *n.* the following.

слежа́ться [*infl.* **-жи́ться**] *v.r., pfv. of* **слёживаться.**

слеже́ние *n., aerospace* tracking; monitoring. —**ста́нция слеже́ния,** tracking station.

слёживаться *v.r. impfv.* [*pfv.* **слежа́ться**] **1,** to become firmly packed. **2,** to become rumpled (*from lying around a long time*).

сле́жка *n.* surveillance: установи́ть сле́жку за (+ *instr.*), to place under surveillance.

слеза́ [*pl.* **слёзы, слёз, слеза́м**] *n.* tear: быть в слеза́х, to be in tears.

слеза́ть *v. impfv.* [*pfv.* **слезть**] (*with* **с** + *gen.*) **1,** to climb down (from). **2,** to dismount (from). **3,** *colloq.* to get off (a train, bus, etc.). **4,** *colloq.* (*of paint, skin, etc.*) to come off.

слези́нка [*gen. pl.* **-нок**] *n.* tear; teardrop.

слези́ться *v.r. impfv.* (*of one's eyes*) to water; tear.

слезли́вый *adj.* **1,** easily moved to tears. **2,** tearful. **3,** *fig.* overly sentimental; maudlin.

слёзный *adj.* **1,** tear (*attrib.*); lachrymal: слёзный прото́к, tear duct. **2,** *colloq.* plaintive.

слезоточи́вый *adj.* (*of one's eyes*) teary. —**слезоточи́вый газ,** tear gas.

слезть [*infl. like* **лезть**] *v., pfv. of* **слеза́ть.**

слепе́нь [*gen.* **-пня́**] *n.m.* horsefly.

слепе́ц [*gen.* **-пца́**] *n.* blind man.

слепи́ть[1] *v. impfv.* [*pres.* **слеплю́, слепи́шь**] **1,** *obs.* to blind. **2,** to dazzle.

слепи́ть[2] [*infl.* **слеплю́, сле́пишь**] *v., pfv. of* **лепи́ть** (*in sense #2*) *and* **слепля́ть.** —**слепи́ться,** *refl., pfv. of* **слепля́ться.**

слепля́ть *v. impfv.* [*pfv.* **слепи́ть**] to glue together; paste together. —**слепля́ться,** *refl.* to stick together; become stuck.

сле́пнуть *v. impfv.* [*pfv.* **осле́пнуть;** *past* **слеп** *or* **сле́пнул, сле́пла**] to go blind; lose one's eyesight.

сле́по *adv.* blindly.

слепо́й *adj.* blind. —*n.* blind man.

сле́пок [*gen.* **-пка**] *n.* cast; mold.

слепорождённый *adj.* blind from birth.

слепота́ *n.* blindness.

слепы́ш [*gen.* **-пыша́**] *n.* mole rat.

сле́сарный *adj.* metalworking (*attrib.*); locksmith (*attrib.*). *Also,* **сле́сарский.**

сле́сарь [*pl.* **слесаря́** *or* **сле́сари**] *n.m.* **1,** metalworker. **2,** locksmith.

слёт *n.* **1,** flight (*of birds*). **2,** *fig.* gathering; meeting; rally.

слета́ть[1] *v. impfv.* [*pfv.* **слете́ть**] **1,** (*with* **с** + *gen.*) to fly down (from). **2,** to fly away. **3,** (*with* **с** + *gen.*) to slip off; fall off. **4,** *colloq.* to jump down. **5,** *fig.* (*of a feeling*) to pass; disappear. **6,** *in* **слета́ть с губ/уст/языка́,** to escape one's lips. —**слета́ться,** *refl.* to fly in (*from many places*); come flying in.

слета́ть[2] *v. pfv.* to fly (*to a certain place and return*).

слете́ть [*infl.* **-чу́, -ти́шь**] *v., pfv. of* **слета́ть**[1]. —**слете́ться,** *refl., pfv. of* **слета́ться.**

слечь *v. pfv.* [*infl. like* **лечь**] to take ill; take to one's bed.

сли́ва *n.* **1,** plum. **2,** plum tree.

слива́ть *v. impfv.* [*pfv.* **слить**] **1,** to pour off; pour out. **2,** to pour together. **3,** *fig.* to combine; merge. —**слива́ться,** *refl.* **1,** (*of rivers*) to meet; converge. **2,** (*of organizations*) to merge. **3,** (*of sounds, colors, etc.*) to blend. Слива́ться с фо́ном, to melt into the background.

сли́вки [*gen.* **-вок**] *n. pl.* cream. —**сли́вки о́бщества,** the cream of society.

сли́вовый *adj.* plum (*attrib.*).

сли́вочник *n.* creamer; cream pot.

сли́вочный *adj.* **1,** cream (*attrib.*). **2,** creamy. —**сли́вочное моро́женое,** ice cream. —**сли́вочный сыр,** cream cheese.

слива́нка *n.* plum brandy.

слиза́ть [*infl.* **слижу́, сли́жешь**] *v., pfv. of* **сли́зывать.**

сли́зень [*gen.* **-зня**] *n.m., zool.* slug.

сли́зистый *adj.* **1,** slimy. **2,** *anat.* mucous: сли́зистая оболо́чка, mucous membrane.

слизня́к [*gen.* **-няка́**] *n., zool.* slug.

сли́зывать *v. impfv.* [*pfv.* **слиза́ть**] to lick off.

слизь *n.f.* **1,** mucus. **2,** [*also,* **расти́тельная слизь**] mucilage. **3,** slime.

слиня́лый *adj., colloq.* faded.

слиня́ть *v. pfv., colloq.* to fade.

слипа́ться *v.r. impfv.* [*pfv.* **сли́пнуться**] **1,** to stick together. **2,** [*impfv. only*] (*of one's eyes*) to be heavy with sleep: у меня́ глаза́ слипа́ются, I can hardly keep my eyes open.

сли́пнуться [*past* **сли́пся, сли́плась**] *v.r., pfv. of* **слипа́ться.**

сли́тно *adv.* **1,** together. **2,** (*of a way of spelling*) as one word.

сли́тный *adj.* **1,** continuous; unbroken. **2,** (*of spelling*) as one word.

сли́ток [*gen.* **-тка**] *n.* **1,** ingot; bar. **2,** *pl.* bullion: зо́лото в сли́тках, gold bullion.

слить [*infl.* **солью́, сольёшь;** *past fem.* **слила́**] *v., pfv. of* **слива́ть.** —**сли́ться,** *refl.* [*past* **сли́лся, -ла́сь, -ло́сь**] *pfv. of* **слива́ться.**

слича́ть *v. impfv.* [*pfv.* **сличи́ть**] to compare (against each other).

сли́шком *adv.* **1,** too. **2,** (*with certain verbs*) too much; excessively. —**сли́шком мно́го,** too much; too many.

слия́ние *n.* **1,** blending (*of styles, colors, etc.*). **2,** confluence (*of rivers*). **3,** merger; amalgamation; union.

слобода́ [*pl.* **сло́боды, слобо́д, слобода́м**] *n., hist.* settlement inhabited by tradesmen or free peasants.

слова́к *n.m.* [*fem.* **-ва́чка**] Slovak.

слова́рный *adj.* **1,** dictionary (*attrib.*). **2,** lexical.

слова́рь [*gen.* **-варя́**] *n.m.* **1,** dictionary. **2,** vocabulary.

слова́цкий *adj.* Slovak.

слове́нец [*gen.* **-нца**] *n.m.* [*fem.* **-нка**] Slovene. —**слове́нский,** *adj.* Slovenian.

слове́сник *n.* **1,** teacher of Russian language and literature. **2,** *obs.* philologist.

слове́сность *n.f., obs.* **1,** literature. **2,** philology.

слове́сный *adj.* **1,** verbal; oral. **2,** *obs.* philological.

слове́чко [*gen. pl.* **-чек**] *n., dim. of* **сло́во.** —**замо́лвить** *or* **заки́нуть слове́чко за** (+ *acc.*), to put in a word for.

сло́вник *n.* word list (*for a dictionary*); subject list (*for an encyclopedia*).

сло́вно *conj.* **1,** as if; as though. **2,** like.

сло́во [*pl.* **слова́, слов, слова́м**] *n.* **1,** word. **2,** one's word: сдержа́ть (своё) сло́во, to keep one's word. **3,** the floor: проси́ть сло́ва, to ask for the floor. —**в двух слова́х,** in a few words; briefly. —**други́ми слова́ми,** in other words. —**игра́ слов,** play on words. —**к сло́ву (сказа́ть),** by the way. —**на слова́х, 1,** orally. **2,** in words. —**одни́м сло́вом,** in a word. —**от сло́ва**

до сло́ва, from beginning to end. —**по слова́м** (+ *gen.*), according to. —**слов нет,** *colloq.* there is no denying; it must be said that... —**сло́во в сло́во,** word for word. —**сло́во за́ слово,** gradually; as the conversation progressed. —**сло́вом,** in a word. —**с пе́рвого сло́ва,** right at the outset (of the conversation). —**челове́к сло́ва,** a man of his word.

словоохо́тливый *adj.* talkative; loquacious.

словосочета́ние *n.* combination of words. —**усто́йчивое словосочета́ние,** set expression.

слог [*pl.* **сло́ги, слого́в, слога́м**] *n.* **1,** syllable. **2,** *obs.* style.

слогово́й *adj.* syllabic.

слоёный *adj.* puff (*attrib.*); flaky. —**слоёный пиро́г,** puff pastry. —**слоёное те́сто,** puff paste.

сложе́ние *n.* **1,** *math.* addition. **2,** build; physique.

сложённый *adj.* built: хорошо́ сложённый ю́ноша, well-built young man.

сложи́ть [*infl.* **сложу́, сло́жишь**] *v., pfv. of* **скла́дывать** *and* **слага́ть.** —**сложи́ться,** *refl., pfv. of* **скла́дываться.**

сло́жно *adv.* in a complicated way.

сложноподчинённый *adj., in* **сложноподчинённое предложе́ние,** complex sentence.

сложносочинённый *adj., in* **сложносочинённое предложе́ние,** compound sentence.

сло́жность *n.f.* **1,** complexity. **2,** *pl.* difficulties. —**в о́бщей сло́жности,** in all; a total of; all told.

сло́жный *adj.* **1,** complex; complicated. **2,** difficult. **3,** intricate. **4,** (*of words, interest, etc.*) compound.

слои́стый *adj.* stratified; laminated. —**слои́стые облака́,** strati.

слой [*pl.* **слои́, слоёв**] *n.* **1,** layer. **2,** coat (*of paint*). **3,** *geol.* stratum. **4,** (social) stratum: все слои́ населе́ния, all strata (*or* segments) of the population.

сло́йка [*gen. pl.* **сло́ек**] *n.* puff (*piece of pastry*).

слом *n.* tearing down; dismantling; demolition.

слома́ть *v., pfv. of* **лома́ть.** —**слома́ться,** *refl., pfv. of* **лома́ться** (*in sense #1*).

сломи́ть *v. pfv.* [*infl.* **сломлю́, сло́мишь**] **1,** to break; smash; shatter. **2,** to defeat; crush. **3,** *fig.* to break (a person, one's spirit, will, resistance, etc.). **4,** *in* **сломя́ го́лову,** at breakneck speed; like mad. —**сломи́ться,** *refl., colloq.* to break.

слон [*gen.* **слона́**] *n.* **1,** elephant. **2,** *chess* bishop. **3,** *in* **морско́й слон,** sea elephant; elephant seal. —**де́лать из му́хи слона́,** to make a mountain out of a molehill.

слонёнок [*gen.* **-нка;** *pl.* **-ня́та, -ня́т**] *n.* baby elephant; young elephant.

слони́ха *n.* she-elephant.

слоно́вость *n.f.* elephantiasis.

слоно́вый *adj.* elephant (*attrib.*). —**слоно́вая боле́знь,** elephantiasis. —**слоно́вая кость,** ivory.

слоня́ться *v.r. impfv., colloq.* to loiter; drift (*from place to place*).

сло́пать *v., pfv. of* **ло́пать.**

слуга́ [*pl.* **слу́ги**] *n.m.* servant; manservant.

служа́нка [*gen. pl.* **-нок**] *n.* servant; maid.

слу́жащий *n., decl. as an adj.* employee; office worker.

слу́жба *n.* **1,** service. **2,** work; job. **3,** church service. —**сослужи́ть слу́жбу,** *see* **сослужи́ть.**

служе́бный *adj.* **1,** office (*attrib.*); official. **2,** auxiliary; secondary.

служе́ние *n.* serving; service.

служи́тель *n.m.* **1,** *obs.* servant. **2,** attendant. —**служи́тель ку́льта,** clergyman.

служи́ть *v. impfv.* [*pfv.* **послужи́ть;** *pres.* **служу́, слу́жишь**] **1,** to serve. **2,** (*with dat.*) to serve; be in the service of. **3,** (*with instr.*) to serve (as); function (as). **4,** *v.t.* [*impfv. only*] *eccl.* to officiate at; conduct (a service, mass, etc.). **5,** [*impfv. only*] (*of a dog*) to beg.

слупи́ть *v., pfv. of* **лупи́ть.**

слух *n.* **1,** (sense of) hearing. **2,** ear for music: игра́ть по слу́ху, to play by ear. Абсолю́тный слух, absolute/perfect pitch. **3,** rumor. —**ни слу́ху ни ду́ху** (*with* **о** *or* **от**), there hasn't been a word from... —**превраща́ться в слух,** to be all ears; listen with rapt attention.

слухово́й *adj.* hearing (*attrib.*); auditory. —**слухово́й аппара́т,** hearing aid. —**слухово́е окно́,** dormer window. —**слухово́й рожо́к; слухова́я тру́бка,** ear trumpet.

слу́чай *n.* **1,** case: в тако́м слу́чае, in that case. **2,** opportunity; chance. **3,** incident; occurrence: несча́стный слу́чай, an accident. **4,** chance; luck: де́ло слу́чая, a matter of chance. —**во вся́ком слу́чае,** in any case; at any rate. —**в кра́йнем слу́чае,** if worst comes to worst; as a last resort. —**в лу́чшем слу́чае,** at best. —**в проти́вном слу́чае,** otherwise; failing which. —**в слу́чае** (+ *gen.*), in case of; in the event of. —**в слу́чае чего́, 1,** in which case. **2,** in the event of trouble. —**в том слу́чае, е́сли...,** in case... —**в ху́дшем слу́чае,** at worst. —**на вся́кий слу́чай,** just in case. —**на слу́чай** (+ *gen.*), in case of; so as to be prepared for. —**на слу́чай, е́сли...,** in case...; so as to be prepared when... —**ни в ко́ем слу́чае,** under no circumstances. —**от слу́чая к слу́чаю,** from time to time. —**по слу́чаю, 1,** (*with gen.*) on the occasion of. **2,** (*with gen.*) on account of; owing to. **3,** by chance; by luck. —**при слу́чае,** when the opportunity presents itself.

случа́йно *adv.* **1,** by chance; by accident; accidentally. **2,** *in questions,* by any chance.

случа́йность *n.f.* **1,** (*with gen.*) accidental nature (*of something*). **2,** chance occurrence; accident: чи́стая случа́йность, pure accident.

случа́йный *adj.* [*short form* **-ча́ен, -ча́йна**] **1,** chance; accidental; random. **2,** (*of earnings, expenses, etc.*) incidental.

случа́ть *v. impfv.* [*pfv.* **случи́ть**] to mate (animals).

случа́ться *v.r. impfv.* [*pfv.* **случи́ться**] **1,** to happen; occur. **2,** (*with* **с** + *instr.*) to happen to: что случи́лось с ним?, what happened to him? **3,** *impers.* (*with dat. and inf.*) to happen to; have occasion to. **4,** *colloq.* to happen to be; turn up.

случи́ть *v., pfv. of* **случа́ть.**

случи́ться *v.r., pfv. of* **случа́ться.**

слу́шание *n.* **1,** listening. **2,** attending (*a lecture*); taking (*a course*). **3,** *law* hearing.

слу́шатель *n.m.* **1,** listener. **2,** student. **3,** *pl.* audience.

слу́шать *v. impfv.* **1,** to listen (to). **2,** [*pfv.* **послу́шать**] *fig.* to listen to; heed. **3,** to hear (a case). **4,** [*pfv.* **прослу́шать**] to attend (a lecture); take (a course). —**слу́шаю!, 1,** (*when answering the phone*) hello! **2,** (*on receiving an order*) very well!; I understand!

слу́шаться *v.r. pfv.* [*pfv.* **послу́шаться**] **1,** (*with gen.*) to obey. **2,** (*with gen.*) to heed (advice). **3,** [*impfv. only*] *law* (*of a case*) to be heard.

слыть *v. impfv.* [*pfv.* **прослы́ть;** *pres.* **слыву́, слывёшь;** *past fem.* **слыла́**] (*with instr.*) to be reputed to be; have a reputation for.

слыха́ть *v. impfv., colloq., used in the past tense,* to hear.

слы́шать *v. impfv.* [*pfv.* **услы́шать;** *pres.* **слы́шу, слы́шишь**] to hear. —**слы́шаться,** *refl.* [*pfv.* **послы́шаться**] **1,** to be heard. **2,** [*impfv. only*] *fig.* to be felt; be sensed.

слы́шимость *n.f.* **1,** audibility. **2,** (*on radio or TV*) reception. **3,** (*on the telephone*) connection.

слы́шно *adv.* audibly. —*adj., used predicatively* **1,** audible: его́ не слы́шно, he can't be heard. Мне ничего́ не слы́шно, I can't hear a thing. Слы́шно, как му́ха пролети́т, you could hear a pin drop. **2,** heard; rumored: что слы́шно?, what's new?

слы́шный *adj.* [*short form* **слы́шен, -шна́, -шно**] audible.

слюда́ *n.* mica. —**слюдяно́й,** *adj.* mica (*attrib.*).

слюна́ *n.* saliva.

слю́ни [*gen.* **слюне́й**] *n. pl., colloq.* saliva. —**пуска́ть слю́ни,** to drool; drivel; slobber. —**распуска́ть слю́ни,** *colloq.* **1,** to start crying. **2,** to complain; whine. **3,** to be moved.

слюни́ть *v. impfv.* [*pfv.* **послюни́ть**] to moisten with saliva.

слю́нки [*gen. pl.* **-нок**] *n. pl., colloq.* = **слю́ни.** —**у меня́ слю́нки теку́т,** my mouth is watering.

слю́нный *adj.* salivary.

слюня́вый *adj., colloq.* driveling.

сля́коть *n.f.* slush. —**сля́котный,** *adj.* slushy.

сма́зать [*infl.* **сма́жу, сма́жешь**] *v., pfv. of* **сма́зывать.**

сма́зка *n.* **1,** grease. **2,** greasing; lubrication.

смазли́вый *adj., colloq.* pretty; good-looking.

сма́зочный *adj.* lubrication (*attrib.*); lubricating: сма́зочный материа́л, lubricant.

сма́зчик *n.* grease monkey.

сма́зывание *n.* **1,** oiling; greasing; lubrication. **2,** painting; swabbing. **3,** blurring; slurring over.

сма́зывать *v. impfv.* [*pfv.* **сма́зать**] **1,** to oil; grease; lubricate. **2,** to paint; swab. **3,** to wipe off. **4,** *colloq.* to blur (a picture). **5,** *fig., colloq.* to slur over; gloss over.

смак *n., colloq.* relish; gusto: есть со сма́ком, to eat with relish/gusto.

смакова́ть *v. impfv.* [*pres.* **-ку́ю, -ку́ешь**] *colloq.* to savor; relish.

сма́нивать *v. impfv.* [*pfv.* **смани́ть**] *colloq.* **1,** to entice. **2,** to lure away.

смани́ть [*infl.* **сманю́, сма́нишь**] *v., pfv. of* **сма́нивать.**

смастери́ть *v., pfv. of* **мастери́ть.**

сма́тывать *v. impfv.* [*pfv.* **смота́ть**] **1,** to wind; wind in. **2,** (*with* **с** + *gen.*) to wind off; unwind (from). **3,** *in* **сма́тывать у́дочки,** *colloq.* to take off; vamoose. —**сма́тываться,** *refl., colloq.* **1,** to take off; vamoose. **2,** (*with* **в** + *acc.*) to run down to; dash down to (*and return*).

сма́хивать *v. impfv.* **1,** [*pfv.* **смахну́ть**] to brush off; brush away. **2,** [*impfv. only*] (*with* **на** + *acc.*) *colloq.* to look like; resemble.

сма́чивать *v. impfv.* [*pfv.* **смочи́ть**] to moisten.

сма́чный *adj., colloq.* tasty. —**сма́чно,** *adv., colloq.* with relish; with gusto.

смежа́ть *v. impfv.* [*pfv.* **смежи́ть**] to close (one's eyes).

сме́жный *adj.* **1,** adjacent; contiguous; adjoining. **2,** allied; related. —**сме́жность,** *n.f.* contiguity.

смека́листый *adj., colloq.* clever; sharp; quick-witted.

смека́лка *n., colloq.* shrewdness; native intelligence.

смека́ть *v. impfv.* [*pfv.* **смекну́ть**] *colloq.* to catch on; get the point.

смеле́ть *v. impfv.* [*pfv.* **осмеле́ть**] to become bolder; grow bolder.

сме́ло *adv.* **1,** boldly. **2,** *colloq.* with full confidence; safely.

сме́лость *n.f.* boldness; daring; audacity; temerity.

сме́лый *adj.* bold; daring; audacious.

смельча́к [*gen.* **-чака́**] *n.* daredevil.

сме́на *n.* **1,** changing; replacement. Сме́на карау́ла, changing of the guard. **2,** alternation (*of the seasons, day and night, etc.*). **3,** shift (*of work or duty*); session (*of school*). **4,** change; set: две сме́ны белья́, two changes/sets of underwear. **5,** a replacement: найти́ сме́ну, to find a replacement. **6,** the rising generation. —**идти́** *or* **приходи́ть на сме́ну** (+ *dat.*), to replace; take the place of.

смени́ть [*infl.* **сменю́, сме́нишь**] *v., pfv. of* **сменя́ть**[1]. —**смени́ться,** *refl., pfv. of* **сменя́ться.**

сме́нный *adj.* **1,** shift (*attrib.*). **2,** removable; replaceable.

сменя́емый *adj.* removable; replaceable.

сменя́ть[1] *v. impfv.* [*pfv.* **смени́ть**] **1,** to change. **2,** to replace; relieve; remove. **3,** to replace; take the place of. —**сменя́ться,** *refl.* **1,** to be replaced. **2,** (*with* **с** + *gen.*) to be relieved of. **3,** (*with instr.*) to give way to: ле́то смени́лось о́сенью, summer gave way to autumn.

сменя́ть[2] *v. pfv., colloq.* to exchange; trade.

смерде́ть *v. impfv.* [*pres.* **-ржу́, -рди́шь**] to stink.

смерза́ться *v.r. impfv.* [*pfv.* **смёрзнуться**] to freeze together.

смёрзнуться [*past* **смёрзся, смёрзлась**] *v.r., pfv. of* **смерза́ться.**

сме́рить *v. pfv., colloq.* to measure. —**сме́рить (кого́-нибудь) взгля́дом** *or* **глаза́ми,** to look over (from head to toe).

смерка́ться *v.r. impfv.* [*pfv.* **сме́ркнуться**] *impers.* to get dark: смерка́ется, it is getting dark; dusk is falling.

смерте́льно *adv.* **1,** mortally; fatally; to death. **2,** terribly: смерте́льно уста́л, terribly tired. Смерте́льно ску́чно, deadly dull.

смерте́льный *adj.* **1,** deadly; mortal; fatal; lethal. **2,** (*of an insult*) grievous. **3,** (*of boredom, exhaustion, etc.*) utter.

сме́ртник *n.* prisoner condemned to death.

сме́ртность *n.f.* death rate; mortality. —**де́тская сме́ртность,** infant mortality.

сме́ртный *adj.* **1,** death (*attrib.*). **2,** mortal. —*n.* mortal: просты́е сме́ртные, mere mortals. —**сме́ртная казнь,** the death penalty; capital punishment.

смертоно́сный *adj.* lethal; fatal; mortal.

смерть [*pl.* **сме́рти, -те́й, -тя́м**] *n.f.* death. —**до́ сме́рти,** to death: мне ску́чно до́ сме́рти, I am bored to death. —**при́ сме́рти,** near death.

смерч *n.* **1,** whirlwind. **2,** tornado. **3,** waterspout.

смеси́тель *n.m.* mixer; blender.

смести́ [*infl. like* **мести́**] *v., pfv. of* **смета́ть**[1].

смести́ть [*infl.* **-щу́, -сти́шь**] *v., pfv. of* **смеща́ть.**

смесь *n.f.* mixture; blend.

сме́та *n.* estimate.

смета́на *n.* sour cream.

сметáть[1] *v. impfv.* [*pfv.* **смести́**] **1,** to sweep away; sweep off. **2,** *fig.* (*of a fire, wind, etc.*) to sweep away.

сметáть[2] *v. pfv.* **1,** [*infl.* **-тáю, -тáешь**] *pfv. of* **метáть**[2] *and* **смётывать** (*in sense #1*). **2,** [*infl.* **смечу́, смéчешь**] *pfv. of* **смётывать** (*in sense #2*).

смётка *n., colloq.* quick-wittedness; savvy.

смётливый *adj.* bright; clever; quick-witted.

смéтный *adj.* estimated.

смётывать *v. impfv.* [*pfv.* **сметáть**] **1,** to baste together. **2,** to stack (hay, straw, etc.).

сметь *v. impfv.* [*pfv.* **посмéть**] to dare: никтó не смел возрази́ть, no one dared raise an objection. —**как вы смéете!,** how dare you! —**не смéйте** (+ *inf.*)!, don't you dare...!

смех *n.* laughter; laugh. —**для** *or* **рáди смéха,** (just) for fun. —**как** (*or* **слóвно**) **нá смех,** as if to mock someone; as if to rub it in. —**не до смéху** (+ *dat.*), (one is) in no mood for laughter. —**поднимáть нá смех,** to hold up to ridicule. —**умирáть сó смеху,** to die laughing.

смехотвóрный *adj.* laughable; ludicrous; ridiculous.

смéшанный *adj.* **1,** mixed. **2,** hybrid.

смешáть *v., pfv. of* **мешáть** (*in sense #3*) *and* **смéшивать.** —**смешáться,** *refl., pfv. of* **мешáться** *and* **смéшиваться.**

смешéние *n.* **1,** mixing. **2,** mixture; blend. **3,** confusion. —**смешéние языкóв,** babel of tongues.

смéшивание *n.* mixing.

смéшивать *v. impfv.* [*pfv.* **смешáть**] **1,** to mix; blend. **2,** to mix up (*objects previously in order*). **3,** to get (two persons or things) mixed up; confuse with each other. —**смéшиваться,** *refl.* **1,** to mix; blend; merge. **2,** (*with* **с** + *instr.*) to blend in (with); melt (into); disappear (into). **3,** (*of objects*) to get mixed up. **4,** *colloq.* (*of a person*) to become confused; get mixed up.

смеши́ть *v. impfv.* [*pfv.* **насмеши́ть** *or* **рассмеши́ть**] to make (someone) laugh.

смешли́вый *adj.* easily moved to laughter.

смешнó *adv.* in a funny way. —*adj., used predicatively* funny: э́то не смешнó, that is not funny. Мне не смешнó, I do not find it funny; I am not amused.

смешнóй *adj.* **1,** funny; amusing. **2,** ridiculous; ludicrous. —**до смешнóго,** ridiculously; to the extreme.

смешóк [*gen.* **-шкá**] *n., colloq.* **1,** chuckle. **2,** *pl.* taunts; digs.

смещáть *v. impfv.* [*pfv.* **смести́ть**] **1,** to displace. **2,** to remove (*from office*).

смещéние *n.* **1,** removal; dismissal; displacement. **2,** *in* смещéние поня́тий, confusion of (two) concepts.

смея́ться *v.r. impfv.* [*pres.* **смею́сь, смеёшься**] **1,** to laugh. **2,** (*with dat.*) to laugh at: смея́ться шу́тке, to laugh at a joke. **3,** (*with* **над**) to make fun of. **4,** (*with* **над**) to laugh off; shrug off. **5,** *colloq.* to joke.

сми́ловаться *v.r. pfv.* [*infl.* **-луюсь, -луешься**] *obs.* (*with* **над**) to have pity (on); take pity (on); have mercy (on).

смирéние *n.* **1,** humility. **2,** meekness. **3,** (sense of) resignation.

смирéнный *adj.* humble; meek. —**смирéнно,** *adv.* humbly. —**смирéнность,** *n.f.* humility.

смири́тельный *adj., in* **смири́тельная рубáшка,** strait jacket.

смири́ть *v., pfv. of* **смиря́ть.** —**смири́ться,** *refl., pfv. of* **смиря́ться.**

сми́рно *adv.* quietly; still: сидéть сми́рно, to sit still. —*interj., mil.* attention! —**стóйка сми́рно,** position of attention.

сми́рный *adj.* quiet; mild-mannered.

смиря́ть *v. impfv.* [*pfv.* **смири́ть**] to suppress; repress; curb. —**смиря́ться,** *refl.* **1,** to submit; give in. **2,** (*with* **с** + *instr.*) to reconcile oneself (to).

смóква *n.* fig.

смóкинг *n.* tuxedo; dinner jacket.

смокóвница *n.* fig tree.

смолá [*pl.* **смóлы**] *n.* **1,** resin. **2,** pitch; tar.

смолёный *adj.* tarred.

смоли́стый *adj.* resinous.

смоли́ть *v. impfv.* [*pfv.* **вы́смолить**] to pitch; tar.

смолкáть *v. impfv.* [*pfv.* **смóлкнуть**] **1,** to fall silent. **2,** (*of noise, sounds, etc.*) to die away; stop; cease.

смóлкнуть [*past* **смолк, -ла**] *v., pfv. of* **смолкáть.**

смóлоду *adv.* **1,** since one's youth. **2,** in one's youth.

смолóть *v., pfv. of* **молóть.**

смолчáть *v. pfv.* [*infl.* **-чу́, -чи́шь**] *colloq.* to be silent; hold one's tongue.

смоль *n.f., in* **чёрный как смоль,** jet-black.

смолянóй *adj.* resin (*attrib.*); pitch (*attrib.*); tar (*attrib.*).

смонти́ровать *v., pfv. of* **монти́ровать.**

сморкáть *v. impfv.* [*pfv.* **вы́сморкать**], *in* **сморкáть нос,** to blow one's nose. —**сморкáться,** *refl.* to blow one's nose.

сморóдина *n.* currants. —**сморóдинный,** *adj.* currant (*attrib.*); made of currants.

сморчóк [*gen.* **-чкá**] *n.* morel (*mushroom*).

смóрщенный *adj.* wrinkled.

смóрщивать *v. impfv.* [*pfv.* **смóрщить**] to wrinkle. —**смóрщиваться,** *refl.* **1,** to become wrinkled. **2,** to shrivel.

смóрщить *v., pfv. of* **мóрщить** *and* **смóрщивать.** —**смóрщиться,** *refl., pfv. of* **мóрщиться** (*in senses #2 & #3*) *and* **смóрщиваться.**

смотáть *v., pfv. of* **смáтывать.** —**смотáться,** *refl., pfv. of* **смáтываться.**

смотр *n.* **1,** [*2nd loc.* **смотру́;** *pl.* **смотры́**] review; parade. **2,** [*no 2nd loc.; pl.* **смóтры**] public showing.

смотрéть *v. impfv.* [*pfv.* **посмотрéть;** *pres.* **смотрю́, смóтришь**] **1,** to look. **2,** (*with* **на** + *acc.*) to look at. **3,** to look over; have a look at; examine. **4,** to watch; see (television, a movie, game, etc.). **5,** (*with* **на** + *acc.*) *fig.* to regard; look upon. **6,** [*impfv. only*] (*with* **в** *or* **на** + *acc.*) to look out on; face. **7,** [*impfv. only*] to appear; peep out. **8,** (*with* **за** + *instr.*) to look after; keep an eye on. **9,** [*impfv. only*] (*with instr.*) *colloq.* to look like. —**смотри́(те), 1,** watch out!; take care! **2,** see how!; look how! —**смотря́ где,** it depends (on) where. —**смотря́ как,** it depends. —**смотря́ когдá,** it depends (on) when. —**смотря́ по** (+ *dat.*), depending on.

смотрéться *v.r. impfv.* [*pfv.* **посмотрéться;** *pres.* **смотрю́сь, смóтришься**] to look at oneself: смотрéться в зéркало, to look at oneself in the mirror.

смотри́тель *n.m.* guard; watchman; keeper.

смотровóй *adj.* **1,** observation (*attrib.*): смотровáя вы́шка, observation tower. **2,** *mil.* inspection (*attrib.*); review (*attrib.*).

смочи́ть [*infl.* **смочу́, смóчишь**] *v., pfv. of* **смáчивать.**

смочь *v., pfv. of* **мочь.**

смошéнничать *v., pfv. of* **мошéнничать.**

смрад *n.* stench. —**смра́дный,** *adj.* stinking.
сму́глый *adj.* dark; swarthy; dark-complexioned.
сму́та *n.* **1,** *obs.* (civil) strife. **2,** *colloq.* dissension. **3,** distress.
смути́ть [*infl.* **-щу́, -ти́шь**] *v., pfv. of* **смуща́ть.** —**смути́ться,** *refl., pfv. of* **смуща́ться.**
сму́тно *adv.* vaguely; dimly.
сму́тный *adj.* **1,** dim; hazy; vague. **2,** troubled. **3,** marked by civil strife. —**сму́тное вре́мя,** *hist.* The Time of Troubles (1605-13).
смутья́н *n., colloq.* fomenter of civil strife; agitator.
смуща́ть *v. impfv.* [*pfv.* **смути́ть**] **1,** to embarrass; disconcert. **2,** to trouble; bother; disturb; perturb. —**смуща́ться,** *refl.* to be embarrassed.
смуще́ние *n.* embarrassment.
смыва́ть *v. impfv.* [*pfv.* **смыть**] to wash away; wash off. —**смыва́ться,** *refl.* **1,** to wash off; come off. **2,** *colloq.* to disappear; take off.
смыка́ть *v. impfv.* [*pfv.* **сомкну́ть**] to close (ranks, one's eyes, etc.). —**смыка́ться,** *refl.* **1,** to close. **2,** to close in. **3,** (*with* **с** + *instr.*) to join; make contact with. **4,** *fig.* to close ranks; unite.
смысл *n.* **1,** sense. **2,** meaning. —**в смы́сле** (+ *gen.*), **1,** in the sense of. **2,** as regards. —**нет смы́сла** (+ *inf.*), there is no sense (*or* no point) in...
смы́слить *v. impfv., colloq.* to understand.
смыслово́й *adj.* semantic.
смыть [*infl.* **смо́ю, смо́ешь**] *v., pfv. of* **смыва́ть.** —**смы́ться,** *refl., pfv. of* **смыва́ться.**
смы́чка *n.* **1,** joining; linking; coupling. **2,** *fig.* joining together; unifying.
смычко́вый *adj.* (*of musical instruments*) played with a bow.
смычо́к [*gen.* **-чка́**] *n., music* bow.
смышлёный *adj., colloq.* bright; clever; smart.
смягча́ть *v. impfv.* [*pfv.* **смягчи́ть**] **1,** to soften. **2,** to alleviate; mitigate; assuage. **3,** to tone down. —**смягча́ться,** *refl.* **1,** to soften; become soft. **2,** to abate; relent; ease. **3,** (*of the weather*) to become mild.
смягче́ние *n.* **1,** softening. **2,** mitigation.
смягчи́ть *v., pfv. of* **смягча́ть.** —**смягчи́ться,** *refl., pfv. of* **смягча́ться.**
смяте́ние *n.* **1,** confusion. **2,** panic.
смяте́нный *adj., obs.* troubled.
смять *v. pfv.* [*infl.* **сомну́, сомнёшь**] **1,** *pfv. of* **мять** (*in senses #2 & #3*). **2,** to trample upon; trample down. **3,** *mil.* to crush; overrun. **4,** *fig.* to crush; overwhelm. —**смя́ться,** *refl., pfv. of* **мя́ться** (*in sense #1*).
снабди́ть [*infl.* **-бжу́, -бди́шь**] *v., pfv. of* **снабжа́ть.**
снабжа́ть *v. impfv.* [*pfv.* **снабди́ть**] (*with instr.*) to supply (with); furnish (with); provide (with).
снабже́ние *n.* supply; supplying; provision.
сна́добье *n., colloq.* medicinal herb.
сна́йпер *n.* **1,** sharpshooter. **2,** sniper.
снару́жи *adv.* **1,** from the outside; on the outside. **2,** outwardly.
снаря́д *n.* **1,** shell; projectile; missile. **2,** apparatus; device; machine. —**гимнасти́ческие снаря́ды,** gymnastic apparatus.
снаряди́ть [*infl.* **-жу́, -ди́шь**] *v., pfv. of* **снаряжа́ть.**
снаря́дный *adj.* shell (*attrib.*); ammunition (*attrib.*).
снаряжа́ть *v. impfv.* [*pfv.* **снаряди́ть**] **1,** to equip; outfit. **2,** *colloq.* to send; dispatch.
снаряже́ние *n.* **1,** equipping; outfitting. **2,** equipment; outfit.
снасть [*pl.* **сна́сти, -сте́й, -стя́м**] *n.f.* tackle: рыболо́вная снасть, fishing tackle.
снача́ла *adv.* **1,** at first; in the beginning. **2,** first (*before doing something else*). **3,** over again; from the beginning.
сна́шивать *v. impfv.* [*pfv.* **сноси́ть**] to wear out (clothes). —**сна́шиваться,** *refl.* (*of clothes*) to wear out.
снег [*2nd loc.* **снегу́;** *pl.* **снега́**] *n.* snow. —**как снег на́ голову,** out of a clear blue sky.
снеги́рь [*gen.* **-гиря́**] *n.m.* bullfinch.
снегово́й *adj.* **1,** snow (*attrib.*). **2,** (*of mountains*) snowcapped.
снегоочисти́тель *n.m.* snowplow.
снегопа́д *n.* snowfall.
снегосту́п *n.* snowshoe.
снегохо́д *n.* snowmobile.
снегу́рочка *n.* snow maiden. *Also,* **снегу́рка.**
снеда́ть *v. impfv.* **1,** *obs., colloq.* to eat. **2,** *fig.* to gnaw; consume; torment.
снедь *n.f., obs.* food.
снежи́нка [*gen. pl.* **-нок**] *n.* snowflake.
снежи́ть *v. impfv., colloq.* to snow.
сне́жный *adj.* **1,** snow (*attrib.*). **2,** snowy. —**сне́жная ба́ба,** snowman.
снежо́к [*gen.* **-жка́**] *n.* **1,** light snow. **2,** snowball. —**игра́ть в снежки́,** to throw snowballs.
снести́ [*infl. like* **нести́**] *v., pfv. of* **нести́** (*in sense #10*) *and* **сноси́ть**[1]. —**снести́сь,** *refl., pfv. of* **нести́сь** (*in sense #5*) *and* **сноси́ться**[1].
снижа́ть *v. impfv.* [*pfv.* **сни́зить**] **1,** to lower; reduce. **2,** to bring down; land (an airplane). —**снижа́ться,** *refl.* **1,** (*of prices, temperature, etc.*) to go down; come down; drop; fall. **2,** (*of an airplane*) to land.
сниже́ние *n.* **1,** lowering; reduction. **2,** descent (*of an airplane*).
сни́зить [*infl.* **-жу, -зишь**] *v., pfv. of* **снижа́ть.** —**сни́зиться,** *refl., pfv. of* **снижа́ться.**
снизойти́ [*infl.* **снизойду́, снизойдёшь;** *past* **снизошёл, снизошла́**] *v., pfv. of* **снисходи́ть.**
сни́зу *adv.* **1,** from below. **2,** from the bottom. —**сни́зу до́верху,** from top to bottom. —**смотре́ть на** (+ *acc.*) **сни́зу вверх,** to look up to someone.
сни́кнуть *v. pfv.* [*past* **сник, -ла**] **1,** (*of plants*) to droop. **2,** *fig.* to die down. **3,** *fig., colloq.* to feel depressed.
снима́ть *v. impfv.* [*pfv.* **снять**] **1,** to take down; remove. **2,** to take off; remove (clothing, jewelry, make-up, etc.). **3,** to withdraw (a motion, one's candidacy, etc.). **4,** to remove; drop (from an agenda, from production, etc.). **5,** to lift (a ban or siege); dismiss (a charge); remit (a punishment). **6,** to dismiss (from a job); remove (from office). **7,** to gather in (a harvest). **8,** to photograph; take a picture of. **9,** to rent. —**снима́ть коло́ду,** to cut the cards. —**снима́ть ко́пию с** (+ *gen.*), to make a copy of. —**снима́ть ме́рку с** (+ *gen.*), to take someone's measurements. —**снима́ть показа́ния** (+ *gen.*), to take evidence from. —**снима́ть тру́бку,** to pick up the receiver (*of a telephone*).
снима́ться *v.r. impfv.* [*pfv.* **сня́ться**] **1,** (*with* **с** + *gen.*) to come off (of); come loose (from). **2,** (*with* **с** +*gen.*) to leave; depart (from). **3,** to be photographed; have one's picture taken. —**снима́ться с ла́геря,** to break camp. —**снима́ться с я́коря,** to weigh anchor.

сни́мок [*gen.* **-мка**] *n.* picture; photograph; snapshot.
сниска́ть *v. pfv.* [*infl.* **снищу́, сни́щешь**] to gain; win.
снисходи́тельность *n.f.* **1,** condescension. **2,** leniency.
снисходи́тельный *adj.* **1,** condescending. **2,** lenient.
снисходи́ть *v. impfv.* [*pfv.* **снизойти́**; *pres.* **-хожу́, -хо́дишь**] **1,** (*with* **к, до,** *or inf.*) to condescend (to); deign (to). **2,** (*with* **к**) to show sympathy (toward); be tolerant (of).
снисхожде́ние *n.* **1,** condescension. **2,** leniency.
сни́ться *v.r. impfv.* [*pfv.* **присни́ться**] (*with dat.*) to appear in one's dreams: вы мне сни́лись, I dreamt (*or* had a dream) about you. Мне сни́лось, что..., I dreamt that...
сноб *n.* snob. —**снобизм,** *n.* snobbery; snobbishness.
сно́ва *adv.* again; once again; over again; anew.
снова́ть *v. impfv.* [*pres.* **сную́, снуёшь**] **1,** (*of ships*) to ply back and forth. **2,** to scamper about.
сновиде́ние *n.* dream.
сногсшиба́тельный *adj., colloq.* stunning; staggering.
сноп [*gen.* **снопа́**] *n.* **1,** sheaf. **2,** shaft (*of light*).
сноровистый *adj., colloq.* clever; smart.
сноро́вка *n.* skill; knack; ability.
снос *n.* **1,** *aero.; naut.* drift. **2,** tearing down; demolition. **3,** *colloq.* wear: э́тому сно́су нет, you can't wear it out. —**быть на сно́сях,** *colloq.* to be about to give birth.
сноси́ть[1] *v. impfv.* [*pfv.* **снести́**; *pres.* **сношу́, сно́сишь**] **1,** to carry down. **2,** to take; deliver. **3,** to cut off; chop off. **4,** (*of the wind*) to blow off; blow away; (*of water*) to wash away. **5,** to tear down (a building). **6,** to endure. **7,** *cards* to discard. —**сноси́ться,** *refl.* (*with* **с** + *instr.*), to communicate (with); get in touch (with).
сноси́ть[2] *v. pfv.* [*infl.* **сношу́, сно́сишь**] **1,** *pfv. of* **сна́шивать. 2,** *colloq.* to carry (*to a certain place and back*). —**сноси́ться,** *refl., pfv. of* **сна́шиваться.**
сно́ска [*gen. pl.* **-сок**] *n.* footnote.
сно́сно *adv.* **1,** fairly well; tolerably well. **2,** so-so.
сно́сный *adj.* **1,** tolerable; bearable. **2,** *colloq.* tolerable; passable; fairly good.
снотво́рный *adj.* **1,** taken to induce sleep: снотво́рная табле́тка, sleeping pill. **2,** *fig.* soporific.
снoxа́ [*pl.* **сно́хи**] *n.* daughter-in-law.
сноше́ние *n., usu. pl.* relations; dealings; intercourse.
сня́тие *n.* **1,** removal. **2,** dismissal. **3,** gathering in (*of a harvest*). **4,** lifting (*of a ban, siege, etc.*). **5,** making (*of copies*).
снято́й *adj., in* **снято́е молоко́,** skim milk.
снять [*infl.* **сниму́, сни́мешь**; *past fem.* **сняла́**] *v., pfv. of* **снима́ть.** —**сня́ться,** *refl.* [*past* **сня́лся, -ла́сь, -ло́сь**] *pfv. of* **снима́ться.**
со *prep.* = **с.**
со- *prefix* **1,** = **с-. 2,** *corresponds to English prefix* co-: соа́втор, coauthor; сосуществова́ние, coexistence.
соа́втор *n.* coauthor. —**соа́вторство,** *n.* coauthorship.
соба́ка *n.* **1,** dog. **2,** *in* **морска́я соба́ка,** dogfish. —**вот где соба́ка зары́та!,** so that's what it's all about! —**он на э́том соба́ку съел,** he knows this subject inside out.
соба́чий [*fem.* **-чья**] *adj.* **1,** dog (*attrib.*). **2,** *fig., colloq.* a dog's: соба́чья жизнь, a dog's life. —**соба́чий хо́лод,** brutal cold.
соба́чка [*gen. pl.* **-чек**] *n.* **1,** little dog; doggy. **2,** trigger. **3,** pawl; pallet.
соба́чник *n., colloq.* dog lover.
собесе́дник *n.* **1,** person to whom one was speaking. **2,** (*after an adj.*) person to talk to.
собесе́дование *n.* conversation; discussion.
собира́ние *n.* gathering; collecting.
собира́тель *n.m.* collector.
собира́тельный *adj., gram.* collective.
собира́тельство *n.* **1,** collecting (*as a hobby*). **2,** *anthropology* gathering.
собира́ть *v. impfv.* [*pfv.* **собра́ть**] **1,** to gather (people, firewood, information, etc.). **2,** to collect (books, taxes, etc.). **3,** to pick (fruit); gather in (a harvest). **4,** to assemble; put together (a machine, collection, etc.). **5,** to put together; pack: собира́ть ве́щи в я́щик, to pack things into a box. **6,** to receive; poll (votes). **7,** to gather; take in (a garment). **8,** *colloq.* to get (someone) ready to go somewhere: собира́ть дете́й в шко́лу, to get the children ready for school. **9,** *in* собира́ть на стол, *colloq.* to set the table. **10,** to collect (one's thoughts); summon up (one's strength, courage, etc.).
собира́ться *v.r. impfv.* [*pfv.* **собра́ться**] **1,** to gather; assemble. **2,** to prepare; get ready: собира́ться в доро́гу/о́тпуск, to get ready for a trip; get ready to go on vacation. **3,** (*of a storm*) to be gathering; be in the offing. **4,** [*impfv. only*] (*with inf.*) to intend (to). **5,** [*impfv. only*] (*with inf.*) to be about to. **6,** [*pfv. only*] (*with inf.*) to make up one's mind (to). **7,** (*with* **с** + *instr.*) to collect (one's thoughts); summon up (one's strength, courage, etc.).
соблаговоли́ть *v. pfv.* (*with inf.*) *obs.* to deign (to).
собла́зн *n.* temptation.
соблазни́тель *n.m.* **1,** tempter. **2,** seducer.
соблазни́тельный *adj.* **1,** tempting. **2,** seductive.
соблазня́ть *v. impfv.* [*pfv.* **соблазни́ть**] **1,** to tempt. **2,** to seduce. —**соблазня́ться,** *refl.* to be tempted.
соблюда́ть *v. impfv.* [*pfv.* **соблюсти́**] to observe; abide by.
соблюде́ние *n.* observance.
соблюсти́ [*infl.* **-блюду́, -блюдёшь**] *v., pfv. of* **блюсти́** *and* **соблюда́ть.**
собо́й *also,* **собо́ю** *pron., instr. of* **себя́.**
соболе́знование *n.* condolence; condolences.
соболе́зновать *v. impfv.* [*pres.* **-ную, -нуешь**] (*with dat.*) to commiserate (with).
собо́лий [*fem.* **-лья**] *adj.* sable (*attrib.*).
соболи́ный *adj.* sable (*attrib.*).
со́боль *n.m.* sable.
собо́р *n.* **1,** cathedral. **2,** *hist.* assembly: зе́мский собо́р, zemski sobor (*legislative assembly in old Russia*). **3,** *relig.* council: вселе́нский собо́р, ecumenical council.
собо́рный *adj.* cathedral (*attrib.*).
собо́рование *n.* extreme unction.
собо́ю *pron.* = **собо́й.**
собра́ние *n.* **1,** meeting. **2,** assembly. **3,** collection. —**собра́ние сочине́ний,** collected works.
со́бранный *adj.* **1,** tensed up; intense; concentrated. **2,** straight; erect. **3,** precise; efficient.
собра́т [*pl.* **собра́тья, собра́тьев** *or* **собра́тий**] *n.* **1,** colleague. **2,** *colloq.* counterpart.
собра́ть [*infl. like* **брать**] *v., pfv. of* **собира́ть.** —**собра́ться,** *refl.* [*past* **собра́лся, -ла́сь, -ло́сь** *or* **-лось, -ли́сь** *or* **-лись**] *pfv. of* **собира́ться.**

со́бственник *n.* owner; proprietor.
со́бственнический *adj.* **1,** proprietary. **2,** acquisitive; possessive.
со́бственно *particle* **1,** actually; in fact. **2,** proper: со́бственно го́род, the city proper. —**со́бственно говоря́,** strictly speaking.
собственнору́чный *adj.* handwritten. Собственнору́чная по́дпись, autograph. —**собственнору́чно,** *adv.* with one's own hands.
со́бственность *n.f.* **1,** property. **2,** ownership.
со́бственный *adj.* one's own. —**в со́бственном смы́сле,** in the true (*or* literal) sense. —**и́мя со́бственное,** proper noun. —**со́бственной персо́ной,** in person.
собуты́льник *n., colloq.* drinking companion.
собы́тие *n.* event.
сова́ [*pl.* **со́вы**] *n.* owl.
сова́ть *v. impfv.* [*pfv.* **су́нуть;** *pres.* **сую́, суёшь**] to stick; slip; thrust. —**сова́ться,** *refl.* (*with* **в** + *acc.*) *colloq.* **1,** to plunge (into). **2,** to force one's way (into). **3,** to butt (into); poke one's nose (into).
совере́н *n.* sovereign (*British coin*).
соверша́ть *v. impfv.* [*pfv.* **соверши́ть**] **1,** to make (a trip, deal, mistake, etc.). **2,** to commit (a crime, sin, aggression, etc.). **3,** to carry out (a mission, raid, etc.). **4,** to accomplish (a feat, miracle, etc.).
соверше́ние *n.* **1,** accomplishment; completion. **2,** commission; perpetration (*of a crime*).
соверше́нно *adv.* completely; entirely; absolutely; perfectly; utterly.
совершенноле́тие *n.* majority; coming of age. —**совершенноле́тний,** *adj.* of age.
соверше́нный *adj.* **1,** perfect. **2,** absolute; utter. —**соверше́нный вид,** *gram.* perfective aspect.
соверше́нство *n.* perfection. —**в соверше́нстве,** perfectly; to perfection.
соверше́нствование *n.* improvement; perfecting.
соверше́нствовать *v. impfv.* [*pfv.* **усоверше́нствовать;** *pres.* **-ствую, -ствуешь**] to improve; perfect; refine.
соверши́ть *v., pfv. of* **соверша́ть.**
со́вестить *v. impfv.* [*pres.* **-щу, -стишь**] *colloq.* to shame; chide. —**со́веститься,** *refl.* [*pfv.* **посо́веститься**] *colloq.* to be ashamed.
со́вестливый *adj.* conscientious; scrupulous.
со́вестно *adj., used predicatively (with dat.)* ashamed: мне бы́ло со́вестно, I was ashamed.
со́весть *n.f.* conscience. —**на со́весть,** conscientiously. —**по со́вести (говоря́),** to tell the truth; to be honest; in all honesty.
сове́т *n.* **1,** advice; counsel. **2,** council. **3,** soviet: Верхо́вный Сове́т, the Supreme Soviet.
сове́тник *n.* adviser.
сове́товать *v. impfv.* [*pfv.* **посове́товать;** *pres.* **-тую, -туешь**] (*with dat.*) to advise. —**сове́товаться,** *refl.* (*with* **с** + *instr.*) to consult; seek the advice of.
советбло́г *n.* specialist on the Soviet Union; Kremlinologist.
сове́тский *adj.* Soviet. —**Сове́тский Сою́з,** the Soviet Union.
сове́тчик *n.* adviser.
совеща́ние *n.* conference.
совеща́тельный *adj.* consultative; deliberative. —**пра́во совеща́тельного го́лоса,** voice but no vote. —**член с совеща́тельным го́лосом,** nonvoting member.
совеща́ться *v.r. impfv.* **1,** to deliberate. **2,** (*with* **с** + *instr.*) to confer (with).
сови́ный *adj.* **1,** owl's. **2,** owlish.
совлада́ть *v. pfv.* (*with* **с** + *instr.*) *colloq.* to cope with; handle; control. —**совлада́ть с собо́й,** to control oneself; get control of oneself.
совладе́лец [*gen.* **-льца**] *n.* co-owner; joint owner.
совладе́ние *n.* joint ownership.
совмести́мый *adj.* compatible. —**совмести́мость,** *n.f.* compatibility.
совмести́тельство *n.* holding of more than one job. Рабо́тать по совмести́тельству, to hold down two jobs.
совмести́ть [*infl.* **-щу́, -сти́шь**] *v., pfv. of* **совмеща́ть.**
совме́стно *adv.* jointly; together.
совме́стный *adj.* joint; combined. —**совме́стное обуче́ние,** coeducation.
совмеща́ть *v. impfv.* [*pfv.* **совмести́ть**] to combine.
Совнарко́м *n., contr. of* **Сове́т Наро́дных Комисса́ров,** Council of People's Commissars; Sovnarkom; (*replaced in 1946 by the Council of Ministers*).
совнархо́з *n., contr. of* **сове́т наро́дного хозя́йства,** council of the national economy; sovnarkhoz (*regional economic councils established in 1957*).
сово́к [*gen.* **-вка́**] *n.* scoop. —**садо́вый сово́к,** trowel. —**сово́к для му́сора,** dustpan.
совокупле́ние *n.* copulation; coition.
совокупля́ться *v.r. impfv.* to copulate.
совоку́пно *adv., obs.* jointly.
совоку́пность *n.f.* aggregate; sum total.
совоку́пный *adj., obs.* joint; combined.
совпада́ть *v. impfv.* [*pfv.* **совпа́сть**] **1,** to coincide. **2,** to agree; tally.
совпаде́ние *n.* **1,** coincidence. **2,** identity; concurrence; harmony (*of interests, opinions, etc.*). **3,** combination (*of circumstances*).
совпа́сть [*infl. like* **пасть**] *v., pfv. of* **совпада́ть.**
соврати́тель *n.m.* seducer.
соврати́ть [*infl.* **-щу́, -ти́шь**] *v., pfv. of* **совраща́ть.**
совра́ть *v., pfv. of* **врать.**
совраща́ть *v. impfv.* [*pfv.* **соврати́ть**] **1,** to pervert; **2,** to seduce.
совраще́ние *n.* perversion; seduction.
совреме́нник *n.* contemporary.
совреме́нность *n.f.* **1,** modernity. **2,** the present.
совреме́нный *adj.* **1,** contemporary. **2,** modern.
совсе́м *adv.* **1,** quite. **2,** completely; entirely. —**не совсе́м,** not entirely. —**совсе́м не,** not at all; not in the least.
совхо́з *n.* state farm (*contr. of* **сове́тское хозя́йство**).
согла́сие *n.* **1,** consent; assent. **2,** agreement. **3,** harmony.
согласи́тельный *adj.* conciliation (*attrib.*): согласи́тельная коми́ссия, conciliation committee.
согласи́ться [*infl.* **-шу́сь, -си́шься**] *v.r., pfv. of* **соглаша́ться.**
согла́сно *adv.* in harmony. —*prep., with dat. or* **с** + *instr.* according to; in accordance with.
согла́сный *adj.* [*short form* **-сен, -сна**] **1,** (*with* **с** + *instr.*) in agreement: я с ва́ми согла́сен (согла́сна), I agree with you. **2,** (*with* **на** + *acc.*) agreeable: он согла́сен на все усло́вия, he agrees (*or* is agree-

able) to all the conditions. **3,** harmonious. **4,** *phonet.* consonantal: согла́сная бу́ква, consonant. —*n.* consonant.

согласова́ние *n.* **1,** coordination. **2,** *gram.* agreement. Согласова́ние времён, sequence of tenses.

согласо́ванный *adj.* coordinated; concerted. —**согласо́ванность,** *n.f.* coordination.

согласова́ть [*infl* **-су́ю, -су́ешь**] *v., pfv. of* **согласо́вывать.**

согласова́ться *v.r. impfv. & pfv.* [*pres.* **-су́ется**] (*with* **с** + *instr.*) **1,** to be in conformance (with); be in keeping (with). **2,** *gram.* to agree (with).

согласо́вывать *v. impfv.* [*pfv.* **согласова́ть**] **1,** to coordinate. **2,** *gram.* to make agree.

соглаша́тель *n.m.* compromiser; appeaser. —**соглаша́тельский,** *adj.* of compromise; of appeasement. —**соглаша́тельство,** *n.* policy of compromise; appeasement.

соглаша́ться *v.r. impfv.* [*pfv.* **согласи́ться**] **1,** (*with* **с** + *instr.*) to agree (with). **2,** (*with inf. or* **на** + *acc.*) to agree (to); consent (to).

соглаше́ние *n.* agreement.

согна́ть [*infl.* **сгоню́, сго́нишь;** *past fem.* **согнала́**] *v., pfv. of* **сгоня́ть.**

со́гнутый *adj.* **1,** bent. **2,** bent over; stooped.

согну́ть *v., pfv. of* **гнуть** *and* **сгиба́ть.** —**согну́ться,** *refl., pfv. of* **гну́ться** *and* **сгиба́ться.**

согрева́ние *n.* warming; heating.

согрева́ть *v. impfv.* [*pfv.* **согре́ть**] to warm; heat. —**согрева́ться,** *refl.* to get warm; warm up.

согреши́ть *v., pfv. of* **греши́ть.**

со́да *n.* soda: каусти́ческая со́да, caustic soda.

соде́йствие *n.* assistance; help.

соде́йствовать *v. impfv. & pfv.* [*pres.* **-ствую, -ствуешь**] (*with dat.*) **1,** to assist. **2,** to further; promote; contribute to.

содержа́ние *n.* **1,** support; maintenance; upkeep. **2,** content: фо́рма и содержа́ние, form and content. Бога́тое содержа́ние белка́, high protein content. **3,** *colloq.* contents (*of a container*). **4,** contents (*of a book, letter, etc.*); subject matter. **5,** table of contents. **6,** pay; wages; salary.

содержа́нка [*gen. pl.* **-нок**] *n.* kept woman.

содержа́тель *n.m., obs.* owner; operator.

содержа́тельный *adj.* rich in content; informative; meaty.

содержа́ть *v. impfv.* [*pres.* **-держу́, -де́ржишь**] **1,** to contain. **2,** to support (a family, children, etc.). **3,** to keep (*in a certain state*): содержа́ть в испра́вности, to keep in working order. **4,** to keep; (forcibly) confine: содержа́ть под аре́стом, to keep under arrest. **5,** *obs.* to own; operate (a business). —**содержа́ться,** *refl.* **1,** to be kept; be maintained. **2,** to be contained: в мя́се соде́ржатся белки́, meat contains proteins.

содержи́мое *n., decl. as an adj.* contents.

со́довый *adj.* soda (*attrib.*).

содо́м *n., colloq.* uproar; commotion.

содра́ть [*infl.* **сдеру́, сдерёшь;** *past fem.* **содрала́**] *v., pfv. of* **драть** (*in sense #4*) *and* **сдира́ть.**

содрога́ние *n.* shudder.

содрога́ться *v.r. impfv.* [*pfv.* **содрогну́ться**] to shudder.

содру́жество *n.* **1,** cooperation; harmony. **2,** association; union. —**Брита́нское содру́жество на́ций,** British Commonwealth of Nations.

со́евый *adj.* soybean (*attrib.*). —**со́евые бобы́,** soybeans.

соедине́ние *n.* **1,** joining; uniting. **2,** linking; connecting. **3,** joint. **4,** *chem.* compound. **5,** *mil.* large unit (*division-size or larger*).

соединённый *adj.* united. —**Соединённые Шта́ты,** the United States.

соедини́тельный *adj.* connecting. —**соедини́тельная ткань,** connective tissue.

соединя́ть *v. impfv.* [*pfv.* **соедини́ть**] **1,** to connect; hook up. **2,** to unite. Соединя́ть си́лы, to join forces. **3,** to link; connect; join. **4,** to combine. —**соединя́ться,** *refl.* **1,** to unite; be united. **2,** to be linked; be connected. **3,** to be combined.

сожале́ние *n.* **1,** regret. **2,** pity. —**к сожале́нию,** unfortunately.

сожале́ть *v. impfv.* **1,** (*with* **о** *or a dependent clause*) to regret. **2,** (*with* **о**) *obs.* to pity; feel sorry for.

сожже́ние *n.* burning.

сожи́тель *n.m.* [*fem.* **-ница**] **1,** roommate. **2,** *colloq.* lover. —**сожи́тельство,** *n.* cohabitation.

сожи́тельствовать *v. impfv.* [*pres.* **-ствую, -ствуешь**] to live together.

сожра́ть *v., pfv. of* **жрать.**

созва́ниваться *v.r. impfv.* [*pfv.* **созвони́ться**] (*with* **с** + *instr.*) *colloq.* to call (someone) on the telephone; be in touch by phone.

созва́ть [*infl. like* **звать**] *v., pfv. of* **созыва́ть** *and* **сзыва́ть.**

созве́здие *n.* constellation.

созвони́ться *v.r., pfv. of* **созва́ниваться.**

созву́чие *n.* **1,** *music* consonance. **2,** harmony; concord. **3,** assonance.

созву́чный *adj.* **1,** (*of sounds*) harmonious; assonant. **2,** (*with dat.*) in keeping with; in tune with.

создава́ть *v. impfv.* [*pfv.* **созда́ть;** *pres.* **-даю́, -даёшь**] **1,** to create. **2,** *short form past passive part. only* (*with* **для**), made (for); cut out (for): со́зданы друг для дру́га, made for each other; не со́здан для э́того, not cut out for this. —**создава́ться,** *refl.* to be created; arise; develop. У меня́ создало́сь впечатле́ние, что..., I got the impression that...

созда́ние *n.* **1,** creation (*act of creating*). **2,** creation; work. **3,** creature.

созда́тель *n.m.* creator; originator.

созда́ть [*infl. like* **дать;** *past* **со́здал, создала́, со́здало**] *v., pfv. of* **создава́ть.** —**созда́ться,** *refl.* [*past* **-да́лся, -дала́сь, -дало́сь** *or* **-да́лось**] *pfv. of* **создава́ться.**

созерца́ние *n.* contemplation. —**созерца́тельный,** *adj.* contemplative.

созерца́ть *v. impfv.* to contemplate.

созида́ние *n.* creation. —**созида́тель,** *n.m.* creator. —**созида́тельный,** *adj.* creative.

созида́ть *v. impfv.* to create.

сознава́ть *v. impfv.* [*pfv.* **созна́ть;** *pres.* **-знаю́, -знаёшь**] to realize; recognize; be conscious of; be aware of. —**сознава́ться,** *refl.* (*with* **в** + *prepl.*) to confess (to).

созна́ние *n.* **1,** consciousness: приходи́ть в созна́ние, to regain consciousness. Без созна́ния, unconscious. **2,** awareness; realization; recognition; consciousness. **3,** *obs.* confession.

созна́тельно *adv.* consciously; deliberately.

созна́тельность *n.f.* consciousness; awareness: кла́ссовая созна́тельность, class consciousness; полити́ческая созна́тельность, political awareness.

созна́тельный *adj.* **1,** conscious. **2,** deliberate.

созна́ть [*infl.* **-зна́ю, -зна́ешь**] *v., pfv. of* **сознава́ть.** —**созна́ться,** *refl., pfv. of* **сознава́ться.**

созрева́ние *n.* ripening; maturation.

созрева́ть *v. impfv.* [*pfv.* **созре́ть**] to ripen; mature.

созре́ть *v., pfv. of* **зреть**[1] *and* **созрева́ть.**

созы́в *n.* calling; convening.

созыва́ть *v. impfv.* [*pfv.* **созва́ть**] **1,** to call together; invite; summon. **2,** to call; convene.

соизволя́ть *v. impfv.* [*pfv.* **соизво́лить**] (*with inf.*) *obs.* to deign (to).

соизмери́мый *adj.* commensurable.

соиска́ние *n.* (*with gen.*) competition (*for an award or degree*).

соиска́тель *n.m.* competitor; rival.

со́йка [*gen. pl.* **со́ек**] *n.* jay (*bird*).

сойти́ [*infl.* **сойду́, сойдёшь;** *past* **сошёл, сошла́, сошло́**] *v., pfv. of* **сходи́ть.** —**сойти́сь,** *refl., pfv. of* **сходи́ться.**

сок *n.* **1,** juice. **2,** sap. —**в по́лном соку́,** in the prime of life.

сока́мерник *n.* cellmate.

соковыжима́лка [*gen. pl.* **-лок**] *n.* squeezer; juicer.

со́кол *n.* falcon. —**гол как соко́л** (*with different stress*), poor as a church mouse.

соколи́ный *adj.* falcon's. —**соколи́ная охо́та,** falconry.

сократи́ть [*infl.* **-щу́, -ти́шь**] *v., pfv. of* **сокраща́ть.** —**сократи́ться,** *refl., pfv. of* **сокраща́ться.**

сокраща́ть *v. impfv.* [*pfv.* **сократи́ть**] **1,** to reduce; curtail. **2,** to shorten. **3,** to abridge; condense. **4,** to abbreviate. **5,** *colloq.* to dismiss; fire. **6,** *math.* to cancel. —**сокраща́ться,** *refl.* **1,** to become *or* grow shorter. **2,** to be shortened. **3,** to be reduced. **4,** *physiol.* to contract.

сокраще́ние *n.* **1,** reduction; curtailment. **2,** shortening. **3,** abridgment; condensation. **4,** abbreviation. **5,** contraction (*of muscles*). **6,** *math.* cancellation. **7,** *colloq.* discharge; dismissal.

сокращённо *adv.* for short.

сокрове́нный *adj.* **1,** secret; hidden. **2,** *fig.* (*of one's thoughts, feelings, etc.*) innermost.

сокро́вище *n.* treasure. —**ни за каки́е сокро́вища,** not for (anything in) the world.

сокро́вищница *n.* treasure house.

сокруша́ть *v. impfv.* [*pfv.* **сокруши́ть**] **1,** to shatter; smash; destroy. **2,** to distress; upset. —**сокруша́ться,** *refl.* [*impfv. only*] (*with* **о**) to grieve; lament; be distressed (over).

сокруше́ние *n.* **1,** smashing; destruction. **2,** distress.

сокрушённый *adj.* grieving; grief-stricken. —**сокрушённо,** *adv.* sorrowfully.

сокруши́тельный *adj.* **1,** (*of a blow*) crushing; crippling; shattering. **2,** (*of a feeling*) overwhelming.

сокруши́ть *v., pfv. of* **сокруша́ть.**

сокры́тие *n.* concealment.

солга́ть *v., pfv. of* **лгать.**

солда́т [*gen. pl.* **-да́т**] *n.* soldier. —**солда́тик,** *n.* toy (*or* tin) soldier. —**солда́тка,** *n.* soldier's wife. —**солда́тский,** *adj.* soldier's.

солева́ренный *adj., in* **солева́ренный заво́д,** saltworks. *Also,* **солева́рный.**

солева́рня [*gen. pl.* **-рен**] *n.* saltworks.

солево́й *adj.* saline.

соле́ние *n.* salting; pickling.

солено́ид *n.* solenoid.

солёность *n.f.* salinity; saltiness.

солёный *adj.* **1,** salt (*attrib.*): солёная вода́, salt water. **2,** salty. **3,** salted; pickled. **4,** *fig., colloq.* spicy; racy; risqué. *See also* **со́лон.**

соле́нье *n., usu. pl.* salted foods.

солеци́зм *n.* solecism.

солидаризи́роваться *v.r. impfv. & pfv.* [*pres.* **-руюсь, -руешься**] (*with* **с** + *instr.*) to express one's solidarity with; make common cause with.

солида́рность *n.f.* solidarity.

солида́рный *adj.* **1,** united; as one; of one mind. **2,** (*with* **с** + *instr.*) in full agreement (with); at one (with).

соли́дно *adv.* **1,** solidly. **2,** in a serious tone or manner. **3,** in a sizable amount: соли́дно зараба́тывать, to earn good money.

соли́дный *adj.* [*short form* **-ден, -дна**] **1,** solid; firm. **2,** sound; thorough. **3,** reputable; well-established. **4,** imposing; impressive. **5,** mature; middle-aged. **6,** *colloq.* large; stout. **7,** *colloq.* sizable; considerable.

соли́ст *n.m.* [*fem.* **соли́стка**] soloist.

солите́р (тэ) *n.* large diamond; solitaire.

солитёр *n.* tapeworm.

соли́ть *v. impfv.* [*pfv.* **посоли́ть;** *pres.* **солю́, со́лишь** *or* **соли́шь**] **1,** to salt. **2,** to pickle.

со́лка *n.* salting; pickling.

со́лнечно *adv.* like the sun. —*adj., used predicatively* sunny: бы́ло со́лнечно и тепло́, it was sunny and warm.

со́лнечный *adj.* **1,** sun (*attrib.*); solar. **2,** sunny. —**со́лнечное пятно́,** sunspot. —**со́лнечный свет,** sunlight; sunshine. —**со́лнечное сплете́ние,** solar plexus. —**со́лнечный уда́р,** sunstroke. —**со́лнечные часы́,** sundial.

со́лнце (сонц) *n.* sun.

солнцезащи́тный *adj.* serving as protection against the sun: солнцезащи́тные очки́, sunglasses.

солнцепёк *n.* blazing sun; heat of the sun.

солнцестоя́ние *n.* solstice.

со́ло *n. indecl.* solo.

солове́й [*gen.* **-вья́**] *n.* nightingale.

соловьи́ный *adj.* nightingale (*attrib.*); nightingale's.

со́лод *n.* malt.

соло́дка *n.* licorice.

солодо́вый *adj.* malt (*attrib.*). —**солодо́вый са́хар,** maltose.

соло́ма *n.* straw.

соло́менный *adj.* **1,** straw (*attrib.*). **2,** (*of a roof*) thatched. **3,** straw-colored. —**соло́менная вдова́,** grass widow.

соло́минка [*gen. pl.* **-нок**] *n.* a straw. —**хвата́ться за соло́минку,** to grasp at a straw.

со́лон *adj., short form of* **солёный, 1,** salty: у меня́ во рту со́лоно, I have a salty taste in my mouth. **2,** *fig.* involving misfortune or adversity: ему́ со́лоно (*or* со́лон) пришло́сь, he came to grief. —**не со́лоно хлеба́вши,** having accomplished nothing.

солоне́ц [*gen.* **-нца́**] *n.* dark alkaline soil.

солони́на *n.* corned beef.

соло́нка [*gen. pl.* **-нок**] *n.* salt shaker; saltcellar.

со́лоно *adj. see* **со́лон.**
солонова́тый *adj.* brackish.
солонча́к [*gen.* **-чака́**] *n.* saline soil; salt marsh.
соль[1] *n.f.* **1,** salt. **2,** (*with gen.*) *colloq.* the point: вся соль расска́за, the whole point of the story.
соль[2] *n. neut. indecl., music* sol; G.
со́льный *adj.* solo.
сольфе́джио *n. indecl.* solfeggio.
соля́нка *n.* **1,** saltwort. **2,** a thick soup with meat or fish.
соляно́й *adj.* salt (*attrib.*); saline.
соля́ный *adj., in* **соля́ная кислота́,** hydrochloric acid.
соля́рий *n.* solarium.
сом [*gen.* **сома́**] *n.* sheatfish.
somати́ческий *adj.* somatic.
со́мкнутый *adj.* (*of a formation, order, etc.*) close.
сомкну́ть *v., pfv. of* **смыка́ть.** —**сомкну́ться,** *refl., pfv. of* **смыка́ться.**
сомнева́ться *v.r. impfv.* (*with* **в** + *prepl. or a dependent clause*) to doubt; have doubts; be in doubt. Вы мо́жете не сомнева́ться в э́том, you can be sure of that.
сомне́ние *n.* doubt. —**без (вся́кого) сомне́ния,** without a doubt. —**вне (вся́кого) сомне́ния,** beyond (any) doubt.
сомни́тельно *adj., used predicatively* doubtful: о́чень сомни́тельно, что́бы..., it is very doubtful whether...
сомни́тельный *adj.* **1,** doubtful; dubious; questionable. **2,** shady; suspicious.
сомно́житель *n.m., math.* factor.
сон [*gen.* **сна**] *n.* **1,** sleep. **2,** dream. —**ви́деть сон,** to have a dream. —**ви́деть (что́-** *or* **кого́-нибудь) во сне,** to have a dream about. —**сквозь сон,** in one's sleep; while half asleep. —**сон в ру́ку,** the dream came true. —**со сна,** being half asleep (*or* awake): он со сна ничего́ не по́нял, he was too sleepy to understand anything. —**у меня́ сна ни в одно́м глазу́,** I am not the least bit sleepy.
сона́та *n.* sonata.
соне́т *n.* sonnet.
сонли́вый *adj.* sleepy; drowsy. —**сонли́вость,** *n.f.* sleepiness; drowsiness.
сонм *n.* **1,** huge throng. **2,** (*with gen.*) multitude (of).
со́нный *adj.* **1,** sleepy; drowsy. **2,** sleeping. —**со́нная боле́знь,** sleeping sickness.
со́ня *n.* dormouse. —*n.m. & f., colloq.* sleepyhead.
соobража́ть *v. impfv.* [*pfv.* **сообрази́ть**] **1,** to think; reflect. **2,** to figure out. Хорошо́ сообража́ть, to be quick to figure things out; be quick-witted. **3,** [*impfv. only*] (*with* **в** + *prepl.*) *colloq.* to know something about (a subject).
соображе́ние *n.* **1,** ability to reason. **2,** *usu. pl.* thoughts; views (*on a subject*). **3,** *usu. pl.* considerations; reasons: по фина́нсовым соображе́ниям, for financial reasons. **4,** *obs.* thinking; thought: поступа́ть без соображе́ния, to act without thinking/thought. —**принима́ть в соображе́ние,** to take into consideration.
сообрази́тельный *adj.* clever; quick-witted. —**сообрази́тельность,** *n.f.* cleverness; quickness of wit.
сообрази́ть [*infl.* **-жу́, -зи́шь**] *v., pfv. of* **сообража́ть.**
сообра́зно *prep., with dat. or* **с** + *instr.* In accordance with; in conformity with.
сообра́зность *n.f.* conformity.
сообра́зный *adj.* (*with* **с** + *instr.*) conforming to; in keeping with. —**ни с чем не сообра́зный,** absurd; ridiculous.
сообразова́ть *v. impfv. & pfv.* [*pres.* **-зу́ю, -зу́ешь**] (*with* **с** + *instr.*) to make (something) conform (to). —**сообразова́ться,** *refl.* (*with* **с** + *instr.*) **1,** to conform to. **2,** to take account of.
сообща́ *adv.* jointly; together; in concert.
сообща́ть *v. impfv.* [*pfv.* **сообщи́ть**] **1,** to report; announce; convey: сообща́ть изве́стие, to report the news; сообща́ть реше́ние *or* о реше́нии, announce a decision. Газе́ты сообща́ют, что..., the newspapers report that... **2,** (*with dat.*) to inform; tell. **3,** to impart; transmit. —**сообща́ться,** *refl.* [*impfv. only*] **1,** to be reported. **2,** (*with* **с** + *instr.*) to communicate (with). **3,** (*with* **с** + *instr.*) to be linked (with). **4,** (*of rooms*) to connect.
сообще́ние *n.* **1,** report; message; communication. **2,** communication(s). Пути́ сообще́ния, communications (*railway, road, etc.*).
соо́бщество *n.* association (*of people*). —**в соо́бществе с,** in the company of.
сообщи́ть *v., pfv. of* **сообща́ть.**
соо́бщник *n.* accomplice.
соорудить [*infl.* **-жу́, -ди́шь**] *v., pfv. of* **сооружа́ть.**
сооружа́ть *v. impfv.* [*pfv.* **сооруди́ть**] to erect; build.
сооруже́ние *n.* **1,** erection; construction. **2,** building; structure. **3,** *mil.* installation; *pl.* works.
соотве́тственно *adv.* **1,** accordingly. **2,** respectively.—*prep., with dat. or* **с** + *instr.* according to; in accordance with.
соотве́тственный *adj.* **1,** (*with dat.*) corresponding (to). **2,** appropriate; proper.
соотве́тствие *n.* accordance; conformity. —**в соотве́тствии с** (+ *instr.*), in accordance with. —**приводи́ть в соотве́тствие с,** to bring into conformity (*or* into line) with.
соотве́тствовать *v. impfv.* [*pres.* **-ствую, -ствуешь**] (*with dat.*) to correspond (to); conform (to).
соотве́тствующий *adj.* **1,** corresponding. **2,** appropriate; proper; suitable. —**соотве́тствующим о́бразом,** accordingly.
соoте́чественник *n.* compatriot; fellow countryman.
соотнести́ [*infl. like* **нести́**] *v., pfv. of* **соотноси́ть.**
соотноси́тельный *adj.* correlative.
соотноси́ть *v. impfv.* [*pfv.* **соотнести́**; *pres.* **-ношу́, -но́сишь**] to correlate. —**соотноси́ться,** *refl.* [*impfv. only*] to correspond.
соотноше́ние *n.* **1,** correlation. **2,** ratio. —**соотноше́ние сил,** correlation of forces; balance of forces.
сопе́рник *n.* rival.
сопе́рничать *v. impfv.* (*with* **с** + *instr.*) **1,** to compete (with). **2,** to vie (with). **3,** to compare (with); rival; equal.
сопе́рничество *n.* rivalry.
сопе́ть *v. impfv.* [*pres.* **-плю́, -пи́шь**] to sniffle; wheeze.
со́пка [*gen. pl.* **-пок**] *n.* **1,** hill or mountain with a rounded summit (*in the Asian USSR*). **2,** volcano (*on Kamchatka Peninsula*).
со́пли [*gen.* **сопле́й**] *n. pl., vulg.* snot.
сопли́вый *adj., colloq.* snotty.
сопло́ [*pl.* **со́пла, со́пел** *or* **сопл**] *n.* nozzle.
сопоста́вить [*infl.* **-влю, -вишь**] *v., pfv. of* **сопоставля́ть.**
сопоставле́ние *n.* comparison.

сопоставля́ть *v. impfv.* [*pfv.* **сопоста́вить**] to compare; contrast.

сопра́но *n. neut. indecl.* soprano (*voice*). —*n. fem. indecl.* soprano (*singer*). —**сопра́нный; сопра́новый,** *adj.* soprano.

сопреде́льный *adj.* neighboring; adjacent; contiguous.

сопредседа́тель *n.m.* co-chairman.

сопре́ть *v., pfv. of* **преть.**

соприкаса́ться *v.r. impfv.* [*pfv.* **соприкосну́ться**] **1,** to touch; border (each other); be contiguous. **2,** (*with* **с** + *instr.*) to border; adjoin. **3,** (*with instr.*) to touch; bump: соприкосну́ться лба́ми, to touch/bump foreheads.

соприкоснове́ние *n.* **1,** contiguity. **2,** contact. —**то́чки соприкоснове́ния,** things in common; areas of common interest.

соприкосну́ться *v.r., pfv. of* **соприкаса́ться.**

сопроводи́тельный *adj.* accompanying. —**сопроводи́тельное письмо́,** covering letter.

сопроводи́ть [*infl.* **-жу́, -ди́шь**] *v., pfv. of* **сопровожда́ть.**

сопровожда́ть *v. impfv.* [*pfv.* **сопроводи́ть**] to accompany. —**сопровожда́ться,** *refl.* [*impfv. only*] (*with instr.*) to be accompanied (by).

сопровожде́ние *n.* **1,** (act of) accompanying: в сопровожде́нии (+ *gen.*), accompanied by; без сопровожде́ния, unaccompanied. **2,** *music* accompaniment. **3,** *mil.* escort.

сопротивле́ние *n.* resistance.

сопротивля́емость *n.f.* resistance (*ability to resist*).

сопротивля́ться *v.r. impfv.* (*with dat.*) to resist.

сопряжённый *adj.* (*with* **с** + *instr.*) involving; entailing: э́то сопряжено́ с больши́ми расхо́дами, it involves/entails great expense.

сопу́тствовать *v. impfv.* [*pres.* **-ствую, -ствуешь**] (*with dat.*) to accompany. Ему́ во всём сопу́тствует уда́ча, he is successful at everything he tries.

сопу́тствующий *adj.* attendant; concomitant.

сор *n.* rubbish; refuse; litter. —**выноси́ть сор из избы́,** to wash one's dirty linen in public; tell tales out of school.

соразме́рить *v., pfv. of* **соразмеря́ть.**

соразме́рно *prep., with dat. or* **с** + *instr.* commensurate with.

соразме́рный *adj.* **1,** commensurate; proportionate. **2,** well-proportioned. —**соразме́рность,** *n.f.* proportion; balance.

соразмеря́ть *v. impfv.* [*pfv.* **соразме́рить**] to make commensurate (with); balance.

сора́тник *n.* comrade in arms.

сорване́ц [*gen.* **-нца́**] *n., colloq.* hoodlum; brat; (*of a girl*) tomboy.

сорва́ть [*infl. like* **рвать**] *v., pfv. of* **срыва́ть.** —**сорва́ться,** *refl., pfv. of* **срыва́ться.**

сорвиголова́ [*infl. like* **голова́**] *n.m. & f., colloq.* daredevil.

сорганизова́ть *v. pfv.* [*infl.* **-зу́ю, -зу́ешь**] *colloq.* to organize.

со́рго *n. indecl.* sorghum.

соревнова́ние *n.* **1,** competition. **2,** *pl., sports* competition; contest.

соревнова́ться *v.r. impfv.* [*pres.* **-ну́юсь, -ну́ешься**] to compete.

сориенти́роваться *v.r., pfv. of* **ориенти́роваться** (*in sense #1*).

сори́нка [*gen. pl.* **-нок**] *n.* speck of dust.

сори́ть *v. impfv.* [*pfv.* **насори́ть**] **1,** to litter. **2,** [*impfv. only*] (*with instr.*) to squander: сори́ть деньга́ми, to toss money around.

со́рный *adj.* rubbish (*attrib.*); refuse (*attrib.*). —**со́рная трава́,** weed; weeds.

сорня́к [*gen.* **-няка́**] *n.* weed.

соро́дич *n.* **1,** relative. **2,** fellow countryman.

со́рок [*gen., dat., instr., & prepl.* **сорока́**] *numeral* forty.

соро́ка *n.* magpie.

сорокале́тие *n.* **1,** fortieth anniversary; fortieth birthday. **2,** forty-year period.

сорокале́тний *adj.* **1,** forty-year (*attrib.*). **2,** forty-year-old.

сороково́й *ordinal numeral* fortieth.

сороконо́жка [*gen. pl.* **-жек**] *n., colloq.* centipede.

сорокопу́т *n.* shrike.

соро́чка [*gen. pl.* **-чек**] *n.* **1,** shirt. Ночна́я соро́чка, nightgown; nightshirt. **2,** chemise. **3,** back (*of a playing card*). —**роди́ться в соро́чке,** to be born with a silver spoon in one's mouth.

сорт [*pl.* **сорта́**] *n.* **1,** sort; kind. **2,** quality; grade: пе́рвого со́рта, top-quality; high-grade.

сортирова́ть *v. impfv.* [*pfv.* **рассортирова́ть;** *pres.* **-ру́ю, -ру́ешь**] to sort; assort.

сортиро́вка *n.* sorting.

сортиро́вочный *adj.* sorting (*attrib.*). —**сортиро́вочная ста́нция,** *R.R.* switchyard.

сортиро́вщик *n.* sorter.

сортово́й *adj.* high-quality.

соса́ние *n.* sucking.

соса́тельный *adj.* sucking (*attrib.*).

соса́ть *v. impfv.* [*pres.* **сосу́, сосёшь**] to suck.

сосва́тать *v., pfv. of* **сва́тать.**

сосе́д [*pl.* **сосе́ди, -дей, -дям**] *n.m.* [*fem.* **-се́дка**] neighbor. —**сосе́дний,** *adj.* neighboring; adjacent; next. —**сосе́дский,** *adj.* the neighbors'.

сосе́дство *n.* **1,** proximity. **2,** *obs.* neighbors. —**по сосе́дству с,** adjacent to; adjoining.

соси́ска [*gen. pl.* **-сок**] *n.* frankfurter.

со́ска [*gen. pl.* **-сок**] *n.* **1,** nipple (*of a nursing bottle*). **2,** pacifier.

соска́бливать *v. impfv.* [*pfv.* **соскобли́ть**] to scrape off.

соска́кивать *v. impfv.* [*pfv.* **соскочи́ть**] (*with* **с** + *gen.*) **1,** to jump off; jump down (from). **2,** to come off.

соска́льзывать *v. impfv.* [*pfv.* **соскользну́ть**] **1,** to slide down. **2,** to slip off.

соскобли́ть [*infl.* **-скоблю́, -ско́блишь** *or* **-скобли́шь**] *v., pfv. of* **соска́бливать.**

соскользну́ть *v., pfv. of* **соска́льзывать.**

соскочи́ть [*infl.* **-скочу́, -ско́чишь**] *v., pfv. of* **соска́кивать.**

соску́читься *v.r. pfv.* **1,** to become bored. **2,** = **скуча́ть** (*in sense #2*).

сослага́тельный *adj., in* **сослага́тельное наклоне́ние,** subjunctive mood.

сосла́ть [*infl.* **сошлю́, сошлёшь**] *v., pfv. of* **ссыла́ть.** —**сосла́ться,** *refl., pfv. of* **ссыла́ться.**

со́слепа *also,* **со́слепу** *adv., colloq.* because one is unable to see; because of one's poor eyesight.

сосло́вие *n.* estate; class. —**дворя́нское сосло́вие,** the nobility. —**духо́вное сосло́вие,** the clergy.

—**крестья́нское сосло́вие,** the peasantry. —**купе́ческое сосло́вие,** the merchants.

сосло́вный *adj.* class (*attrib.*).

сослужи́вец [*gen.* **-вца**] *n.* colleague; fellow worker.

сослужи́ть *v. pfv.* [*infl.* **-служу́, -слу́жишь**], *in* **сослужи́ть слу́жбу** (+ *dat.*), **1,** to do (someone) a favor. **2,** (*with* **хоро́шую**) to stand in good stead; (*with* **плоху́ю**) to do (someone) a disservice; not serve (someone) well.

сосна́ [*pl.* **со́сны, со́сен**] *n.* pine; pine tree. —**сосно́вый,** *adj.* pine (*attrib.*).

сосну́ть *v. pfv., colloq.* to take a nap.

сосня́к [*gen.* **-няка́**] *n.* pine forest.

сосо́к [*gen.* **-ска́**] *n.* nipple; teat.

сосредото́чение *n.* (act of) concentration. —**сосредото́ченность,** *n.f.* (degree of) concentration.

сосредото́ченный *adj.* **1,** concentrated. **2,** lost in concentration. **3,** (*of a look*) intent; (*of attention*) rapt.

сосредото́чивать *v. impfv.* [*pfv.* **сосредото́чить**] to concentrate. —**сосредото́чиваться,** *refl.* **1,** to be concentrated. **2,** (*with* **на** + *prepl.*) to concentrate (on).

соста́в *n.* **1,** composition; make-up. **2,** staff; personnel. Ли́чный соста́в, personnel. **3,** *in certain expressions,* strength: чи́сленный соста́в, numerical strength. В по́лном соста́ве, at full strength. **4,** trains; cars: това́рный соста́в, freight cars; подвижно́й соста́в, rolling stock. **5,** (chemical) compound. **6,** *in* соста́в исполни́телей, *theat.* cast. **7,** *in* соста́в преступле́ния, corpus delicti. —**в соста́ве** (+ *gen.*), consisting of: коми́ссия в соста́ве трёх челове́к, a committee of three. —**входи́ть в соста́в** (+ *gen.*), to form a part of; be a member of.

состави́тель *n.m.* compiler.

соста́вить [*infl.* **-влю, -вишь**] *v., pfv. of* **составля́ть.** —**соста́виться,** *refl., pfv. of* **составля́ться.**

составле́ние *n.* **1,** compilation. **2,** drawing up; drafting. **3,** formation.

составля́ть *v. impfv.* [*pfv.* **соста́вить**] **1,** to put together (*in one place*). **2,** to form (a group, collection, opinion, etc.). **3,** to compile (a list, dictionary, etc.). **4,** to compose; draft; draw up. **5,** to be; represent; constitute. **6,** to total; amount; come to. **7,** *in* составля́ть компа́нию (+ *dat.*), to keep (someone) company. —**составля́ться,** *refl.* **1,** to be formed. **2,** to be built up; accumulate.

составно́й *adj.* **1,** compound; composite. **2,** component; constitutent: составна́я часть, component/constituent part. **3,** sectional. —**составна́я карти́нка,** jigsaw puzzle.

соста́рить *v., pfv. of* **ста́рить.** —**соста́риться,** *refl., pfv. of* **ста́риться.**

состоя́ние *n.* **1,** state; condition: состоя́ние здоро́вья, state of health; в плохо́м состоя́нии, in poor condition. **2,** fortune: нажива́ть состоя́ние, to make a fortune. —**быть в состоя́нии** (+ *inf.*), to be in a position to.

состоя́тельность *n.f.* **1,** wealth. **2,** soundness (*of an argument*).

состоя́тельный *adj.* **1,** well-to-do. **2,** well-founded.

состоя́ть *v. impfv.* [*pres.* **-стою́, -стои́шь**] **1,** (*with* **из**) to consist of. **2,** (*with instr. or various prepositions*) to be (*with reference to one's status*): состоя́ть чле́ном (+ *gen.*), to be a member of; состоя́ть в бра́ке, to be married. **3,** (*with* **в** + *prepl.*) to belong to. **4,** (*with* **в** + *prepl.*) to be; consist of; lie in: ра́зница состои́т в том, что..., the difference is that...

состоя́ться *v.r. pfv.* [*infl.* **-стои́тся**] to take place; be held.

сострада́ние *n.* compassion. —**сострада́тельный,** *adj.* compassionate.

сострига́ть *v. impfv.* [*pfv.* **остри́чь**] to cut off; clip off.

состри́ть *v. pfv.* to crack; make a wisecrack.

состри́чь [*infl. like* **стричь**] *v., pfv. of* **сострига́ть.**

состро́ить *v. pfv., colloq.* to make (a face).

состря́пать *v., pfv. of* **стря́пать.**

состяза́ние *n.* competition; contest; match.

состяза́ться *v.r. impfv.* to compete.

сосу́д *n.* **1,** vessel; container. **2,** *anat.* vessel. —**сосу́дистый,** *adj.* vascular.

сосу́лька [*gen. pl.* **-лек**] *n.* icicle.

сосу́н [*gen.* **-суна́**] *n.* suckling. *Also,* **сосуно́к** [*gen.* **-нка́**].

сосуществова́ние *n.* coexistence.

сосуществова́ть *v. impfv.* [*pres.* **-ству́ю, -ству́ешь**] to coexist.

сосчита́ть *v., pfv. of* **счита́ть** (*in sense #1*).

сот *n., gen. pl. of* **сто:** не́сколько сот, several hundred.

со́тая *n., decl. as an adj.* hundredth: одна́ со́тая, one-hundredth.

сотворе́ние *n.* creation (*of the world*). —**от сотворе́ния ми́ра,** since the world began; since the beginning of time.

сотвори́ть *v., pfv. of* **твори́ть.**

со́тенный *adj., colloq.* hundred-ruble (*attrib.*).

соте́рн (тэ) *n.* sauterne.

votка́ть *v., pfv. of* **ткать.**

со́тня [*gen. pl.* **-тен**] *n.* **1,** one hundred. **2,** *pl.* (*with gen.*) hundreds (of): со́тни ты́сяч люде́й, hundreds of thousands of people.

сотова́рищ *n.* associate; colleague.

со́товый *adj.* of or from a honeycomb.

сотру́дник *n.* **1,** collaborator; colleague; associate. **2,** employee. **3,** (*with gen.*) contributor (*to a newspaper, magazine, etc.*). —**нау́чный сотру́дник,** research assistant.

сотру́дничать *v. impfv.* **1,** (*with* **с** + *instr.*) to cooperate (with); collaborate (with). **2,** (*with* **в** + *prepl.*) to contribute to; write for (a publication).

сотру́дничество *n.* **1,** cooperation; collaboration. **2,** (*with* **в** + *prepl.*) contributing (to a publication).

сотряса́ть *v. impfv.* [*pfv.* **сотрясти́**] to shake; rock. —**сотряса́ться,** *refl.* to shake; tremble.

сотрясе́ние *n.* **1,** shaking; vibration. **2,** shock; impact. —**сотрясе́ние мо́зга,** brain concussion.

сотрясти́ [*infl. like* **трясти́**] *v., pfv. of* **сотряса́ть.** —**сотрясти́сь,** *refl., pfv. of* **сотряса́ться.**

со́ты *n. pl.* [*sing.* **сот**] honeycomb.

со́тый *ordinal numeral* hundredth.

со́ус *n.* sauce; gravy; dressing. —**со́усник,** *n.* gravy boat.

соуча́стие *n.* complicity. —**соуча́стник,** *n.* accomplice.

соучени́к [*gen.* **-ника́**] *n.m.* [*fem.* **-ни́ца**] fellow classmate.

софа́ [*pl.* **со́фы**] *n.* sofa.

софи́зм *n.* sophism. —**софи́ст,** *n.* sophist. —**софи́стика,** *n.* sophistry. —**софисти́ческий,** *adj.* sophistic.

соха́ [*pl.* **со́хи**] *n.* old wooden plow.

со́хнуть *v. impfv.* [*pfv.* **вы́сохнуть;** *past* **сох** *or* **со́хнул, со́хла**] **1,** to dry; become dry. **2,** to dry up. **3,** to wither. **4,** *colloq.* to grow thin.

сохране́ние *n.* **1,** preservation; conservation. **2,** keeping; retention. **3,** safekeeping: отдава́ть на сохране́ние, to turn over for safekeeping.

сохрани́ть *v., pfv. of* **сохраня́ть.** —**сохрани́ться,** *refl., pfv. of* **сохраня́ться.**

сохра́нность *n.f.* **1,** safety. **2,** state of preservation. —**в сохра́нности,** safe; intact.

сохра́нный *adj.* **1,** safe: в сохра́нном ме́сте, in a safe place. **2,** safe; unharmed.

сохраня́ть *v. impfv.* [*pfv.* **сохрани́ть**] **1,** to preserve; maintain. **2,** to keep; retain. **3,** to conserve. **4,** to protect. **5,** *in* **сохраня́ть за собо́й,** to reserve. —**сохраня́ться,** *refl.* **1,** to be preserved; remain; survive. **2,** (*of food*) to keep; not spoil. **3,** *colloq.* (*of a person*) to be well-preserved.

соцве́тие *n.* raceme.

социализа́ция *n.* socialization.

социализи́ровать *v. impfv. & pfv.* [*pres.* **-рую, -руешь**] to socialize.

социали́зм *n.* socialism. —**социали́ст,** *n.* socialist. —**социалисти́ческий,** *adj.* socialist; socialistic.

социа́льный *adj.* social.

социоло́гия *n.* sociology. —**социо́лог,** *n.* sociologist. —**социологи́ческий,** *adj.* sociological.

соче́льник *n.* **1,** Christmas Eve. **2,** Twelfth Night.

сочета́ние *n.* combination. —**в сочета́нии с,** in conjunction with.

сочета́ть *v. impfv. & pfv.* to combine. —**сочета́ться,** *refl.* **1,** to be combined. **2,** to match; go well together; (*with* **с** + *instr.*) go well with.

сочине́ние *n.* **1,** (act of) composing. **2,** (literary) work. **3,** composition (*written for school*).

сочини́тель *n.m.* **1,** *archaic* writer; composer. **2,** *colloq.* liar; storyteller.

сочини́тельный *adj., gram.* coordinate: сочини́тельный сою́з, coordinate conjunction.

сочиня́ть *v. impfv.* [*pfv.* **сочини́ть**] **1,** to compose. **2,** to make up; concoct; invent.

сочи́ть *v. impfv.* to exude. —**сочи́ться,** *refl.* to ooze; trickle.

со́чный *adj.* **1,** juicy; succulent. **2,** *fig.* rich; lush. —**со́чность,** *n.f.* juiciness; succulence.

сочу́вственный *adj.* sympathetic. —**сочу́вственно,** *adv.* sympathetically.

сочу́вствие *n.* sympathy.

сочу́вствовать *v. impfv.* [*pres.* **-ствую, -ствуешь**] (*with dat.*) **1,** to sympathize (with); feel sorry for; feel for. **2,** to sympathize (with); be in sympathy (with).

со́шка [*gen. pl.* **-шек**] *n.* prop; support (*for a gun*). —**ме́лкая со́шка,** small fry; pipsqueak.

сошни́к [*gen.* **-ника́**] *n.* plowshare.

сощу́рить *v., pfv. of* **щу́рить.** —**сощу́риться,** *refl., pfv. of* **щу́риться.**

сою́з *n.* **1,** union. **2,** alliance. **3,** *gram.* conjunction. —**в сою́зе с,** in league with.

сою́зник *n.m.* [*fem.* **-ница**] ally. Фра́нция – наш сою́зник (*or* на́ша сою́зница), France is our ally.

сою́зный *adj.* **1,** union (*attrib.*). **2,** federal. **3,** allied.

со́я *n.* **1,** soybean (*plant*). **2,** *colloq.* soy sauce.

спаге́тти *n. neut. indecl.* spaghetti.

спад *n.* **1,** falling off; decline. **2,** *econ.* recession; slump. **3,** receding (*of water*).

спада́ть *v. impfv.* [*pfv.* **спасть**] **1,** (*with* **с** + *gen.*) to fall off; fall down from. **2,** (*of water, swelling, etc.*) to go down. **3,** [*impfv. only*] to hang down. **4,** to subside; abate.

спазм *also,* **спа́зма** *n.* spasm. —**спазмати́ческий,** *adj.* spasmodic.

спа́ивать *v. impfv.* **1,** [*pfv.* **спая́ть**] to solder (together); *fig.* unite. **2,** [*pfv.* **споить**] *colloq.* to make drunk; make a drunkard of.

спа́йка *n.* **1,** soldering. **2,** soldered joint. **3,** *fig.* unity; cohesion.

спали́ть *v., pfv. of* **пали́ть** (*in sense #2*).

спа́льный *adj.* sleeping (*attrib.*). —**спа́льное ме́сто,** berth.

спа́льня [*gen. pl.* **-лен**] *n.* bedroom.

спание́ль *n.m.* spaniel.

спаньё *n., colloq.* sleeping.

спа́ренный *adj.* dual; twin.

спа́ржа *n.* asparagus. —**спа́ржевый,** *adj.* asparagus (*attrib.*).

спа́ривание *n.* mating.

спа́ривать *v. impfv.* [*pfv.* **спа́рить**] **1,** to pair; couple. **2,** to mate. —**спа́риваться,** *refl.* **1,** *colloq.* to pair off. **2,** to mate.

спартакиа́да *n.* Spartacist Games.

спарта́нец [*gen.* **-нца**] *n.m.* [*fem.* **-нка**] Spartan. —**спарта́нский,** *adj.* Spartan.

спа́рывать *v. impfv.* [*pfv.* **споро́ть**] to remove; take off (*by cutting the stitches*).

спаса́ние *n.* saving; rescuing.

спаса́тель *n.m.* **1,** rescue worker. **2,** lifeguard.

спаса́тельный *adj.* rescue (*attrib.*). —**спаса́тельный жиле́т,** life jacket. —**спаса́тельный круг,** life buoy. —**спаса́тельная ло́дка** *or* **шлю́пка,** lifeboat. —**спаса́тельный по́яс,** life belt; life preserver.

спаса́ть *v. impfv.* [*pfv.* **спасти́**] to save; rescue. —**спаса́ться,** *refl.* **1,** to be saved. **2,** to escape.

спасе́ние *n.* **1,** saving; rescue. **2,** escape. **3,** salvation.

спаси́бо *particle* thank you; thanks. Большо́е (вам) спаси́бо!, thank you very much! —**за (одно́) спаси́бо,** without asking anything in return. —**и на том спаси́бо,** we should be grateful at least for that.

спаси́тель *n.m.* **1,** savior; rescuer. **2,** *relig.* Savior.

спаси́тельный *adj.* that which saves; bringing salvation.

спасова́ть *v., pfv. of* **пасова́ть.**

спасти́ [*infl.* **спасу́, спасёшь;** *past* **спас, спасла́, спасло́**] *v., pfv. of* **спаса́ть.** —**спасти́сь,** *refl., pfv. of* **спаса́ться.**

спасти́ческий *adj.* spastic.

спасть [*infl. like* **пасть**] *v., pfv. of* **спада́ть.**

спать *v. impfv.* [*pres.* **сплю, спишь, спит, спим, спи́те, спят;** *past fem.* **спала́**] to sleep. —**спа́ться,** *refl.* [*past* **спало́сь**] *impers.* (*with dat.*) *colloq.* to be able to sleep: мне не спи́тся, I can't fall asleep; мне пло́хо спало́сь, I didn't sleep well.

спа́янный *adj.* united; close-knit. —**спа́янность,** *n.f.* unity; cohesion.

спая́ть *v., pfv. of* **спа́ивать** (*in sense #1*).

спева́ться *v.r. impfv.* [*pfv.* **спе́ться**] **1,** to achieve harmony in singing. **2,** *colloq.* to get along.

спе́вка *n.* choir practice.

спекта́кль *n.m.* show; performance.

спектр *n.* spectrum. —**спектра́льный,** *adj.* spectral.

спектроско́п *n.* spectroscope. —**спектроскопи́ческий,** *adj.* spectroscopic.
спекули́ровать *v. impfv.* [*pres.* **-рую, -руешь**] (*with instr. or* **на** + *prepl.*) **1,** to speculate (in). **2,** to exploit; capitalize (on); take advantage of.
спекуля́нт *n.* **1,** speculator. **2,** *fig.* exploiter; opportunist.
спекуляти́вный *adj.* **1,** speculative. **2,** (*of prices*) artificially high.
спекуля́ция *n.* **1,** speculation. **2,** (*with* **на** + *prepl.*) taking advantage of.
спелена́ть *v., pfv. of* **пелена́ть.**
спе́лый *adj.* ripe. —**спе́лость,** *n.f.* ripeness.
сперва́ *adv., colloq.* first; at first.
спе́реди *adv.* **1,** in front. **2,** from the front. —*prep., with gen.* in (*or* from) the front of.
спере́ть *v. pfv.* [*infl.* **сопру́, сопрёшь;** *past* **спёр, -ла**] *colloq.* to steal; swipe.
спе́рма *n.* sperm.
спёртый *adj., colloq.* (*of air*) close; stuffy.
спеси́вый *adj.* haughty; arrogant; high and mighty.
спесь *n.f.* haughtiness; arrogance. —**сбива́ть спесь с** (+ *gen.*), to take (someone) down a peg.
спеть[1] *v. impfv.* [*pfv.* **поспе́ть;** *pres.* **спе́ет**] to ripen; become ripe.
спеть[2] [*infl.* **спою́, споёшь**] *v., pfv. of* **петь.** —**спе́ться,** *refl., pfv. of* **спева́ться.**
спех *n., colloq.* hurry. —**мне не к спе́ху,** I'm in no hurry.
специализа́ция *n.* specialization.
специализи́ровать *v. impfv. & pfv.* [*pres.* **-рую, -руешь**] to make specialized; assign a specialty to. —**специализи́роваться,** *refl.* (*with* **в** + *prepl. or* **по**) to specialize (in).
специали́ст *n.* specialist; expert.
специа́льно *adv.* **1,** specially: специа́льно подгото́влен, specially trained. **2,** especially: специа́льно для вас, especially for you.
специа́льность *n.f.* **1,** specialty; field of specialization: рабо́тать по специа́льности, to work in one's field. **2,** profession: инжене́р по специа́льности, an engineer by profession.
специа́льный *adj.* **1,** special. **2,** specialized.
специ́фика *n.* (specific) nature.
спецификáция *n.* specification.
специфи́ческий *adj.* specific.
спе́ция *n.* spice.
спецоде́жда *n.* overalls.
спе́шивать *v. impfv.* [*pfv.* **спе́шить**] to order to dismount; force to dismount. —**спе́шиваться,** *refl.* to dismount.
спе́шить *v., pfv. of* **спе́шивать.** —**спе́шиться,** *refl., pfv. of* **спе́шиваться.**
спеши́ть *v. impfv.* [*pfv.* **поспеши́ть**] **1,** to hurry; rush. **2,** [*impfv. only*] to be in a hurry. **3,** (*with inf.*) to hasten (to). **4,** [*impfv. only*] (*of a timepiece*) to be fast. —**не спеша́,** at a leisurely pace; deliberately.
спе́шка *n., colloq.* hurry; rush; haste. —**в спе́шке,** in one's (*or* everyone's) haste.
спе́шно *adv.* in a hurry; hastily.
спе́шность *n.f.* **1,** urgency. **2,** haste.
спе́шный *adj.* **1,** urgent; pressing. **2,** hurried; hasty. —**спе́шная по́чта,** special delivery.
спива́ться *v.r. impfv.* [*pfv.* **спи́ться**] to take to drink; become an alcoholic.
спидо́метр *n.* speedometer.
спи́кер *n.* speaker (*of the House of Commons or House of Representatives*).
спи́ливать *v. impfv.* [*pfv.* **спили́ть**] **1,** to saw down. **2,** to saw off.
спили́ть [*infl.* **спилю́, спи́лишь**] *v., pfv. of* **спи́ливать.**
спина́ [*acc.* **спи́ну;** *pl.* **спи́ны**] *n.* back. —**за спино́й** (+ *gen.*), behind someone's back. —**спино́й к,** with one's back to.
спи́нка [*gen. pl.* **-нок**] *n.* **1,** *dim. of* **спина́. 2,** back (*of a garment, piece of furniture, etc.*).
спинно́й *adj.* spinal; dorsal. —**спинно́й мозг,** spinal cord. —**спинно́й хребе́т,** spine; backbone; spinal column.
спинномозгово́й *adj.* spinal.
спира́ль *n.f.* spiral. —**спира́льный,** *adj.* spiral.
спири́т *n.* spiritualist (*one who believes in communication with the dead*). —**спирити́зм,** *n.* spiritualism. —**спирити́ческий,** *adj.* spiritualistic.
спиритуали́зм *n., philos.* spiritualism. —**спиритуали́ст,** *n.* spiritualist.
спирт *n.* **1,** alcohol: древе́сный спирт, wood alcohol. **2,** spirits: камфа́рный спирт, spirits of camphor. —**нашаты́рный спирт,** liquid ammonia.
спиртно́е *n., decl. as an adj., colloq.* alcohol.
спиртно́й *adj.* alcoholic.
спирто́вка [*gen. pl.* **-вок**] *n.* spirit lamp.
спиртово́й *adj.* spirit (*attrib.*); alcohol (*attrib.*).
списа́ть [*infl.* **спишу́, спи́шешь**] *v., pfv. of* **спи́сывать.** —**списа́ться,** *refl., pfv. of* **спи́сываться.**
спи́сок [*gen.* **-ска**] *n.* list.
спи́сывать *v. impfv.* [*pfv.* **списа́ть**] **1,** to copy. **2,** (*with* **с** + *gen.*) to base on (*when writing or painting*): спи́сан с живо́го лица́, based on a real-life person. **3,** (*with* **у**) to copy (from); crib (from). **4,** *finance* to write off. —**спи́сываться,** *refl.* (*with* **с** + *instr.*) to write to; get in touch with (*by mail*).
спито́й *adj., colloq.* (*of tea or coffee*) weak.
спи́ться [*infl.* **сопью́сь, сопьёшься;** *past* **спи́лся, спила́сь, спило́сь**] *v.r., pfv. of* **спива́ться.**
спи́хивать *v. impfv.* [*pfv.* **спихну́ть**] *colloq.* **1,** to push off. **2,** *fig.* to shove aside; kick out.
спи́ца *n.* **1,** spoke. **2,** knitting needle.
спич *n.* (short) speech.
спи́чечница *n.* **1,** *obs.* matchbox. **2,** matchbox holder.
спи́чечный *adj.* match (*attrib.*): спи́чечная коро́бка, matchbox.
спи́чка [*gen. pl.* **-чек**] *n.* match.
сплав *n.* **1,** alloy. **2,** floating (*of timber*).
спла́вить [*infl.* **-влю, -вишь**] *v., pfv. of* **сплавля́ть.**
сплавля́ть *v. impfv.* [*pfv.* **спла́вить**] **1,** to fuse; alloy. **2,** *fig.* to bind together; forge together. **3,** to float (something) downstream. **4,** *colloq.* to get rid of; unload.
сплавно́й *adj.* (*of timber*) floating.
сплани́ровать *v., pfv. of* **плани́ровать.**
спла́чивать *v. impfv.* [*pfv.* **сплоти́ть**] **1,** to fasten together; join. **2,** *fig.* to rally; unite. **3,** *in* спла́чивать ряды́, to close ranks. —**спла́чиваться,** *refl.* **1,** to cluster (together). **2,** *fig.* to rally; unite; be united.
сплёвывать *v. impfv.* [*pfv.* **сплю́нуть**] to spit; spit out.
сплести́ [*infl. like* **плести́**] *v., pfv. of* **плести́** *and* **сплета́ть.** —**сплести́сь,** *refl., pfv. of* **сплета́ться.**
сплета́ть *v. impfv.* [*pfv.* **сплести́**] **1,** to weave. **2,** to

entwine; intertwine. —**сплета́ться,** *refl.* **1,** to become entwined; become tangled. **2,** *fig.* to become intertwined.

сплете́ние *n.* **1,** junction. **2,** tangle. **3,** *anat.* plexus: со́лнечное сплете́ние, solar plexus. **4,** *fig.* combination: сплете́ние обстоя́тельств, combination of circumstances. —**сплете́ние лжи,** web of lies.

спле́тник *n.m.* [*fem.* **-ница**] gossip (*person*).

спле́тничать *v. impfv.* [*pfv.* **наспле́тничать**] to gossip.

спле́тня [*gen. pl.* **-тен**] *n.* gossip; item of gossip.

сплеча́ *adv.* **1,** with a full sweep of the arm. **2,** in haste; without thought. —**руби́ть сплеча́,** to shoot from the hip.

сплоти́ть [*infl.* **-чу́, -ти́шь**] *v., pfv. of* **спла́чивать.** —**сплоти́ться,** *refl., pfv. of* **спла́чиваться.**

сплохова́ть *v. pfv.* [*infl.* **-ху́ю, -ху́ешь**] *colloq.* to make a blunder.

сплоче́ние *n.* rallying; uniting.

сплочённость *n.f.* unity; solidarity; cohesion.

сплочённый *adj.* **1,** solid. **2,** united.

сплошно́й *adj.* **1,** solid; continuous; unbroken. **2,** complete; total. **3,** *colloq.* pure; utter; sheer.

сплошь *adv.* all over; completely. —**сплошь и** (*or* **да) ря́дом,** *colloq.* very often.

сплутова́ть *v., pfv. of* **плутова́ть.**

сплыва́ть *v. impfv.* [*pfv.* **сплыть**] *colloq.* **1,** to swim downstream; float downstream. **2,** to overflow; run over. —**бы́ло да сплы́ло,** it came and it went; it's gone for good.

сплыть [*infl. like* **плыть**] *v., pfv. of* **сплыва́ть.**

сплю́нуть *v., pfv. of* **сплёвывать.**

сплю́снутый *adj.* flat; flattened. *Also,* **сплю́щенный.**

сплю́щивать *v. impfv.* [*pfv.* **сплю́щить**] to flatten. —**сплю́щиваться,** *refl.* to become flat; flatten out.

спляса́ть *v., pfv. of* **пляса́ть.**

сподви́жник *n.* associate; comrade-in-arms.

сподру́чный *adj., colloq.* convenient; handy.

спозара́нку *adv., colloq.* early in the morning.

спои́ть [*infl.* **спою́, спо́ишь** *or* **спои́шь**] *v., pfv. of* **спа́ивать** (*in sense #2*).

споко́йно *adv.* calmly; peacefully. —*adj., used predicatively* quiet; peaceful: здесь споко́йно, it is quiet/peaceful here. —**спи́те споко́йно!,** sleep well! —**у меня́ на душе́ споко́йно,** my mind is at ease.

споко́йный *adj.* [*short form* **-ко́ен, -ко́йна**] **1,** calm; tranquil; quiet; peaceful. **2,** (*of light, color, etc.*) restful. **3,** *colloq.* comfortable. —**споко́йной но́чи!,** good night!

споко́йствие *n.* **1,** quiet; calm; tranquillity. **2,** public order. **3,** composure; equanimity.

спола́скивать *v. impfv.* [*pfv.* **сполосну́ть**] *colloq.* to rinse; rinse out.

сполза́ть *v. impfv.* [*pfv.* **сползти́**] **1,** to climb down; crawl down. **2,** to slip off; slip down. **3,** to trickle down. **4,** to slope down. **5,** (*of an expression, smile, etc.*) to fade (from one's face).

сползти́ [*infl. like* **ползти́**] *v., pfv. of* **сполза́ть.**

сполна́ *adv.* in full.

сполосну́ть *v., pfv. of* **спола́скивать.**

споло́х *n.* **1,** flash of lightning. **2,** *pl.* northern lights.

сponта́нный *adj.* spontaneous.

спор *n.* **1,** argument. **2,** dispute; controversy. —**спо́ру нет,** there is no question; there's no denying.

спо́ра *n.* spore.

спораdи́ческий *adj.* sporadic.

спо́рить *v. impfv.* [*pfv.* **поспо́рить**] **1,** to argue. **2,** to deny: не спо́рю, что..., I don't deny that... **3,** *colloq.* to bet. **4,** (*with* **с** *or* **про́тив**) *fig.* to fight. **5,** to compete.

спори́ться *v.r. impfv., colloq.* to go well; work out well; turn out well.

спо́рный *adj.* **1,** controversial. **2,** debatable; moot. **3,** unsettled; outstanding. **4,** disputed.

споро́ть [*infl.* **спорю́, спо́решь**] *v., pfv. of* **спа́рывать.**

спорт *n.* sports.

спорти́вный *adj.* sports (*attrib.*); sporting; athletic. —**из спорти́вного интере́са,** for the fun of it.

спортсме́н *n.m.* [*fem.* **-ме́нка**] athlete; sportsman. —**спортсме́нский,** *adj.* sportsmanlike.

спорхну́ть *v. pfv.* **1,** to fly away; flit away. **2,** to land suddenly.

спо́рщик *n.* person who likes to argue.

спо́рый *adj., colloq.* **1,** (*of work, movements, etc.*) smooth. **2,** profitable.

спорынья́ *n.* ergot.

спо́соб *n.* way; method.

спосо́бность *n.f.* **1,** ability. **2,** *usu. pl.* (*with* **к**) aptitude (for); faculty (for). У́мственные спосо́бности, mental faculties. **3,** capacity; power: пропускна́я спосо́бность, carrying capacity; покупа́тельная спосо́бность, purchasing power.

спосо́бный *adj.* [*short form* **-бен, -бна**] **1,** able; bright; talented. **2,** (*with* **к**) good (at); having a gift (for). **3,** (*with* **к, на,** *or inf.*) capable (of).

спосо́бствовать *v. impfv.* [*pres.* **-ствую, -ствуешь**] (*with dat.*) to further; promote; contribute to.

спотыка́ться *v.r. impfv.* [*pfv.* **споткну́ться**] to stumble; trip.

спохвати́ться [*infl.* **-хвачу́сь, -хва́тишься**] *v.r., pfv. of* **спохва́тываться.**

спохва́тываться *v.r. impfv.* [*pfv.* **спохвати́ться**] *colloq.* to remember suddenly.

спра́ва *adv.* **1,** from the right. **2,** to (*or* on) the right.

справедли́во *adv.* fairly; justly.

справедли́вость *n.f.* justice; fairness. —**справедли́вости ра́ди,** in all fairness. —**отда́ть справедли́вость** (+ *dat.*), to give credit to; give (someone) his due.

справедли́вый *adj.* **1,** just; fair. **2,** just; justifiable; justified. **3,** correct; valid.

спра́вить [*infl.* **-влю, -вишь**] *v., pfv. of* **справля́ть.** —**спра́виться,** *refl., pfv. of* **справля́ться.**

спра́вка [*gen. pl.* **-вок**] *n.* **1,** *usu. pl.* reference: для спра́вок, for reference purposes. **2,** information. **3,** certificate. —**наводи́ть спра́вки о,** to make inquiries about.

справля́ть *v. impfv.* [*pfv.* **спра́вить**] *colloq.* to celebrate (an occasion). Справля́ть сва́дьбу, to hold a wedding. —**справля́ться,** *refl.* **1,** (*with* **о**) to inquire (about). **2,** (*with* **в** + *prepl.*) to consult (a book, dictionary, etc.). **3,** (*with* **с** + *instr.*) to cope with; handle.

спра́вочник *n.* reference book; directory.

спра́вочный *adj.* reference (*attrib.*); information (*attrib.*); inquiry (*attrib.*).

спра́шивать *v. impfv.* [*pfv.* **спроси́ть**] **1,** (*with acc. or* **у**) to ask (someone). **2,** (*with acc. or* **о**) to ask (about). **3,** to ask for. **4,** to ask for (someone); ask to see. **5,** to call on (a pupil). **6,** *colloq.* to ask; charge (a price). **7,** (*with* **с** + *gen.*) *colloq.* to hold accountable. —**спра́-**

шиваться, *refl.* **1**, (*with* **у**) *colloq.* to ask permission (of). **2**, [*impfv. only*] *impers.*: спра́шивается, one may ask; the question arises.

спрессова́ть *v., pfv. of* **прессова́ть**.

спринт *n.* sprint. —**спри́нтер**, *n.* sprinter.

спринцева́ть *v. impfv.* [*pres.* **-цу́ю, -цу́ешь**] to syringe.

спринцо́вка *n.* **1**, syringing. **2**, syringe.

спрова́живать *v. impfv.* [*pfv.* **спрова́дить**] *colloq.* to escort out; send on one's way; send packing.

спровоци́ровать *v., pfv. of* **провоци́ровать**.

спроекти́ровать *v., pfv. of* **проекти́ровать**.

спрос *n., econ.* demand: спрос и предложе́ние, supply and demand. —**без спро́са; без спро́су**, without permission.

спроси́ть [*infl.* **спрошу́, спро́сишь**] *v., pfv. of* **спра́шивать**. —**спроси́ться**, *refl., pfv. of* **спра́шиваться**.

спросо́нок *adv., colloq.* half-awake; being only half-awake.

спроста́ *adv., colloq.* **1**, out of naïveté. **2**, on the spur of the moment; just like that.

спрут *n.* octopus.

спры́гивать *v. impfv.* [*pfv.* **спры́гнуть**] (*with* **с** + *gen.*) to jump off; jump down (from).

спры́скивать *v. impfv.* [*pfv.* **спры́снуть**] *colloq.* to sprinkle.

спряга́ть *v. impfv.* [*pfv.* **проспряга́ть**] to conjugate (a verb).

спряже́ние *n., gram.* conjugation.

спрясть *v., pfv. of* **прясть**.

спря́тать *v., pfv. of* **пря́тать**. —**спря́таться**, *refl., pfv. of* **пря́таться**.

спу́гивать *v. impfv.* [*pfv.* **спугну́ть**] to frighten off; frighten away.

спуд *n., in* **под спу́дом**, hidden; under wraps; **из-под спу́да**, from hiding; from under wraps.

спуск *n.* **1**, lowering. **2**, descent; going down. **3**, descent; slope. —**не дава́ть спу́ска** (+ *dat.*), *colloq.* to give someone no quarter.

спуска́ть *v. impfv.* [*pfv.* **спусти́ть**] **1**, to lower; let down. **2**, to launch (a ship). **3**, to release; let loose. **4**, to let the air out of; let the water out of. **5**, *v.i.* (*of a tire*) to go flat. **6**, *colloq.* to pardon; forgive. **7**, *colloq.* to sell; unload. **8**, *colloq.* to squander; throw away. **9**, *in* спуска́ть куро́к, to pull the trigger. **10**, *in* спуска́ть пе́тлю, to drop a stitch. —**спуска́ться**, *refl.* **1**, to go down; descend. **2**, (*of a plane, bird, etc.*) to land. **3**, to sail downstream. **4**, (*of fog, dusk, etc.*) to descend; fall. **5**, [*impfv. only*] to hang down. **6**, [*impfv. only*] to slope down.

спускно́й *adj.* drain (*attrib.*): спускно́й кран, drain cock.

спусково́й *adj.* = **спускно́й**. —**спусково́й крючо́к**, trigger.

спусти́ть [*infl.* **спущу́, спу́стишь**] *v., pfv. of* **спуска́ть**. —**спусти́ться**, *refl., pfv. of* **спуска́ться**.

спустя́ *prep., with acc.* after.

спу́танный *adj.* **1**, tangled. **2**, confused; muddled; incoherent.

спу́тать *v., pfv. of* **пу́тать**. —**спу́таться**, *refl., pfv. of* **пу́таться**.

спу́тник *n.* **1**, traveling companion. **2**, satellite.

спья́на *also,* **спья́ну** *adv., colloq.* while drunk.

спя́тить *v. pfv.* [*infl.* **спя́чу, спя́тишь**] *colloq.* to go crazy; go nuts.

спя́чка *n.* **1**, [*usu.* **зи́мняя спя́чка**] hibernation. **2**, *colloq.* drowsiness; lethargy.

сраба́тывать *v. impfv.* [*pfv.* **срабо́тать**] *colloq.* **1**, to make; turn out. **2**, (*of a device, machine, etc.*) to work; operate. —**сраба́тываться**, *refl.* **1**, (*of a machine*) to wear out. **2**, to achieve harmony in work.

срабо́танность *n.f.* **1**, harmony in work. **2**, wear (and tear).

срабо́тать *v., pfv. of* **сраба́тывать**. —**срабо́таться**, *refl., pfv. of* **сраба́тываться**.

сравне́ние *n.* **1**, comparison. **2**, simile. —**по сравне́нию с; в сравне́нии с**, compared to; in comparison with. —**не идёт (ни) в (како́е) сравне́ние с**, cannot compare to.

сра́внивать *v. impfv.* **1**, [*pfv.* **сравни́ть**] to compare. **2**, [*pfv.* **сравня́ть**] to make equal. Сравня́ть счёт, to tie the score. **3**, [*pfv.* **сровня́ть**] to even; level. Сровня́ть с землёй, to raze to the ground.

сравни́мый *adj.* comparable. —**ни с чем не сравни́мый**, incomparable; in a class by itself.

сравни́тельно *adv.* **1**, comparatively. **2**, (*with* **с** + *instr.*) compared to.

сравни́тельный *adj.* comparative.

сравни́ть *v., pfv. of* **сра́внивать** (*in sense #1*). —**сравни́ться**, *refl.* (*with* **с** + *instr.*) to compare: никто́ не мо́жет сравни́ться с ней, no one can compare to her.

сравня́ть *v., pfv. of* **равня́ть** *and* **сра́внивать** (*in sense #2*). —**сравня́ться**, *refl.* (*with* **с** + *instr.*) to become the equal of; achieve equality with.

сража́ть *v. impfv.* [*pfv.* **срази́ть**] **1**, to strike down. **2**, *fig.* (*of news*) to stagger. —**сража́ться**, *refl.* to fight (*in batttle*).

сраже́ние *n.* battle.

срази́ть [*infl.* **-жу́, -зи́шь**] *v., pfv. of* **сража́ть**. —**срази́ться**, *refl., pfv. of* **сража́ться**.

сра́зу *adv.* **1**, at once; immediately; right away. **2**, all at once. **3**, just: сра́зу за (+ *instr.*), just beyond *or* behind. —**сра́зу по́сле** (+ *gen.*), **1**, right after. **2**, just past.

срам *n., colloq.* shame.

срами́ть *v. impfv.* [*pfv.* **осрами́ть**; *pres.* **-млю́, -ми́шь**] *colloq.* to shame; disgrace.

срамни́к [*gen.* **-ника́**] *n., colloq.* shameless person.

срамно́й *adj., obs.* indecent.

сраста́ние *n.* knitting (*of bones*).

сраста́ться *v.r. impfv.* [*pfv.* **срасти́сь**] to grow together; (*of bones*) knit.

срасти́сь [*infl. like* **расти́**] *v.r., pfv. of* **сраста́ться**.

срасти́ть [*infl.* **-щу́, -сти́шь**] *v., pfv. of* **сра́щивать**.

сраще́ние *n.* **1**, joining together. **2**, growing together.

сра́щивание *n.* **1**, setting (*of a bone*). **2**, joining; splicing. **3**, *fig.* merging.

сра́щивать *v. impfv.* [*pfv.* **срасти́ть**] **1**, to set (a broken bone). **2**, to join together; splice. **3**, *fig.* to merge; intertwine.

сре́бреник *n.* ancient silver coin; piece of silver.

среда́ *n.* **1**, [*acc.* **сре́ду**] Wednesday. **2**, [*acc.* **среду́**] surroundings; environment; *physics* medium. —**окружа́ющая среда́**, the environment.

среди́ *prep., with gen.* **1**, in the middle of. **2**, among. —**среди́ (***or* **средь) бе́ла дня**, in broad daylight.

среди́на *n.* = **середи́на**. —**среди́нный**, *adj.* = **середи́нный**.

сре́дне *adv., colloq.* fair; so-so.

средне- *prefix* **1**, central: среднеазиа́тский, Central

Asian. **2,** middle: среднеангли́йский язы́к, Middle English.

средневеко́вье *n.* the Middle Ages. —**средневеко́вый,** *adj.* medieval.

сре́днее *n., decl. as an adj.* average: вы́ше/ни́же сре́днего, above/below average. —**в сре́днем,** on the average.

сре́дний *adj.* **1,** middle. **2,** medium. **3,** average; mean. **4,** average; mediocre. **5,** *gram.* neuter. **6,** (*of school or education*) secondary. —**сре́дние века́,** the Middle Ages. —**сре́дних лет,** middle-aged. —**сре́дней руки́,** ordinary; of no particular distinction.

средото́чие *n.* focus; focal point; center; hub.

сре́дство *n.* **1,** means; way. **2,** *pl.* means: сре́дства произво́дства, means of production; челове́к со сре́дствами, man of means. **3,** *pl.* funds. **4,** medication; preparation; remedy: возбужда́ющее сре́дство, stimulant; сре́дство от ка́шля, cough remedy; сре́дство от насеко́мых, insecticide.

средь *prep.* = **среди́.**

срез *n.* **1,** cut; slice; section. **2,** microscopic section.

сре́зать [*infl.* **сре́жу, сре́жешь**] *v., pfv. of* **ре́зать** (*in sense #6*) *and* **среза́ть.** —**сре́заться,** *refl., pfv. of* **среза́ться.**

среза́ть *v. impfv.* [*pfv.* **сре́зать**] **1,** to cut off; cut away. **2,** to strike down; cut down. **3,** *fig.* to reduce; cut down. **4,** to cut off (*while speaking*). **5,** to slice (a ball). **6,** *colloq.* to flunk (a student). **7,** *in* сре́зать у́гол, to take a shortcut. —**среза́ться,** *refl.* (*with* **на** + *prepl.*) to flunk (an examination).

сре́зывать *v. impfv.* = **среза́ть.**

срисова́ть [*infl.* **-су́ю, -су́ешь**] *v., pfv. of* **срисо́вывать.**

срисо́вывать *v. impfv.* [*pfv.* **срисова́ть**] to copy.

сровня́ть *v., pfv. of* **ровня́ть** *and* **сра́внивать** (*in sense #3*).

сродни́ *adv.* (*with dat.*) *colloq.* **1,** related (to). **2,** *fig.* akin (to).

сродни́ть *v., pfv. of* **родни́ть.** —**сродни́ться,** *refl.* (*with* **с** + *instr.*) **1,** to become close to. **2,** to get used to.

сро́дный *adj.* related.

сродство́ *n.* relationship; affinity.

сро́ду *adv., colloq.* **1,** since one was born; always. **2,** (*fol. by* **не**) never (in one's whole life).

срок *n.* **1,** (period of) time: в коро́ткий срок, in a short time. Срок ожида́ния, waiting period. **2,** term: избира́ться сро́ком на четы́ре го́да, to be elected for a four-year term. **3,** date: намеча́ть срок, to set the date. **4,** deadline. —**в срок; к сро́ку,** in time; on time; on schedule. —**до сро́ка; ра́ньше сро́ка,** ahead of time; ahead of schedule. —**кра́йний/после́дний/преде́льный срок,** deadline.

сро́чно *adv.* **1,** urgently. **2,** immediately; without delay.

сро́чность *n.f.* **1,** urgency. **2,** *colloq.* hurry.

сро́чный *adj.* **1,** urgent; pressing: сро́чное де́ло, urgent matter. Сро́чный зака́з, rush order. **2,** prompt. **3,** for a fixed period: сро́чная слу́жба, service for a fixed period; regular tour of duty.

сруб *n.* **1,** felling (of timber): продава́ть на сруб, to sell for timber. **2,** frame; framework. **3,** log cabin.

сруба́ть *v. impfv.* [*pfv.* **сруби́ть**] to chop down; fell.

сруби́ть *v. pfv.* [*infl.* **срублю́, сру́бишь**] **1,** *pfv. of* **сруба́ть. 2,** to build (*of logs*).

срыв *n.* failure; breakdown; collapse.

срыва́ть *v. impfv.* [*pfv.* **сорва́ть**] **1,** to tear off; tear away. **2,** to pick; pluck. **3,** to frustrate; disrupt; thwart; foil. **4,** *fig., colloq.* to win (applause); steal (a kiss); wangle (money). **5,** (*with* **на** + *prepl.*) to vent (one's feelings) on. **6,** *in* сорва́ть банк, to break the bank. **7,** *in* сорва́ть го́лос, to strain one's voice. **8,** [*pfv.* **срыть**] to level with the ground; raze to the ground. —**срыва́ться,** *refl.* **1,** to come off; come loose. **2,** (*with* **с** + *gen.*) to fall (from); slip (from). **3,** to break loose. **4,** (*with* **с** + *gen.*) to spring up (from); depart suddenly (from). **5,** (*of sounds*) to ring out; resound. **6,** *fig., colloq.* to fail; fall through. **7,** (*of one's voice*) to break. **8,** *in* срыва́ться с губ *or* с языка́, to escape one's lips.

срыть [*infl.* **сро́ю, сро́ешь**] *v., pfv. of* **срыва́ть** (*in sense #8*).

сря́ду *adv., colloq.* in a row; consecutively.

сса́дина *n.* scratch; abrasion.

ссади́ть [*infl.* **ссажу́, сса́дишь**] *v., pfv. of* **сса́живать.**

сса́живать *v. impfv.* [*pfv.* **ссади́ть**] **1,** to scratch. **2,** to help down; help (someone) get down. **3,** to put off; make (someone) get off.

ссо́ра *n.* quarrel. —**быть в ссо́ре (с),** to have had a falling-out (with).

ссо́рить *v. impfv.* [*pfv.* **поссо́рить**] to cause a quarrel between. —**ссо́риться,** *refl.* to quarrel.

ссо́хнуться [*past* **ссо́хся, -лась**] *v.r., pfv. of* **ссыха́ться.**

СССР *abbr. of* **Сою́з Сове́тских Социалисти́ческих Респу́блик,** Union of Soviet Socialist Republics; USSR

ссу́да *n.* loan. —**безвозвра́тная ссу́да,** outright grant.

ссуди́ть [*infl.* **ссужу́, ссу́дишь**] *v., pfv. of* **ссужа́ть.**

ссужа́ть *v. impfv.* [*pfv.* **ссуди́ть**] to loan; lend.

ссуту́лить *v., pfv. of* **суту́лить.** —**ссуту́литься,** *refl., pfv. of* **суту́литься.**

ссыла́ть *v. impfv.* [*pfv.* **сосла́ть**] to banish; exile. —**ссыла́ться,** *refl.* (*with* **на** + *acc.*) **1,** to cite; quote; refer (to); allude (to). **2,** to cite (*as an excuse*); plead; allege.

ссы́лка [*gen. pl.* **-лок**] *n.* **1,** reference: перекрёстная ссы́лка, cross reference. **2,** exile; banishment.

ссы́лочный *adj.* reference (*attrib.*).

ссы́льный *adj.* in exile. —*n.* exile.

ссы́пать [*infl.* **ссы́плю, ссы́плешь**] *v., pfv. of* **ссыпа́ть.**

ссыпа́ть *v. impfv.* [*pfv.* **ссы́пать**] to pour.

ссыха́ться *v.r. impfv.* [*pfv.* **ссо́хнуться**] **1,** to shrink. **2,** to warp; become warped. **3,** to cake; become caked.

стабилиза́тор *n.* stabilizer.

стабилиза́ция *n.* stabilization.

стабилизи́ровать *v. impfv. & pfv.* [*pres.* **-рую, -руешь**] to stabilize. —**стабилизи́роваться,** *refl.* to stabilize; become stabilized.

стаби́льность *n.f.* stability.

стаби́льный *adj.* stable. —**стаби́льный учёбник,** standard textbook.

ста́вень [*gen.* **-вня**] *n.m.* shutter.

ста́вить *v. impfv.* [*pfv.* **поста́вить;** *pres.* **-влю, -вишь**] **1,** to stand; place; set; put. **2,** to install. **3,** to apply (*to a part of one's body*). **4,** to affix (a seal, signature, etc.). **5,** to stage; produce; put on. **6,** to bet; stake. **7,** *with various nouns,* to set: ста́вить реко́рд, to set a record; ста́вить часы́/буди́льник, to set a watch/alarm clock/; ста́вить себе́ зада́чу, to set a task for oneself; ста́вить себе́ це́лью, to set as one's goal.

—**ста́вить вопро́с,** to pose a question. —**ста́вить в приме́р,** to hold up as an example. —**ста́вить диа́гноз,** to make a diagnosis. —**ста́вить отме́тки,** to give grades. —**ста́вить усло́вия,** to lay down conditions.

ста́вка *n.* **1,** stake; stakes. **2,** rate: ста́вка проце́нта, rate of interest. **3,** wage. **4,** *fig.* reliance: де́лать ста́вку на (+ *acc.*), to count on. **5,** *mil.* headquarters.

ста́вленник *n.* protégé.

ста́вня [*gen. pl.* **-вен**] *n.* shutter.

стадиа́льный *adj.* occurring in stages. *Also,* **стади́йный.**

стадио́н *n.* stadium.

ста́дия *n.* stage. —**по ста́диям,** in stages.

ста́дный *adj.* (*of animals*) living in herds; gregarious. —**ста́дный инсти́нкт,** herd instinct.

ста́до [*pl.* **стада́**] *n.* herd; flock.

стаж *n.* length of service. Слу́жащий с больши́м ста́жем, employee with a long record of service. Надба́вка к зарпла́те за стаж, pay increase for length of service.

стажёр *n.* person undergoing on-the-job training.

стажиро́вка *n.* practical training; on-the-job training.

ста́ивать *v. impfv.* [*pfv.* **ста́ять**] to melt.

ста́йка [*gen. pl.* **ста́ек**] *n., dim. of* **ста́я,** small flock; small group.

стака́н *n.* glass: стака́н воды́, glass of water.

стакка́то *adv.* staccato.

ста́ксель *n.m.* staysail.

сталагми́т *n.* stalagmite.

сталакти́т *n.* stalactite.

сталева́р *n.* steelworker.

сталелите́йный *adj.* pert. to the making of steel: сталелите́йный заво́д, steel mill.

сталелите́йщик *n.* steelworker.

сталеплави́льный *adj.* pert. to the melting of steel: сталеплави́льная печь, steel-melting furnace.

ста́лкивать *v. impfv.* [*pfv.* **столкну́ть**] **1,** to push off; push away; push down; push into. **2,** to cause to collide. **3,** *colloq.* to bring together. —**ста́лкиваться,** *refl.* (*with* **с** + *instr.*) **1,** to collide. **2,** *fig.* to clash. **3,** to run into; encounter.

сталь *n.f.* steel. —**стально́й,** *adj.* steel; of steel.

stаме́ска [*gen. pl.* **-сок**] *n.* chisel.

стан *n.* **1,** figure; build. **2,** mill: прока́тный стан, rolling mill. **3,** camp. —**но́тный стан,** *music* staff.

станда́рт *n.* **1,** standard. **2,** *fig.* stereotype.

стандартиза́ция *n.* standardization.

стандартизи́ровать *v. impfv. & pfv.* [*pres.* **-рую, -руешь**] to standardize. *Also,* **стандартизова́ть** [*pres.* **-зу́ю, -зу́ешь**].

станда́ртный *adj.* **1,** standard; standardized. **2,** *fig.* standard; conventional.

стани́на *n.* mount; base.

станио́ль *n.m.* tin foil.

стани́ца *n.* **1,** large Cossack village. **2,** flock (*of birds*).

станко́вый *adj.* machine (*attrib.*). —**станко́вый пулемёт,** heavy *or* medium machine gun.

станови́ться *v.r. impfv.* [*pfv.* **стать;** *pres.* **становлю́сь, стано́вишься**] **1,** to stand: ста́ньте передо мной, stand in front of me. **2,** (*with instr.*) to become; get: стать друзья́ми, to become friends. Стать хо́лодно, to get cold. Стать лу́чше, to get better. —**стать в о́чередь,** to get on line. —**стать в по́зу,** to strike a pose. —**стать на коле́ни,** to kneel (down). —**стать на́ ноги,** to get on one's feet. —**стать на путь** (+ *gen.*), to embark on a path of... —**стать на сто́рону** (+ *gen.*), to side with; take the side of. *See also* **стать.**

становле́ние *n.* (*with gen.*) formation (of): становле́ние хара́ктера, formation of character.

станово́й *adj., pre-rev.* district (*attrib.*). —**станово́й хребе́т; станова́я жи́ла,** backbone; mainstay.

стано́к [*gen.* **-нка́**] *n.* **1,** machine; machine tool: печа́тный стано́к, printing press; тка́цкий стано́к, loom; тока́рный стано́к, lathe. **2,** gun mount.

стано́чник *n.* machine operator; machine tool operator.

станс *n.* stanza.

станцио́нный *adj.* station (*attrib.*).

ста́нция *n.* **1,** station: железнодоро́жная/запра́вочная ста́нция, railroad/filling station. **2,** *R.R.* yard: това́рная ста́нция, freight yard; сортиро́вочная ста́нция, switchyard. —**телефо́нная ста́нция,** telephone exchange.

ста́птывать *v. impfv.* [*pfv.* **стопта́ть**] **1,** to wear down (shoes, heels, etc.). **2,** *colloq.* to trample. —**ста́птываться,** *refl.* (*of shoes, heels, etc.*) to wear down; become worn down.

стара́ние *n.* effort: прилага́ть все стара́ния, to exert every effort.

стара́тель *n.m.* prospector for gold; gold digger.

стара́тельный *adj.* diligent; assiduous; painstaking. —**стара́тельно,** *adv.* diligently; painstakingly. —**стара́тельность,** *n.f.* diligence; application.

стара́ться *v.r. impfv.* [*pfv.* **постара́ться**] to try; endeavor.

старе́ние *n.* aging.

старе́ть *v. impfv.* [*pfv.* **постаре́ть**] **1,** to grow old; get old; age. **2,** [*impfv. only*] to become obsolete; become antiquated.

ста́рец [*gen.* **-рца**] *n.* (venerable) old man.

стари́к [*gen.* **-рика́**] *n.* old man.

старина́ *n.f.* **1,** ancient times; olden times: в старину́, in ancient/olden times. **2,** old ways; old customs: по старине́, the old way; the traditional way. **3,** relic of the past. —*n.m., colloq.* old man!; old boy! —**тряхну́ть старино́й,** to relive one's youth.

стари́нка *n., in* **по стари́нке,** the old way.

стари́нный *adj.* **1,** old; ancient. **2,** antique.

ста́рить *v. impfv.* [*pfv.* **соста́рить**] to age; make old. —**ста́риться,** *refl.* to age; grow old.

старичо́к [*gen.* **-чка́**] *n.* little old man.

старове́р *n., hist.* Old Believer.

староде́вний *adj.* **1,** (*of times*) olden. **2,** (*of an object, custom, etc.*) very old.

старожи́л *n.* long-time resident.

старозаве́тный *adj.* **1,** old-fashioned. **2,** antiquated.

старомо́дный *adj.* old-fashioned.

старообра́зный *adj.* old-looking.

старообря́дец [*gen.* **-дца**] *n., hist.* Old Believer.

ста́роста *n.m.* **1,** village elder. **2,** monitor (*in school*). —**церко́вный ста́роста,** churchwarden.

ста́рость *n.f.* old age. —**на ста́рости лет,** in one's old age.

старт *n.* **1,** *sports* start. **2,** starting line. **3,** *aero.* takeoff. **4,** blast-off.

ста́ртер *n., mech. & sports* starter.

стартова́ть *v. impfv. & pfv.* [*pres.* **-ту́ю, -ту́ешь**] **1,** *sports* to start. **2,** *aero.* to take off. **3,** (*of a space vehicle*) to blast off.

ста́ртовый *adj.* **1,** *sports* starting. **2,** launching: ста́ртовая площа́дка, launching pad.
стару́ха *n.* old woman.
стару́шка [*gen. pl.* **-шек**] *n.* old woman.
ста́рческий *adj.* **1,** of old age. **2,** senile.
ста́рше *adj., comp. of* **ста́рый** *and* **ста́рший.**
старшекла́ссник *n.* pupil in his senior year.
старшеку́рсник *n.* senior (*in college*).
ста́рший *adj., used only as a modifier* **1,** older; elder. **2,** oldest; eldest. **3,** senior; head. —*n.* **1,** chief; man in charge. **2,** *pl.* adults. **3,** *pl.* one's elders. —**ста́рший лейтена́нт,** first lieutenant.
старшина́ [*pl.* **старши́ны**] *n.m.* **1,** *mil.* master sergeant. **2,** *naval* petty officer. **3,** *pre-rev.* foreman (*of a shop, jury, etc.*). —**старшина́ дипломати́ческого ко́рпуса,** dean of the diplomatic corps.
старшинство́ *n.* seniority.
ста́рый *adj.* old. —**ста́рое,** *n.* the old; the past.
старьё *n., colloq.* old things, junk.
старьёвщик *n.* old-clothes dealer; junkman.
ста́скивать *v. impfv.* [*pfv.* **стащи́ть**] **1,** to pull off; drag off. **2,** to pull into; drag into.
стасова́ть *v., pfv. of* **тасова́ть.**
ста́тика *n.* statics.
стати́ст *n., theat.* extra; supernumerary.
стати́стик *n.* statistician. —**стати́стика,** *n.* statistics. —**статисти́ческий,** *adj.* statistical.
стати́ческий *adj., physics; electricity* static.
стати́чный *adj.* static (*not in motion*).
ста́тный *adj.* graceful; shapely.
ста́тус *n.* status.
ста́тус-кво́ *n.m. indecl.* status quo.
стату́т *n.* statute.
статуэ́тка [*gen. pl.* **-ток**] *n.* statuette; figurine.
ста́туя *n.* statue.
стать[1] *v. pfv.* [*infl.* **ста́ну, ста́нешь**] **1,** *pfv. of* **станови́ться. 2,** (*of a watch, machine, etc.*) to stop; stop running. **3,** (*of a river*) to freeze over. **4,** [*past tense only*] (*with inf.*) to begin (to); start. **5,** [*future tense only*] (*with inf.*) *indicates the future:* он не ста́нет есть, he won't eat. **6,** (*with* **с** + *instr.*) to happen (to); become (of). **7,** *impers.* (*with* **не**) to die: его́ не ста́ло, he died; he was no more. **8,** *colloq.* to cost. —**во что бы то ни ста́ло,** at all costs. —**ста́ло быть,** consequently.
стать[2] [*pl.* **ста́ти, -те́й, -тя́м**] *n.f.* figure; build. —**под стать** (+ *dat.*), **1,** right (for). **2,** like. **3,** befitting; becoming. —**с како́й ста́ти?,** why?; what for?
ста́ться *v.r. pfv.* [*infl.* **ста́нется**] (*with* **с** + *instr.*) *colloq.* to happen (to); become (of).
статья́ [*gen. pl.* **-те́й**] *n.* **1,** article. **2,** article; clause; paragraph (*of a constitution, treaty, etc.*). **3,** entry (*in a dictionary*). **4,** item: статья́ расхо́да, expense item. —**по всем статья́м,** in all respects.
стаха́новец [*gen.* **-вца**] *n.* Stakhanovite. —**стаха́новский,** *adj.* Stakhanovite (*attrib.*).
стациона́р *n.* permanent establishment: больница-стациона́р, permanent hospital.
стациона́рный *adj.* **1,** stationary. **2,** permanent. —**стациона́рный больно́й,** hospital patient (*as opposed to an outpatient*).
стача́ть *v., pfv. of* **тача́ть.**
ста́чечник *n.* striker. —**ста́чечный,** *adj.* strike (*attrib.*).
ста́чивать *v. impfv.* [*pfv.* **сточи́ть**] to dull (a cutting instrument) through long use: сточённая бри́тва, dull razor.
ста́чка [*gen. pl.* **-чек**] *n.* strike.
стащи́ть [*infl.* **стащу́, ста́щишь**] *v., pfv. of* **тащи́ть** (*in sense #5*) *and* **ста́скивать.**
ста́я *n.* flock (*of birds*); school (*of fish*); pack (*of dogs*).
ста́ять [*infl.* **ста́ет**] *v., pfv. of* **ста́ивать.**
ствол [*gen.* **ствола́**] *n.* **1,** trunk (*of a tree*). **2,** barrel (*of a gun*).
створ *n.* = **ство́рка.**
створа́живать *v. impfv.* [*pfv.* **створо́жить**] to curdle. —**створа́живаться,** *refl.* (*of a substance*) to curdle.
ство́рка [*gen. pl.* **-рок**] *n.* **1,** leaf; fold (*of a door, gate, mirror, etc.*). **2,** valve (*of a mollusk*).
створо́жить *v., pfv. of* **створа́живать.** —**створо́житься,** *refl., pfv. of* **створа́живаться.**
ство́рчатый *adj.* folding. —**ство́рчатое окно́,** casement window.
стеари́н *n.* stearin.
стеати́т *n.* steatite.
сте́бель [*gen.* **-бля;** *pl.* **сте́бли, -бле́й, -бля́м**] *n.m.* stem; stalk.
стёганка [*gen. pl.* **-нок**] *n., colloq.* quilted jacket.
стёганый *adj.* quilted. —**стёганое одея́ло,** quilt.
стега́ть *v. impfv.* **1,** [*pfv.* **вы́стегать**] to quilt. **2,** [*pfv.* **отстега́ть** *and* **стегну́ть**] to whip; lash.
стежо́к [*gen.* **-жка́**] *n.* stitch.
стезя́ *n., obs.* path; way; road.
стека́ть *v. impfv.* [*pfv.* **стечь**] to flow down. —**стека́ться,** *refl.* **1,** to flow together. **2,** *fig.* to flock together; congregate; throng.
стеклене́ть *v. impfv.* [*pfv.* **остеклене́ть**] **1,** to become like glass. **2,** (*of one's eyes*) to become glassy.
стекло́ [*pl.* **стёкла, стёкол**] *n.* glass. —**око́нное стекло́,** windowpane. —**пере́днее стекло́,** windshield. —**увеличи́тельное стекло́,** magnifying glass.
стекловолокно́ *n.* fiberglass.
стеклоду́в *n.* glass blower.
стеклоочисти́тель *n.m.* windshield wiper.
стекля́нный *adj.* **1,** glass. **2,** (*of a stare*) glassy.
стекля́рус *n.* bugles; bugle beads.
стеко́льный *adj.* glass (*attrib.*): стеко́льный заво́д, glassworks.
стеко́льщик *n.* glazier.
стели́ть *v. impfv.* [*pres.* **стелю́, сте́лешь**] = **стлать.** —**стели́ться,** *refl.* = **стла́ться.**
стелла́ж [*gen.* **-лажа́**] *n.* **1,** shelves. **2,** rack.
сте́лька [*gen. pl.* **-лек**] *n.* insole; inner sole. —**пьян как сте́лька; пьян в сте́льку,** *colloq.* dead drunk.
стемне́ть *v., pfv. of* **темне́ть** (*in sense #2*).
стена́ [*acc.* **сте́ну;** *pl.* **сте́ны, стен, стена́м**] *n.* wall. —**стена́ в сте́ну,** right next door. —**жить** *or* **сиде́ть в четырёх стена́х,** to sit home all the time. —**лезть на́ стену,** *see* **лезть.**
стена́ть *v. impfv., obs.* to moan; groan.
стенгазе́та *n.* wall newspaper.
стенд (тэ) *n.* stand.
сте́ндовый (тэ) *adj., in* **сте́ндовая стрельба́,** trapshooting.
сте́нка [*gen. pl.* **-нок**] *n.* **1,** *dim. of* **стена́. 2,** side (*of a container*). **3,** *anat.* wall. —**поста́вить к сте́нке,** *colloq.* to execute; shoot.
стенно́й *adj.* wall (*attrib.*). —**стенно́й шкаф,** built-in closet.

стенобитный *adj., hist.* used to batter down walls: стенобитный таран, battering-ram.
стенограмма *n.* transcript (of a lecture, report, etc.) taken down in shorthand.
стенограф *n.* stenographer.
стенографировать *v. impfv.* [*pres.* **-рую, -руешь**] to take down in shorthand.
стенографист *n.m.* [*fem.* **-фистка**] stenographer.
стенография *n.* shorthand; stenography. —**стенографический,** *adj.* shorthand (*attrib.*); stenographic.
стенокардия *n.* angina pectoris.
стенопись *n.f.* mural; mural painting.
стеньга *n.* topmast.
степенный *adj.* sedate; staid.
степень [*pl.* **степени, -ней, -ням**] *n.f.* **1,** extent; degree: в значительной степени, to a considerable extent. **2,** academic degree. **3,** *gram.* degree. **4,** *math.* power: десять в пятой степени, ten to the fifth power. —**в высшей степени** (+ *adj.*), extraordinarily; most. —**ни в малейшей степени,** not in the least.
степной *adj.* steppe (*attrib.*).
степь [*2nd loc.* **степи;** *pl.* **степи, -пей, -пям**] *n.f.* steppe.
стервятник *n.* Egyptian vulture.
стереометрия *n.* solid geometry.
стереоскоп *n.* stereoscope. —**стереоскопический,** *adj.* stereoscopic. —**стереоскопия,** *n.* stereoscopy.
стереотип *n.* stereotype.
стереотипировать *v. impfv. & pfv.* [*pres.* **-рую, -руешь**] *printing* to stereotype.
стереотипный *adj.* stereotyped.
стереофонический *adj.* stereophonic.
стереть [*infl.* **сотру, сотрёшь;** *past* **стёр, -ла**] *v., pfv. of* **стирать.** —**стереться,** *refl., pfv. of* **стираться.**
стеречь *v. impfv.* [*pres.* **стерегу, стережёшь, ...стерегут;** *past* **стерёг, стерегла, стерегло**] to guard; watch.
стержень [*gen.* **-жня**] *n.m.* **1,** rod; bar. **2,** pivot. **3,** *fig.* core; heart.
стержневой *adj.* (*of a question or issue*) key; pivotal.
стерилизатор *n.* sterilizer. —**стерилизация,** *n.* sterilization.
стерилизовать *v. impfv. & pfv.* [*pres.* **-зую, -зуешь**] to sterilize.
стерильный *adj.* sterile; sterilized. —**стерильность,** *n.f.* sterility.
стерлинг *n.* sterling. Фунт стерлингов, the pound sterling. —**стерлинговый,** *adj.* sterling (*attrib.*).
стерлядь [*pl.* **стерляди, -дей, -дям**] *n.f.* sterlet (*fish*).
стерня *n.* **1,** harvested field (*with only the stubble remaining*). **2,** stubble. *Also,* **стернь,** *n.f.*
стероид *n.* steroid.
стерпеть *v. pfv.* [*infl.* **стерплю, стерпишь**] to bear; endure. —**стерпеться,** *refl.* (*with* **с** + *instr.*) *colloq.* to get used to; come to accept.
стёртый *adj.* **1,** effaced. **2,** worn smooth. **3,** *fig.* trite.
стеснение *n.* **1,** uneasiness; inhibition; constraint. **2,** constriction; feeling of tightness. **3,** *usu. pl.* restrictions; constraints.
стеснённый *adj.* **1,** crowded together. **2,** (*of breathing*) labored. **3,** uneasy; inhibited. **4,** straitened: в стеснённых обстоятельствах, in straitened circumstances. **5,** (*fol. by* **в** + *prepl.*) short of; squeezed (for): стеснён(ный) в средствах, squeezed for money.
стеснительность *n.f.* shyness, diffidence.
стеснительный *adj.* **1,** tight-fitting; constricting. **2,** confining; restrictive. **3,** shy; inhibited.
стеснить *v., pfv. of* **теснить** (*in sense #2*) *and* **стеснять.** —**стесниться,** *refl., pfv. of* **тесниться** (*in sense #1*) *and* **стесняться** (*in senses #3 & #4*).
стеснять *v. impfv.* [*pfv.* **стеснить**] **1,** to crowd; cramp. **2,** to hinder; hamper. **3,** to confine; restrict. **4,** to constrain; inhibit. **5,** to constrict. **6,** (*with* **себя**) to stint: не стеснять себя в средствах, not stint oneself. —**стесняться,** *refl.* **1,** [*impfv. only*] to feel uneasy; feel awkward; feel self-conscious. **2,** [*pfv.* **постесняться**] (*with inf.*) to be afraid (to); be ashamed (to); (*with gen.*) by shy (in the presence of); be afraid (of). **3,** [*pfv.* **стесниться**] to crowd; crowd together; be crowded together. **4,** [*pfv.* **стесниться**] (*with* **в** + *prepl.*) to spare; use sparingly: не стесняться в средствах, not stint oneself; не стесняться в выражениях, not mince words.
стетоскоп *n.* stethoscope.
стечение *n.* **1,** flowing together. **2,** coming together; gathering (*of people*). **3,** combination (*of circumstances*).
стечь [*infl. like* **течь**] *v., pfv. of* **стекать.** —**стечься,** *refl., pfv. of* **стекаться.**
стибрить *v. pfv., colloq.* to swipe; pilfer; filch.
стилет *n.* stiletto.
стилизация *n.* stylization.
стилизовать *v. impfv. & pfv.* [*pres.* **-зую, -зуешь**] to stylize.
стилист *n.* stylist. —**стилистика,** *n.* stylistics. —**стилистический,** *adj.* stylistic.
стиль *n.m.* **1,** style. **2,** *swimming* stroke.
стильный *adj.* **1,** period (*attrib.*): стильная мебель, period furniture. **2,** *colloq.* stylish; chic.
стиляга *n.m. & f.* stilyaga (*young man or woman adopting modish clothes and often evading social responsibility*).
стимул *n.* stimulus; incentive.
стимулирование *n.* stimulation.
стимулировать *v. impfv. & pfv.* [*pres.* **-рую, -руешь**] to stimulate.
стипендия *n.* grant; scholarship.
стиральный *adj.* washing (*attrib.*): стиральная машина, washing machine. —**стиральный порошок,** soap powder; detergent.
стирать *v. impfv.* [*pfv.* **стереть**] **1,** to wipe off. **2,** to erase. **3,** to rub; chafe; irritate. **4,** [*pfv.* **выстирать**] to wash; launder. —**стираться,** *refl.* [*pfv.* **стереться**] **1,** to be effaced; be obliterated; wear away. **2,** to become worn down; wear thin. **3,** [*impfv. only*] to wash: рубашка не стирается, the shirt is not washable.
стирка *n.* wash; washing; laundering. —**отдавать (что-нибудь) в стирку,** to have (something) washed; send out to be laundered.
стирол *n.* styrene.
стискивать *v. impfv.* [*pfv.* **стиснуть**] **1,** to squeeze. **2,** to hem in. **3,** to constrict. **4,** to grit (one's teeth).
стих [*gen.* **стиха**] *n.* **1,** verse. **2,** *pl.* poetry; poems.
стихарь [*gen.* **-харя**] *n.m.* surplice.
стихать *v. impfv.* [*pfv.* **стихнуть**] **1,** to grow still; become silent. **2,** to die down; subside; abate.
стихийность *n.f.* spontaneity.
стихийный *adj.* **1,** elemental. **2,** spontaneous. —**стихийное бедствие,** natural disaster.

стихи́я *n.* element. —**быть в свое́й стихи́и,** to be in one's element.

сти́хнуть [*past* **стих, -ла**] *v., pfv. of* **стиха́ть.**

стихоплёт *n., colloq.* rhymer; rhymester.

стихосложе́ние *n.* versification.

стихотворе́ние *n.* short poem.

стихотво́рный *adj.* **1,** poetical. **2,** in verse.

стишо́к [*gen.* **-шка́**] *n., dim. of* **стих.**

стлать *v. impfv.* [*pfv.* **постла́ть;** *pres.* **стелю́, сте́лешь**] to lay (a tablecloth, carpet, etc.); make (a bed). —**стла́ться,** *refl.* [*impfv. only*] **1,** to stretch; extend. **2,** (*of a plant*) to creep.

сто [*gen., dat., instr., & prepl.* **ста;** *gen. pl.* **сот**] *numeral* hundred.

стог [*2nd loc.* **стогу́;** *pl.* **стога́**] *n.* stack: стог се́на, haystack.

сто́ик *n.* stoic.

сто́имость *n.f.* **1,** cost. **2,** *econ.* value: приба́вочная сто́имость, surplus value.

сто́ить *v. impfv.* **1,** to cost. **2,** (*with gen.*) to be worth: сто́ить больши́х де́нег, to be worth a lot of money. Не сто́ит труда́, it's not worth the trouble. **3,** (*with gen.*) to be worthy of. **4,** (*with inf.*) to be worth (while): кни́гу сто́ит проче́сть, the book is worth (while) reading. Не сто́ит с ним спо́рить, it is not worth arguing with him. **5,** (*with gen.*) to take (a certain amount of effort): ему́ сто́ило больши́х уси́лий (+ *inf.*), it took great effort on his part to... —**сто́ит то́лько** (+ *inf.*), one has only to...

стоици́зм *n.* stoicism.

стои́ческий *adj.* stoical. —**стои́чески,** *adv.* stoically.

сто́йка [*gen. pl.* **сто́ек**] *n.* **1,** [*also,* **сто́йка сми́рно**] position of attention. **2,** handstand. **3,** post; upright; stanchion. **4,** strut; prop. **5,** counter; bar.

сто́йкий *adj.* **1,** durable; hardy; long-lasting. **2,** *chem.* stable. **3,** *fig.* steadfast; staunch.

сто́йко *adv.* **1,** stoically. **2,** firmly. Сто́йко держа́ться, to stand firm; stand fast.

сто́йкость *n.f.* **1,** durability; hardinesss. **2,** *fig.* fortitude; steadfastness.

сто́йло *n.* stall.

стойми́ *adv.* upright.

сток *n.* **1,** flow; drainage. **2,** drain; gutter.

сто́кер *n.* stoker (*machine*).

стокра́т *adv., archaic* a hundred times. —**стокра́тный,** *adj.* hundredfold: в стокра́тном разме́ре, a hundredfold.

стол [*gen.* **стола́**] *n.* **1,** table. **2,** board; meals: кварти́ра и стол, room and board. **3,** food; cooking. **4,** diet. **5,** department; office; bureau: стол зака́зов, order department. —**пи́сьменный стол,** desk.

столб [*gen.* **столба́**] *n.* **1,** pole; post; pillar. **2,** column (*of air, smoke, etc.*). —**позвоно́чный столб,** spinal column.

столбене́ть *v. impfv.* [*pfv.* **остолбене́ть**] *colloq.* to freeze (*from terror, shock, etc.*).

столбе́ц [*gen.* **-бца́**] *n.* column (*of print, figures, etc.*).

сто́лбик *n.* **1,** small column. **2,** column (*of print, figures, etc.*). **3,** *in* сто́лбик рту́ти, column of mercury. **4,** *bot.* style.

столбня́к [*gen.* **-няка́**] *n.* **1,** tetanus. **2,** *colloq.* stupor; trance.

столе́тие *n.* **1,** century. **2,** centenary; centennial.

столе́тний *adj.* **1,** hundred-year (*attrib.*). **2,** hundred-year-old. —**столе́тняя война́,** the Hundred Years' War. —**столе́тний юбиле́й,** hundredth anniversary.

столе́тник *n.* century plant.

сто́лик *n.* small table.

столи́ца *n.* capital (*city*). —**столи́чный,** *adj.* of a capital; capital (*attrib.*).

столкнове́ние *n.* **1,** collision. **2,** clash; conflict.

столкну́ть *v., pfv. of* **ста́лкивать.** —**столкну́ться,** *refl., pfv. of* **ста́лкиваться.**

столкова́ться *v.r. pfv.* [*infl.* **-ку́юсь, -ку́ешься**] *colloq.* to agree; reach agreement.

столова́ться *v.r. impfv.* [*pres.* **-лу́юсь, -лу́ешься**] to board; take meals.

столо́вая *n., decl. as an adj.* **1,** dining room. **2,** dining hall.

столо́вый *adj.* **1,** table (*attrib.*). **2,** dining-room (*attrib.*). —**столо́вая гора́,** mesa. —**столо́вая ло́жка,** tablespoon; soupspoon. —**столо́вые прибо́ры,** tableware; flatware.

столо́чь *v. pfv.* [*infl. like* **толо́чь**] *colloq.* to pound; crush; pulverize.

столп [*gen.* **столпа́**] *n.* **1,** *obs.* = **столб. 2,** *fig.* pillar: столпы́ о́бщества, the pillars of society.

столпи́ться *v.r. pfv.* to crowd; congregate.

столпотворе́ние *n., in* **вавило́нское столпотворе́ние, 1,** chaos. **2,** babel.

столь *adv.* so: э́то не столь ва́жно, it's not so important.

сто́лько *adv.* so much; so many. —**сто́лько (же)..., ско́лько (и),** as much as; as many as.

столя́р [*gen.* **-яра́**] *n.* joiner; cabinetmaker.

столя́рничать *v. impfv.* to be a cabinetmaker.

столя́рный *adj.* joiner's.

стоматоло́гия *n.* stomatology; dentistry. —**стомато́лог,** *n.* stomatologist; dentist.

стон *n.* groan; moan.

стона́ть *v. impfv.* [*pres.* **стону́, сто́нешь**] to groan; moan.

стоп *interj.* stop!

стопа́ [*pl.* **стопы́** *in sense #1;* **сто́пы** *in other senses*] *n.* **1,** foot. **2,** *pros.* foot: метри́ческая стопа́, metric foot. **3,** pile (*of objects*). **4,** ream (*of paper*). —**идти́ по стопа́м** (+ *gen.*), to follow in the footsteps of. —**направля́ть свои́ стопы́,** to wend one's way.

сто́пка [*gen. pl.* **-пок**] *n.* **1,** pile. **2,** small glass (*for wine or vodka*).

сто́пор *n., mech.* stop; catch.

сто́порить *v. impfv.* [*pfv.* **засто́порить**] to stop (an engine, machine, etc.). —**сто́пориться,** *refl.* **1,** to stop; jam; become inoperative. **2,** *fig., colloq.* to come to a standstill.

сто́порный *adj., mech.* stop (*attrib.*); arresting; locking.

стопроце́нтный *adj.* one-hundred-percent (*attrib.*).

стоп-сигна́л *n.* stoplight; brake light.

стопта́ть [*infl.* **стопчу́, сто́пчешь**] *v., pfv. of* **ста́птывать.** —**стопта́ться,** *refl., pfv. of* **ста́птываться.**

сторгова́ться *v.r. pfv.* [*infl.* **-гу́юсь, -гу́ешься**] to agree on a price (*after bargaining*).

сторицей *also,* **сторицею** *adv.* many times over: окупа́ться сто́рицей, to pay for itself many times over.

сто́рож [*pl.* **сторожа́**] *n.* watchman; guard.

сторожево́й *adj.* watch (*attrib.*); sentry (*attrib.*). —**сторожева́я ба́шня** (*or* **вы́шка**), watchtower. —**сторожево́й ка́тер,** patrol boat. —**сторожево́й пёс,** watchdog.

сторожи́ть *v. impfv.* to guard; watch.

сторо́жка [*gen. pl.* **-жек**] *n.* hut; cabin; lodge (*of a watchman, warden, etc.*).

сторона́ [*acc.* **сто́рону;** *pl.* **сто́роны, сторо́н, сторона́м**] *n.* **1,** side. **2,** direction: в ту сто́рону, in that direction; that way. **3,** *fig.* aspect: положи́тельная сторона́, positive aspect. **4,** *law* party. **5,** land; country. —**в стороне́ (от),** apart (from); aloof (from). —**в сто́рону,** aside. —**в сто́рону** (+ *gen.*), in the direction of. —**на все четы́ре сто́роны,** wherever one wishes to go. —**на стороне́,** elsewhere; in another place. —**на́ сторону,** (*with verbs of selling*) on the side.—**по ту сто́рону** (+ *gen.*), on the other side (of). —**со всех сторо́н, 1,** on all sides; from all sides. **2,** from all aspects. —**с одно́й стороны́..., с друго́й стороны́...,** on the one hand..., on the other hand... —**со стороны́, 1,** from a distance; without being directly involved. **2,** from elsewhere; from another place. —**со стороны́** (+ *gen.*), **1,** from the direction of. **2,** on the part of. Со свое́й стороны́ я..., for my part, I... О́чень ми́ло с ва́шей стороны́, very kind on your part; very kind of you. **3,** (*of relatives*) on the side of. —**стороно́й, 1,** by: проходи́ть стороно́й, to pass by; bypass. **2,** on one side: обходи́ть (что́-нибудь) стороно́й, to sidestep. **3,** *fig.* indirectly; secondhand. —**встать** *or* **стать на сто́рону** (+ *gen.*), to side with; take the side of. —**держа́ться** *or* **остава́ться в стороне́,** to remain aloof; remain on the sidelines.

сторони́ться *v.r. impfv.* [*pfv.* **посторони́ться;** *pres.* **сторони́сь, сторо́нишься**] **1,** to stand aside; step aside; make way. **2,** [*impfv. only*] (*with gen.*) to avoid; shun.

сторо́нний *adj., obs.* = **посторо́нний.** —**сторо́нний наблюда́тель,** outside/detached observer.

сторо́нник *n.* supporter; advocate.

сторублёвка [*gen. pl.* **-вок**] *n., colloq.* hundred-ruble note.

сторублёвый *adj.* **1,** hundred-ruble (*attrib.*). **2,** costing *or* worth one hundred rubles.

стоскова́ться *v.r. pfv.* [*infl.* **-ку́юсь, -ку́ешься**] (*with* **по** + *dat., but prepl. with pers. pronouns*) *colloq.* to miss; long for.

сточи́ть [*infl.* **сточу́, сто́чишь**] *v., pfv. of* **ста́чивать.**

сто́чный *adj.* drainage (*attrib.*). —**сто́чные во́ды,** sewage. —**сто́чная кана́ва,** gutter. —**сто́чная труба́,** sewer.

стошни́ть *v. pfv., impers.* to vomit; throw up: меня́ стошни́ло, I threw up.

сто́я *adv.* (*used after verbs*) standing up; on one's feet.

стоя́к [*gen.* **-яка́**] *n.* upright post.

стоя́ние *n.* standing: до́лгое стоя́ние в о́череди, a long stand in line.

стоя́нка [*gen. pl.* **-нок**] *n.* **1,** stop. **2,** stopping place. **3,** stand (*for taxis, carriages, etc.*). **4,** parking (*of cars*). **5,** parking lot.

стоя́ть *v. impfv.* [*pres.* **стою́, стои́шь**] **1,** to stand; be standing. **2,** to stand; be situated: дом стои́т на холму́, the house stands (*or* sits) on a hill. **3,** to be: маши́на стои́т в гараже́, the car is in the garage. Стоя́ть у вла́сти, to be in power. ♦*Also in many other constructions:* стои́т си́льный моро́з, there is a heavy frost. Пого́да стоя́ла тёплая, the weather was warm. Зима́ стоя́ла холо́дная, it was a cold winter. Стоя́л коне́ц ию́ня, it was late June. Стоя́ла тишина́, it was quiet. **4,** to stop; cease to function: мои́ часы́ стоя́т, my watch has stopped. Рабо́та стои́т, work has stopped; work is at a standstill. **5,** (*with* **за** + *acc.*) to stand for; favor; be in favor of. —**стой!; сто́йте!, 1,** stop! **2,** wait a minute! —**стоя́ть на своём,** to stand one's ground.

стоя́чий *adj.* **1,** standing; upright; erect. **2,** (*of water*) stagnant.

сто́ящий *adj., colloq.* worthwhile.

страви́ть [*infl.* **стравлю́, стра́вишь**] *v., pfv. of* **стра́вливать.**

стра́вливать *v. impfv.* [*pfv.* **страви́ть**] **1,** to set (two animals) against each other. **2,** *colloq.* to provoke a fight or argument between (two people).

страда́ *n.* **1,** extra hard work performed at harvest time. **2,** *fig.* hard work. **3,** season of hard work.

страда́лец [*gen.* **-льца**] *n.* sufferer.

страда́льческий *adj.* of suffering.

страда́ние *n.* suffering.

страда́тельный *adj., gram.* passive: страда́тельный зало́г, passive voice.

страда́ть *v. impfv.* [*pfv.* **пострада́ть**] **1,** to suffer: страда́ть от жары́, to suffer from the heat; страда́ть бессо́нницей, to suffer from insomnia. Страда́ть за свои́ убежде́ния, to suffer for one's beliefs. **2,** [*impfv. only*] (*with* **за** + *acc.*) to feel for. **3,** [*impfv. only*] *colliq.* to be poor; be deficient: у него́ страда́ет орфогра́фия, he is poor at spelling. *See also* **пострада́ть.**

стра́дный *adj.* (*of time*) busy; hectic.

страж *n., obs.* guard; guardian.

стра́жа *n.* **1,** *obs.* guard; watch. **2,** (*with* **под**) custody: быть под стра́жей, to be in custody; брать под стра́жу, take into custody; содержа́ть под стра́жей, hold in custody. —**быть на стра́же, 1,** to be on guard. **2,** (*with gen.*) to guard; be guarding.

страна́ [*pl.* **стра́ны**] *n.* country. —**страна́ све́та,** cardinal point; point of the compass.

страни́ца *n.* page.

стра́нник *n.* wanderer.

стра́нно *adv.* strangely. —*adj., used predicatively* strange: как ни стра́нно, strange as it seems.

стра́нность *n.f.* **1,** strangeness. **2,** *usu. pl.* peculiarity; quirk; eccentricity.

стра́нный *adj.* strange; odd. —**стра́нное де́ло,** it is strange; it's a strange thing.

странове́дение *n.* area studies.

стра́нствие *n.* traveling; wandering. *Also,* **стра́нствование.**

стра́нствовать *v. impfv.* [*pres.* **-ствую, -ствуешь**] to wander; roam.

стра́стно *adv.* **1,** passionately. **2,** ardently.

страстно́й *adj.* pert. to the week before Easter. —**страстна́я неде́ля,** holy week. —**страстно́й четве́рг,** Holy Thursday. —**страстна́я пя́тница,** Good Friday.

стра́стность *n.f.* passion; ardor.

стра́стный *adj.* **1,** passionate; impassioned. **2,** ardent; fervent. **3,** avid; enthusiastic.

страсть [*pl.* **стра́сти, -сте́й, -стя́м**] *n.f.* **1,** passion. **2,** *usu. pl., colloq.* horrors. —*adv.* [*usu. fol. by* **как** *or* **како́й**] *colloq.* awfully (much); terribly (much).

стратаге́ма *n.* stratagem.

страте́гия *n.* strategy. —**страте́г,** *n.* strategist. —**стратеги́ческий,** *adj.* strategic.

стратифика́ция *n.* stratification.

стратосфе́ра *n.* stratosphere.

стра́ус *n.* ostrich. —**стра́усовый,** *adj.* ostrich (*attrib.*).
страх *n.* fear. —**на свой страх,** at one's risk. —**под стра́хом сме́рти,** on pain of death.
страхова́ние *n.* insurance.
страхова́ть *v. impfv.* [*pfv.* **застрахова́ть**] **1,** to insure. **2,** *fig.* to safeguard. —**страхова́ться,** *refl.* to insure oneself; (*with* **от**) take out insurance (against).
страхо́вка *n.* insurance.
страхово́й *adj.* insurance (*attrib.*).
страхо́вщик *n.* insurer.
страши́лище *n., colloq.* fright; horrible sight.
страши́ть *v. impfv.* to frighten. —**страши́ться,** *refl.* (*with gen.*) to be afraid (of); fear.
стра́шно *adv.* terribly; awfully. —*adj., used predicatively* **1,** terrible; horrible; awful. **2,** (*with dat.*) afraid: мне стра́шно, I am afraid.
стра́шный *adj.* terrible; horrible; dreadful; frightful; awful.
стре́жень [*gen.* **-жня**] *n.m.* part of a river where the current is strongest.
стрекоза́ [*pl.* **-ко́зы**] *n.* dragonfly; darning needle.
стре́кот *n.* chirping. *Also,* **стрекота́ние.**
стрекота́ть *v. impfv.* [*pres.* **-кочу́, -ко́чешь**] to chirp.
стрела́ [*pl.* **стре́лы**] *n.* **1,** arrow. **2,** boom (*of a derrick*). —**стрело́й,** straight (*or* swift) as an arrow.
стреле́ц [*gen.* **-льца́**] *n.* **1,** *hist.* member of a special military corps in the 16th and 17th centuries; strelets. **2,** *cap.* Sagittarius.
стре́лка [*gen. pl.* **-лок**] *n.* **1,** *dim. of* **стрела́. 2,** arrow (*pointing to something*). **3,** hand (*of a clock or watch*): мину́тная стре́лка, minute hand. **4,** needle (*of a compass, dial, etc.*). **5,** *R.R.* switch. **6,** spit (*of land*).
стрелко́вый *adj.* **1,** rifle (*attrib.*); shooting (*attrib.*). **2,** *mil.* rifle (*attrib.*). —**стрелко́вое де́ло,** musketry. —**стрелко́вое ору́жие,** small arms.
стреловидный *adj.* **1,** arrow-shaped. **2,** *aero.* swept-back.
стрело́к [*gen.* **-лка́**] *n.* **1,** shot; marksman: хоро́ший стрело́к, a good shot. **2,** *mil.* gunner.
стре́лочник *n., R.R.* switchman.
стрельба́ [*pl.* **стре́льбы**] *n.* **1,** shooting; firing. **2,** *pl.* firing practice. —**откры́ть стрельбу́,** to open fire; start shooting.
стре́льбище *n.* firing range.
стрельну́ть *v. pfv.* **1,** to fire a shot. **2,** *colloq.* to dash; dart (*away or out of sight*).
стре́льчатый *adj.* arched. —**стре́льчатое окно́,** lancet window.
стре́ляный *adj.* **1,** shot; killed. **2,** (*of a weapon*) having been fired; (*of a shell or cartridge*) spent. **3,** having been under fire. —**стре́ляный воробе́й,** *colloq.* old hand.
стреля́ть *v. impfv.* [*pfv.* **вы́стрелить**] **1,** to shoot; fire: не стреля́йте!, don't shoot! **2,** (*with* **в** + *acc. or* **по**) to shoot at; fire at. **3,** (*with* **из**) to fire (a weapon). **4,** [*impfv. only*] to shoot (and kill): стреля́ть у́ток, to shoot ducks. **5,** [*impfv. only*] to crackle. **6,** [*impfv. only*] (*with instr.*) *colloq.* to crack (a whip). **7,** [*impfv. only*] *impers., colloq.* to have a shooting pain: у меня́ стреля́ет в у́хе, I have a shooting pain in my ear. —**стреля́ть глаза́ми, 1,** to glance around. **2,** to make eyes.
стремгла́в *adv.* headlong.
стреми́тельный *adj.* **1,** very fast; rapid. **2,** dynamic; energetic. —**стреми́тельно,** *adv.* rapidly; headlong.
стреми́ться *v.r. impfv.* [*pres.* **стремлю́сь, стреми́шься**] **1,** (*with* **к**) to seek; aim for; strive for; aspire to. **2,** (*with inf.*) to try (to). **3,** (*with* **в** *or* **на** + *acc.*) to try to get to (a place); try to get into (a school or college). **4,** *obs.* to rush.
стремле́ние *n.* **1,** (*with* **к**) striving (for). **2,** aspiration. **3,** longing; yearning; urge.
стремни́на *n.* rapids (*on a river*).
стре́мя [*gen., dat., & prepl.* **стре́мени;** *instr.* **стре́менем;** *pl.* **стремена́, стремя́н, стремена́м**] *n. neut.* stirrup.
стремя́нка [*gen. pl.* **-нок**] *n.* stepladder.
стрено́жить *v., pfv. of* **трено́жить.**
стре́пет *n.* little bustard.
стрептоко́кк *n.* streptococcus.
стрептомици́н *n.* streptomycin.
стресс *n.* (emotional) stress.
стреха́ [*pl.* **стре́хи**] *n.* eaves.
стригу́щий *adj., in* **стригу́щий лиша́й,** ringworm.
стриж [*gen.* **стрижа́**] *n.* swift (*bird*).
стри́женый *adj.* **1,** (*of hair*) short; closely cropped; (*of a person*) with closely cropped hair. **2,** (*of sheep*) shorn. **3,** (*of a lawn, trees, etc.*) trimmed.
стри́жка [*gen. pl.* **-жек**] *n.* **1,** clipping. **2,** shearing. **3,** haircut. —**маши́нка для стри́жки,** clippers.
стрипти́з *n.* striptease.
стрихни́н *n.* strychnine.
стричь *v. impfv.* [*pfv.* **остри́чь;** *pres.* **стригу́, стрижёшь, ...стригу́т;** *past* **стриг, -ла**] **1,** to cut (one's hair, beard, etc.). **2,** to give (someone) a haircut. **3,** to shear; trim; clip. —**стри́чься,** *refl.* **1,** to cut one's hair. **2,** to get a haircut. **3,** to wear one's hair a certain way: стри́чься ко́ротко, to wear one's hair short.
стробоско́п *n.* stroboscope.
строга́льный *adj.* (*of a machine or tool*) planing. —**строга́льщик,** *n.* planer.
строга́ть *v. impfv.* [*pfv.* **вы́строгать**] to plane (wood).
стро́гий *adj.* [*comp.* **стро́же**] **1,** (*of a person, rule, etc.*) strict. **2,** (*of rules, measures, etc.*) stringent. **3,** (*of a look, voice, etc.*) stern. **4,** (*of criticism, a sentence, etc.*) severe.
стро́го *adv.* **1,** strictly: стро́го говоря́, strictly speaking; стро́го воспреща́ется, strictly forbidden. **2,** severely.
стро́гость *n.f.* **1,** strictness. **2,** severity.
строево́й *adj.* **1,** *mil.* drill (*attrib.*): строево́й расчёт, drill team. **2,** *mil.* front-line: строево́й офице́р, front-line officer. **3,** (*of material*) building: строево́й лес, lumber; timber. —**строева́я подгото́вка,** drill. —**строева́я сто́йка,** position of attention.
строе́ние *n.* **1,** a building. **2,** (*with gen.*) structure (of).
строи́тель *n.m.* builder. —**строи́тельный,** *adj.* building (*attrib.*); construction (*attrib.*).
строи́тельство *n.* **1,** (act of) building; construction. **2,** construction project. **3,** construction site.
стро́ить *v. impfv.* [*pfv.* **постро́ить**] **1,** to build; construct. **2,** (*with* **на** + *prepl.*) to base (on). **3,** to make (plans, assumptions, etc.). **4,** to organize; plan. **5,** [*impfv. only*] to make (an expression on one's face): стро́ить гла́зки, to make eyes; стро́ить грима́сы, to make faces. **6,** *mil.* to form. **7,** *in* стро́ить себе́ иллю́зии, to create illusions for oneself; delude oneself. **8,** *in* **стро́ить из себя́** (+ *acc.*), to make oneself out to be. —**стро́иться,** *refl.* **1,** to be built. **2,** to build a house for oneself. **3,** (*with* **на** + *prepl.*) to be based (on). **4,** *mil.* to form; line up.

строй *n.* **1,** [*2nd loc.* **строю́**; *pl.* **строи́, строёв**] *mil.* formation. **2,** system: общéственный строй, social system. **3,** tone; pitch; key (*of a musical instrument*). **4,** *gram.* structure. **5,** pattern: строй мышлéния, pattern of thinking. —**вводи́ть в строй,** to put into service; put into operation. —**вступа́ть в строй,** to go into operation. —**выбыва́ть из стро́я,** *see* **выбыва́ть.** —**выводи́ть из стро́я,** to put out of operation; put out of commission. —**выходи́ть из стро́я,** to break down; be disabled. —**прогоня́ть кого́-нибудь сквозь строй,** to make someone run the gauntlet.

стро́йка [*gen. pl.* **стро́ек**] *n.* **1,** (act of) building; construction. **2,** construction project. **3,** construction site.

стро́йный *adj.* **1,** graceful; slender; trim; svelte. **2,** (*of rows or columns*) regular; even. **3,** logical; coherent; consistent. **4,** harmonious.

строка́ [*acc.* **строку́** *or* **стро́ку**; *pl.* **стро́ки, строк, строка́м**] *n.* line (*of writing*). —**чита́ть мéжду строк,** to read between the lines.

стро́нций *n.* strontium.

стропи́ло *n.* rafter.

стропти́вый *adj.* obstinate; contrary.

строфа́ [*pl.* **стро́фы**] *n.* stanza.

строчи́ть *v. impfv.* [*pres.* **строчу́, стро́чишь** *or* **строчи́шь**] **1,** [*pfv.* **прострочи́ть**] to stitch. **2,** [*pfv.* **настрочи́ть**] *colloq.* to scribble; dash off. **3,** [*impfv. only*] *colloq.* to fire in rapid succession; blaze away.

стро́чка [*gen. pl.* **-чек**] *n.* **1,** = **строка́. 2,** stitch: ажу́рная стро́чка, hemstitch.

строчно́й *adj.* (*of a letter*) small; lower-case. *Also,* **стро́чный.**

струг *n.* plane (*tool*).

стру́жка [*gen. pl.* **-жек**] *n.* **1,** *usu. pl.* shavings. **2,** excelsior. —**мы́льная стру́жка,** soap flakes.

струи́ться *v.r. impfv.* to stream; pour.

стру́йка [*gen. pl.* **стру́ек**] *n.* **1,** stream; trickle. **2,** wisp (*of smoke*).

стру́йный *adj.* jet (*attrib.*). —**стру́йное тече́ние,** jet stream.

структу́ра *n.* structure. —**структу́рный,** *adj.* structural.

струна́ [*pl.* **стру́ны**] *n.* **1,** string (*of a musical instrument, tennis racket, etc.*). **2,** *fig.* chord: задéть чувстви́тельную струну́, to strike a sensitive chord. —**игра́ть на сла́бых стру́нах (кого́-нибудь),** to play on someone's weaknesses.

стру́нка [*gen. pl.* **-нок**] *n.* = **струна́.** —**вы́тянуться** *or* **стать в стру́нку,** to stand at attention. —**ходи́ть по стру́нке (у),** to toe the line (for).

стру́нный *adj.* **1,** string (*attrib.*): стру́нный квартéт, string quartet. **2,** (*of a musical instrument*) stringed.

струп [*pl.* **стру́пья, стру́пьев**] *n.* scab.

стру́сить *v., pfv. of* **тру́сить.**

стручко́вый *adj.* leguminous. —**стручко́вый горо́х,** peas in the pod. —**стручко́вый пéрец,** red pepper. —**стручко́вая фасо́ль,** string beans.

стручо́к [*gen.* **-чка́**] *n.* pod.

струя́ [*pl.* **стру́и**] *n.* spurt; jet; stream; current. —**бить струёй,** to spurt; jet.

стря́пать *v. impfv.* [*pfv.* **состря́пать**] *colloq.* **1,** to cook. **2,** *fig.* to cook up.

стряпня́ *n., colloq.* **1,** cooking. **2,** concoction.

стряса́ть *v. impfv.* [*pfv.* **стрясти́**] to shake off.

стрясти́ [*infl. like* **трясти́**] *v., pfv. of* **стряса́ть.** —**стрясти́сь,** *refl.* (*with* **с** + *instr.*) *colloq.* (*of a misfortune*) to happen to; befall.

стря́хивать *v. impfv.* [*pfv.* **стряхну́ть**] **1,** to shake off. **2,** to shake down (a thermometer).

студéнт *n.m.* [*fem.* **-дéнтка**] student. —**студéнческий,** *adj.* student (*attrib.*); students'.

студéнчество *n.* **1,** students. **2,** student days; student life.

студёный *adj., colloq.* very cold; freezing; icy.

сту́день [*gen.* **-дня**] *n.m.* aspic (*of meat or fish*).

студи́ть *v. impfv.* [*pfv.* **остуди́ть**; *pres.* **стужу́, сту́дишь**] *colloq.* to cool; chill.

сту́дия *n.* studio.

сту́жа *n., colloq.* severe cold.

стук *n.* **1,** knock: стук в дверь, knock at the door. **2,** clatter.

сту́кать *v. impfv.* [*pfv.* **сту́кнуть**] **1,** to knock; rap. **2,** to hit; strike. Сту́кнуть кулако́м по́ столу, to bang one's fist on the table. —**сту́каться,** *refl.* (*with instr.*) to bang; bump; knock: сту́кнуться голова́ми, to bump heads. Сту́кнуться голово́й о дверь, to bang one's head on the door. *See also* **сту́кнуть.**

стука́ч [*gen.* **-кача́**] *n., colloq.* informer; stool pigeon.

сту́кнуть *v. pfv.* **1,** *pfv. of* **сту́кать. 2,** *colloq.* (*of time*) to come. **3,** *impers.* (*with dat.*) *colloq., indicating attainment of a certain age:* ему́ ужé сту́кнуло сéмьдесят лет, he is already seventy. —**сту́кнуться,** *refl., pfv. of* **сту́каться.**

стул *n.* **1,** [*pl.* **сту́лья, сту́льев**] chair. **2,** *med.* stool. —**сидéть мéжду двух сту́льев,** to fall between two stools.

стульча́к [*gen.* **-чака́**] *n.* toilet seat.

сту́льчик *n., dim. of* **стул.** —**высо́кий дéтский сту́льчик,** highchair.

сту́па *n.* mortar (*bowl*).

ступа́ть *v. impfv.* [*pfv.* **ступи́ть**] **1,** to step. **2,** [*impfv. only*] to walk. —**нога́ не ступа́ет (куда́-нибудь),** not set foot in (a certain place). *See also* **ступи́ть.**

ступéнчатый *adj.* stepped; graded.

ступéнь *n.f.* **1,** step (*on a staircase*). **2,** *fig.* step; stage. **3,** *fig.* level.

ступéнька [*gen. pl.* **-нек**] *n.* **1,** step (*on a staircase*). **2,** rung (*of a ladder*).

ступи́ть *v. pfv.* [*infl.* **ступлю́, сту́пишь**] **1,** *pfv. of* **ступа́ть. 2,** (*with* **на** + *acc.*) to set foot on.

ступи́ца *n.* hub (*of a wheel*).

сту́пка [*gen. pl.* **-пок**] *n.* = **сту́па.**

ступня́ *n.* **1,** foot. **2,** sole (*of the foot*).

сту́пор *n.* stupor.

стуча́ть *v. impfv.* [*pfv.* **постуча́ть**; *pres.* **-чу́, -чи́шь**] **1,** to knock; rap. **2,** (*of one's teeth*) to chatter; (*of one's heart*) to throb. —**стуча́ться,** *refl.* to knock; rap.

стушева́ться *v.r., pfv. of* **тушева́ться** *and* **стушёвываться.**

стушёвываться *v.r. impfv.* [*pfv.* **стушева́ться**] *colloq.* **1,** to become indistinct; fade away. **2,** to withdraw into the background. **3,** (*with* **пéред**) to be overshadowed (by). **4,** to become flustered.

стуши́ть *v., pfv. of* **туши́ть** (*in sense #2*).

стыд [*gen.* **стыда́**] *n.* shame.

стыди́ть *v. impfv.* [*pfv.* **пристыди́ть**; *pres.* **стыжу́, стыди́шь**] to shame; put to shame. —**стыди́ться,** *refl.* [*pfv.* **постыди́ться**] (*with gen.*) to be ashamed (of).

стыдли́вый *adj.* bashful; modest; self-conscious. —**стыдли́вость,** *n.f.* bashfulness; modesty.

сты́дно *adj., used predicatively* it is a shame. —**сты́дно!**, shame on you! —**мне сты́дно**, I am ashamed. —**как вам не сты́дно!**, aren't you ashamed!
сты́дный *adj.* shameful.
стык *n.* **1**, joint. **2**, junction.
стыкова́ться *v.r. pfv.* [*infl.* **-ку́ется**] (*of space vehicles*) to dock.
стыко́вка *n.* docking (*of space vehicles*).
сты́нуть *v. impfv.* [*past* **стыл, сты́ла**] = **стыть.**
стыть *v. impfv.* [*pfv.* **осты́ть;** *pres.* **сты́ну, сты́нешь**] **1**, to cool off; get cold. **2**, to freeze; become frozen. **3**, *fig.* (*of an emotion*) to cool.
сты́чка [*gen. pl.* **-чек**] *n.* **1**, skirmish; clash. **2**, *colloq.* squabble; altercation.
стю́ард *n.* steward (*aboard ship or aloft*). —**стюарде́сса**, (дэ) *n.* stewardess.
стяг *n.* banner; standard.
стя́гивать *v. impfv.* [*pfv.* **стяну́ть**] **1**, to tighten; draw tight. **2**, to gather; concentrate. **3**, to pull off; remove. —**стя́гиваться**, *refl.* **1**, to tighten; become tight. **2**, to assemble; congregate.
стяжа́тель *n.m.* money-grubber. —**стяжа́тельство**, *n.* making money.
стяжа́ть *v. impfv. & pfv.* **1**, to amass (wealth). **2**, to win; gain (fame, respect, etc.).
стяну́ть *v. pfv.* [*infl.* **стяну́, стя́нешь**] **1**, *pfv. of* **стя́гивать. 2**, *colloq.* to swipe; pilfer. —**стяну́ться**, *refl., pfv. of* **стя́гиваться.**
суахи́ли *n.m. indecl.* Swahili.
субаре́нда *n.* sublease.
суббо́та *n.* **1**, Saturday. **2**, Sabbath.
суббо́тний *adj.* **1**, Saturday (*attrib.*). **2**, Sabbath (*attrib.*).
суббо́тник *n.* voluntary unpaid work performed on days off (*originally on Saturday*).
субконтине́нт *n.* subcontinent.
сублима́т *n.* sublimate. —**сублима́ция**, *n., chem.* sublimation.
сублими́ровать *v. impfv. & pfv.* [*pres.* **-рую, -руешь**] *chem.* to sublimate.
субордина́ция *n.* deference to rank: соблюда́ть субордина́цию, to defer to rank.
субподря́д *n.* subcontract. —**субподря́дчик**, *n.* subcontractor.
субсиди́ровать *v. impfv. & pfv.* [*pres.* **-рую, -руешь**] to subsidize.
субси́дия *n.* subsidy.
субста́нция *n.* substance.
субстра́т *n.* substratum.
субти́льный *adj., colloq.* frail; delicate.
субти́тр *n., motion pictures* subtitle.
субтро́пики [*gen.* **-ков**] *n. pl.* subtropics. —**субтропи́ческий**, *adj.* subtropical.
субъе́кт *n.* **1**, subject. **2**, *colloq.* fellow; person; character.
субъективи́зм *n.* **1**, subjectivism. **2**, subjectivity.
субъекти́вный *adj.* subjective. —**субъекти́вность**, *n.f.* subjectivity.
сува́льда *n.* tumbler (*of a lock*).
сувени́р *n.* souvenir.
суверéн *n.* sovereign. —**суверените́т**, *n.* sovereignty. —**сувере́нный**, *adj.* sovereign.
сугли́нок [*gen.* **-нка**] *n.* loam. —**сугли́нистый**, *adj.* loamy.
сугро́б *n.* snowdrift.
сугу́бо *adv.* especially; particularly.
сугу́бый *adj.* **1**, *obs.* double. **2**, special; particular.
суд [*gen.* **суда́**] *n.* **1**, court (*of law*). **2**, trial: суд над ке́м-нибудь, the trial of... **3**, judgment; verdict. **4**, *in* **вое́нный суд**, court-martial. **5**, *in* **стра́шный суд**, Judgment Day. —**пока́ суд да де́ло**, in the meantime; while we're waiting.
суда́к [*gen.* **-дака́**] *n.* pike perch.
суда́рыня *n., obs.* madam.
су́дарь *n.m., obs.* sir.
суда́чить *v. impfv., colloq.* to gossip.
суде́бный *adj.* **1**, court (*attrib.*). **2**, legal; judicial. **3**, forensic. —**суде́бная оши́бка**, miscarriage of justice. —**суде́бный проце́сс**, trial.
суде́йский *adj.* **1**, judge's. **2**, referee's; umpire's.
суди́лище *n.* (unfair) trial.
суди́мость *n.f., law* previous conviction.
суди́ть *v. impfv.* [*pres.* **сужу́, су́дишь**] **1**, (*often with* **о**) to judge. **2**, to try (*in court*). **3**, *sports* to referee; umpire. **4**, *in* **су́дя по** (+ *dat., but prepl. with pers. pronouns*) judging by. —**суди́ться**, *refl.* **1**, to go to court. **2**, (*with* **с** + *instr.*) to sue. **3**, to be tried (*in court*). *See also* **суждено́.**
су́дно *n.* **1**, [*pl.* **суда́, судо́в**] vessel; ship. **2**, [*pl.* **су́дна, су́ден**], *in* **подкладно́е су́дно**, bedpan.
су́дный *adj., obs.* of a court; judicial. —**Су́дный день**, Judgment Day.
судове́рфь *n.f.* shipyard.
судовладе́лец [*gen.* **-льца**] *n.* shipowner.
судово́й *adj.* ship (*attrib.*); ship's.
судо́к [*gen.* **-дка́**] *n.* **1**, gravy boat. **2**, cruet stand. **3**, *pl.* set of interlocking pots for carrying food.
судомо́йка [*gen. pl.* **-мо́ек**] *n.* (woman) dishwasher. —**судомо́йня**, *n.* [*gen. pl.* **-мо́ен**] scullery.
судопроизво́дство *n.* legal proceedings.
су́дорога *n.* **1**, cramp. **2**, convulsion.
су́дорожный *adj.* **1**, convulsive. **2**, *fig.* feverish; frantic; hectic.
судострое́ние *n.* shipbuilding. —**судострои́тель**, *n.m.* shipbuilder. —**судострои́тельный**, *adj.* shipbuilding (*attrib.*).
судоустро́йство *n.* judicial system.
судохо́дный *adj.* **1**, shipping (*attrib.*). **2**, navigable. —**судохо́дность**, *n.f.* navigability.
судохо́дство *n.* shipping; navigation.
судьба́ [*pl.* **су́дьбы, су́деб, су́дьбам**] *n.* **1**, fate; fortune; destiny. **2**, (one's) fate; (one's) lot. —**во́лею суде́б**, by the will of fate. —**каки́ми судьба́ми?**, what brings you here? —**не судьба́**, **1**, it was not to be; it was not in the cards. **2**, (*with dat. and inf.*) (one was) not fated (*or* destined) to: ему́ не судьба́ возврати́ться, he was not destined to return.
судья́ [*pl.* **су́дьи, суде́й, су́дьям**] *n.m.* **1**, judge. **2**, *sports* referee; umpire.
суеве́рие *n.* superstition. —**суеве́рный**, *adj.* superstitious.
суета́ *n.* **1**, fuss; bustle. **2**, trifle; triviality. —**суета́ суе́т**, vanity of vanities.
суети́ться *v.r. impfv.* [*pres.* **суечу́сь, суети́шься**] to bustle about.
суетли́вый *adj.* **1**, restless; fidgety. **2**, bustling.
сужде́ние *n.* judgment; opinion.
суждено́ *short form neut. of past passive part. of* **суди́ть**, fated; destined: нам не суждено́ бы́ло вы́играть, we were not fated to win.

сужéние *n.* narrowing; contraction; constriction.
сýживать *v. impfv.* [*pfv.* **сýзить**] **1,** to narrow. **2,** to take in (a garment). —**сýживаться,** *refl.* to narrow; become narrow; contract.
сýзить [*infl.* **сýжу, сýзишь**] *v., pfv. of* **сýживать.** —**сýзиться,** *refl., pfv. of* **сýживаться.**
сук [*gen.* **сукá;** *2nd loc.* **сукý;** *pl.* **сýчья, сýчьев** *or* **сукú, сукóв**] *n.* **1,** bough. **2,** knot (*in wood*).
сýка *n.* bitch. —**сýкин,** *adj., in* **сýкин сын,** *vulg.* son of a bitch.
сукнó [*pl.* **сýкна, сýкон**] *n.* smooth woolen cloth. —**класть под сукнó,** to shelve; pigeonhole.
сукóнка [*gen. pl.* **-нок**] *n.* cloth; rag.
сукóнный *adj.* **1,** cloth (*attrib.*). **2,** (*of language, speech, etc.*) dull; vapid; uninspired.
сулемá *n.* mercuric chloride; corrosive sublimate.
сулúть *v. impfv.* [*pfv.* **посулúть**] **1,** *obs.* to promise. **2,** [*impfv. only*] to portend; augur.
султáн *n.* **1,** sultan. **2,** plume. **3,** column (*of steam, smoke, etc.*).
султанáт *n.* sultanate.
султáнка [*gen. pl.* **-нок**] *n.* red mullet.
сульфаниламúдный *adj., in* **сульфаниламúдные препарáты,** sulfa drugs.
сульфáт *n.* sulfate.
сульфúд *n.* sulfide.
сумá *n., obs.* bag. —**ходúть с сумóй,** to beg for a living.
сумасбрóд *n.* nut; screwball.
сумасбрóдный *adj.* **1,** crazy; touched; unbalanced. **2,** mad; wild; reckless. —**сумасбрóдство,** *n.* erratic behavior.
сумасшéдший *adj.* mad; crazy; insane. —*n.* madman; insane person. —**сумасшéдший дом,** insane asylum.
сумасшéствие *n.* madness; insanity.
суматóха *n.* bustle; tumult; commotion.
суматóшный *adj., colloq.* **1,** bustling. **2,** tumultuous; hectic. *Also,* **суматóшливый.**
сумáх *n.* sumac.
сумбýр *n.* confusion. —**сумбýрный,** *adj.* confused.
сýмеречный *adj.* **1,** twilight (*attrib.*). **2,** (*of light*) dim; dull.
сýмерки [*gen.* **-рек**] *n. pl.* twilight; dusk.
сумéть *v. pfv.* (*with inf.*) to be able; manage; succeed.
сýмка [*gen. pl.* **-мок**] *n.* **1,** bag: сýмка для покýпок, shopping bag. **2,** handbag; purse; pocketbook. **3,** *zool.* pouch. —**санитáрная сýмка,** first-aid kit.
сýмма *n.* **1,** sum; total. **2,** sum; amount (*of money*).
суммáрный *adj.* **1,** total. **2,** general; generalized.
суммúровать *v. impfv. & pfv.* [*pres.* **-рую, -руешь**] **1,** to add up; total. **2,** to sum up; summarize.
сýмочка [*gen. pl.* **-чек**] *n.* handbag; purse; pocketbook.
сýмрак *n.* semidarkness. —**сýмрачный,** *adj.* gloomy.
сýмчатый *adj. & n.* marsupial.
сумя́тица *n., colloq.* **1,** bustle; commotion. **2,** confusion; turmoil.
сундýк [*gen.* **-дукá**] *n.* trunk; chest.
сýнуть *v., pfv. of* **совáть.** —**сýнуться,** *refl., pfv. of* **совáться.**
суп [*pl.* **супы́**] *n.* soup.
супермáркет *n.* supermarket.
супероблóжка [*gen. pl.* **-жек**] *n.* dust jacket.
супертáнкер *n.* supertanker.
сýпесь *n.f.* loam. *Also,* **сýпесок** [*gen.* **-ска**].
супинáтор *n.* arch support.
сýпить *v. impfv.* [*pres.* **сýплю, сýпишь**] *colloq.* to knit (one's brows).
сýпник *n.* soup tureen. *Also,* **сýпница.**
суповóй *adj.* soup (*attrib.*). —**суповáя лóжка,** soup ladle.
супрýг *n.* husband; spouse. —**супрýга,** *n.* wife; spouse. —**супрýги,** *n. pl.* husband and wife; married couple.
супрýжеский *adj.* marital; matrimonial; married; conjugal. —**супрýжество,** *n.* married life; matrimony.
сургýч [*gen.* **-гучá**] *n.* sealing wax. —**сургýчный,** *adj.* of sealing wax.
сурдúнка *n., music* mute. —**под сурдúнку,** quietly; secretly; on the sly.
сурéпица *n.* rape (*plant*). —**сурéпный,** *adj.* rape (*attrib.*): сурéпное мáсло, rape oil.
сýрик *n.* red lead.
сурóво *adv.* **1,** severely. **2,** sternly.
сурóвость *n.f.* severity; harshness.
сурóвый *adj.* **1,** (*of climate, winter, etc.*) harsh; severe; rigorous. **2,** (*of life, truth, measures, etc.*) harsh. **3,** (*of punishment, a sentence, etc.*) harsh; severe. **4,** (*of a person, look, voice, etc.*) stern. **5,** (*of cloth*) unbleached.
сурóк [*gen.* **-ркá**] *n.* marmot; woodchuck; ground hog.
суррогáт *n.* substitute: суррогáт сáхара, sugar substitute. —**суррогáтный,** *adj.* substitute; ersatz.
сурьмá *n.* antimony.
сусáльный *adj., in* **сусáльное зóлото,** gold leaf; **сусáльное серебрó,** silver leaf.
сýслик *n.* a kind of ground squirrel; suslik.
сýсло *n.* mash. —**виногрáдное сýсло,** new wine.
сустáв *n., anat.* joint.
суставнóй *adj.* of the joints. —**суставнóй ревматúзм,** rheumatic fever.
сутенёр *n.* gigolo.
сýтки [*gen.* **-ток**] *n. pl.* twenty-four-hour period; day: трóе сýток, three days (and nights). —**крýглые сýтки,** round the clock.
сýтолока *n.* bustle; commotion.
сýточный *adj.* a day's. —**сýточные,** *n. pl.* per diem.
сутýлить *v. impfv.* [*pfv.* **ссутýлить**] to hunch: сутýлить спúну, to hunch one's back. —**сутýлиться,** *refl.* to stoop; slouch.
сутýлый *adj.* round-shouldered; stooped. —**сутýлость,** *n.f.* stoop; slouch.
суть[1] *n.f.* essence. —**по сýти дéла,** in essence; as a matter of fact. —**суть дéла,** the heart (*or* crux) of the matter.
суть[2] *v., archaic, 3rd person of* **быть:** такúе дéйствия суть нéчто инóе, чем..., such actions are something different from...
суфлé *n. neut. indecl.* soufflé.
суфлёр *n., theat.* prompter.
суфлúровать *v. impfv.* [*pres.* **-рую, -руешь**] *theat.* (*with dat.*) to prompt.
суфражúстка [*gen. pl.* **-ток**] *n.* suffragette.
сýффикс *n.* suffix.
сухáрь [*gen.* **-харя́**] *n.m.* zwieback; rusk.
сухáя *n., decl. as an adj., sports, colloq.* shutout.
сýхо *adv.* **1,** dryly: сказáть сýхо, to say dryly. **2,** coldly: принять гостéй сýхо, to receive the guests coldly. —*adj., used predicatively* dry: бы́ло сýхо, it was dry.

суховéй *n.* hot dry wind.
сухожи́лие *n.* tendon.
сухо́й *adj.* [*comp.* **су́ше**] **1,** dry. **2,** dried. **3,** dried-up. **4,** arid. **5,** thin; skinny. **6,** cold; aloof. **7,** (*of a reception, tone, etc.*) cold; chilly. **8,** dry; dull. —**вы́йти сухи́м из воды́,** to emerge unscathed. —**держа́ть по́рох сухи́м,** to keep one's powder dry. *See also* **суха́я.**
сухопа́рый *adj., colloq.* lean; skinny.
сухопу́тный *adj.* land (*attrib.*); ground (*attrib.*); overland.
сухосто́й *n.* dead trees.
су́хость *n.f.* **1,** dryness. **2,** coldness; aloofness.
сухоща́вый *adj., colloq.* lean; skinny.
сучёный *adj.* twisted.
сучи́ть *v. impfv.* [*pres.* **сучу́, су́чишь**] **1,** to twist. **2,** (*with instr.*) *colloq.* to flap.
сучкова́тый *adj.* **1,** knotty. **2,** gnarled.
сучо́к [*gen.* **-чка́**] *n.* **1,** twig. **2,** knot (*in wood*). —**без сучка́, без задо́ринки,** without a hitch.
су́ша *n.* land; dry land.
су́ше *adj., comp. of* **сухо́й.**
суше́ние *n.* drying.
сушёный *adj.* dried.
суше́нье *n.* dried fruit.
суши́лка [*gen. pl.* **-лок**] *n.* **1,** dryer. **2,** drying room.
суши́льный *adj.* drying (*attrib.*).
суши́льня [*gen. pl.* **-лен**] *n.* drying room.
суши́ть *v. impfv.* [*pfv.* **вы́сушить;** *pres.* **сушу́, су́шишь**] to dry; make dry. —**суши́ться,** *refl.* to dry; become dry.
су́шка [*gen. pl.* **-шек**] *n.* **1,** drying. **2,** bagel.
сушь *n.f., colloq.* **1,** dry spell. **2,** dry place; dry land. **3,** dry reading matter.
суще́ственно *adv.* substantially.
суще́ственный *adj.* **1,** substantial; fundamental. **2,** vital; essential. —**суще́ственным о́бразом,** substantially.
существи́тельный *adj., in* **и́мя существи́тельное,** noun. —**существи́тельное,** *n.* noun.
существо́ *n.* **1,** essence; gist. **2,** being; creature. —**по существу́, 1,** in essence; in effect; essentially. **2,** to the point: говори́ть по существу́, to speak to the point.
существова́ние *n.* existence.
существова́ть *v. impfv.* [*pres.* **-тву́ю, -тву́ешь**] to exist.
су́щий *adj.* **1,** *obs.* existing. **2,** *colloq.* pure; utter; downright; absolute.
су́щность *n.f.* essence. —**в су́щности, 1,** essentially; in essence. **2,** *in* в су́щности говоря́, as a matter of fact; as a practical matter. —**по са́мой свое́й су́щности,** by its (their) very nature.
сфабрикова́ть *v. pfv.* [*infl.* **-ку́ю, -ку́ешь**] *colloq.* **1,** to forge. **2,** *pfv. of* **фабрикова́ть** (*in sense #3*).
сфальши́вить *v., pfv. of* **фальши́вить.**
сфантази́ровать *v., pfv. of* **фантази́ровать** (*in sense #2*).
сфе́ра *n.* **1,** sphere. **2,** *fig.* sphere; realm; domain. **3,** *pl.* circles: деловы́е сфе́ры, business circles. —**сфе́ра влия́ния,** sphere of influence.
сфери́ческий *adj.* spherical.
сферо́ид *n.* spheroid. —**сфероида́льный,** *adj.* spheroidal.
сфинкс *n.* sphinx.
сформирова́ть *v., pfv. of* **формирова́ть.** —**сформирова́ться,** *refl., pfv. of* **формирова́ться.**
сформова́ть *v., pfv. of* **формова́ть.**
сформули́ровать *v., pfv. of* **формули́ровать.**
сфотографи́ровать *v., pfv. of* **фотографи́ровать.** —**сфотографи́роваться,** *refl., pfv. of* **фотографи́роваться.**
схвати́ть [*infl.* **схвачу́, схва́тишь**] *v., pfv. of* **хвата́ть** (*in sense #1*) *and* **схва́тывать.** —**схвати́ться,** *refl., pfv. of* **хвата́ться** (*in sense #1*) *and* **схва́тываться.**
схва́тка [*gen. pl.* **-ток**] *n.* **1,** fight; skirmish. **2,** *pl.* cramps; pains.
схва́тывать *v. impfv.* [*pfv.* **схвати́ть**] **1,** to seize; grab. **2,** *colloq.* to catch (a cold, illness, etc.). **3,** (*of an illness*) to strike: его́ схвати́ла пода́гра, he was stricken with gout. **4,** *fig., colloq.* to grasp; comprehend. **5,** *fig.* (*of an artist, portrait, etc.*) to capture. —**схва́тываться,** *refl.* **1,** (*with* **за** + *acc.*) to seize; grab; grasp; snatch. **2,** to fight; battle; (*with* **с** + *instr.*) grapple (with); come to grips (with).
схе́ма *n.* **1,** diagram; chart. **2,** outline. **3,** *electronics* circuit.
схемати́ческий *adj.* **1,** schematic; diagrammatic. **2,** sketchy.
схи́зма *n.* schism.
схитри́ть *v., pfv. of* **хитри́ть.**
схлы́нуть *v. pfv.* **1,** (*of water*) to rush back; sweep back. **2,** *fig.* (*of emotions*) to subside.
сход *n.* **1,** going down; descent. **2,** coming off. **3,** *colloq.* descent; slope. **4,** *pre-rev.* meeting; assembly.
сходи́ть[1] *v. impfv.* [*pfv.* **сойти́;** *pres.* **схожу́, схо́дишь**] **1,** to go down; descend. **2,** to get off; disembark. **3,** (*with* **с** + *gen.*) to go off (a road, tracks, etc.). **4,** (*of paint, dirt, skin, etc.*) to come off; peel off. **5,** (*with* **за** + *acc.*) to pass for; be taken for. **6,** *colloq.* to go; come off: всё сошло́ хорошо́, everything went well. —**сходи́ть на бе́рег,** to go ashore. —**сходи́ть на нет,** to come to naught. —**сходи́ть с рук,** to go unnoticed; go unpunished; (*with dat.*) get away with: э́то сходи́ло ему́ с рук, he got away with it. —**сходи́ть с ума́,** to go out of one's mind; lose one's mind; go mad.
сходи́ть[2] *v. pfv.* [*infl.* **схожу́, схо́дишь**] to go (*to a certain place and return*).
сходи́ться *v.r. impfv.* [*pfv.* **сойти́сь;** *pres.* **схожу́сь, схо́дишься**] **1,** to meet. **2,** to gather. **3,** (*with* **с** + *instr.*) to become friends (with); become intimate (with). **4,** to coincide. **5,** to tally. **6,** *colloq.* to agree. —**сходи́ться** (*or* **не сходи́ться**) **во вку́сах,** to have similar (*or* different) tastes. —**сходи́ться** (*or* **не сходи́ться**) **хара́ктерами,** to be compatible (*or* incompatible).
схо́дка [*gen. pl.* **-док**] *n., pre-rev.* meeting; assembly.
схо́дни [*gen.* **-ней**] *n. pl.* gangplank.
схо́дный *adj.* **1,** similar. **2,** *colloq.* (*of a price*) fair; reasonable.
схо́дство *n.* similarity; likeness; resemblance.
схо́жесть *n.f., colloq.* similarity; resemblance.
схо́жий *adj., colloq.* similar.
сца́пать *v. pfv., colloq.* to grab; grab hold of.
сцара́пывать *v. impfv.* [*pfv.* **сцара́пать**] to scrape off.
сцеди́ть [*infl.* **сцежу́, сце́дишь**] *v., pfv. of* **сце́живать.**
сце́живать *v. impfv.* [*pfv.* **сцеди́ть**] to strain off.
сце́на *n.* **1,** stage: выступа́ть на сце́не, to appear on (the) stage. **2,** scene: фина́льная сце́на, the final scene. **3,** *colloq.* scene: устро́ить сце́ну, to make a

scene. —**сойти́ со сце́ны, 1,** to retire from the stage. **2,** (*of a play*) no longer be performed. **3,** *fig.* to pass from the scene. —**уйти́ со сце́ны,** to retire from the stage. —**яви́ться/появи́ться/вы́ступить на сце́ну,** to appear on the scene.

сцена́рий *n.* scenario. —**сценари́ст,** *n.* scenario writer.

сцени́ческий *adj.* stage (*attrib.*); scenic.

сцени́чный *adj.* suitable for the stage.

сцепи́ть [*infl.* **сцеплю́, сце́пишь**] *v., pfv. of* **сцепля́ть.** —**сцепи́ться,** *refl., pfv. of* **сцепля́ться.**

сцепле́ние *n.* **1,** coupling. **2,** clutch. **3,** *fig.* combination (of circumstances).

сцепля́ть *v. impfv.* [*pfv.* **сцепи́ть**] to couple. —**сцепля́ться,** *refl.* **1,** to engage; mesh. **2,** *colloq.* to grapple; be locked in combat.

сцепно́й *adj.* coupling (*attrib.*).

счастли́вец [*gen.* **-вца**] *n.m.* [*fem.* **-вица**] lucky person.

счастли́во *also,* **сча́стливо** *adv.* **1,** happily. **2,** luckily: счастли́во отде́латься, to get off lucky. —*interj.* good luck!; all the best!

счастли́вчик *n., colloq.* = **счастли́вец.**

счастли́вый *adj.* [*short form* **сча́стлив** *or* **счастли́в**] **1,** happy. **2,** lucky; fortunate. —**счастли́вого пути́!,** bon voyage!

сча́стье *n.* **1,** happiness. **2,** (good) luck; (good) fortune. Ва́ше сча́стье, что..., you are lucky/fortunate that... —**к сча́стью; по сча́стью,** fortunately. —**на сча́стье, 1,** for (good) luck. **2,** (*with gen.*) luckily for. На моё сча́стье, luckily for me.

счесть [*infl.* **сочту́, сочтёшь;** *past* **счёл, сочла́, сочло́**] *v., pfv. of* **счита́ть** (*in sense #3*). —**сче́сться,** *refl., pfv. of* **счита́ться** (*in sense #4*).

счёт [*2nd loc.* **на счету́;** *pl.* **счета́,** *except in sense #6*] *n.* **1,** counting: вести́ счёт (+ *dat.*), to keep count of. **2,** calculation; reckoning. **3,** account. **4,** bill; (*in a restaurant*) check. **5,** *sports* score. **6,** *pl.* accounts; scores: своди́ть счёты с, to settle scores with. —**без счёту,** countless. —**в два счёта,** *colloq.* in a jiffy. —**в коне́чном счёте,** in the final analysis. —**в счёт** (+ *gen.*), against; to be applied against. —**за счёт** (+ *gen.*), **1,** by using; by taking from. **2,** at the expense of. —**на счёт, 1,** (*with gen.*) at the expense of. **2,** (*with a possessive pronoun*) about; concerning. —**на счету́,** *in* **ка́ждый ... на счету́,** every ... counts. —**на хоро́шем счету́ у,** in good standing with; in the good graces of. —**на э́тот счёт,** on this point; on that score. —**счёту нет** (+ *dat.*), more than one knows what to do with.

счётный *adj.* **1,** calculating (*attrib.*): счётная маши́на, adding machine. **2,** accounts (*attrib.*): счётная кни́га, accounts book.

счетово́д *n.* bookkeeper; accountant. —**счетово́дный,** *adj.* bookkeeping (*attrib.*); accounting (*attrib.*). —**счетово́дство,** *n.* bookkeeping; accounting.

счётчик *n.* **1,** meter: га́зовый счётчик, gas meter. **2,** counter (*person*). —**счётчик Ге́йгера,** Geiger counter.

счёты [*gen.* **-тов**] *n. pl.* abacus.

счисле́ние *n.* **1,** *obs.* calculation; computation. **2,** *math.* numbering: десяти́чная систе́ма счисле́ния, decimal system. **3,** *naut.* reckoning: счисле́ние пути́, dead reckoning.

счи́стить [*infl.* **-щу, -стишь**] *v., pfv. of* **счища́ть.**

счи́танные *adj.* only a few.

счита́ть *v. impfv.* **1,** [*pfv.* **сосчита́ть**] to count: счита́ть до десяти́, to count to ten. Не счита́я..., not counting... **2,** to do arithmetic: счита́ть в уме́, to do figures in one's head. **3,** [*pfv.* **счесть**] (*with instr. or* **за** + *acc.*) to consider; regard; look upon: счита́ть что́-нибудь ну́жным, to consider something necessary; счита́ть за честь, to consider it an honor. **4,** to believe; think; feel: я счита́ю, что..., I believe that... —**счита́ться,** *refl.* **1,** [*pfv.* **посчита́ться**] (*with* **с** + *instr.*) to consider; take into consideration; take into account. Не счита́ться с, to ignore. **2,** (*with instr.*) to be considered; be regarded. **3,** *passive of* **счита́ть:** э́то не счита́ется, that doesn't count. Счита́ется, что..., it is believed (*or* thought) that... **4,** [*pfv.* **сче́сться**] (*with* **с** + *instr.*) *colloq.* to settle (up) with.

счи́тывание *n., computer science* reading; readout.

счища́ть *v. impfv.* [*pfv.* **счи́стить**] to clear away.

США *abbr. of* **Соединённые Шта́ты Аме́рики,** United States of America; USA.

сшиба́ть *v. impfv.* [*pfv.* **сшиби́ть**] *colloq.* **1,** to knock off. **2,** to knock down. —**сшиба́ться,** *refl., colloq.* **1,** to collide. **2,** to get into a fight.

сшиби́ть [*infl.* **-бу́, -бёшь;** *past* **сшиб, -ла**] *v., pfv. of* **сшиба́ть.** —**сшиби́ться,** *refl., pfv. of* **сшиба́ться.**

сшива́ть *v. impfv.* [*pfv.* **сшить**] **1,** to sew together. **2,** *med.* to suture. **3,** to join together; fasten together. **4,** to make (*by fastening together planks*).

сшить [*infl.* **сошью́, сошьёшь**] *v., pfv. of* **шить** *and* **сшива́ть.**

съеда́ть *v. impfv.* [*pfv.* **съесть**] to eat; eat up.

съеде́ние *n.* being eaten alive. —**отдава́ть** *or* **оставля́ть на съеде́ние** (+ *dat.*), **1,** to leave to be eaten alive by. **2,** *fig.* to leave at the mercy of.

съедо́бный *adj.* edible.

съёживаться *v.r. impfv.* [*pfv.* **съёжиться**] **1,** to shrivel; shrink. **2,** to huddle up; cringe. **3,** to become haggard.

съёжиться *v.r., pfv. of* **ёжиться** *and* **съёживаться.**

съезд *n.* convention; congress.

съе́здить *v. pfv.* [*infl.* **съе́зжу, съе́здишь**] to go (*to a place and return*); make a trip (to).

съезжа́ть *v. impfv.* [*pfv.* **съе́хать**] (*with* **с** + *gen.*) **1,** to go down; ride down; drive down. **2,** to go off; drive off. **3,** *obs.* to leave; drive off. **4,** *colloq.* to move out. **5,** *colloq.* to come off; slip off. —**съезжа́ться,** *refl.* **1,** to meet; run into each other. **2,** to gather; assemble.

съёмка [*gen. pl.* **-мок**] *n.* **1,** taking down; removal. **2,** survey; surveying: возду́шная съёмка, aerial survey. **3,** shooting (*of a picture*).

съёмный *adj.* removable; detachable.

съёмочный *adj., motion pictures* shooting (*attrib.*). —**съёмочная площа́дка,** (movie) set.

съёмщик *n.* tenant; renter.

съестно́й *adj.* food (*attrib.*). —**съестно́е,** *n.* food; victuals.

съесть [*infl. like* **есть**] *v., pfv. of* **есть** (*in sense #1*) *and* **съеда́ть.**

съе́хать [*infl.* **съе́ду, съе́дешь**] *v., pfv. of* **съезжа́ть.** —**съе́хаться,** *refl., pfv. of* **съезжа́ться.**

съязви́ть *v., pfv. of* **язви́ть** (*in sense #3*).

сы́воротка *n.* **1,** whey. **2,** *med.* serum.

сы́гранность *n.f.* coordination; teamwork.

сыгра́ть *v. pfv.* **1,** *pfv. of* **игра́ть. 2,** *in* сыгра́ть шу́тку с, to play a joke/trick on. —**сыгра́ться,** *refl.* to play well together; develop teamwork.

сы́змала *also,* **сы́змалу** *adv., colloq.* since childhood.
сы́знова *adv., colloq.* all over again; anew; afresh.
сын [*pl.* **сыновья́, -ве́й, -вья́м**] *n.* son.
сыни́шка *n.m., dim. of* **сын.**
сыно́вний *adj.* filial.
сыно́к [*gen.* **-нка́**] *n., colloq.* **1,** son. **2,** sonny.
сы́пать *v. impfv.* [*pres.* **сы́плю, сы́плешь**] **1,** to pour (a dry substance). **2,** (*with acc. or instr.*) to shower; rain (blows, insults, etc.); spout (words, information, etc.). **3,** *v.i.* (*of rain, snow, etc.*) to fall; come down. **4,** *in* сы́пать деньга́ми, to toss money around. —**сы́паться,** *refl.* **1,** (*of a dry substance*) to pour; spill. **2,** to flake off; peel off. **3,** to fly about. **4,** (*of rain, snow, etc.*) to fall; come down. **5,** *fig.* to rain down; stream in; pour in.
сыпно́й *adj., in* **сыпно́й тиф,** typhus.
сыпня́к [*gen.* **-няка́**] *n., colloq.* typhus.
сыпу́чий *adj.* friable; crumbly; loose. —**ме́ры сыпу́чих тел,** dry measures. —**сыпу́чий песо́к,** quicksand.
сыпь *n.f.* rash.
сыр [*pl.* **сыры́**] *n.* cheese.
сыре́ть *v. impfv.* [*pfv.* **отсыре́ть**] to become damp.
сыре́ц [*gen.* **-рца́**] *n., usu. used in compounds,* product in its raw state: шёлк-сыре́ц, raw silk.
сы́рник *n.* cheese pancake.
сы́рный *adj.* cheese (*attrib.*).
сыроваре́ние *n.* cheese making.
сыроéжка [*gen. pl.* **-жек**] *n.* a variety of mushroom; russula.
сыро́й *adj.* **1,** damp. **2,** (*of food*) raw; uncooked; (*of water*) unboiled. **3,** not completely cooked or baked; half-done. **4,** in rough form; unfinished.
сы́ромять *n.f.* rawhide. —**сыромя́тный,** *adj.* rawhide.
сы́рость *n.f.* dampness.
сырьё *n.* raw material(s).
сыск *n., pre-rev.* criminal investigation.
сыска́ть *v. pfv.* [*infl.* **сыщу́, сы́щешь**] *colloq.* to find.
сыскно́й *adj., pre-rev.* of criminal investigation.
сы́тно *adv.* heartily. Сы́тно поéсть, have a hearty meal.
сы́тный *adj.* (*of food or a meal*) filling.
сы́тость *n.f.* satiety.
сы́тый *adj.* full (*from eating*). —**сыт по го́рло, 1,** stuffed to the gills. **2,** (*with instr.*) sick and tired of.
сыч [*gen.* **сыча́**] *n.* little owl.
сычу́г [*gen.* **-чуга́**] *n.* **1,** fourth stomach of a ruminant animal. **2,** rennet.
сычу́жина *n.* rennin.
сычу́жный *adj.* rennet (*attrib.*). —**сычу́жный ферме́нт,** rennin.
сы́щик *n.* detective.
сэконо́мить *v., pfv. of* **эконо́мить.**
сэр *n.* sir.
сэт *n., tennis* set.
сюда́ *adv., expressing direction* here; this way.
сюже́т *n.* **1,** subject; subject matter. **2,** *lit.* plot. **3,** *colloq.* topic.
сюже́тный *adj.* **1,** of a plot: сюже́тное разви́тие, development of a plot. **2,** having a strong plot.
сюзере́н *n.* suzerain. —**сюзерените́т,** *n.* suzerainty. —**сюзере́нный,** *adj.* suzerain.
сюи́та *n., music* suite.
сюрпри́з *n.* a surprise. —**сюрпри́зный,** *adj.* surprise (*attrib.*).
сюрреали́зм *n.* surrealism. —**сюрреали́ст,** *n.* surrealist. —**сюрреалисти́ческий,** *adj.* surrealistic.
сюрту́к [*gen.* **-тука́**] *n.* frock coat.
сюсю́канье *n., colloq.* lisp; lisping.
сюсю́кать *v. impfv., colloq.* to lisp.
сяк *adv., in* **так и сяк; то так то сяк, 1,** this way or that; one way or the other. **2,** fair; so-so.
сям *adv., in* **там и сям; то там то сям,** here and there.

Т

Т, т *n. neut.* nineteenth letter of the Russian alphabet.
та *adj., fem. of* **тот.**
таба́к [*gen.* **-бака́**] *n.* tobacco. —**де́ло таба́к,** *colloq.* things are in a bad way; things are in a sorry state.
табаке́рка [*gen. pl.* **-рок**] *n.* snuffbox.
табаково́д *n.* tobacco grower. —**табаково́дство,** *n.* tobacco growing. —**табаково́дческий,** *adj.* tobacco-growing.
таба́чный *adj.* tobacco (*attrib.*).
та́бель *n.m.* **1,** table; chart. **2,** [*also,* **та́бель успева́емости**] report card. **3,** sign-out board. —*n.f., in* **та́бель о ра́нгах,** *hist.* Table of Ranks.
та́бельный *adj.* shown on a table. —**та́бельная доска́,** time board. —**та́бельные часы́,** time clock.
та́бельщик *n.* one who records the hours worked by employees; timekeeper.
табле́тка [*gen. pl.* **-ток**] *n.* tablet; pill.
табли́ца *n.* table: табли́ца умноже́ния, multiplication table.
табли́чка [*gen. pl.* **-чек**] *n.* tablet; plaque.
табли́чный *adj.* tabular.
табло́ *n. indecl.* (electronic) indicator panel; scoreboard.
табльдо́т *n.* table d'hôte.
та́бор *n.* gypsy band.
табу́ *n. neut. indecl.* taboo.
табуля́тор *n.* tabulating machine; tabulator.
табу́н [*gen.* **-буна́**] *n.* herd; flock. —**табу́нщик,** *n.* herdsman.
табуре́т *n.* stool.
табуре́тка [*gen. pl.* **-ток**] *n.* stool.
та́волга *n.* meadowsweet.

тавpёный *adj.* branded.
таври́ть *v. impfv.* to brand (cattle).
тавpó [*pl.* **тáвра, тавр, таврáм**] *n.* brand (*on cattle*).
тавтолóгия *n.* tautology. —**тавтологи́ческий,** *adj.* tautological; redundant.
тагáн *n.* trivet.
таджи́к *n.m.* [*fem.* **-жи́чка**] Tadzhik. —**таджи́кский,** *adj.* Tadzhik.
таёжный *adj.* of the taiga; in the taiga.
таз [*2nd loc.* **тазу́;** *pl.* **тазы́**] *n.* **1,** basin. Умывáльный таз, washbasin. **2,** pelvis.
тáзовый *adj.* pelvic. —**тáзовая кость,** hipbone.
таи́нственность *n.f.* mystery.
таи́нственный *adj.* **1,** mysterious. **2,** secret.
тáинство *n.* **1,** *obs.* secret; mystery. **2,** sacrament.
таи́ть *v. impfv.* **1,** to conceal; hide. **2,** to harbor (a thought, feeling, grudge, etc.). **3,** *in* **таи́ть в себé,** *fig.* to hold; be fraught with. —**таи́ться,** *refl.* **1,** to hide; be hiding. **2,** to lurk. **3,** to withhold information; not tell the whole story.
тайгá *n.* taiga.
тайкóм *adv.* secretly; surreptitiously; on the sly. —**тайкóм от,** without the knowledge of; without telling.
тайм *n.* period (*of a game*).
тáйна *n.* **1,** secret: глубóкая тáйна, a deep secret. Держáть (чтó-нибудь) в тáйне, to keep (something) secret. **2,** mystery.
тайни́к [*gen.* **-никá**] *n.* **1,** hiding place; cache. **2,** hideout; hideaway. —**в тайникáх сéрдца,** in the innermost recesses of one's heart.
тáйно *adv.* secretly; in secret.
тáйнопись *n.f.* secret writing.
тáйный *adj.* secret.
тáйский *adj.* Thai.
тайфу́н *n.* typhoon.
так *adv.* **1,** this way; that way; like this; like that: не говори́те так, don't talk like that. **2,** (*before short-form adjectives*) so: э́то не так стрáшно, it's not so terrible. **3,** so; true; correct: э́то не совсéм так, that is not entirely correct. **4,** then; in that case. —*particle* so; then; thus; therefore. —**не так,** wrong; amiss: чтó-то не так, something is wrong. —**не так ли?,** isn't that so?; don't you think so? —**так же,** (in) the same way. —**так же... как и,** as... as. —**так и быть,** so be it. —**так и не** (+ *verb*), never. —**так и так,** either way. —**так как,** since; inasmuch as. —**так себé,** so-so. —**так что,** so; and so.
такелáж *n., naut.* rigging.
тáкже *adv.* also; too; as well.
-таки *particle, used for emphasis.* —**всё-таки,** still; all the same. —**опя́ть-таки,** *see* **опя́ть.**
такóв *indef. pron.* [*fem.* **таковá;** *neut.* **таковó;** *pl.* **таковы́**] **1,** such/that is; such/those are: таковы́ фáкты, such are the facts; those are the facts. **2,** like that; the same; alike: все моряки́ таковы́, all sailors are like that. —**и был такóв,** *colloq.* and off he went; and away he went.
таковóй *indef. pron.* such; the same: за отсу́тствием таковóго, in the absence of the same. —**как таковóй,** as such.
такóй *indef. adj.* such; such a: такóй человéк, such a person; таки́е вéщи, such things. —*indef. pron.* the sort of person: он такóй, что..., he is the sort of person who... —*adv.* (*used before long-form adjectives only*) so; such: онá такáя краси́вая, she is so beautiful; такáя краси́вая дéвушка, such a beautiful girl. —**и всё такóе,** *colloq.* and all that. —**кто такóй?,** who is it? Кто вы такóй?, who are you? —**таки́м óбразом,** *see* **óбраз.** —**такóе,** such a thing. —**такóй же,** the same. —**такóй же** (+ *adj.*) **как,** as... as. —**что ж (тут) такóе (*or* такóго)?,** what of it? —**что такóе?,** what's the matter?; what's going on? —**что такóе** (+ *nom.*), what is a...? —**что э́то такóе?,** what is this?
такóй-то *adj.* **1,** so-and-so. **2,** such and such.
тáкса *n.* **1,** (set) rate. **2,** dachshund.
такси́ *n. neut. indecl.* taxi; cab.
таксóметр *n.* taximeter.
таксомотóр *n.* taxi.
таксонóмия *n.* taxonomy. —**таксономи́ческий,** *adj.* taxonomic.
такт *n.* **1,** *music* bar; measure. **2,** rhythm; beat; time: в такт, in time. В такт му́зыке, in time to the music. Отбивáть такт, to beat time. Сби́ться с тáкта, to lose the beat. **3,** tact.
тáк-таки *particle, colloq.* **1,** still; anyway. **2,** really. —**тáк-таки всё,** absolutely everything.
тáктик *n.* tactician.
тáктика *n.* tactics. —**такти́ческий,** *adj.* tactical.
такти́чный *adj.* tactful. —**такти́чно,** *adv.* tactfully. —**такти́чность,** *n.f.* tactfulness; tact.
талáнт *n.* talent. —**талáнтливый,** *adj.* talented.
талисмáн *n.* talisman.
тáлия *n.* waist.
тáллий *n.* thallium.
талму́д *n.* Talmud. —**талмуди́зм,** *n.* dogmatism; fundamentalism; talmudism.
талмуди́ст *n.* **1,** Talmudic scholar. **2,** dogmatist; fundamentalist. —**талмуди́стский,** *adj.* dogmatic; doctrinaire. —**талмуди́ческий,** *adj.* Talmudic.
талóн *n.* coupon. —**посáдочный талóн,** boarding pass.
тáлый *adj.* melting; melted.
тальк *n.* **1,** talc; talcum. **2,** talcum powder. —**тáльковый,** *adj.* talc (*attrib.*); talcum (*attrib.*).
там *adv.* there; in that place. —**там, где,** where; the place where. —**там же,** in that place; (*in footnotes*) ibid.
тамадá *n.m.* toastmaster.
тамари́нд *n.* tamarind.
тамари́ск *n.* tamarisk.
тáмбур *n.* **1,** vestibule. **2,** platform (*of a railway car*). **3,** chain stitch.
тамбури́н *n.* tambourine.
тáмбурный *adj., in* **тáмбурный шов; тáмбурная стрóчка,** chain stitch.
тамóженник *n.* customs official. —**тамóженный,** *adj.* customs (*attrib.*).
тамóжня *n.* customs; custom house.
тáмошний *adj., colloq.* of that place; local.
тампóн *n.* tampon.
тамтáм *n.* tom-tom.
танáгра *n.* tanager.
тáнгенс *n., trig.* tangent. —**тангенциáльный,** *adj.* tangential.
тáнго *n. indecl.* tango.
тáндем (дэ) *n.* tandem.
тáнец [*gen.* **-нца**] *n.* **1,** dance. **2,** *pl.* dance (*affair with dancing*): пойти́ на тáнцы, to go to a dance.
тани́н *n.* tannin. —**тани́нный,** *adj.* tannic.
танк *n.* **1,** *mil.* tank. **2,** tank; cistern.

та́нкер *n.* tanker.
танке́тка [*gen. pl.* **-ток**] *n.* **1,** *mil.* light tank. **2,** wedge heel. **3,** *pl.* wedge-heeled shoes.
танки́ст *n.* member of a tank crew.
та́нковый *adj., mil.* tank (*attrib.*).
танта́л *n.* tantalum.
танцева́льный *adj.* dance (*attrib.*); dancing (*attrib.*): танцева́льный ве́чер, dance.
танцева́ть *v. impfv.* [*pres.* **-цу́ю, -цу́ешь**] to dance.
танцо́вщик *n.m.* [*fem.* **-щица**] (ballet) dancer.
танцо́р *n.* dancer.
тапёр *n.* pianist engaged for a dance.
тапио́ка *n.* tapioca.
тапи́р *n.* tapir.
та́почки [*gen.* **-чек**] *n. pl.* [*sing.* **та́почка**] **1,** slippers. **2,** sneakers.
та́ра *n.* **1,** container (*for safeguarding or transporting*). **2,** wrapping material; packing material. **3,** *comm.* tare.
тараба́нить *v. impfv., colloq.* to clatter.
тараба́рщина *n., colloq.* gibberish.
тарака́н *n.* cockroach.
тара́н *n.* **1,** battering-ram. **2,** *mech.* ram.
тара́нить *v. impfv.* [*pfv.* **протара́нить**] to ram.
таранта́с *n.* large four-wheeled carriage; tarantass.
тара́нтул *n.* tarantula.
тара́нь *n.f.* roach (*fish*).
тарара́м *n., colloq.* uproar; hubbub; hullabaloo.
тарата́йка [*gen. pl.* **-та́ек**] *n.* two-wheeled carriage.
тарато́рить *v. impfv., colloq.* to jabber; chatter.
тарахте́ть *v. impfv.* [*pres.* **-хчу́, -хти́шь**] *colloq.* **1,** to clatter. **2,** *fig.* to chatter.
тара́щить *v. impfv.* [*pfv.* **вы́таращить**] *colloq., in* **тара́щить глаза́,** to stare; gape.
таре́лка [*gen. pl.* **-лок**] *n.* **1,** plate; dish. **2,** *pl.* cymbals. —**быть в своей таре́лке,** to be in one's element. —**быть не в своей таре́лке, 1,** to be out of sorts; be not quite oneself. **2,** to feel ill at ease; feel uneasy.
таре́лочка [*gen. pl.* **-чек**] *n., dim. of* **таре́лка.** —**стрельба́ по таре́лочкам,** trapshooting.
тари́ф *n.* **1,** tariff. **2,** rate. —**тари́фный,** *adj.* tariff (*attrib.*).
та́ры-ба́ры *n. pl. indecl., colloq.* chatter; tittle-tattle.
таска́ть *v. impfv.* **1,** *indeterm. of* **тащи́ть. 2,** to carry. **3,** *colloq.* to wear (for a long time). **4,** (*with* **за** + *acc.*) *colloq.* to pull (by): таска́ть (кого́-нибудь) за́ уши, to pull (someone) by the ears. —**таска́ться,** *refl., colloq.* **1,** to wander; amble. **2,** (*with* **по**) to make the rounds of. **3,** to hang around. **4,** (*with* **с** + *instr.*) to carry around (*on one's person*). **5,** (*with* **за** + *instr.*) to chase after (women). **6,** (*with* **с** + *instr.*) to have an affair (with).
тасова́ть *v. impfv.* [*pfv.* **стасова́ть;** *pres.* **-су́ю, -су́ешь**] to shuffle (cards).
тасо́вка *n.* shuffling; shuffle (*of cards*).
ТАСС *n.m.* Tass (*abbr. of* **Телегра́фное Аге́нство Сове́тского Сою́за**).
тата́рин [*pl.* **тата́ры, тата́р**] *n.m.* [*fem.* **тата́рка**] Tatar. —**тата́рский,** *adj.* Tatar.
татуи́ровать *v. impfv. & pfv.* [*pres.* **-рую, -руешь**] to tattoo.
татуиро́вка *n.* **1,** tatooing. **2,** tattoo.
тафта́ *n.* taffeta. —**тафтяно́й,** *adj.* taffeta.
тахо́метр *n.* tachometer.
тахта́ *n.* ottoman; divan.
тача́нка [*gen. pl.* **-нок**] *n.* **1,** light open carriage. **2,** machine-gun cart.
тача́ть *v. impfv.* [*pfv.* **вы́тачать** *or* **стача́ть**] to stitch.
та́чка [*gen. pl.* **-чек**] *n.* wheelbarrow.
тащи́ть *v. impfv.* [*pfv.* **потащи́ть;** *pres.* **тащу́, та́щишь**] **1,** to pull; draw; tow. **2,** to drag; haul; lug. **3,** [*pfv.* **вы́тащить**] to pull out. **4,** [*pfv.* **вы́тащить**] to drag (someone) somewhere against his will. **5,** [*pfv.* **вы́тащить** *or* **стащи́ть**] *colloq.* to swipe; pilfer. —**тащи́ться,** *refl.* **1,** to drag along; trail along (the ground). **2,** *colloq.* to drag oneself along. **3,** *colloq.* to go (somewhere) reluctantly; drag oneself. *See also* **таска́ть.**
та́яние *n.* melting.
та́ять *v. impfv.* [*pfv.* **раста́ять;** *pres.* **та́ю, та́ешь**] **1,** to melt; thaw. **2,** (*of clouds, smoke, etc.*) to dissipate. **3,** *fig.* to fade; wane; dwindle; ebb. **4,** *fig.* to fade from view. **5,** [*impfv. only*] (*of a person*) to waste away.
тварь *n.f., obs.* **1,** creature. **2,** wretch; bum.
тверде́ть *v. impfv.* [*pfv.* **затверде́ть**] to harden; become hard.
тверди́ть *v. impfv.* [*pres.* **твержу́, тверди́шь**] **1,** to repeat (*or* keep saying) over and over again; (*with* **о**) talk endlessly about. **2,** [*pfv.* **затверди́ть** *or* **вы́твердить**] to memorize (*through repetition*).
твёрдо *adv.* firmly; firm. Твёрдо вы́учить, to learn thoroughly. Твёрдо запо́мнить, to remember well.
твёрдока́менный *adj.* callous; insensitive; hard-boiled.
твердоло́бый *adj., colloq.* **1,** thickheaded. **2,** dyed-in-the-wool.
твёрдость *n.f.* **1,** hardness; firmness. **2,** *fig.* resoluteness; steadfastness.
твёрдый *adj.* [*comp.* **твёрже**] **1,** hard. **2,** solid. **3,** firm. **4,** fixed; set. **5,** *fig.* steadfast; resolute. —**твёрдый знак,** hard sign (ъ).
тверды́ня *n.* **1,** stronghold. **2,** *fig.* bulwark.
твёрже *adj., comp. of* **твёрдый.**
твид *n.* tweed.
твой [*infl. like* **мой**] *poss. adj. & pron.* your; yours (*familiar*).
творе́ние *n.* **1,** *obs.* creation; creating. **2,** creation; product; work. **3,** *obs.* creature; being.
творе́ц [*gen.* **-рца́**] *n.* creator; maker.
твори́тельный *adj., in* **твори́тельный паде́ж,** instrumental case.
твори́ть *v. impfv.* [*pfv.* **сотвори́ть**] **1,** to create. **2,** to perform; do. **3,** *in* твори́ть чудеса́, to work miracles. —**твори́ться,** *refl.* [*impfv. only*] *colloq.* to be going on.
творо́г [*gen.* **-рога́**] *n.* **1,** curds. **2,** cottage cheese. *Also,* **тво́рог** [*gen.* **тво́рога**].
творо́жник *n.* curd pancake; cottage-cheese pancake.
тво́рческий *adj.* creative.
тво́рчество *n.* **1,** creative activity. **2,** works (*of an author*).
те *adj., pl. of* **тот.**
т.е. *abbr. of* **то есть,** that is; i.e.
теа́тр *n.* **1,** theater: идти́ в теа́тр, to go to the theater. **2,** *mil.* theater: теа́тр вое́нных де́йствий, theater of (military) operations.
театра́л *n.m.* [*fem.* **-тра́лка**] theatergoer; playgoer.
театра́льный *adj.* **1,** theater (*attrib.*); theatrical. **2,** overly dramatic; histrionic. —**театра́льность,** *n.f.* theatrics; histrionics.
тебе́ *pron., dat. & prepl. of* **ты.**
тебя́ *pron., gen. & acc. of* **ты.**

тевтóн *n.* Teuton. —**тевтóнский,** *adj.* Teutonic.
тезáурус *n.* thesaurus.
тéзис (тэ) *n.* thesis.
тёзка [*gen. pl.* **-зок**] *n.m. & f.* namesake.
теи́зм (тэ) *n.* theism. —**теи́ст,** *n.* theist. —**теисти́ческий,** *adj.* theistic.
текст *n.* **1,** text. **2,** *music* words; lyrics; libretto.
тексти́ль *n.m.* textiles. —**тексти́льный,** *adj.* textile (*attrib.*). —**тексти́льщик,** *n.* textile worker.
текстовóй *adj.* textual.
текстуáльный *adj.* **1,** textual. **2,** literal; word-for-word.
текýчесть *n.f.* **1,** fluidity. **2,** fluctuation. **3,** turnover (*of personnel*).
текýчий *adj.* **1,** fluid; flowing; running. **2,** fluctuating; constantly changing.
текýщий *adj.* **1,** current; present. **2,** routine; everyday. —**текýщий ремóнт,** routine repairs; preventive maintenance. —**текýщий счёт,** (liquid) bank account; checking account.
телеви́дение *n.* television. —**телевизиóнный,** *adj.* television (*attrib.*).
телеви́зор *n.* television set.
телéга *n.* cart; wagon.
телегрáмма *n.* telegram.
телегрáф *n.* **1,** telegraph. **2,** telegraph office.
телеграфи́ровать *v. impfv. & pfv.* [*pres.* **-рую, -руешь**] to telegraph; wire; cable.
телеграфи́ст *n.* telegraph operator; telegrapher. —**телеграфи́я,** *n.* telegraphy.
телегрáфный *adj.* telegraph (*attrib.*); telegraphic.
телéжка [*gen. pl.* **-жек**] *n.* light cart; handcart.
телезри́тель *n.m.* (television) viewer.
телекáмера *n.* television camera.
телемéтр *n.* telemeter. —**телеметри́я,** *n.* telemetry.
телёнок [*gen.* **-нка;** *pl.* **телята, телят**] *n.* calf.
телеобъекти́в *n.* telephoto lens.
телеолóгия *n.* teleology. —**телеологи́ческий,** *adj.* teleological.
телепáтия *n.* telepathy. —**телепати́ческий,** *adj.* telepathic.
телепередáча *n.* **1,** television transmission. **2,** telecast.
телескóп *n.* telescope. —**телескопи́ческий,** *adj.* telescopic. —**телескóпный,** *adj.* telescope (*attrib.*).
телéсный *adj.* **1,** bodily; corporal. **2,** flesh-colored. **3,** corporeal.
телестýдия *n.* television studio.
телетáйп *n.* teletype.
телефóн *n.* telephone. —**телефóн-автомáт,** *n.* public telephone; pay phone.
телефони́ровать *v. impfv. & pfv.* [*pres.* **-рую, -руешь**] (*with dat.*) to telephone; phone; call.
телефони́ст *n.m.* [*fem.* **-и́стка**] telephone operator.
телефони́я *n.* telephony.
телефóнный *adj.* **1,** telephone (*attrib.*). **2,** telephonic.
телéц [*gen.* **-льцá**] *n.* **1,** *obs.* calf. **2,** *cap.* Taurus.
тели́ться *v.r. impfv.* [*pfv.* **отели́ться;** *pres.* **тéлится**] to calve.
тёлка [*gen. pl.* **-лок**] *n.* heifer.
теллýр *n.* tellurium.
тéло [*pl.* **телá, тел, телáм**] *n.* body. —**держáть в чёрном тéле,** to work (someone) to the bone. —**душóй и тéлом,** utterly; totally; body and soul. —**ни душóй ни тéлом не виновáт,** completely innocent.
телогрéйка [*gen. pl.* **-грéек**] *n.* padded jacket.
телодвижéние *n.* body movement; gesture.
телосложéние *n.* build; physique.
телохрани́тель *n.m.* bodyguard.
тéльный *adj., colloq.* worn next to the skin.
тéльце *n.* **1,** [*pl.* **тéльца, тéлец**] little body. **2,** [*pl.* **тельцá, телéц**] corpuscle.
теля́тина *n.* veal.
теля́чий [*fem.* **-чья**] *adj.* **1,** calf (*attrib.*); calf's. **2,** veal (*attrib.*). —**теля́чий востóрг,** childish glee.
тем *adj., instr. sing. & dat. pl. of* **тот.** —*adv., used with comp. degree of adjectives* **1,** so much the: тем лýчше, so much the better. **2,** (*with* **чем**) the... the: чем рáньше, тем лýчше, the sooner the better. —**тем бóлее,** *see* **бóлее.** —**тем не мéнее,** nevertheless. —**тем сáмым,** thus; thereby.
тéма *n.* **1,** subject; topic; theme. **2,** *music* theme: тéма с вариáциями, theme with variations.
темáтика *n.* subject matter. —**темати́ческий,** *adj.* thematic; topical.
тембр (тэ) *n.* timbre.
тéмень *n.f., colloq.* darkness.
темнéть *v. impfv.* **1,** [*pfv.* **потемнéть**] to become dark; darken. **2,** [*pfv.* **стемнéть**] *impers.* to get dark: темнéет, it is getting dark. **3,** [*impfv. only*] (*of anything dark*) to appear; loom.
темни́ть *v. impfv.* to darken; make darker.
темни́ца *n., obs.* prison; dungeon.
темнó *adj., used predicatively* dark: в кóмнате бы́ло темнó, it was dark in the room.
тёмно- *prefix, used with colors,* dark: тёмно-зелёный, dark green.
темноволóсый *adj.* dark-haired.
темнокóжий *adj.* dark-skinned.
темнотá *n.* dark; darkness.
тёмный *adj.* **1,** dark. **2,** gloomy; dismal. **3,** obscure; vague. **4,** shady; unsavory; suspicious. **5,** ignorant.
темп *n.* **1,** *music* tempo. **2,** pace; rate; tempo.
тéмпера (тэ) *n.* tempera; distemper.
темперáмент *n.* **1,** temperament. **2,** zest; verve; vibrancy. Человéк с темперáментом, spirited/vibrant person.
темперáментный *adj.* **1,** temperamental. **2,** spirited; vibrant.
температýра *n.* temperature.
температýрить *v. impfv., colloq.* to have a temperature.
температýрный *adj.* temperature (*attrib.*).
темь *n.f., colloq.* darkness.
тéмя [*gen., dat., & prepl.* **тéмени;** *instr.* **тéменем**] *n. neut.* top of the head.
тенденциóзность (тэ, дэ) *n.f.* **1,** tendentiousness. **2,** biased attitude; biased approach.
тенденциóзный (тэ, дэ) *adj.* **1,** tendentious. **2,** biased; slanted.
тендéнция (тэ, дэ) *n.* **1,** tendency. **2,** bias.
тéндер (тэ, дэ) *n.* **1,** *R.R.* tender. **2,** *naut.* cutter.
теневóй *adj.* shady. —**теневáя сторонá** (+ *gen.*), the dark side (of).
тенёта [*gen.* **-нёт**] *n. pl.* net; snare.
тени́стый *adj.* shady.
тéннис (тэ) *n.* tennis. —**теннис́ист,** *n.* tennis player.
тéнниска (тэ) [*gen. pl.* **-сок**] *n., colloq.* sport shirt; polo shirt.
тéннисный (тэ) *adj.* tennis (*attrib.*).

те́нор [*pl.* **тенора́**] *n.* tenor. —**теноро́вый,** *adj.* tenor (*attrib.*).

тент (тэ) *n.* awning.

тень [*2nd loc.* **тени́;** *pl.* **те́ни, тене́й, теня́м**] *n.f.* **1,** shade. **2,** shadow. **3,** *fig.* trace (of sadness, doubt, etc.) on one's face. **4,** *fig.* grain; particle (*of truth*); shadow; particle (*of doubt*). **5,** ghost. —**броса́ть тень на** (+ *acc.*), to cast aspersions on. —**держа́ться в тени́,** to remain in the background. —**от него́ оста́лась одна́ тень,** he is only a shadow of his former self.

теокра́тия (тэ) *n.* theocracy. —**теократи́ческий,** *adj.* theocratic.

теоло́гия (тэ) *n.* theology. —**телеологи́ческий,** *adj.* theological.

теоре́ма *n.* theorem.

теоретизи́ровать *v. impfv.* [*pres.* **-рую, -руешь**] to theorize.

теоре́тик *n.* theoretician; theorist.

теорети́ческий *adj.* theoretical. —**теорети́чески,** *adv.* theoretically.

тео́рия *n.* theory. —**в тео́рии,** in theory; theoretically.

теосо́фия (тэ) *n.* theosophy. —**теосо́ф,** *n.* theosophist. —**теосо́фский; теософи́ческий,** *adj.* theosophical.

тепе́решний *adj., colloq.* present; today's; present-day. Тепе́решняя жизнь, life today.

тепе́рь *adv.* now.

тепле́ть *v. impfv.* [*pfv.* **потепле́ть**] to become warm; get warm; warm up.

те́плиться *v.r. impfv.* to flicker; glimmer.

тепли́ца *n.* hothouse; greenhouse. —**тепли́чный,** *adj.* hothouse (*attrib.*).

тепло́ *n.* **1,** warmth. **2,** *physics* heat. —*adv.* warmly. —*adj., used predicatively* warm: сего́дня тепло́, it is warm today; мне тепло́, I am warm.

теплова́тый *adj.* tepid; lukewarm.

теплово́з *n.* diesel locomotive.

теплово́й *adj.* heat (*attrib.*); thermal; caloric. —**теплово́й уда́р,** heatstroke.

теплокро́вный *adj.* warm-blooded.

тепломе́р *n.* calorimeter.

теплопрово́дный *adj.* heat-conducting.

теплосто́йкий *adj.* heat-resistant.

теплота́ *n.* **1,** heat. **2,** warmth.

теплохо́д *n.* motor ship.

теплу́шка [*gen. pl.* **-шек**] *n., colloq.* heated freight car used to carry people.

тёплый *adj.* **1,** warm. **2,** *fig.* warm; cordial. —**тёплое месте́чко,** soft job.

теплы́нь *n.f., colloq.* warm weather; mild weather.

терапе́вт *n.* internist. —**терапевти́ческий,** *adj.* therapeutic.

терапи́я *n.* **1,** internal medicine. **2,** therapy.

те́рбий *n.* terbium.

тереби́ть *v. impfv.* [*pres.* **-блю́, -би́шь**] **1,** to pull at; tug at. **2,** *fig., colloq.* to pester; nag.

те́рем [*pl.* **терема́**] *n.* tower in old Russian mansions where women were kept in seclusion.

тере́ть *v. impfv.* [*pres.* **тру, трёшь;** *past* **тёр, -ла**] **1,** to rub. **2,** to grate; grind. **3,** to chafe (*trans. & intrans.*). —**тере́ться,** *refl.* [*pfv.* **потере́ться**] **1,** *colloq.* to rub oneself. **2,** (*with* **о** + *acc.*) to rub against. **3,** *fig., colloq.* to hang around.

терза́ние *n.* torment; anguish; agony.

терза́ть *v. impfv.* **1,** to tear apart; tear to pieces. **2,** to torment. —**терза́ться,** *refl.* to suffer; be tormented.

тёрка [*gen. pl.* **-рок**] *n.* grater.

те́рмин *n.* term: техни́ческий те́рмин, technical term.

термина́л *n.* computer terminal.

терминоло́гия *n.* terminology.

терми́т *n.* **1,** termite. **2,** Thermit.

терми́ческий *adj.* thermal.

термодина́мика *n.* thermodynamics. —**термодинами́ческий,** *adj.* thermodynamic.

термо́метр *n.* thermometer.

термопа́ра *n.* thermocouple.

те́рмос (тэ) *n.* thermos (bottle).

термоста́т (тэ) *n.* thermostat.

термоя́дерный *adj.* thermonuclear.

тёрн *n.* **1,** blackthorn. **2,** sloe; sloes.

терни́стый *adj.* **1,** *obs.* thorny. **2,** *fig.* thorny; full of pitfalls: терни́стый путь, thorny path.

терно́вник *n.* blackthorn.

терпели́вый *adj.* patient. —**терпели́во,** *adv.* patiently. —**терпели́вость,** *n.f.* patience; forbearance.

терпе́ние *n.* patience.

терпе́ть *v. impfv.* [*pres.* **терплю́, те́рпишь**] **1,** to endure; bear; stand. **2,** to tolerate; stand; put up with. **3,** [*pfv.* **потерпе́ть**] to suffer; sustain (a defeat, losses, etc.). **4,** *in* вре́мя те́рпит, there is plenty of time; вре́мя не те́рпит, there is no time to be lost. —**терпе́ться,** *refl.* [*impfv. only*] *used negatively with the dative case and inf.* to be impatient (to); be unable to wait (to): ему́ не терпе́лось нача́ть, he couldn't wait to begin.

терпи́мо *adv.* with tolerance: относи́ться терпи́мо к, to be tolerant of. —*adj., used predicatively, colloq.* tolerable; bearable.

терпи́мость *n.f.* tolerance. —**дом терпи́мости,** brothel.

терпи́мый *adj.* **1,** tolerant. **2,** tolerable.

те́рпкий *adj.* [*comp.* **те́рпче**] tart; acrid; astringent. —**те́рпкость,** *n.f.* astringency; acerbity.

террако́та (тэ) *n.* terra cotta.

террако́товый (тэ) *adj.* **1,** terra-cotta. **2,** reddish brown.

терра́са *n.* terrace. —**терра́сный,** *adj.* terraced.

территориа́льный *adj.* territorial.

террито́рия *n.* **1,** territory. **2,** premises; grounds (*of a building, factory, etc.*).

терро́р *n.* terror.

терроризи́ровать *v. impfv. & pfv.* [*pres.* **-рую, -руешь**] to terrorize.

террори́зм *n.* terrorism. —**террори́ст,** *n.* terrorist. —**террористи́ческий,** *adj.* terrorist (*attrib.*).

тёртый *adj.* **1,** grated. **2,** *fig., colloq.* experienced; worldly-wise. —**тёртый кала́ч,** experienced person; old hand.

те́рция (тэ) *n., music* third.

терье́р (тэ) *n.* terrier.

теря́ть *v. impfv.* [*pfv.* **потеря́ть**] **1,** to lose. **2,** to waste (time, words, etc.). **3,** to shed (leaves). **4,** *v.i.* (*with* **в** + *prepl.*) to lose; suffer; be the worse for: теря́ть в ве́се, to lose weight; теря́ть в перево́де, to suffer in translation; теря́ть в чьём-нибудь мне́нии, to go down in someone's estimation. —**теря́ть го́лову,** to lose one's head. Не теря́ть головы́, to keep one's head. —**теря́ть из виду** (*or* **из ви́да**), to lose sight of; lose track of. —**теря́ть си́лу, 1,** to lose one's vigor.

2, to expire; become invalid. —**теря́ть управле́ние, 1,** (*with instr.*) to lose control (of). **2,** to go out of control.
теря́ться *v.r. impfv.* [*pfv.* **потеря́ться**] **1,** to be lost; get lost. **2,** [*impfv. only*] (*of one's eyesight, memory, etc.*) to fail; fade. **3,** to become flustered; panic.
тёс *n.* boards; planks.
теса́к [*gen.* **-сака́**] *n.* cutlass.
теса́ние *n.* cutting; hewing.
тёсаный *adj.* cut; hewn.
теса́ть *v. impfv.* [*pres.* **тешу́, те́шешь**] to cut; hew.
тесёмка [*gen. pl.* **-мок**] *n.* braid.
теси́на *n.* board; plank.
тёска *n.* cutting; hewing.
тесло́ [*pl.* **тёсла, тёсел**] *n.* adz.
тесни́на *n.* **1,** gorge; ravine. **2,** defile.
тесни́ть *v. impfv.* **1,** [*pfv.* **потесни́ть**] to crowd; cramp. **2,** [*pfv.* **стесни́ть**] to constrict (the throat, chest, etc.). *Also impers.:* мне тесни́т грудь, I feel a tightness in my chest. **3,** [*impfv. only*] (*of clothes*) to be too tight. —**тесни́ться,** *refl.* **1,** [*pfv.* **стесни́ться**] to crowd; cluster. **2,** to crowd together; move closer to each other. **3,** to be crowded (together). **4,** to jostle each other.
те́сно *adv.* **1,** close together. **2,** closely: те́сно свя́занный, closely connected. —*adj., used predicatively* **1,** crowded: здесь те́сно, it is crowded here. **2,** tight: мне те́сно в плеча́х, it feels tight in the shoulders.
теснота́ *n.* crowded conditions; close quarters.
те́сный *adj.* [*short form* **те́сен, тесна́, те́сно**] **1,** crowded; cramped. **2,** tight; compact; close. **3,** *fig.* close; intimate. **4,** (*of clothes*) tight.
тесо́вый *adj.* board (*attrib.*); plank (*attrib.*).
те́сто *n.* dough. —**из друго́го те́ста,** of a different breed; made of different stuff.
тесть *n.m.* father-in-law (*wife's father*).
тесьма́ *n.* braid.
тётенька *n., colloq.* aunt; aunty.
те́терев [*pl.* **тетерева́**] *n.* black grouse.
тетеревя́тник *n.* [*often* **я́стреб-тетеревя́тник**] goshawk.
тетёрка [*gen. pl.* **-рок**] *n.* female black grouse; gray hen.
тете́ря *n.* **1,** *regional* black grouse. **2,** *colloq., in* **со́нная тете́ря,** sleepyhead; **лени́вая тете́ря,** lazybones.
тетива́ *n.* bowstring.
тётка [*gen. pl.* **-ток**] *n.* aunt.
тетра́дка [*gen. pl.* **-док**] *n.* notebook.
тетра́дный *adj.* notebook (*attrib.*).
тетра́дь *n.f.* notebook.
тётушка *n., dim. of* **тётка** *and* **тётя.**
тётя [*gen. pl.* **-тей**] *n.* aunt.
те́фтели [*gen.* **-лей**] *n. pl.* meatballs.
техне́ций *n.* technetium.
те́хник *n.* technician.
те́хника *n.* **1,** technology. **2,** technique. **3,** (technical) equipment.
те́хникум *n.* technical school.
техни́ческий *adj.* technical. —**техни́чески,** *adv.* technically.
техно́лог *n.* **1,** technologist. **2,** production engineer.
технологи́ческий *adj.* **1,** technological. **2,** production (*attrib.*): технологи́ческий пото́к, production line. —**технологи́ческая ка́рта,** production chart; flow sheet.
техноло́гия *n.* technology; engineering.
тече́ние *n.* **1,** flow; flowing. **2,** current: по тече́нию; про́тив тече́ния, with/against the current (*or* tide). Вверх/вниз по тече́нию, upstream/downstream. **3,** *fig.* course (*of events, an illness, etc.*). **4,** *fig.* trend; tendency. —**в тече́ние** (+ *gen.*), **1,** in the course of; during. **2,** for; over a period of. **3,** within (a certain amount of time). —**с тече́нием вре́мени,** with the passage of time; in due course of time.
те́чка *n.* heat (*in animals*).
те́чь[1] *v. impfv.* [*pres.* **теку́, течёшь, ...теку́т;** *past* **тёк, текла́, текло́**] **1,** to flow. **2,** to stream. **3,** to leak. **4,** *fig.* (*of time, life, etc.*) to pass; flow by. —**у меня́ из носу течёт,** my nose is running. —**у меня́ кровь течёт из носу,** my nose is bleeding.
течь[2] *n.f.* leak: дать течь, to spring a leak.
те́шить *v. impfv.* [*pfv.* **поте́шить**] *colloq.* **1,** to amuse; entertain. **2,** to gratify; please. **3,** to console. —**те́шиться,** *refl.* **1,** to amuse oneself. **2,** (*with* **над**) *colloq.* to make fun of; poke fun at. **3,** (*with instr.*) to console oneself (in *or* by); take consolation (in).
тёща *n.* mother-in-law (*wife's mother*).
тиа́ра *n.* tiara.
тибе́тский *adj.* Tibetan.
ти́гель [*gen.* **-гля**] *n.m.* crucible.
тигр *n.* tiger.
тигрёнок [*gen.* **-нка;** *pl.* **тигря́та, тигря́т**] *n.* tiger cub.
тигри́ца *n.* tigress.
тигро́вый *adj.* tiger (*attrib.*); tiger's.
тик *n.* **1,** (nervous) tic. **2,** teak (*wood*). **3,** ticking (*cloth*).
ти́канье *n.* ticking (*of a clock*).
ти́кать *v. impfv.* (*of a clock*) to tick.
ти́ккер *n.* ticker.
ти́ковый *adj.* **1,** teak (*attrib.*). **2,** made with ticking.
ти́льда *n.* tilde.
тимиа́н *n.* = **тимья́н.**
тимофе́евка *n.* timothy; timothy grass.
тимпа́н *n., music* timpani.
тимья́н *also,* **тимиа́н** *n.* thyme.
ти́на *n.* pond scum. —**ти́нистый,** *adj.* filled with pond scum.
тинкту́ра *n.* tincture.
тип *n.* **1,** type. **2,** phylum. **3,** [*acc.* **ти́па**] *colloq.* character; odd person.
типа́ж [*gen.* **типажа́**] *n.* model; prototype.
типи́ческий *adj.* typical.
типи́чно *adv.* typically. —*adj., used predicatively* typical: э́то типи́чно для него́, that's typical of him.
типи́чный *adj.* typical.
типово́й *adj.* **1,** model. **2,** standard; standardized.
типо́граф *n.* printer; typographer. —**типогра́фия,** *n.* printing house. —**типогра́фский,** *adj.* typographic(al); printer's.
типу́н [*gen.* **-пуна́**] *n.* pip (*bird disease*).
тир *n.* shooting gallery.
тира́да *n.* tirade.
тира́ж [*gen.* **тиража́**] *n.* **1,** drawing (*in a lottery*). **2,** circulation (*of a periodical*). **3,** printing (*of a book*); number of copies printed. —**вы́йти в тира́ж,** to be no longer able to work; be ready for retirement.
тира́н *n.* tyrant.
тира́нить *v. impfv.* **1,** to tyrannize; oppress. **2,** to torment.
тирани́я *n.* tyranny. —**тирани́ческий,** *adj.* tyrannical.
тира́нство *n.* tyranny.

тира́нствовать *v. impfv.* [*pres.* **-ствую, -ствуешь**] to be a tyrant.
тирé (рэ) *n. neut. indecl.* dash.
тис *n.* yew.
ти́скать *v. impfv.* [*pfv.* **ти́снуть**] *colloq.* to squeeze; press.
тиски́ [*gen.* **-скóв**] *n. pl.* vise: зажа́ть в тиски́, to grip in a vise.
тиснéние *n.* **1,** stamping; embossing. **2,** imprint; design.
тиснёный *adj.* stamped; embossed.
ти́снуть *v., pfv. of* **ти́скать.**
тита́н *n.* **1,** titan. **2,** titanium. **3,** large boiler. —**титани́ческий,** *adj.* titanic.
титр *n., motion pictures* title; subtitle.
ти́тул *n.* title.
титулóванный *adj.* titled.
титулова́ть *v. impfv. & pfv.* [*pres.* **-лу́ю, -лу́ешь**] to call; address (someone) by his title.
ти́тульный *adj., printing* title (*attrib.*): ти́тульный лист, title page.
тиф *n.* typhus. —**брюшнóй тиф,** typhoid. —**возвра́тный тиф,** relapsing fever. —**сыпнóй тиф,** typhus.
тифóзный *adj.* typhoid; typhus (*attrib.*).
ти́хий *adj.* [*comp.* **ти́ше**] **1,** soft; low. **2,** quiet; still. **3,** calm; tranquil. **4,** quiet; retiring. **5,** slow.
ти́хо *adv.* **1,** quietly. **2,** softly. **3,** slowly. —*adj., used predicatively* quiet: здесь ти́хо, it is quiet here.
тихомóлком *adv., colloq.* quietly; without making a sound.
тихóнько *adv., colloq.* quietly; softly.
тихóня *n.m. & f., colloq.* timid person; meek person.
ти́ше *adj., comp. of* **ти́хий.** —*adv., comp. of* **ти́хо.** —*interj.* quiet!; please be quiet!
тишина́ *n.* quiet; silence; stillness.
тишь [*2nd loc.* **тиши́**] *n.f.* quiet; stillness. —**тишь да гладь,** peace and quiet.
тка́ный *adj.* woven.
ткань *n.f.* **1,** cloth; fabric. **2,** *anat.* tissue.
тканьё *n.* **1,** weaving. **2,** cloth. **3,** woven design.
ткать *v. impfv.* [*pfv.* **сотка́ть;** *pres.* **тку, ткёшь;** *past fem.* **ткала́** *or* **тка́ла**] **1,** to weave. **2,** *in* ткать паути́ну, to spin a web.
тка́цкий *adj.* weaving (*attrib.*); weaver's. —**тка́цкий станóк,** loom.
ткач [*gen.* **ткача́**] *n.m.* [*fem.* **-чи́ха**] weaver.
ткну́ть *v., pfv. of* **ты́кать.** —**ткну́ться,** *refl., pfv. of* **ты́каться.**
тлéние *n.* **1,** rotting; decay. **2,** smoldering.
тлéнный *adj.* mortal.
тлетвóрный *adj.* **1,** noxious. **2,** *fig.* pernicious; deleterious.
тлеть *v. impfv.* **1,** to rot; decay. **2,** to smolder. —**тлéться,** *refl., colloq.* to smolder.
тля *n.* plant louse.
тмин *n.* caraway. —**тми́нный,** *adj.* caraway (*attrib.*).
то *dem. adj. & pron., neut. of* **тот,** that: в то врéмя, at that time. То бы́ли незабыва́емые мину́ты, those were unforgettable moments. —*conj.* then: éсли он не хóчет, то не уговáривайте егó, if he does not want to, then don't try to persuade him. —**а то; не то,** or; or else; otherwise. —**а то и,** or maybe: человéк двéсти, а то и бóльше, some 200 people, or maybe more. —**и то,** and even; at that. —**не то..., не то,** half... half; a combination of... —**не то что; не то чтóбы,** it is not (so much) that... —**то есть,** that is; that is to say. —**то ли..., то ли,** either..., or; a combination of... —**то..., то,** now..., now: он живёт то в гóроде, то в дерéвне, he divides his time between the city and the country. —**то, что...,** **1,** what... **2,** the fact that...
тобóй *also,* **тобóю** *pron., instr. of* **ты.**
това́р *n.* **1,** goods; merchandise. **2,** commodity.
това́рищ *n.* **1,** comrade. **2,** friend. **3,** (*with* **по**) fellow: това́рищ по рабóте, fellow worker. —**това́рищ по несча́стью,** comrade in distress; fellow sufferer. —**това́рищ по ору́жию,** comrade in arms.
това́рищеский *adj.* comradely; friendly.
това́рищество *n.* **1,** comradeship; fellowship. **2,** company; society; association.
това́рный *adj.* **1,** goods (*attrib.*); commodity (*attrib.*). **2,** *R.R.* freight (*attrib.*): това́рный пóезд, freight train.
товарообмéн *n.* barter.
товарооборóт *n.* commodity turnover.
тóга *n.* toga.
тогда́ *adv.* **1,** then; at that time. **2,** then; in that case. —**тогда́ как,** while; whereas. —**тогда́, когда́...,** when...
тогда́шний *adj., colloq.* of that time; at that time.
тогó (vo) *adj., gen. of* **тот.**
тождéственный *adj.* identical. —**тождéственность,** *n.f.* identity; sameness.
тóждество *n.* identity: тóждество взгля́дов, identity of views.
тóже *adv.* **1,** also; too. **2,** (*with neg. verbs*) either: я тóже не зна́ю, I don't know either.
той *adj., fem. gen., dat., prepl., & instr. of* **тот.**
ток *n.* **1,** current (*of air, water, etc.*). **2,** *electricity* current. **3,** [*2nd loc.* **току́;** *pl.* **тока́**] threshing floor. **4,** mating (*of birds*). **5,** [*2nd. loc.* **току́;** *pl.* **тока́**] mating ground. **6,** toque. —**ток крóви,** bloodstream.
тока́рный *adj.* lathe (*attrib.*). —**тока́рный станóк,** lathe.
тóкарь [*pl.* **тóкари** *or* **токаря́**] *n.m.* lathe operator; turner.
токова́ние *n.* mating call.
токова́ть *v. impfv.* [*pres.* **-ку́ет**] (*of a bird*) to utter its mating call.
токоприёмник *n.* trolley (*device for conducting current*).
токсеми́я *n.* toxemia.
токсиколóгия *n.* toxicology. —**токсикóлог,** *n.* toxicologist. —**токсикологи́ческий,** *adj.* toxicological.
токси́н *n.* toxin.
токси́ческий *adj.* toxic.
тол *n.* TNT; trinitrotoluene.
толи́ка *n.* (*with gen.*) *colloq.* small amount (of). —**ма́лую толи́ку,** a little; tiny bit.
толк *n.* **1,** sense. **2,** good; use. **3,** *pl.* talk; rumors. **4,** sect; group. —**бéз толку, 1,** without making any sense. **2,** for nothing; to no purpose. —**взять в толк,** to understand; figure out. —**знать толк в** (+ *prepl.*), to know well; be a connoisseur of. —**сбива́ть с тóлку,** to confuse. —**сбива́ться с тóлку,** to become confused. —**с тóлком,** showing good sense; intelligently. *See also* **тóлком.**
толка́ние *n.* pushing. —**толка́ние ядра́,** *sports* shot-put.
толка́ть *v. impfv.* [*pfv.* **толкну́ть**] **1,** to push; shove. **2,** to poke; prod. **3,** (*with* **на** + *acc.*) to incite (to);

put up to. **4,** *in* **толкáть ядрó,** *sports* to put the shot. —**толкáться,** *refl.* **1,** [*impfv. only*] to push one another; jostle; shove. **2,** (*with* **о** + *acc.*) *colloq.* to strike (against). **3,** (*with* **в** + *acc.*) *colloq.* to knock on the door of; try to get into. **4,** [*impfv. only*] *colloq.* to knock about; idle; loaf.

толкáч [*gen.* **-качá**] *n., colloq.* person who cuts through red tape; fixer; expediter.

толкнýть *v., pfv. of* **толкáть.** —**толкнýться,** *refl., pfv. of* **толкáться.**

толковáние *n.* **1,** interpretation. **2,** commentary.

толковáтель *n.m.* interpreter; commentator.

толковáть *v. impfv.* [*pres.* **-кýю, -кýешь**] **1,** to interpret. **2,** *colloq.* to explain. **3,** *colloq.* to talk; converse.

толкóвый *adj.* **1,** intelligent; clever. **2,** clear; intelligible. —**толкóвый словáрь,** defining dictionary.

тóлком *adv., colloq.* **1,** plainly; clearly. **2,** in earnest: засéсть тóлком за урóки, to sit down to one's lessons in earnest. **3,** properly. Тóлком всё разглядéть, to have a good look around. Никтó тóлком не знал, nobody really knew.

толкотня́ *n., colloq.* crush (*of people*).

толкýчий *adj., in* **толкýчий рынок,** *colloq.* flea market. —**толкýчка,** *n., colloq.* flea market.

толокнó *n.* oatmeal.

толóчь *v. impfv.* [*pfv.* **растолóчь** *or* **истолóчь;** *pres.* **толкý, толчёшь, ...толкýт;** *past* **толóк, толклá, толклó**] **1,** to pound; crush; pulverize. **2,** *in* **толóчь вóду в стýпе,** to waste one's time; beat the air. —**толóчься,** *refl.* [*impfv. only*] *colloq.* **1,** to move about (*in a small area*). **2,** to crowd; mill about. **3,** to hang around.

толпá [*pl.* **тóлпы**] *n.* crowd.

толпи́ться *v.r. impfv.* to crowd; throng.

толстéть *v. impfv.* [*pfv.* **потолстéть**] to get fat; put on weight.

толсти́ть *v. impfv., colloq.* to make (someone) look fat.

толстóвка [*gen. pl.* **-вок**] *n.* long belted blouse (*as worn by Tolstoy*).

толстогýбый *adj.* thick-lipped.

толстокóжий *adj.* thick-skinned. —**тостокóжее живóтное,** pachyderm.

толстосýм *n., colloq.* rich man; moneybags.

толстýха *n., colloq.* fat woman.

тóлстый *adj.* [*comp.* **тóлще**] **1,** thick. **2,** fat; stout. **3,** (*of cloth*) heavy. —**тóлстая кишкá,** large intestine.

толстя́к [*gen.* **-стякá**] *n., colloq.* fat man.

толуóл *n.* toluene.

толчёный *adj.* ground: толчёный миндáль, ground almonds.

толчея́ *n., colloq.* crush (*of people*).

толчóк [*gen.* **-чкá**] *n.* **1,** push; shove. **2,** jolt; bump. **3,** shock; tremor. **4,** *fig.* spur; impetus. **5,** *weightlifting* clean and jerk.

тóлща *n.* **1,** thick mass; layer. **2,** *fig.* the masses.

тóлще *adj., comp. of* **тóлстый.**

толщинá *n.* **1,** thickness. **2,** corpulence.

толь *n.m.* tarred roofing paper.

тóлько *adv.* **1,** only: тóлько три дня, only three days. **2,** not until; not till: тóлько в послéднюю минýту, not until/till the last minute. **3,** alone: тóлько в э́том годý, this year alone. **4,** just: он тóлько пришёл, he just arrived. **5,** (*with* **не**) *used in exclamations for emphasis:* где тóлько он не бывáл!, where *hasn't* he been?; is there anywhere he hasn't been? Чегó тóлько не придýмывают лю́ди!, what people won't think of! —*conj.* only: с удовóльствием, тóлько не сегóдня, with pleasure, only not today. —*particle* just: подýмать тóлько!, just think! Вы тóлько попрóбуйте э́тот кóфе!, just taste this coffee! —**да и тóлько,** *see* **да.** —**едвá тóлько,** = **как тóлько.** —**как тóлько,** as soon as. —**лишь тóлько,** = **как тóлько.** —**оди́н тóлько,** *see* **оди́н.** —**стóит тóлько** (+ *inf.*), one has only to... —**тóлько бы, 1,** if only. **2,** (*with* **не** + *inf.*) one must simply not; the one thing we must not do is... —**тóлько и,** the only thing: об э́том тóлько и говори́ли, it was all they talked about. —**тóлько что,** just: я тóлько что пришёл, I just arrived.

том[1] *adj., prepl. of* **тот.**

том[2] [*pl.* **томá**] *n.* volume.

томагáвк *n.* tomahawk.

томáт *n.* tomato. —**томáтный,** *adj.* tomato (*attrib.*).

тóмик *n., dim. of* **том.**

томи́тельный *adj.* **1,** oppressive; agonizing. **2,** tedious; tiring.

томи́ть *v. impfv.* [*pfv.* **истоми́ть;** *pres.* **томлю́, томи́шь**] **1,** to tire; exhaust. **2,** (*of heat, thirst, etc.*) to oppress. —**томи́ться,** *refl.* [*impfv. only*] **1,** to suffer. **2,** to languish (*in prison, captivity, etc.*). **3,** (*with* **по**) to pine (for).

томлéние *n.* **1,** anguish; suffering. **2,** languor.

тóмность *n.f.* languor.

тóмный *adj.* languid; languorous.

томý *adj., dat. of* **тот.** —**томý назáд,** ago.

тон [*pl.* **тонá** *or* **тóны**] *n.* **1,** (musical) tone. **2,** tone of voice. **3,** tone; shade. **4,** *fig.* tone; tenor: тон письмá, the tone of the letter. **5,** form: э́то считáется дурны́м тóном, it is considered poor form. —**в тон, 1,** (*with dat.*) in harmony with; in tune with; in keeping with. **2,** in the same tone of voice; in kind. —**не в тон,** off key. —**повы́сить тон,** to raise one's voice. —**попáсть в тон,** to strike the right note. —**сбáвить тон,** to quiet down.

тонáльность *n.f., music* key: тонáльность до диéз, key of C sharp.

тонáльный *adj.* tonal.

тóненький *adj., colloq.* thin.

тонзýра *n.* tonsure.

тонизи́ровать *v. impfv.* [*pres.* **-рую, -руешь**] *physiol.* to tone up.

тони́ческий *adj.* tonic.

тóнкий *adj.* [*comp.* **тóньше;** *superl.* **тончáйший**] **1,** thin. **2,** (*of thread, linen, etc.*) fine. **3,** (*of the senses*) keen. **4,** (*of food, wines, etc.*) fine. **5,** fine; subtle; nice. **6,** astute; keen; perceptive.

тóнко *adv.* **1,** thinly; thin. **2,** finely. **3,** subtly.

тонкокóжий *adj.* thin-skinned.

тóнкость *n.f.* **1,** thinness. **2,** fineness. **3,** subtlety. **4,** keenness (*of the senses*). **5,** fine point; subtlety; nicety. —**до тóнкостей,** minutely; down to the fine points.

тóнна *n.* ton.

тоннáж *n.* tonnage.

туннéль (нэ) *n.m.* tunnel.

тóнус *n., physiol.* tone: мы́шечный тóнус, muscle tone.

тонýть *v. impfv.* [*pres.* **тонý, тóнешь**] **1,** [*pfv.* **потонýть**] to sink. **2,** [*pfv.* **утонýть**] to drown.

тóньше *adj., comp. of* **тóнкий.**

топáз *n.* topaz. —**топáзовый,** *adj.* topaz.

то́пать *v. impfv.* [*pfv.* **то́пнуть**] (*with instr.*) to stamp (one's feet).

топи́ть *v. impfv.* [*pres.* **топлю́, то́пишь**] **1,** to heat (a building). **2,** to stoke (a furnace). **3,** [*pfv.* **расто-пи́ть**] to melt. **4,** [*pfv.* **потопи́ть**] to sink. **5,** [*pfv.* **уто-пи́ть**] to drown. —**топи́ться,** *refl.* **1,** (*of a stove*) to burn; be lit. **2,** to melt. **3,** [*pfv.* **утопи́ться**] to drown oneself.

то́пка *n.* **1,** heating. **2,** melting. **3,** furnace.

то́пкий *adj.* [*comp.* **то́пче**] swampy; marshy.

топлёный *adj.* **1,** melted. **2,** baked.

то́пливо *n.* fuel. —**то́пливный,** *adj.* fuel (*attrib.*).

то́пнуть *v., pfv. of* **то́пать.**

топогра́фия *n.* topography. —**топо́граф,** *n.* topographer. —**топографи́ческий,** *adj.* topographical.

то́полевый *adj.* poplar (*attrib.*).

тополо́гия *n.* topology.

то́поль [*pl.* **тополя́**] *n.m.* poplar.

топо́р [*gen.* **топора́**] *n.* ax.

топо́рик *n.* hatchet.

топори́ще *n.* ax handle.

топо́рный *adj.* **1,** of an ax; ax (*attrib.*). **2,** (*of a piece of furniture*) crudely made. **3,** (*of workmanship*) crude. **4,** (*of a person*) unpolished; unrefined; uncouth.

топо́рщить *v. impfv.* to make (hair, fur, etc.) stand on end. —**топо́рщиться,** *refl.* (*of one's hair*) to bristle; (*of material*) to pucker.

то́пот *n.* tramp; tramping; stamping; clatter.

топота́ть *v. impfv.* [*pres.* **-почу́, -по́чешь**] *colloq.* **1,** [*also,* **топота́ть нога́ми**] to stamp one's feet. **2,** to tramp along.

то́псель *n.m.* topsail.

топта́ние *n.* trampling. —**топта́ние на ме́сте,** marking time.

топта́ть *v. impfv.* [*pres.* **топчу́, то́пчешь**] **1,** to trample; trample down. **2,** to stamp out (a fire). **3,** *colloq.* to soil; track dirt on. **4,** *in* **топта́ть в грязь,** to drag through the mud. —**топта́ться,** *refl.* **1,** to shift from foot to foot. **2,** *colloq.* to walk about; hang about. **3,** *in* **топта́ться на ме́сте,** to mark time.

топча́к [*gen.* **-чака́**] *n.* treadmill.

топь *n.f.* swamp; marsh; bog.

то́ра *n.* Torah.

то́рба *n.* feedbag.

торг [*2nd loc.* **торгу́;** *pl.* **торги́**] *n.* **1,** trade. **2,** bargaining. **3,** deal. **4,** *obs.* market. **5,** *pl.* auction.

торга́ш [*gen.* **-гаша́**] *n., colloq.* petty tradesman; huckster.

торгова́ть *v. impfv.* [*pres.* **-гу́ю, -гу́ешь**] **1,** to do business. **2,** (*of a store*) to be open (for business). **3,** (*with instr.*) to deal in; sell. **4,** (*with* **с** + *instr.*) to trade (with another country). —**торгова́ться,** *refl.* to bargain; haggle; dicker.

торго́вец [*gen.* **-вца**] *n.* merchant; tradesman. У́личный торго́вец, street vendor.

торго́вля *n.* trade; business; commerce.

торго́вый *adj.* **1,** trade (*attrib.*); commercial. **2,** (*of a ship, fleet, etc.*) merchant. —**торго́вая пала́та,** chamber of commerce. —**торго́вый центр,** shopping center.

тореадо́р *n.* toreador.

торе́ц [*gen.* **-рца́**] *n.* **1,** butt end. **2,** (wooden) paving block.

торже́ственно *adv.* **1,** with great solemnity. **2,** solemnly. —**торже́ственность,** *n.f.* solemnity.

торже́ственный *adj.* **1,** solemn. **2,** festive; gala. **3,** ceremonial. **4,** triumphal.

торжество́ *n.* **1,** celebration; *pl.* festivities. **2,** triumph; victory. **3,** (feeling of) triumph; exultation.

торжествова́ть *v. impfv.* [*pfv.* **восторжествова́ть;** *pres.* **-ству́ю, -ству́ешь**] **1,** (*with* **над**) to triumph (over). **2,** [*impfv. only*] to rejoice; exult. **3,** [*impfv. only*] *obs.* to celebrate (a holiday, victory, etc.).

торжеству́ющий *adj.* triumphant; exultant.

то́ри *n.m. indecl.* Tory.

то́рий *n.* thorium.

торма́шки *n.pl., in* **вверх торма́шки** *and* **вверх торма́шками, 1,** head over heels. **2,** upside-down; topsy-turvy.

торможе́ние *n.* braking.

то́рмоз *n.* **1,** [*pl.* **тормоза́**] brake. **2,** [*pl.* **то́рмозы**] *fig.* brake; obstacle; hindrance.

тормози́ть *v. impfv.* [*pfv.* **затормози́ть;** *pres.* **-мо-жу́, -мози́шь**] **1,** to brake; apply the brakes (to). **2,** *fig.* to hinder; hamper; impede; retard.

тормозно́й *adj.* brake (*attrib.*): тормозно́й башма́к, brake shoe. —**тормозно́й конду́ктор,** brakeman. —**тормозна́я ракéта,** retro-rocket.

тормоши́ть *v. impfv., colloq.* **1,** to pull at; tug at. **2,** *fig.* to bother; pester.

то́рный *adj.* (*of a road*) even; smooth; worn down; well-trodden.

торова́тый *adj., obs.* generous.

торопи́ть *v. impfv.* [*pfv.* **поторопи́ть;** *pres.* **торо-плю́, торо́пишь**] **1,** to hurry (up); rush. **2,** to hasten; speed up. —**торопи́ться,** *refl.* **1,** to hurry; rush. **2,** to be in a hurry.

торопли́вый *adj.* **1,** hasty; hurried. **2,** always in a hurry; bustling. —**торопли́во,** *adv.* hastily; hurriedly. —**торопли́вость,** *n.f.* haste; hurry.

торо́с *n.* hummock (*in an ice field*).

торпе́да *n.* torpedo.

торпеди́ровать *v. impfv. & pfv.* [*pres.* **-рую, -руешь**] to torpedo.

торпе́дный *adj.* torpedo (*attrib.*). —**торпе́дный ка́-тер,** PT boat.

торс *n.* torso.

торт *n.* cake.

торф *n.* peat. —**торфяно́й,** *adj.* peat (*attrib.*).

торча́ть *v. impfv.* [*pres.* **-чу́, -чи́шь**] **1,** to stick out; jut out; protrude. **2,** *colloq.* to hang around. —**тор-ча́ть пе́ред глаза́ми,** to be ever present; never go away.

торчко́м *adv., colloq.* on end; erect; upright.

торше́р *n.* floor lamp.

тоска́ *n.* **1,** melancholy. **2,** boredom; ennui. **3,** (*with* **по**) longing (for); yearning (for); nostalgia (for).

тосkли́вый *adj.* **1,** melancholy; depressed. **2,** dreary; dismal; depressing.

тоскова́ть *v. impfv.* [*pres.* **-ку́ю, -ку́ешь**] **1,** to be melancholy; be depressed. **2,** (*with* **по** + *dat., but prepl. for pers. pronouns*) to miss; long for. —**тоско-ва́ть по до́му,** to be homesick.

тост *n.* toast: предлага́ть тост, to propose a toast.

то́стер (тэ) *n.* toaster.

тот [*fem.* **та;** *neut.* **то;** *pl.* **те;** *gen.* **того́, той, тех;** *dat.* **тому́, той, тем;** *acc. fem.* **ту;** *instr.* **тем, той, те́ми;** *prepl.* **том, той, тех**] *dem. adj.* **1,** that: в тот день, on that day. **2,** (*with* **кото́рый**) the... that: э́та та кни́га, кото́рую вы иска́ли?, is this the book you were looking for? **3,** the right: э́то тот дом?, is this the right house? Я набрáл не тот нóмер, I dialed the wrong number. **4,** the other; the far: по ту стóрону (+ *gen.*), on the other side of. —*dem. pron.* **1,** that one; that. **2,** the latter. **3,** (*fol. by* **кто**) he (who); the one (who). **4,** (*fol. by* **котóрый**) the one (that). —**и тот и другóй,** both. —**не тот, так другóй,** if not one, then the other. —**ни тот ни другóй,** neither; neither one. —**тот или инóй,** some... or other; one... or another. —**тот же; тот сáмый; тот же сáмый,** the same. *See also* **то** *and* **тем.**

тотализáтор *n.* **1,** totalizator; pari-mutuel machine. **2,** pari-mutuel betting.

тоталитарúзм *n.* totalitarianism. —**тоталитáрный,** *adj.* totalitarian.

тотáльный *adj.* total. —**тотáльная войнá,** total war.

тотéм (тэ) *n.* totem. —**тотемúзм,** *n.* totemism.

тó-то *particle, colloq.* **1,** that's just the point. **2,** aha!; what did I tell you! **3,** that is why; that is how. **4,** how!: тó-то бы́ло красúво, how beautiful it was!

тóтчас *adv.* immediately; at once.

точéние *n.* sharpening.

точёный *adj.* **1,** sharpened. **2,** shaped in a lathe. **3,** *fig.* (*of features*) chiseled.

точúлка [*gen. pl.* **-лок**] *n.* **1,** sharpener. **2,** *colloq.* pencil sharpener.

точúло *n.* grindstone; whetstone.

точúльный *adj.* sharpening (*attrib.*). —**точúльный кáмень,** grindstone; whetstone. —**точúльный ремéнь,** strop.

точúльщик *n.* grinder; knife grinder.

точúть *v. impfv.* [*pres.* **точý, тóчишь**] **1,** [*pfv.* **наточúть**] to sharpen; hone. **2,** [*pfv.* **вы́точить**] to turn (*in a lathe*). **3,** to eat away. **4,** (*of water*) to wear away. **5,** *fig.* to oppress; wear down. —**точúть зýбы на** (+ *acc.*), to have it in for; bear a grudge against.

тóчка [*gen. pl.* **-чек**] *n.* **1,** dot. **2,** point (*in space*): сáмая высóкая тóчка, the highest point. Отправнáя тóчка, starting point. **3,** period. **4,** *in* **две тóчки,** colon; **тóчка с запятóй,** semicolon. **5,** *in* **тóчка кипéния/замерзáния,** boiling/freezing point. **6,** *in* **тóчка зрéния,** point of view; viewpoint. **7,** sharpening. —*interj.* enough!; that will do! —**бить в однý тóчку,** to concentrate on one thing. —**до тóчки,** thoroughly; down to the last detail. —**доходúть до тóчки,** to reach the breaking point; reach the end of one's rope; be at the end of one's tether. —**мёртвая тóчка,** *see* **мёртвый.** —**попáсть в (сáмую) тóчку,** to hit the nail on the head. —**стáвить тóчку на** (+ *prepl.*), to finish; close the books on. —**стáвить тóчки над "и",** to dot the "i's" and cross the "t's". —**тóчка в тóчку,** perfectly; to the letter.

тóчно *adv.* exactly; precisely; accurately. —*conj.* **1,** like; as. **2,** as if; as though. —**так тóчно!,** *mil.* yes, sir!

тóчность *n.f.* **1,** exactness; precision. **2,** accuracy. **3,** punctuality. —**в тóчности,** exactly; precisely; to the letter. —**с тóчностью до,** within.

тóчный *adj.* **1,** exact; precise. **2,** accurate. **3,** punctual. —**тóчные прибóры,** precision instruments.

точь-в-точь *adv.* exactly.

тошнúть *v. impfv., impers.* to be nauseous; feel nauseous: меня тошнúт, I feel nauseous.

тóшно *adj., used predicatively* nauseating; sickening: мне тóшно смотрéть на э́то, it sickens me to look at it.

тошнотá *n.* nausea. —**тошнотвóрный,** *adj.* nauseating; sickening.

тóшный *adj., colloq.* **1,** nauseating. **2,** bothersome; tiresome.

тощáть *v. impfv.* [*pfv.* **отощáть**] *colloq.* to become very thin; become gaunt; waste away.

тóщий *adj.* **1,** emaciated; gaunt. **2,** empty. **3,** poor; meager.

тпру *interj.* whoa!

травá [*pl.* **трáвы**] *n.* **1,** grass. **2,** herb. —**сóрная травá,** weed; weeds.

травúнка [*gen. pl.* **-нок**] *n.* blade of grass.

травúть *v. impfv.* [*pres.* **травлю́, трáвишь**] **1,** [*pfv.* **вы́травить**] to exterminate; poison. **2,** [*pfv.* **потравúть**] to trample (down). **3,** [*pfv.* **затравúть**] to hunt (down); *fig.* hound; persecute. **4,** [*pfv.* **вы́травить**] to etch. **5,** [*pfv.* **вы́травить**] *naut.* to let out; pay out (a rope, cable, etc.). —**травúться,** *refl.* [*impfv. only*] *colloq.* to take poison.

травлéние *n.* etching.

трáвля *n.* **1,** hunt; hunting. **2,** *fig.* hounding; persecution.

трáвма *n.* injury; trauma. —**травматúческий,** *adj.* traumatic. —**травматолóгия,** *n.* traumatology.

травмúровать *v. impfv. & pfv.* [*pres.* **-рую, -руешь**] **1,** to injure; damage. **2,** to traumatize.

травоя́дный *adj.* herbivorous.

травянúстый *adj.* **1,** herbaceous. **2,** grassy. **3,** *fig., colloq.* tasteless.

травянóй *adj.* **1,** grass (*attrib.*). **2,** grassy.

трагéдия *n.* tragedy.

трагúзм *n.* tragedy; tragic element.

трáгик *n.* tragedian.

трагикомéдия *n.* tragicomedy. —**трагикомúческий,** *adj.* tragicomic.

трагúческий *adj.* tragic. —**трагúчески,** *adv.* tragically.

трагúчный *adj.* tragic. —**трагúчно,** *adv.* tragically. —**трагúчность,** *n.f.* tragedy; tragic nature.

традúция *n.* tradition. —**традициóнный,** *adj.* traditional.

траектóрия *n.* trajectory. —**траектóрия полёта,** flight path.

тракт *n., obs.* highway. —**желýдочно-кишéчный тракт,** alimentary canal. —**пищеварúтельный тракт,** digestive tract.

трактáт *n.* **1,** treatise; tract. **2,** treaty.

трактúр *n., obs.* tavern; inn. —**трактúрщик,** *n., obs.* innkeeper.

трактовáть *v. impfv.* [*pres.* **-тýю, -тýешь**] **1,** to interpret. **2,** (*with* **о**) to treat; discuss (a certain subject).

трактóвка *n.* treatment; interpretation.

трáктор [*pl.* **трáкторы** *or* **трактора́**] *n.* tractor. —**трактори́ст,** *n.* tractor driver. —**трáкторный,** *adj.* tractor (*attrib.*).

трал *n.* trawl.

трáлить *v. impfv.* to trawl.

трáльщик *n.* **1,** trawler. **2,** minesweeper.

трамбовáть *v. impfv.* [*pfv.* **утрамбовáть;** *pres.* **-бýю, -бýешь**] to beat down; smooth down.

трамвáй *n.* streetcar; trolley; tram. —**трамвáйный,** *adj.* streetcar (*attrib.*); trolley (*attrib.*); tram (*attrib.*).

трамплúн *n.* **1,** diving board; springboard. **2,** *fig.* springboard; starting point. —**лы́жный трамплúн,** ski jump.

транжи́р *n., colloq.* spendthrift.
транжи́рить *v. impfv.* [*pfv.* **растранжи́рить**] *colloq.* to squander.
транзи́стор *n.* transistor.
транзи́т *n.* transit. —**транзи́тный,** *adj.* transit (*attrib.*).
транс *n.* trance.
трансатланти́ческий *adj.* transatlantic.
трансконтинента́льный *adj.* transcontinental.
транскри́пция *n., ling.; music* transcription.
трансли́ровать *v. impfv. & pfv.* [*pres.* **-рую, -руешь**] to transmit; broadcast.
транслитера́ция *n.* transliteration.
транслитери́ровать *v. impfv. & pfv.* [*pres.* **-рую, -руешь**] to transliterate.
трансля́ция *n.* transmission; broadcast. —**трансляцио́нный,** *adj.* transmission (*attrib.*); broadcasting.
трансокеа́нский *adj.* transoceanic.
транспара́нт *n.* **1,** lined paper (*placed under unlined paper*). **2,** banner; streamer.
транспони́ровать *v. impfv. & pfv.* [*pres.* **-рую, -руешь**] *music* to transpose.
транспониро́вка *n., music* transposition.
тра́нспорт *n.* **1,** transport. **2,** transportation. **3,** shipment; consignment. **4,** supply ship; troopship; troop transport.
транспо́рт *n., bookkeeping* carrying forward.
транспорта́бельный *adj.* transportable.
транспортёр *n.* **1,** conveyor. **2,** *mil.* transporter; carrier.
транспорти́р *n.* protractor.
транспорти́ровать *v. impfv. & pfv.* [*pres.* **-рую, -руешь**] **1,** to transport. **2,** *bookkeeping* to carry forward.
транспортиро́вка *n.* transporting; transportation.
тра́нспортник *n.* transport worker.
тра́нспортный *adj.* transport (*attrib.*).
транссиби́рский *adj.* trans-Siberian.
трансформа́тор *n.* **1,** *electricity* transformer. **2,** *theat.* quick-change artist.
трансформа́ция *n.* transformation.
трансформи́ровать *v. impfv. & pfv.* [*pres.* **-рую, -руешь**] to transform; convert.
трансцендента́льный *adj.* transcendental.
трансценде́нтный *adj.* **1,** *philos.* transcendent. **2,** *math.* transcendental.
транше́йный *adj.* trench (*attrib.*). —**транше́йная стопа́,** trench foot.
транше́я *n.* trench.
трап *n.* **1,** ship's ladder. **2,** boarding ramp.
тра́пеза *also,* **трапе́за** *n.* food; meal (*originally referring to that served in a monastery*).
тра́пезная *also,* **трапе́зная** *n., decl. as an adj.* refectory (*in a monastery*).
тра́пезный *also,* **трапе́зный** *adj.* meal (*attrib.*); dining (*attrib.*).
трапе́ция *n.* **1,** *geom.* trapezoid. **2,** trapeze.
тра́сса *n.* **1,** route. **2,** path (*of a bullet, missile, etc.*). **3,** road; highway.
трасса́нт *n., comm.* drawer.
трасси́ровать *v. impfv. & pfv.* [*pres.* **-рую, -руешь**] to trace (*on a map or chart*).
трасси́рующий *adj.* tracer (*attrib.*): трасси́рущая пу́ля, tracer bullet.
тра́та *n.* **1,** spending. **2,** expenditure; expense. **3,** (*preceded by an adj.*) waste: пуста́я тра́та вре́мени, waste of time.
тра́тить *v. impfv.* [*pfv.* **истра́тить** *or* **потра́тить;** *pres.* **тра́чу, тра́тишь**] **1,** to spend (money). **2,** to expend (time, energy, etc.). **3,** to use up. **4,** to waste. —**тра́титься,** *refl.* **1,** to spend money. **2,** to be spent.
тра́улер *n.* trawler.
тра́ур *n.* **1,** mourning. **2,** mourning clothes. —**наде́ть тра́ур,** to go into mourning. —**носи́ть тра́ур по** (+ *dat.*), to be in mourning for.
тра́урница *n.* mourning cloak (*butterfly*).
тра́урный *adj.* **1,** mourning (*attrib.*); funeral (*attrib.*). **2,** *fig.* mournful; sorrowful.
трафаре́т *n.* **1,** stencil. **2,** *fig.* stereotype.
трафаре́тный *adj.* **1,** stenciled. **2,** *fig.* conventional; stereotyped.
трах *interj.* bang!
трахе́я *n.* trachea. —**трахе́йный,** *adj.* tracheal.
тра́хнуть *v. pfv., colloq.* **1,** to fire; shoot. **2,** (*of a sound, shot, etc.*) to ring out. **3,** to bang; smash; whack. —**тра́хнуться,** *refl., colloq.* (*with* **о** + *acc.*) to bang (into *or* against).
трахо́ма *n.* trachoma.
тре́ба *n.* **1,** sacrifice; offering. **2,** religious ceremony (*wedding, christening, etc.*) performed by a clergyman.
тре́бование *n.* **1,** demand. **2,** *pl.* requirements: отвеча́ть тре́бованиям, to meet the requirements. **3,** requisition; order.
тре́бовательный *adj.* demanding; exacting.
тре́бовать *v. impfv.* [*pfv.* **потре́бовать;** *pres.* **тре́бую, тре́буешь**] **1,** (*with gen., acc., or* **что́бы**) to demand. **2,** (*with acc.*) to demand to see (a permit, passport, etc.). **3,** (*with gen.*) to require; need; call for. **4,** (*with acc.*) to summon; send for; call in. —**тре́боваться,** *refl.* to be needed; be required.
требуха́ *n.* entrails.
трево́га *n.* **1,** alarm: быть в трево́ге, to be alarmed. **2,** alarm signal: бить трево́гу, to sound the alarm. **3,** alert: поднима́ть по трево́ге, to place on the alert.
трево́жить *v. impfv.* **1,** [*pfv.* **встрево́жить**] to alarm; worry; trouble. **2,** [*pfv.* **потрево́жить**] to disturb; interrupt. —**трево́житься,** *refl.* [*pfv.* **встрево́житься**] to become alarmed; become worried.
трево́жный *adj.* **1,** anxious; uneasy; troubled. **2,** of alarm: трево́жный взгляд, a look of alarm. **3,** alarming. **4,** alarm (*attrib.*): трево́жный сигна́л, alarm signal.
треволне́ние *n., colloq.* **1,** worry; agitation. **2,** *pl.* vicissitudes.
тре́звенник *n., colloq.* teetotaler.
трезве́ть *v. impfv.* [*pfv.* **отрезве́ть**] to sober up; become sober.
трезво́н *n.* **1,** sound of church bells. **2,** long ringing of a bell. **3,** *fig., colloq.* talk; gossip. **4,** *fig., colloq.* row; ruckus.
трезво́нить *v. impfv.* **1,** to ring; sound; peal. **2,** *fig., colloq.* to trumpet; proclaim. **3,** (*with* **о**) *colloq.* to spread rumors (about).
тре́звость *n.f.* **1,** sobriety. **2,** temperance; abstinence. —**тре́звость ума́,** cool-headedness.
трезву́чие *n., music* triad.
тре́звый *adj.* **1,** sober; not drunk. **2,** *colloq.* who does not drink; teetotaling. **3,** *fig.* sober; realistic.
трезу́бец [*gen.* **-бца**] *n.* trident.
трек *n., sports* track. —**тре́ковый,** *adj.* track (*attrib.*).

трель *n.f.* trill; warble.
трелья́ж *n.* **1,** trellis. **2,** three-leaf mirror.
тре́моло *n. indecl.* tremolo.
тре́нер *n.* trainer; coach.
тре́нзель *n.m.* snaffle.
тре́ние *n.* **1,** rubbing; rubbing together. **2,** friction. **3,** *pl., fig.* friction; conflict.
трениро́ванный *adj.* trained.
тренирова́ть *v. impfv.* [*pfv.* **натренирова́ть;** *pres.* **-ру́ю, -ру́ешь**] to train; coach. —**тренирова́ться,** *refl.* to train; undergo training.
трениро́вка *n.* **1,** training. **2,** practice; workout. —**трениро́вочный,** *adj.* training (*attrib.*).
трено́га *n.* **1,** tripod. **2,** three-legged shackle (*for a horse*).
трено́гий *adj.* three-legged.
трено́жить *v. impfv.* [*pfv.* **стрено́жить**] to hobble (a horse).
трено́жник *n.* tripod.
тре́нькать *v. impfv., colloq.* to strum.
трепа́к [*gen.* **-пака́**] *n.* trepak.
трепа́ло *n.* scutch; swingle. *Also,* **трепа́лка.**
трёпаный *adj., colloq.* **1,** torn; tattered; ragged; frayed. **2,** disheveled; unkempt.
трепа́ть *v. impfv.* [*pres.* **треплю́, тре́плешь**] **1,** [*pfv.* **потрепа́ть**] to dishevel (*by pulling or tugging at*). **2,** [*pfv.* **потрепа́ть**] (*of the wind*) to blow about. **3,** [*pfv.* **потрепа́ть**] (*with* **по** + *dat.*) to pat; stroke. **4,** [*pfv.* **истрепа́ть**] *colloq.* to fray; wear out. **5,** [*impfv. only*] (*with* **за** + *acc.*) to pull (someone's hair, ears, etc.). **6,** [*impfv. only*] *colloq.* to whip; whack. **7,** [*impfv. only*] (*of illness, fever, etc.*) to rack. **8,** [*impfv. only*] to scutch. **9,** *in* трепа́ть не́рвы (+ *dat.*), to jangle someone's nerves. **10,** *in* трепа́ть языко́м, *colloq.* to babble; chatter. —**трепа́ться,** *refl.* **1,** [*impfv. only*] to flutter. **2,** [*pfv.* **истрепа́ться**] *colloq.* to become frayed; wear out.
тре́пет *n.* **1,** quivering; trembling. **2,** tremor; palpitation. **3,** *fig.* trepidation.
трепета́ние *n.* **1,** quivering; trembling. **2,** palpitation.
трепета́ть *v. impfv.* [*pres.* **трепещу́, трепе́щешь**] **1,** to quiver. **2,** (*of one's heart*) to palpitate. **3,** to flicker. **4,** to tremble (*with an emotion*).
тре́петно *adv.* **1,** with a quiver. **2,** with trepidation.
тре́петный *adj.* **1,** quivering; fluttering; flickering. **2,** of trepidation; trembling. **3,** timid; fearful.
трёпка [*gen. pl.* **-пок**] *n., colloq.* **1,** beating; thrashing. **2,** scolding; bawling out; dressing-down. —**трёпка не́рвов,** strain on one's nerves.
треск *n.* **1,** crack; cracking sound. **2,** crackle; crackling sound. **3,** *colloq.* fuss; hullabaloo. —**провали́ться с тре́ском,** to fail ignominiously; be a complete flop.
треска́ *n.* cod; codfish.
тре́скаться *v.r. impfv.* [*pfv.* **потре́скаться**] **1,** to crack. **2,** to chap; become chapped.
тресково́й *adj.* cod (*attrib.*); codfish (*attrib.*).
трескотня́ *n., colloq.* **1,** crackle; rattle. **2,** chirping (*of insects*). **3,** *fig.* chatter.
треску́чий *adj., colloq.* **1,** crackling. **2,** (*of a sound*) grating; harsh. **3,** (*of frost*) sharp; harsh. **4,** *fig.* high-flown; high-sounding; pretentious.
тре́снуть *v. pfv.* **1,** *v.i.* to crack; burst. **2,** *colloq.* to bang (on *or* against). **3,** *colloq.* to hit; smack. —**тре́снуться,** *refl., colloq.* to bang: тре́снуться голово́й о перекла́дину, to bang one's head on a crossbar.
трест *n., econ.* trust.
трете́йский *adj.* of arbitration: трете́йский суд, court of arbitration.
тре́тий [*fem.* **-тья**] *ordinal numeral* third. —**тре́тьего дня,** the day before yesterday. *See also* **тре́тье.**
трети́ровать *v. impfv.* [*pres.* **-рую, -руешь**] to slight; snub.
трети́чный *adj.* tertiary.
треть [*pl.* **тре́ти, -те́й, -тя́м**] *n.f.* a third: две тре́ти, two thirds (2/3).
тре́тье *n., decl. as an adj.* third course; dessert.
третьесо́ртный *adj.* third-rate.
третьестепе́нный *adj.* **1,** insignificant. **2,** third-rate.
треуго́лка [*gen. pl.* **-лок**] *n.* cocked hat.
треуго́льник *n.* triangle. —**треуго́льный,** *adj.* triangular.
трефно́й *adj.* (*of food*) non-kosher. —**трефно́е,** *n.* non-kosher food.
тре́фовый *also,* **трефо́вый** *adj., cards* of clubs: тре́фовый туз, ace of clubs.
тре́фы [*gen.* **треф**] *n. pl., cards* clubs.
трёхвале́нтный *adj.* trivalent.
трёхгла́вый *adj.* three-headed. —**трёхгла́вая мы́шца,** triceps.
трёхгоди́чный *adj.* three-year (*attrib.*).
трёхгодова́лый *adj.* three-year-old.
трёхгра́нник *n.* trihedron. —**трёхгра́нный,** *adj.* trihedral.
трёхдне́вный *adj.* three-day (*attrib.*).
трёхколёсный *adj.* three-wheel(ed). —**трёхколёсный велосипе́д,** tricycle.
трёхко́мнатный *adj.* three-room.
трёхле́тие *n.* **1,** third anniversary; third birthday. **2,** three-year period.
трёхле́тний *adj.* **1,** three-year (*attrib.*). **2,** three-year-old.
трёхме́рный *adj.* three-dimensional.
трёхме́сячный *adj.* **1,** three-month (*attrib.*). **2,** three-month-old.
трёхнеде́льный *adj.* **1,** three-week (*attrib.*). **2,** three-week-old.
трёхсло́жный *adj.* three-syllable.
трёхсотле́тие *n.* three-hundredth anniversary; tercentenary. —**трёхсотле́тний,** *adj.* three-hundred-year (*attrib.*); tercentenary.
трёхсо́тый *ordinal numeral* three-hundredth.
трёхсторо́нний *adj.* **1,** three-sided. **2,** trilateral; tripartite; three-way.
трёхцве́тный *adj.* three-colored; tricolored.
трёхчасово́й *adj.* **1,** three-hour (*attrib.*). **2,** *colloq.* three-o'clock (*attrib.*).
трёхчле́н *n.* trinomial. —**трёхчле́нный,** *adj.* trinomial.
трёхэта́жный *adj.* three-story.
треща́ние *n.* **1,** cracking; crackling. **2,** chirping. **3,** chattering.
треща́ть *v. impfv.* [*pres.* **трещу́, трещи́шь**] **1,** to crack. **2,** to crackle. **3,** to chirp. **4,** to ring loudly; make a racket. **5,** *colloq.* to chatter. **6,** *colloq.* (*of one's head*) to be splitting. **7,** *fig.* to be on the verge of collapse.
тре́щина *n.* **1,** crack; split. **2,** fissure. **3,** *fig.* rift; split; breach. —**дать тре́щину,** to crack.
трещо́тка [*gen. pl.* **-ток**] *n.* **1,** rattle (*for making a noise*). **2,** ratchet. **3,** *colloq.* chatterbox.
три [*gen. & prepl.* **трёх;** *dat.* **трём;** *instr.* **тремя́**] *numeral* three.
триа́да *n.* triad.

триангуля́ция *n.* triangulation.
триа́совый *adj.* Triassic.
трибу́н *n.* tribune.
трибу́на *n.* **1,** speaker's rostrum. **2,** grandstand; stands.
трибуна́л *n.* tribunal.
тривиа́льный *adj.* trite; banal. —**тривиа́льность,** *n.f.* banality.
тригономе́трия *n.* trigonometry. —**тригонометри́ческий,** *adj.* trigonometric.
три́девять *numeral, colloq., in* **за три́девять земе́ль,** at the other end of the world.
тридцатиле́тний *adj.* **1,** thirty-year (*attrib.*). **2,** thirty-year-old.
тридца́тый *ordinal numeral* thirtieth.
три́дцать [*gen., dat., & prepl.* **-цати́;** *instr.* **-цатью́**] *numeral* thirty.
три́жды *adv.* three times; thrice.
тризм *n.* lockjaw.
трико́ *n. indecl.* **1,** tricot. **2,** tights.
трикота́ж *n.* **1,** knitted fabric. **2,** knitted wear.
трикота́жный *adj.* **1,** knitting (*attrib.*). **2,** knitted.
триктра́к *n.* backgammon.
трили́стник *n.* trefoil; shamrock.
триллио́н *n.* trillion (*U.S.*); billion (*Brit.*).
трило́гия *n.* trilogy.
триме́стр *n.* trimester.
трина́дцатый *ordinal numeral* thirteenth.
трина́дцать *numeral* thirteen.
тринитротолуо́л *n.* trinitrotoluene.
три́о *n. indecl.* trio.
трио́д *n.* triode.
трио́ль *n.f., music* triplet.
три́ппер *n.* gonorrhea.
три́птих *n.* triptych.
три́ста [*gen.* **трёхсо́т;** *dat.* **трёмста́м;** *instr.* **тремяста́ми;** *prepl.* **трёхста́х**] *numeral* three hundred.
три́тий *n.* tritium.
трито́н *n., zool.* triton; newt.
триумви́р *n.* triumvir. —**триумвира́т,** *n.* triumvirate.
триу́мф *n.* triumph. —**триумфа́льный,** *adj.* triumphal.
трихи́на *n.* trichina.
трихинеллёз *n.* trichinosis.
тро́гательный *adj.* touching; moving; poignant. —**тро́гательность,** *n.f.* poignancy.
тро́гать *v. impfv.* [*pfv.* **тро́нуть**] **1,** to touch. **2,** bother; disturb. **3,** to touch; move; affect (*emotionally*). **4,** *v.i.* to start moving. —**тро́гаться,** *refl.* **1,** to start moving. **2,** [*often* **тро́нуться в путь**] to set out; start out. **3,** (*of ice*) to begin to break up. **4,** to be touched; be moved (*emotionally*). *See also* **тро́нуть.**
тро́е [*infl. like* **дво́е**] *collective numeral* three.
троекра́тный *adj.* done or happening three times; three-time.
тро́ица *n.* **1,** Trinity. **2,** *colloq.* Whitsunday.
тро́ицын *adj., in* **тро́ицын день,** Whitsunday.
тро́йка *n.* **1,** the numeral 3. **2,** *colloq.* anything numbered 3. **3,** troika. **4,** a grade of "three", signifying "satisfactory". **5,** *cards* three. **6,** *colloq.* [*also,* **костю́м-тро́йка**] three-piece suit.
тройно́й *adj.* triple; threefold; three-way.
тро́йня *n.* triplets.
тро́йственный *adj.* **1,** triple. **2,** tripartite.
тролле́йбус *n.* trolley bus. —**тролле́йбусный,** *adj.* trolley-bus (*attrib.*).
тролль *n.m., folklore* troll.
тромб *n.* blood clot. —**тромбо́з,** *n.* thrombosis.
тромбо́н *n.* trombone. —**тромбони́ст,** *n.* trombonist.
трон *n.* throne. —**тро́нный,** *adj.* throne (*attrib.*).
тро́нутый *adj.* **1,** [*short form only*] touched; moved (*emotionally*). **2,** *colloq.* touched in the head; wacky.
тро́нуть *v. pfv.* **1,** *pfv. of* **тро́гать. 2,** to touch; affect: тро́нутый моро́зом, touched (*or* nipped) by the frost. —**тро́нуться,** *refl.* **1,** *pfv. of* **тро́гаться. 2,** *colloq.* to be slightly touched (*or* wacky).
троп *n.* trope.
тропа́ [*pl.* **тро́пы, троп, тропа́м** *or* **тро́пам**] *n.* path.
тро́пик *n.* **1,** tropic: тро́пик Ра́ка, Tropic of Cancer; тро́пик Козеро́га, Tropic of Capricorn. **2,** *pl.* tropics.
тропи́нка [*gen. pl.* **-нок**] *n.* path.
тропи́ческий *adj.* tropical. —**тропи́ческий по́яс,** Torrid Zone.
тропосфе́ра *n.* troposphere.
трос *n.* rope; cable.
трости́нка [*gen. pl.* **-нок**] *n.* thin reed.
тростни́к [*gen.* **-ника́**] *n.* reed; rush; cane. —**са́харный тростни́к,** sugar cane.
тростнико́вый *adj.* **1,** reed (*attrib.*); rush (*attrib.*); cane (*attrib.*). **2,** overgrown with reeds; reedy.
тро́сточка [*gen. pl.* **-чек**] *n.* cane; walking stick.
трость [*pl.* **тро́сти, -сте́й, -стя́м**] *n.f.* cane; walking stick.
троти́л *n.* trinitrotoluene.
тротуа́р *n.* sidewalk; pavement.
трофе́й *n.* **1,** trophy; memento. **2,** *pl.* spoils; booty. —**трофе́йный,** *adj.* captured (*in war*).
трохе́й *n.* trochee. —**трохеи́ческий,** *adj.* trochaic.
трою́родный *adj., denoting relationships of cousins:* трою́родный брат; трою́родная сестра́, second cousin.
троя́кий *adj.* triple; threefold.
троя́нский *adj.* Trojan.
труба́ [*pl.* **тру́бы**] *n.* **1,** pipe. Дымова́я труба́, chimney; smokestack. **2,** trumpet. **3,** *anat.* tube. —**вы́лететь в трубу́,** *colloq.* to go broke. —**пусти́ть в трубу́,** *colloq.* **1,** to bankrupt; ruin. **2,** to squander; dissipate.
трубаду́р *n.* troubadour.
труба́ч [*gen.* **-бача́**] *n.* trumpeter; trumpet player.
труби́ть *v. impfv.* [*pfv.* **протруби́ть;** *pres.* **трублю́, труби́шь**] **1,** (*with* **в** + *acc.*) to blow (a trumpet). **2,** to sound; signal; announce. **3,** to sound; blare. **4,** (*with* **о**) *colloq.* to trumpet; crow about.
тру́бка [*gen. pl.* **-бок**] *n.* **1,** tube; pipe. **2,** receiver (*of a telephone*). Возьми́те тру́бку!, pick up the phone! Я переда́м тру́бку (+ *dat.*), I'll put... on. **3,** pipe (*for smoking*). **4,** fuse. **5,** roll (*of material*).
трубкозу́б *n.* aardvark.
тру́бный *adj.* **1,** pipe (*attrib.*). **2,** trumpet (*attrib.*).
трубопрово́д *n.* conduit; pipeline.
трубочи́ст *n.* chimney sweep.
тру́бочный *adj.* pipe (*attrib.*): тру́бочный таба́к, pipe tobacco.
тру́бчатый *adj.* tubular.
труд [*gen.* **труда́**] *n.* **1,** labor. **2,** effort; trouble; difficulty: не сто́ит труда́, it's not worth the trouble. **3,** (written) work (*usually of a scientific nature*). —**дать себе́ (***or* **взять на себя́) труд,** to take the trouble. —**с трудо́м, 1,** with difficulty. **2,** hardly; scarcely; barely.

труди́ться *v.r. impfv.* [*pres.* **тружу́сь, тру́дишься**] **1,** to work; labor; toil. **2,** *colloq.* to bother; take the trouble.

тру́дно *adv.* with difficulty. Тру́дно произноси́мое сло́во, a difficult (*or* hard) word to pronounce. —*adj., used predicatively* difficult; hard: тру́дно сказа́ть, it is difficult/hard to say. Мне тру́дно пове́рить э́тому, I find that hard to believe.

тру́дность *n.f.* difficulty.

тру́дный *adj.* [*short form* **-ден, -дна́, -дно**] difficult; hard.

трудово́й *adj.* **1,** labor (*attrib.*). **2,** working. **3,** earned: трудовы́е дохо́ды, earned income. —**трудова́я кни́жка,** work-record book.

трудоде́нь [*gen.* **-дня́**] *n.m.* workday (*unit of payment on collective farms*).

трудоёмкий *adj.* **1,** labor-intensive. **2,** time-consuming.

трудолюби́вый *adj.* hard-working; industrious. —**трудолю́бие,** *n.* industry; industriousness.

трудоспосо́бный *adj.* able to work; able-bodied. —**трудоспосо́бность,** *n.f.* ability to work.

трудоустро́йство *n.* job placement.

трудя́щийся *adj.* working; laboring. —*n.* worker; laborer.

тру́женик *n.* worker; toiler.

труни́ть *v. impfv.* (*with* **над**) *colloq.* to make fun of; kid.

труп *n.* dead body; corpse; cadaver.

трупиа́л *n.* oriole.

тру́пный *adj.* **1,** of or like a corpse. **2,** (*of an odor*) putrid. —**тру́пное окочене́ние,** rigor mortis. —**тру́пный яд,** ptomaine.

тру́ппа *n.* company; troupe.

трус *n.m.* [*fem.* **-си́ха**] coward.

тру́сики [*gen.* **-ков**] *n. pl.* **1,** shorts. **2,** undershorts; underpants; panties.

тру́сить *v. impfv.* [*pfv.* **стру́сить;** *pres.* **тру́шу, тру́сишь**] to be a coward; be afraid; get cold feet.

труси́ть *v. impfv.* [*pres.* **трушу́, труси́шь**] *colloq.* to trot; jog.

труси́ха *n., fem. of* **трус.**

трусли́вый *adj.* cowardly.

тру́сость *n.f.* cowardice.

трусца́ *n., colloq.* trot.

трусы́ [*gen.* **-со́в**] *n. pl.* **1,** shorts. **2,** undershorts; underpants.

трут *n.* tinder.

тру́тень [*gen.* **-тня**] *n.m.* drone.

труха́ *n.* **1,** dust; flakes; bits (*of hay, straw, rotted wood, etc.*). **2,** *fig.* trash; rubbish.

трухля́вый *adj.* moldering; rotten.

трущо́ба *n.* **1,** thicket. **2,** out-of-the-way place. **3,** slum.

трын-трава́ *predicate* (*with dat.*) *colloq.* all the same: ему́ всё трын-трава́, it's all the same to him.

трюи́зм *n.* truism.

трюк *n.* trick; stunt. —**трю́ковый,** *adj.* trick (*attrib.*).

трюм *n.* hold (*of a ship*).

трюмо́ *n. indecl.* pier glass.

трю́фель [*pl.* **трю́фели, -ле́й, ля́м**] *n.m.* **1,** truffle. **2,** *pl.* chocolate truffles.

тряпи́чник *n.* ragman.

тряпи́чный *adj.* rag (*attrib.*).

тря́пка [*gen. pl.* **-пок**] *n.* **1,** rag. **2,** *pl., colloq.* clothes; finery. **3,** *colloq.* milksop; weakling.

тряпьё *n.* rags.

тряси́на *n.* quagmire.

тря́ска *n.* bumpiness; shaking.

тря́ский *adj.* **1,** (*of a vehicle*) that shakes a lot; shaky. **2,** (*of a road*) bumpy.

трясогу́зка [*gen. pl.* **-зок**] *n.* wagtail (*bird*).

трясти́ *v. impfv.* [*pfv.* **тряхну́ть;** *pres.* **трясу́, трясёшь;** *past* **тряс, трясла́, трясло́**] **1,** to shake: трясти́ де́рево, to shake a tree; трясти́ голово́й, to shake one's head. **2,** to shake out. **3,** *impers.* (*of a person*) to be shaking: его́ всего́ трясёт, he is shaking all over. **4,** (*of a vehicle*) to shake. —**трясти́сь,** *refl.* **1,** to shake. **2,** to tremble. **3,** *colloq.* to bounce along. **4,** (*with* **над**) *colloq.* to guard with one's life; watch like a hawk.

тсс *interj.* hush!

тсу́га *n.* hemlock (*tree*).

ту *adj., fem. acc. of* **тот.**

туале́т *n.* **1,** dress; clothes. **2,** toilet; grooming. **3,** dressing table; vanity. **4,** rest room; washroom.

туале́тный *adj.* toilet (*attrib.*). —**туале́тный сто́лик,** dressing table; vanity.

ту́ба *n.* tuba.

туберкулёз *n.* tuberculosis. —**туберкулёзный,** *adj.* tubercular; tuberculous.

тубеpо́за *n.* tuberose.

туви́нец [*gen.* **-нца**] *n.m.* [*fem.* **-нка**] Tuvinian (*one of a people inhabiting southern Siberia*). —**туви́нский,** *adj.* Tuvinian.

ту́го *adv.* **1,** tight; tightly. **2,** *colloq.* with difficulty; slowly. —*adj., used predicatively, colloq.* short of: с деньга́ми мне ту́го, I am short of money.

тугоду́м *n., colloq.* dimwit.

туго́й *adj.* [*comp.* **ту́же**] **1,** tight; taut. **2,** tightly filled; stuffed. **3,** slow to grasp things; dense; dull. —**туго́й на де́ньги,** tight with one's money. —**туго́й на язы́к,** slow of speech; inarticulate. —**туго́й на́ ухо,** hard of hearing.

тугоу́хий *adj.* hard of hearing; partially deaf.

туда́ *adv., expressing direction,* there: посмотри́те туда́!, look over there! Положи́те э́то туда́!, put it (over) there! —**не туда́,** to the wrong place; in the wrong direction. Вы не туда́ попа́ли, you've got the wrong number (*on the telephone*). —**ни туда́ ни сюда́,** neither backward nor forward; unable to move. —**туда́ и обра́тно,** there and back. Биле́т туда́ и обра́тно, round-trip ticket. Пое́здка туда́ и обра́тно, round trip. —**туда́ и сюда́,** back and forth.

туда́-сюда́ *adv., colloq.* **1,** here and there; around and about. **2,** all right; so-so; passable.

ту́же *adj., comp. of* **туго́й.**

тужи́ть *v. impfv.* [*pres.* **тужу́, ту́жишь**] *colloq.* to grieve.

ту́житься *v.r. impfv., colloq.* to exert oneself; make a great effort.

тужу́рка [*gen. pl.* **-рок**] *n.* man's double-breasted jacket.

туз [*gen. & acc.* **туза́**] *n.* **1,** *cards* ace. **2,** *colloq.* bigwig.

тузе́мец [*gen.* **-мца**] *n.m.* [*fem.* **-мка**] native. —**тузе́мный,** *adj.* native; indigenous.

тузи́ть *v. impfv.* [*pfv.* **оттузи́ть;** *pres.* **тужу́, тузи́шь**] *colloq.* to thrash; pommel.

тука́н *n.* toucan.

ту́кать *v. impfv.* [*pfv.* **ту́кнуть**] *colloq.* **1,** to slam. **2,** to tap; clack. —**ту́каться,** *refl.* (*with* **о** + *acc.*) *colloq.* to bang into.

ту́лий *n.* thulium.
ту́ловище *n.* trunk; torso.
тулу́п *n.* sheepskin coat.
тулья́ [*gen. pl.* **-ле́й**] *n.* crown (*of a hat*).
тума́к [*gen.* **-мака́;** *acc.* **тума́к** *or* **-мака́**] *n., colloq.* punch; wallop; clout.
тума́н *n.* fog.
тума́нить *v. impfv.* [*pfv.* **затума́нить**] to cloud; obscure. —**тума́ниться,** *refl.* **1,** to be obscured by fog. **2,** (*of one's eyes*) to become dim; (*of the senses*) to become muddled.
тума́нность *n.f.* **1,** fog; fogginess. **2,** *fig.* vagueness; obscurity. **3,** *astron.* nebula.
тума́нный *adj.* **1,** foggy; misty. **2,** *fig.* hazy; vague.
ту́мба *n.* **1,** curbside stone or post. **2,** stand; pedestal.
ту́мбочка [*gen. pl.* **-чек**] *n.* night table.
тунг *n.* tung tree. —**ту́нговый,** *adj.* tung (*attrib.*): ту́нговое ма́сло, tung oil.
ту́ндра *n.* tundra. —**ту́ндровый,** *adj.* tundra (*attrib.*).
туне́ц [*gen.* **-нца́**] *n.* tuna.
тунея́дец [*gen.* **-дца**] *n.* parasite; sponger. —**тунея́дство,** *n.* parasitism.
туни́ка *n.* tunic (*worn in ancient times*).
тунне́ль (нэ) *n.m.* tunnel.
тупе́ть *v. impfv.* **1,** to become dull. **2,** (*of the senses*) to become clouded.
ту́пик *n.* puffin (*bird*).
тупи́к [*gen.* **тупика́**] *n.* **1,** blind alley; dead-end street. **2,** *fig.* impasse; deadlock. —**зайти́ в тупи́к,** to reach an impasse; be deadlocked. —**ста́вить в тупи́к,** to put on the spot; throw for a loss. —**стать в тупи́к,** to be on the spot; be at a loss.
тупи́ть *v. impfv.* [*pfv.* **иступи́ть** *or* **затупи́ть;** *pres.* **туплю́, ту́пишь**] to blunt; dull; take the edge off. —**тупи́ться,** *refl.* to dull; become dull.
тупи́ца *n.m. & f., colloq.* dimwit; dullard; dolt.
тупоголо́вый *adj., colloq.* dimwitted; thickheaded.
тупо́й *adj.* **1,** dull; blunt. **2,** (*of pain, sounds, etc.*) dull. **3,** (*of a person*) dull; obtuse. **4,** (*of a look, expression, etc.*) vacant; blank. —**тупо́й у́гол,** obtuse angle. —**тупо́е ударе́ние,** grave accent.
ту́пость *n.f.* **1,** dullness; bluntness. **2,** dullness; obtuseness.
тупоу́мие *n.* dullness; obtuseness. —**тупоу́мный,** *adj.* thickheaded; dimwitted.
тур *n.* **1,** turn (*in dancing*). **2,** round (*of a tournament, negotiations, etc.*). **3,** stage; phase. **4,** aurochs.
тура́ *n., chess* rook; castle.
турба́за *n.* tourist center. —**молодёжная турба́за,** youth hostel.
турби́на *n.* turbine. —**турби́нный,** *adj.* turbine (*attrib.*).
турбовинтово́й *adj.* turboprop (*attrib.*).
турбореакти́вный *adj.* turbojet (*attrib.*).
туре́цкий *adj.* Turkish. —**туре́цкий бараба́н,** bass drum. —**туре́цкий горо́х,** chickpea.
тури́зм *n.* tourism. —**тури́ст,** *n.* tourist.
туристи́ческий *adj.* **1,** tourist (*attrib.*). **2,** walking (*attrib.*); hiking (*attrib.*): туристи́ческий похо́д, walking tour; hiking expedition.
тури́стский *adj.* tourist (*attrib.*).
туркме́н [*gen. pl.* **-ме́н**] *n.m.* [*fem.* **-ме́нка**] Turkmen (*one of a people inhabiting the Turkmen S.S.R.*). —**туркме́нский,** *adj.* Turkmen.
турмали́н *n.* tourmaline.
ту́рман *n.* tumbler pigeon.
турне́ (нэ) *n. neut. indecl.* tour.
турни́к [*gen.* **-ника́**] *n., sports* horizontal bar.
турнике́т *n.* turnstile.
турни́р *n.* tournament.
ту́рок [*gen.* **ту́рка;** *gen. pl.* **ту́рок**] *n.m.* [*fem.* **турча́нка**] Turk.
турухта́н *n.* ruff (*bird*).
ту́скло *adv.* dimly.
ту́склость *n.f.* dullness; dimness.
ту́склый *adj.* **1,** (*of light*) dim. **2,** (*of metals*) dull; lackluster. **3,** dreary; overcast. **4,** *fig.* colorless; insipid.
тускне́ть *v. impfv.* [*pfv.* **потускне́ть**] **1,** to grow dim; lose its luster. **2,** *fig.* to fade; wane. **3,** [*impfv. only*] (*with* **пе́ред**) to pale (before).
тут *adv., expressing location,* here. —**(быть) тут как тут,** *colloq.* to appear like clockwork; be Johnny on the spot. —**не тут-то бы́ло,** it was not to be. —**там и тут,** here and there. —**тут же,** then and there; there and then.
ту́товник *n.* mulberry tree.
ту́товый *adj.* mulberry (*attrib.*). —**ту́товый шелкопря́д,** silkworm. —**ту́товая я́года,** mulberry.
ту́фелька [*gen. pl.* **-лек**] *n.* **1,** small shoe; fancy shoe. **2,** paramecium.
ту́фля [*gen. pl.* **-фель**] *n.* shoe: ту́фли на высо́ких каблука́х, high-heeled shoes. —**дома́шние ту́фли,** (bedroom) slippers.
ту́хлый *adj.* rotten; spoiled; tainted.
тухля́тина *n., colloq.* **1,** food which has spoiled or become rotten. **2,** foul odor from such food.
ту́хнуть *v. impfv.* [*past* **тух** *or* **ту́хнул, ту́хла**] **1,** [*pfv.* **поту́хнуть**] (*of something burning*) to go out. **2,** [*pfv.* **проту́хнуть**] to spoil; rot.
ту́ча *n.* cloud; storm cloud.
тучне́ть *v. impfv.* [*pfv.* **потучне́ть**] to grow fat; put on weight.
ту́чность *n.f.* **1,** obesity; corpulence. **2,** richness; fertility.
ту́чный *adj.* **1,** fat; stout; obese. **2,** (*of soil*) rich; fertile. **3,** (*of grass, grain, a meadow, etc.*) lush.
туш *n.* flourish (*of trumpets*).
ту́ша *n.* carcass.
туше́ *n. neut. indecl.* touch (*when playing a musical instrument*).
тушева́ть *v. impfv.* [*pfv.* **затушева́ть;** *pres.* **-шу́ю, -шу́ешь**] **1,** to shade; add shading to. **2,** *fig.* to soften; tone down. —**тушева́ться,** *refl.* [*pfv.* **стушева́ться**] *colloq.* to become flustered.
тушёвка *n.* shading.
туше́ние *n.* **1,** extinguishing. **2,** stewing.
тушёный *adj.* stewed.
туши́ть *v. impfv.* [*pres.* **тушу́, ту́шишь**] **1,** [*pfv.* **потуши́ть**] to put out; extinguish (a fire, candle, etc.); turn out; turn off (a light). **2,** [*pfv.* **стуши́ть**] to stew; braise.
тушка́нчик *n.* jerboa.
тушь *n.f.* **1,** India ink. **2,** mascara.
тща́тельный *adj.* careful; painstaking. —**тща́тельно,** *adv.* carefully; painstakingly. —**тща́тельность,** *n.f.* care.
тщеду́шие *n.* frailty. —**тщеду́шный,** *adj.* frail.
тщесла́вие *n.* vanity. —**тщесла́вный,** *adj.* vain.
тщётный *adj.* vain; futile. —**тщётно,** *adv.* vainly; in vain. —**тщётность,** *n.f.* futility.

тщи́ться *v.r. impfv.* (*with inf.*) to try (to); endeavor (to); take pains (to).

ты [*gen. & acc.* **тебя́**; *dat. & prepl.* **тебе́**; *instr.* **тобо́й** *or* **тобо́ю**] *pers. pron., 2nd person sing.* you (*familiar*). —**быть с** (+ *instr.*) **на ты,** to address each other as "ты" (*as opposed to* "вы").

ты́кать[1] *v. impfv.* [*pfv.* **ткнуть;** *pres.* **ты́чу, ты́чешь**] *colloq.* **1,** to stick; thrust. **2,** to poke; jab. —**ты́каться,** *refl., colloq.* **1,** (*with* **в** + *acc.*) to bang into. **2,** (*with instr.*) to stick; poke (one's nose, head, etc.) into. **3,** to rush about; bustle about.

ты́кать[2] *v. impfv.* [*pres.* **ты́каю, ты́каешь**] *colloq.* to address someone using the familiar pronoun **ты.**

ты́ква *n.* pumpkin. —**ты́квенный,** *adj.* pumpkin (*attrib.*).

тыл [*2nd loc.* **тылу́;** *pl.* **тылы́**] *n., mil.* **1,** rear. **2,** rear services. —**тылово́й,** *adj.* rear.

ты́льный *adj.* rear; back. —**ты́льная сторона́ руки́,** back of the hand.

тын *n.* paling; fence.

ты́сяча *numeral* thousand.

тысячекра́тный *adj.* thousandfold.

тысячеле́тие *n.* **1,** millennium. **2,** thousandth anniversary.

тысячеле́тний *adj.* **1,** thousand-year (*attrib.*). **2,** thousand-year-old.

ты́сячная *n., decl. as an adj.* thousandth: одна́ ты́сячная, one-thousandth.

ты́сячный *ordinal numeral* thousandth. —*adj.* consisting of many thousands: ты́сячная толпа́, a crowd of many thousands.

тычи́нка *n.* stamen.

тычо́к [*gen.* **-чка́**] *n., colloq.* **1,** poke; jab. **2,** something sticking up in the air.

тьма *n.* **1,** darkness. **2,** (*with gen.*) *colloq.* a host (of); a multitude (of).

тьфу *interj.* bah!; phooey!

тюбете́йка [*gen. pl.* **-те́ек**] *n.* skullcap (*worn in Central Asia*).

тю́бик *n.* tube (*for glue, toothpaste, etc.*).

тю́бинг *n.* tubing; piping.

тюк [*gen.* **тюка́**] *n.* **1,** bale. **2,** bundle.

тю́кать *v. impfv.* [*pfv.* **тю́кнуть**] *colloq.* to bang.

тю́левый *adj.* tulle.

тюле́невый *adj.* **1,** seal (*attrib.*). **2,** sealskin.

тюле́ний [*fem.* **-нья**] *adj.* seal (*attrib.*).

тюле́нь *n.m.* seal (*sea animal*).

тюль *n.m.* tulle.

тюльпа́н *n.* tulip. —**тюльпа́нный,** *adj.* tulip (*attrib.*).

тюрба́н *n.* turban.

тюрбо́ *n. indecl.* turbot.

тюре́мный *adj.* prison (*attrib.*); jail (*attrib.*). —**тюре́мное заключе́ние,** imprisonment.

тюре́мщик *n.* jailer.

тю́ркский *adj.* Turkic.

тюрьма́ [*pl.* **тю́рьмы, тю́рем**] *n.* jail; prison.

тюфя́к [*gen.* **тюфяка́**] *n.* straw mattress.

тя́вкать *v. impfv.* [*pfv.* **тя́вкнуть**] to yelp.

тяг *n., in* **дать тя́гу,** *colloq.* to take to one's heels; make tracks.

тя́га *n.* **1,** pulling; towing. **2,** pulling power; traction. **3,** thrust (*of an engine*). **4,** rod: соедини́тельная тя́га, connecting rod. **5,** draft (*of a chimney*). **6,** (*with* **к**) bent (for); craving (for).

тяга́ться *v.r. impfv.* [*pfv.* **потяга́ться**] (*with* **с** + *instr.*) to compete (with); contend (with); vie (with).

тяга́ч [*gen.* **тягача́**] *n.* tractor (*for hauling trailers*). —**артиллери́йский тяга́ч,** artillery mover. —**тяга́ч с прице́пом,** tractor-trailer.

тя́гло *n.* **1,** *hist.* tax; impost; assessment. **2,** [*also,* **живо́е тя́гло**] draft animals.

тя́гловый *adj.* **1,** *hist.* taxed. **2,** (*of animals*) draft.

тя́глый *adj.* (*of animals*) draft.

тя́говый *adj.* **1,** tractive. **2,** used to haul: тя́говый кана́т, hauling rope.

тя́гостный *adj.* **1,** burdensome; onerous. **2,** painful; distressing.

тя́гость *n.f.* burden: быть в тя́гость (+ *dat.*), to be a burden (to).

тягота́ [*pl.* **тя́готы**] *n.* **1,** burden. **2,** *pl.* (*with gen.*) the rigors (of): тя́готы пути́, the rigors of traveling.

тяготе́ние *n.* **1,** *physics* gravity. **2,** (*with* **к**) gravitation (toward). **3,** (*with* **к**) *fig.* bent (for); liking (for).

тяготе́ть *v. impfv.* **1,** (*with* **к**) to gravitate (toward); be drawn (to). **2,** (*with* **над**) to hang over; tower over. **3,** *fig.* (*with* **над**) to hang over; weigh upon.

тяготи́ть *v. impfv.* [*pres.* **-гощу́, -готи́шь**] **1,** to burden; weigh down. **2,** (*of an article of clothing*) to bother; make uncomfortable. —**тяготи́ться,** *refl.* (*with instr.*) to be burdened (by); feel (something) as a burden.

тягу́честь *n.f.* **1,** stretchability. **2,** malleability. **3,** viscosity.

тягу́чий *adj.* **1,** stretchable. **2,** malleable; ductile. **3,** viscous. **4,** *fig.* slow; drawn-out. **5,** *fig.* dull; boring; monotonous.

тя́жба *n., obs.* lawsuit; litigation.

тяжеле́ть *v. impfv.* to become heavy; grow heavy.

тяжело́ *adv.* **1,** heavily. **2,** gravely; seriously; severely. —*adj., used predicatively* (*often with dat.*) **1,** hard; difficult. **2,** miserable; wretched. **3,** grievous; painful.

тяжелоатле́т *n.* **1,** wrestler. **2,** weightlifter.

тяжелове́с *n., sports* heavyweight.

тяжелове́сный *adj.* heavy; ponderous.

тяжёлый *adj.* **1,** heavy. **2,** hard; difficult. **3,** grave; serious; severe. **4,** painful; grievous; distressing. **5,** (*of thoughts, a feeling, odor, etc.*) oppressive. **6,** (*of a style of writing*) ponderous.

тя́жесть *n.f.* **1,** weight. **2,** load. **3,** *physics* gravity. **4,** heaviness. **5,** gravity; severity.

тя́жкий *adj.* **1,** *obs.* heavy. **2,** grave; severe. **3,** distressing. —**пусти́ться во все тя́жкие, 1,** to let oneself go. **2,** to go all out.

тяну́ть *v. impfv.* [*pfv.* **потяну́ть;** *pres.* **тяну́, тя́нешь**] **1,** to pull; tug. **2,** to haul; tow. **3,** to stretch; extend. **4,** to draw; attract. **5,** *colloq.* to drag (someone) somewhere against his will. **6,** (*with* **с** + *instr.*) to delay: тяну́ть с отве́том, to delay in answering. **7,** [*impfv. only*] to drag out; prolong. **8,** [*impfv. only*] to sustain; prolong (a note, song, etc.). **9,** (*of a chimney*) to draw. **10,** to sustain oneself; subsist. **11,** *usu. impers.* to blow gently; waft. **12,** to weigh (so much). **13,** *impers.* to long to: его́ тя́нет домо́й, he is longing to go home. —**тяну́ться,** *refl.* [*impfv. only*] **1,** to stretch. **2,** to stretch; extend (*over a distance*). **3,** [*pfv.* **потяну́ться**] (*with* **за** *or* **к**) to reach for; reach out for. **4,** to follow along; follow in succession. **5,** to move slowly along. **6,** to last; drag on. **7,** (*with* **к**) to be drawn toward. **8,** (*of clouds, smoke, etc.*) to drift. **9,** (*with* **за** + *instr.*) *colloq.* to try to keep up with.

тяну́чка *n.* taffy.

тя́пка [*gen. pl.* **-пок**] *n.* chopping knife; cleaver.

тя́тя *n.m., colloq.* dad; pop.

У

У, у *n. neut.* twentieth letter of the Russian alphabet.

у *prep., with gen.* **1,** by; at; near: стоя́ть у окна́, to stand at/by/near the window. **2,** at the home of: жить у родны́х, to live with one's relatives. **3,** *indicating possession:* у меня́ три бра́та, I have three brothers. **4,** from: узна́ть что́-нибудь у сосе́да, to find out something from one's neighbor.

у- *prefix* **1,** *indicating movement away:* убега́ть, to run away. **2,** *indicating the imparting of a quality or attribute:* удлиня́ть, to lengthen; углубля́ть, to deepen. **3,** *indicating reduction:* убавля́ть, to reduce; ушива́ть, to take in. **4,** *indicating covering of a surface:* усыпа́ть, to strew; bestrew; устила́ть, to cover; overlay.

уба́вить [*infl.* **-влю, -вишь**] *v., pfv. of* **убавля́ть.** **уба́виться,** *refl., pfv. of* **убавля́ться.**

убавля́ть *v. impfv.* [*pfv.* **уба́вить**] **1,** to reduce; lower. **2,** *in* убавля́ть в ве́се, *colloq.* to lose weight. —**убавля́ться,** *refl.* **1,** to be reduced in size; become smaller. **2,** to decrease; diminish.

убаю́кать *v., pfv. of* **баю́кать** *and* **убаю́кивать.**

убаю́кивать *v. impfv.* [*pfv.* **убаю́кать**] **1,** to lull to sleep. **2,** *fig.* to lull.

убега́ть *v. impfv.* [*pfv.* **убежа́ть**] **1,** to run away; flee. **2,** to escape. **3,** [*impfv. only*] (*of inanimate objects*) to extend; retreat; disappear (into the distance).

убеди́тельно *adv.* **1,** convincingly; persuasively. **2,** earnestly: убеди́тельно прошу́ вас, I urge you; I beg you.

убеди́тельность *n.f.* persuasiveness.

убеди́тельный *adj.* **1,** convincing; persuasive. **2,** (*of a request*) urgent; earnest.

убеди́ть [*infl.* **-ди́шь, -ди́т;** *1st person sing. not used*] *v., pfv. of* **убежда́ть.** —**убеди́ться,** *refl., pfv. of* **убежда́ться.**

убежа́ть [*infl. like* **бежа́ть**] *v., pfv. of* **убега́ть.**

убежда́ть *v. impfv.* [*pfv.* **убеди́ть**] **1,** (*with* **в** + *prepl.*) to convince (of). **2,** (*with inf.*) to persuade (to). **3,** [*impfv. only*] to try to persuade; urge. —**убежда́ться,** *refl.* (*with* **в** + *prepl. or a dependent clause*) **1,** to become convinced (of *or* that). **2,** to make sure (of *or* that). **3,** *in* **сам убеди́ться,** to see for oneself.

убежде́ние *n.* **1,** persuasion. **2,** belief; conviction.

убеждённо *adv.* with conviction. —**убеждённость,** *n.f.* conviction; certainty.

убеждённый *adj.* **1,** convinced. **2,** staunch; confirmed.

убе́жище *n.* **1,** refuge. **2,** asylum: пра́во убе́жища, right of asylum. **3,** *mil.* shelter; dugout.

убере́чь *v. pfv.* [*infl. like* **бере́чь**] to protect.

убива́ть *v. impfv.* [*pfv.* **уби́ть**] to kill. —**убива́ться,** *refl., colloq.* **1,** to be killed. **2,** to hurt oneself. **3,** [*impfv. only*] to work oneself to the bone; "kill oneself". **4,** [*impfv. only*] to grieve; mourn.

уби́йственный *adj.* **1,** deadly. **2,** murderous; unbearable. **3,** (*of a result or consequences*) disastrous. **4,** (*of news, criticism, a look, etc.*) devastating.

уби́йство *n.* murder; assassination.

уби́йца *n.m. & f.* killer; murderer; assassin.

убира́ть *v. impfv.* [*pfv.* **убра́ть**] **1,** to take away; remove. **2,** to put away. **3,** to delete; take out. **4,** to clean up; tidy up; straighten up. **5,** *in* убра́ть со стола́, to clear the table. **6,** to make (a bed). **7,** *colloq.* to take in (a garment). **8,** to gather in; harvest. **9,** to decorate; adorn. —**убира́ться,** *refl., colloq.* **1,** to clear out; beat it; vamoose. **2,** to clean up; tidy up.

уби́тый *adj.* **1,** killed; murdered. **2,** *fig.* crushed (*in spirit*): уби́тый го́рем, heartbroken; broken-hearted. —*n.* dead man; person who has been killed. —**спать как уби́тый,** to sleep like a log.

уби́ть [*infl.* **убью́, убьёшь**] *v., pfv. of* **убива́ть.** —**уби́ться,** *refl., pfv. of* **убива́ться.**

ублажа́ть *v. impfv.* [*pfv.* **ублажи́ть**] *colloq.* to indulge; cater to.

ублю́док [*gen.* **-дка**] *n., colloq.* **1,** cur; mongrel. **2,** cur (*contemptible person*).

убо́гий *adj.* **1,** wretched; squalid. **2,** crippled; disfigured. **3,** *fig.* empty; sterile.

убо́гость *n.f.* **1,** utter poverty; squalor. **2,** *fig.* emptiness; sterility; poverty.

убо́жество *n.* **1,** utter poverty; squalor. **2,** *fig.* emptiness; sterility; poverty. **3,** *obs.* physical disability; deformity.

убо́й *n.* slaughtering; slaughter (*of animals*). —**корми́ть (как) на убо́й,** to stuff to the gills. —**посыла́ть (кого́-нибудь) на убо́й,** to send off to be slaughtered.

убо́йный *adj.* **1,** (*of animals*) to be slaughtered; intended for slaughter; (*of a place*) slaughtering (*attrib.*). **2,** *mil.* (*of power, energy, etc.*) destructive; lethal.

убо́р *n., archaic* attire. —**головно́й убо́р,** headdress.

убо́ристый *adj.* (*of writing, type, etc.*) close.

убо́рка *n.* **1,** cleaning up; tidying up. **2,** gathering in; harvesting.

убо́рная *n., decl. as an adj.* **1,** lavatory; washroom. **2,** *theat.* dressing room.

убо́рочный *adj.* harvesting (*attrib.*). —**убо́рочная маши́на,** harvester.

убо́рщик *n.* janitor; porter. —**убо́рщица,** *n.* cleaning woman; maid.

убра́нство *n.* **1,** furnishings. **2,** *obs.* dress; attire.
убра́ть [*infl. like* **брать**] *v., pfv. of* **убира́ть.** —**убра́ться,** *refl., pfv. of* **убира́ться.**
убыва́ть *v. impfv.* [*pfv.* **убы́ть**] **1,** to decrease; wane; recede; subside. **2,** to leave; take leave.
у́быль *n.f.* **1,** decrease. **2,** loss. —**идти́ на у́быль,** to wane; ebb; subside.
убы́ток [*gen.* **-тка**] *n.* **1,** loss: продава́ть в убы́ток (*or* с убы́тком), to sell at a loss. **2,** *pl.* losses; damages.
убы́точный *adj.* unprofitable.
убы́ть [*infl.* **убу́ду, убу́дешь;** *past* **у́был, убыла́, у́было**] *v., pfv. of* **убыва́ть.**
уважа́емый *adj.* **1,** respected; honored. **2,** (*in direct address or salutations*) dear.
уважа́ть *v. impfv.* to respect.
уваже́ние *n.* respect. —**с уваже́нием,** sincerely yours (*in letters*).
уважи́тельный *adj.* **1,** valid; legitimate. **2,** respectful; deferential.
ува́жить *v. pfv., colloq.* **1,** to comply with; honor (a request). **2,** to humor; be nice to.
у́валень [*gen.* **-льня**] *n.m., colloq.* lout; lummox.
ува́риваться *v.r. impfv.* [*pfv.* **увари́ться**] *colloq.* to be thoroughly cooked.
увари́ться [*infl.* **ува́рится**] *v.r., pfv. of* **ува́риваться.**
уве́домить [*infl.* **-млю, -мишь**] *v., pfv. of* **уведомля́ть.**
уведомле́ние *n.* notification; notice.
уведомля́ть *v. impfv.* [*pfv.* **уве́домить**] to notify; inform.
увезти́ [*infl. like* **везти́**] *v., pfv. of* **увози́ть.**
увекове́чение *n.* immortalization; perpetuation.
увекове́чивать *v. impfv.* [*pfv.* **увекове́чить**] **1,** to immortalize. **2,** to perpetuate.
увеличе́ние *n.* **1,** increase. **2,** magnification; *photog.* enlargement.
увели́чивать *v. impfv.* [*pfv.* **увели́чить**] **1,** to increase. **2,** to magnify; *photog.* enlarge. —**увели́чиваться,** *refl.* to increase; grow.
увеличи́тель *n.m., photog.* enlarger.
увеличи́тельный *adj.* magnifying. —**увеличи́тельный аппара́т,** enlarger. —**увеличи́тельное стекло́,** magnifying glass.
увели́чить *v., pfv. of* **увели́чивать.** —**увели́читься,** *refl., pfv. of* **увели́чиваться.**
увенча́ть *v., pfv. of* **венча́ть** (*in sense #1*) *and* **уве́нчивать.** —**увенча́ться,** *refl., pfv. of* **венча́ться** (*in sense #1*) *and* **уве́нчиваться.**
уве́нчивать *v. impfv.* [*pfv.* **увенча́ть**] to crown. —**уве́нчиваться,** *refl.* **1,** *obs.* to be crowned. **2,** (*with instr.*) to culminate (in): увенча́ться успе́хом, to succeed; be crowned with success.
увере́ние *n.* assurance.
уве́ренность *n.f.* **1,** confidence. **2,** assurance; certainty.
уве́ренный *adj.* [*short form* **уве́рен, -ена**] **1,** sure; certain; confident. **2,** [*usu. short form*] (*with* **в** + *prepl.*) sure (of); certain (of).
уве́рить *v., pfv. of* **уверя́ть.** —**уве́риться,** *refl., pfv. of* **уверя́ться.**
уверну́ться *v.r., pfv. of* **увёртываться.**
уве́ровать *v. pfv.* [*infl.* **-рую, -руешь**] (*with* **в** + *acc.*) to come to believe (in).
увёртка [*gen. pl.* **-ток**] *n., colloq.* subterfuge; dodge; ruse; trick.
увёртливый *adj.* shifty; evasive.
увёртываться *v.r. impfv.* [*pfv.* **уверну́ться**] (*with* **от**) to evade; dodge.
увертю́ра *n., music* overture.
уверя́ть *v. impfv.* [*pfv.* **уве́рить**] to assure. —**уверя́ться,** *refl.* **1,** to make sure. **2,** to become convinced.
увеселе́ние *n.* entertainment; amusement.
увеселительный *adj.* amusement (*attrib.*); entertainment (*attrib.*); pleasure (*attrib.*).
увеселя́ть *v. impfv.* to entertain; amuse.
уве́систый *adj.* weighty; heavy.
увести́ [*infl. like* **вести́**] *v., pfv. of* **уводи́ть.**
уве́чить *v. impfv.* to mutilate; maim.
уве́чье *n.* (serious) injury.
уве́шивать *v. impfv.* [*pfv.* **уве́шать**] to hang; cover with hangings: уве́шать сте́ну карти́нами, to hang a wall with pictures.
увеща́ние *n.* admonition; exhortation; remonstrance.
увещева́ть *v. impfv.* to admonish; exhort; remonstrate. *Also,* **увеща́ть.**
увива́ть *v. impfv.* [*pfv.* **уви́ть**] to wind around; twine around. —**увива́ться,** *refl.* [*impfv. only*] *colloq.* to hang around.
увида́ть *v. pfv., used only in the past tense, colloq.* to see; catch sight of. —**увида́ться,** *refl., colloq.* to see each other.
уви́деть *v. pfv.* [*infl.* **уви́жу, уви́дишь**] **1,** *pfv. of* **ви́деть. 2,** to catch sight of. —**уви́деться,** *refl., pfv. of* **ви́деться.**
уви́ливать *v. impfv.* [*pfv.* **увильну́ть**] (*with* **от**) *colloq.* **1,** to avoid; dodge. **2,** to evade; get out of (*doing something*). **3,** [*impfv. only*] to try to get out of.
уви́ть [*infl. like* **вить**] *v., pfv. of* **увива́ть.**
увлажне́ние *n.* **1,** moistening. **2,** moisture.
увлажня́ть *v. impfv.* [*pfv.* **увлажни́ть**] to moisten; dampen; humidify.
увлека́тельный *adj.* fascinating; absorbing.
увлека́ть *v. impfv.* [*pfv.* **увле́чь**] **1,** to carry away; carry off. **2,** *fig.* to carry away; engross. **3,** *fig.* to fascinate; enthrall. **4,** *fig.* to enchant; captivate. —**увлека́ться,** *refl.* **1,** (*with instr.*) to develop an enthusiasm for. **2,** (*with instr.*) to become engrossed in; be wrapped up in. **3,** (*with instr.*) to fall for; become infatuated with. **4,** to get carried away.
увлека́ющийся *adj.* easily carried away; easily falling in love.
увлече́ние *n.* **1,** enthusiasm. **2,** (*with instr.*) passion (for); fascination (with). **3,** (*with instr.*) infatuation (with); crush (on).
увлечённый *adj.* enthusiastic. —**увлечённо,** *adv.* with enthusiasm.
увле́чь [*infl. like* **влечь**] *v., pfv. of* **увлека́ть.** —**увле́чься,** *refl., pfv. of* **увлека́ться.**
уво́д *n.* **1,** evacuation; withdrawal. **2,** theft.
уводи́ть *v. impfv.* [*pfv.* **увести́;** *pres.* **увожу́, уво́дишь**] **1,** to lead away; take away. **2,** to carry off; steal.
уво́з *n.* **1,** carting away. **2,** abduction.
увози́ть *v. impfv.* [*pfv.* **увезти́;** *pres.* **увожу́, уво́зишь**] **1,** to take away (*by conveyance*). **2,** to abduct.
увола́кивать *v. impfv.* [*pfv.* **уволо́чь**] *colloq.* **1,** to drag away. **2,** to carry off; abduct. **3,** to make off with; steal.
уво́лить *v., pfv. of* **увольня́ть.** —**уво́литься,** *refl., pfv. of* **увольня́ться.**
уволо́чь [*infl. like* **волочь**] *v., pfv. of* **увола́кивать.**

увольне́ние *n.* discharge; dismissal.
увольни́тельный *adj., in* **увольни́тельная запи́ска; увольни́тельное свиде́тельство,** pass; written leave of absence.
увольня́ть *v. impfv.* [*pfv.* **уво́лить**] **1,** to dismiss; discharge; lay off; fire. **2,** (*with* **от**) to spare (from); relieve (of). —**увольня́ться,** *refl.* **1,** to be discharged; get one's discharge. **2,** to be released; be excused.
увы́ *interj.* alas!
увяда́ть *v. impfv.* [*pfv.* **увя́нуть**] to fade; wither.
увя́дший *adj.* faded; withered.
увяза́ть[1] [*infl.* **увяжу́, увя́жешь**] *v., pfv. of* **увя́зывать.** —**увяза́ться,** *refl., pfv. of* **увя́зываться.**
увяза́ть[2] *v. impfv.* [*pfv.* **увя́знуть;** *pres.* **-за́ю, -за́ешь**] **1,** to get stuck. **2,** *fig.* to become mired; get bogged down.
увя́зка *n.* **1,** tying up. **2,** *fig.* coordination; tying together.
увя́знуть [*past* **увя́з, -ла**] *v., pfv. of* **вя́знуть** *and* **увяза́ть**[2].
увя́зывать *v. impfv.* [*pfv.* **увяза́ть**] **1,** to tie up; pack up. **2,** *fig.* to coordinate; reconcile; square. —**увя́зываться,** *refl.* **1,** (*with* **с** + *instr.*) to tie in with. **2,** (*with* **за** + *instr.*) *colloq.* to follow; haunt; dog.
увя́нуть [*past* **увя́л, увя́ла**] *v., pfv. of* **вя́нуть** *and* **увяда́ть.**
угада́ть *v., pfv. of* **уга́дывать.**
уга́дчик *n., colloq.* guesser.
уга́дывать *v. impfv.* [*pfv.* **угада́ть**] to guess.
уга́дываться *v.r. impfv.* to be sensed; be felt; be seen.
уга́р *n.* **1,** carbon-monoxide fumes. **2,** carbon-monoxide poisoning. **3,** *fig.* ecstasy; fever; intoxication.
уга́рный *adj.* **1,** carbon-monoxide (*attrib.*); containing carbon monoxide. **2,** *fig.* feverish; frenzied. —**уга́рный газ,** carbon monoxide.
угаса́ние *n.* fading; waning; dying out.
угаса́ть *v. impfv.* [*pfv.* **уга́снуть**] **1,** to go out; die out. **2,** *fig.* to fade; wane; ebb.
уга́снуть [*past* **уга́с, -ла**] *v., pfv. of* **га́снуть** *and* **угаса́ть.**
углево́д *n.* carbohydrate.
углеводоро́д *n.* hydrocarbon.
углекислота́ *n.* carbonic acid.
углеки́слый *adj.* carbonate (of): углеки́слый ка́льций, calcium carbonate; углеки́слый на́трий, sodium carbonate. —**углеки́слый газ,** carbon dioxide. —**углеки́слая соль,** carbonate.
углеко́п *n., obs.* coal miner.
углеро́д *n.* carbon.
углеро́дистый *adj.* **1,** carbon: углеро́дистая сталь, carbon steel. **2,** carbide (of): углеро́дистый ка́льций, calcium carbide.
углова́тый *adj.* **1,** angular. **2,** *fig.* awkward.
углово́й *adj.* **1,** corner (*attrib.*). **2,** angular: углова́я ско́рость, angular velocity.
углуби́ть [*infl.* **-блю́, -би́шь**] *v., pfv. of* **углубля́ть.** —**углуби́ться,** *refl., pfv. of* **углубля́ться.**
углубле́ние *n.* **1,** deepening. **2,** hollow; depression; dip.
углублённый *adj.* **1,** sunken. **2,** *fig.* in-depth. **3,** *fig.* (*with* **в** + *acc.*) engrossed (in).
углубля́ть *v. impfv.* [*pfv.* **углуби́ть**] to deepen. —**углубля́ться,** *refl.* **1,** to deepen; become deeper. **2,** (*with* **в** + *acc.*) to go deep (into); sink (into). **3,** *fig.* (*with* **в** + *acc.*) to go deep into; delve (into). **4,** *fig.* (*with* **в** + *acc.*) to become absorbed (in). **5,** *in* **углуби́ться в себя́,** to withdraw into oneself.
угляде́ть *v. pfv.* [*infl.* **-жу́, -ди́шь**] *colloq.* **1,** to see; spot. **2,** (*with* **за** + *instr.*) to look after; keep an eye on.
угна́ть [*infl. like* **гнать**] *v., pfv. of* **угоня́ть.** —**угна́ться,** *refl.* (*with* **за** + *instr.*) [*usu. in neg. sentences*] to keep up (with); keep pace (with).
угнезди́ться *v.r. pfv., colloq.* to nestle.
угнета́тель *n.m.* oppressor.
угнета́ть *v. impfv.* **1,** to oppress. **2,** to depress.
угнете́ние *n.* **1,** oppression. **2,** depression; dejection.
угнетённый *adj.* **1,** oppressed. **2,** depressed.
угова́ривать *v. impfv.* [*pfv.* **уговори́ть**] **1,** to persuade. **2,** [*impfv. only*] to try to persuade; coax. —**угова́риваться,** *refl., colloq.* to agree; arrange.
угово́р *n.* **1,** *often pl.* persuasion; attempt at persuasion: угово́ры на него́ не де́йствуют, attempts to persuade him are useless. **2,** *colloq.* agreement; arrangement; understanding.
уговори́ть *v., pfv. of* **угова́ривать.** —**уговори́ться,** *refl., pfv. of* **угова́риваться.**
уго́да *n., in* **в уго́ду** (+ *dat.*), (in order) to please.
угоди́ть *v. pfv.* [*infl.* **угожу́, угоди́шь**] **1,** *pfv. of* **угожда́ть. 2,** (*with various prepositions*) *colloq.* to fall (into); step (into); land (in); end up (in). **3,** (*with* **в** + *acc.*) *colloq.* to hit; strike: пу́ля угоди́ла ему́ в плечо́, the bullet struck him in the shoulder. **4,** (*with instr.*) *colloq.* to cause to strike; bang: угоди́ть голово́й в стекло́, to bang into the glass with one's head.
уго́дливый *adj.* obsequious. —**уго́дливость,** *n.f.* obsequiousness.
уго́дник *n.* **1,** *colloq.* sycophant. **2,** saint.
уго́дничать *v. impfv.* (*with* **пе́ред**) *colloq.* to curry favor (with); play up to.
уго́дничество *n.* obsequiousness; servility.
уго́дно *predicate (with dat.)* wished; desired: что вам уго́дно?, what would you like? Как вам уго́дно, as you wish; just as you like. Ско́лько душе́ уго́дно, as much as one's heart desires. —*particle* any-; -ever one likes: что уго́дно, anything/whatever you like; где (*or* куда́) уго́дно, anywhere/wherever you like. Како́й уго́дно (+ *noun*), any ...you like. —**е́сли уго́дно,** perhaps.
уго́дный *adj.* (*with dat.*) pleasing (to).
уго́дье *n., often pl.* land (*with reference to its use*): травяно́е уго́дье, grassland; лесны́е уго́дья, forests.
угожда́ть *v. impfv.* [*pfv.* **угоди́ть**] (*with dat. or* **на** + *acc.*) to please. *See also* **угоди́ть.**
у́гол [*gen.* **угла́;** *2nd loc.* **углу́**] *n.* **1,** corner: в углу́, in the corner; на углу́, on the (street) corner. **2,** angle. **3,** place to live: име́ть свой у́гол, to have a home of one's own. **4,** (*with an adj.*) remote place: глухо́й у́гол, out-of-the-way place; медве́жий у́гол, godforsaken place. —**за угло́м,** around the corner. —**из-за угла́, 1,** from around the corner. **2,** from behind; without warning. —**из угла́ в у́гол,** (*with verbs of walking or pacing*) up and down; back and forth. —**под угло́м в** (+ *acc.*), at an angle of. —**по угла́м,** (*with verbs of talking or whispering*) in secret; in the corridors.
уголёк [*gen.* **-лька́**] *n.* small piece of coal.
уголо́вник *n.* criminal.
уголо́вный *adj.* criminal: уголо́вное пра́во, criminal law.
уголо́вщина *n., colloq.* **1,** criminal act. **2,** criminals; the underworld.
уголо́к [*gen.* **-лка́**] *n.* **1,** *dim. of* **у́гол. 2,** cozy corner;

nook. —**кра́сный уголо́к,** recreation and reading room.

у́голь [*gen.* **у́гля** *or* **угля́**; *pl.* **у́гли, у́глей** *or* **угле́й, у́глям** *or* **угля́м**] *n.m.* **1,** coal. **2,** (piece of) coal: горя́чие у́гли, live coals; live embers. —**быть** *or* **си́деть как на у́гольях,** to be on tenterhooks.

уго́льник *n.* **1,** try square. **2,** triangle (*drawing instrument*).

у́гольный *adj.* coal (*attrib.*). —**у́гольная кислота́,** carbonic acid.

у́гольщик *n.* coal miner.

угомони́ть *v. pfv., colloq.* to calm; calm down. —**угомони́ться,** *refl., colloq.* to calm down; become calm.

уго́н *n.* **1,** driving away; sending away. **2,** hijacking (*of an aircraft*).

угоня́ть *v. impfv.* [*pfv.* **угна́ть**] **1,** to drive away. **2,** *colloq.* to steal (cattle). **3,** to hijack (an aircraft).

угора́здить *v. pfv., colloq., impers.* **1,** to make; prompt; possess: как э́то вас угора́здило сде́лать э́то?, what on earth made you do it? **2,** (*used sarcastically*) to manage to: его́ угора́здило заболе́ть, he managed to get sick.

угора́ть *v. impfv.* [*pfv.* **угоре́ть**] **1,** to be overcome by fumes; get carbon-monoxide poisoning. **2,** *colloq.* to go mad.

угоре́лый *adj., colloq.* mad; crazy. —**бежа́ть как угоре́лый,** to run like mad.

угоре́ть [*infl.* **-рю́, -ри́шь**] *v., pfv. of* **угора́ть.**

у́горь [*gen.* **угря́**] *n.m.* **1,** eel. **2,** blackhead; *pl.* acne.

угости́ть [*infl.* **-щу́, -сти́шь**] *v., pfv. of* **угоща́ть.** —**угости́ться,** *refl., pfv. of* **угоща́ться.**

угото́вить *v. pfv.* [*infl.* **-влю, -вишь**] *obs.* to prepare.

угоща́ть *v. impfv.* [*pfv.* **угости́ть**] to treat: угоща́ть друзе́й обе́дом, to treat one's friends to dinner. —**угоща́ться,** *refl., colloq.* **1,** to partake oneself. Угоща́йтесь, пожа́луйста!, help yourself! **2,** (*with instr.*) to help oneself to.

угоще́ние *n.* **1,** entertaining; treating. **2,** food; refreshments.

угрева́тый *adj.* covered with blackheads; pimply.

угрожа́ть *v. impfv.* (*with dat.*) to threaten: угрожа́ть кому́-нибудь ору́жием, to threaten someone with a weapon. Стране́ угрожа́ет го́лод, the country is threatened with (*or* faces) famine.

угрожа́ющий *adj.* threatening; menacing.

угро́за *n.* threat; menace. —**ста́вить под угро́зу,** to endanger; jeopardize.

угрызе́ние *n., in* **угрызе́ния со́вести,** pangs of conscience.

угрю́мый *adj.* **1,** sullen; gloomy; morose. **2,** bleak; forbidding. —**угрю́мость,** *n.f.* sullenness; gloominess; moroseness.

уда́в *n.* boa (*snake*).

удава́ться *v.r. impfv.* [*pfv.* **уда́ться;** *pres.* **удаётся**] **1,** to be successful; be a success; turn out well. **2,** *impers.* (*with dat. and inf.*) to succeed: ему́ удало́сь доста́ть биле́ты, he succeeded in getting the tickets.

удави́ть *v. pfv.* [*infl.* **удавлю́, уда́вишь**] to strangle. —**удави́ться,** *refl., colloq.* to hang oneself.

удавле́ние *n.* strangling; strangulation.

удале́ние *n.* **1,** withdrawal. **2,** removal. **3,** extraction. **4,** distance.

удалённый *adj.* remote. —**удалённость,** *n.f.* remoteness; distance.

удале́ц [*gen.* **-льца́**] *n.* daring person.

удали́ть *v., pfv. of* **удаля́ть.** —**удали́ться,** *refl., pfv. of* **удаля́ться.**

удало́й *also,* **уда́лый** *adj.* **1,** bold; daring. **2,** dashing.

у́даль *n.f.* boldness; daring; bravado.

удальство́ *n., colloq.* = **у́даль.**

удаля́ть *v. impfv.* [*pfv.* **удали́ть**] **1,** to move away; move farther away. **2,** to remove; take away. **3,** to remove; force to leave: удаля́ть ученика́ из кла́сса, to send a pupil out of the room. **4,** to remove; extract (a tooth, splinter, etc.). —**удаля́ться,** *refl.* **1,** to move away. Удаля́ться от те́мы, to wander from the subject. **2,** (*with* **от**) to get away (from); isolate oneself (from). **3,** to withdraw; retire.

уда́р *n.* **1,** blow. **2,** stroke (*of a clock, bell, etc.*). **3,** *mil.* attack; thrust; strike; blow. **4,** *sports* shot; stroke. **5,** bolt (*of thunder or lightning*). **6,** *med.* stroke. **7,** *in* уда́р судьбы́, stroke of bad luck. —**быть в уда́ре,** *colloq.* to be in good form. —**быть под уда́ром,** to be vulnerable; be under the gun. —**ста́вить под уда́р,** to endanger; jeopardize.

ударе́ние *n.* **1,** accent; stress. **2,** accent mark. **3,** *fig.* emphasis: де́лать ударе́ние на (+ *prepl.*), to stress; emphasize.

уда́рить *v., pfv. of* **ударя́ть.** —**уда́риться,** *refl., pfv. of* **ударя́ться.**

уда́рник *n.* **1,** firing pin. **2,** drummer. **3,** shock worker; pace-setting worker.

уда́рный *adj.* **1,** striking (*attrib.*); percussion (*attrib.*). **2,** shock (*attrib.*): уда́рная волна́/брига́да, shock wave/brigade. **3,** urgent. **4,** (*of a syllable*) stressed.

ударя́ть *v. impfv.* [*pfv.* **уда́рить**] **1,** to strike; hit: уда́рить ло́шадь кнуто́м, to strike the horse with a whip. Уда́рить кого́-нибудь по лицу́, to slap someone in the face. **2,** (*with instr.*) to bang; pound: уда́рить кулако́м по́ столу, to bang/pound one's fist on the table. **3,** (*of an illness, emotion, etc.*) to strike. **4,** (*with* **на** + *acc. or* **по**) to attack. *Also intrans.:* уда́рить со всех сторо́н, to attack from all sides. **5,** *fig.* (*with* **по**) to strike a blow against; combat. **6,** (*with* **в** + *acc.*) to beat (a drum); ring (a bell); sound (an alarm). **7,** to ring out; resound. Уда́рил гром, there was a clap of thunder. **8,** (*of a clock*) to strike (a certain hour). —**не уда́рить лицо́м в грязь,** not disgrace oneself. —**ударя́ть в го́лову** (+ *dat.*), (*of alcoholic beverages*) to go to one's head. —**уда́рить по рука́м,** to strike a bargain.

ударя́ться *v.r. impfv.* [*pfv.* **уда́риться**] **1,** (*with* **о** *or* **в** + *acc.*) to strike; bang (into *or* against); bump (into). Ло́дка уда́рилась о скалу́, the boat struck a rock. Уда́риться голово́й о дверь, to bang one's head on the door. **2,** (*with* **в** + *acc.*) *colloq.* to break into; burst into; give way to (tears, panic, etc.). —**уда́риться в кра́йность,** to go to an extreme.

уда́ться [*infl. like* **дать;** *past* **уда́лся, -ла́сь, -ло́сь**] *v.r., pfv. of* **удава́ться.**

уда́ча *n.* **1,** success. **2,** good luck.

уда́чливый *adj.* **1,** lucky. **2,** successful.

уда́чник *n., colloq.* lucky man.

уда́чно *adv.* **1,** successfully. **2,** well. **3,** aptly. —*adj., used predicatively* fortunate: уда́чно, что..., it is fortunate that...

уда́чный *adj.* **1,** successful. **2,** apt; appropriate; felicitous.

удва́ивать *v. impfv.* [*pfv.* **удво́ить**] **1,** to double. **2,** *fig.* to redouble. —**удва́иваться,** *refl.* to double.

удвое́ние *n.* doubling; redoubling.

удво́ить *v., pfv. of* **удва́ивать.** —**удво́иться,** *refl., pfv. of* **удва́иваться.**

уде́л *n.* **1,** *hist.* princely domain. **2,** fate; lot; destiny.

удели́ть [*infl.* **уделю́, удели́шь**] *v., pfv. of* **уделя́ть.**

уде́льный *adj., physics* specific: уде́льная теплота́, specific heat. —**уде́льный вес, 1,** specific gravity. **2,** relative amount (*as against a total*); proportion; percentage.

уделя́ть *v. impfv.* [*pfv.* **удели́ть**] **1,** to spare (a small amount of something). **2,** to give; devote (time, attention, etc.).

у́держ *n., colloq., in* **без у́держу, 1,** without restraint; with abandon. **2,** (*with verbs of crying*) uncontrollably. —**ему́** (*or* **на него́**) **нет у́держу,** there is nothing to stop him; there is no holding him back. —**не знать у́держу,** to know no restraint.

удержа́ние *n.* **1,** keeping; retention. **2,** holding back; withholding. **3,** deduction; withholding (*of money*).

удержа́ть [*infl.* **удержу́, уде́ржишь**] *v., pfv. of* **уде́рживать.** —**удержа́ться,** *refl., pfv. of* **уде́рживаться.**

уде́рживать *v. impfv.* [*pfv.* **удержа́ть**] **1,** to hold up; keep from falling. **2,** to restrain; hold back. **3,** to keep; retain. **4,** to deduct; withhold. —**уде́рживаться,** *refl.* **1,** to keep one's feet. **2,** to hold out. **3,** to restrain oneself. **4,** (*with* **от**) to keep (from); help: я не мог удержа́ться от сме́ха, I couldn't help laughing.

удесятеря́ть *v. impfv.* [*pfv.* **удесятери́ть**] to increase tenfold.

удешеви́ть [*infl.* **-влю́, -ви́шь**] *v., pfv. of* **удешевля́ть.**

удешевля́ть *v. impfv.* [*pfv.* **удешеви́ть**] to reduce the price of.

удиви́тельно *adv.* **1,** surprisingly; remarkably. **2,** marvelously. **3,** extremely. —*adj., used predicatively* surprising: удиви́тельно, что... it is surprising that...

удиви́тельный *adj.* **1,** surprising. **2,** wonderful; marvelous. **3,** remarkable.

удиви́ть [*infl.* **-влю́, -ви́шь**] *v., pfv. of* **удивля́ть.** —**удиви́ться,** *refl., pfv. of* **удивля́ться.**

удивле́ние *n.* surprise: к моему́ удивле́нию, to my surprise. —**на удивле́ние, 1,** first-rate. **2,** splendidly. **3,** *fol. by an adj. or adv.* surprisingly. **4,** *in* всем на удивле́ние, to the surprise of everyone.

удивлённый *adj.* surprised. —**удивлённо,** *adv.* in surprise.

удивля́ть *v. impfv.* [*pfv.* **удиви́ть**] to surprise. —**удивля́ться,** *refl.* (*with dat.*) to be surprised (at).

удила́ [*gen.* **уди́л**] *n. pl.* bit. —**закуси́ть удила́,** to take the bit in one's teeth.

уди́лище *n.* fishing rod.

уди́льщик *n.* angler.

удира́ть *v. impfv.* [*pfv.* **удра́ть**] *colloq.* to take off; run away.

уди́ть *v. impfv.* [*pres.* **ужу́, у́дишь**] to fish for: уди́ть ры́бу, to fish. —**уди́ться,** *refl.* (*of fish*) to bite.

удлине́ние *n.* **1,** lengthening. **2,** extension.

удлинённый *adj.* **1,** lengthened. **2,** oblong; elongated.

удлини́тель *n.m.* extension cord. —**удлини́тельный,** *adj.* extension (*attrib.*): удлини́тельный шнур, extension cord.

удлиня́ть *v. impfv.* [*pfv.* **удлини́ть**] **1,** to lengthen; make longer. **2,** to extend; prolong. —**удлиня́ться,** *refl.* to lengthen; become (*or* get) longer.

удму́рт *n.m.* [*fem.* **удму́ртка**] Udmurt (*one of a people inhabiting central European Russia*). —**удму́ртский,** *adj.* Udmurt.

удо́бно *adv.* comfortably. —*adj., used predicatively* **1,** (*with dat.*) comfortable: вам удо́бно?, are you comfortable? **2,** (*with dat.*) convenient: когда́ вам бу́дет удо́бно?, when will it be convenient for you? **3,** all right: удо́бно ли спроси́ть его́ об э́том?, is it all right to ask him about it?

удо́бный *adj.* [*short form* **-бен, -бна**] **1,** comfortable. **2,** convenient.

удо́бо- *prefix* easy to: удобочита́емый, easy to read; удобоисполни́мый, easy to carry out.

удобовари́мый *adj.* digestible. —**удобовари́мость,** *n.f.* digestiblity.

удобре́ние *n.* **1,** fertilization. **2,** fertilizer.

удобря́ть *v. impfv.* [*pfv.* **удо́брить**] to fertilize (soil).

удо́бство *n.* **1,** comfort. **2,** convenience: со все́ми удо́бствами, with all the conveniences.

удовлетворе́ние *n.* satisfaction; gratification.

удовлетворённый *adj.* satisfied; contented. —**удовлетворённость,** *n.f.* satisfaction; contentment.

удовлетвори́тельно *adv.* **1,** satisfactorily. **2,** (*as a school grade*) "satisfactory".

удовлетвори́тельный *adj.* satisfactory.

удовлетворя́ть *v. impfv.* [*pfv.* **удовлетвори́ть**] **1,** to satisfy; make (someone) content. **2,** to satisfy; assuage (one's hunger, curiosity, etc.). **3,** to grant; comply with (a wish, request, etc.). **4,** to meet; satisfy: удовлетворя́ть тре́бование, to meet a demand. Удовлетворя́ть тре́бованиям, to meet/satisfy/answer the requirements. **5,** (*with instr.*) to supply (with); furnish (with). —**удовлетворя́ться,** *refl.* (*with instr.*) to be satisfied (with).

удово́льствие *n.* pleasure. С удово́льствием!, with pleasure!; I'll be glad to! К о́бщему удово́льствию, to everyone's delight. —**жить в своё удово́льствие,** to live a life of ease.

удово́льствоваться *v.r., pfv. of* **дово́льствоваться.**

удо́д *n.* hoopoe.

удо́й *n.* **1,** yield of milk. **2,** milking.

удо́йный *adj.* (*of a cow*) giving much milk.

удорожа́ть *v. impfv.* [*pfv.* **удорожи́ть**] to raise the price of.

удоста́ивать *v. impfv.* [*pfv.* **удосто́ить**] **1,** (*with gen.*) to award; confer (a title, degree, etc.). **2,** (*with instr.*) to favor (with): он не удосто́ил нас отве́том, he did not favor us with an answer. —**удоста́иваться,** *refl.* **1,** (*with gen.*) to be awarded; be given; be granted (something). **2,** (*with inf.*) to have the honor of; have the good fortune to.

удостовере́ние *n.* **1,** certification; attestation. **2,** certificate. —**удостовере́ние ли́чности,** identity card.

удостоверя́ть *v. impfv.* [*pfv.* **удостове́рить**] **1,** to certify; attest. **2,** to witness (a signature). —**удостоверя́ться,** *refl.* (*with* **в** + *prepl. or a dependent clause*) to make sure (of *or* that).

удосто́ить *v., pfv. of* **удоста́ивать.** —**удосто́иться,** *refl., pfv. of* **удоста́иваться.**

удосу́живаться *v.r. impfv.* [*pfv.* **удосу́житься**] *colloq.* to find time (to); get around to.

удочеря́ть *v. impfv.* [*pfv.* **удочери́ть**] to adopt (a girl).

у́дочка [*gen. pl.* **-чек**] *n.* fishing rod (*with the line attached*). —**заки́нуть у́дочку,** to drop a hint; put out a feeler. —**пойма́ть на у́дочку,** to trick; hoodwink. —**попа́сться на у́дочку,** to swallow (*or* take) the bait.

удра́ть [*infl. like* **драть**] *v., pfv. of* **удира́ть.**

удружи́ть *v. pfv.* (*with dat.*) *colloq.* to do (someone) a favor.

удруча́ть *v. impfv.* [*pfv.* **удручи́ть**] to depress; dispirit.

удручённый *adj.* depressed; dejected; despondent.

удручи́ть *v., pfv. of* **удруча́ть.**

удуша́ть *v. impfv.* [*pfv.* **удуши́ть**] **1,** to suffocate; smother. **2,** *fig.* to stifle.

удуше́ние *n.* suffocation; asphyxiation.

удуши́ть [*infl.* **удушу́, уду́шишь**] *v., pfv. of* **удуша́ть.**

уду́шливый *adj.* stifling. —**уду́шливый газ,** choking gas.

уду́шье *n.* difficulty in breathing.

уедине́ние *n.* solitude; seclusion.

уединённый *adj.* solitary; secluded.

уединя́ть *v. impfv.* [*pfv.* **уедини́ть**] to seclude; isolate. —**уединя́ться,** *refl.* to withdraw; seclude oneself; closet oneself.

уе́зд *n., hist.* district. —**уе́здный,** *adj.* district (*attrib.*).

уезжа́ть *v. impfv.* [*pfv.* **уе́хать**] to leave; go away; depart (*by conveyance*).

уе́хать [*infl.* **уе́ду, уе́дешь**] *v., pfv. of* **уезжа́ть.**

уж[1] *adv.* = **уже́.** —*particle, used for emphasis:* э́то уж про́сто безобра́зие, it's simply disgraceful; не так уж хо́лодно сего́дня, it's not all that cold today.

уж[2] [*gen.* **ужа́**] *n.* any of several kinds of nonpoisonous snakes. —**обыкнове́нный уж,** grass snake. —**водяно́й уж,** water snake.

ужа́лить *v., pfv. of* **жа́лить.**

у́жас *n.* **1,** horror; terror. **2,** *pl.* horrors: у́жасы войны́, the horrors of war. **3,** *colloq.* horrible thing; horrible situation: про́сто у́жас!, it's simply horrible!

ужаса́ть *v. impfv.* [*pfv.* **ужасну́ть**] to terrify; horrify. —**ужаса́ться,** *refl.* to be terrified; be horrified.

ужа́сно *adv.* terribly; awfully. —*adj., used predicatively* terrible; awful: э́то ужа́сно, that's terrible; that's awful.

ужасну́ть *v., pfv. of* **ужаса́ть.** —**ужасну́ться,** *refl., pfv. of* **ужаса́ться.**

ужа́сный *adj.* terrible; horrible; frightful; awful; dreadful.

у́же *adj., comp. of* **у́зкий.**

уже́ *adv.* **1,** already. **2,** (*in interr. sentences*) yet. —**уже́ не,** no longer; any longer; anymore.

уже́ние *n.* fishing; angling.

ужива́ться *v.r. impfv.* [*pfv.* **ужи́ться**] (*with* **с** + *instr.*) to get along (with).

ужи́вчивый *adj.* easygoing; easy to get along with.

ужи́мка [*gen. pl.* **-мок**] *n., usu. pl.* grimace.

у́жин *n.* supper.

у́жинать *v. impfv.* [*pfv.* **поу́жинать**] to have supper.

ужи́ться [*infl. like* **жить;** *past* **ужи́лся, -ла́сь, -ло́сь**] *v.r., pfv. of* **ужива́ться.**

узаконе́ние *n.* **1,** legalization. **2,** *obs.* law; statute.

узако́нивать *v. impfv.* [*pfv.* **узако́нить**] to legalize; legitimize. *Also,* **узаконя́ть.**

узбе́к *n.m.* [*fem.* **-бе́чка**] *n.* Uzbek. —**узбе́кский,** *adj.* Uzbek.

узда́ [*pl.* **у́зды**] *n.* **1,** bridle. **2,** *fig.* restraint; check: держа́ть в узде́, to keep in check.

узде́чка [*gen. pl.* **-чек**] *n.* bridle.

у́зел [*gen.* **узла́**] *n.* **1,** knot. **2,** junction. **3,** *fig.* hub. **4,** bundle; pack. **5,** node. **6,** *naut.* knot (*measure of speed*). **7,** *mech.* unit.

узело́к [*gen.* **-лка́**] *n.* **1,** small knot. **2,** nodule.

у́зенький *adj., colloq.* narrow.

у́зкий *adj.* [*short form* **у́зок, узка́, у́зко, у́зки** *or* **узки́;** *comp.* **у́же**] **1,** narrow. **2,** (*of clothes, shoes, etc.*) tight: ю́бка мне узка́, the skirt is tight on me. **3,** *fig.* narrow-minded. —**у́зкое ме́сто,** bottleneck.

у́зко *adv.* **1,** tightly. **2,** *fig.* from a narrow perspective. —*adj., used predicatively* narrow; tight: здесь у́зко, it is narrow/tight in here.

узкоколе́йный *adj., R.R.* narrow-gauge.

узколо́бый *adj.* narrow-minded.

узлова́тый *adj.* (*of a rope, thread, etc.*) full of knots; knotted.

узлово́й *adj.* **1,** junction (*attrib.*): узлова́я ста́нция, (railway) junction. **2,** *fig.* key; pivotal: узлово́й вопро́с, key/ pivotal question.

узнава́ние *n.* recognition.

узнава́ть *v. impfv.* [*pfv.* **узна́ть;** *pres.* **узнаю́, узнаёшь**] **1,** to recognize. **2,** to find out; learn. **3,** to try to find out; inquire. **4,** to experience; know. **5,** to get to know.

узна́ть [*infl.* **узна́ю, узна́ешь**] *v., pfv. of* **узнава́ть.**

у́зник *n.* prisoner.

узо́р *n.* pattern; design. —**узо́рчатый,** *adj.* having a design; figured.

у́зость *n.f.* narrowness.

узре́ть *v. pfv.* [*infl.* **узрю́, у́зришь** *or* **узри́шь**] **1,** *pfv. of* **зреть**[2]. **2,** to see; realize; perceive.

узурпа́тор *n.* usurper. —**узурпа́ция,** *n.* usurpation.

узурпи́ровать *v. impfv. & pfv.* [*pres.* **-рую, -руешь**] to usurp.

у́зы [*gen.* **уз**] *n. pl.* bonds; ties: у́зы дру́жбы, bonds/ ties of friendship.

уйгу́р *n.m.* [*fem.* **-гу́рка**] Uigur (*one of a people inhabiting Central Asia and China*). —**уйгу́рский,** *adj.* Uigur.

у́йма *n., colloq.* (*with gen.*) a lot (of); heaps (of); tons (of).

уйти́ [*infl.* **уйду́, уйдёшь;** *past* **ушёл, ушла́, ушло́**] *v., pfv. of* **уходи́ть.**

ука́з *n.* decree; edict; ukase. —**не ука́з** (+ *dat.*), not such that it (*or* one) must be obeyed: никто́ ему́ не ука́з, he doesn't take orders from anyone.

указа́ние *n.* **1,** indication; indicating. **2,** *usu. pl.* instructions; directions.

ука́занный *adj.* indicated: на ука́занном ме́сте, at the place indicated.

указа́тель *n.m.* **1,** indicator; pointer. **2,** index. **3,** directory.

указа́тельный *adj.* serving to indicate. —**указа́тельное местоиме́ние,** demonstrative pronoun. —**указа́тельный па́лец,** index finger. —**указа́тельный столб,** signpost.

указа́ть [*infl.* **укажу́, ука́жешь**] *v., pfv. of* **ука́зывать.**

ука́зка [*gen. pl.* **-зок**] *n.* **1,** pointer. **2,** *colloq.* orders: по ука́зке (+ *gen.*), on orders from.

ука́зчик *n., colloq.* one who gives orders.

ука́зывать *v. impfv.* [*pfv.* **указа́ть**] **1,** to point (in a certain direction); (*with* **на** + *acc.*) point to; point at. **2,** to point out; indicate (a road, place, etc.). **3,** (*with* **на** + *acc.*) to point out (mistakes, shortcomings, etc.). **4,** to indicate (one's name, certain information, etc.).

уката́ть *v., pfv. of* **ука́тывать**[1]

укати́ть [*infl.* **укачу́, ука́тишь**] *v., pfv. of* **ука́тывать**[2]. —**укати́ться,** *refl., pfv. of* **ука́тываться.**

ука́тывать[1] *v. impfv.* [*pfv.* **уката́ть**] **1,** to roll (a surface). **2,** to wear (a road) smooth.

ука́тывать[2] *v. impfv.* [*pfv.* **укати́ть**] **1,** *v.t.* to roll away; remove by rolling. **2,** *v.i., colloq.* to leave; take off. —**ука́тываться,** *refl.* **1,** to roll away. **2,** *colloq.* (*of a vehicle*) to drive off.

ука́чивать *v. impfv.* [*pfv.* **укача́ть**] **1,** to rock to sleep. **2,** *impers.* to experience motion sickness: меня укача́ло, I became seasick, carsick, etc.

укла́д *n.* **1,** mode; tenor: укла́д жи́зни, way/mode/tenor of life. **2,** system: феода́льный укла́д, feudal system.

укла́дка *n.* **1,** laying. **2,** piling; stacking. **3,** arranging; setting (*of one's hair*).

укла́дчик *n.* **1,** packer. **2,** layer (*of floors, tracks, etc.*).

укла́дывать *v. impfv.* [*pfv.* **уложи́ть**] **1,** to lay; lay down (gently). **2,** [*also,* **укла́дывать спать**] to put to bed. **3,** to order to bed; (*of an illness*) lay up. **4,** to pile up; stack. **5,** to arrange; set (one's hair). **6,** to pack. **7,** to lay; cover (a surface with a certain material). **8,** *colloq.* to kill. —**укла́дываться,** *refl.* **1,** [*pfv.* **уложи́ться**] *colloq.* to pack; pack up. **2,** [*pfv.* **уложи́ться**] (*with* **в** + *acc. or prepl.*) to fit (into); go (into). **3,** [*pfv.* **уле́чься**] to go to sleep. **4,** [*pfv.* **уле́чься**] (*of objects*) to lie correctly; lie as desired. *See also* **уле́чься.**

укло́н *n.* **1,** slope; incline. **2,** *fig.* bias; slant. **3,** *fig.* (political) deviation. —**под укло́н,** downhill; downward.

уклоне́ние *n.* **1,** deviation; digression. **2,** evasion; avoidance.

уклони́ться [*infl.* **уклоню́сь, укло́нишься**] *v.r., pfv. of* **уклоня́ться.**

укло́нчивый *adj.* evasive. —**укло́нчивость,** *n.f.* evasiveness.

уклоня́ться *v.r. impfv.* [*pfv.* **уклони́ться**] (*with* **от**) **1,** to dodge; duck. **2,** to evade; avoid. **3,** to deviate (from); digress (from).

уклю́чина *n.* oarlock.

уко́л *n.* **1,** prick. **2,** *med.* injection. **3,** *fig.* gibe; dig.

уколо́ть *v. pfv.* [*infl.* **уколю́, уко́лешь**] **1,** to prick. **2,** *fig.* to wound; pique.

укомплектова́ние *n.* **1,** manning; staffing. **2,** bringing up to full strength.

укомплектова́ть *v., pfv. of* **комплектова́ть.**

уко́р *n.* reproach. —**уко́ры со́вести,** pangs of conscience. —**не в уко́р будь ска́зано,** no criticism implied.

укора́чивать *v. impfv.* [*pfv.* **укороти́ть**] to shorten.

укорени́вшийся *adj.* deep-seated; ingrained.

укореня́ть *v. impfv.* [*pfv.* **укорени́ть**] **1,** to root; implant. **2,** *fig.* to root; ingrain. —**укореня́ться,** *refl.* **1,** to take root. **2,** *fig.* to become ingrained.

укори́зна *n.* reproach. —**укори́зненный,** *adj.* of reproach; reproachful.

укори́ть *v., pfv. of* **укоря́ть.**

укороти́ть [*infl.* **-чу́, -ти́шь**] *v., pfv. of* **укора́чивать.**

укоря́ть *v. impfv.* [*pfv.* **укори́ть**] (*with* **в** + *prepl.*) to reproach (for).

укра́дкой *adv.* stealthily; furtively.

украи́нец [*gen.* **-нца**] *n.m.* [*fem.* **-нка**] Ukrainian. —**украи́нский,** *adj.* Ukrainian.

укра́сить [*infl.* **-шу, -сишь**] *v., pfv. of* **украша́ть.**

укра́сть *v., pfv. of* **красть.**

украша́ть *v. impfv.* [*pfv.* **укра́сить**] to decorate; adorn; embellish.

украше́ние *n.* **1,** (act of) decorating; decoration. **2,** decoration; adornment; embellishment; ornament.

укрепи́ть [*infl.* **-плю́, -пи́шь**] *v., pfv. of* **укрепля́ть.** —**укрепи́ться,** *refl., pfv. of* **укрепля́ться.**

укрепле́ние *n.* **1,** strengthening; consolidation; reinforcement. **2,** *mil.* fortification.

укрепля́ть *v. impfv.* [*pfv.* **укрепи́ть**] **1,** to strengthen; reinforce. **2,** to fortify. **3,** to consolidate. **4,** to invigorate. **5,** to build up (one's strength, confidence, etc.). **6,** to tighten (discipline). —**укрепля́ться,** *refl.* **1,** to become stronger. **2,** to take up a fortified position. **3,** *fig.* to become firmly established. **4,** *fig.* (*with* **в** + *prepl.*) to become firm (in): укрепи́ться в свои́х убежде́ниях, to become firm in one's beliefs. Укрепи́ться в наме́рении (+ *inf.*), to become ever more determined to...

укро́мный *adj.* secluded.

укро́п *n.* dill.

укроти́тель *n.m.* tamer: укроти́тель львов, lion tamer.

укроти́ть [*infl.* **-щу́, -ти́шь**] *v., pfv. of* **укроща́ть.**

укроща́ть *v. impfv.* [*pfv.* **укроти́ть**] **1,** to tame. **2,** to curb; restrain; subdue.

укроще́ние *n.* **1,** taming. **2,** curbing; restraining; subduing.

укрупне́ние *n.* **1,** enlargement. **2,** amalgamation.

укрупня́ть *v. impfv.* [*pfv.* **укрупни́ть**] to combine into larger units.

укрыва́тельство *n.* concealment (*of a crime*); harboring; hiding (*of a criminal*).

укрыва́ть *v. impfv.* [*pfv.* **укры́ть**] **1,** to cover. **2,** to conceal; harbor; shelter. —**укрыва́ться,** *refl.* **1,** to cover oneself up. **2,** to take cover; take shelter; take refuge. **3,** to escape one's notice: от него́ ничто́ не укро́ется, nothing escapes him.

укры́тие *n.* **1,** concealment. **2,** shelter. —**под укры́тием** (+ *gen.*), under cover of.

укры́ть [*infl.* **укро́ю, укро́ешь**] *v., pfv. of* **укрыва́ть.** —**укры́ться,** *refl., pfv. of* **укрыва́ться.**

у́ксус *n.* vinegar. —**у́ксусница,** *n.* vinegar cruet.

уксуснoки́слый *adj., in* **уксуснoки́слая соль,** acetate.

у́ксусный *adj.* vinegar (*attrib.*); acetic. —**у́ксусная кислота́,** acetic acid.

уку́поривать *v. impfv.* [*pfv.* **уку́порить**] **1,** to cork up. **2,** *colloq.* to pack.

уку́с *n.* bite; sting.

укуси́ть [*infl.* **укушу́, уку́сишь**] *v., pfv. of* **куса́ть.**

уку́тывать *v. impfv.* [*pfv.* **уку́тать**] (*with* **в** + *acc.*) to wrap (in).

ула́вливать *v. impfv.* [*pfv.* **улови́ть**] **1,** to catch; perceive; detect. **2,** to grasp (the meaning of something). **3,** *colloq.* to entice. **4,** *colloq.* to seize: улови́ть моме́нт, to seize the moment. **5,** to pick up (a radio signal).

ула́дить [*infl.* **-жу, -дишь**] *v., pfv. of* **ула́живать.** —**ула́диться,** *refl., pfv. of* **ула́живаться.**

ула́живание *n.* settlement; reconciliation; adjustment.

ула́живать *v. impfv.* [*pfv.* **ула́дить**] **1,** to settle (a matter). **2,** to settle; reconcile; compose; adjust (differences). —**ула́живаться,** *refl.* to be settled.

ула́мывать *v. impfv.* [*pfv.* **улома́ть**] *colloq.* **1,** to persuade; induce; prevail upon. **2,** [*impfv. only*] to try to persuade.

у́лей [*gen.* **у́лья**] *n.* beehive.
улепётывать *v. impfv.* [*pfv.* **улепетну́ть**] *colloq.* to take to one's heels; skedaddle.
улета́ть *v. impfv.* [*pfv.* **улете́ть**] to fly away; fly off.
улете́ть [*infl.* **-чу́, -ти́шь**] *v., pfv. of* **улета́ть.**
улету́чиваться *v.r. impfv.* [*pfv.* **улету́читься**] **1,** to evaporate. **2,** *colloq.* to vanish.
уле́чься *v.r. pfv.* [*infl. like* **лечь**] **1,** *pfv. of* **укла́дываться** (*in senses #3 & #4*). **2,** (*of dust*) to settle. **3,** *fig.* to subside; die down.
улизну́ть *v. pfv., colloq.* to slip away; sneak away; steal away.
ули́ка *n.* piece of evidence; *pl.* evidence.
ули́тка [*gen. pl.* **-ток**] *n.* snail.
у́лица *n.* street. —**на у́лице; на у́лицу,** outside; outdoors. —**с у́лицы,** from outside; from outdoors.
улича́ть *v. impfv.* [*pfv.* **уличи́ть**] **1,** to convict; prove guilty. **2,** (*with* **в** + *prepl.*) to catch (*in the act of doing something*).
у́личка [*gen. pl.* **-чек**] *n., colloq.* small street; narrow street.
у́личный *adj.* street (*attrib.*).
уло́в *n.* catch (*quantity caught*).
улови́мый *adj.* perceptible; audible.
улови́ть [*infl.* **уловлю́, уло́вишь**] *v., pfv. of* **ула́вливать.**
уло́вка [*gen. pl.* **-вок**] *n.* trick; ruse.
уложе́ние *n., hist.* code of law.
уложи́ть [*infl.* **уложу́, уло́жишь**] *v., pfv. of* **укла́дывать.** —**уложи́ться,** *refl., pfv. of* **укла́дываться** (*in senses #1 & #2*).
улома́ть *v., pfv. of* **ула́мывать.**
у́лочка [*gen. pl.* **-чек**] *n., colloq.* small street; narrow street.
улуча́ть *v. impfv.* [*pfv.* **улучи́ть**] to find (time); seize (a moment).
улучша́ть *v. impfv.* [*pfv.* **улу́чшить**] to improve; better. —**улучша́ться,** *refl.* to improve; get better.
улучше́ние *n.* **1,** improvement; improving. **2,** *pl.* improvements.
улу́чшить *v., pfv. of* **улучша́ть.** —**улу́чшиться,** *refl., pfv. of* **улучша́ться.**
улыба́ться *v.r. impfv.* [*pfv.* **улыбну́ться**] **1,** to smile. **2,** (*with dat.*) *fig.* to smile on: судьба́ ему́ улыбну́лась, fortune smiled on him. **3,** [*impfv. only*] (*with dat.*) *colloq.* to appeal to: мысль мне не улыба́ется, the idea doesn't appeal to me.
улы́бка [*gen. pl.* **-бок**] *n.* smile.
улыбну́ться *v.r., pfv. of* **улыба́ться.**
улы́бчивый *adj., colloq.* smiling.
ультима́тум *n.* ultimatum.
ультра- *prefix* ultra-.
ультразвуково́й *adj.* ultrasonic.
ультрамари́н *n.* ultramarine. —**ультрамари́новый,** *adj.* ultramarine.
ультрасовреме́нный *adj.* ultramodern.
ультрафиоле́товый *adj., in* **ультрафиоле́товые лучи́,** ultraviolet rays.
улюлю́ *interj.* halloo!
улюлю́кать *v. impfv.* to halloo.
ум [*gen.* **ума́**] *n.* **1,** mind. **2,** intellect. —**без ума́,** (*with verbs of loving*) madly. —**без ума́ от,** crazy about. —**в своём уме́,** in one's right mind. —**в уме́, 1,** in one's mind. **2,** in one's head: счита́ть в уме́, to do figures in one's head. —**из ума́ вон,** completely slipped one's mind. —**на уме́,** on one's mind. —**себе́ на уме́,** shrewd; crafty. —**с умо́м,** *colloq.* intelligently. —**сходи́ть с ума́,** to go out of one's mind; go mad.
умале́ние *n.* belittling; derogation.
умали́ть *v., pfv. of* **умаля́ть.**
умалишённый *adj.* mad; insane. —*n.* madman; lunatic. —**дом умалишённых,** insane asylum.
ума́лчивать *v. impfv.* [*pfv.* **умолча́ть**] (*with* **о**) to keep silent (about); say nothing (about); fail to mention.
умаля́ть *v. impfv.* [*pfv.* **умали́ть**] **1,** to belittle; minimize. **2,** to detract from; diminish.
ума́сливать *v. impfv.* [*pfv.* **ума́слить**] *colloq.* to butter up.
ума́ять *v. pfv., colloq.* to exhaust; wear out. —**ума́яться,** *refl., colloq.* to become exhausted; become worn out.
у́мбра *n.* umber.
уме́лец [*gen.* **-льца**] *n.* skilled craftsman.
уме́лый *adj.* able; skillful. —**уме́ло,** *adv.* ably; skillfully.
уме́ние *n.* ability; skill.
уменьша́емое *n., decl. as an adj., math.* minuend.
уменьша́ть *v. impfv.* [*pfv.* **уме́ньшить** *or* **уменьши́ть**] to reduce; decrease; lessen. —**уменьша́ться,** *refl.* to decrease; diminish; decline.
уменьше́ние *n.* reduction; decrease; decline; diminution.
уменьши́тельный *adj., gram.* diminutive. —**уменьши́тельное и́мя,** familiar first name (*e.g.* То́ля *for* Анато́лий).
уме́ньшить *also,* **уменьши́ть** *v., pfv. of* **уменьша́ть.** —**уме́ньшиться; уменьши́ться,** *refl., pfv. of* **уменьша́ться.**
уме́ренный *adj.* **1,** moderate. **2,** temperate. —**уме́ренность,** *n.f.* moderation.
умере́ть [*infl.* **умру́, умрёшь;** *past* **у́мер, умерла́, у́мерло**] *v., pfv. of* **умира́ть.**
уме́рить *v., pfv. of* **умеря́ть.**
умертви́ть [*infl.* **умерщвлю́, умертви́шь**] *v., pfv. of* **умерщвля́ть.**
уме́рший *n., decl. as an adj.* the deceased.
умерщвле́ние *n.* killing. —**умерщвле́ние пло́ти,** mortification of the flesh.
умерщвля́ть *v. impfv.* [*pfv.* **умертви́ть**] **1,** to kill. **2,** to deaden. —**умерщвля́ть плоть,** to mortify the flesh.
умеря́ть *v. impfv.* [*pfv.* **уме́рить**] to moderate; temper.
умести́ть [*infl.* **-щу́, сти́шь**] *v., pfv. of* **умеща́ть.** —**умести́ться,** *refl., pfv. of* **умеща́ться.**
уме́стно *adv.* appropriately; aptly.—*adj., used predicatively* appropriate: бы́ло бы уме́стно (+ *inf.*), it would be appropriate to...; it would be a good idea to...
уме́стность *n.f.* timeliness; relevance; pertinence.
уме́стный *adj.* appropriate; timely; relevant; pertinent.
уме́ть *v. impfv.* (*with inf.*) to know how (to); be able (to).
умеща́ть *v. impfv.* [*pfv.* **умести́ть**] to fit; get: умести́ть всё в чемода́н(е), to fit/get everything into the suitcase. —**умеща́ться,** *refl.* to fit; go (into *or* onto).
умиле́ние *n.* deep feeling; deep emotion. Слёзы умиле́ния, tears of emotion. —**приходи́ть в умиле́ние,** to be deeply moved.
умили́тельный *adj.* moving; touching; affecting.
умили́ть *v., pfv. of* **умиля́ть.** —**умили́ться,** *refl., pfv. of* **умиля́ться.**
уми́лостивить *v. pfv.* [*infl.* **-влю, -вишь**] to placate; mollify.

уми́льный *adj.* **1,** touching; affecting. **2,** ingratiating; obsequious.

умиля́ть *v. impfv.* [*pfv.* **умили́ть**] to move; touch; affect. —**умиля́ться,** *refl.* to be moved; be touched.

умира́ние *n.* dying..

умира́ть *v. impfv.* [*pfv.* **умере́ть**] to die.

умира́ющий *adj.* dying. —*n.* dying man.

умиротворе́ние *n.* pacification; appeasement.

умиротворя́ть *v. impfv.* [*pfv.* **умиротвори́ть**] to pacify; appease.

умля́ут *n.* umlaut.

умне́ть *v. impfv.* [*pfv.* **поумне́ть**] to become wiser; grow wiser.

у́мник *n., colloq.* **1,** clever man; clever child. **2,** smart aleck; wise guy.

у́мница *n.m. & f., colloq.* clever person.

у́мничать *v. impfv., colloq.* to show off one's intelligence.

умножа́ть *v. impfv.* [*pfv.* **умно́жить**] **1,** *math.* to multiply. **2,** to increase; augment. —**умножа́ться,** *refl.* to multiply; increase in number.

умноже́ние *n.* **1,** *math.* multiplication. **2,** increase.

умно́жить *v., pfv. of* **мно́жить** *and* **умножа́ть.** —**умно́житься,** *refl., pfv. of* **мно́житься** *and* **умножа́ться.**

у́мный *adj.* [*short form* **умён, умна́, у́мно** *or* **умно́, у́мны** *or* **умны́**] intelligent; clever; smart.

умозаключа́ть *v. impfv.* [*pfv.* **умозаключи́ть**] to conclude; deduce.

умозаключе́ние *n.* conclusion; deduction.

умозаключи́ть *v., pfv. of* **умозаключа́ть.**

умозре́ние *n.* speculation; conjecture.

умозри́тельный *adj.* speculative.

умоисступле́ние *n.* frenzy: припа́док умоисступле́ния, fit of frenzy.

умоли́ть *v. pfv.* [*infl.* **умолю́, умо́лишь**] to persuade; prevail upon.

у́молк *n., in* **без у́молку,** endlessly; incessantly.

умолка́ть *v. impfv.* [*pfv.* **умо́лкнуть**] **1,** to fall silent. **2,** (*of noise, sounds, etc.*) to die away; stop; cease.

умо́лкнуть [*past* **умо́лк, -ла**] *v., pfv. of* **умолка́ть.**

умолча́ние *n.* **1,** silence; keeping silent. **2,** *pl.* (deliberate) omissions; things left unsaid.

умолча́ть [*infl.* **-чу́, -чи́шь**] *v., pfv. of* **ума́лчивать.**

умоля́ть *v. impfv.* to beg; plead with; implore; beseech; entreat.

умонастрое́ние *n.* frame of mind.

умопомеша́тельство *n.* mental derangement; insanity.

умопомраче́ние *n.* daze; trance; stupor.

умопомрачи́тельный *adj., colloq.* stunning; stupendous; fantastic.

умо́ра *n., colloq.* a scream; a riot: э́то умо́ра, it's a scream/riot.

умори́тельный *adj., colloq.* screamingly funny; hilarious.

умори́ть *v. pfv., colloq.* **1,** to kill. **2,** to exhaust; wear out. —**умори́ть го́лодом,** to starve (someone) to death. —**умори́ть со́ смеху,** to have (someone) in stitches.

у́мственный *adj.* mental; intellectual. —**у́мственно,** *adv.* mentally: у́мственно отста́лый, mentally retarded.

умудря́ть *v. impfv.* [*pfv.* **умудри́ть**] to make wiser. —**умудря́ться,** *refl.* **1,** to become wiser. **2,** (*with inf.*) *colloq.* to manage (to); contrive (to).

умча́ть *v. pfv.* [*infl.* **умчу́, умчи́шь**] to whisk away. —**умча́ться,** *refl.* to dash away; speed away.

умыва́льник *n.* washstand; washbasin; washbowl.

умыва́льный *adj.* wash (*attrib.*); washing (*attrib.*).

умыва́ние *n.* washing.

умыва́ть *v. impfv.* [*pfv.* **умы́ть**] to wash. —**умыва́ться,** *refl.* to wash (one's hands and face).

у́мысел [*gen.* **-сла**] *n.* design; intention; purpose. Злой у́мысел, malicious intent. —**с у́мыслом,** on purpose; deliberately.

умы́ть [*infl.* **умо́ю, умо́ешь**] *v., pfv. of* **умыва́ть.** —**умы́ться,** *refl., pfv. of* **умыва́ться.**

умы́шленный *adj.* intentional; deliberate; premeditated. —**умы́шленно,** *adv.* deliberately; intentionally; purposely.

умягча́ть *v. impfv.* [*pfv.* **умягчи́ть**] **1,** to soften. **2,** *fig.* to mollify.

умя́ть [*infl.* **умну́, умнёшь**] *v., pfv. of* **умина́ть.**

унаво́зить *v., pfv. of* **наво́зить.**

унасле́довать *v. pfv.* [*infl.* **-дую, -дуешь**] to inherit.

унести́ [*infl. like* **нести́**] *v., pfv. of* **уноси́ть.** —**унести́сь,** *refl., pfv. of* **уноси́ться.**

униа́т *n.* Uniat. —**униа́тский,** *adj.* Uniat.

универма́г *n.* department store (*contr. of* **универса́льный магази́н**).

универса́льность *n.f.* universality.

универса́льный *adj.* **1,** universal. **2,** all-round. **3,** multi-purpose; all-purpose. —**универса́льный магази́н,** department store. —**универса́льное сре́дство,** panacea.

университе́т *n.* university. —**университе́тский,** *adj.* university (*attrib.*).

унижа́ть *v. impfv.* [*pfv.* **уни́зить**] **1,** to humiliate. **2,** to degrade; humble; abase. —**унижа́ться,** *refl.* **1,** to humble oneself. **2,** (*with* **до**) to stoop to.

униже́ние *n.* **1,** humiliation. **2,** degradation; abasement. **3,** indignity.

уни́женный *adj.* **1,** humiliated. **2,** humble; abject.

униза́ть [*infl.* **унижу́, уни́жешь**] *v., pfv. of* **уни́зывать.**

унизи́тельный *adj.* humiliating; degrading.

уни́зить [*infl.* **-жу, -зишь**] *v., pfv. of* **унижа́ть.** —**уни́зиться,** *refl., pfv. of* **унижа́ться.**

уни́зывать *v. impfv.* [*pfv.* **униза́ть**] to stud (*with jewels*).

уника́льный *adj.* unique.

у́никум *n.* unique person; unique object.

унима́ть *v. impfv.* [*pfv.* **уня́ть**] **1,** to quiet; calm; pacify. **2,** to stop; suppress. —**унима́ться,** *refl.* **1,** to quiet down; calm down. **2,** to stop; subside; abate; die down.

унисо́н *n.* unison. —**в унисо́н,** in unison.

унита́з *n.* toilet.

унифика́ция *n.* standardization.

унифици́ровать *v. impfv. & pfv.* [*pres.* **-рую, -руешь**] to standardize.

уничижи́тельный *adj.* pejorative.

уничтожа́ть *v. impfv.* [*pfv.* **уничто́жить**] **1,** to destroy; annihilate; obliterate; wipe out. **2,** to eliminate; abolish; do away with.

уничтожа́ющий *adj.* **1,** destructive; devastating. **2,** *fig.* scathing; devastating; withering.

уничтоже́ние *n.* **1,** destruction; annihilation. **2,** elimination; abolition.

уничто́жить *v., pfv. of* **уничтожа́ть.**

у́ния *n.* union (*of countries or churches*).

уноси́ть *v. impfv.* [*pfv.* **унести́;** *pres.* **уношу́, уно́сишь**] **1,** to carry away; carry off. **2,** *fig.* to take (lives). **3,** *colloq.* to make off with. **4,** *in* **уноси́ть но́ги,** to escape; get away. —**уноси́ться,** *refl.* **1,** to speed away; dash off. **2,** *fig.* (*of thoughts*) to go back. **3,** *fig.* (*of time*) to fly by.

у́нтер-офице́р *n.* noncommissioned officer.

у́нция *n.* ounce.

унива́ть *v. impfv.* to lose heart; be dejected; be discouraged.

уны́лый *adj.* **1,** downcast; despondent; dejected. **2,** cheerless; dreary; dismal.

уны́ние *n.* despondency; dejection.

уня́ть [*infl.* **уйму́, уймёшь;** *past* **уня́л, уняла́, уня́ло**] *v., pfv. of* **унима́ть.** —**уня́ться,** *refl., pfv. of* **унима́ться.**

упа́д *n., in* **до упа́ду,** till one is about to drop.

упа́док [*gen.* **-дка**] *n.* decline; decay. —**упа́док ду́ха,** despondency; depression. —**упа́док сил,** weakness; loss of strength.

упа́дочничество *n.* decadence. —**упа́дочнический,** *adj.* decadent.

упа́дочный *adj.* **1,** decadent. **2,** depressed: упа́дочное настрое́ние, depression.

упакова́ть [*infl.* **-ку́ю, -ку́ешь**] *v., pfv. of* **пакова́ть** *and* **упако́вывать.** —**упакова́ться,** *refl., pfv. of* **упако́вываться.**

упако́вка *n.* **1,** packing. **2,** packing material. —**упако́вочный,** *adj.* packing (*attrib.*).

упако́вщик *n.* packer.

упако́вывать *v. impfv.* [*pfv.* **упакова́ть**] to pack. —**упако́вываться,** *refl.* to pack; get packed; pack one's things.

упасти́ *v. pfv.* [*infl. like* **спасти́**] *archaic* to save. —**упаси́ бог!; бо́же упаси́!, 1,** God forbid!; heaven forbid! **2,** perish the thought!

упа́сть [*infl. like* **пасть**] *v., pfv. of* **па́дать.**

упека́ть *v. impfv.* [*pfv.* **упе́чь**] *colloq.* **1,** to bake thoroughly. **2,** to send away; banish. **3,** *in* упека́ть в тюрьму́, to toss into jail.

упере́ть [*infl. like* **пере́ть**] *v., pfv. of* **упира́ть.** —**упере́ться,** *refl., pfv. of* **упира́ться.**

упе́чь [*infl. like* **печь**] *v., pfv. of* **упека́ть.**

упива́ться *v.r. impfv.* [*pfv.* **упи́ться**] **1,** *colloq.* to get drunk. **2,** (*with instr.*) to delight in; revel in.

упира́ть *v. impfv.* [*pfv.* **упере́ть**] **1,** to place firmly (on *or* against): упира́ть ле́стницу в сте́ну, to place a ladder against the wall. **2,** to fix (one's eyes on something): упира́ть взгляд в дверь, to fix one's eyes on the door. **3,** *v.i.* (*with* **на** + *acc.*) *colloq.* to emphasize; lay stress on. —**упира́ться,** *refl.* **1,** (*with instr.*) to give a push with. **2,** (*with instr.*) to plant firmly (on *or* against): упира́ться нога́ми в зе́млю, to plant one's feet firmly on the ground. **3,** (*with instr.*) *colloq.* to fix (one's eyes on something): упере́ться взгля́дом в дверь, to fix one's eyes on the door. **4,** (*with* **в** + *acc.*) *colloq.* to run into; come up against. **5,** *fig., colloq.* to balk; resist.

уписа́ть [*infl.* **упишу́, упи́шешь**] *v., pfv. of* **упи́сывать.**

упи́сывать *v. impfv.* [*pfv.* **уписа́ть**] *colloq.* to eat; gobble up.

упи́танный *adj.* well-fed; fat; plump.

упи́ться [*infl. like* **пить;** *past* **упи́лся, -ла́сь, -ло́сь**] *v.r., pfv. of* **упива́ться.**

упла́та *n.* payment.

уплати́ть [*infl.* **уплачу́, упла́тишь**] *v., pfv. of* **упла́чивать.**

упла́чивать *v. impfv.* [*pfv.* **уплати́ть**] to pay.

уплотне́ние *n.* **1,** packing down; compression. **2,** hard spot. **3,** *in* уплотне́ние рабо́чего дня, tightening up the schedule of the working day.

уплотни́тель *n.m.* seal.

уплотня́ть *v. impfv.* [*pfv.* **уплотни́ть**] **1,** to pack down (dirt, sand, etc.). **2,** to make more compact; make more crowded. **3,** *fig.* to crowd more into: уплотня́ть рабо́чий день, to crowd more into the working day. —**уплотня́ться,** *refl.* **1,** to be packed down. **2,** to become more crowded. **3,** to give up part of one's living space.

уплыва́ть *v. impfv.* [*pfv.* **уплы́ть**] **1,** to swim away. **2,** to sail away; sail off. **3,** to float away. **4,** (*of time*) to slip by.

уплы́ть [*infl. like* **плыть**] *v., pfv. of* **уплыва́ть.**

упова́ние *n., obs.* hope.

упова́ть *v. impfv., obs.* **1,** to hope. **2,** (*with* **на** + *acc.*) to hope for. **3,** (*with* **на** + *acc.*) to count on.

уподо́бить [*infl.* **-блю, -бишь**] *v., pfv. of* **уподобля́ть.** —**уподо́биться,** *refl., pfv. of* **уподобля́ться.**

уподобля́ть *v. impfv.* [*pfv.* **уподо́бить**] to liken: уподобля́ть поли́тику ша́хматам, to liken politics to chess. —**уподобля́ться,** *refl.* (*with dat.*) to become like; come to resemble.

упое́ние *n.* rapture; ectasy.

упои́тельный *adj.* ravishing; intoxicating.

упоко́й *n., in* **за упоко́й** (+ *gen.*), for the repose of.

уполза́ть *v. impfv.* [*pfv.* **уползти́**] **1,** to crawl away. **2,** to move away (*slowly*); drift away.

уползти́ [*infl. like* **ползти́**] *v., pfv. of* **уполза́ть.**

уполномо́ченный *adj.* authorized. —*n.* authorized agent; representative; plenipotentiary.

уполномо́чивать *v. impfv.* [*pfv.* **уполномо́чить**] to authorize; empower.

уполномо́чие *n., in* **по уполномо́чию** (+ *gen.*), by authority of.

уполномо́чить *v., pfv. of* **уполномо́чивать.**

упомина́ние *n.* mentioning; mention: при (одно́м) упомина́нии (+ *gen. or with* **о**), at the (very) mention of.

упомина́ть *v. impfv.* [*pfv.* **упомяну́ть**] to mention.

упо́мнить *v. pfv., colloq.* to remember.

упомяну́ть [*infl.* **-мяну́, -мя́нешь**] *v., pfv. of* **упомина́ть.**

упо́р *n.* **1,** support: для упо́ра, for support. **2,** prop; support. —**в упо́р,** pointblank. —**де́лать упо́р на** (+ *acc. or prepl.*), to emphasize; lay stress on.

упо́рный *adj.* stubborn; persistent.

упо́рство *n.* stubbornness; persistence; perseverance.

упо́рствовать *v. impfv.* [*pres.* **-ствую, -ствуешь**] **1,** to be stubborn. **2,** to persist; persevere.

упорхну́ть *v. pfv.* to fly away; flit away.

упоря́доченный *adj.* orderly; efficient; well organized.

упоря́дочить *v. pfv.* to put in order; put right; normalize.

употреби́тельный *adj.* widely-used; in common use.

употреби́ть [*infl.* **-блю́, -би́шь**] *v., pfv. of* **употребля́ть.** —**употреби́ться,** *refl., pfv. of* **употребля́ться.**

употребле́ние *n.* use.

употребля́ть *v. impfv.* [*pfv.* **употреби́ть**] to use. —**употребля́ться,** *refl.* to be used.

упра́ва *n.* **1,** *pre-rev.* council; board. **2,** *colloq.* justice: иска́ть упра́вы, to seek justice. Найти́ упра́ву на (+ *acc.*), to see justice done in the case of.

управи́тель *n.m., obs.* manager; steward.

упра́виться [*infl.* **-влюсь, -вишься**] *v.r., pfv. of* **управля́ться.**

управле́ние *n.* **1,** (*with instr.*) management (of); administration (of). **2,** (*with instr.*) driving (a car); steering (a ship); conducting (an orchestra). **3,** *mech.* control: дистанцио́нное управле́ние, remote control. Рыча́г управле́ния, control lever. **4,** government: ме́стное управле́ние, local government. **5,** (governmental) board; bureau; administration; agency; directorate.

управле́нческий *adj.* administrative.

управля́емый *adj.* guided; управля́емый снаря́д, guided missile.

управля́ть *v. impfv.* (*with instr.*) **1,** to operate (a machine); drive (a car). **2,** to manage; administer; run. **3,** to rule; govern. **4,** to control. **5,** to conduct (an orchestra). **6,** *gram.* to govern. —**управля́ться,** *refl.* [*pfv.* **упра́виться**] *colloq.* **1,** (*with* **с** + *instr.*) to finish (with). **2,** (*with* **с** + *instr.*) to cope with; deal with; handle. **3,** [*impfv. only*] (*of a vehicle*) to ride; handle (*a certain way*).

управля́ющий *n., decl. as an adj.* manager.

упражне́ние *n.* exercise.

упражня́ть *v. impfv.* to exercise; train. —**упражня́ться,** *refl.* (*with* **в** *or* **на** + *prepl.*) to practice.

упраздне́ние *n.* abolition.

упраздня́ть *v. impfv.* [*pfv.* **упраздни́ть**] to abolish.

упра́шивать *v. impfv.* to beg; entreat.

упрева́ть *v. impfv.* [*pfv.* **упре́ть**] *colloq.* to be well-cooked.

упрежда́ть *v. impfv.* [*pfv.* **упреди́ть**] *obs.* **1,** to warn. **2,** to anticipate. —**упрежда́ющий уда́р,** preemptive strike.

упрёк *n.* reproach; rebuke; reproof. —**ста́вить (что́-нибудь) в упрёк** (+ *dat.*), to hold something against someone.

упрека́ть *v. impfv.* [*pfv.* **упрекну́ть**] (*with* **в** + *prepl.*) to reproach; rebuke: упрека́ть кого́-нибудь в неблагода́рности, to reproach someone for his (her) ingratitude.

упре́ть *v., pfv. of* **упрева́ть.**

упроси́ть *v. pfv.* [*infl.* **упрошу́, упро́сишь**] to persuade; talk into; prevail upon.

упрости́ть [*infl.* **-щу́, -сти́шь**] *v., pfv. of* **упроща́ть.**

упро́чение *n.* strengthening; consolidation.

упро́чивать *v. impfv.* [*pfv.* **упро́чить**] to strengthen; consolidate. —**упро́чиваться,** *refl.* to become firmly established.

упроща́ть *v. impfv.* [*pfv.* **упрости́ть**] **1,** to simplify. **2,** to oversimplify.

упроще́ние *n.* simplification. —**упрощённый,** *adj.* simplified. —**упроще́нство; упроще́нчество,** *n.* oversimplification. —**упроще́нческий,** *adj.* oversimplified; simplistic.

упру́гий *adj.* elastic; resilient; springy. —**упру́гость,** *n.f.* elasticity; resilience.

упря́жка [*gen. pl.* **-жек**] *n.* **1,** team (*of horses, dogs, etc.*). **2,** harness.

упряжно́й *adj.* harness (*attrib.*). —**упряжна́я ло́шадь,** draft horse.

у́пряжь *n.f.* harness.

упря́мец [*gen.* **-мца**] *n., colloq.* stubborn person.

упря́миться *v.r. impfv.* [*pfv.* **заупря́миться;** *pres.* **-млюсь, -мишься**] to be stubborn; balk.

упря́мство *n.* stubbornness; obstinacy.

упря́мый *adj.* **1,** stubborn; obstinate. **2,** persistent.

упря́тать [*infl.* **упря́чу, упря́чешь**] *v., pfv. of* **упря́тывать.**

упря́тывать *v. impfv.* [*pfv.* **упря́тать**] *colloq.* **1,** to hide; put away. **2,** *in* упря́тывать в тюрьму́, to toss into prison.

упуска́ть *v. impfv.* [*pfv.* **упусти́ть**] **1,** to lose hold of; let slip out of one's hands. **2,** to let slip by; miss; lose (a chance, opportunity, etc.). —**упуска́ть из виду,** to lose sight of; overlook; fail to realize.

упусти́ть [*infl.* **упущу́, упу́стишь**] *v., pfv. of* **упуска́ть.**

упуще́ние *n.* omission; oversight.

упы́рь [*gen.* **упыря́**] *n.m., colloq.* vampire.

ура́ *interj.* hurrah!; hurray!

уравне́ние *n.* **1,** equalization. **2,** *math.* equation.

ура́внивать *v. impfv.* **1,** [*pfv.* **уравня́ть**] to equalize; make equal. **2,** [*pfv.* **уровня́ть**] to level; even.

уравни́тельный *adj.* **1,** equalizing. **2,** applied equally to all.

уравнове́сить [*infl.* **-шу, -сишь**] *v., pfv. of* **уравнове́шивать.**

уравнове́шенный *adj.* **1,** balanced. **2,** *fig.* even-tempered. —**уравнове́шенность,** *n.f.* even temper.

уравнове́шивать *v. impfv.* [*pfv.* **уравнове́сить**] **1,** to balance. **2,** *fig.* to counterbalance; offset.

уравня́ть *v., pfv. of* **ура́внивать** (*in sense #1*).

урага́н *n.* hurricane.

уразумева́ть *v. impfv.* [*pfv.* **уразуме́ть**] to understand.

ура́н *n.* **1,** uranium. **2,** *cap.* Uranus.

ура́новый *adj.* uranium (*attrib.*).

урва́ть [*infl. like* **рвать**] *v., pfv. of* **урыва́ть.**

урду́ *n.m. indecl.* Urdu.

урегули́рование *n.* settlement.

урегули́ровать *v. pfv.* [*infl.* **-рую, -руешь**] to settle (an issue, dispute, etc.).

уре́зать [*infl.* **уре́жу, уре́жешь**] *v., pfv. of* **уре́зывать** *and* **уреза́ть.**

урезо́нивать *v. impfv.* [*pfv.* **урезо́нить**] *colloq.* **1,** to bring to reason. **2,** [*impfv. only*] to reason with; try to persuade.

уре́зывать *v. impfv.* [*pfv.* **уре́зать**] **1,** *colloq.* to shorten (*by cutting off a part*). **2,** to reduce; cut; curtail. **3,** to abridge (someone's rights). **4,** *in* **уре́зывать себя́ в** (+ *prepl.*), to stint oneself (in). *Also,* **уреза́ть.**

уреми́я *n.* uremia. —**уреми́ческий,** *adj.* uremic.

уре́тра *n.* urethra.

у́рна *n.* **1,** urn. **2,** refuse container. —**избира́тельная у́рна,** ballot box.

у́ровень [*gen.* **-вня**] *n.m.* **1,** level: у́ровень мо́ря, sea level. **2,** *fig.* standard: жи́зненный у́ровень, standard of living. **3,** level (*instrument*). —**быть на у́ровне,** *colloq.* to be up to the mark; be up to par. —**идти́ в у́ровень с ве́ком,** to keep up with the times.

уровня́ть *v., pfv. of* **ура́внивать** (*in sense #2*).

уро́д *n.* **1,** freak; monster. **2,** ugly person. **3,** monstrosity.

уроди́ть *v. pfv.* [*infl.* **-жу́, -ди́шь**] to bear; yield. —**уроди́ться,** *refl.* **1,** to come up; grow; ripen. **2,** *colloq.* to be born. **3,** (*with* **в** + *acc.*) *colloq.* to take after; resemble.

уро́дливость *n.f.* **1,** ugliness. **2,** deformity.

уро́дливый *adj.* **1,** deformed; misshapen. **2,** extremely ugly; hideous. **3,** *fig.* wrong; improper; distorted.

уро́довать *v. impfv.* [*pfv.* **изуро́довать;** *pres.* **-дую, -дуешь**] **1,** to disfigure. **2,** *fig.* to corrupt.

уро́дский *adj., colloq.* ugly; hideous.

уро́дство *n.* **1,** deformity. **2,** ugliness. **3,** abnormality.

урожа́й *n.* harvest; crop.

урожа́йность *n.f.* productivity; yield.

урожа́йный *adj.* **1,** (*of ground, soil, etc.*) productive; fertile. **2,** (*of crops*) high-yield. **3,** (*of a year, season, etc.*) good (*for crops*); productive.

урождённая *adj.* née.

уроже́нец [*gen.* **-нца**] *n.m.* [*fem.* **-нка**] native.

уро́к *n.* lesson.

уроло́гия *n.* urology. —**уро́лог,** *n.* urologist. —**урологи́ческий,** *adj.* urological.

уро́н *n.* **1,** damage; harm. **2,** losses; casualties.

урони́ть [*infl.* **уроню́, уро́нишь**] *v., pfv. of* **роня́ть.**

уро́чище *n.* natural boundary.

уро́чный *adj.* **1,** *obs.* fixed; set; agreed-upon. **2,** usual; customary.

урча́ние *n.* rumbling.

урча́ть *v. impfv.* [*pres.* **-чу́, -чи́шь**] to rumble.

урыва́ть *v. impfv.* [*pfv.* **урва́ть**] *colloq.* **1,** to snatch; grab. **2,** *fig.* to find (time).

уры́вками *adv., colloq.* in snatches; by fits and starts.

урю́к *n.* dried apricots.

ус [*pl.* **усы́**] *n.* **1,** whisker (*of an animal*). **2,** *bot.* runner. —**кито́вый ус,** whalebone. *See also* **усы́.**

усади́ть [*infl.* **усажу́, уса́дишь**] *v., pfv. of* **уса́живать.**

уса́дка *n.* shrinkage.

уса́дьба [*gen. pl.* **-деб**] *n.* **1,** country estate. **2,** farmstead.

уса́живать *v. impfv.* [*pfv.* **усади́ть**] **1,** to seat; sit; offer a seat to. **2,** (*with* **за** + *acc.*) to sit (someone) down to. **3,** to plant (with). —**уса́живаться,** *refl.* [*pfv.* **усе́сться**] **1,** to sit down; take a seat. **2,** (*with* **за** + *acc. or inf.*) to sit down to; settle down to.

уса́тый *adj.* **1,** with a mustache. **2,** (*of an animal*) having whiskers.

уса́ч [*gen.* **усача́**] *n., colloq.* man with a (big) mustache.

усва́ивать *v. impfv.* [*pfv.* **усво́ить**] **1,** to master. **2,** to acquire (a habit, instinct, etc.). **3,** to adopt (a custom, manner, etc.). **4,** to digest; assimilate.

усвое́ние *n.* **1,** mastering. **2,** acquiring. **3,** assimilation.

усво́ить *v., pfv. of* **усва́ивать.**

усе́ивать *v. impfv.* [*pfv.* **усе́ять**] to dot; stud: не́бо усе́яно звёздами, the sky is studded with stars.

усека́ть *v. impfv.* [*pfv.* **усе́чь**] to truncate.

усе́рдие *n.* zeal.

усе́рдный *adj.* **1,** zealous. **2,** diligent.

усе́рдствовать *v. impfv.* [*pres.* **-ствую, -ствуешь**] **1,** to show great zeal; work hard. **2,** (*with inf.*) to take pains (to).

усе́сться [*infl. like* **сесть**] *v.r., pfv. of* **уса́живаться.**

усе́чь [*infl. like* **сечь;** *past* **усе́к, -ла́, -ло́**] *v., pfv. of* **усека́ть.**

усе́ять [*infl.* **усе́ю, усе́ешь**] *v., pfv. of* **усе́ивать.**

усиде́ть *v. pfv.* [*infl.* **-жу́, -ди́шь**] **1,** to keep one's seat. **2,** to sit; stay (*in one place*). **3,** *colloq.* to keep a job.

усидчивый *adj.* assiduous. —**усидчивость,** *n.f.* assiduousness.

у́сик *n.* **1,** small mustache. **2,** *zool.* feeler. **3,** *bot.* tendril.

усиле́ние *n.* **1,** strengthening; reinforcement. **2,** intensification. **3,** amplification (*of sound*).

уси́ленно *adv.* **1,** with great force. **2,** hard; diligently; in earnest: уси́ленно гото́виться к экза́менам, to study hard for one's examinations. **3,** *colloq.* with great effort; with great difficulty.

уси́ленный *adj.* **1,** increased; extra. **2,** intense; strenuous. **3,** (*of requests, questions, etc.*) repeated; persistent.

уси́ливать *v. impfv.* [*pfv.* **уси́лить**] **1,** to strengthen; reinforce. **2,** to increase; intensify. **3,** to amplify (sound). —**уси́ливаться,** *refl.* **1,** to become stronger. **2,** to increase; become more intense. **3,** (*of rain*) to come down harder. **4,** [*impfv. only*] (*with inf.*) *obs.* to strive (to); endeavor (to).

уси́лие *n.* effort: прилага́ть все уси́лия, to make every effort. —**де́лать над собо́й уси́лие,** to force oneself.

усили́тель *n.m.* amplifier; booster.

уси́лить *v., pfv. of* **уси́ливать.** —**уси́литься,** *refl., pfv. of* **уси́ливаться.**

ускака́ть *v. pfv.* [*infl.* **ускачу́, уска́чешь**] **1,** to skip away; hop away. **2,** to gallop off.

ускольза́ть *v. impfv.* [*pfv.* **ускользну́ть**] **1,** to slip out: ускользну́ть из рук, to slip out of one's hands. **2,** to slip away; sneak away; steal away. **3,** (*with* **от**) to elude; evade; give (someone) the slip. **4,** *in* ускользну́ть от чьего́-нибудь внима́ния, to escape one's notice. **5,** (*with* **от**) *colloq.* to avoid giving (an answer, explanation, etc.).

ускоре́ние *n.* acceleration.

ускори́тель *n.m.* **1,** accelerator. **2,** *rocketry* booster.

ускоря́ть *v. impfv.* [*pfv.* **уско́рить**] **1,** to accelerate; speed up; quicken. **2,** to hasten; bring on sooner. —**ускоря́ться,** *refl.* **1,** to pick up speed; accelerate. **2,** to be speeded up.

усла́вливаться *v.* = **усло́вливаться.**

усла́да *n., obs.* pleasure; delight.

услади́ть [*infl.* **-жу́, -ди́шь**] *v., pfv. of* **услажда́ть.**

услажда́ть *v. impfv.* [*pfv.* **услади́ть**] *obs.* **1,** to delight; bring pleasure to. **2,** to brighten up. **3,** to relieve; mitigate.

усла́ть [*infl.* **ушлю́, ушлёшь**] *v., pfv. of* **усыла́ть.**

уследи́ть *v. pfv.* [*infl.* **-жу́, -ди́шь**] (*with* **за** + *instr.*) **1,** to keep an eye on. **2,** to follow; keep track of.

усло́вие *n.* **1,** condition: непреме́нное усло́вие, essential condition. Ста́вить усло́вия, to lay down conditions. **2,** *pl.* conditions: усло́вия труда́, working conditions. **3,** *pl.* terms; provisions (*of a treaty, contract, etc.*): на льго́тных усло́виях, on favorable terms. **4,** *obs.* agreement: заключи́ть усло́вие, to conclude an agreement. —**в усло́виях** (+ *gen.*), under conditions of... —**ни при каки́х усло́виях,** under no circumstances. —**при про́чих ра́вных усло́виях,** other things being equal. —**при таки́х усло́виях,** under such conditions. —**при усло́вии, что...,** on condition that; provided.

усло́виться [*infl.* **-влюсь, -вишься**] *v.r., pfv. of* **усло́вливаться.**

усло́вленный *adj.* **1,** agreed-upon. **2,** [*short form only*] agreed: как усло́влено, as agreed.

усло́вливаться *v.r. impfv.* [*pfv.* **усло́виться**] to agree; arrange: усло́виться встре́титься, to agree/ arrange to meet. Усло́виться о цене́, to agree on the price.

усло́вно *adv.* conditionally; tentatively. Он получи́л год усло́вно, he was given a year on probation; he was given a one-year suspended sentence.

усло́вность *n.f.* convention; conventionality.

усло́вный *adj.* **1,** agreed-upon; prearranged. **2,** conventional. **3,** conditional; provisional. **4,** relative. **5,** (*of a line*) imaginary. **6,** *art* symbolic. **7,** *gram.* conditional. —**усло́вный пригово́р,** suspended sentence. —**усло́вный рефле́кс,** conditioned reflex.

усложне́ние *n.* complication.

усложня́ть *v. impfv.* [*pfv.* **усложни́ть**] to complicate. —**усложня́ться,** *refl.* to become complicated.

услу́га *n.* **1,** favor; good turn: оказа́ть услу́гу (+ *dat.*), to do (someone) a favor. Плоха́я услу́га, disservice; ill turn. **2,** *pl.* services: предлага́ть свои́ услу́ги, to offer one's services. **3,** *pl.* facilities. —**к ва́шим услу́гам,** at your disposal.

услу́живать *v. impfv.* [*pfv.* **услужи́ть**] (*with dat.*) **1,** to help; oblige; accommodate; do something for. **2,** [*impfv. only*] *obs.* to serve; be a servant to.

услужи́ть [*infl.* **услужу́, услу́жишь**] *v., pfv. of* **услу́живать.**

услу́жливый *adj.* obliging; helpful; accommodating.

услыха́ть *v. pfv.* [*infl. like* **слы́шать**] = **услы́шать.**

услы́шать *v., pfv. of* **слы́шать.**

усма́тривать *v. impfv.* [*pfv.* **усмотре́ть**] **1,** (*with* **за** + *instr.*) to look after; keep an eye on. **2,** (*with* **в** + *prepl.*) to see (in); see (as): усма́тривать в ко́м-нибудь сопе́рника, to see someone as a rival. **3,** *colloq.* to see; spot.

усмеха́ться *v.r. impfv.* [*pfv.* **усмехну́ться**] to smile; grin.

усме́шка *n.* **1,** smile; grin. **2,** sneer; smirk.

усмире́ние *n.* **1,** suppression. **2,** pacification.

усмиря́ть *v. impfv.* [*pfv.* **усмири́ть**] **1,** to pacify; quiet. **2,** to suppress; put down.

усмотре́ние *n.* discretion; judgment.

усмотре́ть [*infl.* **усмотрю́, усмо́тришь**] *v., pfv. of* **усма́тривать.**

усну́ть *v. pfv.* to fall asleep.

усоверше́нствование *n.* **1,** improvement; refinement. **2,** advanced training: ку́рсы усоверше́нствования, advanced training program.

усоверше́нствовать *v., pfv. of* **соверше́нствовать.**

усомни́ться *v.r. pfv.* (*with* **в** + *prepl.*) to doubt; have doubts about.

усоно́гий *adj., in* **усоно́гий рак,** barnacle.

усо́пший *adj., obs.* deceased. —*n., obs.* the deceased.

усо́хнуть [*past* **усо́х, -ла**] *v., pfv. of* **усыха́ть.**

успева́емость *n.f.* progress (*in one's studies*). —**та́бель успева́емости,** report card.

успева́ть *v. impfv.* [*pfv.* **успе́ть**] **1,** (*with inf.*) to have time (to). **2,** (*with* **на** + *acc. or* **к**) *colloq.* to be on time (for). **3,** (*with* **в** + *prepl.*) *obs.* to be successful (in). **4,** [*impfv. only*] to make progress (*in one's studies*).

успе́ние *n., relig.* **1,** death; passing. **2,** Assumption. —**успе́нский,** *adj.* Assumption (*attrib.*): Успе́нский собо́р, Cathedral of the Assumption.

успе́ть *v., pfv. of* **успева́ть.** —**успе́ется,** *impers., colloq.* there's plenty of time!

успе́х *n.* **1,** success. **2,** *pl.* progress: де́лать успе́хи, to make progress. —**как ва́ши успе́хи?,** how are you getting along? —**с тем же успе́хом,** might (just) as well.

успе́шный *adj.* successful. —**успе́шно,** *adv.* successfully. —**успе́шность,** *n.f.* success.

успока́ивать *v. impfv.* [*pfv.* **успоко́ить**] **1,** to calm; calm down. **2,** to quiet; quiet down (a child, group, etc.). **3,** to relieve; soothe (pain); calm (one's nerves); settle (one's stomach). **4,** to allay (suspicion, doubts, etc.). —**успока́иваться,** *refl.* **1,** to calm down. **2,** (*of pain, a storm, etc.*) to subside; abate. **3,** *colloq.* to be satisfied.

успокое́ние *n.* **1,** calming; quieting; soothing. **2,** peace of mind; tranquillity.

успоко́ительный *adj.* **1,** calming; soothing. **2,** reassuring. —**успоко́ительное сре́дство,** sedative; tranquilizer.

успоко́ить *v., pfv. of* **успока́ивать.** —**успоко́иться,** *refl., pfv. of* **успока́иваться.**

уста́ [*gen.* **уст**] *n.pl., obs.* mouth. —**из пе́рвых уст,** firsthand. —**из уст** (+ *gen.*), from the mouth of; from. —**из уст в уста́,** by word of mouth. —**у всех на уста́х,** on everyone's lips.

уста́в *n.* **1,** regulations; statutes. **2,** charter: уста́в ООН, United Nations Charter. **3,** *mil.* manual: боево́й уста́в, field manual.

устава́ть *v. impfv.* [*pfv.* **уста́ть;** *pres.* **устаю́, устаёшь**] to tire; get tired. —**не устава́я,** tirelessly.

уста́вить [*infl.* **-влю, -вишь**] *v., pfv. of* **уставля́ть.** —**уста́виться,** *refl., pfv. of* **уставля́ться.**

уставля́ть *v. impfv.* [*pfv.* **уста́вить**] *colloq.* **1,** to place; arrange. **2,** (*with instr.*) to cover (with); fill (with); cram (with). **3,** to point; direct; aim. —**уставля́ться,** *refl., colloq.* **1,** (*with* **в** + *acc.*) to fit (into); go (into). **2,** (*with instr.*) to be crowded (with); be crammed (with). **3,** (*with* **на** + *acc.*) to stare (at).

уста́вный *adj.* regulation; prescribed.

уста́лость *n.f.* fatigue.

уста́лый *adj.* tired.

у́сталь *n.f., obs.* = **уста́лость.** —**без у́стали,** tirelessly. —**не знать у́стали,** to be tireless; be indefatigable.

устана́вливать *v. impfv.* [*pfv.* **установи́ть**] **1,** to install. **2,** to establish. **3,** to set; fix. —**устана́вливаться,** *refl.* **1,** to be established. **2,** to be formed. **3,** to set in.

установи́ть [*infl.* **-новлю́, -но́вишь**] *v., pfv. of* **устана́вливать.** —**установи́ться,** *refl., pfv. of* **устана́вливаться.**

устано́вка [*gen. pl.* **-вок**] *n.* **1,** placing; mounting; installation. **2,** plant; unit: силова́я устано́вка, power plant; холоди́льная устано́вка, refrigeration unit; бурова́я устано́вка, drilling rig; дождева́льная устано́вка, sprinkler system. **3,** mount: оруди́йная устано́вка, gun mount. **4,** launcher: раке́тная устано́вка, rocket launcher. **5,** adjustment: то́нкая устано́вка, fine adjustment. **6,** setting: устано́вка высотоме́ра, altimeter setting. **7,** directive; instructions. **8,** precept; tenet: идеологи́ческие устано́вки, ideological precepts/tenets.

установле́ние *n.* establishment.

устарева́ть *v. impfv.* [*pfv.* **устаре́ть**] to become obsolete; become antiquated.

устаре́вший *adj.* obsolete; outmoded; outdated; out-of-date; antiquated. *Also,* **устаре́лый.**

устаре́ть *v., pfv. of* **устарева́ть.**

уста́ть [*infl.* **уста́ну, уста́нешь**] *v., pfv. of* **устава́ть.**

устерега́ть *v. impfv.* [*pfv.* **устере́чь**] *colloq.* to guard.

устере́чь [*infl. like* **стере́чь**] *v., pfv. of* **устерега́ть.**
устила́ть *v. impfv.* [*pfv.* **устла́ть**] to cover; overlay.
устла́ть [*infl.* **устелю́, усте́лешь**] *v., pfv. of* **устила́ть.**
у́стный *adj.* oral; verbal. —**у́стно,** *adv.* orally; verbally.
усто́й *n.* **1,** abutment (*of a bridge*). **2,** foundation. **3,** *pl., fig.* foundation; basis. **4,** *colloq.* cream forming on the surface of milk.
усто́йчивый *adj.* stable; steady. —**усто́йчивость,** *n.f.* stability.
устоя́ть *v. pfv.* [*infl.* **устою́, устои́шь**] **1,** to remain on one's feet; keep one's balance. **2,** to hold out; stand firm; stand one's ground. **3,** (*with* **пе́ред** *or* **про́тив**) to withstand; resist. —**устоя́ться,** *refl.* **1,** (*of liquids*) to settle. **2,** *fig.* to become fixed; become firmly established: устоя́вшиеся взгля́ды, set views.
устра́ивать *v. impfv.* [*pfv.* **устро́ить**] **1,** to arrange; organize. **2,** to arrange; settle; put in order. **3,** to place (in a job, school, etc.). **4,** to put up (in lodgings). **5,** to build; make; construct. **6,** *colloq.* to make; create (a scene, scandal, etc.). **7,** *colloq.* to suit: э́то меня́ вполне́ устра́ивает, that suits me fine. —**устра́иваться,** *refl.* **1,** to work out: всё устро́илось, everything worked out. **2,** to settle down (in a comfortable place): устро́иться на дива́не, to settle down on the couch. **3,** to get settled (in a house or apartment). **4,** to get a job. **5,** to manage; make out; get along; get by.
устране́ние *n.* removal; elimination.
устраня́ть *v. impfv.* [*pfv.* **устрани́ть**] to remove; eliminate. —**устраня́ться,** *refl.* **1,** (*with* **от**) to withdraw (from); retire (from). **2,** to disappear.
устраша́ть *v. impfv.* [*pfv.* **устраши́ть**] to frighten; scare. —**устраша́ться,** *refl.* to be frightened.
устреми́ть [*infl.* **-млю́, -ми́шь**] *v., pfv. of* **устремля́ть.** —**устреми́ться,** *refl., pfv. of* **устремля́ться.**
устремле́ние *n.* **1,** surge; onrush. **2,** aspiration.
устремля́ть *v. impfv.* [*pfv.* **устреми́ть**] to direct; fix (one's gaze, attention, etc.). —**устремля́ться,** *refl.* **1,** to rush; dash; (*with* **вниз**) swoop down. **2,** (*with* **на** + *acc. or* **к**) to be directed (toward); (*of one's eyes*) be fixed (on); (*of a person*) concentrate (on).
у́стрица *n.* oyster. —**у́стричный,** *adj.* oyster (*attrib.*).
устрои́тель *n.m.* organizer.
устро́ить *v., pfv. of* **устра́ивать.** —**устро́иться,** *refl., pfv. of* **устра́иваться.**
устро́йство *n.* **1,** arranging; organizing. **2,** arrangement; layout. **3,** (political or social) system. **4,** mechanism; device.
усту́п *n.* ledge.
уступа́ть *v. impfv.* [*pfv.* **уступи́ть**] **1,** *v.t.* to yield; give up; let have; cede. **2,** *v.i.* (*with dat.*) to yield (to); succumb (to); give in (to); give way (to). **3,** *v.i.* (*with dat.*) to be inferior (to); be second (to). **4,** *v.t., colloq.* to sell (*at a reduced price*); let go; let have: уступи́ть что́-нибудь за шесть до́лларов, to let something go for six dollars. **5,** *v.t., colloq.* to deduct; take off (*from a price*): уступи́ть два рубля́, to deduct/take off/two rubles.
уступи́тельный *adj., gram.* concessive.
уступи́ть [*infl.* **уступлю́, усту́пишь**] *v., pfv. of* **уступа́ть.**
усту́пка [*gen. pl.* **-пок**] *n.* **1,** yielding; giving up. **2,** concession: идти́ на (*or* де́лать) усту́пки, to make concessions. **3,** discount; reduction.
усту́пчивый *adj.* amenable; compliant.
устыди́ть *v. pfv.* [*infl.* **-жу́, -ди́шь**] to shame; put to shame. —**устыди́ться,** *refl.* (*with gen.*) to be ashamed (of).
у́стье [*gen. pl.* **у́стьев**] *n.* **1,** mouth (*of a river*). **2,** opening; mouth.
усугуби́ть [*infl.* **-блю́, -би́шь**] *v., pfv. of* **усугубля́ть.** *Also,* **усугу́бить** [*infl.* **-блю, -бишь**].
усугубля́ть *v. impfv.* [*pfv.* **усугуби́ть** *or* **усугу́бить**] **1,** to increase; heighten; intensify; redouble. **2,** to (further) aggravate; make (even) worse.
усы́ [*gen.* **усо́в**] *n. pl.* [*sing.* **ус**] **1,** mustache. **2,** whiskers (*of an animal*).
усыла́ть *v. impfv.* [*pfv.* **усла́ть**] to send away.
усынови́ть [*infl.* **-влю́, -ви́шь**] *v., pfv. of* **усыновля́ть.**
усыновле́ние *n.* adoption (*of a child*).
усыновля́ть *v. impfv.* [*pfv.* **усынови́ть**] to adopt (a child).
усыпа́льница *n.* burial vault.
усы́пать [*infl.* **усы́плю, усы́плешь**] *v., pfv. of* **усыпа́ть.**
усыпа́ть *v. impfv.* [*pfv.* **усы́пать**] **1,** to strew; bestrew. **2,** *fig.* to stud: не́бо усы́пано звёздами, the sky is studded with stars.
усыпи́тельный *adj.* soporific.
усыпи́ть [*infl.* **-плю́, -пи́шь**] *v., pfv. of* **усыпля́ть.**
усыпля́ть *v. impfv.* [*pfv.* **усыпи́ть**] **1,** to put to sleep; lull to sleep. **2,** *fig.* to lull (someone's attention); allay (suspicions).
усыпля́ющий *adj.* = **усыпи́тельный.**
усыха́ть *v. impfv.* [*pfv.* **усо́хнуть**] **1,** to wither. **2,** *colloq.* to become wizened.
ута́ивать *v. impfv.* [*pfv.* **утаи́ть**] **1,** to conceal; hold back; withhold. **2,** to hide. **3,** to steal; appropriate.
ута́йка *n., colloq.* concealment. —**без ута́йки,** without concealing anything; without holding anything back.
ута́птывать *v. impfv.* [*pfv.* **утопта́ть**] to trample down.
ута́скивать *v. impfv.* [*pfv.* **утащи́ть**] **1,** to carry away; drag away. **2,** *colloq.* to drag (someone) somewhere against his will. **3,** *colloq.* to make off with; steal.
утащи́ть [*infl.* **утащу́, ута́щишь**] *v., pfv. of* **ута́скивать.**
у́тварь *n.f.* utensils.
утверди́тельный *adj.* affirmative. —**утверди́тельно,** *adv.* affirmatively; in the affirmative.
утверди́ть [*infl.* **-жу́, -ди́шь**] *v., pfv. of* **утвержда́ть.** —**утверди́ться,** *refl., pfv. of* **утвержда́ться.**
утвержда́ть *v. impfv.* [*pfv.* **утверди́ть**] **1,** [*impfv. only*] to maintain; assert; claim; contend. **2,** to approve; confirm; ratify. **3,** to establish firmly. **4,** (*with* **в** + *prepl.*) to convince (of). Утверди́ть кого́-нибудь во мне́нии, что..., to reinforce someone's opinion that... —**утвержда́ться,** *refl.* **1,** to become firmly established. **2,** (*with* **в** + *prepl.*) to become firm in (one's views, intention, etc.).
утвержде́ние *n.* **1,** assertion; claim; contention. **2,** approval; confirmation.
утека́ть *v. impfv.* [*pfv.* **уте́чь**] **1,** (*of a liquid or gas*) to leak; escape. **2,** (*of time*) to pass; fly by. —**мно́го воды́ утекло́ с тех пор,** a lot of water has flown under the bridge since then.
утёнок [*gen.* **-нка;** *pl.* **утя́та, утя́т**] *n.* duckling. —**га́дкий утёнок,** ugly duckling.
утепля́ть *v. impfv.* [*pfv.* **утепли́ть**] **1,** to warm; heat. **2,** to winterize.
утере́ть [*infl. like* **тере́ть**] *v., pfv. of* **утира́ть.**

утерпе́ть *v. pfv.* [*infl.* **утерплю́, уте́рпишь**] to restrain oneself.
утéря *n.* loss (*of papers, documents, etc.*).
утеря́ть *v. pfv.* to lose; mislay.
утёс *n.* cliff.
утёсистый *adj.* **1,** rocky; craggy. **2,** steep; precipitous.
утéха *n., colloq.* **1,** pleasure; delight; fun. **2,** comfort; consolation.
утéчка *n.* **1,** loss; leakage. **2,** *fig.* outflow; drain.
утéчь [*infl. like* **течь**] *v., pfv. of* **утека́ть.**
утеша́ть *v. impfv.* [*pfv.* **утéшить**] to console; comfort. —**утеша́ться,** *refl.* **1,** to console oneself. **2,** (*with instr.*) to take consolation (in). **3,** to calm down; pull oneself together.
утешéние *n.* consolation; comfort; solace.
утеши́тель *n.m.* comforter.
утеши́тельный *adj.* comforting; consoling. —**утеши́тельный приз,** consolation prize.
утéшить *v., pfv. of* **утеша́ть.** —**утéшиться,** *refl., pfv. of* **утеша́ться.**
утилиза́ция *n.* utilization.
утилизи́ровать *v. impfv. & pfv.* [*pres.* **-рую, -руешь**] to utilize.
утилитари́зм *n.* utilitarianism. —**утилита́рный,** *adj.* utilitarian.
ути́ль *n.m.* scrap. —**ути́льный,** *adj.* scrap (*attrib.*).
утильсырьё *n.* = **ути́ль.**
ути́ный *adj.* duck (*attrib.*); duck's.
утира́ть *v. impfv.* [*pfv.* **утерéть**] **1,** to wipe away (tears, sweat, etc.). **2,** to wipe (one's face, brow, etc.). —**утерéть нос** (+ *dat.*), *colloq.* to show up; get the better of.
утиха́ть *v. impfv.* [*pfv.* **ути́хнуть**] to subside; abate; die down; calm down.
ути́хнуть [*past* **ути́х, -ла**] *v., pfv. of* **утиха́ть.**
утихоми́ривать *v. impfv.* [*pfv.* **утихоми́рить**] *colloq.* to calm; pacify; placate. —**утихоми́риваться,** *refl., colloq.* **1,** to calm down. **2,** to abate.
у́тка [*gen. pl.* **у́ток**] *n.* **1,** duck. **2,** *fig.* canard. **3,** *colloq.* bedpan.
уткну́ть *v. pfv., colloq.* **1,** to plant firmly. **2,** to hide; bury. —**уткну́ться,** *refl., colloq.* **1,** (*with* **в** + *acc.*) to bury oneself in (a pillow, book, etc.). **2,** (*with instr. and* **в** + *acc.*) to bury (a part of oneself) in. **3,** (with **в** + *acc.*) to bang into; strike.
утконо́с *n.* (duck-billed) platypus.
утлéгарь *n.m.* jib boom; outrigger.
у́тлый *adj.* **1,** (*of a boat*) rickety. **2,** wretched. **3,** *obs.* decrepit.
уто́к [*gen.* **утка́**] *n., textiles* woof; weft; filling.
утолéние *n.* (*with gen.*) **1,** appeasing (*of hunger*); quenching (*of thirst*). **2,** *fig.* relief (of).
утоли́ть *v., pfv. of* **утоля́ть.**
утолща́ть *v. impfv.* [*pfv.* **утолсти́ть**] to thicken.
утолщéние *n.* bulge.
утоля́ть *v. impfv.* [*pfv.* **утоли́ть**] **1,** to appease; assuage (one's hunger); quench (one's thirst). **2,** *fig.* to relieve; alleviate.
утоми́тельный *adj.* **1,** tiring; fatiguing. **2,** tiresome; dull.
утоми́ть [*infl.* **-млю́, -ми́шь**] *v., pfv. of* **утомля́ть.** —**утоми́ться,** *refl., pfv. of* **утомля́ться.**
утомлéние *n.* fatigue.
утомлённый *adj.* tired.
утомля́ть *v. impfv.* [*pfv.* **утоми́ть**] to tire. —**утомля́ться,** *refl.* to tire; become tired; get tired.
утону́ть [*infl.* **утону́, уто́нешь**] *v., pfv. of* **тону́ть** (*in sense #2*) *and* **утопа́ть.**
утонча́ть *v. impfv.* [*pfv.* **утончи́ть**] **1,** to thin; make thinner. **2,** *fig.* to refine; cultivate.
утончённый *adj.* refined; cultivated. —**утончённость,** *n.f.* refinement.
утончи́ть *v., pfv. of* **утонча́ть.**
утопа́ть *v. impfv.* [*pfv.* **утону́ть**] **1,** to drown. **2,** [*impfv. only*] (*with* **в** + *prepl.*) to be rolling in (money, wealth, etc.); be bathed in (light, verdure, etc.).
утопа́ющий *n., decl. as an adj.* drowning man.
утопи́зм *n.* utopianism.
утопи́ть *v., pfv. of* **топи́ть** (*in sense #5*). —**утопи́ться,** *refl., pfv. of* **топи́ться** (*in sense #3*).
уто́пия *n.* utopia. —**утопи́ческий,** *adj.* utopian.
утоплéние *n.* drowning.
уто́пленник *n.* drowned man.
утопта́ть [*infl.* **утопчу́, уто́пчешь**] *v., pfv. of* **ута́птывать.**
у́точка [*gen. pl.* **-чек**] *n., dim. of* **у́тка.** —**ходи́ть у́точкой,** to waddle.
уточнéние *n.* **1,** making (something) more precise. **2,** a clarification: внести́ уточнéния в проéкт, to make some clarifications in the draft; make some things in the draft more precise.
уточня́ть *v. impfv.* [*pfv.* **уточни́ть**] **1,** to make more precise. **2,** to state more precisely. **3,** to find out more about.
утра́ивать *v. impfv.* [*pfv.* **утро́ить**] to triple; treble. —**утра́иваться,** *refl.* to triple; increase threefold.
утрамбова́ть *v., pfv. of* **трамбова́ть.**
утра́та *n.* loss.
утра́тить [*infl.* **-чу, -тишь**] *v., pfv. of* **утра́чивать.**
утра́чивать *v. impfv.* [*pfv.* **утра́тить**] to lose.
у́тренний *adj.* morning (*attrib.*).
у́тренник *n.* **1,** morning performance. **2,** early-morning frost.
у́треня *n.* matin; morning prayer.
утри́ровать *v. impfv. & pfv.* [*pres.* **-рую, -руешь**] to exaggerate.
утриро́вка *n.* exaggeration.
у́тро [*gen.* **у́тра** *but* **утра́** *after* **с, до,** *and the time of day; dat.* **у́тру** *but* **утру́** *after* **к**] *n.* morning. Шесть часо́в утра́, six o'clock in the morning. —**к утру́; под у́тро,** toward morning. —**по утра́м,** each morning. —**с утра́ до вéчера,** from morning till night. *See also* **у́тром.**
утро́ба *n.* belly; womb.
утро́бный *adj.* **1,** uterine. **2,** (*of sounds*) deep; from the belly.
утро́ить *v., pfv. of* **утра́ивать.** —**утро́иться,** *refl., pfv. of* **утра́иваться.**
у́тром *adv.* in the morning. —**вчера́/за́втра/сего́дня у́тром,** yesterday/tomorrow/this morning.
утружда́ть *v. impfv.* **1,** to bother; trouble. **2,** to overburden; tire. **3,** *in* утружда́ть себя́, to extend oneself; go to a lot of trouble. —**утружда́ться,** *refl.* = **утружда́ть себя́.** Не утружда́йтесь!, don't trouble yourself!; don't go to a lot of trouble!
утучня́ть *v. impfv.* [*pfv.* **утучни́ть**] to fatten; fatten up.
утю́г [*gen.* **утюга́**] *n.* an iron (*for ironing*).
утю́жить *v. impfv.* [*pfv.* **вы́утюжить**] to iron; press.
утю́жка *n.* ironing; pressing.

утяжеля́ть *v. impfv.* [*pfv.* **утяжели́ть**] to make heavier; increase the weight of.

утяну́ть *v. pfv.* [*infl.* **утяну́, утя́нешь**] *colloq.* **1,** to drag away; drag off. **2,** to drag (someone) somewhere against his will.

уха́ *n.* fish soup.

уха́б *n.* pothole. —**уха́бистый,** *adj.* full of potholes; bumpy.

ухажёр *n., colloq.* **1,** ladies' man; philanderer. **2,** suitor; admirer.

уха́живание *n.* **1,** looking after; caring for; tending. **2,** courting; paying court to. **3,** *pl.* advances.

уха́живать *v. impfv.* (*with* **за** + *instr.*) **1,** to look after; take care of; care for; tend. **2,** to court; pay court to; woo. **3,** to play up to.

у́харь *n.m., colloq.* dashing fellow; gay blade. —**у́харский,** *adj., colloq.* dashing. —**у́харство,** *n., colloq.* bravado; bluster.

у́хать *v. impfv.* [*pfv.* **у́хнуть**] *colloq.* **1,** to cry out; gasp. **2,** (*of an owl*) to hoot. **3,** to make a loud noise; ring out; resound.

ухва́т *n.* oven prongs.

ухвати́ть [*infl.* **ухвачу́, ухва́тишь**] *v., pfv. of* **ухва́тывать.** —**ухвати́ться,** *refl., pfv. of* **ухва́тываться.**

ухва́тка [*gen. pl.* **-ток**] *n., colloq.* **1,** movement of the body. **2,** knack. **3,** manner; way.

ухва́тывать *v. impfv.* [*pfv.* **ухвати́ть**] to grasp. —**ухва́тываться,** *refl.* (*with* **за** + *acc.*) **1,** to grasp; grab hold of. **2,** *fig., colloq.* to tackle (a job, task, etc.). **3,** *fig., colloq.* to jump at (an idea, suggestion, opportunity, etc.).

ухитря́ться *v.r. impfv.* [*pfv.* **ухитри́ться**] (*with inf.*) *colloq.* to manage (to); contrive (to).

ухищре́ние *n.* device; trick.

ухищря́ться *v.r. impfv.* to contrive; scheme.

ухло́пать *v. pfv., colloq.* **1,** to kill. **2,** to squander.

ухмы́лка [*gen. pl.* **-лок**] *n., colloq.* grin; smirk.

ухмыля́ться *v.r. impfv.* [*pfv.* **ухмыльну́ться**] *colloq.* to grin; smirk.

у́хнуть *v., pfv. of* **у́хать.**

у́хо [*pl.* **у́ши, уше́й, уша́м**] *n.* ear. —**во все у́ши слу́шать,** to be all ears. —**в одно́ у́хо вошло́, в друго́е вы́шло,** in one ear and out the other. —**и у́хом не вести́,** not to pay the least attention. —**по́ уши в** (+ *prepl.*), up to one's ears; head over heels (*in work, love, debt, etc.*). —**пропуска́ть ми́мо уше́й,** to ignore; pay no attention to.

ухо́д *n.* **1,** leaving; departure. **2,** quitting: ухо́д с рабо́ты, quitting one's job. **3,** care: ухо́д за ра́неными/маши́ной, care of the wounded; care of a car.

уходи́ть *v. impfv.* [*pfv.* **уйти́;** *pres.* **ухожу́, ухо́дишь**] **1,** to leave; go away: уйти́ из до́ма, to leave the house; уйти́ от жены́, to leave one's wife; уйти́ в шко́лу, to leave for school. **2,** to quit; retire: уйти́ с рабо́ты, to quit one's job; уйти́ со сце́ны, to retire from the stage; уйти́ на пе́нсию, to retire. **3,** (*with* **от**) to escape (from); elude. **4,** (*of time*) to pass. **5,** (*with* **на** + *acc.*) to go into: мно́го рабо́ты ушло́ на э́то, a lot of work went into that. **6,** (*with* **в** + *acc.*) to sink (into). **7,** (*with* **в** + *acc.*) *fig.* to become absorbed (in). **8,** *colloq.* to boil over. —**уходи́ть в себя́,** to withdraw into oneself.

ухудша́ть *v. impfv.* [*pfv.* **уху́дшить**] to worsen; make worse. —**ухудша́ться,** *refl.* to worsen; become worse; deteriorate.

ухудше́ние *n.* worsening; deterioration.

уху́дшить *v., pfv. of* **ухудша́ть.** —**уху́дшиться,** *refl., pfv. of* **ухудша́ться.**

уцеле́ть *v. pfv.* **1,** to escape injury; escape damage. **2,** to survive.

уце́нивать *v. impfv.* [*pfv.* **уцени́ть**] to mark down (merchandise).

уцени́ть [*infl.* **уценю́, уце́нишь**] *v., pfv. of* **уце́нивать.**

уцепи́ть *v. pfv.* [*infl.* **уцеплю́, уце́пишь**] *colloq.* to grab. —**уцепи́ться,** *refl.* (*with* **за** + *acc.*) **1,** to grab hold of. **2,** *fig., colloq.* to jump at (an idea, offer, etc.).

уча́ствовать *v. impfv.* [*pres.* **-ствую, -ствуешь**] (*with* **в** + *prepl.*) **1,** to participate (in); take part (in). **2,** to share (in).

уча́стие *n.* **1,** (*with* **в** + *prepl.*) participation (in). **2,** (*with* **в** + *prepl.*) sharing (in). **3,** (*with* **к**) sympathy (for); concern (for). —**принима́ть уча́стие в** (+ *prepl.*), **1,** to take part in. **2,** to take an interest in (someone); show concern for.

участи́ть [*infl.* **-щу́, -сти́шь**] *v., pfv. of* **учаща́ть.** —**участи́ться,** *refl., pfv. of* **учаща́ться.**

участко́вый *adj.* district (*attrib.*). —*n., colloq.* district militia officer.

уча́стливый *adj.* sympathetic.

уча́стник *n.* participant. Уча́стник конфере́нции, conferee. Уча́стник состяза́ния, contestant.

уча́сток [*gen.* **-стка**] *n.* **1,** plot (*of land*). **2,** section (*of a road, pipeline, etc.*). **3,** area; portion (*of a surface*). **4,** *mil.* sector. **5,** *fig.* area; field; sphere. **6,** district. **7,** *pre-rev.* police district.

у́часть *n.f.* fate; lot.

учаща́ть *v. impfv.* [*pfv.* **участи́ть**] to increase the frequency of; make more frequent. —**учаща́ться,** *refl.* **1,** to become more frequent. **2,** (*of one's pulse*) to quicken.

уча́щийся *n., decl. as an adj.* student; pupil.

учёба *n.* **1,** studies. **2,** training.

учёбник *n.* textbook.

учёбный *adj.* **1,** educational: учёбное заведе́ние, educational institution. **2,** teaching: учёбные посо́бия, teaching aids. **3,** *mil.* training: учёбное по́ле, training ground. —**учёбный год,** school year; academic year. —**учёбный план,** curriculum. —**учёбная стрельба́,** firing practice.

уче́ние *n.* **1,** studies; studying; learning. **2,** apprenticeship. **3,** teaching. **4,** *mil.* exercise. **5,** doctrine. **6,** (*with gen.*) the teachings (of).

учени́к [*gen.* **-ника́**] *n.m.* [*fem.* **-ни́ца**] **1,** pupil. **2,** apprentice. **3,** disciple.

учени́ческий *adj.* **1,** pupil's; pupils'. **2,** crude; amateurish.

учени́чество *n.* **1,** time spent as a student. **2,** apprenticeship.

учёность *n.f.* learning; erudition.

учёный *adj.* **1,** learned; erudite; scholarly. **2,** scientific. **3,** academic. **4,** (*of animals*) trained. —*n.* **1,** scientist. **2,** scholar. —**учёный секрета́рь,** academic secretary. —**учёная сте́пень,** (college) degree.

уче́сть [*infl.* **учту́, учтёшь;** *past* **учёл, учла́, учло́**] *v., pfv. of* **учи́тывать.**

учёт *n.* **1,** stock-taking; inventory. **2,** record: учёт осмóтра, record of inspection. **3,** registration: брать на учёт, to register. Быть *or* состоя́ть на учёте, to be registered; be on the books. **4,** consideration; taking into account: с учётом (+ *gen.*), in consideration of; taking into account.

учетверя́ть *v. impfv.* [*pfv.* **учетвери́ть**] to quadruple. —**учетверя́ться,** *refl.* to quadruple; be quadrupled.

учётный *adj.* **1,** record (*attrib.*); registration (*attrib.*). **2,** *finance* discount (*attrib.*).

учи́лище *n.* (specialized) school: ремéсленное учи́лище, vocational school.

учини́ть [*infl.* **учиню́, учини́шь**] *v., pfv. of* **чини́ть** (*in sense #3*) *and* **учиня́ть.**

учиня́ть *v. impfv.* [*pfv.* **учини́ть**] **1,** to carry out (reprisals); conduct (an interrogation). **2,** *colloq.* to make (a scene); create (a scandal).

учи́тель [*pl.* **учителя́**] *n.m.* [*fem.* **учи́тельница**] teacher.

учи́тельский *adj.* teachers'. —**учи́тельская,** *n.* teachers' room.

учи́тельство *n.* **1,** teaching. **2,** teachers.

учи́тельствовать *v. impfv.* [*pres.* **-ствую, -ствуешь**] to teach; be a teacher.

учи́тывать *v. impfv.* [*pfv.* **учéсть**] **1,** to consider; take into consideration; take into account; take account of. **2,** to take stock of. **3,** *in* учи́тывать вéксель, to discount a note.

учи́ть *v. impfv.* [*pfv.* **вы́учить;** *pres.* **учу́, у́чишь**] **1,** [*pfv. also* **научи́ть**] (*with dat. or inf.*) to teach: учи́ть (когó-нибудь) англи́йскому языку́, to teach (someone) English; учи́ть когó-нибудь плáвать, to teach someone how to swim. **2,** (*with acc.*) to study; learn; memorize (a lesson, role, etc.). —**учи́ться,** *refl.* **1,** [*impfv. only*] (*with dat.*) to study: учи́ться рýсскому языку́, to study Russian. **2,** [*pfv.* **вы́учиться** *or* **научи́ться**] (*with dat. or inf.*) to learn: вы́учиться/научи́ться рýсскому языку́, to learn Russian; учи́ться плáвать, to learn (how) to swim. **3,** [*impfv. only*] to study; be a student.

учреди́тель *n.m.* founder.

учреди́тельный *adj.* constituent: учреди́тельное собрáние, constituent assembly.

учреждáть *v. impfv.* [*pfv.* **учреди́ть**] to found; establish.

учреждéние *n.* **1,** founding; establishment. **2,** institution; establishment: культýрное учреждéние, cultural institution. **3,** (social) institution: отжи́вшее учреждéние, outmoded institution.

учти́вый *adj.* polite; courteous. —**учти́вость,** *n.f.* politeness; courtesy.

учу́ять *v. pfv.* [*infl.* **учу́ю, учу́ешь**] *colloq.* to smell; sense.

ушáнка [*gen. pl.* **-нок**] *n.* cap with earflaps.

ушáстый *adj., colloq.* with big ears.

ушáт *n.* tub (*carried on a pole inserted through handles*).

у́ши *n., pl. of* **у́хо.**

уши́б *n.* injury; bruise.

ушибáть *v. impfv.* [*pfv.* **ушиби́ть**] to hurt; injure; bruise: ушиби́ть себé пáлец, to hurt one's finger. —**ушибáться,** *refl.* to hurt oneself.

ушиби́ть [*infl.* **-бу́, -бёшь;** *past* **уши́б, -ла**] *v., pfv. of* **ушибáть.** —**ушиби́ться,** *refl., pfv. of* **ушибáться.**

уши́бленный *adj.* injured.

ушивáть *v. impfv.* [*pfv.* **уши́ть**] to take in (a garment).

уши́ть [*infl.* **ушью́, ушьёшь**] *v., pfv. of* **ушивáть.**

у́шко [*pl.* **у́шки, у́шек**] *n., dim. of* **у́хо.**

ушкó [*pl.* **ушки́, ушкóв**] *n.* **1,** = **у́шко. 2,** eye (*of a needle*). **3,** tab; hook.

ушни́к [*gen.* **-никá**] *n., colloq.* ear specialist.

ушнóй *adj.* ear (*attrib.*).

ущéлье *n.* gorge; ravine; canyon.

ущеми́ть [*infl.* **-млю́, -ми́шь**] *v., pfv. of* **ущемля́ть.**

ущемлéние *n.* **1,** jamming; catching. **2,** *fig.* restriction; abridgment. **3,** *med.* strangulation.

ущемля́ть *v. impfv.* [*pfv.* **ущеми́ть**] **1,** to jam; catch: ущеми́ть пáлец двéрью, to catch one's finger in the door. **2,** to abridge (someone's rights); restrict (someone's freedom). **3,** to oppress. **4,** to hurt; aggrieve. **5,** to hurt; wound (someone's pride).

ущéрб *n.* harm; damage. —**в ущéрб** (+ *dat.*), to the detriment of. —**на ущéрбе,** on the wane.

ущéрбный *adj.* waning.

ущипну́ть *v. pfv.* to pinch.

уэ́льский *adj.* Welsh.

ую́т *n.* comfort.

ую́тный *adj.* cozy; comfortable.

уязви́мый *adj.* vulnerable. —**уязви́мость,** *n.f.* vulnerability.

уязвля́ть *v. impfv.* [*pfv.* **уязви́ть**] **1,** *obs.* to sting; wound. **2,** *fig.* to hurt; pique.

уясня́ть *v. impfv.* [*pfv.* **уясни́ть**] **1,** (*often with* **себé**) to get a clear idea of. **2,** *obs.* to explain.

Ф, ф *n. neut.* 21st letter of the Russian alphabet.
фа *n. neut., music* fa; F
фáбрика *n.* factory.
фабрикáнт *n.* factory owner; manufacturer.
фабрикáт *n.* manufactured item; finished product.
фабрикáция *n.* manufacture; fabrication.
фабриковáть *v. impfv.* [*pres.* **-кýю, -кýешь**] **1,** *obs.* to manufacture. **2,** *colloq.* to turn out; crank out (*in large numbers*). **3,** [*pfv.* **сфабриковáть**] *colloq.* to fabricate; make up: сфабрикóванные обвинéния, trumped-up charges.
фабрúчный *adj.* **1,** factory (*attrib.*). **2,** factory-made. —*n., obs.* factory worker. —**фабрúчная мáрка,** trademark.
фáбула *n.* plot (*of a story*).
фавн *n.* faun.
фавóр *n.* favor: быть в фавóре у, to be in someone's favor; be in someone's good graces.
фаворúт *n.* favorite.
фаворитúзм *n.* favoritism.
фагóт *n.* bassoon. —**фаготúст,** *n.* bassoonist.
фагоцúт *n.* phagocyte.
фáза *n.* phase.
фазáн *n.* pheasant. —**фазáний,** *adj.* [*fem.* **-нья**] pheasant (*attrib.*); pheasant's.
фáзис *n.* phase.
фáкел *n.* torch.
фáкельный *adj.* of a torch. —**фáкельное шéствие,** torchlight procession.
фáкельщик *n.* **1,** torchbearer. **2,** one who puts something to the torch.
факсúмиле *n. neut. indecl.* facsimile.
факт *n.* fact. Факт, что..., it is a fact that... Факт тот, что..., the fact of the matter is... —**постáвить пéред фáктом,** to present with a fait accompli.
фактúчески *adv.* in fact; to all intents and purposes.
фактúческий *adj.* **1,** actual. **2,** factual. **3,** de facto: фактúческое признáние, de facto recognition. —**фактúческий брак,** common-law marriage.
фáктор *n.* factor.
фактóрия *n.* trading post.
фактýра *n.* **1,** texture; finish. **2,** *art* manner of execution. **3,** *comm.* invoice; bill.
факультатúвный *adj.* optional; elective.
факультéт *n.* university department; faculty.
фал *n.* halyard.
фалáнга *n.* phalanx.
фáлда *n.* tail (*of a coat*); coattail.
фаллúческий *adj.* phallic.
фаллóпиев *adj., in* **фаллóпиевы трýбы,** Fallopian tubes.
фáллос *n.* phallus.
фальсификáция *n.* **1,** falsificaton. **2,** forgery. **3,** adulteration. —**фальсификáтор,** *n.* falsifier.
фальсифицúровать *v. impfv. & pfv.* [*pres.* **-рую, -руешь**] **1,** to falsify. **2,** to distort. **3,** to adulterate.
фальцéт *n.* falsetto. —**фальцéтный,** *adj.* falsetto.
фальшúвить *v. impfv.* [*pfv.* **сфальшúвить;** *pres.* **-влю, -вишь**] **1,** to be insincere; play the hypocrite. **2,** to play or sing off key.
фальшúвка [*gen. pl.* **-вок**] *n., colloq.* forged document; forgery.
фальшúво *adv.* **1,** falsely. **2,** off key.
фальшивомонéтчик *n.* counterfeiter.
фальшúвый *adj.* **1,** false. **2,** forged; counterfeit. **3,** false; insincere.
фальшь *n.f.* **1,** cheating; dishonesty. **2,** falseness; hypocrisy; insincerity. **3,** *music* false note(s); being off key.
фамúлия *n.* last name; family name; surname.
фамúльный *adj.* family (*attrib.*).
фамильярничать *v. impfv.* (*with* **с** + *instr.*) *colloq.* to be overly familiar (with); take liberties (with).
фамильярный *adj.* familiar; unceremonious. —**фамильярно,** *adv.* unceremoniously. —**фамильярность,** *n.f.* familiarity.
фанабéрия *n., colloq.* arrogance; snobbery.
фанатúзм *n.* fanaticism. —**фанáтик,** *n.* fanatic. —**фанатúческий; фанатúчный,** *adj.* fanatic; fanatical.
фанéра *n.* **1,** veneer (*thin layer of wood*). **2,** plywood. —**фанéрный,** *adj.* plywood (*attrib.*).
фант *n., usu. pl.* forfeits (*game*).
фантазёр *n.* dreamer; visionary.
фантазúровать *v. impfv.* [*pres.* **-рую, -руешь**] **1,** to indulge in fantasy. **2,** [*pfv.* **сфантазúровать**] to make up; dream up. **3,** to make things up. **4,** to improvise.
фантáзия *n.* **1,** fantasy; fancy. **2,** imagination. **3,** *colloq.* whim; fancy. **4,** *music* fantasy.
фантасмагóрия *n.* phantasmagoria. —**фантасмагорúческий,** *adj.* phantasmagoric.
фантáст *n.* **1,** visionary. **2,** writer or artist treating the fantastic.
фантáстика *n.* fantasy. —**наýчная фантáстика,** science fiction.
фантастúческий *adj.* fantastic. *Also,* **фантастúчный.**
фантóм *n.* phantom.

фанфа́ра *n.* **1,** trumpet; bugle. **2,** fanfare; flourish.
фанфаро́н *n., colloq.* braggart.
фа́ра *n.* headlight.
фарао́н *n.* **1,** Pharoah. **2,** *cards* faro.
фарва́тер (тэ) *n.* waterway; channel.
Фаренге́йт *n.* Fahrenheit: со́рок гра́дусов по Фаренге́йту, forty degrees Fahrenheit.
фарисе́й *n.* pharisee. —**фарисе́йский,** *adj.* pharisaic.
фармаколо́гия *n.* pharmacology. —**фармако́лог,** *n.* pharmacologist. —**фармакологи́ческий,** *adj.* pharmacological.
фармакопе́я *n.* pharmacopeia.
фармаце́вт *n.* pharmacist. —**фармаце́втика,** *n.* pharmaceutics. —**фармацевти́ческий,** *adj.* pharmaceutical.
фармаци́я *n.* pharmacy (*preparation of drugs*).
фарс *n.* farce. —**фа́рсовый,** *adj.* farcical.
фа́ртинг *n.* farthing.
фа́ртук *n.* apron.
фарфо́р *n.* china; porcelain. —**фарфо́ровый,** *adj.* china; porcelain.
фарцо́вщик *n., colloq.* black marketeer (*reselling merchandise and currency acquired from foreigners*).
фарш *n.* stuffing; filling.
фарширо́ванный *adj.* stuffed.
фарширова́ть *v. impfv.* [*pres.* **-ру́ю, -ру́ешь**] to stuff.
фас *n.* **1,** front (*of one's face*). **2,** *obs.* front (*of an object, building, etc.*). —**в фас; фа́сом,** full face.
фаса́д *n.* **1,** front (*of a building*). **2,** façade.
фасе́тка [*gen. pl.* **-ток**] *n.* facet (*of a gem*). *Also,* **фасе́т.**
фасова́ть *v. impfv.* [*pfv.* **расфасова́ть;** *pres.* **-су́ю, -су́ешь**] to package (food).
фасо́вка *n.* packaging. —**фасо́вочный,** *adj.* packaging (*attrib.*).
фасо́левый *adj.* of (kidney) beans; bean (*attrib.*): фасо́левый суп, bean soup.
фасо́ль *n.f.* **1,** kidney beans. **2,** a (single) kidney bean.
фасо́н *n.* **1,** cut (*of a garment*). **2,** fashion; style. **3,** *colloq.* style; manner.
фасо́нистый *adj., colloq.* fashionable; stylish.
фасо́нный *adj.* shaped.
фат *n.* fop.
фата́ *n.* bridal veil.
фатали́зм *n.* fatalism. —**фатали́ст,** *n.* fatalist.
фаталисти́ческий *adj.* **1,** fatalistic. **2,** fatal; inevitable.
фата́льный *adj.* **1,** fatal. **2,** of resignation: фата́льный вид, air of resignation.
фатова́тый *adj.* foppish.
фатовство́ *n.* foppery.
фа́уна *n.* fauna.
фаши́зм *n.* fascism. —**фаши́ст,** *n.* fascist. —**фаши́стский,** *adj.* fascist.
фаэто́н *n.* phaeton.
фая́нс *n.* glazed pottery; delftware. —**фая́нсовый,** *adj.* made of delftware.
февра́ль [*gen.* **-раля́**] *n.m.* February. —**февра́льский,** *adj.* February (*attrib.*).
федерали́зм *n.* federalism. —**федерали́ст,** *n.* federalist.
федера́льный *adj.* federal.
федерати́вный *adj.* federated; federal.
федера́ция *n.* federation.
феери́ческий *adj.* **1,** *theat.* based on a fairy tale. **2,** *fig.* magical; fabulous. **3,** *colloq.* enchanting.
фее́рия *n.* **1,** *theat.* play or ballet based on a fairy tale. **2,** *fig.* enchanting spectacle.
фейерве́рк *n.* fireworks.
фельдма́ршал *n.* field marshal.
фе́льдшер [*pl.* **фельдшера́**] *n.* medical assistant.
фельето́н *n.* humorous or satirical article. —**фельетони́ст,** *n.* writer of such articles. —**фельето́нный,** *adj.* humorous; satirical.
фемини́зм *n.* feminism. —**фемини́ст; фемини́стка,** *n.* feminist. —**фемини́стский; феминисти́ческий,** *adj.* feminist (*attrib.*).
фен *n.* hair dryer.
фе́никс *n.* phoenix.
фенобарбита́л *n.* phenobarbital.
фено́л *n.* phenol.
фено́мен *n.* phenomenon; marvel; whiz.
феномена́льный *adj.* phenomenal.
фе́нхель *n.m.* fennel.
фео́д *n.* fief.
феода́л *n.* feudal lord. —**феодали́зм,** *n.* feudalism. —**феода́льный,** *adj.* feudal.
ферзь [*gen. & acc.* **ферзя́**] *n.m., chess* queen. —**фе́рзевый,** *adj.* queen's.
фе́рма *n.* **1,** farm. **2,** girder; truss.
ферме́нт *n.* ferment; enzyme.
фе́рмер *n.* farmer. —**фе́рмерский,** *adj.* farmer's; farmers'.
фе́рмерство *n.* **1,** farming. **2,** farmers.
фе́рмий *n.* fermium.
фермуа́р *n., obs.* **1,** clasp. **2,** necklace.
ферроти́пия *n.* ferrotype; tintype.
феру́ла *n.* ferule.
фе́ска [*gen. pl.* **-сок**] *n.* fez.
фестива́ль *n.m.* festival. —**фестива́льный,** *adj.* festival (*attrib.*).
фесто́н *n.* **1,** *pl.* scallops (*on material*). **2,** festoon (*ornamental carving*). —**фесто́нный; фесто́нчатый,** *adj.* scalloped.
фети́ш *n.* fetish.
фетишизи́ровать *v. impfv.* [*pres.* **-рую, -руешь**] to make a fetish of.
фетр *n.* felt. —**фе́тровый,** *adj.* felt.
фехтова́ние *n., sports* fencing. —**фехтова́льный,** *adj.* fencing (*attrib.*). —**фехтова́льщик,** *n.* fencer.
фехтова́ть *v. impfv.* [*pres.* **-ту́ю, -ту́ешь**] *sports* to fence.
фешене́бельный (нэ) *adj.* fashionable; high-class.
фе́я *n.* fairy.
фи *interj.* fie!; tut!; pshaw!
фиа́кр *n.* (hired) carriage.
фиа́лка [*gen. pl.* **-лок**] *n.* violet (*flower*).
фиа́ско *n. indecl.* fiasco.
фи́бра *n.* **1,** *obs.* fiber. **2,** *usu. pl., fig.* fiber: все́ми фи́брами души́, with every fiber of one's soul.
фибро́зный *adj.* fiber (*attrib.*); fibrous.
фи́га *n.* **1,** fig. **2,** fig tree. **3,** *colloq.* fig (*insulting gesture*).
фигля́р *n.* **1,** *obs.* (circus) acrobat; performer of tricks. **2,** *colloq.* buffoon.
фи́говый *adj.* fig (*attrib.*). —**фи́говый листо́к,** fig leaf.
фигу́ра *n.* **1,** figure. **2,** *chess* piece. **3,** *cards* face card.
фигура́льный *adj.* figurative; metaphorical.
фигури́ровать *v. impfv.* [*pres.* **-рую, -руешь**] to figure; appear.

фигури́ст *n.m.* [*fem.* **-и́стка**] figure skater.
фигу́рка [*gen. pl.* **-рок**] *n.* **1,** *dim. of* **фигу́ра. 2,** figurine.
фигу́рный *adj.* **1,** figure (*attrib.*): фигу́рное ката́ние на конька́х, figure skating. **2,** (*of a pattern*) figured.
фи́дер (дэ) *n., electricity* feeder.
фи́зик *n.* physicist.
фи́зика *n.* physics.
физиоло́гия *n.* physiology. —**физио́лог,** *n.* physiologist. —**физиологи́ческий,** *adj.* physiological.
физионо́мия *n.* **1,** face. **2,** facial expression; look. **3,** physiognomy.
физиотерапи́я *n.* physiotherapy; physical therapy. —**физиотерапе́вт,** *n.* (physio)therapist.
физи́чески *adv.* physically.
физи́ческий *adj.* **1,** physical. **2,** physics (*attrib.*); of physics.
физкульту́ра *n.* physical training; physical education (*contr. of* **физи́ческая культу́ра**).
физкульту́рный *adj.* athletic. —**физкульту́рный зал,** gymnasium. —**физкульту́рный костю́м,** gym suit.
фикса́ж *n., photog.* fixing agent; hypo.
фикси́ровать *v. impfv. & pfv.* [*pfv. also* **зафикси́ровать;** *pres.* **-рую, -руешь**] **1,** to fix; set. **2,** to record (*on paper, film, etc.*). **3,** to fix (one's gaze, attention, etc.). **4,** *photog.* to fix.
фикти́вный *adj.* **1,** fictitious. **2,** forged. —**фикти́вный брак,** pro forma marriage (*carried out to meet a certain legal requirement*).
фи́кус *n.* **1,** fig tree. **2,** rubber plant (*ornamental house plant*).
фи́кция *n.* fiction; invention; fabrication.
филакте́рия *n.* phylactery.
филантро́пия *n.* philanthropy. —**филантро́п,** *n.* philanthropist. —**филантропи́ческий,** *adj.* philanthropic.
филармо́ния *n.* philharmonic society. —**филармони́ческий,** *adj.* philharmonic.
филатели́я (тэ) *n.* philately. —**филатели́ст,** *n.* philatelist. —**филателисти́ческий,** *adj.* philatelic.
филе́ *n. neut. indecl.* filet; sirloin.
филёнка [*gen. pl.* **-нок**] *n.* panel. —**филёночный; филёнчатый,** *adj.* paneled.
филёр *n.* detective; agent.
филиа́л *n.* branch (*of a store, institution, etc.*). —**филиа́льный,** *adj.* branch (*attrib.*).
филигра́нный *adj.* **1,** filigree. **2,** *fig.* meticulous.
филигра́нь *n.f.* filigree.
фи́лин *n.* eagle owl.
фили́ппика *n.* philippic.
филиппи́нский *adj.* Philippine.
филоде́ндрон (дэ) *n.* philodendron.
филоло́гия *n.* philology. —**фило́лог,** *n.* philologist. —**филологи́ческий,** *adj.* philological.
филосо́фия *n.* philosophy. —**фило́соф,** *n.* philosopher. —**филосо́фский,** *adj.* philosophic(al).
филосо́фствовать *v. impfv.* [*pres.* **-ствую, -ствуешь**] to philosophize.
фильм *n.* film; movie; motion picture.
фильмоте́ка *n.* film library.
фильтр *n.* filter.
фильтра́ция *n.* filtration; filtering.
фильтрова́льный *adj.* filter (*attrib.*); filtering.
фильтрова́ть *v. impfv.* [*pres.* **-ру́ю, -ру́ешь**] **1,** to filter. **2,** *fig., colloq.* to screen; select.
фимиа́м *n.* incense. —**кури́ть фимиа́м** (+ *dat.*), to sing the praises of.
фина́л *n.* **1,** finale. **2,** *sports* finals; final round. —**финали́ст,** *n.* finalist. —**фина́льный,** *adj.* final.
финанси́ровать *v. impfv. & pfv.* [*pres.* **-рую, -руешь**] to finance.
финанси́ст *n.* financier.
фина́нсовый *adj.* financial; fiscal.
фина́нсы [*gen.* **-сов**] *n. pl.* finance; finances.
фи́ник *n.* date (*fruit*).
финики́йский *adj.* Phoenician.
фи́никовый *adj.* date (*attrib.*). —**фи́никовая па́льма,** date palm.
фини́фть *n.f., obs.* enamel.
фи́ниш *n.* **1,** finish (*of a race*). **2,** finish line.
финиши́ровать *v. impfv. & pfv.* [*pres.* **-рую, -руешь**] *sports* to finish.
фи́нишный *adj.* finish (*attrib.*): фи́нишная ле́нта (*or* ле́нточка), the tape.
фи́нка [*gen. pl.* **-нок**] *n.* **1,** *fem. of* **финн. 2,** *colloq.* knife; dagger.
финн *n.m.* [*fem.* **фи́нка**] Finn.
фи́нно-уго́рский *adj.* Finno-Ugric.
фи́нский *adj.* Finnish.
финт *n., sports* feint.
финти́ть *v. impfv.* [*pres.* **-чу́, -ти́шь**] *colloq.* to be tricky; resort to deception.
финтифлю́шка [*gen. pl.* **-шек**] *n., colloq.* knick-knack.
фиоле́товый *adj.* violet; purple.
фио́рд *n.* fiord.
фи́рма *n.* business firm.
фи́рменный *adj.* company (*attrib.*); house (*attrib.*). —**фи́рменное блю́до,** specialty of the house.
фисгармо́ния *n.* harmonium.
фиска́л *n., colloq.* tattler; talebearer.
фиска́лить *v. impfv., colloq.* to tattle; tell tales.
фиста́шка *n.* pistachio. —**фиста́шковый,** *adj.* pistachio.
фи́стула *also,* **фистула́** *n.* **1,** *med.* fistula. **2,** falsetto.
фити́ль [*gen.* **-тиля́**] *n.m.* wick.
фи́шка [*gen. pl.* **-шек**] *n.* chip (*used in games*).
флаг *n.* flag. —**под фла́гом** (+ *gen.*), **1,** (*of a ship*) flying the flag of. **2,** *fig.* under the banner of. **3,** *fig.* in the guise of.
фла́гман *n.* **1,** flag officer. **2,** flagship.
фла́гманский *adj., in* **фла́гманский кора́бль,** flagship; **фла́гманский самолёт,** lead aircraft.
флагшто́к *n.* flagpole.
фла́жный *adj.* flag (*attrib.*).
флажо́к [*gen.* **-жка́**] *n.* small flag.
флако́н *n.* small bottle.
flama
флама́ндец [*gen.* **-дца**] *n.m.* [*fem.* **-дка**] Fleming. —**флама́ндский,** *adj.* Flemish.
флами́нго *n.m. indecl.* flamingo.
фланг *n., mil.* flank. —**фланго́вый,** *adj.* flanking.
флане́ль *n.f.* flannel. —**флане́левый,** *adj.* flannel.
фла́нец [*gen.* **-нца**] *n.* flange.
флани́ровать *v. impfv.* [*pres.* **-рую, -руешь**] *colloq.* to stroll; saunter.
фланки́ровать *v. impfv. & pfv.* [*pres.* **-рую, -руешь**] *mil.* to flank.
флеби́т *n.* phlebitis.

фле́гма *n.* **1,** phlegm; sluggishness; apathy. **2,** *colloq.* phlegmatic person.
флегма́тик *n.* phlegmatic person. —**флегмати́ческий; флегмати́чный,** *adj.* phlegmatic.
фле́йта *n.* flute. —**флейти́ст,** *n.* flutist.
фле́ксия *n. gram.* inflection. —**флекти́вный,** *adj.* inflected.
флёр *n.* crepe.
фли́гель [*pl.* **флигеля́**] *n.m.* **1,** wing (*of a building*). **2,** annex.
флирт *n.* flirting; flirtation.
флиртова́ть *v. impfv.* [*pres.* **-ту́ю, -ту́ешь**] to flirt.
флокс *n.* phlox.
флома́стер *n.* soft-tip pen.
фло́ра *n.* flora.
флори́н *n.* florin.
флот *n.* **1,** fleet. **2,** navy. —**вое́нно-морско́й флот,** navy. —**возду́шный флот,** air force. —**торго́вый флот,** merchant fleet; merchant marine.
флоти́лия *n.* **1,** flotilla. **2,** fleet: китобо́йная флоти́лия, whaling fleet.
фло́тский *adj.* naval.
флоэ́ма *n.* phloem.
флуоресце́нция *n.* fluorescence.
флуоресци́ровать *v. impfv.* [*pres.* **-рует**] to fluoresce.
флюга́рка [*gen. pl.* **-рок**] *n.* **1,** ship's emblem. **2,** *colloq.* weather vane.
флю́гер [*pl.* **флюгера́**] *n.* weather vane.
флюоресце́нция *n.* = **флуоресце́нция.** —**флюоресци́ровать,** *v.* = **флуоресци́ровать.**
флюс *n.* **1,** gumboil. **2,** *metall.* flux.
фля́га *n.* flask; canteen. *Also,* **фля́жка.**
фо́бия *also,* **фоби́я** *n.* phobia.
фойе́ *n. neut. indecl.* lobby (*of a theater*).
фок *n.* foresail.
фок-ма́чта *n.* foremast.
фокстерье́р (тэ) *n.* fox terrier.
фокстро́т *n.* fox trot.
фо́кус *n.* **1,** *physics; photog.* focus. **2,** *fig.* focal point; center. **3,** trick.
фокуси́ровать *v. impfv. & pfv.* [*pres.* **-рую, -руешь**] to focus.
фо́кусник *n.* magician; conjurer; prestidigitator.
фо́кусничать *v. impfv., colloq.* to play tricks.
фо́кусный *adj.* focal.
фо́кус-по́кус *n., colloq.* hocus-pocus.
фол *n., sports* foul.
фолиа́нт *n.* large book; volume; folio.
фо́лио *n. indecl.* folio.
фолли́кул *n.* follicle.
фо́льга *n.* foil: алюми́ниевая фо́льга, aluminum foil.
фолькло́р *n.* folklore. —**фольклори́ст,** *n.* specialist in folklore.
фон *n.* background.
фона́рик *n., dim. of* **фона́рь.**
фона́рный *adj.* lamp (*attrib.*); lantern (*attrib.*). —**фона́рный столб,** lamppost.
фона́рщик *n., obs.* lamplighter.
фона́рь [*gen.* **-наря́**] *n.m.* **1,** lantern. **2,** (*in combinations*) -light: за́дний/карма́нный/у́личный фона́рь, taillight/flashlight/street light/. **3,** *in* проекцио́нный фона́рь, projector. **4,** bay window; skylight. **5,** *colloq.* black eye.
фонд *n.* **1,** fund: фонд за́работной пла́ты, wage fund. **2,** *pl.* stocks; securities. **3,** fund; foundation: фонд по́мощи, relief fund.
фо́ндовый *adj.* stock (*attrib.*). —**фо́ндовая би́ржа,** stock exchange; stock market.
фоне́ма (нэ) *n.* phoneme. —**фонемати́ческий,** *adj.* phonemic.
фоне́тика (нэ) *n.* phonetics. —**фонети́ческий,** *adj.* phonetic.
фоноло́гия *n.* phonology.
фоноте́ка *n.* record library.
фонта́н *n.* fountain.
фонтани́ровать *v. impfv.* [*pres.* **-рует**] to gush; gush forth.
фонта́нчик *n.* **1,** *dim. of* **фонта́н. 2,** water fountain; drinking fountain.
фо́ра *n., sports* advantage; head start (*given a weaker player*). —**табли́ца фор,** table of handicaps.
форе́йтор *n.* postilion.
форе́ль *n.f.* trout.
фо́рзац *n.* flyleaf.
фо́рма *n.* **1,** form. **2,** shape. **3,** mold. **4,** uniform. —**быть в фо́рме,** to be in good form. —**для фо́рмы,** for form's sake. —**по всей фо́рме, 1,** properly. **2,** really and truly.
формали́зм *n.* formalism. —**формали́ст,** *n.* formalist. —**формалисти́ческий,** *adj.* formalistic.
формальдеги́д *n.* formaldehyde.
форма́льно *adv.* formally; officially; legally.
форма́льность *n.f.* formality; technicality.
форма́льный *adj.* formal.
форма́т *n.* format; size.
форма́ция *n.* **1,** structure. **2,** *geol.* formation.
фо́рменный *adj.* **1,** uniform (*attrib.*). **2,** *obs.* formal; official. **3,** *colloq.* real; regular; downright.
формирова́ние *n.* **1,** forming; formation. **2,** *mil.* unit.
формирова́ть *v. impfv.* [*pfv.* **сфомирова́ть;** *pres.* **-ру́ю, -ру́ешь**] **1,** to form; mold. **2,** to form; organize. —**формирова́ться,** *refl.* **1,** to form; be formed. **2,** to mature; develop.
формова́ть *v. impfv.* [*pfv.* **сформова́ть;** *pres.* **-му́ю, -му́ешь**] to shape; mold; model.
фо́рмула *n.* formula.
формули́ровать *v. impfv. & pfv.* [*pfv. also* **сформули́ровать;** *pres.* **-рую, -руешь**] to word; phrase; formulate.
формулиро́вка *n.* **1,** formulation. **2,** formula. **3,** wording.
формуля́р *n.* **1,** *pre-rev.* record of service. **2,** maintenance log. **3,** charge card (*inserted in a library book*).
форпо́ст *n.* outpost.
форс *n., colloq.* show; swank; ostentation. —**для фо́рса,** to show off.
форси́рованный *adj.* accelerated. —**форси́рованный марш,** *mil.* forced march.
форси́ровать *v. impfv. & pfv.* [*pres.* **-рую, -руешь**] **1,** to speed up. **2,** *mil.* to make a forced crossing of (*e.g.* a river).
форсу́нка [*gen. pl.* **-нок**] *n.* sprayer; injector.
форт [*2nd loc.* **форту́;** *pl.* **форты́**] *n.* fort.
фо́рте (тэ) *adv., music* forte.
фо́ртель *n.m., colloq.* trick.
фортепья́но *n. indecl.* piano. —**фортепья́нный,** *adj.* piano (*attrib.*).
форти́ссимо *adv.* fortissimo.

фортификáция *n.* fortification. —**фортификациóнный,** *adj.* fortification (*attrib.*).
фóрточка [*gen. pl.* **-чек**] *n.* small hinged window pane.
фортýна *n.* fortune.
фóрум *n.* forum.
форшлáг *n., music* grace note.
форштéвень (штэ) [*gen.* **-вня**] *n.m., naut.* stem.
фосгéн *n.* phosgene.
фосфáт *n.* phosphate. —**фосфáтный; фосфáтовый,** *adj.* phosphate (*attrib.*).
фóсфор *n.* phosphorus.
фосфоресцéнция *n.* phosphorescence. —**фосфоресцúрующий,** *adj.* phosphorescent.
фóсфорный *adj.* phosphoric; phosphorous.
фóто *n. indecl., colloq.* photo; photograph.
фотоаппарáт *n.* camera.
фотогенúчный *adj.* photogenic.
фотогравю́ра *n.* photogravure; photoengraving.
фотóграф *n.* photographer.
фотографúровать *v. impfv.* [*pfv.* **сфотографúровать;** *pres.* **-рую, -руешь**] **1,** to photograph; take a picture of. **2,** [*impfv. only*] to take a picture; take pictures. —**фотографúроваться,** *refl.* to be photographed; have one's picture taken.
фотографúческий *adj.* photographic.
фотогрáфия *n.* **1,** photography. **2,** photograph. **3,** photographer's studio.
фотокáрточка [*gen. pl.* **-чек**] *n., colloq.* photograph; snapshot.
фотокóпия *n.* photocopy.
фотолюбúтель *n.m.* amateur photographer.
фотóметр *n.* photometer.
фотóн *n.* photon.
фотосúнтез (тэ) *n.* photosynthesis.
фотоснúмок [*gen.* **-мка**] *n.* photograph; snapshot.
фотостáт *n.* photostat machine.
фотосфéра *n.* photosphere.
фотоэлектрúческий *adj.* photoelectric.
фотоэлемéнт *n.* photoelectric cell; electric eye.
фóфан *n., colloq.* dope; jerk.
фрагмéнт *n.* fragment. —**фрагментáрный,** *adj.* fragmentary.
фрáза *n.* **1,** sentence. **2,** phrase.
фразеолóгия *n.* phraseology. —**фразеологúческий,** *adj.* phraseological.
фразёр *n.* phrasemonger. —**фразёрство,** *n.* phrasemongering.
фрак *n.* tail coat; tails.
фракúйский *adj.* Thracian.
фракциóнный *adj.* **1,** factional. **2,** factious.
фрáкция *n.* (political) faction.
фрамбéзия *n.* yaws.
фрамýга *n.* transom.
франк *n.* **1,** franc (*monetary unit*). **2,** *hist.* Frank.
франкúровать *v. impfv. & pfv.* [*pres.* **-рую, -руешь**] to prepay the postage (on).
франкмасóн *n.* freemason. —**франкмасóнство,** *n.* freemasonry.
франт *n.* dandy; fop.
франтúть *v. impfv.* [*pres.* **-чý, -тúшь**] *colloq.* to dress like a dandy.
франтовáтый *adj., colloq.* foppish.
фрáнций *n.* francium.
францýз *n.m.* [*fem.* **-цýженка**] Frenchman. —**францýзский,** *adj.* French.
фрахт *n.* **1,** freight. **2,** freight charges.
фрахтовáть *v. impfv.* [*pfv.* **зафрахтовáть;** *pres.* **-тýю, -тýешь**] to charter.
фрáчный *adj.* of or for a tail coat; worn with a tail coat.
фрегáт *n.* frigate.
фрéза *also,* **фрезá** *n.* milling cutter.
фрéзерный *adj.* milling (*attrib.*): фрéзерный станóк, milling machine.
фрезеровáние *n.* milling.
фрезеровáть *v. impfv. & pfv.* [*pres.* **-рýю, -рýешь**] to cut; mill (metal).
фрéйлина *n.* lady in waiting.
френолóгия *n.* phrenology.
френч *n.* service jacket.
фрéска [*gen. pl.* **-сок**] *n.* fresco. —**фрéсковый,** *adj.* fresco (*attrib.*).
фривóльный *adj.* ribald.
фриз *n.* frieze.
фрикадéлька (дэ) [*gen. pl.* **-лек**] *n.* ball of minced meat or fish cooked in soup.
фрикасé (сэ) *n. neut. indecl.* fricassee.
фрикатúвный *adj.* fricative.
фронт [*pl.* **фрóнты, фронтóв, фронтáм**] *n.* **1,** *mil.* front. **2,** *meteorology* front: тёплый фронт, warm front. **3,** *fig.* front: едúный фронт, united front. —**стать во фронт,** to stand at attention.
фронтáльный *adj.* frontal.
фронтиспúс *n.* frontispiece.
фронтовúк [*gen.* **-викá**] *n.* front-line soldier.
фронтовóй *adj., mil.* front (*attrib.*); front-line.
фронтóн *n.* pediment.
фрукт *n.* **1,** piece of fruit. **2,** *pl.* fruit.
фруктóвый *adj.* fruit (*attrib.*). —**фруктóвый сад,** orchard.
фрустрáция *n.* frustration.
фтор *n.* fluorine.
фторúд *n.* fluoride.
фтóристый *adj.* fluoride (of): фтóристый нáтрий, sodium fluoride.
фу *interj.* **1,** (*of disgust, contempt, etc.*) ugh! **2,** (*of fatigue, relief, etc.*) whew!
фýга *n., music* fugue.
фугáс *n.* land mine.
фугáска [*gen. pl.* **-сок**] *n., colloq.* **1,** land mine. **2,** demolition bomb.
фугáсный *adj.* high-explosive. —**фугáсная бóмба,** demolition bomb.
фужéр *n.* tall wine glass.
фýкать *v. impfv.* [*pfv.* **фýкнуть**] *colloq.* **1,** to snort. **2,** to blow. **3,** (*of an engine, locomotive, etc.*) to puff.
фуксúн *n.* fuchsin; magenta.
фýксия *n.* fuchsia.
фундáмент *n.* foundation.
фундаментáльный *adj.* **1,** solid; sturdy. **2,** (*of knowledge*) thorough; profound. **3,** (*of research, a work, study, etc.*) basic. —**фундаментáльная библиотéка,** main library.
фундýк [*gen.* **-дукá**] *n.* filbert.
фуникулёр *n.* **1,** funicular railway. **2,** cable car.
функционáльный *adj.* functional.
функционúровать *v. impfv.* [*pres.* **-рую, -руешь**] to function.
фýнкция *n.* function.
фунт *n.* pound (*unit of weight; monetary unit*).

фу́нтик *n., colloq.* cone-shaped paper bag.
фу́ра *n.* **1,** wagon. **2,** van.
фура́ж [*gen.* **-ража́**] *n.* fodder; forage.
фура́жка [*gen. pl.* **-жек**] *n.* service cap.
фура́жный *adj.* forage (*attrib.*); fodder (*attrib.*).
фурго́н *n.* van.
фу́рия *n.* **1,** *myth.* Fury. **2,** *colloq.* shrew; virago.
фуро́р *n.* furor; sensation.
фуру́нкул *n., med.* boil.
фут *n.* foot (*12 inches*).
футбо́л *n.* soccer. —**футболи́ст,** *n.* soccer player.
футбо́лка [*gen. pl.* **-лок**] *n.* sport shirt.
футбо́льный *adj.* soccer (*attrib.*).
футля́р *n.* case: футля́р для очко́в, eyeglass case.
фу́товый *adj.* one foot in length; one-foot (*attrib.*).
футури́зм *n.* futurism. —**футуристи́ческий,** *adj.* futuristic.
фуфа́йка [*gen. pl.* **-фа́ек**] *n.* jersey.
фы́рканье *n.* snorting; snort.
фы́ркать *v. impfv.* [*pfv.* **фы́ркнуть**] **1,** to snort. **2,** (*of an engine, locomotive, etc.*) to puff. **3,** *colloq.* to chuckle. **4,** *colloq.* to grumble. **5,** (*with* **на** + *acc.*) *colloq.* to sneer (at).
фюзеля́ж *n.* fuselage.

Х, х *n. neut.* 22nd letter of the Russian alphabet.
ха́живать *v. impfv., colloq.* to go (*regularly*).
хака́с *n.m.* [*fem.* **-ка́ска**] Khakass (*one of a people inhabiting southern Siberia*). —**хака́сский,** *adj.* Khakass.
ха́ки *n. neut. indecl. & adj.* khaki.
хала́т *n.* **1,** oriental robe. **2,** bathrobe. **3,** (surgeon's) gown; (artist's) smock. —**рабо́чий хала́т,** overalls.
хала́тность *n.f.* **1,** indifference. **2,** negligence.
хала́тный *adj.* indifferent; lackadaisical; negligent.
халва́ *n.* a paste made of nuts, sugar, and oil; halva.
хали́ф *n.* caliph. —**халифа́т,** *n.* caliphate.
халту́ра *n., colloq.* **1,** work performed (*or* money earned) on the side. **2,** hackwork. —**халту́рный,** *adj., colloq.* hack. —**халту́рщик,** *n., colloq.* hack worker; hack.
халцедо́н *n.* chalcedony.
хам *n., colloq.* cad; boor.
хамелео́н *n.* chameleon.
хами́тский *adj.* Hamitic.
ха́мский *adj., colloq.* boorish. —**ха́мство,** *n., colloq.* boorishness.
хан *n.* khan.
хандра́ *n.* melancholy; depression.
хандри́ть *v. impfv.* to be depressed; have the blues; be down in the dumps.
ханжа́ *n.m. & f.* self-righteous person; hypocrite. —**ха́нжеский; ханжеско́й,** *adj.* sanctimonious; self-righteous. —**ха́нжество; ханжество́,** *n.* sanctimony; self-righteousness.
ханжи́ть *v. impfv., colloq.* to play the hypocrite; put on an act.
ха́нство *n.* khanate.
хао́с *n.* chaos. —**хаоти́ческий,** *adj.* chaotic.
хаоти́чный *adj.* chaotic. —**хаоти́чность,** *n.f.* chaotic nature.
ха́пать *v. impfv.* [*pfv.* **ха́пнуть**] *colloq.* **1,** to grab; snatch. **2,** to steal; swipe.
хараки́ри *n. neut. indecl.* hara-kiri.
хара́ктер *n.* **1,** character; personality; disposition. **2,** nature (*of something*): хара́ктер рабо́ты, the nature of the work. **3,** (strength of) character: проявля́ть хара́ктер, to show *or* demonstrate character. Челове́к с хара́ктером, strong-willed person. **4,** character (*in a story, play, etc.*). —**вы́держать хара́ктер,** to stand firm. —**носи́ть (како́й-нибудь) хара́ктер,** to be... (in nature): носи́ть вре́менный хара́ктер, to be temporary (in nature).
характеризова́ть *v. impfv. & pfv.* [*pres.* **-зу́ю, -зу́ешь**] **1,** to describe; characterize. **2,** to be characteristic of; be typical of. —**характеризова́ться,** *refl.* [*impfv. only*] (*with instr.*) to be characterized (by); be marked (by).
характери́стика *n.* **1,** description; characterization. **2,** character reference.
характе́рно *adv.* in one's own distinctive way. —*adj., used predicatively* **1,** (*with* **для**) characteristic (of). **2,** significant: характе́рно, что..., it is significant that...
характе́рный *adj.* **1,** typical; characteristic. **2,** distinctive. **3,** *theat.* character (*attrib.*).
ха́рза *n.* yellow-throated marten.
ха́ркать *v. impfv.* [*pfv.* **ха́ркнуть**] *colloq.* to expectorate; spit. Ха́ркать кро́вью, to spit blood.
ха́ртия *n.* charter. —**Вели́кая ха́ртия во́льностей,** Magna Carta.
харче́вня [*gen. pl.* **-вен**] *n., obs.* (cheap) eating place.
харчи́ [*gen.* **-че́й**] *n. pl., colloq.* food; grub.
харчо́ *n. indecl.* mutton soup.
ха́ря *n., colloq.* face; mug; puss.
ха́та *n.* peasant's hut. —**моя́ ха́та с кра́ю,** it has nothing to do with me.
ха́ять *v. impfv.* [*pres.* **ха́ю, ха́ешь**] *colloq.* to find fault with; run down.
хвала́ *n.* praise.
хвале́бный *adj.* **1,** laudatory. **2,** (*of a song, hymn, etc.*) of praise.
хвалёный *adj.* (much) vaunted; famous.
хвали́ть *v. impfv.* [*pfv.* **похвали́ть;** *pres.* **хвалю́,**

хва́лишь] to praise. —**хвали́ться,** *refl.* (*with instr.*) to boast (about *or* of); brag (about).

хва́статься *v.r. impfv.* [*pfv.* **похва́статься**] (*with instr.*) to boast (about *or* of); brag (about).

хвастли́вый *adj.* boastful. —**хвастли́вость,** *n.f.* boastfulness.

хвастовство́ *n.* boasting; bragging.

хвасту́н [*gen.* **-стуна́**] *n.m.* [*fem.* **-сту́нья**] *colloq.* braggart.

хват *n., colloq.* dashing fellow; gay blade.

хвата́ть *v. impfv.* **1,** [*pfv.* **схвати́ть**] to seize; grab; grasp; snatch. **2,** [*pfv.* **хвати́ть**] *impers.* (*with gen.*) to suffice; be enough; last: вре́мени не хвата́ет, there is not enough time. Этого нам хва́тит на ме́сяц, that will last us a month. Хва́тит!, enough! На сего́дня хва́тит, that will be enough for today. С меня́ хва́тит!, I've had enough! Хва́тит тебе́ пла́кать!, enough of your crying! **3,** [*impfv. only*] (*with* **не**) *impers.* A, to be missing: не хвата́ет двух страни́ц, two pages are missing. B, to miss (someone): мне вас не хвата́ет, I miss you. —**наско́лько хвата́ет глаз,** as far as the eye can see. *See also* **хвати́ть.**

хвата́ться *v.r. impfv.* (*with* **за** + *acc.*) **1,** [*pfv.* **схвати́ться**] to grab; grasp. **2,** [*impfv. only*] to take up; seize upon; embrace. —**хвата́ться за́ голову,** to clutch one's head (*in horror or despair*). —**хвата́ться за соло́минку,** to grasp at a straw. —**хвата́ться за ум,** to come to one's senses.

хвати́ть *v. pfv.* [*infl.* **хвачу́, хва́тишь**] **1,** *pfv. of* **хвата́ть** (*in sense #2*). **2,** *colloq.* to strike; hit. **3,** *colloq.* to experience; suffer. **4,** *colloq.* to drink; guzzle. **5,** *in* **хвати́ть че́рез край,** to go too far; overstate one's case. —**хвати́ться,** *refl.* (*with gen.*) *colloq.* to miss; notice the absence of.

хва́тка *n.* **1,** grip; grasp. **2,** skill. —**мёртвая хва́тка,** mortal grip; iron grip.

хво́йный *adj.* **1,** coniferous. **2,** pine (*attrib.*).

хвора́ть *v. impfv., colloq.* to be ill; be ailing.

хво́рост *n.* **1,** brushwood. **2,** pastry sticks.

хворости́на *n.* switch; stick; rod.

хво́рый *adj., colloq.* sickly; ailing.

хворь *n.f., colloq.* illness; ailment.

хвост [*gen.* **хвоста́**] *n.* **1,** tail. **2,** tail end; tag end. **3,** *colloq.* line; queue: стоя́ть в хвосте́, to stand in line.

хвоста́тый *adj.* having a tail.

хво́стик *n., dim. of* **хвост.** —**с хво́стиком,** plus a little more: пятьдеся́т лет с хво́стиком, fifty plus (years).

хвостово́й *adj.* tail (*attrib.*).

хвощ [*gen.* **хвоща́**] *n.* horsetail (*plant*).

хво́я *n.* **1,** pine needles. **2,** branches of a pine tree.

хе́рес *n.* sherry.

херуви́м *n.* cherub. —**херуви́мский,** *adj.* cherubic.

хе́тты [*gen.* **-тов**] *n. pl.* Hittites. —**хе́ттский,** *adj.* Hittite.

хиба́рка [*gen. pl.* **-рок**] *n.* shanty; hovel. *Also,* **хиба́ра.**

хи́жина *n.* hut; shack.

хиле́ть *v. impfv., colloq.* to fade; decline; become sickly.

хи́лый *adj.* sickly; feeble.

химе́ра *n.* chimera. —**химери́ческий,** *adj.* chimerical.

хи́мик *n.* chemist.

химика́лии [*gen.* **-лий**] *n. pl.* chemicals.

химиотерапи́я *n.* chemotherapy.

хими́ческий *adj.* chemical. —**хими́ческий каранда́ш,** indelible pencil. —**хими́ческая чи́стка,** dry cleaning.

хи́мия *n.* chemistry.

химчи́стка *n., colloq.* **1,** dry cleaning. **2,** dry cleaning establishment; dry cleaner's (*contr. of* **хими́ческая чи́стка**).

хи́на *n.* quinine.

хи́нди *n.m. indecl.* Hindi.

хини́н *n.* quinine.

хи́нный *adj.* quinine (*attrib.*). —**хи́нное де́рево,** cinchona (*tree*).

хире́ть *v. impfv.* [*pfv.* **захире́ть**] *colloq.* **1,** to decline in health. **2,** (*of plants*) to wither.

хирома́нт *n.* palmist; palm reader. —**хирома́нтия,** *n.* palmistry.

хиру́рг *n.* surgeon. —**хирурги́ческий,** *adj.* surgical. —**хирурги́я,** *n.* surgery.

хитре́ц [*gen.* **-треца́**] *n.* cunning person.

хитреца́ *n., colloq.* shrewdness; cunning. *Also,* **хитри́нка.**

хитри́ть *v. impfv.* [*pfv.* **схитри́ть**] **1,** to use cunning; resort to guile. **2,** (*with* **с** + *instr.*) to try to outwit. **3,** *colloq.* to maneuver; contrive.

хи́тро *adv.* **1,** slyly. **2,** *colloq.* cleverly.

хитросплете́ние *n., usu. pl.* **1,** intricacies; complexities. **2,** schemes; stratagems.

хи́трость *n.f.* **1,** cunning; guile. **2,** ingenuity. **3,** ruse; trick. —**не велика́ хи́трость,** it takes no great skill.

хитроу́мие *n.* cleverness.

хитроу́мный *adj.* **1,** clever. **2,** ingenious. **3,** intricate.

хи́трый *adj.* [*short form* **хитёр, хитра́, хи́тро**] **1,** sly; crafty; cunning; wily. **2,** *colloq.* clever; ingenious.

хихи́канье *n.* giggling.

хихи́кать *v. impfv.* to giggle.

хище́ние *n.* theft; embezzlement; misappropriation.

хи́щник *n.* **1,** beast of prey; bird of prey. **2,** *fig.* predator.

хи́щнический *adj.* **1,** (*of instincts, habits, etc.*) predatory. **2,** rapacious. **3,** destructive (*to the environment*).

хи́щничество *n.* **1,** preying on others. **2,** plundering.

хи́щный *adj.* predatory; rapacious. —**хи́щная пти́ца,** bird of prey.

хладнокро́вие *n.* equanimity; composure.

хладнокро́вно *adv.* **1,** calmly. **2,** in cold blood.

хладнокро́вный *adj.* **1,** cool; calm; collected. **2,** (*of an act*) cold-blooded.

хлам *n.* rubbish; refuse; trash.

хлеб *n.* **1,** bread. **2,** loaf of bread. **3,** [*pl.* **хлеба́**] grain.

хлеба́ть *v. impfv.* [*pfv.* **хлебну́ть**] to gulp (down). *See also* **хлебну́ть.**

хле́бец [*gen.* **-бца**] *n.* small loaf of bread.

хле́бница *n.* breadbasket.

хлебну́ть *v. pfv.* **1,** *pfv. of* **хлеба́ть. 2,** *colloq.* to drink; have a drop to drink: хлебну́ть ли́шнего, to have a drop too much to drink. **3,** *fig.* (*with gen.*) *colloq.* to experience; know: хлебну́ть го́ря, to have known much sorrow.

хле́бный *adj.* **1,** bread (*attrib.*). **2,** of grain; grain (*attrib.*). **3,** rich in grain. **4,** *colloq.* profitable; lucrative.

хлебопёк *n.* baker.

хлеборо́б *n.* farmer.

хлебосо́л *n.* hospitable person; good host. —**хлебосо́льный,** *adj.* hospitable. —**хлебосо́льство,** *n.* hospitality.

хлеб-со́ль [*gen.* **хле́ба-со́ли**] *n.m. or f.* **1,** bread and salt (*symbol of hospitality*). **2,** hospitality. —*interj.* hearty appetite!

хлев [*2nd loc.* **хлеву́**; *pl.* **хлева́**] *n.* **1,** barn (*for livestock*). **2,** *colloq.* pigsty.

хлеста́ть *v. impfv.* [*pfv.* **хлестну́ть**; *pres.* **хлещу́, хле́щешь**] **1,** to whip; lash; flog. **2,** (*of rain*) to come down in torrents. **3,** (*with* **в** *or* **о** + *acc.*) to beat against. **4,** *fig.* to flay; castigate; excoriate.

хлёсткий *adj.* [*comp.* **хлёстче**] **1,** (*of a wind*) biting; (*of a sound, blow, etc.*) sharp. **2,** *fig.* biting; scathing; trenchant.

хлестну́ть *v., pfv. of* **хлеста́ть.**

хли́пкий *adj., colloq.* **1,** rickety. **2,** frail. **3,** watery.

хлоп *interj.* bang!

хло́панье *n.* banging; slamming; clapping.

хло́пать *v. impfv.* [*pfv.* **похло́пать** *or* **хло́пнуть**] **1,** to slap; bang: хло́пать кого́-нибудь по спине́, to slap someone on the back; хло́пать кулако́м по́ столу, to bang one's fist on the table. **2,** (*with instr.*) to slam (a door); crack (a whip); flap (one's wings). **3,** (*of a cork*) to pop; (*of a shot*) to ring out. **4,** to clap; applaud; (*with dat.*) applaud (someone). —**хло́пать в ладо́ши,** to clap one's hands. —**хло́пать глаза́ми** *or* **уша́ми,** to look blank.

хло́паться *v.r. impfv.* [*pfv.* **хло́пнуться**] *colloq.* to fall down; flop.

хло́пец [*gen.* **-пца**] *n., colloq.* boy; lad; youth.

хлопково́д *n.* cotton grower. —**хлопково́дство,** *n.* cotton growing. —**хлопково́дческий,** *adj.* cotton-growing.

хло́пковый *adj.* cotton. —**хло́пковое ма́сло,** cottonseed oil.

хлопкоочисти́тельный *adj., in* **хлопкоочисти́тельная маши́на,** cotton gin.

хло́пнуть *v., pfv. of* **хло́пать.** —**хло́пнуться** *refl., pfv. of* **хло́паться.**

хло́пок [*gen.* **-пка**] *n.* cotton.

хлопо́к [*gen.* **-пка́**] *n.* **1,** loud noise; bang; sound (*of a shot*); pop (*of a cork*). **2,** slap; pat (*on the back*). **3,** *pl.* clapping; applause.

хлопота́ть *v. impfv.* [*pfv.* **похлопота́ть**; *pres.* **-почу́, -по́чешь**] **1,** [*impfv. only*] to fuss; bustle about. **2,** (*with* **о**) to seek; try to get. **3,** (*with* **что́бы**) to make efforts (to); try to see to it that. **4,** (*with* **за** + *acc.*) to make efforts; intercede (on behalf of).

хлопотли́вый *adj.* **1,** busy; bustling. **2,** difficult; demanding; onerous.

хло́потный *adj., colloq.* = **хлопотли́вый** (*in sense #2*).

хлопотня́ *n., colloq.* bustling about; feverish activity.

хлопоту́н [*gen.* **-туна́**] *n.m.* [*fem.* **-ту́нья**] *colloq.* hustler; busybody.

хло́поты [*gen.* **хлопо́т**; *dat.* **хлопота́м**] *n. pl.* **1,** chores. **2,** efforts. **3,** worries; cares.

хлопу́шка [*gen. pl.* **-шек**] *n.* **1,** fly swatter. **2,** cracker (*party favor*).

хлопча́тник *n.* cotton plant.

хлопчатобума́жный *adj.* cotton.

хло́пья [*gen.* **-пьев**] *n. pl.* flakes: хло́пья сне́га, snowflakes; кукуру́зные хло́пья, corn flakes.

хлор *n.* chlorine.

хлори́д *n.* chloride.

хлори́рование *n.* chlorination.

хлори́ровать *v. impfv. & pfv.* [*pres.* **-рую, -руешь**] to chlorinate.

хло́ристый *adj.* **1,** chlorous. **2,** *in compounds,* ... chloride: хло́ристый аммо́ний/ка́лий/на́трий, ammonium/potassium/sodium chloride.

хло́рный *adj.* chloric. —**хло́рная и́звесть,** chloride of lime. —**хло́рная кислота́,** perchloric acid.

хлорофи́лл *n.* chlorophyll.

хлорофо́рм *n.* chloroform.

хлороформи́ровать *v. impfv. & pfv.* [*pres.* **-рую, -руешь**] to chloroform.

хлы́нуть *v. pfv.* **1,** to stream; gush; pour; rush. **2,** (*of rain*) to come down in torrents. **3,** (*of a crowd*) to stream; surge.

хлыст [*gen.* **хлыста́**] *n.* **1,** whip. **2,** *hist.* member of a religious sect that practiced flagellation; khlyst.

хлыщ [*gen.* **хлыща́**] *n., colloq.* fop; dandy.

хлю́пать *v. impfv., colloq.* to splash; make a splashing sound. —**хлю́пать но́сом,** to sniff.

хлю́пкий *adj., colloq.* **1,** soggy. **2,** rickety. **3,** frail.

хлябь *n.f.* **1,** *archaic* abyss. **2,** *colloq.* mud.

хля́стик *n.* half-belt (*at the back of a coat*).

хмелёк [*gen.* **-лька́**] *n., dim. of* **хмель.** —**под хмелько́м,** tipsy; high.

хмеле́ть *v. impfv., colloq.* to become tipsy; get high.

хмель *n.m.* **1,** hop (*plant*). **2,** hops. **3,** *colloq.* intoxication: во хмелю́, intoxicated.

хмельно́й *adj.* **1,** intoxicated. **2,** intoxicating. —**хмельно́е,** *n.* alcohol; liquor.

хму́рить *v. impfv.* [*pfv.* **нахму́рить**] **1,** to knit (one's brows). **2,** *in* хму́рить лицо́, to frown. —**хму́риться,** *refl.* **1,** to frown. **2,** to be overcast.

хму́рый *adj.* **1,** (*of a person*) gloomy; somber; sullen. **2,** (*of the weather, sky, etc.*) gloomy; overcast; dismal.

хна *n.* henna.

хны́канье *n., colloq.* whining; whimpering.

хны́кать *v. impfv.* [*pres.* **хны́чу, хны́чешь** *or* **хны́каю, хны́каешь**] *colloq.* to whine; whimper.

хо́бби *n. neut. indecl., colloq.* hobby.

хо́бот *n.* trunk (*of an elephant*).

ход *n.* **1,** motion: за́дний ход, reverse motion. **2,** speed: замедля́ть ход, to reduce one's speed; slow down. **3,** operation (*of a machine*). **4,** [*pl.* **хо́ды** *or* **ходы́**] stroke (*of an engine, piston, etc.*). **5,** *fig.* course; progress: ход собы́тий, course of events. Ход мы́слей, train of thought. **6,** [*pl.* **хо́ды** *or* **ходы́**] move (*in chess*); lead (*in cards*). На сороково́м ходу́, on the fortieth move. **7,** [*pl.* **хо́ды**] *fig.* move; maneuver. **8,** [*pl.* **ходы́**] entrance; door: пара́дный/чёрный ход, front/back door. **9,** [*pl.* **ходы́**] passage; passageway. **10,** *fig.* chance of success: ему́ хо́ду нет, he has no chance. **11,** *obs.* procession. —**в большо́м ходу́,** in great demand. —**в по́лном ходу́,** in full swing. —**в хо́де** (+ *gen.*), in the course of; during. —**дать ход** (+ *dat.*), to start up; set in motion. —**дать хо́ду,** *colloq.* to take to one's heels. —**знать все ходы́ и вы́ходы,** to know all the ins and outs. —**идти́ по́лным хо́дом,** to proceed apace. —**идти́ свои́м хо́дом, 1,** to proceed under one's own power *or* steam. **2,** to proceed at one's own pace. —**на по́лном ходу́,** (at) full speed. —**на ходу́, 1,** in operation. **2,** quickly; on the run. **3,** while something is in motion. —**не дава́ть хо́ду** (+ *dat.*), to give someone no chance. —**пойти́ в ход, 1,** to come into use; come into play. **2,** to become much in demand. —**по́лный ход!,** full speed ahead! —**пусти́ть в ход, 1,** to start; set in motion. **2,** *in* пусти́ть в ход все сре́дства, to move heaven and earth; leave no stone unturned. —**с хо́ду,** without stopping; while in motion.

хода́тай *n.* intercessor.

хода́тайство *n.* **1,** application; solicitation; petition. **2,** intercession.

хода́тайствовать *v. impfv.* [*pfv.* **походатайствовать;** *pres.* **-ствую, -ствуешь**] **1,** (*with* **о**) to apply (for); petition (for); solicit. **2,** (*with* **за** + *acc.*) to intercede (on behalf of).

хо́дики [*gen.* **-ков**] *n.pl., colloq.* wall clock (*driven by weights*).

ходи́ть *v. impfv.* [*pres.* **хожу́, хо́дишь**] **1,** *indeterm. of* **идти́. 2,** to walk; be able to walk. **3,** (*of trains, buses, etc.*) to run; operate. **4,** (*of news, rumors, etc.*) to be going around. **5,** (*with* **в** + *prepl.*) to wear: ходи́ть в очка́х, to wear glasses. **6,** (*with* **за** + *instr.*) to look after; care for.

хо́дкий *adj., colloq.* **1,** agile. **2,** (*of a vehicle, ship, etc.*) fast-moving. **3,** (*of merchandise*) fast-selling. **4,** (*of an expression*) currently popular.

ходово́й *adj.* **1,** *mech.* working; operational. **2,** performance (*attrib.*): ходовы́е испыта́ния, performance tests. Ходовы́е ка́чества маши́ны, performance of a car. **3,** *colloq.* popular; fast-selling. **4,** *colloq.* (*of an expression, anecdote, etc.*) currently popular. —**ходова́я пружи́на,** mainspring (*of a watch*).

ходо́к [*gen.* **-дока́**] *n.* **1,** walker. **2,** *colloq.* regular visitor (to). **3,** (*with* **на** + *acc. or* **по**) *colloq.* person who is adroit (with *or* at). **4,** *obs.* envoy; delegate.

ходу́ли [*gen.* **-лей**] *n. pl.* [*sing.* **ходу́ля**] stilts.

ходу́лочник *n.* stilt (*bird*).

ходу́льный *adj.* stilted.

ходу́н [*gen.* **-дуна́**] *n., colloq.* walker. —**ходи́ть ходуно́м, 1,** to shake violently. **2,** *fig.* to be in a whirl.

ходунки́ [*gen.* **-ко́в**] *n. pl.* walker (*device*).

ходьба́ *n.* walking; walk: полчаса́ ходьбы́, half an hour's walk.

ходя́чий *adj.* **1,** walking. **2,** (*of a sick person*) able to walk; ambulatory. **3,** *fig.* current; currently popular.

хожде́ние *n.* **1,** walking; going: хожде́ние в кино́, going to the movies. **2,** circulation (*of money*). **3,** *fig.* use; currency: име́ть широ́кое хожде́ние, to be in wide use; enjoy wide currency.

хозрасчёт *n.* self-supporting basis; operation without government support (*contr. of* **хозя́йственный расчёт**).

хозя́ин [*pl.* **хозя́ева, хозя́ев**] *n.* **1,** owner. **2,** master. **3,** (*preceded by an adj.*) (good, bad, *etc.*) administrator; manager. **4,** employer; boss. **5,** landlord. **6,** host. —**хозя́ева по́ля,** *sports* the home team. —**хозя́ин своего́ сло́ва,** man of his word.

хозя́йка [*gen. pl.* **-я́ек**] *n., fem. of* **хозя́ин.** —**дома́шняя хозя́йка,** housewife.

хозя́йничать *v. impfv.* **1,** to be in charge; run things. **2,** to keep house. **3,** *colloq.* to throw one's weight around.

хозя́йский *adj.* **1,** master's. **2,** proprietary: хозя́йское отноше́ние к, a proprietary attitude toward. **3,** *fig.* careful: хозя́йским гла́зом, with a careful eye. **4,** *fig.* imperious. —**де́ло хозя́йское,** *colloq.* it's up to you (to decide).

хозя́йственник *n.* administrator; manager.

хозя́йственность *n.f.* efficiency (*in running a household*).

хозя́йственный *adj.* **1,** economic. **2,** household (*attrib.*). **3,** thrifty; economical. —**хозя́йственное мы́ло,** kitchen soap. —**хозя́йственная су́мка,** shopping bag.

хозя́йство *n.* **1,** economy. **2,** [*usu.* **дома́шнее хозя́йство**] housekeeping. **3,** equipment; property. **4,** household equipment. **5,** farm. —**се́льское хозя́йство,** agriculture.

хозя́йствование *n.* management.

хозя́йствовать *v. impfv.* [*pres.* **-ствую, -ствуешь**] **1,** to manage; be a manager. **2,** to keep house.

хозя́йчик *n., colloq.* small proprietor.

хокке́ист *n.* hockey player.

хокке́й *n.* hockey. —**хокке́йный,** *adj.* hockey (*attrib.*).

хо́леный *adj.* well-groomed.

холе́ра *n.* cholera.

холе́рик *n.* temperamental, high-strung person. —**холери́ческий,** *adj.* choleric; temperamental; high-strung.

холе́рный *adj.* cholera (*attrib.*).

холестери́н *n.* cholesterol.

хо́лить *v. impfv.* to take care of.

хо́лка *n.* withers.

холл *n.* **1,** (meeting) hall. **2,** lobby.

холм [*gen.* **холма́**] *n.* hill.

хо́лмик *n.* small hill; knoll.

холми́стый *adj.* hilly.

хо́лод [*pl.* **холода́**] *n.* **1,** cold. **2,** *pl.* cold weather: пе́рвые холода́, first cold weather.

холода́ть *v. impfv., impers.* to get cold; turn cold.

холоде́ть *v. impfv.* [*pfv.* **похолоде́ть**] **1,** to grow cold. **2,** *fig.* to turn cold (*from fear, horror, etc.*).

холоде́ц [*gen.* **-дца́**] *n., colloq.* aspic (*of meat or fish*).

холоди́льник *n.* refrigerator; icebox.

холоди́льный *adj.* refrigeration (*attrib.*); refrigerating.

холоди́ть *v. impfv.* [*pres.* **-жу́, -ди́шь**] to cool; chill.

холо́дненький *adj., colloq.* chilly; nippy.

холодне́ть *v. impfv., impers.* to get cold; turn cold.

хо́лодно *adv.* coldly. —*adj., used predicatively* cold: здесь хо́лодно, it is cold here; мне хо́лодно, I am cold.

холоднова́тый *adj., colloq.* rather cold.

холоднокро́вный *adj., zool.* cold-blooded.

хо́лодность *n.f.* coldness.

холо́дный *adj.* [*short form* **хо́лоден, холодна́, хо́лодно**] **1,** cold. **2,** unheated. **3,** (*of a garment, blanket, etc.*) light; thin; not providing sufficient warmth. —**холо́дное ору́жие,** plain weapon (*sword, bayonet, etc.*).

холодо́к [*gen.* **-дка́**] *n., colloq.* **1,** coolness; chill. **2,** cool breeze. **3,** cool place. **4,** cool (*of the day, evening, etc.*). **5,** *fig.* chill; coolness (*in relations*).

холо́п *n.* **1,** *hist.* serf; bondsman. **2,** *fig.* lackey; stooge.

холо́пский *adj.* **1,** *hist.* serf's. **2,** *fig.* servile.

холо́пство *n.* **1,** *hist.* serfdom. **2,** *fig.* servility.

холо́пствовать *v. impfv.* [*pres.* **-ствую, -ствуешь**] **1,** to be servile. **2,** (*with* **пе́ред**) to kowtow to.

холости́ть *v. impfv.* [*pfv.* **вы́холостить;** *pres.* **-лощу́, -лости́шь**] to castrate; geld (an animal).

холосто́й *adj.* **1,** (*of a man*) single; unmarried. **2,** bachelor (*attrib.*). **3,** *mech.* idle: холосто́й ход, idling. **4,** blank: холосто́й патро́н, blank cartidge.

холостя́к [*gen.* **-стяка́**] *n.* bachelor. —**холостя́цкий,** *adj., colloq.* bachelor (*attrib.*); bachelor's.

холоще́ние *n.* castration.

холощёный *adj.* castrated; gelded.

холст [*gen.* **холста́**] *n.* **1,** linen. **2,** sackcloth; burlap. **3,** *painting* canvas.

холсти́на *n.* = **холст.**

холсти́нка *n.* **1,** piece of cloth. **2,** linen or cotton fabric.

холу́й *n., colloq.* lackey; flunky; stooge.

холщо́вый *adj.* **1,** linen. **2,** burlap.

хо́ля *n., colloq.* loving care. —**жить в хо́ле,** to be lovingly cared for.

хому́т [*gen.* **-мута́**] *n.* collar (*for a horse*).

хомя́к [*gen.* **-мяка́**] *n.* hamster.

хор [*pl.* **хоры́** *or* **хо́ры**] *n.* **1,** chorus. **2,** choir. —**хо́ром,** in a chorus; in unison; all together. *See also* **хо́ры.**

хора́л *n.* chorale.

хорва́т *n.m.* [*fem.* **-ва́тка**] Croat. —**хорва́тский,** *adj.* Croatian.

хо́рда *n., math.* chord.

хоре́й *n.* trochee. —**хоре́йческий,** *adj.* trochaic.

хорёк [*gen.* **-рька́**] *n.* polecat; fitch; ferret.

хореогра́фия *n.* choreography. —**хореóграф,** *n.* choreographer. —**хореографи́ческий,** *adj.* choreographic.

хоре́я *n.* chorea.

хори́ст *n.* member of a choir; chorister.

хорме́йстер *n.* choirmaster.

хорово́д *n.* round dance with singing.

хорово́й *adj.* choral.

хорони́ть *v. impfv.* [*pfv.* **похорони́ть;** *pres.* **-роню́, -ро́нишь**] to bury; inter.

хорохо́риться *v.r. impfv., colloq.* to swagger; bluster.

хоро́шенький *adj.* **1,** pretty; attractive; cute. **2,** *colloq.* good. **3,** *colloq., ironic* fine; nice; pretty: хоро́шенькая исто́рия, a pretty mess.

хороше́нько *adv., colloq.* properly; thoroughly. Хороше́нько отдохну́ть, to have a good rest. Сту́кните хороше́нько!, give a good knock!

хороше́ть *v. impfv.* [*pfv.* **похороше́ть**] to get prettier; become more attractive.

хоро́ший *adj.* [*short form* **хоро́ш, хороша́, хорошо́, хороши́**] **1,** good. **2,** (*short form only, usu. with* **собо́й**) pretty; attractive; good-looking.

хорошо́ *adv.* well: хорошо́ себя́ чу́вствовать, to feel well. Хорошо́ ска́зано!, well said! Хорошо́ па́хнуть, to smell good. —*adj., used predicatively* **1,** good; fine; nice: э́то хорошо́, that's good/nice. Хорошо́, что..., it's a good thing that... **2,** (*with dat.*) satisfied; happy: вам бу́дет хорошо́ там, you'll be happy there; you'll like it there. —*particle* all right; O.K.; very well. —*n. indecl.* "good" (*school grade*).

хо́ры [*gen.* **хо́ров**] *n. pl.* gallery; balcony.

хорь [*gen.* **хоря́**] *n.m.* = **хорёк.**

хорько́вый *adj.* fitch (*attrib.*).

хоте́ть *v. impfv.* [*pres.* **хочу́, хо́чешь, хо́чет, хоти́м, хоти́те, хотя́т**] **1,** to want: что вы хоти́те?, what do you want? **2,** to like; wish: хоти́те ещё ча́шку ко́фе?, would you like another cup of coffee? Де́лайте, как хоти́те, do as you like/wish/please. —**хо́чешь не хо́чешь,** like it or not.

хоте́ться *v.r. impfv.* [*pres.* **хо́чется**] *impers.* (*with dat.*) **1,** to want: мне хо́чется поговори́ть с ним, I want to have a talk with him. **2,** to feel like: ему́ не хо́чется идти́, he doesn't feel like going.

хоть *conj.* **1,** although; though. **2,** if you like. **3,** at least. **4,** even if. **5,** for example. **6,** any-: хоть что, anything; хоть где, anywhere. **7,** *used with an imperative verb in a number of idiomatic expressions:* хоть убе́й, for the life of me; хоть отбавля́й, plenty; ample; more than enough. —**хоть бы, 1,** even if. **2,** if only. —**хоть бы и так,** *colloq.* **1,** what of it?; what if it is? **2,** even so. —**хоть бы что** (+ *dat.*), *colloq.* couldn't care less. —**хоть куда́,** *colloq.* first-rate.

хотя́ *conj.* **1,** although. **2,** though. —**хотя́ бы, 1,** if only. **2,** even if. **3,** at least.

хохла́тый *adj.* crested.

хохла́ч [*gen.* **-лача́**] *n.* hooded seal.

хо́хлиться *v.r. impfv.* [*pfv.* **нахо́хлиться**] **1,** (*of a bird*) to ruffle its feathers. **2,** *fig., colloq.* to sulk.

хохо́л [*gen.* **хохла́**] *n.* **1,** crest (*of a bird*). **2,** topknot. **3,** *obs., colloq.* Ukrainian.

хохоло́к [*gen.* **-лка́**] *n., dim. of* **хохо́л** (*in senses #1 & #2*).

хо́хот *n.* loud laughter.

хохота́ть *v. impfv.* [*pres.* **хохочу́, хохо́чешь**] to laugh loudly.

хохоту́н [*gen.* **-туна́**] *n.m.* [*fem.* **-ту́нья**] *colloq.* merry fellow; one easily moved to laughter.

храбре́ц [*gen.* **-бреца́**] *n.* brave man.

храбри́ться *v.r. impfv., colloq.* to pretend not to be afraid; keep a stiff upper lip.

хра́брый *adj.* brave. —**хра́бро,** *adv.* bravely. —**хра́брость,** *n.f.* bravery.

храм *n.* temple. —**Храм Васи́лия Блаже́нного,** St. Basil's Cathedral (*on Red Square*).

хране́ние *n.* storage; safekeeping. —**ка́мера хране́ния (багажа́),** baggage room.

храни́лище *n.* storehouse; depository; respository.

храни́тель *n.m.* **1,** keeper; custodian. **2,** curator (*of a museum*).

храни́ть *v. impfv.* **1,** to keep: храни́ть письмо́/та́йну, to keep a letter/secret. Храни́ть что́-нибудь в се́йфе, to keep something in a safe. **2,** to maintain (silence, a custom, etc.).

храп *n.* **1,** snore; snoring. **2,** snorting (*of a horse*).

храпе́ть *v. impfv.* [*pres.* **-плю́, -пи́шь**] **1,** to snore. **2,** (*of a horse*) to snort.

храпови́к [*gen.* **-вика́**] *n.* ratchet. —**храпово́й,** *adj.* ratchet (*attrib.*).

храпу́н [*gen.* **-пуна́**] *n., colloq.* snorer.

хребе́т [*gen.* **-бта́**] *n.* **1,** spine; backbone. **2,** mountain range.

хрен *n.* horseradish.

хрестома́тия *n.* reader (*book*).

хризанте́ма (тэ) *n.* chrysanthemum.

хрип *n.* wheeze. —**предсме́ртный хрип,** death rattle.

хрипе́ть *v. impfv.* [*pres.* **-плю́, -пи́шь**] **1,** to wheeze. **2,** to be hoarse.

хри́плый *adj.* hoarse. —**хри́пло,** *adv.* hoarsely; in a hoarse voice.

хри́пнуть *v. impfv.* [*past* **хрип** *or* **хри́пнул, хри́пла**] to become hoarse.

хрипота́ *n.* hoarseness.

христиани́н [*pl.* **-тиа́не, -тиа́н**] *n.m.* [*fem.* **-тиа́нка**] Christian. —**христиа́нский,** *adj.* Christian. —**христиа́нство,** *n.* Christianity.

Христо́с [*gen.* **Христа́**] *n.* Christ.

хром *n.* **1,** chromium. **2,** chrome. **3,** chrome leather.

хромати́чесикй *adj.* chromatic.

хрома́ть *v. impfv.* **1,** to limp. **2,** *colloq.* to be deficient. **3,** *colloq.* to be weak; be poor (*in a certain school subject*): он хрома́ет по орфогра́фии *or* у него́ хрома́ет орфогра́фия, he is poor in spelling. —**хрома́ть на о́бе ноги́,** to flounder.

хроми́рование *n.* chrome plating.
хроми́ровать *v. impfv. & pfv.* [*pres.* **-рую, -руешь**] to plate with chrome; chrome-plate.
хро́мистый *adj.* chrome (*attrib.*): хро́мистая сталь, chrome steel.
хроми́т *n.* chromite.
хро́мовый *adj.* chrome (*attrib.*). —**хро́мовая кислота́,** chromic acid.
хромо́й *adj.* lame. —*n.* lame person.
хромоно́гий *adj.* lame.
хромосо́ма *n.* chromosome.
хромота́ *n.* lameness.
хро́ник *n., colloq.* chronically ill person.
хро́ника *n.* **1,** chronicle. **2,** news items. **3,** newsreel.
хроника́льный *adj.* chronicle (*attrib.*); in chronicle form. —**хроника́льный фильм,** newsreel.
хрони́ческий *adj.* **1,** chronic. **2,** chronically ill.
хроноло́гия *n.* chronology. —**хронологи́ческий,** *adj.* chronological.
хроно́метр *n.* **1,** *obs.* timepiece. **2,** chronometer.
хронометра́ж *n.* time (and motion) study. —**хронометражи́ст,** *n.* time-study man.
хронометри́ровать *v. impfv. & pfv.* [*pres.* **-рую, -руешь**] to time; clock.
хронометри́ст *n.* timer; timekeeper.
хру́пкий *adj.* [*short form* **-пок, -пка́, -пко**] **1,** fragile; brittle. **2,** frail; delicate.
хру́пкость *n.f.* **1,** fragility. **2,** frailty.
хруст *n.* crunch; crunching sound.
хруста́лик *n.* **1,** *colloq.* something made of crystal. **2,** lens of the eye.
хруста́ль [*gen.* **-сталя́**] *n.m.* **1,** crystal. **2,** item made of crystal.
хруста́льный *adj.* **1,** crystal. **2,** like crystal.
хруста́н *n.* dotterel.
хрусте́ть *v. impfv.* [*pfv.* **хру́стнуть;** *pres.* **хрущу́, хрусти́шь**] to crunch.
хрущ [*gen.* **хруща́**] *n.* cockchafer.
хрю́канье *n.* grunting.
хрю́кать *v. impfv.* [*pfv.* **хрю́кнуть**] to grunt.
хряк [*gen.* **хряка́**] *n.* male hog.
хрящ [*gen.* **хряща́**] *n.* cartilage. —**хрящева́тый,** *adj.* cartilaginous. —**хрящево́й,** *adj.* cartilage (*attrib.*).
худе́ть *v. impfv.* [*pfv.* **похуде́ть**] to get thin; lose weight.
ху́до *n., obs., colloq.* harm. —*adv.* badly; poorly: ху́до оде́тый, poorly dressed. —*adj., used predicatively* (*with dat.*) **1,** bad; in a bad way. **2,** unwell: ему́ ху́до, he is not feeling well.
худоба́ *n.* thinness; leanness.
худо́жественность *n.f.* artistic value; artistry.
худо́жественный *adj.* **1,** art (*attrib.*); of art. **2,** artistic. —**худо́жественная литерату́ра,** fiction. —**худо́жественный фильм,** feature film.
худо́жество *n.* **1,** *obs.* art. **2,** *colloq.* trick; prank.
худо́жник *n.m.* [*fem.* **-ница**] **1,** artist. **2,** painter.
худо́й *adj.* **1,** [*comp.* **ху́же**] bad. **2,** [*comp.* **худе́е**] thin; skinny. **3,** [*comp.* **худе́е**] *colloq.* worn; tattered; full of holes. —**на худо́й коне́ц,** *colloq.* if worst comes to worst. *See also* **ху́же.**
худоща́вый *adj.* thin; lean; skinny.
худше́е *n., decl. as an adj.* **1,** the worse: переме́на к ху́дшему, change for the worse. **2,** the worst: пригото́виться к ху́дшему, to be prepared for the worst.
ху́дший *adj., used only as a modifer, comp. and superl. of* **плохо́й** *and* **худо́й,** worse; worst. —**в ху́дшем слу́чае,** at worst.
ху́же *adj., comp. of* **плохо́й** *and* **худо́й,** worse. —*adv., comp. of* **пло́хо** *and* **ху́до,** worse. —**тем ху́же,** so much the worse. —**ху́же всего́,** worst of all. —**ху́же всего́ то, что...,** the worst of it is that...
хула́ *n.* (verbal) abuse.
хулига́н *n.* hooligan; hoodlum.
хулига́нить *v. impfv.* to behave like a hooligan or hoodlum.
хулига́нский *adj.* like that of a hooligan or hoodlum.
хулига́нство *n.* hooliganism; disorderly conduct.
хули́тель *n.m.* detractor.
хули́ть *v. impfv.* to disparage.
ху́нта *n.* junta.
хурма́ *n.* persimmon.
ху́тор [*pl.* **хутора́**] *n.* farm. —**хуторско́й,** *adj.* farm (*attrib.*).

Ц

Ц, ц *n. neut.* 23rd letter of the Russian alphabet.
ца́пать *v. impfv.* [*pfv.* **ца́пнуть**] *colloq.* to grab; snatch.
ца́пля [*gen. pl.* **-пель**] *n.* heron. —**бе́лая ца́пля,** egret.
ца́пнуть *v., pfv. of* **ца́пать.**
цара́пать *v. impfv.* **1,** [*pfv.* **цара́пнуть**] to scratch. **2,** [*pfv.* **нацара́пать**] *colloq.* to scribble; scrawl. —**цара́паться,** *refl.* [*impfv. only*] **1,** to scratch; make scratching sounds; have a tendency to scratch. **2,** to scratch each other.
цара́пина *n.* scratch.
цара́пнуть *v., pfv. of* **цара́пать.**
царе́вич *n.* tsarevitch.
царе́вна [*gen. pl.* **-вен**] *n.* tsarevna.
цареуби́йство *n.* regicide.
цари́зм *n.* tsarism.
цари́ть *v. impfv.* **1,** *obs.* (*of a monarch*) to reign. **2,** *fig.* (*of silence*) to reign; (*of conditions*) to prevail.
цари́ца *n.* **1,** tsarina. **2,** *fig.* (*with gen.*) queen (of):

цари́ца мод, queen of fashion. —**цари́ца ба́ла,** belle of the ball.

ца́рский *adj.* **1,** of the tsar; tsar's. **2,** tsarist. **3,** *fig.* regal.

ца́рственный *adj.* regal; majestic.

ца́рство *n.* **1,** kingdom; realm. **2,** reign. **3,** *fig.* kingdom: живо́тное ца́рство, animal kingdom. —**венча́ние на ца́рство,** coronation.

ца́рствование *n.* reign. —**в ца́рствование** (+ *gen.*), during the reign of.

ца́рствовать *v. impfv.* [*pres.* **-ствую, -ствуешь**] to reign.

царь [*gen.* **царя́**] *n.m.* **1,** tsar. **2,** *fig.* king: царь звере́й, king of beasts.

цвести́ *v. impfv.* [*pres.* **цвету́, цветёшь;** *past* **цвёл, цвела́, цвело́**] **1,** to bloom; blossom; flower. **2,** (*with instr.*) *fig.* to be the picture of (beauty, health, etc.). **3,** *fig.* to flourish.

цвет *n.* **1,** [*pl.* **цвета́**] color. **2,** [*pl.* **цветы́**] (*sing. rare*) flower. —**во цве́те лет,** in one's prime; in the prime of life. —**в по́лном цвету́,** in full bloom.

цвете́ние *n.* blooming; blossoming; flowering.

цвети́стый *adj.* **1,** colorful. **2,** *fig.* flowery; florid.

цветко́вый *adj.* (*of plants*) flowering.

цветни́к [*gen.* **-ника́**] *n.* flower bed; flower garden.

цветно́й *adj.* colored; color (*attrib.*). —**цветна́я капу́ста,** cauliflower. —**цветно́й каранда́ш,** crayon. —**цветны́е мета́ллы,** non-ferrous metals. —**цветно́е стекло́,** stained glass.

цветово́дство *n.* floriculture.

цветово́й *adj.* color (*attrib.*).

цвето́к [*gen.* **-тка́;** *pl.* **цветы́, цвето́в, цвета́м**] *n.* flower.

цветоло́же *n., bot.* receptacle.

цветоно́жка [*gen. pl.* **-жек**] *n., bot.* pedicel.

цвето́чек [*gen.* **-чка**] *n., dim. of* **цвето́к.**

цвето́чница *n.* flower girl.

цвето́чный *adj.* flower (*attrib.*); floral.

цвету́щий *adj.* **1,** flowering; blossoming; blooming. **2,** *fig.* healthy; robust. **3,** *fig.* flourishing; prospering.

цеди́лка [*gen. pl.* **-лок**] *n., colloq.* strainer.

цеди́ть *v. impfv.* [*pres.* **цежу́, це́дишь**] **1,** to strain; filter. **2,** to pour slowly (*through a narrow opening*). **3,** to sip. **4,** *colloq.* to utter (*often slowly and with suppressed anger*).

це́дра *n.* dried lemon or orange peel.

це́зий *n.* cesium.

цейтно́т *n., chess* time trouble.

целе́бный *adj.* **1,** medicinal; curative. **2,** healthful; salubrious.

целево́й *adj.* having a particular purpose. —**целева́я устано́вка,** aim; objective.

целенапра́вленный *adj.* purposeful.

целесообра́зный *adj.* advisable; expedient. —**целесообра́зность,** *n.f.* advisability; expediency.

целеустремлённый *adj.* purposeful.

целико́м *adv.* **1,** whole: проглоти́ть целико́м, to swallow whole. **2,** wholly; entirely. —**целико́м и по́лностью,** completely; fully.

целина́ *n.* virgin land; virgin soil.

цели́нный *adj.* virgin: цели́нные зе́мли, virgin lands.

цели́тельный *adj.* healing; curative.

це́лить *v. impfv.* (*with* **в** + *acc.*) to aim (at). *Also,* **це́литься,** *refl.*

целлофа́н *n.* cellophane. —**целлофа́новый,** *adj.* cellophane.

целлуло́ид *n.* celluloid. —**целлуло́идный,** *adj.* celluloid.

целлюло́за *n.* cellulose. —**целлюло́зный,** *adj.* cellulose.

целова́ть *v. impfv.* [*pfv.* **поцелова́ть;** *pres.* **-лу́ю, -лу́ешь**] to kiss. —**целова́ться,** *refl.* (*of two people*) to kiss.

це́лое *n., decl. as an adj.* **1,** whole; the whole. **2,** *math.* whole number; integer.

целому́дренный *adj.* chaste. —**целому́дрие,** *n.* chastity.

це́лостность *n.f.* unity. —**территориа́льная це́лостность,** territorial integrity.

це́лостный *adj.* unified; integrated.

це́лость *n.f.* **1,** (*with gen.*) the safety (of). **2,** wholeness; unity. —**в це́лости,** intact. —**в це́лости и сохра́нности,** safe and sound.

це́лый *adj.* **1,** whole; entire. **2,** intact; undamaged. **3,** safe; unharmed: цел и невреди́м, safe and sound. —**в це́лом, 1,** on the whole. **2,** as a whole. —**в о́бщем и це́лом,** on the whole; all in all. —**по це́лым дням; це́лыми дня́ми,** for days on end. *See also* **це́лое.**

цель *n.f.* **1,** target; mark. **2,** aim; goal; object; purpose. —**с це́лью; в це́лях** (+ *gen. or with inf.*), with the aim of; for the purpose of. —**с э́той це́лью,** toward this end.

це́льность *n.f.* unity; wholeness.

це́льный *adj.* **1,** whole; of one piece. **2,** single; unified; integrated. **3,** (*of a person, his nature, etc.*) sound; steady; solid. **4,** complete; finished. **5,** (*of milk, blood, etc.*) whole.

Це́льсий *n.* Celsius; Centigrade: де́сять гра́дусов по Це́льсию, ten degrees Celsius/Centigrade.

цеме́нт *n.* cement.

цементи́ровать *v. impfv. & pfv.* [*pres.* **-рую, -руешь**] **1,** to cement. **2,** to casehardon.

цеме́нтный *adj.* cement.

цена́ [*acc.* **це́ну;** *pl.* **це́ны**] *n.* **1,** price. **2,** *fig.* worth. Знать це́ну (+ *dat.*), to know the worth (*or* value) of. —**ценой** (+ *gen.*), at the cost of. —**цены́ нет** (+ *dat.*), priceless.

ценз *n.* requirement: возрастно́й ценз, age requirement.

це́нзор *n.* censor.

цензу́ра *n.* **1,** censorship. **2,** censorship office.

цензу́рный *adj.* **1,** censorship (*attrib.*). **2,** able to pass censorship; printable.

цени́тель *n.m.* judge; connoisseur.

цени́ть *v. impfv.* [*pres.* **ценю́, це́нишь**] **1,** *obs.* to appraise; evaluate. **2,** to judge. **3,** to appreciate. **4,** to value; prize.

це́нник *n.* price list.

це́нность *n.f.* **1,** value. **2,** *pl.* valuables. **3,** *pl.* values.

це́нный *adj.* **1,** valuable. **2,** (*of a parcel*) having a stated value. —**це́нные бума́ги,** securities.

цент *n.* cent.

це́нтнер *n.* centner (*100 kilograms*).

центр *n.* center.

централиза́ция *n.* centralization.

централи́зм *n.* centralism. —**демократи́ческий централи́зм,** democratic centralism.

централизо́ванный *adj.* centralized.

централизова́ть *v. impfv. & pfv.* [*pres.* **-зу́ю, -зу́ешь**] to centralize.
центра́льный *adj.* central.
центробе́жный *adj.* centrifugal: центробе́жная си́ла, centrifugal force.
центрово́й *adj.* center (*attrib.*); central. —*n.* center (*on a basketball team*).
центростреми́тельный *adj.* centripetal.
цеп [*gen.* **цепа́**] *n.* flail.
цепене́ть *v. impfv.* [*pfv.* **оцепене́ть**] to become numb; become rigid.
це́пкий *adj.* [*short form* **це́пок, цепка́, це́пко**] **1,** prehensile; tenacious. **2,** *fig.* keen; perceptive. **3,** (*of one's memory*) retentive. **4,** *fig., colloq.* persistent; dogged.
це́пкость *n.f.* tenacity.
цепля́ться *v.r impfv.* (*with* **за** + *acc.*) to cling (to).
цепно́й *adj.* chain (*attrib.*). —**цепно́е колесо́,** sprocket wheel. —**цепна́я реа́кция,** chain reaction.
цепо́чка [*gen. pl.* **-чек**] *n.* **1,** small chain: цепо́чка для часо́в, watch chain. **2,** row; line; file: цепо́чкой, in a line.
цеппели́н *n.* zeppelin.
цепь [*2nd loc.* **цепи́**; *pl.* **це́пи, цепе́й, цепя́м**] *n.f.* **1,** chain. **2,** *fig.* (*with gen.*) chain (*of mountains, islands, events, etc.*). **3,** *electricity* circuit.
церебра́льный *adj.* cerebral. —**церебра́льный парали́ч,** cerebral palsy.
церемониа́л *n.* ceremonial; ritual. —**церемониа́льный,** *adj.* ceremonial.
церемо́ниться *v.r. impfv.* to stand on ceremony.
церемо́ния *n.* **1,** ceremony. **2,** *pl., colloq.* ceremony; formalities. Без дальне́йших церемо́ний, without further ado. —**церемо́нный,** *adj.* ceremonious.
це́рий *n.* cerium.
церковнославя́нский *adj.* Church Slavonic.
церко́вный *adj.* of the church; church (*attrib.*).
це́рковь [*gen., dat., & prepl.* **це́ркви**; *instr.* **це́рковью**; *pl.* **це́ркви, церкве́й, церква́м**] *n.f.* church.
цесаре́вич *n.* crown prince (*in tsarist Russia*).
цеса́рка [*gen. pl.* **-рок**] *n.* guinea fowl; guinea hen.
цех *n.* **1,** shop (*in a factory*). **2,** *hist.* guild.
цехово́й *adj.* shop (*attrib.*). —**цехово́й профсою́з,** craft union.
цеце́ *n.f. indecl.* [*often* **му́ха цеце́**] tsetse fly.
циа́н *n.* cyanogen.
циани́д *n.* cyanide.
циа́нистый *adj.* cyanic. —**циа́нистый ка́лий,** potassium cyanide.
циа́новый *adj.* cyanic.
циано́з *n.* cyanosis.
цивилиза́ция *n.* civilization.
цивилизо́ванный *adj.* civilized.
цивилизова́ть *v. impfv. & pfv.* [*pres.* **-зу́ю, -зу́ешь**] to civilize.
циви́льный *adj., obs.* civilian.
цига́рка [*gen. pl.* **-рок**] *n., colloq.* hand-rolled cigarette.
циге́йка *n.* fur of the tsigai sheep (*a common variety in the USSR*).
цика́да *n.* cicada.
цикл *n.* cycle.
цикламе́н *n.* cyclamen.
цикли́ческий *adj.* cyclical. *Also,* **цикли́чный.**
цикло́н *n.* cyclone. —**циклони́ческий,** *adj.* cyclonic.
циклотро́н *n.* cyclotron.
цико́рий *n.* chicory. —**цико́рный,** *adj.* chicory (*attrib.*).
цику́та *n.* water hemlock.
цили́ндр *n.* **1,** cylinder. **2,** top hat. —**цилиндри́ческий,** *adj.* cylindrical.
цимба́лы [*gen.* **-ба́л**] *n. pl.* dulcimer.
цинга́ *n.* scurvy.
цини́зм *n.* cynicism. —**ци́ник,** *n.* cynic.
цини́ческий *adj.* = **цини́чный.**
цини́чный *adj.* **1,** cynical. **2,** indecent; off-color. —**цини́чность,** *n.f.* cynicism.
цинк *n.* zinc. —**ци́нковый,** *adj.* zinc (*attrib.*).
ци́нния *n.* zinnia.
цино́вка [*gen. pl.* **-вок**] *n.* mat.
цирк *n.* circus.
цирка́ч [*gen.* **-кача́**] *n., colloq.* circus performer.
цирково́й *adj.* circus (*attrib.*).
цирко́н *n.* zircon.
цирко́ний *n.* zirconium.
циркули́ровать *v. impfv.* [*pres.* **-рую, -руешь**] to circulate.
ци́ркуль *n.m.* pair of compasses (*for drawing*).
циркуля́р *n.* circular; directive.
циркуля́ция *n.* circulation.
цирро́з *n.* cirrhosis.
цирю́льник *n., obs.* barber.
цирю́льня [*gen. pl.* **-лен**] *n., obs.* barbershop.
цисте́рна *n.* **1,** cistern; tank. **2,** tank car.
цитаде́ль (дэ) *n.f.* citadel.
цита́та *n.* quotation.
цити́рование *n.* quoting; citing.
цити́ровать *v. impfv.* [*pfv.* **процити́ровать**; *pres.* **-рую, -руешь**] to quote; cite.
цитоло́гия *n.* cytology. —**цитологи́ческий,** *adj.* cytological.
ци́тра *n.* zither.
цитра́т *n.* citrate.
ци́трус *n.* citrus.
ци́трусовый *adj.* citrus. —**ци́трусовые,** *n. pl.* citrus plants.
цифербла́т *n.* dial (*of an instrument*); face (*of a clock*).
ци́фра *n.* number; numeral; figure.
цифрово́й *adj.* numerical. —**цифрова́я вычисли́тельная маши́на,** digital computer.
ци́церо *n. neut. or m. indecl., typog.* pica.
цо́кать *v. impfv.* [*pfv.* **цо́кнуть**] to clatter; clank.
цо́коль *n.m.* socle.
цо́кот *n.* clatter; clank.
цуг *n.* team of horses harnessed in tandem or in pairs. —**цу́гом,** in tandem.
цука́т *n.* candied fruit; candied peel.
цыга́н [*pl.* **цыга́не, цыга́н, цыга́нам**] *n.m.* [*fem.* **цыга́нка**] Gypsy. —**цыга́нский,** *adj.* Gypsy.
цы́пки [*gen.* **-пок**] *n. pl., colloq.* red spots (*on the skin*).
цыплёнок [*gen.* **-нка**; *pl.* **цыпля́та, цыпля́т**] *n.* chicken; chick.
цы́почки *n. pl.* tiptoes. —**стать на цы́почки,** to stand on one's tiptoes. —**ходи́ть на цы́почках,** to tiptoe.

Ч

Ч, ч *n. neut.* 24th letter of the Russian alphabet.
чаба́н [*gen.* **-бана́**] *n.* shepherd.
чабёр [*gen.* **-бра́**] *n.* savory (*plant*). *Also,* **ча́бер** [*gen.* **-бра**].
чабре́ц *also,* **чебре́ц** [*gen.* **-реца́**] *n.* thyme.
ча́вкать *v. impfv.* **1,** to munch; eat noisily. **2,** to tramp; tread noisily.
чад [*2nd loc.* **чаду́**] *n.* **1,** fumes. **2,** daze: быть (как) в чаду́, to be in a daze.
чади́ть *v. impfv.* [*pfv.* **начади́ть;** *pres.* **чажу́, чади́шь**] **1,** to smoke; emit fumes. **2,** (*with instr.*) to give off (*while smoking, cooking, etc.*).
ча́дный *adj.* **1,** smoky. **2,** smoking. **3,** *fig.* dazed. **4,** *fig.* deadening.
ча́до *n., archaic* offspring; child.
чадра́ *n.* veil worn by Moslem women.
чаёвничать *v. impfv., colloq.* to (leisurely) drink tea.
чаевы́е *n. pl., decl. as an adj.* tip; gratuity.
чаепи́тие *n.* drinking of tea.
чаи́нка [*gen. pl.* **-нок**] *n.* tea leaf.
чай [*2nd gen.* **ча́ю**] *n.* tea. —**дать на чай** (+ *dat.*), to tip (someone).
ча́йка [*gen. pl.* **ча́ек**] *n.* gull; sea gull.
ча́йная *n., decl. as an adj.* tearoom.
ча́йник *n.* teakettle; teapot.
ча́йница *n.* tea caddy.
ча́йный *adj.* tea (*attrib.*). —**ча́йная ло́жка,** teaspoon. —**ча́йная ча́шка,** teacup.
чал *n.* mooring line.
ча́лить *v. impfv.* to moor (a ship).
ча́лка [*gen. pl.* **-лок**] *n.* mooring line.
чалма́ *n.* turban.
ча́лый *adj.* roan.
чан [*pl.* **чаны́**] *n.* vat.
ча́ра *n., archaic* goblet.
ча́рка [*gen. pl.* **-рок**] *n., archaic* cup.
чарова́ть *v. impfv.* [*pres.* **-ру́ю, -ру́ешь**] to charm; captivate.
чаровни́ца *n.* charming woman; enchantress.
чароде́й *n.* **1,** sorcerer; magician. **2,** *fig.* charmer. —**чароде́йка,** *n.* sorceress; *fig.* enchantress. —**чароде́йство,** *n.* sorcery; witchcraft.
чару́ющий *adj.* charming; captivating; enchanting.
ча́ры [*gen.* **чар**] *n. pl.* **1,** *obs.* magic charm. **2,** charm; charms.
час [*gen.* **ча́са,** *but after 2, 3, & 4* **часа́;** *pl.* **часы́, часо́в**] *n.* **1,** hour. **2,** (*in telling time*) o'clock: пять часо́в, five o'clock; в семь часо́в, at seven o'clock. Час дня, 1 P.M.; час но́чи, 1 A.M. —**в до́брый час!,** good luck! —**в кото́ром часу́?,** (at) what time? —**кото́рый (тепе́рь) час?,** what time is it? —**расти́ не по дням, а по часа́м,** to grow by the hour; shoot up like a beanstalk. —**с ча́су на час,** at any hour; at any moment. —**час о́т часу,** by the hour; by the minute: ему́ стано́вится лу́чше час о́т часу, he is getting better by the minute; he is improving steadily. —**час о́т часу не ле́гче!,** things are getting worse by the minute. —**часа́ми,** for hours. *See also* **часы́.**
часо́вня [*gen. pl.* **-вен**] *n.* chapel.
часово́й *adj.* **1,** lasting an hour; hour-long. **2,** hourly; per hour. **3,** *colloq.* one-o'clock (*attrib.*). **4,** clock (*attrib.*); watch (*attrib.*). —*n.* sentry. —**часово́й по́яс,** time zone. —**часова́я стре́кла,** hour hand. —**часовы́е стре́лки,** hands of a clock. —**по часово́й стре́лке,** clockwise. —**про́тив часово́й стре́лки,** counterclockwise.
часовщи́к [*gen.* **-щика́**] *n.* watchmaker.
часте́нько *adv., colloq.* fairly often.
части́ца *n.* **1,** small part. **2,** particle: части́ца пы́ли, particle of dust. **3,** *gram.* particle.
части́чный *adj.* partial. —**части́чно,** *adv.* partly; partially.
ча́стник *n., colloq.* private trader.
ча́стное *n., decl. as an adj.* **1,** *math.* quotient. **2,** the particular.
ча́стность *n.f.* detail. —**в ча́стности,** in particular; specifically.
ча́стный *adj.* **1,** private. **2,** particular; individual. —**ча́стный ито́г,** subtotal. —**ча́стным о́бразом,** privately. *See also* **ча́стное.**
ча́сто *adv.* **1,** often; frequently. **2,** densely; close together.
частоко́л *n.* fence; paling.
частота́ *n.* **1,** frequency: частота́ слу́чаев, frequency of cases. **2,** [*pl.* **часто́ты**] *physics; radio* frequency: ультравысо́кая частота́, ultrahigh frequency.
часто́тный *adj.* frequency (*attrib.*).
часту́шка [*gen. pl.* **-шек**] *n.* ditty; jingle.
ча́стый *adj.* [*comp.* **ча́ще**] **1,** frequent. **2,** quick; rapid; rapid-fire. **3,** dense; thick. **4,** set close together; close. **5,** (*of a comb, sieve, etc.*) fine. **6,** (*of rain*) steady.
часть [*pl.* **ча́сти, часте́й, частя́м**] *n.f.* **1,** part: ра́вные ча́сти, equal parts; запасны́е ча́сти, spare parts. Ча́сти те́ла, parts of the body. **2,** *mil.* unit. **3,** department: уче́бная часть, teaching department. **4,** *colloq.* field; sphere: не по мое́й ча́сти, out of my line/province. —**бо́льшая часть** (+ *gen.*), most (of). —**бо́ль-**

шей частью; по бóльшей части, for the most part. —**по частям,** in parts; piecemeal.
частью *adv.* partly; in part.
часы́ [*gen.* **часóв**] *n. pl.* **1,** clock; watch. **2,** *mil.* sentry duty: стоя́ть на часа́х, to stand guard. **3,** *in* **песóчные часы́,** hourglass; **сóлнечные часы́,** sundial. —**рабóтать как часы́,** to work like clockwork; perform flawlessly.
ча́хлый *adj.* **1,** (*of a person*) sickly. **2,** (*of plants*) withered.
ча́хнуть *v. impfv.* [*pfv.* **зача́хнуть;** *past* **чах** *or* **ча́хнул, ча́хла, ча́хло**] **1,** (*of plants*) to wither; wilt. **2,** (*of persons*) to become weak; fade; waste away.
чахóтка *n., colloq.* consumption; tuberculosis. —**чахóточный,** *adj., colloq.* consumptive.
ча́ша *n.* **1,** drinking bowl (*used in olden times*). Кругова́я ча́ша, loving cup. **2,** large bowl. —**ча́ша весóв,** scale: склони́ть ча́шу весóв в пóльзу (+ *gen.*), to tip the scales in favor of. —**ча́ша терпе́ния,** one's patience.
чашели́стик *n.* sepal.
ча́шечка [*gen. pl.* **-чек**] *n.* **1,** small cup. **2,** *bot.* calyx. —**колéнная ча́шечка,** kneecap.
ча́шка [*gen. pl.* **-шек**] *n.* cup. —**колéнная ча́шка,** kneecap.
ча́ща *n.* dense forest.
ча́ще *adj., comp. of* **ча́стый.** —*adv., comp. of* **ча́сто.** —**ча́ще всегó,** most often; usually.
чащóба *n., colloq.* = **ча́ща.**
ча́яние *n.* hope; expectation. —**па́че ча́яния,** *see* **па́че.**
ча́ять *v. impfv.* [*pres.* **ча́ю, ча́ешь**] *obs.* to expect; hope. —**души́ не ча́ять в** (+ *prepl.*), to idolize; adore; dote upon.
чва́ниться *v.r. impfv.* to swagger; boast.
чванли́вый *adj.* conceited; pretentious.
чва́нный *adj.* arrogant; conceited.
чва́нство *n.* arrogance; conceit.
чебрéц *n.* = **чабрéц.**
чебурéк *n.* mutton pie (*Caucasian dish*).
чегó (vo) *pron., gen. of* **что.** —*adv., colloq.* why?; what for?: чегó я туда́ пойду́?, why should I go there? —**до чегó,** how!: до чегó она́ краси́ва!, how lovely she is! —**пóсле чегó,** after which. —**чегó бы не,** what: чегó бы он не дал за э́то!, what he wouldn't give for that! —**чегó дóброго,** for all one knows.
чей [*fem.* **чья;** *neut.* **чьё;** *pl.* **чьи;** *gen.* **чьегó, чьей, чьих;** *acc. fem.* **чью;** *dat.* **чьему́, чьей, чьим;** *instr.* **чьим, чьей, чьи́ми;** *prepl.* **чьём, чьей, чьих**] *poss. pron.* **1,** *interr.* whose?: чья э́та шля́па?, whose hat is this? **2,** *rel.* whose: человéк, чьё и́мя извéстно всем, a man whose name is known to all.
чéй-либо [*infl. like* **чей**] *indef. pron.* = **чéй-нибудь.**
чéй-нибудь [*infl. like* **чей**] *indef. pron.* someone's; somebody's; anyone's; anybody's.
чéй-то [*infl. like* **чей**] *indef. pron.* someone's; somebody's.
чек *n.* **1,** check. **2,** bill; receipt.
чека́ *n.* pin; linchpin.
Чека́ *n. fem. indecl., contr. of* **Чрезвыча́йная коми́ссия,** Cheka (*Soviet security agency, 1917-22*).
чека́н *n.* stamp; punch; die.
чека́нить *v. impfv.* [*pfv.* **отчека́нить**] **1,** to mint; coin. **2,** to engrave; emboss. **3,** *fig.* to articulate.
чека́нка *n.* **1,** minting (*of coins*); mintage. **2,** embossed design.
чека́нный *adj.* **1,** engraving. **2,** engraved; embossed. **3,** *fig.* precise; crisp.
чеки́ст *n.* member of the Cheka.
чéковый *adj.* check (*attrib.*); checking. —**чéковая кни́жка,** checkbook.
челéста *n.* celesta.
чёлка *n.* bangs (*of hair*): носи́ть чёлку, to wear bangs.
чёлн [*gen.* **челна́;** *pl.* **челны́** *or* **чёлны**] *n.* canoe.
челнóк [*gen.* **-нока́**] *n.* **1,** = **чёлн. 2,** shuttle. —**челнóчный,** *adj.* shuttle (*attrib.*).
челó [*pl.* **чёла**] *n., archaic* forehead; brow. —**бить челóм** (+ *dat.*), **1,** to bow humbly before. **2,** to beseech. **3,** to thank earnestly.
человéк [*gen. pl.* **человéк;** *other pl. forms rarely used*] *n.* **1,** person; man. **2,** man; mankind: человéк – разу́мное существó, man is a rational being.
человеконенави́стник *n.* misanthrope. —**человеконенави́стнический,** *adj.* misanthropic. —**человеконенави́стничество,** *n.* misanthropy.
человекообра́зный *adj.* anthropomorphous; anthropoid.
человекоподóбный *adj.* anthropoid; manlike.
человéко-ча́с [*pl.* **-часы́, -часóв**] *n.* man-hour.
человéческий *adj.* **1,** human. **2,** humane. —**человéческий род,** the human race.
человéчество *n.* mankind; humanity.
человéчный *adj.* humane. —**человéчность,** *n.f.* humaneness; humanity.
чéлюсть *n.f.* **1,** jaw; jawbone. **2,** denture; set of false teeth. —**челюстнóй,** *adj.* jaw (*attrib.*); jawbone (*attrib.*).
чéлядь *n.f.* servants.
чем *pron., instr. of* **что.** —*conj.* **1,** than: лу́чше пóздно, чем никогда́, better late than never. Бóльше чем когда́-либо ра́ньше, more than ever before. **2,** (*with* **тем**) the..., the...: чем ра́ньше, тем лу́чше, the sooner the better. **3,** (*with inf.*) instead of; rather than.
чём *pron., prepl. of* **что.**
чемери́ца *n.* hellebore.
чемода́н *n.* suitcase. —**чемода́нчик,** *n.* small suitcase.
чемпиóн *n.* champion. —**чемпиона́т,** *n.* championship (*tournament*). —**чемпиóнский,** *adj.* championship (*attrib.*). —**чемпиóнство,** *n.* championship.
чему́ *pron., dat. of* **что.**
чепéц [*gen.* **-пца́**] *n.* cap worn indoors by elderly women, usually tied under the chin.
чепуха́ *n., colloq.* **1,** nonsense. **2,** trifling matter. **3,** trifling amount.
чéпчик *n.* **1,** *dim. of* **чепéц. 2,** (baby's) bonnet.
червеобра́зный *adj.* vermiform. —**червеобра́зный отрóсток,** vermiform appendix.
чéрви [*gen.* **-вéй**] *n. pl., cards* hearts.
черви́веть *v. impfv.* [*pfv.* **очерви́веть**] to become wormy.
черви́вый *adj.* worm-eaten; wormy.
червóнец [*gen.* **-нца**] *n.* **1,** *pre-rev.* three-ruble gold coin. **2,** ten-ruble note in use from 1922 through 1947.
червóнный *adj.* **1,** *archaic* red; scarlet. **2,** *cards* of hearts: червóнный туз, ace of hearts. —**червóнное зóлото,** pure gold.
червотóчина *n.* **1,** wormhole. **2,** *fig.* flaw.
чéрвы [*gen.* **черв**] *n. pl.* = **чéрви.**
червь [*gen.* **червя́;** *pl.* **чéрви, червéй, червя́м**] *n.m.* worm.

червя́к [*gen.* **-вяка́**] *n.* = **червь.** —**заморить червяка́,** *colloq.* to have a bite to eat.
червя́чный *adj., mech.* worm (*attrib.*): червя́чная шестерня́, worm gear.
червячо́к [*gen.* **-чка́**] *n.* small worm. —**заморить червячка́,** *colloq.* to have a bite to eat.
черда́к [*gen.* **-дака́**] *n.* attic. —**черда́чный,** *adj.* attic (*attrib.*).
черёд [*gen.* **череда́**] *n., colloq.* **1,** (one's) turn. **2,** time: наста́л черёд (+ *inf.*), the time has come to... —**идти́ свои́м черёдо́м,** to take its normal course.
череда́ *n.* **1,** *obs.* = **черёд. 2,** column; file. **3,** *fig.* sequence; chain. **4,** bur marigold (*flower*).
чередова́ние *n.* alternation.
чередова́ть *v. impfv.* [*pres.* **-ду́ю, -ду́ешь**] to alternate. —**чередова́ться,** *refl.* to alternate; take turns.
че́рез *prep., with acc.* **1,** across: перейти́ че́рез у́лицу, to walk across the street; cross the street. **2,** over: перепры́гнуть че́рез забо́р, to jump over the fence. **3,** through: идти́ че́рез лес, to walk through the forest. **4,** via; by way of: е́хать че́рез Минск, to go by way of Minsk. **5,** in (*expressing time from the present*): я приду́ че́рез де́сять мину́т, I'll come in ten minutes. **6,** after (*an interval of*): верну́ться че́рез год, to return after a year; че́рез де́сять лет по́сле войны́, ten years after the war. **7,** through; with the aid of: говори́ть че́рез перево́дчика, to speak through an interpreter. **8,** *indicating intervals of two:* че́рез день, every other day. Они́ живу́т че́рез дом от нас, they live two houses away from us. **9,** *indicating a specified interval:* печа́тать че́рез два интерва́ла, to double-space. Они́ живу́т че́рез три до́ма отсю́да, they live three houses away.
черёмуха *n.* a kind of cherry tree.
черено́к [*gen.* **-нка́**] *n.* **1,** handle; haft. **2,** cutting; graft.
че́реп [*pl.* **черепа́**] *n.* skull; cranium.
черепа́ха *n.* **1,** turtle; tortoise. **2,** tortoise shell.
черепа́ховый *adj.* **1,** turtle (*attrib.*). **2,** tortoise-shell (*attrib.*).
черепа́ший [*fem.* **-шья**] *adj.* **1,** turtle (*attrib.*); turtle's. **2,** *fig.* snail-like: черепа́шьим ша́гом, at a snail's pace.
черепи́ца *n.* (unglazed) tile. —**черепи́чный,** *adj.* tile (*attrib.*); tiled.
черепно́й *adj.* cranial. —**черепна́я коро́бка,** cranium.
черепо́к [*gen.* **-пка́**] *n.* fragment of pottery. —**разби́ться в черепки́,** to be smashed to smithereens.
чересседе́льник *n.* saddle girth.
чересчу́р *adv.* **1,** too. **2,** (*with verbs*) too much. —**чересчу́р мно́го,** too much; too many.
чере́шневый *adj.* cherry (*attrib.*).
чере́шня [*gen. pl.* **-шен**] *n.* **1,** sweet cherries. **2,** a (single) sweet cherry. **3,** cherry tree.
черешо́к [*gen.* **-шка́**] *n.* **1,** petiole. **2,** = **черено́к.**
черка́ть *also,* **чёркать** *v. impfv.* [*pfv.* **черкну́ть**] *colloq.* **1,** (*with* **по**) to scratch; leave a mark on. **2,** [*impfv. only*] to cross out (a word or words); mark up (a page).
черке́с *n.m.* [*fem.* **черке́шенка**] Circassian. —**черке́сский,** *adj.* Circassian.
черкну́ть *v. pfv., colloq.* **1,** *pfv. of* **черка́ть. 2,** to write; dash off: черкни́те мне не́сколько слов, drop me a line.
черне́ть *v. impfv.* [*pfv.* **почерне́ть**] **1,** to turn black. **2,** [*impfv. only*] (*of anything black*) to appear; loom.
черни́ка *n.* **1,** blueberries; huckleberries; whortleberries. **2,** a single such berry. **3,** a bush yielding any of these berries.
черни́ла [*gen.* **-ни́л**] *n. pl.* ink.
черни́льница *n.* inkwell.
черни́льный *adj.* ink (*attrib.*). —**черни́льный каранда́ш,** indelible pencil. —**черни́льный оре́шек,** gallnut.
черни́ть *v. impfv.* **1,** [*pfv.* **начерни́ть**] to blacken; make black. **2,** [*pfv.* **очерни́ть**] to blacken; slander; defame.
черни́чный *adj.* blueberry (*attrib.*); huckleberry (*attrib.*); whortleberry (*attrib.*).
чёрно-бе́лый *adj.* black-and-white.
черно-бу́рый *adj.* dark brown. —**черно-бу́рая лиси́ца,** silver fox.
черновик [*gen.* **-вика́**] *n.* rough draft; rough copy.
черново́й *adj.* (*of something written*) rough; preliminary.
черного́рец [*gen.* **-рца**] *n.m.* [*fem.* **-рка**] Montenegrin. —**черного́рский,** *adj.* Montenegrin.
чернозём *n.* rich black topsoil of central European Russia; chernozem.
черноко́жий *adj.* dark-skinned; black. —*n.* black man; black.
черннома́зый *adj., colloq.* swarthy; dark-complexioned.
чернорабо́чий *adj.* unskilled. —*n.* unskilled laborer.
черносли́в *n.* prunes.
чернота́ *n.* blackness; darkness.
чёрный *adj.* **1,** black. **2,** (*of a door, yard, staircase, etc.*) back. **3,** *fig.* dark; somber. —*n.* **1,** black; negro. **2,** *neut.* black (clothes): она́ была́ вся в чёрном, she was all in black. **3,** *pl., chess* black: игра́ть чёрными, to be black; play the black pieces. —**бере́чь на чёрный день,** to put aside for a rainy day. —**чёрное де́рево,** ebony. —**чёрная доска́,** blackboard. —**чёрный дрозд,** blackbird. —**чёрные мета́ллы,** ferrous metals. —**чёрная рабо́та,** menial work; dirty work. —**чёрный ры́нок,** black market. —**чёрный спи́сок,** blacklist. —**чёрным по бе́лому,** in black and white; in the clearest possible terms.
чернь *n.f., obs.* rabble; riffraff.
черпа́к [*gen.* **-пака́**] *n.* scoop.
черпа́лка [*gen. pl.* **-лок**] *n., colloq.* scoop.
че́рпать *v. impfv.* [*pfv.* **черпну́ть**] **1,** to draw (water); scoop up (dirt, sand, etc.). **2,** [*impfv. only*] *fig.* to draw; derive; cull.
черстве́ть *v. impfv.* **1,** [*pfv.* **зачерстве́ть** *or* **почерстве́ть**] (*of bread*) to become stale. **2,** [*pfv.* **очерстве́ть**] to become callous; become hardhearted.
чёрствый *adj.* **1,** stale. **2,** callous; hardhearted. —**чёрствость,** *n.f.* callousness.
чёрт [*pl.* **че́рти, черте́й, чертя́м**] *n.* devil. —**до чёрта,** *colloq.* **1,** awfully. **2,** (*with gen.*) plenty (of); galore. —**иди́ к чёрту!,** go to hell! —**к чёрту!,** to hell with it! —**како́го чёрта** (+ *subject & verb*), what the hell is/does...? —**на кой чёрт?,** *colloq.* what the hell for? —**ни черта́,** *colloq.* not a thing. —**чёрт возьми́!; чёрт побери́!,** what the hell? —**чёрт (его́) зна́ет!,** God knows! —**чёрт с** (+ *instr.*), to hell with...!
черта́ *n.* **1,** line. **2,** boundary. В черте́ го́рода, within the city limits. **3,** *pl.* features: черты́ лица́, facial features. **4,** trait; feature; characteristic. —**в о́бщих черта́х,** in general terms; in broad outline.
чертёж [*gen.* **-тежа́**] *n.* drawing; draft; design.
чертёжник *n.* draftsman.

чертёжный *adj.* drawing (*attrib.*).
чертёнок [*gen.* **-нка;** *pl.* **-тенята, -тенят**] *n., colloq.* little devil; imp.
чертить *v. impfv.* [*pfv.* **начертить;** *pres.* **черчу, чертишь**] to draw (a line, figure, map, diagram, etc.).
чёртов *adj.* of the devil; devil's. —**чёртова дюжина,** baker's dozen. —**чёртово колесо,** Ferris wheel.
чертовски *adv., colloq.* awfully: чертовски рад, awfully glad. Чертовски сердит, mad as hell. Чертовски голоден, famished. Чертовски далеко, a hell of a long way.
чертовский *adj.* **1,** of the devil; devilish. **2,** *colloq.* hellish; damnable.
чертовщина *n.* **1,** devils. **2,** *fig., colloq.* something awful or ridiculous.
чертог *n., obs.* **1,** chamber. **2,** palace.
чертополох *n.* thistle.
чёрточка [*gen. pl.* **-чек**] *n.* **1,** line. **2,** hyphen.
чертыхаться *v.r. impfv.* [*pfv.* **чертыхнуться**] *colloq.* to swear; curse.
черчение *n.* drawing. —**техническое черчение,** mechanical drawing.
чесалка [*gen. pl.* **-лок**] *n.* combing (*or* carding) machine.
чесальный *adj.* combing (*attrib.*); carding (*attrib.*).
чесание *n.* combing; carding.
чесать *v. impfv.* [*pfv.* **почесать;** *pres.* **чешу, чешешь**] **1,** to scratch (*to relieve an itch*). **2,** [*impfv. only*] *colloq.* to comb (hair). **3,** [*impfv. only*] to comb; card (flax, cotton, etc.). —**чесать затылок** (*or* **в затылке**), *colloq.* to scratch one's head (*in puzzlement*). —**чесать язык** (*or* **языком**), *colloq.* to babble; prattle.
чесаться *v.r. impfv.* [*pres.* **чешусь, чешешься**] **1,** to itch: у меня чешется спина, my back itches. *Also fig.* у него чешутся руки (+ *inf.*), he is itching to... **2,** [*pfv.* **почесаться**] to scratch oneself (*to relieve itching*). **3,** *colloq.* to comb one's hair.
чеснок [*gen.* **-нока**] *n.* garlic. —**чесночный,** *adj.* garlic (*attrib.*).
чесотка *n.* scabies; mange.
чествование *n.* **1,** honoring. **2,** celebration (*in honor of someone*).
чествовать *v. impfv.* [*pres.* **-ствую, -ствуешь**] to honor; pay tribute to.
честить *v. impfv.* [*pres.* **чещу, честишь**] **1,** *obs.* to honor. **2,** *obs.* to call (by a name or title). **3,** *ironic, colloq.* to curse out; vilify.
честно *adv.* honestly. —**честно говоря,** to be honest...; in all honesty.
честной *adj., obs.* honored.
честность *n.f.* honesty.
честный *adj.* honest. —**честное слово!,** word of honor!; honest to goodness!
честолюбец [*gen.* **-бца**] *n.* ambitious person.
честолюбивый *adj.* ambitious. —**честолюбие,** *n.* ambition.
честь *n.f.* **1,** honor: в честь (+ *gen.*), in honor of. **2,** credit: делать честь (+ *dat.*), to be a credit to. —**отдавать честь** (+ *dat.*), to salute. —**пора и честь знать, 1,** it's time to stop. **2,** it's time we were going. —**с честью,** with distinction; with flying colors. —**честь честью,** properly.
чёт *n., colloq.* even number.
чета *n.* **1,** pair; couple. **2,** married couple. —**не чета** (+ *dat.*), **1,** not the equal of; no match for. **2,** too good for; head and shoulders above.
четверг [*gen.* **-верга**] *n.* Thursday. —**после дождичка в четверг,** *colloq.* who knows when?
четвереньки *n. pl., in* **на четвереньках,** on one's hands and knees; on all fours.
четвёрка *n.* **1,** the numeral 4. **2,** *colloq.* anything numbered 4. **3,** team of four horses. **4,** a grade of "four", signifying "good". **5,** *cards* four.
четверной *adj.* quadruple; fourfold.
четверня *n.* **1,** team of four horses. **2,** *colloq.* quadruplets.
четверо [*gen. & prepl.* **-рых;** *dat.* **-рым;** *instr.* **-рыми**] *collective numeral* four.
четвероногий *adj.* four-legged. —**четвероногое,** *n.* quadruped.
четверостишие *n.* quatrain.
четвертак [*gen.* **-така**] *n., obs.* twenty-five kopecks.
четвёртка [*gen. pl.* **-ток**] *n., obs.* quarter.
четвертной *adj.* **1,** *in* **четвертная нота,** *music* quarter note. **2,** (*of a grade*) for a (school) quarter. **3,** *obs.* twenty-five-ruble. —**четвертная,** *n., obs.* twenty-five-ruble note.
четвертование *n.* (execution by) quartering.
четвертовать *v. impfv. & pfv.* [*pres.* **-тую, -туешь**] to quarter (*as a method of execution*).
четвёртый *ordinal numeral* fourth.
четверть *n.f.* quarter; fourth: три четверти, three quarters; three fourths (¾). Четверть шестого, a quarter past five; без четверти семь, a quarter to seven.
четвертьфинал *n.* quarterfinal. —**четвертьфинальный,** *adj.* quarterfinal.
чётки [*gen.* **-ток**] *n. pl.* rosary (*beads*).
чёткий *adj.* [*short form* **чёток, четка, чётко;** *comp.* **чётче**] **1,** clear; distinct. **2,** clear-cut. **3,** precise. **4,** efficient.
чётко *adv.* **1,** clearly; distinctly. **2,** smartly: чётко шагать, to step smartly.
чёткость *n.f.* **1,** clarity. **2,** precision. **3,** efficiency.
чётный *adj.* (*of a number*) even.
четыре [*gen. & prepl.* **четырёх;** *dat.* **четырём;** *instr.* **четырьмя**] *numeral* four.
четырежды *adv.* four times.
четыреста [*gen.* **четырёхсот;** *dat.* **четырёмстам;** *instr.* **четырьмястами;** *prepl.* **четырёхстах**] *numeral* four hundred.
четырёхгодичный *adj.* four-year (*attrib.*).
четырёхголосный *adj., music* four-part.
четырёхгранник *n.* tetrahedron. —**четырёхгранный,** *adj.* tetrahedral.
четырёхдневный *adj.* four-day (*attrib.*).
четырёхклассный *adj.* (*of schools or courses*) four-year.
четырёхколёсный *adj.* four-wheel(ed).
четырёхкратный *adj.* fourfold; quadruple.
четырёхлетие *n.* **1,** fourth anniversary; fourth birthday. **2,** four-year period.
четырёхлетний *adj.* **1,** four-year (*attrib.*). **2,** four-year-old.
четырёхмесячный *adj.* **1,** four-month (*attrib.*). **2,** four-month-old.
четырёхнедельный *adj.* **1,** four week (*attrib.*). **2,** four-week-old.
четырёхсотлетие *n.* four-hundredth anniversary.

—**четырёхсотле́тний,** *adj.* four-hundred-year (*attrib.*).
четырёхсо́тый *ordinal numeral* four-hundredth.
четырёхсто́пный *adj.* tetrameter. —**четырёхсто́пный стих,** tetrameter. —**четырёхсто́пный ямб,** iambic tetrameter.
четырёхсторо́нний *adj.* four-sided; quadrilateral.
четырёхуго́льник *n.* quadrangle. —**четырёхуго́льный,** *adj.* quadrangular.
четырёхэта́жный *adj.* four-story.
четы́рнадцатый *ordinal numeral* fourteenth.
четы́рнадцать *numeral* fourteen.
чех *n.m.* [*fem.* **че́шка**] Czech.
чехарда́ *n.* leapfrog.
чехо́л [*gen.* **чехла́**] *n.* **1,** cover; slip cover. **2,** case.
чехослова́цкий *adj.* Czechoslovak.
чечеви́ца *n.* **1,** lentil. **2,** *obs.* lens. —**чечеви́чный,** *adj.* lentil (*attrib.*).
чече́нец [*gen.* **-нца**] *n.m.* [*fem.* **-нка**] Chechen (*one of a people inhabiting the Caucasus*). —**чече́нский,** *adj.* Chechen.
чечётка [*gen. pl.* **-ток**] *n.* **1,** tap dance. **2,** redpoll (*bird*).
че́шский *adj.* Czech.
чешу́йчатый *adj.* scaly.
чешуя́ *n.* scales (*of a fish, snake, etc.*).
чи́бис *n.* lapwing, pewit.
чиж [*gen.* **чижа́**] *n.* siskin (*bird*).
чили́ец [*gen.* **-и́йца**] *n.m.* [*fem.* **-и́йка**] Chilean. —**чили́йский,** *adj.* Chilean.
чин [*pl.* **чины́**] *n.* rank; grade. —**чин чи́ном,** properly.
чина́р *also,* **чина́ра** *n.* Oriental plane tree.
чини́ть *v. impfv.* **1,** [*pfv.* **почини́ть;** *pres.* **чиню́, чи́нишь**] to fix; mend; repair. **2,** [*pfv.* **очини́ть;** *pres.* **чиню́, чи́нишь**] to sharpen (a pencil). **3,** [*pfv.* **учини́ть;** *pres.* **чиню́, чини́шь**] to carry out. Чини́ть препя́тствия (+ *dat.*), to put obstacles in someone's way.
чини́ться *v.r. impfv., obs.* to stand on ceremony.
чи́нный *adj.* decorous; sedate. —**чи́нность,** *n.f.* decorum; propriety.
чино́вник *n.* **1,** official; functionary. **2,** bureaucrat.
чино́внический *adj.* **1,** official's; officials'. **2,** bureaucratic.
чино́вничество *n.* **1,** officials; officialdom. **2,** bureaucracy.
чино́вничий [*fem.* **-чья**] *adj.* = **чино́внический.**
чино́вный *adj., obs.* high-ranking.
чи́псы [*gen.* **-сов**] *n. pl.* potato chips.
чи́рей [*gen.* **чи́рья**] *n., colloq.* boil; abscess.
чири́канье *n.* chirping; twittering.
чири́кать *v. impfv.* to chirp; twitter.
чи́ркать *v. impfv.* [*pfv.* **чи́ркнуть**] **1,** (*with* **о** + *acc. or* **по**) to rub (something) against. **2,** (*with instr.*) to strike (a match).
чиро́к [*gen.* **-рка́**] *n.* teal.
чи́сленно *adv.* numerically.
чи́сленность *n.f.* number; size; numerical strength. —**чи́сленностью в** (+ *acc.*), numbering.
чи́сленный *adj.* numerical.
числи́тель *n.m.* numerator.
числи́тельное *n., decl. as an adj., gram.* numeral. *Also,* **и́мя числи́тельное.**
чи́слить *v. impfv.* **1,** *obs.* to count; calculate. **2,** to list; put down; record. **3,** (*with instr.*) to consider; regard (as). —**чи́слиться,** *refl.* **1,** to be listed; be put down; be recorded. **2,** (*with* **за** + *instr.*) to be put down under the name of; *fig.* be attributed to. **3,** to number: в го́роде чи́слится сто ты́сяч челове́к, the city has a population of 100,000. **4,** (*with instr.*) to be considered; be regarded (as).
число́ [*pl.* **чи́сла, чи́сел**] *n.* **1,** number: чётное число́, even number. **2,** number; quantity. **3,** date; day (*of the month*): како́е сего́дня число́?, what is today's date? В после́дних чи́слах декабря́, in the last days of December. **4,** *gram.* number: еди́нственное число́, singular; мно́жественное число́, plural. **5,** *pl., cap., Bib.* (book of) Numbers. —**в том числе́,** including. —**в числе́** (+ *gen.*), among.
числово́й *adj.* numerical.
чи́стик *n.* guillemot (*bird*).
чисти́лище *n.* purgatory.
чи́стильщик *n.* cleaner. —**чи́стильщик сапо́г,** shoeshine boy; bootblack.
чи́стить *v. impfv.* [*pfv.* **почи́стить** *or* **вы́чистить;** *pres.* **чи́щу, чи́стишь**] **1,** to clean. **2,** to clean out; clear out. **3,** to clear (a road); dredge (a river). **4,** [*pfv.* **очи́стить**] to peel; pare. **5,** to shine (shoes); brush (one's teeth). **6,** *fig., colloq.* to purge.
чи́стка *n.* **1,** cleaning. **2,** purge.
чи́сто *adv.* **1,** cleanly; neatly. **2,** purely. **3,** just like: она́ рассужда́ет чи́сто по-же́нски, she reasons just like a woman. —*adj., used predicatively* clean: здесь чи́сто, it is clean here. —**чи́сто-на́чисто,** spotlessly clean.
чистови́к [*gen.* **-вика́**] *n., colloq.* final draft.
чистово́й *adj.* (*of a copy, manuscript, etc.*) final; clean.
чистога́н *n., colloq.* cash.
чистокро́вный *adj.* thoroughbred.
чистописа́ние *n.* penmanship.
чистопло́тный *adj.* clean; neat; tidy; cleanly.
чистопоро́дный *adj.* thoroughbred.
чистосерде́чие *n.* open-heartedness; sincerity. —**чистосерде́чный,** *adj.* open-hearted; sincere.
чистота́ *n.* **1,** cleanliness. **2,** purity.
чи́стый *adj.* [*comp.* **чи́ще**] **1,** clean. **2,** pure. **3,** clear. **4,** (*of income, weight, etc.*) net. **5,** *colloq.* pure; sheer; utter. —**чи́стой** *or* **чисте́йшей воды́,** of the first water; of the first order. —**чи́стое по́ле,** open country.
чита́льный *adj., in* **чита́льный зал,** reading room.
чита́льня [*gen. pl.* **-лен**] *n.* reading room.
чита́тель *n.m.* reader. —**чита́тельский,** *adj.* reader's; readers'.
чита́ть *v. impfv.* [*pfv.* **прочита́ть** *or* **проче́сть**] **1,** to read. **2,** to recite (a poem, prayer, etc.). **3,** to give; deliver (a lecture, sermon, etc.); give; teach (a course). —**чита́ться,** *refl.* [*impfv. only*] **1,** to be read. **2,** to be legible. **3,** (*of a book*) to read (easily, quickly, etc.). **4,** (*used negatively with dat.*) not to feel like reading.
чи́тка *n.* reading.
чих *n., colloq.* sneeze.
чиха́нье *n.* sneezing.
чиха́ть *v. impfv.* [*pfv.* **чихну́ть**] to sneeze.
чи́ще *adj., comp. of* **чи́стый.**
член *n.* **1,** member. **2,** limb (*of the body*). **3,** part (*of a sentence*). **4,** *gram.* article. **5,** *math.* term. —**член-корреспонде́нт,** corresponding/associate member (*of an academy*).
члени́ть *v. impfv.* to divide into parts.

членовреди́тельство *n.* **1,** (deliberate) mutilation (of someone). **2,** self-mutilation.
членоразде́льный *adj.* articulate.
чле́нский *adj.* membership (*attrib.*); чле́нские взно́сы, membership dues.
чле́нство *n.* membership.
чмо́кать *v. impfv.* [*pfv.* **чмо́кнуть**] **1,** [*also,* **чмо́кать губа́ми**] to smack one's lips. **2,** *colloq.* to give (someone) a loud kiss. **3,** to make a squirting sound.
чо́каться *v.r. impfv.* [*pfv.* **чо́кнуться**] to clink glasses (*when making a toast*).
чо́порный *adj.* strait-laced; prim and proper.
чрева́тый *adj.* (*with instr.*) fraught (with): чрева́тый опа́сными после́дствиями, fraught with dangerous consequences.
чре́во *n., archaic* **1,** stomach. **2,** womb.
чревовеща́ние *n.* ventriloquism. —**чревовеща́тель,** *n.m.* ventriloquist.
чреда́ *n., obs.* turn.
чрез *prep.* = **че́рез.**
чрезвыча́йный *adj.* **1,** extraordinary. **2,** emergency: чрезвыча́йное положе́ние, state of emergency. —**чрезвыча́йно,** *adv.* extremely; extraordinarily.
чрезме́рный *adj.* excessive. —**чрезме́рно,** *adv.* excessively.
чте́ние *n.* reading. Чте́ние ле́кций, lecturing.
чтец [*gen.* **чтеца́**] *n.* reader; reciter.
чти́во *n., colloq.* (piece of) literary trash.
чтить *v. impfv.* [*pres.* **чту, чтишь, ...чтят** *or* **чтут**] **1,** to honor. **2,** to revere.
что [*gen.* **чего́;** *dat.* **чему́;** *instr.* **чем;** *prepl.* **чём**] *pron.* **1,** *interr.* what?: что э́то зна́чит?, what does this mean? О чём он говори́т?, what is he talking about? **2,** *rel.* which; that: пе́рвое, что пришло́ мне в го́лову, the first thing that came into my head. Никто́ не подошёл к телефо́ну, что о́чень необы́чно, no one answered the telephone, which is very unusual. **3,** *indef.* (*with* **есть**) quite a lot; quite a bit: а́втору есть что рассказа́ть, the author has quite a lot to tell. Сожале́ть ему́ есть о чём, he has quite a lot to be sorry about. Выбира́ть бы́ло из чего́, there was quite a lot to choose from. —*conj.* that: я уве́рен, что он говори́т пра́вду, I am sure that he is telling the truth. Это так про́сто, что ка́ждый поймёт, it is so simple that anyone can understand it. —*adv.* why?; how come?: что ты тако́й весёлый?, why are you so merry? Что же ты молчи́шь?, why are you (*or* how come you're) so quiet? —**не́ за что!,** don't mention it! —**ни за что, 1,** not for anything. **2,** for nothing; in vain. —**ни к чему́, 1,** of no use. **2,** (*with inf.*) there is no need to. **3,** for no reason. —**ни с чем, 1,** empty-handed. **2,** *in* оста́ться ни с чем, to be left with nothing; be left destitute. —**ну и что?,** *colloq.* well, so what?; what of it? —**что (бы) ни,** whatever: что ни де́лаешь; что бы ты ни де́лал, whatever you do. —**что вы!, 1,** how can you say that! **2,** *in* ну, что вы!, oh go on! **3,** *in* нет, что вы!, not at all! —**что до,** as for. —**что за** (+ *nom.*), **1,** what is?; what are?: что там за кни́ги?, what are those books over there? **2,** what kind of; what sort of: что он за челове́к?, what sort of person is he?; what is he like? —**что к чему́,** (*with verbs of knowing, understanding, etc.*) what's what; what's going on. —**что ли,** perhaps. —**что с ва́ми?,** what's the matter with you? *See also* **чего́** *and* **чем.**
что́бы *also,* **чтоб** *conj.* **1,** *with inf.* in order to; so as to: что́бы приходи́ть во́время, in order to be on time; что́бы не меша́ть гостя́м, so as not to disturb the guests. **2,** *used to introduce a dependent clause:* скажи́те ему́, что́бы он ушёл, tell him to go away. Я не ви́дел, что́бы кто́-нибудь входи́л, I didn't see anyone enter. Она́ лю́бит, что́бы ей льсти́ли, she likes to be flattered. —*particle, used to express a peremptory command:* что́бы э́того бо́льше не́ было!, this must not happen again! —**для того́, что́бы; с тем, что́бы, 1,** (*with inf.*) in order to; so as to. **2,** (*with a dependent clause*) so that; in order that.
что́-либо *indef. pron.* = **что́-нибудь.**
что́-нибудь *indef. pron.* something; anything.
что́-то *indef. pron.* something. —*adv., colloq.* somehow: мне что́-то не спало́сь, I somehow couldn't sleep.
чуб [*pl.* **чубы́**] *n.* forelock.
чуба́рый *adj.* (*of a horse*) dappled.
чува́ш *n.m.* [*fem.* **чува́шка**] Chuvash (*one of a people inhabiting central European Russia*). —**чува́шский,** *adj.* Chuvash.
чу́вственный *adj.* **1,** sense (*attrib.*): чу́вственное восприя́тие, sense perception. **2,** sensual. —**чу́вственность,** *n.f.* sensuality.
чувстви́тельность *n.f.* sensitivity.
чувстви́тельный *adj.* **1,** sensitive. **2,** sentimental. **3,** noticeable; perceptible. **4,** severe; keenly felt. —**чувстви́тельный нерв,** sensory nerve.
чу́вство *n.* **1,** sense: пять чувств, the five senses. Чу́вство ю́мора, sense of humor. **2,** feeling: прия́тное чу́вство, a pleasant feeling. **3,** consciousness. —**лиши́ться чувств,** to lose consciousness. —**привести́ в чу́вство,** to revive; bring around. —**прийти́ в чу́вство,** to regain consciousness; come to. —**упа́сть без чувств,** to faint away.
чу́вствовать *v. impfv.* [*pfv.* **почу́вствовать;** *pres.* **-ствую, -ствуешь**] **1,** to feel. **2,** to sense. **3,** (*with* **себя́**) to feel (*a certain way*): как вы себя́ чу́вствуете?, how do you feel? Чу́вствовать себя́ больны́м, to feel ill. **4,** *in* чу́вствовать за́пах (+ *gen.*), to smell (something). —**чу́вствоваться,** *refl.* **1,** to be felt. **2,** to be sensed.
чугу́н [*gen.* **-гуна́**] *n.* **1,** cast iron. **2,** iron pot. —**чугу́нный,** *adj.* cast-iron.
чугунолите́йный *adj.* iron (*attrib.*). —**чугунолите́йный заво́д,** ironworks.
чуда́к [*gen.* **-дака́**] *n.m.* [*fem.* **-да́чка**] strange person; queer bird.
чудакова́тый *adj.* odd; queer; peculiar; eccentric.
чуда́ческий *adj.* odd; queer; eccentric.
чуда́чество *n.* **1,** peculiarity; quirk. **2,** *pl.* shenanigans; monkey business.
чудеса́ *n., pl. of* **чу́до.**
чуде́сно *adv.* **1,** miraculously. **2,** marvelously; wonderfully. **3,** *as an interj.* wonderful!
чуде́сный *adj.* **1,** miraculous. **2,** wonderful; marvelous.
чуди́ть *v. impfv., colloq.* to behave oddly; act up.
чу́диться *v.r. impfv.* [*pfv.* **почу́диться**] *impers.* to seem: мне чу́дится, it seems to me.
чу́дище *n., obs.* monster.
чу́дно *adv.* **1,** wonderfully; marvelously. **2,** *as an interj.* wonderful!

шеф *n.* **1,** *colloq.* boss; chief. **2,** patron; sponsor. —**шеф-по́вар,** chef.
ше́фство *n.* patronage; sponsorship.
ше́фствовать *v. impfv.* [*pres.* **-ствую, -ствуешь**] (*with* **над**) to be a patron of; sponsor.
ше́я *n.* neck. —**бро́ситься на ше́ю** (+ *dat.*), to throw one's arms around someone's neck. —**ве́шаться на ше́ю** (+ *dat.*), to throw oneself at. —**гнуть ше́ю пе́ред,** to kowtow to. —**по (са́мую) ше́ю,** up to one's neck (*in work, debt, etc.*). —**получи́ть по ше́е,** to get it in the neck. —**сади́ться на ше́ю** (+ *dat.*); **сиде́ть на ше́е у,** to live off; sponge off; be a burden to. —**слома́ть (себе́) ше́ю, 1,** to break one's neck. **2,** *fig.* to fall on one's face.
ши́бкий *adj., colloq.* fast; swift; quick.
ши́бко *adv., colloq.* **1,** fast. **2,** very; very much.
ши́ворот *n., in* **за ши́ворот,** by the scruff of the neck. —**ши́ворот-навы́ворот,** topsy-turvy.
шизофрени́я *n.* schizophrenia. —**шизофре́ник,** *n.* schizophrenic. —**шизофрени́ческий,** *adj.* schizophrenic.
шик *n.* stylishness: одёт с ши́ком, stylishly dressed. Счита́ться ши́ком, to be considered chic.
шика́рно *adv.* **1,** smartly. **2,** *as an interj., colloq.* splendid!
шика́рный *adj.* **1,** smart; chic. **2,** *colloq.* fine; grand.
ши́кать *v. impfv.* [*pfv.* **ши́кнуть**] *colloq.* **1,** (*with* **на** + *acc.*) to shoo away by saying **шш. 2,** (*with* **на** + *acc.*) to hush; say **шш** to. **3,** (*with dat.*) to hiss (a performer).
ши́ллинг *n.* shilling.
ши́ло [*pl.* **ши́лья, ши́льев**] *n.* awl.
шилоклю́вка [*gen. pl.* **-вок**] *n.* avocet (*bird*).
шилохво́сть *n.f.* pintail (*duck*).
шимпанзе́ (зэ) *n.m. indecl.* chimpanzee.
ши́на *n.* **1,** tire. **2,** *med.* splint.
шине́ль *n.f.* overcoat.
шинка́рь [*gen.* **-каря́**] *n.m., obs.* tavern keeper.
шинкова́ть *v. impfv.* [*pres.* **-ку́ю, -ку́ешь**] to chop; shred (cabbage).
ши́нный *adj.* tire (*attrib.*).
шино́к [*gen.* **-нка́**] *n., obs.* tavern.
шинши́лла *n.* chinchilla.
шиньо́н *n.* chignon.
шип [*gen.* **шипа́**] *n.* **1,** thorn. **2,** tenon. **3,** spike; cleat.
шипе́ние *n.* hissing; sizzling; fizzing.
шипе́ть *v. impfv.* [*pres.* **шиплю́, шипи́шь**] to hiss; sizzle; fizz.
шипо́вник *n.* wild rose.
шипу́честь *n.f.* effervescence.
шипу́чий *adj.* sparkling; effervescent. —**шипу́чее,** *n.* sparkling beverage.
шипу́чка *n., colloq.* sparkling beverage.
шипя́щий *adj.* **1,** hissing. **2,** *phonet.* sibilant. —*n., phonet.* sibilant.
ши́ре *adj., comp. of* **широ́кий.**
ширина́ *n.* width; breadth. В три ме́тра ширино́й, three meters wide. Име́ть три ме́тра в ширину́, to be three meters wide.
шири́нка *n., colloq.* fly (*on trousers*).
ши́рить *v. impfv.* **1,** *colloq.* to widen; make wider; open wider. **2,** *fig.* to expand. —**ши́риться,** *refl.* to expand.
ши́рма *n.* **1,** screen. **2,** *fig.* screen; cover.
широ́кий *adj.* [*short form* **широ́к, широка́, широко́** *or* **широ́ко, широки́** *or* **широ́ки;** *comp.* **ши́ре**] **1,** wide; broad. **2,** loose; loose-fitting. **3,** extensive. **4,** generous. **5,** lavish; grand. **6,** *in* широ́кая пу́блика, the general public; широ́кий чита́тель, the general/average reader. **7,** *in* това́ры широ́кого потребле́ния, consumer goods. —**жить на широ́кую но́гу,** to live in grand style.
широко́ *adv.* **1,** widely; wide. **2,** broadly. —**жить широко́,** to live in grand style.
широковеща́ние *n.* broadcasting.
широковеща́тельный *adj.* **1,** broadcasting (*attrib.*). **2,** *fig.* high-sounding.
ширококоле́йный *adj., R.R.* broad-gauge.
широкопле́чий *adj.* broad-shouldered.
широкоуго́льный *adj.* wide-angle.
широта́ [*pl.* **широ́ты**] *n.* **1,** *colloq.* width. **2,** breadth; broad scope; wide range. **3,** latitude.
ширпотре́б *n., colloq.* **1,** mass consumption. **2,** consumer goods.
ширь *n.f.* expanse; open space. —**во всю ширь, 1,** to its full extent. **2,** *fig.* to the fullest.
шить *v. impfv.* [*pfv.* **сшить;** *pres.* **шью, шьёшь**] **1,** to sew. **2,** [*impfv. only*] to embroider. **3,** [*impfv. only*] *colloq.* to have one's clothes made (somewhere). —**он ни шьёт ни по́рет,** he keeps hemming and hawing.
шитьё *n.* **1,** sewing. **2,** needlework. **3,** embroidery.
ши́фер *n.* slate. —**ши́ферный,** *adj.* slate (*attrib.*).
шифо́н *n.* chiffon. —**шифо́новый,** *adj.* chiffon.
шифонье́рка [*gen. pl.* **-рок**] *n.* chiffonier.
шифр *n.* **1,** cipher; code. **2,** call number.
шифрова́льщик *n.* cipher clerk; cryptographer.
шифро́ванный *adj.* in code; coded.
шифрова́ть *v. impfv.* [*pfv.* **зашифрова́ть;** *pres.* **-ру́ю, -ру́ешь**] to encipher; code; encode.
шифро́вка *n.* **1,** enciphering; encoding. **2,** *colloq.* coded message.
шиш [*gen.* **шиша́**] *n., colloq.* **1,** fig (*insulting gesture*). **2,** nothing; nil.
ши́шка [*gen. pl.* **-шек**] *n.* **1,** *bot.* cone. **2,** bump; lump. **3,** *colloq.* big shot.
шишкова́тый *adj.* knobby.
шишкови́дный *adj.* cone-shaped; pineal.
шкала́ [*pl.* **шка́лы**] *n.* **1,** scale; dial. **2,** *fig.* scale: шкала́ за́работной пла́ты, wage scale.
шка́лик *n.* **1,** old Russian unit of liquid measure equal to about ⅛ of a pint. **2,** small vodka glass or bottle of this capacity.
шка́нцы [*gen.* **-нцев**] *n. pl.* quarterdeck.
шкату́лка [*gen. pl.* **-лок**] *n.* small box.
шкаф [*2nd loc.* **шкафу́;** *pl.* **шкафы́**] *n.* closet; cabinet; cupboard. —**кни́жный шкаф,** bookcase. —**несгора́емый шкаф,** safe. —**платяно́й шкаф,** wardrobe.
шка́фик *also,* **шка́фчик** *n.* small closet; small cabinet.
шквал *n.* squall. —**шква́листый,** *adj.* gusty.
шква́рки [*gen.* **-рок**] *n. pl.* cracklings.
шкво́рень [*gen.* **-рня**] *n.m.* pivot; kingbolt; kingpin.
шкив [*pl.* **шкивы́**] *n.* pulley.
шки́пер *n.* skipper; captain.
шко́ла *n.* **1,** school. Шко́ла-интерна́т, boarding school. **2,** schooling; training: пройти́ хоро́шую шко́лу, to receive thorough training.—**суро́вая шко́ла жи́зни,** the bitter experience of life; the school of hard knocks.

чудно́ *adv., colloq.* **1,** strangely; oddly. **2,** *as an interj.* (it is) strange!
чудно́й *adj., colloq.* odd; strange; queer.
чу́дный *adj.* wonderful; marvelous.
чу́до [*pl.* **чудеса́, чуде́с, чудеса́м**] *n.* miracle; wonder. —**чу́дом,** by a miracle. —**чу́до приро́ды,** freak of nature.
чудо́вище *n.* monster.
чудо́вищность *n.f.* (*with gen.*) monstrosity (of); enormity (of).
чудо́вищный *adj.* monstrous.
чудоде́й *n., obs.* miracle worker; magician.
чудоде́йственный *adj.* wonder-working; miraculous.
чудотво́рец [*gen.* **-рца**] *n.* miracle worker. —**чудотво́рный,** *adj.* wonder-working; miraculous.
чужа́к [*gen.* **-жака́**] *n., colloq.* stranger; newcomer.
чужби́на *n.* foreign land; foreign soil.
чужда́ться *v.r. impfv.* (*with gen.*) to avoid; shun; keep away from.
чу́ждый *adj.* **1,** (*often with dat.*) alien (to); foreign (to). **2,** (*with gen.*) devoid (of); free (from).
чужезе́мец [*gen.* **-мца**] *n., obs.* foreigner. —**чужезе́мный,** *adj., obs.* foreign.
чужестра́нец [*gen.* **-нца**] *n., obs.* foreigner. —**чужестра́нный,** *adj., obs.* foreign.
чужо́й *adj.* **1,** someone else's. **2,** foreign; alien. **3,** strange; unfamiliar. —*n.* **1,** stranger. **2,** *neut.* something belonging to someone else.
чу́кча [*gen. pl.* **-чей**] *n.m. & f.* [*fem. also* **чукча́нка**] Chukchi (*one of a people inhabiting northeasternmost Siberia*). —**чуко́тский,** *adj.* Chukchi.
чула́н *n.* storeroom; pantry.
чуло́к [*gen.* **-лка́;** *gen. pl.* **чуло́к**] *n.* stocking. —**чуло́чный,** *adj.* stocking (*attrib.*); hose (*attrib.*).
чума́ *n.* plague.
чума́зый *adj., colloq.* dirty.
чумно́й *adj.* **1,** of the plague; plague (*attrib.*). **2,** afflicted with the plague.—*n.* person afflicted with the plague.
чура́ться *v.r. impfv., colloq.* to avoid.
чурба́н *n.* block (*of wood*).
чу́рка [*gen. pl.* **-рок**] *n.* block (*of wood*); strip (*of metal*).
чу́ткий *adj.* [*short form* **чу́ток, чутка́, чу́тко;** *comp.* **чу́тче**] **1,** keen; sensitive. **2,** (*of sleep*) light. **3,** sympathetic; kind.
чу́тко *adv.* **1,** closely: чу́тко прислу́шиваться, to listen closely. **2,** sympathetically. **3,** *in* чу́тко спать, to be a light sleeper.
чу́ткость *n.f.* **1,** keenness; sensitivity. **2,** sympathy; consideration.
чу́точка *n., colloq., in* **чу́точку,** a little; a bit. —**ни чу́точки,** not a bit; not in the least.
чуть *adv.* **1,** hardly; scarcely; barely. **2,** (just) a little; (very) slightly. —*conj.* as soon as. —**чуть ли не,** almost; nearly; just about: чуть ли не ка́ждый день, almost every day. —**чуть ли не; чуть бы́ло не,** almost; nearly: он чуть не упа́л, he almost fell. —**чуть свет,** at the crack of dawn. —**чуть то́лько,** as soon as. —**чуть что,** at the drop of a hat.
чутьё *n.* **1,** scent; sense of smell (*of an animal*). **2,** *fig.* flair; instinct; feel.
чуть-чу́ть *adv.* a tiny bit. —**чуть-чу́ть не,** = **чуть не.**
чу́чело *n.* **1,** stuffed animal; stuffed bird. **2,** scarecrow.
чу́шка [*gen. pl.* **-шек**] *n., colloq.* baby pig. —**чугу́н в чу́шках,** pig iron.
чушь *n.f., colloq.* nonsense.
чу́ять *v. impfv.* [*pfv.* **почу́ять;** *pres.* **чу́ю, чу́ешь**] **1,** to smell; scent. **2,** *fig.* to sense. —**ног под собо́й не чу́ять, 1,** to be utterly exhausted. **2,** to be walking on air.
чьё *pron., neut. of* **чей.** —**чья,** *pron., fem. of* **чей.**

Ш, ш *n. neut.* 25th letter of the Russian alphabet.
ша́баш *n.* sabbath. —**ша́баш ведьм,** witches' sabbath.
шаба́шить *v. impfv.* [*pfv.* **пошаба́шить**] *colloq.* to quit work; knock off work.
ша́бер *n.* scraper.
шабло́н *n.* **1,** mold. **2,** stencil. **3,** *fig.* stereotype.
шабло́нный *adj.* **1,** standard. **2,** *fig.* stereotyped; trite.
ша́вка [*gen. pl.* **-вок**] *n., colloq.* small dog.
шаг [*gen.* **ша́га,** *but after 2, 3, & 4* **шага́;** *pl.* **шаги́, шаго́в**] *n.* **1,** step: сде́лать шаг, to take a step. **2,** pace: отсчита́ть де́сять шаго́в, to mark off ten paces. **3,** *pl.* (sound of) footsteps. **4,** pace (*rate of speed when walking*): ускорить шаг *or* прибавить ша́гу, to quicken one's pace. **5,** step; action: риско́ванный шаг, risky step. —**два шага́; в двух шага́х (от),** a few steps away (from); a stone's throw (from). —**на ка́ждом шагу́,** at every step; at every turn. —**ни на шаг, 1,** not a step; not one step. **2,** not at all; not a bit. —**ни шагу́,** not a step; not one step. —**у́зки в шагу́,** tight in the seat. —**шаг за ша́гом,** step by step.
шага́ть *v. impfv.* [*pfv.* **шагну́ть**] **1,** to step. **2,** to stride; pace. **3,** *fig.* to progress; make progress.
ша́гом *adv.* at a walk. —**ша́гом марш!,** forward march!
шагоме́р *n.* pedometer.
ша́йба *n.* **1,** *mech.* washer. **2,** *sports* puck.
ша́йка [*gen. pl.* **ша́ек**] *n.* **1,** gang; band. **2,** small washbasin.

шака́л *n.* jackal.
шала́нда *n., naut.* lighter; scow.
шала́ш [*gen.* **-лаша́**] *n.* hut; cabin.
шале́ (пэ) *n. neut. indecl.* chalet.
шале́ть *v. impfv.* [*pfv.* **ошале́ть**] *colloq.* to go crazy.
шали́ть *v. impfv.* to act up; misbehave; be naughty.
шаловли́вый *adj.* **1,** playful. **2,** mischievous. —**шаловли́вость,** *n.f.* playfulness.
шалопа́й *n., colloq.* playboy; good-for-nothing.
ша́лость *n.f.* prank; trick.
шало́т *n.* shallot.
шалу́н [*gen.* **-луна́**] *n.* rascal; imp.
шалфе́й *n.* sage (*plant*).
ша́лый *adj., colloq.* crazy; nuts.
шаль *n.f.* shawl.
шально́й *adj., colloq.* **1,** crazy; mad. **2,** (*of a bullet, bomb, etc.*) stray; random.
шама́н *n.* shaman. —**шама́нство,** *n.* shamanism.
ша́мкать *v. impfv., colloq.* to mumble.
шампа́нское *n., decl. as an adj.* champagne.
шампу́нь *n.m.* shampoo.
шанкр *n.* chancre. —**мя́гкий шанкр,** soft chancre; chancroid. —**твёрдый шанкр,** hard chancre; chancre.
шанс *n.* chance: ша́нсы на успе́х, chances of success.
шансоне́тка [*gen. pl.* **-ток**] *n.* **1,** light comic song. **2,** cabaret singer.
шанта́ж [*gen.* **-тажа́**] *n.* blackmail.
шантажи́ровать *v. impfv.* [*pres.* **-рую, -руешь**] to blackmail.
шантажи́ст *n.* blackmailer.
ша́пка [*gen. pl.* **-пок**] *n.* **1,** cap; hat. **2,** (*with gen.*) shock (*of hair*); clump (*of grass*). **3,** *journalism* headline; masthead.
ша́почка [*gen. pl.* **-чек**] *n., dim. of* **ша́пка.** —**Кра́сная ша́почка,** Little Red Riding Hood.
ша́почник *n.* hatter.
ша́почный *adj.* **1,** hat (*attrib.*). **2,** *in* **ша́почное знако́мство,** nodding acquaintance. —**прийти́ к ша́почному разбо́ру,** to arrive just when everyone is leaving.
шар [*gen.* **ша́ра,** *but after 2, 3, & 4* **шара́**; *pl.* **шары́, шаро́в**] *n.* **1,** sphere. **2,** ball. —**возду́шный шар,** balloon. —**земно́й шар,** the earth; the globe. —**про́бный шар,** trial balloon.
шараба́н *n.* gig (*carriage*).
шара́да *n.* charade.
шара́хать *v. impfv.* [*pfv.* **шара́хнуть**] *colloq.* **1,** to smack. **2,** to shoot. —**шара́хаться,** *refl., colloq.* **1,** to jump aside (*from fear or surprise*). **2,** [*impfv. only*] (*with* **от**) to shun; keep away from.
шарж *n.* caricature; lampoon.
шаржи́ровать *v. impfv.* [*pres.* **-рую, -руешь**] to caricature; lampoon.
ша́рик *n.* **1,** *dim. of* **шар. 2,** marble: игра́ть в ша́рики, to play marbles. —**кровяны́е ша́рики,** blood corpuscles.
ша́риковый *adj.* ball-shaped. —**ша́риковый подши́пник,** ball bearing. —**ша́риковая ру́чка,** ball-point pen.
шарикоподши́пник *n.* ball bearing.
ша́рить *v. impfv.* to feel; fumble; grope; rummage.
ша́рканье *n.* shuffling (*of feet*).
ша́ркать *v. impfv.* [*pfv.* **ша́ркнуть**] **1,** [*impfv. only*] (*with* **по**) to shuffle (along). **2,** (*with instr.*) to shuffle (one's feet).
шарлата́н *n.* charlatan; quack. —**шарлата́нский,** *adj.* quack; fraudulent. —**шарлата́нство,** *n.* quackery; charlatanism.
шарма́нка [*gen. pl.* **-нок**] *n.* barrel organ. —**шарма́нщик,** *n.* organ grinder.
шарни́р *n.* hinge; joint.
шарова́ры [*gen.* **-ва́р**] *n. pl.* **1,** loose trousers gathered at the ankles (*part of the national costume of certain peoples*). **2,** (sports) pants: лы́жные шарова́ры, ski pants.
шарови́дный *adj.* spherical.
шарово́й *adj.* spherical. —**шарово́й шарни́р,** ball-and-socket joint.
шарообра́зный *adj.* spherical.
шарф *n.* scarf.
шасси́ *n. neut. indecl.* **1,** chassis. **2,** *aero.* undercarriage; landing gear.
шата́ние *n.* **1,** swaying; wobbling. **2,** *fig.* wavering; vacillation. **3,** *colloq.* roaming; wandering.
шата́ть *v. impfv.* **1,** to shake; rock. **2,** *impers.* to reel; stagger: его́ шата́ло, he was reeling. —**шата́ться,** *refl.* **1,** to be loose; be unsteady. **2,** to reel; stagger. **3,** to sway. **4,** *colloq.* to roam about; knock about.
шате́н (тэ) *n.m.* [*fem.* **-те́нка**] person with brown hair.
шатёр [*gen.* **-тра́**] *n.* large tent.
ша́ткий *adj.* **1,** shaky; unsteady; rickety; wobbly. **2,** *fig.* shaky; precarious. **3,** *fig.* wavering; vacillating. —**ни ша́тко ни ва́лко,** fair to middling.
шату́н [*gen.* **-туна́**] *n.* connecting rod.
ша́фер [*pl.* **шафера́**] *n.* best man (*at a wedding*).
шафра́н *n.* saffron. —**шафра́нный,** *adj.* saffron (*attrib.*).
шах *n.* **1,** shah. **2,** *chess* check.
шахмати́ст *n.* chess player.
ша́хматный *adj.* **1,** chess (*attrib.*). **2,** like a checkerboard; in checkerboard fashion. **3,** *colloq.* checked; checkered.
ша́хматы [*gen.* **-мат**] *n. pl.* **1,** chess. **2,** chess set.
ша́хта *n.* **1,** mine; pit. **2,** shaft.
шахтёр *n.* miner. —**шахтёрский,** *adj.* miner's; miners'.
ша́хтный *adj.* mine (*attrib.*).
ша́шечница *n., colloq.* checkerboard.
ша́шечный *adj.* for or pert. to checkers; checkers (*attrib.*).
ша́шка [*gen. pl.* **-шек**] *n.* **1,** saber; sword. **2,** checker piece. **3,** *pl.* checkers (*game*). **4,** paving block. **5,** block; slab; cartridge (*containing an explosive charge*). —**дымова́я ша́шка,** smudge pot.
шашлы́к [*gen.* **-лыка́**] *n.* shashlik; shish kebab.
ша́шни [*gen.* **-ней**] *n. pl., colloq.* **1,** tricks; pranks. **2,** (love) affairs.
шва́бра *n.* mop.
шваль *n.f., colloq.* **1,** trash; junk. **2,** good-for-nothing. **3,** riffraff; rabble.
шварто́в *n.* mooring line; *pl.* moorings.
швартова́ть *v. impfv.* [*pfv.* **пришвартова́ть**; *pres.* **-ту́ю, -ту́ешь**] to moor (a ship). —**швартова́ться,** *refl.* to moor; tie up.
швед *n.m.* [*fem.* **шве́дка**] Swede. —**шве́дский,** *adj.* Swedish.
шве́йник *n.* worker in a garment factory.
шве́йный *adj.* sewing (*attrib.*). —**шве́йная маши́на,** sewing machine. —**шве́йная фа́брика,** clothing (*or* garment) factory.
швейца́р *n.* doorman.

швейца́рец [*gen.* **-рца**] *n.m.* [*fem.* **-рка**] Swiss. —**швейца́рский,** *adj.* Swiss.
швец [*gen.* **швеца́**] *n., obs., regional* **1,** tailor. **2,** shoemaker. —**и швец, и жнец, и в дуду́ игре́ц,** jack-of all-trades.
швея́ *n.* seamstress.
шво́рень [*gen.* **-рня**] *n.m.* pivot; kingpin.
швырну́ть *v., pfv. of* **швыря́ть.**
швыро́к [*gen.* **-рка́**] *n.* **1,** toss. **2,** logs; firewood. **3,** object tossed in the air for firing practice.
швыря́ние *n.* tossing; flinging; hurling.
швыря́ть *v. impfv.* [*pfv.* **швырну́ть**] **1,** (*with acc. or instr.*) to toss; fling; hurl. **2,** *impers.* to toss: ло́дку швыря́ло на волна́х, the boat was tossing on the waves. **3,** *in* швыря́ть де́ньги *or* деньга́ми, to toss (*or* throw) money around. —**швыря́ться,** *refl.* [*impfv. only*] (*with instr.*) *colloq.* **1,** to toss; hurl (at one another). **2,** *fig.* to trifle with.
шевели́ть *v. impfv.* [*pfv.* **пошевели́ть** *or* **шевельну́ть**; *pres.* **шевелю́, шеве́лишь** *or* **шевели́шь**] **1,** (*with instr.*) to move; wiggle. **2,** (*with acc.*) to stir. **3,** *in* **шевели́ть мозга́ми,** to use one's brains. —**шевели́ться,** *refl.* **1,** to move; stir. **2,** *fig.* to show signs of life.
шевельну́ть *v., pfv. of* **шевели́ть.** —**шевельну́ться,** *refl., pfv. of* **шевели́ться.**
шевелю́ра *n.* head of hair.
шевио́т *n.* cheviot. —**шевио́товый,** *adj.* cheviot.
шевро́ *n. indecl.* kidskin. —**шевро́вый,** *adj.* kidskin; kid.
шевро́н *n., mil.* chevron; stripe.
шеде́вр (дэ) *n.* masterpiece.
шезло́нг *n.* chaise longue.
ше́йка [*gen. pl.* **ше́ек**] *n.* **1,** *dim. of* **ше́я. 2,** neck; narrow part. —**ше́йка ма́тки,** cervix.
ше́йный *adj.* **1,** neck (*attrib.*). **2,** *anat.* cervical. —**ше́йный плато́к,** neckerchief.
шейх *n.* sheik.
ше́лест *n.* rustle; rustling.
шелесте́ть *v. impfv.* [*pres.* **-ти́т**] to rustle.
шёлк [*pl.* **шелка́**] *n.* silk. —**в долгу́ как в шелку́,** up to one's ears in debt.
шелкови́нка [*gen. pl.* **-нок**] *n.* (piece of) silk thread.
шелкови́стый *adj.* silky; silken.
шелкови́ца *n.* mulberry.
шелкови́чный *adj.* mulberry (*attrib.*). —**шелкови́чный червь,** silkworm.
шелково́дство *n.* sericulture.
шёлковый *adj.* **1,** silk. **2,** (*of hair*) silken. **3,** *fig., colloq.* meek; docile.
шелкопря́д *n.* **1,** silkworm. **2,** moth: непа́рный шелкопря́д, gypsy moth.
шelláк *n.* shellac.
шелохну́ть *v. pfv.* (*with acc. or instr.*) to move (slightly). —**шелохну́ться,** *refl.* to move; stir.
шелуди́вый *adj., colloq.* mangy.
шелуха́ *n.* husk; peel; hull.
шелуши́ть *v. impfv.* to shell; peel; husk. —**шелуши́ться,** *refl.* (*of paint, one's skin, etc.*) to peel.
ше́льма *n.m. & f., colloq.* scoundrel; rascal.
шельме́ц [*gen.* **-мeца́**] *n., colloq.* = **ше́льма.**
шельмова́ть *v. impfv.* [*pfv.* **ошельмова́ть**; *pres.* **-му́ю, -му́ешь**] *colloq.* to disparage; run down.
шемя́кин *adj., in* **шемя́кин суд,** unfair trial.
шепеля́вить *v. impfv.* [*pres.* **-влю, -вишь**] to lisp; pronounce *s* as *sh* and *z* as *zh*.
шепеля́вый *adj.* lisping. —**шепеля́вость,** *n.f.* lisp.
шепну́ть *v., pfv. of* **шепта́ть.**
шёпот *n.* whisper. —**шёпотом,** *adv.* in a whisper.
шептала́ *n.* dried peaches; dried apricots.
шепта́ние *n.* whispering.
шепта́ть *v. impfv.* [*pfv.* **прошепта́ть** *or* **шепну́ть**; *pres.* **шепчу́, ше́пчешь**] to whisper. —**шепта́ться,** *refl.* [*impfv. only*] to whisper (to each other).
шепту́н [*gen.* **-туна́**] *n., colloq.* **1,** whisperer. **2,** spreader of gossip.
щербе́т *n.* sherbet.
шере́нга *n.* **1,** rank; column; file. **2,** (*with gen.*) row (of); line (of).
шери́ф *n.* sheriff.
шерохова́тость *n.f.* **1,** roughness. **2,** rough edge. **3,** *pl., fig.* rough edges; disagreements.
шерохова́тый *adj.* **1,** rough. **2,** *fig.* crude.
шерсти́нка [*gen. pl.* **-нок**] *n.* strand of wool.
шерсти́стый *adj.* woolly.
шерсти́ть *v. impfv.* (*of rough material*) to irritate the skin; itch.
шерсть *n.f.* **1,** wool. **2,** hair; fur (*of an animal*). —**про́тив ше́рсти,** against the grain. —**гла́дить про́тив ше́рсти,** to rub the wrong way.
шерстяно́й *adj.* wool; woolen.
шерша́вить *v. impfv.* to become rough.
шерша́вый *adj.* rough.
ше́ршень [*gen.* **-шня**] *n.m.* hornet.
шест [*gen.* **шеста́**] *n.* pole.
шеста́я *n., decl. as an adj.* sixth: одна́ шеста́я, one-sixth.
ше́ствие *n.* procession. —**замыка́ть ше́ствие,** to bring up the rear.
ше́ствовать *v. impfv.* [*pres.* **-ствую, -ствуешь**] to march; parade.
шестёрка *n.* **1,** the numeral 6. **2,** *colloq.* anything numbered 6. **3,** group of six. **4,** team of six horses. **5,** *cards* six.
шестерня́ *n.* **1,** [*gen. pl.* **-рён**] gear; cogwheel; pinion. **2,** [*gen. pl.* **-не́й**] *colloq.* team of six horses.
ше́стеро *collective numeral* six.
шестидеся́тый *ordinal numeral* sixtieth.
шестидне́вный *adj.* six-day (*attrib.*).
шестикра́тный *adj.* sixfold.
шестиме́сячный *adj.* **1,** six-month (*attrib.*). **2,** six-month-old.
шестисо́тый *ordinal numeral* six-hundredth.
шестиуго́льник *n.* hexagon. —**шестиуго́льный,** *adj.* hexagonal.
шестна́дцатый *ordinal numeral* sixteenth.
шестна́дцать *numeral* sixteen.
шесто́й *ordinal numeral* sixth.
шесто́к [*gen.* **-тка́**] *n.* **1,** hearth (*of a Russian stove*). **2,** perch; roost.
шесть [*gen., dat., & prepl.* **шести́**; *instr.* **шестью́**] *numeral* six.
шестьдеся́т [*gen., dat., & prepl.* **шести́десяти**; *instr.* **шестью́десятью**] *numeral* sixty.
шестьсо́т [*gen.* **шестисо́т**; *dat.* **шестиста́м**; *instr.* **шестьюста́ми**; *prepl.* **шестиста́х**] *numeral* six hundred.
ше́стью *adv.* six times: ше́стью шесть — три́дцать шесть, six times six is 36.

шко́лить *v. impfv.* [*pfv.* **вы́школить**] *colloq.* to school; train; discipline.
шко́льник *n.* schoolboy. —**шко́льница,** *n.* schoolgirl.
шко́льнический *adj.* schoolboy (*attrib.*); typical of a schoolboy.
шко́льничество *n.* schoolboyish behavior; schoolboy pranks; shenanigans.
шко́льный *adj.* school (*attrib.*).
шку́ра *n.* skin; hide; pelt. —**быть в чьей-нибудь шку́ре,** to be in someone's shoes. —**дели́ть шку́ру неуби́того медве́дя,** to count one's chickens before they are hatched. —**драть шку́ру с** (+ *gen.*), **1,** to tan someone's hide. **2,** to exploit mercilessly; bleed white. —**дрожа́ть за свою́ шку́ру,** to worry about one's own skin. —**испы́тывать (что́-нибудь) на свое́й шку́ре,** to experience (something) personally. —**спасти́ свою́ шку́ру,** to save one's skin. —**спусти́ть шку́ру с** (+ *gen.*), to tan someone's hide.
шку́рка *n.* **1,** *dim. of* **шку́ра. 2,** sandpaper.
шку́рник *n., colloq.* self-seeker; one who looks out only for himself.
шку́рный *adj., colloq.* selfish; self-seeking.
шлагба́ум *n.* barrier; gate.
шлак *n.* slag.
шланг *n.* hose.
шлейф *n.* train (*of a dress*).
шлем *n.* **1,** helmet. **2,** *cards* slam.
шлёпанцы *n. pl.* [*sing.* **шлёпанец**] *colloq.* bedroom slippers.
шлёпать *v. impfv.* [*pfv.* **шлёпнуть**] **1,** to smack; slap; spank. **2,** (*with instr.*) to make a noise with. **3,** [*impfv. only*] *colloq.* to shuffle; tramp. **4,** [*impfv. only*] (*with* **по**) *colloq.* to tramp; slosh (through water, mud, etc.). —**шлёпаться,** *refl., colloq.* to tumble; flop; plop.
шлёпка *n., colloq.* spanking.
шлёпнуть *v., pfv. of* **шлёпать.** —**шлёпнуться,** *refl., pfv. of* **шлёпаться.**
шлепо́к [*gen.* **-пка́**] *n.* slap; smack.
шлифова́льный *adj.* polishing (*attrib.*).
шлифова́льщик *n.* polisher.
шлифова́ть *v. impfv.* [*pfv.* **отшлифова́ть;** *pres.* **-фу́ю -фу́ешь**] to polish.
шлифо́вка *n.* polishing. —**шлифо́вщик,** *n.* polisher.
шлюз *n.* **1,** sluice. **2,** lock (*in a canal*). —**шлю́зный,** *adj.* sluice (*attrib.*).
шлюп *n.* sloop.
шлю́пка [*gen. pl.* **-пок**] *n.* boat. —**спаса́тельная шлю́пка,** lifeboat.
шлю́ха *n., colloq.* slut.
шля́па *n.* hat. —**де́ло в шля́пе,** it's in the bag.
шля́пка [*gen. pl.* **-пок**] *n.* **1,** *dim. of* **шля́па. 2,** head (*of a nail*). **3,** cap (*of a mushroom*).
шля́пник *n.* hatter.
шля́пный *adj.* hat (*attrib.*). —**шля́пный ма́стер,** hatter.
шля́ться *v.r. impfv., colloq.* to wander about; gad about; gallivant.
шмель [*gen.* **шмеля́**] *n.m.* bumblebee.
шмы́гать *v. impfv.* [*pfv.* **шмыгну́ть**] **1,** *colloq.* to bustle; scurry. **2,** [*impfv. only*] (*with instr.*) to scrape: шмы́гать нога́ми по́ полу, to scrape one's feet on the floor. —**шмы́гать но́сом,** to sniff the air.
шмыгну́ть *v. pfv.* **1,** *pfv. of* **шмы́гать. 2,** to dart; slip.
шнитт-лу́к *n.* chive.
шни́цель *n.m.* schnitzel.
шно́ркель *n.m.* snorkel.
шнур [*gen.* **шнура́**] *n.* **1,** cord; lace. **2,** electric cord. **3,** fuse.
шнурова́ть *v. impfv.* [*pfv.* **зашнурова́ть;** *pres.* **-ру́ю, -ру́ешь**] to lace; tie.
шнуро́вка *n.* lacing.
шнуро́к [*gen.* **-рка́**] *n.* lace: шнуро́к для боти́нок, shoelace.
шныря́ть *v. impfv., colloq.* **1,** to scurry; scamper. **2,** to poke about; prowl around; snoop about. **3,** *in* шныря́ть глаза́ми, to cast one's eyes about.
шов [*gen.* **шва**] *n.* **1,** seam. **2,** stitch; suture. **3,** *mech.* joint. —**треща́ть по (всем) швам,** to come apart at the seams.
шовини́зм *n.* chauvinism. —**шовини́ст,** *n.* chauvinist. —**шовинисти́ческий,** *adj.* chauvinistic.
шок *n., med.* shock.
шоки́ровать *v. impfv.* [*pres.* **-рую, -руешь**] to shock.
шокола́д *n.* chocolate. —**шокола́дный,** *adj.* chocolate.
шо́мпол [*pl.* **шомпола́**] *n.* ramrod.
шо́рник *n.* saddler; harness-maker.
шо́рный *adj.* saddle (*attrib.*); harness (*attrib.*); saddler's.
шо́рох *n.* rustle; rustling.
шо́рты [*gen.* **шорт**] *n. pl* shorts.
шо́ры [*gen.* **шор**] *n pl.* blinkers; blinders.
шоссе́ (сэ) *n. neut. indecl.* highway.
шоссе́йный (сэ) *adj.* road (*attrib.*); highway (*attrib.*). —**шоссе́йная доро́га,** highway.
шосси́ровать *v. impfv. & pfv.* [*pres.* **-рую, -руешь**] to make into a highway.
шотла́ндец [*gen.* **-дца**] *n.m.* [*fem.* **-дка**] Scot; Scotsman.
шотла́ндка [*gen. pl.* **-док**] *n.* **1,** *fem. of* **шотла́ндец. 2,** tartan; plaid.
шотла́ндский *adj.* Scottish; Scotch.
шофёр *n.* driver; chauffeur. —**шофёрский,** *adj.* driver's; chauffeur's.
шпа́га *n.* sword.
шпага́т *n.* **1,** string; cord; twine. **2,** *gymnastics* split.
шпа́жный *adj.* of a sword.
шпаклева́ть *v. impfv.* [*pfv.* **зашпаклева́ть;** *pres.* **-лю́ю, -лю́ешь**] to putty; seal up.
шпаклёвка *n.* **1,** puttying; sealing up. **2,** putty.
шпа́ла *n.* railroad tie.
шпале́ра *n., usu. pl.* **1,** trellis. **2,** row of trees along a road. **3,** *mil.* rows; columns. **4,** *obs.* wallpaper.
шпанго́ут *n.* frame (*of a ship, airplane, etc.*).
шпа́нка *n.* Spanish fly.
шпа́нский *adj., obs.* Spanish. —**шпа́нская му́шка,** Spanish fly.
шпарга́лка [*gen. pl.* **-лок**] *n., colloq.* pony; crib (*concealed student's notes*).
шпа́рить *v. impfv., colloq.* **1,** to pour boiling water on. **2,** to scald.
шпат *n.* spar. —**алма́зный шпат,** corundum. —**плавико́вый шпат,** fluorspar; fluorite. —**полево́й шпат,** feldspar.
шпа́тель (тэ) *n.m.* **1,** spatula. **2,** palette knife; putty knife.
шпенёк [*gen.* **-нька́**] *n.* peg; prong.
шпигова́ть *v. impfv.* [*pfv.* **нашпигова́ть;** *pres.* **-гу́ю, -гу́ешь**] to lard.

шпик *n.* **1,** small cubes of lard. **2,** *colloq.* sleuth; secret agent.
шпиль *n.m.* **1,** spire; steeple. **2,** capstan.
шпи́лька [*gen. pl.* **-лек**] *n.* **1,** hairpin. **2,** *mech.* pin; stud. **3,** tack; brad. **4,** *fig.* sarcastic comment; dig.
шпина́т *n.* spinach. —**шпина́тный,** *adj.* spinach (*attrib.*).
шпингале́т *n.* latch; catch; bolt.
шпи́ндель (дэ) *n.m.* spindle; shaft.
шпио́н *n.* spy.
шпиона́ж *n.* espionage.
шпио́нить *v. impfv.* to spy.
шпио́нский *adj.* espionage (*attrib.*); spy (*attrib.*).
шпио́нство *n.* spying.
шпиц *n.* **1,** *obs.* spire; steeple. **2,** spitz (*dog*).
шпон *n., printing* lead; slug.
шпо́нка [*gen. pl.* **-нок**] *n., mech.* key; dowel.
шпо́ра *n.* spur.
шпо́рник *n.* delphinium; larkspur.
шприц *n.* (hypodermic) syringe.
шпро́ты [*gen.* **шпрот**] *n. pl.* sprats.
шпу́лька [*gen. pl.* **-лек**] *n.* spool; bobbin.
шпунт [*gen.* **шпунта́**] *n.* groove.
шпыня́ть *v. impfv., colloq.* **1,** to poke; jab. **2,** *fig.* to nag; needle.
шрам *n.* scar.
шрапне́ль *n.f.* shrapnel. —**шрапне́льный,** *adj.* shrapnel (*attrib.*).
шрифт [*pl.* **шрифты́**] *n.* print; type.
штаб [*pl.* **штабы́**] *n., mil.* staff; headquarters.
шта́бель [*pl.* **штабеля́**] *n.m.* pile; stack.
штаб-кварти́ра *n.* headquarters (building).
штабно́й *adj.* staff (*attrib.*). —*n.* staff officer.
штаке́тник *n.* **1,** fence. **2,** pickets (*forming a fence*).
штамп *n.* **1,** *mech.* die. **2,** (rubber) stamp. **3,** imprint. **4,** *fig.* stereotype. **5,** *fig.* cliché.
штампова́льный *adj., mech.* punching; stamping. —**штампова́льный пресс,** punch press.
штампо́ванный *adj.* **1,** pressed; shaped. **2,** *fig.* stock; trite.
штампова́ть *v. impfv.* [*pres.* **-пу́ю, -пу́ешь**] **1,** to stamp. **2,** *mech.* to punch; press; shape. **3,** *fig., colloq.* to grind out.
штампо́вка *n.* **1,** stamping. **2,** punching; pressing.
штампо́вочный *adj., mech.* punching; stamping. —**штампо́вочный пресс,** punch press.
шта́нга *n.* **1,** rod; bar. **2,** *sports* barbell. **3,** *sports* crossbar (*between goal posts*).
штанги́ст *n.* weightlifter.
штанда́рт *n., obs.* standard; banner.
штани́на *n., colloq.* pants leg; trouser leg.
штани́шки [*gen. pl.* **-шек**] *n. pl., colloq.* short pants.
штаны́ [*gen.* **-но́в**] *n. pl., colloq.* trousers; pants.
штат *n.* **1,** state: Соединённые Шта́ты Аме́рики, the United States of America. **2,** (permanent) staff: сокраще́ние шта́тов, staff reduction.
штати́в *n.* **1,** stand; base. **2,** *photog.* tripod.
шта́тный *adj.* staff (*attrib.*); permanent.
шта́тский *adj. & n.* civilian.
ште́вень [*gen.* **-вня**] *n.m.* stem *or* sternpost (*of a ship*).
штемпелева́ть (тэ) *v. impfv.* [*pfv.* **заштемпелева́ть;** *pres.* **-лю́ю, -лю́ешь**] to stamp; postmark.
ште́мпель [*pl.* **штемпеля́**] *n.m.* **1,** rubber stamp. **2,** imprint made with a rubber stamp. —**почто́вый ште́мпель,** postmark.
ште́мпельный (тэ) *adj.* stamp (*attrib.*); stamping (*attrib.*). —**ште́мпельная поду́шка,** stamp pad; ink pad.
ште́псель (тэ) [*pl.* **штепселя́**] *n.m.* **1,** electric plug. **2,** *colloq.* electric outlet.
ште́псельный (тэ) *adj.* of an electric plug or outlet. —**ште́псельная ви́лка,** electric plug. —**ште́псельная розе́тка,** electric outlet.
штибле́ты *n. pl.* [*sing.* **штибле́та**] (men's) shoes; boots.
штилево́й *adj., naut.* calm. —**штилевы́е по́лосы,** *naut.* the doldrums.
штиль *n.m., naut.* calm.
штифт [*gen.* **штифта́**] *n.* pin; peg; dowel.
шток *n., mech.* rod: шток по́ршня, piston rod.
штокро́за *n.* hollyhock.
што́пальный *adj.* darning (*attrib.*): што́пальная игла́, darning needle.
што́пать *v. impfv.* [*pfv.* **зашто́пать**] to darn.
што́пка *n.* **1,** darning. **2,** *colloq.* darning thread.
што́пор *n.* **1,** corkscrew. **2,** *aero.* spin. —**што́пор на хвост,** tailspin.
што́ра *n.* window shade; blind.
шторм *n.* storm; gale (*at sea*).
штормова́ть *v. impfv.* [*pres.* **-му́ю, -му́ешь**] to weather a storm.
штормово́й *adj.* **1,** storm (*attrib.*). **2,** stormy. —**ве́тер штормово́й си́лы,** wind of gale force.
штоф *n.* **1,** damask. **2,** old Russian unit of liquid measure equal to about $2\frac{1}{2}$ pints. **3,** *obs.* wine bottle of this capacity.
што́фный *adj.* damask.
штраф *n.* fine; penalty.
штрафно́й *adj.* **1,** penalty (*attrib.*). **2,** penal.—**штрафно́й бросо́к,** *basketball* free throw. —**штрафно́й уда́р,** *soccer* penalty kick.
штрафова́ть *v. impfv.* [*pfv.* **оштрафова́ть;** *pres.* **-фу́ю, -фу́ешь**] to fine.
штрейкбре́хер *n.* strikebreaker.
штри́пка [*gen. pl.* **-пок**] *n.* strap for fastening trousers to footwear.
штрих [*gen.* **штриха́**] *n.* **1,** stroke (*in drawing*). **2,** *fig.* detail; feature.
штрихова́ть *v. impfv.* [*pfv.* **заштрихова́ть;** *pres.* **-ху́ю, -ху́ешь**] *drawing* to shade; hatch.
штрихо́вка *n., drawing* shading; hatching.
штуди́ровать *v. impfv.* [*pfv.* **проштуди́ровать;** *pres.* **-рую, -руешь**] to study.
шту́ка *n.* **1,** piece; item; unit: пять штук яиц, five eggs. **2,** *colloq.* thing. **3,** *colloq.* trick. —**за шту́ку,** apiece; each.
штука́рь [*gen.* **-каря́**] *n.m., colloq.* jokester; prankster.
штукату́р *n.* plasterer.
штукату́рить *v. impfv.* [*pfv.* **оштукату́рить**] to plaster.
штукату́рка *n.* **1,** plaster. **2,** plastering. —**штукату́рный,** *adj.* plaster (*attrib.*); plastering (*attrib.*).
штурва́л *n.* steering wheel (*of a ship or aircraft*). —**за штурва́лом,** at the helm; at the controls.
штурва́льный *adj.* steering (*attrib.*). —*n.* man at the wheel; helmsman.
штурм *n., mil.* storm; assault.

шту́рман *n.* navigator.
штурмова́ть *v. impfv.* [*pres.* **-му́ю, -му́ешь**] *mil.* to storm.
штурмови́к [*gen.* **-вика́**] *n.* **1,** low-flying attack aircraft. **2,** storm trooper (*in Nazi Germany*).
штурмо́вка *n.* strafing.
штурмово́й *adj.* assault (*attrib.*). —**штурмова́я авиа́ция, 1,** ground-attack aircraft. **2,** ground-attack forces.
шту́цер [*pl.* **штуцера́**] *n.* carbine.
шту́чка [*gen. pl.* **-чек**] *n., dim. of* **шту́ка.**
шту́чный *adj.* by the piece; sold by the piece.
штык [*gen.* **штыка́**] *n.* bayonet. —**встре́тить** *or* **приня́ть в штыки́,** to meet with extreme hostility; be up in arms over.
штыково́й *adj.* bayonet (*attrib.*).
штырь [*gen.* **штыря́**] *n.m.* pin; dowel.
шу́ба *n.* fur coat.
шубе́йка [*gen. pl.* **-бе́ек**] *n., colloq.* short fur coat.
шуга́ *n.* drift ice.
шу́лер [*pl.* **шулера́**] *n.* cardsharp; cheat. —**шу́лерский,** *adj.* cheating; dishonest. —**шу́лерство,** *n.* cheating; foul play.
шум *n.* **1,** noise. **2,** *fig.* fuss: подня́ть шум, to make/raise a fuss. **3,** *fig.* stir; sensation: вы́звать шум; наде́лать шу́ма, to cause a sensation; cause quite a stir. **4,** *in* шум в се́рдце, heart murmur; шум в уша́х, buzzing in one's ears. —**мно́го шу́ма из ничего́,** much ado about nothing.
шуме́ть *v. impfv.* [*pres.* **-млю́, -ми́шь**] **1,** to make (a) noise; be noisy. **2,** *fig., colloq.* to make a fuss. —**у меня́ шуми́т в уша́х,** I have a buzzing in my ears.
шуми́ха *n., colloq.* fuss; uproar; clamor; hullabaloo.
шумли́вый *adj.* **1,** noisy; boisterous. **2,** *colloq.* high-sounding.
шу́мно *adv.* noisily. —*adj., used predicatively* noisy: здесь сли́шком шу́мно, it is too noisy in here.
шу́мный *adj.* **1,** noisy. **2,** lively; bustling. **3,** *fig.* causing a sensation: шу́мный успе́х, huge/sensational success.
шумови́к [*gen.* **-вика́**] *n., theat.* sound-effects man.
шумо́вка [*gen. pl.* **-вок**] *n.* straining spoon; skimmer.
шумово́й *adj.* sound (*attrib.*). —**шумовы́е эффе́кты,** sound effects.
шумо́к [*gen.* **-мка́**] *n., colloq.* slight noise. —**под шумо́к,** secretly; on the sly.
шу́рин *n.* brother-in-law (*wife's brother*).
шуру́п *n.* screw.
шурша́ние *n.* rustling.
шурша́ть *v. impfv.* [*pres.* **-шу́, -ши́шь**] to rustle.
шу́стрый *adj., colloq.* smart; bright.
шут [*gen.* **шута́**] *n.* jester; buffoon.
шути́ть *v. impfv.* [*pfv.* **пошути́ть;** *pres.* **шучу́, шу́тишь**] **1,** to joke; jest: вы шу́тите!, you're joking! **2,** (*with* **с** + *instr.*) to play (with). **3,** (*with* **над**) to make fun of. **4,** [*impfv. only*] (*with instr.*) to trifle with. —**шути́ть с огнём,** to play with fire. —**шу́тки шути́ть,** to joke.
шути́ха *n.* **1,** *fem. of* **шут. 2,** rocket (*firework*).
шу́тка [*gen. pl.* **-ток**] *n.* joke. —**в шу́тку,** in jest; as a joke. —**не до шу́ток,** it's no joke; it's no laughing matter. Ему́ не до шу́ток, he is in no mood for jokes. —**не на шу́тку,** really; genuinely; seriously. —**с ним шу́тки пло́хи,** he is not to be trifled with; you don't fool around with him. —**сыгра́ть шу́тку с,** to play a joke/trick on. —**шу́тки в сто́рону; кро́ме шу́ток,** joking aside.
шутли́вый *adj.* **1,** *colloq.* jocular; full of fun. **2,** (*of a remark, song, etc.*) humorous; facetious.
шутни́к [*gen.* **-ника́**] *n.* joker; jokester.
шутовско́й *adj.* **1,** of a jester. Шутовско́й колпа́к, fool's cap. **2,** mischievous; prankish.
шутовство́ *n.* buffoonery.
шу́точный *adj.* **1,** humorous; facetious. **2,** (*usu. neg.*) trifling: э́то не шу́точное де́ло, it's no trifling (*or* laughing) matter.
шутя́ *adv.* **1,** in jest; for fun. **2,** easily; without any difficulty. —**не шутя́,** seriously; in earnest.
шушу́каться *v.r. impfv., colloq.* to whisper (to each other).
шхе́ры [*gen.* **шхер**] *n. pl.* rocky islets along a rugged coast.
шху́на *n.* schooner.
шш *interj.* shh!

Щ, щ *n. neut.* 26th letter of the Russian alphabet.
щаве́левый *adj.* sorrel (*attrib.*). —**щаве́левая кислота́,** oxalic acid.
щаве́ль [*gen.* **-веля́**] *n.m.* sorrel.
щади́ть *v. impfv.* [*pfv.* **пощади́ть;** *pres.* **щажу́, щади́шь**] **1,** to spare; spare the life of; have mercy on. **2,** to spare: не щади́ть уси́лий, to spare no effort; щади́ть чьё-нибудь самолю́бие, to spare someone's pride.
щебёнка *n., colloq.* = **ще́бень.**
ще́бень [*gen.* **-бня**] *n.m.* macadam. —**щебёночный,** *adj.* macadam(ized).
ще́бет *n.* twitter; chirping. *Also,* **щебета́ние.**
щебета́ть *v. impfv.* [*pres.* **-бечу́, -бе́чешь**] **1,** to twitter; chirp. **2,** *colloq.* to chatter.
щего́л [*gen.* **-гла́**] *n.* goldfinch.
щеголева́тый *adj.* stylish; dapper.

щёголь *n.m.* dandy; fop.
щегольну́ть *v., pfv. of* **щеголя́ть.**
щегольско́й *adj.* **1,** smart; handsome; elegant. **2,** dashing; jaunty.
щегольство́ *n.* **1,** foppery; dandyism. **2,** showing off.
щеголя́ть *v. impfv.* [*pfv.* **щегольну́ть**] **1,** [*impfv. only*] to wear fancy clothes. **2,** (*with* **в** + *prepl.*) *colloq.* to sport. **3,** (*with instr.*) *colloq.* to show off; flaunt.
ще́дрый *adj.* generous. —**ще́дро,** *adv.* generously. —**ще́дрость,** *n.f.* generosity.
щека́ [*acc.* **щёку;** *pl.* **щёки, щёк, щека́м**] *n.* cheek. —**уплета́ть** *or* **упи́сывать за о́бе щеки́,** to eat ravenously; devour; gobble up.
щеко́лда *n.* door latch.
щекота́ние *n.* tickling sensation.
щекота́ть *v. impfv.* [*pfv.* **пощекота́ть;** *pres.* **-кочу́, -ко́чешь**] to tickle.
щеко́тка *n.* **1,** tickling. **2,** tickling sensation. —**боя́ться щеко́тки,** to be ticklish.
щекотли́вый *adj.* ticklish; delicate. —**щекотли́вость,** *n.f.* ticklishness; delicacy.
щеко́тно *adj., used predicatively* tickling: мне щеко́тно, it tickles.
щеко́тный *adj.* causing a tickling sensation.
щели́стый *adj., colloq.* full of cracks.
щёлк *n., colloq.* snap; crack; click.
щёлка [*gen. pl.* **-лок**] *n.* crack; slit.
щёлканье *n.* **1,** snapping; cracking; clicking. **2,** warbling (*of birds*).
щёлкать *v. impfv.* [*pfv.* **щёлкнуть**] **1,** to flick: щёлкнуть кого́-нибудь по́ носу, to give someone a flick on the nose. **2,** (*of a lock, shutter, etc.*) to click. **3,** (*with instr.*) to crack (a whip); snap (one's fingers, a shutter, etc.); click (one's tongue); turn (a key) with a click. **4,** to crack (nuts). **5,** [*impfv. only*] (*of a bird*) to warble.
щелкопёр *n., obs.* hack writer.
щёлок *n.* lye.
щелочно́й *adj.* alkaline. —**щёлочность,** *n.f.* alkalinity.
щёлочь *n.f.* alkali.
щелчо́к [*gen.* **-чка́**] *n.* **1,** flick; fillip. **2,** click; crack. **3,** *colloq.* slight; snub.
щель [*2nd loc.* **щели́;** *pl.* **ще́ли, щеле́й, щеля́м**] *n.f.* **1,** crack; slit. **2,** slot (*for a coin*). **3,** *mil.* slit trench. —**голосова́я щель,** glottis.
щеми́ть *v. impfv.* **1,** to constrict. **2,** to ache; hurt. **3,** *fig.* to oppress; weigh on.
щемя́щий *adj.* oppressive; nagging.
щени́ться *v.r. impfv.* [*pfv.* **ощени́ться**] to have pups.
щено́к [*gen.* **-нка́;** *pl.* **-нки́, -нко́в** *or* **щеня́та, щеня́т**] *n.* pup; puppy.
щепа́ [*pl.* **ще́пы, щеп, щепа́м**] *n.* **1,** chip of wood. **2,** chips; kindling. **3,** shingles (*for a roof*).
щепа́ть *v. impfv.* [*pres.* **щеплю́, ще́плешь**] to chop; cleave.
щепети́льный *adj.* punctilious.
ще́пка [*gen. pl.* **-пок**] *n.* chip; sliver. —**худо́й как ще́пка,** thin as a rail.
щепо́тка [*gen. pl.* **-ток**] *n.* = **щепо́ть.**
щепо́ть *also,* **ще́поть** *n.f.* **1,** three fingers (the thumb, index, and middle finger) held together. **2,** pinch: щепо́ть со́ли, pinch of salt.
щерба́тый *adj.* **1,** chipped. **2,** with teeth missing. **3,** *colloq.* pockmarked.
щерби́на *n.* **1,** chip; nick. **2,** place where a tooth is missing. **3,** pockmark.
щети́на *n.* **1,** bristles. **2,** stubble (*of beard*). —**щети́нистый,** *adj.* bristly.
щети́ниться *v.r. impfv.* [*pfv.* **ощети́ниться**] to bristle.
щётка [*gen. pl.* **-ток**] *n.* **1,** brush. **2,** fetlock.
щёточный *adj.* brush (*attrib.*).
щёчный *adj.* cheek (*attrib.*).
щи [*gen.* **щей**] *n. pl.* cabbage soup. —**попа́сть как кур во́ щи,** to get into a jam; get into hot water.
щи́колотка [*gen. pl.* **-ток**] *n.* ankle.
щипа́ть *v. impfv.* [*pres.* **щиплю́, щи́плешь**] **1,** [*pfv.* **щипну́ть**] to pinch. **2,** [*impfv. only*] to burn; sting. **3,** [*pfv.* **общипа́ть** *or* **ощипа́ть**] to pluck. **4,** [*impfv. only*] to nibble. —**щипа́ться,** *refl.* [*impfv. only*] *colloq.* **1,** to pinch. **2,** to pinch each other.
щипко́вый *adj., in* **щипко́вые инструме́нты,** instruments played by plucking.
щипко́м *adv.* pizzicato.
щипну́ть *v., pfv. of* **щипа́ть** (*of sense #1*).
щипо́к [*gen.* **-пка́**] *n.* pinch; nip; tweak.
щипцы́ [*gen.* **-цо́в**] *n. pl.* tongs. —**хирурги́ческие щипцы́,** forceps. —**щипцы́ для зави́вки,** curling irons. —**щипцы́ для оре́хов,** nutcracker.
щи́пчики [*gen.* **-ков**] *n. pl.* tweezers.
щит [*gen.* **щита́**] *n.* **1,** shield. **2,** screen; guard: щит от гря́зи, mudguard. **3,** board; panel: распредели́тельный щит, switchboard; щит управле́ния, control panel. **4,** shell (*of a turtle*). **5,** *basketball* backboard. —**верну́ться на щите́,** to return home defeated. —**верну́ться со щито́м,** to return home victorious. —**поднима́ть на щит,** to extol; praise to the skies.
щитови́дный *adj.* thyroid: щитови́дная железа́, thyroid gland.
щито́к [*gen.* **-тка́**] *n.* **1,** *dim. of* **щит. 2,** panel. **3,** *sports* shinguard.
щитомо́рдник *n.* copperhead (*snake*).
щу́ка *n.* pike (*fish*).
щуп *n.* **1,** probe. **2,** dipstick.
щу́пальце [*gen. pl.* **-лец**] *n.* tentacle.
щу́пать *v. impfv.* [*pfv.* **пощу́пать**] to feel; touch. —**щу́пать** (+ *acc.*) **глаза́ми,** to look over; scan.
щу́плый *adj., colloq.* puny; thin; frail.
щу́рить *v. impfv.* [*pfv.* **сощу́рить**], *in* **щу́рить глаза́,** to squint. —**щу́риться,** *refl.* to squint.
щу́чий [*fem.* **-чья**] *adj.* pike's. —**как по щу́чьему веле́нию,** as if by magic.

Ъ, ъ *n. neut., called* **твёрдый знак,** 27th letter of the Russian alphabet.

Ы, ы *n. neut.* 28th letter of the Russian alphabet.

Ь, ь *n. neut., called* **мя́гкий знак,** 29th letter of the Russian alphabet.

Э

Э, э *n. neut., also called* **э оборо́тное,** thirtieth letter of the Russian alphabet.
эбе́новый *adj.* ebony. —**эбе́новое де́рево,** ebony.
эбони́т *n.* ebonite; vulcanite.
эвакуа́ция *n.* evacuation. —**эвакуацио́нный,** *adj.* evacuation (*attrib.*).
эвакуи́ровать *v. impfv. & pfv.* [*pres.* **-рую, -руешь**] to evacuate.
эве́н *n.m.* [*fem.* **эве́нка**] Even (*one of a people inhabiting eastern Siberia*).
эве́нк *n.m.* [*fem.* **эвенки́йка**] Evenk (*one of a people inhabiting eastern Siberia*). —**эвенки́йский,** *adj.* Evenki.
эве́нский *adj.* Even: эве́нский язы́к, the Even language (*see* **эве́н**).
эвкали́пт *n.* eucalyptus. —**эвкали́птовый,** *adj.* eucalyptus (*attrib.*).
ЭВМ *abbr. of* **электро́нная вычисли́тельная маши́на,** (electronic) computer.
эволюциони́ровать *v. impfv. & pfv.* [*pres.* **-рую, -руешь**] to evolve.
эволю́ция *n.* evolution. —**эволюцио́нный,** *adj.* evolutionary.
э́врика *interj.* eureka!
эвфеми́зм *n.* euphemism. —**эвфемисти́ческий,** *adj.* euphemistic.
эгалита́рный *adj.* egalitarian.
эги́да *n.* aegis: под эги́дой (+ *gen.*), under the aegis (of).
эгои́зм *n.* egoism; selfishness. —**эгои́ст; эгои́стка,** *n.* egoist; egotist. —**эгоисти́ческий; эгоисти́чный,** *adj.* egoistic; egotistical; selfish.
эготи́зм *n.* egotism.
эдельве́йс (дэ) *n.* edelweiss.
Эде́м (дэ) *n.* Eden.
эй *interj.* hey!
эйнште́йний (тэ) *n.* einsteinium.
эйфори́я *n.* euphoria.
эква́тор *n.* equator. —**экваториа́льный,** *adj.* equatorial.
эквивале́нт *n.* equivalent. —**эквивале́нтность,** *n.f.* equivalence. —**эквивале́нтный,** *adj.* equivalent.
эквилибри́ст *n.* tightrope walker; high-wire artist. —**эквилибри́стика,** *n.* balancing act; tightrope walking.
экзальта́ция *n.* exaltation; ecstasy. —**экзальтиро́ванный,** *adj.* in a state of exaltation; ecstatic.
экза́мен *n.* examination. —**экзамена́тор,** *n.* examiner. —**экзаменацио́нный,** *adj.* examination (*attrib.*).
экзаменова́ть *v. impfv.* [*pfv.* **проэкзаменова́ть;** *pres.* **-ну́ю, -ну́ешь**] to examine. —**экзаменова́ться,** *refl.* to take an examination.
экзеку́ция *n., obs.* **1,** whipping; flogging; corporal punishment. **2,** execution.
экзе́ма (зэ) *n.* eczema.
экземпля́р (зэ) *n.* **1,** copy (*one of many*): в трёх экземпля́рах, in three copies; in triplicate. **2,** specimen: ре́дкий экземпля́р, rare specimen.
экзистенциали́зм *n.* existentialism. —**экзистенциали́ст,** *n.* existentialist. —**экзистенциа́льный,** *adj.* existential(ist).
экзо́тика *n.* exotic things; exotic objects. —**экзоти́ческий,** *adj.* exotic.
экиво́к *n., usu. pl.* ambiguity: говори́ть с экиво́ками, to talk in ambiguities; говори́ть без экиво́ков, to talk straight to the point.
э́кий *adj., colloq.* what a...!
экипа́ж *n.* **1,** carriage. **2,** crew.
экипирова́ть *v. impfv. & pfv.* [*pres.* **-ру́ю, -ру́ешь**] to equip.
экипиро́вка *n.* **1,** equipping. **2,** equipment.
эклекти́зм *n.* eclecticism. —**экле́ктик,** *n.* eclectic. —**эклекти́ческий; эклекти́чный,** *adj.* eclectic.
экле́р *n.* éclair.
эклиптика *n., astron.* ecliptic.
эколо́гия *n.* ecology. —**экологи́ческий,** *adj.* ecological.
эконо́м *n., obs.* **1,** thrifty person. **2,** manager of a household; steward. **3,** economist.
эконо́мика *n.* **1,** economics. **2,** economy (*of a country*). —**экономи́ст,** *n.* economist.
эконо́мить *v. impfv.* [*pfv.* **сэконо́мить;** *pres.* **-млю, -мишь**] **1,** to save: эконо́мить вре́мя, to save time; эконо́мить на материа́лах, to save on materials. **2,** [*impfv. only*] to economize.
экономи́ческий *adj.* economic.
экономи́чный *adj.* (*of a device, method, etc.*) economical.
эконо́мия *n.* **1,** economy; thrift: соблюда́ть эконо́мию, to be economical; economize. **2,** (*with gen.*) saving (of): эконо́мия то́плива, saving of fuel; fuel economy. **3,** savings; amount saved (*by economizing*): эконо́мия соста́вила..., the savings amounted to...
эконо́мка [*gen. pl.* **-мок**] *n., obs.* housekeeper.
эконо́мничать *v. impfv., colloq.* to economize; scrimp; watch one's pennies.
эконо́мный *adj.* economical; thrifty.

экра́н *n.* **1,** screen. **2,** the screen (*motion pictures*). **3,** shield: теплово́й экра́н, heat shield.
экраниза́ция *n.* filming.
экранизи́ровать *v. impfv. & pfv.* [*pres.* **-рую, -руешь**] to make into a movie.
экскава́тор *n.* steam shovel.
э́кскурс *n.* digression.
экскурса́нт *n.* person on an excursion; sightseer.
экску́рсия *n.* **1,** excursion; sightseeing tour. **2,** tourist group; sightseeing party. —**экскурсио́нный,** *adj.* excursion (*attrib.*).
экскурсово́д *n.* tour guide.
экsли́брис *n.* bookplate.
экспанси́вный *adj.* expansive; effusive.
экспансиони́зм *n.* expansionism. —**экспансиони́стский,** *adj.* expansionist.
экспа́нсия *n.* (territorial) expansion.
экспатриа́ция *n.* expatriation. —**экспатриа́нт,** *n.* expatriate.
экспатрии́ровать *v. impfv. & pfv.* [*pres.* **-рую, -руешь**] to expatriate.
экспеди́ция *n.* expedition. —**экспедицио́нный,** *adj.* expeditionary.
экспериме́нт *n.* experiment. —**эксперимента́льный,** *adj.* experimental. —**эксперименти́рование,** *n.* experimentation.
эксперименти́ровать *v. impfv.* [*pres.* **-рую, -руешь**] to experiment.
экспе́рт *n.* expert.
эксперти́за *n.* **1,** examination by experts. **2,** committee of experts.
экспе́ртный *adj.* **1,** expert. **2,** of experts.
эксплуата́тор *n.* exploiter. —**эксплуата́торский,** *adj.* exploiter (*attrib.*); exploiting.
эксплуата́ция *n.* **1,** exploitation. **2,** operation. —**эксплуатацио́нный,** *adj.* operating; operational.
эксплуати́ровать *v. impfv.* [*pres.* **-рую, -руешь**] **1,** to exploit; take advantage of. **2,** to operate; run.
экспози́метр *n., photog.* exposure meter; light meter.
экспози́ция *n.* **1,** layout; display. **2,** *photog.* exposure.
экспона́т *n.* exhibit.
экспоне́нт *n.* **1,** exhibitor. **2,** *math.* exponent.
экспони́ровать *v. impfv. & pfv.* [*pres.* **-рую, -руешь**] **1,** to exhibit. **2,** *photog.* to expose.
экспоно́метр *n., photog.* exposure meter; light meter.
э́кспорт *n.* **1,** export. **2,** exports. —**экспортёр,** *n.* exporter.
экспорти́ровать *v. impfv. & pfv.* [*pres.* **-рую, -руешь**] to export.
э́кспортный *adj.* export (*attrib.*).
экспре́сс *n.* express (*train, ship, bus, etc.*).
экспресси́вный *adj.* expressive.
экспре́ссия *n.* expression; expressiveness.
экспро́мт *n.* something composed on the spur of the moment; something one just dashed off. —**экспро́мтом,** *adv.* impromptu; extemporaneously.
экспроприа́ция *n.* expropriation.
экспроприи́ровать *v. impfv. & pfv.* [*pres.* **-рую, -руешь**] to expropriate.
экста́з *n.* ecstasy. —**экстати́ческий,** *adj.* ecstatic.
экстéрн (тэ) *n.* student allowed to take examinations without attending classes.
экстерриториа́льный *adj.* extraterritorial.
экстравага́нтный *adj.* eccentric; bizarre; outlandish.
экстраги́ровать *v. impfv. & pfv.* [*pres.* **-рую, -руешь**] to extract.
экстра́кт *n.* extract.
экстра́кция *n.* extraction.
экстраордина́рный *adj.* extraordinary.
экстраполи́ровать *v. impfv. & pfv.* [*pres.* **-рую, -руешь**] to extrapolate.
экстраполя́ция *n.* extrapolation.
экстреми́зм *n.* extremism. —**экстреми́ст,** *n.* extremist. —**экстреми́стский,** *adj.* extremist.
э́кстренный *adj.* **1,** urgent. **2,** special. —**э́кстренно,** *adv.* urgently.
эксце́нтрик *n.* **1,** clown. **2,** *obs.* eccentric (person). **3,** *mech.* cam.
эксцентри́ческий *adj.* **1,** = **эксцентри́чный. 2,** *theat.* comical; improbable. **3,** *math.* eccentric.
эксцентри́чный *adj.* eccentric; odd. —**эксцентри́чность,** *n.f.* eccentricity.
эксце́сс *n., usu. pl.* excesses.
эктопла́зма *n.* ectoplasm.
эласти́чный *adj.* **1,** elastic. **2,** supple. —**эласти́чность,** *n.f.* elasticity.
элева́тор *n.* **1,** grain elevator. **2,** lift; hoist.
элега́нтный *adj.* elegant. —**элега́нтно,** *adv.* elegantly. —**элега́нтность,** *n.f.* elegance.
элеги́ческий *adj.* **1,** elegiac. **2,** [*also,* **элеги́чный**] *fig.* melancholy.
эле́гия *n.* **1,** elegy. **2,** *fig.* melancholy.
электризова́ть *v. impfv. & pfv.* [*pfv. also* **наэлектризова́ть;** *pres.* **-зу́ю, -зу́ешь**] **1,** to electrify; charge with electricity. **2,** *fig.* to electrify; thrill.
эле́ктрик *n.* electrician. —**инжене́р-эле́ктрик,** electrical engineer.
элетри́к *adj. indecl.* grayish blue.
электрифика́ция *n.* electrification.
электрифици́ровать *v. impfv. & pfv.* [*pres.* **-рую, -руешь**] to electrify; provide with electric power.
электри́ческий *adj.* electric. —**электри́ческий стул,** electric chair.
электри́чество *n.* electricity.
электри́чка [*gen. pl.* **-чек**] *n., colloq.* **1,** electric railway. **2,** electric train.
электро- *prefix* electric(al): электропо́езд, electric train; электроте́хник, electrical engineer.
электрово́з *n.* electric locomotive.
электро́д *n.* electrode.
электродви́гатель *n.m.* electric motor.
электрока́р *n.* electric (*i.e.* battery-operated) vehicle for carrying loads or baggage.
электрокардиогра́мма *n.* electrocardiogram. —**электрокардио́граф,** *n.* electrocardiograph.
электро́лиз *n.* electrolysis.
электроли́ния *n.* electric power line.
электроли́т *n.* electrolyte.
электромагнети́зм *n.* electromagnetism. —**электромагни́т,** *n.* electromagnet. —**электромагни́тный,** *adj.* electromagnetic.
электромонтёр *n.* electrician.
электро́н *n.* electron.
электро́ника *n.* electronics.
электро́нный *adj.* **1,** electron (*attrib.*). **2,** electronic. —**электро́нная ла́мпа,** electron tube; vacuum tube.
электропита́ние *n.* power supply.
электроста́нция *n.* power station.
электроста́тика *n.* electrostatics. —**электростати́ческий,** *adj.* electrostatic.
электроте́хник *n.* electrical engineer. —**электроте́хника,** *n.* electrical engineering.

электроэне́ргия *n.* electrical energy; electric power.
элеме́нт *n.* **1,** element. **2,** *electricity* cell: сухо́й элеме́нт, dry cell. **3,** *colloq.* character: подозри́тельный элеме́нт, suspicious character.
элемента́рный *adj.* elementary.
элеро́н *n.* aileron.
эликси́р *n.* elixir.
эли́та *n.* elite.
э́ллинский *adj.* Hellenic.
э́ллипс *n.* **1,** ellipse. **2,** = **э́ллипсис.**
э́ллипсис *n., ling.* ellipsis.
эллипсо́ид *n.* ellipsoid.
эллипти́ческий *adj.* elliptical.
эль *n.m.* ale.
эльф *n.* elf.
эма́левый *adj.* enamel (*attrib.*); enameled.
эмалиро́ванный *adj.* enameled.
эмалирова́ть *v. impfv.* [*pres.* **-ру́ю, -ру́ешь**] to enamel.
эма́ль *n.f.* enamel.
эмана́ция *n.* emanation.
эмансипа́тор *n.* emancipator. —**эмансипа́ция,** *n.* emancipation.
эмансипи́ровать *v. impfv. & pfv.* [*pres.* **-рую, -руешь**] to emancipate.
эмба́рго *n. indecl.* embargo.
эмбле́ма *n.* emblem. —**эмблемати́ческий,** *adj.* emblematic.
эмболи́я *n.* embolism.
эмбриоло́гия *n.* embryology. —**эмбрио́лог,** *n.* embryologist.
эмбрио́н *n.* embryo. —**эмбриона́льный,** *adj.* embryonic.
эмигра́нт *n.* émigré; emigrant. —**эмигра́нтский,** *adj.* émigré (*attrib.*).
эмигра́ция *n.* **1,** emigration. **2,** émigrés. —**в эмигра́ции,** abroad; in a foreign land (*to which one has emigrated*).
эмигри́ровать *v. impfv. & pfv.* [*pres.* **-рую, -руешь**] to emigrate.
эми́р *n.* emir. —**эмира́т,** *n.* emirate.
эмисса́р *n.* emissary.
эми́ссия *n.* **1,** *finance* issuance; emission. **2,** *electronics* emission.
эмо́ция *n.* emotion. —**эмоциона́льный,** *adj.* emotional.
эмпири́зм *n.* empiricism. —**эмпи́рик,** *n.* empiricist. —**эмпири́ческий,** *adj.* empirical.
э́му *n.m. indecl.* emu.
эму́льсия *n.* emulsion.
эмфизе́ма (зэ) *n.* emphysema.
эндеми́ческий *adj.* endemic.
эндокри́нный *adj.* endocrine.
эндокриноло́гия *n.* endocrinology.
э́ндшпиль *n.m., chess* end game.
энерге́тика *n.* energy. —**энергети́ческий,** *adv.* energy (*attrib.*).
энерги́чный *adj.* **1,** (*of a person*) energetic. **2,** (*of measures, protests, etc.*) forceful; vigorous; energetic. —**энерги́чно,** *adv.* energetically; vigorously.
эне́ргия *n.* **1,** energy. **2,** (electric) power.
э́нный *adj.* **1,** any; an unspecified; a certain. **2,** *colloq.* unlimited; endless: э́нное коли́чество, an endless amount. —**в э́нной сте́пени,** to the nth degree.
э́нский *adj.* X (*used to designate something that cannot be identified*).
энтери́т *n.* enteritis.
энтомоло́гия *n.* entomology. —**энтомо́лог,** *n.* entomologist. —**энтомологи́ческий,** *adj.* entomological.
энтузиа́зм *n.* enthusiasm. —**энтузиа́ст,** *n.* enthusiast.
энцефали́т *n.* encephalitis.
энци́клика *n.* encyclical.
энциклопе́дия *n.* encyclopedia. —**энциклопеди́ст,** *n.* encyclopedist. —**энциклопеди́ческий,** *adj.* encyclopedic.
эпиго́н *n.* imitator; copier.
эпигра́мма *n.* epigram. —**эпиграммати́ческий,** *adj.* epigrammatic.
эпи́граф *n.* epigraph.
эпиде́мия *n.* epidemic. —**эпидеми́ческий,** *adj.* epidemic.
эпиде́рмис (дэ) *n.* epidermis.
эпизо́д *n.* episode.
эпизоди́ческий *adj.* **1,** episodic. **2,** occasional; sporadic.
э́пик *n.* epic poet.
эпикуре́ец [*gen.* **-е́йца**] *n.* epicurean. —**эпикуре́йский,** *adj.* epicurean.
эпиле́псия *n.* epilepsy. —**эпиле́птик,** *n.* epileptic. —**эпилепти́ческий,** *adj.* epileptic.
эпило́г *n.* epilogue.
эпи́стола *n.* epistle. —**эпистоля́рный,** *adj.* epistolary.
эпита́фия *n.* epitaph.
эпите́лий (тэ) *n.* epithelium. —**эпителиа́льный,** *adj.* epithelial.
эпи́тет *n.* epithet.
эпице́нтр *n.* epicenter.
эпи́ческий *adj.* epic.
эполе́та *n.* epaulet. *Also,* **эполе́т.**
эпопе́я *n.* epic; epic work.
эпо́ха *n.* epoch; age; era. —**эпоха́льный,** *adj.* epochal.
э́ра *n.* era. —**до на́шей э́ры,** B.C.: в двухсо́том году́ до на́шей э́ры, in 200 B.C.—**на́шей э́ры,** A.D.: в двухсо́том году́ на́шей э́ры, in 200 A.D.
э́рбий *n.* erbium.
эрг *n.* erg.
эре́кция *n., physiol.* erection.
э́рика *n.* brier; heath.
Эрмита́ж *n.* the Hermitage Museum (*in Leningrad*).
эро́зия *n.* erosion.
эроти́зм *n.* eroticism.
эро́тика *n.* **1,** sensuality. **2,** erotic literature. —**эроти́ческий,** *adj.* erotic.
эруди́рованный *adj.* erudite.
эруди́ция *n.* erudition. —**эруди́т,** *n.* erudite person.
эрцге́рцог *n.* archduke. —**эрцгерцоги́ня,** *n.* archduchess. —**эрцге́рцогство,** *n.* archduchy.
эска́дра *n., naval* squadron.
эска́дренный *adj.* squadron (*attrib.*). —**эска́дренный миноно́сец,** destroyer.
эскадри́лья [*gen. pl.* **-лий**] *n.* (air) squadron.
эскадро́н *n.* (cavalry) squadron. —**эскадро́нный,** *adj.* squadron (*attrib.*).
эскала́тор *n.* escalator.
эскала́ция *n.* escalation.
эска́рп *n., mil.* escarpment.
эсква́йр *n.* esquire.
эски́з *n.* **1,** sketch. **2,** draft; outline. —**эски́зный,** *adj.* rough; preliminary; in outline form.

эскимó *n. indecl.* ice cream on a stick.
эскимóс *n.m.* [*fem.* **-мóска**] Eskimo. —**эскимóсский,** *adj.* Eskimo.
эскóрт *n., mil.* escort.
эскорти́ровать *v. impfv.* [*pres.* **-рую, -руешь**] *mil.* to escort.
эсми́нец [*gen.* **-нца**] *n., naval* destroyer (*contr. of* **эскáдренный минонóсец**).
эсперáнто *n. indecl.* Esperanto.
эспланáда *n.* esplanade.
эссéнция *n.* **1,** essence: рóмовая эссéнция, essence of rum. **2,** *fig.* essence.
эстакáда *n.* **1,** trestle; overpass. **2,** pier.
эстафéта *n.* **1,** relay race. **2,** baton (*used in a relay race*). —**эстафéтный,** *adj.* relay (*attrib.*); used in a relay race.
эстéтика (тэ) *n.* esthetics. —**эстéт,** *n.* esthete. —**эстети́ческий,** *adj.* esthetic.
эстóнец [*gen.* **-нца**] *n.m.* [*fem.* **-нка**] Estonian. —**эстóнский,** *adj.* Estonian.
эстрагóн *n.* tarragon.
эстрáда *n.* **1,** stage; platform. **2,** vaudeville. —**эстрáдный,** *adj.* vaudeville (*attrib.*).
этáж [*gen.* **этажá**] *n.* floor; story.
этажéрка [*gen. pl.* **-рок**] *n.* bookcase.
э́так *adv., colloq.* **1,** so; like this; like that. **2,** about; approximately; some. —**и так и э́так,** this way and that.
э́такий *adj., colloq.* **1,** such; such a... **2,** what a...!
эталóн *n.* **1,** standard (*of measurement*). **2,** *fig.* model.
этáп *n.* **1,** stage; leg (*of a journey*). **2,** *fig.* stage; phase. **3,** halting place (*for troops, or prisoners going into exile*). **4,** group of prisoners traveling under guard. —**по этáпу,** under guard; under escort.
э́тика *n.* ethics.
этикéт *n.* etiquette.
этикéтка [*gen. pl.* **-ток**] *n.* label.
эти́л *n.* ethyl.
этилéн *n.* ethylene.
этили́рованный *adj.* (*of gasoline*) leaded.
эти́ловый *adj.* ethyl (*attrib.*).
этимолóгия *n.* etymology. —**этимóлог,** *n.* etymologist. —**этимологи́ческий,** *adj.* etymological.
эти́ческий *adj.* ethical. *Also,* **эти́чный.**
этни́ческий *adj.* ethnic.
этногрáфия *n.* ethnography. —**этнóграф,** *n.* ethnographer. —**этнографи́ческий,** *adj.* ethnographic.
этнолóгия *n.* ethnology. —**этнóлог,** *n.* ethnologist. —**этнологи́ческий,** *adj.* ethnological.
э́то *dem. adj., neut. of* **э́тот,** this: э́то слóво, this word. —*dem. pron.* **1,** this; that; it: что э́то?, what is this? Я ужé знал об э́том, I already knew about it. Что вы хоти́те э́тим сказáть?, what do you mean by that? **2,** this is; that is; it is: э́то дуб, this is an oak tree; э́то – жéлуди, these are acorns. Это óчень прóсто, this (that, it) is very simple. **3,** (*of neuter nouns only*) this one. —*particle* **1,** (the one) who: кто э́то звони́л?, who was that who called? Это он вы́болтал секрéт?, was it *he* who spilled the beans? **2,** *used as an intensifier:* что э́то с вáми?, what's the matter with you? Кудá э́то он пошёл?, where on earth has he gone?
э́тот [*fem.* **э́та;** *neut.* **э́то;** *pl.* **э́ти;** *gen.* **э́того, э́той, э́тих;** *dat.* **э́тому, э́той, э́тим;** *acc. fem.* **э́ту;** *instr.* **э́тим, э́той, э́тими;** *prepl.* **э́том, э́той, э́тих**] *dem. adj.* this: э́тот дом, this house; э́та кни́га, this book; э́то слóво, this word; э́ти лю́ди, these people. —*dem. pron.* this one.
этрýсский *adj.* Etruscan.
этю́д *n.* **1,** *art* sketch. **2,** essay. **3,** *music* étude. **4,** chess problem.
эфемéрный *adj.* ephemeral.
эфéс *n.* hilt (*handle of a sword*).
эфиóп *n.m.* [*fem.* **эфиóпка**] Ethiopian. —**эфиóпский,** *adj.* Ethiopian.
эфи́р *n.* **1,** ether (*upper regions of the atmosphere*). **2,** *chem.* ether: эти́ловый эфи́р, ether; ethyl ether. **3,** *radio* air: выходи́ть в эфи́р, to go on the air. Передавáть в эфи́р, to broadcast. —**прямóй эфи́р,** live broadcasting.
эфи́рный *adj.* **1,** ether (*attrib.*). **2,** ethereal. —**эфи́рное мáсло,** essential oil.
эффéкт *n.* **1,** effect. **2,** *pl.* effects: шумовы́е эффéкты, sound effects. —**с эффéктом,** with emphasis; with a flourish.
эффекти́вный *adj.* **1,** effective. **2,** efficient. —**эффекти́вно,** *adv.* effectively; efficiently. —**эффекти́вность,** *n.f.* effectiveness; efficiency.
эффéктный *adj.* striking; showy; flashy.
э́хо *n.* echo.
эхолóт *n.* sonic depth finder.
эшафóт *n.* scaffold.
эшелóн *n.* **1,** *mil.* echelon. **2,** special train.

Ю

Ю, ю *n. neut.* 31st letter of the Russian alphabet.

юбиле́й *n.* anniversary; jubilee. —**юбиле́йный,** *adj.* anniversary (*attrib.*).

юбиля́р *n.* person or institution whose anniversary is being celebrated.

ю́бка [*gen. pl.* **-бок**] *n.* skirt. —**ни́жняя ю́бка,** half slip; petticoat. —**ю́бка клёш,** flared skirt.

ю́бочка [*gen. pl.* **-чек**] *n.* short skirt. —**шотла́ндская ю́бочка,** kilt.

ювели́р *n.* jeweler.

ювели́рный *adj.* **1,** jewelry (*attrib.*); jeweler's (*attrib.*). **2,** *fig.* finely wrought; exquisite.

юг *n.* south.

ю́го-восто́к *n.* southeast. —**ю́го-восто́чный,** *adj.* southeast; southeastern; southeasterly.

ю́го-за́пад *n.* southwest. —**ю́го-за́падный,** *adj.* southwest; southwestern; southwesterly.

югосла́в *n.m.* [*fem.* **-сла́вка**] Yugoslav. —**югосла́вский,** *adj.* Yugoslav; Yugoslavian.

южа́нин [*pl.* **южа́не, южа́н**] *n.m.* [*fem.* **южа́нка**] southerner.

ю́жный *adj.* southern; South; southerly.

ю́зом *adv.* into a skid: пойти́ ю́зом, to skid.

ю́кка *n.* yucca.

юла́ *n.* **1,** top (*toy*). **2,** *colloq.* fidgety person; fidgety child.

юлиа́нский *adj., in* **юлиа́нский календа́рь,** Julian calendar.

юли́ть *v. impfv., colloq.* **1,** to keep moving about. **2,** (*of an insect*) to flit. **3,** (*with* **пе́ред**) to play up to; ingratiate oneself (with). **4,** to equivocate.

ю́мор *n.* humor.

юморе́ска *n.* humoresque.

юмори́ст *n.* humorist. —**юмористи́ческий,** *adj.* humorous.

ю́нга *n.* cabin boy.

юне́ц [*gen.* **юнца́**] *n., colloq.* youth; lad.

ю́нкер *n.* **1,** [*pl.* **ю́нкеры**] junker. **2,** [*pl.* **юнкера́**] *prerev.* military cadet.

ю́ность *n.f.* youth.

ю́ноша [*gen. pl.* **-шей**] *n.m.* youth (*young man*).

ю́ношеский *adj.* **1,** youth (*attrib.*). **2,** youthful.

ю́ношество *n.* **1,** youth; young people. **2,** youth (*time when one is young*).

ю́ный *adj.* young; youthful.

юпи́тер *n.* **1,** Jupiter. **2,** *l.c.* floodlight.

юр *n., in* **на (са́мом) юру́, 1,** in an open (*or* exposed) place. **2,** *colloq.* in the midst (*or* center) of everything.

юриди́ческий *adj.* juridical; legal; judicial. —**юриди́ческий факульте́т,** department/faculty of law; law school.

юрисди́кция *n.* jurisdiction.

юриско́нсульт *n.* legal adviser (*to a company, institution, etc.*).

юриспруде́нция *n.* jurisprudence.

юри́ст *n.* lawyer.

ю́ркий *adj.* **1,** nimble; agile. **2,** *fig., colloq.* clever; sharp.

юркну́ть *also,* **ю́ркнуть** *v. pfv.* to dart; scamper.

юро́дивый *adj.* touched; cracked; crazy.

юро́дство *n.* **1,** madness; derangement. **2,** irrational act.

юро́дствовать *v. impfv.* [*pres.* **-ствую, -ствуешь**] to act like a madman.

юро́к [*gen.* **юрка́**] *n.* brambling.

ю́рский *adj.* Jurassic.

ю́рта *n.* nomad's tent.

юсти́ция *n.* justice. —**мини́стр юсти́ции,** Minister of Justice; (*U.S.*) Attorney General.

ют *n.* quarterdeck.

юти́ться *v.r. impfv.* [*pres.* **ючу́сь, юти́шься**] **1,** to nestle. **2,** to huddle. **3,** to be cooped up.

юфть *n.f.* Russia leather.

Я

Я, я *n. neut.* 32nd letter of the Russian alphabet. —**от А до Я,** from A to Z.

я [*gen. & acc.* **меня́;** *dat. & prepl.* **мне;** *instr.* **мной** *or* **мно́ю**] *pers. pron., 1st person sing.* I.

я́беда *n.m. & f., colloq.* **1,** tattler. **2,** spreader of malicious gossip. —*n.f., obs.* malicious gossip.

я́бедник *n., colloq.* spreader of malicious gossip.

я́бедничать *v. impfv.* [*pfv.* **ная́бедничать**] (*with* **на** + *acc.*) *colloq.* **1,** to tell (on); tattle (on). **2,** to spread malicious gossip (about).

я́бедничество *n., colloq.* spreading of malicious gossip.

я́блоко [*pl.* **я́блоки, я́блок**] *n.* apple. —**в я́блоках,** dappled: се́рый в я́блоках, dapple-gray. —**глазно́е я́блоко,** eyeball. —**я́блоко мише́ни,** bull's-eye. —**я́блоко раздо́ра,** apple of discord; bone of contention.

я́блоновый *adj.* of apple trees. Я́блоневый цвет, apple blossom. Я́блоневый сад, apple orchard. *Also,* **я́блонный.**

я́блоня *n.* apple tree.

я́блочко [*gen. pl.* **-чек**] *n., dim. of* **я́блоко.**

я́блочный *adj.* apple (*attrib.*); of apples.

яви́ть [*infl.* **явлю́, я́вишь**] *v., pfv. of* **являть.** —**яви́ться,** *refl., pfv. of* **явля́ться.**

я́вка [*gen. pl.* **-вок**] *n.* **1,** appearance; attendance. **2,** secret meeting. **3,** secret meeting place.

явле́ние *n.* **1,** phenomenon. **2,** occurrence. **3,** *theat.* scene.

явля́ть *v. impfv.* [*pfv.* **яви́ть**] **1,** to show; reveal. **2,** *in* **явля́ть собо́й,** *colloq.* to be. —**явля́ться,** *refl.* **1,** to appear; report: яви́ться на рабо́ту, to appear at work; report for work. **2,** (*with instr.*) to be: явля́ться по́лной неожи́данностью, to be a complete surprise.

я́вный *adj.* **1,** overt; open: я́вная вражда́, overt/open hostility. **2,** obvious: э́то я́вное недоразуме́ние, this is an obvious (*or* is obviously a) misunderstanding. —**я́вно,** *adv.* obviously.

я́вор *n.* sycamore; Eurasian maple.

я́вочный *adj.* **1,** secret; clandestine. **2,** *in* я́вочный пункт; я́вочная ба́за, *mil.* reporting office (*for recruits*). —**я́вочным поря́дком,** without prior permission.

я́вственный *adj.* clear; distinct.

я́вствовать *v. impfv.* [*pres.* **-ствует**] to be clear; be apparent; be obvious.

явь *n.f.* reality.

ягдта́ш *n.* game bag.

я́гель *n.m.* reindeer moss.

ягнёнок [*gen.* **-нка;** *pl.* **ягня́та, ягня́т**] *n.* lamb.

ягни́ться *v.r. impfv.* [*pfv.* **оягни́ться**] (*of a ewe*) to give birth.

ягня́тник *n.* bearded vulture.

я́года *n.* **1,** berry. **2,** *in* **ви́нная я́года,** fig. —**одного́ по́ля я́года,** birds of a feather.

я́годицы *n. pl.* [*sing.* **я́годица**] buttocks.

я́годник *n.* **1,** berry patch. **2,** berry bush. **3,** *colloq.* one who likes to pick berries.

я́годный *adj.* berry (*attrib.*).

ягуа́р *n.* jaguar.

яд *n.* **1,** poison. **2,** *fig.* venom.

я́дерный *adj.* nuclear.

ядови́тый *adj.* **1,** poison; poisonous; venomous; toxic. **2,** *fig.* venomous; vicious; malicious.

ядохимика́т *n.* pesticide.

ядрёный *adj., colloq.* **1,** (*of a plant*) hearty; (*of a fruit*) juicy. **2,** (*of a person*) robust; vigorous; hale and hearty. **3,** bracing; invigorating.

я́дрица *n.* unground buckwheat.

ядро́ [*pl.* **я́дра, я́дер, я́драм**] *n.* **1,** kernel. **2,** core. **3,** nucleus. **4,** *fig.* heart; core. **5,** *mil.* ball: пу́шечное ядро́, cannon ball. **6,** *sports* shot: толка́ть ядро́, to put the shot.

я́зва *n.* **1,** ulcer; sore. **2,** *fig.* curse; plague. —**сиби́рская я́зва,** anthrax.

я́звенный *adj.* ulcerous. —**я́звенная боле́знь,** peptic ulcer.

язви́тельный *adj.* caustic; biting; cutting; sarcastic.

язви́ть *v. impfv.* [*pres.* **язвлю́, язви́шь**] **1,** *obs.* to sting. **2,** *fig., obs.* to taunt. **3,** [*pfv.* **съязви́ть**] to say sarcastically.

язы́к [*gen.* **языка́**] *n.* **1,** tongue. **2,** language. **3,** clapper (*of a bell*). **4,** *mil.* prisoner (*to be interrogated*). —**найти́ о́бщий язы́к,** to find common ground. —**говори́ть на ра́зных языка́х,** to be speaking different languages; be on different wavelengths.

языка́стый *adj., colloq.* sharp-tongued.

языкове́д *n.* linguist. —**языкове́дение,** *n.* linguistics.

языково́й *adj.* linguistic; language (*attrib.*).

языко́вый *adj.* tongue (*attrib.*).

языкозна́ние *n.* linguistics.

язы́ческий *adj.* heathen; pagan. —**язы́чество,** *n.* paganism.

язычко́вый *adj., phonet.* uvular. —**язычко́вый инструме́нт,** reed instrument.

язы́чник *n.* heathen; pagan.

язычо́к [*gen.* **-чка́**] *n.* **1,** *dim. of* **язы́к. 2,** tongue (of a shoe). **3,** uvula. **4,** *music* reed. **5,** catch; fastener.

язь [*gen.* **язя́**] *n.m.* a fish of the carp family.

яичко [*gen. pl.* **-чек**] *n.* **1,** *dim. of* **яйцó**. **2,** testicle.

яичник *n., anat.* ovary.

яичница *n.* [*also,* **яичница-глазу́нья**] fried eggs. —**яичница-болту́нья,** scrambled eggs.

яичный *adj.* egg (*attrib.*).

яйцеви́дный *adj.* egg-shaped.

яйцевóд *n.* oviduct.

яйцекладу́щий *adj.* oviparous.

яйцеклéтка *n., biol.* ovule.

яйцерóдный *adj.* oviparous.

яйцó [*pl.* **я́йца, яиц, я́йцам**] *n.* egg. —**яйцó-пашóт,** poached egg.

як *n.* yak.

я́кобы *conj.* that (*implying skepticism about a statement*): говоря́т, я́кобы он скóро уезжáет, they say (that) he is leaving soon. —*particle* supposedly; allegedly: письмó, я́кобы напи́санное им, a letter allegedly written by him.

я́корный *adj.* of an anchor. —**я́корное мéсто; я́корная стоя́нка,** (place of) anchorage.

я́корь [*pl.* **якоря́**] *n.m.* **1,** anchor. **2,** *electricity* armature. —**стать на я́корь,** to anchor. —**стоя́ть на я́коре,** to stand/lie at anchor. —**я́корь спасéния,** last hope; last means of salvation.

яку́т *n.m.* [*fem.* **яку́тка**] Yakut (*one of a people inhabiting northeastern Siberia*). —**яку́тский,** *adj.* Yakut.

якшáться *v.r. impfv.* (*with* **с** + *instr.*) *colloq.* to hobnob (with); rub elbows (with).

ял *n.* yawl.

я́лик *n.* skiff; dinghy; wherry.

я́ловый *adj.* (*of cows, sheep, etc.*) dry; giving no milk.

я́ма *n.* hole; pit. —**возду́шная я́ма,** air pocket. —**выгребна́я я́ма,** cesspool. —**долговáя я́ма,** debtors' prison.

ямб *n.* iamb. —**четырёхстóпный ямб,** iambic tetrameter. —**пятистóпный ямб,** iambic pentameter.

ямби́ческий *adj.* iambic.

я́мка [*gen. pl.* **-мок**] *n.* **1,** *dim. of* **я́ма**. **2,** dimple.

я́мочка [*gen. pl.* **-чек**] *n.* dimple.

ямс *n.* yam.

ямщи́к [*gen.* **-щикá**] *n.* stagecoach driver.

янвáрь [*gen.* **января́**] *n.m.* January. —**янвáрский,** *adj.* January (*attrib.*).

я́нки *n.m. indecl.* Yankee.

янтáрь [*gen.* **-таря́**] *n.m.* amber. —**янтáрный,** *adj.* amber.

япóнец [*gen.* **-нца**] *n.m.* [*fem.* **-нка**] Japanese (man): он япóнец, he is Japanese. —**япóнский,** *adj.* Japanese.

яр [*2nd loc.* **яру́**] *n.* **1,** cliff. **2,** ravine.

ярáнга *n.* tent made of reindeer hides.

ярд *n.* yard (*36 inches*).

ярéмный *adj., in* **ярéмная вéна,** jugular vein.

я́ркий *adj.* [*short form* **я́рок, яркá, я́рко;** *comp.* **я́рче**] **1,** bright; brilliant. **2,** *fig.* striking; vivid; graphic. **3,** *fig.* brilliant; outstanding.

я́рко *adv.* **1,** brightly; brilliantly. **2,** clearly; distinctly.

я́рко- *prefix, used with colors,* bright: я́рко-крáсный, bright red.

я́ркость *n.f.* brightness; brilliance.

ярлы́к [*gen.* **-лыкá**] *n.* label; tag.

ярлычóк [*gen.* **-чкá**] *n., dim. of* **ярлы́к.**

я́рмарка [*gen. pl.* **-рок**] *n.* (trade) fair. —**я́рмарочный,** *adj.* fair (*attrib.*).

ярмó [*pl.* **я́рма**] *n.* **1,** yoke (*for oxen*). **2,** *fig.* yoke (*of oppression*).

яровизáция *n.* vernalization.

яровизи́ровать *v. impfv. & pfv.* [*pres.* **-рую, -руешь**] to vernalize.

яровóй *adj.* (*of crops*) spring (*attrib.*): ярова́я пшени́ца, spring wheat.

я́ростный *adj.* **1,** furious. **2,** violent.

я́рость *n.f.* fury; rage.

я́рус *n.* tier. —**я́русный,** *adj.* tiered.

я́рый *adj.* **1,** furious; violent. **2,** fervent; zealous; rabid.

ярь-медя́нка [*gen.* **я́ри-медя́нки**] *n.* verdigris.

я́сельный *adj.* nursery (*attrib.*).

я́сеневый *adj.* ash (*attrib.*).

я́сень *n.m.* ash (*tree*).

я́сли [*gen.* **я́слей**] *n. pl.* **1,** manger. **2,** nursery; day nursery.

ясне́ть *v. impfv.* to become clear; clear up.

я́сно *adv.* clearly. —*adj., used predicatively* clear: всё я́сно?, is everything clear? Сегóдня я́сно, it is a clear day today. —*particle* **1,** I see; I understand. **2,** *colloq.* of course.

ясновидение *n.* clairvoyance. —**ясновúдец,** *n.* [*gen.* **-дца**] clairvoyant (person). —**ясновúдящий,** *adj.* clairvoyant.

я́сность *n.f.* clarity.

я́сный *adj.* [*short form* **я́сен, яснá, я́сно, я́сны** *or* **ясны́**] clear. —**я́сное дéло,** of course; it goes without saying. —**яснée я́сного,** as clear as day; crystal-clear.

я́ства *n. pl.* [*sing.* **я́ство**] food; victuals.

я́стреб [*pl.* **ястребá** *or* **я́стребы**] *n.* hawk.

ястреби́ный *adj.* **1,** hawk's. **2,** hawklike.

ястребóк [*gen.* **-бкá**] *n.* **1,** *dim. of* **я́стреб**. **2,** *colloq.* fighter plane.

ятагáн *n.* scimitar.

ять *n.m.* name of the old letter ѣ of the Russian alphabet, replaced in 1918 by the letter **е**. —**на ять,** *colloq.* **1,** first-rate. **2,** perfectly; to a T.

я́хонт *n., obs.* **1,** ruby. **2,** sapphire.

я́хта *n.* yacht.

яхтсмéн *n.* yachtsman.

ячéйка [*gen. pl.* **ячéек**] *n.* **1,** tiny opening (*one of many*). **2,** socket (*of a tooth*). **3,** cell (*of a communist party*). **4,** foxhole.

ячмéнный *adj.* barley (*attrib.*).

ячмéнь [*gen.* **-меня́**] *n.m.* **1,** barley. **2,** sty (*on one's eye*).

я́чневый *adj.* made of fine-ground barley.

я́шма *n.* jasper. —**я́шмовый,** *adj.* jasper (*attrib.*).

я́щер *n.* pangolin.

я́щерица *n.* lizard.

я́щик *n.* **1,** box. **2,** drawer. **3,** *in* му́сорный я́щик, garbage can; почтóвый я́щик, mailbox. —**отклáдывать в дóлгий я́щик,** to put off indefinitely. —**сыгрáть в я́щик,** *colloq.* to die; kick the bucket.

я́щур *n.* foot-and-mouth disease.

A Glossary of Proper Nouns

CONTINENTS

Africa	А́фрика
America	Аме́рика
Antarctica	Антаркти́да (continent) Анта́рктика (South Polar Region)
Asia	А́зия
Eurasia	Евра́зия
Europe	Евро́па

COUNTRIES

Afghanistan	Афганиста́н
Albania	Алба́ния
Algeria	Алжи́р
Angola	Анго́ла
Argentina	Аргенти́на
Australia	Австра́лия
Austria	А́встрия
Bahrain	Бахре́йн
Bangladesh	Бангладе́ш
Barbados	Барба́дос
Belgium	Бе́льгия
Belize	Бели́з
Benin	Бени́н
Bhutan	Бута́н
Bolivia	Боли́вия
Botswana	Ботсва́на
Brazil	Брази́лия
Bulgaria	Болга́рия
Burma	Би́рма
Burundi	Буру́нди
Cambodia	Камбо́джа
Cameroon	Камеру́н
Canada	Кана́да
Chad	Чад
Chile	Чи́ли
China	Кита́й
Colombia	Колу́мбия
Congo	Ко́нго
Costa Rica	Ко́ста-Ри́ка
Cuba	Ку́ба
Cyprus	Кипр
Czechoslovakia	Чехослова́кия
Denmark	Да́ния
Dominican Republic	Доминика́нская респу́блика
Ecuador	Эквадо́р
Egypt	Еги́пет (*gen.* -пта)
El Salvador	Сальвадо́р
Ethiopia	Эфио́пия
Fiji	Фи́джи
Finland	Финля́ндия
France	Фра́нция
Gabon	Габо́н
Gambia	Га́мбия
Germany	Герма́ния
Ghana	Га́на
Great Britain	Великобрита́ния
Greece	Гре́ция
Guatemala	Гватема́ла
Guinea	Гвине́я
Guyana	Гайа́на
Haiti	Гаи́ти
Honduras	Гондура́с
Hungary	Ве́нгрия
Iceland	Исла́ндия
India	И́ндия
Indonesia	Индоне́зия
Iran	Ира́н
Iraq	Ира́к
Ireland	Ирла́ндия
Israel	Изра́иль (*m.*).
Italy	Ита́лия
Ivory Coast	Бе́рег Слоно́вой Ко́сти
Jamaica	Яма́йка
Japan	Япо́ния
Jordan	Иорда́ния
Kenya	Ке́ния
Korea	Коре́я
Kuwait	Куве́йт
Laos	Лао́с
Lebanon	Лива́н
Lesotho	Лесо́то
Liberia	Либе́рия
Libya	Ли́вия
Luxembourg	Люксембу́рг

Malagasy Republic	Малагаси́йская Респу́блика
Malawi	Мала́ви
Malaysia	Мала́йзия
Mali	Мали́
Malta	Ма́льта
Mauritania	Маврита́ния
Mauritius	Маври́кий
Mexico	Ме́ксика
Mongolia	Монго́лия
Morocco	Маро́кко
Mozambique	Мозамби́к
Namibia	Нами́бия
Nepal	Непа́л
Netherlands	Нидерла́нды
New Zealand	Но́вая Зела́ндия
Nicaragua	Никара́гуа
Niger	Ни́гер
Nigeria	Ниге́рия
Norway	Норве́гия
Oman	Ома́н
Pakistan	Пакиста́н
Panama	Пана́ма
Paraguay	Парагва́й
Peru	Перу́
Philippines	Филиппи́ны
Poland	По́льша
Portugal	Португа́лия
Qatar	Ка́тар
Romania	Румы́ния
Rwanda	Руа́нда
Saudi Arabia	Саудо́вская Ара́вия
Senegal	Сенега́л
Sierra Leone	Сье́рра-Лео́не
Singapore	Сингапу́р
Somalia	Сомали́
South Africa	Ю́жно-Африка́нская Респу́блика
Soviet Union	Сове́тский Сою́з
Spain	Испа́ния
Sri Lanka	Шри Ла́нка
Sudan	Суда́н
Surinam	Сурина́м
Swaziland	Сва́зиленд
Sweden	Шве́ция
Switzerland	Швейца́рия
Syria	Си́рия
Taiwan	Тайва́нь (*m.*)
Tanzania	Танза́ния
Thailand	Таила́нд
Togo	То́го
Trinidad and Tobago	Тринида́д и Тоба́го
Tunisia	Туни́с
Turkey	Ту́рция
Uganda	Уга́нда
United States	Соединённые Шта́ты
Upper Volta	Ве́рхняя Во́льта
Uruguay	Уругва́й
Venezuela	Венесуэ́ла
Vietnam	Вьетна́м
Yemen	Йе́мен
Yugoslavia	Югосла́вия
Zaire	Заи́р
Zambia	За́мбия
Zimbabwe	Зимба́бве

TERRITORIES, REGIONS, PRINCIPALITIES

Andorra	Андо́рра
Armenia	Арме́ния
Bavaria	Бава́рия
Bessarabia	Бессара́бия
Bosnia	Бо́сния
Britanny	Брета́нь (*f.*)
Burgundy	Бургу́ндия
Cape Cod	Кейп-Ко́д
Cape of Good Hope	мыс До́брой Наде́жды
Cornwall	Ко́рнуолл
Crimea	Крым
Croatia	Хорва́тия
Dalmatia	Далма́ция
England	А́нглия
Eritrea	Эритре́я
Estonia	Эсто́ния
Flanders	Фла́ндрия
Galicia	Гали́ция
Georgia	Гру́зия
Gibraltar	Гибралта́р
Greenland	Гренла́ндия
Holland	Голла́ндия
Hong Kong	Гонко́нг
Indochina	Индокита́й
Kashmir	Кашми́р
Labrador	Лабрадо́р
Latvia	Ла́твия
Liechtenstein	Ли́хтенштейн
Lithuania	Литва́
Macao	Мака́о
Macedonia	Македо́ния
Manchuria	Маньчжу́рия
Melanesia	Мелане́зия
Mesopotamia	Месопота́мия
Micronesia	Микроне́зия
Monaco	Мона́ко

New England	Нóвая Áнглия
Normandy	Нормáндия
Oceania	Океáния
Palestine	Палести́на
Patagonia	Патагóния
Persia	Пéрсия
Phoenicia	Финики́я
Polynesia	Полинéзия
Prussia	Прýссия
Punjab	Пенджáб
Russia	Росси́я
Saar	Саáр
San Marino	Сан-Мари́но
Saxony	Саксóния
Scandinavia	Скандинáвия
Scotland	Шотлáндия
Serbia	Сéрбия
Siam	Сиáм
Siberia	Сиби́рь (*f.*)
Silesia	Силéзия
Sinai	Синáйский полуóстров
Slovakia	Словáкия
Slovenia	Словéния
Tibet	Тибéт
Tuscany	Тоскáна
Tyrol	Тирóль (*m.*)
Ukraine	Украи́на
Ulster	Óльстер
Wales	Уэ́льс
Yucatan	Юкатáн

ISLAND GROUPS

Aleutian Islands	Алеýтские островá
Antilles	Анти́льские островá
Azores	Азóрские островá
Bahamas	Багáмские островá
Balearic Islands	Балеáрские островá
Canary Islands	Канáрские островá
Cape Verde Islands	островá Зелёного Мы́са
Channel Islands	Нормáндские островá
Falkland Islands	Фолклéндские островá
Faroe Islands	Фарéрские островá
Galapagos Islands	островá Галáпагос
Leeward Islands	Подвéтренные островá
Maldive Islands	Мальди́вские островá
Mariana Islands	Мариáнские островá
Marshall Islands	Мáршалловы островá
Orkney Islands	Оркнéйские островá
Ryukyu Islands	островá Рюкю́
Samoa	Самóа
Seychelles	Сейшéльские островá
Shetland Islands	Шетлáндские островá
Solomon Islands	Соломóновы островá
Virgin Islands	Вирги́нские островá
Windward Islands	Навéтренные островá

ISLANDS

Antigua	Анти́гуа
Aruba	Арýба
Bali	Бáли
Bermuda	Бермýдские островá
Borneo	Борнéо
Corfu	Кóрфу
Corsica	Кóрсика
Crete	Крит
Curacao	Кюрасáо
Easter Island	óстров Пáсхи
Guadalcanal	Гуадалканáл
Guadeloupe	Гваделýпа
Guam	Гуам
Hokkaido	Хоккáйдо
Honshu	Хóнсю
Iwo Jima	Иводзи́ма
Java	Я́ва
Leyte	Лéйте
Long Island	Лонг-Áйленд
Luzon	Лусóн
Madagascar	Мадагаскáр
Madeira	Мадéйра
Majorca	Мальóрка, Майóрка
Man, Isle of	óстров Мэн
Martinique	Мартини́ка
Mindanao	Минданáо
New Guinea	Нóвая Гвинéя
Okinawa	Окинáва
Puerto Rico	Пуэ́рто-Ри́ко
Réunion	Реюньóн
Rhodes	Рóдос

Sakhalin	Сахали́н
Sardinia	Сарди́ния
Sicily	Сици́лия
Sumatra	Сума́тра
Tahiti	Таи́ти
Tasmania	Тасма́ния
Timor	Тимо́р
Vancouver	Ванку́вер
Zanzibar	Занзиба́р

STATES of the UNION

Alabama	Алаба́ма
Alaska	Аля́ска
Arizona	Аризо́на
Arkansas	Арка́нзас
California	Калифо́рния
Colorado	Колора́до
Connecticut	Конне́ктикут
Delaware	Де́лавэр
Florida	Флори́да
Georgia	Джо́рджия
Hawaii	Гава́йи
Idaho	А́йдахо
Illinois	Иллино́йс
Indiana	Индиа́на
Iowa	Айо́ва
Kansas	Ка́нзас
Kentucky	Кенту́кки
Louisiana	Луизиа́на
Maine	Мэн
Maryland	Мэ́риленд
Massachusetts	Массачу́сетс
Michigan	Мичига́н
Minnesota	Миннесо́та
Mississippi	Миссиси́пи
Missouri	Миссу́ри
Montana	Монта́на
Nebraska	Небра́ска
Nevada	Нева́да
New Hampshire	Нью-Хэ́мпшир
New Jersey	Нью-Дже́рси
New Mexico	Нью-Ме́ксико
New York	Нью-Йо́рк
North Carolina	Се́верная Кароли́на
North Dakota	Се́верная Дако́та
Ohio	Ога́йо
Oklahoma	Оклахо́ма
Oregon	Орего́н
Pennsylvania	Пенсильва́ния
Rhode Island	Род-А́йленд
South Carolina	Ю́жная Кароли́на
South Dakota	Ю́жная Дако́та
Tennessee	Теннесси́
Texas	Теха́с
Utah	Ю́та
Vermont	Вермо́нт
Virginia	Вирги́ния
Washington	Вашингто́н
West Virginia	За́падная Вирги́ния
Wisconsin	Виско́нсин
Wyoming	Вайо́минг

CANADIAN PROVINCES

Alberta	Альбе́рта
British Columbia	Брита́нская Колу́мбия
Manitoba	Манито́ба
New Brunswick	Нью-Бра́нсуик
Newfoundland	Ньюфаундле́нд
Nova Scotia	Но́вая Шотла́ндия
Ontario	Онта́рио
Prince Edward Island	о́стров При́нца Э́дуарда
Quebec	Квебе́к
Saskatchewan	Саска́чеван

CITIES

Acapulco	Акапу́лько
Accra	А́ккра
Addis Ababa	Адди́с-Абе́ба
Albany	О́лбани
Alexandria	Александри́я
Algiers	Алжи́р
Amman	Амма́н
Amsterdam	Амстерда́м
Ankara	Анкара́
Antwerp	Антве́рпен
Archangel	Арха́нгельск
Asunción	Асунсьо́н
Athens	Афи́ны
Atlanta	Атла́нта
Auckland	О́кленд
Baghdad	Багда́д
Baku	Баку́
Baltimore	Ба́лтимор
Bangkok	Бангко́к
Barcelona	Барсело́на
Beirut	Бейру́т
Belfast	Бе́лфаст
Belgrade	Белгра́д

Berlin	Берли́н
Berne	Берн
Bethlehem	Вифлее́м
Birmingham	Би́рмингем
Bogotá	Богота́
Bombay	Бомбе́й
Bonn	Бонн
Bordeaux	Бордо́
Boston	Бо́стон
Brasília	Брази́лия
Brazzaville	Браззави́ль (*m.*)
Brisbane	Бри́сбен
Brussels	Брюссе́ль (*m.*)
Bucharest	Бухаре́ст
Budapest	Будапе́шт
Buenos Aires	Буэ́нос-А́йрес
Buffalo	Бу́ффало
Cairo	Каи́р
Calcutta	Кальку́тта
Calgary	Ка́лгари
Cambridge	Ке́мбридж
Canberra	Ка́нберра
Cannes	Канн
Canterbury	Ке́нтербери
Canton	Канто́н
Capetown	Ке́йптаун
Caracas	Кара́кас
Cardiff	Ка́рдифф
Casablanca	Касабла́нка
Chicago	Чика́го
Cincinnati	Цинцинна́ти
Cleveland	Кли́вленд
Cologne	Кёльн
Colombo	Коло́мбо
Conakry	Ко́накри
Copenhagen	Копенга́ген
Cracow	Кра́ков
Dacca	Да́кка
Dakar	Дака́р
Dallas	Да́ллас
Damascus	Дама́ск
Dar es Salaam	Дар-эс-Сала́м
Denver	Де́нвер
Des Moines	Де-Мо́йн
Detroit	Детро́йт
Djakarta	Джака́рта
Dover	Дувр
Dresden	Дре́зден
Dublin	Ду́блин
Dubrovnik	Дубро́вник
Edinburgh	Э́динбург
Edmonton	Э́дмонтон
Florence	Флоре́нция
Fort Worth	Форт-Уэ́рт
Frankfurt	Фра́нкфурт
Geneva	Жене́ва
Genoa	Ге́нуя
Glasgow	Гла́зго
Gorky	Го́рький
Guadalajara	Гвадалаха́ра

Hague, The	Гаа́га
Haifa	Ха́йфа
Halifax	Га́лифакс
Hamburg	Га́мбург
Hanoi	Хано́й
Hanover	Ганно́вер
Harbin	Харби́н
Havana	Гава́на
Helsinki	Хе́льсинки
Hiroshima	Хироси́ма
Honolulu	Гонолу́лу
Houston	Хью́стон
Indianapolis	Индиана́полис
Irkutsk	Ирку́тск
Istanbul	Стамбу́л
Jericho	Иерихо́н
Jerusalem	Иерусали́м
Johannesburg	Йоха́ннесбург
Kabul	Кабу́л
Kansas City	Ка́нзас-Си́ти
Karachi	Кара́чи
Katmandu	Катманду́
Kazan	Каза́нь (*f.*)
Kharkov	Ха́рьков
Khartoum	Харту́м
Kiev	Ки́ев
Kingston	Ки́нгстон
Kinshasa	Кинша́са
Kishinev	Кишинёв
Kuala Lumpur	Куа́ла-Лу́мпур
Kuibyshev	Ку́йбышев
Kyoto	Кио́то
Lagos	Ла́гос
Lahore	Лахо́р
Lancaster	Ла́нкастер
Las Vegas	Лас-Ве́гас
Leeds	Лидс
Le Havre	Гавр
Leicester	Ле́стер
Leipzig	Ле́йпциг
Leningrad	Ленингра́д
Lhasa	Лха́са
Lima	Ли́ма
Lisbon	Лиссабо́н
Little Rock	Литл-Ро́к
Liverpool	Ливерпу́ль (*m.*)
London	Ло́ндон
Los Angeles	Лос-А́нджелес
Louisville	Лу́исвилл
Luanda	Луа́нда
Lucerne	Люце́рн
Lusaka	Луса́ка
Lvov	Львов
Madrid	Мадри́д
Managua	Мана́гуа
Manchester	Ма́нчестер
Manila	Мани́ла
Marseilles	Марсе́ль (*m.*)

Mecca	Мéкка
Melbourne	Мéльбурн
Memphis	Мéмфис
Mexico City	Мéхико
Miami	Майáми
Milan	Милáн
Milwaukee	Милуóки
Minneapolis	Миннеáполис
Minsk	Минск
Mobile	Мобúл
Montevideo	Монтевидéо
Montreal	Монреáль (*m.*)
Moscow	Москвá
Munich	Мю́нхен
Murmansk	Мýрманск
Nairobi	Найрóби
Naples	Неáполь (*m.*)
Nashville	Нáшвилл
Nassau	Нáссау
Nazareth	Назарéт
Newark	Нью́арк
New Delhi	Дéли
New Orleans	Нóвый Орлеáн
New York	Нью-Йóрк
Nice	Нúцца
Nicosia	Никосúя
Nottingham	Нóттингем
Novosibirsk	Новосибúрск
Nuremberg	Ню́рнберг
Oakland	Óкленд
Odessa	Одéсса
Omaha	Óмаха
Osaka	Óсака
Oslo	Óсло
Ottawa	Оттáва
Oxford	Óксфорд
Paris	Парúж
Peking	Пекúн
Perth	Перт
Philadelphia	Филадéльфия
Phnom Penh	Пномпéнь (*m.*)
Phoenix	Фúникс
Pisa	Пúза
Pittsburgh	Пúтсбург
Plymouth	Плúмут
Port-au-Prince	Порт-о-Прéнс
Portland	Пóртленд
Portsmouth	Пóртсмут
Prague	Прáга
Pretoria	Претóрия
Providence	Прóвиденс
Pyongyang	Пхенья́н
Quebec	Квебéк
Quito	Кúто
Raleigh	Рóли
Rangoon	Рангýн
Rawalpindi	Равалпúнди
Regina	Риджáйна
Reno	Рúно
Reykjavik	Рéйкьявик
Richmond	Рúчмонд
Riga	Рúга
Rio de Janeiro	Рúо-де-Жанéйро
Riyadh	Эр-Рия́д
Rochester	Рóчестер
Rome	Рим
Rotterdam	Рóттердам
Saigon	Сайгóн
St. Louis	Сент-Лýис
St. Paul	Сент-Пóл
Salisbury	Сóлсбери
Salt Lake City	Солт-Лейк-Сúти
Samarkand	Самаркáнд
San Diego	Сан-Диéго
San Francisco	Сан-Францúско
San Juan	Сан-Хуáн
Santiago	Сантья́го
São Paulo	Сан-Пáулу
Seattle	Сиэ́тл
Seoul	Сеýл
Seville	Севúлья
Shanghai	Шанхáй
Sofia	Софúя
Stockholm	Стокгóльм
Sydney	Сúдней
Taipei	Тайбэ́й
Tallin	Тáллин
Tashkent	Ташкéнт
Tbilisi	Тбилúси
Teheran	Тегерáн
Tel Aviv	Тель-Авúв
Tirana	Тирáна
Tokyo	Тóкио
Toronto	Торóнто
Trieste	Триéст
Tripoli	Трúполи
Tulsa	Тáлса
Tunis	Тунúс
Turin	Турúн
Ulan Bator	Улáн-Бáтор
Vancouver	Ванкýвер
Venice	Венéция
Versailles	Версáль (*m.*)
Victoria	Виктóрия
Vienna	Вéна
Vientiane	Вьентья́н
Vilnius	Вúльнюс
Vladivostok	Владивостóк
Volgograd	Волгогрáд

Warsaw	Варша́ва
Washington	Вашингто́н
Wellington	Ве́ллингтон
Wilmington	Уи́лмингтон
Winnipeg	Ви́ннипег
Yerevan	Ерева́н
Yokohama	Йокоха́ма
York	Йорк
Zurich	Цю́рих

SECTIONS OF CITIES

Bronx	Бронкс
Brooklyn	Бру́клин
Coney Island	Ко́ни-А́йленд
Harlem	Га́рлем
Hollywood	Голливу́д
Manhattan	Манха́ттан
Montmartre	Монма́ртр
Queens	Квинс
Soho	Со́хо
Westminster	Ве́стминстер

OCEANS

Arctic	Се́верный Ледови́тый океа́н
Atlantic	Атланти́ческий океа́н
Indian	Инди́йский океа́н
Pacific	Ти́хий океа́н

SEAS

Adriatic	Адриати́ческое мо́ре
Aegean	Эге́йское мо́ре
Aral	Ара́льское мо́ре
Azov, of	Азо́вское мо́ре
Baltic	Балти́йское мо́ре
Bering	Бе́рингово мо́ре
Black	Чёрное мо́ре
Caribbean	Кари́бское мо́ре
Caspian	Каспи́йское мо́ре
Dead	Мёртвое мо́ре
Irish	Ирла́ндское мо́ре
Japan, of	Япо́нское мо́ре
Mediterranean	Средизе́мное мо́ре
North	Се́верное мо́ре
Okhotsk, of	Охо́тское мо́ре
Red	Кра́сное мо́ре
South China	Ю́жно-Кита́йское мо́ре
White	Бе́лое мо́ре
Yellow	Жёлтое мо́ре

LAKES

Albert	Альбе́рт
Baikal	Байка́л
Chad	Чад
Erie	Э́ри
Great Bear	Большо́е Медве́жье о́зеро
Great Salt	Большо́е Солёное о́зеро
Great Slave	Большо́е Нево́льничье о́зеро
Huron	Гуро́н
Ladoga	Ла́дожское о́зеро
Michigan	Мичига́н
Onega	Оне́жское о́зеро
Ontario	Онта́рио
Superior	Ве́рхнее о́зеро
Tanganyika	Танганьи́ка
Titicaca	Титика́ка
Victoria	Викто́рия

RIVERS

Amazon	Амазо́нка
Amur	Аму́р
Columbia	Колу́мбия
Congo	Ко́нго

Danube	Дуна́й
Delaware	Де́лавэр
Dnieper	Днепр
Dniester	Днестр
Don	Дон
Elbe	Э́льба
Euphrates	Евфра́т
Ganges	Ганг
Hudson	Гудзо́н
Indus	Инд
Irrawaddy	Irава́ди
Irtysh	Ирты́ш
Jordan	Иорда́н
Lena	Ле́на
Loire	Луа́ра
Mackenzie	Макке́нзи
Mekong	Меко́нг
Mississippi	Миссиси́пи
Missouri	Миссу́ри
Niger	Ни́гер
Nile	Нил
Ob	Обь
Oder	О́дер
Ohio	Ога́йо
Orinoco	Орино́ко
Paraná	Парана́
Po	По
Potomac	Пото́мак
Rhine	Рейн
Rhone	Ро́на
Rio Grande	Ри́о-Гра́нде
St. Lawrence	Свято́го Лавре́нтия
Seine	Се́на
Susquehanna	Саскуэха́нна
Thames	Те́мза
Tigris	Тигр
Vistula	Ви́сла
Volga	Во́лга
Volta	Во́льта
Yangtze	Янцзы́
Yellow	Жёлтая
Yenisei	Енисе́й
Yukon	Ю́кон
Zambezi	Замбе́зи

GULFS, BAYS, STRAITS, CHANNELS, CANALS

Bengal, Bay of	Бенга́льский зали́в
Bering Strait	Бе́рингов проли́в
Biscay, Bay of	Биска́йский зали́в
Bosp(h)orus	Босфо́р
English Channel	Ла-Ма́нш
Gibraltar, Strait of	Гибралта́рский проли́в
Hudson Bay	Гудзо́нов зали́в
Magellan, Strait of	Магелла́нов проли́в
Mexico, Gulf of	Мексика́нский зали́в
Panama Canal	Пана́мский кана́л
Persian Gulf	Перси́дский зали́в
Suez Canal	Суэ́цкий кана́л

MOUNTAIN RANGES

Adirondack Mountains	Адиро́ндак
Allegheny Mountains	Аллега́ны
Alps	А́льпы
Andes	А́нды
Appalachian Mountains	Аппала́чи
Carpathian Mountains	Карпа́ты
Catskill Mountains	го́ры Ка́тскилл
Caucasus	Кавка́з
Himalayas	Гимала́и
Pyrenees	Пирене́и
Rocky Mountains	Скали́стые го́ры
Ural Mountains	Ура́л

MOUNTAIN PEAKS

Elbrus	Эльбру́с
Etna	Э́тна
Everest	Эвере́ст
Fuji, Fujiyama	Фудзия́ма
Kilimanjaro	Килиманджа́ро
Matterhorn	Ма́ттерхорн
Mauna Loa	Ма́уна-Ло́а

McKinley	Мак-Ки́нли
Mont Blanc	Монбла́н
Pike's Peak	Пайкс-Пик
Popocatepetl	Попокате́петль
Rainier	Рейни́р
Sinai	Сина́й
Vesuvius	Везу́вий
Whitney	У́итни

FAMOUS NAMES

Aesop	Эзо́п
Andropov	Андро́пов
Aristotle	Аристо́тель
Atatürk	Ататю́рк
Attila	Атти́ла
Bach	Бах
Balzac	Бальза́к
Beethoven	Бетхо́вен
Bismarck	Би́смарк
Bolivar	Боли́вар
Brahms	Брамс
Brezhnev	Бре́жнев
Buddha	Бу́дда
Caesar	Це́зарь
Calvin	Кальви́н
Carter	Ка́ртер
Caruso	Кару́зо
Cervantes	Серва́нтес
Chaplin	Ча́плин
Charlemagne	Карл Вели́кий
Chaucer	Чо́сер
Chekhov	Че́хов
Chopin	Шопе́н
Christ	Христо́с
Churchill	Че́рчилль
Cicero	Цицеро́н
Clausewitz	Кла́узевиц
Clemenceau	Клемансо́
Columbus	Колу́мб
Confucius	Конфу́ций
Copernicus	Копе́рник
Cortés	Корте́с
Curie	Кюри́
Dante	Да́нте
Darwin	Да́рвин
da Vinci	да Ви́нчи
Debussy	Дебюсси́
de Gaulle	де Голль
Demosthenes	Демосфе́н
Descartes	Дека́рт
Dickens	Ди́ккенс
Diderot	Дидро́
Diogenes	Диоге́н
Disraeli	Дизрае́ли
Dostoyevsky	Достое́вский
Dvorak	Дво́ржак
Edison	Э́дисон
Einstein	Эйнште́йн
Eisenhower	Эйзенха́уэр
Erasmus	Эра́зм
Faulkner	Фо́лкнер
Flaubert	Флобе́р
Franco	Фра́нко
Franklin	Фра́нклин
Freud	Фрейд
Galileo	Галиле́й
Gandhi	Га́нди
Garibaldi	Гариба́льди
Genghis Khan	Чингисха́н
Goethe	Гёте
Gogol	Го́голь
Grieg	Григ
Gutenberg	Гу́тенберг
Hammarskjöld	Хаммаршёльд
Hannibal	Ганниба́л
Hawthorne	Хо́торн
Haydn	Гайдн
Hegel	Ге́гель
Hemingway	Хемингуэ́й
Hippocrates	Гиппокра́т
Hitler	Ги́тлер
Homer	Гоме́р
Hugo	Гюго́
Jefferson	Дже́фферсон
Joan of Arc	Жа́нна д'Арк
Joyce	Джойс
Kafka	Ка́фка
Keats	Китс
Kennedy	Ке́ннеди
Khrushchev	Хрущёв
Kipling	Ки́плинг
Lenin	Ле́нин
Lincoln	Ли́нкольн
Longfellow	Лонгфе́лло
Luther	Лю́тер
MacArthur	Мака́ртур
Machiavelli	Макиаве́лли
Magellan	Магелла́н
Manet	Мане́

Mao Tse-tung	Мáо Цзэ-дýн	Schweitzer	Швéйцер
Marshall	Мáршалл	Shakespeare	Шекспи́р
Marx	Маркс	Shaw	Шóу
Metternich	Мéттерних	Shostakovich	Шостакóвич
Michelangelo	Микелáнджело	Socrates	Сокрáт
Milton	Ми́льтон	Solzhenitsyn	Солжени́цын
Mohammed	Мухáммед	Sophocles	Софóкл
Molière	Мольéр	Stalin	Стáлин
Monet	Монé	Strauss	Штрáус
Mozart	Мóцарт		
Mussolini	Муссоли́ни	Talleyrand	Талейрáн
		Tamerlane	Тимýр
Napoleon	Наполеóн	Tchaikovsky	Чайкóвский
Newton	Ньютóн	Tennyson	Тéннисон
Nixon	Ни́ксон	Thackeray	Тéккерей
		Tito	Ти́то
Pasternak	Пастернáк	Tolstoy	Толстóй
Pasteur	Пастéр	Trotsky	Трóцкий
Picasso	Пикáссо	Truman	Трýмэн
Plato	Платóн	Turgenev	Тургéнев
Proust	Пруст		
Pushkin	Пýшкин	van Gogh	ван Гог
		Virgil	Верги́лий
Raphael	Рафаэ́ль	Voltaire	Вольтéр
Reagan	Рéйган		
Rembrandt	Рéмбрандт	Wagner	Вáгнер
Renoir	Ренуáр	Washington	Вáшингтон
Robespierre	Робеспьéр	Webster	Уэ́бстер
Rockefeller	Рокфéллер	Whitman	Уи́тмен
Rodin	Родéн	Wilson	Ви́льсон
Roosevelt	Рýзвельт	Wright	Райт
Rousseau	Руссó		
Rubens	Рýбенс	Zola	Золя́